# DICIONÁRIOS GARNIER

1. DICIONÁRIO LATINO-PORTUGUÊS - F.R. dos Santos Saraiva
2. VOCABULÁRIO DA LÍNGUA GREGA - Ramiz Galvão
3. DICIONÁRIO ESPANHOL-PORTUGUÊS - A. Tenório de Albuquerque
4. FRASES E CURIOSIDADES LATINAS - Arthur Vieira de Rezende e Silva
5. DICIONÁRIO ITALIANO-PORTUGUÊS - João Amendola
6. DICIONÁRIO INGLÊS/PORTUGUÊS-PORTUGUÊS/INGLÊS - João Fernandes Valdez e Levindo Castro Lafayete
7. DICIONÁRIO FRANCÊS/PORTUGUÊS-PORTUGUÊS/FRANCÊS - João Fernandes Valdez
8. VOCABULÁRIO LATINO-PORTUGUÊS - Ernesto Faria
9. DICIONÁRIO DAS DIFICULDADES DA LÍNGUA PORTUGUESA - Cândido Jucá (Filho)
10. DICIONÁRIO TÉCNICO INDUSTRIAL - Michel Feutry - Robert M. de Mertzenfeld - Agnès Dollinger

# DICIONÁRIO
## TÉCNICO
## INDUSTRIAL

DICIONÁRIOS GARNIER

Vol. 10

Capa
Cláudio Martins

**LIVRARIA GARNIER**
BELO HORIZONTE
Rua São Geraldo, 67 - Floresta - Cep. 30-150-070
Tel.: (31) 3212-4600 - Fax: (31) 3224-5151

MICHEL FEUTRY
ROBERT M. DE MERTZENFELD
AGNÈS DOLLINGER

# DICIONÁRIO TÉCNICO INDUSTRIAL

*Tratando das áreas de:*
MECÂNICA, METALURGIA, ELETRICIDADE, QUÍMICA,
CONSTRUÇÃO CIVIL E CIÊNCIAS EXATAS.

*INGLÊS – FRANCÊS – ALEMÃO – ESPANHOL – PORTUGUÊS*

LIVRARIA GARNIER

| 118, Rua Benjamin Constant, 118 | 53, Rua São Geraldo, 53 |
| Rio de Janeiro | Belo Horizonte |

*Compilado por:*
MICHEL FEUTRY
*Editor*

*Colaboradores*
ROBERT MERTZ DE MERTZENFELD
*Tradutor técnico – Membro da S.F.T.*

AGNÈS DOLLINGER
*Tradutora técnica diplomada (E.S.I.T.) – Membro da S.F.T.*

*Compilação da parte em português*
JOSHUAH DE BRAGANÇA SOARES
*Tradutor técnico*

*Revisto por*
LUZIA MENDONÇA VENTURA
NILZA AGUA

*Título original:*
DICTIONNAIRE TECHNOLOGIQUE

(c) Copyright 1976 by LA MAISON DU DICTIONNAIRE, Paris.

2001

Direitos de Propriedade Literária adquiridos pela
**LIVRARIA GARNIER**
Belo Horizonte - Rio de Janeiro

Impresso no Brasil
*Printed in Brazil*

# SUMÁRIO

**PRIMEIRA PARTE**

| | |
|---|---|
| Prólogo (em Português) | IX |
| Foreword | X |
| Avant-Propos | XI |
| Vorwort | XII |
| Prólogo (em Espanhol) | XIII |
| Nota Explicativa | XIV |
| Verbetes Numerados | 1 a 373 |
| Suplemento Espanhol | 375 a 563 |

**SEGUNGA PARTE**

| | |
|---|---|
| Índice Francês | 565 a 746 |
| Índice Alemão | 749 a 943 |
| Índice Espanhol | 947 a 1156 |

**TERCEIRA PARTE**

| | |
|---|---|
| Índice Remissivo Português | 1159 a 1336 |

## PRÓLOGO

A obra que tenho a honra de apresentar é o fruto do trabalho realizado por um consultor que contou com a ajuda de dois tradutores especializados na matéria.

Esta obra abrange o vasto campo das indústrias mecânica, metalúrgica e hidráulica de caráter poliglota (Inglês, Francês, Alemão, Espanhol e Português) para satisfazer as exigências de inúmeros tradutores que têm a importante missão de servir de intermediários entre os cientistas e os técnicos.

O trabalho de lexicógrafo requer um esforço contínuo e árduo porque pressupõe uma seleção criteriosa de todos os termos a incluir no dicionário. Essa seleção só pode ser perfeita quando o lexicógrafo consulta muitas obras, estudando o contexto em que a palavra é empregada, sabendo que um mesmo vocábulo pode mudar completamente de sentido conforme o lugar que ocupa na frase e o ramo industrial em que é empregado.

Esses dois passos, escolha e estudo do contexto deverão ser repetidos tantas vezes quantas forem as línguas que formam o dicionário. Daí surge uma séria dificuldade própria das línguas em questão. Sabe-se que o Alemão emprega aglutinações de substantivos e adjetivos além de formar verbos de grande complexidade. O inglês, por sua vez, também aglutina os termos criando formas compostas totalmente distintas da morfologia e da léxica dos grupos lingüísticos latinos. Assim, pois, torna-se necessário seguir um critério para a ordenação alfabética dos verbetes.

Outro problema é o que trazem os neologismos. O enriquecimento do vocabulário que segue "pari passu" a aquisição de novos conhecimentos técnicos e científicos conduz à criação de novas palavras e expressões cunhadas sem obediência lógica a nenhuma regra de modo que o lexicógrafo deve valer-se da imaginação para decifrar o verdadeiro significado de certos termos.

Essas dificuldades todas só podem ser vencidas por tradutores de muita prática no ofício e com um bom conhecimento da matéria que traduzem.

Agradecemos, pois, aos colaboradores do trabalho feito, o terem proporcionado aos seus colegas de classe a utilização de um instrumento indispensável de trabalho.

O humanista Scaliger dizia no século XVI: "Se quiseres enviar um condenado ao suplício não o envies às minas de ferro nem ao verdugo, mas obriga-o a compilar um dicionário".

Não queremos tomar ao pé da letra essa maneira sinistra de descrever a lexicografia, mas sim, congratularmo-nos com os autores reconhecendo o alto valor cultural de seu trabalho.

Dr. A. SLIOSBERG,
Presidente da Associação Francesa de Tradutores

## FOREWORD

The work it is my great privilege to present, is the product of a documentation consultant and of two translators, authorities in their particular fields. It covers the very vast domain of the mechanical, metallurgical and hydraulic industries, and this fact alone gives one an idea of the immense efforts that had to be expended to compile a three-language work of such a magnitude ; this dictionary must in fact meet the requirements of a large number of translators employed in industry, and who serve as irreplaceable intermediaries between scientists and technicians working on both sides of the Rhine, the channel and the Atlantic.

The work of a lexicographer entails continuous and laborious efforts : it comprises first of all the selection of the terms relevant to the contents of the dictionary, and only the reading of large numbers of works and periodicals can assure a more or less exhaustive vocabulary of words and terms. Next one must analyze the context in which the chosen term has been used, and in this connection it should be noted that the same word may have a different meaning, depending on whether it is preceded or followed by a certain adjective or verb. Moreover this same term is liable to mean different things in different industries, or to be used in a sometimes peculiar or even picturesque manner, in the slang of technicians.

These two steps - choice and analysis of contents - must be repeated as many times as the number of languages in the dictionary. This further difficulty is in fact inherent in the two languages used ; for instance the manner in which the words are constructed is different. In German nouns and their adjectives tend to be strung together, or complex verbs built up. In English there is also a tendency to form composite nouns or adjectives, and the French translator must know how to split these up in order to assign them an appropriate alphabetic position, taking into account the first letter of the noun.

Neologisms represent another stumbling block : the enriching of the vocabulary, which goes hand in hand with the acquisition of scientific and technical know-how, impels writers to coin new words ; there are no precise rules governing this coining of new words, and thus full play is given to an at times fanciful imagination. The lexicographer is thus faced with a veritable decoding task.

Outlined above are some of the difficulties that the compilers of this dictionary had to overcome, and it was only their great experience in translating that enabled them successfully to conclude this arduous task.

We must therefore not fail to thank them for having placed at the disposal of their colleagues an essential tool which extends well beyond the various technological and industrial domains, and which appears to be the first and sole three-language technological dictionary published in France. Similarly credit must also be given to the editor for having taken great care to present a work that is both clear and easy to consult.

The classical scholar Scaliger said in the 16th century : « If you wish to punish a condemned man, do not send him to the iron mines, or to the torturer, instead make him compile a dictionary ... » Without taking literally this gloomy manner of imagining lexicography, may I be allowed to congratulate the three authors of this work for their fine performance, and to wish them all the success they deserve.

*Dr. A. SLIOSBERG,*

**President of the French Translators' Association**

## AVANT-PROPOS

L'ouvrage que j'ai le redoutable honneur de présenter est l'oeuvre d'un conseiller en documentation et de deux traducteurs spécialistes en la matière. Il couvre le très vaste domaine des industries de la mécanique, de la métallurgie et de l'hydraulique ; c'est dire la somme de travail qu'il a fallu fournir pour mettre sur pied un ouvrage trilingue - Anglais, Français. Allemand - qui doit satisfaire aux exigences des nombreux traducteurs qui oeuvrent dans l'industrie et qui servent aussi d'intermédiaires irremplaçables entre les scientifiques et les techniciens de part et d'autre du Rhin, de la Manche et de l'Atlantique.

Le travail du lexicographe exige un effort continu et pénible : il comporte tout d'abord la sélection des termes se rapportant à la matière du Dictionnaire, et seule la lecture de nombreux ouvrages et périodiques peut fournir un ensemble terminologique plus ou moins exhaustif ; on doit ensuite étudier le contexte dans lequel le terme choisi est utilisé, et l'on sait que le même mot peut changer de signification selon qu'il est précédé ou suivi de tel qualificatif ou de tel verbe : en outre ce même terme est susceptible d'avoir des sens différents dans divers domaines industriels ou d'être utilisé d'une manière parfois singulière, voire pittoresque dans le jargon des techniciens.

Ces deux démarches - choix et étude du contexte - doivent être répétées autant de fois que le dictionnaire comporte de langues. Il s'agit là d'une nouvelle difficulté inhérente aux deux idiomes utilisés : d'une part la construction des mots ; on sait que l'allemand a tendance à accoler les substantifs et leurs qualificatifs ou forger des verbes complexes ; les Anglophones ont également l'habitude de créer des substantifs ou des adjectifs composés, que le traducteur français doit savoir scinder pour leur assigner une place alphabétique appropriée en tenant compte de la première lettre du substantif.

Les néologismes représentent un autre écueil : l'enrichissement du vocabulaire qui va de pair avec l'acquisition de nouvelles notions scientifiques ou techniques pousse les auteurs à créer des mots nouveaux, et comme aucune règle précise ne préside à cette création, elle est laissée à leur imagination souvent fantaisiste, et demande au lexicographe un véritable effort de décodage.

Telles sont les difficultés que les auteurs de ce dictionnaire avaient à surmonter et seule une longue pratique de la traduction leur ont permis de mener à bonne fin cette tâche ardue.

On ne peut que les remercier d'avoir mis à la disposition de leurs confrères un outil indispensable qui déborde largement sur différents domaines technologiques et industriels et qui semble être le premier et unique dictionnaire technologique trilingue édité en France : à ce titre on doit également des louanges à l'éditeur qui a pris soin de présenter un ouvrage clair et facile à consulter.

L'humaniste Scaliger disait au XVIe siècle : «Si tu veux envoyer un condamné au supplice, ne l'envoie pas aux mines de fer, ni au tortionnaire, fais lui faire un dictionnaire ...» Sans prendre à la lettre cette sombre façon de concevoir la lexicographie, qu'il me soit permis de féliciter les trois auteurs de cet ouvrage pour leur performance et de leur souhaiter tout le succès qu'ils méritent.

Dr A. SLIOSBERG,

Président de la Société Française des Traducteurs

*VORWORT*

*Ich darf Ihnen hiermit ein Werk vorstellen, das von einem Dokumentenberater und zwei Fachübersetzern erarbeitet worden ist. Es umfasst das weite Gebiet der mechanischen Industrien, der Metallurgie und der Hydraulik. Ein ungemeiner Arbeitsaufwand war erforderlich, um ein dreisprachiges Wörterbuch : Englisch - Französisch - Deutsch zu schaffen, das den Bedürfnissen zahlreicher Übersetzer gerecht wird, die in der Industrie und als unentbehrliche Vermittler zwischen den Wissenschaftlern und Technikern zu beiden Seiten des Rheins, des Armelkanals und des Atlantiks tätig sind.*

*Die Arbeit des Lexikographen ist mühselig und langwierig. Zunächst einmal müssen alle Begriffe, die mit dem Wörterbuch im Zusammenhang stehen, ausgewählt werden, und nur die Lektüre zahlreicher Werke und Fachzeitschriften kann eine mehr oder weniger erschöpfende Terminologie liefern. Sodann muss der Kontext, in welchem der gewählte Begriff verwendet worden ist, untersucht werden. Es ist bekannt, dass das gleiche Wort durch ein vor-oder nachgestelltes Adjektiv oder Verb seine Bedeutung ändern kann. Uberdies kann der gleiche Ausdruck in den einzelnen Industriebereichen einen anderen Sinn haben oder manchmal in eigenartiger, bildhafter Weise im Jargon der Techniker gebraucht werden.*

*Diese beiden Verfahren - Auswahl und Studium des Kontextes- müssen so oft wiederholt werden wie das Wörterbuch Sprachen enthält. Hier tritt eine neue Schwierigkeit auf, die mit der Besonderheit der beiden verwendeten Sprachen verbunden ist : zum einen handelt es sich um die Schwierigkeit der Wortkonstruktion. Bekanntlich neigt die deutsche Sprache dazu, die Substantive mit ihren Adjektiven zusammenzuziehen oder komplexe Verben zu schmieden. Der englischen Sprache ist es ebenfalls eigen, zusammengesetzte Substantive oder Adjektive zu formen. Der französische Übersetzer muss daher in der Lage sein, diese Wörter aufzuteilen, um den Begriff unter dem ersten Buchstaben des Substantives im Wörterbuch zu finden.*

*Zum andern stellen die Neuschöpfungen eine schwierige Klippe dar. Die Erweiterung des Wortschatzes Hand in Hand mit neuen wissenschaftlichen oder technischen Erkenntnissen, durch welche die Autoren gezwungen werden, neue Wörter zu schaffen, und da diese Neuschöpfungen keiner festen Regel unterliegen, werden sie der oft von eigenartigen Einfällen geleiteten Vorstellung der Autoren überlassen, so dass der Lexikograph eine wahre Entschlüsselungsarbeit leisten muss.*

*Das sind die Schwierigkeiten, die die Autoren dieses Wörterbuches zu überwinden hatten. Nur eine lange Praxis in der Übersetzung gestattete es ihnen, diese Aufgabe zum guten Ende zu bringen.*

*Deshalb gebührt den Autoren Dank, ihren Kollegen ein unerlässliches Hilfsmittel zur Verfügung zu stellen, das oft über die verschiedenen technologischen und industriellen Bereiche hinausgeht, und das als erstes dreisprachiges technologisches Wörterbuch in Frankreich herausgegeben wird. Hier muss auch dem Verleger gedankt werden, der sich der Mühe unterzogen hat, ein Werk vorzulegen, das übersichtlich und leicht nachzuschlagen ist.*

*Der Humanist Scaliger sagte im 16. Jahrhundert : «Wenn Du einen Verurteilten bestrafen willst, schicke ihn nicht in die Eisenbergwerke noch in die Folterkammer, lasse ihn ein Wörterbuch zusammenstellen...» Ohne diese düstere Auffassung zu teilen, sei es mir gestattet, die drei Autoren dieses Werkes zu ihrer Leistung zu beglückwünschen. Möge ihnen der verdiente Erfolg beschieden sein.*

*Dr. A. SLIOSBERG,*

*Präsident der Société Française des Traducteurs*

# PRÓLOGO

La obra que tengo el honor de presentar es la de un consejero en documentación y la de dos especialistas en la materia. Esta obra cubre el vasto dominio de la industrias dedicadas a la mecánica, metalúrgia, siderurgia e hidráulica, es decir la suma de trabajo necesaria para poder realizar una obra cuatrilingüe — Inglès, Francés, Alemán y Español — la cual debe satisfacer las exigencias de numerosos traductores que trabajan en la industria y que sirven de intermediarios irremplazables entre los científicos y los técnicos.

El trabajo de lexicografía exige un continuado y pesado esfuerzo : Comporta toda la selección términos que se incluyen en el diccionario, y solamente la lectura de numerosas obras y revistas periódicas puede dar a conocer un conjunto de terminología tan completo, estudiando el contexto en el cual la palabra escogida es utilizada, sabiendo que la misma palabra puede cambiar de significación según esté precedida o seguida de algún calificativo o de algún verbo : por contra esta misma palabra es susceptible de tener significado diferente según los dominios industriales o de ser utilizada de una manera singular, o bien característica del lenguaje usual de los técnicos.

Estos dos conceptos deben ser repetidos tantas cuantas veces las lenguas incluidas en el diccionario. Esto presenta una dificultad propia de las lenguas utilizadas : De una parte la construcción de las palabras. Sabemos que el alemán tiene tendencia a reunir los calificativos o inventar verbos complejos. Los ingleses tienen la costumbre de crear substantivos o adjetivos compuestos, que los traductores franceses y españoles deben saber separar para asignarles un lugar alfabético apropiado teniendo en cuenta la primera letra des substantivo.

Los neologismos representan otro defecto : El enriquecimiento del vocabulario que va de la mano con la adquisición de nuevos concimientos científicos o técnicos empujan a los otros a crear palabras nuevas, y como no hay ninguna regla precisa que solucione esta creación, está dejada a la imaginación pidiendo al lexicógrafo un verdadero esfuerzo de desciframiento.

Tales son las dificultades que los autores de este diccionario han tenido que superar y solamento una práctica constante de la traducción les ha permitido llevar a buen fin este árduo trabajo.

Les debemos estar agradecidos por haber puesto a disposición de sus colegas un instrumento indispensable que rebasa ampliamente diversos dominios tecnológicos e industriales y que es, al parecer, el primero y único diccionario tecnológico trilingüe (con suplemento en castellano) editado en Francia. Debemos alabar también al editor por el esmero puesto en presentar una obra clara y fácil de leer.

El humanista Sclaiger decía en el Siglo XVI : «Si quieres enviar a un condenado al suplicio, no le envíes a las minas de hierro ni al verdugo, oblígale a hacer un diccionario...» Sin tomar al pie de la letra esta lóbrega manera de concebir la lexicografía, séame permitido felicitar a los tres autores de esta obra por su esfuerzo y desearles todo el éxito que merecen.

Dr A. SLIOSBERG,
Presidente de la Asiciación Francesa de Traductores

## NOTA EXPLICATIVA

*A ordem seguida obedece a rigorosos critérios de consulta que facilitam de sobremaneira o entendimento dos verbetes.*

*Assim, temos a ordenação do inglês* **antecedida** *de número, depois a tradução simultânea em francês e alemão; na seqüência, a tradução em espanhol.*

*Na segunda parte estão os índices alfabéticos do francês, alemão e espanhol* **precedidos** *do número que remete à primeira parte.*

*Na parte final da obra, a tradução em português antecedida de número remissivo às demais línguas.*

**O Editor**

# PRIMEIRA PARTE

INGLÊS
FRANCÊS
ALEMÃO
ESPANHOL

**ABS**

| | | | |
|---|---|---|---|
| 1 | A.C ALTERNATING CURRENT | COURANT ALTERNATIF | WECHSELSTROM |
| 2 | A.C.-WELDING MACHINE | POSTE DE SOUDAGE A COURANT ALTERNATIF | WECHSELSTROMSCHWEISSMASCHINE |
| 3 | A.C.H.F. ALTERNATING CURRENT WITH HIGH FREQUENCY | COURANT ALTERNATIF HAUTE FREQUENCE | WECHSELSTROM (HOCHFREQUENZER) |
| 4 | ABATING | REDUCTION DE TREMPE | HÄRTUNGSMINDERUNG |
| 5 | ABERRATION OF LIGHT | ABERRATION | ABWEICHUNG, ABERRATION DES LICHTES |
| 6 | ABILITY OF BEING DECOMPOSED | DESTRUCTIBILITE | ZERSETZLICHKEIT |
| 7 | ABNORMAL GRAIN GROWTH | CROISSANCE ANORMALE DES CRISTAUX | KRISTALLWACHSTUM (ABNORMALES) |
| 8 | ABNORMAL STEEL | ACIER ANORMAL | STAHL (ANORMALER) |
| 9 | ABNORMAL WROUGHT IRON | FER MALLEABLE ANORMAL | SCHMIEDEEISEN (ANORMALES) |
| 10 | ABRADE (TO) | ENLEVER (OU USER) EN EMOULANT | ABSCHLEIFEN |
| 11 | ABRADING AGENT | MATIERE A POLIR | POLIERMITTEL |
| 12 | ABRAMSEN STRAIGHTENER | REDRESSEUR (DE TUBES) ABRAMSEN | ABRAMSEN-ROHRRICHTMASCHINE |
| 13 | ABRASION | ABRASION, ENLEVEMENT PAR EMOULAGE | ABSCHLEIFEN, ABRIEB |
| 14 | ABRASION HARDNESS | DURETE DE MEULAGE | SCHLEIFHÄRTE |
| 15 | ABRASION MARKS | MARQUES DE MEULAGE | SCHLEIFSPUREN |
| 16 | ABRASION TESTS | ESSAIS D'USURE | ABSCHLEIFVERSUCH |
| 17 | ABRASIVE | ABRASIF | SCHLEIFMITTEL |
| 18 | ABRASIVE BELT | BANDE ARRASIVE, RUBAN D'EMERI | SCHLEIFBAND |
| 19 | ABRASIVE BRICK | BRIQUE ABRASIVE | SCHLEIFSTEIN |
| 20 | ABRASIVE DISK | MEULE D'EMERI | SCHLEIFSCHMIRGELSCHEIBE |
| 21 | ABRASIVE GRAIN | GRAIN ABRASIF | SCHLEIFKORN |
| 22 | ABRASIVE MATERIAL | MATIERE A POLIR | POLIERMITTEL, SCHLEIFMITTEL |
| 23 | ABRASIVE PARTICLE SIZE | GROSSEUR DES GRAINS D'ABRASIF | SCHLEIFMATERIALKORNGRÖSSE |
| 24 | ABRASIVE POINTS | POINTES ABRASIVES | SCHLEIFSPITZEN |
| 25 | ABRASIVE SHOT | GRENAILLE | GRANALIE |
| 26 | ABRASIVE WHEELS | DISQUES ABRASIFS, MEULES | SCHLEIFKÖRPER, SCHLEIFSCHMIRGELSCHEIBEN |
| 27 | ABSCISSA | ABSCISSE | ABSZISSE |
| 28 | ABSOLUTE ALCOHOL | ALCOOL ABSOLU, ALCOOL ANHYDRE | ALKOHOL (WASSERFREIER), ALKOHOL (ABSOLUTER) |
| 29 | ABSOLUTE DIMENSIONING | COTATION ABSOLUE | BEZUGSMASSSYSTEM |
| 30 | ABSOLUTE HUMIDITY OF THE AIR, MOISTURE CONTENT OF THE AIR | HUMIDITE ABSOLUE DE L'AIR | FEUCHTIGKEITSGEHALT, FEUCHTIGKEIT ABSOLUTE DER LUFT |
| 31 | ABSOLUTE MEASURING SYSTEM | SYSTEME DE MESURE ABSOLUE | MESSWERTERFASSUNG (ABSOLUTE) |
| 32 | ABSOLUTE MOTION | MOUVEMENT ABSOLU | BEWEGUNG (ABSOLUTE) |
| 33 | ABSOLUTE PRESSURE | PRESSION ABSOLUE | DRUCK (ABSOLUTER) |
| 34 | ABSOLUTE REFERENCE POINT | POINT DE REFERENCE ABSOLU | BEZUGSPUNKT (ABSOLUTER) |
| 35 | ABSOLUTE TEMPERATURE | TEMPERATURE ABSOLUE | TEMPERATUR (ABSOLUTE) |
| 36 | ABSOLUTE ZERO POINT | ZERO ABSOLU | NULLPUNKT (ABSOLUTER) |
| 37 | ABSORB (TO), SUCK UP (TO) | ABSORBER | AUFNEHMEN, AUFSAUGEN, ABSORBIEREN |
| 38 | ABSORBABLE | ABSORBABLE | ABSORBIERBAR |
| 39 | ABSORBENT | ABSORBANT | ABSORPTIONSMITTEL |
| 40 | ABSORBER | ABSORBEUR | ABSORBATOR, ABSORBER |
| 41 | ABSORBING CAPACITY FOR HEAT | CAPACITE CALORIFIQUE | WÄRMEAUFNAHMEFÄHIGKET |
| 42 | ABSORBING POWER | POUVOIR ABSORBANT, PUISSANCE ABSORBANTE | AUFSAUGEFÄHIGKEIT, ABSORPTIONSFÄHIGKEIT, ABSORPTIONSVERMÖGEN, ABSORBIERBARKEIT |

**ABS** 2

| | | |
|---|---|---|
| 43 | **ABSORPTIOMETER** | ABSORPTIOMETRE | ABSORPTIOMETER |
| 44 | **ABSORPTION** | ABSORPTION | AUFSAUGEN, AUFSAUGUNG, ABSORPTION |
| 45 | **ABSORPTION BAND** | BANDE D'ABSORPTION | ABSORPTIONSSTREIFEN |
| 46 | **ABSORPTION COEFFICIENT** | COEFFICIENT D'ABSORPTION APPARENT | ABSORPTIONSKOEFFIZIENT |
| 47 | **ABSORPTION CONSTANT** | CONSTANTE D'ABSORPTION | ABSORPTIONSKONSTANTE |
| 48 | **ABSORPTION DYNAMOMETER** | DYNAMOMETRE D'ABSORPTION | ABSORPTIONSDYNAMOMETER |
| 49 | **ABSORPTION EDGE** | BORD OU FLANC DE LA BANDE D'ABSORPTION | ABSORPTIONSKANTE |
| 50 | **ABSORPTION LIMIT** | LIMITE D'ABSORPTION | ABSORPTIONSGRENZE |
| 51 | **ABSORPTION OF HEAT** | ABSORPTION DE CHALEUR | WÄRMEAUFNAHME |
| 52 | **ABSORPTION OF WATER** | ABSORPTION D'EAU | WASSERAUFNAHME |
| 53 | **ABSORPTION RATIO** | RAPPORT D'ABSORPTION | ABSORPTIONSVERHÄLTNIS |
| 54 | **ABSORPTION SPECTRUM** | SPECTRE D'ABSORPTION | ABSORPTIONSSPEKTRUM |
| 55 | **ABSORPTION, BRAKE DYNAMOMETER** | DYNAMOMETRE D'ABSORPTION, DYNAMOMETRE-FREIN | BREMSDYNAMOMETER, ABSORPTIONSDYNAMOMETER |
| 56 | **ABSORPTIVITY** | ABSORPTIVITE | ABSORPTIONSVERMÖGEN |
| 57 | **ABUTMENT** | SUPPORT, APPUI CALE, BUTEE, CULEE | WIDERLAGER |
| 58 | **ABYSSINIAN GOLD** | BRONZE D'ALUMINIUM | GOLD (ABESSINISCHES) |
| 59 | **AC/DC WELDING MACHINE** | POSTE DE SOUDAGE A COURANTS ALTERNATIF ET CONTINU | ALLSTROMSCHWEISSMASCHINE |
| 60 | **ACCELERATED MOTION** | MOUVEMENT ACCELERE | BEWEGUNG (BESCHLEUNIGTE) |
| 61 | **ACCELERATING PUMP** | POMPE DE REPRISE | MEMBRANPUMPE |
| 62 | **ACCELERATION** | ACCELERATION | BESCHLEUNIGUNG |
| 63 | **ACCELERATION OF A FALLING BODY** | ACCELERATION DE VITESSE D'UN CORPS TOMBANT | FALLBESCHLEUNIGUNG |
| 64 | **ACCELERATION OF GRAVITY** | ACCELERATION DE LA PESANTEUR | SCHWEREBESCHLEUNIGUNG |
| 65 | **ACCELERATION OF GRAVITY, GRAVITY ACCELERATION** | ACCELERATION DE LA PESANTEUR | SCHWEREBESCHLEUNIGUNG |
| 66 | **ACCELERATOR** | ACCELERATEUR | BESCHLEUNIGER |
| 67 | **ACCEPTANCE** | RECEPTION | ABNAHME |
| 68 | **ACCEPTANCE (OF MACHINES)** | RECEPTION (DE MACHINES) | ABNAHME (VON MASCHINEN) |
| 69 | **ACCEPTANCE BOUNDARY** | LIMITE D'ACCEPTATION | ABNAHMEGRENZE |
| 70 | **ACCEPTANCE CERTIFICATE** | CERTIFICAT DE RECEPTION | ABNAHMEBESCHEINIGUNG |
| 71 | **ACCEPTANCE TEST** | ESSAI DE RECEPTION | ABNAHMEPRÜFUNG, ABNAHMEVERSUCH |
| 72 | **ACCESSIBILITY** | ACCESSIBILITE | ZUGÄNGLICHKEIT |
| 73 | **ACCESSIBLE** | ACCESSIBLE | ZUGÄNGLICH |
| 74 | **ACCESSORIES** | ACCESSOIRES | ZUBEHÖR, ZUBEHÖRTEILE |
| 75 | **ACCIDENT** | ACCIDENT DU TRAVAIL | UNFALL, BETRIEBSUNFALL |
| 76 | **ACCUMULATOR** | ACCUMULATEUR | SAMMLER, SPEICHER, AKKUMULATOR |
| 77 | **ACCUMULATOR BATTERY** | BATTERIE D'ACCUMULATEURS | SAMMLERBATTERIE, AKKUMULATORENBATTERIE |
| 78 | **ACCUMULATOR CELL, SECONDARY CELL** | ELEMENT D'ACCUMULATEUR | AKKUMULATORZELLE |
| 79 | **ACCUMULATOR LOCOMOTIVE** | LOCOMOTIVE ELECTRIQUE A ACCUMULATEURS | SAMMLERLOKOMOTIVE, AKKUMULATORENLOKOMOTIVE |
| 80 | **ACCUMULATOR METAL** | METAL D'ACCUMULATEUR | AKKUMULATORENMETALL |
| 81 | **ACCUMULATOR PLATE** | PLAQUE D ACCUMULATEUR, LAME D ACCUMULATEUR | AKKUMULATORPLATTE |
| 82 | **ACCURACY** | PRECISION | GENAUIGKEIT |

**3**         **ACI**

| | English | French | German |
|---|---|---|---|
| 83 | ACCURACY OF WORK | PRECISION D'USINAGE | GENAUIGKEIT DER AUSFÜHRUNG |
| 84 | ACETALDEHYDE | ALDEHYDE ACETIQUE, ALDEHYDE ETHYLIQUE, ETHYLAL, HYDRURE D ACETYLE, OXYDE D ETHYLIDENE, HYDRATE DE VINYLE, ACIDE ALDEHYDIQUE | ALDEHYD, AZETALDEHYD, ÄTHYLALDEHYD |
| 85 | ACETATE | ACETATE | ESSIGSAURES SALZ, AZETAT |
| 86 | ACETIC ACID | ACIDE ACETIQUE, VINAIGRE RADICAL | ESSIGSÄURE |
| 87 | ACETIC ANHYDRIDE | ANHYDRIDE ACETIQUE | ESSIGSÄUREANHYDRID |
| 88 | ACETIC ETHER, ETHYL ACETATE | ETHER ACETIQUE, ACETATE D'ETHYLE | ESSIGSÄUREÄTHER, ESSIGSÄUREÄTHYLESTER, ÄTHYLAZETAT |
| 89 | ACETIMETER, ACETOMETER, ACIDIMETER | ACIDIMETRE, PESE-ACIDES | SÄUREMESSER |
| 90 | ACETONE, DIMETHYL KETONE | ACETONE, DIMETHYLCETONE | AZETON, ESSIGGEIST, BRENZESSIGGEIST, DIMETHYLKETON |
| 91 | ACETYL CELLULOSE, CELLULOSE ACETATE | ACETATE, ACETYLE DE CELLULOSE | AZETYLZELLULOSE, ZELLULOSEAZETAT |
| 92 | ACETYL CHLORIDE | CHLORURE D'ACETYLE | AZETYLCHLORID |
| 93 | ACETYLENE | ACETYLENE | AZETYLEN |
| 94 | ACETYLENE CUTTING | COUPAGE A L'ACETYLENE | AZETYLENSCHNEIDVERFAHREN |
| 95 | ACETYLENE LAMP | LAMPE A ACETYLENE | AZETYLENLAMPE |
| 96 | ACETYLENE WELDING | SOUDAGE A L'ACETYLENE | AZETYLENGASSCHWEISSUNG |
| 97 | ACHESON FURNACE | FOURNEAU D'ACHESON | ACHESON-OFEN |
| 98 | ACHROMATIC | ACHROMATIQUE | ACHROMATISCH |
| 99 | ACHROMATISATION | ACHROMATISATION | ACHROMATISIEREN |
| 100 | ACHROMATISE (TO) | ACHROMATISER | ACHROMATISIEREN |
| 101 | ACHROMATISM | ACHROMATISME | ACHROMASIE, ACHROMATISMUS |
| 102 | ACICULAR | ACICULAIRE | NADEL- (KRISTALL-)FÖRMIG, NADELIG, MIT NADELSTRUKTUR |
| 103 | ACICULAR MARTENSITE | MARTENSITE ACICULAIRE | MARTENSIT (NADELFÖRMIGER) |
| 104 | ACID | ACIDE | SÄURE |
| 105 | ACID BESSEMER PIG | FONTE BRUTE BESSEMER | BESSEMER-ROHEISEN |
| 106 | ACID BESSEMER PROCESS | PROCEDE BESSEMER AU CONVERTISSEUR A GARNISSAGE ACIDE | BESSEMER-VERFAHREN |
| 107 | ACID BESSEMER STEEL | ACIER BESSEMER | BESSEMER-STAHL |
| 108 | ACID BOTTOM | SOLE ACIDE | SOHLE (SAURE) |
| 109 | ACID BRITTLENESS | FRAGILITE DE DECAPAGE | BEIZSPRÖDIGKEIT |
| 110 | ACID CORE SOLDER | ETAIN A SOUDER A FONDANT ACIDE | LOT (SAURES) |
| 111 | ACID DIP | BAIN DE DECAPAGE | DEKAPIERBAD |
| 112 | ACID DIPPING | DECAPAGE AU BAIN ACIDULE | BEIZBEHANDLUNG (SAURE) |
| 113 | ACID ELECTRIC STEEL | ACIER ELECTRIQUE ACIDE | ELEKTROSTAHL (SAURER) |
| 114 | ACID FLUX | FONDANT ACIDE | FLUSSMITTEL (SAURES) |
| 115 | ACID FORMING ELEMENT | ELEMENT ACIDIFICATEUR | SÄUREBILDNER |
| 116 | ACID OPEN HEARTH STEEL | ACIER MARTIN PAR LE PROCEDE ACIDE | SIEMENS MARTINSTAHL (SAURER) |
| 117 | ACID PIG | FONTE BESSEMER | BESSEMER-ROHEISEN |
| 118 | ACID POTASSIUM OXALATE | OXALATE ACIDE DE POTASSIUM | KALI (SAURES), KALI (OXALSAURES), KALIUMBIOXALAT |
| 119 | ACID POTASSIUM TARTRATE, CREAM OF TARTAR | TARTRE, BITARTRATE DE POTASSIUM, PIERRE DE VIN, CRISTAUX, CREME DE TARTRE | WEINSTEIN (SAURER), WEINSAURES KALI, KALIUMBITARTRAT |
| 120 | ACID PROCESS | PROCEDE ACIDE | VERFAHREN (SAURES) |

# ACI

**4**

| | | | |
|---|---|---|---|
| 121 | ACID PUMP, GLASS BARREL PUMP | POMPE A ACIDE | SÄUREPUMPE |
| 122 | ACID REACTION | REACTION ACIDE | REAKTION (SAURE) |
| 123 | ACID REFRACTORIES | GARNISSAGE REFRACTAIRE ACIDE | OFENFUTTER (SAURES) |
| 124 | ACID RESISTANT | ANTI-ACIDE RESISTANT AUX ACIDES | SÄUREFEST, SÄUREBESTÄNDIG |
| 125 | ACID RESISTING ALLOYS | ALLIAGES RESISTANT AUX ACIDES | SÄUREFESTE LEGIERUNGEN |
| 126 | ACID SODIUM CARBONATE, SODIUM BICARBONATE | CARBONATE ACIDE DE SODIUM, BICARBONATE DE SOUDE | NATRON (DOPPELTKOHLENSAURES), NATRIUMBIKARBONAT |
| 127 | ACID VAPOURS | VAPEURS ACIDES | SÄUREDÄMPFE |
| 128 | ACID-PROOF | INATTAQUABLE AUX ACIDES | SÄUREBESTÄNDIG, SÄUREFEST |
| 129 | ACIDIC | ACIDE | ACIDISCH |
| 130 | ACIDIFIANT, ACIDIFIC | ACIDIFIANT | SÄUREBILDEND |
| 131 | ACIDIMETRY | ACIDIMETRIE | SÄUREGEHALTSBESTIMMUNG, AZIDIMETRIE |
| 132 | ACIDS | ACIDES | SÄUREN |
| 133 | ACIDULATE (TO) | ACIDULER | ANSÄUERN |
| 134 | ACIDULATED WATER | EAU ACIDULEE | WASSER (ANGESÄUERTES) |
| 135 | ACIERAGE | ACIERAGE | VERSTAHLEN, STAHLUNG |
| 136 | ACOUSTIC | ACOUSTIQUE | AKUSTISCH |
| 137 | ACOUSTICS | ACOUSTIQUE | SCHALLEHRE, AKUSTIK |
| 138 | ACROSS THE GRAIN FIBRES | A CONTREFIL | SENKRECHT ZUR FASER, QUER ZUR FASERRICHTUNG |
| 139 | ACTINIC | ACTINIQUE | AKTINISCH |
| 140 | ACTINIC RAYS | RAYONS ACTINIQUES | STRAHLEN (ARTINISCHE) |
| 141 | ACTINIUM | ACTINIUM | AKTINIUM |
| 142 | ACTINOMETER | ACTINOMETRE | AKTINOMETER, STRAHLENMESSER |
| 143 | ACTION OF A FORCE | ACTION D'UNE FORCE | KRAFTWIRKUNG, EIN WIRKUNG (EINER KRAFT) |
| 144 | ACTIVATION | ACTIVATION | STEIGERUNG DER REAKTIONSFÄHIGKEIT, AKTIVIERUNG |
| 145 | ACTIVATION - ACIERATION | ADDITION DE CARBONE | STAHLBILDUNG, VERWANDLUNG IN STAHL, KOHLENSTOFFZUGABE |
| 146 | ACTIVATION AGENT | ACTIVATEUR | AKTIVATOR |
| 147 | ACTIVATION ENERGY | ENERGIE D'ACTIVATION | AKTIVIERUNGSENERGIE |
| 148 | ACTIVATOR | SUBSTANCE ACTIVATRICE | AKTIVIERUNGSMITTEL, AKTIVATOR, BESCHLEUNIGER |
| 149 | ACTIVE DEPOSIT | DEPOT ACTIF | NIEDERSCHLAG (RADIOAKTIVER) |
| 150 | ACTIVE HYDROGEN | HYDROGENE ATOMIQUE | WASSERSTOFF (ATOMARER) |
| 151 | ACTUAL EFFECTIVE BRAKE HORSE POWER (B.H.P.) | CHEVAL EFFECTIF, PUISSANCE EFFECTIVE EN CHEVAUX, PUISSANCE AU FREIN EN CHEVAUX | PFERDESTÄRKE (NUTZBARE), PFERDESTÄRKE (GEBREMSTE), BREMSPFERDESTÄRKE (EFFEKTIVE), PSE |
| 152 | ACTUAL SIZE | DIMENSION REELLE | GRÖSSE (WIRKLICHE) |
| 153 | ACTUAL, REAL VALUE | VALEUR REELLE | ISTWERT |
| 154 | ACUTANGULAR, ACUTEANGLED | ACUTANGLE | SPITZWINKLIG |
| 155 | ACUTE ANGLE | ANGLE AIGU, ANGLE POINTU, ANGLE VIF | WINKEL (SPITZER) |
| 156 | ACUTE BISECTRIX | BISECTRICE AIGUE | BISEKTRIX (SPITZE) |
| 157 | ACUTE-ANGLED TRIANGLE | TRIANGLE ACUTANGLE | DREIECK (SPITZWINKLIGES) |
| 158 | ADAMANTINE LUSTRE | ECLAT ADAMANTIN | DIAMANTGLANZ |
| 159 | ADAPT PROGRAMMING LANGUAGE | LANGAGE DE PROGRAMMATION ADAPT | ADAPT-PROGRAMMIERSPRACHE |
| 160 | ADAPTER | ADAPTEUR | ADAPTOR, PASSSTÜCK |
| 161 | ADAPTIVE CONTROL | COMMANDE ADAPTIVE | STEUERUNG (ADAPTIVE) |

| | | | |
|---|---|---|---|
| 162 | ADD (TO), SUM (TO), ADMIX (TO) | ADDITIONNER (MATH.), AJOUTER | ZUSAMMENZÄHLEN, ADDIEREN, SUMMIEREN, BEIMISCHEN, BEIMENGEN |
| 163 | ADD WATER (TO) | ADDITIONNER DE L'EAU | VERSETZEN (MIT WASSER), ZUSETZEN (WASSER) |
| 164 | ADDENDUM | HAUTEUR DE FACE, HAUTEUR DE LA TETE D'UNE DENT, SAILLIE SUR LE PRIMITIF | ZAHNKOPFLÄNGE |
| 165 | ADDENDUM ANGLE | ANGLE DE SAILLIE | KOPFWINKEL |
| 166 | ADDENDUM CIRCLE | CERCLE DE TETE, CERCLE EXTERIEUR, CIRCONFERENCE D'ECHANFREINEMENT | KOPFKREIS, KRONENKREIS |
| 167 | ADDENDUM FLANK | CERCLE DE TETE, FLANC DE SAILLIE | KOPFKREIS, KOPFFLANKE |
| 168 | ADDITION AGENT | ELEMENT D'ADDITION, ADDITIF | ZUSATZELEMENT, BADZUSATZ |
| 169 | ADDITION, SUMMATION | ADJUVANT, ADDITION | ZUSATZ, ZUSAMMENZÄHLEN, HINZUFÜGEN, ADDITION, SUMMATION |
| 170 | ADDITIONAL LOSS | PERTE ADDITIONNELLE | VERLUST (ZUSÄTZLICHER), ZUSATZVERLUST |
| 171 | ADDRESS | ADRESSE | ADRESSE |
| 172 | ADHERENCE TEST | CONTROLE D'ADHERENCE | HAFTFÄHIGKEITSVERSUCH |
| 173 | ADHESION | ADHERENCE | HAFTFESTIGKEIT |
| 174 | ADHESION, ADHESIVE POWER | ADHESION, ADHERENCE | ADHÄSIONSKRAFT |
| 175 | ADHESIVE | ADHESIF, ADHERENT | HAFTEND, HAFT- |
| 176 | ADHESIVE PROPERTY | POUVOIR ADHESIF | HAFTVERMÖGEN |
| 177 | ADHESIVE SUBSTANCE | SUBSTANCE ADHESIVE | KLEBEMITTEL, KLEBSTOFF |
| 178 | ADIABATIC | ADIABATIQUE | ADIABATISCH |
| 179 | ADIABATIC CURVE | LIGNE, COURBE ADIABATIQUE, ADIABATIQUE | ADIABATE |
| 180 | ADJACENT ANGLE | ANGLE ADJACENT | NEBENWINKEL |
| 181 | ADJACENT, CONTIGUOUS | ADJACENT, CONTIGU | ANLIEGEND, ANGRENZEND, ANSTOSSEND |
| 182 | ADJUST (TO), REGULATE (TO) | REGLER | EINSTELLEN, REGELN, REGULIEREN, ADJUSTIEREN |
| 183 | ADJUSTABLE | REGLABLE, AJUSTABLE | VERSTELLBAR, NACHSTELLBAR |
| 184 | ADJUSTABLE HAND REAMER | ALESOIR A MAIN REGLABLE | HANDREIBAHLE (EINSTELLBARE) |
| 185 | ADJUSTABLE KEY | COIN, CLAVETTE DE SERRAGE, COIN POUR LE RATTRAPAGE DU JEU, COIN D'EPAISSEUR, CALE DE RATTRAPAGE | STELLKEIL, SPANNKEIL, NACHSTELLKEIL |
| 186 | ADJUSTABLE SNAP-GAUGE LIMIT TIPE | JAUGE-MACHOIRE REGLABLE | GRENZ-RACHENLEHRE (EINSTELLBARE) |
| 187 | ADJUSTABLE STOP | BUTEE REGLABLE | VOLLAST-EINSTELLSCHRAUBE |
| 188 | ADJUSTABLE, EXPANDING REAMER | ALESOIR EXTENSIBLE, A LAMES MOBILES | REIBAHLE (VERSTELLBARE), EXPANSIONSREIBAHLE |
| 189 | ADJUSTANCE DIES | FILIERES | DRAHTZIEHSTEIN |
| 190 | ADJUSTEMENT BY SCREW | REGLAGE PAR VIS | VERSTELLUNG DURCH SCHRAUBE |
| 191 | ADJUSTING NUT | ECROU DE REGLAGE | STELLMUTTER, NACHSTELLMUTTER |
| 192 | ADJUSTING SCREW | VIS DE REGLAGE | STELLSCHRAUBE, EINSTELLSCHRAUBE, ADJUSTIERSCHRAUBE |
| 193 | ADJUSTING SCREW | VIS DE PRESSION | DRUCKSCHRAUBE |
| 194 | ADJUSTING SLEEVE | DOUILLE DE REGLAGE | EINSTELLHÜLSE |
| 195 | ADJUSTMENT, REGULATION | REGLAGE | EINSTELLEN, EINSTELLUNG, REGELUNG, REGULIERUNG, ADJUSTIEREN |
| 196 | ADJUTAGE, AJUTAGE, DISCHARGING TUBE, MOUTHPIECE | AJUTAGE D'ECOULEMENT, EMBOUCHURE, GICLEUR | ANSATZROHR, AUSFLUSSSTUTZEN, MUNDSTÜCK, AUSFLUSSDÜSE |
| 197 | ADMIRALTY GUN METAL | BRONZE DE CANONS | GESCHÜTZBRONZE |

## ADM

| | | | |
|---|---|---|---|
| 198 | ADMIRALTY METAL | LAITON DE MARINE | ADMIRALITÄTSMETALL |
| 199 | ADMISSION LINE | LIGNE D'ADMISSION DE LA VAPEUR | DAMPFEINSTRÖMLINIE, EINSTRÖMLINIE, VOLLDRUCKLINIE |
| 200 | ADMISSION PORT, STEAM PORT | LUMIERE D'ADMISSION | EINLASSSCHLITZ |
| 201 | ADMISSION VALVE, (STREAM) INLET VALVE | SOUPAPE D'ADMISSION | EINLASSVENTIL |
| 202 | ADSORB (TO) | ADSORBER | ADSORBIEREN |
| 203 | ADSORPTION | ADSORPTION | ADSORPTION |
| 204 | ADULTERATE (TO) | ADULTERER, FALSIFIER | VERFÄLSCHEN |
| 205 | ADULTERATION | ADULTERATION, FALSIFICATION, SOPHISTICATION, FRAUDE | FÄLSCHUNG, VERFÄLSCHUNG |
| 206 | ADVANCE | AVANCE | FRÜHEINSTELLUNG |
| 207 | ADZE | HERMINETTE | DÄCHSEL, DECHSEL, TEXEL, KRUMMAXT |
| 208 | AERATE (TO) | AERER UN SABLE | AUFLOCKERN (DEN SAND) |
| 209 | AERATION CELL | DIVISEUR-AERATEUR | BELÜFTUNGSELEMENT, SANDSCHLEUDER |
| 210 | AERATION OF WATER | AERATION DE L'EAU | BELÜFTUNG DES WASSERS |
| 211 | AERATOR | AERATEUR | ENTLÜFTER |
| 212 | AERIAL LINE, CONDUCTOR, OVERHEAD LINE | LIGNE AERIENNE | OBERIRDISCHE LEITUNG, FREILEITUNG, LUFTLEITUNG |
| 213 | AERIAL ROPEWAY, AERIAL CABLEWAY | TRANSPORTEUR AERIEN, TRANSPORTEUR PAR CABLE | LUFTSEILBAHN, DRAHTSEILBAHN |
| 214 | AERODYNAMIC | AERODYNAMIQUE | AERODYNAMISCH |
| 215 | AERODYNAMICS | AERODYNAMIQUE | LUFTBEWEGUNGSLEHRE, AERODYNAMIK |
| 216 | AEROSE | BRONZE (DE) | BRONZEN |
| 217 | AEROSTATICAL | AEROSTATIQUE | AEROSTATISCH |
| 218 | AEROSTATICS | AEROSTATIQUE | LUFTDRUCKLEHRE, AEROSTATIK |
| 219 | AERUGINOUS | ERUGINEUX | GRÜNSPAN, GRÜNSPANÄHNLICH |
| 220 | AERUGO, VERDIGRIS | VERT-DE-GRIS | EDELROST, GRÜNSPAN, PATINA |
| 221 | AFTER-FLOW | REVENU-FLUAGE POSTERIEUR | NACHGLÜHEN, NACHFLIESSEN |
| 222 | AGATE | AGATE | ACHAT |
| 223 | AGE HARDENING | DURCISSEMENT PAR VIEILLISSEMENT | AUSHÄRTUNG, VERGÜTUNG BEI NORMALER TEMPERATUR |
| 224 | AGE-HARDENING | DURCISSEMENT STRUCTURAL | KALT-ODER WARM-AUSHÄRTUNG |
| 225 | AGEING, AGING | VIEILLISSEMENT | ALTERUNG |
| 226 | AGEING, ARTIFICIAL | VIEILLISSEMENT ARTIFICIEL | ALTERUNG (KÜNSTLICHE) |
| 227 | AGGREGATE | AGREGAT | AGGREGAT, GEHÄUSE |
| 228 | AGGREGATE | MATIERE DE MELANGE | ZUSCHLAGSTOFF, FÜLLSTOFF (BAUW.) |
| 229 | AGGREGATION | AGREGATION | ZUSAMMENSETZUNG |
| 230 | AGING RANGE | TEMPERATURES DE VIEILLISSEMENT | ALTERUNGSBEREICH |
| 231 | AGING, CRITICAL | VIEILLISSEMENT COMPLET | ALTERUNG (VOLLSTÄNDIGE) |
| 232 | AGING, INTERRUPTED | VIEILLISSEMENT ECHELONNE | ALTERUNG (STUFENWEISE) |
| 233 | AGING, NATURAL | VIEILLISSEMENT NATUREL | ALTERUNG (NATÜRLICHE) |
| 234 | AGING, PROGRESSIVE | VIEILLISSEMENT PROGRESSIF | ALTERUNG (PROGRESSIVE) |
| 235 | AGING, STRAIN | VIEILLISSEMENT PAR TRAVAIL A FROID | ALTERUNG DURCH KALTBEARBEITUNG |
| 236 | AGITATOR | AGITATEUR | RÜHRWERK, RÜHRAPPARAT, RÜHRER |
| 237 | AGITATOR RECESS | NICHE D'AGITATEUR | RÜHRWERKNISCHE |
| 238 | AGITATOR, STIRRER | AGITATEUR MECANIQUE | RÜHRWERK |
| 239 | AILANTHUS | VERNIS DU JAPON | GÖTTERBAUM, AILANTHUSBAUM |
| 240 | AIR | AIR ATMOSPHERIQUE | LUFT (ATMOSPHÄRISCHE) |

| | | | |
|---|---|---|---|
| 241 | **AIR BELT** | CHAMBRE DE VENT | WINDKAMMER |
| 242 | **AIR BLAST** | JET D'AIR, SOUFFLERIE | LUFTSTRAHL, GEBLÄSE, LUFTSTOSS |
| 243 | **AIR BLAST, WIND** | AIR DE LA SOUFFLERIE | LUFT, GEBLÄSEWIND, WIND |
| 244 | **AIR BLASTING** | NETTOYAGE PAR JETS D'AIR | ABBLASEN MIT PRESSLUFT |
| 245 | **AIR BRICK** | BRIQUE CREUSE | LOCHSTEIN, LOCHZIEGEL, HOHLZIEGEL |
| 246 | **AIR CHAMBER** | ANTIBELIER | LUFTKAMMER |
| 247 | **AIR CHANNELS** | CANAUX DE VENT | WETTERLUTTE, WETTERFANG, LUTTE, WETTERLEITUNG, WINDKANÄLE |
| 248 | **AIR CLASSIFICATION** | TRIAGE PAR COURANT GAZEUX | WINDSICHTUNG |
| 249 | **AIR COMPRESSOR** | COMPRESSEUR D'AIR, POMPE D'AIR | LUFTVERDICHTER, LUFTKOMPRESSOR |
| 250 | **AIR CONDITIONER** | CLIMATISEUR | KLIMAANLAGE |
| 251 | **AIR COOLED ENGINE** | MOTEUR REFROIDI PAR AIR | MOTOR (LUFTGEKÜHLTER) |
| 252 | **AIR COOLING** | REFROIDISSEMENT A L'AIR | LUFTKÜHLUNG |
| 253 | **AIR CURRENT** | COURANT D'AIR | LUFTSTROM |
| 254 | **AIR CUSHION** | MATELAS, COUCHE, COUSSIN D'AIR | LUFTKISSEN, LUFTPOLSTER |
| 255 | **AIR DAMPING** | AMORTISSEMENT PNEUMATIQUE | LUFTDÄMPFUNG |
| 256 | **AIR DASHPOT** | DASHPOT A AIR, AMORTISSEUR PNEUMATIQUE, COUSSIN PNEUMATIQUE | LUFTPUFFER |
| 257 | **AIR DRAUGHT** | TIRAGE D'AIR | ZUG, LUFTZUG |
| 258 | **AIR DRILL** | MARTEAU-PIQUEUR | BOHRHAMMER |
| 259 | **AIR ESCAPE VALVE** | SOUPAPE A AIR | LUFTVENTIL, ENTLÜFTUNGSVENTIL |
| 260 | **AIR FILTER** | FILTRE A AIR | LUFTFILTER |
| 261 | **AIR FURNAGE** | FOUR REVERBERE | FLAMMOFEN |
| 262 | **AIR GAP** | INTERSTICE, ENTREFER | LUFTZWISCHENRAUM, LUFTSPALT, EISENSPALT, LUFTSTRECKE, LUFTABSTAND |
| 263 | **AIR GAP OF A MAGNET** | ENTREFER D'UN AIMANT | LUFTSPALT EINES MAGNETEN |
| 264 | **AIR GAS** | GAZ A L'AIR | LUFTGAS |
| 265 | **AIR GAS THERMOMETER** | THERMOMETRE A GAZ | LUFTTHERMOMETER, GASTHERMOMETER |
| 266 | **AIR GATE** | TRAINEE D'AIR | ENTLÜFTUNGSNUT, ENTLÜFTUNGSRILLE |
| 267 | **AIR HARDENING** | TREMPE A L'AIR | LUFTHÄRTUNG |
| 268 | **AIR HEATER, AIR HEATING** | CHAUFFAGE DE L'AIR, CHAUFFAGE A AIR CHAUD | LUFTHEIZUNG |
| 269 | **AIR HOLE** | EVENT | LUFTLOCH, STEIGER |
| 270 | **AIR INTAKE** | PRISE D'AIR | LUFTEINLASS |
| 271 | **AIR KNOCK-OUT** | EJECTEUR PNEUMATIQUE | AUSWERFER (PNEUMATISCHER) |
| 272 | **AIR LANCE** | SOUFFLETTE | ABBLASHAHN, ZERSTÄUBER |
| 273 | **AIR LIFT PUMP** | EMULSEUR | LUFTDRUCKPUMPE, DRUCKLUFTPUMPE |
| 274 | **AIR LOCK** | SAS A AIR | LUFTSCHLEUSE |
| 275 | **AIR NOZZLE** | BEC DE SOUFFLAGE | PRESSLUFTDÜSE |
| 276 | **AIR NOZZLE, AIR GUN** | SOUFFLETTE A AIR | LUFTPISTOLE, LUFTVENTIL |
| 277 | **AIR OF COMBUSTION** | AIR COMBURANT, COMBURANT | VERBRENNUNGSLUFT |
| 278 | **AIR OPENING IN THE GRATE BARS, AIR SPACE BETWEEN GRATE BARS** | INTERVALLE LIBRE, VIDE ENTRE LES BARREAUX DE LA GRILLE | ROSTSPALT, ROSTFUGE |
| 279 | **AIR OPERATED CHUCK** | MANDRIN PNEUMATIQUE | DRUCKLUFTFUTTER |
| 280 | **AIR PATENTING** | PATENTAGE A L'AIR | LUFTPATENTIEREN |
| 281 | **AIR PIPE LINE** | CONDUITE, CANALISATION, DISTRIBUTION D'AIR | LUFTLEITUNG |
| 282 | **AIR PISTON, PNEUMATIC PISTON** | PISTON A AIR | LUFTKOLBEN |

# AIR

| | | | |
|---|---|---|---|
| 283 | AIR PRESSURE GAUGE | JAUGE PNEUMATIQUE | MESSER (PNEUMATISCHER) |
| 284 | AIR PUMP, VACUUM PUMP | POMPE A AIR, POMPE A VIDE, POMPE PNEUMATIQUE | LUFTPUMPE, VAKUUMPUMPE |
| 285 | AIR QUENCHING | TREMPE A L'AIR | LUFTHÄRTUNG |
| 286 | AIR RAMMER | FOULOIR PNEUMATIQUE | PRESSLUFTSTAMPFER |
| 287 | AIR REHEATER | RECHAUFFEUR D'AIR | LUFTERHITZER |
| 288 | AIR SCALE | ECAILLE | SCHUPPE |
| 289 | AIR SCOOP | PRISE D'AIR | LUFTEINLASS |
| 290 | AIR SEPARATION | SEPARATION PNEUMATIQUE | WINDSICHTUNG |
| 291 | AIR SHAFT | PUITS D'AERATION | LUFTSCHACHT |
| 292 | AIR STRANGLER OU AIR CHOKE | VOLET D'AIR | STARTERKLAPPE |
| 293 | AIR TAP, COCK | ROBINET D'AIR | LUFTHAHN |
| 294 | AIR VESSEL, AIR CHAMBER | RESERVOIR A AIR | WINDKESSEL |
| 295 | AIR-ACETYLENE WELDING | SOUDAGE AERO-ACETYLENIQUE | AZETYLEN-LUFTSCHWEISSEN |
| 296 | AIR-COOLED SURFACE CONDENSER | CONDENSEUR PAR SURFACE AU MOYEN DE L'AIR | OBERFLÄCHENKONDENSATOR MIT LUFTKÜHLUNG |
| 297 | AIR-DRY WOOD, SEASONED TIMBER | BOIS SECHE A L'AIR LIBRE | HOLZ (LUFTTROCKENES), HOLZ (GELAGERTES) |
| 298 | AIR-HARDENNING, SELF HARDENING STEEL | ACIER AUTO-TREMPANT | SELBSTHÄRTERSTAHL |
| 299 | AIR-INJECTION MACHINE | MACHINE A INJECTION PNEUMATIQUE | LUFTEINSPRITZUNGMASCHINE |
| 300 | AIR-REFINING PROCESS | AFFINAGE AU VENT | WINDFRISCHEN |
| 301 | AIR-SETTING BINDER | LIANT DURCISSANT A L'AIR | BINDEMITTEL (LUFTHÄRTENDES) |
| 302 | AIR-SETTING CEMENT | CIMENT DURCISSANT A L'AIR | ZEMENT (LUFTHÄRTENDER) |
| 303 | AIR-TIGHT | ETANCHE A L'AIR, HERMETIQUE | LUFTDICHT |
| 304 | ALABASTER | ALBATRE | ALABASTER |
| 305 | ALARM | APPAREIL D'ALARME | MELDEVORRICHTUNG, ALARMVORRICHTUNG |
| 306 | ALARM SIGNAL | SIGNAL D'ALARME | WARNZEICHEN, ALARMZEICHEN, ALARMSIGNAL |
| 307 | ALARM WHISTLE | SIFFLET D'ALARME, SIFFLET AVERTISSEUR | WARNPFEIFE, ALARMPFEIFE, SIGNALPFEIFE |
| 308 | ALBEDO | ALBEDO | ALBEDO |
| 309 | ALBERT LAY WIRE ROPE | CABLE A CABLAGE ALBERT | DRAHTSEIL IM GLEICHSCHLAG |
| 310 | ALBUMIN | ALBUMINE | EIWEISS, ALBUMIN |
| 311 | ALBUMINISED PAPER | PAPIER ALBUMINE | EIWEISSPAPIER, ALBUMINPAPIER |
| 312 | ALCOHOL ENGINE | MOTEUR A ALCOOL | SPIRITUSMOTOR |
| 313 | ALCOHOL, SPIRIT, SPIRITS OF WINE, ETHYL ALCOHOL | ALCOOL ORDINAIRE, ALCOOL VINIQUE, ALCOOL ETHYLIQUE, HYDRATE D'ETHYLE | WEINGEIST, SPIRITUS, ALKOHOL, ÄTHYLALKOHOL |
| 314 | ALCOHOLIC | ALCOOLIQUE | ALKOHOLISCH |
| 315 | ALCOHOLIC SOLUTION | SOLUTION ALCOOLIQUE | LÖSUNG (ALKOHOLISCHE) |
| 316 | ALCOHOLOMETER | ALCOOMETRE, PESE-ALCOOLS | ALKOHOLMETER |
| 317 | ALDEHYDE | ALDEHYDE | ALDEHYD |
| 318 | ALDER | AUNE, AULNE | ERLE |
| 319 | ALFAMETER | ALFAMETRE | ALFAMETER |
| 320 | ALGEBRA | ALGEBRE | ALGEBRA |
| 321 | ALGEBRAIC | ALGEBRIQUE | ALGEBRAISCH |
| 322 | ALGEBRAIC EQUATION | EQUATION ALGEBRIQUE | GLEICHUNG (ALGEBRAISCHE) |
| 323 | ALIGN (TO) | ALIGNER | AUSRICHTEN |
| 324 | ALIGNMENT | ALIGNEMENT, LIGNE DE FUITE | AUSRICHTEN, INRICHTUNGBRINGEN, FLUCHTLINIE |

| | | | |
|---|---|---|---|
| 325 | **ALINEMENT** | ALIGNEMENT | ABFLUCHTUNG |
| 326 | **ALIPHATIC COMPOUND** | COMBINAISON ALIPHATIQUE | VERBINDUNG (ALIPHATISHE) |
| 327 | **ALIZARIN** | ALIZARINE | ALIZARIN |
| 328 | **ALKALI** | ALCALI | ALKALI |
| 329 | **ALKALI-METALS** | METAUX ALCALINS | ALKALIMETALLE |
| 330 | **ALKALIFY (TO), ALKALISE (TO)** | ALCALINISER, RENDRE ALCALIN | ALKALISCH MACHEN, ALKALISIEREN |
| 331 | **ALKALIMETER** | ALCALIMETRE | ALKALIMETER |
| 332 | **ALKALIMETRIC** | ALCALIMETRIQUE | ALKALIMETRISCH |
| 333 | **ALKALIMETRY** | ALCALIMETRIE | ALKALIMETRIE |
| 334 | **ALKALINE CLEANING** | NETTOYAGE ALCALIN | REINIGUNG (ALKALISCHE) |
| 335 | **ALKALINE EARTH METALS** | METAUX ALCALIN-TERREUX | ERDALKALIMETALLE |
| 336 | **ALKALINE EARTHS, ALKALINE EARTH METALS** | TERRES ALCALINES | ERDEN (ALKALISCHE), ERDALKALIEN |
| 337 | **ALKALINE REACTION** | REACTION ALCALINE | REAKTION (ALKALISCHE), REAKTION (BASISCHE) |
| 338 | **ALKALINE SALT** | SEL ALCALIN | ALKALISALZ, SALZ (ALKALISCHES) |
| 339 | **ALKALINE SOLUTION** | SOLUTION ALCALINE | ALKALILAUGE |
| 340 | **ALKALINTY** | ALCALINITE | ALKALINITÄT, ALKALISCHE BESCHAFFENHEIT, BASIZITÄT |
| 341 | **ALKALOID** | ALCALOIDE | ALKALOID |
| 342 | **ALKANNIN PAPER** | PAPIER D'ORCANETINE, PAPIER D'ANCHUSINE | ALKANNAROTPAPIER |
| 343 | **ALL-ALUMINIUM CONDUCTOR** | CABLE CONDUCTEUR TOUT-ALUMINIUM | GANZ-ALUMINIUMLEITER |
| 344 | **ALL-FLOTATION** | FLOTTATION | SCHWIMMVERFAHREN |
| 345 | **ALL-IRON** | TOUT EN METAUX FERREUX | GANZEISEN |
| 346 | **ALL-MINE PIG** | FER VIRGINAL | FRISCHEISEN |
| 347 | **ALL-WELD-METAL TEST SPECIMEN** | EPROUVETTE DU METAL DEPOSE PUR | SCHWEISSGUT (REINES) |
| 348 | **ALLIGATORING** | PEAU DE CROCODILE | KROKODILNARBUNG, LÄNGSABBLATTERUNG |
| 349 | **ALLOMERIC** | ALLOMERIQUE | ALLOMER |
| 350 | **ALLOMERISM** | ALLOMERIE | ALLOMERISMUS |
| 351 | **ALLOMORPHISM** | ALLOMORPHIE | ALLOMORPHIE |
| 352 | **ALLOMORPHOUS** | ALLOMORPHE | ALLOMORPH |
| 353 | **ALLONABLE STRESS** | CONTRAINTE ADMISSIBLE | BEANSPRUCHUNG (ZULÄSSIGE) |
| 354 | **ALLOTRIOMORPHIC CRYSTAL** | ALLOTRIOMORPHE | ALLOTRIOMORPH |
| 355 | **ALLOTROPIC TRANSFORMATION** | TRANSFORMATION ALLOTROPIQUE | PHASENUMWANDLUNG |
| 356 | **ALLOTROPICALL** | ALLOTROPIQUE | ALLOTROP |
| 357 | **ALLOTROPY** | ALLOTROPIE, ISOMERIE | ALLOTROPIE, ISOMERISMUS |
| 358 | **ALLOWANCE** | JEU, TOLERANCE, SUREPAISSEUR D'USINAGE, JEU DE COIFFAGE | SPIEL, TOLERANZ, BEARBEITUNGSZUGABE, ABMASS SPIELRAUM |
| 359 | **ALLOWANCE, PERMISSIBLE TOLERANCE, MARGIN** | TOLERANCE D'USINAGE, TOLERANCE ADMISE | SPIELRAUM, ZULÄSSIGE ABWEICHUNG, TOLERANZ |
| 360 | **ALLOY** | ALLIAGE | LEGIERUNG |
| 361 | **ALLOY (TO)** | ALLIER | LEGIEREN |
| 362 | **ALLOY BALANCE** | BASCULE POUR ALLIAGE | LEGIERWAAGSCHALE |
| 363 | **ALLOY CASTING** | FONTE ALLIEE | GUSSEISEN (LEGIERTES) |
| 364 | **ALLOY COATING** | REVETEMENT D'ALLIAGE | LEGIERUNGSÜBERZUG, LEGIERUNGSABSCHEIDUNG |
| 365 | **ALLOY CONTAMINATION** | CONTAMINATION D'UN ALLIAGE | LEGIERUNGSKONTAMINATIONVERSEUCHUNG |
| 366 | **ALLOY PLATE** | GALVANISER | GALVANISIEREN |
| 367 | **ALLOY POWDER** | POUDRE ALLIEE | PULVER (LEGIERTES) |

**ALL** 10

| | | | |
|---|---|---|---|
| 368 | ALLOY STEEL | ACIER ALLIE | STAHL (LEGIERTER), SONDERSTAHL |
| 369 | ALLOY STEEL ANGLES | CORNIERES EN ACIER ALLIE | WINKELSTAHL (LEGIERTER) |
| 370 | ALLOY STEEL BILLETS | BILLETTES EN ACIER ALLIE | KNÜPPEL AUS LEGIERTEN STÄHLEN |
| 371 | ALLOY STEEL BUNDLING STRIP | FEUILLARDS EN ACIER ALLIE | BANDSTAHL (WARMGEWALZTER), LEGIERT |
| 372 | ALLOY STEEL CASTINGS | MOULAGES D'ACIER ALLIE | STAHLFORMGUSS AUS LEGIERTEN STÄHLEN |
| 373 | ALLOY STEEL FLATS | PLATS EN ACIER ALLIE | FLACHEISEN AUS LEGIERTEN STÄHLEN |
| 374 | ALLOY STEEL HEXAGONS | HEXAGONES EN ACIER ALLIE | SECHSKANTEISEN AUS LEGIERTEN STÄHLEN |
| 375 | ALLOY STEEL OCTAGONS | BARRES HUIT-PANS EN ACIER ALLIE | ACHTKANTEISEN AUS LEGIERTEN STÄHLEN |
| 376 | ALLOY STEEL ROD WIRE | FIL MACHINE EN ACIER ALLIE | WALZDRAHT AUS LEGIERTEN STÄHLEN |
| 377 | ALLOY STEEL ROUNDS | RONDS EN ACIER ALLIE | RUNDEISEN AUS LEGIERTEN STÄHLEN |
| 378 | ALLOY STEEL SHEET BARS | LARGETS EN ACIER ALLIE | PLATINEN AUS LEGIERTEN STÄHLEN |
| 379 | ALLOY STEEL SQUARES | CARRES EN ACIER ALLIE | VIERKANTSTAHL, LEGIERT |
| 380 | ALLOY STEEL THIN SHEETS | TOLES MINCES EN ACIER ALLIE | BLECHE AUS LEGIERTEN STÄHLEN |
| 381 | ALLOY SYSTEM | SYSTEME DES ALLIAGES | LEGIERUNGSSYSTEM |
| 382 | ALLOY-TREATED STEEL | ACIER FAIBLEMENT ALLIE | STAHL (NIEDRIGLEGIERTER) |
| 383 | ALLOY, ABRASION-RESISTANT | ALLIAGE RESISTANT A L'USURE | LEGIERUNG (VERSCHLEISSFESTE) |
| 384 | ALLOY, ACID RESISTANT | ALLIAGE RESISTANT AUX ACIDES | LEGIERUNG (SÄUREBESTÄNDIGE) |
| 385 | ALLOY, BEARING | ALLIAGE POUR COUSSINETS, ALLIAGE ANTI-FRICTION | LAGERLEGIERUNG |
| 386 | ALLOY, BRAZING | ALLIAGE DE BRASAGE | HARTLÖTLEGIERUNG |
| 387 | ALLOY, CORROSION RESISTANT | ALLIAGE INOXYDABLE, ALLIAGE RESISTANT A LA CORROSION | LEGIERUNG (KORROSIONSBESTÄNDIGE) |
| 388 | ALLOY, DIE CASTING | ALLIAGE POUR COULEE SOUS PRESSION | DRUCKGUSSLEGIERUNG |
| 389 | ALLOY, FUSIBLE | ALLIAGE FUSIBLE | SCHMELZLEGIERUNG |
| 390 | ALLOY, HEAT AND CORROSION RESISTANT | ALLIAGE RESISTANT A LA CHALEUR ET A LA CORROSION | LEGIERUNG (HITZE-UND KORROSIONSBESTÄNDIGE) |
| 391 | ALLOY, HEAT RESISTANT | ALLIAGE RESISTANT A LA CHALEUR | LEGIERUNG (HITZEBESTÄNDIGE) |
| 392 | ALLOY, MAGNET | ALLIAGE MAGNETIQUE | LEGIERUNG (MAGNETISCHE) |
| 393 | ALLOY, REFRACTORY | ALLIAGE REFRACTAIRE | LEGIERUNG (FEUERFISTE) |
| 394 | ALLOYING | ADDITION | ZUSATZ |
| 395 | ALLOYING ELEMENTS | ELEMENTS D'ADDITION | ZUSATZELEMENTE |
| 396 | ALLOYS, ABRASION & CORROSION RESISTANT | ALLIAGES RESISTANTS A L'ABRASION ET A LA CORROSION | LEGIERUNGEN (ABRIED-UND KORROSIONFESTE) |
| 397 | ALMALGAM | AMALGAME | AMALGAM |
| 398 | ALNICO | ALLIAGE MAGNETIQUE 'ALNICO' | ALNICO |
| 399 | ALPHA BRASS | LAITON ALPHA | ALPHA-MESSING |
| 400 | ALPHA PARTICLE | PARTICULE ALPHA | ALPHA-TEILCHEN |
| 401 | ALPHA RADIATOR | RADIATEUR ALPHA | ALPHA-STRAHLER, ALPHA-STRAHLENQUELLE |
| 402 | ALPHA RAYS | RAYONS ALPHA | ALPHA-STRAHLUNG |
| 403 | ALPHA-BETA BRASS | LAITON ALPHA-BETA | ALPHA-BETA-MESSING |
| 404 | ALTERNATE CONES | CONE ET CONTRE-CONE, PAIRE DE CONES LISSES | RIEMENKEGELTRIEB |

| | | | |
|---|---|---|---|
| 405 | ALTERNATE-IMMERSION TEST | ESSAI PAR IMMERSIONS ET EMERSIONS ALTERNEES | WECHSELTAUCHVERSUCH-PRÜFUNG |
| 406 | ALTERNATING ALTERNATE CURRENT (A.C., A.C.) | COURANT ALTERNATIF | WECHSELSTROM |
| 407 | ALTERNATING CURRENT GENERATOR, ALTERNATOR | ALTERNATEUR, DYNAMO, GENERATRICE, MACHINE A COURANT ALTERNATIF | WECHSELSTROMMASCHINE, WECHSELSTROMDYNAMO, WECHSELSTROMGENERATOR, ALTERNATOR |
| 408 | ALTERNATING CURRENT MOTOR | MOTEUR A COURANT ALTERNATIF, ALTERNO-MOTEUR | WECHSELSTROMMOTOR |
| 409 | ALTERNATIVE | ALTERNATIVE | ALTERNATIVE |
| 410 | ALTERNATIVE SOLUTION | VARIANTE | VARIANTE |
| 411 | ALTERNATOR | ALTERNATEUR | WECHSELSTROMGENERATOR |
| 412 | ALUMINA | ALUMINE | ALUMINIUMOXYD, TONERDE |
| 413 | ALUMINA, ALUMINIUM OXIDE | ALUMINE, OXYDE D'ALUMINIUM | TONERDE, ALUMINIUMOXYD |
| 414 | ALUMINATE | ALUMINATE | ALUMINAT |
| 415 | ALUMINIFEROUS | ALUMINIFERE | ALUMINIUMHALTIG |
| 416 | ALUMINIUM | ALUMINIUM | ALUMINIUM |
| 417 | ALUMINIUM ACETATE | ACETATE D'ALUMINIUM | TONERDE (ESSIGSAURE), ALUMINIUMAZETAT |
| 418 | ALUMINIUM ALLOY | ALLIAGE A BASE D'ALUMINIUM | ALUMINIUMLEGIERUNG |
| 419 | ALUMINIUM BRASS | LAITON D'ALUMINIUM | ALUMINIUMMESSING |
| 420 | ALUMINIUM BRONZE | BRONZE D'ALUMINIUM | ALUMINIUMBRONZE |
| 421 | ALUMINIUM CHLORIDE | CHLORURE D'ALUMINIUM, CHLORALUM | ALUMINIUMCHLORID, CHLORALUMINIUM |
| 422 | ALUMINIUM FILE | LIME A ALUMINIUM | ALUMINIUMFEILE |
| 423 | ALUMINIUM HYDROXIDE | ALUMINE HYDRATEE | TONERDEHYDRAT, ALUMINIUMHYDROXYD |
| 424 | ALUMINIUM INGOT METAL | ALUMINIUN EN LINGOT | ALUMINIUMROHBLOCK |
| 425 | ALUMINIUM SILICATE | SILICATE D'ALUMINE | TONERDE (KIESELSAURE), TONERDESILIKAT, ALUMINIUMSILIKAT |
| 426 | ALUMINIUM SULPHATE | SULFATE D'ALUMINIUM | TONERDE (SCHWEFELSAURE), ALUMINUIMSULFAT |
| 427 | ALUMINIUM TUBE | TUBE EN ALUMINIUM | ALUMINIUMROHR |
| 428 | ALUMINIUM WIRE | FIL D'ALUMINIUM | ALUMINIUMDRAHT |
| 429 | ALUMINIZING, ALUMINIZE | ALUMINATION | ALUMINISIEREN, VERALUMINIEREN |
| 430 | ALUMINO | ALUMINO | ALUMINO |
| 431 | ALUMINOTHERMICS | ALUMINOTHERMIE | ALUMINOTHERMIE, THERMIT-VERFAHREN |
| 432 | ALUMINUM | ALUMINIUM | ALUMINIUM |
| 433 | ALUMINUM ALLOY, WROUGHT | ALLIAGE D'ALUMINIUM FORGEABLE | KNETALUMINIUM-LEGIERUNG |
| 434 | ALUMINUM BRONZE | BRONZE D'ALUMINIUM CUPRO-ALUMINIUM | ALUMINIUMBRONZE |
| 435 | ALUMINUM CASTING ALLOY | ALLIAGE D'ALUMINIUM POUR MOULAGE | GUSSALUMINIUM |
| 436 | ALUMINUM FOIL | FEUILLE D'ALUMINIUM | ALUMINIUMFOLIE |
| 437 | ALUMINUM FORGING ALLOY | ALLIAGE D'ALUMUNIUM FORGEABLE | ALUMINIUM-SCHMIEDE-LEGIERUNG |
| 438 | ALUMINUM OXIDE | ALUMINE | TONERDE |
| 439 | ALUMINUM-BASE ALLOY | ALLIAGE A BASE D'ALUMINIUM | LEGIERUNG MIT ALUMINIUM ALS GRUNDMETALL |
| 440 | ALUMINUM-BERYLLIUM ALLOY | ALLIAGE D'ALUMINIUM-BERYLLIUM | ALUMINIUM-BERYLLIUM-LEGIERUNG |
| 441 | ALUMINUM-COATED SHEET | TOLE (D'ACIER) ALUMINEE | ALITIERTES (STAHL-)BLECH |
| 442 | ALUMINUM-KILLED STEEL | ACIER CALME A L'ALUMINIUM | STAHL (ALUMINIUM-BERUHIGTER) |
| 443 | ALUMINUM-SILICATE REFRACTORY CEMENT | CIMENT REFRACTAIRE AU SILICATE D'ALUMINIUM | MÖRTEL (ALUMINIUM-SILIKAT-FEUERFESTER) |
| 444 | ALUMINUM, ALUMINIUM | ALUMINIUM | ALUMINIUM |

# AMA 12

| | English | French | German |
|---|---|---|---|
| 445 | AMALGAM | AMALGAME | AMALGAM |
| 446 | AMALGAMATE (TO) | AMALGAMER | AMALGAMIEREN |
| 447 | AMALGAMATION | AMALGAMATION | AMALGAMIERUNG, AMALGAMATION, AMALGAMIEREN |
| 448 | AMALGAMATION PROCESS | PROCEDE D'AMALGAMATION | AMALGAMIERUNGSVERFAHREN |
| 449 | AMBER | AMBRE JAUNE, ARBRE SUCCIN | BERNSTEIN |
| 450 | AMBIENT AIR | AIR AMBIANT | AUSSENLUFT |
| 451 | AMERICAN STANDARD THREAD, SELLERS THREAD | PAS SYSTEME SELLERS | SELLERSGEWINDE |
| 452 | AMMETER, AMPEREMETER | AMPEREMETRE, COULOMBMETRE | STROMMESSER, STROMZEIGER, AMPEREMETER |
| 453 | AMMONIA | GAZ AMMONIAC, AMMONIAQUE | AMMONIAKGAS |
| 454 | AMMONIA | AMMONIAC | AMMONIAK |
| 455 | AMMONIA SODA, SOLVAY SODA | SOUDE A L'AMMONIAQUE, SOUDE SOLVAY, SEL SOLVAY | AMMONIAKSODA, SOLVAYSODA |
| 456 | AMMONIACAL LIQUOR, GAS LIQUOR | EAU AMMONIACALE DU GAZ | GASWASSER, AMMONIAKWASSER |
| 457 | AMMONIACAL SOLUTION | SOLUTION AMMONIACALE | LÖSUNG (AMMONIAKALISCHE) |
| 458 | AMMONIUM ACETATE | ACETATE D'AMMONIUM | AMMONIAK (ESSIGSAURES), AMMONIUMAZETAT |
| 459 | AMMONIUM BICARBONATE | BICARBONATE D'AMMONIUM | AMMONIAK (DOPPELTKOHLENSAURES), AMMONIUMBIKARBONAT |
| 460 | AMMONIUM BISULPHITE | BISULFITE D'AMMONIAQUE | AMMONIAK (SAURES), AMMONIAK (SCHWEFLIGSAURES), AMMONIUMBISULFIT |
| 461 | AMMONIUM CARBONATE, SAL VOLATILE | CARBONATE D'AMMONIUM, SEL VOLATIL D'ANGLETERRE | HIRSCHHORNSALZ, AMMONIUMKARBONAT, AMMONIAK (KOHLENSAURES) |
| 462 | AMMONIUM CHLORIDE, SAL AMMONIAC | CHLORURE D'AMMONIUM, HYDROCHLORATE, CHLORHYDRATE D'AMMONIAQUE, SEL AMMONIAC, MURIATE D'AMMONIAQUE | SALMIAK, AMMONIUMCHLORID, CHLORAMMONIUM |
| 463 | AMMONIUM FLUORIDE | FLUORURE D'AMMONIUM | FLUORAMMONIUM, AMMONIUMFLUORID |
| 464 | AMMONIUM HYDROSULPHIDE, SULPHHYDRATE OF AMMONIUM | SULFHYDRATE D'AMMONIUM | AMMONIUMSULFHYDRAT, AMMONIUMHYDROSULFID |
| 465 | AMMONIUM NITRATE | NITRATE D'AMMONIUM, NITRUM FLAMMANS | AMMONIAK (SALPETERSAURES), AMMONIUMNITRAT, AMMONIAKSALPETER, FLAMMENDER SALPETER |
| 466 | AMMONIUM NITRITE | NITRITE D'AMMONIUM | AMMONIAK (SALPETRIGSAURES), AMMONIUMNITRIT |
| 467 | AMMONIUM OXALATE | OXALATE D'AMMONIAQUE | AMMONIAK (OXALSAURES), AMMONIUMOXALAT |
| 468 | AMMONIUM PERSULPHATE | PERSULFATE D'AMMONIAQUE | AMMONIAK (ÜBERSCHWEFELSAURES), AMMONIUMPERSULFAT |
| 469 | AMMONIUM PHOSPHATE | PHOSPHATE D'AMMONIUM | AMMONIAK (PHOSPHORSAURES), AMMONIUMPHOSPHAT |
| 470 | AMMONIUM STANNIC CHLORIDE, PINK SALT | CHLORURE DOUBLE D'ETAIN ET D'AMMONIUM | PINKSALZ, AMMONIUMZINNCHLORID |
| 471 | AMMONIUM SULPHATE | SULFATE D'AMMONIUM | AMMONIAK (SCHWEFELSAURES), AMMONIUMSULFAT |
| 472 | AMMONIUM SULPHIDE | SULFURE D'AMMONIUM | AMMONIUMSULFID, SCHWEFELAMMONIUM |
| 473 | AMMONIUM TARTRATE | TARTRATE D'AMMONIAQUE | AMMONIAK (WEINSAURES), AMMONIUMTARTRAT |
| 474 | AMMUNITION | MUNITION | MUNITION |
| 475 | AMORPHOUS | AMORPHE | AMORPH |

| | | | |
|---|---|---|---|
| 476 | **AMORPHOUS SULPHUR** | SOUFRE AMORPHE | SCHWEFEL (AMORPHER) |
| 477 | **AMOUNT OF CONTRACTION** | RETRAIT, COEFFICIENT DE RETRAIT | SCHWINDMASS, UNTERMASS, SCHRUMPFMASS, |
| 478 | **AMPERAGE** | NOMBRE D'AMPERES, AMPERAGE, INTENSITE DU COURANT | AMPEREZAHL, STROMSTÄRKE |
| 479 | **AMPERE** | AMPERE | AMPERE |
| 480 | **AMPERE TURN** | AMPERE-TOUR | AMPEREWINDUNG |
| 481 | **AMPERE-HOUR (AMP.HR)** | AMPERE-HEURE, A-H | AMPERESTUNDE |
| 482 | **AMPERE-MINUTE** | AMPERE-MINUTE | AMPEREMINUTE |
| 483 | **AMPERE-SECOND** | AMPERE-SECONDE | AMPERESEKUNDE |
| 484 | **AMPHOTERIC METAL** | AMPHOTERE | AMPHOTER |
| 485 | **AMPLIFIER** | AMPLIFICATEUR | VERSTÄRKER |
| 486 | **AMPLITUDE** | AMPLITUDE | SCHWINGUNGSWEITE, AUSSCHLAG, AMPLITUDE |
| 487 | **AMYL ACETATE** | ACETATE D'AMYLE, ESSENCE DE POIRE | AMYLAZETAT |
| 488 | **AMYL ACOHOL** | ALCOOL AMYLIQUE | AMYLALKOHOL, PENTHYLALKOHOL, AMYLOXYDHYDRAT |
| 489 | **ANAEROBIC** | ANAEROBIQUE | ANAEROB |
| 490 | **ANALOG** | ANALOGIQUE | ANALOG |
| 491 | **ANALYSE (TO)** | ANALYSER | ANALYSIEREN |
| 492 | **ANALYSER** | ANALYSEUR | ANALYSATOR |
| 493 | **ANALYSIS** | ANALYSE | ANALYSE |
| 494 | **ANALYTICAL** | ANALYTIQUE | ANALYTISCH |
| 495 | **ANALYTICAL CHEMISTRY** | CHIMIE ANALYTIQUE | CHEMIE (ANALYTISCHE) |
| 496 | **ANALYTICAL DETERMINATION** | DETERMINATION ANALYTIQUE | BESTIMMUNG (ANALYTISCHE) |
| 497 | **ANASTIGMAT** | ANASTIGMAT | ANASTIGMAT |
| 498 | **ANATOMICAL ALLOY** | ALLIAGE OSTEOPLASTIQUE | OSTEOPLASTIKLEGIERUNG |
| 499 | **ANCHERING** | ANCRAGE | ANKERUNG |
| 500 | **ANCHOR** | ANCRE (CONSTR.) | MAUERANKER, ANKER |
| 501 | **ANCHOR BOLT** | BOULON D'ANCRAGE | ANKERSCHRAUBE, FUNDAMENTANKER |
| 502 | **ANCHOR PLATE** | CONTREPLAQUE (SCELLEE DANS LE SOL) | ANKERPLATTE (IM FUNDAMENT) |
| 503 | **ANEMOMETER** | ANEMOMETRE | WINDMESSER, ANEMOMETER |
| 504 | **ANEROID BAROMETER** | BAROMETRE ANEROIDE, BAROMETRE METALLIQUE, ANEROIDE | FEDERBAROMETER, METALLBAROMETER, DOSENBAROMETER, ANEROID BAROMETER |
| 505 | **ANGLE** | ANGLE (GEOM.) | WINKEL (GEOM.) |
| 506 | **ANGLE (IRON)** | CORNIERE | WINKELEISEN, WINKELPROFIL |
| 507 | **ANGLE AT THE CENTRE** | ANGLE AU CENTRE | ZENTRIWINKEL |
| 508 | **ANGLE BEARING** | PALIER AVEC PLAN DE SEPARATION INCLINE | LAGER (SCHRÄG), LAGER (SCHIEF GESCHNITTENES), SCHRÄGLAGER |
| 509 | **ANGLE BOX SPANNER** | CLEF TUBULAIRE COURBE | HÜLSENSCHLÜSSEL, AUFSTECKSCHLÜSSEL, SCHLÜSSEL (GEKRÖPFTER) |
| 510 | **ANGLE BRACKET** | EQUERRE D'ASSEMBLAGE | ECKWINKEL |
| 511 | **ANGLE COCK** | ROBINET D'ANGLE | WINKELHAHN |
| 512 | **ANGLE FLANGE** | BRIDE ANGULAIRE | WINKELFLANSCH |
| 513 | **ANGLE GAUGE** | CALIBRE D'ANGLES | WINKELLEHRE |
| 514 | **ANGLE IRON** | FER CORNIERE, CORNIERE, FER EN L, EQUERRE | WINKELEISEN, L-EISEN |
| 515 | **ANGLE OF ADVANCE, ANGULAR ADVANCE, ANGLE OF LEAD** | ANGLE D'AVANCE, ANGLE DE DECALAGE EN AVANCE | VOREILWINKEL |

# ANG

14

| | | | |
|---|---|---|---|
| 516 | **ANGLE OF CHAMFER** | CHANFREIN D'ENTREE | ABSCHRÄGWINKEL |
| 517 | **ANGLE OF CONTACT** | ANGLE D'ENROULEMENT, ANGLE DE CONTACT | ANSCHMIEGUNGSWINKEL, UMSCHLINGUNGSWINKEL, GREIFWINKEL |
| 518 | **ANGLE OF DEFLECTION** | ANGLE DE DEVIATION | AUSSCHLAGWINKEL |
| 519 | **ANGLE OF FLEXURE** | ANGLE DE FLEXION | BIEGEWINKEL |
| 520 | **ANGLE OF INCIDENCE** | ANGLE D'INCIDENCE | EINFALLWINKEL |
| 521 | **ANGLE OF INCLINATION** | ANGLE D'INCLINAISON | NEIGUNGSWINKEL |
| 522 | **ANGLE OF LAG, ANGULAR LAG** | ANGLE DE RETARD, ANGLE DE DECALAGE EN ARRIERE | NACHEILWINKEL, VERZÖGERUNGSWINKEL |
| 523 | **ANGLE OF PHASE LAG** | ANGLE DE DEPHASAGE EN ARRIERE | PHASENNACHEILWINKEL |
| 524 | **ANGLE OF PHASE LEAD** | ANGLE DE DEPHASAGE EN AVANCE | PHASENVOREILWINKEL |
| 525 | **ANGLE OF REFLECTION** | ANGLE DE REFLEXION | REFLEXIONSWINKEL |
| 526 | **ANGLE OF REFRACTION** | ANGLE DE REFRACTION | BRECHUNGSWINKEL |
| 527 | **ANGLE OF REPOSE, ANGLE OF FRICTION, LIMITING ANGLE OF RESISTANCE** | ANGLE DE FROTTEMENT | REIBUNGSWINKEL |
| 528 | **ANGLE OF ROTATION** | ANGLE DE ROTATION | DREHUNGSWINKEL |
| 529 | **ANGLE OF TAPER OF KEY** | ANGLE DE CALAGE | AUFKEILWINKEL |
| 530 | **ANGLE OF THREAD** | ANGLE DU FILET | FLANKENWINKEL DES GEWINDES |
| 531 | **ANGLE OF THREAD** | ANGLE DE L'INCLINAISON DU FILET | STEIGUNGSWINKEL EINER SCHRAUBE |
| 532 | **ANGLE OF TWIST** | ANGLE DE TORSION | VERDREHUNGSWINKEL, DRILLUNG |
| 533 | **ANGLE PLATE** | EQUERRE D'ABLOCAGE | WINKELPLATTE |
| 534 | **ANGLE VALVE** | ROBINET D'EQUERRE, SOUPAPE D'EQUERRE | ECKVENTIL |
| 535 | **ANGLE VISE** | ETAU INCLINABLE | SINUS-SCHRAUBSTROCK |
| 536 | **ANGSTROM UNIT** | ANGSTROM | ANGSTRÖM |
| 537 | **ANGULAR ACCELERATION** | ACCELERATION ANGULAIRE | WINKELBESCHLEUNIGUNG, DREHBESCHLEUNIGUNG |
| 538 | **ANGULAR BALL BEARING** | ROULEMENT A BILLES A CHARGE RADIALE ET AXIALE COMBINEE, ROULEMENT A BILLES A POUSSEE AXIALE ET LATERALE COMBINEE | KUGELSCHULTERLAGER, KUGELDRUCK- UND TRAGLAGER |
| 539 | **ANGULAR CUT** | COUPE ANGULAIRE | WINKELSCHNITT |
| 540 | **ANGULAR CUTTERS** | FRAISES CONIQUES | WINKELFRÄSER |
| 541 | **ANGULAR DISPLACEMENT** | DEPLACEMENT ANGULAIRE, DECALAGE | WINKELVERSCHIEBUNG |
| 542 | **ANGULAR DISTORTION** | RETRAIT ANGULAIRE | WINKELSCHRUMPFUNG |
| 543 | **ANGULAR MILLING CUTTER** | FRAISE ANGULAIRE, FRAISE CONIQUE | WINKELFRÄSER, KEGELFRÄSER |
| 544 | **ANGULAR NOTION** | MOUVEMENT ANGULAIRE | WINKELBEWEGUNG |
| 545 | **ANGULAR TRIANGULAR THREAD, VEE-SHAPED THREAD, V-THREAD** | FILET TRIANGULAIRE | GEWINDE (SCHARFES), GEWINDE (SCHARFGÄNGIGES), DREIECK GEWINDE |
| 546 | **ANGULAR VELOCITY** | VITESSE ANGULAIRE | WINKELGESCHWINDIGKEIT, KREISFREQUENZ |
| 547 | **ANGULAR-THREADED TRIANGULAR-THREADED SCREW, VEE-THREADED V-THREADED SCREW** | VIS A FILET TRIANGULAIRE | SCHRAUBE MIT DREIECKGEWINDE, SCHRAUBE (SCHARFGÄNGIGE) |
| 548 | **ANHYDRIDE** | ANHYDRIDE | ANHYDRID |
| 549 | **ANHYDRITE, ANHYDROUS SULPHATE OF CALCIUM** | ANHYDRIT, SULFATE ANHYDRE DE CHAUX | ANHYDRIT, KALK (WASSERFREIER SCHWEFELSAURER), WASSERFREIES KALZIUMSULFAT |
| 550 | **ANHYDROUS** | ANHYDRE | WASSERFREI (CHEM.) |

|  | | | |
|---|---|---|---|
| 551 | ANHYDROUS SODIUM CARBONATE, SODA ASH | SEL DE SOUDE, CARBONATE DE SOUDE ANHYDRE | SODA (GEGLÜHTE) (KALZINIERTE), SODASALZ (KALZINIERTES), NATRIUMKARBONAT (WASSERFREIES) |
| 552 | ANILINE | ANILINE, PHENYLAMINE | ANILIN, AMIDOBENZOL, PHENYLAMIN |
| 553 | ANILINE OIL | ANILINE DU COMMERCE | ANILINÖL, ROHANILIN |
| 554 | ANIMAL CHARCOAL, BONE CHARCOAL | CHARBON ANIMAL | KNOCHENKOHLE |
| 555 | ANIMAL OIL | HUILE ANIMALE | ÖL (TIERISCHES) |
| 556 | ANION | ANION | SAUERSTOFFION, ANION |
| 557 | ANIONIC FLOTATION | FLOTTATION ANIONIQUE | FLOTATION (ANIONISCHE), SCHWIMMAUFBEREITUNG (ANIONISCHE) |
| 558 | ANISOTROPIC | ANISOTROPE | ANISOTROP |
| 559 | ANISOTROPY, ANISOTROPISM | ANISOTROPIE | ANISOTROPIE |
| 560 | ANNEAL (TO), NORMALISE THE STEEL (TO) | RECUIRE L'ACIER | STAHL AUSGLÜHEN, STAHL NORMALISIBREN |
| 561 | ANNEALED BLACK WIRE | FIL RECUIT | DRAHT (GEGLÜHTER) |
| 562 | ANNEALING | RECUIT | AUSGLÜHEN, GLÜHFRISCHEN, TEMPERN, GLÜHEN |
| 563 | ANNEALING BOX | CAISSE DE RECUIT | GLÜHKISTE |
| 564 | ANNEALING FURNACE | FOUR A RECUIRE, FOUR DE RECUIT, FOUR DE REVENU | GLÜHOFEN |
| 565 | ANNEALING PLANT | INSTALLATION DE RECUIT | GLÜHANLAGE |
| 566 | ANNEALING POT | POT A RECUIRE | GLÜHTOPF |
| 567 | ANNEALING POTS | CAISSE DE RECUIT | GLÜHKISTE |
| 568 | ANNEALING PROCESS | TRAITEMENT DE RECUIT | GLÜHEN, TEMPERN |
| 569 | ANNEALING RESISTANCE | RESISTANCE A L'ETAT DE RECUIT | GLÜHFESTIGKEIT |
| 570 | ANNEALING TWINS | BANDE A JUMEAUX | ZWILLINGSBAND |
| 571 | ANNEALING, BLACK | RECUIT EN NOIR | SCHWARZGLÜHEN |
| 572 | ANNEALING, BLUE | BLEUISSAGE | BLAUGLÜHEN |
| 573 | ANNEALING, BRIGHT | RECUIT BLANC | BLANKGLÜHEN |
| 574 | ANNEALING, CONTINUOUS | RECUIT CONTINU | DURCHLAUFBANDGLÜHEN |
| 575 | ANNEALING, FLAME | RECUIT AU CHALUMEAU | OBERFLÄCHENGLÜHUNG |
| 576 | ANNEALING, FULL | RECUIT COMPLET | AUSGLÜHEN (VOLLSTÄNDIGES) |
| 577 | ANNEALING, INTERMEDIATE | RECUIT INTERMEDIAIRE | ZWISCHENGLÜHEN |
| 578 | ANNEALING, INVERSE | RECUIT INVERSE | GLÜHFRISCHEN (INVERSES) |
| 579 | ANNEALING, ISOTHERMAL | RECUIT ISOTHERMIQUE | GLÜHUNG (ISOTHERME) |
| 580 | ANNEALING, LOCAL | RECUIT SELECTIF | SELEKTIVES FRISCHGLÜHEN |
| 581 | ANNEALING, NORMALISING THE STEEL | RECUIT DE L'ACIER | AUSGLÜHEN, NORMALISIEREN DES STAHLS |
| 582 | ANNEALING, PERIODIC | RECUIT PERIODIQUE | KREISLAUFGLÜHUNG |
| 583 | ANNEALING, RELIEF | RECUIT DE RELAXATION | GLÜHEN (ENTSPANNENDES) |
| 584 | ANNEALING, STRESS-RELIEF | RECUIT DE DETENTE | GLÜHEN (SPANNUNGSFREIES) |
| 585 | ANNEX, EXTENSION | ANNEXE D'UN BATIMENT, BATIMENT ANNEXE | ANBAU |
| 586 | ANNUAL RING | CERCLE ANNUEL, CRUE, COUCHE ANNUELLE | JAHRESRING |
| 587 | ANNULAR CROSS SECTION | SECTION ANNULAIRE | QUERSCHNITT (RINGFÖRMIGER), QUERSCHNITT (KREISRINGFÖRMIGER) |
| 588 | ANNULAR, RING-SHAPED | ANNULAIRE | RINGFÖRMIG |
| 589 | ANNULUS | ANNEAU, COURONNE CIRCULAIRE | KREISRING |
| 590 | ANODE | ANODE | ANODE |
| 591 | ANODE BUTT | BOUT ANODIQUE | ANODENBRENNFLECK |
| 592 | ANODE CLEANING | PURIFICATION ANODIQUE | REINIGUNG (ANODISCHE) |

## ANO

16

| | | | |
|---|---|---|---|
| 593 | **ANODE COPPER** | CUIVRE ANODIQUE | ANODENKUPFER |
| 594 | **ANODE CORROSION EFFICIENCY** | COEFFICIENT DE CORROSION ANODIQUE | KORROSIONSKOEFFIZIENT (ANODISCHE) |
| 595 | **ANODE DROP** | CHUTE ANODIQUE | ANODENFALL, SPANNUNGSABFALL AN DER ANODE |
| 596 | **ANODE EFFECT** | EFFET D'ANODE | ANODENEFFEKT |
| 597 | **ANODE EFFICIENCY** | RENDEMENT ANODIQUE | ANODENWIRKUNGSGRAD |
| 598 | **ANODE INSOLUBLE** | ANODE INSOLUBLE | ANODE (UNLÖSLICHE) |
| 599 | **ANODE LAYER** | COUCHE (DE PROTECTION) ANODIQUE, REVETEMENT (ENDUIT) ANODIQUE | ÜBERZUG (ANODISCHER) |
| 600 | **ANODE MUD, ANODE SLIME** | BOUE D'ANODE | ANODENRÜCKSTAND, ANODENSCHLAMM |
| 601 | **ANODE PICKLING** | DECAPAGE ANODIQUE | ANODENBEIZUNG |
| 602 | **ANODE, POSITIVE ELECTRODE** | ELECTRODE POSITIVE, ANODE | ELEKTRODE (POSITIVE), ANODE |
| 603 | **ANODIC** | ANODIQUE | ANODISCH |
| 604 | **ANODIC POLARIZATION** | POLARISATION ANODIQUE | ANODENPOLARISATION |
| 605 | **ANODIZING** | OXYDATION ANODIQUE TRAITEMENT ANODIQUE | ELOXIEREN |
| 606 | **ANOLYTE** | ANOLYTE, SOLUTION ANODIQUE | ANOLYT, ANODENFLÜSSIGKEIT |
| 607 | **ANTHRACENE** | ANTHRACENE | ANTHRAZEN |
| 608 | **ANTHRACENE OIL** | HUILE ENTHRACENIQUE, HUILE A ANTHRACENE | ANTHRAZENÖL |
| 609 | **ANTHRACITE** | ANTHRACITE, HOUILLE ECLATANTE | ANTHRAZIT |
| 610 | **ANTI-AIRCRAFT GUN** | CANON ANTI-AERIEN | FLAK-GESCHÜTZ |
| 611 | **ANTI-CATHODE** | ANTI CATHODE | ANTIKATHODE |
| 612 | **ANTI-FREEZE SOLUTION** | ANTIGEL | FROSTSCHUTZMITTEL |
| 613 | **ANTI-KNOCK FUEL** | CARBURANT ANTI-DETONNANT | KRAFTSTOFF (KLOPFFESTER) |
| 614 | **ANTI-MAGNETIC** | ANTIMAGNETIQUE | ANTIMAGNETISCH |
| 615 | **ANTI-PIPING COMPOUND** | COUVERTE | ABDECKMITTEL |
| 616 | **ANTI-PITTING AGENT** | AGENT ANTI-PIQURE | PORENVERMUTTUNGSMITTEL |
| 617 | **ANTI-SEIZURE PROPERTIES** | PROPRIETES ANTI-FRICTION | ANTIFRIKTIONSWIRKUNG |
| 618 | **ANTIFRICTION BEARING** | ROULEMENT A BILLES, ROULEMENT A GALETS | WÄLZLAGER |
| 619 | **ANTIFRICTION METAL** | ALLIAGE, METAL ANTIFRICTION, ANTIFRICTION | ANTIFRIKTIONSMETALL |
| 620 | **ANTILOGARITHM** | ANTILOGARITHME | GEGENLOGARITHMUS, ANTILOGARITHMUS |
| 621 | **ANTIMONIAL LEAD** | PLOMB AIGRE, PLOMB ANTIMONIAL | ANTIMONBLEI |
| 622 | **ANTIMONITE, STIBNITE** | STIBINE | ANTIMONGLANZ, ANTIMONIT, GRAUSPIESSGLANZERZ |
| 623 | **ANTIMONY** | ANTIMOINE | ANTIMON, SPIESSGLANZ |
| 624 | **ANTIMONY PENTACHLORIDE** | PENTACHLORURE D'ANTIMOINE | ANTIMONPENTACHLORID, ANTIMONSUPERCHLORID |
| 625 | **ANTIMONY PENTASULPHIDE** | SULFURE DOREE, SOUFFRE DORE D'ANTIMOINE, PENTASULFURE D'ANTIMOINE | FÜNFFACH-SCHWEFELANTIMON, GOLDSCHWEFEL, ANTIMONPENTASULFID, SULFURAURAT |
| 626 | **ANTIMONY TRICHLORIDE, BUTTER OF ANTIMONY** | TRICHLORURE D'ANTIMOINE, BEURRE D'ANTIMOINE LIQUIDE | ANTIMONTRICHLORID, ANTIMONCHLORÜR, CHLORANTIMON, SPLESSGLANZBUTTER, ANTIMONBUTTER |
| 627 | **ANTIMONY TRISULPHIDE** | PROTOSULFURE, TRISULFURE D'ANTIMOINE | DREIFACH-SCHWEFELANTIMON, ANTIMONTRISULFID, ANTIMONSULFÜR |
| 628 | **ANTISEPTIC** | ANTISEPTIQUE, ASEPTISANT, ANTIPUTRIDE | FÄULNISWIDRIG, ANTISEPTISCH |

**17**                         **ARC**

| 629 | **ANTISEPTIC** | ANTISEPTIQUE, ANTIPUTRIDE, AGENT ANTIPUTREFIANT | FÄULNIṢVERHINDERNDES MITTEL, ABTÖTENDES MITTEL, ANTISEPTISCHES MITTEL, ANTISEPTIKUM |
|---|---|---|---|
| 630 | **ANVIL** | ENCLUME | AMBOSS |
| 631 | **ANVIL CUTTER, ANVIL CHISEL** | TRANCHET D'ENCLUME, CASSE-FER | ABSCHROT, ABSCHRÖTER |
| 632 | **ANVIL STAKE** | TAS, TASSEAU | SCHLAGSTÖCKCHEN, STÖCKEL, AMBOSSSTÖCKEL , POLIERSTOCK |
| 633 | **ANVIL STAND BLOCK** | BILLOT, CHABOTTE D'ENCLUME | AMBOSSSTOCK, AMBOSSUNTERSATZ |
| 634 | **APERIODIC** | APERIODIQUE | APERIODISCH |
| 635 | **APERIODIC DEAD BEAT INSTRUMENT, CRITICALLY DAMPED INSTRUMENT** | INSTRUMENT APERIODIQUE | INSTRUMENT (GEDÄMPFTES), INSTRUMENT (APERIODISCHES) |
| 636 | **APERIODIC MOTION** | MOUVEMENT APERIODIQUE | BEWEGUNG (APERIODISCHE) |
| 637 | **APERIODICITY** | APERIODICITE | APERIODIZITÄT |
| 638 | **APEX, VERTEX** | SOMMET, APEX | SCHEITEL, SPITZE (GEOM.) |
| 639 | **APLANAT** | APLANAT | APLANAT |
| 640 | **APOCHROMATIC** | APOCHROMATIQUE | APOCHROMATISCH |
| 641 | **APPARATUS** | APPAREIL | GERÄT, APPARAT |
| 642 | **APPARENT DENSITY** | DENSITE APPARENTE | DURCHSCHNITTLICHE DICHTE, SCHEINDICHTE |
| 643 | **APPARENT RADIATION CONSTANT** | CONSTANTE DE RADIATION APPARENTE | STRAHLUNGSKONSTANTE (SCHEINBARE) |
| 644 | **APPEARANCE OF CRACKS** | FORMATION DE FISSURES | RISSBILDUNG |
| 645 | **APPLICANT FOR A PATENT** | DEMANDEUR D'UN BREVET | PATENTBEWERBER, BEWERBER UM EIN PATENT, PATENTANMELDER |
| 646 | **APPLICATION FOR A PATENT** | DEMANDE, REQUETE DE BREVET | PATENTANMELDUNG, EINREICHUNG EINES PATENTGESUCHES |
| 647 | **APPLICATION OF A FORCE** | APPLICATION D'UNE FORCE | ANGREIFEN, ANGRIFF EINER KRAFT |
| 648 | **APPLIED CHEMISTRY** | CHIMIE APPLIQUEE | CHEMIE (ANGEWANDTE) |
| 649 | **APPLIED RESEARCH** | RECHERCHE APPLIQUEE | FORSCHUNG (ANGEWANDTE) |
| 650 | **APPLY A BRAKE (TO)** | SERRER, APPLIQUER UN FREIN | BREMSE ANZIEHEN (EINE) |
| 651 | **APPLY FOR A PATENT (TO)** | DEMANDER UN BREVET | EIN PATENT ANMELDEN, EIN PATENTGESUCH EINREICHEN |
| 652 | **APPROXIMATE CALCULATION** | CALCUL APPROXIMATIF, APPROXIMATION | ANNÄHERUNGSRECHNUNG |
| 653 | **APPROXIMATE VALUE** | VALEUR APPROCHEE | NÄHERUNGSWERT, ANGENÄHERTER WERT |
| 654 | **APPROXIMATIVE FORMULA** | FORMULE APPROXIMATIVE, D'APPROXIMATION | NÄHERUNGSFORMEL |
| 655 | **APRON** | TABLIER | BLECHSCHUTZ |
| 656 | **APT PROGRAMMING LANGUAGE** | LANGAGE DE PROGRAMMATION APT | APT-PROGRAMMIERSPRACHE |
| 657 | **AQUA FORTIS** | EAU FORTE | ÄTZE, GELBBRENNSÄURE |
| 658 | **AQUA REGIA, NITROHYDROCHLORIC NITROMURITICACID** | EAU REGALE | KÖNIGSWASSER, SALPETERSALZSÄURE |
| 659 | **AQUEOUS ALCOHOL** | ALCOOL AQUEUX | ALKOHOL (WÄSSERIGER) |
| 660 | **AQUEOUS AMMONIA SOLUTION** | SOLUTION AMMONIACALE, ALCALI VOLATIL, AMMONIAC | SALMIAKGEIST, AMMONIAKFLÜSSIGKEIT, ÄTZAMMONIAK, SALMIAKSPIRITUS |
| 661 | **AQUEOUS SOLUTION** | SOLUTION AQUEUSE | LÖSUNG (WÄSSRIGE) |
| 662 | **ARBOR** | SUPPORT METALLIQUE DE NOYAU | METALLKERNSTÜTZE |
| 663 | **ARBOR TYPE CUTTERS** | FRAISES ARBREES | AUFSTECKFRÄSER |
| 664 | **ARC** | ARC D'UNE COURBE | BOGEN |
| 665 | **ARC BLOW** | SOUFFLAGE MAGNETIQUE DE L'ARC | BLASWIRKUNG (MAGNETISCHE) |
| 666 | **ARC BRAZING** | BRASAGE FORT A L'ARC | LICHTBOGEN-HARTLÖTEN |
| 667 | **ARC DIRECT-ARC FURNACE** | FOUR ELECTRIQUE A ARC DIRECT | LICHTBOGENOFEN (DIREKTER) |

**ARC** 18

| | | | |
|---|---|---|---|
| 668 | ARC FURNACE | FOUR A ARC ELECTRIQUE | LICHTBOGENOFEN |
| 669 | ARC FURNACE INDIRECT | FOUR A ARC INDIRECT | LICHTBOGENOFEN (INDIREKTER) |
| 670 | ARC FURNACE, CARBON | FOUR A ARC ELECTRIQUE A ELECTRODES DE CHARBON | KOHLEELEKTRODEN-LICHTBOGENOFEN |
| 671 | ARC FURNACE, SMOOTHERED ARC | FOUR ELECTRIQUE A ARC DIRECT | LICHTBOGENOFEN (DIREKTER) |
| 672 | ARC LAMP | LAMPE A ARC | BOGENLAMPE |
| 673 | ARC LIGHT | LUMIERE DE L'ARC VOLTAIQUE | BOGENLICHT |
| 674 | ARC OF CIRCLE | ARC DE CERCLE, ARC CIRCULAIRE | KREISBOGEN |
| 675 | ARC OF CONTACT | ARC D'ENROULEMENT, COURBE DE CONTACT | UMSPANNUNGSBOGEN, UMSCHLINGUNGSBOGEN, EINGRIFFSBOGEN |
| 676 | ARC STREAM VOLTAGE | TENSION (VOLTAGE) DE L'ARC | LICHTBOGENSPANNUNG |
| 677 | ARC STRIKE | COUP DE SOUDURE POINT D'AMORCAGE DE L'ARC | ZÜNDSTELLE |
| 678 | ARC THICKNESS | EPAISSEUR A L'ARC | ZAHNSTÄRKE (IM ROLLKREIS) |
| 679 | ARC TRUE VOLTAGE | TENSION DE SERVICE DE L'ARC | LICHTBOGEN-ARBEITSSPANNUNG |
| 680 | ARC WELDER | MACHINE DE SOUDAGE A L'ARC | LICHTBOGEN-SCHWEISSMASCHINE |
| 681 | ARC WELDING | SOUDURE A L'ARC ELECTRIQUE | LICHTBOGENSCHWEISSUNG |
| 682 | ARC WELDING CONTACT | SOUDAGE AU CONTACT | KONTAKT SCHWEISSEN, LICHTBOGENSCHWEISSEN |
| 683 | ARC WELDING INERT, GAS SHIELDED | SOUDAGE A L'ARC EN ATMOSPHERE INERTE | SCHUTZGAS SCHWEISSEN, LICHTBOGENSCHWEISSEN |
| 684 | ARC WELDING SUBMERGED | SOUDAGE A L'ARC SUBMERGE, PROCEDE 'UNIONMELT' | SCHWEISSEN MIT VERDECKTEN LICHTBOGEN, UNTERPULVER-SCHWEISSEN |
| 685 | ARC WELDING, ALTERNATING CURRENT | SOUDAGE A L'ARC A COURANT ALTERNATIF | LICHTBOGENSCHWEISSEN MIT WECHSELSTROM |
| 686 | ARC WELDING, DIRECT CURRENT | SOUDAGE A L'ARC A COURANT CONTINU | GLEICHSTROM-LICHTBOGENSCHWEISSEN |
| 687 | ARCH BRICK | VOUSSOIR, VOUSSEAU | GEWÖLBESTEIN |
| 688 | ARCH-BUTTRESS | ARC-BOUTANT | STREBEBOGEN |
| 689 | ARCHIMEDEAN DRILL, BRACE, PERSIAN DRILL | DRILLE | DRILLBOHRER |
| 690 | ARCHIMEDEAN SPIRAL, SPIRAL OF ARCHIMEDES | SPIRALE ARCHIMEDIENNE, SPIRALE D'ARCHIMEDE | SPIRALE ARCHIMEDISCHE |
| 691 | ARCHITECT | ARCHITECTE | ARCHITEKT |
| 692 | ARCHITECTURAL BRONZE | BRONZE ARCHITECTURAL | BAUBRONZE |
| 693 | ARCHITECTURAL DRAWING | DESSIN D'ARCHITECTURE | BAUZEICHNUNG |
| 694 | AREA | SURFACE | FLÄCHE |
| 695 | AREA OF CIRCLE | AIRE DU CERCLE | KREISFLÄCHE, KREISINHALT |
| 696 | AREA OF ENGAGEMENT | SURFACE D'ENGRENEMENT | EINGRIFFSFLÄCHE |
| 697 | AREA OF SURFACE | AIRE | INHALT EINER FLÄCHE, FLÄCHENINHALT |
| 698 | AREAL COORDINATES | COORDONNEES PLANES | KOORDINATEN-EBENE |
| 699 | ARGILLACEOUS MARL | MARNE ARGILEUSE | TONMERGEL |
| 700 | ARGILLITE | ARGILLITE | TONSCHIEFER, ARGILLIT |
| 701 | ARGON | ARGON | ARGON |
| 702 | ARITHMETIC | ARITHMETIQUE | ARITHMETIK |
| 703 | ARITHMETICAL MEAN | MOYENNE ARITHMETIQUE | MITTEL (ARITHMETISCHES) |
| 704 | ARITHMETICAL PROGRESSION | PROGRESSION ARITHMETIQUE | REIHE (ARITHMETISCHE) |
| 705 | ARM OF A FLYWHEEL, OF A PULLEY | BRAS D'UN VOLANT, BRAS D'UNE POULIE | ARM (EINES SCHWUNGRADES), ARM (EINER RIEMENSCHEIBE) |
| 706 | ARM OF LEVER, LEVER ARM | BRAS DE LEVIER DE LA FORCE | HEBELARM, KRAFTARM |
| 707 | ARMATURE | INDUIT, ARMATURE | ANKER EINER GLEICHSTROMMASCHINE |

**19** **ASB**

| | | | |
|---|---|---|---|
| 708 | **ARMATURE CORE PLATE** | TOLE POUR LES INDUITS DES DYNAMOS | ANKERBLECH, DYNAMOBLECH |
| 709 | **ARMATURE WINDING MACHINE** | MACHINE A BOBINER LES INDUITS | ANKERWICKELMASCHINE |
| 710 | **ARMATURE, KEEPER OF A MAGNET** | ARMATURE, ARMURE, CONTACT D'UN AIMANT | ANKER EINES MAGNETEN, MAGNETANKER |
| 711 | **ARMCO INGOT IRON** | FER ARMCO | ARMCO-LISEN |
| 712 | **ARMOUR PLATE** | PLAQUE DE BLINDAGE | PANZERPLATTE |
| 713 | **ARMOURED CABLE** | CABLE ARME | PANZERKABEL |
| 714 | **ARMOURED HOSE** | TUBE FLEXIBLE CERCLE EN ACIER, TUBE FLEXIBLE AVEC ARMATURE EN FIL DE FER | SCHLAUCH (GEPANZERTER) |
| 715 | **ARMOURING OF A CABLE** | ARMATURE, REVETEMENT D'UN CABLE | BEWEHRUNG, ARMATUR EINES KABELS, KABELARMATUR |
| 716 | **AROMATIC COMPOUNDS** | COMPOSES AROMATIQUES | VERBINDUNGEN (AROMATISCHE) |
| 717 | **ARRANGEMENT OF RIVETS** | DISTRIBUTION DES RIVETS | GRUPPIERUNG DER NIETE, NIETVERTEILUNG |
| 718 | **ARREST POINT** | POINT DE TRANSFORMATION | UMWANDLUNGSPUNKT |
| 719 | **ARROW** | FLECHE | RICHTUNGSPFEIL |
| 720 | **ARSENIATE** | ARSENIATE | ARSENSÄURESALZ, ARSENIAT |
| 721 | **ARSENIC** | ARSENIC | ARSEN |
| 722 | **ARSENIC ACID** | ACIDE ARSENIQUE | ARSENSÄURE |
| 723 | **ARSENIC PENTOXIDE** | ANHYDRIDE ARSENIQUE | ARSENPENTOXYD, ARSENSÄUREANHYDRID |
| 724 | **ARSENIC TRICHLORIDE** | TRICHLORURE D'ARSENIQUE | ARSENTRICHLORID, CHLORARSEN |
| 725 | **ARSENICAL COPPER** | CUIVRE ARSENICAL | ARSENKUPFER |
| 726 | **ARSENIDE** | ARSENIURE | ARSENMETALL, ARSENID |
| 727 | **ARSENIOUS OXIDE, WHITE ARSENIC** | ARSENIQUE BLANC, ACIDE, ANHYDRIDE ARSENIEUX | ARSENIK (WEISSER), SÄURE (ARSENIGE), ARSENIGS ÄUREANHYDRID, ARSENTRIOXYD |
| 728 | **ARSENIOUS SULPHIDE** | TRISULFURE D'ARSENIC, ORPIMENT | ARSENTRISULFID, ARSENSUPERSULFÜR, AURIPIGMENT, OPERMENT, RAUSCHGELB, ARSENIK (GELBES) |
| 729 | **ARSENITE** | ARSENITE | ARSENIGSÄURESALZ, ARSENIT |
| 730 | **ARSENIURETTED HYDROGEN** | HYDROGENE ARSENIE, ARSENIURE D'HYDROGENE | ARSENWASSERSTOFF |
| 731 | **ARTIFICIAL AGING** | VIEILLISSEMENT ARTIFICIEL | ALTERUNG (KÜNSTLICHE) |
| 732 | **ARTIFICIAL FUEL** | COMBUSTIBLE ARTIFICIEL | BRENNSTOFF (KÜNSTLICHER) |
| 733 | **ARTIFICIAL ILLUMINATION LIGHTING** | ECLAIRAGE ARTIFICIEL | BELEUCHTUNG (KÜNSTLICHE) |
| 734 | **ARTIFICIAL LIGHT** | LUMIERE ARTIFICIELLE | LICHT (KÜNSTLICHES) |
| 735 | **ARTIFICIAL MAGNET** | AIMANT ARTIFICIEL | MAGNET (KÜNSTLICHER) |
| 736 | **ARTIFICIAL SILK** | SOIE ARTIFICIELLE | KUNSTSEIDE |
| 737 | **ARTIFICIAL STONE** | PIERRE ARTIFICIELLE | STEIN (KÜNSTLICHER), KUNSTSTEIN |
| 738 | **ARTIFICIAL VENTILATION** | VENTILATION ARTIFICIELLE | LÜFTUNG (KÜNSTLICHE) |
| 739 | **AS CAST** | BRUT DE COULEE | ROHGEGOSSEN |
| 740 | **AS CONDITION** | ETAT BRUT | ROH |
| 741 | **AS DELIVERED** | A L'ETAT DE LIVRAISON | IM LIEFERZUSTAND |
| 742 | **AS FORGED** | BRUT DE FORGE | ROHGESCHMIEDET |
| 743 | **AS QUENCHED** | BRUT DE TREMPE | IM ABGESCHRECKTEN ZUSTAND |
| 744 | **AS ROLLED** | BRUT DE LAMINAGE | IM GEWALZTEN ZUSTAND |
| 745 | **AS WELDED** | A L'ETAT DE SOUDAGE | IM SCHWEISSZUSTAND |
| 746 | **ASBESTOS** | AMIANTE | ASBEST |
| 747 | **ASBESTOS CARD, ASBESTOS MILLBOARD** | CARTON D'AMIANTE | ASBESTPAPPE, PRESSASBEST |
| 748 | **ASBESTOS CLOTH** | TOILE, TISSU D'AMIANTE | ASBESTGEWEBE |

**ASB** 20

| | | | |
|---|---|---|---|
| 749 | **ASBESTOS CORD** | FIL, BOUDIN D'AMIANTE | ASBESTSCHNUR |
| 750 | **ASBESTOS FELT** | FEUTRE D'AMIANTE | ASBESTFILZ |
| 751 | **ASBESTOS GASKET** | TRESSE, CORDON D'AMIANTE, AMIANTE TRESSE EN CORDELETTE | ASBESTZOPF |
| 752 | **ASBESTOS PAPER** | PAPIER D'AMIANTE | ASBESTPAPIER |
| 753 | **ASBESTOS RING** | ANNEAU D'AMIANTE | ASBESTRING |
| 754 | **ASBESTOS STRIP** | BANDE D'AMIANTE | ASBESTSTREIFEN |
| 755 | **ASBESTOS, AMIANTHUS** | AMIANTE, ASBESTE | ASBEST, AMIANT |
| 756 | **ASCENDING PIPE LINE** | CONDUITE ASCENDANTE | STEIGENDE LEITUNG |
| 757 | **ASCENT, ACCLIVITY, RISING GRADIENT** | RAMPE | STEIGUNG, ANSTIEG |
| 758 | **ASH CONTENT** | TENEUR EN CENDRES, POURCENTAGE DE CENDRES | ASCHENGEHALT |
| 759 | **ASH PIT** | CENDRIER | ASCHENRAUM, ASCHENFALL |
| 760 | **ASHES** | CENDRE, CENDRES | ASCHE |
| 761 | **ASHLAR** | PIERRE DE TAILLE | WERKSTEIN, HAUSTEIN, QUADER |
| 762 | **ASHLAR WORK** | MACONNERIE EN PIERRES DE TAILLE | QUADERMAUERWERK |
| 763 | **ASPHALT (TO)** | ASPHALTER, BITUMER | ASPHALTIEREN |
| 764 | **ASPHALT MASTIC, ROCK ASPHALT MASTIC** | MASTIC D'ASPHALTE | ASPHALTMASTIX |
| 765 | **ASPHALTED FELT** | FEUTRE ASPHALTE | ASPHALTFILZ |
| 766 | **ASPHALTED TUBE** | TUBE PROTEGE PAR UN RECOUVREMENT DE JUTE ASPHALTE | ASPHALTIERTES ROHR |
| 767 | **ASPHALTING** | ASPHALTAGE | ASPHALTIEREN |
| 768 | **ASPHALTUM** | ASPHALTE, BITUME SOLIDE | ASPHALT, ERDPECH |
| 769 | **ASPIRATOR** | ASPIRATEUR | ASPIRATOR |
| 770 | **ASSEMBLING BAY** | HALLE DE MONTAGE | MONTAGEHALLE |
| 771 | **ASSEMBLING BOLT** | BOULON D'ASSEMBLAGE | VERBINDUNGSBOLZEN, VERBINDUNGSSCHRAUBE |
| 772 | **ASSEMBLING DRAWING** | PLAN DE MONTAGE | MONTAGEZEICHNUNG |
| 773 | **ASSEMBLING SHOP** | ATELIER, HALLE DE MONTAGE | MONTAGEHALLE |
| 774 | **ASTATIC** | ASTATIQUE | ASTATISCH |
| 775 | **ASTATIC GOVERNOR** | REGULATEUR ASTATIQUE | REGLER (ASTATISCHER) |
| 776 | **ASTERISM** | ASTERISME | ASTERISMUS |
| 777 | **ASYMMETRICAL CELL** | ELEMENT ASYMETRIQUE | ELEMENT (ASYMMETRISCHES) |
| 778 | **ASYMMETRICAL, DISSYMMETRICAL** | ASYMETRIQUE, DISSYMETRIQUE | UNSYMMETRISCH, ASYMMETRISCH, NICHT SPIEGELGLEICH |
| 779 | **ASYMMETRY, DISSYMMETRY** | ASYMETRIE, DISSYMETRIE | ASYMMETRIE |
| 780 | **ASYMPTOTE** | ASYMPTOTE | ASYMPTOTE |
| 781 | **ASYMPTOTIC** | ASYMPTOTE, ASYMPTOTIQUE | ASYMPTOTISCH |
| 782 | **ASYNCHRONISM** | ASYNCHRONISME | ASYNCHRONISMUS |
| 783 | **ASYNCHRONOUS MOTOR** | MOTEUR ASYNCHRONE | ASYNCHRONMOTOR |
| 784 | **ASYNCHRONOUS, NONSYNCHRONOUS** | ASYNCHRONE | ASYNCHRON |
| 785 | **ATHERMANCY** | ATHERMANEITE | UNDURCHLÄSSIGKEIT FÜR WÄRMESTRAHLEN |
| 786 | **ATHERMANOUS** | ATHERMANE | UNDURCHLÄSSIG FÜR WÄRMESTRAHLEN, ATHERMAN |
| 787 | **ATMOSPHERE** | ATMOSPHERE | ATMOSPHÄRE |
| 788 | **ATMOSPHERE (ATM.)** | ATMOSPHERE (UNITE DE PRESSION) | ATMOSPHÄRE (MASSEINHEIT) |
| 789 | **ATMOSPHERE PREPARED** | ATMOSPHERE ARTIFICIELLE | ATMOSPHÄRE (PRÄPARIERTE) |
| 790 | **ATMOSPHERE PROTECTIVE** | ATMOSPHERE PROTECTRICE | SCHUTZATMOSPHÄRE |

| | | | |
|---|---|---|---|
| 791 | ATMOSPHERE SPECIAL PURPOSE | ATMOSPHERE A USAGE SPECIAL | SONDERZWECKATMOSPHÄRE |
| 792 | ATMOSPHERIC ACTION | ACTIONS ATMOSPHERIQUES | WITTERUNGSEINFLÜSSE |
| 793 | ATMOSPHERIC AGENTS | AGENTS ATMOSPHERIQUES | ATMOSPHÄRILIEN |
| 794 | ATMOSPHERIC BAROMETRIC PRESSURE, PRESSURE OF THE ATMOSPHERE | PRESSION ATMOSPHERIQUE, PRESSION BAROMETRIQUE, PRESSION DE X CM DE MERCURE | LUFTDRUCK, DRUCK (ATMOSPHÄRISCHER) |
| 795 | ATMOSPHERIC CORROSION | CORROSION ATMOSPHERIQUE | KORROSION (ATMOSPHÄRISCHE) |
| 796 | ATMOSPHERIC ELECTRICITY | ELECTRICITE ATMOSPHERIQUE | LUFTELEKTRIZITÄT, ELEKTRIZITÄT (ATMOSPHÄRISCHE) |
| 797 | ATMOSPHERIC ESCAPE VALVE | SOUPAPE D'ECHAPPEMENT | AUSPUFFVENTIL |
| 798 | ATMOSPHERIC LINE | LIGNE ATMOSPHERIQUE | LINIE (ATMOSPHÄRISCHE) |
| 799 | ATMOSPHERIC PRESSURE HEAD | MASSELOTTE A NOYAU | |
| 800 | ATOM | ATOME | ATOM |
| 801 | ATOMIC (HYDROGEN) ARC WELDING | SOUDAGE ARCATOM (A L'ARC PROTEGE, A L'HYDROGENE ATOMIQUE) | SCHUTZGAS-LICHTBOGEN-SCHWEISSEN (ATOMARES) |
| 802 | ATOMIC HEAT | CHALEUR ATOMIQUE | ATOMWÄRME |
| 803 | ATOMIC NUMBER | NOMBRE ATOMIQUE | ATOMZAHL |
| 804 | ATOMIC PLANE | PLAN RETICULAIRE | NETZEBENE, GITTEREBENE |
| 805 | ATOMIC THEORY | THEORIE ATOMIQUE | ATOMTHEORIE |
| 806 | ATOMIC VOLUME | VOLUME ATOMIQUE | ATOMVOLUMEN |
| 807 | ATOMIC WEIGHT | POIDS ATOMIQUE | ATOMGEWICHT |
| 808 | ATOMISE A LIQUID (TO) | PULVERISER (UN LIQUIDE) | ZERSTÄUBEN (EINE FLÜSSIGKEIT) |
| 809 | ATOMISER | PULVERISATEUR, DISPERSEUR DE LIQUIDES | ZERSTÄUBER |
| 810 | ATOMISING A LIQUID | PULVERISATION D'UN LIQUIDE | ZERSTÄUBEN EINER FLÜSSIGKEIT |
| 811 | ATOMIZATION | ATOMISATION, PULVERISATION | ZERSTÄUBUNG |
| 812 | ATTACHMENT | ELEMENT D'APPOINT, ACCESSOIRE | ZUSATZEINRICHTUNG |
| 813 | ATTACK | ATTAQUE | ANGRIFF |
| 814 | ATTENDANCE | CONDUITE (D'UNE MACHINE) | WARTUNG, BEDIENUNG |
| 815 | ATTRACTION | ATTRACTION | ANZIEHUNG |
| 816 | AUDIBLE SIGNAL | SIGNAL ACOUSTIQUE | HÖRBARES ZEICHEN, HÖRSIGNAL, SIGNAL (AKUSTISCHES) |
| 817 | AUER METAL | ALLIAGE D'AUER | AUER METALL, MISCHMETALL |
| 818 | AUGER | TARIERE | ZIMMERMANNBOHRER |
| 819 | AUGITE | AUGITE | AUGIT |
| 820 | AUGITE SYENITE | AUGITE-SYENITE | AUGITSYENIT |
| 821 | AURIC CHLORIDE, CHLORIDE OF GOLD, GOLD TRICHLORIDE | TRICHLORURE D'OR | GOLDTRICHLORID, CHLORGOLD, GOLDCHLORID, AURICHLORID |
| 822 | AURIFEROUS | AURIFERE | GOLDHALTIG |
| 823 | AUROUS CHLORIDE | CHLORURE D'OR | GOLDMONOCHLORID, GOLDCHLORÜR, AUROCHLORID |
| 824 | AUSTEMPERING | TREMPE ETAGEE BAINITIQUE, TREMPE EN ETAPES | ZWISCHENSTUFENVERGÜTUNG, AUSTEMPERUNG, ZWISCHENSTUFENHÄRTUNG |
| 825 | AUSTENITE | AUSTENITE | AUSTENIT |
| 826 | AUSTENITIC STEEL | ACIER AUSTENITIQUE | STAHL (AUSTENITISCHER) |
| 827 | AUSTENITIZING | AUSTENITISATION | AUSTENITISIERUNG |
| 828 | AUTO-STARTER | DEMARREUR AUTOMATIQUE | AUTOSTARTER |
| 829 | AUTOCLAVE, DIGESTER | AUTOCLAVE, DIGESTEUR, MARMITE AUTOCLAVE, MARMITE DE PAPIN | DRUCKKESSEL, DAMPFFASS, DAMPFKOCHTOPF, PAPINSCHER TOPF, DIGESTOR, AUTOKLAV |
| 830 | AUTOFRETTAGE | SOUMISSION A UNE PRE-TENSION | KALTRECKEN, VORSPANNEN |
| 831 | AUTOGEN WELDING | SOUDURE AUTOGENE | AUTOGEN-SCHWEISSUNG |

**AUT** 22

| | | | |
|---|---|---|---|
| 832 | AUTOGENOUS CUTTING | DECOUPAGE AUTOGENE | SCHNEIDEN (AUTOGENES) |
| 833 | AUTOGENOUS CUTTING MACHINE | MACHINE A DECOUPER AUTOGENE | SCHNEIDMASCHINE, SAUERSTOFFSCHNEID-MASCHINE (AUTOGENE) |
| 834 | AUTOGENOUS SOLDERING WELDING | SOUDURE AUTOGENE, AUTOSOUDURE | SCHWEISSUNG (AUTOGENE) |
| 835 | AUTOGENOUS WELDING | SOUDAGE AUTOGENE | AUTOGENSCHWEISSEN |
| 836 | AUTOMATIC ACCELERATION | ACCELERATION AUTOMATIQUE | BESCHLEUNIGUNG (AUTOMATISCHE) |
| 837 | AUTOMATIC ACTION MOVEMENT | AUTOMATICITE | ARBEITEN (SELBSTTÄTIGES), SELBSTTÄTIGKEIT |
| 838 | AUTOMATIC CHOKE | STARTER AUTOMATIQUE | LUFTKAPPENVERSTELLUNG (AUTOMATISCHE) |
| 839 | AUTOMATIC CYCLE | CYCLE AUTOMATIQUE | ARBEITSABLAUF (SELBSTTÄTIGER) |
| 840 | AUTOMATIC CYCLE LATH | TOUR A CYCLES AUTOMATIQUES | DREHMASCHINE MIT AUTOMATISCHEN ARBEITSABLAUFEN |
| 841 | AUTOMATIC DECELERATION | DECELERATION AUTOMATIQUE | VERZÖGERUNG (AUTOMATISCHE) |
| 842 | AUTOMATIC FEED LEVER | LEVIER D'AVANCE AUTOMATIQUE | VORSCHUBHEBEL (SELBSTTÄTIGER) |
| 843 | AUTOMATIC GOVERNOR | REGULATEUR AUTOMATIQUE | REGLER (SELBSTTÄTIGER) |
| 844 | AUTOMATIC IGNITION | ALLUMAGE AUTOMATIQUE | SELBSTZÜNDUNG |
| 845 | AUTOMATIC ISOLATING VALVE | ROBINET D'ISOLEMENT | SELBSTSCHLUSSVENTIL, ROHRBRUCHVENTIL |
| 846 | AUTOMATIC LATHE, AUTOMATIC SCREW MACHINE | TOUR AUTOMATIQUE | DREHBANK (SELBSTTÄTIGE), AUTOMAT, DREHAUTOMAT |
| 847 | AUTOMATIC LEVEL CONTROL | STABILISATEUR AUTOMATIQUE | SELBSTSTABILISIERUNGSSYSTEM |
| 848 | AUTOMATIC LUBRICATION | GRAISSAGE MECANIQUE, GRAISSAGE AUTOMATIQUE | SCHMIERUNG (SELBSTTÄTIGE) |
| 849 | AUTOMATIC MACHINE WELDING | SOUDAGE AUTOMATIQUE | AUTOMATENSCHWEISSEN |
| 850 | AUTOMATIC PROGRAMMING | PROGRAMMATION AUTOMATIQUE | PROGRAMMIEREN (MASCHINELLES) |
| 851 | AUTOMATIC SELF-ACTING LUBRICATOR | GRAISSEUR AUTOMATIQUE | SELBSTÖLER, SCHMIERVORRICHTUNG (SELBSTTÄTIGE) |
| 852 | AUTOMATIC VALVE | SOUPAPE AUTOMATIQUE, SOUPAPE DESMODROMIQUE | VENTIL (UNGESTEUERTES), VENTIL (SELBSTTÄTIGES) |
| 853 | AUXILIARY ENGINE | MACHINE AUXILIAIRE | HILFSMASCHINE |
| 854 | AUXILIARY FUNCTION | FONCTION AUXILIAIRE | HILFSFUNKTION |
| 855 | AVERAGE MEAN TEMPERATURE | TEMPERATURE MOYENNE | TEMPERATUR (MITTLERE), DURCHSCHNITTSTEMPERATUR |
| 856 | AVIATION SNIPS | CISAILLES ARTICULEES | FAUSTSCHERE |
| 857 | AXE | HACHE | AXT |
| 858 | AXES AT RIGHT ANGLES INTERSECTING | AXES D'EQUERRE | ACHSEN (SICH RECHTWINKLIG SCHNEIDENDE) |
| 859 | AXIAL COMPONENT | COMPOSANTE AXIALE | AXIALKOMPONENTE |
| 860 | AXIAL DISPLACEMENT | DEPLACEMENT AXIAL, DEPLACEMENT LONGITUDINAL, DEPLACEMENT PARALLELE A L'AXE | LÄNGSVERSCHIEBUNG, VERSCHIEBUNG (AXIALE) |
| 861 | AXIAL FLOW PUMP | POMPE HELICOIDALE | SCHRAUBENPUMPE |
| 862 | AXIAL FLOW TURBINE | TURBINE AXIALE, TURBINE PARALLELE | AXIALTURBINE |
| 863 | AXIAL RATIO IN CRYSTALS | AXE DE SYMETRIE DES CRISTAUX | KRISTALLSYMMETRIEACHSE |
| 864 | AXIS | AXE | KOORDINATENACHSE |
| 865 | AXIS OF A CRYSTAL | AXE D'UN CRISTAL | KRISTALLACHSE |
| 866 | AXIS OF A PIPE TUBE | AXE D'UN TUYAU | ROHRACHSE |
| 867 | AXIS OF OSCILLATION | AXE D'OSCILLATION | SCHWINGUNGSACHSE |
| 868 | AXIS OF ROTATION | AXE DE ROTATION | DREHACHSE, UMDREHUNGSACHSE |
| 869 | AXIS OF SYMMETRY | AXE DE SYMETRIE | SCHWERPUNKTACHSE, SYMMETRIBACHSE |
| 870 | AXIS OF THE WELD | AXE DE SOUDURE | NAHTACHSE |

| | | | |
|---|---|---|---|
| 871 | AXIS OF THE WELD BEAD | AXE DU CORDON DE SOUDURE | SCHWEISSRAUPENACHSE |
| 872 | AXIS OF X | AXE DES ABCISSES, AXE DES X | ABSZISSENACHSE, X-ACHSE |
| 873 | AXIS OF Y | AXE DES ORDONNEES, AXE DES Y | ORDINATENACHSE, Y-ACHSE |
| 874 | AXIS, CENTRE LINE | AXE GEOMETRIQUE | ACHSE, MITTELLINIE, ZENTRALLINIE |
| 875 | AXLE | ESSIEU OU ARBRE | ACHSE, WELLE |
| 876 | AXLE BEARING | BOITE D'ESSIEU | ACHSLAGER |
| 877 | AXLE BOX | BOITE D'ESSIEU, BOITE A GRAISSE, BOITE A HUILE, BOITE DE GRAISSAGE | ACHSLAGER, ACHSBÜCHSE |
| 878 | AXLE BOX DRILLING MACHINE | PERCEUSE POUR BOITE D'ESSIEU | ACHSLAGERBOHRMASCHINE |
| 879 | AXLE GREASE | GRAISSE DE VOITURE, CAMBOUIS | WAGENFETT, WAGENSCHMIERE |
| 880 | AXLE JOURNAL LATHE | TOUR POUR FUSEE D'ESSIEU | ACHSSCHENKELDREHBANK |
| 881 | AXLE LATHE | TOUR A ESSIEUX | ACHSENDREHBANK |
| 882 | AXLE NECK | FUSEE D'ESSIEU | ACHSSCHENKEL |
| 883 | AXLE WRENCH | CLEF DE CHAPEAU, CLEF D'ESSIEU | ACHSKAPPENSCHLÜSSEL, RADMUTTERSCHLÜSSEL |
| 884 | AXLE, AXLE TREE | ESSIEU | ACHSE, RADACHSE |
| 885 | AXONOMETRIC PERSPECTIVE | PERSPECTIVE AXONOMETRIQUE | PERSPEKTIVE (AXONOMETRISCHE) |
| 886 | AZURITE, BLUE CARBONATE OF COPPER | AZURITE | KUPFERLASUR, BERGBLAU |
| 887 | B.S.I. (BRITSH STANDARDS INSTITUTION) | INSTITUT BRITANNIQUE DE NORMALISATION | NORMENINSTITUT (ENGLISCHES) |
| 888 | BABBITT ('S METAL) | METAL ANTIFRICTION, METAL BLANC | WEISSMETALL |
| 889 | BABBITT METAL | REGULE, ANTIFRICTION | LAGER-WEISSMETAL |
| 890 | BACK | DOS | RÜCKEN |
| 891 | BACK DOOR | HAYON, PORTE, PORTIERE ARRIERE | HINTERTÜR |
| 892 | BACK FIRING | RETOUR DE LA FLAMME | ZURÜCKSCHLAGEN DER FLAMME |
| 893 | BACK OFF (TO), RELIEVE (TO) | DEPOUILLER, DEGAGER | HINTERDREHEN |
| 894 | BACK PRESSURE OPERATION | MARCHE EN CONTRE-PRESSION | GEGENDRUCKBETRIEB |
| 895 | BACK PRESSURE VALVE | VALVE DE CONTREPRESSION | GEGENDRUCKVENTIL |
| 896 | BACK REFLECTION | REFLEXION EN RETOUR | RÜCKSTRAHLUNG |
| 897 | BACK SAW | SCIE A DOS | RÜCKENSÄGE |
| 898 | BACK STOP | BUTEE | GEGENHALTER |
| 899 | BACK WINDOW | LUNETTE ARRIERE | RÜCKFENSTER |
| 900 | BACK-FILLING | REMBLAI, REMBLAYAGE | HINTERFÜLLUNG |
| 901 | BACK-STEP SEQUENCE | SOUDURE A PAS DE PELERIN | PILGERSCHRITTSCHWEISSVERFAHREN |
| 902 | BACK-STRIP, BACKING-STRIP | FEUILLARD-SUPPORT, PLAT-SUPPORT | KUPFERFLACHPROFIL, BANDSTAHL |
| 903 | BACK-UP ROLLS | CYLINDRES DE SUPPORT | STÜTZWALZEN |
| 904 | BACK-UP WELD | CORDON SUPPORT (A L'ENVERS) | STÜTZRAUPE, WURZELSEITIGE GEGENNAHT |
| 905 | BACKED OFF CUTTER, RELIEVED TOOTH MILLING CUTTER | FRAISE A DENTS DEPOUILLEES, FRAISE A DENTS DEGAGEES, FRAISE A PROFIL CONSTANT | FRÄSER MIT HINTERDREHTEN ZÄHNEN |
| 906 | BACKFIRE | RETOUR DE FLAMME | FLAMMENRÜCKSCHLAG, RÜCKSCHLAG, RÜCKZÜNDUNG |
| 907 | BACKHAND WELDING | SOUDAGE A DROITE | RECHTSSCHWEISSUNG |
| 908 | BACKING LIGHTS | FEUX DE RECUL | RÜCKLICHT |
| 909 | BACKING MATERAIL | METAL SUPPORT | GRUNDWERKSTOFF |
| 910 | BACKING OFF, RELIEVING | DEPOUILLE, DEGAGEMENT | HINTERDREHEN |
| 911 | BACKING RING | CONTRE-JOINT | STÜTZRING |
| 912 | BACKING SAND | SABLE DE COUVERTURE | FÜLLSAND |

# BAC 24

| | | | |
|---|---|---|---|
| 913 | BACKING-OFF LATHE, RELIEVING LATHE | TOUR A DEPOUILLER, A DEGAGER | HINTERDREHBANK |
| 914 | BACKLASH | JEU ENTRE DENTS | FLANKENSPIELRAUM |
| 915 | BACKLASH ELIMINATOR | MECANISME DE REPRISE DES JEUX | SPIELVERRINGERUNGSEINRICHTUNG |
| 916 | BACKLASH, LOST MOTION | JEU INUTILE, JEU PERNICIEUX, JEU NUISIBLE | GANG (TOTER) |
| 917 | BACKREST | DOSSIER | RÜCKENLEHNE |
| 918 | BACKSTEP WELDING | SOUDAGE EN PAS DE PELERIN | GEGENSCHRITTSCHWEISSEN |
| 919 | BACKWARD MOVEMENT | MOUVEMENT DANS LE SENS RETROGRADE, MOUVEMENT DE RECUL, RECUL | RÜCKWÄRTSBEWEGUNG, BEWEGUNG (RÜCKLÄUFIGE) |
| 920 | BAD WELD | SOUDAGE MAL FAIT, SOUDURE MAL FAITE | SCHWEISSVERBINDUG (SCHLECHTE) |
| 921 | BAFFLE | DEFLECTEUR, CHICANE, TOLE DEFLECTRICE | LEITBLECH, ABLEITBLECH |
| 922 | BAFFLE PLATE, BAFFLER, DEFLECTOR | CHICANE | LEITBLECH, VERTEILUNGSWAND |
| 923 | BAG MOULDING PROCESS | PROCEDE DE MOULAGE AU MOYEN DU SAC EN CAOUTCHOUC | GUMMISACKVERFAHREN |
| 924 | BAGASSE | BAGASSE | BAGASSE |
| 925 | BAINITE | BAINITE | BAINITE, ZWISCHENSTUFENGEFÜGE |
| 926 | BAKED CLAY | ARGILE CUITE | TON (GEBRANNTER) |
| 927 | BAKED CORE | NOYAU ETUVE | TROCKENKERN |
| 928 | BAKING | SECHAGE | TROCKNUNG |
| 929 | BALANCE | EQUILIBRE | AUSGLEICH |
| 930 | BALANCE (TO), COUNTERBALANCE (TO) | EQUILIBRER, CONTRE-BALANCER, COMPENSER | AUSWUCHTEN, AUSGLEICHEN, AUSBALANCIEREN |
| 931 | BALANCE, SCALES | BALANCE, BASCULE | WAAGE |
| 932 | BALANCED ECONOMY | ECONOMIE SAINE, ECONOMIE EN EQUILIBRE | WIRSTSCHAFT (GESUNDE) |
| 933 | BALANCED FILTERS | FILTRES SYMETRIQUES | FILTER (SYMMETRISCHE) |
| 934 | BALANCED VALVE, EQUILIBRIUM VALVE | SOUPAPE EQUILIBREE, VALVE EQUILIBREE | VENTIL (ENTLASTETES), VENTIL (AUSBALANCIERTES) |
| 935 | BALANCING | EQUILIBRAGE | BALANCIEREN |
| 936 | BALANCING A VALVE | EQUILIBRAGE D'UNE SOUPAPE | ENTLASTUNG EINES VENTILS |
| 937 | BALANCING APPARATUS | APPAREIL D'EQUILIBRAGE | AUSWUCHTMASCHINE |
| 938 | BALANCING CYLINDER | CYLINDRE D'EQUILIBRAGE | AUSGLEICHZYLINDER |
| 939 | BALANCING DRUM | CYLINDRE D'EQUILIBRAGE | AUSGLEICHZYLINDER |
| 940 | BALANCING MACHINE | MACHINE A EQUILIBRER | AUSWUCHTMASCHINE |
| 941 | BALANCING THE MASSES | EQUILIBRAGE DES MASSES | MASSENAUSGLEICH |
| 942 | BALANCING, COUNTERBALANCING, EQUILIBRATION | EQUILIBRAGE, EQUILIBRATION | AUSWUCHTUNG, AUSGLEICHUNG, AUSBALANCIERUNG |
| 943 | BALATA | BALATA | BALATAHARZ, BALATA |
| 944 | BALATA BELT | COURROIE EN BALATA | BALATARIEMEN |
| 945 | BALE | BALLE (DE MARCHANDISE) | BALLEN |
| 946 | BALE PICK-UP | RAMASSE-BALLES | HEUBÜNDLER |
| 947 | BALE TRUCK | DIABLE, CABROUET | SACKKARREN, BALLENKARREN, STECHKARREN |
| 948 | BALERS, HIGH, LOW DENSITY, STATIONARY AND PICK-UP | BOTTELEUSES MECANIQUES A TOUTE DENSITE | BINDERMASCHINEN ALLER ARTEN |
| 949 | BALK, JOIST | POUTRE EN BOIS | BALKEN (HÖLZERNER) |
| 950 | BALL | BILLE | KUGEL |
| 951 | BALL (OR LUMP) OF STEEL | LOUPE, MASSE D'ACIER, GUEUSE | STAHLDEUL |
| 952 | BALL AND SOCKET BEARING | PALIER A TOURILLON SPHERIQUE | KUGELZAPFENLAGER |

| | | | |
|---|---|---|---|
| 953 | BALL AND SOCKET JOINT, SPHERICAL JOINT | JOINT SPHERIQUE, GENOU, JOINT A ROTULE | KUGELGELENK |
| 954 | BALL BEARING | PALIER A ROULEMENT A BILLES, ROULEMENT A BILLES, COUSSINET A BILLES, ROULEMENT | KUGELLAGER |
| 955 | BALL BEARING CUP | CAGE DE ROULEMENT A BILLES | KUGELLAGERSCHALE |
| 956 | BALL BURNISHING | POLISSAGE A BILLES | KUGELPOLIEREN |
| 957 | BALL CAGE | CAGE A BILLES | KÄFIG EINES KUGELLAGERS, KUGELKÄFIG |
| 958 | BALL JOINT SUSPENSION | SUSPENSION A ROTULE | KUGELGELENKAUFHÄNGUNG |
| 959 | BALL MILL | BROYEUR A BOULETS | KUGELMÜHLE |
| 960 | BALL PANE HAMMER | MARTEAU A PANNE BOMBEE, MARTEAU ARRONDI | HAMMER MIT KUGELFINNE |
| 961 | BALL PEEN | PANNE RONDE | KUGELFINNE |
| 962 | BALL PEEN HAMMER | MARTEAU A PANNE RONDE | HAMMER MIT KUGELFINNE |
| 963 | BALL PLANE | PANNE BOMBEE, PANNE SPHERIQUE | KUGELFINNE |
| 964 | BALL RACE | ANNEAU DE ROULEMENT, BAGUE DE ROULEMENT | KUGELRING, LAUFRING |
| 965 | BALL RACE WAY | CHEMIN DE ROULEMENT DES BILLES | KUGELBAHN, KUGELSPUR (EINES LAGERS) |
| 966 | BALL THRUST BEARING | BUTEE A BILLES | KUGELDRUCKLAGER |
| 967 | BALL THRUST TESTING MACHINE | APPAREIL A BILLER | KUGELDRUCKPRÜFAPPARAT |
| 968 | BALL VALVE | VANNE A BOISSEAU SPHERIQUE, ROBINET A BOISSEAU SPHERIQUE (A BOULE), SOUPAPE A BOULET, SOUPAPE-BILLE | KUGELVENTIL, KUGELHAHN |
| 969 | BALLAST | BALLAST | SCHÜTTUNG, MASSE (AUFGBSCHÜTTETE) |
| 970 | BALLAST UNIT | CLAPET | VENTIL |
| 971 | BALLASTING | BALLASTAGE | SCHÜTTUNG, ANSCHÜTTEN |
| 972 | BAMBOO CANE | BAMBOU | BAMBUSROHR |
| 973 | BANCA TIN | ETAIN DE BANCA | BANKAZINN |
| 974 | BAND | BANDE, RUBAN | BAND |
| 975 | BAND PULLEY | POULIE A CORDE | SCHNURSCHEIBE |
| 976 | BAND TENSION INDICATOR | INDICATEUR DE TENSION DU RUBAN | BANDSPANNUNGSANZEIGER |
| 977 | BAND-SAWING MACHINE | SCIE A RUBAN | BANDSÄGEMASCHINE |
| 978 | BAND, ENDLESS, RIBBON SAW | SCIE A RUBAN, SCIE A LAME SANS FIN | BANDSÄGE |
| 979 | BANDED STRUCTURE | STRUCTURE ZONALE | ZEILENSTRUKTUR |
| 980 | BANDS | BANDES, RUBANS, FEUILLARDS | BÄNDER, STREIFEN |
| 981 | BAR | BARRE | STAB |
| 982 | BAR AND TUBE DRAWING MACHINE | MACHINE A ETIRER LES BARRES ET LES TUBES | STANGEN-UND ROHRZIEHMASCHINE |
| 983 | BAR AUTOMATICS | TOUR AUTOMATIQUE TRAVAILLANT EN BARRE | STANGENDREHAUTOMAT |
| 984 | BAR IRON, STEEL BAR | BARREAUX VERGES DE FER, FER EN BARREAUX EN VERGES, ACIER EN BARRES | STABEISEN |
| 985 | BAR MAGNET | AIMANT EN FORME DE BARREAU, BARREAU AIMANTE | STABMAGNET |
| 986 | BAR, MEMBER (OF LATTICEWORK) | BARRE, POUTRELLE | STAB (EINES FACHWERKES) |
| 987 | BARBED WIRE | RONCE ARTIFICIELLE, FIL BARBELE | STACHELDRAHT |
| 988 | BARBED WIRE MACHINE | MACHINE A FIL BARBELE | STACHELDRAHTMASCHINE |
| 989 | BARE ELECTRODE | ELECTRODE NUE | ELEKTRODE (NACKTE) |

# BAR

26

| | | | |
|---|---|---|---|
| 990 | **BARE WIRE** | FIL NU | DRAHT (NACKTER), DRAHT (BLANKER), DRAHT (NICHT ISOLIERTER ELEKTR.) |
| 991 | **BARGE** | BARGE, PENICHE | LASTKAHN |
| 992 | **BARIUM** | BARYUM | BARIUM |
| 993 | **BARIUM ACETATE** | ACETATE DE BARYUM | BARYT, BARIUMAZETAT (ESSIGSAURES) |
| 994 | **BARIUM ALUMINATE** | ALUMINATE DE BARYTE | BARIUMALUMINAT |
| 995 | **BARIUM CARBIDE** | CARBURE DE BARYUM | BARIUMKARBID |
| 996 | **BARIUM CARBONATE** | CARBONATE DE BARYUM | BARIUM (KOHLENSAURES), BARIUMKARBONAT |
| 997 | **BARIUM CHLORIDE** | CHLORURE DE BARYUM | CHLORBARIUM, BARIUMCHLORID |
| 998 | **BARIUM DIOXIDE** | BIOXYDE DE BARYUM | BARIUMSUPEROXYD, BARIUMHYPEROXYD, BARIUMDIOXYD |
| 999 | **BARIUM FLUORIDE** | FLUORURE DE BARYUM | BARUIMFLUORID, FLUOBARIUM |
| 1000 | **BARIUM HYDROXIDE** | HYDRATE DE BARYTE, HYDRATE DE BARYUM | BARIUMHYDROXYD, BARIUMOXYDHYDRAT, BARYTHYDRAT, BARYT (KAUSTISCHER), ÄTZBARYT |
| 1001 | **BARIUM NITRATE** | AZOTATE DE BARYUM | BARYT (SALPETERSAURER), BARIUMNITRAT |
| 1002 | **BARIUM PLATINOCYANIDE** | PLATINOCYANURE DE BARYUM | BARIUMPLATINZYANÜR |
| 1003 | **BARIUM SULPHATE, PERMANENT WHITE, BLANC FIXE** | SULFATE DE BARYUM, BLANC FIXE, BLANC DE BARYTE | BARIUM (SCHWEFELSAURES), BARIUMSULFAT, BARYTWEISS, NEUWEISS, MINERALWEISS, PERMANENTWEISS, SCHNEEWEISS |
| 1004 | **BARIUM SULPHIDE** | SULFURE DE BARYUM | SCHWEFELBARIUM, BARIUMSULFID |
| 1005 | **BARK** | COUCHE INTERMEDIAIRE DECARBUREE | ZWISCHENSCHICHT (ENTKOHLTE) |
| 1006 | **BARN** | UNITE DE SURFACE NUCLEAIRE, BARN | BARN |
| 1007 | **BAROGRAPH** | BAROMETRE ENREGISTREUR | BAROGRAPH |
| 1008 | **BAROMETER** | BAROMETRE | BAROMETER |
| 1009 | **BAROMETRIC** | BAROMETRIQUE | BAROMETRISCH |
| 1010 | **BAROMETRIC CONDENSER** | CONDENSEUR BAROMETRIQUE | KONDENSATOR (BAROMETRISCHER) |
| 1011 | **BAROSCOPE** | BAROSCOPE | BAROSKOP |
| 1012 | **BARREL BURNISHING** | POLISSAGE AU TAMBOUR | FASSPOLIEREN |
| 1013 | **BARREL DRILLING MACHINE** | MACHINE A ALESER EN CREUX | HOHLBOHRMASCHINE |
| 1014 | **BARREL FINISHING** | FINISSAGE AU TONNEAU | TROMMELN |
| 1015 | **BARREL OF A PUMP, PUMP BARREL** | CYLINDRE, CORPS DE POMPE | PUMPENZYLINDER |
| 1016 | **BARREL PLATING** | REVETEMENT GALVANIQUE AU TAMBOUR, GALVANOPLASTIE AU TONNEAU | ÜBERZUG IN FÄSSER (GALVANISCHER), TROMMELGALVANISIERUNG |
| 1017 | **BARREL-SHAPED ROLLER** | ROULEAU RENFLE | ROLLE (TONNENFÖRMIGE) |
| 1018 | **BARRING ENGINE** | SERVOMOTEUR DE LANCEMENT, SERVOMOTEUR DE DEMARRAGE | ANLASSMASCHINE, DREHMASCHINE, SCHALTMASCHINE |
| 1019 | **BARYTA WATER** | EAU DE BARYTE | BARYTWASSER |
| 1020 | **BARYTA, BARIUM MONOXIDE** | BARYTE, PROTOXYDE DE BARYUM | BARYT, BARIUMMONOXYD, SCHWERERDE |
| 1021 | **BARYTES, HEAVY SPAR** | BARYTINE, BARYTITE, SPATH PESANT | SCHWERSPAT, BARYT (SCHWEFELSAURER) |
| 1022 | **BASALT** | BASALTE | BASALT |
| 1023 | **BASALTIC TUFF** | BASALTIQUE | BASALTTUFF |
| 1024 | **BASE** | BASE (CHIM.) | BASE (CHEM.) |
| 1025 | **BASE** | BASE (D'UN SOLIDE) | GRUNDFLÄCHE |
| 1026 | **BASE** | BASE, SOCLE, FACE D'APPUI | BASE, UNTERBAU, GRUNDPLATTE, BERÜHRUNGSFLÄCHE |

| | | | |
|---|---|---|---|
| 1027 | **BASE** | BASE | GRUNDLINIE, BASIS (GEOM.) |
| 1028 | **BASE BOTTOM OF THREAD** | FOND, RACINE, BASE D'UN FILET | GRUND, BASIS EINES GEWINDES, GEWINDEBASIS, GEWINDEGRUND |
| 1029 | **BASE BULLION** | PLOMB IMPUR, PLOMB NON RAFFINE | BLEI (UNREINLICHES), BLEI UNRAFFINIERTES) |
| 1030 | **BASE CIRCLE, FUNDAMENTAL CIRCLE** | CERCLE DE BASE, CERCLE PRIMITIF | GRUNDKREIS |
| 1031 | **BASE METAL** | METAL NON PRECIEUX | METALL (UNEDLES) |
| 1032 | **BASE METAL** | METAL DE BASE | GRUNDMETALL |
| 1033 | **BASE OF A LOGARITHM** | BASE D'UN LOGARITHME | GRUNDZAHL, BASIS EINES LOGARITHMUS |
| 1034 | **BASE OF BEARING** | PATIN D'UN PALIER | LAGERFUSS |
| 1035 | **BASE OF COLUMN** | SOUBASSEMENT D'UNE COLONNE | FUSS EINER SÄULE, SÄULENFUSS |
| 1036 | **BASE OF TOOTH** | RACINE DE LA DENT | ZAHNWURZEL |
| 1037 | **BASE PLATE, BED PLATE, FOUNDATION PLATE** | PLAQUE DE FOND, PLAQUE DE FONDATION, PLAQUE D'ASSISE, PLAQUE DE BASE, SOCLE EN FONTE | GRUNDPLATTE EINER MASCHINE |
| 1038 | **BASE-FORMING ELEMENT** | ELEMENT BASIQUE | ELEMENT (BASENBILDENDES) |
| 1039 | **BASE-METAL TEST SPECIMEN** | EPROUVETTE DE METAL DE BASE | GRUNDMETALLPROBESTÜCK, PRÜFSTÜCK |
| 1040 | **BASE-PLATE** | EMBASE | UNTERPLATTE |
| 1041 | **BASE, FOOT** | PIED, SUPPORT | FUSSGESTELL |
| 1042 | **BASIC** | BASIQUE | BASISCH |
| 1043 | **BASIC BESSEMER PROCESS** | PROCEDE BASIQUE, PROCEDE THOMAS | THOMAS-VERFAHREN |
| 1044 | **BASIC BESSEMER STEEL** | ACIER THOMAS | THOMASSTAHL |
| 1045 | **BASIC BOTTOM & LINING** | SOLE ET GARNISSAGE BASIQUES | BODENSTEIN (BASISCHER) UND FUTTER (BASISCHES) |
| 1046 | **BASIC FLUX** | FLUX BASIQUE | FLUSS (BASISCHER) |
| 1047 | **BASIC OPEN HEARTH STEEL** | ACIER MARTIN PAR LE PROCEDE BASIQUE | SIEMENSMARTINSTAHL (BASISCHER) |
| 1048 | **BASIC OPEN-HEARTH STEEL** | ACIER SUR SOLE BASIQUE, ACIER MARTIN | SIEMENS-MARTIN-STAHL (BASISCHER) |
| 1049 | **BASIC PIG** | FONTE THOMAS | THOMASROHEISEN, ROHEISEN (BASISCHES) |
| 1050 | **BASIC PROCESS** | PROCEDE BASIQUE | VERFAHREN (BASISCHES) |
| 1051 | **BASIC REFRACTORIES** | REFRACTAIRES BASIQUES | OFENFUTTER (BASISCHES) |
| 1052 | **BASIC RESEARCH** | RECHERCHE PURE | GRUNDLAGENFORSCHUNG |
| 1053 | **BASIC SIZE** | COTE DE BASE | GRUNDMASS |
| 1054 | **BASIC SLAG** | SCORIES BASIQUES | THOMASSCHLACKE |
| 1055 | **BASICITY** | BASICITE | BASIZITÄT |
| 1056 | **BAST, PHLOEM** | LIBER | BAST |
| 1057 | **BASTARD FILE** | LIME A TAILLE BATARDE | BASTARDFEILE, VORFEILE |
| 1058 | **BASTARD SAWING OF TIMBER** | SCIAGE PARALLELE, SCIAGE EN LONG, DEBIT A LA SCIE DE LONG, GRAND DEBIT DU BOIS | SEHNENSCHNITT, FLADERSCHNITT, TANGENTIATLSCHNITT DES HOLZES |
| 1059 | **BATCH** | LOT DE COULEE | SATZ, GICHT, EINZELLOS |
| 1060 | **BATCH FURNACE** | FOUR A CHARGER, FOUR NON CONTINU | CHARGENOFEN, EÏNSATZOFEN |
| 1061 | **BATCHED GEAR** | ROCHET | KLINGWERK |
| 1062 | **BATH** | BAIN | BAD |
| 1063 | **BATH MIXING TAP** | ROBINET DE BAIGNOIRE | MISCHBATTERIE FÜR BADEWANNEN |
| 1064 | **BATH VOLTAGE** | COURANT DU BAIN | BADSTROM |
| 1065 | **BATTER** | INCLINAISON, OBLIQUITE | SCHRÄGE, NEIGUNG |

**BAT** 28

| | | | |
|---|---|---|---|
| 1066 | **BATTERY** | BATTERIE D'ACCUMULATEURS | BATTERIE |
| 1067 | **BATTERY BOX** | BAC DE BATTERIE | BATTERIEKASTEN |
| 1068 | **BATTERY MAIN SWITCH** | ROBINET DE BATTERIE | BATTERIESCHALTER |
| 1069 | **BATTERY OF BOILERS** | BATTERIE DE CHAUDIERES | KESSELBATTERIE |
| 1070 | **BAUSCHINGER EFFECT** | EFFET BAUSCHINGER | BAUSCHINGER-EFFEKT |
| 1071 | **BAUXITE** | BAUXITE | BAUXIT |
| 1072 | **BAY** | HALLE | HALLE |
| 1073 | **BAYER PROCESS** | PROCEDE BAYER | BAYER-VERFAHREN |
| 1074 | **BAYONET JOINT** | EMMANCHEMENT, FERMETURE A BAIONNETTE, BAIONNETTE | BAJONETTVERSCHLUSS |
| 1075 | **BE IN COMPRESSION (TO), TENSION** | TRAVAILLER A LA COMPRESSION, TRAVAILLER A LA TRACTION | BEANSPRUCHT WERDEN (AUF DRUCK), BEANSPRUCHT WERDEN (AUF ZUG) |
| 1076 | **BE IN EQUILIBRIUM (TO)** | EQUILIBRER (S') | AUFHEBEN (SICH), GLEICHGEWICHT SEIN (MIT) |
| 1077 | **BE IN GEAR (TO), GEAR TOGETHER (TO), GEAR WITH (TO)...** | ENGRENER ENSEMBLE, S'ENGRENER | INEINANDERGREIFEN, IM EINGRIFF STEHEN |
| 1078 | **BE IN SHEAR (TO), BE SUBJECT TO SHEARING STRESS (TO)** | CISAILLER, ETRE SOUMIS A UN EFFORT DE CISAILLEMENT, TRAVAILLER AU CISAILLEMENT | SCHUBBEANSPRUCHTWERDEN |
| 1079 | **BE ON FULL LOAD (TO)** | MARCHER A PLEINE CHARGE | VOLLBELASTET LAUFEN |
| 1080 | **BE ON LIGHT LOAD (TO)** | MARCHER A CHARGE INCOMPLETE | UNTERBELASTET LAUFEN |
| 1081 | **BE ON NO-LOAD (TO)** | MARCHER A VIDE | UNBELASTET, LEERLAUFEN |
| 1082 | **BEAD** | BOUDIN, CORDON DE SOUDURE | WULST, SCHWEISSRAUPE |
| 1083 | **BEAD** | BORD RABATTU, TOMBE | BÖRDEL, KREMPE |
| 1084 | **BEAD (TO)** | RABATTRE, TOMBER, RETROUSSER LES BORDS DES TOLES, RABATTRE LA COLLERETTE DES TUBES | KREMPEN, UMBÖRDELN |
| 1085 | **BEAD WELD** | SOUDURE LINEAIRE DE FRACTION | STRICHNAHT, ZUGNAHT |
| 1086 | **BEADED IRON** | FER POUR CLOTURE | GELÄNDER-EISEN |
| 1087 | **BEADED TUBE** | TUBE A COLLET RABATTU, TUBE A BORD RABATTU | BÖRDELROHR |
| 1088 | **BEADING** | RABATTEMENT, TOMBAGE, RETROUSSEMENT DES BORDS DES TOLES, RABATTEMENT DE LA COLLERETTE DES TUBES, BORDELAGE | KREMPEN, BÖRDELN, UMBÖRDELN, UMBÖRDELUNG |
| 1089 | **BEADING MACHINE** | MACHINE A FAIRE LES BOURRELETS | WULSTMASCHINE |
| 1090 | **BEAK HORN** | BIGORNE, CORNE D'ENCLUME | AMBOSSHORN |
| 1091 | **BEAK IRON, BECK IRON** | BIGORNE | SPERRHORN |
| 1092 | **BEAKER** | BECHER | BECHERGLAS |
| 1093 | **BEAM** | FAISCEAU, FAISCEAU ELECTRONIQUE, POUTRELLE, POUTRE | ELEKTRONENBÜNDEL, TRÄGER, BÜNDEL |
| 1094 | **BEAM AND CRANK MECHANISM** | MECANISME A MANIVELLE, DISPOSITIF BIELLE ET MANIVELLE | KURBELGETRIEBE |
| 1095 | **BEAM BALANCE** | BALANCE A FLEAU | BALKENWAAGE |
| 1096 | **BEAM COMPASSES, TRAMMELS** | COMPAS A VERGE | STANGENZIRKEL |
| 1097 | **BEAM FIXED AT ONE END, FREELY SUPPORTED AT OTHER** | POUTRE ENCASTREE A UNE EXTREMITE ET REPOSANT A L'AUTRE SUR UN APPUI | TRÄGER (HALBEINGESPANNTER, EINSEITIG EINGESPANNTER) |
| 1098 | **BEAM SUPPORTED AT BOTH ENDS** | POUTRE REPOSANT SOUTENUE LIBREMENT SUR DEUX APPUIS | TRÄGER (FREI AUFLIEGENDER) |
| 1099 | **BEAM, GIRDER** | POUTRE | TRÄGER (BAUW.) |

**BEL**

| | | | |
|---|---|---|---|
| 1100 | **BEARING** | COUSSINET, PALIER | LAGERSCHALE, LAGER, KOLBENSTANGENLAGER |
| 1101 | **BEARING AREA** | SURFACE PORTANTE | LAGEFLÄCHE, AUFLAGEFLÄCHE |
| 1102 | **BEARING BALL** | BILLE POUR ROULEMENTS | KUGEL EINES KUGELLAGERS |
| 1103 | **BEARING BRACKET** | CHAISE DE PALIER | LAGERBOCK |
| 1104 | **BEARING CAP** | CHAPEAU DE PALIER | LAGERDECKEL |
| 1105 | **BEARING FRICTION** | FROTTEMENT DANS LES PALIERS | LAGERREIBUNG |
| 1106 | **BEARING METAL, BOX METAL** | METAL POUR COUSSINET, COMPOSITION POUR COUSSINET, ALLIAGE POUR COUSSINET | LAGERMETALL |
| 1107 | **BEARING NECK** | PORTEE D'UN ARBRE | LAGERHALS EINER WELLE |
| 1108 | **BEARING NEEDLES** | AIGUILLES POUR ROULEMENTS | ROLLENLAGERNADELN |
| 1109 | **BEARING PLATE, STRUCTURAL** | TOLE DE CONSTRUCTION | BAUSTAHLBLECH |
| 1110 | **BEARING PRESSURE, REACTION** | PRESSION SUR LES SURFACES D'APPUI, REACTION DES APPUIS | AUFLAGERDRUCK, FLÄCHENDRUCK, STÜTZDRUCK. LAGERDRUCK, AUFLAGEPRESSUNG ; ACHSDRUCK |
| 1111 | **BEARING RACE** | CHEMIN DE ROULEMENT. | LAUFRING |
| 1112 | **BEARING ROLLER** | ROULEAU, GALET POUR ROULEMENTS | ROLLE EINES ROLLENLAGERS |
| 1113 | **BEARING SHELL** | COQUILLE DE COUSSINET | LAGERSCHALE |
| 1114 | **BEARING SPRING** | RESSORT DE SUSPENSION | TRAGFEDER |
| 1115 | **BEARING SURFACE** | SURFACE PORTANTE, SURFACE D'APPUI | FLÄCHE (TRAGENDE), TRAGFLÄCHE, AUFLAGEFLÄCHE |
| 1116 | **BEARING SURFACE FOR ROTATING SHAFT** | SURFACE DE PORTEE D'UN TOURILLON, PORTEE D'UN MANETON | LAUFFLÄCHE, AUFLAGERFLÄCHE EINES ZAPFENS, ZAPFENLAUFFLÄCHE |
| 1117 | **BEARING, SHAFT BEARING** | PALIER, ROULEMENT | LAGER, WELLENLAGER, ZAPFENLAGER |
| 1118 | **BEARING, SUPPORT** | APPUI, SUPPORT (CONSTR.) | LAGER, LAGERUNG, AUFLAGER |
| 1119 | **BEAT** | BATTEMENT | SCHWEBUNG |
| 1120 | **BEATING** | BATTEMENT DES METAUX | METALLHÄMMERN |
| 1121 | **BEAVER, THREADER** | FILIERE A TUBES | GEWINDEKLUPPE |
| 1122 | **BECOME CONCENTRATED (TO)** | CONCENTRER (SE) | ANREICHERN (SICH) |
| 1123 | **BECOME DEMAGNETISED (TO), RETURN TO THE UNMAGNETISED STATE (TO)** | DESAIMANTER (SE) | UNMAGNETISCH WERDEN |
| 1124 | **BECOME ELECTRIC (TO)** | ELECTRISER (S') | ELEKTRISCH WERDEN |
| 1125 | **BECOME LENGTHENED (TO), STRETCH (TO)** | ALLONGER (S') | LÄNGEN (SICH) |
| 1126 | **BECOME MAGNETIC (TO)** | AIMANTER (S') | MAGNETISCH WERDEN |
| 1127 | **BED PLATE** | PLAQUE D'APPUI, SEMELLE | AUFLAGERPLATTE (BAUW.), GRUNDPLATTE |
| 1128 | **BEEF TALLOW** | SUIF DES BOEUFS | RINDSTALG |
| 1129 | **BEESWAX** | CIRE D'ABEILLES | BIENENWACHS |
| 1130 | **BEILBY LAYER** | COUCHE DE BEILBY | BEILBY-SCHICHT |
| 1131 | **BELL CRANK LEVER, BENT LEVER** | LEVIER COUDE, LEVIER A SONNETTE, EQUERRE | WINKELHEBEL |
| 1132 | **BELL FURNAGE** | FOUR A CLOCHE | HAUBENOFEN |
| 1133 | **BELL HOUSING** | CARTER D'EMBRAYAGE | KUPPLUNGSGEHÄUSE |
| 1134 | **BELL METAL** | BRONZE DE CLOCHE | GLOCKENMETALL, GLOCKENSPEISE, GLOCKENBRONZE |
| 1135 | **BELL TYPE FURNACE** | FOUR A CLOCHE | HAUBENOFEN |
| 1136 | **BELL VALVE** | SOUPAPE A CLOCHE, SOUPAPE DE CORNOUAILLES | GLOCKENVENTIL, KRONENVENTIL |
| 1137 | **BELL, ALARM BELL** | SONNERIE, TIMBRE-AVERTISSEUR | KLINGELVORRICHTUNG, LÄUTWERK |

# BEL

30

| | | | |
|---|---|---|---|
| 1138 | **BELLOW VALVE** | ROBINET A SOUFFLET | VENTIL MIT FALTENBALG-ABDICHTUNG, BLASEBALGHAHN |
| 1139 | **BELLOWS** | SOUFFLET, SOUFFLET DE FORGE | FALTENBALG, BLASEBALG |
| 1140 | **BELT** | COURROIE | RIEMEN |
| 1141 | **BELT CONVEYOR LOADING** | CHARGEMENT PAR CONVOYEUR A BANDE | FÖRDERBANDBELADUNG |
| 1142 | **BELT COUPLING, UNITING THE JOINTS OF BELTS** | JONCTIONNEMENT DES COURROIES, LIAISONS DE COURROIE, REUNION DES COURROIE ATTACHE DES COURROIES | RIEMENVERBINDUNG, VERBINDEN DER RIEMENENDEN |
| 1143 | **BELT CUT ALONG THE SPINE** | OUTILLAGE EN ECHINE | RIEMEN AUS WIRBELBAHNEN |
| 1144 | **BELT DRIVE OR GEARING** | TRANSMISSION PAR COURROIES, DISPOSITIF POULIE ET COURROIE | RIEMENTRIEB, RIEMENANTRIEB |
| 1145 | **BELT DRIVEN MACHINE** | MACHINE A COMMANDE PAR COURROIE | MASCHINE FÜR RIEMENANTRIEB |
| 1146 | **BELT FASTENER** | AGRAFE POUR COURROIES | RIEMENVERBINDER, RIEMENSCHLOSS, RIEMENKLAMMER |
| 1147 | **BELT FLYWHEEL, FLYWHEEL PULLEY** | VOLANT-POULIE, POULIE-VOLANT | RIEMENSCHEIBENSCHWUNGRAD |
| 1148 | **BELT FURNACE** | FOUR A BANDE | FÖRDERBANDOFEN |
| 1149 | **BELT GEARING FOR SKEW, NON-PARALLEL SHAFTS** | RENVOI D'ANGLE | WINKELRIEMENGETRIEBE |
| 1150 | **BELT GUIDE** | GUIDE-COURROIE | RIEMENFÜHRER |
| 1151 | **BELT JOINT** | JONCTION, REUNION, ATTACHE DES COURROIES | RIEMENVERBINDUNG |
| 1152 | **BELT PULLEY** | POULIE A COURROIE | RIEMENSCHEIBE |
| 1153 | **BELT PUNCH** | EMPORTE-PIECE POUR COURROIE | RIEMENLOCHZANGE |
| 1154 | **BELT REVERSING GEAR, REVERSING GEAR OPERATED WITH BELTS** | DISPOSITIF DE CHANGEMENT DE SENS DE MARCHE PAR COURROIE | RIEMENWENDEGETRIEBE |
| 1155 | **BELT RIVET** | RIVET POUR COURROIES | RIEMENNIET |
| 1156 | **BELT SCREW** | BOULON POUR COURROIES | RIEMENSCHRAUBE |
| 1157 | **BELT SHIFTER, BELT STRIKING GEAR** | MECANISME DE DEBRAYAGE DE LA COURROIE | RIEMENAUSRÜCKER, RIEMENSCHALTER |
| 1158 | **BELT SHIFTING** | DEPLACEMENT DE LA COURROIE, PASSAGE DE LA COURROIE D'UNE POULIE SUR L'AUTRE | RIEMENVERSCHIEBUNG, RIEMENSCHALTUNG |
| 1159 | **BELT SHIPPER** | PASSE-COURROIE, MONTE-COURROIE, PORTE-COURROIE | RIEMENAUFLEGER |
| 1160 | **BELT SHIPPING** | MISE EN PLACE, MONTAGE DE LA COURROIE | AUFLEGEN DES RIEMENS |
| 1161 | **BELT STRETCHER** | TENDEUR DE COURROIES | RIEMENSPANNER, SPANNROLLE |
| 1162 | **BELT TENSION** | TENSION DE LA COURROIE | RIEMENSPANNUNG |
| 1163 | **BELT; STRAP** | COURROIE MOTRICE, DE COMMANDE | RIEMEN, TREIBRIEMEN |
| 1164 | **BELT, BAND CONVEYOR** | TRANSPORTEUR A COURROIE, TRANSPORTEUR A TAPIS ROULANT, TOILE TRANSPORTEUSE | GURTFÖRDERER, FÖRDERGURT, FÖRDERBAND, LAUFENDES BAND, TRANSPORTBAND, BANDTRANSPORTEUR, TRAINEUR |
| 1165 | **BELTING (THICKNESS OF)** | COURROIE (EPAISSEUR D'UNE) | RIEMENS (SCHICHT EINES) |
| 1166 | **BELTING OF SO MANY PLIES** | COURROIE A X PLIS, COURROIE EN X EPAISSEURS | RIEMEN (X-FACHER), RIEMEN AUS X LAGEN |
| 1167 | **BENCH** | ETABLI, BANC | BANK, WERKBANK |
| 1168 | **BENCH DRILLING MACHINE** | PERCEUSE D'ETABLI | TISCHBOHRMASCHINE, WERKBANKBOHRMASCHINE, BANKBOHRMASCHINE |
| 1169 | **BENCH MOLDING** | MOULAGE A LA TABLE | BANKFORMUNG |
| 1170 | **BENCH TEST** | ESSAI AU BANC | PRÜFSTANDVERSUCH |
| 1171 | **BENCH VISE** | ETAU D'ETABLI | BANKSCHRAUBSTOCK |

| | | | |
|---|---|---|---|
| 1172 | **BEND** | COUDE | ROHRBOGEN |
| 1173 | **BEND (TO)** | PLIER, CINTRER, COURBER | BIEGEN |
| 1174 | **BEND (TO), DEFLECT (TO)** | FLECHIR | DURCHBIEGEN (SICH) |
| 1175 | **BEND A PIPE (TO)** | CINTRER UN TUYAU, COUDER UN TUYAU, COURBER UN TUYAU | BIEGEN (EIN ROHR) |
| 1176 | **BEND RADIUS** | RAYON DE COURBURE | BIEGERADIUS |
| 1177 | **BEND TEST** | ESSAI DE FLEXION ESSAI DE PLIAGE | BIEGEPROBE |
| 1178 | **BEND TEST, FACE** | ESSAI DE FLEXION DE LA FACE DE LA SOUDURE | BIEGEPROBE AN DER OBERFLÄCHE DER SCHWEISSTELLE |
| 1179 | **BEND TEST, ROOT** | ESSAI DE PLIAGE A L'ENVERS | BIEGEVERSUCH MIT DER WURZEL IN DER ZUGZONE |
| 1180 | **BEND, PIPE BEND** | COUDE ROND | KRÜMMER, ROHRKRÜMMER, BOGENSTÜCK, BOGENROHR |
| 1181 | **BENDER** | PLIEUSE | BIEGEGLIED |
| 1182 | **BENDING** | PLIAGE, CINTRAGE, COURBAGE, FLEXION | BIEGEN, BIEGUNG |
| 1183 | **BENDING BRAKE** | JOUE DE CINTRAGE | BIEGEBACKE |
| 1184 | **BENDING MACHINE** | MACHINE A CINTRER | BIEGEMASCHINE, BIEGEPRESSE |
| 1185 | **BENDING MOMENT** | MOMENT FLECHISSANT, MOMENT DE FLEXION | BIEGEMOMENT, BIEGUNGSMOMENT |
| 1186 | **BENDING ROLLS** | MACHINE A ROULER, CYLINDRE A CINTRER, CYLINDRE DE CINTRAGE | WALZENBIEGEMASCHINE, BIEGEWALZWERK, RUNDMASCHINE, BIEGEWALZE, BIEGUNGSWALZE |
| 1187 | **BENDING STRAIN** | EFFORT DE FLEXION | BIEGEBEANSPRUCHUNG |
| 1188 | **BENDING STRENGTH** | RESISTANCE AU PLIAGE, RESISTANCE AU CINTRAGE | BIEGEFESTIGKEIT |
| 1189 | **BENDING TEST** | ESSAI A LA FLEXION, ESSAI DE PLIAGE, ESSAI DE CINTRAGE | BIEGEVERSUCH, BIEGEPROBE |
| 1190 | **BENDING TEST IMPACT TEST ON NOTCHED BAR, NICK BEND TEST** | ESSAI DE FLEXION PAR CHOC SUR BARREAUX ENTAILLES, ESSAI DE CHOC SUR ENTAILLE | EINKERBBIEGEPROBE, KERBSCHLAGPROBE, SCHLAGBIEGEPROBE MIT EINGEKERBTEN PROBESTÜCKEN |
| 1191 | **BENDING TRANSVERSE STRAIN** | EFFORT DE FLEXION, EFFORT TRANSVERSAL, TRAVAIL A LA FLEXION | BEANSPRUCHUNG AUF BIEGUNG, BIEGEBEANSPRUCHUNG |
| 1192 | **BENDING TRANSVERSE STRENGTH** | RESISTANCE A LA FLEXION TRANSVERSALE | BIEGEFESTIGKEIT |
| 1193 | **BENDING TRANVERSE STRESS** | EFFORT DE FLEXION PAR UNITE DE SECTION | BIEGESPANNUNG |
| 1194 | **BENT PIPE** | TUYAU CINTRE, COUDE, COL DE CYGNE | ROHR (GEKRÜMMTES) |
| 1195 | **BENT SPANNER, SKEW SPANNER** | CLEF COUDEE | WENDESCHLÜSSEL, SCHRAUBENSCHLÜSSEL MIT SCHRÄGEM MAUL |
| 1196 | **BENT WOOD** | BOIS BOUGE | HOLZ (GEBOGENES) |
| 1197 | **BENT, OUT OF TRUTH** | FAUSSE | VERBOGEN |
| 1198 | **BENZALDEHYDE, OIL OF BITTER ALMONDS** | BENZALDEHYDE, ALDEHYDE BENZYLIQUE, ESSENCE D'AMANDES AMERES | BENZALDEHYD, BENZOYLWASSERSTOFF, BITTERMANDELÖL |
| 1199 | **BENZENE** | BENZINE, BENZENE | BENZOL, STEINKOHLENBENZIN |
| 1200 | **BENZENE SULPHONIC ACID** | ACIDE BENZOSULFONIQUE, ACIDE PHENYLSULFUREUX | BENZOLSULFOSÄURE |
| 1201 | **BENZIDINE (PARADIAMIDODIPHENYL)** | BENZIDINE | BENZIDIN, P-DIAMIDODIPHENYL |
| 1202 | **BENZOIC ACID** | ACIDE BENZOIQUE | BENZOESÄURE |
| 1203 | **BENZOIN** | BENJOIN | BENZOEHARZ |
| 1204 | **BENZOLE** | BENZOL | ROHBENZOL |
| 1205 | **BENZOPHENONE** | BENZOPHENONE | BENZOPHENON |

**BER** 32

| | | | |
|---|---|---|---|
| 1206 | BERLIN BLUE, PRUSSIAN BLUE, FERRIC FERROCYANIDE | BLEU DE PRUSSE, BLEU DE BERLIN | BLAU (BERLINER), PREUSSISCHBLAU, FERRIFERROZYANID |
| 1207 | BERYLLIUM | BERYLLIUM | BERYLLIUM |
| 1208 | BERYLLIUM BRONZE | BRONZE AU BERYLLIUM | BERYLLIUMBRONZE |
| 1209 | BERYLLIUM COPPER | CUPRO-BERYLLIUM | BERYLLIUMBRONZE |
| 1210 | BERYLLIUM, GLUCINUM | GLUCINIUM | BERYLLIUM |
| 1211 | BESSEMER AFTER-BLOW | SURSOUFFLAGE BESSEMER | BESSEMER-NACHBLASEN |
| 1212 | BESSEMER CONVERTER | CONVERTISSEUR BESSEMER | BESSEMER-BIRNE, BESSEMER-KONVERTER, BESSEMER-OFEN |
| 1213 | BESSEMER PIG | FONTE BESSEMER | BESSEMER-ROHEISEN |
| 1214 | BESSEMER PROCESS | PROCEDE BESSEMER | BESSEMER-VERFAHREN |
| 1215 | BESSEMER STEEL | ACIER BESSEMER | BESSEMER-STAHL |
| 1216 | BETA BRASS | LAITON BETA | BETAMESSING |
| 1217 | BETA PARTICLE | PARTICULE BETA | BETATEILCHEN |
| 1218 | BETA RAYS | RAYONS BETA | BETASTRAHLEN |
| 1219 | BETA STRUCTURE | STRUCTURE BETA | BETASTRUKTUR |
| 1220 | BETTS PROCESS | PROCEDE BETTS | BETTS-VERFAHREN |
| 1221 | BEVEL | BIAIS, BISEAU | ABSCHRÄGUNG |
| 1222 | BEVEL (TO) | BISEAUTER, TAILLER EN BIAIS, TAILLER EN SIFFLET | ABSCHRÄGEN |
| 1223 | BEVEL ANGLE | ANGLE DU CHANFREIN, BIAIS | KANTENABSCHRÄGWINKEL, ABSCHRÄGUNGSWINKEL |
| 1224 | BEVEL FRICTION GEAR | TRANSMISSION PAR CONES DE FRICTION | REIBKEGELGETRIEBE |
| 1225 | BEVEL FRICTION GEAR WHEEL | ROUE DE FRICTION CONIQUE, CONE DE FRICTION | REIBKEGELRAD |
| 1226 | BEVEL GEAR | PIGNON CONIQUE | KEGELRAD |
| 1227 | BEVEL GEARING | ENGRENAGE CONIQUE, ENGRENAGE D'ANGLE | KEGELRADGETRIEBE, WINKELRÄDERGETRIEBE |
| 1228 | BEVEL SQUARE, ANGLE BEVEL | FAUSSE EQUERRE, SAUTERELLE, ANGLOIR | SCHMIEGE, SCHRÄGMASS, SCHRÄGMESSER, SCHRÄGWINKEL, STELLWINKEL |
| 1229 | BEVEL WHEEL | ROUE CONIQUE, ROUE D'ANGLE | KEGELRAD, RAD (KONISCHES), WINKELRAD |
| 1230 | BEVEL WHEEL DRIVE | COMMANDE PAR ENGRENAGE CONIQUE | KEGELRADANTRIEB |
| 1231 | BEVELLING | CHANFREINAGE, BISEAUTAGE | ABSCHRÄGUNG, ABSCHRÄGEN |
| 1232 | BEZEL | BAGUE PERIPHERIQUE | DECKRING |
| 1233 | BI-POLAR ELECTRODE | ELECTRODE BIPOLAIRE | ELEKTRODE (ZWEIPOLIGE) |
| 1234 | BIB COCK | ROBINET A BEC COURBE | HAHN MIT ABLAUF, UNTERLAUFHAHN, ZAPFHAHN |
| 1235 | BIB COCK, FAUCET | ROBINET DE PUISAGE | AUSLAUFVENTIL |
| 1236 | BICHROMATE DIP FINISH | TRAITEMENT AU BICHROMATE | BICHROMATBEHANDLUNG |
| 1237 | BICONCAVE DOUBLE-CONCAVE LENS, CONCAVO-CONCAVE LENS | LENTILLE BICONCAVE | LINSE (BIKONKAVE) |
| 1238 | BICONVEX DOUBLE-CONVEX LENS, CONVEXO-CONVEX LENS | LENTILLE BICONVEXE | LINSE (BIKONVEXE) |
| 1239 | BICYCLE CHAIN | CHAINE DE BICYCLETTE | FAHRRADKETTE |
| 1240 | BIFILAR SUSPENSION | SUSPENSION BIFILAIRE | AUFHÄNGUNG (BIFILARE) |
| 1241 | BIFURCATED RIVETS | RIVETS | ZWEIKNOPFNIETSTIFTE |
| 1242 | BIG END BRASSES, CRANK PIN BEARING | COUSSINET DE TETE DE BIELLE | KURBELZAPFENLAGER |
| 1243 | BILLET | BILLE, BILLETTE, BUCHE | KNÜPPEL, SCHEIT, HOLZSCHEIT |
| 1244 | BILLET AND SHEET SHEARING MACHINES | CISAILLES POUR BILLETTES ET LARGETS | KNÜPPEL U. PLATINENSCHERE |

| 33 | | | BLA |
|---|---|---|---|

| 1245 | BILLET MILL | LAMINOIR A BILLETTES | KNÜPPELWALZWERK |
|---|---|---|---|
| 1246 | BILLET SHEARS | CISAILLES POUR BILLETTES | KNÜPPELSCHERE |
| 1247 | BINARY ALLOY | ALLIAGE BINAIRE | LEGIERUNG (BINÄRE) |
| 1248 | BINARY DECIMALCODE | CODE BINAIRE DECIMAL | BINÄR-DEZIMALCODE |
| 1249 | BINARY DIGIT OR BIT | BIT, POSITION BINAIRE | BIT, BINÄRSTELLE, BINÄRZEICHEN |
| 1250 | BINDER | LIANT, LUBRIFIANT | PRESSMITTEL, PRESSZUSATZ, BINDEMITTEL |
| 1251 | BINDERS AND HARVESTERS | MOISSONNEUSES ET M. LIEUSES | MÄHBINDER UND ERNTEMASCHINEN |
| 1252 | BINDING HOOP | FRETTE | SCHRUMPFRING |
| 1253 | BINDING MATERIAL, CEMENT | SUBSTANCE AGGLUTINANTE, MATIERE AGGLUTINANTE, AGGLOMERANT, LIANT, LEIN (GEOL.): CIMENT | BINDEMITTEL |
| 1254 | BINDING POST | BORNE DE RACCORDEMENT | ANSCHLUSSKLEMME |
| 1255 | BINDING WIRE | FIL DE LIGATURE | BINDEDRAHT, WICKELDRAHT |
| 1256 | BINOCULAR MICROSCOPE | MICROSCOPE BINOCULAIRE | MIKROSKOP (BINOKULARES) |
| 1257 | BINOMIAL COEFFICIENT | COEFFICIENT BINOMIAL | BINOMIALKOEFFIZIENT |
| 1258 | BINOMIAL DISTRIBUTION | LOI BINOMIALE | BINOMIALVERTEILUNG |
| 1259 | BINOMIAL EQUATION | EQUATION BINOME | GLEICHUNG (ZWEIGLIEDRIGE), GLEICHUNG (BINOMISCHE) |
| 1260 | BINOMIAL SERIES | SERIE BINOMIALE | REIHE (BINOMISCHE), BINOMIALREIHE |
| 1261 | BIPLANE | BIPLAN | DOPPELDECKER |
| 1262 | BIQUADRATIC EQUATION | EQUATION BIQUADRATIQUE, EQUATION BICARREE, EQUATION DU QUATRIEME DEGRE | GLEICHUNG VIERTEN GRADES, GLEICHUNG (BIQUADRATISCHE) |
| 1263 | BIRD-EYE | MICROFISSURE | MIKRORISS, MIKROBRUCH |
| 1264 | BIRD'S EVE VIEW | PERSPECTIVE, VUE A VOL D'OISEAU | VOGELPERSPEKTIVE |
| 1265 | BIREFRINGENT | BIREFRINGENT | DOPPELBRECHEND |
| 1266 | BISECT (TO) | PARTAGER, DIVISER EN DEUX, BISSECTER | HALBIEREN (MATH.) |
| 1267 | BISECTION | BISSECTION | HALBIEREN (MATH.) |
| 1268 | BISECTRIX | BISSECTRICE | WINKELHALBIERENDE, HALBIERUNGSLINIE EINES WINKELS |
| 1269 | BISMUTH | BISMUTH | WISMUT |
| 1270 | BISMUTH CHLORIDE | TRICHLORURE DE BISMUTH | WISMUTCHLORID, CHLORWISMUT |
| 1271 | BISMUTH NITRATE | AZOTATE, NITRATE DE BISMUTH | WISMUT (SALPETERSAURES), WISMUTNITRAT |
| 1272 | BISMUTH OXIDE | OXYDE DE BISMUTH | WISMUTSESQUIOXYD |
| 1273 | BISMUTH OXYNITRATE | AZOTATE DE BISMUTHYLE | WISMUTNITRAT (BASISCHES), WISMUTSUBNITRAT |
| 1274 | BISMUTH SOLDER | SOUDURE AU BISMUTH | WISMUTLOT |
| 1275 | BISMUTHINE, BISMUTH TRISULPHIDE | BISMUTHINE | WISMUTGLANZ, BISMUTIN |
| 1276 | BISQUE, BISCUIT | BISCUIT | BISKUIT, BISKUITGUT |
| 1277 | BITE ANGLE | ANGLE D'ATTAQUE | GREIFWINKEL |
| 1278 | BITE OF THE ROPE | COINCEMENT DE LA CORDE DANS LA GORGE | KLEMMEN DES SEILES IN DER RILLE |
| 1279 | BITTINESS | GRANULATION, GRUMELAGE | KORNBINDUNG |
| 1280 | BITUMEN | BRAI GRAS NATUREL | ASPHALT-TEER, ASPHALT-GOUDRON, BITUMEN |
| 1281 | BITUMINOUS | BITUMINEUX | BITUMENHALTIG, BITUMINÖS |
| 1282 | BITUMINOUS COAL, SOFT FAT COAL | HOUILLE GRASSE | FETTKOHLE |
| 1283 | BITUMINOUS PAINT VARNISH, TAR VARNISH | VERNIS AU BITUME, VERNIS JAPON | ASPHALTLACK |

**BLA** 34

| | | | |
|---|---|---|---|
| 1284 | BLACK ANNEALED IRON WIRE | FIL DE FER RECUIT NOIR | EISENDRAHT (SCHWARZGEGLÜHTER) |
| 1285 | BLACK BODY | CORPS NOIR | KÖRPER (SCHWARZER) |
| 1286 | BLACK BOLT | BOULON BRUT | BOLZEN (ROHER), SCHRAUBE (UNBEARBEITETE), SCHRAUBE SCHWARZE |
| 1287 | BLACK COPPER | CUIVRE NOIR BRUT | SCHWARZKUPFER, ROHKUPFER |
| 1288 | BLACK HEAT (OF A) | PORTE AU ROUGE NAISSANT | SCHWARZROTGLÜHEND |
| 1289 | BLACK HOOP AND STRIP | BANDES NOIRES | SCHWARZBLECHE |
| 1290 | BLACK NUT | ECROU BRUT DE FORGE | MUTTER (ROHE), MUTTER (SCHWARZE), MUTTER (UNBEARBEITETE) |
| 1291 | BLACK OIL | HUILE MINERALE BRUNE | MINERALÖL UNGEREINIGTES |
| 1292 | BLACK PIG IRON | FONTE GRAPHITIQUE | ROHEISEN (SCHWARZES) |
| 1293 | BLACK PINE | PIN NOIR D'AUTRICHE | SCHWARZKIEFER |
| 1294 | BLACK PLATE | TOLE NOIRE | BLECH (SCHWARZES) |
| 1295 | BLACK RED HEAT | ROUGE NAISSANT | SCHWARZROTGLUT |
| 1296 | BLACK SHEET | TOLE NOIRE, TOLE TERNE, FER NOIR | SCHWARZBLECH, BLECH (GLATTES) |
| 1297 | BLACKING | NOIR DE FONDERIE | FORMSCHWÄRZE |
| 1298 | BLACKSMITH'S TONGS, SMITH'S TONGS, PLIERS | TENAILLE, PINCE DE FORGERON | SCHMIEDEZANGE |
| 1299 | BLADE | LAME | KLINGE, BLATT |
| 1300 | BLADE OF A CUTTING TOOL | LAME D'UN OUTIL TRANCHANT, LAME TRANCHANTE | KLINGE EINES SCHNEIDWERKZEUGS |
| 1301 | BLANK | LOPIN, PIECE BRUTE, EBAUCHE | BLANKETT, ROHLING |
| 1302 | BLANK BOLT | BOULON NON FILETE | BOLZEN OHNE GEWINDE |
| 1303 | BLANK END OF PIPE | BOUT DE TUBE FERME | ROHRENDE (BLINDES) |
| 1304 | BLANK FLANGE | BRIDE DE RECOUVREMENT, BRIDE PLEINE, BRIDE OBTURATRICE, FAUSSE BRIDE | BLINDFLANSCH, DECKELFLANSCH, FLANSCHENDECKEL |
| 1305 | BLANK HOLDER | SUPPORT DE PIECE A ESTAMPER | GEGENHALTER |
| 1306 | BLANK LINER | COLONNE PERDUE NON-PERFOREE | ROHR (NICHTGELOCHTES), ROHR (VERLORENES) |
| 1307 | BLANK NUT | ECROU CARRE A SOUDER | VIERKANTMUTTER (SCHWEISSBARE) |
| 1308 | BLANK NUT, NUT BLANK | ECROU NON TARAUDE | MUTTER OHNE GEWINDE |
| 1309 | BLANKING | COUPE | SCHNEIDEARBEIT |
| 1310 | BLANKING DIE | MATRICE A DISQUE | PLATINENSCHNITT |
| 1311 | BLAST FURNACE | HAUT FOURNEAU | HOCHOFEN |
| 1312 | BLAST FURNACE SLAG, CINDER, SCORIA | SCORIE DES HAUTS-FOURNEAUX, LAITIER | HOCHOFENSCHLACKE |
| 1313 | BLAST FURNACE WASTE GAS | GAZ DE HAUT FOURNEAU | GICHTGAS, HOCHOFENGAS |
| 1314 | BLAST MAIN | CONDUITE DE VENT | WINDLEITUNG |
| 1315 | BLAST, AIR BLAST | COURANT D'AIR FORCE, VENT | GEBLÄSEWIND, WIND |
| 1316 | BLASTING | SABLAGE | SANDSTRAHLEN |
| 1317 | BLEACHING POWDER, CHLORIDE OF LIME | CHLORURE DE CHAUX | CHLORKALK, BLEICHKALK, BLEICHPULVER |
| 1318 | BLEEDER | PURGEUR | ABLASSHAHN |
| 1319 | BLEEDER SCREW | VIS DE PURGE | ENTLÜFTUNGSSCHRAUBE |
| 1320 | BLEEDER VENT | EVENT AUTOMATIQUE | LUFTABZUG (AUTOMATISCHER) |
| 1321 | BLEEDING | MIGRATION, DEGORGEMENT, SAIGNEE | AUSBLUTEN, DURCHSCHLAGEN |
| 1322 | BLEEDING OF THE MOLM | RETRAIT AU MOULE | FORMVERSATZ |
| 1323 | BLEND (TO) | MELANGER, DOSER | MISCHEN |
| 1324 | BLENDE, ZINC BLENDE, SPHALERITE | BLENDE, SPHALERITE, FAUSSE GALENE | ZINKBLENDE, BLENDE, SPHALERIT |

| | | | |
|---|---|---|---|
| 1325 | **BLENDING** | MELANGE, DOSAGE, MELANGE DE DIVERSES FRACTIONS DE POUDRES D'UNE MEME SUBSTANCE | MISCHEN, VERSCHNEIDEN, MISCHUNG, BLENDUNG |
| 1326 | **BLIND FLANGE** | BRIDE PLEINE, TAMPON OBTURATEUR | BLINDFLANSCH |
| 1327 | **BLISTER** | POQUETTE, PUSTULE | WANZE |
| 1328 | **BLISTER BAR** | BARRE EN ACIER CEMENTE | ZEMENTSTAHLSTAB |
| 1329 | **BLISTER COPPER** | CUIVRE A SOUFFLURES | ROHKUPFER (KUPFER, BLASIGES) |
| 1330 | **BLISTERING** | CLOQUAGE, SOUFFLURES, PUSTULES, BOURSOUFLURES | BLASENBILDUNG, BLASEN |
| 1331 | **BLOATING** | GONFLEMENT, MOUSSAGE | AUFBLÄHEN |
| 1332 | **BLOCK** | BLOC (D'INFORMATIONS) | BLOCK, SATZ, |
| 1333 | **BLOCK** | CHAPE DE POULIE | FLASCHE, KLOBEN, ROLLENKLOBEN, SCHERE |
| 1334 | **BLOCK ADDRESS FORMAT** | FORMAT A ADRESSES DE BLOCS | SATZADRESSEEINGABEFORMAT |
| 1335 | **BLOCK BRAKE** | FREIN A SABOT | KLOTZBREMSE |
| 1336 | **BLOCK CHAIN** | CHAINE PLATE | BLOCKKETTE |
| 1337 | **BLOCK DELETE** | SAUT DE BLOC, SUPPRESSION | SATZUNTERDRÜCKUNG |
| 1338 | | | |
| 1339 | **BLOCK TIN** | ETAIN EN SAUMONS | BLOCKZINN |
| 1340 | **BLOCK, CLICHE** | CLICHE TYPOGRAPHIQUE | DRUCKSTOCK, KLISCHEE |
| 1341 | **BLOCKING** | EBAUCHAGE, PREFORMAGE | VORFORMUNG |
| 1342 | **BLOCKING CONDENSER** | CONDENSATEUR DE BLOCAGE, CONDENSATEUR D'ARRET | VERBLOCKUNGSKONDENSATOR, SPERRKONDENSATOR |
| 1343 | **BLOCKING DIE** | EBAUCHE DE FORGEAGE PREALABLE | VORSCHMIEDEGESENK |
| 1344 | **BLONDIN** | BLONDIN | KABELKRAN |
| 1345 | **BLOOM** | LOUPE (MET.) | LUPPE, PUDDELLUPPE |
| 1346 | **BLOOM** | BLOOM | VORBLOCK, VORGEWALZTER BLOCK |
| 1347 | **BLOOMING** | VOILE, LOUCHE | HAUCHBILDUNG, SCHLEIERBILDUNG |
| 1348 | **BLOOMING MILL** | TRAIN EBAUCHEUR, LAMINOIR A BLOOMS | VORWALZWERK, VORBLOCKWALZWERK |
| 1349 | **BLOOMS** | EBAUCHES | ROHLINGE, LUPPEN |
| 1350 | **BLOTTING PAPER** | PAPIER BUVARD, BUVARD | LÖSCHPAPIER, FLIESSPAPIER |
| 1351 | **BLOW** | SOUFFLURE | BLASE, OBERFLÄCHENPORE |
| 1352 | **BLOW (TO), FUSE (TO)** | FONDRE (LE COUPE-CIRCUIT FOND) | DURCHBRENNEN (SICHERUNG) |
| 1353 | **BLOW HOLE** | SOUFFLURE, POCHE DE RETRAITE | GASBLASE, BLASIGE STELLE IM GUSS, GUSSBLASE, GASEINSCHLUSS, BLASE |
| 1354 | **BLOW OFF** | DECOLLEMENT | ABLÖSUNG |
| 1355 | **BLOW PIPE** | CHALUMEAU | LÖTROHR |
| 1356 | **BLOW PIPE TEST ANALYSIS** | ANALYSE AU CHALUMEAU | LÖTROHRPROBE |
| 1357 | **BLOW-OFF COCK, SLUDGE COCK** | ROBINET DE VIDANGE | ABBLASEHAHN, AUSBLASEHAHN, AUSLAUFHAHN, SCHLAMMHAHN |
| 1358 | **BLOW-OFF VALVE** | SOUPAPE DE VIDANGE, SOUPAPE DE DECHARGE, SOUPAPE D'EVACUATION | ABBLASEVENTIL, AUSBLASEVENTIL, ABLASSVENTIL, SCHLAMMVENTIL |
| 1359 | **BLOW-OFF VALVE** | VANNE D'EXTRACTION, ROBINET D'EXTRACTION | ZAHNSTANGENSCHIEBER, ABSCHLAMMVENTIL |
| 1360 | **BLOW-OUT PREVENTER** | VANNE D'ERUPTION | ERUPTIONSABSPERRVORRICHTUNG |
| 1361 | **BLOWER** | SOUFFLERIE, APPAREIL SOUFFLANT | GEBLÄSE |
| 1362 | **BLOWHOLES** | SOUFFLURES | BLASEN, LUNKER |
| 1363 | **BLOWING ENGINE** | MACHINE SOUFFLANTE | GEBLÄSEMASCHINE |
| 1364 | **BLOWING OFF A BOILER** | VIDANGE D'UNE CHAUDIERE | ABBLASEN EINES KESSELS |

# BLO

| | | | |
|---|---|---|---|
| 1365 | **BLOWN GLASS** | VERRE SOUFFLE | GLAS (GEBLASENES) |
| 1366 | **BLOWN METAL** | METAL PREAFFINE | VORMETALL |
| 1367 | **BLOWPIPE** | CONDUITE DE VENT | WINDLEITUNG |
| 1368 | **BLUE (TO) THE STEEL** | BLEUIR L'ACIER | STAHL (DEN) BLAU ANLAUFENLASSEN |
| 1369 | **BLUE DIP** | BAIN BLEU, BAIN DE CHLORURE DE MERCURE | BLAUBRENNE, QUECKSILBERCHLORIDBAD |
| 1370 | **BLUE HEAT** | BLEU (CHAUDE) | BLAUGLUT |
| 1371 | **BLUE HEAT (OF A)** | CHAUFFE AU BLEU | BLAUWARM |
| 1372 | **BLUE HEAT TEST** | ESSAI DE RESISTANCE AU CHAUD BLEU | BLAUBRUCHPROBE |
| 1373 | **BLUE LINE, BLACK LINE PHOTOTYPE** | REPRODUCTION AU FERROPRUSSIATE EN BLEU SUR FOND BLANC | WEISSPAUSE, LICHTPAUSE (POSITIVE) |
| 1374 | **BLUE POWDER** | POUDRE DE ZINC OXYDE | ZINKSTAUB |
| 1375 | **BLUE PRINT, WHITE LINE PHOTOTYPE, CYANOTYPE** | BLEU, REPRODUCTION AU FERRO-PRUSSIATE EN BLANC SUR FOND BLEU | BLAUPAUSE, LICHTPAUSE (NEGATIVE) |
| 1376 | **BLUE VITRIOL, CHALCANTHITE** | VITRIOL BLEU, BLEU DE CHYPRE, COUPEROSE BLEUE | KUPFERVITRIOL, VITRIOL (BLAUER) |
| 1377 | **BLUING** | BLEUISSAGE | BLAUUNG |
| 1378 | **BLUSHING** | VOILE, LOUCHE | WEISSANLAUFEN |
| 1379 | **BOARD** | PLANCHE MINCE | BRETT |
| 1380 | **BOARD DROP HAMMER** | MARTEAU-PELIN A PLANCHE, MOUTON A PLANCHE | BRETTFALLHAMMER |
| 1381 | **BOARD, MILLBOARD** | CARTON | PAPPE, PAPPDECKEL |
| 1382 | **BOAT NAIL** | CLOU A BATEAU | SCHIFFSNAGEL |
| 1383 | **BOATSWAIN CHAIR** | NACELLE, SIEGE SUSPENDU | HÄNGESITZ |
| 1384 | **BOBBIN** | BOBINE | SPULE |
| 1385 | **BODY** | CORPS, CARROSSERIE | KÖRPER, KAROSSERIE, GEHÄUSE |
| 1386 | **BODY AT REST** | CORPS AU REPOS | KÖRPER (RUHENDER) |
| 1387 | **BODY CLEARANCE** | DETALONNAGE | HINTERFRÄSEN |
| 1388 | **BODY CLEARANCE ANGLE** | ANGLE DE DETALONNAGE DU CORPS | HINTERFRÄSWINKEL |
| 1389 | **BODY COLOUR, OPAQUE COLOUR** | COULEUR OPAQUE | FARBE (DECKENDE), DECKFARBE |
| 1390 | **BODY FILE** | LIME-FRAISE | FRÄSVORRICHTUNG |
| 1391 | **BODY FORMING MACHINE** | MACHINE A COURBER | RUNDMASCHINE |
| 1392 | **BODY IN MOTION, MOVING BODY** | CORPS EN MOUVEMENT, CORPS MOBILE | KÖRPER (BEWEGTER) |
| 1393 | **BODY OF A PIGMENT** | PROPRIETE COUVRANTE, PROPRIETE DE COUVRIR D'UNE COULEUR | DECKKRAFT EINER FARBE |
| 1394 | **BODY OF A SCREW** | NOYAU D'UNE VIS | KERN EINER SCHRAUBE, SCHRAUBENKERN |
| 1395 | **BODY OF AN OIL** | CONSISTANCE D'UNE HUILE | KONSISTENZ EINES ÖLES |
| 1396 | **BODY OF UNIFORM STRENGTH** | PRISME D'EGALE RESISTANCE | KÖRPER VON GLEICHEM WIDERSTAND |
| 1397 | **BODY SEAT RING** | SIEGE DE CORPS DE VANNE | VENTILKÖRPERSITZ |
| 1398 | **BODY SHOP** | ATELIER DE CARROSSERIE, ATELIER DE TOLERIE | KAROSSERIEWERKSTATT |
| 1399 | **BODY-CENTERED** | CENTRE CUBIQUE | KUBISCHRAUMZENTRIERT |
| 1400 | **BOHEMIAN GLASS** | VERRE BLANC DE BOHEME | GLAS (BÖHMISCHES), KALIKALKGLAS |
| 1401 | **BOIL (TO)** | BOUILLIR, ETRE EN EBULLITION | KOCHEN, SIEDEN |
| 1402 | **BOIL-OFF RATE** | TAUX D'EVAPORATION | VERDUNSTUNGSHÖHE |
| 1403 | **BOIL-OFF TEST** | ESSAI DE DEPERDITION THERMIQUE | WÄRMEVERLUSTPRÜFUNG |

| | | | |
|---|---|---|---|
| 1404 | BOIL-OUT | VAPEUR D'EBULLITION, BUEE | SIEDEDAMPF, DUNST |
| 1405 | BOIL-OUT NOZZLE | EVACUATION DE LA VAPEUR D'EBULLITION | SIEDEDAMPFABLASSDÜSE |
| 1406 | BOILER | CHAUDIERE | KOCHKESSEL, KOCHER |
| 1407 | BOILER BODY OF A STILL | CUCURBITE | DESTILLIERBLASE |
| 1408 | BOILER COATING | MATIERE CALORIFUGE POUR CHAUDIERES | KESSELABDECKUNGSMATERIAL, KESSELISOLIERMATERIAL |
| 1409 | BOILER DRILLING MACHINE | PERCEUSE DE CHAUDIERES | KESSELBOHRMASCHINE |
| 1410 | BOILER EXPLOSION, BURSTING OF A BOILER | EXPLOSION D'UNE CHAUDIERE | BERSTEN, EXPLOSION EINES KESSELS, KESSELEXPLOSION |
| 1411 | BOILER FITTINGS, BOILER MOUNTINGS | GARNITURES DE CHAUDIERES, APPAREILS ACCESSOIRES, ACCESSOIRES DE CHAUDIERES | KESSELAUSRÜSTUNG, KESSELZUBEHÖR, KESSELARMATUR |
| 1412 | BOILER FLUE | TUBE FOYER, CARNEAU INTERIEUR D'UNE CHAUDIERE | FLAMMROHR |
| 1413 | BOILER HOUSE | BATIMENT DES CHAUDIERES, BATIMENT DE GENERATEUR | KESSELHAUS |
| 1414 | BOILER INSPECTION | INSPECTION, VISITE DE LA CHAUDIERE | KESSELUNTERSUCHUNG |
| 1415 | BOILER MAKER, BOILER SMITH | CHAUDRONNIER EN TOLE, CHAUDRONNIER EN FER | KESSELSCHMIED |
| 1416 | BOILER PLATE | TOLE DE CHAUDIERE | KESSELBLECH |
| 1417 | BOILER PRESSURE | PRESSION DANS UNE CHAUDIERE | KESSELDRUCK |
| 1418 | BOILER ROOM | SALLE DES CHAUDIERES, SALLE DE CHAUFFERIE, CHAUFFERIE | KESSELRAUM |
| 1419 | BOILER SHELL | CORPS CYLINDRIQUE D'UNE CHAUDIERE | KESSELMANTEL |
| 1420 | BOILER SHOP SMITHY | ATELIER DE CHAUDRONNERIE EN FER | KESSELSCHMIEDE |
| 1421 | BOILER TEST, PRESSURE TEST OF BOILER | ESSAI DE LA CHAUDIERE SOUS PRESSION | KESSELDRUCKPROBE |
| 1422 | BOILER TUBE | TUBE DE CHAUDIERE | DAMPFKESSELROHR, KESSELROHR |
| 1423 | BOILER WORKS | GROSSE CHAUDRONNERIE, CHAUDRONNERIE EN FER | KESSELFABRIK |
| 1424 | BOILING POINT | POINT D'EBULLITION | SIEDEPUNKT |
| 1425 | BOILING POINT (WITH A HIGT) | EBULLITION ELEVE (A POINT D') | SCHWERSIEDEND |
| 1426 | BOILING POINT (WITH A LOW) | EBULLITION BAS (A POINT D') | LEICHTSIEDEND |
| 1427 | BOILING TEMPERATURE | TEMPERATURE D'EBULLITION | SIEDEHITZE, SIEDETEMPERATUR |
| 1428 | BOILING WATER | EAU BOUILLANTE | WASSER (KOCHENDES), WASSER (SIEDENDES) |
| 1429 | BOILING, EBULLITION | EBULLITION | SIEDEN, KOCHEN |
| 1430 | BOLE | BOL | BOLUS |
| 1431 | BOLOMETER | BOLOMETRE | BOLOMETER, STRAHLENMESSER |
| 1432 | BOLT | VERROU, BOULON | RIEGEL, QUERRIEGEL, SCHRAUBE UND MUTTER, BOLZEN |
| 1433 | BOLT CIRCLE | CERCLE DES TROUS DE BOULONS | LOCHKREIS, SCHRAUBENKREIS |
| 1434 | BOLT DIAMETER | DIAMETRE DU BOULON | BOLZENDURCHMESSER |
| 1435 | BOLT DOWN (TO) | BOULONNER | VERBOLZEN |
| 1436 | BOLT HEAD, SCREW HEAD | TETE D'UNE VIS, TETE D'UN BOULON | KOPF EINER SCHRAUBE, SCHRAUBENKOPF |
| 1437 | BOLT HOLE | TROU DE BOULON | SCHRAUBENLOCH |
| 1438 | BOLT-CIRCLE DIAMETER | DIAMETRE DE PERCAGE | LOCHKREUZDURCHMESSER |
| 1439 | BOLT-DRILLING DIAMETER | BRIDE-DIAMETRE DE PERCAGE | BOHRDURCHMESSER |
| 1440 | BOLT-HOLE DIAMETER | DIAMETRE DU TROU DE BOULON | BOLZENBOHRUNGSDURCHMESSER |

**BOL** 38

| | | | |
|---|---|---|---|
| 1441 | **BOLT, SCREW BOLT, BOLT AND NUT** | BOULON LIBRE | MUTTERSCHRAUBE, DURCHSTECKSCHRAUBE,SCHRAUBE (DURCHGEHENDE) |
| 1442 | **BOLTED CONNECTION** | ASSEMBLAGE PAR VIS, RACCORD A ECROUS | SCHRAUBENVERBINDUNG |
| 1443 | **BOLTING** | BOULONNERIE, BOULONNAGE | VERBOLZUNG |
| 1444 | **BOND** | APPAREIL DE CONSTRUCTON | MAUERVERBAND, VERBAND |
| 1445 | **BOND** | AGGLUTINANT, LIANT | GRÜNSANDBINDER, BINDEMITTEL |
| 1446 | **BONDED TENDONS** | CABLES INJECTES | GLIEDER (VORGERSPANNTE) |
| 1447 | **BONE BLACK** | NOIR ANIMAL, NOIR D'IVOIRE | BEINSCHWARZ |
| 1448 | **BONE DUST, MEAL, CRUSHED BONE** | OS PULVERISES, POUDRE D'OS | KNOCHENMEHL |
| 1449 | **BONE GLUE** | COLLE FORTE DES OS, OSSEINE | KNOCHENLEIM |
| 1450 | **BONE OIL; NEAT'S FOOT OIL** | HUILE DE PIED DE BOEUF, HUILE DE PIED DE MOUTON | KLAUENFETT, KLAUENÖL ; KNOCHENÖL |
| 1451 | **BONNET** | CAPOT, CAPOT-MOTEUR, CHAPEAU | MOTORHAUBE, HAUBE |
| 1452 | **BONNET FLANGE** | BRIDE DE CHAPEAU | ÜBERWURFFLANSCH, HAUBENFLANSCH |
| 1453 | **BONNET STUD BOLT** | TIGE FILETEE DE CHAPEAU | HAUBENGEWINDEBOLZEN |
| 1454 | **BONNET, CAP** | CHAPEAU | AUFSATZ |
| 1455 | **BONNET, HOOD** | HOTTE | RAUCHFANG |
| 1456 | **BOOSTER** | SURPRESSEUR, SURCOMPRESSEUR, SURVOLTEUR, AMORCE | ÜBERVERDICHTER, ZUSATZDYNAMO, ZUSATZMASCHINE |
| 1457 | **BOOSTER BRAKE** | SERVO-FREIN | SERVO-BREMSE |
| 1458 | **BOOT** | COFFRE, MALLE | KOFFERRAUM |
| 1459 | **BORAX, SODIUM BIBORATE, TINCAL** | BORAX, BIBORATE DE SODIUM, BORATE DE SOUDE ANHYDRE | BORAX, NATRON (BORSAURES), NATRIUMBIBORAT |
| 1460 | **BORDER CURVE** | COURBE LIMITE | GRENZKURVE |
| 1461 | **BORE** | ALESAGE, ALESAGE DE CYLINDRE | BOHRUNG, ZYLINDER |
| 1462 | **BORE (TO)** | ALESER | AUSBOHREN |
| 1463 | **BORE HOLE** | TROU DE SONDAGE | BOHRLOCH (IM GESTEIN) |
| 1464 | **BORE INTERNAL DIAMETER OF A PIPE** | DIAMETRE INTERIEUR D'UN TUYAU | LICHTE WEITE EINES ROHRES, ROHRWEITE |
| 1465 | **BORE LINER** | CHEMISE DE CYLINDRE | ZYLINDERLAUFBÜCHSE |
| 1466 | **BORE ON THE LATHE (TO)** | ALESER AU TOUR | AUSDREHEN |
| 1467 | **BORIC (BORACIC) ACID** | ACIDE BORIQUE | BORSÄURE, BORAXSÄURE |
| 1468 | **BORING** | FORAGE, PERCAGE, ALESAGE | BOHREN, AUSBOHREN |
| 1469 | **BORING AND TURNING MILL, VERTICAL LATHE** | TOUR EN L'AIR A PLATEAU HORIZONTAL | PLANDREHBANK MIT WAAGERECHTER PLANSCHEIBE, KARUSSELLDREHBANK |
| 1470 | **BORING BARS** | BARRES DE FORAGE | BOHRSTANGEN |
| 1471 | **BORING MACHINE** | MACHINE A ALESER, ALESEUSE | AUSBOHRMASCHINE, BOHRMASCHINE |
| 1472 | **BORING MILL** | PERCEUSE | BOHRWERK |
| 1473 | **BORING ON THE LATHE** | ALESAGE AU TOUR | AUSDREHEN |
| 1474 | **BORING RESTS** | LUNETTES D'ALESAGE | BOHR-LÜNETTEN |
| 1475 | **BORING TEST, DRILL TEST** | ESSAI DE FORAGE, ESSAI DE PERCAGE | BOHRVERSUCH |
| 1476 | **BORINGS** | COPEAUX DE FORAGE | BOHRSPÄNE |
| 1477 | **BORON** | BORE | BOR |
| 1478 | **BORON ALLOYS** | ALLIAGE AU BORE | BORLEGIERUNG |
| 1479 | **BORON CARBIDE** | CARBURE DE BORE | BORKARBID |
| 1480 | **BORT** | BORT | BORT |
| 1481 | **BOSS, NAVE, HUB** | MOYEU | NABE |
| 1482 | **BOSSING** | BATTRE EN FORME | KLOPFEN (IN DIE FORM) |

| | | | |
|---|---|---|---|
| 1483 | **BOTT** | TAMPON BOUCHON | STOPFEN |
| 1484 | **BOTTLE GLASS** | VERRE A BOUTEILLES | FLASCHENGLAS |
| 1485 | **BOTTLE JACK** | VERIN A BOUTEILLE | FLASCHENWINDE |
| 1486 | **BOTTOM BOARD** | PLAQUE DE FOND | GRUNDPLATTE |
| 1487 | **BOTTOM BRASS** | DEMI-COUSSINET INFERIEUR, COQUILLE INFERIEURE | LAGERSCHALE (UNTERE), UNTERSCHALE |
| 1488 | **BOTTOM CASTING** | COULEE EN SOURCE | GIESSEN (STEIGENDES) |
| 1489 | **BOTTOM CLEARANCE** | JEU A FOND DES DENTS, JEU DU FOND DE LA DENT | KOPFSPIEL EINES ZAHNRADES |
| 1490 | **BOTTOM CURB ANGLE** | CORNIERE DE PIED DE BAC | KESSELBODENWINKELEISEN |
| 1491 | **BOTTOM DEAD CENTER** | POINT MORT BAS | TOTPUNKT (UNTER) |
| 1492 | **BOTTOM DRAIN** | BONDE DE FOND | BODENABLAUF |
| 1493 | **BOTTOM DRAIN VALVE** | ROBINET DE FOND DE CUVE | BODENVENTIL |
| 1494 | **BOTTOM END OF CYLINDER, CYLINDER BOTTOM** | FOND DU CYLINDRE | ZYLINDERBODEN |
| 1495 | **BOTTOM NOZZLE** | TUBULURE DE FOND | BODENDÜSE |
| 1496 | **BOTTOM POURING LADLE** | POCHE A QUENOUILLE | STOPFENPFANNE |
| 1497 | **BOTTOM SWAGE** | ETAMPE, MATRICE DE DESSOUS | UNTERGESENK |
| 1498 | **BOTTOM VIEW** | VUE DE BAS EN HAUT, VUE PAR-DESSOUS | FROSCHPERSPEKTIVE |
| 1499 | **BOTTOMING TAP** | TARAUD FINISSEUR | FERTIGSCHNEIDER |
| 1500 | **BOUNDARY** | JOINT, CONTOUR DE GRAIN | KRONGRENZE |
| 1501 | **BOURDON PRESSURE GAUGE** | MANOMETRE A TUBE, MANOMETRE BOURDON | RÖHRENFEDERMANOMETER |
| 1502 | **BOURNONITE, ENDELLIONITE, WHEEL ORE** | BOURNONITE | RÄDELERZ, BOURNONIT |
| 1503 | **BOW COMPASSES, SPRING BOWS, COMPASSES** | COMPAS-BALUSTRE | FEDERZIRKEL |
| 1504 | **BOW DRILL, FIDDLE DRILL** | ARCHET | ROLLENBOHRER |
| 1505 | **BOW SAW, TURNING SAW** | SCIE A CHANTOURNER | SCHWEIFSÄGE |
| 1506 | **BOWING** | MANQUE DE PLANEITE | BALLIGKEIT |
| 1507 | **BOX** | BUIS | BUCHSBAUM |
| 1508 | **BOX CASTING** | MOULAGE EN CHASSIS | KASTENGUSS |
| 1509 | **BOX CONNECTING ROD END** | TETE DE BIELLE A CAGE FERMEE | SCHUBSTANGENKOPF (GESCHLOSSENER) |
| 1510 | **BOX COUPLING, MUFF COUPLING, BUTT COUPLING** | ACCOUPLEMENT A MANCHON | MUFFENKUPPLUNG |
| 1511 | **BOX FRAME** | CHASSIS-CAISSON | KASTENRAHMEN |
| 1512 | **BOX NUT, CAP NUT** | ECROU A CHAPEAU, ECROU BORGNE, ECROU CREUX | MUTTER (GESCHLOSSENE), ÜBERWURFMUTTER, BUCHSENMUTTER, KAPPENMUTTER |
| 1513 | **BOX PIN** | GOUJON DE CENTRAGE | ZENTRIERSTIFT, FÜHRUNGSSTIFT |
| 1514 | **BOX PISTON** | PISTON EVIDE | HOHLKOLBEN |
| 1515 | **BOX SPANNER** | CLEF A DOUILLE, CLEF TUBULAIRE, CLEF EN BOUT | STECKSCHLÜSSEL |
| 1516 | **BRACE** | RENFORT, ENTRETOISE (CHARPENTE), BRACON (ELEMENT DE CHARPENTE METALLIQUE) | QUERVERSTREBUNG, VERSTREBUNG, STREBE |
| 1517 | **BRACE (TO)** | METTRE DES CONTREFICHES | VERSTREBEN |
| 1518 | **BRACE WITH SCREW** | VILEBREQUIN A VIS DE PRESSION | BOHRKURBEL |
| 1519 | **BRACE, BREAST BRACE** | VILEBREQUIN (OUTIL A PERCER) | BRUSTLEIER, BOHRWINDE, FAUSTLEIER |
| 1520 | **BRACES** | TIRANTS (DE SPHERE), CROISILLONS DE CHARPENTE, BRACONS DE CHARPENTE | KREUZSTREBEN, VERANKERUNG |

**BRA**       40

| | | | |
|---|---|---|---|
| 1521 | **BRACING** | MISE DE CONTREFICHES | VERSTREBEN |
| 1522 | **BRACKET** | ATTACHE, CONSOLE, SUPPORT | HALTERUNG, KONSOLE, TRÄGER, STÜTZE, TRAGSTÜTZE |
| 1523 | **BRACKET PEDESTAL, WALL BEARING, WALL HANGER** | PALIER MURAL, PALIER CONSOLE | WANDLAGER, KONSOLLAGER |
| 1524 | **BRACKISH WATER** | EAU SAUMATRE | BRACKWASSER |
| 1525 | **BRAGG'S METHOD** | METHODE DE BRAGG, LOI DE BRAGG | GESETZ (BRAGGSCHES), GESETZ VON BRAGG |
| 1526 | **BRAIDED COVERING** | GARNITURE EN TRESSE | GEFLECHTÜBERZUG |
| 1527 | **BRAIDED ROPE** | CORDE TRESSEE | SEIL (GEFLOCHTENES) |
| 1528 | **BRAILED WIRE** | FIL TRESSE | DRAHT (GEFLOCHTENER), DRAHT (UMKLÖPPELTER), DRAHT UMFLOCHTENER |
| 1529 | **BRAKE** | FREIN, JOUE DE CINTRAGE | BREMSE, BIEGEBACKE |
| 1530 | **BRAKE (TO)** | FREINER | BREMSEN |
| 1531 | **BRAKE BLOCK** | SABOT DE FREIN | BREMSKLOTZ |
| 1532 | **BRAKE CYLINDER, BRAKE DRUM** | TAMBOUR, CYLINDRE A FREIN | BREMSZYLINDER, BREMSTROMMEL |
| 1533 | **BRAKE DRUM** | TAMBOUR DE FREIN | BREMSTROMMEL |
| 1534 | **BRAKE FLUID TANK** | RESERVOIR DE LIQUIDE DE FREIN | BREMSFLÜSSIGKEITSBEHÄLTER |
| 1535 | **BRAKE HORSE POWER** | PUISSANCE AU FREIN | BREMSLEISTUNG |
| 1536 | **BRAKE JAW** | MACHOIRE DE FREIN | BREMSBACKE |
| 1537 | **BRAKE LEVER** | LEVIER DE FREIN | BREMSHEBEL |
| 1538 | **BRAKE LINING** | GARNITURE DE FREIN | BREMSBELAG |
| 1539 | **BRAKE LINKAGE** | TRINGLERIE DE FREIN | BREMSGESTÄNGE |
| 1540 | **BRAKE POWER** | PUISSANCE EFFECTIVE, PUISSANCE AU FREIN | WIRKLICHLEISTUNG, BREMSLEISTUNG |
| 1541 | **BRAKE RING** | BAGUE DE FREINAGE | BREMSRING |
| 1542 | **BRAKE SHOE** | SEGMENT DE FREIN | BREMSBACKE |
| 1543 | **BRAKE SHOE, BRAKE BLOCK** | SABOT DE FREIN | BREMSKLOTZ, BREMSBACKE |
| 1544 | **BRAKE STRAP** | BANDE DE FREIN, RUBAN DE FREIN, COLLIER DE FREIN | BREMSBAND |
| 1545 | **BRAKE SYSTEM** | CIRCUIT DE FREINAGE | BREMSKREIS |
| 1546 | **BRAKE TEST** | ESSAI AU FREIN | BREMSVERSUCH |
| 1547 | **BRAKE WEIGHT** | CONTREPOIDS DU FREIN | BREMSGEWICHT |
| 1548 | **BRAKE WHEEL** | POULIE DE FREIN | BREMSSCHEIBE |
| 1549 | **BRAKING** | FREINAGE, SERRAGE DU FREIN, MANOEUVRE DU FREIN | BREMSEN |
| 1550 | **BRAKING ACTION** | ACTION DU FREIN | BREMSWIRKUNG |
| 1551 | **BRAKING FORCE** | PUISSANCE DE FREINAGE, EFFORT TANGENTIEL DU FREIN | BREMSKRAFT |
| 1552 | **BRAKING RESISTANCE** | RESISTANCE AU FREINAGE | BREMSWIDERSTAND |
| 1553 | **BRALE** | PRESSE BRINELL | BRINELL-PRESSE, BRINELL-HÄRTEPRÜFER |
| 1554 | **BRANCH CONNECTION** | DERIVATION, BRANCHEMENT | ROHRANSCHLUSS |
| 1555 | **BRANCH OF A CURVE** | BRANCHE D'UNE COURBE | AST, ZWEIG, ZUG EINER KURVE |
| 1556 | **BRANCH OFF (TO)** | SE BRANCHER | ABZWEIGEN |
| 1557 | **BRANCH PIECE** | TUBULURE DE BRANCHEMENT | STUTZEN, ROHRSTUTZEN, ABZWEIGSTUTZEN, ROHRANSATZ, ANSCHLUSSSTUTZEN |
| 1558 | **BRANCH PIPE** | TUBE DE DERIVATION | ABZWEIGROHR, ABZWEIG |
| 1559 | **BRANCH TEE** | RACCORD T | T-STUCK,T-VERSCHRAUBUNG |
| 1560 | **BRAND, BRANDING LETTER, STAMP** | ALPHABET A FRAPPER, CHIFFRES ET LETTRES A CHAUD/FROID | STEMPEL, SCHRIFTSTEMPEL |
| 1561 | **BRASILIAN SPLITTING TEST** | ESSAI D'ECRASEMENT SUR CYLINDRE DE BETON MASSIF | ZYLINDERSPALTVERSUCH |

| | | |
|---|---|---|
| 1562 | **BRASS** | LAITON, CUIVRE JAUNE | MESSING, GELBKUPFER, GELBGUSS |
| 1563 | **BRASS BILLET** | BILLETTE DE LAITON | MESSINGKNÜPPEL |
| 1564 | **BRASS BRIGHT DIP** | BAIN DE BRILLANTAGE | GLÄNZBAD (CHEMISCHES) |
| 1565 | **BRASS BUSH OF STUFFING BOX** | BAGUE DE FOND | GRUNDBÜCHSE |
| 1566 | **BRASS FOUNDRY** | FONDERIE DE CUIVRE, ROBINETTERIE | MESSINGGIESSEREI |
| 1567 | **BRASS PLATING** | PLACAGE AU LAITON | VERMESSINGUNG |
| 1568 | **BRASS ROD WIRE** | FIL LAMINE DE LAITON, FIL MACHINE DE LAITON | MESSINGWALZDRAHT |
| 1569 | **BRASS SHEET, STRIP** | TOLE DE LAITON | MESSINGBLECH |
| 1570 | **BRASS TUBE** | TUBE EN LAITON | MESSINGROHR |
| 1571 | **BRASS WIRE** | FIL DE LAITON, FIL D'ARCHAL | MESSINGDRAHT |
| 1572 | **BRASSES** | COUSSINET EN DEUX PIECES, COUSSINET EN COQUILLES | LAGERSCHALE (GETEILTE) |
| 1573 | **BRAZE (TO)** | SOUDER FORT, BRASER | HARTLÖTEN |
| 1574 | **BRAZED-ON TIPS** | MISES BRASEES | SPITZEN (AUFGELÖTETE) |
| 1575 | **BRAZIERS' COPPER** | CUIVRE DE BRASAGE | HARTLÖTKUPFER |
| 1576 | **BRAZING** | BRASAGE, BRASEMENT, SOUDURE FORTE, BRASURE | HARTLÖTEN, HARTLÖTUNG |
| 1577 | **BRAZING FURNAGE** | FOURNEAU A BRASER | HARTLÖTOFEN |
| 1578 | **BRAZING INSERTS** | INSERTIONS DE BRASAGE | HARTLÖTUNGSEINLAGEN |
| 1579 | **BREADTH OF TOOTH** | LONGUEUR/LARGEUR DE LA DENT | ZAHNBREITE |
| 1580 | **BREAK (TO), CRUSH (TO), STAMP (TO)** | CONCASSER | ZERKLEINERN |
| 1581 | **BREAKDOWN** | PERTURBATION, DERANGEMENT DANS LE SERVICE, PANNE | BETRIEBSSTÖRUNG, PANNE, STÖRUNG |
| 1582 | **BREAKDOWN VOLTAGE** | TENSION DE CLAQUAGE | DURCHBRUCHSPANNUNG |
| 1583 | **BREAKING DOWN** | EBAUCHAGE | VORARBEIT, VORWALZEN |
| 1584 | **BREAKING LENGTH** | LONGUEUR DE RUPTURE | REISSLÄNGE |
| 1585 | **BREAKING LOAD** | CHARGE DE RUPTURE | BRUCHLAST |
| 1586 | **BREAKING WEIGHT LOAD** | CHARGE-LIMITE D'ELASTICITE | BRUCHBELASTUNG |
| 1587 | **BREAKING-IN** | RODAGE (D'UNE VOITURE) | EINFAHRZEIT |
| 1588 | **BREAKING, CRUSHING, STAMPING** | CONCASSAGE | ZERKLEINERN, ZERKLEINERUNG |
| 1589 | **BREAKOUT** | PERCEE | DURCHBRUCH |
| 1590 | **BREAST PLATE** | PLAQUE DE CONSCIENCE (DE VILLEBREQUIN), PLASTRON | BOHRBRETT, BRUSTBRETT, DRILLBRETT, BRUSTSCHEIBE |
| 1591 | **BREATHER** | RENIFLARD | ENTLÜFTERROHR |
| 1592 | **BREATHER TANK** | RESERVOIR TAMPON | ZWISCHENLAGERBEHÄLTER |
| 1593 | **BREATHER VALVE, RELIEF VALVE, SAFETY VALVE** | SOUPAPE DE SECURITE, RESPIRATION RENIFLARD | SICHERHEITSVENTIL, SCHNÜFFELVENTIL |
| 1594 | **BREATHING LOSS** | PERTE PAR RESPIRATION | ATMUNGSVERLUST |
| 1595 | **BREECHES PIPE** | CULOTTE | HOSENROHR, GABELROHR |
| 1596 | **BRICK** | BRIQUE | BACKSTEIN, MAUERSTEIN, ZIEGELSTEIN, MAUERZIEGEL |
| 1597 | **BRICK (TO)** | MACONNER | MAUERN |
| 1598 | **BRICK EARTH** | TERRE A BRIQUES | ZIEGELERDE |
| 1599 | **BRICK FOUNDATION** | FONDATION EN BRIQUES, FONDATION EN MACONNERIE | ZIEGELSTEINFUNDAMENT |
| 1600 | **BRICKED IN, SET IN MASONRY** | ENGAGE DANS UNE MACONNERIE | EINGEMAUERT |
| 1601 | **BRICKLAYING** | MACONNERIE | MAUERN |
| 1602 | **BRICKWORK** | MACONNERIE EN BRIQUES, BRIQUETAGE | ZIEGELMAUERWERK |
| 1603 | **BRIDGE APPROACH** | APPONTEMENT | ZUFAHRT |

**BRI** 42

| | | | |
|---|---|---|---|
| 1604 | BRIDGING | COURONNEMENT, FORMATION DE PONT | SCHLACKENKRANZBILDUNG, BRÜCKENBILDUNG |
| 1605 | BRIGG'S PIPE THREAD, AMERICAN STANDARD PIPE THREAD | PAS SYSTEME BRIGGS POUR TUBES | BRIGGS'SCHES GEWINDE |
| 1606 | BRIGHT ANNEALED WIRE | FIL RECUIT BLANC | BLANKGLÜHDRAHT |
| 1607 | BRIGHT BOLT | BOULON DECOLLETE, VIS DECOLLETEE | SCHRAUBENBOLZEN (BLANKER), SCHRAUBENBOLZEN (BEARBEITETER) |
| 1608 | BRIGHT DIP | BAIN DE BRILLANTAGE | GELBBRENNE |
| 1609 | BRIGHT DIP FINISH | BAIN DE BRILLANTAGE | GLANZBRENNE |
| 1610 | BRIGHT HARD DRAWN WIRE | FIL DE FER CLAIR CRU | (BLANKGEZOGENER) EISENDRAHT |
| 1611 | BRIGHT METALLIC SURFACE | SURFACE METALLIQUE POLIE | METALLFLÄCHE (BLANKE) |
| 1612 | BRIGHT NUT | ECROU DECOLLETE | MUTTER (BLANKE), MUTTER (BEARBEITETE) |
| 1613 | BRIGHT RED HEAT | ROUGE CLAIR, ROUGE VIF | HELLROTGLUT |
| 1614 | BRIGHT RED HOT | CHAUFFE AU ROUGE CLAIR | HELLROTGLÜHEND |
| 1615 | BRIGHTENER | AGENT DE BRILLANTAGE | GLANZMITTEL, GLANZZUSATZ |
| 1616 | BRIGHTNESS, BRILLIANCY | ECLAT LUMINEUX | HELLIGKEIT |
| 1617 | BRINE | EAU SALEE, SAUMURE | SOLE, SALZSOLE |
| 1618 | BRINELL BALL TEST | ESSAI PAR EMPREINTE DE BILLE, ESSAI PAR LA BILLE DE BRINELL, BILLAGE | KUGELDRUCKVERSUCH NACH BRINELL, EINDRUCKVERSUCH, BRINELLPROBE |
| 1619 | BRINELL HARDNESS NUMBER | CHIFFRE DE DURETE BRINELL, DURETE BRINELL | KUGELDRUCKHÄRTE, BRINELLHÄRTE |
| 1620 | BRINELL TEST | ESSAI BRINELL | KUGELDRUCKVERSUCH, BRINELL'SCHER |
| 1621 | BRINGING A TOOL INTO POSITION | MISE AU POINT D'UN OUTIL | ANSETZEN, ANSTELLEN EINES WERKZEUGES |
| 1622 | BRIQUETTE | BRIQUETTE DE FERRO ALLIAGE | FERROLEGIERUNGSBRIKETT |
| 1623 | BRIQUETTE, PATENT FUEL | AGGLOMERE, BRIQUETTE | BRIKETT, PRESSLING |
| 1624 | BRITANNIA METAL | METAL BRITANNIQUE | BRITANNIAMETALL |
| 1625 | BRITISH THERMAL UNIT | CALORIE ANGLAISE | KALORIE (ENGLISCHE) |
| 1626 | BRITISH THERMAL UNIT (B.TH.U.) | UNITE THERMIQUE ANGLAISE | WÄRMEEINHEIT (BRITISCHE) |
| 1627 | BRITTLE | CASSANT | BRÜCHIG, SPRÖDE |
| 1628 | BRITTLENESS | FRAGILITE, MANQUE DE SOUPLESSE | ZERBRECHLICHKEIT, SPRÖDIGKEIT |
| 1629 | BRITTLENESS OF IRON | FRAGILITE DU FER | SPRÖDIGKEIT DES EISENS |
| 1630 | BRITTLENESS, ACID | FRAGILITE PAR DECAPAGE | BEIZUNGSVERSPRÖDIGKEIT |
| 1631 | BRITTLENESS, BLUE | FRAGILITE AU BLEU | BLAUBRÜCHIGKEIT |
| 1632 | BRITTLENESS, NOTCH | FRAGILITE D'ENTAILLE | KERBSPRÖDIGKEIT |
| 1633 | BRITTLENESS, RHEOTROPIC | FRAGILITE RHEOTROPIQUE | RHEOTROPE SPRÖDIGKEIT |
| 1634 | BRITTLENESS, TEMPER | FRAGILITE DE REVENU | ANLASSPRÖDIGKEIT |
| 1635 | BROACH (TO), REAM (TO), OPEN OUT THE RIVET HOLES (TO) | ALESER LES TROUS DE RIVET | AUFREISSEN (DIE NIETLÖCHER) |
| 1636 | BROACH, REAMER, RYMER, RIMER, RHYMER | ALESOIR, EQUARRISSOIR | REIBAHLE, RÄUMER, AUSREIBER, AUFREIBER |
| 1637 | BROACHING | BROCHAGE | RÄUMEN |
| 1638 | BROACHING, REAMING, OPENING OUT THE RIVET HOLES | ALESAGE DES TROUS DE RIVET | AUFREIBEN DER NIETLÖCHER |
| 1639 | BROAD FLANGE GIRDER | POUTRE A LARGES AILES | BREITFLANSCHTRÄGER |
| 1640 | BROAD FLANGE TEE IRON | FER EN T A LARGES AILES | T-EISEN (BREITFÜSSIGES) |
| 1641 | BROAD FLANGED BEAMS | POUTRELLES A LARGES AILES | BREITFLANSCHTRÄGER |
| 1642 | BROADSIDE MILL | LAMINOIR TRANSVERSAL | QUERWALZWERK |
| 1643 | BROADSIDE ROLLS | CYLINDRES TRANSVERSAUX | QUERWALZEN |
| 1644 | BROKEN STONE | PIERRES CONCASSEES, PIERRAILLE | SCHOTTER, STEINSCHLAG, KLEINSCHLAG |

| | | | |
|---|---|---|---|
| 1645 | **BROMARGYRITE, SILVER BROMIDE** | BROMARGYRITE, BROMITE, BROMARGURE, BROMYRITE, ARGENT BROMURE, ARGENT VERT | BROMSILBER, SILBERBROMID, BROMIT, BROMARGYRIT |
| 1646 | **BROMATE** | BROMATE | BROMAT |
| 1647 | **BROMIC ACID** | ACIDE BROMIQUE | BROMSÄURE |
| 1648 | **BROMIDE** | BROMURE | BROMMETALL, BROMID |
| 1649 | **BROMINE** | BROME | BROM |
| 1650 | **BRONZE** | BRONZE | BRONZE |
| 1651 | **BRONZE (TO)** | BRONZER | BRONZIEREN |
| 1652 | **BRONZE POWDER** | POUDRE DE BRONZE, BRONZE EN POUDRE | BRONZEPULVER |
| 1653 | **BRONZE TUBE** | TUBE EN BRONZE | BRONZEROHR |
| 1654 | **BRONZE WIRE** | FIL DE BRONZE | BRONZEDRAHT |
| 1655 | **BRONZE, ACID** | BRONZE RESISTANT AUX ACIDES | BRONZE (SÄUREBESTÄNDIGE) |
| 1656 | **BRONZE, ALPHA** | BRONZE ALPHA | ALPHA-BRONZE |
| 1657 | **BRONZE, COMMERCIAL** | BRONZE DE QUALITE COMMERCIALE, BRONZE DU COMMERCE | HANDELSGÜTEBRONZE |
| 1658 | **BRONZE, GUN METAL** | BRONZE | ROTGUSS |
| 1659 | **BRONZE, HARDWARE** | BRONZE POUR VISSERIE | SCHRAUBENBRONZE |
| 1660 | **BRONZE, PLASTIC** | BRONZE PLASTIQUE, BRONZE DE COUSSINET | LAGERBRONZE |
| 1661 | **BRONZE, SPRING** | BRONZE DE RESSORT | FEDERBRONZE |
| 1662 | **BRONZE, STATUARY** | BRONZE STATUAIRE | BILDHAVERBRONZE |
| 1663 | **BRONZE, TRIM** | BRONZE ORNEMENTAL | ZIERBRONZE |
| 1664 | **BRONZING** | BRONZAGE | BRONZIEREN |
| 1665 | **BROWN COAL** | LIGNITE PARFAIT | BRAUNKOHLE |
| 1666 | **BROWN COAL BRIQUETTE** | AGGLOMERE DE LIGNITE | BRAUNKOHLENBRIKETT |
| 1667 | **BROWN COAL TAR** | GOUDRON DE LIGNITE | BRAUNKOHLENTEER |
| 1668 | **BROWN COAL TAR OIL** | HUILE DE GOUDRON DE LIGNITE | BRAUNKOHLENTEERÖL, PARAFFINGASÖL, DEUTSCHES GASÖL, ROTÖL, GELBÖL |
| 1669 | **BRUSH COPPER** | CUIVRE A BALAI | BÜRSTENKUPFERBLECH |
| 1670 | **BUBBLE OF AIR, AIR BUBBLE** | BULLE D'AIR | LUFTBLASE |
| 1671 | **BUBBLE OF GAS, GAS BUBBLE** | BULLE DE GAZ | GASBLASE |
| 1672 | **BUBBLING** | BULLAGE | BLASENBILDUNG |
| 1673 | **BUCKET** | PISTON A CLAPET, PISTON ELEVATOIRE | VENTILKOLBEN |
| 1674 | **BUCKET** | SEAU, GODET | EIMER |
| 1675 | **BUCKET CONVEYOR** | CONVOYEUR, TRANSPORTEUR A GODETS | FÖRDERKETTE, BECHERKETTE, BECHERKABEL, KONVEYOR |
| 1676 | **BUCKET ELEVATOR** | ELEVATEUR A GODETS, NORIA | BECHERWERK, SCHÖPFWERK, PATERNOSTERWERK |
| 1677 | **BUCKET OF A WATER WHEEL** | AUBE, PALETTE D'UNE ROUE HYDRAULIQUE | SCHAUFEL EINES WASSERRADES |
| 1678 | **BUCKET SEAT** | SIEGE BAQUET | KÜBELSITZ |
| 1679 | **BUCKLED PLATE** | TOLE BOMBEE, TOLE EMBOUTIE | BUCKELPLATTE, TROGBLECH |
| 1680 | **BUCKLES** | PLIS | FALTEN |
| 1681 | **BUCKLING** | LAMBAGE (DE TOLES) | KNICKUNG |
| 1682 | **BUCKLING STRENGTH** | RESISTANCE AU FLAMBAGE | KNICKFESTIGKEIT |
| 1683 | **BUCKRAKES** | RATEAUX-AMMEULONNEURS | SCHOBERRECHEN |
| 1684 | **BUFF WHEEL** | DISQUE EN BUFFLE | LEDERPOLIERSCHEIBE |
| 1685 | **BUFFALO HIDE** | PEAU DE BUFFLE, BUFFLE | BÜFFELLEDER |

**BUF** 44

| | | | |
|---|---|---|---|
| 1686 | BUFFER | TAMPON, BUTOIR, POLISSOIR | PUFFER, BUFFER, POLIERMASCHINE |
| 1687 | BUFFER BATTERY | BATTERIE-TAMPON | PUFFERBATTERIE |
| 1688 | BUFFER SPRING | RESSORT AMORTISSEUR DES CHOCS | PUFFERFEDER |
| 1689 | BUFFER STORAGE | MEMOIRE INTERMEDIAIRE | PUFFER-SPEICHER |
| 1690 | BUFFERS | SELS DE POLISSAGE | SCHWABBELSALZE |
| 1691 | BUFFING | EMEULAGE | SCHWABBELN |
| 1692 | BUFFING COMPOUND | COMPOSITION DE POLISSAGE A LA MEULE | SCHWABBELMITTEL |
| 1693 | BUFFING WHEEL | DISQUE POLISSEUR | POLIERSCHEIBE, SCHWABBELSCHEIBE |
| 1694 | BUILD (TO) | CONSTRUIRE | BAUEN |
| 1695 | BUILD-UP | SUREPAISSEUR | AUFMASS, ÜBERDICKE |
| 1696 | BUILD-UP SEQUENCE | PROCESSUS DE RECHARGEMENT | AUFTRAGSPROZESS |
| 1697 | BUILDING BLOCKS | PARPAINGS, BRIQUES CREUSES | BAUSTEINE |
| 1698 | BUILDING CONTRACTOR | ENTREPRENEUR DE BATIMENT | BAUUNTERNEHMER |
| 1699 | BUILDING SITE | EMPLACEMENT, TERRAIN A BATIR | BAUGRUND |
| 1700 | BUILDING STONE | PIERRE A BATIR | BAUSTEIN |
| 1701 | BUILDING UP | EPAISSISSEMENT | VERSTÄRKUNG |
| 1702 | BUILT-IN BEAM | POUTRE ENCASTREE | EINBAUTRÄGER |
| 1703 | BUILT-IN BEAM, BEAM WITH ENDS FIXED | POUTRE ENCASTREE A SES DEUX EXTREMITES | BEIDERSEITIG EINGESPANNTER TRÄGER |
| 1704 | BUILT-IN MEMBER | ELEMENT DE CHARPENTE INCORPORE | BAUTEIL (EINGEBAUTES) |
| 1705 | BUILT-UP | RAPPORTE, ACCUMULATION | ZUGEBAUT, SPEICHERUNG |
| 1706 | BUILT-UP CRANK | MANIVELLE EN PLUSIEURS PIECES | KURBEL (GEBAUTE), ZUSAMMENGEBAUTE |
| 1707 | BUILT-UP EDGE | COPEAU ADHERENT | AUFBAUSCHNEIDE |
| 1708 | BUILT-UP FLANGE | BRIDE RAPPORTEE | FLANSCHRING |
| 1709 | BUILT-UP PISTON | PISTON DE DEUX PIECES | KOLBEN (GETEILTER), ZWEITEILIGER |
| 1710 | BUILT-UP PLATE | PLAQUE MODELE | MODELLPLATTE |
| 1711 | BULB | PLONGEUR (DE THERMOMETRE), BULBE | FÜHLER, TAUCHROHR |
| 1712 | BULB ANGLE IRON | FER CORNIERE A BOUDIN | WULSTWINKEL, WINKELWULSTEISEN |
| 1713 | BULB ANGLES | CORNIERES A BOUDIN | WINKELWULSTEISEN |
| 1714 | BULB BAR | FER PLAT A BOUDIN | FLACHWULSTEISEN |
| 1715 | BULB HEAD RAILS | RAILS A BOUDIN | DOPPELKOPFSCHIENEN |
| 1716 | BULB IRON | FER A BOUDIN | WULSTEISEN |
| 1717 | BULB OF A THERMOMETER | AMPOULE DU THERMOMETRE | THERMOMETERKUGEL |
| 1718 | BULB PIPETTE | PIPETTE A CYLINDRE | VOLLPIPETTE |
| 1719 | BULB TEE | FER EN T A BOUDIN, FER A BOUDIN A PATIN | T-WULST, FLANSCHWULSTEISEN |
| 1720 | BULGE | BOMBEMENT, BOMBE, CONVEXITE, GONFLEMENT, BOSSE | AUSBAUCHUNG, AUSBEULUNG, WÖLBUNG, BEULE |
| 1721 | BULGE (TO) | SE GONFLER | AUSBAUCHEN (SICH) |
| 1722 | BULGED | BOMBE | AUSGEBAUCHT |
| 1723 | BULGING | BOMBAGE, ELARGISSEMENT | AUFWEITUNG, AUFWÖLBUNG, AUFWULSTUNG, AUSBAUCHUNG |
| 1724 | BULK DENSITY | DENSITE AU REMPLISSAGE | FÜLLDICHTE |
| 1725 | BULK SPECIFIC GRAVITY | DENSITE APPARENTE | SCHEINDICHTE |
| 1726 | BULKHEAD | CLOISON | SCHOTT, TRENNWAND |
| 1727 | BULL BLOCK | BANC A TREFILER LES GROS FILS | GROBZUG |
| 1728 | BULL LADLE | POCHE DE GRUE DE COULEE | KRANPFANNE, KRANGIESSPFANNE |

|  |  |  |  |
|---|---|---|---|
| 1729 | **BULLION** | METAL NOBLE EN BARRES | EDELMETALLBARREN |
| 1730 | **BULLION BAR** | BARRE DE METAL NOBLE | EDELMETALLBAR |
| 1731 | **BULLOCK GEAR, HORSE GEAR, CATTLE GEAR** | MANEGE, BARITEL | GÖPEL, ROSSWERK |
| 1732 | **BUMPER** | PILETTE MECANIQUE, PARE-CHOC | PLASTSTAMPFER (MECHANISCHER), STOSSFÄNGER |
| 1733 | **BUMPING SCREEN** | CRIBLE A SECOUSSES | STOSSSIEB |
| 1734 | **BUMPING TOOL** | OUTIL A MAIN DE MARTELAGE | SCHLICHTHAMMER |
| 1735 | **BUND** | CAVALIER | TANKWALL |
| 1736 | **BUNDLE** | BOTTE (DE TUBES OU PROFILES) | ROHR-ODER FORMSTAHLBÜNDEL |
| 1737 | **BUNDLE (TO)** | BOTTELER | BÜNDELN |
| 1738 | **BUNDLE OF HOOP IRON** | BOTTE DE FEUILLARD | BUND VON BANDEISEN |
| 1739 | **BUNKER BED** | COUCHETTE, LIT-PLACARD | SCHLAFKOJE |
| 1740 | **BUNKER, COAL BUNKER** | RESERVOIR, SOUTE A CHARBON | BUNKER, KOHLENBUNKER |
| 1741 | **BUNSEN BURNER** | BRULEUR BUNSEN, BEC BUNSEN | BUNSENBRENNER |
| 1742 | **BUOYANCY** | POUSEE DE BAS EN HAUT, FORCE ASCENSIONNELLE, FLOTTABILITE | AUFTRIEB, SCHWIMMFÄHIGKEIT |
| 1743 | **BURETTE** | BURETTE | BÜRETTE |
| 1744 | **BURIED PIPE-LINES** | BRANCHEMENTS SOUTERRAINS | FERNROHRLEITUNG (EINGEERDETE) |
| 1745 | **BURN (TO)** | BRULER | VERBRENNEN, BRENNEN |
| 1746 | **BURN (TO), OVERHEAT THE IRON (TO)** | BRULER LE FER | EISEN (DAS) ÜBERHITZEN, VERBRENNEN (DAS) |
| 1747 | **BURN-UP** | COMBUSTION NUCLEAIRE | ABBRAND |
| 1748 | **BURNED INGOT** | LINGOT BRULE | VERBRANNTER BLOCK |
| 1749 | **BURNER** | BRULEUR | BRENNER |
| 1750 | **BURNING** | BRULURE | VERBRENNEN |
| 1751 | **BURNING FIRING GASEOUS FUELS** | CHAUFFAGE AU GAZ | GASFEUERUNG, VERFEUERN GASFÖRMIGER BRENNSTOFFE |
| 1752 | **BURNING FIRING OIL FUEL, OIL FIRING** | CHAUFFAGE AU PETROLE, CHAUFFAGE AU NAPHTE, CHAUFFAGE A HUILE LOURDE | ÖLFEUERUNG, VERFEUERN VON ÖL |
| 1753 | **BURNING FIRING PULVERISED COAL** | CHAUFFAGE AU CHARBON PULVERISE | KOHLENSTAUBFEUERUNG, VERFEUERN VON KOHLENSTAUB |
| 1754 | **BURNING OVERHEATING THE IRON** | BRULEMENT DU FER | ÜBERHITZUNG, VERBRENNEN DES EISENS |
| 1755 | **BURNISH** | POLI PARFAIT, BRUNI, BRUNISSURE | HOCHGLANZ |
| 1756 | **BURNISH (TO)** | BRILLANTER, POLIR BRILLANT, BRUNIR | HOCHGLANZPOLIEREN |
| 1757 | **BURNISHER** | BRUNISSOIR | POLIEREISEN, POLIERSTAHL, GLÄTTZAHN |
| 1758 | **BURNISHING** | BRUNISSAGE, GALETAGE | BRÄUNUNG, BRÜNIERUNG, PRÄGEPOLIEREN, HOCHGLANZPOLIEREN |
| 1759 | **BURNISHING BALLS** | BILLES A POLIR, BILLES POUR BRUNISSAGE | POLIERKUGELN |
| 1760 | **BURNT BRICK** | BRIQUE CUITE | ZIEGEL (GEBRANNTER) |
| 1761 | **BURNT DEPOSIT** | DEPOT BRULE | NIEDERSCHLAG (ANGEBRANNTER) |
| 1762 | **BURNT IRON** | FER BRULE | EISEN (VERBRANNTES) |
| 1763 | **BURNT STEEL** | ACIER BRULE | STAHL (VERBRANNTER) |
| 1764 | **BURR** | BAVURE, EBARBURE, EBARBE, BARBE, BARBURE | GRAT, BART |
| 1765 | **BURR REMOVER FOR TUBES, TUBE BURR REMOVER** | FRAISE EBARBEUSE | ROHRFRÄSER |
| 1766 | **BURRING** | EBAVURAGE | ENTGRATEN, ABGRATEN |
| 1767 | **BURSTING** | ECLATEMENT | PLATZEN |

**BUR**

46

| | | | |
|---|---|---|---|
| 1768 | **BURSTING OF A PIPE** | ECLATEMENT, RUPTURE D'UN TUYAU | AUFPLATZEN EINES ROHRES |
| 1769 | **BURSTING OF A PULLEY, OF A FLYWHEEL** | ECLATEMENT D'UNE POULIE, ECLATEMENT D'UN VOLANT | BERSTEN, EXPLOSION EINER SCHEIBE, EXPLOSION EINES SCHWUNGRADES |
| 1770 | **BUS BAR** | BARRE COLLECTRICE, RAIL DE CONTACT, BARRE OMNIBUS | STROMSCHIENE, SAMMELSCHIENE |
| 1771 | **BUSH OF BEARING** | COUSSINET EN UNE SEULE PIECE | LAGERBÜCHSE, LAGERHÜLSE, BÜCHSE, LAGERSCHALE (UNGETEILTE) |
| 1772 | **BUSHELLING** | EMPAQUETAGE, MISE EN BOTTES | PAKETIEREN |
| 1773 | **BUSHING** | BAGUE, REDUCTION MALE-FEMELLE, DOUILLE, MANCHON | LAGERSCHALE, LAGERBÜCHSE, REDUZIERSTÜCK, HÜLSE |
| 1774 | **BUSTLE PIPE** | CONDUIT ANNULAIRE DE VENT CHAUD | HEISSINDLEITUNG, RINGLEITUNG, WINDRING |
| 1775 | **BUTANE** | BUTANE, HYDRURE DE BUTYLE | BUTAN |
| 1776 | **BUTT JOINT** | JOINT BOUT A BOUT | STOSSVERBINDUNG, STUMPF, STUMPFSTOSSVERBINDUNG |
| 1777 | **BUTT JOINT, DOUBLE WELDED** | JOINT ABOUTE SOUDE DES DEUX COTES | STUMPFSTOSS (BEIDERSEITIG GESCHWEISSTER) |
| 1778 | **BUTT JOINT, JUMP JOINT** | ASSEMBLAGE, JONCTION BOUT A BOUT | STOSSVERBINDUNG |
| 1779 | **BUTT JOINT, SINGLE WELDER** | JOINT ABOUTE SOUDE D'UN SEUL COTE | STUMPFSTOSS (EINSEITIG GESCHWEISSTER) |
| 1780 | **BUTT OF TANNED HIDE** | CUIR DU CROUPON | KERNLEDER |
| 1781 | **BUTT RIVETED JOINT** | RIVURE A BANDE DE RECOUVREMENT | LASCHENNIETUNG, BANDNIETUNG |
| 1782 | **BUTT STRAP JOINT, FISHED JOINT, WELDED JOINT** | ASSEMBLAGE A COUVRE-JOINTS, JOINT A ECLISSES | ÜBERLASCHUNG, STOSS (MIT LASCHE), ÜBERLASCHTER STOSS |
| 1783 | **BUTT STRIP STRAP, COVERING STRIP, WELT, FISHPLATE, COVER STRAP** | BANDE DE RECOUVREMENT COUVRE-JOINT, ECLISSE | LASCHE, STOSSLASCHE, STOSSPLATTE |
| 1784 | **BUTT WELD** | SOUDURE BOUT A BOUT, SOUDURE PAR RAPPROCHEMENT | STOSSNAHT, STUMPF-(SCHWEISS- )NAHT |
| 1785 | **BUTT WELD (TO)** | SOUDER PAR CONTACT, SOUDER PAR ENCOLLAGE | STUMPFSCHWEISSEN |
| 1786 | **BUTT WELD, - THROAT OF** | EPAISSEUR D'UNE SOUDURE BOUT A BOUT | STUMPFNAHTDICKE |
| 1787 | **BUTT WELD, CLOSED DOUBLE BEVEL** | SOUDURE EN K SANS ECARTEMENT | K-NAHT OHNE LUFTSPALT |
| 1788 | **BUTT WELD, CLOSED DOUBLE JOINTS** | SOUDURE DOUBLE FERMEE | DOPPELNAHT OHNE LUFTSPALT |
| 1789 | **BUTT WELD, CLOSED SINGLE BEVEL** | SOUDURE EN DEMI-V SANS ECARTEMENT | HALB-V-NAHT OHNE LUFTSPALT |
| 1790 | **BUTT WELD, CLOSED SINGLE JOINT** | JOINT DE SOUDURE EN J FERMEE | J-NAHTVERBINDUNG |
| 1791 | **BUTT WELD, CLOSED SQUARE** | SOUDURE EN I SANS ECARTEMENT DES BORDS | I-NAHTVERBINDUNG (I-STOSS) OHNE LUFTSPALT |
| 1792 | **BUTT WELD, CONCAVE** | SOUDURE CONCAVE | HOHLNAHT (KONCAVE), SCHWEISSNAHT (LEICHTE) |
| 1793 | **BUTT WELD, DOUBLE BEVEL** | CHANFREIN (SOUDURE) EN K | K-NAHT |
| 1794 | **BUTT WELD, FLASH** | SOUDURE PAR ETINCELAGE | ABBRENNSTUMPFSCHWEISSUNG |
| 1795 | **BUTT WELD, JUMP** | SOUDURE (ASSEMBLAGE) EN T | T-NAHT |
| 1796 | **BUTT WELD, OPEN DOUBLE BEVEL** | SOUDURE EN K AVEC ECARTEMENT | K-NAHT MIT LUFTSPALT |
| 1797 | **BUTT WELD, OPEN SINGLE BEVEL** | SOUDURE EN DEMI-V AVEC ECARTEMENT | HALB-V-NAHT MIT LUFTSPALT |
| 1798 | **BUTT WELD, OPEN SINGLE JOINT** | SOUDURE EN J AVEC ECARTEMENT | J-NAHT MIT LUFTSPALT |
| 1799 | **BUTT WELD, RESISTANCE** | SOUDURE BOUT A BOUT PAR RESISTANCE | WIDERSTANDSSTUMPFNAHT |
| 1800 | **BUTT WELD, SINGLE BEVEL** | CHANFREIN EN DEMI-V | HALB-V-NAHT |
| 1801 | **BUTT WELD, TEE** | SOUDURE (ASSEMBLAGE) EN T | T-NAHT |

| | | | |
|---|---|---|---|
| 1802 | **BUTT WELDED JOINT, JUMP WELD** | SOUDURE PAR RAPPROCHEMENT, SOUDURE PAR ENCOLLAGE | SCHWEISSUNG (STUMPFE) |
| 1803 | **BUTT WELDED PIPE** | TUBE SOUDE BOUT A BOUT | ROHRVERBINDUNG (STUMPFGESCHWEISSTE) |
| 1804 | **BUTT WELDED TUBE** | TUBE SOUDE PAR RAPPROCHEMENT, TUBE A RAPPROCHEMENT | ROHR (STUMPFGESCHWEISSTES) |
| 1805 | **BUTT WELDING** | SOUDAGE PAR RAPPROCHEMENT, SOUDAGE BOUT A BOUT (PAR RESISTANCE) | STUMPFSCHWEISSEN |
| 1806 | **BUTT WELDING, FLASH** | SOUDAGE EN BOUT PAR ETINCELAGE | ABBRENNSTUMPFSCHWEISSEN |
| 1807 | **BUTT WELDING, RESISTANCE** | SOUDAGE EN BOUT PAR RESISTANCE | WIDERSTANDSSTUMPFSCHWEISSEN |
| 1808 | | | |
| 1809 | **BUTT-WELDED JOINT** | SOUDURE BOUT A BOUT | STUMPFNAHT |
| 1810 | **BUTT-WELDING ENDS, SOCKET-WELDING ENDS** | ORIFICES A SOUDER (EN BOUT, A L'INTERIEUR) | VORSCHWEISSENDEN, EINSCHWEISSENDEN |
| 1811 | **BUTTERFLY VALVE** | VANNE A PAPILLON | DROSSELKLAPPE |
| 1812 | **BUTTON** | FOND DE POCHE | PFANNENBÄR |
| 1813 | **BUTTON HEAD, ROUND HEAD, CUP HEAD, SPHERICAL HEAD, SEGMENTAL HEAD OF SCREW BOLT** | TETE RONDE D'UNE VIS | RUNDSCHRAUBENKOPF |
| 1814 | **BUTTRESS THREAD** | FILET TRAPEZOIDAL | TRAPEZFÖRMIGES, GEWINDE (HALBIERTES), TRAPEZGEWINDE |
| 1815 | **BUTTRESS THREADED SCREW** | VIS A FILET TRAPEZOIDAL | SCHRAUBE MIT TRAPEZGEWINDE |
| 1816 | **BUTYLENE** | BUTYLENE | BUTYLEN |
| 1817 | **BUTYRIC ACID** | ACIDE BUTYRIQUE | BUTTERSÄURE |
| 1818 | **BY-PASS** | CONDUITE DE DERIVATION, BY-PASS | NEBENSCHLUSS, UMFÜHRUNG |
| 1819 | **BY-PASS VALVE, AUXILIARY VALVE** | SOUPAPE DE DERIVATION | UMFÜHRUNGSVENTIL, HILFSVENTIL, ENTLASTUNGSVENTIL, ZUSATZVENTIL, UMLAUFVENTIL, UMGEHUNGSVENTIL, ZIRKULATIONSVENTIL |
| 1820 | **BY-PRODUCT** | SOUS-PRODUIT, PRODUIT SECONDAIRE | NEBENERZEUGNIS, NEBENPRODUKT |
| 1821 | **BYPASS** | DERIVATION, BY-PASS | UMGEHUNG, NEBENSCHLUSS |
| 1822 | **C-SPANNER** | CLEF A CROCHET | HAKENSCHLÜSSEL, NUTENSCHLÜSSEL |
| 1823 | **C-SPRING, CEE SPRING, COACH SPRING** | RESSORT EN C | BÜGELFEDER |
| 1824 | **CAB OVER ENGINE** | CABINE AVANCEE | FRONT FÜHRERHAUS |
| 1825 | **CABLE** | CABLE ELECTRIQUE | LEITUNGSKABEL |
| 1826 | **CABLE RAILWAY** | CHEMIN DE FER FUNICULAIRE, FUNICULAIRE | SEILBAHN, GLEISSEILBAHN |
| 1827 | **CABLE TERMINAL** | COSSE | LEITUNGSSCHUH |
| 1828 | **CABLE TWISTING** | CABLAGE | KABELVERSEILUNG |
| 1829 | **CABLE, CABLE-LAID ROPE** | GRELIN | KABEL, TAU |
| 1830 | **CABLE, WIRE** | TELEGRAMME | TELEGRAMM |
| 1831 | **CADMIUM** | CADMIUM | KADMIUM |
| 1832 | **CADMIUM PLATING** | CADMIAGE | KADMIEREN |
| 1833 | **CAESIUM** | CESIUM, CAESIUM | ZÄSIUM |
| 1834 | **CAKE** | LINGOT DE DEPART | AUSGANGSBLOCK |
| 1835 | **CAKING COAL** | HOUILLE COLLANTE | KOHLE (BACKENDE) |
| 1836 | **CALAMINE, SMITHSONITE** | CALAMINE, SIMITHSONITE | ZINKSPAT, GALMEI (EDLER), KALAMIN, SMITHSONI |
| 1837 | **CALC SINTER** | CONCRETION CALCAIRE | KALKSINTER |

**CAL** 48

| | | | |
|------|------|------|------|
| 1838 | CALCAREOUS TUFA | TUF CALCAIRE | TUFFSTEIN, KALKTUFF |
| 1839 | CALCINATION | CALCINATION, GRILLAGE | KALZINIEREN, RÖSTUNG, KALZINIERUNG |
| 1840 | CALCINATION OF ORES | CALCINATION DES MINERAIS | GLÜHEN, KALZINIEREN VON ERZEN |
| 1841 | CALCINE ORES (TO) | CALCINER LES MINERAIS | ERZE GLÜHEN, KALZINIEREN |
| 1842 | CALCINED MAGNESIA | MAGNESIE CALCINEE | MAGNESIA (GEBRANNTE) |
| 1843 | CALCINING FURNACE, KILN | FOUR DE CALCINATION | KALZINIEROFEN |
| 1844 | CALCITE | CALCITE | KALZIT |
| 1845 | CALCITE, CALCAREOUS SPAR | SPATH CALCAIRE, CALCITE | KALKSPAT, KALZIT |
| 1846 | CALCIUM | CALCIUM | KALZIUM |
| 1847 | CALCIUM BICARBONATE, CALCIUM ACID CARBONATE | BICARBONATE DE CALCIUM | KALZIUM (DOPPELTKOHLENSAURES), KALZIUMBIKARBONAT |
| 1848 | CALCIUM CARBIDE | CARBURE, ACETYLURE DE CALCIUM | KALZIUMKARBID, KARBID |
| 1849 | CALCIUM CARBONATE, CARBONATE OF LIME | CARBONATE DE CHAUX | KALK (KOHLENSAURER), KALZIUM (KOHLENSAURES), KALZIUMKARBONAT |
| 1850 | CALCIUM CHLORIDE | CHLORURE DE CALCIUM | CHLORKALZIUM, KALZIUMCHLORID |
| 1851 | CALCIUM HYDROXIDE, SLAKED LIME | CHAUX ETEINTE, CHAUX HYDRATEE, HYDRATE DE CHAUX | KALK (GELÖSCHTER), KALZIUMHYDROXYD, KALKHYDRAT |
| 1852 | CALCIUM MONO SULPHIDE, CANTON'S PHOSPHORUS | MONOSULFURE DE CALCIUM | SCHWEFELKALZIUM (EINFACH), KALZIUMSULFID, CANTONSPHOSPHOR |
| 1853 | CALCIUM OXALATE | OXALATE DE CALCIUM | KALK (OXALSAURER), KALZIUMOXALAT |
| 1854 | CALCIUM OXIDE, QUICK LIME | CHAUX VIVE, CHAUX ANHYDRE, OXYDE DE CALCIUM | ÄTZKALK, KALK (GEBRANNTER), KALZIUMOXYD |
| 1855 | CALCIUM PHOSPHATE | PHOSPHATE DE CALCIUM, PHOSPHATE TRICALCIQUE | KALK (PHOSPHORSAURER), KALZIUMPHOSPHAT |
| 1856 | CALCIUM SULFATE | SULFATE DE CALCIUM | KALZIUMSULFAT |
| 1857 | CALCULATE (TO) | CALCULER | BERECHNEN |
| 1858 | CALCULATED THEORETICAL VALUE | VALEUR THEORIQUE, VALEUR CALCULEE | WERT (ERRECHNETER), WERT (RECHNERISCHER), SOLLWERT |
| 1859 | CALCULATING MACHINE | MACHINE ARITHMETIQUE, MACHINE A CALCULER | RECHENMASCHINE |
| 1860 | CALCULATION | CALCUL | BERECHNUNG |
| 1861 | CALIBRATE (TO) | CALIBRER, JAUGER | KALIBRIEREN |
| 1862 | CALIBRATED CHAINS | CHAINES CALIBREES | KETTEN (KALIBRIERTE) |
| 1863 | CALIBRATING (OF A TANK) | ETALONNAGE (D'UN RESERVOIR) | EICHUNG (EINES BEHÄLTERS) |
| 1864 | CALIBRATING AND DIE-FORGING PRESS | PRESSE MECANIQUE A CALIBRER ET A MATRICER | KALIBRIER-UND GESENKSCHMIEDE-PRESSE |
| 1865 | CALIBRATING MACHINE | MACHINE A CALIBRER | KALIBRIERMASCHINE |
| 1866 | CALIBRATING SPRING | RESSORT TARE | KALIBRIERTE FEDER |
| 1867 | CALIBRATION | ETALONNAGE, CALIBRAGE, JAUGEAGE | EICHUNG, KALIBRIERUNG, KALIBRIEREN |
| 1868 | CALIBRATION CAPACITOR | CONDENSATEUR-ETALON | EICHKONDENSATOR |
| 1869 | CALIBRATION ERROR | ERREUR D'ETALONNAGE | EICHFEHLER |
| 1870 | CALIPER | MAITRE A DANSER | GREIFZIRKEL |
| 1871 | CALIPER GAUGE WITH DEPTH GAUGE | CALIBRE A COULISSE AVEC REGLE DE PROFONDEUR | SCHUBLEHRE MIT TIEFENMASSSTAB |
| 1872 | CALKING HAMMER | MARTEAU A MATER | STEMMHAMMER |
| 1873 | CALLIPER | COMPAS D'EPAISSEUR | KALIBER |
| 1874 | CALLIPERS | COMPAS DE CALIBRE | TASTER, TASTZIRKEL, GREIFZIRKEL |
| 1875 | CALLIPERS | MICROMETRE, PALMER | MIKROMETERLEHRE |
| 1876 | CALOMEL HALFICELL | ELECTRODE AU CALOMEL | KALOMELELEKTRODE |
| 1877 | CALORIMETER | CALORIMETRE | KALORIMETER |
| 1878 | CALORIMETRIC | CALORIMETRIQUE | KALORIMETRISCH |

**49** **CAP**

| | | | |
|---|---|---|---|
| 1879 | CALORIMETRIC BOMB | BOMBE CALORIMETRIQUE | BOMBE (KALORIMETRISCHE), BOMBENKALORIMETER |
| 1880 | CALORIMETRIC DETERMINATION | ANALYSE CALORIMETRIQUE | BESTIMMUNG (KALORIMETRISCHE) |
| 1881 | CALORIMETRY | CALORIMETRIE | KALORIMETRIE |
| 1882 | CALORIZING | CALORISATION | KALORISIERUNG |
| 1883 | CAM | CAME EXCENTRIQUE BOSSE, BOSSAGE | EXZENTER (UNRUNDE SCHEIBE, HUBSCHEIBE),NOCKE, MITTNEHMER, NOCKEN, DAUMEN, KNAGGE |
| 1884 | CAM ACTION | LEVEE DE CAME | NOCKENHUB |
| 1885 | CAM FOLLOWER | GALET DE POUSSOIR | STÖSSEL |
| 1886 | CAM GEAR MOTION | MECANISME A CAME | KURVENTRIEB, EXZENTERTRIEBWERK |
| 1887 | CAM PIN | DOIGT INCLINE | NOCKENANLAUFSCHRÄGER |
| 1888 | CAM SHAFT | ARBRE A CAME S, ARBRE PORTE-CAMES | DAUMENWELLE |
| 1889 | CAMBER | BOMBAGE, CAMBRAGE, CARROSSAGE, ANGLE DE CARROSSAGE | RADSTURZ, STURZ (WINKEL), WÖLBUNG, BOMBIERUNG |
| 1890 | CAMEL HAIR | POIL, POILS DE CHAMEAU | KAMELHAAR |
| 1891 | CAMEL HAIR BELT | COURROIE EN POILS DE CHAMEAU | KAMELHAARRIEMEN |
| 1892 | CAMEL-BACK | BANDE DE RECHAPAGE | ROHLAUFSTREIFEN |
| 1893 | CAMPHOR | CAMPHRE | KAMPFER |
| 1894 | CAMPHOR OIL | HUILE DE CAMPHRE | KAMPFERÖL |
| 1895 | CAMROLLER, FOLLOWER | GALET, MOLETTE DE LA CAME | NOCKENROLLE, EXZENTERROLLE |
| 1896 | CAMSHAFT | ARBRE A CAMES | NOCKENWELLE |
| 1897 | CAMSHAFT LATHE | TOUR A ARBRE A CAMES | NOCKENWELLENDREHBANK |
| 1898 | CANADIAN ASBESTOS | AMIANTE, FIBRE DU CANADA | KANADAFASER |
| 1899 | CANDLE | CHANDELLE, BOUGIE | KERZE |
| 1900 | CANDLE POWER | INTENSITE EN BOUGIES | KERZENSTÄRKE |
| 1901 | CANNEL COAL | CANNEL-COAL | CANNELKOHLE, KENNELKOHLE, KANNELKOHLE, GASKOHLE (ECHTE) |
| 1902 | CANT | CHANFREIN | ABSCHRÄGUNG |
| 1903 | CANT FILE | LIME A BISEAU, LIME A BARRETTES | BARETTFEILE |
| 1904 | CANTILEVER | POUTRE ENCASTREE A UNE EXTREMITE, POUTRE EN PORTE-A-FAUX | FREITRÄGER |
| 1905 | CANTILEVER BEAM | POUTRE EN PORTE-A-FAUX, POUTRE NON ENTRETOISEE | FREITRÄGER |
| 1906 | CANVAS | TOILE A VOILE | SEGELTUCH |
| 1907 | CANVAS BELT | COURROIE EN CHANVRE | HANFRIEMEN |
| 1908 | CANVAS HOSE | TUYAU EN TOILE DE CHANVRE | HANFSCHLAUCH |
| 1909 | CAOT (TO) | ENDUIRE | ÜBERZIEHEN |
| 1910 | CAP | BOUCHON FEMELLE, BOUCHON, CAPUCHON, CHAPEAU | KAPPE, DECKEL, VERSCHLUSSDECKEL |
| 1911 | CAP OF A SPHERICAL TANK | CALOTTE (D'UNE SPHERE) | KUGELKAPPE, KUGELHAUBE, KUGELSCHALE, KUGELKALOTTE |
| 1912 | CAP OF BEARING | CHAPEAU, COUVERCLE DU PALIER | LAGERDECKEL |
| 1913 | CAP SCREW | VIS A TETE | KOPFSCHRAUBE |
| 1914 | CAPABLE OF BEING CAST | SUSCEPTIBLE D'ETRE COULE, QUI PEUT SE COULER | GIESSBAR |
| 1915 | CAPABLE OF BEING ROLLED | SUSCEPTIBLE D'ETRE LAMINE; QUI SE LAMINE FACILEMENT | WALZBAR |
| 1916 | CAPACITOR | CONDENSATEUR, CONDENSEUR (DE VAPEUR) | KONDENSATOR |

# CAP

| | | | |
|---|---|---|---|
| 1917 | CAPACITY | PUISSANCE, CAPACITE (ELECTR.), CAPACITE, CONTENANCE | KAPAZITÄT (ELEKTR.), FASSUNGSVERMÖGEN, AUFNAHMEFÄHIGKEIT, KAPAZITÄT |
| 1918 | CAPACITY TO RESIST SHOCKS, RESISTANCE TO SHOCK | RESISTANCE AU CHOC, RESILIENCE | STOSSFESTIGKEIT, WIDERSTANDSFÄHIGKEIT GEGENSTOSS |
| 1919 | CAPE CHISEL | BEDANE | KREUZMEISSEL |
| 1920 | CAPILLARITY, CAPILLARY ACTION | CAPILLARITE | HAARRÖHRCHENWIRKUNG, KAPILLARITÄT |
| 1921 | CAPILLARY | TUBE CAPILLAIRE | HAARROHR, KAPILLARROHR |
| 1922 | CAPILLARY ACTION | ASPIRATION PAR CAPILLARITE | KAPILLARWIRKUNG |
| 1923 | CAPILLARY CONSTANT | CONSTANTE CAPILLAIRE | KAPILLARKONSTANTE |
| 1924 | CAPILLARY DEPRESSION | DEPRESSION CAPILLAIRE | KAPILLARDEPRESSION |
| 1925 | CAPILLARY ELEVATION | ASCENSION, ELEVATION CAPILLAIRE | KAPILLARELEVATION |
| 1926 | CAPITAL OF COLUMN | CHAPITEAU D'UNE COLONNE | KAPITÄL EINER SÄULE, SÄULENKAPITÄL |
| 1927 | CAPPING | FORMATION D'UNE CROUTE | DECKELBILDUNG |
| 1928 | CAPPING STRIPS | BANDES DE METAL DE RECOUVREMENT | ABDECKLEISTEN |
| 1929 | CAPSTAN | CABESTAN | SPILL |
| 1930 | CAPSTAN HEADED SCREW, TOMMY SCREW | VIS A BROCHE, VIS A LEVIER | KNEBELSCHRAUBE |
| 1931 | CAPSTAN LATHE | TOUR A REVOLVER | REVOLVERVERDREHBANK |
| 1932 | CAR TIPPING GEAR | BASCULEUR DE WAGONS | KIPPER, WAGENKIPPER |
| 1933 | CARBIDE | CARBURE | KARBID |
| 1934 | CARBIDE PRECIPITATION | PRECIPITATION DE CARBURE | KARBIDAUSSCHEIDUNG |
| 1935 | CARBIDE TIPPED REAMER | ALESOIR A MISE DE CARBURE | REIBAHLE (HARTMETALLBESTÜCKTE) |
| 1936 | CARBIDE-TIPPED DRILL | FORET A MISE EN CARBURE | BOHRER (HARTMETALLBESTÜCKTER) |
| 1937 | CARBOHYDRATE | HYDRATE DE CARBONE | KOHLEHYDRAT |
| 1938 | CARBOLIC ACID, PHENOL | PHENOL, ACIDE PHENIQUE, ACIDE CARBOLIQUE | KARBOLSÄURE, PHENOL, BENZOPHENOL, PHENYLSÄURE, PHENYLALKOHOL, MONOXYBENZOL, STEINKOHLENKREOSOT |
| 1939 | CARBOLINEUM | CARBOLINEUM, CARBONYLE | KARBOLINEUM |
| 1940 | CARBON | CARBONE | KOHLENSTOFF |
| 1941 | CARBON ARC | ARC AVEC ELECTRODE DE CARBONE | KOHLELICHTBOGEN |
| 1942 | CARBON ARC CUTTING | COUPAGE A L'ARC AU CARBONE | KOHLELICHTBOGENSCHNEIDEN |
| 1943 | CARBON ARC WELDING | SOUDAGE A L'ARC AVEC ELECTRODE AU CARBONE | KOHLE(LICHTBOGEN)SCHWEISSEN |
| 1944 | CARBON ARC, UNSHIELDED | ARC NON PROTEGE AVEC ELECTRODE AU CHARBON | UNGESCHÜTZTER KOHLELICHTBOGEN |
| 1945 | CARBON ARC,SHIELDED | ARC PROTEGE AVEC ELECTRODE AU CHARBON | SCHUTZGASLICHTBOGEN |
| 1946 | CARBON BRUSH | BALAI AU CHARBON | KOHLEBÜRSTE |
| 1947 | CARBON CONTENT | TENEUR EN CARBONE, DOSAGE DU CARBONE, PROPORTION DE CARBONE | KOHLENSTOFFGEHALT |
| 1948 | CARBON DIOXIDE, CARBONIC ACID GAS, CARBONIC ANHYDRIDE | ANHYDRIDE CARBONIQUE, GAZ CARBONIQUE | KOHLENSÄURE, KOHLENDIOXYD |
| 1949 | CARBON DIOXYDE AND HYDROGEN | ACIDE CARBONIQUE | KOHLENSÄURE |
| 1950 | CARBON ELECTRODE | ELECTRODE DE CHARBON | KOHLELEKTRODE |
| 1951 | CARBON FILAMENT LAMP, CARBON INCANDESCENT LAMP | LAMPE A FILAMENT DE CARBONE | KOHLEFADENGLÜHLAMPE |
| 1952 | CARBON MONOXIDE, CARBONIC OXIDE | OXYDE DE CARBONE | KOHLENMONOXYD |

| | | | |
|---|---|---|---|
| 1953 | **CARBON RESTORATION** | RECARBURATION, REGENERATION DES PIECES DECARBURISEES | AUFKOHLUNG, RÜCKOHLUNG |
| 1954 | **CARBON STEEL** | ACIER AU CARBONE | KOHLENSTOFFSTAHL, STAHL (UNLEGIERTER) |
| 1955 | **CARBON STEEL BLOOMS** | BLOOMS EN ACIER AU CARBONE | BLÖCKE AUS KOHLENSTOFFSTAHL |
| 1956 | **CARBON STEEL SHEET BARS** | LARGETS EN ACIER AU CARBONE | PLATINEN AUS LEGIERTEN STÄHLEN |
| 1957 | **CARBON STEEL, HIGH** | ACIER DUR A HAUTE TENEUR EN CARBONE | HARTSTAHL, STAHL (KOHLENSTOFFEICHER) |
| 1958 | **CARBON STEEL, LOW** | ACIER DOUX | FLUSSTAHL, STAHL (WEICHER) |
| 1959 | **CARBON STEEL, MEDIUM** | ACIER DEMI-DOUX | STAHL (HALBHARTER) |
| 1960 | **CARBON TETRACHLORIDE** | TETRACHLORURE DE CARBONE | TETRACHLORKOHLENSTOFF |
| 1961 | **CARBON-FREE** | EXEMPT DE CARBONE | KOHLENSTOFFREI |
| 1962 | **CARBON, COMBINED** | CARBONE COMBINE | KOHLENSTOFF (GEBUNDENER) |
| 1963 | **CARBON, DISSOLVED** | CARBONE DISSOUS | KOHLENSTOFF (GELÖSTER) |
| 1964 | **CARBON, DISULPHIDE** | SULFURE DE CARBONE | SCHWEFELKOHLENSTOFF, KOHLENDISULFID, SCHWEFELALKOHOL |
| 1965 | **CARBON, TEMPER** | CARBONE DE REVENU, POURCENTAGE DE CHARBON | AUSLASSKOHLENSTOFF, KOHLENSTOFFGEHALT |
| 1966 | **CARBONACEOUS** | CARBONE | KOHLENSTOFFARTIG KOHLENSTOFFHALTIG |
| 1967 | **CARBONADO, BLACK DIAMOND** | CARBONADO | KARBONAT, CARBONADO, DIAMANT (SCHWARZER) |
| 1968 | **CARBONATE** | CARBONATE | SALZ (KOHLENSAURES), KARBONAT |
| 1969 | **CARBONIFEROUS LIMESTONE** | CALCAIRE CARBONIFERE | KOHLENKALK |
| 1970 | **CARBONISATION** | CARBONISATION | VERKOHLUNG, KARBONISATION |
| 1971 | **CARBONISE (TO)** | CARBONISER, CHARBONNER | VERKOHLEN, KARBONISIEREN |
| 1972 | **CARBONITRIDING** | CARBONITRURATION | KARBONITRIEREN |
| 1973 | **CARBONITRIDING ATMOSPHERE** | ATMOSPHERE DE CARBONITRURATION | KARBONITRIERUNGSATMOSPHÄRE |
| 1974 | **CARBONIZATION** | CARBONISATION | KARBONISIERUNG, VERKOHLUNG |
| 1975 | **CARBONIZING** | CARBONISATION, COKEFACTION | VERKOHLUNG, VERKOKUNG |
| 1976 | **CARBONYL** | CARBONYLE | KARBONYL |
| 1977 | **CARBONYL IRON** | FER DE CARBONYLE | KARBONYLEISEN |
| 1978 | **CARBONYL NICKEL** | NICKEL AU CARBONYLE | KARBONYLNICKEL |
| 1979 | **CARBONYL POWDER** | POUDRE DE CARBONYLE | KARBONYLPULVER |
| 1980 | **CARBORUNDUM, CARBON SILICIDE** | CARBORUNDUN, CARBURE DE SILICIUM, SILICIURE DE CARBONE | KARBORUND, KARBORUNDUM, SILIZIUMKARBID |
| 1981 | **CARBOY** | TOURIE, DAME-JEANNE, BONBONNE | KORBFLASCHE, BALLON, DEMIJOHN |
| 1982 | **CARBURATOR (U.S), CARBURETTOR (G.B)** | CARBURATEUR | VERGASER |
| 1983 | **CARBURETTED ALCOHOL** | ALCOOL CARBURE | KRAFTSPIRITUS, MOTORENSPIRITUS, ALKOHOL (KARBURIERTER) |
| 1984 | **CARBURETTER, CARBURETOR** | CARBURATEUR | VERGASER, KARBURATOR |
| 1985 | **CARBURISATION OF IRON** | CARBURATION DU FER | KOHLUNG DES EISENS |
| 1986 | **CARBURISE THE IRON (TO)** | CARBURER LE FER | EISEN (DAS) KOHLEN |
| 1987 | **CARBURIZING** | CEMENTATION PAR LE CARBONE | ZEMENTIEREN (MIT KOHLENSTOFF), AUFKOHLEN, EINSATZHÄRTUNG |
| 1988 | **CARBURIZING COMPOUNDS** | CARBURANTS | AUFKOHLUNGSMITTEL, EINSATZMITTEL |
| 1989 | **CARBURIZING CONTAINERS** | BOITES DE CEMENTATION | EINSATZKASTEN |
| 1990 | **CARBURIZING FLAME** | FLAMME CARBURANTE | FLAMME (KARBURIERENDE), FLAMME (AUFKOHLENDE) |
| 1991 | **CARBURIZING FURNACE** | FOUR DE CARBURISATION | KARBURIEROFEN |
| 1992 | **CARBURIZING, GAS** | CEMENTATION PAR GAZ | ZEMENTATION IN GASATMOSPHÄRE |

# CAR

| | | | |
|---|---|---|---|
| 1993 | **CARBURIZING, HOMOGENEOUS** | CEMENTATION HOMOGENE | ZEMENTIERUNG (GLEICHARTIGE) |
| 1994 | **CARBURIZING, LIQUID** | BAIN DE CEMENTATION | EINSATZBAD |
| 1995 | **CARBURIZING, SELECTIVE** | CEMENTATION SELECTIVE | ZEMENTIERUNG (SELEKTIVE) |
| 1996 | **CARBURIZING,BOX** | CEMENTATION EN CAISSE | KASTENZEMENTIERUNG, KISTENZEMENTIERUNG |
| 1997 | **CARDAN COUPLING** | CARDAN | KARDANKUPPLUNG |
| 1998 | **CARDAN'S SUSPENSION** | SUSPENSION A LA CARDAN | AUFHÄNGUNG (KARDANISCHE) |
| 1999 | **CARDBOARD** | CARTON LEGER, CARTE | KARTON, FEINPAPPE |
| 2000 | **CARDINAL STRAIN** | DEFORMATION PRINCIPALE | HAUPTVERFORMUNG |
| 2001 | **CARDIOID** | CARDIOIDE | HERZKURVE, KARDIOIDE |
| 2002 | **CARMINE PAPER** | PAPIER CARMIN | KARMINPAPIER |
| 2003 | **CARNAUBA WAX** | CIRE DE CARNAUBA | CARNAUBAWACHS |
| 2004 | **CARNOT'S CYCLE** | CYCLE DE CARNOT | KREISPROZESS (CARNOTSCHER) |
| 2005 | **CARPENTER** | CHARPENTIER | ZIMMERMANN |
| 2006 | **CARPENTRY** | CHARPENTERIE | ZIMMEREI |
| 2007 | **CARRIAGE PLANING MACHINE** | MACHINE A RABOTER A TABLE MOBILE | TISCHHOBELMASCHINE |
| 2008 | **CARRIAGE SPRING** | RESSORT DE VOITURE | WAGENFEDER |
| 2009 | **CARROT WEDGE** | BROCHE CONIQUE | KEGELSPINDEL, KONUSSTIFT |
| 2010 | **CARRYING AXLE** | ESSIEU PORTEUR | TRAGACHSE |
| 2011 | **CARRYING CAPACITY** | CAPACITE DE CHARGE | TRAGFÄHIGKEIT |
| 2012 | **CARRYING PLATE** | PLATEAU DE DEMOTTAGE | TROCKENPLATTE |
| 2013 | **CART** | CHARRETTE | KARREN, KARRE |
| 2014 | **CARTESIAN COORDINATES** | COORDONNEES CARTESIENNES | KOORDINATE (KARTESISCHE) |
| 2015 | **CARTRIDGE** | CARTOUCHE | PATRONE |
| 2016 | **CARTRIDGE BRASS** | LAITON POUR CARTOUCHES | PATRONENMESSING |
| 2017 | **CARTS, FARM** | TOMBERAUX | ACKERWAGEN |
| 2018 | **CASCADE** | CASCADE | KASKADE |
| 2019 | **CASE** | COUCHE SUPERFICIELLE, SURFACE | OBERFLÄCHENSCHICHT, OBERFLÄCHE |
| 2020 | **CASE DEPTH** | PROFONDEUR DE LA COUCHE CEMENTEE | DICKE DER ZEMENTIERSCHICHT |
| 2021 | **CASE HARDENING** | TREMPE DE SURFACE, CEMENTATION | EINSETZEN, EINSATZHÄRTUNG, OBERFLÄCHENARTUNG |
| 2022 | **CASE HARDENING POWDER** | CEMENT | EINSATZPULVER |
| 2023 | **CASE HARDENING, SURFACE HARDENING** | CEMENTATION DES PIECES EN ACIER DOUX , CEMENTATION PARTIELLE, TREMPE EN SURFACE | EINSATZHÄRTUNG, OBERFLÄCHENHÄRTUNG |
| 2024 | **CASEHARDENING MATERIALS** | CARBURANTS, CEMENTS | AUFKOHLUNGSMITTEL, EINSATZMITTEL |
| 2025 | **CASEIN** | CASEINE | KASEIN |
| 2026 | **CASING** | CARTER | EINKAPSELUNG, GEHÄUSE (EINES MASCHINENTEILS) |
| 2027 | **CASING TESTER** | CALIBRE POUR TUBES | ROHRKALIBER |
| 2028 | **CASSETTE** | CASSETTE | KASSETTE |
| 2029 | **CASSINIAN OVAL** | CASSINOIDE, LEMNISCATE, ELLIPSE DE CASSINI | KURVE (CASSINISCHE), ELLIPSE |
| 2030 | **CAST (TO)** | FONDRE, COULER, MOULER | GIESSEN, VERGIESSEN |
| 2031 | **CAST BRASS** | LAITON COULE | GUSSMESSING |
| 2032 | **CAST COATING** | REVETEMENT FONDU | GUSSPLATTIERUNG |
| 2033 | **CAST HOLE** | TROU VENU DE FONTE | LOCH (GEGOSSENES) |
| 2034 | **CAST IRON** | FONTE DE FER, FONTE | GUSSEISEN, GUSS, GRAUGUSS |
| 2035 | **CAST IRON PIPE** | TUYAU EN FONTE | ROHR (GUSSEISERNES), GUSSEISENROHR |

| | | | |
|---|---|---|---|
| 2036 | CAST IRON THERMIT | THERMITE DE FONTE | GUSSEISENTHERMIT |
| 2037 | CAST IRON, ALLOY | FONTE ALLIEE | GUSSEISEN (LEGIERTES) |
| 2038 | CAST IRON, CHILLED | FONTE DE COQUILLE, FONTE TREMPEE | HARTGUSS, KOKILLENGUSS, SCHALENHARTGUSS |
| 2039 | CAST IRON, CORROSION RESISTANT | FONTE RESISTANTE A LA CORROSION | GUSSEISEN (KORROSIONSBESTÄNDIGES) |
| 2040 | CAST IRON, DUCTILE | FONTE DUCTILE | GUSSEISEN MIT KUGELGRAPHIT |
| 2041 | CAST IRON, GRAY | FONTE GRISE | GRAUGUSS, GUSSEISEN MIT LAMELLENGRAPHIT |
| 2042 | CAST IRON, HIGH STRENTCH | FONTE A GRANDE RESISTANCE | FESTIGKEITSGUSS, QUALITÄTSGUSS |
| 2043 | CAST IRON, MALLEABLE | FONTE MALLEABLE | TEMPERGUSS |
| 2044 | CAST IRON, MOTTLED | FONTE TRUITEE | GUSSEISEN (MELIERTES) |
| 2045 | CAST IRON, NODULAR | FONTE DUCTILE, FONTE A GRAPHITE SPHEROIDAL | GUSSEISEN MIT KUGELGRAPHIT |
| 2046 | CAST IRON, PEARLITIC | FONTE PERLITIQUE | GUSSEISEN (PERLITISCHES) |
| 2047 | CAST IRON, PEARLITIC MALLEABLE | FONTE MALLEABLE PERLITIQUE | SCHMIEDEISEN (PERLITISCHES) |
| 2048 | CAST IRON, WEAR RESISTANT | FONTE RESISTANTE A L'USURE | GUSSEISEN (VERSCHLEISSFESTES) |
| 2049 | CAST IRON, WHITE | FONTE BLANCHE | GUSSEISEN (WEISSES) |
| 2050 | CAST METAL | METAL COULE | GUSSMETALL |
| 2051 | CAST NAIL | CLOU FONDU | NAGEL (GEGOSSENER) |
| 2052 | CAST PLATE | PLAQUE-MODELE | MODELLGUSSPLATTE |
| 2053 | CAST SHELL PROCESS | ETIRAGE A FROID DE TUBES COULES SANS SOUDURE | KALTZIEHEN VON NAHTLOSGEGOSSENEN RÖHREN |
| 2054 | CAST SOLID, CAST WHOLE | VENU DE FONTE, VENU DE FONDERIE, VENUE A LA COULEE | ZUSAMMENGEGOSSEN, IN EINEM STÜCK GEGOSSEN |
| 2055 | CAST STEEL | ACIER MOULE, FONTE D'ACIER | STAHLGUSS |
| 2056 | CAST STEEL WHEEL CENTER | CENTRE DE ROUE EN ACIER FONDU | STAHLGUSSRADSTERN |
| 2057 | CAST STEEL, CRUCIBLE CAST STEEL | ACIER FONDU AU CREUSET | GUSSSTAHL, TIEGELGUSSSTAHL |
| 2058 | CAST STRUCTURE | STRUCTURE DES ALLIAGES | GEFÜGE DER LEGIERUNGEN |
| 2059 | CAST TOOTH | DENT BRUTE DE FONTE | ZAHN (UNBEARBEITETER) |
| 2060 | CAST WELD ASSEMBLY | ASSEMBLAGE PAR SOUDURE DE PIECES MOULEES | GUSSTÜCKENZUSAMMENSCHWEISSEN |
| 2061 | CAST-IRON GROWTH | GONFLEMENT DE LA FONTE | GUSSEISENQUELLUNG |
| 2062 | CAST-IRON PIPE | CONDUITE EN FONTE | GUSSEISEN-ROHRLEITUNG |
| 2063 | CAST-ON FLANGE | BRIDE VENUE DE FONTE | FLANSCH (ANGEGOSSENER) |
| 2064 | CASTABILITY | COULABILITE | VERGIESSBARKEIT, FLIESSVERMÖGEN |
| 2065 | CASTABILITY TEST | ESSAI DE COULABILITE | VERGIESSBARKEITSVERSUCH |
| 2066 | CASTER | CHASSE | NACHLAUF |
| 2067 | CASTER (ANGLE) | CHASSE (ANGLE DE) | NACHLAUF (WINKEL) |
| 2068 | CASTING | COULEE, COULAGE, FONTE, MOULAGE | GIESSEN, VERGIESSEN, GUSS |
| 2069 | CASTING | LINGOT, PIECE MOULEE | GUSSSTÜCK |
| 2070 | CASTING (OPERATION) | COULEE (OPERATION) | GIESSEN |
| 2071 | CASTING BAY | CHANTIER DE COULEE, HALLE DE COULEE | GIESSHALLE, GIESSEREI |
| 2072 | CASTING CARS | WAGONS CIGARES/POCHES | GIESSPFANNENWAGEN |
| 2073 | CASTING COPPER | CUIVRE AFFINE | GUSSKUPFER |
| 2074 | CASTING FREE FROM INTERNAL STRESSES | FONTE SANS TENSIONS INTERNES | GUSS (SPANNUNGSFREIER) |
| 2075 | CASTING FREE FROM PIPES | FONTE SANS RETASSURES | GUSS (LUNKERFREIER) |
| 2076 | CASTING HEAT BATCH | COULEE (LOT DE...) | SCHMELZE, GICHT |
| 2077 | CASTING HOUSE OR BAY | HALLE DE COULEE | GIESSHALLE |

| | | | |
|---|---|---|---|
| 2078 | **CASTING STRAINS** | TENSION DE COULAGE | GUSSSPANNUNG |
| 2079 | **CASTING, CAST WORK, FOUNDER'S WORK** | PIECE DE FONTE MOULEE, PIECE DE FONDERIE | GUSSSTÜCK |
| 2080 | **CASTINGS** | PIECES COULEES (OU MOULEES) | GUSSTÜCKE |
| 2081 | **CASTINGS STRAINS** | TENSION DE COULEE | GUSSSPANNUNG |
| 2082 | **CASTINGS, CORROSION RESISTANT** | PIECES MOULEES(OU COULEES) RESISTANT A LA CORROSION | GUSSTÜCKE (KORROSIONSBESTÄNDIGE) |
| 2083 | **CASTINGS, GRAY IRON** | PIECES MOULEES EN FONTE GRISE | GRAUGUSSSTÜCKE |
| 2084 | **CASTINGS, HEAT-RESISTING** | PIECES MOULEES RESISTANTES AUX TEMPERATURES ELEVEES | GUSSTÜCKE (HITZEBESTÄNDIGE) |
| 2085 | **CASTLE NUT, CASTELLATED NUT** | ECROU CRENELE, ECROU A CRENEAUX, ECROU A ENTAILLES, ECROU A FENETRES | KRONENMUTTER |
| 2086 | **CASTOR OIL** | HUILE DE RICIN | RIZINUSÖL, KASTORÖL |
| 2087 | **CAT-HEAD** | MANCHON DE CENTRAGE | ZENTRIERRING |
| 2088 | **CAT'S-EYES** | OEIL DE CHAT | KATZENAUGE |
| 2089 | **CATACAUSTIC CURVE** | CAUSTIQUE PAR REFLEXION | BRENNLINIE DURCH REFLEXION, KATAKAUSTISCHE LINIE |
| 2090 | **CATALYSIS, CATALYTIC ACTION** | CATALYSE | KATALYSE |
| 2091 | **CATALYST** | CATALYSEUR | KATALYSATOR |
| 2092 | **CATALYTIC** | CATALYTIQUE | KATALYTISCH |
| 2093 | **CATCH** | SAILLIE | NASE |
| 2094 | **CATCH, DETEND, STOP PAWL, PAWL** | CLIQUET D'ARRET, DOIGT D'ENCLIQUETAGE, DOIGT DE RETENUE, CHIEN | SPERRKLINKE, SPERRKEGEL, SPERRHAKEN |
| 2095 | **CATENARY** | CHAINETTE (GEOM.) | KETTENLINIE |
| 2096 | **CATHETOMETER** | CATHETOMETRE | KATHETOMETER |
| 2097 | **CATHODE** | CATHODE | KATODE |
| 2098 | **CATHODE CLEANING** | NETTOYAGE CATHODIQUE | KATODISCHE REINIGUNG |
| 2099 | **CATHODE COPPER** | CUIVRE ELECTROLYTIQUE | ELEKTROLYTKUPFER |
| 2100 | **CATHODE DROP** | CHUTE (DE TENSION) CATHODIQUE | KATODENSPANNUNGSABFALL |
| 2101 | **CATHODE EFFICIENCY** | RENDEMENT CATHODIQUE | KATODENWIRKUNGSGRAD |
| 2102 | **CATHODE LAYER** | REVETEMENT CATHODIQUE | ÜBERZUG (KATODISCHER) |
| 2103 | **CATHODE PICKLING** | DECAPAGE CATHODIQUE | KATODENBEIZUNG |
| 2104 | **CATHODE RAYS** | RAYONS CATHODIQUES | ELEKTRONENSTRAHLEN, KATODENSTRAHLEN |
| 2105 | **CATHODE-ARY TUBE** | TUBE CATHODIQUE, TUBE A RAYONS CATHODIQUES | ELEKTRONENSTRAHLRÖHRE, KATODENSTRAHLRÖHRE |
| 2106 | **CATHODE, KATHODE, NEGATIVE ELECTRODE** | ELECTRODE NEGATIVE, CATHODE | ELEKTRODE (NEGATIVE), KATHODE |
| 2107 | **CATHODIC CORROSION** | CORROSION CATHODIQUE | KORROSION, (KATODISCHE) |
| 2108 | **CATHODIC POLARIZATION** | POLARISATION CATHODIQUE | KATODENPOLARISATION |
| 2109 | **CATHODIC PROTECTION** | PROTECTION CATHODIQUE | KORROSIONSSCHUTZ (GALVANISCHER), SCHUTZ (KATODISCHER) |
| 2110 | **CATHODIC VACUUM ETCHING** | GRAVURE CATHODIQUE | ÄTZEN (KATODISCHES), GLIMMEN (KATODISCHES) |
| 2111 | **CATHOLYTE** | CATHOLYTE | KATOLYT |
| 2112 | **CATION, KATHION** | CATION, ION HYDROGENE | WASSERSTOFFION, KATION |
| 2113 | **CAULK (TO), FULLER (TO)** | MATER | VERSTEMMEN |
| 2114 | **CAULKING TOOL, FULLERING TOOL** | MATOIR | STEMMEISSEL |
| 2115 | **CAULKING, FULLERING** | MATAGE | VERSTEMMEN, VERSTEMMUNG |
| 2116 | **CAUSTIC CURVE** | CAUSTIQUE (OPT.) | BRENNLINIE |
| 2117 | **CAUSTIC DIP** | BAIN D'HYDROXYDE DE SODIUM | NATRIUMHYDROXYDBAD |
| 2118 | **CAUSTIC EMBRITTLEMENT** | FRAGILITE CAUSTIQUE | LAUGENSPRÖDIGKEIT |

**CEN**

| | | | |
|------|------|------|------|
| 2119 | **CAUSTIC LIQUOR, CAUSTIC SOLUTION** | LIQUIDE CAUSTIQUE | ÄTZLAUGE |
| 2120 | **CAUSTIC SODA IYE, CAUSTIC SODA SOLUTION** | LESSIVE, SOLUTION DE SOUDE CAUSTIQUE | NATRONLAUGE, ÄTZNATRONLAUGE |
| 2121 | **CAUSTIC SURFACE** | SURFACE CAUSTIQUE | BRENNFLÄCHE |
| 2122 | **CAVETTO** | CAVET, GORGE | HOHLKEHLE |
| 2123 | **CAVITATION** | CAVITATION | HOHLRAUMBILDUNG, HOHLSOGBILDUNG, KAVITATION |
| 2124 | **CAVITY** | COUCHE D'AIR, RETASSURE | LUFTSCHICHT, LUNKER |
| 2125 | **CAVITY, HOLLOW SPACE** | ESPACE CREUX, CREUX, CAVITE | HOHLRAUM |
| 2126 | **CELL** | PILE ELECTRIQUE | ZELLE (ELEKTR.) |
| 2127 | **CELL CAVITY** | CAVITE DE CELLULE | ELEMENTHOHLRAUM |
| 2128 | **CELL CONSTANT** | CONSTANTE D'UNE CELLULE ELECTROLYTIQUE | ELEKTROLYTZELLENKONSTANTE |
| 2129 | **CELLULAR RADIATOR** | RADIATEUR NID D'ABEILLES | ZELLENKÜHLER |
| 2130 | **CELLULOID** | CELLULOID | ZELLULOID, ZELLHORN |
| 2131 | **CELLULOSE** | CELLULOSE | ZELLSTOFF, ZELLULOSE |
| 2132 | **CELLULOSE ACETATE ACETYL CELLULOSE** | ACEJATE DE CELLULOSE | AZETYLZELLULOSE, ZELLULOSEAZETAT |
| 2133 | **CEMENT** | CIMENT | ZEMENT |
| 2134 | **CEMENT (TO)** | CIMENTER (COUVRIR D'UNE COUCHE DE CIMENT), CEMENTER, ACIERER (MET.), MASTIQUER, LUTER | VERPUTZEN MIT ZEMENT, ZEMENTIEREN, VERKITTEN |
| 2135 | **CEMENT CONCRETE** | BETON DE CIMENT | ZEMENTBETON |
| 2136 | **CEMENT COPPER** | CUIVRE CEMENTATOIRE, CUIVRE DE CEMENT, CUIVRE REGENERE, CEMENT DE CUIVRE | ZEMENTKUPFER |
| 2137 | **CEMENT MORTAR** | MORTIER DE CIMENT | ZEMENTMÖRTEL |
| 2138 | **CEMENT STEEL, BLISTER STEEL** | ACIER CEMENTE, ACIER DE CEMENTATION, ACIER DE CARBURATION | ZEMENTSTAHL, BLASENSTAHL, EINSATZSTAHL |
| 2139 | **CEMENT, CASE HARDENING COMPOUND,** | CEMENT, AGENT DE CEMENTATION, POUDRE CARBURANTE | HÄRTEPULVER |
| 2140 | **CEMENT, GLUE FOR LEATHER** | COLLE POUR COURROIES | LEDERLEIM |
| 2141 | **CEMENTATION** | CEMENTATION | EINSATZHÄRTEN, ZEMENTIEREN, ZEMENTIERUNG |
| 2142 | **CEMENTATION, CONVERTING** | CEMENTATION (DES BARRES DE FER), ACIERATION, ACIERAGE | ZEMENTSTAHLHERSTELLUNG, ZEMENTATION, ZEMENTIEREN |
| 2143 | **CEMENTED BELT JOINT** | JONCTION DES COURROIES PAR COLLAGE | RIEMENVERBINDUNG (GELEIMTE) |
| 2144 | **CEMENTED CARBIDE CUTTING FOOLS** | OUTILS A MISES EN CARBURE | HARTMETALLSCHNEIDWERKZEUG |
| 2145 | **CEMENTED GLUED BELT** | COURROIE COLLEE | RIEMEN (GELEIMTER) |
| 2146 | **CEMENTING** | MASTICAGE, CIMENTATION (RECOUVREMENT D'UNE COUCHE DE CIMENT) | KITTEN, VERKITTEN; VERPUTZEN MIT ZEMENT, ZEMENTIEREN |
| 2147 | **CEMENTITE** | CEMENTITE | ZEMENTIT |
| 2148 | **CENTER** | CENTRE | MITTELPUNKT |
| 2149 | **CENTER BOLT** | BOULON ETOQUIAU | FEDERBOLZEN |
| 2150 | **CENTER LATHE** | TOUR A POINTE | SPITZENDREHBANK |
| 2151 | **CENTER LINE** | FIBRE NEUTRE, AXE | NEUTRALE FASER, MITTELLINIE, ACHSE |
| 2152 | **CENTER REST** | APPUI MEDIAN | MITTELAUFLAGER |
| 2153 | **CENTERING PIN** | PION DE CENTRAGE | ZENTRIERSTIFT |
| 2154 | **CENTERING RING** | BAGUE DE CENTRAGE | ZENTRIERRING |
| 2155 | **CENTERLESS CYLINDRICAL GRINDING MACHINE** | RECTIFIEUSE POUR SURFACES DE REVOLUTION SANS CENTRE | AUSSEN-RUND SCHLEIF-MASCHINE (SPITZENLOSE) |

**CEN** 56

| | | | |
|---|---|---|---|
| 2156 | CENTERLESS GRINDING | RECTIFICATION SANS POINTE(S) | SCHLEIFEN (SPITZENLOSES) |
| 2157 | CENTIGRADE SCALE, CELSIUS SCALE | ECHELLE CENTIGRADE, ECHELLE DE CELSIUS | CELSIUSSKALA |
| 2158 | CENTIMETRE | CENTIMETRE | ZENTIMETER |
| 2159 | CENTIMETRE-GRAMME-SECOND SYSTEM, C.G.S. UNITS | SYSTEME CENTIMETRE-GRAMME-SECONDE, SYSTEME C.G.S. | MASSSYSTEM (ABSOLUTES), GRAMM-ZENTIMETER-SEKUNDE-SYSTEM, G.C.S.-SYSTEM, ZENTIMETER-GRAMM-SEKUNDE-SYSTEM |
| 2160 | CENTRAL HEATING | CHAUFFAGE CENTRAL | ZENTRALHEIZUNG |
| 2161 | CENTRAL LOAD | CHARGE CENTRALE | BELASTUNG (ZENTRISCHE), BELASTUNG (ZENTRALE), BELASTUNG MITTIGE |
| 2162 | CENTRE | CENTRE | MITTELPUNKT (GEOM.) |
| 2163 | CENTRE (TO) | CENTRER | EINMITTELN, MITTEN, ZENTRIEREN |
| 2164 | CENTRE BIT | FORET A CENTRE, FORET A TETON, MECHE A CENTRE, MECHE A TROIS POINTES | ZENTRUMBOHRER |
| 2165 | CENTRE DISTANCE | ENTRAXE | ACHSABSTAND |
| 2166 | CENTRE HEAD | INSTRUMENT A CENTRER | ZENTRIERVORRICHTUNG |
| 2167 | CENTRE OF CURVATURE | CENTRE DE COURBURE | KRÜMMUNGSMITTELPUNKT |
| 2168 | CENTRE OF GRAVITY | CENTRE DE GRAVITE | SCHWERPUNKT, MASSENMITTELPUNKT |
| 2169 | CENTRE OF MOTION | CENTRE DE ROTATION | DREHPUNKT |
| 2170 | CENTRE OF OSCILLATION | CENTRE D'OSCILLATION | SCHWINGUNGSMITTELPUNKT |
| 2171 | CENTRE OF RIVET | CENTRE DU RIVET | NIETMITTE |
| 2172 | CENTRE PUNCH | POINTEAU DE CENTRAGE | KÖRNER, ANKÖRNER |
| 2173 | CENTRE SQUARE, RADIUS FLINDER | EQUERRE A TRACER LES CENTRES | MITTELPUNKTSUCHER, ZENTRIERWINKEL |
| 2174 | CENTRELESS GRINDER | MACHINE A MEULER SANS POINTES | SCHLEIFMASCHINE (SPITZENLOSE) |
| 2175 | CENTRIFUGAL BRAKE | FREIN CENTRIFUGE | SCHLEUDERBREMSE, ZENTRIFUGALBREMSE |
| 2176 | CENTRIFUGAL CASTING | COULEE CENTRIFUGE | SCHLEUDERGUSS |
| 2177 | CENTRIFUGAL CLUTCH | EMBRAYAGE CENTRIFUGE | FLIEHKRAFTKUPPLUNG |
| 2178 | CENTRIFUGAL COMPRESSOR, TURBO-COMPRESSOR | TURBO-COMPRESSEUR, COMPRESSEUR CENTRIFUGE | KREISELVERSICHTER, SCHAUFELVERDICHTER, TURBOKOMPRESSOR |
| 2179 | CENTRIFUGAL FAN | VENTILATEUR A FORCE CENTRIFUGE | SCHLEUDERGEBLÄSE, ZENTRIFUGGALGEBLÄSE |
| 2180 | CENTRIFUGAL FORCE | FORCE CENTRIFUGE | FLIEHKRAFT, ZENTRIFUGALKRAFT |
| 2181 | CENTRIFUGAL GOVERNOR | REGULATEUR CENTRIFUGE | FLIEHKRAFTREGLER |
| 2182 | CENTRIFUGAL LUBRICATOR | GRAISSEUR CENTRIFUGE | SCHMIERGEFÄSS (UMLAUFENDES), ZENTRIFUGALÖLER |
| 2183 | CENTRIFUGAL MOMENT | MOMENT CENTRIFUGE | ZENTRIFUGALMOMENT |
| 2184 | CENTRIFUGAL PUMP | POMPE CENTRIFUGE | KREISELPUMPE, SCHLEUDERPUMPE, ZENTRIFUGALPUMPE |
| 2185 | CENTRIFUGAL TYPE GOVERNOR, BALL GOVERNOR | REGULATEUR A FORCE CENTRIFUGE, REGULATEUR DE WATT, REGULATEUR A BOULES | FLIEHKRAFTREGLER, ZENTRIFUGALREGLER |
| 2186 | CENTIGRADE CELSIUS THERMOMETER | THERMOMETRE CENTIGRADE | THERMOMETER (HUNDERTTEILIGES), CELESIUSTHERMOMETER |
| 2187 | CENTRING | CENTRAGE | EINMITTELN, ZENTRIEREN |
| 2188 | CENTRING AND SPOT-FACING MACHINE | MACHINE A CENTRER ET A DRESSER | ZENTRIER-U. PLANDREHMASCHINE |
| 2189 | CENTRIPETAL ACCELERATION | ACCELERATION CENTRIPETE | ZENTRIPETALBESCHLEUNIGUNG |
| 2190 | CENTRIPETAL FORCE | FORCE CENTRIPETE | ZENTRIPETALKRAFT |
| 2191 | CENTROID | CENTRE DE SURFACE | FLÄCHENMITTELPUNKT |

| | | | |
|---|---|---|---|
| 2192 | **CERAMIC METAL** | CERMET, MELANGE DE CARBURES FRITTES | CERMET, METALL-KERAMIKMISCHUNG (GESINTERTE) |
| 2193 | **CERAMICS** | CERAMIQUE | KERAMIK |
| 2194 | **CERESINE, CERASIN** | CIRE MINERALE, CERESINE | ZERESIN, OZOZEROTIN |
| 2195 | **CERIUM** | CERIUM | ZERIUM, ZER, CER |
| 2196 | **CERUSSITE, CARBONATE OF LEAD** | CERUSSITE | BLEISPAT, BLEIKARBONAT, WEISSBLEIERZ, ZERUSSIT |
| 2197 | **CESIUM** | CESIUM | CESIUM, ZÄSIUM |
| 2198 | **CETANE NUMBER** | INDICE DE CETANE | CETANZAHL |
| 2199 | **CHAFF CUTTERS** | HACHE PAILLES | STROHHÄCKSLER |
| 2200 | **CHAFING FATIGUE** | FATIGUE PAR CONTACTS DE FROTTEMENT | REIBUNGERMÜDUNG |
| 2201 | **CHAIN** | CHAINE | KETTE |
| 2202 | **CHAIN BARREL** | TAMBOUR A CHAINE, TAMBOUR POUR CHAINE-CABLE | KETTENTROMMEL |
| 2203 | **CHAIN BRAKE** | FREIN A CHAINE | KETTENBREMSE |
| 2204 | **CHAIN CASE** | CARTER DE CHAINES | KETTENKÄSTEN |
| 2205 | **CHAIN DOTTED LINE** | LIGNE UN TRAIT | LINIE (STRICHPUNKTIERTE) |
| 2206 | **CHAIN DRIVE** | COMMANDE PAR CHAINE | KETTENANTRIEB |
| 2207 | **CHAIN DRIVE, CHAIN GEARING** | TRANSMISSION PAR CHAINES | KETTENTRIEB |
| 2208 | **CHAIN DRIVE, DRIVING, DRIVE BY CHAINS** | COMMANDE PAR CHAINE | KETTENRADANTRIEB |
| 2209 | **CHAIN GRATE** | GRILLE A CHAINE | KETTENROST |
| 2210 | **CHAIN INTERMITTENT FILLET WELD** | SOUDURE D'ANGLE A RANGEES ALTERNEES SYMETRIQUES | KEHLNÄHTE (SYMMETRISCH VERSETZTE) |
| 2211 | **CHAIN LINK** | MAILLON DE CHAINE | KETTENGLIED |
| 2212 | **CHAIN LUBRICATION** | GRAISSAGE A CHAINETTE | KETTENSCHMIERUNG |
| 2213 | **CHAIN PULLEY BLOCK** | PALAN A CHAINE | KETTENFLASCHENZUG |
| 2214 | **CHAIN RIVET** | RIVET DE CHAINE | KETTENNIET |
| 2215 | **CHAIN RIVETED JOINT** | RIVURE EN CHAINE | PARALLELNIETUNG, KETTENNIETUNG |
| 2216 | **CHAIN SAW** | SCIE A CHAINETTE | KETTENSÄGE |
| 2217 | **CHAIN SHEAVE, SHEAVE WHEEL (FOR CHAIN)** | POULIE A CHAINE, POULIE A EMPREINTES, ROUE A EMPREINTES, BARBOTIN | KETTENROLLE |
| 2218 | **CHAIN TENSION ADJUSTER** | TENDEUR DE CHAINE | KETTENSPANNER |
| 2219 | **CHAIN TIGHTENER** | TENDEUR DE CHAINE | KETTENSPANNER |
| 2220 | **CHAIN WHEEL VALVE** | VOLANT A CHAINE ADAPTABLE | KETTENRADSCHIEBER |
| 2221 | **CHAIN-TYPE SULFIDE** | SULFURE EN CHAINE | SULFID (KETTENFÖRMIGES) |
| 2222 | **CHAIN, SERIES OF OPERATIONS, PROCESSES IN A FACTORY** | SUITE, GAMME DES OPERATIONS | ARBEITSGANG, FABRIKATIONSGANG |
| 2223 | **CHAINWHEEL** | VOLANT A CHAINE | KETTENRAD |
| 2224 | **CHALK** | CRAFE | KREIDE |
| 2225 | **CHALK MARL** | MARNE CALCAIRE | KALKMERGEL |
| 2226 | **CHALKING** | FARINAGE, PULVERISATION | ABKREIDEN, VERPULVERUNG |
| 2227 | **CHALKY WATER** | EAU CALCAIRE | WASSER (KALKHALTIGES) |
| 2228 | **CHAMBER ACID** | ACIDE DES CHAMBRES | KAMMERSÄURE |
| 2229 | **CHAMBER CHEST OF SLIDE VALVE** | BOITE, CHAMBRE DE DISTRIBUTION, BOITE A SOUPAPE, CHAPELLE | GEHÄUSE EINES SCHIEBERS, GEHÄUSE EINES VENTILS, VENTILKASTEN, VENTILKAMMER |
| 2230 | **CHAMFER (TO)** | CHANFREINER, ABATTRE UN ANGLE | ABFASEN, ABKANTEN, ABRÄNDERN |
| 2231 | **CHAMFERED EDGE** | CHANFREIN | KANTE (ABGEFASTE), ABFASUNG |
| 2232 | **CHAMFERED SET HAMMER** | CHASSE A BISEAU | SCHRÄGER SETZHAMMER, BALLHAMMER |

# CHA

58

| 2233 | CHAMFERING | CHANFREINAGE | ABFASEN, ABKANTEN, ABSCHRÄGUNG |
| 2234 | CHAMOIS LEATHER, WASH LEATHER | PEAU DE NETTOYAGE, PEAU DE CHAMOIS | PUTZLEDER, WASCHLEDER, SÄMISCHLEDER |
| 2235 | CHAMOTTE | CHAMOTTE | SCHAMOTTE |
| 2236 | CHANGE OF DIRECTION | CHANGEMENT DE DIRECTION | RICHTUNGSÄNDERUNG, RICHTUNGSWECHSEL |
| 2237 | CHANGE OF PRESSURE | CHANGEMENT DE PRESSION | DRUCKÄNDERUNG |
| 2238 | CHANGE OF STATE | CHANGEMENT D'ETAT | ZUSTANDSÄNDERUNG |
| 2239 | CHANGE OF TEMPERATURE | CHANGEMENT DE TEMPERATURE | TEMPERATURWECHSEL, TEMPERATURÄNDERUNG |
| 2240 | CHANGE OF VOLUME | CHANGEMENT DE VOLUME | VOLUMENÄNDERUNG |
| 2241 | CHANGE OVER (TO) | INVERTIR, CHANGER LE SENS DU COURANT, COMMUTER | UMSCHALTEN (ELEKTR.) |
| 2242 | CHANGE SPEED GEAR | MECANISME DE CHANGEMENT DE VITESSE | WECHSELGETRIEBE |
| 2243 | CHANGE WHEEL, SPARE WHEEL | ROUE DE RECHANGE, ROUE DE SECOURS | WECHSELRAD, RESERVERAD, ERSATZRAD |
| 2244 | CHANGE-OVER SWITCH, THROW-OVER SWITCH | COMMUTATEUR | UMSCHALTER (ELEKTR.) |
| 2245 | CHANGE, ALTERATION OF SPEED | CHANGEMENT DE VITESSE, CHANGEMENT DE MULTIPLICATION | GESCHWINDIGKEITSÄNDERUNG |
| 2246 | CHANGING OVER | COMMUTATION, CHANGEMENT DU SENS D'UN COURANT | UMSCHALTEN (ELEKTR.) |
| 2247 | CHANGING ROOM | BARAQUE DE VESTIAIRE | UMKLEIDEBUDE |
| 2248 | CHANNEL | FER EN U, FER A GORGE, CANAL | RILLENEISEN, U-EISEN, KANAL |
| 2249 | CHANNEL BEAM/IRON | POUTRELLE EN U | U-TRÄGER |
| 2250 | CHANNEL IRON | FER EN E, FER EN U, FER A BRANCARDS | E-EISEN, U-EISEN |
| 2251 | CHANNEL; (HYDR.:), FLUME, RACE | RIGOLE, CANIVEAU, BIER | GERINNE, RINNE |
| 2252 | CHANNELED PLATE | TOLE STRIEE, TOLE CANNELEE | KANALBLECH |
| 2253 | CHAPLET | SUPPORT D'AME SUPPORT DE NOYAU | KERNSTÜTZE |
| 2254 | CHAPMANIZING | PROCEDE CHAPMAN | CHAPMAN-VERFAHREN |
| 2255 | CHARACTER | CARACTERE | ZEICHEN |
| 2256 | CHARACTERISTIC CURVE | CARACTERISTIQUE | KENNLINIE, CHARAKTERISTIK |
| 2257 | CHARACTERISTIC INDEX OF A LOGARITHM | CARACTERISTIQUE D'UN LOGARITHME | KENNZIFFER EINES LOGARITHMUS |
| 2258 | CHARCOAL PIG IRON | FONTE AU CHARBON DE BOIS | HOLZKOHLENROHEISEN |
| 2259 | CHARGE | CHARGE, CHARGE ELECTRIQUE | BESCHICKUNG, LADUNG, (ELEKTR.) |
| 2260 | CHARGE A METALLURGICAL FURNACE (TO) | CHARGER UN FOUR METALLURGIQUE | BESCHICKEN (EINEN METALLURGISCHEN OFFEN) |
| 2261 | CHARGE AN ACCUMULATOR (TO) | CHARGER UN ACCUMULATEUR | LADEN (EINEN AKKHUMULATOR) |
| 2262 | CHARGE, VOLUME OF CHARGE | CYLINDREE | LADUNG, ZYLINDERINHALT |
| 2263 | CHARGING | ALIMENTATION, CHARGEMENT | BESCHICKUNG |
| 2264 | CHARGING A METALLURGICAL FURNACE | CHARGEMENT D'UN FOUR METALLURGIQUE | BESCHICKUNG EINES METALLURGISCHEN OFENS |
| 2265 | CHARGING AN ACCUMULATOR | CHARGEMENT D'UN ACCUMULATEUR | LADEN EINES AKKUMULATORS |
| 2266 | CHARGING CURRENT | COURANT DE CHARGE | LADESTROM |
| 2267 | CHARGING INDICATEUR | INDICATEUR DE CHARGE | LADEKONTROLLAMPE |
| 2268 | CHARGING MACHINE, FURNACE | MACHINE A CHARGER LES FOURS | OFENBESCHICKUNGSMASCHINE |
| 2269 | CHARGING, FILLING | REMPLISSAGE, CHARGEMENT | FÜLLEN, FÜLLUNG |
| 2270 | CHARPY IMPACT TEST | ESSAI DE CHOC DE CHARPY (SUR EPROUVETTE ENTAILLEE) | KERBSCHLAGVERSUCH, CHARPY SCHLAGPROBE |

| | | | |
|---|---|---|---|
| 2271 | **CHARPY MACHINE** | MOUTON-PENDULE CHARPY | PENDELHAMMER FÜR SCHLAGVERSUCHE |
| 2272 | **CHARRED LEATHER** | CUIR BRULE, CALCINE, CARBONISE | LEDER (GERÖSTETES) |
| 2273 | **CHART** | TABLEAU, ABAQUE | TABELLE |
| 2274 | **CHASER, COMB TOOL** | PEIGNE POUR LES PAS DE VIS | STRÄHLER, GEWINDESTRÄHLER, GEWINDESTAHL, SCHRAUBSTAHL |
| 2275 | **CHASSIS** | CHASSIS | FAHRGESTELL |
| 2276 | **CHATTER MARKS** | MARQUES DE VIBRATION | RATTERMARKEN |
| 2277 | **CHATTERING OF THE VALVE** | VIBRATIONS, AFFOLEMENT DE LA SOUPAPE | FLATTERN, KLAPPERN DES VENTILS |
| 2278 | **CHECK** | CRIQUE, FELURE, FISSURE | RISS |
| 2279 | **CHECK A MEASUREMENT MADE (TO)** | VERIFIER LES MESURES | NACHMESSEN |
| 2280 | **CHECK ANALYSIS** | ANALYSE DE CONTROLE, VERIFICATION DE LA COMPOSITION CHIMIQUE, CONTRE-ANALYSE | KONTROLLANALYSE, PRÜFUNGSANALYSE |
| 2281 | **CHECK BOLT** | BOULON DE BLOCAGE | GEGENSCHRAUBE |
| 2282 | **CHECK MARKS** | MARQUES SUPERFICIELLES EN FORME DE V | ZIEHSPUREN (V-FÖRMIGE) |
| 2283 | **CHECK VALVE** | CLAPET DE RETENUE | RÜCKSCHLAGKLAPPE |
| 2284 | **CHECK VALVE, BACK PRESSURE VALVE, RETAINING VALVE, NON-RETURN VALVE** | SOUPAPE, CLAPET DE RETENUE | RÜCKSCHLAGVENTIL, RÜCKSCHLAGKLAPPE |
| 2285 | **CHECKERED PLATE** | TOLE GAUFREE, TOLE STRIEE | RIFFELBLECH |
| 2286 | **CHECKING** | FAIENCAGE, FORMATION DE CIRQUES | SPRUNGBILDUNG, RISSBILDUNG |
| 2287 | **CHEEK** | PART CENTRALE | TEIL (ZENTRALER) |
| 2288 | **CHEESE CLOTH** | MOUSSELINE | MULL |
| 2289 | **CHELATING AGENT** | AGENT DE CHELATION | CHELATBILDUNGSMITTEL |
| 2290 | **CHEMICAL** | CHIMIQUE | CHEMISCH |
| 2291 | **CHEMICAL ACTION** | PROCEDE CHIMIQUE | VORGANG (CHEMISCHER), PROZESS |
| 2292 | **CHEMICAL AFFINITY** | AFFINITE CHIMIQUE | VERWANDTSCHAFT, AFFINITÄT (CHEMISCHE) |
| 2293 | **CHEMICAL ANALYSIS** | ANALYSE CHIMIQUE | ANALYSE (CHEMISCHE) |
| 2294 | **CHEMICAL BALANCE** | BALANCE D'ANALYSE, TREBUCHET POUR ANALYSES | WAAGE (CHEMISCHE), ANALYSENWAAGE |
| 2295 | **CHEMICAL BEHAVIOUR** | PROPRIETES, CARACTERISTIQUES CHIMIQUES | VERHALTEN (CHEMISCHES) |
| 2296 | **CHEMICAL CHANGE** | TRANSFORMATION CHIMIQUE, ALTERATION CHIMIQUE | UMWANDLUNG (CHEMISCHE), VERÄNDERUNG (CHEMISCHE) |
| 2297 | **CHEMICAL COATING** | REVETEMENT CHIMIQUE | ÜBERZUG (CHEMISCHER) |
| 2298 | **CHEMICAL COMPONENT** | CONSTITUANT CHIMIQUE | KOMPONENTE (CHEMISCHE), BESTANDTEIL |
| 2299 | **CHEMICAL COMPOSITION** | COMPOSITION CHIMIQUE | ZUSAMMENSETZUNG (CHEMISCHE) |
| 2300 | **CHEMICAL COMPOUND** | COMBINAISON CHIMIQUE | VERBINDUNG (CHEMISCHE) |
| 2301 | **CHEMICAL CONSTITUTION** | CONSTITUTION CHIMIQUE | AUFBAU (CHEMISCHER), KONSTITUTION (CHEMISCHE) |
| 2302 | **CHEMICAL CORROSION** | CORROSION CHIMIQUE | KORROSION (CHEMISCHE) |
| 2303 | **CHEMICAL CUTTING FLUIDS** | FLUIDES DE COUPE CHIMIQUES, FLUIDES DE COUPE SYNTHETIQUES | SCHNEIDFLÜSSIGKEITEN (CHEMISCHE) |
| 2304 | **CHEMICAL DIP BRAZING** | BRASAGE AU TREMPE BRASAGE PAR IMMERSION | TAUCHLÖTEN |
| 2305 | **CHEMICAL ENERGY** | ENERGIE CHIMIQUE | ENERGIE (CHEMISCHE), REAKTIONSENERGIE |
| 2306 | **CHEMICAL ENGINEER** | INGENIEUR-CHIMISTE | INGENIEURCHEMIKER |

**CHE**       **60**

| | | | |
|---|---|---|---|
| 2307 | CHEMICAL EQUILIBRIUM | EQUILIBRE CHIMIQUE | GLEICHGEWISCHT (CHEMISCHES) |
| 2308 | CHEMICAL EQUIVALENT | EQUIVALENT CHIMIQUE | ÄQUIVALENT (CHEMISCHES), ÄQUIVALENTGEWICHT |
| 2309 | CHEMICAL FINISHING PROCESS | PROCEDE DE FINITION CHIMIQUE DE SURFACE | OBERFLÄCHENENDBEARBEITUNG (CHEMISCHE) |
| 2310 | CHEMICAL FORMULA | FORMULE CHIMIQUE | FORMEL (CHEMISCHE) |
| 2311 | CHEMICAL LEAD | PLOMB PUR | BLEI (REINES) |
| 2312 | CHEMICAL REACTION | REACTION CHIMIQUE | EINWIRKUNG (CHEMISCHE), REAKTION (CHEMISCHE) |
| 2313 | CHEMICAL STABILITY | STABILITE (CHIM.) | BESTÄNDIGKEIT (CHEM.) |
| 2314 | CHEMICAL SURFACE TREATING PROCESSES | PROCEDES CHIMIQUES DE TRAITEMENT DE SURFACE | OBERFLÄCHEN-BEHANDLUNGSVERFAHREN (CHEMISCHES) |
| 2315 | CHEMICAL SYMBOL | SYMBOLE (CHIM.) | ZEICHEN (CHEMISCHES), SYMBOL (CHEMISCHES) |
| 2316 | CHEMICAL WOOD PULP | PATE CHIMIQUE DE BOIS | HOLZZELLSTOFF |
| 2317 | CHEMICALLY COMBINED | CHIMIQUEMENT COMBINE | CHEMISCH GEBUNDEN |
| 2318 | CHEMICALLY COMBINED WATER, WATER OF CONSTITUTION | EAU DE CONSTITUTION, EAU CHIMIQUE | WASSER (GEBUNDENES), KONSTITUTIONSWASSER |
| 2319 | CHEMICALLY PURE | CHIMIQUEMENT PUR | CHEMISCH REIN |
| 2320 | CHEMICALS | PRODUITS CHIMIQUES | CHEMIKALIEN |
| 2321 | CHEMIST | CHIMISTE | CHEMIKER |
| 2322 | CHEMISTRY | CHIMIE | CHEMIE |
| 2323 | CHEMONUCLEAR REACTOR | REACTEUR DE RADIOCHIMIE | RADIOCHEMIEREAKTOR |
| 2324 | CHEMPUR TIN | ETAIN CHIMIQUEMENT PUR | ZINN (CHEMISCH REINES) |
| 2325 | CHEQUERED PLATE | TOLE STRIEE | RIFFELBLECH, BLECH (GERIFFELTES), BLECH (GERIPPTES) |
| 2326 | CHERRY RED HEAT | CHAUDE ROUGE-CERISE, ROUGE CERISE, COULEUR CERISE | KIRSCHROTGLUT |
| 2327 | CHERRY RED HOT | CHAUFFE, PORTE AU ROUGE CERISE | KIRSCHROTGLÜHEND |
| 2328 | CHESTNUT COAL, NUTS | GAILLETINS, TETES DE MOINEAU, NOISETTES | NUSSKOHLE |
| 2329 | CHIEF DRAUGHTSMAN | INGENIEUR-CONSTRUCTEUR EN CHEF | CHEFKONSTRUKTER |
| 2330 | CHILI SALPETRE, CALICHE, SODIUM NITRATE | SALPETRE, NITRATE DU CHILI, AZOTATE DE SODIUM, CALICHE | CHILISALPETER, PERUSALPETER, NATRONSALPETER, SALPETERSAURES NATRON, NATRIUMNITRAT |
| 2331 | CHILL | COQUILLE | KOKILLE, SCHALE |
| 2332 | CHILL (TO) | TREMPER (FONTE), REFROIDIR, TREMPER | ABSCHRECKEN, ABKÜHLEN |
| 2333 | CHILL CAST PIG | FER BRUT COULE EN COQUILLE | ROHEISEN IN KOKILLENGUSS |
| 2334 | CHILL CASTING | COULEE EN COQUILLE, FONTE EN COQUILLE | SCHALENGUSS, KOKILLENGUSS |
| 2335 | CHILLED CASTING | FONTE EN COQUILLE | HARTGUSS, SCHALENGUSS, KAPSELGUSS, KOKILLENGUSS |
| 2336 | CHILLED IRON | FONTE (DURCIE) | ROHEISEN (HARTGEGOSSEN) |
| 2337 | CHILLED STIFT METAL | METAL FONDU EN COQUILLE SANS DEFORMATION | METALL (VERFORMUNGSFREIES, IN METALLFORM GEGOSSENES |
| 2338 | CHILLING | TREMPE | ABSCHRECKEN, ABSCHRECKHÄRTUNG |
| 2339 | CHIMNEY STACK, FUNNEL | CHEMINEE | KAMIN, ESSE, SCHLOT, SCHORNSTEIN |
| 2340 | CHINA CLAY, KAOLIN | KAOLIN, CAOLIN | PORZELLANTON, PORZELLANERDE, KAOLIN |
| 2341 | CHINESE SCRIPT | ECRITURE CHINOISE | SCHRIFT (CHINESISCHE) |
| 2342 | CHINESE VEGETABLE TALLOW | SUIF VEGETAL DE CHINE | CHINESISCHER TALG |
| 2343 | CHIP | COPEAU, COPEAU DE BURINAGE | SPAN, MEISSELSPAN |

| | | | |
|---|---|---|---|
| 2344 | **CHIP (TO), CHISEL (TO)** | BURINER | MEISSELN |
| 2345 | **CHIP TEST** | ANALYSE DE COPEAUX | SPANANALYSE |
| 2346 | **CHIP, CHIPPING, SHAVING** | COPEAU | SPAN |
| 2347 | **CHIPPING** | BURINAGE, PIQUAGE AU MARTEAU | AUSHAUEN, ABKLOPPEN, MEISSELN |
| 2348 | **CHIPS OF METAL, METAL SHAVINGS** | COPEAUX METALLIQUES | METALLSPÄNE |
| 2349 | **CHISEL** | BURIN, CISEAU | MEISSEL |
| 2350 | **CHISEL-SHAPED SOLDERING IRON** | FER A SOUDER A TETE CARREE | HAMMERLÖTKOLBEN |
| 2351 | **CHLORATE** | CHLORATE | CHLORSÄURESALZ, CHLORAT |
| 2352 | **CHLORIDE** | CHLORURE | CHLORMETALL, CHLORID |
| 2353 | **CHLORINATION** | CHLORURATION | CHLORIERUNG |
| 2354 | **CHLORINE** | CHLORE | CHLOR |
| 2355 | **CHLORINE MONOXIDE** | ANHYDRIDE HYPOCHLOREUX | CHLORMONOXYD, UNTERCHLORIGSÄUREANHYDRID |
| 2356 | **CHLOROFORM, TRICHLORMETHANE** | CHLOROFORME | CHLOROFORM |
| 2357 | **CHOKE** | STARTER | DROSSELKLAPPE |
| 2358 | **CHOKE (TO)** | BOUCHER (SE), OBSTRUER (S'), ENGORGER (S') | VERSTOPFEN (SICH) |
| 2359 | **CHOKE TUBE** | DIFFUSEUR OU BUSE | LUFTTRICHTER |
| 2360 | **CHOKED FILTER SURFACE** | SURFACE FILTRANTE SATUREE | FILTERFLÄCHE (ÜBERSÄTTIGTE) |
| 2361 | **CHOKED PIPE** | TUYAU BOUCHE, TUYAU ENGORGE | ROHR (VERSTOPFTES) |
| 2362 | **CHOKING** | OBSTRUCTION, ENGORGEMENT | VERSTOPFEN, VERSTOPFUNG |
| 2363 | **CHONITE, HARD RUBBER, VULCANITE** | CAOUTCHOUC DURCI, EBONITE | HARTGUMMI, EBONIT, VULKANIT |
| 2364 | **CHORD OF CIRCLE** | CORDE D'UN CERCLE | KREISSEHNE |
| 2365 | **CHORDAL TOOTH THICKNESS** | EPAISSEUR DE DENT A LA CORDE | ZAHNSTÄRKE |
| 2366 | **CHROMATE** | CHROMATE | CHROMSÄURESALZ, CHROMAT |
| 2367 | **CHROMATE DIP** | CHROMATATION | CHROMATIEREN |
| 2368 | **CHROMATIC** | CHROMATIQUE | CHROMATISCH |
| 2369 | **CHROMATIC ABERRATION** | ABERRATION CHROMATIQUE, ABERRATION DE REFRANGIBILITE | ABWEICHUNG (CHROMATISCHE), ABERRATION (CHROMATISCHE) |
| 2370 | **CHROME ALUM** | ALUN DE CHROME | CHROMALAUN, KALICHROMALAUN, SCHWEFELSAURES CHROMOXYDKALL |
| 2371 | **CHROME BRICK** | BRIQUE DE CHROMITE | CHROMERZSTEIN, CHROMITSTEIN |
| 2372 | **CHROME GREEN** | VERT EMERAUDE | CHROMGRÜN |
| 2373 | **CHROME ORE** | CHROMITE | CHROMIT, CHROMEISENSTEIN |
| 2374 | **CHROME RED** | ROUGE DE CHROME | CHROMROT |
| 2375 | **CHROME YELLOW, LEAD CHROMATE** | CHROMATE DE PLOMB, JAUNE DE CHROME | CHROMGELB, BLEI (CHROMSAURES), BLEICHROMAT |
| 2376 | **CHROME-NICKEL STEEL** | ACIER CHROME-NICKEL | CHROMNICKELSTAHL |
| 2377 | **CHROME-TANNED LEATHER** | CUIR CHROME, TANNE AU CHROME | LEDER (CHROMGARES) |
| 2378 | **CHROME-TUNGSTEN STEEL** | ACIER AU CHROME-TUNGSTENE | CHROM-WOLFRAMSTAHL |
| 2379 | **CHROMIC ACID** | ACIDE CHROMIQUE | CHROMSÄURE |
| 2380 | **CHROMIC ACID ANODIZING** | OXIDATION ANODIQUE A L'ACIDE CHROMIQUE | OXYDATION (CHROMSAURE ANODISCHE) |
| 2381 | **CHROMIC CHLORIDE** | SESQUICHLORURE DE CHROME, CHLORURE CHROMIQUE | CHROMCHLORID |
| 2382 | **CHROMIC OXYDE** | SESQUIOXYDE DE CHROME | CHROMOXYD |
| 2383 | **CHROMIC TRIOXIDE** | ANHYDRIDE CHROMIQUE | CHROMSÄUREANHYDRID, CHROMTRIOXYD |
| 2384 | **CHROMITE** | CHROMITE | CHROMEISENSTEIN, CHROMIT |
| 2385 | **CHROMIUM** | CHROME | CHROM |
| 2386 | **CHROMIUM NICKEL STEEL** | ACIER AU NICKEL-CHROME | CHROMNICKELSTAHL |
| 2387 | **CHROMIUM PAINT** | MATIERE COLORANTE A BASE DE CHROME | CHROMFARBE |

**CHR** 62

| | | | |
|---|---|---|---|
| 2388 | **CHROMIUM PLATING** | CHROMAGE ELECTROLYTIQUE | VERCHROMUNG (ELEKTROLYTISCHE) |
| 2389 | **CHROMIUM STEEL, CHROME STEEL** | ACIER CHROME | CHROMSTAHL |
| 2390 | **CHROMIZING** | CEMENTATION PAR LE CHROME | INCHROMIEREN |
| 2391 | **CHROMOUS CHLORIDE** | CHLORURE CHROMEUX | CHROMCHLORÜR |
| 2392 | **CHRYSOLITE** | CHRYSOLITHE | CHRYSOLITH |
| 2393 | **CHUCK** | MANDRIN DE TOUR, MANDRIN | DREHBANKFUTTER, SPANNFUTTER |
| 2394 | **CHUCK JAWS** | MORS DOUX POUR MANDRINS | DREHFUTTER-BACKEN |
| 2395 | **CHUTE** | COULOIR, GLISSIERE, GOUTTIERE, GOULOTTE, DECHARGE | RUTSCHE, FÖRDERRINNE, BAHN (ABSCHÜSSIGE) |
| 2396 | **CIGARETTE LIGHTER** | ALLUME-CIGARETTE | ZIGARETTENANZÜNDER |
| 2397 | **CINDER** | CENDRE, LAITIER, SCORIE | ASCHE, SCHLACKE |
| 2398 | **CINDER COOLER** | REFRIGERANT DE CENDRES | ASCHENKÜHLER |
| 2399 | **CINDER NOTCH** | BEC DE PASSAGE DU LAITIER | SCHLACKENLOCH, SCHLACKENFORM |
| 2400 | **CINNABAR** | CINABRE | ZINNOBER, BERGZINNOBER, MERKURBLENDE, ZINNABARIT |
| 2401 | **CIRCLE** | CERCLE | KREIS |
| 2402 | **CIRCLE OF CURVATURE** | CERCLE DE COURBURE | KRÜMMUNGSKREIS |
| 2403 | **CIRCLE SHEARS** | CISAILLE CIRCULAIRE | KREISSCHERE |
| 2404 | **CIRCLE, CIRCUMFERENCE PERIPHERY OF CIRCLE** | CIRCONFERENCE, PERIPHERIE DU CERCLE | KREIS, KREISLINIE, KREISUMFANG, PERIPHERIE |
| 2405 | **CIRCLIP F. GUDGEON PIN** | ARRET D'AXE DE PISTON | SICHERUNGSRING F. KOLBENBOLZEN |
| 2406 | **CIRCUIT** | CIRCUIT ELECTRIQUE | STROMKREIS |
| 2407 | **CIRCUIT BREAKER** | DISJONCTEUR | AUSLÖSER, AUSSCHALTER |
| 2408 | **CIRCULAR CHART RECORDER** | ENREGISTREUR A DIAGRAMME CIRCULAIRE | KREISBLATTSCHREIBER |
| 2409 | **CIRCULAR CONE** | CONE CIRCULAIRE, CONE A BASE CIRCULAIRE | KREISKEGEL |
| 2410 | **CIRCULAR CROSS SECTION** | SECTION CIRCULAIRE | QUERSCHNITT (KREISFÖRMIGER) |
| 2411 | **CIRCULAR CYLINDER** | CYLINDRE A BASE CIRCULAIRE | KREISZYLINDER |
| 2412 | **CIRCULAR ELECTRODE** | MOLETTE (OU GALET) DE SOUDAGE | ELEKTRODENROLLE, SCHWEISSROLLE |
| 2413 | **CIRCULAR FUNCTION** | FONCTION CIRCULAIRE, FONCTION CYCLIQUE | KREISFUNKTION |
| 2414 | **CIRCULAR GLASS** | GLACE RONDE, VOYANT ROND | SCHAUGLAS (RUNDES) |
| 2415 | **CIRCULAR GROOVE** | RAINURE ANNULAIRE, RAINURE CIRCULAIRE | RINGNUT |
| 2416 | **CIRCULAR INTERPOLATION** | INTERPOLATION CIRCULAIRE | INTERPOLATION (ZIRKULARE) |
| 2417 | **CIRCULAR KNIFE** | COUTEAU CIRCULAIRE | KREISMESSER, SCHEIBENMESSER |
| 2418 | **CIRCULAR MAIN, RING MAIN** | CONDUITE CIRCULAIRE | RINGLEITUNG |
| 2419 | **CIRCULAR MEASURE** | MESURE DE L'ARC INTERCEPTE | BOGENMASS |
| 2420 | **CIRCULAR MILLING MACHINE** | FRAISEUSE CIRCULAIRE | RUNDFRÄSMASCHINE, KREISFRÄSMASCHINE |
| 2421 | **CIRCULAR MOTION** | MOUVEMENT CIRCULAIRE | BEWEGUNG (KREISFÖRMIGE), KREISSEHNE |
| 2422 | **CIRCULAR PENDULUM** | PENDULE CIRCULAIRE | KREISPENDEL |
| 2423 | **CIRCULAR PITCH, CIRCUMFERENTIAL PITCH** | PAS CIRCONFERENTIEL | UMFANGSTEILUNG, ZAHNTEILUNG, TEILKREIS |
| 2424 | **CIRCULAR PLATES** | PLATEAUX CIRCULAIRES | RUNDTISCHE |
| 2425 | **CIRCULAR POLISHING BRUSH** | BROSSE CIRCULAIRE A POLIR | BÜRSTENSCHEIBE |
| 2426 | **CIRCULAR PROTRACTOR** | RAPPORTEUR CERCLE ENTIER | VOLLKREISTRANSPORTEUR |
| 2427 | **CIRCULAR SAW** | SCIE CIRCULAIRE, DISQUE-SCIE | KREISSÄGE |
| 2428 | **CIRCULAR SAWING MACHINE** | SCIE CIRCULAIRE | KREISSÄGEMASCHINE |
| 2429 | **CIRCULAR SHEARS** | CISAILLE CIRCULAIRE | KREISSCHERE |

| | | | |
|---|---|---|---|
| 2430 | CIRCULAR SPIRIT LEVEL, BOX SPIRIT LEVEL | NIVEAU SPHERIQUE | DOSENLIBELLE |
| 2431 | CIRCULAR TOOTH THICKNESS | EPAISSEUR CIRCULAIRE DE LA DENT | ZAHNSTÄRKE IM ROLLKREIS |
| 2432 | CIRCULATE (TO) | CIRCULER | UMLAUFEN, ZIRKULIEREN |
| 2433 | CIRCULATION | CIRCULATION | UMLAUF, ZIRKULATION |
| 2434 | CIRCULATION OF WATER | CIRCULATION D'EAU | WASSERUMLAUF, WASSERZIRKULATION |
| 2435 | CIRCUM-CIRCLE, CIRCUMSCRIBED CIRCLE | CERCLE CIRCONSCRIT, CIRCONFERENCE CIRCONSCRITE | KREIS (UMGESCHRIEBENER), KREIS (UMLIEGENDER), UMKREIS |
| 2436 | CIRCUMSCRIBED POLYGON | POLYGONE CIRCONSCRIT | POLYGON (UMSCHRIEBENES), TANGENTENPOLYGON |
| 2437 | CISSING | RETRAIT, RETRACTION, RAMPAGE | PERLEN, BLASENBILDUNG |
| 2438 | CISSOID | CISSOIDE | ZISSOIDE, EFEUBLATTKURVE |
| 2439 | CISTERN | CITERNE | ZISTERNE |
| 2440 | CISTERN BAROMETER | BAROMETRE A CUVETTE | GEFÄSSBAROMETER |
| 2441 | CITRIC ACID | ACIDE CITRIQUE | ZITRONENSÄURE |
| 2442 | CIVIL ARCHITECTURE | ARCHITECTURE | HOCHBAU, ARCHITEKTUR |
| 2443 | CIVIL ENGINEER | INGENIEUR-CONSTRUCTEUR, INGENIEUR DES CONSTRUCTIONS CIVILES | BAUINGENIEUR |
| 2444 | CIVIL ENGINEERING | GENIE CIVIL, CONSTRUCTIONS CIVILES, TRAVAUX PUBLICS | TIEFBAU, BAUINGENIEURWESEN |
| 2445 | CLAD PLATE | TOLE PLAQUEE | BLECH (PLATTIERTES) |
| 2446 | CLAD STEEL | ACIER PLAQUE | STAHL (PLATTIERTER) |
| 2447 | CLADDING | DOUBLAGE, PLACAGE | PLATTIERUNG |
| 2448 | CLAMP | COLLIER | SPANNSCHELLE |
| 2449 | CLAMP COUPLING, SPLIT COMPRESSION COUPLING | MANCHON D'ACCOUPLEMENT CYLINDRIQUE, MANCHON A BOULONS NOYES, MANCHON A COQUILLES | SCHALENKUPPLUNG |
| 2450 | CLAMP, CLIP, U-BOLT | ETRIER | BÜGEL |
| 2451 | CLAMP, CRAMP FOR JOINERS, SCREW CLAMP FOR WOOD WORKERS | SERRE-JOINTS, PRESSE DE MENUISIER, PRESSE A COLLER | LEIMZWINGE |
| 2452 | CLAMP, CRAMP, SCREW CLAMP | SERRE-JOINTS, SERGENT, PRESSE A VIS | SCHRAUBZWINGE |
| 2453 | CLAMPING SCREW | VIS D'ARRET, VIS, ECROU DE SERRAGE | KLEMMSCHRAUBE, SPANNSCHRAUBE |
| 2454 | CLAPPER BOX | CHAPE DU BATTANT PORTE-OUTIL | MEISSELKLAPPENHALTER |
| 2455 | CLARIFICATION, CLARIFYING | CLARIFICATION | KLÄREN |
| 2456 | CLARIFY (TO) | CLARIFIER | KLÄREN |
| 2457 | CLASP NAIL | CLOU A CROCHET | HAKENNAGEL |
| 2458 | CLASS OF IRON, BRAND OF IRON | ESPECE DE FER, CATEGORIE DE FER | EISENSORTE |
| 2459 | CLASS, VARIETY OF STEEL | CATEGORIE SORTE D'ACIER | STAHLSORTE |
| 2460 | CLASSIFICATION | CLASSEMENT | KLASSIERUNG |
| 2461 | CLAW CLUTCH, CLAW COUPLING, JAW COUPLING, DOG CLUTCH | EMBRAYAGE, ACCOUPLEMENT A GRIFFES, ACCOUPLEMENT A DENTS | ZAHNKUPPLUNG, KLAUENKUPPLUNG |
| 2462 | CLAW HAMMER | MARTEAU A PANNE FENDUE, MARTEAU A DENT | KLAUENHAMMER, HAMMER MIT GESPALTENER FINNE |
| 2463 | CLAW OF A HAMMER | PANNE FENDUE, PANNE A PIED DE BICHE | FINNE (GESPALTENE), KLAUE EINES HAMMERS |
| 2464 | CLAW OF DOG CLUTCH | GRIFFE, DENT | KLAUE, KUPPLUNGSKLAUE |
| 2465 | CLAY | ARGILE | TON, PELIT, LEHM |

**CLA** 64

| | | | |
|---|---|---|---|
| 2466 | CLAY GROUND | TERRAIN ARGILEUX | LEHMBODEN |
| 2467 | CLAY IRONSTONE BAND, ARGILLACEOUS IRON ORE | LIMONITE ARGILEUSE, OCRE JAUNE | BRAUNEISENSTEIN (TONIGER), TONEISENSTEIN |
| 2468 | CLAY RING | BAGUE, BOURRELET EN TERRE GLAISE | TONRING |
| 2469 | CLEAN (TO), TRIM (TO), FETTLE CASTINGS (TO) | DESABLER, EBARBER, ECROUTER LES PIECES COULEES | PUTZEN (GUSSSTÜCKE) |
| 2470 | CLEAN METALLIC SURFACE | SURFACE METALLIQUE DECAPEE | OBERFLÄCHE (METALLREINE) |
| 2471 | CLEANER | PRODUIT DE NETTOYAGE | REINIGUNGSMITTEL |
| 2472 | CLEANER, ALKALINE | NETTOYANT ALCALIN | REINIGER (ALKALISCHER) |
| 2473 | CLEANER, SOLVENT | DEGRAISSEUR AU SOLVANT | FETTLÖSUNGSMITTEL, REINIGUNGSMITTEL |
| 2474 | CLEANING | NETTOYAGE DU METAL, DEGRAISSAGE | METALLREINIGUNG, ENTFETTUNG |
| 2475 | CLEANING AND POLISHING COMPOUNDS | PRODUITS DE NETTOYAGE ET DE POLISSAGE | REINIGUNGS- UND POLIERMITTEL |
| 2476 | CLEANING DIP | BAIN DE DECAPAGE PRELIMINAIRE | VORBRENNE |
| 2477 | CLEANING OIL | HUILE DE NETTOYAGE | PUTZÖL |
| 2478 | CLEANING, TRIMMING, FETTLING CASTINGS | EBARBAGE, DESABLAGE, ECROUTAGE DES PIECES COULEES | PUTZEN DER GUSSSTÜCKE |
| 2479 | CLEAR CUT SHARP IMAGE | IMAGE NETTE | BILD (SCHARFES) |
| 2480 | CLEAR OIL, PALE OIL | HUILE MINERALE BLONDE | MINERALÖL (GEREINIGTES), MINERALÖL (RAFFINNIERTES) |
| 2481 | CLEAR SPACE | VIDE LIBRE | ABSTAND (LICHTER) |
| 2482 | CLEARANCE | ESPACE NUISIBLE, ESPACE MORT, ESPACE NEUTRE | RAUM (TOTER), RAUM (SCHÄDLICHER), TOTRAUM |
| 2483 | CLEARANCE | JEU, JEU DE COIFFAGE, TOLERANCE | SPIEL, SPIELRAUM DER KERNMARKE, TOLERANZ |
| 2484 | CLEARANCE ANGLE, ANGLE OF CLEARANCE, ANGLE OF RELIEF | ANGLE D'INCIDENCE (D'UN OUTIL) | ANSTELLUNGSWINKEL, RÜCKENWINKEL |
| 2485 | CLEAT | TAQUET | TREIBKEIL, KNAGGE, ANSCHLAG |
| 2486 | CLEAVABLE ROCK | ROCHE CLIVABLE | GESTEIN (SPALTBARES) |
| 2487 | CLEAVAGE | CLIVAGE | SPALTUNG, SPALTFLÄCHE |
| 2488 | CLEAVAGE PLANE | PLAN DE CLIVAGE | SPALTFLÄCHE |
| 2489 | CLENCH THE RIVET HEADS TO | ECRASER LES RIVETS, RABBATRE L'EXCES DE LA TIGE DU RIVET | NIETE STAUCHEN |
| 2490 | CLENCHING THE RIVET HEADS | ECRASEMENT DES RIVETS | STAUCHEN DER NIETE |
| 2491 | CLEVIS | JUMELLE | SCHÄKEL |
| 2492 | CLEVIS PIN | GOUPILLE A TETE | GABELBOLZEN |
| 2493 | CLICK | DOIGT D'ENCLIQUETAGE | SCHALTKLINKE |
| 2494 | CLICK AND DETENT MOTION | ENCLIQUETAGE DOUBLE | DOPPELKLINKENGETRIEBE |
| 2495 | CLICK-WHEEL | ROUE A ROCHET | SPERRAD |
| 2496 | CLICK, RATCHET PAWL | CLIQUET | SCHALTLINKE, SCHLUBKLINKE, SCHIEBEKLINKE, SCHUBFALLE |
| 2497 | CLIMB MILLING | FRAISAGE EN AVALANT | FRÄSEN (GLEICHLÄUFIGES) |
| 2498 | CLIMBING ABILITY | TENUE DE ROUTE EN COTE | STEIGVERMÖGEN |
| 2499 | CLIMBING OF THE BELT | MONTEE DE LA COURROIE | KLETTERN DES RIEMENS |
| 2500 | CLINKER | MACHEFER (FOND), BRIQUE DURE ET TRES CUITE | KOHLENSCHLACKE, HERDSCHLACKE, KESSELSCHLACKE; KLINKER |
| 2501 | CLINOGRAPHIC PARALLEL PROJECTION | PROJECTION OBLIQUE | PARALLELPROJEKTION (SCHIEFE), PARALLELPROJEKTION (KLINOGRAPHISCHE) |
| 2502 | CLIP | ATTACHE | KLAMMER |
| 2503 | CLIP PULLEY | POULIE A GRIFFES | GREIFERSCHEIBE |
| 2504 | CLIPPING | EBARBAGE | ENTGRATUNG, ENTGRATEN |

**65**          **CLU**

| | | | |
|---|---|---|---|
| 2505 | **CLOCK-BRASS** | LAITON POUR HORLOGES | UHRENMESSING |
| 2506 | **CLOCKWISE** | DANS LE SENS DES AIGUILLES D'UNE MONTRE | RECHTSDREHEND, IM UHRZEIGERSINN |
| 2507 | **CLOCKWISE ROTATION** | ROTATION A DROITE | RECHTSDREHUNG |
| 2508 | **CLOCKWISE WOUND, RIGHT-HANDRED WOUND, DEXTRORSE** | ENROULE A DROITE, DEXTRORSUM | RECHTSGEWUNDEN, RECHTSGEWICKELT |
| 2509 | **CLOCKWORK** | MOUVEMENT D'HORLOGERIE | UHRWERK |
| 2510 | **CLOGGING** | COLMATAGE, ENCRASSEMENT | ABLAGERUNG, VERSCHMUTZEN, ANSETZEN VON SCHMUTZ |
| 2511 | **CLOSE GRAINED IRON** | FER A GRAIN FIN, FER A GRAIN SERRE | FEINKORNEISEN, EISEN (KLEINLUCKIGES) |
| 2512 | **CLOSE JOINTED TUBES** | TUBES RAPPROCHES | ROHRE MIT OFFENER NAHT |
| 2513 | **CLOSE LAID WIRE ROPE** | CABLE CLOS | SEIL (VERSCHLOSSENES), SEIL (VOLLSCHLÄCHTIGES) |
| 2514 | **CLOSE PACKED** | STRUCTURE COMPACTE (A) | DICHTGEPACKT |
| 2515 | **CLOSE THE CIRCUIT TO** | FERMER LE CIRCUIT ELECTRIQUE | STROMKREIS (DEN) SCHLIESSEN |
| 2516 | **CLOSE UP THE RIVETS TO** | FACONNER, FORMER LA TETE DU RIVET, RIVER | SCHLIESSKOFF (DEN) BILDEN |
| 2517 | **CLOSED CELL FOAM** | MOUSSE A CELLULES FERMEES | SCHAUMSTOFF (GESCHLOSSENZELLIGER) |
| 2518 | **CLOSED CHAIN CLOSED RING CYCLIC HYDROCARBONS** | HYDROCARBURES DE LA SERIE AROMATIQUE | KOHLENWASSERSTOFFE DER KARBOREIHE, ISOZYKLISCHE KOHLENWASSERSTOFFE |
| 2519 | **CLOSED CORNER JOINT** | ASSEMBLAGE EN ANGLE | ECKVERBAND |
| 2520 | **CLOSED CURVE** | COURBE FERMEE | KURVE (GESCHLOSSENE) |
| 2521 | **CLOSED DIES** | ESTAMPES FERMEES | STEMPEL (GESCHLOSSENE) |
| 2522 | **CLOSED DOUBLE-BEVEL BUTT WELD** | SOUDURE EN K SANS ECARTEMENT | ECKNAHTVERBINDUNG OHNE LUFTSPALT |
| 2523 | **CLOSED DOUBLE-J BUTT WELD** | SOUDURE DOUBLE J FERMEE | DOPPEL-J-NAHT OHNE LUFTSPALT |
| 2524 | **CLOSED DOUBLE-U GROOVE WELD** | SOUDURE DE BORD EN DOUBLE U FERMEE | DOPPEL-U-FUGENNAHT OHNE LUFTSPALT |
| 2525 | **CLOSED DOUBLE-V GROOVE WELD** | SOUDURE DE BORD EN DOUBLE-V SANS ECARTEMENT | X-FUGENNAHT OHNE LUFTSPALT |
| 2526 | **CLOSED PASS** | CANNELURE EMBOITEE, CANNELURE FERMEE | FLACHKABBER (GESCHLOSSENES), KABBER, KASTENKABBER |
| 2527 | **CLOSED PASSES** | CANNELURES FERMEES | WALZNUTEN (GESCHLOSSENE) |
| 2528 | **CLOSED SINGLE-BEVEL BUTT WELD** | SOUDURE EN DEMI-V SANS ECARTEMENT | HALB-V-NAHT OHNE LUFTSPALT |
| 2529 | **CLOSED SINGLE-J BUTT WELD** | SOUDURE EN J SANS ECARTEMENT | J-NAHT OHNE LUFTSPALT |
| 2530 | **CLOSED SINGLE-U GROOVE WELD** | SOUDURE DE BORD EN U FERMEE | U-FUGENNAHT OHNE LUFTSPALT |
| 2531 | **CLOSED SINGLE-V GROOVE WELD** | SOUDURE DE BORD EN V SANS ECARTEMENT | V-FUGENNAHT OHNE LUFTSPALT |
| 2532 | **CLOSED SQUARE BUTT WELD** | SOUDURE EN I SANS ECARTEMENT | I-NAHT OHNE LUFTSPALT |
| 2533 | **CLOSED-LOOP SYSTEM** | SYSTEME A BOUCLE DE RETOUR | RÜCKFÜHRUNGSREGELSYSTEM |
| 2534 | **CLOSED, TUBE PRESSURE GAUGE** | MANOMETRE A AIR COMPRIME | HEBERMANOMETER |
| 2535 | **CLOSING CYLINDER** | PISTON DE FERMETURE DU MOULE | SCHLIESSKOLBEN (FORM) |
| 2536 | **CLOSING LINE SIDE** | LIGNE DE FERMETURE | SCHLUSSLINIE |
| 2537 | **CLOSING OF THE VALVE** | FERMETURE DE LA SOUPAPE | VENTILSCHLUSS |
| 2538 | **CLOTH MOP** | MECHE EN LISIERE DE DRAP | SCHWABBEL |
| 2539 | **CLOTH ROLLS** | ROULEAUX DE POLISSAGE DRAPES | POLIERROLLEN (STOFFBEKLEIDETE) |
| 2540 | **CLOUDBURST TREATMENT** | TRAITEMENT AU JET DE SABLE | STRAHLSANDBLASEN |
| 2541 | **CLOUDING** | TROUBLE, LOUCHISSEMENT | TRÜBUNG, SCHLEIERBILDUNG |
| 2542 | **CLUSTER** | AMAS DE GUINIER-PRESTON | CLUSTER |
| 2543 | **CLUSTER MILL** | LAMINOIR A SIX CYLINDRES | SECHSROLLENWALZWERK |
| 2544 | **CLUTCH** | EMBRAYAGE | KUPPLUNG |

**CLU** 66

| | | | |
|---|---|---|---|
| 2545 | CLUTCH FACING | GARNITURE D'EMBRAYAGE | KUPPLUNGSBELAG |
| 2546 | CLUTCH HOUSING | CARTER D'EMBRAYAGE | KUPPLUNGSGEHÄUSE |
| 2547 | CLUTCH PEDAL | PEDALE D'EMBRAYAGE | KUPPLUNGSFUSSHEBEL |
| 2548 | CLUTCH RELEASE | DEBRAYAGE | AUSRÜCKEN |
| 2549 | CLUTCH THRUST BEARING | BUTEE DE DEBRAYAGE | KUPPLUNGSDRUCKLAGER |
| 2550 | CLUTRIATE (TO) | LAVER (LES MINERAIS) | SCHLÄMMEN |
| 2551 | CLYBURN SPANNER | CLEF A MOLETTE | ROLLGABELSCHLÜSSEL |
| 2552 | COACH SCREW | VIS A BOIS A TETE CARREE | WAGENSCHRAUBE |
| 2553 | COACH, CARRIAGE BOLT | BOULON DE CHARRONNAGE, BOULON DE CARROSSERIE | SCHLOSSSCHRAUBE |
| 2554 | COACHWORK NAILS | CLOUS DE CARROSSERIE | KAROSSERIENAGEL |
| 2555 | COAGULATE (TO) | SE COAGULER | GERINNEN, KOAGULIEREN |
| 2556 | COAGULATION | COAGULATION | GERINNEN, KOAGULIEREN |
| 2557 | COAGULUM | COAGULUM | GERINNSEL, KOAGULUM |
| 2558 | COAL | CHARBON, HOUILLE, CHARBON DE TERRE, CHARBON FOSSILE | KOHLE, STEINKOHLE |
| 2559 | COAL BREAKER | CONCASSEUR A CHARBON | KOHLENBRECHER |
| 2560 | COAL BRIQUETTE | AGGLOMERE DE HOUILLE | STEINKOHLENBRIKETT |
| 2561 | COAL BUNKER | SOUTE A CHARBON | KOHLENBUNKER |
| 2562 | COAL DISTRICT | REGION HOUILLERE | KOHLENGEBIET |
| 2563 | COAL DUST | POUSSIER DE HOUILLE | STAUBKOHLE |
| 2564 | COAL FIRING, FIRING, BURNING COAL | CHAUFFAGE AU CHARBON | KOHLENFEUERUNG, VERFEUERN VON KOHLEN |
| 2565 | COAL FURNACE, FURNACE FOR COAL | FOYER A CHARBON, FOYER A HOUILLE | KOHLENFEUERUNG (ANLAGE) |
| 2566 | COAL MINE, COAL PIT, COLLIERY | MINE DE HOUILLE, HOUILLERE, CHARBONNAGE | KOHLENBERGWERK, KOHLENGRUBE, KOHLENZECHE |
| 2567 | COAL TAR DYE | MATIERE COLORANTE DERIVEE DU GOUDRON DE HOUILLE | TEERFARBSTOFF |
| 2568 | COAL TAR OIL, SOLVENT NAPHTHA | HUILE DE GOUDRON DE HOUILLE | STEINKOHLENTEERÖL |
| 2569 | COAL TAR PITCH | BRAI SEC MINERAL | STEINKOHLENTEERPECH |
| 2570 | COAL TAR, GAS TAR | GOUDRON DE HOUILLE, GOUDRON DE GAZ, BRAI LIQUIDE | STEINKOHLENTEER, GASTEER |
| 2571 | COALESCED COPPER | CUIVRE ELECTROLYTIQUE COALESCE | KOALESZIERTES ELEKTROLYTKUPFER |
| 2572 | COALESCENCE | COALESCENCE | VERWACHSUNG, ZUSAMMENBALLUNG, KOALESZENZ |
| 2573 | COARSE GRAIN | GROS GRAIN | GROBKORN |
| 2574 | COARSE GRAINED SAND | SABLE A GROS GRAIN | SAND (GROBKÖRNIGER) |
| 2575 | COARSE PITCH THREAD | FILET A GRAND DIAMETRE | GROBGEWINDE, GEWINDE (GROBES) |
| 2576 | COARSE THREAD | GROS FILET | GROBGEWINDE |
| 2577 | COARSE-GRAINED STEEL | ACIER A GROS GRAIN | STAHL (GROBKÖRNIGER) |
| 2578 | COARSE-MESHED | A GRANDES MAILLES | WEITMASCHIG, GROBMASCHIG |
| 2579 | COARSE-STRAND WIRE ROPE | CABLE METALLIQUE EN GROS FILS | SEIL (GROBDRÄHTIGES) |
| 2580 | COARSELY GROUND POWDER | POUDRE GROSSIEREMENT BROYEE, GROSSE POUDRE | PULVER (GROBGEMAHLENES) |
| 2581 | COAT OF LACQUER | COUCHE DE LAQUE | LACKANSTRICH, LACKIERUNG |
| 2582 | COAT OF OIL PAINT | COUCHE DE COULEUR A L'HUILE | ÖLFARBENANSTRICH |
| 2583 | COAT OF PAINT | PEINTURE, ENDUIT | FARBANSTRICH, FARBÜBERZUG |
| 2584 | COATED ELECTRODE | ELECTRODE ENROBEE | MANTELELEKTRODE, ELEKTRODE (UMHÜLLTE) |
| 2585 | COATED PARTICLES | PARTICULES ENROBEES | TEILCHEN (UMHÜLLTE) |
| 2586 | COATED SHEETS | TOLES ENROBEES | BLECHE (UMHÜLLTE) |
| 2587 | COATING | REVETEMENT, ENROBAGE | AUFTRAG, ÜBERZUG, UMHÜLLUNG |

| | | | |
|---|---|---|---|
| 2588 | **COATING, ANODIZED** | REVETEMENT ANODIQUE | ÜBERZUG (ANODISCHER) |
| 2589 | **COATING, ORGANIC** | PRODUIT DE REVETEMENT | ANSTRICHMITTEL |
| 2590 | **COATINGS** | COUCHES, RECOUVREMENT, REVETEMENT | BESCHICHTUNG, SCHICHT, ÜBERZUG |
| 2591 | **COATINGS, CHROMATE** | COUCHE DE CHROMATE | CHROMATSCHICHT |
| 2592 | **COATINGS, DIPPED** | REVETEMENTS PAR TREMPE | TAUCHÜBERZUG |
| 2593 | **COATINGS, ELECTROPLATED** | REVETEMENTS ELECTROLYTIQUES OU GALVANOPLASTIQUES | ELEKTROPLATTIERUNG |
| 2594 | **COATINGS, ENAMELED** | REVETEMENTS EMAILLES | EMAILLEÜBERZUG |
| 2595 | **COATINGS, LACQUER** | REVETEMENT PAR PEINTURE | LACKÜBERZUG |
| 2596 | **COATINGS, METALLIC** | REVETEMENT METALLIQUE | METALLÜBERZUG |
| 2597 | **COATINGS, NON-METALLIC** | REVETEMENT NON-METALLIQUE | ÜBERZUG (NICHTMETALLISCHE) |
| 2598 | **COATINGS, OXIDE** | REVETEMENT D'OXYDE | OXYDBELAG |
| 2599 | **COATINGS, PAINT** | PEINTURES | FARBAUFTRAG |
| 2600 | **COATINGS, PHOSPHATE** | PHOSPHATATION | PHOSPHATISIERUNG |
| 2601 | **COATINGS, ROST-INHIBITING** | REVETEMENT ANTI-ROUILLE | ROSTSCHUTZMITTEL |
| 2602 | **COATINGS, TIN** | REVETEMENT D'ETAIN | ZINNÜBERZUG |
| 2603 | **COATINGS, VITREOUS** | REVETEMENT VITREUX | ÜBERGLASUNG |
| 2604 | **COATINGS, ZINC** | ZINGAGE | VERZINKUNG |
| 2605 | **COAXIAL, COAXAL** | COAXIAL | GLEICHACHSIG, KOAXIAL |
| 2606 | **COB COAL, COBBLES** | GAILLETTE, GAILLETTERIE | WÜRFELKOHLE |
| 2607 | **COBALT** | COBALT | KOBALT |
| 2608 | **COBALT CARBONYL** | COBALT-CARBONYLE | KOBALT-KARBONYL |
| 2609 | **COBALT CHLORIDE** | CHLORURE DE COBALT | KOBALTCHLORÜR, KOBALTOCHLORID, CHLORKOBALT |
| 2610 | **COBALT NITRATE** | AZOTATE DE COBALT | KOBALT (SALPETERSAURER), KOBALTNITRAT |
| 2611 | **COBALT OXIDE** | SESQUIOXYDE DE COBALT | KOBALTOXYD |
| 2612 | **COBALT STEEL** | ACIER AU COBALT | KOBALTSTAHL |
| 2613 | **COBALT-CHROME STEEL** | ACIER AU COBALT-CHROME | KOBALT-CHROMSTAHL |
| 2614 | **COBALTITE, COBALT GLANCE** | COBALTINE | KOBALTGLANZ, GLANZKOBALT |
| 2615 | **COBALTOUS SULPHATE** | SULFATE DE COBALT | KOBALTOXYDUL (SCHWEFELSAURES), KOBALTOXYDULSULFAT, KOBALTOSULFAT, KOBALTVITRIOL |
| 2616 | **COBWEBBING** | TOILE D'ARAIGNEE | FADENZIEHEN |
| 2617 | **COCK** | SOUPAPE, CLAPET, VANNE, ROBINET | KUGELHAHN, VENTIL, KLAPPE, HAHN |
| 2618 | **COCK LEVER, PLUG VALVE WRENCH** | CLEF DE MANOEUVRE (POUR ROBINET A BOISSEAU) | HAHNSCHLÜSSEL |
| 2619 | **COCKLES** | ONDULATIONS | WELLIGGRAT, WÖLBUNG |
| 2620 | **COCONUT OIL** | HUILE DE COCO, BEURRE DE COCO | KOKOSNUSSÖL, KOKOSFETT, KOKOSTALG |
| 2621 | **COEFFICIENT** | COEFFICIENT | BEIWERT, KENNZAHL, KOEFFIZIENT |
| 2622 | **COEFFICIENT OF CONDUCTIVITY FOR HEAT** | COEFFICIENT DE CONDUCTIBILITE CALORIFIQUE | WÄRMELEITZAHL |
| 2623 | **COEFFICIENT OF CONTRACTION** | COEFFICIENT DE CONTRACTION | KONTRAKTIONSZAHL |
| 2624 | **COEFFICIENT OF CORROSION** | COEFFICIENT DE CORROSION | KORROSIONSKOEFFIZIENT |
| 2625 | **COEFFICIENT OF CUBICAL EXPANSION** | COEFFICIENT DE DILATATION CUBIQUE | RAUMAUSDEHNUNGSZAHL |
| 2626 | **COEFFICIENT OF DISCHARGE** | COEFFICIENT D'ECOULEMENT | AUSFLUSSZAHL |
| 2627 | **COEFFICIENT OF ELECTRICAL RESISTIVITY** | COEFFICIENT DE RESISTIVITE ELECTRIQUE | WIDERSTANDS-BEIWERT (ELEKTRISCHER) |
| 2628 | **COEFFICIENT OF EXPANSION** | COEFFICIENT DE DILATATION | AUSDEHNUNGSZAHL |
| 2629 | **COEFFICIENT OF FRICTION** | COEFFICIENT DE FROTTEMENT | REIBUNGSKOEFFIZIENT |

| | | | |
|---|---|---|---|
| 2630 | **COEFFICIENT OF LINEAR EXPANSION** | COEFFICIENT DE DILATATION LINEAIRE | LÄNGENAUSDEHNUNGSZAHL |
| 2631 | **COEFFICIENT OF PROPORTIONALITY** | COEFFICIENT DE PROPORTIONNALITE | PROPORTIONALITÄTSFAKTOR |
| 2632 | **COEFFICIENT OF RESISTANCE** | COEFFICIENT DE RESISTANCE | WIDERSTANDSZAHL |
| 2633 | **COEFFICIENT OF ROLLING FRICTION** | COEFFICIENT DE ROULEMENT | REIBUNGSKOEFFIZIENT FÜR ROLLENDE REIBUNG |
| 2634 | **COEFFICIENT OF SLIDING FRICTION** | COEFFICIENT DE GLISSEMENT | REIBUNGSKOEFFIZIENT FÜR GLEITENDE REIBUNG |
| 2635 | **COEFFICIENT OF SUPERFICIAL EXPANSION** | COEFFICIENT DE DILATATION SUPERFICIELLE | FLÄCHENAUSDEHNUNGSZAHL |
| 2636 | **COEFFICIENT OF THERMAL EXPANSION** | COEFFICIENT DE DILATATION | AUSDEHNUNGSKOEFFIZIENT |
| 2637 | **COEFFICIENT OF THERMOELECTRIC EFFECT** | COEFFICIENT D'EFFET THERMOELECTRIQUE COUPLE THERMOELECTRIQUE | EFFEKT-KOEFFIZIENT (THERMOELEKTRISCHER) |
| 2638 | **COEFFICIENT OF VELOCITY** | COEFFICIENT DE VITESSE | GESCHWINDIGKEITSZAHL |
| 2639 | **COERCITIVE FORCE** | FORCE COERCITIVE | KOERZITIVEFELD, KOERZITIVKRAFT |
| 2640 | **COERCIVE** | COERCITIF | KOERZITIV |
| 2641 | **COERCIVITY** | FORCE COERCITIVE | KOERZITIVKRAFT |
| 2642 | **COGGING** | LAMINAGE DE LINGOTS | BLOCKWALZEN |
| 2643 | **COHESION** | COHERENCE | STANDFESTIGKEIT |
| 2644 | **COHESION, COHESIVE POWER** | COHESION, FORCE DE COHESION | KOHÄSION, KOHÄSTONSKRAFT, KOHÄRENZ |
| 2645 | **COIL** | ROULEAU, BOBINE, SERPENTIN | SPULE, ROHRSCHLANGE, BUND, ROLLE |
| 2646 | **COIL OF A SPIRAL** | SPIRE, TOUR DE SPIRE | WINDUNG EINER SPIRALE |
| 2647 | **COIL SPRING** | RESSORT HELICOIDAL | SCHRAUBENFEDER |
| 2648 | **COIL WINDING** | BOBINAGE | SPULENWICKLUNG |
| 2649 | **COILED SPRING SUBJECTED TO BENDING** | RESSORT DE FLEXION A ENROULEMENT | BIEGEFEDER (GEWUNDENE) |
| 2650 | **COILING** | ENROULEMENT | AUFROLLEN |
| 2651 | **COINING** | ESTAMPAGE, MATRICAGE, MONNAYAGE, CALIBRAGE | PRÄGEN, MÜNZEN, KALIBRIEREN |
| 2652 | **COINING DIE** | MATRICE D'ESTAMPAGE | PRÄGESTEMPEL |
| 2653 | **COINING PRESS** | PRESSE MONETAIRE | PRÄGEPRESSE |
| 2654 | **COIR** | FIBRE DE COCO, BOURRE DE COCO | KOKOSFASER |
| 2655 | **COKE** | COKE | KOKS |
| 2656 | **COKE (TO)** | COKEFIER, TRANSFORMER EN COKE | VERKOKEN |
| 2657 | **COKE BLAST FURNACE PIG IRON** | FONTE AU COKE (DE HAUT-FOURNEAU) | HOCHOFEN-ROHEISEN |
| 2658 | **COKE BREAKER** | CONCASSEUR A COKE, CASSE-COKE | KOKSBRECHER |
| 2659 | **COKE BREEZE, DUST COKE** | POUSSIER DE COKE, ESCARBILLE, BRAISETTE | LÖSCHE, KOKSLÖSCHE, KOKSABRIEB |
| 2660 | **COKE FILTER** | FILTRE A COKE | KOKSFILTER |
| 2661 | **COKE OVEN** | FOUR A COKE | KOKSOFEN |
| 2662 | **COKE OVEN COKE, HARD COKE** | COKE METALLURGIQUE, COKE DE FOUR | ZECHENKOKS, HÜTTENKOKS, GIESSEREIKOKS, SCHMELZKOKS |
| 2663 | **COKE OVEN GAS** | GAZ DE FOUR A COKE | KOKEREIGAS, KOKSOFENGAS |
| 2664 | **COKE PIG IRON** | FONTE AU COKE BOIS | KOKSROHEISEN |
| 2665 | **COKE WORKS** | USINE DE CARBONISATION DE LA HOUILLE | KOKEREI, VERKOKUNGSANSTALT |
| 2666 | **COKING** | COKEFACTION, COKEFICATION, TRANSFORMATION EN COKE | VERKOKUNG |

| | | | |
|---|---|---|---|
| 2667 | COLD BEND TEST | ESSAI DE CINTRAGE A FROID, ESSAI DE PLIAGE A FROID | KALTBIEGEPROBE |
| 2668 | COLD BENDING | PLIAGE A FROID, CINTRAGE A FROID | KALTBIEGUNG |
| 2669 | COLD BLAST IRON | FONTE A L'AIR FROID | ROHEISEN (KALT ERBLASENES) |
| 2670 | COLD CHAMBER MACHINE | MACHINE A CHAMBRE FROIDE | KALTKAMMER-DRUCKGIESSMASCHINE |
| 2671 | COLD CHAMBER PRESSURE CASTING | FONTE EN CHAMBRE FROIDE | KALTKAMMER- DRUCKGIESSEN |
| 2672 | COLD CHISEL | CISEAU A FROID | FLACHMEISSEL |
| 2673 | COLD COINING | ESTAMPAGE A FROID | KALTPRESSEN |
| 2674 | COLD CRACK | FELURE A FROID | KALTRISS, SPANNUNGSKALTRISS |
| 2675 | COLD DRAW (TO) | ETIRER A FROID | KALTZIEHEN |
| 2676 | COLD DRAWING | ETIRAGE A FROID | KALTZIEHEN |
| 2677 | COLD DRAWN | ETIRE A FROID | KALT GEZOGEN |
| 2678 | COLD DRAWN TUBES | TUBES ETIRES A FROID | RÖHRE (KALTGEZOGENE) |
| 2679 | COLD FINISHING | FINISSAGE A FROID | KALTNACHPRESSEN |
| 2680 | COLD FLOW | FLUAGE A FROID | KALTFLIESSEN |
| 2681 | COLD FORGING | FORGEAGE A FROID | KALTSCHMIEDEN |
| 2682 | COLD FORMING | PROFILAGE A FROID | KALTFORMUNG, KALTPROFILIEREN |
| 2683 | COLD GALVANIZING | GALVANISATION A FROID | VERZINKUNG (ELEKTROLYTISCHE) |
| 2684 | COLD HAMMER (TO) | MARTELER A FROID, ECROUIR | KALTHÄMMERN |
| 2685 | COLD HAMMERING | MARTELAGE A FROID, ECROUISSAGE | KALTHÄMMERN |
| 2686 | COLD HEADING | REFOULEMENT A FROID, FACONNEMENT DES TETES A FROID | KALTSTAUCHEN, KALTANKÖPFEN |
| 2687 | COLD INSPECTION | EXAMEN A FROID | KALTPRÜFUNG |
| 2688 | COLD IRON SAW | SCIE A FROID | KALTSÄGE |
| 2689 | COLD PIERCING | PENETRATION A FROID | KALTDURCHBOHRUNG |
| 2690 | COLD PRESSING | PRESSAGE A FROID | KALTPRESSEN |
| 2691 | COLD REDUCING | DEGAUCHISSAGE A FROID | HERUNTERWALZEN |
| 2692 | COLD RIVET (TO) | RIVER A FROID | KALTNIETEN |
| 2693 | COLD RIVETING | RIVURE A FROID | KALTNIETEN |
| 2694 | COLD ROLL (TO) | LAMINER A FROID | KALTWALZEN |
| 2695 | COLD ROLLED BARS | BARRES LAMINEES A FROID | KALTGEWALZTER STABSTAHL |
| 2696 | COLD ROLLED PLATE | TOLE LAMINEE A FROID | BLECH (KALTGEWALZTES) |
| 2697 | COLD ROLLED STEEL | ACIER ECROUI | STAHL (KALTGERECKTER) |
| 2698 | COLD ROLLING | LAMINAGE A FROID | KALTWALZEN |
| 2699 | COLD SAWING | SCIAGE A FROID | KALTSÄGEN |
| 2700 | COLD SERVICE INSULATION | ISOLATION A FROID | KÄLTEISOLIERUNGSMITTEL |
| 2701 | COLD SET | TRANCHE A FROID | KALTSCHROTMEISSEL |
| 2702 | COLD SHORT IRON | FER CASSANT A FROID, FER AIGRE | EISEN (KALTBRÜCHIGES) |
| 2703 | COLD SHORTNESS | FRAGILITE A FROID | KALTBRÜCHIGKEIT |
| 2704 | COLD SHORTNESS OF IRON | AIGREUR DU FER | KALTBRÜCHIGKEIT DES EISENS |
| 2705 | COLD SHUT | BRASURE A FROID | KALTLÖTSTELLE, KALTSCHWEISSE |
| 2706 | COLD SHUT | GOUTTE FROIDE | KALTGUSS |
| 2707 | COLD SPRUING | DECAPAGE A FROID | KALTABSPRITZEN |
| 2708 | COLD STRIP MILL | TRAIN DE LAMINAGE A FROID | KALTWALZWERK |
| 2709 | COLD TEST | ESSAI A FROID | KALTVERSUCH |
| 2710 | COLD TREATMENT OF METALS | TRAITEMENT DES METAUX A FROID | KALTBEHANDLUNG |
| 2711 | COLD TRIMMING | EBARBAGE A FROID | KALTABGRATEN |
| 2712 | COLD WELDING | SOUDURE A FROID, SOUDAGE A FROID | KALTSCHWEISSEN |

**COL** 70

| | | | |
|---|---|---|---|
| 2713 | **COLD WORKING** | ECROUISSAGE, USINAGE A FROID, TRAVAIL A FROID | KALTBEARBEITUNG, KALTVERFORMUNG |
| 2714 | **COLD-DRAWN TUBING** | TUBE ETIRE A FROID | ROHR (KALTGEZOGENES) |
| 2715 | **COLD-DRAWN WIRE** | FIL ETIRE A FROID | DRAHT (KALTGEZOGENER) |
| 2716 | **COLD-ROLLED** | LAMINE A FROID | KALTGEWALZT |
| 2717 | **COLD, CHIPPING CHISEL** | CISEAU A FROID | KALTMEISSEL, BANKMEISSEL |
| 2718 | **COLLAPSIBILITY** | APTITUDE AU DEBOURRAGE | AUSSTOSSFÄHIGKEIT |
| 2719 | **COLLAPSIBLE TOP** | CAPOTE PLIANTE | KLAPPVERDECK |
| 2720 | **COLLAR** | ETRIER, COLLIER | BÜGEL, KLEMMSCHELLE |
| 2721 | **COLLAR GAUGE, RING GAUGE** | LUNETTE, BAGUE DE CALIBRE, LUNETTE VERIFICATRICE, TAMPON FILETE FEMELLE | KALIBERRING |
| 2722 | **COLLAR STEP BEARING** | CRAPAUDINE A PIVOT ANNULAIRE | RINGSPURLAGER |
| 2723 | **COLLAR SURFACE OF THRUST BEARING** | JOUE DU COUSSINET D'UNE BUTEE | RINGFLÄCHE EINES KAMMLAGERS |
| 2724 | **COLLAR, FAST COLLAR** | EMBASE, RONDELLE D'UN ARBRE | BUNDRING, WELLENBUND |
| 2725 | **COLLECTING PIPE** | TUYAU COLLECTEUR | SAMMELROHR |
| 2726 | **COLLECTOR PLATES** | PLAQUES COLLECTIVES | SAMMELPLATTEN |
| 2727 | **COLLET** | MANDRIN | SPANNDORN |
| 2728 | **COLLET CHUCK** | DOUILLE DE SERRAGE | ZANGENFUTTER |
| 2729 | **COLLETS** | MANDRIN ET PINCES PORTE-FRAISE | ZANGENFUTTER |
| 2730 | **COLLIMATE (TO)** | COLLIMATER | RICHTEN, EINSTELLEN |
| 2731 | **COLLIMATION** | COLLIMATION | KOLLIMATION |
| 2732 | **COLLIMATOR** | COLLIMATEUR | SPALTROHR, KOLLIMATOR |
| 2733 | **COLLODION** | COLLODION | KOLLODIUM, KLEBÄTHER |
| 2734 | **COLLOID** | COLLOIDE | KOLLOID |
| 2735 | **COLLOIDAL** | COLLOIDAL | KOLLOIDAL |
| 2736 | **COLLOIDAL PARTICLES** | PARTICULES COLLOIDALES | KOLLOIDTEILCHEN |
| 2737 | **COLOPHONY** | COLOPHANE, POIX SECHE, BRAI SEC | KOLOPHONIUM |
| 2738 | **COLOR METALLOGRAPHY** | METALLOGRAPHIE EN COULEURS | FARBMETALLOGRAPHIE |
| 2739 | **COLORIMETRIC SPECTROMETRY** | SPECTROSCOPIE COLORIMETRIQUE | ANALYSE (KOLORIMETRISCHE) |
| 2740 | **COLORING** | COLORATION | FÄRBUNG |
| 2741 | **COLOUR** | COULEUR (PHYS.) | FARBE (PHYS.) |
| 2742 | **COLOUR A DRAWING (TO)** | LAVER UN DESSIN | ZEICHNUNG (EINE) AUSTUSCHEN, ZEICHNUNG (EINE) ANLEGEN |
| 2743 | **COLOUR BRUSH** | PINCEAU | PINSEL, TUSCHPINSEL |
| 2744 | **COLOUR OF INCANDESCENCE** | TEMPERATURE DE FORGEAGE, CHALEUR DE FORGE | GLÜHFARBE |
| 2745 | **COLOURED PENCIL** | CRAYON DE COULEUR, PASTEL | FARBSTIFT |
| 2746 | **COLOURLESS GLASS** | VERRE INCOLORE | GLAS (FARBLOSES) |
| 2747 | **COLUMBIUM** | NIOBIUM | NIOB |
| 2748 | **COLUMN** | POTEAU, COLONNE | SÄULE, PFEILER |
| 2749 | **COLUMN HEAD** | TETE DE POTEAU | SÄULENKOPF |
| 2750 | **COLUMN OF LIQUID, LIQUID COLUMN** | COLONNE LIQUIDE | FLÜSSIGKEITSSÄULE |
| 2751 | **COLUMN OF MERCURY** | COLONNE DE MERCURE, COLONNE BAROMETRIQUE | QUECKSILBERSÄULE |
| 2752 | **COLUMN OF WATER** | COLONNE D'EAU | WASSERSÄULE |
| 2753 | **COLUMN PIPE** | COLONNE MONTANTE, CONDUITE VERTICALE | STEIGLEITUNG |
| 2754 | **COLUMN SUPPORTED FRAME** | CHARPENTE A POTEAUX | STÄNDERTRAGWERK |
| 2755 | **COLUMN TYPE DRILLING MACHINE** | PERCEUSE SUR BATI OU MONTANT, PERCEUSE A COLONNE | STÄNDERBOHRMASCHINE |

| | | | |
|---|---|---|---|
| 2756 | COLUMN WITH BOTH ENDS HINGED | POTEAU AVEC LES DEUX EXTREMITES GUIDEES | TRÄGER (BEIDERSEITSEINGESPANNTER) |
| 2757 | COLUMNAR CRYSTALS | CRISTAL BASALTIQUE | STENGELKRISTALL |
| 2758 | COLUMNAR STRUCTURE | STRUCTURE BASALTIQUE | STENGELGEFÜGE |
| 2759 | COLUMNED FRAME | CHARPENTE A POTEAUX | SÄULENGERÜST |
| 2760 | COMB GAUGE | JAUGE DE FILETAGE | GEWINDEKONTROLLEHRE |
| 2761 | COMBINATION | COMBINAISON (MATH.) | KOMBINATION (MATH.) |
| 2762 | COMBINATION DIE | MOULE A EMPREINTES MULTIPLES | KOMPOUNDSCHNITT |
| 2763 | COMBINATION DRILL AND COUNTERSINK | FORET A CENTRER | ZENTRIERBOHRER (KOMBINIERTER) |
| 2764 | COMBINATION PLIERS | PINCE MOTORISTE | MAULRINGSCHLÜSSEL |
| 2765 | COMBINE DIAGRAMS (TO) | RANKINISER, TOTALISER LES DIAGRAMMES | DIAGRAMME RANKINISIEREN |
| 2766 | COMBINE HARVESTERS AND ACCESSORY EQUIPMENT | MOISSONNEUSES-BATTEUSES | MÄHDRESCHER UND ZUSÄTZLICHE ANLAGE |
| 2767 | COMBINED CARBON | CARBONE COMBINE AU FER | KOHLENSTOFF (CHEMISCH GEBUNDENER IM EISEN) |
| 2768 | COMBINED SUCTION AND PRESSURE FAN | VENTILATEUR ASPIRANT ET SOUFFLANT | SAUG- UND DRUCKLÜFTER, SAUG- UND DRUCKVENTILATOR |
| 2769 | COMBINING MIXING CONE NOZZLE | TUYERE CONVERGENTE, AJUTAGE CONVERGENT, CONVERGENT (D'UNE TUYERE) | MISCHDÜSE |
| 2770 | COMBINING THE DIAGRAMS | RANKINISATION DES DIAGRAMMES | RANKINISIEREN VON DIAGRAMMEN |
| 2771 | COMBINING WEIGHT PROPORTION | PROPORTIONS DEFINIES | VERBINDUNGSGEWICHT |
| 2772 | COMBUSTIBLE | COMBUSTIBLE | BRENNBAR |
| 2773 | COMBUSTIBLENESS, COMBUSTIBILITY | COMBUSTIBILITE | BRENNBARKEIT, VERBRENNLICHKEIT |
| 2774 | COMBUSTION | COMBUSTION | VERBRENNUNG |
| 2775 | COMBUSTION AND EXPANSION STROKE | COURSE DE DETENTE, COURSE DE COMBUSTION | AUSDEHNUNGSHUB, EXPANSIONSHUB |
| 2776 | COMBUSTION CHAMBER | CHAMBRE DE COMBUSTION | VERBRENNUNGSRAUM, KAMMER |
| 2777 | COMBUSTION CHAMBER OF A FURNACE | CHAMBRE DE COMBUSTION D'UN FOYER | VERBRENNUNGSRAUM EINER FEUERUNG |
| 2778 | COMBUSTION CHAMBER OF AN INTERNAL COMBUSTION ENGINE, EXPLOSION CHAMBER, FIRING CHAMBER, LIGHTING CHAMBER | CHAMBRE D'EXPLOSIONS D'UN MOTEUR | VERBRENNUNGSRAUM EINES MOTORS |
| 2779 | COMBUSTION, COMPLETE | COMBUSTION COMPLETE | VERBRENNUNG (VOLLSTÄNDIGE) |
| 2780 | COMMAND | ORDRE | BEFEHL, KOMMANDO |
| 2781 | COMMERCIAL EFFICIENECY | RENDEMENT INDUSTRIEL, RENDEMENT COMMERCIAL, RENDEMENT ECONOMIQUE | WIRKUNGSGRAD (WIRTSCHAFTLICHER), WIRKUNGSGRAD (KOMMERZIELLER) |
| 2782 | COMMERCIAL POWER LINE | SECTEUR | NETZANSCHLUSS |
| 2783 | COMMERCIAL UTILISATION OF AN INVENTION | APPLICATION INDUSTRIELLE D'UNE INVENTION | VERWERTUNG (GEWERBLICHE) EINER ERFINDUNG |
| 2784 | COMMERCIAL VEHICLE | VEHICULE UTILITAIRE | NUTZFAHRZEUG |
| 2785 | COMMERCIAL ZINC, SPELTER | ZINC DU COMMERCE, ZINC BRUT | ROHZINK, HÜTTENZINK, HANDELSZINK |
| 2786 | COMMINUTION | PULVERISATION, CONCASSAGE | FEINZERKLEINERUNG |
| 2787 | COMMON ALUM, POTASH CRYSTAL ALUM | ALUN ORDINAIRE, ALUN POTASSIQUE | ALAUN, KALIALAUN, KALIUMALUMINIUMSULFAT |
| 2788 | COMMON BRIGGIAN LOGARITHM | LOGARITHME VULGAIRE, LOGARITHME DECIMAL | LOGARITHMUS (GEMEINER), LOGARITHMUS (BRIGG'SSCHER) |
| 2789 | COMMON DENOMINATOR | DENOMINATEUR COMMUN | NENNER (GEMEINSCHAFTLICHER), HAUPTNENNER, GENERALNENNER |
| 2790 | COMMON SALT, SODIUM CHLORIDE | SEL COMMUN, SEL MARIN, CHLORURE DE SODIUM | KOCHSALZ, SIEDESALZ, NATRIUMCHLORID, CHLORNATRIUM |

# COM                                                72

| | | | |
|------|------|------|------|
| 2791 | **COMPACT** | COMPRIME, AGGLOMERE | PRESSKÖRPER, PRESSLING |
| 2792 | **COMPACT COKE** | COKE DENSE | KOKS (KOMPAKTER) |
| 2793 | **COMPANION DIMENSIONS** | COTES DE RACCORDEMENT | ANSCHLUSSMASSE |
| 2794 | **COMPARATOR** | COMPARATEUR | KOMPARATOR |
| 2795 | **COMPARATORS** | COMPARATEURS | VERGLEICHER |
| 2796 | **COMPARISON BLOCKS** | CALES DE COMPARAISON | DICKENVERGLEICHER |
| 2797 | **COMPARISON MEASUREMENT** | MESURE COMPARATIVE | VERGLEICHSMESSUNG |
| 2798 | **COMPARTMENT** | COMPARTIMENT, CASE, CAISSON | ABTEIL, ABTEILUNG, FACH, RAUM, KASTEN |
| 2799 | **COMPASS** | BOUSSOLE | KOMPASS |
| 2800 | **COMPASS CARD** | ROSE DES VENTS | WINDROSE |
| 2801 | **COMPASS PLANE** | RABOT CINTRE | SCHIFFHOBEL |
| 2802 | **COMPASS SAW, KEYHOLE SAW, PAD SAW, LOCK SAW** | SCIE A GUICHET | STICHSÄGE, SPITZSÄGE, LOCHSÄGE |
| 2803 | **COMPASSES WITH INK POINT, PEN POINT** | COMPAS A TIRE-LIGNE | ZIEHFEDERZIRKEL |
| 2804 | **COMPASSES WITH PENCIL POINT** | COMPAS A PORTE-CRAYON | BLEISTIFTZIRKEL |
| 2805 | **COMPASSES WITH REMOVABLE LEGS** | COMPAS A PIECES DE RECHANGE | EINSATZZIRKEL |
| 2806 | **COMPATIBILITY** | COMPATIBILITE | VERTRÄGLICKEIT (GEGENSEITIGE) |
| 2807 | **COMPENSATE (TO)** | COMPENSER | AUSGLEICHEN, KOMPENSIEREN |
| 2808 | **COMPENSATED PENDULUM** | PENDULE COMPENSATEUR, PENDULE COMPENSE, COMPENSATEUR | KOMPENSATIONSPENDEL |
| 2809 | **COMPENSATION** | COMPENSATION | AUSGLEICH, AUSGLEICHUNG, KOMPENSIERUNG, KOMPENSATION |
| 2810 | **COMPLEMENT OF AN ANGLE** | COMPLEMENT D'UN ANGLE | KOMPLEMENT EINES WINKELS |
| 2811 | **COMPLEMENTARY ANGLE** | ANGLE COMPLEMENTAIRE | KOMPLEMENTWINKEL |
| 2812 | **COMPLEMENTARY COLOUR** | COULEUR COMPLEMENTAIRE | ERGÄNZUNGSFARBE, KOMPLEMENTÄRFARBE |
| 2813 | **COMPLEX NUMBER** | NOMBRE COMPLEXE | ZAHL (KOMPLEXE) |
| 2814 | **COMPLEX VARIABLE** | VARIABLE COMPLEXE | KOMPLEXE VERÄNDERLICHE |
| 2815 | **COMPONENT** | COMPOSANT | KOMPONENTE |
| 2816 | **COMPONENT FORCE** | FORCE COMPOSANTE | TEILKRAFT |
| 2817 | **COMPONENT OF A FORCE** | COMPOSANTE | SEITENKRAFT, TEILKRAFT, KOMPONENTE |
| 2818 | **COMPOSITE DIE** | MATRICE COMPOSITE | GESENK (ZWEITEILIGES) |
| 2819 | **COMPOSITE ELECTRODE** | ELECTRODE COMPOSITE | VERBUNDELEKTRODE |
| 2820 | **COMPOSITE NUMBER** | NOMBRE COMPOSE | ZAHL (ZUSAMMENGESETZTE) |
| 2821 | **COMPOSITE PLATE** | DEPOT ELECTROLYTIQUE A PLUSIEURS COUCHES | AUFLAGE (MEHRSCHICHT-ELEKTROLYTISCHE) |
| 2822 | **COMPOSITE STRENGTH** | RESISTANCE COMPLEXE, RESISTANCE COMPOSEE | FESTIGKEIT (ZUSAMMENGESETZTE) |
| 2823 | **COMPOSITION** | COMPOSITION | ZUSAMMENSETZUNG, KOMPOSITION |
| 2824 | **COMPOSITION BRASS** | LAITON ROUGE | ROTMESSING |
| 2825 | **COMPOSITION OF FORCES** | COMPOSITION DES FORCES | ZUSAMMENSETZUNG VON KRÄFTEN |
| 2826 | **COMPOSITION PLANE** | PLAN D'ACCOLEMENT (MACLE) | ZWILLINGSFLÄCHE |
| 2827 | **COMPOUND** | PATE A POLIR, COMPOSITION CHIMIQUE | MASSE, POLIERPASTE, VERBINDUNG (CHEMISCHE) |
| 2828 | **COMPOUND COMPACT** | EBAUCHE A PLUSIEURS CONSTITUANTS | MEHRSTOFFPRESSLING |
| 2829 | **COMPOUND ENGINE** | MACHINE COMPOUND | VERBUNDDAMPFMASCHINE, COMPOUNDMASCHINE |
| 2830 | **COMPOUND GAUGE** | MANO-VACUOMETRE | MANO-VAKUUMMETER |
| 2831 | **COMPOUND GIRDER** | POUTRE MIXTE OU COMPOSEE | VERBUNDTRÄGER, VERSTEIFTER WALZTRÄGER |

| | | | |
|---|---|---|---|
| 2832 | **COMPOUND OIL, MIXED OIL** | HUILE MIXTE, HUILE COMPOUND | MISCHÖL, COMPOUNDÖL |
| 2833 | **COMPOUND SCREW, DIFFERENTIAL SCREW** | VIS DIFFERENTIELLE | DIFFERENTIALSCHRAUBE |
| 2834 | **COMPOUND SPRING, LAMINATED SPRING** | RESSORT A PLUSIEURS LAMES, RESSORT A LAMES ETAGEES | FEDER (ZUSAMMENGESETZTE), FEDER (GESCHICHTETE), BLATTFEDERWERK |
| 2835 | **COMPOUND WOUND MOTOR** | MOTEUR COMPOUND | VERBUNDMOTOR, DOPPELSCHLUSSMOTOR, COMPOUNDMOTOR |
| 2836 | **COMPOUND, MULTI- STAGE COMPRESSOR** | COMPRESSEUR COMPOUND, COMPRESSEUR ETAGE | VERBUNDVERDICHTER, STUFENVERDICHTER, COMPOUNDVERDICHTER |
| 2837 | **COMPRESS (TO)** | COMPRIMER | VERDICHTEN, KOMPRIMIEREN |
| 2838 | **COMPRESS A SPRING (TO)** | COMPRIMER UN RESSORT | FEDER (EINE) ZUSAMMENDRÜCKEN |
| 2839 | **COMPRESSED AIR** | AIR COMPRIME | LUFT (VERDICHTETE) (KOMPRIMIERTE), DRUCKLUFT, PRESSLUFT |
| 2840 | **COMPRESSED AIR BRAKE** | FREIN A AIR COMPRIME | LUFTDRUCKBREMSE, DRUCKLUFTBREMSE |
| 2841 | **COMPRESSED AIR CYLINDER** | CYLINDRE A AIR | DRUCKLUFTZYLINDER |
| 2842 | **COMPRESSED AIR DRIVE** | COMMANDE PNEUMATIQUE | DRUCKLUFTANTRIEB, ANTRIEB MIT DRUCKLUFT |
| 2843 | **COMPRESSED AIR ENGINE** | MOTEUR A AIR COMPRIME, AERO-MOTEUR | PRESSLUFTMOTOR, DRUCKLUFTMOTOR |
| 2844 | **COMPRESSED AIR LOCOMOTIVE** | LOCOMOTIVE A AIR COMPRIME | DRUCKLUFTLOKOMOTIVE, PRESSLUFTLOKOMOTIVE |
| 2845 | **COMPRESSED AIR PIPING** | CONDUITE, TUYAUTERIE, DISTRIBUTION D'AIR COMPRIME | DRUCKLUFTLEITUNG, PRESSLUFTLEITUNG |
| 2846 | **COMPRESSED AIR TEST** | EPREUVE A L'AIR COMPRIME | DRUCKLUFTPROBE |
| 2847 | **COMPRESSED GAS** | GAZ COMPRIME | GAS (VERDICHTETES), GAS (KOMPRIMIERTES) |
| 2848 | **COMPRESSED OXYGEN BLOW PIPE** | CHALUMEAU A OXYGENE COMPRIME | BRENNER, LÖTBRENNER FÜR VERDICHTETEN SAUERSTOFF |
| 2849 | **COMPRESSED STEEL** | ACIER COMPRIME | PRESSSTAHL, STAHL (KOMPRIMIERTER) |
| 2850 | **COMPRESSED STEEL SHAFT** | ARBRE EN ACIER COMPRIME | WELLE (KOMPRIMIERTE) |
| 2851 | **COMPRESSIBILITY** | COMPRESSIBILITE | VERDICHTBARKEIT |
| 2852 | **COMPRESSIBILITY, ELASTICITY OF BULK OF VOLUME** | COMPRESSIBILITE | ZUSAMMENDRÜCKBARKEIT, KOMPRESSIBILITÄT, VOLUMENELASTIZITÄT |
| 2853 | **COMPRESSIBLE** | COMPRESSIBLE | ZUSAMMENDRÜCKBAR, KOMPRIMIERBAR |
| 2854 | **COMPRESSION** | COMPRESSION | VERDICHTUNG, KOMPRESSION |
| 2855 | **COMPRESSION BAR** | BARRE TRAVAILLANT A LA COMPRESSION | DRUCKSTAB, GEDRÜCKTER STAB |
| 2856 | **COMPRESSION CHAMBER** | CHAMBRE DE COMBUSTION | VERBRENNUNGSRAUM |
| 2857 | **COMPRESSION LINE** | LIGNE DE COMPRESSION | KOMPRESSIONSLINIE |
| 2858 | **COMPRESSION OF THE AIR** | COMPRESSION DE L'AIR | LUFTVERDICHTUNG |
| 2859 | **COMPRESSION PRESSURE** | PRESSION DE COMPRESSION | KOMPRESSIONSDRUCK |
| 2860 | **COMPRESSION RATIO** | TAUX DE COMPRESSION, RAPPORT DE COMPRESSION, RAPPORT VOLUMETRIQUE | VERDICHTUNGSVERHÄLTNIS |
| 2861 | **COMPRESSION RING** | SEGMENT DE COMPRESSION | KOLBENRING, KOMPRESSIONSRING |
| 2862 | **COMPRESSION SPRING, SPRING FOR COMPRESSION** | RESSORT DE COMPRESSION | DRUCKFEDER |
| 2863 | **COMPRESSION STRAIN** | EFFORT DE COMPRESSION | DRUCKBEANSPRUCHUNG |
| 2864 | **COMPRESSION STROKE** | TEMPS DE COMPRESSION, COURSE DE COMPRESSION | VERDICHTUNGSHUB |
| 2865 | **COMPRESSION TEST** | ESSAI DE COMPRESSION | DRUCKPROBE |
| 2866 | **COMPRESSION-IGNITION ENGINE** | MOTEUR DIESEL | SELBSTENTZÜNDUNGSMOTOR |
| 2867 | **COMPRESSION-RING** | SEGMENT D'ETANCHEITE | VERDICHTUNGSRING |

# COM
74

| 2868 | **COMPRESSIVE FORCE** | FORCE DE COMPRESSION | DRUCKKRAFT |
|---|---|---|---|
| 2869 | **COMPRESSIVE STRAIN** | EFFORT DE COMPRESSION, TRAVAIL A LA COMPRESSION | BEANSPRUCHUNG AUF DRUCK, DRUCKBEANSPRUCHUNG |
| 2870 | **COMPRESSIVE STRENGTH** | RESISTANCE A LA COMPRESSION | DRUCKFESTIGKEIT |
| 2871 | **COMPRESSIVE STRESS** | EFFORT DE COMPRESSION PAR UNITE DE SECTION | DRUCKSPANNUNG |
| 2872 | **COMPRESSIVE TEST** | ESSAI A LA COMPRESSION | DRUCKVERSUCH |
| 2873 | **COMPRESSIVE YIELD STRENGTH** | LIMITE D'ECRASEMENT | QUETSCHGRENZE |
| 2874 | **COMPRESSOR** | COMPRESSEUR | VERDICHTER, KOMPRESSOR |
| 2875 | **COMPUTER DIRECTED NUMERICAL CONTROL** | COMMANDE DIRECTE PAR CALCULATEUR | RECHNERSTEUERUNG (DIREKTE) |
| 2876 | **COMSUMPTION OF ENERGY** | DEPENSE D'ENERGIE DE FORCE MOTRICE, CONSOMMATION D'ENERGIE | KRAFTAUFWAND, ARBEITSAUFWAND, KRAFTVERBRAUCH, ENERGIEVERBRAUCH |
| 2877 | **CONCAVE** | CONCAVE | KONKAV |
| 2878 | **CONCAVE FILLET WELD** | SOUDURE D'ANGLE CONCAVE, SOUDURE EN CONGE | HOHLKEHLNAHT |
| 2879 | **CONCAVE MIRROR** | MIROIR CONCAVE | HOHLSPIEGEL, KONKAVSPIEGEL |
| 2880 | **CONCAVITY** | CONCAVITE | HOHLWÖLBUNG |
| 2881 | **CONCENTRATE** | CONCENTRE | KONZENTRAT |
| 2882 | **CONCENTRATE (TO)** | CONCENTRER | ANREICHERN |
| 2883 | **CONCENTRATED STRONG SOLUTION** | SOLUTION CONCENTREE, SOLUTION FORTE | LÖSUNG (KONZENTRIERTE), LÖSUNG (ANGEREICHERTE) |
| 2884 | **CONCENTRATED SULPHURIC ACID** | ACIDE SULFURIQUE CONCENTRE | SCHWEFELSÄURE (KONZENTRIERTE), PFANNENSÄURE |
| 2885 | **CONCENTRATING A SOLUTION BY VAPORISATION** | CONCENTRATION D'UNE SOLUTION PAR EVAPORATION | EINDAMPFEN EINER LÖSUNG |
| 2886 | **CONCENTRATION** | CONCENTRATION | ANREICHERUNG, KONZENTRATION |
| 2887 | **CONCENTRATION CELL** | ELEMENT A DEUX LIQUIDES | KONZENTRATIONSELEMENT |
| 2888 | **CONCENTRATION CELL CORROSION** | CORROSION DE LA PILE DE CONCENTRATION | KONZENTRATIONSELEMENT-KORROSION |
| 2889 | **CONCENTRATION POLARIZATION** | POLARISATION (D'UN ELECTRODE) PAR CHUTE DE CONCENTRATION | KONZENTRATIONS POLARISATION (EINER ELEKTRODE) |
| 2890 | **CONCENTRIC CIRCLES** | CERCLES CONCENTRIQUES | KREISE (KONZENTRISCHE) |
| 2891 | **CONCENTRICITY** | CONCENTRICITE | KONZENTRIZITÄT |
| 2892 | **CONCHOID** | CONCHOIDE | KONCHOIDE, MUSCHELLINIE |
| 2893 | **CONCHOIDAL FRACTURE** | CASSURE CONCHOIDALE | BRUCHFLÄCHE (MUSCHELIGE), BRUCH (MUSCHELIGER) |
| 2894 | **CONCRETE** | BETON | BETON, STEINMÖRTEL, GROBMÖRTEL |
| 2895 | **CONCRETE (TO), LAY CONCRETE (TO)** | BETONNER | BETONIEREN |
| 2896 | **CONCRETE FOUNDATION** | FONDATION, ASSISE, MASSIF EN BETON | BETONFUNDAMENT |
| 2897 | **CONCRETE IRON SHEARS** | CISAILLE POUR FERS A BETON | BETONEISENSCHERE |
| 2898 | **CONCRETE PIPE** | TUYAU EN CIMENT | BETONROHR, ZEMENTROHR |
| 2899 | **CONCRETE PRE-STRESSING** | PRECONTRAINTE DU BETON | BETONVORSPANNUNG |
| 2900 | **CONCRETE SLAB** | DALLE DE BETON (SUPPORT D'UN RESERVOIR) | BETON-(DECKEN-)PLATTE, SOHLE, FUNDAMENTPLATTE |
| 2901 | **CONCRETE WORKS** | OUVRAGES EN BETON | BETONARBEITEN |
| 2902 | **CONCRETING** | BETONNAGE | BETONIEREN |
| 2903 | **CONCURRENT FORCES** | FORCES CONCOURANTES | KRÄFTE MIT GEMEINSAMEM ANGRIFFSPUNKT |
| 2904 | **CONCURRENT HEATING** | CHAUFFAGE SUPPLEMENTAIRE | HEIZUNG (ZUSÄTZLICHE) |
| 2905 | **CONDENSATE** | CONDENSAT | KONDENSAT |
| 2906 | **CONDENSATION** | CONDENSATION | KONDENSATION |

| | | | |
|---|---|---|---|
| 2907 | **CONDENSE (TO)** | SE CONDENSER | NIEDERSCHLAGEN, KONDENSIEREN (SICH) |
| 2908 | **CONDENSER** | CONDENSATEUR (ELECTR.), CONDENSEUR (CHIM.), CONDENSEUR (OPT.) | KONDENSATOR (ELEKTR.), VERFLÜSSIGER, KONDENSATOR (CHEM.), KONDENSOR (OPT.) |
| 2909 | **CONDENSER LENS** | LENTILLE CONVERGENTE | SAMMELLINSE |
| 2910 | **CONDENSING CONVERGING LENS, CONVEX LENS** | LENTILLE CONVERGENTE, LENTILLE A BORD MINCE | SAMMELLINSE, LINSE (KONVEXE) |
| 2911 | **CONDENSING STEAM ENGINE** | MACHINE AVEC CONDENSATION | KONDENSATIONSDAMPFMASCHINE |
| 2912 | **CONDITIONING** | ENLEVEMENT DE LA COUCHE SUPERFICIELLE | BESEITIGUNG DER OBERFLÄCHENSCHICHT |
| 2913 | **CONDUCT (TO) (ELECTRICITY, HEAT)** | CONDUIRE (L'ELECTRICITE, LA CHALEUR) | LEITEN (ELEKTRIZITÄT, WÄRME) |
| 2914 | **CONDUCTING MEDIUM** | MILIEU CONDUCTEUR | MEDIUM (LEITENDES) |
| 2915 | **CONDUCTING SALTS** | SELS AUGMENTANT LA CONDUCTIBILITE D'UNE SOLUTION | LEITSALZE |
| 2916 | **CONDUCTION** | CONDUCTION | ÜBERTRAGUNG |
| 2917 | **CONDUCTION OF HEAT** | CONDUCTION DE LA CHALEUR | WÄRMELEITUNG |
| 2918 | **CONDUCTIVE** | CONDUCTEUR (DE LA CHALEUR DE L'ELECTRICITE) | LEITEND (WÄRME, ELEKTRIZITÄT) |
| 2919 | **CONDUCTIVITY** | CONDUCTIBILITE, CONDUCTIVITE | LEITFÄHIGKEIT |
| 2920 | **CONDUCTIVITY FOR HEAT, THERMAL CONDUCTIVITY** | CONDUCTIBILITE THERMIQUE CALORIFIQUE | WÄRMELEITFÄHIGKEIT, WÄRMELEITVERMÖGEN |
| 2921 | **CONDUCTOR** | CONDUCTEUR (ELECTR.) | LEITER (ELEKTR.) |
| 2922 | **CONDUCTOR WIRE** | FIL CONDUCTEUR, CONDUCTEUR D'ELECRICITE, FIL ELECTRIQUE | LEITUNGSDRAHT |
| 2923 | **CONE** | DARD DE LA FLAMME | FLAMMENKEGEL |
| 2924 | **CONE** | CONE (GEOM.) | KEGEL, KONUS (GEOM.) |
| 2925 | **CONE BELT** | COURROIE TRAPEZOIDALE | KEILRIEMEN |
| 2926 | **CONE BRAKE** | FREIN A CONE | KEGELBREMSE |
| 2927 | **CONE CLUTCH** | EMBRAYAGE A CONE | KEGELKUPPLUNG |
| 2928 | **CONE COUPLING** | ACCOUPLEMENT PAR CONE | KEGELKUPPLUNG |
| 2929 | **CONE EXTRACTORS** | EXTRACTEURS DE CONES | KEGELAUSZIEHER |
| 2930 | **CONE FRICTION CLUTCH** | EMBRAYAGE A CONES | KEGELREIBUNGSKUPPLUNG |
| 2931 | **CONE KEY** | FRETTE | RINGKEIL, HÜLSENKEIL, HÜLSENKEGEL, SPANNHÜLSE |
| 2932 | **CONE OF RAYS, LUMINOUS CONE** | CONE LUMINEUX | LICHTKEGEL |
| 2933 | **CONFOCAL** | CONFOCAL | KONFOKAL |
| 2934 | **CONGLOMERATE** | CONGLOMERAT | KONGLOMERAT |
| 2935 | **CONGO RED** | ROUGE CONGO | KONGOROT |
| 2936 | **CONGO RED PAPER** | PAPIER AU ROUGE CONGO | KONGOPAPIER |
| 2937 | **CONGRUENCE** | CONGRUENCE | KONGRUENZ (GEOM.) |
| 2938 | **CONGRUENT MELTING** | FUSION CONGRUENTE | SCHMELZEN (KONGRUENTES) |
| 2939 | **CONGRUENT TRANSFORMATION** | TRANSFORMATION CONGRUENTE | ÜBERGANG (KONGRUENTER) |
| 2940 | **CONIC SECTION** | CONIQUE, SECTION CONIQUE | KEGELSCHNITT |
| 2941 | **CONICAL GUIDE** | CONE GALOPIN | KEGELTROMMEL |
| 2942 | **CONICAL HELICAL SPRING** | RESSORT CONIQUE | KEGELFEDER, SCHRAUBENFEDER (KEGELIGE) |
| 2943 | **CONICAL PENDULUM GOVERNOR** | REGULATEUR CONIQUE | KEGELPENDELREGLER |
| 2944 | **CONICAL PISTON, MARINE TYPE PISTON** | PISTON CONIQUE | TRICHTERKOLBEN, KOLBEN (KONISCHER), MARINEKOLBEN |
| 2945 | **CONICAL RING** | BAGUE CONIQUE | KEILRING |
| 2946 | **CONICAL RIVET, RIVET WITH CONICAL HEAD WITH STAFF POINT HAMMERED POINT** | RIVET A TETE CONIQUE, RIVET A TETE CHANFREINEE | NIET MIT DREIECKPROFILKOPF, NIET MIT GEHÄMMERTEM KOPF |

**CON** 76

| | | | |
|---|---|---|---|
| 2947 | **CONICAL ROOF** | TOIT CONIQUE | KEGELDACH |
| 2948 | **CONICAL SHAPE** | CONICITE | KEGELFORM |
| 2949 | **CONICAL SURFACE** | SURFACE LATERALE D'UN CONE | MANTELFLÄCHE EINES KEGELS |
| 2950 | **CONICAL TRANSITION SECTION** | ELEMENTS DE REDUCTION TRONCONIQUES | REDUZIER-ELEMENTE (KEGELSTUMPFE) |
| 2951 | **CONICAL VALVE, MITRE VALVE** | SOUPAPE A SIEGE CONIQUE | KEGELSITZVENTIL |
| 2952 | **CONJUGATE** | CONJUGUE | KONJUGIERT (MATH.) |
| 2953 | **CONJUGATE AXIS OF HYPERBOLA** | AXE NON TRANSVERSE D'UNE HYPERBOLE | NEBENACHSE DER HYPERBEL |
| 2954 | **CONJUGATE DIAMETER** | DIAMETRE CONJUGUE | DURCHMESSER (ZUGEORDNETER), DURCHMESSER (KONJUGIERTER) |
| 2955 | **CONNECT (TO)** | RACCORDER, RELIER (ELECTR.) | ANSCHLIESSEN (ELEKTR.) |
| 2956 | **CONNECT IN PARALLEL (TO)** | MONTER EN PARALLELE, GROUPER EN QUANTITE | SCHALTEN NEBENEINANDER, SCHALTEN PARALLEL |
| 2957 | **CONNECT IN SERIES (TO)** | MONTER EN TENSION, GROUPER EN SERTIE | SCHALTEN IN REIHE, SCHALTEN HINTEREINANDER |
| 2958 | **CONNECTING** | RACCORDEMENT (ELECTR.) | ANSCHLIESSEN (ELEKTR.) |
| 2959 | **CONNECTING BOLT** | BOULON DE LIAISON | VERBINDUNGSSCHRAUBE |
| 2960 | **CONNECTING PIPE** | TUYAU DE COMMUNICATION, TUYAU DE RACCORDEMENT | ANSCHLUSSROHR, VERBINDUNGSROHR |
| 2961 | **CONNECTING RING** | BAGUE DE RACCORD | ZWISCHENRING |
| 2962 | **CONNECTING ROD** | BIELLE, TRIANGLE DE LIAISON, BARRE DE CONNEXION, TIGE DE RACCORDEMENT | PLEUELSTANGE, KOLBENSTANGE, VERBINDUNGSSTANGE, SCHUBSTANGE, TREIBSTANGE |
| 2963 | **CONNECTING ROD END** | TETE DE BIELLE | SCHUBSTANGENKOPF, PLEUELKOPF |
| 2964 | **CONNECTING WALKWAY** | PASSERELLE DE LIAISON | VERBINDUNGSSTEG |
| 2965 | **CONNECTION** | RACCORD | VERBINDUNG |
| 2966 | **CONNECTION** | RACCORD (ELECTR.) | ANSCHLUSS (ELEKTR.) |
| 2967 | **CONSERVATION OF ENERGY** | CONSERVATION DE L'ENERGIE | ERHALTUNG DER ENERGIE |
| 2968 | **CONSISTENCY** | CONSISTANCE | KONSISTENZ |
| 2969 | **CONSTANT** | CONSTANTE | KONSTANTE, FESTWERT |
| 2970 | **CONSTANT CURRENT WELDING SOURCE** | GENERATRICE DE SOUDAGE POUR COURANT CONSTANT | SCHWEISSGENERATOR FÜR KONSTANTEN STROM |
| 2971 | **CONSTANT CUTTING SPEED** | VITESSE DE COUPE CONSTANTE | SCHNITTGESCHWINDIGKEIT (KONSTANTE) |
| 2972 | **CONSTANT DEFLECTION TEST** | ESSAI DE FLEXION CONSTANTE | DURCHBIEGUNGS PRÜFUNG (KONSTANTE) |
| 2973 | **CONSTANT FORCE** | FORCE CONSTANTE | KRAFT (GLEICHBLEIBENDE), KRAFT (KONTINUIERLICHE) |
| 2974 | **CONSTANT LOAD TEST** | ESSAI DE CHARGE CONSTANTE | DAUERLASTPRÜFUNG |
| 2975 | **CONSTANT OF GRAVITATION** | INTENSITE DE LA PESANTEUR | GRAVITATIONSKONSTANTE |
| 2976 | **CONSTANT PRESSURE** | PRESSION CONSTANTE | DRUCK (GLEICHBLEIBENDER), DRUCK (KONSTANTER) |
| 2977 | **CONSTANT TEMPERATURE** | TEMPERATURE CONSTANTE | TEMPERATUR (GLEICHBLEIBENDE), TEMPERATUR (KONSTANTE) |
| 2978 | **CONSTANT VOLTAGE** | TENSION CONSTANTE | DAUERSPANNUNG |
| 2979 | **CONSTANT VOLTAGE WELDING SOURCE** | SOURCE DE COURANT A TENSION CONSTANTE (POUR SOUDAGE) | KONSTANTSPANNUNGSSTROMQUELLE |
| 2980 | **CONSTANTAN** | CONSTANTAN | KONSTANTAN |
| 2981 | **CONSTITUENT** | CONSTITUANT, COMPOSANT | ELEMENTARBESTANDTEIL |
| 2982 | **CONSTITUENT METAL COMPONENT OF AN ALLOY** | CONSTITUANT, COMPOSANT D'UN ALLIAGE, METAL CONSTITUANT | BESTANDTEIL EINER LEGIERUNG |
| 2983 | **CONSTITUENT, COMPONENT** | COMPOSANT (CHIM.) | BESTANDTEIL, KOMPONENTE (CHEM.) |
| 2984 | **CONSTITUTION DIAGRAM** | DIAGRAMME DE PHASES | ZUSTANDSDIAGRAMM |

| | | | |
|---|---|---|---|
| 2985 | CONSTRAINED MOTION, DEFINITELY, FULLY CONTROLLED MOTION, POSITIVE MOTION | MOUVEMENT A COMMANDE POSITIVE, MOUVEMENT A COMMANDE MECANIQUE | BEWEGUNG (ZWANGSLÄUFIGE) |
| 2986 | CONSTRUCTION | CONSTRUCTION, MONTAGE | KONSTRUKTION, ERBAUUNG |
| 2987 | CONSTRUCTION HUT | BARAQUE DE CHANTIER | BAUSTELLENBARACKE |
| 2988 | CONSTRUCTIONAL METALS, COMMON | METAUX DE CONSTRUCTION (ORDINAIRES) | BAUMETALLE (GEWÖHNLICHE) |
| 2989 | CONSULTING ENGINEER | INGENIEUR-CONSEIL | INGENIEUR (BERATENDER) |
| 2990 | CONSUMABLE ELECTRODE, CONSUTRODE | ELECTRODE FUSIBLE | ELEKTRODE (SCHMELZBARE), CONSUTRODE |
| 2991 | CONSUMABLE INSERT RING | JOINT FUSIBLE | ABSCHMELZVERBINDUNGSRING |
| 2992 | CONSUMED WEIGHT | POIDS CONSOMME | GEWICHT (VERBRAUCHTES) |
| 2993 | CONSUMPTION OF CURRENT | CONSOMMATION DE COURANT | STROMVERBRAUCH |
| 2994 | CONSUMPTION OF FUEL | CONSOMMATION DE COMBUSTIBLE | BRENNSTOFFVERBRAUCH |
| 2995 | CONSUMPTION OF STEAM, STEAM CONSUMPTION DEMAND | CONSOMMATION, DEPENSE DE VAPEUR | DAMPFVERBRAUCH |
| 2996 | CONTACT | CONTACT A LA MASSE (ELECT.), CONTACT (GEN.) | KONTAKT (ELEKTR.) BERÜHRUNG (ALLG.) |
| 2997 | CONTACT ARC | ARC DE CONTACT | GREIFBOGEN |
| 2998 | CONTACT AREA | SURFACE DE CONTACT | GREIFOBERFLÄCHE |
| 2999 | CONTACT BAR | BARRE DE CONTACT | KONTAKTBACKE |
| 3000 | CONTACT BREAKER | GRAINS DE CONTACT (RUPTEUR) | KONTAKTUNTERBRECHER |
| 3001 | CONTACT CONDUCTOR | ELECTRODE A CONTACT | KONTAKTELEKTRODE |
| 3002 | CONTACT CORROSION | CORROSION PAR CONTACT | BERÜHRUNGSKORROSION |
| 3003 | CONTACT JAW | JOUE DE CONTACT | KONTAKTBLOCK |
| 3004 | CONTACT PLATING | DEPOT PAR CONTACT | KONTAKTPLATTIERUNG |
| 3005 | CONTACT POINT | POINT DE CONTACT | BERÜHRUNGSPUNKT |
| 3006 | CONTACT POINT INSERT | POINTE DE RECHANGE | AUFSATZSPITZE |
| 3007 | CONTACT POTENTIAL | POTENTIEL DE CONTACT | KONTAKTPOTENTIAL |
| 3008 | CONTACT ROLLER | GALET DE CONTACT | KONTAKTROLLE |
| 3009 | CONTACTS POINT | PLOT | UNTERBRECHERKONTAKT |
| 3010 | CONTAINER, RECELVER, TANK, DRUM | RECIPIENT | BEHÄLTER |
| 3011 | CONTENTS | TENEUR, PROPORTION, DOSAGE | GEHALT, MENGENVERHÄLTNIS |
| 3012 | CONTINOUS LUBRICATION | GRAISSAGE CONTINU | SCHMIERUNG (BESTÄNDIGE) |
| 3013 | CONTINOUS PAPER | PAPIER CONTINU | PAPIER (ENDLOSES) |
| 3014 | CONTINOUS SINTERING | FRITTAGE CONTINU | SINTERN (KONTINUIERLICHES) |
| 3015 | CONTINOUS SYSTEM OF ROPE DRIVING | TRANSMISSION SUR POULIES MULTIPLES | KREISSEILTRIEB |
| 3016 | CONTINOUS WELD | SOUDAGE CONTINU | DURCHLAUFSCHWEISSEN |
| 3017 | CONTINUITY | CONTINUITE | KONTINUITÄT, STETIGER VERLAUF, STETIGKEIT |
| 3018 | CONTINUOUS BEAM | POUTRE CONTINUE | TRÄGER (DURCHGEHENDER), TRÄGER (DURCHLAUFENDER) |
| 3019 | CONTINUOUS CASTING | COULEE CONTINUE | GIESSEN (KONTINUIERLICHES) |
| 3020 | CONTINUOUS CHAIN PASSENGER LIFT | ASCENSEUR CONTINU | PATERNOSTERAUFZUG |
| 3021 | CONTINUOUS CURRENT GENERATOR, DYNAMO | DYNAMO, GENERATRICE, MACHINE A COURANT CONTINU | GLEICHSTROMMASCHINE, GLEICHSTROMDYNAMO, GLEICHSTROMGENERATOR |
| 3022 | CONTINUOUS CURRENT MOTOR | MOTEUR A COURANT CONTINU | GLEICHSTROMMOTOR |
| 3023 | CONTINUOUS DIRECT CURRENT (C.C., D.C.) | COURANT CONTINU | GLEICHSTROM |
| 3024 | CONTINUOUS DISTILLATION | DISTILLATION CONTINUE | DESTILLATION (STETIGE) |
| 3025 | CONTINUOUS FUNCTION | FONCTION CONTINUE | FUNKTION (STETIGE) |

**CON** 78

| | | | |
|---|---|---|---|
| 3026 | **CONTINUOUS FURNACE** | FOUR CONTINU | DURCHLAUFOFEN, OFEN (KONTINUIERLICHER) |
| 3027 | **CONTINUOUS GALVANIZING** | GALVANISATION EN CONTINU | VERZINKEN (KONTINUIERLICHES) |
| 3028 | **CONTINUOUS HOT DIP** | TREMPE CONTINUE A CHAUD | EINTAUCH-VERFAHREN (KONTINUIERLICHES) |
| 3029 | **CONTINUOUS INGOT CASTING** | COULEE CONTINUE | STRANGGIESSEN |
| 3030 | **CONTINUOUS MILL** | TRAIN CONTINU (DE LAMINOIR) | WALZSTRASSE (KONTINUIERLICHE) |
| 3031 | **CONTINUOUS MOTION** | MOUVEMENT CONTINU | BEWEGUNG (STETIGE) |
| 3032 | **CONTINUOUS PATH** | COMMANDE CONTINUE | STETIGBAHNSTEUERUNG |
| 3033 | **CONTINUOUS PHASE** | PHASE CONTINUE, PHASE DISPERSIVE | PHASE (DISPERSIVE), PHASE (KONTINUIERLICHE) |
| 3034 | **CONTINUOUS PRODUCTION, PROGRESSIVE MANUFACTURE, MANUFACTURE ON THE FLOW PRINCIPE, MASS PRODUCTION WITH CONSECUTIVE OPERATIONS** | TRAVAIL A LA CHAINE, OPERATIONS A LA CHAINE | FLIESSARBEIT |
| 3035 | **CONTINUOUS ROLLING** | LAMINAGE CONTINU | WALZEN (KONTINUIERLICHES) |
| 3036 | **CONTINUOUS SPECTRUM** | SPECTRE CONTINU | SPEKTRUM (KONTINUIERLICHES) |
| 3037 | **CONTINUOUS WELD/WELDING** | SOUDURE CONTINUE | NAHT (DURCHLAUFENDE) |
| 3038 | **CONTINUOUS WORKING, CONTINUOUS RUNNING** | FONCTIONNEMENT CONTINU, SERVICE CONTINU | DAUERBETRIEB, BETRIEB (UNUNTERBROCHENER) |
| 3039 | **CONTOUR CONTROL SYSTEM** | COMMANDE DE CONTOURNAGE | BAHNSTEUERUNG |
| 3040 | **CONTOUR GRINDING** | FRAISAGE DES CONTOURS | UMRISSFRÄSEN |
| 3041 | **CONTOUR SHAPING** | FORMATION DU MODELE | MODELLFORMUNG |
| 3042 | **CONTRACTED** | RETRECI | VERENGT, EINGESCHNÜRT |
| 3043 | **CONTRACTION** | RETRAIT, STRICTION | SCHRUMPFUNG |
| 3044 | **CONTRACTION OF A JET, STREAM OF LIQUID** | CONTRACTION DE LA VEINE FLUIDE, ETRANGLEMENT DE LA VEINE LIQUIDE | EINSCHNÜRUNG, KONTRAKTION EINES FLÜSSIGKEITSSTRAHLES |
| 3045 | **CONTRACTION OF AREA** | CONTRACTION, RETRECISSEMENT, STRICTION | EINSCHNÜRUNG, VERENGERUNG, KONTRAKTION |
| 3046 | **CONTRACTION OF RIVET SHANK** | CONTRACTION DE LA TIGE DU RIVET | ZUSAMMENZIEHEN, SCHRUMPFEN DES NIETSCHAFTES |
| 3047 | **CONTRACTION RULE** | REGLE A RETRAIT | SCHWINDMASSSTAB |
| 3048 | **CONTROL** | CONTROLE, COMMANDE | KONTROLL, STEUERUNG |
| 3049 | **CONTROL (TO)** | MANOEUVRER, COMMANDER | STEUERN |
| 3050 | **CONTROL ARM** | BRAS DE SUSPENSION | SCHWINGARM |
| 3051 | **CONTROL CABLE** | CABLE DE COMMANDE | STEUERSEIL |
| 3052 | **CONTROL DEVICE** | DISPOSITIF DE CONTROLE | REGELVORRICHTUNG |
| 3053 | **CONTROL GAUGE** | JAUGE DE CONTROLE | LEHRGERÄT |
| 3054 | **CONTROL PANEL** | TABLEAU DE COMMANDE | BEDIENUNGSTAFEL |
| 3055 | **CONTROLLED ATMOSPHERE FURNACE** | FOUR A ATMOSPHERE CONTROLEE | SCHUTZGASOFEN |
| 3056 | **CONTROLLED COOLING** | REFROIDISSEMENT COMMANDE | KÜHLUNG (GESTEUERTE) |
| 3057 | **CONTROLLER** | ORGANE DE COMMANDE | STEUERUNG |
| 3058 | **CONTRUCTION CLIP ANGLE** | GOUSSET, CORNIERE SUPPORT | BEFESTIGUNGSWINKEL |
| 3059 | **CONVECTION** | CONVECTION (CHALEUR RAYONNANTE) | KONVEKTION |
| 3060 | **CONVECTION OF HEAT** | CONVECTION, CONVEXION | FORTFÜHRUNG DER WÄRME, KONVEKTION DER WÄRME |
| 3061 | **CONVENTIONAL MILLING** | FRAISAGE CLASSIQUE | FRÄSEN, (GEGENLÄUFIGES) |
| 3062 | **CONVERGE (TO)** | CONVERGER | ZUSAMMENLAUFEN, KONVERGIEREN |
| 3063 | **CONVERGENCE** | CONVERGENCE | KONVERGENZ |
| 3064 | **CONVERGENT** | CONVERGENT | ZUSAMMENLAUFEND, KONVERGENT |
| 3065 | **CONVERGENT SERIES** | SERIE CONVERGENTE | REIHE (KONVERGENTE) |

| | | | |
|---|---|---|---|
| 3066 | **CONVERGING MOUTHPIECE** | AJUTAGE CONVERGENT, EMBOUCHURE CONVERGENTE | AUSFLUSSSTUTZEN (SICH VERENGERNDER) |
| 3067 | **CONVERSION** | TRANSFORMATION, CONVERSION | UMRECHNUNG |
| 3068 | **CONVERSION OF IRON INTO STEEL** | TRANSFORMATION DU FER EN ACIER | EISEN-STAHLUMWANDLUG |
| 3069 | **CONVERSION TABLE** | TABLE DE TRANSFORMATION, DE CONVERSION | UMRECHNUNGSTAFEL |
| 3070 | **CONVERSION TRANSFORMATION OF ENERGY** | TRANSFORMATION D'ENERGIE | UMWANDLUNG VON ENERGIE, ENERGIEUMWANDLUNG |
| 3071 | **CONVERTER** | CONVERTISSEUR, COMMUTATRICE | UMFORMER, STROMUMFORMER, KONVERTERBIRNE |
| 3072 | **CONVERTER MOUTH/NOSE** | BEC DU CONVERTISSEUR | KONVERTERHUT |
| 3073 | **CONVERTIBLE (CAR)** | VOITURE DECAPOTABLE | KABRIOLETT |
| 3074 | **CONVERTING CEMENTATION FURNACE** | FOUR DE CEMENTATION | ZEMENTIEROFEN |
| 3075 | **CONVERTING POT** | CAISSE DE CEMENTATION | GLÜHKISTE, ZEMENTIERKISTE |
| 3076 | **CONVEX** | CONVEXE | KONVEX |
| 3077 | **CONVEX FILLET WELD** | SOUDURE D'ANGLE CONVEXE | VOLLKEHLNAHT, WÖLBKEHLNAHT |
| 3078 | **CONVEX MIRROR** | MIROIR CONVEXE | SPIEGEL (ERHABENER), KONVEXSPIEGEL |
| 3079 | **CONVEXITY RATIO** | RAPPORT DE CONVEXITE | KONVEXITÄTSVERHÄLTNIS WÖLBUNGSVERHÄLTNIS |
| 3080 | **CONVEYOR, CONVEYING MACHINERY, HANDLING APPLIANCE** | APPAREIL DE MANUTENTION, TRANSPORTEUR | FÖRDEREINRICHTUNG |
| 3081 | **COOL (TO)** | REFROIDIR (SE), REFRIGERER | ABKÜHLEN (SICH) |
| 3082 | **COOL TIME** | TEMPS DE REFROIDISSEMENT | ABKÜHLUNGSZEIT |
| 3083 | **COOLANT** | REFRIGERANT, FLUIDE DE REFROIDISSEMENT | KÜHLMITTEL |
| 3084 | **COOLED PISTON** | PISTON REFROIDI | KOLBEN (GEKÜHLTER) |
| 3085 | **COOLING** | REFROIDISSEMENT, REFRIGERATION | KÜHLEN, ABKÜHLEN, KÜHLUNG |
| 3086 | **COOLING AGENT** | AGENT FRIGORIFIQUE, AGENT DE REFRIGERATION | KÜHLMITTEL, KÄLTEMITTEL |
| 3087 | **COOLING CURVE** | COURBE DE REFROIDISSEMENT | ABKÜHLUNGSKURVE |
| 3088 | **COOLING FAN** | VENTILATEUR DE REFROIDISSEMENT | KÜHLLUFTGEBLASE |
| 3089 | **COOLING PLANT FOR WATER OF CONDENSATION** | INSTALLATION POUR LE REFROIDISSEMENT DES EAUX DE CONDENSATION, REFRIGERANT POUR LES EAUX DE CONDENSATION | RÜCKKÜHLANLAGE |
| 3090 | **COOLING POND** | BASSIN REFROIDISSANT | KÜHLTEICH |
| 3091 | **COOLING STRESSES** | EFFORTS DE REFROIDISSEMENT | ABKÜHLUNGSSPANNUNGEN |
| 3092 | **COOLING SURFACE** | SURFACE DE REFROIDISSEMENT, DE REFRIGERATION, SURFACE REFROIDISSANTE | KÜHLFLÄCHE |
| 3093 | **COOLING SYSTEM** | REFROIDISSEMENT, CIRCUIT DE REFROIDISSEMENT | KÜHLUNG, KÜHLSYSTEM |
| 3094 | **COOLING TOWER** | TOUR DE REFROIDISSEMENT | KÜHLTURM |
| 3095 | **COOLING WATER** | EAU DE REFROIDISSEMENT, EAU DE REFRIGERATION | KÜHLWASSER |
| 3096 | **COOLING-DOWN** | RETOUR A LA TEMPERATURE AMBIANTE | RÜCKKÜHLUNG ZU UMGEBUNGSTEMPERATUR |
| 3097 | **COORDINATE DIMENSIONING** | COTATION ABSOLUE | BEZUGSMASSSYSTEM |
| 3098 | **COORDINATE DRILLING AND BORING MACHINE** | PERCEUSE-ALESEUSE A COORDONNEES | KOORDINATEN-BOHR-U. AUSBOHR-MASCHINE |
| 3099 | **COORDINATE LOCATING** | REPERAGE PAR COORDONNEES | KOORDINATENSYSTEM |
| 3100 | **COORDINATES** | COORDONNEES | KOORDINATEN |
| 3101 | **COPAIBA** | BAUME DE COPAHU, COPAHU | KOPAIVABALSAM |

**COP** 80

| | | | |
|---|---|---|---|
| 3102 | COPAL GUM | COPAL, COPALE | KOPAL |
| 3103 | COPAL VARNISH | VERNIS AU COPAL | KOPALLACK |
| 3104 | COPE | PARTIE DE DESSUS | FORMOBERTEIL |
| 3105 | COPE AND DRAG PATTERN | MODELE EN DEUX | MODELL (ZWEITEILIGES) |
| 3106 | COPER WIRE | FIL DE CUIVRE | KUPFERDRAHT |
| 3107 | COPING | GRUGEAGE | AUSKLINKEN |
| 3108 | COPING SAW | SCIE A GRUGER | BOGENSÄGE |
| 3109 | COPOLA SPARK ARRESTOR | PARE-ETINCELLES | FUNKENFÄNGER |
| 3110 | COPPER | CUIVRE (CUIVRE ROUGE) | KUPFER |
| 3111 | COPPER ALLOY | ALLIAGE A BASE DE CUIVRE | KUPFERLEGIERUNG |
| 3112 | COPPER ANODE | ANODE DE CUIVRE | KUPFERANODE |
| 3113 | COPPER BAR | BARRE DE CUIVRE | KUPFERSTAB |
| 3114 | COPPER COINAGE | MONNAIES DE CUIVRE | KUPFERMÜNZEN |
| 3115 | COPPER CYANIDE | CYANURE DE CUIVRE | ZYANKUPFER, KUPFERZYANID |
| 3116 | COPPER FLAT WIRE | FIL PLAT EN CUIVRE, FIL DE CUIVRE PLAT | KUPFERFLACHDRAHT |
| 3117 | COPPER FOIL | FEUILLE MINCE DE CUIVRE | KUPFERFOLIE |
| 3118 | COPPER GLANCE, VITREOUS COPPER ORE, CHALCOCITE, REDRUTHITE | CHALCOSINE, CUIVRE VITREUX, CUIVRE SUFURE GRIS | KUPFERGLANZ |
| 3119 | COPPER HAMMER | MASSE, MASSETTE EN CUIVRE | KUPFERHAMMER |
| 3120 | COPPER INGOT | LINGOT DE CUIVRE | KUPFERBARREN, KUPFERBLOCK |
| 3121 | COPPER MATT, REGULUS OF COPPER | MATTE DE CUIVRE | KUPFERSTEIN, KUPFERLECH |
| 3122 | COPPER ORE | MINERAI DE CUIVRE | KUPFERERZ |
| 3123 | COPPER PLATE | PLAQUE DE CUIVRE | KUPFERPLATTE |
| 3124 | COPPER PLATE (TO) | CUIVRER | VERKUPFERN |
| 3125 | COPPER PLATING | CUIVRAGE | VERKUPFERUNG |
| 3126 | COPPER PYRITES, CHALCOPYRITES | PYRITE CUIVREUSE, CUIVRE PYRITEUX, CHALCOPYRITE | KUPFERKIES, CHALKOPYRIT |
| 3127 | COPPER SHEET | TOLE DE CUIVRE | KUPFERBLECH |
| 3128 | COPPER SHOT | GRENAILLE DE CUIVRE | KUPFERSCHROT |
| 3129 | COPPER SLAB | LINGOT PLAT DE CUIVRE | KUPFERFLACHBLOCK |
| 3130 | COPPER STEEL | ACIER AU CUIVRE | KUPFERSTAHL |
| 3131 | COPPER STRIP | LAME DE CUIVRE, BANDE DE CUIVRE | KUPFERSTREIFEN |
| 3132 | COPPER TUBE | TUYAU EN CUIVRE | KUPFERROHR |
| 3133 | COPPER WIRE | FIL DE CUIVRE | KUPFERDRAHT |
| 3134 | COPPER-ASBESTOS GASKET | JOINT METALLOPLASTIQUE | KUPFERASBESTDICHTUNG |
| 3135 | COPPERSMITH | CHAUDRONNIER EN CUIVRE | KUPFERSCHMIED |
| 3136 | COPPERSMITHING | CHAUDRONNERIE | KUPFERSCHMIEDEN |
| 3137 | COPPERWELD | COPPERWELD | COPPERWELD |
| 3138 | COPYING LATHE | TOUR A COPIER, TOUR A REPRODUIRE | KOPIERDREHMASCHINE, FORMDREHBANK, KOPIERDREHBANK, SCHABLONENDREHBANK, FASSONDREHBANK |
| 3139 | COPYING MACHINE | MACHINE A REPRODUIRE | KOPIERMASCHINE |
| 3140 | CORBEL | CORBEAU | KRAGSTÜCK, KONSOLE |
| 3141 | CORD DRIVE, BAND DRIVE | TRANSMISSION COURROIES DE CHASSE | SCHNURTRIEB |
| 3142 | CORE | CAROTTE, NOYAU, AME, NOYAU MAGNETIQUE | MASSEKERN, BOHRKERN, KERN, ADER, SEELE |
| 3143 | CORE BAR | ARMATURE DE NOYAU | KERNSTANGE |
| 3144 | CORE BEARING BLOCK | POINT DE GUIDAGE DES NOYAUX | KERNFÜHRUNGSBLOCK |
| 3145 | CORE BINDER | LIANT DE NOYAUTAGE | TROCKENSANDBINDER, KERNBINDER |

| | | | |
|---|---|---|---|
| 3146 | **CORE BLOWING-MACHINE** | MACHINE A SOUFFLER LES NOYAUX | KERNBLASMASCHINE |
| 3147 | **CORE BOX** | BOITE A NOYAUX | KERNKASTEN |
| 3148 | **CORE DRIER** | COQUILLE DE SECHAGE | TROCKENSCHALE |
| 3149 | **CORE DRILL** | FORET ALESEUR | SPIRALSENKER |
| 3150 | **CORE GRINDER** | MACHINE A MEULER LES NOYAUX | KERNSCHLEIFMASCHINE |
| 3151 | **CORE GUM** | COLLE A NOYAUX | KERNKLEBEMITTEL |
| 3152 | **CORE HOOK** | CROCHET A NOYAUX | KERNHAKEN |
| 3153 | **CORE KNOCK-OUT MACHINE** | MACHINE A DENOYAUTER, MACHINE A DEBOURRER | AUSSCHLAGRÜTTLER |
| 3154 | **CORE MAKING MACHINE** | MACHINE A MOULER LES NOYAUX | KERNFORMMASCHINE |
| 3155 | **CORE OF A PACKING** | NOYAU D'UNE GARNITURE | EINLAGE EINER PACKUNG |
| 3156 | **CORE OF CROSS SECTION** | NOYAU DE LA SECTION | KERN EINES QUERSCHNITTES |
| 3157 | **CORE OIL** | HUILE A NOYAUX | KERNÖL |
| 3158 | **CORE OVEN** | ETUVE | KERNTROCKENOFEN |
| 3159 | **CORE PACKING** | JOINT A INSERTION | PACKUNG MIT EINLAGE |
| 3160 | **CORE PLATE** | SEGMENT DE TOLE (D'INDUIT) | ANKERSCHNITT, TRAFOBLECH, ROTOR PLATTE |
| 3161 | **CORE PRINT** | PORTEE DE MODELE | KERNMARKE |
| 3162 | **CORE ROD** | POINCON, BROCHE (FRITTAGE) | DORN, KERN |
| 3163 | **CORE SAND** | SABLE A NOYAUX | KERNSAND |
| 3164 | **CORE STRAINER** | NOYAU FILTRE | SIEBKERN |
| 3165 | **CORE STRUCTURE** | STRUCTURE DU COEUR | KERNGEFÜGE |
| 3166 | **CORE VENTS** | TIRAGE D'AIR DES NOYAUX | LUFTSTECHEN, ENTLÜFTUNG |
| 3167 | **CORE, CENTRE OF A ROPE** | AME D'UN CABLE | SEELE EINES SEILES |
| 3168 | **CORED BAR** | BARRE A NOYAU FUSIBLE | STAB MIT SCHMELZKERN |
| 3169 | **CORED CRYSTAL** | CRISTAL INHOMOGENE | KRISTALL (INHOMOGENER) |
| 3170 | **CORED STRUCTURE** | HETEROGENEITE | UNGLEICHARTIGKEIT |
| 3171 | **COREWASH** | ENDUIT POUR NOYAUX | SCHLICHTE |
| 3172 | **CORING** | SEGREGATION, MICROSEGREGATION | SEIGERUNG, ENTMISCHUNG, MIKROSEIGERUNG |
| 3173 | **CORK** | LIEGE, BOUCHON | KORK |
| 3174 | **CORK BRICK** | BRIQUE EN LIEGE | KORKSTEIN |
| 3175 | **CORK SLAB** | PLAQUE DE LIEGE | KORKPLATTE |
| 3176 | **CORK STOPPLE** | BOUCHON DE LIEGE | PFROPFEN, KORKSTOPFEN, KORK |
| 3177 | **CORN AND SEED DRESSING AND CLEANING MACHINERY** | TARARES CRIBLEURS T. TRIEURS | SAATGUT UND GETREIDEREINIGUNGS-MASCHINEN |
| 3178 | **CORNER DRILLING MACHINE** | MACHINE A PERCER LES TROUS A ANGLE | ECKBOHRMASCHINE |
| 3179 | **CORNER JOINT** | CONTRE-FICHE, JOINT EN ANGLE EXTERIEUR | GEGENSTREBE, WINKELSTOSSVERBINDUNG |
| 3180 | **CORNERING STABILITY** | TENUE DE ROUTE EN VIRAGE | KURVENFESTIGKEIT |
| 3181 | **CORRECTION** | CORRECTION | BERICHTIGUNG |
| 3182 | **CORRODE (TO)** | ATTAQUER, CORRODER | ANFRESSEN, ANGREIFEN |
| 3183 | **CORROSION** | CORROSION | VERROTTUNG, ANFRESSUNG, KORROSION |
| 3184 | **CORROSION AND HEAT RESISTING STEELS** | ACIERS RESISTANT A LA CORROSION ET A LA CHALEUR | STÄHLE (KORROSIONS- UNDWÄRMEBESTÄNDIGE) |
| 3185 | **CORROSION CREVICE** | CORROSION FISSURANTE | SPALTKORROSION |
| 3186 | **CORROSION EMBRITTLEMENT** | FRAGILITE PAR CORROSION | KORROSIONSSPRÖDIGKEIT |
| 3187 | **CORROSION FATIGUE** | FATIGUE PAR CORROSION | KORROSIONSERMÜDUNG |
| 3188 | **CORROSION FATIGUE LIMIT** | LIMITE DE FATIGUE PAR CORROSION | KORROSIONSERMÜDUNGSGRENZE |
| 3189 | **CORROSION INHIBITOR** | PRODUIT ANTI-ROUILLE | ROSTSCHUTZMITTEL |

# COR

82

| | | | |
|---|---|---|---|
| 3190 | **CORROSION PIT** | PIQURE DE CORROSION | KORROSIONSNARBE |
| 3191 | **CORROSION PREVENTION** | PROTECTION CONTRE LA CORROSION | KORROSIONSSCHUTZ, KORROSIONSVERHÜTUNG |
| 3192 | **CORROSION PRODUCT SOLVENTS** | SOLVANTS POUR CORROSIFS | LÖSUNGSMITTEL FÜR KORROSION |
| 3193 | **CORROSION RATE** | VITESSE DE CORROSION | KORROSIONSGESCHWINDIGKEIT |
| 3194 | **CORROSION RESISTANCE** | RESISTANCE A LA CORROSION | KORROSIONSBESTÄNDIGKEIT |
| 3195 | **CORROSION STRESS** | CORROSION SOUS TENSION | SPANNUNGSKORROSION |
| 3196 | **CORROSIVE** | CORROSIF, MORDANT | ÄTZEND |
| 3197 | **CORROSIVE SUBSTANCE** | SUBSTANCE CORROSIVE, CORROSIF, CORRODANT | ÄTZMITTEL |
| 3198 | **CORRUGATED SHEET IRON** | TOLE ONDULEE | WELLBLECH |
| 3199 | **CORRUGATED TUBE** | TUBE PLISSE | WELLROHR |
| 3200 | **CORRUGATED WIRE NETTING** | GRILLAGE ONDULE | SCHLANGENROST |
| 3201 | **CORUNDUM** | CORINDON | KORUND |
| 3202 | **COSECANT** | COSECANTE | KOSEKANTE |
| 3203 | **COSINE** | COSINUS | KOSINUS |
| 3204 | **COST OF HANDLING** | FRAIS DE MANUTENTION | FÖRDERKOSTEN |
| 3205 | **COST OF PACKING, PACKING COSTS** | FRAIS D'EMBALLAGE | VERPACKUNGSKOSTEN |
| 3206 | **COST OF POWER** | FRAIS DE FORCE MOTRICE | KRAFTBEDARFSKOSTEN |
| 3207 | **COST OF PRODUCTION** | FRAIS DE PRODUCTION, FRAIS DE FABRICATION | SELBSTKOSTEN, GESTEHUNGSKOSTEN, HERSTELLUNGSKOSTEN, PRODUKTIONSKOSTEN |
| 3208 | **COST OF REPAIRS** | FRAIS DE REPARATION | AUSBESSERUNGSKOSTEN, WIEDERHERSTELLUNGSKOSTEN, REPARATURKOSTEN |
| 3209 | **COST OF TRANSPORTATION, FREIGHT CHARGES** | FRAIS DE TRANSPORT | BEFÖRDERUNGSKOSTEN, VERSANDKOSTEN, FRACHTKOSTEN, FRACHT, TRANSPORTKOSTEN |
| 3210 | **COST PRICE** | PRIX DE REVIENT | SELBSTKOSTENPREIS, GESTEHUNGSPREIS |
| 3211 | **COTANGENT** | COTANGENTE | KOTANGENTE |
| 3212 | **COTTER** | CLE, CLEF, CLAVETTE-CLEF | VORSTECKER, VORSTECKKEIL, VORSTECKSTIFT, |
| 3213 | **COTTER PIN** | CLAVETTE D'ARRET | SETZKEIL, SPLINT |
| 3214 | **COTTER WAY** | TROU DE GOUPILLE | KEILLOCH |
| 3215 | **COTTER, COTTAR** | CLAVETTE EN COIN, CLAVETTE TRANSVERSALE, CHEVILLE D'ASSEMBLAGE | QUERKEIL |
| 3216 | **COTTING BLOWPIPE** | CHALUMEAU A DECOUPER | SCHNEIDBRENNER |
| 3217 | **COTTON** | COTON | BAUMWOLLE |
| 3218 | **COTTON BELT** | COURROIE EN COTON | BAUMWOLLRIEMEN |
| 3219 | **COTTON COVERED WIRE, SILK COVERED WIRE** | FIL GUIPE | UMSPONNENER DRAHT |
| 3220 | **COTTON GASKET** | TRESSE EN COTON | BAUMWOLLZOPF |
| 3221 | **COTTON ROPE** | CABLE EN COTON | BAUMWOLLSEIL |
| 3222 | **COTTON SEED OIL** | HUILE DE COTON | BAUMWOLLSAMENÖL, COTTONÖL, NIGGERÖL |
| 3223 | **COTTON WASTE** | COTON A NETTOYER | PUTZWOLLE |
| 3224 | **COTTRELL BARRIER** | BARRIERE DE COTTRELL | COTTRELL-SCHRANKE |
| 3225 | **COULOMB** | COULOMB | COULOMB |
| 3226 | **COULOMB MODULUS** | MODULE DE COULOMB | SCHUBMODUL |
| 3227 | **COULOMETER** | VOLTAMETRE | COULOMETER, VOLTAMETER |
| 3228 | **COUMPOUND WOUND GENERATOR DYNAMO** | DYNAMO COMPOUND | VERBUNDDYNAMO, DOPPELSCHLUSSDYNAMO, COMPOUNDDYNAMO |
| 3229 | **COUNTER** | COMPTEUR | ZÄHLVORRICHTUNG, ZÄHLER |

| | | | |
|---|---|---|---|
| 3230 | **COUNTER CURRENT** | COURANTS DE SENS CONTRAIRE, CONTRE-COURANT | GEGENSTROM |
| 3231 | **COUNTER ELECTROMOTIVE FORCE** | FORCE CONTRE-ELECTROMOTRICE | KRAFT (GEGENELEKTROMOTORISCHE), GEGEN-EMK |
| 3232 | **COUNTER PRESSURE** | CONTRE-PRESSION | GEGENDRUCK |
| 3233 | **COUNTER SHAFT** | ARBRE DE RENVOI | VORGELEGEWELLE, GEGENWELLE |
| 3234 | **COUNTER SINKING** | FRAISAGE, CHANFREINAGE | VERSENKEN |
| 3235 | **COUNTER WEIGHTED CRANKSHAFT** | VILEBREQUIN A CONTREPOIDS | KURBELWELLE MIT GEGENGEWICHT |
| 3236 | **COUNTER-BORING** | CHAMBRAGE | VERSENKEN |
| 3237 | **COUNTER-CLOCKWISE** | EN SENS INVERSE DES AIGUILLES D'UNE MONTRE | LINKSDREHEND, ENTGEGENGESETZT DEM UHRZEIGERSINN |
| 3238 | **COUNTER-CLOCKWISE ROTATION** | ROTATION A GAUCHE | LINKSDREHUNG |
| 3239 | **COUNTER-CLOCKWISE WOUND, LEFT-HANDED WOUND, SINISTRORSE** | ENROULE A GAUCHE, SINISTRORSUM, SENESTRORSUM | LINKSGEWUNDEN, LINKSGEWICKELT |
| 3240 | **COUNTER-SHAFT** | ARBRE DE RENVOI | VORGELEGEWELLE |
| 3241 | **COUNTERBORE** | FORET ALESEUR | ZYLINDERSENKER |
| 3242 | **COUNTERBORING** | CHAMBRAGE | VERSENKEN |
| 3243 | **COUNTERMOVEMENT, MOVEMENT IN THE OPPOSITE DIRECTION** | MOUVEMENT EN SENS CONTRAIRE | BEWEGUNG (GEGENLÄUFIGE), GEGENBEWEGUNG |
| 3244 | **COUNTERSHAFT AND ACCESSORIES , INTERMEDIATE GEARING** | TRANSMISSION INTERMEDIAIRE, RENVOI DE MOUVEMENT | VORGELEGE |
| 3245 | **COUNTERSINK** | FORET A FRAISER, FRAISE POUR LOGEMENT DE TETES DE VIS, FORET CHAMPIGNON | VERSENKBOHRER, VERSENKER, KRAUSKOPF |
| 3246 | **COUNTERSINK A RIVET HEAD, A SCREW HEAD (TO)** | NOYER UNE TETE DE RIVET, NOYER UNE TETE DE VIS, FRAISER UN TROU DE RIVET, FRAISER UN TROU DE VIS | VERSENKEN (EINEN NIETKOPF), VERSENKEN (EINEN SCHRAUBENKOPF), EINLASSEN (EINEN SCHRAUBENKOPF) |
| 3247 | **COUNTERSINKING A RIVET HEAD, A SCREW HEAD** | FRAISAGE D'UN TROU DE RIVET, FRAISSAGE D'UN TROU A VIS | VERSENKEN (EINLASSEN EINES NIETKOPFES, EINES SCHRAUBENKOPFES), EINLASSEN (EINES NIETKOPFES, EINE SCHRAUBENKOPFES) |
| 3248 | **COUNTERSUNK HEAD SCREW** | VIS A TETE NOYEE | SENKSCHRAUBE |
| 3249 | **COUNTERSUNK RIVET, RIVET WITH COUNTERSUNK POINT** | RIVET A TETE FRAISEE AVEC BOMBE | HALBVERSENKNIET, NIET MIT HALBVERSENKTEM KOPF |
| 3250 | **COUNTERSUNK SCREW HEAD** | TETE FRAISEE, TETE NOYEE D'UNE VIS | VERSENKTER SCHRAUBENKOPF |
| 3251 | **COUNTERWEIGHT, COUNTERPOISE WEIGHT, BALANCE WEIGHT** | CONTREPOIDS | GEGENGEWICHT, AUSGLEICHGEWICHT, BELASTUNGSGEWICHT |
| 3252 | **COUPLE** | COUPLE, PAIRE | PAAR |
| 3253 | **COUPLE (TO)** | ACCOUPLER | KUPPELN |
| 3254 | **COUPLING** | ACCOUPLEMENT, EMMANCHEMENT, MANCHONNAGE, ASSEMBLAGE, JONCTION, REUNION, RACCORD, EMBRAYAGE, COUPLAGE | KUPPELN, VERBINDEN, VERBINDUNG, VERSCHRAUBUNG, KUPPLUNG |
| 3255 | **COUPLING FLANGE** | PLATEAU D'ACCOUPLEMENT, BRIDE D'ACCOUPLEMENT | KUPPLUNSFLANSCH, KUPPLUNGSSCHEIBE |
| 3256 | **COUPLING ROD** | BIELLE D'ACCOUPLEMENT | KUPPELSTANGE |
| 3257 | **COUPLING SLEEVE** | MANCHON D'ACCOUPLEMENT | MUFFE, KUPPLUNGSMUFFE |
| 3258 | **COUPLING, SOCKET** | MANCHON | MUFFE |
| 3259 | **COURSE OF BRICKS** | ASSISE DE BRIQUES | ZIEGESTEINSCHICHT |
| 3260 | **COURSE RING OF A BOILER SHELL** | VIROLE D'UNE CHAUDIERE | SCHUSS EINES KESSELS, KESSELSCHUSS |
| 3261 | **COVARIANCE** | COVARIANCE | MITVERÄNDERUNG |
| 3262 | **COVER (PLATE)** | TAMPON (COUVERCLE D'UN TAMPON) | VERSCHLUSS (EINES MANNLOCHS) |

# COV 84

| | | | |
|---|---|---|---|
| 3263 | **COVER (TO), LAG (TO), CLOTH A PIPE (TO)** | ENVELOPPER UN TUYAU, ENTOURER UN TUYAU | VERKLEIDEN (EIN ROHR), UMHÜLLEN (EIN ROHR) |
| 3264 | **COVER COAT** | ENDUIT DE FINITION, GLACURE | AUSSENPUTZ |
| 3265 | **COVER GLASS, COVER SLIP** | COUVRE-OBJET | DECKGLAS |
| 3266 | **COVER OF SLIDE VALVE CHEST, VALVE COVER** | COUVERCLE D'UN ROBINET, COUVERCLE D'UNE SOUPAPE | DECKEL, HAUBE EINES SCHIEBERS, HAUBE EINES VENTILS |
| 3267 | **COVER PLATE** | PLAQUE DE RECOUVREMENT, TAMPON | DECKPLATTE, ABDECKPLATTE, FLANGEABDECKUNG |
| 3268 | **COVER STRIP** | RUBAN METALLIQUE DE PROTECTION | SCHUTZSTREIFEN AUS METALL |
| 3269 | **COVER, LID, CAP** | COUVERCLE | DECKEL |
| 3270 | **COVERED CAM** | CAME A RAINURE | EXZENTER (GESCHLOSSENES) |
| 3271 | **COVERED ELECTRODE** | ELECTRODE ENROBEE | MANTELELEKTRODE |
| 3272 | **COVERED WIRE** | FIL RECOUVERT | DRAHT (UMMANTELTER) |
| 3273 | **COVERING POWER** | POUVOIR COUVRANT | DECKFÄHIGKEIT |
| 3274 | **COVERING, CLEADING** | ENVELOPPE, REVETEMENT EXTERIEUR, CHEMISE | VERKLEIDUNG, UMHÜLLUNG |
| 3275 | **COWHIDE** | CUIR DE BOEUF, CUIR DE VACHE | RINDLEDER |
| 3276 | **COWL** | AUVENT | HAUBE, WINDFANG |
| 3277 | **COWSTALL EQUIPMENT** | INSTALLATIONS D'ETABLES | KUHSTALL-AUSSTATTUNGEN |
| 3278 | **CRACK** | FENTE, CRIQUE, FISSURE, RUPTURE, GERCE, COUPURE, CREVASSE, DECHIRURE, TAPURE | RISS, SPRUNG, SPALTE, BRUCH |
| 3279 | **CRACK (TO)** | FENDILLER (SE) | RISSIG WERDEN |
| 3280 | **CRACK AND FLAW DETECTOR** | DETECTEUR DE CRIQUES ET FELURES | RISS- UND FEHLERDETEKTOR |
| 3281 | **CRACK AT THE EDGE** | FENDILLEMENT SUR LES BORDS | KANTENRISS, QUERRISS |
| 3282 | **CRACK IN HARDENED STEEL** | GERCURE, GERCE, TAPURE DE L'ACIER TREMPE | HÄRTERISS |
| 3283 | **CRACK/MICROCRACK** | PAILLE, FISSURE (MICROFISSURE) | RISS |
| 3284 | **CRACKING** | CRAQUAGE OU CRACKING, FISSURATION, FISSURAGE, CRIQUAGE | KRACKEN, RISSBILDUNG, RISS |
| 3285 | **CRACKING PROCESS** | DISTILLATION AVEC CRACKING, CRACKING | KRACKUNG, KRACKVERFAHREN, CRACKINGDESTILLATION |
| 3286 | **CRACKING ROUND THE RIVET HOLES** | FENDILLEMENT DES TROUS DE RIVET | RISSIGWERDEN DER NIETLÖCHER |
| 3287 | **CRACKING TOWER** | TOUR DE CRAQUAGE | KRACKTURM |
| 3288 | **CRADDLE** | BERCEAU, SUPPORT | SATTELBEFESTIGUNG |
| 3289 | **CRAFTSMAN, SKILLED WORKMAN** | OUVRIER PROFESSIONNEL, OUVRIER EXPERIMENTE | GELERNTER ARBEITER |
| 3290 | **CRANE** | GRUE | KRAN |
| 3291 | **CRANE JIB** | FLECHE DE GRUE | KRANAUSLEGER |
| 3292 | **CRANE LADLE** | POCHE DE GRUE DE COULEE | KRANGIESSPFANNE |
| 3293 | **CRANE RAIL** | RAIL DE PONT ROULANT | LAUFSCHIENE, KRANSCHIENE |
| 3294 | **CRANES** | GRUES AGRICOLES | ACKERKRÄNE |
| 3295 | **CRANK** | MANIVELLE | KURBEL |
| 3296 | **CRANK ARM** | BRAS DE MANIVELLE | KURBELARM |
| 3297 | **CRANK BOSS, BOSS OF CRANK** | MOYEU DE LA MANIVELLE | KURBELNABE, KURBELAUGE |
| 3298 | **CRANK CIRCLE PATH** | CERCLE DECRIT PAR LA MANIVELLE | KURBELKREIS |
| 3299 | **CRANK END, LARGE END, BIG END OF CONNECTING ROD** | GROSSE TETE DE BIELLE | KURBELENDE DER SCHUBSTANGE |
| 3300 | **CRANK HANDLE** | MANETON, MANCHON DE MANIVELLE A BRAS | KURBELGRIFF |

**85**           **CRI**

| | | | |
|---|---|---|---|
| 3301 | **CRANK LEVER** | BRAS DE MANIVELLE | KURBELARM |
| 3302 | **CRANK PIN** | BOUTON DE MANIVELLE, MANETON | KURBELZAPFEN |
| 3303 | **CRANK SHAFT BEARING, MAIN BEARING** | PALIER DE L'ARBRE MANIVELLE, PALIER DE L'ARBRE DE COUCHE, PALIER DE VILEBREQUIN | KURBELWELLENLAGER, HAUPTLAGER |
| 3304 | **CRANK WEB** | FLASQUE D'UN ARBRE COUDE | KURBELWANGE |
| 3305 | **CRANK WITH LOOSE SLEEVE, HANDLE** | MANIVELLE A MANCHON | HEFTKURBEL |
| 3306 | **CRANKCASE** | CARTER-MOTEUR | KURBELGEHAÜSE |
| 3307 | **CRANKCASE BREATHER** | RENIFLARD | KURBELGEHAÜSE ENTLÜFTUNG |
| 3308 | **CRANKCASE SLUDGE** | CAMBOUIS | SCHMIERE (ALTE) |
| 3309 | **CRANKED SHAFT** | ARBRE COUDE, ARBRE A VILEBREQUIN, ARBRE-MANIVELLE | KURBELWELLE, WELLE (GEKRÖPFTE) |
| 3310 | **CRANKING MOTOR** | DEMARREUR | ANLASSER |
| 3311 | **CRANKPIN** | MANETON DE VILEBREQUIN, MANETON | KURBELWELLENZAPFEN |
| 3312 | **CRANKPIN TURNING RINGS** | ANNEAUX A TOURILLONNER | ZAPFENDREHRINGE |
| 3313 | **CRANKSHAFT** | VILEBREQUIN | KURBELWELLE |
| 3314 | **CRANKSHAFT BEARING** | PALIER DE VILEBREQUIN | KURBELWELLENLAGER |
| 3315 | **CRANKSHAFT GEAR** | PIGNON DE VILLEBREQUIN | KURBELWELLENZAHNRAD |
| 3316 | **CRANKSHAFT LATHE** | TOUR A ARBRE COUDE | KURBELWELLENDREHBANK |
| 3317 | **CRATER** | CRATERE | KRATER |
| 3318 | **CRAZE** | FISSURE CAPILLAIRE, MICROCRIQUE | HAARRISS |
| 3319 | **CRAZING** | CRAQUELURE SUPERFICIELLE | OBERFLÄCHENHAARRISSE |
| 3320 | **CREASE** | PLI | FALTE |
| 3321 | **CREASING HAMMER** | MARTEAU A SUAGE | SICKENHAMMER, STEKENHAMMER |
| 3322 | **CREASING IRON** | SUAGE | SICKENSTOCK, SIEKENSTOCK |
| 3323 | **CREASING MACHINE** | MACHINE A BORDER | SICKENMASCHINE |
| 3324 | **CREEP (ING)** | FLUAGE (METAUX) | KRIECHEN |
| 3325 | **CREEP LIMIT** | LIMITE (CONVENTIONNELLE) DE FLUAGE | DAUERSTANDGRENZE, KRIECHGRENZE (KONVENTIONELLE) |
| 3326 | **CREEP RATE** | VITESSE DE FLUAGE | KRIECHGESCHWINDIGKEIT |
| 3327 | **CREEP STRENGHT DEPENDING ON TIME** | RESISTANCE AU FLUAGE POUR UNE DUREE FINIE | ZEITSTANDFESTIGKEIT |
| 3328 | **CREEP STRENGTH** | RESISTANCE AU FLUAGE | ZEITSTANDFESTIGKEIT |
| 3329 | **CREEPING IN BELTS** | CONTRACTION DE LA COURROIE | EINKRIECHEN DES RIEMENS |
| 3330 | **CREEPING OF A SOLUTION** | GRIMPEMENT D'UNE SOLUTION | KRIECHEN, ÜBERKRIECHEN EINER LÖSUNG |
| 3331 | **CREOSOTE OIL** | CREOSOTE | KREOSOT, KREOSOTÖL |
| 3332 | **CREOSOTING** | CREOSOTAGE | KREOSOTIEREN |
| 3333 | **CREST** | SOMMET DU FILET | GEWINDESPITZE |
| 3334 | **CREST OF WAVE, WAVE CREST** | CRETE DE L'ONDE | WELLENBERG |
| 3335 | **CRESTCLEARANCE** | JEU A LA CRETE | SPITZENSPIEL |
| 3336 | **CRIMP (TO)** | ONDULER, PLISSER | FALTEN VERFORMEN |
| 3337 | **CRIPPLING** | DEFORMATION PERMANENTE | FORMÄNDERUNG (BLEIBENDE) |
| 3338 | **CRIPPLING BUCKLING LOAD** | CHARGE DE RUPTURE AU FLAMBAGE | KNICKLAST, KNICKBELASTUNG |
| 3339 | **CRIPPLING BUCKLING STRAIN** | EFFORT DE FLAMBAGE, EFFORT DE COMPRESSION SUR PIECES LONGUES | BEANSPRUCHUNG AUF KNICKUNG, KNICKBEANSPRUCHUNG |
| 3340 | **CRIPPLING BUCKLING STRENGTH** | RESISTANCE AU FLAMBAGE | KNICKFESTIGKEIT |
| 3341 | **CRIPPLING BUCKLING STRESS** | EFFORT DE FLAMBAGE PAR UNITE DE SECTION | KNICKSPANNUNG |
| 3342 | **CRIPPLING BUCKLING TEST** | ESSAI AU FLAMBAGE | KNICKVERSUCH |

# CRI

| | | | |
|---|---|---|---|
| 3343 | CRIPPLING, BUCKLING | FLAMBAGE, FLAMBEMENT | KNICKUNG, KNICKEN |
| 3344 | CRITICAL AGING | VIEILLISSEMENT CRITIQUE | ALTERUNG (KRITISCHE) |
| 3345 | CRITICAL ANGLE | ANGLE LIMITE | GRENZWINKEL (OPT.) |
| 3346 | CRITICAL HUMIDITY | HUMIDITE CRITIQUE | FEUCHTIGKEIT (KRITISCHE) |
| 3347 | CRITICAL POINT | POINT CRITIQUE, POINT DE TRANSFORMATION | PUNKT (KRITISCHER), HALTEPUNKT, UMWANDLUNGSPUNKT |
| 3348 | CRITICAL PRESSURE | PRESSION CRITIQUE | DRUCK (KRITISCHER) |
| 3349 | CRITICAL STATE | ETAT CRITIQUE | ZUSTAND (KRITISCHER), GRENZZUSTAND |
| 3350 | CRITICAL STRAIN | DEFORMATION CRITIQUE | SPANNUNG (KRITISCHE) |
| 3351 | CRITICAL STRESS | TENSION CRITIQUE | BEANSPRUCHUNG (KRITISCHE) |
| 3352 | CRITICAL TEMPERATURE | TEMPERATURE CRITIQUE | TEMPERATUR (KRITISCHE) |
| 3353 | CRITICAL VELOCITY | VITESSE CRITIQUE | GESCHWINDIGKEIT (KRITISCHE) |
| 3354 | CRITICAL VOLUME | VOLUME CRITIQUE | VOLUMEN (KRITISCHES) |
| 3355 | CROCUS | ROUGE D'ANGLETERRE | ROT (PARISER) |
| 3356 | CROP | CHUTE | ABFALLENDE, SCHOPPENDE |
| 3357 | CROPPING | EBOUTAGE | SCHOPFEN |
| 3358 | CROPPING SHEARS | CISAILLE A DECOUPER LA CHUTE | SCHOPFSCHERE |
| 3359 | CROSS | CROIX | KREUZSTÜCK |
| 3360 | CROSS ARCHES FRAME | CHARPENTE A CROISILLONS | KREUZSTREBENTRAGWERK |
| 3361 | CROSS BAR | TRAVERSE | QUERBALKEN, QUERRIEGEL |
| 3362 | CROSS COUNTRY VEHICLE | VEHICULE TOUS TERRAINS | GELÄNDEWAGEN |
| 3363 | CROSS CURRENT | COURANTS CROISES | KREUZSTROM |
| 3364 | CROSS CUT CHISEL | BEDANE, BEC-D'ANE | KREUZMEISSEL |
| 3365 | CROSS CUT SAW | SCIE A TRONCONNER, SCIE PASSE-PARTOUT, PASSE-PARTOUT | SCHROTSÄGE, TRECKSÄGE, BAUCHSÄGE, QUERSÄGE |
| 3366 | CROSS HATCHED COATINGS | APPLICATION EN PASSES CROISEES | KREUZAUFTRAGUNG |
| 3367 | CROSS MEMBER | TRAVERSE | QUERTRÄGER |
| 3368 | CROSS PIPE | CROIX A QUATRE DIRECTIONS | KREUZROHR, KREUZSTÜCK, VIERWEGESTÜCK |
| 3369 | CROSS PLANE | PANNE EN TRAVERS | QUERFINNE |
| 3370 | CROSS PRESS | PRESSE DE COULEE | SPANNVORRICHTUNG |
| 3371 | CROSS SECTION | SECTION EFFICACE | WIRKUNGSQUERSCHNITT |
| 3372 | CROSS SECTION IRON | FER EN CROIX | KREUZEISEN |
| 3373 | CROSS SECTION OF FRACTURE | SECTION DE RUPTURE, PLAN DE RUPTURE | BRUCHQUERSCHNITT |
| 3374 | CROSS SECTION OF PASSAGE | SECTION DE PASSAGE, SECTION LIBRE | DURCHFLUSSQUERSCHNITT, DURCHGANGSQUERSCHNITT, DURCHTRITTSQUERSCHNITT |
| 3375 | CROSS SECTION UNDER COMPRESSION | SECTION SOUMISE A UN EFFORT DE COMPRESSION | QUERSCHNITT (GEDRÜCKTER), DRUCKQUERSCHNITT |
| 3376 | CROSS SECTION UNDER TENSION | SECTION SOUMISE A UN EFFORT DE TRACTION | QUERSCHNITT (GEZOGENER), ZUGQUERSCHNITT |
| 3377 | CROSS SECTION, TRANSVERSE SECTION | COUPE TRANSVERSALE, PROFIL TRANSVERSAL | QUERPROFIL |
| 3378 | CROSS SECTION, TRANSVERSE SECTION | SECTION TRANSVERSALE | QUERSCHNITT |
| 3379 | CROSS SLIDE | CHARIOT TRANSVERSAL | QUERSCHLITTEN |
| 3380 | CROSS SLIP | DEVIATION | QUERGLEITUNG |
| 3381 | CROSS STEEL | FER EN CROIX | KREUZPROFILEISEN |
| 3382 | CROSS STRIP | CORDON D'ECRASEMENT | STAUCHSTREIFEN |
| 3383 | CROSS WIRES, SPIDER LINES | RETICULE | FADENKREUZ |
| 3384 | CROSS-ROLLING | LAMINAGE TRANSVERSAL | QUERWALZEN |

**CRY**

87

| | | | |
|---|---|---|---|
| 3385 | CROSS-WIRE WELDING | SOUDAGE DE FILS EN CROIX | KREUZDRAHTSCHWEISSEN |
| 3386 | CROSSED ARM GOVERNOR, PARABOLIC GOVERNOR, PARABOLIC GOVERNOR | REGULATEUR A BRAS CROISES, REGULATEUR FARCOT | REGLER MIT GEKREUZTEN STANGEN |
| 3387 | CROSSED BELT | COURROIE CROISEE, COURROIE RENVERSEE | RIEMENTRIEB (GEKREUZTER), RIEMENTRIEB (GESCHRÄNKTER), KREUZTRIEB |
| 3388 | CROSSHEAD | ENTRETOISE, CROSSETTE | QUERHAUPT, KOPFPLATTE, KREUZKOPF |
| 3389 | CROSSHEAD END SMALL END OF CONNECTING ROD | PIED DE BIELLE, EXTREMITE DE LA BIELLE ARTICULEE AU PISTON | KREUZKOPFENDE DER SCHUBSTANGE |
| 3390 | CROSSHEAD PIN BRASSES | COUSSINET DE PIED DE BIELLE | KREUZKOPFZAPFENLAGER |
| 3391 | CROSSHEAD PIN, CROSSHEAD GUDGEON, GUDGEON PIN | TOURILLON DE CROSSE, TOURILLON A FOURCHETTE, TOURILLON-AXE POUR CHAPE-FOURCHETTE | KREUZKOPFZAPFEN |
| 3392 | CROSSING FILE, TUMBLER FILE | LIME FEUILLE DE SAUGE | VOGELZUNGE |
| 3393 | CROSSING POINT | POINT DE CROISEMENT | KREUZUNGSPUNKT |
| 3394 | CROW BAR, PINCH BAR | GRAND LEVIER, PINCE | BRECHSTANGE |
| 3395 | CROW'S FEET, TICKS, ARROW HEADS | FLECHE DE COTE | MASSPFEIL |
| 3396 | CROWN | GALBE, CONVEXITE, VOUSSURE, CERCLE DE TETE | BALLIGKEIT, WÖLBUNG, KRANZ |
| 3397 | CROWN GLASS | CROWN-GLASS | KRONGLAS, CROWNGLAS |
| 3398 | CROWN OF PULLEY | BOMBEMENT DE LA JANTE D'UNE POULIE | WÖLBUNG EINER RIEMENSCHEIBE, SCHEIBENWÖLBUNG |
| 3399 | CROWN WHEEL | COURONNE DENTEE, ROUE DE CHAMP | KRONRAD |
| 3400 | CROWN-FACED PULLEY, PULLEY WITH CROWN FACE CONVEX RIM | POULIE BOMBEE | RIEMENSCHEIBE (BALLIGE), RIEMENSCHEIBE (GEWÖLBTE) |
| 3401 | CRUCIBLE | CREUSET (DE HAUT FOURNEAU) | TIEGEL, HERD, SCHMEIZTIEGEL |
| 3402 | CRUCIBLE FURNACE | FOURNEAU A CALEBASSE, FOURNEAU A CREUSET | TIEGELOFEN |
| 3403 | CRUCIBLE LIFTER | BRANCARD DE CREUSET | TRAGSCHERE, TIEGELSCHERE |
| 3404 | CRUCIBLE PROCESS | PROCEDE AU CREUSET | TIEGELSCHMELZVERFAHREN |
| 3405 | CRUCIBLE TONGS | PINCE A CREUSET | SCHMELZTIEGELZANGE, TIEGELZANGE |
| 3406 | CRUDE | BRUT | ROHERDÖL |
| 3407 | CRUDE (OIL) TANK | RESERVOIR A PETROLE BRUT | ROHÖLTANK |
| 3408 | CRUDE BENZINE | ESSENCE MINERALE BRUTE | ROHBENZIN |
| 3409 | CRUDE LEAD | PLOMB D'OEUVRE | WERKBLEL |
| 3410 | CRUDE METAL | METAL BRUT | TIEGELGUSSSSTAHL |
| 3411 | CRUDE OIL | PETROLE BRUT | ROHERDÖL |
| 3412 | CRUDE PETROLEUM, CRUDE OIL | PETROLE BRUT, HUILE BRUTE DE PETROLE | ROHPETROLEUM, ROHÖL |
| 3413 | CRUDE RUBBER | CAOUTCHOUC BRUT, VIERGE | ROHGUMMI |
| 3414 | CRUDE STEEL | ACIER BRUT | ROHSTAHL |
| 3415 | CRUDE TURPENTINE | TEREBENTHINE | TERPENTIN |
| 3416 | CRUISING RANGE | AUTONOMIE | FAHRBEREICH |
| 3417 | CRUISING SPEED | VITESSE DE CROISIERE | REISEGESCHWINDIGKEIT |
| 3418 | CRUMBLING, DESINTEGRATION | EFFRITEMENT, DESINTEGRATION | ZERSTÄUBUNG, ZERFALL |
| 3419 | CRUSHER | MACHINE A BROYER, BROYEUR, MACHINE A CONCASSER, CONCASSEUR, MACHINE A ECRASER | ZERKLEINERUNGSMASCHINE, BRECHMASCHINE |
| 3420 | CRUSHING | ECRASEMENT | STAUCHUNG |
| 3421 | CRUST | CROUTE | SALZKRUSTE |

**CRY** 88

| | | | |
|---|---|---|---|
| 3422 | **CRYOHYDRATE** | CRYOHYDRATE | KRYOHYDRAT |
| 3423 | **CRYOLITHE** | CRYOLITHE | EISTEIN, GRÖNTARNSPAT, KRYOLITH |
| 3424 | **CRYSTAL** | CRISTAL (MIN.) | KRISTALL |
| 3425 | **CRYSTAL ANALYSIS** | ANALYSE (DETERMINATION) DE STRUCTURE CRISTALLINE | KRISTALLSTRUKTUR-ANALYSE |
| 3426 | **CRYSTAL ELONGATION** | ALLONGEMENT DES CRISTAUX | KRISTALLDEHNUNG |
| 3427 | **CRYSTAL FACE** | PLAN DE CRISTAL, FACE CRISTALLINE | KRISTALLFLÄCHE |
| 3428 | **CRYSTAL GLASS** | CRISTAL (VERRE) | KRISTALLGLAS |
| 3429 | **CRYSTAL SPOTS** | TACHE PAR CRISTAUX DE SULFURE DE CUIVRE | METALLSULFITFLECK |
| 3430 | **CRYSTAL STRUCTURE** | STRUCTURE CRISTALLINE | KRISTALLSTRUKTUR |
| 3431 | **CRYSTAL SYSTEM** | SYSTEME DES CRISTAUX | KRISTALLSYSTEM, SYNGONIE |
| 3432 | **CRYSTAL UNIT** | CRISTAL OSCILLATEUR | SCHWINGQUARZ |
| 3433 | **CRYSTALLINE** | CRISTALLIN | KRISTALLINISCH |
| 3434 | **CRYSTALLINE STRUCTURE, CRYSTALLINE TEXTURE** | TEXTURE CRISTALLINE | GEFÜGE (KRISTALLINISCHES) |
| 3435 | **CRYSTALLINE SULPHUR** | SOUFRE CRISTALLISE | SCHWEFEL (KRISTALLINISCHER) |
| 3436 | **CRYSTALLISABILITY** | CRISTALLISABILITE | KRISTALLISIERBARKEIT |
| 3437 | **CRYSTALLISABLE** | CRISTALLISABLE | KRISTALLISIERBAR |
| 3438 | **CRYSTALLISATION** | CRISTALLISATION | KRISTALLISATION, KRISTALLBILDUNG |
| 3439 | **CRYSTALLISE (TO)** | CRISTALLISER | KRISTALLISIEREN |
| 3440 | **CRYSTALLITE** | CRISTALLITE | KRISTALLIT |
| 3441 | **CRYSTALLOGRAM** | CRISTALLOGRAMME, DIAGRAMME DE DIFFRACTION A RAYONS X | KRISTALLOGRAMM, RÖNTGENBEUGUNGSBILD |
| 3442 | **CRYSTALLOGRAPHY** | CRISTALLOGRAPHIE | KRISTALLOGRAFIE |
| 3443 | **CRYSTALLOID** | CRISTALLOIDE | KRISTALLOID |
| 3444 | **CUBATURE** | CUBAGE (EVALUATION EN UNITES CUBES) | INHALTSBERECHNUNG EINES KÖRPERS, RAUMINHALTSBERECHNUNG, KÖRPERINHALTSBERECHNUNG, KUBATUR |
| 3445 | **CUBE** | CUBE (GEOM.) | WÜRFEL, KUBUS, DRITTE POTENZ |
| 3446 | **CUBE (TO), FIND THE CUBIC CONTENTS (TO)** | CUBER | KÖRPERINHALT (DEN) BERECHNEN, KUBIEREN |
| 3447 | **CUBE ROOT** | RACINE CUBIQUE | KUBIKWURZEL, DRITTE WURZEL |
| 3448 | **CUBIC CAPACITY** | CYLINDREE | ZYLINDERINHALT |
| 3449 | **CUBIC CENTIMETRE** | CENTIMETRE CUBE | KUBIKZENTIMETER |
| 3450 | **CUBIC CRYSTALS** | CRISTAL CUBIQUE | KRISTALL (ISOMETRISCHER), KRISTALL (KUBISCHER), KRISTALL (REGULÄRER) |
| 3451 | **CUBIC DECIMETRE** | DECIMETRE CUBE | KUBIKDEZIMETER |
| 3452 | **CUBIC EQUATION** | EQUATION CUBIQUE, EQUATION DU TROISIEME DEGRE | GLEICHUNG DRITTEN GRADES, GLEICHUNG (KUBISCHE) |
| 3453 | **CUBIC FOOT** | PIED CUBE ANGLAIS | KUBIKFUSS (ENGLISCHER) |
| 3454 | **CUBIC INCH** | POUCE CUBE ANGLAIS | KUBIKZOLL (ENGLISCHER) |
| 3455 | **CUBIC METRE** | METRE CUBE | KUBIKMETER |
| 3456 | **CUBIC MILLIMETRE** | MILLIMETRE CUBE | KUBIKMILLIMETER |
| 3457 | **CULTIVATORS, RIGID TINE, SPRING-LOADED TINE, SPRING TINE** | CULTIVATEURS, VIBROCULTEURS | BODENBEARBEITUNGSGERÄTE, WÜHLGRUBBER, FEDERZINKENEGGEN |
| 3458 | **CUP LEATHER** | CUIR EMBOUTI | LEDERSTULP, LEDERMANSCHETTE |
| 3459 | **CUP LEATHER PACKING** | GARNITURE EN CUIR EMBOUTI | LEDERSTULPDICHTUNG, MANSCHETTENDICHTUNG |
| 3460 | **CUP SHAKE IN TIMBER** | ROULURE DU BOIS | RINGKLUFT, KERNSCHÄLE DES HOLZES |

| | | | |
|---|---|---|---|
| 3461 | **CUP SPRING** | RONDELLE BELLEVILLE | BELLEVILLE FEDER |
| 3462 | **CUP TEST MACHINE** | APPAREIL D'ESSAI DE DUCTILITE | DUKTILITÄTSPRÜFMASCHINE |
| 3463 | **CUPELLATION** | COUPELLATION | KUPELLATION |
| 3464 | **CUPOLA** | CUBILOT | KUPOL.. |
| 3465 | **CUPOLA CONTROL EQUIPEMENT** | REGULATEUR DE DEBIT DE VENT | LUFTSTROMREGLER |
| 3466 | **CUPOLA FURNACE** | CUBILOT, FOURNEAU A LA WILKINSON | KUPPELOFEN, KUPOLOFEN |
| 3467 | **CUPOLA MALLEABLE IRON** | FONTE MALLEABLE DE CUBILOT | KUPOLOFENTEMPERGUSS |
| 3468 | **CUPOLA METAL** | METAL DE CUBILOT | KUPOLOFENMETALL |
| 3469 | **CUPPING** | EMBOUTISSAGE EN COUPE DE FILS, EMBOUTISSAGE PROFOND | TIEFZIEHEN |
| 3470 | **CUPRIC CARBONATE** | CARBONATE DE CUIVRE | KUPFER (KOHLENSAURES), KUPFERKARBONAT |
| 3471 | **CUPRIC HYDROXYDE** | OXYDE CUIVRIQUE HYDRATE | KUPFERHYDROXYD, KUPRIHYDROXYD, KUPFEROXYDHYDRAT |
| 3472 | **CUPRIC NITRATE** | NITRATE DE CUIVRE | KUPFER (SALPETERSAURES), KUPFERNITRAT, KUPRINITRAT |
| 3473 | **CUPRIC NITRITE** | NITRITE DE CUIVRE | KUPFER (SALPETRIGSAURES), KUPFERNITRIT, KUPRONITRAT |
| 3474 | **CUPRIC OXIDE** | OXYDE CUIVRIQUE | KUPFEROXYD |
| 3475 | **CUPRIC SULPHATE** | SULFATE DE CUIVRE | KUPFER (SCHWEFELSAURES), KUPFERSULFAT |
| 3476 | **CUPRITE, RED OXIDE OF COPPER** | CUIVRE OXYDULE | ROTKUPFERERZ |
| 3477 | **CUPRO-NICKEL** | CUPRO-NICKEL | KUPFERNICKEL |
| 3478 | **CUPROUS CHLORIDE** | CHLORURE CUIVREUX | KUPFERCHLORÜR, KUPROCHLORID |
| 3479 | **CUPROUS OXIDE** | OXYDE CUIVREUX | KUPFEROXYDUL |
| 3480 | **CURB WEIGHT** | POIDS EN ORDRE DE MARCHE | LEISTUNGSGEWICHT (FAHRFERTIG) |
| 3481 | **CURCUMIN** | CURCUMINE | KURKUMAGELB, KURKUMIN |
| 3482 | **CURD SOAP** | SAVON BLANC ORDINAIRE | KERNSEIFE |
| 3483 | **CURE** | PRISE, DURCISSEMENT | AUSHÄRTEN |
| 3484 | **CURING** | PRISE (DU CIMENT), VULCANISATION | ZEMENTAUSHÄRTUNG, VULKANISIEREN |
| 3485 | **CURLING DIE** | OUTIL DE ROULAGE | ROLLWERKZEUG |
| 3486 | **CURRENT** | COURANT | STROM |
| 3487 | **CURRENT COORDINATES** | COORDONNEES COURANTES | KOORDINATEN (LAUFENDE) |
| 3488 | **CURRENT DENSITY** | DENSITE DU COURANT | STROMDICHTE |
| 3489 | **CURRENT EFFICIENCY** | RENDEMENT EN COURANT | STROMAUSBEUTE |
| 3490 | **CURRENT METER** | INSTRUMENT POUR LA DETERMINATION DE LA VITESSE D'UN COURANT | STRÖMUNGSMESSER |
| 3491 | **CURRENT REGULATOR** | REGULATEUR DE COURANT, REGULATEUR D'INTENSITE | STROMREGLER |
| 3492 | **CURTAINING** | DRAPERIES/COULURES EN FESTONS | VORHÄNGEBILDUNG |
| 3493 | **CURTATE CYCLOID** | CYCLOIDE RACCOURCIE | ZYKLOIDE (VERKÜRZTE) |
| 3494 | **CURVATURE** | COURBURE, CINTRE | KRÜMMUNG |
| 3495 | **CURVE OF DIAGRAM, GRAPH** | COURBE D'UN DIAGRAMME | SCHAULINIE, DIAGRAMMLINIE, DIAGRAMMKURVE |
| 3496 | **CURVE, SWEEP** | COURBE | KURVE, KRUMME LINIE |
| 3497 | **CURVED ARM OF PULLEY** | BRAS PARABOLIQUE D'UNE POULIE | SCHEIBENARM (GESCHWUNGENER) |
| 3498 | **CURVED SURFACE, CURVED FACE** | SURFACE COURBE | FLÄCHE (GEKRÜMMTE), FLÄCHE (KRUMME) |
| 3499 | **CURVILINEAR** | CURVILIGNE | KRUMMLINIG |
| 3500 | **CURVILINEAR MOTION** | MOUVEMENT CURVILIGNE | BEWEGUNG (KRUMMLINIGE) |
| 3501 | **CURVOMETER** | CURVIMETRE | MESSRAD, KURVIMETER |

# CUT

90

| | | | |
|---|---|---|---|
| 3502 | **CUSP OF A CURVE** | POINT DE REBROUSSEMENT | SPITZE EINER KURVE |
| 3503 | **CUT** | COUPE | SCHNITT |
| 3504 | **CUT (TO)** | COUPER (GEOM.), TAILLER | DURCHSCHNEIDEN (GEOM.), SCHNEIDEN |
| 3505 | **CUT BY THE AUTOGENOUS PROCESS (TO)** | DECOUPER A L'AUTOGENE, DECOUPER AU CHALUMEAU | AUTOGENSCHNEIDEN |
| 3506 | **CUT EDGE** | RIVE CISAILLEE | KANTE (GESCHNITTENE) |
| 3507 | **CUT FILES (TO)** | TAILLER LES LIMES | FEILEN HAUEN |
| 3508 | **CUT GEAR WHEEL** | ROUE A DENTS TAILLEES, ENGRENAGE TAILLE | ZAHNRAD (BEARBEITETES), ZAHNRAD (GESCHNITTENES) |
| 3509 | **CUT INTO THE REQUISITE SIZE (TO)** | DEBITER AUX DIMENSIONS VOULUES | ABLÄNGEN |
| 3510 | **CUT OFF (TO)** | DECOLLETER, TRONCONNER, DECOUPER | ABSTECHEN |
| 3511 | **CUT OFF THE RIVET HEADS (TO)** | DERIVER, CHASSER LES RIVETS | ENTNIETEN, ABNIETEN, NIETE (DIE) HERAUSSCHLAGEN |
| 3512 | **CUT OUTSIDE SCREW THREADS (TO)** | FILETER | AUSSENGEWINDESCHNEIDEN |
| 3513 | **CUT PLATES (TO)** | DECOUPER DES TOLES | SCHNEIDEN (BLECHE) |
| 3514 | **CUT TOOTH** | DENT TAILLEE | ZAHN (BEARBEITETER) |
| 3515 | **CUT WITH THE ANVIL CHISEL (TO)** | COUPER AU TRANCHET, TRANCHER | ABSCHROTEN |
| 3516 | **CUT-OUT RELAY** | DISJONCTEUR | SCHALTSCHÜTZ |
| 3517 | **CUT, KERF OF A SAW, SAW KERF, SAW CUT** | TRAIT DE SCIE | SÄGESCHNITT, SÄGEEINSCHNITT, SÄGESCHNITTFUGE, SCHNITTFUGE EINER SÄGE |
| 3518 | **CUT, TEETH OF A FILE** | TAILLE, DENTS, DENTURE D'UNE LIME | FEILENHIEB, HIEB EINER FEILE |
| 3519 | **CUTTER** | FRAISE | FRÄSER |
| 3520 | **CUTTER ARBOR** | ARBRE PORTE-FRAISE | FRÄSERSPINDEL |
| 3521 | **CUTTER COMPENSATION** | CORRECTION D'OUTIL | WERKZEUGKORREKTUR |
| 3522 | **CUTTERS, BLOWERS** | ENSILEUSES | SILIERMASCHINEN |
| 3523 | **CUTTING** | COUPE, COUPAGE, TAILLE, TAILLAGE | SCHNEIDEN |
| 3524 | **CUTTING ANGLE** | ANGLE D'ATTAQUE, ANGLE DE COUPE | SCHNEIDWINKEL |
| 3525 | **CUTTING ATTACHMENT** | DISPOSITIF DE COUPE | SCHNEIDEINSATZ |
| 3526 | **CUTTING DEPTH** | PROFONDEUR DE COUPE | SCHNITTIEFE |
| 3527 | **CUTTING DOWN** | POLISSAGE DE LA SURFACE | OBERFLÄCHENPOLIERUNG |
| 3528 | **CUTTING EDGE OF A TOOL** | TRANCHANT D'UN OUTIL, ARETE COUPANTE | SCHNEIDE, SCHNEIDKANTE EINES WERKZEUGS |
| 3529 | **CUTTING FILES** | TAILLAGE DES LIMES | FEILENHAUEN |
| 3530 | **CUTTING FLUID** | FLUIDE DE COUPE | SCHNEIDFLÜSSIGKEIT |
| 3531 | **CUTTING HEAD** | TETE DE FRAISAGE (OU DE COUPE) | FRÄSKOPF |
| 3532 | **CUTTING NIPPERS, NIPPING PLIERS** | PINCE COUPANTE, TENAILLE A MORS COUPANTS | BEISSZANGE, KNEIPZANGE, KNEIFZANGE, ZWICKZANGE, DRAHTZWICKZANGE |
| 3533 | **CUTTING OFF** | DECOLLETAGE, TRONCONNAGE, TRONCONNEMENT, DECOUPAGE | ABSTECHEN |
| 3534 | **CUTTING OIL** | HUILE DE COUPE | SCHNEIDÖL |
| 3535 | **CUTTING OUTSIDE SCREW THREADS** | FILETAGE | SCHNEIDEN EINES AUSSENGEWINDES |
| 3536 | **CUTTING STROKE** | COURSE DE TRAVAIL, COURSE UTILE (D'UNE MACHINE-OUTIL) | ARBEITSGANG, SCHNITTGANG (EINER WERKZEUGSMASCHINE) |
| 3537 | **CUTTING TIP** | BUSE DE COUPE | SCHNEIBRENNERDÜSE |
| 3538 | **CUTTING TOOL** | OUTIL TRANCHANT, OUTIL COUPANT, OUTIL A TAILLANT | SCHNEIDWERKZEUG |

| | | | |
|---|---|---|---|
| 3539 | **CUTTING TORCH** | CHALUMEAU | SCHNEIDBRENNER |
| 3540 | **CUTTING-OFF LATHE** | TOUR A DECOLLETER | ABSTECHBANK |
| 3541 | **CUTTING-OFF MACHINE** | MACHINE A TRONCONNER, TRONCONNEUSE | ABSTECHMASCHINE |
| 3542 | **CUTTING-OFF WHEEL** | DISQUE A COUPER, DISQUE DE COUPER | SCHNEIDSCHEIBE, TRENNSCHEIBE |
| 3543 | **CUTTINGS** | COPEAUX | SPÄNE |
| 3544 | **CYANATE** | CYANATE | ZYANSÄURESALZ, ZYANAT |
| 3545 | **CYANIC ACID** | ACIDE CYANIQUE | ZYANSÄURE |
| 3546 | **CYANIDATION** | EXTRACTION DE L'OR PAR CYANURATION | CYANIDLAUGEREI, CYANIDLAUGUNGSVERFAHREN |
| 3547 | **CYANIDE** | CYANURE | ZYANMETALL, ZYANID, CYANID |
| 3548 | **CYANIDE SLIMES** | PARTICULES DE METAUX NOBLES | EDELMETALLTEILCHEN |
| 3549 | **CYANIDING** | CIRCULATION AU CYANURE, ENDURCISSEMENT AU CYANURE | ZYANSALZBARHÄRTUNG |
| 3550 | **CYANIDING FURNACE** | FOUR A CYANURATION | ZYANIDVERFAHRENOFEN |
| 3551 | **CYANOGEN** | CYANOGENE | ZYAN |
| 3552 | **CYANURIC ACID** | ACIDE CYANURIQUE | ZYANURSÄURE, TRIZYANSÄURE |
| 3553 | **CYCLE** | CYCLE, CYCLE DE TRAVAIL | PERIODE, ZYCLUS |
| 3554 | **CYCLE OF OPERATIONS , CYCLIC PROCESS** | CYCLE | KREISPROZESS |
| 3555 | **CYCLIC CURVE** | CYCLIQUE | KURVE (ZYKLISCHE) |
| 3556 | **CYCLIC PERMUTATION** | PERMUTATION CYCLIQUE | VERTAUSCHUNG (ZYKLISCHE) |
| 3557 | **CYCLOID** | CYCLOIDE | RADLINIE, ZYKLOIDE |
| 3558 | **CYCLOIDAL GEAT TEETH** | ENGRENAGE CYCLOIDAL | ZYKLOIDENVERZAHNUNG |
| 3559 | **CYCLOMETER DIAL COUNTER** | COMPTEUR A CHIFFRES, COMPTEURS A FENETRES | ZÄHLWERK MIT SPRINGENDEN ZAHLEN, SPRINGENDES ZÄHLWERK |
| 3560 | **CYCLONE** | CYCLONE PULVERISATEUR | ZYKLON |
| 3561 | **CYLINDER** | CYLINDRE (GEOM.) | ZYLINDER, WALZE (GEOM.) |
| 3562 | **CYLINDER BARREL** | FUT DE CYLINDRE | ZYLINDERLAUFBÜCHSE |
| 3563 | **CYLINDER BIT, HALF ROUND BIT** | FORET OU MECHE A CANON | KANONENBOHRER |
| 3564 | **CYLINDER BLOCK** | BLOC-CYLINDRES | ZYLINDERBLOCK |
| 3565 | **CYLINDER BORE** | ALESAGE DU CYLINDRE | ZYLINDERBOHRUNG |
| 3566 | **CYLINDER CAPACITY** | CYLINDREE | ZYLINDERINHALT |
| 3567 | **CYLINDER COVER** | COUVRE CULBUTEURS, COUVERCLE DU CYLINDRE | ZYLINDERKKOPFDECKEL, ZYLINDERDECKEL |
| 3568 | **CYLINDER GRINDER** | MACHINE A RECTIFIER L'INTERIEUR DES CYLINDRES | ZYLINDERSCHLEIFMASCHINE |
| 3569 | **CYLINDER HEAD** | TETE DU CYLINDRE, CULASSE | ZYLINDERKOPF |
| 3570 | **CYLINDER HEAD GASKET** | JOINT DE CULASSE | ZYLINDERKOPFDICHTUNG |
| 3571 | **CYLINDER LINER** | GARNITURE INTERIEURE DU CYLINDRE, CHEMISE DU CYLINDRE | EINSATZZYLINDER, ZYLINDERLAUFBÜCHSE, ZYLINDEREINSATZ, ZYLINDERFUTTER |
| 3572 | **CYLINDER OIL** | HUILE POUR CYLINDRES | ZYLINDERÖL |
| 3573 | **CYLINDER RECORDER** | ENREGISTREUR A TAMBOUR | TROMMELSCHREIBER |
| 3574 | **CYLINDER SCREW HEAD, CHEESE SCREW HEAD** | TETE CYLINDRIQUE D'UNE VIS | ZYLINDRISCHER SCHRAUBENKOPF |
| 3575 | **CYLINDER VALVE FOR COMPRESSED GAS** | ROBINET DE BOUTEILLE (DE GAZ COMPRIME) | ABSPERRVENTIL FÜR GASFLASCHEN |
| 3576 | **CYLINDRAL MOUTHPIECE** | AJUTAGE CYLINDRIQUE | ZYLINDRISCHER AUSFLUSSSTUTZEN |
| 3577 | **CYLINDRICAL** | CYLINDRIQUE | ZYLINDRISCH |
| 3578 | **CYLINDRICAL BOILER** | CHAUDIERE CYLINDRIQUE | WALZENKESSEL |
| 3579 | **CYLINDRICAL CAM, DRUM CAM** | TAMBOUR, CYLINDRE A RAINURE | SCHLITZTROMMEL, NUTENTROMMEL |
| 3580 | **CYLINDRICAL COORDINATES** | COORDONNEES CYLINDRIQUES | ZYLINDERKOORDINATEN |

**CYL** 92

| | | | |
|---|---|---|---|
| 3581 | CYLINDRICAL GAUGE, PLUG AND COLLAR GAUGE, PLUG AND RING GAUGE | TAMPON ET BAGUE, TAMPON ET LUNETTE DE CALIBRE, CALIBRE MALE ET FEMELLE | LEHRBOLZEN, LEHRDORN UND LOCHLEHRE, KALIBER UND KALIBERRING |
| 3582 | CYLINDRICAL GRADUATED MEASURE | CYLINDRE GRADUE | MESSZYLINDER |
| 3583 | CYLINDRICAL GRINDER | MACHINE A RECTIFIER LES PIECES CYLINDRIQUES | RUNDSCHLEIFMASCHINE |
| 3584 | CYLINDRICAL GUIDE | GLISSIERE CYLINDRIQUE | RUNDFÜHRUNG |
| 3585 | CYLINDRICAL HELICAL SPRING | RESSORT A BOUDIN CYLINDRIQUE | SCHRAUBENFEDER (ZYLINDRISCHE) |
| 3586 | CYLINDRICAL PIPE | TUYAU CYLINDRIQUE | ROHR (ZYLINDRISCHES) |
| 3587 | CYLINDRICAL PLUG GAUGES | CALIBRES MALES CYLINDRIQUES | MESSDORN (ZYLINDRISCHER) |
| 3588 | CYLINDRICAL RING | ANNEAU CYLINDRIQUE, TORE CIRCULAIRE | RING (ZYLINDRISCHER) |
| 3589 | CYLINDRICAL ROLLER | GALET CYLINDRIQUE | ZYLINDERROLLE |
| 3590 | CYLINDRICAL SURFACE | SURFACE LATERALE D'UN CYLINDRE | MANTELFLÄCHE EINES ZYLINDERS |
| 3591 | CYLINDRICAL WHEEL | ROUE CYLINDRIQUE, ROUE DROITE | RAD (ZYLINDRISCHES) |
| 3592 | D-SLIDE VALVE | TIROIR A COQUILLE | MUSCHELSCHIEBER, D-SCHIEBER, DREIWEGSCHIEBER |
| 3593 | D'COMER BAR | BARRE DE DEVERSOIR | FALLROHR |
| 3594 | DAILY WAGES | SALAIRE, PRIX A LA JOURNEE | TAGELOHN |
| 3595 | DAIRY MACHINERY, APPLIANCES, PLANT AND EQUIPMENT | MACHINES DE LAITERIE | MOLKEREIMASCHINEN UND ZUSATZGERÄTE |
| 3596 | DAM PLATE | PLAQUE DE DAME | WALLPLATTE, SCHLACKENBLECH |
| 3597 | DAM, BARRAGE | BARRAGE D'UNE VALLEE | TALSPERRE |
| 3598 | DAMMAR | GOMME DAMMAR, DAMMAR | DAMMARHARZ |
| 3599 | DAMP AIR, MOIST AIR | AIR HUMIDE | FEUCHTE LUFT |
| 3600 | DAMPED OSCILLATION | VIBRATION AMORTIE | SCHWINGUNG (GEDÄMPFTE) |
| 3601 | DAMPENER | AMORTISSEUR | DÄMPFER |
| 3602 | DAMPER | DAMPER, AMORTISSEUR (ELECTR.) | DÄMPFER, SCHWINGUNGSDÄMPFER |
| 3603 | DAMPER, REGISTER | REGISTRE DE TIRAGE, REGISTRE DE FUMEE | LUFTSCHIEBER, RAUCHSCHIEBER, ZUGREGLER, ESSENKLAPPE, SCHORNSTEINKLAPPE |
| 3604 | DAMPING | ATTENUATION, AMORTISSEMENT | DÄMPFUNG |
| 3605 | DAMPING CAPACITY | CAPACITE D'AMORTISSEMENT | DÄMPFUNGSVERMÖGEN, DÄMPFUNGSFÄHIGKEIT |
| 3606 | DAMPING OF OSCILLATIONS | AMORTISSEMENT DE VIBRATIONS | DÄMPFUNG, BERUHIGUNG VON SCHWINGUNGEN |
| 3607 | DANDY (US) | FOUR DE PREMIER ALLIAGE | FRISCHEREIÖFEN |
| 3608 | DANGER OF FIRE | DANGER, RISQUE, CHANCES D'INCENDIE | FEUERSGEFAHR |
| 3609 | DANGEROUS SECTION | SECTION DANGEREUSE | QUERSCHNITT (GEFÄHRLICHER) |
| 3610 | DASH BOARD | TABLEAU DE BORD | INSTRUMENTENBRETT |
| 3611 | DASHPOT | CATARACTE, DASHPOT | PUFFERVORRICHTUNG, ZEITREGLER, KATARAKT |
| 3612 | DATA | DONNEES | DATEN |
| 3613 | DATA BOOK | RECUEIL DE DONNEES | DATENREGISTER |
| 3614 | DATA REPORTS | DOSSIER TECHNIQUE | BERICHT (TECHNISCHER) |
| 3615 | DATA SHEETS | FICHES TECHNIQUES | KENNBLATT (TECHNISCHES) |
| 3616 | DATE OF APPLICATION FOR A PATENT | JOUR, DATE DU DEPOT DE LA DEMANDE DE BREVET | TAG DER ANMELDUNG, ANMELDUNGSDATUM EINER ERFINDUNG |
| 3617 | DATE OF SEALING THE PATENT | JOUR DE LA SIGNATURE DU BREVET, DATE DE L'ACCORD DU BREVET | TAG DER ERTEILUNG EINES PATENTES |
| 3618 | DAVIT | POTENCE | SCHWENKKRAN |
| 3619 | DAVIT ARM | BRAS DE POTENCE | SCHWENKKRANARM |
| 3620 | DAY SHIFT | TRAVAIL DE JOUR | TAGSCHICHT |

**93** **DEC**

| | | | |
|---|---|---|---|
| 3621 | DAY WORK | TRAVAIL A LA JOURNEE | LOHNARBEIT |
| 3622 | DAYLIGHT | LUMIERE DU JOUR | TAGESLICHT |
| 3623 | DE-AERATION OF WATER | DEGAZAGE DE L'EAU | ENTLÜFTUNG DES WASSERS |
| 3624 | DEAD AXLE | ESSIEU FIXE | ACHSE (FESTSTEHENDE) |
| 3625 | DEAD CENTER | ARETE TERMINALE | TOTPUNKT |
| 3626 | DEAD CENTRE POINT | POINT MORT | TOTER PUNKT, TOTPUNKT |
| 3627 | DEAD CONDUCTOR | CONDUCTEUR SANS COURANT, CONDUCTEUR SANS TENSION | LEITER (STROMLOSER), LEITER (SPANNUNGSLOSER) |
| 3628 | DEAD DIP | DECAPAGE MAT | MATTBEIZEN, MATTBRENNEN |
| 3629 | DEAD HEAD, HEAD METAL | MASSELOTTE | KOPF (VERLORENER) |
| 3630 | DEAD HOLE | TROU EN CUL DE SAC, TROU BORGNE | LOCH (BLINDES), LOCH (NICHT DURCHGEHENDES), BLINDLOCH |
| 3631 | DEAD LOAD | CHARGE MORTE | LAST (TOTE) |
| 3632 | DEAD LOAD (SAFETY) VALVE, COWBURN VALVE | SOUPAPE DE SURETE A CHARGE DIRECTE | VENTIL MIT UNMITTELBARER GEWICHTSBELASTUNG |
| 3633 | DEAD LOAD, PERMANENT CONSTANT LOAD, STEADY QUIESCENT LOAD | CHARGE PERMANENTE | BELASTUNG (RUHENDE), BELASTUNG (STÄNDIGE), BELASTUNG (STETIGE), DAUERBELASTUNG, LAST (TOTE) |
| 3634 | DEAD MELTING | CHAUFFAGE AU-DESSUS DU POINT DE FUSION | ÜBERSCHMELZEN |
| 3635 | DEAD POINT | POINT MORT | TOTPUNKT |
| 3636 | DEAD ROASTING | GRILLAGE TOTAL | TOTALRÖSTUNG |
| 3637 | DEAD WEIGHT | POIDS PROPRE, POIDS MORT | GEWICHT (TOTES), EIGENGEWICHT, EIGENLAST |
| 3638 | DEAD WEIGHT BRAKE | FREIN A LEVIER ET CONTREPOIDS | LÜFTUNGSBREMSE, LÖSUNGSBREMSE, GEWICHTSHEBELBREMSE |
| 3639 | DEAD-BURNED MAGNESITE | MAGNESITE MORTE | MAGNESIT (TOTGEBRANNTER) |
| 3640 | DEADEN A SHOCK (TO) | AMORTIR UN CHOC | DÄMPFEN (EINEN STOSS) |
| 3641 | DEAFENING | MATIERE IMPERMEABLE AU SON, MATIERE ETOUFFANT LE BRUIT | SCHALLDÄMPFENDES MITTEL, SCHALLDICHTER STOFF |
| 3642 | DEBURRING | EBAVURAGE, EBARBAGE | ABGRATEN |
| 3643 | DEBYE-SCHERRER METHOD | METHODE DE DEBYE-SCHERRER | DEBYE-SCHERRER METHODE, PULVERMETHODE |
| 3644 | DECAGON | DECAGONE | ZEHNECK |
| 3645 | DECAGRAMME | DECAGRAMME | DEKAGRAMM |
| 3646 | DECALESCENCE | DECALESCENCE | DEKALESZENZ |
| 3647 | DECALITRE | DECALITRE | DEKALITER |
| 3648 | DECAMETRE | DECAMETRE | DEKAMETER |
| 3649 | DECANT (TO), POUR OFF (TO) | DECANTER | ABGIESSEN, ABKLÄREN, DEKANTIEREN |
| 3650 | DECANTING, POURING OFF | DECANTATION | ABKLÄREN, ABGIESSEN, DEKANTIEREN |
| 3651 | DECARBONISATION | DECARBONISATION | ENTKOHLEN, ENTKOHLUNG |
| 3652 | DECARBONISE (TO) | DECARBONISER | ENTKOHLEN |
| 3653 | DECARBURISATION OF IRON | DECARBURATION DU FER | ENTKOHLEN DES EISENS |
| 3654 | DECARBURISE THE IRON (TO) | DECARBURER LE FER | ENTKOHLEN (EISEN) |
| 3655 | DECARBURIZATION | DECARBURATION | ENTKOHLUNG |
| 3656 | DECAY | DECROISSANCE | ABNAHME |
| 3657 | DECIGRAMME | DECIGRAMME | DEZIGRAMM |
| 3658 | DECILITRE | DECILITRE | DEZILITER |
| 3659 | DECIMAL | DECIMALE | DEZIMALE, DEZIMALSTELLE |
| 3660 | DECIMAL BALANCE, DECIMAL WEIGHING MACHINE | BALANCE, BASCULE, BASCULE AU DIXIEME (AU 10) | DEZIMALWAAGE |
| 3661 | DECIMAL CODE | CODE DECIMAL | DEZIMALKODE |

# DEC

| 3662 | DECIMAL FRACTION | FRACTION DECIMALE | DEZIMALBRUCH |
|---|---|---|---|
| 3663 | DECIMAL INTERNATIONAL CANDIE, BOUGIE DECIMALE | BOUGIE DECIMALE | DEZIMALKERZE, KERZE (INTERNATIONALE), STANDARDKERZE, NORMKERZE |
| 3664 | DECIMAL NUMBER | NOMBRE DECIMAL | DEZIMALZAHL |
| 3665 | DECIMAL SYSTEM | SYSTEME DECIMAL | DEZIMALSYSTEM |
| 3666 | DECIMETRE | DECIMETRE | DEZIMETER |
| 3667 | DECK | TOIT, VOILE, PONT | DECKE, DACH |
| 3668 | DECLINATION, DEVIATION OF THE MAGNETIC NEEDLE | DECLINAISON MAGNETIQUE | ABWEICHUNG DER MAGNETNADEL, DEKLINATION |
| 3669 | DECOCTION | DECOCTION | ABKOCHUNG, ABSUD |
| 3670 | DECODER | DECODEUR | DEKODIERER |
| 3671 | DECOMPOSABLE | DECOMPOSABLE | ZERLEGBAR, ZERSETZBAR |
| 3672 | DECOMPOSE (TO) | DECOMPOSER | ZERLEGEN (CHEM.) |
| 3673 | DECOMPOSE (TO) | DECOMPOSER (SE) | ZERSETZEN (SICH) |
| 3674 | DECOMPOSITION | DECOMPOSITION (CHIM.) | ZERSETZUNG, ZERLEGUNG (CHEM.) |
| 3675 | DECOMPOSITION POTENTIAL | TENSION DE DECOMPOSITION | ZERSETZUNGSPANNUNG |
| 3676 | DECOMPOSITION, SPLITTING UP OF LIGHT | DECOMPOSITION DE LA LUMIERE | ZERLEGUNG DES LICHTS |
| 3677 | DECREASE OF SPEED | DIMINUTION, CHUTE DE VITESSE | GESCHWINDIGKEITSABNAHME |
| 3678 | DECREASE THE VELOCITY (TO) | REDUIRE LA VITESSE | GESCHWINDIGKEIT VERRINGERN, GESCHWINDIGKEITVERMINDERN |
| 3679 | DECREASING SPEED | VITESSE DECROISSANTE | GESCHWINDIGKEIT (ABNEHMENDE) |
| 3680 | DECTECTIVE MATERIAL | VICE DE MATIERE | MATERIALFEHLER |
| 3681 | DEDENDUM | HAUTEUR DU FLANC, HAUTEUR DU PIED DE DENT, CREUX SOUS LE PRIMITIF | ZAHNFUSSLÄNGE, ZAHNFUSSHÖHE |
| 3682 | DEDUSTING | DEPOUSSIERAGE | ENTSTAUBEN |
| 3683 | DEEP DRAWING | EMBOUTISSAGE PROFOND | TIEFZIEHEN |
| 3684 | DEEP ETCH TEST | ESSAI DE MACRO-ATTAQUE | TIEFBEIZPROBE |
| 3685 | DEEP ETCHING | ATTAQUE PROFONDE | TIEFBEIZEN |
| 3686 | DEEP HOLE DRILL | FORET POUR PERCAGE PROFOND | TIEFLOCHBOHRER |
| 3687 | DEEP HOLE DRILLING AND BORING MACHINE | MACHINE A FORER ET ALESER LES TROUS PROFONDS | TIEFLOCH-BOHRMASCHINE |
| 3688 | DEEP STAMPING STRIPS | FEUILLARDS D'ACIER POUR EMBOUTISSAGE PROFOND | TIEFZIEHBANDSTAHL |
| 3689 | DEEP WELL PUMP | POMPE POUR PUITS PROFONDS | TIEFBRUNNENPUMPE |
| 3690 | DEEP-DRAWING BRASS | LAITON A QUALITE D'EMBOUTISSAGE | TIEFZIEHQUALITÄTSMESSING |
| 3691 | DEFECT | DEFAUT | FEHLER |
| 3692 | DEFECT FLAW IN THE MATERIAL | VICE, DEFAUT DE MATIERE | MATERIALFEHLER, FEHLER, FEHLERHAFTE STELLE IM MATERIAL |
| 3693 | DEFECT IN MANUFACTURE | DEFAUT DE FABRICATION, VICE DE CONSTRUCTION, FAUTE D'EXECUTION | HERSTELLUNGSFEHLER, FABRIKATIONSFEHLER |
| 3694 | DEFECTIVE DESIGN | VICE DE CONCEPTION | ENTWURFSMANGEL |
| 3695 | DEFECTIVE OPERATION | VICE DE FONCTIONNEMENT | FEHLERHAFTER BETRIEB |
| 3696 | DEFECTIVE, FAULTY, CONDEMNED WORK | REBUTS DE FABRICATION, PIECES DEFECTUEUSES | AUSSCHUSS, AUSSCHUSSWARE |
| 3697 | DEFINITE INTEGRAL | INTEGRALE DEFINIE | INTEGRAL (BESTIMMTES) |
| 3698 | DEFLECTION | DEFORMATION (FLECHE), FLEXION, FLECHE | VERFORMUNG, DURCHBIEGUNG, BIBGUNG |
| 3699 | DEFLECTION OF A POINTER | DEVIATION, DEFLECTION, ELONGATION DE L'AIGUILLE | ZEIGERAUSSCHLAG |

| | | | |
|---|---|---|---|
| 3700 | **DEFLECTION, BENDING, FLEXURE** | FLEXION TRANSVERSALE, FLECHISSEMENT | BIEGUNG, DURCHBIEGUNG |
| 3701 | **DEFLECTION, SET** | FLECHE (MEC.) | DURCHBIEGUNG (MASS) |
| 3702 | **DEFLECTOR** | DEFLECTEUR | ABLEITBLECH |
| 3703 | **DEFLOCCULATED GRAPHITE** | GRAPHITE DEFLOCULE | GRAPHIT (AUSGEFLOCKTER), FLOCKENGRAPHIT |
| 3704 | **DEFOGGING** | DESEMBUAGE | ENTNEBELUNG |
| 3705 | **DEFORMABILITY** | DEFORMABILITE, CAPACITE DE DEFORMATION, PLASTICITE | VERFORMBARKEIT, FORMÄNDERUNGSVERMÖGEN |
| 3706 | **DEFORMATION BAND** | BANDE DE DEFORMATION | VERFORMUNGSBAND, DEFORMATIONSBAND |
| 3707 | **DEFORMATION, CHANGE OF FORM SHAPE** | DEFORMATION, CHANGEMENT DE FORME | FORMÄNDERUNG |
| 3708 | **DEFROSTER** | DEGIVREUR | ENTFROSTER |
| 3709 | **DEGASIFYING ALLOY** | ALLIAGE DEGAZEUR | ENTGASUNGSLEGIERUNG |
| 3710 | **DEGASSING** | DEGAZAGE | ENTGASUNG |
| 3711 | **DEGRAS** | DEGRAS, GRAISSE DES TANNEURS | DEGRAS |
| 3712 | **DEGREASING** | DEGRAISSAGE | ENTFETTUNG |
| 3713 | **DEGREASING COMPOUND** | COMPOSITION DE DEGRAISSAGE | ENTFETTUNGSMITTEL |
| 3714 | **DEGREE** | DEGRE | GRAD |
| 3715 | **DEGREE BAUME** | DEGRE BAUME | GRAD BAUME |
| 3716 | **DEGREE CENTIGRADE** | DEGRE CENTIGRADE | GRAD CELSIUS, CELSIUSGRAD |
| 3717 | **DEGREE ENGLER** | DEGRE ENGLER | ENGLERGRAD |
| 3718 | **DEGREE FAHRENHEIT** | DEGRE FAHRENHEIT | GRAD FAHRENHEIT, FAHRENHEITGRAD |
| 3719 | **DEGREE OF CYCLIC IRREGULARITY** | COEFFICIENT DE REGULARITE, REGULARITE CYCLIQUE | GLEICHFÖRMIGKEITSGRAD, UNGLEICHFÖRMIGKEITSGRAD |
| 3720 | **DEGREE OF HARDNESS** | DEGRE DE DURETE | HÄRTEGRAD, HÄRTESTUFE, HÄRTEMASS |
| 3721 | **DEGREE OF PRECISION** | DEGRE DE PRECISION, DEGRE D'EXACTITUDE | GENAUIGKEITSGRAD |
| 3722 | **DEGREE OF SATURATION** | DEGRE DE SATURATION | SÄTTIGUNGSGRAD |
| 3723 | **DEGREE OF SENSITIVENESS** | COEFFICIENT DE SENSIBILITE | EMPFINDLICHKEITSGRAD, UNEMPFLINDLICHKEITSGRAD |
| 3724 | **DEGREE REAUMUR** | DEGRE REAUMUR | GRAD REAUMUR, REAUMURGRAD |
| 3725 | **DEGREE TWADDELL** | DEGRE TWADDELL | GRAD TWADDELL |
| 3726 | **DEGREES OF FREEDOM** | DEGRES DE LIBERTE | FREIHEITSGRADE |
| 3727 | **DEHYDRATE (TO)** | DESHYDRATER, DESHYDRATER (SE) | HYDRATWASSER ENTZIEHEN (DAS), HYDRATWASSER VERLIEREN (DAS) |
| 3728 | **DEHYDRATION** | DESHYDRATATION | WASSERENTZIEHUNG (CHEM.) |
| 3729 | **DEIONIZATION** | DESIONISATION | ENTIONISIERUNG |
| 3730 | **DELAY** | RETARD | VERSPÄTUNG |
| 3731 | **DELAY IN DELIVERY** | RETARD DE LIVRAISON | LIEFERUNGSVERZUG |
| 3732 | **DELIQUESCE (TO)** | TOMBER EN DELIQUESCENCE | ZERFLIESSEN, DELIQUESZIEREN |
| 3733 | **DELIQUESCENCE** | DELIQUESCENCE | ZERFLIESSLICHKEIT, DELIQUESZENZ |
| 3734 | **DELIQUESCENT** | DELIQUESCENT | ZERFLIESSEND, ZERFLIESSLICH |
| 3735 | **DELIVERY OF HEAT** | CESSION DE CHALEUR | WÄRMEABGABE, WÄRMEABFUHR |
| 3736 | **DELIVERY PIPES** | TUYAUTERIE, TUYAU A PRESSION, TUYAU DE REFOULEMENT, TUBULURE DE DEVERSEMENT | DRUCKLEITUNG, DRUCKROHRLEITUNG |
| 3737 | **DELIVERY TERMS** | CONDITIONS DE LIVRAISON | LIEFERUNGSBEDINGUNGEN |
| 3738 | **DELIVERY TUBE, DELIVERY NOZZLE, DELIVERY CONE** | TUYERE DIVERGENTE, AJUTAGE DIVERGENT, TUYERE DE REFOULEMENT | DRUCKDÜSE |

| | | | |
|---|---|---|---|
| 3739 | **DELIVERY VALVE, DISCHARGE VALVE** | SOUPAPE DE REFOULEMENT, CLAPET DE REFOULEMENT | DRUCKVENTIL, DRUCKKLAPPE |
| 3740 | **DELTA IRON** | FER DELTA | DELTA-EISEN |
| 3741 | **DELTA METAL** | METAL ALLIAGE DELTA | DELTAMETALL |
| 3742 | **DEMAGNETISATION** | DESAIMANTATION | ENTMAGNETISIEREN |
| 3743 | **DEMAGNETISE (TO)** | DESAIMANTER | ENTMAGNETISIEREN |
| 3744 | **DEMAGNETIZERS** | DEMAGNETISEURS | ENTMAGNETISIERUNGSAPPARATE |
| 3745 | **DEMAND OF FUEL** | COMBUSTIBLE NECESSAIRE | BRENNSTOFFBEDARF |
| 3746 | **DEMAND OF POWER** | ENERGIE, FORCE NECESSAIRE, PUISSANCE REQUISE | KRAFTBEDARF |
| 3747 | **DENATURING AGENT** | DENATURANT | VERGÄLLUNGSMITTEL, DENATURIERUNGSMITTEL |
| 3748 | **DENDRITE** | DENDRITE | DENDRIT, TANNENBAUMKRISTALL |
| 3749 | **DENDRITIC POWDER** | POUDRE DENTRIDIQUE | PULVER (DENDRITISCHES) |
| 3750 | **DENDRITIC STRUCTURE** | STRUCTURE DENDRITIQUE | STRUKTUR (DENDRITISCHE) |
| 3751 | **DENICKELIFICATION** | DENICKELAGE | ENTNICKELUNG |
| 3752 | **DENOMINATOR** | DENOMINATEUR | NENNER |
| 3753 | **DENSIFICATION** | DENSIFICATION | VERDICHTUNG |
| 3754 | **DENSIFIER** | MOYEN D'HOMOGENEISATION | HOMOGENISIERUNGSMITTEL |
| 3755 | **DENSIMETER** | DENSIMETRE | DENSIMETER |
| 3756 | **DENSITY** | DENSITE | DICHTE, GEWICHT (SPEZIFISCHES) |
| 3757 | **DENSITY OF A GAS** | DENSITE D'UN GAZ | GASDICHTE |
| 3758 | **DENSITY OF A LIQUID** | DENSITE D'UN LIQUIDE | FLÜSSIGKEITSDICHTE |
| 3759 | **DENSITY RATIO** | RAPPORT DE DENSITE | DICHTEVERHÄLNIS |
| 3760 | **DENT** | BOSSE RENTRANTE, DEFONCEMENT | EINBEULUNG |
| 3761 | **DENT AND INDENT** | ADENT | ZAHN UND EINZAHNUNG |
| 3762 | **DEOXIDATION** | DESOXYDATION, DESOXYGENATION | SAUERSTOFFENTZIEHUNG, DESOXYDATION |
| 3763 | **DEOXIDISE (TO)** | DESOXYDER, DESOXYGENER | SAUERSTOFF ENTZIEHEN (DEN), DESOXYDIEREN |
| 3764 | **DEOXIDIZED COPPER** | CUIVRE DESOXYDE | KUPFER (DESOXYDIERTES) |
| 3765 | **DEOXIDIZER** | DESOXYDANT | DESOXYDATIONSMITTEL |
| 3766 | **DEOXIDIZING** | DESOXYDATION | DESOXYDATION |
| 3767 | **DEPLETION** | ABAISSEMENT DE CONCENTRATION | KONZENTRATIONSHERABSETZUNG |
| 3768 | **DEPOLARISATION** | DEPOLARISATION | DEPOLARISATION |
| 3769 | **DEPOLARISE (TO)** | DEPOLARISER | DEPOLARISIEREN |
| 3770 | **DEPOLARISER** | DEPOLARISANT | DEPOLARISATOR |
| 3771 | **DEPOLARIZATION** | DEPOLARISATION | DEPOLARISATION |
| 3772 | **DEPOLARIZER** | DEPOLARISANT, DEPOLARISATEUR | DEPOLARISATOR |
| 3773 | **DEPOSIT** | SEDIMENT | ABLAGERUNG (GEOL.) |
| 3774 | **DEPOSIT ATTACK** | CORROSION DUE A DES DEPOTS | BELAGKORROSION |
| 3775 | **DEPOSIT METAL** | METAL D'APPORT, METAL DE RECHARGE | AUFTRAGSMETALL |
| 3776 | **DEPOSITED METAL** | METAL FONDU APPLIQUE | SCHWEISSGUT (EINGEBRACHTES) |
| 3777 | **DEPOSITION EFFICIENCY** | RAPPORT DE DISTRIBUTION DU METAL | NIEDERSCHLAGSVERTEILUNGSVERHÄLTNIS |
| 3778 | **DEPRESSION** | DEPRESSION | UNTERDRUCK |
| 3779 | **DEPTH** | PROFONDEUR | TIEFE |
| 3780 | **DEPTH DRILLING** | FORAGE EN PROFONDEUR | TIEFBOHRUNG |
| 3781 | **DEPTH GAUGE** | CALIBRE DE PROFONDEUR, PIED A PROFONDEUR | TIEFENMASS, TIEFENLEHRE, AUSDREHWINKEL, LOCHWINKEL, SCHUBWINKEL |
| 3782 | **DEPTH OF CUT** | PROFONDEUR DE COUPE | SCHNITTIEFE |

| | | | |
|---|---|---|---|
| 3783 | **DEPTH OF GAP** | PROFONDEUR DU COL DE CYGNE | AUSLADUNGSTIEFE |
| 3784 | **DEPTH OF THREAD** | PROFONDEUR DU FILET | GANGTIEFE EINER SCHRAUBE, GEWINDETIEFE |
| 3785 | **DEPTH OF TOOTH** | HAUTEUR TOTALE DE LA DENT | ZAHNLÄNGE |
| 3786 | **DERIVATIVE** | DERIVE | DERIVAT |
| 3787 | **DERRICK BARGES** | BARGES DE MANUTENTION | BOHRTURM PONTON |
| 3788 | **DERRICK CRANE** | GRUE DERRICK, DERRICK | DERRICKKRAN |
| 3789 | **DESACTIVATION** | DESACTIVATION | ENTAKTIVIERUNG |
| 3790 | **DESCALING DIP** | BAIN DE DECALAMINAGE | ENTZUNDERUNGSBAD |
| 3791 | **DESCENDING PIPE LINE** | CONDUITE DESCENDANTE | LEITUNG (FALLENDE) |
| 3792 | **DESCENT, DECLIVITY, FALLING GRADIENT** | PENTE, DECLIVITE | GEFÄLLE (NEIGUNG) |
| 3793 | **DESEAMING** | ELIMINATION DES DEFAUTS SUPERFICIELS | ENTFERNUNG DER OBERFLÄCHENFEHLER |
| 3794 | **DESIGN (OF A PROJECT)** | TRACE, CONCEPTION, PLAN, PROJET, CALCUL, ETUDE | ENTWURF, KONZEPTION, PLANUNG, GESTALTUNG, BAUART, AUFBAU, ENTWICKELN |
| 3795 | **DESIGN (TO)** | ETUDIER, TRACER, CALCULER | ENTWERFEN, KONSTRUIEREN, AUSRECHNEN |
| 3796 | **DESIGN OFFICE/ENGINEERING OFFICE** | BUREAU D'ETUDE | KONSTRUKTIONSBÜRO |
| 3797 | **DESIGN SKETCH** | CROQUIS DE PRINCIPE | ENTWURFSZEICHNUNG |
| 3798 | **DESIGN TEMPERATURE** | TEMPERATURE DE CALCUL, TEMPERATURE D'ETUDE | TEMPERATUR (GERECHNETE) |
| 3799 | **DESIGNING** | ETUDE | ENTWERFEN, KONSTRUIEREN, KONSTRUKTION |
| 3800 | **DESIGNING DEPARTMENT, OFFICE** | BUREAU D'ETUDES | KONSTRUKTIONSBÜRO |
| 3801 | **DESILVERISE (TO)** | DESARGENTER | ENTSILBERN |
| 3802 | **DESILVERISING** | DESARGENTAGE | ENTSILBERUNG |
| 3803 | **DESLAGGING** | EVACUATION DU LAITIER | SCHLACKENABZUG |
| 3804 | **DESSICATOR** | DESSICCATEUR | EXSIKKATOR |
| 3805 | **DESTRUCTIVE DISTILLATION** | DISTILLATION AVEC DECOMPOSITION | ZERSETZUNGSDESTILLATION, SPALTUNGSDESTILLATION, DESTRUKTIVE DESTILLATION |
| 3806 | **DESTRUCTIVE TESTING** | ESSAI DESTRUCTIF | PRÜFUNG (ZERSTÖRENDE) |
| 3807 | **DESURFACING** | ENLEVEMENT DE COUCHES SUPERFICIELLES | OBERFLÄCHENGLÄTTUNG |
| 3808 | **DETACHABLE, REMOVABLE** | AMOVIBLE | ABNEHMBAR |
| 3809 | **DETAIL DRAWING** | DESSIN DE DETAIL | EINZELZEICHNUNG, STÜCKZEICHNUNG, DETAILZEICHNUNG |
| 3810 | **DETAIL OF DESIGN** | DETAIL DE CONSTRUCTION | KONSTRUKTIONSEINZELHEIT |
| 3811 | **DETAIL PART, COMPONENT** | PIECE DETACHEE | EINZELTEIL |
| 3812 | **DETAILED DRAWING** | PLAN DETAILLE | AÜSFÜHRUNGSZEICHNUNG |
| 3813 | **DETERGENT** | DETERGENT | REINIGUNGSMITTEL |
| 3814 | **DETERMINANT** | DETERMINANT | DETERMINANTE |
| 3815 | **DEVELOP (TO)** | DEVELOPPER (GEOM.) | ABWICKELN (GEOM.) |
| 3816 | **DEVELOPABLE** | DEVELOPPABLE | ABWICKELBAR (GEOM.) |
| 3817 | **DEVELOPABLE SURFACE, TORSE** | SURFACE DEVALOPPABLE, DEVELOPPABLE | FLÄCHE (ABWICKELBARE) |
| 3818 | **DEVELOPMENT OF GAS** | DEGAGEMENT DE GAZ | GASENTWICKLUNG |
| 3819 | **DEVIATION** | ECART, DEVIATION | ABWEICHUNG, REGELABWEICHUNG, ABLENKUNG (PHYS.) |
| 3820 | **DEVICE, CONTRIVANCE, ARRANGEMENT, APPLIANCE** | DISPOSITIF | VORRICHTUNG |
| 3821 | **DEVIL** | POT A FEU, BRASERO | FEUERTOPF |

**DEV** 98

| | | | |
|---|---|---|---|
| 3822 | DEVIL'S CLAW | CROCHET DE CHAINE | KROPFEISEN, |
| 3823 | DEVITRIFICATION | DEVITRIFICATION | ENTGLASUNG |
| 3824 | DEW POINT | POINT DE CONDENSATION | TAUPUNKT |
| 3825 | DEXTRINE, BRITISH GUM | DEXTRINE | STÄRKEGUMMI, DEXTRIN |
| 3826 | DEXTRO-TARTARIC ACID | ACIDE TARTRIQUE DEXTROGYRE | RECHTSWEINSÄURE |
| 3827 | DEXTROROTATORY, DEXTROGYRATE | DEXTROGYRE | RECHTSDREHEND |
| 3828 | DIABASE | DIABASE | DIABAS, GRÜNSTEIN |
| 3829 | DIACAUSTIC CURVE | CAUSTIQUE PAR REFRACTION, DIACAUSTIQUE | BRENNLINIE DURCH REFRAKTION, DIAKAUSTISCHE LINIE |
| 3830 | DIAGNOSTIC ROUTINE | PROGRAMME DIAGNOSTIQUE | DIAGNOSEPROGRAMM, FEHLERSUCHPROGRAMM |
| 3831 | DIAGONAL | DIAGONAL, DIAGONALE | DIAGONAL, DIAGONALE, ECKENLINIE |
| 3832 | DIAGONAL CUTTING PLIERS | PINCE COUPANTE DIAGONALE | SEITENSCHNEIDER |
| 3833 | DIAGONAL SCALE | ECHELLE DE PROPORTION | TRANSVERSALMASSSTAB |
| 3834 | DIAGRAM | DIAGRAMME, GRAPHIQUE, ABAQUE | SCHAUBILD, DIAGRAMM |
| 3835 | DIAGRAMM OF FORCES | DIAGRAMME DES FORCES | KRÄFTEPLAN |
| 3836 | DIAGRAMMATIC DRAWING | CROQUIS SCHEMATIQUE, SCHEMA | ZEICHNUNG (SCHEMATISCHE) |
| 3837 | DIAL | DISQUE, INDICATEUR, CADRAN DIVISE | ZIFFERBLATT, RAHMEN |
| 3838 | DIAL BORE GAUGE | COMPARATEUR A CADRAN POUR ALESAGES | BOHRUNGSMESSGERÄT MIT SKALA |
| 3839 | DIAL FEED MECHANICAL PRESS | PRESSE MECANIQUE A PLATEAU REVOLVER | REVOLVERPRESSEN (MECHANISCHE) |
| 3840 | DIAL INDICATEUR | INDICATEUR A CADRAN | RINGSKALA-ANZEIGER |
| 3841 | DIAL SCALE | ECHELLE ANNULAIRE | RINGSKALA |
| 3842 | DIAL TEST INDICATOR | PALPEUR A CADRAN | MESSUHR |
| 3843 | DIAL TRAIN | MINUTERIE | ZEIGERWERK |
| 3844 | DIALYSE (TO) | DIALYSER | DIALYSIEREN |
| 3845 | DIALYSER | DIALYSEUR | DIALYSATOR |
| 3846 | DIALYSIS | DIALYSE | DIALYSE |
| 3847 | DIAMAGNETIC | DIAMAGNETIQUE | DIAMAGNETISCH |
| 3848 | DIAMAGNETISM | DIAGMAGNETISME | DIAMAGNETISMUS |
| 3849 | DIAMETER | DIAMETRE | DURCHMESSER |
| 3850 | DIAMETER AT BOTTOM OF THREAD, INTERNAL DIAMETER OF THREAD | DIAMETRE INTERIEUR, PETIT DIAMETRE DU FILET, DIAMETRE DU NOYAU, DIAMETRE A FOND DE FILET | INNERER GEWINDEDURCHMESSER, KERNDURCHMESSER EINER SCHRAUBE |
| 3851 | DIAMETER INCREMENT | COMPLEMENT DIAMETRAL | DICKENWACHSTUM |
| 3852 | DIAMETER OF A BOLT, OF A SCREW; EXTERNAL DIAMETER OF THREAD | DIAMETRE EXTERIEUR, GRAND DIAMETRE DU FILET | GEWINDEDURCHMESSER (ÄUSSERER) |
| 3853 | DIAMETER OF BOLT CIRCLE | DIAMETRE (DU CERCLE) DE PERCAGE | LOCHKREISDURCHMESSER |
| 3854 | DIAMETER OF BOLT HOLE | DIAMETRE DE TROU DE BOULON | SCHRAUBENLOCHDURCHMESSER |
| 3855 | DIAMETER OF BORE | DIAMETRE D'ALESAGE, ALESAGE | BOHRUNG, BOHRUNGSDURCHMESSER |
| 3856 | DIAMETER OF CHAIN LINK BAR | DIAMETRE DE LA BARRE DE FER D'UN MAILLON | KETTENEISENSTÄRKE |
| 3857 | DIAMETER OF HOLE | DIAMETRE DU TROU | LOCHWEITE |
| 3858 | DIAMETER OF PIPE | DIAMETRE D'UN TUYAU | ROHRDURCHMESSER |
| 3859 | DIAMETER OF RIVET | DIAMETRE DU RIVET | NIETSTÄRKE |
| 3860 | DIAMETER OF WIRE, SIZE OF WIRE | DIAMETRE D'UN FIL, EPAISSEUR D'UN FIL | DRAHTSTÄRKE |

| | | | |
|---|---|---|---|
| 3861 | **DIAMETRAL PITCH** | PAS DIAMETRAL, DIAMETRE PRIMITIF, MODULE DE DENTURE | DURCHMESSERTEILUNG, VERHÄLTNISZÄHNEZAHL, DURCHMESSER DES TEILKREISES |
| 3862 | **DIAMOND** | DIAMANT | DIAMANT |
| 3863 | **DIAMOND DUST** | POUDRE DE DIAMANT, EGRISE | DIAMANTSTAUB |
| 3864 | **DIAMOND GRINDING WHEEL** | MEULE-DIAMANT | DIAMANTSCHLEIFSCHEIBE |
| 3865 | **DIAMOND HARDNESS** | ESSAI DE DURETE | DIAMANTHÄRTEPROBE |
| 3866 | **DIAMOND TOOL** | OUTIL DIAMANTE | DIAMANTWERKZEUG, SPITZSTAHL |
| 3867 | **DIAMOND WHEEL** | MEULE DIAMANTEE | DIAMANTSCHLEIFSCHEIBE |
| 3868 | **DIAPHANEITY** | DIAPHANEITE | LICHTDURCHLÄSSIGKEIT, DIAPHANITÄT |
| 3869 | **DIAPHANOUS** | DIAPHANE | LICHTDURCHLÄSSIG, DIAPHAN |
| 3870 | **DIAPHRAGM** | MEMBRANE, DIAPHRAGME, CLOISON | SCHWINGPLATTE, MEMBRAN, DIAPHRAGMA, SCHEIDEWAND |
| 3871 | **DIAPHRAGM** | DIAPHRAGME (OPT.) | BLENDE, DIAPHRAGMA |
| 3872 | **DIAPHRAGM OPERATED CONTROL VALVE** | ROBINET REGULATEUR A MEMBRANE, VANNE DE CONTROLE | MEMBRAN-REGELVENTIL |
| 3873 | **DIAPHRAGM PRESSURE GAUGE** | MANOMETRE A PLAQUE | PLATTENFEDERMANOMETER |
| 3874 | **DIAPHRAGM PUMP** | POMPE A DIAPHRAGME, A MEMBRANE | MEMBRANPUMPE |
| 3875 | **DIAPHRAGM SPRING** | RESSORT DIAPHRAGME | MEMBRANFEDER |
| 3876 | **DIAPHRAGM VALVE** | ROBINET A MEMBRANE | MEMBRAN-VENTIL |
| 3877 | **DIAPHRAHM (TO)** | DIAPHRAGMER | ABBLENDEN |
| 3878 | **DIATHERMANCY** | DIATHERMANEITE, DIATHERMANSIE | DURCHLÄSSIGKEIT FÜR WÄRMESTRAHLEN, DIATHERMANITÄT, DIATHERMANSIE |
| 3879 | **DIATHERMANOUS** | DIATHERMANE, DIATHERMIQUE | DURCHLÄSSIG FÜR WÄRMESTRAHLEN, DIATHERMAN |
| 3880 | **DIATOMACEOUS EARTH** | TERRE DE DIATOMEES | DIATOMEENERDE, KIESELGUR |
| 3881 | **DIATOMIC, DIVALENT** | DIATOMIQUE, DIVALENT, BIATOMIQUE | ZWEIWERTIG, ZWEIATOMIG |
| 3882 | **DIBASIC** | DIBASIQUE | ZWEIBASISCH |
| 3883 | **DIE** | MOULE, FILIERE, ESTAMPE, MATRICE, COQUILLE, MOULE METALLIQUE | PRÄGESTEMPEL, MATRIZE, KOKILLE, PRESSRING, FORM |
| 3884 | **DIE BLOCK** | PORTE-ESTAMPE | STEMPELBLOCK |
| 3885 | **DIE BODY** | PARTIE FIXE, CORPS DE L'ESTAMPE | FESTER STEMPELTEIL |
| 3886 | **DIE CASTING** | COULEE SOUS PRESSION | DRUCKGIESSVERFAHREN, DRUCKGUSS |
| 3887 | **DIE CUSHIONS** | SERRE-FLANS | NIEDERHALTER |
| 3888 | **DIE LINES** | MARQUE DE L'ESTAMPE | MATRIZENSPUR, TEILFUGE |
| 3889 | **DIE METAL** | METAL POUR MATRICES | GESENKMETALL |
| 3890 | **DIE SET** | MONTURE D'ESTAMPE A GUIDAGE A COLONNES | SÄULEFÜHRUNGSGESTELL |
| 3891 | **DIE SHIFT** | DEPLACEMENT DE L'ESTAMPE | STEMPELVERSCHIEBUNG |
| 3892 | **DIE SINKING** | FRAISAGE DES MATRICES | GESENKFRÄSEN |
| 3893 | **DIE STAMP** | POINCON (D'INSPECTION) | PRÜFSTEMPEL, KONTROLLSTEMPEL |
| 3894 | **DIE STAMPING** | MATRICAGE (DEFAUT DE SURFACE DE TOLE), MARQUAGE DES TOLES AU POINCON, POINCONNAGE | PRÄGUNG, GESENKSCHMIEDEN |
| 3895 | **DIE STOCK, SCREW STOCK** | MONTURE D'UNE FILIERE A COUSSINETS | KLUPPENHALTER |
| 3896 | **DIE, SCREW DIES, SCREWING DIES** | COUSSINETS DE FILIERE | SCHNEIDBACKEN, GEWINDESCHNEIDBACKEN |

# DIE 100

| | | | |
|---|---|---|---|
| 3897 | DIE, SWAGE | MATRICE ETAMPE ESTAMPE DE FORGERON | GESENK |
| 3898 | DIELECTRIC | DIELECTRIQUE, ISOLANT, NON CONDUCTEUR | NICHTLEITER, DIELEKTRISCH, NICHTLEITEND, DIELEKTRIKUM |
| 3899 | DIELECTRIC COEFFICIENT CONSTANT, INDUCTIVE CAPACITY, INDUCTIVITY, PERMITTIVITY | CONSTANTE DIELECTRIQUE | DIELEKTRIZITÄTSKONSTANTE |
| 3900 | DIELECTRIC STRENGHT | RESISTANCE DIELECTRIQUE OU DISRUPTIVE | DURCHSCHLAGSFESTIGKEIT |
| 3901 | DIESEL ENGINE | MOTEUR DIESEL, DIESEL | DIESELMASCHINE, DIESELMOTOR |
| 3902 | DIFFERENCE | DIFFERENCE | DIFFERENZ (MATH.) |
| 3903 | DIFFERENCE GAUGE | JAUGE LIMITE DE TOLERANCE | TOLERANZLEHRE |
| 3904 | DIFFERENCE OF TEMPERATURE | DIFFERENCE DE TEMPERATURE | TEMPERATURUNTERSCHIED |
| 3905 | DIFFERENCE, LIMIT GAUGE | CALIBRE DE TOLERANCE | GRENZLEHRE, DIFFENRENZLEHRE, TOLERANZLEHRE, DOPPELKALIBER, ZWIESELKALIBER, TOLERANZKALIBER |
| 3906 | DIFFERENTIAL | DIFFERENTIEL | DIFFERENTIAL |
| 3907 | DIFFERENTIAL BRAKE | FREIN DIFFERENTIEL | DIFFERENTIALBREMSE |
| 3908 | DIFFERENTIAL CALCULUS | CALCUL DIFFERENTIEL | DIFFERENTIALRECHUNG |
| 3909 | DIFFERENTIAL COEFFICIENT | COEFFICIENT DIFFERENTIEL | DIFFERENTIALKOEFFIZIENT |
| 3910 | DIFFERENTIAL CROWNWHEEL | GRANDE COURONNE DE DIFFERENTIEL | DIFFERENTIALANTRIEBS-KEGELRAD |
| 3911 | DIFFERENTIAL DYNAMOMETER | DYNAMOMETRE DIFFERENTIEL | DIFFERENTIALDYNAMOMETER |
| 3912 | DIFFERENTIAL EQUATION | EQUATION DIFFERENTIELLE | DIFFERENTIALGLEICHUNG |
| 3913 | DIFFERENTIAL GEAR | MOUVEMENT, MECANISME, TRAIN DIFFERENTIEL, DIFFERENTIEL, ENGRENAGE DIFFERENTIEL | DIFFERENFIALGETRIEBE |
| 3914 | DIFFERENTIAL HARDENING | TREMPE DIFFERENTIELLE, TREMPE LOCALISEE | ABSCHRECKEN (ÖRTLICH BEGRENZTES) |
| 3915 | DIFFERENTIAL HEATING | CHAUFFAGE SELECTIF | SELEKTIVE ERHITZUNG |
| 3916 | DIFFERENTIAL QUOTIENT | QUOTIENT DIFFERENTIEL | DIFFERENTIALQUOTIENT |
| 3917 | DIFFERENTIAL SIDE GEAR WHEEL | ROUE DE DIFFERENTIEL | HINTERACHSWELLENRAD |
| 3918 | DIFFERENTIAL SPIDER PINION | SATELLITE DE DIFFERENTIEL | AUSGLEICHSKEGELRAD |
| 3919 | DIFFERENTIAL THERMAL ANALYSIS | ANALYSE THERMIQUE SELECTIVE | ANALYSE (SELEKTIVE THERMISCHE) |
| 3920 | DIFFERENTIAL THERMOMETER | THERMOMETRE DIFFERENTIEL | DIFFERENTIALTHERMOMETER |
| 3921 | DIFFERENTIAL U-TUBE GAUGE | MANOMETRE DIFFERENTIEL | DIFFERENTIALMANOMETER |
| 3922 | DIFFERENTIATE (TO) | DIFFERENCIER | DIFFERENZIEREN (MATH.) |
| 3923 | DIFFERENTIATION | DIFFERENCIATION | DIFFERENTIATION (MATH.) |
| 3924 | DIFFRACTION | DIFFRACTION | DIFFRAKTION, BRECHUNG, BEUGUNG |
| 3925 | DIFFRACTION GRATING | RESEAU DE DIFFRACTION | BEUGUNGSGITTER |
| 3926 | DIFFRACTION PATTERN | DIAGRAMME DE DIFFRACTION RX | RÖNTGEN-REFLEXE |
| 3927 | DIFFUSED LIGHT | LUMIERE DIFFUSE | LICHT (ZERSTREUTES), LICHT (DIFFUSES) |
| 3928 | DIFFUSER | DIFFUSEUR | AUSWURFKEGEL, DIFFUSER |
| 3929 | DIFFUSION | DIFFUSION | DIFFUSION |
| 3930 | DIFFUSION COATINGS | REVETEMENTS DE DIFFUSION | DIFFUSIONSÜBERZÜGE |
| 3931 | DIFFUSION COEFFICIENT | COEFFICIENT DE DIFFUSION | DIFFUSIONSKOEFFIZIENT |
| 3932 | DIFFUSION OF GASES | DIFFUSION DES GAZ | DIFFUSION VON GASEN |
| 3933 | DIFFUSION OF LIGHT | DIFFUSION DE LA LUMIERE | STREUUNG, DIFFUSION DES LICHTES |
| 3934 | DIFFUSION ZONE | ZONE DE DIFFUSION | DIFFUSIONGEBIET |
| 3935 | DIFFUSIVE SURFACE | SURFACE DIFFUSIVE | FLÄCHE (LICHTZERSTREUENDE) |
| 3936 | DIFFUSIVITY | DIFFUSIBILITE | DIFFUSIONSVERMÖGEN |
| 3937 | DIGEST (TO) | FAIRE DIGERER, METTRE A DIGERER | DIGERIEREN |

| | | | |
|---|---|---|---|
| 3938 | DIGESTER | LESSIVEUR | DAMPFKOCHTOPF |
| 3939 | DIGESTION | DIGESTION (CHIM.) | DIGERIEREN, DIGESTION |
| 3940 | DIGIT | CHIFFRE, POSITION | ZEICHEN, ZAHL, STELLE |
| 3941 | DIGITAL | NUMERIQUE | DIGITAL, NUMERISCH |
| 3942 | DIGITAL INPUT DATA | INFORMATION D'ENTREE NUMERIQUE | DATEN (NUMERISCH EINGEGEBENE) |
| 3943 | DIGITIZER | CODEUR NUMERIQUE | CODIERER |
| 3944 | DIHEDRAL ANGLE | DIEDRE, ANGLE DIEDRE | EBENENWINKEL |
| 3945 | DIKE | LEVEE DE TERRE | DEICH |
| 3946 | DIKES | CAVALIERS | ERDAUFSCHÜTTUNG |
| 3947 | DILATABILITY, EXPANSIBILITY | DILATABILITE | AUSDEHNUNGSFÄHIGKEIT |
| 3948 | DILATABLE, EXPANSIBLE | DILATABLE | AUSDEHNUNGSFÄHIG |
| 3949 | DILATATION | DILATATION | DILATATION, DEHNUNG |
| 3950 | DILATOMETER | DILATOMETRE | DILATOMETER |
| 3951 | DILUENT | DILUANT | VERDÜNNUNGSMITTEL |
| 3952 | DILUTE A SOLUTION (TO) | DILUER, ETENDRE UNE SOLUTION | VERDÜNNEN (EINE LÖSUNG) |
| 3953 | DILUTE SOLUTION | SOLUTION DILUEE, ETENDUE | VERDÜNNTE LÖSUNG |
| 3954 | DILUTION OF A SOLUTION | DILUTION D'UNE SOLUTION | VERDÜNNEN, VERDÜNNUNG EINER LÖSUNG |
| 3955 | DIM LIGHT | LUMIERE DIFFUSE | STREULICHT |
| 3956 | DIMENSION FIGURED | COTE | MASSZAHL, MASSBEZEICHNUNG, EINGESCHRIEBENES MASS |
| 3957 | DIMENSION LINE | LIGNE DE COTE | MASSLINIE |
| 3958 | DIMENSIONAL STABILITY | STABILITE DIMENSIONNELLE | FORMBESTÄNDIGKEIT |
| 3959 | DIMENSIONED DRAWING, DRAWING WITH DIMENSIONS | DESSIN COTE | MASSZEICHNUNG, ZEICHNUNG MIT EINGESCHRIEBENEN MASSEN |
| 3960 | DIMENSIONS, MEASUREMENTS | DIMENSIONS | ABMESSUNGEN, MASSE, AUSMASSE, DIMENSIONEN |
| 3961 | DIMETRIC PROJECTION | PROJECTION DIMETRIQUE | PROJEKTION (DIMETRISCHE) |
| 3962 | DIMINISHING REDUCING SOCKET | MANCHON DE REDUCTION D'ALESAGE | ÜBERGANGSMUFFE, ABSATZMUFFE, REDUKTIONSMUFFE |
| 3963 | DIMMER SWITCH | INVERSEUR-PHARE-CODE | DUNKELSCHALTER |
| 3964 | DIODE | DIODE | DIODE |
| 3965 | DIODE LAMP | LAMPE DIODE | ZWEIELEKTRODENLAMPE |
| 3966 | DIORITE | DIORITE | DIORIT |
| 3967 | DIP | IMMERSION, BAIN | BAD |
| 3968 | DIP (TO), IMMERGE (TO), IMMERSE (TO) | PLONGER, IMMERGER | EINTAUCHEN |
| 3969 | DIP BRAZING | SOUDURE FORTE PAR IMMERSION | TAUCHHARTLÖTUNG |
| 3970 | DIP COATING | APPLICATION D'UN REVETEMENT PAR TREMPAGE | TAUCHAUFTRAG |
| 3971 | DIP HATCH | TROU DE JAUGE | MESSSTABLOCH |
| 3972 | DIP HATCH AND VENT COMBINED | TROU DE JAUGE COMBINE AVEC EVENT | MESSSTAB-UND LUFTLOCH |
| 3973 | DIP TANK | CUVE DE TREMPAGE | TAUCHBEHÄLTER, TANK |
| 3974 | DIPHENYLAMINE | DIPHENYLAMINE | DIPHENYLAMIN |
| 3975 | DIPPING | IMMERSION, TREMPE | IMMERSION, TAUCHEN |
| 3976 | DIPPING BASKET | CORBEILLE DE TREMPAGE | TAUCHKORB |
| 3977 | DIPPING PROCESS | METHODE AU TREMPE | EINTAUCHVERFAHREN |
| 3978 | DIPPING, IMMERSION | IMMERSION, TREMPE | EINTAUCHEN |
| 3979 | DIPSTICK | JAUGE D'HUILE | ÖLMESSSTAB |
| 3980 | DIRECT ACTING | A ACTION DIRECTE | UNMITTELBAR, DIREKT WIRKEND |

# DIR
102

| | | | |
|---|---|---|---|
| 3981 | **DIRECT COMPUTER CONTROL** | COMMANDE DIRECTE PAR CALCULATEUR | RECHNERSTEUERUNG (DIREKTE) |
| 3982 | **DIRECT COUPLED MACHINE** | MACHINE A ACCOUPLEMENT DIRECT, MACHINE A MANCHONNAGE DIRECT | MASCHINE (DIREKTGEKUPPELTE) |
| 3983 | **DIRECT DRIVE** | PRISE DIRECTE | GANG (DIREKTER) |
| 3984 | **DIRECT EXTRUSION** | FILAGE DIRECT | VORWÄRTSFLIESSPRESSEN |
| 3985 | **DIRECT NUMERICAL CONTROL** | COMMANDE DIRECTE PAR CALCULATEUR | RECHNERSTEUERUNG, (DIREKTE) |
| 3986 | **DIRECT READING DIAL CALIPER** | PIED A COULISSE A CADRAN | SCHUBLEHRE MIT DIREKTER ABLESUNG |
| 3987 | **DIRECT SPRING LOADED (SAFETY) VALVE** | SOUPAPE DE SURETE A CHARGE DIRECTE A RESSORT | VENTIL MIT UNMITTELBARER FEDERBELASTUNG |
| 3988 | **DIRECT-CONTACT CONDENSER** | CONDENSEUR PAR MELANGE | MISCHKONDENSATOR |
| 3989 | **DIRECTION INDICATOR LIGHTS** | CLIGNOTANTS, FEUX DE DIRECTION | FAHRTRICHTUNGSANZEIGER, BLINKLICHTER |
| 3990 | **DIRECTION OF A FORCE** | DIRECTION D'UNE FORCE | KRAFTRICHTUNG, RICHTUNG EINER KRAFT |
| 3991 | **DIRECTION OF MOTION** | DIRECTION DE MOUVEMENT | BEWEGUNGSRICHTUNG |
| 3992 | **DIRECTION OF ROTATION** | SENS DE ROTATION | DREHRICHTUNG, DREHSINN |
| 3993 | **DIRECTION OF THE FIBRES** | DIRECTION DES FIBRES | FASERRICHTUNG |
| 3994 | **DIRECTIONAL PROPERTIES** | ORIENTATION DES CRISTAUX | KRISTALLORIENTIERUNG |
| 3995 | **DIRECTOR** | DIRECTEUR, INTERPOLATEUR | STEUERDIREKTOR, INTERPOLATOR |
| 3996 | **DIRECTRIX** | DIRECTRICE | LEITLINIE, DIREKTRIX |
| 3997 | **DIRT COLLECTION** | PRISE DE POUSSIERES | SCHMUTZANHAFTUNG |
| 3998 | **DIRT SAND INCLUSION** | GRAINS CONTENUS DANS LA FONTE | SANDEINSCHLUSS IM GUSS |
| 3999 | **DISAGGREGATE (TO)** | DESINTEGRER, DESAGREGER | AUFLOCKERN, AUFSCHLIESSEN |
| 4000 | **DISAGGREGATION** | DESINTEGRATION, DESAGREGATION | AUFLOCKERUNG, AUFSCHLIESSUNG |
| 4001 | **DISC BRAKE** | FREIN A DISQUE | SCHEIBENBREMSE |
| 4002 | **DISC CLUTCH** | EMBRAYAGE A DISQUE | LAMELLENKUPPLUNG |
| 4003 | **DISC CRANK, CRANK DISC, CRANK PLATE** | PLATEAU-MANIVELLE | KURBELSCHEIBE |
| 4004 | **DISC FLYWHEEL** | VOLANT EN DISQUE, DISQUE-VOLANT | SCHWUNGSCHEIBE |
| 4005 | **DISC FRICTION GEAR** | TRANSMISSION PAR PLATEAUX | PLANSCHEIBENGETRIEBE |
| 4006 | **DISC GRINDER** | PONCEUSE | SCHLEIFSCHEIBE |
| 4007 | **DISC HARROWS** | PULVERISEURS A DISQUES | SCHEIBENEGGEN |
| 4008 | **DISC HOLDER** | PORTE-CLAPET | KEGELHALTERUNG |
| 4009 | **DISC LOCKNUT** | ECROU DE CLAPET | KEGELMUTTER |
| 4010 | **DISC SANDER** | PONCEUSE | SCHLEIFSCHEIBE |
| 4011 | **DISC VALVE** | SOUPAPE A SIEGE PLAN, SOUPAPE A DISQUE | EBENES VENTIL, TELLERVENTIL, SCHEIBENVENTIL, PLATTENVENTIL |
| 4012 | **DISC WHEEL** | ROUE A CENTRE PLEIN, ROUE A VOILE, ROUE A DISQUE | SCHEIBENRAD |
| 4013 | **DISC WHEEL CENTRE** | TOILE D'UNE ROUE, D'UN VOLANT | RADSCHEIBE |
| 4014 | **DISC, COMPOSITION DISC** | DISQUE (DE CLAPET) | DICHTSCHEIBE |
| 4015 | **DISC, DISK** | DISQUE | SCHEIBE |
| 4016 | **DISC, PLUG** | CLAPET (DE ROBINET) | KEGEL |
| 4017 | **DISCHARGE** | DECHARGE | ENTLADUNG |
| 4018 | **DISCHARGE (TO), EMPTY (TO)** | VIDER, DECHARGER | ENTLEEREN |
| 4019 | **DISCHARGE AN ACCUMULATOR (TO)** | DECHARGER UN ACCUMULATEUR | AKKUMULATOR ENTLADEN (EINEN) |
| 4020 | **DISCHARGE CROSS SECTION, CROSS SECTION APERTURE OF DISCHARGE ORIFICE** | SECTION DE L'ORIFICE D'ECOULEMENT | AUSFLUSSQUERSCHNITT |

**DIS** 103

| | | | |
|---|---|---|---|
| 4021 | DISCHARGE HEAD, DELIVERY HEAD OF A PUMP | HAUTEUR DE REFOULEMENT D'UNE POMPE | DRUCKHÖHE EINER PUMPE |
| 4022 | DISCHARGE PIPE-LINE | CONDUITE DE REFOULEMENT | ABLASSROHRLEITUNG |
| 4023 | DISCHARGE, DELIVERY, QUANTITY DISCHARGED | VOLUME QUI PASSE AU TRAVERS D'UN ORIFICE PAR SECONDE | AUSFLUSSMENGE, ABFLUSSMENGE |
| 4024 | DISCHARGE, EMPTYING | VIDANGE, DECHARGE | ENTLEERUNG |
| 4025 | DISCHARGING AN ACCUMULATOR | DECHARGE D'UN ACCUMULATEUR | ENTLADUNG EINES AKKUMULATORS |
| 4026 | DISCOLORATION | ALTERATION DE LA TEINTE | VERFÄRBUNG |
| 4027 | DISCONNECTABLE | DEMONTABLE | AUSEINANDERNEHMBAR, ZERLEGBAR |
| 4028 | DISCONNECTION | DEBRAYAGE | AUSRÜCKUNG |
| 4029 | DISCRIMINANT | DISCRIMINANT | DISKRIMINANTE |
| 4030 | DISENGAGE THE CATCH (TO) | DECLIQUETER, DECLENCHER | AUSKLINKEN |
| 4031 | DISENGAGEMENT RELEASE OF A CATCH | DECLENCHEMENT, DECLIQUETAGE | AUSKLINKEN |
| 4032 | DISENGAGING COUPLING | ACCOUPLEMENT DEBRAYAGE | AUSLÖSUNGSKUPPLUNG |
| 4033 | DISENGAGING COUPLING CLUTCH | ACCOUPLEMENT A DEBRAYAGE | EIN-UND AUSRÜCKKUPPLUNG, LÖSBARE KUPPLUNG, VERSCHIEBBARE KUPPLUNG, AUSRÜCKBARE KUPPLUNG |
| 4034 | DISENGAGING GEAR | MECANISME DE DEBRAYAGE, MECANISME D'EMBRAYAGE | AUSRÜCKVORRICHTUNG, EINRÜCKVORRICHTUNG |
| 4035 | DISENGAGING LEVER | LEVIER DE DEBRAYAGE, LEVIER DE DESEMBRAYAGE | AUSRÜCKHEBEL, ABSTELLHEBEL |
| 4036 | DISHED BOTTOM | FOND BOMBE | BODEN (GEWÖLBTER) |
| 4037 | DISHED DISC WHEEL | ROUE A VOILE BOMBE | SCHEIBENRAD (GEWÖLBTES) |
| 4038 | DISHED HEAD | FOND EMBOUTI | KESSELBODEN (GEWÖLBTER), KLOPPERBODEN |
| 4039 | DISHED ROOF | TOIT BOMBE | BOGENDACH |
| 4040 | DISHING | EMBOUTISSAGE | KÜMPELARBEIT |
| 4041 | DISINCRUSTANT, SCALE SOLVENT | DESINCRUSTANT CURATIF, TARTRIFUGE, ANTI-TARTRE | KESSELSTEINLÖSUNGSMITTEL |
| 4042 | DISINFECTANT | DESINFECTANT | DESINFEKTIONSMITTEL |
| 4043 | DISINTEGRATE (TO), CRUMBLE (TO) | EFFRITER (S'), DESAGREGER (SE) | ZERSTÄUBEN, ZERFALLEN |
| 4044 | DISINTEGRATION | DESINTEGRATION | ZERBRÖCKLUNG, ZERFALLEN |
| 4045 | DISINTEGRATOR | CONCASSEUR | SCHLEUDERMÜHLE, DESINTEGRATOR |
| 4046 | DISK CLUTCH | EMBRAYAGE A DISQUES | LAMELLENKUPPLUNG |
| 4047 | DISLOCATION | DISLOCATION | DISLOKATION, VERSETZUNG |
| 4048 | DISMOUNTABLE GAUGE | JAUGE DEMONTABLE | LEHRE (ZUSAMMENSTELLBARE) |
| 4049 | DISPERSED PHASE | PHASE DISPERSEE | DISPERSIONSPHASE |
| 4050 | DISPERSING AGENT | DISPERSANT, AGENT DE DISPERSION | DISPERGIERUNGSMITTEL, DISPERSIONSMITTEL |
| 4051 | DISPERSION | DISPERSION | ZERSTREUUNG, DISPERSION |
| 4052 | DISPLACEABLE | DEPLACABLE | VERSCHIEBBAR |
| 4053 | DISPLACEMENT (CEN); | DEPLACEMENT (CEN), VOLUME DEPLACE (PHYS.) | VERSCHIEBUNG, FORTRÜCKUNG (ALLG.), VOLUMEN (VERDRÄNGTES) (PHYS.) |
| 4054 | DISPLACEMENT OF A LIQUID | DEPLACEMENT D'UN LIQUIDE | VERDRÄNGUNG EINER FLÜSSIGKEIT |
| 4055 | DISPLACEMENT OF THE SHAFT CENTER LINES OF THE AXES OF THE SHAFTS | DESAXAGE | ACHSENVERSCHIEBUNG |
| 4056 | DISPOSITION, ARRANGEMENT | DISPOSITION | ANORDNUNG |
| 4057 | DISRUPTIVE STRENGTH | RESISTANCE DISRUPTIVE | ZERREISSFESTIGKEIT, DURCHSCHLAGSFESTIGKEIT |
| 4058 | DISSOCIATION | DISSOCIATION | SPALTUNG, DISSOZIATION |
| 4059 | DISSOLUTION | DISSOLUTION (ACTION) (CHIM.) | LÖSEN, AUFLÖSEN (CHEM.) |
| 4060 | DISSOLUTION | DISSOLUTION | AUFLÖSUNG |

**DIS**

104

| | | | |
|---|---|---|---|
| 4061 | **DISSOLVE (TO)** | DISSOUDRE, FONDRE (CHIM.), DISSOUDRE (SE) | AUFLÖSEN (SICH) (CHEM.), LÖSEN (SICH) |
| 4062 | **DISSOLVING POWER** | POUVOIR DISSOLVANT | LÖSUNGSVERMÖGEN, AUFLÖSUNGSVERMÖGEN |
| 4063 | **DISTANCE** | CHEMIN, DISTANCE, PARCOURS, TRAJET; ECARTEMENT, ESPACEMENT | WEG (MECH.); ENTFERNUNG, ABSTAND, DISTANZ |
| 4064 | **DISTANCE BETWEEN BEARINGS** | ECARTEMENT DES PALIERS | LAGERENTFERNUNG |
| 4065 | **DISTANCE BETWEEN CENTERS** | DISTANCE ENTRE POINTES, ENTRAXE, DISTANCE D'AXE EN AXE | SPITZENWEITE, ACHSABSTAND |
| 4066 | **DISTANCE FROM EDGE OF PLATE TO CENTRE OF RIVET** | DISTANCE DU CENTRE DU RIVET AU BORD DE LA TOLE | RANDENTFERNUNG, RANDABSTAND DER NIETE, ABSTAND DER NIETE VOM BLECHRAND |
| 4067 | **DISTANCE PIECE** | ENTRETOISE | ABSTANDHÜLSE, STÜCK |
| 4068 | **DISTANCE PIECE** | PIECE D'ECARTEMENT, ENTRETOISE | ABSTANDHALTER, DISTANZSTÜCK, ABSTANDHÜLSE |
| 4069 | **DISTANT READING THERMOMETER** | TELE-THERMOMETRE | FERNTHERMOMETER |
| 4070 | **DISTIL (TO)** | DISTILLER | DESTILLIEREN |
| 4071 | **DISTILLATE** | PRODUIT DE DISTILLATION, DISTILLATION | DESTILLAT, DESTILLATIONSERZEUGNIS |
| 4072 | **DISTILLATION** | DISTILLATION (ACTION) | DESTILLATION |
| 4073 | **DISTILLATION IN STEAM** | DISTILLATION A LA VAPEUR D'EAU | DESTILLATION MIT WASSERDAMPF |
| 4074 | **DISTILLATION OF COAL** | DISTILLATION DE LA HOUILLE | ENTGASUNG DER KOHLE |
| 4075 | **DISTILLATION UNDER REDUCED PRESSURE** | DISTILLATION DANS LE VIDE, VASE CLOS | DESTILLATION IM VAKUUM, VAKUUMDESTILLATION |
| 4076 | **DISTILLED WATER** | EAU DISTILLEE | WASSER (DESTILLIERTES) |
| 4077 | **DISTORTION** | ABERRATION, DISTORSION | ABWEICHUNG, VERFORMUNG, VERZERRUNG |
| 4078 | **DISTRIBUTED LOAD** | CHARGE REPARTIE | LAST (VERTEILTE) |
| 4079 | **DISTRIBUTING MAIN** | CONDUCTEUR DE RESEAU, CABLE DE DISTRIBUTION | VERTEILUNGSLEITUNG |
| 4080 | **DISTRIBUTING NETWORK** | RESEAU DE CONDUCTEURS ELECTRIQUES, RESEAU DE DISTRIBUTION ELECTRIQUE | LEITUNGSNETZ, STROMLEITUNGSNETZ, STROMVERTEILUNGSNETZ |
| 4081 | **DISTRIBUTION OF LOAD** | REPARTITION D'UNE CHARGE | LASTVERTEILUNG |
| 4082 | **DISTRIBUTION OF MASSES** | REPARTITION DES MASSES | MASSENVERTEILUNG |
| 4083 | **DISTRIBUTION OF TEMPERATURE** | DISTRIBUTION DE LA TEMPERATURE | TEMPERATURVERTEILUNG |
| 4084 | **DISTRIBUTOR** | DISTRIBUTEUR | VERTEILER |
| 4085 | **DISTRIBUTOR ARM** | DOIGT D'ALLUMEUR | VERTEILERLÄUFER |
| 4086 | **DISTRIBUTOR HEAD** | BOITIER DE DISTRIBUTION, DISTRIBUTEUR | VERTEILERKOPF, VERTEILERKASTEN |
| 4087 | **DISTRIBUTORS : FERTILISER** | DISTRIBUTEURS D'ENGRAIS | DÜNGERSTREUER |
| 4088 | **DISTRIBUTORS : TRAILER AND LORRY ATTACHMENTS** | DISTRIBUTEURS VEHICULES POUR ATTACHEMENT | ANHÄNGEVORRICHTUNGEN FÜR WAGEN |
| 4089 | **DISTRIBUTORS AND SPREADERS, LIME** | DISTRIBUTEURS DE CHAUX | KALKSTREUER |
| 4090 | **DITCHING AND DRAINING PLANT AND EQUIPMENT** | SOUS-SOLEUSES ET CHARRUES RIGOLEUSES | ENTWÄSSERUNGSGERÄTE UND GRABENPFLÜGE |
| 4091 | **DIVERGE (TO)** | DIVERGER | AUSEINANDERLAUFEN, DIVERGIEREN |
| 4092 | **DIVERGENCE, DIVERGENCY** | DIVERGENCE | DIVERGENZ |
| 4093 | **DIVERGENT** | DIVERGENT | AUSEINANDERLAUFEND, DIVERGENT |
| 4094 | **DIVERGENT SERIES** | SERIE DIVERGENTE | REIHE (DIVERGENTE) |
| 4095 | **DIVERGING LENS, CONCAVE LENS** | LENTILLE DIVERGENTE, LENTILLE A BORD EPAIS | HOHLLINSE, ZERSTREUUNGSLINSE, LINSE (KOKAVE), VERKLEINERUNGSGLAS |

| | | | |
|---|---|---|---|
| 4096 | **DIVERGING MOUTHPIECE** | AJUTAGE DIVERGENT, EMBOUCHURE DIVERGENTE | AUSFLUSSSTUTZEN (SICH ERWEITERNDER) |
| 4097 | **DIVIDE (TO)** | DIVISER (MATH.) | TEILEN, DIVIDIEREN |
| 4098 | **DIVIDED JOURNAL BEARING** | PALIER EN DEUX PARTIES, PALIER EN COQUILLES | LAGER (GETEILTES) |
| 4099 | **DIVIDEND** | DIVIDENDE | DIVIDEND |
| 4100 | **DIVIDER** | DIVISEUR, COMPAS | STAHLLINEAL MIT TEILUNG, TEILGERÄT |
| 4101 | **DIVIDERS** | COMPAS DROIT A POINTES, COMPAS A POINTES SECHES | SCHARNIERZIRKEL (GERADER), SPITZZIRKEL |
| 4102 | **DIVIDING ENGINE** | MACHINE A DIVISER | TEILMASCHINE |
| 4103 | **DIVIDING ENGINE FOR CIRCLES** | MACHINE A DIVISER LES CERCLES | KREISTEILMASCHINE |
| 4104 | **DIVIDING ENGINE FOR STRAIGHT LINES** | MACHINE A DIVISER LES LIGNES DROITES | LÄNGENTEILMASCHINE |
| 4105 | **DIVIDING HEAD** | APPAREIL DIVISEUR | TEILSCHEIBE |
| 4106 | **DIVIDING PLATE** | PLATEAU DIVISEUR | TEILSCHEIBE |
| 4107 | **DIVISION** | DIVISION (MATH.) | TEILUNG, DIVISION |
| 4108 | **DIVISION OF A CIRCLE** | DIVISION DU CERCLE | KREISTEILUNG |
| 4109 | **DIVISION PLATE** | PLATEAU DIVISEUR, PLATEAU DIVISE, A DIVISIONS, PLATE-FORME A DIVISER | TEILSCHEIBE |
| 4110 | **DIVISION WALL, PARTITION WALL** | CLOISON, DIAPHRAGME | ZWISCHENWAND, TRENNUNGSWAND, SCHEIDEWAND |
| 4111 | **DIVISOR** | DIVISEUR | DIVISOR |
| 4112 | **DODECAHEDRON** | DODECAEDRE | ZWÖLFFLACH, ZWÖLFFLÄCHERN, DODBKAEDER |
| 4113 | **DOG CLUTCH** | EMBRAYAGE A GRIFFES | KLAUENKUPPLUNG |
| 4114 | **DOLERITE** | DOLERITE | DOLERIT |
| 4115 | **DOLLY** | CONTRE-BOUTEROLLE | VORHALTER, GEGENHALTER, NIETPFANNE |
| 4116 | **DOLLY** | TAS, CHARIOT, DISQUE EN LISIERE DE TISSU, MEULE FLEXIBLE | SCHWABBELSCHEIBE, PLANIERKOLBEN, MONTAGEGESTELL, TRAGGESTELL |
| 4117 | **DOLOMITE, MAGNESIAN LIMESTONE, CALCIUM MAGNESIUM CARBONATE** | DOLOMIE, DOLOMITE | DOLOMIT |
| 4118 | **DOME CAP NUT** | ECROU BORGNE | HUTMUTTER |
| 4119 | **DOME LIGHT** | PLAFONNIER | DECKENLEUCHTE |
| 4120 | **DOME ROOF** | TOIT BOMBE | KUPPELDACH |
| 4121 | **DOME-ROOF TANK** | RESERVOIR A TOIT BOMBE | TANK MIT GEWÖLBTEM DECKEL |
| 4122 | **DOOR AND WINDOW IRONS** | FERS D'HUISSERIE | BESCHLÄGE FÜR TÜREN UND FENSTER |
| 4123 | **DOOR LOCK** | SERRURE DE PORTIERE | TÜRSCHLOSS |
| 4124 | **DORMANT SCRAP** | FERRAILLES DE PROTECTION PROPRE | HÜTTENSCHROTT |
| 4125 | **DOTTED BROKEN LINE** | LIGNE POINTILLEE, LIGNE PONCTUEE, TRAIT PONCTUE | LINIE (GESTRICHELTE), LINIE (PUNKTIERTE) |
| 4126 | **DOTTING PEN, WHEEL PEN** | TIRE-LIGNE A POINTILLER | PUNKTIERFEDER |
| 4127 | **DOUBLE ARMED PULLEY** | POULIE A BRASSURE DOUBLE | RIEMENSCHEIBE MIT DOPPELSPEICHEN |
| 4128 | **DOUBLE BELT** | COURROIE DOUBLE | DOPPELRIEMEN |
| 4129 | **DOUBLE BLOCK BRAKE** | FREIN A DEUX SABOTS, FREIN A DEUX MACHOIRES | DOPPELKLOTZBREMSE, DOPPELBACKENBREMSE |
| 4130 | **DOUBLE BUTT STRAP RIVETED JOINT, BUTT RIVETED JOINT WITH TWO WELTS** | RIVURE A DEUX COUVRE-JOINTS, RIVURE A DOUBLE COUVRE-JOINT | LASCHENNIETUNG (ZWEISEITIGE), LASCHENNIETUNG (DOPPELSEITIGE), DOPPELLASCHENNIETUNG |
| 4131 | **DOUBLE CRANKED LEVER, T-LEVER** | LEVIER A TROIS BRAS | HEBEL (DREIARMIGER) |

**DOU** 106

| | | | |
|---|---|---|---|
| 4132 | DOUBLE CUT | TAILLE CROISEE | KREUZHIEB |
| 4133 | DOUBLE CUT FILE, CROSS CUT FILE | LIME A DOUBLE TAILLE, LIME A TAILLE CROISEE | FEILE ZWEIHIEBIGE, DOPPELSCHNITTFEILE |
| 4134 | DOUBLE CUT, CROSS CUT OF A FILE | TAILLE CROISEE, DOUBLE TAILLE D'UNE LIME | KREUZHIEB, ZWEIFACHER HIEB EINER FELLE |
| 4135 | DOUBLE DECIMETRE | DOUBLE DECIMETRE | ANLEGEMASSSTAB |
| 4136 | DOUBLE DECOMPOSITION | DOUBLE DECOMPOSITION | WECHSELZERSETZUNG, UMSETZUNG (CHEMISCHE) |
| 4137 | DOUBLE ENDED PLUG LIMIT GAUGE | JAUGE-TAMPON DOUBLE A LIMITES | GRENZLEHRDORN |
| 4138 | DOUBLE FEEDING | ALIMENTATION DOUBLE | ZUFUHR (DOPPELTE) |
| 4139 | DOUBLE FLANGE | DOUBLE BRIDE | DOPPELFLANSCH |
| 4140 | DOUBLE FRAME HAMMER | MARTEAU DE FORGE DOUBLE CORPS | DOPPELSAÜLESCHMIEDEHAMMER |
| 4141 | DOUBLE FULL FILLET JOINT | JOINT SOUDE A DOUBLE CLIN | DOPPELKEHLNAHT |
| 4142 | DOUBLE GEAR | DOUBLE HARNAIS, DOUBLE TRAIN D'ENGRENAGES | DOPPELGETRIEBE |
| 4143 | DOUBLE HELICAL SPUR WHEEL, HERRINGBONE GEAR WHEEL | ROUE A CHEVRONS | WINKELRAD, PFEILRAD |
| 4144 | DOUBLE HELICAL TOOTH, HERRINGBONE TOOTH | DENT A CHEVRON, CHEVRON | WINKELZAHN, PFEILZAHN |
| 4145 | DOUBLE INTEGRAL | INTEGRALE DOUBLE | DOPPELINTEGRAL |
| 4146 | DOUBLE IRON PLANE, PLANE WITH TOP, BACK IRON | RABOT A CONTRE-FER | DOPPELHOBEL |
| 4147 | DOUBLE LEVER | LEVIER DOUBLE, A DEUX BRAS | HEBEL (DOPPELARMIGER), HEBEL ZWEIARMIGER, DOPPELHE |
| 4148 | DOUBLE MEMBER SNAP GAUGE | JAUGE-FOURCHE A TOLERANCES | GRENZ-RACHENLEHRE (DOPPELSEITIGE) |
| 4149 | DOUBLE NIPPLE | MAMELON A DEUX FILETS | DOPPELNIPPEL |
| 4150 | DOUBLE RACK IN FRAME | CADRE A CREMAILLERES, CADRE DENTE | KULISSENZAHNSTANGE |
| 4151 | DOUBLE REFRACTION | DOUBLE REFRACTION | DOPPELBRECHUNG |
| 4152 | DOUBLE RIVETED JOINT | RIVURE DOUBLE, RIVURE A DEUX RANGS | NIETUNG (ZWEIREIHIGE), NIETUNG (DOPPELTE) |
| 4153 | DOUBLE SALT | SEL DOUBLE | DOPPELSALZ |
| 4154 | DOUBLE SEATED VALVE | ROBINET A SOUPAPE DOUBLE | DOPPELSITZVENTIL |
| 4155 | DOUBLE SHEAR RIVETED JOINT | RIVURE A DEUX COUPES | NIETUNG (ZWEISCHNITTIGE) |
| 4156 | DOUBLE SHEAR STEEL | ACIER, FER DOUBLE CORROYE, FER FORT SUPERIEUR | STAHL (ZWEIMAL GEÄRBTER), DOPPELGÄRBSTAHL |
| 4157 | DOUBLE SIDED MECHANICAL PRESS | PRESSE MECANIQUE A ARCADE | DOPPELSTÄNDER PRESSE (MECHANISCHE) |
| 4158 | DOUBLE SOCKET | MANCHON POUR RACCORDER DEUX TUYAUX COUPES | ÜBERSCHIEBER, ÜBERSCHIEBMUFFE, DOPPELMUFFE |
| 4159 | DOUBLE STANDARD | MONTANT DOUBLE, MONTANT JUMELE | DOPPELSTÄNDER |
| 4160 | DOUBLE TWISTED AUGER | MECHE TORSE, MECHE A COUTEAUX RENVERSES | SCHLANGENBOHRER |
| 4161 | DOUBLE WALL TANK | RESERVOIR A DOUBLE PAROI | TANK, DOPPELWANDIGER |
| 4162 | DOUBLE WEDGE DISC | OPERCULE DOUBLE | ZWEITEILIGER KEIL |
| 4163 | DOUBLE-ACTING | DOUBLE EFFET (A) | DOPPELTWIRKEND |
| 4164 | DOUBLE-ACTING PISTON | PISTON A DOUBLE EFFET | KOLBEN (DOPPELTWIRKENDER) |
| 4165 | DOUBLE-ACTING STEAM ENGINE | MACHINE A DOUBLE EFFET | DAMPFMASCHINE (DOPPELTWIRKENDE) |
| 4166 | DOUBLE-BEAT VALVE, CORNISH VALVE | SOUPAPE A DOUBLE SIEGE | VENTIL (DOPPELSITZIGES), DOPPELSITZVENTIL |
| 4167 | DOUBLE-ENDED SPANNER | CLEF A FOURCHE DOUBLE, CLEF DE CALIBRE DOUBLE | SCHRAUBENSCHLÜSSEL (DOPPELMÄULIGER), DOPPELSCHLÜSSEL |

| | | | |
|---|---|---|---|
| 4168 | **DOUBLE-EXPANSION ENGINE** | MACHINE A DOUBLE EXPANSION | ZWEIFACH-EXPANSIONSMASCHINE |
| 4169 | **DOUBLE-FACED HAMMER** | MARTEAU A DEUX TETES | FLÄCHENHAMMER, HAMMER MIT ZWEI BAHNEN |
| 4170 | **DOUBLE-WALLED** | DOUBLE PAROI (A) | DOPPELWANDIG |
| 4171 | **DOUBLE-WELDED LAP JOINT** | JOINT A RECOUVREMENT SOUDE DES DEUX COTES | BEIDERSEITIG GESCHWEISSTE ÜBERLAPPUNGSVERBINDUNG |
| 4172 | **DOUBLET** | DOUBLET | DUBLETT, DOUBLET |
| 4173 | **DOUBLING-OVER TEST** | ESSAI DE PLIAGE | FALTVERSUCH |
| 4174 | **DOUBLING-PLATE** | PLATINE (PETITE PLAQUE METALLIQUE) | ZWISCHENPLATTE, PLATINE |
| 4175 | **DOVETAIL** | QUEUE D'ARONDE, QUEUE D'HIRONDE, TENON D'AGRAFAGE | SCHWALBENSCHWANZ |
| 4176 | **DOVETAIL CUTTERS** | FRAISES POUR QUEUE D'ARONDE | SCHWALBENSCHWANZFRÄSER |
| 4177 | **DOVETAILED** | QUEUE D'ARONDE (A) | SCHWALBENSCHWANZFÖRMIG |
| 4178 | **DOVETAILED JOINT** | ASSEMBLAGE A QUEUE D'ARONDE | SCHWALBENSCHWANZVERBINDUNG |
| 4179 | **DOVETAILING MACHINE** | MACHINE A FAIRE LES TENONS EN QUEUE D'ARONDE | ZINKENSCHNEIDMASCHINE |
| 4180 | **DOWEL** | GOUJON EN BOIS, CHEVILLE | DÜBEL, BOLZEN |
| 4181 | **DOWEL PIN** | GOUJON | PASSSTIFT, PASSBOLZEN |
| 4182 | **DOWN MILLING** | FRAISAGE EN DESCENDANT | GLEICHLÄUFIGES FRÄSEN |
| 4183 | **DOWN PIPE** | TUYAU, TUBE DE DESCENTE | FALLROHR |
| 4184 | **DOWN STREAM** | EN AVAL, D'AVAL | STROMABWÄRTS, MIT DEM STROM |
| 4185 | **DOWN-COMER BAR** | BARRE DE DEVERSOIR | FALLROHR |
| 4186 | **DOWN-GATE** | DESCENTE DE COULEE | EINGUSSKANAL, EINLAUF |
| 4187 | **DOWN-STROKE DESCENT OF PISTON** | DESCENTE DU PISTON, COURSE DESCENDANTE DU PISTON | KOLBENNIEDERGANG |
| 4188 | **DOWNCOMERS BELOW TRAYS** | DEVERSOIR DES PLATEAUX | FALLROHR UNTER SCHEIBEN |
| 4189 | **DOWNDRAFT CARBURETTOR** | CARBURATEUR INVERSE | FALLSTROMVERGASER |
| 4190 | **DOWNHAND POSITION** | SOUDURE EN POSITION A PLAT | SCHWEISSUNG (WAAGERECHTE) |
| 4191 | **DOWNTIME** | TEMPS MORT | STILLSTANDZEIT |
| 4192 | **DOWNWARD VERTICAL POSITION** | SOUDURE EN POSITION VERTICALE DESCENDANTE | ABWÄRTSSCHWEISSUNG |
| 4193 | **DOWNWARDS PULLED DIE** | MATRICE A DESCENTE COMMANDEE | ABZUGSMANTELMATRIZE |
| 4194 | **DOWSON GAS, MIXED SEMI-WATER GAS** | GAZ PAUVRE | MISCHGAS, KRAFTGAS, DOWSONGAS, SAUGGAS, HALBWASSERGAS |
| 4195 | **DRAFT (TO)** | DESSINER, TRACER | ZEICHNEN |
| 4196 | **DRAFT (U.S) - DRAUGHT (GB)** | TIRAGE, REDUCTION CONICITE, DEPOUILLE | ZUG, ANZUG, SCHRÄGE |
| 4197 | **DRAFT ANGLE** | ANGLE DE RETRAIT | AUSZIEHWINKEL |
| 4198 | **DRAFTING OFFICE** | BUREAU DE DESSIN | ZEICHENBÜRO |
| 4199 | **DRAG** | PARTIE DE DESSOUS (DE MOULE) | FORMUNTERTEIL |
| 4200 | **DRAG COEFFICIENT** | COEFFICIENT DE TRAINEE | WIDERSTANDSBEIWERT (LUFT) |
| 4201 | **DRAG-IN** | SOLUTION ADHERENTE | EINGESCHLEPPTE LOSÜNG, EÏNTRAG |
| 4202 | **DRAG-OUT** | SOLUTION ENTRAINEE | HERAUSGESCHLEPPTE LÖSUNG, AUSTRAG |
| 4203 | **DRAGON'S BLOOD** | SANG-DRAGON | DRACHENBLUT |
| 4204 | **DRAIN (TO)** | VIDER, VIDANGER, DRAINER, PURGER | ENTWÄSSERN |
| 4205 | **DRAIN COCK** | ROBINET PURGEUR, ROBINET DE VIDANGE | ABLASSVENTIL, ABLASSHAHN |
| 4206 | **DRAIN PIPE** | PURGE | ENTLEERUNGSROHR |
| 4207 | **DRAIN PIPE, DISCHARGE PIPE, WASTE PIPE** | TUYAU D'ECOULEMENT, TUYAU D'EVACUATION, TUYAU DE DECHARGE, TUYAU DE DEBIT | ABFLUSSROHR, ABLEITUNGSROHR |

**DRA** 108

| 4208 | DRAIN PLUG | BOUCHON DE VIDANGE | ABLASSSCHRAUBE |
|---|---|---|---|
| 4209 | DRAIN THE SOIL (TO) | DRAINER UNE TERRE HUMIDE | BODEN ENTWÄSSERN |
| 4210 | DRAINAGE | DRAINAGE, ASSECHEMENT, ECOULEMENT | ENTWÄSSERN, TROCKENLEGUNG |
| 4211 | DRAUGHT GAUGE | MANOMETRE POUR DETERMINATIONS ANEMOMETRIQUES | ZUGMESSER (FÜR SCHORNSTEINE UND GEBLÄSE) |
| 4212 | DRAUGHT OF A CHIMNEY, CHIMNEY DRAUGHT | TIRAGE D'UNE CHEMINEE | ZUG EINES SCHORNSTEINS, SCHORNSTEINZUG, KAMINZUG |
| 4213 | DRAUGHTSMAN | DESSINATEUR | ZEICHNER |
| 4214 | DRAUGHTSMAN, DESIGNER | MECANICIEN-CONSTRUCTEUR | KONSTRUKTEUR, KONSTRUKTIONSINGENIEUR |
| 4215 | DRAW (TO) | TIRER | ZIEHEN |
| 4216 | DRAW A PERPENDICULAR (TO) | ABAISSER UNE PERPENDICULAIRE, ABAISSER UNE VERTICALE | FÄLLEN (EIN LOT) |
| 4217 | DRAW BAR | BARRE, CROCHET D'ATTELAGE | ZUGHAKEN, ZUGSTANGE |
| 4218 | DRAW BENCH | BANC D'ETIRAGE | ZIEHBANK, DRAHTZIEHBANK |
| 4219 | DRAW DOWN (TO) | ECROUIR | RECKEN, STRECKEN (EISEN) |
| 4220 | DRAW INTO WIRE(TO) | TREFILER, ETIRER EN FIL | DRAHTZIEHEN, AUSZIEHEN (ZU DRAHT) |
| 4221 | DRAW KNIFE | PLANE | ZIEHMESSER, ZIEHKLINGE, SCHNITZMESSER |
| 4222 | DRAW ON (TO), PULL ON A WHEEL (TO), DRAW ON A PULLEY (TO) | SERRER UNE ROUE, SERRER UNE POULIE SUR L'ARBRE | AUFPRESSEN (EIN RAD), AUFPRESSEN (EINE RIEMENSCHEIBE), AUFZIEHEN (EIN RAD), AUFZIEHEN (EINE RIEMENSCHEIBE) |
| 4223 | DRAW PLATE | FILIERE, FILIERE DE TREFILAGE | DRAHTZIEHEISEN, ZIEHEISEN |
| 4224 | DRAW TUBES (TO) | ETIRER LES TUBES | ROHRE ZIEHEN |
| 4225 | DRAW-OFF | SOUTIRAGE-VIDANGE | ENTNAHME |
| 4226 | DRAW-OFF NOZZLE WITH PERIPHERICAL SUMP | TUBULURE DE PURGE AVEC CUVETTE PERIPHERIQUE | ENTLEERUNGSSTUTZEN MIT UMFANGSWANNE |
| 4227 | DRAW-OFF PAN | CAISSON DE SOUTIRAGE | ANZAPFUNGSTANK |
| 4228 | DRAWABILITY | ETIRABILITE | ZIEHBARKEIT |
| 4229 | DRAWING | DESSIN, PLAN | ZEICHNUNG |
| 4230 | DRAWING | TREFILAGE, ETIRAGE, ETIRAGE A FROID, FILAGE, RETIRURE, REFROIDISSEMENT LENT, REVENU | ZIEHEN, DRAHTZIEHEN,SCHWINDUNG, LANGSAMES ABKÜHLEN, ABLASSEN, TEMPERN |
| 4231 | DRAWING BOARD | PLANCHE A DESSIN | REISSBRETT, ZEICHENBRETT |
| 4232 | DRAWING BRASS | LAITON D'ETIRAGE | ZIEHMESSING |
| 4233 | DRAWING COMPOUND | GRAISSE D'ETIRAGE | ZIEHFETT |
| 4234 | DRAWING DIE | ANNEAU, MATRICE A ETIRER | ZIEHWERKZEUG, ZIEHRING |
| 4235 | DRAWING DOWN | ECROUISSAGE | RECKEN, STRECKEN DES EISENS |
| 4236 | DRAWING INSTRUMENTS | OUTILS ET INSTRUMENTS DE DESSIN, OUTILLAGE DU DESSINATEUR | ZEICHENGERÄT, ZEICHENUTENSILIEN |
| 4237 | DRAWING MACHINE | DEMOULEUSE | ABHEBEFORMMASCHINE |
| 4238 | DRAWING OFFICE | BUREAU DE DESSIN | ZEICHENSAAL, ZEICHENBÜRO |
| 4239 | DRAWING OUT DEVICE | DISPOSITIF A RETIRER | AUSZIEHVORRICHTUNG |
| 4240 | DRAWING PAPER | PAPIER A DESSIN | ZEICHENPAPIER |
| 4241 | DRAWING PEN | TIRE-LIGNE | REISSFEDER, ZIEHFEDER |
| 4242 | DRAWING PIN | PUNAISE | REISSZWECKE, HEFTZWEKE, REISSNAGEL, HEFTSTIFT |
| 4243 | DRAWING TABLE OR DESK | TABLE A DESSIN, TABLE DE DESSINATEUR | ZEICHENTISCH |
| 4244 | DRAWING TOOL | OUTIL A ETIRER, OUTIL A TREFILER | ZIEHWERKZEUG |

**109**      **DRI**

| | | | |
|---|---|---|---|
| 4245 | **DRAWING, DRAFT** | DESSIN (REPRESENTATION GRAPHIQUE) | ZEICHNUNG |
| 4246 | **DRAWING, DRAFTING** | DESSIN (ART DU DESSINATEUR) | ZEICHNEN |
| 4247 | **DRAWN** | ETIRE | GESCHRECKT |
| 4248 | **DRAWN BARS** | BARRES ETIREES | STABSTAHL (GEZOGENER) |
| 4249 | **DRAWN HALF ROUNDS** | DEMI-RONDS TREFILES | HALBRUNDSTAHL (GEZOGENER) |
| 4250 | **DRAWN SHEETS** | TOLES ETIREES | BLECHE (GESTRECKTE) |
| 4251 | **DRAWN STEEL** | ACIER ETIRE | STAHL (GEZOGENER) |
| 4252 | **DRAWN WIRE** | FIL ETIRE, FIL TREFILE | DRAHT (GEZOGENER), STRECKDRAHT |
| 4253 | **DRESS ORES (TO)** | TRAITER MECANIQUEMENT LES MINERAIS | ERZE AUFBEREITEN |
| 4254 | **DRESSER** | EBARBEUR | GUSSPUTZER |
| 4255 | **DRIED SAND** | SABLE SEC | SAND (TROCKENER) |
| 4256 | **DRIER** | ETUVE, SECHOIR, SICCATIF | TROCKENSCHRANK, SIKKATIV |
| 4257 | **DRIER, SICCATIVE** | SICCATIF | TROCKENSTOFF, SIKKATIV |
| 4258 | **DRIERS : GRAIN** | SECHOIRS A GRAINS | GETREIDETROCKNER |
| 4259 | **DRIERS : GRASS AND GREEN CROP** | SECHOIRS A FOURRAGES | GRASTROCKNER |
| 4260 | **DRIFT** | MANDRIN, BROCHE | DORN, EINTREIBDORN |
| 4261 | **DRIFT (OR TAPER) PUNCH** | BROCHE D'ASSEMBLAGE | DURCHTREIBER |
| 4262 | **DRIFT A RIVET HOLE (TO)** | ELARGIR AU MANDRIN, MANDRINER UN TROU DE RIVET | NIETLOCH AUFDORNEN (EIN) |
| 4263 | **DRILL** | FORET, MECHE | BOHRER |
| 4264 | **DRILL (TO)** | PERCER, FORER | BOHREN |
| 4265 | **DRILL BIT** | TREPAN | BOHRSTANGE, BOHRKRONE |
| 4266 | **DRILL CHUCK** | MANCHON PORTE-MECHE | BOHRFUTTER |
| 4267 | **DRILL GAUGE** | CALIBRE DE PERCAGE, GABARIT DE PERCAGE | BOHRLEHRE, BOHRERLEHRE |
| 4268 | **DRILL JIGS** | GABARITS DE PERCAGE | BOHRUNGSSTEUERVORRICHTUNG |
| 4269 | **DRILL POINT SIZE** | DIAMETRE DE LA POINTE DU FORET | BOHRERSPITZENDURCHMESSER |
| 4270 | **DRILL STEELS FOR ROCK DRILLS** | ACIERS DE TARIERES POUR FORAGES | BOHRSTÄHLE FÜR GESTEINS-BOHRUNGEN |
| 4271 | **DRILL, BIT** | FORET, MECHE | BOHRER |
| 4272 | **DRILLABLE LINER** | COLONNE PERDUE FORABLE | PERFORIERBARES VERLORENES ROHR |
| 4273 | **DRILLED HOLE** | TROU FORE, TROU ALESE | LOCH (GEBOHRTES), BOHRLOCH |
| 4274 | **DRILLED PLATE** | TOLE A TROUS FORES | BLECH MIT GEBOHRTEN LÖCHERN |
| 4275 | **DRILLED RIVET HOLE** | TROU DE RIVET PERCE, FORE | NIETLOCH GEBOHRTES |
| 4276 | **DRILLER** | PERCEUR -MECANICIEN, FOREUR | BOHRER (ARBEITER) |
| 4277 | **DRILLING** | PERCAGE, TARAUDAGE, FORAGE | BOHREN, BOHRUNG |
| 4278 | **DRILLING HEAD STOCK** | POUPEE DE PERCAGE | BOHRSPINDELSTOCK |
| 4279 | **DRILLING MACHINE** | MACHINE A FORER, FOREUSE, MACHINE A PERCER, PERCEUSE, ALESEUSE | BOHRMASCHINE |
| 4280 | **DRILLING OIL** | HUILE POUR FORER | BOHRÖL |
| 4281 | **DRINKING WATER** | EAU POTABLE, EAU DE BOISSON | TRINKWASSER |
| 4282 | **DRIP** | GOUTTE | TROPFEN |
| 4283 | **DRIP CUP, DRIP PAN, OIL COLLECTOR, OIL TRAY** | CUVETTE D'EGOUTTAGE | TROPFSCHALE, ÖLSCHALE, AUFFANGSCHALE, ÖLSCHIFF, ÖLFÄNGER |
| 4284 | **DRIP FEED LUBRICATION, DROP FEED LUBRICATION** | GRAISSAGE PAR COMPTE-GOUTTES | TROPFSCHMIERUNG |
| 4285 | **DRIP MOULDING** | GOUTTIERE | TROPFRINNE |
| 4286 | **DRIP MOULDING PLIERS** | PINCE DE JET D'EAU | REGENRINNENZANGE |

# DRI

**110**

| | | | |
|---|---|---|---|
| 4287 | DRIP OIL FEED | GRAISSAGE COMPTE-GOUTTES | TROPFÖLSCHMIERUNG |
| 4288 | DRIVE | CARRE D'ENTRAINEMENT | MITNEHMERSTANGENEINSATZ |
| 4289 | DRIVE (TO) | COMMANDER, ACTIONNER, METTRE EN MOUVEMENT | ANTREIBEN |
| 4290 | DRIVE AXLE | ESSIEU MOTEUR | TREIBACHSE |
| 4291 | DRIVE BY FRICTION (TO) | ENTRAINER PAR FROTTEMENT | REIBUNG MITNEHMEN (DURCH) |
| 4292 | DRIVE IN (TO), HAMMER IN A NAIL (TO) | ENFONCER UN CLOU | EINTREIBEN (EINEN NAGEL), EINSCHLAGEN (EINEN NAGEL) |
| 4293 | DRIVE IN A KEY (TO) | ENFONCER UN COIN, FORCER UNE CLAVETTE DANS SA RAINURE | EINTREIBEN (EINEN KEIL) |
| 4294 | DRIVE LINE | TRANSMISSION | KRAFTÜBERTRAGUNG |
| 4295 | DRIVE OUT A KEY (TO) | CHASSER UNE CLAVETTE, DECALER | AUSTREIBEN (EINEN KEIL) |
| 4296 | DRIVE SHAFT | ARBRE DE TRANSMISSION | ANTRIEBSWELLE |
| 4297 | DRIVE, DRIVING | COMMANDE, ATTAQUE | ANTREIBEN, ANTRIEB |
| 4298 | DRIVEN PULLEY, FOLLOWING PULLEY | POULIE COMMANDEE, POULIE CONDUITE, POULIE MENEE, POULIE ENTRAINEE, POULIE RECEPTRICE | GETRIEBENE SCHEIBE, ANGETRIEBENE SCHEIBE |
| 4299 | DRIVEN SHAFT | ARBRE MENE, CONDUIT, ARBRE RECEPTEUR | WELLE (ANGETRIEBENE) |
| 4300 | DRIVEN WHEEL, FOLLOWER | ROUE MENEE, CONDUITE, ROUE RECEPTRICE | RAD (ANGETRIEBENES) |
| 4301 | DRIVER | TAQUET, SAILLANT, ENTRAINEUR, DOIGT, TOC D'ENTRAINEMENT | MITNEHMER |
| 4302 | DRIVER'S LICENCE | PERMIS DE CONDUIRE | FÜHRERSCHEIN |
| 4303 | DRIVING | ENTRAINEMENT | ANTRIEB |
| 4304 | DRIVING BY FRICTION | ENTRAINEMENT (PAR FROTTEMENT) | MITNEHMEN (DURCH REIBUNG) |
| 4305 | DRIVING CHAIN | CHAINE DE TRANSMISSION | TRIEBKETTE |
| 4306 | DRIVING CHAIN, DRIVE CHAIN | CHAINE DE TRANSMISSION, CHAINE MOTRICE | TRIEBKETTE, TREIBKETTE |
| 4307 | DRIVING FIT | EMMANCHEMENT, AJUSTAGE, MONTAGE BLOQUE | TREIBSITZ |
| 4308 | DRIVING FLASK | FLACON DESSECHANT, FLACON SECHEUR | TROCKENFLASCHE, TROCKENGLAS |
| 4309 | DRIVING GEAR | MECANISME DE COMMANDE, COMMANDE, ORGANE DE COMMANDE | TRIEB, ANTRIEBVORRICHTUNG, ANTRIEBMECHANISMUS |
| 4310 | DRIVING IN OF A KEY | ENCASTREMENT, CALAGE D'UNE CLAVETTE | EINTREIBEN EINES KEILS |
| 4311 | DRIVING MECHANISM | MECANISME DE COMMANDE | TRIEBWERK |
| 4312 | DRIVING OUT A KEY | DECALAGE (ACTION D'OTER LES CALES) | AUSTREIBEN EINES KEILS |
| 4313 | DRIVING PULLEY | POULIE MOTRICE, POULIE CONDUCTRICE, POULIE MENANTE, POULIE DE COMMANDE, POULIE D'ATTAQUE | TREIBENDE SCHEIBE, ANTRIEBSCHEIBE |
| 4314 | DRIVING ROPE, TRANSMISION ROPE | CABLE DE TRANSMISSION, CORDE-COURROIE | ANTRIEBSEIL, TRIEBWERKSEIL, TRANSMISSIONSSEIL, TREIBSEIL |
| 4315 | DRIVING SHAFT | ARBRE MOTEUR, ARBRE DE COMMANDE | TRIEBWELLE, WELLE (TREIBENDE), ANTRIEBWELLE, STEUERWELLE |
| 4316 | DRIVING SIDE LEADING SIDE TIGHT SIDE OF A BELT, ROPE ETC. | BRIN CONDUCTEUR, BRIN MENANT, MENEUR, BRIN MOTEUR, BRIN TENDU (D'UNE COURROIE SANS FIN) | TRUMM (ZIEHENDES), TRUMM (AUFLAUFENDES) |
| 4317 | DRIVING SPINDLE | BIELLE DE COMMANDE | ANTRIEBSPINDEL |

| | | | |
|---|---|---|---|
| 4318 | **DRIVING WHEEL, DRIVER** | ROUE MOTRICE, ROUE DE COMMANDE, ROUE MENANTE, ROUE CONDUCTRICE | TRIEBRAD, TREIBENDES RAD |
| 4319 | **DRIVINGS, DRIVE BY BELTS** | COMMANDE PAR COURROIE | RIEMENANTRIEB, RIEMENBETRIEB |
| 4320 | **DROP (TO), FALL INTO GEAR (TO)** | RETOMBER (CLIQUET) | EINFALLEN (KLINKE) |
| 4321 | **DROP BOTTLE** | COMPTE-GOUTTES | TROPFFLASCHE |
| 4322 | **DROP CENTER RIM** | JANTE A BASE CREUSE | TIEFBETTFELGE |
| 4323 | **DROP FEED LUBRICATOR, DRIP FEED LUBRICATOR** | GRAISSEUR COMPTE-GOUTTES | TROPFÖLER, ÖLTROPFAPPARAT |
| 4324 | **DROP FORGING** | PIECE MATRICEE | GESENKSCHMIEDESTÜCK |
| 4325 | **DROP FORGING HAMMER** | MARTEAU-PILON, MOUTON | FALLHAMMER |
| 4326 | **DROP HAMMER** | MOUTON, MARTEAU-PILON | FALLHAMMER, FALLWERK, GLEISHAMMER, PRISMENHAMMER, RAHMENHAMMER, PARALLELHAMMER, STEMPELHAMMER |
| 4327 | **DROP STAMPER** | MARTEAU-PILON, MOUTON A CHUTE LIBRE | FALLHAMMER |
| 4328 | **DROP TEST** | ESSAI DE CHOC (CHUTE), ESSAI DE FLEXION PAR CHOC, ESSAI DE CHOC SUR BARREAUX NON ENTAILLES | SCHLAGBIEGEPROBE, SCHLAGVERSUCH, FALLVERSUCH |
| 4329 | **DROP WEIGHT** | POIDS DU MOUTON | FALLGEWICHT |
| 4330 | **DROP WEIGHT TEST** | ESSAI DE CHUTE DE POIDS | GEWICHTSFALLVERSUCH |
| 4331 | **DROSS** | ECUME, CRASSE | SCHAUM, KRÄTZE, GEKRÄTZ |
| 4332 | **DROSS HOLE** | TROU A CRASSE | SCHLACKENLOCH |
| 4333 | **DRUM** | POULIE-TAMBOUR, TAMBOUR | RIEMENTROMMEL, TROMMEL |
| 4334 | **DRUM BRAKE** | FREIN A TAMBOUR | TROMMELBREMSE |
| 4335 | **DRUM CLEANING** | NETTOYAGE AU TAMBOUR | TROMMELN |
| 4336 | **DRUM LADLE** | POCHE-TONNEAU | TROMMELPFANNE, GIESSTROMMEL |
| 4337 | **DRUNKEN SAW** | SCIE OSCILLANTE | TAUMELSÄGE |
| 4338 | **DRY (TO), DESICCATE (TO), GROW DRY (TO)** | SECHER, DESSECHER | TROCKNEN |
| 4339 | **DRY AIR** | AIR SEC | LUFT (TROCKNE) |
| 4340 | **DRY AIR PUMP** | POMPE A AIR SEC | LUFTPUMPE (TROCKNE) |
| 4341 | **DRY ANALYSIS** | ANALYSE PAR VOIE SECHE | ANALYSE AUF TROCKENEM WEGE |
| 4342 | **DRY BINDER** | LIANT SEC | TROCKENBINDER |
| 4343 | **DRY CELL** | PILE SECHE | TROCKENELEMENT |
| 4344 | **DRY COAL** | HOUILLE SECHE A LONGUE FLAMME | KOHLE (TROCKNE), SANDKOHLE, SINTERKOHLE |
| 4345 | **DRY COMPRESSOR** | COMPRESSEUR SEC | VERDICHTER (TROCKENER) |
| 4346 | **DRY DISTILLATION** | DISTILLATION SECHE | DESTILLATION (TROCKENE) |
| 4347 | **DRY DRAWING** | ETIRAGE BRILLANT | GLANZZIEHEN |
| 4348 | **DRY LINER** | CHEMISE SECHE | LAUFBÜCHSE (TROCKENE) |
| 4349 | **DRY METALLURGY** | THERMOMETALLURGIE | PYROMETALLURGIE |
| 4350 | **DRY OXIDATION** | OXYDATION (OU CORROSION) SECHE | OXIDATION (ODER KORROSION) TROCKENE |
| 4351 | **DRY STEAM** | VAPEUR SECHE | DAMPFTROCKNER |
| 4352 | **DRY STRENGTH** | STABILITE A SEC | TROCKENFESTIGKEIT |
| 4353 | **DRY-SAND CASTING** | COULEE EN SABLE SEC, ETUVE | TROCKENGUSS |
| 4354 | **DRY-SAND MOULDING** | MOULAGE ETUVE, MOULAGE EN SABLE ETUVE, MOULAGE EN SABLE SEC | TROCKENSANDFORMEN |
| 4355 | **DRYING APPARATUS, DRIER** | SECHOIR | TROCKNER, TROCKENVORRICHTUNG |
| 4356 | **DRYING CHAMBER** | SECHEUR, APPAREIL SECHEUR | TROCKENKAMMER |
| 4357 | **DRYING OIL** | HUILE SICCATIVE | ÖL (TROCKNENDES), TROCKENÖL |

**DRY** 112

| | | | |
|---|---|---|---|
| 4358 | DRYING STOVE | ETUVE | TROCKENSCHRANK, TROCKENKASTEN, TROCKENOFEN |
| 4359 | DRYING, DESICCATION | SECHAGE, DESSICCATION | TROCKNEN |
| 4360 | DUAL BARREL CARBURETTOR | CARBURATEUR A DOUBLE CORPS | DOPPELVERGASER |
| 4361 | DUCTILE | DUCTILE | DEHNBAR, STRECKBAR, ZIEHBAR, SCHMIEGSAM-STRECKBAR |
| 4362 | DUCTILE CAST IRON | FONTE A GRAPHITE SPEROIDAL | KUGELGRAPHIT-GUSSEISEN |
| 4363 | DUCTILITY | DUCTILITE | DUKTILITÄT, DEHNBARKEIT, STRECKBARKEIT, ZIEHBARKEIT |
| 4364 | DUG PEAT | TOURBE MOTTIERE | HANDSTICHTORF |
| 4365 | DULL BLUNT CUTTING EDGE | ARETE TRANCHANTE EMOUSSEE | SCHNEIDE (STUMPFE) |
| 4366 | DULL CHROMIUM PLATE | CHOMAGE MAT | MATTVERCHROMUNG |
| 4367 | DULL RED HEAT | ROUGE SOMBRE | DUNKELROTGLUT |
| 4368 | DULL RED HOT | CHAUFFE AU ROUGE SOMBRE | DUNKELROTGLÜHEND |
| 4369 | DULLING | TERNISSEMENT | GLANZVERLUST |
| 4370 | DUMMY | PRE-MODELE, MAQUETTE | VORMODELL |
| 4371 | DUMMY BLOCK | BILLETTE | PRESSBLOCK (IN DER STRANGPRESSE) |
| 4372 | DUMMY PASS | CANNELURE, PASSE A VIDE | BLINDSTICH, BLINDKALIBER |
| 4373 | DUMMY ROLL | CYLINDRE A VIDE | BLINDWALZE |
| 4374 | DUMP TEST | ESSAI D'ECRASEMENT | STAUCHVERSUCH |
| 4375 | DUMP TRUCK | CAMION A BENNE BASCULANTE | KIPPER |
| 4376 | DUMPING | DEVERSEMENT | KIPPEN |
| 4377 | DUNT | FISSURE | HAARRISS |
| 4378 | DUPLEX ALLOY | ALLIAGE DUPLEX, ALLIAGE BINAIRE | BIMETALLLEGIERUNG |
| 4379 | DUPLEX MANUFACTURING MILLING MACHINE | FRAISEUSE DUPLEX A GRAND RENDEMENT | HOCHLEISTUNGSDUPLEXFRÄSMASCHINE |
| 4380 | DUPLEX PRACTICE | PROCEDE DUPLEX | DUPLEXVERFAHREN |
| 4381 | DUPLEX PUMP | POMPE DUPLEX | DUPLEXPUMPE |
| 4382 | DUPLEX SPOT WELDER | MACHINE DE SOUDAGE DOUBLE POINT | DOPPELPUNKTSCHWEISSMASCHINE |
| 4383 | DUPLICATE MOLDING | SURMOULAGE | FORMEN NACH DEM GUSSSTÜCK |
| 4384 | DUPLICATE TEST | CONTRE-ESSAI, CONTRE-EPROUVETTE | GEGENPROE |
| 4385 | DURABILITY | CONSERVABILITE, STABILITE, DURABILITE | HALTBARKEIT, DAUERHAFTIGKEIT |
| 4386 | DURABLE | DURABLE | DAUERHAFT |
| 4387 | DURALUMIN | DURALUMIN | DURALUMIN |
| 4388 | DURVILLE POURING | COULEE TRANQUILLE | GIESSEN (WIRBELFREIES) |
| 4389 | DUST | POUSSIERE | STAUB |
| 4390 | DUST ARRESTOR | ASPIRATEUR DE POUSSIERES | STAUBFÄNGER, GICHTSTAUBSAMMLER |
| 4391 | DUST COLLECTING UNITS | APPAREILS DE DEPOUSSIERAGE | ENTSTAUBUNGSAPPARATE |
| 4392 | DUST COLLECTION BY EXHAUST VENTILATION | CAPTAGE DU GAZ ET DEPOUSSIERAGE | GASABZUG UND STAUBABSAUGUNG |
| 4393 | DUST PROOF | A L'ABRI DE LA POUSSIERE | STAUBDICHT |
| 4394 | DUSTING | POUDRAGE AU SULFURE | EINSTAUBEN MIT SCHWEFEL, SCHWEFELBESTÄUBUNG |
| 4395 | DUTY CYCLE | REGIME D'UTILISATION | AUSLASTUNGSGRAD |
| 4396 | DWELL | ARRET TEMPORISE | VERWEILZEIT |
| 4397 | DYE | COLORANT | FARBSTOFF |
| 4398 | DYNAMIC STRESS | CONTRAINTE DYNAMIQUE | BEANSPRUCHUNG (DYNAMISCHE) |
| 4399 | DYNAMICAL | DYNAMIQUE | DYNAMISCH |

| | | |
|---|---|---|
| 4400 | **DYNAMICS** | DYNAMIQUE | DYNAMIK |
| 4401 | **DYNAMITE** | DYNAMITE | DYNAMIT |
| 4402 | **DYNAMO (GB)** | DYNAMO | LICHTMASCHINE |
| 4403 | **DYNAMOMETER** | DYNAMOMETRE | FEDERWAAGE, LEISTUNGSMESSER, KRAFTMESSER, DYNAMOMETER |
| 4404 | **DYNAMOMETRICAL** | DYNAMOMETRIQUE | DYNAMOMETRISCH |
| 4405 | **DYNE** | DYNE | DYN, DYNE |
| 4406 | **DYNODE** | DYNODE | DYNODE |
| 4407 | **DYSPROSIUM** | DYSPROSIUM | DYSPROSIUM |
| 4408 | **EAR** | CORNE D'EMBOUTISSAGE, PLI | ECKE, FALTE |
| 4409 | **EARTH** | TERRE, MASSE (TERRE) | ERDE, MASSE |
| 4410 | **EARTH (TO), GROUND (TO)** | METTRE A LA TERRE, RELIER A LA TERRE (ELECTR.) | ERDEN |
| 4411 | **EARTH CABLE** | CABLE DE MASSE | MASSEKABEL |
| 4412 | **EARTH COLOUR, MINERAL DYE** | MATIERE COLORANTE MINERALE | ERDFARBE, MINERALFARBE |
| 4413 | **EARTH WAX, MINERAL WAX, OZOKERITE** | CIRE FOSSILE, OZOKERITE | ERDWACHS, BERGWACHS, BERGTALG, OZOKERIT |
| 4414 | **EARTH-MOVING EQUIPMENT** | EQUIPEMENT POUR NIVELER LE SOL | BAGGER, SCHÜRFRAUPE |
| 4415 | **EARTH, EARTH CONNECTION ; GROUND** | TERRE (ELECTR.), CONTACT A LA TERRE | ERDE, ERDLEITUNG, ERDUNG, ERDSCHLUSS |
| 4416 | **EARTHENWARE PIPE** | TUYAU EN POTERIE, EN TERRE CUITE | TONROHR |
| 4417 | **EARTHING** | MISE A LA TERRE | ERDUNG |
| 4418 | **EARTHING BOSS** | BOSSAGE DE MISE A LA TERRE | ERDKONTAKT |
| 4419 | **EARTHING LUG** | TAQUET DE MISE A LA TERRE | ERDUNGSKLEMME |
| 4420 | **EARTHWORK** | TERRASSEMENTS | ERDBAUTEN, ERDARBEITEN |
| 4421 | **EARTHY FRACTURE** | CASSURE TERREUSE | BRUCH (ERDIGER) |
| 4422 | **EAU DE LABARRAQUE (SODIUM HYPOCHLORITE SOLUTION)** | EAU DE LABARRAQUE (SOLUTION DE CHLORURE DE SOUDE) | LABARRAQUESCHE LAUGE, EAU DE LABARRAQUE (NATRIUMHYPOCHLORITLÖSUNG, CHLORSODALÖSUNG) |
| 4423 | **EBONY** | EBENE | EBENHOLZ |
| 4424 | **ECCENTRIC** | EXCENTRIQUE, EXCENTRE | AUSSERMITTIG, EXZENTRISCH |
| 4425 | **ECCENTRIC (ADJ.)** | EXCENTRIQUE | EXZENTER |
| 4426 | **ECCENTRIC CIRCLES** | CERCLES EXCENTRIQUES | KREISE (EXZENTRISCHE) |
| 4427 | **ECCENTRIC CRANK MOTION** | MECANISME A MANIVELLE EXCENTRIQUE | KURBELTRIEB (GESCHRÄNKTER), KURBELTRIEB (EXZENTRISCHER) |
| 4428 | **ECCENTRIC LOAD** | CHARGE EXCENTRIQUE | BELASTUNG (EXZENTRISCHE), BELASTUNG (AUSSERMITTIGE) |
| 4429 | **ECCENTRIC PISTON RING** | SEGMENT DE PISTON EXCENTRE | KOLBENRING (EXZENTRISCHER) |
| 4430 | **ECCENTRIC PRESS** | PRESSE A EXCENTRIQUE | EXZENTERPRESSE |
| 4431 | **ECCENTRIC ROD** | TIGE, BARRE D'EXCENTRIQUE | EXZENTERSTANGE |
| 4432 | **ECCENTRIC ROD END** | TETE DE LA TIGE D'EXCENTRIQUE | EXZENTERSTANGENKOPF |
| 4433 | **ECCENTRIC SHEAVE** | EXCENTRIQUE, EXCENTRIQUE CIRCULAIRE A COLLIER | EXZENTER, KREISEXZENTER, SCHEIBENKURBEL |
| 4434 | **ECCENTRIC SHEAVE PULLEY** | DISQUE D' EXCENTRIQUE, POULIE D' EXCENTRIQUE | EXZENTERSCHEIBE |
| 4435 | **ECCENTRIC STRAP HOOP** | COLLIER, BAGUE D'EXCENTRIQUE | EXZENTERBÜGEL, EXZENTERRING |
| 4436 | **ECCENTRICITY** | EXCENTRICITE | EXZENTRIZITÄT |
| 4437 | **ECONOMIZER** | ECONOMISEUR (DE CARBURANT) | KRAFTSTOFFSPARER, RAUCHGASVORWÄRMER, EKONOMISER |
| 4438 | **EDDY CURRENT** | COURANT DE FOUCAULT | WIRBELSTROM |
| 4439 | **EDDY CURRENT BRAKE** | FREIN A COURANTS DE FOUCAULT | WIRBELSTROMBREMSE |

| | | | |
|---|---|---|---|
| 4440 | EDDY CURRENTS, FOUCAULT CURRENTS | COURANTS DE FOUCAULT | WIRBELSTRÖME, FOUCAULTSCHE STRÖME |
| 4441 | EDGE | BORD, ARETE, RIVE, REBORD | KANTE, RAND, BLECHRAND |
| 4442 | EDGE CAM, PLATE CAM | CAME, EXCENTRIQUE A ONDES | UNRUNDE SCHEIBE, KURVENSCHEIBE |
| 4443 | EDGE DISLOCATION | DISLOCATION-COIN | STUFENVERSETZUNG |
| 4444 | EDGE FINDER | DISPOSITIF DE REPERAGE DES RIVES | KANTENDETEKTIONSVORRICHTUNG |
| 4445 | EDGE JOINT | JOINT SUR TRANCHES | ECKVERBAND |
| 4446 | EDGE MILLING CUTTER | FRAISE AXIALE | PLANFRÄSER, AXIALFRÄSER |
| 4447 | EDGE OF HOLE | ARETE D'UN TROU | LOCHKANTE, LOCHRAND |
| 4448 | EDGE OF REGRESSION | ARETE DE REBROUSSEMENT | RÜCKKEHRKANTE |
| 4449 | EDGE PREPARATION | PREPARATION DES BORDS | KANTENVORBEREITUNG |
| 4450 | EDGE RUNNER | MEULE VERTICALE, MOULIN A MEULES VERTICALES | KOLLERGANG, ROLLQUESTSCHE |
| 4451 | EDGER | MATRICE RONDE ET DIVISEE CAGE REFOULEUSE | RUNDGESENK, VERTEILGESENK, STAUCHGERÜST |
| 4452 | EDGING | REFOULEMENT | STAUCHEN |
| 4453 | EDGING MACHINES | PLIEUSES | ABKANTMASCHINEN |
| 4454 | EDGING MILL | CAGE REFOULEUSE | STAUCHGERÜST |
| 4455 | EDGING PASS | CANNELURE, PASSE REFOULEUSE | STAUCHKALIBER, STAUCHSTICH |
| 4456 | EDGING ROLL | CAGE A CYLINDRES VERTICAUX, CYLINDRE DE REFOULEMENT | VERTIKALGERÜST, STAUCHWALZE |
| 4457 | EFFECTIVE HEAT | CHALEUR UTILE, CHALEUR EFFECTIVE | NUTZWÄRME |
| 4458 | EFFECTIVE POWER | PUISSANCE EFFECTIVE, PUISSANCE AU FREIN | LEISTUNG (TATSÄCHLICHE), NUTZLEISTUNG, BREMSLEISTUNG |
| 4459 | EFFECTIVE PRESSURE | PRESSION REELLE, PRESSION ABSOLUE | ARBEITSDRUCK, DRUCK (ABSOLUTER) |
| 4460 | EFFECTIVE SECTION | SECTION CHARGEE | QUERSCHNITT (WIRKSAMER) |
| 4461 | EFFERVESCENCE | EFFERVESCENCE, BOUILLONNEMENT, MOUSSAGE | AUFBRAUSEN, SCHÄUMEN, AUFWALLEN |
| 4462 | EFFERVESCING STEEL | ACIER EFFERVESCENT, ACIER NON CALME | STAHL (UNBERUHIGTER) |
| 4463 | EFFICIENCY | RENDEMENT, EFFET UTILE | LEISTUNG, WIRKUNGSGRAD, GÜTEVERHÄLTNIS, NUTZEFFEKT |
| 4464 | EFFLORESCENCE | EFFLORESCENCE | AUSBLÜHUNG, AUSWITTERUNG, EFFLORESZENZ |
| 4465 | EFFUSION | EFFUSION | EFFUSION, AUSSTRÖMUNG |
| 4466 | EFFUSION OF GASES | EFFUSION DES GAZ | AUSFLUSS, EFFUSION VON GASEN |
| 4467 | EIGHTH BEND | COUDE AU 1/2 | ACHTELKRÜMMER |
| 4468 | EJECT | EJECTER, DEMOULER | AUSWERFEN, AUSSTOSSEN |
| 4469 | EJECTOR | EJECTEUR | EJEKTOR, AUSWERFER |
| 4470 | EJECTOR CONDENSER | CONDENSEUR PAR EJECTION, EJECTO-CONDENSEUR | STRAHLKONDENSATOR |
| 4471 | EJECTOR/KNOCK-OUT | DEFOURNEMENT PAR EXTRACTEUR A BRAS | ARMAUSWURF |
| 4472 | EJECTOR, EXHAUSTER | EJECTEUR, ELEVATEUR | EJEKTOR |
| 4473 | ELASTIC | ELASTIQUE | FEDERND, ELASTISCH |
| 4474 | ELASTIC AFTEREFFECT | ELASTICITE DE SUITE | NACHWIRKUNG (ELASTISCHE) |
| 4475 | ELASTIC CONSTANTS | CONSTANTES D'ELASTICITE | ELASTIZITÄTSKONSTANTEN |
| 4476 | ELASTIC COUPLING | ACCOUPLEMENT ELASTIQUE, MANCHON ELASTIQUE | KUPPLUNG (ELASTISCHE) |
| 4477 | ELASTIC DEFLECTION | FLEXION ELASTIQUE | DURCHBIEGUNG (ELASTISCHE), DURCHFEDERUNG |
| 4478 | ELASTIC DEFORMATION | DEFORMATION ELASTIQUE | FORMÄNDERUNG (ELASTISCHE) |

**115**     **ELE**

| | | | |
|---|---|---|---|
| 4479 | **ELASTIC DIAPHGRAM** | DIAPHRAGME ELASTIQUE, MEMBRANE | FEDERMEMBRAN |
| 4480 | **ELASTIC FORCE OF A GAS** | FORCE ELASTIQUE D'UN GAZ | SPANNKRAFT EINES GASES |
| 4481 | **ELASTIC LIMIT, LIMIT OF ELASTICITY** | LIMITE ELASTIQUE, LIMITE D'ELASTICITE | BRUCHGRENZE, ELASTIZITÄTSGRENZE |
| 4482 | **ELASTIC METALLIC PACKING** | GARNITURE, JOINT PLASTIQUE | METALLPACKUNG (NACHGIEBIGE) |
| 4483 | **ELASTIC MODULUS** | MODULE D'ELASTICITE | ELASTIZITÄTSMODUL |
| 4484 | **ELASTIC SOLID** | SOLIDE ELASTIQUE | FESTSTOFF (ELASTISCHER) |
| 4485 | **ELASTIC STRAIN** | DEFORMATION ELASTIQUE | FORMÄNDERUNG (ELASTISCHE) |
| 4486 | **ELASTIC WASHER** | RONDELLE ELASTIQUE | FEDERRING, UNTERLEGRING (FEDERNDER) |
| 4487 | **ELASTICITY** | ELASTICITE | ELASTIZITÄT, FEDERKRAFT, FEDERWIRKUNG, EIGENFEDERUNG |
| 4488 | **ELASTICITY OF COMPRESSION** | ELASTICITE DE COMPRESSION | DRUCKELASTIZITÄT |
| 4489 | **ELASTICITY OF FLEXURE** | ELASTICITE DE FLEXION | BIEGUNGSELASTIZITÄT |
| 4490 | **ELASTICITY OF TORSION** | ELASTICITE DE TORSION | TORSIONSELASTIZITÄT |
| 4491 | **ELASTICY OF ELONGATION** | ELASTICITE DE TRACTION | ZUGELASTIZITÄT |
| 4492 | **ELATED TANK** | RESERVOIR SURELEVE | HOCHBEHÄLTER, HOCHRESERVOIR |
| 4493 | **ELBOW** | COUDE | KNIESTÜCK |
| 4494 | **ELECTRIC ARC** | ARC VOLTAIQUE | LICHTBOGEN (ELEKTR.) |
| 4495 | **ELECTRIC ARC FURNACE** | FOUR A ARC | ELEKTROLICHTBOGENOFEN, LICHBOGEN(ELEKTRO)OFEN |
| 4496 | **ELECTRIC BLOW PIPE** | CHALUMEAU ELECTRIQUE | LÖTROHR (ELEKTRISCHES) |
| 4497 | **ELECTRIC BOILER** | CHAUDIERE ELECTRIQUE | ELEKTRODAMPFKESSEL, DAMPFKESSEL (ELEKTRISCH GEHEIZTER) |
| 4498 | **ELECTRIC BRAZING** | BRASAGE DUR ELECTRIQUE | ELEKTROHARTLÖTEN |
| 4499 | **ELECTRIC COIL** | BOBINE | SPULE |
| 4500 | **ELECTRIC CURRENT** | COURANT ELECTRIQUE | STROM (ELEKTRISCHER) |
| 4501 | **ELECTRIC DENSITY, CURRENT DENSITY** | DENSITE ELECTRIQUE, DENSITE DE COURANT | DICHTE (ELEKTRISCHE), STROMDICHTE |
| 4502 | **ELECTRIC DISCHARGE** | DECHARGE ELECTRIQUE | ENTLADUNG (ELEKTRISCHE) |
| 4503 | **ELECTRIC DRIVING** | COMMAMDE ELECTRIQUE | ANTRIEB (ELEKTRISCHER) |
| 4504 | **ELECTRIC ELECTROSTATIC FIELD** | CHAMP ELECTRIQUE | FELD (ELECTRISCHES) |
| 4505 | **ELECTRIC FIELD** | CHAMP ELECTRIQUE | FELD (ELEKTRISCHES), SPANNUNGSFELD |
| 4506 | **ELECTRIC FIELD INTENSITY** | INTENSITE DE CHAMP | FELDSTÄRKE |
| 4507 | **ELECTRIC FURNACE** | FOUR ELECTRIQUE | OFEN (ELEKTRISCHER), ELEKTROOFEN, ELEKTROSTAHLOFEN |
| 4508 | **ELECTRIC FURNACE ANNEALING** | RECUIT AU FOUR ELECTRIQUE | GLÜHEN IN DEM ELEKTROOFEN |
| 4509 | **ELECTRIC FURNACE IRON** | FONTE ELECTRIQUE | ELEKTROGUSSEISEN |
| 4510 | **ELECTRIC FURNACE PIG IRON** | FONTE AU FOUR ELECTRIQUE | ELEKTROGUSSEISEN |
| 4511 | **ELECTRIC FURNACE STEEL** | ACIER ELABORE AU FOUR ELECTRIQUE, ACIER ELECTRIQUE | ELEKTROSTAHL |
| 4512 | **ELECTRIC GENERATING CENTRAL STATION, POWER HOUSE, POWER STATION; ELECTRICITY WORKS** | USINE CENTRALE ELECTRIQUE, CENTRALE ELECTRIQUE | ELEKTRIZITÄTSWERK, ELEKTRISCHE ZENTRALE |
| 4513 | **ELECTRIC HEATING** | CHAUFFAGE ELECTRIQUE | HEIZUNG (ELEKTRISCHE) |
| 4514 | **ELECTRIC IGNITION** | ALLUMAGE ELECTRIQUE | ZÜNDUNG (ELEKTRISCHE) |
| 4515 | **ELECTRIC INDUCTION FURNACE** | FOUR ELECTRIQUE A INDUCTION | INDUKTIONSOFEN |
| 4516 | **ELECTRIC LAMP** | LAMPE ELECTRIQUE | LAMPE (ELEKTRISCHE) |
| 4517 | **ELECTRIC LIGHT** | LUMIERE ELECTRIQUE | LICHT (ELEKTRISCHES) |
| 4518 | **ELECTRIC LIGHTING** | ECLAIRAGE ELECTRIQUE | BELEUCHTUNG (ELEKTRISCHE) |
| 4519 | **ELECTRIC LIGHTING MAINS** | LIGNE D'ECLAIRAGE | LICHTLEITUNG (ELEKTRISCHE) |
| 4520 | **ELECTRIC LOCOMOTIVE** | LOCOMOTIVE ELECTRIQUE | LOKOMOTIVE (ELEKTRISCHE) |

**ELE** 116

| | | | |
|---|---|---|---|
| 4521 | ELECTRIC LONG-DISTANCE LINE MAINS | LIGNE DE TRANSPORT A GRANDE DISTANCE | FERNLEITUNG (ELEKTRISCHE) |
| 4522 | ELECTRIC MACHINE | MACHINE ELECTRIQUE | MASCHINE (ELEKTRISCHE) |
| 4523 | ELECTRIC MAINS | LIGNE, CANALISATION ELECTRIQUE, LIGNE CONDUCTRICE | LEITUNG (ELEKTRISCHE) |
| 4524 | ELECTRIC MOTORS, GENERATING EQUIPMENT, WELDING SETS AND LIGHTING PLANT. | MOTEURS ELECTRIQUES, GROUPES ELECTROGENES | ELEKTROMOTOREN, MASCHINENSÄTZE, SCHWEISS- UND BELEUCHTUNGSANLAGEN |
| 4525 | ELECTRIC POWER | COURANT ELECTRIQUE ENERGIE | STROM (ELEKTRISCHER) |
| 4526 | ELECTRIC POWER MAINS, TRANSMISSION LINE | LIGNE DE TRANSPORT DE FORCE | KRAFTLEITUNG (ELEKTRISCHE) |
| 4527 | ELECTRIC REGULATOR | REGULATEUR ELECTRIQUE | REGLER (ELEKTRISCHER) |
| 4528 | ELECTRIC RESISTANCE | RESISTANCE ELECTRIQUE | WIDERSTAND (ELEKTRISCHER) |
| 4529 | ELECTRIC SHOCK | COMMOTION, CHOC, SECOUSSE ELECTRIQUE | SCHLAG (ELEKTRISCHER) |
| 4530 | ELECTRIC SOLDERING IRON | FER A SOUDER ELECTRIQUE | LÖTKOLBEN-(ELEKTRISCHER) |
| 4531 | ELECTRIC SPARK MACHINING | ELECTROEROSION, ETINCELAGE ELECTRIQUE | FUNKENEROSION |
| 4532 | ELECTRIC STEEL | ACIER AU FOUR ELECTRIQUE | ELEKTROSTAHL |
| 4533 | ELECTRIC WELDING | SOUDAGE (A L'ARC) ELECTRIQUE | ELEKTROSCHWEISSEN, SCHWEISSEN (ELEKTRISCHES), SCHWEISSUNG (ELEKTRISCHE) |
| 4534 | ELECTRICAL ACCUMULATOR, STORAGE BATTERY, SECONDARY BATTERY | ACCUMULATEUR ELECTRIQUE, PILE SECONDAIRE, BATTERIE | ELEKTRISCHER SAMMLER, AKKUMULATOR, SEKUNDÄRELEMENT, BATTERIE |
| 4535 | ELECTRICAL COMPARATOR | COMPARATEUR ELECTRIQUE | VERGLEICHER (ELEKTRISCHER) |
| 4536 | ELECTRICAL CONDUCTIVITY | CONDUCTIBILITE ELECTRIQUE | LEITFÄHIGKEIT (ELEKTRISCHE) |
| 4537 | ELECTRICAL CONDUCTOR | CONDUCTEUR ELECTRIQUE | LEITER (ELEKTRISCHER) |
| 4538 | ELECTRICAL CONTACT METALS | METAUX UTILISES COMME CONTACT ELECTRIQUE | KONTAKTMETALLE (ELEKTRISCHE) |
| 4539 | ELECTRICAL ENERGY | ENERGIE, TRAVAIL ELECTRIQUE | ENERGIE (ELEKTRISCHE) |
| 4540 | ELECTRICAL ENGINEER | INGENIEUR-ELECTRICIEN | ELEKTROINGENIEUR |
| 4541 | ELECTRICAL ENGINEERING | ELECTRICITE INDUSTRIELLE | ELEKTROINGENIEURWESEN |
| 4542 | ELECTRICAL EQUIPMENT | EQUIPEMENT ELECTRIQUE | ANLAGE (ELEKTRISCHE) |
| 4543 | ELECTRICAL FITTER | MONTEUR-ELECTRICIEN | ELEKTROMONTEUR |
| 4544 | ELECTRICAL GRADE SHEET | TOLE ELECTRIQUE, TOLE DE TRANSFORMATEUR | ELEKTROBLECH, TRANSFORMATORENBLECH |
| 4545 | ELECTRICAL INSULATION | ISOLATION ELECTRIQUE | ISOLATION, ISOLIERUNG |
| 4546 | ELECTRICAL LOAD(ING) | PUISSANCE/ALIMENTATION | LAST (ELEKTRISCHE) |
| 4547 | ELECTRICAL OSCILLATION | OSCILLATION ELECTRIQUE | SCHWINGUNG (ELEKTRISCHE) |
| 4548 | ELECTRICAL RESISTIVITY | RESISTANCE SPECIFIQUE, RESISTIVITE | WIDERSTAND (SPEZIFISCHER), WIDERSTANDSFÄHIGKEIT |
| 4549 | ELECTRICAL VALVE | VALVE ELECTRIQUE, ELEMENT REDRESSEUR | VENTIL (ELEKTRISCHES) |
| 4550 | ELECTRICALLY MADE PIG IRON | FONTE ELECTRIQUE | ELEKTROROHEISEN |
| 4551 | ELECTRICIAN | ELECTRICIEN | ELEKTROTECHNIKER |
| 4552 | ELECTRICITY | ELECTRICITE | ELEKTRIZITÄT |
| 4553 | ELECTRICTY METER, SUPPLY METER | COMPTEUR D'ELECTRICITE | STROMZÄHLER, ELEKTRIZITÄTSZÄHLER |
| 4554 | ELECTRIFICATION | ELECTRIFICATION | ELEKTRIFIZIERUNG |
| 4555 | ELECTRIFY (TO) | ELECTRIFIER | ELEKTRIFIZIEREN |
| 4556 | ELECTRO DRILL | FLEURET ELECTRIQUE, FORET ELECTRIQUE | ELEKTROBOHRMASCHINE |
| 4557 | ELECTRO FORMING | ELECTRO-FORMAGE | GALVANOPLASTIK |

| | | | |
|---|---|---|---|
| 4558 | **ELECTRO REFINING** | AFFINAGE ELECTROLYTIQUE | VEREDELUNG (ELEKTROLYTISCHE), VERGÜTUNG (ELEKTROLYTISCHE) |
| 4559 | **ELECTRO-BAND MACHINING** | COUPE PAR ELECTRO-EROSION | FUNKENEROSIONSCHNITT |
| 4560 | **ELECTRO-CHEMICAL** | ELECTROCHIMIQUE | ELEKTROCHEMISCH |
| 4561 | **ELECTRO-CHEMISTRY** | ELECTROCHIMIE | ELEKTROCHEMIE |
| 4562 | **ELECTRO-DEPOSITION** | RECOUVREMENT D'UN METAL PAR VOIE ELECTRO-CHIMIQUE | GALVANISIERUNG |
| 4563 | **ELECTRO-DYNAMIC** | ELECTRODYNAMIQUE | ELEKTRODYNAMISCH |
| 4564 | **ELECTRO-DYNAMOMETER** | ELECTRODYNAMOMETRE | ELEKTRODYNAMOMETER |
| 4565 | **ELECTRO-EROSION** | ELECTRO-EROSION | ELEKTROEROSION |
| 4566 | **ELECTRO-GALVANISING** | ZINGAGE ELECTROCHIMIQUE ELECTROLYTIQUE | VERZINKUNG (KALTE), VERZINKUNG (ELEKTROLYSTISCHE), VERZINKUNG GALVANISCHE |
| 4567 | **ELECTRO-MAGNET** | ELECTRO-AIMANT | ELEKTROMAGNET |
| 4568 | **ELECTRO-STATIC** | ELECTROSTATIQUE | ELEKTROSTATISCH |
| 4569 | **ELECTRO-TYPING** | ELECTROTYPIE | ELEKTROTYPIE |
| 4570 | **ELECTROANALYSIS** | ELECTROANALYSE | ELEKTROANALYSE, ANALYSE (ELEKTROLYTISCHE) |
| 4571 | **ELECTROCHEMICAL EQUIVALENT** | EQUIVALENT ELECTROCHIMIQUE | ÄQUIVALENT (ELEKTROCHEMISCHES) |
| 4572 | **ELECTROCHEMICAL VALVE** | REDRESSEUR ELECTROCHIMIQUE | GLEICHRICHTER (ELEKTROCHEMISCHER) |
| 4573 | **ELECTROCHEMISTRY** | ELECTRO-CHIMIE | ELEKTROCHEMIE |
| 4574 | **ELECTRODE** | ELECTRODE | ELEKTRODE |
| 4575 | **ELECTRODE HOLDER** | PORTE-ELECTRODE | ELEKTRODENHALTER, ELEKTRODENZANGE |
| 4576 | **ELECTRODE METAL** | METAL DE L'ELECTRODE | ELEKTRODENMETALL |
| 4577 | **ELECTRODE POTENTIAL** | POTENTIEL D'ELECTRODE | ELEKTRODENPOTENTIAL |
| 4578 | **ELECTRODE STUB** | BOUT D'ELECTRODE | ELEKTRODENREST |
| 4579 | **ELECTRODE TIP** | POINTE DE L'ELECTRODE | ELEKTRODENSPITZE, ELEKTRODENARBEITSFLÄCHE |
| 4580 | **ELECTRODEPOSITION** | DEPOT ELECTROLYTIQUE | ABSCHEIDUNG (ELEKTROLYTISCHE) |
| 4581 | **ELECTRODISSOLUTION** | DISSOLUTION ELECTROLYTIQUE | AUFLÖSUNG (ELEKTROLYSTISCHE) |
| 4582 | **ELECTROEXTRACTION** | EXTRACTION ELECTROLYTIQUE | EXTRAKTION (ELEKTROLYTISCHE) |
| 4583 | **ELECTROGALVANIZING** | GALVANISATION (OU ZINGAGE) ELECTROLYTIQUE | VERSINKUNG (GALVANISCHE) |
| 4584 | **ELECTROLIMIT GAGE** | CALIBRE LIMITE (OU DE TOLERANCE) | ELEKTROGRENZLEHRE |
| 4585 | **ELECTROLYSE (TO)** | ELECTROLYSER | ELEKTROLYSIEREN |
| 4586 | **ELECTROLYSIS** | ELECTROLYSE | ELEKTROLYSE |
| 4587 | **ELECTROLYTE** | ELECTROLYTE | ELEKTROLYT |
| 4588 | **ELECTROLYTIC CELL** | CELLULE (OU CUVE) ELECTROLYTIQUE | BAD (ELEKTROLYTISCHES), ELEKTROLYSEUR |
| 4589 | **ELECTROLYTIC CLEANING** | DEGRAISSAGE ELECTROLYTIQUE | REINIGUNG (ELEKTROLYTISCHE) |
| 4590 | **ELECTROLYTIC CONDENSER** | CONDENSATEUR ELECTROLYTIQUE | ELEKTROLYTKONDENSATOR |
| 4591 | **ELECTROLYTIC COPPER** | CUIVRE ELECTROLYTIQUE | ELEKTROLYTKUPFER |
| 4592 | **ELECTROLYTIC DEPOSIT** | DEPOT GALVANIQUE | NIEDERSCHLAG (GALVANISCHER) |
| 4593 | **ELECTROLYTIC DEPOSITION** | DEPOT ELECTROLYTIQUE, DEPOSITION ELECTROLYTIQUE | ABSCHEIDUNG (ELEKTROLYTICHE), FÄLLUNG (ELEKTROLYTISCHE) |
| 4594 | **ELECTROLYTIC DETERMINATION** | ANALYSE ELECTROLYTIQUE | BESTIMMUNG (ELEKTROLYTISCHE) |
| 4595 | **ELECTROLYTIC DISSOCIATION** | DISSOCIATION ELECTROLYTIQUE | DISSOZIATION (ELEKTROLYTISCHE) |
| 4596 | **ELECTROLYTIC DISSOCIATION, IONISATION** | DECOMPOSITION ELECTROLYTIQUE, IONISATION | DISSOZIATION (ELEKTROLYTISCHE), IONISATION |
| 4597 | **ELECTROLYTIC FURNACE** | FOUR A CREUSET | TIEGELOFEN |
| 4598 | **ELECTROLYTIC GOLD** | OR ELECTROLYTIQUE | ELEKTROLYTGOLD |

**ELE**  118

| | | | |
|---|---|---|---|
| 4599 | ELECTROLYTIC MANGANESE | MANGANESE ELECTROLYTIQUE | MANGAN (ELEKTROLYTISCHES) |
| 4600 | ELECTROLYTIC NICKEL | NICKEL ELECTROLYTIQUE | ELEKTROLYTNICKEL, KATHODENNICKEL |
| 4601 | ELECTROLYTIC OXIDATION | OXYDATION ELECTROLYTIQUE | OXYDATION (ELEKTROCHEMISCHE) |
| 4602 | ELECTROLYTIC PARTING | SEPARATION ELECTROLYTIQUE | SCHEIDUNG (ELEKTROLYTISCHE) |
| 4603 | ELECTROLYTIC PICKLING | DECAPAGE ELECTROLYTIQUE | BEIZUNG (ELEKTROLYTISCHE) |
| 4604 | ELECTROLYTIC POLARIZATION | POLARISATION ELECTROLYTIQUE | POLARISATION (ELEKTROLYTISCHE) |
| 4605 | ELECTROLYTIC POLISHING | POLISSAGE ELECTROLYTIQUE | POLIEREN (ELEKTROLYTISCHES), ELEKTROPOLIEREN |
| 4606 | ELECTROLYTIC RECTIFIER | REDRESSEUR (OU DETECTEUR) ELECTROLYTIQUE | ELEKTROLYTGLEICHRICHTER |
| 4607 | ELECTROLYTIC REDUCTION | REDUCTION ELECTROLYTIQUE, NEGATIVATION | REDUKTION (ELEKTROLYTISCHE) |
| 4608 | ELECTROLYTIC SILVER | ARGENT ELECTROLYTIQUE | ELEKTROLYTSILBER |
| 4609 | ELECTROLYTIC SOLUTION TENSION | TENSION DE SOLUTION ELECTROLYTIQUE | LÖSUNGSSPANNUNG |
| 4610 | ELECTROLYTIC TOUGH PITCH COPPER | CUIVRE ELECTROLYTIQUE A OXYDE CUIVREUX | CUPROOXYD ELEKTROLYT (KUPFER ENTHALTENDES) |
| 4611 | ELECTROMAGNET | ELECTRO-AIMANT | ELEKTROMAGNET |
| 4612 | ELECTROMAGNETIC | ELECTROMAGNETIQUE | ELEKTROMAGNETISCH |
| 4613 | ELECTROMAGNETIC BRAKE | FREIN ELECTROMAGNETIQUE | BREMSE (ELEKTRISCHE), BREMSE (ELEKTROMAGNETISCHE) |
| 4614 | ELECTROMAGNETIC HARDNESS ANALYZER | APPAREIL ELECTRO MAGNETIQUE POUR ESSAI DE DURETE | HÄRTEPRÜFER (ELEKTROMAGNETISCHER) |
| 4615 | ELECTROMAGNETIC INDUCTION | INDUCTION MAGNETOELECTRIQUE | INDUKTION (ELEKTROMAGNETISCHE) |
| 4616 | ELECTROMAGNETIC LEAKAGE | DISPERSION ELECTROMAGNETIQUE | STREUUNG (ELEKTROMAGNETISCHE) |
| 4617 | ELECTROMAGNETIC PERCUSSIVE WELDING | SOUDAGE PAR PERCUSSION ELECTROMAGNETIQUE | SCHLAGSCHWEISSEN (ELEKTROMAGNETISCHES) |
| 4618 | ELECTROMAGNETIC SEPARATION | SEPARATION ELECTROMAGNETIQUE | SCHEIDUNG (ELEKTROMAGNETISCHE) |
| 4619 | ELECTROMAGNETIC WELDING | SOUDAGE PAR INDUCTION | INDUKTIONSSCHWEISSEN |
| 4620 | ELECTROMAGNETISM | ELECTROMAGNETISME | ELEKTROMAGNETISMUS |
| 4621 | ELECTROMETALLURGY | ELECTRO-METALLURGIE | ELEKTROMETALLURGIE |
| 4622 | ELECTROMOTIVE FORCE (E.M.F., EMF) | FORCE ELECTROMOTRICE, F E M | KRAFT (ELEKTROMOTORISCHE), EMK |
| 4623 | ELECTROMOTOR, ELECTRIC MOTOR | MOTEUR ELECTRIQUE, ELECTROMOTEUR | ELEKTROMOTOR |
| 4624 | ELECTRON | ELECTRON | ELEKTRON |
| 4625 | ELECTRON BEAM | FAISCEAU D'ELECTRONS | ELEKTRONENSTRAHL |
| 4626 | ELECTRON BEAM FOCUSING LENS | LENTILLE DE CONCENTRATION DES ELECTRONS | ELEKTRONENSTRAHLKONZENTRATIONS-LINSE |
| 4627 | ELECTRON BEAM WELDING (EBW) | SOUDAGE PAR BOMBARDEMENT ELECTRONIQUE | ELEKTRONENSTRAHLSCHWEISSEN |
| 4628 | ELECTRON GUN | CANON A ELECTRONS | ELEKTRONENSTRAHLER, ELEKTRONENKANONE |
| 4629 | ELECTRON MICROSCOPE | MICROSCOPE ELECTRONIQUE | ELEKTRONENMIKROSKOP |
| 4630 | ELECTRON-BEAM WELDING | SOUDAGE PAR BOMBARDEMENT D'ELECTRONS | ELEKTRONENSTRAHLSCHWEISSEN |
| 4631 | ELECTRONEGATIVE | ELECTRONEGATIF | NEGATIVELEKTRISCH, ELEKTRONEGATIV |
| 4632 | ELECTRONIC COMPARATOR | COMPARATEUR ELECTRONIQUE | VERGLEICHER (ELEKTRONISCHER) |
| 4633 | ELECTRONIC IGNITION | ALLUMAGE ELECTRONIQUE | ELEKTRONIKZÜNDUNG |
| 4634 | ELECTRONIC RECTIFIER | REDRESSEUR ELECTRONIQUE | GLEICHRICHTER (ELEKTRONISCHER) |
| 4635 | ELECTRONIC REGULATOR | REGULATEUR ELECTRONIQUE | REGLER (ELEKTRONISCHER) |
| 4636 | ELECTRONIC TUBES | TUBES ELECTRONIQUES | ELEKTRONENRÖHREN |
| 4637 | ELECTRONICS | ELECTRONIQUE | ELEKTRONIK |

| | | | |
|---|---|---|---|
| 4638 | **ELECTROOSMOSIS** | ELECTRO-OSMOSE | ELEKTRO-OSMOSIS |
| 4639 | **ELECTROPHORESIS, CATAPHORESIS** | ELECTROPHORESE, CATAPHORESE | ELEKTROPHORESE, KATAPHORESE |
| 4640 | **ELECTROPLATING** | GALVANOSTEGIE, ELECTROCHIMIE, GALVANOPLASTIE | GALVANOSTEGIE, ELEKTROPLATTIERUNG |
| 4641 | **ELECTROPOSITIVE** | ELECTROPOSITIF | POSITIVELEKTRISCH, ELEKTROPOSITIV |
| 4642 | **ELECTROSTATIC FORCE** | FORCE ELECTROSTATIQUE | KRAFT (ELEKTROSTATISCHE) |
| 4643 | **ELECTROSTATIC GENERATOR** | GENERATEUR ELECTROSTATIQUE | GENERATOR (ELEKTROSTATISCHER) |
| 4644 | **ELECTROSTATIC INDUCTION** | INDUCTION ELECTROSIATIQUE | INDUKTION (ELEKTROSTATISCHE) |
| 4645 | **ELECTROSTATIC PERCUSSIVE WELDING** | SOUDAGE PAR PERCUSSION A CONDENSATEUR | KONDENSATORSTOSSENTLADUNGS-SCHWEISSEN |
| 4646 | **ELECTROSTATIC SEPARATION** | SEPARATION ELECTROSTATIQUE | TRENNUNG (ELEKTROSTATISCHE) |
| 4647 | **ELECTROTECHNICAL** | ELECTROTECHNIQUE | ELEKTROTECHNISCH |
| 4648 | **ELECTROTECHNICS, ELECTROTECHNOLOGY** | ELECTROTECHNIQUE | ELEKTROTECHNIK |
| 4649 | **ELECTROTHERMAL EFFICIENCY** | RENDEMENT ELECTROTHERMIQUE | WIRKUNGSGRAD (ELEKTROTHERMISCHER) |
| 4650 | **ELECTROTHERMICS** | ELECTROTHERMIQUE | ELEKTROTHERMIE, ELEKTROWÄRMELEHRE |
| 4651 | **ELECTROTYPING** | GALVANOPLASTIE | GAVALNOPLASTIK |
| 4652 | **ELECTROWINNING** | EXTRACTION ELECTROLYTIQUE | EXTRAKTION (ELEKTROLYTISCHE) |
| 4653 | **ELECTRUM** | ELECTRUM, ELECTRE | ELEKTRUM |
| 4654 | **ELEMENT** | ELEMENT, CORPS SIMPLE | ELEMENT, GRUNDSTOFF, ELEMENT (CHEMISCHES) |
| 4655 | **ELEMENTARY ANALYSIS** | ANALYSE ELEMENTAIRE | ELEMENTARANALYSE |
| 4656 | **ELEMI** | ELEMI, RESINE ELEMI | ELEMIHARZ |
| 4657 | **ELETRO-ANALYSIS** | ELECTROANALYSE | ELEKTROANALYSE |
| 4658 | **ELEVATED TEMPERATURE** | TEMPERATURE ELEVEE | TEMPERATUR (ERHÖHTE) |
| 4659 | **ELEVATION, VERTICAL SECTION** | ELEVATION, PROJECTION VERTICALE | AUFRISS, VERTIKALPROJEKTION |
| 4660 | **ELEVATOR** | ELEVATEUR (U.S. = ASCENSEUR) | ELEVATOR (U.S. = AUFZUG, LIFT) |
| 4661 | **ELEVATORS AND LOADERS : HAY AND STRAW** | ELEVATEURS DE FOIN ET DE PAILLE | FÖRDERUNGSANLAGE (HEU UND STROH) |
| 4662 | **ELIMINATE (TO)** | ELIMINER (MATH.) | ELIMINIEREN (MATH.) |
| 4663 | **ELIMINATE HEAT (TO)** | ELIMINER, ENLEVER DE LA CHALEUR | WÄRME ABFÜHREN |
| 4664 | **ELIMINATION** | ELIMINATION (MATH.) | ELIMINATION (MATH.) |
| 4665 | **ELIMINATION OF AIR FROM A PIPE LINE** | EVACUATION DE L'AIR D'UNE CONDUITE | ENTLÜFTUNG EINER ROHRLEITUNG |
| 4666 | **ELIMINATION OF HEAT** | SOUSTRACTION DE LA CHALEUR | ABLEITUNG VON WÄRME, WÄRMEABLEITUNG |
| 4667 | **ELIMINATION, REMOVAL** | ELIMINATION, ENLEVEMENT | ENTFERNUNG, ENTFERNEN, BESEITIGUNG |
| 4668 | **ELINVAR** | ELINVAR | ELINVARLEGIERUNG |
| 4669 | **ELLIPSE** | ELLIPSE, OVALE | ELLIPSE |
| 4670 | **ELLIPSOGRAPH, ELLIPTIC TRAMMEL** | ELLIPSOGRAPHE | ELLIPSENZIRKEL, ELLIPSOGRAPH |
| 4671 | **ELLIPSOID** | ELLIPSOIDE | ELLIPSOID |
| 4672 | **ELLIPSOID OF REVOLUTION** | ELLIPSOIDE DE ROTATION, ELLIPSOIDE DE REVOLUTION | DREHUNGSELLIPSOID, UMDREHUNGSELLIPSOID, ROTATIONSELLIPSOID |
| 4673 | **ELLIPSOIDAL HEAD** | TETE GOUTTE DE SUIF D'UNE VIS | KORBBOGENKOPF |
| 4674 | **ELLIPTIC CROSS SECTION** | SECTION ELLIPTIQUE | QUERSCHNITT (ELLIPTISCHER) |
| 4675 | **ELLIPTIC CYLINDER** | CYLINDRE A BASE ELLIPTIQUE | ZYLINDER (ELLIPTISCHER) |
| 4676 | **ELLIPTIC INTEGRAL** | INTEGRALE ELLIPTIQUE | INTEGRAL (ELLIPTISCHES) |

# ELL 120

| 4677 | ELLIPTICAL OVAL GEAR WHEEL | ROUE ELLIPTIQUE, ENGRENAGE ELLIPTIQUE | ELLIPSENRAD |
|------|---|---|---|
| 4678 | ELLIPTICAL, OVAL WIRE | FIL OVALE, FIL ELLIPTIQUE | DRAHT (EIRUNDER), DRAHT (OVALER), DRAHT (ELLIPTISCHER) |
| 4679 | ELONGATION | ALLONGEMENT | DEHNUNG, AUSDEHNUNG |
| 4680 | ELONGATION, LONGITUDINAL EXTENSION | ALLONGEMENT | LÄNGSDEHNUNG |
| 4681 | ELUTRIATION | DECANTATION, LAVAGE (DU SABLE), TRIAGE PAR COURANT GAZEUX, LEVIGATION | SCHLÄMMUNG, SCHLÄMMEN |
| 4682 | EMBED IN CONCRETE (TO) | ENCASTRER DANS LE BETON | EINBETONIEREN |
| 4683 | EMBEDDABILITY | DEGRE D'ENCROUTEMENT | EINDRINGUNGSGRAD, EINSCHLIESSUNGSGRAD |
| 4684 | EMBOSSING | BOSSELAGE | RELIEFARBEIT |
| 4685 | EMBRITTLEMENT | FRAGILITE, ACCROISSEMENT DE LA FRAGILITE | SPRÖDIGKEIT, BRÜCHIGWERDEN, SPRÖDIGWERDEN, VERSPRÖDUNG. |
| 4686 | EMBRYO | EMBRYON, GERME | KEIM |
| 4687 | EMERGENCY BRAKE | FREIN DE SECOURS | NOTBREMSE |
| 4688 | EMERGENCY LIGHTING | ECLAIRAGE PROVISOIRE, ECLAIRAGE DE SECOURS | HILFSBELEUCHTUNG, NOTBELEUCHTUNG |
| 4689 | EMERGENCY LIGHTS | ECLAIRAGE DE SECOURS | NOTBELEUCHTUNG |
| 4690 | EMERGENCY LINE | LIGNE DE SECOURS, CANALISATION DE SECOURS | NOTLEITUNG (ELEKTR.) |
| 4691 | EMERGENT RAY | RAYON EMERGENT | STRAHL (AUSTRETENDER) |
| 4692 | EMERY ABRASIVE | EMERI | SCHMIRGEL |
| 4693 | EMERY CLOTH | TOILE EMERI | SCHMIRGELLEINEN, SCHMIRGELLEINWAND |
| 4694 | EMERY GRIND (TO) | POLIR A L'EMERI | ABSCHMIRGELN |
| 4695 | EMERY GRINDING | POLISSAGE A L'EMERI | SCHMIRGELN, ABSCHMIRGELN |
| 4696 | EMERY PAPER | PAPIER D' EMERI | SCHMIRGELPAPIER |
| 4697 | EMERY POWDER | POUDRE D'EMERI | SCHMIRGELPULVER |
| 4698 | EMERY WHEEL, EMERY GRINDER, EMERY BUFF | MEULE D'EMERI | SCHMIRGELSCHEIBE |
| 4699 | EMERY, CORUNDUM | EMERI, CORINDON | SCHMIRGEL, KORUND |
| 4700 | EMISSION | EMISSION | EMISSION |
| 4701 | EMISSIVE POWER, EMISSIVITY | POUVOIR EMISSIF | AUSSTRAHLUNGSVERMÖGEN, EMISSIONSVERMÖGEN |
| 4702 | EMISSIVITY | POUVOIR RAYONNANT | STRAHLUNGSVERMÖGEN |
| 4703 | EMIT RAYS (TO) | EMETTRE DES RAYONS | STRAHLEN AUSSENDEN, AUSSTRAHLEN |
| 4704 | EMPIRICAL FORMULA | FORMULE BRUTE | ERFAHRUNGSFORMEL, EMPIRISCHE FORMEL |
| 4705 | EMPTYING/OUTLET/SUCTION NOZZLE | TUBULURE DE SORTIE/ D'ASPIRATION | AUSGANGS-ROHRSTUTZEN |
| 4706 | EMULSIFIED OIL | HUILE EMULSIONNEE | EMULSIONSÖL |
| 4707 | EMULSIFY (TO), EMULSIONISE (TO) | EMULSIONNER | EMULGIEREN |
| 4708 | EMULSION | EMULSION | EMULSION |
| 4709 | ENAMEL | EMAIL | GLASFLUSS, SCHMELZ, EMAIL, EMAILLE |
| 4710 | ENAMEL (TO) | EMAILLER | EMAILLIEREN |
| 4711 | ENAMEL PAINT | PEINTURE VERNISSANTE | SCHMELZFARBE, EMAILFARBE |
| 4712 | ENAMELLING | EMAILLAGE | EMAILLIEREN, EMAILLIERUNG |
| 4713 | ENANTIOTROPIC | ENANTIOTROPIQUE | ENANTIOTROPISCH |
| 4714 | ENCASED BEAM | POUTRE ENROBEE | EINBETONIERTER TRÄGER |

**121**                                                                                     **ENG**

| | | | |
|---|---|---|---|
| 4715 | **ENCLOSED MOTOR** | MOTEUR A CARTER, MOTEUR BLINDE OU CUIRASSE | MOTOR (GEKAPSELTER), MOTOR (GESCHLOSSENER) |
| 4716 | **ENCODING** | CODAGE | KODIERUNG |
| 4717 | **END ELEVATION, END VIEW** | VUE DE FACE POSTERIEURE | RÜCKANSICHT |
| 4718 | **END GRAIN SAWING OF TIMBER** | SCIAGE VERTICAL, SCIAGE CONTRE FIL, SCIAGE EN TRAVERS, TRONCONNAGE DU BOIS | HIRNSCHNITT, QUERSCHNITT DES HOLZES |
| 4719 | **END GRAIN TIMBER, CROSS GRAIN TIMBER, TIMBER CUT A CROSS THE GRAIN** | BOIS TAILLE CONTRE LE FIL | HIRNHOLZ |
| 4720 | **END JOURNAL BEARING, END OUTER BEARING** | PALIER D'EXTREMITE | STIRNLAGER |
| 4721 | **END JOURNAL, JOURNAL AT END OF SHAFT** | TOURILLON FRONTAL, TOURILLON D EXTREMITE | STIRNZAPFEN |
| 4722 | **END MILLING CUTTER** | FRAISE EN BOUT, FRAISE RADIALE, FRAISE FRONTALE, FRAISE DE FACE, FRAISE A SURFACER | STIRNFRÄSER, RADIALFRÄSER |
| 4723 | **END MILLS** | FRAISES EN BOUT | SCHAFTFRÄSER |
| 4724 | **END OF PROGRAM** | FIN DE PROGRAMME | PROGRAMMENDE |
| 4725 | **END OF TAPE (EOT)** | FIN DE BANDE | LOCHSTREIFENENDE |
| 4726 | **END PEDESTAL BRACKET** | CHAISE EN BOUT | WINKELARM, WINKELKONSOLE, QUERKONSOLE |
| 4727 | **END PLAY** | JEU AXIAL | SPIELRAUM (AXIALER) |
| 4728 | **END WALL** | PAROI FRONTALE | STIRNWAND, KOPFWAND |
| 4729 | **END-CENTERED** | A FACES CENTREES | FLÄCHENZENTRIERT |
| 4730 | **END-OF-BLOCK (EOB)** | FIN DE BLOC | BLOCKENDE |
| 4731 | **END-OF-LINE** | FIN DE LIGNE | LINIENENDE |
| 4732 | **ENDLESS CHAIN** | CHAINE SANS FIN | KETTE (ENDLOSE) |
| 4733 | **ENDLESS ROPE** | CABLE SANS FIN | SEIL (ENDLOSES) |
| 4734 | **ENDLONG THRUST PRESSURE** | POUSSEE AXIALE, POUSSEE LONGITUDINALE | LÄNGSSCHUB, AXIALSCHUB, AXIALDRUCK |
| 4735 | **ENDLONG, SIDE PLAY IN THE SHAFT, LATERAL FLOAT OF THE SHAFT** | JEU LATERAL DES ARBRES | SPIEL (SEITLICHES) DER WELLE |
| 4736 | **ENDOSMOSE** | ENDOSMOSE | ENDOSMOSE |
| 4737 | **ENDOTHERMIC** | ENDOTHERMIQUE | WÄRMEVERZEHREND, ENDOTHERMISCH, ENDOTHERM |
| 4738 | **ENDURANCE** | ENDURANCE | DAUERHAFTIGKEIT |
| 4739 | **ENDURANCE CRACK** | FISSURE DE FATIGUE / D'ENDURANCE | DAUERRISS, ERMÜDUNGSRISS |
| 4740 | **ENDURANCE FAILURE, ENDURANCE FRACTURE** | RUPTURE DE FATIGUE / D'ENDURANCE | DAUERBRUCH |
| 4741 | **ENDURANCE LIMIT** | LIMITE D'ENDURANCE | DAUERFESTIGKEIT |
| 4742 | **ENDURANCE RATIO** | RAPPORT : LIMITE DE FATIGUE, RESISTANCE DE RUPTURE PAR FRACTION | DAUERFESTIGKEITSVERHÄLTNIS, SCHWELLFESTIGKEITSVERHÄLTNIS |
| 4743 | **ENDURANCE TEST** | ESSAI DE FATIGUE / D'ENDURANCE | DAUERVERSUCH, ERMÜDUNGSVERSUCH |
| 4744 | **ENERGIZER** | SUBSTANCE ACTIVATRICE | SUBSTANZ (AKTIVIERENDE) |
| 4745 | **ENERGY** | ENERGIE | ARBEITSVERMÖGEN, ENERGIE |
| 4746 | **ENERGY EFFICIENCY** | EFFICACITE ENERGETIQUE | WIRKUNGSGRAD (ENERGETISCHER) |
| 4747 | **ENERGY INPUT, ENERGY PUT IN** | ENERGIE, PUISSANCE ABSORBEE, PUISSANCE RECUEILLIE, TRAVAIL CONSOMME | AUFGEWANDTE ENERGIE, ZUGEFÜHRTE LEISTUNG, ARBEIT, AUFGENOMMENE LEISTUNG, AUFNAHME |
| 4748 | **ENERGY OF DISCHARGE** | ENERGIE D'ECOULEMENT | AUSSTRÖMUNGSENERGIE |
| 4749 | **ENGAGE THE CATCH (TO)** | ENCLIQUETER, ENCLENCHER | EINKLINKEN |
| 4750 | **ENGAGE WITH (TO)** | ENGAGER, ENGRENER | EINGREIFEN |

**ENG** 122

| 4751 | ENGAGEMENT OF A CATCH PAWL | ENCLANCHEMENT, ENCLENCHEMENT | EINKLINKEN |
| 4752 | ENGAGING | ENGRENEMENT | EINGRIFF |
| 4753 | ENGINE HOUSE, POWER HOUSE | BATIMENT DES MACHINES | MASCHINENGEBÄUDE, MASCHINENHAUS |
| 4754 | ENGINE MOUNTING | SUPPORT MOTEUR | MOTORAUFHÄNGUNG |
| 4755 | ENGINE OIL, MACHINE OIL | HUILE POUR MACHINES | MASCHINENÖL |
| 4756 | ENGINE PART | ORGANE DE MACHINE | TRIEBWERK |
| 4757 | ENGINE ROOM | SALLE DES MACHINES, COMPARTIMENT MOTEUR | MASCHINENHALLE, MOTORRAUM, MASCHINENRAUM |
| 4758 | ENGINE SHAFT | ARBRE DE COUCHE, ARBRE PREMIER MOTEUR | MASCHINENWELLE |
| 4759 | ENGINE WORKED WITH SUPERHEATED STEAM | MACHINE A VAPEUR SURCHAUFFEE | HEISSDAMPFMASCHINE |
| 4760 | ENGINE-BRAKE | FREIN-MOTEUR | MOTOR-BREMSE |
| 4761 | ENGINEER | INGENIEUR | INGENIEUR |
| 4762 | ENGINEER-IN-CHIEF, CHIEF ENGINEER | INGENIEUR EN CHEF | OBERINGENIEUR |
| 4763 | ENGINEERING CAST IRON | FONTE MECANIQUE | MASCHINENGUSS, GUSS FÜR DEN MASCHINENBAU |
| 4764 | ENGINEERING WORKS FACTORY | ATELIER, ETABLISSEMENT DE CONSTRUCTON DE MACHINES, USINE DE CONSTRUCTON MECANIQUE | MASCHINENBAUANSTALT, MASCHINENFABRIK |
| 4765 | ENGINEMAN | MACHINISTE, CONDUCTEUR DE MACHINE, MECANICIEN | MASCHINIST, MASCHINENFÜHRER, MASCHINENWÄRTER |
| 4766 | ENGINES (PETROL, VAPORISING OIL, DIESEL) | MOTEURS FIXES ET MOBILES | MOTOREN (BENZIN, KEROSIN UND DIESEL) |
| 4767 | ENGRAVERS' COPPER | CUIVRE POUR GRAVURE | GRAVIERKUPFER |
| 4768 | ENLARGEMENT (ENLARGED PORTION) OF A PIPE | EPANOUISSEMENT D'UN TUBE | ERWEITERUNG, ERWEITERTER TEIL (EINES ROHRES) |
| 4769 | ENLARGEMENT OF A DRAWING | AGRANDISSEMENT D'UN DESSIN | VERGRÖSSERUNG EINER ZEICHNUNG |
| 4770 | ENRICHED BLAST | VENT ENRICHI D'OXYGENE | WIND (SAUERSTOFFANGEREICHERTER) |
| 4771 | ENTRAINED AIR | AIR PARASITE, RENTREE D'AIR | FALSCHLUFT |
| 4772 | ENTRAPPED SLAG | INCLUSION DE SCORIE | SCHLACKENEINSCHLUSS |
| 4773 | ENTROPY | ENTROPIE | ENTROPIE |
| 4774 | ENTRY SIDE | COTE D'ENTREE, COTE D INTRODUCTION | EINSTECKSEITE, EINTRITTSEITE |
| 4775 | ENTRY TABLE | LIGNE DE ROULEAUX D'AMENEE | ZUFUHRROLLGANG |
| 4776 | ENVELOPE | ENVELOPPE (GEOM.) | EINHÜLLENDE, HÜLLKURVE, UMHÜLLUNGSKURVE, ENVELOPPE |
| 4777 | ENVELOPE FLAME | PANACHE | BEIFLAMME |
| 4778 | EPICYCLIC GEAR TRAIN | TRAIN EPICYCLOIDAL | UMLAUFVORGELEGE, EPIZYKELVORGELEGE |
| 4779 | EPICYCLOID | EPICYCLOIDE | EPIZYKLOIDE |
| 4780 | EPICYCLOIDAL GEAR | DENTS A FLANCS EPICYCLOIDAUX, ENGRENAGE EPICYCLOIDAL | EPIZYKLOIDENVERZAHNUNG |
| 4781 | EQUAL SIDED ANGLE IRON | CORNIERE A AILES EGALES | WINKELEISEN (GLEICHSCHENKLIGES) |
| 4782 | EQUATION | EQUATION | GLEICHUNG |
| 4783 | EQUATION OF STATE | EQUATION D'ETAT | ZUSTANDSGLEICHUNG |
| 4784 | EQUI-AXED CRYSTALS | CRISTAUX EQUIAXES | KRISTALLE (GLEICHGERICTETE) |
| 4785 | EQUILATERAL TRIANGLE | TRIANGLE EQUILATERAL | DREIECK GLEICHSEITIGES |
| 4786 | EQUILIBRIUM | EQUILIBRE | GLEICHGEWICHT |
| 4787 | EQUILIBRIUM CONSTANT | CONSTANTE D'EQUILIBRE | GLEICHGEWICHTSKONSTANTE |
| 4788 | EQUILIBRIUM DIAGRAM | DIAGRAMME D'EQUILIBRE | GLEICHGEWICHTSDIAGRAMM |

| | | | |
|---|---|---|---|
| 4789 | **EQUILIBRIUM ELECTRODE POTENTIAL** | TENSION D'EQUILIBRE D'UNE ELECTRODE | GLEICHGEWICHTSPOTENTIAL EINER ELEKTRODE |
| 4790 | **EQUILIBRIUM REACTION POTENTIAL** | TENSION D'EQUILIBRE D'UNE REACTION | STATISCHES GLEICHGEWICHTSPOTENTIAL EINER REAKTION |
| 4791 | **EQUILIBRIUM TEMPERATURE** | TEMPERATURE D'EQUILIBRE | GLEICHGEWICHTSTEMPERATUR |
| 4792 | **EQUILIBRIUM VALUE** | VALEUR D'EQUILIBRE | GLEICHGEWICHTSWERT |
| 4793 | **EQUILIBRIUM, BALANCE** | EQUILIBRE | GLEICHGEWICHT |
| 4794 | **EQUIPMENT** | OUTILLAGE | WERKSGERÄT |
| 4795 | **EQUIVALENCE** | EQUIVALENCE | GLEICHWERTIGKEIT |
| 4796 | **EQUIVALENT** | EQUIVALENT | GLEICHWERTIG, AEQUIVALENT |
| 4797 | **EQUIVALENT CONDUCTIVITY** | CONDUCTIBILITE EQUIVALENTE | ÄQUIVALENTE LEITFÄHIGKEIT |
| 4798 | **EQUIVALENT RESISTIVITY** | RESISTIVITE EQUIVALENTE | ÄQUIVALENTE WIDERSTANDSFÄHIGKEIT |
| 4799 | **ERASE (TO), RUB OUT (TO)** | GRATTER, EFFACER | AUSKRATZEN, RADIEREN, AUSRADIEREN, WEGRADIEREN |
| 4800 | **ERASER, ERASING KNIFE** | GRATTOIR DE BUREAU, GRATTOIR DE DESSINATEUR | RADIERMESSER |
| 4801 | **ERASING RUBBER** | GOMME-GRATTOIR | RADIERGUMMI |
| 4802 | **ERASING, RUBBING OUT** | GRATTAGE | RADIEREN |
| 4803 | **ERASURE** | GRATTAGE (RESULTAT) | RADIERSTELLE, RASUR |
| 4804 | **ERBIUM** | ERBIUM | ERBIUM |
| 4805 | **ERECT (TO)** | MONTER | AUFSTELLEN, ZUSAMMENBAUEN, MONTIEREN |
| 4806 | **ERECT A PERPENDICULAR (TO)** | ELEVER UNE VERTICALE, ELEVER UNE PERPENDICULAIRE | SENKRECHTE ERRICHTEN (EINE) |
| 4807 | **ERECTED CONCURRENTLY OR CONSEQUENTLY** | MONTE SIMULTANEMENT OU EN CONTINUITE | GLEICHZEITIG UND FORTLAUFEND MONTIERT |
| 4808 | **ERECTING** | MONTAGE | AUFSTELLUNG, MONTAGE |
| 4809 | **ERECTING EQUIPMENT** | MATERIEL DE MONTAGE | MONTAGEMATERIAL |
| 4810 | **ERECTING MATERIAL** | MATERIEL DE MONTAGE | MONTAGEAUSRÜSTUNG |
| 4811 | **ERECTING SHOP** | ATELIER DE MONTAGE | MONTAGEHALLE, MONTIERWERKSTATT |
| 4812 | **ERECTING TOOLS** | OUTILLAGE DE MONTAGE | MONTAGEWERKZEUG |
| 4813 | **ERECTION** | MONTAGE | MONTAGE, AUFBAU |
| 4814 | **ERECTION DRAWING** | PLAN DE MONTAGE | MONTAGEZEICHNUNG |
| 4815 | **ERECTION WORK** | MONTAGE | MONTAGE |
| 4816 | **ERECTOR** | MONTEUR | AUFSTELLER, MONTEUR |
| 4817 | **ERECTOR'S TOOLS** | OUTILLAGE DU MONTEUR | MONTAGEWERKZEUG |
| 4818 | **ERG** | ERG, DYNE-CENTIMETRE | ERG |
| 4819 | **ERICHSEN CUP-TEST MACHINE** | MACHINE D'ESSAI D'EMBOUTISSAGE D'ERICHSEN | ERICHSEN-TIEFZIEHVERSUCHSMASCHINE |
| 4820 | **EROSION** | EROSION, USURE | VERSCHLEISS, EROSION |
| 4821 | **ERRATIC, BOULDER** | BLOC ERRATIQUE | FINDLING, BLOCK ERRATISCHER |
| 4822 | **ERROR** | ERREUR | FEHLER |
| 4823 | **ERROR COUNTER** | COMPTEUR D'ERREURS | FEHLERZÄHLER |
| 4824 | **ERROR IN CALCULATION** | ERREUR DE CALCUL | RECHENFEHLER |
| 4825 | **ERROR IN DESIGN** | ERREUR DE CONCEPTION DU CONSTRUCTEUR | KONSTRUKTIONSFEHLER |
| 4826 | **ERROR IN READING** | ERREUR DE LECTURE | ABLESEFEHLER |
| 4827 | **ERROR IN VALUATION** | ERREUR D'APPRECIATION | SCHÄTZUNGSFEHLER |
| 4828 | **ERROR OF COLLIMATION** | ERREUR DE COLLIMATION | KOLLIMATIONSFEHLER |
| 4829 | **ERROR OF OBSERVATION** | ERREUR D'OBSERVATION | BEOBACHTUNGSFEHLER |
| 4830 | **ERROR REGISTER** | COMPTEUR D'ERREURS | FEHLERZÄHLER |

**ESC** 124

| | | | |
|---|---|---|---|
| 4831 | ERYTHROSIN, IODEOSIN | ERYTHROSINE, TETRAIOD-FLUORESCEINE, PRIMEROSE SOLUBLE | TETRAJODFLUORESZEIN, BLAUSTICHIGES EOSIN, ERYTHROSIN, DIANTHIN, JODEOSIN |
| 4832 | ESCAPE (TO) | ECOULER (S'), ECHAPPER (S') | AUSSTRÖMEN, ENTWEICHEN |
| 4833 | ESCAPE OF STEAM, OF GASES | ECHAPPEMENT DE VAPEUR, ECHAPPEMENT DE GAZ | ENTWEICHEN, AUSSTRÖMEN VON DAMPF, VON GASEN |
| 4834 | ESCRIBED CIRCLE | CERCLE EXINSCRIT | ANGESCHRIEBENER KREIS, ANKREIS |
| 4835 | ESCUTCHEON PLATE | RONDELLE PROTECTRICE, CACHE-ENTREE | SCHLÜSSELLOCHDECKEL |
| 4836 | ESSENTIAL VOLATILE OIL | HUILE VOLATILE, HUILE ESSENTIELLE | ÖL (FLÜCHTIGES) |
| 4837 | ESTER | ETHER COMPOSE | ESTER, ZUSAMMENGESETZTER ÄTHER, SÄUREÄTHER |
| 4838 | ESTIMATE OF THE COST | DEVIS, ESTIMATION | KOSTENANSCHLAG, VORANSCHLAG |
| 4839 | ETCH (TO) | ATTAQUER A L'ACIDE | ÄTZEN |
| 4840 | ETCH BANDS | BANDES REVELEES PAR ATTAQUE CHIMIQUE | ÄTZUNG HERVORTRETENDE BÄNDER (DURCH) |
| 4841 | ETCH CRACKS | CRIQUES D'ATTAQUE CHIMIQUE | ÄTZRISSE |
| 4842 | ETCH FIGURES | FIGURES D'ATTAQUE A L'ACIDE | ÄTZFIGUREN |
| 4843 | ETCH PITS | PIQURES DE CORROSION | STOCKFLECKEN |
| 4844 | ETCHANT | REACTIF | ÄTZMITTEL |
| 4845 | ETCHED FIGURE, CORROSION FIGURE | FIGURE DE CORROSION | ÄTZFIGUR, KRAFTWIRKUNGSFIGUR |
| 4846 | ETCHING | ATTAQUE (COR.), ATTAQUE A L'ACIDE | ÄTZEN, ÄTZUNG |
| 4847 | ETCHING REAGENT | CAUSTIQUE, CORROSIF, REACTIF D'ATTAQUE A L'ACIDE | ÄTZFLÜSSIGKEIT, ÄTZMITTEL |
| 4848 | ETHANE, DIMETHYL | ETHANE, HYDRURE D'ETHYLE, DIMETHYLE | ÄTHAN, ÄTHYLWASSERSTOFF, DIMETHYL |
| 4849 | ETHYL CHLORIDE | CHLORURE D'ETHYLE, ETHER CHLORHYDRIQUE | ÄTHYLCHLORID, CHLORÄTHYL, MONOCHLORÄTHAN, CHLORWASSERSTOFFÄTHER, SALZÄTHER |
| 4850 | ETHYL NITRATE | AZOTATE, NITRATE D'ETHYLE, ETHER NITRIQUE, ETHER AZOTIQUE | SALPETERSÄUREÄTHER, ÄTHYLNITRAT |
| 4851 | ETHYLENE, OLEFIANT GAS | ETHYLENE, HYDROGENE BICARBONE, ETHENE, GAZ OLEFIANT | SCHWERES KOHLENWASSERSTOFFGAS, ÄTHYLEN, ÖLBILDENDES GAS |
| 4852 | EUDIOMETER | EUDIOMETRE | GASPRÜFER, EUDIOMETER |
| 4853 | EUPRIC CHLORIDE | CHLORURE CUIVRIQUE | KUPFERCHLORID |
| 4854 | EUROPIUM | EUROPIUM | EUROPIUM |
| 4855 | EUTECTIC | EUTECTIQUE | EUTEKTIKUM, EUTEKTISCH |
| 4856 | EUTECTIC MELTING | FUSION EUTECTIQUE | SCHMELZUNG (EUTEKTISCHE) |
| 4857 | EUTECTIC MIXTURE | MELANGE EUTECTIQUE | MISCHUNG EUTEKTISCHE |
| 4858 | EUTECTIC TEMPERATURE | TEMPERATURE EUTECTIQUE | TEMPERATUR (EUTEKTISCHE) |
| 4859 | EUTECTOID | EUTECTOIDE | EUTEKTOID |
| 4860 | EUTECTOID REACTION | REACTION EUTECTOIDE | EUTEKTOIDE REAKTION |
| 4861 | EVAPORABLE, VAPORISABLE | EVAPORABLE | VERDAMPFBAR |
| 4862 | EVAPORATE (TO), VAPORISE (TO) | EVAPORER, VAPORISER, EVAPORER (S') | VERDAMPFEN |
| 4863 | EVAPORATE IN THE OPEN AIR (TO) | EVAPORER (S') A L'AIR LIBRE | VERDUNSTEN |
| 4864 | EVAPORATING DISH | CAPSULE | ABDAMPFSCHALE |
| 4865 | EVAPORATING TEMPERATURE | TEMPERATURE DE VAPORISATION | VERDAMPFUNGSTEMPERATUR |
| 4866 | EVAPORATION LOSS | PERTE PAR EVAPORATION | VERDAMPFUNGSVERLUST |
| 4867 | EVAPORATION, VAPORISATION | EVAPORATION, VAPORISATION | VERDAMPFEN |

| | | | |
|---|---|---|---|
| 4868 | EVAPORATIVE CONDENSER | CONDENSEUR A EVAPORATION | VERDUNSTUNGSKONDENSATOR, VERDAMPFUNGSKONDENSATOR |
| 4869 | EVAPORATOR | APPAREIL EVAPORATEUR | ABDAMPFVORRICHTUNG, VERDAMPFER |
| 4870 | EVAPORATOR BODY | CAISSE OU CORPS D'UN EVAPORATEUR | VERDAMPFERKÖRPER |
| 4871 | EVEN FRACTURE | CASSURE UNIE, RABOTEUSE | BRUCH (EBENER) |
| 4872 | EVEN NUMBER | NOMBRE PAIR | ZAHL (GERADE) |
| 4873 | EVOLUTE | DEVELOPPEE, EVOLUTE | EVOLUTE |
| 4874 | EVOLUTION OF HEAT | DEGAGEMENT DE CHALEUR | WÄRMEENTWICKLUNG |
| 4875 | EXACT MEASUREMENT | MESURAGE EXACT, PRECIS | FEINMESSUNG |
| 4876 | EXAMINATION | EXAMEN, CONTROLE | ÜBERPRÜFUNG |
| 4877 | EXAMINATION BY SECTIONING | INSPECTION PAR TREPANAGE | ROHRKONTROLLE DURCH TRENNUNG |
| 4878 | EXCESS | EXCES | ÜBERSCHUSS |
| 4879 | EXCESS FLOW VALVE | LIMITEUR OU REGULATEUR DE DEBIT | STROMBEGRENZUNGSVENTIL |
| 4880 | EXCESS OF WORK | EXCES DE TRAVAIL | MEHRARBEIT |
| 4881 | EXCESS VOLTAGE | SURVOLTAGE | ÜBERSPANNUNG (ELEKTR.) |
| 4882 | EXCESS-ACETYLENE FLAME | FLAMME REDUCTRICE | REDUKTIONSFLAMME |
| 4883 | EXCESS-OXYGEN FLAME | FLAMME OXYDANTE | OXYDATIONSFLAMME |
| 4884 | EXCHANGE OF HEAT | ECHANGE DE CHALEUR | WÄRMEAUSTAUSCH |
| 4885 | EXCITATION | EXCITATION | ERREGUNG (PHYS.) |
| 4886 | EXCITATION ANODE | ANODE D'EXCITATION | ERREGERANODE |
| 4887 | EXCITE (TO) | EXCITER | ERREGEN |
| 4888 | EXCITER | EXCITATRICE | ERREGERMASCHINE |
| 4889 | EXFOLIATION | AFFOUILLEMENT, ECAILLEMENT | ABBLÄTTERUNG, HÄUTUNG |
| 4890 | EXHAUST | ECHAPPEMENT (DES GAZ D'UN MOTEUR) | AUSPUFF, AUSLASS |
| 4891 | EXHAUST GAS | GAZ D'ECHAPPEMENT | AUSPUFFGAS |
| 4892 | EXHAUST LINE | LIGNE D'ECHAPPEMENT DE LA VAPEUR | DAMPFAUSSTRÖMLINIE, AUSSTRÖMLINIE |
| 4893 | EXHAUST MANIFOLD | COLLECTEUR D'ECHAPPEMENT | AUSPUFFSAMMELROHR |
| 4894 | EXHAUST PIPE | TUYAU D'ECHAPPEMENT, TUBULURE D ECHAPPEMENT | AUSPUFFROHR |
| 4895 | EXHAUST PORT, EDUCTION PORT | LUMIERE D'ECHAPPEMENT | AUSLASSSCHLITZ |
| 4896 | EXHAUST STEAM | VAPEUR D'ECHAPPEMENT | ABDAMPF |
| 4897 | EXHAUST STEAM PIPE | TUYAU D'ECHAPPEMENT DE VAPEUR | ABDAMPFROHR, DAMPFAUSLASSROHR, DAMPFABLEITUNGSROHR |
| 4898 | EXHAUST STROKE | COURSE D'ECHAPPEMENT | AUSPUFFHUB |
| 4899 | EXHAUST VALVE | SOUPAPE D'ECHAPPEMENT, SOUPAPE D EMISSION | AUSLASSVENTIL |
| 4900 | EXHAUSTER | EXTRACTEUR, EXHAUSTEUR | ABSAUGER, EXHAUSTOR |
| 4901 | EXOTHERMIC | EXOTHERMIQUE | WÄRMEGEBEND, EXOTHERMISCH, EXOTHERM |
| 4902 | EXPAND (TO) | DETENDRE (SE) | AUSDEHNEN (SICH), EXPANDIEREN |
| 4903 | EXPAND A TUBE (TO) | ELARGIR UN TUBE AU MANDRIN, MANDRINER UN TUBE | AUFWEITEN (EIN ROHR), AUFTREIBEN (EIN ROHR), AUFDORNEN (EIN ROHR) |
| 4904 | EXPANDED METAL | METAL DEPLOYE | STRECKMETALL |
| 4905 | EXPANDED TUBE | TUBE DUDGEONNE | ROHR (EINGEWALZTES) |
| 4906 | EXPANDING CHUCKS | MANDRINS EXPANSIBLES | SPREIZBARE DORNE |
| 4907 | EXPANDING MANDREL | MANDRIN DE MONTAGE EXPANSIBLE | SPREIZDORN |

# EXP

126

| | | | |
|---|---|---|---|
| 4908 | EXPANDING OF TUBES | DUDGEONNAGE, SERTISSAGE DES TUYAUX AU DUDGEON | EINWALZEN VON ROHREN |
| 4909 | EXPANDING PULLEY | POULIE EXTENSIBLE, POULIE A EXPANSION | EXPANSIONSRIEMENSCHEIBE |
| 4910 | EXPANDING ROLLER | GALET TENDEUR | SPANNROLLE |
| 4911 | EXPANDING TEST | ESSAI DE MANDRINAGE | AUFTREIBEPROBE, AUFWEITEPROBE |
| 4912 | EXPANSION | AUGMENTATION DE VOLUME | VOLUMEN-AUFNAHME |
| 4913 | EXPANSION BEND | TUBE COMPENSATEUR, COMPENSATEUR DE DILATATION, COUDE, LYRE DE COMPENSATION, CINTRE DE DILATATION, LYRE DE DILATATION | AUSGLEICHROHR, DEHNUNGSROHR, FEDERROHR, KOMPENSATIONSROHR, LYRA, ROHRBOGENAUSGLEICHER |
| 4914 | EXPANSION COEFFICIENT | COEFFICIENT DE DILATION | AUSDEHNUNGSKOEFFIZIENT |
| 4915 | EXPANSION COUPLING | MANCHON DE DILATATION | AUSDEHNUNGSKUPPLUNG, KUPPLUNG (LÄNGSBEWEGLICHE) |
| 4916 | EXPANSION CURVE, CURVE OF EXPANSION | COURBE DE DETENTE | EXPANSIONSKURVE |
| 4917 | EXPANSION HAND REAMER | ALESOIR A MAIN EXPANSIBLE | HAND (NACHSTELLBARE) |
| 4918 | EXPANSION JOINT | JOINT DE DILATATION | AUSDEHNUNGSFUGE, AUSGLEICHFUGE, TEMPERATURFUGE, DEHNUNGSDICHTUNG, DEHNUNGSFUGE |
| 4919 | EXPANSION OF A METAL | DILATATION D'UN METAL | METALLAUSDEHNUNG |
| 4920 | EXPANSION OF GAS | DETENTE DES GAZ | GASEXPANSION |
| 4921 | EXPANSION OF STEAM, OF A GAS | DETENTE DE LA VAPEUR, DETENTE D UN GAZ | EXPANSION, AUSDEHNUNG VON DAMPF ODER GAS |
| 4922 | EXPANSION PIECE | PIECE DE COMPENSATION | AUSDEHNUNGSSTÜCK |
| 4923 | EXPANSION REAMER | ALESOIR EXPANSIBLE | REIBAHLE (NACHSTELLBARE) |
| 4924 | EXPANSION STEAM ENGINE, ENGINE | MACHINE A DETENTE, MACHINE A EXPANSION | EXPANSIONSDAMPFMASCHINE |
| 4925 | EXPANSION TURBINE | TURBINE A DETENTE | EXPANSIONSTURBINE |
| 4926 | EXPANSION VALVE | SOUPAPE DE DETENTE | EXPANSIONSVENTIL |
| 4927 | EXPECTED VALUE | ESPERANCE MATHEMATIQUE | ERWARTUNGSWERT |
| 4928 | EXPERIMENT (TO) | FAIRE DES ESSAIS | VERSUCHE MACHEN, EXPERIMENTIEREN |
| 4929 | EXPERIMENTAL DETERMINATION | DETERMINATION EXPERIMENTALE | BESTIMMUNG (EXPERIMENTELLE) |
| 4930 | EXPERT | EXPERT | SACHVERSTÄNDIGER, GUTACHTER |
| 4931 | EXPERT'S REPORT | EXPERTISE | GUTACHTEN |
| 4932 | EXPIRATION OF A PATENT | EXPIRATION D'UN BREVET | ABLAUF EINES PATENTES, PATENTABLAUF |
| 4933 | EXPLODE (TO) | EXPLOSER | BERSTEN, ZERKNALLEN, EXPLODIEREN |
| 4934 | EXPLODED VIEW | VUE ECLATEE | ANSICHT (EXPLODIERTE) |
| 4935 | EXPLOSION | EXPLOSION | EXPLOSION, BERSTEN, ZERKNALL |
| 4936 | EXPLOSION PRESSURE | PRESSION EXPLOSIVE | VERPUFFUNGSDRUCK, VERBRENNUNGSDRUCK, EXPLOSIONSDRUCK |
| 4937 | EXPLOSIVE | EXPLOSIF | EXPLOSIV, SPRENGSTOFF, EXPLOSIVSTOFF |
| 4938 | EXPLOSIVE COMBUSTIBLE MIXTURE | MELANGE EXPLOSIF, MELANGE TONNANT, MELANGE DETONANT | GEMISCH (BRENNBARES), GEMISCH (ZÜNDFÄHIGES), GEMISCH (ENTZÜNDLICHES) |
| 4939 | EXPONENT | EXPOSANT | EXPONENT |
| 4940 | EXPONENT OF DISCHARGE | EXPOSANT D'ECOULEMENT | AUSFLUSSEXPONENT |
| 4941 | EXPONENTIAL DISTRIBUTION | LOI EXPONENTIELLE | EXPONENTIALVERTEILUNG |
| 4942 | EXPONENTIAL FUNCTION | FONCTION EXPONENTIELLE | EXPONENTIALFUNKTION |
| 4943 | EXPONENTIAL SERIES | SERIE EXPONENTIELLE | EXPONENTIALREIHE |
| 4944 | EXPOSURE | EXPOSITION, TEMPS DE POSE | BELICHTUNG, AUFNAHME |

**127** **FAB**

| | | | |
|---|---|---|---|
| 4945 | EXTENDING HANDLE | RALLONGE DE MANCHE | TELESKOPSTEIL |
| 4946 | EXTENSION | EXTENSION | DEHNUNG |
| 4947 | EXTENSION BAR | RALLONGE | VERLÄNGERUNGSTAB |
| 4948 | EXTENSION BY HEAT, EXPANSION DUE TO HEAT | DILATATION SOUS L'INFLUENCE DE LA CHALEUR | WÄRMEAUSDEHNUNG, AUSDEHNUNG DURCH WÄRME |
| 4949 | EXTENSOMETER | EXTENSOMETRE | DEHNUNGSMESSER |
| 4950 | EXTERNAL ANGLE | ANGLE EXTERNE | AUSSENWINKEL |
| 4951 | EXTERNAL BURR REMOVER FOR TUBES | FRAISE EBARBEUSE FEMELLE, FRAISE D'EXTERIEUR POUR TUBES | ROHRFRÄSER ZUM AUSSENFRÄSEN |
| 4952 | EXTERNAL CHASER | PEIGNE POUR L'EXTERIEUR, PEIGNE A FILETER | AUSSENSTRÄHLER |
| 4953 | EXTERNAL CYLINDRICAL GRINDING MACHINE | RECTIFIEUSE POUR SURFACES DE REVOLUTION EXTERIEURES | AUSSEN-RUNDSCHLEIF-MASCHINE |
| 4954 | EXTERNAL FORCE | FORCE EXTERIEURE, EFFORT EXTERIEUR, CHARGE | ÄUSSERE KRAFT |
| 4955 | EXTERNAL GAUGE | JAUGE D'EXTERIEUR | AUSSENLEHRE |
| 4956 | EXTERNAL GEARING | ENGRENAGE EXTERIEUR | GETRIEBE MIT AUSSENVERZAHNUNG, AUSSENGETRIEBE |
| 4957 | EXTERNAL GRINDING | RECTIFICATION EXTERIEURE | AUSSENSCHLIFF |
| 4958 | EXTERNAL OUTSIDE DIAMETER | DIAMETRE EXTERIEUR | DURCHMESSER (ÄUSSERER) |
| 4959 | EXTERNAL TEETH | DENTURE EXTERIEURE | AUSSENVERZAHNUNG |
| 4960 | EXTERNAL THREAD | FILET EXTERIEUR | AUSSENGEWINDE |
| 4961 | EXTERNAL THREADING | FILETAGE EXTERIEUR | AUSSENGEWINDE |
| 4962 | EXTERNAL WORK | TRAVAIL EXTERIEUR | ÄUSSERE ARBEIT |
| 4963 | EXTERNALLY RIBBED TUBE | TUBE A AILETTES EXTERIEURES | RIPPENROHR MIT AUSSENRIPPEN |
| 4964 | EXTRACT | EXTRAIT | AUSZUG, EXTRAKT |
| 4965 | EXTRACTION LIQUOR | LIQUIDE D'EXTRACTION | AUSLAUGEFLÜSSIGKEIT |
| 4966 | EXTRACTION OF METALS | EXTRACTION DES METAUX | GEWINNUNG VON METALLEN |
| 4967 | EXTRACTOR | EXTRACTEUR (CHIM.) | AUSLAUGER, EXTRAKTIONSAPPARAT |
| 4968 | EXTREME VALUE DISTRIBUTION | LOI DES VALEURS EXTREMES | GRENZWERTVERTEILUNG |
| 4969 | EXTRUDED MOULDINGS | MOULURES FILEES | ZIERLEISTEN (STRANGGEPRESSTE) |
| 4970 | EXTRUSION | FILAGE, EXTRUSION, FILAGE A FROID | ZIEHEN, FLIESSPRESSEN, KALTSPRITZEN, STRANGPRESSEN |
| 4971 | EXTRUSION BILLET | EBAUCHE POUR PRESSE A FILER | STRANGPRESSENROHLING |
| 4972 | EXTRUSION PRESS | PRESSE A FILER | FLIESSPRESSE |
| 4973 | EYE BOLT | PITON | RINGBOLZEN, ÖSENSCHRAUBE |
| 4974 | EYE HOOK | CROC, CROCHET A OEIL | ÖSENHAKEN |
| 4975 | EYE OF A HAMMER | OEIL D'UN MARTEAU | AUGE EINES HAMMERS, ÖHR EINES HAMMERS, ÖSE EINES HAMMERS |
| 4976 | EYE OF CONNECTING ROD | OEIL DE LA BIELLE | SCHUBSTANGENAUGE |
| 4977 | EYE-PIECE, OCULAR | SYSTEME OCULAIRE, OCULAIRE | OKULAR |
| 4978 | EYE, BORE OF A WHEEL, OF A PULLEY | ALESAGE D'UNE ROUE, ALESAGE D'UNE POULIE | BOHRUNG EINES RADES, BOHRUNG EINER RIEMENSCHEIBE |
| 4979 | EYED RIVET SNAP, EYED RIVETING SET | BOUTEROLLE A MANCHE OU A OEIL | SCHELLHAMMER |
| 4980 | EYELET | OEIL, OEILLET | ÖSE, AUGE |
| 4981 | FABRIC BELT | COURROIE EN FIBRES TEXTILES | FASERSTOFFRIEMEN, TEXTILRIEMEN |
| 4982 | FABRICATED VESSEL | APPAREIL CHAUDRONNE | BEHÄLTER (TIEFGEZOGENER) |
| 4983 | FABRICATION | FACONNAGE, USINAGE | ERZEUGUNG, HERSTELLUNG |
| 4984 | FABRICATION DRAWING | PLAN D'EXECUTION | AUSFÜHRUNGSZEICHNUNG |
| 4985 | FABRICATION JIG | MONTAGE D'USINAGE BATI MANNEQUIN | WERKSTÜCKAUFNAHME |
| 4986 | FABRICATION NUMBER | NUMERO DE CONSTRUCTION | FABRIKNUMMER |

**FAB** 128

| | | | |
|---|---|---|---|
| 4987 | FABRICATION REQUIREMENTS | EXIGENCES D'USINAGE | VERARBEITUNGSANFORDERUNGEN |
| 4988 | FABRICATION TOLERANCES | TOLERANCES D'USINAGE | VERARBEITUNGSTOLERANZEN |
| 4989 | FACE | FACE D'ATTAQUE | STIRNFLÄCHE |
| 4990 | FACE ANGLE | ANGLE DE TETE | KOPFKEGELWINKEL |
| 4991 | FACE CENTRED CUBIC | CUBIQUE A FACE CENTREE | KUBISCH-FLÄCHEN-ZENTRIERT |
| 4992 | FACE MILLING COTTERS | FRAISES A DEUX TAILLES EN BOUT | STIRNFRÄSER |
| 4993 | FACE OF A HAMMER | TETE D'UN MARTEAU, PLANCHE DU MARTEAU | HAMMERBAHN, BAHN EINES HAMMERS |
| 4994 | FACE OF A NUT | PAN D'UN ECROU | SEITENFLÄCHE EINER MUTTER |
| 4995 | FACE OF ANVIL, ANVIL FACE | TABLE D'ENCLUME | AMBOSSBAHN |
| 4996 | FACE OF SLIDE VALVE | GLACE DU TIROIR | SCHIEBERSPIEGEL |
| 4997 | FACE OF TOOTH | FACE DE LA DENT | ZAHNFLANKE (ÜBER DEM TEILKREIS) |
| 4998 | FACE OF WELD | SUPERFICIE DE LA SOUDURE | SCHWEISSNAHTOBERFLÄCHE |
| 4999 | FACE PLATE | PLAQUE CIRCULAIRE, PLAQUE FRONTALE | PLANSCHEIBE |
| 5000 | FACE SHIELD | ECRAN DE SOUDAGE | GESICHTSSCHUTZMASKE |
| 5001 | FACE SURFACING LATHE | TOUR EN L'AIR | PLANDREHBANK, KOPFDREHBANK, SCHEIBENDREHBANK |
| 5002 | FACE-CENTERED. | A FACES CENTREES | FLÄCHENZENTRIERT |
| 5003 | FACED FLANGE | BRIDE TOURNEE | FLANSCH (BEARBEITETER) |
| 5004 | FACING BRICK | PIERRE DE PAREMENT, BRIQUE DE PAREMENT | VERBLENDER, VERBLENDSTEIN |
| 5005 | FACING LATHE | TOUR EN L'AIR | PLANDREHBANK, KOPFDREHBANK |
| 5006 | FACING SAND | SABLE DE CONTACT | MODELLSAND |
| 5007 | FACING STRIP | PORTEE D'ASSEMBLAGE DRESSEE (D'UNE PIECE DE FONDERIE) | ARBEITSLEISTE |
| 5008 | FACTOR | FACTEUR | FAKTOR (MATH.) |
| 5009 | FACTOR OF SAFETY, MARGIN OF SAFETY | COEFFICIENT DE SECURITE, FACTEUR DE SECURITE | SICHERHEITSGRAD, SICHERHEITSZUGABE, SICHERHEITSKOEFFIZIENT, SICHERHEITSFAKTOR |
| 5010 | FACTORY | USINE | WERK |
| 5011 | FACTORY ACCEPTANCE GAUGE | JAUGE DE REVISION | REVISIONSLEHRE, WERKSTATTABNAHMELEHRE |
| 5012 | FACTORY BUILDING | BATIMENT D'USINE | FABRIKGEBÄUDE |
| 5013 | FACTORY, MANUFACTORY, WORKS, MILL | FABRIQUE, MANUFACTURE, USINE, ETABLISSEMENT DE FABRICATION | FABRIK |
| 5014 | FADING | DECOLORATION | VERBLASSEN |
| 5015 | FAGOT | PAQUET DE FER A SOUDER | SCHWEISSPAKET |
| 5016 | FAGOT SCRAP | MITRAILLES PAQUETEES | PAKETIERSCHROTT |
| 5017 | FAGOT, PILE | PAQUET, TROUSSE (METALLURGIE) | SCHWEISSPAKET, PAKET |
| 5018 | FAGOTING | PAQUETAGE | PAKETIEREN |
| 5019 | FAHRENHEIT SCALE | ECHELLE FAHRENHEIT | FAHRENHEITSKALA |
| 5020 | FAHRENHEIT THERMOMETER | THERMOMETRE FAHRENHEIT | FAHRENHEITTHERMOMETER |
| 5021 | FAILURE OF AN ENGINE | RATE D'UN MOTEUR | VERSAGEN EINES MOTORS |
| 5022 | FALL DIMINUTION OF TEMPERATURE | ABAISSEMENT DE LA TEMPERATURE, BAISSE DE TEMPERATURE | TEMPERATURABNAHME, TEMPERATURERNIEDRIGUNG, TEMPERATURRÜCKGANG |
| 5023 | FALL, LOOSE END (IN LIFTING TACKLE) | EXTREMITE LIBRE, BRIN GARANT DU CABLE, GARANT (D'UN PALAN) | TRUMM (FREIES), ZUGTRUMM (EINES FLASCHENZUGS) |
| 5024 | FALLING FREELY | A CHUTE LIBRE | FREIFALLEND |

| | | | |
|---|---|---|---|
| 5025 | **FALLING TEMPERATURE** | TEMPERATURE ABAISSANTE | TEMPERATUR (ABNEHMENDE), TEMPERATUR (SINKENDE), TEMPERATUR (FALLENDE) |
| 5026 | **FALSE BOTTOM** | DOUBLE FOND, FAUX FOND | BODEN (FALSCHER), DOPPELBODEN, BLINDBODEN, ZWISCHENBODEN |
| 5027 | **FALSE CORE** | NOYAU EXTERIEUR, FAUX NOYAU | KERNSTÜCK |
| 5028 | **FAMILY OF CURVES** | FAISCEAU DE COURBES | SCHAR VON KURVEN, KURVENSCHAR |
| 5029 | **FAN BELT** | COURROIE DE VENTILATEUR | VENTILATORRIEMEN |
| 5030 | **FAN BLADES** | PALES DE VENTILATEUR | VENTILATORFLÜGELBLATT |
| 5031 | **FAN BRAKE** | FREIN, MOULINET A PALETTES, MOULINET DYNAMOMETRIQUE | FLÜGELBREMSE |
| 5032 | **FAN PULLEY** | POULIE DE VENTILATEUR | VENTILATORRIEMENSCHEIBE |
| 5033 | **FAN, VENTILATOR** | VENTILATEUR | LÜFTER, VENTILATOR, WINDFLÜGEL |
| 5034 | **FANTAIL** | CARNEAU DE RACCORDEMENT | VERBINDUNGSKANAL |
| 5035 | **FARAD** | FARAD | FARAD |
| 5036 | **FARADAY CAGE** | CAGE DE FARADAY | FARADAYSCHER KÄFIG |
| 5037 | **FAST FIXED RIGID PERMANENT COUPLING** | ACCOUPLEMENT FIXE, ACCOUPLEMENT RIGIDE | KUPPLUNG (FESTE) |
| 5038 | **FAST IDLE** | RALENTI ACCELERE | LEERLAUF (SCHNELLER), LEERLAUF (ERHÖHTER) |
| 5039 | **FAST PIPE FLANGE** | BRIDE FIXE | FLANSCH (FESTER) |
| 5040 | **FAST PULLEY** | POULIE FIXE | RIEMENSCHEIBE (FESTE), FESTSCHEIBE, LASTSCHEIBE, VOLLSCHEIBE |
| 5041 | **FASTEN (TO), FIX (TO)** | FIXER | BEFESTIGEN |
| 5042 | **FASTENER** | ORGANE DE FIXATION | BEFESTIGUNGSELEMENT |
| 5043 | **FASTENING SCREW** | VIS OU BOULON DE FIXATION, VIS OU BOULON DE MONTAGE | BEFESTIGUNGSSCHRAUBE |
| 5044 | **FASTENING, FIXING** | FIXAGE, FIXATION | BEFESTIGUNG |
| 5045 | **FAT** | GRAISSE | FETT (CHEM.) |
| 5046 | **FAT RICH LIME** | CHAUX GRASSE | KALK (FETTER), FETTKALK |
| 5047 | **FATIGUE** | FATIGUE | ERMÜDUNG |
| 5048 | **FATIGUE CRACK** | FISSURE PAR FATIGUE | ERMÜDUNGSRISS |
| 5049 | **FATIGUE EXPERIMENT, TEST FOR FATIGUE (OF A MATERIAL) ; RELIABILITY TEST (OF A MACHINE OR ENGINE)** | ESSAI AUX CHOCS REPETES, ESSAI D'ENDURANCE | DAUERVERSUCH |
| 5050 | **FATIGUE LIMIT** | LIMITE D'ENDURANCE OU DE FATIGUE | DAUERGRENZE |
| 5051 | **FATIGUE OF MATERIALS** | FATIGUE D'UN MATERIEL | ERMÜDUNG DES MATERIALS |
| 5052 | **FATIGUE RESISTANCE** | RESISTANCE A LA FATIGUE | DAUERFESTIGKEIT |
| 5053 | **FATIGUE STRENGTH** | LIMITE DE FATIGUE, RESISTANCE-LIMITE D'ENDURANCE | DAUERSCHWINGFESTIGKEIT |
| 5054 | **FATIGUE TESTING** | ESSAI DE RESISTANCE A LA FATIGUE | ERMÜDUNGSVERSUCH |
| 5055 | **FATTY ACID** | ACIDE GRAS | FETTSÄURE |
| 5056 | **FAULT, FLAW IN A CASTING** | DEFAUT DE COULAGE, PAILLE | GUSSFEHLER |
| 5057 | **FAULTY, DEFECTIVE, DETERIORATED, DAMAGED** | DEFECTUEUX, ENDOMMAGE, DETERIORE | SCHADHAFT |
| 5058 | **FAYING SURFACE** | SURFACE D'AFFLEUREMENT | ANLAGEFLÄCHE, PASSFLÄCHE |
| 5059 | **FEATHER KEY** | LANGUETTE | FEDER, LÄNGSFEDER, FEDERKEIL, LÄNGSNASE |
| 5060 | **FEATHER WING RIB OF VALVE** | AILETTE DE LA SOUPAPE | FÜHRUNGSRIPPE, FÜHRUNGSLEISTE, FLÜGEL EINES VENTILS |
| 5061 | **FEATHER.** | STRIE | SCHLIERE |

**FEE** 130

| | | | |
|---|---|---|---|
| 5062 | FEATHERED BOLT, LIP BOLT, SNUG HEAD BOLT | BOULON A ERGOT | NASENSCHRAUBE |
| 5063 | FEED | ALIMENTATION, AVANCE | ZUSCHIEBUNG, VORSCHUB, SPEISUNG, ZUFÜHRUNG |
| 5064 | FEED (TO) | ALIMENTER | SPEISEN |
| 5065 | FEED CHANGE LEVER | LEVIER SELECTEUR DES AVANCES | VORSCHUBWÄHLHEBEL |
| 5066 | FEED COCK | ROBINET D'ALIMENTATION | FÜLLHAHN, SPEISEHAHN, |
| 5067 | FEED GEAR MECHANISM | MECANISME DES AVANCEMENTS | VORSCHUBMECHANISMUS |
| 5068 | FEED OF A TOOL | AVANCE D'UN OUTIL | VORSCHUB EINES WERKZEUGS |
| 5069 | FEED PER TOOTH | AVANCE PAR DENT | VORSCHUB JE ZAHN |
| 5070 | FEED PIPE | TUYAU D'ALIMENTATION | SPEISEROHR, SPEISELEITUNG |
| 5071 | FEED PUMP | POMPE D'ALIMENTATION | SPEISEPUMPE |
| 5072 | FEED REGULATOR | ALIMENTATEUR AUTOMATIQUE | SPEISEREGLER |
| 5073 | FEED REVERSE LEVER | LEVIER D'INVERSION DE L'AVANCE | VORSCHUBUMSTEUERHEBEL |
| 5074 | FEED ROLLER | CYLINDRE D'ALIMENTATION, CYLINDRE ENTRAINEUR | SPEISEWALZE, LIEFERWALZE, ZUFÜHRWALZE |
| 5075 | FEED TANK | BAC D'ALIMENTATION | SPEISEBEHÄLTER |
| 5076 | FEED VALVE | SOUPAPE D'ALIMENTATION | SPEISEVENTIL |
| 5077 | FEED WATER | EAU D'ALIMENTATION | SPEISEWASSER |
| 5078 | FEED WATER HEATER | RECHAUFFEUR D'EAU D'ALIMENTATION | SPEISEWASSER-VORWÄRMER |
| 5079 | FEED-RATE OVERRIDE | CORRECTION DE VITESSE D'AVANCE | VORSCHUBGESCHWINDIGKEITSKORREKTUR |
| 5080 | FEEDBACK LOOP | BOUCLE DE RETOUR | RÜCKFÜHRKREIS |
| 5081 | FEEDER | ARTERE, CABLE PRINCIPAL, FEEDER | SPEISELEITUNG, HAUPTLEITUNG (ELEKTR.) |
| 5082 | FEEDING | ALIMENTATION | BRENNSTOFFZUFÜHRUNG |
| 5083 | FEEDING ARRANGEMENT, FEED APPARATUS | APPAREIL D'ALIMENTATION | SPEISEVORRICHTUNG |
| 5084 | FEEDING NOZZLE | TUBULURE D'ALIMENTATION | SPEISEDÜSE |
| 5085 | FEEDRATE NUMBER (FRN) | CODE DE VITESSE D'AVANCE | VORSCHUBZAHL |
| 5086 | FEELER GAUGE | CALIBRE D'EPAISSEUR | EINSTELLLEHRE |
| 5087 | FELDSPAR | FELDSPATH | FELDSPAT |
| 5088 | FELLOE | JANTE D'UNE ROUE | FELGE, RADFELGE |
| 5089 | FELSPAR | FELDSPATH | FELDSPAT |
| 5090 | FELT | FEUTRE | FILZ |
| 5091 | FEMALE GAUGE | JAUGE D'EXTERIEUR | AUSSENLEHRE |
| 5092 | FEMALE INTERNAL SCREW THREAD | FILET, FILETAGE INTERIEUR, FILETAGE FEMELLE | INNENGEWINDE, MUTTERGEWINDE |
| 5093 | FENCE OF A PLANE | JOUE D'UN RABOT | ANSCHLAG EINES HOBELS |
| 5094 | FENCING | CLOTURE | ZAUN |
| 5095 | FENDER | AILE | KOTFLÜGEL |
| 5096 | FENDER WASHER | RONDELLE D'AILE | KOTFLÜGELSCHEIBE |
| 5097 | FERMENT | FERMENT | GÄRSTOFF, GÄRUNGSSTOFF |
| 5098 | FERMENTATION | FERMENTATION | GÄRUNG, FERMENTATION |
| 5099 | FERRIC ACETATE | ACETATE FERRIQUE | EISENOXYD (ESSIGSAURES), FERRIAZETAT |
| 5100 | FERRIC CHLORIDE | CHLORURE FERRIQUE | EISENCHLORID, FERRICHLORID |
| 5101 | FERRIC HYDROXIDE | PEROXYDE HYDRATE DE FER | EISENHYDROXYD, FERRIHYDROXYD, FERRIHYDRAT, EISENOXYDHYDRAT |
| 5102 | FERRIC OXIDE | OXYDE DE FER | EISENOXYD |
| 5103 | FERRIC SULFATE | SULFATE FERRIQUE | FERRISULFAT |
| 5104 | FERRITE | FERRITE | FERRIT |

|  |  |  |  |
|---|---|---|---|
| 5105 | **FERRITE GHOST** | BANDE DE FERRITE LIBRE | FERRITBAND (FREIES) |
| 5106 | **FERRO-ALUMINIUM** | FERRO-ALUMINIUM | ALUMINIUMEISEN, FERROALUMINIUM |
| 5107 | **FERRO-BORON** | FERRO-BORE | BOREISEN, FERROBOR |
| 5108 | **FERRO-CHROME** | FERRO-CHROME | CHROMEISEN, FERROCHROM |
| 5109 | **FERRO-CONCRETE PIPE** | TUYAU EN CIMENT ARME | ZEMENTROHR MIT EISENEINLAGE |
| 5110 | **FERRO-MANGANESE** | FERRO-MANGANESE | MANGANEISEN, EISENMANGAN, FERROMANGAN |
| 5111 | **FERRO-MOLYBDENUM** | FERRO-MOLYBDENE | MOLYBDÄNEISEN, FERROMOLYBDÄN |
| 5112 | **FERRO-NICKEL** | FERRO-NICKEL | NICKELEISEN, FERRONICKEL |
| 5113 | **FERRO-SILICON, SILICEOUS IRON** | FERRO-SILICIUM | SILIZIUMEISEN, FERROSILIZIUM |
| 5114 | **FERRO-TITANIUM** | FERRO-TITANE | TITANEISEN, FERROTITAN |
| 5115 | **FERRO-TUNGSTEN** | FERRO-TUNGSTENE | WOLFRAMEISEN, FERROWOLFRAM |
| 5116 | **FERRO-VANADIUM** | FERRO-VANADIUM | VANADIUMEISEN, FERROVANADIUM |
| 5117 | **FERROALLOYS** | FERROALLIAGES | EISENLEGIERUNGEN |
| 5118 | **FERROMAGNETIC** | FERROMAGNETIQUE | FERROMAGNETISCH |
| 5119 | **FERROPRUSSIATE PAPER** | PAPIER AU FERRO-PRUSSIATE, PAPIER PRUSSIATE, PAPIER CYANOFER, CYANOTYPE, PAPIER BLEU POUR PHOTOCALQUE | BLAUDRUCKPAPIER, EISENBLAUPAPIER, EISENZYANPAPIER |
| 5120 | **FERROUS ACETATE** | ACETATE FERREUX | ESSIGSAURES EISENOXYDUL, FERROAZETAT |
| 5121 | **FERROUS CHLORIDE** | CHLORURE FERREUX | EISENCHLORÜR, FERROCHLORID, EINFACHCHLOREISEN |
| 5122 | **FERROUS MANGANESE ORES** | MINERAIS DE MANGANESE FERREUX | EISENHALTIGES MANGANERZ |
| 5123 | **FERROUS METALLURGY** | METALLURGIE DU FER | METALLURGIE DES EISENS |
| 5124 | **FERROUS OXALATE** | OXALATE FERREUX | EISENOXALAT, FERROOXALAT, EISEN (OXALSAURES), OXYDUL |
| 5125 | **FERROUS OXYDE** | OXYDE FERREUX, PROTOXYDE DE FER | EISENOXYDUL, FERROOXYD |
| 5126 | **FERROUS SCRAP** | FERRAILLE | EISENSCHROTT |
| 5127 | **FERRUGINOUS** | FERRUGINEUX | EISENHALTIG |
| 5128 | **FERRULE** | VIROLE | ZWINGE, SPERRING |
| 5129 | **FETTLING** | EBARBAGE | ENTGRATEN, PUTZEN |
| 5130 | **FETTLING, CLEANING SHOP** | ATELIER DE DESABLAGE, ATELIER D'EBARBAGE, ATELIER D'ECROUTAGE | GUSSPUTZEREI, PUTZEREI |
| 5131 | **FIBER** | FIBRE | FASER |
| 5132 | **FIBER DIAGRAM (X-R.)** | AXE DE FIBRE | FASERACHSE |
| 5133 | **FIBER DIRECTION** | DIRECTION DES FIBRES | FASERRICHTUNG |
| 5134 | **FIBER STRESS** | EFFORT DANS LA FIBRE | FASERSPANNUNG |
| 5135 | **FIBERING** | STRUCTURE FIBREUSE | FASERSTRUKTUR |
| 5136 | **FIBRE** | FIBRE | FASER |
| 5137 | **FIBROUS** | FIBREUX | FASERIG |
| 5138 | **FIBROUS FRACTURE** | CASSURE FIBREUSE | BRUCH (FASERIGER), BRUCH (SEHNIGER) |
| 5139 | **FIBROUS IRON** | FER NERVEUX, FER A NERF | EISEN (SEHNIGES) |
| 5140 | **FIBROUS MATERIAL** | MATIERE FIBREUSE | FASERSTOFF |
| 5141 | **FIBROUS STRUCTURE, TEXTURE** | TEXTURE FIBREUSE | GEFÜGE (FASERIGES) |
| 5142 | **FIELD GUN CARRIAGE** | AFFUT DE CAMPAGNE | FELDLAFETTE |
| 5143 | **FIELD OF VIEW** | CHAMP VISUEL, CHAMP DE VISION | GESICHTSFELD, SEHFELD |
| 5144 | **FIELD STRENGTH INTENSITY** | INTENSITE DU CHAMP | FELDSTÄRKE, FELDDICHTE, FELDINTENSITÄT |
| 5145 | **FIELD SUPERINTENDENT** | CHEF DE CHANTIER | BAULEITER |

**FIF** 132

| | | | |
|---|---|---|---|
| 5146 | FIELD WELD | SOUDURE EXECUTEE SUR CHANTIER | BAUSTELLENSCHWEISSNAHT |
| 5147 | FIFTH ROOT | RACINE CINQUIEME | WURZEL (FÜNFTE) |
| 5148 | FILE | LIME | FEILE |
| 5149 | FILE (TO) | LIMER | FEILEN |
| 5150 | FILE CLEANING CARD | CARDE, BROSSE A LIMES | FEILENBÜRSTE |
| 5151 | FILE CUTTER | TAILLEUR DE LIMES | FEILENHAUER |
| 5152 | FILE HARDNESS TESTING | ESSAI DE DURETE A LA LIME | FEILENHÄRTEPROBE |
| 5153 | FILING | LIMAGE | FEILEN |
| 5154 | FILING MACHINE | MACHINE A LIMER | FEILMASCHINE |
| 5155 | FILINGS | LIMAILLE | FEILSPÄNE, FEILICHT |
| 5156 | FILL (TO), CHARGE (TO) | REMPLIR, CHARGER | FÜLLEN |
| 5157 | FILLER | CHARGE CHIMIQUE | FÜLLSTOFF |
| 5158 | FILLER CAP | BOUCHON DE REMPLISSAGE | EINFÜLLVERSCHLUSS |
| 5159 | FILLER METAL | METAL, ALLIAGE D'APPORT | FÜLLMETALL, ZUSATZWERKSTOFF |
| 5160 | FILLER PLATE SLIDE | COULISSEAU D'OBTURATION | ABSPERRUNGSSTÖSSEL |
| 5161 | FILLET | CONGE | HOHLKEHLE |
| 5162 | FILLET WELD | SOUDAGE EN ANGLE, SOUDAGE EN CONGE | KEHLNAHTSCHWEISSEN |
| 5163 | FILLING LOSS | PERTE PAR REMPLISSAGE | FÜLLVERLUST |
| 5164 | FILLING MATERIAL | MATIERE DE REMPLISSAGE | FÜLLSTOFF, AUSFÜLLMASSE |
| 5165 | FILLISTER HEAD SCREW | VIS A TETE CYLINDRIQUE | ZYLINDERSCHRAUBE |
| 5166 | FILM | COUCHE, FILM, PELLICULE | SCHICHT, FILM |
| 5167 | FILM OF OIL | PELLICULE GRASSE, MINCE COUCHE D'HUILE DE GRAISSAGE | SCHMIERSCHICHT |
| 5168 | FILM OF OXIDE | PELLICULE D'OXYDE | OXYDHAUT |
| 5169 | FILM OF WATER | PELLICULE D'EAU | WASSERHAUT |
| 5170 | FILM THICKNESS | EPAISSEUR DE FILM | FILMDICKE |
| 5171 | FILM, THIN LAYER | PELLICULE | HAUT, SCHICHT (DÜNNE) |
| 5172 | FILTER | FILTRE | FILTER |
| 5173 | FILTER (TO), STRAIN (TO) | FILTRER | FILTERN, FILTRIEREN |
| 5174 | FILTER AID | ADJUVANT DE FILTRATION | FILTERHILFSSTOFF |
| 5175 | FILTER CARTRIDGE | CARTOUCHE FILTRANTE | FILTERSIEB, FILTEREINSATZ |
| 5176 | FILTER CLOTH | ETOFFE FILTRANTE | FILTERTUCH |
| 5177 | FILTER PAPER | PAPIER A FILTRER | FILTERPAPIER, FILTRIERPAPIER |
| 5178 | FILTER TANK | BASSIN DE FILTRATION | FILTERBECKEN |
| 5179 | FILTERING MATERIAL | MATIERE FILTRANTE | FILTERSTOFF, FILTRIERMATERIAL |
| 5180 | FILTERPRESS | FILTRE-PRESSE | FILTERPRESSE |
| 5181 | FILTRATE | FILTRAT, LIQUIDE FILTRE | FILTRAT, DURCHLAUF |
| 5182 | FILTRATION, FILTERING | FILTRATION, FILTRAGE | FILTERN, FILTRIEREN, FILTRATION |
| 5183 | FIN | AILETTE, AILERON | RIPPE |
| 5184 | FIN, BURR | BAVURE (D'UNE PIECE MOULEE) | GUSSNAHT |
| 5185 | FINAL DRAWING | PLAN DEFINITIF | ZEICHNUNG (ENDGÜLTIGE) |
| 5186 | FINAL DRIVE | TRANSMISSION AUX ROUES | RADANTRIEB |
| 5187 | FINAL POSITION | POSITION FINALE | ENDLAGE, ENDSTELLUNG |
| 5188 | FINAL PRESSURE, TERMINAL PRESSURE | PRESSION FINALE | ENDDRUCK |
| 5189 | FINAL PRODUCT | PRODUIT FINAL | ENDERZEUGNIS, ENDPRODUKT |
| 5190 | FINAL STATE | ETAT FINAL | ENDZUSTAND |
| 5191 | FINAL TEMPERATURE | TEMPERATURE FINALE | ENDTEMPERATUR |
| 5192 | FINAL VALUE | VALEUR FINALE | ENDWERT |
| 5193 | FINAL VELOCITY | VITESSE FINALE | ENDGESCHWINDIGKEIT |

| | | | |
|---|---|---|---|
| 5194 | **FINAL YIELD** | RENDEMENT FINAL | ENDAUSBEUTE |
| 5195 | **FINE** | AMENDE | GELDSTRAFE |
| 5196 | **FINE BORING MACHINE** | ALESEUSE DE PRECISION | FEINBOHRMASCHINE |
| 5197 | **FINE FLUTED REAMER** | ALESOIR A FINES RAINURES | REIBAHLE (GERIFFELTE) |
| 5198 | **FINE GOLD** | OR FIN | FEINGOLD |
| 5199 | **FINE GRAINED SAND** | SABLE A GRAIN FIN | SAND (FEINKÖRNIGER) |
| 5200 | **FINE GRAINED STRUCTURE** | STRUCTURE A GRAINS FINS | GEFÜGE (FEINKÖRNIGES) |
| 5201 | **FINE PITCH THREAD** | FILET A PAS FIN | FEINGEWINDE, FEINES GEWINDE |
| 5202 | **FINE SILVER** | ARGENT FIN | FEINSILBER |
| 5203 | **FINE STRUCTURE** | STRUCTURE FINE (R.X.) | FEINSTRUKTUR |
| 5204 | **FINE THREAD** | FILET FIN | FEINGEWINDE |
| 5205 | **FINE WIRE** | FIL FIN, FIL MINCE | FEINDRAHT |
| 5206 | **FINE-MESHED** | A MAILLES SERREES | ENGMASCHIG, FEINMASCHIG |
| 5207 | **FINE-STRAND WIRE ROPE** | CABLE METALLIQUE EN FILS FINS | SEIL (FEINDRÄHTIGES) |
| 5208 | **FINENESS** | FINESSE | FEINHEIT |
| 5209 | **FINENESS OF AN ALLOY** | DEGRE DE FIN D'UN ALLIAGE | FEINGEHALT, REINGEHALT EINER LEGIERUNG |
| 5210 | **FING STRUCTURE** | STRUCTURE FINE | FEINSTRUKTUR |
| 5211 | **FINGER BAR** | CLAVETTE, BARRETTE, DOIGT | KEIL, BEFESTIGUNGSKEIL |
| 5212 | **FINGERNAILING** | DEFORMATIONS EN DEMI-LUNE DU CORDON DE SOUDURE | HALBMONDFÖRMIGE SCHWEISSNAHT-VERZERRUNGEN |
| 5213 | **FINISH** | ETAT DE SURFACE, FINISSAGE | OBERFLÄCHENBESCHAFFENHEIT |
| 5214 | **FINISH (TO)** | PARACHEVER, FINIR, RETOUCHER | NACHBEARBEITEN, SCHLICHTEN |
| 5215 | **FINISH ROLLING** | LAMINAGE FINISSEUR | FERTIGWALZEN, AUSWALZEN |
| 5216 | **FINISH WELDING** | SOUDAGE-FINITION | FERTIGSCHWEISSEN |
| 5217 | **FINISH, LAST COAT OF PAINT** | COUCHE SUPERFICIELLE (DE PEINTURE) | DECKANSTRICH |
| 5218 | **FINISHED PRODUCT** | PRODUIT FINI / PLAT / LONG | FERTIGERZEUGNIS |
| 5219 | **FINISHER** | MATRICE FINISSEUSE, CAGE FINISSEUSE | FERTIGGESENK, FERTIGGERÜST |
| 5220 | **FINISHING AND CLEANING** | PARACHEVEMENT | FERTIGBEARBEITUNG |
| 5221 | **FINISHING DIE** | DERNIERE FILIERE | ENDSTEIN |
| 5222 | **FINISHING MILL** | LAMINOIR FINISSEUR | FERTIGWALZWERK |
| 5223 | **FINISHING OPERATION** | FINISSAGE | FERTIGUNGSARBEIT |
| 5224 | **FINISHING POLISH** | FINISSAGE A LA MEULE | FERTIGSCHLEIFEN |
| 5225 | **FINISHING ROLLERS** | CAGE FINISSEURS | FERTIGWALZE |
| 5226 | **FINISHING TAPER REAMER** | ALESOIR FINISSEUR CONIQUE | KEGELSCHLICHTBOHRER |
| 5227 | **FINISHING TEMPERATURE** | TEMPERATURE DE FINISSAGE | FERTIGUNGSTEMPERATUR |
| 5228 | **FINISHING TOOL** | OUTIL A FINIR | SCHLICHTSTAHL |
| 5229 | **FINISHING TRAIN** | TRAIN FINISSEUR | FERTIGSTRASSE |
| 5230 | **FINISHING WASHER** | RONDELLE DECORATIVE | ZIERRING |
| 5231 | **FINITE DECIMAL FRACTION** | FRACTION DECIMALE TERMINEE | DEZIMALBRUCH (ENDLICHER) |
| 5232 | **FINITE SERIES** | SERIE FINIE | REIHE (ENDLICHE) |
| 5233 | **FINNED RADIATOR** | RADIATEUR A AILETTES | RIPPENROHRKÜHLER |
| 5234 | **FINNED TUBE** | TUYAU A AILETTES | RIPPENROHR |
| 5235 | **FIRE (TO)** | CHAUFFER | HEIZEN, FEUERN |
| 5236 | **FIRE (TO), START UP A BOILER (TO)** | ALLUMER LE FOYER D'UNE CHAUDIERE | ANHEIZEN, ANFEUERN (EINEN KESSEL) |
| 5237 | **FIRE BAR, GRATE BAR, FURNACE BAR** | BARREAU DE GRILLE | ROSTSTAB |
| 5238 | **FIRE BOX** | BOITE A FEU | FEUERBÜCHSE |

**FIR**                                                                134

| | | | |
|---|---|---|---|
| 5239 | FIRE BRICK | BRIQUE REFRACTAIRE | STEIN (FEUERFESTER), SCHAMOTTESTEIN |
| 5240 | FIRE CHECK | CRIQUE A CHAUD | BRANDRISS, WARMRISS |
| 5241 | FIRE CLAY | TERRE REFRACTAIRE | TON (FEUERFESTER), SCHAMOTTE |
| 5242 | FIRE DOOR | PORTE DU FOYER | FEUERTÜR, HEIZTÜR |
| 5243 | FIRE GILDING | DORURE AU FEU | FEUERVERGOLDUNG |
| 5244 | FIRE HYDRANT | BOUCHE D'INCENDIE | UNTERFLURHYDRANT |
| 5245 | FIRE REFINING | AFFINAGE AU FEU | VEREDELUNG (THERMISCHE), VERGÜTUNG (THERMISCHE) |
| 5246 | FIRE SCALE | COUCHE D'OXYDE DE CUIVRE | KUPFEROXIDSCHICHT |
| 5247 | FIRE TEST (OIL) | POINT DE COMBUSTION, POINT DE FEU (HUILE) | BRENNPUNKT (EINES ÖLES) |
| 5248 | FIRE TUBE | TUBE DE FUMEE | RAUCHROHR |
| 5249 | FIRE TUBE BOILER | CHAUDIERE IGNITUBULAIRE, CHAUDIERE A TUBES DE FUMEE, CHAUDIERE TUBULAIRE | HEIZRÖHRENKESSEL, RAUCHRÖHRENKESSEL |
| 5250 | FIRE-REFINED COPPER | CUIVRE AFFINE AU FEU | KUPFER (THERMISCH VEREDELTES), KUPFER (THERMISCH VERGÜTETES) |
| 5251 | FIRE-WALL | CLOISON PARE-FEU, TABLIER DU MOTEUR | SPRITZWAND |
| 5252 | FIREBRICK | BRIQUE REFRACTAIRE | FEUERFESTERZIEGEL, FEUERZIEGEL |
| 5253 | FIRECLAY | ARGILE REFRACTAIRE | FEUERTON |
| 5254 | FIRECLAY BRICK | BRIQUE REFRACTAIRE ALUMINEUSE | SCHAMOTTESTEIN |
| 5255 | FIRECLAY MORTAR | CIMENT REFRACTAIRE | SCHAMOTTEMÖRTEL |
| 5256 | FIRELESS LOCOMOTIVE | LOCOMOTIVE SANS FOYER | FEUERLOSE LOKOMOTIVE |
| 5257 | FIREPROOF, REFRACTORY | REFRACTAIRE, IGNIFUGE | FEUERBESTÄNDIG, FEUERFEST, FEUERSICHER |
| 5258 | FIREWOOD, FUEL WOOD | BOIS DE CHAUFFAGE, BOIS A BRULER | BRENNHOLZ |
| 5259 | FIRING | CHAUFFAGE | HEIZEN, HEIZUNG, FEUERN |
| 5260 | FIRING ORDER | ORDRE D'ALLUMAGE | ZÜNDFOLGE |
| 5261 | FIRING TOOL | ATTIRAIL DE CHAUFFE | FEUERUNGSGERÄT |
| 5262 | FIRING UP, STOKING | CHARGEMENT, ALIMENTATION D'UN FOYER | BESCHICKUNG EINER FEUERUNG |
| 5263 | FIRING, STARTING A BOILER | ALLUMAGE DU FOYER D'UNE CHAUDIERE | ANHEIZEN EINES KESSELS, ANFEUERN EINES KESSELS |
| 5264 | FIRMER CHISEL | FERMOIR | STEMMEISEN, STEMMBEITEL |
| 5265 | FIRST FILTER | FILTRE PREPARATOIRE, PREMIER FILTRE | VORFILTER |
| 5266 | FIRST FORMED RIVET HEAD | PREMIERE TETE DE RIVET | SETZKOPF |
| 5267 | FIRST RUNNINGS | TETE DE DISTILLATION | VORLAUF (DER DESTILLATION) |
| 5268 | FIRST TAP, ENTERING TAP, TAPER TAP | TARAUD CONIQUE, TARAUD EBAUCHEUR | GEWINDEVORSCHNEIDER |
| 5269 | FISH BOLT | BOULON D'ECLISSE | LASCHENBOLZEN |
| 5270 | FISH PLATES | ECLISSES | VERBINDUNGSLASCHEN |
| 5271 | FISH TAIL | CAVITE EN V | V-LUNKER |
| 5272 | FISH-BELLIED | A VENTRE DE POISSON | FISCHBAUCHFÖRMIG |
| 5273 | FISSURE | GERCURE | BORSTE |
| 5274 | FISSURING | FENDILLEMENT | SPRUNG-BILDUNG |
| 5275 | FIT | AJUSTAGE, MONTAGE, EMMANCHEMENT | PASSUNG |
| 5276 | FIT (TO) | AJUSTER | EINPASSEN, ANPASSEN, JUSTIEREN |
| 5277 | FIT PIPES INTO EACH OTHER TO | EMBOITER, ABOUCHER DES TUYAUX, ASSEMBLER DES TUYAUX PAR EMBOITEMENT | ROHRE INEINANDERSTECKEN |

| | | | |
|---|---|---|---|
| 5278 | FITTER | AJUSTEUR, AJUSTEUR-MECANICIEN | MASCHINENSCHLOSSER, SCHLOSSER |
| 5279 | FITTER'S HAMMER | MARTEAU D'AJUSTEUR | MONTIERHAMMER |
| 5280 | FITTING | RACCORD, AJUSTAGE | ANSCHLUSS, EINPASSEN, JUSTIEREN |
| 5281 | FITTING PIPES INTO EACH OTHER | EMBOITEMENT, EMBOITAGE, EMMANCHEMENT DE TUBES | INEINANDERSTECKEN VON ROHREN |
| 5282 | FITTING SHOP | ATELIER D'AJUSTAGE | SCHLOSSERWERKSTATT, TEILMONTAGE-WERKSTATT |
| 5283 | FITTINGS | ACCESSOIRES, GARNITURES, ARMATURE | ZUBEHÖR, ARMATUREN, ARMATUR, AUSRÜSTUNG |
| 5284 | FIXED AT BOTH ENDS | ENCASTRE AUX DEUX EXTREMITES | BEIDERSEITIG EINGESPANNT |
| 5285 | FIXED AT ONE END | ENCASTRE PAR UNE EXTREMITE | EINSEITIG EINGESPANNT |
| 5286 | FIXED BEAM. | POUTRE ENCASTREE | EINGESPANNTER TRÄGER |
| 5287 | FIXED BLOCK | POULIE FIXE (D'UN PALAN) | FLASCHE (FESTE), ROLLE |
| 5288 | FIXED BLOCK FORMAT | FORMAT A BLOC FIXE | EINGABEFORMAT (FESTES) |
| 5289 | FIXED CARBON | CARBONE COMBINE | GEBUNDENER KOHLENSTOFF |
| 5290 | FIXED CIRCLE | CERCLE FIXE | KREIS (FESTER) |
| 5291 | FIXED CRANE | GRUE FIXE, STATIONNAIRE | KRAN (STANDFESTER) (ORTSFESTER) |
| 5292 | FIXED CYCLE | CYCLE FIXE | FESTER ZYKLUS |
| 5293 | FIXED GAUGE | CALIBRE FIXE | SCHABLONE (FIXE) |
| 5294 | FIXED OIL | HUILE GRASSE, HUILE FIXE | ÖL (FETTES) |
| 5295 | FIXED POINT | POINT FIXE, APPUI FIXE | FESTPUNKT, FIXPUNKT |
| 5296 | FIXED ROOF | TOIT FIXE | FESTDACH |
| 5297 | FIXED SEQUENTIAL FORMAT | FORMAT A SEQUENCE FIXE | EINGABEFORMAT IN FESTER WORTFOLGESCHREIBWEISE |
| 5298 | FIXED-BED MILLING MACHINE | FRAISEUSE A BANC FIXE | FESTBETTFRÄSMASCHINE |
| 5299 | FIXED, RIGID VICE JAW | MACHOIRE FIXE D'UN ETAU | SCHRAUBSTOCKBACKEN (FESTER) |
| 5300 | FIXING THE TEST BAR | ENCASTREMENT, FIXATION D'UNE EPROUVETTE | EINSPANNEN EINES PROBESTABES |
| 5301 | FIXTURE | MONTAGE | AUFSPANNVORRICHTUNG |
| 5302 | FLAG, FLAGSTONE | DALLE | FUSSBODENPLATTE |
| 5303 | FLAKE | FLOCON, LAMELLE | FLOCKE, LAMELLE |
| 5304 | FLAKE CRACK | TAPURE, CRIQUE DE TENSION, GERCURE | SPANNUNGSRISS |
| 5305 | FLAKE GRAPHITE | GRAPHITE LAMELLAIRE | FLOCKENGRAPHIT, SCHUPPENGRAPHIT |
| 5306 | FLAKING | ECAILLAGE | ABBLÄTTERUNG |
| 5307 | FLAME BLOWPIPE | CHALUMEAU | SCHWEISSBRENNER, SCHNEIDBRENNER |
| 5308 | FLAME BRIDGE | PONT DE CHAUFFE | FEUERBRÜCKE |
| 5309 | FLAME CHIPPING | NETTOYER AU CHALUMEAU | BRENNPUTZEN, FLAMMPUTZEN |
| 5310 | FLAME CLEANING | DECALAMINAGE AU CHALUMEAU | FLAMMENENTZUNDERUNG |
| 5311 | FLAME CONDITIONING TORCH | CHALUMEAU DEROUILLEUR | ENTROSTUNG SBRENNER |
| 5312 | FLAME CUTTER | CHALUMEAU COUPEUR | SCHNEIDBRENNER (AUTOGEN) |
| 5313 | FLAME DESCALING | DECALAMINAGE A LA FLAMME | ENTZUNDERUNG (THERMISCHE) |
| 5314 | FLAME FAILURE CONTROLLER | CONTROLEUR DE FLAMME | FLAMMENWÄCHTER |
| 5315 | FLAME HARDENING | TREMPE AU CHALUMEAU | AUTOGENE OBERFLÄCHENHÄRTUNG, BRENNHÄRTEN |
| 5316 | FLAME IGNITION | ALLUMAGE A FLAMME | FLAMMENZÜNDUNG |
| 5317 | FLAME PLATING | PLACAGE A LA FLAMME | FLAMMPLATTIERUNG |
| 5318 | FLAME SHAPING | COUPAGE A LA FLAMME | AUTOGENE FORMGEBUNG |
| 5319 | FLAME SOFTENING | RECUIT A LA FLAMME | THERMISCHE ERWEICHUNG |
| 5320 | FLAME SPECTROSCOPY | SPECTROSCOPIE DE LA FLAMME | FLAMMENSPEKTROSKOPIE |
| 5321 | FLAME-ARRESTOR | ARRETE-FLAMMES | FLAMMEN-LÖSCHER |

**FLA** 136

| | | | |
|---|---|---|---|
| 5322 | **FLAME-PROOF** | ANTIDEFLAGRANT | FLAMMENSICHER |
| 5323 | **FLANGE** | BRIDE, FLASQUE | FLANSCH, LAGERDECKEL |
| 5324 | **FLANGE (TO)** | EMBOUTIR | KÜMPELN |
| 5325 | **FLANGE ADAPTER.** | ADAPTATEUR DE BRIDE | FLANSCHANPASSSTÜCK |
| 5326 | **FLANGE BACK-FACE** | DOS DE LA FACE DE BRIDE | FLANSCHRÜCKFLÄCHE |
| 5327 | **FLANGE FACE** | FACE DE BRIDE | FLANSCHFLÄCHE |
| 5328 | **FLANGE HOLES** | TROUS DE BRIDE | FLANSCHBOHRUNGEN |
| 5329 | **FLANGE HUB** | MOYEU D'UNE BRIDE | FLANSCHNABE |
| 5330 | **FLANGE OF A TEE IRON** | AILE (D'UN FER A T) | FLANSCH EINES EISENS |
| 5331 | **FLANGE OF A WHEEL** | BOURRELET D'UNE ROUE | SPURKRANZ EINES RADES |
| 5332 | **FLANGE OF PULLEY** | REBORD, JOUE D'UNE POULIE | BORDSCHEIBE EINER RIEMENSCHEIBE |
| 5333 | **FLANGE ROLLING MACHINE** | MACHINE A MANDRINER LES BRIDES | FLANSCHENAUFWALZMASCHINE |
| 5334 | **FLANGE TURNING LATHE** | TOUR A BRIDES | FLANSCHENDREHBANK |
| 5335 | **FLANGE WELD** | SOUDURE SUR BORDS RELEVES | BÖRDELNAHT |
| 5336 | **FLANGED BELT PULLEY** | POULIE AVEC JOUES, POULIE AVEC REBORDS | RIEMENSCHEIBE MIT BORD SCHEIBE |
| 5337 | **FLANGED BRANCH PIECE** | TUBULURE A BRIDE, TUBULURE A COLLET DE RACCORDEMENT | FLANSCHSTUTZEN |
| 5338 | **FLANGED COUPLING, FACE PLATE COUPLING** | ACCOUPLEMENT PAR MANCHON A PLATEAU, ACCOUPLEMENT A PLATEAUX BOULONNES | SCHEIBENKUPPLUNG, FLANSCHENKUPPLUNG |
| 5339 | **FLANGED ENDS** | ORIFICES A BRIDES | FLANSCHENANSCHLUSS, GEFLANSCHTE ENDEN |
| 5340 | **FLANGED HEX (AGONAL) NUT** | ECROU HEXAGONAL (6-PANS) A EMBASE | SECHSKANTBUNDMUTTER |
| 5341 | **FLANGED NOZZLE** | TUBULURE A BRIDE | ROHRSTUTZEN |
| 5342 | **FLANGED NUT** | ECROU A EMBASE | BUNDMUTTER |
| 5343 | **FLANGED PIPE** | TUYAU A BRIDES | FLANSCHENROHR |
| 5344 | **FLANGED PIPE JOINT** | ASSEMBLAGE A BRIDES | FLANSCHENVERSCHRAUBUNG, FLANSCHENVERBINDUNG |
| 5345 | **FLANGING** | EMBOUTISSAGE | KÜMPELN |
| 5346 | **FLANGING MACHINE** | MACHINE A EMBOUTIR, EMBOUTISSEUSE, MACHINE A RETROUSSER, SERTISSEUSE | KÜMPELMASCHINE, BÖRDELMASCHINE, KREMPMASCHINE |
| 5347 | **FLANGING TEST** | ESSAI DE RABATTEMENT | BÖRDELPROBE |
| 5348 | **FLANK** | FLANC | FLANKE |
| 5349 | **FLANK CLEARANCE** | JEU ENTRE LES POINTS DE CONTACT DES DENTS | FLANKENSPIEL (ZAHNRÄDERN) |
| 5350 | **FLANK OF THREAD** | FLANC DU FILET | FLANKE EINES GEWINDES |
| 5351 | **FLANK SHOULDER OF TOOTH** | FLANC DE LA DENT | ZAHNFLANKE (UNTER DEM TEILKREIS) |
| 5352 | **FLANNEL** | FLANELLE | FLANELL |
| 5353 | **FLAP VALVE, CLACK VALVE** | CLAPET, SOUPAPE A CLAPET, SOUPAPE A CHARNIERE, DISTRIBUTEUR, OBTURATEUR A LEVEE ANGULAIRE | KLAPPE, KLAPPENVENTIL |
| 5354 | **FLAPPING** | RUPTURE DE LA COUCHE DE SCORIES | AUFBRECHEN DER SCHLACKENSCHICHT |
| 5355 | **FLARE** | TORCHERE | FACKEL |
| 5356 | **FLARE (TO)** | ELARGIR, S'ELARGIR, S'ETENDRE | AUFWEITEN, SICH ERWEITERN |
| 5357 | **FLASH** | BAVURE, ARETE (DE SOUDURE) DUE AU REFOULEMENT | GRAT, STAUCHGRAT, SCHWEISSRIPPE |
| 5358 | **FLASH (BUTT) WELDING** | SOUDAGE PAR ETINCELAGE | ABBRENNSCHWEISSEN |

| | | | |
|---|---|---|---|
| 5359 | **FLASH (TO), BURST FORTH INTO FLAME (TO)** | JETER DE LA FLAMME | AUFFLAMMEN |
| 5360 | **FLASH BAKER** | ETUVE A SECHAGE RAPIDE | SCHNELLTROCKNER, BLITZTROCKNER |
| 5361 | **FLASH COATING** | METALLISATION AU PISTOLET | METALLSPRITZEN |
| 5362 | **FLASH HEAT** | ECHAUFFEMENT RAPIDE | ANWÄRMHITZE (KURZE) |
| 5363 | **FLASH POINT** | POINT D'INFLAMMATION, POINT DE FLAMME | FLAMMPUNKT |
| 5364 | **FLASH TRIM (TO)** | EBARBER, EBAVURER | ENTGRATEN |
| 5365 | **FLASHBACK** | RENTREE DE FLAMME | FLAMMENRÜCKSCHLAG |
| 5366 | **FLASHER LIGHTS** | CLIGNOTANTS | BLINKLEUCHTE |
| 5367 | **FLASHING** | PLAGE D'OXYDE, INCRUSTATION DE CALAMINE | ZUNDERFLECK, ABSATZSTELLEN |
| 5368 | **FLASHING POINT** | POINT D'ECLAIR, POINT D'INFLAMMABILITE | FLAMMPUNKT |
| 5369 | **FLASK** | CHASSIS DE MOULAGE | FORMKASTEN |
| 5370 | **FLASK** | BALLON (CHIM.) | KOLBEN, GLASKOLHEN |
| 5371 | **FLASK ANNEALING** | RECUIT EN CAISSE | KASTENGLÜHEN |
| 5372 | **FLASK PIN (US)** | GOUPILLE DE CHASSIS | FORMKASTENSTIFT |
| 5373 | **FLAT ARCH** | ARC EN ANSE DE PANIER | KORBBOGEN |
| 5374 | **FLAT BAR** | BARRE PLATE | FLACHSTAB |
| 5375 | **FLAT BAR IRON, FLATS** | FER PLAT, PLATS, FER EN BANDES, BANDELETTE | FLACHEISEN, UNIVERSALEISEN |
| 5376 | **FLAT BULB IRON** | FER PLAT A BOUDIN | FLACHWULSTEISEN |
| 5377 | **FLAT CHISEL** | BURIN | FLACHMEISSEL |
| 5378 | **FLAT CURVE SWEEP** | COURBE APLATIE, COURBE A GRAND RAYON | FLACHE KURVE |
| 5379 | **FLAT DISC WHEEL** | ROUE A VOILE DROIT | SCHEIBENRAD (GERADES) |
| 5380 | **FLAT DRILL** | FORET A LANGUE D'ASPIC, LANGUE D'ASPIC, MECHE PLATE | SPITZBOHRER |
| 5381 | **FLAT FILE** | LIME PLATE | FLACHFEILE |
| 5382 | **FLAT FLANGE** | BRIDE PLATE | FLANSCH (GLATTER) |
| 5383 | **FLAT FOUR ENGINE** | MOTEUR A 4 CYLINDRES OPPOSES HORIZONTAUX | VIER-ZYLINDER-BOXER-MOTOR |
| 5384 | **FLAT GUIDE** | GLISSIERE PLATE | FLACHFÜHRUNG |
| 5385 | **FLAT HEAD SCREW** | VIS A TETE PLÀTE | SENKSCHRAUBE |
| 5386 | **FLAT HEADED BOLTS** | BOULONS A TETE PLATE | SCHEIBENBOLZEN |
| 5387 | **FLAT HEARTH TYPE MIXER** | MELANGEUR A SOLE PLATE | FLACHHERDMISCHER |
| 5388 | **FLAT KEY** | CLAVETTE PLATE, CLAVETTE A MEPLAT, CLAVETTE POSEE A PLAT | FLACHKEIL |
| 5389 | **FLAT OF THREAD** | TRONCATURE D'UN FILET | ABFLACHUNG DES GEWINDES |
| 5390 | **FLAT PILE** | LIME PLATE POINTUE | FLACHFEILE |
| 5391 | **FLAT ROLL** | CYLINDRE LISSE | FLACHWALZE |
| 5392 | **FLAT ROLLED STEEL** | ACIERS LAMINES PLATS | FLACHSTAHL |
| 5393 | **FLAT ROPE** | CABLE PLAT | FLACHSEIL, BANDSEIL |
| 5394 | **FLAT SCREW HEAD** | TETE PLATE D'UNE VIS | SCHRAUBENKOPF (FLACHER) |
| 5395 | **FLAT SHEET** | TOLE DRESSEE | BLECH (GERICHTETES) |
| 5396 | **FLAT SPIRAL SPRING** | RESSORT SPIRALE | SPIRALFEDER, SCHNECKENFEDER |
| 5397 | **FLAT TUBULAR WOVEN BELTING** | COURROIE EN TISSU TUBULAIRE | SCHLAUCHGEWEBERIEMEN |
| 5398 | **FLAT TWIN ENGINE** | MOTEUR A 2 CYLINDRES OPPOSES HORIZONTAUX | ZWEIZYLINDER-BOXER-MOTOR |
| 5399 | **FLAT WASHER** | RONDELLE PLATE | FLACHSCHEIBE |
| 5400 | **FLAT WEDGE** | COIN PLAT | FLACHKEIL |

# FLA

| | | | |
|---|---|---|---|
| 5401 | **FLAT WELD** | CORDON DE SOUDURE PLAT | RAUPE (FLACHE) |
| 5402 | **FLAT WIRE** | FIL PLAT, FIL RECTANGULAITRE, FIL MEPLAT | FLACHDRAHT, DRAHT (RECHTECKIGER) |
| 5403 | **FLAT WIRE PLIERS** | PINCE PLATE | FLACHZANGE, DRAHTZANGE (FLACHE) |
| 5404 | **FLAT-FACED PULLEY, PULLEY WITH STRAIGHT RIM FLAT FACE** | POULIE DROITE, CYLINDRIQUE | RIEMENSCHEIBE GERADE |
| 5405 | **FLATTEN (TO)** | PLANER | AUSBEULEN |
| 5406 | **FLATTENED** | APLATI | ABGEFLACHT, ABGEPLATTET |
| 5407 | **FLATTENED-STRAND WIRE ROPE** | CABLE METALLIQUE A TORONS MEPLATS | DRAHTSEIL (FLACHLITZIGES) |
| 5408 | **FLATTENING** | LISSAGE, POLISSAGE | ABPLATTEN, ABFLACHEN, GLÄTTEN |
| 5409 | **FLATTENING TEST** | ESSAI D'APLATISSEMENT | STRECKPROBE, AUSBREITEPROBE |
| 5410 | **FLATTER** | CHASSE A PARER | FLACHHAMMER, GERADER SETZHAMMER |
| 5411 | **FLAW** | DEFAUT, AMORCE DE CRIQUE | ANRISS, FEHLER, DEFEKT |
| 5412 | **FLAX** | LIN | FLACHS |
| 5413 | **FLAX TOW** | ETOUPE DE LIN | FLACHSWERG |
| 5414 | **FLESH SIDE OF LEATHER** | COTE CHAIR DU CUIR | FLEISCHSEITE DES LEDERS |
| 5415 | **FLEXIBILITY, PLIABILITY** | FLEXIBILITE, SOUPLESSE | BIEGSAMKEIT, BIEGBARKEIT |
| 5416 | **FLEXIBLE CONNECTION** | FIXATION, LIAISON, JOINT SOUPLE | VERBINDUNG (NACHGIEBIGE) |
| 5417 | **FLEXIBLE COUPLING** | MANCHON FLEXIBLE, ACCOUPLEMENT FLEXIBLE | KUPPLUNG (BEWEGLICHE), KUPPLUNG (NACHGIEBIGE), KUPPLUNG (ELASTISCHE) |
| 5418 | **FLEXIBLE JOINT PIPE, ARTICULATED PIPE, PIPE WITH BALL JOINT** | TUYAU A JOINT SPHERIQUE | GELENKROHR |
| 5419 | **FLEXIBLE METAL HOSE TUBING** | TUYAU METALLIQUE FLEXIBLE | METALLSCHLAUCH |
| 5420 | **FLEXIBLE SHAFT** | ARBRE FLEXIBLE, TRANSMISSION FLEXIBLE | WELLE (BIEGSAME) |
| 5421 | **FLEXILBLE PIPE** | TUYAU METALLIQUE FLEXIBLE | METALLSCHLAUCH |
| 5422 | **FLEXION** | FLEXION | BIEGUNG |
| 5423 | **FLEXURAL RIGIDITY** | RIGIDITE A LA FLEXION | BIEGESTEIFIGKEIT |
| 5424 | **FLEXURAL STRENGTH** | RESISTANCE A LA FLEXION | BIEGEFESTIGKET |
| 5425 | **FLEXURAL STRESS** | TENSION DE FLEXION | BIEGESPANNUNG |
| 5426 | **FLEXURE** | FLECHE, DEFORMATION PAR FLEXION | BIEGUNG, DURCHBIEGUNG |
| 5427 | **FLINT** | FLINT, PIERRE A FUSIL, SILEX PYROMAQUE, PIERRE A BRIQUET | FEUERSTEIN, FLINT |
| 5428 | **FLINT GLASS, LEAD GLASS** | FLINT-GLASS | FLINTGLAS |
| 5429 | **FLIP-FLOP** | BASCULE BINAIRE | KIPPSCHALTUNG (BI-STABILE) |
| 5430 | **FLOAT** | FLOTTEUR | SCHWIMMER |
| 5431 | **FLOAT CHAMBER** | CUVE A NIVEAU CONSTANT | SCHWIMMERKAMMER |
| 5432 | **FLOAT TRAP** | PURGEUR D'EAU CONDENSEE A FLOTTEUR | SCHWIMMERKONDENSTOPF |
| 5433 | **FLOAT VALVE** | ROBINET A FLOTTEUR, SOUPAPE A FLOTTEUR | SCHWIMMERHAHN, SCHWIMMERVENTIL |
| 5434 | **FLOATING** | NUANCAGE, FUSEES | AUSSCHWIMMEN |
| 5435 | **FLOATING AXE** | ESSIEU-FLOTTANT | SCHWEBEACHSE |
| 5436 | **FLOATING BODY** | CORPS FLOTTANT | KÖRPER (SCHWIMMENDER) |
| 5437 | **FLOATING DIE** | MATRICE FLOTTANTE | SCHWEBEMANTELMATRIZE |
| 5438 | **FLOATING PLUG** | MANDRIN FLOTTANT | PENDELDORN, PENDELFUTTER |
| 5439 | **FLOATING ROOF TANK** | RESERVOIR A TOIT FLOTTANT | SCHWIMMDACHTANK |
| 5440 | **FLOATING ZERO** | ZERO FLOTTANT | NULLPUNKT (BELIEBIGER) |
| 5441 | **FLOCCULATION** | FLOCULATION | AUSFLOCKUNG |

| | | | |
|---|---|---|---|
| 5442 | **FLOOD LUBRICATION, LUBRICATION BY THE CIRCULATING SYSTEM** | GRAISSAGE SOUS PRESSION A CIRCULATION CONTINUE, GRAISSAGE A POMPE ET CIRCULATION D'HUILE | UMLAUFSCHMIERUNG, ZIRKULATIONSSCHMIERUNG, SPÜLSCHMIERUNG |
| 5443 | **FLOODING** | NUANCAGE, FUSEES | AUSSCHWIMMEN |
| 5444 | **FLOOR COUNTERSHAFT** | RENVOI FIXE AU SOL | FUSSBODENVORGELEGE |
| 5445 | **FLOOR MOULDING** | MOULAGE SUR LE SOL, MOULAGE EN FOSSE | FORMUNG AUF DEM BODEN |
| 5446 | **FLOOR PAN ASSEMBLY** | PLANCHER DE VOITURE | BODENBLECH, BODENBRETT |
| 5447 | **FLOOR PLATE, FOOT PLATE** | TOLE POUR REVETEMENT DE SOL | FUSSBODENBELAGBLECH, BELAGBLECH FÜR FUSSBÖDEN |
| 5448 | **FLOOR STAND** | COLONNE DE MANOEUVRE | FLURSÄULE |
| 5449 | **FLOOR-PLATE** | PLATELAGE | BODENPLATTE |
| 5450 | **FLOORING** | PLANCHER COUVERTURE DE PLANCHER, COUVERTURE DE SOL | FUSSBODEN (BELAG), FUSSBODENBELAG |
| 5451 | **FLOORING/FLOOR-PLATE** | PLATELAGE | BODENBELAG |
| 5452 | **FLOTATION** | FLOTTATION | FLOTATION, SCHWIMMAUFBEREITUNG |
| 5453 | **FLOUR (EMERY)** | POTEE D'EMERI | SCHMIRGEL (GESCHLÄMMTER) |
| 5454 | **FLOW** | ECOULEMENT | FLIESSEN |
| 5455 | **FLOW GAUGE** | CALIBRE A DEBIT | DURCHFLUSSMESSER |
| 5456 | **FLOW LIMIT** | LIMITE D'ECOULEMENT, LIMITE ELASTIQUE | FLIESSGRENZE |
| 5457 | **FLOW LINE** | LIGNE D'ECOULEMENT | FLIESSLINIE, FLIESSMARK |
| 5458 | **FLOW METER** | DEBITMETRE | DURCHFLUSSMESSER, MENGENMESSER |
| 5459 | **FLOW RATE** | VITESSE DE FLUAGE, TEMPS D'ECOULEMENT, DEBIT | FLIESSGESCHWINDIGKEIT, FLIESSZEIT, LEISTUNG, DURCHFLUSSGRÖSSE |
| 5460 | **FLOW STRESS** | EFFORT DE FLUAGE | SCHUBSPANNUNG |
| 5461 | **FLOW STRUCTURE** | STRUCTURE DUE A LA DEFORMATION PLASTIQUE | VERSCHIEBUNGSTRUKTUR, FLIESSTEXTUR |
| 5462 | **FLOW VELOCITY** | VITESSE D'ECOULEMENT | STRÖMUNGSGESCHWINDIGKEIT |
| 5463 | **FLOWABILITY** | FLUIDITE | FLIESSFÄHIGKEIT |
| 5464 | **FLOWERS OF SULPHUR, SUBLIMED SULPHUR** | FLEUR DE SOUFRE, SOUFRE SUBLIME | SCHWEFELBLUMEN, SCHWEFELBLÜTE |
| 5465 | **FLOWING OF THE MATERIAL, PLASTIC YIELDING OF THE MATERIAL** | ECOULEMENT DU MATERIAU | FLIESSEN DES MATERIALS |
| 5466 | **FLOWING WATER** | EAU COURANTE | WASSER (STRÖMENDES), WASSER (FLIESSENDES) |
| 5467 | **FLUE** | CARNEAU | RAUCHKANAL, RAUCHFANG |
| 5468 | **FLUE BOILER** | CHAUDIERE A FOYER INTERIEUR, CHAUDIERE A TUBE FOYER | FLAMMROHRKESSEL |
| 5469 | **FLUE DUST** | ESCARBILLES, POUSSIERE DE GUEULARD, POUSSIERES DE GAZ DE HAUT FOURNEAU | GICHTSTAUB |
| 5470 | **FLUE GASES** | GAZ DU FOYER, GAZ DE LA COMBUSTION | RAUCHGASE, VERBRENNUNGSGASE, FEUERGASE |
| 5471 | **FLUID** | TRES FLUIDE, TRES MOBILE | DÜNNFLÜSSIG, LEICHTFLÜSSIG |
| 5472 | **FLUID DRIVE** | TRANSMISSION HYDRAULIQUE | HYDRAULISCHE ÜBERTRAGUNG |
| 5473 | **FLUID FRICTION** | FROTTEMENT INTERIEUR DES LIQUIDES | REIBUNG (INNERE), FLÜSSIGKEITSREIBUNG, ZÄHIGKEITSREIBUNG |
| 5474 | **FLUIDITY, LIQUIDITY** | FLUIDITE | FLÜSSIGKEITSGRAD DÜNNFLÜSSIGKEIT, LEICHTFLÜSSIGKEIT |
| 5475 | **FLUIDIZER** | FONDANT | FLUSSMITTEL, SCHLACKENZUSCHLAG |
| 5476 | **FLUORESCENCE** | FLUORESCENCE | FLUORESZENZ |

# FLU

**140**

| | | | |
|---|---|---|---|
| 5477 | **FLUORESCENT SCREEN** | ECRAN LUMINEUX, ECRAN FLUORESCENT | LEUCHTSCHIRM, FLUORESZENZSCHIRM |
| 5478 | **FLUORINE** | FLUOR | FLUOR |
| 5479 | **FLUORSPAR, CALCIUM FLUORIDE** | FLUORINE, SPATH FLUOR, FLUORURE DE CALCIUM, CHAUX FLUATEE, FLUSSPATH | FLUSSSPAT, FLUORKALZIUM, KALZIUMFLUORID |
| 5480 | **FLUSH HEADLIGHT** | PHARE ENCASTRE | SCHEINWERFER (EINGELASSENER) |
| 5481 | **FLUSH WELD** | SOUDURE BOUT A BOUT SANS SUREPAISSEUR | FLACHNAHT |
| 5482 | **FLUSH, FAIR** | AFFLEURE | BÜNDIG |
| 5483 | **FLUTE** | GOUJURE, GORGE | SPANNUT, AUSKEHLUNG |
| 5484 | **FLUTED** | CANNELE, STRIE | RIEFIG, GERIEFT, GERIFFELT |
| 5485 | **FLUTED REAMER** | ALESOIR A RAINURES, ALESOIR A CANNELURES | REIBAHLE (GENUTETE) |
| 5486 | **FLUTED ROLLER** | CYLINDRE CANNELE, STRIE | RIFFELWALZE |
| 5487 | **FLUTED SPECTRUM** | SPECTRE CANNELE | BANDSPEKTRUM |
| 5488 | **FLUTING** | RUPTURE PAR FLEXION | BIEGEBRUCH |
| 5489 | **FLUX** | FONDANT | FLUSSMITTEL, ZUSCHLAG |
| 5490 | **FLUX FOR SOLDERING** | FONDANT POUR SOUDER | LÖTAUFBRINGEMITTEL, AUFBRINGEMITTEL, LÖTFLUSSMITTEL |
| 5491 | **FLUX OIL** | HUILE DE FLUXAGE | STELLÖL |
| 5492 | **FLUXED ELECTRODE** | ELECTRODE ENROBE | ELEKTRODE (UMMANTELTE) |
| 5493 | **FLY ASH** | CENDRES VOLANTES | FLUGASCHE |
| 5494 | **FLYCUTTER** | OUTIL A TREPANER | SCHLAGFRÄSER |
| 5495 | **FLYING SHEARS** | CISAILLE VOLANTE, CISAILLE A PORTE A FAUX | SCHERE (FLIBGENDE) |
| 5496 | **FLYWHEEL** | VOLANT-MOTEUR | SCHWUNGRAD |
| 5497 | **FLYWHEEL IN HALVES** | VOLANT EN DEUX SEGMENTS | SCHWUNGRAD (ZWEITEILIGES) |
| 5498 | **FLYWHEEL PIT** | FOSSE DU VOLANT | SCHWUNGRADGRUBE |
| 5499 | **FOAM** | MOUSSE | SCHAUM |
| 5500 | **FOCAL LENGTH DISTANCE** | DISTANCE FOCALE, LONGUEUR FOCALE | BRENNWEITE |
| 5501 | **FOCAL PLANE** | PLAN FOCAL | BRENNEBENE |
| 5502 | **FOCUS** | FOYER (OPT. ET GEOM.) | BRENNPUNKT, FOKUS |
| 5503 | **FOCUS-FILM DISTANCE** | DISTANCE FOCALE | BRENNWEITE, BRENNPUNKTABSTAND |
| 5504 | **FOCUSED BEAM** | FAISCEAU FOCALISE, FAISCEAU CONCENTRE | GEBÜNDELTER STRAHL |
| 5505 | **FOCUSSING** | MISE AU POINT D UN INSTRUMENT D OPTIQUE | FOKUSSIEREN, EINSTELLEN, EINSTELLUNG EINES OPTISCHEN INSTRUMENTS |
| 5506 | **FOG LIGHTS** | PHARE DE BROUILLARD | NEBELLAMPE |
| 5507 | **FOGGING** | ASSOMBRISSEMENT | BLINDWERDEN |
| 5508 | **FOIL** | FEUILLE, FEUILLE DE METAL | FOLIE, METALFOLIE |
| 5509 | **FOIL OF METAL** | FEUILLE MINCE DE METAL | BLATTMETALL, FOLIE |
| 5510 | **FOLD** | REPLIURE DE LAMINAGE | ÜBERWALZUNGSFEHLER |
| 5511 | **FOLD (DOUBLED PART)** | PLI, REPLI (TRAVAIL DES TOLES) | FALZ (BLECHBEARBEITUNG) |
| 5512 | **FOLDING FOOT RULE** | METRE PLIANT | GELENKMASSSTAB, KLAPPMASSSTAB, FALTMASSSTAB, GLIEDERMASSSTAB, ZOLLSTOCK |
| 5513 | **FOLIUM OF DESCARTES** | FOLIUM DE DESCARTES | BLATT (DESCARTESSCHES), FOLIUM KARTESISCHES |
| 5514 | **FOLLOWER REST** | LUNETTE MOBILE, LUNETTE A SUIVRE | BRILLE (LAUFENDE) |
| 5515 | **FOLLOWING EDGE** | ARETE DE SORTIE | AUSTRITTKANTE |

| | | | |
|---|---|---|---|
| 5516 | FOLLOWING SIDE OF A BELT, SLACK SIDE; LOOSE SIDE, ROPE ETC. | BRIN CONDUIT, BRIN MENE, BRIN MOU, BRIN LACHE, BRIN SORTANT (D UNE COURROIE SANS FIN) | TRUMM (GEZOGENES), TRUMM (RÜCKLAUFENDES), TRUMM (LOSES, ABLAUFENDES) TRUMM |
| 5517 | FOOD PROCESSING INDUSTRY | INDUSTRIE DE L'ALIMENTATION | LEBENSMITTELINDUSTRIE |
| 5518 | FOOT | PIED ANGLAIS | FUSS (ENGLISCHER) |
| 5519 | FOOT BRAKE | FREIN A PIED, A PEDALE | FUSSBREMSE |
| 5520 | FOOT LATHE | TOUR A PEDALE | FUSSTRITTDREHBANK |
| 5521 | FOOT LEVER, PEDAL | LEVIER A PEDALE | FUSSHEBEL, TRITTHEBEL |
| 5522 | FOOT POUND (F.P., FT-LB.) | LIVRE-PIED | FUSSPFUND |
| 5523 | FOOT VALVE | CLAPET DE FOND, CLAPET DE PIED, CLAPET-CREPINE | FUSSVENTIL, BODENVENTIL, GEGENDRUCKVENTIL, FUSSVENTIL |
| 5524 | FOOTSTEP BEARING, PIVOT BEARING, STEP BEARING | PALIER VERITICAL, PALIER DE PIED; CRAPAUDINE | SPURLAGER, FUSSLAGER, STÜTZLAGER |
| 5525 | FORAGE AND SILAGE HARVESTERS | FAUCHEUSES A FOURRAGES | MÄHHÄCKSLER |
| 5526 | FORCE DIAGRAM | DIAGRAMME DES FORCES, DIAGRAMME DES EFFORTS | KRÄFTEPLAN |
| 5527 | FORCE FIT, PRESS FIT | EMMANCHEMENT A LA PRESSE, AJUSTAGE A LA PRESSE, MONTAGE A LA PRESSE | PRESSSITZ |
| 5528 | FORCE OF A SPRING | FORCE D'UN RESSORT | SPANNKRAFT EINER FEDER |
| 5529 | FORCE OF ATTRACTION, ATTRACTIVE FORCE | FORCE ATTRACTIVE | ANZIEHUNGSKRAFT |
| 5530 | FORCE OF REPULSION, REPULSIVE FORCE | FORCE REPULSIVE | ABSTOSSUNGSKRAFT |
| 5531 | FORCE PUMP, PRESSURE PUMP | POMPE FOULANTE | DRUCKPUMPE |
| 5532 | FORCE, EFFORT | FORCE, EFFORT | KRAFT |
| 5533 | FORCED DRAUGHT | TIRAGE FORCE | DRUCKZUG |
| 5534 | FORCED FLOW | COURANT FORCE | STRÖMUNG (AUFGEZWUNGENE) |
| 5535 | FORCED VIBRATION | OSCILLATIONS FORCEES | SCHWINGUNG (ERZWUNGENE) |
| 5536 | FORCEPS | PINCETTE | PINZETTE, FEDERZANGE |
| 5537 | FORCES ACTING IN OPPOSITE DIRECTIONS | FORCES OPPOSEES EN DIRECTION | KRÄFTE (ENTGEGENGESETZT GERICHTETE) |
| 5538 | FORCES ACTING IN THE SAME DIRECTION | FORCES DE MEME SENS | KRÄFTE (GLEICHGERICHTETE) |
| 5539 | FOREHAND WELDING | SOUDURE POUSSEE VERS LA GAUCHE | LINKSSCHWEISSUNG |
| 5540 | FOREIGN PATENT | BREVET ETRANGER | AUSLANDSPATENT |
| 5541 | FOREMAN | CONTREMAITRE | WERKFÜHRER, WERKMEISTER, MEISTER |
| 5542 | FORGE (TO) | FORGER | SCHMIEDEN |
| 5543 | FORGE COAL, SMITHY COAL | HOUILLE MARECHALE, CHARBON DE FORGE | SCHMIEDEKOHLE |
| 5544 | FORGE PIG | FONTE D'AFFINAGE | PUDDELROHEISEN |
| 5545 | FORGE TEST | ESSAI DE FORGEAGE | SCHMIEDEPROBE |
| 5546 | FORGE WELDING | SOUDAGE A LA FORGE | SCHMIEDESCHWEISSUNG |
| 5547 | FORGE, BLACK SMITH'S SHOP, SMITHY | FORGE, ATELIER DE FORGE | SCHMIEDE, SCHMIEDEWERKSTATT |
| 5548 | FORGE, FORGE FIRE, SMITH'S FIRE, BLACKSMITH'S HEARTH | FORGE, FORGE DE MARECHALE, FEU DE FORGE | SCHMIEDEFEUER, SCHMIEDEESSE, SCHMIEDEHERD |
| 5549 | FORGED CARBON STEEL FITTING | RACCORD ACIER FORGE | SCHMIEDESTAHLANSCHLUSS |
| 5550 | FORGED CRANK | MANIVELLE FORGEE, MANIVELLE COUDEE A LA FORGE, MANIVELLE VENUE DE FORGE | KURBEL (GESCHMIEDETE) |
| 5551 | FORGED EYEBAR | BARRE A OEILLETS | AUGENSTAB (GESCHMIEDETER) |

**FOR**

**142**

| | | | |
|---|---|---|---|
| 5552 | **FORGED IN THE SOLID** | FORGE D'UNE PIECE DANS LA MASSE | GESCHMIEDET (AUS DEM VOLLEN) |
| 5553 | **FORGED SCRAP IRON** | FER DE RIBLONS, FER DE MASSE, MITRAILLE | ABFALLEISEN |
| 5554 | **FORGED STEEL** | ACIER FORGE | SCHMIEDESTAHL, STAHL (GESCHMIEDETER) |
| 5555 | **FORGING** | FORGEAGE | SCHMIEDEN |
| 5556 | **FORGING (FORGED WORK)** | PIECE FORGEE, PIECE TRAVAILLEE A LA FORGE, PIECE DE FORGE | SCHMIEDESTÜCK |
| 5557 | **FORGING (MAKING FORGED WORK)** | FORGEAGE | SCHMIEDEN |
| 5558 | **FORGING BRASS** | LAITON A FORGER | SCHMIEDEMESSING |
| 5559 | **FORGING HAMMER** | MARTEAU DE FORGE, MARTEAU MECANIQUE | SCHMIEDEHAMMER (MECHANISCHER) |
| 5560 | **FORGING HEAT** | TEMPERATURE DE FORGEAGE | SCHMIEDETEMPERATUR |
| 5561 | **FORGING MACHINE** | MACHINE A FORGER, MACHINE A REFOULER | SCHMIEDEMASCHINE, STAUCHMASCHINE |
| 5562 | **FORGING PRESS** | PRESSE A FORGER | SCHMIEDEPRESSE |
| 5563 | **FORGING ROLLS** | LAMINOIR A FORGER | SCHMIEDEWALZWERK |
| 5564 | **FORGING STRAINS** | EFFORTS DUS AU FORGEAGE | SCHMIEDESPANNUNG |
| 5565 | **FORGING TEMPERATURE** | TEMPERATURE DE FORGEAGE | SCHMIEDETEMPERATUR |
| 5566 | **FORGINGS** | FERS FORGES | SCHMIEDESTÜCKE |
| 5567 | **FORK JOINT** | CHAPE, CARDAN | GABELGELENK |
| 5568 | **FORKED CONNECTING ROD END** | PIED DE LA BIELLE A FOURCHETTE, CHAPE-FOURCHETTE | SCHUBSTANGENKOPF (GEGABELTER), SCHUBSTANGENGABEL |
| 5569 | **FORKED LEVER** | LEVIER A FOURCHE | HEBEL (GEGABELTER) |
| 5570 | **FORM** | MOULE | FORM |
| 5571 | **FORM (TO), SHAPE (TO)** | FACONNER, PROFILER | FORMEN, FORM GEBEN |
| 5572 | **FORM FACTOR** | FACTEUR DE FORME | FORMFAKTOR |
| 5573 | **FORMALDEHYDE, FORMIC ALDEHYDE** | ALDEHYDE FORMIQUE, ALDEHYDE METHYLIQUE, FORMOL, FORMALDEHYDE, METHANAL, OXYDE DE METHYLENE | FORMALIN, FORMALDEHYD, FORMOL |
| 5574 | **FORMAT** | FORMAT | FORMAT |
| 5575 | **FORMATION OF MILDEW** | FORMATION DE LA MOISISSURE | SCHIMMELBILDUNG |
| 5576 | **FORMATION VOLTAGE** | TENSION DE FORMATION | FORMIERUNGSSPANNUNG |
| 5577 | **FORMED CUTTERS** | FRAISES-MERES | FORMFRÄSER |
| 5578 | **FORMIC ACID** | ACIDE FORMIQUE | AMEISENSÄURE, FORMYLSÄURE |
| 5579 | **FORMING** | CINTRAGE, FORMAGE, FORMATION | FORMGEBUNG, FORMIERUNG |
| 5580 | **FORMING DIE** | ESTAMPE D'EMBOUTISSAGE | PRÄGESTEMPEL |
| 5581 | **FORMING, SHAPING** | FACONNAGE | FORMEN, FORMGEBUNG |
| 5582 | **FORMULA** | FORMULE | FORMEL |
| 5583 | **FORMULA (CONSTITUTIONAL), FORMULA (RATIONAL)** | FORMULE DE CONSTITUTION | RATIONELLE FORMEL, KONSTITUTIONSFORMEL |
| 5584 | **FORWARD MOVEMENT** | MOUVEMENT D'AVANCE, AVANCEMENT | VORWÄRTSBEWEGUNG |
| 5585 | **FORWARD STROKE OF PISTON** | COURSE AVANT, COURSE ALLER, COURSE DIRECTE DU PISTON, AVANCE, MARCHE EN AVANT DU PISTON | KOLBENHINGANG |
| 5586 | **FOSSIL FUEL** | COMBUSTIBLE FOSSILE | BRENNSTOFF (FOSSILER) |
| 5587 | **FOUL (TO)** | GENER MUTUELLEMENT (SE) | HINDERN, (SICH BEI DER BEWEGUNG GEGENSEITIG) KOLLIDIEREN |
| 5588 | **FOUL ELECTROLYTE** | ELECTROLYTE IMPUR | ELEKTROLYT (VERBRAUCHTER) |
| 5589 | **FOUNDATION** | FONDATION, MASSIF DE FONDATION | UNTERBAU, FUNDAMENT, ERDUNG, FUNDIERUNG |

| | | | |
|---|---|---|---|
| 5590 | **FOUNDATION BOLT, HOLDDOWN BOLT, TIE BOLT** | BOULON DE FONDATION | ANKERBOLZEN, ANKERSCHRAUBE, ANKER, FUNDAMENTSCHRAUBE, FUNDAMENTBOLZEN |
| 5591 | **FOUNDER** | FONDEUR, OUVRIER FONDEUR | GIESSER |
| 5592 | **FOUNDING** | FONDERIE (ART), FONDERIE, COULEE | GIESSEREI, GIESSKUNST, GIESSEN |
| 5593 | **FOUNDRY** | FONDERIE | GUSSWERK, GIESSEREI |
| 5594 | **FOUNDRY ALLOY** | PRE-ALLIAGE | VORLEGIERUNG |
| 5595 | **FOUNDRY COKE** | COKE DE CUBILOT | GIESSEREIKOKS, KUPOLOFENKOKS |
| 5596 | **FOUNDRY PIG (IRON)** | FONTE DE MOULAGE, FONTE GRISE | GIESSEREIROHEISEN ROHEISEN (GRAUES) |
| 5597 | **FOUNDRY SHOP** | FONDERIES (ETABLISSEMENT) | GIESSEREI, GIESSHAUS |
| 5598 | **FOUNDRYMEN'S NAILS** | POINTES POUR FONDERIE | FORMERSTIFTE |
| 5599 | **FOUR DOOR SEDAN** | BERLINE 4 PORTES | VIERTÜRIGE LIMOUSINE |
| 5600 | **FOUR STROKE CYCLE ENGINE, FOUR STROKE ENGINE** | MOTEUR A QUATRE TEMPS | VIERTAKTMOTOR |
| 5601 | **FOUR WHEEL DRIVE** | PROPULSION A 4 ROUES MOTRICES | VIERRADANTRIEB |
| 5602 | **FOUR-CUSPED HYPOCYCLOID** | ASTROIDE | STERNKURVE, ASTROIDE, HYPOZYKLOIDE (VIERSPITZIGE) |
| 5603 | **FOUR-CYCLE ENGINE** | MOTEUR A QUATRE TEMPS | VIERTAKTMOTOR |
| 5604 | **FOUR-JAW INDEPENDENT CHUCK** | MANDRIN A QUATRE MORS INDEPENDANTS | VIERBACKENFUTTER |
| 5605 | **FOUR-WAY COCK** | ROBINET A QUATRE VOIES | VIERWEGHAHN |
| 5606 | **FOUR-WAY VALVE** | ROBINET A QUATRE VOIES | VIERWEGVENTIL |
| 5607 | **FOURDRINIER WIRE** | FIL DE BRONZE PHOSPHOREUX | FOURDRINIERDRAHT |
| 5608 | **FOURTH POWER** | QUATRIEME PUISSANCE | POTENZ (VIERTE) |
| 5609 | **FOURTH ROOT** | RACINE BIQUADRATIQUE | WURZEL (VIERTE), WURZEL (BIQUADRATISCHE) |
| 5610 | **FOXEY TIMBER** | BOIS A COEUR POURRI, BOIS POUILLEUX | HOLZ (ROTFAULES), HOLZ (KERNFAULES) |
| 5611 | **FRACTION** | FRACTION DE DISTILLATION | FRAKTION (EINER DESTILLATION) |
| 5612 | **FRACTIONAL DISTILLATION** | DISTILLATION FRACTIONNEE | DESTILLATION (STUFENWEISE), DESTILLATION (UNTERBROCHENE), DESTILLATION (FRAKTIONIERTE) |
| 5613 | **FRACTIONAL NUMBER** | FRACTION, NOMBRE FRACTIONNAIRE | BRUCH, ZAHL (GEBROCHENE) |
| 5614 | **FRACTIONATING TOWER** | TOUR DE FRACTIONNEMENT | FRAKTIONIERTURM |
| 5615 | **FRACTIONISE (TO), FRACTIONATE (TO)** | FRACTIONNER | DESTILLIEREN (STUFENWEISE), FRAKTIONIEREN |
| 5616 | **FRACTOGRAPHY** | THEORIE DES CASSURES | BRUCHTHEORIE, FRAKTOGRAPHIE |
| 5617 | **FRACTURE** | CASSURE, RUPTURE | BRUCH |
| 5618 | **FRACTURE STRESS** | EFFORT DE RUPTURE | BRUCHSPANNUNG |
| 5619 | **FRACTURE TEST** | ESSAI DE RUPTURE | BRUCHPROBE |
| 5620 | **FRACTURED SURFACE, SURFACE OF FRACTURE** | SECTION DE RUPTURE, CASSURE | BRUCH, BRUCHFLÄCHE |
| 5621 | **FRAGILE** | FRAGILE | ZERBRECHLICH |
| 5622 | **FRAGILITY** | FRAGILITE | ZERBRECHLICHKEIT |
| 5623 | **FRAGMENTATION OF GRAINS** | FRAGMENTATION DE GRAINS | KORNVERSTÜCKELUNG |
| 5624 | **FRAME** | CHARPENTE, CHASSIS, CADRE, CARCASSE | GERÜST, GERIPPE, FAHRGESTELL, POLGEHÄUSE, GESTELL, RAHMEN |
| 5625 | **FRAME HORN** | BRANCARD | BODENLÄNGSTRÄGER |
| 5626 | **FRAME OF AN ENGINE, FRAME OF A MACHINE** | BATI D'UNE MACHINE | MASCHINENRAHMEN |
| 5627 | **FRAME RAIL** | LONGERON | RAHMENLÄNGSTRÄGER |
| 5628 | **FRAME SAW** | SCIE A REFENDRE | ÖRTERSÄGE, SPANNSÄGE, TISCHLERSÄGE |

**FRA** 144

| | | | |
|---|---|---|---|
| 5629 | **FRAME SAWING MACHINE, RECIPROCATING SAW** | SCIE A CADRE, A CHASSIS, SCIERIE A MOUVEMENT ALTERNATIF, MACHINE ALTERNATIVE A SCIER | GATTERSÄGE |
| 5630 | **FRAMEWORK** | CHARPENTE, OSSATURE | BALKENWERK, RAHMENWERK |
| 5631 | **FRAUNHOFER LINES** | RAIES DE FRAUNHOFER | FRAUNHOFERSCHE LINIEN |
| 5632 | **FREE CYANIDE** | CYANURE LIBRE | ZYANID (FREIES) |
| 5633 | **FREE FALL** | CHUTE LIBRE | FREIFALL |
| 5634 | **FREE FLOW** | COURANT LIBRE | STRÖMUNG (FREIE) |
| 5635 | **FREE FROM ACID, ACIDLESS** | EXEMPT D'ACIDE | SÄUREFREI |
| 5636 | **FREE FROM ASH** | EXEMPT DE CENDRES | ASCHEFREI |
| 5637 | **FREE FROM DUST (TO)** | DEPOUSSIERER | ENTSTAUBEN |
| 5638 | **FREE FROM SLAG, SLAGLESS** | SANS SCORIES | SCHLACKENFREI |
| 5639 | **FREE MACHINING STEEL** | ACIER DE DECOLLETAGE RAPIDE | AUTOMATENSTAHL |
| 5640 | **FREE MAGNETISM** | MAGNETISME LIBRE | MAGNETISMUS (FREIER) |
| 5641 | **FREE STANDING ACCESSWAY** | ESCALIER DROIT | TREPPE (GERADE) |
| 5642 | **FREE VENT** | EVENT LIBRE | LUFTABZUG (FREIER) |
| 5643 | **FREE VIBRATION** | OSCILLATION LIBRE | SCHWINGUNG (FREIE) |
| 5644 | **FREE WHEEL** | ROUE LIBRE | FREILAUFRAD |
| 5645 | **FREE-CUTTING BRASS** | LAITON DE DECOLLETAGE | AUTOMATENMESSING |
| 5646 | **FREE-STANDING ACCESSWAY** | ESCALIER DROIT | TANKZUGANGSLEITER |
| 5647 | **FREE, NATIVE, VIRGIN** | NATIF, A L'ETAT NATIF, VIERGE (MIN.) | GEDIEGEN (MIN.) |
| 5648 | **FREEHAND DRAWING** | DESSIN A MAIN LEVEE | FREIHANDZEICHNUNG, HANDZEICHNUNG |
| 5649 | **FREELY SUSPENDED** | SUSPENDU LIBREMENT | FREI AUFGEHÄNGT |
| 5650 | **FREELY, SIMPLY SUPPORTED** | REPOSANT LIBREMENT | FREI AUFLIEGEND, FREI GELAGERT |
| 5651 | **FREEWHEEL** | ROUE LIBRE | FREILAUF |
| 5652 | **FREEWHEELING MECHANISM** | MECANISME DE ROUE LIBRE | FREILAUFMECHANISMUS |
| 5653 | **FREEZING** | SOLIDIFICATION | ERSTARRUNG |
| 5654 | **FREEZING MIXTURE** | MELANGE REFRIGERANT | KÄLTEMISCHUNG |
| 5655 | **FREEZING OF FURNACE** | CONGELATION DU FOUR | EINFRIEREN DES OFENS |
| 5656 | **FREEZING POINT** | POINT DE CONGELATION, POINT DE SOLIDIFICATION | GEFRIERPUNKT, ERSTARRUNGSPUNKT |
| 5657 | **FREEZING PREVENTIVE** | ANTI-GEL | FROSTSCHUTZMITTEL |
| 5658 | **FREEZING RANGE** | INTERVALLE DE SOLIDIFICATION, ZONE DE SOLIDIFICATION | ERSTARRUNGS-BEREICH, ERSTARRUNGS-INTERVALL |
| 5659 | **FRENCH CHALK** | STEATITE, TALC | SPECKSTEIN, TALKUM |
| 5660 | **FRENCH CURVES** | REGLE COURBE, PISTOLET | KURVENLINEAL, KURVENSCHIENE |
| 5661 | **FREQUENCY** | FREQUENCE | PERIODENZAHL, FREQUENZ |
| 5662 | **FREQUENCY FUNCTION** | FREQUENCE EMPIRIQUE | HÄUFIGKEITSFUNKTION |
| 5663 | **FRESH WATER** | EAU DOUCE | SÜSSWASSER |
| 5664 | **FRESH-WATER LIMESTONE** | CALCAIRE GROSSIER, CALCAIRE D'EAU DOUCE | GROBKALK |
| 5665 | **FRET SAW** | SCIE A DECOUPER, MACHINE A CHANTOURNER, SAUTEUSE | LAUBSÄGE |
| 5666 | **FRETTING** | CORROSION PAR FROTTEMENT | PASSFLÄCHENKORROSION, REIBUNGSOXYDATION |
| 5667 | **FRETTING CORROSION** | CORROSION DES FACES EN CONTACT, OXYDATION PAR FROTTEMENT | FASSFLÄCHENKORROSION, REIBUNGSOXYDATION |
| 5668 | **FRICTION** | FRICTION, FROTTEMENT | REIBUNG |
| 5669 | **FRICTION BRAKE** | FREIN A FRICTION | REIBUNGSBREMSE |
| 5670 | **FRICTION COEFFICIENT** | COEFFICIENT DE FROTTEMENT | REIBUNGSZAHL |

**145** **FUE**

| | | | |
|---|---|---|---|
| 5671 | FRICTION CONE | CONE DE FRICTION | REIBUNGSKEGEL |
| 5672 | FRICTION COUPLING | EMBRAYAGE A FRICTION, ACCOUPLEMENT A FRICTION | REFBUNGSKUPPLUNG |
| 5673 | FRICTION DISC | PLATEAU DE FRICTION | REIBSCHEIBE, FRIKTIONSSCHEIBE |
| 5674 | FRICTION GEAR | ENGRENAGE A FRICTION | REIBGETRIEBE |
| 5675 | FRICTION GRIPPING PAWL | CLIQUET DE FROTTEMENT | KLEMMBACKE, KLEMMKLINKE, REIBUNGSKLINKE |
| 5676 | FRICTION GRIPPING PAWL MOTION | ENCLIQUETAGE A FROTTEMENT | REIBUNGSGESPERRE, REIBUNGSSCHALTWERK, KLEMMGESPERRE, KLEMMBACKENSCHALTGETRIEBE |
| 5677 | FRICTION OF MOTION, KINETIC FRICTION | FROTTEMENT PENDANT LE MOUVEMENT, FROTTEMENT EN MARCHE | REIBUNG DER BEWEGUNG |
| 5678 | FRICTION OF REPOSE, OF REST, STATIC FRICTION | FROTTEMENT AU DEPART, FROTTEMENT AU DEMARRAGE | REIBUNG (RUHENDE), REIBUNG DER RUHE, HAFTREIBUNG |
| 5679 | FRICTION ROLLER | GALET DE FRICTION | REIBROLLE |
| 5680 | FRICTION SAWING | SCIAGE PAR FRICTION | REIBUNGSSÄGEN |
| 5681 | FRICTION STRAP BRAKE, BAND BRAKE, RIBBON BRAKE | FREIN A BANDE, FREIN A RUBAN, FREIN A COLLIER, FREIN A ENROULEMENT | BANDBREMSE |
| 5682 | FRICTION WHEEL | ROUE DE FRICTION | REIBRAD |
| 5683 | FRICTIONAL FORCE, FORCE OF FRICTION | FORCE DU FROTTEMENT | REIBUNGSKRAFT |
| 5684 | FRICTIONAL GEARING | TRANSMISSION PAR FRICTION | REIBUNGSGETRIEBE |
| 5685 | FRICTIONAL LOSS | PERTE DUE AU FROTTEMENT | REIBUNGSVERLUST |
| 5686 | FRICTIONAL RESISTANCE | RESISTANCE DU FROTTEMENT | REIBUNGSWIDERSTAND |
| 5687 | FRICTIONAL SURFACE | SURFACE FROTTANTE | REIBUNGSFLÄCHE |
| 5688 | FRICTIONLESS | SANS FROTTEMENT | REIBUNGSLOS |
| 5689 | FRINGE LINES | LIGNES LIMITES | GRENZLINIEN |
| 5690 | FRITTING | FRITTAGE | SINTERUNG |
| 5691 | FRONT AXLE | ESSIEU AVANT | VORDERACHSE |
| 5692 | FRONT BODY PANEL | TABLIER | QUERWAND |
| 5693 | FRONT CROSS MEMBER | TRAVERSE AVANT | VORDERQUERTRÄGER |
| 5694 | FRONT ELEVATION, FRONT VIEW | VUE DE FACE | VORDERANSICHT |
| 5695 | FRONT END ASSEMBLY | AUVENT | WINDLAUF |
| 5696 | FRONT END GEOMETRY | GEOMETRIE DU TRAIN AVANT | VORDERACHSGEOMETRIE |
| 5697 | FRONT OPERATED LATHE | TOUR FRONTAL (TOUR EN L'AIR) | DREHMASCHINE MIT FRONTBEDIENUNG |
| 5698 | FRONT RAKE, TOP RAKE | ANGLE DE DEPOUILLE, ANGLE DE DEGAGEMENT DU COPEAU | BRUSTWINKEL |
| 5699 | FRONT WHEEL DRIVE | TRACTION AVANT | VORDERRADANTRIEB |
| 5700 | FROST SHAKE IN TIMBER | GELIVURE DU BOIS | EISKLUFT, FROSTRISS DES HOLZES |
| 5701 | FROSTED GROUND GLASS | VERRE DEPOLI | MATTGLAS |
| 5702 | FROSTING | GIVRAGE | EISBLUMENBILDUNG |
| 5703 | FROTHING | BULLAGE | SCHAUMBILDUNG |
| 5704 | FRUIT AND VEGETABLE GRADING AND WASHING MACHINERY | LAVEUSES ET TRIEURS DE RACINES ET DE FRUITS | SORTIER-UND WASCHMASCHINEN FÜR FRÜCHTE UND GEMÜSE |
| 5705 | FUEL | COMBUSTIBLE | BRENNMITTEL, BRENNSTOFF, HEIZSTOFF |
| 5706 | FUEL BUNKER | SOUTE A MAZOUT | ÖLBUNKER |
| 5707 | FUEL ECONOMY | ECONOMIE DE COMBUSTIBLE | BRENNSTOFFERSPARNIS |
| 5708 | FUEL FILTER | FILTRE A CARBURANT, FILTRE A COMBUSTIBLE | KRAFTSTOFFILTER |
| 5709 | FUEL GAS | GAZ DE CHAUFFAGE, GAZ COMBUSTIBLE | HEIZGAS, BRENNGAS |

**FUE**

146

| | | | |
|---|---|---|---|
| 5710 | FUEL GAUGE | INDICATEUR DE NIVEAU D'ESSENCE | KRAFTSTOFFSTANDMESSER |
| 5711 | FUEL INJECTION PUMP | POMPE D'INJECTION | EINSPRITZPUMPE |
| 5712 | FUEL INJECTION PUMP HOUSING | CARTER DE POMPE D'INJECTION | EINSPRITZPUMPEN-GEHÄUSE |
| 5713 | FUEL LIFT PUMP | POMPE D'ALIMENTATION | FÖRDERPUMPE |
| 5714 | FUEL OIL | MAZOUT, FUEL, HUILE LOURDE (POUR FORCE MOTRICE) | HEIZÖL, SCHWERÖL, TREIBÖL |
| 5715 | FUEL PUMP | POMPE D'ALIMENTATION | KRAFTSTOFFPUMPE |
| 5716 | FUEL TANK | RESERVOIR, RESERVOIR DE CARBURANT, RESERVOIR D'ESSENCE | KRAFTSTOFFBEHÄLTER |
| 5717 | FULCRUM | CENTRE DE ROTATION, POINT D'ARTICULATION | DREHPUNKT, GELENKPUNKT |
| 5718 | FULL ADMISSON TURBINE | TURBINE A ADMISSION TOTALE | VOLLTURBINE |
| 5719 | FULL ANNEALING | RECUIT A GROSGRAIN | HOCHGLÜHEN |
| 5720 | FULL FILLET JOINT | JOINT SOUDE A SIMPLE CLIN | EINZELKEHLNAHT |
| 5721 | FULL HARDENING | DURCISSEMENT A COEUR | DURCHHÄRTUNG |
| 5722 | FULL LOAD | PLEINE CHARGE | BELASTUNG (VOLLE) |
| 5723 | FULL SIZE (TO) | EN GRANDEUR NATURELLE, EN GRANDEUR D'EXECUTION | NATÜRLICHER GRÖSSE (IN), MASSSTAB NATÜRLICHEM (IN), ORIGINALGRÖSSE (IN) |
| 5724 | FULL SIZE DRAWING | DESSIN EN GRANDEUR NATURELLE, DESSIN NATURE | ZEICHNUNG IN NATÜRLICHER GRÖSSE |
| 5725 | FULL, UNBROKEN, SOLID LINE | LIGNE PLEINE | LINIE (AUSGEZOGENE) |
| 5726 | FULLER | ESTAMPE A DEGROSSIR, ESTAMPE A ETIRER | STRECKGESENK |
| 5727 | FULLER'S EARTH | TERRE A FOULON | WALKERDE, FULLERERDE, BLEICHERDE |
| 5728 | FULLERING | DEGORGEMENT | EINSCHNÜRUNG |
| 5729 | FULLERING TOOL | DEGORGEOIR | SETZHAMMER (RUNDER) |
| 5730 | FULLY MANUFACTURED ARTICLE, FINISHED PRODUCT, WORK, FULLY MANUFACTURED PRODUCT | PIECE FINIE, PRODUIT FINI, FABRIQUE | FERTIGERZEUGNIS, GANZFABRIKAT |
| 5731 | FULMINIC ACID | ACIDE FULMINIQUE | KNALLSÄURE |
| 5732 | FUMES | FUMEES | RAUCHGASE |
| 5733 | FUMING NORDHAUSEN SULPHURIC ACID, DISULPHURIC PYROSULPHURIC ACID | ACIDE SULFURIQUE FUMANT, ACIDE DE NORDHAUSEN, ACIDE DE SAXE | SCHWEFELSÄURE (RAUCHENDE), NORDHÄUSER VITRIOLÖL, OLEUM |
| 5734 | FUNCTION (MATH.) | FONCTION (MATH.) | FUNKTION (MATH.) |
| 5735 | FUNDAMENTAL RESEARCH | RECHERCHE FONDAMENTALE | GRUNDLAGENFORSCHUNG |
| 5736 | FUNDAMENTAL VIBRATION | VIBRATION PROPRE, VIBRATION FONDAMENTALE | GRUNDSCHWINGUNG, EIGENSCHWINGUNG, FUNDAMENTALSCHWINGUNG |
| 5737 | FUNICULAR LINK STRING POLYGON | POLYGONE FUNICULAIRE, POLYGONE ARTICULE | SEILECK, SEILZUG, SEILPOLYGON |
| 5738 | FUNNEL | ENTONNOIR | TRICHTER |
| 5739 | FURNACE | FOUR, FOURNEAU | OFEN |
| 5740 | FURNACE BRAZING | BRASAGE AU FOUR | OFENHARTLÖTEN |
| 5741 | FURNACE CHROME | CHROME A FOUR | CHROMERZMÖRTEL |
| 5742 | FURNACE COOLING | REFROIDISSEMENT DU FOUR | OFENKÜHLUNG |
| 5743 | FURNACE FLUE | CARNEAU DE FUMEE | FEUERKANAL, FEUERZUG, HEIZKANAL |
| 5744 | FURNACE FOR GASEOUS FUEL, GASEOUS FUEL FURNACE | FOYER A GAZ | GASFEUERUNG |
| 5745 | FURNACE FOR OIL FUEL, OIL FUEL FURNACE | FOYER A PETROLE, FOYER A HUILE LOURDE | ÖLFEUERUNG |

| | | | |
|---|---|---|---|
| 5746 | **FURNACE FOR PULVERISED COAL, PULVERISED COAL FURNACE** | FOYER A CHARBON PULVERISE | KOHLENSTAUBFEUERUNG |
| 5747 | **FURNACE INSTALLATION** | FOYER DE CHAUDIERE, FOUR DE CHAUFFERIE | FEUERUNGSANLAGE |
| 5748 | **FURNACE LINING** | GARNISSAGE DU FOUR | OFENFUTTER |
| 5749 | **FURNACE SHELL** | CHEMISE DU FOUR | OFENMANTEL |
| 5750 | **FURTHER TREATMENT, WORKING, MACHINING** | USINAGE ULTERIEUR | WEITERVERARBEITUNG |
| 5751 | **FUSE** | FUSIBLE | SICHERUNG |
| 5752 | **FUSE BOX** | BOITE A FUSIBLES | SICHERUNGSKASTEN |
| 5753 | **FUSED ALUMINA** | ELECTRO-CORINDON | ELEKTROKUNSTKORUND |
| 5754 | **FUSEL OIL** | HUILE DE POMMES DE TERRE | FUSELÖL |
| 5755 | **FUSIBILITY** | FUSIBILITE | SCHMELZBARKEIT |
| 5756 | **FUSIBLE** | FUSIBLE, LIQUEFIABLE | SCHMELZBAR |
| 5757 | **FUSIBLE ALLOY** | ALLIAGE FUSIBLE | LEGIERUNG (LEICHT SCHMELZBARE), SCHMELZLEGIERUNG |
| 5758 | **FUSIBLE PLUG, SAFETY PLUG** | BOUCHON, PLOMB FUSIBLE, FUSIBLE | SCHMELZPFROPFEN |
| 5759 | **FUSING MELTING POINT** | POINT DE FUSION | SCHMELZPUNKT |
| 5760 | **FUSION** | FUSION | SCHMELZEN |
| 5761 | **FUSION RANGE** | ZONE DE FUSION | SCHMELZBEREICH |
| 5762 | **FUSION WELDING** | SOUDAGE PAR FUSION | SCHMELZSCHWEISSEN |
| 5763 | **FUSION ZONE** | ZONE DE FUSION | SCHMELZZONE |
| 5764 | **FUSION, MELTING** | FUSION IGNEE, LIQUEFACTION | SCHMELZEN, SCHMELZUNG |
| 5765 | **GABBRO** | GABBRO | GABBRO |
| 5766 | **GADGET** | DISPOSITIF ACCESSOIRE | ÜBERFLÜSSIGE ZUTAT |
| 5767 | **GADOLINIUM** | GADOLINIUM | GADOLINIUM |
| 5768 | **GAGE** | INDICATEUR, JAUGE, ETALON, GABARIT | EICHMASS, LEHRE, MESSGERÄT |
| 5769 | **GAGE BLOCKS** | TAMPONS DE CONTROLE, ETALONS, CALIBRES, JAUGES, GABARITS | PARALLELENDMASS, LEHRE |
| 5770 | **GAGE CALIBRATION** | ETALONNAGE D'UNE JAUGE | PEILEICHUNG |
| 5771 | **GAGE PRESSURE** | PRESSION MANOMETRIQUE | DRUCK (MANOMETRISCHER), MESSERDRUCK |
| 5772 | **GAGGER** | CROCHET, TIRETTE, TIRANT D'ENLEVEMENT | SANDHAKEN, AUSHEBEBAND |
| 5773 | **GAIN** | GAIN | VERSTÄRKUNG |
| 5774 | **GAIN IN SPACE** | REDUCTION DES EMPLACEMENTS | PLATZERSPARNIS, RAUMERSPARNIS |
| 5775 | **GALENA, LEAD GLANCE, LEAD SULPHIDE** | PLOMB SULFURE, GALENE | BLEIGLANZ, GALENIT, SCHWEFELBLEI |
| 5776 | **GALLERY, PLAFTORM** | PLATEFORME, PASSERELLE | BÜHNE, BEDIENUNGSBÜHNE |
| 5777 | **GALLIC ACID** | ACIDE GALLIQUE | GALLUSSÄURE, TRIOXYBENZOESÄURE |
| 5778 | **GALLING** | USURE PAR FROTTEMENT, GRIPPAGE | FRESSEN, ANFRESSUNG |
| 5779 | **GALLIUM** | GALLIUM | GALLIUM |
| 5780 | **GALLO TANNIC ACID, TANNIN** | ACIDE TANNIQUE, ACIDE DIGALLIQUE, TANNIN | GERBSTOFF, GALLUSGERBSÄURE, TANNIN |
| 5781 | **GALLON** | GALLON (MESURE ANGLAISE) | GALLONE |
| 5782 | **GALVANIC CELL** | PILE GALVANIQUE, PILE HYDRO-ELECTRIQUE, ELEMENT GALVANIQUE, COUPLE ELECTRO-CHIMIQUE | ELEMENT (GALVANISCHES), ZELLE (GALVANISCHE) |
| 5783 | **GALVANIC CORROSION** | CORROSION GALVANIQUE | KORROSION (GALVANISCHE) |
| 5784 | **GALVANISE (TO)** | GALVANISER, ZINGUER | VERZINKEN |
| 5785 | **GALVANISED SHEET IRON** | TOLE GALVANISEE, TOLE ZINGUEE | BLECH (VERZINKTES), BLECH (GALVANISIERTES) |

# GAL 148

| 5786 | GALVANISED WIRE | FIL GALVANISE, FIL ZINGUE | DRAHT (VERZINKTER), DRAHT (GALVANISIERTER) |
|---|---|---|---|
| 5787 | GALVANISING BY DIPPING, HOT COMMON ORDINARY GALVNISING | GALVANISATION, ZINGAGE | VERZINKUNG (HEISSE), FEUERVERZINKUNG |
| 5788 | GALVANIZED STRIPS | BANDES GALVANISEES | EISENBLECHE (VERZINKTE) |
| 5789 | GALVANIZING | GALVANISATION, ZINGAGE | GALVANISIEREN, VERZINKEN |
| 5790 | GALVANIZING EMBRITTLEMENT | FRAGILITE AU ZINGAGE | VERSPRÖDUNG BEIM VERZINKEN |
| 5791 | GALVANOMETER | GALVANOMETRE | GALVANOMETER |
| 5792 | GALVANOPLASTIC | GALVANOPLASTIQUE | GALVANOPLASTISCH |
| 5793 | GAMBOGE | GOMME-GUTTE | GUMMIGUTT |
| 5794 | GAMMA FUNCTION | FONCTION GAMMA | GAMMA-FUNKTION |
| 5795 | GAMMA IRON | FER GAMMA | GAMMA-EISEN |
| 5796 | GAMMA RAYS | RAYONS GAMMA | GAMMA-STRAHLEN |
| 5797 | GAMMA STRUCTURE | STRUCTURE GAMMA | GAMMA-STRUKTUR |
| 5798 | GAMMA-GRAPH | GAMMA-GRAPHIE | GAMMA-STRAHLENBILD |
| 5799 | GANG DRILL | PERCEUSE A TETES MULTIPLES | MEHRSPINDEL-BOHRMASCHINE |
| 5800 | GANG MILLING | FRAISAGE EN TRAIN | SATZFRÄSER |
| 5801 | GANG TOOLS | PORTE-OUTIL A PLUSIEURS OUTILS | MEISSELSATZ |
| 5802 | GANGUE | GANGUE, ROCHE-MERE | GANGART, GANGGESTEIN, GANGMINERAL, NEBENGESTEIN |
| 5803 | GANISTER | GANNISTER, BRIQUE DINAS | GANISTER, FLICKMASSE, KALKDINAS |
| 5804 | GANTRY CRANE, GOLIATH CRANE | PONT-ROULANT DE CHANTIER/DE GARE | BOCKKRAN, GERÜSTKRAN |
| 5805 | GAP SIZED GRADING | MELANGE DE GRAIN SANS GRAINS INTERMEDIAIRES | KORNGEMISCH OHNE MITTELKORN |
| 5806 | GAPING OF A JOINT | BAILLEMENT, BEANT D'UN JOINT | KLAFFEN EINER FUGE |
| 5807 | GARNET | GRENAT | GRANAT |
| 5808 | GAS | CORPS GAZEUX, GAZ, FLUIDE GAZEUX | GASFÖRMIGER KÖRPER, GAS |
| 5809 | GAS ANALYSIS | ANALYSE DES GAZ | GASANALYSE |
| 5810 | GAS BRAZING | BRASAGE AU CHALUMEAU | GASLÖTEN, FLAMMLÖTEN |
| 5811 | GAS BURNER | BRULEUR A GAZ, BEC A GAZ | GASBRENNER |
| 5812 | GAS CARBON | CHARBON DE CORNUE | RETORTENKOHLE, RETORTENGRAPHIT |
| 5813 | GAS COAL | HOUILLE A GAZ | GASKOHLE |
| 5814 | GAS COCK | ROBINET A GAZ | GASHAHN |
| 5815 | GAS CONSTANT | CONSTANTE D'UN GAZ | GASKONSTANTE |
| 5816 | GAS CURRENT | COURANT GAZEUX | GASSTROM |
| 5817 | GAS CUTTING | COUPAGE A L'AUTOGENE, COUPAGE AU CHALUMEAU, OXYCOUPAGE | BRENNSCHNEIDEN |
| 5818 | GAS CYANIDING | CEMENTATION A L'AZOTE | NITROZEMENTIERUNG |
| 5819 | GAS ENGINE | MOTEUR A ESSENCE | GASKRAFTMASCHINE, GASMOTOR |
| 5820 | GAS FLARE | TORCHERE | GASFACKEL |
| 5821 | GAS FLUE | CARNEAU A GAZ | GASABZUG |
| 5822 | GAS GOUGING | RAINURAGE A LA FLAMME | AUTOGENE RILLUNG |
| 5823 | GAS GROOVES | ONDULATIONS DUES AU GAZ | GASRILLEN |
| 5824 | GAS HEATED SOLDERING IRON | FER A SOUDER AU GAZ | GASLÖTKOLBEN |
| 5825 | GAS HOLE | SOUFFLURE | GASEINSCHLUSS, GASBLASE |
| 5826 | GAS LAMP | LAMPE A GAZ D'ECLAIRAGE | GASLAMPE, LEUCHTGASLAMPE |
| 5827 | GAS LIGHT | LUMIERE DU GAZ | GASLICHT |
| 5828 | GAS LIGHTING | ECLAIRAGE AU GAZ | GASBELEUCHTUNG |
| 5829 | GAS METER | COMPTEUR A GAZ | GASMESSER, GASUHR |

| | | | |
|---|---|---|---|
| 5830 | **GAS NITRIDING** | NITRURATION GAZEUSE | GASNITRIEREN |
| 5831 | **GAS OIL** | GAZOLE | GASÖL |
| 5832 | **GAS PICKLING** | DECAPAGE AU GAZ | GASBEIZUNG |
| 5833 | **GAS PIPE** | TUYAU A GAZ | GASROHR |
| 5834 | **GAS PIPE LINE** | CONDUITE DE GAZ, DISTRIBUTION DE GAZ | GASLEITUNG |
| 5835 | **GAS PLIERS, GAS TONGS** | PINCES A GAZ | GASROHRZANGE |
| 5836 | **GAS POCKET** | INCLUSION DE GAZ, SOUFFLURE | GASEINSCHLUSS, GASBLASE |
| 5837 | **GAS PRESSURE** | PRESSION DU GAZ | GASDRUCK |
| 5838 | **GAS PRODUCER** | GAZOGENE, GENERATEUR A GAZ | GASERZEUGER, GASGENERATOR |
| 5839 | **GAS PURIFICATION** | EPURATION DES GAZ | GASREINIGUNG |
| 5840 | **GAS QUENCHING** | TREMPE AU GAZ | GASHÄRTUNG |
| 5841 | **GAS RECUPERATION WITHOUT COMBUSTION** | CAPTAGE DES GAZ SANS COMBUSTION | GASABZUG OHNE VERBRENNUNG MIT WIEDERGEWINNUNG |
| 5842 | **GAS TAKE** | COLLECTEUR DE GAZ | GASFANG |
| 5843 | **GAS THREAD** | PAS POUR TUBES A GAZ | GASROHRGEWINDE |
| 5844 | **GAS TURBINE** | TURBINE A GAZ | GASTURBINE |
| 5845 | **GAS WASHING BOTTLE** | BARBOTEUR POUR LAVAGES, FLACON LAVEUR | GASWASCHFLASCHE |
| 5846 | **GAS WATER-HEATER** | CHAUFFE EAU A GAZ | DURCHLAUFERHITZER |
| 5847 | **GAS WELDING** | SOUDURE AUTOGENE | GASSCHWEISSEN |
| 5848 | **GAS WORKS** | USINE A GAZ | GASFABRIK, GASWERK, GASANSTALT |
| 5849 | **GAS WORKS COKE** | COKE DE GAZ, COKE D'USINE A GAZ | GASKOKS |
| 5850 | **GAS-ELECTRIC GENERATOR** | GENERATRICE A GAZ | GASDYNAMO |
| 5851 | **GAS-FIRED FURNACE** | FOUR CHAUFFE AU GAZ | OFEN (GASGEHEIZTER) |
| 5852 | **GAS-SHIELD ARC WELDING** | SOUDAGE A L'ARC SOUS PROTECTION GAZEUSE | SCHUTZGAS-LICHTBOGENSCHWEISSEN |
| 5853 | **GAS-TIGHT** | ETANCHE AUX GAZ | GASDICHT |
| 5854 | **GASEOUS FUEL** | COMBUSTIBLE GAZEUX | BRENNSTOFF (GASFÖRMIGER) |
| 5855 | **GASEOUS INCLUSION** | INCLUSION GAZEUSE | GASEINSCHLUSS |
| 5856 | **GASEOUS MIXTURE** | MELANGE GAZEUX | GASGEMISCH |
| 5857 | **GASEOUS STATE** | ETAT GAZEUX | AGGREGAT- ZUSTAND (GASFÖRMIGER) |
| 5858 | **GASHING** | AMORCAGE (DE COUPE) | VORFRÄSEN |
| 5859 | **GASHOLDER, GASOMETER** | GAZOMETRE | GASBEHÄLTER, GASGLOCKE, GASOMETER |
| 5860 | **GASIFIABLE** | GAZEIFIABLE | VERGASBAR |
| 5861 | **GASIFICATION** | GAZEIFICATION | VERGASUNG |
| 5862 | **GASIFY (TO)** | GAZEIFIER | VERGASEN |
| 5863 | **GASKET** | TRESSE, JOINT, JOINT D'ETANCHEITE | ZOPF FÜR PACKUNGEN, DICHTUNGSZOPF, PACKUNGSZOPF, DICHTUNG, DICHTFLANSCH |
| 5864 | **GASOLINE, PETROL** | ESSENCE | BENZIN |
| 5865 | **GASSING** | GAZEIFICATION | VERGASUNG |
| 5866 | **GATE** | ATTAQUE DE COULEE | AUSCHNITT |
| 5867 | **GATE VALVE** | VANNE, VANNE A PASSAGE DIRECT | ABSPERRSCHIEBER, DURCHGANGSVENTIL |
| 5868 | **GATED PATTERN** | MODELE A ENTONNOIRS | MODELL MIT EINGUSSTRICHTERN |
| 5869 | **GATHERING STOCK** | AUGMENTATION DE LA SECTION TRANSVERSALE | QUERSCHNITTSVERGRÖSSERUNG |
| 5870 | **GATING SYSTEM** | SYSTEME DE COULEE ET D'ALIMENTATION | ANSCHNITTSYSTEM |

# GAU

**150**

| 5871 | GAUGE (METR), GAUGE (RAILWAY) | JAUGE, CALIBRE, INSTRUMENT DE VERIFICATION, VERIFICATEUR (METR), ECARTEMENT DE LA VOIE (CH. DE FER) | LEHRE, KALIBER (METR), SPURWEITE (EISENBAHN) |
|------|-------------------------------|----------------------------------------------------------------------------------------------------|----------------------------------------------|
| 5872 | GAUGE (TO) | ETALONNER, TARER, TIMBRER | EICHEN |
| 5873 | GAUGE BLOCKS | CALES-ETALONS | LEHRSTÜCKE |
| 5874 | GAUGE CALIBRATION | ETALONNAGE D'UNE JAUGE | PEILEICHUNG |
| 5875 | GAUGE COCK, GAUGE VALVE | ROBINET DE JAUGE | PROBIERHAHN, PROBIERVENTIL |
| 5876 | GAUGE FLOAT | FLOTTEUR (DE JAUGE) | SCHWIMMER |
| 5877 | GAUGE HEAD | TETE DE JAUGE | PEILKOPF |
| 5878 | GAUGE LENGTH | LONGUEUR DE REFERENCE | BEZUGSLÄNGE |
| 5879 | GAUGE MARK | REPERE | ENDMARKE |
| 5880 | GAUGE OF SHEET METAL | NUMERO DE JAUGE D'UNE TOLE | BLECHNUMMER |
| 5881 | GAUGE OF WIRE | NUMERO DE JAUGE D'UN FIL | DRAHTNUMMER |
| 5882 | GAUGE PRESSURE | PRESSION RELATIVE | ÜBERDRUCK |
| 5883 | GAUGE TAP | BOUCHON DE JAUGE | KALIBERSTOPFEN |
| 5884 | GAUGE-BLOCK BUILD-UP | MONTAGE DE CALES-ETALONS | LEHRSTÜCKENMONTAGE |
| 5885 | GAUGER'S PLATFORM | PLATEFORME DE JAUGEAGE | PEILBÜHNE |
| 5886 | GAUGING | ETALONNAGE, ETALONNEMENT, TARAGE, TIMBRE | EICHEN, EICHUNG |
| 5887 | GAUSSIAN DISTRIBUTION | DISTRIBUTION GAUSSIENNE | GAUSSSCHE VERTEILUNG |
| 5888 | GAUZE | GAZE, TOILE METALLIQUE | GAZE, DRAHTGEWEBE |
| 5889 | GEAR | ENGRENAGE, PIGNON | ZAHNRAD |
| 5890 | GEAR BOX | CARTER D'ENGRENAGE, BOITE DE VITESSE | RÄDERKASTEN, SCHALTGETRIEBE |
| 5891 | GEAR CUTTING MACHINE | MACHINE A TAILLER LES ENGRENAGES, TAILLEUSE D'ENGRENAGES | ZAHNRADSCHNEIDEMASCHINE |
| 5892 | GEAR DRIVE | COMMANDE PAR ENGRENAGE | ZAHNRADANTRIEB |
| 5893 | GEAR DRIVEN MACHINE | MACHINE A COMMANDE PAR ENGRENAGE | MASCHINE MIT ZAHNRADANTRIEB |
| 5894 | GEAR MILLING MACHINE | FRAISEUSE A TAILLER LES ENGRENAGES | RÄDERFRÄSMASCHINE |
| 5895 | GEAR PUMP | POMPE A ENGRENAGE | ZAHNRADPUMPE |
| 5896 | GEAR RATIO | RAPPORTS D'ENGRENAGES | ÜBERSETZUNGSVERHÄLTNIS |
| 5897 | GEAR RATIO OF A TRAIN OF WHEELS | RAPPORT D'ENGRENAGE | RÄDERÜBERSETZUNG (VERHÄLTNIS) |
| 5898 | GEAR TOOTH MILLING CUTTER, HOB | FRAISE A TAILLER LES ENGRENAGES | ZAHNRADFRÄSER |
| 5899 | GEAR TOOTH VERNIER | PIED A DENTURE | ZAHNMESS-SCHIEBLEHRE |
| 5900 | GEAR TOOTH VERNIER CALIPER | PIED A COULISSE A VERNIER POUR DENTS DE PIGNON | ZAHNRAD-NONIUSSCHUBLEHRE |
| 5901 | GEAR TRAIN, TRAIN OF GEARS OF GEARING OF WHEELS, WHEEL TRAIN | TRAIN D'ENGRENAGES, JEU D'ENGRENAGES | RÄDERGRUPPE, RÄDERGETRIEBE (ZUSAMMENGESETZTES) |
| 5902 | GEAR WHEEL TESTING MACHINE | BANC POUR VERIFIER LES ENGRENAGES | ZAHNRÄDERPRÜFMASCHINE |
| 5903 | GEAR WHEEL, TOOTHED WHEEL | ROUE DENTEE, ROUE D'ENGRENAGE | ZAHNRAD |
| 5904 | GEAR-WHEEL STEEL | ACIER POUR ENGRENAGES | ZAHNRADSTAHL |
| 5905 | GEARED BRACE, HAND DRILL | VILEBREQUIN A ENGRENAGE | RÄDERBOHRER, ECKENBOHRER, ECKBOHRWINDE |
| 5906 | GEARED FLYWHEEL | VOLANT DENTE, VOLANT ENGRENAGE | SCHWUNGRAD (GEZAHNTES), SCHWUNGRAD (VERZAHNTES) |
| 5907 | GEARING | HARNAIS D'ENGRENAGES, ENGRENAGES | RÄDERGETRIEBE, ZAHNRADGETRIEBE |

| | | | |
|---|---|---|---|
| 5908 | **GEARING DOWN** | DEMULTIPLICATION | UNTERSETZUNG |
| 5909 | **GEARING UP** | MULTIPLICATION | ÜBERSETZUNG |
| 5910 | **GEARING, MESHING** | ENGRENEMENT | EINGRIFF, INEINANDERGREIFEN, KÄMMEN VON ZAHNRÄDERN |
| 5911 | **GEIGER COUNTER** | COMPTEUR GEIGER | GEIGER-ZÄHLER |
| 5912 | **GEL** | GEL | GEL |
| 5913 | **GELATINE** | GELATINE PURE | GELATINE |
| 5914 | **GENERAL LAYOUT** | DISPOSITION GENERALE, PLAN DE DISPOSITION | DISPOSITIONSZEICHNUNG, GRUNDRISS |
| 5915 | **GENERAL MANAGER** | DIRECTEUR D'USINE | FABRIKDIREKTOR |
| 5916 | **GENERATE (TO), PRODUCE (TO) (STEAM, GAS)** | PRODUIRE (DE LA VAPEUR, DES GAZ) | ERZEUGEN, (DAMPF, GAS) |
| 5917 | **GENERATE AN ELECTRIC CURRENT (TO)** | PRODUIRE UN COURANT ELECTRIQUE | ELEKTRISCHEN STROM ERZEUGEN |
| 5918 | **GENERATING CONE** | CONE GENERATEUR, CONE COMPLEMENTAIRE | ERGÄNZUNGSKEGEL |
| 5919 | **GENERATING FUNCTION** | FONCTION GENERATRICE (DES MOMENTS) | ERZEUGENDE FUNKTION |
| 5920 | **GENERATING PLANT** | INSTALLATION GENERATRICE DE COURANT | STROMERZEUGUNGSANLAGE |
| 5921 | **GENERATING ROLLING MOVING CIRCLE** | CERCLE ROULANT, CERCLE MOBILE | ROLLENDER KREIS, ROLLKREIS, WÄLZKREIS |
| 5922 | **GENERATION OF POWER** | PRODUCTION D'ENERGIE | ENERGIEERZEUGUNG |
| 5923 | **GENERATION OF STEAM, STEAM RAISING** | GENERATION DE VAPEUR | DAMPFERZEUGUNG |
| 5924 | **GENERATOR, DYNAMOELECTRIC MACHINE** | DYNAMO, GENERATRICE DE COURANT | DYNAMOMASCHINE, DYNAMOELEKTRISCHE MASCHINE, GENERATOR (ELEKTRISCHER), STROMERZEUGER, LICHTMASCHINE |
| 5925 | **GENERATOR, GENERATING LINE** | GENERATRICE (GEOM.) | ERZEUGENDE, GENERATRIX |
| 5926 | **GEOMETRIC REPRESENTATION** | REPRESENTATION GEOMETRIQUE | DARSTELLUNG (GEOMETRISCHE) |
| 5927 | **GEOMETRICAL** | GEOMETRIQUE | GEOMETRISCH |
| 5928 | **GEOMETRICAL DRAWING** | DESSIN GEOMETRIQUE | ZEICHNUNG (GEOMETRISCHE) |
| 5929 | **GEOMETRICAL MEAN** | MOYENNE GEOMETRIQUE | MITTEL (GEOMETRISCHES) |
| 5930 | **GEOMETRICAL PROGRESSION** | PROGRESSION GEOMETRIQUE | REIHE (GEOMETRISCHE) |
| 5931 | **GEOMETRY** | GEOMETRIE | GEOMETRIE |
| 5932 | **GERMAN SILVER** | ARGENTAN, MAILLECHORT, ARGENTAL, ARGENT ALLEMAND, ARGENT DE CHINE | NEUSILBER, ARGENTAN, WEISSKUPFER, PACKFONG |
| 5933 | **GERMANIUM** | GERMANIUM | GERMANIUM |
| 5934 | **GERMINATION** | GERMINATION, FORMATION DE GERMES | KEIMBILDUNG |
| 5935 | **GERMINATIVE CONDITION** | CONDITION CRITIQUE DE DEFORMATION | SPANNUNGSZUSTAND (KRITISCHER) |
| 5936 | **GEYSER** | GEYSER (NATURE) | GEISER |
| 5937 | **GIB** | CONTRE-CLAVETTE | GEGENKEIL, KEILBEILAGE, BEILAGE |
| 5938 | **GIB AND COTTER** | CLAVETTE ET CONTRE-CLAVETTE | DOPPELKEIL |
| 5939 | **GIBHEADED KEY** | CLAVETTE A TALON, CLAVETTE A TETE, CLAVETTE A MENTONNET | NASENKEIL |
| 5940 | **GIBS** | LARDONS | LEISTEN |
| 5941 | **GILD (TO)** | DORER | VERGOLDEN |
| 5942 | **GILDING** | DORURE | VERGOLDEN, VERGOLDUNG |
| 5943 | **GILDING METAL** | ALLIAGE CUIVRE-ZINC | KUPFERZINKLEGIERUNG |
| 5944 | **GIMLET** | VRILLE, AVANT-CLOU | NAGELBOHRER, BORBOHRER |

**GIR** 152

| | | | |
|---|---|---|---|
| 5945 | GIN TRIPORD FORM, SHEAR LEGS, SHEAR POLES, SHEERS, SHEARS | CHEVRE A TROIS PIEDS, GIBET | HEBEBOCK, DREIBEIN |
| 5946 | GIRDER | POUTRE | TRÄGER |
| 5947 | GIRDER FLANGE | SEMELLE D'UNE POUTRE | TRÄGERFUSSPLATTE |
| 5948 | GIRTH SEAM | SOUDURE HORIZONTALE | RUNDNAHTSCHWEISSUNG |
| 5949 | GIVE (TO), YIELD (TO) | CEDER | NACHGEBEN |
| 5950 | GIVE OFF HEAT (TO) | DEPENSER DE LA CHALEUR | WÄRME ABGEBEN |
| 5951 | GIVEN QUANTITY | DONNEE | GRÖSSE (GEGEBENE) |
| 5952 | GLACIAL ACETIC ACID | ACIDE ACETIQUE CRISTALLISABLE | EISESSIG |
| 5953 | GLAND | PRESSE-ETOUPE, CHAPEAU DE LA BOITE A ETOUPE | STOPFBÜCHSE |
| 5954 | GLAND COCK | ROBINET A BOURRAGE | PACKHAHN, STOPFBÜCHSENHAHN |
| 5955 | GLAND FLANGE | BRIDE DE FOULOIR | STOPFBÜCHSENFLANSCH |
| 5956 | GLASS | VERRE | GLAS |
| 5957 | GLASS BRICK STONE | PIERRE DE VERRE | GLASBAUSTEIN |
| 5958 | GLASS CLOTH | TOILE VERREE | GLASLEINWAND |
| 5959 | GLASS HALF CELL | ELECTRODE DE VERRE | GLAS-HALBZELLE |
| 5960 | GLASS MEASURE, GRADUATED MEASURING CYLINDER | TUBE CYLINDRIQUE GRADUE | MESSZYLINDER |
| 5961 | GLASS PAPER | PAPIER DE VERRE | GLASPAPIER |
| 5962 | GLASS POWDER | VERRE PILE | GLASMEHL |
| 5963 | GLASS SHEET | PLAQUE DE VERRE | GLASTAFEL, GLASPLATTE, GLASSCHEIBE |
| 5964 | GLASS TILE | TUILE EN VERRE | GLASZIEGEL |
| 5965 | GLASS TUBE | TUBE EN VERRE | GLASRÖHRE |
| 5966 | GLASS WOOL | LAINE DE VERRE, VERRE FILE | GLASWOLLE |
| 5967 | GLAUBER'S SALT | SEL DE GLAUBER | GLAUBERSALZ |
| 5968 | GLAZE | GLACURE, COUVERTE | GLASUR |
| 5969 | GLAZE (TO) | GLACER, VITRER | GLASIEREN, VERGLASEN |
| 5970 | GLAZED BRICK | BRIQUE VERNISSEE, BRIQUE EMAILLEE | GLASURSTEIN |
| 5971 | GLAZIER'S PUTTY | MASTIC DES VITRIERS | GLASERKITT |
| 5972 | GLAZING | GLACURE, EMOUSSAGE, GLACAGE, VITRAGE | GLASUR, ABSCHLEIFEN, VERGLASEN, GLASIEREN |
| 5973 | GLIDE | GLISSEMENT | GLEIT |
| 5974 | GLIDE MODULUS, COEFFICIENT OF TRANSVERSE ELASTICITY OF RIGIDITY | COEFFICIENT D'ELASTICITE DE CISAILLEMENT, MODULE D'ELASTICITE TRANVERSALE | GLEITMASS, GLEITMODUL, SCHUBELASTIZITÄTSMODUL |
| 5975 | GLIDE PLANE | PLAN DE GLISSEMENT | GLEITEBENE |
| 5976 | GLISSETTE | GLISSETTE | GLEITKURVE |
| 5977 | GLOBE VALVE | ROBINET A SOUPAPE, ROBINET DROIT | ABSPERRVENTIL, KUGELVENTIL, DURCHGANGSVENTIL |
| 5978 | GLOBOID WORM | VIS GLOBIQUE | GLOBOIDSCHRAUBE, GLOBOIDSCHNECKE |
| 5979 | GLOBULAR POWDER | POUDRE GLOBULAIRE | PULVER (KUGELIGES) |
| 5980 | GLOVE COMPARTMENT | BOITE A GANTS | HANDSCHUHKASTEN |
| 5981 | GLOW | CHAUDE | GLÜHHITZE |
| 5982 | GLOW (TO) | PORTER AU ROUGE | GLÜHEN |
| 5983 | GLOWING | INCANDESCENT | GLÜHEND |
| 5984 | GLUE | COLLE | LEIM |
| 5985 | GLUE (TO) | COLLER | LEIMEN |
| 5986 | GLUED JOINT | JOINT COLLE | LEIMVERBAND |
| 5987 | GLUING | COLLAGE | LEIMEN |

| | | |
|---|---|---|
| 5988 | **GLYCERINE, GLYCEROL** | GLYCERINE | GLYZERIN, ÖLSÜSS |
| 5989 | **GNEISS** | GNEISS | GNEIS |
| 5990 | **GNOMONIC PROJECTION** | PROJECTION GNOMOMIQUE | PROJEKTION (GNOMONISCHE) |
| 5991 | **GO-NO GO GAUGE** | CALIBRE PASSE-PASSE PAS | GUT-UND-AUSSCHUSS-GRENZLEHRE |
| 5992 | **GOGGLES** | LUNETTES DE PROTECTION | SCHUTZBRILLEN |
| 5993 | **GOLD** | OR | GOLD |
| 5994 | **GOLD BEATING** | BATTEMENT D'OR | BLATTGOLDSCHLÄGEREI |
| 5995 | **GOLD BRONZE** | BRONZE D'OR | GOLDBRONZE |
| 5996 | **GOLD COINAGE** | OR DE MONNAIE | MÜNZGOLD |
| 5997 | **GOLD CYANIDE** | CYANURE D'OR | ZYANGOLD, GOLDZYANID |
| 5998 | **GOLD DUST** | POUSSIERE D'OR | GOLDSTAUB |
| 5999 | **GOLD FILLED** | DOUBLE | DOUBLE, DUBLEE |
| 6000 | **GOLD LEAF** | FEUILLE D'OR, OR BATTU | BLATTGOLD |
| 6001 | **GOLD PAINT** | LAQUE DE BRONZE | BRONZELACK |
| 6002 | **GOLD PLATING** | DORAGE | GOLDPLATTIERUNG |
| 6003 | **GOLDSMITHING** | ORFEVRERIE | GOLDSCHMIEDEKUNST |
| 6004 | **GONIOMETER** | GONIOMETRE | GONIOMETER, WINKELMESSER |
| 6005 | **GOOD WELD** | SOUDURE BIEN FAITE | SCHWEISSVERBINDUNG (GUTE) |
| 6006 | **GOODNESS OF FIT TEST** | TEST D'AJUSTEMENT | PASSUNGSPRÜFUNG |
| 6007 | **GOODS LIFT, HOIST** | MONTE-CHARGE | LASTENAUFZUG, WARENAUFZUG, AUFZUG |
| 6008 | **GOOSE FLESH** | PEAU D'ORANGE | APFELSINEN(SCHALEN-)EFFEKT |
| 6009 | **GOOSENECK** | COL DE CYGNE | S-BOGEN |
| 6010 | **GOUGE** | GOUGE DE MENUISIER | HOHLEISEN |
| 6011 | **GOUGING** | GOUGEAGE | FLÄMMHOBELN |
| 6012 | **GOUGING MACHINE** | MACHINE A DECOUPER | DEKUPIERMASCHINE |
| 6013 | **GOVERNOR** | REGULATEUR | DREHZAHLREGLER |
| 6014 | **GOVERNOR ARM** | BRAS/BRANCHE DE REGULATEUR | REGLERARM, KUGELARM, PENDELARM |
| 6015 | **GOVERNOR BALL** | BOULE/SPHERE DU REGULATEUR | REGLERKUGEL, SCHWUNGKUGEL, SCHWINGGEWICHT |
| 6016 | **GOVERNOR HOUSING** | CARTER DE REGULATEUR | REGLERGEHÄUSE |
| 6017 | **GOVERNOR SLEEVE** | MANCHON/DOUILLE DU REGULATEUR | REGLERMUFFE, REGLERHÜLSE |
| 6018 | **GOVERNOR SPINDLE** | TIGE VERTICALE, AXE DU REGULATEUR | REGLERSPINDEL, REGLERWELLE |
| 6019 | **GOVERNOR SPRING** | RESSORT DE REGULATEUR | REGLERFEDER |
| 6020 | **GRACE PERIOD** | FRANCHISE (DELAI AVANT) | KARENZZEIT |
| 6021 | **GRADE** | GRADE, DEGRE, NIVEAU | GRAD, STUFE |
| 6022 | **GRADE OF STEEL** | NUANCE/QUALITE DE L'ACIER | STAHLSORTE |
| 6023 | **GRADING ANALYSIS** | ANALYSE GRANULOMETRIQUE | KORNVERTEILUNGSBESTIMMUNG |
| 6024 | **GRADUAL CHANGE OF TEMPERATURE/OF SPEED** | VARIATION PROGRESSIVE DE TEMPERATURE/DE VITESSE | ÄNDERUNG (ALLMÄHLICHE DER TEMPERATUR), ÄNDERUNG DER GESCHWIDIGKEIT |
| 6025 | **GRADUATE (TO)** | GRADUER | GRADEINTEILUNG VERSEHEN (MIT), GRADUIEREN |
| 6026 | **GRADUATED CIRCLE, LIMB** | CERCLE GRADUE, CERCLE DIVISE, LIMBE | TEILKREIS, LIMBUS |
| 6027 | **GRADUATED DIAL** | CADRAN GRADUE | SKALENSCHEIBE |
| 6028 | **GRADUATED STRAIGHT PIPETTE** | PIPETTE DROITE GRADUEE | MESSPIPETTE |
| 6029 | **GRAIN** | GRAIN (MESURE ANGLAISE) | GRAIN |
| 6030 | **GRAIN** | CRISTAL, GRAIN | KORN, KRISTALL |
| 6031 | **GRAIN (WITH THE), FIBRES (ALONG THE)** | FIBRES (DANS LE SENS) | FASER (PARALLEL ZUR), FASERN (IN DER RICHTUNG) |

## GRA

| | | | |
|---|---|---|---|
| 6032 | GRAIN ASSORTMENT | GRANULOMETRIE | KORNUNG |
| 6033 | GRAIN BOUNDARIES | LIMITE/JOINT DE GRAIN | KORNGRENZE |
| 6034 | GRAIN ELEVATORS CONVEYORS | ELEVATEURS DE GRAINS/AERO ENGRANGEURS | GETREIDEFÖRDERER UND HEBER |
| 6035 | GRAIN GROWTH | GROSSISSEMENT DU GRAIN, CROISSANCE DES GRAINS | KORNWASCHSTUM |
| 6036 | GRAIN ORIENTED SHEET | TOLE A GRAIN ORIENTE | BLECH (KORNORIENTIERTES) |
| 6037 | GRAIN REFINEMENT | AFFINEMENT DU GRAIN | KORNVERFEINERUNG |
| 6038 | GRAIN SIDE, HAIR SIDE OF LEATHER | COTE FLEUR DU CUIR, COTE POIL DU CUIR, FLEUR DU CUIR | HAARSEITE, NARBENSEITE DES LEDERS |
| 6039 | GRAIN SIZE | GROSSEUR DU GRAIN | KORNGRÖSSE |
| 6040 | GRAIN SIZE DISTRIBUTION | GRANULOMETRIE | KÖRNUNG, KORNGRÖSSENVERTEILUNG |
| 6041 | GRAIN STRUCTURE | STRUCTURE DU GRAIN | KORNSTRUKTUR |
| 6042 | GRAIN TIN | ETAIN EN GRENAILLES/EN GRAINS | ZINN IN KÖRNERN, GRANALIENZINN, GRANULIERTES ZINN |
| 6043 | GRAINING | GRANULATION | KÖRNUNG |
| 6044 | GRAM MOLECULE | MOLECULE-GRAMME | GRAMMOLEKÜL, GRAMMOL, MOL |
| 6045 | GRAMME CALORIE | PETITE CALORIE, CALORIE GRAMME-DEGRE | GRAMMKALORIE |
| 6046 | GRAMME, GRAM | GRAMME | GRAMM |
| 6047 | GRANITE | GRANIT | GRANIT |
| 6048 | GRANITE SURFACE PLATEAU | MARBRE | ABRICHTPLATTE |
| 6049 | GRANT OF A PATENT | DELIVRANCE D'UN BREVET, ACCORD DU BREVET | PATENTERTEILUNG, ERTEILUNG EINES PATENTS |
| 6050 | GRANULAR | GRANULAIRE | KÖRNIG |
| 6051 | GRANULAR FRACTURE | CASSURE GRENUE | BRUCH (KÖRNIGER), BRUCH (GRIESIGER) |
| 6052 | GRANULAR STRUCTURE | STRUCTURE GRANULAIRE | STRUKTUR (KÖRNIGE) |
| 6053 | GRANULAR STRUCTURE, TEXTURE | TEXTURE GRENUE | GEFÜGE (KÖRNIGES) |
| 6054 | GRANULATED METAL | METAL A GRENAILLES | GRANALIEN, KÖRNER |
| 6055 | GRANULATED SLAG | LAITIER GRANULE | SCHLACKE (GEKÖRNTE), SCHLACKE (GRANULIERTE) |
| 6056 | GRANULATING PIT | PUITS A GRANULATION DU LAITIER | GRANULIERGRUBE |
| 6057 | GRANULATION | GRANULATION | GRANULIERUNG, KÖRNUNG |
| 6058 | GRAPE SUGAR, GLUCOSE, DEXTROSE | SUCRE DE RAISIN, GLUCOSE | TRAUBENZUCKER, KARTOFFELZUCKER, STÄRKEZUCKER, GLUKOSE, GLYKOSE, DEXTROSE |
| 6059 | GRAPHIC CARBON, GRAPHITIC CARBON | CARBONE A L'ETAT GRAPHITOIDE | KOHLENSTOFF (GRAPHITISCHER) |
| 6060 | GRAPHIC SOLUTION, GRAPHICAL CONSTRUCTION | SOLUTION GRAPHIQUE, CALCUL GRAPHIQUE | LÖSUNG (ZEICHNERISCHE) |
| 6061 | GRAPHIC STATICS | GRAPHOSTATIQUE, STATIQUE GRAPHIQUE | STATIK (GRAPHISCHE) |
| 6062 | GRAPHITE | GRAPHITE | GRAPHIT |
| 6063 | GRAPHITE OIL GREASE | HUILE GRAPHITEE, GRAISSE GRAPHITEE, GRAISSE AMELIOREE, CAMBOUIS | GRAPHITÖL, GRAPHITSCHMIERE |
| 6064 | GRAPHITE PLUMBAGO CRUCIBLE | CREUSET EN GRAPHITE | GRAPHITTIEGEL |
| 6065 | GRAPHITE PYROMETER | PYROMETRE A GRAPHITE | GRAPHITPYROMETER |
| 6066 | GRAPHITIZATION | GRAPHITISATION | GRAPHITIERUNG, TEMPERKOHLEABSCHEIDUNG |
| 6067 | GRAPHITIZER | GRAPHITISANT | GRAPHITIERUNGSMITTEL |
| 6068 | GRATE AREA, GRATE SURFACE | SURFACE DE GRILLE | ROSTFLÄCHE |
| 6069 | GRATE BARS | BARRES POUR GRILLAGES | ROSTSTÄHLE |

| | | | |
|---|---|---|---|
| 6070 | **GRATE, FURNACE GRATE** | GRILLE | FEUERROST |
| 6071 | **GRATING** | GRILLAGE | GITTER |
| 6072 | **GRATUATED HYDROMETER** | AREOMETRE A POIDS CONSTANT | SKALENARÄOMETER |
| 6073 | **GRAVEL** | GRAVIER | KIES |
| 6074 | **GRAVEL FILTER** | FILTRE A GRAVIER | KIESFILTER |
| 6075 | **GRAVEL WIRE NETTING** | GRILLE A GRAVIER | KIESROST |
| 6076 | **GRAVELLY SOIL** | TERRAIN GRAVELEUX | KIESBODEN |
| 6077 | **GRAVIMETRIC ANALYSIS** | ANALYSE GRAVIMETRIQUE, ANALYSE PONDERALE | GEWICHTSANALYSE, BESTIMMUNG (GRAVIMETRISCHE) |
| 6078 | **GRAVITATION, GRAVITY** | GRAVITE, PESANTEUR | SCHWERE, SCHWERKRAFT, GRAVITATION |
| 6079 | **GRAVITY CASTING** | COULEE SOUS PRESSION PAR GRAVITE | SCHWERKRAFTDRUCKGUSS, STANDGUSS |
| 6080 | **GRAVITY DROP HAMMER** | MARTEAU-PILON | FREIFALLHAMMER |
| 6081 | **GRAVITY INCLINE, INCLINED PLANE, SELF-ACTING INCLINE D PLANE** | PLAN INCLINE, PLAN AUTOMOTEUR | BREMSBERG |
| 6082 | **GRAVITY ROLLER CONVEYOR** | TRANSPORTEUR PAR GRAVITE A ROULEAUX | ROLLENFÖRDERER, ROLLENTRANSPORTER, ROLLBAHN, ROLLGANG |
| 6083 | **GRAY BODY** | CORPS GRIS | GRAUSTRAHLER |
| 6084 | **GREASE (TO)** | GRAISSER (ENDUIRE DE GRAISSE) | EINFETTEN |
| 6085 | **GREASE BOX** | BOITE A GRAISSE | ACHSBÜCHSE, SCHMIERBÜCHSE |
| 6086 | **GREASE FITTING** | GRAISSEUR | SCHMIERNIPPEL |
| 6087 | **GREASING, GREASE LUBRICATION** | GRAISSAGE (ENDUCTION A LA GRAISSE), GRAISSAGE A LA GRAISSE CONSISTANCE, GRAISSAGE AU SUIF | EINFETTEN, FETTSCHMIERUNG, STARRSCHMIERUNG |
| 6088 | **GREEN** | AGGLOMERE | PRESSLING, PRESSKÖRPER |
| 6089 | **GREEN CARBONATE OF COPPER, MALACHITE** | MALACHITE | MALACHIT |
| 6090 | **GREEN COMPACT** | EBAUCHE DE COMPACT | GRÜNLING |
| 6091 | **GREEN CROP LOADERS** | RAMASSEUSES DE FOURRAGES | GRÜNFUTTERLADER |
| 6092 | **GREEN GOLD** | OR VERT | GOLD (GRÜNES) |
| 6093 | **GREEN VITRIOL, COPPERAS, FERROUS SULPHATE** | VITRIOL VERT, VITRIOL MARTIAL, SULFATE DE FER, COUPEROSE VERTE | EISENVITRIOL, VITRIOL (GRÜNES), FERROSULFAT, EISENOXYDULSUFAT, SCHWEFELSAURES EISENOXYDUL |
| 6094 | **GREY PIG IRON, GREY IRON, GREY PIG** | FONTE GRISE | ROHEISEN (GRAUES), GRAUGUSS |
| 6095 | **GREYWACKE, GRAUWACKE** | GRAUWACKE | GRAUWACKE |
| 6096 | **GRID** | GRILLE, GRILLAGE, RESEAU D'ELECTRIFICATION | GITTER, ROST, STROMVERSORGUNGSNETZ |
| 6097 | **GRID ACCUMULATOR** | ACCUMULATEUR A GRILLAGE | GITTERAKKUMULATOR |
| 6098 | **GRID BAR IRON, FIRE BAR IRON** | FER A BARREAUX DE GRILLE | ROSTSTABEISEN |
| 6099 | **GRID-LINE** | QUADRILLAGE | LINIENNETZ (QUADRATISCHES) |
| 6100 | **GRIDIRON VALVE** | TIROIR A GRILLE | GITTERSCHIEBER, SPALTSCHIEBER, ROSTSCHIEBER |
| 6101 | **GRILL-FLOORING** | CAILLEBOTIS, PLATELAGE | GITTERROST |
| 6102 | **GRILL-FLOORING TREADS** | MARCHES EN CAILLEBOTIS | GITTERROSTSTUFEN |
| 6103 | **GRIND (TO), CRUSH (TO)** | BROYER, PULVERISER, REDUIRE EN POUDRE | MAHLEN |
| 6104 | **GRIND IN (TO)** | RODER A L'EMERI | EINSCHLEIFEN, EINSCHMIRGELN |
| 6105 | **GRINDER** | AIGUISEUR, AFFUTEUR, REMOULEUR, RECTIFIEUR | SCHLEIFER |
| 6106 | **GRINDING** | MEULAGE, RODAGE, BROYAGE FIN (FRITTAGE), ABRASION, RECTIFICATION | SCHLEIFEN, MAHLEN, FEINVERKLEINERUNG, SCHLIFF |

# GRI

156

| | | | |
|---|---|---|---|
| 6107 | GRINDING AGENT, ABRASIVE MATERIAL, ABRADING AGENT | MATIERE A AIGUISER, SUBSTANCE USANTE | SCHLEIFMITTEL, SCHÄRFMITTEL |
| 6108 | GRINDING AND LAPPING COMPOUNDS | PATE A SURFACER ET A RODER | OBERFLÄCHEN-U. EINSCHLEIFMASSE |
| 6109 | GRINDING COOLANT | REFRIGERANT DE MEULAGE | SCHLEIFKÜHLMITTEL |
| 6110 | GRINDING FLOUR | POUDRE ABRASIVE | SCHLEIFPULVER |
| 6111 | GRINDING IN | RODAGE A L'EMERI | EINSCHLEIFEN, EINSCHMIRGEIN |
| 6112 | GRINDING LUBRICANT | LUBRIFIANT DE RODAGE | SCHLEIFSCHMIERSTOFF |
| 6113 | GRINDING MACHINE | MACHINE A MEULER, MACHINE A DRESSER, MEULEUSE, MACHINE A RECTIFIER A LA MEULE | SCHLEIFMASCHINE (ZUM PUTZEN UND SCHLICHTEN), FEINSCHLEIFMASCHINE, PRÄZISIONSSCHLEIFMASCHINE |
| 6114 | GRINDING PLATE | MARBRE | SCHLEIFPLATTE |
| 6115 | GRINDING WHEEL | ROUE A MEULER, MEULE | SCHLEIFSCHEIBE |
| 6116 | GRINDING WHEEL BALANCING DEVICES | APPAREIL A EQUILIBRER LES MEULES | SCHLEIFSCHEIBEN-AUSGLEICHAPPARATE |
| 6117 | GRINDING, CRUSHING | BROYAGE, TRITURATION, PULVERISATION | MAHLEN |
| 6118 | GRINDSTONE | MEULE EN GRES, MEULE D'AFFUTAGE | SCHLEIFSTEIN, SCHLEIFSCHEIBE |
| 6119 | GRINNING | POUVOIR OPACIFIANT INSUFFISANT | UNGENÜGENDE DECKKRAFT |
| 6120 | GRIP | MORDACHES | FINSPANNBACKEN, PRESSBACKEN |
| 6121 | GRIP DIE | MANDRIN DE SERRAGE | SPANNBACKE |
| 6122 | GRIPPING JAW | MACHOIRE (D'ETAU) | SCHRAUBSTOCKBACKE |
| 6123 | GRIT | GRENAILLE FINE, ABRASIF | GRIT |
| 6124 | GRIT BLASTING | GRENAILLAGE (FIN) | SCHLEUDERSTRAHLEN, METALLSANDSTRAHLUNG |
| 6125 | GROG | ARGILE CALCINEE FONDUE, COULIS REFRACTAIRE | TON (GEBRANNTER), SCHAMOTTE (GEMAHLENE) |
| 6126 | GROG FIRECLAY MORTAR | COULIS REFRACTAIRE | SCHAMOTTEMÖRTEL |
| 6127 | GROOVE | RAINURE, GORGE, JOINT | NUT, FUGE, RILLE, RINNE |
| 6128 | GROOVE (TO) | RAINER, RAINURER | NUTEN, MIT EINER NUT VERSEHEN |
| 6129 | GROOVE ANGLE | ANGLE D'OUVERTURE DE LA RAINURE | FUGENÖFFNUNGSWINKEL |
| 6130 | GROOVE FACE | BORD A SOUDER | FUGENFLANKE |
| 6131 | GROOVE OF SHEAVE PULLEY | GORGE D'UNE POULIE | SEILSCHEIBENRILLE |
| 6132 | GROOVE RADIUS | RAYON D'ECARTEMENT ENTRE LES BORDS | FUGENRADIUS |
| 6133 | GROOVE WELD | SOUDURE DE BORD | FUGENNAHT |
| 6134 | GROOVED DISC CAM | CAME A RAINURE | NUTENSCHEIBE |
| 6135 | GROOVED PULLEY | POULIE A GORGE | SEILSCHEIBE |
| 6136 | GROOVED-SERRATED ROLLER | CYLINDRE CANNELE | WALZE (GERIFFELTE), PROFILWALZE |
| 6137 | GROOVING | RAINURAGE, RAINAGE | NUTEN |
| 6138 | GROOVING MACHINE | MACHINE A RAINER, MACHINE A CANNELER, RAINEUSE | RIFFELMASCHINE |
| 6139 | GROOVING PLANE | BOUVET FEMELLE | NUTHOBEL |
| 6140 | GROOWED PULLEY | POULIE A GORGE | RILLENSCHEIBE |
| 6141 | GROSS WEIGHT | POIDS BRUT | BRUTTOGEWICHT |
| 6142 | GROUND AND POLISHED SURFACE | SURFACE POLIE | SCHLIFFFLÄCHE |
| 6143 | GROUND CLEARANCE | GARDE AU SOL | BODENFREIHEIT |
| 6144 | GROUND CORK | ROGNURES DE LIEGE, POUDRE DE LIEGE | KORKSCHROT, KORKKLEIN, KORKMEHL |
| 6145 | GROUND GLASS, FOCUSING SCREEN | VERRE DEPOLI, GLACE DEPOLIE (PHOT.) | MATTSCHEIBE, VISIERSCHEIBE |
| 6146 | GROUND IN STOPPER | BOUCHON A L'EMERI | STÖPSEL (EINGESCHLIFFENER) |

**GUN**

157

| | | | |
|---|---|---|---|
| 6147 | GROUND WATER | EAUX SOUTERRAINES, NAPPE D'EAU SOUTERRAINE | GRUNDWASSER |
| 6148 | GROUND WATER LEVEL | NIVEAU DE L'EAU SOUTERRAINE | GRUNDWASSERSPIEGEL |
| 6149 | GROUNDING OF A TANK, EARTHING OF A TANK | MISE A LA TERRE | ERDUNG |
| 6150 | GROUP DRIVE | COMMANDE PAR GROUPES | GRUPPENANTRIEB |
| 6151 | GROUP OF MACHINES | GROUPE DE MACHINES | MASCHINENSATZ, MASCHINENAGGREGAT |
| 6152 | GROUT | LAIT DE CIMENT, COULIS | ZEMENTMILCH |
| 6153 | GROUT (TO) | COULER, BOURRER, SCELLER DE CIMENT | VERGIESSEN (MIT MÖRTEL, ZEMENT) |
| 6154 | GROUTING | COULAGE DE CIMENT | VERGIESSEN (MIT ZEMENT, MÖRTEL) |
| 6155 | GROWTH | GONFLEMENT, CROISSANCE | WACHSEN, WACHSTUM |
| 6156 | GRUB SCREW | VIS SANS TETE | SCHNITTSCHRAUBE, MADENSCHRAUBE, WURMSCHRAUBE, GEWINDESTIFT |
| 6157 | GUARD CRADLE, NET, CATCH NET | FILET PROTECTEUR | SCHUTZNETZ |
| 6158 | GUDGEON PIN | AXE DE PISTON | KOLBENBOLZEN |
| 6159 | GUDGEON, PIN FOR FORKED END OF A ROD | AXE D'ARTICULATION D'UNE FOURCHE | GABELZAPFEN |
| 6160 | GUIDE | GLISSIERE, GUIDE, PLAQUE DE GARDE, GUIDAGE | GLEITBAHN, FÜHRUNG, ABSTREIFPLATTE |
| 6161 | GUIDE PULLEY | GALET-GUIDE, GALET DE GUIDAGE, POULIE DE RENVOI, POULIE-GUIDE | LEITROLLE, FÜHRUNGSROLLE |
| 6162 | GUIDE RAIL | RAIL-GUIDE | GLEITSCHIENE, FÜHRUNGSSCHIENE |
| 6163 | GUIDE RING | BAGUE DE GUIDAGE | FÜHRUNGSRING |
| 6164 | GUIDE ROD | TIGE DE GUIDAGE, TRINGLE DE GUIDAGE, BARRE DE GUIDAGE | FÜHRUNGSSTANGE |
| 6165 | GUIDE SCREW | VIS-MERE | LEITSPINDEL |
| 6166 | GUIDE SURFACE | SURFACE DE GUIDAGE | FÜHRUNGSBAHN |
| 6167 | GUIDE VANE, STATIONARY BLADE OF A TURBINE | AUBE DIRECTRICE, AUBE FIXE D'UNE TURBINE | LEITSCHAUFEL EINER TURBINE |
| 6168 | GUIDE WHEEL, GUIDE RING OF A TURBINE | SATELLITE, COURONNE FIXE, COURONNE DIRECTRICE D'UNE TURBINE | LEITRAD, LEITRAD EINER TURBINE |
| 6169 | GUIDES, SLIDE BARS, GUIDE BARS, MOTION BARS (FOR CROSSHEAD) | GLISSIERE DE CROSSE, GUIDE DE LA CROSSE | GERADFÜHRUNG (DAMPFM.), GLEITBAHN (DAMPFM.), GLEITSCHIENE (DAMPFM.) |
| 6170 | GUILLOTINE SHEARS | CISAILLES A GUILLOTINE | RAHMENBLECHSCHERE |
| 6171 | GUINIER-PRESTON ZONES | ZONE DE GUINIER-PRESTON | GUINIER-PRESTON ZONE |
| 6172 | GUM ARABIC, GUM ACACIA | GOMME ARABIQUE | GUMMI (ARABISCHES) |
| 6173 | GUM RESIN | GOMME-RESINE | GUMMIHARZ, SCHLEIMHARZ |
| 6174 | GUM TRAGACANTH, GUM DRAGON | GOMME ADRAGANTE | TRAGANT, GUMMITRAGANT, TRAGANTGUMMI |
| 6175 | GUN CARRIAGE | AFFUT | LAFETTE |
| 6176 | GUN COTTON, PYROXYLIN, CELLULOSE HEXANITRATE, NITROCELLULOSE | FULMICOTON, COTONPOUDRE, NITROCELLULOSE, CELLULOSE NITREE, PYROXYLE, PYROXYLINE, XYLOIDINE | SCHIESSBAUMWOLLE, NITROZELLULOSE, PYROXYLIN, ZELLULOSENITRAT |
| 6177 | GUN DRILL | FORET A CANON | KANONENBOHRER |
| 6178 | GUN METAL | BRONZE A CANON | KANONENGUT, KANONENMETALL, GESCHÜTZBRONZE |
| 6179 | GUN SPRAYING | PEINTURE AU PISTOLET | FARBSPRITZVERFAHREN |
| 6180 | GUN WELDING MACHINE | PISTOLET DE SOUDAGE PAR POINTS | STOSSPUNKTER |

**GUS** 158

| | | | |
|---|---|---|---|
| 6181 | GUNPOWDER, BLACK POWDER | POUDRE NOIRE | SCHIESSPULVER |
| 6182 | GUSSET | GOUSSET | ECKBLECH, ZWICKEL |
| 6183 | GUT BAND | COURROIE EN BOYAUX | DARMSAITENRIEMEN |
| 6184 | GUTTA PERCHA | GOMME PLASTIQUE, GOMME DE SUMATRA, GOMME GETTANIA | GUTTAPERCHA |
| 6185 | GUTTER | CANAL DE TROP-PLEIN, RIGOLE, GOUTTIERE | ÜBERLAUFROHR, RINNE |
| 6186 | GUY CABLES | TRIRANTS | HALTESEILE, ANKERSEILE |
| 6187 | GUY, STAY ROPE | HAUBAN | ANKERDRAHT, VERANKERUNGSDRAHT, SPANNDRAHT |
| 6188 | GYPSUM CEMENT MOLD | MOULE EN PLATRE | GIPSFORM |
| 6189 | GYPSUM CEMENT PATTERN | MODELE EN PLATRE | GIPSMODELL |
| 6190 | GYPSUM, HYDROUS SULPHATE OF CALCIUM | SULFATE DE CALCIUM, GYPSE, PIERRE A PLATRE | GIPS, SCHWEFELSAURER KALK, KALZIUMSULFAT |
| 6191 | GYROSCOPE | GYROSCOPE | KREISEL |
| 6192 | GYROSCOPIC ACTION | ACTION GYROSCOPIQUE | KREISELWIRKUNG |
| 6193 | GYROSCOPIC MOTION | MOUVEMENT GYROSCOPIQUE | KREISELBEWEGUNG |
| 6194 | H-IRON | FER EN DOUBLE T, FER EN I | DOPPEL-T-EISEN, I-EISEN |
| 6195 | HACKLY FRACTURE | CASSURE HACHEE, CASSURE CROCHUE | BRUCH (ZACKIGER), BRUCH (HAKIGER) |
| 6196 | HACKSAW | SCIE A METAUX | BÜGELSÄGE |
| 6197 | HACKSAW BLADE | LAME POUR SCIE A METAUX | METALLSÄGEBLATT |
| 6198 | HACKSAWING MACHINE | MACHINE A SCIER ALTERNATIVE | BÜGELSÄGEMASCHINE |
| 6199 | HAFNIUM | HAFNIUM | HAFNIUM |
| 6200 | HAIR BELT | COURROIE EN POILS, COURROIE EN CRIN | HAARRIEMEN |
| 6201 | HAIR COMPASSES | COMPAS A CHEVEU, COMPAS DE PRECISION | HAARZIRKEL |
| 6202 | HAIR CRACK | FISSURE CAPILLAIRE/MICROCRIQUE | HAARRISS |
| 6203 | HALATION | FORMATION DE HALO | LICHTHOFBILDUNG |
| 6204 | HALF CELL | DEMI-CELLULE, HEMICELLULE | HALBZELLE |
| 6205 | HALF OF THE COUPLING | DEMI-MANCHON | KUPPLUNGSHÄLFTE, KUPPELSCHEIBE |
| 6206 | HALF SIDE MILLING CUTTERS | FRAISES A UNE TAILLE LATERALE | SCHEIBENFRÄSER MIT EINSEITIGER STIRNVERZAHNUNG |
| 6207 | HALF-CROSSED QUATERING BELT | COURROIE DEMI-CROISEE, COURROIE TORDUE | RIEMENTRIEB (HALBGESCHRÄNSKTER), HALBKREUZRIEMENTRIEB |
| 6208 | HALF-ROUND FILE | LIME DEMI-RONDE | HALBRUNDFEILE |
| 6209 | HALF-ROUND IRON | PROFILE MI-ROND | HALBRUNDPROFILEISEN |
| 6210 | HALF-ROUND TIMBER | BOIS MI-PLAT | HALBHOLZ |
| 6211 | HALF-VALUE THICKNESS | COUCHE DE DEMI-ATTENUATION | HALBWERTSCHICHT |
| 6212 | HALF-WAVE RECTIFICATION | RECTIFICATION DEMI-ONDE | HALBWELLENGLEICHRICHTEN |
| 6213 | HALO | HALO | HALO |
| 6214 | HALOGEN | HALOGENE | SALZBILDNER, HALOGEN |
| 6215 | HAMMER | MARTEAU | HAMMER |
| 6216 | HAMMER (TO) | MARTELER | HÄMMERN |
| 6217 | HAMMER SCALE, FORGE SCALE | BATTITURES, PAILLE DE FER, MARTELURES, SCORIES DE FORGE | GLÜHSPAN, ZUNDER, HAMMERSCHLAG, SCHMIEDESINTER |
| 6218 | HAMMER WELD | SOUDAGE A LA FORGE | HAMMERSCHWEISSEN |
| 6219 | HAMMER-HARDENING | ECROUISSAGE | HÄRTEN |
| 6220 | HAMMERED | MARTELE | GEHÄMMERT |
| 6221 | HAMMERED METALWORK | METAL MARTELLE | METALL (GEHÄMMERTES) |
| 6222 | HAMMERED STEEL | ACIER BATTU | HAMMERSTAHL |

**159**  HAN

| 6223 | HAMMERING | MARTELAGE | HÄMMERN |
|------|-----------|-----------|---------|
| 6224 | HAMMERING SHARP CLOSING OF THE VALVE | CHOC DE LA SOUPAPE | VENTILSCHLAG, SCHLAGEN, ANPRALL DES VENTILS |
| 6225 | HAMMERMANN | FORGERON A MAIN | ZUSCHLÄGER |
| 6226 | HAND | AIGUILLE (DE MANOMETRE) | ZEIGER |
| 6227 | HAND BRAKE | FREIN A MAIN | HANDBREMSE |
| 6228 | HAND BURNISHING | POLISSAGE A LA MAIN | HANDGLANZSCHLEIFEN |
| 6229 | HAND CAPSTAN | CABESTAN A BRAS | GANGSPILL |
| 6230 | HAND CART | CHARRETTE A BRAS | HANDKARREN |
| 6231 | HAND CRANK | MANIVELLE A MAIN | HANDKURBEL, GRIFFKURBEL |
| 6232 | HAND CUTTING | COUPE A LA MAIN | HANDSCHNEIDEN |
| 6233 | HAND DRIVING | COMMANDE A LA MAIN | HANDANTRIEB, ANTRIEB VON HAND, HANDBETRIEB |
| 6234 | HAND FILE | LIME A MAIN | HANDFEILE |
| 6235 | HAND HAMMER | MARTEAU A MAIN | SCHMIEDEHAMMER, HANDHAMMER, BANKHAMMER, FAUSTHAMMER |
| 6236 | HAND HOLE | TROU A MAIN, TROU DE BRAS | HANDLOCH |
| 6237 | HAND LABOUR, MANUAL LABOUR | TRAVAIL MANUEL | HANDARBEIT |
| 6238 | HAND LADLE | POCHE DE COULEE A MAIN | HANDPFANNE |
| 6239 | HAND LEVER | LEVIER A POIGNEE | HANDHEBEL |
| 6240 | HAND MADE | TRAVAILLE A LA MAIN | HANDGEFERTIGT, HANDGEARBEITET |
| 6241 | HAND OPERATED, MOVED BY MANUAL POWER, ACTUATED BY HAND | A COMMANDE A LA MAIN | HAND ANGETRIEBEN, HANDBETRIEB (FÜR) |
| 6242 | HAND PART PROGRAMMING | PROGRAMMATION MANUELLE DE PIECE | HAND-TEILEPROGRAMM |
| 6243 | HAND PRINTING | ECRITURE PERPENDICULAIRE, ECRITURE DROITE | STEILSCHRIFT |
| 6244 | HAND PUMP | POMPE A MAIN, A BRAS | HANDPUMPE |
| 6245 | HAND RAILLING | FER MAIN-COURANTE | HANDLEISTENEISEN |
| 6246 | HAND RAMMER | FOULOIR A MAIN | HANDSTAMPFER |
| 6247 | HAND REAMER | ALESOIR A MAIN | HANBREIBAHLE |
| 6248 | HAND RIVETING | RIVETAGE A LA MAIN, RIVETAGE AU MARTEAU | HANDNIETUNG |
| 6249 | HAND SAW | SCIE A MAIN | HANDSÄGE |
| 6250 | HAND SHANK LADLE | POCHE A MAIN A MANCHE | STIELPFANNE |
| 6251 | HAND SHEARS | CISAILLES A MAIN | HANDSCHERE |
| 6252 | HAND SHIELD | MASQUE, ECRAN | HANDSCHIRM |
| 6253 | HAND TOOL | OUTIL A MAIN | HANDWERKZEUG |
| 6254 | HAND VICE | ETAU A MAIN | FEILKLOBEN, HANDKLOBEN |
| 6255 | HAND WHEEL | VOLANT DE MANOEUVRE | HANDRAD |
| 6256 | HAND WINCH | TREUIL A BRAS, TREUIL A MANIVELLE | HANDWINDE |
| 6257 | HAND WORKED TAP | TARAUD A MAIN | HANDGEWINDEBOHRER |
| 6258 | HAND-DRILL | CHIGNOLE | HANDBOHRMASCHINE |
| 6259 | HAND-RAIL | GARDE-CORPS | TREPPENGELÄNDER |
| 6260 | HAND-WARM PREHEATING | DEGOURDISSAGE (PRECHAUFFAGE AVANT SOUDAGE) | ANWÄRMEN, VORWÄRMEN |
| 6261 | HAND-WROUGHT | FORGE A LA MAIN | HANDGESCHMIEDET |
| 6262 | HANDLE | POIGNEE, MANCHE | HANDGRIFF, HANDHABE |
| 6263 | HANDLE OF A TOOL | MANCHE D'UN OUTIL | HEFT EINES WERKZEUGES, GRIFF EINES WERKZEUGS |
| 6264 | HANDLING HOLES | TROUS DE MANIPULATION | ANGREIFLÖCHER |

# HAN
**160**

| | | | |
|---|---|---|---|
| 6265 | **HANDRAIL IRON** | FER A MAIN COURANTE | HANDLÄUFEREISEN, HANDLEISTENEISEN, GELÄNDEREISEN |
| 6266 | **HANDRAIL POST** | MONTANT DE GARDE-CORPS | GELÄNDERSTÜTZE |
| 6267 | **HANDWHEEL** | VOLANT A MAIN | HANDRAD |
| 6268 | **HANDWHEEL RETAINING NUT** | ECROU DE VOLANT | HANDRADMUTTER |
| 6269 | **HANDY, MANAGEABLE** | MANIABLE | HANDLICH |
| 6270 | **HANGER WITH DOUBLE SUPPORT** | PALIER PENDANT FERME | HÄNGELAGER (GESCHLOSSENES) |
| 6271 | **HANGER WITH SINGLE SUPPORT** | PALIER PENDANT OUVERT | HÄNGELAGER (OFFENES) |
| 6272 | **HANSGIRG PROCESS** | PROCEDE HANSGIRG | VERFAHREN (HANSGIRGSCHE) |
| 6273 | **HARD BURNT STOCK BRICK** | BRIQUE DURE | HARTBRANDSTEIN |
| 6274 | **HARD DRAWN** | TREMPE PRODUITE PAR ETIRAGE A FROID | HÄRTUNGSGRAD BEIM KALTZIEHEN |
| 6275 | **HARD GREASE** | GRAISSE CONSISTANTE | STARRFETT, FETT KONSISTENTES, STARRSCHMIERE |
| 6276 | **HARD LEAD** | PLOMB ANTIMONIEUX, PLOMB DURCI, METAL BLANC DUR | HARTBLEI, ANTIMONBLEI, WEISSMETALL (HARTES) |
| 6277 | **HARD METAL** | METAL DUR | HARTMETALL |
| 6278 | **HARD SETTING** | POSE DE PLAQUETTES DE COUPE METAL DUR | HARTMETALLBESTÜCKUNG |
| 6279 | **HARD SOLDER, BRAZING METAL** | BRASURE, SOUDURE FORTE (COMPOSITION FUSIBLE) | HARTLOT, SCHLAGLOT, STRENGLOT |
| 6280 | **HARD STEEL** | ACIER DUR | STAHL (HARTER), HARTSTAHL |
| 6281 | **HARD WATER** | EAU DURE, EAU CALCAIRE | WASSER (HARTES), WASSER (KALKHALTIGES) |
| 6282 | **HARD WOOD** | BOIS DUR, LOURD | HARTHOLZ, HARTES HOLZ |
| 6283 | **HARD-SURFACING** | RECHARGEMENT DUR | HARTMETALL-AUFTRAGSCHWEISSUNG |
| 6284 | **HARD-SURFACING ALLOY** | ALLIAGE DE RECHARGEMENT DUR | HARTMETALL-AUFTRAGSLEGIERUNG |
| 6285 | **HARDEN A METAL (TO)** | TREMPER UN METAL | METALL HÄRTEN (EIN) |
| 6286 | **HARDEN IN THE AIR (TO)** | DURCIR, FAIRE PRISE, SE SOLIDIFIER A L'AIR (CIMENT) | AN DER LUFT ERHÄRTEN (ZEMENT) |
| 6287 | **HARDEN UNDER WATER (TO)** | DURCIR, FAIRE PRISE, SE SOLIDIFIER DANS L'EAU (CIMENT) | IM WASSER ERHÄRTEN (ZEMENT) |
| 6288 | **HARDENABILITY** | APTITUDE A LA TREMPE, TREMPABILITE | HÄRTBARKEIT |
| 6289 | **HARDENED STEEL** | ACIER TREMPE | STAHL (GEHÄRTETER) |
| 6290 | **HARDENER** | DURCISSEUR (ALLIAGE) | HÄRTUNGSMITTEL |
| 6291 | **HARDENING** | DURCISSEMENT, TREMPE | HÄRTUNG, AUSHÄRTUNG |
| 6292 | **HARDENING (CEMENT, MORTAR)** | DURCISSEMENT, SOLIDIFICATION | ERHÄRTEN, ERHÄRTUNG (MÖRTEL, ZEMENT) |
| 6293 | **HARDENING (METALS)** | TREMPE DES METAUX | HÄRTEN VON METALLEN |
| 6294 | **HARDENING BATH, MIXTURE** | BAIN DE TREMPE | HÄRTUNGSBAD, HÄRTUNGSFLÜSSIGKEIT |
| 6295 | **HARDENING OIL** | HUILE DE TREMPE | HÄRTEÖL |
| 6296 | **HARDENING QUALITY OF A METAL** | FACULTE DE PRENDRE BIEN LA TREMPE | HÄRTBARKEIT EINES METALLES |
| 6297 | **HARDNESS** | DURETE | HÄRTE |
| 6298 | **HARDNESS OF WATER** | DURETE DE L'EAU, DEGRE HYDROTIMETRIQUE | HÄRTE DES WASSERS |
| 6299 | **HARDNESS TEMPER OF STEEL** | DEGRE DE TREMPE DE L'ACIER | HÄRTEGRAD DES STAHLES |
| 6300 | **HARDNESS TEST, HARDNESS TESTING** | ESSAI DE DURETE | HÄRTEPRÜFUNG, HÄRTEPROBE |
| 6301 | **HARDWOOD** | BOIS FEUILLU | HARTHOLZ |
| 6302 | **HARMONIC MOTION** | MOUVEMENT PENDULAIRE | SINUSSCHWINGUNG, SCHWINGUNGZ HARMONISCHE BEWEGUNG |

**161** **HEA**

| | | | |
|---|---|---|---|
| 6303 | HARROWS : CHAIN, ZIG-ZAG, FLEXIBLE, SADDLE-BACK, ETC. | HERSES (A CHAINE, HERSES A ZIG-ZAG, HERSES FLEXIBLE) | EGGEN (GLEIDEREGGEN, ZIGZAGEGGEN) |
| 6304 | HATCH (TO) | HACHURER | SCHRAFFIEREN |
| 6305 | HATCHET | HACHETTE, HACHEREAU, HACHERON | BEIL |
| 6306 | HATCHING | HACHURE | SCHRAFFUR, SCHRAFFIERUNG |
| 6307 | HAULAGE HOOKS | CROCHETS DE TRACTION | ZUGHAKEN |
| 6308 | HAVING A HIGH MELTING POINT | A POINT DE FUSION ELEVE | HOCHSCHMELZEND |
| 6309 | HAWSER-LAID ROPE | AUSSIERE | SEIL (TROSSWEISE GESCHLAGENES) |
| 6310 | HAY FORKS : GRABS AND STACKERS | DECHARGEURS A GRIFFES (MAT. ET GRUE) | HEUGABELN UND GREIFER |
| 6311 | HAY MAKERS : COMBINE | RATELEUSES RAMASSEUSES | HEUMÄHDRESCHBINDER |
| 6312 | HAY RAKES | RATEAUX | HEURECHEN |
| 6313 | HAZE | VOILE | SCHLEIERBILDUNG |
| 6314 | HEAD | FOND, EXTREMITE, PRESSION (CHAUD.) | TANKBODEN, KOPF, DRUCK |
| 6315 | HEAD LOSS | PERTE DE CHARGE | DRUCKVERLUST |
| 6316 | HEAD OF A DRUM | FOND D'UN BALLON | KESSELTROMMELBODEN |
| 6317 | HEAD OF A HAMMER | CORPS DU MARTEAU | HAMMERKOPF, KOPF EINES HAMMERS |
| 6318 | HEAD OF KEY, KEY HEAD | TALON D'UNE CLAVETTE, TETE D'UNE CLAVETTE, NEZ D'UNE CLAVETTE, MENTONNET D'UNE CLAVETTE | KEILNASE |
| 6319 | HEAD RACE | CANAL D'ARRIVEE, BIEF D'AMONT | ZULEITUNGSKANAL, OBERWASSERKANAL |
| 6320 | HEAD REST | APPUIE-TETE | KOPFLEHNE |
| 6321 | HEAD SHAFT HANGER, HANG DOWN | PALIER PENDANT, PENDANT, PALIER A POTENCE | HÄNGELAGER, DECKENLAGER |
| 6322 | HEAD WATER | EAU D'AMONT | OBERWASSER |
| 6323 | HEAD, PRESSURE HEAD, STATIC HEAD | CHARGE D'EAU | DRUCKHÖHE (HÖHE DER FLÜSSIGKEITSSÄULE) |
| 6324 | HEADER | BOUTISSE | BINDER (BAUW.) |
| 6325 | HEADING TOOL | CLOUTIERE, CLOUERE, CLOUIERE, CLOUTERE, CLOUVIERE | NAGELEISEN |
| 6326 | HEADLAMP | PHARE, PROJECTEUR | SCHEINWERFER |
| 6327 | HEADLIGHT | PHARE | SCHEINWERFER |
| 6328 | HEADSTOCK | POUPEE DE TOUR, POUPEE FIXE | REITSTOCK, SPINDELSTOCK |
| 6329 | HEART CAM | CAME, EXCENTRIQUE EN COEUR | HERZSCHEIBE, HERZEXZENTER |
| 6330 | HEART-SHAPED THIMBLE | COSSE OVALE | HERZKAUSCHE |
| 6331 | HEARTH | CREUSET, SOLE | HERD |
| 6332 | HEARTH FURNACE | FOUR A SOIE | HERDOFEN |
| 6333 | HEAT | CHALEUR, PIQUEE, COULEE | HITZE, WÄRME, ABSTICH, SCHMELZE |
| 6334 | HEAT (TO), RUN HOT (TO) | ECHAUFFER, RECHAUFFER | WARMLAUFEN, HEISSLAUFEN, ERHITZEN, ERWÄRMEN |
| 6335 | HEAT ABSORPTION CAPACITY, ABSORBING CAPACITY FOR HEAT | CAPACITE CALORIFIQUE | WÄRMEAUFNAHMEFÄHIGKEIT, WÄRMEKAPAZITÄT |
| 6336 | HEAT ACCUMULATOR | ACCUMULATEUR THERMIQUE DE CHALEUR | WÄRMESPEICHER, WÄRMEAKKUMULATOR |
| 6337 | HEAT BALANCE | BILAN CALORIFIQUE, BILAN THERMIQUE | WÄRMEBILANZ |
| 6338 | HEAT BUILD UP | ECHAUFFEMENT INTERNE | WÄRMEENTWICKLUNG |
| 6339 | HEAT CAPACITY | CAPACITE CALORIFIQUE | WÄRMEKAPAZITÄT |
| 6340 | HEAT CONDUCTOR | CONDUCTEUR DE LA CHALEUR | WÄRMELEITER |
| 6341 | HEAT CONSTANT | CONSTANTE CALORIFIQUE | WÄRMEKONSTANTE |

**HEA** 162

| | | | |
|---|---|---|---|
| 6342 | HEAT CONTENT | CAPACITE CALORIQUE | WÄRMEINHALT |
| 6343 | HEAT DUE TO FRICTION | CHALEUR PRODUITE PAR FROTTEMENT | REIBUNGSWÄRME |
| 6344 | HEAT ENERGY | ENERGIE CALORIFIQUE, ENERGIE THERMIQUE | WÄRMEENERGIE |
| 6345 | HEAT ENGINE, THERMODYNAMIC ENGINE | MACHINE, MOTEUR THERMIQUE | WÄRMEKRAFTMASCHINE |
| 6346 | HEAT ENTROPY DIAGRAM | DIAGRAMME ENTROPIQUE | WÄRMEDIAGRAMM, TS-DIAGRAMM, ENTROPIEDIAGRAMM |
| 6347 | HEAT EQUIVALENT OF THE WORK DONE | EQUIVALENT CALORIFIQUE DU TRAVAIL | KALORISCHES ARBEITSÄQUIVALENT, WÄRMEWERT DER ARBEITSEINHEIT |
| 6348 | HEAT EVOLVED, ABSORBED IN REACTIONS | NOMBRE DE CALORIES DEGAGEES DANS UNE REACTION, CHALEUR DEGAGEE DANS UNE REACTION | WÄRMETÖNUNG |
| 6349 | HEAT EXCHANGER | ECHANGEUR DE CHALEUR, ECHANGEUR THERMIQUE | WÄRMEAUSTAUSCHER |
| 6350 | HEAT EXCHANGER TUBE | TUBE D'ECHANGEUR THERMIQUE | WÄRMETAUSCHERROHR |
| 6351 | HEAT IN CONTACT WITH AIR (TO) | CHAUFFER EN PRESENCE, CHAUFFER AU CONTACT DE L'AIR | UNTER LUFTZUTRITT ERHITZEN |
| 6352 | HEAT INSULATOR | SUBSTANCE CALORIFUGE, CALORIFUGE | WÄRMESCHUTZSTOFF, WÄRMESCHUTZMITTEL |
| 6353 | HEAT LOSS | PERTE DE CHALEUR, PERTE THERMIQUE | WÄRMEVERLUST |
| 6354 | HEAT OF ABSORPTION | CHALEUR D'ABSORPTION | ABSORPTIONSWÄRME |
| 6355 | HEAT OF CARBURIZATION | CHALEUR DE CARBURATION | KARBONISIERUNGSWÄRME |
| 6356 | HEAT OF COMBUSTION | CHALEUR DE COMBUSTION | VERBRENNUNGSWÄRME |
| 6357 | HEAT OF DECOMPOSITION | CHALEUR DE DECOMPOSITION | ZERSETZUNGSWÄRME |
| 6358 | HEAT OF DISSOCIATION | CHALEUR DE DISSOCIATION | DISSOZIATIONSWÄRME |
| 6359 | HEAT OF EVAPORATION | CHALEUR D'EVAPORATION | VERDAMPFUNGSWÄRME, VERDUNSTUNGSWÄRME |
| 6360 | HEAT OF FUSION | CHALEUR DE FUSION, TEMPERATURE DE FUSION | SCHMELZWÄRME |
| 6361 | HEAT OF OXIDATION | CHALEUR D'OXYDATION | OXYDATIONSWÄRME |
| 6362 | HEAT OF REDUCTION | CHALEUR DE REDUCTION | REDUKTIONSWÄRME |
| 6363 | HEAT OF SUBLIMATION | CHALEUR DE SUBLIMATION | SUBLIMATIONSWÄRME |
| 6364 | HEAT OF TRANSFORMATION | CHALEUR DE TRANSFORMATION | UMWANDLUNGSWÄRME |
| 6365 | HEAT OF TRANSITION | CHALEUR LATENTE | WÄRME (LATENTE) |
| 6366 | HEAT OF VAPORIZATION | CHALEUR DE VAPORISATION | VERDAMPFUNGSWÄRME, VERDUNSTUNGSWÄRME |
| 6367 | HEAT OUT OF CONTACT WITH AIR (TO) | CHAUFFER EN VASE CLOS | ERHITZEN (UNTER LUFTABSCHLUSS) |
| 6368 | HEAT PENETRATION | PENETRATION DE LA CHALEUR | WÄRMEEINDRINGTIEFE |
| 6369 | HEAT RAY | RAYON CALORIFIQUE | WÄRMESTRAHL |
| 6370 | HEAT SET FREE, HEAT EVOLVED | CHALEUR DEGAGEE | WÄRME (FREIGEWORDENE) |
| 6371 | HEAT TINTING | COLORATION THERMIQUE | WÄRMETÖNUNG |
| 6372 | HEAT TRANSFER | TRANSMISSION, TRANSFERT DE CHALEUR | WÄRMEÜBERGANG, WÄRMEÜBERTRAGUNG |
| 6373 | HEAT TRANSFER COEFFICIENT | COEFFICIENT DE CONDUCTIBILITE CALORIFIQUE | WÄRMEÜBERGANGSZAHL |
| 6374 | HEAT TRANSMISSION | TRANSMISSION DE CHALEUR, TRANSPORT DE CHALEUR | WÄRMEÜBERGANG, WÄRMEÜBERTRAGUNG |
| 6375 | HEAT TREATING | TRAITEMENT THERMIQUE | WÄRMEBEHANDLUNG, VERGÜTUNG |
| 6376 | HEAT TREATING PLANT | INSTALLATION DE REVENU | VERGÜTEANLAGE |
| 6377 | HEAT TREATMENT, THERMAL TREATMENT | TRAITEMENT THERMIQUE | WARMBEHANDLUNG, GLÜHBEHANDLUNG |
| 6378 | HEAT VALUE | POUVOIR CALORIFIQUE | HEIZWERT |

| | | | |
|---|---|---|---|
| 6379 | **HEAT WAVE** | ONDE CALORIFIQUE | WÄRMEWELLE |
| 6380 | **HEAT-AFFECTED ZONE** | ZONE INFLUENCEE PAR LA CHALEUR | WÄRMEEINFLUSSZONE |
| 6381 | **HEAT-PRODUCING LOSSES** | PERTES THERMOGENES | WÄRMEERZEUGENDE VERLUSTE |
| 6382 | **HEAT-TIME** | TEMPS D'ECOULEMENT DE COURANT, TEMPS DE SOUDAGE EFFECTIF | STROMZEIT |
| 6383 | **HEAT-TREATABLE ALLOY** | ALLIAGE DE TRAITEMENT | VERGÜTUNGSLEGIERUNG |
| 6384 | **HEATED PISTON** | PISTON CHAUFFE | KOLBEN (GEHEIZTER) |
| 6385 | **HEATER** | RECHAUFFEUR | ANWÄRMER, ERHITZER |
| 6386 | **HEATER FILAMENT** | FILAMENT | GLÜHDRAHT |
| 6387 | **HEATER PLUG** | BOUGIE DE PRECHAUFFAGE | GLÜHKERZE |
| 6388 | **HEATER PLUG RESISTANCE** | RESISTANCE DE BOUGIE DE PRECHAUFFAGE | GLÜHKERZENWIDERSTAND |
| 6389 | **HEATER PLUG SWITCH** | COMMUTATEUR DES BOUGIES DE PRECHAUFFAGE | GLÜHANLASSSCHALTER |
| 6390 | **HEATING** | CHAUFFAGE, CHAUFFE | ERHITZEN, ERWÄRMEN, ERWÄRMUNG |
| 6391 | **HEATING BLOWPIPE** | CHALUMEAU DE PRECHAUFFAGE | ANWÄRMBRENNER |
| 6392 | **HEATING CALORIFIC THERMAL VALUE, FUEL VALUE** | PUISSANCE CALORIFIQUE, POUVOIR CALORIFIQUE | HEIZWERT |
| 6393 | **HEATING GATE** | TROU DE SOUFFLAGE | BLASLOCH |
| 6394 | **HEATING INSTALLATION** | INSTALLATION DE CHAUFFAGE CENTRAL | HEIZUNGSANLAGE |
| 6395 | **HEATING OF BUILDINGS** | CHAUFFAGE DES BATIMENTS | HEIZUNG VON GEBÄUDEN |
| 6396 | **HEATING PIPE** | TUYAU DE CHAUFFAGE CENTRAL | HEIZUNGSROHR |
| 6397 | **HEATING STEAM** | VAPEUR DE CHAUFFAGE | HEIZDAMPF |
| 6398 | **HEATING SURFACE, GENERATING SURFACE** | SURFACE DE CHAUFFE | HEIZFLÄCHE |
| 6399 | **HEATING TORCH** | CHALUMEAU DE CHAUFFAGE | ANWÄRMBRENNER |
| 6400 | **HEATING UP, FIRING OF BEARINGS** | ECHAUFFEMENT DES COUSSINETS | WARMLAUFEN, HEISSLAUFEN DER LAGER |
| 6401 | **HEAVY CURRENT** | COURANT DE GRANDE INTENSITE, COURANT FORT | STARKSTROM |
| 6402 | **HEAVY DUTY GEAR WHEEL** | ENGRENAGE DE FORCE, ENGRENAGE DE GRANDE FATIGUE | KRAFTZAHNRAD |
| 6403 | **HEAVY DUTY OIL** | HUILE SPECIALE, HUILE H.D. | HEAV DUTY ÖL, H.D. ÖL |
| 6404 | **HEAVY DUTY PLAIN MOLLING CUTTERS** | FRAISES SIMPLES POUR TRAVAUX LOURDS | FRÄSER (EINFACHER) FÜR SCHWERE SCHNITTE |
| 6405 | **HEAVY DUTY TRUCK (U.S.)** | CAMION POIDS LOURD | SCHWERKRAFTLASTWAGEN |
| 6406 | **HEAVY FORGING** | PIECE DE GROSSE FORGE | SCHMIEDESTÜCK (SCHWERES) |
| 6407 | **HEAVY METAL** | METAL LOURD | SCHWERMETALL |
| 6408 | **HEAVY OIL, THICK OIL** | HUILE LOURDE, MAZOUT | SCHWERÖL, MASUT |
| 6409 | **HEAVY PLATE** | TOLE FORTE | GROBBLECH |
| 6410 | **HEAVY PLATE MILL** | LAMINOIR POUR TOLES FORTES | GROBWALZWERK |
| 6411 | **HEAVY PLATE PRESS** | PRESSE POUR TOLES FORTES | GROBBLECHPRESSE |
| 6412 | **HEAVY RUNNING** | MARCHE LOURDE | GANG (SCHWERER), GANG (HARTER), GANG (STOSSENDER) |
| 6413 | **HEAVY SECTIONS** | PROFILES LOURDS | PROFILE, SCHWERE |
| 6414 | **HEAVY WATER** | EAU LOURDE | SCHWERWASSER |
| 6415 | **HECTOLITRE** | HECTOLITRE | HEKTOLITER |
| 6416 | **HECTOWATT** | HECTOWATT | HEKTOWATT |
| 6417 | **HECTOWATT/HOUR** | HECTOWATT-HEURE | HECTOWATTSTUNDE |

**HEF** 164

| | | | |
|---|---|---|---|
| 6418 | **HEDGE CLIPPERS AND CUTTERS** | MACHINES POUR COUPER LES HAIES | HECKENSCHNEIDER |
| 6419 | **HEFNER CANDIE** | BOUGIE, ETALON HEFNER | HEFNERKERZE |
| 6420 | **HEIGHT** | HAUTEUR | HÖHE |
| 6421 | **HEIGHT FALLEN THROUGH** | HAUTEUR DE CHUTE | FALLHÖHE |
| 6422 | **HEIGHT OF THE BAROMETER, BAROMETRIC HEIGHT** | NIVEAU BAROMETRIQUE | BAROMETERSTAND |
| 6423 | **HEIGHT UNDER CROSS-RAIL** | HAUTEUR SOUS TRAVERSE | HÖHE UNTER QUERBALKEN |
| 6424 | **HELIARC TORCH** | TORCHE A HELIUM | HELIARC-BRENNER |
| 6425 | **HELICAL GEAR WHEEL** | ROUE HELICOIDALE, ENGRENAGE HELICOIDAL | SCHRÄGZAHNRAD, SPIRALZAHNSTIRNRAD, SCHRAUBENRAD |
| 6426 | **HELICAL MOTION** | MOUVEMENT HELICOIDAL | BEWEGUNG AUF EINER SCHRAUBENLINIE, SCHRAUBENBEWEGUNG |
| 6427 | **HELICAL SPRING** | RESSORT A BOUDIN, RESSORT EN HELICE | SCHRAUBENFEDER |
| 6428 | **HELICOIDAL SURFACE** | SURFACE HELICOIDALE, HELICOIDE | SCHRAUBENFLÄCHE |
| 6429 | **HELIUM** | HELIUM | HELIUM |
| 6430 | **HELIX** | HELICE | SCHRAUBENLINIE, SCHNECKE |
| 6431 | **HELIX ANGLE** | ANGLE HELICOIDAL | STEIGUNGSWINKEL |
| 6432 | **HELMET SHIELD** | CASQUE, MASQUE DE SOUDAGE | SCHUTZHAUBE |
| 6433 | **HELVE** | MANCHE D'UNE HACHE | HELM EINER AXT, HELM EINES BEILES |
| 6434 | **HEMATITE** | HEMATITE | HÄMATIT |
| 6435 | **HEMATITE PIG IRON** | FONTE HEMATITE | HÄMATITROHEISEN |
| 6436 | **HEMIHEDRAL CRYSTAL** | CRISTAL HEMIEDRIQUE | HEMIEDERKRISTALL |
| 6437 | **HEMIMORPHIC CRYSTAL** | CRISTAL HEMIMORPHE | KRISTALL (HEMIMORPHER) |
| 6438 | **HEMISPHERE** | DEMI-SPHERE, HEMISPHERE | HALBKUGEL |
| 6439 | **HEMP** | CHANVRE, FILASSE DE CHANVRE | HANF |
| 6440 | **HEMP CORE** | AME EN CHANVRE | HANFSEELE |
| 6441 | **HEMP GASKET** | TRESSE EN CHANVRE | HANFZOPF |
| 6442 | **HEMP GASKET GREASED WITH TALLON** | TRESSE DE CHANVRE SUIFFEE | HANFZOPF (GEFETTETER) |
| 6443 | **HEMP ROPE** | CABLE DE CHANVRE, CORDE DE CHANVRE | HANFSEIL |
| 6444 | **HEMP TOW** | ETOUPE DE CHANVRE | HANFWERG |
| 6445 | **HEMPEN PACKING** | BOURRAGE, GARNITURE EN CHANVRE | HANFPACKUNG, HANFDICHTUNG, HANFLIDERUNG |
| 6446 | **HEMPSEED OIL** | HUILE DE CHENEVIS | HANFÖL |
| 6447 | **HERMETICALLY CLOSED, SEALED** | HERMETIQUEMENT CLOS, FERME | LUFTDICHT, HERMETISCH VERSCHLOSSEN |
| 6448 | **HERRINGBONE GEARS** | ENGRENAGES A CHEVRONS | PFEILZAHNRÄDER |
| 6449 | **HESSIAN, PACKING CANVAS** | TOILE D'EMBALLAGE, TOILE DE JUTE | PACKLEINWAND |
| 6450 | **HETEROCHROMATIC X-RADIATION** | RAYONNEMENT HETEROGENE | HETEROGENE STRAHLUNG |
| 6451 | **HETEROGENEOUS** | HETEROGENE | HETEROGEN |
| 6452 | **HETEROGENEOUS TEXTURE** | TEXTURE HETEROGENE | GEFÜGE (UNGLEICHARTIGES), GEFÜGE (INHOMOGENES), GEFÜGE (HETEROGENES) |
| 6453 | **HEXAGON** | HEXAGONE | SECHSECK |
| 6454 | **HEXAGON BAR** | FER HEXAGONAL | SECHSKANTEISEN |
| 6455 | **HEXAGON NUT** | ECROU A SIX PANS | SECHSKANTMUTTER |
| 6456 | **HEXAGON NUT ANGLE GAUGE** | EQUERRE A SIX PANS | SECHSKANTWINKEL, SECHSKANTE |
| 6457 | **HEXAGON-HEAD SCREW** | VIS, BOULON A TETE A SIX PANS | SECHSKANTSCHRAUBE |

165 HIG

| | | | |
|---|---|---|---|
| 6458 | HEXAGONAL CLOSE-PACKED STRUCTURE | STRUCTURE HEXAGONALE COMPACTE | HEXAGONAL-DICHTGEPACKTE STRUKTUR |
| 6459 | HEXAGONAL CRYSTAL | CRISTAL HEXAGONAL | HEXAGONALER KRISTALL |
| 6460 | HEXAGONAL PRISM | PRISME HEXAGONAL | PRISMA (SECHSSEITIGES) |
| 6461 | HEXAGONAL SCREW HEAD, BOLT HEAD | TETE A SIX PANS D'UNE VIS | SECHSKANTSCHRAUBENKOPF |
| 6462 | HEXAGONAL WIRE | FIL HEXAGONAL | SECHSKANTDRAHT |
| 6463 | HEXAHEDRON | HEXAEDRE | SECHSFLACH, SECHSFLÄCHNER, HEXAEDER |
| 6464 | HIGH AND LOW SPOTS | IMPERFECTIONS DE SURFACE | UNEBENHEITEN |
| 6465 | HIGH BREAST WHEEL | ROUE DE POITRINE | WASSERRAD (RÜCKENSCHLÄCHTIGES), BRUSTRAD |
| 6466 | HIGH EFFICIENCY ENGINE | MACHINE A GRAND RENDEMENT, MACHINE A GRAND DEBIT | HOCHLEISTUNGSMASCHINE |
| 6467 | HIGH FREQUENCY | HAUTE FREQUENCE | HOCHFREQUENZ |
| 6468 | HIGH FREQUENCY CURRENT | COURANT A HAUTE FREQUENCE | HOCHFREQUENZSTROM |
| 6469 | HIGH FREQUENCY FURNACE | FOUR A HAUTE FREQUENCE | HOCHFREQUENZOFEN |
| 6470 | HIGH HELIX DRILL | FORET A HELICE SERREE | SPIRALBOHRER MIT GROSSEM DRALLWINKEL |
| 6471 | HIGH HELIX PLAIN MILLING CUTTERS | FRAISES SIMPLES A HELICE RAPIDE | SPIRALFRÄSER MIT GROSSEM DRALLWINKEL |
| 6472 | HIGH LIGHTS | POINTS BRILLANTS | GLANZPUNKTE, GLANZLICHTER |
| 6473 | HIGH PRESSURE | HAUTE PRESSION, FORTE PRESSION | DRUCK (HOHER), HOCHDRUCK |
| 6474 | HIGH SPEED STEEL | ACIER RAPIDE | SCHNELLDREHSTAHL |
| 6475 | HIGH SPEED STEEL CUTTING FOOLS | OUTILS EN ACIER RAPIDE | SCHNEIDWERKZEUGE AUS SCHNELLSTAHL |
| 6476 | HIGH TEMPERATURE | HAUTE TEMPERATURE | TEMPERATUR (HOHE) |
| 6477 | HIGH VACUUM | VIDE POUSSE | HOCHVAKUUM |
| 6478 | HIGH VOLTAGE | HAUTE TENSION | HOCHSPANNUNG |
| 6479 | HIGH VOLTAGE PRESSURE TENSION | HAUTE TENSION, HAUT VOLTAGE | HOCHSPANNUUG (ELEKT.) |
| 6480 | HIGH-BRASS | LAITON DE QUALITE | MESSING (HOCHWERTIGES) |
| 6481 | HIGH-DENSITY ALLOY | ALLIAGE A HAUTE DENSITE | LEGIERUNG GROSSER DICHTE |
| 6482 | HIGH-DENSITY METAL | METAL A HAUTE DENSITE | METALL GROSSER DICHTE |
| 6483 | HIGH-GRADE | A HAUTE TENEUR | HOCHPROZENTIG |
| 6484 | HIGH-GRADE FUEL | COMBUSTIBLE DE TRES BONNE QUALITE | BRENNSTOFF (HOCHWERTIGER) |
| 6485 | HIGH-GRADE ORE | MINERAI RICHE, MINERAI DE HAUTE TENEUR | ERZ (REICHES) |
| 6486 | HIGH-GRADE STEEL | ACIER DE QUALITE SUPERIEURE, ACIER SUPERIEUR | STAHL (HOCHWERTIGER) |
| 6487 | HIGH-PRESSURE BOILER | CHAUDIERE A HAUTE PRESSION | HOCHDRUCKKESSEL |
| 6488 | HIGH-PRESSURE CYLINDER | CYLINDRE A HAUTE PRESSION | HOCHDRUCKZYLINDER |
| 6489 | HIGH-PRESSURE HOT WATER HEATING | CHAUFFAGE PAR L'EAU CHAUDE A HAUTE PRESSION | HOCHDRUCKWASSERHEIZUNG, HEISSWASSERHEIZUNG |
| 6490 | HIGH-PRESSURE PIPING | CONDUITE POUR HAUTE PRESSION | HOCHDRUCKLEITUNG |
| 6491 | HIGH-PRESSURE STEAM | VAPEUR A HAUTE PRESSION | HOCHDRUCKDAMPF, HOCH GESPANNTER DAMPF |
| 6492 | HIGH-PRESSURE STEAM ENGINE | MACHINE A HAUTE PRESSION | HOCHDRUCKDAMPFMASCHINE |
| 6493 | HIGH-PRESSURE STEAM HEATING | CHAUFFAGE PAR LA VAPEUR A HAUTE PRESSION | HOCHDRUCKDAMPFHEIZUNG |
| 6494 | HIGH-PRESSURE TURBINE | TURBINE A HAUTE PRESSION | HOCHDRUCKTURBINE |
| 6495 | HIGH-SPEED DRILLING MACHINE | PERCEUSE A GRANDE VITESSE | SCHNELLBOHRMASCHINE |
| 6496 | HIGH-SPEED ENGINE | MACHINE A GRANDE VITESSE, MACHINE A MARCHE RAPIDE | SCHNELLAUFENDE MASCHINE, SCHNELLÄUFER |

**HIG** 166

| | | | |
|------|------|------|------|
| 6497 | HIGH-SPEED STEEL | ACIER RAPIDE | SCHNELLARBEITSSTAHL, SCHNELLDREHSTAHL |
| 6498 | HIGH-TEMPERATURE OXIDATION | OXYDATION A TEMPERATURE ELEVEE | OXYDATION BEI HOCHTEMPERATUR |
| 6499 | HIGH-TEMPERATURE TESTING | ESSAI A HAUTE TEMPERATURE | PRÜFUNG BEI HOCHTEMPERATUR |
| 6500 | HIGH-TENSION CURRENT | COURANT A HAUTE TENSION | HOCHSPANNUNGSSTROM, STROM (HOCHGESPANNTER) |
| 6501 | HIGH-TENSION LINE | LIGNE A HAUTE TENSION | HOCHSPANNUNGSLEITUNG |
| 6502 | HIGH-TENSION MOTOR | MOTEUR A HAUTE TENSION | HOCHSPANNUNGSMOTOR |
| 6503 | HIGHLY INFLAMMABLE | INFLAMMABLE, DANGEREUX | FEUERGEFÄHRLICH |
| 6504 | HINDERED CONTRACTION | RETRAIT CONTRARIE | SCHWINDUNG (BEHINDERTE) |
| 6505 | HINGE | CHARNIERE, BRAS D'ARTICULATION | GELENKBAND, SCHARNIER, FÜHRUNGSARM |
| 6506 | HINGE BUCKLE | PLI CHARNIERE | SCHARNIERHEBEL |
| 6507 | HINGE PILLAR | MONTANT DE PORTE | TÜRPFOSTEN |
| 6508 | HINGE PIN | CHARNIERE (MALE) | SCHARNIERSTIFT |
| 6509 | HINGED BOLT | BOULON A CHARNIERE, BOULON A BASCULE | KLAPPSCHRAUBE, SCHARNIERSCHRAUBE |
| 6510 | HINGED LID COVER | COUVERCLE A CHARNIERE | KLAPPDECKEL, AUFKLAPPBARER DECKEL |
| 6511 | HINGED, TAIL VICE | ETAU ORDINAIRE, ETAU A PIED, ETAU DU NORD | FLASCHENSCHRAUBSTOCK |
| 6512 | HOB | PLATEAU DE FOUR, FRAISE-MERE | OFENPLATTE, ABWALZFRÄSEN |
| 6513 | HOBBING | FINITION A LA FRAISE-MERE | ABWÄLZ-FRASEN |
| 6514 | HOBRED CAVITY | DECOUPAGE A L'EMPORTE-PIECE | LOCHEISENHOHLRÄUME |
| 6515 | HOES, TRACTOR TRAILED AND MOUNTED. | HOUES (A TRACTEUR TRAINEE OU MONTEE) | HAUEN (DURCH TRAKTOREN ANGETRIEBEN) |
| 6516 | HOIST | PALAN | HEBEZEUG |
| 6517 | HOIST (TO), WIND (TO) | MONTER, LEVER | AUFWINDEN, HOCHWINDEN |
| 6518 | HOISTING CHAIN | CHAINE-CABLE, CHAINE DE LEVAGE | LASTKETTE, HUBKETTE |
| 6519 | HOISTING DEVICE, LIFTING MECHANISM, APPLIANCE | APPAREIL DE LEVAGE, ENGIN | HEBEMASCHINE, HEBEZEUG |
| 6520 | HOISTING ROPE | CABLE DE LEVAGE, CABLE D'EXTRACTION | FÖRDERSEIL |
| 6521 | HOLD | ARRET DE SUSPENSION | HALT (WAHLWEISER) |
| 6522 | HOLD DOWN | GOUPILLE DE RETENUE | STELLSPINDEL |
| 6523 | HOLD TIME | TEMPS DE MAINTIEN DE L'EFFORT | NACHHALTEZEIT |
| 6524 | HOLD UP (TO) | TENIR LE COUP, TENIR (RIVETAGE), SOUTENIR LE TAS | VORHALTEN, GEGENHALTEN |
| 6525 | HOLD-OPEN MECHANISM | MECANISME DE RETENUE EN POSITION D'OUVERTURE | OFFENHALTUNGSVORRICHTUNG |
| 6526 | HOLDING | MAINTIEN | WARMHALTEN |
| 6527 | HOLDING FURNACE | FOUR DE MAINTIEN | WARMHALTEOFEN |
| 6528 | HOLDING TIME | MAINTIEN EN TEMPERATURE | HALTEZEIT |
| 6529 | HOLDING-UP HAMMER | CONTRE-BOUTEROLLE A MANCHE | VORHALTHAMMER |
| 6530 | HOLE | TROU, ORIFICE, LACUNE | LOCH, BOHRUNG, ÖFFNUNG |
| 6531 | HOLE GAUGE | TAMPON DE CONTROLE D'ALESAGE | BOHRUNGSLEHRE |
| 6532 | HOLE-IN-THE-DIE | CALIBRE DE MATRICE | LOCHRINGÖFFNUNG |
| 6533 | HOLED CIRCULAR NUT | ECROU A TROUS, ECROU A ENCOCHES | LOCHMUTTER |
| 6534 | HOLIDAY DETECTOR | BALAI ELECTRIQUE | LÜCKENSUCHGERÄT |
| 6535 | HOLIDAY TEST | ESSAI (OU CONTROLE) AU BALAI ELECTRIQUE | PRÜFUNG MIT DEM LÜCKENSUCHGERÄT |
| 6536 | HOLIDAYS | LACUNES (AFNOR), MANQUES (AFNOR) | BLANKE STELLE |

| | | | |
|---|---|---|---|
| 6537 | **HOLLOW** | CONGE DE RACCORDEMENT, ARRONDI | ABRUNDUNGSBOGEN, AUSRUNDUNG |
| 6538 | **HOLLOW BODY** | CORPS CREUX | HOHLKÖRPER |
| 6539 | **HOLLOW CASTING** | PIECE DE MOULAGE CREUSE | HOHLGUSS |
| 6540 | **HOLLOW CYLINDER** | CYLINDRE CREUX | HOHLZYLINDER |
| 6541 | **HOLLOW HALF-ROUND IRON** | FER DEMI-ROND CREUX | HALBRUNDEISEN (HOHLES) |
| 6542 | **HOLLOW KEY, SADDLE KEY** | CLAVETTE A FRICTION, CLAVETTE CREUSE, CLAVETTE EVIDEE | HOHLKEIL |
| 6543 | **HOLLOW OF WAVE, WAVE HOLLOW TROUGH** | CREUX, VIDE ENTRE LES ONDES | WELLENTAL |
| 6544 | **HOLLOW PLANE** | MOUCHETTE | LEISTENHOBEL |
| 6545 | **HOLLOW PUNCH** | DECOUPOIR, EMPORTE-PIECE CYLINDRIQUE | LOCHEISEN, LOCHSTAHL, AUSSCHLAGEISEN, AUSSCHLAGSTAHL, AUSSCHLAGPUNZE |
| 6546 | **HOLLOW SET, SMITH'S GOUGE** | GOUGE DE FORGERON | HALBRUNDER MEISSEL |
| 6547 | **HOLLOW SHAFT** | ARBRE CREUX | WELLE (HOHLE) |
| 6548 | **HOLLOW SPACE BETWEEN TEETH** | CREUX DE LA DENT, VIDE ENTRE DEUX DENTS | ZAHNLÜCKE |
| 6549 | **HOLLOW SPHERE** | SPHERE CREUSE | HOHLKUGELWALZE |
| 6550 | **HOLLOW SQUARE SECTION** | SECTION RECTANGULAIRE CREUSE, SECTION A NERVURES | QUERSCHNITT (HOHLRECHTECKIGER) |
| 6551 | **HOLMIUM** | HOLMIUM | HOLMIUM |
| 6552 | **HOLOHEDRAL CRYSTAL** | CRISTAL HOLOEDRE | HOLOEDERKRISTALL |
| 6553 | **HOLSTING, WINDING** | LEVAGE | AUFWINDEN, HOCHWINDEN |
| 6554 | **HOME SCRAP** | FERAILLES DE PRODUCTION PROPRE | HÜTTENSCHROTT |
| 6555 | **HOMOGENEOUS** | HOMOGENE | HOMOGEN, GLEICHMÄSSIG |
| 6556 | **HOMOGENEOUS BONDING** | UNION HOMOGENE | VERBINDUNG (HOMOGENE) |
| 6557 | **HOMOGENEOUS EQUATION** | EQUATION HOMOGENE | GLEICHUNG (HOMOGENE) |
| 6558 | **HOMOGENEOUS MATTER** | SUBSTANCE HOMOGENE | GRUNDSTOFF (HOMOGENE) |
| 6559 | **HOMOGENEOUS RADIATION** | RAYONNEMENT HOMOGENE | STRAHLUNG (HOMOGENE) |
| 6560 | **HOMOGENEOUS TEXTURE** | TEXTURE HOMOGENE | GEFÜGE (GLEICHARTIGES), GEFÜGE (HOMOGENES) |
| 6561 | **HOMOGENIZING** | HOMOGENEISATION | HOMOGENISIERUNG |
| 6562 | **HOMOLOGOUS SERIES** | SERIE HOMOLOGUE | REIHE (HOMOLOGE) (CHEM.) |
| 6563 | **HONEYCOMBED POROUS SPONGY BLOWN CASTING** | FONTE A SOUFFLURES | GUSS (BLASIGER) |
| 6564 | **HONING** | RECTIFICATION INTERIEURE, RODAGE AU LIQUIDE | HONEN, ZIEHSCHLEIFEN |
| 6565 | **HONING AND LAPPING MACHINE** | MACHINE A RODER | ZIEHSCHLEIF- U. LÄPPMASCHINE |
| 6566 | **HOOD** | CAPOT DE VOITURE | HAUBE |
| 6567 | **HOOF DUST, CRUSHED HOOFS** | SABOTS D'ANIMAUX RAPES | KLAUENMEHL, HUFMEHL |
| 6568 | **HOOK** | CROCHET | HAKEN |
| 6569 | **HOOK BOLT** | BOULON A CROCHET | HAKENSCHRAUBE |
| 6570 | **HOOK LINK CHAIN, WIDE LINK CHAIN, LADDER CHAIN** | CHAINE DE VAUCANSON | HAKENKETTE, VAUCANSONSCHE KETTE |
| 6571 | **HOOK WRENCH, HAND HOOK** | GRIFFE DE FORGERON | RICHTHAKEN, RICHTHORN |
| 6572 | **HOOKE'S JOINT COUPLING, UNIVERSAL COUPLING** | MANCHON ARTICULE UNIVERSEL | UNIVERSAL-GELENKKUPPLUNG |
| 6573 | **HOOKE'S JOINT, UNIVERSAL JOINT** | JOINT DE CARDAN, ARTICULATION A CARDAN, CARDAN, JOINT UNIVERSEL, CHARNIERE UNIVERSELLE | KREUZGELENK, KARDANGELENK, KARDANISCHES GELENK, UNIVERSALGELENK, HOOKESCHER SCHLÜSSEL |
| 6574 | **HOOKE'S LAW** | LOI DE HOOKE | HOOKESCHES GESETZ |
| 6575 | **HOOP IRON** | FEUILLARD DE FER, FER FEUILLARD | BANDEISEN |
| 6576 | **HOOP STRESS** | CONTRAINTE CIRCONFERENTIELLE | UMFANGSSPANNUNG |

# HOR

**168**

| | | | |
|---|---|---|---|
| 6577 | **HOPPER** | TREMIE | FÜLLTRICHTER, SCHÜTTRUMPF |
| 6578 | **HORIZONTAL** | HORIZONTAL | LIEGEND, WAAGRECHT, HORIZONTAL |
| 6579 | **HORIZONTAL BOILER** | CHAUDIERE HORIZONTALE | KESSEL (LIEGENDER) |
| 6580 | **HORIZONTAL BULLET DRUM** | RESERVOIR BALLON | BOILER (WAAGERECHTER) |
| 6581 | **HORIZONTAL DRILLING MACHINE** | PERCEUSE HORIZONTALE | BOHRMASCHINE (LIEGENDE), HORIZONTALBOHRMASCHINE |
| 6582 | **HORIZONTAL ENGINE** | MACHINE HORIZONTALE | MASCHINE (LIEGENDE) |
| 6583 | **HORIZONTAL FILLET WELD** | SOUDURE EN ANGLE A PLAT | HORIZONTALKEHLNAHTSCHWEISSEN |
| 6584 | **HORIZONTAL GRATE** | GRILLE HORIZONTALE | PLANROST |
| 6585 | **HORIZONTAL LINE** | LIGNE HORIZONTALE | WAAGERECHTE, HORIZONTALE |
| 6586 | **HORIZONTAL NECK JOURNAL BEARING** | SUPPORT, APPUI INTERMEDIAIRE D'UN ARBRE | HALSLAGER EINER LIEGENDEN WELLE |
| 6587 | **HORIZONTAL SHAFT** | ARBRE HORIZONTAL | WELLE (LIEGENDE) |
| 6588 | **HORIZONTAL SPINDLE GRINDER** | MACHINE A MEULER A AXE HORIZONTAL | WAAGERECHTSPINDELSCHLEIFBOCK |
| 6589 | **HORIZONTAL SPINDLE MILLING MACHINE** | FRAISEUSE HORIZONTALE | LIEGENDE FRÄSMASCHINE, FRÄSMASCHINE (HORIZONTALE), FRÄSMASCHINE (WAAGERECHTE) |
| 6590 | **HORIZONTAL THRUST** | POUSSEE HORIZONTALE | HORIZONTALSCHUB |
| 6591 | **HORIZONTAL WELDING** | SOUDURE EN CORNICHE | SCHWEISSEN (WAAGERECHTES) |
| 6592 | **HORN** | AVERTISSEUR SONORE, KLAXON, BRAS DE L'ELECTRODE | HORN, HUPE, ELEKTRODENARM |
| 6593 | **HORN BLOCK** | PLAQUE DE GARDE | ACHSENGABEL |
| 6594 | **HORN CENTRE** | CENTRE A COMPAS | ZENTRUMSCHEIBE (FÜR ZIRKEL) |
| 6595 | **HORN CLIPPINGS** | CORNE RAPEE | HORNSPÄNE |
| 6596 | **HORN OF PLATEN SPACING** | DISTANCE ENTRE LES BRAS | ARMABSTAND |
| 6597 | **HORN OF SADDLE SUPPORT** | EXTREMITE DU BERCEAU | SATTELENDE |
| 6598 | **HORNBLENDE** | HORNBLENDE, AMPHIBOLE | HORNBLENDE |
| 6599 | **HORNBLENDE ASBESTOS, AMPHIBOLE ASBESTOS** | AMIANTE | HORNBLENDEASBEST |
| 6600 | **HORNGATE** | ATTAQUE EN CORNICHON | HORNEINGUSS, HORNZULAUF |
| 6601 | **HORSE NAILS** | CLOUS DE FER A CHEVAL | HUFNÄGEL |
| 6602 | **HORSE POWER (H.P.)** | CHEVAL-VAPEUR | PFERDESTÄRKE, PFERDEKRAFT |
| 6603 | **HORSE-POWER/HOUR (H.P.-HR., H.P.-HR.)** | CHEVAL-HEURE | PFERDESTÄRKE-STUNDE |
| 6604 | **HORSEHAIR** | CRIN DE CHEVAL | ROSSHAAR, PFERDEHAAR |
| 6605 | **HORSESHOE IRON** | FER CAVALIER | HUFSTABEISEN |
| 6606 | **HORSESHOE MAGNET** | AIMANT EN U, EN FER A CHEVAL | HUFEISENMAGNET |
| 6607 | **HORSESHOE STEP GAUGE** | JAUGE-MACHOIRE A UNE BRANCHE POUR COTES 'MINI' ET 'MAXI' | EINSEITIGE GRENZRACHENLEHRE MIT ZWEI MESSSTELLEN FÜR 'GUT' UND 'AUSSCHUSSSEITE' |
| 6608 | **HORSESHOE, SNAP, CALLIPER GAUGE** | CALIBRE EN FER A CHEVAL | OFFENE LEHRE, LOCHLEHRE, TASTERLEHRE, RACHENLEHRE, KLINKE |
| 6609 | **HOSE** | DURITE | VERBINDUNG |
| 6610 | **HOSE CLAMP** | COLLIER DE SERRAGE (POUR TUYAU) | SCHLAUCHSCHELLE |
| 6611 | **HOSE CLIP** | COLLIER A VIS POUR TUYAUX FLEXIBLES | SCHLAUCHSCHELLE, SCHLAUCHKLEMME, SCHLAUCHKLAMMER |
| 6612 | **HOSE COUPLING** | RACCORD POUR TUYAUX FLEXIBLES | SCHLAUCHKUPPLUNG |
| 6613 | **HOSE DRAIN NOZZLE** | TUBULURE POUR PURGE SOUPLE | ABLASSSCHLAUCH-STUTZEN |
| 6614 | **HOSE PIPE** | TUBE FLEXIBLE, BOYAU | SCHLAUCH |
| 6615 | **HOT AIR ENGINE** | MOTEUR A AIR CHAUD | HEISSLUFTMASCHINE, LUFTMOTOR |
| 6616 | **HOT AIR HEATING** | CHAUFFAGE A AIR CHAUD | LUFTHEIZUNG |
| 6617 | **HOT BED** | BANC REFROIDISSEUR | KÜHLBETT, WARMLAGER |

|  |  |  |  |
|---|---|---|---|
| 6618 | HOT BEND TEST | ESSAI DE PLIAGE A CHAUD | WARMBIEGEPROBE |
| 6619 | HOT BENDING | FLEXION A CHAUD, PLIAGE A CHAUD | WARMBIEGUNG |
| 6620 | HOT BLAST IRON | FONTE A L'AIR CHAUD | ROHEISEN (HEISS ERBLASENES) |
| 6621 | HOT CRACK | RUPTURE A CHAUD, CRIQUE A CHAUD | WARMBRUCH, WARMRISS |
| 6622 | HOT CUTTING | COUPAGE A CHAUD | WARMSCHNEIDEN |
| 6623 | HOT DRAW (TO) | ETIRER A CHAUD | WARMZIEHEN |
| 6624 | HOT DRAWING | ETIRAGE A CHAUD, TREFILAGE A CHAUD | WARMZIEHEN |
| 6625 | HOT EMBRITTLEMENT | FRAGILISATION A CHAUD | WARMVERSPRÖDUNG |
| 6626 | HOT FORGING | FORGEAGE A CHAUD | WARMSCHMIEDEN |
| 6627 | HOT FORMING | FACONNAGE A CHAUD, FORMAGE A CHAUD | WARMFORMUMG, |
| 6628 | HOT GALVANIZING | GALVANISATION PAR TREMPE | FEUERVERZINKUNG |
| 6629 | HOT HARDNESS | DURETE A CHAUD | HÄRTE BEI HOCHTEMPERATUR |
| 6630 | HOT IRON SAW | SCIE A CHAUD, SCIE POUR METAUX AU ROUGE | WARMSÄGE, HEISSSÄGE |
| 6631 | HOT METAL | METAL EN ETAT DE FUSION, METAL EN FUSION | METALL IM SCHMELZZUSTAND |
| 6632 | HOT PRESSING | ESTAMPAGE A CHAUD | WARMPRESSEN |
| 6633 | HOT QUENCHING | TREMPE ECHELONNEE | STUFENHÄRTUNG |
| 6634 | HOT RIVET (TO) | RIVER A CHAUD | WARMNIETEN |
| 6635 | HOT RIVETING | RIVURE A CHAUD | WARMNIETEN |
| 6636 | HOT ROLL (TO) | LAMINER A CHAUD | WARMWALZEN |
| 6637 | HOT ROLLED PLATE | TOLE LAMINEE A CHAUD | BLECH (WARMGEWALZTES) |
| 6638 | HOT ROLLING | LAMINAGE A CHAUD | WARMWALZEN |
| 6639 | HOT SERVICE THERMAL INSULATION | CALORIFUGEAGE | WÄRMEDÄMMUNG |
| 6640 | HOT SET | TRANCHE A CHAUD | WARMSCHROTMEISSEL |
| 6641 | HOT SHORTNESS | FRAGILITE A CHAUD | MESSBRÜCHIGKEIT, WARMBRÜCHIGKEIT |
| 6642 | HOT SPOT | POINT CHAUD | STELLE (HEISSE), STELLE (WARME) |
| 6643 | HOT STAMPING | ETAMPAGE A CHAUD | WARMGESENKDRÜCKEN |
| 6644 | HOT SURFACE | SURFACE TRES POREUSE | OBERFLÄCHE (SAUGENDE) |
| 6645 | HOT TEAR | CRIQUE DE RETRAIT | WARMRISS, SCHWINDUNGSRISS |
| 6646 | HOT TEST | ESSAI DE RESISTANCE A CHAUD | WARMVERSUCH |
| 6647 | HOT TRIMMING | EBARBAGE A CHAUD | HEISSFERTIGPUTZEN |
| 6648 | HOT WATER HEATING | CHAUFFAGE PAR L'EAU CHAUDE | WASSERHEIZUNG |
| 6649 | HOT WATER PIPE LINE | CONDUITE D'EAU CHAUDE | WARMWASSERLEITUNG |
| 6650 | HOT WORKING | TRAVAIL A CHAUD, USINAGE A CHAUD | WARMBEARBEITUNG |
| 6651 | HOT-BLAST MAIN | CONDUITE DE VENT CHAUD | HEISSWINDLEITUNG |
| 6652 | HOT-CATHODE TUBE | TUBE A CATHODE CHAUDE | GLÜHKATODENRÖHRE |
| 6653 | HOT-DIP GALVANIZING | GALVANISATION A CHAUD | FEUERTAUCHVERZINKEN |
| 6654 | HOT-FACE TEMPERATURE | TEMPERATURE SUPERFICIELLE MAXIMALE | MAXIMALE OBERFLÄCHENTEMPERATUR |
| 6655 | HOT-FINISHING | FINISSAGE A CHAUD | WARMVERGÜTUNG |
| 6656 | HOT-ROLLING | LAMINAGE A CHAUD | WARMWALZEN |
| 6657 | HOT-SAWING | SCIAGE A CHAUD | WARMSÄGEN |
| 6658 | HOT-SHORT | CASSANT A CHAUD | WARMBRÜCHIG |
| 6659 | HOTDIP COATING PROCESS | PROCEDE DE REVETEMENT EN BAIN CHAUD | SCHMELZTAUCHVERFAHREN |
| 6660 | HOUSING | LOGEMENT, BOITIER | LAGER, GEHÄUSE |

# HUB

| | | | |
|---|---|---|---|
| 6661 | HUB | MOYEU | NABE |
| 6662 | HUB CAP | ENJOLIVEUR DE ROUE | RAD(NABEN)KAPPE |
| 6663 | HUB FLANGE | BRIDE A MOYEU | NABENFLANSCH |
| 6664 | HUMECTANT | HUMIDIFIANT | BEFEUCHTER |
| 6665 | HUMIC ACID | ACIDE HUMIQUE | HUMUSSÄURE |
| 6666 | HUMIDITY MOISTURE OF THE AIR, ATMOSPHERIC MOISTURE | ETAT HYGROMETRIQUE DE L'AIR, HUMIDITE DE L'AIR | LUFTFEUCHTIGKEIT |
| 6667 | HUMUS, VEGETABLE MOULD | HUMUS | HUMUS |
| 6668 | HUNDREDWEIGHT (CWT.) (100 LBS) | QUINTAL (50 KGS ENV.) | ZENTNER (50 KGS ENV.) |
| 6669 | HUNG ON KNIFE EDGE | SUSPENDU SUR UN COUTEAU | AUF EINER SCHNEIDE GELAGERT |
| 6670 | HUNTING | POMPAGE | PENDELN |
| 6671 | HUNTING OF GOVERNOR | OSCILLATIONS DU REGULATEUR | TANZEN DES REGLERS |
| 6672 | HYDRANT | BOUCHE D'ARROSAGE, BOUCHE D'EAU | SCHACHTHYDRANT, HYDRANT |
| 6673 | HYDRATE, HYDROXIDE | HYDRATE, HYDROXYDE | HYDRAT, HYDROXYD |
| 6674 | HYDRATED | HYDRATE | WASSERHALTIG |
| 6675 | HYDRATION WATER, WATER OF HYDRATION | EAU D'HYDRATATION | HYDRATWASSER |
| 6676 | HYDRAULIC | HYDRAULIQUE | HYDRAULISCH |
| 6677 | HYDRAULIC ACCUMULATOR | ACCUMULATEUR HYDRAULIQUE | DRUCKWASSERSPEICHER, AKKUMULATOR (HYDRAULISCHER) |
| 6678 | HYDRAULIC BRAKE | AMORTISSEUR A LIQUIDE, FREIN HYDRAULIQUE, FREIN HYDROPNEUMATIQUE | FLÜSSIGKEITSBREMSE |
| 6679 | HYDRAULIC CHUCKS | MANDRINS HYDRAULIQUES | FUTTER (HYDRAULISCHE) |
| 6680 | HYDRAULIC COMPRESSOR | COMPRESSEUR HYDRAULIQUE | VERDICHTER (HYDRAULISCHER) |
| 6681 | HYDRAULIC COUPLING | ACCOUPLEMENT HYDRAULIQUE, EMBRAYAGE HYDRAULIQUE | KUPPLUNG (HYDRAULISCHE) |
| 6682 | HYDRAULIC DRAWING PRESS | PRESSE HYDRAULIQUE A EMBOUTIR | ZIEHPRESSE (HYDRAULISCHE) |
| 6683 | HYDRAULIC DRIVE | COMMANDE HYDRAULIQUE | DRUCKWASSERANTRIEB, ANTRIEB (HYDRAULISCHER) |
| 6684 | HYDRAULIC EFFICIENCY | RENDEMENT HYDRAULIQUE | WIRKUNGSGRAD (HYDRAULISCHER) |
| 6685 | HYDRAULIC ENGINEERING | CONSTRUCTION HYDRAULIQUE | WASSERBAU |
| 6686 | HYDRAULIC FIELD | REMBLAI HYDRAULIQUE | SPÜLVERSATZ |
| 6687 | HYDRAULIC FORGING PRESS, HYDRAULIC HAMMER | PRESSE A FORGER HYDRAULIQUE, PRESSE HYDRAULIQUE A MARTEAU-PILON | SCHMIEDEPRESSE (HYDRAULISCHE), DRUCKWASSERSCHMIEDEPRESSE |
| 6688 | HYDRAULIC JACK | VERIN HYDRAULIQUE | HEBEBOCK (HYDRAULISCHER), DAUMENKRAFT |
| 6689 | HYDRAULIC LIME | CHAUX HYDRAULIQUE | WASSERKALK, KALK (HYDRAULISCHER) |
| 6690 | HYDRAULIC MORTAR | MORTIER HYDRAULIQUE | WASSERMÖRTEL, MÖRTEL (HYDRAULISCHER) |
| 6691 | HYDRAULIC MOTOR, WATER MOTOR | MOTEUR HYDRAULIQUE, MACHINE HYDRAULIQUE | WASSERKRAFTMASCHINE, WASSERMOTOR, MOTOR (HYDRAULISCHER) |
| 6692 | HYDRAULIC POWER PLANT | USINE HYDRAULIQUE, CENTRALE HYDRAULIQUE | WASSERKRAFTANLAGE |
| 6693 | HYDRAULIC PRESS | PRESSE HYDRAULIQUE | DRUCKWASSERPRESSE, PRESSE (HYDRAULISCHE) |
| 6694 | HYDRAULIC RAM | BELIER HYDRAULIQUE | WIDDER (HYDRAULISCHER), STOSSHEBER |
| 6695 | HYDRAULIC TEST, WATER PRESSURE TEST | EPREUVE HYDRAULIQUE | DRUCKWASSERPROBE, WASSERDRUCKPROBE, PROBE (HYDRAULISCHE) |
| 6696 | HYDRAULIC TURBINE, WATER TURBINE | TURBINE HYDRAULIQUE | WASSERTURBINE |

| | | | |
|---|---|---|---|
| 6697 | **HYDRAULICALLY OPERATED VALVE** | SOUPAPE A COMMANDE HYDRAULIQUE | VENTIL (HYDRAULISCH BETÄTIGTES) |
| 6698 | **HYDRAULICS** | HYDRAULIQUE | HYDRAULIK |
| 6699 | **HYDRID PROCESS** | PROCEDE A PARTIR DES PRODUITS RESULTANT DE LA DECOMPOSITION DE L'HYDRURE. | HYBRID-VERFAHREN |
| 6700 | **HYDRO-ELECTRIC GENERATOR** | GENERATRICE HYDROELECTRIQUE | WASSERDYNAMO |
| 6701 | **HYDRO-ELECTRIC POWER STATION** | USINE HYDROELECTRIQUE | ZENTRALE (WASSERELEKTRISCHE), ZENTRALE (HYDROELKTRISCHE) |
| 6702 | **HYDRO-EXTRACT (TO)** | ESSORER PAR FORCE CENTRIFUGE | AUSSCHLEUDERN, ZENTRIFUGIEREN |
| 6703 | **HYDRO-EXTRACTOR, CONTRIFUGAL MACHINE** | ESSOREUSE CENTRIFUGE | SCHLEUDER, TROCKENSCHLEUDER, ZENTRIFUGE |
| 6704 | **HYDROBROMIC ACID** | ACIDE BROMHYDRIQUE | BROMWASSERSTOFFSÄURE |
| 6705 | **HYDROCARBON** | CARBURE D'HYDROGENE, HYDROCARBURE | KOHLENWASSERSTOFF, HYDROKARBÜR |
| 6706 | **HYDROCHLORIC ACID, MURIATIC ACID, HYDROGEN CHLORIDE, SPIRITS OF SALT** | ACIDE CHLORHYDRIQUE, HYDROCHLORIQUE, MURIATIQUE, ESPRIT DE SEL | SALZSÄURE, CHLORWASSERSTOFFSÄURE |
| 6707 | **HYDROCYANIC ACID, PRUSSIC ACID** | ACIDE CYANHYDRIQUE, ACIDE PRUSSIQUE | ZYANWASSERSTOFF, BLAUSÄURE, ZYANWASSERSTOFFSÄURE |
| 6708 | **HYDRODYNAMIC** | HYDRODYNAMIQUE | HYDRODYNAMISCH |
| 6709 | **HYDRODYNAMIC DAMPENER** | FREIN HYDRAULIQUE | DÄMPFUNGVORRICHTUNG (HYDRODYNAMISCHE) |
| 6710 | **HYDRODYNAMICS** | HYDRODYNAMIQUE | HYDRODYNAMIK |
| 6711 | **HYDROFLUORIC ACID** | ACIDE FLUORHYDRIQUE | FLUORWASSERSTOFFSÄURE, FLUSSSPATSÄURE, FLUSSSÄURE |
| 6712 | **HYDROGEN** | HYDROGENE | WASSERSTOFF |
| 6713 | **HYDROGEN EMBRITTLEMENT** | FRAGILITE DE DECAPAGE | BEIZSPRÖDIGKEIT |
| 6714 | **HYDROGEN FLAME** | FLAMME D'HYDROGENE | WASSERSTOFFFLAMME |
| 6715 | **HYDROGEN ION CONCENTRATION** | CONCENTRATION DES IONS HYDROGENE | WASSERSTOFFIONENKONZENTRATION |
| 6716 | **HYDROGEN PEROXIDE, HYDROGEN DIOXIDE** | EAU OXYGENEE, BIOXYDE D'HYDROGENE | WASSERSTOFFSUPEROXYD |
| 6717 | **HYDROGEN SULPHIDE, SULPHURETTED HYDROGEN** | ACIDE SULFHYDRIQUE, HYDROGENE SULFURE, GAZ PUANT | SCHWEFELWASSERSTOFF, WASSERSTOFFSULFID |
| 6718 | **HYDROGEN TYPE CORROSION** | CORROSION AVEC DEGAGEMENT D'HYDROGENE | KORROSION UNTER WASSERSTOFFENTWICKLUNG |
| 6719 | **HYDROLYSIS** | HYDROLYSE | HYDROLYSE |
| 6720 | **HYDROMECHANICS** | MECANIQUE DES CORPS LIQUIDES | HYDROMECHANIK |
| 6721 | **HYDROMETALLURGY** | HYDROMETALLURGIE | HYDROMETALLURGIE |
| 6722 | **HYDROMETER** | AREOMETRE, PESE-LIQUEURS | SENKWAAGE, SCHWIMMWAAGE, ARÄOMETER, GRAVIMETER |
| 6723 | **HYDROMETER WITH SCALE PANS** | AREOMETRE A POIDS VARIABLE | GEWICHTSARÄOMETER |
| 6724 | **HYDROPHILIC** | HYDROPHILE | HYDROPHIL |
| 6725 | **HYDROSTATIC BALANCE** | BALANCE HYDROSTATIQUE | WAAGE (HYDROSTATISCHE) |
| 6726 | **HYDROSTATIC FLUID PRESSURE** | PRESSION HYDROSTATIQUE | FLÜSSIGKEITSDRUCK, DRUCK (HYDROSTATISCHER) |
| 6727 | **HYDROSTATIC TESTING** | ESSAI HYDROSTATIQUE | PROBE (HYDROTATISCHE) |
| 6728 | **HYDROSTATICS** | HYDROSTATIQUE | HYDROSTATIK |
| 6729 | **HYGROMETER** | HYGROMETRE | FEUCHTIGKEITSMESSER, HYGROMETER |
| 6730 | **HYGROSCOPIC** | HYGROMETRIQUE, AVIDE D'EAU | WASSERAUFSAUGEND, WASSERANZIEHEND, WASSERGIERIG, HYGROSKOPISCH |
| 6731 | **HYGROSCOPIC MOISTURE** | EAU HYGROMETRIQUE | WASSER (HYGROSKOPISCHES), FEUCHTIGKEIT (HYGROSKOPISCHE) |

**HYP** 172

| 6732 | HYGROSCOPICITY | HYGROMETRICITE | HYGROSKOPISCHE EIGENSCHAFT, WASSERGIER, HYGROSKOPIZITÄT |
| 6733 | HYPER-EUTECTOID | HYPEREUTECTOIDE | ÜBEREUTEKTOID |
| 6734 | HYPERBOLA | HYPERBOLE | HYPERBEL |
| 6735 | HYPERBOLIC | HYPERBOLIQUE | HYPERBOLISCH |
| 6736 | HYPERBOLIC CYLINDER | CYLINDRE HYPERBOLIQUE | ZYLINDER HYPERBOLISCHER |
| 6737 | HYPERBOLIC FUNCTION | FONCTION HYPERBOLIQUE | HYPERBELFUNKTION |
| 6738 | HYPERBOLIC SPIRAL | SPIRALE HYPERBOLIQUE | SPIRALE (HYPERBOLISCHE) |
| 6739 | HYPERBOLOID OF ONE SHEET | HYPERBOLOIDE A UNE NAPPE | HYPERBOLOID (EINSCHALIGES) |
| 6740 | HYPERBOLOID OF TWO SHEETS | HYPERBOLOIDE A DEUX NAPPES | HYPERBOLOID (ZWEISCHALIGES) |
| 6741 | HYPO-EUTECTOID | HYPOEUTECTOIDE | UNTEREUTEKTOID |
| 6742 | HYPOCHLOROUS ACID | ACIDE HYPOCHLOREUX | SÄURE (UNTERCHLORIGE) |
| 6743 | HYPOCYCLOID | HYPOCYCLOIDE | HYPOZYKLOIDE |
| 6744 | HYPOCYCLOIDAL GEAR | DENTS A FLANCS HYPOCYCLOIDAUX, ENGRENAGE HYPOCYCLOIDAL | HYPOZYKLOIDENVERZAHNUNG |
| 6745 | HYPOID GEARS | ENGRENAGES HYPOIDES | HYPOIDGETRIEBE |
| 6746 | HYPOTENUSE | HYPOTENUSE | HYPOTENUSE |
| 6747 | HYSTERESIS | HYSTERESIS | REIBUNG (MAGNETISCHE), HYSTERESIS, HYSTERESE |
| 6748 | I BEAM | POUTRELLE EN I | I-TRÄGER |
| 6749 | ICE CALORIMETER | CALORIMETRE A FUSION DE LA GLACE | EISKALORIMETER |
| 6750 | ICE MAKING MACHINE | MACHINE A GLACE | EISMASCHINE |
| 6751 | IDIOMORPHIC CRYSTAL | CRISTAL IDIOMORPHE | KRISTALL (IDIOMORFER) |
| 6752 | IDLE RUNNING | MARCHE A VIDE | LEERLAUF |
| 6753 | IDLE TIME | TEMPS MORT | LEERZEIT, LEERLAUFZET |
| 6754 | IDLE WHEEL, IDLER | ROUE INTERMEDIAIRE, ROUE DE TRANSPORT, POULIE FOLLE | ZWISCHENTRIEBRAD, ÜBERTRAGUNGSRAD, TRANSPORTRAD |
| 6755 | IDLING | RALENTI | LEERLAUF |
| 6756 | IDLING SHAFT | ARBRE DE RENVOI, ARBRE INTERMEDIAIRE | VORGELEGEWELLE |
| 6757 | IGNITE (TO) | ALLUMER, ENFLAMMER (S') | ANZÜNDEN, ENTZÜNDEN |
| 6758 | IGNITER | ALLUMEUR | ZÜNDVORRICHTUNG, ZÜNDER |
| 6759 | IGNITING POINT | POINT D'ALLUMAGE, D'INFLAMMATION | ZÜNDPUNKT |
| 6760 | IGNITION | INFLAMMATION, IGNITION, ALLUMAGE | ENTZÜNDUNG, ENTFLAMMUNG, ZÜNDUNG |
| 6761 | IGNITION COIL | BOBINE D'ALLUMAGE | ZÜNDSPULE |
| 6762 | IGNITION DISTRIBUTOR | ALLUMEUR, DISTRIBUTEUR D'ALLUMAGE | ZÜNDVERTEILER |
| 6763 | IGNITION LOSS | PERTES AU FEU | GLÜHVERLUST |
| 6764 | IGNITION POINT | POINT D'INFLAMMATION, POINT DE FLAMME | ENTZÜNDUNGSPUNKT, FLAMMPUNKT |
| 6765 | IGNITION RESIDUE | RESIDU DE CALCINATION, IMBRULES | GLÜHRÜCKSTAND |
| 6766 | IGNITION SWITCH | CONTRACTEUR D'ALLUMAGE | ZÜNDSCHALTER |
| 6767 | IGNITION TEMPERATURE | TEMPERATURE D'ALLUMAGE, D'INFLAMMATION | ENTZÜNDUNGSTEMPERATUR |
| 6768 | IGNITION TIMING | REGLAGE DE L'ALLUMAGE | ZÜNDZEITVERSTELLUNG |
| 6769 | IGNITION WARNING-LIGHT | TEMOIN D'ALLUMAGE | ZÜNDUNGPRÜFLAMPE |
| 6770 | IGNITION, FIRING | ALLUMAGE (DANS LES MOTEURS A EXPLOSION) | ZÜNDUNG |
| 6771 | ILLINIUM | ILLINIUM, PROMETHEUM | PROMETHIUM |

| | | | |
|---|---|---|---|
| 6772 | **ILLUMINANT** | APPAREIL D'ECLAIRAGE | BELEUCHTUNGSKÖRPER |
| 6773 | **ILLUMINATED BODY** | CORPS ECLAIRE | BELEUCHTETER KÖRPER |
| 6774 | **ILLUMINATING DEVICE** | DISPOSITIF D'ECLAIRAGE | BELEUCHTUNGSVORRICHTUNG |
| 6775 | **ILLUMINATING GAS, COAL GAS** | GAZ D'ECLAIRAGE, GAZ LUMIERE | LEUCHTGAS |
| 6776 | **ILLUMINATING POWER** | POUVOIR ECLAIRANT | LEUCHTKRAFT |
| 6777 | **ILLUMINATION** | INTENSITE D' ECLAIREMENT | BELEUCHTUNGSSTÄRKE, BELEUCHTUNG |
| 6778 | **ILLUSTRATION** | ILLUSTRATION, FIGURE | ABBILDUNG |
| 6779 | **IMAGE** | IMAGE | BILD (OPT.) |
| 6780 | **IMAGE POINT** | POINT D'IMAGE | BILDPUNKT |
| 6781 | **IMAGINARY NUMBER** | NOMBRE IMAGINAIRE | ZAHL (IMAGINÄRE) |
| 6782 | **IMCOMPLETE FUSION** | MANQUE DE FUSION | BINDEFEHLER |
| 6783 | **IMPACT** | CHOC | SCHLAG, STOSS |
| 6784 | **IMPACT EXTRUSION** | EXTRUSION PAR CHOC | SCHLAGFLIESSPRESSEN |
| 6785 | **IMPACT STRENGTH** | RESILIENCE, RESISTANCE AU CHOC | STOSSFESTIGKEIT, SCHLAGFESTIGKEIT |
| 6786 | **IMPACT TEST** | ESSAI DE RESISTANCE AU CHOC, ESSAI DE RUPTURE AU CHOC, ESSAI PAR CHOC | SCHLAGVERSUCH, STOSSVERSUCH |
| 6787 | **IMPACT TESTING MACHINE** | MOUTON-PENDULE DE CHARPY | CHARPY-PRÜFMASCHINE, PENDELHAMMER |
| 6788 | **IMPACT VALVE** | RESILIENCE | KERBSCHLAGZÄHIGKEIT |
| 6789 | **IMPALPABLE POWDER, FINELY GROUND POWDER** | POUDRE IMPALPABLE, SUBSTANCE FINEMENT BROYEE, SUBSTANCE EN POUDRE FINE | PULVER (FEINGEMAHLENES) |
| 6790 | **IMPART (TO), GIVE A FINE EDGE (TO)** | AFFILER, DONNER LE FIL A UN INSTRUMENT TRANCHANT | ABZIEHEN, NACHSCHÄRFEN |
| 6791 | **IMPART TO, APPLY A PRESERVATIVE SKIN** | APPLIQUER UNE COUCHE PROTECTRICE | SCHUTZSCHICHT AUFBRINGEN, SCHUTZSCHICHT (EINE) AUFTRAGEN |
| 6792 | **IMPARTING APPLICATION OF A PRESERVATIVE SKIN** | APPLICATION D'UNE COUCHE PROTECTRICE | AUFBRINGEN EINER SCHUTZSCHICHT, AUFTRAGEN EINER SCHUTZSCHICHT |
| 6793 | **IMPARTING, GIVING A FINE EDGE** | AFFILAGE | ABZIEHEN, NACHSCHÄRFEN |
| 6794 | **IMPEDANCE, APPARENT RESISTANCE** | IMPEDANCE, RESISTANCE APPARENTE | SCHEINWIDERSTAND, WIDERSTAND (SCHEINBARER), IMPEDANZ |
| 6795 | **IMPELLER** | ROTOR, TURBINE, TURBINE DE POMPE CENTRIFUGE | LAUFRAD, VERDICHTERRAD |
| 6796 | **IMPERMEABILITY TO WATER** | IMPERMEABILITE A L'EAU | WASSERUNDURCHLÄSSIGKEIT |
| 6797 | **IMPERMEABILITY, IMPERVIOUSNESS** | IMPERMEABILITE | DICHTHEIT, UNDURCHLÄSSIGKEIT |
| 6798 | **IMPERMEABLE, IMPERVIOUS** | IMPERMEABLE | UNDURCHLÄSSIG |
| 6799 | **IMPINGEMENT ATTAK** | CORROSION SOUS EROSION | AUFPRALLKORROSION |
| 6800 | **IMPONDERABLE** | IMPONDERABLE | UNWÄGBAR |
| 6801 | **IMPOVERISHMENT** | APPAUVRISSEMENT | VERARMUNG |
| 6802 | **IMPREGNATE (TO)** | IMPREGNER, IMBIBER | DURCHTRÄNKEN, IMPRÄGNIEREN |
| 6803 | **IMPREGNATED PAPER GAS PIPE** | TUYAU A GAZ EN PAPIER IMPREGNE DE BITUME | ASPHALTROHR, PAPIERROHR |
| 6804 | **IMPREGNATING MEDIUM AGENT** | AGENT D'IMPREGNATION | TRÄNKUNGSMITTEL, IMPRÄGNIERUNGSMITTEL |
| 6805 | **IMPREGNATION** | IMPREGNATION, IMBIBITION, INFILTRATION | TRÄNKEN, DURCHTRÄNKEN, IMPRÄGNIEREN, TRÄNKUNG |
| 6806 | **IMPRESSION, CURVED DEPRESSION** | EMPREINTE | EINDRUCK, EINPRÄGUNG |
| 6807 | **IMPROPER FRACTION** | EXPRESSION FRACTIONNAIRE | BRUCH (UNECHTER) |
| 6808 | **IMPROVE THE STEEL BY HEAT TREATMENT (TO)** | CORRIGER L'ACIER PAR UN REVENU | STAHL VERGÜTEN (DEN) |
| 6809 | **IMPULSE** | IMPULSION, MOUVEMENT MOTEUR | ANTRIEB EINER KRAFT, IMPULS |

**IMP** 174

| | | | |
|------|------|------|------|
| 6810 | IMPULSE, ACTION TURBINE | TURBINE A ACTION, TURBINE A IMPULSION, TURBINE A LIBRE DEVIATION | DRUCKTURBINE, AKTIONSTURBINE |
| 6811 | IMPULSIVE FORCE | FORCE IMPULSIVE | STOSSKRAFT, MOMENTANKRAFT |
| 6812 | IMPULSIVE SUDDEN LOAD | CHARGE PERIODIQUE | BELASTUNG (STOSSWEISE), BELASTUNG (PULSIEREND) |
| 6813 | IMPURITIES, ADMIXTURES | CORPS ETRANGERS, SUBSTANCES ETRANGERES, IMPURETES | BEIMENGUNGEN, UNREINIGKEITEN, VERUNREINIGUNGEN, FREMDSTOFFE |
| 6814 | IMPURITY | IMPURETE | UNREINHEIT |
| 6815 | IN DIRECT RATIO | EN RAISON DIRECTE | VERHÄLTNIS (IN GERADEM), VERHÄLTNIS (IN DIREKTEM) |
| 6816 | IN INVERSE RATIO | EN RAISON INVERSE | VERHÄLTNIS (IN UMGEKEHRTEM) |
| 6817 | IN THE FORM OF VAPOUR | SOUS FORME DE VAPEUR | DAMPFFÖRMIG |
| 6818 | IN UNCOMBINED CONDITION | NON COMBINE, A L'ETAT LIBRE | UNGEBUNDEN, ZUSTAND (IN UNGEBUNDENEM), ZUSTAND (IN FREIEM) (CHEM.) |
| 6819 | IN WORKING ORDER | EN ETAT DE SERVICE | BETRIEBSFÄHIG, BETRIEBSFÄHIGEM ZUSTAND (IN) |
| 6820 | INACCESSIBILITY | INACCESSIBILITE | UNZUGÄNGLICHKEIT |
| 6821 | INACCESSIBLE | INACCESSIBLE | UNZUGÄNGLICH |
| 6822 | INCANDESCENCE | INCANDESCENCE | GLÜHUNG |
| 6823 | INCANDESCENCE, WHITE HEAT | CHALEUR BLANCHE, BLANC EBLOUISSANT, BLANC INCANDESCENT | WEISSGLUT |
| 6824 | INCANDESCENT | CHAUFFE A BLANC, PORTE A INCANDESCENCE | WEISSGLÜHEND |
| 6825 | INCANDESCENT ELECTRIC LAMP, GLOW LAMP | LAMPE A INCANDESCENCE | GLÜHLAMPE |
| 6826 | INCANDESCENT ELECTRIC LIGHT | LUMIERE A INCANDESCENCE | GLÜHLICHT |
| 6827 | INCANDESCENT GAS | GAZ INCANDESCENT | GAS (GLÜHENDES) |
| 6828 | INCANDESCENT GAS LAMP | LAMPE A GAZ, LAMPE A INCANDESCENCE | GASGLÜHLICHTLAMPE |
| 6829 | INCANDESCENT GAS LIGHT | LUMIERE DU GAZ A INCANDESCENCE | GASGLÜHLICHT |
| 6830 | INCH | POUCE ANGLAIS | ZOLL (ENGLISCHER) |
| 6831 | INCIDENCE | INCIDENCE | EINSTRAHLUNG |
| 6832 | INCIDENT RAY | RAYON INCIDENT | STRAHL (AUFTREFFENDER), STRAHL (EINFALLENDER) |
| 6833 | INCIPIENT CRACK | AMORCE DE CRIQUE, AMORCE DE FISSURE | ANRISS |
| 6834 | INCIPIENT FRACTURE | FENTE SUPERFICIELLE | ANBRUCH, ANRISS |
| 6835 | INCLINABLE, TILTING | INCLINABLE, BASCULANT | KIPPBAR, UMKIPPBAR, UMBIEGBAR |
| 6836 | INCLINATION, INCLINE, GRADIENT, SLOPE | INCLINAISON, PENTE | NEIGUNG |
| 6837 | INCLINED GRATE | GRILLE INCLINEE | SCHRÄGROST. SCHÜTTROST |
| 6838 | INCLINED PLANE | PLAN INCLINE | EBENE (SCHIEFE) |
| 6839 | INCLINED TOOTH CLUTCH | EMBRAYAGE A DENTURE CONIQUE | KEGELKUPPLUNG |
| 6840 | INCLUSION | INCLUSION | EINSCHLUSS |
| 6841 | INCLUSION STRINGERS | INCLUSION ALLONGEE | LANGGESTRECKETER EINSCHLUSS |
| 6842 | INCOMBUSTIBILITY | INCOMBUSTIBILITE | UNVERBRENNBARKEIT, UNVERBRENNLICHKEIT |
| 6843 | INCOMBUSTIBLE | IMCOMBUSTIBLE | NICHT BRENNBAR, UNVERBRENNBAR, UNVERBRENNLICH |
| 6844 | INCOMING SUPPLY | ALIMENTATION ARRIVEE | ANKOMMENDER STROM |
| 6845 | INCOMPLETE COMBUSTION | COMBUSTION INCOMPLETE | VERBRENNUNG (UNVOLLKOMMENE) |
| 6846 | INCOMPRESSIBILITY | INCOMPRESSIBILITE | UNZUSAMMENDDRÜCKBARKEIT |

**175**  **IND**

| | | |
|---|---|---|
| 6847 | **INCOMPRESSIBLE** | INCOMPRESSIBLE | UNZUSAMMENDRÜCKBAR, NICHT ZUSAMMENDRÜCKBAR, UNKOMPRIMIERBAR |
| 6848 | **INCREASE OF PRESSURE** | AUGMENTATION DE LA PRESSION | DRUCKSTEIGERUNG, DRUCKANSTIEG, DRUCKZUNAHME |
| 6849 | **INCREASE OF SPEED** | ACCROISSEMENT DE VITESSE | GESCHWINDIGKEITZUNAHME |
| 6850 | **INCREASE OF STRENGTH** | AUGMENTATION DE LA RESISTANCE | VERFESTIGUNG |
| 6851 | **INCREASE THE VELOCITY (TO)** | AUGMENTER LA VITESSE, ACCELERER | GESCHWINDIGKEIT ERHÖHEN, GESCHWINDIGKEIT STEIGERN |
| 6852 | **INCREASING SPEED** | VITESSE CROISSANTE | GESCHWINDIGKEIT (ZUNEHMENDE) |
| 6853 | **INCREMENTAL COLLAPSE** | DEFORMATION PROGRESSIVE | VERFORMUNG (STUFENLOSE) |
| 6854 | **INCREMENTAL DIMENSION** | COTATION RELATIVE | KETTENMASSSYSTEM |
| 6855 | **INCREMENTAL PRESSURE** | AUGMENTATION DE PRESSION | STEIGDRUCK |
| 6856 | **INCRUSTATION, FOULING** | FORMATION D'INCRUSTATIONS, ENTARTRAGE | KRUSTENBILDUNG; KESSELSTEINBILDUNG |
| 6857 | **INCRUSTED, FOULED** | INCRUSTE, ENTARTRE | VERKRUSTET |
| 6858 | **INDEFINITE INTEGRAL** | INTEGRALE INDEFINIE | INTEGRAL (UNBESTIMMTES) |
| 6859 | **INDENTATION** | EMPREINTE DE DURETE | HÄRTE-EINDRUCK |
| 6860 | **INDENTATION HARDNESS** | DURETE VICKERS | VICKERSHÄRTE |
| 6861 | **INDENTATION TEST** | ESSAI DE DURETE PAR EMPREINTE DE BILLE | KUGELDRUCKHÄRTEPRÜFUNG |
| 6862 | **INDENTED** | DENTELE | GEZÄHNELT, AUSGEZACKT, ZACKIG |
| 6863 | **INDEPENDENT MACHINE** | MACHINE A COMMANDE INDEPENDANTE | MASCHINE MIT EINZELANTRIEB |
| 6864 | **INDEX** | INDICE (MATH.) | INDEX (MATH.) |
| 6865 | **INDEX CRANK** | MANIVELLE D'INDEXAGE | INDEXHANDKURBEL |
| 6866 | **INDEX OF REFRACTION, REFRACTIVE INDEX** | INDICE DE REFRACTION | BRECHUNGSZAHL, BRECHUNGSEXPONENT, BRECHUNGSINDEX |
| 6867 | **INDEX PLATE** | SECTEUR GRADUE | TEILPLATTE |
| 6868 | **INDEX, POINTER, FINGER, INDICATOR** | INDICE, AIGUILLE INDICATRICE | ZEIGER (EINES INSTRUMENTS) |
| 6869 | **INDEXING HEADS** | MECANISME D'INDEXAGE | INDEXSCHALTEINRICHTUNG |
| 6870 | **INDEXING PLATES** | PLATEAUX DIVISEURS | TEILSCHEIBEN |
| 6871 | **INDIAN INK, CHINESE INK** | ENCRE DE CHINE | TUSCHE, AUSZIEHTUSCHE |
| 6872 | **INDICATED EFFICIENCY** | RENDEMENT INDIQUE | WIRKUNGSGRAD (INDIZIERTER) |
| 6873 | **INDICATED HORSE POWER (I.H.P.)** | CHEVAL NOMINAL | PFERDESTÄRKE (INDIZIERTE), PSI |
| 6874 | **INDICATED HORSEPOWER** | PUISSANCE INDIQUEE (OU FISCALE) | PFERDESTÄRKE (ANGEGEBENE) |
| 6875 | **INDICATED POWER** | PUISSANCE INDIQUEE | LEISTUNG (INDIZIERTE) |
| 6876 | **INDICATED WORK** | TRAVAIL INDIQUE | ARBEIT (INDIZIERTE) |
| 6877 | **INDICATING MICROMETER** | MICROMETRE A CADRAN | SKALENSCHEIBENMIKROMETER |
| 6878 | **INDICATOR** | INDICATEUR DE PRESSION | INDIKATOR (DAMPFM.) |
| 6879 | **INDICATOR** | INDICATEUR, REACTIF INDICATEUR | INDIKATOR (CHEM.) |
| 6880 | **INDICATOR CARD** | PAPIER D'INDICATEUR | INDIKATORPAPIER |
| 6881 | **INDICATOR DIAGRAM, DIAGRAM OF WORK** | DIAGRAMME D'INDICATEUR, DIAGRAMME DE TRAVAIL | ARBEITSDIAGRAMM, INDIKATORDIAGRAMM, SPANNUNGSDIAGRAMM, DRUCKVOLUMENDIAGRAMM, PV-DIAGRAMM |
| 6882 | **INDIFFERENT NEUTRAL EQUILIBRIUM** | EQUILIBRE INDIFFERENT | GLEICHGEWICHT (INDIFFERENTES) |
| 6883 | **INDIRECT ACTING** | A ACTION INDIRECTE | INDIREKT WIRKEND |
| 6884 | **INDIRECT EXTRUSION** | FILAGE AVEC REMONTEE DE MATIERES | RÜCKWÄRTSFLIESSPRESSEN |
| 6885 | **INDIUM** | INDIUM | INDIUM |
| 6886 | **INDIVIDUAL DRIVE** | COMMANDE INDIVIDUELLE | EINZELANTRIEB |
| 6887 | **INDOOR LIGHTING** | ECLAIRAGE INTERIEUR | INNENBELEUCHTUNG |
| 6888 | **INDUCE (TO)** | INDUIRE | INDUZIEREN |

# IND 176

| | | | |
|---|---|---|---|
| 6889 | **INDUCED CURRENT** | COURANT D'INDUCTION | INDUKTIONSSTROM, STROM (INDUZIERTER) |
| 6890 | **INDUCED DRAUGHT** | TIRAGE INDUIT | SAUGZUG |
| 6891 | **INDUCTANCE** | INDUCTANCE | SELBSTINDUKTIONSWIDERSTAND, INDUKTANZ |
| 6892 | **INDUCTION** | INDUCTION | INDUKTION |
| 6893 | **INDUCTION BRAZING** | BRASAGE PAR INDUCTION | INDUKTIONSHARTLÖTEN |
| 6894 | **INDUCTION COIL** | BOBINE D'INDUCTION | SELBSTINDUKTIONSSPULE |
| 6895 | **INDUCTION FURNACE** | FOUR A INDUCTION | INDUKTIONSOFEN |
| 6896 | **INDUCTION HARDENING** | TREMPE PAR INDUCTION | INDUKTIONSHÄRTUNG |
| 6897 | **INDUCTION HEATING** | CHAUFFAGE PAR INDUCTION | INDUKTIONSHEIZUNG |
| 6898 | **INDUCTOR** | INDUCTEUR | ERREGERWICKLUNG |
| 6899 | **INDUSTRIAL FUMES** | FUMEES INDUSTRIELLES | INDUSTRIELLE RAUCHGASE |
| 6900 | **INDUSTRIAL FURNACE** | FOUR INDUSTRIEL | INDUSTRIEOFEN |
| 6901 | **INDUSTRIAL ORGANISATION, ADMINISTRATION** | ORGANISATION DES USINES | FABRIKORGANISATION |
| 6902 | **INDUSTRIAL WASTE WATER, MILL EFFLUENTS** | EAUX RESIDUAIRES | FABRIKABWÄSSER, INDUSTRIEABWÄSSER |
| 6903 | **INDUSTRY** | INDUSTRIE | INDUSTRIE |
| 6904 | **INELASTIC** | INELASTIQUE | UNELASTISCH |
| 6905 | **INERT GAS** | GAZ INERTE, GAZ DE PROTECTION | EDELGAS, INDIFFERENTES GAS, INAKTIVES GAS, SCHUTZGAS |
| 6906 | **INERT-GAS TUNGSTEN-ARC WELDING** | SOUDAGE T.I.G (A L'ARC DE TUNGSTENE SOUS GAZ INERTE) | WOLFRAM-INERTGAS-SCHWEISSEN |
| 6907 | **INERTIA** | INERTIE, FORCE, EFFORT D'INERTIE | TRÄGHEIT, TRÄGHEITSKRAFT, BEHARRUNGSVERMÖGEN |
| 6908 | **INFANT MORTALITY** | DEFAILLANCE PRECOCE | ZEIT DER ANFANGSAUSFÄLLE |
| 6909 | **INFINITE SERIES** | SERIE INFINIE | REIHE (UNENDLICHE) |
| 6910 | **INFINITELY GREAT** | INFINIMENT GRAND | UNENDLICH GROSS |
| 6911 | **INFINITELY SMALL** | INFINIMENT PETIT | UNENDLICH KLEIN |
| 6912 | **INFINITESIMAL CALCULUS** | CALCUL INFINITESIMAL | INFINITESIMALRECHNUNG |
| 6913 | **INFLAMMABILITY** | INFLAMMABILITE | ENTFLAMMBARKEIT, ENTZÜNDBARKEIT, ZÜNDFÄHIGKEIT |
| 6914 | **INFLAMMABLE** | INFLAMMABLE | ENTFLAMMBAR, ENTZÜNDBAR |
| 6915 | **INFLOW SUPPLY OF WATER** | ARRIVEE D'EAU, ENTREE D'EAU | ZUFLUSS, WASSERZUFLUSS |
| 6916 | **INFRINGEMENT OF A PATENT** | ATTEINTE PORTEE AUX DROITS DU BREVETE | PATENTVERLETZUNG, VERLETZUNG EINES PATENTES |
| 6917 | **INFUSIBILITY** | INFUSIBILITE | UNSCHMELZBARKEIT |
| 6918 | **INFUSIBLE** | INFUSIBLE | UNSCHMELZBAR |
| 6919 | **INGOT** | LINGOT | BLOCK, METALLBLOCK, ROHBLOCK |
| 6920 | **INGOT CAR** | CAR A LINGOTS (TRANSPORT DE LINGOT) | BLOCKWAGEN |
| 6921 | **INGOT IRON** | FER FONDU | FLUSSEISEN |
| 6922 | **INGOT LATHE** | TOUR A LINGOT | BLOCKDREHBANK |
| 6923 | **INGOT MOLD** | LINGOTIERE | BLOCKFORM, STAHLWERKSKOKILLE |
| 6924 | **INGOT STEEL** | ACIER FONDU | FLUSSSTAHL |
| 6925 | **INGOTISM** | SEGREGATION MAJEURE | BLOCKSEIGERUNG |
| 6926 | **INHIBIT (TO)** | EMPECHER, LIMITER, RETARDER | HEMMEN, HINDERN, VERZÖGERN |
| 6927 | **INHIBITOR** | INHIBITEUR | INHIBITOR, HEMMSTOFF |
| 6928 | **INITIAL CREEP** | FREINAGE INITIAL | ANFANGSKRIECHEN |
| 6929 | **INITIAL PRESSURE** | PRESSION INITIALE | ANFANGSDRUCK |
| 6930 | **INITIAL STATE** | ETAT INITIAL | ANFANGSZUSTAND |

| | | | |
|---|---|---|---|
| 6931 | **INITIAL TEMPERATURE** | TEMPERATURE INITIALE | ANFANGSTEMPERATUR, AUSGANGSTEMPERATUR |
| 6932 | **INITIAL VALUE** | VALEUR INITIALE | ANFANGSWERT |
| 6933 | **INITIAL VELOCITY** | VITESSE INITIALE | ANFANGSGESCHWINDIGKEIT |
| 6934 | **INJECT (TO)** | INJECTER, PROJETER DANS... | EINSPRITZEN |
| 6935 | **INJECTION** | INJECTION | EINSPRITZEN, EINSPRITZUNG |
| 6936 | **INJECTION ORDER** | ORDRE D'INJECTION | EINSPRITZFOLGE |
| 6937 | **INJECTION VALVE** | SOUPAPE D'INJECTION | EINSPRITZVENTIL |
| 6938 | **INJECTOR** | INJECTEUR, GIFFARD | EINSPRITZDÜSE, INJEKTOR |
| 6939 | **INK ERASER** | GOMME A ENCRE | TINTENGUMMI |
| 6940 | **INK IN (TO)** | PASSER A L'ENCRE, ENCRER | MIT TUSCHE AUSZIEHEN |
| 6941 | **INKED-IN DRAWING** | DESSIN PASSE A L'ENCRE | ZEICHNUNG (AUSGEZOGENE) |
| 6942 | **INKING IN** | PASSAGE A L'ENCRE | AUSZIEHEN MIT TUSCHE |
| 6943 | **INLET** | ENTREE, ADMISSION | EINGANG, ZUFLUSS, EINLASS |
| 6944 | **INLET CONNECTING TERMINAL** | BORNE D'ARRIVEE | EINGANGSKLEMME |
| 6945 | **INLET MANIFOLD** | COLLECTEUR D'ADMISSION | ANSAUG-ROHR, SAUGROHR |
| 6946 | **INLET NOZZLE / FILLING NOZZLE** | TUBULURE D'ARRIVEE, TUBULURE D'ENTREE | EINGANGS-ROHRSTUTZEN |
| 6947 | **INLET OPENING** | ORIFICE D'ADMISSION, ORIFICE D'ENTREE, ORIFICE D'ARRIVEE, ORIFICE D'ADDUCTION, ORIFICE D'INTRODUCTION | EINLASSÖFFNUNG, EINFLUSSÖFFNUNG |
| 6948 | **INLET PIPE** | TUBULURE D'ADMISSION | SAUGLEITUNG |
| 6949 | **INLET VALVE** | SOUPAPE D'ADMISSION | EINLASSVENTIL |
| 6950 | **INLET VELOCITY, VELOCITY OF APPROACH** | VITESSE D'ARRIVEE, VITESSE A L'ARRIVEE, VITESSE D'ENTREE | ZUSTRÖMGESCHWINDIGKEIT, ZUFLUSSGESCHWINDIGKEIT, EINTRITTGESCHWINDIGKEIT |
| 6951 | **INNER CONE** | DARD | INNENKONUS |
| 6952 | **INNER FLAME CONE** | DARD INTERIEUR | FLAMMENKEGEL (INNERER) |
| 6953 | **INNER RACE OF BALL BEARING** | BAGUE INTERIEURE D'UN ROULEMENT A BILLES | RING (INNERER) EINES KUGELLAGERS, INNENRING |
| 6954 | **INNER SURFACE OF A PIPE** | SURFACE INTERIEURE D'UN TUYAU | INNENWANDUNG EINES ROHRES |
| 6955 | **INNER TUBE** | CHAMBRE A AIR | LUFTSCHLAUCH |
| 6956 | **INOCULATION** | INOCULATION | IMPFUNG |
| 6957 | **INORGANIC MATTER** | MATIERE INORGANIQUE | ANORGANISCHER STOFF, UNORGANISCHER STOFF |
| 6958 | **INORGANIC MINERAL CHEMISTRY** | CHIMIE MINERALE OU INORGANIQUE | CHEMIE (ANORGANISCHE) |
| 6959 | **INOXIDISABLE, UNOXIDISABLE** | INOXYDABLE | NICHT OXYDIERBAR |
| 6960 | **INPUT MEDIUM** | SUPPORT D'INFORMATION D'ENTREE | EINGABEDATENTRÄGER |
| 6961 | **INSCRIBABLE QUADRILATERAL** | QUADRILATERE INSCRIPTIBLE | KREISVIERECK |
| 6962 | **INSCRIBED ANGLE** | ANGLE INSCRIT, ANGLE DANS LE SEGMENT | PERIPHERIEWINKEL |
| 6963 | **INSCRIBED CIRCLE** | CERCLE INSCRIT, CIRCONFERENCE INSCRITE | EINGESCHRIEBENER KREIS, EINLIEGENDER KREIS, INKREIS |
| 6964 | **INSCRIBED POLYGON** | POLYGONE INSCRIT | POLYGON (EINGESCHRIEBENES), SEHNENPOLYGON |
| 6965 | **INSERT** | INSERTION, PIECE RAPPORTEE, INSERT | EINLAGE, EINSATZSTÜCK |
| 6966 | **INSERT DIE** | MATRICE AMOVIBLE | EINSATZMATRIZE, EINSATZGELENK |
| 6967 | **INSERT THE RIVETS (TO)** | POSER LES RIVETS | NIETEN EINSETZEN (DIE), NIETEN EINZIEHEN (DIE) |
| 6968 | **INSERTED BEAM** | POUTRE ENCASTREE | EINBAUTRÄGER |
| 6969 | **INSERTED NOZZLE** | TUBULURE ENCASTREE | ROHRSTUTZEN (EINGELASSENER) |
| 6970 | **INSERTED PIECE** | PIECE RAPPORTEE | STÜCK (EINGESETZTES) |

**INS** 178

| | | | |
|---|---|---|---|
| 6971 | **INSERTED TOOTH MILLING CUTTER** | FRAISE A DENTS RAPPORTEES, A LAMES RAPPORTEES | FRÄSER MIT EINGESETZTEN ZÄHNEN, MESSERKOPF |
| 6972 | **INSERTING THE RIVETS** | POSE DES RIVETS | EINSETZEN DER NIETEN, EINZIEHEN DER NIETEN |
| 6973 | **INSERTION RUBBER** | CAOUTCHOUC AVEC TOILE INTERCALEE | GUMMI MIT GEWEBEEINLAGE |
| 6974 | **INSIDE** | COTE INTERIEUR | INNENSEITE |
| 6975 | **INSIDE CALLIPERS** | COMPAS DE DIAMETRE INTERIEUR, MAITRE A DANSER | LOCHTASTER, INNENTASTER, LOCHZIRKEL, HOHLZIRKEL, TANZMEISTER |
| 6976 | **INSIDE CRANK, CENTRE CRANK** | COUDE D'UN ARBRE, MANIVELLE DU VILEBREQUIN | KURBEL (GEKRÖPFTE), MITTENKURBEL, KRÖPFUNG DER WELLE, KRUMMACHSE |
| 6977 | **INSIDE DIAMETER** | DIAMETRE INTERIEUR | INNENDURCHMESSER |
| 6978 | **INSIDE LENGTH OF CHAIN LINK** | PAS D'UNE CHAINE | KETTENTEILUNG, BAULÄNGE EINES KETTENGLIEDES, INNERE, GLIEDERLÄNGE |
| 6979 | **INSIDE MICROMETER CALIPERS** | CALIBRES MICROMETRIQUES D'INTERIEUR | INNENTASTER (MIKROMETRISCHER) |
| 6980 | **INSIDE SCREW GATE VALVE** | VANNE A VIS INTERIEURE | ABSPERRSCHIEBER MIT INNENSPINDEL, ABSPERRSCHIEBER MIT INNENLIEGENDEM SPINDELGEWINDE |
| 6981 | **INSIDE SCREW STEM** | TIGE A VIS INTERIEURE | SPINDEL MIT INNENLIEGENDEM GEWINDE |
| 6982 | **INSIDE WIDTH OF CHAIN LINK** | LARGEUR INTERIEURE D'UN MAILLON | INNERE LICHTE EINER KETTE, GLIEDERBREITE EINER KETTE |
| 6983 | **INSOLUBILITY** | INSOLUBILITE | UNLÖSLICHKEIT |
| 6984 | **INSOLUBLE** | INSOLUBLE | UNLÖSLICH |
| 6985 | **INSPECTION** | INSPECTION | INSPEKTION, REVISION |
| 6986 | **INSPECTION LINE** | LIGNE D'INSPECTION | PRÜFSTRASSE |
| 6987 | **INSPECTION OR EXAMINATION** | CONTROLE | PRÜFUNG |
| 6988 | **INSTALLATION** | INSTALLATION INTERIEURE | INSTALLATION |
| 6989 | **INSTANTANEOUS MOMENTARY VIRTUAL CENTRE** | CENTRE INSTANTANE DE ROTATION | MOMENTANZENTRUM |
| 6990 | **INSTANTANEOUS VALUE** | VALEUR INSTANTANEE | MOMENTANWERT |
| 6991 | **INSTRUCTION** | INSTRUCTION | ANWEISUNG, BEFEHL |
| 6992 | **INSTRUCTIONS FOR USE** | INSTRUCTION, MODE D'EMPLOI | GEBRAUCHSANWEISUNG |
| 6993 | **INSTRUMENT PANEL** | TABLEAU DE BORD | INSTRUMENTENBRETT |
| 6994 | **INSULATE (TO)** | ISOLER | ISOLIEREN |
| 6995 | **INSULATED TANK** | RESERVOIR CALORIFUGE | TANK (WÄRMEISOLIERTER) |
| 6996 | **INSULATED WIRE** | FIL ISOLE | DRAHT (ISOLIERTER) |
| 6997 | **INSULATING COMPOUND, NON-CONDUCTING COMPOSITION** | COMPOSE ISOLANT | ISOLIERMASSE, SCHUTZMASSE |
| 6998 | **INSULATING MATERIAL, INSULATION** | CALORIFUGE, MATIERE ISOLANTE, ISOLANT | ISOLIERSTOFF, ISOLIERMITTEL, ISOLIERMATERIAL |
| 6999 | **INSULATING OIL** | HUILE POUR ISOLEMENT | ISOLIERÖL |
| 7000 | **INSULATING PROPERTY** | POUVOIR ISOLANT | ISOLIERVERMÖGEN |
| 7001 | **INSULATING TAPE** | RUBAN ISOLANT | ISOLIERBAND |
| 7002 | **INSULATING TUBE** | TUBE ISOLANT | ISOLIERROHR |
| 7003 | **INSULATION** | ISOLATION THERMIQUE, ISOLEMENT, ISOLATION | ISOLIERUNG, WÄRMESCHUTZ, KÄLTESCHUTZ, ISOLIEREN |
| 7004 | **INSULATION FROM SOUND** | ISOLATION CONTRE LE BRUIT, LE SON | ISOLIERUNG GEGEN SCHALL |
| 7005 | **INSULATION RESISTANCE** | RESISTANCE D'ISOLEMENT | ISOLIERFESTIGKEIT |
| 7006 | **INSULATOR** | ISOLANT, ISOLATEUR | ISOLIERKÖRPER, ISOLATOR |
| 7007 | **INTAKE MANIFOLD** | COLLECTEUR D'ADMISSION | ANSAUGLEITUNG |
| 7008 | **INTAKE STROKE** | TEMPS D'ADMISSION | EINLASSHUB, SAUGHUB |

| | | | |
|---|---|---|---|
| 7009 | **INTEGRAL** | INTEGRALE | INTEGRAL |
| 7010 | **INTEGRAL BEAM** | POUTRE INCORPOREE | BALKEN (EINGEBAUTER) |
| 7011 | **INTEGRAL CALCULUS** | CALCUL INTEGRAL | INTEGRALRECHNUNG |
| 7012 | **INTEGRAL NUMBER** | NOMBRE ENTIER | ZAHL (GANZE), ZAHL (NATÜRLICHE) |
| 7013 | **INTEGRAPH** | INTEGRAPHE | INTEGRAPH |
| 7014 | **INTEGRATE (TO)** | INTEGRER | INTEGRIEREN |
| 7015 | **INTEGRATION** | INTEGRATION | INTEGRATION |
| 7016 | **INTEGRATOR** | INTEGRATEUR | INTEGRATOR |
| 7017 | **INTENSIFYING SCREEN** | ECRAN RENFORCATEUR | VERSTÄRKERFOLIE |
| 7018 | **INTENSITY** | INTENSITE | INTENSITÄT |
| 7019 | **INTENSITY OF RADIATION** | INTENSITE DE RADIATION, INTENSITE LUMINEUSE | STRAHLUNGSINTENSITÄT, AUSSTRAHLUNGSSTÄRKE |
| 7020 | **INTENSITY REGULATOR** | REGULATEUR D'INTENSITE | STROMSTÄRKEREGLER |
| 7021 | **INTENSITY STRENGTH OF CURRENT** | INTENSITE D'UN COURANT | STROMSTÄRKE |
| 7022 | **INTERCALATE (TO), INSERT (TO)** | INTERCALER, INSERER | EINSCHALTEN, EINSCHIEBEN |
| 7023 | **INTERCALATION, INSERTION** | INTERCALATION, INSERTION | EINSCHALTEN, EINSCHIEBEN |
| 7024 | **INTERCEPT RAYS (TO)** | INTERCEPTER DES RAYONS | STRAHLEN AUFFANGEN |
| 7025 | **INTERCHANGEABILITY** | INTERCHANGEABILITE | AUSTAUSCHBARKEIT, AUSWECHSELBARKEIT |
| 7026 | **INTERCHANGEABLE** | INTERCHANGEABLE | AUSWECHSELBAR, AUSTAUSCHBAR |
| 7027 | **INTERCHANGEABLE GEARS** | ROUES D'ASSORTIMENT, DE SERIE | SATZRÄDER, RÄDER (AUSTAUSCHBARE) |
| 7028 | **INTERCHANGEABLE MANUFACTURE** | INTERCHANGEABILITE DE FABRICATION | AUSTAUSCHBARKEIT |
| 7029 | **INTERCOMMUNICATING POROSITY** | POROSITE A COMMUNICATION INTERNE | VERBUNDPOROSITÄT |
| 7030 | **INTERCRYSTALLINE CORROSION** | CORROSION INTERCRISTALLINE, CORROSION INTERGRANULAIRE | KORROSION (INTERKRISTALLINE), KORNGRENZENBRUCH |
| 7031 | **INTERDENDRITIC ATTACK** | ATTAQUE INTERDENDRITIQUE | ANGRIFF (INTERDENDRITISCHER) |
| 7032 | **INTERFACE** | INTERFACE | ZWISCHENFLÄCHE |
| 7033 | **INTERFACIAL TENSION** | TENSION SUPERFICIELLE | OBERFLÄCHENSPANNUNG |
| 7034 | **INTERFACIAL ZONE** | ZONE DE SURFACE DE SEPARATION | TRENNUNGSFLÄCHENGEBIET |
| 7035 | **INTERFERENCE** | INTERFERENCE | INTERFERENZ |
| 7036 | **INTERFERENCE BAND** | BANDE D'INTERFERENCE | INTERFERENZSTREIFEN |
| 7037 | **INTERFERENCE COLOUR** | COULEUR D'INTERFERENCE | INTERFERENZFARBE |
| 7038 | **INTERFERENCE COMPARATOR** | COMPARATEUR INTERFERENTIEL | INTERFERENZKOMPARATOR |
| 7039 | **INTERFERENCE FIGURE** | FIGURE D'INTERFERENCE | INTERFERENZFIGUR |
| 7040 | **INTERFERENCE FRINGE** | FRANGE D'INTERFERENCE | INTERFERENZSTREIFEN |
| 7041 | **INTERGRANULAR CORROSION** | CORROSION INTERCRISTALLINE, CORROSION FISSURANTE | KORROSION (INTERKRISTALLINE) |
| 7042 | **INTERGRANULAR FRACTURE** | CASSURE INTERGRANULAIRE | KORNGRENZENBRUCH |
| 7043 | **INTERMEDIARY PRODUCT** | PRODUIT INTERMEDIAIRE | ZWISCHENERZEUGNIS, ZWISCHENPRODUKT |
| 7044 | **INTERMEDIATE BEARING, AUXILIARY BEARING** | PALIER AUXILIAIRE, PALIER SECONDAIRE | NEBENLAGER |
| 7045 | **INTERMEDIATE BELT GEARING, BELT COUNTERSHAFT** | RENVOI A COURROIE | RIEMENVORGELEGE |
| 7046 | **INTERMEDIATE COOLER** | REFROIDISSEUR INTERNE | KÜHLKÖRPER (EINGEGOSSENER) |
| 7047 | **INTERMEDIATE GIRDER** | RAIDISSEUR INTERMEDIAIRE | ZWISCHENTRÄGER |
| 7048 | **INTERMEDIATE LANDING** | PALIER INTERMEDIAIRE | ZWISCHENPODEST |
| 7049 | **INTERMEDIATE SHAFT, SUBSIDARY SHAFT** | ARBRE INTERMEDIAIRE, ARBRE TROISIEME MOTEUR | ZWISCHENWELLE, HILFSWELLE, ÜBERTRAGUNGSWELLE |

**INT** 180

| | | | |
|---|---|---|---|
| 7050 | INTERMEDIATE TOOTHED GEARING, GEARED COUNTERSHAFT | ENGRENAGE INTERMEDIAIRE, RENVOI A ENGRENAGES, HARNAIS D'ENGRENAGES | RÄDERVORGELEGE, ZAHNRADVORGELEGE |
| 7051 | INTERMEDIATE VALUE | VALEUR INTERMEDIAIRE | ZWISCHENWERT |
| 7052 | INTERMETALLIC COMPOUND | COMPOSE INTERMETALLIQUE | INTERMETALLISCHE VERBINDUNG |
| 7053 | INTERMITTENT MOTION | MOUVEMENT INTERMITTENT, MOUVEMENT DISCONTINU, MOUVEMENT SACCADE | BEWEGUNG (AUSSETZENDE), BEWEGUNG (UNTERBROCHENE), BEWEGUNG (STOSSWEISE), BEWEGUNG (RUCKWEISE), BEWEGUNG (INTERMITTIERENDE) |
| 7054 | INTERMITTENT WELD | SOUDURE INTERMITTENTE | NAHT (UNTERBROCHENE) |
| 7055 | INTERMITTENT WELDING | SOUDURE DISCONTINUE | NAHT (UNTERBROCHENE) |
| 7056 | INTERMITTENT WORKING, INTERMITTENT RUNNING | FONCTIONNEMENT INTERMITTENT, SERVICE INTERMITTENT | BETRIEB (AUSSETZENDER), BETRIEB (INTERMITTIERENDER) |
| 7057 | INTERNAL ANGLE | ANGLE INTERIEUR, ANGLE INTERNE | INNENWINKEL |
| 7058 | INTERNAL ANNULAR GEARING | ENGRENAGE INTERIEUR | GETRIEBE MIT INNENVERZAHNUNG, INNENGETRIEBE |
| 7059 | INTERNAL BURR REMOVER FOR TUBES | FRAISE EBARBEUSE MALE, FRAISE D'INTERIEUR POUR TUBES | ROHRFRÄSER ZUM INNENFRÄSEN |
| 7060 | INTERNAL CHASER | PEIGNE POUR L'INTERIEUR, PEIGNE A TARAUDER | INNENSTRÄHLER |
| 7061 | INTERNAL COMBUSTION ENGINE | MOTEUR A COMBUSTION INTERNE, MOTEUR A EXPLOSIONS | VERBRENNUNGSMOTOR |
| 7062 | INTERNAL COMBUSTION ENGINE | MOTEUR A COMBUSTION INTERNE | VERBRENNUNGSMOTOR |
| 7063 | INTERNAL DISPLACEMENT | DEPLACEMENT INTERNE | VERSCHIEBUNG (INNERE) |
| 7064 | INTERNAL FORCE | FORCE INTERIEURE | KRAFT (INNERE) |
| 7065 | INTERNAL FRICTION | FRICTION INTERNE, FROTTEMENT INTERNE | REIBUNG (INNERE), DÄMPFUNG (INNERE) |
| 7066 | INTERNAL GAUGE | JAUGE D'INTERIEUR | LOCHLEHRE |
| 7067 | INTERNAL GEARS | ENGRENAGES INTERIEURS | INNENGETRIEBE |
| 7068 | INTERNAL GRINDER | MACHINE A RECTIFIER LES SURFACES INTERIEURES | HOHLSCHLEIFMASCHINE, INNENSCHLEIFMASCHINE |
| 7069 | INTERNAL GRINDING | RECTIFICATION INTERIEURE | INNENSCHLIFF |
| 7070 | INTERNAL HEATING | CHALEUR INTERNE | WÄRME (INNERE) |
| 7071 | INTERNAL INSIDE DIAMETER | DIAMETRE INTERIEUR | DURCHMESSER (INNERER) |
| 7072 | INTERNAL RESISTANCE | RESISTANCE INTERNE | WIDERSTAND (INNERER) |
| 7073 | INTERNAL SHRINKAGE | CAVITE, RETASSURE | INNENLUNKER |
| 7074 | INTERNAL STRESS | TENSION INTERNE | SPANNUNG (INNERE) |
| 7075 | INTERNAL STRESSES IN CASTINGS, STRESSES SET UP IN CASTINGS | TENSIONS INTERNES DANS LA FONTE | GUSSSPANNUNG |
| 7076 | INTERNAL TAPER GAUGE | JAUGE-TAMPON CONIQUE | KEGELLEHRDORN |
| 7077 | INTERNAL TEETH | DENTURE INTERIEURE | INNENVERZAHNUNG |
| 7078 | INTERNAL THREAD | FILET (AGE) INTERIEUR, TARAUDAGE (INTERIEUR) | INNENGEWINDE |
| 7079 | INTERNAL TOOTHED WHEEL, ANNULAR WHEEL | ROUE A DENTURE INTERIEURE | HOHLZAHNRAD |
| 7080 | INTERNAL WELDING | SOUDAGE INTERIEUR | INNENSCHWEISSEN |
| 7081 | INTERNAL WORK | TRAVAIL INTERIEUR | ARBEIT (INNERE) |
| 7082 | INTERNALLY RIBBED TUBE | TUBE A AILETTES INTERIEURES | RIPPENROHR MIT INNENRIPPEN |
| 7083 | INTERNATIONAL METRIC TAREAD | FILET METRIQUE INTERNATIONAL | GEWINDE (INTERNATIONALES METRISCHES) |
| 7084 | INTERNATIONAL STANDARD THREAD, MILLIMETRE PITCH THREAD, METRIC THREAD | PAS SYSTEME INTERNATIONAL A BASE METRIQUE (S.I.) | GEWINDE (METRISCHES, INTERNATIONALES), S-I-GEWINDE |
| 7085 | INTERPASS ANNEALING | RECUIT INTERMEDIAIRE ENTRE DEUX ETIRAGES | GLÜHEN ZWISCHEN ZWEI ZÜGEN |

**181**          **ION**

| | | | |
|---|---|---|---|
| 7086 | **INTERPASS TEMPERATURE** | TEMPERATURE DE LA PASSE INTERMEDIAIRE | ZWISCHENLAGENTEMPERATUR |
| 7087 | **INTERPLANAR DISTANCE** | DISTANCE RETICULAIRE | NETZEBENEN-ABSTAND |
| 7088 | **INTERPOLATE (TO)** | INTERPOLER | EINSCHALTEN, INTERPOLIEREN |
| 7089 | **INTERPOLATION** | INTERPOLATION | EINSCHALTUNG, INTERPOLATION |
| 7090 | **INTERRUPT THE ELECTRIC CURRENT (TO), BREAK (TO)** | COUPER LE COURANT, INTERROMPRE LE CIRCUIT ELECTRIQUE | ELEKTRISCHEN STROM UNTERBRECHEN (DEN) |
| 7091 | **INTERRUPTED AGING** | VIEILLISSEMENT INTERROMPU | ALTERUNG (UNTERBROCHENE) |
| 7092 | **INTERRUPTION OF SERVICE, STOPPAGE OF WORK** | INTERRUPTION DE SERVICE, ARRET D'USINE, CHOMAGE | BETRIEBSUNTERBRECHUNG |
| 7093 | **INTERRUPTION OF THE ELECTRIC CURRENT, BREAK** | INTERRUPTION DE PASSAGE DU COURANT ELECTRIQUE | STROMUNTERBRECHUNG, UNTERBRECHUNG DES ELEKTRISCHEN STROMES |
| 7094 | **INTERSECT (TO)** | COUPER (SE) (GEOM.) | SCHNEIDEN (SICH) (GEOM.) |
| 7095 | **INTERSECTING PLANE** | PLAN D'INTERSECTION | SCHNITTEBENE |
| 7096 | **INTERSECTING SHAFTS** | ARBRES CONCOURANTS | SCHNEIDENDE WELLEN (SICH) |
| 7097 | **INTERSECTION RADIOGRAPHIC CONTROL** | RADIO DES NOEUDS DE SOUDURE | RADIOGRAMM EINER SCHWEISSNAHT |
| 7098 | **INTERSTAND** | CAGE MEDIANE | MITTEL-(WALZ-)GERÜST |
| 7099 | **INTERURBAN BUS** | AUTOCAR | ÜBERLANDBUS |
| 7100 | **INTERVAL** | ARRET DE SERVICE, REPOS | BETRIEBSPAUSE, ARBEITSPAUSE |
| 7101 | **INTERVAL, SPACE OF TIME** | INTERVALLE | ZWISCHENZEIT, ZEITSTRECKE, INTERVALL |
| 7102 | **INTIMATE THOROUGH MIXING** | MELANGE INTIME | INNIGES MISCHEN, DURCHMISCHEN |
| 7103 | **INTRA-RED RAYS** | RAYONS INFRA-ROUGES | STRAHLEN (INFRAROTE) |
| 7104 | **INTRINSIC BRIGHTNESS** | INTENSITE LUMINEUSE PAR UNITE DE SURFACE | LEUCHTDICHTE, FLÄCHENHELLIGKEIT |
| 7105 | **INVAR** | METAL INVAR, INVAR | INVAR |
| 7106 | **INVARIANT** | INVARIANT | INVARIANTE |
| 7107 | **INVENTION** | INVENTION | ERFINDUNG |
| 7108 | **INVENTOR** | INVENTEUR, AUTEUR D'UNE INVENTION | ERFINDER |
| 7109 | **INVERSE CHILL** | TREMPE INVERSE | HARTGUSS (UMGEKEHRTER) |
| 7110 | **INVERSION** | INVERSION (MATH.) | UMKEHRUNG, INVERSION |
| 7111 | **INVERTED PLUG VALVE** | ROBINET A BOISSEAU RENVERSE | HAHN (SELBSTDICHTENDER) |
| 7112 | **INVERTED TROUGH IRON** | FER POUR TABLIERS DE PONT, FER ZORES | BELAGEISEN, ZORESEISEN |
| 7113 | **INVERTED WELDING** | SOUDAGE AU PLAFOND | ÜBERKOPFSCHWEISSEN |
| 7114 | **INVESTIGATION, EXAMINATION, RESEARCH WITH THE MICROSCOPE, MICROSCOPIC EXAMINATION** | EXAMEN MICROSCOPIQUE | UNTERSUCHUNG (MIKROSKOPISCHE), BEOBACHTUNG |
| 7115 | **INVESTMENT CASTING** | MOULAGE A CIRE PERDUE | GIESSEN MIT VERLORENER GIESSFORM, INVESTMENTGUSS |
| 7116 | **INVESTMENT PATTERN** | MODELE A CIRE PERDUE | AUSSCHMELZMODELL |
| 7117 | **INVOLUTE** | DEVELOPPANTE | EVOLVENTE, INVOLUTE |
| 7118 | **INVOLUTE OF THE CIRCLE** | DEVELOPPANTE DU CERCLE | KREISEVOLVENTE |
| 7119 | **INVOLUTE TEETH** | ENGRENAGE A DEVELOPPANTE DE CERCLE | EVOLVENTENVERZAHNUNG |
| 7120 | **IODINE** | IODE | JOD |
| 7121 | **ION** | ION | ION |
| 7122 | **ION CONCENTRATION** | CONCENTRATION D'IONS | IONENKONZENTRATION |
| 7123 | **ION MIGRATION** | MIGRATION D'IONS | IONENWANDERUNG |
| 7124 | **IONIZATION** | IONISATION | IONISATION, IONISIERUNG |

**ION** 182

| 7125 | IONIZATION CHAMBER | CHAMBRE D'IONISATION | IONISATIONSKAMMER |
|---|---|---|---|
| 7126 | IONIZATION CHAMBER CURRENT | COURANT DE LA CHAMBRE D'IONISATION | KAMMERSTROM (IONISATION) |
| 7127 | IONIZATION METHOD | METHODE D'IONISATION | IONISATIONSMETHODE |
| 7128 | IONIZED REGION | ZONE IONISEE | ZONE (IONISIERTE) |
| 7129 | IONOGEN | IONOGENE | IONOGEN |
| 7130 | IONOGEN SOLVENT | SOLVANT IONOGENE | LÖSUNGSMITTEL (IONISIERENDES) |
| 7131 | IRIDIUM | IRIDIUM | IRIDIUM |
| 7132 | IRIS DIAPHRAGM | DIAPHRAGME IRIS | IRISBLENDE |
| 7133 | IRON | FER | EISEN |
| 7134 | IRON ACETATE | ACETATE DE FER | ESSIGSAURES EISEN, EISENAZETAT |
| 7135 | IRON ALUM | ALUN DE FER | EISENALAUN |
| 7136 | IRON AND SECTION IRON SHEARING MACHINE | MACHINE A CISAILLER LES FERS ET PROFILES | EISEN- UND FORMSTAHLSCHEREN |
| 7137 | IRON ANGLES FROM REROLLED SCRAP | CORNIERES DE FER AU PAQUET | WINKELEISEN AUS PAKETEISEN |
| 7138 | IRON CARBIDE | CARBURE DE FER | EISENKARBID |
| 7139 | IRON CARBON DIAGRAM | DIAGRAMME FER-CARBURE | EISEN-KOHLENSTOFF-DIAGRAMM |
| 7140 | IRON CARBONYL | CARBONYLE DE FER | EISENKARBONYL |
| 7141 | IRON CEMENT | MASTIC DE FER, MASTIC POUR FONTE | ROSTKITT, EISENKITT |
| 7142 | IRON FOUNDRY | FONDERIE DE FER/DE FONTE | EISENGIESSEREI |
| 7143 | IRON ORE | MINERAI DE FER | EISENERZ |
| 7144 | IRON OXIDE | OXYDE DE FER | EISENOXYD |
| 7145 | IRON POWDER | POUDRE DE FER | EISENPULVER |
| 7146 | IRON PYRITES, IRON DISULPHIDE | PYRITE JAUNE, MARTIALE | SCHWEFELKIES, EISENKIES, PYRIT |
| 7147 | IRON ROPE | CABLE EN FILS DE FER | EISENDRAHTSEIL |
| 7148 | IRON SESQUIOXIDE, FERRIC OXIDE, COLCOTHAR | PEROXYDE, SESQUIOXYDE DE FER, OXYDE FERRIQUE, ROUGE DE PRUSSE, ROUGE ANGLAIS, ROUGE A POLIR, COLCOTHAR | ENGLISCHROT, POLIERROT, KOLKOTHAR, EISENSESQUIOXYD, EINSEMENNIGE |
| 7149 | IRON SILICATE | SILICATE DE FER | EISENSILIKAT |
| 7150 | IRON SLEEPER | TRAVERSE EN FER | EISENSCHWELLE |
| 7151 | IRON SPONGE | EPONGE DE FER | EISENSCHWAMM |
| 7152 | IRON STEEL STRUCTURE | CONSTRUCTION METALLIQUE, CHARPENTE METALLIQUE | EISENBAU, EISENKONSTRUKTION |
| 7153 | IRON SULFIDE | SULFURE FERREUX/FERRIQUE | EISENSULFID |
| 7154 | IRON TOOTH | DENT EN FONTE | EISENZAHN |
| 7155 | IRON WIRE | FIL DE FER | EISENDRAHT |
| 7156 | IRON-BASE ALLOY | ALLIAGE DE FER | EISENLEGIERUNG |
| 7157 | IRON, CAST IRON | FONTE | GUSSEISEN |
| 7158 | IRONING | EMBOUTISSAGE PROFOND | TIEFZIEHEN |
| 7159 | IRONWORK (FITTINGS, MOUNTINGS) | FERRURE | BESCHLAG, EISENBESCHLAG, BESCHLÄGE |
| 7160 | IRONWORKS | FORGE (USINE) | EISENHÜTTE, EISENWERK |
| 7161 | IRRADIATION | IRRADIATION | BESTRAHLUNG |
| 7162 | IRRATIONAL NUMBER | NOMBRE IRRATIONNEL/ INCOMMENSURABLE | ZAHL (IRRATIONALE) |
| 7163 | IRREGULAR | IRREGULIER | UNREGELMÄSSIG |
| 7164 | IRREGULAR POLYGON | POLYGONE IRREGULIER | POLYGON (UNREGELMÄSSIGES), POLYGON (IRREGULÄRES) |
| 7165 | IRREGULAR RUNNING | MARCHE IRREGULIERE, BOITEMENT | GANG (UNRUHIGER) |
| 7166 | IRREGULAR TRACE, LINE WITH SHARP TURNS | LIGNE BRISEE | LINIE (GEBROCHENE) |

| | | | |
|---|---|---|---|
| 7167 | **IRREGULARITY OF MOTION** | IRREGULARITE DU MOUVEMENT | UNGLEICHFÖRMIGKEIT DER BEWEGUNG |
| 7168 | **IRREVERSIBILITY** | IRREVERSIBILITE, NON-REVERSIBILITE | NICHTUMKEHRBARKEIT |
| 7169 | **IRREVERSIBLE** | IRREVERSIBLE, NON-REVERSIBLE | NICHT UMKEHRBAR |
| 7170 | **IRREVERSIBLE CHANGE OF STATE** | CHANGEMENT D'ETAT NON REVERSIBLE | ZUSTANDSÄNDERUNG (NICHTUMKEHRBARE) |
| 7171 | **IRREVERSIBLE ELECTROLYTIC PROCESS** | REACTION ELECTROLYTIQUE IRREVERSIBLE | REAKTION (IRREVERSIBEL ELEKTROLYTISCHE) |
| 7172 | **IRRIGATION PLANT** | MATERIEL D'IRRIGATION | BEWÄSSERUNGSANLAGEN |
| 7173 | **ISENTROPIC LINE** | LIGNE ISENTROPIQUE | ISENTROPE |
| 7174 | **ISINGLASS, FISH GLUE** | COLLE DE POISSON, ICHTYOCOLLE | HAUSENBLASE, FISCHLEIM |
| 7175 | **ISO ELECTRIC POINT** | POINT ISO-ELECTRIQUE | PUNKT (ISOELEKTRISCHER) |
| 7176 | **ISOBAR** | ISOBARE | ISOBARE |
| 7177 | **ISOBAR, ISOPIESTIC LINE** | COURBE ISOBARIQUE | LINIE GLEICHEN DRUCKES, ISOBARE |
| 7178 | **ISOCHRONISM** | ISOCHRONISME | ISOCHRONISMUS |
| 7179 | **ISOCHRONOUS** | ISOCHRONE | ISOCHRON |
| 7180 | **ISOCHRONOUS GOVERNOR** | REGULATEUR ISOCHRONE | REGLER (ISOCHRONER) |
| 7181 | **ISOCLINIC LINE** | LIGNE ISOCLINE | ISOKLINE |
| 7182 | **ISODYNAMIC LINE** | LIGNE ISODYNAME, LIGNE ISODYNAMIQUE | KURVE (ISODYNAME), KURVE (ISODYNAMISCHE) |
| 7183 | **ISOLATED, CONCENTRATED LOAD** | CHARGE ISOLEE | EINZELLAST |
| 7184 | **ISOLATION** | ISOLATION | ISOLIERUNG, ABTRENNUNG |
| 7185 | **ISOMERICAL** | ISOMERE | ISOMER |
| 7186 | **ISOMERISM** | ISOMERIE | ISOMERISMUS, ISOMERIE |
| 7187 | **ISOMETRIC LINE, ISOPLERE** | ISOPLERE, LIGNE COURBE DE VOLUME CONSTANT | LINIE GLEICHEN RAUMINHALTES, ISOPLERE |
| 7188 | **ISOMETRIC PROJECTION** | PROJECTION ISOMETRIQUE | PROJEKTION (ISOMETRISCHE) |
| 7189 | **ISOMORPHISM** | ISOMORPHIE | ISOMORPHIE, ISOMORPHISMUS |
| 7190 | **ISOMORPHOUS** | ISOMORPHE | ISOMORPH |
| 7191 | **ISOMORPHOUS MIXTURE** | ISOMORPHISME | HOMÖOMORPHIE, ISOMORPHISMUS |
| 7192 | **ISOSCELES TRIANGLE** | TRIANGLE ISOCELE | DREIECK (GLEICHSCHENKLIGES) |
| 7193 | **ISOTHERMAL CURVE** | LIGNE COURBE ISOTHERMIQUE | ISOTHERME |
| 7194 | **ISOTHERMAL HEAT TREATING** | TRAITEMENT ISOTHERME | BEHANDLUNG (ISOTHERMISCHE) |
| 7195 | **ISOTHERMAL QUENCHING** | TREMPE ISOTHERME | HÄRTUNG (ISOTHERMISCHE) |
| 7196 | **ISOTHERMAL TRANSFORMATION** | TRANSFORMATION ISOTHERME | UMWANDLUNG (ISOTHERMISCHE) |
| 7197 | **ISOTOPES** | ISOTOPES | ISOTOPEN |
| 7198 | **ISOTROPIC** | ISOTROPE | ISOTROP |
| 7199 | **IVORY** | IVOIRE | ELFENBEIN |
| 7200 | **IZOD IMPACT TEST** | ESSAI IZOD | IZOD-PROBE |
| 7201 | **JACK PLANE** | RIFLARD | SCHROPPHOBEL, SCHROBHOBEL, SCHRUPPHOBEL, SCHROTHOBEL, SCHURFHOBEL, SCHÜRFHOBEL |
| 7202 | **JACK SHAFT** | ARBRE INTERMEDIAIRE | ZWISCHENWELLE |
| 7203 | **JACKET** | FRETTE | SCHRUMPFRING |
| 7204 | **JACKET COOLING** | REFROIDISSEMENT PAR CHEMISE D'EAU | ABKÜHLUNG MIT WASSERMANTEL |
| 7205 | **JACKETED VALVE** | VANNE A ENVELOPPE CHAUFFANTE | HEIZMANTELSCHIEBER |
| 7206 | **JACKING BRACKET LUGS** | PATTES DE LEVAGE PAR VERINS | HEBESTUTZEN |
| 7207 | **JACKING SHOE** | SABOT POUR DISPOSITIF DE LEVAGE | SCHUH FÜR HEBEVORRICHTUNG |
| 7208 | **JACOBS COLLET CHUCK** | MANDRIN EXPANSIBLE JACOBS | JACOBS-SPREIZZANGENFUTTER |

**JAM** 184

| | | | |
|---|---|---|---|
| 7209 | JAG BOLT | BOULON DE SCELLEMENT A BARBELURES | STEINSCHRAUBE MIT AUFGEHAUENEN KANTEN |
| 7210 | JAM (TO) | COINCER (SE) | KLEMMEN (SICH), ECKEN, HÄNGENBLEIBEN |
| 7211 | JAMB | MONTANT LATERAL D'ENTREE | TÜRSTEIN |
| 7212 | JAMMING | COINCEMENT, PINCEMENT | ECKEN, KLEMMEN |
| 7213 | JAPAN WAX | CIRE DU JAPON | WACHS (JAPANISCHES) |
| 7214 | JAPANNING | REVETEMENT AVEC VERNIS FIN | BRANDLACKIEREN |
| 7215 | JARRING MACHINE | MACHINE A MOULER RAPIDE A SECOUSSES | RÜTTELFORMMASCHINE |
| 7216 | JAW OF WRENCH | MACHOIRE DE CLEF, PAND D'UNE CLEF | BACKEN EINES SCHRAUBENSCHLÜSSELS |
| 7217 | JENA GLASS | VERRE D'IENA | JENAER GLAS |
| 7218 | JET | GICLEUR | DÜSE |
| 7219 | JET CARRIER | PORTE-GICLEUR | DÜSENTRÄGER |
| 7220 | JET CONDENSER | CONDENSEUR PAR INJECTION | EINSPRITZKONDENSATOR |
| 7221 | JET OF FLUID | JET LIQUIDE | FLÜSSIGKEITSSTRAHL |
| 7222 | JET PIERCING | PERCAGE PAR JET DE FLAMME | STRAHLDÜSENBOHREN |
| 7223 | JET PUMP | INJECTEUR | STRAHLPUMPE |
| 7224 | JIB CRANE | GRUE A FLECHE | AUSLEGERKRAN |
| 7225 | JIB LENGTH | LONGUEUR DE LA FLECHE | AUSLERGERLÄNGE |
| 7226 | JIB OF A CRANE | FLECHE PRINCIPALE D'UNE GRUE | HAUPTAUSLEGER |
| 7227 | JIG | DISPOSITIF DE FIXATION, DISPOSITIF DE SERRAGE | EINSPANNVORRICHTUNG |
| 7228 | JIG BORING MACHINE | MACHINE A POINTER | LEHRENBOHRMASCHINE |
| 7229 | JOB | AFFAIRE | ARBEIT, GESCHÄFT |
| 7230 | JOBBING FOUNDRY | FONDERIE SUR MODELES | KUNDENGIESSEREI |
| 7231 | JOGGLE JOINT | RENVOI A LA CHASSE | ZAPFENFUGE |
| 7232 | JOGGLING MACHINES | MACHINES A COUDER | KRÖPFMASCHINEN |
| 7233 | JOINER | MENUISIER | SCHREINER, TISCHLER |
| 7234 | JOINER'S BENCH | ETABLI, BANC DE MENUISIER | HOBELBANK |
| 7235 | JOINER'S SHOP | MENUISERIE (ATELIER) | SCHREINEREI, TISCHLEREI (WERKSTÄTTE) |
| 7236 | JOINERY | MENUISERIE | TISCHLEREI, SCHREINEREI (HANDWERK) |
| 7237 | JOINT | JOINT SOUDE | SCHWEISSVERBINDUNG |
| 7238 | JOINT (MEC.) | JOINT (POINT DE JONCTION), ARTICULATION (MEC.) | STOSSSTELLE, STOSS, FUGE, GELENK (MECH.) |
| 7239 | JOINT DISTRIBUTION FUNCTION | FONCTION DE REPARTITION COMPOSEE | VERTEILUNG (MEHRDIMENSIONALE) |
| 7240 | JOINT GEOMETRY | GEOMETRIE DU JOINT | VERBINDUNGSGEOMETRIE |
| 7241 | JOINT OF BEARING | JOINT DE SEPARATION D'UN PALIER | LAGERFUGE, TEILFUGE, TRENNUNGSFUGE EINES LAGERS |
| 7242 | JOINT PIN, LINK PIN | TOURILLON D'ARTICULATION | GELENKZAPFEN, GELENKBOLZEN |
| 7243 | JOINT PIPES WITH FLANGES (TO), CONNECT PIPES IN LINE WITH FLANGES (TO) | BRIDER DES TUYAUX | ROHRE DURCH FLANSCHEN VERBINDEN |
| 7244 | JOINT UP PIPES (TO) | RACCORDER DES TUYAUX | ROHRE VERBINDEN |
| 7245 | JOINTER PLANE | VARLOPE | RAUHBANK, LANGHOBEL |
| 7246 | JOINTER, JOINTING MACHINE | MACHINE A FAIRE LES JOINTS | FÜGEMASCHINE |
| 7247 | JOINTING MATERIAL, PACKING MATERIAL | MATIERE POUR JOINT, JOINT, BOURRAGE | DICHTUNGSMITTEL, DICHTUNGSSTOFF, DICHTUNGSMATERIAL |
| 7248 | JOINTING PIPES, CONNECTING TOGETHER LENGTHS OF PIPING | RACCORDEMENT DE TUYAUX | VERBINDEN VON ROHREN |

**KEY**

**185**

| | | | |
|---|---|---|---|
| 7249 | JOLT AND JUMBLE TEST | ESSAI DE CHOC ET BALLOTTEMENT | STOSS-UND RÜTTELPRÜFUNG |
| 7250 | JOLT MOLDING MACHINE | MACHINE A MOULER A SECOUSSES | RÜTTELFORM-MASCHINE |
| 7251 | JOLT ROLL-OVER MOLDING MACHINE | MACHINE A MOULER A SECOUSSES AVEC PLAQUE REVERSIBLE | UMROLL-RÜTTELFORM MASCHINE |
| 7252 | JOLT-SQUEEZE MACHINE | MACHINE A SERRAGE PAR SECOUSSE ET PRESSION SANS DEMOULAGE | RÜTTELPRESS-FORMMASCHINE OHNE ENTFORMUNG |
| 7253 | JOLT-SQUEEZE STRIPPER MACHINE | MACHINE A MOULER A SECOUSSES ET A SERRAGE COMBINES AVEC DEMOULAGE | RÜTTELPRESSFORMMASCHINE |
| 7254 | JOMINY TEST | ESSAI JOMINY, ESSAI DE REBONDISSEMENT BRUSQUE | JOMINY-PROBE, STIRNABSCHRECKPROBE |
| 7255 | JOULE | JOULE, VOLT-COULOMB | JOULE |
| 7256 | JOURNAL | PORTEE, TOURILLON | DREHZAPFEN, ZAPFEN, TRAGZAPFEN |
| 7257 | JOURNAL BEARING | PALIER A CHARGE RADIALE/ TRANSVERSALE | TRAGLAGER, QUERDRUCKLAGER |
| 7258 | JOURNAL FRICTION | FROTTEMENT DES TOURILLONS | ZAPFENREIBUNG |
| 7259 | JOURNAL PRESSURE | PRESSION/REACTION SUR LES TOURILLONS | ZAPFENDRUCK |
| 7260 | JUMP SCAFFOLD | ECHAFAUDAGE VOLANT | SPRUNGGERÜST |
| 7261 | JUMP SEAT | STRAPONTIN | KLAPPSITZ |
| 7262 | JUMP TEST | ESSAI D'ECRASEMENT | STAUCHVERSUCH |
| 7263 | JUMP UP (TO), UPSET (TO) | ECRASER, REFOULER | ZUSAMMENSTAUCHEN |
| 7264 | JUMPER CABLE | CABLE VOLANT | SCHALTDRAHT |
| 7265 | JUMPING UP, UPSETTING | ECRASEMENT, REFOULEMENT, REFOULAGE | ZUSAMMENSTAUCHEN |
| 7266 | JUNK RING | COUVERCLE DU PISTON | KOLBENDECKEL |
| 7267 | JURASSIC LIMESTONE | CALCAIRE JURASSIQUE | JURAKALK |
| 7268 | JUTE | JUTE | JUTE |
| 7269 | K-FACTOR (THERMAL CONDUCTIVITY) | COEFFICIENT CALORIFIQUE (OU DE CONDUCTIVITE THERMIQUE) | WÄRMELEITZAHL |
| 7270 | KAHLBAUM IRON | FER KAHLBAUM | KAHLBAUM-EISEN |
| 7271 | KALDO PROCESS | PROCEDE FOUR KALDO | KALDOVERFAHREN |
| 7272 | KALE CUTTERS | COUPE-RAVES | BLATTKOHLSCHNEIDER |
| 7273 | KEELBLOCK | LINGOT-EPROUVETTE (EN FORME DE QUILLE DE NAVIRE) | KIELBLOCK, KIELKLOTZ |
| 7274 | KERF | SAIGNEE | SCHNITTFUGE |
| 7275 | KEROSENE OIL, PARAFFIN OIL, COMMON LAMP OIL, ILLUMINATING OIL | HUILE LAMPANTE DE PETROLE, HUILE D'ECLAIRAGE, PETROLE LAMPANT, KEROSENE | LEUCHTÖL, LEUCHTPETROLEUM |
| 7276 | KEY | CHEVILLE, CLAVETTE, CLAVETTE LONGITUDINALE | DÜBEL, KEIL, LÄNGSKEIL |
| 7277 | KEY (TO), WEDGE (TO) | CLAVETER, CALER | VERKEILEN |
| 7278 | KEY DRIFT | CHASSE-CLAVETTE | KEILTREIBER |
| 7279 | KEY ON TO (TO) | CLAVETER, CALER SUR... | AUFKEILEN |
| 7280 | KEY PLATE | CLAME D'ASSEMBLAGE | SPANNFINGER |
| 7281 | KEY WAY MILLING MACHINE | MACHINE A FRAISER LES RAINURES | LANGLOCHFRÄSMASCHINE, KEILNUTENFRÄSMASCHINE, NUTENFRÄSMASCHINE |
| 7282 | KEY WAY, KEY BED, KEY SCATING | RAINURE, CANNELURE, LOGEMENT D'UNE CLAVETTE, MORTAISE A CLAVETTE, RAINURE DE CLAVETAGE | KEILNUT, KEILRILLE |
| 7283 | KEY-SEAT GAUGE | JAUGE POUR RAINURE DE CLAVETTE | KEILNUTENSCHABLONE |

# KEY

186

| | | | |
|---|---|---|---|
| 7284 | KEY, FIXED SPANNER | CLEF DE CALIBRE, CLEF A FOURCHE | SCHRAUBENSCHLÜSSEL (GEWÖHNLICHER) |
| 7285 | KEYED JOINT, COTTERED JOINT | ASSEMBLAGE PAR CLAVETTE | KEILVERBINDUNG |
| 7286 | KEYHEAD | TALON DE CLAVETTE | KEILNASE |
| 7287 | KEYHOLE | TROU DE COULEE | SCHLÜSSELOCH, STICHLOCH |
| 7288 | KEYING | CLAVETAGE | KEILVERBINDUNG |
| 7289 | KEYSEAT CLAMPS | BRIDES DE MORTAISAGE | KEILNUTENFLANSCHEN |
| 7290 | KEYSEAT RULES | REGLES DE MORTAISAGE | KEILNUTENSCHABLONE |
| 7291 | KEYWAY | RAINURE DE CLAVETTE | KEILNUT |
| 7292 | KIESELGUHR, DIATOM EARTH, DIATOMITE, MOUNTAIN MEAL, FOSSIL MEAL | KIESELGUHR, TRIPOLI SILICEUX, FARINE FOSSILE, SILICE FARINEUSE, TERRE POURRIE, TERRE D'INFUSOIRES | KIESELGUR, INFUSORIENERDE, DIATOMEENERDE |
| 7293 | KILLED SPIRITS, SOLUTION OF ZINC CHLORIDE | EAU A SOUDER, LIQUIDE DE DECAPAGE, ESPRIT DE SEL DENATURE | LÖTWASSER |
| 7294 | KILLED STEEL | ACIER CALME | BERUHIGTER STAHL |
| 7295 | KILN | FOUR DE CALCINATION | BRENNOFEN |
| 7296 | KILODYNE | KILODYNE | KILODYN |
| 7297 | KILOGRAMME | KILOGRAMME | KILOGRAMM, KILO |
| 7298 | KILOGRAMME CALORIE, MAJOR CALORIE | GRANDE CALORIE, CALORIE KILOGRAMME-DEGRE | KILOGRAMMLKALORIE |
| 7299 | KILOGRAMMETRE (KGM) | KILOGRAMMETRE | METERKILOGRAMM, KILOGRAMMETER, MKG |
| 7300 | KILOMETER | KILOMETRE | KILOMETER |
| 7301 | KILOVOLT | KILOVOLT | KILOVOLT |
| 7302 | KILOVOLT-AMPERE | KILOVOLT-AMPERE | KILOVOLTAMPERE |
| 7303 | KILOWATT | KILOWATT | KILOWATT |
| 7304 | KILOWATT/OUR (KW/HR), BOARD OF TRADE UNIT (B.T.U.), KELVIN | KILOWATT-HEURE | KILOWATTSTUNDE |
| 7305 | KINEMATICAL | CINEMATIQUE | KINEMATISCH |
| 7306 | KINEMATICS | CINEMATIQUE | GETRIEBELEHRE, KINEMATIK |
| 7307 | KINETIC | CINETIQUE | KINETISCH |
| 7308 | KINETIC ENERGY | ENERGIE CINETIQUE, ENERGIE ACTUELLE, PUISSANCE, FORCE VIVE | ENERGIE DER BEWEGUNG, ENERGIE (KINETISCHE), ENERGIE DYNAMISCHE, LEBENDIGE KRAFT, WUCHT |
| 7309 | KINETIC FRICTION | FROTTEMENT CINETIQUE | REIBUNGSGRENZE |
| 7310 | KINETICS | CINETIQUE | BEWEGUNGSLEHRE, KINETIK |
| 7311 | KING PIN | AXE (DE PIVOT), AXE DE PIVOTEMENT | ACHSSCHENKELBOLZEN |
| 7312 | KING PIN INCLINATION ANGLE | ANGLE D'INCLINATION DES PIVOTS | STURZ |
| 7313 | KINK | NOEUD, COQUE | KINKE, KNICK |
| 7314 | KINK BAND | BANDE DE PLIAGE | KNICKBAND |
| 7315 | KINKING | DEFORMATION EN GENOU | KNICKUNG |
| 7316 | KIP = KILOPOUND (US) | KIP = 1000 LIVRES = 453,59 KG | KIP = 1000 PFD = 453,59 KG |
| 7317 | KISH | ECUME DE GRAPHITE | GARSCHAUMGRAPHIT |
| 7318 | KLINGERIT | KLINGERITE | KLINGERIT |
| 7319 | KNEE-AND-COLUMN MILLING MACHINE | FRAISEUSE A CONSOLE ET COLONNE | KONSOL-UND SÄULENFRÄSMASCHINE |
| 7320 | KNEE, ELBOW | COUDE D'EQUERRE | KNIEROHR, KNIESTÜCK |
| 7321 | KNEE, SHOULDER | EPAULEMENT | KRÖPFUNG |
| 7322 | KNEETYPE MILLING MACHINE | MACHINE A FRAISER A CONSOLE | KONSOLFRÄSMASCHINE |
| 7323 | KNIFE | COUTEAU | MESSER |

| | | | |
|---|---|---|---|
| 7324 | **KNIFE (EDGED) FILE** | LIME-COUTEAU | MESSERFEILE |
| 7325 | **KNIFE-EDGE BEARING** | SUPPORT A COUTEAU, COUTEAU | SCHNEIDENLAGER |
| 7326 | **KNIFE-EDGE SUSPENSION** | SUSPENSION A COUTEAU | SCHNEIDENAUFHÄNGUNG |
| 7327 | **KNOCK-ON** | COLLISION (DE NEUTRONS AVEC DES ATOMES) | ANSTOSS |
| 7328 | **KNOCK-OUT** | DECOCHAGE | AUSSCHLAGEN, AUSLEEREN |
| 7329 | **KNOCKED-DOWN** | DEMONTE, PIECES DETACHEES (EN) | ZERLEGT |
| 7330 | **KNOCKING** | DETONATION, COGNEMENT | KNALL, KLOPFEN |
| 7331 | **KNOCKING OF THE PUMP** | TAPAGE D'UNE POMPE | SCHLAGEN DER PUMPE |
| 7332 | **KNOCKOUT BAR** | CHASSE-POINTE | DURCHSCHLAG |
| 7333 | **KNOCKOUT PIN (US)** | BARRE DE PIQUAGE | STOSSEISEN, BRECHSTANGE |
| 7334 | **KNOCKOUT PLATE (US)** | GRILLE DE DECOCHAGE | AUSSCHLAGROST, AUSLEERROST |
| 7335 | **KNOWN QUANTITY** | QUANTITE CONNUE | GRÖSSE (BEKANNTE) |
| 7336 | **KNUCKLE JOINT** | FERMETURE A GRENOUILLERE, ROTULE | KNIEHEBELVERCHLUSS, KNOCHENGELENK |
| 7337 | **KNURL DRIVE** | COMMAMDE PAR VIS MOLETEE | RÄNDELSCHRAUBENANTRIEB |
| 7338 | **KNURLING** | MOLETAGE | KORDELUNG, RÄNDELUNG |
| 7339 | **KRYPTON** | KRYPTON | KRYPTON |
| 7340 | **KYANISING** | IMPREGNATION DU BOIS AU SUBLIME CORROSIF PAR LE PROCEDE KYAN | KYANISIEREN DES HOLZES |
| 7341 | **L.O.I= LOSS ON IGNITION** | PERTE AU ROUGE, PERTE AU FEU | GLÜHVERLUST |
| 7342 | **L.P.G (LIQUEFIED PETROLEUM GAS)** | GAZ LIQUEFIE | FLÜSSIGGAS |
| 7343 | **LABILE** | LABILE | LABIL |
| 7344 | **LABORATORY** | LABORATOIRE | LABORATORIUM |
| 7345 | **LABORATORY SET** | JEU DE LABORATOIRE | LABORGERÄTESATZ |
| 7346 | **LABOUR COSTS, COST OF LABOUR** | FRAIS, PRIX DE MAIN-D'OEUVRE | ARBEITSKOSTEN |
| 7347 | **LABYRINTH PACKING** | GARNITURE, JOINT A LABYRINTHE, JOINT A CHICANE | LABYRINTHDICHTUNG |
| 7348 | **LACED BELT JOINT** | JONCTION DES COURROIES PAR LANIERES EN CUIR | RIEMENVERBINDUNG (GENÄHTE) |
| 7349 | **LACED LEATHER BELT FLEXIBLE COUPLING** | MANCHON A BANDE DE COURROIE | BANDKUPPKLUNG, RIEMENKUPPLUNG, LEDERRIEMENKUPPLUNG |
| 7350 | **LACED SEWED BELT** | COURROIE COUSUE | RIEMEN (GENÄHTER) |
| 7351 | **LACK OF FUSION** | COLLAGE | BINDEFEHLER |
| 7352 | **LACK OF UNIFORMITY IN THE MATERIAL** | INHOMOGENEITE D'UN MATERIEL | UNGLEICHFÖRMIGKEIT DES MATERIALS |
| 7353 | **LACQUER (TO), VARNISH (TO), COAT WITH LACQUER (TO)** | LAQUER, VERNIR | LACKIEREN |
| 7354 | **LACQUER, SPIRIT VARNISH** | LAQUE, VERNIS A L'ALCOOL | SPIRITUSLACK, LACK (ALKOHOLISCHER), WEINGEISTLAK, WEINGEISTFIRNIS, SPIRITUSFIRNIS, ALKOHOLFIRNIS |
| 7355 | **LACTIC ACID** | ACIDE LACTIQUE | MILCHSÄURE |
| 7356 | **LADLE** | POCHE DE COULEE | PFANNE, GIESSPFANNE |
| 7357 | **LADLE ADDITION** | ADDITION EN POCHE | PFANNENZUSATZ |
| 7358 | **LADLE ANALYSIS** | ANALYSE DE COULEE | PFANNENANALYSE |
| 7359 | **LADLE BRICK** | BRIQUE DE POCHE | PFANNENZIEGEL, PFANNENSTEIN |
| 7360 | **LADLE CHILL** | SOLIDIFICATION DE LA MASSE FONDUE DANS LA POCHE | ERSTARRUNG DER SCHMELZE IN DER PFANNE |
| 7361 | **LADLE LIP** | BEC DE COULEE DE LA POCHE | PFANNENAUSGUSS |
| 7362 | **LADLE MAN, LADLE POURER** | COULEUR | PFANNENFÜHRER |
| 7363 | **LADLE NOSE** | BEC DE LA POCHE DE COULEE | PFANNENAUSGUSS |
| 7364 | **LAEVO-TARTARIC ACID** | ACIDE TARTRIQUE LEVOGYRE | LINKSWEINSÄURE |

# LAG
188

| | | | |
|---|---|---|---|
| 7365 | **LAEVOROTATORY, LAEVOGYRATE** | LEVOGYRE | LINKSDREHEND |
| 7366 | **LAG (TO)** | RETARDER | NACHEILEN |
| 7367 | **LAGGING** | REVETEMENT CALORIFUGE | WÄRMESCHUTZ |
| 7368 | **LAGGING OF PHASE** | DEPHASAGE, DECALAGE EN ARRIERE | PHASENNACHEILUNG |
| 7369 | **LAGGING OF PIPES, PIPE COVERING** | RECOUVREMENT DE TUYAUX, ENVELOPPE DE TUYAUX | ROHRVERKLEIDUNG, VERKLEIDEN, UMHÜLLEN VON ROHREN |
| 7370 | **LAKE COPPER** | CUIVRE NATIF, CUIVRE DU LAC SUPERIEUR | KUPFER (GEDIEGENES), OBERSEE KUPFER, KUPFER VON LAKE-SUPERIOR-ERZEN |
| 7371 | **LAMELLA** | LAMELLE | LAMELLE |
| 7372 | **LAMELLAR** | LAMELLAIRE | LAMELLAR |
| 7373 | **LAMELLAR STRUCTURE** | STRUCTURE LAMELLAIRE | BLÄTTRIGE STRUKTUR |
| 7374 | **LAMINAR TEXTURE** | TEXTURE LAMELLEUSE | GEFÜGE (BLÄTTRIGES) |
| 7375 | **LAMINATED** | LAMINE | LAMELLIERT, GESCHICHTET |
| 7376 | **LAMINATED BELT, BELT MADE UP OF BUILT-ON EDGE STRIPS** | COURROIE EN LANIERES DE CUIR TRAVAILLANT SUR CHAMP | HOCHKANTRIEMEN, LEDERHOCKANTRIEMEN |
| 7377 | **LAMINATED COMPOUND MAGNET, MAGNETIC BATTERY** | AIMANT A LAMES SUPERPOSEES | BLÄTTERMAGNET, LAMELLENMAGNET, MAGNETISCHES MAGAZIN |
| 7378 | **LAMINATED FRACTURE** | CASSURE LAMELLAIRE | BRUCH (BLÄTTRIGER) |
| 7379 | **LAMINATED METAL** | METAL STRATIFIE | MEHRSCHICHTMETALL |
| 7380 | **LAMINATED RECTANGULAR PLATE SPRING** | RESSORT RECTANGULAIRE A LAMES SUPERPOSEES | RECHTECKFEDER (GESCHICHTETE) |
| 7381 | **LAMINATED TRIANGULAR PLATE SPRING** | RESSORT TRIANGULAIRE A LAMES SUPERPOSEES | DREIECKFEDER (GESCHICHTETE) |
| 7382 | **LAMINATION** | STRATIFICATION, FEUILLETAGE (DEDOUBLEMENT DES BORDS) DE TOLE | LAGE, SCHICHTUNG, DOPPLUNG |
| 7383 | **LAMINATION CRACK** | FISSURE CRIQUE DE LAMINAGE | LAGENRISS, SCHICHTENRISS, WALZSPLITTER |
| 7384 | **LAMP** | LAMPE | LAMPE |
| 7385 | **LAMP, BULB** | AMPOULE | LAMPE, BIRNE |
| 7386 | **LAMPBLACK** | NOIR DE FUMEE, NOIR A NOIRCIR | KIENRUSS |
| 7387 | **LANCE CUTTING** | OXYCOUPAGE | BRENNSCHNEIDEN |
| 7388 | **LANDING** | PALIER | TREPPENABSATZ |
| 7389 | **LANG LAY** | CABLAGE, TORSION LANG | ALBERTSCHLAG |
| 7390 | **LANG LAY WIRE ROPE** | CABLE METALLIQUE A FILS PARALLELES, CABLE A CABLAGE LANG OU ALBERT | DRAHTSEIL NACH ALBERTSCHLAG, GLEICHSCHLAGRAHTSEIL |
| 7391 | **LANOLINE** | LANOLINE | LANOLIN |
| 7392 | **LANTERN RING** | LANTERNE D'UNE VANNE, LANTERNE DE PRESSE-ETOUPE | ZWISCHENRING, AUFSATZRING, LATERNE EINES SCHIEBERS |
| 7393 | **LANTERN WHEEL** | LANTERNE | LATERNE, DREHLING |
| 7394 | **LANTHANUM** | LANTHANE | LANTHAN |
| 7395 | **LAP** | REPLIURE DE LAMINAGE, REPLI | ÜBERWALZUNGSFEHLER |
| 7396 | **LAP JOINT** | ASSEMBLAGE PAR RECOUVREMENT | ÜBERLAPPUNG, ÜBERLAPPTER STOSS |
| 7397 | **LAP JOINT** | JOINT A RECOUVREMENT, ASSEMBLAGE PAR RECOUVREMENT | ÜBERLAPPUNGSVERBINDUNG, ÜBERLAPPTER STOSS |
| 7398 | **LAP JOINT FLANGE** | BRIDE TOURNANTE | ÜBERLAPPUNGSFLANSCH |
| 7399 | **LAP OF SLIDE VALVE** | RECOUVREMENT DU TIROIR | ÜBERDECKUNG DES SCHIEBERS, ÜBERLAPPUNG DES SCHIEBERS |
| 7400 | **LAP RIVETED JOINT** | RIVURE A RECOUVREMENT | ÜBERBLATTUNGSNIETUNG, ÜBERLAPPUNGSNIETUNG |

| | | | |
|---|---|---|---|
| 7401 | **LAP SEAM WELDING** | SOUDAGE CONTINU PAR RECOUVREMENT | ÜBERLAPPNAHTSCHWEISSEN |
| 7402 | **LAP SPOT WELDING** | SOUDAGE PAR POINTS A RECOUVREMENT | ÜBERLAPPUNGSPUNKTNAHT |
| 7403 | **LAP WELD** | SOUDAGE PAR RECOUVREMENT | NAHT (ÜBERLAPPTE) |
| 7404 | **LAP WELD (TO)** | SOUDER EN BISEAU | ÜBERLAPPT SCHWEISSEN |
| 7405 | **LAP WELDED JOINT** | SOUDURE PAR RECOUVREMENT, SOUDURE EN BISEAU | ÜBERLAPPTE SCHWEISSUNG, ÜBERLAPPUNGSSCHWEISSUNG, SCHWEISSVERBINDUNG (ÜBERLAPPTE) |
| 7406 | **LAP WELDED TUBE** | TUBE SOUDE PAR RECOUVREMENT, TUBE A RECOUVREMENT | ROHR (ÜBERLAPPT GESCHWEISSTES) |
| 7407 | **LAPPING** | REPRISES VISIBLES, RODAGE | ANSÄTZE, LÄPPEN |
| 7408 | **LAPSE OF A PATENT** | DECHEANCE D'UN BREVET | ERLÖSCHEN EINES PATENTES |
| 7409 | **LARD OIL** | HUILE DE GRAISSE, HUILE DE SAINDOUX | SPECKÖL, SCHMALZÖL, LARDÖL |
| 7410 | **LARGE GAS ENGINE** | MOTEUR A ESSENCE DE GRANDE PUISSANCE | GROSSGASMASCHINE |
| 7411 | **LARGE RAKE ANGLE** | GRANDE PENTE DE COUPE EFFECTIVE | WEITERSPANNWINKEL |
| 7412 | **LARGE WATER-CAPACITY BOILER, BOILER WITH LARGE WATER SPACE** | CHAUDIERE A GRAND VOLUME | GROSSWASSERRAUMKESSEL |
| 7413 | **LAST RUNNINGS** | QUEUE DE DISTILLATION | NACHLAUF DER DESTILLATION |
| 7414 | **LATCH** | LOQUET | FALLKLINKE, FALLE |
| 7415 | **LATENT HEAT** | CHALEUR LATENTE | WÄRME (LATENTE) |
| 7416 | **LATENT HEAT OF VAPORISATION** | CHALEUR LATENTE DE VAPORISATION | VERDAMPFUNGSWÄRME (LATENTE) |
| 7417 | **LATENT MAGNETISM** | MAGNETISME LATENT | MAGNETISMUS (GEBUNDENER) |
| 7418 | **LATERAL BUCKLING** | GAUCHISSEMENT LATERAL | VERWERFUNG (SEITLICHE), VERZIEHEN (SEITLICHES) |
| 7419 | **LATERAL DEVIATION** | DEVIATION LATERALE | ABLENKUNG (SEITLICHE) |
| 7420 | **LATERAL DISPLACEMENT** | DEPLACEMENT LATERAL, DEPLACEMENT PERPENDICULAIRE A L'AXE | QUERVERSCHIEBUNG |
| 7421 | **LATERAL EXPANSION** | DILATATION LATERALE | QUERDEHNUNG, QUERAUSBAUCHUNG |
| 7422 | **LATERAL PRESSURE** | PRESSION LATERALE | DRUCK (SEITLICHER), SEITENDRUCK |
| 7423 | **LATERAL TRANSLATION** | DEPORT LATERAL | VERSCHIEBUNG (SEITLICHE) |
| 7424 | **LATERAL TRANSVERSE CONTRACTION** | STRICTION | QUERKONTRAKTION |
| 7425 | **LATEX LATICES** | LATEX | LATEX |
| 7426 | **LATH; BATTEN** | LATTE | HOLZLATTE |
| 7427 | **LATHE** | TOUR | DREHBANK |
| 7428 | **LATHE WITH LEADING SCREW** | TOUR A COMMANDES PAR VIS-MERE | LEITSPINDELDREHBANK |
| 7429 | **LATTICE** | RESEAU CRISTALLIN, TREILLIS METALLIQUE | GITTER |
| 7430 | **LATTICE CONSTANTS** | CONSTANTES DU RESEAU | GITTERKONSTANTE |
| 7431 | **LATTICE GIRDER** | POUTRE EN TREILLIS | FACHWERKTRÄGER, GITTERTRÄGER |
| 7432 | **LATTICE PLANE** | PLAN RETICULAIRE | NETZEBENE |
| 7433 | **LATTICE WORK** | TREILLIS | FACHWERK |
| 7434 | **LATTICE-DISTORTION THEORY** | THEORIE DE LA DISTORSION DU RESEAU | GITTERVERZERRUNGSTHEORIE |
| 7435 | **LAUE DIAGRAMME** | DIAGRAMME DE LAUE | RÜCKAUFNAHME LAUEDIAGRAMM |
| 7436 | **LAUNDER** | CANAL DE COULEE | ABSTICHRINNE |
| 7437 | **LAVA** | LAVE | LAVA |
| 7438 | **LAVE METHOD** | METHODE DE LAVE | LAVE-VERFAHREN |

# LAY

190

| | | | |
|---|---|---|---|
| 7439 | LAWN MOWERS AND CUTTERS | TONDEUSES A GAZON | RASENMÄHER |
| 7440 | LAY BARGES | BARGES DE POSE | VERLEGESCHIFF |
| 7441 | LAY PIPES (TO) | POSER DES TUYAUX | ROHRE VERLEGEN |
| 7442 | LAYER | COUCHE | SCHICHT, LAGE |
| 7443 | LAYER CORROSION | CORROSION PAR INFILTRATION STRATIFIEE | SCHICHTKORROSION |
| 7444 | LAYER LINE | STRATE | SCHICHTLINIE |
| 7445 | LAYOUT | COMPARAISON DE DIMENSIONS | VERGLEICH VON ABMESSUNGEN |
| 7446 | LEACHING | LESSIVAGE | AUSLAUGUNG |
| 7447 | LEAD | PLOMB | BLEI |
| 7448 | LEAD (TO) | AVANCER | VOREILEN |
| 7449 | LEAD ACETATE PAPER | PAPIER A L'ACETATE DE PLOMB | BLEIZUCKERPAPIER |
| 7450 | LEAD ACETATE, SUGAR OF LEAD | ACETATE DE PLOMB | BLEIESSIGSÄURE, BLEIAZETAT, BLEIZUCKER |
| 7451 | LEAD ALLOY | ALLIAGE A BASE DE PLOMB | BLEILEGIERUNG |
| 7452 | LEAD ASSY | FAISCEAU DE FILS | KABELBÜNDEL |
| 7453 | LEAD BASE ALLOY | ALLIAGE AU PLOMB | BLEILEGIERUNG |
| 7454 | LEAD BATH | BAIN DE PLOMB | BLEIBAD |
| 7455 | LEAD BATTERY | ACCUMULATEUR AU PLOMB | BLEIAKKUMULATOR |
| 7456 | LEAD BRONZE | BRONZE AU PLOMB | BLEIBRONZE |
| 7457 | LEAD CAST | REPRODUCTION EN PLOMB FONDU | BLEIABGUSS |
| 7458 | LEAD CHLORIDE | CHLORURE DE PLOMB | CHLORBLEI, BLEICHLORID |
| 7459 | LEAD COATED WIRE | FIL PLOMBE | DRAHT (VERBLEITER) |
| 7460 | LEAD COVERED SHEET IRON | TOLE PLOMBEE | BLECH (VERBLEITES) |
| 7461 | LEAD DIOXIDE | DIOXYDE DE PLOMB, OXYDE PUCE | BLEISUPEROXYD, BLEIDIOXYD, BLEIPEROXYD |
| 7462 | LEAD FOIL | FEUILLE DE PLOMB, PLOMB EN FEUILLES | BLEIFOLIE |
| 7463 | LEAD HAMMER | MASSETTE EN PLOMB | BLEIHAMMER |
| 7464 | LEAD JOINT FOR PIPING | JOINT A BAGUE DE PLOMB MATEE POUR TUYAUTERIES | BLEIDICHTUNG FÜR ROHRE |
| 7465 | LEAD ORE | MINERAI DE PLOMB | BLEIERZ |
| 7466 | LEAD PAINT | MATIERE COLORANTE A BASE DE PLOMB | BLEIFARBE |
| 7467 | LEAD PENCIL DRAWING | DESSIN AU CRAYON | BLEISTIFTZEICHNUNG |
| 7468 | LEAD PIPE | TUYAU EN PLOMB | BLEIROHR |
| 7469 | LEAD PIPE COATED WITH TIN | TUYAU EM PLOMB ETAME A L'INTERIEUR | MANTELROHR |
| 7470 | LEAD RING | BAGUE EN PLOMB | BLEIRING |
| 7471 | LEAD SCREW | VIS MERE | LEITSPINDEL |
| 7472 | LEAD SHOT | GRENAILLE DE PLOMB | SCHROT, BLEISCHROT |
| 7473 | LEAD SUPHATE | SULFATE DE PLOMB | BLEI (SCHWEFESAURES), BLEISULFAT |
| 7474 | LEAD THIOSULFATE | HYPOSULFITE DE PLOMB | BLEI (UNTERSCHWEFLIGSAURES), BLEITHIOSULFAT |
| 7475 | LEAD TIN SOLDER | SOUDURE CLAIRE | BLEI-ZINNLOT |
| 7476 | LEAD WELDING | SOUDAGE DE PLOMB | BLEISCHWEISSEN |
| 7477 | LEAD WIRE | FIL DE PLOMB | BLEIDRAHT |
| 7478 | LEAD, BLACK LEAD PENCIL | CRAYON | ZEICHENSTIFT, BLEISTIFT |
| 7479 | LEADED | PLOMBE | VERBLEIT |
| 7480 | LEADEN SEAL | PLOMB (SCEAU EN PLOMB) | PLOMBE |
| 7481 | LEADING DIMENSIONS | DONNEES PRINCIPALES, DIMENSIONS D'ENCOMBREMENT | HAUPTMASSE, HAUPTABMESSUNGEN |

| | | | |
|---|---|---|---|
| 7482 | **LEADING HAND** | CHEF D'EQUIPE | VORARBEITER |
| 7483 | **LEADING OF PHASE** | DEPHASAGE, DECALAGE EN AVANCE | PHASENVOREILUNG |
| 7484 | **LEADWORKING** | PLOMBERIE | BLEIVERARBEITUNG |
| 7485 | **LEAF SPRING** | RESSORT A LAMES | BLATTFEDER |
| 7486 | **LEAK** | FUITE AUX JOINTS | UNDICHTIGKEIT, UNDICHTE STELLE, LECK |
| 7487 | **LEAK (TO)** | FUIR | LECKEN, LECK SEIN, RINNEN, TROPFEN |
| 7488 | **LEAK, SEEPAGE** | FUITE, SUINTEMENT | LECK, VERSICKERUNG |
| 7489 | **LEAKAGE** | COULURE | LECKSTELLE |
| 7490 | **LEAKAGE CURRENT** | COURANT DE FUITE, COURANT DE DISPERSION | STREUSTROM, VERLUSTSTROM |
| 7491 | **LEAKINESS** | INETANCHEITE, ETANCHEITE (MANQUE D') | UNDICHTIGKEIT, UNDICHTHEIT |
| 7492 | **LEAKING** | FUITE, COULAGE (D'UN LIQUIDE) | LECKEN, TROPFEN, RINNEN |
| 7493 | **LEAKY** | PERD (QUI), FUIT (QUI) | UNDICHT |
| 7494 | **LEATHER** | CUIR | LEDER |
| 7495 | **LEATHER BELT** | COURROIE EN CUIR | LEDERRIEMEN |
| 7496 | **LEATHER CHAIN BELT, LEATHER LINK BELT** | COURROIE EN CUIR A MAILLONS | GLIEDERRIEMEN AUS LEDER, LEDERGLIEDERRIEMEN, KETTENBAND |
| 7497 | **LEATHER CLIPPINGS** | ROGNURES DE CUIR | LEDERABFÄLLE |
| 7498 | **LEATHER DIAPHRAGM** | DIAPHRAGME EN CUIR | LEDERMEMBRAN |
| 7499 | **LEATHER HOSE** | TUYAU EN CUIR | LEDERSCHLAUCH |
| 7500 | **LEATHER LACE, BELT LACE** | LANIERE POUR COURROIES | NÄHRIEMEN, BINDERIEMEN |
| 7501 | **LEATHER LINK FLEXIBLE COUPLING** | MANCHON A LANIERES DE CUIR | LEDERLASCHENKUPPLUNG |
| 7502 | **LEATHER PACKING** | GARNITURE EN CUIR | LEDERPACKUNG, LEDERDICHTUNG |
| 7503 | **LEATHER STRAP** | COURROIE EN CUIR | LEDERRIEMEN |
| 7504 | **LEDEBURITE** | LEDEBURITE | LEDEBURIT |
| 7505 | **LEE** | COTE SOUS LE VENT | LEESEITE |
| 7506 | **LEFT HAND SCREW** | VIS FILETEE A GAUCHE | SCHRAUBE (LINKSGÄNGIGE) |
| 7507 | **LEFT-HAND OFFSET** | DECALAGE A GAUCHE | LINKSVERSCHIEBUNG |
| 7508 | **LEFT-HAND THREAD** | PAS A GAUCHE | GEWINDE (LINKSGÄNGIGES), LINKSGEWINDE |
| 7509 | **LEFT-HANDED HELICAL TEETH** | DENTURE A PAS INCLINE A GAUCHE | VERZAHNUNG (LINKSSTEIGENDE) |
| 7510 | **LEFT-HANDED SCREW** | VIS A GAUCHE | SCHRAUBE (LINKSGÄNGIGE) |
| 7511 | **LEFT-LAID ROPE** | CABLE TORDU A GAUCHE | SEIL (LINKSGESCHLAGENES) |
| 7512 | **LEG OF AN ANGLE** | COTE D'UN ANGLE | SCHENKEL EINES WINKELS |
| 7513 | **LEGEND** | LEGENDE | LEGENDE |
| 7514 | **LEMNISCATE** | LEMNISCATE | LEMNISKATE, SCHLEIFENKURVE |
| 7515 | **LENARD RAYS** | RAYONS DE LENARD | LENARD-STRAHLEN |
| 7516 | **LENGTH** | LONGUEUR | LÄNGE |
| 7517 | **LENGTH OF ARC** | LONGUEUR D'ARC | BOGENLÄNGE |
| 7518 | **LENGTH OF OVERHANG** | LONGUEUR LIBRE | FREILÄNGE |
| 7519 | **LENGTH OF PISTON STROKE, STROKE TRAVEL OF PISTON** | COURSE DU PISTON, JEU DU PISTON | KOLBENHUB, KOLBENWEG, HUB, HUBLÄNGE, HUBHÖHE EINES KOLBENS |
| 7520 | **LENGTH OF WELD** | LONGUEUR DU CORDON | SCHWEISSNAHTLÄNGE |
| 7521 | **LENGTHENING BAR** | RALLONGE D'UN COMPAS | ZIRKELVERLÄNGERUNG, VERLÄNGERUNGSSTÜCK FÜR ZIRKEL |
| 7522 | **LENS** | LENTILLE | LINSE |
| 7523 | **LEONARD EFFECT** | EFFET LEONARD, SOUFFLURE | LEONARD-EFFEKT, GASBLASE |
| 7524 | **LETTERING OF A DRAWING** | INDICATIONS D'UN DESSIN | BESCHRIFTUNG EINER ZEICHNUNG |

# LEV
192

| 7525 | LEVEL | NIVEAU | NIVEAU (HÖHENLAGE) |
|------|-------|--------|--------------------|
| 7526 | LEVEL GAUGE | INDICATEUR DE NIVEAU | STANDPEILER |
| 7527 | LEVEL SURFACE, EQUIPOTENTIAL SURFACE | SURFACE DE NIVEAU, SURFACE EQUIPOTENTIELLE | SCHICHTFLÄCHE, EQUIPOTENTIALFLÄCHE, NIVEAUFLÄCHE |
| 7528 | LEVELLING ACTION | EFFET D'EGALISATION | VERLAUFEFFEKT |
| 7529 | LEVELLING SCREW, FOOT SCREW | VIS EGALISATRICE | FUSSSCHRAUBE, NIVELLIERSCHRAUBE |
| 7530 | LEVER | LEVIER | HEBEL |
| 7531 | LEVER ARM | BRAS DE LEVIER | HEBELARM |
| 7532 | LEVER BRAKE | FREIN A LEVIER | HEBELBREMSE |
| 7533 | LEVER JACK | CRIC A LEVIER | HEBELADE |
| 7534 | LEVER PRESS | PRESSE A LEVIER | HEBELPRESSE |
| 7535 | LEVER WEIGHT (SAFETY) VALVE | SOUPAPE DE SURETE A LEVIER ET CONTREPOIDS | VENTIL MIT HEBELGEWICHTSBELASTUNG |
| 7536 | LEVERAGE | RAPPORT DES BRAS DE LEVIER, LONGUEUR DU BRAS DE LEVIER | HEBELÜBERSETZUNG (VERHÄLTNIS) |
| 7537 | LEVIGATION | LEVIGATIONS, DEBOURBAGE | ABSCHLÄMMEN |
| 7538 | LIBERATION TANK | BAIN DE DECOMPOSITION DE L ELECTROLYTE | ELECTROLYTREINIGUNGSBAD |
| 7539 | LICENCE | LICENCE D'EXPLOITATION | LIZENZ (PATENTRECHTLICHE) |
| 7540 | LICENSEE | CONCESSIONNAIRE DE LICENCE | LIZENZINHABER |
| 7541 | LIFE | DUREE | LEBENSDAUER |
| 7542 | LIFT (TO), RAISE A LOAD (TO) | SOULEVER, ELEVER UN FARDEAU | HEBEN (EINE LAST) |
| 7543 | LIFT CHECK VALVE | CLAPET DE RETENUE A SOUPAPE | RÜCKSCHLAGKLAPPE, RÜCKSCHAGVENTIL |
| 7544 | LIFT OF VALVE, VALVE LIFT | SOULEVEMENT DE LA SOUPAPE, LEVEE DE LA SOUPAPE | VENTILHUB, VENTILAUSSCHLAG |
| 7545 | LIFT PUMP | POMPE ELEVATOIRE | HUBPUMPE |
| 7546 | LIFT ROPE | CABLE D'ASCENSEUR | AUFZUGSEIL |
| 7547 | LIFT VALVE, POPPET, MUSHROOM VALVE | SOUPAPE A CLAPET, SOUPAPE CHAMPIGNON | HUBVENTIL |
| 7548 | LIFTER | HAPPE | TIEGELZANGE |
| 7549 | LIFTING | DETREMPAGE | AUFZIEHEN |
| 7550 | LIFTING CYLINDER | CYLINDRE DE LEVAGE | HUBZYLINDER |
| 7551 | LIFTING HEIGHT OF A CRANE | HAUTEUR DE LEVAGE D'UNE GRUE | HUBHÖHE, FÖRDERHÖHE EINES KRANS |
| 7552 | LIFTING HOOK | CROCHET DE LEVAGE | LASTHAKEN |
| 7553 | LIFTING LEVER | LEVIER DE PURGE LIBRE | ANLÜFTHEBEL |
| 7554 | LIFTING MAGNET | ELECTRO-AIMANT PORTEUR | LASTMAGNET, HUBMAGNET, TRAGMAGNET |
| 7555 | LIFTING PISTON | PISTON DE LEVAGE | HUBKOLBEN, HEBEKOLBEN |
| 7556 | LIFTING SCREW | VIS DE RELEVAGE | ABDRÜCKSCHRAUBE |
| 7557 | LIFTING TONGS | PINCE (D'UN APPAREIL DE LEVAGE) | LASTZANGE |
| 7558 | LIFTING TRUNNION | TOURILLON CROCHET DE LEVAGE | HEBEHAKEN |
| 7559 | LIFTING, RAISING A LOAD | SOULEVEMENT D'UN FARDEAU, ASCENSION D'UNE CHARGE | HEBEN EINER LAST |
| 7560 | LIGHT | LUMIERE | LICHT |
| 7561 | LIGHT FILLET WELD | SOUDURE D'ANGLE CONCAVE, SOUDURE EN CONGE | HOHLKEHLNAHT |
| 7562 | LIGHT LOAD | CHARGE INCOMPLETE, CHARGE INFERIEURE A LA NORMALE | UNTERBELASTUNG, UNTERLAST |
| 7563 | LIGHT LORRY | CAMIONNETTE | KLEINLASTWAGEN |
| 7564 | LIGHT METAL | METAL LEGER, ALLIAGE LEGER | LEICHTMETALL |

| | | | |
|---|---|---|---|
| 7565 | **LIGHT METAL TURNING LATHE** | TOUR POUR METAUX LEGERS | LEICHTMETALLDREHBANK |
| 7566 | **LIGHT PHENOMENON** | PHENOMENE LUMINEUX | ICHTERSCHEINUNG, LICHTPHÄNOMEN |
| 7567 | **LIGHT RUNNING** | MARCHE DOUCE | GANG (WEICHER), GANG (LEICHTER), GANG (STOSSFREIER) |
| 7568 | **LIGHT SOURCE** | SOURCE LUMINEUSE | LICHTQUELLE |
| 7569 | **LIGHT SPEED** | VITESSE DE LA LUMIERE | LICHTGESCHWINDIGKEIT |
| 7570 | **LIGHT THIN OIL** | HUILE LEGERE | LEICHTÖL |
| 7571 | **LIGHT WAVE** | ONDE LUMINEUSE | LICHTWELLE |
| 7572 | **LIGHT-TIGHT** | IMPERMEABLE A LA LUMIERE | LICHTUNDURCHLÄSSIG, LICHTDICHT |
| 7573 | **LIGHTING FLARE** | FUSEE ECLAIRANTE | LEUCHTBOMBE |
| 7574 | **LIGHTING, ILLUMINATION** | ECLAIRAGE, ILLUMINATION | BELEUCHTUNG |
| 7575 | **LIGHTNING ARRESTER** | PARAFOUDRE | BLITZSCHUTZVORRICHTUNG |
| 7576 | **LIGHTNING CONDUCTOR** | PARATONNERRE | BLITZABLEITER |
| 7577 | **LIGNIN, LIGNONE** | LIGNINE, LIGNONE, LIGNOSE | LIGNIN |
| 7578 | **LIGNITE** | LIGNITE, LIGNEUX | LIGNIT |
| 7579 | **LIGNITE WAX** | CIRE DE LIGNITE, CIRE DE PARAFFINE | MONTANWACHS |
| 7580 | **LIGROIN, LIGHT PETROLEUM** | LIGROINE, BENZOLINE | LIGROIN |
| 7581 | **LIKE, SIMILAR POLES** | POLES SEMBLABLES | POLE (GLEICHNAMIGE) |
| 7582 | **LIME** | CHAUX | KALK |
| 7583 | **LIME TITANIA TYPE COATING** | REVETEMENT PAR COMPOSITION KB TI | KB-TI-MISCHTYP-ÜBERZUG |
| 7584 | **LIME TYPE COATING** | ENROBAGE BASIQUE | KALKBASISCHE UMHÜLLUNG |
| 7585 | **LIME WATER** | EAU DE CHAUX | KALKWASSER |
| 7586 | **LIMESTONE** | CALCAIRE | KALKSTEIN |
| 7587 | **LIMIT** | TOLERANCE LIMITE, LIMITE | GRENZMASS |
| 7588 | **LIMIT OF ELASTICITY** | LIMITE ELASTIQUE | ELASTIZITÄTSGRENZE |
| 7589 | **LIMIT OF ERROR** | LIMITE D'ERREURS | FEHLERGRENZE |
| 7590 | **LIMIT OF PROPORTIONALITY** | LIMITE D'ELASTICITE PROPORTIONNELLE | PROPORTIONALITÄTSGRENZE, GLEICHMASSGRENZE |
| 7591 | **LIMIT OF SATURATION** | LIMITE DE SATURATION | SÄTTIGUNGSGRENZE |
| 7592 | **LIMIT OF TEMPERATURE** | LIMITE DE TEMPERATURE | TEMPERATURGRENZE |
| 7593 | **LIMIT PRESSURE** | PRESSION LIMITE | GRENZDRUCK |
| 7594 | **LIMIT VALUE** | VALEUR LIMITE | GRENZWERT |
| 7595 | **LIMITS** | LIMITES DE TOLERANCE | TOLERANZGRENZE, GRENZEN |
| 7596 | **LIMONITE, BOG IRON ORE, BROWN HAEMATITE** | LIMONITE, HEMATITE BRUNE | BRAUNEISENSTEIN, BRAUNEISENERZ, RASENEISENERZ, SUMPFERZ, LIMONIT |
| 7597 | **LINE** | LIGNE, RAIE | LINIE |
| 7598 | **LINE (TO)** | REVETIR, DOUBLER | AUSFÜTTERN, AUSKLEIDEN |
| 7599 | **LINE FOCUS** | SOURCE LINEAIRE | STRICHFOKUS |
| 7600 | **LINE INTEGRAL** | INTEGRALE LINEAIRE | LINIENINTEGRAL |
| 7601 | **LINE OF COLLIMATION** | LIGNE DE COLLIMATION | KOLLIMATIONSLINIE, ABSEHLINIE, ZIELLINIE |
| 7602 | **LINE OF CONTACT ACTION** | LIGNE D'ENGRENEMENT | EINGRIFFSLINIE |
| 7603 | **LINE OF FORCE** | LIGNE DE FORCE | KRAFTLINIE |
| 7604 | **LINE OF GAUGE MARK** | LIGNE DE TRUSQUINAGE | PARALLELREISSLINIE |
| 7605 | **LINE OF INTERSECTION** | LIGNE D'INTERSECTION | SCHNITTLINIE |
| 7606 | **LINE OF RAILS** | VOIE FERREE, CHEMIN DE ROULEMENT | GLEIS |
| 7607 | **LINE OF SHAFTING** | LIGNE D'ARBRES, LIGNE DE TRANSMISSION | WELLENSTRANG |
| 7608 | **LINE POLE** | POTEAU DE LIGNE ELECTRIQUE | LEITUNGSMAST |

**LIN**  194

| | | | |
|---|---|---|---|
| 7609 | **LINE SHAFT DRIVE** | COMMANDE PAR ARBRE DE TRANSMISSION | WELLENANTRIEB, TRANSMISSIONSANTRIEB |
| 7610 | **LINE SPECTRUM** | SPECTRE DISCONTINU | LINIENSPEKTRUM |
| 7611 | **LINEAR ACCELERATION** | ACCELERATION LINEAIRE | BESCHLEUNIGUNG (LINEARE) |
| 7612 | **LINEAR EXPANSION, EXTENSION** | ALLONGEMENT LONGITUDINAL, DILATATION LINEAIRE | LANGSDEHNUNG, AUSDEHNUNG (LINEAIRE) |
| 7613 | **LINEAR INTERPOLATION** | INTERPOLATION LINEAIRE | INTERPOLATION (LINEAIRE) |
| 7614 | **LINEAR PERSPECTIVE** | PERSPECTIVE LINEAIRE | PERSPEKTIVE (MATHEMATISCHE), PERSPEKTIVE (LINEARE) |
| 7615 | **LINEAR PITCH** | PAS LINEAIRE | GERADLINIGE LÄNGSTEIGUNG |
| 7616 | **LINEAR SIMPLE EQUATION** | EQUATION LINEAIRE, EQUATION DU PREMIER DEGRE | GLEICHUNG ERSTEN GRADES, GLEICHUNG (LINEARE) |
| 7617 | **LINEAR VELOCITY** | VITESSE LINEAIRE | GESCHWINDIGKEIT (LINEARE) |
| 7618 | **LINED LADLE** | POCHE GARNIE, POCHE BRIQUETEE | GIESSPFANNE (GEMAUERTE) |
| 7619 | **LINEN** | TOILE | LEINEN, LEINWAND |
| 7620 | **LINER** | COLONNE PERDUE, GARNITURE | ROHR (VERLORENES), EINLEGESTREIFEN |
| 7621 | **LINER, SHIM** | FEUILLE DE CLINQUANT, CLINQUANT D'EPAISSEUR | FUGEINLAGE, ZWISCHENLAGE, BEILAGEBLECH, PASSBLECH |
| 7622 | **LINES OF LUDERS** | LIGNES DE LUDERS | LÜDERSFLIESSFIGUREN |
| 7623 | **LINING** | GARNISSAGE, FOURRURE, CALORIFUGEAGE, REVETEMENT, REVETEMENT INTERIEUR, CHEMISE, DOUBLAGE, DOUBLURE | FUTTER, WÄRMEISOLIERUNGSBEKLEIDUNG, AUSFÜTTERUNG, AUSKLEIDUNG, FÜTTERN, AUSFÜTTERN, AUSKLEIDEN |
| 7624 | **LINING FOR BEARINGS** | FOURRURE DUN PALIER, GARNITURE DE METAL ANTIFRICTION, REVETEMENT D'ANTIFRICTION | LAGERFUTTER |
| 7625 | **LINK BLOCK, DIE BLOCK** | COULISSEAU MOBILE, CURSEUR, VOYAGEUR | GELENKSTEIN, KULISSENSTEIN |
| 7626 | **LINK MOTION** | DISTRIBUTION PAR COULISSE | KULISSENSTEUERUNG |
| 7627 | **LINK OF CHAIN** | CHAINON, MAILLON, ANNEAU, MAILLE D'UNE CHAINE | KETTENGLIED, SCHAKE |
| 7628 | **LINKAGE** | SYSTEME ARTICULE | GELENKSYSTEM |
| 7629 | **LINKED, FLEXIBLY CONNECTED** | ARTICULE | GELENKIG VERBUNDEN |
| 7630 | **LINOLEUM** | LINOLEUM | LINOLEUM |
| 7631 | **LINSEED OIL** | HUILE DE LIN | LEINÖL |
| 7632 | **LIP** | BEC DE COULEE | PFANNENAUSGUSS |
| 7633 | **LIPS** | LEVRES DE COUPES | SCHNEIDLIPPEN |
| 7634 | **LIQUATED SURFACE** | SURFACE DE LIQUATION | OBERFLÄCHE (AUSGESEIGERTE) |
| 7635 | **LIQUATION, ELIQUATION** | LIQUATION, SEGREGATION | SAIGERUNG, SEIGERUNG |
| 7636 | **LIQUEFACTION OF A GAS** | LIQUEFACTION D'UN GAZ | VERFLÜSSIGUNG EINES GASES |
| 7637 | **LIQUEFIED GAS** | GAZ LIQUEFIE | GAS (VERFLÜSSIGTES) |
| 7638 | **LIQUEFIED PETROLEUM GAS (L.P.G)** | GAZ DE PETROLE LIQUEFIE | FLÜSSIGGAS |
| 7639 | **LIQUEFLABLE** | LIQUEFIABLE | VERFLÜSSIGBAR |
| 7640 | **LIQUEFY A GAS (TO)** | LIQUEFIER UN GAZ | GAS VERFLÜSSIGEN (EIN) |
| 7641 | **LIQUID** | LIQUIDE, CORPS LIQUIDE, FLUIDE, FLUIDE LIQUIDE | KÖRPER (FLÜSSIGER), FLÜSSIGKEIT |
| 7642 | **LIQUID** | LIQUIDE | TROPFBAR, FLÜSSIG |
| 7643 | **LIQUID AIR** | AIR LIQUIDE | LUFT (FLÜSSIGE) |
| 7644 | **LIQUID AMMONIA** | AMMONIAQUE | AMMONIAK |
| 7645 | **LIQUID CARBON DIOXYDE** | ACIDE CARBONIQUE LIQUIDE, GAZ CARBONIQUE LIQUEFIE | KOHLENSÄURE (FLÜSSIGE) |
| 7646 | **LIQUID CARBURIZING** | CEMENTATION EN BAIN | BADZEMENTIEREN |
| 7647 | **LIQUID CHARGE** | CHARGE LIQUIDE | EINSATZ (FLÜSSIGER) |

| | | | |
|---|---|---|---|
| 7648 | **LIQUID CONTRACTION** | CONTRACTION DE REFROIDISSEMENT | ABKÜHLUNGSSCHRUMPFUNG |
| 7649 | **LIQUID DAMPING** | AMORTISSEMENT PAR LIQUIDE | FLÜSSIGKEITSDÄMPFUNG |
| 7650 | **LIQUID FUEL, OIL FUEL** | COMBUSTIBLE LIQUIDE | BRENNSTOFF (FLÜSSIGER) |
| 7651 | **LIQUID HARDENING** | TREMPE EN BAIN DE SEL | SALZBADHÄRTUNG |
| 7652 | **LIQUID HEAD** | CHARGE HYDROSTATIQUE | DRUCK (HYDROSTATISCHER), BELASTUNG (HYDROSTATISCHE) |
| 7653 | **LIQUID HONING** | HONAGE AU JET DE VAPEUR | STRAHLHONVERFAHREN |
| 7654 | **LIQUID LEVEL REGULATOR** | REGULATEUR DE NIVEAU | NIVEAU REGLER |
| 7655 | **LIQUID LEVEL-CONTROLLER** | CONTROLEUR DE NIVEAU | NIVEAUSTANDSREGLER |
| 7656 | **LIQUID PENETRANT EXAMINATION** | EXAMEN PAR RESSUAGE | SEIGERUNGSPRÜFUNG |
| 7657 | **LIQUID STATE** | ETAT LIQUIDE | AGGREGAT-ZUSTAND (FLÜSSIGER) |
| 7658 | **LIQUID TIGHT COMPARTMENTS** | CAISSONS ETANCHES | SENKKASTEN (FLÜSSIGKEITSDICHTER) |
| 7659 | **LIQUID VEIN TRANSFER** | TRANSFERT PAR VEINE LIQUIDE | METALLÜBERGANG (FLÜSSIGER) |
| 7660 | **LIQUIDS** | LIQUIDES | FLÜSSIGKEITEN |
| 7661 | **LIQUIDUS** | LIQUIDUS, LIGNE DU LIQUIDUS | LIQUIDUSLINIE |
| 7662 | **LIST OF PARTS** | NOMENCLATURE DES PIECES | STÜCKLISTE |
| 7663 | **LITHARGE, LEAD MONOXIDE** | PROTOXYDE DE PLOMB, LITHARGE | BLEIGLÄTTE, BLEIOXYD |
| 7664 | **LITHIUM** | LITHIUM | LITHIUM |
| 7665 | **LITHIUM CARBONATE** | CARBONATE DE LITHIUM | LITHIUMKARBONAT |
| 7666 | **LITHIUM CHLORIDE** | CHLORURE DE LITHIUM | LITHIUMCHLORID |
| 7667 | **LITHIUM FLUORIDE** | FLUORURE DE LITHIUM | LITHLUMFLUORID |
| 7668 | **LITMUS PAPER** | PAPIER DE TOURNESOL | LACKMUSPAPIER |
| 7669 | **LITRE** | LITRE | LITER |
| 7670 | **LIVE CONDUCTOR, CURRENT CARRYING CONDUCTOR** | CONDUCTEUR PARCOURU, TRAVERSE PAR UN COURANT | STROMFÜHRENDER LEITER, LEITER (UNTER SPANNUNG STEHENDER) |
| 7671 | **LIVE LOAD** | CHARGE VIVE | LAST (BEWEGLICHE) |
| 7672 | **LIVE LOAD, VARIABLE INTERMITTENT FLUCTUATING LOAD** | CHARGE VARIABLE, CHARGE INTERMITTENTE | BELASTUNG (WECHSELNDE), BELASTUNG (UNSTETE), BELASTUNG (INTERMITTIERENDE) |
| 7673 | **LIVE STEAM** | VAPEUR FRAICHE | FRISCHDAMPF |
| 7674 | **LIVER OF SULPHUR** | FOIE DE SOUFRE | SCHWEFELLEBER |
| 7675 | **LIVERING** | EPAISSISSEMENT (PEINTURE) | VERDICKUNG |
| 7676 | **LIXIVIATE (TO)** | LESSIVER, LIXIVIER | AUSLAUGEN |
| 7677 | **LIXIVIATION** | LESSIVAGE, LIXIVIATION | AUSLAUGEN, AUSLAUGUNG |
| 7678 | **LNG(LIQUEFIED NATURAL GAS) TANK** | RESERVOIR DE GNL | TANK FÜR FLÜSSIGES ERDGAS |
| 7679 | **LOAD (ING)** | CHARGE, SOLLICITATIONS, EFFORT EXTERIEUR | BELASTUNG, BEANSPRUCHUNG, LAST, AUFLAST, LADUNG |
| 7680 | **LOAD (TO)** | CHARGER (RESISTANCE DES MATERIAUX) | BELASTEN |
| 7681 | **LOAD BRAKE** | FREIN DE RETENUE | LASTDRUCKBREMSE, SENKSPERRBREMSE |
| 7682 | **LOAD CARRYING CAPACITY** | CAPACITE DE CHARGE | TRAGFÄHIGKEIT |
| 7683 | **LOAD DIAGRAM** | PLAN DE CHARGE | BELASTUNGSDIAGRAMM |
| 7684 | **LOAD DISTRIBUTION** | REPARTITION DES CHARGES | LASTVERTEILUNG |
| 7685 | **LOAD WITHOUT IMPACT** | CHARGE SANS CHOCS | BELASTUNG (STOSSFREIE) |
| 7686 | **LOADED ENGINE** | MOTEUR SOUS TENSION | MOTOR (BELASTETER) |
| 7687 | **LOADERS : GRASS AND GREEN CROP** | CHARGEUR (OU CHARGEUSE) POUR FOURRAGE VERT | GRÜNFUTTERLADER |
| 7688 | **LOADERS AND HOISTS (SACK, BAG AND SUGAR BEET)** | CHARGEURS DE SACS ET DE BETTERAVES | HEBEMASCHINEN (SÄCKE, BÜNDEL UND ZUCKE PRÜBEN) |
| 7689 | **LOADERS, MANURE** | CHARGEURS DE FUMIER | DÜNGERLADER |

# LOA

196

| | | | |
|---|---|---|---|
| 7690 | **LOADING AGENT** | MATIERE CHARGEANTE | BESCHWERUNGSMITTEL |
| 7691 | **LOAM** | TERRE GLAISE, GLAISE | LEHM |
| 7692 | **LOAM BRICK** | BRIQUE CRUE, BRIQUE SECHEE A L'AIR | LEHMSTEIN, LEHMPATZEN, LUFTZIEGEL |
| 7693 | **LOAM MOLD** | MOULE EN TERRE GLAISE | LEHMFORM |
| 7694 | **LOCAL CELL** | PILE LOCALE | LOKALELEMENT |
| 7695 | **LOCAL CORROSION** | CORROSION LOCALE | LOKALANGRIFF, LOKALKORROSION |
| 7696 | **LOCAL HEATING** | CHAUFFAGE PARTIEL | LOKALHEIZUNG |
| 7697 | **LOCAL QUENCHING** | TREMPE PARTIELLE | HÄRTEN (PARTIELLES) |
| 7698 | **LOCK** | ECLUSE | SCHLEUSE |
| 7699 | **LOCK (TO)** | VERROUILLER | VERRIEGELN, SPERREN |
| 7700 | **LOCK A NUT (TO), A KEY** | BLOQUER UN ECROU, BLOQUER UNE CLAVETTE | SICHERN (EINEN KEIL), SICHERN (EINE MUTTER) |
| 7701 | **LOCK ANGLE** | ANGLE DE BRAQUAGE | EINSCHLAGWINKEL |
| 7702 | **LOCK NUT, CHECK NUT, JAM NUT** | ECROU DE SURETE, CONTRE-ECROU, ECROU DE BLOCAGE | STELLMUTTER, KONTERMUTTER, GEGENMUTTER, SICHERHEITSMUTTER |
| 7703 | **LOCK WASHER** | RONDELLE FREIN, RONDELLE DE SERRAGE, RONDELLE DE BLOCAGE | UNTERLAGSCHEIBE (FERERNDE), SICHERUNGSSCHEIBE |
| 7704 | **LOCKING A KEY** | BLOCAGE, FIXATION D'UN COIN DE SERRAGE | KEILSICHERUNG |
| 7705 | **LOCKING DEVICE** | DISPOSITIF DE BLOCAGE, ENCLIQUETAGE | FESTSTELLVORRICHTUNG, SPERRE, ARRETIERUNG |
| 7706 | **LOCKING LEVER** | MANETTE DE COMMANDE | STELLHEBEL, FESTSTELLHEBEL |
| 7707 | **LOCKING OF BOLTS AND NUTS** | BLOCAGE, CONSOLIDATION, IMMOBILISATION DES ECROUS ET BOULONS | SICHERUNG VON SCHRAUBEN, SCHRAUBENSICHERUNG |
| 7708 | **LOCKING SCREW** | VIS DE BLOCAGE | SICHERUNGSSCHRAUBE |
| 7709 | **LOCKING STOP GEAR** | MECANISME D'ARRET | SPERRWERK, GESPERRE |
| 7710 | **LOCKING, BOLTING** | VERROUILLAGE | VERRIEGELUNG, VERIEGEIN |
| 7711 | **LOCKING, CLAMPING** | BLOCAGE, ASSUJETTISSEMENT | SICHERUNG GEGEN VERSCHIEBEN, LAGENSICHERUNG |
| 7712 | **LOCOMOTION** | LOCOMOTION | ORTSVERÄNDERUNG, FORTBEWEGUNG |
| 7713 | **LOCOMOTIVE** | LOCOMOTIVE | LOKOMOTIVE |
| 7714 | **LOCOMOTIVE BOILER** | CHAUDIERE TYPE LOCOMOTIVE | LOKOMOTIVKESSEL |
| 7715 | **LOCUS** | LIEU GEOMETRIQUE | ORT (GEOMETRISCHER) |
| 7716 | **LOESS** | LOESS | LÖSS |
| 7717 | **LOG** | PROFIL, COUPE, DIAGRAMME, GRAPHIQUE, RELEVE | DIAGRAMM |
| 7718 | **LOGARITHM** | LOGARITHME | LOGARITHMUS |
| 7719 | **LOGARITHMIC SERIES** | SERIE LOGARITHMIQUE | REIHE (LOGARITHMISCHE) |
| 7720 | **LOGARITHMIC SPIRAL** | SPIRALE LOGARITHMIQUE | SPIRALE (LOGARITHMISCHE) |
| 7721 | **LOGARITHMIC TABLE, TABLE OF LOGARITHMS** | TABLE DES LOGARITHMES | LOGARITHMENTAFEL |
| 7722 | **LOGOCYCLIC CURVE, STROPHOID, FOLLATE** | STROPHOIDE | STROPHOIDE |
| 7723 | **LOGS, UNHEWN TIMBER** | BOIS EN GRUME | GANZHOLZ |
| 7724 | **LONG FLAME COAL** | HOUILLE A LONGUE FLAMME | KOHLE (LANGLFAMMIGE) |
| 7725 | **LONG LEVER** | ANSPECT | HEBEBAUM |
| 7726 | **LONG NIPPLE** | LONGUE-VIS | LANGNIPPEL |
| 7727 | **LONG RUN WORK** | FABRICATION EN GRANDES SERIES | GROSSSERIENANFERTIGUNG |
| 7728 | **LONG-DISTANCE NETWORK** | RESEAU A GRANDE DISTANCE | FERNLEITUNGSNETZ |
| 7729 | **LONG-LINE CURRENT EFFECT** | EFFET DE LIGNE DE TRANSMISSION | LANGLEITUNGSEFFEKT |

**197** **LOW**

| | | | |
|---|---|---|---|
| 7730 | **LONG-LINK CHAIN** | CHAINE A MAILLONS LONGS | KETTE (LANGGLIEDRIGE) |
| 7731 | **LONG-STROKE ENGINE** | MACHINE A GRANDE COURSE | MASCHINE (LANGHÜBIGE) |
| 7732 | **LONG-THROW CRANK** | MANIVELLE A GRANDE COURSE | KURBEL (LANGHÜBIGE) |
| 7733 | **LONGITUDINAL AXIS** | AXE LONGITUDINAL | LÄNGSACHSE |
| 7734 | **LONGITUDINAL BAR** | LONGRINE | LÄNGSRIEGEL |
| 7735 | **LONGITUDINAL DUCTILITY** | DUCTILITE LONGITUDINALE | LÄNGSDUKTILITÄT |
| 7736 | **LONGITUDINAL PITCH OF RIVETS** | DISTANCE DES RIVETS DE CENTRE A CENTRE EN LIGNE CONTINUE | LÄNGSNIETTEILUNG |
| 7737 | **LONGITUDINAL SEAM WELDING** | SOUDAGE LONGITUDINAL | LÄNGSNAHTSCHWEISSEN |
| 7738 | **LONGITUDINAL SECTION** | PROFIL EN LONG, COUPE LONGITUDINALE | LÄNGSSCHNITT, LÄNGENPROFIL |
| 7739 | **LONGITUDINAL VIBRATION** | OSCILLATION LONGITUDINALE | LÄNGESCHWINGUNG |
| 7740 | **LONGITUDINALLY RUBBED TUBE, TUBE RIBBED IN ITS LONGITUDINAL SECTION** | TUBE A NERVURES LONGITUDINALES, TUBE SERVE | RIPPENROHR MIT LÄNGSRIPPEN |
| 7741 | **LOOP OF A CURVE** | LACET, NOEUD D'UNE COURBE | SCHLEIFE EINER KURVE |
| 7742 | **LOOP OF A ROPE** | BOUCLE D'UNE CORDE | SEILSCHLINGE |
| 7743 | **LOOSE COLLAR, SET COLLAR** | BAGUE D'ARRET, BAGUE AMOVIBLE, RONDELLE GOUPILLEE | STELLRING |
| 7744 | **LOOSE PATTERN** | MODELE DEMONTABLE | MODELL (ZELEGBARES) |
| 7745 | **LOOSE PIECE** | PARTIE DEMONTABLE | TEIL (LOSER) |
| 7746 | **LOOSE PIPE FLANGE** | BRIDE FOLLE | FLANSCH (LOSER), ÜBERWURFFLANSCH |
| 7747 | **LOOSE PULLEY** | POULIE FOLLE | LOSSCHEIBE, LEERSCHEIBE, RIEMENSCHEIBE (LOSE) |
| 7748 | **LOOSE PULLEY BUSH** | DOUILLE POUR POULIE FOLLE | LEERLAUFBÜCHSE |
| 7749 | **LOOSELY MOUNTED ON THE SHAFT** | PLACE FOU (SUR L'ARBRE) | LOSE AUFGESETZT (AUF DIE WELLE) |
| 7750 | **LOOSEN A KEY (TO)** | DECLAVETER | LOSKEILEN, EINEN KEIL LÖSEN |
| 7751 | **LOOSENING A KEY** | DEMONTAGE D'UNE CLAVETTE, DECLAVETAGE | LÖSEN EINES KEILS, LÖSUNG EINES KEILS |
| 7752 | **LORRY (GB)** | CAMION | LASTWAGEN |
| 7753 | **LORRY, TRUCK (U.S.A.)** | CAMION A RIDELLES | LASTKRAFTWAGEN |
| 7754 | **LOSS** | PERTE | VERLUST |
| 7755 | **LOSS BY FRICTION** | PERTE DE FROTTEMENT | REIBUNGSVERLUST |
| 7756 | **LOSS DUE TO LEAKAGE** | PERTE PAR FUITES | UNDICHTIGKEITSVERLUST |
| 7757 | **LOSS DUE TO SHOCK** | PERTE PAR CHOCS | STOSSVERLUST |
| 7758 | **LOSS OF ENERGY** | PERTE D'ENERGIE | KRAFTVERLUST, ENERGIEVERLUST |
| 7759 | **LOSS OF HEAD** | PERTE DE CHARGE | WIDERSTANDSVERLUST, DRUCKVERLUST |
| 7760 | **LOSS OF HEAT** | PERTE DE CHALEUR, DEPERDITION DE CHALEUR | WÄRMEVERLUST |
| 7761 | **LOSS OF IGNITION** | PERTE AU FEU | ABBRANDVERLUST |
| 7762 | **LOSS OF OUTPUT** | PERTE DE PUISSANCE | LEISTUNGSVERLUST |
| 7763 | **LOSS OF PRESSURE** | PERTE DE PRESSION | DRUCKVERLUST |
| 7764 | **LOSS OF WEIGHT** | PERTE DE POIDS | GEWICHTSVERLUST |
| 7765 | **LOSS OF WORK** | PERTE DE TRAVAIL | ARBEITSVERLUST |
| 7766 | **LOT** | LOT | LOS |
| 7767 | **LOW ANGLE BOUNDARY (OR SUB-BOUNDARY)** | SOUS-JOINT A FAIBLE | |
| 7768 | **LOW BRASS** | LAITON DE FAIBLE ALLIAGE | MESSING (NIEDRIGLEGIERTES) |
| 7769 | **LOW BREAST WHEEL** | ROUE DE COTE (HYDRAULIQUE) | WASSERRAD (MITTELSCHLÄCHTIGES) |
| 7770 | **LOW CARBON STEEL** | ACIER A FAIBLE TENEUR EN CARBONE, ACIER DOUX | STAHL (KOHLENSTOFFARMER), STAHL (WEICHER) |

**LOW** 198

| | | | |
|---|---|---|---|
| 7771 | LOW FREQUENCY | FAIBLE FREQUENCE | NIEDERFREQUENZ |
| 7772 | LOW FREQUENCY FURNACE | FOUR A INDUCTION A BASSE FREQUENCE | NIEDERFREQUENZOFEN |
| 7773 | LOW MELTING TEMPERATURE ALLOYS | ALLIAGES FUSIBLES | LEGIERUNGEN (NIEDRIG SCHMELZENDE) |
| 7774 | LOW PRESSURE | BASSE PRESSION | DRUCK (NIEDERER), NIEDERDRUCK |
| 7775 | LOW TEMPERATURE | BASSE TEMPERATURE | TEMPERATUR (NIEDRIGE), TEMPERATUR (TIEFE) |
| 7776 | LOW TEMPERATURE CARBONISATION | DISTILLATION DES COMBUSTIBLES A BASSE TEMPERATURE, CARBONISATION INCOMPLETE | SCHWELEN, SCHWELEREI |
| 7777 | LOW TENSION CURRENT | COURANT A BASSE TENSION | NIEDERSPANNUNGSSTROM, NIEDRIGGESPANNTER STROM |
| 7778 | LOW VOLTAGE PRESSURE TENSION | BASSE TENSION | NIEDERSPANNUNG (EL.) |
| 7779 | LOW-DENSITY METAL | METAL LEGER | LEICHTMETALL |
| 7780 | LOW-GRADE INFERIOR FUEL | MAUVAIS COMBUSTIBLE | BRENNSTOFF MINDERWERTIGER |
| 7781 | LOW-GRADE ORE | MINERAI PAUVRE, MINERAI DE BASSE TENEUR | ERZ (ARMES) |
| 7782 | LOW-PRESSURE BOILER | CHAUDIERE A BASSE PRESSION | NIEDERDRUCKKESSEL |
| 7783 | LOW-PRESSURE CYLINDER | CYLINDRE A BASSE PRESSION | NIEDERDRUCKZYLINDER |
| 7784 | LOW-PRESSURE HOT WATER HEATING | CHAUFFAGE PAR L'EAU CHAUDE A BASSE PRESSION | NIEDERDRUCKWASSERHEIZUNG, WARMWASSERHEIZUNG |
| 7785 | LOW-PRESSURE STEAM | VAPEUR A BASSE PRESSION | NIEDERDRUCKDAMPF, NIEDRIG GESPANNTER DAMPF, DAMPF VON NIEDRIGER SPANNUNG |
| 7786 | LOW-PRESSURE STEAM ENGINE | MACHINE A PRESSION ORDINAIRE | NIEDERDRUCKDAMPFMASCHINE |
| 7787 | LOW-PRESSURE STEAM HEATING | CHAUFFAGE PAR LA VAPEUR A BASSE PRESSION | NIEDERDRUCKDAMPFHEIZUNG |
| 7788 | LOW-PRESSURE TURBINE | TURBINE A BASSE PRESSION | NIEDERDRUCKTURBINE |
| 7789 | LOW-SPEED ENGINE | MACHINE A PETITE VITESSE, MACHINE A MARCHE LENTE | MASCHINE (LANGSAMLAUFENDE) |
| 7790 | LOW-TEMPERATURE JOINING | ASSEMBLAGE A BASSE TEMPERATURE | NIEDRIGTEMPERATURVERBINDUNG |
| 7791 | LOW-TENSION MOTOR | MOTEUR A BASSE TENSION | NIEDERSPANNUNGSMOTOR |
| 7792 | LOWENHERZ, DELISLE THREAD | PAS SYSTEME LOWENHERZ | LÖWENHERZGEWINDE |
| 7793 | LOWER A LOAD (TO) | ABAISSER UN FARDEAU | LAST SENKEN (EINE) |
| 7794 | LOWER PUNCH | POINCON INFERIEUR | UNTERSTEMPEL |
| 7795 | LOWER RAIL OR MID-BAR | SOUS-LISSE | MITTELSTANGE |
| 7796 | LOWER SAW GUIDE | GUIDE-RUBAN INFERIEUR | GATTERSTAB (UNTERER) |
| 7797 | LOWERING A LOAD | DESCENTE D'UN FARDEAU | SENKEN EINER LAST |
| 7798 | LOWERING OF THE WATER LEVEL | DENIVELLEMENT, DENIVELLATION | SENKUNG, ABSENKUNG DES WASSERSPIEGELS |
| 7799 | LOZENGE RIVETED JOINT | RIVURE EN LOSANGE | NIETUNG (VERJÜNGTE) |
| 7800 | LUBRICANT | LUBRIFIANT | SCHMIERMITTEL, SCHMIERSTOFF, SCHMIERMATERIAL |
| 7801 | LUBRICATE (TO) | LUBRIFIER, GRAISSER | SCHMIEREN |
| 7802 | LUBRICATED PLUG VALVE | ROBINET A BOISSEAU LUBRIFIE | HAHN MIT GEHÄUSESCHMIERUNG, HAHNVENTIL (GEÖLTES) |
| 7803 | LUBRICATING | LUBRIFICATION, GRAISSAGE | SCHMIERUNG |
| 7804 | LUBRICATING FAT GREASE | GRAISSE DE LUBRIFICATION | SCHMIERFETT |
| 7805 | LUBRICATING OIL | HUILE LUBRIFIANTE, HUILE DE GRAISSAGE | SCHMIERÖL |
| 7806 | LUBRICATING PROPERTY | POUVOIR LUBRIFIANT, QUALITE LUBRIFIANTE | SCHMIERWERT |
| 7807 | LUBRICATING WICK | MECHE DE GRAISSAGE | SCHMIERDOCHT |

| | | | |
|---|---|---|---|
| 7808 | **LUBRICATION** | LUBRIFICATION, GRAISSAGE | SCHMIEREN, SCHMIERUNG |
| 7809 | **LUBRICATION EFFECTED BY A MECHANICAL LUBRICATOR** | GRAISSAGE PAR OLEO-COMPRESSEUR | ZENTRALSCHMIERUNG |
| 7810 | **LUBRICATION GROOVE, OIL GROOVE, GREASE CHANNEL** | RIGOLE DE GRAISSAGE, PATTE D'ARAIGNEE | SCHMIERNUT |
| 7811 | **LUBRICATION SCREW** | BOULON GRAISSEUR | SCHMIERSCHRAUBE |
| 7812 | **LUBRICATOR, OIL FEED** | GRAISSEUR, GRAISSAGE, ORGANE DE LUBRIFICATION | SCHMIERVORRICHTUNG, SCHMIERGEFÄSS |
| 7813 | **LUBRICITY UNCTUOUSNESS OF A LUBRICANT** | ONCTUOSITE DU LUBRIFIANT | SCHLÜPFRIGKEIT EINES SCHMIERSTOFFES, LUBRIZITÄT |
| 7814 | **LUBRIFICATION** | GRAISSAGE | SCHMIERUNG |
| 7815 | **LUDER'S LINES** | LIGNES DE LUDERS, LIGNES D'HARTMANN | LINIEN (LÜDERSCHE) |
| 7816 | **LUG** | BERCEAU | SITZ (ANGEGOSSENER) |
| 7817 | **LUG, CAR (ON A CASTING)** | OREILLE, ATTACHE, BRIDE, PATTE | AUGE (ANGEGOSSENES) |
| 7818 | **LUMEN** | LUMEN | LUMEN |
| 7819 | **LUMINESCENCE** | LUMINESCENCE | LUMINESZENZ |
| 7820 | **LUMINOUS FLAME** | FLAMME ECLAIRANTE, FLAMME REDUCTRICE, FEU DE REDUCTION | FLAMME (LEUCHTENDE) |
| 7821 | **LUMINOUS FLUX** | FLUX LUMINEUX | LICHTSTROM |
| 7822 | **LUMINOUS INTENSITY, INTENSITY OF LIGHT** | INTENSITE LUMINEUSE | LICHSTÄRKE, LICHTINTENSITÄT |
| 7823 | **LUMINOUS POINT** | POINT LUMINEUX | PUNKT (LEUCHTENDER) |
| 7824 | **LUMINOUS RAY, RAY OF LIGHT, BEAM** | RAYON LUMINEUX | LICHTSTRAHL |
| 7825 | **LUMINOUS VIBRATION** | VIBRATION LUMINEUSE | LICHTSCHWINGUNG |
| 7826 | **LUMP COAL** | CHARBON GROS | STÜCKKOHLE, GROBKOHLE |
| 7827 | **LUMP FUEL** | COMBUSTIBLE EN GROS MORCEAUX | BRENNSTOFF (STÜCKIGER) |
| 7828 | **LUNAR CAUSTIC, SILVER NITRATE** | NITRATE D'ARGENT, AZOTATE D'ARGENT, PIERRE INFERNALE | HÖLLENSTEIN, SILBERNITRAT |
| 7829 | **LUNE** | CROISSANT | KREISSICHELSTÜCK, KREISBOGENSICHEL |
| 7830 | **LUSTRE** | ECLAT (MIN.) | GLANZ (MIN.) |
| 7831 | **LUTE (TO)** | LUTTER | ABDICHTEN |
| 7832 | **LUTE OF A PIPE, LOOP OF A PIPE** | LYRE (D'UN TUYAU) | ROHRBOGEN |
| 7833 | **LUTECIUM** | LUTECIUM | CASSIOPEIUM, LUTETIUM |
| 7834 | **LUX** | LUX | LUX |
| 7835 | **LYE** | LESSIVE | LAUGE |
| 7836 | **MACERATE (TO)** | MACERER | MAZERIEREN |
| 7837 | **MACERATION** | MACERATION | MAZERATION |
| 7838 | **MACHINABILITY** | USINABILITE | BEARBEITBARKEIT |
| 7839 | **MACHINE** | MACHINE DE TRAVAIL, MACHINE RECEPTRICE | MASCHINE, ARBEITSMASCHINE |
| 7840 | **MACHINE BOLT** | BOULON FAIT A LA MACHINE, BOULON MECANIQUE | MASCHINENSCHRAUBE |
| 7841 | **MACHINE CUT NAIL** | CLOU DECOUPE | NAGEL (GESCHNITTENER), SCHNITTNAGEL |
| 7842 | **MACHINE CUTTING** | DECOUPAGE A LA MACHINE | MASCHINABSCHNEIDEN |
| 7843 | **MACHINE DRAWING** | DESSIN DE MACHINE | MASCHINENZEICHNUNG |
| 7844 | **MACHINE FINISHING** | FINISSAGE A LA MACHINE | FERTIGBEARBEITUNG (MASCHINELLE) |
| 7845 | **MACHINE FOR MAKING BENDING TESTS** | MACHINE POUR ESSAIS DE FLEXION | BIEGEMASCHINE (FÜR VERSUCHE), BIEGEPRESSE (FÜR VERSUCHE) |

**MAC**

**200**

| | | | |
|---|---|---|---|
| 7846 | **MACHINE FOR MAKING TENSILE TESTS** | DYNAMOMETRE, BAN DE TRACTION, APPAREIL POUR LES RUPTURES A LA TRACTION | ZERREISSMASCHINE |
| 7847 | **MACHINE FORGING** | FORGEAGE A LA MACHINE | MASCHINENSCHMIEDEN |
| 7848 | **MACHINE FOUNDATION** | FONDATION D'UNE MACHINE | FUNDAMENT EINER MASCHINE, MASCHINENFUNDAMENT |
| 7849 | **MACHINE GRINDING** | MEULAGE A LA MACHINE | MASCHINENSCHLEIFEN |
| 7850 | **MACHINE MADE** | TRAVAILLE A LA MACHINE | MECHANISCH, MASCHINELL, MASCHINEN HERGESTELLT (MIT) |
| 7851 | **MACHINE MOLDING** | MOULAGE MECANIQUE | MASCHINENFORMUNG |
| 7852 | **MACHINE PART, ENGINE DETAIL** | ELEMENT, ORGANE, PIECE DE MACHINE, ORGANE, PIECE MECANIQUE | MASCHINENTEIL |
| 7853 | **MACHINE REAMER** | ALESOIR DE MACHINE | MASCHINENREIBAHLE |
| 7854 | **MACHINE RIVETING** | RIVETAGE MECANIQUE | MASCHINENNIETUNG |
| 7855 | **MACHINE SHOP** | ATELIER DE MACHINES, SALLE DES MACHINES, ATELIER DE MECANIQUE | MASCHINENHALLE, MASCHINENWERKSTATT |
| 7856 | **MACHINE SHOP** | ATELIER DE MECANIQUE | MASCHINENWERKSTATT |
| 7857 | **MACHINE STEEL** | ACIER A OUTILS | WERKZEUGSTAHL |
| 7858 | **MACHINE TAP** | TARAUD A LA MACHINE, TARAUDEUSE | MASCHINENGEWINDEBOHRER |
| 7859 | **MACHINE TOOL** | MACHINE-OUTIL | WERKZEUGMASCHINE |
| 7860 | **MACHINE WORK** | TRAVAIL MECANIQUE (TRAVAIL FAIT A LA MACHINE) | MASCHINENARBEIT |
| 7861 | **MACHINED** | USINE | BEARBEITET |
| 7862 | **MACHINERY** | MACHINERIE | MASCHINENEINRICHTUNG |
| 7863 | **MACHINERY CASTINGS** | FONTE MECANIQUE | MASCHINENGUSS |
| 7864 | **MACHINING** | USINAGE | BEARBEITUNG |
| 7865 | **MACHINING ALLOWANCE** | SUREPAISSEUR D'USINAGE | BEARBEITUNGSZUGABE |
| 7866 | **MACHINING STEP** | DEGRE D'USINAGE | BEARBEITUNGSSTUFE |
| 7867 | **MACHINING WIDTH** | LARGEUR D'USINAGE | ARBEITSBREITE |
| 7868 | **MACHINIST** | OUVRIER MECANICIEN, OUVRIER DE MACHINE -OUTIL | MASCHINENARBEITER |
| 7869 | **MACRO STRUCTURE** | STRUCTURE A GROS GRAINS, MACROSTRUCTURE | GROBGEFÜGE |
| 7870 | **MACROETCHING** | ATTAQUE MACROGRAPHIQUE | MAKROÄTZUNG |
| 7871 | **MACROGRAPHY** | MACROGRAPHIE | MAKROGRAPHIE |
| 7872 | **MACROSCOPIC** | MACROSCOPIQUE | MAKROSKOPISCH |
| 7873 | **MACROSCOPIC EXAMINATION** | OBSERVATION MACROSCOPIQUE A L'OEIL NU | BEOBACHTUNG (MAKROSKOPISCHE), UNTERSUCHUNG (MAKROSKOPISCHE) |
| 7874 | **MACROSCOPIC STRESS** | EFFORT MACROSCOPIQUE | BEANSPRUCHUNG (MAKROSKOPISCHE) |
| 7875 | **MACROSECTION** | SECTION MACROSCOPIQUE | QUERSCHNITT (MAKROSKOPISCHER) |
| 7876 | **MACROSEGREGATION** | MACROSEGREGATION | MAKROSEIGERUNG |
| 7877 | **MAGNAFLUX TESTING METHOD** | MAGNETOSCOPIE | MAGNETPULVER-PRÜFVERFAHREN |
| 7878 | **MAGNALIUM** | MAGNALIUM | MAGNALIUM |
| 7879 | **MAGNESIA, MAGNESIUM OXIDE** | MAGNESIE, OXYDE DE MAGNESIUM | MAGNESIA, MAGNESIUMOXYD |
| 7880 | **MAGNESITE** | GLOBERTITE, MAGNESITE | MAGNESIT, TALKSPAT, BITTERSPAT |
| 7881 | **MAGNESITE BRICK** | AGGLOMERE MAGNESIEN | MAGNESITSTEIN |
| 7882 | **MAGNESIUM** | MAGNESIUM | MAGNESIUM |
| 7883 | **MAGNESIUM BICARBONATE** | BICARBONATE DE MAGNESIUM | ZWEIFACHKOHLENSÄURE, DOPPELTKOHLENSAURE MAGNESIA, MAGNESIUMBIKARBONAT |

| | | | |
|---|---|---|---|
| 7884 | **MAGNESIUM CARBONATE, CARBONATE OF MAGNESIA** | CARBONATE DE MAGNESIE | MAGNESIAKOHLENSÄURE, MAGNESIUMKARBONAT |
| 7885 | **MAGNESIUM CHLORIDE** | CHLORURE DE MAGNESIUM | MAGNESIUMCHLORID, CHLORMAGNESIUM |
| 7886 | **MAGNESIUM FLUORIDE** | FLUORURE DE MAGNESIUM | MAGNESIUMFLUORID, FLUORMAGNESIUM |
| 7887 | **MAGNESIUM HYDROXIDE** | HYDRATE DE MAGNESIE | MAGNESIUMHYDROXYD |
| 7888 | **MAGNESIUM SILICATE** | SILICATE DE MAGNESIUM | MAGNESIA-KIESELSÄURE, MAGNESIUMSILIKAT |
| 7889 | **MAGNESIUM SULPHATE, SULPHATE OF MAGNESIA, EPSOM SALT** | SULFATE DE MAGNESIUM, SEL ANGLAIS, SEL D'EPSOM, SEL DE SEDLITZ | BITTERSALZ, MAGNESIA-SCHWEFELSÄURE, MAGNESIUMSULFAT (ENGLISCHES), SEDLITZERSALZ, EPSOMER SALZ |
| 7890 | **MAGNESIUM-BASE ALLOY** | ALLIAGE A BASE DE MAGNESIUM | MAGNESIUMLEGIERUNG |
| 7891 | **MAGNET** | AIMANT | MAGNET |
| 7892 | **MAGNET STEEL** | ACIER POUR AIMANTS | MAGNETSTAHL |
| 7893 | **MAGNETIC** | MAGNETIQUE | MAGNETISCH |
| 7894 | **MAGNETIC ANALYSIS** | ANALYSE MAGNETIQUE | ANALYSE (MAGNETISCHE) |
| 7895 | **MAGNETIC ATTRACTION** | ATTRACTION MAGNETIQUE | ANZIEHUNG (MAGNETISCHE) |
| 7896 | **MAGNETIC BRAKE** | FREIN MAGNETIQUE | BREMSE (MAGNETISCHE) |
| 7897 | **MAGNETIC CHUCK BLOCKS** | CALES MAGNETIQUES DE FIXATION | MAGNETSPANNFUTTER |
| 7898 | **MAGNETIC CHUCKS** | MANDRINS MAGNETIQUES | MAGNETFUTTER |
| 7899 | **MAGNETIC DENSITY, FLUX DENSITY** | DENSITE MAGNETIQUE | DICHTE (MAGNETISCHE) |
| 7900 | **MAGNETIC ENERGY** | ENERGIE MAGNETIQUE | ENERGIE (MAGNETISCHE) |
| 7901 | **MAGNETIC FIELD** | CHAMP MAGNETIQUE | FELD (MAGNETISCHES) |
| 7902 | **MAGNETIC FIGURES** | SPECTRE MAGNETIQUE | FEILSPÄNKURVEN, KRAFTLINIENBILD |
| 7903 | **MAGNETIC FLUX** | FLUX MAGNETIQUE | MAGNETISCHE STRÖMUNG, MAGNETISCHER KRAFTFLUSS, KRAFTLINIENFLUSS, KRAFTLINIENSTROM |
| 7904 | **MAGNETIC FORCE** | FORCE MAGNETIQUE | KRAFT (MAGNETISCHE) |
| 7905 | **MAGNETIC GAUGE** | JAUGE MAGNETIQUE | MESSER (MAGNETISCHER) |
| 7906 | **MAGNETIC HYSTERESIS** | MAGNETISATION | MAGNETISIERUNG |
| 7907 | **MAGNETIC HYSTERESIS LOSS** | PERTES DE MAGNETISATION | MAGNETISIERUNGSVERLUSTE |
| 7908 | **MAGNETIC INDUCTION** | INDUCTION MAGNETIQUE | INDUKTION (MAGNETISCHE) |
| 7909 | **MAGNETIC NEEDLE** | AIGUILLE AIMANTEE | MAGNETNADEL |
| 7910 | **MAGNETIC PARTICLE INSPECTION (MAGNAFLUX)** | MAGNETOSCOPIE | MAGNETOSKOPIE |
| 7911 | **MAGNETIC PERMEABILITY** | PERMEABILITE MAGNETIQUE | DURCHLÄSSIGKEIT (MAGNETISCHE), PERMEABILITÄT (MAGNETISCHE) |
| 7912 | **MAGNETIC PLATES** | PLATEAUX MAGNETIQUES | MAGNET-PLANSCHEIBEN |
| 7913 | **MAGNETIC POLE** | POLE MAGNETIQUE | MAGNETPOL |
| 7914 | **MAGNETIC PYRITES, PYRRHOTITE** | PYRRHOTINE, PYRITE MAGNETIQUE | MAGNETKIES, PYRRHOTIN |
| 7915 | **MAGNETIC REPULSION** | REPULSION MAGNETIQUE | ABSTOSSUNG (MAGNETISCHE) |
| 7916 | **MAGNETIC SATURATION** | SATURATION MAGNETIQUE | SÄTTIGUNG (MAGNETISCHE) |
| 7917 | **MAGNETIC SEPARATION** | SEPARATION MAGNETIQUE | TRENNUNG (MAGNETISCHE) |
| 7918 | **MAGNETIC SUSCEPTIBILITY** | SUSCEPTIBILITE MAGNETIQUE | SUSZEPTIBILITÄT (MAGNETISCHE), MAGNETISIERUNGSKOEFFIZIENT |
| 7919 | **MAGNETIC TAPE** | BANDE MAGNETIQUE | MAGNETBAND |
| 7920 | **MAGNETIC TRANSFORMATION TEMPERATURE** | POINT DE CURIE | CURIEPUNKT |
| 7921 | **MAGNETIC TRIM HAMMER** | MARTEAU DE TAPISSIER AIMANTE | MAGNETHAMMER |
| 7922 | **MAGNETISABLE** | MAGNETISABLE | MAGNETISIERBAR |
| 7923 | **MAGNETISATION** | AIMANTATION | MAGNETISIEREN, MAGNETISIERUNG |
| 7924 | **MAGNETISE (TO)** | AIMANTER | MAGNETISIEREN |

# MAG 202

| | | | |
|---|---|---|---|
| 7925 | MAGNETISING FORCE | FORCE MAGNETISANTE | KRAFT (MAGNETISIERENDE) |
| 7926 | MAGNETISM | MAGNETISME | MAGNETISMUS, MAGNETISM |
| 7927 | MAGNETITE, FERROSOFERRIC OXIDE, MAGNETIC OXIDE OF IRON, LOADSTONE | MAGNETITE, FER OXYDULE, MINERAI DE FER MAGNETIQUE | MAGNETEISENSTEIN, MAGNETEISENERZ, MAGNETIT, MAGNETISCH, EISENOXYD, EISENOXYDULOXYD, MAGNETSTEIN |
| 7928 | MAGNETIZATION | MAGNETISATION, AIMANTATION | MAGNETISIERUNG |
| 7929 | MAGNETIZING FORCE | FORCE MAGNETOMOTRICE SPECIFIQUE | MAGNETOMOTORISCHE KRAFT |
| 7930 | MAGNETO-ELECTRIC MACHINE | MACHINE MAGNETO-ELECTRIQUE, MAGNETO | MASCHINE (MAGNETELEKTRISCHE) |
| 7931 | MAGNETOGRAPHIC INSPECTION | EXAMEN MAGNETOGRAPHIQUE | PRÜFUNG (MAGNETOGRAPHISCHE) |
| 7932 | MAGNETOMOTIVE FORCE (M M F) | FORCE MAGNETOMOTRICE | KRAFT (MAGNETOMOTORISCHE) |
| 7933 | MAGNETOSTRICTION | MAGNETOSTRICTION | MAGNETOSTRIKTION |
| 7934 | MAGNETTE CLUTCH | EMBRAYAGE MAGNETIQUE | KUPPLUNG (MAGNETISCHE), KUPPUNG (ELEKTROMAGNETISCHE) |
| 7935 | MAGNIFICATION | GROSSISSEMENT, AGRANDISSEMENT | VERGRÖSSERUNG (OPT.) |
| 7936 | MAGNIFYING GLASS | LOUPE, VERRE GROSSISSANT | LUPE, VERGRÖSSERUNGSGLAS |
| 7937 | MAGNIFYING POWER | GROSSISSEMENT, POUVOIR GROSSISSANT | VERGRÖSSERUNGSKRAFT |
| 7938 | MAGNIFYING POWER OF A LENS | GROSSISSEMENT D'UNE LENTILLE | VERGRÖSSERUNG EINER LINSE |
| 7939 | MAGNITUDE OF A FORCE | GRANDEUR, INTENSITE D'UNE FORCE | GRÖSSE EINER KRAFT, INTENSITÄT EINER KRAFT |
| 7940 | MAIN (ELECTRIC) POWER SUPPLY | ALIMENTATION, RESEAU | HAUPTSPEISELEITUNG |
| 7941 | MAIN BEARING | COUSSINET DE PALIER, PALIERS DE VILEBREQUIN | HAUPTLAGER, GRUNDLAGER |
| 7942 | MAIN JET | GICLEUR PRINCIPAL | HAUPTDÜSE |
| 7943 | MAIN SHAFT (GB) | ARBRE PRIMAIRE OU PRINCIPAL | HAUPTWELLE, ABTRIEBSWELLE |
| 7944 | MAIN SHAFTING, LINE SHAFTING | ARBRE PRINCIPAL, TRANSMISSION PRINCIPALE, ARBRE DE TRANSMISSION, ARBRE D'ATTAQUE, ARBRE SECOND MOTEUR, ARBRE DEUXIEME MOTEUR | HAUPTWELLE, TRIEBWERKSWELLE, TRANSMISSIONSWELLE |
| 7945 | MAINTENANCE COSTS, COST OF UPKEEP, OF MAINTENANCE | FRAIS D'ENTRETIEN | INSTANDHALTUNGSKOSTEN, UNTERHALTUNGSKOSTEN |
| 7946 | MAINTENANCE, UPKEEP | ENTRETIEN | UNTERHALTUNG, INSTANDHALTUNG, WARTUNG |
| 7947 | MAJOR AXIS OF ELLIPSE | GRAND AXE D'UNE ELLIPSE | GROSSE ACHSE EINER ELLIPSE |
| 7948 | MAKE (TO), MANUFACTURE (TO) | FABRIQUER, MANUFACTURER | HERSTELLEN, ERZEUGEN, FABRIZIEREN |
| 7949 | MAKE AND BREAK COMPONENT | CONJONCTEUR-DISJONCTEUR | RÜCKSTROMSCHALTELEMENT |
| 7950 | MAKE CONTACT (TO) | REALISER, ETABLIR UN CONTACT | KONTAKT HERSTELLEN (EINEN) |
| 7951 | MAKE FLUSH (TO) | AFFLEURER | BÜNDIG MACHEN |
| 7952 | MAKE MALLEABLE CASTINGS (TO) | MALLEABILISER LA FONTE | TEMPERN |
| 7953 | MAKE TIGHT (TO), CAULK (TO) | RENDRE ETANCHE, ETANCHER | ABDICHTEN |
| 7954 | MAKING TIGHT, CAULKING | ETANCHEMENT | ABDICHTEN, DICHTEN |
| 7955 | MALE EXTERNAL SCREW THREAD | FILETAGE EXTERIEUR, FILETAGE MALE | AUSSENGEWINDE, BOLZENGEWINDE, VATERGEWINDE |
| 7956 | MALE TAPER GAUGE | JAUGE-TAMPON CONIQUE | KEGELLEHRDORN |
| 7957 | MALE-FEMALE FACING | EMBOITEMENT SIMPLE (M ET F) | VOR-UND RÜCKSPRUNG |
| 7958 | MALLEABILITY, FORGEABILITY | MALLEABILITE, FORGEABILITE | HÄMMERBARKEIT, SCHMIEDBARKEIT |
| 7959 | MALLEABLE CAST IRON, MALLEABLE CASTING | FONTE MALLEABLE | GUSS (SCHMIEDBARER), TEMPERGUSS, TEMPERSTAHLGUSS, WEICHGUSS |
| 7960 | MALLEABLE, FORGEABLE | MALLEABLE, FORGEABLE | HÄMMERBAR, SCHMIEDBAR |

| | | | |
|---|---|---|---|
| 7961 | **MALLEABLEIZING** | MALLEABILISATION | SCHMIEDBARMACHEN |
| 7962 | **MALLET, WOODEN HAMMER** | MAILLET EN BOIS | SCHLÄGEL, HOLZHAMMER |
| 7963 | **MAN HOLE** | TROU D'HOMME, OUVERTURE, JOINT AUTOCLAVE | MANNLOCH |
| 7964 | **MANDREL** | POUPEE (DE TOUR), MANDRIN DE MONTAGE, MANDRIN DE REPRISE | DORN, AUFNAHMEDORN |
| 7965 | **MANE HAIR** | POILS DE LA CRINIERE, CRINS | MÄHNENHAAR |
| 7966 | **MANGANESE** | MANGANESE | MANGAN |
| 7967 | **MANGANESE BRONZE** | BRONZE AU MANGANESE, LAITON AU MANGANESE | MANGANBRONZE |
| 7968 | **MANGANESE STEEL** | ACIER AU MANGANESE | MANGANSTAHL |
| 7969 | **MANGANESE-KILLED STEEL** | ACIER CALME AU MANGANESE | STAHL MIT MANGAN (BERUHIGTER) |
| 7970 | **MANGANIC OXIDE** | SESQUIOXYDE DE MANGANESE | MANGAN-SESQUIOXYD |
| 7971 | **MANGANIFEROUS** | MANGANESIFERE | MANGANHALTIG |
| 7972 | **MANGANOUS CHLORIDE** | CHLORURE MANGANEUX | MANGANCHLORÜR, MANGANOCHLORID, CHLORMANGAN |
| 7973 | **MANGANOUS OXIDE** | PROTOXYDE DE MANGANESE | MANGANOXYDUL, MANGANMONOXYD |
| 7974 | **MANGANOUS SULPHATE** | SULFATE MANGANEUX | MANGANOSULFAT |
| 7975 | **MANGLE WHEEL** | ROUE DENTEE INTERROMPUE | MANGELRAD, WENDERAD |
| 7976 | **MANHOLE** | TROU D'HOMME | EINSTEIGELOCH |
| 7977 | **MANHOLE COVER** | TAMPON DE TROU D'HOMME | MANNLOCHDECKEL |
| 7978 | **MANHOLE NECK** | COLLET DE TROU D'HOMME | MANNLOCHRING |
| 7979 | **MANIFOLD** | COLLECTEUR | SAMMELLEITUNG |
| 7980 | **MANILLA HEMP** | CHANVRE DE MANILLE, MANILLE, ABACA | MANILAHANF |
| 7981 | **MANILLA ROPE** | CORDE EN MANILLE | MANILAHANFSEIL |
| 7982 | **MANIPULATOR** | MACHINE DE MANIPULATION, CULBUTEUR DE LINGOTS | KANTVORRICHTUNG |
| 7983 | **MANNESMANN TUBE** | TUBE MANNESMANN | MANNESMANNROHR |
| 7984 | **MANOMETRIC, PRESSURE EFFICIENCY** | RENDEMENT MANOMETRIQUE | WIRKUNGSGRAD (MANOMETRISCHER) |
| 7985 | **MANTISSA** | MANTISSE | MANTISSE |
| 7986 | **MANTLE** | ENVELOPPE, GAINE | MANTEL |
| 7987 | **MANUAL DATA INPUT** | INTRODUCTION MANUELLE DES DONNEES | DATENEINGABE (MANUELLE) |
| 7988 | **MANUAL WELD** | SOUDURE DEPOSEE A LA MAIN | NAHT (HANDGESCHWEISSTE) |
| 7989 | **MANUFACTURE** | FABRICATION, CONSTRUCTION, PRODUIT MANUFACTURE | HERSTELLUNG, FABRIKATION, ERZEUGNIS, FABRIKAT |
| 7990 | **MANUFACTURE OF BRIQUETTES** | AGGLOMERATION, FABRICATION DES AGGLOMERES | BRIKETTIERUNG |
| 7991 | **MANUFACTURE OF COKE** | FABRICATION DU COKE, CARBONISATION DE LA HOUILLE | KOKEREI, KOKSBRENNEREI, KOKSFABRIKATION |
| 7992 | **MANUFACTURER, MAKER** | FABRICANT, INDUSTRIEL, CONSTRUCTEUR | HERSTELLER, ERZEUGER, FABRIKANT |
| 7993 | **MANUFACTURER'S DATA REPORT** | ETAT DESCRIPTIF DU CONSTRUCTEUR | HERSTELLERBESCHREIBUNG |
| 7994 | **MANUFACTURING RANGE** | GAMME DE FABRICATION, PROGRAMME DE FABRICATION | FERTIGUNGSUMFANG, FERTIGUNGSBEREICH, FERTIGUNGSPROGRAMM |
| 7995 | **MANURE SPREADERS : FARMYARD** | EPANDEURS DE FUMIER | DÜNGERAUSBREITEMASCHINEN |
| 7996 | **MANUSCRIPT** | MANUSCRIT | MANUSKRIPT |
| 7997 | **MANWAY** | TROU D'HOMME, T.H. | MANNLOCH |
| 7998 | **MANWAY NECK** | MANCHON DE T.H., COLLET DE T.H. | MANNLOCHRING |
| 7999 | **MAPPING PEN** | PLUME A DESSIN | ZEICHENFEDER |
| 8000 | **MARAGING STEEL** | ACIER AUTOTREMPANT | STAHL (NATURHARTER), SS-STAHL, MARTENSIT, STAHL (AUSHÄRTENDER) |

# MAR

204

| | | | |
|---|---|---|---|
| 8001 | **MARBLE** | MARBRE | MARMOR |
| 8002 | **MARGINAL PLATE** | TOLE MARGINALE | RANDBLECH |
| 8003 | **MARINE BOILER** | CHAUDIERE MARINE | SCHIFFSKESSEL |
| 8004 | **MARINE CHAINS** | CHAINES DE MARINE | SCHIFFSKETTEN |
| 8005 | **MARINE ENGINE** | MOTEUR MARIN, MACHINE MARINE | SCHIFFSMASCHINE |
| 8006 | **MARINE GLUE** | GLU MARINE | MARINELEIM |
| 8007 | **MARINE PATTERN CONNECTING ROD END** | TETE DE BIELLE A CAGE OUVERTE | OFFENER SCHUBSTANGENKOPF, MARINEKOPF, SCHIFFSKOPF |
| 8008 | **MARK (TO)** | REPERER, MARQUER | ANZEICHNEN, MARKIEREN |
| 8009 | **MARK OF A SCALE** | TRAIT D'UNE ECHELLE | TEILSTRICH, GRADSTRICH |
| 8010 | **MARK OUT (TO), SET OUT (TO), LINE OUT (TO), LAY OUT (TO), SCRIBE (TO)** | TRACER, MARQUER | ANREISSEN, VORREISSEN |
| 8011 | **MARK WITH THE CENTRE PUNCH (TO)** | MARQUER UN REPERE, REPERER, AMORCER AU MOYEN D'UN COUP DE POINTEAU | ANKÖRNEN |
| 8012 | **MARK, GUILDING MARK** | REPERE | ZEICHEN, MERKZEICHEN |
| 8013 | **MARKER OUT, LINER OUT** | TRACEUR-MECANICIEN | ANREISSER, VORREISSER (ARBEITER) |
| 8014 | **MARKET LEAD, SOFT LEAD** | PLOMB MARCHAND, PLOMB DOUX | WEICHBLEI, HÜTTENBLEI, KAUFBLEI |
| 8015 | **MARKING** | REPERAGE, MARQUAGE | ANZEICHNEN, MARKIEREN |
| 8016 | **MARKING GAUGE** | TRUSQUIN A POINTE, CALIBRE DE TRACAGE | PARALLELMASS, STREICHMASS, REISSMASS, PARALLELREISSER, STREICHMODELL, REISSMODELL, ANDREISSSCHABLONE |
| 8017 | **MARKING OUT, SETTING OUT, LINING OUT, LAYING OUT, SCRIBING** | TRACAGE, TRACE | ANREISSEN, VORREISSEN |
| 8018 | **MARKING-OUT OF PLATES** | TRACAGE DES TOLES | BLECHANREISSEN |
| 8019 | **MARL** | MARNE | MERGEL |
| 8020 | **MARSEILLE SOAP** | SAVON DE MARSEILLE | MARSEILLER SEIFE |
| 8021 | **MARTEMPERING** | TREMPE EN BAIN CHAUD, TREMPE MARTENSITIQUE | WARMBADHÄRTUNG |
| 8022 | **MARTENSITE** | MARTENSITE | HARDENIT, MARTENSIT |
| 8023 | **MARTIN-SIEMENS STEEL, OPEN HEARTH STEEL** | ACIER SIEMENS- MARTIN | SIEMENS-MARTINSTAHL |
| 8024 | **MASH WELD** | SOUDURE A L'ECRASEMENT | ROLLENQUETSCHNAHT |
| 8025 | **MASONRY** | MACONNERIE, OUVRAGE DE MACONNERIE | MAUERWERK |
| 8026 | **MASS** | MASSE (MEC.) | MASSE |
| 8027 | **MASS EFFECT** | EFFET DE MASSE, SENSIBILITE A L'EPAISSEUR | MASSENEFFEKT |
| 8028 | **MASS PRODUCTION, BULK PRODUCTION** | CONSTRUCTION, PRODUCTION, FABRICATION, CONFECTION, TRAVAIL EN GRANDE SERIE | MASSENHERSTELLUNG, MASSENFABRIKATION |
| 8029 | **MASS SPECTROMETER** | SPECTROMETRE DE MASSE | MASSENSPEKTROMETER |
| 8030 | **MASS-ABSORPTION COEFFICIENT** | COEFFICIENT D'ABSORPTION MASSIQUE | MASSENABSORPTIONSKOEFFIZIENT |
| 8031 | **MASSICOT, LEAD MONOXIDE** | MASSICOT | MASSICOT, BLEIOXYD (GELBES), BLEIGELB, NEUGELB, KÖNIGSGELB |
| 8032 | **MASTER** | MODELE ETALON | MUSTERMODELL |
| 8033 | **MASTER BLOCK** | PORTE-ESTAMPES, PORTE-POINCONS | STEMPELHALTER |
| 8034 | **MASTER FORM** | PIECE DE REFERENCE | KOPIERMODELL, BEZUGSFORMSTÜCK |
| 8035 | **MASTER GAUGE** | JAUGE DE REFERENCE | PRÜFLEHRE |
| 8036 | **MASTER SET** | JEU ETALON | BEZUGSGERÄTESATZ |
| 8037 | **MASTER-CYLINDER** | MAITRE-CYLINDRE | HAUPTZYLINDER |

|  |  |  |  |
|---|---|---|---|
| 8038 | **MASTIC** | MASTIC, LUT | KITT |
| 8039 | **MASTIC RESIN** | MASTIC EN LARMES, MASTIC EN GRAINS | MASTIX |
| 8040 | **MASURIUM** | MASURIUM,TECHNETIUM | MASURIUM, TECHNETIUM |
| 8041 | **MASUT** | MAZOUT | MASUT |
| 8042 | **MATCH (TO)** | ASSORTIR, ACCOSTER | ZUSAMMENPASSEN, ANHAFTEN |
| 8043 | **MATCH LINE** | FACE DE REFERENCE | BEZUGSKANTE |
| 8044 | **MATCH PLATE PATTERN** | PLAQUE MODELE DOUBLE FACE | WENDEPLATTE, MODELLPLATTE (ZWEISEITIGE) |
| 8045 | **MATCH PLATES (TO) (DURING ERECTION)** | ACCOSTER DES TOLES (MONTAGE) | BLECHE ANEINANDERLEGEN |
| 8046 | **MATCHING (OF PLATES)** | ACCOSTAGE DE TOLES | BLECHANHAFTUNG |
| 8047 | **MATCHING PLANE** | BOUVET A FOURCHEMENT | SPUNDHOBEL |
| 8048 | **MATE, HELPER** | AIDE | HILFSARBEITER |
| 8049 | **MATERIAL COSTS, COST OF MATERIALS** | FRAIS DE MATIERE, FRAIS DE CONSOMMATION | MATERIALKOSTEN |
| 8050 | **MATERIAL OF CONSTRUCTION ENGINEERING** | MATERIEL DE CONSTRUCTION | BAUSTOFF, MATERIAL, BAUMATERIAL |
| 8051 | **MATHEMATICAL INSTRUMENTS** | INSTRUMENTS DE MATHEMATIQUES, BOITE DE COMPAS | REISSZEUG |
| 8052 | **MATHEMATICAL TABLE** | BAREME | RECHENTAFEL, RECHENTABELLE |
| 8053 | **MATHEMATICS** | MATHEMATIQUE | MATHEMATIK |
| 8054 | **MATING FLANGE** | CONTREBRIDE | GEGENFLANSCH |
| 8055 | **MATRIX** | MATRICE, MASSE PRINCIPALE | GRUNDMASSE, MATRIZE |
| 8056 | **MATRIX BRASS** | LAITON DE BASE | GRUNDMESSING |
| 8057 | **MATRIX METAL** | METAL DE BASE | GRUNDMETALL |
| 8058 | **MATTE** | MATTE | LECH, STEIN |
| 8059 | **MATTE DIP** | BAIN DE DECAPAGE MAT, BAIN DE BLANCHIMENT | MATTBRENNE |
| 8060 | **MATTE SURFACE** | SURFACE MATE | OBERFLÄCHE (GLANZLOSE) |
| 8061 | **MATTER IN SOLUTION** | MATIERES EN DISSOLUTION | LÖSUNGSSTOFFE |
| 8062 | **MATTER IN SUSPENSION, SUSPENDED MATTER** | MATIERES EN SUSPENSION | SCHWEBESTOFFE, SINKSTOFFE |
| 8063 | **MAXIMUM AND MINIMUM THERMOMETER** | THERMOMETRE A MAXIMA ET MINIMA | MAXIMUM-UND MINIMUM-THERMOMETER |
| 8064 | **MAXIMUM DEFLECTION** | FLECHE MAXIMUM | DURCHBIEGUNG (GRÖSSTE) |
| 8065 | **MAXIMUM LOAD, PEAK LOAD** | CHARGE MAXIMUM | SPITZENLAST, SPITZENBELASTUNG, HÖCHSTBELASTUNG |
| 8066 | **MAXIMUM OUTPUT** | PUISSANCE MAXIMUM | HÖCHSTLEISTUNG |
| 8067 | **MAXIMUM SPEED** | VITESSE MAXIMUM | HÖCHSTGESCHWINDIGKEIT |
| 8068 | **MAXIMUM TEMPERATURE** | TEMPERATURE MAXIMUM | HÖCHSTTEMPERATUR, MAXIMALTEMPERATUR |
| 8069 | **MAXIMUM VALUE** | VALEUR MAXIMUM | HÖCHSTWERT, GRÖSSTWERT, MAXIMALWERT |
| 8070 | **MAXIMUM WEIGHT** | POIDS MAXIMUM | HÖCHSTGEWICHT, MAXIMALGEWICHT |
| 8071 | **MCQUAID-EHN TEST** | TEST DE MCQUAID-EHN | MCQUAID-EHN-PRÜFUNG |
| 8072 | **MEAN** | MOYEN | MITTEL |
| 8073 | **MEAN AVERAGE VALUE** | VALEUR MOYENNE | WERT (MITTLERER), MITTELWERT, DURCHSCHNITTSWERT |
| 8074 | **MEAN DEVIATION** | ECART MOYEN | ABWEICHUNG (DURCHSCHNITTLICHE) |
| 8075 | **MEAN PRESSURE** | PRESSION MOYENNE | DRUCK (MITTLERER) |
| 8076 | **MEAN SPECIFIC HEAT** | CHALEUR SPECIFIQUE MOYENNE | WÄRME (MITTLERE SPEZIFISCHE) |
| 8077 | **MEASURE** | MESURE | MASS |

# MEA

| 8078 | MEASURE (TO) | MESURER | MESSEN, AUSMESSEN, ABMESSEN |
|---|---|---|---|
| 8079 | MEASURE OF CAPACITY | MESURE DE CAPACITE | HOHLMASS |
| 8080 | MEASURE OF LENGTH, LINEAR MEASURE | MESURE LINEAIRE | LÄNGENMASS |
| 8081 | MEASURE OF SURFACE, SQUARE MEASURE | MESURE DE SURFACE | FLÄCHENMASS |
| 8082 | MEASURE OF VOLUME, CUBIC SOLID MEASURE | MESURE DE VOLUME | KÖRPERMASS |
| 8083 | MEASURE THE POWER BY A BRAKE TEST (TO) | MESURER LA PUISSANCE DES FREINS | LEISTUNG ABBREMSEN (DIE) |
| 8084 | MEASURE WITH THE PLANIMETER (TO) | PLANIMETRER | PLANIMETRIEREN |
| 8085 | MEASURE, MEASURING ROD, RULE | REGLE GRADUEE | MASSSTAB, MESSSTAB |
| 8086 | MEASUREMENT OF TEMPERATURE | MESURE DE LA TEMPERATURE | TEMPERATURMESSUNG |
| 8087 | MEASUREMENT WITH THE PLANIMETER | PLANIMETRAGE | PLANIMETRIERUNG |
| 8088 | MEASUREMENT, MEASURING | MESURAGE | MESSUNG, MESSEN |
| 8089 | MEASURING ERROR, ERROR IN MEASUREMENT | ERREUR DE MESURE | MESSFEHLER |
| 8090 | MEASURING INSTRUMENT APPLIANCE | INSTRUMENT DE MESURE | MESSGERÄT, MESSINSTRUMENT |
| 8091 | MEASURING POINT | POINT DE MESURE | MESSPUNKT |
| 8092 | MEASURING TAPE | METRE A RUBAN, RUBAN, ROULETTE D'ARPENTAGE | MESSBAND, BANDMASS, ROLLBANDMASS |
| 8093 | MECHANICAL | MECANIQUE | MECHANISCH |
| 8094 | MECHANICAL ADVANTAGE | GAIN DE TRAVAIL, BENEFICE DANS LE TRAVAIL | ARBEITSGEWINN, GEWINN AN ARBEIT |
| 8095 | MECHANICAL CHUCKS | MANDRINS MECANIQUES | FUTTER (MECHANISCHES) |
| 8096 | MECHANICAL CLEANING | NETTOYAGE MECANIQUE | REINIGUNG (MECHANISCHE) |
| 8097 | MECHANICAL COMPARATOR | COMPARATEUR MECANIQUE | VERGLEICHER (MECHANISCHER) |
| 8098 | MECHANICAL DRAUGHT | TIRAGE ARTIFICIEL, TIRAGE A SOUFFLERIE | ZUG (KÜNSTLICHER) |
| 8099 | MECHANICAL DRAWING | DESSIN INDUSTRIEL | ZEICHNUNG (TECHNISCHE) |
| 8100 | MECHANICAL EFFICIENCY | RENDEMENT MECANIQUE, RENDEMENT ORGANIQUE | WIRKUNGSGRAD (MECHANISCHER) |
| 8101 | MECHANICAL ENERGY | ENERGIE MECANIQUE | ARBEITSVERMÖGEN (MECHANISCHES), ENERGIE (MECHANISCHE) |
| 8102 | MECHANICAL ENGINEER | INGENIEUR-MECANICIEN | MASCHINENBAUINGENIEUR |
| 8103 | MECHANICAL ENGINEERING | CONSTRUCTION MECANIQUE, CONSTRUCTION, FABRICATION DES MACHINES | MASCHINENBAU |
| 8104 | MECHANICAL EQUIVALENT OF HEAT | EQUIVALENT MECANIQUE DE LA CHALEUR | WÄRMEÄQUIVALENT (MECHANISCHES) |
| 8105 | MECHANICAL FORCE FEED LUBRICATOR | GRAISSEUR MOLLERUP, APPAREIL DE GRAISSAGE SOUS PRESSION MECANIQUE | SCHMIERPRESSE |
| 8106 | MECHANICAL HANDLING OF MATERIALS IN THE WORKS, WORKS TRANSPORT | MANUTENTION MECANIQUE | FÖRDERUNG, BEFÖRDERUNG, TRANSPORT IM WERK |
| 8107 | MECHANICAL METALLURGY | METALLURGIE MECANIQUE | METALLURGIE (MECHANISCHE) |
| 8108 | MECHANICAL PLATING | PLACAGE MECANIQUE | PLATTIERUNG (MECHANISCHE) |
| 8109 | MECHANICAL PROPERTIES | CARACTERISTIQUES MECANIQUES | EIGENSCHAFTEN (MECHANISCHE) |
| 8110 | MECHANICAL STOKER | CHARGEUR, FOYER AUTOMATIQUE | SELSTTÄTIGE MECHANISCHE ROSTBESCHICKUNGSVORRICHTUNG |
| 8111 | MECHANICAL STOKING | CHAUFFAGE MECANIQUE | SELBSTTÄTIGE MECHANISCHE ROSTBESCHICKUNG |
| 8112 | MECHANICAL TESTING | ESSAIS MECANIQUES | PRÜFUNG (MECHANISCHE) |

|      |                                                              |                                                       |                                                                          |
|------|--------------------------------------------------------------|-------------------------------------------------------|--------------------------------------------------------------------------|
| 8113 | **MECHANICAL TWINS**                                         | MACLE DE DEFORMATION                                  | VERZERRUNGSZWILLINGSKRISTALL                                             |
| 8114 | **MECHANICAL VIBRATION**                                    | VIBRATION MECANIQUE                                  | SCHWINGUNG (MECHANISCHE)                                                 |
| 8115 | **MECHANICAL WELDING**                                      | SOUDAGE MECANIQUE (AUTOMATIQUE)                      | MASCHINENSCHWEISSEN                                                      |
| 8116 | **MECHANICAL WOOD PULP**                                    | PATE MECANIQUE DE BOIS                               | HOLZSTOFF, HOLZSCHLIFF                                                   |
| 8117 | **MECHANICAL WORK**                                         | TRAVAIL MOTEUR, TRAVAIL MECANIQUE                    | ARBEIT (MECHANISCHE)                                                     |
| 8118 | **MECHANICAL-OPTICAL COMPARATOR**                           | COMPARATEUR OPTICO-MECANIQUE                         | VERGLEICHER (OPTISCH-MECHANISCHER)                                       |
| 8119 | **MECHANICALLY DRIVEN OPERATED, OPERATED BY MACHINERY, POWER DRIVEN, ACTUATED BY POWER** | COMMANDE MECANIQUE, COMMANDE PAR MOTEUR | MECHANISCH, MASCHINELL ANGETRIEBEN, FÜR MASCHINENBETRIEB |
| 8120 | **MECHANICALLY OPERATED VALVE**                             | SOUPAPE COMMANDEE                                    | VENTIL (GESTEUERTES)                                                     |
| 8121 | **MECHANICS** •                                             | MECANIQUE                                            | MECHANIK                                                                 |
| 8122 | **MECHANISM, GEAR, MOTION**                                 | MECANISME, MOUVEMENT                                 | GETRIEBE, TRIEBWEK, MECHANISMUS                                          |
| 8123 | **MEDIAL SECTION**                                          | DIVISION D'UNE LIGNE EN MOYENNE ET EXTREME RAISON   | SCHNITT (GOLDENER)                                                       |
| 8124 | **MEDIAN LINE**                                             | MEDIANE                                              | MITTELLINIE, SCHWERLINIE, SEITENHALBIERENDE, MEDIANE, TRANSVERSALE       |
| 8125 | **MEDIUM OIL**                                              | HUILE MOYENNE                                        | MITTELÖL                                                                 |
| 8126 | **MEDIUM WATER-CAPACITY BOILER, BOILER WITH MEDIUM WATER SPACE** | CHAUDIERE A MOYEN VOLUME                      | MITTELWASSERRAUMKESSEL                                                   |
| 8127 | **MEDIUM-PRESSURE BOILER**                                  | CHAUDIERE A MOYENNE PRESSION                         | MITTELDRUCKKESSEL                                                        |
| 8128 | **MEDULLARY RAY**                                           | RAYON MEDULLAIRE                                     | MARKSTRAHL                                                               |
| 8129 | **MEGADYNE**                                                | MEGADYNE                                             | MEGADYN                                                                  |
| 8130 | **MEGAVOLT**                                                | MEGAVOLT                                             | MEGAVOLT                                                                 |
| 8131 | **MEGERG**                                                  | MEGERG                                               | MEGERG                                                                   |
| 8132 | **MEGOHM**                                                  | MEGOHM                                               | MEGOHM                                                                   |
| 8133 | **MELAPHYRE**                                               | MELAPHYRE                                            | MELAPHYR                                                                 |
| 8134 | **MELT**                                                    | FUSION, COULEE                                       | SCHMELZE                                                                 |
| 8135 | **MELT (TO), FUSE TO)**                                     | FONDRE, LIQUEFIER, PASSER A L'ETAT LIQUIDE           | SCHMELZEN                                                                |
| 8136 | **MELTING**                                                 | FUSION                                               | SCHMELZEN                                                                |
| 8137 | **MELTING BATH / MOLTEN POOL**                              | BAIN DE FUSION                                       | SCHMELZBAD                                                               |
| 8138 | **MELTING FURNACE**                                         | FOUR DE FUSION                                       | SCHMELZOFEN                                                              |
| 8139 | **MELTING LEE**                                             | GLACE FONDANTE                                       | EIS SCHMELZENDES                                                         |
| 8140 | **MELTING LOSS**                                            | PERTES DE FUSION                                     | SCHMELZVERLUSTE                                                          |
| 8141 | **MELTING POINT**                                           | POINT DE FUSION                                      | SCHMELZPUNKT                                                             |
| 8142 | **MELTING POT**                                             | CREUSET                                              | SCHMELZTOPF                                                              |
| 8143 | **MELTING RANGE**                                           | INTERVALLE DE FUSION                                 | SCHMELZBEREICH                                                           |
| 8144 | **MELTING RATE**                                            | VITESSE DE FUSION                                    | SCHMELZGESCHWINDIGKEIT                                                   |
| 8145 | **MEMBER**                                                  | MEMBRURE, ELEMENT                                    | BAUGLIED, ELEMENT                                                        |
| 8146 | **MEMORY**                                                  | MEMOIRE                                              | SPEICHER                                                                 |
| 8147 | **MENISCUS LENS, CONCAVO-CONVEX LENS**                      | MENISQUE CONVERGENT                                  | LINSE (KONKAVKONVEXE)                                                    |
| 8148 | **MERCHANT IRON, COMMERCIAL IRON**                          | FER MARCHAND                                         | HANDELSEISEN                                                             |
| 8149 | **MERCHANT SHAPES**                                         | PROFILES MARCHANDS                                   | HANDELSPROFILE                                                           |
| 8150 | **MERCURIAL BAROMETER**                                     | BAROMETRE A MERCURE                                  | QUECKSILBERBAROMETER                                                     |
| 8151 | **MERCURIAL PRESSURE GAUGE, MERCURY GAUGE**                 | MANOMETRE A MERCURE                                  | QUECKSILBERMANOMETER                                                     |
| 8152 | **MERCURIAL THERMOMETER**                                   | THERMOMETRE A MERCURE                                | QUECKSILBERTHERMOMETER                                                   |

**MER** 208

| | | | |
|---|---|---|---|
| 8153 | MERCURIC CHLORIDE, CORROSIVE SUBLIMATE | CHLORURE MERCURIQUE, BICHLORURE DE MERCURE, SUBLIME CORROSIF | QUECKSILBERCHLORID, MERKURICHLORID, SUBLIMAT |
| 8154 | MERCURIC FULMINATE | FULMINATE DE MERCURE | KNALLQUECKSILBER |
| 8155 | MERCURIC IODIDE | IODURE DE MERCURE | QUECKSILBERJODID, MERKURIJODID, ZWEIFACHJODQUECKSILBER, ROTES JODQUECKSILBER, JODZINNOBER, JODINROT |
| 8156 | MERCURIC NITRATE | NITRATE DE MERCURE, AZOTATE MERCURIQUE | QUECKSILBEROXYD SALPETERSAURES, QUECKSILBEROXYDNITRAT, MERKURINITRAT |
| 8157 | MERCURIC OXIDE, RED PRECIPITATE | OXYDE DE MERCURE, OXYDE MERCURIQUE | QUECKSILBEROXYD, MERKURIOXYD, ROTES PRÄZIPITAT, ROTOXID |
| 8158 | MERCURIC SULPHATE | SULFATE MERCURIQUE | QUECKSILBEROXYDSULFAT, MERKURISULFAT |
| 8159 | MERCUROUS CHLORIDE, CALOMEL | CHLORURE MERCUREUX, PROTOCHLORURE DE MERCURE, CALOMEL | QUECKSILBERCHLORÜR, MERKUROCHLORID, KALOMEL |
| 8160 | MERCUROUS NITRATE | NITRATE MERCUREUX, AZOTATE MERCUREUX | QUECKSILBEROXYDUL (SALPETERSAURES), MERKURONITRAT, QUECKSILBEROXYDULNITRAT |
| 8161 | MERCUROUS OXIDE | PROTOXYDE DE MERCURE, OXYDE MERCUREUX | QUECKSILBEROXYDUL, MERKUROOXYD |
| 8162 | MERCUROUS SULPHATE | SULFATE MERCUREUX | QUECKSILBEROXYDULSULFAT, MERKUROSULFAT |
| 8163 | MERCURY AIR PUMP | POMPE A MERCURE | QUECKSILBERLUFTPUMPE |
| 8164 | MERCURY ARC RECTIFIER | REDRESSEUR A VAPEUR DE MERCURE | QUECKSILBERDAMPF-GLEICHRICHTER |
| 8165 | MERCURY CELL | CELLULE AU MERCURE | QUECKSILBERZELLE |
| 8166 | MERCURY SWITCH | CONTACTEUR A MERCURE | QUECKSILBER-SCHALTER |
| 8167 | MERCURY VAPOUR LAMP | LAMPE A VAPEUR DE MERCURE | QUECKSILBERDAMPFLAMPE |
| 8168 | MERCURY, QUICKSILVER | MERCURE | QUECKSILBER |
| 8169 | MESH | MAILLE (D'UN CRIBLE) | SIEBMASCHE, MASCHE |
| 8170 | MESH OF A SIEVE MESH OF A STEEL FABRIC | MAILLE D'UN TAMIS, MAILLE D'UNE TOILE METALLIQUE | MASCHENGRÖSSE |
| 8171 | MESHED, IN MESH, IN GEAR | EN PRISE | IM EINGRIFF |
| 8172 | METACENTRE | METACENDRE | METAZENTRUM |
| 8173 | METAL | METAL | METALL |
| 8174 | METAL ARC | ARC METALLIQUE | METALL-LICHTBOGEN |
| 8175 | METAL ARC CUTTING | COUPAGE A L'ARC METALLIQUE | METALL-LICHTBOGENSCHNEIDEN |
| 8176 | METAL ARC WELDING | SOUDAGE A L'ARC ELECTRIQUE | METALL-LICHTBOGENSCHWEISSEN |
| 8177 | METAL CLAD CABLE | CABLE A GAINE METALLIQUE | KABEL MIT METALLMANTEL |
| 8178 | METAL CUTTING MACHINE | MACHINE-OUTIL A TRAVAILLER LES METAUX, MACHINE A METAUX | METALLBEARBEITUNGSMASCHINE |
| 8179 | METAL DISTRIBUTION RATIO | RAPPORT DE DISTRIBUTION DU METAL | NIEDERSCHLAGSVERTEILUNGSVERHÄLTNIS |
| 8180 | METAL ELECTRODE | ELECTRODE METALLIQUE | METALLELEKTRODE, SCHWEISSDRAHT |
| 8181 | METAL FILAMENT LAMP | LAMPE A FILAMENT METALLIQUE | METALLDRAHTLAMPE, METALLFADENLAMPE |
| 8182 | METAL FOG | BROUILLARD METALLIQUE | METALLNEBEL |
| 8183 | METAL FOR MEDALS, COINAGE BRONZE | BRONZE DES MONNAIES | MÜNZENBRONZE, MEDAILLENBRONZE |
| 8184 | METAL LEAF | FEUILLE METALLIQUE | METALLFOLIE |
| 8185 | METAL POWDER | METAL PULVERISE | METALLPULVER |
| 8186 | METAL SAW, HACK SAW | SCIE A MONTURE METALLIQUE, SCIE A METAUX | BÜGELSÄGE, BOGENSÄGE, METALLSÄGE |

| | | | |
|---|---|---|---|
| 8187 | **METAL SCREW** | VIS A METAUX | METALLSCHRAUBE |
| 8188 | **METAL SHOE** | SABOT MAGNETIQUE | MAGNETBREMSKLOTZ |
| 8189 | **METAL SPINNING, BURNISHING** | REPOUSSE, REPOUSSAGE, EMBOUTISSAGE | METALLDRÜCKEN, DRÜCKEN, METALLDRÜCKEREI |
| 8190 | **METAL SPRAYING** | METALLISATION | METALLSPRITZEN |
| 8191 | **METAL TURNING LATHE** | TOUR A METAUX | METALLDREHBANK |
| 8192 | **METAL WORKING** | TRAVAIL DES METAUX, USINAGE DES METAUX | METALLBEARBEITUNG |
| 8193 | **METAL-SLITTING SAN** | FRAISE-SCIE , SCIE A MORTAISER | SCHLITZSÄGE |
| 8194 | **METALLIC COATING, COAT OF METAL** | REVETEMENT METALLIQUE | METALLÜBERZUG, ÜBERZUG (METALLISCHER) |
| 8195 | **METALLIC LUSTRE** | ECLAT METALLIQUE | METALLGLANZ, GLANZ (METALLISCHER) |
| 8196 | **METALLIC PACKING** | GARNITURE METALLIQUE | PACKUNG (METALLISCHE), METALLPACKUNG, METALLIDERUNG |
| 8197 | **METALLIFEROUS** | METALLIFERE | METALLHALTIG |
| 8198 | **METALLIFEROUS MINE** | MINE METALLIQUE | ERZGRUBE, ERZBERGWERK |
| 8199 | **METALLISED PAPER** | PAPIER METALLISE | PAPIER (METALLISIERTES) |
| 8200 | **METALLIZED COATING** | REVETEMENT METALLISE | ÜBERZUG (METALLBEDAMPFTER) |
| 8201 | **METALLIZING** | METALLISATION | METALL-AUFSPRITZEN |
| 8202 | **METALLOGRAPHIC** | METALLOGRAPHIQUE | METALLOGRAPHISCH |
| 8203 | **METALLOGRAPHY** | METALLOGRAPHIE | METALLOGRAPHIE |
| 8204 | **METALLOGRAPIC ETCHING** | ATTAQUE METALLOGRAPHIQUE | METALLOGRAPHISCHE ÄTZUNG |
| 8205 | **METALLOID** | METALLOIDE | METALLOID |
| 8206 | **METALLURGICAL** | METALLURGIQUE | HÜTTENMÄNNISCH, METALLURGISCH |
| 8207 | **METALLURGICAL FURNACE** | FOUR METALLURGIQUE | OFEN (METALLURGISCHER) |
| 8208 | **METALLURGY** | METALLURGIE | HÜTTENWESEN, METALLURGIE |
| 8209 | **METALLURGY OF IRON** | METALLURGIE DU FER, SIDERURGIE | EISENHÜTTENWESEN |
| 8210 | **METAPHOSPHORIC ACID** | ACIDE METAPHOSPHORIQUE | METAPHOSPHORSÄURE |
| 8211 | **METASILICIC ACID** | ACIDE METASILICIQUE | METAKIESELSÄURE |
| 8212 | **METASTABLE** | METASTABLE | METASTABIL |
| 8213 | **METEORIC WATER** | EAU METEORIQUE | NIEDERSCHLAGWASSER, METEORISCHES WASSER |
| 8214 | **METER** | COMPTEUR | ZÄHLER (FLÜSSIGKEITS-) |
| 8215 | **METHANE, MARSH GAS, LIGHT CARBURETTED HYDROGEN** | METHANE, FORMENE, PROTOCARBURE D'HYDROGENE, HYDRURE METHYLIQUE, GAZ DES MARAIS | METHAN, GRUBENGAS, SUMPFAGS, LEICHTES KOHLENWASSERSTOFFGAS |
| 8216 | **METHOD** | METHODE | VERFAHREN |
| 8217 | **METHOD OF GEARING, MODE OF DRIVING** | MODE D'ATTAQUE | ANTRIEBART |
| 8218 | **METHOD OF MANUFACTURE, OF PRODUCTION** | PROCEDE DE FABRICATION | HERSTELLUNGSVERFAHREN, FABRIKATIONSVERFAHREN |
| 8219 | **METHOD OF MEASUREMENT** | METHODE DE MESURE | MESSVERFAHREN |
| 8220 | **METHOD OF WORKING, MODE OF OPERATION** | METHODE, MODE OPERATOIRE, METHODE DE TRAVAIL | ARBEITSWEISE, ARBEITSVERFAHREN, ARBEITSMETHODE |
| 8221 | **METHYL CHLORIDE** | CHLORURE DE METHYLE | METHYLCHLORID, CHLORMETHYL |
| 8222 | **METHYL ETHER** | ETHER OXYDE METHYLIQUE, OXYDE DE METHYLE | METHYLÄTHER, HOLZÄTHER, METHYLOXYD, METHYLENHYDRAT |
| 8223 | **METHYL ORANGE, HELIANTHINE, TROPAEOLINE D** | HELIANTHINE, METHYLORANGE | METHYLORANGE, HELIANTHIN |
| 8224 | **METHYLATED SPIRIT, DENATURED ALCOHOL** | ALCOOL DENATURE | ALKOHOL (VERGÄLLTER), WEINGEIST, DENATURIERTER SPIRITUS |
| 8225 | **METRE** | METRE (UNITE DE MESURE) | METER |

# MET

**210**

| | | | |
|---|---|---|---|
| 8226 | **METRE** | METRE, METRE DROIT, METRE RIGIDE | METERMASS, METERMASSSTAB |
| 8227 | **METRIC MEASURE** | MESURE METRIQUE | MASS (METRISCHES) |
| 8228 | **METRIC MICROMETER** | MICROMETRE METRIQUE | MIKROMETER (METRISCHER) |
| 8229 | **METRIC SYSTEM** | SYSTEME METRIQUE | SYSTEM (METRISCHES) |
| 8230 | **METRIC TAPER PLUG GAUGE** | JAUGE-TAMPON AU CONE METRIQUE | KEGELLEHRHÜLSE (METRISCHE) |
| 8231 | **MICA** | MICA | GLIMMER |
| 8232 | **MICA-SCHIST** | MICASCHISTE | GLIMMESCHIEFER |
| 8233 | **MICANITE** | MICANITE | MIKANIT |
| 8234 | **MICRO FISSURES** | MICROFISSURES | MIKRORISSE |
| 8235 | **MICRO SEGREGATION** | SEGREGATION MINEURE | MIKROSEIGERUNG |
| 8236 | **MICRO-SET ADJUSTABLE CENTRE** | CONTREPOINTE MICROMETRIQUE | KÖRNERSPITZE (MIKROMETRISCHE EINSTELLBARE) |
| 8237 | **MICROAMMETER** | MICROAMPEREMETRE | MIKROAMPEREMETER |
| 8238 | **MICROAMPERE** | MICROAMPERE | MIKROAMPERE |
| 8239 | **MICROBEAM** | FOYER FIN (TUBE DE RAYONS | |
| 8240 | **MICROBORE BORING BAR** | BARRE D'ALESAGE MICROMETRIQUE | MIKROBOHRWERKZEUG |
| 8241 | **MICROCOSMICSALT, SODIUM AMMONIUM PHOSPHATE** | SEL DE PHOSPHORE, PHOSPHATE DE SODIUM ET D'AMMONIUM, SEL MICROCOSMIQUE | NATRIUMAMMONIUMPHOSPHAT, PHOSPHORSALZ |
| 8242 | **MICROFARAD** | MICROFARAD | MIKROFARAD |
| 8243 | **MICROGRAPHIC** | MICROGRAPHIQUE | MIKROGRAPHISCH |
| 8244 | **MICROGRAPHY** | MICROGRAPHIE | MIKROAUFNAHME |
| 8245 | **MICROHARDNESS** | MICRODURETE | MIKROHÄRTE |
| 8246 | **MICROHARDNESS TESTING** | ESSAI DE MICRODURETE | MIKROHÄRTEPRÜFUNG |
| 8247 | **MICROHM** | MICROHM | MIKROHM |
| 8248 | **MICROINCH** | MICRO POUCE | MILLIONSTEL ZOLL |
| 8249 | **MICROMETER** | PALMER, MICROMETRE | BÜGELMESSSCHRAUBE, MILROMETER |
| 8250 | **MICROMETER CALIPER STAND** | PORTE-MICROMETRE | MIKROMETERHALTER |
| 8251 | **MICROMETER CALIPERS** | CALIBRES MICROMETRIQUES | LEHRE (MIKROMETRISCHE) |
| 8252 | **MICROMETER DEPTH GAUGE** | MICROMETRE DE PROFONDEUR | TIEFENMIKROMETER |
| 8253 | **MICROMETER DIAL** | ECHELLE CIRCULAIRE MICROMETRIQUE | MIKROMETERRUNDSKALA |
| 8254 | **MICROMETER EYEPIECE** | OCULAIRE-MICROMETRE | OKULARMIKROMETER |
| 8255 | **MICROMETER SCREW** | VIS MICROMETRIQUE | MIKROMETERSCHRAUBE |
| 8256 | **MICROMETRIC GAUGE** | JAUGE MICROMETRIQUE | MILLIMETERTASTER |
| 8257 | **MICRON** | MILLIEME DE MILLIMETRE, MICRON | MIKROMILLIMETER |
| 8258 | **MICROPHOTOGRAPH** | MICROGRAPHIE | MIKROPHOTOGRAMM |
| 8259 | **MICROSCOPE** | MICROSCOPE | MIKROSKOP |
| 8260 | **MICROSCOPIC EXAMINATION** | EXAMEN MICROSCOPIQUE | UNTERSUCHUNG (MIKROSKOPISCHE) |
| 8261 | **MICROSECTION** | COUPE MICROGRAPHIQUE | MIKROSCHLIFF |
| 8262 | **MICROSTRUCTURE** | MICROSTRUCTURE | FEINGEFÜGE, MIKROGEFÜGE |
| 8263 | **MICROTOME** | MICROTOME | MIKROTOM |
| 8264 | **MICROVOLT** | MICROVOLT | MIKROVOLT |
| 8265 | **MID POSITION** | POSITION INTERMEDIAIRE, DE MILIEU, MI-POSITION | MITTELLAGE, MITTELSTELLUNG |
| 8266 | **MIDDLE CUT FILE** | LIME A TAILLE MOYENNE | MITTELHIEBFEILE |
| 8267 | **MIDDLINGS** | FRAGMENTS MENUS | GRUBENKLEIN (MITTELGROSSES) |
| 8268 | **MIGRATION** | MIGRATION | WANDERUNG |
| 8269 | **MILD ABRASIVE** | ABRASIF DOUX | SCHLEIFMITTEL (MILDES) |
| 8270 | **MILD CARBON STEEL** | ACIER DOUX, ACIER A BAS CARBONE | STAHL (KOHLENSTOFFARMER), STAHL (WEICHER) |

| | | | |
|---|---|---|---|
| 8271 | **MILDEW** | MOISISSURE | SCHIMMEL |
| 8272 | **MILE** | MILLE (ANGLAIS) | MEILE (ENGLISCHE) |
| 8273 | **MILK GLASS** | VERRE OPAQUE | MILCHGLAS |
| 8274 | **MILK OF LIME** | LAIT DE CHAUX | KALKMILCH |
| 8275 | **MILKING MACHINES** | MACHINES A TRAIRE | MOLKMASCHINEN |
| 8276 | **MILL (TO)** | FRAISER | FRÄSEN |
| 8277 | **MILL A SCREW HEAD (TO)** | MOLETTER UNE TETE DE VIS | SCHRAUBENKOPF RÄNDELN (EINEN), SCHRAUBENKOPF KORDIEREN (EINEN) |
| 8278 | **MILL FINISHING** | FINISSAGE AU LAMINOIR | WALZFERTIGUNG |
| 8279 | **MILL SCALE** | PAILLE, BATITURE | WALZZUNDER |
| 8280 | **MILLED NUT** | ECROU MOLETE | RÄNDELMUTTER, MUTTER (GERÄNDELTE) |
| 8281 | **MILLED SCREW HEAD** | TETE MOLETEE D'UNE VIS | SCHRAUBENKOPF (GERÄNDELTER) |
| 8282 | **MILLER INDICES** | INDICES DE MILLER | INDIZES (MILLERSCHE) |
| 8283 | **MILLI AMMETER** | MILLIAMPERE/METRE | MILLIAMPEREMETER |
| 8284 | **MILLIAMPERE** | MILLIAMPERE | MILLIAMPERE |
| 8285 | **MILLIGRAMME** | MILLIGRAMME | MILLIGRAMM |
| 8286 | **MILLIMETRE** | MILLIMETRE | MILLIMETER |
| 8287 | **MILLING** | BROYAGE, FRAISAGE, MOLETAGE | MAHLEN, FRÄSEN, RÄNDELN |
| 8288 | **MILLING A SCREW HEAD** | MOLETAGE D'UNE TETE DE VIS | RÄNDELN EINES SCHRAUBENKOPFES, KORDIEREN EINES SCHRAUBENKOPFES |
| 8289 | **MILLING CUTTER** | FRAISE | FRÄSER, FRÄSE |
| 8290 | **MILLING DOWELS, HOLDING TABLES** | DES DE FRAISAGE, TABLES DE FIXATION | FRÄSSTIFTE, SPANNTISCHE |
| 8291 | **MILLING MACHINE** | FRAISEUSE, MACHINE A FRAISER | FRÄSMASCHINE |
| 8292 | **MILLING MACHINIST** | FRAISEUR | FRÄSER (ARBEITER) |
| 8293 | **MILLING SHOP** | ATELIER DE FRAISAGE | FRÄSEREI |
| 8294 | **MILLIVOLT** | MILLIVOLT | MILLIVOLT |
| 8295 | **MILLS/COMBINE** | MOULINS/COMBINE | MÜHLEN/(KOMBINIERT) |
| 8296 | **MILLS/CRUSHING AND GRINDING** | MOULINS/APLATISSEURS | QUETSCH-UND SCHROTMÜHLEN |
| 8297 | **MILLS/HAMMER** | MOULINS/BROYEUR | HAMMERMÜHLEN |
| 8298 | **MILLSTONE** | MEULE DE MOULIN | MÜHLSTEIN, MAHLSTEIN |
| 8299 | **MILLSTONE GRIT** | PIERRE MEULIERE, MEULIERE | MÜHLSTEIN (GEOL.) |
| 8300 | **MINE** | MINE | BERGWERK, GRUBE, ZECHE |
| 8301 | **MINERAL** | MINERAL | MINERAL |
| 8302 | **MINERAL ACID** | ACIDE MINERAL | MINERALSÄURE |
| 8303 | **MINERAL DEPOSIT** | GISEMENT MINERAL, GITE MINIER | LAGERSTÄTTE EINES MINERALS |
| 8304 | **MINERAL OIL** | HUILE MINERALE | MINERALÖL |
| 8305 | **MINETTE** | MINETTE | MINETTE |
| 8306 | **MINIMUM TEMPERATURE** | TEMPERATURE MINIMUM | TEMPERATUR (TIEFSTE), MINIMALTEMPERATUR |
| 8307 | **MINIMUM VALUE** | VALEUR MINIMUM | MINDESTWERT, KLEINSTWERT, MINIMALWERT |
| 8308 | **MINIMUM VALUE OF UPPER YIELD POINT** | LIMITE ELASTIQUE MINIMALE GARANTIE | MINDESTSTRECKGRENZE |
| 8309 | **MINIMUM WAVELENGTH** | LONGUEUR D'ONDE MINIMALE | GRENZWELLENLÄNGE |
| 8310 | **MINIMUM WEIGHT** | POIDS MINIMUM | MINDESTGEWICHT, MINIMALGEWICHT |
| 8311 | **MINING** | EXPLOITATION MINIERE, INDUSTRIE MINIERE | BERGBAU |
| 8312 | **MINING ENGINEER** | INGENIEUR DES MINES | BERGINGENIEUR |
| 8313 | **MINOR AXIS OF ELLIPSE** | PETIT AXE D'UNE ELLIPSE | ACHSE (KLEINE) EINER ELLIPSE |
| 8314 | **MINOR DIAMETER** | DIAMETRE INTERIEUR | KERNDURCHMESSER |

# MIN

212

| | | | |
|---|---|---|---|
| 8315 | MINOR OF A DETERMINANT | DETERMINANT MINEUR | UNTERDETERMINANTE |
| 8316 | MINUEND | MINUENDE | MINUEND |
| 8317 | MINUS MESH | GROSSEUR DE GRAIN MINIMALE | MINUSKORNGRÖSSE |
| 8318 | MINUS-PRESSURE, VACUUM STEAM HEATING | CHAUFFAGE PAR LA VAPEUR A UNE PRESSION INFERIEURE A LA PRESSION ATMOSPHERIQUE | VAKUUMHEIZUNG |
| 8319 | MISCELLANEOUS FONCTION | FONCTION AUXILIAIRE | HILFSFUNKTION |
| 8320 | MISCH METAL | MISCHMETAL | MISCHMETALL |
| 8321 | MISRUN | MAL VENUE, REBUT | SCHLECHTAUSGELAUFEN |
| 8322 | MISTRIMMED FORGING | PIECE FORGEE A EBAVURAGE EXCESSIF | SCHMIEDESTÜCK (ÜBERENTGRATETES) |
| 8323 | MITRE GEARS | ENGRENAGES CONCOURANTS | KEGELRADPAAR MIT ÜBERSETZUNGS-VERHÄLTNIS 1:1 |
| 8324 | MITRE JOINT | ASSEMBLAGE A ONGLET | GEHRFUGE, STOSS AUF GEHRUNG, GEHRSTOSS |
| 8325 | MITRE SQUARE | EQUERRE A ONGLET | GEHRMASS, ACHTELWINKELMASS, GEHRDREIECK |
| 8326 | MITRE, MITER | ONGLET | GEHRUNG |
| 8327 | MIX | MELANGE | GEMISCH, MISCHUNG |
| 8328 | MIX (TO) | MELANGER, AGITER | MISCHEN, RÜHREN |
| 8329 | MIXED CRYSTALS | CRISTAUX MIXTES | MISCHKRISTALLE |
| 8330 | MIXED FLOW TURBINE | TURBINE MIXTE, TURBINE AMERICAINE | TURBINE (GEMISCHTE) |
| 8331 | MIXER -MIXING DRUM | MELANGEUR | MISCHER, MISCHTROMMEL |
| 8332 | MIXERS, FOOD AND CONCRETE | MELANGEURS | NÄHRMITTEL- UND BETONMISCHMASCHINEN |
| 8333 | MIXING LADLE | POCHE MELANGEUSE | MISCHERPFANNE |
| 8334 | MIXING MACHINE | MELANGEUR, MALAXEUR | MISCHMASCHINE |
| 8335 | MIXING VALVE | ROBINET MELANGEUR | MISCHVENTIL |
| 8336 | MIXING, MIXTURE | MELANGE (ACTION), MELANGE (CHIMIQUE) | PULVERMISCHUNG, MISCHEN, MISCHUNG |
| 8337 | MIXTURE (AIR AND FUEL) | MELANGE CARBURE | KRAFTSTOFFLUFTGEMISCH |
| 8338 | MODEM, MODULATOR, DEMODULATOR | MODEM, MODULATEUR, DEMODULATEUR | MODEM, MODULATOR, DEMODULATOR |
| 8339 | MODULUS | MODULE | MODUL |
| 8340 | MODULUS COEFFICIENT OF ELASTICITY, ELASTIC MODULUS, YOUNG'S MODULUS, STRETCH MODULUS | COEFFICIENT DE RESISTANCE A L'ALLONGEMENT, MESURE DE L'ELASTICITE | ELASTIZITÄTSMODUL, ELASTIZITÄTSMASS |
| 8341 | MODULUS OF ELASTICITY | MODULE D'ELASTICITE | ELASTIZITÄTSMODUL, SCHWUNGSZAHL |
| 8342 | MODULUS OF RIGIDITY | MODULE DE CISAILLEMENT, MODULE DE GLISSEMENT | GLEITMODUL, SCHUBELASTIZITÄTSMODUL |
| 8343 | MODULUS OF RUPTURE | MODULE DE RUPTURE | BRUCHMODUL |
| 8344 | MOE DRAINERS, DITCH CUTTERS | SOUS-SOLEUSES, CHARRUES RIGOLEURSE | GRABENPFLÜGE, MASCHINEN FÜR MAULWURFS DRÄNUNG |
| 8345 | MOHR'S CLIP | PINCE DE MOHR | QUETSCHHAHN |
| 8346 | MOHS SCALE | ECHELLE DE DURETE DE MOHS | HÄRTESKALA (MOHSCHE) |
| 8347 | MOISTEN (TO) | HUMECTER, MOUILLER | ANFEUCHTEN |
| 8348 | MOISTENING, DAMPING | HUMIDIFICATION, MOUILLAGE | ANFEUCHTEN |
| 8349 | MOISTURE-PROOF | IMPERMEABLE A L'HUMIDITE, HYDROFUGE | WASSERABWEISEND |
| 8350 | MOLAR CONDUCTIVITY | CONDUCTANCE MOL(ECUL)AIRE | LEITFÄHIGKEITSMOLARE |
| 8351 | MOLAR RESISTIVITY | RESISTANCE MOL(ECUL)AIRE | WIDERSTANDSMOLARE |
| 8352 | MOLD (U.S) MOULD (GB) | MOULE | FORM |

| | | | |
|---|---|---|---|
| 8353 | **MOLD CAVITY** | CAVITE DU MOULE | FORMENHOHLRAUM |
| 8354 | **MOLD JACKET (U.S), SLIP JACKET** | JAQUETTE | GIESSRAHMEN, SCHUTZRAHMEN |
| 8355 | **MOLD WASH** | ENDUIT POUR LINGOTIERES | FORMSCHLICHTE |
| 8356 | **MOLD WEIGHT** | POIDS DE CHARGE | BELASTUNGSGEWICHT, BESCHWEREISEN |
| 8357 | **MOLDERS'RULE** | SONDE DE MOULEUR | TIEFENMASS |
| 8358 | **MOLDING MACHINE** | MACHINE A MOULER | FORMMASCHINE |
| 8359 | **MOLECULAR ATTRACTION** | ATTRACTION MOLECULAIRE | ANZIEHUNG (MOLEKULARE) |
| 8360 | **MOLECULAR FORCE** | FORCE MOLECULAIRE | MOLEKULARKRAFT |
| 8361 | **MOLECULAR STRUCTURE** | STRUCTURE MOLECULAIRE | MOLEKÜLSTRUKTUR |
| 8362 | **MOLECULAR VOLUME** | VOLUME MOLECULAIRE | MOLEKULARVOLUMEN |
| 8363 | **MOLECULAR WEIGHT** | POIDS MOLECULAIRE | MOLEKULARGEWICHT |
| 8364 | **MOLECULE** | MOLECULE | MOLEKEL, MOLEKÜL |
| 8365 | **MOLTEN METAL** | MATIERE EN FUSION, METAL EN FUSION | SCHMELZE, SCHMELZFUSS |
| 8366 | **MOLYBDENITE, MOLYBDENITE GLANCE** | MOLYBDENITE | MOLYBDÄNGLANZ |
| 8367 | **MOLYBDENUM** | MOLYBDENE | MOLYBDÄN |
| 8368 | **MOLYBDENUM STEEL** | ACIER AU MOLYBDENE | MOLYBDÄNSTAHL |
| 8369 | **MOLYBDIC ACID** | ACIDE MOLYBDIQUE | MOLYBDÄNSÄURE |
| 8370 | **MOMENT OF A FORCE** | MOMENT D'UNE FORCE | MOMENT EINER KRAFT |
| 8371 | **MOMENT OF FRICTION** | MOMENT DU FROTTEMENT | REIBUNGSMOMENT |
| 8372 | **MOMENT OF INERTIA** | MOMENT D'INERTIE | TRÄGHEITSMOMENT |
| 8373 | **MOMENT OF MOMENTUM** | MOMENT DE LA QUANTITE DE MOUVEMENT | SCHWUNGMOMENT |
| 8374 | **MOMENT OF RESISTANCE** | MOMENT RESISTANT, COUPLE RESISTANT, COUPLE REACTION | WIDERSTANDSMOMENT |
| 8375 | **MOMENT OF STABILITY** | MOMENT DE STABILITE | STABILITÄTSMOMENT |
| 8376 | **MOMENTUM, QUANTITY OF MOTION** | QUANTITE DE MOUVEMENT | BEWEGUNGSGRÖSSE |
| 8377 | **MONATOMIC, MONOVALENT** | MONOATOMIQUE, UNIVALENT | EINWERTIG, EINATOMIG |
| 8378 | **MOND GAS** | GAZ MOND | MONDGAS |
| 8379 | **MONEL METAL** | METAL MONEL, MONEL | MONELMETALL |
| 8380 | **MONKEY COOLER** | REFROIDISSEUR DU TROU DE LAITIER | SCHLACKENFORMKÜHLER, KÜHLKASTEN |
| 8381 | **MONKEY WALL** | PAROI DE LA BOITE DE REFROIDISSEMENT | KÜHLKASTENKOPFWAND |
| 8382 | **MONOCHROMATIC EMISSIVITY** | POUVOIR EMISSIF MONOCHROMATIQUE | EMISSIONSVERMÖGEN (MONOCHROMATISCHES) |
| 8383 | **MONOCHROMATIC RADIATION** | RAYONNEMENT MONOCHROMATIQUE | STRAHLUNG (MONOCHROMATISCHE) |
| 8384 | **MONOCLINIC CRYSTAL** | CRISTAL MONOCLINIQUE | KRISTALL (MONOKLINER) |
| 8385 | **MONOLITHIC LINING** | GARNITURE MONOLITHIQUE | OFENFUTTER (MONOLITHISCHES) |
| 8386 | **MONOTECTOID REACTION** | REACTION MONOTECTOIDE | MONOTEKTOIDE REAKTION |
| 8387 | **MONOTRON** | MONOTRON | MONOTRON |
| 8388 | **MONOTROPIC** | MONOTROPE | MONOTROP |
| 8389 | **MONTEJUS** | MONTE-JUS | SAFTHEBER, MONTEJUS |
| 8390 | **MOORING** | MOUILLAGE | ANKERPLATZ |
| 8391 | **MORDANT** | MORDANT | BEIZE |
| 8392 | **MORSE TAPER PLUG GAUGE** | JAUGE-TAMPON AU CONE MORSE | MORSEKEGELLEHRDORN |
| 8393 | **MORSE TAPER RING GAUGE** | CALIBRE DE CONICITE NORMAL | MORSEKEGELLEHRE |
| 8394 | **MORTAR** | MORTIER (A CONSTRUIRE) | MÖRTEL |
| 8395 | **MORTAR** | MORTIER (VASE EN PORCELAINE, EN AGATE) | REIBSCHALE |
| 8396 | **MORTAR** | MORTIER (VASE EN BRONZE) | MÖRSER |
| 8397 | **MORTAR GUN CARRIAGE** | AFFUT DE MORTIER | MÖRSERLAFETTE |

# MOR

214

| | | | |
|---|---|---|---|
| 8398 | **MORTISE CHISEL** | BEDANE DE MENUISIER | LOCHBEITEL |
| 8399 | **MORTISE GAUGE** | TRUSQUIN D'ASSEMBLAGE | ZAPFENSTREICHMASS |
| 8400 | **MORTISE WHEEL, COG WHEEL** | ROUE A DENTS EN BOIS | KAMMZAHNRAD, HOLZEISENRAD |
| 8401 | **MORTISE, MORTICE** | MORTAISE | ZAPFENLOCH |
| 8402 | **MORTISING MACHINE** | MORTAISEUSE A BOIS | STEMMASCHINE |
| 8403 | **MOSAIC STRUCTURE** | STRUCTURE MOSAIQUE | MOSAIKSTRUKTUR |
| 8404 | **MOSSY ZINC** | GRENAILLE DE ZINC | ZINKGRIES |
| 8405 | **MOTHER LIQUOR** | EAU MERE, BITTERN | MUTTERLAUGE |
| 8406 | **MOTION** | MOUVEMENT | BEWEGUNG |
| 8407 | **MOTION OF TRANSLATION** | MOUVEMENT DE TRANSLATION | BEWEGUNG (FORTSCHREITENDE), TRANSLATIONSBEWEGUNG |
| 8408 | **MOTIVE AGENT** | AGENT MOTEUR | TREIBMITTEL, BETRIEBSSTOFF |
| 8409 | **MOTIVE POWER** | PUISSANCE MOTRICE, FORCE MOTRICE | TRIEBKRAFT, BETRIEBSKRAFT |
| 8410 | **MOTOR BUS** | AUTOBUS | STADTOMNIBUS |
| 8411 | **MOTOR CAR, AUTOMOBILE, AUTOCAR** | VOITURE AUTOMOBILE, AUTOMOBILE, AUTO | KRAFTWAGEN, AUTOMOBIL, AUTO |
| 8412 | **MOTOR COACH** | AUTOCAR | REISEOMNIBUS |
| 8413 | **MOTOR GENERATOR** | MOTEUR-GENERATEUR, GROUPE MOTEUR-GENERATEUR | MOTORGENERATOR |
| 8414 | **MOTOR LORRY, MOTOR TRUCK, AUTOTRUCK** | CAMION AUTOMOBILE, AUTOMOBILE INDUSTRIELLE | LASTKRAFTWAGEN, LASTAUTO |
| 8415 | **MOTOR OIL** | HUILE POUR MOTEUR | MOTORÖL |
| 8416 | **MOTOR OPERATED GATE VALVE** | VANNE MOTORISEE | MOTORSCHIEBER |
| 8417 | **MOTOR OPERATED VALVE** | ROBINET A MOTEUR | MOTORVENTIL |
| 8418 | **MOTOR STARTER** | DEMARREUR | ANLASSER (ELEKTR.) |
| 8419 | **MOTOR TUNE-UP** | MISE AU POINT | MOTOREINSTELLUNG |
| 8420 | **MOTTLED IRON** | FONTE TRUITEE | ROHEISEN (HALBIERTES), ROHEISEN (MELIERTES) |
| 8421 | **MOTTLING** | LIQUETURE | TÜPPELUNG |
| 8422 | **MOULD** | CALIBRE POUR PROFILS, LINGOTIERE | FORMKALIBER, GUSSFORM |
| 8423 | **MOULD (FOUND.), MOULD** | MOULE (FOND.), TERRE VEGETALE | GUSSFORM (GIESS.), DAMMERDE |
| 8424 | **MOULD (TO)** | MOULER | ABFORMEN |
| 8425 | **MOULDED BRICK** | BRIQUE PROFILEE | FORMSTEIN |
| 8426 | **MOULDED CONCRETE** | BETON MOULE | GUSSBETON |
| 8427 | **MOULDER** | MOULEUR, OUVRIER MOULEUR | FORMER |
| 8428 | **MOULDING** | MOULAGE (REPRODUCTION A L'AIDE D'UN MOULE) | FORMEN, ABFORMEN |
| 8429 | **MOULDING MACHINE** | MACHINE A MOULER, MACHINE A MOULURER | FORMMASCHINE, SANDFORMMASCHINE, KEHLMASCHINE |
| 8430 | **MOULDING SAND** | SABLE DE MOULAGE, SABLE DE FONDERIE | FORMSAND |
| 8431 | **MOUNT A TRACING (TO)** | MONTER UN CALQUE | PAUSE AUFZIEHEN (EINE) |
| 8432 | **MOUNTED ON A POINTED PIVOT** | REPOSANT, SUSPENDU SUR UN PIVOT | GELAGERT (AUF EINER SPITZE) |
| 8433 | **MOUTH BLOW PIPE** | CHALUMEAU A BOUCHE | BLASLÖTROHR, LÖTROHR MIT MUNDSTÜCK |
| 8434 | **MOUTH OF A PLANE** | LUMIERE D'UN RABOT | KEILLOCH EINES HOBELS |
| 8435 | **MOVABLE BLOCK** | POULIE MOBILE (D'UN PALAN) | FLASCHE (LOSE), ROLLE |
| 8436 | **MOVABLE PLATEN** | CHARIOT D'ECRASEMENT | STAUCHSCHLITTEN |
| 8437 | **MOVABLE VICE JAW** | MACHOIRE MOBILE D'UN ETAU | SCHRAUBSTOCKBACKEN (BEWEGLICHER) |
| 8438 | **MOVEMENT, MOTION** | MOUVEMENT | BEWEGUNG |

| | | |
|---|---|---|
| 8439 | **MOWERS : TRACTOR TRAILED, MOUNTED AND SEMI-MOUNTED** | FAUCHEUSES A TRACTEUR-TRAINEES/MONTEES | MÄHMASCHINEN (DURCH TRAKTOREN ANGETRIEBEN) UND HALBSATTELMÄHMASCHINEN |
| 8440 | **MUCILAGE** | MUCILAGE, EXTRAIT MUCILAGINEUX | AUFQUELLUNG |
| 8441 | **MUCK BAR** | BARRE DE FER BRUT, FER EBAUCHE | ROHSCHIENE |
| 8442 | **MUD HOLE** | TROU DE VIDANGE | SCHLAMMLOCH |
| 8443 | **MUD-FLAP** | PARE-BOUE | SCHMUTZFÄNGER |
| 8444 | **MUD, SLUDGE** | BOUE, BOUES | SCHLAMM |
| 8445 | **MUDDY** | BOUEUX | SCHLAMMIG |
| 8446 | **MUDDY WATER** | EAU BOUEUSE | WASSER (SCHLAMMIGES) |
| 8447 | **MUFFLE, CHAMBER FURNACE** | FOUR A MOUFLE | MUFFELOFEN |
| 8448 | **MUFFLER (U.S)** | SILENCIEUX, POT D'ECHAPPEMENT | SCHALLDÄMPFER, AUSPUFFTOPF, AUSPUFFGERÄUSCHDÄMPFER |
| 8449 | **MULLER** | MALAXEUR | MISCHKOLLERGANG |
| 8450 | **MULLING (U.S.)** | FROTTAGE | KOLLERN |
| 8451 | **MULLING MACHINE** | FROTTEUR | MISCHKOLLERGANG |
| 8452 | **MULTI HOLE TYPE NOZZLE** | INJECTEUR A TROUS | MEHRLOCHDÜSE |
| 8453 | **MULTI-CYLINDER ENGINE** | MOTEUR POLYCYLINDRIQUE | MEHRZYLINDERMASCHINE |
| 8454 | **MULTI-DISC BRAKE** | FREIN A LAME, FREIN A DISQUE | LAMELLENBREMSE |
| 8455 | **MULTI-PASS WELDING** | SOUDAGE A PASSES MULTIPLES | MEHRLAGENSCHWEISSEN |
| 8456 | **MULTI-PURPOSE MACHINE** | MACHINE MULTIPLE | MEHRZWECKMACHINE |
| 8457 | **MULTI-ROLLER PROFILING MACHINE** | MACHINE A PROFILER A GALETS MULTIPLES | MEHRROLLENPROFILIERMASCHINE |
| 8458 | **MULTI-SPINDLE DRILLING HEAD** | TETE DE PERCAGE MULTIBROCHES | BOHRKÖPFE (MEHRSPINDLIGE) |
| 8459 | **MULTI-SPINDLE HEAD** | TETE MULTI-BROCHES | MEHRSPINDELBOHRKOPF |
| 8460 | **MULTI-SPINDLE IN LINE DRILLING MACHINE** | PERCEUSE MULTIBROCHE EN LIGNE | MEHRSPINDLIGE BOHRMASCHINE IN REIHENANORDNUNG |
| 8461 | **MULTI-STAGE (TRANSFER) PRESSES** | PRESSES TRANSFERT A POINCONS MULTIPLES | STUFENPRESSEN (MECHANISCHE) |
| 8462 | **MULTIPHASE, POLYPHASE CURRENT** | COURANT POLYPHASE | MEHRPHASENSTROM |
| 8463 | **MULTIPLE BELT** | COURROIE MULTIPLE, COURROIE A PLUSIEURS EPAISSEURS | MEHRFACHRIEMEN |
| 8464 | **MULTIPLE ELECTRODE SPOT WELDING** | SOUDAGE PAR POINTS MULTIPLES | VIELPUNKTSCHWEISSEN |
| 8465 | **MULTIPLE INTEGRAL** | INTEGRALE MULTIPLE | INTEGRAL (MEHRFACHES), INTEGRAL (VIELFACHES) |
| 8466 | **MULTIPLE MOLD** | MOULE MULTIPLE | MEHRFACHFORM |
| 8467 | **MULTIPLE PORT PLUG** | ROBINET DE DISTRIBUTEUR | MEHRWEGEVENTIL |
| 8468 | **MULTIPLE PROJECTION WELDING** | SOUDAGE PAR BOSSAGES MULTIPLES | MEHRFACHBUCKELSCHWEISSEN |
| 8469 | **MULTIPLE SPINDLE AUTOMATIC LATHE** | TOUR AUTOMATIQUE A BROCHES MULTIPLES | MEHRSPINDELAUTOMAT |
| 8470 | **MULTIPLE SPINDLE DRILLING MACHINE** | MACHINE A PERCER A BROCHES MULTIPLES | BOHRMASCHINE (MEHRSPINDLIGE) |
| 8471 | **MULTIPLE SPINDLE MILLING MACHINE** | FRAISEUSE MULTIPLE | FRÄSMASCHINE MIT MEHREREN SPINDELN |
| 8472 | **MULTIPLE SYSTEM** | SYSTEME MULTIPLE | MEHRFACHSYSTEM |
| 8473 | **MULTIPLE SYSTEM OF ROPE DRIVING** | TRANSMISSION PAR POULIE A GORGES MULTIPLES | SEILTRIEB (MEHRFACHER) |
| 8474 | **MULTIPLE THREADED SCREW** | VIS A PLUSIEURS FILETS | SCHRAUBE (MEHRGÄNGIGE) |
| 8475 | **MULTIPLE VALVE (COAXIAL)** | SOUPAPE ETAGEE | VENTIL (MEHRSTÖCKIGES), STUFENVENTIL, ETAGENVENTIL |
| 8476 | **MULTIPLE VALVE (COPLANAR)** | SOUPAPE MULTIPLE | VENTIL (MEHRFACHES), GRUPPENVENTIL |

# MUL 216

| | | | |
|---|---|---|---|
| 8477 | MULTIPLE-EXPANSION ENGINE | MACHINE A MULTIPLE EXPANSION | MEHRFACHEXPANSIONSMASCHINE |
| 8478 | MULTIPLE-THROW CRANK SHAFT | VILEBREQUIN A PLUSIEURS COUDES | WELLE (MEHRKURBELIGE), KURBELWELLE (MEHRFACH GEKRÖPFTE) |
| 8479 | MULTIPLICAND | MULTIPLICANDE | MULTIPLIKAND |
| 8480 | MULTIPLICATION | MULTIPLICATION | VERVIELFACHEN, MULTIPLIKATION |
| 8481 | MULTIPLICATION, REPRODUCTION | REPRODUCTION | VERVIELFÄLTIGEN, REPRODUZIEREN |
| 8482 | MULTIPLIER | MULTIPLICATEUR | MULTIPLIKATOR |
| 8483 | MULTIPLY (TO) | MULTIPLIER | VERVIELFACHEN, MULTIPLIZIEREN |
| 8484 | MULTIPLY (TO), REPRODUCE (TO) | REPRODUIRE | VERVIELFÄLTIGEN, REPRODUZIEREN |
| 8485 | MULTISPINDLE FINISHING LATHE | TOUR DE REPRISE MULTIBROCHES | NACHDREHMASCHINE (MEHRSPINDLIGE) |
| 8486 | MUNTZ METAL, YELLOW PATENT METAL | METAL MUNTZ | MUNTZMETALL, SCHMIEDEMESSING |
| 8487 | MUSCHELKALK | CALCAIRE COQUILLIER, MUSCHELKALK | MUSCHELKALK |
| 8488 | MUSHY STAGE | ETAT PATEUX | TEIGZUSTAND |
| 8489 | MUTUAL INDUCTION | INDUCTION MUTUELLE | INDUKTION (GEGENSEITIGE), INDUKTION (WECHSELSEITIGE) |
| 8490 | NAGELFLUH | POUDINGUE | NAGELFLUH |
| 8491 | NAIL | CLOU | NAGEL |
| 8492 | NAIL (TO) | CLOUER | NAGELN |
| 8493 | NAPHTHA | NAPHTE | NAPHTHA |
| 8494 | NAPHTHALENE | NAPHTALINE, NAPHTALENE | NAPHTHALIN, STEINKOHLENTEERKAMPFER, NAPHTHYLWASSERSTOFF |
| 8495 | NAPHTHOL | NAPHTOL | NAPHTHOL (A-NAPHTHOL, SS-NAPHTHOL) |
| 8496 | NARROW EDGE MILLING CUTTER | FRAISE A DISQUE | SCHEIBENFRÄSER |
| 8497 | NASCENT | NAISSANT, LIBERANT (SE) (CHIM.) | FREIWERDEND (CHEM.) |
| 8498 | NATIVE ALLOY | ALLIAGE NATUREL | LEGIERUNG (NATÜRLICHE) |
| 8499 | NATURAL ABRASIVE | ABRASIF NATUREL | SCHLEIFMITTEL (NATÜRLICHES) |
| 8500 | NATURAL AGING | VIEILLISSEMENT NATUREL | ALTERUNG (NATÜRLICHE) |
| 8501 | NATURAL DRAUGHT | TIRAGE NATUREL | ZUG (NATÜRLICHER) |
| 8502 | NATURAL EVAPORATION | EVAPORATION A L'AIR LIBRE | VERDUNSTUNG |
| 8503 | NATURAL FUEL | COMBUSTIBLE NATUREL | BRENNSTOFF (NATÜRIICHER) |
| 8504 | NATURAL GAS | GAZ NATUREL | NATURGAS, ERDGAS |
| 8505 | NATURAL LIGHTING | ECLAIRAGE NATUREL | BELEUCHTUNG (NATÜRLICHE) |
| 8506 | NATURAL MAGNET | AIMANT NATUREL, PIERRE D'AIMANT | MAGNET (NATÜRLICHER) |
| 8507 | NATURAL STONE | PIERRE NATURELLE | STEIN (NATÜRLICHER), NATURSTEIN |
| 8508 | NATURAL VENTILATION | VENTILATION NATURELLE | LÜFTUNG (NATÜRLICHE) |
| 8509 | NATURAL, HYPERBOLIC LOGARITHM | LOGARITHME NATUREL, LOGARITHME HYPERBOLIQUE | LOGARITHMUS (NATÜRLICHER), LOGARITHMUS (HYPERBOLISCHER) |
| 8510 | NAVAL ARCHITECTURE | CONSTRUCTION NAVALE | SCHIFFBAU |
| 8511 | NAVAL BRASS | LAITON ALPHA-BETA, LAITON DE L'AMIRAUTE | SONDERMESSING (SEEWASSERFESTES) |
| 8512 | NECK | CONGE, COL | KEHLE, HALS |
| 8513 | NECK JOURNAL | TOURILLON INTERMEDIAIRE | HALSZAPFEN, WELLENHALS |
| 8514 | NECK NOZZLE | TUBULURE A COLLET | HALSSTUTZEN |
| 8515 | NECKING | EXECUTION D'UNE GORGE, STRICTION | STECHEN, EINSCHNÜRUNG |
| 8516 | NECKING DOWN | STRICTION | EINHALSUNG |
| 8517 | NEEDLE | PARTICULE ACICULAIRE | TEILCHEN (NADELFÖRMIGES) |
| 8518 | NEEDLE BEARING | ROULEMENT A AIGUILLES | NADELLAGER |

| | | | |
|---|---|---|---|
| 8519 | **NEEDLE FILE** | LIME AIGUILLE | NADELFEILE |
| 8520 | **NEEDLE LUBRICATOR** | GRAISSEUR A TIGE, GRAISSEUR A EPINGLETTE, GODET EN VERRE A TIGE | STIFTÖLER, NADELÖLER |
| 8521 | **NEEDLE POINT** | BRANCHE PORTE-AIGUILLE D'UN COMPAS | NADELEINSATZ FÜR ZIRKEL |
| 8522 | **NEEDLE VALVE** | ROBINET A POINTEAU (A AIGUILLE), POINTEAU | NADELVENTIL, SCHWIMMERNADELVENTIL |
| 8523 | **NEEDLED STEEL** | ACIER A STRUCTURE ACICULAIRE | STAHL MIT NADELIGER STRUKTUR |
| 8524 | **NEGATIVE (PHOTOGRAPHIC)** | EPREUVE NEGATIVE, CLICHE PHOTOGRAPHIQUE | NEGATIV (PHOTOGRAPHISCHES) |
| 8525 | **NEGATIVE ACCELERATION, RETARDATION** | ACCELERATION NEGATIVE | BESCHLEUNIGUNG (NEGATIVE), VERZÖGERUNG |
| 8526 | **NEGATIVE ELECTRICITY** | ELECTRICITE NEGATIVE | ELEKTRIZITÄT (NEGATIVE) |
| 8527 | **NEGATIVE HARDENING** | TREMPE NEGATIVE | NEGATIVE HÄRTUNG |
| 8528 | **NEGATIVE HEAT OF FORMATION** | CHALEUR DE DECOMPOSITION | TRENNUNGSWÄRME |
| 8529 | **NEGATIVE MATRIX** | MATRICE NEGATIVE | NEGATIVE |
| 8530 | **NEGATIVE PLATE** | PLAQUE NEGATIVE | PLATTE (NEGATIVE), MINUSPLATTE |
| 8531 | **NEGATIVE POLE** | POLE NEGATIF | POL (NEGATIVER) |
| 8532 | **NEGATIVE SIGN** | SIGNE NEGATIF | VORZEICHEN (NEGATIVES), MINUSZEICHEN |
| 8533 | **NEODYMIUM** | NEODYME | NEODYM |
| 8534 | **NEODYMIUM** | NEODYMIUM | NEODYM |
| 8535 | **NEON** | NEON | NEON |
| 8536 | **NEON LAMP** | LAMPE AU NEON | NEONLAMPE |
| 8537 | **NEPHELOMETRY** | ANALYSE NEPHELOMETRIQUE | TRÜBUNGSANALYSE |
| 8538 | **NEST OF TUBES** | FAISCEAU TUBULAIRE | ROHRBÜNDEL, RÖHRENBÜNDEL |
| 8539 | **NETWORK STRUCTURE** | STRUCTURE RETICULAIRE | NETZSTRUKTUR, NETZGEFÜGE |
| 8540 | **NEUMANN BANDS** | BANDES DE NEUMANN | LINIEN (NEUMANNSCHE) |
| 8541 | **NEUTRAL AXIS LINE** | AXE NEUTRE | NULLACHSE, ACHSE (NEUTRALE), NULLINIE |
| 8542 | **NEUTRAL FIBRE** | FIBRE NEUTRE | FASER (NEUTRALE) |
| 8543 | **NEUTRAL FLAME** | FLAMME NEUTRE, FLAMME NORMALE | NORMALFLAMME |
| 8544 | **NEUTRAL LAYER OF FIBRES** | COUCHE DES FIBRES INVARIABLES | FASERSCHICHT (NEUTRALE), NULLSCHICHT |
| 8545 | **NEUTRAL LINE** | LIGNE NEUTRE | NULLEITUNG |
| 8546 | **NEUTRAL NORMAL SALT** | SEL NEUTRE | SALZ (NEUTRALES) |
| 8547 | **NEUTRAL POINT** | ZONE NEUTRE | FLIESSSCHEIDE |
| 8548 | **NEUTRALISATION** | NEUTRALISATION | NEUTRALISATION, ABSTUMPFUNG |
| 8549 | **NEUTRALISE (TO)** | NEUTRALISER | NEUTRALISIEREN, ABSTUMPFEN |
| 8550 | **NEW ZEALAND FLAX** | LIN DE LA NOUVELLE-ZELANDE | NEUSEELANDHANF |
| 8551 | **NIB** | COMPACT TERMINE | FERTIGER PRESSLING |
| 8552 | **NIBBLING** | GRIGNOTAGE | DEKUPIEREN, KNABBERN |
| 8553 | **NIBBLING MACHINE** | GRIGNOTEUSE | AUSHAUMASCHINE |
| 8554 | **NICK (TO), NOTCH (TO)** | ENTAILLER, PRATIQUER UNE SAIGNEE DANS UNE PIECE, SAIGNER | KERBEN, EINKERBEN |
| 8555 | **NICK-BREAK TEST** | ESSAI DE FLEXION SUR EPROUVETTE ENTAILLEE | KERBBIEGEVERSUCH |
| 8556 | **NICKEL** | NICKEL | NICKEL |
| 8557 | **NICKEL ALLOY** | ALLIAGE A BASE DE NICKEL | NICKELLEGIERUNG |
| 8558 | **NICKEL AMMONIUM SULPHATE** | SULFATE DOUBLE DE NICKEL ET D'AMMONIAQUE | SCHWEFELSAURES NICKELOXYDULAMMONIAK, NICKELAMMONIUMSULFAT |

**NIC** 218

| 8559 | NICKEL BRASS | LAITON AU NICKEL | NICKELMESSING |
| 8560 | NICKEL BRONZE | BRONZE AU NICKEL | NICKELBRONZE |
| 8561 | NICKEL CARBONYL | CARBONYLE DE NICKEL | NICKELKOHLENOXYD, KOHLENOXYDNICKEL, NICKELKARBONYL |
| 8562 | NICKEL CHLORIDE | CHLORURE NICKELEUX | NICKELCHLORÜR, CHLORNICKEL |
| 8563 | NICKEL MATTE | MATTE DE NICKEL | NICKELSTEIN |
| 8564 | NICKEL ORE | MINERAI DE NICKEL | NICKELERZ |
| 8565 | NICKEL OXIDE | PROTOXYDE DE NICKEL | NICKELOXYDUL |
| 8566 | NICKEL PLATE (TO) | NICKELER | VERNICKELN |
| 8567 | NICKEL PLATING | NICKELAGE, PLAQUAGE AU NICKEL | VERNICKELUNG, NICKELPLATTIERUNG |
| 8568 | NICKEL SHOT | GRENAILLE DE NICKEL | NICKELSCHROT |
| 8569 | NICKEL SILVER | ARGENTAN, ALPACCA, MAILLECHORT | NEUSILBER, ALPAKA, ARGENTAN |
| 8570 | NICKEL STEEL | ACIER AU NICKEL | NICKELSTAHL |
| 8571 | NICKEL SULPHATE | SULFATE DE NICKEL | SCHWEFELSAURES NICKELOXYDUL, NICKELSULFAT, NICKELVITRIOL |
| 8572 | NICKEL-ALUMINIUM BRONZE | BRONZE DE NICKEL ET ALUMINIUM | NICKELALUMINIUMBRONZE |
| 8573 | NICKEL-CLAD STEEL | ACIER NICKELE | STAHL (NICKELPLATTIERTER) |
| 8574 | NICKELIC OXIDE | OXYDE DE NICKEL | NICKELOXYD |
| 8575 | NIGHT SHIFT | TRAVAIL DE NUIT, TACHE DE NUIT | NACHTSCHICHT |
| 8576 | NIOBIUM, COLUMBIUM | NIOBIUM | NIOBIUM |
| 8577 | NIP ANGLE | ANGLE D'ATTAQUE | GREIFWINKEL |
| 8578 | NIPPLE | MAMELON, RACCORD MALE | NIPPEL |
| 8579 | NITRATE | NITRATE, AZOTATE | SALPETERSAURES SALZ, NITRAT |
| 8580 | NITRIC ACID, ACQUA FORTIS | ACIDE AZOTIQUE, ACIDE NITRIQUE, EAU FORTE | SALPETERSÄURE, SCHEIDEWASSER, AQUA FORTIS, STICKSTOFFSÄURE |
| 8581 | NITRIC OXIDE | BIOXYDE D'AZOTE, OXYDE AZOTIQUE | STICKSTOFF MONOXYD, STICKOXYD, SALPETERGAS |
| 8582 | NITRIDING | TREMPE PAR NITRURATION | NITRIERHÄRTUNG |
| 8583 | NITRIDING ATMOSPHERE | ATMOSPHERE DE NITRURATION | NITRIERATMOSPHÄRE |
| 8584 | NITRIDING FURNACE | FOUR A NITRURATION | NITRIEROFEN |
| 8585 | NITRIDING STEEL | ACIER DE NITRURATION | NITRIERSTAHL |
| 8586 | NITRITE | NITRITE, AZOTITE | SALPETRIGSAURES SALZ, NITRIT |
| 8587 | NITROBENZENE, ESSENCE OF MIRBANE | NITROBENZINE, NITROBENZENE, ESSENCE DE MIRBANE | MIRBANÖL, NITROBENZOL |
| 8588 | NITROGEN | AZOTE, NITROGENE | STICKSTOFF |
| 8589 | NITROGEN HARDENING | NITRURATION | NITRIERUNG |
| 8590 | NITROGEN PENTOXIDE | ACIDE AZOTIQUE ANHYDRE, ANHYDRIDE AZOTIQUE | STICKSTOFFPENTOXYD, SALPETERSSÄUREANHYDRID |
| 8591 | NITROGEN TETROXIDE, PEROXIDE | AZOTYLE, HYPOAZOTIDE, ANHYDRIDE, HYPOAZOTIQUE, PEROXYDE D'AZOTE | STICKSTOFFPEROXYD, STICKSTOFFTETROXYD, STICKSTOFFDIOXYD, UNTERSALPETERSÄURE |
| 8592 | NITROGEN TRIOXIDE | ANHYDRIDE AZOTEUX | STICKSTOFFTRIOXYD, STICKSTOFFSESQUIOXYD, SALPETRIGSÄUREANHYDRID |
| 8593 | NITROGLYCERINE | NITROGLYCERINE, TRINITRINE | NITROGLYZERIN |
| 8594 | NITROMETER | NITROMETRE | NITROMETER |
| 8595 | NITROSULPHURIC ACID | MELANGE SULFONITRIQUE | MISCHSÄURE, NITRIERSÄURE |
| 8596 | NITROUS ACID | ACIDE AZOTEUX | SÄURE (SALPETRIGE) |
| 8597 | NITROUS OXYDE | PROTOXYDE D'AZOTE, OXYDE AZOTEUX | STICKSTOFFOXYDUL |
| 8598 | NO-LOAD CONDITIONS, RUNNING LIGHT | MARCHE A VIDE | LEERLAUF |

| | | | |
|---|---|---|---|
| 8599 | **NO-LOAD LOSS** | PERTE A VIDE | LEERLAUFVERLUST |
| 8600 | **NO-LOAD RESISTANCE** | RESISTANCE DANS LA MARCHE A VIDE | LEERLAUFWIDERSTAND |
| 8601 | **NO-LOAD WORK** | TRAVAIL A VIDE | LEERLAUFARBEIT |
| 8602 | **NOBLE METAL** | METAL NOBLE OU PRECIEUX | EDELMETALL |
| 8603 | **NOBLE PRECIOUS METAL** | METAL PRECIEUX | EDELMETALL, METALL EDLES |
| 8604 | **NODE CIRCLE (FOR CALCULATION OF PRESSURE TANK FRAMES)** | CERCLE DE POINT NEUTRE (CALCUL DES CHARPENTES DE RESISTANCE SOUS PRESSION) | TOTLAGEKREIS |
| 8605 | **NODE OF OSCILLATION, VIBRATION NODE** | NOEUD DE VIBRATION, NOEUD D'OSCILLATION | SCHWINGUNGSKNOTEN |
| 8606 | **NODULAR** | SPHEROIDAL, NODULAIRE | KNOLLIG, KNODIG, NODULAR, KUGELIG |
| 8607 | **NODULAR CAST-IRON** | FONTE NODULAIRE | KUGELGRAPHITGUSSEISEN |
| 8608 | **NOISE** | BRUIT | GERÄUSCH |
| 8609 | **NOISELESS QUIET SILENT RUNNING** | MARCHE SILENCIEUSE | GANG (GERÄUSCHLOSER) |
| 8610 | **NOISY RUNNING** | MARCHE BRUYANTE | GANG (GERÄUSCHVOLLER) |
| 8611 | **NOMINAL DIAMETER** | DIAMETRE NOMINAL | NENNDURCHMESSER, SOLLDURCHMESSER |
| 8612 | **NOMINAL DIMENSION** | DIMENSION NOMINALE | NENNABMESSUNG |
| 8613 | **NOMINAL PRESSURE** | PRESSION NOMINALE | NENNDRUCK (ND) |
| 8614 | **NOMINAL PRESSURE RATING** | TIMBRE D'UN RESERVOIR (A. PRESSION) | GENEHMIGUNGSDRUCK |
| 8615 | **NOMINAL SIZE** | DIMENSION NOMINALE, ORIFICE NOMINAL | NENNMASS, NENNWEITE (NW) |
| 8616 | **NOMINAL VALUE** | VALEUR NOMINALE | NENNWERT |
| 8617 | **NOMOGRAM** | ABAQUE | FLUCHTLINIENTAFEL |
| 8618 | **NON CONSUMABLE ELECTRODE** | ELECTRODE NON-CONSOMMABLE | ELEKTRODE (NICHTSCHMELZENDE) |
| 8619 | **NON FERROUS ALLOY** | ALLIAGE NON-FERREUX | NICHTEISENLEGIERUNG |
| 8620 | **NON METALLIC INCLUSIONS** | INCLUSIONS NON-METALLIQUES | EINSCHLÜSSE (NICHTMETALLISCHE) |
| 8621 | **NON REACTIVE** | INERTE | INERT |
| 8622 | **NON REFRACTORY ALLOY** | ALLIAGE NON REFRACTAIRE | LEGIERUNG (NICHT-FEUERFESTE) |
| 8623 | **NON RISING STEM** | TIGE FIXE | SPINDEL (NICHTSTEIGENDE) |
| 8624 | **NON RISING STEM GATE VALVE** | VANNE A TIGE FIXE | ABSPERRSCHIEBER MIT NICHTSTEIGENDER SPINDEL |
| 8625 | **NON-ADJUSTABLE GAUGE** | JAUGE (NON- VARIABLE) | LEHRE (UNVERSTELLBARE) |
| 8626 | **NON-CAKING FREE BURNING COAL** | HOUILLE NON COLLANTE | KOHLE (NICHTBACKENDE) |
| 8627 | **NON-CONDENSING STEAM ENGINE** | MACHINE SANS CONDENSATION, ECHAPPEMENT LIBRE | AUSPUFFDAMPFMASCHINE |
| 8628 | **NON-CONDUCTIVE OF HEAT, HEAT INSULATING** | CALORIFUGE | ISOLIEREND GEGEN WÄRME, WÄRMESCHUTZ- |
| 8629 | **NON-CONSTRAINED MOTION, NON-DEFINITELY CONTROLLED MOTION, NON-POSITIVE, FORCE-CLOSED MOTION** | MOUVEMENT A COMMANDE ELASTIQUE | BEWEGUNG (KRAFTSCHLÜSSIGE) |
| 8630 | **NON-DESTRUCTIVE TESTING** | ESSAI NON DESTRUCTIF | PRÜFUNG (ZERSTÖRUNGSFREIE) |
| 8631 | **NON-FERROUS** | NON-FERREUX | NICHTEISEN- |
| 8632 | **NON-FERROUS METAL** | METAL AUTRE QUE LE FER, PETIT METAL | NICHTEISENMATALL |
| 8633 | **NON-FREEZE COATED PALLET** | CLAPET ANTIGEL | FROSTSCHUTZVENTIL |
| 8634 | **NON-LIABILITY TO FREEZE** | INCONGELABILITE | FROSTBESTÄNDIGKEIT |
| 8635 | **NON-LIABLE TO FREEZE** | INCONGELABLE | KÄLTEBESTÄNDIG, FROSTBESTÄNDIG |
| 8636 | **NON-LUMINOUS FLAME** | FLAMME INCOLORE, FLAMME OXYDANTE, FEU D'OXYDATION | FLAMME (NICHTLEUCHTENDE) |
| 8637 | **NON-MAGNETIC** | AMAGNETIQUE | UNMAGNETISCH |

# NON

**220**

| | | | |
|---|---|---|---|
| 8638 | NON-MAGNETIC STEEL | ACIER NON MAGNETIQUE | STAHL (UNMAGNETISIERBARER) |
| 8639 | NON-METAL | NON-METALLIQUE | NICHT-METALLISCH |
| 8640 | NON-METAL, METALLOID | METALLOIDE | METALLOID |
| 8641 | NON-METALLIC COATING | REVETEMENT NON-METALLIQUE | ÜBERZUG (NICHT-METALLISCHER) |
| 8642 | NON-POSITIVE DRIVE | COMMANDE ELASTIQUE | ANTRIEB (KRAFTSCHLÜSSIGER) |
| 8643 | NON-PRESSURE WELDING | SOUDAGE PAR FUSION | SCHMELZSCHWEISSEN |
| 8644 | NON-RUSTING STEEL | ACIER INOXYDABLE | STAHL (NICHTROSTENDER) |
| 8645 | NON-SLIP DIFFERENTIAL | SYSTEME ANTI-DERAPANT | GLEITSCHUTZDIFFERENTIAL |
| 8646 | NON-SPINNING ROPE | CABLE ANTIGIRATOIRE | SEIL (DRALLFREIES) |
| 8647 | NON-UNIFORM MOTION | MOUVEMENT NON UNIFORME | BEWEGUNG (UNGLEICHFÖRMIGE) |
| 8648 | NON-UNIFORMLY ACCELERATED MOTION | MOUVEMENT NON UNIFORMEMENT ACCELERE | BEWEGUNG (UNGLEICHFÖRMIG BESCHLEUNIGTE) |
| 8649 | NON-UNIFORMLY RETARDED MOTION | MOUVEMENT NON UNIFORMEMENT RETARDE | BEWEGUNG (UNGLEICHFÖRMIG VERZÖGERTE) |
| 8650 | NONMETALLIC MOULD | MOULE NON-METALLIQUE | FORM (NICHT-METALLISCHE) |
| 8651 | NOOSE, RUNNING KNOT | NOEUD COULANT | SCHLAUFE, ZUGKNOTEN |
| 8652 | NORMAL | NORMALE (GEOM.) | WINKELRECHT, NORMAL (GEOM.) |
| 8653 | NORMAL ACCELERATION | ACCELERATION NORMALE | NORMALBESCHLEUNIGUNG |
| 8654 | NORMAL CROSS SECTION | SECTION NORMALE, SECTION DROITE | NORMALSCHNITT |
| 8655 | NORMAL LOAD | CHARGE NORMALE | GRUNDLAST, GRUNDBELASTUNG |
| 8656 | NORMAL MAGNESIUM PHOSPHATE | PHOSPHATE DE MAGNESIE | PHOSPHORSAURE MAGNESIA, MAGNESIUMPHOSPHAT |
| 8657 | NORMAL PRESSURE | PRESSION NORMALE | NORMALDRUCK |
| 8658 | NORMAL RATED OUTPUT | DEBIT NORMAL | NENNLEISTUNG, REGELLEISTUNG, NORMALLEISTUNG |
| 8659 | NORMAL RATED VOLTAGE | VOLTAGE NORMAL | NENNSPANNUNG, BETRIEBSSPANNUNG (ELEKTR.) |
| 8660 | NORMAL SEGREGATION | SEGREGATION MAJEURE | BLOCKSEIGERUNG |
| 8661 | NORMAL STRESS | CHARGE NORMALE | NORMALSPANNUNG |
| 8662 | NORMAL TO A CURVE | NORMALE D'UNE COURBE | NORMALE EINER KURVE |
| 8663 | NORMAL WORKING SPEED | VITESSE DE REGIME, VITESSE NORMALE DE FONCTIONNEMENT, REGIME DE VITESSE | BETRIEBSGESCHWINDIGKEIT |
| 8664 | NORMALIZING | RECUIT DE NORMALISATION | NORMALGLÜHEN |
| 8665 | NORTH SEEKING POLE OF A MAGNET | POLE NORD D'UN AIMANT | NORDPOL EINES MAGNETEN |
| 8666 | NOSE (OF A TOOL) | BEC (D'UN OUTIL) | STAHLSPITZE |
| 8667 | NOSE, PROJECTION | NEZ, TALON | NASE |
| 8668 | NOTCH | ENTAILLE | KERBE |
| 8669 | NOTCH BRITTLENESS | FRAGILITE D'ENTAILLE | KERBSPRÖDIGKEIT |
| 8670 | NOTCH SENSITIVITY | SENSIBILITE A L'EFFET D'ENTAILLE | KERBEMPFINDLICHKEIT |
| 8671 | NOTCH TOUGHNESS | TENACITE A L'ENTAILLE, RESILIENCE | KERBZÄHIGKEIT, KERBSCHLAGZÄHIGKEIT |
| 8672 | NOTCH, NICK | ENTAILLE, ECHANCRURE, ENCOCHE, CRAN | KERBE, EINKERBUNG, RAST |
| 8673 | NOTCHED BAR IMPACT TEST | ESSAI DE CHOC SUR BARREAU ENTAILLE, ESSAI DE RESILIENCE | KERBSCHLAGPROBE |
| 8674 | NOTCHED INGOT | LINGOT ENTAILLE | VORGEKERBTER BLOCK |
| 8675 | NOTCHED TEST BAR | EPROUVETTE AVEC ENTAILLE, BARREAU ENTAILLE | PROBESTAB MIT EINKERBUNG |
| 8676 | NOTCHING | ENCOCHAGE | KERBEN |
| 8677 | NOTCHING MACHINE | GRUGEOIR | AUSKLINKMASCHINE |
| 8678 | NOWEL | MOULE DE DESSOUS | UNTERKASTEN |

**221** OCH

| | | | |
|---|---|---|---|
| 8679 | NOZZLE | TUBULURE, PIETEMENT, LANCE, AJUSTAGE CONIQUE | STUTZEN, STRAHLROHR, DÜSE |
| 8680 | NOZZLE DISTANCE/HEIGHT | HAUTEUR DE BUSE | DÜSENHÖHE |
| 8681 | NOZZLE DRILLING MACHINE | MACHINE A PERCER LES TUYERES | DÜSENBOHRMASCHINE |
| 8682 | NOZZLE HOLDER | PORTE-INJECTEUR | DÜSENHALTER |
| 8683 | NOZZLE NECK | TUBULURE A COLLET | FLANSCHROHRSTUTZEN |
| 8684 | NOZZLE NEEDLE | AIGUILLE D'INJECTEUR | DÜSENNADEL |
| 8685 | NOZZLE OF A BLOWER | TUYERE, BUSE | GEBLÄSEDÜSE, DÜSE EINES GEBLÄSES |
| 8686 | NOZZLE SPRING | RESSORT D'INJECTEUR | DÜSENFEDER |
| 8687 | NUCLEATION | GERMINATION | KERNBILDUNG, KEIMBILDUNG |
| 8688 | NUCLEUS | GERME (DE CRISTAL), CRISTALLIN | KERN, KRISTALLKERN, KEIM |
| 8689 | NUMBER OF A LOGARITHM | NOMBRE D'UN LOGARITHME | NUMERUS EINES LOGARITHMUS |
| 8690 | NUMBER OF REVOLUTIONS PER MINUTE, R. P. M. | NOMBRE DE TOURS, TOURS A LA MINUTE | DREHZAHL, UMDREHUNGSZAHL, UMLAUFZAHL, TOURENZAHL |
| 8691 | NUMBER OF TEETH | NOMBRE DE DENTS | ZÄHNEZAHL |
| 8692 | NUMBER OF THREADS | NOMBRE DE FILETS | GEWINDEGANGZAHL, GANGZAHL EINES GEWINDES |
| 8693 | NUMERATOR | NUMERATEUR | ZÄHLER, (MATH.) |
| 8694 | NUMERIC SOLUTION | SOLUTION PAR LE CALCUL | LÖSUNG (RECHNERISCHE), LÖSUNG (ZAHLENMÄSSIGE) |
| 8695 | NUMERICAL CONTROL SYSTEM | SYSTEME DE COMMANDE NUMERIQUE | STEUERUNGS-SYSTEM (NUMERISCHES) |
| 8696 | NUMERICAL DATA | DONNEES NUMERIQUES | ANZEIGE (DIGITALE), DATEN |
| 8697 | NUMERICAL VALUE | VALEUR NUMERIQUE | ZAHLENWERT |
| 8698 | NUT | ECROU | MUTTER, SCHRAUBENMUTTER |
| 8699 | NUT AUTOMATIC LATHE | TOUR A DECOLLETER LES ECROUS | MUTTERAUTOMAT |
| 8700 | NUT FORGED IN THE PRESS | ECROU EMBOUTI | MUTTER (GEDRÜCKTE), MUTTER (GEPRESSTE) |
| 8701 | NUT LOCK, BOLT LOCK | MECANISME D'ARRET DES ECROUS, FREIN D'ECROU | SCHRAUBENSICHERUNGSVORRICHTUNG |
| 8702 | NUTATION | NUTATION | NUTATION |
| 8703 | O-RING | JOINT TORIQUE | O-RING, TORUSRING |
| 8704 | OAK-TANNED LEATHER | CUIR TANNE A L'ECORCE DE CHENE | LOHGARES, ROTGARES LEDER |
| 8705 | OBELISK | OBELISQUE | OBELISK, SPITZSÄULE |
| 8706 | OBJECT POINT | POINT D'OBJET | OBJEKTPUNKT |
| 8707 | OBJECTION AGAINST A PATENT | ACTION EN NULLITE RELATIVE A UN BREVET | EINSPRUCH GEGEN EIN PATENT, PATENTEINSPRUCH |
| 8708 | OBJECTIVE | VERRE, SYSTEME OBJECTIF, OBJECTIF | OBJEKTIV |
| 8709 | OBLIQUE CONE | CONE OBLIQUE | KEGEL (SCHIEFER) |
| 8710 | OBLIQUE COORDINATES | COORDONNEES OBLIQUES | KOORDINATEN (SCHIEFWINKLIGE) |
| 8711 | OBLIQUE CROSS SECTION | SECTION OBLIQUE | SCHNITT (SCHIEFER) |
| 8712 | OBLIQUE CYLINDER | CYLINDRE OBLIQUE | ZYLINDER (SCHIEFER) |
| 8713 | OBLIQUE PARALLELOPIPED | PARALLELEPIPEDE OBLIQUE | PARALLELEPIPED (SCHIEFES) |
| 8714 | OBLONG HOLE, SLOT HOLE (ROUNDING AT THE ENDS) | MORTAISE A EXTREMITES ARRONDIES, TROU OBLONG | LANGLOCH |
| 8715 | OBROUND | OBLONG | ELLIPSOID |
| 8716 | OBSIDIAN | OBSIDIENNE | OBSIDIAN |
| 8717 | OBTUSE ANGLE | ANGLE OBTUS | WINKEL (STUMPFER) |
| 8718 | OBTUSE-ANGLED TRIANGLE | TRIANGLE OBTUSANGLE | DREIECK (STUMPFWINKLIGES) |
| 8719 | OCCLUSION | OCCLUSION (CHIM.) | OKKLUSION (CHEM.), VERSTOPFUNG |

**OCT** 222

| | | | |
|---|---|---|---|
| 8720 | OCHRE | OCRE, SANGUINE, BOL DIARMENIE, CRAIE ROUGE | OCKER |
| 8721 | OCTAGON | OCTOGONE, OCTANGLE | ACHTECK |
| 8722 | OCTAHEDRON | OCTAEDRE | ACHTFLACH, ACHTFLÄCHNER, OKTAEDER |
| 8723 | OCTANE RATING | INDICE D'OCTANE | OKTANZAHL |
| 8724 | OCTANT | OCTANT | ACHTELKREIS, OKTANT |
| 8725 | ODD NUMBER | NOMBRE IMPAIR | ZAHL (UNGERADE) |
| 8726 | ODONTOGRAPH | ODONTOGRAPHE | ZAHNFLANKENZIRKEL, ODONTOGRAPH |
| 8727 | OF ONE DIMENSION | DIMENSION (A UNE) | EINDIMENSIONAL |
| 8728 | OF THREE DIMENSIONS | DIMENSIONS (A TROIS) | DREIDIMENSIONAL |
| 8729 | OF TWO DIMENSIONS | DIMENSION (A DEUX) | ZWEIDIMENSIONAL |
| 8730 | OFF CENTER | DESAXE, DECALE, DECENTRE | EXZENTRISCH, VERSCHOBEN |
| 8731 | OFF CENTERED | DECALE, HORS D'AXE | SEITLICH VERSCHOBEN |
| 8732 | OFF HEAT | COULEE RATEE | FEHLSCHMELZE |
| 8733 | OFF IRON | FONTE DE TRANSITION | ÜBERGANGSROHEISEN |
| 8734 | OFF TIME | TEMPS DE REPOS, COUPURE DE COURANT | STROMPAUSE |
| 8735 | OFF-LINE OPERATION | TRAITEMENT INDIRECT | OFF-LINE-BETRIEB |
| 8736 | OFF-LOADING PORT | PORT DE DECHARGEMENT (DE NAVIRES MARCHANDS) | ENTLADEHAFEN, ENTLADESTATION |
| 8737 | OFF-SET (JOINT) | DEFAUT D'ALIGNEMENT OU DENIVELLATION (D'UN JOINT SOUDE) | VERSETZUNG |
| 8738 | OFF-SHORE | EN MER, AU LARGE | OFF-SHORE, SCHELF...., KÜSTENNAHE..... |
| 8739 | OFF-SHORE QUALITY STEEL | ACIER POUR PLATE-FORME DE FORAGE EN MER | STAHL FÜR KÜSTENNAHE ÖL BOHRUNG |
| 8740 | OFFICIAL TEST | EPREUVE OFFICIELLE | PRÜFUNG (AMTLICHE) |
| 8741 | OGEE-ARCH | ARC EN DOS D'ANE | ESELRÜCKENBOGEN |
| 8742 | OHM | OHM | OHM |
| 8743 | OIL | HUILE | ÖL |
| 8744 | OIL (TO) | GRAISSER A L'HUILE, HUILER | ÖLEN |
| 8745 | OIL BATH | BAIN D'HUILE | ÖLBAD |
| 8746 | OIL BATH AIR CLEANER | FILTRE A AIR A BAIN D'HUILE | ÖLBADLUFTFILTER |
| 8747 | OIL BATH RETURN GAUGE | JAUGE AVEC RENVOI A BAIN D'HUILE | GEGENSTROMMESSER IN ÖLBAD |
| 8748 | OIL BUNKERS | SOUTES A COMBUSTIBLE | ÖLBUNKER |
| 8749 | OIL CAN | BURETTE DE GRAISSAGE, BURETTE A HUILE | ÖLKANNE, SCHMIERKANNE |
| 8750 | OIL CONTROL RING | SEGMENT RACLEUR | ÖLABSTREIFRING |
| 8751 | OIL COOLER | REFROIDISSEUR D'HUILE | ÖLKÜHLER |
| 8752 | OIL COOLING | REFROIDISSEMENT A L'HUILE | ÖLKÜHLUNG |
| 8753 | OIL CUP, GREASE CUP | GODET GRAISSEUR, GODET HUILEUR, GODET DE GRAISSAGE | SCHMIERBÜCHSE, SCHMIERKELCH, SCHMIERNAPF, ÖLVASE |
| 8754 | OIL CUSHION | MATELAS D'HUILE | ÖLPOLSTER (DÄMPFUNG) |
| 8755 | OIL DASHPOT | FREIN HYDRAULIQUE, FREIN A HUILE | ÖLBREMSE, ÖLPUFFER |
| 8756 | OIL ENGINE | MOTEUR A CARBURANT | ÖLMASCHINE |
| 8757 | OIL FILTER | FILTRE A HUILE | ÖLFILTER |
| 8758 | OIL GAS | GAZ D'HUILE, GAZ RICHE | ÖLGAS, FETTGAS, REICHGAS |
| 8759 | OIL GROOVE | PATTE D'ARAIGNEE | ÖLNUT |
| 8760 | OIL HARDENING | TREMPE A L'HUILE, TREMPE DOUCE | ÖLHÄRTUNG |

| | | | |
|---|---|---|---|
| 8761 | **OIL HOLE** | ORIFICE DE GRAISSAGE, TROU GRAISSEUR | SCHMIERLOCH, SCHMIERBOHRUNG |
| 8762 | **OIL HOLE DRILL** | FORET A CANALISATION D'HUILE | SCHMIERBOHRER |
| 8763 | **OIL IMPELLER** | TURBINE DE RETOUR D'HUILE | ÖLFLÜGELRAD |
| 8764 | **OIL LEVEL DIPSTICK** | JAUGE D'HUILE | ÖLMESSSTAB |
| 8765 | **OIL OF TURPENTINE** | ESSENCE DE TEREBENTHINE | TERPENTINÖL |
| 8766 | **OIL PAINT, OIL COLOUR** | PEINTURE A L'HUILE | ÖLFARBE |
| 8767 | **OIL PAN** | CARTER D'HUILE (INFERIEUR) | KURBELGEHÄUSE-UNTERTEIL |
| 8768 | **OIL PRESSURE INDICATOR, GAUGE** | INDICATEUR DE PRESSION D'HUILE | ÖLDRUCKMESSER |
| 8769 | **OIL PUMP** | POMPE DE GRAISSAGE, POMPE HYDRAULIQUE, POMPE A HUILE | HYDRAULIKPUMPE, ÖLPUMPE, SCHMIERÖLPUMPE |
| 8770 | **OIL PUMP STRAINER** | CREPINE D'HUILE | ÖLPUMPENSIEB |
| 8771 | **OIL PUTTY** | MASTIC A L'HUILE | ÖLKITT |
| 8772 | **OIL QUENCHING** | TREMPE A L'HUILE | ÖLHÄRTUNG |
| 8773 | **OIL RESERVOIR CHAMBER** | RESERVOIR D'HUILE | ÖLSPEICHER |
| 8774 | **OIL RING** | BAGUE DE GRAISSAGE | ÖLRING, SCHMIERRING |
| 8775 | **OIL SCRAPER-RING** | SEGMENT RACLEUR | ÖLABSTREIFRING |
| 8776 | **OIL SEAL** | JOINT (DE RETENUE) D'HUILE | ÖLFANGRING |
| 8777 | **OIL SEPARATION** | EXTRACTION DE L'HUILE | ENTÖLUNG, ÖLABSCHEIDUNG |
| 8778 | **OIL SEPARATOR** | SEPARATEUR D'HUILE | ENTÖLER, ÖLABSCHEIDER |
| 8779 | **OIL SEPARATOR FOR STEAM** | DESHUILEUR DE VAPEUR | ABDAMPF-ENTÖLER, ÖLABSCHEIDER |
| 8780 | **OIL SHALE** | SCHISTE BITUMINEUX, NAPHTOSCHISTE | ÖLSCHIEFER |
| 8781 | **OIL STONE, HONE** | PIERRE A HUILE | ÖLSTEIN |
| 8782 | **OIL SUMP** | CARTER D'HUILE (INFERIEUR) | KURBELGEHÄUSE-UNTERTEIL, ÖLWANNE |
| 8783 | **OIL SUPPLY** | AMENEE D'HUILE | ÖLZUFÜHRUNG |
| 8784 | **OIL SYRINGE** | SERINGUE A HUILE | ÖLSPRITZE |
| 8785 | **OIL TESTER, OIL TESTING MACHINE** | MACHINE A ESSAYER LES HUILES | ÖLPRÜFMASCHINE |
| 8786 | **OIL VARNISH, BOILED OIL** | HUILE DE LIN A VERNIS, HUILE DE LIN BOUILLIE, VERNIS A L'HUILE | LEINÖLFIRNIS |
| 8787 | **OIL VISCOSITY INDEX** | INDICE DE VISCOSITE | ÖLVISKOSITÄTSINDEX |
| 8788 | **OILED PAPER** | PAPIER HUILE | ÖLPAPIER |
| 8789 | **OILING POINT** | POINT A LUBRIFIER | SCHMIERSTELLE |
| 8790 | **OILING RING** | BAGUE DE GRAISSAGE | SCHMIERRING |
| 8791 | **OILING, OIL LUBRICATION** | GRAISSAGE A L'HUILE, HUILAGE | ÖLSCHMIERUNG, ÖLEN |
| 8792 | **OILPROOF** | INATTAQUABLE A L'HUILE | ÖLFEST |
| 8793 | **OLD PROCESS** | PROCEDE OLD | OLD VERFAHREN (OXYGENE-LINZ-DONAWITZ) |
| 8794 | **OLDHAM'S COUPLING** | JOINT D'OLDHAM, JOINT A DOUBLE TOURNEVIS | KREUZSCHEIBENKUPPLUNG, OLDHAMKUPPLUNG |
| 8795 | **OLEIC ACID** | ACIDE OLEIQUE | ÖLSÄURE, OLEINSÄURE, STEARINÖL |
| 8796 | **OLIVINE** | OLIVINE, PERIDOT | OLIVIN |
| 8797 | **OLSEN CUP TEST** | ESSAI D'EMBOUTISSAGE ERICKSEN | ERICHSEN-TIEFZIEHVERSUCH, EINBEULVERSUCH |
| 8798 | **ON-COST** | FRAIS GENERAUX | UNKOSTEN (ALLGEMEINE) |
| 8799 | **ON-LINE OPERATION** | TRAITEMENT DIRECT | ON-LINE-BETRIEB |
| 8800 | **ON-SITE ERECTION** | MONTAGE SUR CHANTIER | BAUSTELLENMONTAGE |
| 8801 | **OOLITIC LIMESTONE** | CALCAIRE OOLITHIQUE, PISOLITHIQUE | OOLITHKALK, ROGENSTEIN |
| 8802 | **OPACITY, OPAQUENESS** | OPACITE | UNDURCHSICHTIGKEIT |
| 8803 | **OPAQUE** | OPAQUE | UNDURCHSICHTIG |

# OPE

224

| | | | |
|---|---|---|---|
| 8804 | **OPEN BELT** | COURROIE DROITE, COURROIE OUVERTE | RIEMENTRIEB (OFFENER) |
| 8805 | **OPEN CAM** | EXCENTRIQUE PLAN | EXZENTER (OFFENES) |
| 8806 | **OPEN CHAIN HYDROCARBONS** | HYDROCARBURES DE LA SERIE GRASSE | KOHLENWASSERSTOFFE DER FETTREIHE |
| 8807 | **OPEN CHANNEL** | CONDUITE LIBRE, CANAL DECOUVERT | LEITUNGSKANAL |
| 8808 | **OPEN CIRCUIT VOLTAGE** | TENSION A VIDE | LEERLAUFSPANNUNG |
| 8809 | **OPEN CORNER JOINT** | SOUDURE D'ANGLE OUVERTE | ECKNAHTVERBINDUNG MIT LUFTSPALT |
| 8810 | **OPEN DIES** | MATRICE OUVERTE | GESENK (OFFENES) |
| 8811 | **OPEN DOUBLE-BEVEL BUTT WELD** | SOUDURE EN K AVEC ECARTEMENT | K-NAHT MIT LUFTSPALT |
| 8812 | **OPEN DOUBLE-J BUTT WELD** | SOUDURE DOUBLE OUVERTE | DOPPEL-J-NAHT MIT LUFTSPALT |
| 8813 | **OPEN FIRE** | FEU NU | OFFENESFEUER, FREIES FEUER |
| 8814 | **OPEN FRONT MECHANICAL PRESS** | PRESSE MECANIQUE A BATI COL DE CYGNE | EINSTÄNDERPRESSE (MECHANISCHE) |
| 8815 | **OPEN HEARTH FURNACE** | FOUR MARTIN | SIEMENS-MARTIN-OFEN |
| 8816 | **OPEN HEARTH STEEL** | ACIER MARTIN | SIEMENS-MARTIN-STAHL, MARTIN-STAHL |
| 8817 | **OPEN LOOP SYSTEM** | SYSTEME DE COMMANDE EN BOUCLE OUVERTE | STEUERKETTE |
| 8818 | **OPEN MOTOR** | MOTEUR OUVERT, MOTEUR NON PROTEGE | OFFENER MOTOR |
| 8819 | **OPEN PIG IRON** | FER A GROS GRAIN | GROBKORNEISEN, GROSSLUCKIGES EISEN |
| 8820 | **OPEN SAND CASTING** | MOULAGE A DECOUVERT | HERDGUSS |
| 8821 | **OPEN SIDE PLANING MACHINE** | MACHINE A RABOTER OUVERTE SUR LE COTE, MACHINE A RABOTER A UN SEUL MONTANT | TISCHHOBELMASCHINE (EINSEITIG OFFENE), EINSTÄNDERHOBELMASCHINE, EINPILASTERHOBELMASCHINE |
| 8822 | **OPEN SINGLE-BEVEL BUTT WELD** | SOUDURE EN DEMI-V AVEC ECARTEMENT | HALB-V-HAHT MIT LUFTSPALT |
| 8823 | **OPEN SINGLE-J-BUTT WELD** | SOUDURE EN J AVEC ECARTEMENT | J-NAHT MIT LUFTSPALT |
| 8824 | **OPEN SQUARE BUTT WELD** | SOUDURE EN I AVEC ECARTEMENT | I-NAHT MIT LUFTSPALT |
| 8825 | **OPEN STEEL** | ACIER SEMI-CALME | STAHL (UNVOLLSTÄNDIG DESOXYDIERTER) |
| 8826 | **OPEN THE CIRCUIT (TO)** | OUVRIR LE CIRCUIT ELECTRIQUE | STROMKREIS ÖFFNEN (DEN) |
| 8827 | **OPEN TUBE PRESSURE GAUGE** | MANOMETRE A AIR LIBRE | GEFÄSSMANOMETER |
| 8828 | **OPEN-FRONT HYDRAULIC PRESS** | PRESSE HYDRAULIQUE A COL DE CYGNE | EINSTÄNDERPRESSE (HYDRAULISCHE) |
| 8829 | **OPEN-HEARTH FURNACE** | FOUR MARTIN | SIEMENS-MARTIN-OFEN |
| 8830 | **OPEN-HEARTH PROCESS** | PROCEDE SIEMENS-MARTIN | SIEMENS-MARTINS-VERFAHREN |
| 8831 | **OPENING** | EVIDEMENT | AUSSPARUNG |
| 8832 | **OPENING OF THE VALVE** | OUVERTURE DE LA SOUPAPE | VENTILERÖFFNUNG |
| 8833 | **OPERATING BRAKE** | LEVIER DE MANOEUVRE | STEUERHEBEL |
| 8834 | **OPERATING CONDITIONS** | CONDITIONS DE SERVICE | BETRIEBSVERHÄLTNISSE |
| 8835 | **OPERATING INSTRUCTIONS** | INSTRUCTIONS, REGLES DE SERVICE | BEDIENUNGSVORSCHRIFTEN |
| 8836 | **OPERATING TEMPERATURE** | TEMPERATURE DE SERVICE, TEMPERATURE DE TRAVAIL | BETRIEBSTEMPERATUR, ARBEITSTEMPERATUR |
| 8837 | **OPERATION** | EXPLOITATION, FONCTIONNEMENT, SERVICE | BETRIEB |
| 8838 | **OPERATION NOMBER** | NUMERO D'OPERATION EN COURS | NUMMER DES ARBEITSGANGES |
| 8839 | **OPERATOR'S STAND** | POSTE, STAND DE L'OUVRIER | ARBEITSPLATZ, ARBEITSSTAND |
| 8840 | **OPTICAL** | OPTIQUE | OPTISCH |
| 8841 | **OPTICAL AXIS** | AXE OPTIQUE | ACHSE (OPTISCHE) |
| 8842 | **OPTICAL COMPARATOR** | COMPARATEUR OPTIQUE | VERGLEICHER (OPTISCHER) |

**OSC**

| | | | |
|---|---|---|---|
| 8843 | **OPTICAL FLAT** | PLAN OPTIQUE | PLANFLÄCHE (OPTISCHE) |
| 8844 | **OPTICAL INSTRUMENT** | INSTRUMENT D'OPTIQUE | INSTRUMENT (OPTISCHES) |
| 8845 | **OPTICAL PYROMETER** | PYROMETRE OPTIQUE | PYROMETER (OPTISCHES) |
| 8846 | **OPTICAL PYROMETRY** | PYROMETRIE OPTIQUE | GLÜHFADENPYROMETRIE |
| 8847 | **OPTICAL READERS** | LECTEURS OPTIQUES | ABLESEGERÄTE (OPTISCHE) |
| 8848 | **OPTICAL SYSTEM** | SYSTEME OPTIQUE | SYSTEM (OPTISCHES) |
| 8849 | **OPTICS** | OPTIQUE | OPTIK |
| 8850 | **OPTIONAL STOP** | ARRET FACULTATIF | HALT (WAHLWEISER) |
| 8851 | **ORANGE PEEL EFFECT** | EFFET DE PEAU D'ORANGE | ORANGENSCHALENEFFEKT, APPELSINENSCHALENEFFEKT |
| 8852 | **ORDER OF MAGNITUDE** | ORDRE DE GRANDEUR | BEDEUTUNG, GRÖSSENORDNUNG |
| 8853 | **ORDINARY ETHER, DIETHYL ETHER** | ETHER ORDINAIRE, ETHER SULFURIQUE, OXYDE D'ETHYLE | ÄTHER, ÄTHYLÄTHER, SCHWEFELÄTHER |
| 8854 | **ORDINARY LIME MORTAR** | MORTIER AERIEN | KALKMÖRTEL, LUFTMÖRTEL |
| 8855 | **ORDINARY LINK CHAIN, OPEN LINK CHAIN** | CHAINE ORDINAIRE | GLIEDERKETTE, SCHAKENKETTE |
| 8856 | **ORDINARY SULPHURIC ACID** | ACIDE SULFURIQUE COMMERCIAL | SCHWEFELSÄURE (ROHE), HANDELSSCHWEFELSÄURE |
| 8857 | **ORDINARY WORKING CONDITIONS** | REGIME | BETRIEBSZUSTAND (NORMALER) |
| 8858 | **ORDINATE** | ORDONNEE | ORDINATE |
| 8859 | **ORE** | MINERAI | ERZ |
| 8860 | **ORE BRIQUETTE** | BRIQUETTE DE MINERAI, MINERAI BRIQUETTE | ERZBRIKETT, ERZZIEGEL, ERZPRESSSTEIN, BRIKETTIERTES ERZ |
| 8861 | **ORE DRESSING** | ENRICHISSEMENT DU MINERAI, TRAITEMENT MECANIQUE, PREPARATION DES MINERAIS | AUFBEREITUNG VON ERZEN, ERZANREICHERUNG |
| 8862 | **ORE ROASTING** | GRILLAGE DU MINERAI | ERZRÖSTEN |
| 8863 | **ORES AND FLUXES** | MINERAIS ET FONDANTS | ERZ UND SCHMELZMITTEL |
| 8864 | **ORGANIC ACID** | ACIDE ORGANIQUE | SÄURE (ORGANISCHE) |
| 8865 | **ORGANIC CHEMISTRY** | CHIMIE ORGANIQUE | CHEMIE (ORGANISCHE) |
| 8866 | **ORGANIC MATTER** | MATIERE ORGANIQUE | STOFF (ORGANISCHER) |
| 8867 | **ORIENTATION** | ORIENTATION | ORIENTIERUNG |
| 8868 | **ORIGIN OF COORDINATES** | ORIGINE DES COORDONNEES | ANFANGSPUNKT DER KOORDINATEN, NULLPUNKT DER KOORDINATEN, URSPRUNG DER KOORDINATEN, KOORDINATENANFANG |
| 8869 | **ORNAMENTAL, ECCENTRIC TURNING** | TOURNAGE DES SURFACES FIGUREES | PASSIGDREHEN, UNRUNDDREHEN |
| 8870 | **ORTHOGRAPHIC PARALLEL PROJECTION** | PROJECTION ORTHOGONALE | PARALLELPROJEKTION (RECHTWINKLIGE), PARALLELPROJEKTION ORTHOGONALE, PARALLELPROJEKTION ORTHOGRAPHISCHE |
| 8871 | **ORTHOHEXAGONAL CRYSTAL AXES** | AXES CRISTALLINS ORTHOHEXAGONAUX | KRISTALLACHSEN (ORTHOHEXAGONALE) |
| 8872 | **ORTHOMORPHIC CONFORM PROJECTION REPRESENTATION** | REPRESENTATION CONFORME | WINKELTREUE KONFORME ABBILDUNG |
| 8873 | **ORTHOPHOSPHORIC ACID** | ACIDE ORTHOPHOSPHORIQUE | PHOSPHORSÄURE, ORTHOPHOSPHORSÄURE, KNOCHENSÄURE |
| 8874 | **ORTHORHOMBIC CRYSTALS** | CRISTAUX ORTHORHOMBIQUES | KRISTALLE (ORTHORHOMBISCHE) |
| 8875 | **ORTHOSILICIC ACID** | ACIDE ORTHOSILICIQUE | ORTHOKIESELSÄURE |
| 8876 | **ORTHOTUNGSTIC ACID** | ACIDE TUNGSTIQUE | WOLFRAMSÄURE, SCHEELSÄURE, TUNGSTEINSÄURE |
| 8877 | **OSCILLATE (TO), VIBRATE (TO)** | OSCILLER, VIBRER | SCHWINGEN, OSZILLIEREN |
| 8878 | **OSCILLATING CAM** | CAME OSCILLANTE | SCHWINGNOCKEN |
| 8879 | **OSCILLATING CRYSTAL METHOD** | METHODE DE CRISTAL OSCILLANT | SCHWINGKRISTALLMETHODE |

# OSC

226

| | | | |
|---|---|---|---|
| 8880 | OSCILLATING ENGINE | MACHINE A CYLINDRE OSCILLANT | DAMPFMASCHINE MIT SCHWINGENDEM ZYLINDER, OSZILLIERENDE DAMPFMASCHINE |
| 8881 | OSCILLATING MOTION, VIBRATING MOTION | MOUVEMENT OSCILLATOIRE | BEWEGUNG (SCHWINGENDE), SCHWINGBEWEGUNG |
| 8882 | OSCILLATING PISTON | PISTON OSCILLANT | KOLBEN (SCHWINGENDER), SCHWINGKOLBEN |
| 8883 | OSCILLATION DUE TO RESONANCE | VIBRATIONS DUES A LA RESONANCE | RESONANZCHWINGUNG |
| 8884 | OSCILLATION, VIBRATION | OSCILLATION, VIBRATION | SCHWINGUNG, OSZILLATION |
| 8885 | OSCILLOGRAPH | OSCILLOGRAPHE | OSZILLOGRAPH |
| 8886 | OSCILLOSCOPE | OSCILLOSCOPE | OSZILLOSKOP |
| 8887 | OSCULATING PLANE | PLAN OSCULATEUR | SCHMIEGUNGSEBENE |
| 8888 | OSMIRIDIUM | OSMIRIDIUM | OSMIRIDIUM |
| 8889 | OSMIUM | OSMIUM | OSMIUM |
| 8890 | OSMOSIS | OSMOSE | OSMOSE |
| 8891 | OSMOTIC PRESSURE | PRESSION OSMOTIQUE | DRUCK (OSMOTISCHER) |
| 8892 | OUT OF GEAR | DESENGRENE | AUSSER EINGRIFF |
| 8893 | OUT OF LINE WITH THE AXIAL CENTRE | DESAXE | AUSSERACHSIG, DEZENTRIERT |
| 8894 | OUT-OF-ROUNDNESS | FAUX-ROND | UNRUNDHEIT |
| 8895 | OUT-OF-SQUARE | HORS D'EQUERRE | NICHT RECHTWINKELIG |
| 8896 | OUT-PUT | DEBIT | LEISTUNG |
| 8897 | OUTDOOR LIGHTING | ECLAIRAGE EXTERIEUR | AUSSENBELEUCHTUNG |
| 8898 | OUTER RACE OF BALL BEARING | BAGUE EXTERIEURE D'UN ROULEMENT A BILLES | ÄUSSERER RING, AUSSENRING EINES KUGELLAGERS |
| 8899 | OUTFLOW DISCHARGE OF WATER | ECOULEMENT D'EAU | ABFLUSS, WASSERABFLUSS |
| 8900 | OUTLET | SORTIE | AUSGANG, ABFLUSS |
| 8901 | OUTLET NOZZLE | TUBULURE DE SORTIE | AUSLASSSTUTZEN |
| 8902 | OUTLET OPENING , DISCHARGE ORIFICE | ORIFICE DE DECHARGE, ORIFICE DE SORTIE, ORIFICE D'ECHAPPEMENT, ORIFICE D'ECOULEMENT | AUSLASSÖFFNUNG, AUSFLUSSÖFFNUNG, AUSFLUSSMÜNDUNG |
| 8903 | OUTLET VELOCITY, VELOCITY OF DISCHARGE | VITESSE DE SORTIE, VITESSE A LA SORTIE, VITESSE D'ECOULEMENT | ABSTRÖMGESCHWINDIGKEIT, ABFLUSSGESCHWINDIGKEIT, AUSFLUSSGESCHWINDIGKEIT, AUSTRITTGESCHWINDIGKEIT |
| 8904 | OUTLET WEIR | BARRAGE DE SORTIE | FLUCHTSCHLEUSE |
| 8905 | OUTLINE DRAWING | DESSIN AU TRAIT, DESSIN LINEAIRE, PLAN D'ENSEMBLE, PLAN DE MASSE | STRICHZEICHNUNG, LINEARZEICHNUNG |
| 8906 | OUTLINE OF A CAM | PROFIL, CONTOUR D'UNE CAME | BEGRENZUNGSKURVE EINES EXZENTERS |
| 8907 | OUTLINE, CONTOUR, BOUNDARY OF A FIGURE | CONTOUR | UMRISS, UMRISSLINIE, KONTUR |
| 8908 | OUTPUT | DEBIT | LEISTUNG |
| 8909 | OUTPUT GOVERNOR | REGULATEUR DE PUISSANCE, REGULATEUR DE DEBIT | LEISTUNGSREGLER |
| 8910 | OUTPUT SHAFT | ARBRE SECONDAIRE | ABTRIEBSWELLE |
| 8911 | OUTSIDE | COTE EXTERIEUR | AUSSENSEITE |
| 8912 | OUTSIDE CALLIPERS | COMPAS D'EPAISSEUR | AUSSENTASTER, DICKZIRKEL |
| 8913 | OUTSIDE DIAMETER | DIAMETRE EXTERIEUR | AUSSENDURCHMESSER |
| 8914 | OUTSIDE SCREW GATE VALVE | VANNE A VIS EXTERIEURE | ABSPERRSCHIEBER MIT AUSSENSPINDEL, APSPERRSCHIEBER MIT AUSSENLIEBGENDEM SPINDELGEWINDE |

| | | | |
|---|---|---|---|
| 8915 | **OUTSIDE SCREW STEM** | TIGE A VIS EXTERIEURE | SPINDEL MIT AUSSENLIEGENDEM GEWINDE |
| 8916 | **OVAL BAR IRON, OVALS** | FER OLIVE, OLIVES | OVALEISEN |
| 8917 | **OVAL CROSS SECTION** | SECTION OVALE | QUERSCHNITT (EIRUNDER), QUERSCHNITT OVALER |
| 8918 | **OVAL ELLIPTICAL FLANGE** | BRIDE OVALE | FLANSCH (OVALER) |
| 8919 | **OVAL TURNING LATHE** | TOUR A OVALES | OVALDREHBANK |
| 8920 | **OVEN** | FOUR | OFEN |
| 8921 | **OVER DRIVE** | MULTIPLICATEUR DE VITESSE | ÜBERSETZUNGSGETRIEBE |
| 8922 | **OVER-ALL DIMENSIONS** | DIMENSIONS HORS-TOUT | AUSSENMASSE |
| 8923 | **OVERAGING** | SURVIEILLISSEMENT | ÜBERALTERUNG |
| 8924 | **OVERALL HEIGHT** | HAUTEUR DE CONSTRUCTION, HAUTEUR TOTALE | BAUHÖHE |
| 8925 | **OVERALL LENGTH** | LONGUEUR TOTALE, LONGUEUR DE CONSTRUCTION | BAULÄNGE, GESAMTLÄNGE, FABRIKATIONSLÄNGE |
| 8926 | **OVERALL WIDTH** | LARGEUR DE CONSTRUCTION, LARGEUR TOTALE | BAUBREITE |
| 8927 | **OVERALL, TOTAL EFFICIENCY** | RENDEMENT TOTAL | GESAMTWIRKUNGSGRAD, RESULTIERENDER WIRKUNGSGRAD |
| 8928 | **OVERBALANCE (TO)** | SURPASSER, EMPORTER SUR...(L') | ÜBERWIEGEN |
| 8929 | **OVERCOME A RESISTANCE (TO)** | VAINCRE UNE RESISTANCE | WIDERSTAND ÜBERWINDEN (EINEN) |
| 8930 | **OVERDRIVE** | VITESSE SURMULTIPLIEE | SCHNELLGANG |
| 8931 | **OVERFALL** | DEVERSOIR, TROP PLEIN | ÜBERFALL |
| 8932 | **OVERFLOW PIPE** | TUYAU DE TROP-PLEIN, TROP-PLEIN | ÜBERFALLROHR, ÜBERLAUFROHR |
| 8933 | **OVERFLOW VALVE** | SOUPAPE DE TROP PLEIN | SCHLABBERVENTIL, ÜBERSTRÖMVENTIL |
| 8934 | **OVERHANG** | PORTE-A-FAUX | ÜBERHANG |
| 8935 | **OVERHANGING CYLINDER** | CYLINDRE EN PORTE-A-FAUX | ZYLINDER (FREITRAGENDER), ZYLINDER (FREIHÄNGENDER), ZYLINDER (SCHWEBENDER) |
| 8936 | **OVERHANGING, OVERHUNG** | PORTE-A-FAUX | FLIEGEND GELAGERT, FREISCHWEBEND, ÜBERHÄNGEND, ÜBERSTEHEND, FREIHÄNGEND |
| 8937 | **OVERHAUL (TO)** | REVOIR, REVISER | NACHSEHEN, ÜBERHOLEN |
| 8938 | **OVERHEAD CABLE** | CABLE AERIEN | LUFTKABEL |
| 8939 | **OVERHEAD CAMSHAFT** | ARBRE A CAMES EN TETE | NOCKENWELLE, (OBENLIEGENDE) |
| 8940 | **OVERHEAD COUNTERSHAFT** | RENVOI DE PLAFOND | DECKENVORGELEGE |
| 8941 | **OVERHEAD POSITION** | SOUDURE EN POSITION PLAFOND | ÜBERKOPFSCHWEISSUNG |
| 8942 | **OVERHEAD TRAVELLER, TRAVELLING CRANE** | PONT-ROULANT D'USINE | LAUFKRAN |
| 8943 | **OVERHEAD VALVES** | SOUPAPES EN TETE | VENTILE (HÄNGENDE) |
| 8944 | **OVERHEAD WELD** | SOUDURE AU PLAFOND | ÜBERKOPFSCHWEISSNAHT |
| 8945 | **OVERHEATED STEEL** | ACIER SURCHAUFFE | STAHL, (ÜBERHITZTER) |
| 8946 | **OVERHEATING** | SURCHAUFFE | UBERHITZUNG |
| 8947 | **OVERHUNG OVERHANGING CRANK, OUTSIDE CRANK** | MANIVELLE FRONTALE, MANIVELLE EN BOUT, MANIVELLE EN PORTE-A-FAUX | STIRNKURBEL, ENDKURBEL, FLIEGEND ANGEORDNETE KURBEL |
| 8948 | **OVERLAP** | DEPASSEMENT, RECOUVREMENT, SUREPAISSEUR, BAVURE | ÜBERLAGERUNG, ÜBERLAPPUNG, NAHTÜBERHÖHUNG |
| 8949 | **OVERLAP (OF A WELD)** | BAVURE (DE SOUDURE) | ÜBERLAPPUNG |
| 8950 | **OVERLAP (TO), LAP (TO)** | CHEVAUCHER | ÜBEREINANDERLIEGEN, ÜBEREINANDERGREIFEN, ÜBEREINANDERSTEHEN |
| 8951 | **OVERLAPPING, OVERLAP** | RECOUVREMENT, CHEVAUCHEMENT | ÜBEREINANDERGREIFEN, ÜBERLAPPEN, ÜBERLAPPUNG |

# OVE
228

| | | | |
|---|---|---|---|
| 8952 | **OVERLAY** | SURCOUCHE | AUFTRAGSSCHWEISSZUSATZ, ÜBERLAGERUNG |
| 8953 | **OVERLOAD** | SURCHARGE | ÜBERLAST, ÜBERBELASTUNG, ÜBERLADUNG |
| 8954 | **OVERLOAD (TO)** | SURCHARGER | ÜBERBELASTEN |
| 8955 | **OVERPRESSURE** | PRESSION SUPERIEURE A LA PRESSION AUTORISEE, SURPRESSION | ÜBERNORMALDRUCK, ÜBERDRUCK |
| 8956 | **OVERRIDER** | BUTOIR DE PARE-CHOCS | STOSSSTANGENHORN |
| 8957 | **OVERRUNNING CLUTCH** | EMBRAYAGE A ROUE LIBRE | FREILAUFKUPPLUNG |
| 8958 | **OVERSEER, OVERLOOKER** | SURVEILLANT | FABRIKAUFSEHER, AUFSEHER |
| 8959 | **OVERSHOOT** | DEPASSEMENT | ÜBERFAHREN |
| 8960 | **OVERSHOT WATER WHEEL** | ROUE PAR-DESSUS, ROUE A AUGETS, NORIA | OBERSCHLÄCHTIGES WASSERRAD |
| 8961 | **OVERSIZE** | SURCROIT DE DIMENSION | ÜBERGRÖSSE, ÜBERMASS |
| 8962 | **OVERSTRAIN A MATERIAL (TO)** | SURCHARGER, FATIGUER UN MATERIEL | MATERIAL ÜBERANSTRENGEN (EIN) |
| 8963 | **OVERSTRESSING** | SURCHARGE | ÜBERLASTUNG, ÜBERBEANSPRUCHUNG |
| 8964 | **OVERTIME** | HEURES SUPPLEMENTAIRES | ÜBERSTUNDEN |
| 8965 | **OVERTURNING** | RENVERSEMENT (CALCUL SOUS SEISMES) | UMSTÜRZEN, UMKEHRUNG |
| 8966 | **OVERTURNING MOMENT** | MOMENT DE RENVERSEMENT | KIPPMOMENT |
| 8967 | **OVERVOLTAGE** | SURVOLTAGE | ÜBERSPANNUNG |
| 8968 | **OXALATE** | OXALATE | OXALSAURES SALZ, OXALAT |
| 8969 | **OXALIC ACID** | ACIDE OXALIQUE | OXALSÄURE, ÄTHANDISÄURE, KLEESÄURE, SAUERKLEESÄURE |
| 8970 | **OXIDATION** | OXYDATION | OXYDATION, OXYDIERUNG |
| 8971 | **OXIDE** | OXYDE | OXYD |
| 8972 | **OXIDISABLE, SUSCEPTIBLE OF OXIDATION** | OXYDABLE | OXYDIERBAR |
| 8973 | **OXIDISE (TO), OXIDATE (TO), CONVERT INTO AN OXYDE (TO)** | OXYDER, OXYDER (S') | OXYDIEREN |
| 8974 | **OXIDISING AGENT** | OXYDANT | OXYDATIONSMITTEL |
| 8975 | **OXIDISING FLAME** | DARD DE CHALUMEAU, FLAMME OXYDANTE | STICHFLAMME, FLAMME (OXIDIERENDE) |
| 8976 | **OXY-ACETYLENE DESEAMING** | ELIMINATION DES DEFAUTS DE SURFACE AU CHALUMEAU | AUTOGENES BRENNSCHNEIDEN, BRENNPUTZEN (FLÄMMEN) |
| 8977 | **OXYACETYLENE CUTTING** | OXYCOUPAGE | AZETYLEN-SAUERSTOFF BRENNSCHNEIDEVERFAHREN |
| 8978 | **OXYACETYLENE PRESSURE WELDING** | SOUDAGE AUTOGENE PAR PRESSION | AUTOGEN-PRESS-SCHWEISSEN |
| 8979 | **OXYACETYLENE WELDING** | SOUDURE OXY-ACETYLENIQUE, SOUDAGE AUTOGENE | SAUERSTOFF-AZETYLEN-, AUTOGENSCHWEISSEN |
| 8980 | **OXYGEN** | OXYGENE | SAUERSTOFF |
| 8981 | **OXYGEN LANCE** | LANCE A OXYGENE | SAUERSTOFFLANZE |
| 8982 | **OXYGEN PROCESS** | PROCEDE A L'OXYGENE | SAUERSTOFFVERFAHREN |
| 8983 | **OXYGEN-FREE HIGH CONDUCTIVITY COPPER** | CUIVRE EXEMPT D'OXYGENE A HAUTE CONDUCTIVITE | LEITKUPFER OHNE SAUERSTOFF |
| 8984 | **OXYGENIZATION** | OXYGENATION, OXYDATION | OXYDIEREN |
| 8985 | **OXYHYDROGEN** | GAZ OXHYDRIQUE | KNALLGAS |
| 8986 | **OXYHYDROGEN BLOW PIPE** | CHALUMEAU OXHYDRIQUE | KNALLGASGEBLÄSE, SAUERSTOFFGEBLÄSE |
| 8987 | **OXYHYDROGEN LIGHT, LIMELIGHT** | LUMIERE OXHYDRIQUE, LUMIERE DE DRUMMOND | KALKLICHT, DRUMMONDSCHES LICHT |

| | | | |
|---|---|---|---|
| 8988 | **OXYHYDROGEN WELDING** | SOUDURE OXHYDRIQUE | SAUERSTOFF-WASSERSTOFF-SCHWEISSUNG, SCHWEISSUNG (HYDROOXYGENE |
| 8989 | **OZONE** | OZONE | OZON |
| 8990 | **PACK (TO), INSERT PACKING MATERIAL (TO)** | GARNIR DE MATIERE DE JOINT | PACKEN, VERPACKEN, LIDERN |
| 8991 | **PACK (TO), MAKE UP INTO A PACKAGE (TO)** | EMBALLER | VERPACKEN |
| 8992 | **PACK CARBURIZING** | CEMENTATION A LA POUDRE | PULVERZEMENTIEREN |
| 8993 | **PACK FILM** | PELLICULE RIGIDE, PLATE, FILM RIGIDE | PLANFILM |
| 8994 | **PACK ROLLING** | LAMINAGE EN PAQUET | PAKETWALZEN |
| 8995 | **PACKAGING** | CONDITIONNEMENT | VERPACKUNG |
| 8996 | **PACKED OILS** | HUILES CONDITIONNEES | AUFBEREITETE ÖLE |
| 8997 | **PACKED PLUG VALVE** | ROBINET A BOISSEAU | STOPFENHAHN, PACKHAHN, HAHNVENTIL |
| 8998 | **PACKING** | GARNITURE DE JOINT, GARNITURE DE SOUPAGE | DICHTUNG, PACKUNG |
| 8999 | **PACKING** | EMBALLAGE, ENROBAGE | VERPACKUNG, UMHÜLLUNG |
| 9000 | **PACKING COLLAR** | BAGUE DE FOND | GRUNDRING |
| 9001 | **PACKING GLAND** | DOUILLE-FOULOIR (DE PRESSE-ETOUPE) | DICHTUNGSBÜCHSE, STOPFBÜCHSE |
| 9002 | **PACKING GLAND FLANGE** | BRIDE DE PRESSE-ETOUPE | STOPFBÜCHSENBRILLE |
| 9003 | **PACKING LIST** | ETAT DE COLISAGE | KOLLISPEZIFIKATION |
| 9004 | **PACKING MATERIAL** | GARNITURE, BOURRAGE | PACKMATERIAL |
| 9005 | **PACKING NUT** | ECROU DE PRESSE-ETOUPE | STOPFBÜCHSENMUTTER |
| 9006 | **PACKING PIECE** | PIECE D'AJUSTAGE | PASSSTÜCK |
| 9007 | **PACKING RING** | BAGUE DE GARNITURE, BAGUE D'ETANCHEITE | DICHTUNGSRING, LIDERUNGSRING, PACKUNGSRING |
| 9008 | **PACKING SPACE** | BOITE A BOURRAGE, BOITE A GARNITURES, BOISSEAU DE LA BOITE A ETOUPE | STOPFBÜCHSTOPF, STOPFBÜCHSGEHÄUSE, PACKUNGSRAUM |
| 9009 | **PACKING, JOINT** | GARNITURE, BOURRAGE | LIDERUNG, DICHTUNG, PACKUNG |
| 9010 | **PACKLESS VALVE** | ROBINET SANS PRESSE-ETOUPE | VENTIL (STOPFBÜCHSLOSES) |
| 9011 | **PAD** | SOLE DE HAUT-FOURNEAU, ASPERITE, TAMPON, ASSISE, GALETTE | HOCHOFENBODEN, RAUHIGKEIT, STOPFEN, TRAGBELAG |
| 9012 | **PADTYPE NOZZLE** | TUBULURE AUTORENFORCEE | ROHRSTUTZEN (SELBSTVERSTEIFTER) |
| 9013 | **PAINT** | PEINTURE | ANSTRICH |
| 9014 | **PAINT (TO), COAT WITH PAINT (TO)** | PEINTURER, ENDUIRE | ANSTREICHEN |
| 9015 | **PAINT, COLOUR** | COULEUR, PEINTURE | ANSTRICHFARBE |
| 9016 | **PAINTED PIPE** | TUBE PROTEGE PAR UNE PEINTURE | ROHR (ANGESTRICHENES), ROHR (GESTRICHENES) |
| 9017 | **PAINTER'S TROLLEY** | NACELLE DE PEINTRE | SCHWERARBEITSSITZ, ANSTRICHGONDEL |
| 9018 | **PAINTING** | PEINTURE, PEINTURAGE | ANSTRICH, ANSTREICHEN |
| 9019 | **PAINTING BRUSH** | BROSSE, PINCEAU | MALPINSEL |
| 9020 | **PAINTING BY SPRAYING** | PEINTURE AU PISTOLET | SPRITZLACKIEREN |
| 9021 | **PAINTING DEFECTS** | DEFAUTS DE PEINTURE | ANSTRICHMÄNGEL |
| 9022 | **PAIR OF COMPASSES** | COMPAS | ZIRKEL |
| 9023 | **PALLADIUM** | PALLADIUM | PALLADIUM |
| 9024 | **PALLET** | CLAPET DE SOUPAPE | VENTILKLAPPE |
| 9025 | **PALLETIZED TRUCKS** | CAMIONS TRANSPALETTES | PALETTEN-HUBLASTWAGEN |
| 9026 | **PALLETIZING** | PALETTISATION | PALETTIEREN |
| 9027 | **PALM OIL** | HUILE DE PALME | PALMÖL, PALMBUTTER, PALMFETT |

**PAN** 230

| | | | |
|---|---|---|---|
| 9028 | PALMITIC ACID | ACIDE PALMITIQUE | PALMITINSÄURE |
| 9029 | PAN | RECIPIENT PLAT, CUVE DE FOUR | SCHALE, HERDWANNE |
| 9030 | PAN HEAD RIVET | RIVET A TETE TRONCONIQUE | NIET MIT TRAPEZPROFILKOPF |
| 9031 | PANE, PEEN, PENE, PEAN, PLEND OF A HAMMER | PANNE DU MARTEAU | HAMMERFINNE, HAMMERPINNE, FINNE, PINNE EINES HAMMERS |
| 9032 | PANEL | PLAQUE, MAILLE, PLANCHE, PANNEAU | KUNSTSTOFFPLATTE, RAHMENFÜLLUNG, TAFEL |
| 9033 | PANTOGRAPH | PANTOGRAPHE | STORCHSCHNABEL, PANTOGRAPH |
| 9034 | PAPER PULLEY | POULIE EN CARTON | RIEMENSCHEIBE AUS PAPIER, PAPIERRIEMENSCHEIBE |
| 9035 | PAPER PULP | PATE A PAPIER | PAPIERSTOFF, PAPIERZEUG |
| 9036 | PAPIER MACHE | PAPIER MACHE, PAPIER POURRI | PAPIERMACHE |
| 9037 | PARA RUBBER | CAOUTCHOUC DE PARA | PARAKAUTSCHUK, PARAGUMMI |
| 9038 | PARABOLA | PARABOLE | PARABEL |
| 9039 | PARABOLIC CYLINDER | CYLINDRE PARABOLIQUE | ZYLINDER (PARABOLISCHER) |
| 9040 | PARABOLIC INTERPOLATION | INTERPOLATION PARABOLIQUE | PARABELINTERPOLATION |
| 9041 | PARABOLIC MIRROR | MIROIR PARABOLIQUE | PARABOLSPIEGEL |
| 9042 | PARABOLOID OF REVOLUTION | PARABOLOIDE DE REVOLUTION | UMDREHUNGSPARABOLOID, DREHUNGSPARABOLOID, ROTATIONSPARABOLOID |
| 9043 | PARAFFIN | PARAFFINE | PARAFFIN |
| 9044 | PARAFFIN OIL | HUILE LOURDE DE PARAFFINE, HUILE PARAFFINE | PARAFFINÖL |
| 9045 | PARAFFIN WAX | CIRE DE PARAFFINE | HARTPARAFFIN |
| 9046 | PARAFFIN, PETROLEUM ENGINE | MOTEUR A PETROLE | PETROLEUMMOTOR |
| 9047 | PARALLAX | PARALLAXE | PARALLAXE |
| 9048 | PARALLAX ERROR | ERREUR PARALLACTIQUE | PARALLAXENFEHLER |
| 9049 | PARALLEL | PARALLELE | PARALLELE |
| 9050 | PARALLEL (ADJ) | PARALLELE | PARALLEL |
| 9051 | PARALLEL CONNECTION, CONNECTION IN PARALLEL | MONTAGE, GROUPEMENT, COUPLAGE EN QUANTITE, MONTAGE EN SURFACE, MONTAGE EN PARALLELE | NEBENEINANDERSCHALTUNG, PARALLELSCHALTUNG |
| 9052 | PARALLEL DISC WITH SPRING | OPERCULE PARALLELE A SERRAGE PAR RESSORT | PARALLELSCHIEBER MIT FEDERVERSCHLUSS |
| 9053 | PARALLEL DISC WITH WEDGE | OPERCULE PARALLELE A SERRAGE MECANIQUE | PARALLELSCHIEBER MIT MECHANISCHEM VERSCHLUSS |
| 9054 | PARALLEL ENTRY | ENTREE EN PARALLELE | PARALLELANZEIGE |
| 9055 | PARALLEL FLOW | COURANT A FILETS PARALLELES | STRÖMUNG (GEORDNETE), STRÖMUNG (LAMINARE), PARALLELSTRÖMUNG, SCHICHTENSTRÖMUNG |
| 9056 | PARALLEL FORCES | FORCES PARALLELES | KRÄFT (PARALLELE) |
| 9057 | PARALLEL MOTION | PARALLELOGRAMME ARTICULE | PARALLELOGRAMMGETRIEBE |
| 9058 | PARALLEL PROJECTION | PROJECTION PARALLELE | PARALLELPROJEKTION |
| 9059 | PARALLEL RULER | REGLE A TRACER DES PARALLELES | PARALLELLINEAL |
| 9060 | PARALLEL SEAT GATE VALVE | VANNE A SIEGES PARALLELES | PARALLELSCHIEBER |
| 9061 | PARALLEL SEAT GATE VALVE WITH SPRING | VANNE A LIBRE DILATATION | PARALLELSCHIEBER (SELBSTDICHTENDER) |
| 9062 | PARALLEL SEAT GATE VALVE, WITH WEDGE | VANNE A BLOCAGE MECANIQUE | SCHIEBER MIT MECHANISCHER ABSPERRUNG |
| 9063 | PARALLEL SEATS | SIEGES PARALLELES | SITZE (PARALLELE) |
| 9064 | PARALLEL SHAFTS | ARBRES PARALLELES | WELLEN (PARALLELE) |
| 9065 | PARALLEL THREAD | FILETAGE CYLINDRIQUE | GEWINDE (ZYLINDRISCHES) |
| 9066 | PARALLEL VICE | ETAU A SERRAGE PARALLELE | PARALLELSCHRAUBSTOCK |
| 9067 | PARALLEL, BLUNT FILE | LIME LARGE, LIME PLATE MAIN | STUMPFFEILE |

| | | |
|---|---|---|
| 9068 | **PARALLELEPIPED, PARALLELOPIPED** | PARALLELEPIPEDE | PARALLELEPIPED |
| 9069 | **PARALLELISM** | PARALLELISME | PARALLELITÄT |
| 9070 | **PARALLELOGRAM** | PARALLELOGRAMME | PARALLELOGRAMM |
| 9071 | **PARALLELOGRAM OF FORCES** | PARALLELOGRAMME DES FORCES | PARALLELOGRAMM DER KRÄFTE, KRÄFTEPARALLELOGRAMM |
| 9072 | **PARALLELOGRAM OF VELOCITIES** | PARALLELOGRAMME DES VITESSES | PARALLELOGRAMM DER GESCHWINDIGKEITEN, GESCHWINDIGKEITSPARALLELOGRAMM |
| 9073 | **PARAMAGNETIC** | PARAMAGNETIQUE | PARAMAGNETISCH |
| 9074 | **PARAMAGNETISM** | PARAMAGNETISME | PARAMAGNETISMUS |
| 9075 | **PARAMETER** | PARAMETRE, CARACTERISTIQUE | KENNWERT, PARAMETER, GITTERKONSTANTE |
| 9076 | **PARCEL PLATING** | GALVANISATION PARTIELLE | ÜBERZUG (TEILWEISER) |
| 9077 | **PARCHMENT** | PARCHEMIN | PERGAMENT |
| 9078 | **PARCHMENT PAPER, ARTIFICIAL IMITATION PARCHMENT** | PARCHEMIN VEGETAL, PAPIER-PARCHEMIN, PAPYRINE | PERGAMENTPAPIER, PERGAMENT (VEGETABILISCHES) |
| 9079 | **PARENT METAL** | METAL DE BASE | MUTTERWERKSTOFF, GRUNDMETALL |
| 9080 | **PARING CHISEL** | CISEAU POUR MENUISIER | STECHBEITEL |
| 9081 | **PARITY CHECK** | CONTROLE DE PARITE | PARITÄTSPRÜFUNG |
| 9082 | **PARKING BRAKE** | FREIN DE STATIONNEMENT, FREIN A MAIN | FESTSTELLBREMSE, HANDBREMSE, FESTSTELLBREMSE |
| 9083 | **PART** | PIECE | TEIL |
| 9084 | **PART PROGRAMMING** | PROGRAMMATION DE PIECE | TEILEPROGRAMM |
| 9085 | **PARTIAL ADMISSION TURBINE** | TURBINE A ADMISSION PARTIELLE | PARTIALTURBINE |
| 9086 | **PARTIAL DIFFERENTIAL EQUATION** | EQUATION DIFFERENTIELLE PARTIELLE | PARTIELLE DIFFERENTIALGLEICHUNG |
| 9087 | **PARTIAL PRESSURE** | PRESSION PARTIELLE | TEILDRUCK |
| 9088 | **PARTICLE** | PARTICULE | TEILCHEN |
| 9089 | **PARTICLE SIZE** | GROSSEUR DE LA PARTICULE | TEILCHENGRÖSSE |
| 9090 | **PARTICLE SIZE DISTRIBUTION** | COMPOSITION GRANULOMETRIQUE | KORNGRÖSSENVERTEILUNG |
| 9091 | **PARTING** | PRECIPITATION | SCHEIDUNG |
| 9092 | **PARTING COMPOUND** | LUBRIFIANT DE MOULE | TRENNMITTEL |
| 9093 | **PARTING LINE** | LIGNE DE JOINT, PLAN DE JOINT | TRENNLINIE |
| 9094 | **PARTING SAND** | SABLE ISOLANT | STREUSAND |
| 9095 | **PARTS LIST** | NOMENCLATURE | TEILLISTE |
| 9096 | **PASS** | OPERATION, PASSE, COUCHE | ARBEITSGANG, LAGE |
| 9097 | **PASS SEQUENCE** | SEQUENCE DES CALIBRES | KALIBERFOLGE, STICHFOLGE |
| 9098 | **PASSAGE OF HEAT** | PASSAGE DE LA CHALEUR | WÄRMEÜBERGANG |
| 9099 | **PASSAGE OF LIGHT** | PASSAGE DE LA LUMIERE | LICHTDURCHGANG |
| 9100 | **PASSAGE OPENING** | ORIFICE DE PASSAGE | DURCHLASSÖFFNUNG, DURCHFLUSSÖFFNUNG, DURCHGANGSÖFFNUNG |
| 9101 | **PASSENGER LIFT** | ASCENSEUR | PERSONENAUFZUG, AUFZUG |
| 9102 | **PASSING LIGHT** | FEU DE DEPASSEMENT | ÜBERHOLUNGSLEUCHTE |
| 9103 | **PASSIVATING** | BAIN DE PASSIVATION | PASSIVIERBAD |
| 9104 | **PASSIVATING FILM** | PELLICULE PASSIVANTE | PASSIVIERUNGSSCHICHT |
| 9105 | **PASSIVATION** | PASSIVATION | PASSIVIERUNG |
| 9106 | **PASSIVATOR** | PASSIVANT | PASSIVIERUNGSMITTEL |
| 9107 | **PASSIVITY** | PASSIVITE | PASSIVITÄT |
| 9108 | **PASTE SOLDER** | PATE A SOUDER | LÖTPASTE |
| 9109 | **PATCH** | RAPIECAGE, RAPIECEMENT (RESULTAT) | FLICKEN |
| 9110 | **PATCH (TO)** | RAPIECER | FLICKEN |

# PAT

232

| | | | |
|---|---|---|---|
| 9111 | **PATCHING** | RAPIECAGE, RAPIECEMENT (ACTION) | FLICKEN |
| 9112 | **PATENT** | BREVET D'INVENTION | PATENT, ERFINDUNGSPATENT |
| 9113 | **PATENT (TO)** | BREVETER | PATENTIEREN, PATENTRECHTLICH SCHÜTZEN |
| 9114 | **PATENT AGENT** | AGENT DE BREVETS D'INVENTION | PATENTANWALT |
| 9115 | **PATENT FEES** | TAXES DE BREVET | PATENTGEBÜHREN |
| 9116 | **PATENT LAW** | BREVETS D'INVENTION (LOI SUR LES) | PATENTGESETZ |
| 9117 | **PATENT LEATHER** | CUIR VERNI | GLANZLEDER |
| 9118 | **PATENT LEVELING** | PLANAGE | STRECKRICHTEN |
| 9119 | **PATENT MEDICINE** | SPECIALITE PHARMACEUTIQUE | SPEZIALITÄT (PHARMAZEUTISCHE) |
| 9120 | **PATENT OFFICE** | BREVETS D'INVENTION (BUREAU DES) | PATENTAMT |
| 9121 | **PATENT PRIVILEGES, RIGHTS** | DROITS DU BREVETE | PATENTRECHTE |
| 9122 | **PATENTABLE INVENTION** | INVENTION BREVETABLE, SUSCEPTIBLE D'ETRE BREVETEE | ERFINDUNG (PATENTFÄHIGE), ERFINDUNG (SCHUTZFÄHIGE) |
| 9123 | **PATENTEE** | BREVETE | PATENTINHABER, INHABER EINES PATENTS |
| 9124 | **PATENTING** | PATENTAGE | PATENTIEREN |
| 9125 | **PATH OF FLOW** | TRAJET SUIVI PAR UN FLUIDE | STRÖMUNGSWEG |
| 9126 | **PATHOGENIC ORGANISM** | MICROBE PATHOGENE | KRANKHEITSKEIM, KRANKHEITSERREGER |
| 9127 | **PATINA, PATINA FINISCH** | PATINE | PATINA, EDELROST |
| 9128 | **PATTERN** | GABARIT, MODELE, DIAGRAMME DE RX | SCHABLONE, MODELL, MUSTER, RÖNTGENBILD ODER DIAGRAM |
| 9129 | **PATTERN FOR CASTING** | MODELE POUR FONTE | GUSSMODELL |
| 9130 | **PATTERN MAKER** | OUVRIER MODELEUR | MODELLSCHREINER, MODELLTISCHLER |
| 9131 | **PATTERN MAKING** | MENUISERIE DE MODELES (ART) | MODELLTISCHLEREI (HERSTELLUNG VON MODELLEN) |
| 9132 | **PATTERN SHOP** | MENUISERIE DE MODELES (ATELIER) | MODELLTISCHLEREI (WERKSTÄTTE) |
| 9133 | **PATTERN, MODEL** | MODELE | MODELL |
| 9134 | **PATTERNED SURFACE** | PEAU D'ORANGE (AFNOR) | APFELSINEN-(SCHALEN-)EFFEKT |
| 9135 | **PATTERNMAKING** | MODELAGE | MODELLHERSTELLUNG |
| 9136 | **PAVEMENT, PAVING** | PAVE, DALLAGE | PFLASTER, PFLASTERUNG |
| 9137 | **PAVING STONE** | PAVE (PIERRE) | PFLASTERSTEIN |
| 9138 | **PAWL AND RATCHET MOTION** | ENCLIQUETAGE A ROCHET | ZAHNGESPERRE, KLINKENGETRIEBE, SCHALTGETRIEBE, SCHALTMECHANISMUS, KLINKEN, SCHALTWERK |
| 9139 | **PAYLOAD** | CHARGE UTILE | LADEFÄHIGKEIT |
| 9140 | **PEA COAL** | GRAINS POUR GAZOGENES | PERLKOHLE, ERBSKOHLE |
| 9141 | **PEA CUTTER AND CORN SWATHER** | RECOLTEUSES DE POIS | ERBSENSCHNEIDER |
| 9142 | **PEAR-SHAPED FLASK** | BALLON A FOND PLAT | STEHKOLBEN |
| 9143 | **PEARL ASH** | PERLASSE | PERLASCHE, POTTASCHE (GEREINIGTE) |
| 9144 | **PEARLITE** | PERLITE | PERLIT |
| 9145 | **PEARLITIC STEEL** | ACIER PERLITIQUE | STAHL (PERLITISCHER) |
| 9146 | **PEARLY LUSTRE** | ECLAT NACRE, PERLE | PERLMUTTERGLANZ |
| 9147 | **PEAT** | TOURBE | TORF |
| 9148 | **PEAT BRICK** | BRIQUE EN TOURBE | TORFSTEIN |
| 9149 | **PEAT BRIQUETTE, BRIQUETTED PEAT** | AGGLOMERE DE TOURBE | TORFBRIKETT |
| 9150 | **PEAT SLAB** | PLAQUE DE TOURBE | TORFPLATTE |

PER

| | | | |
|---|---|---|---|
| 9151 | **PEAT TURF** | MOTTE DE TOURBE | TORFSODE, TORFKUCHEN |
| 9152 | **PEBBLE** | CAILLOU | KIESELSTEIN |
| 9153 | **PEBBLE TRAP** | PIEGE A CAILLOUX | STEINFÄNGER |
| 9154 | **PEDESTAL BEARING** | PALIER A CHAISE SUR LE SOL | BOCKLAGER |
| 9155 | **PEEL** | CROUTE | SCHALE |
| 9156 | **PEELING** | ECROUTAGE, ECAILLAGE, DECOLLEMENT | SCHÄLEN, ABBLÄTTERN ABLÖSEN |
| 9157 | **PEENING** | MARTELAGE, PANNAGE | HÄMMERN, DRESSIEREN, GLÄTTEN |
| 9158 | **PEEP HOLE** | REGARD | SCHAULOCH |
| 9159 | **PEG** | GOUPILLE | HALTESTEIN, HALTESTIFT |
| 9160 | **PEN POINT** | BRANCHE TIRE-LIGNE D'UN COMPAS | ZIEHFEDEREINSATZ, TINTENEINSATZ, TUSCHEINSATZ FÜR ZIRKEL |
| 9161 | **PENCIL** | PLUME, STYLET, STYLET TRACEUR, TRACEUR, CRAYON (D'UN APPAREIL ENREGISTREUR) | SCHREIBSTIFT (EINER REGISTRIERVORRICHTUNG) |
| 9162 | **PENCIL BUNDLE OF RAYS OF LIGHT** | FAISCEAU LUMINEUX, PINCEAU LUMINEUX | LICHTSTRAHLENBÜNDEL |
| 9163 | **PENCIL ERASER** | GOMME A CRAYON | BLEISTIFTGUMMI |
| 9164 | **PENCIL OF RAYS** | FAISCEAU DE RAYONS | STRAHLENBÜNDEL |
| 9165 | **PENCIL POINT** | BRANCHE PORTE-CRAYON, PORTE-CRAYON D'UN COMPAS | BLEISTIFTEINSATZ FÜR ZIRKEL |
| 9166 | **PENDANT BRACKET, HANG DOWN BRACKET** | CHAISE PENDANTE A DEUX JAMBES, CHAISE EN U | HÄNGEBOCK |
| 9167 | **PENDULUM** | PENDULE | PENDEL |
| 9168 | **PENDULUM GOVERNOR** | REGULATEUR PENDULE | PENDELREGLER |
| 9169 | **PENETRATING OIL** | LIQUIDE PENETRANT | ÖL (ROSTLÖSENDES) |
| 9170 | **PENETRATION** | PENETRATION | DURCHDRINGUNG |
| 9171 | **PENETROMETER** | PENETROMETRE | PENETROMETER |
| 9172 | **PENTAGON** | PENTAGONE | FÜNFECK |
| 9173 | **PENTAGONAL PRISM** | PRISME PENTAGONAL | PRISMA (FÜNFSEITIGES) |
| 9174 | **PENTAGONAL PYRAMID** | PYRAMIDE PENTAGONALE | PYRAMIDE (FÜNFSEITIGE) |
| 9175 | **PENTAHEDRON** | PENTAEDRE | FÜNFFLACH, FÜNFFLÄCHNER, PENTAEDER |
| 9176 | **PENTANE (NORMAL)** | PENTANE NORMAL | PENTAN (NORMALES) |
| 9177 | **PENUMBRA** | PENOMBRE | HALBSCHATTEN |
| 9178 | **PEPPER BLISTERS** | POROSITES SUPERFICIELLES | OBERFLÄCHENPOREN |
| 9179 | **PERCENTAGE BY VOLUME** | VOLUME (POUR CENT DU) | RAUMTEIL, RAUMPROZENT, VOLUMPROZENT |
| 9180 | **PERCENTAGE BY WEIGHT** | POIDS (POUR CENT DU) | GEWICHTSTEIL, GEWICHTSPROZENT |
| 9181 | **PERCOLATING WATER** | EAU D'INFILTRATION | SICKERWASSER |
| 9182 | **PERCUSSION PRESS** | PRESSE MECANIQUE A FRAPPER | SCHLAGPRESSE (MECHANISCHE) |
| 9183 | **PERCUSSIVE WELDING** | SOUDURE PAR PERCUSSION | SCHLAGSCHWEISSEN |
| 9184 | **PERFECT COMBUSTION** | COMBUSTION PARFAITE | VOLLKOMMENE VERBRENNUNG |
| 9185 | **PERFECT GAS** | GAZ PARFAIT | GAS (VOLLKOMMENES) |
| 9186 | **PERFORATE (TO)** | PERFORER, PERCER DES TROUS | DURCHLOCHEN, PERFORIEREN |
| 9187 | **PERFORATED LINER** | COLONNE PERDUE A TROUS | LOCHLINER |
| 9188 | **PERFORATED PULLEY** | POULIE A JANTE PERFOREE | RIEMENSCHEIBE (DURCHLOCHTE), RIEMENSCHEIBE MIT DURCHLOCHTEM KRANZ |
| 9189 | **PERFORATED SHEET** | TOLE PERFOREE, TOLE AJOUREE, TOLE DECOUPEE A JOUR | BLECH (GELOCHTES), BLECH (PERFORIERTES) |
| 9190 | **PERIMETER** | PERIMETRE | UMFANG (GEOM.) |
| 9191 | **PERIODIC** | PERIODIQUE | PERIODISCH |
| 9192 | **PERIODIC DECIMAL FRACTION** | FRACTION DECIMALE PERIODIQUE | DEZIMALBRUCH (PERIODISCHER) |

**PER** 234

| | | | |
|---|---|---|---|
| 9193 | **PERIODIC INSPECTION OF BOILERS** | SURVEILLANCE DES CHAUDIERES | DAMPFKESSELÜBERWACHUNG, KESSELKONTROLLE |
| 9194 | **PERIODIC MOTION** | MOUVEMENT PERIODIQUE | BEWEGUNG (PERIODISCHE) |
| 9195 | **PERIODICAL INTERMITTENT LUBRICATION** | GRAISSAGE INTERMITTENT | SCHMIERUNG (UNTERBROCHENE) |
| 9196 | **PERIODICITY** | PERIODICITE | PERIODIZITÄT |
| 9197 | **PERIPHERAL RESISTANCE** | RESISTANCE SUIVANT LA TANGENTE | UMFANGSWIDERSTAND |
| 9198 | **PERIPHERAL SPEED, CIRCUMFERENTIAL VELOCITY** | VITESSE PERIPHERIQUE, VITESSE CIRCONFERENTIELLE | UMFANGSGESCHWINDIGKEIT |
| 9199 | **PERITECTIC REACTION** | REACTION PERITECTIQUE | REAKTION (PERITEKTISCHE) |
| 9200 | **PERLITIC CAST IRON** | FONTE PERLITIQUE | PERLITGUSS |
| 9201 | **PERMALLOY** | PERMALLOY | PERMALLOY |
| 9202 | **PERMANENT DEFORMATION** | DEFORMATION PERMANENTE | VERFORMUNG (BLEIBENDE) |
| 9203 | **PERMANENT HARDNESS OF WATER** | DURETE PERMANENTE DE L'EAU | BLEIBENDE HÄRTE DES WASSERS, PERMANENTE HÄRTE DES WASSERS, MINERALSÄURE HÄRTE DES WASSERS |
| 9204 | **PERMANENT MAGNET** | AIMANT PERMANENT | DAUERMAGNET |
| 9205 | **PERMANENT MAGNETIC CHUCK** | PLATEAU A AIMANTS PERMANENTS | DAUERMAGNET-SPANNPLATTE |
| 9206 | **PERMANENT MAGNETISM** | MAGNETISME PERMANENT | MAGNETISMUS (PERMANENTER) |
| 9207 | **PERMANENT MOLD** | COQUILLE | KOKILLE, DAUERFORM |
| 9208 | **PERMANENT MOLD CASTING** | COULEE EN COQUILLE | KOKILLENGUSS |
| 9209 | **PERMANENT SERVICE** | SERVICE CONTINU | DAUERBETRIEB |
| 9210 | **PERMANENT SET** | DEFORMATION PERMANENTE | FORMÄNDERUNG (BLEIBENDE) |
| 9211 | **PERMEABILITY, PERVIOUSNESS** | PERMEABILITE | PERMEABILITÄT, DURCHLÄSSIGKEIT, DURCHDRINGLICHKEIT |
| 9212 | **PERMEABLE TO AIR** | PERMEABLE A L'AIR | LUFTDURCHLÄSSIG |
| 9213 | **PERMEABLE, PERVIOUS** | PERMEABLE | DURCHLÄSSIG |
| 9214 | **PERMEAMETER** | PERMEAMETRE | PERMEAMETER |
| 9215 | **PERMISSIBLE ALLOWABLE WORKING STRESS** | CHARGE ADMISE | BEANSPRUCHUNG (ZULÄSSIGE), SPANNUNG (ZULÄSSIGE) |
| 9216 | **PERMUTATION** | PERMUTATION | VERTAUSCHUNG, VERSETZUNG, PERMUTATION |
| 9217 | **PERPENDICULAR** | VERTICALE, PERPENDICULAIRE, APLOMB (D') | LOT, SENKRECHTE, LOTRECHTE, VERTIKALE |
| 9218 | **PERPENDICULAR SIDE OF RIGHT-ANGLED TRIANGLE** | COTE DE L'ANGLE DROIT | KATHETE |
| 9219 | **PERPENDICULARITY** | PERPENDICULARITE, APLOMB | RICHTUNG (SENKRECHTE), STELLUNG |
| 9220 | **PERSPECTIVE** | PERSPECTIF, PERSPECTIVE | PERSPEKTIVISCH, PERSPEKTIVE |
| 9221 | **PESTLE** | PILON DE MORTIER | MÖRSERKEULE, STÖSSEL, REIBER |
| 9222 | **PETROL ; GASOLINE (U.S.)** | CARBURANT, ESSENCE, ESSENCE MINERALE, PETROLE, GAZOLINE | KRAFTSTOFF, BENZIN, PETROLEUMBENZIN |
| 9223 | **PETROL ENGINE (GASOLINE ENGINE) (U.S.)** | MOTEUR A ESSENCE DE PETROLE | BENZINMOTOR |
| 9224 | **PETROL LAMP** | LAMPE A ESSENCE MINERALE | BENZINLAMPE |
| 9225 | **PETROL LOCOMOTIVE** | LOCOMOTIVE A ESSENCE, LOCOMOTION A BENZINE | BENZINLOKOMOTIVE |
| 9226 | **PETROLEUM** | PETROLE | PETROLEUM, ERDÖL |
| 9227 | **PETROLEUM LAMP, KEROSENE LAMP** | LAMPE A PETROLE | PETROLEUMLAMPE |
| 9228 | **PETROLEUM SPIRIT** | ETHER DE PETROLE, GAZOLINE | PETROLIEUMÄTHER, GASÄTHER, GASOLIN |
| 9229 | **PETROLEUM, ROCK OIL** | PETROLE, HUILE DE PIERRE | PETROLEUM, ERDÖL, STEINÖL |
| 9230 | **PEWTER** | ETAIN DUR, METAL ANGLAIS | HARTZINN, PEWTER |
| 9231 | **PH, PH-VALUE** | PH. | PH-WERT |
| 9232 | **PHASE** | PHASE | PHASE |

| | | | |
|---|---|---|---|
| 9233 | **PHASE ANGLE** | ANGLE DE DEPHASAGE, ANGLE DE DECALAGE | PHASENVERSCHIEBUNGSWINKEL |
| 9234 | **PHASE DISPLACEMENT** | DEPHASAGE, DECALAGE DES PHASES | PHASENVERSCHIEBUNG |
| 9235 | **PHASE METER, INDICATOR, POWER FACTOR INDICATOR, METER** | INDICATEUR DE PHASES | PHASENMESSER, PHASENINDIKATOR, LEISTUNGSFAKTORMESSER |
| 9236 | **PHASE RULE** | REGLE DES PHASES | PHASENGESETZ |
| 9237 | **PHASE SHIFT** | DECALAGE DE PHASE | PHASENVERSCHIEBUNG |
| 9238 | **PHENOLPHTHALEIN** | PHENOLPHTALEINE, PHTALEINE DU PHENOL | PHENOLPHTALEIN |
| 9239 | **PHENOLPHTHALEIN PAPER** | PAPIER A LA PHENOIPHTALEINE | PHENOLPHTALEINPAPIER |
| 9240 | **PHENOMENON** | PHENOMENE | VORGANG |
| 9241 | **PHOENIX COLUMN SECTION, PILLAR IRON** | FER EN QUART DE ROND | QUADRANTEISEN |
| 9242 | **PHONAUTOGRAPH** | PHONAUTOGRAPHE | VIBROGRAPH, PHONAUTOGRAPH |
| 9243 | **PHONOLITE** | OLIVINE, PERIDOT | PHONOLITH |
| 9244 | **PHOSPHATE** | PHOSPHATE | PHOSPHORSAURES SALZ, PHOSPHAT |
| 9245 | **PHOSPHATE COATINGS** | COUCHE DE PHOSPHATE | PHOSPHATÜBERZUG |
| 9246 | **PHOSPHOR BRONZE** | BRONZE PHOSPHOREUX | PHOSPHORBRONZE, ZINNBRONZE |
| 9247 | **PHOSPHORESCENCE** | PHOSPHORESCENCE | PHOSPHORESZENZ |
| 9248 | **PHOSPHORESCENT** | PHOSPHORESCENT | PHOSPHORESZIEREND |
| 9249 | **PHOSPHORIC OXIDE** | ANHYDRIDE PHOSPHORIQUE | PHOSPHORSÄUREANHYDRID, PHOSPHORPENTOXYD |
| 9250 | **PHOSPHORIZED COPPER** | CUIVRE PHOSPHOREUX | PHOSPHORKUPFER |
| 9251 | **PHOSPHORS** | SUBSTANCES PHOSPHORESCENTES | SUBSTANZEN (SELBSTLEUCHTENDE) |
| 9252 | **PHOSPHORUS** | PHOSPHORE | PHOSPHOR |
| 9253 | **PHOSPHORUS COPPER** | CUIVRE PHOSPHOREUX | PHOSPHORKUPFER |
| 9254 | **PHOSPHORUS PENTACHLORIDE** | PENTACHLORURE DE PHOSPHORE | PHOSPHORPENTACHLORID, PHOSPHORSUPERCHLORID |
| 9255 | **PHOSPHORUS TRIBROMIDE** | TRIBOMURE DE PHOSPHORE | PHOSPHORBROMÜR, PHOSPHORTRIBROMID |
| 9256 | **PHOSPHORUS TRICHLORIDE** | TRICHLORURE DE PHOSPHORE | PHOSPHORTRICHLORID, PHOSPHORCHLORÜR |
| 9257 | **PHOTO PRINTING PAPER** | PAPIER PHOTOCALQUE | LICHTPAUSPAPIER |
| 9258 | **PHOTO-DIODE** | PHOTO-DIODE | FOTODIODE |
| 9259 | **PHOTO-ELECTRIC CELL** | PILE PHOTO-ELECTRIQUE | ZELLE (PHOTOELEKTRISCHE) |
| 9260 | **PHOTOCELL** | CELLULE PHOTO-ELECTRIQUE | PHOTOZELLE (LICHTELEKTRISCHE) |
| 9261 | **PHOTOCONDUCTIVE CELL** | CELLULE PHOTO-CONDUCTRICE | PHOTOWIDERSTAND |
| 9262 | **PHOTOGRAPH (TO)** | PHOTOGRAPHIER | PHOTOGRAPHISCH AUFNEHMEN, PHOTOGRAPHIEREN |
| 9263 | **PHOTOGRAPH, PHOTOGRAPHIC IMAGE PICTURE** | PHOTOGRAPHIE, REPRODUCTION PHOTOGRAPHIQUE | LICHTBILD, PHOTOGRAPHIE |
| 9264 | **PHOTOGRAPHIC CAMERA** | CHAMBRE NOIRE | APPARAT (PHOTOGRAPHISCHER), KAMERA |
| 9265 | **PHOTOGRAPHY** | PHOTOGRAPHIE | PHOTOGRAPHIEREN, PHOTOGRAPHIE |
| 9266 | **PHOTOMACROGRAPH** | MACROPHOTOGRAPHIE | MAKROPHOTOGRAPHIE |
| 9267 | **PHOTOMETER** | PHOTOMETRE | HELLIGKEITSMESSER, LICHTSTÄRKEMESSER, PHOTOMETER |
| 9268 | **PHOTOMETER BENCH** | BANC PHOTOMETRIQUE | PHOTOMETERBANK, BANK (OPTISCHE) |
| 9269 | **PHOTOMETRIC** | PHOTOMETRIQUE | PHOTOMETRISCH |
| 9270 | **PHOTOMETRIC UNIT** | UNITE DE LUMIERE, ETALON PHOTOMETRIQUE | LICHTEINHEIT, EINHEIT PHOTOMETRISCHE |
| 9271 | **PHOTOMETRY** | PHOTOMETRIE | LICHTISTÄRKEMESSUNG, PHOTOMETRIE |

**PHO** 236

| | | | |
|---|---|---|---|
| 9272 | PHOTOMICROGRAPH | MICROPHOTOGRAMME | MIKROPHOTOGRAMM |
| 9273 | PHOTOMISSIVE CELL | CELLULE PHOTO-EMISSIVE | EMISSIONSPHOTOZELLE |
| 9274 | PHOTOMULTIPLIER | PHOTOMULTIPLICATEUR | PHOTOVERVIELFACHER |
| 9275 | PHOTON | PHOTON | PHOTON |
| 9276 | PHOTOTYPE, SUN COPY, SUN PRINT | PHOTOCALQUE, PHOTOCOPIE | LICHTPAUSE |
| 9277 | PHOTOVOLTAIC CELL | CELLULE PHOTOVOLTAIQUE | SPERRSCHICHTPHOTOZELLE |
| 9278 | PHYLLITE | PHYLLITE | URTONSCHIEFER, PHYLLIT |
| 9279 | PHYSICAL | PHYSIQUE | PHYSIKALISCH |
| 9280 | PHYSICAL CHANGE | CHANGEMENT D'ETAT PHYSIQUE, ALTERNATION PHYSIQUE | UMWANDLUNG (PHYSISCHE), VERÄNDERUNG (PHYSIKALISCHE) |
| 9281 | PHYSICAL CHEMISTRY | CHIMIE PHYSIQUE | CHEMIE (PHYSIKALISCHE) |
| 9282 | PHYSICAL METALLURGY | METALLURGIE PHYSIQUE | METALLURGIE (PHYSIKALISCHE) |
| 9283 | PHYSICAL PROPERTIES | PROPRIETES PHYSIQUES | EIGENSCHAFTEN (PHYSIKALISCHE) |
| 9284 | PHYSICAL TESTING | ESSAI PHYSIQUE | PRÜFUNG (PHYSIKALISCHE) |
| 9285 | PHYSICS | PHYSIQUE | PHYSIK |
| 9286 | PHYSIO- CHEMICAL ENGINEERING | CHIMIE INDUSTRIELLE OU TECHNOLOGIQUE | CHEMIE (TECHNISCHE) |
| 9287 | PIANO WIRE, MUSIC WIRE | CORDE A PIANO, FIL D'ACIER POUR CORDES A PIANO | KLAVIERSAITENDRAHT |
| 9288 | PICKLE, PICKLING | DECAPAGE A L'ACIDE, DECAPAGE CHIMIQUE | BEIZEN, DEKAPIEREN |
| 9289 | PICKLING DIP | BAIN DE DECAPAGE, BAIN DE MORDANCAGE | BEIZBAD, BEIZLÖSUNG |
| 9290 | PICKLING SOLUTION | SOLUTION ACIDE, BAIN DE DECAPAGE A L'ACIDE | BEIZLÖSUNG |
| 9291 | PICRIC ACID | ACIDE PICRIQUE, ACIDE CARBAZOTIQUE | PIKRINSÄURE, TRINITROPHENOL |
| 9292 | PIECE OF TUBE, SECTION OF TUBING | TRONCON DE TUYAU | ROHRSTÜCK |
| 9293 | PIECE OF WORK | PIECE D'USINAGE, PIECE A TRAVAILLER | WERKSTÜCK, ARBEITSSTÜCK |
| 9294 | PIECE WORK | TRAVAIL AUX PIECES, TRAVAIL A LA TACHE | STÜCKARBEIT, AKKORDARBEIT |
| 9295 | PIECE WORK WAGES | SALAIRE AUX PIECES, SALAIRE A LA TACHE | STÜCKLOHN, AKKORDLOHN |
| 9296 | PIERCING MACHINE | PERCEUSE | LOCHMASCHINE |
| 9297 | PIEZOELECTRICITY | PIEZO-ELECTRICITE | PIEZOELEKTRIZITÄT |
| 9298 | PIG | GUEUSE | ROHEISENMASSEL |
| 9299 | PIG IRON | FONTE BRUTE, FONTE CRUE | GUSSEISEN, ROHEISEN, ROHGUSS |
| 9300 | PIG SKIN | PEAU DE PORC | SCHWEINSLEDER |
| 9301 | PIG TALL HOOK | CROCHET A QUEUE DE COCHON | SAUSCHWANZHAKEN |
| 9302 | PIG, SOW | GUEUSE | MASSEL |
| 9303 | PIGMENT, COLOUR, DYE | COLORANT, MATIERE COLORANTE, COULEUR | FARBE, FARBSTOFF |
| 9304 | PILE | PILE | STAPEL |
| 9305 | PILE CAP | DALLE SUPPORT / SUR PIEUX | PFAHLKAPPE, SOHLE AUF PFÄHLEN |
| 9306 | PILE DRIVING | BATTAGE DE PIEUX | PFAHLEINTREIBEN, EINRAMMEN |
| 9307 | PILE WOOD (TO) | EMPILER LE BOIS | AUFSTAPELN (HOLZ) |
| 9308 | PILING FURMACE | FOUR A RECHAUFFER EN PAQUETS | PAKETWÄRMOFEN |
| 9309 | PILING WOOD | EMPILAGE DU BOIS | AUFSTAPELN DES HOLZES |
| 9310 | PILL PRESS | PRESSE A PASTILLES, PASTILLEUSE | TABLETTENMASCHINE |
| 9311 | PILLAR | PILIER | PFEILER |
| 9312 | PILLAR DRILLING MACHINE, PILLAR TYPE DRILLING MACHINE | PERCEUSE A COLONNE, FOREUSE A COLONNE | SÄULENBOHRMASCHINE |

**PIP**

237

| 9313 | PILLOW, BODY OF BEARING | CORPS DU PALIER | LAGERKÖRPER |
| 9314 | PIMPLING | GRANULATION SUPERFICIELLE | PICKELBILDUNG |
| 9315 | PIN | PIVOT, GOUPILLE, CHEVILLE, GOUJON AIGUILLE, AXE | ZAPFEN, BOLZEN, STIFT, WELLE |
| 9316 | PIN DRILL, PLUG CENTRE BIT | FORET A TETON CYLINDRIQUE | ZAPFENBOHRER |
| 9317 | PIN HEAD BLISTER | TETE D'EPINGLE | NADELSTAPEL |
| 9318 | PIN JOINT | ARTICULATION A TOURILLON | ZAPFENGELENK, BOLZENGELENK |
| 9319 | PIN OF CENTRE CRANK | BOUTON DE VILEBREQUIN, MANETON | KRUMMZAPFEN |
| 9320 | PIN OF ROLLER CHAIN | GOUJON D'ASSEMBLAGE, SOIE, PIVOT, D'UNE CHAINE A ROULEAUX | BOLZEN, INNENBOLZEN EINER ROLLENKETTE, KETTENBOLZEN |
| 9321 | PIN RIVETING | RIVETAGE A TIGE, RIVETAGE A RIVET SANS TETE | STIFTNIETUNG |
| 9322 | PIN SPANNER, FORK SPANNER | CLEF A GRIFFES EN BOUT | GABELSCHLÜSSEL, STIFTSCHLÜSSEL |
| 9323 | PIN STAVE OF LANTERN WHEEL | FUSEAU D'UN ENGRENAGE A LANTERNE | TRIEBSTOCK |
| 9324 | PIN WHEEL | PIGNON A FUSEAUX | ZAPFENZAHNRAD, TRIEBSTOCKRAD, STIFTRAD |
| 9325 | PIN WHEEL AND PINION GEAR | ENGRENAGE A POINT, ENGRENAGE A FUSEAUX, ENGRENAGE A LANTERNE | TRIEBSTOCKGETRIEBE, STOCKGETRIEBE |
| 9326 | PIN-PUNCH | CHASSE-GOUPILLE | SPLINTTREIBER |
| 9327 | PINACOID | PINACOIDE | PINAKOID |
| 9328 | PINCERS | TENAILLE | NAGELZANGE |
| 9329 | PINCH EFFECT | EFFET DE PINCEMENT | EINSCHNÜRUNGSEFFEKT, PINCHEFFEKT |
| 9330 | PINCH PASS | LAMINAGE A FAIBLE PRESSION | KALTNACHWALZUNG |
| 9331 | PINE TREE CRYSTALS | DENDRITE | DENDRIT |
| 9332 | PINHOLE | TROU D'AXE OU DE GOUPILLE | STIFTLOCH, SPLINTLOCH |
| 9333 | PINHOLE POROSITY | PIQURE | SPLINTLOCH |
| 9334 | PINHOLING | PIQURES | KRATERBILDUNG |
| 9335 | PINION | PIGNON | RITZEL, ZAHNRAD KLEINERE |
| 9336 | PINION DRIVE | LANCEUR | ANLASSER, RITZEL |
| 9337 | PINT | PINT | PINT |
| 9338 | PINTLE TYPE NOZZLE | INJECTEUR A TETON | ZAPFENDÜSE |
| 9339 | PIPE | TUBE, TUYAU, CANALISATION | ROHR, SCHLAUCH, LEITUNG, TREIBSTOFFSYSTEM |
| 9340 | PIPE (IN CASTINGS) | RETASSURE | LUNKER, LUNGER, SAUGTRICHTER |
| 9341 | PIPE BENDING | CINTRAGE D'UN TUBE | BIEGEN EINES ROHRES |
| 9342 | PIPE CAST HORIZONTALLY | TUBE COULE HORIZONTAL | ROHR (LIEGEND GEGOSSENES) |
| 9343 | PIPE CAST UPRIGHT ON END | TUBE COULE DEBOUT | ROHR (STEHEND GEGOSSENES) |
| 9344 | PIPE CLAMP | COLLIER DE FIXATION (POUR TUBE) | ROHRSCHELLE |
| 9345 | PIPE CLIP | COLLIER POUR TUBES, COLLIER POUR SCELLEMENT DANS LES MURS | ROHRSCHELLE |
| 9346 | PIPE COIL | SERPENTIN | ROHRSCHLANGE |
| 9347 | PIPE CONNECTION | JOINT DE TUBES | ROHRVERBINDUNG |
| 9348 | PIPE CUTTER | COUPE-TUBES | ROHRABSCHNEIDER |
| 9349 | PIPE CUTTING MACHINE | MACHINE A COUPER LES TUBES | ROHRABSCHNEIDEMASCHINE |
| 9350 | PIPE FITTINGS | RACCORD POUR TUBES | FORMSTÜCK FÜR ROHRLEITUNGEN, ROHRFORMSTÜCK, FASSONROHR |
| 9351 | PIPE FLANGE | BRIDE RONDELLE DE TUBE, BRIDE DE TUBE | FLANSCH EINES ROHRES, ROHRFLANSCH |
| 9352 | PIPE FLARING MACHINE | MACHINE A ELARGIR LES TUBES | ROHRWEITEMASCHINE |

# PIP

238

| | | | |
|---|---|---|---|
| 9353 | PIPE FRACTURE, FRACTURE OF A PIPE | RUPTURE, BRIS D'UN TUBE | ROHRBRUCH |
| 9354 | PIPE HOOK | CROCHET POUR TUBES | ROHRHAKEN |
| 9355 | PIPE JOINT | JOINT POUR TUYAUTERIE | ROHRDICHTUNG |
| 9356 | PIPE LAYING | POSE DE TUBES | VERLEGEN VON ROHREN |
| 9357 | PIPE LINE, PIPING, TUBING, SERIES OF PIPES | TUYAUTAGE, TUYAUTERIE, TUYAU DE CONDUITE, CONDUITE | ROHRLEITUNG, ROHRSTRECKE, ROHRSTRANG, RÖHRENFAHRT, RÖHRENTOUR |
| 9358 | PIPE MILL | LAMINOIR A TUBES | RÖHRENWALZWERK |
| 9359 | PIPE STANDARDS | STANDARDS POUR TUYAUTERIES | ROHRNORMALIEN |
| 9360 | PIPE THREAD | PAS POUR TUBES | ROHRGEWINDE |
| 9361 | PIPE THREAD CUTTING MACHINE | MACHINE A TARAUDER ET FILETER LES TUBES | ROHRGEWINDE-SCHNEIDEMASCHINE |
| 9362 | PIPE TONGS | PINCES A TUBES | ROHRZANGE |
| 9363 | PIPE VICE | ETAU A TUBES | ROHRSCHRAUBSTOCK |
| 9364 | PIPE WELDED BY THE AUTOGENOUS PROCESS | TUBE SOUDE A L'AUTOGENE | ROHR (AUTOGEN GESCHWEISSTES) |
| 9365 | PIPE WITH BRANCH CONNECTIONS | TUBE A RACCORDS | ABZWEIGROHR |
| 9366 | PIPE WRENCH, TUBE WRENCH | CLEF A TUBES, CLEF CROCODILE, MACHOIRE DE CROCODILE | ROHRSCHLÜSSEL |
| 9367 | PIPECLAY | TERRE DE PIPE | PFEIFENTON, PFEIFENERDE |
| 9368 | PIPETTE | PIPETTE | PIPETTE |
| 9369 | PISTOL GRIP HAND HACKSAW | SCIE A METAUX A POIGNEE PISTOLET | PISTOLENGRIFFMETALLSÄGE |
| 9370 | PISTON | PISTON | KOLBEN (MASCHINENB.) |
| 9371 | PISTON ACCELERATION | ACCELERATION DU PISTON | KOLBENBESCHLEUNIGUNG |
| 9372 | PISTON BLOWER | VENTILATEUR A PISTON | KOLGENGEBLÄSE |
| 9373 | PISTON BODY HEAD | CORPS DU PISTON | KOLBENKÖRPER |
| 9374 | PISTON COMPRESSOR | COMPRESSEUR A PISTON | KOLBENVERDICHTER |
| 9375 | PISTON PACKING | GARNITURE DE PISTON | KOLBENDICHTUNG |
| 9376 | PISTON PIN | AXE DE PISTON | KOLBENBOLZEN |
| 9377 | PISTON PRESSURE | PRESSION SUR LE PISTON | KOLBENDRUCK |
| 9378 | PISTON PUMP | POMPE A PISTON | KOLBENPUMPE |
| 9379 | PISTON RING | BAGUE, SEGMENT DE PISTON | KOLBENRING |
| 9380 | PISTON RING WITH BUTT JOINT | BAGUE DE PISTON AVEC FENTE D'EQUERRE | KOLBENRING MIT SENKRECHTER STOSSFUGE |
| 9381 | PISTON RING WITH INCLINED JOINT | BAGUE DE PISTON A JOINT EN BISEAU | KOLBENRING MIT SCHRÄGER STOSSFUGE |
| 9382 | PISTON RING WITH LAP JOINT | BAGUE DE PISTON AVEC JOINT (FENTE) A RECOUVREMENT | KOLBENRING MIT TREPPENSTOSS, KOLBENRING MIT ÜBERLAPPTER STOSSFUGE |
| 9383 | PISTON ROD | TIGE DU PISTON | KOLBENSTANGE |
| 9384 | PISTON ROD END | EXTREMITE, QUEUE DE LA TIGE DU PISTON | KOLBENSTANGENENDE |
| 9385 | PISTON ROD GUIDE | GUIDE DE LA TIGE DU PISTON | KOLBENSTANGENFÜHRUNG |
| 9386 | PISTON ROD PACKING | GARNITURE, BOURRAGE DE TIGE DE PISTON | KOLBENSTANGENPACKUNG, STANGENDICHTUNG |
| 9387 | PISTON ROD WITH TAIL ROD | TIGE DE PISTON TRAVERSANTE, BILATERALE | KOLBENSTANGE (DURCHLAUFENDE), KOLBENSTANGE (DURCHGEHENDE) |
| 9388 | PISTON SPEED VELOCITY | VITESSE DU PISTON | KOLBENGESCHWINDIGKEIT |
| 9389 | PISTON STROKE, STROKE OF PISTON | COUP DE PISTON | KOLBENHUB, HUB EINES KOLBENS, KOLBENBEWEGUNG |
| 9390 | PISTON VALVE | TIROIR CYLINDRIQUE, TIROIR A PISTON, TIROIR EQUILIBRE, PISTON DISTRIBUTEUR | KOLBENSCHIEBER |

## 239 PLA

| | | | |
|---|---|---|---|
| 9391 | **PISTON WITH TAIL ROD** | PISTON A CONTRE-TIGE, PISTON A DOUBLE TIGE | KOLBEN (SCHWEBENDER, VON DER STANGE GETRAGENER), FREISCHWEBENDER KOLBEN |
| 9392 | **PISTON WITHOUT TAIL ROD** | PISTON A TIGE UNIQUE | KOLBEN (AUFLIEGENDER), KOLBEN (VON DER ZYLINDERWAND GETRAGENER), SELBSTTRAGENDER KOLBEN, SCHLEIFKOLBEN |
| 9393 | **PIT** | PIQURE | GRÜBCHEN |
| 9394 | **PIT CASTING** | COULEE EN FOSSE | GRUBENGUSS |
| 9395 | **PIT PLANING MACHINE** | MACHINE A RABOTER A FOSSE | GRUBENHOBELMASCHINE |
| 9396 | **PIT SAND** | SABLE DE CARRIERE | GRUBENSAND |
| 9397 | **PIT WATER** | EAU DE PUITS DE MINE | GRUBENWASSER, BERGWERKSWASSER |
| 9398 | **PIT, SHAFT OF A MINE** | PUITS (D'UNE MINE) | SCHACHT, GRUBENSCHACHT |
| 9399 | **PITCH** | PAS DE FILETAGE | GEWINDESTEIGUNG, TEILUNG |
| 9400 | **PITCH** | POIX | PECH, SCHIFFSPECH, SCHUSTERPECH |
| 9401 | **PITCH ANGLE** | ANGLE PRIMITIF | TEILKEGELWINKEL |
| 9402 | **PITCH CHAIN WHEEL, SPROCKET WHEEL, LARGE SPROCKET** | ROUE, PIGNON DE CHAINE | KETTENZAHNRAD |
| 9403 | **PITCH CIRCLE** | CERCLE PRIMITIF DE DENTURE | ZAHNTEILKREIS |
| 9404 | **PITCH CIRCLE, PITCH LINE, PRIMITIVE CIRCLE CIRCUMFERENCE, PITCH CIRCOMFERENCE** | CERCLE PRIMITIF, CIRCONFERENCE PRIMITIVE | TEILKREIS |
| 9405 | **PITCH COAL** | LIGNITE NOIR | PECHKOHLE |
| 9406 | **PITCH CONE** | CONE PRIMITIF | GRUNDKEGEL |
| 9407 | **PITCH DIAMETER** | DIAMETRE PRIMITIF, DIAMETRE A FLANC DE FILET | TEILKREISDURCHMESSER, FLANKENDURCHMESSER |
| 9408 | **PITCH OF GEAR, PITCH OF TEETH** | PAS DE L'ENGRENAGE | ZAHNTEILUNG |
| 9409 | **PITCH OF RIVETS** | DISTANCE DE CENTRE A CENTRE DES RIVETS | NIETTEILUNG |
| 9410 | **PITCH OF THREAD** | PAS DE L'HELICE, PAS DE VIS | GANGHÖHE EINER SCHRAUBE |
| 9411 | **PITCHBLENDE** | PECHBLENDE, PECHURANE | PECHBLENDE |
| 9412 | **PITCHED CHAIN** | CHAINE CALIBREE | KETTE (KALIBRIERTE), KETTE (ADJUSTIERTE) |
| 9413 | **PITH** | MOELLE DU BOIS | MARK DES HOLZES |
| 9414 | **PITMAN ARM** | LEVIER DE COMMANDE | LENKSTOCKHEBEL |
| 9415 | **PITOT TUBE** | TUBE DE PITOT | PITOTROHR |
| 9416 | **PITS** | PIQURES | ÄTZGRÜBCHEN |
| 9417 | **PITTING** | PIQURE DE LAMINAGE | WALZNARBE |
| 9418 | **PITTING CORROSION** | CORROSION LOCALISEE | LOCHFRASS |
| 9419 | **PIVOT** | PIVOT | ZAPFEN, ANGEL |
| 9420 | **PIVOT** | TOURILLON, PIVOT | ZAPFEN, WELLENZAPFEN |
| 9421 | **PIVOT, JOURNAL OF FOOTSTEP BEARING** | PIVOT (D'UN ARBRE VERTICAL), PIVOT, TOURILLON D'APPUI, TOURILLON DE BUTEE POUR CRAPAUDINE | SPURZAPFEN, STÜTZZAPFEN |
| 9422 | **PIVOTED** | PIVOTANT | DREHBAR, AUF ZAPFEN GELAGERT |
| 9423 | **PLACE OF ERECTION OF INSTALLATION** | LIEU D'ETABLISSEMENT, LIEU D'INSTALLATION, LIEU DE MONTAGE | AUFSTELLUNGSORT |
| 9424 | **PLAIN CYLINDRICAL JOURNAL BEARING** | PALIER A COUSSINETS LISSES, ROULEMENT LISSE | GLEITLAGER |
| 9425 | **PLAIN MANDREL** | MANDRIN DE MONTAGE LISSE | DORN (FESTER) |
| 9426 | **PLAIN SLIDE VALVE** | TIROIR PLAT, PLAN | FLACHSCHIEBER |
| 9427 | **PLAIN STEEL** | ACIER AU C. | STAHL |

**PLA** 240

| | | | |
|---|---|---|---|
| 9428 | PLAIN TURNING LATHE | TOUR A CYLINDRER, TOUR PARALLELE | PARALLELDREHBANK, EGALISIERBANK |
| 9429 | PLAIN VICE | ETAU SIMPLE | SCHRAUBSTOCK (EINFACHER) |
| 9430 | PLAN OF SITE, GENERAL PLAN | PLAN, DESSIN, VUE D'ENSEMBLE | LAGEPLAN, ÜBERSICHTSPLAN, SITUATIONSPLAN |
| 9431 | PLAN RING GAUGE | CALIBRE FEMELLE LISSE | LEHRRING (NORMALE) |
| 9432 | PLANE | RABOT | HOBEL |
| 9433 | PLANE | PLAN | EBENE (GEOM.) |
| 9434 | PLANE (TO) | RABOTER | HOBELN |
| 9435 | PLANE CURVE | COURBE PLANE | KURVE (EBENE) |
| 9436 | PLANE IRON, CUTTING IRON OF A PLANE | FER DU RABOT | HOBELEISEN, HOBELSTAHL, HOBELMESSER, HOBELSTICHEL |
| 9437 | PLANE MIRROR | MIROIR PLAN | SPIEGEL (EBENER) |
| 9438 | PLANE OF PROJECTION | PLAN DE PROJECTION | PROJEKTIONSEBENE |
| 9439 | PLANE OF REFRACTION | PLAN DE REFRACTION | BRECHUNGSEBENE |
| 9440 | PLANE OF SYMETRY | PLAN DE SYMETRIE | SYMMETRIEEBENE |
| 9441 | PLANE SURFACE, FLAT FACE | SURFACE PLANE | FLÄCHE (EBENE) |
| 9442 | PLANE-FACING AND SURFACING MACHINE | MACHINE A DRESSER ET A SURFACER | ABRICHT- U. FLÄCHENSCHLEIFMASCHINE |
| 9443 | PLANER | RABOTEUSE, RABOTEUR, OUVRIER RABOTEUR | HOBELMASCHINE, HOBLER |
| 9444 | PLANET WHEEL | PIGNON, ROUE SATELLITE, SATELLITE, ROUE PLANETAIRE | PLANETENRAD |
| 9445 | PLANETARY | PLANETAIRE | PLANETARISCH |
| 9446 | PLANETARY GEAR | ENGRENAGE EPICYCLIQUE, TRAIN PLANETAIRE | PLANETENGETRIEBE |
| 9447 | PLANETARY MOTION | MOUVEMENT PLANETAIRE, SATELLITE | PLANETENBEWEGUNG |
| 9448 | PLANIMETER | PLANIMETRE | PLANIMETER |
| 9449 | PLANIMETRY | PLANIMETRIE | PLANIMETRIE |
| 9450 | PLANING | RABOTAGE, RABOTEMENT | HOBELN |
| 9451 | PLANING MACHINE | MACHINE A RABOTER, PLANEUSE | HOBELMASCHINE |
| 9452 | PLANING MACHINE, PLANER | MACHINE A RABOTER, RABOTEUSE | HOBELMASCHINE |
| 9453 | PLANING-MILLING MACHINE | RABOTEUSE-FRAISEUSE | HOBEL-UND FRÄSMASCHINE |
| 9454 | PLANISHING | PLANAGE | PLANIEREN, GLÄTTEN |
| 9455 | PLANISHING HAMMER | MARTEAU A PLANER | SCHLICHTHAMMER, PLANIERHAMMER |
| 9456 | PLANISHING MILL | LAMINOIR A POLIR | GLÄTTWALZWERK |
| 9457 | PLANK, DEAL | PLANCHE FORTE, MADRIER | BOHLE |
| 9458 | PLANO-CONCAVE LENS | LENTILLE PLAN-CONCAVE | LINSE (PLANKONKAVE) |
| 9459 | PLANO-CONVEX LENS | LENTILLE PLAN-CONVEXE | LINSE (PLANKONVEXE) |
| 9460 | PLANO-MILLER, PLANER TYPE MILLING MACHINE, SLAB MILLER, SLABBING MACHINE | FRAISEUSE-RABOTEUSE | LANGFRÄSMASCHINE IN HOBELMASCHINENFORM |
| 9461 | PLANT | INSTALLATION INDUSTRIELLE OU USINE | WERKE, ANLAGEN |
| 9462 | PLANT ECONOMY, ECONOMY OF AN UNDERTAKING, ENTERPRISE | PROSPERITE ECONOMIQUE D'UNE ENTREPRISE, RENTABILITE | WIRTSCHAFTLICHKEIT EINES BETRIEBES |
| 9463 | PLASTER | ENDUIT (MACON.) | PUTZ, VERPUTZ |
| 9464 | PLASTER (TO) | ENDUIRE (MACON.) | VERPUTZEN (BAUW.) |
| 9465 | PLASTER MOLD | MOULE EN PLATRE | GIPSFORM |
| 9466 | PLASTER OF PARIS | PLATRE | GIPS (GEBRANNTER) |
| 9467 | PLASTIC BODY | CORPS PLASTIQUE | KÖRPER (BILDSAMER), KÖRPER (FORMBARER), KÖRPER (PLASTISCHER) |

| | | | |
|---|---|---|---|
| 9468 | **PLASTIC COATED WIRE** | FIL GAINE DE PLASTIQUE | DRAHT (KUNSTSTOFFUMKLEIDETER) |
| 9469 | **PLASTIC DEFORMATION** | DEFORMATION PLASTIQUE | VERFORMUNG (PLASTISCHE) |
| 9470 | **PLASTIC FIRECLAY** | ARGILE PLASTIQUE | FORMENTON |
| 9471 | **PLASTIC FLOW** | FLUAGE PLASTIQUE, DEFORMATION PLASTIQUE | FLIESSEN (PLASTISCHES), KRIECHEN |
| 9472 | **PLASTIC INSULATED CABLE** | CABLE ISOLE AU P.V.C. | KABEL (KUNSTSTOFFISOLIERTES) |
| 9473 | **PLASTIC REFRACTORY** | REFRACTAIRE PLASTIQUE | PLASTMASSE (FEUERFESTE) |
| 9474 | **PLASTICITY** | PLASTICITE | BILDSAMKEIT, PLASTIZITÄT |
| 9475 | **PLASTICIZER** | PLASTIFIANT | WEICHMACHER |
| 9476 | **PLASTICS** | MATIERES PLASTIQUES | KUNSTSTOFFE |
| 9477 | **PLATE** | PLAQUE, TOLE FORTE, TOLE EPAISSE | PLATTE, GROBBLECH |
| 9478 | **PLATE (FLANGING QUALITY), SOFT SHEETS** | TOLE POUR EMBOUTISSAGE | BÖRDELBLECH |
| 9479 | **PLATE (TO)** | PLAQUER | BEPLATTEN, PLATTIEREN |
| 9480 | **PLATE BENDING MACHINE** | MACHINE A CINTRER LES TOLES | BLECHBIEGEMASCHINE |
| 9481 | **PLATE BENDING PRESS** | PRESSE PLIEUSE | BLECHABKANTPRESSE |
| 9482 | **PLATE CAM, DISC CAM** | CAME A DISQUE, CAME A PLATEAU | SCHEIBENEXZENTER |
| 9483 | **PLATE EDGE** | RIVE DE TOLE | BLECHRAND, BLECHKANTE |
| 9484 | **PLATE EDGE PLANING MACHINE** | MACHINE A CHANFREINER LES TOLES | BLECHKANTENHOBELMASCHINE |
| 9485 | **PLATE FLATTENING MACHINE** | MACHINE A PLANER LES TOLES | BLECHRICHTMASCHINE |
| 9486 | **PLATE FRICTION CLUTCH, DISC FRICTION CLUTCH** | EMBRAYAGE A LAMES, A DISQUES | PLANSCHEIBENKUPPLUNG, LAMELLENKUPPLUNG |
| 9487 | **PLATE GAUGE** | CALIBRE D'UNE TOLE | BLECHDICKE |
| 9488 | **PLATE GIRDER** | POUTRE COMPOSEE | VERBUNDTRÄGER |
| 9489 | **PLATE GIRDER STIFFENER** | RAIDISSEUR DE POUTRES EN TOLE, ENTRETOISE | VERSTEIFUNGSBLECH |
| 9490 | **PLATE GIRDER, BUILT-UP GIRDER** | POUTRE COMPOSEE | BLECHTRÄGER |
| 9491 | **PLATE GLASS** | VERRE A GLACES | SPIEGELGLAS |
| 9492 | **PLATE LEAF OF A SPRING** | LAME, FEUILLE D'UN RESSORT | FEDERBLATT |
| 9493 | **PLATE LEFT-OVER** | CHUTE (RESTE) DE TOLE | BLECHABFALL |
| 9494 | **PLATE SHEARING MACHINE** | CISAILLE A TOLES | BLECHSCHERMASCHINE, BLECHSCHERE |
| 9495 | **PLATE SPRING** | RESSORT A LAME | BLATTFEDER |
| 9496 | **PLATE TRIMMING** | EBARBAGE DE TOLE EN BISEAU | BLECHKANTENABSCHRÄGUNG |
| 9497 | **PLATE-CAMS** | CAMES-DISQUES | STEUERSCHEIBEN |
| 9498 | **PLATELET** | PLAQUETTE | PLÄTTCHEN |
| 9499 | **PLATEN AREA** | PLATINE DE FIXATION | AUFSPANNPLATTE |
| 9500 | **PLATES LAY-OUT SEQUENCE** | TOLES (ORDRE DE MISE EN PLACE DES) | BLECHEINLEGEFOLGE |
| 9501 | **PLATES OVERLAPPING** | RECOUVREMENT DE TOLES | PLATTENÜBERLAPPUNG |
| 9502 | **PLATFORM / LANDING** | PALIER | TREPPENABSATZ, BÜHNE |
| 9503 | **PLATING** | PLACAGE, REVETEMENT METALLIQUE PAR GALVANOPLASTIE | GALVANISCHER UEBERZUG, BEPLATTUNG, PLATTIEREN |
| 9504 | **PLATING LAY-OUT DRAWING** | PLAN DE LA TOLERIE | BLECHKONSTRUKTIONSZEICHNUNG |
| 9505 | **PLATING RACK** | CHARIOT DE SUSPENSION POUR PIECES A TREMPER | EINHÄNGEGESTELL |
| 9506 | **PLATING SALTS** | SELS POUR BAINS | BADZUSÄTZE |
| 9507 | **PLATINIC CHLORIDE** | CHLORURE PLATINIQUE | PLATINCHLORID, PLATINTETRACHLORID, CHLORPLATIN |
| 9508 | **PLATINITE** | ACIER PLATINITE, PLATINITE | PLATINID |

**PLA**

242

| | | | |
|---|---|---|---|
| 9509 | PLATINOUS CHLORIDE | CHLORURE PLATINEUX | PLATINCHLORÜR |
| 9510 | PLATINUM | PLATINE (METAL) | PLATIN |
| 9511 | PLATINUM BLACK | NOIR DE PLATINE | PLATINMOHR, PLATINSCHWARZ |
| 9512 | PLATINUM CRUCIBLE | CREUSET EN PLATINE | PLATINTIEGEL |
| 9513 | PLATINUM WIRE | FIL DE PLATINE | PLATINDRAHT |
| 9514 | PLATINUM-BLACK | MOUSSE DE PLATINE | PLATINMOHR |
| 9515 | PLATINUM-IRIDIUM | PLATINE IRIDIE | PLATIN-IRIDIUM |
| 9516 | PLAY, CLEARANCE | JEU (MOUVEMENT), JEU DE MONTAGE, JEU UTILE, CHASSE | SPIEL (RAUM) |
| 9517 | PLENUM SYSTEM VENTILATION | VENTILATION PAR PULSION | DRUCKLÜFTUNG, PULSIONSVENTILATION |
| 9518 | PLIANT, PLIABLE, FLEXIBLE | FLEXIBLE | BIEGSAM, BIEGBAR |
| 9519 | PLOT (TO) | TRACER GRAPHIQUEMENT | AUFZEICHNEN |
| 9520 | PLOT A DIAGRAM (TO) | TRACER, RELEVER UN DIAGRAMME | DIAGRAMM AUFZEICHNEN (EIN) |
| 9521 | PLOTTING A DIAGRAM | TRACE D'UN DIAGRAMME | AUFZEICHNEN EINES DIAGRAMMES |
| 9522 | PLOUGH | GUILLAUME | SIMSHOBEL, GESIMSHOBEL |
| 9523 | PLOUGHS DISC (TRAILED OR MOUTED) | CHARRUES A DISQUES (TRAINEES OU PORTEES) | SCHEIBENPFLÜGE UND ANBAUPFLÜGE |
| 9524 | PLOUGHS MOULDBOARD, TRACTOR MOUNTED | CHARRUES PORTEES | SCHARPFLÜGE UND SCHLEPPERPFLÜGE |
| 9525 | PLOUGHS MOULDBOARD, TRACTOR TRAILED | CHARRUES TRAINEES | PFLÜGE DURCH TRAKTOREN ANGETRIEBENE |
| 9526 | PLOUGHS ONE-WAY, TRAILED OR MOUNTED | CHARRUES, BRABANT (TRAINEES OU PORTEES) | KEHRPFLÜGE UND ANHANGEPFLÜGE |
| 9527 | PLOUGHS RIDGING | CHARRUES BILLONEUSES | HÄUFEPFLÜGE |
| 9528 | PLOW STEEL | ACIER A CHARRUE | PATENT-PFLUGSTAHL |
| 9529 | PLUG | BOUCHON, FICHE DE PRISE DE COURANT, OBTURATEUR, TAMPON | STOPFENSTECKER, STOPFEN, KÜKEN, VERSCHLUSSSTÜCK, ABSPERRSTÜCK, PFLOCK, PFROPFEN |
| 9530 | PLUG COCK | ROBINET A CLEF | KEGELHAHN |
| 9531 | PLUG GAGE | TAMPON | LEHRDORN |
| 9532 | PLUG OF A COCK | CLEF, NOIX DE ROBINET | KÜKEN, WIRBEL, REIBER, SCHLÜSSEL, KONUS EINES HAHNES, HAHNKÜKEN, HAHNKEGEL, HAHNWIRBEL, HAHNSCHLÜSSEL, HAHNREIBER |
| 9533 | PLUG SQUARE | CARRE (POUR CLEF) | VIERKANT |
| 9534 | PLUG TAP, PARALLEL TAP | TARAUD CYLINDRIQUE, TARAUD FINISSEUR | GEWINDENACHSCHNEIDER |
| 9535 | PLUG VALVE | ROBINET A BOISSEAU | HAHNVENTIL |
| 9536 | PLUG WELD | SOUDURE EN BOUCHON | LOCHNAHTSCHWEISSUNG |
| 9537 | PLUG WELDING | SOUDAGE DE TROUS DE RIVETS | NIETLOCHSCHWEISSEN |
| 9538 | PLUMB BOB, BOB | PLOMB (DU FIL A PLOMB) | SENKELGEWICHT, SENKELBIRNE |
| 9539 | PLUMB LINE | FIL A PLOMB, APLOMB, PLOMB | SENKEL, SENKLOT, LOT |
| 9540 | PLUMB RULE | NIVEAU A FIL | BLEILOT, BLEIWAAGE |
| 9541 | PLUMBAGO | PLOMBAGINE, GRAPHITE | GRAPHIT |
| 9542 | PLUMBAGO, BLACK LEAD | PLOMBAGINE, MINE DE PLOMB | GRAPHIT, PLUMBAGO |
| 9543 | PLUMMER BLOCK, PILLOW BLOCK | PALIER A PATIN | STEHLAGER |
| 9544 | PLUNGER | POINCON | STEMPEL |
| 9545 | PLUNGER | PISTON PLONGEUR, PLONGEUR | TAUCHKOLBEN, ROHRKOLBEN, MÖNCHSKOLBEN, PLUNSCHER, PLUNGER |
| 9546 | PLUNGER PUMP | POMPE A PISTON PLONGEUR | TAUCHKOLBENPUMPE, PLUNSCHEPUMPE, PLUNGERPUMPE |
| 9547 | PLUNGER SPRING WITH RETAINER | RESSORT DE PISTON AVEC CUVETTE | KOLBENFEDER MIT TELLER |
| 9548 | PLUS MESH | REFUS DE CRIBLAGE | SIEBRÜCKSTAND |

**243**                                          **POL**

| | | | |
|---|---|---|---|
| 9549 | **PNEUMATIC** | PNEUMATIQUE | PNEUMATISCH |
| 9550 | **PNEUMATIC CHUCKS** | MANDRINS PNEUMATIQUES | FUTTER (PNEUMATISCHE) |
| 9551 | **PNEUMATIC DROP HAMMER** | MARTEAU PNEUMATIQUE | DRUCKLUFTHAMMER |
| 9552 | **PNEUMATIC FORGING HAMMER** | MARTEAU-PILON | SCHMIEDEHAMMER |
| 9553 | **PNEUMATIC HAMMER** | MARTEAU PNEUMATIQUE, MARTEAU A AIR COMPRIME | PRESSLUFTHAMMER, DRUCKLUFTHAMMER, LUFTHAMMER |
| 9554 | **PNEUMATIC KNOCKOUT** | EJECTEUR PNEUMATIQUE, DECOCHAGE, DEMOULAGE | AUSWERFER, AUSSCHLAGEN |
| 9555 | **PNEUMATIC RIVETING HAMMER** | MARTEAU A RIVER PNEUMATIQUE, MARTEAU MECANIQUE A AIR COMPRIME | SCHLAGNIETHAMMER, PRESSLUFTNIETHAMMER, DRUCKLUFTNIETHAMMER |
| 9556 | **PNEUMATIC TOOL** | OUTIL PNEUMATIQUE | PRESSLUFTWERKZEUG |
| 9557 | **PNEUMATICALLY OPERATED VALVE** | SOUPAPE A COMMANDE PNEUMATIQUE | PRESSLUFTVENTIL, VENTIL (PNEUMATISCH GESTEUERTES) |
| 9558 | **PNEUMATICS** | PNEUMATIQUE | MECHANIK DER LUFT, AEROMECHANIK |
| 9559 | **POINT** | POINT | PUNKT |
| 9560 | **POINT IN SPACE** | POINT DANS L'ESPACE | RAUMPUNKT |
| 9561 | **POINT OF APPLICATION** | POINT D'APPLICATION | ANGRIFFSPUNKT |
| 9562 | **POINT OF CONTACT** | POINT DE CONTACT, POINT DE TANGENCE | BERÜHRUNGSSTELLE, BERÜHRUNGSPUNKT |
| 9563 | **POINT OF FRACTURE** | POINT DE RUPTURE | BRUCHSTELLE |
| 9564 | **POINT OF INFLECTION** | POINT D'INFLEXION | WENDEPUNKT, INFLEXIONSPUNKT (GEOM.) |
| 9565 | **POINT OF INTERSECTION** | POINT D'INTERSECTION, POINT DE RENCONTRE, POINT DE CONCOURS | SCHNITTPUNKT, TREFFPUNKT |
| 9566 | **POINT OF REFERENCE** | POINT DE REPERE | BEZUGSPUNKT |
| 9567 | **POINT OF SUPPORT** | POINT D'APPUI | STÜTZPUNKT, UNTERSTÜTZUNGSPUNKT |
| 9568 | **POINT OF SUSPENSION** | POINT DE SUSPENSION | AUFHÄNGEPUNKT |
| 9569 | **POINT OF TOOTH** | TETE DE LA DENT | ZAHNKOPF, ZAHNKRONE |
| 9570 | **POINT SUSPENSION** | SUSPENSION A PIVOT | SPITZENAUFHÄNGUNG |
| 9571 | **POINT TOOL** | GRAIN D'ORGE | SPITZSTAHL |
| 9572 | **POINT-TO-POINT CONTROL** | COMMANDE POINT-A-POINT | PUNKTSTEUERUNG |
| 9573 | **POINTED SOLDERING IRON** | FER A SOUDER DROIT | SPITZLÖTKOLBEN |
| 9574 | **POINTS** | CONTACTS | KONTAKTSTÜCKE |
| 9575 | **POKE A FIRE (TO)** | RINGARDER | SCHÜREN |
| 9576 | **POKE WELDING** | SOUDAGE PAR POINTS AU PISTOLET, SOUDAGE A LA CAROTTE | PUNKTSCHWEISSEN MIT HANDBETÄTIGTER SCHWEISSENELEKTRODE |
| 9577 | **POLAR** | POLAIRE | POLARE |
| 9578 | **POLAR COORDINATES** | COORDONNEES POLAIRES | POLARKOORDINATEN |
| 9579 | **POLAR DISTANCE** | DISTANCE POLAIRE | POLABSTAND |
| 9580 | **POLAR RAY** | RAYON POLAIRE | SEILSTRAHL, POLSTRAHL |
| 9581 | **POLAR TRIANGLE** | TRIANGLE POLAIRE | POLARDREIECK |
| 9582 | **POLARISATION** | POLARISATION | POLARISATION |
| 9583 | **POLARISATION MICROSCOPE** | MICROSCOPE POLARISANT | POLARISATIONSMIKROSKOP |
| 9584 | **POLARISCOPE** | POLARISCOPE | POLARISATIONSAPPARAT, POLARISKOP |
| 9585 | **POLARISED LIGHT** | LUMIERE POLARISEE | LICHT (POLARISIERTES) |
| 9586 | **POLARISER** | PRISME POLARISATEUR, POLARISEUR | POLARISATOR, POLARISATIONSPRISMA |
| 9587 | **POLARITY** | POLARITE | POLARITÄT |
| 9588 | **POLARITY INDICATOR** | INDICATEUR DU SENS DE COURANT | STROMRICHTUNGSANZEIGER |

## POL

244

| | | | |
|---|---|---|---|
| 9589 | POLARIZATION | POLARISATION | POLARISATION |
| 9590 | POLAROGRAPHY | POLAROGRAPHIE | POLAROGRAPHIE |
| 9591 | POLE | POLE (ELECTR.) | POL (ELEKTRISCHER) |
| 9592 | POLE | POLE | POL (GEOM.) |
| 9593 | POLE FACES | MASSES POLAIRES | POLSCHUHEN |
| 9594 | POLE FINDING PAPER | PAPIER CHERCHEUR DE POLES, PAPIER POLE | POLSUCHPAPIER |
| 9595 | POLE OF A MAGNET | POLE D'UN AIMANT | MAGNETPOL, POL EINES MAGNETEN |
| 9596 | POLE STRENGTH, STRENGTH OF POLE | INTENSITE DE POLE, FORCE POLAIRE | POLSTÄRKE |
| 9597 | POLING | TRAVAIL A LA PERCHE | POLEN |
| 9598 | POLISH (TO), BUFF (TO) | POLIR | GLANZ SCHLEIFEN, BLANK SCHLEIFEN, POLIEREN |
| 9599 | POLISHABLE | POLI (QUI PREND BIEN LE), POLI (SUSCEPTIBLE D'UN BEAU), POLI (SUSCEPTIBLE DE PRENDRE UN) | POLIERBAR |
| 9600 | POLISHING | POLISSAGE | POLIEREN |
| 9601 | POLISHING AGENT | MATIERE A POLIR, MATIERE ABRASIVE, ABRASIF | SCHLEIFMITTEL, POLIERMITTEL |
| 9602 | POLISHING CYLINDER DRUM | TONNEAU A POLIR | SCHEUERTROMMEL, POLIERTROMMEL, POLIERFASS, POLIERTONNE |
| 9603 | POLISHING MACHINE | MACHINE A POLIR | POLIERMASCHINE |
| 9604 | POLISHING WHEEL | ROUE POLISSEUSE, MEULE, MEUBLE A POLIR | POLIERSCHEIBE |
| 9605 | POLISHING, BUFFING | POLISSAGE | SCHLEIFEN, GLANZSCHLEIFEN, BLANKSCHLEIFEN, POLIEREN |
| 9606 | POLONIUM | POLONIUM | POLONIUM |
| 9607 | POLYCHROMATIC | POLYCHROME | VIELFARBIG |
| 9608 | POLYCRYSTALLINE METAL | METAL POLYCRISTALLIN | POLYKRISTALLINES METALL |
| 9609 | POLYGON | POLYGONE | VIELECK, POLYGON |
| 9610 | POLYGON OF FORCES | POLYGONE DES FORCES | KRAFTECK, KRÄFTEPOLYGON |
| 9611 | POLYGONAL TRACE | LIGNE POLYGONALE | POLYGONZUG |
| 9612 | POLYHEDRON | POLYEDRE | VIELFLACH, POLYEDER |
| 9613 | POLYMER, POLYMERIC | POLYMERE | POLYMEREKÖRPER, POLYMER |
| 9614 | POLYMERISATION | POLYMERISATION | POLYMERISATION |
| 9615 | POLYMERISE (TO) | POLYMERISER (SE) | POLYMERISIEREN (SICH) |
| 9616 | POLYMERISM | POLYMERIE | POLYMERIE |
| 9617 | POLYMORPHISM | POLYMORPHISME | METALL (POLYKRISTALLINES) |
| 9618 | POLYTROPIC CURVE | COURBE POLYTROPIQUE | KURVE (POLYTROPISCHE), POLYTROPE |
| 9619 | PONDERABLE | PONDERABLE | WÄGBAR |
| 9620 | PONTON MANHOLE | TROU D'HOMME, TROU DE VISITE D'UN CAISSON | PONTONSMANNLOCH |
| 9621 | PONTOON DECK ROOF | CAISSON (TOIT A...) | SCHWIMMBRÜCKENDACH |
| 9622 | PONY ROUGHING MILL | CAGE DEGROSSISSEUSE | VORSTRECKGERÜST |
| 9623 | POOR LIME | CHAUX MAIGRE | KALK (MAGERER), MAGERKALK |
| 9624 | POPPY SEED OIL | HUILE D'OEILLETTE | MOHNÖL |
| 9625 | PORCELAIN | PORCELAINE | PORZELLAN |
| 9626 | PORCELAIN CRUCIBLE | CREUSET EN PORCELAINE | PORZELLANTIEGEL |
| 9627 | PORE | PORE | PORE |
| 9628 | PORE FORMING MATERIAL | PRODUIT FORMANT DES POROSITES, POROGENE | MATERIAL (PORENERZEUGENDES) |
| 9629 | POROSITY | POROSITE, PIQUAGE | POROSITÄT, GASPORE, PORIGKEIT |
| 9630 | POROUS | POREUX | PORIG, PORÖS |

|      |                                          |                                                              |                                              |
|------|------------------------------------------|--------------------------------------------------------------|----------------------------------------------|
| 9631 | **PORPHYRITIC TUFF**                     | TUF PORPHYRITIQUE                                            | PORPHYRTUFF                                   |
| 9632 | **PORPHYRY**                             | PORPHYRE                                                      | PORPHYR                                       |
| 9633 | **PORT**                                 | ORIFICE                                                       | ÖFFNUNG                                       |
| 9634 | **PORT SIZE, ORIFICE SIZE**              | ORIFICE DE PASSAGE                                           | DURCHGANGSWEITE                               |
| 9635 | **PORTABLE**                             | MOBILE, ROULANT                                             | FAHRBAR                                       |
| 9636 | **PORTABLE DRILLING MACHINE**            | MACHINE A PERCER, PERCEUSE PORTATIVE                         | BOHRMASCHINE (FAHRBARE) (TRAGBARE)            |
| 9637 | **PORTABLE FORGE**                       | FORGE PORTATIVE, FORGE VOLANTE                               | FELDSCHMIEDE                                  |
| 9638 | **PORTABLE PUMP**                        | POMPE PORTATIVE                                             | PUMPE (TRAGBARE)                              |
| 9639 | **PORTABLE RAILWAY**                     | CHEMIN DE FER A VOIE ETROITE, VOIE PORTATIVE, VOIE DECAUVILLE, DECAUVILLE | FELDBAHN                      |
| 9640 | **PORTABLE STEAM ENGINE, LOCOMOBILE**    | LOCOMOBILE                                                   | LOKOMOBILE                                    |
| 9641 | **PORTAL CRANE**                         | GRUE A PORTIQUE, PORTIQUE                                   | PORTALKRAN                                    |
| 9642 | **PORTAL MILLING MACHINE**               | FRAISEUSE A PORTIQUE                                        | PORTALFRÄSWERKE                               |
| 9643 | **PORTION OF SHAFT**                     | TRONCON D'ARBRE                                             | WELLENSTÜCK                                   |
| 9644 | **PORTLAND CEMENT**                      | CIMENT DE PORTLAND                                          | PORTLANDZEMENT                                |
| 9645 | **POSITION OF CRANK**                    | POSITION DE LA MANIVELLE                                    | KURBELSTELLUNG                                |
| 9646 | **POSITION OF DEAD CENTRE**              | POSITION AU POINT MORT                                      | TOTPUNKTLAGE, TOTPUNKTSTELLUNG               |
| 9647 | **POSITION OF EQUILIBRIUM**              | POSITION D'EQUILIBRE                                        | GLEICHGEWICHTSLAGE                            |
| 9648 | **POSITION OF REST**                     | POSITION DE REPOS                                           | RUHELAGE                                      |
| 9649 | **POSITION SENSOR**                      | CAPTEUR DE POSITION                                         | WEGMESSGERÄT                                  |
| 9650 | **POSITIONING CONTROL**                  | COMMANDE DE POSITIONNEMENT                                  | POSITIONSSTEUERUNG                            |
| 9651 | **POSITIONING TIME**                     | TEMPS DE POSITIONNEMENT                                     | POSITIONIERZEIT                               |
| 9652 | **POSITIVE ACCELERATION**                | ACCELERATION POSITIVE                                       | BESCHLEUNIGUNG (POSITIVE)                     |
| 9653 | **POSITIVE DISPLACEMENT PUMP**           | POMPE VOLUMETRIQUE                                          | VERDRÄNGERPUMPE                               |
| 9654 | **POSITIVE DRIVE**                       | COMMANDE POSITIVE, COMMANDE MECANIQUE                       | ANTRIEB (ZWANGSLAÜFIGER)                      |
| 9655 | **POSITIVE ELECTRICITY**                 | ELECTRICITE POSITIVE                                        | ELEKTRIZITÄT (POSITIVE)                       |
| 9656 | **POSITIVE HEAT OF FORMATION**           | CHALEUR DE FORMATION, CHALEUR DE COMBINAISON                | BILDUNGSWÄRME                                 |
| 9657 | **POSITIVE ION**                         | CATION                                                      | KATION                                        |
| 9658 | **POSITIVE PLATE**                       | PLAQUE POSITIVE                                             | PLATTE (POSITIVE), PLUSPLATTE                 |
| 9659 | **POSITIVE POLE**                        | POLE POSITIF                                                | POL (POSITIVER)                               |
| 9660 | **POSITIVE RAYS**                        | LUMIERE ANODIQUE                                           | ANODENSTRAHLUNG                               |
| 9661 | **POSITIVE SIGN**                        | SIGNE POSITIF                                               | VORZEICHEN (POSITIVES), PLUSZEICHEN          |
| 9662 | **POSITRON**                             | ELECTRON POSITIF                                           | POSITRON                                      |
| 9663 | **POST HANGER, STANCHION BRACKET PEDESTAL** | PALIER-CONSOLE SUR COLONNE                              | SÄULENLAGER                                   |
| 9664 | **POST HOLE BORERS**                     | VRILLES                                                     | BOHRMASCHINEN FÜR MASTEN                      |
| 9665 | **POST PROCESSOR**                       | POST-PROCESSEUR                                             | POST-PROZESSOR                                |
| 9666 | **POST WELD HEAT TREATMENT**             | TRAITEMENT DE DETENTE APRES SOUDAGE                         | WÄRMENACHBEHANDLUNG                           |
| 9667 | **POST-WELDING HEAT TREATMENT**          | RECUIT DE DETENTE                                           | WÄRMEBEHANDLUNG NACH DEM SCHWEISSEN          |
| 9668 | **POSTHEATING**                          | POSTCHAUFFAGE                                               | NACHWÄRMEN                                    |
| 9669 | **POT FURNAGE**                          | FOUR A CREUSET                                              | TIEGELSCHMELZOFEN                             |
| 9670 | **POTASH HARDENING**                     | CEMENTATION AU PRUSSIATE DE POTASSE, CEMENTATION AU PRUSSIATE JAUNE | EINBRENNHÄRTUNG                      |

# POT

246

| | | | |
|---|---|---|---|
| 9671 | POTASH LYE, CAUSTIC POTASH SOLUTION | SOLUTION DE POTASSE CAUSTIQUE, LESSIVE DE POTASEE | KALILAUGE, ÄTZKALILAUGE, ÄTZALKALISCHE LÖSUNG |
| 9672 | POTASSIUM | POTASSIUM | KALIUM |
| 9673 | POTASSIUM ACETATE | ACETATE DE POTASSE | ESSIGSAURES KALI, KALIUMAZETAT |
| 9674 | POTASSIUM ALUMINATE | ALUMINATE DE POTASSIUM | KALIUMALUMINAT |
| 9675 | POTASSIUM ANTIMONYL TARTRATE, TARTAR EMETIC | TARTRATE DE POTASSE ET D'ANTIMOINE, EMETIQUE, TARTRE STIBIE | BRECHWEINSTEIN, WEINSAURES ANTIMONOXYDKALI |
| 9676 | POTASSIUM BICARBONATE, BICARBONATE OF POTASH, POTASSIUM HYDROGEN CARBONATE | BICARBONATE DE POTASSE | SAURES KOHLENSAURES KALI, DOPPELT KOHLENSAURES KALI, KALIUMBIKARBONAT, KALIUMHYDROKARBONAT |
| 9677 | POTASSIUM BICHROMATE | BICHROMATE DE POTASSIUM | KALIUMBICHROMAT, KALIUMDICHROMAT, ROTES CHROMKALI, ROTES CHROMSAURES KALI, DOPPELTCHROMSAURES KALI, ROTES CHROMSALZ |
| 9678 | POTASSIUM BROMIDE | BROMURE DE POTASSIUM | BROMKALIUM, KALIUMBROMID |
| 9679 | POTASSIUM CARBONATE, POTASH | CARBONATE NEUTRE DE POTASSE, POTASSE | POTTASCHE, KOHLENSAURES KALI, KALIUMKARBONAT |
| 9680 | POTASSIUM CHLORATE | CHLORATE DE POTASSIUM | CHLORSAURES KALI, KALIUMCHLORAT |
| 9681 | POTASSIUM CHLORIDE | CHLORURE DE POTASSIUM | CHLORKALIUM, KALIUMCHLORID |
| 9682 | POTASSIUM CHROMATE | CHROMATE NEUTRE DE POTASSIUM | NEUTRALES KALIUMCHROMAT, GELBES CHROMKALI, GELBES CHROMSAURES . KALI |
| 9683 | POTASSIUM CYANIDE | CYANURE DE POTASSIUM | ZYANKALI, BLAUSAURES KALI, KALIUMZYANID |
| 9684 | POTASSIUM FERRICYANIDE, RED PRUSSIATE OF POTASH | FERRICYANURE DE POTASSIUM, PRUSSIATE ROUGE | ROTES BLUTLAUGENSALZ, FERRIZYANKALIUM, KALIUMEISENZYANID, ROTES ZYANEISENKALIUM |
| 9685 | POTASSIUM FERROCYANIDE, YELLOW PRUSSIATE OF POTASH | FERROCYANURE DE POTASSIUM, CYANOFERRURE DE POTASSIUM, PRUSSIATE JAUNE | GELBES BLUTLAUGENSALZ, FERROZYANKALIUM, GELBES ZYANEISENKALIUM, KALIUMEISENZYANÜR |
| 9686 | POTASSIUM FLUORIDE | FLUORURE DE POTASSIUM | KALIUMFLUORID, FLUORKALIUM |
| 9687 | POTASSIUM HYDROXIDE, POTASSIUM HYDRATE, CAUSTIC POTASH | POTASSE CAUSTIQUE, HYDRATE DE POTASSIUM | ÄTZKALI, KALIUMHYDROXYD, KALIUMOXYDHYDRAT, KALIHYDRAT |
| 9688 | POTASSIUM HYPOCHLORITE SOLUTION | CHLORURE DE POTASSE (SOLUTION DE) | JAVELLESCHE LAUGE, EAU DE JAVEL, KALIUMHYPOCHLORITLÖSUNG |
| 9689 | POTASSIUM IODIDE | IODURE DE POTASSIUM | JODKALIUM, KALIUMJODID |
| 9690 | POTASSIUM IODIDE STARCH PAPER | PAPIER IODOAMIDONNE | JODKALIUMSTÄRKEPAPIER |
| 9691 | POTASSIUM NITRITE | AZOTITE, NITRITE DE POTASSE, POTASSE AZOTEUSE, NITREUSE | SALPETRIGSAURES KALI, KALIUMNITRIT |
| 9692 | POTASSIUM OXALATE | OXALATE NEUTRE DE POTASSIUM | OXALSAURES KALI, NEUTRALES KALIUMOXALAT |
| 9693 | POTASSIUM PERCARBONATE | PERCARBONATE DE POTASSE | KALIUMPERKARBONAT, ÜBERKOHLENSAURES KALIUM |
| 9694 | POTASSIUM PERCHLORATE | PERCHLORATE DE POTASSE | ÜBERCHLORSAURES KALI, KALIUMPERCHLORAT |
| 9695 | POTASSIUM PERMANGANATE, PERMANGANATE OF POTASH | PERMANGANATE DE POTASSE | ÜBERMANGANSAURES, HYPERMANGANSAURES KALI, KALIUMPERMANGANAT |
| 9696 | POTASSIUM PHOSPHATE | PHOSPHATE DE POTASSIUM | PHOSPHORSAURES KALI, KALIUMPHOSPHAT |
| 9697 | POTASSIUM POLYSULPHIDE | POLYSULFURE DE POTASSIUM | KALIUMPOLYSULFID, POLYSULFID DES KALIUMS |
| 9698 | POTASSIUM SILICATE | SILICATE DE POTASSE | KALIWASSERGLAS, KIESELSAURES KALIUM, KALIUMSILIKAT |

| | | | |
|---|---|---|---|
| 9699 | **POTASSIUM SULPHATE** | SULFATE DE POTASSE | SCHWEFELSAURES KALI, KALIUMSULFAT |
| 9700 | **POTASSIUM SULPHIDE** | SULFURE DE POTASSE | SCHWEFELKALIUM |
| 9701 | **POTASSIUM SULPHOCYANATE** | SULFOCYANURE DE POTASSIUM | RHODANKALIUM, KALIUMRHODANID, SCHWEFELZYANKALIUM, KALIUMSULFOZYANAT |
| 9702 | **POTATO COVERER** | BUTTEUSES POUR POMMES DE TERRE | MASCHINEN ZUM BEDECKEN DER KARTOFFELPFLANZEN |
| 9703 | **POTATO ELEVATOR DIGGERS AND SHAKERS** | ARRACHEUSES DE TUBERCULES | KARTOFFELRODER |
| 9704 | **POTATO HARVESTERS** | RECOLTEUSES DE POMMES DE TERRE | KARTOFFELERNTEMASCHINEN |
| 9705 | **POTATO PLANTERS** | PLANTEUSES DE POMMES DE TERRE | KARTOFFELLEGEMASCHINEN |
| 9706 | **POTATO SORTERS** | TRIEURS DE POMMES DE TERRE | KARTOFFELSORTIERMASCHINEN |
| 9707 | **POTATO SPINNERS AND DIGGERS** | ARRACHEUSES DE POMMES DE TERRE | KARTOFFELPFLÜGE |
| 9708 | **POTENTIAL** | POTENTIEL | POTENTIAL, SPANNUNG |
| 9709 | **POTENTIAL DIFFERENCE, DIFFERENCE OF POTENTIAL** | DIFFERENCE DE POTENTIEL, TENSION AUX ELECTRODES | SPANNUNGSUNTERSCHIED, POTENTIALDIFFERENZ, ELEKTRODENSPANNUNG |
| 9710 | **POTENTIAL ENERGY** | ENERGIE POTENTIELLE, ENERGIE LATENTE | ENERGIE (POTENTIELLE), ENERGIE (STATISCHE) |
| 9711 | **POTENTIOMETER** | POTENTIOMETRE | POTENTIOMETER |
| 9712 | **POUND (TO)** | PILER, ECRASER | ZERSTOSSEN |
| 9713 | **POURED ASPHALT** | ASPHALTE COULE | GUSSASPHALT |
| 9714 | **POURED CONCRETE** | BETON COULE DANS DES TROUS | SCHÜTTBETON |
| 9715 | **POURING** | COULEE | GUSS, GIESSEN |
| 9716 | **POURING CUP** | ENTONNOIR DE COULEE | GIESSTRICHTER |
| 9717 | **POURING/TEEMING** | SORTIE EN LINGOTIERE | KOKILLENAUSTRITT, ABGUSS |
| 9718 | **POWDER COMPACTING PRESS** | PRESSE A COMPRIMER LES POUDRES | METALLPULVERPRESSE |
| 9719 | **POWDER CUTTING** | DECOUPAGE A LA POUDRE | PULVERBRENNSCHNEIDEN |
| 9720 | **POWDER METALLURGY** | METALLURGIE DES POUDRES | PULVERMETALLURGIE |
| 9721 | **POWDER METHOD** | METHODE DES POUDRES | PULVERMETHODE |
| 9722 | **POWDER WELDING** | SOUDAGE SOUS POUDRE | PULVERSPRITZSCHWEISSEN |
| 9723 | **POWDERED ASPHALT** | ASPHALTE EN POUDRE | ASPHALTSTEINPULVER |
| 9724 | **POWDERED BRICK** | BRIQUE PILEE | ZIEGELMEHL, SCHAMOTTEMEHL |
| 9725 | **POWDERED MAGNESIA** | MAGNESIE EN POUDRE | MAGNESIA (GEMAHLENE) |
| 9726 | **POWDERED PEAT** | POUSSIER DE TOURBE, TOURBE MENUE | TORFMULL, TORFMEHL |
| 9727 | **POWDERED PUMICE** | POUDRE DE PONCE | BIMSSAND |
| 9728 | **POWDERY, PULVEROUS, PULVERULENT** | PULVERULENT | PULVERFÖRMIG, PULVERIG, IN PULVERFORM |
| 9729 | **POWER** | PUISSANCE (MATH.) | POTENZ (MATH.) |
| 9730 | **POWER** | PUISSANCE, EFFET, DEBIT | ARBEITSLEISTUNG, EFFEKT, KRAFT, LEISTUNG |
| 9731 | **POWER BRAKES** | FREINS ASSISTES, SERVO-FREINS | SERVOBREMSEN |
| 9732 | **POWER DRILL** | CHIGNOLE, PERCEUSE ELECTRIQUE | HANDBOHRMASCHINE (ELEKTRISCHE) |
| 9733 | **POWER DRIVE** | FORCE MOTRICE | KRAFTANTRIEB |
| 9734 | **POWER DRIVING** | COMMANDE MECANIQUE, COMMANDE PAR MOTEUR | MASCHINENANTRIEB, MASCHINENBETRIEB, MECHANISCHER ANTRIEB MASCHINELLER |
| 9735 | **POWER FACTOR** | FACTEUR DE PUISSANCE | LEISTUNGSFAKTOR |
| 9736 | **POWER GAS** | GAZ POUR ACTIONNER LES MOTEURS | KRAFTGAS |

# POW

248

| | | | |
|---|---|---|---|
| 9737 | POWER GENERATION | PRODUCTION D'ENERGIE | KRAFTERZEUGUNG |
| 9738 | POWER OF MEN, MAN POWER | FORCE DE L'HOMME | MENSCHENKRAFT |
| 9739 | POWER PLANT | INSTALLATION POUR LA PRODUCTION DE FORCE MOTRICE | KRAFTANLAGE |
| 9740 | POWER RIVETING | RIVETAGE POUR CONSTRUCTIONS METALLIQUES, RIVURE DE FORCE, RIVURE D'ASSEMBLAGE DE FORCE | KRAFTNIETUNG |
| 9741 | POWER SEAT | SIEGE A REGLAGE AUTOMATIQUE | SITZ (SELBSTEINSTELLENDER) |
| 9742 | POWER STATION | USINE DE FORCE MOTRICE, STATION GENERATRICE, STATION CENTRALE | KRAFTWERK, KRAFTSTATION, KRAFTZENTRALE |
| 9743 | POWER STEERING | DIRECTION ASSISTEE, SERVO-DIRECTION | SERVOLENKUNG |
| 9744 | POWER SUPPLY, SUPPLY OF POWER | DISTRIBUTION DE FORCE MOTRICE | KRAFTVERSORGUNG |
| 9745 | POWER TAKE-OFF | PRISE DE FORCE | ZAPFWELLE |
| 9746 | POWER TRANSMISSION | TRANSMISSION DE PUISSANCE | KRAFTÜBERTRAGUNG |
| 9747 | POWER, MACHINE SAW, SAWING MACHINE, SAW DRIVEN BY MACHINERY | MACHINE A SCIER, SCIERIE MECANIQUE, SCIE MECANIQUE | GESTELLSÄGE, MASCHINENSÄGE |
| 9748 | POZZOLANA, PUZZUOLANA | POUZZOLANE, POZZOLANE | PUZZOLANERDE |
| 9749 | POZZUOLANIC CEMENT | CIMENT POUZZOLANIQUE | PUZZOLANZEMENT |
| 9750 | PRASEODYMIUM | PRASEODYME | PRASEODYM |
| 9751 | PRE-FILTER | PREFILTRE | VORFILTER |
| 9752 | PRE-SET TOOLING | USINAGE PREREGLE | BEARBEITUNG (VOREINGESTELLTE) |
| 9753 | PRECAUTIONS | PRECAUTIONS | VORSICHTSMASSREGEIN |
| 9754 | PRECESSION | PRECESSION | PRÄZESSION |
| 9755 | PRECICION GRINDING | AFFUTAGE DE PRECISION | MASSSCHLEIFEN |
| 9756 | PRECIOUS METAL | METAL PRECIEUX | EDELMETALL |
| 9757 | PRECIPITABLE | PRECIPITABLE | AUSFÄLLBAR |
| 9758 | PRECIPITANT | PRECIPITANT | FÄLLMITTEL |
| 9759 | PRECIPITATE | PRECIPITE | NIEDERSCHLAG, BODENSATZ, PRÄZIPITAT |
| 9760 | PRECIPITATE (TO) | PRECIPITER, SEPARER (SE), PRECIPITER (SE) | AUSFÄLLEN, SICH ABSCHEIDEN, SICH AUSSCHEIDEN |
| 9761 | PRECIPITATION | PRECIPITATION | FÄLLEN, AUSFÄLLEN, NIEDERSCHLAG, AUSSCHEIDUNG |
| 9762 | PRECIPITATION HARDENING | DURCISSEMENT PAR PRECIPITATION | AUSSCHEIDUNGSHÄRTUNG |
| 9763 | PRECISION | PRECISION | GENAUIGKEIT |
| 9764 | PRECISION BALANCE | BALANCE DE PRECISION | FEINWAAGE, PRÄZISIONSWAAGE |
| 9765 | PRECISION CASTING | MOULAGE DE PRECISION | PRÄZISIONSGUSS, WACHSAUSSCHMELZGUSS |
| 9766 | PRECISION GAUGE | JAUGE DE PRECISION | PRÄZISIONSLEHRE |
| 9767 | PRECISION GRADUATED SCALE | REGLE DIVISEE DE PRECISION | PRÄZISIONSMASSSTAB |
| 9768 | PRECISION HEIGHT GAUGE | CALIBRE DE HAUTEUR DE PRECISION | PRÄZISIONSHÖHENMESSER |
| 9769 | PRECISION INDEXING HEAD | DIVISEUR DE PRECISION | GENAUIGKEITSTEILGERÄT |
| 9770 | PRECISION MACHINE | MACHINE DE PRECISION | PRÄZISIONSMASCHINE |
| 9771 | PREFERRED ORIENTATION | ORIENTATION PREFERENTIELLE | ORIENTIERUNG (VORZUGSWEISE) |
| 9772 | PREFORM | PREFORME | VORFORMLING |
| 9773 | PREFORMING | PREFORMAGE | VORFORMUNG |
| 9774 | PREHEAT (TO) | CHAUFFER PREALABLEMENT | VORWÄRMEN |
| 9775 | PREHEATER | RECHAUFFEUR | VORWÄRMER |
| 9776 | PREHEATING | EBULLITION PREALABLE, PRECHAUFFAGE | VORWÄRMEN |

| | | | |
|---|---|---|---|
| 9777 | **PREHEATING FURNACE** | FOUR PRECHAUFFEUR | VORWÄRMOFEN |
| 9778 | **PREIGNITION** | ALLUMAGE PREMATURE | FRÜHZÜNDUNG |
| 9779 | **PRELIMINARY TEST** | ESSAI PRELIMINAIRE | VORVERSUCH |
| 9780 | **PRELIMINARY TREATMENT** | TRAITEMENT PREPARATOIRE, PRELIMINAIRE | VORBEHANDLUNG |
| 9781 | **PRELOAD PRESTRESSING DEVICE** | DISPOSITIF DE PRECONTRAINTE | VORSPANNVORRICHTUNG |
| 9782 | **PRELOAD, PRESTRESSING, PRESTRESS** | PRECHARGE, PRECONTRAINTE | VORBELASTUNG, VORSPANNUNG |
| 9783 | **PREPACKED GRAVEL LINER** | CREPINE PREGRAVILLONNEE | LINER (KIESBEDECKTER) |
| 9784 | **PREPARATION** | PREPARATION, PRODUIT | PRÄPARAT |
| 9785 | **PREPARATION OF A SOLUTION** | PREPARATION D'UNE SOLUTION | ANSETZEN EINER LÖSUNG |
| 9786 | **PREPARATORY FUNCTION** | FONCTION PREPARATOIRE | WEGBEDINGUNG |
| 9787 | **PREPARATORY WORK, PRELIMINARY OPERATIONS** | TRAVAUX PREPARATOIRES, TRAVAUX PRELIMINAIRES, OPERATIONS PREPARATOIRES, OPERATIONS PRELIMINAIRES | VORARBEITEN |
| 9788 | **PREPARE (TO) A SOLUTION** | PREPARER UNE SOLUTION | ANSETZEN (EINE LÖSUNG) |
| 9789 | **PRESELECTOR** | PRESELECTEUR | VORWÄHLER |
| 9790 | **PRESERVATION OF TIMBER** | CONSERVATION DU BOIS | KONSERVIERUNG DES HOLZES |
| 9791 | **PRESERVATIVE** | AGENT DE CONSERVATION | KONSERVIERUNGSMITTEL |
| 9792 | **PRESERVATIVE COATINGS** | REVETEMENTS DE PROTECTION | SCHUTZÜBERZÜGE |
| 9793 | **PRESERVATIVE SKIN, PROTECTIVE COATING** | COUCHE PROTECTRICE | SCHUTZSCHICHT, SCHUTZÜBERZUG, SCHUTZANSTRICH |
| 9794 | **PRESINTERING** | PREFRITTAGE | VORSINTERUNG, VORSINTERN |
| 9795 | **PRESS** | PRESSE | PRESSE |
| 9796 | **PRESS BLOWERS** | SOUFFLETTES | PRESSLUFT-AUSWURFVORRICHTUNGEN |
| 9797 | **PRESS BUTTON, PUSH BUTTON** | POUSSOIR, BOUTON-POUSSOIR, BOUTON D'INTERRUPTEUR, BOUTON ELECTRIQUE | DRUCKKNOPF, KONTAKTKNOPF |
| 9798 | **PRESS FORGING** | FORGEAGE A LA PRESSE | PRESSSCHMIEDEN |
| 9799 | **PRESS SINTERING (HOT PRESSING)** | FRITTAGE SOUS PRESSION | DRUCKSINTERN |
| 9800 | **PRESS WITH THE FORGING MACHINE (TO)** | FORGER A LA PRESSE | PRESSEN (MIT DER SCHMIEDEPRESSE) |
| 9801 | **PRESS-SPAHN, PRESS BOARD, FULLER BOARD, GLAZED BOARD, PRESS PAPER** | PRESSSPAHN | PRESSSPAN, GLANZPAPPE, GLANZDECKEL |
| 9802 | **PRESSED CORK SLAB** | PLAQUE DE LIEGE AGGLOMERE | KORKPLATTE (GEPRESSTE) |
| 9803 | **PRESSED FLANGE** | BRIDE A COLLET RABATTU, COLLERETTE | BÖRDELFLANSCH |
| 9804 | **PRESSED PEAT** | TOURBE COMPRIMEE | PRESSTORF, MASCHINENTORF |
| 9805 | **PRESSED STEEL PULLEY** | POULIE EN TOLE EMBOUTIE | RIEMENSCHEIBE AUS GEPRESSTEM BLECH |
| 9806 | **PRESSING** | COMPRESSION, PRESSAGE | PRESSEN |
| 9807 | **PRESSING WITH THE FORGING MACHINE** | FORGEAGE A LA PRESSE | PRESSEN (MIT DER SCHMIEDEPRESSE) |
| 9808 | **PRESSURE** | PRESSION, TENSION | DRUCK, SPANNUNG |
| 9809 | **PRESSURE ABOVE ATMOSPHERIC** | PRESSION MANOMETRIQUE | ÜBERDRUCK |
| 9810 | **PRESSURE ANGLE, ANGLE OF OBLIQUITY OF PRESSURE** | ANGLE DE PRESSION | EINGRIFFSWINKEL |
| 9811 | **PRESSURE BELOW ATMOSPHERIC** | DEPRESSION | UNTERDRUCK |
| 9812 | **PRESSURE CASTING** | MOULAGE SOUS PRESSION, COULEE SOUS PRESSION | DRUCKGUSS |
| 9813 | **PRESSURE CONTROLLER** | CONTROLEUR DE PRESSION | DRUCKREGLER |
| 9814 | **PRESSURE DIFFERENCE** | DIFFERENCE DE PRESSION | DRUCKUNTERSCHIED |
| 9815 | **PRESSURE DROP** | CHUTE DE PRESSION | DRUCKABFALL |

# PRE

250

| | | | |
|---|---|---|---|
| 9816 | **PRESSURE DUE TO FRICTION** | PRESSION DUE AU FROTTEMENT | REIBUNGSDRUCK |
| 9817 | **PRESSURE FAN** | VENTILATEUR SOUFFLANT, VENTILATEUR REFOULANT | BLASENDER LÜFTER, VENTILATOR, DRUCKLÜFTER |
| 9818 | **PRESSURE FEED LUBRICATION, FORCED LUBRICATION, LUBRICATION BY THE PRESSURE SYSTEM** | GRAISSAGE SOUS PRESSION | DRUCKSCHMIERUNG, PRESSSCHMIERUNG, |
| 9819 | **PRESSURE GAS PRODUCER** | GAZOGENE A VENT SOUFFLE | DRUCKGASGENERATOR |
| 9820 | **PRESSURE GAUGE** | MANOMETRE, INDICATEUR DE PRESSION | MANOMETER, DRUCKMESSER |
| 9821 | **PRESSURE GAUGE, MANOMETER** | MANOMETRE | DRUCKMESSER, MANOMETER |
| 9822 | **PRESSURE IN A PIPE LINE** | PRESSION INTERIEURE DANS UNE CONDUITE | DRUCK (INNERER), LEITUNGSDRUCK |
| 9823 | **PRESSURE LOAD** | CHARGE DE FORGEAGE | DRUCKBELASTUNG |
| 9824 | **PRESSURE LUBRICATION** | GRAISSAGE SOUS PRESSION | DRUCKSCHMIERUNG |
| 9825 | **PRESSURE OF FLOW** | PRESSION DU COURANT | STRÖMUNGSDRUCK |
| 9826 | **PRESSURE ON EDGES** | PRESSION SUR LES ARETES | KANTENPRESSUNG |
| 9827 | **PRESSURE PIPE** | CONDUIT DE PRESSION | DRUCKROHRLEITUNG |
| 9828 | **PRESSURE RATING, STAMPING OF A VALVE** | TIMBRE D'UNE SOUPAPE, TIMBRAGE | DRUCK (ZULÄSSIGER) |
| 9829 | **PRESSURE RELIEF CONTROLLER** | DISPOSITIF DE CONTROLE DE PRESSION | DRUCKREGLER |
| 9830 | **PRESSURE RING** | BAGUE DE PRESSION | DRUCKRING |
| 9831 | **PRESSURE SCREW** | VIS DE PRESSION | DRUCKSCHRAUBE |
| 9832 | **PRESSURE SETTING** | PRESSION DE REGLAGE | REGELDRUCK |
| 9833 | **PRESSURE STAGE** | ETAGE DE PRESSION | DRUCKSTUFE |
| 9834 | **PRESSURE STROKE** | COURSE DE REFOULEMENT | DRUCKHUB |
| 9835 | **PRESSURE SWITCH** | MANOSTAT | DRUCKSCHALTER, MANOSTAT |
| 9836 | **PRESSURE TEST** | EPREUVE DE PRESSION | DRUCKPROBE |
| 9837 | **PRESSURE THERMIT WELDING** | SOUDAGE ALUMINOTHERMIQUE PAR PRESSION | PRESS SCHWEISSEN (ALUMINOTHERMISCHES), THERMITPRESSSCHWEISSEN |
| 9838 | **PRESSURE TIGHT WELDING** | SOUDURE RESISTANTE A LA PRESSION | NAHT (DRUCKFESTE) |
| 9839 | **PRESSURE VESSEL** | APPAREIL CHAUDRONNE SOUS PRESSION, RECIPIENT SOUS PRESSION | BEHÄLTER (UNTER DRUCK TIEFGEZOGENER), DRUCKGEFÄSS |
| 9840 | **PRESSURE WATER PIPING** | CONDUITE D'EAU SOUS PRESSION, D'EAU FORCEE | DRUCKWASSERLEITUNG |
| 9841 | **PRESSURE WATER, WATER UNDER PRESSURE** | EAU SOUS PRESSION | DRUCKWASSER |
| 9842 | **PRESSURE WELDING** | SOUDAGE PAR PRESSION | PRESSSCHWEISSEN |
| 9843 | **PRESSURE-VACUUM VALVE** | SOUPAPE PRESSION-DEPRESSION | SAUG-DRUCKVENTIL |
| 9844 | **PRICK PUNCH** | POINCON DE TRACAGE | KÖRNER |
| 9845 | **PRIMARY BATTERY, GALVANIC BATTERY** | BATTERIE DE PILES | BATTERIE (GALVANISCHE) |
| 9846 | **PRIMARY CELL** | PILE PRIMAIRE | PRIMÄRELEMENT |
| 9847 | **PRIMARY COLOUR** | COULEUR SIMPLE | GRUNDFARBE, ERSTFARBE |
| 9848 | **PRIMARY CONSTITUENT** | ELEMENT PRO-EUTECTIQUE | VOR-EUTEKTISCHER BESTANDTEIL |
| 9849 | **PRIMARY CRYSTALLIZATION** | CRISTALLISATION PRIMAIRE | KRISTALLISATION (PRIMÄRE) |
| 9850 | **PRIMARY CURRENT RATIO** | TAUX DE COURANT PRIMAIRE | PRIMÄRSTROMVERHÄLTNIS |
| 9851 | **PRIMARY GRAPHITE** | CHARBON GRAPHITIQUE | GRAPHITKOHLE |
| 9852 | **PRIMARY MATERIAL** | PRODUIT PRIMAIRE | AUSGANGSSTOFF, GRUNDSTOFF |
| 9853 | **PRIMARY METAL** | METAL VIERGE OU NAISSANT | METALL (GEDIEGENES) |
| 9854 | **PRIMARY STRENGTH** | RESISTANCE PRIMITIVE | URSPRUNGSFESTIGKEIT |

| | | |
|---|---|---|
| 9855 | **PRIME** | APPRET | GRUNDIERLACK |
| 9856 | **PRIME A FORCE PUMP (TO), FETCH A LIFT PUMP (TO)** | AMORCER UNE POMPE | PUMPE ANSAUGEN (EINE) ANHEBEN LASSEN |
| 9857 | **PRIME COAT** | COUCHE PRIMAIRE, COUCHE DE FOND | UNTERSCHICHT, GRUNDSCHICHT |
| 9858 | **PRIME COST, INITIAL COST; COST OF INSTALLATION** | FRAIS DE PREMIER ETABLISSEMENT | ANSCHAFFUNGSKOSTEN, ANLAGEKOSTEN |
| 9859 | **PRIME MOVER, ENGINE, MOTOR** | MACHINE MOTRICE, MOTEUR, TRACTEUR | MASCHINE, ANTRIEBMACHINE, KRAFTMACHINE, MOTOR, TRAKTOR |
| 9860 | **PRIME NUMBER** | NOMBRE PREMIER | GRUNDZAHL, PRIMZAHL |
| 9861 | **PRIMER BRASS** | ALLIAGE CUIVRE-ZING | KUPFERZINKLEGIERUNG |
| 9862 | **PRIMES** | PRODUITS DE PREMIERE QUALITE | PRODUKTE (ERSTKLASSIGE) |
| 9863 | **PRIMING** | PRIMAGE (ENTRAINEMENT DE L'EAU PAR LA VAPEUR) | MITREISSEN VON WASSER IM DAMPF |
| 9864 | **PRIMING COAT, FIRST COAT OF PAINT** | COUCHE DE BASE, PEINTURE SOUS-JACENTE, PREMIERE COUCHE DE PEINTURE | GRUNDANSTRICH, GRUNDIERUNG |
| 9865 | **PRIMITIVE TRANSLATION** | TRANSLATION PRIMITIVE | PRIMITIVE TRANSLATION |
| 9866 | **PRINCIPAL AXIS** | AXE PRINCIPAL | HAUPTACHSE |
| 9867 | **PRINCIPAL DYNAMO** | DYNAMO, GENERATRICE | HAUPTDYNAMO, HAUPTMASCHINE |
| 9868 | **PRINCIPAL SECTION** | SECTION PRINCIPALE | HAUPTSCHNITT |
| 9869 | **PRINCIPAL STRESS** | TENSION PRINCIPALE | HAUPTSPANNUNG |
| 9870 | **PRINT** | EPREUVE, COPIE (PHOT.) | ABZUG (PHOT.) |
| 9871 | **PRINTED CIRCUIT (PC)** | CIRCUIT IMPRIME (C.I.) | SCHALTUNG (GEDRÜCKTE) |
| 9872 | **PRINTER** | IMPRIMANTE | DRUCKER |
| 9873 | **PRINTING ROLL KNURLING MACHINE** | MACHINE A MOLETER LES CYLINDRES D'IMPRIMERIE | DRUCKWALZENRÄNDELMASCHINE |
| 9874 | **PRINTING, COPYING FRAME** | CHASSIS POUR BLEUS | LICHTPAUSAPPARAT |
| 9875 | **PRISM** | PRISME | PRISMA |
| 9876 | **PRISM WITH OBLIQUE CROSS SECTION** | PRISME A SECTION OBLIQUE | PRISMA (SCHIEF ABGESCHNITTENES) |
| 9877 | **PRISMATIC PLANE** | PLAN PRISMATIQUE | EBENE (PRISMATISCHE) |
| 9878 | **PRISMATIC SPECTRUM** | SPECTRE PRODUIT PAR PRISME | PRISMENSPEKTRUM |
| 9879 | **PRISMATICAL** | PRISMATIQUE | PRISMATISCH |
| 9880 | **PRISMOID** | PRISMATOIDE | PRISMATOID |
| 9881 | **PROBABILITY DISTRIBUTION** | FONCTION DE DISTRIBUTION | WAHRSCHEINLICHKEITSVERTEILUNG |
| 9882 | **PROBE** | PALPEUR | SONDE, MESSFÜHLER |
| 9883 | **PROCESS** | PROCESSUS, PROCEDE | VORGANG, VERFAHREN |
| 9884 | **PROCESS ANNEALLING** | RECUIT INTERMEDIAIRE D'USINAGE | ZWISCHENGLÜHUNG |
| 9885 | **PROCESS BOOK** | MANUEL DE FABRICATION | HERSTELLUNGSHANDBUCH |
| 9886 | **PROCESS METALLURGY** | METALLURGIE D'EXTRACTION | EXTRAKTIONSMETALLURGIE |
| 9887 | **PROCESS OF MANUFACTURE** | PROCEDE D'USINAGE | ARBEITSVORGANG, ARBEITSPROZESS |
| 9888 | **PROCESSING INDUSTRY** | INDUSTRIE DE TRANSFORMATION | VEREDLUNGSINDUSTRIE |
| 9889 | **PROCESSOR** | PROCESSEUR | PROZESSOR |
| 9890 | **PRODUCER GAS** | GAZ DE GAZOGENE | GENERATORGAS, MAGERES GAS, SCHWACHGAS |
| 9891 | **PRODUCT** | PRODUIT (MATH.) | PRODUKT (MATH.) |
| 9892 | **PRODUCT** | PRODUIT | PRODUKT, ERZEUGNIS |
| 9893 | **PRODUCT OF COMBUSTION** | PRODUIT DE COMBUSTION | VERBRENNUNGSERZEUGNIS, VERBRENNUNGSPRODUKT |
| 9894 | **PRODUCTION GENERATION OF AN ELECTRIC CURRENT** | PRODUCTION DE COURANT | STROMERZEUGUNG |
| 9895 | **PRODUCTION OF COLD** | PRODUCTION DU FROID | KÄLTEERZEUGUNG |

**PRO** 252

| 9896 | **PRODUCTION OF HEAT** | PRODUCTION DE CHALEUR | WÄRMEERZEUGUNG |
|---|---|---|---|
| 9897 | **PRODUCTIVITY** | PRODUCTIVITE | ERTRAGSFÄHIGKEIT, PRODUKTIVITÄT |
| 9898 | **PROFILE** | PROFIL, COUPE | SCHNITT, PROFIL, SEITENANSICHT |
| 9899 | **PROFILE MILLING CUTTER** | FRAISE DE FORME, FRAISE PROFILEE | FORMFRÄSER, PROFILFRÄSER, FASSONFRÄSER |
| 9900 | **PROFILE MILLING MACHINE** | FRAISEUSE-FACONNEUSE, FRAISEUSE A COPIER | FORMFRÄSMASCHINE, PROFILFRÄSMASCHINE, KOPIERFRÄSMASCHINE |
| 9901 | **PROFILING MACHINE FOR WOOD** | TOUPIE | HOLZFRÄSMASCHINE, KREISELFRÄSER |
| 9902 | **PROGRAM** | PROGRAMME | PROGRAMM |
| 9903 | **PROGRAM STOP** | ARRET PROGRAMME | PROGRAMMIERTER HALT |
| 9904 | **PROGRAMMING** | PROGRAMMATION | PROGRAMMIEREN |
| 9905 | **PROGRESS** | AVANCEMENT | ARBEITSFORTSCHRITT |
| 9906 | **PROGRESSIVE AGING** | VIEILLISSEMENT PROGRESSIF | PROGRESSIVE ALTERUNG |
| 9907 | **PROGRESSIVE CYLINDRICAL PLUG GAUGE** | TAMPON A ECHELONS DE TOLERANCE | GRENZLEHRDORN |
| 9908 | **PROGRESSIVE INDUCTION SEAM WELDING** | BRASAGE PAR INDUCTION PROGRESSIVE | PROGRESSIVINDUKTIONSSCHWEISSEN |
| 9909 | **PROJECT (TO)** | PROJETER | PROJIZIEREN |
| 9910 | **PROJECTING** | SAILLANT | VORSPRINGEND, VORSTEHEND |
| 9911 | **PROJECTING PLATE** | TOLE EN SAILLIE | VORSPRINGENDES BLECH |
| 9912 | **PROJECTION** | PROJECTION | PROJEKTION |
| 9913 | **PROJECTION** | SAILLIE | VORSPRUNG, ÜBERKRAGUNG, AUSLADUNG |
| 9914 | **PROJECTION LENS** | LENTILLE DIVERGENTE | PROJEKTIV |
| 9915 | **PROJECTION WELD** | JOINT DE SOUDURE PAR BOSSAGES | BUCKELSCHWEISSNAHT |
| 9916 | **PROJECTION WELDING** | SOUDAGE PAR BOSSAGES | BUCKELSCHWEISSEN |
| 9917 | **PROJECTION, SET OFF** | RESSAUT, SAILLIE | AUSKRAGUNG, VORKRAGUNG, AUSLADUNG |
| 9918 | **PROLATE CYCLOID** | CYCLOIDE RALLONGEE | ZYKLOIDE (GEDEHNTE), ZYKLOIDE (VERLÄNGERTE) |
| 9919 | **PROLONGATION OF A PATENT** | PROLONGATION DE DUREE D'UN BREVET | PATENTVERLÄGERUNG, VERLÄNGERUNG EINES PATENTES |
| 9920 | **PRONY BRAKE** | FREIN DYMAMOMETRIQUE DE PRONY | ZAUM (PRONYSCHER) |
| 9921 | **PROOF** | EPREUVE, ESSAI | VERSUCH |
| 9922 | **PROOF STRENGTH** | LIMITE ELASTIQUE CONVENTIONNELLE OU APPARENTE | PRÜFDEHNGRENZE |
| 9923 | **PROOF STRESS** | LIMITE D'ALLONGEMENT, LIMITE ELASTIQUE CONVENTIONNELLE | DEHNGRENZE |
| 9924 | **PROOF TEST** | ESSAI NON DESTRUCTIF | VERSUCH (ZERSTÖRUNGSFREIER) |
| 9925 | **PROP, STAY** | ETAI | STÜTZE, STEIFE |
| 9926 | **PROPAGATION OF WAVES** | PROPAGATION D'ONDES | FORTPFLANZUNG VON WELLEN |
| 9927 | **PROPANE** | PROPANE, HYDRURE DE PROPYLE | PROPAN |
| 9928 | **PROPELLER BLADE** | AILE D'UNE HELICE | SCHRAUBENFLÜGEL |
| 9929 | **PROPELLER FAN, HELICAL, SCREW BLOWER** | VENTILATEUR A HELICE | SCHRAUBENGEBLÄSE, SCHNECKENGEBLÄSE, AXIALGEBLÄSE |
| 9930 | **PROPELLER SHAFT** | ARBRE D'ENTRAINEMENT, ARBRE D'HELICE | TREIBWELLE, SCHRAUBENWELLE |
| 9931 | **PROPELLER-MIXER** | HELICO-MELANGEUR | SPIRALMISCHER |
| 9932 | **PROPER FRACTION** | FRACTION PROPRE, PURE | BRUCH (ECHTER) |
| 9933 | **PROPORTION** | PROPORTION (MATH.) | VERHÄLTNIS, VERHÄLTNISGLEICHUNG, PROPORTION |

| | | | |
|---|---|---|---|
| 9934 | **PROPORTION OF MIXTURE** | PROPORTION, DOSAGE DU MELANGE | MISCHUNGSVERHÄLTNIS |
| 9935 | **PROPORTIONAL** | PROPORTIONNEL | VERHÄLTNISGLEICH, PROPORTIONAL, VERHÄLTNISSMÄSSIG |
| 9936 | **PROPORTIONAL LIMIT** | LIMITE (D'ELASTICITE) PROPORTIONNELLE | PROPORTIONALITÄTSGRENZE |
| 9937 | **PROPORTIONAL REDUCTION COMPASSES** | COMPAS DE REDUCTION | REDUKTIONSZIRKEL, PROPORTIONALZIRKEL |
| 9938 | **PROPORTIONALITY** | PROPORTIONNALITE | PROPORTIONALITÄT |
| 9939 | **PROPYLENE** | PROPYLENE | PROPYLEN |
| 9940 | **PROTACTINIUM** | PROTACTINIUM | PROTAKTINIUM |
| 9941 | **PROTECTED MOTOR** | MOTEUR PROTEGE | GESCHÜTZTER MOTOR |
| 9942 | **PROTECTING SLEEVE** | MANCHON PROTECTEUR | SCHUTZMUFFE |
| 9943 | **PROTECTION** | PROTECTION | SCHUTZ |
| 9944 | **PROTECTION CAP** | COUVERCLE PROTECTEUR | SCHUTZKAPPE, SCHUTZDECKEL |
| 9945 | **PROTECTION FROM RUST** | PROTECTION CONTRE LA ROUILLE | ROSTSCHUTZ |
| 9946 | **PROTECTION OF INDUSTRIAL PROPERTY** | PROTECTION DE LA PROPRIETE INDUSTRIELLE | SCHUTZ DES GEWERBLICHEN EIGENTUMS |
| 9947 | **PROTECTIVE ATMOSPHERE** | ATMOSPHERE PROTECTRICE | SCHUTZATMOSPHÄRE |
| 9948 | **PROTECTIVE CASING** | CAGE, BOITE, ENVELOPPE PROTECTRICE | SCHUTZGEHÄUSE |
| 9949 | **PROTECTIVE COVERING** | REVETEMENT PROTECTEUR | SCHUTZHÜLLE |
| 9950 | **PROTECTIVE FILM** | COUCHE PROTECTRICE | DECKSCHICHT |
| 9951 | **PROTECTIVE GRATING** | TREILLIS DE PROTECTION, TREILLAGE PROTECTEUR | SCHUTZGITTER |
| 9952 | **PROTECTIVE MATERIAL** | MATIERE PROTECTRICE | SCHUTZSTOFF |
| 9953 | **PROTECTIVE WALL** | PAROI PROTECTRICE | SCHUTZWAND |
| 9954 | **PROTON** | PROTON | PROTON |
| 9955 | **PROTOTYPE** | PROTOTYPE | URMUSTER |
| 9956 | **PROTRACTOR** | RAPPORTEUR | GRADBOGEN, WINKELMESSER, TRANSPORTEUR |
| 9957 | **PSEUDO-ASTATIC GOVERNOR** | REGULATEUR PSEUDO-ASTATIQUE | REGLER (PSEUDOASTATISCHER) |
| 9958 | **PSEUDOBINARY SYSTEM** | SYSTEME QUASI-BINAIRE | SYSTEM (QUASIBINÄRES) |
| 9959 | **PSEUDOCARBURIZING** | CEMENTATION BRILLANTE | BLINDAUFKOHLEN |
| 9960 | **PSYCHROMETER, WET AND DRY BULB HYGROMETER** | PSYCHROMETRE | PSYCHROMETER |
| 9961 | **PUDDLE** | BAIN DE FUSION | SCHWEISSBAD |
| 9962 | **PUDDLED IRON** | FER PUDDLE | PUDDELEISEN |
| 9963 | **PUDDLED STEEL** | ACIER PUDDLE | PUDDELSTAHL |
| 9964 | **PUDDLING** | PUDDLER | PUDDELN |
| 9965 | **PUDDLING FURNACE** | FOUR DE PUDDLAGE | PUDDELOFEN |
| 9966 | **PUG MILL** | MALAXEUR | LEHMMÜHLE |
| 9967 | **PULL AT RIGHT ANGLES TO THE FIBRES** | TRACTION NORMALEMENT A LA DIRECTION DES FIBRES | ZUG SENKRECHT ZUR FASER |
| 9968 | **PULL IN THE DIRECTION OF THE FIBRES** | TRACTION DANS LA DIRECTION DES FIBRES | ZUG PARALLEL ZUR FASER |
| 9969 | **PULL THE RIVET HOLES INTO LINE COINCIDENCE WITH EACH OTHER (TO)** | FAIRE CORRESPONDRE LES TROUS DE RIVETS, ASSURER LA CONCORDANCE DES TROUS DE RIVETS | NIETLÖCHER AUFEINANDERPASSEN DIE |
| 9970 | **PULL, TENSION** | TRACTION | ZUG (MECH.) |
| 9971 | **PULLEY (FOR LIFTING WEIGHTS)** | POULIE (APPAREIL DE LEVAGE) | ROLLE (ALS HEBEZEUG) |
| 9972 | **PULLEY BLOCK** | MOUFLE | FLASCHENZUG |
| 9973 | **PULLEY BLOCKS, LIFTING TACKLE, BLOCKS AND TACKLE, PULLEY TACKLE, LIFTING BLOCKS** | PALAN, MOUFLES, POULIES MOUFLEES | FLASCHENZUG, ROLLENZUG, KLOBENZUG, ZUG |

PUL 254

| | | | |
|---|---|---|---|
| 9974 | PULLEY OUT OF TRUTH | POULIE MAL TOURNEE | UNRUNDE RIEMENSCHEIBE |
| 9975 | PULLEY TURNING LATHE | FOUR A POULIES | RIEMENSCHEIBENDREHBANK |
| 9976 | PULLEY WITH CURVED ARMS | POULIE A BRAS COURBES, POULIE A BRAS PARABOLIQUES | RIEMENSCHEIBE MIT GESCHWEIFTEN ARMEN |
| 9977 | PULLEY WITH STRAIGHT ARMS | POULIE A BRAS DROITS | RIEMENSCHEIBE MIT GERADEN ARMEN |
| 9978 | PULSATION WELDING | SOUDAGE PAR PULSATION | PULSATIONSSCHWEISSVERFAHREN |
| 9979 | PULSE | IMPULSION | IMPULS |
| 9980 | PULSOMETER | PULSOMETRE | DAMPFDRUCKPUMPE, PULSOMETER |
| 9981 | PULVERISABLE | PULVERISABLE | PULVERISIERBAR |
| 9982 | PULVERISE (TO), POWDER (TO) | PULVERISER | PULVERISIEREN |
| 9983 | PULVERISED | PULVERISE | GEPULVERT, PULVERISIERT |
| 9984 | PULVERISED POWDERED COAL | CHARBON PULVERISE, POUDRE DE CHARBON | KOHLENSTAUB |
| 9985 | PULVERIZATION | PULVERISATION | PULVERISIERUNG, FEINSTMAHLUNG |
| 9986 | PUMICE | PIERRE PONCE | NATURBIMSSTEIN |
| 9987 | PUMICE (TO) | PONCER | ABBIMSEN |
| 9988 | PUMICE STONE | PIERRE PONCE, PONCE | BIMSSTEIN, BIMS |
| 9989 | PUMICEOUS TUFF | TUF PONCEUX | BIMSSTEINTUFF |
| 9990 | PUMICING | PONCAGE | BIMSEN, ABBIMSEN |
| 9991 | PUMP | POMPE | PUMPE |
| 9992 | PUMP CYLINDER | CYLINDRE DE POMPE | PUMPZYLINDER |
| 9993 | PUMP INJECTOR | INJECTEUR DE POMPE | EINSPRITZROHR |
| 9994 | PUMP OILER, OIL CAN WITH FORCE PUMP | BURETTE A PISTON | VENTILÖLKANNE |
| 9995 | PUMP PLUNGER | PISTON DE POMPE | PUMPENELEMENT |
| 9996 | PUMPING SETS | POMPES | PUMPANLAGEN |
| 9997 | PUNCH | POINCON, PERCOIR POUR TOLE | STEMPEL, DURCHSCHLAG, LOCHSTEMPEL, MÖNCH, LOCHER |
| 9998 | PUNCH (TO), STAMP OUT (TO) | DECOUPER, POINCONNER | STANZEN, SCHNEIDEN, AUSSCHNEIDEN |
| 9999 | PUNCH HOLES (TO) | POINCONNER | LOCHEN, LÖCHER STANZEN |
| 10000 | PUNCH PLIERS | EMPORTE-PIECE, PINCE EMPORTE-PIECE | LOCHZANGE |
| 10001 | PUNCH PRESS | POINCONNEUSE, PERFOREUSE | LOCHPRESS, LOCHSTANZE |
| 10002 | PUNCHED CARD | CARTE PERFOREE | LOCHKARTE |
| 10003 | PUNCHED PLATE | TOLE A TROUS POINCONNES | BLECH MIT GESTANZTEN LÖCHERN |
| 10004 | PUNCHED RIVET HOLE | TROU DE RIVET POINCONNE | NIETLOCH (GESTANZTES), NIETLOCH (GELOCHTES) |
| 10005 | PUNCHED TAPE | BANDE PERFOREE | LOCHSTREIFEN |
| 10006 | PUNCHING | PERCAGE, POINCONNAGE | LOCHEN, STANZEN, AUSSTANZEN |
| 10007 | PUNCHING AND SHEARING MACHINE | MACHINE A POINCONNER ET A CISAILLER, POINCONNEUSE-CISAILLE | LOCHMASCHINE MIT SCHERE |
| 10008 | PUNCHING HOLES | POINCONNAGE | LOCHEN, STANZEN VON LÖCHERN |
| 10009 | PUNCHING MACHIME | MACHINE A POINCONNER, POINCONNEUSE, POINCONNEUSE-DECOUPEUSE | LOCHMASCHINE, LOCHSTANZE, STANZE, STANZE (AUSSCHNEIDEMASCHINE) |
| 10010 | PUNCHING TEST, DRIFT TEST | ESSAI DE POINCONNAGE, ESSAI A LA PERFORATION | LOCHVERSUCH, AUFDORNPROBE |
| 10011 | PUNCHING UNIT | UNITE DE POINCONNAGE | STANZEINHEIT |
| 10012 | PUNCHING, STAMPING OUT | DECOUPAGE, POINCONNAGE | STANZEN, SCHNEIDEN, AUSSCHNEIDEN |
| 10013 | PUNCTURE OF INSULATION | PERFORATION PAR DECHARGE DISRUPTIVE | DURCHSCHLAG (ELEKTR.) |

| | | | |
|---|---|---|---|
| 10014 | **PURCHASE CRAB, WINCH** | TREUIL A ENGRENAGE | RÄDERWINDE |
| 10015 | **PURCHASE INSPECTION GAUGE** | JAUGE DE RECEPTION | ABNAHMELEHRE |
| 10016 | **PURE RESEARCH** | RECHERCHE PURE | GRUNDLAGENFORSCHUNG |
| 10017 | **PURGING** | EFFET DE NETTOYAGE | REINIGUNGSWIRKUNG |
| 10018 | **PURIFICATION OF GAS** | EPURATION DES GAZ | GASREINIGUNG |
| 10019 | **PURIFICATION OF WATER** | PURIFICATION DE L'EAU | REINIGUNG DES WASSERS, WASSERREINIGUNG |
| 10020 | **PURIFIER** | PURGEUR, EPURATEUR | REINIGER |
| 10021 | **PUSH ALONG THE FIBRES** | COMPRESSION DANS LA DIRECTION DES FIBRES | DRUCK PARALLEL ZUR FASER |
| 10022 | **PUSH AT RIGHT ANGLES TO THE FIBRES** | COMPRESSION NORMALEMENT A LA DIRECTION DES FIBRES | DRUCK SENKRECHT ZUR FASER |
| 10023 | **PUSH BENCH** | BANC D'ETIRAGE | ZIEHBANK |
| 10024 | **PUSH HEATING FURNACE** | FOUR A SECOUSSES | STOSSOFEN |
| 10025 | **PUSH IN FIT** | EMMANCHEMENT, AJUSTAGE, MONTAGE LACHE | SCHIEBESITZ |
| 10026 | **PUSH ROD** | TIGE DU CULBUTEUR | STOSSTANGE |
| 10027 | **PUSH-WELDING** | SOUDAGE A LA CAROTTE | HAND-STOSSELEKTRODENSCHWEISSEN |
| 10028 | **PUSH, COMPRESSION** | COMPRESSION | DRUCK, ZUSAMMENDRÜCKEN |
| 10029 | **PUSHER** | POUSSOIR | STOSSVORRICHTUNG |
| 10030 | **PUSHER-TYPE FURNACE** | FOUR POUSSANT | STOSSOFEN, DURCHSTOSSOFEN |
| 10031 | **PUSHROD** | TIGE DE CULBUTEURS | STÖSSELSTANGE |
| 10032 | **PUT A SPRING IN TENSION (TO)** | TENDRE UN RESSORT, BANDER UN RESSORT | FEDER SPANNEN (EINE) |
| 10033 | **PUT TO THROW INTO GEAR (TO), ENGAGE (TO)** | EMBRAYER | EINSCHALTEN, EINRÜCKEN, EINGRIFF BRINGEN IN, EINKUPPELN |
| 10034 | **PUT TO THROW OUT OF GEAR (TO), DISENGAGE (TO)** | DEBRAYER, DESEMBRAYER, DESENGRENER | AUSSCHALTEN, AUSRÜCKEN, AUSKUPPELN, ENTKUPPELN, LOSKUPPELN |
| 10035 | **PUTREFACTION** | PUTREFACTION (ACTION), POURRITURE (ETAT) | FÄULNIS |
| 10036 | **PUTREFY (TO)** | PUTREFIER (SE), FERMENTER, POURRIR | FAULEN, IN FÄULNIS ÜBERGEHEN |
| 10037 | **PUTTY** | MASTIC | KITT, DICHTUNGSMASSE |
| 10038 | **PYRAMID** | PYRAMIDE | PYRAMIDE |
| 10039 | **PYRAMID HARDNESS** | DURETE VICKERS A LA PYRAMIDE | VICKERS-PYRAMIDHÄRTE |
| 10040 | **PYRAMIDAL PLANE SYSTEM** | SYSTEME PYRAMIDAL | PYRAMIDENSYSTEM |
| 10041 | **PYRIDINE** | PYRIDINE | PYRIDIN |
| 10042 | **PYRO-ELECTRIC** | PYROELECTRIQUE | PYROELEKTRISCH |
| 10043 | **PYRO-ELECTRICITY** | PYROELECTRICITE | KRISTALLELEKTRIZITÄT, PYROELEKTRIZITÄT |
| 10044 | **PYROCONDUCTIVITY** | CONDUCTIVITE THERMO-ELECTRIQUE | LEITFÄHIGKEIT (THERMO-ELEKTRISCHE) |
| 10045 | **PYROGALLOL, PYROGALLIC ACID, TRIHYDROXYBENZENE** | ACIDE PYROGALLIQUE, PYROGALLOL | PYROGALLUSSÄURE, PYROGALLOL |
| 10046 | **PYROLIGNEOUS ACID** | ACIDE PYROLIGNEUX | HOLZESSIG, HOLZSÄURE |
| 10047 | **PYROLUSITE, MANGANESE DIOXIDE** | BIOXYDE DE MANGANESE, PEROXYDE DE MANGANESE | BRAUNSTEIN, PYROLUSIT, MANGANDIOXYD, MANGANSUPEROXYD, MANGANHYPEROXYD |
| 10048 | **PYROMETALLURGY** | PYROMETALLURGIE | PYROMETALLURGIE |
| 10049 | **PYROMETER** | PYROMETRE | HITZEMESSER, PYROMETER |
| 10050 | **PYROMETRIC CONE** | CONE PYROMETRIQUE | SEGERKEGEL, SCHMELZKEGEL, PYROMETERKEGEL |
| 10051 | **PYROMETRIC CONE EQUIVALENT** | EQUIVALENT DU CONE PYROMETRIQUE | PYROMETERKEGEL-FALLPUNKT |

**PYR**

256

| | | |
|---|---|---|
| 10052 | **PYROMETRY** | PYROMETRIE | PYROMETRIE |
| 10053 | **PYROPHORIC ALLOY** | ALLIAGE PYROPHORIQUE | ZÜNDLEGIERUNG |
| 10054 | **PYROPHOSPHORIC ACID** | ACIDE PYROPHOSPHORIQUE | PYROPHOSPHORSÄURE, PARAPHOSPHORSÄURE |
| 10055 | **QUADRANGULAR PRISM** | PRISME QUADRANGULAIRE, QUADRILATERE | VIERSEITIGES PRISMA |
| 10056 | **QUADRANT** | QUADRANT | VIERTELKREIS, QUADRANT |
| 10057 | **QUADRATIC EQUATION** | EQUATION QUADRATIQUE, EQUATION DU SECOND DEGRE | GLEICHUNG ZWEITEN GRADES, GLEICHUNG (QUADRATISCHE) |
| 10058 | **QUADRILATERAL, QUADRANGLE** | QUADRANGLE, QUADRILATERE | VIERECK |
| 10059 | **QUADRUPLE-EXPANSION ENGINE** | MACHINE A QUADRUPLE EXPANSION | VIERFACHEXPANSIONSMASCHINE |
| 10060 | **QUADRUPLE-SEAT VALVE** | SOUPAPE A QUADRUPLE SIEGE | VENTIL (VIERSITZIGES) |
| 10061 | **QUALIMETER** | PENETROMETRE | QUALIMETER |
| 10062 | **QUALITATIVE ANALYSIS** | ANALYSE QUALITATIVE | ANALYSE (QUALITATIVE) |
| 10063 | **QUALITY CONTROL** | CONTROLE DE QUALITE | QUALITÄTSKONTROLLE, GÜTEPRÜFUNG |
| 10064 | **QUANTITATIVE ANALYSIS** | ANALYSE QUANTITATIVE, DOSAGE | ANALYSE (QUANTITATIVE), MENGENBESTIMMUNG |
| 10065 | **QUANTITY** | GRANDEUR, QUANTITE | GRÖSSE, (MATH.) |
| 10066 | **QUANTITY AMOUNT OF HEAT** | QUANTITE DE CHALEUR | WÄRMEMENGE |
| 10067 | **QUANTITY OF ELECTRICITY** | QUANTITE D'ELECTRICITE | ELEKTRIZITÄTSMENGE |
| 10068 | **QUANTITY OF MOTION** | QUANTITE DE MOUVEMENT | BEWEGUNGSGRÖSSE |
| 10069 | **QUANTITY PASSING** | DEBIT | DURCHFLUSSMENGE |
| 10070 | **QUANTITY TO BE MEASURED** | QUANTITE MESUREE | MESSGRÖSSE |
| 10071 | **QUANTUM EFFICIENCY** | RENDEMENT QUANTIQUE | QUANTENAUSBEUTE |
| 10072 | **QUANTUM LIMIT** | LONGUEUR D'ONDES CRITIQUE | GRENZWELLENLÄNGE |
| 10073 | **QUARRY** | CARRIERE | STEINBRUCH |
| 10074 | **QUARTER BEND** | COUDE ROND A ANGLE DROIT, COUDE ROND AU 1/4 | NORMALKRÜMMER |
| 10075 | **QUARTER SAWING OF TIMBER** | SCIAGE HOLLANDAIS, SCIAGE PAR RAYONNEMENT, DEBIT AU COIN DU BOIS | SPIEGELSCHNITT, RADIALSCHNITT DES HOLZES |
| 10076 | **QUARTER TIMBER** | QUARTIER, BOIS EN QUARTIERS | VIERTELHOLZ, KREUZHOLZ |
| 10077 | **QUARTZ** | QUARTZ | QUARZ |
| 10078 | **QUARTZ FIBRE** | FILAMENT DE QUARTZ | QUARZFADEN |
| 10079 | **QUARTZ GLASS** | VERRE DE QUARTZ | QUARZGLAS |
| 10080 | **QUARTZ MERCURY LAMP** | LAMPE A VAPEUR DE MERCURE EN QUARTZ | QUARZQUECKSILBERLAMPE |
| 10081 | **QUARTZ PORPHYRY** | PORPHYRE QUARTZIFERE | QUARZPORPHYR |
| 10082 | **QUARTZ SAND, SILICEOUS SAND** | SABLE QUARTZEUX, SILICEUX | QUARZSAND |
| 10083 | **QUARTZITE** | QUARTZITE | QUARZIT |
| 10084 | **QUATERNARY ALLOY** | ALLIAGE QUATERNAIRE | LEGIERUNG (QUATERNÄRE) |
| 10085 | **QUATERNARY EUTECTIC ALLOY** | ALLIAGE QUATERNAIRE EUTECTIQUE | LEGIERUNG (QUATERNÄRE EUTEKTISCHE) |
| 10086 | **QUATREFOIL** | QUATRE-FEUILLES | VIERBLATT |
| 10087 | **QUENCH AGING** | VIEILLISSEMENT PAR REFROIDISSEMENT RAPIDE | ABSCHRECKALTERUNG |
| 10088 | **QUENCH AND HOT BEND TEST, BENDING TEST AFTER QUENCHING** | FLEXION EFFECTUE SUR DES ACIERS TRAITES AVEC DES TREMPES (ESSAI DE...) | ABSCHRECKBIEGEPROBE |
| 10089 | **QUENCH HARDENING** | DURCISSEMENT PAR TREMPE | ABSCHRECKHÄRTUNG |
| 10090 | **QUENCH TANK** | CUVE DE TREMPE | ABSCHRECKBEHÄLTER |
| 10091 | **QUENCH THE STEEL (TO)** | REFROIDIR BRUSQUEMENT L'ACIER | STAHL ABSCHRECKEN (DEN) |

| | | | |
|---|---|---|---|
| 10092 | **QUENCHED AND TEMPERED** | TREMPE ET REVENU | HÄRTEN UND ANLASSEN, VERGÜTUNG |
| 10093 | **QUENCHED AND TEMPERED STEEL** | ACIER CALME ET TREMPE, ACIER TREMPE ET REVENU | STAHL (BERUHIGTER UND GEHÄRTETER), STAHL (VERGÜTETER) |
| 10094 | **QUENCHING** | TREMPE | ABSCHRECKEN (FONTE) |
| 10095 | **QUENCHING AND TEMPERING** | TREMPE ET REVENU | VERGÜTUNG |
| 10096 | **QUENCHING BATH** | BAIN DE TREMPE | HÄRTEBAD |
| 10097 | **QUENCHING CRACK** | CRIQUE, FISSURE DE TREMPE | HÄRTERISS |
| 10098 | **QUENCHING MEDIUM** | MILIEU DE TREMPE | ABSCHRECKMITTEL |
| 10099 | **QUENCHING OIL** | HUILE DE TREMPE | HÄRTEÖL |
| 10100 | **QUENCHING THE STEEL** | REFROIDISSEMENT BRUSQUE DE L'ACIER | ABSCHRECKEN DES STAHLES |
| 10101 | **QUESTIONNAIRE** | QUESTIONNAIRE | FRAGEBOGEN |
| 10102 | **QUICK CURVE SWEEP, SHARP CURVE** | COURBE VIVE, COURBE RAIDE, COURBE A PETIT RAYON, COURBE A FAIBLE RAYON | KURVE (STEILE) |
| 10103 | **QUICK OPENING GATE VALVE** | VANNE A MANOEUVRE RAPIDE | SCHNELLÖFFNUNGS-SCHIEBER |
| 10104 | **QUICK OPERATING VALVE** | ROBINET A MANOEUVRE RAPIDE | SCHNELLSCHLUSSVENTIL |
| 10105 | **QUICK PITCH THREAD** | FILET A PAS ALLONGE, FILET A PAS RAPIDE | GEWINDE MIT STARKER STEIGUNG |
| 10106 | **QUICK RETURN CRANK MOTION** | MECANISME POUR RETOUR RAPIDE, RETOUR RAPIDE | SCHNELLRÜCKLAUFGETRIEBE, RASCHER RÜCKLAUF |
| 10107 | **QUICK SETTING CEMENT** | CIMENT A PRISE RAPIDE | ZEMENT (SCHNELL BINDENDER) |
| 10108 | **QUICK-CHANGE ADAPTOR** | ADAPTEUR POUR ECHANGE RAPIDE | SCHNELLWECHSELEINRICHTUNG |
| 10109 | **QUIESCENT POURING (DURVILLE PROCESS)** | COULEE TRANQUILLE (PROCEDE DURVILLE) | GIESSEN (WIRBELFREIES) (DURVILLE-VERFAHREN) |
| 10110 | **QUINHYDRONE HALF-CELL** | QUINHYDRONE (HEMI-CELLULE A LA) | CHINHYDRONELEKTRODE |
| 10111 | **QUINTAL (METRIC)** | QUINTAL METRIQUE | DOPPELZENTNER, METRISCHER ZENTNER, METERZENTNER |
| 10112 | **QUINTIC EQUATION** | EQUATION QUINTIQUE, EQUATION DU CINQUIEME DEGRE | GLEICHUNG FÜNFTEN GRADES |
| 10113 | **QUOTE (TO)** | CITER | ANFÜHREN, ZITIEREN |
| 10114 | **QUOTIENT** | QUOTIENT | QUOTIENT |
| 10115 | **RABBET PLANE, REBATE PLANE** | FEUILLERET | FALZHOBEL |
| 10116 | **RABBLE** | RINGARD | SCHÜREISEN |
| 10117 | **RACE (TO)** | EMBALLER, EMBALLER (S') | DURCHGEHEN (MASCHINE) |
| 10118 | **RACING** | EMBALLEMENT D'UN MOTEUR | DURCHGEHEN EINER MASCHINE |
| 10119 | **RACK** | CREMAILLERE | ZAHNSTANGE |
| 10120 | **RACK AND PINION** | CREMAILLERE ET PIGNON, ENGRENAGE PAR ROUE DENTEE ET CREMAILLERE | ZAHNSTANGENGETRIEBE |
| 10121 | **RACK AND PINION JACK** | CRIC, LEVE-ROUE | ZAHNSTANGENWINDE, WAGENWINDE |
| 10122 | **RACK COMPASSES** | COMPAS A CREMAILLERE | BOGENZIRKEL MIT GEZAHNTEM BOGEN |
| 10123 | **RACK INDEXING ATTACHMENT** | MECANISME D'INDEXAGE POUR CREMAILLERE | ZAHNSTANGENTEILVORRICHTUNG |
| 10124 | **RACK LINK OU CONTROL ROD** | TIGE DE CREMAILLERE | ZAHNSTANGE |
| 10125 | **RADIAL** | RADIAL | RADIAL |
| 10126 | **RADIAL (PLY) TYRE** | PNEU A CARCASSE RADIALE | RADIALREIFEN |
| 10127 | **RADIAL ACCELERATION** | ACCELERATION CENTRIFUGE | FLIEHKRAFTBESCHLEUNIGUNG |
| 10128 | **RADIAL ARM** | BRAS RADIAL | AUSLEGERARM |
| 10129 | **RADIAL ARM DRILLING MACHINE** | MACHINE A PERCER RADIALE | RADIALBOHRMASCHINE |

# RAD
258

| | | | |
|---|---|---|---|
| 10130 | **RADIAL BALL BEARING** | ROULEMENT A BILLES A CHARGE RADIALE, ROULEMENT A POUSSEE LATERALE | KUGELQUERDRUCKLAGER, RADIALKUGELLAGER |
| 10131 | **RADIAL BEAM / RAFTER** | POUTRE RAYONNANTE | RADIALTRÄGER, TRÄGER (EINGESPANNTER) |
| 10132 | **RADIAL COMPONENT** | COMPOSANTE RADIALE | RADIALKOMPONENTE |
| 10133 | **RADIAL DISPLACEMENT** | DEPLACEMENT RADIAL | RADIALE VERSCHIEBUNG |
| 10134 | **RADIAL DRILL PRESS, RADIAL DRILLING MACHINE** | PERCEUSE RADIALE | RADIALBOHRMASCHINE |
| 10135 | **RADIAL ENGINE** | MOTEUR EN ETOILE | STERNMOTOR |
| 10136 | **RADIAL FLOW TURBINE** | TURBINE RADIALE | RADIALTURBINE |
| 10137 | **RADIAL PROJECTION** | PROJECTION CENTRALE | ZENTRALPROJEKTION |
| 10138 | **RADIAN** | RADIAN | RADIAN |
| 10139 | **RADIANT ENERGY** | ENERGIE DE RAYONNEMENT | ENERGIE (STRAHLENDE) |
| 10140 | **RADIANT HEAT** | CHALEUR RADIANTE, CHALEUR RAYONNANTE | STRAHLUNGSWÄRME, WÄRME (STRAHLENDE) |
| 10141 | **RADIATE (TO)** | RAYONNER | STRAHLEN |
| 10142 | **RADIATING SURFACE** | SURFACE RAYONNANTE | FLÄCHE (STRAHLENDE), EMMISSIONSFLÄCHE |
| 10143 | **RADIATION** | RADIATION, RAYONNEMENT | AUSSTRAHLUNG, RADIATION, STRAHLENEMISSION |
| 10144 | **RADIATION CONSTANT** | CONSTANTE DE RADIATION | STRAHLUNGSKONSTANTE |
| 10145 | **RADIATION LOSS** | PERTE DE CHALEUR PAR RAYONNEMENT | STRAHLUNGSWÄRMEVERLUST |
| 10146 | **RADIATION OF HEAT** | RAYONNEMENT DE LA CHALEUR | WÄRMESTRAHLUNG |
| 10147 | **RADIATION OF LIGHT, LUMINOUS RADIATION** | RAYONNEMENT IRRADIATION DE LA LUMIERE | LICHTSTRAHLUNG |
| 10148 | **RADIATOR** | RADIATEUR | KÜHLER |
| 10149 | **RADIATOR (FOR COOLING)** | RADIATEUR DE REFROIDISSEMENT | KÜHLER (FÜR MOTOREN) |
| 10150 | **RADIATOR (FOR HEATING)** | RADIATEUR DE CHAUFFAGE | HEIZKÖRPER, HEIZELEMENT, RADIATOR |
| 10151 | **RADIATOR CAP** | BOUCHON DE RADIATEUR | KÜHLERVERSCHRAUBUNG |
| 10152 | **RADIATOR COWL** | CALANDRE DE RADIATEUR | KÜHLERVERKLEIDUNG |
| 10153 | **RADIATOR VALVE** | ROBINET DE RADIATEUR | HEIZUNGS-REGULIERVENTIL |
| 10154 | **RADICAL** | RADICAL | RADIKAL (CHEM.) |
| 10155 | **RADIO METALLURGY** | RADIOMETALLOGRAPHIE | ROENTGENMETALLOGRAPHIE |
| 10156 | **RADIO SUPRESSOR** | ANTI-PARASITE | STÖRSCHUTZ |
| 10157 | **RADIOACTIVE** | RADIO-ACTIF | RADIOAKTIV |
| 10158 | **RADIOACTIVE SUBSTANCES** | SUBSTANCES RADIOACTIVES | SUBSTANZEN (RADIOAKTIVE) |
| 10159 | **RADIOACTIVE, RADIUM EMANATION, NITON** | RADON, EMANATION | EMANATION DES RADIUMS |
| 10160 | **RADIOACTIVITY** | RADIO-ACTIVITE | RADIOAKTIVITÄT |
| 10161 | **RADIOGRAPH** | RADIOGRAPHIE | ROENTGENBILD |
| 10162 | **RADIOGRAPHIC INSPECTION** | EXAMEN RADIOGRAPHIQUE | ROENTGENUNTERSUCHUNG |
| 10163 | **RADIOGRAPHY** | RADIOGRAPHIE | RÖNTGENPHOTOGRAPHIE, RADIOGRAPHIE |
| 10164 | **RADIOLOGY** | RADIOLOGIE | RADIOLOGIE, STRAHLENKUNDE |
| 10165 | **RADIUM** | RADIUM | RADIUM |
| 10166 | **RADIUS** | RAYON | HALBMESSER, RADIUS |
| 10167 | **RADIUS CUTTING** | CHANTOURNAGE | AUSKEHLEN |
| 10168 | **RADIUS OF CURVATURE** | RAYON DE COURBURE | KRÜMMUNGSHALBMESSER, BIEGEHALBMESSER, ABRUNDUNGSHALBMESSER, WÖLBHALBMESSER |
| 10169 | **RADIUS OF INERTIA, RADIUS OF GYRATION** | RAYON DE GIRATION, RAYON DE ROTATION | TRÄGHEITSHALBMESSER, DREHUNGSHALBMESSER |

| | | | |
|---|---|---|---|
| 10170 | **RADIUS VECTOR** | RAYON VECTEUR | FAHRSTRAHL, LEITSTRAHL, RADIUSVEKTOR |
| 10171 | **RAG** | PIQURE | WALZNARBE |
| 10172 | **RAG BOLT, LEWIS BOLT** | BOULON DE SCELLEMENT | STEINSCHRAUBE |
| 10173 | **RAG WHEEL** | DISQUE EN DRAP | TUCHSCHEIBE, SCHWABBELSCHEIBE |
| 10174 | **RAGGED ROLL** | CYLINDRE RUGUEUX | WALZE (RAUHE) |
| 10175 | **RAIL** | RAIL | SCHIENE, FAHRSCHIENE |
| 10176 | **RAIL AND FISH PLATE DRILLING MACHINE** | MACHINE A PERCER RAILS ET ECLISSES | SCHIENEN U. LASCHENBOHRMASCHINE |
| 10177 | **RAIL STEEL PRODUCTS** | PRODUITS EN ACIER A RAIL | SCHIENENSTAHL (UMGEWALZTER) |
| 10178 | **RAIN SPOTTING** | TACHES D'EAU (DE PLUIE) | REGENWASSERFLECKEN |
| 10179 | **RAIN WATER** | EAU PLUVIALE | REGENWASSER |
| 10180 | **RAISE TO A POWER (TO)** | ELEVER A UNE PUISSANCE | ERHEBEN (IN EINE POTENZ, POTENZIEREN |
| 10181 | **RAISED PATTERN PLATE** | TOLE LARMEE | TRÄNENBLECH |
| 10182 | **RAISED WATER LEVEL** | RETENUE D'EAU | STAU, ANSTAUUNG |
| 10183 | **RAISED-UP FLANGE** | BRIDE A FACE SURELEVEE | FLANSCH (ÜBERHÖHTER) |
| 10184 | **RAISING TEST** | ESSAI D'EMBOUTISSAGE | TREIBPROBE |
| 10185 | **RAISING THE SPEED** | AUGMENTATION DE VITESSE | GESCHWINDIGKEITSERHÖHUNG, STEIGERUNG DER GESCHWINDIGKEIT |
| 10186 | **RAKE ANGLE** | ANGLE DE COUPE | SPANWINKEL, BRUSTWINKEL |
| 10187 | **RAKER SET** | DENTURE AVOYEE | SÄGEVERZAHNUNG (GESCHRÄNKTE) |
| 10188 | **RAM** | COULISSEAU, PISTON DE VERIN | STÖSSEL, SCHLITTEN, ARBEITSZYLINDER |
| 10189 | **RAM (TO), TAMP (TO)** | DAMER | FESTSTAMPFEN |
| 10190 | **RAM-TYPE VERTICAL RILLING-MACHINE** | FRAISEUSE RADIALE A COULISSE | RÄUMMASCHINE (SENKRECHTE) |
| 10191 | **RAM'S HORN** | CROCHET DOUBLE, CROCHET A TETE DE BELIER | DOPPELHAKEN, WIDDERKOPF |
| 10192 | **RAMIE FIBRE, CHINA GRASS, RHEA** | RAMIE, CHINA-GRASS | RAMIE, RAMIEFASER |
| 10193 | **RAMMED CONCRETE** | BETON DAME | STAMPFBETON |
| 10194 | **RAMMING** | SERRE, SERRAGE | STAMPFEN |
| 10195 | **RAMMING, TAMPING** | DAMAGE | STAMPFEN, FESTSTAMPFEN |
| 10196 | **RAMSBOTTOM PISTON** | PISTON SUEDOIS, PISTON RAMSBOTTOM | SCHWEDISCHER KOLBEN, RAMSBOTTOMKOLBEN |
| 10197 | **RANCID OIL** | HUILE RANCE | ÖL (RANZIGES) |
| 10198 | **RANDOM ACCESS** | ACCES DIRECT | ZUGRIFF (DIREKTER) |
| 10199 | **RANDOMLY ORIENTAETED** | ORIENTE AU HASARD | REGELLOS ORIENTIERT |
| 10200 | **RANGE** | GAMME | BEREICH |
| 10201 | **RANGE OF A MEASURING INSTRUMENT** | ETENDUE DE L'ECHELLE D'UN INSTRUMENT | MESSBEREICH, ANZEIGEBEREICH EINES INSTRUMENTS |
| 10202 | **RANGE OF SOUND** | PORTEE DU SON | REICHWEITE DES SCHALLES |
| 10203 | **RANKINE DIAGRAM** | DIAGRAMME RANKINISE, TOTALISE | DIAGRAMM (RANKINISIERTES) |
| 10204 | **RAPE SEED OIL; COLZA OIL** | HUILE DE COLZA, HUILE DE NAVETTE | RÜBÖL |
| 10205 | **RAPID COMBUSTION** | COMBUSTION VIVE | VERBRENNUNG (LEBHAFTE) |
| 10206 | **RAPID STEEL DRILL** | MECHE A COUPE RAPIDE | SCHNELLBOHRER |
| 10207 | **RAPID TOOL STEEL** | ACIER RAPIDE A OUTILS | WERKZEUGSCHNELLSTAHL |
| 10208 | **RAPID TRAVERSE** | AVANCE RAPIDE | SCHNELLGANG |
| 10209 | **RAPIDLY ROTATING, REVOLVING SHAFT** | ARBRE A GRANDE VITESSE | WELLE (SCHNELLAUFENDE) |
| 10210 | **RARE EARTHS** | TERRES RARES | ERDEN (SELTENE) |
| 10211 | **RAREFACTION OF A GAS** | RAREFACTION D'UN GAZ | VERDÜNNUNG EINES GASES |

# RAR

| | | | |
|---|---|---|---|
| 10212 | **RAREFACTION OF AIR** | RAREFACTION DE L'AIR | LUFTVERDÜNNUNG |
| 10213 | **RAREFIED AIR** | AIR RAREFIE | LUFT (VERDÜNNTE) |
| 10214 | **RAREFY A GAS (TO)** | RAREFIER UN GAZ | VERDÜNNEN (EIN GAS) |
| 10215 | **RASP** | RAPE | RASPEL |
| 10216 | **RAT TAIL FILE** | LIME QUEUE DE RAT | RATTENSCHWANZ |
| 10217 | **RATATING MOORING SYSTEM** | FLOTTEUR DE STOCKAGE ET D'ACCOSTAGE | MOORINGSYSTEM (DREHBARES) |
| 10218 | **RATCHET** | CLIQUET (MECANISME POUR TRANSFORMER UN MOUVEMENT ALTERNATIF EN MOUVEMENT CONTINU) | RATSCHE, RÄTSCHE, KNARRE |
| 10219 | **RATCHET BRACE** | CLIQUET POUR PERCER, RACCAGNAC | BOHRKNARRE, BOHRRATSCHE |
| 10220 | **RATCHET EFFECT** | EFFET DE CLIQUET | SPERRKLINKEEFFEKT |
| 10221 | **RATCHET GEAR COUPLING** | ACCOUPLEMENT, MANCHON A CLIQUETS | FREILAUFKUPPLUNG |
| 10222 | **RATCHET JACK** | VERIN A CLIQUET | SCHRAUBENWINDE MIT RATSCHE |
| 10223 | **RATCHET LEVER** | LEVIER A CLIQUET | SPERRADHEBEL, SCHALTHEBEL, KLINKENHEBEL |
| 10224 | **RATCHET SPANNER** | CLEF A CLIQUET | KNARRENSCHRAUBENSCHLÜSSEL |
| 10225 | **RATCHET WHEEL, DOG WHEEL** | ROUE A ROCHET, ROCHET, ROUE DENTEE A CLIQUET | KLINKENRAD, SCHALTRAD, SPERRAD |
| 10226 | **RATE** | TAUX, VITESSE | SATZ, VERHÄLTNIS, GESCHWINDIGKEIT |
| 10227 | **RATE OF COMBUSTION** | VITESSE DE COMBUSTION | BRENNGESCHWINDIGKEIT |
| 10228 | **RATE OF DELIVERY OF A PUMP** | DEBIT D'UNE POMPE | FÖRDERMENGE, LIEFERMENGE EINER PUMPE |
| 10229 | **RATE OF DEPOSITION** | VITESSE DE DEPOT | ABSCHEIDUNGSGESCHWINDGKEIT |
| 10230 | **RATE OF FLAME PROPAGATION** | VITESSE DE PROPAGATION DE LA FLAMME | ZÜNDGESCHWINDIGKEIT |
| 10231 | **RATE OF HEATING** | MONTEE EN TEMPERATURE | TEMPERATURANSTIEG |
| 10232 | **RATE OF OIL FLOW** | VITESSE D'ECOULEMENT D'HUILE | ÖLDURCHLÄSSIGKEITSMASS |
| 10233 | **RATED HORSE POWER** | PUISSANCE FISCALE, PUISSANCE NOMINALE | STEUERLEISTUNG |
| 10234 | **RATIO** | RAPPORT, QUOTIENT | VERHÄLTNIS |
| 10235 | **RATIONAL NUMBER** | NOMBRE RATIONNEL, COMMENSURABLE | ZAHL (RATIONALE) |
| 10236 | **RATTAN CANE** | ROTIN, JONC DES INDES | ROHR (SPANISCHES) |
| 10237 | **RAW HIDE** | CUIR BRUT, CUIR VERT | ROHHAUT |
| 10238 | **RAW HIDE PINION** | PIGNON EN CUIR VERT | ROHHAUTRITZEL |
| 10239 | **RAW MATERIAL** | MATIERE PREMIERE | ROHSTOFF, ROHMATERIAL |
| 10240 | **RAW UNTREATED WATER** | EAU ORDINAIRE | ROHWASSER |
| 10241 | **RAYING** | IRRADIATION | BESTRAHLUNG |
| 10242 | **RAYS** | RAYONS | STRAHLEN |
| 10243 | **RE-ENTRANT CORNER ANGLE** | ANGLE RENTRANT | ECKE (EINSPRINGENDE), WINKEL (EINSPRINGENDER) |
| 10244 | **RE-ERECT (TO)** | REMONTER | WIEDERZUSAMMENSETZEN |
| 10245 | **RE-ERECTION** | REMONTAGE | WIEDERZUSAMMENSETZUNG |
| 10246 | **RE-UTILISATION** | REUTILISATION, REEMPLOI | WIEDERVERWERTUNG, WIEDERVERWENDUNG |
| 10247 | **REACTANCE** | REACTANCE | BLINDWIDERSTAND, REAKTANZ |
| 10248 | **REACTION** | FORCE REACTIVE, REACTION | RÜCKWIRKUNG, GEGENKRAFT, REAKTION |
| 10249 | **REACTION LIMIT** | LIMITE DE REACTION | REAKTIONSGRENZE |

| | | | |
|---|---|---|---|
| 10250 | **REACTION, PRESSURE TURBINE** | TURBINE A REACTION, TURBINE A PRESSION INTERIEURE | ÜBERDRUCKTURBINE, REAKTIONSTURBINE |
| 10251 | **REACTOR (NUCL.)** | REACTEUR | REAKTOR (KERN) |
| 10252 | **READ (TO)** | LIRE | LESEN |
| 10253 | **READ-OUT** | VISUALISATION, AFFICHAGE | ANZEIGE |
| 10254 | **READING** | LECTURE | ABLESEN, ABLESUNG |
| 10255 | **READJUST (TO)** | RETOUCHER LE REGLAGE | NACHSTELLEN |
| 10256 | **READJUSTEMENT** | RETOUCHE DE REGLAGE, REGLAGE CONSECUTIF | NACHSTELLEN, NACHSTELLUNG |
| 10257 | **REAGENT** | REACTIF | REAGENS |
| 10258 | **REAL FOCUS** | FOYER REEL | BRENNPUNKT (WIRKLICHER), BRENNPUNKT (REELLER) |
| 10259 | **REAL IMAGE** | IMAGE REELLE | BILD (WIRKLICHES), BILD (REELLES) |
| 10260 | **REAL NUMBER** | NOMBRE REEL | ZAHL (IRRATIONALE) |
| 10261 | **REAL STRENGTH** | RESISTANCE EFFECTIVE | WIRKWIDERSTAND |
| 10262 | **REALGAR** | BISULFURE D'ARSENIC, REALGAR | ARSENDISULFID, ARSENSULFÜR, ROTES SCHWEFELARSEN, REALGAR, RAUSCHROT, ROTER ARSENIK |
| 10263 | **REAMER** | ALESOIR | REIBAHLE |
| 10264 | **REAMER HOLDER** | PORTE-ALESOIRS | REIBAHLENHALTER |
| 10265 | **REAR AXLE** | PONT ARRIERE (MOTEUR), ESSIEU ARRIERE (NON-MOTEUR) | HINTERACHSE |
| 10266 | **REAR VIEW MIRROR** | RETROVISEUR | RÜCKBLICKSPIEGEL |
| 10267 | **REAUMUR SCALE** | ECHELLE DE REAUMUR | REAUMURSKALA |
| 10268 | **REAUMUR THERMOMETER** | THERMOMETRE REAUMUR | THERMOMETER (ACHTZIGTEILIGES), REAUMURTHERMOMETER |
| 10269 | **REBATE, RABBET** | FEUILLURE | FALZ (BAUWESEN) |
| 10270 | **REBORE (TO)** | REALESER, RECTIFIER AVEC L'ALESOIR | NACHBOHREN |
| 10271 | **REBORING** | REALESAGE, RECTIFICATION A L'ALESOIR | NACHBOHREN |
| 10272 | **REBOUND** | REBONDISSEMENT | RÜCKSPRUNG, RÜCKPRALL |
| 10273 | **REBOUND (TO)** | REBONDIR | ZURÜCKPRALLEN, ZURÜCKSPRINGEN |
| 10274 | **RECALESCENCE** | DEGAGEMENT DE CHALEUR, RECALESCENCE | WÄRMEENTWICKLUNG, REKALESZENZ |
| 10275 | **RECARBURISING THE IRON** | RECARBURATION DU FER | RÜCKKOHLUNG DES EISENS |
| 10276 | **RECARBURIZER** | RECARBURANT | RÜCKKOHLUNGSMITTEL |
| 10277 | **RECEIVER** | RECIPIENT (D'UNE CORNUE), MATRAS | VORLAGE, RETORTENVORLAGE |
| 10278 | **RECEIVER SET** | POSTE RECEPTEUR | RADIOEMPFÄNGER |
| 10279 | **RECESS** | EVIDEMENT, NICHE | AUSSPARUNG, NISCHE |
| 10280 | **RECIPROCAL** | QUANTITE RECIPROQUE | WERT (REZIPROKER) |
| 10281 | **RECIPROCAL LATTICE** | RESEAU RECIPROQUE | GITTER (REZIPROKES) |
| 10282 | **RECIPROCAL MILLING** | FRAISAGE RECIPROQUE | PENDELFRÄSER |
| 10283 | **RECIPROCATING MOTION, TO-AND-FRO MOTION** | MOUVEMENT DE VA-ET-VIENT, MOUVEMENT ALTERNATIF, MOUVEMENT PENDULAIRE | BEWEGUNG (HIN-UND HERGEHENDE) |
| 10284 | **RECIPROCATING PUMP** | POMPE A PISTON A MOUVEMENT RECTILIGNE ET ALTERNATIF | PUMPE MIT GERADLINIG HIN UND HERGEHENDEM KOLBEN, KOLBENPUMPE |
| 10285 | **RECIPROCATING STEAM ENGINE** | MACHINE A PISTON | KOLBENDAMPFMASCHINE |
| 10286 | **RECOIL** | CHOC EN RETOUR, CHOC EN ARRIERE | RÜCKSCHLAG, RÜCKSTOSS |
| 10287 | **RECONDITIONING** | REMISE EN ETAT | WIEDERINSTANDSETZUNG |
| 10288 | **RECORD (TO), REGISTER (TO)** | ENREGISTRER | AUFZEICHNEN, REGISTRIEREN |

**REC** 262

| | | | |
|---|---|---|---|
| 10289 | **RECORDER, RECORDING INSTRUMENT** | ENREGISTREUR, INSTRUMENT ENREGISTREUR | SCHREIBER, SELBSTAUFZEICHNENDES INSTRUMENT, REGISTRIERENDES INSTRUMENT, SELBSTSCHREIBER |
| 10290 | **RECORDING DRUM** | TAMBOUR, CYLINDRE TOURNANT D'UN ENREGISTREUR | TROMMEL, WALZE EINER REGISTRIERVORRICHTUNG, REGISTRIERTROMMEL, REGISTRIERWALZE |
| 10291 | **RECORDING DYNAMOMETER, DYNAMOGRAPH** | DYNAMOGRAPHE | DYNAMOMETER MIT SCHREIBVORRICHTUNG, DYNAMOGRAPH |
| 10292 | **RECORDING REGISTERING PRESSURE GAUGE** | MANOMETRE ENREGISTREUR | MANOMETER (REGISTRIERENDES) |
| 10293 | **RECORDING REGISTERING THERMOMETER, THERMOMETROGRAPH** | THERMOMETRE ENREGISTREUR, THERMOGRAPHE | THERMOMETER (AUFZEICHNENDES), THERMOMETER SCHREIBENDES, THERMOMETER REGISTRIERENDES, THERMOGRAPH |
| 10294 | **RECORDING, SELF REGISTERING APPARATUS** | APPAREIL ENREGISTREUR | SCHREIBWERK, SCHREIBZEUG, SCHREIBVORRICHTUNG, REGISTRIERVORRICHTUNG |
| 10295 | **RECOVER (TO)** | RECUPERER | WIEDERGEWINNEN, ZURÜCKGEWINNEN |
| 10296 | **RECOVERY** | RECUPERATION, RESTAURATION | RÜCKGEWINNUNG, WIEDERVERWERTUNG, WIEDERGEWINNUNG, ZURÜCKGEWINNUNG |
| 10297 | **RECRYSTALLISATION** | RECRISTALLISATION | REKRISTALLISATION |
| 10298 | **RECRYSTALLIZATION TEMPERATURE** | TEMPERATURE DE RECRISTALLISATION | REKRISTALLISATIONSTEMPERATUR |
| 10299 | **RECTANGLE** | RECTANGLE | RECHTECK |
| 10300 | **RECTANGULAR COORDINATE ELECTRO-DISCHARGE JIG-BORING MACHINE** | MACHINE A POINTER PAR ETINCELAGE EN COORDONNEES RECTANGULAIRES | FUNKENEROSIONS-LEHRENBOHR-MASCHINE (IN RECHTECKIGEN KOORDINATEN ARBEITEND) |
| 10301 | **RECTANGULAR COORDINATES** | COORDONNEES ORTHOGONALES, COORDONNEES RECTANGULAIRES | KOORDINATEN (RECHTWINKLIGE) |
| 10302 | **RECTANGULAR CROSS SECTION** | SECTION RECTANGULAIRE | QUERSCHNITT (RECHTECKIGER) |
| 10303 | **RECTANGULAR LOAD** | CHARGE RECTANGULAIRE | RECHTECKLAST |
| 10304 | **RECTANGULAR MESH** | MAILLE RECTANGULAIRE | RECHTECKMASCHE |
| 10305 | **RECTANGULAR PARALLELOPIPED** | PARALLELEPIPEDE RECTANGLE | PARALLELEPIPED (RECHTWINKLIGES), RECHTKANT |
| 10306 | **RECTANGULAR PLATE SPRING** | RESSORT RECTANGULAIRE A LAME PLATE | RECHTECKFEDER |
| 10307 | **RECTANGULAR PLATE SPRING WITH END TAPERED** | RESSORT A LAME RECTANGULAIRE A PROFIL PARABOLOIDE | RECHTECKFEDER (ZUGESCHÄRFTE) |
| 10308 | **RECTANGULAR PROTRACTOR** | RAPPORTEUR A FORME D'EQUERRE | WINKELTRANSPORTEUR |
| 10309 | **RECTANGULAR SQUARE SCREW HEAD BOLT HEAD** | TETE CARREE D'UNE VIS | VIERKANTSCHRAUBENKOPF |
| 10310 | **RECTANGULAR, RIGHT-ANGLED** | RECTANGLE | RECHTWINKLIG |
| 10311 | **RECTIFICATION** | RECTIFICATION (CHIM.) | REKTIFIKATION (CHEM.) |
| 10312 | **RECTIFICATION** | REDRESSEMENT, DEMODULATION | GLEICHRICHTUNG, DEMODULATION |
| 10313 | **RECTIFIED SPIRIT** | ALCOOL RECTIFIE | ALKOHOL (REKTIFIZIERTER) |
| 10314 | **RECTIFIER** | REDRESSEUR DE COURANT | GLEICHRICHTER |
| 10315 | **RECTIFIER ANODE** | PLAQUE DE REDRESSEUR | GLEICHRICHTERANODE |
| 10316 | **RECTIFIER CATHODE** | CATHODE DE REDRESSEUR | GLEICHRICHTERKATODE |
| 10317 | **RECTIFIER TUBE** | TUBE REDRESSEUR | GLEICHRICHTERRÖHRE |
| 10318 | **RECTIFY (TO)** | RECTIFIER (CHIM.) | REKTIFIZIEREN (CHEM.) |
| 10319 | **RECTILINEAR** | RECTILIGNE | GERADLINIG |
| 10320 | **RECTILINEAR MOTION** | MOUVEMENT RECTILIGNE | BEWEGUNG (GERADLINIGE) |
| 10321 | **RECUPERATIVE FURNACE** | FOUR A REGENERATION | REKUPERATIVOFEN |
| 10322 | **RECUPERATOR** | RECUPERATEUR | REKUPERATOR |

| | | | |
|---|---|---|---|
| 10323 | **RECUT FILES (TO)** | RETAILLER LES LIMES | FEILEN AUFHAUEN |
| 10324 | **RECUTTING FILES** | RETAILLAGE DES LIMES | FEILENAUFHAUEN |
| 10325 | **RED BRASS** | LAITON ROUGE | ROTMESSING |
| 10326 | **RED BRONZE** | BRONZE AU ZING | ROTGUSS |
| 10327 | **RED FUMES** | FUMEES ROUSSES | RAUCH (BRAUNER) |
| 10328 | **RED HARDNESS** | DURETE A CHAUD | WARMHÄRTE |
| 10329 | **RED HEAT** | CHAUDE, CHALEUR ROUGE, ROUGE | ROTGLUT |
| 10330 | **RED HEAT (OF A)** | ROUGE AU FEU, CHAUFFE AU ROUGE | ROTWARM, ROTGLÜHEND |
| 10331 | **RED HEAT TEST** | ESSAI DE RESISTANCE AU CHAUD ROUGE | ROTBRUCHPROBE |
| 10332 | **RED LEAD PUTTY** | MASTIC AU MINIUM, MASTIC ROUGE | MENNIGEKITT, MINIUMKITT |
| 10333 | **RED LEAD, MINIUM** | MINIUM, OXYDE SALIN DE PLOMB | BLEIMENNIGE, ROTES BLEIOXYD |
| 10334 | **RED PHOSPHORUS** | PHOSPHORE ROUGE | ROTER PHOSPHOR, AMORPHER PHOSPHOR |
| 10335 | **RED RUST** | ROUILLE | ROST (EISENOXYD) |
| 10336 | **RED SANDSTONE** | GRES ROUGE | SANDSTEIN (ROTER) |
| 10337 | **RED SHORT** | CASSANT A CHAUD | WARMBRÜCHIG |
| 10338 | **RED SHORT IRON, HOT SHORT IRON** | FER CASSANT A CHAUD, FER DE COULEUR, FER METIS | EISEN (ROTBRÜCHIGES) |
| 10339 | **RED SHORTNESS** | FRAGILITE A CHAUD | WARMBRÜCHIGKEIT |
| 10340 | **REDDLE, RED CHALK** | TERRE RUBRIQUE, RUBRIQUE | RÖTEL |
| 10341 | **REDISTILLED ZINC** | ZINC REFONDU | ZINK (UMGESCHMOLZENES) |
| 10342 | **REDUCE (TO)** | REDUIRE (CHIM.) | REDUZIEREN (CHEM.) |
| 10343 | **REDUCED SCALE** | ECHELLE REDUITE | MASSSTAB (IN VERJÜNGTEM), MASSSTÄBLICH VERKLEINERT |
| 10344 | **REDUCED TEMPERATURE** | TEMPERATURE REDUITE | TEMPERATUR (HERABGESETZTE) |
| 10345 | **REDUCING** | REDUCTEUR, REDUCTRICE | REDUZIEREND, REDUKTIONS..., REDUZIER... |
| 10346 | **REDUCING AGENT** | REDUCTEUR, AGENT REDUCTEUR | REDUKTIONSMITTEL |
| 10347 | **REDUCING ATMOSPHERE** | ATMOSPHERE REDUCTRICE | REDUKTIONSATMOSPHÄRE |
| 10348 | **REDUCING COUPLING** | REDUCTION FEMELLE-FEMELLE | REDUZIERMUFFE |
| 10349 | **REDUCING FLAME** | FLAMME REDUCTRICE | FLAMME (REDUZIERENDE) |
| 10350 | **REDUCING FLANGE** | BRIDE A REDUCTION | ÜBERGANGSFLANSCH, REDUKTIONSFLANSCH |
| 10351 | **REDUCING NIPPLE** | MANCHON REDUCTEUR | REDUZIERNIPPEL |
| 10352 | **REDUCING PIPE, REDUCER, REDUCING PIECE** | TUBE DE REDUCTION, RACCORD CONIQUE | ÜBERGANGSROHR, VERJÜNGUNGSROHR, REDUKTIONSROHR |
| 10353 | **REDUCING ROLLS** | TRAIN REDUCTEUR | REDUZIERWALZSTRASSE |
| 10354 | **REDUCING TEMPERATURE** | TEMPERATURE DE REDUCTION | REDUKTIONSTEMPERATUR |
| 10355 | **REDUCING VALVE, PRESSURE REGULATOR, PRESSURE REGULTATING VALVE** | SOUPAPE DE REDUCTION, REDUCTEUR DE PRESSION, DETENDEUR | DRUCKMINDERVENTIL, DRUCKREGLER, DRUCKMINDERER, DRUCKMINDERUNGSVENTIL, REDUZIERVENTIL |
| 10356 | **REDUCTION** | REDUCTION (CHIM.) | REDUKTION (CHEM.) |
| 10357 | **REDUCTION** | DEMULTIPLICATION | UNTERSETZUNG |
| 10358 | **REDUCTION CONE** | CONE DE REDUCTION | EINSATZFUTTER |
| 10359 | **REDUCTION FURNACE** | FOUR REDUCTEUR | REDUZIEROFEN |
| 10360 | **REDUCTION GEAR RATIO** | RAPPORT DE REDUCTION | UNTERSETZUNGSVERHÄLTNIS |
| 10361 | **REDUCTION OF AREA** | STRICTION | EINSCHNÜRUNG, KONTRAKTION |
| 10362 | **REDUCTION OF AREA OF CROSS SECTION** | DIMINUTION, REDUCTION DE LA SECTION TRANSVERSALE | QUERSCHNITTSVERMINDERUNG |
| 10363 | **REDUCTION OF SPEED, REDUCING THE SPEED** | REDUCTION DE VITESSE | GESCHWINDIGKEITSVERMINDERUNG, HERABSETZUNG DER GESCHWINDIGKEIT |

# REE 264

| | | | |
|---|---|---|---|
| 10364 | **REDUNDANCY** | REDONDANCE | REDUNDANZ |
| 10365 | **REED COMPARATOR** | COMPARATEUR A LAMES | LAMELLENVERGLEICHSMESSER |
| 10366 | **REFERENCE GAUGE** | RAPPORTEUR FIXE, JAUGE DE REFERENCE | PRÜFLEHRE |
| 10367 | **REFERENCE MARK** | INDICE DE RAPPEL | BEZUGSZEICHEN |
| 10368 | **REFERENCE POINT** | POINT DE REFERENCE | BEZUGSPUNKT |
| 10369 | **REFERENCE TEMPERATURE** | TEMPERATURE DE REPERE | BEZUGSTEMPERATUR |
| 10370 | **REFINE (TO)** | AFFINER | REINIGEN, LÄUTERN, RAFFINIEREN |
| 10371 | **REFINE A METAL (TO)** | AFFINER UN METAL | METALL VEREDELN (EIN) |
| 10372 | **REFINED** | PURIFIE, RAFFINE | RAFFINIERT |
| 10373 | **REFINED OIL** | HUILE EPUREE | ÖL (GELÄUTERTES), ÖL (RAFFINIERTES) |
| 10374 | **REFINED PRODUCT** | PRODUIT DE RAFFINAGE | RAFFINAT |
| 10375 | **REFINERY** | RAFFINERIE | RAFFINERIE |
| 10376 | **REFINERY FLARE** | TORCHERE DE RAFFINERIE | RAFFINERIEFACKEL |
| 10377 | **REFINING** | AFFINAGE, RAFFINAGE | AFFINIEREN, VEREDELUNG, REINIGEN, LÄUTERN, RAFFINIEREN |
| 10378 | **REFINING A METAL** | RAFFINAGE D'UN METAL | VEREDELUNG EINES METALLS |
| 10379 | **REFINING FURNACE** | FOUR D'AFFINAGE | FRISCHOFEN |
| 10380 | **REFINING PROCESS** | PROCEDE D'AFFINAGE | FRISCHVERFAHREN |
| 10381 | **REFINING REMPERATURE** | TEMPERATURE D'AFFINAGE | FRISCHUNGSTEMPERATUR |
| 10382 | **REFLECT (TO)** | REFLETER, REFLECHIR | ZURÜCKSTRAHLEN, ZURÜCKWERFEN, REFLEKTIEREN |
| 10383 | **REFLECTED LIGHT** | LUMIERE REFLECHIE | LICHT (ZURÜCKGEWORFENES), LICHT (REFLEKTIERTES) |
| 10384 | **REFLECTED RAY** | RAYON REFLECHI | STRAHL (ZUÜCKGEWORFENER), STRAHL (REFLEKTIERTER) |
| 10385 | **REFLECTING SURFACE** | SURFACE REFLECHISSANTE | FLÄCHE (ZURÜCKSTRAHLENDE), FLÄCHE (REFLEKTIERENDE) |
| 10386 | **REFLECTING TELESCOPE** | TELESCOPE | SPIEGELFERNROHR, TELESKOP |
| 10387 | **REFLECTION** | DIFFRACTION, REFLEXION | REFLEKTION, REFLEXION |
| 10388 | **REFLECTION GRATING** | RESEAU DE REFLEXION | REFLEXIONSGITTER |
| 10389 | **REFLECTION LOSS** | PERTE PAR REFLEXION | REFLEXIONSVERLUST |
| 10390 | **REFLECTION OF LIGHT** | REFLEXION DE LA LUMIERE | RÜCKSTRAHLUNG, REFLEXION DES LICHTES |
| 10391 | **REFLECTION RATIO** | RAPPORT DE REFLEXION | REFLEXIONSVERHÄLTNIS |
| 10392 | **REFLECTIVE, REFLECTING POWER** | POUVOIR REFLECHISSANT | RÜCKSTRAHLUNGSVERMÖGEN, REFLEXIONSVERMÖGEN |
| 10393 | **REFLECTIVITY** | POUVOIR REFLECHISSANT | REFLEXIONSVERMÖGEN |
| 10394 | **REFLECTOR** | REFLECTEUR | REFLEKTOR, LICHTSPIEGEL |
| 10395 | **REFLEX GAUGE** | INDICATEUR A REFRACTION | REFLEXIONS-WASSERSTANDSANZEIGER |
| 10396 | **REFLEX GLASS** | GLACE A REFRACTION | REFLEXIONSGLAS |
| 10397 | **REFRACTED RAY** | RAYON REFRACTE, BRISE | STRAHL (GEBROCHENER) |
| 10398 | **REFRACTING TELESCOPE, REFRACTOR** | LUNETTE D'APPROCHE | FERNROHR |
| 10399 | **REFRACTION** | REFRACTION | STRAHLENBRECHUNG |
| 10400 | **REFRACTION OF LIGHT** | REFRACTION DE LA LUMIERE | BRECHUNG DES LICHTES, LICHTBRECHUNG, REFRAKTION |
| 10401 | **REFRACTIVE MEDIUM** | MILIEU REFRACTIF, REFRINGENT | MEDIUM (STRAHLENBRECHENDES) |
| 10402 | **REFRACTIVE, REFRACTING** | REFRINGENT | LICHTBRECHEND |
| 10403 | **REFRACTIVITY** | POUVOIR REFRINGENT | LICHTBRECHUNGSVERMÖGEN, REFRAKTIONSVERMÖGEN |
| 10404 | **REFRACTOMETER** | REFRACTOMETRE | REFRAKTOMETER |

| | | | |
|---|---|---|---|
| 10405 | **REFRACTORINESS** | PROPRIETE REFRACTAIRE | FEUERFESTIGKEIT, FEUERBESTÄNDIGKEIT |
| 10406 | **REFRACTORY MORTAR** | COULIS, MORTIER REFRACTAIRE | MÖRTEL (FEUERFESTER) |
| 10407 | **REFRIGERATING MACHINE** | MACHINE FRIGORIFIQUE, MACHINE A FROID | KÄLTEMASCHINE |
| 10408 | **REFRIGERATING PLANT** | INSTALLATION DE REFRIGERATION | KÜHLANLAGE |
| 10409 | **REFRIGERATOR** | REFRIGERANT, REFRIGERATEUR | KÜHLER |
| 10410 | **REGENERATIVE FURNACE** | FOYER A RECUPERATION INTERMITTENTE, FOUR A REGENERATION | REGENERATIVFEUERUNG, REKUPERATIVOFEN |
| 10411 | **REGENERATIVE HEAT** | CHALEUR EMMAGASINEE | SPEICHERWÄRME |
| 10412 | **REGENERATOR** | REGENERATEUR, RECUPERATEUR, SYSTEME SIEMENS | REGENERATOR, WÄRMESPEICHER |
| 10413 | **REGISTER, REGISTERING FACE, RING** | BAGUE DE CENTRAGE | ZENTRIERRING, ZENTRIERLEISTE |
| 10414 | **REGULAR LAY** | CABLAGE ALTERNATIF, TORSION ALTERNATIVE | KREUZSCHLAG |
| 10415 | **REGULAR LAY WIRE ROPE** | CABLE METALLIQUE TORDU ALTERNATIF | KREUZGESCHLAGENES DRAHTSEIL, SPIRALSEIL |
| 10416 | **REGULAR POLYGON** | POLYGONE REGULIER | POLYGON (REGELMÄSSIGES), POLYGON (REGULÄRES) |
| 10417 | **REGULARITY OF MOTION** | REGULARITE DU MOUVEMENT | GLEICHFÖRMIGKEIT DER BEWEGUNG |
| 10418 | **REGULATING DEVICE** | DISPOSITIF DE REGLAGE | REGELVORRICHTUNG |
| 10419 | **REGULATION OF PRESSURE** | REGLAGE DE LA PRESSION | DRUCKREGLUNG |
| 10420 | **REGULATOR** | DETENDEUR | DRUCKMINDERER |
| 10421 | **REGULATOR, GOVERNOR** | REGULATEUR DE VITESSE, MODERATEUR | REGLER, REGULATOR |
| 10422 | **REGULUS** | REGULE | LAGERMETALL |
| 10423 | **REGULUS OF ANTIMONY** | REGULE D'ANTIMOINE | ANTIMONREGULUS |
| 10424 | **REHEAT (TO)** | RECHAUFFER | WIEDERERHITZEN |
| 10425 | **REHEATING** | RECHAUFFAGE, RECHAUFFEMENT | WIEDERERHITZEN, NACHWÄRMEN |
| 10426 | **REHEATING FURNACE** | FOUR A RECUIRE | NACHWÄRMOFEN |
| 10427 | **REINFORCEMENT OF WELD** | RENFORCEMENT DE LA SOUDURE | SCHWEISSNAHTÜBERHÖHUNG |
| 10428 | **REINFORCEMENT WELD** | SOUDAGE DE RENFORCEMENT | VERSTÄRKUNGSSCHWEISSNAHT |
| 10429 | **REINFORCING** | RENFORT | VERSTÄRKUNG |
| 10430 | **REINFORCING PLATE** | TOLE DE RENFORT, TOLE DOUBLANTE | VERSTÄRKUNGSBLECH |
| 10431 | **REJECTION** | REFUS DE RECEPTION, REBUT | ABNAHMEVERWEIGERUNG, ZÜRÜCKWEISUNG |
| 10432 | **RELATIVE HUMIDITY** | HUMIDITE RELATIVE | FEUCHTIGKEIT (RELATIVE) |
| 10433 | **RELATIVE HUMIDITY OF THE AIR** | DEGRE HYGROMETRIQUE DE L'AIR, HUMIDITE RELATIVE DE L'AIR | FEUCHTIGKEITSGRAD, RELATIVE FEUCHTIGKEIT DER LUFT |
| 10434 | **RELATIVE MOTION** | MOUVEMENT RELATIF | BEWEGUNG (GEGENSEITIGE), BEWEGUNG (RELATIVE) |
| 10435 | **RELAXATION** | RELAXATION, DETENTE | ENTSPANNUNG |
| 10436 | **RELEASE A BRAKE (TO)** | DESSERRER UN FREIN | LÖSEN (EINE BREMSE) |
| 10437 | **RELEASING CAM** | DOIGT DE DECLENCHEMENT | AUSLÖSEDAUMEN, AUSLÖSEFINGER |
| 10438 | **RELEASING LEVER** | LEVIER DE DECLENCHEMENT | AUSLÖSCHEBEL |
| 10439 | **RELIABILITY, SAFETY OF SERVICE** | SECURITE DE BON FONCTIONNEMENT, FIDELITE DE SERVICE, FIABILITE | BETRIEBSSICHERHEIT, ZUVERLÄSSIGKEIT |
| 10440 | **RELIABLE, SAFE** | FONCTIONNEMENT SUR (DE) | BETRIEBSSICHER |
| 10441 | **RELIEF VALVE** | SOUPAPE DE DECHARGE, CLAPET DE DECHARGE | DRUCKBEGRENZUNGSVENTIL, ÜBERDRUCKVENTIL |
| 10442 | **RELIEVING ARCH** | ARC DE SOUTENEMENT | STÜTZBOGEN |
| 10443 | **RELIEVING LATHE** | TOUR A DETALONNER | HINTERDREHBANK |

# REM

**266**

| | | | |
|---|---|---|---|
| 10444 | **RELUCTANCE, MAGNETIC RESISTANCE** | RESISTANCE MAGNETIQUE, RELUCTANCE | WIDERSTAND (MAGNETISCHER), RELUKTANZ |
| 10445 | **REMANENCE, REMANENT FLUX, REMANENT RESIDUAL MAGNETISM** | REMANENCE, MAGNETISME REMANENT, MAGNETISME RESIDUEL, AIMANTATION REMANENTE, AIMANTATION RESIDUELLE | RÜCKSTAND (MAGNETISCHER), MAGNETISMUS (REMANENTER), REMANENZ |
| 10446 | **REMELT (TO)** | REFONDRE | EINSCHMELZEN, UMSCHMELZEN |
| 10447 | **REMELTING** | REFONTE | EINSCHMELZEN, UMSCHMELZEN |
| 10448 | **REMOTE CONTROL** | COMMANDE A DISTANCE, TELECOMMANDE | FERNSTEUERUNG |
| 10449 | **REMOTE CONTROL GAUGING** | JAUGEAGE A DISTANCE, TELEJAUGEAGE | FERNEICHUNG, FERNMESSUNG |
| 10450 | **REMOVABLE CRANK** | MANIVELLE AMOVIBLE | EINSTECKKURBEL |
| 10451 | **REMOVAL AND REPLACE** | DEPOSE ET REMONTAGE | ABBAUEN UND ERSETZEN |
| 10452 | **REMOVAL EXTRACTION OF DUST** | EVACUATION DES POUSSIERES | ENTSTAUBEN, ENTSTAUBUNG |
| 10453 | **REMOVAL OF WASTE WATER** | EVACUATION DES EAUX RESIDUAIRES | ABWÄSSERBESEITIGUNG |
| 10454 | **REMOVAL, ELIMINATION OF THE IRON IN THE WATER** | ELIMINATION DU FER DE L'EAU | ENTEISENUNG DES WASSERS |
| 10455 | **REMOVE GASES (TO)** | EVACUER LES GAZ, DEGAZER | GASE ABFÜHREN |
| 10456 | **RENDER SOLUBLE (TO)** | SOLUBILISER | LÖSLICH MACHEN |
| 10457 | **RENEW A MACHINE PART (TO)** | RENOUVELER UN ORGANE DE MACHINE | MASCHINENTEIL ERNEUERN (EINEN) |
| 10458 | **RENEWAL OF A MACHINE PART** | RENOUVELLEMENT D'UN ORGANE DE MACHINE | ERNEUERUNG EINES MASCHINENTEILS |
| 10459 | **REPAIR** | REPARATION | AUSBESSERUNG, WIEDERINSTANDSETZUNG, REPARATUR |
| 10460 | **REPAIR (TO), MEND (TO)** | REPARER | AUSBESSERN, WIEDERINSTANDSETZEN, REPARIEREN |
| 10461 | **REPAIRING SHOP** | ATELIER D'ENTRETIEN, ATELIER DE REPARATION | REPARATURWERKSTÄTTE |
| 10462 | **REPETITION WORK** | CONSTRUCTION, FABRICATION, PRODUCTION, CONFECTION, TRAVAIL EN SERIE | REIHENANFERTIGUNG, SERIENBAU, SERIENFABRIKATION |
| 10463 | **REPLACE (TO), INERCHANGE (TO)** | REMPLACER, RECHANGER | AUSWECHSELN, AUSTAUSCHEN |
| 10464 | **REPLACEMENT OF A MACHINE PART** | RECHANGE D'UN ORGANE DE MACHINE | AUSWECHSLUNG EINES MASCHINENTEILS, AUSTAUSCH EINES MASCHINENTEILS |
| 10465 | **REPLICA** | EMPREINTE | ABDRUCK |
| 10466 | **REPRACTORIES** | MATERIAUX REFRACTAIRES | STOFFE (FEUERFESTE) |
| 10467 | **REPRODUCTION** | REPRODUCTION (RESULTAT) | VERVIELFÄLTIGUNG, REPRODUKTION, KOPIE |
| 10468 | **REPULSION** | REPULSION | ABSTOSSUNG |
| 10469 | **REQUIRED QUANTITY** | GRANDEUR CHERCHEE | GRÖSSE (GESUCHTE) |
| 10470 | **REROLLING** | RELAMINAGE | NACHWALZEN |
| 10471 | **RESERVOIR** | RESERVOIR | SAMMELBEHÄLTER |
| 10472 | **RESIDUAL ELASTICITY, ELASTIC AFTERWORKING** | ELASTICITE RESIDUELLE | NACHWIRKUNG (ELASTISCHE) |
| 10473 | **RESIDUAL INDUCTION** | REMANENCE | INDUKTION (REMANENTE) |
| 10474 | **RESIDUAL STRESS** | CONTRAINTE RESIDUELLE | EIGENSPANNUNG |
| 10475 | **RESIDUE** | RESIDU | RÜCKSTAND |
| 10476 | **RESIDUE OF COMBUSTION** | RESIDU DE LA COMBUSTION | VEBRENNUNGSRÜCKSTAND |
| 10477 | **RESILIENCE** | RESILENCE, RESISTANCE VIVE | FORMÄNDERUNG (ELASTISCHE), KERRSCHLAGZÄHIGKEIT |
| 10478 | **RESIN, ROSIN** | RESINE | HARZ |

**RES**

| | | | |
|---|---|---|---|
| 10479 | **RESINIFEROUS** | RENFERMANT DE LA RESINE | HARZHALTIG |
| 10480 | **RESINIFICATION, GUMMING** | RESINIFICATION | VERHARZUNG, VERHARZEN |
| 10481 | **RESINIFY (TO), GUM (TO)** | RESINIFIER (SE) | VERHARZEN |
| 10482 | **RESINOUS CEMENT** | MASTIC RESINEUX, MASTIC A LA RESINE | HARZKITT |
| 10483 | **RESINOUS WOOD, TIMBER FROM CONIFEROUS TREES** | BOIS RESINEUX | NADELHOLZ |
| 10484 | **RESISTANCE / RESISTOR** | RESISTANCE, FORCE RESISTANCE | BESTÄNDIGKEIT, FESTIGKEIT, WIDERSTAND, WIDERSTANDSKRAFT |
| 10485 | **RESISTANCE AIR-FURNACE** | FOUR A ARC A RESISTANCE | LICHT BOGEN-WIDERSTANDSOFEN |
| 10486 | **RESISTANCE ALLOYS** | ALLIAGES POUR RESISTANCES ELECTRIQUES | WIDERTANDSLEGIERUNGEN |
| 10487 | **RESISTANCE BRAZING** | BRASAGE PAR RESISTANCE | WIDERSTANDSHARTLÖTEN |
| 10488 | **RESISTANCE BUTT WELDING** | SOUDAGE EN BOUT PAR RESISTANCE | WIDERSTANDSSTUMPFSCHWEISSUNG |
| 10489 | **RESISTANCE DIAGRAM** | DIAGRAMME DES RESISTANCES | WIDERSTANDSDIAGRAMM |
| 10490 | **RESISTANCE FURNACE** | FOUR ELECTRIQUE A RESISTANCE | WIDERSTANDSOFEN (ELEKTRISCHER) |
| 10491 | **RESISTANCE OF A CONDUCTOR** | RESISTANCE D'UN CONDUCTEUR | LEITUNGSWIDERSTAND (ELEKTR.) |
| 10492 | **RESISTANCE OF THE AIR, AIR RESISTANCE, WIND RESISTANCE** | RESISTANCE DE L'AIR | LUFTWIDERSTAND, LUFTREIBUNG |
| 10493 | **RESISTANCE SPOT WELDING** | SOUDAGE PAR POINTS PAR RESISTANCE | WIDERSTANDSPUNKTSCHWEISSEN |
| 10494 | **RESISTANCE STRAIN GAUGE** | JAUGE DE CONTRAINTE A RESISTANCE | WIDERSTANDSDEHNUNGSMESSTREIFEN |
| 10495 | **RESISTANCE THERMOMETER, PYROMETER** | PYROMETRE A RESISTANCE, PYROMETRE ELECTRIQUE | WIDERSTANDSTHERMOMETER, PLATINTHERMOMETER, WIDERSTANDSPYROMETER |
| 10496 | **RESISTANCE TO ACIDS** | INATTAQUABILITE AUX ACIDES | SÄUREFESTIGKEIT, SÄUREBESTÄNDIGKEIT |
| 10497 | **RESISTANCE TO MOTION** | RESISTANCE AU MOUVEMENT, RESISTANCE PASSIVE | SCHÄDLICHER WIDERSTAND, VERLUSTWIDERSTAND, BEWEGUNGSWIDERSTAND |
| 10498 | **RESISTANCE TO SLIPPING, RESISTANCE OF SLIDING FRICTION** | RESISTANCE AU GLISSEMENT | GLEITWIDERSTAND |
| 10499 | **RESISTANCE TO WEAR** | RESISTANCE A L'USURE | VERSCHLEISSFESTIGKEIT, VERSCHLEISSWIDERSTAND |
| 10500 | **RESISTANCE WELDING** | SOUDAGE PAR RESISTANCE | WIDERSTANDSSCHWEISSEN, WIDERSTANDSSCHWEISSUNG |
| 10501 | **RESISTANCE WIRE** | FIL POUR RESISTANCES ELECTRIQUES | WIDERSTANDSDRAHT |
| 10502 | **RESISTIBILITY** | RESISTANCE | WIDERSTANDSFÄHIGKEIT, WIDERSTANDSVERMÖGEN, BESTÄNDIGKEIT |
| 10503 | **RESISTIVITY, SPECIFIC RESISTANCE** | RESISTIVITE, RESISTANCE SPECIFIQUE ELECTRIQUE | LEITWIDERSTAND (SPEZIFISCHER) |
| 10504 | **RESOLUTION** | RESOLUTION | AUFLÖSUNG |
| 10505 | **RESOLUTION OF FORCES** | DECOMPOSITION DES FORCES | ZERLEGUNG VON KRÄFTEN |
| 10506 | **RESONANCE** | RESONANCE | MITSCHWINGEN, RESONANZ |
| 10507 | **RESQUARING** | CISAILLAGE | ZUSCHNEIDEN |
| 10508 | **RESTART (TO)** | REMETTRE EN MARCHE | GANG SETZEN (WIEDER IN) |
| 10509 | **RESTARTING** | REMISE EN MARCHE | WIEDERINGANGSETZEN |
| 10510 | **RESTRAINER** | INHIBITEUR | SPARBEIZE |
| 10511 | **RESTRIKING** | RECTIFICATION | NACHRICHTEN |
| 10512 | **RESULT OF TEST, TEST RESULT** | RESULTAT D'UNE EPREUVE | VERSUCHSERGEBNIS, PRÜFUNGSERGEBNIS, PRÜFUNGSRESULTAT |

# RET

| | | | |
|---|---|---|---|
| 10513 | **RESULTANT** | RESULTANTE | MITTELKRAFT, RESULTIERENDE, RESULTANTE |
| 10514 | **RETAINER NUT** | ECROU D'ARRET | SICHERUNGSSCHRAUBENMUTTER |
| 10515 | **RETAINING RING** | BAGUE DE RETENUE | SPRENGRING |
| 10516 | **RETAINING STRIP** | BAGUETTE DE RETENUE | HALTESTREIFEN |
| 10517 | **RETARDATION OF BOILING** | RETARD A L'EBULLITION | SIEDEVERZUG |
| 10518 | **RETARDED MOTION** | MOUVEMENT RETARDE | BEWEGUNG (VERZÖGERTE) |
| 10519 | **RETARDED VALVE CLOSING** | RETARD A LA FERMETURE DE LA SOUPAPE | VENTILSCHLUSS (VERSPÄTETER) |
| 10520 | **RETENTION OF HARDNESS** | DURETE APRES REVENU | ANLASSHÄRTE |
| 10521 | **RETENTION OF SHAPE** | RESISTANCE A LA DEFORMATION | FORMBESTÄNDIGKEIT |
| 10522 | **RETEST** | CONTRE-ESSAI | WIEDERHOLUNGSVERSUCH |
| 10523 | **RETORT** | CORNUE | RETORTE, DESTILLIERKOLBEN |
| 10524 | **RETORT FURNACE** | FOUR A CORNUE | RETORTENOFEN, KAMMEROFEN |
| 10525 | **RETORT WITH TUBULURE** | CORNUE TUBULEE | RETORTE (TUBULIERTE) |
| 10526 | **RETRACTING RELEASE, RETURN SPRING** | RESSORT DE RAPPEL | RÜCKZUGFEDER, RÜCKZIEHFEDER |
| 10527 | **RETROFIT** | MONTAGE ULTERIEUR | NACHAUSRÜSTUNG |
| 10528 | **RETURN CRANK, FLY CRANK** | CONTREMANIVELLE | GEGENKURBEL |
| 10529 | **RETURN IDLE NON-CUTTING STROKE** | COURSE A VIDE (D'UNE MACHINE-OUTIL) | LEERGANG (EINER WERKZEUGMASCHINE) |
| 10530 | **RETURN STROKE OF PISTON** | COURSE DE RETOUR, COURSE RETROGRADE DU PISTON, RETOUR, MARCHE EN ARRIERE DU PISTON | KOLBENRÜCKGANG, KOLBENRÜCKKEHR |
| 10531 | **REVEAL MOULDINGS** | ENJOLIVEURS | ZIERLEISTEN |
| 10532 | **REVERBERATORY FURNACE** | FOUR A REVERBERE | HERDGLÜHOFEN, FLAMMOFEN, REVERBERIEROFEN |
| 10533 | **REVERSAL TIME** | TEMPS D'INVERSION | UMSTELLZEIT |
| 10534 | **REVERSE (TO)** | RENVERSER LE SENS DE LA MARCHE | UMSTEUERN, UMKEHREN (DIE BEWEGUNG) |
| 10535 | **REVERSE-BEND TEST** | ESSAI DE FLEXION ALTERNEE | HIN-UND HERBIEGEVERSUCH |
| 10536 | **REVERSED FEEDBACK** | CONTRE-REACTION | GEGENKOPPLUNG |
| 10537 | **REVERSIBILITY** | REVERSIBILITE | UMKEHRBARKEIT |
| 10538 | **REVERSIBLE** | REVERSIBLE | UMKEHRBAR |
| 10539 | **REVERSIBLE CHANGE OF STATE** | CHANGEMENT D'ETAT REVERSIBLE | ZUSTANDSÄNDERUNG (UMKEHRBARE) |
| 10540 | **REVERSIBLE MOTOR** | MOTEUR REVERSIBLE | MOTOR (UMKEHRBARER) |
| 10541 | **REVERSING AN ENGINE, REVERSAL OF AN ENGINE** | RENVERSEMENT DE LA MARCHE D'UNE MACHINE | UMSTEUERUNG EINER MASCHINE |
| 10542 | **REVERSING COUNTERSHAFT** | DISPOSITIF DE CHANGEMENT DE SENS DE MARCHE POUR TRANSMISSION | UMKEHRVORGELEGE |
| 10543 | **REVERSING ENGINE** | MACHINE A VAPEUR REVERSIBLE | UMKEHRDAMPFMASCHINE, DAMPFMASCHINE MIT UMKEHRUNG, UMSTEUERUNG, REVERSIERDAMPFMASCHINE |
| 10544 | **REVERSING GEAR** | MECANISME DE CHANGEMENT DE MARCHE | WENDEGETRIEBE, KEHRGETRIEBE |
| 10545 | **REVERSING GEAR OPERATED WITH BEVEL WHEELS** | DISPOSITIF DE CHANGEMENT DE SENS DE MARCHE PAR ENGRENAGE CONIQUE | KEGELRÄDERWENDEGETRIEBE |
| 10546 | **REVERSING GEAR OPERATED WITH FRICTION DISCS, (CONES)** | DISPOSITIF DE CHANGEMENT DE SENS DE MARCHE PAR ROUE DE FRICTION | REIBRÄDERWENDEGETRIEBE |
| 10547 | **REVERSING GEAR OPERATED WITH SPUR WHEELS** | DISPOSITIF DE CHANGEMENT DE SENS DE MARCHE PAR ENGRENAGE DROIT | STIRNRÄDERWENDEGETRIEBE |

| | | | |
|---|---|---|---|
| 10548 | **REVERSING GEARS** | INVERSEUR DE MARCHE | UMSTEUERGETRIEBE |
| 10549 | **REVERSING LEVER** | LEVIER DE CHANGEMENT DE MARCHE | UMSTEUERHEBEL |
| 10550 | **REVERSING SHAFT, WEIGH SHAFT** | ARBRE DE CHANGEMENT DE MARCHE, ARBRE DE RELEVAGE, ARBRE DE DISTRIBUTION | STEUERWELLE, UMSTEUERWELLE |
| 10551 | **REVERSING SHEAVE** | POULIE DE RENVOI | UMLENKSCHEIBE |
| 10552 | **REVERSING THE MOTION** | INVERSION DE MOUVEMENT | UMKEHRUNG EINER BEWEGUNG, BEWEGUNGSUMKEHR |
| 10553 | **REVERSING VALVE** | CLAPET INVERSEUR | UMSCHALTVENTIL |
| 10554 | **REVERSION** | REVERSION | RÜCKBILDUNG |
| 10555 | **REVETED BELT JOINT** | JONCTION DES COURROIES PAR RIVET | RIEMENVERBINDUNG (GENIETETE) |
| 10556 | **REVOLUTION COUNTER, ENGINE COUNTER, REVOLUTION INDICATOR** | COMPTEUR DE TOURS, COMPTE-TOURS, TACHYMETRE | DREHZAHLMESSER, UMLAUFZÄHLER, TOURENZÄHLER |
| 10557 | **REVOLUTION, TURN** | TOUR, REVOLUTION | UMLAUF, UMDREHUNG, TOUR, UMLAUFBEWEGUNG |
| 10558 | **REVOLUTIONS PER MINUTE (R.P.M.)** | REGIME DE ROTATION, REGIME | DREHZAHL |
| 10559 | **REVOLVING GRATE** | GRILLE ROTATIVE, GRILLE TOURNANTE | DREHROST |
| 10560 | **REVOLVING HEAD CENTRE** | CONTREPOINTE TOURNANTE | REITSTOCKSPITZE (UMLAUFENDE) |
| 10561 | **REVOLVING ROTATING MASS** | MASSE EN ROTATION, MASSE TOURNANTE | SCHWUNGMASSE |
| 10562 | **RHEOLOGY** | RHEOLOGIE | RHEOLOGIE, FLIESSKUNDE |
| 10563 | **RHEOSTAT** | RHEOSTAT | WIDERSTANDSREGLER, REGELWIDERSTAND, REGULIERWIDERSTAND, RHEOSTAT |
| 10564 | **RHODIUM** | RHODIUM | RHODIUM |
| 10565 | **RHOMBOHEDRAL CRYSTAL** | CRISTAL RHOMBOEDRIQUE | KRISTALL (RHOMBOEDRISHER) |
| 10566 | **RHOMBOHEDRON** | RHOMBOEDRE | RAUTENFLÄCHNER, RHOMBOEDER |
| 10567 | **RHOMBOID** | RHOMBOIDE | RHOMBOID |
| 10568 | **RHOMBUS, LOZENGE, DIAMOND** | LOSANGE, RHOMBE | RAUTE, RHOMBUS |
| 10569 | **RIB** | NERVURE, RENFORT | RIPPE, VERSTEIFUNG |
| 10570 | **RIB OF A PIPE** | NERVURE D'UN TUBE | ROHRRIPPE, VERSTÄRKUNGSRIPPE EINES ROHRES |
| 10571 | **RIBBED GILLED TUBE** | TUBE A AILERONS, TUBE A AILETTES, TUBES A NERVURES | ROHR (GERIPPTES), RIPPENROHR |
| 10572 | **RIDDLE** | CRIBLE, TAMIS | SIEB |
| 10573 | **RIDGERS : 2, 3, AND 4 ROW** | PORTES-BILLONNEUSES | FURCHENZIEHER (2-, 3-, UND 4-REIHIG) |
| 10574 | **RIFFLED SHEET** | TOLE STRIEE | RIFFELBLECH |
| 10575 | **RIFFLER, BOW FILE** | RIFLOIR | RIFFELFEILE |
| 10576 | **RIFFLES** | STRIES | RIFFEL |
| 10577 | **RIGHT ANGLE** | ANGLE DROIT, EQUERRE (D') | WINKEL (RECHTER) |
| 10578 | **RIGHT CONE** | CONE DROIT, VERTICAL | KEGEL (GERADER) |
| 10579 | **RIGHT CYLINDER** | CYLINDRE DROIT | ZYLINDER (GERADER) |
| 10580 | **RIGHT HAND SCREW** | VIS FILETEE A DROITE | SCHRAUBE (RECHTSGÄNGIGE) |
| 10581 | **RIGHT PARALLELOPIPED** | PARALLELEPIPEDE DROIT | PARALLELEPIPED (GERADES), PARALLELEPIPED (NORMALES) |
| 10582 | **RIGHT-ANGLED TRIANGLE** | TRIANGLE RECTANGLE | DREIECK (RECHTWINKLIGES) |
| 10583 | **RIGHT-HAND OFFSET** | DECALAGE A DROITE | RECHTSVERSCHIEBUNG |
| 10584 | **RIGHT-HAND SCREW** | VIS A DROITE | SCHRAUBE (RECHTSGÄNGIGE) |
| 10585 | **RIGHT-HAND THREAD** | PAS A DROITE, FILET A DROITE | GEWINDE (RECHTSÄNGIGES), RECHTSGEWINDE |

**RIG** 270

| | | | |
|---|---|---|---|
| 10586 | RIGHT-HANDED HELICAL TEETH | DENTURE A PAS INCLINE A DROITE | VERZAHNUNG (RECHTSSTEIGENDE) |
| 10587 | RIGHT-LAID ROPE | CABLE TORDU A DROITE | SEIL (RECHTSGESCHLAGENES) |
| 10588 | RIGID BODY | CORPS RIGIDE | KÖRPER (STARRER) |
| 10589 | RIGID CONNECTION | FIXATION RIGIDE, LIAISON RIGIDE, JOINT RIGIDE, ASSEMBLAGE RIGIDE | VERBINDUNG (STARRE) |
| 10590 | RIGID DRILLS | PERCEUSES RIGIDES | STARRBOHRMASCHINEN |
| 10591 | RIGIDITY, STIFFNESS | RIGIDITE, RAIDEUR | STEIFIGKEIT |
| 10592 | RIM | JANTE | RADKRANZ |
| 10593 | RIM OF FLYWHEEL | JANTE DE VOLANT | SCHWUNGRADKRANZ |
| 10594 | RIM OF GEAR WHEEL | JANTE (COURONNE) D'UNE ROUE D'ENGRENAGE | KRANZ EINES ZAHNRADES, ZAHNKRANZ |
| 10595 | RIM OF PULLEY | JANTE D'UNE POULIE | KRANZ EINER RIEMENSCHEIBE, SCHEIBENKRANZ |
| 10596 | RIM OF WHEEL | COURONNE D'UNE ROUE | RADKRANZ |
| 10597 | RIM VENT | EVENT D'ETANCHEITE | RANDLUFTÖFFNUNG |
| 10598 | RIMMED STEEL | ACIER EFFERVESCENT, ACIER FRETTE | RANDSTAHL, SINTERSTAHL, STAHL (UNBERUHIGTER) |
| 10599 | RIMMING, OR RIMMED STEEL | ACIER EFFERVESCENT, ACIER PARTIELLEMENT DESOXYDE, ACIER MOUSSEUX | SINTERSTAHL |
| 10600 | RING | ANNEAU, BAGUE | RING |
| 10601 | RING LUBRICATION OILING | GRAISSAGE A BAGUE | RINGSCHMIERUNG, ABSTREIFSCHMIERUNG |
| 10602 | RING OILED BEARING | PALIER GRAISSEUR A BAGUE | RINGSCHMIERLAGER |
| 10603 | RING SEGMENT | SEGMENT D'ANNEAU CIRCULAIRE | RINGSTÜCK |
| 10604 | RING TYPE JOINT | JOINT ANNULAIRE | RINGDICHTUNG |
| 10605 | RING VALVE, ANNULAR VALVE | SOUPAPE ANNULAIRE | RINGVENTIL |
| 10606 | RING-SHAPED ANNULAR PIVOT | PIVOT ANNULAIRE | RINGSPURZAPFEN |
| 10607 | RINSE (TO) | RINCER, LAVER A GRANDE EAU | SPÜLEN |
| 10608 | RINSING | RINCAGE | SPÜLEN |
| 10609 | RIP SAW | SCIE DE LONG | SPALTSÄGE, KRANSÄGE, DIELENSÄGE, BRETTSÄGE, LÄNGENSÄGE |
| 10610 | RIPPING FENCE | GUIDE A REFENDRE | LANGSÄGEFÜHRUNG |
| 10611 | RISE | LEVEE, HAUSSE, HAUTEUR D'ASCENSION | ANSTEIG, STEIGHÖHE, (MECH.) |
| 10612 | RISE INCREASE IN TEMPERATURE, TEMPERATURE RISE | AUGMENTATION OU ELEVATION DE LA TEMPERATURE | TEMPERATURZUNAHME, TEMPERATURSTEIGERUNG, TEMPERATURERHÖHUNG, TEMPERATURANSTIEG |
| 10613 | RISE OF AN ARCH | FLECHE, SAGETTE, AFFAISSEMENT | BOGENHÖHE, PFEILHÖHE, STICHHÖHE, STICH |
| 10614 | RISER | COLONNE MONTANTE, EVANT, CONTRE-MARCHE | STEIGLEITUNG, STEIGTRICHTER, FUTTER |
| 10615 | RISER, RISING MAIN | TUYAU D'ASCENSION, TUYAU ELEVATOIRE, TUYAU VERTICAL, MONTANT | STEIGROHR |
| 10616 | RISING STEM | TIGE MONTANTE | SPINDEL (STEIGENDE) |
| 10617 | RISING STEM GATE VALVE | VANNE A TIGE MONTANTE | ABSPERRSCHIEBER MIT STEIGENDER SPINDEL |
| 10618 | RISING TEMPERATURE | TEMPERATURE CROISSANTE | TEMPERATUR (STEIGENDE), TEMPERATUR (ZUNEHMENDE) |
| 10619 | RIVER SAND | SABLE DE RIVIERE | FLUSSSAND |
| 10620 | RIVER WATER | EAU FLUVIALE, EAU DE RIVIERE | FLUSSWASSER |
| 10621 | RIVET | RIVET | NIET |

| | | | |
|---|---|---|---|
| 10622 | **RIVET AT EDGE OF PLATE** | RIVET AU BORD DE LA TOLE | RANDNIET |
| 10623 | **RIVET FORGE** | FOUR A CHAUFFER LES RIVETS | NIETWÄRMEOFEN |
| 10624 | **RIVET HEAD** | TETE DE RIVET | NIETKOPF |
| 10625 | **RIVET HOLE** | TROU DES TOLES A ASSEMBLER, TROU DE RIVET | NIETLOCH |
| 10626 | **RIVET SNAP, RIVETING SET** | BOUTEROLLE A MAIN, CHASSE-RIVET | SETZEISEN, SCHELLEISEN, DÖPPER |
| 10627 | **RIVET STEEL** | ACIER A RIVETS | NIETEISEN |
| 10628 | **RIVET TAIL, RIVET POINT, TAIL POINT CLOSING HEAD** | RIVURE | SCHLIESSKOPF |
| 10629 | **RIVET TO** | RIVETER | VERNIETEN |
| 10630 | **RIVET TONGS** | TENAILLE A RIVETS | NIETZANGE |
| 10631 | **RIVET WELDING** | SOUDAGE DES RIVETS | NIETSCHWEISSEN |
| 10632 | **RIVET WITH CYLINDRICAL HEAD** | RIVET A TETE CYLINDRIQUE | NIET MIT ZYLINDRISCHEM KOPF |
| 10633 | **RIVET WITH ELLIPSOIDAL HEAD** | RIVET A TETE GOUTTE DE SUIF | NIET MIT KORBBOGENKOPF |
| 10634 | **RIVET WITH FLAT HEAD** | RIVET A TETE PLATE | NIET MIT FLACHEM KOPF |
| 10635 | **RIVET WITH FLUSH HEAD, FLUSH COUNTERSUNK RIVET** | RIVET A TETE NOYEE, RIVET A TETE PERDUE, RIVET A TETE FRAISEE, RIVET A TETE AFFLEUREE | NIET MIT VERSENKTEM KOPF, SENKNIET, VERSENKTES NIET, NIET MIT BÜNDIGEM KOPF |
| 10636 | **RIVET WITH SEGMENTAL HEAD** | RIVET A TETE RONDE | NIET MIT HALBRUNDKOPF |
| 10637 | **RIVET WITH SNAP HEAD, CUP HEAD, BUTTON HEAD, SPHERICAL HEAD** | RIVET A TETE HEMISPHERIQUE | NIET MIT RUNDKOPF, NIET MIT SCHELLKOPF |
| 10638 | **RIVETED FLANGE** | BRIDE RIVETEE | AUFGENIETETER FLANSCH, NIETFLANSCH |
| 10639 | **RIVETED JOINT, RIVET JOINT** | ASSEMBLAGE PAR RIVETS, RIVURE, CLOUURE | NIETVERBINDUNG, NIETUNG |
| 10640 | **RIVETED PIPE** | TUYAU RIVE | GENIETETES ROHR |
| 10641 | **RIVETER** | RIVEUR, OUVRIER RIVEUR | NIETER |
| 10642 | **RIVETER, RIVETING MACHINE** | MACHINE A RIVETER, RIVEUSE | NIETMASCHINE |
| 10643 | **RIVETING** | RIVETAGE | NIETEN, VERNIETEN, NIETUNG |
| 10644 | **RIVETING HAMMER** | MARTEAU-RIVOIR, RIVOIR, MARTEAU A RIVER | NIETHAMMER |
| 10645 | **RIVETING MACHINE** | MACHINE A RIVER | NIETMASCHINE |
| 10646 | **RIVETS** | RIVETS | NIETE |
| 10647 | **ROAD OIL** | ESSENCE CRAQUEE | STRASSENÖL |
| 10648 | **ROAST ORES (TO)** | GRILLER LES MINERAIS | ERZE RÖSTEN |
| 10649 | **ROASTING FURNACE** | FOUR DE GRILLAGE | RÖSTOFEN |
| 10650 | **ROASTING ORES** | GRILLAGE DES MINERAIS | RÖSTEN VON ERZEN |
| 10651 | **ROCK** | ROCHE | GESTEIN |
| 10652 | **ROCK CRYSTAL** | CRISTAL DE ROCHE | BERGKRISTALL |
| 10653 | **ROCK SALT** | SEL GEMME | STEINSALZ |
| 10654 | **ROCKER ARM, ROCKER LEVER** | CULBUTEUR | KIPPHEBEL |
| 10655 | **ROCKING GRATE** | GRILLE A SECOUSSES, GRILLE A BARREAUX MOBILES, GRILLE OSCILLANTE | SCHÜTTELROST |
| 10656 | **ROCKING LEVER** | LEVIER OSCILLANT | SCHWINGHEBEL |
| 10657 | **ROCKING SHAFT** | ARBRE OSCILLANT | SCHWINGENDE WELLE |
| 10658 | **ROCKING SHEAR** | CISAILLE BASCULANTE | KIPPSCHERE |
| 10659 | **ROCKWELL HARDNESS TEST** | ESSAI DE DURETE ROCKWELL | ROCKWELL-HÄRTEPRÜFUNG |
| 10660 | **ROD** | BARRE, BARREAU, BAGUETTE, TIGE | STAB, STANGE |
| 10661 | **ROD GAUGE** | CALIBRE D'ALESAGE | STICHMASS, ZYLINDERMASS |
| 10662 | **ROD OF PLANIMETER** | BRANCHE DE LA POINTE TRACANTE DU PLANIMETRE | FAHRARM DES PLANIMETERS |

# ROE

272

| | | | |
|---|---|---|---|
| 10663 | **ROD, BAR** | TRINGLE, TIGE, BARRE | STANGE |
| 10664 | **ROENTGENOGRAPHY** | RADIOGRAPHIE | ROENTGENBILD |
| 10665 | **ROLL (TO)** | LAMINER, ROULER | WALZEN, AUSWALZEN, ROLLEN |
| 10666 | **ROLL DOWN** | REDUIRE PAR LAMINAGE | AUSWALZEN |
| 10667 | **ROLL FILM** | PELLICULE EN BOBINE | FILM ROLLEN |
| 10668 | **ROLL FORGING** | FORGEAGE PAR LAMINAGE, PROFILAGE | WALZSCHMIEDEN PROFILWALZEN |
| 10669 | **ROLL LINE** | TRAIN DE LAMINOIR | WALZENSTRASSE |
| 10670 | **ROLL TRAIN** | TRAIN DE LAMINAGE | WALZENSTRASSE |
| 10671 | **ROLL, ROLLER, CYLINDER** | CYLINDRE, ROULEAU, TAMBOUR, GALET | WALZE, ROLLE, ZYLINDER |
| 10672 | **ROLLED FLANGE** | BRIDE MANDRINEE | FLANSCH (AUFGEWALZTER), WALZFLANSCH |
| 10673 | **ROLLED GOLD** | DOUBLE D'OR | GOLDDUBLEE, WALZGOLD |
| 10674 | **ROLLED PLATE** | TOLE LAMINEE | BLECH (GEWALZTES) |
| 10675 | **ROLLED SECTION** | FER LAMINE PROFILE | WALZPROFIL |
| 10676 | **ROLLED STEEL, ROLLED IRON, ROLLED BARS** | FER LAMINE | WALZEISEN |
| 10677 | **ROLLED TUBE** | TUBE LAMINE | ROHR (GEWALZTES) |
| 10678 | **ROLLED WIRE** | FIL LAMINE | WALZDRAHT, DRAHT (GEWALZTER) |
| 10679 | **ROLLER** | ROULEAU, GALET | ROLLE |
| 10680 | **ROLLER BEARING** | ROULEMENT A GALETS (A ROULEAUX), PALIER A GALETS (A ROULEAUX) | ROLLENLAGER, WALZENLAGER |
| 10681 | **ROLLER BEARING WITH BARREL-SHAPED ROLLERS** | ROULEMENT A ROTULE SUR ROULEAUX | ROLLENLAGER MIT TONNENFÖRMIGEN ROLLEN, TONNENLAGER |
| 10682 | **ROLLER BEARING WITH CYLINDRICAL ROLLERS** | ROULEMENT A GALETS CYLINDRIQUES | ROLLENLAGER MIT ZYLINDRISCHEN ROLLEN |
| 10683 | **ROLLER BEARING WITH TAPER ROLLERS** | ROULEMENT A GALETS CONIQUES | ROLLENLAGER MIT KEGELROLLEN |
| 10684 | **ROLLER CHAIN** | CHAINE A ROULEAUX | ROLLENKETTE |
| 10685 | **ROLLER LEVELER** | DRESSEUSE A GALETS | ROLLENRICHTMASCHINE |
| 10686 | **ROLLER LEVER, ROLLING LEVER** | LEVIER ROULANT | WÄLZHEBEL |
| 10687 | **ROLLER MILL** | BROYEUR A CYLINDRES | WALZENMÜHLE |
| 10688 | **ROLLER OF A CHAIN** | ROULEAU D'UNE CHAINE | BÜCHSE EINER ROLLENKETTE |
| 10689 | **ROLLER RACE WAY, ROLLER PATH** | CHEMIN DE ROULEMENT DES GALETS | ROLLENBAHN (EINES LAGERS) |
| 10690 | **ROLLER SADDLE SUPPORT** | BERCEAU A GALETS | ROLLENTROMMELSATTEL |
| 10691 | **ROLLER STEP BEARING** | BUTEE A ROULEAUX (A GALETS) | ROLLENSPURLAGER, WALZENSPURLAGER |
| 10692 | **ROLLER TAPPET** | POUSSOIR A GALET | ROLLENSTÖSSEL |
| 10693 | **ROLLER THREAD GAUGE** | JAUGE-MACHOIRE POUR FILETS | GRENZGEWINDERACHENLEHRE MIT MESSROLLEN |
| 10694 | **ROLLER TYPE SADDLE SUPPORT** | BERCEAU A GALETS | SCHLITTEN MIT ROLLEN |
| 10695 | **ROLLERS, FLAT, RING AND RIDGE** | ROULEAUX, GALETS (POUR MISE SUR CHAMP) | GLATTWALZEN, ACKERWALZEN, ROLLEN |
| 10696 | **ROLLING** | LAMINAGE, ROULEMENT | WALZEN, AUSWALZEN, ROLLEN |
| 10697 | **ROLLING CURVE, ROULETTE** | ROULETTE, COURBE ROULANTE | ROLLKURVE |
| 10698 | **ROLLING DIRECTION** | SENS DE LAMINAGE | WALZRICHTUNG |
| 10699 | **ROLLING FLANGE** | BRIDE A MANDRINER | WALZFLANSCH |
| 10700 | **ROLLING FRICTION** | FROTTEMENT DE ROULEMENT | REIBUNG (ROLLENDE) |
| 10701 | **ROLLING MILL** | LAMINOIR, TRAIN DE LAMINOIR | WALZENSTRASSE, WALZSTRECKE, WALZWERK |
| 10702 | **ROLLING MOTION** | MOUVEMENT DE ROULEMENT | BEWEGUNG (ROLLENDE), ROLLBEWEGUNG |

|  |  |  |  |
|---|---|---|---|
| 10703 | **ROLLING RESISTANCE** | RESISTANCE AU ROULEMENT | ROLLWIDERSTAND |
| 10704 | **ROLLING STAND** | CAGE DE CYLINDRES | WALZGERÜST |
| 10705 | **ROLLING SURFACE** | SURFACE DE ROULEMENT | WÄLZFLÄCHE |
| 10706 | **ROLLING, TRAVELLING DYNAMIC LOAD, MOVING WEIGHT** | CHARGE ROULANTE, MOBILE | VERKEHRSLAST, LAST (WANDERNDE), LAST (FAHRENDE), LAST (BEWEGLICHE) |
| 10707 | **ROMAN CEMENT** | CIMENT ROMAIN | ROMANZEMENT |
| 10708 | **ROOF** | TOIT | DACH |
| 10709 | **ROOF LIGHT** | PLAFONNIER | DECKENLEUCHTE |
| 10710 | **ROOF MANHOLE** | TROU D'HOMME DE TOIT | DACH-MANNLOCH |
| 10711 | **ROOF NOZZLE** | TUBULURE DE TOIT | DACHSTUTZEN |
| 10712 | **ROOFING FELT** | CARTON BITUME OU ASPHALTE | DACHPAPPE, TEERPAPPE |
| 10713 | **ROOM TEMPERATURE** | TEMPERATURE AMBIANTE, TEMPERATURE NORMALE, ORDINAIRE DE LA SALLE | ZIMMERWÄRME, RAUMTEMPERATUR |
| 10714 | **ROOT** | RACINE (MATH.) | WURZEL, (MATH.) |
| 10715 | **ROOT AND TURNIP CUTTERS AND CLEANERS** | COUPE-RACINES | REINIGUNGS- UND SCHNEIDEMASCHINEN FÜR WURZELN UND RÜBEN |
| 10716 | **ROOT ANGLE** | ANGLE DE PIED | ZAHNFUSSWINKEL |
| 10717 | **ROOT CIRCLE** | CERCLE DE PIED | FUSSKREIS |
| 10718 | **ROOT CONE** | CONE DE PIED | ZAHNFUSSKEGEL |
| 10719 | **ROOT DIAMETER** | DIAMETRE DE PIED | KERNDURCHMESSER |
| 10720 | **ROOT EDGE** | FLANC DE BASE, RACINE | WURZELFLANKE |
| 10721 | **ROOT FACE** | FLANC DE RACINE | STEGFLANKE |
| 10722 | **ROOT LIFTERS** | SOULEVEUSES DE RACINES | ERNTEMASCHINEN FÜR HACKFRÜCHTE |
| 10723 | **ROOT LINE CIRCLE** | CERCLE DE PIED, CERCLE DE FOND, CERCLE DE CREUX, CIRCONFERENCE D'EVIDEMENT | WURZELKREIS, FUSSKREIS |
| 10724 | **ROOT OF A TOOTH** | PIED DE DENT | ZAHNWURZEL |
| 10725 | **ROOT OF TOOTH** | PIED DE LA DENT | ZAHNFUSS |
| 10726 | **ROOT OF WELD** | RACINE DE LA SOUDURE | NAHTWURZEL |
| 10727 | **ROOT OPENING** | LARGEUR DE LA SOUDURE DE BASE | WURZELSPALT |
| 10728 | **ROOT RADIUS** | RAYON D'ECARTEMENT ENTRE LES BORDS | FUGENRADIUS |
| 10729 | **ROOT'S BLOWER** | VENTILATEUR SYSTEME ROOT | ROOTGEBLÄSE |
| 10730 | **ROPE** | CORDE, CABLE | SEIL |
| 10731 | **ROPE BLOCK** | MOUFLE A CORDE | TAUKLOBEN |
| 10732 | **ROPE BRAKE** | FREIN A CORDE | SEILBREMSE |
| 10733 | **ROPE DIAMETER** | DIAMETRE D'UN CABLE | SEILSTÄRKE, SEILDICKE, SEILDURCHMESSER |
| 10734 | **ROPE DRIVE OR GEARING** | TRANSMISSION PAR CABLES, TRANSMISSION PAR CORDES COURROIES, TRANSMISSION FUNICULAIRE | SEILTRIEB |
| 10735 | **ROPE DRIVE, DRIVING, DRIVE BY ROPES** | COMMANDE PAR CABLE | SEILANTRIEB |
| 10736 | **ROPE DRIVEN MACHINE** | MACHINE A COMMANDE PAR CABLE | MASCHINE FÜR SEILANTRIEB |
| 10737 | **ROPE DRUM** | TAMBOUR D'ENROULEMENT | SEILTROMMEL |
| 10738 | **ROPE FLYWHEEL** | VOLANT A GORGES | SEILSCHEIBENSCHWUNGRAD |
| 10739 | **ROPE LAYING, TWISTING** | COMMETTAGE, CABLAGE | SEILSCHLAG, VERSEILEN |
| 10740 | **ROPE LINE** | BRIN DE CABLE | SEILSTRANG |

# ROP

274

| | | | |
|---|---|---|---|
| 10741 | **ROPE PULLEY BLOCK** | PALAN A CORDE | SEILFLASCHENZUG |
| 10742 | **ROPE WHEEL, ROPE SHEAVE, SHEAVE WHEEL (FOR ROPE)** | POULIE A CABLE, POULIE POUR CABLE DE TRANSMISSION | SEILSCHEIBE, SEILROLLE |
| 10743 | **ROPE WIRE** | FIL POUR CABLE | SEILDRAHT |
| 10744 | **ROPE YARN** | FIL DE CARET | SEILGARN, SEILFADEN |
| 10745 | **ROPINESS** | CORDAGE | VERDICKUNG (FASERIGE) |
| 10746 | **ROSE** | POMME D'ARROSOIR | BRAUSE |
| 10747 | **ROSE REAMER** | ALESOIR EN BOUT | VERSENKER |
| 10748 | **ROSETTE COPPER** | CUIVRE ROSETTE | ROSETTENKUPFER |
| 10749 | **ROSIN OIL, RESIN OIL** | HUILE DE RESINE, HUILE DE PIN | HARZÖL |
| 10750 | **ROSOLIC ACID** | ACIDE ROSOLIQUE | ROSOLSÄURE |
| 10751 | **ROTARY BLOWER FAN** | VENTILATEUR A PISTON ROTATIF | KAPSELGEBLÄSE, FLÜGELGEBLÄSE |
| 10752 | **ROTARY COOLER** | REFROIDISSEUR CIRCULAIRE | UMLAUFKÜHLER |
| 10753 | **ROTARY CULTIVATORS HOES AND TILLERS** | MOTOCULTEURS A FRAISES ROTATIVES | HACKFRÄSEN UND BODENFRÄSEN |
| 10754 | **ROTARY ENGINE** | MOTEUR A PISTONS ROTATIFS | UMLAUFMOTOR |
| 10755 | **ROTARY FILE** | LIME ROTATIVE | DREHFEILE |
| 10756 | **ROTARY PISTON** | PISTON ROTATIF | DREHKOLBEN |
| 10757 | **ROTARY PRESS** | PRESSE ROTATIVE | KARUSSELLPRESSE |
| 10758 | **ROTARY PUMP** | POMPE A ROTOR, POMPE ROTATIVE, POMPE A PALETTES ROTATIVES | ZENTRIFUGALPUMPE, DREHKOLBENPUMPE, ROTATIONSPUMPE, KAPSELPUMPE, WALZENPUMPE, WÜRGELPUMPE, KREISKOLBENPUMPE |
| 10759 | **ROTARY SHEARS** | CISAILLES ROTATIVES | SCHERE (ROTIERENDE) |
| 10760 | **ROTARY SLIDE VALVE** | DISTRIBUTEUR GLISSANT A ROBINET, ROBINET DISTRIBUTEUR TOURNANT, OBTURATEUR, DISTRIBUTEUR OSCILLANT, VALVE OSCILLANTE | DREHSCHIEBER |
| 10761 | **ROTARY STEAM ENGINE** | MACHINE ROTATIVE | ROTIERENDE DAMPFMASCHINE, ROTATIONSDAMPFMASCHINE, DAMPFMASCHINE MIT UMLAUFENDEM KOLBEN |
| 10762 | **ROTARY TABLE** | PLATEAU TOURNANT | DREHTISCH |
| 10763 | **ROTATE (TO), REVOLVE (TO)** | TOURNER | DREHEN (SICH), UMLAUFEN, ROTIEREN |
| 10764 | **ROTATING SHAFT** | ARBRE ROTATIF | UMLAUFENDE WELLE, ROTIERENDE WELLE, DREHENDE WELLE (SICH) |
| 10765 | **ROTATION; REVOLUTION** | ROTATION | UMDREHUNG, DREHUNG, ROTATION |
| 10766 | **ROTATORY MOTION, MOTION OF ROTATION** | MOUVEMENT ROTATOIRE, MOUVEMENT DE ROTATION | DREHBEWEGUNG, BEWEGUNG (DREHENDE) |
| 10767 | **ROTOR** | ROTOR | LÄUFER, ROTOR |
| 10768 | **ROTTEN TIMBER** | BOIS CARIE | HOLZ (MORSCHES) |
| 10769 | **ROTTENNESS** | DECOMPOSITION | FÄULNIS, ZERSETZUNG |
| 10770 | **ROTTING OF TIMBER, DECAY IN TIMBER** | CARIE, NECROSE, POURRITURE DU BOIS | FÄULNIS DES HOLZES |
| 10771 | **ROUGH BORE (TO), DRILL (TO)** | PERCER, FORER PREALABLEMENT | VORBOHREN |
| 10772 | **ROUGH CALCULATION** | CALCUL RAPIDE APPROCHE | ÜBERSCHLÄGIGE RECHNUNG, ÜBERSCHLAGSRECHNUNG |
| 10773 | **ROUGH CAST GEAR WHEEL** | ROUE D'ENGRENAGE BRUTE DE FONDERIE, ENGRENAGE BRUT DE FONTE, ROUE A DENTURE BRUTE | ZAHNRAD (ROH GEGOSSENES) |
| 10774 | **ROUGH CUT FILE, RUBBER FILE** | LIME A GROSSE TAILLE, LIME A TAILLE RUDE, LIME FORTE | GROBFEILE, ARMFEILE, STROHFEILE |

| | | | |
|---|---|---|---|
| 10775 | **ROUGH DOWN (TO)** | DEGROSSIR, EBAUCHER | SCHRUPPEN, ZURICHTEN, VORBEARBEITEN, GROBEN BEARBEITEN (AUS DEM), ROHEN BEARBEITEN (AUS DEM) |
| 10776 | **ROUGH FLANGE** | BRIDE BRUTE DE FONTE | FLANSCH (ROHER), FLANSCH (UNBEARBEITETER) |
| 10777 | **ROUGH GRINDING** | DEGROSSISSAGE A LA MEULE | VORSCHLEIFEN |
| 10778 | **ROUGH ROLLED, COGGED** | BRUT DE LAMINAGE | VORGEWALZT |
| 10779 | **ROUGH SURFACE** | SURFACE RUGUEUSE | FLÄCHE (RAUHE) |
| 10780 | **ROUGH TUBE** | TUBE RUGUEUX | ROHR (RAUHES) |
| 10781 | **ROUGH WEIGHT** | POIDS BRUT | ROHGEWICHT, BRUTTOGEWICHT |
| 10782 | **ROUGH-DRILLED HOLE** | AVANT-TROU | LOCH (VORGEBOHRTES) |
| 10783 | **ROUGHEN (TO)** | RENDRE RUGUEUX | AUFRAUHEN |
| 10784 | **ROUGHENED SURFACE** | SURFACE RUGUEUSE | FLÄCHE (GERAUHTE) |
| 10785 | **ROUGHING** | EBAUCHAGE | ROHBEARBEITUNG |
| 10786 | **ROUGHING DOWN** | DEGROSSISSAGE, EBAUCHAGE | BEARBEITUNG, AUS DEM GROBEN, BEARBEITUNG AUS DEM ROHEN, VORBEARBEITUNG, ZURICHTEN, SCHRUPPEN, SCHRUPPARBEIT |
| 10787 | **ROUGHING DOWN OR SHINGLING** | CAGE DEGROSSISEURS | VORWALZE |
| 10788 | **ROUGHING LATHE** | TOUR A EBAUCHER | SCHRUPPDREHBANK |
| 10789 | **ROUGHING MILL** | TRAIN EBAUCHEUR | VORSTRASSE |
| 10790 | **ROUGHING TAPER REAMER** | ALESOIR EBAUCHEUR CONIQUE | VORREIBAHLE (KONISCHE) |
| 10791 | **ROUGHING TOOL** | OUTIL A DEGROSSIR | SCHRUPPSTAHL |
| 10792 | **ROUGHNESS** | RUGOSITE, ASPERITE | RAUHIGKEIT |
| 10793 | **ROUND AN EDGE (TO)** | ARRONDIR UNE ARETE | KANTE RUNDEN (EINE), ABRUNDEN |
| 10794 | **ROUND BACKED ANGLE** | FER CORNIERE A ANGLE ARRONDI | WINKELEISEN (INNEN VOLL), ABGERUNDET |
| 10795 | **ROUND BAR IRON** | FER ROND | RUNDEISEN, RUNDSTAB |
| 10796 | **ROUND FILE** | LIME RONDE | RUNDFEILE |
| 10797 | **ROUND FLANGE** | BRIDE RONDE | FLANSCH (RUNDER) |
| 10798 | **ROUND FLASK** | BALLON ORDINAIRE | RUNDKOLBEN |
| 10799 | **ROUND HAND** | ECRITURE RONDE | RUNDSCHRIFT |
| 10800 | **ROUND PLANE** | RABOT ROND | KEHLHOBEL |
| 10801 | **ROUND ROPE** | CABLE ROND | RUNDSEIL |
| 10802 | **ROUND THREAD** | FILET ROND | GEWINDE (RUNDES), KORDELGEWINDE |
| 10803 | **ROUND TIMBER** | RONDIN, BOIS EN RONDINS | RUNDHOLZ |
| 10804 | **ROUND WIRE** | FIL ROND | RUNDDRAHT, DRAHT (RUNDER) |
| 10805 | **ROUND WIRE PLIERS** | PINCE RONDE | RUNDZANGE, DRAHTZANGE (RUNDE) |
| 10806 | **ROUND-HAND PEN** | PLUME DE RONDE | RUNDSCHRIFTFEDER |
| 10807 | **ROUND-THREADED SCREW** | VIS A FILET ROND | SCHRAUBE MIT RUNDGEWINDE, RUNDGÄNGIGE SCHRAUBE |
| 10808 | **ROUNDED EDGE** | ARETE ARRONDIE | KANTE (ABGERUNDETE) |
| 10809 | **ROUNDING OF THREAD** | ARRONDI DU FILET | ABRUNDUNG DES GEWINDES |
| 10810 | **ROUTE** | ITINERAIRE MARITIME, PARCOURS | SEEWEG, FAHRT |
| 10811 | **ROUTINE** | PROGRAMME D'ORDINATEUR | RECHNERPROGRAMM |
| 10812 | **ROW** | LIGNE | ZEILE |
| 10813 | **ROW OF RIVETS** | LIGNE DE RIVETS, RANG DE RIVETS | NIETREIHE |
| 10814 | **RPM** | REVOLUTIONS PAR MINUTE, TOUR MINUTE | DREHZAHL, TOURENZAHL, UMDREHUNGEN PRO MINUTE, U/MIN |
| 10815 | **RUB THE RUST OFF (TO)** | DEROUILLER | ENTROSTEN |
| 10816 | **RUBBER** | CAOUTCHOUC | GUMMI |

# RUB

| | | | |
|---|---|---|---|
| 10817 | **RUBBER BELT** | COURROIE EN CAOUTCHOUC, COURROIE EN TISSU CAOUTCHOUTE | GUMMIRIEMEN |
| 10818 | **RUBBER CLOTH** | TISSU CAOUTCHOUTE, TOILE CAOUTCHOUTEE, ETOFFE CAOUTCHOUTEE | GUMMISTOFF |
| 10819 | **RUBBER DIAPHRAGM** | DIAPHRAGME EN CAOUTCHOUC | GUMMIMEMBRAN |
| 10820 | **RUBBER GASKET** | JOINT A BAGUE DE CAOUTCHOUC | GUMMIRINGDICHTUNG, DICHTUNG MIT GUMMIRING |
| 10821 | **RUBBER HOSE** | TUYAU (FLEXIBLE) DE CAOUTCHOUC | GUMMISCHLAUCH |
| 10822 | **RUBBER INSULATING TAPE** | RUBAN CAOUTCHOUTE | GUMMIISOLIER BAND |
| 10823 | **RUBBER RING** | BAGUE EN CAOUTCHOUC, RONDELLE EN CAOUTCHOUC | GUMMIRING |
| 10824 | **RUBBER STOPPER** | BOUCHON DE CAOUTCHOUC | GUMMIPFROPFEN, KAUTSCHUKSTOPFEN |
| 10825 | **RUBBER, INDIA-RUBBER, CAOUTCHOUC** | CAOUTCHOUC, GOMME ELASTIQUE | KAUTSCHUK, FEDERHARZ |
| 10826 | **RUBBING OFF THE RUST** | DEROUILLEMENT | ENTROSTEN |
| 10827 | **RUBBLE STONE** | MOELLON | BRUCHSTEIN |
| 10828 | **RUBBLE WORK** | MACONNERIE EN MOELLONS | BRUCHSTEINMAUERWERK |
| 10829 | **RUBIDIUM** | RUBIDIUM | RUBIDIUM |
| 10830 | **RUHMKORFF COIL** | BOBINE DE RUHMKORFF | RUHMKORFF-INDUKTOR |
| 10831 | **RULER** | REGLE DE DESSINATEUR | LINEAL |
| 10832 | **RUN** | COUCHE, PASSE | LAGE |
| 10833 | **RUN AT A HIGH SPEED (TO)** | MARCHER A GRANDE VITESSE | SCHNELLAUFEN |
| 10834 | **RUN AT A LOW SPEED (TO)** | MARCHER A PETITE VITESSE | LANGSAMLAUFEN |
| 10835 | **RUN IN AN ENGINE (TO)** | RODER UN MOTEUR | EINLAUFEN LASSEN (EINE MASCHINE) |
| 10836 | **RUN OUT** | BAVURE | GRAT |
| 10837 | **RUN OUT BEARING** | FONDRE (LE COUSSINET FOND) | AUSGELAUFENES LAGER, AUSGESCHMOLZENES |
| 10838 | **RUN OUT TABLE** | TRAIN DE ROULEAUX DE SORTIE | AUSLAUFROLLGANG |
| 10839 | **RUN PIPE** | COLLECTEUR | TRANSPORTROHR |
| 10840 | **RUN UNTRUE (TO)** | TOURNER FAUX-ROND | UNRUND LAUFEN |
| 10841 | **RUN-OF-MINE COAL, ROUGH COAL** | TOUT-VENANT, HOUILLE TOUT-VENANT | FÖRDERKOHLE |
| 10842 | **RUN-OFF PLATE** | TOLE TECHNOLOGIQUE | AUSLAUFBLECH |
| 10843 | **RUNDOWN TANK** | RESERVOIR DE RECETTE | EMPFANGSTANK |
| 10844 | **RUNNER** | GALET DE ROULEMENT, COULEE, CANAL DE COULEE | LAUFROLLE, GUSSRINNE |
| 10845 | **RUNNER GATE** | COULEE, ATTAQUE | ANGUSS |
| 10846 | **RUNNING BACKWARD, GOING ASTERN** | MARCHE ARRIERE | RÜCKWÄRTSGANG |
| 10847 | **RUNNING FIT** | EMMANCHEMENT, AJUSTAGE, MONTAGE TOURNANT | LAUFSITZ |
| 10848 | **RUNNING FORWARD, GOING AHEAD** | MARCHE AVANT | VORWÄRTSGANG |
| 10849 | **RUNNING METRE, METRE RUN** | METRE COURANT | METER (LAUFENDES) |
| 10850 | **RUNNING OF AN ENGINE** | MARCHE, FONCTIONNEMENT, ALLURE D'UNE MACHINE | GANG EINER MASCHINE |
| 10851 | **RUNNING PART (IN LIFTING TACKLE)** | BRIN COURANT, COURANT D'UN PALAN | LAUFENDES TRUMM EINES FLASCHENZUGES |
| 10852 | **RUNNING SCREW** | VIS DE TRANSLATION | BEWEGUNGSSCHRAUBE |
| 10853 | **RUNNING SIDE DRIVING FACE OF A BELT** | COTE INTERIEUR D'UNE COURROIE | LAUFSEITE EINES RIEMENS |
| 10854 | **RUNNING WHEEL** | ROUE PORTEUSE, GALET DE ROULEMENT | LAUFRAD |

| | | | |
|---|---|---|---|
| 10855 | **RUNNING-IN** | RODAGE | EINFAHRZEIT |
| 10856 | **RUNS, RUNNING** | COULURES | LÄUFER |
| 10857 | **RUNWAY (FOR A RODF ROLLING LADDER)** | CHEMIN DE ROULEMENT (POUR ECHELLE ROULANTE DE TOIT) | FAHRFLÄCHE-LAUFBAHN, ROLLBAHN (FÜR ROLLEITER) |
| 10858 | **RUPTURE** | FRACTURE, RUPTURE, ARRACHEMENT | BRUCH |
| 10859 | **RUPTURE (TO), REND (TO)** | DECHIRER (SE) | REISSEN, EINREISSEN, AUFREISSEN |
| 10860 | **RUPTURE DISC** | MEMBRANE D'ECLATEMENT, DISQUE DE RUPTURE | SICHERHEITSMEMBRANE, BRUCHSCHEIBE |
| 10861 | **RUPTURE, FRACTURE** | RUPTURE, BRIS | BRUCH, BRECHEN |
| 10862 | **RUSSIAN OIL OF TURPENTINE** | ESSENCE DE TEREBENTHINE RUSSE | KIENÖL |
| 10863 | **RUST** | ROUILLE | ROST |
| 10864 | **RUST (TO)** | ROUILLER (SE) | VERROSTEN |
| 10865 | **RUST FORMATION, FORMATION OF RUST** | FORMATION DE ROUILLE | ROSTEN, VERROSTEN, ROSTBILDUNG |
| 10866 | **RUST INHIBITOR** | PRODUIT ANTI-ROUILLE | ROSTSCHUTZMITTEL |
| 10867 | **RUST JOINT** | JOINT AU MASTIC DE FONTE | ROSTDICHTUNG |
| 10868 | **RUST PREVENTING** | PRESERVANT DE LA ROUILLE | ROSTVERHÜTEND |
| 10869 | **RUST PREVENTING AGENT** | PRESERVATIF CONTRE LA ROUILLE, ANTI-ROUILLE | ROSTSCHUTZMITTEL |
| 10870 | **RUST PREVENTIVE (AGENT)** | PRODUIT ANTI-ROUILLE | ROSTSCHUTZMITTEL |
| 10871 | **RUST PROOFING** | PROTECTION CONTRE LA ROUILLE | ROSTSCHUTZ |
| 10872 | **RUST REMOVING DIP** | BAIN DE DEROUILLAGE | ENTROSTUNGSBAD |
| 10873 | **RUSTY** | ROUILLE | ROSTIG, VERROSTET |
| 10874 | **RUTHENIUM** | RUTHENIUM | RUTHENIUM |
| 10875 | **S.S. (STAINLESS STEEL) STRAP** | FEUILLARD INOX | STAHLBAND (ROSTFREIES) |
| 10876 | **SADDLE** | PIECE D'APPUI | SATTEL |
| 10877 | **SADDLE SUPPORT** | BERCEAU | STÜTZGESTELL, SATTELHALTER |
| 10878 | **SAFE EDGED FILE** | LIME A COTES LISSES | ANSATZFEILE |
| 10879 | **SAFE LOAD, WORKING LOAD** | CHARGE PRATIQUE, CHARGE DE SECURITE | BETRIEBSBELASTUNG |
| 10880 | **SAFE WORKING STRESS** | EFFORT ADMISSIBLE | BEANSPRUCHUNG (ZULÄSSIGE) |
| 10881 | **SAFETY APPLIANCE** | DISPOSITIF PROTECTEUR, DISPOSITIF DE SURETE, DISPOSITIF DE SECURITE, APPAREIL DE PROTECTION | SCHUTZVORRICHTUNG, SICHERHEITSVORRICHTUNG |
| 10882 | **SAFETY BELT** | CEINTURE DE SECURITE | SICHERHEITSGURT |
| 10883 | **SAFETY BRAKE** | FREIN DE SECURITE | SICHERHEITSBREMSE |
| 10884 | **SAFETY COUPLING** | MANCHON DE SURETE | SICHERHEITSKUPPLUNG |
| 10885 | **SAFETY FACTOR** | COEFFICIENT DE SECURITE | SICHERHEITSFAKTOR |
| 10886 | **SAFETY FUSE** | COUPE-CIRCUIT DE SURETE, PLOMB FUSIBLE, FUSIBLE DES COUPE-CIRCUIT, PLOMB DE SURETE | SICHERUNG (ELEKTR.) |
| 10887 | **SAFETY HEAD** | DISQUE DE RUPTURE | BRECHSICHERUNG |
| 10888 | **SAFETY HOOK** | CROCHET DE SURETE | SICHERHEITSHAKEN |
| 10889 | **SAFETY RULES** | MESURES DE SECURITE | SICHERHEITSVORSCHRIFTEN |
| 10890 | **SAFETY VALVE WITH HIGH LIFT** | SOUPAPE DE SURETE A GRANDE LEVEE | HOCHHUBSICHERHEITSVENTIL |
| 10891 | **SAFETY VALVE, RELIEF VALVE** | SOUPAPE DE SURETE | SICHERHEITSVENTIL |
| 10892 | **SAG** | EXCENTRATION, FLECHISSEMENT, COULURE POCHE, DEGOULINAGE | DURCHHÄNGEN, NASENBILDUNG |
| 10893 | **SAG (TO)** | FLECHIR | DURCHHÄNGEN |
| 10894 | **SAG, SAGGING** | FLECHISSEMENT | DURCHHANG |
| 10895 | **SAGGING (OR SAGS)** | COULURES | VORHÄNGEBILDUNG |

**SAL** 278

| | | | |
|---|---|---|---|
| 10896 | SALAMANDER | LOUP | OFENSAU |
| 10897 | SALARY | APPOINTEMENTS, SALAIRE | GEHALT |
| 10898 | SALES ENGINEER | INGENIEUR CHARGE DES VENTES | VERKAUFSINGENIEUR |
| 10899 | SALICYLIC ACID | ACIDE SALICYLIQUE | SALIZYLSÄURE |
| 10900 | SALIENT ANGLE | ANGLE SAILLANT | VORSPRINGENDE ECKE |
| 10901 | SALINOMETER | PESE-SELS | SALZSPINDEL, SALZWAAGE, SOLWAAGE, SALINOMETER |
| 10902 | SALOON | CONDUITE INTERIEURE, BERLINE | INNENLENKER, INNENSTEUERLIMOUSINE |
| 10903 | SALPETRE, NITRE, POTASSIUM NITRATE | SALPETRE, NITRE, NITRATE, AZOTATE DE POTASSIUM | SALPETER, KALISALPETER, SALPETERSAURES KALI, KALIUMNITRAT |
| 10904 | SALT | SEL (CHIM.) | SALZ (CHEM.) |
| 10905 | SALT BATH | BAIN DE SEL | SALZBAD |
| 10906 | SALT CONTENT | TENEUR EN SEL | SALZGEHALT |
| 10907 | SALT OF SORREL, SALT OF LEMON | SEL D'OSEILLE | SAUERKLEESALZ, KLEESALZ |
| 10908 | SALT SOLUTION | SOLUTION SALINE | SALZLÖSUNG |
| 10909 | SALT SPRAY TEST | ESSAI AU BROUILLARD SALIN | SALZSPRÜHNEBELPRÜFUNG |
| 10910 | SALT WATER | EAU SALINE | WASSER (SALZHALTIGES), SALZWASSER |
| 10911 | SALT-BATH BRAZING | BRASAGE AU BAIN SALIN | SALZBADLÖTEN |
| 10912 | SALT-BATH FURNACE | FOUR A BAIN DE SEL | SALZBADOFEN |
| 10913 | SALT-BATH HARDENING | TREMPE AU BAIN DE SEL | SALZBADHÄRTUNG |
| 10914 | SAMARIUM | SAMARIUM | SAMARIUM |
| 10915 | SAMPLE, SPECIMEN | ECHANTILLON, SPECIMEN | PROBE, PROBESTÜCK, MUSTER |
| 10916 | SAMPLING | PRISE D'UN ECHANTILLON, ECHANTILLONNAGE | ENTNAHME EINER PROBE, PROBENEHMEN, AUSWAHL, PROBEENTNAHME |
| 10917 | SAND | SABLE | SAND |
| 10918 | SAND BATH | BAIN DE SABLE | SANDBAD |
| 10919 | SAND BLAST (TO) | SABLER | SANDSTRAHL BEARBEITEN (MIT), ABSANDEN |
| 10920 | SAND BLAST APPARATUS | MACHINE AU JET DE SABLE, SABLEUSE | SANDSTRAHLGEBLÄSE |
| 10921 | SAND BLASTING | SABLAGE | BEARBEITEN MIT SANDSTRAHL, ABSANDEN, SANDTRAHLUNG |
| 10922 | SAND CASTING | COULEE EN SABLE | SANDGUSS |
| 10923 | SAND FILTER | FILTRE A SABLE | SANDFILTER |
| 10924 | SAND MOLD | MOULE EN SABLE | SANDFORM |
| 10925 | SAND PAPER | PAPIER SABLE | SANDPAPIER |
| 10926 | SAND PAPERING MACHINE, GLASS PAPERING MACHINE | MACHINE A PONCER AU PAPIER DE VERRE | SANDPAPIERMASCHINE |
| 10927 | SANDARACH | SANDARAQUE, RESINE DE VERNIS | SANDARAK |
| 10928 | SANDSTONE | GRES (GEOL.) | SANDSTEIN |
| 10929 | SANDWICH ROLLING | LAMINAGE EN SANDWICH, LAMINAGE STRATIFIE | SANDWICHWALZEN |
| 10930 | SANDY SOIL | TERRAIN SABLEUX | SANDBODEN |
| 10931 | SANITRY FACILITIES | INSTALLATIONS SANITAIRES, EQUIPEMENT SANITAIRE | EINRICHTUNG (SANITÄRE) |
| 10932 | SAPONIFIABLE | SAPONIFIABLE | VERSEIFBAR |
| 10933 | SAPONIFICATION | SAPONIFICATION | SEIFENBILDUNG, VERSEIFUNG |
| 10934 | SAPONIFY (TO) | SAPONIFIER | VERSEIFEN |
| 10935 | SAPONITE | SAPONITE, PIERRE DE SAVON | SEIFENSTEIN, SAPONIT |
| 10936 | SAPWOOD, ALBURNUM | AUBIER | SPLINT, SPLINTHOLZ |
| 10937 | SASH BAR IRON | FER (MOULURE) A VITRAGES | SPROSSENEISEN |

| | | | |
|---|---|---|---|
| 10938 | **SATIN FINISH** | FINI SATINE | MATTGESCHLIFFEN |
| 10939 | **SATURATE (TO)** | SATURER | SÄTTIGEN |
| 10940 | **SATURATED HYDROCARBONS** | HYDROCARBURES SATURES, HYDROCARBURES PARAFFINIQUES | KOHLENWASSERSTOFFE (GESÄTTIGTE) |
| 10941 | **SATURATED SOLUTION** | SOLUTION SATUREE | LÖSUNG (GESÄTTIGTE) |
| 10942 | **SATURATED STEAM** | VAPEUR SATUREE, SATURANTE | DAMPF (GESÄTTIGTER), SATTDAMPF |
| 10943 | **SATURATION** | SATURATION | SÄTTIGUNG |
| 10944 | **SATURATION PRESSURE** | PRESSION DE SATURATION | SÄTTIGUNGSDRUCK |
| 10945 | **SATURATION TEMPERATURE** | TEMPERATURE DE SATURATION | SÄTTIGUNGSTEMPERATUR |
| 10946 | **SAUCER** | GODET (DU DESSINATEUR) | TUSCHNAPF, TUSCHSCHALE |
| 10947 | **SAVING OF LABOUR** | ECONOMIE DANS LE TRAVAIL, ECONOMIE DE MAIN-D'OEUVRE | ARBEITSERSPARNIS |
| 10948 | **SAVING OF POWER** | ECONOMIE DE FORCE MOTRICE | KRAFTERSPARNIS |
| 10949 | **SAVING OF TIME, ECONOMY OF TIME** | ECONOMIE DE TEMPS, GAIN DE TEMPS | ZEITERSPARNIS |
| 10950 | **SAW** | SCIE | SÄGE |
| 10951 | **SAW (TO)** | SCIER | SÄGEN |
| 10952 | **SAW BLADE** | LAME DE SCIE | SÄGEBLATT |
| 10953 | **SAW DUST** | SCIURE DE BOIS , BRAN DE SCIE | SÄGEMEHL, SÄGESPÄNE |
| 10954 | **SAW FILE** | LIME A SCIES | SÄGEFEILE |
| 10955 | **SAW FILER'S CLAMP, VICE** | ETAU D'AFFUTAGE POUR SCIES | SÄGEFEILKLUPPE |
| 10956 | **SAW MILL** | SCIERIE (USINE) | SÄGEWERK |
| 10957 | **SAW SET** | TOURNE-A-GAUCHE POUR AVOYER, TOURNE-A-GAUCHE POUR DONNER DU PAS/DE VOIE A UNE SCIE | SCHRÄNKEISEN |
| 10958 | **SAW SETTING** | MISE EN VOIE DES DENTS D'UNE SCIE, AVOYAGE D'UNE SCIE | SCHRÄNKEN, AUSSETZEN DER SÄGEZÄHNE |
| 10959 | **SAW TOOTH** | DENT DE SCIE | SÄGEZAHN |
| 10960 | **SAW TOOTH CLUTCH** | EMBRAYAGE A DENTS DE SCIE | SÄGEZAHNKUPPLUNG |
| 10961 | **SAWING** | SCIAGE | SÄGEN |
| 10962 | **SAWN TIMBER** | BOIS DEBITE | SCHNITTHOLZ |
| 10963 | **SAWS AND SAW BENCHES** | SCIES A BUCHES | SÄGEN UND SÄGEBÄNKE |
| 10964 | **SCAB** | ECAILLE | SCHUPPE |
| 10965 | **SCAFFOLD** | ECHAFAUDAGE | GERÜST, ARBEITSGERÜST, BAUGERÜST |
| 10966 | **SCALAR PRODUCT** | PRODUIT SCALAIRE | PRODUKT (SKALARES) |
| 10967 | **SCALAR QUANTITY** | SCALAIRE | SKALAR |
| 10968 | **SCALE** | ECHELLE, ECAILLE | MASSSTAB, SCHUPPE |
| 10969 | **SCALE** | DEPOTS CALCAIRES, INCRUSTATIONS DES CHAUDIERES, CALCAIRE, TARTRE DES CHAUDIERES | KESSELSTEIN |
| 10970 | **SCALE (ON A LARGER)** | REPRODUCTION (EN GRAND) | MASSSTAB (IN VERGRÖSSERTEM), MASSSTÄBLICH VERGRÖSSERT |
| 10971 | **SCALE (TO), REMOVE THE SCALE (TO)** | DESINCRUSTER, DETARTRER | KESSELSTEIN ENTFERNEN |
| 10972 | **SCALE BEAM, BEAM OF A BALANCE** | FLEAU DE BALANCE | WAAGEBALKEN |
| 10973 | **SCALE OF A DRAWING** | ECHELLE D'UN PLAN | MASSSTAB EINER ZEICHNUNG, ZEICHNUNGSMASSSTAB |
| 10974 | **SCALE OF HARDNESS** | ECHELLE, GAMME DE DURETE | HÄRTESKALA |
| 10975 | **SCALE OFF (TO), PEEL OFF (TO), FLAKE (TO)** | ECAILLER (S') | ABBLÄTTERN |
| 10976 | **SCALE PAN** | PLATEAU D'UNE BALANCE | WAAGSCHALE, GEWICHTSSCHALE |
| 10977 | **SCALE PIT** | FOSSE A BATTITURES | SINTERGRUBE |

**SCA** 280

| | | | |
|---|---|---|---|
| 10978 | SCALE PREVENTIVE, ANTI-INCRUSTATOR | DESINCRUSTANT PREVENTIF, SUBSTANCE ANTI-INCRUSTANTE, DETARTRANT | KESSELSTEINVERHÜTUNGSMITTEL |
| 10979 | SCALE REMOVING | DECALAMINAGE | ENTZUNDERUNG |
| 10980 | SCALE RESISTANCE | INOXYDABILITE | ZUNDERBESTÄNDIGKEIT |
| 10981 | SCALE, DIVISION, GRADUATION | DIVISION, GRADUATION, ECHELLE | TEILUNG, GRADEINTEILUNG, SKALA |
| 10982 | SCALE, RATIO OF DIMENSIONS | ECHELLE (MOYEN DE COMPARAISON) | MASSSTAB, GRÖSSENVERHÄLTNIS |
| 10983 | SCALED PROPORTIONAL DRAWING, DRAWING TO SCALE | DESSIN A L'ECHELLE | ZEICHNUNG (MASSSTÄBLICHE) |
| 10984 | SCALENE TRIANGLE | TRIANGLE SCALENE | DREIECK (UNGLEICHSEITIGES) |
| 10985 | SCALING | ECAILLAGE | ABBLÄTTERUNG |
| 10986 | SCALING HAMMER | MARTEAU A EBARBER LA FONTE, MARTEAU A PIQUER LES CHAUDIERES | GUSSPUTZHAMMER, KESSELSTEINHAMMER |
| 10987 | SCALING, REMOVAL OF SCALE | DESINCRUSTATION, DETARTRAGE | KESSELSTEINENTFERNUNG |
| 10988 | SCALPING | ECROUTAGE | SCHÄLUNG |
| 10989 | SCALY FLAKE GRAPHITE | GRAPHITE EN PAILLETTES | SCHUPPENGRAPHIT |
| 10990 | SCAN | BALAYER | ABTASTEN |
| 10991 | SCANDIUM | SCANDIUM | SKANDIUM |
| 10992 | SCANNING | BALAYAGE | ZONENABTASTEN |
| 10993 | SCARF | DECRIQUER (AU CHALUMEAU) | FLÄMMEN |
| 10994 | SCATTERING | DIFFUSION | STREUUNG |
| 10995 | SCAVENGER | ELIMINATEUR D'IMPURETES | REIN1GUNGSMITTEL |
| 10996 | SCHEELE'S GREEN | VERT DE SCHEELE, ARSENITE DE CUIVRE | GRÜN (SCHEELESCHES), SCHWEDISCHGRÜN, MINERALGRÜN |
| 10997 | SCHEELITE | SCHEELITE, SCHEELIN CALCAIRE | SCHEELIT |
| 10998 | SCHELLAC VARNISH | VERNIS A LA GOMME-LAQUE | SCHELLACKFIRNIS |
| 10999 | SCHIST | SCHISTE | SCHIEFER (GEOL.) |
| 11000 | SCHWEINFURTH GREEN | VERT DE SCHWEINFURT | SCHWEINFURTERGRÜN |
| 11001 | SCIENTIFIC MANAGEMENT | DIRECTION/ORGANISATION SCIENTIFIQUE DES ATELIERS | BETRIEBSFÜHRUNG (WISSENCHAFTLICHE) |
| 11002 | SCLEROMETER | SCLEROMETRE | RITZHÄRTEPRÜFER, SKLEROMETER |
| 11003 | SCLEROSCOPE HARDNESS | DURETE SHORE | KUGELFALLHÄRTE, SHOREHÄRTE |
| 11004 | SCORIFICATION | SCORIFICATION | VERSCHLACKUNG |
| 11005 | SCOUR (TO), PICKLE A METAL (TO) | DECAPER, DEROCHER, DEGRAISSER UN METAL | ABBEIZEN (EIN METALL), BLANKBEIZEN, ENTZUNDERN, DEKAPIEREN |
| 11006 | SCOURING, PICKLING A METAL | DECAPAGE, DEROCHAGE, DEGRAISSAGE D'UN METAL | BEIZEN, ABBEIZEN, BLANKBEIZEN, ENTZUNDERN, DEKAPIEREN EINES METALLES |
| 11007 | SCRAP, SCRAP IRON | RIBLONS DE FER, ROGNURES DE FER, FERRAILLE, MITRAILLE | ALTEISEN, SCHROTT |
| 11008 | SCRAPE (TO) | GRATTER, RACLER, CURER | SCHABEN |
| 11009 | SCRAPE, SCRAPER | GRATTOIR, RACLOIR, RACLETTE, ROGNOIR, CURETTE | SCHABER |
| 11010 | SCRAPER | TRANSPORTEUR A RACLETTES | KRATZER, SCHLEPPER, SCHLEPPKETTE, SEILFÖRDERER, SCHLEPPSEIL |
| 11011 | SCRAPING | GRATTAGE, RACLAGE, CURAGE | SCHABEN, KRATZEN |
| 11012 | SCRAPING MACHINE | MACHINE A GRATTER | SCHABEMASCHINE |
| 11013 | SCRATCH | GRIFFE | RITZ |
| 11014 | SCRATCH BRUSH | BROSSE METALLIQUE | KRATZBÜRSTE, PUTZBÜRSTE |
| 11015 | SCRATCH HARDNESS | RESISTANCE A L'ABRASION | KRATZFESTIGKEIT |
| 11016 | SCRATCH-BRUSH FINISH | FINISSAGE A LA BROSSE METALLIQUE | METALLBÜRSTEN-FERTIGBEARBEITUNG |
| 11017 | SCRATCHING TEST | ESSAI SCLEROMETRIQUE | RITZVERSUCH |

| | | | |
|---|---|---|---|
| 11018 | **SCREEN** | ECRAN, TAMIS | SCHIRM, SIEB |
| 11019 | **SCREEN (OPT.)** | ECRAN (OPT.) | SCHIRM (OPT.) |
| 11020 | **SCREEN ANALYSIS** | ANALYSE GRANULOMETRIQUE | SIEBANALYSE |
| 11021 | **SCREW** | VIS, BOULON A VIS | SCHRAUBE |
| 11022 | **SCREW (TO)** | VISSER, SERRER A VIS | VERSCHRAUBEN, ANSCHRAUBEN, FESTSCHRAUBEN, ZUSAMMENSCHRAUBEN |
| 11023 | **SCREW AUGER, TWISTED AUGER** | MECHE STYRIENNE, MECHE FACON SUISSE | SCHNECKENBOHRER |
| 11024 | **SCREW AXIS** | AXE DE SYMETRIE | SYMMETRIEACHSE |
| 11025 | **SCREW CAP, CAP WITH A FEMALE THREAD** | BOUCHON FILETE, BOUCHON FEMELLE, BOUCHON TARAUDE | VERSCHLUSSKAPPE, SCHRAUBVERSHLUSS, SCHRAUBKAPPE |
| 11026 | **SCREW COUPLING** | MANCHON A VIS | SCHRAUBENKUPPLUNG, GEWINDEKUPPLUNG |
| 11027 | **SCREW CURRENT METER** | MOULINET HYDRAULIQUE (POUR LA MESURE DE LA VITESSE D'ECOULEMENT D'UN COURANT D'EAU) | WASSERMESSFLÜGEL, WASSERMESSSCHRAUBE, HYDROMETRISCHER FLÜGEL |
| 11028 | **SCREW CUTTING** | FILETAGE (OPERATION) | SCHRAUBENSCHNEIDEN |
| 11029 | **SCREW CUTTING LATHE** | TOUR A FILETER | GEWINDEDREHBANK |
| 11030 | **SCREW CUTTING, SCREW THREADING, CUTTING SCREW THREADS** | CREUSAGE, CREUSEMENT D'UN FILET | SCHNEIDEN EINES GEWINDES, GEWINDESCHNEIDEN |
| 11031 | **SCREW DISLOCATION** | DISLOCATION-VIS (EN HELICE) | SCHRAUBENVERSETZUNG |
| 11032 | **SCREW DOLLY** | TAS AVEC CONTRE-BOUTEROLLE, TURC | NIETWINDE |
| 11033 | **SCREW DOWN COCK** | ROBINET A VIS DE PRESSION | NIEDERSCHRAUBHAHN |
| 11034 | **SCREW GAUGE** | PALMER | SCHRAUBLEHRE |
| 11035 | **SCREW JACK** | VERIN, CRIC MECANIQUE, CRIC A VIS | WINDE, WAGENHEBER, SCHRAUBENHEBER, SCHRAUBENWINDE |
| 11036 | **SCREW MILLING MACHINE, THREAD MILLER** | MACHINE A FRAISER LES VIS | GEWINDEFRÄSMASCHINE |
| 11037 | **SCREW ON (TO)** | VISSER SUR, MONTER A VIS | AUFSCHRAUBEN |
| 11038 | **SCREW PITCH GAUGE** | JAUGE DE FILETAGE | GEWINDEKONTROLLEHRE |
| 11039 | **SCREW PLATE, DIE PLATE** | FILIERE SIMPLE, FILIERE A TRUELLE | SCHNEIDEISEN, GEWINDEEISEN, SCHNEIDKLINGE, SCHRAUBENBLECH |
| 11040 | **SCREW PRESS** | PRESSE A VIS, BALANCIER A VIS | SPINDELPRESSE, SCHRAUBENPRESSE |
| 11041 | **SCREW PROPELLER, PROPELLER** | PROPULSEUR, HELICE PROPULSIVE | ANTRIEBSCHRAUBE, TREIBSCHRAUBE, PROPELLER |
| 11042 | **SCREW PUMP** | POMPE HELICOIDALE | SCHRAUBENPUMPE |
| 11043 | **SCREW SPIKE** | TIRE-FOND | SCHWELLENSCHRAUBE, SCHIENENSCHRAUBE |
| 11044 | **SCREW TAP** | TARAUD | GEWINDEBOHRER |
| 11045 | **SCREW THREAD** | FILET, PAS DE VIS, FILETAGE | GEWINDE, SCHRAUBENGEWINDE |
| 11046 | **SCREW THREAD (TO), CUT SCREW THREADS (TO)** | CREUSER UN FILER | GEWINDE SCHNEIDEN |
| 11047 | **SCREW THREAD GAUGE** | CALIBRE DE FILETAGE | GEWINDELEHRE |
| 11048 | **SCREW THREAD MICROMETER COMPARATOR** | COMPARATEUR MICROMETRIQUE POUR FILETAGES | MIKROMETRISCHER SCHRAUBENGEWINDE-KOMPARATOR |
| 11049 | **SCREW THREAD PLUG GAUGE** | TAMPON D'ALESAGE, TAMPON FILETE MALE | GEWINDELEHRDORN |
| 11050 | **SCREW THREAD RING GAUGE** | BAGUE TARAUDEE DU CALIBRE DE FILETAGE | GEWINDELEHRMUTTER |
| 11051 | **SCREW WITH CYLINDRICAL HEAD, CHEESE HEAD SCREW** | VIS A TETE RONDE | RUNDKOPFSCHRAUBE, SCHRAUBE MIT ZYLINDERKOPF |

**SCR**

282

| | | | |
|---|---|---|---|
| 11052 | **SCREW WRENCH, MONKEY WRENCH, ADJUSTABLE SPANNER** | CLEF AJUSTABLE, CLEF ANGLAISE | SCHRAUBENSCHLÜSSEL (VERSTELLBARER), SCHRAUBENSCHLÜSSEL (ENGLISCHER), UNIVERSALSCHRAUBENSCHLÜSSEL |
| 11053 | **SCREWED ENDS (FEMALE)** | ORIFICES TARAUDES (FEMELLES) | MUFFENANSCHLUSS |
| 11054 | **SCREWED ENDS (MALE)** | ORIFICES FILETES (MALES) | GEWINDEWEITEN |
| 11055 | **SCREWED FLANGE** | BRIDE A VISSER | GEWINDEFLANSCH |
| 11056 | **SCREWED HOLE** | TROU FILETE, ECROU | GEWINDELOCH |
| 11057 | **SCREWED HOOK** | CROCHET A VIS, PITON-VIS | SCHRAUBENHAKEN |
| 11058 | **SCREWED JOINT, THREADED CONNECTION** | RACCORD VISSE | SCHRAUBVERBINDUNG, VERSCHRAUBUNG |
| 11059 | **SCREWED PIPE** | TUBE TARAUDE, TUBE FILETE | GEWINDEROHR |
| 11060 | **SCREWED PLUG, PLUG WITH A MALE THREAD** | BOUCHON VISSE, BOUCHON A VIS, BOUCHON FILETE, BOUCHON MALE | VERSCHLUSSPFROPFEN, VERSCHLUSSSCHRAUBE ,GEWINDEPFROPFEN |
| 11061 | **SCREWED SOCKET** | MANCHON TARAUDE, MANCHON FEMELLE, ECROU A RACCORD, RACCORD FILETE | SCHRAUBMUFFE, GEWINDEMUFFE |
| 11062 | **SCREWED SPINDLE** | TIGE FILETEE | SPINDEL, SCHRAUBENSPINDEL, GEWINDESPINDEL |
| 11063 | **SCREWED-ON FLANGE** | BRIDE VISSEE | FLANSCH (AUFGESCHRAUBTER) |
| 11064 | **SCREWED, SCREWING FLANGE** | BRIDE TARAUDEE | GEWINDEFLANSCH |
| 11065 | **SCREWING** | VISSAGE | VERSCHRAUBEN, ANSCHRAUBEN, FESTSCHRAUBEN, ZUSAMMENSCHRAUBEN |
| 11066 | **SCREWING MACHINE, SCREW CUTTING MACHINE** | MACHINE A VISSER, MACHINE A FILETER ET TARAUDER, FILETEUSE, TARAUDEUSE | SCHRAUBENSCHNEIDMASCHINE, GEWINDESCHNEIDMASCHINE |
| 11067 | **SCREWING ON** | MONTAGE A VIS | AUFSCHRAUBEN |
| 11068 | **SCRIBER, SCRIBING IRON** | POINTE A TRACER, TRACERET, TRACOIR | VORREISSER, REISSNADEL, ANREISSNADEL, ANREISSSPITZE |
| 11069 | **SCRIBING BLOCK, SURFACING GAUGE** | TRUSQUIN A MARBRE | STREICHMASS (STEHENDES) |
| 11070 | **SEA LEVEL** | NIVEAU DE LA MER | MEERESSPIEGEL, MEERESHÖHE, SEEHÖHE |
| 11071 | **SEA SAND, MARINE SAND** | SABLE DE MER | MEERESSAND, SEESAND, DÜNENSAND |
| 11072 | **SEA WATER** | EAU DE MER | MEERWASSER, SEEWASSER |
| 11073 | **SEAL PAN** | CUVETTE | PLATTENABDICHTUNGSSCHALE |
| 11074 | **SEAL PAN (OF TRAYS)** | CUVETTE DE PLATEAUX | BECKEN DES ABSTELLTISCHES |
| 11075 | **SEAL PLATE** | PLAQUETTE | DICHTPLÄTTCHEN |
| 11076 | **SEAL WELD** | SOUDAGE ETANCHE | DICHTSCHWEISSEN |
| 11077 | **SEAL WITH LEAD (TO)** | PLOMBER (MARQUER D'UN SCEAU EN PLOMB) | PLOMBIEREN, MIT EINER PLOMBE VERSEHEN |
| 11078 | **SEALANT** | BOURRAGE PLASTIQUE ETANCHE, JOINT PLASTIQUE | KUNSTSTOFF-DICHTPACKUNG |
| 11079 | **SEALED BEAM** | BLOC OPTIQUE, MONOBLOC | SEALED-BEAM SCHEINMERFER |
| 11080 | **SEALINE** | CANALISATION EN MER OUVERTE, CONDUITE EN MER | SEEROHRLEITUNG |
| 11081 | **SEALING** | ETANCHEITE | ABDICHTUNG |
| 11082 | **SEALING LIQUID** | LIQUIDE OBTURATEUR | SPERRFLÜSSIGKEIT |
| 11083 | **SEAM** | SOUDURE | FUGE, NAHT |
| 11084 | **SEAM OF RIVETED JOINT** | LIGNE DE JONCTION DES TOLES | NIETNAHT |
| 11085 | **SEAM OF TUBE** | SOUDURE D'UN TUBE | NAHT EINES ROHRES, ROHRNAHT |
| 11086 | **SEAM WELDING** | SOUDURE CONTINE, SOUDAGE EN LIGNE CONTINUE A LA MOLETTE | NAHTSCHWEISSUNG, ROLLEN(NAHT)SCHWEISSEN |
| 11087 | **SEAM-FOLDING MACHINE** | PLIEUSE | FALZBIEGEMASCHINE |
| 11088 | **SEAMING MACHINE** | SERTISSEUSE | FALZMASCHINE |

| | | | |
|---|---|---|---|
| 11089 | **SEAMLESS PIPE, SEAMLESS TUBES, SEAMLESS WELDLESS TUBE** | TUBE SANS SOUDURE | ROHR (NAHTLOSES) |
| 11090 | **SEARCH UNIT** | PALPEUR | FÜHLER |
| 11091 | **SEARCHLIGHT** | PROJECTEUR DE LUMIERE | SCHEINWERFER |
| 11092 | **SEASON CRACK** | CRIQUE DE VIEILLISSEMENT, CRAQUELURE SAISONNIERE | ALTERSRISS |
| 11093 | **SEASON CRACKING** | CORROSION INTERCRISTALLINE DES LAITONS 70/30 | SPANNUNGSRISSKORROSION |
| 11094 | **SEASON TIMBER (TO)** | SECHER LES BOIS A L'AIR LIBRE | HOLZ AUSTROCKNEN, HOLZ AN DER LUFT TROCKNEN |
| 11095 | **SEASONING (TIMBER)** | DESSECHAGE/DESSICCATION DES BOIS A L'AIR LIBRE | TROCKNEN DES HOLZES AN DER LUFT, AUSTROCKNEN DES HOLZES |
| 11096 | **SEAT BELT** | CEINTURE DE SECURITE | SITZGURT |
| 11097 | **SEAT RING** | SIEGE DE SOUPAPE | VENTILSITZ |
| 11098 | **SEAT, SEATING** | SIEGE | SITZ, SITZFLÄCHE |
| 11099 | **SECANT** | SECANTE | SEKANTE |
| 11100 | **SECOND CUT FILE** | LIME A TAILLE DEMI-DOUCE | HALBSCHLICHTFEILE |
| 11101 | **SECOND FILTER** | SECOND FILTRE | FEINFILTER |
| 11102 | **SECOND TAP** | TARAUD DEMI-CONIQUE, TARAUD INTERMEDIAIRE | GEWINDEMITTELSCHNEIDER |
| 11103 | **SECONDARY COLOUR** | COULEUR COMPOSEE | ZWEITFARBE, MISCHFARBE |
| 11104 | **SECONDARY CREEP** | FLUAGE SECONDAIRE | SEKUNDÄRES KRIECHEN, ZWEITES KRIECHSTADIUM |
| 11105 | **SECONDARY HARDENING** | TREMPE SECONDAIRE | SEKUNDÄRE HÄRTUNG |
| 11106 | **SECONDARY INCLUSION** | INCLUSION SECONDAIRE | EINSCHLUSS (SEKUNDÄRER) |
| 11107 | **SECONDARY METAL** | METAL DE RECUPERATION | UMSCHMELZMETALL |
| 11108 | **SECONDARY SPECTRUM** | SPECTRE SECONDAIRE | NEBENSPEKTRUM |
| 11109 | **SECONDARY STRESS** | CONTRAINTE SECONDAIRE | NEBENSPANNUNG |
| 11110 | **SECONDARY WELDING CURRENT** | COURANT SECONDAIRE DE SOUDAGE | SEKUNDÄRSCHWEISSSTROM |
| 11111 | **SECTION** | SECTION, COUPE TRANSVERSALE | QUERSCHNITT |
| 11112 | **SECTION (ON LINE AB), SECTIONAL VIEW** | COUPE D'UN DESSIN | SCHNITT, DURCHSCHNITT NACH A-B |
| 11113 | **SECTION FOR MICROSCOPIC RESEARCH** | OBJET A EXAMINER AU MICROSCOPE SOUS FORME DE COUPE MINCE | SCHLIFF FÜR MIKROSKOPIE, DÜNNSCHLIFF |
| 11114 | **SECTION IRON(S) OR SHAPE(S) STRUCTURAL(S)** | PROFILE(S) | FORMSTAHL |
| 11115 | **SECTION MODULUS** | MODULE D'INERTIE | WIDERSTANDSMOMENT |
| 11116 | **SECTION OF A BEAM** | SECTION (DROITE OU OBLIQUE) D'UNE POUTRE | SENKRECHTER ODER SCHRÄGER ABSCHNITT EINES BALKENS |
| 11117 | **SECTION OF A PRESSURE VESSEL** | ELEMENT D'UN RECIPIENT A PRESSION | DRUCKLUFTBEHÄLTERGLIED |
| 11118 | **SECTION OF A STRAIGHT LINE** | SEGMENT D'UNE DROITE | STRECKE (GEOM.) |
| 11119 | **SECTION, SECTIONAL IRON** | FER PROFILE FACONNE, PROFILE | FORMEISEN, PROFILEISEN, FASSONEISEN |
| 11120 | **SECTIONAL AREA** | SURFACE, AIRE DE LA SECTION | QUERSCHNITTFLÄCHE |
| 11121 | **SECTIONAL AREA OF VALVE PASSAGE** | SECTION DE PASSAGE D'UNE SOUPAPE, AIRE DE L'OUVERTURE MASQUEE PAR LA SOUPAPE | SPALTQUERSCHNITT EINES VENTILS |
| 11122 | **SECTIONAL DRAWING** | DESSIN EN COUPE, COUPE, SECTION | SCHNITTZEICHNUNG |
| 11123 | **SECTIONAL GROOVE** | CALIBRE DE PROFILAGE | PROFILKALIBER |
| 11124 | **SECTIONAL PLAN, PLAN** | PLAN, PROJECTION HORIZONTALE | GRUNDRISS, HORIZONTALPROJEKTION |
| 11125 | **SECTIONAL STEEL** | ACIER PROFILE | PROFILSTAHL |

# SEC

| | | | |
|---|---|---|---|
| 11126 | **SECTOR OF CIRCLE** | SECTEUR D'UN CERCLE, SECTEUR CIRCULAIRE | KREISAUSSCHNITT, KREISSEKTOR |
| 11127 | **SECTOR OF SPHERE, SPHERICAL SECTOR** | SECTEUR SPHERIQUE | KUGELAUSSCHNITT, KUGELSEKTOR |
| 11128 | **SEDAN** | BERLINE | INNENLENKER |
| 11129 | **SEED BARROWS AND BROADCASTERS** | SEMOIRS A LA VOLEE | KARREN UND BREITSÄMASCHINEN |
| 11130 | **SEED CHARGE** | AGENT PRECIPITANT | FÄLLMITTEL |
| 11131 | **SEED LAC** | GOMME-LAQUE EN GRAINS | KÖRNERLACK, LACK IN KÖRNERN |
| 11132 | **SEEDERS AND SEEDER UNITS** | SEMOIRS POUR PORTES OUTILS | SÄMASCHINEN |
| 11133 | **SEEDING TRANSPLANTERS AND SISAL PLANTERS** | REPIQUEUSES | PIKIERMASCHINEN UND SISALPFLANZMASCHINEN |
| 11134 | **SEGER CONE** | CONE PYROMETRIQUE (DE SEGER), MONTRE DE SEGER, MONTRE FUSIBLE | SEGERKEGEL, SCHMELZKEGEL, BRENNKEGEL |
| 11135 | **SEGMENT** | SEGMENT | AUSSCHNITT |
| 11136 | **SEGMENT OF CIRCLE** | SEGMENT D'UN CERCLE | KREISABSCHNITT, KREISSEGMENT |
| 11137 | **SEGMENT OF SPHERE** | CALOTTE SPHERIQUE, SEGMENT SPHERIQUE A UNE BASE | KUGELHAUBE, KUGELSCHALE, KALOTTE |
| 11138 | **SEGMENTAL FLYWHEEL** | VOLANT EN PLUSIEURS SEGMENTS | SCHWUNGRAD (MEHRSTELLIGES) |
| 11139 | **SEGREGATION** | TRI, SEGREGATION | AUSSONDERUNG |
| 11140 | **SEIZE (TO)** | GRIPPER | FRESSEN, EINFRESSEN (SICH) |
| 11141 | **SEIZING** | GRIPPAGE, GRIPPEMENT | FRESSEN, EINFRESSEN, FESTFRESSEN |
| 11142 | **SELECTIVE ANNEALING** | RECUIT SELECTIF | AUSGLÜHEN (SELEKTIVES) |
| 11143 | **SELECTIVE CARBURIZING** | CEMENTATION SELECTIVE | AUFKOHLUNG (SELEKTIVE) |
| 11144 | **SELECTIVE FLOTATION** | FLOTTATION SELECTIVE | SCHWIMMAUFBEREITUNG (SELEKTIVE) |
| 11145 | **SELECTIVE HARDENING** | TREMPE PARTIELLE | TEILHÄRTUNG |
| 11146 | **SELENIUM** | SELENIUM | SELEN |
| 11147 | **SELF- LUMINOUS BODY** | CORPS LUMINEUX | KÖRPER (SELBSTLEUCHTENDER) |
| 11148 | **SELF-ACTING, AUTOMATIC** | AUTOMATIQUE | SELBSTTÄTIG, AUTOMATISCH |
| 11149 | **SELF-ACTUATING CLUTCH** | ACCOUPLEMENT AUTOMATIQUE | KUPPLUNG (SELBSTEINRÜCKENDE) |
| 11150 | **SELF-ADJUSTING BEARING** | PALIER AUTO-REGULATEUR | LAGER (SICH SELBSTEINSTELLENDES |
| 11151 | **SELF-CONTAINED MACHINE** | MACHINE ISOLEE | MASCHINE (FREISTEHENDE) |
| 11152 | **SELF-DRIVING CHUCKS** | MANDRINS AUTO-ENTRAINEURS | FUTTER (SELBSTTÄTIGE) |
| 11153 | **SELF-EXCITATION** | AUTO-EXCITATION | SELBSTERREGUNG, EIGENERREGUNG |
| 11154 | **SELF-HARDENING STEEL** | ACIER AUTO-TREMPANT | SELBSTHÄRTESTAHL |
| 11155 | **SELF-HEATING SOLDERING IRON** | FER A SOUDER A CHAUFFAGE AUTOMATIQUE | SELBSTWÄRMENDER LÖTKOLBEN, LÖTKOLBEN MIT SELBSTBEHEIZUNG |
| 11156 | **SELF-INDUCTION** | AUTO-INDUCTION, SELF-INDUCTION, INDUCTION PROPRE | SELBSTINDUKTION |
| 11157 | **SELF-LOCKING** | BLOCAGE AUTOMATIQUE (A) | SELBSTHEMMEND, SELBSTSPERREND |
| 11158 | **SELF-LUBRICATING BEARING** | COUSSINET AUTO-GRAISSEUR | LAGER (SELBSTSCHMIERENDES) |
| 11159 | **SELF-RELEASING TAPER** | CONE AUTO-DEMONTABLE | KEGEL (SELBSTLÖSENDER) |
| 11160 | **SELF-SUPPORTING CONICAL ROOF TANK** | RESERVOIR A TOIT CONIQUE AUTOPORTANT | TANK MIT SELBSTTRAGENDEM KONUSDACH |
| 11161 | **SELF-SUPPORTING FRAME** | CHARPENTE AUTOPORTANTE | GERIPPE (SELBSTTRAGENDES), KONSTRUKTION (SELBSTTRAGENDE), GERÜST (SELBSTTRAGENDES) |
| 11162 | **SELF-TAPPING SCREW** | VIS AUTOTARAUDEUSE | SCHRAUBE (SELBSTSCHNEIDENDE) |
| 11163 | **SELF-TAPPING WASHER** | RONDELLE AUTOTARAUDEUSE | SCHEIBE (SELBSTSCHNEIDENDE) |
| 11164 | **SELLERS COUPLING** | MANCHON D'ACCOUPLEMENT SELLERS | KLEMMKUPPLUNG, SELLERSKUPPLUNG |
| 11165 | **SEMI-ANTHRACITE, STEAM COAL** | HOUILLE ANTHRACITEUSE, HOUILLE MAIGRE A COURTE FLAMME | KOHLE (ANTHRAZITISCHE) |

| | | | |
|---|---|---|---|
| 11166 | SEMI-AUTOMATIC ARC WELD | SOUDAGE SEMI-AUTOMATIQUE A L'ARC | LICHTBOGEN-SCHWEISSEN (TEILAUTOMATISCHES) |
| 11167 | SEMI-AXIS | DEMI-AXE | HALBACHSE (GEOM.) |
| 11168 | SEMI-BITUMINOUS COAL, LEAN MEAGER COAL | HOUILLE MAIGRE | KOHLE (MAGERE) |
| 11169 | SEMI-CIRCULAR (ADJ) | DEMI-CIRCULAIRE | HALBKREISFÖRMIG |
| 11170 | SEMI-CIRCULAR, HALF-ROUND CROSS SECTION | SECTION MI-RONDE, SEMI-CIRCULAIRE | QUERSCHNITT (HALBRUNDER) |
| 11171 | SEMI-DIESEL (OIL INJECTION ENGINE, MIXED-CYCLE ENGINE) | MOTEUR SEMI-DIESEL, SEMI-DIESEL | HALBDIESELMOTOR |
| 11172 | SEMI-JIG BORING MACHINE | SEMI-POINTEUSE | HALBLEHRENBOHRMASCHINE |
| 11173 | SEMI-KILLED STEEL | ACIER SEMI-CALME | STAHL (HALBBERUHIGTER) |
| 11174 | SEMI-MANUFACTURED GOODS | PRODUIT SEMI-OUVRE | HALBZEUG, HALBFABRIKAT |
| 11175 | SEMI-PORTABLE STEAM ENGINE, STATIONARY LOCOMOBILE | MACHINE A VAPEUR DEMI-FIXE | LOKOMOBILE (FESTSTEHENDE), LOKOMOBILE (ORTSFESTE), LOKOMOBILE (STATIONÄRE) |
| 11176 | SEMI-ROTARY WING PUMP | POMPE A PISTON OSCILLANT | PUMPE MIT SCHWINGENDEM ODER OSZILLIERENDEM KOLBEN, FLÜGELPUMPE |
| 11177 | SEMI-STEEL | FONTE ACIEREE | GUSSEISEN MIT STAHLZUSATZ |
| 11178 | SEMI-TRAILER | SEMI-REMORQUE | SATTELSCHLEPPER |
| 11179 | SEMICIRCLE | DEMI-CERCLE | HALBKREIS |
| 11180 | SEMICIRCULAR PROTRACTOR | RAPPORTEUR DEMI-CERCLE | HALBKREISTRANSPORTEUR |
| 11181 | SENDZIMIR MILL | LAMINOIR SENDZIMIR | SENDZIMIRWALZWERK |
| 11182 | SENSE OF A FORCE | SENS D'UNE FORCE | KRAFTSINN, SINN EINER KRAFT |
| 11183 | SENSE OF MOTION | SENS DU MOUVEMENT, SENS DE LA MARCHE | BEWEGUNGSSINN |
| 11184 | SENSIBLE HEAT | CHALEUR SENSIBLE | WÄRME (FÜHLBARE) |
| 11185 | SENSING AND SORTING MACHINES | TRIEUSES ELECTRONIQUES | ABTAST-UND-SORTIERMASCHINEN |
| 11186 | SENSITIVE DRILLING MACHINE | MACHINE A PERCER SENSITIVE | GEFÜHLSBOHRMASCHINE |
| 11187 | SENSITIVE PLATE | PLAQUE SENSIBLE, PLAQUE PHOTOGRAPHIQUE | PLATTE (LICHTEMPFINDLICHE), PLATTE (PHOTOGRAPHISCHE) |
| 11188 | SENSITIVENESS OF AN INSTRUMENT | SENSIBILITE D'UN INSTRUMENT | EMPFINDLICHKEIT EINES INSTRUMENTS |
| 11189 | SEPARATE (TO) | SEPARER (CHIM.) | ABSCHEIDEN (CHEM.) |
| 11190 | SEPARATE EXCITATION | EXCITATION SEPAREE, INDEPENDANTE | FREMDERREGUNG, SONDERERREGUNG, ÄUSSERE ERREGUNG |
| 11191 | SEPARATION | SEPARATION (CHIM.) | ABSCHEIDUNG, ABSCHEIDEN |
| 11192 | SEPARATION OF A MIXTURE | SEPARATION D'UN MELANGE | ENTMISCHUNG |
| 11193 | SEQUENCE NUMBER | NUMERO DE SEQUENCE | SATZNUMMER |
| 11194 | SEQUENTIAL | SEQUENTIEL | SEQUENTIELL |
| 11195 | SEQUESTRATION | CHELATION | CHELATBILDUNG |
| 11196 | SERIAL | SERIE (EN) | SERIEN- |
| 11197 | SERIAL NUMBER | NUMERO D'ORDRE DE LA FABRICATION | FABRIKNUMMER |
| 11198 | SERIAL PRODUCTION | PRODUCTION EN SERIE | SERIENPRODUKTION |
| 11199 | SERIES CONNECTION, CONNECTION IN SERIES | MONTAGE, GROUPEMENT, COUPLAGE EN SERIE, COUPLAGE EN TENSION | REIHENSCHALTUNG, SERIENSCHALTUNG, HINTEREINANDERSCHALTUNG |
| 11200 | SERIES SPOT WELD | SOUDAGE PAR POINTS EN SERIE PAR RESISTANCE | SERIENPUNKTNAHT |
| 11201 | SERIES WOUND GENERATOR DYNAMO | DYNAMO EN SERIE | HAUPTSCHLUSSDYNAMO, REIHENSCHLUSSDYNAMO, SERIENDYNAMO, DYNAMO (IN SERIE GESCHALTETER |
| 11202 | SERIES WOUND MOTOR | MOTEUR-SERIE | HAUPTSCHLUSSMOTOR, REIHENSCHLUSSMOTOR, SERIENMOTOR |

**SER** 286

| | | | |
|---|---|---|---|
| 11203 | **SERIES, PROGRESSION** | SERIE, SUITE, PROGRESSION | REIHE |
| 11204 | **SERPENTINE** | SERPENTINE, OPHITE | FELS (SERPENTIN) |
| 11205 | **SERPENTINE ASBESTOS, CHRYSOTILE** | CHRYSOTILE | SERPENTINASBEST |
| 11206 | **SERRATED ROLLER** | CYLINDRE CANNELE, STRIE | RIFFELWALZE |
| 11207 | **SERUM ALBUMIN** | ALBUMINE DU SERUM | BLUTALBUMIN |
| 11208 | **SERVICE CONDITIONS** | CONDITIONS D'EMPLOI | BETRIEBSBEDINGUNGEN |
| 11209 | **SERVICE INSTRUCTIONS** | INSTRUCTIONS RELATIVES AU TRAVAIL, REGLEMENTS D'USINE | BETRIEBSVORSCHRIFTEN |
| 11210 | **SERVO-MECHANISM** | SERVO-MECANISME | SERVO-STEUERUNG |
| 11211 | **SERVOMOTOR** | SERVO-MOTEUR | HILFSMOTOR, SERVOMOTOR |
| 11212 | **SESAME OIL** | HUILE DE SESAME | SESAMÖL |
| 11213 | **SET** | JEU, SERIE, ASSORTIMENT (DE PIECES), GROUPE (DE MACHINES ELECTRIQUES) | SATZ, GARNITUR |
| 11214 | **SET (TO)** | FAIRE PRISE | ABBINDEN, ANZIEHEN (ZEMENT) |
| 11215 | **SET A BOILER IN MASONRY (TO)** | ENTOURER UNE CHAUDIERE DE MACONNERIE | KESSEL EINMAUERN (EINEN) |
| 11216 | **SET A VALVE (TO)** | TARER UNE SOUPAPE | TARIEREN |
| 11217 | **SET CHISEL, ROD CHISEL** | TRANCHE | SCHROTMEISSEL, SETZMEISSEL |
| 11218 | **SET HAMMER** | CHASSE (OUTIL DE FORGERON) | SETZHAMMER |
| 11219 | **SET OF WEIGHTS** | ASSORTIMENT, SERIE, JEU DE POIDS | GEWICHTSATZ |
| 11220 | **SET PIN** | GOUPILLE DE BLOCAGE, GOUPILLE DE CLAVETAGE, GOUPILLE DE RETENUE, PRISONNIER | HALTESTIFT, STIFTSCHRAUBE |
| 11221 | **SET POINT** | VALEUR DE REGLAGE | SOLLWERT |
| 11222 | **SET SCREW** | VIS POINTEAU POUR ARRET DE BAGUES | STELLSCHRAUBE, FESTSTELLSCHRAUBE |
| 11223 | **SET SQUARE** | EQUERRE A DESSIN | DREIECK, WINKEL |
| 11224 | **SET THE TEETH OF A SAW (TO)** | DONNER LA VOIE A UNE SCIE, AVOYER UNE SCIE | SÄGEZÄHNE SCHRÄNKEN, SÄGEZÄHNE AUSSETZEN (DIE) |
| 11225 | **SETTING GAUGE** | JAUGE D'AJUSTAGE | EINSTELLLEHRE |
| 11226 | **SETTING OF CEMENT** | PRISE DU CIMENT | ABBINDEN DES ZEMENTS |
| 11227 | **SETTLE (TO)** | DEPOSER (SE) | ABSETZEN (SICH) |
| 11228 | **SETTLING** | SEDIMENTATION, DECANTATION | ABSETZEN, ABLAGERUNG |
| 11229 | **SETTLING TANK** | RESERVOIR DE DECANTATION, CUVE DE DECANTATION | KLÄRGEFÄSS, KLÄRBOTTICH |
| 11230 | **SEWAGE WATER** | EAUX D'EGOUTS | ABWÄSSER VON STÄDTEN |
| 11231 | **SEXE OF AN AXE** | OEIL D'UNE HACHE | HELMLOCH EINER AXT |
| 11232 | **SHACKLE** | MANILLE D'ASSEMBLAGE | SCHÄKEL |
| 11233 | **SHACKLES** | JUMELLES | FEDERGEHÄNGE |
| 11234 | **SHADE (TO)** | OMBRER | SCHATTIEREN |
| 11235 | **SHADED DRAWING** | DESSIN OMBRE | ZEICHNUNG (SCHATTIERTE) |
| 11236 | **SHADING** | OMBRE | SCHATTIERUNG |
| 11237 | **SHADING** | ACTION D'OMBRER | SCHATTIEREN |
| 11238 | **SHADOWGRAPH** | PROJECTEUR D'OMBRE | SCHATTENAUFNAHMEAPPARAT |
| 11239 | **SHAFT** | ARBRE (MEC.) | WELLE (MASCHB.), ACHSE |
| 11240 | **SHAFT COUPLING** | ACCOUPLEMENT D'ARBRES | WELLENKUPPLUNG, KUPPLUNG |
| 11241 | **SHAFT FURNACE** | FOUR A CUVE, FOUR A MANCHE | SCHACHTOFEN |
| 11242 | **SHAFT GOVERNOR** | REGULATEUR PLAN, REGULATEUR SUR L'ARBRE | ACHSENREGLER, FLACHREGLER |
| 11243 | **SHAFT OF COLUMN** | FUT D'UNE COLONNE | STAMM EINER SÄULE, SÄULENSTAMM |

| | | | |
|---|---|---|---|
| 11244 | **SHAFT OR HANDLE OF A HAMMER** | MANCHE D'UN MARTEAU | HAMMERSTIEL, STIEL EINES HAMMERS |
| 11245 | **SHAFT STRAIGHTENER** | MACHINE A DRESSER LES ARBRES | WELLENRICHTMASCHINE |
| 11246 | **SHAFT TURNING LATHE** | TOUR A ARBRES | WELLENDREHBANK |
| 11247 | **SHAFT WITH OVERHANGING ENDS** | ARBRE EN PORTE-A-FAUX DES DEUX COTES | WELLE MIT ÜBERSTEHENDEN ENDEN |
| 11248 | **SHAFTING** | TRANSMISSION | WELLENLEITUNG, TRANSMISSION |
| 11249 | **SHAFTS AT RIGHT ANGLES (OR INCLINED) AND NOT INTERSECTING** | ARBRES (PERPENDICULAIRES, OBLIQUES) SITUES DANS DES PLANS DIFFERENTS | WELLEN (SICH KREUZENDE, GESCHRÄNKTE) |
| 11250 | **SHAKE IN TIMBER** | GERCE, GERCURE DU BOIS, CRIQUE DANS LE BOIS | RISS IM HOLZ |
| 11251 | **SHAKE-OUT** | DEMOULAGE | AUSSCHLAGEN |
| 11252 | **SHAKING SCREEN** | CRIBLE OSCILLANT | SCHÜTTELSIEB |
| 11253 | **SHAKING TRAY, PAN (SHAKING)** | TRANSPORTEUR, GOUTIERE A SECOUSSES | SCHÜTTELRINNE, WIPPE, SCHWINGE |
| 11254 | **SHAKING-DOWN** | AGITATION DU BAIN | RÜHREN |
| 11255 | **SHALE OIL TAR** | GOUDRON DE SCHISTE | SCHIEFERTEER |
| 11256 | **SHALE OIL, SCHIST OIL** | HUILE DE SCHISTE | SCHIEFERÖL |
| 11257 | **SHANK** | TIGE, QUEUE | SCHAFT |
| 11258 | **SHANK LADLE** | POCHE DE COULEE A ANSE | GABELGIESSPFANNE |
| 11259 | **SHANK MILLING CUTTER** | FRAISE A QUEUE | SCHAFTFRÄSER, FINGERFRÄSER |
| 11260 | **SHANK OF BOLT SCREW** | TIGE D'UNE VIS, TIGE D'UN BOULON | SCHAFT, BOLZEN EINER SCHRAUBE, SCHRAUBENSCHAFT, SCHRAUBENBOLZEN |
| 11261 | **SHANK OF CONNECTING ROD** | CORPS DE LA BIELLE | SCHAFT DER SCHUBSTANGE |
| 11262 | **SHANK OF KEY** | CORPS D'UNE CLAVETTE, TIGE D'UNE CLAVETTE | KEILBOLZEN |
| 11263 | **SHANK OF RIVET** | CORPS DU RIVET, TIGE DU RIVET, FUT DU RIVET | NIETSCHAFT, NIETBOLZEN |
| 11264 | **SHAPE** | FORME | FORM |
| 11265 | **SHAPED PART** | PIECE FACONNEE | FORMSTÜCK |
| 11266 | **SHAPED PLATES** | TOLES DECOUPEES | BLECH (ZUGESCHNITTENES) |
| 11267 | **SHAPERS** | ETAUX-LIMEUR | WAAGERECHTSTOSSMASCHINEN |
| 11268 | **SHAPING** | FACONNAGE | FORMGEBUNG |
| 11269 | **SHAPING MACHINE** | ETAU-LIMEUR | FEILMASCHINE, SHAPINGMASCHINE, WAAGRECHTSTOSSMASCHINE |
| 11270 | **SHARK SKIN, SHAGREEN** | PEAU DE CHIEN | FISCHHAUT |
| 11271 | **SHARP BACKED ANGLE** | FER CORNIERE A ANGLE VIF | WINKELEISEN (INNEN SCHARF) |
| 11272 | **SHARP EDGE** | ARETE VIVE | KANTE (SCHARFE) |
| 11273 | **SHARPEN (TO), WHET (TO), GRIND (TO)** | AIGUISER, MEULER, EMOUDRE, AFFUTER, RECTIFIER, REPASSER | SCHÄRFEN, SCHARFSCHLEIFEN |
| 11274 | **SHARPENING MACHINE** | AFFUTEUSE | SCHÄRFMASCHINE |
| 11275 | **SHARPENING, WHETTING, GRINDING** | AIGUISAGE, MEULAGE, EMOULAGE, AFFUTAGE, RECTIFICATION | SCHLEIFEN, SCHÄRFEN, SCHARFSCHLEIFEN |
| 11276 | **SHARPNESS OF IMAGE** | NETTETE D'UNE IMAGE | BILDSCHÄRFE |
| 11277 | **SHAVINGS, CHIPS, CHIPPINGS** | ALESURES | BOHRSPÄNE |
| 11278 | **SHAVINGS, CHIPS, METAL SHAVINGS** | COPEAUX | SPÄNE |
| 11279 | **SHEAR** | CISAILLE, CISAILLEMENT | SCHERE, SCHUB |
| 11280 | **SHEAR (TO)** | CISAILLER (COUPER AVEC DES CISAILLES) | ABSCHEREN, MIT DER SCHERE ABSCHNEIDEN |
| 11281 | **SHEAR ANGLE** | ANGLE DE CISAILLEMENT | SCHERWINKEL |
| 11282 | **SHEAR BLADE** | LAME D'UNE CISAILLE | SCHERBLATT, SCHERMESSER, SCHERKLINGE, SCHERBACKEN, DRUCKBACKEN EINER SCHERE |
| 11283 | **SHEAR PIN** | GOUPILLE DE CISAILLEMENT | ABSCHERSTIFT |

# SHE

**288**

| | | | |
|---|---|---|---|
| 11284 | SHEAR PLANE | PLAN DE CISAILLEMENT | SCHERFLÄCHE |
| 11285 | SHEAR STRENGTH | RESISTANCE AU CISAILLEMENT | SCHERFESTIGKEIT |
| 11286 | SHEAR STRESS | TENSION DE CISAILLEMENT | SCHUBVERFORMUNG |
| 11287 | SHEAR TEST | ESSAI DE CISAILLEMENT | SCHERVERSUCH |
| 11288 | SHEAR, SHEARING, SLIDE | CISAILLEMENT, GLISSEMENT TRANSVERSAL | GLEITUNG, SCHIEBUNG, SCHUB (FESTIGKEITSL.) |
| 11289 | SHEARINESS | EMBUS | EINSAUGUNG |
| 11290 | SHEARING | CISAILLEMENT, CISAILLAGE | SCHERUNG, ABSCHEREN, SCHNEIDEN |
| 11291 | SHEARING FORCE | FORCE DE CISAILLEMENT | SCHERKRAFT, SCHUBKRAFT, QUERKRAFT, TRANSVERSALKRAFT |
| 11292 | SHEARING MACHINE | CISAILLE MECANIQUE, MACHINE A CISAILLER, CISAILLEUSE | MASCHINENSCHERE |
| 11293 | SHEARING OF THE RIVET | RUPTURE DU RIVET PAR CISAILLEMENT | ABSCHEREN DES NIETES |
| 11294 | SHEARING PIN | GOUPILLE DE CISAILLEMENT | ABSCHERBOLZEN |
| 11295 | SHEARING STRAIN | EFFORT DE CISAILLEMENT, EFFORT TRANCHANT, TRAVAIL AU CISAILLEMENT | BEANSPRUCHUNG AUF SCHUB, ABSCHERUNG, SCHUBBEANSPRUCHUNG, SCHERBEANSPRUCHUNG |
| 11296 | SHEARING STRESS | EFFORT DE CISAILLEMENT PAR UNITE DE SECTION, CONTRAINTE DE CISAILLEMENT | SCHERSPANNUNG, SCHUBSPANNUNG |
| 11297 | SHEARS | CISAILLE, CISAILLES | SCHERE |
| 11298 | SHEAT | TOLE | BLECH |
| 11299 | SHEATHED ELECTRODE | ELECTRODE BLINDEE | ELEKTRODE (BLECHUMHÜLLTE) |
| 11300 | SHEATHED WIRE | FIL GAINE | DRAHT (UMHÜLLTER) |
| 11301 | SHEAVE, PULLEY OF A TACKLE | POULIE, REA D'UN MOUFLE | ROLLE EINES FLASCHENZUGS |
| 11302 | SHED (FOR STORAGE) | HANGAR, PARC COUVERT | LAGERSCHUPPEN, SCHUPPEN |
| 11303 | SHEEL | ENVELOPPE, CHEMISE, COQUILLE | MANTEL, HÜLSE, SCHALE, KOKILLE |
| 11304 | SHEET | TOLE FINE | FEINBLECH, STURZBLECH |
| 11305 | SHEET (METAL) | TOLE | BLECH |
| 11306 | SHEET BAR | LARGET, PLATINE | PLATINE, VORBLECH |
| 11307 | SHEET BRASS | LAITON EN FEUILLES | MESSINGBLECH |
| 11308 | SHEET COPPER | CUIVRE EN FEUILLES | KUPFERBLECH |
| 11309 | SHEET IRON | TOLE DE FER | EISENBLECH |
| 11310 | SHEET IRON COVER | CAPOT EN TOLE | BLECHMANTEL |
| 11311 | SHEET IRON METAL GAUGE, PLATE GAUGE | JAUGE POUR TOLES | BLECHLEHRE |
| 11312 | SHEET IRON PIPE | TUYAU EN TOLE | BLECHROHR |
| 11313 | SHEET IRON PLATE | FEUILLE DE TOLE | BLECHTAFEL |
| 11314 | SHEET LEAD | PLOMB EN FEUILLES | BLEIBLECH, WALZBLEI |
| 11315 | SHEET METAL | TOLE, FEUILLE METALLIQUE, PLAQUE METALLIQUE | BLECH |
| 11316 | SHEET METAL LEVELLING MACHINE | MACHINE A PLANER ET DRESSER LES TOLES | BLECHRICHTMASCHINE |
| 11317 | SHEET METAL PERFORATING MACHINES | MACHINES A PERFORER LES TOLES | BLECHPERFORIERMASCHINEN |
| 11318 | SHEET METAL PLANING MACHINE | MACHINES A PLANER LES TOLES | BLECHPLANIERMASCHINEN |
| 11319 | SHEET METAL SCORING MACHINE | MACHINE A ENTAILLER LES TOLES | BLECHRITZMASCHINE |
| 11320 | SHEET METAL WORKING MACHINES | MACHINES A TRAVAILLER LA TOLE | BLECHBEARBEITUNGSMASCHINEN |
| 11321 | SHEET MILL / STRIP MILL | TRAIN A BANDES | BLECHSTREIFENWALZWERK |
| 11322 | SHEET OF FELT | PLAQUE EN FEUTRE | FILZPLATTE |
| 11323 | SHEET OR BAND METAL SHEARING MACHINE | MACHINE A CISAILLER LES METAUX EN FEUILLES OU EN BANDES | BLECH- ODER BANDMETALLSCHERMASCHINE |

289 SHO

| 11324 | SHEET ROLLING MILL | TRAIN (DE LAMINOIRS) A TOLES FINES | BLECHWALZSTRASSE |
|---|---|---|---|
| 11325 | SHEET STEEL | TOLE D'ACIER | STAHLBLECH |
| 11326 | SHEET TIN | ETAIN EN FEUILLES | ZINNBLECH |
| 11327 | SHEET ZINC | FEUILLE DE ZINC, ZINC EN FEUILLES | ZINKBLECH |
| 11328 | SHEETING | EXFOLIATION | ABBLÄTTERUNG |
| 11329 | SHEETING RUBBER, SHEETING NEOPRENE | FEUILLE DE CAOUTCHOUC (NEOPRENE) | GUMMI- (ODER NEOPREN-) ISOLIERUNG |
| 11330 | SHELL | ROBE | WANDUNG |
| 11331 | SHELL EXTENSION | REHAUSSE ....DE TOIT FLOTTANT | AUFSATZ FÜR SCHWIMMDACH |
| 11332 | SHELL MANHOLE | TROU D'HOMME DE ROBE | INNERWANDUNGSMANNLOCH |
| 11333 | SHELL MOLDING | MOULAGE EN COQUILLE | MASKENFORMEN |
| 11334 | SHELL OF A COCK | BOISSEAU D'UN ROBINET | GEHÄUSE EINES HAHNES, HAHNGEHÄUSE |
| 11335 | SHELL PLATE | TOLE DE ROBE | MANTELBLECH |
| 11336 | SHELL REAMER | ALESOIR/FRAISE CREUX | AUFSTECKREIBAHLE |
| 11337 | SHELL-END MILLS | FRAISES EN BOUT ALESEES | WALZENSTIRNFRÄSER |
| 11338 | SHELLAC | GOMME-LAQUE, LAQUE EN ECAILLES, LAQUE EN PLAQUES, LAQUE EN FEUILLES, LAQUE PLATE | SCHELLACK |
| 11339 | SHELLING | ECAILLAGE | ABBLÄTTERUNG |
| 11340 | SHERARDISE (TO) | SHERARDISER | SHERARDISIEREN |
| 11341 | SHERARDISING | SHERARDISATION | SHERARDISIEREN |
| 11342 | SHIELD | ECRAN DE PROTECTION, BOUCLIER | SCHUTZSCHILD, SCHUTZVORRICHTUNG |
| 11343 | SHIELD PLATE | TOLE DE RENFORT OU DOUBLANTE, TOLE DE BLINDAGE | VERSTÄRKUNGSBLECH, PANZERBLECH, SCHUTZBLECH |
| 11344 | SHIELDED ELECTRODE | ELECTRODE ENROBEE | ELEKTRODE (DICKUMHÜLLTE) |
| 11345 | SHIELDED METAL ARC WELDING | SOUDAGE A L'ARC METALLIQUE SOUS GAZ PROTECTEUR | METALL-LICHTBOGEN-SCHWEISSEN MIT UMHÜLLTER ELEKTRODE |
| 11346 | SHIELDING | ECRAN, PROTECTION | SCHUTZVORRICHTUNG, SCHIRM |
| 11347 | SHIFT | JOURNEE DE TRAVAIL | SCHICHT (ARBEITSZEIT) |
| 11348 | SHIFT SQUAD | EQUIPE D'OUVRIERS | SCHICHT (ARBEITERGRUPPE) |
| 11349 | SHIFT THE BELT (TO) | DEPLACER LA COURROIE | RIEMEN SCHALTEN (DEN), RIEMEN VERSCHIEBEN (DEN) |
| 11350 | SHIFT WORK | TRAVAIL EN (DEUX OU TROIS) EQUIPES | SCHICHTARBEIT |
| 11351 | SHIM | RONDELLE D'EPAISSEUR | UNTERLEGBLECH |
| 11352 | SHIM-PLATE | CALE D'EPAISSEUR | EINLAGE, ZWISCHENLAGESCHEIBE, BEILEGESCHEIBE |
| 11353 | SHIMMY | SHIMMY | FLATTERN |
| 11354 | SHINGLE | GALETS (GEOL.) | GERÖLLE, GESCHIEBE |
| 11355 | SHINGLING | COMPRESSION, SERRAGE, TASSEMENT | VERDICHTUNG |
| 11356 | SHIP PLATE | TOLE (POUR CONSTRUCTION) NAVALE | SCHIFFSBLECH |
| 11357 | SHIP THE BELT (TO) | MONTER, INSTALLER LA COURROIE, METTRE EN PLACE LA COURROIE | RIEMEN AUFLEGEN (DEN) |
| 11358 | SHOCK ABSORBER | AMORTISSEUR DE CHOCS | DÄMPFER, STOSSDÄMPFER |
| 11359 | SHOCK, IMPACT, PERCUSSION | CHOC, PERCUSSION, A-COUP, SECOUSSE, HEURT | STOSS (MECH.) |
| 11360 | SHOE | SABOT | SCHUH |
| 11361 | SHOP DRAWING | PLAN D'EXECUTION (ATELIER) | WERKSTATTZEICHNUNG |

## SHO                                    290

| 11362 | SHOP WELDING | SOUDAGE EN ATELIER | WERKSTATTSCHWEISSEN |
|---|---|---|---|
| 11363 | SHOP, WORKING DRAWING | EPURE D'UNE PIECE MECANIQUE | WERKZEICHNUNG, ARBEITSZEICHNUNG |
| 11364 | SHOP, WORKSHOP | ATELIER | WERKSTATT |
| 11365 | SHORE | CHANDELLE (ETAI VERTICAL) | STÜTZE, TRAGSTANGE |
| 11366 | SHORE'S SCLEROSCOPE | SCLEROSCOPE, REBONDIMETRE, APPAREIL SHORE | HÄRTEPRÜFER, SKLEROSKOP NACH SHORE |
| 11367 | SHORE'S SCLEROSCOPE TEST | ESSAI PAR REBONDISSEMENT DES BILLES (APPAREIL SHORE) | KUGELFALLPROBE NACH SHORE |
| 11368 | SHORT BRITTLE IRON | FER CASSANT | EISEN (SPRÖDES), EISEN (BRÜCHIGES) |
| 11369 | SHORT CIRCUIT | COURT-CIRCUIT | KURZSCHLUSS |
| 11370 | SHORT CIRCUIT TRANSFER | TRANSFERT PAR COURT-CIRCUIT | KURZSCHLUSSÜBERTRAGUNG |
| 11371 | SHORT FLAME COAL | HOUILLE A COURTE FLAMME | KOHLE (KURZFLAMMIGE) |
| 11372 | SHORT-CIRCUIT | COURT-CIRCUIT | KURZSCHLUSS |
| 11373 | SHORT-LINK CHAIN, CLOSE-LINK CHAIN | CHAINE A MAILLONS COURTS, CHAINE A MAILLONS SERRES | KETTE (KURZGLIEDRIGE) |
| 11374 | SHORT-STROKE ENGINE | MACHINE A FAIBLE COURSE | MASCHINE (KURZHÜBIGE) |
| 11375 | SHORT-THROW CRANK | MANIVELLE A FAIBLE COURSE | KURBEL (KURZHÜBIGE) |
| 11376 | SHORTENING | RACCOURCISSEMENT | VERKÜRZUNG VERKÜRZEN |
| 11377 | SHORTENING A ROPE, A BELT | RACCOURCISSEMENT D'UN CABLE, RACCOURCISSEMENT D'UNE COURROIE | KÜRZUNG EINES SEILES, KÜRZUNG EINES RIEMENS |
| 11378 | SHORTNESS | FRAGILITE | BRÜCHIGKEIT |
| 11379 | SHOT | MITRAILLE, GRENAILLE | SCHROT, GRANULAT |
| 11380 | SHOT BLASTING | GRENAILLAGE | STAHLSANDBLASEN, SCHROTSTRAHLPUTZEN |
| 11381 | SHOT PEENING | DECAPAGE PAR GRENAILLAGE | KUGELSTRAHLEN |
| 11382 | SHOTBLASTING | GRENAILLAGE (GROS) | GRANALIEN BLASEN |
| 11383 | SHOULDER | EPAULEMENT | ABSATZ, SCHULTER, STUFE |
| 11384 | SHOULDER OF A SHAFT | EPAULEMENT D'UN ARBRE, COLLET D'UN ARBRE, BUTEE D'UN ARBRE | ANLAUF EINER WELLE, BRUST EINER WELLE, SCHULTER EINER WELLE |
| 11385 | SHOVEL | PELLE | SCHAUFEL, SCHIPPE |
| 11386 | SHOVEL (TO) | PELLETER | SCHAUFELN |
| 11387 | SHOWER VALVE | ROBINET DE DOUCHE | DUSCHVENTIL, BRAUSEVENTIL |
| 11388 | SHRINK (TO) | SE RETRECIR, SE CONTRACTER | EINSCHRUMPFEN, SCHWINDEN |
| 11389 | SHRINK FIT | EMMANCHEMENT, MONTAGE A LA PRESSE A CHAUD | SCHRUMPFSITZ, WARMSITZ |
| 11390 | SHRINK ON (TO) | POSER, EMMANCHER, FRETTER A CHAUD | WARM AUFZIEHEN, AUFSCHRUMPFEN |
| 11391 | SHRINK RING | FRETTE POSEE A CHAUD, COLLIER POSE A CHAUD, ANNEAU MIS A CHAUD, BAGUE DE SERRAGE | SCHRUMPFRING, SCHWINDRING |
| 11392 | SHRINKAGE | CONTRACTION, RETRAIT | SCHWINDUNG, SCHRUMPFUNG, SCHWINDEN |
| 11393 | SHRINKAGE CAVITY | RETASSURE | LUNKER |
| 11394 | SHRINKAGE CONTRACTION OF A METAL (IN COOLING DOWN) | RETASSEMENT | SCHWINDEN EINES METALLS BEIM ERSTARREN |
| 11395 | SHRINKAGE CRACK | TAPURE DE RETRAIT | SCHWINDUNGSRISS |
| 11396 | SHRINKAGE OF THE WOOD | RETRAIT DU BOIS | SCHWINDEN DES HOLZES |
| 11397 | SHRINKAGE, SHRINKING | RETRECISSEMENT, RETRACTION, CONTRACTION (PENDANT LE REFROIDISSEMENT) | SCHRUMPFEN, EINSCHRUMPFEN, SCHWINDEN |
| 11398 | SHRINKING ON | FRETTAGE, EMMANCHEMENT A CHAUD | AUFSCHRUMPFEN, WARMAUFZIEHEN |

|  |  |  |  |
|---|---|---|---|
| 11399 | **SHRIVELLING** | RIDAGE | KRÄUSELN |
| 11400 | **SHROUD** | JOUE D'UNE ROUE D'ENGRENAGE, EPAULEMENT D'UNE ROUE D'ENGRENAGE | SEITENSCHEIBE EINES ZAHNRADES, BORDSCHEIBE EINES ZAHNRADES |
| 11401 | **SHROUD LAID ROPE** | GRELIN COMPOSE DE QUATRE AUSSIERES | KUGELWEISE GESCHLAGENES SEIL |
| 11402 | **SHROUDED GEAR WHEEL** | ROUE D'ENGRENAGE EPAULEE, ROUE D'ENGRENAGE AVEC JOUES | VERSTEIFTES ZAHNRAD, ZAHNRAD MIT BORDSCHEIBEN |
| 11403 | **SHUNT** | DERIVATION, SHUNT | NEBENSCHLUSS |
| 11404 | **SHUNT WOUND GENERATOR DYNAMO** | DYNAMO-SHUNT, DYNAMO EN DERIVATION | NEBENSCHLUSSDYNAMO |
| 11405 | **SHUNT WOUND MOTOR** | MOTEUR-SHUNT, MOTEUR EN DERIVATION | NEBENSCHLUSSMOTOR |
| 11406 | **SHUT DOWN A MACHINE (TO)** | METTRE UNE MACHINE HORS SERVICE | AUSSER BETRIEB SETZEN (EINE MASCHINE), STILL SETZEN |
| 11407 | **SHUT OFF A PIPE (TO)** | FERMER L'INTRODUCTION, OBTURER L'ADMISSION DANS UNE TUYAUTERIE | AUSSCHALTEN (EINE ROHRLEITUNG), ABSCHALTEN EINE ROHRLEITUNG, ABSPERREN EINE ROHRLEITUNG |
| 11408 | **SHUT OFF C●CK / VALVE** | ROBINET D'ARRET | ABSTELLHAHN, ABSPERRHAHN |
| 11409 | **SHUT-DOWNS** | ARRETS DE TRAVAIL | STILLEGUNG |
| 11410 | **SHUTTING DOWN A MACHINE** | MISE HORS SERVICE D'UNE MACHINE | AUSSERBETRIEBSETZUNG EINER MASCHINE, STILLSETZEN EINER MASCHINE |
| 11411 | **SIDE DELIVERY RAKES** | RATEAUX A DEVERSEMENT LATERAL | SCHWADENMÄHER |
| 11412 | **SIDE MILLING CUTTER** | FRAISE DISQUE | SCHEIBENFRÄSER |
| 11413 | **SIDE OF A BELT, OF A CHAIN** | BRIN D'UNE COURROIE, BRIN D'UNE CHAINE SANS FIN | TRUMM EINES RIEMENS, TRUMM EINES KETTENTRIEBS |
| 11414 | **SIDE OF POLYGON** | COTE D'UN POLYGONE | SEITE EINES POLYGONS, POLYGONSEITE |
| 11415 | **SIDE PLANING MACHINE** | MACHINE A RABOTER LATERALE | SEITENHOBELMASCHINE |
| 11416 | **SIDE PLATE OF A ROLLER CHAIN** | FLASQUE D'UNE CHAINE A ROULEAUX, JOUE D'UNE CHAINE A ROULEAUX | SEITENLASCHE, LASCHE EINER ROLLENKETTE |
| 11417 | **SIDE RABBET PLANE** | GUILLAUME DE COTE | WANDHOBEL, WANGENHOBEL |
| 11418 | **SIDE RAKE ANGLE** | ANGLE DE PENTE LATERALE | SPANWINKEL |
| 11419 | **SIDE STRAIN** | ONDULATIONS | WELLIGKEIT |
| 11420 | **SIDE VIEW, LONGITUDINAL ELEVATION** | VUE DE COTE, PROFIL (A DROITE, A GAUCHE) | SEITENANSICHT |
| 11421 | **SIDERITE, SPATHIC IRON ORE, CHALYBITE** | SIDEROSE, FER SPATHIQUE | SPATEISENSTEIN, EISENSPAT, SIDERIT |
| 11422 | **SIEVE, RIDDLE, SCREEN** | CRIBLE, TAMIS, SAS | SIEB |
| 11423 | **SIFT (TO), SCREEN (TO)** | CRIBLER, TAMISER, SASSER | SIEBEN, ABSIEBEN, DURCHSIEBEN |
| 11424 | **SIFTING, SCREENING** | CRIBLAGE, TAMISAGE | SIEBEN |
| 11425 | **SIGHT FEED LUBRICATOR** | GRAISSEUR A DEBIT VISIBLE | SCHAUÖLER |
| 11426 | **SIGHT FLOW INDICATOR, SIGHT GLASS** | CONTROLEUR DE CIRCULATION | DURCHFLUSSANZEIGER |
| 11427 | **SIGHT HOLE** | REGARD | SCHAUÖFFNUNG, SCHAULOCH, SCHAUGLAS |
| 11428 | **SIGMA WELDING** | SOUDAGE A L'ARC METALLIQUE SOUS PROTECTION DE GAZ INERTE | SIGMA-SCHWEISSEN |
| 11429 | **SIGN** | SIGNE | VORZEICHEN |
| 11430 | **SILAGE MAKING MACHINERY** | ENSILEUSES | GÄRFUTTERZUBEREITUNGSMASCHINEN |
| 11431 | **SILENCER, MUFFLER** | POT D'ECHAPPEMENT, SILENCIEUX | AUSPUFFTOPF, SCHALLDÄMPFER |
| 11432 | **SILENT CHAIN** | CHAINE SILENCIEUSE | ZAHNKETTE, KETTE (GERÄUSCHLOSE) |

# SIL

292

| | | | |
|---|---|---|---|
| 11433 | **SILENT RATCHET MOTION** | ENCLIQUETAGE SILENCIEUX | STUMMES GESPERRE |
| 11434 | **SILICA** | SILICE | SILIZIUMDIOXYD, KIESELERDE |
| 11435 | **SILICA BRICK** | BRIQUE SILICEUSE | SILIKASTEIN, DINASSTEIN |
| 11436 | **SILICA, SILICON DIOXIDE, SILICIC ACID** | SILICE, ANHYDRIDE, ACIDE SILICIQUE | KIESELSÄURE, KIESELSÄUREANHYDRID, KIESELERDE, SILIZIUMDIOXYD |
| 11437 | **SILICATE** | SILICATE | KIESELSAURES SALZ, SILIKAT |
| 11438 | **SILICEOUS ELECTRIC CALAMINE, HEMIMORPHITE** | ZINC SILICATE | KIESELGALMEI, KIESELZINKERZ |
| 11439 | **SILICEOUS MARL** | MARNE SILICEUSE | MERGEL (KIESELIGER) |
| 11440 | **SILICO-SPIEGEL** | SILICO-SPIEGEL | SILIZIUMMANGANEISEN, SILIKOSPIEGEL |
| 11441 | **SILICOFLUORIC ACID** | ACIDE FLUOSILICIQUE | KIESELFLUORWASSERSTOFFSÄURE, KIESELFLUSSSÄURE |
| 11442 | **SILICON** | SILICIUM | SILIZIUM |
| 11443 | **SILICON BRASS** | LAITON SILICEUX | SILIZIUMMESSING |
| 11444 | **SILICON BRONZE** | BRONZE SILICEUX | SILIZIUMBRONZE |
| 11445 | **SILICON CARBIDE** | CARBURE DE SILICIUM | SILIZIUMKARBID |
| 11446 | **SILICON COPPER** | CUIVRE SILICEUX | SILIZIUMKUPFER |
| 11447 | **SILICON STEEL** | ACIER AU SILICIUM | SILIZIUMSTAHL |
| 11448 | **SILICON STEEL SHEET** | TOLE ELECTRIQUE | ELEKTROBLECH |
| 11449 | **SILICON STEEL, SILICEOUS STEEL** | ACIER AU SILICIUM | SILIZIUMSTAHL |
| 11450 | **SILICON-MANGANESE STEEL** | ACIER MANGANO-SILICEUX | SILIZIUM-MANGANSTAHL |
| 11451 | **SILIECOUS LIMESTONE** | CALCAIRE SILICEUX | KIESELKALK |
| 11452 | **SILK** | SOIE | SEIDE |
| 11453 | **SILKING** | NUANCAGE | STREIFIGKEIT |
| 11454 | **SILKY FRACTURE** | CASSURE SOYEUSE | BRUCH (SEIDIGER) |
| 11455 | **SILKY LUSTRE** | ECLAT SOYEUX | SEIDENGLANZ, ATLASGLANZ |
| 11456 | **SILOCONE** | SILICONE | SILIKON |
| 11457 | **SILTING UP OF A PIPE** | ENVASEMENT D'UNE CONDUITE | VERSCHLAMMEN EINER ROHRLEITUNG |
| 11458 | **SILVER** | ARGENT | SILBER |
| 11459 | **SILVER (TO)** | ARGENTER | VERSILBERN |
| 11460 | **SILVER ALLOY BRAZING** | BRASURE A L'ALLIAGE D'ARGENT | SILBERHARTLÖTEN |
| 11461 | **SILVER CHLORIDE** | ARGENT CHLORURE, CHLORURE D'ARGENT | CHLORSILBER, SILBERCHLORID |
| 11462 | **SILVER CYANIDE** | CYANURE D'ARGENT | ZYANSILBER, SILBERZYANID |
| 11463 | **SILVER FULMINATE** | FULMINATE D'ARGENT | KNALLSILBER |
| 11464 | **SILVER IODIDE** | IODURE D'ARGENT | JODSILBER, SILBERJODID |
| 11465 | **SILVER PLATING** | ARGENTURE | VERSILBERUNG |
| 11466 | **SILVER SOLDER** | SOUDURE A L'ARGENT, PAILLON D'ARGENT | SILBERSCHLAGLOT |
| 11467 | **SILVER SULPHATE** | SULFATE D'ARGENT | SCHWEFELSAURES SILBER, SILBERSULFAT |
| 11468 | **SILVER-BEARING COPPER** | CUIVRE ARGENTIFERE | KUPFER (SILBERHALTIGES) |
| 11469 | **SILVERING** | ARGENTURE | VERSILBERN, VERSILBERUNG |
| 11470 | **SIMILARITY** | SIMILITUDE | ÄHNLICHKEIT (GEOM.) |
| 11471 | **SIMPLE INTEGRAL** | INTEGRALE SINGULIERE | INTEGRAL (SINGULÄRES) |
| 11472 | **SIMPLE PISTON ROD** | TIGE DE PISTON UNILATERALE | KOLBENSTANGE (EINSEITIGE) |
| 11473 | **SIMPLE STEEL** | ACIER AU CARBONE | KOHLENSTOFFSTAHL |
| 11474 | **SIMPLY FREELY SUPPORTED AT BOTH ENDS** | SOUTENU, REPOSANT LIBREMENT SUR DEUX APPUIS | GESTÜTZT (BEIDERSEITIG), FREI AUFLIEGEND |
| 11475 | **SINE** | SINUS | SINUS |

|  |  |  |  |
|---|---|---|---|
| 11476 | **SINE CURVE** | COURBE SINUEUSE | SINUSKURVE |
| 11477 | **SINGLE BELT** | COURROIE SIMPLE | EINFACHRIEMEN |
| 11478 | **SINGLE BUTT STRAP RIVETED JOINT, BUTT RIVETED JOINT WITH ONE WELD** | RIVURE A UNE SEULE BANDE DE RECOUVREMENT, RIVURE A PLAT-JOINT, RIVURE A COUVRE-JOINT SIMPLE | EINSEITIGE LASCHENNIETUNG |
| 11479 | **SINGLE COLLAR THRUST BEARING** | PALIER DE BUTEE A UNE SEULE EMBASE | EINRINGDRUCKLAGER |
| 11480 | **SINGLE CRYSTAL** | MONOCRISTAL | EINKRISTALL |
| 11481 | **SINGLE CUT FILE, FLOAT CUT FILE** | ECOUENNE, ECOUANE, ECOINE | FEILE (EINHIEBIGE) |
| 11482 | **SINGLE CUT, FLOAT CUT OF A FILE** | TAILLE SIMPLE D'UNE LIME | EINFACHER HIEB EINER FEILE |
| 11483 | **SINGLE FORCE** | FORCE UNIQUE | EINZELKRAFT |
| 11484 | **SINGLE PART** | PIECE DETACHEE | EINZELTEIL |
| 11485 | **SINGLE PASS WELDING** | SOUDURE MONOPASSE | SCHWEISSNAHT (EINLAGIGE) |
| 11486 | **SINGLE PURPOSE MACHINE** | MACHINE POUR TRAVAUX SPECIAUX | MASCHINE FÜR SONDERZWECKE, SPEZIALMASCHINE |
| 11487 | **SINGLE RIVETED JOINT** | RIVURE SIMPLE, RIVURE A SIMPLE CLOUURE, RIVURE A UN RANG, CLOUURE SIMPLE | NIETUNG (EINREIHIGE), NIETUNG (EINFACHE) |
| 11488 | **SINGLE SEATED VALVE** | ROBINET A SOUPAPE SIMPLE | EINSITZVENTIL |
| 11489 | **SINGLE SHEAR RIVETED JOINT** | RIVURE A UNE COUPE | NIETUNG (EINSCHNITTIGE) |
| 11490 | **SINGLE SHEAR STEEL** | ACIER, FER CORROYE, FER FORT | GÄRBSTAHL |
| 11491 | **SINGLE VALVE** | SOUPAPE UNIQUE | VENTIL (EINFACHES) |
| 11492 | **SINGLE WEDGE DISC** | OPERCULE SIMPLE | KEIL (EINTEILIGER) |
| 11493 | **SINGLE-ACTING** | EFFET SIMPLE (A) | EINFACHWIRKEND |
| 11494 | **SINGLE-ACTING PISTON** | PISTON A SIMPLE EFFET | KOLBEN EINFACHWIRKENDER |
| 11495 | **SINGLE-ACTING STEAM ENGINE** | MACHINE A SIMPLE EFFET | DAMPFMASCHINE EINFACHWIRKENDE |
| 11496 | **SINGLE-ACTION TOOL** | OUTIL A SIMPLE EFFET | WERKZEUG (EINFACHWIRKENDES) |
| 11497 | **SINGLE-BEAT VALVE** | SOUPAPE A SIMPLE SIEGE | EINSITZIGES VENTIL, EINSITZVENTIL |
| 11498 | **SINGLE-CYLINDER ENGINE** | MACHINE MONOCYLINDRIQUE | EINZYLINDERMASCHINE |
| 11499 | **SINGLE-ENDED SPANNER** | CLEF A FOURCHE SIMPLE, CLEF DE CALIBRE SIMPLE | SCHRAUBENSCHLÜSSEL (EINFACHER), SCHRAUBENSCHLÜSSEL (EINMAULIGER) |
| 11500 | **SINGLE-EXPANSION ENGINE** | MACHINE A SIMPLE EXPANSION | EINFACHEXPANSIONSMASCHINE |
| 11501 | **SINGLE-PHASE, MONOPHASE, ONE-PHASE, UNIPHASE CURRENT** | COURANT MONOPHASE | EINPHASENSTROM |
| 11502 | **SINGLE-THREADED SCREW** | VIS A UN FILET | SCHRAUBE (EINGÄNGIGE) |
| 11503 | **SINGLE-THROW CRANK SHAFT** | ARBRE COUDE SIMPLE | WELLE (EINKURBELIGE), EINFACH GEKRÖPFTE KURBELWELLE |
| 11504 | **SINGLE-WELDED LAP JOINT** | JOINT A RECOUVREMENT SOUDE D'UN SEUL COTE | EINSEITIG GESCHWEISSTE ÜBERLAPPUNGSVERBINDUNG |
| 11505 | **SINK HOLE** | RETASSURE | LUNKER |
| 11506 | **SINKHEAD** | MASSELOTTE | GIESSKOPF |
| 11507 | **SINKING** | PENETRATION | EINSINKEN |
| 11508 | **SINKING (ROLLING) MILL** | LAMINOIR REDUCTEUR | REDUZIERWALZWERK |
| 11509 | **SINTER (TO)** | FRITTER, S'AGGLOMERER | ZUSAMMENSINTERN |
| 11510 | **SINTERED CARBIDE ALLOY** | ALLIAGE DUR AUX CARBURES FRITTES | HARTMETALLLEGIERUNG |
| 11511 | **SINTERING** | FRITTAGE | SINTERUNG, SINTERN |
| 11512 | **SINTERING FURNACE** | FOUR A FRITTER | SINTEROFEN |
| 11513 | **SINUSOID** | SINUOIDE | SINUSOIDE |
| 11514 | **SIPHON** | SIPHON (DE MANOMETRE) | WASSERSACKROHR |
| 11515 | **SIPHON BAROMETER** | BAROMETRE A SIPHON | HEBERBAROMETER |

# SIP

| 294 | | | |
|---|---|---|---|
| 11516 | SIPHON LUBRICATOR, SIPHON OIL CUP | GRAISSEUR A MECHE | DOCHTÖLER |
| 11517 | SIPHON, SYPHON | SIPHON, SYPHON | HEBER, SAUGHEBER, SIPHON |
| 11518 | SIREN, HOOTER | TROMPE, SIRENE D'ALARME | SIRENE |
| 11519 | SITE HUT | BARAQUE DE CHANTIER | BAUSTELLENBUDE |
| 11520 | SITE SUPERINTENDENT | CHEF DE CHANTIER | BAUSTELLENLEITER |
| 11521 | SIX LIGHT SALOON | LIMOUSINE | LIMOUSINE |
| 11522 | SIZE OF GRAIN | GROSSEUR DU GRAIN | KORNGRÖSSE |
| 11523 | SIZE OF MESH | ECARTEMENT DES MAILLES | MASCHENWEITE |
| 11524 | SIZING | CALIBRAGE, FINISSAGE DIMENSIONNEL, TRIAGE | KALIBRIERUNG, MASSABFERTIGUNG, SORTIERUNG |
| 11525 | SIZING PRESS | PRESSE A CALIBRER | KALIBRIERPRESSE |
| 11526 | SKELETON PATTERN | MODELE SQUELETTE | SKELETT-MODELL |
| 11527 | SKELP | BANDE A TUBES | RÖHRENSTREIFEN |
| 11528 | SKETCH | CROQUIS | SKIZZE, ENTWURFZEICHNUNG |
| 11529 | SKETCH (TO) | CROQUER, DESSINER A GRANDS TRAITS | SKIZZIEREN |
| 11530 | SKETCH PAPER, SQUARED PAPER, CROSS SECTION PAPER | PAPIER QUADRILLE | PAPIER (KARIERTES), GITTERPAPIER, NETZPAPIER |
| 11531 | SKETCH PLATE | TOLE MARGINALE | RANDBLECH |
| 11532 | SKETCH, HAND SKETCH | CROQUIS | SKIZZE |
| 11533 | SKETCHING | ACTION DE CROQUER | SKIZZIEREN |
| 11534 | SKEW BEVEL WHEEL | ENGRENAGE HYPERBOLOIDE, ENGRENAGE A DENTURE SPIRALE | HYPERBELRAD, HYPERBOLOIDRAD |
| 11535 | SKEW, GAUCHE SURFACE | SURFACE GAUCHE | WINDSCHIEFE FLÄCHE |
| 11536 | SKIMMER (SPOON) | ECUMOIRE | SCHAUMLÖFFEL |
| 11537 | SKIMP | MANQUE | MÄNGEL |
| 11538 | SKIN | CROUTE DE LA FONTE | GUSSHAUT |
| 11539 | SKIN GLUE | COLLE DES PEAUX | LEDERLEIM, HAUT-LEIM |
| 11540 | SKIN PACKAGING | EMBALLAGE MOULANT | SKINPACKUNG, HAUTPACKUNG |
| 11541 | SKIN PASS | PASSE DE DECALAMINAGE (LAMINAGE), PASSE DE FINISSAGE | KALTSTICH, POLIERSTICH |
| 11542 | SKIN PASS | PASSE DE FINISSAGE | POLIERSTICH |
| 11543 | SKIN ROLL | PASSE DE DRESSAGE, PASSE DE DEGAUCHISSAGE | RICHTSTICH |
| 11544 | SKIN, SKIN DUE TO ROLLING | PELLICULE, COUCHE SUPERFICIELLE, CROUTE DE LAMINAGE | FILM, RANDSCHICHT, WALZHAUT |
| 11545 | SKINNING | FORMATION DE PEAUX | HAUTBILDUNG |
| 11546 | SKIP | INSTRUCTION DE SAUT, INTERRUPTION | ÜBERSPRINGUNSBEFEHL, UNSTETIGKEIT |
| 11547 | SKIRT | JUPE | EINFASSUNG |
| 11548 | SKIRT OF A COVER-PLATE | MANCHETTE D'UN TAMPON | DECKELMANSCHETTE, MUFFE |
| 11549 | SKIRT OF A TANK | JUPE (D'UN RESERVOIR) | SCHÜRZE |
| 11550 | SKULL | LOUP | BÄR |
| 11551 | SLAB | DALLE, BRAME | PLATTE, BRAMME |
| 11552 | SLAB / SLABBING MILL | BRAME (TRAIN A BRAMES) | BRAMME (BRAMMENSTRASSE) |
| 11553 | SLAB BENDING | BRAMES (CINTRAGE DES) | BRAMMENBIEGEN |
| 11554 | SLAB SHEARS | CISAILLES A BRAMES | BRAMMENSCHERE |
| 11555 | SLABBING MILL | LAMINOIR A BRAMES | BRAMMENWALZWERK |
| 11556 | SLABBING MILL(S) | TRAIN(S) A BRAMES | BRAMMEN-STRASSE |
| 11557 | SLACK COAL , FINE SMALL COAL | HOUILLE MENUE, MENUS DE HOUILLLE | FEINKOHLE, GRUSKOHLE, KOHLENGRUS |

| | | | |
|---|---|---|---|
| 11558 | **SLACKEN A BOLT SCREW (TO)** | DESSERRER UN ECROU, DESSERRER UNE VIS | SCHRAUBE LOCKERN (EINE) |
| 11559 | **SLACKEN BACK (TO), WORK LOOSE OUT (TO)** | DESSERRER (SE) | LOCKER WERDEN, LOCKERN (SICH) |
| 11560 | **SLACKING BACK, WORKING LOOSE** | DESSERRAGE, DEBLOCAGE | LOCKERUNG, LOCKERWERDEN |
| 11561 | **SLAG** | LAITIER, SCORIE | SCHLACKE |
| 11562 | **SLAG BEARING** | CONTENANT DES SCORIES | SCHLACKENHALTIG |
| 11563 | **SLAG BRICK** | MOELLON EN LAITIER | SCHLACKENSTEIN |
| 11564 | **SLAG CEMENT** | CIMENT DE LAITIER, CIMENT DE MACHEFER | SCHLACKENZEMENT |
| 11565 | **SLAG CONCRETE** | BETON DE LAITIER, BETON DE MACHEFER | SCHLACKENBETON |
| 11566 | **SLAG WOOL, MINERAL WOOL, SILICATE COTTON** | LAINE MINERALE | SCHLACKENWOLLE |
| 11567 | **SLAG, CINDER INCLUSION** | SCORIE EMPRISONNEE | SCHLACKE (EINGESCHLOSSENE), SCHLACKE (EINGEWALZTE) |
| 11568 | **SLAKE THE LIME (TO)** | ETEINDRE LA CHAUX | KALK LÖSCHEN |
| 11569 | **SLAKING THE LIME** | EXTINCTION DE LA CHAUX, HYDRATATION DE LA CHAUX | LÖSCHEN DES KALKES |
| 11570 | **SLAT CONVEYOR** | TRANSPORTEUR A TABLIER METALLIQUE, TRANSPORTEUR A PALETTES | PLATTENFÖRDERER |
| 11571 | **SLATE** | ARDOISE | SCHIEFER (BAUW.) |
| 11572 | **SLEDGE HAMMER** | MASSE, COGNEE | SCHMIEDEHAMMER |
| 11573 | **SLEDGE, SLEDGE HAMMER** | MARTEAU A FRAPPER DEVANT, FRAPPE-DEVANT | ZUSCHLAGHAMMER, VORSCHLAGHAMMER |
| 11574 | **SLEEPER** | TRAVERSE DE VOIE | SCHWELLE, EISENBAHNSCHWELLE |
| 11575 | **SLEEPER SCREWS** | TIREFONDS | SCHIENENSCHRAUBEN |
| 11576 | **SLEEVE** | FOURREAU, MANCHETTE, DOUILLE | HÜLSE, MANSCHETTE |
| 11577 | **SLEEVE COUPLING, FRICTION CLIP COUPLING** | MANCHON A FRETTES | HÜLSENKUPPLUNG |
| 11578 | **SLEEVE GOVERNOR** | REGULATEUR A MANCHON, REGULATEUR A DOUILLE | MUFFENREGLER |
| 11579 | **SLEEVE VALVE** | SOUPAPE A CLOCHE INTERIEURE, SOUPAPE A MANCHON | ROHRVENTIL |
| 11580 | **SLENDERNESS** | ELANCEMENT | SCHLANKHEIT |
| 11581 | **SLENDERNESS OF A BEAM** | ELANCEMENT D'UNE POUTRE | SCHLANKHEIT (EINES TRÄGERS) |
| 11582 | **SLENDERNESS RATIO** | RAPPORT D'ELANCEMENT | SCHLANKHEITSGRAD |
| 11583 | **SLEWING CRANE** | GRUE PIVOTANTE | DREHKRAN, SCHWENKKRAN |
| 11584 | **SLICING LATHE** | TOUR A DECOLLETER | ABSTECHDREHMASCHINE |
| 11585 | **SLIDE** | SURFACE DE GLISSEMENT, COULISSEAU, GLISSOIRE | GLEITFLÄCHE, GLEITSTÜCK |
| 11586 | **SLIDE (TO)** | GLISSER, COULISSER | GLEITEN |
| 11587 | **SLIDE BLOCK, GUIDE BLOCK, SLIPPER BLOCK, SLIPPER OF CROSSHEAD** | PATIN, GLISSOIR, BLOC DE LA CROSSE | SCHUH, GLEITSCHUH, FÜHRUNGSSCHUH, GLEITKLOTZ DES KREUZKOPFES |
| 11588 | **SLIDE FACE** | GLISSIERE | GLEITBAHN, GLEITFLÄCHE |
| 11589 | **SLIDE OF A MICROSCOPE** | LAME DE VERRE | OBJEKTTRÄGER, GLAS |
| 11590 | **SLIDE REST LATHE** | TOUR A CHARIOTER, TOUR A CHARIOT | SUPPORTDREHBANK |
| 11591 | **SLIDE RULE** | REGLE A CALCUL | RECHENSCHIEBER |
| 11592 | **SLIDE VALVE** | DISTRIBUTEUR, OBTURATEUR GLISSANT, APPAREIL DE DISTRIBUTION A GLISSEMENT, TIROIR, ROBINET | SCHIEBER |
| 11593 | **SLIDE VALVE DIAGRAM** | DIAGRAMME DE DISTRIBUTION | SCHIEBERDIAGRAMM |

**SLI** 296

| | | | |
|---|---|---|---|
| 11594 | SLIDE VALVE GEAR | DISTRIBUTION PAR TIROIR | SCHIEBERSTEUERUNG |
| 11595 | SLIDING | GLISSEMENT | GLEITEN |
| 11596 | SLIDING BEARING | PALIER COULISSANT | GLEITLAGER, SCHLITTENLAGER |
| 11597 | SLIDING CALIPER | PIED A COULISSE | SCHUBLEHRE |
| 11598 | SLIDING CHANGE GEAR | ENGRENAGE BALADEUR | SCHIEBERÄDERGETRIEBE |
| 11599 | SLIDING CLUTCH SLEEVE | MANCHON D'EMBRAYAGE, MANCHON MOBILE | AUSRÜCKMUFFE, VERSCHIEBBARE KUPPLUNGSMUFFE |
| 11600 | SLIDING FIT | EMMANCHEMENT, AJUSTAGE, MONTAGE GLISSANT, EMMANCHEMENT GRAS, EMMANCHEMENT COULISSANT | GLEITSITZ |
| 11601 | SLIDING FRICTION | FROTTEMENT DE GLISSEMENT | REIBUNG (GLEITENDE) |
| 11602 | SLIDING GEAR TRAIN | TRAIN BALADEUR | ZAHNRADSATZ (VERSCHIEBBARER) |
| 11603 | SLIDING LATHE | FOUR A CHARIOTER | ZUGSPINDELDREHMASCHINE |
| 11604 | SLIDING LID COVER | COUVERCLE A GLISSIERE | SCHIEBEDECKEL |
| 11605 | SLIDING MOTION | MOUVEMENT DE GLISSEMENT | BEWEGUNG (GLEITENDE), GLEITBEWEGUNG |
| 11606 | SLIDING PLATE SUPPORT | BERCEAU A PATINS | UNTERGESTELL MIT GLEITSCHUH, SCHLITTEN MIT GLEITPLATTEN |
| 11607 | SLIDING SCALE | ECHELLE MOBILE | LOHNSKALA (GLEITENDE) |
| 11608 | SLIDING SURFACE | SURFACE DE GLISSEMENT | GLEITFLÄCHE |
| 11609 | SLIME | BOUE | SCHLAMM |
| 11610 | SLING | ELINGUE | SCHLINGE |
| 11611 | SLIP (PING) | GLISSEMENT | GLEITUNG |
| 11612 | SLIP (TO) | PATINER, GLISSER | GLEITEN, SCHLÜPFEN |
| 11613 | SLIP BANDS | BANDES DE GLISSEMENT | GLEITLINIEN, STREIFEN |
| 11614 | SLIP CLUTCH | EMBRAYAGE A FRICTION | REIBUNGSKUPPLUNG |
| 11615 | SLIP CRACK | CRIQUE DE CLIVAGE | SCHIEFERBRUCH |
| 11616 | SLIP FORM (CONCRETE) | COFFRAGE GLISSANT (POUR BETON) | GLEITVERSCHALUNG |
| 11617 | SLIP JOINT | JOINT COULISSANT | AUSDEHNUNGSKUPPLUNG |
| 11618 | SLIP RING | BAGUE COLLECTRICE, COLLECTEUR | SCHLEIFRING, KOLLEKTOR |
| 11619 | SLIPPING CLUTCH | EMBRAYAGE PROGRESSIF A FRICTION | RUTSCHKUPPLUNG |
| 11620 | SLIPPING OF THE BELT | GLISSEMENT DE LA COURROIE, PATINAGE DE LA COURROIE | GLEITEN DES RIEMENS, RUTSCHEN DES RIEMENS, SCHLÜPFEN DES RIEMENS, GLEITSCHLUPF |
| 11621 | SLIPPING, SKIDDING OF WHEELS | PATINAGE DES ROUES | SCHLÜPFEN DER RÄDER |
| 11622 | SLITTING | FENDAGE | SPALTEN |
| 11623 | SLITTING FILE, FEATHER EDGE FILE | LIME A LOSANGE | EINSTREICHFEILE, SCHRAUBENKOPFFEILE, SCHWERTFEILE |
| 11624 | SLIVER | CROUTE | SCHALE |
| 11625 | SLIVER ORE | MINERAI D'ARGENT | SILBERERZ |
| 11626 | SLIVERS | ARRACHEMENTS | WALZSPLITTER |
| 11627 | SLOPE | TALUS, PENTE, INCLINAISON | BÖSCHUNG, ABHANG, NEIGUNG |
| 11628 | SLOPING SCREEN | CRIBLE POUR LE SABLE, POUR LA TERRE | DURCHWURFSIEB, SANDSIEB, ERDSIEB, WURFGITTER |
| 11629 | SLOT | FENTE | SPALT |
| 11630 | SLOT (TO) | MORTAISER | STOSSEN, NUTEN STOSSEN |
| 11631 | SLOT AND CRANK | MANIVELLE A COULISSE, COULISSE ET MANIVELLE | KURBELSCHLEIFE |
| 11632 | SLOT DRILLS | FRAISES A RAINURES, FRAISES A COUTEAUX | NUTENFRÄSER |
| 11633 | SLOT LINK, REVERSING LINK | COULISSE | SCHLEIFE, SCHWINGE, KULISSE |
| 11634 | SLOT MILLING CUTTER | FRAISE POUR RAINURES | NUTENFRÄSER |

| | | | |
|---|---|---|---|
| 11635 | **SLOT WELD** | SOUDURE A ENTAILLE | SCHLITZNAHT |
| 11636 | **SLOT WELDING** | SOUDAGE A ENTAILLE | SCHLITZSCHWEISSEN |
| 11637 | **SLOTTED HEAD SCREW** | VIS A TETE FENDUE | SCHLITZSCHRAUBE |
| 11638 | **SLOTTED LEVER** | LEVIER A COULISSE | SCHLITZHEBEL, KULISSENHEBEL |
| 11639 | **SLOTTED LINER** | COLONNE PERDUE A FENTES | LINER (GESCHLITZER) |
| 11640 | **SLOTTERS** | MORTAISEUSES | SENKRECHTSTOSSMASCHINEN |
| 11641 | **SLOTTING** | MORTAISAGE | STOSSEN, NUTENSTOSSEN |
| 11642 | **SLOTTING ATTACHEMENT** | APPAREIL A MORTAISER | STOSSAPPARATE |
| 11643 | **SLOTTING MACHINE** | MACHINE A MORTAISER, MORTAISEUSE | STOSSMASCHINE, VERTIKALHOBELMASCHINE, NUTSTOSSMASCHINE |
| 11644 | **SLOW COMBUSTION** | COMBUSTION LENTE | VERBRENNUNG (LANGSAME) |
| 11645 | **SLOW DOWN AN ENGINE (TO)** | RALENTIR LA MARCHE D'UNE MACHINE | VERLANGSAMEN (DEN GANG EINER MASCHINE) |
| 11646 | **SLOW IDLING JET** | GICLEUR DE RALENTI | LEERLAUFDÜSE |
| 11647 | **SLOW PITCH THREAD** | FILET A PETIT PAS | GEWINDE MIT SCHWACHER STEIGUNG |
| 11648 | **SLOW SETTING CEMENT** | CIMENT A PRISE LENTE | ZEMENT (LANGSAM BINDENDER) |
| 11649 | **SLOWING DOWN AN ENGINE** | RALENTISSEMENT DE LA MARCHE | VERLANGSAMEN DES GANGES |
| 11650 | **SLOWLY ROTATING, REVOLVING SHAFT** | ARBRE A PETITE VITESSE | WELLE (LANGSAMLAUFENDE) |
| 11651 | **SLUG** | EBAUCHE | ROHLING |
| 11652 | **SLUICE** | VANNE | SCHÜTZ, SCHÜTZE |
| 11653 | **SLUICE VALVE, GATE VALVE** | ROBINET-VANNE | ABSPERRSCHIEBER |
| 11654 | **SLURRY** | BOUE | SCHLAMM |
| 11655 | **SLUSH** | BOUE | SCHLAMM |
| 11656 | **SLUSH CASTING PROCESS** | PROCEDE DE MOULAGE INVERSE | STÜRZGUSSVERFAHREN |
| 11657 | **SMALL COKE** | GRESILLON DE COKE | KOKSKLEIN |
| 11658 | **SMALL GAS ENGINE** | MOTEUR A GAZ DE FAIBLE PUISSANCE | KLEINGASMASCHINE |
| 11659 | **SMALL HAND SAW** | SCIE EGOINE | FUCHSSCHWANZ |
| 11660 | **SMALL IRONWARE** | QUINCAILLERIE | KLEINEISENWAREN |
| 11661 | **SMALL MOTOR, FRATIONAL HORSEPOWER MOTOR** | MOTEUR DE FAIBLE PUISSANCE | KLEINMOTOR |
| 11662 | **SMALL SPROCKET** | NOIX POUR CHAINES, NOIX D'ENTRAINEMENT POUR CHAINES-CABLES | KETTENNUSS |
| 11663 | **SMALL WATER-CAPACITY BOILER, BOILER WITH SMALL WATER SPACE** | CHAUDIERE A FAIBLE VOLUME | KLEINWASSERRAUMKESSEL |
| 11664 | **SMELT (TO), MELT DOWN FROM THE DRE (TO)** | TRAITER LES MINERAIS | VERHÜTTEN |
| 11665 | **SMELTER** | FOUR A FONDRE | SCHMELZOFEN |
| 11666 | **SMELTING** | FUSION, TRAITEMENT DES MINERAIS | SCHMELZEN, VERHÜTTUNG |
| 11667 | **SMELTING FURNACE** | FOUR, FOURNEAU DE FUSION | SCHMELZOFEN |
| 11668 | **SMELTING WORKS** | USINE METALLURGIQUE | HÜTTENWERK |
| 11669 | **SMITH FORGING** | FORGEAGE A LA MAIN, PIECE FORGEE A LA MAIN | HANDSCHMIEDEN |
| 11670 | **SMITH HAMMER FORGING** | PIECE FORGEE AU MARTEAU | FREIFORMSCHMIEDESTÜCK |
| 11671 | **SMITH, BLACKSMITH** | FORGERON | SCHMIED, GROBSCHMIED |
| 11672 | **SMOKE** | FUMEE | RAUCH |
| 11673 | **SMOKE CONSUMING** | FUMIVORE | RAUCHVERZEHREND |
| 11674 | **SMOKE CONSUMING FURNACE** | FOYER FUMIVORE | FEUERUNG FÜR RAUCHFREIE VERBRENNUNG |

# SMO

298

| | | | |
|---|---|---|---|
| 11675 | SMOKE FORMATION | FORMATION DE LA FUMEE | RAUCHBILDUNG, RAUCHENTWICKLUNG |
| 11676 | SMOKE NUISANCE | NUISANCE PAR LA FUMEE | RAUCHBELÄSTIGUNG |
| 11677 | SMOKE PREVENTION | SUPPRESSION DE LA FUMEE | RAUCHVERHÜTUNG |
| 11678 | SMOKY FLAME | FLAMME FULIGINEUSE | FLAMME (RUSSENDE) |
| 11679 | SMOOTH (TO) | LISSER | GLÄTTEN |
| 11680 | SMOOTH CUT FILE | LIME A TAILLE DOUCE, LIME FINE | FEINHIEBFEILE, SCHLICHTFEILE |
| 11681 | SMOOTH EVEN RUNNING | MARCHE REGULIERE | GANG (RUHIGER) |
| 11682 | SMOOTH FINISH, FINISHING | ACHEVEMENT, PARACHEVEMENT, FINISSAGE, FINITION, RETOUCHE | NACHARBEITEN, NACHBEARBEITUNG, FERTIGBEARBEITUNG, SCHLICHTEN |
| 11683 | SMOOTH FRACTURE | CASSURE NETTE | BRUCH (GLATTER) |
| 11684 | SMOOTH PLAIN TUBE | TUBE LISSE | ROHR (GLATTES) |
| 11685 | SMOOTH STARTING | DEMARRAGE DOUX, DEMARRAGE SANS A-COUPS | ANLAUF (STOSSFREIER) |
| 11686 | SMOOTHING | LISSAGE | GLÄTTEN |
| 11687 | SMOOTHING PLANE | RABOT A REPASSER | SCHLICHTHOBEL |
| 11688 | SMOULDER (TO) | BRULER SANS FLAMME, COUVER | SCHWELEN |
| 11689 | SNAGGING | EBARBAGE, MEULAGE | PUTZEN |
| 11690 | SNAP ACTION SWITH | INTERRUPTEUR A ACTION INSTANTANEE | SPRINGSCHALTER, SCHNAPPSCHALTER |
| 11691 | SNAP HOOK | PORTE-MOUSQUETON, MOUSQUETON | KARABINERHAKEN |
| 11692 | SNAP RING | JONC D'ARRET | SPRENGRING |
| 11693 | SNAP-GAUGES | CALIBRES-MACHOIRES | RACHENLEHRE |
| 11694 | SNIFTING VALVE | RENIFLARD | SCHNARCHVENTIL, SCHNÜFFELVENTIL, SCHNÜFFLER, LUFTANSAUGEVENTIL |
| 11695 | SNOW LOAD | CHARGE DE NEIGE | SCHNEELAST |
| 11696 | SNOW-CHAINS | CHAINES DE NEIGE | SCHNEEKETTEN |
| 11697 | SOAK CLEANING | NETTOYAGE PAR IMMERSION | EINTAUCHREINIGUNG |
| 11698 | SOAKING FURNACE | FOUR D'EGALISATION | AUSGLEICHOFEN |
| 11699 | SOAKING PIT | PIT A TREMPER | DURCHWEICHUNGSGRUBE |
| 11700 | SOAKING TEMPERATURE | TEMPERATURE DE RECUIT | DURCHWÄRMETEMPERATUR |
| 11701 | SOAP | SAVON | SEIFE |
| 11702 | SOAP SUDS | EAU DE SAVON, EAU SAVONNEUSE | SEIFENWASSER, SEIFENLAUGE, SEIFENLÖSUNG |
| 11703 | SOAPSTONE, STEATITE | STEATITE, CRAIE DE BRIANCON | SPECKSTEIN, STEATIT |
| 11704 | SOCKET CHISEL | CISEAU A DOUILLE | ROHRMEISSEL |
| 11705 | SOCKET OF A PIPE | MANCHON DE RACCORD | MUFFE, ROHRMUFFE |
| 11706 | SOCKET OF A ROPE | AGRAFE DE JONCTION POUR CABLES | SEILSCHLOSS |
| 11707 | SOCKET PIPE | TUYAU A EMBOITEMENT | MUFFENROHR |
| 11708 | SOCKET WELDING FITTING | RACCORD A EMBOITEMENT POUR SOUDURE | EINFÜGESCHWEISSFITTING |
| 11709 | SOCKET WRENCH | CLE A DOUILLE | STECKSCHLÜSSEL |
| 11710 | SOCKETED END OF PIPE | BOUT FEMELLE D'UN TUYAU | MUFFENENDE EINES ROHRES |
| 11711 | SODA CRYSTALS, CRYSTALLISED SODIUM CARBONATE | CRISTAUX DE SOUDE | KRISTALLISIERTE SODA, KRISTALLSODA, GEWÄSSERTES NATRIUMKARBONAT |
| 11712 | SODA LYE | LESSIVE DE SOUDE | SODALAUGE |
| 11713 | SODA, SODIUM CARBONATE | SOUDE, CARBONATE DE SODIUM | SODA, NATRIUMKARBONAT |
| 11714 | SODIUM | SODIUM | NATRIUM |
| 11715 | SODIUM ACETATE | ACETATE DE SODIUM, DE SOUDE | NATRIUM (ESSIGSAURES), NATRIUMAZETAT |

| | | | |
|---|---|---|---|
| 11716 | **SODIUM ALUMINATE** | ALUMINATE DE SODIUM | TONERDENATRON, NATRIUMALUMINAT |
| 11717 | **SODIUM BISULPHATE** | SULFATE ACIDE DE SOUDE | NATRIUM (SAURES), NATRIUM (SCHWEFELSAURES), NATRIUMBISULFAT |
| 11718 | **SODIUM BISULPHITE** | SULFITE ACIDE, BISULFITE DE SODIUM | NATRON (SCHWEFLIGSAURES), NATRON (DOPPELTSCHWEFLIGSAURES), NATRIUMBISULFIT |
| 11719 | **SODIUM CITRATE** | CITRATE DE SODIUM | NATRON (ZITRONENSAURES), NATRIUMZITRAT |
| 11720 | **SODIUM CYANIDE** | CYANURE DE SODIUM | ZYANNATRIUM, NATRIUMZYANID |
| 11721 | **SODIUM FLUORIDE** | FLUORURE DE SODIUM | FLUORNATRIUM |
| 11722 | **SODIUM HYDROXIDE, CAUSTIC SODA** | SOUDE CAUSTIQUE, HYDRATE DE SODIUM | ÄTZNATRON, NATRIUMHYDROXYD, NATRIUMOXYDHYDRAT, NATRONHYDRAT, KAUSTISCHE SODA |
| 11723 | **SODIUM LINE** | RAIE DU SODIUM | NATRIUMLINIE |
| 11724 | **SODIUM MONOXIDE** | OXYDE DE SODIUM | NATRON, NATRIUMOXYD |
| 11725 | **SODIUM NITRITE** | AZOTITE, NITRITE DE SOUDE, SOUDE AZOTEUSE, SOUDE NITREUSE | NATRIUM (SALPETRIGSAURES), NATRIUMNITRIT |
| 11726 | **SODIUM OXALATE** | OXALATE DE SODIUM | NATRIUM (OXALSAURES), NATRIUM, NATRIUMOXALAT |
| 11727 | **SODIUM PEROXIDE** | BIOXYDE DE SODIUM | NATRIUMSUPEROXYD, NATRIUMPEROXYD |
| 11728 | **SODIUM PHOSPHATE** | PHOSPHATE DE SODIUM | NATRON (PHOSPHORSAURES), NATRIUMPHOSPHAT |
| 11729 | **SODIUM POTASSIUM TARTRATE, SEIGNETTE'S SALT, ROCHELLE SALT** | TARTRATE DE POTASSE ET DE SOUDE, SEL DE SEIGNETTE | KALINATRON (WEINSAURES), ROCHELLESALZ, SCHWANENSALZ, SEIGNETTESALZ, NATRONWEINSTEIN, KALIUMNATRIUMTARTRAT |
| 11730 | **SODIUM PYROPHOSPHATE** | PYROPHOSPHATE DE SOUDE | NATRIUMPYROPHOSPHAT, PYROPHOSPHORSAURES NATRON |
| 11731 | **SODIUM SILICATE** | SILICATE DE SOUDE | NATRONWASSERGLAS, KIESELSAURES NATRIUM, NATRIUMSILIKAT |
| 11732 | **SODIUM STANNATE** | STANNATE DE SODIUM | NATRIUM (ZINNSAURES), NATRIUMSTANNAT, SODASTANNAT, ZINNOXYDNATRON, ZINNSODA, PRÄPARIERSALZ |
| 11733 | **SODIUM SULPHATE** | SULFATE NEUTRE DE SODIUM | NATRON (SCHWEFELSAURES), NATRIUMSULFAT |
| 11734 | **SODIUM SULPHITE** | SULFITE DE SOUDE | NATRON (SCHWEFLIGSAURES), NATRIUMSULFIT |
| 11735 | **SODIUM TANNATE** | TANNATE DE SODIUM | NATRIUM (GERBSAURES), NATRIUMTANNAT |
| 11736 | **SODIUM THIOSULPHATE HYPOSULPHITE** | HYPOSULFITE DE SODIUM | NATRON (UNTERSCHWEFLIGSAURES), NATRIUMTHIOSULFAT, NATRIUMHYPOSULFIT |
| 11737 | **SODIUM TUNGSTATE** | TUNGSTATE DE SOUDE | NATRIUM (WOLFRAMSAURES), NATRIUMWOLFRAMAT |
| 11738 | **SOFT FLOWING METAL** | METAL MOU, TENDRE | WEICHMETALL |
| 11739 | **SOFT PACKING** | GARNITURE SOUPLE | PACKUNG (WEICHE) |
| 11740 | **SOFT SOAP** | SAVON MOU, SAVON VERT, SAVON NOIR, SAVON DE POTASSE | SCHMIERSEIFE |
| 11741 | **SOFT SOLDER (TO)** | SOUDER A L'ETAIN | WEICH LÖTEN |
| 11742 | **SOFT SOLDER, PLUMBER'S SOLDER** | SOUDURE A L'ETAIN | WEICHLOT, SCHNELLOT, WEISSLOT, ZINNLOT, LÖTZINN |
| 11743 | **SOFT SOLDERING** | SOUDURE A L'ETAIN | WEICHLÖTEN |
| 11744 | **SOFT STEEL** | ACIER DOUX | STAHL (WEICHER), FLUSSEISEN, FLUSSSTAHL |
| 11745 | **SOFT WATER** | EAU PURE, EAU PEU CHARGEE | WEICHES WASSER |

# SOF 300

| | | | |
|---|---|---|---|
| 11746 | SOFT WOOD | BOIS LEGER, BOIS TENDRE, BOIS BLANC | WEICHHOLZ, WEICHES HOLZ |
| 11747 | SOFT-FACED HAMMER | MARTEAU A TETE PLASTIQUE | KUNSTSTOFFBAHNHAMMER |
| 11748 | SOFTEN THE WATER (TO) | EPURER, PURIFIER LES EAUX D'ALIMENTATION PAR VOIE CHIMIQUE | WASSER ENTHÄRTEN |
| 11749 | SOFTENING | ADOUCISSEMENT | ENTHÄRTUNG |
| 11750 | SOFTENING POINT | POINT D'AFFAISSEMENT | ERWEICHUNGSPUNKT |
| 11751 | SOIL BEARING CAPACITY | PORTANCE DU SOL | TRAGFÄHIGKEIT DES BODENS |
| 11752 | SOIL SURVEY | ETUDE DE TERRAIN, ETUDE DE SOL | BODENUNTERSUCHUNG, TRAGFÄHIGKEIT DES BODENS |
| 11753 | SOLAR OIL | HUILE SOLAIRE | SOLARÖL, BRAUNKOHLENBENZIN |
| 11754 | SOLAR SPECTRUM | SPECTRE SOLAIRE | SONNENSPEKTRUM |
| 11755 | SOLDER | ALLIAGE FUSIBLE POUR SOUDER OU BRASER, SOUDURE (COMPOSITION FUSIBLE) | LOT, LÖTMITTEL |
| 11756 | SOLDER (TO) | SOUDER | LÖTEN |
| 11757 | SOLDER EMBRITTLEMENT | FRAGILITE PAR PENETRATION DE SOUDURE | VERSPRÖDUNG DURCH EINDRINGEN VON LOT |
| 11758 | SOLDERED BRAZED FLANGE | BRIDE BRASEE, RONDELLE BRASEE | FLANSCH (AUFGELÖTETER) |
| 11759 | SOLDERED BRAZED JOINT | ASSEMBLAGE PAR SOUDURE | LÖTVERBINDUNG |
| 11760 | SOLDERED BRAZED PIPE | TUBE BRASE | ROHR (GELÖTETES) |
| 11761 | SOLDERED SEAM | SOUDURE (TRAVAIL FAIT EN SOUDANT AVEC INTERPOSITION D'UN ALLIAGE) | LÖTSTELLE |
| 11762 | SOLDERING | SOUDAGE, SOUDURE, BRASAGE | LÖTEN, LÖTUNG |
| 11763 | SOLDERING FURNACE | FOUR A SOUDER | LÖTOFEN |
| 11764 | SOLDERING IRON | FER A SOUDER | LÖTKOLBEN |
| 11765 | SOLDERING IRON BIT, COPPER BIT | FER A SOUDER | LÖTKOLBEN, LÖTEISEN |
| 11766 | SOLDERING LAMP | LAMPE A SOUDER | LÖTLAMPE |
| 11767 | SOLDERING TONGS | PINCE, TENAILLE A SOUDER | LÖTZANGE |
| 11768 | SOLDERING WITH THE BLOW PIPE | SOUDURE AU CHALUMEAU | FLAMMENLÖTUNG |
| 11769 | SOLDERING WITH THE SOLDERING BIT | SOUDURE AU FER A SOUDER | KOLBENLÖTUNG |
| 11770 | SOLE LEATHER | CUIR FORT | SOHLLEDER |
| 11771 | SOLE OF A PLANE | SEMELLE D'UN RABOT | SOHLE EINES HOBELS |
| 11772 | SOLE PLATE | SEMELLE DE PALIER | SOHLPLATTE (FÜR LAGER) |
| 11773 | SOLENOID | SOLENOIDE | SOLENOID |
| 11774 | SOLENOID VALVE | SOUPAPE ELECTROMAGNETIQUE, SOLENOIDE, ROBINET ELECTROMAGNETIQUE, VALVE ELECTROMAGNETIQUE | MAGNETVENTIL |
| 11775 | SOLID | SOLIDE, CORPS SOLIDE | FESTKÖRPER, KÖRPER (FESTER) |
| 11776 | SOLID ANGLE | ANGLE SOLIDE | WINKEL (KÖRPERLICHER) |
| 11777 | SOLID BEARING | PALIER FERME | LAGER (EINTEILIGES) |
| 11778 | SOLID BORING BAR | BARRE D'ALESAGE MONOPIECE | BOHRSTANGE (EINTEILIGE) |
| 11779 | SOLID BOSS | MOYEU D'UNE SEULE PIECE | NABE (UNGETEILTE) |
| 11780 | SOLID BRICK | BRIQUE PLEINE | VOLLSTEIN, VOLLZIEGEL |
| 11781 | SOLID DIE | FILIERE RONDE MONOBLOC | GEWINDESCHNEIDKOPF (RUNDER) |
| 11782 | SOLID DRAWN TUBE | TUBE ETIRE | ROHR (GEZOGENES) |
| 11783 | SOLID END MILLS | FRAISES EN BOUT PLEINES | SCHAFTFRÄSER |
| 11784 | SOLID FLYWHEEL | VOLANT D'UNE SEULE PIECE | SCHWUNGRAD (EINTEILIGES) |
| 11785 | SOLID FUEL | COMBUSTIBLE SOLIDE | BRENNSTOFF (FESTER) |
| 11786 | SOLID HALF-ROUND IRON | FER DEMI-ROND PLEIN | HALBRUNDEISEN (VOLLES) |

| | | |
|---|---|---|
| 11787 | **SOLID JET** | JET COMPACT | STRAHL (ZUSAMMENHALTENDER) |
| 11788 | **SOLID JOURNAL BEARING, DEAD EYE BEARING** | PALIER EN UNE SEULE PIECE | LAGER (EINTEILIGES), LAGER (GESCHLOSSENES), AUGENLAGER, FROSCHLAGER |
| 11789 | **SOLID MANDREL** | MANDRIN LISSE | DORN (FESTER) |
| 11790 | **SOLID OF REVOLUTION** | CORPS DE REVOLUTION | DREHUNGSKÖRPER, UMDREHUNGSKÖRPER, ROTATIONSKÖRPER |
| 11791 | **SOLID PISTON** | PISTON PLEIN | SCHEIBENKOLBEN, EINSCHEIBENKOLBEN, TELLERKOLBEN |
| 11792 | **SOLID PULLEY** | POULIE EN UNE PIECE | RIEMENSCHEIBE (UNGETEILTE) (GANZE) |
| 11793 | **SOLID SHAFT** | ARBRE PLEIN | WELLE (VOLLE), WELLE (MASSIVE), RIEMENSCHEIBE |
| 11794 | **SOLID SOLUTION** | SOLUTION SOLIDE | MISCHKRISTALL, LÖSUNG (FESTE) |
| 11795 | **SOLID STATE** | ETAT SOLIDE | ZUSTAND (FESTER), FESTER AGGREGAT-ZUSTAND |
| 11796 | **SOLID WEDGE DISC** | OPERCULE MONOBLOC (COIN) | KEIL (MASSIVER) |
| 11797 | **SOLIDIFICATION** | SOLIDIFICATION | ERSTARRUNG, ERSTARREN |
| 11798 | **SOLIDIFICATION FRONT** | FRONT DE SOLIDIFICATION, FRONT DE CRISTALLISATION | ERSTARRUNGSFRONT, KRISTALLISATIONSFRONT |
| 11799 | **SOLIDIFICATION OF A LIQUID** | SOLIDIFICATION D'UN LIQUIDE | ERSTARRUNG EINER FLÜSSIGKEIT |
| 11800 | **SOLIDIFICATION POINT** | POINT DE SOLIDIFICATION | ERSTARRUNGSPUNKT |
| 11801 | **SOLIDIFICATION RANGE** | INTERVALLE DE SOLIDIFICATION | ERSTARRUNGSBEREICH |
| 11802 | **SOLIDIFICATION SHRINKAGE** | CONTRACTION DE SOLIDIFICATION | ERSTARRUNGSSCHWINDUNG |
| 11803 | **SOLIDIFY (TO)** | SOLIDIFIER (SE) PAR REFROIDISSEMENT | ERSTARREN |
| 11804 | **SOLIDIFYING POINT** | POINT DE SOLIDIFICATION, POINT DE PRISE | ERSTARRUNGSPUNKT, STOCKPUNKT |
| 11805 | **SOLIDUS** | SOLIDUS | SOLIDUS, SOLIDUSLINIE |
| 11806 | **SOLUBILITY** | SOLUBILITE | LÖSLICHKEIT |
| 11807 | **SOLUBLE** | SOLUBLE | LÖSLICH |
| 11808 | **SOLUBLE GLASS, WATER GLASS** | VERRE SOLUBLE, VERRE LIQUIDE | WASSERGLAS |
| 11809 | **SOLUBLE IN WATER** | SOLUBLE DANS L'EAU | WASSERLÖSLICH |
| 11810 | **SOLUBLE OIL** | HUILE SOLUBLE | ÖL (WASSERLÖSLICHES) |
| 11811 | **SOLUTION** | SOLUTION | LÖSUNG, AUFLÖSUNG |
| 11812 | **SOLUTION HEAT TREATMENT** | RECUIT DE MISE EN SOLUTION | LÖSUNGSGLÜHEN |
| 11813 | **SOLVE (TO)** | RESOUDRE, DISSOUDRE | AUFLÖSEN (MATH.) |
| 11814 | **SOLVENT** | DISSOLVANT, SOLVANT | LÖSUNGSMITTEL |
| 11815 | **SONIC TESTING** | ESSAI ACOUSTIQUE | PRÜFUNG (AKUSTISCHE) |
| 11816 | **SOOT** | SUIE | RUSS |
| 11817 | **SORBITE** | SORBITE | SORBIT |
| 11818 | **SOUND VIBRATION** | VIBRATION SONORE | SCHALLSCHWINGUNG |
| 11819 | **SOUND WAVE** | ONDE SONORE | SCHALLWELLE |
| 11820 | **SOUND WOOD** | BOIS SAIN | HOLZ (GESUNDES) |
| 11821 | **SOUNDNESS OF A WELD** | HOMOGENEITE D'UNE SOUDURE | FEHLERFREIHEIT DER SCHWEISSNAHT |
| 11822 | **SOUR CRUDE** | PETROLE BRUT SULFUREUX | ERDÖL (SCHWEFELHALTIGES) |
| 11823 | **SOURCE OF ELECTRIC CURRENT** | SOURCE D'ELECTRICITE | STROMQUELLE |
| 11824 | **SOURCE OF ENERGY** | SOURCE D'ENERGIE | ENERGIEQUELLE |
| 11825 | **SOURCE OF ERROR** | CAUSE D'ERREUR, SOURCE D'ERREURS | FEHLERQUELLE |
| 11826 | **SOURCE OF LIGHT, LUMINOUS SOURCE** | SOURCE LUMINEUSE | LICHTQUELLE |
| 11827 | **SOUTH SEEKING POLE OF A MAGNET** | POLE SUD D'UN AIMANT | SÜDPOL EINES MAGNETEN |

**SPA** 302

| | | | |
|---|---|---|---|
| 11828 | SPACE LATTICE | RESEAU SPATIAL | RAUMGITTER |
| 11829 | SPACE OCCUPIED, REQUIRED | ENCOMBREMENT | PLATZBEDARF, RAUMBEDARF, RAUMBEANSPRUCHUNG |
| 11830 | SPALLING | ECAILLAGE | ABBLÄTTERUNG |
| 11831 | SPAN | PORTEE (DISTANCE ENTRE DEUX POINTS D'APPUI), TROUEE | TRAGWEITE, SPANNWEITE, STÜTZWEITE |
| 11832 | SPANNER GAP, WIDTH OF JAWS, GAP OF SPANNER | OUVERTURE DE CLEF | SCHRAUBENSCHLÜSSELWEITE, SCHLÜSSELWEITE |
| 11833 | SPANNER, SCREW KEY | CLEF A ECROUS | SCHRAUBENSCHLÜSSEL, MUTTERSCHLÜSSEL |
| 11834 | SPARE PART, REPAIR PART, REPLACEMENT PART | PIECE DE RECHANGE, PIECE INTERCHANGEABLE | ERSATZTEIL |
| 11835 | SPARE WHEEL | ROUE DE SECOURS | RESERVERAD, ERSATZRAD |
| 11836 | SPARK | ETINCELLE | FUNKE |
| 11837 | SPARK ADVANCE | CORRECTEUR D'AVANCE | ZÜNDVERSTELLUNG |
| 11838 | SPARK PLUG | BOUGIE D'ALLUMAGE | ZÜNDKERZE |
| 11839 | SPARK PLUG BARREL OR BODY | CULOT DE BOUGIE | ZÜNDKERZENGEHÄUSE |
| 11840 | SPARK TEST | ESSAI A L'ETINCELLE | FUNKENPROBE |
| 11841 | SPARKING PLUG | BOUGIE D'ALLUMAGE | ZÜNDKERZE |
| 11842 | SPATTER | CRACHEMENT, ECLABOUSSURE, PERLE DE SOUDURE | SPRITZEN, SCHWEISSPERLE |
| 11843 | SPATTER LOSS | PERTES PAR CRACHEMENT | SPRITZVERLUSTE |
| 11844 | SPATULA | SPATULE | SPACHTEL |
| 11845 | SPECIAL BRANCH | DOMAINE, BRANCHE, SPECIALITE | FACHGEBIET, SONDERGEBIET, SPEZIALGEBIET |
| 11846 | SPECIAL PLATE, SHAPED PLATE, PROFILED SHEET IRON | TOLE FACONNEE, TOLE PROFILEE | FORMBLECH |
| 11847 | SPECIAL SECTION WIRE | FIL PROFILE | FORMDRAHT, FASSONDRAHT, PROFILDRAHT |
| 11848 | SPECIAL STEEL | ACIER SPECIAL | SONDERSTAHL |
| 11849 | SPECIALITY, SPECIAL ARTICLE OF MANUFACTURE | PRODUIT SPECIAL | SONDERERZEUGNIS, SPEZIALARTIKEL |
| 11850 | SPECIFIC GRAVITY | POIDS SPECIFIQUE, DENSITE | GEWICHT (SPEZIFISCHES), EINHEITSGEWICHT |
| 11851 | SPECIFIC GRAVITY FLASK, PYKNOMETER | PYCNOMETRE | PYKNOMETER |
| 11852 | SPECIFIC HEAT | CHALEUR SPECIFIQUE | WÄRME (SPEZIFISCHE) |
| 11853 | SPECIFIC PRESSURE | PRESSION EN KILOGRAMMES PAR UNITE DE SURFACE | DRUCK (SPEZIFISCHER) |
| 11854 | SPECIFIC VOLUME | VOLUME SPECIFIQUE | VOLUMEN (SPEZIFISCHES) |
| 11855 | SPECIFICATION | CAHIER DES CHARGES | LASTENHEFT |
| 11856 | SPECIFICATION OF A PATENT | DESCRIPTION, MEMOIRE DESCRIPTIF DU BREVET | PATENTSCHRIFT, PATENTBESCHREIBUNG |
| 11857 | SPECIFIED SIZE | DIMENSIONS NOMINALES | NENNMASS |
| 11858 | SPECIMEN | EPROUVETTE DE METAL | PROBE |
| 11859 | SPECTRAL COLOURS | COULEURS SPECTRALES | SPEKTRALFARBEN |
| 11860 | SPECTROGRAPH | SPECTROGRAPHE | SPEKTROGRAPH |
| 11861 | SPECTROGRAPHE ANALYSIS | ANALYSE SPECTRALE | SPEKTRALANALYSE |
| 11862 | SPECTROSCOPE, SPECTROMETER, SPECTROGRAPH | SPECTROSCOPE, SPECTROMETRE | SPEKTROSKOP, SPEKTROMETER, SPEKTROGRAPH, SPEKTRALAPPARAT |
| 11863 | SPECTRUM | SPECTRE | SPEKTRUM, WELLENBAND |
| 11864 | SPECTRUM ANALYSIS | ANALYSE SPECTRALE | SPEKTRALANALYSE |
| 11865 | SPECULAR IRON, HEMATITE, HAEMATITE | OLIGISTE, FER SPECULAIRE, HEMATITE ROUGE | EISENGLANZ, ROTEISENERZ, ROTEISENSTEIN, HÄMATIT |
| 11866 | SPECULAR SURFACE | SURFACE MIROITANTE | FLÄCHE (SPIEGELNDE) |

| | | | |
|---|---|---|---|
| 11867 | **SPECULUM METAL** | BRONZE POUR MIROIRS DE TELESCOPES | SPIEGELMETALL, SPIEGELBRONZE |
| 11868 | **SPEED** | VITESSE | GESCHWINDIGKEIT |
| 11869 | **SPEED INDICATOR, TACHOMETER, TACHYMETER** | TACHYMETRE | GESCHWINDIGKEITSMESSER, TACHOMETER |
| 11870 | **SPEED OF IGNITION** | VITESSE D'INFLAMMATION | ZÜNDGESCHWINDIGKEIT, ENTZÜNDUNGSGESCHWINDIGKEIT |
| 11871 | **SPEED PULLEY, BELT SPEED CONE, CONE PULLEY, STEPPED PULLEY, STEP CONE, CONE** | POULIE ETAGEE, CONE A ETAGES, POIRE DE VITESSE, CONE D'ATTAQUE, CONE DE TRANSMISSION | STUFENSCHEIBE |
| 11872 | **SPEED REDUCER** | REDUCTEUR DE VITESSE | GESCHWINDIGKEITSREGLER |
| 11873 | **SPEED REDUCTION GEAR** | REDUCTEUR DE VITESSE, ENGRENAGE DEMULTIPLICATEUR | REDUKTIONSGETRIEBE |
| 11874 | **SPEED REGULATOR** | REGULATEUR DE VITESSE | GESCHWINDIGKEITSREGLER, DREHZAHLREGLER |
| 11875 | **SPEED, VELOCITY** | VITESSE | GESCHWINDIGKEIT |
| 11876 | **SPEED, VELOCITY OF ROTATION** | VITESSE DE ROTATION | UMDREHUNGSGESCHWINDIGKEIT, UMLAUFGESCHWINDIGKEIT, DREHGESCHWINDIGKEIT |
| 11877 | **SPEEDOMETER** | COMPTEUR DE VITESSE | GESCHWINDIGKEITSMESSER |
| 11878 | **SPEISS** | MATTE | ROHSTEIN, LECH |
| 11879 | **SPELTER** | ZINC (COMMERCIAL) | HANDELSZINK |
| 11880 | **SPELTER SOLDER** | SOUDURE JAUNE | MESSINGLOT |
| 11881 | **SPERM OIL** | HUILE DE BLANC DE BALEINE | WALRATÖL |
| 11882 | **SPERMACETI** | SPERMACETI, BLANC DE BALEINE | WALRAT |
| 11883 | **SPHERE** | SPHERE, GLOBE | KUGEL (GEOM.) |
| 11884 | **SPHERICAL** | SPHERIQUE | KUGELFÖRMIG, KUGELIG, SPHÄRISCH |
| 11885 | **SPHERICAL ABERRATION** | ABERRATION DE SPHERICITE | ABWEICHUNG (SPHÄRISCHE), ABERRATION (SPHÄRISCHE) |
| 11886 | **SPHERICAL ANGLE** | FUSEAU SPHERIQUE | KUGELZWEIECK, KUGELWINKEL |
| 11887 | **SPHERICAL CALOTTE** | CALOTTE SPHERIQUE | KUGELSCHALE |
| 11888 | **SPHERICAL MIRROR** | MIROIR SPHERIQUE | KUGELSPIEGEL, SPIEGEL (SPHÄRISCHER) |
| 11889 | **SPHERICAL MOTION** | MOUVEMENT SPHERIQUE | KUGELBEWEGUNG, BEWEGUNG (SPHÄRISCHE) |
| 11890 | **SPHERICAL THRUST BEARING** | CRAPAUDINE A BILLES | KUGELSPURLAGER |
| 11891 | **SPHERICAL TRIANGLE** | TRIANGLE SPHERIQUE | KUGELDREIECK, DREIECK (SPHÄRISCHES) |
| 11892 | **SPHERICAL WEDGE** | ONGLET SPHERIQUE | KUGELKEIL |
| 11893 | **SPHERICAL, JOURNAL, PIVOT** | TOURILLON, PIVOT SPHERIQUE | KUGELZAPFEN |
| 11894 | **SPHEROIDAL CAST IRON** | FONTE A GRAPHITE SPHEROIDAL, FONTE NODULAIRE, FONTE DUCTILE | GUSSEISEN MIT KUGELGRAPHIT |
| 11895 | **SPHEROIDAL GRAPHITE IRON** | FONTE A GRAPHITE SPHEROIDAL | GUSSEISEN MIT KUGELGRAPHIT |
| 11896 | **SPHEROIDIZING** | GLOBULISATION, SPHEROIDISATION | KUGELBILDUNG |
| 11897 | **SPHEROMETER** | SPHEROMETRE | KRÜMMUNGSMESSER, SPHÄROMETER |
| 11898 | **SPIEGEL IRON** | SPIEGEL | SPIEGELEISEN |
| 11899 | **SPIEGELEISEN, SPIEGEL** | SPIEGEL, SPIEGELEISEN, FONTE SPECULAIRE | SPIEGELEISEN |
| 11900 | **SPIGOT AND SOCKET JOINT** | JOINT A EMBOITEMENT | MUFFENVERBINDUNG |
| 11901 | **SPIGOTED END OF PIPE** | BOUT MALE D'UN TUYAU | MANTELENDE EINES ROHRES, SCHWANZENDE EINES ROHRES, SPITZENDE EINES ROHRES, ZOPFENDE EINES ROHRES |
| 11902 | **SPIKES** | CROCHETS | HAKENNÄGEL |
| 11903 | **SPILLS** | SOUFFLURES | BLASEN |

## SPI 304

| 11904 | SPINDLE | MANDRIN, AXE, BROCHE | DORN, SPINDEL, ASCHE (KLEINE) |
|---|---|---|---|
| 11905 | SPINDLE BEARING | CRAPAUDINE, PALIER D'UN TOURILLON | ZAPFENLAGER |
| 11906 | SPINDLE BORE | PASSAGE DE BROCHE | SPINDEL-DURCHLASS |
| 11907 | SPINDLE NUT, DISC BUSHING | ECROU D'OPERCULE | SPINDELVERSCHRAUBUNG |
| 11908 | SPINDLE OIL | HUILE MINERALE POUR BROCHES | SPINDELÖL |
| 11909 | SPINDLE SPEEDS | VITESSE DE BROCHE | SPINDELDREHZAHLEN |
| 11910 | SPINDLE SUPPORT | SUPPORT DE FUSEE | SPINDELHALTER |
| 11911 | SPINNING AND PLANISHING LATHE | TOUR A REPOUSSER ET A LISSER | DRUCK-UND PLANIERMASCHINE |
| 11912 | SPIRAL | SPIRALE | SPIRALE |
| 11913 | SPIRAL CAM | CAME A PLATEAU COURBE | SCHEIBE (GEWUNDENE), SCHEIBE (KRUMME) |
| 11914 | SPIRAL CHUTE | TOBOGGAN | WENDELRUTSCHE, SPIRALRUTSCHE, TOBOGGAN |
| 11915 | SPIRAL FLUTED REAMER | ALESOIR A RAINURES HELICOIDALES, A RAINURES TORSES | SPIRALGENUTETE REIBAHLE |
| 11916 | SPIRAL GEARING | COUPLE DE ROUES HELICOIDALES | SCHRAUBENRADGETRIEBE |
| 11917 | SPIRAL MILLING CUTTER | FRAISE A DENTURE HELICOIDALE | FRÄSER MIT SCHRAUBENFÖRMIGEN SCHNEIDEN, SPIRALFRÄSER |
| 11918 | SPIRAL RIVETED | RIVETE EN SPIRALE | SPIRALFÖRMIG GENIETET |
| 11919 | SPIRAL STAIRWAY | ESCALIER HELICOIDAL | WENDELTREPPE |
| 11920 | SPIRAL WELDED TUBE | TUBE SOUDE EN SPIRALE, EN HELICE | ROHR (SPIRALGESCHWEISSTES) |
| 11921 | SPIRAL WELDING | SOUDAGE EN SPIRALE | SCHWEISSEN (SPIRALFÖRMIGES) |
| 11922 | SPIRIT ALCOHOL THERMOMETER | THERMOMETRE A ALCOOL | WEINGEISTTHERMOMETER, ALKOHOLTHERMOMETER |
| 11923 | SPIRIT LAMP | LAMPE A ALCOOL | SPIRITUSLAMPE, SPIRITUSBRENNER |
| 11924 | SPLASH CONE | CONE DE DEFLECTION (DANS RESERVOIR) | UMLENKKONUS, ABLENKKEGEL |
| 11925 | SPLASH LUBRICATION | GRAISSAGE PAR BARBOTAGE | TAUCHBADSCHMIERUNG, TAUCHSCHMIERUNG |
| 11926 | SPLASH PANEL | DOUBLURE | ABLENKPLATTE |
| 11927 | SPLASH-APRON | GARDE-BOUE | KÜHLERSPRITZBLECH |
| 11928 | SPLASHED OIL, WASTE OIL | HUILE PROJETEE, HUILE VERSEE | ÖL (VERSPRITZTES) |
| 11929 | SPLASHINGS | ECLABOUSSURES DE METAL | METALLTROPFEN |
| 11930 | SPLICE | EPISSURE | SPLEISS |
| 11931 | SPLICE A ROPE (TO) | EPISSURER | SPLEISSEN (EIN SEIL), SPLISSEN (EIN SEIL) |
| 11932 | SPLICE MEMBER | ELEMENTS A COUVRE-JOINTS | STOSSLASCHENTEIL, LASCHENVERBINDUNGEN |
| 11933 | SPLICE OF A ROPE | EPISSURE (RESULTAT) | SPLISS, SEILSPLISS |
| 11934 | SPLICING A ROPE | EPISSURE (ACTION) | SPLEISSEN, SPLISSEN, SEILVERSPLEISSUNG |
| 11935 | SPLINED SHAFT | ARBRE CANNELE | KEILWELLE |
| 11936 | SPLINTERY FRACTURE | CASSURE CEROIDE, ECAILLEUSE, ESQUILLEUSE | BRUCH (SPLITTRIGER) |
| 11937 | SPLIT | FENTE | SPALT |
| 11938 | SPLIT BOSS | MOYEU EN DEUX PIECES | NABE (GETEILTE), NABE (GESCHLITZTE), KLEMMNABE |
| 11939 | SPLIT COLLAR | BAGUE D'ARRET EN DEUX PIECES | STELLRING (ZWEITEILIGER), KLEMMRING |
| 11940 | SPLIT COTTER PIN | GOUPILLE FENDUE | SPLINT |
| 11941 | SPLIT FLYWHEEL | VOLANT FENDU | SCHWUNGRAD (GESPRENGTES) |

|       |                              |                              |                              |
|-------|------------------------------|------------------------------|------------------------------|
| 11942 | **SPLIT NUT** | ECROU FENDU, ECROU A FENTE | MUTTER (GESCHLITZTE), MUTTER (GETEILTE), MUTTER (AUFGESCHNITTENE), SCHLITZMUTTER |
| 11943 | **SPLIT PIN** | GOUPILLE FENDUE | SPLINT |
| 11944 | **SPLIT PISTON RING** | BAGUE DE PISTON FENDUE | KOLBENRING (GESPALTENER), KOLBENRING (GESCHLITZTER) |
| 11945 | **SPLIT PULLEY** | POULIE EN DEUX PIECES, POULIE FENDUE | RIEMENSCHEIBE (GETEILTE) |
| 11946 | **SPLIT UP (TO)** | DEDOUBLER, SCINDER | SPALTEN (CHEM.) |
| 11947 | **SPLIT-BEARINGS** | DEMI-COUSSINETS | SCHALENLAGER (GETEILTES) |
| 11948 | **SPLITTING OF THE WOOD** | ECLATEMENT DU BOIS | REISSEN DES HOLZES |
| 11949 | **SPLITTING TEST** | ESSAI D'ECRASEMENT, ESSAI DE CISAILLEMENT | SCHERVERSUCH, STAUCHVERSUCH |
| 11950 | **SPLITTING UP** | DEDOUBLEMENT | SPALTEN (CHEM.) |
| 11951 | **SPOKE CENTRE WHEEL, SPIDER WHEEL** | ROUE A RAYONS | SPEICHENRAD |
| 11952 | **SPONGE CLOTH, WIPER** | CHIFFON A NETTOYER, CHIFFON D'ESSUYAGE | PUTZTUCH, PUTZLAPPEN |
| 11953 | **SPONGE IRON** | PAILLE DE FER | SCHWAMMEISEN |
| 11954 | **SPONGY LEAD** | PLOMB SPONGIEUX | BLEISCHWAMM |
| 11955 | **SPONGY PLATINUM, PLATINUM SPONGE** | MOUSSE DE PLATINE, EPONGE DE PLATINE | PLATINSCHWAMM |
| 11956 | **SPONTANEOUS COMBUSTION, IGNITION** | COMBUSTION, INFLAMMATION SPONTANEE, AUTO-INFLAMMATION | SELBSTENTZÜNDUNG |
| 11957 | **SPOON BIT, SHELL AUGER** | MECHE, FORET A CUILLER | LÖFFELBOHRER |
| 11958 | **SPOT TEST** | ESSAI A LA GOUTTE | TROPFPROBE |
| 11959 | **SPOT WELDING** | SOUDURE PAR POINTS | PUNKTSCHWEISSUNG, PUNKTSCHWEISSUNG |
| 11960 | **SPOT-FACING** | FINITION PARTIELLE, LAMAGE | TEILFERTIGUNG, STIRNSENKUNG |
| 11961 | **SPOTTING OUT** | FORMATION DES TACHES | AUSSCHLAGBILDUNG |
| 11962 | **SPRAY GUN** | PISTOLET A PROJETER, PISTOLET DE PULVERISATION | SPRITZPISTOLE |
| 11963 | **SPRAY NOZZLE** | TUYERE DE PULVERISATION | STREUDÜSE |
| 11964 | **SPRAY NOZZLE** | TUYERE DE PULVERISATION | SPRÜHDÜSE |
| 11965 | **SPRAY PAINTING** | PEINTURE PAR PULVERISATION AU PISTOLET | SPRITZLACKIERUNG |
| 11966 | **SPRAY QUENCHING** | TREMPE PAR PULVERISATION | SPRÜHHÄRTUNG |
| 11967 | **SPRAYER** | PULVERISATEUR | SPRITZDUSE ZERSTÄUBER, SPRITZER |
| 11968 | **SPRAYING** | PROJECTION, PULVERISATION | SPRITZEN |
| 11969 | **SPRAYING AND DUSTING MACHINES (HAND AND KNAPSACK)** | POUDREUSES PORTATIVES | RÜCKENSTÄUBER UND RÜCKENSPRITZGRERÄTE |
| 11970 | **SPRAYING AND DUSTING MACHINES FRUIT AND HOPS** | POUDREUSES SOUFREUSES | ZERSTÄUBUNGS-UND SPRITZMASCHINEN (FRÜCHTE UND HOPFEN) |
| 11971 | **SPRAYING AND DUSTING MACHINES GRASS AND CROPS** | POUDREUSES PULVERISATEURS | ZERSTÄUBUNGS-UND SPRITZMASCHINEN (GRAS UND GETREIDE) |
| 11972 | **SPRAYING PROCESS** | PROCEDE PAR ASPERSION | SPRITZVERFAHREN |
| 11973 | **SPREADER** | ECARTEUR | ABSTANDHALTER |
| 11974 | **SPRING** | RESSORT, RESSORT ANTAGONISTE | FEDER, GEGENFEDER |
| 11975 | **SPRING AND WIRE TESTING MACHINE** | MACHINE A ESSAYER LES RESSORTS ET LES FILS | FEDER-UND DRAHT-PRÜFMASCHINE |
| 11976 | **SPRING BALANCE** | PESON A RESSORT, BALANCE A RESSORT | FEDERWAAGE |
| 11977 | **SPRING BLADE** | LAME DE RESSORT | FEDERBLATT |
| 11978 | **SPRING BRASS** | LAITON DE RESSORT | FEDERMESSING |

# SPR

306

| | | | |
|---|---|---|---|
| 11979 | **SPRING COLLET CHUCK** | DOUILLE A RESSORT | ZANGENSPANNFUTTER |
| 11980 | **SPRING DASHPOT** | BOITE A RESSORT | FEDERPUFFER |
| 11981 | **SPRING FACTOR** | FACTEUR DE VIBRATION | SCHWINGUNGSFAKTOR |
| 11982 | **SPRING GREASE BOX** | COMPRESSEUR A GRAISSE | FEDERSCHMIERBÜCHSE |
| 11983 | **SPRING IN TENSION, LOADED SPRING** | RESSORT CHARGE, TENDU, BANDE | FEDER (GESPANNTE) |
| 11984 | **SPRING LOADED GOVERNOR** | REGULATEUR A RESSORT | FEDERKRAFTREGLER |
| 11985 | **SPRING LOADED LEVER (SAFETY) VALVE, SPRING BALANCE VALVE** | SOUPAPE DE SURETE A LEVIER ET A RESSORT | VENTIL MIT HEBELFEDERBELASTUNG |
| 11986 | **SPRING LOADED SAFETY VALVE** | SOUPAPE DE SURETE A RESSORT | SICHERHEITSVENTIL (FEDERBELASTETES) |
| 11987 | **SPRING PAWL CATCH** | CLIQUET A RESSORT | FEDERKLINKE |
| 11988 | **SPRING PLATE** | COUPELLE DE RESSORT | FEDERPLATTE, FEDERTELLER |
| 11989 | **SPRING PRESSURE GAUGE** | MANOMETRE METALLIQUE, MANOMETRE A RESSORT | FEDERMANOMETER |
| 11990 | **SPRING RING** | CERCLE ELASTIQUE, CIRCLIP | SPANNRING, FEDERRING, SELBSTSPANNENDER KOLBENRING, SPREIZRING, SELBSTSPANNER |
| 11991 | **SPRING SHACKLE** | JUMELLE DE RESSORT | FEDERLASCHE |
| 11992 | **SPRING STEEL, STEEL FOR SPRINGS** | ACIER A RESSORT | FEDERSTAHL |
| 11993 | **SPRING SUBJECTED TO BENDING** | RESSORT DE FLEXION | BIEGEFEDER, BIEGUNGSFEDER |
| 11994 | **SPRING SUBJECTED TO TORSION** | RESSORT DE TORSION | DREHUNGSFEDER, TORSIONSFEDER |
| 11995 | **SPRING WASHER** | RONDELLE GROWER | FEDERRING |
| 11996 | **SPRING WATER** | EAU DE SOURCE | QUELLWASSER |
| 11997 | **SPRING WIRE** | FIL POUR RESSORT | FEDERDRAHT |
| 11998 | **SPRING-LOADED SAFETY VALVE** | SOUPAPE DE SURETE A RESSORT | SICHERHEITSVENTIL MIT FEDERBELASTUNG, FEDERSICHERHEITSVENTIL |
| 11999 | **SPRINGING OFF OF RIVET HEADS** | RUPTURE DES TETES DE RIVET | ABSPRINGEN DER NIETKÖPFE, ABREISSEN DER NIETKÖPFE |
| 12000 | **SPRINKLE (TO)** | ARROSER | EINSPRENGEN, BESPRENGEN, BENETZEN |
| 12001 | **SPRINKLING** | ARROSAGE | EINSPRENGEN, BESPRENGEN, BENETZEN |
| 12002 | **SPROCKET CHAIN, FLAT LINK CHAIN, PLATE LINK CHAIN, GALLE'S CHAIN** | CHAINE GALLE | GELENKKETTE, LASCHENKETTE, GALLESCHE KETTE |
| 12003 | **SPRUE** | ENTONNOIR, DESCENTE DE COULEE | EINGUSSTRICHTER |
| 12004 | **SPRUE, GATE, GEAT, GIT** | JET DE COULEE | ANGUSS, GUSSZAPFEN |
| 12005 | **SPUN YARN** | BITORD | SCHIEMANNSGARN |
| 12006 | **SPUR AND HELICAL GEAR CUTTING MACHINES** | MACHINES A TAILLER LES ENGRENAGES DROITS ET HELICOIDAUX | VERZAHNMASCHINEN FÜR STIRN- U. SCHRÄGVERZAHNUNGEN |
| 12007 | **SPUR FRICTION GEAR WHEEL** | ROUE DE FRICTION CYLINDRIQUE | REIBRAD (ZYLINDRISCHES) |
| 12008 | **SPUR GEARING** | ENGRENAGE DROIT, ENGRENAGE CYLINDRIQUE | STIRNRÄDERGETRIEBE |
| 12009 | **SPUR WHEEL** | ROUE D'ENGRENAGE DROITE, ROUE D'ENGRENAGE CYLINDRIQUE | STIRNRAD |
| 12010 | **SPUR WHEEL DRIVE** | COMMANDE PAR ENGRENAGE DROIT | STIRNRADANTRIEB |
| 12011 | **SPUR WHEEL PULLEY BLOCK** | PALAN A ENGRENAGE DROIT | STIRNRADFLASCHENZUG |
| 12012 | **SQUAB** | DOSSIER | SITZRÜCKENLEHNE |
| 12013 | **SQUARE** | CARRE (DEUXIEME PUISSANCE), CARRE (GEOM.) | ZWEITE POTENZ, QUADRAT (GEOM.) |
| 12014 | **SQUARE** | EQUERRE | WINKELMASS, WINKELHAKEN, WINKEL |
| 12015 | **SQUARE BAR IRON** | FER CARRE | QUADRATEISEN, VIERKANTEISEN |

| | | | |
|---|---|---|---|
| 12016 | **SQUARE CENTIMETRE** | CENTIMETRE CARRE | QUADRATZENTIMETER |
| 12017 | **SQUARE CROSS SECTION** | SECTION CARREE | QUERSCHNITT (QUADRATISCHER) |
| 12018 | **SQUARE DECIMETRE** | DECIMETRE CARRE | QUADRATDEZIMETER |
| 12019 | **SQUARE FILE** | LIME CARREE, CARREE, CARREAU, CARRELET, LIME QUATRE-QUARTS, LIME 4/4 | VIERKANTFEILE |
| 12020 | **SQUARE FOOT** | PIED CARRE ANGLAIS | QUADRATFUSS (ENGLISCHER) |
| 12021 | **SQUARE INCH** | POUCE CARRE ANGLAIS | QUADRATZOLL (ENGLISCHER) |
| 12022 | **SQUARE METRE** | METRE CARRE | QUADRATMETER |
| 12023 | **SQUARE MILLIMETRE** | MILLIMETRE CARRE | QUADRATMILLIMETER |
| 12024 | **SQUARE NUT** | ECROU CARRE | VIERKANTMUTTER |
| 12025 | **SQUARE PIECE** | CARRE | VIERKANT |
| 12026 | **SQUARE PYRAMID** | PYRAMIDE QUADRANGULAIRE, QUADRILATERE | PYRAMIDE (VIERSEITIGE) |
| 12027 | **SQUARE ROOT** | RACINE CARREE | QUADRATWURZEL, WURZEL (ZWEITE) |
| 12028 | **SQUARE ROPE** | CABLE A SECTION CARREE | VIERKANTSEIL, QUADRATSEIL |
| 12029 | **SQUARE SHAFT** | ARBRE CARRE | VIERKANTWELLE |
| 12030 | **SQUARE THREAD** | FILET CARRE | GEWINDE (FLACHES), GEWINDE (FLACHGÄNGIGES), FLACHGEWINDE, RECHTECKGEWINDE |
| 12031 | **SQUARE YARD** | YARD CARRE | QUADRATYARD (ENGLISCHES) |
| 12032 | **SQUARE-GROOVE WELD** | SOUDURE SUR BORDS DROITS | I-STUMPFNAHT |
| 12033 | **SQUARE-HEADED SCREW** | VIS A TETE CARREE, BOULON A TETE CARREE | VIERKANTSCHRAUBE |
| 12034 | **SQUARE-THREADED SCREW** | VIS A FILET CARRE | SCHRAUBE MIT FLACHGEWINDE, FLACHGÄNGIGE SCHRAUBE |
| 12035 | **SQUARED TIMBER** | BOIS EQUARRI | KANTHOLZ |
| 12036 | **SQUARING** | QUADRATURE | QUADRATUR |
| 12037 | **SQUARING SHEAR** | CISAILLE A EBOUTER | KOPFSCHERE |
| 12038 | **SQUEEZE INTERVAL** | RETARD DE SOUDAGE | SCHWEISSVERZÖGERUNGSZEIT |
| 12039 | **SQUEEZE OUT (TO), PRESS OUT (TO)** | EXPRIMER, EXTRAIRE | AUSPRESSEN |
| 12040 | **SQUIRREL CAGE OF A ROLLER BEARING** | CAGE D'UN ROULEMENT A GALETS | KÄFIG EINES ROLLENLAGERS, ROLLENKÄFIG |
| 12041 | **STABILITY** | STABILITE | STANDFESTIGKEIT, STANDSICHERHEIT, STABILITÄT |
| 12042 | **STABILIZER SHAFT** | STABILISATEUR | STABILISATOR |
| 12043 | **STABILIZING** | STABILISATION | STABILISIERUNG |
| 12044 | **STABILIZING ANNEAL** | RECUIT DE DETENTE | GLÜHEN (SPANNUNGSFREIES) |
| 12045 | **STABLE EQUILIBRIUM** | EQUILIBRE STABLE | GLEICHGEWICHT[3] (STABILES) |
| 12046 | **STACK** | CUVE | SCHACHT |
| 12047 | **STAGE OF A MISCROSCOPE** | PORTE-OBJET | OBJEKTTISCH |
| 12048 | **STAGGERED** | QUINCONE (EN), ALTERNE | GEGENEINANDER VERSETZT |
| 12049 | **STAGGERED INTERMITTENT FILLET WELD** | SOUDURE D'ANGLE DISCONTINUE A RANGEES ALTERNEES | KEHLNAHT (UNTERBROCHENE VERSETZTE) |
| 12050 | **STAGNANT WATER** | EAU STAGNANTE, EAU DORMANTE | WASSER, (TOTES) WASSER (STEGEBDES), WASSER (STAGNIERENDES), TOTWASSER |
| 12051 | **STAINLESS STEEL** | ACIER INOXYDABLE | EISEN (NICHT-ROSTENDES), STAHL (ROSTFREIER), NIROSTAHL |
| 12052 | **STAIR-HORSE** | LIMON | TREPPENWANGE |
| 12053 | **STAIRWAY** | ESCALIER | TREPPE |
| 12054 | **STALAGMOMETRY** | STALAGMOMETRIE | STALAGMOMETRIE |
| 12055 | **STAMP** | PILON DE BOCARD | STEMPEL, POCHSTEMPEL |

# STA 308

| | | | |
|---|---|---|---|
| 12056 | **STAMP (TO)** | ESTAMPER, ETAMPER, MATRICER | STANZEN, PRÄGEN |
| 12057 | **STAMP MILL** | BOCARD, MOULIN A BOCARDS | POCHWERK, STAMPFWERK |
| 12058 | **STAMPED LINK CHAIN** | CHAINE DECOUPEE | BANDKETTE |
| 12059 | **STAMPING** | ESTAMPAGE, ETAMPAGE, MATRICAGE | GESENKSCHMIEDEN, STANZEN, PRÄGEN |
| 12060 | **STAMPING MACHINE, PRESS** | ESTAMPEUSE, ETAMPEUSE | STANZE, PRÄGWERK, PRÄGEPRESSE |
| 12061 | **STAMPING TEST** | ESSAI D'ESTAMPAGE | STANZPROBE, PRÄGEPROBE |
| 12062 | **STANCHION, POST, UPRIGHT** | MONTANT, POTEAU | STÄNDER, PFOSTEN |
| 12063 | **STANCHION, UPRIGHT, POST** | MONTANT | TREPPENPFOSTEN |
| 12064 | **STAND FOR PEDESTAL BEARING** | CHAISE SUR LE SOL | STEHBOCK, LAGERSTUHL, LAGERBOCK |
| 12065 | **STAND OF ROLLS** | CAGE DE LAMINOIR | WALZGERÜST |
| 12066 | **STAND PIPE** | TUYAU DE PRISE D'EAU | STANDROHR, HYDRANTENSTANDROHR |
| 12067 | **STAND PIPE, PIEZOMETER** | PIEZOMETRE | STANDROHR, PIEZOMETER |
| 12068 | **STAND-BY ....** | DE RESERVE | RESERVE-, HILFS- |
| 12069 | **STAND-BY COMPRESSOR** | COMPRESSEUR DE RESERVE | HILFSKOMPRESSOR, HILFSVERDICHTER |
| 12070 | **STAND-BY ENGINE** | MACHINE DE RESERVE, MOTEUR DE RESERVE | AUSHILFSMASCHINE, RESERVEMASCHINE |
| 12071 | **STANDARD** | NORME, DIMENSION NORMALE, STANDARD | NORM, NORMALE |
| 12072 | **STANDARD CUBIC FOOT** | PIED CUBE NORMALISE | KUBIKFUSS (GENORMTER) |
| 12073 | **STANDARD DESIGN** | MODELE STANDARD, CONCEPTION STANDARD | STANDARDMODELL |
| 12074 | **STANDARD DEVIATION** | ECART TYPE | STANDARDABWEICHUNG |
| 12075 | **STANDARD FILLET WELD** | SOUDURE D'ANGLE A CORDON PLAT | FLACHKEHLNAHT |
| 12076 | **STANDARD GAUGE** | ETALON, CALIBRE NORMAL | EICHMASS, NORMALLEHRE |
| 12077 | **STANDARD MEASURE** | MESURE ETALON, MESURE DE CONTROLE, ETALON | NORMALMASS |
| 12078 | **STANDARD OF AN ENGINE, A MACHINE** | MONTANT D'UNE MACHINE | MASCHINENSTÄNDER |
| 12079 | **STANDARD OF REFERENCE** | GRANDEUR DE COMPARAISON | BEZUGSGRÖSSE |
| 12080 | **STANDARD PRESSURE GAUGE** | MANOMETRE ETALON | KONTROLLMANOMETER |
| 12081 | **STANDARD ROD** | METRE ETALON | NORMALMASSSTAB |
| 12082 | **STANDARD SAMPLE** | ETALON NORMALISE | NORMPROBE |
| 12083 | **STANDARD SECTION** | PROFIL NORMAL | NORMALPROFIL |
| 12084 | **STANDARD SOLUTION** | LIQUEUR TITREE, LIQUEUR NORMALE | NORMALLÖSUNG, MASSFLÜSSIGKEIT, TITRIERTE LÖSUNG, TITERFLÜSSIGKEIT |
| 12085 | **STANDARD THERMOMETER** | THERMOMETRE ETALON | NORMALTHERMOMETER |
| 12086 | **STANDARD TYPE** | TYPE STANDARD | NORMALMODELL |
| 12087 | **STANDARD TYPE PLUG GAUGE** | JAUGE TAMPON NORMALE | NORMAL LEHRDORN |
| 12088 | **STANDARD TYPE SOLID SNAP GAUGE** | JAUGE MACHOIRE NORMALE | NORMALRACHENLEHRE |
| 12089 | **STANDARD WIRE GAUGE (S. W. G.), BIRMINGHAM WIRE GAUGE (B. W. G.)** | JAUGE ANGLAISE, JAUGE DE BIRMINGHAM POUR FILS METALLIQUES | DRAHTLEHRE (ENGLISCHE) (B. W. G.) |
| 12090 | **STANDARDISE (TO)** | UNIFIER, NORMALISER, STANDARDISER | NORMEN, NORMALISIEREN |
| 12091 | **STANDARDIZATION** | UNIFICATION, NORMALISATION, STANDARDISATION | NORMUNG, NORMALISIERUNG |
| 12092 | **STANDING PART (IN LIFTING TACKLE)** | BRIN DORMANT, DORMANT (DU CABLE D'UN PALAN) | TRUMM (FESTES), TRUMM (STEHENDES), TRUMM (EINES FLASCHENZUGS) |
| 12093 | **STANDPIPE** | COLONNE MONTANTE | STANDROHR |
| 12094 | **STANDSTILL OF AN ENGINE** | ARRET D'UNE MACHINE (ETAT) | STILLSTAND EINER MASCHINE |

| | | | |
|---|---|---|---|
| 12095 | **STANNATE** | STANNATE | ZINNSÄURESALZ, STANNAT |
| 12096 | **STANNIC CHLORIDE** | CHLORURE STANNIQUE, TETRACHLORURE, BICHLORURE D'ETAIN | ZWEIFACH-CHLORZINN, ZINNTETRACHLORID, STANNICHLORID |
| 12097 | **STANNIC HYDROXIDE** | ACIDE STANNIQUE | ZINNSÄURE, ZINNOXYDHYDRAT, ZINNHYDROXYD |
| 12098 | **STANNIC OXIDE** | OXYDE STANNIQUE, BIOXYDE D'ETAIN, POTEE D'ETAIN | ZINNASCHE, ZINNDIOXYD, ZINNSÄUREANHYDRID |
| 12099 | **STANNIC SULPHIDE** | SULFURE STANNIQUE, BISULFURE D'ETAIN, OR MUSIF | ZINNDTSULFID, MUSIVGOLD |
| 12100 | **STANNOUS CHLORIDE** | CHLORURE STANNEUX, PROTOCHLORURE D'ETAIN, SEL D'ETAIN | ZINNSALZ, ZINNCHLORÜR, STANNOCHLORID, EINFACH-CHLORZINN, ZINNDICHLORID |
| 12101 | **STANNOUS HYDROXIDE** | HYDRATE STANNEUX | METAZINNSÄURE |
| 12102 | **STANNOUS OXIDE** | OXYDE STANNEUX | ZINNOXYDUL, STANNOOXYD |
| 12103 | **STANNOUS SULPHIDE** | SULFURE STANNEUX | ZINNMONOSULFID, ZINNSULFÜR |
| 12104 | **STAPLE / FINGER BAR** | CAVALIER DE FOND | DRAHTKLAMMER |
| 12105 | **STAPLE, DOG** | CRAMPON, CLAMEAU | KLAMMER, KLAMMERHAKEN, KRAMPE |
| 12106 | **STAPLE, WIRE STAPLE** | CAVALIER | DRAHTÖSE, KRAMPE |
| 12107 | **STAR POLYGON** | POLYGONE ETOILE | STERNPOLYGON |
| 12108 | **STAR SHAKE IN TIMBER** | CADRANURE, CADRAN DU BOIS | STRAHLENRISS, SPIEGELKLUFT DES HOLZES |
| 12109 | **STAR WHEEL** | ROUE ETOILEE | STERNRAD |
| 12110 | **STAR-SHAPED CROSS SECTION** | SECTION ETOILEE | QUERSCHNITT (STERNFÖRMIGER) |
| 12111 | **STARCH** | AMIDON, FECULE | STÄRKE |
| 12112 | **STARCH PASTE** | PATE, COLLE D'AMIDON, EMPOIS | KLEISTER, STÄRKEKLEISTER |
| 12113 | **START (TO)** | DEMARRER | ANLAUFEN (MASCHINE) |
| 12114 | **START AN ENGINE (TO), SET A MACHINE IN MOTION (TO)** | METTRE EN MARCHE, METTRE EN TRAIN, METTRE EN ROUTE UNE MACHINE, LANCER UN MOTEUR | ANLASSEN (EINE MASCHINE), ANLAUFEN LASSEN (EINE MASCHINE), IN GANG SETZEN (EINE MASCHINE) |
| 12115 | **START/STOP BUTTON** | BOUTON MARCHE/ARRET | START/STOP DRUCKKNOPF |
| 12116 | **STARTER** | DEMARREUR | ANLASSER |
| 12117 | **STARTERSWITCH** | COMMANDE DE DEMARREUR | ANLASSSCHALTER |
| 12118 | **STARTING** | MISE EN MARCHE, MISE EN SERVICE, DEMARRAGE | INBETRIEBSETZUNG, ANLAUF |
| 12119 | **STARTING GEAR** | APPAREIL DE MISE EN MARCHE | ANLASSVORRICHTUNG |
| 12120 | **STARTING LEVER** | LEVIER DE DEMARRAGE | ANLASSHEBEL |
| 12121 | **STARTING MOTOR** | MOTEUR DE DEMARRAGE | ANLASSMOTOR |
| 12122 | **STARTING OF AN ENGINE, OF A MACHINE** | DEMARRAGE D'UN MOTEUR | ANLAUFEN, ANLAUF EINER MASCHINE |
| 12123 | **STARTING PERIOD** | PERIODE DE DEMARRAGE OU DE MISE EN MARCHE D'UNE USINE | ANLAUFPERIODE |
| 12124 | **STARTING POINT OF A MOTION** | POINT DE DEPART D'UN MOUVEMENT | AUSGANGSPUNKT EINER BEWEGUNG |
| 12125 | **STARTING POINTS** | HYPOTHESES DE BASE | ANHALTSPUNKTE |
| 12126 | **STARTING POSITION** | POSITION DE DEPART | ANFANGSLAGE, AUSGANGSLAGE, ANFANGSSTELLUNG |
| 12127 | **STARTING PUNCH** | CHASSE-CLOU | NAGELTREIBER |
| 12128 | **STARTING RESISTANCE** | RESISTANCE AU DEMARRAGE | ANLASSWIDERSTAND, ANLAUFWIDERSTAND |
| 12129 | **STARTING TORQUE** | COUPLE DE DEMARRAGE | ANZUGMOMENT |
| 12130 | **STARTING UP AN ENGINE, A MACHINE** | MISE EN MARCHE, MISE EN TRAIN, MISE EN ROUTE D'UNE MACHINE, LANCEMENT D'UN MOTEUR | ANLASSEN, INGANGSETZEN EINER MASCHINE |

# STA

**310**

| | | | |
|---|---|---|---|
| 12131 | STARTING VALVE | VALVE DE DEMARRAGE | ANLASSVENTIL |
| 12132 | STATE OF EQUILIBRIUM | ETAT D'EQUILIBRE | GLEICHGEWICHTSZUSTAND |
| 12133 | STATIC | STATIQUE | STATISCH |
| 12134 | STATIC FRICTION | FROTTEMENT STATIQUE | HAFTREIBUNG |
| 12135 | STATIC GOVERNOR | REGULATEUR STATIQUE | REGLER (STATISCHER) |
| 12136 | STATIC LIQUID HEAD | PRESSION STATIQUE | DRUCK (STATISCHER) |
| 12137 | STATIC PRESSURE | PRESSION STATIQUE | DRUCK (RUHENDER), DRUCK (STATISCHER) |
| 12138 | STATICAL LOAD | CHARGE STATIQUE | BELASTUNG (STATISCHE) |
| 12139 | STATICAL MOMENT | MOMENT STATIQUE | MOMENT (STATISCHES) |
| 12140 | STATICS | STATIQUE | GLEICHGEWICHTSLIEHRE, STATIK |
| 12141 | STATION WAGON | COMMERCIALE, BREAK | KOMBINATIONS-KRAFTWAGEN, KOMBIWAGEN |
| 12142 | STATIONARY HEART FURNACE | FOUR STATIONNAIRE FIXE | OFEN (FESTSTEGENDER) |
| 12143 | STATIONARY LAND BOILER | CHAUDIERE INDUSTRIELLE | LANDDAMPFKESSEL |
| 12144 | STATIONARY STEAM ENGINE, LAND ENGINE | MACHINE A VAPEUR FIXE | DAMPFMASCHINE (ORTSFESTE), DAMPFMASCHINE (FESTSTEHENDE), DAMPFMASCHINE (STATIONÄRE) |
| 12145 | STATIONARY WAVE | ONDE STATIONNAIRE | WELLE (STEHENDE) (PHYS.) |
| 12146 | STATOR | STATOR | STÄNDER, STATOR (ELEKTR.) |
| 12147 | STATUARY BRONZE, ART BRONZE | BRONZE D'ART, BRONZE STATUAIRE | KUNSTBRONZE, STATUENBRONZE |
| 12148 | STAUFFER LUBRICATOR | GRAISSEUR STAUFFER, STAUFFER | STAUFFERBÜCHSE |
| 12149 | STAVE | DOUVE | DAUBE |
| 12150 | STAY (TO), PROP (TO) | ETAYER, SOUTENIR, ENTRETOISER, ETANCONNER | AUSSTEIFEN, ABSTEIFEN |
| 12151 | STAY BOLT | ENTRETOISE | STEHBOLZEN, DISTANZBOLZEN |
| 12152 | STAYING WITH RIBS | RENFORCEMENT PAR DES NERVURES | RIPPENVERSTEIFUNG |
| 12153 | STAYING, PROPPING | ETAIEMENT, ETAYAGE, ETAYEMENT, SOUTENEMENT, ENTRETOISEMENT | ABSTEIFEN, ABSTEIFUNG |
| 12154 | STEADY REST | LUNETTE FIXE | BRILLE (FESTSTEHENDE) |
| 12155 | STEAM | VAPEUR | DAMPF |
| 12156 | STEAM ACCUMULATOR | ACCUMULATEUR DE VAPEUR | DAMPFSPEICHER |
| 12157 | STEAM BATH | BAIN DE VAPEUR | DAMPFBAD |
| 12158 | STEAM BOILER, ENGINE BOILER | CHAUDIERE A VAPEUR, GENERATEUR DE VAPEUR | DAMPFKESSEL |
| 12159 | STEAM BRAKE | FREIN A VAPEUR | DAMPFBREMSE |
| 12160 | STEAM CALORIMETER | CALORIMETRE A CONDENSATION | DAMPFKALORIMETER |
| 12161 | STEAM COIL, HEATING COIL | SERPENTIN CHAUFFE PAR LA VAPEUR | HEIZSCHLANGE, DAMPFSCHLANGE |
| 12162 | STEAM CYLINDER | CYLINDRE A VAPEUR | ZYLINDER EINER DAMPFMASCHINE, DAMPFMASCHINEN-ZYLINDER |
| 12163 | STEAM DOME | DOME DE PRISE DE VAPEUR | DAMPFDOM, DAMPFSAMMLER |
| 12164 | STEAM ENGINE | MACHINE A VAPEUR, MOTEUR A VAPEUR | DAMPFKRAFTMASCHINE |
| 12165 | STEAM ENGINE WORKED NON-EXPANSIVELY WITHOUT CUT OFF | MACHINE A PLEINE PRESSION | VOLLDRUCKDAMPFMASCHINE |
| 12166 | STEAM HAMMER | MARTEAU-PILON, MARTEAU A VAPEUR | DAMPFHAMMER |
| 12167 | STEAM HEATING | CHAUFFAGE PAR LA VAPEUR | DAMPFHEIZUNG |
| 12168 | STEAM JACKET | CHEMISE, ENVELOPPE DE VAPEUR | DAMPFMANTEL |
| 12169 | STEAM JENNY | GENERATEUR A VAPEUR | DAMPFERZEUGER |
| 12170 | STEAM JET | JET DE VAPEUR | DAMPFSTRAHL |

| | | | |
|---|---|---|---|
| 12171 | **STEAM JET AIR PUMP** | INJECTEUR DE VAPEUR | DAMPFSTRAHLLUFTPUMPE |
| 12172 | **STEAM JET BLOWER** | EJECTEUR, SOUFFLERIE DE VAPEUR | DAMPFSTRAHLGEBLÄSE |
| 12173 | **STEAM LOCOMOTIVE** | LOCOMOTIVE A VAPEUR | DAMPFLOKOMOTIVE |
| 12174 | **STEAM METER** | COMPTEUR DE VAPEUR | DAMPFVERBRAUCHMESSER |
| 12175 | **STEAM NOZZLE** | TUYERE A VAPEUR | DAMPFDÜSE |
| 12176 | **STEAM PASSAGE, PORT, STEAMWAY** | LUMIERE (D'UN CYLINDRE A VAPEUR) | DAMPFWEG, DAMPFKANAL |
| 12177 | **STEAM PIPE** | TUYAU A VAPEUR, TUBE DE VAPEUR | DAMPFLEITUNGSROHR |
| 12178 | **STEAM PIPING, PIPE LINE** | CONDUITE, TUYAUTERIE, CANALISATION DE VAPEUR | DAMPFLEITUNG |
| 12179 | **STEAM PISTON** | PISTON A VAPEUR | DAMPFKOLBEN |
| 12180 | **STEAM POWER PLANT** | INSTALLATION DE MACHINE A VAPEUR | DAMPFKRAFTANLAGE, DAMPFMASCHINENANLAGE |
| 12181 | **STEAM PRESSURE** | PRESSION DE LA VAPEUR | DAMPFSPANNUNG, DAMPFDRUCK |
| 12182 | **STEAM PRESSURE TEST** | ESSAI DE LA CHAUDIERE, EPREUVE A CHAUD DE LA CHAUDIERE | DAMPFDRUCKPROBE |
| 12183 | **STEAM PUMP** | POMPE A VAPEUR | DAMPFPUMPE |
| 12184 | **STEAM SEPARATOR, STEAM DRYER** | SEPARATEUR DE VAPEUR | DAMPFABSCHEIDER, DAMPFTROCKENER |
| 12185 | **STEAM SPACE OF A BOILER** | CHAMBRE DE VAPEUR D'UNE CHAUDIERE | DAMPFRAUM EINES KESSELS |
| 12186 | **STEAM STOP VALVE** | SOUPAPE D'ARRET DE VAPEUR | DAMPFABSPERRVENTIL |
| 12187 | **STEAM SUPPLY VALVE** | SOUPAPE DE PRISE DE VAPEUR, ROBINET DE PRISE DE VAPEUR | DAMPFENTNAHMEVENTIL |
| 12188 | **STEAM TRAP** | SEPARATEUR D'EAU, PURGEUR D'EAU CONDENSEE | WASSERABSCHEIDER, KONDENSWASSERABSCHEIDER, KONDENSTOPF, ENTWÄSSERUNGSTOPF, WASSERSAMMLER, KONDENSATIONSWASSERABLEITER |
| 12189 | **STEAM TURBINE** | TURBINE A VAPEUR | DAMPFTURBINE |
| 12190 | **STEAM WHISTLE** | SIFFLET A VAPEUR | DAMPFPFEIFE |
| 12191 | **STEAM-ELECTRIC GENERATOR** | GENERATRICE A VAPEUR | DAMPFDYNAMO |
| 12192 | **STEAM, AQUEOUS VAPOUR, WATER VAPOUR** | VAPEUR D'EAU | WASSERDAMPF |
| 12193 | **STEAMTIGHT** | ETANCHE (A LA VAPEUR) | DAMPFDICHT |
| 12194 | **STEARIC ACID** | ACIDE STEARIQUE | STEARINSÄURE |
| 12195 | **STEARINE, STEARIN** | STEARINE | STEARIN |
| 12196 | **STEEL** | ACIER | STAHL |
| 12197 | **STEEL BAND TAPE** | BANDE D'ACIER | STAHLBAND |
| 12198 | **STEEL BARS - STEEL RODS FOR CONCRETE REINFORCEMENT** | FERS A BETON | BETONEISEN |
| 12199 | **STEEL BEAM, IRON GIRDER** | POUTRE EN FER | TRÄGER (EISERNER), EISENTRÄGER |
| 12200 | **STEEL BELT** | COURROIE EN ACIER | STAHLBANDRIEMEN |
| 12201 | **STEEL CABLE** | CABLE EN ACIER, CABLE EN GRELIN | STAHLKABEL |
| 12202 | **STEEL CASTING** | ACIER MOULE, ACIER COULE | STAHLFORMGUSS |
| 12203 | **STEEL CONCRETE, REINFORCED, ARMOURED CONCRETE, FERROCONCRETE** | BETON, CIMENT ARME | EISENBETON, BETON (BEWEHRTER), BETON (ARMIERTER) |
| 12204 | **STEEL CYLINDER** | TUBE D'ACIER (POUR GAZ LIQUEFIES) | STAHLFLASCHE |
| 12205 | **STEEL FACE (TO), STEEL (TO)** | ACIERER | STÄHLEN, VERSTÄHLEN, ANSTÄHLEN |
| 12206 | **STEEL FACING, STEELING** | ACIERAGE | STÄHLEN, VERSTÄHLEN, ANSTÄHLEN |
| 12207 | **STEEL FOUNDRY** | FONDERIE D'ACIER | STAHLGIESSEREI |

**STE** 312

| | | | |
|---|---|---|---|
| 12208 | STEEL FRAME | CHARPENTE METALLIQUE | EISENKONSTRUKTION, STAHLKONSTRUKTION, STAHLGERIPPE |
| 12209 | STEEL FREE FROM BLISTERS | ACIER SANS SOUFFLURES | STAHL (BLASENFREIER) |
| 12210 | STEEL INGOT | LINGOT D'ACIER | STAHLBARREN, STAHLBLOCK, ROHSTAHLBLOCK |
| 12211 | STEEL MILL | ACIERIE | STAHLWERKE |
| 12212 | STEEL PIPE | TUBE D'ACIER | STAHLROHR |
| 12213 | STEEL PLATE | TOLE D'ACIER | STAHLBLECH |
| 12214 | STEEL PROCESSING | ELABORATION DE L'ACIER | STAHLERZEUGUNG |
| 12215 | STEEL ROPE | CABLE EN ACIER, CABLE EN FILIN | STAHLDRAHTSEIL |
| 12216 | STEEL SHEET | FEUILLARD (TOLE MINCE) | BANDSTAHL |
| 12217 | STEEL STRANDS / OR WIRE ROPES | TORONS EN ACIER POUR CABLES | STAHLLITZEN |
| 12218 | STEEL STRUCTURE | CONSTRUCTION EN ACIER / METALLIQUE | STAHLBAU, STAHLGERÜST, STAHLKONSTRUKTION |
| 12219 | STEEL TUBE | TUBE EN ACIER | STAHLROHR |
| 12220 | STEEL TYRES FOR LOCOMOTIVES | BANDAGES DE ROUE | EISENBAHNRADREIFEN |
| 12221 | STEEL WIRE | FIL D'ACIER | STAHLDRAHT |
| 12222 | STEEL WORKS | ACIERIE | STAHLWERK |
| 12223 | STEEL, CARBON STEEL | ACIER | STAHL |
| 12224 | STEELY IRON | FER ACIEREUX, ACIER EXTRA-DOUX | EISEN (STAHLARTIGES) |
| 12225 | STEELYARD, ROMAN BALANCE | BASCULE ROMAINE, BASCULE ROMAINE (A CURSEUR) | LAUFGEWICHTSWAAGE, SCHNELLWAAGE, STELLIT (RÖMISCHE) |
| 12226 | STEERING | CONDUITE, MANOEUVRE | STEUERUNG |
| 12227 | STEERING ARM | LEVIER D'ATTAQUE DE DIRECTION | LENKSTOCKHEBEL |
| 12228 | STEERING COLUMN | COLONNE DE DIRECTION | LENKSAÜLE |
| 12229 | STEERING GEAR | BOITIER DE DIRECTION | LENKGETRIEBE |
| 12230 | STEERING KNUCKLE | SUPPORT DE FUSEE | ACHSSCHENKEL |
| 12231 | STEERING KNUCKLE TIE ROD | BARRE D'ACCOUPLEMENT | SPURSTANGE |
| 12232 | STEERING LINKAGE | TIMONERIE, TRINGLERIE DE DIRECTION | LENKGESTÄNGE |
| 12233 | STEERING WHEEL | VOLANT DE DIRECTION | STEUERRAD, LENKRAD |
| 12234 | STELLITE | STELLITE | STELLIT |
| 12235 | STEM THERMOMETER | THERMOMETRE GRADUE SUR TIGE | STABTHERMOMETER, STOCKTHERMOMETER |
| 12236 | STEM, ROD, SPINDLE OF SLIDE VALVE | QUEUE DE ROBINET, TIGE DE SOUPAPE | SPINDEL, STANGE EINES SCHIEBERS, STANGE EINES VENTILS |
| 12237 | STEM, SPINDLE | TIGE | SPINDEL, SCHAFT |
| 12238 | STENCIL | POCHOIR | SCHABLONE |
| 12239 | STEP | MARCHE, DEGRE, STADE, PAS, GRADIN | STUFE, SCHRITT, ABSATZ |
| 12240 | STEP ANNEALING | RECUIT ECHELONNE | STUFENGLÜHEN |
| 12241 | STEP BEARING | CRAPAUDINE | SPURLAGER |
| 12242 | STEP HARDENING | TREMPE ETAGEE | STUFENHÄRTUNG |
| 12243 | STEP QUENCHING | TREMPE ETAGEE MARTENSITIQUE | MARTENSITHÄRTUNG (GESTAFFELTE) |
| 12244 | STEP-DOWN TRANSFORMER | TRANSFORMATEUR DEVOLTEUR, TRANSFORMATEUR REDUCTEUR DE POTENTIEL | ABSPANNTRANSFORMATOR, ABWÄRTSTRANSFORMATOR |
| 12245 | STEP-UP TRANSFORMER | TRANSFORMATEUR SURVOLTEUR, TRANSFORMATEUR AMPLIFICATEUR DE POTENTIEL | AUFWÄRTSTRANSFORMATOR |
| 12246 | STEPPED | A GRADINS, EN GRADINS, ECHELONNE | STUFENFÖRMIG, ABGESTUFT, TREPPENFÖRMIG, STUFEN... |
| 12247 | STEPPED GEARING | ENGRENAGE A DENTURE CROISEE, ENGRENAGE A DENTS RECROISEES | STUFENRAD |

| | | | |
|---|---|---|---|
| 12248 | **STEPPED GRATE** | GRILLE A GRADINS, GRILLE A ETAGES | TREPPENROST, STUFENROST |
| 12249 | **STEPPED QUENCHING** | TREMPE INTERROMPUE | HÄRTEN (GEBROCHENES) |
| 12250 | **STEREOMETRICAL** | STEREOMETRIQUE | STEREOMETRISCH |
| 12251 | **STEREOMETRY** | STEREOMETRIE | STEREOMETRIE |
| 12252 | **STERILISING THE WATER** | STERILISATION DE L'EAU | ENTKEIMUNG DES WASSERS |
| 12253 | **STERLING SILVER** | ARGENT A 92/5% | SILBER (92/5% FEIN) |
| 12254 | **STICK LAC** | GOMME-LAQUE EN BRANCHES | STOCKLACK, STANGENLACK, GUMMILACK, LACK IN STANGENFORM |
| 12255 | **STICK SULPHUR, ROLL SULPHUR** | SOUFRE EN CANON | SCHWEFELSTANGEN, STANGENSCHWEFEL |
| 12256 | **STIFFENER** | ELEMENT RAIDISSEUR | VERSTEIFUNGSELEMENT |
| 12257 | **STIFFENING PLATE** | PLAQUE DE RENFORT, TOLE DE RENFORT | VERSTEIFUNGSPLATTE |
| 12258 | **STIFFNESS OF A ROPE, OF A BELT** | RAIDEUR D'UNE CORDE, RAIDEUR D'UNE COURROIE | STEIFIGKEIT EINES SEILES, STEIFHEIT EINES RIEMENS |
| 12259 | **STILL, DISTILLING APPARATUS** | APPAREIL DISTILLATOIRE, ALAMBIC | DESTILLIERVORRICHTUNG |
| 12260 | **STIRRING ROD** | AGITATEUR, BAGUETTE EN VERRE | RÜHRSTAB |
| 12261 | **STIRRUP** | ETRIER, DEMI-CERCLE | BÜGEL |
| 12262 | **STOCK OF A PLANE** | FUT DE RABOT | HOBELKASTEN |
| 12263 | **STOCK OF MATERIAL** | STOCK, EXISTENCE | LAGERVORRAT, LAGERBESTAND, LAGER |
| 12264 | **STOCK SHEARS, BLOCK SHEARS** | CISAILLES D'ETABLI | STOCKSCHERE |
| 12265 | **STOCK YARD** | CHANTIER, DEPOT, PARC NON COUVERT | LAGERPLATZ |
| 12266 | **STOCKS AND DIES** | FILIERE A COUSSINETS | KLUPPE, SCHNEIDKLUPPE, GEWINDESCHNEID-KLUPPE |
| 12267 | **STOICHIOMETRIC** | STOECHIOMETRIQUE | STÖCHIOMETRISCH |
| 12268 | **STOICHIOMETRY** | STOECHIOMETRIE | STÖCHIOMETRIE |
| 12269 | **STOKE (TO), FIRE UP (TO)** | CHARGER UN FOYER, ALIMENTER UN FOYER | BESCHICKEN (EINE FEUERUNG) |
| 12270 | **STOKE-HALL** | CHAUFFERIE | FEUERRAUM, HEIZRAUM |
| 12271 | **STOKER, FIRE STOKER** | CHAUFFEUR | HEIZER |
| 12272 | **STOKER, FIREMAN** | CHAUFFEUR | HEIZER, KESSELWÄRTER |
| 12273 | **STONE BREAKER** | CONCASSEUR A MACHOIRES | STEINBRECHER, STEINBRECHMASCHINE |
| 12274 | **STONE CEMENT** | MASTIC A PIERRE | STEINKITT |
| 12275 | **STONE SHIELD** | PARE-PIERRE | STEINSCHLAGGITTER |
| 12276 | **STONEWARE** | GRES CERAME | STEINZEUG[9] |
| 12277 | **STONEWARE PIPE** | TUBE EN GRES | STEINZEUGROHR |
| 12278 | **STOP** | BUTEE, BUTOIR, DISPOSITIF D'ARRET, ARRET, TAQUET, TOC LIMITANT LA COURSE | ANSCHLAG, ANSCHLAGVORRICHTUNG, HUBBEGRENZER |
| 12279 | **STOP A LEAK (TO)** | AVEUGLER UNE FUITE | VERSTOPFEN (EINE UNDICHTE STELLE) |
| 12280 | **STOP AN ENGINE (TO)** | ARRETER UNE MACHINE | ABSTELLEN (EINE MASCHINE), ANHALTEN (EINE MASCHINE) |
| 12281 | **STOP COCK** | ROBINET D'ARRET | ABSPERRHAHN, DURCHGANGSHAHN |
| 12282 | **STOP VALVE** | SOUPAPE D'ARRET | ABSPERRVENTIL |
| 12283 | **STOP WATCH** | CHRONOMETRE A STOP, COMPTE-SECONDES | STOPPUHR |
| 12284 | **STOPPER** | BOUCHON DE COULEE | ABSTICHVERSCHLUSS-STOPFEN |
| 12285 | **STOPPER, STOPPLE** | BOUCHON | STOPFEN, STÖPSEL |
| 12286 | **STOPPING AN ENGINE** | ARRET D'UNE MACHINE | ABSTELLEN EINER MASCHINE, ANHALTEN EINER MASCHINE |

# STO
314

| | | | |
|---|---|---|---|
| 12287 | **STOPPING OFF** | ISOLATION | ABDECKUNG |
| 12288 | **STORAGE** | EMMAGASINAGE, MAGASINAGE | EINLAGERUNG |
| 12289 | **STORAGE MEDIUM** | SUPPORT D'INFORMATION | DATENTRÄGER |
| 12290 | **STORAGE OF ENERGY** | ACCUMULATION/EMMAGASINAGE D'ENERGIE | SPEICHERUNG, AUFSPEICHERUNG VON ENERGIE |
| 12291 | **STORAGE OF HEAT** | ACCUMULATION/EMMAGASINAGE DE CHALEUR | WÄRMEAUFSPEICHERUNG, AUFSPEICHREUNG VON VÄRME |
| 12292 | **STORAGE TANKS** | RESERVOIRS DE STOCKAGE | LAGER, SAMMELBEHÄLTER |
| 12293 | **STORE** | DEPOT (ENDROIT) | LAGERRAUM |
| 12294 | **STORE (TO)** | EMMAGANISER, ENTREPOSER, STATIONNER, STOCKER | EINLAGERN, AUFSPEICHERN |
| 12295 | **STORE ENERGY (TO)** | EMMAGASINER DE L'ENERGIE | ENERGIE AUFSPEICHERN |
| 12296 | **STORE HEAT (TO)** | ACCUMULER LA CHALEUR, EMMAGASINER LA CHALEUR | WÄRME AUFSPEICHERN |
| 12297 | **STOREHOUSE, WAREHOUSE, MAGAZINE, DEPOT** | MAGASIN | LAGER, LAGERHAUS, SPEICHER, MAGAZIN |
| 12298 | **STOREKEEPER** | MAGASINIER, MANUTENTIONNAIRE | LAGERVERWALTER |
| 12299 | **STORING** | EMMAGASINAGE | LAGERUNG, EINLAGERN, AUFSPEICHERN |
| 12300 | **STOVE** | FOUR, FOURNEAU | OFEN |
| 12301 | **STRADDLE MILLING CUTTER** | FRAISAGE EN DUPLEX | SCHEIBENFRÄSERPAAR |
| 12302 | **STRAIGHT ARM OF PULLEY** | BRAS DROIT D'UNE POULIE | SCHEIBENARM (GERADER) |
| 12303 | **STRAIGHT EDGE** | REGLE DE JAUGE | RICHTSCHIENE, RICHTLINEAL |
| 12304 | **STRAIGHT FLUTED DRILL** | FORET A COUTURE DROITE | BOHRER (GERADEGENUTETER) |
| 12305 | **STRAIGHT FLUTED REAMER** | ALESOIR A RAINURES DROITES | REIBAHLE (GERADEGENUTETE) |
| 12306 | **STRAIGHT LEVER** | LEVIER DROIT | HEBEL (GERADARMIGER) |
| 12307 | **STRAIGHT MILLING CUTTER** | FRAISE A DENTURE DROITE | FRÄSER MIT GERADEN SCHNEIDEN |
| 12308 | **STRAIGHT PANE SLEDGE HAMMER** | MARTEAU A DEVANT, PANNE EN LONG | KREUZSCHLAG, KREUZHAMMER, LÄNGSFINNE |
| 12309 | **STRAIGHT PIPE** | TUBE DROIT | ROHR (GERADES) |
| 12310 | **STRAIGHT RIGHT LINE** | LIGNE DROITE, DROITE | GERADE, GERADE LINIE |
| 12311 | **STRAIGHT SET** | DENTURE DROITE | GERADVERZAHNUNG |
| 12312 | **STRAIGHT SPRING SUBJECTED TO BENDING** | RESSORT DE FLEXION DROIT | BIEGEFEDER (GERADE) |
| 12313 | **STRAIGHT TOOTH CLUTCK** | EMBRAYAGE A DENTURE DROITE | GERADVERZAHNUNGSKUPPLUNG |
| 12314 | **STRAIGHT-CUT CONTROL** | COMMANDE PARAXIALE | STRECKENSTEUERUNG |
| 12315 | **STRAIGHT-LINE MOTION** | GUIDE DU MOUVEMENT RECTILIGNE | GERADFÜHRUNG |
| 12316 | **STRAIGHT-SIDED MECHANICAL PRESS** | PRESSE MECANIQUE A MONTANT | PRESSE (GERADSEITIGE MECHANISCHE) |
| 12317 | **STRAIGHT-WAY VALVE** | SOUPAPE DROITE | DURCHGANGSVENTIL |
| 12318 | **STRAIGHTEN (TO)** | REDRESSER, DEGAUCHIR | RICHTEN, GERADERICHTEN, AUSRICHTEN |
| 12319 | **STRAIGHTENING** | REDRESSAGE, DEGAUCHISSAGE, DRESSAGE, DEGAUCHISSEMENT | DRESSIEREN, RICHTEN, GERADERICHTEN, AUSRICHTEN |
| 12320 | **STRAIGHTENING MACHINE** | MACHINE A REDRESSER, BANC A RECTIFIER | RICHTMASCHINE |
| 12321 | **STRAIGHTENING PLATE** | MARBRE | RICHTPLATTE |
| 12322 | **STRAIN** | DEFORMATION, CONTRAINTE | VERFORMUNG, SPANNUNG |
| 12323 | **STRAIN A BODY (TO), SUBJECT A BODY TO STRAINING FORCES (TO)** | SOUMETTRE UN CORPS A UNE CHARGE, EXERCER UN EFFORT SUR UN CORPS | BEANSPRUCHEN (EINEN KÖRPER) |
| 12324 | **STRAIN AGING** | VIEILLISSEMENT PAR LES EFFORTS | STAUCHALTERUNG, RECKALTERUNG |
| 12325 | **STRAIN GAUGE** | EXTENSOMETRE | DEHNUNGSMESSER |
| 12326 | **STRAIN HARDENING** | ECROUISSAGE (DEFORMATION) | KALTHÄRTUNG |

| | | | |
|---|---|---|---|
| 12327 | **STRAIN-AGEING** | VIEILLISSEMENT PAR DEFORMATION | VERFORMUNGSALTERUNG |
| 12328 | **STRAIN-DEFORMATION** | VIEILLISSEMENT PAR DEFORMATION | VERFORMUNGSALTERUNG |
| 12329 | **STRAIN-GAGE** | JAUGE DE CONTRAINTE (A FIL RESISTANT) | DEHNUNGSMESSSTREIFE |
| 12330 | **STRAIN-RATE** | VITESSE DE DEFORMATION | VERFORMUNGGESCHWINDIGKEIT |
| 12331 | **STRAIN, INTENSITY OF STRAIN, UNIT STRAIN** | EFFORT, ACTION D'UNE FORCE EXTERIEURE, SOLLICITATION, CHARGE, TRAVAIL | BEANSPRUCHUNG, INANSPRUCHNAHME |
| 12332 | **STRAINER** | CREPINE, SUCETTE | SEIHER, SAUGKORB, SAUGKOPF, SAUGSIEB |
| 12333 | **STRAINER, SEDIMENT SEPARATOR** | FILTRE | SCHMUTZFÄNGER, FILTER |
| 12334 | **STRAINING, TIGHTENING, JOCKEY, BINDER, TENSION PULLEY** | GALET, ROULEAU, TENDEUR, ROULEAU, POULIE DE TENSION, TENDEUR A GALET | SPANNROLLE |
| 12335 | **STRAITS TIN, MALACCA TIN** | ETAIN DE MALACCA | MALAKKAZINN |
| 12336 | **STRAND** | TORON | LITZE |
| 12337 | **STRAND (TO)** | TORONNER | VERLITZEN |
| 12338 | **STRAND OF A CABLE-LAID ROPE** | CORDON D'UN CABLE | STRANG EINES TAUES, SCHENKEL EINES TAUES |
| 12339 | **STRAND OF A ROPE** | TORON D'UNE CORDE | LITZE EINES SEILES, SEILLITZE |
| 12340 | **STRANDING** | TORONNAGE | VERLITZEN |
| 12341 | **STRANDING MACHINE** | TORONNEUSE | DRAHTSEILHERSTELLUNGSMASCHINE |
| 12342 | **STRANGLER** | DISPOSITIF DE DEPART A FROID | STARTERKLAPPE |
| 12343 | **STRAP** | FEUILLARD | STAHLBAND |
| 12344 | **STRAP AND SCREW BRAKE** | FREIN A VIS | SCHRAUBENBREMSE, SPINDELBREMSE |
| 12345 | **STRAP CONNECTING ROD END** | CHAPE DE LA TETE DE BIELLE | KAPPENKOPF EINER SCHUBSTANGE |
| 12346 | **STRAP FORK, BELT FORK** | FOURCHE DE DEBRAYAGE, FOURCHE GUIDE-COURROIE, FOURCHETTE | RIEMENGABEL |
| 12347 | **STRAP TYPE HINGE** | CHARNIERE TYPE PENTURE | BANDSCHARNIER |
| 12348 | **STRAW FIBRE** | FIBRE DE PAILLE | STROHFASER |
| 12349 | **STRAY CURRENT** | COURANT VAGABOND | STREUSTROM |
| 12350 | **STRAY CURRENT CORROSION** | CORROSION PAR COURANT VAGABOND | IRRSTROMKORROSION |
| 12351 | **STREAM LINE** | FILET FLUIDE, LIGNE AERODYNAMIQUE | STROMLINIE |
| 12352 | **STRENGTH** | RESISTANCE, FORCE | FESTIGKEIT, KRAFT |
| 12353 | **STRENGTH IN FATIGUE, ENDURANCE AGAINST REPEATED STRESSES** | RESISTANCE AUX CHOCS REPETES | SCHWINGUNGSFESTIGKEIT |
| 12354 | **STRENGTH OF A SOLUTION** | TITRE D'UNE SOLUTION | TITER EINER LÖSUNG |
| 12355 | **STRENGTH OF MATERIALS** | RESISTANCE DES MATERIAUX | MATERIALFESTIGKEIT, FESTIGKEIT DES MATERIALS |
| 12356 | **STRENGTH TEST** | EPREUVE DE RESISTANCE | FESTIGKEITSPRÜFUNG |
| 12357 | **STRENGTH WELD** | SOUDURE PORTANTE | NAHT (TRAGENDE) |
| 12358 | **STRENGTHEN (TO), STIFFENT (TO)** | RENFORCER | VERSTEIFEN |
| 12359 | **STRENGTHENING, STIFFENING** | RENFORCEMENT, RENFORT | VERSTEIFEN, VERSTEIFUNG |
| 12360 | **STRESS CONCENTRATION** | CONCENTRATION DE LA CONTRAINTE | SPANNUNGSKONZENTRATION |
| 12361 | **STRESS CORROSION** | CORROSION SOUS TENSION | SPANNUNGSKORROSION |
| 12362 | **STRESS RELIEF ANNEALING** | RECUIT DE DETENTE | SPANNUNGSFREIGLÜHEN |
| 12363 | **STRESS RELIEVING** | RECUIT DE RELAXATION | ENTSPANNUNGSGLÜHEN |
| 12364 | **STRESS-CORROSION CRACKING** | FISSURATION PAR CORROSION SOUS TENSION | KORROSIONSRISSBILDUNG DURCH LATENTE SPANNUNGEN |
| 12365 | **STRESS-STRAIN CURVE** | COURBE EFFORT-DEFORMATION | DEHNUNGSKURVE |

# STR 316

| | | | |
|---|---|---|---|
| 12366 | **STRESS-STRAIN DIAGRAM** | COURBE CHARGE-ALLONGEMENT, GRAPHIQUE DE LA RESISTANCE MECANIQUE | SPANNUNGS-DEHNUNGSKURVE, SPANNUNGSDIAGRAMM |
| 12367 | **STRESS, INTENSITY OF STRESS, UNIT STRESS** | CHARGE PAR UNITE DE SECTION, TENSION INTERIEURE, EFFORT INTERIEUR MOLECULAIRE, CONTRAINTE | SPANNUNG, BEANSPRUCHUNG |
| 12368 | **STRESSED SURFACE** | SURFACE CHARGEE | BELASTUNGSFLÄCHE, SPANNUNGSFLÄCHE |
| 12369 | **STRETCHER** | PANNERESSE | LÄUFER (BAUW.) |
| 12370 | **STRETCHER STRAIN** | TENSION D'ETIRAGE | RECKSPANNUNG |
| 12371 | **STRETCHER STRAIN MARKINGS** | LIGNES DE LUDERS | FLIESSFIGUREN, LUDERSLINIEN |
| 12372 | **STRETCHER/LEVELLER** | MACHINE A DRESSER, PLANEUSE | SPANNMASCHINE |
| 12373 | **STRETCHING FORCE** | EFFORT DE TENSION | SPANNKRAFT |
| 12374 | **STRETCHING OF A BELT, OF A ROPE** | ALLONGEMENT D'UNE COURROIE, ALLONGEMENT D'UN CABLE | LÄNGUNG EINES RIEMENS, EINES SEILES |
| 12375 | **STRIKE** | COUP | SCHLAG, AUFSCHLAG |
| 12376 | **STRING BEAD** | CORDON SOUDE RECTILIGNE | STRICHRAUPE |
| 12377 | **STRINGER** | LIMON | TREPPENWANGE |
| 12378 | **STRIP** | FEUILLARD | STREIFEN |
| 12379 | **STRIP A SCREW THREAD (TO)** | ABIMER UN FILET | ÜBERDREHEN (EIN GEWINDE) |
| 12380 | **STRIP CHART RECORDER** | ENREGISTREUR A DEROULEMENT CONTINU | BANDSCHREIBER |
| 12381 | **STRIPPING AGENTS** | SOLVANTS DE DECAPAGE | BEIZMITTEL |
| 12382 | **STRIPPING BATH** | BAIN DE DECAPAGE | BEIZBAD |
| 12383 | **STRIPPING CRANE** | PONT ROULANT DEMOULEUR | STRIPPERKRAN |
| 12384 | **STRIPPING PLATE** | PEIGNE | ABSTREIFPLATTE |
| 12385 | **STROBOSCOPE** | STROBOSCOPE | STROBOSKOP |
| 12386 | **STROBOSCOPIC METHOD** | METHODE STROBOSCOPIQUE | STROBOSKOPISCHE METHODE |
| 12387 | **STROKE** | TEMPS, COURSE | ARBEITSTAKT, HUB |
| 12388 | **STRONG BACK** | U DE MONTAGE | U-MONTAGETEIL |
| 12389 | **STRONTIUM** | STRONTIUM | STRONTIUM |
| 12390 | **STRONTIUM FLUORIDE** | FLUORURE DE STRONTIUM | STRONTIUMFLUORID |
| 12391 | **STRUCTURAL COMPONENT** | ELEMENT STRUCTURAL | STRUKTURELEMENT |
| 12393 | **STRUCTURAL STEEL** | ACIER DE CONSTRUCTION | BAUSTAHL, KONSTRUKTIONSSTAHL |
| 12394 | **STRUCTURE** | STRUCTURE | STRUKTUR, GEFÜGE |
| 12395 | **STRUCTURE, TEXTURE** | CONSTRUCTION (EDIFICE), STRUCTURE, TEXTURE, GRAIN | BAUWERK, BAU, KONSTRUKTION, GEFÜGE, STRUKTUR |
| 12396 | **STRUT, BRACE** | CONTREFICHE, JAMBE DE FORCE | STREBE |
| 12397 | **STUD** | GOUJON | STIFTSCHRAUBE, BOLZENZAPFEN, STIFT, DÜBEL |
| 12398 | **STUD BOLT** | BOULON A TIGE ENTIEREMENT FILETEE | GEWINDEBOLZEN |
| 12399 | **STUD BOLT, STUD, DOUBLE-ENDED BOLT** | GOUJON, BOULON PRISONNIER, PRISONNIER | STIFTSCHRAUBE |
| 12400 | **STUD GUN** | PISTOLETS A GOUJONS | DRUCKLUFTNIETHAMMER |
| 12401 | **STUD LATHE** | TOUR A BOULONS | BOLZENDREHBANK |
| 12402 | **STUD OF CHAIN LINK** | ETANCON, ETAI, ENTRETOISE D'UN CHAINON | STEG EINER KETTE, KETTENSTEG |
| 12403 | **STUDDED CHAIN, STAYED LINK CHAIN** | CHAINE A ETANCONS, CHAINE A MAILLES ETANCONNEES, CHAINE-CABLE A ETAIS | STEGKETTE |
| 12404 | **STUDDED TYRE** | PNEU A CRAMPONS, PNEU A CLOUS | GLEITSCHUTZREIFEN |
| 12405 | **STUFFING BOX** | PRESSE-ETOUPE, BOITE A ETOUPE | STOPFBÜCHSE, STOPFBÜCHSRAUM |

| | | | |
|---|---|---|---|
| 12406 | **STUFFING BOX PACKING** | GARNITURE DE PRESSE-ETOUPE, GARNITURE DE BOITE A BOURRAGE | STOPFBÜCHSENPACKUNG |
| 12407 | **STUMPF UNIFLOW ENGINE** | MACHINE A EQUICOURANT, MACHINE STUMPF | GLEICHSTROMDAMPFMASCHINE |
| 12408 | **SUBBOUNDARY** | SOUS-JOINT | UNTERVERBINOUNG |
| 12409 | **SUBDIVISION** | SUBDIVISION | UNTERTEILUNG |
| 12410 | **SUBDIVISION OF LABOUR** | DIVISION DU TRAVAIL | ARBEITSTEILUNG |
| 12411 | **SUBLIMATE (TO)** | SUBLIMER | SUBLIMIEREN |
| 12412 | **SUBLIMATION** | SUBLIMATION | SUBLIMATION |
| 12413 | **SUBMERGE (TO)** | SUBMERGER | UNTERTAUCHEN |
| 12414 | **SUBMERGED-ARC WELDING** | SOUDAGE A L'ARC SUBMERGE | UNTERPULVERSCHWEISSEN |
| 12415 | **SUBROUTINE** | SOUS-PROGRAMME | UNTERPROGRAMM |
| 12416 | **SUBSCALING** | SOUS-COUCHE (D'OXYDE) | UNTERLAGE, UNTEROXYDSCHICHT |
| 12417 | **SUBSEQUENT TREATMENT, AFTER-TREATMENT** | TRAITEMENT ULTERIEUR | NACHBEHANDLUNG |
| 12418 | **SUBSIDENCE** | AFFAISSEMENT | EINSINKEN |
| 12419 | **SUBSTANCE, MATTER** | MATIERE, SUBSTANCE | STOFF, SUBSTANZ, MATERIE |
| 12420 | **SUBSTITUTE** | SUCCEDANE | ERSATZ, ERSATZSTOFF |
| 12421 | **SUBSTITUTION** | SUBSTITUTION (MATH.) | SUBSTITUTION (MATH.) |
| 12422 | **SUBSTRATE** | METAL DE BASE | SUBSTRAT |
| 12423 | **SUBSTRUCTURE** | SOUS-STRUCTURE | SUBSTRUKTUR |
| 12424 | **SUBTRACT** | SOUSTRAIRE, RETRANCHER | ABZIEHEN, SUBTRAHIEREN |
| 12425 | **SUBTRACTION** | SOUSTRACTION | ABZIEHEN, SUBTRAKTION |
| 12426 | **SUBTRAHEND** | NOMBRE A SOUSTRAIRE | SUBTRAHEND |
| 12427 | **SUCK (TO)** | ASPIRER | ANSAUGEN |
| 12428 | **SUCTION** | ASPIRATION | SAUGEN, ANSAUGEN, ANSAUGUNG |
| 12429 | **SUCTION FAN** | VENTILATEUR ASPIRANT | SAUGENDER LÜFTER, VENTILATOR, SAUGLÜFTER |
| 12430 | **SUCTION GAS PRODUCER** | GAZOGENE A ASPIRATION | SAUGGASGENERATOR |
| 12431 | **SUCTION GOVERNOR** | REGULATEUR A DEPRESSION | UNTERDRUCKREGLER |
| 12432 | **SUCTION HEAD, SUCTION LIFT OF A PUMP** | HAUTEUR D'ASPIRATION D'UNE POMPE | SAUGHÖHE EINER PUMPE |
| 12433 | **SUCTION PIPE** | TUYAU D'ASPIRATION | SAUGROHR, SAUGLEITUNG |
| 12434 | **SUCTION PUMP** | POMPE ASPIRANTE | SAUGPUMPE |
| 12435 | **SUCTION STROKE** | COURSE D'ASPIRATION | SAUGHUB |
| 12436 | **SUCTION VALVE** | SOUPAPE, CLAPET D'ASPIRATION | SAUGVENTIL, SAUGKLAPPE |
| 12437 | **SUDDEN CHANGE OF TEMPERATURE** | VARIATION BRUSQUE DE TEMPERATURE | ÄNDERUNG (PLÖTZLICHE) DER TEMPERATUR |
| 12438 | **SUGAR BEET DOWN THE ROW THINNER** | DEMARIEUSE POUR BETTERAVES A SUCRE | ZUCKERRÜBENLICHTMASCHINEN |
| 12439 | **SUGAR BEET HARVESTERS** | RECOLTEUSES DE BETTERAVES | ZUCKERRÜBENVOLLERNTEGERÄTE |
| 12440 | **SUGAR BEET PLOUGHS AND LIFTERS** | SOULEVEUSES DE BETTERAVES | ZUCKERRÜBENHEBER UND PFLÜGE |
| 12441 | **SUGAR BEET TOPPERS** | MACHINES A ETETER LES BETTERAVES | ZUCKERRÜBENKÖPFER |
| 12442 | **SULFIDE EMBRITTLEMENT** | FATIGUE PAR L'HYDROGENE SULFURE | ERMÜDUNG DURCH SCHWEFELWASSERSTOFF |
| 12443 | **SULL** | COUCHE D'OXYDE FERREUX | EISENOXYDSCHICHT |
| 12444 | **SULPHATE** | SULFATE | SULFAT |
| 12445 | **SULPHATE SODA, LEBLANC SODA** | SOUDE LEBLANC | LEBLANC-SODA, SULFATSODA |
| 12446 | **SULPHIDE** | SULFURE | SULFID |
| 12447 | **SULPHIDE OF IRON** | SULFURE DE FER | EISENSULFID |
| 12448 | **SULPHITE** | SULFITE | SULFIT |

**SUL** 318

| | | | |
|---|---|---|---|
| 12449 | **SULPHUR** | SOUFRE | SCHWEFEL |
| 12450 | **SULPHUR DIOXIDE, SULPHUROUS ANHYDRIDE** | ACIDE, ANHYDRIDE, OXYDE SULFUREUX | SÄURE (SCHWEFLIGE), SCHWEFLIGSÄUREANHYDRID, SCHWEFELDIOXYD |
| 12451 | **SULPHUR MONOCHLORIDE** | CHLORURE DE SOUFRE | SCHWEFELCHLORÜR, SCHWEFELMONOCHLORID, CHLORSCHWEFEL |
| 12452 | **SULPHUR TRIOXIDE, SULPHURIC ANHYDRIDE** | ANHYDRIDE SULFURIQUE | SCHWEFELSÄUREANHYDRID, WASSERFREIE SCHWEFELSÄURE, SCHWEFELTRIOXYD |
| 12453 | **SULPHURIC ACID, OIL OF VITRIOL, HYDROGEN SULPHATE** | ACIDE SULFURIQUE, ACIDE VITRIOLIQUE, VITRIOL, HUILE DE VITRIOL | SCHWEFELSÄURE |
| 12454 | **SUM** | SOMME | SUMME |
| 12455 | **SUMMIT OF THREAD** | SOMMET, DESSUS D'UN FILET | KOPF, SPITZE EINES GEWINDES, GEWINDEKOPF, GEWINDESPITZE |
| 12456 | **SUN AND PLANET WHEELS MOTION** | MOUVEMENT, TRAIN PLANETAIRE | PLANETENGETRIEBE, UMLAUFGETRIEBE |
| 12457 | **SUN WHEEL** | ROUE CENTRALE D'UN TRAIN PLANETAIRE | SONNENRAD |
| 12458 | **SUNK KEY** | CLAVETTE NOYEE | KEIL (VERSENKTER), NUTKEIL |
| 12459 | **SUPER ALLOY** | ALLIAGE HAUTE-TEMPERATURE | SUPERLEGIERUNG |
| 12460 | **SUPER HEATING** | SURCHAUFFAGE | ÜBERHITZUNG |
| 12461 | **SUPER SATURATION** | SURSATURATION | ÜBERSÄTTIGUNG |
| 12462 | **SUPER STEEL** | ACIER FIN | EDELSTAHL |
| 12463 | **SUPERCOOL (TO)** | REFROIDIR AU-DESSOUS DE LA TEMPERATURE DE CONDENSATION, REFROIDIR AU DESSOUS DU POINT DE CONGELATION | UNTERKÜHLEN |
| 12464 | **SUPERCOOLED LIQUID** | LIQUIDE SURFONDU | UNTERKÜHLTE FLÜSSIGKEIT, ÜBERSCHMOLZENE FLÜSSKIGKEIT |
| 12465 | **SUPERCOOLING, SUPERFUSION** | SURFUSION, SURREFROIDISSEMENT | UNTERKÜHLEN, ÜBERSCHMELZEN |
| 12466 | **SUPERFICIAL EXPANSION, EXTENSION** | DILATATION SUPERFICIELLE | FLÄCHENAUSDEHNUNG |
| 12467 | **SUPERFINE CUT FILE, DEAD SMOOTH CUT FILE** | LIME A TAILLE TRES DOUCE | FEINSCHLICHTFEILE |
| 12468 | **SUPERHEAT (TO)** | SURCHAUFFER | ÜBERHITZEN |
| 12469 | **SUPERHEATED STEAM** | VAPEUR SURCHAUFFEE | DAMPF (ÜBERHITZTER) |
| 12470 | **SUPERHEATED WATER** | EAU SURCHAUFFEE | WASSER (ÜBERHITZTES) |
| 12471 | **SUPERHEATED, GASEOUS STEAM** | VAPEUR SURCHAUFFEE | DAMPF (ÜBERHITZTER), HEISSDAMPF |
| 12472 | **SUPERHEATER** | SURCHAUFFEUR | ÜBERHITZER, DAMPFÜBERHITZER |
| 12473 | **SUPERHEATING** | SURCHAUFFAGE, SURCHAUFFE | ÜBERHITZEN |
| 12474 | **SUPERINTEND (TO), SUPERVISE (TO)** | SURVEILLER | BEAUFSICHTIGEN, ÜBERWACHEN |
| 12475 | **SUPERLATTICE** | SURSTRUCTURE, SUPER-RESEAU | ÜBERSTRUKTUR |
| 12476 | **SUPERPOSITION OF VIBRATIONS** | SUPERPOSITION DE VIBRATIONS | ÜBERLAGERUNG VON SCHWINGUNGEN |
| 12477 | **SUPERSATURATE (TO)** | SURSATURER | ÜBERSÄTTIGEN |
| 12478 | **SUPERSATURATED SOLUTION** | SOLUTION SURSATUREE | LÖSUNG (ÜBERSÄTTIGTE) |
| 12479 | **SUPERSATURATION** | SURSATURATION | ÜBERSÄTTIGUNG |
| 12480 | **SUPERSONIC INSPECTION** | ESSAI AUX ULTRA-SONS | ULTRASCHALLPRÜFUNG |
| 12481 | **SUPERVISION, SUPERINTENDENCE** | SURVEILLANCE | BEAUFSICHTIGUNG, ÜBERWACHUNG, AUFSICHT |
| 12482 | **SUPPLEMENT OF AN ANGLE** | SUPPLEMENT D'UN ANGLE | SUPPLEMENT EINES WINKELS |
| 12483 | **SUPPLEMENTARY ANGLE** | ANGLE SUPPLEMENTAIRE | SUPPLEMENTWINKEL |
| 12484 | **SUPPLY CABLES** | CABLES D'ALIMENTATION | SPEISELEITUNG |

| | | | |
|---|---|---|---|
| 12485 | **SUPPLY HEAT (TO)** | ENVOYER DE LA CHALEUR, FOURNIR DE NOUVELLES CALORIES | WÄRME ZUFÜHREN |
| 12486 | **SUPPLY OF AIR, AIR SUPPLY** | ADMISSION D'AIR, INTRODUCTION D'AIR | LUFTZUFUHR |
| 12487 | **SUPPLY OF ELECTRICAL ENERGY, ELECTRIC SUPPLY** | DISTRIBUTION PUBLIQUE D'ENERGIE ELECTRIQUE | ELEKTRIZITÄTSVERSORGUNG, STROMVERSORGUNG, STROMLIEFERUNG |
| 12488 | **SUPPLY OF HEAT** | FOURNITURE DE CHALEUR | WÄRMEZUFUHR |
| 12489 | **SUPPLY PIPE** | TUYAU ADDUCTEUR, TUYAU D'AMENEE D'ARRIVEE, CONDUITE D'ARRIVEE DU COMBUSTIBLE | ZUFLUSSROHR, ZULEITUNGSROHR, ZULAUFLEITUNG |
| 12490 | **SUPPORT** | SUPPORT, APPUI | STÜTZE, STÄNDER, GESTELL, TRÄGER, HALTER, BOCK, UNTERLAGE, UNTERSATZ |
| 12491 | **SUPPORT (TO)** | APPUYER, SUPPORTER, MONTER | LAGERN, STÜTZEN |
| 12492 | **SUPPORT RING** | COURONNE SUPPORT DE PLATEAU | STÜTZRING |
| 12493 | **SUPPORTING** | SOUTENENENT, MONTAGE | LAGERN, LAGERUNG, STÜTZEN |
| 12494 | **SUPPORTING DATA** | DONNEES JUSTIFICATIVES | UNTERLAGEN |
| 12495 | **SUPPORTING PLATE** | TOLE-SUPPORT | STÜTZBLECH |
| 12496 | **SURFACE** | SURFACE | FLÄCHE |
| 12497 | **SURFACE (TO)** | SURFACER | PLANDREHEN |
| 12498 | **SURFACE ANALYZER** | RUGOSIMETRE ENREGISTREUR | OBERFLÄCHENPRÜFGERÄT |
| 12499 | **SURFACE CONDENSER** | CONDENSEUR PAR SURFACE | OBERFLÄCHENKONDENSATOR |
| 12500 | **SURFACE CONDITION** | ETAT DE SURFACE | OBERFLÄCHENBESCHAFFENHEIT |
| 12501 | **SURFACE CRACK** | FISSURE SUPERFICIELLE, GERCURE | HAUTRISS, OBERFLÄCHENRISS |
| 12502 | **SURFACE DEFECT** | DEFAUT DE SURFACE | OBERFLÄCHENFEHLER |
| 12503 | **SURFACE DEVIATION** | IRREGULARITE DE SURFACE | OBERFLÄCHENUNEBENHEIT |
| 12504 | **SURFACE FINISH** | ETAT DE SURFACE | OBERFLÄCHENBESCHAFFENHEIT |
| 12505 | **SURFACE GRINDER** | MACHINE A RECTIFIER LES SURFACES PLANES | FLÄCHENSCHLEIFMASCHINE, PLANSCHLEIFMASCHINE |
| 12506 | **SURFACE GRINDING** | RECTIFICATION DE SURFACE | PLANSCHLEIFEN, FLÄCHENSCHLEIFEN |
| 12507 | **SURFACE GRINDING MACHINE** | RECTIFIEUSE POUR SURFACE PLANES | FLÄCHENSCHLEIFMASCHINE |
| 12508 | **SURFACE HARDENING** | TREMPE SUPERFICIELLE | OBERFLÄCHENHÄRTUNG |
| 12509 | **SURFACE INDICATOR** | RUGOSIMETRE | OBERFLÄCHENPRÜFGERÄT |
| 12510 | **SURFACE OF CONTACT** | SURFACE DE CONTACT | BERÜHRUNGSFLÄCHE |
| 12511 | **SURFACE OF CUT** | COUPE, SURFACE DE LA COUPE, AIRE DE LA SECTION TRANSVERSALE | SCHNITTFLÄCHE |
| 12512 | **SURFACE OF IMPRESSION** | SURFACE DE L'EMPREINTE | EINDRUCKFLÄCHE |
| 12513 | **SURFACE OF REVOLUTION** | SURFACE DE REVOLUTION | DREHUNGSFLÄCHE, UMDREHUNGSFLÄCHE, ROTATIONSFLÄCHE |
| 12514 | **SURFACE OF THE TIP OF THE TOOTH** | SOMMET DE LA DENT | ZAHNSCHEITEL, ZAHNRÜCKEN |
| 12515 | **SURFACE PLANING MACHINE** | MACHINE A DEGAUCHIR, DEGAUCHISSEUSE | ABRICHTHOBELMASCHINE |
| 12516 | **SURFACE PLATE, MARKING OFF TABLE** | MARBRE A DRESSER, TABLE DRESSEE | RICHTPLATTE, ANREISSPLATTE |
| 12517 | **SURFACE PRESSURE** | PRESSION SUPERFICIELLE | OBERFLÄCHENDRUCK |
| 12518 | **SURFACE ROUGHNESS** | RUGOSITE DE SURFACE | OBERFLÄCHENRAUHIGKEIT |
| 12519 | **SURFACE TENSION** | TENSION SUPERFICIELLE | OBERFLÄCHENSPANNUNG |
| 12520 | **SURFACE WATER** | EAU SUPERFICIELLE, EAU DE SURFACE, EAU DU JOUR | OBERFLÄCHENWASSER, TAGWASSER |
| 12521 | **SURFACE, AREA** | SURFACE | FLÄCHE, OBERFLÄCHE |

# SUR

320

| | | | |
|---|---|---|---|
| 12522 | **SURFACING** | SURFACAGE, CHARIOTAGE TRANSVERSAL | PLANDREHEN |
| 12523 | **SURFACTANT** | AGENT DE TRAITEMENT DE SURFACE | OBERFLÄCHENBEHANDLUNGSMITTEL |
| 12524 | **SUSPENDED DECK** | TOIT SUSPENDU | HÄNGEDECKE |
| 12525 | **SUSPENDED DECK TANK** | RESERVOIR A TOIT SUSPENDU | HÄNGEDACHTANK |
| 12526 | **SUSPENSION** | SUSPENSION | AUFHÄNGUNG |
| 12527 | **SUSPENSION HOOK** | CROCHET DE SUSPENSION | AUFHÄNGEHAKEN |
| 12528 | **SUSPENSION-BRIDGE** | PONT SUSPENDU | HÄNGEBRÜCKE |
| 12529 | **SWABBING** | ENDUCTION | ANSTREICHEN |
| 12530 | **SWAGE (TO)** | ESTAMPER, ETAMPER A CHAUD | SCHMIEDEN (IM GESENK) |
| 12531 | **SWAGE BLOCK** | ETAMPE | GESENKPLATTE, LOCHPLATTE, GESENKKLOTZ, GESENKSTOCK |
| 12532 | **SWAGING** | ESTAMPAGE, MATRICAGE | GESENKSCHMIEDEN |
| 12533 | **SWAGING MACHINE** | MACHINE A RETREINDRE | REDUZIERMASCHINE |
| 12534 | **SWAGING, DROP FORGING, DIE FORGING** | ESTAMPAGE, ETAMPAGE A CHAUD | GESENKSCHMIEDEN |
| 12535 | **SWAN NECK, S-PIPE** | COL DE CYGNE | ROHR (GEKRÖPFTES), S-ROHR, S-STÜCK |
| 12536 | **SWARF** | COPEAU | SPAN, FEILSPÄNE, ABFALL |
| 12537 | **SWATH TURNERS** | VIRE-ANDAINS | SCHWADENWENDER |
| 12538 | **SWAY** | DEPLACEMENT LATERAL, ROULIS | SEITENNEIGUNG |
| 12539 | **SWAY BAR** | BARRE STABILISATRICE | DREHSTABSTABILISATOR |
| 12540 | **SWEATING** | SUINTEMENT, EXSUDATION | AUSSCHWITZUNG |
| 12541 | **SWEEPS** | RAMASSE FOIN | HEURAFFER |
| 12542 | **SWELL (TO)** | GONFLER, FOISONNER | AUFQUELLEN |
| 12543 | **SWELLING** | GONFLEMENT (PAR LES GAZ DE FISSION) | SCHWELLUNG, AUFWACHSEN |
| 12544 | **SWELLING OF WOOD** | GONFLEMENT DU BOIS | QUELLEN DES HOLZES |
| 12545 | **SWING CHECK VALVE** | CLAPET DE RETENUE A BATTANT | RÜCKFLUSSVENTIL MIT KLAPPE, RÜCKSCHLAGKLAPPE |
| 12546 | **SWING JOINT, SWIVEL JOINT** | GENOUILLERE | KNIESTÜCK |
| 12547 | **SWING OVER BED** | DIAMETRE ADMIS AU-DESSUS DU BANC | ZUGELASSENER DREHDURCHMESSER ÜBER BETT |
| 12548 | **SWING VIBRATION OSCILLATION OF A PENDULUM** | OSCILLATION D'UN PENDULE | PENDELSCHWINGUNG |
| 12549 | **SWINGING ARM** | BRAS OSCILLANT | SCHWENKARM |
| 12550 | **SWINGING ARM DRILL** | PERCEUSE A BRAS ARTICULE | GELENKSPINDELBOHRMASCHINE |
| 12551 | **SWIRL CHAMBER** | CHAMBRE DE TURBULENCE | WIRBELKAMMER |
| 12552 | **SWISS THREAD, THURY THREAD** | PAS SYSTEME THURY | NORMALGEWINDE (SCHWEIZER) |
| 12553 | **SWITCH** | INTERRUPTEUR, INTERRUPTEUR-CONJONCTEUR, INTERRUPTEUR-DISJONCTEUR, CONTACTEUR ELECTRIQUE | SCHALTER, EINSCHALTER, AUSSCHALTER (ELEKT.) |
| 12554 | **SWITCH OFF (TO), SWITCH OUT (TO), CUT OUT (TO)** | METTRE HORS CIRCUIT | AUSSCHALTEN (ELEKTR.), ABSCHALTEN (ELEKTR.) |
| 12555 | **SWITCH ON (TO), SWITCH IN (TO), CUT IN (TO)** | METTRE EN CIRCUIT | EINSCHALTEN (ELEKTR.) |
| 12556 | **SWITCH POINT** | CHANGEMENT DE VOIE, AIGUILLAGE | WEICHE |
| 12557 | **SWITCHBOARD** | TABLEAU DISTRIBUTEUR, STANDARD TELEPHONIQUE, TABLEAU GENERAL | SCHALTTAFEL, SCHALTBRETT |
| 12558 | **SWITCHGEAR** | APPAREILS DE DISTRIBUTION (ELECTR.) | SCHALTANLAGE |

| | | | |
|---|---|---|---|
| 12559 | **SWITCHING OFF, SWITCHING OUT, CUTTING OUT** | MISE HORS CIRCUIT | AUSSCHALTEN, ABSCHALTEN (ELEKTR.) |
| 12560 | **SWITCHING ON, SWITCHING IN, CUTTING IN** | MISE EN CIRCUIT | EINSCHALTEN (ELEKTR.) |
| 12561 | **SWIVEL** | EMERILLON | WIRBEL (EINES HAKENS, EINER KETTE) |
| 12562 | **SWIVEL BASE VISE** | ETAU ORIENTABLE, ETAU PIVOTANT | SCHRAUBSTOCK (SCHWENKBARER) |
| 12563 | **SWIVEL BEARING, SELLERS BEARING** | PALIER, COUSSINET A ROTULE | KUGELSCHALENLAGER, SELLERSLAGER |
| 12564 | **SWIVEL HOOK** | CROCHET PIVOTANT | WIRBELHAKEN |
| 12565 | **SYENITE** | SYENITE | SYENIT |
| 12566 | **SYMMETRICAL** | SYMETRIQUE | SYMMETRISCH, SPIEGELGLEICH |
| 12567 | **SYMMETRY** | SYMETRIE | SYMMETRIE |
| 12568 | **SYNCHRO** | SYNCHRO | DREHMELDER |
| 12569 | **SYNCHRONISM** | SYNCHRONISME | SYNCHRONISMUS |
| 12570 | **SYNCHRONOUS** | SYNCHRONE | SYNCHRON |
| 12571 | **SYNCHRONOUS MOTOR** | MOTEUR SYNCHRONE | SYNCHRONMOTOR |
| 12572 | **SYNTHESIS** | SYNTHESE | SYNTHESE |
| 12573 | **SYNTHETIC** | SYNTHETIQUE | SYNTHETISCH |
| 12574 | **SYNTONY** | SYNTONIE | ABSTIMMUNG, SYNTONIE |
| 12575 | **SYSTEM OF COORDINATES** | SYSTEME DE COORDONNEES | ACHSENKREUZ, KOORDINATENSYSTEM |
| 12576 | **SYSTEM OF LENSES** | SYSTEME DE LENTILLES | LINSENSYSTEM |
| 12577 | **SYSTEM OF LEVERS** | SYSTEME ENSEMBLE DE LEVIERS | HEBELWERK, GESTÄNGE |
| 12578 | **SYSTEM OF MEASURES** | SYSTEME DE MESURE | MASSSYSTEM |
| 12579 | **SYSTEM OF PIPES** | RESEAU DE TUYAUX | ROHRNETZ |
| 12580 | **SYSTEM OF WEIGHTS** | SYSTEME DE POIDS | GEWICHTSSYSTEM |
| 12581 | **T.SQUARE, TEE-SQUARE** | TE DE DESSIN, EQUERRE DOUBLE | REISSSCHIENE, KREUZWINKEL, DOPPELTER ANSCHLAGWINKEL |
| 12582 | **T-SLOT CUTTERS** | FRAISES POUR RAINURES EN T | T-SPANN-NUTEN FRÄSER |
| 12583 | **TAB SEQUENTIAL FORMAT** | FORMAT A TABULATION | EINGABEFORMAT IN TABULATOR-SCHREIBWEISE |
| 12584 | **TABLE** | TABLE, TABLEAU (SERIE DE NOMBRES) | TAFEL, TABELLE |
| 12585 | **TABLE CROSS-TRAVEL** | COURSE TRANSVERSALE DE LA TABLE | TISCH-QUERBEWEGUNG |
| 12586 | **TACHOGRAPH** | TACHYMETRE ENREGISTREUR | GESCHWINDIGKEITSSCHREIBER, TACHOGRAPH |
| 12587 | **TACHOMETER** | TACHYMETRE, COMPTE-TOURS | TACHOMETER |
| 12588 | **TACK** | CLOU SEMENCE, SEMENCE | ZWECKE (NAGEL) |
| 12589 | **TACK WELD** | SOUDAGE PROVISOIRE PAR POINTS DE POINTAGE | HEFTSCHWEISSEN |
| 12590 | **TACK-WELDING** | SOUDURE PROVISOIRE PAR POINTS | HEFTSCHWEISSEN |
| 12591 | **TACKINESS** | POISSAGE | KLEBRIGKEIT |
| 12592 | **TACKING RIVET** | BROCHE POUR ASSEMBLAGE PROVISOIRE DES TOLES, BOULON D'ASSEMBLAGE PROVISOIRE | HEFTNIET |
| 12593 | **TAGGER** | TOLE TRES MINCE | FEINBLECH (SEHR DÜNNES) |
| 12594 | **TAIL HAIR** | CRIN, POILS DE QUEUE DE CHEVAL | SCHWEIFHAAR |
| 12595 | **TAIL LIGHT** | FEUX ARRIERE | SCHLUSSLATERNE |
| 12596 | **TAIL RACE** | CANAL DE DECHARGE, CANAL DE FUITE, BIEF D'AVAL | ABLAUFKANAL, UNTERWASSERKANAL |
| 12597 | **TAIL WATER** | EAU D'AVAL | UNTERWASSER |
| 12598 | **TAILINGS** | RESIDUS | BERGE, RÜCKSTÄNDE |

# TAK

322

| | | | |
|---|---|---|---|
| 12599 | **TAILSTOCK** | CONTRE-POINTE, POUPEE MOBILE | REITSTOCK |
| 12600 | **TAKE TO PIECES (TO), DISMANTLE (TO)** | DEMONTER, DESASSEMBLER | ZERLEGEN, AUSEINANDERNEHMEN, DEMONTIEREN |
| 12601 | **TAKE UP A FORCE (TO) (PULL, PUSH)** | RECEVOIR UNE FORCE | AUFNEHMEN (EINE KRAFT) |
| 12602 | **TAKE UP THE SLACK OF A BELT (TO)** | RETENDRE UNE COURROIE | NACHSPANNEN (EINEN RIEMEN) |
| 12603 | **TAKE UP THE WEAR OF A BEARING (TO), OF A COUPLING** | COMPENSER LE JEU D'UN COUSSINET, RATTRAPER LE JEU D'EMBRAYAGE, RACHETER L'USURE | NACHSTELLEN EIN LAGER, EINE KUPPLUNG |
| 12604 | **TAKING TO PIECES, DISMANTLING** | DEMONTAGE, DESASSEMBLAGE | ZERLEGEN, ZERLEGUNG, AUSEINANDERNEHMEN, DEMONTAGE |
| 12605 | **TAKING UP THE SLACK OF A BELT** | ACTION DE RETENDRE UNE COURROIE | NACHSPANNEN EINES RIEMENS |
| 12606 | **TAKING UP THE WEAR OF A BEARING, OF A COUPLING** | RATTRAPAGE DU JEU, RECALAGE (D'UN COUSSINET) | NACHSTELLEN EINES LAGERS, NACHSTELLEN EINER KUPPLUNG |
| 12607 | **TALC POWDER** | TALC EN POUDRE | TALKPULVER, TALKUM |
| 12608 | **TALC, FRENCH CHALK** | TALC | TALK |
| 12609 | **TALLOW, SUET** | SUIF | TALG, UNSCHLITT |
| 12610 | **TAMPED ASPHALT** | ASPHALTE COMPRIME | STAMPFASPHALT |
| 12611 | **TAMPER** | MASSE, DEMOISELLE, DAME | ERDRAMMER |
| 12612 | **TAN CAKE** | TAN COMPRIME, TAN EN MOTTES | LOHKÄSE, LOHKUCHEN |
| 12613 | **TANDEM STEAM ENGINE** | MACHINE TANDEM | TANDEMDAMPFMASCHINE |
| 12614 | **TANG, SHANK OF A TOOL** | SOIE, QUEUE D'UN OUTIL | ANGEL EINES WERKZEUGS |
| 12615 | **TANGENT (OF AN ANGLE)** | TANGENTE | TANGENTE, TANGENS |
| 12616 | **TANGENT (TO A CURVE)** | TANGENTE (GEOM.) | TANGENTE, BERÜHRUNGSLINIE |
| 12617 | **TANGENT AT THE VERTEX** | TANGENTE AU SOMMET | SCHEITELTANGENTE |
| 12618 | **TANGENT KEY** | CLAVETTE TANGENTIELLE | TANGENTIALKEIL |
| 12619 | **TANGENT SCREW** | VIS TANGENTE | TANGENTENSCHRAUBE |
| 12620 | **TANGENTIAL ACCELERATION** | ACCELERATION TANGENTIELLE | TANGENTIALBESCHLEUNIGUNG |
| 12621 | **TANGENTIAL FLOW TURBINE** | TURBINE TANGENTIELLE | TANGENTIALTURBINE |
| 12622 | **TANGENTIAL FORCE** | FORCE TANGENTIELLE | UMFANGSKRAFT, TANGENTIALKRAFT |
| 12623 | **TANGENTIAL SPEED** | VITESSE TANGENTIELLE | GESCHWINDIGKEIT (TANGENTIALE) |
| 12624 | **TANGENTIAL STRESS** | EFFORT TANGENTIEL | TANGENTIALSPANNUNG |
| 12625 | **TANK** | RESERVOIR | BEHÄLTER, TANK |
| 12626 | **TANK CAR** | WAGON-RESERVOIR, WAGON-CITERNE | KESSELWAGEN, ZISTERNENWAGEN |
| 12627 | **TANK FARM** | PARC DE STOCKAGE D'HYDROCARBURE | TANKLAGER |
| 12628 | **TANK PAD** | ASSISE DE RESERVOIR | TANKUNTERBAU |
| 12629 | **TANK PIT** | CUVETTE DE RETENTION D'UN RESERVOIR | TANKGRUBE |
| 12630 | **TANK SHELL** | ROBE DU RESERVOIR | BEHÄLTERMANTEL |
| 12631 | **TANK WITH BOTTOM CONE-DOWN** | RESERVOIR A FOND CONCAVE | BEHÄLTER, TANK MIT KONKAVEM BODEN |
| 12632 | **TANK WITH BOTTOM CONE-UP** | RESERVOIR A FOND CONVEXE | BEHÄLTER, TANK MIT KONVEXEM BODEN |
| 12633 | **TANNATE** | TANNATE | SALZ (GERBSAURES), TANNAT |
| 12634 | **TANTALUM** | TANTALE | TANTAL |
| 12635 | **TANYARD REFUSE** | TAN EPUISE | LOHE (VERBRAUCHTE) |
| 12636 | **TAP (TO), CUT THREADS IN HOLES (TO)** | TARAUDER | BOHREN (GEWINDE), SCHNEIDEN (INNENGEWINDE) |
| 12637 | **TAP HOLE** | TROU DE COULEE | ABSTICHLOCH |
| 12638 | **TAP WRENCH** | TOURNE-A-GAUCHE | WINDEISEN, WENDEEISEN |

**323** **TAR**

| | | | |
|---|---|---|---|
| 12639 | TAP, PLUG | COUVERCLE, ROBINET | STÖPSEL, HAHN |
| 12640 | TAP, SCREW TAP | TARAUD | GEWINDEBOHRER |
| 12641 | TAPE | RUBAN, BANDE | BAND |
| 12642 | TAPE BLOCK VALVE | VANNE D'ARRET | ABSPERRSCHIEBER |
| 12643 | TAPE FEED | ENTREE DES DONNEES PAR BANDE | LOCHSTREIFENEINGABE |
| 12644 | TAPE RECORDER | MAGNETOPHONE | TONBANDGERÄT |
| 12645 | TAPE-HOLE / TAPPING HOLE | SORTIE DE COULEE (TROU) | STICHLOCH, ABSTICHLOCH |
| 12646 | TAPER | CONICITE, DELARDAGE | KONIZITÄT, ABKANTEN |
| 12647 | TAPER CONNECTING PIECE | RACCORD CONIQUE | MUFFE (KONISCHE) |
| 12648 | TAPER FILE | LIME POINTUE | SPITZFEILE |
| 12649 | TAPER FIT | EMMANCHEMENT A CONE, EMMANCHEMENT CONIQUE | KEGELSITZ |
| 12650 | TAPER HAND REAMER | ALESOIR A MAIN CONIQUE | KEGELHANDREIBAHLE |
| 12651 | TAPER MANDREL | MANDRIN CONIQUE | KONUSDORN |
| 12652 | TAPER MICROMETER | MICROMETRE DE CONICITE, MICRO-PALPEUR DE CONICITE | KONIZITÄTSMIKROMETER |
| 12653 | TAPER OF KEY | SERRAGE DE CLAVETTE | KEILANSTELLUNG |
| 12654 | TAPER OF WEDGE | PENTE, CONICITE D'UNE CLAVETTE | ANZUG, STEIGUNG, NEIGUNG EINES KEILS |
| 12655 | TAPER PIN | GOUPILLE CONIQUE | KEGELSTIFT, STIFT (KONISCHER) |
| 12656 | TAPER PLUG GAUGE | JAUGE-TAMPON CONIQUE, CALIBRE MALE CONIQUE | KEGELLEHRDORN |
| 12657 | TAPER PLUG GAUGE WITH DRIVING PILOT | JAUGE-TAMPON CONIQUE AVEC TETON | KEGELLEHRDORN MIT MITNEHMER-LAPPEN |
| 12658 | TAPER REAMER | ALESOIR CONIQUE | KEGELREIBAHLE, REIBAHLE (KONISCHE), REIBAHLE (KEGELIGE) |
| 12659 | TAPER RING GAUGES | CALIBRES FEMELLES CONIQUES | KEGELLEHRHÜLSEN |
| 12660 | TAPER ROLLER | GALET CONIQUE, ROULEAU CONIQUE | KEGELROLLE, KEGELWALZE |
| 12661 | TAPER ROPE | CABLE DIMINUE, CABLE A SECTION DECROISSANTE, CABLE CONIQUE | SEIL (VERJÜNGTES) |
| 12662 | TAPER SEAT GATE VALVE | VANNE A SIEGES OBLIQUES | KEILSCHIEBER |
| 12663 | TAPER SEATS | SIEGES OBLIQUES | SITZE (SCHRÄGE) |
| 12664 | TAPER SHANK | QUEUE CONIQUE | KEGELSCHAFT |
| 12665 | TAPER SUNK KEY | CLAVETTE CONIQUE | TREIBKEIL |
| 12666 | TAPER THREAD | FILETAGE CONIQUE | GEWINDE (KONISCHES) |
| 12667 | TAPER-SHANK MANDREL | MANDRIN A QUEUE CONIQUE | KEGELSCHAFTSPANNDORN |
| 12668 | TAPER, CONICAL TURNING | CHARIOTAGE, TOURNAGE CONIQUE, TOURNAGE DES SURFACES CONIQUES | KEGELIGDREHEN, KONISCHDREHEN |
| 12669 | TAPERED CONE | CONE LISSE, POULIE-CONE | RIEMENKEGEL, RIEMENKONUS, KEGELTROMMEL, KEGELSCHEIBE, RIEMENKONOID |
| 12670 | TAPERED ROD | BARRE A SECTION DECROISSANTE | VERJÜNGTER STAB |
| 12671 | TAPERING OF A PLATE | DELARDAGE D'UNE TOLE | ABKANTEN |
| 12672 | TAPPET | POUSSOIR, MENTONNET | STÖSSEL, HEBLING |
| 12673 | TAPPET CLEARANCE | JEU DES SOUPAPES | STÖSSELSPIEL |
| 12674 | TAPPET ROLLER | GALET DE POUSSOIR | STÖSSEL |
| 12675 | TAPPING | PERCAGE, DEBOUCHAGE | ABSTECHE, KUPOLOFENABSTICH |
| 12676 | TAPPING ATTACHMENT | APPAREIL A TARAUDER | GEWINDESCHNEIDVORRICHTUNG |
| 12677 | TAPPING MACHINE | TARAUDEUSE | INNENGEWINDESCHNEIDMASCHINE |
| 12678 | TAPPING, CUTTING THREADS IN HOLES | TARAUDAGE | BOHREN, EINES GEWINDES, GEWINDEBOHREN, SCHNEIDEN EINES INNENGEWINDES |
| 12679 | TAR | GOUDRON | TEER |

**TAR**                                                                              **324**

| | | | |
|---|---|---|---|
| 12680 | TAR (TO) | GOUDRONNER | TEEREN |
| 12681 | TAR OIL | HUILE DE GOUDRON | TEERÖL |
| 12682 | TARGET | ANTICATHODE, CIBLE, OBJECTIF | ANTIKATHODE, FANGELEKTRODE, ZIEL |
| 12683 | TARGET AREA | SURFACE DE LA CIBLE (OFFERTE AUX RAYONNEMENTS) | AUFPRALLAFLÄCHE |
| 12684 | TARGET TUBE | TUBE A RAYONS-X | ROENTGENRÖHRE |
| 12685 | TARNISH (TO) | TERNIR (SE), OXYDER (S') | ANLAUFEN, MATTIEREN, GLANZ (VERLIEREN DEN) |
| 12686 | TARPAULIN COVERED LORRY | CAMION BACHE | LASTKRAFTWAGEN MIT PLANE UND SPRIEGEL |
| 12687 | TARRED PIPE | TUBE PROTEGE PAR GOUDRONNAGE | ROHR (GETEERTES) |
| 12688 | TARRED ROPE | CORDE NOIRE, CORDE GOUDRONNEE | SEIL (GETEERTES) |
| 12689 | TARRING | GOUDRONNAGE | TEEREN |
| 12690 | TARTARIC ACID, DIOXY-SUCINIC ACID | ACIDE TARTARIQUE | WEINSÄURE, WEINSTEINSÄURE, DIOXYBERNSTEINSÄURE |
| 12691 | TARTRATE | TARTRATE | WEINSAURES SALZ, TARTRAT |
| 12692 | TAXE A READING (TO) | LIRE | ABLESEN |
| 12693 | TEA-POT LADLE | POCHE THEIERE | SIPHONPFANNE |
| 12694 | TECHNICAL | TECHNIQUE | TECHNISCH |
| 12695 | TECHNICS | TECHNIQUE | TECHNIK |
| 12696 | TEDDERS | FANEUSES | GABELHEUWENDER |
| 12697 | TEE | TE | TEESTÜCK |
| 12698 | TEE IRON, TEE BAR, T-IRON | FER EN T | T-EISEN |
| 12699 | TEE PIPE, T-PIECE | TE A TROIS DIRECTIONS | T-STÜCK, DREIWEGESTÜCK |
| 12700 | TEE-BAR | PROFILE EN T | T-TRÄGER |
| 12701 | TEE-HEADED BOLT | BOULON A TETE DE MARTEAU | HAMMERKOPFSCHRAUBE |
| 12702 | TEE-JOINT | ASSEMBLAGE EN T | FLANKENKEHLNAHT, T-MUFFE |
| 12703 | TEEMING | COULEE, MOULAGE SORTIE EN LINGOTIERE | GIESSEN, ABGUSS |
| 12704 | TEETH | DENTURE | VERZAHNUNG |
| 12705 | TELEDYNAMIC CABLE, FLY ROPE | CABLE TELEDYNAMIQUE | FERNTRIEBSEIL |
| 12706 | TELEDYNAMIC TRANSMISSION GEAR | TRANSMISSION PAR CABLE TELEDYNAMIQUE | FERNTRIEB, SEILFERNTRIEB |
| 12707 | TELEGRAPH | TELEGRAPHE | TELEGRAPH |
| 12708 | TELEGRAPH WIRE | FIL TELEGRAPHIQUE | TELEGRAPHENDRAHT |
| 12709 | TELEGRAPHY | TELEGRAPHIE | TELEGRAPHIE |
| 12710 | TELEPHONE | TELEPHONE | FERNSPRECHER, TELEPHON |
| 12711 | TELEPHONE WIRE | FIL TELEPHONIQUE | FERNSPRECHERDRAHT, TELEPHONDRAHT |
| 12712 | TELEPHONY | TELEPHONIE | FERNSPRECHWESEN, TELEPHONIE |
| 12713 | TELESCOPE GAUGES | CALIBRES TELESCOPIQUES | TELESKOPLEHRE |
| 12714 | TELETHERMOMETER | PYROMETRE A DISTANCE | FERNTHERMOMETER |
| 12715 | TELL-TALE HOLE | TROU TEMOIN | BEOBACHTUNGSÖFFNUNG, ANZEIGEEINRICHTUNG |
| 12716 | TELLURIUM | TELLURE | TELLUR |
| 12717 | TEMPER (TO) | FAIRE REVENIR, ADOUCIR | ANLASSEN, TEMPERN |
| 12718 | TEMPER (TO) (MORTAR, CEMENT) | DELAYER, GACHER, MALAXER (DU MORTIER, DU CIMENT) | ANMACHEN (MÖRTEL, ZEMENT), ANRÜHREN (MÖRTEL, ZEMENT) |
| 12719 | TEMPER (TO), LET DOWN THE STEEL (TO) | FAIRE REVENIR, DETREMPER L'ACIER | ANLASSEN (DEN STAHL), NACHLASSEN (DEN STAHL) |
| 12720 | TEMPER ROLLING | DRESSAGE | DRESSIEREN |
| 12721 | TEMPERATURE | TEMPERATURE | WÄRMEGRAD, TEMPERATUR |

| | | | |
|---|---|---|---|
| 12722 | **TEMPERATURE CONTROL DEVICE, THERMOSTAT** | THERMOSTAT | THERMOSTAT |
| 12723 | **TEMPERATURE CURVES** | COURBES DE TEMPERATURE | TEMPERATURKURVEN |
| 12724 | **TEMPERATURE DROP** | CHUTE DE TEMPERATURE | WÄRMEGEFÄLLE, TEMPERATURGEFÄLLE |
| 12725 | **TEMPERATURE GRAPHS** | RELEVES DE TEMPERATURE | TEMPERATURDIAGRAMME |
| 12726 | **TEMPERATURE INDICATOR** | INDICATEUR DE TEMPERATURE, THERMOMETRE | THERMOMETER |
| 12727 | **TEMPERATURE OF IGNITION, IGNITION TEMPERATURE** | TEMPERATURE D'INFLAMMATION | ENTZÜNDUNGSTEMPERATUR, ZÜNDTEMPERATUR |
| 12728 | **TEMPERATURE OF THE AIR** | TEMPERATURE DE L'AIR | LUFTTEMPERATUR |
| 12729 | **TEMPERATURE OF THE AMBIENT AIR** | TEMPERATURE AMBIANTE | TEMPERATUR (DER UMGEBENDEN LUFT), UMGEBUNGSTEMPERATUR |
| 12730 | **TEMPERATURE RANGE** | GAMME DE TEMPERATURE | TEMPERATURBEREICH |
| 12731 | **TEMPERING** | REVENU | ANLASS |
| 12732 | **TEMPERING COLOUR** | COULEUR, TEINTE DE REVENU, TEINTE DE RECUIT | ANLAUFFARBE, ANLASSFARBE |
| 12733 | **TEMPERING, LETTING DOWN OF THE STEEL** | REVENU, DETREMPE DE L'ACIER | ANLASSEN, NACHLASSEN DES STAHLES |
| 12734 | **TEMPLATE, TEMPLET** | GABARIT, PROFIL, PATRON, TROUSSEAU | SCHABLONE |
| 12735 | **TEMPORARY HARDNESS OF WATER** | DURETE TEMPORAIRE DE L'EAU | HÄRTE DES WASSERS (SCHNINDENDE), HÄRTE DES WASSERS (VORÜBERGEHENDE), HÄRTE DES WASSERS (TEMPORÄRE) |
| 12736 | **TEMPORARY STORAGE** | MEMOIRE TEMPORAIRE | PUFFERSPEICHER |
| 12737 | **TENACITY** | TENACITE | ZÄHIGKEIT |
| 12738 | **TENACITY OF NOTCHED BAR** | TENACITE DES BARREAUX ENTAILLES | KERBZÄHIGKEIT |
| 12739 | **TENDONS** | CABLES | VORSPANNUNGSKABEL |
| 12740 | **TENON** | TENON | ZAPFEN (TISCHLEREI) |
| 12741 | **TENON SAW, PANEL SAW** | SCIE A ARASER, SCIE A TENONS, SCIE A CHEVILLES | ZAPFENSÄGE |
| 12742 | **TENONING MACHINE** | MACHINE A FAIRE LES TENONS | ZAPFENSCHNEIDMASCHINE |
| 12743 | **TENSILE** | MECANIQUE (ESSAI) | ZUG |
| 12744 | **TENSILE DEFORMATION** | DEFORMATION PAR TRACTION | ZUGVERFORMUNG |
| 12745 | **TENSILE FORCE** | FORCE DE TRACTION | ZUGKRAFT (FESTIGKEITSL.) |
| 12746 | **TENSILE PROPERTIES** | CARACTERISTIQUES MECANIQUES | FESTIGKEITSEIGENSCHAFTEN |
| 12747 | **TENSILE STRAIN** | EFFORT DE TRACTION, TRAVAIL A LA TRACTION | ZUGSPANNUNG, BEANSPRUCHUNG AUF ZUG, ZUGBEANSPRUCHUNG |
| 12748 | **TENSILE STRENGHT TEST** | ESSAI DE TRACTION | ZUGVERSUCH |
| 12749 | **TENSILE STRENGTH** | RESISTANCE A LA TRACTION, CHARGE DE RUPTURE | ZUGFESTIGKEIT, BRUCHLAST |
| 12750 | **TENSILE STRESS** | CONTRAINTE DE TRACTION (FORCE), EFFORT DE TRACTION PAR UNITE DE SECTION | ZUGSPANNUNG |
| 12751 | **TENSILE TEST** | ESSAI A LA TRACTION | ZUGVERSUCH, ZERREISSVERSUCH |
| 12752 | **TENSILE TESTING MACHINE** | MACHINE D'ESSAI DE TRACTION | ZERREISS(PRÜF)MASCHINE |
| 12753 | **TENSION** | TENSION | SPANNUNG |
| 12754 | **TENSION BAR ROD** | BARRE TRAVAILLANT A LA TENSION | ZUGSTAB, STAB (GEZOGENER) |
| 12755 | **TENSION BOLT** | BOUTON DE TENSION | ZUGBOLZEN |
| 12756 | **TENSION CARRIAGE** | CHASSIS-TENDEUR, RAIL-TENDEUR | SPANNSCHLITTEN, SPANNWAGEN |
| 12757 | **TENSION IMPACT** | ENERGIE DU CHOC | SCHLAGSTÄRKE |
| 12758 | **TENSION SCREW** | VIS DE TENSION | ZUGSCHRAUBE |

# TER 326

| | | | |
|------|------|------|------|
| 12759 | **TENSION SPRING, SPRING FOR TENSION** | RESSORT DE TRACTION | ZUGFEDER |
| 12760 | **TERBIUM** | TERBIUM | TERBIUM |
| 12761 | **TERM OF PATENT, DURATION OF A PATENT** | DUREE DU BREVET | DAUER EINES PATENTRECHTES |
| 12762 | **TERMINAL** | BORNE, POUPEE (ELECTR.), BORNE DE RACCORDEMENT | KLEMME (ELEKTR.) |
| 12763 | **TERMINAL POST** | BORNE | ANSCHLUSSPOL |
| 12764 | **TERMINAL VOLTAGE** | DIFFERENCE DE POTENTIEL AUX BORNES, TENSION, VOLTAGE AUX BORNES | KLEMMENSPANNUNG |
| 12765 | **TERMINALS** | COSSES | KLEMMEN |
| 12766 | **TERNARY SYSTEM** | SYSTEME TERNAIRE | DREISTOFFSYSTEM |
| 12767 | **TERRACOTTA** | TERRE CUITE | TERRAKOTTA |
| 12768 | **TERRAZZO MOSAIC** | TERRAZZO | TERRAZZO |
| 12769 | **TESSELATED PLATE** | TOLE GAUFREE | WAFFELBLECH, WARZENBLECH |
| 12770 | **TEST** | ESSAI, EPREUVE | PROBE, PRÜFUNG, VERSUCH |
| 12771 | **TEST BAR LATHE** | TOUR A EPROUVETTES | PROBESTABDREHBANK |
| 12772 | **TEST BAR, SPECIMEN BAR** | EPROUVETTE, BARREAU-EPROUVETTE, BARRE SOUMISE AUX ESSAIS | PROBESTAB |
| 12773 | **TEST BENCH, TEST BED** | POSTE D'ESSAI, BANC DE CONTROLE, BANC D'ESSAI, TABLE D'EXAMEN | PRÜFSTAND, VERSUCHSTAND, PROBIERSTAND |
| 12774 | **TEST BY REPEATED FLEXURE** | ESSAI DE FLEXION ALTERNE, ESSAI DES FILS AU PLIAGE | HIN- UND HERBIEGEPROBE |
| 12775 | **TEST CERTIFICATE** | CERTIFICAT D'EPREUVE | PRÜFUNGSZEUGNIS |
| 12776 | **TEST COCK, TRY COCK** | ROBINET DE JAUGE | PRÜFHAHN, PROBIERHAHN |
| 12777 | **TEST COUPON** | LINGOT EPROUVETTE | PROBEBLOCK |
| 12778 | **TEST DRILLING** | FORAGE D'ESSAI, SONDAGE | VERSUCHSBOHRUNG |
| 12779 | **TEST GAUGE** | JAUGE DE CONTROLE | PRÜFLEHRE |
| 12780 | **TEST GLASS, TEST TUBE** | EPROUVETTE | REAGENZGLAS, PRÜFGLAS, PROBIERGLAS |
| 12781 | **TEST LOAD, PROOF LOAD** | CHARGE D'ESSAI | PROBEBELASTUNG |
| 12782 | **TEST OF RAW MATERIALS** | ESSAI DES MATERIAUX | WERKSTOFFPRÜFUNG, MATERIALPRÜFUNG, PRÜFUNG DES MATERIALS |
| 12783 | **TEST PAPER** | PAPIER REACTIF | REAGENZPAPIER |
| 12784 | **TEST PIECE, TEST SAMPLE** | EPROUVETTE | PROBESTÜCK, PRÜFSTÜCK |
| 12785 | **TEST PLUG** | TAMPON, FICHE D'ESSAI | PRÜFSTÖPSEL |
| 12786 | **TEST PRESSURE** | PRESSION D'EPREUVE, PRESSION D'ESSAI | PRÜFDRUCK, PROBEDRUCK |
| 12787 | **TEST PUMP** | POMPE D'EPREUVE | PRÜFPUMPE |
| 12788 | **TEST SAMPLE** | EPROUVETTE | PROBE(STÜCK) |
| 12789 | **TEST SPECIMEN, TEST PIECE** | EPROUVETTE (MORCEAU D'ESSAI) | PROBESTÜCK, VERSUCHSSTÜCK |
| 12790 | **TEST TANK** | RESERVOIR DE JAUGEAGE | PRÜFTANK |
| 12791 | **TEST-TUBE** | EPROUVETTE (CHIM) | REAGENZGLAS |
| 12792 | **TEST, EXPERIMENT** | ESSAI, EPREUVE, EXPERIENCE, EXAMEN | VERSUCH, EXPERIMENT |
| 12793 | **TESTING MACHINE** | MACHINE A ESSAYER, APPAREIL D'ESSAI | FESTIGKEITS-PRÜFMASCHINE |
| 12794 | **TESTING TRACK** | PISTE D'ESSAI | PROBEFAHRBAHN |
| 12795 | **TETRAGONAL** | QUADRATIQUE | TETRAGONAL |
| 12796 | **TETRAHEDRITE, FAHLERZ, GREY COPPER ORE** | CUIVRE GRIS, PANABASE | FAHLERZ |

| | | | |
|---|---|---|---|
| 12797 | **TETRAHEDRON** | TETRAEDRE | VIERFLACH, VIERFLÄCHNER, TETRAEDER |
| 12798 | **TETRATOMIC, TETRAVALENT** | TETRATOMIQUE, QUADRIVALENT | VIERWERTIG, VIERATOMIG |
| 12799 | **TEXTILE FIBRE** | FIBRE TEXTILE | SPINNFASER, GESPINSTFASER, TEXTILFASER |
| 12800 | **TEXTURE** | TEXTURE, STRUCTURE | GEFÜGE, STRUKTUR |
| 12801 | **THALLIUM** | THALLIUM | THALLIUM |
| 12802 | **THAT CAN BE WORKED UP INTO...** | MANUFACTURABLE | VERARBEITBAR |
| 12803 | **THERMAL CAPACITY** | CAPACITE THERMIQUE | WÄRMEKAPAZITÄT |
| 12804 | **THERMAL CONDUCTIVITY** | CONDUCTIVITE THERMIQUE | WÄRMELEITFÄHIGKEIT |
| 12805 | **THERMAL CONTRACTION** | RETRAIT THERMIQUE | WÄRMESCHWINDUNG |
| 12806 | **THERMAL EFFICIENCY** | RENDEMENT THERMIQUE | WÄRMEWIRKUNGSGRAD, THERMISCHER WIRKUNGSGRAD |
| 12807 | **THERMAL ELECTROMOTIVE FORCE** | FORCE ELECTROMOTRICE THERMIQUE | KRAFT (THERMOELEKTROMOTORISCHE) |
| 12808 | **THERMAL EXPANSION** | DILATATION THERMIQUE | WÄRMEAUSDEHNUNG |
| 12809 | **THERMAL EXPANSION COEFFICIENT** | COEFFICIENT DE DILATATION THERMIQUE | WÄRMEAUSDEHNUNGSKOEFFIZIENT |
| 12810 | **THERMAL INSOLATION** | ISOLATION THERMIQUE | ISOLIERUNG (THERMISCHE) |
| 12811 | **THERMAL RADIATION** | RAYONNEMENT DE LA CHALEUR | WÄRMESTRAHLUNG |
| 12812 | **THERMAL SHOCK** | CHOC THERMIQUE | TEMPERATURSCHOCK, WÄRMESTOSS |
| 12813 | **THERMAL SHOCK RESISTANCE** | RESISTANCE AUX VARIATIONS DE TEMPERATURE OU AU CHOC THERMIQUE | TEMPERATURWECHSELBESTÄNDIGKEIT |
| 12814 | **THERMAL STRESS** | TENSION THERMIQUE | WÄRMESPANNUNG |
| 12815 | **THERMAL TREATMENT** | TRAITEMENT THERMIQUE | WÄRMEBEHANDLUNG |
| 12816 | **THERMAL UNIT, UNIT OF HEAT** | UNITE DE CHALEUR, UNITE THERMIQUE | WÄRMEEINHEIT |
| 12817 | **THERMIT** | THERMIT | THERMIT |
| 12818 | **THERMIT ALUMINOTHERMIC WELDING** | SOUDURE AVEC APPORT DE FER-THERMIT, SOUDURE ALUMINOTHERMIQUE | THERMITSCHWEISSUNG, ALUMINOTHERMISCHE SCHWEISSUNG |
| 12819 | **THERMIT WELDING** | SOUDAGE PAR ALUMINOTHERMIE | THERMITSCHWEISSUNG |
| 12820 | **THERMO ELECTRIC PILE** | PILE THERMOELECTRIQUE, PILE THERMIQUE | THERMOSÄULE |
| 12821 | **THERMO- ELECTRIC COUPLE** | COUPLE THERMOELECTRIQUE, ELEMENT DE PILE THERMOELECTRIQUE | THERMOELEMENT |
| 12822 | **THERMO-CHEMISTRY** | THERMOCHIMIE | THERMOCHEMIE |
| 12823 | **THERMO-ELECTRIC** | THERMO-ELECTRIQUE | THERMOELEKTRISCH |
| 12824 | **THERMO-ELECTRIC CURRENT** | COURANT THERMOELECTRIQUE | THERMOSTROM, THERMOELEKTRISCHER STROM |
| 12825 | **THERMO-ELECTRIC PYROMETER** | PYROMETRE THERMOELECTRIQUE | PYROMETER (THERMOELEKTRISCHES) |
| 12826 | **THERMO-ELECTRICITY** | THERMO-ELECTRICITE | THERMOELEKTRIZITÄT |
| 12827 | **THERMOCOUPLE** | COUPLE THERMO-ELECTRIQUE, THERMOCOUPLE | THERMOELEMENT |
| 12828 | **THERMODYNAMIC (ADJ)** | THERMODYNAMIQUE | THERMODYNAMISCH |
| 12829 | **THERMODYNAMICS** | THERMODYNAMIQUE | MECHANISCHE WÄRMELEHRE, THERMODYNAMIK |
| 12830 | **THERMOELECTRIC EFFECT** | EFFET THERMOELECTRIQUE | SEEBECK-EFFEKT |
| 12831 | **THERMOELECTRIC POWER** | FORCE THERMOELECTRIQUE | KRAFT (THERMOELEKTRISCHE) |
| 12832 | **THERMOGRAPH** | THERMOGRAPHE | WÄRMESCHREIBER |
| 12833 | **THERMOMETER** | THERMOMETRE | THERMOMETER, WÄRMEMESSER |
| 12834 | **THERMOMETER F. WATER** | INDICATEUR DE TEMPERATURE | WASSERTHERMOMETER |

**THE**         328

| | | | |
|---|---|---|---|
| 12835 | THERMOMETRIC SCALE | ECHELLE THERMOMETRIQUE | THERMOMETEREINTEILUNG, THERMOMETERSKALA, TEMPERATURSKALA |
| 12836 | THERMOPILE | PILE THERMO-ELECTRIQUE | THERMOSÄULE |
| 12837 | THERMOSCOPE | THERMOSCOPE | THERMOSKOP |
| 12838 | THERMOSTAT | THERMOSTAT | KÜHLLUFTREGLER, THERMOSTAT |
| 12839 | THERMOSTATIC TRAP | PURGEUR D'EAU CONDENSEE A DILATATION | KONDENSTOPF (THERMOSTATISCHER) |
| 12840 | THERMOSTATIC VALVE | REGULATEUR DE TEMPERATURE | TEMPERATUR-REGELVENTIL, TEMPERATURREGLER |
| 12841 | THICK-WALLED | PAROI EPAISSE (A) | DICKWANDIG, STARKWANDIG |
| 12842 | THICKENER | SUBSTANCE EPAISSISSANTE | VERDICKER |
| 12843 | THICKNESS | EPAISSEUR | DICKE, STÄRKE |
| 12844 | THICKNESS OF A PIPE | EPAISSEUR DE LA PAROI (DU METAL) D'UN TUBE | WANDDICKE EINES ROHRES, WANDSTÄRKE EINES ROHRES |
| 12845 | THICKNESS OF SHEET METAL | EPAISSEUR D'UNE TOLE | BLECHSTÄRKE, BLECHDICKE |
| 12846 | THICKNESS OF TOOTH | EPAISSEUR DE LA DENT | ZAHNHÖHE, ZAHNDICKE, ZAHNSTÄRKE |
| 12847 | THICKNESSING MACHINE | MACHINE A RABOTER TIRANT LES BOIS D'EPAISSEUR | DICKENHOBELMASCHINE |
| 12848 | THIMBLE | COSSE | KAUSCHE, SEILKAUSCHE |
| 12849 | THIN DRAWN WIRE | FIL METALLIQUE FIN | DRAHT (FEINER), DRAHT (FEINGEZOGNER), FEINDRAHT |
| 12850 | THIN PLATE | TOLE FINE | FEINBLECH |
| 12851 | THIN-WALLED | PAROI MINCE (A) | DÜNNWANDIG |
| 12852 | THIOSULPHATE | HYPOSULFITE, THIOSULFATE | SALZ (UNTERSCHWEFLIGSAURES), THIOSULFAT, HYPOSULFIT |
| 12853 | THIOSULPHURIC, HYPOSULPHUROUS ACID | ACIDE HYPOSULFUREUX, ACIDE THIOSULFURIQUE | UNTERSCHWEFLIGE SÄURE, THIOSCHWEFELSÄURE |
| 12854 | THIXOTROPY | THIXOTROPIE | THIXOTROPIE |
| 12855 | THOMAS BASIC STEEL | ACIER THOMAS | THOMASSTAHL |
| 12856 | THORIUM | THORIUM | THORIUM |
| 12857 | THREAD | FILETAGE, PAS DE VIS | GEWINDE |
| 12858 | THREAD CLEARANCE, CLEARANCE PLAY AT THE APEX OF MALE THREAD | JEU A FOND DE FILET | SPITZENSPIEL IM GEWINDE |
| 12859 | THREAD CUTTING LATHE | TOUR A FILETER | GEWINDEDREHBANK |
| 12860 | THREAD GAUGES | JAUGES POUR FILETAGES | GEWINDE LEHREN |
| 12861 | THREAD PLUG GAUGE, SINGLE ENDED TYPE | JAUGE NORMALE - TAMPON FILETE | NORMALGEWINDELEHRDORN |
| 12862 | THREAD PLUG GAUGES | CALIBRES MALES POUR FILETAGES | GEWINDELEHRDORN |
| 12863 | THREAD RING GAUGE | JAUGE NORMALE BAGUE FILETEE | NORMALGEWINDELEHRRING |
| 12864 | THREAD ROOT | FOND DE FILET | GEWINDEKERN |
| 12865 | THREAD TOOL GAUGE | GABARIT POUR OUTILS A FILETER | GEWINDESTAHLLEHRE |
| 12866 | THREADED FLANGE | BRIDE TARAUDEE | GEWINDEFLANSCH |
| 12867 | THREADED MANDREL | MANDRIN FILETE | GEWINDEDORN |
| 12868 | THREADING | TARAUDAGE, FILETAGE | GEWINDESCHNEIDEN, INNENGEWINDE |
| 12869 | THREADING MACHINE | MACHINE A FILETER | AUSSENGEWINDESCHNEIDMASCHINE |
| 12870 | THREE SQUARE FILE | LIME TIERS-POINT | FEILE (DREIKANTIGE) |
| 12871 | THREE-AXLE LORRY | VEHICULE A TROIS ESSIEUX | LASTKRAFTWAGEN (DREIACHSIG) |
| 12872 | THREE-CENTRE, THREE-ARC CURVE, COMPOUND CURVE | ANSE DE PANIER | KORBBOGENLINIE |
| 12873 | THREE-CYLINDER ENGINE | MACHINE A TROIS CYLINDRES | DREIZYLINDERMASCHINE |
| 12874 | THREE-JAW UNIVERSAL CHUCK | MANDRIN UNIVERSEL A TROIS MORS | DREIBACKENFUTTER |

| | | | |
|---|---|---|---|
| 12875 | **THREE-PHASE GENERATOR, ALTENATOR** | GENERATRICE A COURANT TRIPHASE | DREIPHASENDYNAMO, DREHSTROMDYNAMO, DREHSTROMMASCHINE |
| 12876 | **THREE-PHASE MOTOR** | MOTEUR TRIPHASE, MOTEUR A CHAMP TOURNANT | DREHSTROMMOTOR, DREIPHASENMOTOR |
| 12877 | **THREE-PHASE, TRIPHASE CURRENT** | COURANT TRIPHASE | DREIPHASENSTROM, DREHSTROM |
| 12878 | **THREE-PLY BELT** | COURROIE TRIPLE | RIEMEN (DREIFACHER) |
| 12879 | **THREE-THREADED, TREBLE-THREADED SCREW** | VIS A TROIS FILETS | SCHRAUBE (DREIGÄNGIE) |
| 12880 | **THREE-THROW CRANK SHAFT** | VILEBREQUIN A TROIS COUDES | WELLE (DREIKURBELIGE), KURBELWELLE (DREIFACH GEKRÖPFTE) |
| 12881 | **THREE-WAY COCK** | ROBINET A TROIS VOIES | DREIWEGHAHN |
| 12882 | **THREE-WAY VALVE** | SOUPAPE A TROIS VOIES, ROBINET A TROIS VOIES | DREIWEGEVENTIL, WECHSELVENTIL, UMSTELLVENTIL |
| 12883 | **THREE-WIRE METHOD** | METHODE DITE A TROIS FILS | DREIFADENMETHODE |
| 12884 | **THRESHING MACHINES** | BATTEUSES | DRESCHMASCHINEN |
| 12885 | **THROAT DEPTH** | EPAISSEUR DE LA SOUDURE | ELEKTRODENARMAUSLADUNG |
| 12886 | **THROAT OF FILLET WELD** | EPAISSEUR D'UNE SOUDURE EN ANGLE | KEHLNAHTDICKE |
| 12887 | **THROAT OPENING** | LARGEUR D'UNE SOUDURE | FENSTERÖFFNUNG |
| 12888 | **THROTTLE** | VOLET DE GAZ, PAPILLON | DROSSELKLAPPE |
| 12889 | **THROTTLE (TO)** | ETRANGLER | DROSSELN |
| 12890 | **THROTTLE VALVE, BUTTERFLY VALVE** | PAPILLON DE REGLAGE, REGULATEUR, VALVE A PAPILLON | DROSSELKLAPPE, REGELVENTIL |
| 12891 | **THROTTLING** | ETRANGLEMENT | DROSSELUNG, DROSSELN |
| 12892 | **THROUGH HARDENING** | DURCISSEMENT A COEUR | DURCHHÄRTUNG |
| 12893 | **THROUGH HOLE** | TROU TRAVERSANT LA PIECE | LOCH (DURCHGEHENDES) |
| 12894 | **THROW OF AN ECCENTRIC** | COURSE DE L'EXCENTRIQUE, COURSE DE LA CAME | EXZENTERHUB |
| 12895 | **THROW OFF THE BELT (TO)** | DESCENDRE LA COURROIE | ABWERFEN (DEN RIEMEN) |
| 12896 | **THROWAWAY INSERTS** | PLAQUETTES UNISERVICE | WEGWERFPLATTEN |
| 12897 | **THROWING INTO GEAR, ENGAGEMENT** | EMBRAYAGE | EINSCHALTEN, EINSCHALTUNG, EINRÜCKEN, EINRÜCKUNG, EINKUPPELN, EINKUPPLUNG |
| 12898 | **THROWING OUT OF GEAR, DISENGAGEMENT** | DEBRAYAGE, DESEMBRAYAGE, DESENGRENAGE | AUSSCHALTEN, AUSSCHALTUNG, AUSRÜCKEN, AUSRÜCKUNG, AUSKUPPELN, AUSKUPPLUNG, ENTKUPPELN, ENTKUPPLUNG |
| 12899 | **THROWING POWER** | ACTION EN PROFONDEUR | TIEFENSTREUUNG |
| 12900 | **THRUST BALL BEARING** | PALIER DE BUTEE A BILLES | AXIALKUGELLAGER |
| 12901 | **THRUST BALL BEARING, BALL THRUST BEARING** | BUTEE A BILLES, ROULEMENT A BILLES A CHARGE AXIALE | KUGELSTÜTZLAGER, KUGELSPURLAGER, STÜTZKUGELLAGER, KUGELDRUCKLAGER |
| 12902 | **THRUST BEARING** | PALIER A CHARGE AXIALE, PALIER DE BUTEE, BUTEE | LÄNGSDRUCKLAGER, DRUCKLAGER, AXIALLAGER |
| 12903 | **THRUST BLOCK, MULTIPLE COLLAR THRUST BEARING** | PALIER DE BUTEE A CANNELURES, COUSSINET A CANNELURES | KAMMLAGER, SCHEIBENLAGER, VIELRINNDRUCKLAGER |
| 12904 | **THRUST COLLAR** | COLLET, EMBASE D'UN PIVOT CANNELE, BAGUE DE BUTEE, BAGUE D'ARRET | KAMM, RING, DRUCKRING, SPURRING, SPURKRANZ EINES DRUCKLAGERS, STELLRING |
| 12905 | **THRUST DISC** | GRAIN, CULOT D'UNE CRAPAUDINE | SPURPLATTE, SPURPFANNE |
| 12906 | **THRUST JOURNAL** | TOURILLON A CANNELURES, TOURILLON DE BUTEE CANNELE | KAMMZAPFEN, SCHEIBENZAPFEN |
| 12907 | **THRUST OF THE GROUND** | POUSSEE DES TERRES | ERDDRUCK |
| 12908 | **THRUST ON CROWN OF AN ARCH** | POUSSEE AU SOMMET | SCHEITELDRUCK |
| 12909 | **THRUST SCREW** | VIS DE BUTEE | GEGENDRUCKSCHRAUBE |
| 12910 | **THULIUM** | THULIUM | THULIUM |

**THU** 330

| | | | |
|---|---|---|---|
| 12911 | THUMB NUT, FLY NUT, WING NUT | ECROU A OREILLES, ECROU PAPILLON, VIS VIOLON | FLÜGELMUTTER |
| 12912 | THUMB SCREW, WING SCREW | VIS AILEE, VIS A OREILLES | FLÜGELSCHRAUBE |
| 12913 | THYRISTOR | THYRISTOR | THYRISTOR |
| 12914 | TIE (TO), ANCHOR (TO) | ACCROCHER, ANCRER | VERANKERN |
| 12915 | TIE ROD | BARRE D'ACCOUPLEMENT | SPURSTANGE |
| 12916 | TIE-BAR | BARRE D'ACCOUPLEMENT | SPURSTANGE |
| 12917 | TIE, TIE ROD | TIRANT | ZUGSTANGE, ZUGANKER |
| 12918 | TIEING, ANCHORING | ACCROCHAGE, ANCRAGE | VERANKERUNG, VERANKERN |
| 12919 | TIES OF BRACES | HAUBANS DE SPHERE | ANKERZUGSTANGE, ANKERZUGSEILE |
| 12920 | TIGHT | ETANCHE | DICHT, DICHTHALTEND, DICHTSCHLIESSEND |
| 12921 | TIGHT JOINT | JOINT ETANCHE | FUGE (DICHTE) |
| 12922 | TIGHT JOINT RIVETING, RIVETING FOR TIGHT JOINTS | RIVET D'ETANCHEITE | HEFTNIETUNG, VERSCHLUSSNIETUNG, DICHTUNGSNIETUNG |
| 12923 | TIGHT ROPE | CORDE TENDUE | SEIL (GESPANNTES) |
| 12924 | TIGHTEN A KEY (TO) | SERRER UN COIN | ANZIEHEN (EINEN KEIL) |
| 12925 | TIGHTEN A SCREW NUT (TO) | SERRER UN ECROU, SERRER UNE VIS | ANZIEHEN (EINE SCHRAUBE) |
| 12926 | TIGHTEN THE STUFFING BOX (TO), SCREW DOWN THE GLAND (TO) | SERRER LA BOITE A ETOUPE | ANZIEHEN (DIE STOPFB:UCHSE) |
| 12927 | TIGHTEN UP (TO), PULL UP A SCREW (TO) | SERRER A BLOC UN ECROU, SERRER A FOND UN ECROU | FEST ANZIEHEN (EINE SCHRAUBE), SCHARF ANZIEHEN (EINE SCHRAUBE) |
| 12928 | TIGHTENING A KEY | SERRAGE D'UN COIN | ANZUG EINES KEILES, ANZIEHEN EINES KEILES |
| 12929 | TIGHTENING BY KEYS | SERRAGE PAR COIN | KEILVERSPANNUNG |
| 12930 | TIGHTENING BY SCREW BOLTS | SERRAGE PAR ECROUS | SCHRAUBENVERSPANNUNG |
| 12931 | TIGHTENING TORQUE | COUPLE DE SERRAGE | ANZUGSDREHMOMENT |
| 12932 | TIGHTNESS | ETANCHEITE | DICHTIGKEIT, DICHTHALTEN |
| 12933 | TILE, PAVING TILE, FLOOR TILE, WALL TILE | CARREAU (CONSTR.) | FLIESE |
| 12934 | TILE, ROOFING TILE | TUILE | ZIEGEL, DACHZIEGEL |
| 12935 | TILTING LADLE | POCHE DE COULEE A RENVERSEMENT | KIPPFANNE |
| 12936 | TILTING MOMENT | MOMENT BASCULANT | KIPPMOMENT |
| 12937 | TIMBER | BOIS DE CONSTRUCTION, BOIS DE CHARPENTE | WERKHOLZ, NUTZHOLZ, BAUHOLZ |
| 12938 | TIMBER CUT LONGITUDINALLY THROUGH THE MEDULLARY RAYS | BOIS DE MAILLE | SPIEGELHOLZ |
| 12939 | TIMBER CUT WITH THE GRAIN | BOIS DE FIL | LANGHOLZ, LÄNGENHOLZ |
| 12940 | TIMBER FREE FROM KNOTS | BOIS SANS NOEUDS | HOLZ (ASTFREIES) |
| 12941 | TIMBER SLEEPER | TRAVERSE EN BOIS | HOLZSCHWELLE |
| 12942 | TIMBER WORK | CHARPENTE, CONSTRUCTION EN BOIS | HOLZBAU, HOLZKONSTRUKTION |
| 12943 | TIME | TEMPS | ZEIT |
| 12944 | TIME CONSTANT | CONSTANTE DE TEMPS | ZEITKONSTANTE |
| 12945 | TIME OF SWING | DUREE D'UNE OSCILLATION | SCHWINGUNGSDAUER |
| 12946 | TIME RECORDER | COMPTE-SECONDES, COMPTEUR A POINTAGES, HORLOGE POINCONNEUSE | STECHUHR |
| 12947 | TIMING CASE | CARTER DE DISTRIBUTION | STEUERGEHÄUSE |
| 12948 | TIMING CHAIN | CHAINE DE DISTRIBUTION | STEUERKETTE |
| 12949 | TIMING GEAR | PIGNON DE DISTRIBUTION | VENTILSTEUERUNGS-ZAHNRAD |
| 12950 | TIMING GEAR CHAIN | CHAINE DE DISTRIBUTION | STEUERKETTE |

| | | | |
|---|---|---|---|
| 12951 | TIMING MARKS | REPERES DE CALAGE | EINSTELLUNGSANGELPUNKTE |
| 12952 | TIMING SETTING | CALAGE DE LA DISTRIBUTION | STEUERUNGSEINSTELLUNG |
| 12953 | TIN | ETAIN | ZINN |
| 12954 | TIN (TO) | ETAMER | VERZINNEN |
| 12955 | TIN FOIL | FEUILLE D'ETAIN, PAILLON D'ETAIN | BLATTZINN, ZINNFOLIE, STANNIOL |
| 12956 | TIN ORE | MINERAI D'ETAIN | ZINNERZ |
| 12957 | TIN PLATE | FER-BLANC, TOLE ETAMEE | WEISSBLECH |
| 12958 | TIN SOLDER | SOUDAGE TENDRE | WEICHLÖTEN |
| 12959 | TIN STONE, CASSITERITE | CASSITERITE | ZINNSTEIN, KASSITERIT |
| 12960 | TIN TUBE | TUYAU EN ETAIN | ZINNROHR |
| 12961 | TIN, CAN | BIDON (POUR HUILE, ESSENCE, ECT.) | KANISTER, BLECHKANNE |
| 12962 | TINNED WIRE | FIL ETAME, FIL GALVANISE | DRAHT (VERZINNTER) |
| 12963 | TINNING | ETAMAGE | VERZINNUNG, VERZINNEN |
| 12964 | TINSMITH, WHITESMITH | FERBLANTIER | KLEMPNER, SPENGLER |
| 12965 | TINTED DRAWING, WASH DRAWING, DRAWING WITH COLOURS WASHED IN | DESSIN LAVE, LAVIS | ZEICHNUNG (GETUSCHTE), TUSCHZEICHNUNG |
| 12966 | TIP OF A NOZZLE | BUSE, EMBOUCHURE | DÜSE, MUNDSTÜCK |
| 12967 | TIPPING LORRY | VEHICULE A BENNE BASCULANTE | KIPPER |
| 12968 | TIRATION | TITRAGE | TITRIEREN, TITRIERUNG, TITRATION |
| 12969 | TISSUE PAPER | PAPIER PELURE, PAPIER JOSEPH, PAPIER DE SOIE | SEIDENPAPIER |
| 12970 | TITANIUM | TITANE | TITAN |
| 12971 | TITANIUM DIOXIDE | ANHYDRIDE TITANIQUE | TITANDIOXYD, TITANSÄUREANHYDRID |
| 12972 | TITANIUM STEEL | ACIER AU TITANE | TITANSTAHL |
| 12973 | TITRATE (TO) | TITRER | TITRIEREN |
| 12974 | TITRATION | TITRAGE | TITRIERUNG |
| 12975 | TOE-IN | PINCEMENT | VORSPUR |
| 12976 | TOE-OUT | OUVERTURE | VORSPUR (NEGATIVE) |
| 12977 | TOE-PLATE | ARRETE-PIEDS | FUSSLEISTE |
| 12978 | TOGGLE BRAKE | FREIN A GENOUILLERE | KNIEHEBELBREMSE |
| 12979 | TOGGLE JOINT, MECHANISM | LEVIER A GENOUILLERE, GENOUILLERE, LEVIER ARTICULE | KNIEHEBEL, KNIEHEBELVERBINDUNG |
| 12980 | TOGGLE LEVER PRESS | PRESSE A GENOUILLERES | KNIEHEBELPRESSE |
| 12981 | TOGGLES | SERRE-BARRES | STANGEN-SPANNZANGEN |
| 12982 | TOLERANCE | TOLERANCE | TOLERANZ |
| 12983 | TOLUENE, TOLUOL | TOLUENE, METHYLBENZENE, TOLUOL, HYDRURE DE BENZYLE, HYDRURE DE CRESYLE, | TOLUOL, METHYLBENZOL, BENZYLWASSERSTOFF |
| 12984 | TOMBAC, RED BRASS | TOMBAC | ROTGUSS, ROTMESSING, ROTMETALL, TOMBAK, MASCHINENBRONZE |
| 12985 | TOMMY | BROCHE, LEVIER DE VIS | SCHRAUBENHEBEL |
| 12986 | TON (METRIC) | TONNE (1000 KG) | TONNE (1000 KG) |
| 12987 | TONGS, PLIERS, PLYERS, PINCERS, NIPPERS | TENAILLE (S), PINCES (S) | ZANGE |
| 12988 | TONGUE (TO) | RAINER ET LANGUETTER, BOUVETER | SPUNDEN, NUT UND FEDER VERSEHEN (MIT) |
| 12989 | TONGUE AND GROOVE | LANGUETTE ET RAINURE | FEDER UND NUT, SPUND |
| 12990 | TONGUE-GROOVE FACING | EMBOITEMENT DOUBLE (M ET F) | FEDER UND NUT |
| 12991 | TONGUING | ASSEMBLAGE PAR RAINURE ET LANGUETTE, BOUVETAGE | SPUNDEN |

# TON                                          332

| 12992 | TONGUING AND GROOVING MACHINE | MACHINE A BOUVETER, MACHINE A FAIRE LES RAINURES ET LANGUETTES | SPUNDMASCHINE |
|---|---|---|---|
| 12993 | TONGUING PLANE | BOUVET MALE | FEDERHOBEL |
| 12994 | TOOL | OUTIL | WERKZEUG |
| 12995 | TOOL ANGLE | ANGLE DE L'OUTIL, ANGLE TAILLANT, TRANCHANT, ANGLE DE COIN, ANGLE D'AFFUTAGE | ZUSCHÄRFUNGSWINKEL, MEISSELWINKEL |
| 12996 | TOOL BAG | SAC A OUTILS | WERKZEUGTASCHE |
| 12997 | TOOL BOX | BOITE A OUTILS | WERKZEUGKOFFER |
| 12998 | TOOL CABINET | ARMOIRE A OUTILS | WERKZEUGSCHRANK |
| 12999 | TOOL CHANGE TIME | TEMPS DE CHANGEMENT D'OUTIL | WERKZEUGWECHSELZEIT |
| 13000 | TOOL CHANGER | CHANGEUR D'OUTILS | WERKZEUGWECHSELVORRICHTUNG |
| 13001 | TOOL FUNCTION | FONCTION OUTIL | WERKZEUGBEFEHL |
| 13002 | TOOL GRINDER, TOOL GRINDING MACHINE | MACHINE A AFFUTER LES OUTILS, AFFUTEUSE | WERKZEUGSCHLEIFMASCHINE, SCHÄRFMASCHINE |
| 13003 | TOOL HEAD | PORTE-OUTIL | STÖSSELKOPFSTAHLHALTER |
| 13004 | TOOL HOLDER TURRETS | TOURELLES PORTE-OUTILS | STAHLHALTER-REVOLVERKÖPFE |
| 13005 | TOOL HOLDERS | PORTE-OUTILS | STAHLHALTER |
| 13006 | TOOL MAKING | FABRICATION D'OUTILS A TAILLANTS, TAILLANDERIE | WERKZEUGFABRIKATION |
| 13007 | TOOL OFFSET | CORRECTION DE POSITION D'OUTIL | WERKZEUGVERSATZ |
| 13008 | TOOL SMITH | OUVRIER TREMPEUR, TREMPEUR D'OUTILLAGE | ZEUGSCHMIED, WERKZEUGSCHLOSSER |
| 13009 | TOOL STEEL | ACIER A OUTILS | WERKZEUGSTAHL |
| 13010 | TOOL-POST | MONTANT PORTE-OUTIL | STAHLHALTER |
| 13011 | TOOL, CUTTER | OUTIL COUPANT (D'UNE MACHINE OUTIL) | STAHL, SCHNEIDSTAHL, STICHEL |
| 13012 | TOOLBARS | PORTE OUTILS | ACKERSCHIENEN |
| 13013 | TOOLING CLAMPS | BRIDES D'USINAGE | BEARBEITUNGSFLANSCHE |
| 13014 | TOOLMAKERS'S HAMMER | MARTEAU D'OUTILLEUR | WERKZEUGBAUHAMMER |
| 13015 | TOOLS | OUTILLAGE | HANDWERKSZEUG, WERKZEUGAUSRÜSTUNG |
| 13016 | TOOTH | DENT | ZAHN |
| 13017 | TOOTH DEPTH | HAUTEUR DE DENT | ZAHNHÖHE |
| 13018 | TOOTH FLANK | FLANC DE DENT | ZAHNFLANKE |
| 13019 | TOOTH PROFILE, OUTLINE OF TOOTH | PROFIL D'UNE DENT | ZAHNFORM, ZAHNPROFIL |
| 13020 | TOOTH SHAPE | PROFIL DE DENTURE | ZAHNPROFIL |
| 13021 | TOOTHED GEARING, WHEEL GEARING | ENGRENAGE | RÄDERGETRIEBE, ZAHNRADGETRIEBE, ZAHNTRIEB |
| 13022 | TOOTHED RACK | CREMAILLERE | ZAHNSTANGE |
| 13023 | TOOTHED RIM | COURONNE DENTEE | ZAHNKRANZ |
| 13024 | TOOTHED SEGMENT, TOOTHED SECTOR | SECTEUR DENTE | ZAHNBOGEN, ZAHNSEKTOR, VERZAHNTER SEKTOR, GEZAHNTER SEKTOR |
| 13025 | TOOTHED WHEEL DRIVE, GEAR WHEEL DRIVE | COMMANDE PAR ENGRENAGES, PAR ROUE DENTEE | RÄDERANTRIEB, ZAHNRADANTRIEB |
| 13026 | TOOTHING | DENTURE | VERZAHNUNG |
| 13027 | TOOTHING PLANE | RABOT DENTE A DENTS | ZAHNHOBEL |
| 13028 | TOP ANGLE , CURB ANGLE | CORNIERE DE TETE(D'UN RESERVOIR) | OBERWINKELEISEN |
| 13029 | TOP BOLTING BAR | PLAT DE MAINTIEN | BEFESTIGUNSFLACHEISEN |
| 13030 | TOP BRASS | DEMI-COUSSINET SUPERIEUR, COQUILLE SUPERIEURE, CONTRE-COUSSINET | LAGERSCHALE (OBERE), OBERSCHALE |
| 13031 | TOP CASTING | COULEE DIRECTE | FALLENDGIESSEN |

| | | | |
|---|---|---|---|
| 13032 | **TOP DEAD CENTER** | POINT MORT HAUT (P.M.H) | TOTPUNKT (OBERER) |
| 13033 | **TOP IRON, BACK IRON, NON-CUTTING IRON OF A PLANE** | CONTRE-FER | DECKPLATTE, DECKEL, KAPPE EINES HOBELEISENS |
| 13034 | **TOP PISTON-RING** | SEGMENT DE FEU | KOMPRESSIONSRING (OBERER) |
| 13035 | **TOP RAIL** | LISSE | HANDLEISTE, HANDLAUF |
| 13036 | **TOP SWAGE** | ETAMPE, MATRICE DE DESSUS | OBERGESENK |
| 13037 | **TOP VIEW, PLAN** | VUE DE HAUT EN BAS | AUFSICHTSBILD, DRAUFSICHTSBILD |
| 13038 | **TOPAZ** | TOPAZE | TOPAS |
| 13039 | **TOPOCHEMISTRY** | TOPOCHIMIE | TOPOCHEMIE |
| 13040 | **TOPPED CRUDE** | PETROLE BRUT TOPPE | TOPPRÜCKSTAND |
| 13041 | **TOPPING FILE** | LIME OLIVE | FEILE MIT ZWEI RUNDEN KANTEN |
| 13042 | **TORCH** | TORCHE, CHALUMEAU | BRENNER, FACKEL |
| 13043 | **TORE, TORUS, ANCHOR RING** | TORE | RINGKÖRPER, (GEOM.) |
| 13044 | **TORICONICAL HEAD** | FOND TORICONIQUE | KEGELSENKKOPF |
| 13045 | **TORISPHERICAL HEAD** | FOND EN ANSE DE PANIER | KORBBOGENBODEN, BODEN (FLACHGEWÖLBTER) |
| 13046 | **TORISPHERICAL ROOF** | TOIT SURBAISSE | DACH (FLACHEWÖLBTES) |
| 13047 | **TORISPHERICAL ROOF TANK** | RESERVOIR A TOIT SURBAISSE | TIEFBEHÄLTER |
| 13048 | **TORQUE** | COUPLE MOTEUR, COUPLE | DREHMOMENT |
| 13049 | **TORQUE WRENCH** | CLE, BRAS DYNAMOMETRIQUE | DREHMOMENTSCHRAUBENSCHLÜSSEL |
| 13050 | **TORQUEMETER** | COUPLE METRE | DREHMOMENTMESSER |
| 13051 | **TORSION** | TORSION | TORSION |
| 13052 | **TORSION BALANCE** | BALANCE DE TORSION | VERDREHUNGSWAAGE, TORSIONSWAAGE |
| 13053 | **TORSION BAR** | BARRE DE TORSION | DREHSTAB |
| 13054 | **TORSION, TWISTING, TWIST** | TORSION | DREHUNG, VERDREHUNG, VERDRILLUNG, TORSION |
| 13055 | **TORSIONAL FORCE** | FORCE DE TORSION | TORSIONSKRAFT |
| 13056 | **TORSIONAL STRAIN** | EFFORT DE TORSION, TRAVAIL A LA TORSION | TORSION, DREHBEANSPRUCHUNG, VERDREHUNGSBEANSPRUCHUNG, TORSONSBEANSPRUCHUNG |
| 13057 | **TORSIONAL STRENGTH** | RESISTANCE A LA TORSION | VERDREHUNGSFESTIGKEIT, DREHUNGSFESTIGKEIT, TORSIONSFESTIGKEIT |
| 13058 | **TORSIONAL STRESS** | EFFORT DE TORSION PAR UNITE DE SECTION | DREHSPANNUNG, TORSIONSSPANNUNG |
| 13059 | **TORSIONAL TEST** | ESSAI A LA TORSION | VERDREHUNGSVERSUCH |
| 13060 | **TOTAL INTERNAL REFLEXION** | REFLEXION TOTALE | REFLEXION (TOTALE) |
| 13061 | **TOTAL LIFT OF A PUMP** | HAUTEUR D'ELEVATION D'UNE POMPE | FÖRDERHÖHE EINER PUMPE |
| 13062 | **TOTAL LOAD** | CHARGE TOTALE | GESAMTBELASTUNG |
| 13063 | **TOTAL LOST MOTION** | JEU TOTAL PERDU | GESAMTTOTGANG |
| 13064 | **TOTAL OUTPUT** | DEBIT TOTAL | GESAMTLEISTUNG |
| 13065 | **TOTAL PRESSURE** | PRESSION TOTALE | GESAMTDRUCK |
| 13066 | **TOUCH (TO)** | TOUCHER (GEOM.) | BERÜHREN (GEOM.) |
| 13067 | **TOUGH** | TENACE | ZÄH |
| 13068 | **TOUGH IRON** | FER TENACE | ZÄHES EISEN |
| 13069 | **TOUGH PITCH COPPER** | CUIVRE A OXYDE CUIVREUX | KUPFER (CUPRIOXYD-ENTHALTENDES) |
| 13070 | **TOUGH PITCH COPPER, REFINED COPPER** | CUIVRE AFFINE | KUPFER (HAMMERGARE), KUPFER (RAFFINIERTES) RAFFINADEKUPFER |
| 13071 | **TOUGHNESS** | TENACITE, RESILIENCE | RESILIENZ, ZÄHIGKEIT |
| 13072 | **TOURMALINE** | TOURMALINE | TURMALIN |
| 13073 | **TOW, OAKUM** | ETOUPE | WERG |
| 13074 | **TOWN REFUSE** | ORDURES | MÜLL |

**TRA** 334

| | | | |
|---|---|---|---|
| 13075 | **TOWN WATER** | EAU DE DISTRIBUTION | LEITUNGSWASSER |
| 13076 | **TRACE** | TRACE | SPUR |
| 13077 | **TRACE (TO)** | CALQUER | PAUSEN, DURCHPAUSEN |
| 13078 | **TRACER** | CALQUEUR | PAUSER |
| 13079 | **TRACER OF PLANIMETER** | POINTE TRACANTE DU PLANIMETRE | FAHRSTIFT DES PLANIMETERS |
| 13080 | **TRACER-CONTROLLED MILLING MACHINES** | FRAISEUSE A COMMANDE PAR DISPOSITIF DE COPIAGE | FRÄSMASCHINE (FÜHLERGESTEUERTE) |
| 13081 | **TRACHYTE** | TRACHYTE | TRACHYT |
| 13082 | **TRACING** | CALQUAGE, DECALQUE, CALQUE | PAUSEN, DURCHPAUSEN, PAUSE |
| 13083 | **TRACING CLOTH** | TOILE A CALQUER | PAUSLEINWAND, ZEICHENLEINWAND |
| 13084 | **TRACING PAPER** | PAPIER CALQUE, PAPIER TRANSPARENT | PAUSPAPIER |
| 13085 | **TRACK, TRACKING WIDTH** | VOIE, PISTE, GORGE DE ROULEMENT | SPUR, SPURWEITE, LAUFRILLE |
| 13086 | **TRACKING CHECK** | VERIFICATION DU PARALLELISME | RADAUSFLUCHTUNGSKONTROLLE |
| 13087 | **TRACKING CONTROL** | GUIDE DE CENTRAGE | ZENTRIERFÜHRUNG |
| 13088 | **TRACTION** | TRACTION DES VEHICULES | ZUGFÖRDERUNG, TRAKTION |
| 13089 | **TRACTIVE EFFORT, FORCE** | EFFORT DE TRACTION | ZUGKRAFT (EINES TRAKTORS) |
| 13090 | **TRACTIVE, PORTATIVE FORCE OF A MAGNET, TRACTIVE LIFTING POWER OF A MAGNET** | PUISSANCE DE LEVAGE D'UN AIMANT | TRAGKRAFT, ZUGKRAFT EINES MAGNETEN |
| 13091 | **TRACTOR** | TRACTEUR | ZUGMASCHINE |
| 13092 | **TRACTOR AND TRAILER UNIT** | VEHICULE ARTICULE | SATTELZUG |
| 13093 | **TRACTOR HALF TRACK** | TRACTEUR AGRICOLE DEMI TRAC | HALBRAUPENSCHLEPPER |
| 13094 | **TRACTOR TRACKLAYING** | TRACTEUR AGRICOLE A CHENILLES | RAUPENSCHLEPPER |
| 13095 | **TRACTOR WHEELED** | TRACTEUR AGRICOLE A ROUES | ACKERRADSCHLEPPER |
| 13096 | **TRACTOR, HORTICULTURAL** | TRACTEUR MARAICHERS | TRAKTOREN, GÄRTNEREI- |
| 13097 | **TRACTOR, TRACTION ENGINE** | TRACTEUR | ZUGWAGEN, ZUGMASCHINE, SCHLEPPER, TRAKTOR |
| 13098 | **TRACTORY, TRACTRIX** | TRACTRICE, TRACTOIRE | SCHLEPPKURVE, TRAKTRIX |
| 13099 | **TRADE BALANCE** | BALANCE DU COMMERCE EXTERIEUR | AUSSENHANDELSBILANZ |
| 13100 | **TRADE MARK** | MARQUE DE FABRIQUE, MARQUE DE COMMERCE | FABRIKMARKE, WARENZEICHEN, SCHUTZMARKE |
| 13101 | **TRADE NAME** | NOM COMMERCIAL | HANDELSBEZEICHNUNG, HANDELSÜBLICHE BEZEICHNUNG |
| 13102 | **TRAILERS** | REMORQUES | ANHÄNGER |
| 13103 | **TRAIN OIL, WHALE OIL, BLUBBER OIL** | HUILE DE POISSON, HUILE DE BALEINE | TRAN, FISCHTRAN, FISCHÖL |
| 13104 | **TRAJECTORY** | TRAJECTOIRE | BAHN, TRAJEKTORIE |
| 13105 | **TRAMMELS** | COMPAS A VERGE | STANGENZIRKEL |
| 13106 | **TRAMP IRON** | FER DANS LE BROYEUR | EISEN IM BRECHGUT |
| 13107 | **TRANSCENDENTAL EQUATION** | EQUATION TRANSCENDANTE | GLEICHUNG (TRANSZENDENTE) |
| 13108 | **TRANSDUCER** | TRANSDUCTEUR, CAPTEUR | TRANSDUCER, TRANSDUKTOR |
| 13109 | **TRANSFER** | DECALCOMANIE | ABZIEHBILD |
| 13110 | **TRANSFER LADLE** | POCHE-TONNEAU | TRANSPORTPFANNE |
| 13111 | **TRANSFERENCE, TRANSMISSION OF HEAT** | TRANSMISSION DE LA CHALEUR | WÄRMEÜBERTRAGUNG |
| 13112 | **TRANSFORM (TO), CONVERT ERNERGY (TO)** | TRANSFORMER L'ENERGIE | ENERGIE UMWANDELN |
| 13113 | **TRANSFORMATION RANGE** | DOMAINE DE TRANSFORMATION | UMWANDLUNGSBEREICH |
| 13114 | **TRANSFORMATION TEMPERATURE** | TEMPERATURE DE TRANSFORMATION | UMWANDLUNGSTEMPERATUR |

| | | |
|---|---|---|
| 13115 | **TRANSFORMER** | TRANSFORMATEUR, TRANSFORMATEUR DE POTENTIEL | UMWANDLER, UMSPANNER, TRANSFORMATOR |
| 13116 | **TRANSFORMER PLATE** | TOLE POUR TRANSFORMATEURS | TRANSFORMATORBLECH |
| 13117 | **TRANSGRANULAR FRACTURE** | CASSURE TRANSCRISTALLINE | BRUCH (TRANSKRISTALLINER) |
| 13118 | **TRANSIENT CREEP** | FLUAGE TRANSITOIRE | VORLÄUFIGES FLIESSEN |
| 13119 | **TRANSISTOR** | TRANSISTOR | TRANSISTOR |
| 13120 | **TRANSITION LATTICE** | RESEAU DE TRANSLATION | TRANSLATIONSGITTER |
| 13121 | **TRANSITION PART** | ELEMENT OU PARTIE TRONCONIQUE, REDUCTION | REDUZIERANSCHLUSS |
| 13122 | **TRANSITION POINT** | POINT DE TRANSITION | ÜBERGANGSPUNKT |
| 13123 | **TRANSLATION** | DEPLACEMENT, TRANSLATION, TRADUCTION | PARALLELVERSCHIEBUNG, UMSETZUNG, ÜBERSETZUNG, TRANSLATION |
| 13124 | **TRANSLUCENCE** | TRANSLUCIDITE | TRANSPARENZ |
| 13125 | **TRANSLUCENT** | TRANSLUCIDE | DURCHSCHEINEND, TRANSPARENT |
| 13126 | **TRANSMISSION COMPONENTS** | ORGANES DE TRANSMISSION | ANTRIEBSELEMENTE |
| 13127 | **TRANSMISSION DYNAMOMETER** | DYNAMOMETRE DE TRANSMISSION | TRANSMISSIONSDYNAMOMETER |
| 13128 | **TRANSMISSION GEAR WHEEL** | ENGRENAGE DE TRANSMISSION | ARBEITSRAD, TRIEBWERKSRAD |
| 13129 | **TRANSMISSION OF ELECTRICAL ENERGY** | TRANSMISSION D'ENERGIE ELECTRIQUE | KRAFTÜBERTRAGUNG (ELEKTRISCHE) |
| 13130 | **TRANSMISSION OF MOTION** | TRANSMISSION D'UN MOUVEMENT | ÜBERTRAGUNG EINER BEWEGUNG, BEWEGUNGSÜBERTRAGUNG |
| 13131 | **TRANSMISSION OF POWER BY GEARING** | TRANSMISSION PAR ENGRENAGE | RÄDERÜBERSETZUNG, KRAFTÜBERTRAGUNG DURCH RÄDER |
| 13132 | **TRANSMISSION OF POWER BY LEVERS** | TRANSMISSION PAR LEVIER | HEBELÜBERSETZUNG, KRAFTÜBERTRAGUNG DURCH HEBEL |
| 13133 | **TRANSMISSION OF POWER ELECTRICALLY OVER LONG DISTANCES,** | TRANSMISSION D'ELECTRICITE, TRANSPORT D'ENERGIE ELECTRIQUE A GRANDE DISTANCE | FERNKRAFTÜBERTRAGUNG (ELEKTRISCHE), FERNÜBERTRAGUNG VON ELEKTRISCHER ENERGIE, ÜBERTRAGUNG VON ELEKTRISCHER ENERGIE |
| 13134 | **TRANSMISSION OF POWER, POWER TRANSMISSION** | TRANSPORT DE L'ENERGIE, TRANSMISSION DE PUISSANCE | KRAFTÜBERTRAGUNG, ENERGIETRANSPORT |
| 13135 | **TRANSMISSION, CONVEYANCE OF ENERGY OVER LONG DISTANCES** | TRANSPORT D'ENERGIE A GRANDE DISTANCE, DISTRIBUTION A DISTANCE DE L'ENERGIE | FERNLEITUNG VON ENERGIE |
| 13136 | **TRANSMUTATION OF ELEMENTS** | TRANSMUTATION (CHIM.) | UMWANDLUNG, ELEMENTUMWANDLUNG |
| 13137 | **TRANSPARENCY** | TRANSPARENCE | DURCHSICHTIGKEIT |
| 13138 | **TRANSPARENT** | TRANSPARENT | DURCHSICHTIG |
| 13139 | **TRANSPARENT MEDIUM** | MILIEU TRANSPARENT | MEDIUM (DURCHSICHTIGES) |
| 13140 | **TRANSPORTATION, TRANSPORT** | TRANSPORT | BEFÖRDERUNG, VERSAND, TRANSPORT |
| 13141 | **TRANSPORTER** | PONT TRANSBORDEUR, TRANSBORDEUR | BRÜCKENKRAN, VERLADEBRÜCKE |
| 13142 | **TRANSVERSE AXIS** | AXE TRANSVERSAL | QUERACHSE |
| 13143 | **TRANSVERSE AXIS OF HYPERBOLA** | AXE FOCAL, AXE TRANSVERSE D'UNE HYPERBOLE | HAUPTACHSE DER HYPERBEL |
| 13144 | **TRANSVERSE ELASTICITY** | ELASTICITE DE CISAILLEMENT, ELASTICITE TRANSVERSALE | SCHUBELASTIZITÄT |
| 13145 | **TRANSVERSE PITCH OF RIVETS** | RIVETS (DISTANCE DES) DE CENTRE A CENTRE D'UNE LIGNE A L'AUTRE | QUERNIETTEILUNG |
| 13146 | **TRANSVERSE VIBRATION** | VIBRATION, OSCILLATION TRANSVERSALE | QUERSCHWINGUNG |
| 13147 | **TRANSVERSELY RIBBED TUBE, TUBE RIBBED IN ITS TRANSVERSE SECTION** | TUBE A NERVURES TRANSVERSALES | RIPPENROHR MIT QUERRIPPEN |
| 13148 | **TRAPEZIUM** | TRAPEZE | TRAPEZ |

**TRA** 336

| | | | |
|---|---|---|---|
| 13149 | **TRAPEZOID** | TRAPEZOIDE | TRAPEZOID |
| 13150 | **TRAPEZOIDAL LOAD** | CHARGE TRAPEZOIDALE | TRAPEZLAST |
| 13151 | **TRAPEZOIDAL PLATE SPRING** | RESSORT TRAPEZOIDAL | TRAPEZFEDER |
| 13152 | **TRASS** | TRASS | TRASS |
| 13153 | **TRAVEL INDICATOR** | INDICATEUR D'OUVERTURE | ANZEIGEVORRICHTUNG, ZEIGER |
| 13154 | **TRAVEL OF THE VALVE** | JEU D'UNE SOUPAPE | VENTILSPIEL |
| 13155 | **TRAVELLING CRAB** | CHARIOT D'UN PONT-ROULANT, CHARIOT PORTE-PALAN | LAUFKATZE |
| 13156 | **TRAVELLING CRANE** | PONT ROULANT | LAUFKRAN |
| 13157 | **TRAVELLING CRANE BEAM** | POUTRE DE PONT ROULANT | LAUFKRANTRÄGER |
| 13158 | **TRAVELLING MOTION** | TRANSLATION | FAHRBEWEGUNG |
| 13159 | **TRAVELLING NUT** | ECROU MOBILE | WANDERMUTTER |
| 13160 | **TRAVELLING POISE** | CURSEUR D'UNE BALANCE | LAUFGEWICHT, LÄUFER EINER WAAGE |
| 13161 | **TRAVELLING PORTABLE CRANE** | GRUE MOBILE, GRUE ROULANTE | FAHRBARER KRAN |
| 13162 | **TRAVERSE (TO)** | CYLINDRER, CHARIOTER UNE SURFACE CYLINDRIQUE | ABDREHEN, LANGDREHEN, PARALLELDREHEN, EGALISIEREN |
| 13163 | **TRAVERSE HANDWHEEL** | VOLANT DE CHARIOTAGE | SCHLITTENKREUZBEWEGUNGS-HANDRAD |
| 13164 | **TRAVERSING** | CYLINDRAGE, CHARIOTAGE D'UNE SURFACE CYLINDRIQUE, CHARIOTAGE LONGITUDINAL | ABDREHEN, LANGDREHEN, PARALLELDREHEN, EGALISIEREN |
| 13165 | **TRAVERSING SCREW JACK** | VERIN A CHARIOT | SCHLITTENWINDE |
| 13166 | **TRAVERTINE** | TRAVERTIN | TRAVERTIN |
| 13167 | **TRAY** | PLATEAU | TABLETT |
| 13168 | **TRAY MANWAY** | TRAPPE DE VISITE DE PLATEAU | TABLETTENMANNLOCH |
| 13169 | **TRAY SPACING** | ECARTEMENT DES PLATEAUX | TABLETTABSTAND |
| 13170 | **TRAY SUPPORT RING** | COURONNE-SUPPORT DE PLATEAUX | TABLETTRINGHALTER |
| 13171 | **TRAYS TOWER** | TOUR A PLATEAUX | FRAKTIONIERTURM |
| 13172 | **TREAD** | MARCHE, CHAPE, BANDE DE ROULEMENT | STUFE, REIFENLAUFFLÄCHE |
| 13173 | **TREAD OF A WHEEL** | SURFACE DE ROULEMENT D'UNE ROUE | LAUFFLÄCHE EINES RADES |
| 13174 | **TREADLE, FOOT BOARD** | PEDALE | TRITT, TRETSCHEMEL |
| 13175 | **TREATMENT FOR MAKING MALLEABLE IRON CASTINGS** | MALLEABILISATION DE LA FONTE | GLÜHFRISCHEN, TEMPERN |
| 13176 | **TREBLE HELICAL SPUR WHEEL** | ENGRENAGE A DOUBLES CHEVRONS | DOPPELWINKELZAHNRAD, DOPPELPFEILZAHNRAD |
| 13177 | **TREBLE RIVETED JOINT** | RIVURE TRIPLE A TRIPLE CLOUURE, RIVURE A TROIS RANGS | NIETUNG (DREIREIHIGE) |
| 13178 | **TREBLE SHEAR RIVETED JOINT** | RIVURE A TROIS COUPES | NIETUNG (DREISCHNITTIGE) |
| 13179 | **TREENAIL** | CHEVILLE EN BOIS | HOLZNAGEL |
| 13180 | **TRELLIS WORK** | TREILLAGE | FLECHTWERK |
| 13181 | **TREND** | ALLURE (COURBE) | LAUF, VERLAUF |
| 13182 | **TREPANNING MACHINE** | MACHINE A FORER | HOHLBOHRMASCHINE |
| 13183 | **TREPEZOIDAL CROSS SECTION** | SECTION TRAPEZOIDALE | QUERSCHNITT (TRAPEZF:ORMIGER) |
| 13184 | **TRIAL ERECTION** | MONTAGE A BLANC | VERSUCHSMONTAGE |
| 13185 | **TRIANGLE** | TRIANGLE | DREIECK (GEOM.) |
| 13186 | **TRIANGLE OF FORCES** | TRIANGLE DE FORCES | KRÄFTEDREIECK |
| 13187 | **TRIANGULAR COMPASSES** | COMPAS A TROIS BRANCHES | ZIRKEL (DREISPITZIGER), DREISCHENKELZIRKEL |
| 13188 | **TRIANGULAR CROSS SECTION** | SECTION TRIANGULAIRE | QUERSCHNITT (DREIECKIGER) |
| 13189 | **TRIANGULAR FILE, THREE-SQUARE, THREE-CORNERED FILE** | LIME TIERS-POINT, LIME TROIS-QUARTS | DREIKANTFEILE |

| | | | |
|---|---|---|---|
| 13190 | TRIANGULAR LOAD | CHARGE TRIANGULAIRE | DREIECKLAST |
| 13191 | TRIANGULAR PLATE SPRING | RESSORT TRIANGULAIRE | DREIECKFEDER |
| 13192 | TRIANGULAR PRISM | PRISME TRIANGULAIRE | PRISMA (DREISEITIGES) |
| 13193 | TRIANGULAR PYRAMID | PYRAMIDE TRIANGULAIRE | PYRAMIDE (DREISEITIGE) |
| 13194 | TRIANGULAR ROPE | CABLE A SECTION TRIANGULAIRE | DREIKANTSEIL |
| 13195 | TRIANGULAR STRAND WIRE ROPE | CABLE A TORONS TRIANGULAIRES | DREIKANTLITZENSEIL |
| 13196 | TRIANGULAR WIRE | FIL TRIANGULAIRE | DRAHT (DREIKANTIGER) |
| 13197 | TRIATOMIC, TRIVALENT | TRIATOMIQUE, TRIVALENT | DREIWERTIG, DREIATOMIG |
| 13198 | TRIBASIC | TRIBASIQUE | DREIBASISCH |
| 13199 | TRICLINIC CRYSTAL SYSTEM | SYSTEME TRICLINIQUE | KRISTALLSYSTEM (TRIKLINE) |
| 13200 | TRIGONOMETRICAL | TRIGONOMETRIQUE | TRIGONOMETRISCH |
| 13201 | TRIGONOMETRY | TRIGONOMETRIE | TRIGONOMETRIE |
| 13202 | TRIHEDRON | TRIEDRE | DREIKANT, DREIFLACH, TRIEDER |
| 13203 | TRILINEAR COORDINATES | COORDONNEES DANS L'ESPACE | RAUMKOORDINATEN |
| 13204 | TRIM (TO) | PARER, ROGNER | BESCHNEIDEN |
| 13205 | TRIM A PLATE (TO) | EBARBER UNE TOLE | BLECH (EIN) ENTGRATEN, ABGRATEN (EIN BLECH) |
| 13206 | TRIM OFF THE BURR (TO) | ENLEVER LES BAVURES, EBARBER | ABGRATEN |
| 13207 | TRIMANGANIC, TRIMANGANESE TETROXIDE | OXYDE SALIN DE MANGANESE | MANGANOXYDULOXYD, ROTES MANGANOXYD |
| 13208 | TRIMETRIC PROJECTION | PROJECTION TRIMETRIQUE | PROJEKTION (TRIMETRISCHE) |
| 13209 | TRIMMING | ACTION DE PARER, ROGNAGE, EBARBAGE | BESCHNEIDEN, ABGRATEN |
| 13210 | TRIMMING OFF THE BURR | ENLEVEMENT DES BAVURES, EBARBAGE, EBARBEMENT, EBAVURAGE | ABGRATEN |
| 13211 | TRIMMING PRESS | PRESSE A EBARBER | ABGRATPRESSE |
| 13212 | TRINIDAD ASPHALT | ASPHALTE DE TRINIDAD | TRINIDADASPHALT |
| 13213 | TRINOMIAL EQUATION | EQUATION TRINOME | GLEICHUNG (DREIGLIEDRIGE), GLEICHUNG (TRINOMISCHE) |
| 13214 | TRIP DOGS | CRABOTS ENCLENCHEURS/ DECLENCHEURS | ANSCHLAGBOLZEN |
| 13215 | TRIPLE INTEGRAL | INTEGRALE TRIPLE | INTEGRAL (DREIFACHES) |
| 13216 | TRIPLE POINT | POINT TRIPLE | TRIPELPUNKT |
| 13217 | TRIPLE-EXPANSION ENGINE | MACHINE A TRIPLE EXPANSION | DREIFACHEXPANSIONSMASCHINE |
| 13218 | TRIPOD JACK | VERIN A TREPIED | DREIFUSSWINDE |
| 13219 | TRIPOD STAND, STAND | TREPIED | STÄNDER, STATIV |
| 13220 | TRIPOLI | TRIPOLI | TRIPEL, POLIERSCHIEFER |
| 13221 | TRIPPING, JUMPING CAM | DISQUE A CAMES | DAUMENSCHEIBE, KNAGGENSCHEIBE, NOCKENSCHEIBE |
| 13222 | TRITURATE (TO) RUB TO POWDER (TO) | TRITURER | ZERREIBEN |
| 13223 | TROCHOID | TROCHOIDE | TROCHOIDE |
| 13224 | TROLLEY BEAMS | PORTIQUE DE ROULEMENT | PORTALKRAN |
| 13225 | TROLLEY BUS | TROLLEYBUS | OBUS |
| 13226 | TROMMEL, REVOLVING SCREEN | TROMMEL | TROMMELSIEB |
| 13227 | TROOSTITE | TROOSTITE | TROOSTIT |
| 13228 | TROUGH, TUB, VAT | BAC, BACHE, AUGE, CUVE | TROG, BOTTICH |
| 13229 | TRUCK CAB | CABINE DE CAMION | FÜHRERHAUS |
| 13230 | TRUCK, TRANSVEYOR, TROLLEY | CHARIOT (POUR MANUTENTION D'ATELIER ET MAGASIN) | FÖRDERKARREN, TRANSPORTKARREN |
| 13231 | TRUCKS TROLLEYS | CHARIOTS A BRAS | HANDKARREN, ROLLBÖCKE |
| 13232 | TRUE UP (TO) | DRESSER (RENDRE PLAN) | ABRICHTEN |

**TRU** 338

| | | | |
|---|---|---|---|
| 13233 | TRUEING DEVICES | APPAREILS A DIAMANTER | ABRICHTAPPARATE |
| 13234 | TRUING UP | DRESSAGE (ACTION DE RENDRE PLAN) | ABRICHTEN, RICHTEN |
| 13235 | TRUNCATED CONE | TRONC DE CONE, CONE TRONQUE | KEGEL (ABGESTUMPFTER), KEGELSTUMPF |
| 13236 | TRUNCATED CONICAL SPRING | RESSORT TRONCONIQUE | KEGELSTUMPFFEDER |
| 13237 | TRUNCATED PARALLELIPIPED | TRONC DE PARALLELEPIPEDE | PARALLELEPIPED (ABGESTUMPFTES) |
| 13238 | TRUNCATED PYRAMID | TRONC DE PYRAMIDE | PYRAMIDE (ABGESTUMPFTE), PYRAMIDENSTUMPF |
| 13239 | TRUNK (U.S.) | COFFRE, MALLE | KOFFERRAUM |
| 13240 | TRUNK LID | COUVERCLE DU COFFRE | KOFFERRAUMDECKEL |
| 13241 | TRUNK PISTON | PISTON SANS TIGE | TRUNKKOLBEN |
| 13242 | TRUNNION | TOURILLON SERVANT D'AXE DE ROTATION, ARTICULATION | DREHZAPFEN, SCHWENKZAPFEN |
| 13243 | TRUSSES | FERMES, ARMATURE, TRAVERSE | TRAGBALKEN |
| 13244 | TRUSSES FRAME | CHARPENTE A FERMES | BUNDGESPÄRRE |
| 13245 | TRY SQUARE | EQUERRE A EPAULEMENT A CHAPEAU | ANSCHLAGWINKEL |
| 13246 | TUBE (TYRE) | CHAMBRE A AIR | REIFENSCHLAUCH |
| 13247 | TUBE CLEANER, SCRAPER | BROSSE RACLETTE POUR TUBES | ROHRREINIGER |
| 13248 | TUBE CUTTER, PIPE CUTTER | COUPE-TUBE | ROHRABSCHNEIDER |
| 13249 | TUBE DRAWING | ETIRAGE DES TUBES | ZIEHEN VON ROHREN |
| 13250 | TUBE EXPANDER | MANDRIN A ELARGIR LES TUBES | ROHRAUFWEITEDORN |
| 13251 | TUBE IGNITION | ALLUMAGE PAR INCANDESCENCE | GLÜHROHRZÜNDUNG |
| 13252 | TUBE MILL | TUBE BROYEUR | ROHRMÜHLE |
| 13253 | TUBE OF FORCE | TUBE DE FORCE | KRAFTRÖHRE |
| 13254 | TUBE PLATE | PLAQUE TUBULAIRE | ROHRPLATTE |
| 13255 | TUBE STEM OF A THERMOMETER | TUBE CAPILLAIRE, TIGE DU THERMOMETRE | THERMOMETERRÖHRE |
| 13256 | TUBE VICE, PIPE VICE | ETAU A TUBES, ETAU DE TUYAUTEUR | ROHRSCHRAUBSTOCK |
| 13257 | TUBE, PIPE | TUYAU, TUBE | ROHR, RÖHRE |
| 13258 | TUBULAR BRACING | RENFORCEMENT EN TUBES, ENTRETOISAGE EN TUBES | VERSTEIFUNGSROHR |
| 13259 | TUBULAR SPIRIT LEVEL | NIVEAU A BULLE D'AIR | LIBELLE, RÖHRENLIBELLE, WASSERWAAGE, NIVEAU |
| 13260 | TUFA, TUFF | TUF | TUFF |
| 13261 | TUMBLING BARREL | TAMBOUR DE NETTOTAGE, TONNEAU DE NETTOYAGE, TONNEAU DE FINISSAGE | REINIGUNGSTROMMEL, PUTZTROMMEL |
| 13262 | TUNGSTEN | TUNGSTENE | WOLFRAM |
| 13263 | TUNGSTEN BRONZE | BRONZE AU TUNGSTENE | WOLFRAMBRONZE |
| 13264 | TUNGSTEN FILAMENT LAMP | LAMPE A FILAMENT DE TUNGSTENE | WOLFRAMDRAHTLAMPE |
| 13265 | TUNGSTEN STEEL | ACIER AU TUNGSTENE | WOLFRAMSTAHL |
| 13266 | TUNGSTEN TRIOXIDE | ANHYDRIDE TUNGSTIQUE | WOLFRAMSÄUREANHYDRID, WOLFRAMTRIOXYD |
| 13267 | TURBINE | TURBINE | TURBINE |
| 13268 | TURBINE PLATES | AUBES DE TURBINES | TURBINENSCHAUFELN |
| 13269 | TURBINE PUMP | POMPE CENTRIFUGE | ZENTRIFUGALPUMPE, TURBOPUMPE |
| 13270 | TURBO-BLOWER | TURBO-VENTILATEUR | KREISELGEBLÄSE, TURBOGEBLAŠE |
| 13271 | TURBO-GENERATOR | TURBO-GENERATEUR | TURBODYNAMO, TURBOGENERATOR |
| 13272 | TURBOCHARGER | TURBO-COMPRESSEUR | TURBOKOMPRESSOR |
| 13273 | TURBULENCE | TURBULENCE | TURBULENZ |

| | | | |
|---|---|---|---|
| 13274 | **TURBULENT FLOW** | COURANT TURBULENT | STRÖMUNG (TURBULENTE), STRÖMUNG (UNGEORDNETE), STRÖMUNG (WIRBELIGE) |
| 13275 | **TURMERIC PAPER** | PAPIER DE CURCUMA | KURKUMAPAPIER |
| 13276 | **TURN (TO) (ON THE LATHE)** | TOURNER, TRAVAILLER AU TOUR | DREHEN (AUF DER DREHBANK) |
| 13277 | **TURN CAMBERED SURFACES (TO)** | TOURNER DES SURFACES BOMBEES | BALLIGDREHEN |
| 13278 | **TURN OF A HELIX** | TOUR D'UNE HELICE | WINDUNG EINER SCHRAUBENLINIE |
| 13279 | **TURN OF A THREAD** | REVOLUTION DU FILET | GANG EINES GEWINDES, GEWINDEGANG |
| 13280 | **TURN ORNAMENTAL (TO), ECCENTRIC WORK** | TOURNER DES SURFACES FIGUREES | PASSIG DREHEN, UNRUND DREHEN |
| 13281 | **TURN SPHERICAL SURFACES (TO)** | TOURNER DES SURFACES SPHERIQUES, TOURNER DES CORPS RONDS | KUGELIG DREHEN |
| 13282 | **TURN TAPER (TO),CONICAL** | TOURNER DES SURFACES OBLIQUES/ RAMPANTES | DREHEN (KEGELIG), DREHEN (KONISCH) |
| 13283 | **TURN UP WITH A SHOVEL (TO)** | REMUER A LA PELLE | UMSCHAUFELN |
| 13284 | **TURN-KEY JOB** | CLE EN MAIN (AFFAIRE) | SCHLÜSSELFERTIG |
| 13285 | **TURNBUCKLE** | TENDEUR A VIS | SPANNSCHLOSS, SCHRAUBENSCHLOSS, SPANNVORRICHTUNG, NACHSPANNVORRICHTUNG |
| 13286 | **TURNER** | TOURNEUR | DREHER |
| 13287 | **TURNING (ON THE LATHE)** | TOURNAGE, TRAVAIL AU TOUR | DREHEN (AUF DER DREHBANK) |
| 13288 | **TURNING CAMBERED SURFACES** | TOURNAGE DES SURFACES BOMBEES | BALLIGDREHEN |
| 13289 | **TURNING LATHE** | TOUR (MACHINE-OUTIL) | DREHBANK, WELLENDREHBANK |
| 13290 | **TURNING SHOP, TURNERY** | ATELIER DE TOURNAGE | DREHEREI |
| 13291 | **TURNING SPHERICAL SURFACES** | TOURNAGE DES SURFACES SPHERIQUES DES CORPS RONDS | KUGELDREHEN |
| 13292 | **TURNING TOOL, LATHE TOOL** | OUTIL DE TOUR | DREHSTAHL, DREHSTICHEL, STAHL |
| 13293 | **TURNINGS** | TOURNURES | DREHSPÄNE |
| 13294 | **TURNSCREW, SCREW DRIVER** | TOURNEVIS | SCHRAUBENZIEHER |
| 13295 | **TURNTABLE** | PLAQUE TOURNANTE | DREHSCHEIBE |
| 13296 | **TURPENTINE VARNISH** | VERNIS A L'ESSENCE | TERPENTINÖLLACK |
| 13297 | **TURRET LATHE** | TOUR REVOLVER | REVOLVERDREHMASCHINE |
| 13298 | **TURRET SINGLE SPINDLE AUTOMATIC LATHE** | TOUR MONOBROCHE AUTOMATIQUE A TOURELLE | EINSPINDEL-AUTOMAT MIT REVOLVERKOPF |
| 13299 | **TUYERE** | TUYERE D'AMENEE DE L'AIR SOUS PRESSION | WINDFORM, BLASFORM |
| 13300 | **TWIN** | MACLE | ZWILLING |
| 13301 | **TWIN ENGINE** | MOTEUR A CYLINDRES JUMELES | ZWILLINGSMASCHINE |
| 13302 | **TWINNING** | MACLAGE | ZWILLINGSBILDUNG |
| 13303 | **TWIST (TO)** | COMMETTRE LES TORONS, CABLER | VERSEILEN |
| 13304 | **TWIST DRILL** | FORET HELICOIDAL, FORET HELICOIDE, FORET A HELICE, FORET AMERICAIN | SPIRALBOHRER |
| 13305 | **TWIST OF A ROPE** | TORS, TORSION D'UNE CORDE | DRALL EINES SEILES |
| 13306 | **TWIST TEST** | ESSAI DE TORSION | VERDREHUNGSPROBE |
| 13307 | **TWISTED CURVE, CURVE IN SPACE** | COURBE DANS L'ESPACE, COURBE GAUCHE, COURBE A DOUBLE COURBURE | RAUMKURVE, RÄUMLICHE KURVE, GEWUNDENE KURVE, KURVE DOPPELTER KRÜMMUNG |
| 13308 | **TWISTING MOMENT, TURNING MOMENT, TORQUE** | MOMENT TORDANT, MOMENT DU COUPLE | DREHMOMENT |
| 13309 | **TWISTING OFF A SCREW THREAD** | RUPTURE BRUSQUE DU CORPS D'UNE VIS | ABWÜRGEN (EINER SCHRAUBE) |
| 13310 | **TWISTING TEST** | ESSAI DE FLEXION TOURNANTE | VERWINDEPROBE |

# TWO

340

| | | | |
|---|---|---|---|
| 13311 | **TWO PACK PAINT SYSTEM** | SYSTEME DE PEINTURE A DEUX COMPOSANTS | ZWEIKOMPONENTENLACK |
| 13312 | **TWO STROKE CYCLE ENGINE** | MOTEUR A DEUX TEMPS | ZWEITAKTMOTOR |
| 13313 | **TWO-CYLINDER ENGINE** | MACHINE A DEUX CYLINDRES | ZWEIZYLINDERDAMPFMASCHINE |
| 13314 | **TWO-PHASE, BIPHASE CURRENT** | COURANT DIPHASE | ZWEIPHASENSTROM |
| 13315 | **TWO-THREAD, DOUBLE THREADED SCREW** | VIS A DEUX FILETS | SCHRAUBE (ZWEIGÄNGIGE), SCHRAUBE (DOPPELGÄNGIGE) |
| 13316 | **TWO-THROW CRANK SHAFT** | ARBRE VILEBREQUIN A DEUX COUDES | ZWEIKURBELIGE WELLE, DOPPELT GEKRÖPFTE KURBELWELLE |
| 13317 | **TWO-WAY COCK** | ROBINET A DEUX VOIES | ZWEIWEGEHAHN |
| 13318 | **TWO-WAY VALVE** | SOUPAPE A DEUX VOIES | ZWEIWEGEVENTIL |
| 13319 | **TYPE METAL** | METAL PROPRE A LA FABRICATION DES CARACTERES D'IMPRIMERIE | SCHRIFTMETALL |
| 13320 | **TYPE, MODEL** | TYPE | BAUART, AUSFÜHRUNGSFORM, TYP, KONSTRUKTION, MODELL |
| 13321 | **TYRE TURNING LATHE** | TOUR A BANDAGES | RADREIFENDREHBANK |
| 13322 | **TYRE, TIRE** | BANDAGE DE ROUE, PNEU | RADREIFEN |
| 13323 | **U-BEND** | COUDE EN U, COUDE A 180 | DOPPELKRÜMMER, U-ROHR, RÜCKBOGEN |
| 13324 | **U-BOLT** | COLLIER DE TUBE, ETRIER | ROHRSCHELLE, BÜGELSCHRAUBE |
| 13325 | **U-TUBE** | TUBE COUDE A DEUX BRANCHES COMMUNIQUANT ENTRE ELLES | RÖHREN (KOMMUNIZIERENDE) |
| 13326 | **ULLAGE** | CREUX DE LA SPHERE | LEERRAUM |
| 13327 | **ULTIMATE BREAKING STRENGTH** | RESISTANCE A LA RUPTURE, RESISTANCE, TENACITE EXTREME | BRUCHFESTIGKEIT |
| 13328 | **ULTIMATE COMPRESSIVE CRUSHING STRENGTH** | RESISTANCE A LA COMPRESSION, RESISTANCE A L'ECRASEMENT, RESISTANCE AU RACCOURCISSEMENT | DRUCKFESTIGKEIT |
| 13329 | **ULTIMATE ELONGATION, ELONGATION UP TO THE BREAKING STRAIN** | ALLONGEMENT PROPORTIONNEL A LA LIMITE D'ELASTICITE | BRUCHDEHNUNG |
| 13330 | **ULTIMATE SHEARING STRENGTH** | RESISTANCE AU CISAILLEMENT, RESISTANCE A LA RUPTURE TRANSVERSALE, RESISTANCE AU GLISSEMENT TRANSVERSAL | SCHUBFESTIGKEIT, SCHERFESTIGKEIT |
| 13331 | **ULTIMATE TENSILE STRENGTH** | RESISTANCE A LA TRACTION, RESISTANCE A L'ALLONGEMENT, RESISTANCE A L'EXTENSION, CHARGE DE RUPTURE | ZUGFESTIGKEIT, BRUCHLAST, BRUCHBELASTUNG, BRUCHFESTIGKEIT |
| 13332 | **ULTRA-RED RAYS** | RAYONS ULTRA-ROUGES | STRAHLEN (ULTRAROTE) |
| 13333 | **ULTRA-VIOLET RAYS** | RAYONS ULTRA-VIOLETS | STRAHLEN (ULTRAVIOLETTE) |
| 13334 | **ULTRAMARINE** | OUTREMER | ULTRAMARIN, LASURBLAU, AZURBLAU |
| 13335 | **ULTRAMICROSCOPE** | ULTRAMICROSCOPE | ULTRAMIKROSKOP |
| 13336 | **ULTRAMICROSCOPIC TEST** | EXAMEN A L'ULTRAMICROSCOPE | UNTERSUCHUNG (ULTRAMIKROSKOPISCHE), BEOBACHTUNG (ULTRAMIKROSKOPISCHE) |
| 13337 | **ULTRASONIC EXAMINATION, ULTRASONIC INSPECTION** | CONTROLE AUX ULTRA-SONS | ULTRASCHALLUNTERSUCHUNG, ULTRASCHALLPRÜFUNG |
| 13338 | **ULTRASONIC WELDING** | SOUDAGE PAR ULTRASONS | ULTRASCHALLSCHWEISSEN |
| 13339 | **UMBRA** | OMBRE PORTEE | SCHLAGSCHATTEN |
| 13340 | **UNANNEALED, BRIGHT, HARD DRAWN WIRE** | FIL CLAIR | DRAHT (UNGEGLÜHTER), DRAHT (HARTGEZOGENER), DRAHT (BLANKER) |
| 13341 | **UNBALANCE, WANT, LACK OF BALANCE** | BALOURD, DESEQUILIBRE | UNSYMMETRIE, UNGLEICHGEWICHT, UNBALANZ |
| 13342 | **UNBREAKABILITY** | FRAGILITE (NON-) | UNZERBRECHLICHKEIT |

| | | | |
|---|---|---|---|
| 13343 | **UNBREAKABLE** | INCASSABLE | UNZERBRECHLICH |
| 13344 | **UNBURNT** | IMBRULE | UNVERBRANNT |
| 13345 | **UNCOMBINED CARBON, TEMPER CARBON** | CARBONE NON COMBINE AU FER | TEMPERKOHLE |
| 13346 | **UNDAMPED OSCILLATION** | VIBRATION NON AMORTIE | SCHWINGUNG (UNGEDÄMPFTE) |
| 13347 | **UNDER COOLING** | REFROIDISSEMENT (SOUS-) | UNTERKÜHLUNG |
| 13348 | **UNDER FILLING** | MANQUE DE MATIERE | STOFFMANGEL |
| 13349 | **UNDER SIZE** | DIMENSION INFERIEURE AUX PRESCRIPTIONS | UNTERMASS |
| 13350 | **UNDERBEAD-CRACK** | FISSURE SOUS CORDON | UNTERNAHTRISS |
| 13351 | **UNDERCUT** | COUPE INFERIEURE A LA COTE, CANIVEAU (SOUDURE) | UNTERSCHNITT, EINBRANDKERBEN |
| 13352 | **UNDERFILM CORROSION** | CORROSION SOUS-JACENTE | UNTERROSTUNG |
| 13353 | **UNDERGROUND CABLE; UNDERGROUND CONDUIT** | LIGNE SOUTERRAINE, CANALISATION ELECTRIQUE | LEITUNG (UNTERIRDISCHE) |
| 13354 | **UNDERGROUND PIPING** | CONDUITE SOUTERRAINE, CANALISATION | ROHRLEITUNG (UNTERIRDISCHE) |
| 13355 | **UNDERSHOT WATER WHEEL** | ROUE PAR-DESSOUS | WASSERRAD (UNTERSCHLÄCHTIGES) |
| 13356 | **UNEQUAL SIDED ANGLE IRON** | CORNIERE A AILES INEGALES | WINKELEISEN (UNGLEICHSCHENKLIGES) |
| 13357 | **UNEVEN FRACTURE** | CASSURE INEGALE | BRUCH (UNEBENER) |
| 13358 | **UNGULA** | ONGLET CYLINDRIQUE | ZYLINDERHUF |
| 13359 | **UNHARDENED** | DURCI (NON-), TREMPE (NON-) | UNGEHÄRTET |
| 13360 | **UNIFLOW CURRENT** | COURANTS DE MEME SENS | GLEICHSTROM (VON FLÜSSIGKEITEN) |
| 13361 | **UNIFORM ACCELERATION** | ACCELERATION UNIFORME | BESCHLEUNIGUNG (GLEICHBLEIBENDE) |
| 13362 | **UNIFORM MOTION** | MOUVEMENT UNIFORME | BEWEGUNG (GLEICHFÖRMIGE) |
| 13363 | **UNIFORM VELOCITY** | VITESSE UNIFORME CONSTANTE | GESCHWINDIGKEIT (UNVERÄNDERLICHE), GESCHWINDIGKEIT (KONSTANTE) |
| 13364 | **UNIFORMITY OF THE MATERIAL** | HOMOGENEITE D'UN MATERIEL | GLEICHFÖRMIGKEIT DES MATERIALS |
| 13365 | **UNIFORMLY ACCELERATED MOTION** | MOUVEMENT UNIFORMEMENT ACCELERE | BEWEGUNG (GLEICHMÄSSIG BESCHLEUNIGTE) |
| 13366 | **UNIFORMLY DISTRUBUTED LOAD** | CHARGE UNIFORMEMENT REPARTIE | LAST (GLEICHMÄSSIG VERTEILTE) |
| 13367 | **UNIFORMLY RETARDED MOTION** | MOUVEMENT UNIFORMEMENT RETARDE | BEWEGUNG (GLEICHMÄSSIG VERZÖGERTE) |
| 13368 | **UNION** | UNION, RACCORD | VERSCHRAUBUNG |
| 13369 | **UNION, PIPE UNION** | RACCORD TROIS PIECES, RACCORD-UNION, ECROU DE RAPPEL | ROHRVERSCHRAUBUNG |
| 13370 | **UNIT ELONGATION** | ALLONGEMENT RELATIF | DEHNUNG (RELATIVE) |
| 13371 | **UNIT LOAD** | CHARGE PAR UNITE DE SURFACE | FLÄCHENEINHEITSLAST |
| 13372 | **UNIT OF AREA** | UNITE DE SURFACE | FLÄCHENEINHEIT |
| 13373 | **UNIT OF LENGTH** | UNITE DE LONGUEUR | LÄNGENEINHEIT |
| 13374 | **UNIT OF MASS** | UNITE DE MASSE | MASSENEINHEIT |
| 13375 | **UNIT OF MEASURE** | UNITE DE MESURE | MASSEINHEIT |
| 13376 | **UNIT OF TIME** | UNITE DE TEMPS | ZEITEINHEIT |
| 13377 | **UNIT OF VOLUME SPACE** | UNITE DE VOLUME, UNITE DE CAPACITE | RAUMEINHEIT |
| 13378 | **UNIT OF WEIGHT** | UNITE DE POIDS | GEWICHTSEINHEIT |
| 13379 | **UNIT OF WORK** | UNITE DE TRAVAIL D'ENERGIE | ARBEITSEINHEIT, ENERGIEEINHEIT |
| 13380 | **UNIT VECTOR** | VECTEUR UNITAIRE | EINHEITSVEKTOR |
| 13381 | **UNITIZED BODY** | CARROSSERIE PORTANTE | KAROSSERIE (SELBSTTRAGENDE) |
| 13382 | **UNIVERSAL CHUCK** | MANDRIN UNIVERSEL | UNIVERSALFUTTER |

# UNI
**342**

| | | | |
|---|---|---|---|
| 13383 | **UNIVERSAL CYLINDRICAL GRINDING MACHINE** | MACHINE UNIVERSELLE A RECTIFIER LES SURFACES DE REVOLUTION | UNIVERSAL-RUNDSCHLEIFMASCHINE |
| 13384 | **UNIVERSAL GRINDING MACHINE** | AFFUTEUSE UNIVERSELLE | UNIVERSALSCHLEIFMASCHINE |
| 13385 | **UNIVERSAL JOINT** | JOINT A CARDAN | KARDANGELENK |
| 13386 | **UNIVERSAL MILL** | LAMINOIR UNIVERSEL | UNIVERSALSTAHLWALZWERK |
| 13387 | **UNIVERSAL MILLING MACHINE** | FRAISEUSE UNIVERSELLE | UNIVERSALFRÄSMASCHINE |
| 13388 | **UNIVERSAL TESTING MACHINE** | MACHINE D'ESSAIS UNIVERSELLE | UNIVERSALPRÜFMASCHINE |
| 13389 | **UNIVERSAL VISE** | ETAU UNIVERSEL | UNIVERSALSCHRAUBSTOCK |
| 13390 | **UNIVERSAL WELDING HEAD** | TETE DE SOUDAGE UNIVERSELLE | UNIVERSALSCHWEISSKOPF |
| 13391 | **UNKNOWN QUANTITY** | QUANTITE INCONNUE, INCONNUE | GRÖSSE (UNBEKANNTE), UNBEKANNTE |
| 13392 | **UNLIKE OPPOSITE POLES** | POLES DISSEMBLABLES, POLES DE NOM CONTRAIRE | POLE (UNGLEICHNAMIGE) |
| 13393 | **UNSATURATED HYDROCARBONS** | HYDROCARBURES NONSATURES (HYDROCARBURES ETHYLENIQUES, HYDROCARBURES ACETYLENIQUES) | KOHLENWASSERSTOFFE (UNGESÄTTIGTE) |
| 13394 | **UNSATURATED SOLUTION** | SOLUTION NON SATUREE | LÖSUNG (UNGESÄTTIGTE) |
| 13395 | **UNSCREW (TO)** | DEVISSER, DEMONTER UN BOULON | ABSCHRAUBEN, LOSSCHRAUBEN, AUFSCHRAUBEN |
| 13396 | **UNSCREWING** | DEVISSAGE | ABSCHRAUBEN, LOSSCHRAUBEN, AUFSCHRAUBEN |
| 13397 | **UNSHIELDED METALARC WELDING** | SOUDAGE A L'ARC METALLIQUE SANS GAZ PROTECTEUR | METALL-LICHTBOGENSCHWEISSEN OHNE SCHUTZGAS |
| 13398 | **UNSKILLED LABOURER** | OUVRIER NON SPECIALISE, MANOEUVRE DE SERVICE | ARBEITER (UNGELERNTER) |
| 13399 | **UNSOLDER (TO)** | DESSOUDER | LOSLÖTEN |
| 13400 | **UNSOLDERING** | DESSOUDAGE | LOSLÖTEN |
| 13401 | **UNSTABLE EQUILIBRIUM** | EQUILIBRE INSTABLE | GLEICHGEWICHT (LABILES) |
| 13402 | **UNWIELDY, UNMANAGEABLE** | MANIABLE (PEU) | UNHANDLICH |
| 13403 | **UNWIND** | RATTRAPAGE DE JEU | NACHSTELLEN |
| 13404 | **UNWIND (TO), UNCOIL (TO)** | DEROULER | ABWICKELN, ABWINDEN |
| 13405 | **UNWINDING, UNCOILING** | DEROULEMENT | ABWICKELN, ABWINDEN |
| 13406 | **UP AND DOWN STOKE, FORWARD AND RETURN STROKE OF PISTON** | COURSE COMPLETE (ALLER ET RETOUR) DU PISTON | KOLBENSPIEL |
| 13407 | **UP STREAM** | AMONT (EN), AMONT (D') | STROMAUFWÄRTS, GEGEN DEN STROM |
| 13408 | **UP-MILLING** | FRAISAGE EN REMONTANT | GLEICHLÄUFIGES FRÄSEN |
| 13409 | **UP-STROKE, ASCENT OF PISTON** | MONTEE DU PISTON, COURSE ASCENDANTE, COURSE MONTANTE DU PISTON | KOLBENAUFGANG |
| 13410 | **UP-TIME** | TEMPS ACTIF | ARBEITSZEIT |
| 13411 | **UPPER DEAD CENTER (U.D.C.)** | POINT MORT HAUT (P.M.H.) | TOTPUNKT (OBERER) |
| 13412 | **UPRIGHT DRILLING MACHINE** | PERCEUSE SUR COLONNE STANDARD | STÄNDERBOHRMASCHINE |
| 13413 | **UPSET BUTT WELD** | SOUDURE BOUT A BOUT PAR RESISTANCE | WIDERSTANDSSTUMPFSCHWEISSEN |
| 13414 | **UPSET FORCING** | REFOULEMENT | STAUCHEN |
| 13415 | **UPSETTING MACHINE** | MACHINE A REFOULER | STAUCHMASCHINE |
| 13416 | **UPSETTING TEST** | ESSAI D'ECRASEMENT, ESSAI DE COMPRESSION | STAUCHVERSUCH |
| 13417 | **UPSETTING WITH ELECTRIC RESISTANCE HEATING** | REFOULEMENT AVEC CHAUFFAGE PAR EFFET JOULE | ELEKTROSTAUCHVERFAHREN |
| 13418 | **UPTAKE** | CARNEAU | FUCHS (EINER FEUERUNGSANLAGE) |

| | | | |
|---|---|---|---|
| 13419 | **UPWARD VERTICAL POSITION** | SOUDURE EN POSITON VERTICALE MONTANTE | SENKRECHTE SCHWEISSUNG, AUFWÄRTSSCHWEISSUNG |
| 13420 | **URANIUM** | URANIUM | URAN |
| 13421 | **URBAN BUS** | AUTOBUS | STADTBUS |
| 13422 | **USEFUL CROSS SECTION** | SECTION UTILE | QUERSCHNITT (NUTZBARER) |
| 13423 | **USEFUL DIAMETER** | DIAMETRE UTILE | NUTZDURCHMESSER |
| 13424 | **USEFUL LENGTH** | LONGUEUR UTILE | LÄNGE (NUTZBARE), NUTZLÄNGE |
| 13425 | **USEFUL LOAD** | CHARGE UTILE | NUTZLAST |
| 13426 | **USEFUL RESISTANCE** | RESISTANCE UTILE | NUTZWIDERSTAND |
| 13427 | **USEFUL ROLLING WIDTH** | LARGEUR UTILE DE LAMINAGE | WALZNUTZBREITE |
| 13428 | **USEFUL WORK** | TRAVAIL UTILE | ARBEIT (NUTZBARE), NUTZARBEIT |
| 13429 | **UTILISATION** | UTILISATION | AUSNUTZUNG, NUTZBARMACHUNG, VERWERTUNG |
| 13430 | **UTILISE (TO)** | UTILISER | AUSNÜTZEN, NUTZBAR MACHEN, VERWERTEN |
| 13431 | **V-BELT** | COURROIE TRAPEZOIDALE | KEILRIEMEN |
| 13432 | **V-SHAPED GOUGE** | GOUGE TRIANGULAIRE | GEISSFUSS (STEMMEISEN) |
| 13433 | **VACANCY** | LACUNE | LÜCKE, LEERSTELLE |
| 13434 | **VACUUM** | VIDE, DEPRESSION ATMOSPHERIQUE, PRESSION | LUFTLEERER, RAUM, VAKUUM, UNTERDRUCK |
| 13435 | **VACUUM BOX** | BOITE A VIDE | VAKUUMKASTEN |
| 13436 | **VACUUM BRAKE** | FREIN A VIDE, FREIN A DEPRESSION | LUFTSAUGEBREMSE, VAKUUMBREMSE, UNTERDRUCKBRENSE |
| 13437 | **VACUUM BREAKER** | SOUPAPE CASSE-VIDE | RÜCKSCHLAGVENTIL |
| 13438 | **VACUUM CAN (G.B.), VACUUM BOX (U.S.A.)** | BOITE A VIDE | VAKUUMGEHÄUSE |
| 13439 | **VACUUM CASTING** | MOULAGE SOUS VIDE | VAKUUMFORMEN |
| 13440 | **VACUUM CHAMBER** | CHAMBRE A VIDE, ENCEINTE A VIDE | VAKUUMKAMMER |
| 13441 | **VACUUM ENVIRONNMENT** | ATMOSPHERE RAREFIEE | ATMOSPHÄRE (VERDÜNNTE) |
| 13442 | **VACUUM GAUGE** | INDICATEUR DU VIDE, VACUOMETRE | LUFTLEEREMESSER, UNTERDRUCKMESSER, VAKUUMMETER |
| 13443 | **VACUUM HEAT TREATMENT** | TRAITEMENT THERMIQUE SOUS VIDE | VAKUUM WÄRMEBEHANDLUNG |
| 13444 | **VACUUM MELTING** | FUSION SOUS VIDE | VAKUUMSCHMELZEN |
| 13445 | **VACUUM METALLIZING** | METALLISATION SOUS VIDE | VAKUMMETALLISIERUNG |
| 13446 | **VACUUM METALLURGY** | METALLURGIE SOUS VIDE | VAKUUMMETALLURGIE |
| 13447 | **VACUUM REFINING** | RAFFINAGE SOUS VIDE | VAKUUMRAFFINIERUNG |
| 13448 | **VACUUM SINTERING** | FRITTAGE SOUS VIDE | VAKUUMSINTERUNG |
| 13449 | **VACUUM SPACE** | CHAMBRE A VIDE | VAKUUMKAMMER |
| 13450 | **VACUUM SYSTEM VENTILATION** | VENTILATION PAR APPEL | SAUGLÜFTUNG, ASPIRATIONSVENTILATION |
| 13451 | **VACUUM TANK** | BASSIN A VIDE | VAKUUMKESSEL |
| 13452 | **VALENCE, VALENCY** | VALENCE | WERTIGKEIT, VALENZ |
| 13453 | **VALVE** | VALVE, LAMPE, SOUPAPE, CLAPET, OBTURATEUR, DISTRIBUTEUR | VENTIL, RÖHRE, MEMBRANVENTIL |
| 13454 | **VALVE BODY** | CORPS D'UNE SOUPAPE | VENTILKÖRPER |
| 13455 | **VALVE COCK** | ROBINET-VALVE A SOUPAPE | VENTILHAHN |
| 13456 | **VALVE CONTROL** | EPURE DE DISTRIBUTION | VENTILSTEUERUNG |
| 13457 | **VALVE DIAGRAM** | DIAGRAMME D'OUVERTURE ET DE FERMETURE D'UNE SOUPAPE | VENTILDIAGRAMM |
| 13458 | **VALVE EFFECT** | EFFET DE SOUPAPE | VENTILWIRKUNG |
| 13459 | **VALVE FLAP** | CLAPET D'UNE SOUPAPE | VENTILKLAPPE |

**VAL** 344

| 13460 | VALVE GEAR | DISTRIBUTION PAR SOUPAPE, APPAREIL DE DISTRIBUTION DE LA VAPEUR | VENTILSTEUERUNG, STEUERUNG (DAMPFM.) |
| 13461 | VALVE GUARD | ARRET, BUTEE D'UNE SOUPAPE | HUBBEGRENZER EINES VENTILS, VENTILFÄNGER |
| 13462 | VALVE GUIDE | GUIDE DE SOUPAPE | VENTILFÜHRUNG |
| 13463 | VALVE HEAD | TETE D'UNE SOUPAPE | TELLER (EINES VENTILS), VENTILTELLER |
| 13464 | VALVE HOOD / CAP | BOUCHON DE VALVE | VENTILVERSCHRAUBUNG |
| 13465 | VALVE LEVER | LEVIER DE SOUPAPE | VENTILHEBEL |
| 13466 | VALVE LIFTER | POUSSOIR DE SOUPAPE | VENTILSTÖSSEL |
| 13467 | VALVE LUBRICATOR | GRAISSEUR A SOUPAPE | VENTILÖLER |
| 13468 | VALVE SEAT | SIEGE DE SOUPAPE | VENTILSITZ |
| 13469 | VALVE SETTING / RATING | TARAGE DE SOUPAPE | VENTILEINSTELLUNGTARIEREN |
| 13470 | VALVE SPRING | RESSORT DE SOUPAPE | VENTILFEDER |
| 13471 | VALVE TIMING | DISTRIBUTION | STEUERUNG |
| 13472 | VALVE TUBE | SOUPAPE | VENTILRÖHRE |
| 13473 | VALVE-CLEARANCE ADJUSTER | CALIBRE DE REGLAGE DE SOUPAPE | VENTILLEHRE |
| 13474 | VAN | FOURGON | LIEFERWAGEN |
| 13475 | VANADIUM | VANADIUM | VANADIUM, VANADIN |
| 13476 | VANADIUM STEEL | ACIER AU VANADIUM | VANADIUMSTAHL |
| 13477 | VANE | AILETTES DE REFROIDISSEMENT | KÜHLERRIPPE |
| 13478 | VANE PUMP | POMPE A PALETTES | FLÜGELPUMPE |
| 13479 | VANE WHEEL, BLADE WHEEL | ROUE A PALETTES A AILETTES, ROUE A AUBES | FLÜGELRAD |
| 13480 | VANE, BLADE, BUCKET OF A TURBINE, TURBINE BUCKET | AUBE D'UNE TURBINE | SCHAUFEL EINER TURBINE |
| 13481 | VAPOR LOCK | BOUCHON DE VAPEUR | DAMPFBLASENBILDUNG |
| 13482 | VAPOR-PLATTING | RECOUVREMENT PAR DECOMPOSITION D'UN GAZ | DAMPFMETALLISIEREN |
| 13483 | VAPORIZATION | VAPORISATION | VERDAMPFEN |
| 13484 | VAPOUR | VAPEUR | DAMPF |
| 13485 | VAPOUR ABSORPTION PLANT | INSTALLATION D'EVACUATION, ELIMINATION DES BUEES | ENTNEBELUNGSANLAGE, ENTDUNSTUNGSANLAGE |
| 13486 | VAPOUR DEGREASING | DEGRAISSAGE A LA VAPEUR | ENTFETTEN IM TRIDAMPF |
| 13487 | VAPOUR DEPOSITION | METALLISATION SOUS VIDE | BEDAMPFEN (METALLDAMPF) |
| 13488 | VARIABLE | VARIABLE | VERÄNDERLICHE, VARIABLE |
| 13489 | VARIABLE BLOCK FORMAT | FORMAT A BLOC VARIABLE | EINGABEFORMAT IN VARIABLER SATZSCHREIBWEISE |
| 13490 | VARIABLE MOTION | MOUVEMENT VARIE | BEWEGUNG (VARIABLE), BEWEGUNG (VERÄNDERLICHE) |
| 13491 | VARIABLE PRESSURE | PRESSION VARIABLE | DRUCK (VERÄNDERLICHER) |
| 13492 | VARIABLE SPEED DRIVE ASSEMBLY | ENSEMBLE DE COMMANDE A VITESSE VARIABLE | REGELANTRIEBSTEUERUNG |
| 13493 | VARIABLE SPEED UNIT | VARIATEUR DE VITESSE | DREHZAHLREGLER |
| 13494 | VARIABLE VELOCITY | VITESSE VARIEE, VARIABLE | GESCHWINDIGKEIT (VERÄNDERLICHE) |
| 13495 | VARIATION | VARIATION | SCHWANKUNG |
| 13496 | VARIATION (MATH) | VARIATION (MATH.) | VARIATION (MATH.) |
| 13497 | VARIATION FLUCTUATION OF PRESSURE | VARIATIONS DE PRESSION | DRUCKSCHWANKUNG |
| 13498 | VARIATION OF TEMPERATURE | VARIATION DE TEMPERATURE | WÄRMESCHWANKUNG, TEMPERATURSCHWANKUNG |
| 13499 | VARIATIONS OF SPEED, FLUCTUATIONS IN SPEED | VARIATIONS DE VITESSE, FLUCTUATIONS DE VITESSE | GESCHWINDIGKEITSSCHWANKUNGEN |

| | | |
|---|---|---|
| 13500 | **VARIATIONS OF WATER LEVEL** | VARIATIONS DE NIVEAU D'EAU | VERÄNDERUNG DES WASSERSPIEGELS, SCHWANKUNGEN DES WASSERSTANDES, NIVEAUSCHWANKUNGEN |
| 13501 | **VARIEGATED COPPER ORE, PEACOCK COPPER** | CUIVRE PANACHE | BUNTKUPFERERZ |
| 13502 | **VARIEGATED SANDSTONE** | GRES BIGARRE | BUNTSANDSTEIN |
| 13503 | **VARIETY OF TIMBER** | ESPECE DE BOIS, ESSENCE DE BOIS | HOLZART |
| 13504 | **VARNISH** | VERNIS | FIRNIS |
| 13505 | **VARNISH COATING** | VERNISSAGE | DECKLACK, ÜBERZUGSLACK |
| 13506 | **VARNISHED PAPER** | PAPIER GOMME/LAQUE | SCHELLACKPAPIER, PAPIER (GEFIRNISSTES), PAPIER (LACKIERTES) |
| 13507 | **VARYING ACCELERATION** | ACCELERATION NON UNIFORME | BESCHLEUNIGUNG (UNGLEICHFÖRMIGE) |
| 13508 | **VASELINE, PETROLEUM JELLY** | VASELINE, GRAISSE MINERALE, COSMOLINE, PETREOLINE, PETROLEINE, PIMELEINE | MINERALFETT, VASELIN |
| 13509 | **VECTOR PRODUCT** | PRODUIT VECTORIEL | VEKTORPRODUKT, PRODUKT (VEKTORISCHES) |
| 13510 | **VECTOR QUANTITY** | VECTEUR | VEKTOR |
| 13511 | **VEE-BELT, V-BELT** | COURROIE DE SECTION TRIANGULAIRE, COURROIE TRAPEZOIDALE | KEILRIEMEN |
| 13512 | **VEGETABLE OIL** | HUILE VEGETALE | PFLANZENÖL, ÖL (VEGETABILISCHES) |
| 13513 | **VELOCITY CURVE** | COURBE DE VITESSE | GESCHWINDIGKEITSIKURVE |
| 13514 | **VELOCITY DIAGRAM** | DIAGRAMME DES VITESSES | GESCHWINDIGKEITSDIAGRAMM |
| 13515 | **VELOCITY HEAD** | CHARGE DE LA VITESSE | STAUHÖHE, GESCHWINDIGKEITSHÖHE |
| 13516 | **VELOCITY OF FLOW** | VITESSE DU COURANT | STRÖMUNGSGESCHWINDIGKEIT |
| 13517 | **VELOCITY OF LIGHT** | VITESSE DE LA LUMIERE | LICHTGESCHWINDIGKEIT |
| 13518 | **VELOCITY OF PASSAGE** | VITESSE DE PASSAGE | DURCHFLUSSGESCHWINDIGKEIT |
| 13519 | **VELOCITY OF PROPAGATION** | VITESSE DE PROPAGATION | FORTPFLANZUNGSGESCHWINDIGKEIT |
| 13520 | **VELOCITY OF SOUND WAVES** | VITESSE DU SON | SCHALLGESCHWINDIGKEIT |
| 13521 | **VELOCITY OF TRANSFORMATION** | VITESSE DE TRANSFORMATION | TRANSFORMATIONSGESCHWINDIGKEIT |
| 13522 | **VELOCITY RATIO** | RAPPORT DES VITESSES | ÜBERSETZUNGSVERHÄLTNIS |
| 13523 | **VELOCITY STAGE** | ETAGE DE VITESSE | GESCHWINDIGKEITSSTUFE |
| 13524 | **VENEER** | FEUILLET, FEUILLE DE PLACAGE, PLACAGE | FURNIERHOLZ |
| 13525 | **VENEER CUTTING MACHINE** | MACHINE A FAIRE LES FEUILLES DE PLACAGE | SPANHOBELMASCHINE, FURNIERHOBELMASCHINE |
| 13526 | **VENEER SAW** | SCIE A PLACAGE | KLOBSÄGE, FURNIERSÄGE |
| 13527 | **VENICE TURPENTINE** | TEREBENTHINE DE VENISE | TERPENTIN (VENEZIANER), LÄRCHENTERPENTIN |
| 13528 | **VENT** | EVENT, TROU D'AIR | ÖFFNUNG, ENTLÜFTER, LÜFTUNGSÖFFNUNG |
| 13529 | **VENTILATED MOTOR** | MOTEUR BLINDE VENTILE | MOTOR (VENTILIERTER) |
| 13530 | **VENTILATION** | VENTILATION, AERAGE, AERATION | LÜFTUNG, VENTILATION |
| 13531 | **VENTILATION WINDOW, VENTILATOR WINDOW** | DEFLECTEUR | AUSSTELLFENSTER, SCHWENKFENSTER |
| 13532 | **VENTURI METER, TUBE** | COMPTEUR VENTURI, COMPTEUR D'EAU VENTURI, TUBE DE VENTURI | VENTURIMESSER, VENTURIROHR, WASSERMESSER (VENTURISCHER) |
| 13533 | **VERDIGRIS** | VERT-DE-GRIS, VERDET, ACETATE DE CUIVRE | GRÜNSPAN, KUPFERAZETAT |
| 13534 | **VERIFICATION** | VERIFICATION | PRÜFUNG |

# VER

| | | | |
|---|---|---|---|
| 13535 | **VERMILLON, MERCURIC SULPHIDE** | SULFURE ROUGE DE MERCURE, VERMILLON | ZINNOBER, ZINNOBERROT, VERMILLON |
| 13536 | **VERNIER** | VERNIER | NONIUS, VERNIER |
| 13537 | **VERNIER CALLIPERS, CALLIPER RULE** | PIED, COMPAS A COULISSE | SCHUBLEHRE, SCHIEBLEHRE |
| 13538 | **VERNIER DEPTH GAUGE** | CALIBRE A COULISSE DE PROFONDEUR | TIEFENLEHRE |
| 13539 | **VERNIER DEPTH GAUGE WITH FINE MICROMETER ADJUSTMENT** | CALIBRE A COULISSE DE PROFONDEUR A FIXATION MICROMETRIQUE | TIEFENLEHRE MIT MIKROMETERSCHRAUBE |
| 13540 | **VERNIER MICROMETER** | MICROMETRE A VERNIER | MIKROMETERSCHRAUBE |
| 13541 | **VERNIER SCALE** | ECHELLE VERNIER | SCHIEBELEHRE |
| 13542 | **VERSUS** | FONCTION DE (EN) | ABHÄNGIGKEIT VON (IN) |
| 13543 | **VERTEX CORNER OF POLYGON** | SOMMET D'UN POLYGONE | ECKE EINES POLYGONS |
| 13544 | **VERTICAL BOILER** | CHAUDIERE VERTICALE | KESSEL (STEHENDER) |
| 13545 | **VERTICAL BORING AND TURNING MILL** | TOUR VERTICAL | KARUSSELLDREHMASCHINE |
| 13546 | **VERTICAL ENGINE** | MACHINE VERTICALE | MASCHINE (STEHENDE) |
| 13547 | **VERTICAL NECK JOURNAL BEARING** | PALIER INTERMEDIAIRE, COLLIER POUR ARBRES VERTICAUX | HALSLAGER EINER STEHENDEN WELLE |
| 13548 | **VERTICAL SPINDLE MILLING MACHINE** | FRAISEUSE VERTICALE | FRÄSMASCHINE (STEHENDE), FRÄSMASCHINE VERTIKALE, SENKRECHTFRÄSMASCHINE |
| 13549 | **VERTICAL TRAVEL** | COURSE VERTICALE | BEWEGUNG (SENKRECHTE) |
| 13550 | **VERTICAL UPRIGHT SHAFT** | ARBRE VERTICAL | WELLE (STEHENDE), WELLE (SENKRECHTE), KÖNIGSWELLE |
| 13551 | **VERTICAL, UPRIGHT** | VERTICAL | STEHEND, AUFRECHT, VERTIKAL |
| 13552 | **VERTICAL, UPRIGHT DRILLING MACHINE** | MACHINE A PERCER VERTICALE | BOHRMASCHINE (STEHENDE), VERTIKALBOHRMASCHINE |
| 13553 | **VESSELS CONNECTED BY U-TUBE** | VASES COMMUNICANTS | GEFÄSSE (KOMMUNIZIERENDE) |
| 13554 | **VIBRATION** | VIBRATION | SCHWINGUNG |
| 13555 | **VIBRATION DAMPER** | AMORTISSEUR DE VIBRATIONS | SCHWINGUNGSDÄMPFER |
| 13556 | **VIBRATION DUE TO BENDING STRESS** | VIBRATION DUE A DES EFFORTS DE FLEXION | BIEGUNGSSCHWINGUNG |
| 13557 | **VIBRATION DUE TO TORSIONAL STRESS, TORSIONAL VIBRATION** | VIBRATION DUE A DES EFFORTS DE TORSION | DREHSCHWINGUNG, VERDREHUNGSSCHWINGUNG, TORSIONSSCHWINGUNG |
| 13558 | **VIBRATION OF A SPRING** | OSCILLATION D'UN RESSORT | SCHWINGUNG EINER FEDER |
| 13559 | **VIBRATIONS** | VIBRATIONS, TREPIDATIONS, EBRANLEMENTS | ERSCHÜTTERUNGEN |
| 13560 | **VIBRATIONS OF ETHER** | VIBRATIONS DE L'ETHER | ÄTHERSCHWINGUNGEN |
| 13561 | **VICE** | ETAU | SCHRAUBSTOCK |
| 13562 | **VICE CLAWS, CLAMPS** | MORDACHE A CHARNIERE | SPANNKLUPPE |
| 13563 | **VICE CLAWS, VICE CLAMPS** | MORDACHE D'UN ETAU | BACKENFUTTER EINES SCHRAUBSTOCKS |
| 13564 | **VICE JAW, CHECK** | MACHOIRE, MORS, MORD D'UN ETAU | BACKEN EINES SCHRAUBSTOCKS |
| 13565 | **VICE JAWS FOR WHEEL-WRIGHT, TYRE SMITH'S VICE** | ETAU A CHANFREIN, TENAILLE A CHANFREIN | REIFKLOBEN |
| 13566 | **VICKERS HARDNESS** | DURETE VICKERS | VICKERSHÄRTE |
| 13567 | **VIEW** | VUE | ANSICHT |
| 13568 | **VIEWING SCREEN** | ECRAN DE PROJECTION | LEUCHTSCHIRM |
| 13569 | **VIOLLE STANDARD** | ETALON VIOLLE, VIOLLE | PLATINEINHEIT (DER LICHTSTÄRKE) |
| 13570 | **VIRGIN METAL** | METAL VIERGE | METALL (GEDIEGENES) |
| 13571 | **VIRTUAL FOCUS** | FOYER VIRTUEL IMAGINAIRE | BRENNPUNKT (SCHEINBARER), BRENNPUNKT (VIRTUELLER) |

**347** **VUL**

| | | | |
|---|---|---|---|
| 13572 | VIRTUAL IMAGE | IMAGE VIRTUELLE | SCHEINBILD, BILD (VIRTUELLES) |
| 13573 | VIRTUAL VELOCITY | VITESSE VIRTUELLE | GESCHWINDIGKEIT (VIRTUELLE) |
| 13574 | VISCO SI METER | VISCOSIMETRE | ZÄHIGKEITSMESSER, VISKOSIMETER |
| 13575 | VISCOSE | VISCOSE | VISKOSE |
| 13576 | VISCOSITY | VISCOSITE | ZÄHFLÜSSIGKEIT, DICKFLÜSSIGKEIT, VISKOSITÄT, ZÄHIGKEIT |
| 13577 | VISCOUS | VISQUEUX | DICKFLÜSSIG, SCHWERFLÜSSIG, STRENGFLÜSSIG, ZÄHFLÜSSIG, KLEBRIG, VISKOS |
| 13578 | VISCOUS FLOW | FLUAGE VISQUEUX | FLIESSEN, LAMINÄRE STRÖMUNG |
| 13579 | VISE | ETAU | SCHRAUBSTOCK |
| 13580 | VISIBLE SIGNAL | SIGNAL OPTIQUE | ZEICHEN (SICHTBARES), SICHTSIGNAL, SIGNAL (OPTISCHES) |
| 13581 | VISUAL ANGLE | ANGLE OPTIQUE, ANGLE VISUEL | GESICHTSWINKEL |
| 13582 | VITREOUS | VITREUX | GLASIG |
| 13583 | VITREOUS GLASSY LUSTRE | ECLAT VITREUX | GLASGLANZ |
| 13584 | VITRIFICATION | VITRIFICATION | SINTERUNG, VERGLASUNG |
| 13585 | VOID | LACUNE | FEHLSTELLE |
| 13586 | VOLATILE CONSTITUENT | PARTIE CONSTITUANTE VOLATILE | BESTANDTEIL (FLÜCHTIGER) |
| 13587 | VOLATILISATION | VOLATILISATION | VERFLÜCHTIGUNG |
| 13588 | VOLATILISE (TO) | VOLATILISER | VERFLÜCHTIGEN |
| 13589 | VOLATILITY | VOLATILITE | FLÜCHTIGKEIT |
| 13590 | VOLCANIC TUFA | TUF VOLCANIQUE | TUFF (VULKANISCHER) |
| 13591 | VOLT | VOLT | VOLT |
| 13592 | VOLT-AMPERE | VOLT-AMPERE | VOLT-AMPERE |
| 13593 | VOLTAGE | TENSION DU COURANT, NOMBRE DE VOLTS, VOLTAGE | SPANNUNG, VOLTZAHL |
| 13594 | VOLTAGE POTENTIAL DROP, FALL DROP OF POTENTIAL | PERTE, CHUTE DE TENSION, CHUTE DE POTENTIEL | SPANNUNGSABFALL, SPANNUNGSGEFÄLLE, SPANNUNGSVERLUST, POTENTIALGEFÄLLE |
| 13595 | VOLTAGE REGULATOR, POTENTIAL REGULATOR | REGULATEUR DE TENSION, D'INTENSITE, REGULATEUR DE COURANT | SPANNUNGSREGLER, SPANNUNGSREGULATOR |
| 13596 | VOLTAIC PILE | PILE VOLTAIQUE, DE VOLTA | SÄULE (VOLTASCHE) |
| 13597 | VOLTMETER | VOLTMETRE | SPANNUNGSMESSER, SPANNUNGSZEIGER, VOLTMETER |
| 13598 | VOLUME | VOLUME, CUBAGE | RAUMINHALT, VOLUMEN |
| 13599 | VOLUME OF STROKE | VOLUME ENGENDRE PAR LE DEPLACEMENT DU PISTON | HUBVOLUMEN |
| 13600 | VOLUME REGULATOR | REGULATEUR DE DEBIT | MENGENREGLER |
| 13601 | VOLUMETRIC ANALYSIS | ANALYSE VOLUMETRIQUE | MASSANALYSE (VOLUMETRISCHE) |
| 13602 | VOLUMETRIC EFFICIENCY | RENDEMENT VOLUMETRIQUE | WIRKUNGSGRAD (RÄUMLICHER), WIRKUNGSGRAD (VOLUMETRISCHER) |
| 13603 | VOLUMETRIC EXPANSION, EXTENSION | DILATATION CUBIQUE | AUSDEHNUNG (RÄUMLICHE), RAUMAUSDEHNUNG |
| 13604 | VOLUMMETER | DEBITMETRE | MENGENMESSER |
| 13605 | VOLUTE SPRING, CONICAL HELICAL SPRING OF RECTANGULAR CROSS SECTION | RESSORT CONIQUE A SECTION RECTANGULAIRE, RESSORT CONIQUE A LAME PLATE | KEGELFEDER MIT RECHTECKIGEM QUERSCHNITT |
| 13606 | VORTEX, WHIRL, EDDY | TOURBILLON, REMOUS | WIRBEL, (PHYS.) |
| 13607 | VULCANISATION | VULCANISATION | VULKANISIEREN |
| 13608 | VULCANISE (TO) | VULCANISER | VULKANISIEREN |
| 13609 | VULCANISED FIBRE | FIBRE VULCANISEE, FIBRE | FIBER, VULKANFIBER |
| 13610 | VULCANISED RUBBER | CAOUTCHOUC VULCANISE | KAUTSCHUK (VULKANISIERTER), WEICHKAUTSCHUK, WEICHGUMMI |

**WAD** 348

| | | | |
|---|---|---|---|
| 13611 | VULGAR FRACTION | FRACTION ORDINAIRE | BRUCH (GEMEINER) |
| 13612 | WADDING | OUATE | WATTE |
| 13613 | WAGES | PAIE, PAIEMENT, SALAIRE | LOHN, ARBEITSLOHN |
| 13614 | WAGON DRILL | SONDEUSE SUR CAMION | BOHRWAGEN |
| 13615 | WAIVER | RENONCIATION, DEROGATION | VERZICHT, ABWEICHUNG |
| 13616 | WALKWAY , GANGAY | PASSERELLE | BEDIENUNGSGANG, LAUFSTEG |
| 13617 | WALL BOX | NICHE | MAUERKASTEN |
| 13618 | WALL BRACKET | CHAISE D'APPLIQUE, CHAISE-CONSOLE, CONSOLE | WANDARM, WANDLAGERSTUHL, WANDKONSOLE |
| 13619 | WALL COUNTERSHAFT | RENVOI MURAL, RENVOI FIXE CONTRE UN MUR | WANDVORGELEGE |
| 13620 | WALL ENGINE, WALL DRILLING MACHINE | MACHINE A VAPEUR MURALE | WANDDAMPFMASCHINE, WANDBOHRMASCHINE |
| 13621 | WALL PLATE | CONTREPLAQUE, PLAQUE D'ANCRAGE | ANKERPLATTE, WANDPLATTE, MAUERPLATTE, WANDBETT, ANKERROSETTE |
| 13622 | WALL PLUG AND SOCKET | CONTACT A FICHE | STECKKONTAKT, STÖPSELKONTAKT |
| 13623 | WALL SLEWING CRANE | GRUE A POTENCE | WANDDREHKRAN |
| 13624 | WALLS OF A HOLE | FACE D'UN TROU | LOCHWAND, LOCHLEIBUNG |
| 13625 | WARDING FILE | LIME D'ENTREE | SCHLÜSSELFEILE |
| 13626 | WARNING ORDER | ORDRE DE FONCTIONNEMENT | BETRIEBFOLGE |
| 13627 | WARP | CHAINE D'UN TISSU | KETTE EINES GEWEBES |
| 13628 | WARP (TO), WIND (TO) | GAUCHIR, BOMBER, DEJETER (SE), DEVERSER (SE), VOILER (SE) | WERFEN (SICH), VERZIEHEN (SICH) |
| 13629 | WARPING, WINDING | GAUCHISSEMENT, DEFORMATION, DEFORMATION PAR ENROULEMENT | UMWICKLUNG, WERFEN, VERZIEHEN, KRUMMZIEHEN |
| 13630 | WASH STAND TAP | ROBINET DE LAVABO | STANDVENTIL |
| 13631 | WASHER | RONDELLE | UNTERLAGSCHEIBE |
| 13632 | WASHING | DELAVAGE | WASCHEN |
| 13633 | WASHING BOTTLE FLASK | PISSETTE | SPRITZFLASCHE |
| 13634 | WASTE GAS | GAZ PERDU | ABGAS |
| 13635 | WASTE HEAT | CHALEUR PERDUE | ABWÄRME |
| 13636 | WASTE OIL | HUILE D'EGOUTTAGE, HUILE EN EXCES | ÖL (ABLAUFENDES), TROPFÖL |
| 13637 | WASTE PRODUCTS | DECHETS | ABFÄLLE, ABFALLSTOFFE |
| 13638 | WASTE WATER PURIFICATION | EPURATION, PURIFICATION DES EAUX RESIDUAIRES | ABWÄSSERREINIGUNG |
| 13639 | WATCHMAKER'S LATHE | FOUR D'HORLOGER | DREHSTUHL |
| 13640 | WATER | EAU | WASSER |
| 13641 | WATER BATH | BAIN-MARIE | WASSERBAD (CHEM.) |
| 13642 | WATER BEARING SOIL | SOL AQUIFERE | BODEN (WASSERFÜHRENDER) |
| 13643 | WATER CALORIMETER | CALORIMETRE A EAU | WASSERKALORIMETER |
| 13644 | WATER COCK | ROBINET A EAU | WASSERHAHN |
| 13645 | WATER CONTENT, PERCENTAGE OF WATER | PROPORTION D'EAU, TENEUR EN EAU | WASSERGEHALT |
| 13646 | WATER COOLING | REFROIDISSEMENT A L'EAU | WASSERKÜHLUNG |
| 13647 | WATER DESCALING | DECALAMINAGE A L'EAU | WASSERENTZUNDERUNG |
| 13648 | WATER DISPLACING FILM | FILM ANTI-MOUILLANT | HYDROPHOBIERUNGSFILM |
| 13649 | WATER FOR INDUSTRIAL PURPOSES | EAU INDUSTRIELLE | NUTZWASSER, BRAUCHWASSER, BETRIEBSWASSER, WIRTSCHAFTSWASSER |
| 13650 | WATER FREE FROM BACTERIA | EAU EXEMPTE DE MICROBES, EAU STERILISEE | WASSER (KEIMFREIES) |
| 13651 | WATER GAS | GAZ A L'EAU | WASSERGAS |

| | | | |
|---|---|---|---|
| 13652 | **WATER GAUGE, GAUGE GLASS** | INDICATEUR DE NIVEAU, NIVEAU D'EAU | WASSERSTANDSANZEIGER, WASSERSTANDSGLAS, WASSERSTAND |
| 13653 | **WATER HAMMER** | COUP DE BELIER | WASSERSCHLAG, WIDDERSTOSS |
| 13654 | **WATER HARDENING** | TREMPE A L'EAU | WASSERHÄRTUNG |
| 13655 | **WATER JACKET CHAMBER** | CHEMISE D'EAU | WASSERMANTEL, KÜHLMANTEL |
| 13656 | **WATER JET** | JET D'EAU | WASSERSTRAHL |
| 13657 | **WATER JET AIR PUMP** | INJECTEUR HYDRAULIQUE | WASSERSTRAHLLUFTPUMPE |
| 13658 | **WATER JET BLOWER** | EJECTEUR HYDRAULIQUE | WASSERSTRAHLGEBLÄSE |
| 13659 | **WATER LEVEL** | NIVEAU D'EAU (HAUTEUR D'UN LIQUIDE) | WASSERSPIEGEL, WASSERSTAND |
| 13660 | **WATER LEVEL MARK** | MARQUE REPERE DE NIVEAU D'EAU | WASSERSTANDMARKE |
| 13661 | **WATER METER** | COMPTEUR A EAU | WASSERMESSER, WASSERUHR |
| 13662 | **WATER OF CONDENSATION** | EAU DE CONDENSATION | NIEDERSCHLAGWASSER, KONDENSWASSER, KONDENSAT |
| 13663 | **WATER OF CRYSTALLISATION** | EAU DE CRISTALLISATION | KRISTALLWASSER |
| 13664 | **WATER PAINT** | PEINTURE A L'EAU | WASSERFARBE |
| 13665 | **WATER PIPE** | TUYAU DE CONDUITE, TUYAU DE DISTRIBUTION D'EAU | WASSERLEITUNGSROHR |
| 13666 | **WATER PIPING MAIN** | CONDUITE, CANALISATION, DISTRIBUTION D'EAU | WASSERLEITUNG |
| 13667 | **WATER PISTON, HYDRAULIC PISTON** | PISTON A EAU, PISTON DE MOTEUR HYDRAULIQUE | WASSERKOLBEN |
| 13668 | **WATER POWER, HYDRAULIC POWER** | FORCE HYDRAULIQUE | WASSERKRAFT |
| 13669 | **WATER PRESSURE** | PRESSION D'EAU, PRESSION HYDRAULIQUE | WASSERDRUCK |
| 13670 | **WATER PRESSURE ENGINE** | MACHINE A COLONNE D'EAU | WASSERSÄULENMASCHINE |
| 13671 | **WATER PROOF** | INATTAQUABLE A L'EAU, IMPERMEABLE | WASSERBESTÄNDIG, WASSERFEST |
| 13672 | **WATER QUENCHING** | TREMPE A L'EAU | WASSERHÄRTUNG |
| 13673 | **WATER QUENCHING FOLLOWED BY TEMPERING** | TREMPE A L'EAU SUIVIE DE REVENU | WASSERVERGÜTEN |
| 13674 | **WATER REPELLENT PRODUCT** | PRODUIT HYDROFUGE | MITTEL (WASSERABWEISENDES) |
| 13675 | **WATER SEAL** | JOINT HYDRAULIQUE | WASSERVERSCHLUSS |
| 13676 | **WATER SOFTENING** | EPURATION CHIMIQUE DES EAUX D'ALIMENTATION | ENTHÄRTEN DES WASSERS, WASSERENTHÄRTUNG |
| 13677 | **WATER SPACE OF A BOILER** | CHAMBRE A EAU D'UNE CHAUDIERE | WASSERRAUM EINES KESSELS |
| 13678 | **WATER SUPPLY** | ALIMENTATION EN EAU, DISTRIBUTION D'EAU | WASSERVERSORGUNG |
| 13679 | **WATER TANK** | RESERVOIR A EAU | WASSERBEHÄLTER |
| 13680 | **WATER TOWER** | CHATEAU D'EAU | WASSERTURM |
| 13681 | **WATER TUBE** | TUBE D'EAU | WASSERROHR (DAMPFKESSEL) |
| 13682 | **WATER TUBE BOILER** | CHAUDIERE A TUBES D'EAU, CHAUDIERE A VAPORISATION RAPIDE, CHAUDIERE MULTITUBULAIRE, CHAUDIERE INEXPLOSIBLE | WASSERRÖHRENKESSEL |
| 13683 | **WATER-COOLED** | REFROIDI PAR L'EAU, REFROIDISSEMENT D'EAU (A) | WASSERGEKÜHLT |
| 13684 | **WATER-COOLED SURFACE CONDENSER** | CONDENSEUR PAR SURFACE AU MOYEN DE L'EAU | OBERFLÄCHENKONDENSATOR MIT WASSERKÜHLUNG |
| 13685 | **WATER-REPELLENT** | HYDROFUGE | WASSERABWEISEND |
| 13686 | **WATER-TIGHT, STANCH, STAUNCH** | ETANCHE A L'EAU | WASSERDICHT |
| 13687 | **WATERING CAN POT** | ARROSOIR | GIESSKANNE |
| 13688 | **WATERPROOF** | ETANCHE A L'EAU | WASSERDICHT |

# WAT

| | | | |
|---|---|---|---|
| 13689 | **WATERPROOF (TO)** | IMPERMEABILISER | WASSERDICHT MACHEN |
| 13690 | **WATERPROOF CLOTH** | TISSU IMPERMEABLE | GEWEBE (WASSERDICHTES) |
| 13691 | **WATERPROOFING** | IMPERMEABILISATION | WASSERDICHTMACHEN |
| 13692 | **WATERWHEEL** | ROUE, RECEPTEUR HYDRAULIQUE | WASSERRAD |
| 13693 | **WATERWORKS** | INSTALLATION DE DISTRIBUTION D'EAU | WASSERWERK, WASSERVERSORGUNGSANLAGE |
| 13694 | **WATT** | WATT | WATT |
| 13695 | **WATT-HOUR (W/HR)** | WATT-HEURE | WATTSTUNDE |
| 13696 | **WATT-MINUTE** | WATT-MINUTE | WATTMINUTE |
| 13697 | **WATT-SECOND** | WATT-SECONDE | WATTSEKUNDE |
| 13698 | **WATTMETER** | WATTMETRE | WATTMETER |
| 13699 | **WAVE** | ONDE | WELLE (PHYS.) |
| 13700 | **WAVE LENGTH** | LONGUEUR D'ONDE | WELLENLÄNGE |
| 13701 | **WAVINESS** | ONDULATION | WELLIGKEIT |
| 13702 | **WAX** | CIRE | WACHS |
| 13703 | **WAX PAATERN** | MODELE EN CIRE | WACHSMODELL |
| 13704 | **WAXED THREAD** | FIL POISSE | PECHGARN, PECHDRAHT |
| 13705 | **WEAK CURRENT** | COURANT DE FAIBLE INTENSITE | SCHWACHSTROM |
| 13706 | **WEAK SOLUTION** | SOLUTION FAIBLE | LÖSUNG (SCHWACHE) |
| 13707 | **WEAKENING OF CROSS SECTION** | AFFAIBLISSEMENT DE LA SECTION | SCHWÄCHUNG, VERSCHWÄCHUNG DES QUERSCHNITTS |
| 13708 | **WEAKENING OF THE MATERIAL** | AFFAIBLISSEMENT DU MATERIEL | SCHWÄCHUNG DES MATERIALS |
| 13709 | **WEAR** | USURE | VERSCHLEISS, ABNÜTZUNG |
| 13710 | **WEAR AND TEAR** | USURE NORMALE, CONSOMMATION | ABNÜTZUNG (NATÜRLICHE), VERSCHLEISS |
| 13711 | **WEAR BLOCKS** | CALES D'USURE | VERSCHLEISSPLATTEN |
| 13712 | **WEAR BY RUBBING** | USURE PAR FROTTEMENT | ABRIEB |
| 13713 | **WEAR DOWN (TO), OFF, OUT** | USER (S') | ABNÜTZEN (SICH), VERSCHLEISSEN |
| 13714 | **WEAR FEST** | ESSAI D'USURE | VERSCHLEISSPRÜFUNG |
| 13715 | **WEAR HARDENING** | ECROUISSAGE | KALTHÄRTUNG |
| 13716 | **WEAR PLATE** | TOLE D'USURE | VERSCHLEISSBLECH |
| 13717 | **WEAR RESISTANCE** | RESISTANCE A L'USURE | VERSCHLEISSFESTIGKEIT |
| 13718 | **WEAR RESISTING STEEL** | ACIER RESISTANT A L'USURE | STAHL (VERSCHLEISSFESTER) |
| 13719 | **WEARING OVAL OF A BEARING** | OVALISATION D'UN COUSSINET | UNRUNDWERDEN EINES LAGERS |
| 13720 | **WEATHER SHIELD** | JOINT SECONDAIRE D'ETANCHEITE | SPRITZWASSERSCHUTZ |
| 13721 | **WEATHER SIDE** | COTE DU VENT | LUVSEITE |
| 13722 | **WEATHER STRIP** | CAOUTCHOUC D'ETANCHEITE | DICHTUNGSSTREIFEN |
| 13723 | **WEATHER-PROOF** | INALTERABLE, INATTAQUABLE AUX INTEMPERIES | WETTERBESTÄNDIG, WETTERFEST |
| 13724 | **WEAVE BEAD** | PASSE LARGE | PENDELRAUPE |
| 13725 | **WEAVING MOTION** | MOUVEMENT ALTERNATIF, VA-ET-VIENT. | BEWEGUNG (HIN-UND HERGEHENDE) |
| 13726 | **WEB** | AME | STEG, KERN |
| 13727 | **WEB CRIPPLING OF A PLATE GIRDER** | DEFORMATION PERMANENTE DE L'AME D'UNE POUTRE | DURCHBIEGUNG (BLEIBENDE) EINES TRÄGERSTEGS |
| 13728 | **WEB LEG OF AN ANGLE IRON** | AILE, BRANCHE D'UN FER CORNIERE | SCHENKEL EINES WINKELEISENS |
| 13729 | **WEB OF A BEAM** | AME D'UNE POUTRELLE | STEG |
| 13730 | **WEB, CENTRE WEB, STEM** | AME D'UN FER PROFILE | STEG EINES FORMEISENS |
| 13731 | **WEDGE** | COIN, CALE, CALE D'EPAISSEUR, EPAISSEUR | KEIL, UNTERLAGKEIL, ZWISCHENKEIL |
| 13732 | **WEDGE FRICTION WHEEL** | ROUE DE FRICTION (A JANTE EN FORME DE COIN) | KEILRAD, RILLENRAD |

| | | | |
|---|---|---|---|
| 13733 | WEDGE OF A PLANE | COIN DU RABOT | HOBELKEIL |
| 13734 | WEDGE PRESS | PRESSE A COIN | KEILPRESSE |
| 13735 | WEDGE SHAPE | SECTION CONIQUE | QUERSCHNITT (KEILFÖRMIGER) |
| 13736 | WEDGE SURFACE FRICTION GEAR | TRANSMISSION PAR ROUES DE FRICTION, ENGRENAGE A COIN | KEILRÄDERGETRIEBE |
| 13737 | WEDGE-SHAPED | CUNEIFORME | KEILFÖRMIG |
| 13738 | WEDGE-SHAPED BRICK | BRIQUE CIRCULAIRE ARRONDIE CINTREE | KEILSTEIN |
| 13739 | WEDGE, KEY, COTTER | COIN, CALE, CLAVETTE | KEIL |
| 13740 | WEDGING | CLAVETAGE, CALAGE | VERKEILUNG, VERKEILEN |
| 13741 | WEED THISTLE AND BRACKEN CUTTERS | COUPE CHARDONS ET FOUGERES | UNKRAUTDISTEL-UND FARNKRAUTSCHNEIDER |
| 13742 | WEEDERS AND TILLERS | SARCLEUSES | JÄTMASCHINEN UND ACKERFRÄSEN |
| 13743 | WEFT | TRAME | SCHUSS EINES GEWEBES, EINSCHLAG EINES GEWEBES |
| 13744 | WEIGH (TO) | PESER | ABWIEGEN, WÄGEN |
| 13745 | WEIGHBRIDGE, WEIGH-BRIDGE FOR RAILWAY WAGONS, WAGON WEIGHING MACHINE | PONT A BASCULE | GLEISWAAGE, BRÜCKENWAAGE |
| 13746 | WEIGHING | PESAGE, PESEE | WÄGUNG, WÄGEN, WIEGEN |
| 13747 | WEIGHT | POIDS | GEWICHT |
| 13748 | WEIGHT PER METER | POIDS AU METRE | METERGEWICHT |
| 13749 | WEIGHT-LOADED SAFETY VALVE | SOUPAPE DE SURETE A CONTRE-POIDS | GEWICHTSSICHERHEITSVENTIL, SICHERHEITSVENTIL MIT GEWICHTSBELASTUNG |
| 13750 | WEIGHTED JOCKEY PULLEY (LENIX TYPE) | ENROULEUR DE COURROIE LENIX LENEVEU | SPANNROLLE NACH LENIX |
| 13751 | WEIGHTED LEVER | LEVIER A CONTREPOIDS | HEBEL (BELASTETER), GEWICHTSHEBEL |
| 13752 | WEIGHTED PENDULUM GOVERNOR, LOADED WATT GOVERNOR, PORTER GOVERNOR, CENTRE WEIGHTED GOVERNOR | REGULATEUR A MASSE CENTRALE, REGULATEUR PORTER | GEWICHTSREGLER |
| 13753 | WEIR | DEVERSOIR, BARRAGE | STAUANLAGE, WEHR |
| 13754 | WEIR CREST | CRETE D'UN DEVERSOIR | WEHRKANTE, ÜBERFALLKANTE, WEHRKRONE |
| 13755 | WELD (TO) | SOUDER | SCHWEISSEN, ZUSAMMENSCHWEISSEN |
| 13756 | WELD BEAD | CORDON DE SOUDURE | SCHWEISSRAUPE |
| 13757 | WELD BUILT-UP | SOUDURE EN PASSES SUPERPOSEES | MEHRLAGENSCHWEISSUNG |
| 13758 | WELD BY THE AUTOGENOUS PROCESS (TO) | SOUDER A L'AUTOGENE | AUTOGENSCHWEISSEN |
| 13759 | WELD DECAY | CORROSION DE SOUDURE | KORROSION DER SCHWEISSNAHT |
| 13760 | WELD DEFECTS | DEFAUTS DE LA SOUDURE | NAHTFEHLER, SCHWEISSFEHLER |
| 13761 | WELD DEPOSIT METAL | METAL DEPOSE | SCHWEISSGUT |
| 13762 | WELD DEPOSIT OVERLAY | RECHARGEMENT D'UNE SOUDURE | AUFTRAGSCHWEISSUNG |
| 13763 | WELD METAL | METAL DE SOUDURE | SCHWEISSGUT |
| 13764 | WELD NUGGET | LENTILLE DE SOUDURE | SCHWEISSLINSE |
| 13765 | WELD STEEL | ACIER SOUDE | SCHWEISSSTAHL |
| 13766 | WELD-IRON | FER SOUDE | SCHWEISSEISEN |
| 13767 | WELD, WELDED JOINT | SOUDAGE, SOUDURE, JOINT SOUDE | SCHWEISSUNG, SCHWEISSVERBINDUNG |
| 13768 | WELDABILITY | SOUDABILITE | SCHWEISSBARKEIT |
| 13769 | WELDABLE | SOUDABLE | SCHWEISSBAR |
| 13770 | WELDED CHAIN | CHAINE A MAILLES SOUDEES | KETTE (GESCHWEISSTE) |

# WEL 352

| | | | |
|---|---|---|---|
| 13771 | **WELDED COLLAR** | BAGUE SOUDEE | AUFGESCHWEISSTER BUND, VORSCHWEISSBUND |
| 13772 | **WELDED CONNECTION** | LIAISON SOUDEE | SCHWEISSVERBINDUNG |
| 13773 | **WELDED FLANGE** | BRIDE, RONDELLE SOUDEE | FLANSCH (AUFGESCHWEISSTER), VORSCHWEISSFLANSCH |
| 13774 | **WELDED JOINT / SEAM** | JOINT SOUDE | SCHWEISSVERBINDUNG |
| 13775 | **WELDED PIPE** | TUBE SOUDE | ROHR (GESCHWEISSTES) |
| 13776 | **WELDED SEAM** | JOINT SOUDE, SOUDURE | SCHWEISSNAHT |
| 13777 | **WELDED TUBE** | TUBE SOUDE | ROHR (GESCHWEISSTES) |
| 13778 | **WELDER** | SOUDEUR | SCHWEISSER |
| 13779 | **WELDING** | SOUDURE, SOUDAGE | SCHWEISSEN, SCHWEISSUNG |
| 13780 | **WELDING CURRENT** | INTENSITE DU COURANT DE SOUDAGE | SCHWEISSSTROMSTÄRKE |
| 13781 | **WELDING FITTING** | RACCORD A SOUDER | SCHWEISSFITTING |
| 13782 | **WELDING GUN POSITION** | POSITION DU PISTOLET DE SOUDAGE | STELLUNG (LAGE) DER SCHWEISSPISTOLE |
| 13783 | **WELDING HEAD** | TETE DE SOUDAGE | SCHWEISSKOPF |
| 13784 | **WELDING HEAT** | BLANC SOUDANT, CHAUDE SUANTE, CHALEUR SOUDANTE | SCHWEISSHITZE, SCHWEISSWÄRME |
| 13785 | **WELDING JIG** | GABARIT DE SOUDAGE | SCHWEISSVORRICHTUNG |
| 13786 | **WELDING MACHINE** | MACHINE A SOUDER | SCHWEISSMASCHINE |
| 13787 | **WELDING PARAMETERS** | PARAMETRES DE SOUDAGE | SCHWEISSPARAMETER |
| 13788 | **WELDING PERIOD** | DUREE DU CYCLE DE SOUDAGE | SCHWEISSSPIELZEIT |
| 13789 | **WELDING ROD** | FIL A SOUDER, ELECTRODE | SCHWEISSDRAHT, SCHWEISSELEKTRODE |
| 13790 | **WELDING SEQUENCE** | SUCCESSION DES OPERATIONS DE SOUDAGE | SCHWEISSFOLGE |
| 13791 | **WELDING SYMBOLS** | SYMBOLES DE SOUDAGE | SCHWEISSNAHTSINNBILDER |
| 13792 | **WELDING TEST** | ESSAI DE SOUDABILITE | SCHWEISSVERSUCH |
| 13793 | **WELDING WIRE** | FIL (BAGUETTE) A SOUDER | SCHWEISSDRAHT, SCHWEISSSTAB |
| 13794 | **WELDING-NECK FLANGE, SLIP-ON WELDING FLANGE** | BRIDE A SOUDER (EN BOUT, A L'INTERIEUR) | VORSCHWEISSFLANSCH, EINSCHWEISSFLANSCH |
| 13795 | **WELDMENT** | CONSTRUCTION SOUDEE | SCHWEISSKONSTRUKTION |
| 13796 | **WELL WATER** | EAU DE PUITS | BRUNNENWASSER |
| 13797 | **WELL-SINKER'S CEMENT** | MASTIC DES FONTAINIERS | BRUNNENMACHERKITT |
| 13798 | **WESTON DIFFERENTIAL PULLEY BLOCK** | PALAN DIFFERENTIEL, PALAN WESTON | DIFFERENTIALFLASCHENZUG |
| 13799 | **WET AIR PUMP** | POMPE A AIR HUMIDE | LUFTPUMPE (NASSE) |
| 13800 | **WET ANALYSIS** | ANALYSE PAR VOIE HUMIDE | ANALYSE AUF NASSEM WEGE |
| 13801 | **WET COMPRESSOR** | COMPRESSEUR HUMIDE | VERDICHTER (NASSER), WASSERSÄULENVERDICHTER |
| 13802 | **WET CORROSION** | CORROSION HUMIDE | FEUCHTIGKEITSKORROSION |
| 13803 | **WET DRAWING** | PASSE HUMIDE | NASSZUG |
| 13804 | **WET LINER** | CHEMISE HUMIDE | LAUFBÜCHSE (NASSE) |
| 13805 | **WET STEAM** | VAPEUR HUMIDE | NASSDAMPF |
| 13806 | **WETNESS OF STEAM** | HUMIDITE DE LA VAPEUR | DAMPFNÄSSE |
| 13807 | **WETTING** | HUMECTATION | FEUCHTEN |
| 13808 | **WETTING AGENT** | AGENT MOUILLANT | BENETZUNGSMITTEL |
| 13809 | **WHEATSTONE'S BRIDGE** | PONT DE WHEATSTONE | BRÜCKENVIERECK, BRÜCKE WHEATSTONESCHE |
| 13810 | **WHEEL** | ROUE, VOLANT | HANDRAD, RAD |
| 13811 | **WHEEL ARM** | RAYONS D'UNE ROUE | RADARM, RADSPEICHE |
| 13812 | **WHEEL BARROW** | BROUETTE | SCHUBKARREN |

| | | | |
|---|---|---|---|
| 13813 | **WHEEL BASE** | ECARTEMENT DES ESSIEUX | ACHSSTAND, RADSTAND |
| 13814 | **WHEEL CENTRE, SPIDER** | BRASSURE (D'UNE ROUE) | RADSTERN |
| 13815 | **WHEEL GUARD COVER** | COUVRE-ROUES, CARTER D'ENGRENAGES | RADVERDECK |
| 13816 | **WHEEL LATHE** | TOUR POUR ROUES | RÄDERDREHBANK |
| 13817 | **WHEEL OF PLANIMETER** | TAMBOUR, ROULETTE DU PLANIMETRE | MESSROLLE DES PLANIMETERS |
| 13818 | **WHEEL RIM** | JANTE DE ROUE | RADFELGE |
| 13819 | **WHEEL TOOTH** | DENT D'ENGRENAGE | RADZAHN |
| 13820 | **WHEEL VANE, MOVING BLADE OF A TURBINE** | AUBE RECEPTRICE, AUBE MOBILE D'UNE TURBINE | LAUFRADSCHAUFEL EINER TURBINE |
| 13821 | **WHEEL WORK** | ROUAGE | RÄDERWERK |
| 13822 | **WHEEL-RIM PROFILING MACHINE** | MACHINE A PROFILER LES JANTES DE ROUES | RADKRANZPROFILIERMASCHINE |
| 13823 | **WHEEL, ROTOR OF A TURBINE** | COURONNE MOBILE, ROUE D'UNE TURBINE | LAUFRAD EINER TURBINE, TURBINENRAD |
| 13824 | **WHETSTONE** | PIERRE A AFFUTER, PIERRE A AFFILER, PIERRE A AIGUISER | SCHLEIFSTEIN, ABZIEHSTEIN |
| 13825 | **WHIPPING OF A BELT** | FOUETTEMENT D'UNE COURROIE, FLOTTEMENT D'UNE COURROIE, BALLANT D'UNE COURROIE | FLATTERN DES RIEMENS, PEITSCHEN DES RIEMENS, SCHLAGEN DES RIEMENS |
| 13826 | **WHIRLED THERMOMETER, SING THERMOMETER** | THERMOMETRE-FRONDE | SCHLEUDERTHERMOMETER |
| 13827 | **WHIRLING** | TOURBILLONNEMENT | WIRBELUNG |
| 13828 | **WHISKER** | FIL (CROISSANCE EN FILAMENT), FIL MONOCRISTALLIN | WHISKER-WACHSTUM, FADENKRISTALL |
| 13829 | **WHISTLE** | SIFFLET | PFEIFE |
| 13830 | **WHITE CAST IRON, WHITE IRON, WHITE PIG** | FONTE BLANCHE | ROHEISEN (WEISSES) |
| 13831 | **WHITE GOLD** | OR BLANC | WEISSGOLD |
| 13832 | **WHITE HEAT** | INCANDESCENCE | WEISSGLUT |
| 13833 | **WHITE IRONWOOD** | BOIS DE FER-BLANC, BOIS DE SABLE, SIDEROXYLE | EISENHOLZ |
| 13834 | **WHITE LEAD, BASIC CARBONATE OF LEAD** | CERUSE, BLANC DE PLOMB, BLANC D'ARGENT, BLANC DE CERUSE | BLEIWEISS, BLEI (BASISCH), BLEI (KOHLENSAURES) |
| 13835 | **WHITE MEAL TURNINGS** | METAL BLANC DEFLOCULE | FLOCKEN VON WEISSMETALL |
| 13836 | **WHITE METAL** | METAL, ALLIAGE BLANC, METAL ANTI-FRICTION | WEISSMETALL |
| 13837 | **WHITE METAL LINING** | GARNITURE ANTI-FRICTION | WEISSMETALLAUSGUSS |
| 13838 | **WHITE OILS** | HUILES BLANCHES | WEISSES MINERALÖL |
| 13839 | **WHITE UNTARRED ROPE** | CORDE NON GOUDRONNEE | SEIL (UNGESTEURTES) |
| 13840 | **WHITE-WALLED TYRES** | PNEUS A FLANCS BLANCS | WEISSWANDREIFEN |
| 13841 | **WHITING** | BLANC DE MEUDON, BLANC DE TROYES, BLANC D'ESPAGNE | SCHLÄMMKREIDE |
| 13842 | **WHITING** | CHARGE NEUTRE, CRAIE, KAOLIN (POUR LES PNEUS) | KREIDE |
| 13843 | **WHITWORTH MEASURING MACHINE** | MACHINE A MESURER WHITWORTH | MESSMASCHINE VON WHITWORTH |
| 13844 | **WHITWORTH THREAD, ENGLISH STANDARD THREAD, COMMON THREAD** | PAS WHITWORTH, PAS ANGLAIS | GEWINDE (WHITWORTHSCHES) |
| 13845 | **WHOLE DEPTH** | HAUTEUR DE DENT | ZAHNHÖHE, ZAHNTIEFE |
| 13846 | **WICK** | MECHE (D'UNE LAMPE, D'UN GRAISSEUR) | DOCHT |
| 13847 | **WICK SIPHON LUBRICATION** | GRAISSAGE PAR MECHE | DOCHTSCHMIERUNG |
| 13848 | **WIDE EDGE MILLING CUTTER, HOB** | FRAISE CYLINDRIQUE, FRAISE RECTILIGNE | MANTELFRÄSER, WALZENFRÄSER, ZYLINDERFRÄSER |

**WID** 354

| | | | |
|---|---|---|---|
| 13849 | WIDE FLANGED BEAM | POUTRELLE A LARGES AILES | BREITFLANSCHTRÄGER |
| 13850 | WIDTH | LARGEUR | BREITE |
| 13851 | WINCH, CRAB | TREUIL | WINDE, BOCKWINDE |
| 13852 | WINCHES | TREUILS | ACKERWINDEN |
| 13853 | WIND (TO), COIL (TO) | ENROULER | AUFWICKELN, AUFWINDEN |
| 13854 | WIND CORD | BOURRELET D'ETANCHEITE | FENSTERDICHTUNGSCHNUR |
| 13855 | WIND ENGINE, WIND MILL | MOTEUR A VENT, MOTEUR EOLIEN PNEUMATIQUE, MOULIN A VENT | WINDKRAFTMASCHINE, WINDMOTOR |
| 13856 | WIND GIRDER | POUTRE RAIDISSEUSE, POUTRE AU VENT | VERSTEIFUNGSBALKEN |
| 13857 | WIND LOAD | CHARGE DUE AU VENT | WINDBELASTUNG |
| 13858 | WIND PRESSURE | POUSSEE, PRESSION DU VENT | WINDDRUCK |
| 13859 | WIND TURBINE, AIR TURBINE | TURBINE A AIR | WINDTURBINE |
| 13860 | WIND VANE | GIROUETTE | WINDFAHNE |
| 13861 | WIND WHEEL | ROUE ATMOSPHERIQUE | WINDRAD |
| 13862 | WINDING, COILING | ENROULEMENT, BOBINAGE | WICKLUNG, AUFWICKELN, AUFWINDEN |
| 13863 | WINDLASS | TREUIL SIMPLE | HASPEL |
| 13864 | WINDOW | FENETRE | FENSTER |
| 13865 | WINDOW FRAME | CHASSIS DE FENETRE | FENSTERRAHMEN |
| 13866 | WINDOW GLASS | VERRE A VITRES | FENSTERGLAS |
| 13867 | WINDOW REGULATOR | LEVE-GLACE | FENSTERKURBEL |
| 13868 | WINDOW RIM CHANNEL | GLISSIERE (DE FENETRE) | FENSTERFÜHRUNG |
| 13869 | WINDROWER | ABATTEURS POUR MOISSONNAGE | MASCHINEN ZUM AUFZIEHEN DES HEUES IN SCHWADEN |
| 13870 | WINDSHIELD-WASHER | LAVE-GLACE | SCHEIBENWASCHER |
| 13871 | WINDSHIELD-WIPER | ESSUIE-GLACE | SCHEIBENWISCHER |
| 13872 | WINDSHIELD, WINDSCREEN | PARE-BRISE | WINDSCHUTZSCHEIBE |
| 13873 | WINDUP | JEU | GANG (TOTER) |
| 13874 | WING | AILE | KOTFLÜGEL |
| 13875 | WING PLATFORM | PLATE-FORME EN PORTE-A-FAUX | PLATTFORM (AUSKRAGENDE) |
| 13876 | WING, QUADRANT COMPASSES | COMPAS A QUART DE CERCLE | BOGENZIRKEL |
| 13877 | WINNING EXTRACTION OF COAL | EXTRACTION DE LA HOUILLE | GEWINNUNG DER KOHLE |
| 13878 | WIPER | CAME | HEBEDAUMEN, DÄUMLING |
| 13879 | WIPER RING | BAGUE LARMIER | ÖL-ABSTREIFRING |
| 13880 | WIRE | FIL METALLIQUE | DRAHT |
| 13881 | WIRE (TO) | POSER UN FIL CONDUCTEUR | VERLEGEN (EINEN LEITUNGSDRAHT) |
| 13882 | WIRE BAR | FIL EN VERGE POUR TREFILERIE | DRAHTBARREN, STANGENDRAHT |
| 13883 | WIRE BENDING MACHINE | MACHINE A PLIER LES FILS | DRAHTBIEGEMASCHINE |
| 13884 | WIRE BRUSH | BROSSE EN FILS METALLIQUES, BROSSE METALLIQUE | DRAHTBÜRSTE |
| 13885 | WIRE CHAIN MAKING-MACHINE | MACHINE A FAIRE LES CHAINES EN FIL DE FER | DRAHTKETTENMASCHINE |
| 13886 | WIRE CUTTER | COUPE-FIL | DRAHTSCHNEIDER |
| 13887 | WIRE DRAW DIE | FILIERE A TREFILER | DRAHTZIEHSTEIN |
| 13888 | WIRE DRAWING | ETIRAGE EN FIL, TREFILERIE | ZIEHEN VON DRAHT, DRAHTZIEHEN |
| 13889 | WIRE DRAWING MACHINE | MACHINE A TREFILER | DRAHTZIEHMASCHINE |
| 13890 | WIRE EDGE | MORFIL | SCHLEIFGRAT |
| 13891 | WIRE FACK MACHINE | FRAPPEUR DE POINTES | DRAHTSTIFTSCHLAGMASCHINE |
| 13892 | WIRE GAUGE | JAUGE POUR FILS METALLIQUES, JAUGE DE TREFILERIE | DRAHTLEHRE |
| 13893 | WIRE GAUZE | TOILE METALLIQUE, GAZE METALLIQUE | DRAHTGEWEBE, DRAHTGAZE |

| | | | |
|---|---|---|---|
| 13894 | **WIRE GLASS, FERROGLAS** | VERRE ARME, VERRE A FIL DE FER NOYE | DRAHTGLAS, GLAS (NICHT SPLITTERNDES) |
| 13895 | **WIRE NAIL, FRENCH NAIL** | POINTE DE PARIS | DRAHTSTIFT, PARISER STIFT, DRAHTNAGEL |
| 13896 | **WIRE NETTING** | TREILLIS METALLIQUE | DRAHTNETZ, DRAHTGEFLECHT |
| 13897 | **WIRE NETTING MACHINE** | MACHINE A FAIRE LES GRILLAGES | DRAHTFLECHTMASCHINEN |
| 13898 | **WIRE REEL** | COURONNE DE FIL, DEVIDOIR | DRAHTHASPEL, DRAHTABSPULER |
| 13899 | **WIRE ROPE** | CABLE METALLIQUE | DRAHTSEIL, KABEL |
| 13900 | **WIRE SPEED** | VITESSE DU FIL | DRAHTABSPULGESCHWINDIGKEIT |
| 13901 | **WIRE SPRING COILING MACHINE** | MACHINE A ENROULER LES RESSORTS A BOUDIN | DRAHTFEDERNWINDEMASCHINE |
| 13902 | **WIRE STRAND** | TORON METALLIQUE | DRAHTLITZE |
| 13903 | **WIRE WINDING, UNWINDING MACHINE** | ENROULEUSE, DEROULEUSE DE FIL | DRAHTAUF-U.ABWICKELMASCHINE |
| 13904 | **WIRE WORKING MACHINE** | MACHINE A TRAVAILLER LES FILS METALLIQUES | DRAHTVERARBEITUNGSMASCHINE |
| 13905 | **WIRE WORKS** | TREFILERIE (FABRIQUE) | DRAHTZIEHEREI |
| 13906 | **WIRE-DRAWING** | TREFILAGE | DRAHTZIEHEN |
| 13907 | **WIRELESS TELEGRAPHY, RADIOTELEGRAPHY** | TELEGRAPHIE SANS FIL, RADIOTELEGRAPHIE | TELEGRAPHIE (DRAHTLOSE) |
| 13908 | **WIRELESS TELEPHONY, RADIOTELEPHONY** | TELEPHONIE SANS FIL, RADIOTELEPHONIE | TELEPHONIE (DRAHTLOSE) |
| 13909 | **WIRING** | POSE D'UN FIL CONDUCTEUR | VERLEGUNG EINES LEITUNGSDRAHTES |
| 13910 | **WITHDRAW HEAT FROM.. (TO)** | SOUSTRAIRE DE LA CHALEUR | WÄRME ENTZIEHEN |
| 13911 | **WITHERITE** | WITHERITE, CARBONATE NATUREL DE BARYTE | BARYT (KOHLENSAURER), WITHERIT |
| 13912 | **WOLFRAM** | WOLFRAM | WOLFRAMIT |
| 13913 | **WOOD** | BOIS | HOLZ |
| 13914 | **WOOD CHARCOAL** | CHARBON DE BOIS | HOLZKOHLE |
| 13915 | **WOOD LAGGING** | REVETEMENT EN BOIS | HOLZVERSCHALUNG, HOLZVERKLEIDUNG |
| 13916 | **WOOD MEAL** | POUDRE DE BOIS | HOLZMEHL |
| 13917 | **WOOD SAW** | SCIE A BOIS | HOLZSÄGE |
| 13918 | **WOOD SCREW** | VIS METALLIQUE A BOIS | HOLZSCHRAUBE |
| 13919 | **WOOD SHAVINGS** | COPEAUX (DE BOIS) | HOBELSPÄNE |
| 13920 | **WOOD SPIRIT, METHYL ALCOHOL** | ALCOOL METHYLIQUE, HYDRATE DE METHYLE, METHYLENE, ESPRIT DE BOIS | HOLZGEIST, HOLZALKOHOL, HOLZSPIRITUS, HOLZNAPHTA, METHYLALKOHOL, KARBINOL, METHANOL |
| 13921 | **WOOD TAR** | GOUDRON DE BOIS, GOUDRON VEGETAL | HOLZTEER |
| 13922 | **WOOD TURNING LATHE** | TOUR A BOIS | HOLZDREHBANK |
| 13923 | **WOOD WOOL** | LAINE DE BOIS, COPEAUX DE FIBRES DE BOIS | HOLZWOLLE |
| 13924 | **WOOD WORKING** | TRAVAIL DU BOIS | HOLZBEARBEITUNG |
| 13925 | **WOOD WORKING MACHINE** | MACHINE-OUTIL A TRAVAILLER LE BOIS, MACHINE A BOIS | HOLZBEARBEITUNGSMASCHINE |
| 13926 | **WOODEN HAMMER** | MAILLET | HOLZHAMMER |
| 13927 | **WOODEN LINING** | CHEMISE, FOURRURE EN BOIS | HOLZFUTTER |
| 13928 | **WOODEN PIPE** | TUYAU EN BOIS | HOLZROHR, HOLZRÖHRE |
| 13929 | **WOODRUFF KEY** | CLAVETTE DEMI-RONDE, CLAVETTE WOODRUFF, CLAVETTE-DISQUE | SEGMENTKEIL, WOODRUFFKEIL, SCHEIBENFEDER |
| 13930 | **WOODRUFF KEYSEAT CUTTERS** | FRAISES A RAINURE WOODRUFF | FRÄSER FÜR WOODRUFFKEILE |
| 13931 | **WOODWORKING MACHINERY** | MACHINES A BOIS | HOLZBEARBEITUNGSMASCHINEN |
| 13932 | **WOOL** | LAINE (DE MOUTON) | SCHAFWOLLE |

# WOR 356

| | | | |
|---|---|---|---|
| 13933 | WOOL FAT, YOLK, SUINT | SUINT | WOLLFETT |
| 13934 | WORD | MOT | DATENWORT |
| 13935 | WORD ADDRESS FORMAT | FORMAT A ADRESSES | EINGABEFORMAT IN ADRESSSCHREIBWEISE |
| 13936 | WORK (MOMENTUM) | TRAVAIL | ARBEIT |
| 13937 | WORK (TO), MACHINE (TO) | TRAVAILLER, TRAITER, USINER, OUVRAGER | BEARBEITEN |
| 13938 | WORK AN INVENTION ON A COMMERCIAL SCALE (TO) | EXPLOITER, METTRE EN EXPLOITATION UNE INVENTION | AUSNUTZEN (EINE ERFINDUNG) |
| 13939 | WORK DISTRIBUTION | REPARTITION DU TRAVAIL | ARBEITSVERTEILUNG |
| 13940 | WORK DONE, OUTPUT | TRAVAIL EFFECTUE | ARBEIT (GELEISTETE), ARBEIT (ABGEGEBENE), LEISTUNG (ABGEGEBENE) |
| 13941 | WORK OF COMPRESSION | TRAVAIL DE COMPRESSION | VERDICHTUNGSARBEIT |
| 13942 | WORK OF FRICTION, WORK LOST EXPANDED IN FRICTION | TRAVAIL DU FROTTEMENT | REIBUNGSARBEIT |
| 13943 | WORK ROOM | LIEU DE TRAVAIL, ATELIER | ARBEITSRAUM |
| 13944 | WORK TO OVERCOME RESISTANCE, WORK AGAINST RESISTANCE | TRAVAIL RESISTANT | WIDERSTANDSARBEIT |
| 13945 | WORK-HOLDING JAW | MACHOIRE DE BLOCAGE | FESTSPANNEINRICHTUNG |
| 13946 | WORKABILITY, EASE OF WORKING | USINABILITE, FACILITE DU TRAVAIL | BEARBEITBARKEIT |
| 13947 | WORKABLE | FACILE A TRAVAILLER | BEARBEITBAR, BEARBEITUNGSFÄHIG |
| 13948 | WORKING AN INVENTION ON A COMMERCIAL SCALE | EXPLOITATION D'UNE INVENTION | AUSNUTZUNG EINER ERFINDUNG |
| 13949 | WORKING CONDITIONS, CONDITIONS OF SERVICE | CONDITIONS DE SERVICE | BETRIEBSVERHÄLTNISSE |
| 13950 | WORKING COST, EXPENSES | FRAIS D'EXPLOITATON | BETRIEBSKOSTEN |
| 13951 | WORKING DEPTH | HAUTEUR D'ACTION | EINGRIFFSTIEFE |
| 13952 | WORKING DEPTH IN TOOTHED GEARING | PROFONDEUR D'ENGRENEMENT | EINGRIFFSTIEFE |
| 13953 | WORKING ELEMENT | ORGANE TRAVAILLANT | BESTANDTEIL (ARBEITENDER) |
| 13954 | WORKING ENGINE CYLINDER | CYLINDRE MOTEUR, CYLINDRE DE TRAVAIL | ZYLINDER, ARBEITSZYLINDER |
| 13955 | WORKING GAUGE | JAUGE DE FABRICATION | ARBEITSLEHRE |
| 13956 | WORKING LOAD | CHARGE ADMISSIBLE | BELASTUNG (ZULÄSSIGE) |
| 13957 | WORKING PRESSURE | PRESSION DE REGIME, PRESSION DE SERVICE, TENSION DE SERVICE | BETRIEBSDRUCK |
| 13958 | WORKING STRESS | TAUX DE TRAVAIL | BELASTBARKEIT IM GEBRAUCH |
| 13959 | WORKING, MACHINING | TRAVAIL, TRAITEMENT, USINAGE | BEARBEITEN, BEARBEITUNG |
| 13960 | WORKMAN, WORKER, HAND | OUVRIER, TRAVAILLEUR | ARBEITER |
| 13961 | WORKMANSHIP | MAIN-D'OEUVRE | AUSFÜHRUNG, ARBEIT |
| 13962 | WORKPEOPLE | PERSONNEL OUVRIER | ARBEITERSCHAFT |
| 13963 | WORKS MANAGEMENT | DIRECTION DES USINES, DIRECTION DES ATELIERS, DIRECTION DU TRAVAIL | BETRIEBSFÜHRUNG |
| 13964 | WORKS MANAGER | CHEF DE FABRICATION, CHEF DE SERVICE, CHEF D'ATELIER | BETRIEBSFÜHRER, BETRIEBSLEITER |
| 13965 | WORKS RAILWAY | VOIE FERREE D'ATELIER | FABRIKBAHN |
| 13966 | WORKS SIDING | EMBRANCHEMENT INDUSTRIEL | FABRIKANSCHLUSSGLEIS, ANSCHLUSSGLEIS, INDUSTRIEGLEIS |
| 13967 | WORKSHOP GAUGE | JAUGE DE FABRICATION | ARBEITSLEHRE |
| 13968 | WORKSHOP, SHOP | ATELIER | WERKSTATT, WERKSTÄTTE |
| 13969 | WORM | VIS SANS FIN | SCHNECKE |

| | | | |
|---|---|---|---|
| 13970 | **WORM CONVEYOR** | TRANSPORTEUR A HELICE, VIS TRANSPORTEUSE, VIS D'ARCHIMEDE | FÖRDERSCHNECKE, TRANSPORTSCHNECKE, SCHNECKE |
| 13971 | **WORM CUTTER** | FRAISE MERE | SCHNECKENFRÄSER |
| 13972 | **WORM GEAR MILLING CUTTER, WORM HOB, MILLING CUTTER HOB FOR WORM GEAR** | FRAISE POUR TAILLER DES ENGRENAGES HELICOIDAUX | SCHNECKENFRÄSER |
| 13973 | **WORM GEAR PULLEY BLOCK** | PALAN A VIS TANGENTE, PALAN A VIS SANS FIN | SCHRAUBENFLASCHENZUG, SCHNECKENFLASCHENZUG |
| 13974 | **WORM GEARING** | ENGRENAGE, MECANISME A VIS SANS FIN, COUPLE DE ROUE ET VIS TANGENTE | SCHNECKENRADGETRIEBE, SCHRAUBGETRIEBE, WURMGETRIEBE |
| 13975 | **WORM WHEEL** | ROUE A VIS SANS FIN | SCHNECKENRAD, MUTTERRAD |
| 13976 | **WORM-EATEN** | VERMOULU | WURMSTICHIG |
| 13977 | **WORM-EATEN TIMBER** | BOIS VERMOULU | HOLZ (WURMSTICHIGES) |
| 13978 | **WORM, COOLING COIL** | SERPENTIN DE REFROIDISSEMENT | KÜHLSCHLANGE |
| 13979 | **WORM, ENDLESS SCREW, PERPETUAL SCREW** | VIS SANS FIN | SCHNECKE, WURM, SCHRAUBE OHNE ENDE, ZYLINDERSCHRAUBE |
| 13980 | **WORN OUT BEARING** | COUSSINET OVALISE PAR L'USURE, COUSSINET USE | LAGER (UNRUNDGEWORDENES), LAGER (AUSGELAUFENES) |
| 13981 | **WORN OUT, WORN DOWN SCREW THREAD** | FILET FOIRE, FILET JARETE | GEWINDE (AUSGELEIERTES) |
| 13982 | **WORN OUT, WORN DOWN, WORN OFF, WORN AWAY** | USAGE | ABGENUTZT |
| 13983 | **WOVEN BELT** | COURROIE TISSEE | RIEMEN (GEWEBTER) |
| 13984 | **WRAPPING PAPER** | PAPIER D'EMBALLAGE | EINWICKELPAPIER, PACKPAPIER |
| 13985 | **WRINKLING** | FRISAGE | FALTENBILDUNG |
| 13986 | **WRIST PIN** | GOUPILLE | ANLENKBOLZEN |
| 13987 | **WROUGHT BRASS** | ARCOT | ROHMESSING |
| 13988 | **WROUGHT IRON, MALLEABLE IRON** | FER DOUX, FER FORGE | SCHMIEDEEISEN |
| 13989 | **WROUGHT IRON, MALLEABLE IRON PIPE** | TUYAU EN FER | ROHR (SCHMIEDEEISERNES) |
| 13990 | **WROUGHT NAIL** | CLOU FORGE | NAGEL (GESCHMIEDETER) |
| 13991 | **WULFENITE, LEAD MOLYBDATE** | MELINOSE, WULFENITE | MOLYBDÄNBLEISPAT, GELBBLEIERZ, WULFENIT |
| 13992 | **WULFF NET** | ABAQUE, RESEAU DE WULFF (STEREOGRAPHIQUE) | ABAKUS (WULFFSCHER) |
| 13993 | **X-RAY ANALYSIS** | EXAMEN RADIOGRAPHIQUE | RÖNTGENANALYSE |
| 13994 | **X-RAY APPARATUS** | APPAREIL RADIOGRAPHIQUE | RÖNTGENAPPARAT |
| 13995 | **X-RAY BEAM** | FAISCEAU DE RAYONS X | RÖNTGENSTRAHLENBÜNDEL |
| 13996 | **X-RAY CRYSTALLOGRAPHY** | RADIO-CRISTALLOGRAPHIE | RÖNTGENKRISTALLOGRAPHIE |
| 13997 | **X-RAY DIFFRACTION PATTERN** | DIAGRAMME DE DIFFRACTION DES RAYONS X. | RÖNTGENBEUGUNGSDIAGRAMM |
| 13998 | **X-RAY EXAMINATION** | CONTROLE RADIOGRAPHIQUE | RÖNTGENUNTERSUCHUNG |
| 13999 | **X-RAY FLUORESCENT ANALYSIS** | ANALYSE FLUORESCENTE | RÖNTGEN-FLUORESZENZ-ANALYSE |
| 14000 | **X-RAY SPECTROGRAPH** | SPECTROMETRE A RAYONS X | RÖNTGENSPEKTROMETER |
| 14001 | **X-RAY SPECTRUM** | SPECTRE DES RAYONS X | RÖNTGENSPEKTRUM |
| 14002 | **X-RAY TUBE** | TUBE A RAYONS X | RÖNTGENRÖHRE |
| 14003 | **X-RAYS** | RAYONS X | RÖNTGENSTRAHLEN |
| 14004 | **XENON** | XENON | XENON |
| 14005 | **XEROGRAPHY** | XEROGRAPHIE | XEROGRAPHIE |
| 14006 | **XYLENE** | XYLENE, XYLOL | XYLOL |
| 14007 | **YARD** | YARD | YARD |
| 14008 | **YELLOW BRASS** | LAITON | MESSING |

**YIE** 358

| | | | |
|---|---|---|---|
| 14009 | **YELLOW PHOSPHORUS** | PHOSPHORE BLANC | PHOSPHOR (GELBWEISSER), PHOSPHOR (KRISTALLINISCHER) |
| 14010 | **YIELD** | RENDEMENT | ARBEITSLEISTUNG |
| 14011 | **YIELD POINT, BREAKING DOWN POINT** | LIMITE D'ECOULEMENT, LIMITE TARDIVE, LIMITE ELASTIQUE | FLIESSGRENZE, STRECKGRENZE |
| 14012 | **YIELD STRENGTH** | LIMITE D'ECOULEMENT, LIMITE ELASTIQUE | STRECKGRENZE, FLIESSGRENZE, STRECKFESTIGKEIT |
| 14013 | **YIELD STRESS** | LIMITE ELASTIQUE | STRECKGRENZE, ELASTIZITÄTSGRENZE |
| 14014 | **YOKE** | ARCADE | BÜGEL |
| 14015 | **YOKE BONNET** | CHAPEAU A ARCADE | BÜGELAUFSATZ |
| 14016 | **YOKE BUSHING, YOKE SLEEVE** | DOUILLE D'ARCADE | AUFSATZBUCHSE |
| 14017 | **YOKE OF A MAGNET** | CULASSE D'UN AIMANT | JOCH EINES MAGNETEN |
| 14018 | **YOKE RETAINING NUT** | ECROU DE DOUILLE D'ARCADE | BÜGELVERSCHRAUBUNG |
| 14019 | **YTTERBIUM** | YTTERBIUM | YTTERBIUM |
| 14020 | **YTTRIUM** | YTTRIUM | YTTRIUM |
| 14021 | **ZAMAK** | ZAMAK | FEINZINKLEGIERUNG |
| 14022 | **ZAPON ENAMEL** | VERNIS ZAPON | ZAPONLACK |
| 14023 | **ZED BAR, Z-BAR** | FER EN Z | Z-EISEN |
| 14024 | **ZERO DEVIATION** | DEVIATION NULLE | NULLPUNKTABWEICHUNG |
| 14025 | **ZERO MARK LINE** | TRAIT ZERO | NULLMARKE, NULLSTRICH |
| 14026 | **ZERO OFFSET** | DECALAGE DU POINT D'ORIGINE | NULLPUNKTVERSATZ |
| 14027 | **ZERO POINT** | ZERO (D'UNE ECHELLE), POINT ZERO | NULLPUNKT |
| 14028 | **ZERO POSITION** | POSITION DE ZERO | NULLSTELLUNG |
| 14029 | **ZERO PRESSURE LINE** | LIGNE DE NULLE PRESSION (DU DIAGRAMME D'INDICATEUR) | NULLINIE (INDIKATOR-DIAGRAMM) |
| 14030 | **ZERO RESET** | REMISE A ZERO | NULLRÜCKSTELLUNG |
| 14031 | **ZERO SHIFT** | DECALAGE DU POINT D'ORIGINE | NULLPUNKTVERSATZ |
| 14032 | **ZERO SYNCHRONIZATION** | REMISE A ZERO | NULLRÜCKSTELLUNG |
| 14033 | **ZERO-SUPPRESSION** | SUPPRESSION DES ZEROS | NULLUNTERDRÜCKUNG |
| 14034 | **ZIGZAG RIVETED JOINT** | RIVURE EN QUINCONCE | ZICKZACKNIETUNG, NIETUNG (VERSETZTE) |
| 14035 | **ZINC** | ZINC | ZINK |
| 14036 | **ZINC ACETATE** | ACETATE DE ZINC | ZINK (ESSIGSAURES), ZINKAZETAT |
| 14037 | **ZINC CARBONATE** | CARBONATE DE ZINC | ZINK (KOHLENSAURES), ZINKKARBONAT |
| 14038 | **ZINC CHLORIDE** | CHLORURE DE ZINC | ZINK (SALZSAURES), ZINKCHLORID, CHLORZINK |
| 14039 | **ZINC CHROMATE** | CHROMATE DE ZINC, JAUNE DE ZINC | ZINK (CHROMSAURES), ZINKCHROMAT, ZINKCHROMGELB |
| 14040 | **ZINC CUTTINGS** | ROGNURES DE ZINC | ZINKSPÄNE |
| 14041 | **ZINC CYANIDE** | CYANURE DE ZINC | ZYANZINK |
| 14042 | **ZINC ORE** | MINERAI DE ZINC | ZINKERZ |
| 14043 | **ZINC OXIDE, ZINC WHITE** | OXYDE DE ZINC, BLANC DE ZINC, BLANC DE NEIGE | ZINKOXYD, ZINKWEISS |
| 14044 | **ZINC PLATING** | ZINGAGE, GALVANISATION | VERZINKUNG |
| 14045 | **ZINC SPRAYING** | METALLISATION AU ZINC | SPRITZVERZINKEN |
| 14046 | **ZINC SULPHATE, WHITE VITRIOL** | SULFATE DE ZINC, VITRIOL BLANC, COUPEROSE BLANCHE | ZINKVITRIOL, VITRIOL (WEISSER), ZINKSCHWEFEL (SAURER), ZINKSULFAT |
| 14047 | **ZINC TUBE** | TUYAU EN ZINC | ZINKROHR |
| 14048 | **ZINC WIRE** | FIL DE ZINC | ZINKDRAHT |
| 14049 | **ZIRCONIUM** | ZIRCONIUM | ZIRKONIUM |
| 14050 | **ZONE MELTING** | FUSION PAR ZONE | ZONENSCHMELZEN |

| | | |
|---|---|---|
| 14051 **ZONE OF SPHERE** | ZONE SPHERIQUE, SEGMENT SPHERIQUE A DEUX BASES | KUGELSCHICHT, KUGELZONE |

**VER**  360

| | | | |
|---|---|---|---|
| 13535 | **VERMILLON, MERCURIC SULPHIDE** | SULFURE ROUGE DE MERCURE, VERMILLON | ZINNOBER, ZINNOBERROT, VERMILLON |
| 13536 | **VERNIER** | VERNIER | NONIUS, VERNIER |
| 13537 | **VERNIER CALLIPERS, CALLIPER RULE** | PIED, COMPAS A COULISSE | SCHUBLEHRE, SCHIEBLEHRE |
| 13538 | **VERNIER DEPTH GAUGE** | CALIBRE A COULISSE DE PROFONDEUR | TIEFENLEHRE |
| 13539 | **VERNIER DEPTH GAUGE WITH FINE MICROMETER ADJUSTMENT** | CALIBRE A COULISSE DE PROFONDEUR A FIXATION MICROMETRIQUE | TIEFENLEHRE MIT MIKROMETERSCHRAUBE |
| 13540 | **VERNIER MICROMETER** | MICROMETRE A VERNIER | MIKROMETERSCHRAUBE |
| 13541 | **VERNIER SCALE** | ECHELLE VERNIER | SCHIEBELEHRE |
| 13542 | **VERSUS** | FONCTION DE (EN) | ABHÄNGIGKEIT VON (IN) |
| 13543 | **VERTEX CORNER OF POLYGON** | SOMMET D'UN POLYGONE | ECKE EINES POLYGONS |
| 13544 | **VERTICAL BOILER** | CHAUDIERE VERTICALE | KESSEL (STEHENDER) |
| 13545 | **VERTICAL BORING AND TURNING MILL** | TOUR VERTICAL | KARUSSELLDREHMASCHINE |
| 13546 | **VERTICAL ENGINE** | MACHINE VERTICALE | MASCHINE (STEHENDE) |
| 13547 | **VERTICAL NECK JOURNAL BEARING** | PALIER INTERMEDIAIRE, COLLIER POUR ARBRES VERTICAUX | HALSLAGER EINER STEHENDEN WELLE |
| 13548 | **VERTICAL SPINDLE MILLING MACHINE** | FRAISEUSE VERTICALE | FRÄSMASCHINE (STEHENDE), FRÄSMASCHINE VERTIKALE, SENKRECHTFRÄSMASCHINE |
| 13549 | **VERTICAL TRAVEL** | COURSE VERTICALE | BEWEGUNG (SENKRECHTE) |
| 13550 | **VERTICAL UPRIGHT SHAFT** | ARBRE VERTICAL | WELLE (STEHENDE), WELLE (SENKRECHTE), KÖNIGSWELLE |
| 13551 | **VERTICAL, UPRIGHT** | VERTICAL | STEHEND, AUFRECHT, VERTIKAL |
| 13552 | **VERTICAL, UPRIGHT DRILLING MACHINE** | MACHINE A PERCER VERTICALE | BOHRMASCHINE (STEHENDE), VERTIKALBOHRMASCHINE |
| 13553 | **VESSELS CONNECTED BY U-TUBE** | VASES COMMUNICANTS | GEFÄSSE (KOMMUNIZIERENDE) |
| 13554 | **VIBRATION** | VIBRATION | SCHWINGUNG |
| 13555 | **VIBRATION DAMPER** | AMORTISSEUR DE VIBRATIONS | SCHWINGUNGSDÄMPFER |
| 13556 | **VIBRATION DUE TO BENDING STRESS** | VIBRATION DUE A DES EFFORTS DE FLEXION | BIEGUNGSSCHWINGUNG |
| 13557 | **VIBRATION DUE TO TORSIONAL STRESS, TORSIONAL VIBRATION** | VIBRATION DUE A DES EFFORTS DE TORSION | DREHSCHWINGUNG, VERDREHUNGSSCHWINGUNG, TORSIONSSCHWINGUNG |
| 13558 | **VIBRATION OF A SPRING** | OSCILLATION D'UN RESSORT | SCHWINGUNG EINER FEDER |
| 13559 | **VIBRATIONS** | VIBRATIONS, TREPIDATIONS, EBRANLEMENTS | ERSCHÜTTERUNGEN |
| 13560 | **VIBRATIONS OF ETHER** | VIBRATIONS DE L'ETHER | ÄTHERSCHWINGUNGEN |
| 13561 | **VICE** | ETAU | SCHRAUBSTOCK |
| 13562 | **VICE CLAWS, CLAMPS** | MORDACHE A CHARNIERE | SPANNKLUPPE |
| 13563 | **VICE CLAWS, VICE CLAMPS** | MORDACHE D'UN ETAU | BACKENFUTTER EINES SCHRAUBSTOCKS |
| 13564 | **VICE JAW, CHECK** | MACHOIRE, MORS, MORD D'UN ETAU | BACKEN EINES SCHRAUBSTOCKS |
| 13565 | **VICE JAWS FOR WHEEL-WRIGHT, TYRE SMITH'S VICE** | ETAU A CHANFREIN, TENAILLE A CHANFREIN | REIFKLOBEN |
| 13566 | **VICKERS HARDNESS** | DURETE VICKERS | VICKERSHÄRTE |
| 13567 | **VIEW** | VUE | ANSICHT |
| 13568 | **VIEWING SCREEN** | ECRAN DE PROJECTION | LEUCHTSCHIRM |
| 13569 | **VIOLLE STANDARD** | ETALON VIOLLE, VIOLLE | PLATINEINHEIT (DER LICHTSTÄRKE) |
| 13570 | **VIRGIN METAL** | METAL VIERGE | METALL (GEDIEGENES) |
| 13571 | **VIRTUAL FOCUS** | FOYER VIRTUEL IMAGINAIRE | BRENNPUNKT (SCHEINBARER), BRENNPUNKT (VIRTUELLER) |

| | | | |
|---|---|---|---|
| 13572 | **VIRTUAL IMAGE** | IMAGE VIRTUELLE | SCHEINBILD, BILD (VIRTUELLES) |
| 13573 | **VIRTUAL VELOCITY** | VITESSE VIRTUELLE | GESCHWINDIGKEIT (VIRTUELLE) |
| 13574 | **VISCO SI METER** | VISCOSIMETRE | ZÄHIGKEITSMESSER, VISKOSIMETER |
| 13575 | **VISCOSE** | VISCOSE | VISKOSE |
| 13576 | **VISCOSITY** | VISCOSITE | ZÄHFLÜSSIGKEIT, DICKFLÜSSIGKEIT, VISKOSITÄT, ZÄHIGKEIT |
| 13577 | **VISCOUS** | VISQUEUX | DICKFLÜSSIG, SCHWERFLÜSSIG, STRENGFLÜSSIG, ZÄHFLÜSSIG, KLEBRIG, VISKOS |
| 13578 | **VISCOUS FLOW** | FLUAGE VISQUEUX | FLIESSEN, LAMINÄRE STRÖMUNG |
| 13579 | **VISE** | ETAU | SCHRAUBSTOCK |
| 13580 | **VISIBLE SIGNAL** | SIGNAL OPTIQUE | ZEICHEN (SICHTBARES), SICHTSIGNAL, SIGNAL (OPTISCHES) |
| 13581 | **VISUAL ANGLE** | ANGLE OPTIQUE, ANGLE VISUEL | GESICHTSWINKEL |
| 13582 | **VITREOUS** | VITREUX | GLASIG |
| 13583 | **VITREOUS GLASSY LUSTRE** | ECLAT VITREUX | GLASGLANZ |
| 13584 | **VITRIFICATION** | VITRIFICATION | SINTERUNG, VERGLASUNG |
| 13585 | **VOID** | LACUNE | FEHLSTELLE |
| 13586 | **VOLATILE CONSTITUENT** | PARTIE CONSTITUANTE VOLATILE | BESTANDTEIL (FLÜCHTIGER) |
| 13587 | **VOLATILISATION** | VOLATILISATION | VERFLÜCHTIGUNG |
| 13588 | **VOLATILISE (TO)** | VOLATILISER | VERFLÜCHTIGEN |
| 13589 | **VOLATILITY** | VOLATILITE | FLÜCHTIGKEIT |
| 13590 | **VOLCANIC TUFA** | TUF VOLCANIQUE | TUFF (VULKANISCHER) |
| 13591 | **VOLT** | VOLT | VOLT |
| 13592 | **VOLT-AMPERE** | VOLT-AMPERE | VOLT-AMPERE |
| 13593 | **VOLTAGE** | TENSION DU COURANT, NOMBRE DE VOLTS, VOLTAGE | SPANNUNG, VOLTZAHL |
| 13594 | **VOLTAGE POTENTIAL DROP, FALL DROP OF POTENTIAL** | PERTE, CHUTE DE TENSION, CHUTE DE POTENTIEL | SPANNUNGSABFALL, SPANNUNGSGEFÄLLE, SPANNUNGSVERLUST, POTENTIALGEFÄLLE |
| 13595 | **VOLTAGE REGULATOR, POTENTIAL REGULATOR** | REGULATEUR DE TENSION, D'INTENSITE, REGULATEUR DE COURANT | SPANNUNGSREGLER, SPANNUNGSREGULATOR |
| 13596 | **VOLTAIC PILE** | PILE VOLTAIQUE, DE VOLTA | SÄULE (VOLTASCHE) |
| 13597 | **VOLTMETER** | VOLTMETRE | SPANNUNGSMESSER, SPANNUNGSZEIGER, VOLTMETER |
| 13598 | **VOLUME** | VOLUME, CUBAGE | RAUMINHALT, VOLUMEN |
| 13599 | **VOLUME OF STROKE** | VOLUME ENGENDRE PAR LE DEPLACEMENT DU PISTON | HUBVOLUMEN |
| 13600 | **VOLUME REGULATOR** | REGULATEUR DE DEBIT | MENGENREGLER |
| 13601 | **VOLUMETRIC ANALYSIS** | ANALYSE VOLUMETRIQUE | MASSANALYSE (VOLUMETRISCHE) |
| 13602 | **VOLUMETRIC EFFICIENCY** | RENDEMENT VOLUMETRIQUE | WIRKUNGSGRAD (RÄUMLICHER), WIRKUNGSGRAD (VOLUMETRISCHER) |
| 13603 | **VOLUMETRIC EXPANSION, EXTENSION** | DILATATION CUBIQUE | AUSDEHNUNG (RÄUMLICHE), RAUMAUSDEHNUNG |
| 13604 | **VOLUMMETER** | DEBITMETRE | MENGENMESSER |
| 13605 | **VOLUTE SPRING, CONICAL HELICAL SPRING OF RECTANGULAR CROSS SECTION** | RESSORT CONIQUE A SECTION RECTANGULAIRE, RESSORT CONIQUE A LAME PLATE | KEGELFEDER MIT RECHTECKIGEM QUERSCHNITT |
| 13606 | **VORTEX, WHIRL, EDDY** | TOURBILLON, REMOUS | WIRBEL, (PHYS.) |
| 13607 | **VULCANISATION** | VULCANISATION | VULKANISIEREN |
| 13608 | **VULCANISE (TO)** | VULCANISER | VULKANISIEREN |
| 13609 | **VULCANISED FIBRE** | FIBRE VULCANISEE, FIBRE | FIBER, VULKANFIBER |
| 13610 | **VULCANISED RUBBER** | CAOUTCHOUC VULCANISE | KAUTSCHUK (VULKANISIERTER), WEICHKAUTSCHUK, WEICHGUMMI |

# WAD                                                    362

| | | | |
|---|---|---|---|
| 13611 | VULGAR FRACTION | FRACTION ORDINAIRE | BRUCH (GEMEINER) |
| 13612 | WADDING | OUATE | WATTE |
| 13613 | WAGES | PAIE, PAIEMENT, SALAIRE | LOHN, ARBEITSLOHN |
| 13614 | WAGON DRILL | SONDEUSE SUR CAMION | BOHRWAGEN |
| 13615 | WAIVER | RENONCIATION, DEROGATION | VERZICHT, ABWEICHUNG |
| 13616 | WALKWAY , GANGAY | PASSERELLE | BEDIENUNGSGANG, LAUFSTEG |
| 13617 | WALL BOX | NICHE | MAUERKASTEN |
| 13618 | WALL BRACKET | CHAISE D'APPLIQUE, CHAISE-CONSOLE, CONSOLE | WANDARM, WANDLAGERSTUHL, WANDKONSOLE |
| 13619 | WALL COUNTERSHAFT | RENVOI MURAL, RENVOI FIXE CONTRE UN MUR | WANDVORGELEGE |
| 13620 | WALL ENGINE, WALL DRILLING MACHINE | MACHINE A VAPEUR MURALE | WANDDAMPFMASCHINE, WANDBOHRMASCHINE |
| 13621 | WALL PLATE | CONTREPLAQUE, PLAQUE D'ANCRAGE | ANKERPLATTE, WANDPLATTE, MAUERPLATTE, WANDBETT, ANKERROSETTE |
| 13622 | WALL PLUG AND SOCKET | CONTACT A FICHE | STECKKONTAKT, STÖPSELKONTAKT |
| 13623 | WALL SLEWING CRANE | GRUE A POTENCE | WANDDREHKRAN |
| 13624 | WALLS OF A HOLE | FACE D'UN TROU | LOCHWAND, LOCHLEIBUNG |
| 13625 | WARDING FILE | LIME D'ENTREE | SCHLÜSSELFEILE |
| 13626 | WARNING ORDER | ORDRE DE FONCTIONNEMENT | BETRIEBFOLGE |
| 13627 | WARP | CHAINE D'UN TISSU | KETTE EINES GEWEBES |
| 13628 | WARP (TO), WIND (TO) | GAUCHIR, BOMBER, DEJETER (SE), DEVERSER (SE), VOILER (SE) | WERFEN (SICH), VERZIEHEN (SICH) |
| 13629 | WARPING, WINDING | GAUCHISSEMENT, DEFORMATION, DEFORMATION PAR ENROULEMENT | UMWICKLUNG, WERFEN, VERZIEHEN, KRUMMZIEHEN |
| 13630 | WASH STAND TAP | ROBINET DE LAVABO | STANDVENTIL |
| 13631 | WASHER | RONDELLE | UNTERLAGSCHEIBE |
| 13632 | WASHING | DELAVAGE | WASCHEN |
| 13633 | WASHING BOTTLE FLASK | PISSETTE | SPRITZFLASCHE |
| 13634 | WASTE GAS | GAZ PERDU | ABGAS |
| 13635 | WASTE HEAT | CHALEUR PERDUE | ABWÄRME |
| 13636 | WASTE OIL | HUILE D'EGOUTTAGE, HUILE EN EXCES | ÖL (ABLAUFENDES), TROPFÖL |
| 13637 | WASTE PRODUCTS | DECHETS | ABFÄLLE, ABFALLSTOFFE |
| 13638 | WASTE WATER PURIFICATION | EPURATION, PURIFICATION DES EAUX RESIDUAIRES | ABWÄSSERREINIGUNG |
| 13639 | WATCHMAKER'S LATHE | FOUR D'HORLOGER | DREHSTUHL |
| 13640 | WATER | EAU | WASSER |
| 13641 | WATER BATH | BAIN-MARIE | WASSERBAD (CHEM.) |
| 13642 | WATER BEARING SOIL | SOL AQUIFERE | BODEN (WASSERFÜHRENDER) |
| 13643 | WATER CALORIMETER | CALORIMETRE A EAU | WASSERKALORIMETER |
| 13644 | WATER COCK | ROBINET A EAU | WASSERHAHN |
| 13645 | WATER CONTENT, PERCENTAGE OF WATER | PROPORTION D'EAU, TENEUR EN EAU | WASSERGEHALT |
| 13646 | WATER COOLING | REFROIDISSEMENT A L'EAU | WASSERKÜHLUNG |
| 13647 | WATER DESCALING | DECALAMINAGE A L'EAU | WASSERENTZUNDERUNG |
| 13648 | WATER DISPLACING FILM | FILM ANTI-MOUILLANT | HYDROPHOBIERUNGSFILM |
| 13649 | WATER FOR INDUSTRIAL PURPOSES | EAU INDUSTRIELLE | NUTZWASSER, BRAUCHWASSER, BETRIEBSWASSER, WIRTSCHAFTSWASSER |
| 13650 | WATER FREE FROM BACTERIA | EAU EXEMPTE DE MICROBES, EAU STERILISEE | WASSER (KEIMFREIES) |
| 13651 | WATER GAS | GAZ A L'EAU | WASSERGAS |

| | | | |
|---|---|---|---|
| 13652 | **WATER GAUGE, GAUGE GLASS** | INDICATEUR DE NIVEAU, NIVEAU D'EAU | WASSERSTANDSANZEIGER, WASSERSTANDSGLAS, WASSERSTAND |
| 13653 | **WATER HAMMER** | COUP DE BELIER | WASSERSCHLAG, WIDDERSTOSS |
| 13654 | **WATER HARDENING** | TREMPE A L'EAU | WASSERHÄRTUNG |
| 13655 | **WATER JACKET CHAMBER** | CHEMISE D'EAU | WASSERMANTEL, KÜHLMANTEL |
| 13656 | **WATER JET** | JET D'EAU | WASSERSTRAHL |
| 13657 | **WATER JET AIR PUMP** | INJECTEUR HYDRAULIQUE | WASSERSTRAHLLUFTPUMPE |
| 13658 | **WATER JET BLOWER** | EJECTEUR HYDRAULIQUE | WASSERSTRAHLGEBLÄSE |
| 13659 | **WATER LEVEL** | NIVEAU D'EAU (HAUTEUR D'UN LIQUIDE) | WASSERSPIEGEL, WASSERSTAND |
| 13660 | **WATER LEVEL MARK** | MARQUE REPERE DE NIVEAU D'EAU | WASSERSTANDMARKE |
| 13661 | **WATER METER** | COMPTEUR A EAU | WASSERMESSER, WASSERUHR |
| 13662 | **WATER OF CONDENSATION** | EAU DE CONDENSATION | NIEDERSCHLAGWASSER, KONDENSWASSER, KONDENSAT |
| 13663 | **WATER OF CRYSTALLISATION** | EAU DE CRISTALLISATION | KRISTALLWASSER |
| 13664 | **WATER PAINT** | PEINTURE A L'EAU | WASSERFARBE |
| 13665 | **WATER PIPE** | TUYAU DE CONDUITE, TUYAU DE DISTRIBUTION D'EAU | WASSERLEITUNGSROHR |
| 13666 | **WATER PIPING MAIN** | CONDUITE, CANALISATION, DISTRIBUTION D'EAU | WASSERLEITUNG |
| 13667 | **WATER PISTON, HYDRAULIC PISTON** | PISTON A EAU, PISTON DE MOTEUR HYDRAULIQUE | WASSERKOLBEN |
| 13668 | **WATER POWER, HYDRAULIC POWER** | FORCE HYDRAULIQUE | WASSERKRAFT |
| 13669 | **WATER PRESSURE** | PRESSION D'EAU, PRESSION HYDRAULIQUE | WASSERDRUCK |
| 13670 | **WATER PRESSURE ENGINE** | MACHINE A COLONNE D'EAU | WASSERSÄULENMASCHINE |
| 13671 | **WATER PROOF** | INATTAQUABLE A L'EAU, IMPERMEABLE | WASSERBESTÄNDIG, WASSERFEST |
| 13672 | **WATER QUENCHING** | TREMPE A L'EAU | WASSERHÄRTUNG |
| 13673 | **WATER QUENCHING FOLLOWED BY TEMPERING** | TREMPE A L'EAU SUIVIE DE REVENU | WASSERVERGÜTEN |
| 13674 | **WATER REPELLENT PRODUCT** | PRODUIT HYDROFUGE | MITTEL (WASSERABWEISENDES) |
| 13675 | **WATER SEAL** | JOINT HYDRAULIQUE | WASSERVERSCHLUSS |
| 13676 | **WATER SOFTENING** | EPURATION CHIMIQUE DES EAUX D'ALIMENTATION | ENTHÄRTEN DES WASSERS, WASSERENTHÄRTUNG |
| 13677 | **WATER SPACE OF A BOILER** | CHAMBRE A EAU D'UNE CHAUDIERE | WASSERRAUM EINES KESSELS |
| 13678 | **WATER SUPPLY** | ALIMENTATION EN EAU, DISTRIBUTION D'EAU | WASSERVERSORGUNG |
| 13679 | **WATER TANK** | RESERVOIR A EAU | WASSERBEHÄLTER |
| 13680 | **WATER TOWER** | CHATEAU D'EAU | WASSERTURM |
| 13681 | **WATER TUBE** | TUBE D'EAU | WASSERROHR (DAMPFKESSEL) |
| 13682 | **WATER TUBE BOILER** | CHAUDIERE A TUBES D'EAU, CHAUDIERE A VAPORISATION RAPIDE, CHAUDIERE MULTITUBULAIRE, CHAUDIERE INEXPLOSIBLE | WASSERRÖHRENKESSEL |
| 13683 | **WATER-COOLED** | REFROIDI PAR L'EAU, REFROIDISSEMENT D'EAU (A) | WASSERGEKÜHLT |
| 13684 | **WATER-COOLED SURFACE CONDENSER** | CONDENSEUR PAR SURFACE AU MOYEN DE L'EAU | OBERFLÄCHENKONDENSATOR MIT WASSERKÜHLUNG |
| 13685 | **WATER-REPELLENT** | HYDROFUGE | WASSERABWEISEND |
| 13686 | **WATER-TIGHT, STANCH, STAUNCH** | ETANCHE A L'EAU | WASSERDICHT |
| 13687 | **WATERING CAN POT** | ARROSOIR | GIESSKANNE |
| 13688 | **WATERPROOF** | ETANCHE A L'EAU | WASSERDICHT |

**WAT** 364

| | | | |
|---|---|---|---|
| 13689 | WATERPROOF (TO) | IMPERMEABILISER | WASSERDICHT MACHEN |
| 13690 | WATERPROOF CLOTH | TISSU IMPERMEABLE | GEWEBE (WASSERDICHTES) |
| 13691 | WATERPROOFING | IMPERMEABILISATION | WASSERDICHTMACHEN |
| 13692 | WATERWHEEL | ROUE, RECEPTEUR HYDRAULIQUE | WASSERRAD |
| 13693 | WATERWORKS | INSTALLATION DE DISTRIBUTION D'EAU | WASSERWERK, WASSERVERSORGUNGSANLAGE |
| 13694 | WATT | WATT | WATT |
| 13695 | WATT-HOUR (W/HR) | WATT-HEURE | WATTSTUNDE |
| 13696 | WATT-MINUTE | WATT-MINUTE | WATTMINUTE |
| 13697 | WATT-SECOND | WATT-SECONDE | WATTSEKUNDE |
| 13698 | WATTMETER | WATTMETRE | WATTMETER |
| 13699 | WAVE | ONDE | WELLE (PHYS.) |
| 13700 | WAVE LENGTH | LONGUEUR D'ONDE | WELLENLÄNGE |
| 13701 | WAVINESS | ONDULATION | WELLIGKEIT |
| 13702 | WAX | CIRE | WACHS |
| 13703 | WAX PAATERN | MODELE EN CIRE | WACHSMODELL |
| 13704 | WAXED THREAD | FIL POISSE | PECHGARN, PECHDRAHT |
| 13705 | WEAK CURRENT | COURANT DE FAIBLE INTENSITE | SCHWACHSTROM |
| 13706 | WEAK SOLUTION | SOLUTION FAIBLE | LÖSUNG (SCHWACHE) |
| 13707 | WEAKENING OF CROSS SECTION | AFFAIBLISSEMENT DE LA SECTION | SCHWÄCHUNG, VERSCHWÄCHUNG DES QUERSCHNITTS |
| 13708 | WEAKENING OF THE MATERIAL | AFFAIBLISSEMENT DU MATERIEL | SCHWÄCHUNG DES MATERIALS |
| 13709 | WEAR | USURE | VERSCHLEISS, ABNÜTZUNG |
| 13710 | WEAR AND TEAR | USURE NORMALE, CONSOMMATION | ABNÜTZUNG (NATÜRLICHE), VERSCHLEISS |
| 13711 | WEAR BLOCKS | CALES D'USURE | VERSCHLEISSPLATTEN |
| 13712 | WEAR BY RUBBING | USURE PAR FROTTEMENT | ABRIEB |
| 13713 | WEAR DOWN (TO), OFF, OUT | USER (S') | ABNÜTZEN (SICH), VERSCHLEISSEN |
| 13714 | WEAR FEST | ESSAI D'USURE | VERSCHLEISSPRÜFUNG |
| 13715 | WEAR HARDENING | ECROUISSAGE | KALTHÄRTUNG |
| 13716 | WEAR PLATE | TOLE D'USURE | VERSCHLEISSBLECH |
| 13717 | WEAR RESISTANCE | RESISTANCE A L'USURE | VERSCHLEISSFESTIGKEIT |
| 13718 | WEAR RESISTING STEEL | ACIER RESISTANT A L'USURE | STAHL (VERSCHLEISSFESTER) |
| 13719 | WEARING OVAL OF A BEARING | OVALISATION D'UN COUSSINET | UNRUNDWERDEN EINES LAGERS |
| 13720 | WEATHER SHIELD | JOINT SECONDAIRE D'ETANCHEITE | SPRITZWASSERSCHUTZ |
| 13721 | WEATHER SIDE | COTE DU VENT | LUVSEITE |
| 13722 | WEATHER STRIP | CAOUTCHOUC D'ETANCHEITE | DICHTUNGSSTREIFEN |
| 13723 | WEATHER-PROOF | INALTERABLE, INATTAQUABLE AUX INTEMPERIES | WETTERBESTÄNDIG, WETTERFEST |
| 13724 | WEAVE BEAD | PASSE LARGE | PENDELRAUPE |
| 13725 | WEAVING MOTION | MOUVEMENT ALTERNATIF, VA-ET-VIENT. | BEWEGUNG (HIN-UND HERGEHENDE) |
| 13726 | WEB | AME | STEG, KERN |
| 13727 | WEB CRIPPLING OF A PLATE GIRDER | DEFORMATION PERMANENTE DE L'AME D'UNE POUTRE | DURCHBIEGUNG (BLEIBENDE) EINES TRÄGERSTEGS |
| 13728 | WEB LEG OF AN ANGLE IRON | AILE, BRANCHE D'UN FER CORNIERE | SCHENKEL EINES WINKELEISENS |
| 13729 | WEB OF A BEAM | AME D'UNE POUTRELLE | STEG |
| 13730 | WEB, CENTRE WEB, STEM | AME D'UN FER PROFILE | STEG EINES FORMEISENS |
| 13731 | WEDGE | COIN, CALE, CALE D'EPAISSEUR, EPAISSEUR | KEIL, UNTERLAGKEIL, ZWISCHENKEIL |
| 13732 | WEDGE FRICTION WHEEL | ROUE DE FRICTION (A JANTE EN FORME DE COIN) | KEILRAD, RILLENRAD |

| | | | |
|---|---|---|---|
| 13733 | WEDGE OF A PLANE | COIN DU RABOT | HOBELKEIL |
| 13734 | WEDGE PRESS | PRESSE A COIN | KEILPRESSE |
| 13735 | WEDGE SHAPE | SECTION CONIQUE | QUERSCHNITT (KEILFÖRMIGER) |
| 13736 | WEDGE SURFACE FRICTION GEAR | TRANSMISSION PAR ROUES DE FRICTION, ENGRENAGE A COIN | KEILRÄDERGETRIEBE |
| 13737 | WEDGE-SHAPED | CUNEIFORME | KEILFÖRMIG |
| 13738 | WEDGE-SHAPED BRICK | BRIQUE CIRCULAIRE ARRONDIE CINTREE | KEILSTEIN |
| 13739 | WEDGE, KEY, COTTER | COIN, CALE, CLAVETTE | KEIL |
| 13740 | WEDGING | CLAVETAGE, CALAGE | VERKEILUNG, VERKEILEN |
| 13741 | WEED THISTLE AND BRACKEN CUTTERS | COUPE CHARDONS ET FOUGERES | UNKRAUTDISTEL-UND FARNKRAUTSCHNEIDER |
| 13742 | WEEDERS AND TILLERS | SARCLEUSES | JÄTMASCHINEN UND ACKERFRÄSEN |
| 13743 | WEFT | TRAME | SCHUSS EINES GEWEBES, EINSCHLAG EINES GEWEBES |
| 13744 | WEIGH (TO) | PESER | ABWIEGEN, WÄGEN |
| 13745 | WEIGHBRIDGE, WEIGH-BRIDGE FOR RAILWAY WAGONS, WAGON WEIGHING MACHINE | PONT A BASCULE | GLEISWAAGE, BRÜCKENWAAGE |
| 13746 | WEIGHING | PESAGE, PESEE | WÄGUNG, WÄGEN, WIEGEN |
| 13747 | WEIGHT | POIDS | GEWICHT |
| 13748 | WEIGHT PER METER | POIDS AU METRE | METERGEWICHT |
| 13749 | WEIGHT-LOADED SAFETY VALVE | SOUPAPE DE SURETE A CONTRE-POIDS | GEWICHTSSICHERHEITSVENTIL, SICHERHEITSVENTIL MIT GEWICHTSBELASTUNG |
| 13750 | WEIGHTED JOCKEY PULLEY (LENIX TYPE) | ENROULEUR DE COURROIE LENIX LENEVEU | SPANNROLLE NACH LENIX |
| 13751 | WEIGHTED LEVER | LEVIER A CONTREPOIDS | HEBEL (BELASTETER), GEWICHTSHEBEL |
| 13752 | WEIGHTED PENDULUM GOVERNOR, LOADED WATT GOVERNOR, PORTER GOVERNOR, CENTRE WEIGHTED GOVERNOR | REGULATEUR A MASSE CENTRALE, REGULATEUR PORTER | GEWICHTSREGLER |
| 13753 | WEIR | DEVERSOIR, BARRAGE | STAUANLAGE, WEHR |
| 13754 | WEIR CREST | CRETE D'UN DEVERSOIR | WEHRKANTE, ÜBERFALLKANTE, WEHRKRONE |
| 13755 | WELD (TO) | SOUDER | SCHWEISSEN, ZUSAMMENSCHWEISSEN |
| 13756 | WELD BEAD | CORDON DE SOUDURE | SCHWEISSRAUPE |
| 13757 | WELD BUILT-UP | SOUDURE EN PASSES SUPERPOSEES | MEHRLAGENSCHWEISSUNG |
| 13758 | WELD BY THE AUTOGENOUS PROCESS (TO) | SOUDER A L'AUTOGENE | AUTOGENSCHWEISSEN |
| 13759 | WELD DECAY | CORROSION DE SOUDURE | KORROSION DER SCHWEISSNAHT |
| 13760 | WELD DEFECTS | DEFAUTS DE LA SOUDURE | NAHTFEHLER, SCHWEISSFEHLER |
| 13761 | WELD DEPOSIT METAL | METAL DEPOSE | SCHWEISSGUT |
| 13762 | WELD DEPOSIT OVERLAY | RECHARGEMENT D'UNE SOUDURE | AUFTRAGSCHWEISSUNG |
| 13763 | WELD METAL | METAL DE SOUDURE | SCHWEISSGUT |
| 13764 | WELD NUGGET | LENTILLE DE SOUDURE | SCHWEISSLINSE |
| 13765 | WELD STEEL | ACIER SOUDE | SCHWEISSSTAHL |
| 13766 | WELD-IRON | FER SOUDE | SCHWEISSEISEN |
| 13767 | WELD, WELDED JOINT | SOUDAGE, SOUDURE, JOINT SOUDE | SCHWEISSUNG, SCHWEISSVERBINDUNG |
| 13768 | WELDABILITY | SOUDABILITE | SCHWEISSBARKEIT |
| 13769 | WELDABLE | SOUDABLE | SCHWEISSBAR |
| 13770 | WELDED CHAIN | CHAINE A MAILLES SOUDEES | KETTE (GESCHWEISSTE) |

**WEL** 366

| | | | |
|---|---|---|---|
| 13771 | WELDED COLLAR | BAGUE SOUDEE | AUFGESCHWEISSTER BUND, VORSCHWEISSBUND |
| 13772 | WELDED CONNECTION | LIAISON SOUDEE | SCHWEISSVERBINDUNG |
| 13773 | WELDED FLANGE | BRIDE, RONDELLE SOUDEE | FLANSCH (AUFGESCHWEISSTER), VORSCHWEISSFLANSCH |
| 13774 | WELDED JOINT / SEAM | JOINT SOUDE | SCHWEISSVERBINDUNG |
| 13775 | WELDED PIPE | TUBE SOUDE | ROHR (GESCHWEISSTES) |
| 13776 | WELDED SEAM | JOINT SOUDE, SOUDURE | SCHWEISSNAHT |
| 13777 | WELDED TUBE | TUBE SOUDE | ROHR (GESCHWEISSTES) |
| 13778 | WELDER | SOUDEUR | SCHWEISSER |
| 13779 | WELDING | SOUDURE, SOUDAGE | SCHWEISSEN, SCHWEISSUNG |
| 13780 | WELDING CURRENT | INTENSITE DU COURANT DE SOUDAGE | SCHWEISSSTROMSTÄRKE |
| 13781 | WELDING FITTING | RACCORD A SOUDER | SCHWEISSFITTING |
| 13782 | WELDING GUN POSITION | POSITION DU PISTOLET DE SOUDAGE | STELLUNG (LAGE) DER SCHWEISSPISTOLE |
| 13783 | WELDING HEAD | TETE DE SOUDAGE | SCHWEISSKOPF |
| 13784 | WELDING HEAT | BLANC SOUDANT, CHAUDE SUANTE, CHALEUR SOUDANTE | SCHWEISSHITZE, SCHWEISSWÄRME |
| 13785 | WELDING JIG | GABARIT DE SOUDAGE | SCHWEISSVORRICHTUNG |
| 13786 | WELDING MACHINE | MACHINE A SOUDER | SCHWEISSMASCHINE |
| 13787 | WELDING PARAMETERS | PARAMETRES DE SOUDAGE | SCHWEISSPARAMETER |
| 13788 | WELDING PERIOD | DUREE DU CYCLE DE SOUDAGE | SCHWEISSSPIELZEIT |
| 13789 | WELDING ROD | FIL A SOUDER, ELECTRODE | SCHWEISSDRAHT, SCHWEISSELEKTRODE |
| 13790 | WELDING SEQUENCE | SUCESSION DES OPERATIONS DE SOUDAGE | SCHWEISSFOLGE |
| 13791 | WELDING SYMBOLS | SYMBOLES DE SOUDAGE | SCHWEISSNAHTSINNBILDER |
| 13792 | WELDING TEST | ESSAI DE SOUDABILITE | SCHWEISSVERSUCH |
| 13793 | WELDING WIRE | FIL (BAGUETTE) A SOUDER | SCHWEISSDRAHT, SCHWEISSSTAB |
| 13794 | WELDING-NECK FLANGE, SLIP-ON WELDING FLANGE | BRIDE A SOUDER (EN BOUT, A L'INTERIEUR) | VORSCHWEISSFLANSCH, EINSCHWEISSFLANSCH |
| 13795 | WELDMENT | CONSTRUCTION SOUDEE | SCHWEISSKONSTRUKTION |
| 13796 | WELL WATER | EAU DE PUITS | BRUNNENWASSER |
| 13797 | WELL-SINKER'S CEMENT | MASTIC DES FONTAINIERS | BRUNNENMACHERKITT |
| 13798 | WESTON DIFFERENTIAL PULLEY BLOCK | PALAN DIFFERENTIEL, PALAN WESTON | DIFFERENTIALFLASCHENZUG |
| 13799 | WET AIR PUMP | POMPE A AIR HUMIDE | LUFTPUMPE (NASSE) |
| 13800 | WET ANALYSIS | ANALYSE PAR VOIE HUMIDE | ANALYSE AUF NASSEM WEGE |
| 13801 | WET COMPRESSOR | COMPRESSEUR HUMIDE | VERDICHTER (NASSER), WASSERSÄULENVERDICHTER |
| 13802 | WET CORROSION | CORROSION HUMIDE | FEUCHTIGKEITSKORROSION |
| 13803 | WET DRAWING | PASSE HUMIDE | NASSZUG |
| 13804 | WET LINER | CHEMISE HUMIDE | LAUFBÜCHSE (NASSE) |
| 13805 | WET STEAM | VAPEUR HUMIDE | NASSDAMPF |
| 13806 | WETNESS OF STEAM | HUMIDITE DE LA VAPEUR | DAMPFNÄSSE |
| 13807 | WETTING | HUMECTATION | FEUCHTEN |
| 13808 | WETTING AGENT | AGENT MOUILLANT | BENETZUNGSMITTEL |
| 13809 | WHEATSTONE'S BRIDGE | PONT DE WHEATSTONE | BRÜCKENVIERECK, BRÜCKE WHEATSTONESCHE |
| 13810 | WHEEL | ROUE, VOLANT | HANDRAD, RAD |
| 13811 | WHEEL ARM | RAYONS D'UNE ROUE | RADARM, RADSPEICHE |
| 13812 | WHEEL BARROW | BROUETTE | SCHUBKARREN |

367 WID

| 13813 | WHEEL BASE | ÉCARTEMENT DES ESSIEUX | ACHSSTAND, RADSTAND |
| 13814 | WHEEL CENTRE, SPIDER | BRASSURE (D'UNE ROUE) | RADSTERN |
| 13815 | WHEEL GUARD COVER | COUVRE-ROUES, CARTER D'ENGRENAGES | RADVERDECK |
| 13816 | WHEEL LATHE | TOUR POUR ROUES | RÄDERDREHBANK |
| 13817 | WHEEL OF PLANIMETER | TAMBOUR, ROULETTE DU PLANIMETRE | MESSROLLE DES PLANIMETERS |
| 13818 | WHEEL RIM | JANTE DE ROUE | RADFELGE |
| 13819 | WHEEL TOOTH | DENT D'ENGRENAGE | RADZAHN |
| 13820 | WHEEL VANE, MOVING BLADE OF A TURBINE | AUBE RECEPTRICE, AUBE MOBILE D'UNE TURBINE | LAUFRADSCHAUFEL EINER TURBINE |
| 13821 | WHEEL WORK | ROUAGE | RÄDERWERK |
| 13822 | WHEEL-RIM PROFILING MACHINE | MACHINE A PROFILER LES JANTES DE ROUES | RADKRANZPROFILIERMASCHINE |
| 13823 | WHEEL, ROTOR OF A TURBINE | COURONNE MOBILE, ROUE D'UNE TURBINE | LAUFRAD EINER TURBINE, TURBINENRAD |
| 13824 | WHETSTONE | PIERRE A AFFUTER, PIERRE A AFFILER, PIERRE A AIGUISER | SCHLEIFSTEIN, ABZIEHSTEIN |
| 13825 | WHIPPING OF A BELT | FOUETTEMENT D'UNE COURROIE, FLOTTEMENT D'UNE COURROIE, BALLANT D'UNE COURROIE | FLATTERN DES RIEMENS, PEITSCHEN DES RIEMENS, SCHLAGEN DES RIEMENS |
| 13926 | WHIRLED THERMOMETER, SING THERMOMETER | THERMOMETRE-FRONDE | SCHLEUDERTHERMOMETER |
| 13827 | WHIRLING | TOURBILLONNEMENT | WIRBELUNG |
| 13828 | WHISKER | FIL (CROISSANCE EN FILAMENT), FIL MONOCRISTALLIN | WHISKER-WACHSTUM, FADENKRISTALL |
| 13829 | WHISTLE | SIFFLET | PFEIFE |
| 13830 | WHITE CAST IRON, WHITE IRON, WHITE PIG | FONTE BLANCHE | ROHEISEN (WEISSES) |
| 13831 | WHITE GOLD | OR BLANC | WEISSGOLD |
| 13832 | WHITE HEAT | INCANDESCENCE | WEISSGLUT |
| 13833 | WHITE IRONWOOD | BOIS DE FER-BLANC, BOIS DE SABLE, SIDEROXYLE | EISENHOLZ |
| 13834 | WHITE LEAD, BASIC CARBONATE OF LEAD | CERUSE, BLANC DE PLOMB, BLANC D'ARGENT, BLANC DE CERUSE | BLEIWEISS, BLEI (BASISCH), BLEI (KOHLENSAURES) |
| 13835 | WHITE MEAL TURNINGS | METAL BLANC DEFLOCULE | FLOCKEN VON WEISSMETALL |
| 13836 | WHITE METAL | METAL, ALLIAGE BLANC, METAL ANTI-FRICTION | WEISSMETALL |
| 13837 | WHITE METAL LINING | GARNITURE ANTI-FRICTION | WEISSMETALLAUSGUSS |
| 13838 | WHITE OILS | HUILES BLANCHES | WEISSES MINERALÖL |
| 13839 | WHITE UNTARRED ROPE | CORDE NON GOUDRONNEE | SEIL (UNGESTEURTES) |
| 13840 | WHITE-WALLED TYRES | PNEUS A FLANCS BLANCS | WEISSWANDREIFEN |
| 13841 | WHITING | BLANC DE MEUDON, BLANC DE TROYES, BLANC D'ESPAGNE | SCHLÄMMKREIDE |
| 13842 | WHITING | CHARGE NEUTRE, CRAIE, KAOLIN (PCUR LES PNEUS) | KREIDE |
| 13843 | WHITWORTH MEASURING MACHINE | MACHINE A MESURER WHITWORTH | MESSMASCHINE VON WHITWORTH |
| 13844 | WHITWORTH THREAD, ENGLISH STANDARD THREAD, COMMON THREAD | PAS WHITWORTH, PAS ANGLAIS | GEWINDE (WHITWORTHSCHES) |
| 13845 | WHOLE DEPTH | HAUTEUR DE DENT | ZAHNHÖHE, ZAHNTIEFE |
| 13846 | WICK | MECHE (D'UNE LAMPE, D'UN GRAISSEUR) | DOCHT |
| 13847 | WICK SIPHON LUBRICATION | GRAISSAGE PAR MECHE | DOCHTSCHMIERUNG |
| 13848 | WIDE EDGE MILLING CUTTER, HOB | FRAISE CYLINDRIQUE, FRAISE RECTILIGNE | MANTELFRÄSER, WALZENFRÄSER, ZYLINDERFRÄSER |

**WID** 368

| | | |
|---|---|---|
| 13849 | WIDE FLANGED BEAM | POUTRELLE A LARGES AILES | BREITFLANSCHTRÄGER |
| 13850 | WIDTH | LARGEUR | BREITE |
| 13851 | WINCH, CRAB | TREUIL | WINDE, BOCKWINDE |
| 13852 | WINCHES | TREUILS | ACKERWINDEN |
| 13853 | WIND (TO), COIL (TO) | ENROULER | AUFWICKELN, AUFWINDEN |
| 13854 | WIND CORD | BOURRELET D'ETANCHEITE | FENSTERDICHTUNGSCHNUR |
| 13855 | WIND ENGINE, WIND MILL | MOTEUR A VENT, MOTEUR EOLIEN PNEUMATIQUE, MOULIN A VENT | WINDKRAFTMASCHINE, WINDMOTOR |
| 13856 | WIND GIRDER | POUTRE RAIDISSEUSE, POUTRE AU VENT | VERSTEIFUNGSBALKEN |
| 13857 | WIND LOAD | CHARGE DUE AU VENT | WINDBELASTUNG |
| 13858 | WIND PRESSURE | POUSSEE, PRESSION DU VENT | WINDDRUCK |
| 13859 | WIND TURBINE, AIR TURBINE | TURBINE A AIR | WINDTURBINE |
| 13860 | WIND VANE | GIROUETTE | WINDFAHNE |
| 13861 | WIND WHEEL | ROUE ATMOSPHERIQUE | WINDRAD |
| 13862 | WINDING, COILING | ENROULEMENT, BOBINAGE | WICKLUNG, AUFWICKELN, AUFWINDEN |
| 13863 | WINDLASS | TREUIL SIMPLE | HASPEL |
| 13864 | WINDOW | FENETRE | FENSTER |
| 13865 | WINDOW FRAME | CHASSIS DE FENETRE | FENSTERRAHMEN |
| 13866 | WINDOW GLASS | VERRE A VITRES | FENSTERGLAS |
| 13867 | WINDOW REGULATOR | LEVE-GLACE | FENSTERKURBEL |
| 13868 | WINDOW RIM CHANNEL | GLISSIERE (DE FENETRE) | FENSTERFÜHRUNG |
| 13869 | WINDROWER | ABATTEURS POUR MOISSONNAGE | MASCHINEN ZUM AUFZIEHEN DES HEUES IN SCHWADEN |
| 13870 | WINDSHIELD-WASHER | LAVE-GLACE | SCHEIBENWASCHER |
| 13871 | WINDSHIELD-WIPER | ESSUIE-GLACE | SCHEIBENWISCHER |
| 13872 | WINDSHIELD, WINDSCREEN | PARE-BRISE | WINDSCHUTZSCHEIBE |
| 13873 | WINDUP | JEU | GANG (TOTER) |
| 13874 | WING | AILE | KOTFLÜGEL |
| 13875 | WING PLATFORM | PLATE-FORME EN PORTE-A-FAUX | PLATTFORM (AUSKRAGENDE) |
| 13876 | WING, QUADRANT COMPASSES | COMPAS A QUART DE CERCLE | BOGENZIRKEL |
| 13877 | WINNING EXTRACTION OF COAL | EXTRACTION DE LA HOUILLE | GEWINNUNG DER KOHLE |
| 13878 | WIPER | CAME | HEBEDAUMEN, DÄUMLING |
| 13879 | WIPER RING | BAGUE LARMIER | ÖL-ABSTREIFRING |
| 13880 | WIRE | FIL METALLIQUE | DRAHT |
| 13881 | WIRE (TO) | POSER UN FIL CONDUCTEUR | VERLEGEN (EINEN LEITUNGSDRAHT) |
| 13882 | WIRE BAR | FIL EN VERCE POUR TREFILERIE | DRAHTBARREN, STANGENDRAHT |
| 13883 | WIRE BENDING MACHINE | MACHINE A PLIER LES FILS | DRAHTBIEGEMASCHINE |
| 13884 | WIRE BRUSH | BROSSE EN FILS METALLIQUES, BROSSE METALLIQUE | DRAHTBÜRSTE |
| 13885 | WIRE CHAIN MAKING-MACHINE | MACHINE A FAIRE LES CHAINES EN FIL DE FER | DRAHTKETTENMASCHINE |
| 13886 | WIRE CUTTER | COUPE-FIL | DRAHTSCHNEIDER |
| 13887 | WIRE DRAW DIE | FILIERE A TREFILER | DRAHTZIEHSTEIN |
| 13888 | WIRE DRAWING | ETIRAGE EN FIL, TREFILERIE | ZIEHEN VON DRAHT, DRAHTZIEHEN |
| 13889 | WIRE DRAWING MACHINE | MACHINE A TREFILER | DRAHTZIEHMASCHINE |
| 13890 | WIRE EDGE | MORFIL | SCHLEIFGRAT |
| 13891 | WIRE FACK MACHINE | FRAPPEUR DE POINTES | DRAHTSTIFTSCHLAGMASCHINE |
| 13892 | WIRE GAUGE | JAUGE POUR FILS METALLIQUES, JAUGE DE TREFILERIE | DRAHTLEHRE |
| 13893 | WIRE GAUZE | TOILE METALLIQUE, GAZE METALLIQUE | DRAHTGEWEBE, DRAHTGAZE |

| | | | |
|---|---|---|---|
| 13894 | WIRE GLASS, FERROGLAS | VERRE ARME, VERRE A FIL DE FER NOYE | DRAHTGLAS, GLAS (NICHT SPLITTERNDES) |
| 13895 | WIRE NAIL, FRENCH NAIL | POINTE DE PARIS | DRAHTSTIFT, PARISER STIFT, DRAHTNAGEL |
| 13896 | WIRE NETTING | TREILLIS METALLIQUE | DRAHTNETZ, DRAHTGEFLECHT |
| 13897 | WIRE NETTING MACHINE | MACHINE A FAIRE LES GRILLAGES | DRAHTFLECHTMASCHINEN |
| 13898 | WIRE REEL | COURONNE DE FIL, DEVIDOIR | DRAHTHASPEL, DRAHTABSPULER |
| 13899 | WIRE ROPE | CABLE METALLIQUE | DRAHTSEIL, KABEL |
| 13900 | WIRE SPEED | VITESSE DU FIL | DRAHTABSPULGESCHWINDIGKEIT |
| 13901 | WIRE SPRING COILING MACHINE | MACHINE A ENROULER LES RESSORTS A BOUDIN | DRAHTFEDERNWINDEMASCHINE |
| 13902 | WIRE STRAND | TORON METALLIQUE | DRAHTLITZE |
| 13903 | WIRE WINDING, UNWINDING MACHINE | ENROULEUSE, DEROULEUSE DE FIL | DRAHTAUF-U.ABWICKELMASCHINE |
| 13904 | WIRE WORKING MACHINE | MACHINE A TRAVAILLER LES FILS METALLIQUES | DRAHTVERARBEITUNGSMASCHINE |
| 13905 | WIRE WORKS | TREFILERIE (FABRIQUE) | DRAHTZIEHEREI |
| 13906 | WIRE-DRAWING | TREFILAGE | DRAHTZIEHEN |
| 13907 | WIRELESS TELEGRAPHY, RADIOTELEGRAPHY | TELEGRAPHIE SANS FIL, RADIOTELEGRAPHIE | TELEGRAPHIE (DRAHTLOSE) |
| 13908 | WIRELESS TELEPHONY, RADIOTELEPHONY | TELEPHONIE SANS FIL, RADIOTELEPHONIE | TELEPHONIE (DRAHTLOSE) |
| 13909 | WIRING | POSE D'UN FIL CONDUCTEUR | VERLEGUNG EINES LEITUNGSDRAHTES |
| 13910 | WITHDRAW HEAT FROM.. (TO) | SOUSTRAIRE DE LA CHALEUR | WÄRME ENTZIEHEN |
| 13911 | WITHERITE | WITHERITE, CARBONATE NATUREL DE BARYTE | BARYT (KOHLENSAURER), WITHERIT |
| 13912 | WOLFRAM | WOLFRAM | WOLFRAMIT |
| 13913 | WOOD | BOIS | HOLZ |
| 13914 | WOOD CHARCOAL | CHARBON DE BOIS | HOLZKOHLE |
| 13915 | WOOD LAGGING | REVETEMENT EN BOIS | HOLZVERSCHALUNG, HOLZVERKLEIDUNG |
| 13916 | WOOD MEAL | POUDRE DE BOIS | HOLZMEHL |
| 13917 | WOOD SAW | SCIE A BOIS | HOLZSÄGE |
| 13918 | WOOD SCREW | VIS METALLIQUE A BOIS | HOLZSCHRAUBE |
| 13919 | WOOD SHAVINGS | COPEAUX (DE BOIS) | HOBELSPÄNE |
| 13920 | WOOD SPIRIT, METHYL ALCOHOL | ALCOOL METHYLIQUE, HYDRATE DE METHYLE, METHYLENE, ESPRIT DE BOIS | HOLZGEIST, HOLZALKOHOL, HOLZSPIRITUS, HOLZNAPHTA, METHYLALKOHOL, KARBINOL, METHANOL |
| 13921 | WOOD TAR | GOUDRON DE BOIS, GOUDRON VEGETAL | HOLZTEER |
| 13922 | WOOD TURNING LATHE | TOUR A BOIS | HOLZDREHBANK |
| 13923 | WOOD WOOL | LAINE DE BOIS, COPEAUX DE FIBRES DE BOIS | HOLZWOLLE |
| 13924 | WOOD WORKING | TRAVAIL DU BOIS | HOLZBEARBEITUNG |
| 13925 | WOOD WORKING MACHINE | MACHINE-OUTIL A TRAVAILLER LE BOIS, MACHINE A BOIS | HOLZBEARBEITUNGSMASCHINE |
| 13926 | WOODEN HAMMER | MAILLET | HOLZHAMMER |
| 13927 | WOODEN LINING | CHEMISE, FOURRURE EN BOIS | HOLZFUTTER |
| 13928 | WOODEN PIPE | TUYAU EN BOIS | HOLZROHR, HOLZRÖHRE |
| 13929 | WOODRUFF KEY | CLAVETTE DEMI-RONDE, CLAVETTE WOODRUFF, CLAVETTE-DISQUE | SEGMENTKEIL, WOODRUFFKEIL , SCHEIBENFEDER |
| 13930 | WOODRUFF KEYSEAT CUTTERS | FRAISES A RAINURE WOODRUFF | FRÄSER FÜR WOODRUFFKEILE |
| 13931 | WOODWORKING MACHINERY | MACHINES A BOIS | HOLZBEARBEITUNGSMASCHINEN |
| 13932 | WOOL | LAINE (DE MOUTON) | SCHAFWOLLE |

# WOR

370

| | | | |
|---|---|---|---|
| 13933 | **WOOL FAT, YOLK, SUINT** | SUINT | WOLLFETT |
| 13934 | **WORD** | MOT | DATENWORT |
| 13935 | **WORD ADDRESS FORMAT** | FORMAT A ADRESSES | EINGABEFORMAT IN ADRESSSCHREIBWEISE |
| 13936 | **WORK (MOMENTUM)** | TRAVAIL | ARBEIT |
| 13937 | **WORK (TO), MACHINE (TO)** | TRAVAILLER, TRAITER, USINER, OUVRAGER | BEARBEITEN |
| 13938 | **WORK AN INVENTION ON A COMMERCIAL SCALE (TO)** | EXPLOITER, METTRE EN EXPLOITATION UNE INVENTION | AUSNUTZEN (EINE ERFINDUNG) |
| 13939 | **WORK DISTRIBUTION** | REPARTITION DU TRAVAIL | ARBEITSVERTEILUNG |
| 13940 | **WORK DONE, OUTPUT** | TRAVAIL EFFECTUE | ARBEIT (GELEISTETE), ARBEIT (ABGEGEBENE), LEISTUNG (ABGEGEBENE) |
| 13941 | **WORK OF COMPRESSION** | TRAVAIL DE COMPRESSION | VERDICHTUNGSARBEIT |
| 13942 | **WORK OF FRICTION, WORK LOST EXPANDED IN FRICTION** | TRAVAIL DU FROTTEMENT | REIBUNGSARBEIT |
| 13943 | **WORK ROOM** | LIEU DE TRAVAIL, ATELIER | ARBEITSRAUM |
| 13944 | **WORK TO OVERCOME RESISTANCE, WORK AGAINST RESISTANCE** | TRAVAIL RESISTANT | WIDERSTANDSARBEIT |
| 13945 | **WORK-HOLDING JAW** | MACHOIRE DE BLOCAGE | FESTSPANNEINRICHTUNG |
| 13946 | **WORKABILITY, EASE OF WORKING** | USINABILITE, FACILITE DU TRAVAIL | BEARBEITBARKEIT |
| 13947 | **WORKABLE** | FACILE A TRAVAILLER | BEARBEITBAR, BEARBEITUNGSFÄHIG |
| 13948 | **WORKING AN INVENTION ON A COMMERCIAL SCALE** | EXPLOITATION D'UNE INVENTION | AUSNUTZUNG EINER ERFINDUNG |
| 13949 | **WORKING CONDITIONS, CONDITIONS OF SERVICE** | CONDITIONS DE SERVICE | BETRIEBSVERHÄLTNISSE |
| 13950 | **WORKING COST, EXPENSES** | FRAIS D'EXPLOITATON | BETRIEBSKOSTEN |
| 13951 | **WORKING DEPTH** | HAUTEUR D'ACTION | EINGRIFFSTIEFE |
| 13952 | **WORKING DEPTH IN TOOTHED GEARING** | PROFONDEUR D'ENGRENEMENT | EINGRIFFSTIEFE |
| 13953 | **WORKING ELEMENT** | ORGANE TRAVAILLANT | BESTANDTEIL (ARBEITENDER) |
| 13954 | **WORKING ENGINE CYLINDER** | CYLINDRE MOTEUR, CYLINDRE DE TRAVAIL | ZYLINDER, ARBEITSZYLINDER |
| 13955 | **WORKING GAUGE** | JAUGE DE FABRICATION | ARBEITSLEHRE |
| 13956 | **WORKING LOAD** | CHARGE ADMISSIBLE | BELASTUNG (ZULÄSSIGE) |
| 13957 | **WORKING PRESSURE** | PRESSION DE REGIME, PRESSION DE SERVICE, TENSION DE SERVICE | BETRIEBSDRUCK |
| 13958 | **WORKING STRESS** | TAUX DE TRAVAIL | BELASTBARKEIT IM GEBRAUCH |
| 13959 | **WORKING, MACHINING** | TRAVAIL, TRAITEMENT, USINAGE | BEARBEITEN, BEARBEITUNG |
| 13960 | **WORKMAN, WORKER, HAND** | OUVRIER, TRAVAILLEUR | ARBEITER |
| 13961 | **WORKMANSHIP** | MAIN-D'OEUVRE | AUSFÜHRUNG, ARBEIT |
| 13962 | **WORKPEOPLE** | PERSONNEL OUVRIER | ARBEITERSCHAFT |
| 13963 | **WORKS MANAGEMENT** | DIRECTION DES USINES, DIRECTION DES ATELIERS, DIRECTION DU TRAVAIL | BETRIEBSFÜHRUNG |
| 13964 | **WORKS MANAGER** | CHEF DE FABRICATION, CHEF DE SERVICE, CHEF D'ATELIER | BETRIEBSFÜHRER, BETRIEBSLEITER |
| 13965 | **WORKS RAILWAY** | VOIE FERREE D'ATELIER | FABRIKBAHN |
| 13966 | **WORKS SIDING** | EMBRANCHEMENT INDUSTRIEL | FABRIKANSCHLUSSGLEIS, ANSCHLUSSGLEIS, INDUSTRIEGLEIS |
| 13967 | **WORKSHOP GAUGE** | JAUGE DE FABRICATION | ARBEITSLEHRE |
| 13968 | **WORKSHOP, SHOP** | ATELIER | WERKSTATT, WERKSTÄTTE |
| 13969 | **WORM** | VIS SANS FIN | SCHNECKE |

| | | | |
|---|---|---|---|
| 13970 | **WORM CONVEYOR** | TRANSPORTEUR A HELICE, VIS TRANSPORTEUSE, VIS D'ARCHIMEDE | FÖRDERSCHNECKE, TRANSPORTSCHNECKE, SCHNECKE |
| 13971 | **WORM CUTTER** | FRAISE MERE | SCHNECKENFRÄSER |
| 13972 | **WORM GEAR MILLING CUTTER, WORM HOB, MILLING CUTTER HOB FOR WORM GEAR** | FRAISE POUR TAILLER DES ENGRENAGES HELICOIDAUX | SCHNECKENFRÄSER |
| 13973 | **WORM GEAR PULLEY BLOCK** | PALAN A VIS TANGENTE, PALAN A VIS SANS FIN | SCHRAUBENFLASCHENZUG, SCHNECKENFLASCHENZUG |
| 13974 | **WORM GEARING** | ENGRENAGE, MECANISME A VIS SANS FIN, COUPLE DE ROUE ET VIS TANGENTE | SCHNECKENRADGETRIEBE, SCHRAUBGETRIEBE, WURMGETRIEBE |
| 13975 | **WORM WHEEL** | ROUE A VIS SANS FIN | SCHNECKENRAD, MUTTERRAD |
| 13976 | **WORM-EATEN** | VERMOULU | WURMSTICHIG |
| 13977 | **WORM-EATEN TIMBER** | BOIS VERMOULU | HOLZ (WURMSTICHIGES) |
| 13978 | **WORM, COOLING COIL** | SERPENTIN DE REFROIDISSEMENT | KÜHLSCHLANGE |
| 13979 | **WORM, ENDLESS SCREW, PERPETUAL SCREW** | VIS SANS FIN | SCHNECKE, WURM, SCHRAUBE OHNE ENDE, ZYLINDERSCHRAUBE |
| 13980 | **WORN OUT BEARING** | COUSSINET OVALISE PAR L'USURE, COUSSINET USE | LAGER (UNRUNDGEWORDENES), LAGER (AUSGELAUFENES) |
| 13981 | **WORN OUT, WORN DOWN SCREW THREAD** | FILET FOIRE, FILET JARETE | GEWINDE (AUSGELEIERTES) |
| 13982 | **WORN OUT, WORN DOWN, WORN OFF, WORN AWAY** | USAGE | ABGENUTZT |
| 13983 | **WOVEN BELT** | COURROIE TISSEE | RIEMEN (GEWEBTER) |
| 13984 | **WRAPPING PAPER** | PAPIER D'EMBALLAGE | EINWICKELPAPIER, PACKPAPIER |
| 13985 | **WRINKLING** | FRISAGE | FALTENBILDUNG |
| 13986 | **WRIST PIN** | GOUPILLE | ANLENKBOLZEN |
| 13987 | **WROUGHT BRASS** | ARCOT | ROHMESSING |
| 13988 | **WROUGHT IRON, MALLEABLE IRON** | FER DOUX, FER FORGE | SCHMIEDEEISEN |
| 13989 | **WROUGHT IRON, MALLEABLE IRON PIPE** | TUYAU EN FER | ROHR (SCHMIEDEEISERNES) |
| 13990 | **WROUGHT NAIL** | CLOU FORGE | NAGEL (GESCHMIEDETER) |
| 13991 | **WULFENITE, LEAD MOLYBDATE** | MELINOSE, WULFENITE | MOLYBDÄNBLEISPAT, GELBBLEIERZ, WULFENIT |
| 13992 | **WULFF NET** | ABAQUE, RESEAU DE WULFF (STEREOGRAPHIQUE) | ABAKUS (WULFFSCHER) |
| 13993 | **X-RAY ANALYSIS** | EXAMEN RADIOGRAPHIQUE | RÖNTGENANALYSE |
| 13994 | **X-RAY APPARATUS** | APPAREIL RADIOGRAPHIQUE | RÖNTGENAPPARAT |
| 13995 | **X-RAY BEAM** | FAISCEAU DE RAYONS X | RÖNTGENSTRAHLENBÜNDEL |
| 13996 | **X-RAY CRYSTALLOGRAPHY** | RADIO-CRISTALLOGRAPHIE | RÖNTGENKRISTALLOGRAPHIE |
| 13997 | **X-RAY DIFFRACTION PATTERN** | DIAGRAMME DE DIFFRACTION DES RAYONS X. | RÖNTGENBEUGUNGSDIAGRAMM |
| 13998 | **X-RAY EXAMINATION** | CONTROLE RADIOGRAPHIQUE | RÖNTGENUNTERSUCHUNG |
| 13999 | **X-RAY FLUORESCENT ANALYSIS** | ANALYSE FLUORESCENTE | RÖNTGEN-FLUORESZENZ-ANALYSE |
| 14000 | **X-RAY SPECTROGRAPH** | SPECTROMETRE A RAYONS X | RÖNTGENSPEKTROMETER |
| 14001 | **X-RAY SPECTRUM** | SPECTRE DES RAYONS X | RÖNTGENSPEKTRUM |
| 14002 | **X-RAY TUBE** | TUBE A RAYONS X | RÖNTGENRÖHRE |
| 14003 | **X-RAYS** | RAYONS X | RÖNTGENSTRAHLEN |
| 14004 | **XENON** | XENON | XENON |
| 14005 | **XEROGRAPHY** | XEROGRAPHIE | XEROGRAPHIE |
| 14006 | **XYLENE** | XYLENE, XYLOL | XYLOL |
| 14007 | **YARD** | YARD | YARD |
| 14008 | **YELLOW BRASS** | LAITON | MESSING |

**YIE** 372

| | | |
|---|---|---|
| 14009 | YELLOW PHOSPHORUS | PHOSPHORE BLANC | PHOSPHOR (GELBWEISSER), PHOSPHOR (KRISTALLINISCHER) |
| 14010 | YIELD | RENDEMENT | ARBEITSLEISTUNG |
| 14011 | YIELD POINT, BREAKING DOWN POINT | LIMITE D'ECOULEMENT, LIMITE TARDIVE, LIMITE ELASTIQUE | FLIESSGRENZE, STRECKGRENZE |
| 14012 | YIELD STRENGTH | LIMITE D'ECOULEMENT, LIMITE ELASTIQUE | STRECKGRENZE, FLIESSGRENZE, STRECKFESTIGKEIT |
| 14013 | YIELD STRESS | LIMITE ELASTIQUE | STRECKGRENZE, ELASTIZITÄTSGRENZE |
| 14014 | YOKE | ARCADE | BÜGEL |
| 14015 | YOKE BONNET | CHAPEAU A ARCADE | BÜGELAUFSATZ |
| 14016 | YOKE BUSHING, YOKE SLEEVE | DOUILLE D'ARCADE | AUFSATZBUCHSE |
| 14017 | YOKE OF A MAGNET | CULASSE D'UN AIMANT | JOCH EINES MAGNETEN |
| 14018 | YOKE RETAINING NUT | ECROU DE DOUILLE D'ARCADE | BÜGELVERSCHRAUBUNG |
| 14019 | YTTERBIUM | YTTERBIUM | YTTERBIUM |
| 14020 | YTTRIUM | YTTRIUM | YTTRIUM |
| 14021 | ZAMAK | ZAMAK | FEINZINKLEGIERUNG |
| 14022 | ZAPON ENAMEL | VERNIS ZAPON | ZAPONLACK |
| 14023 | ZED BAR, Z-BAR | FER EN Z | Z-EISEN |
| 14024 | ZERO DEVIATION | DEVIATION NULLE | NULLPUNKTABWEICHUNG |
| 14025 | ZERO MARK LINE | TRAIT ZERO | NULLMARKE, NULLSTRICH |
| 14026 | ZERO OFFSET | DECALAGE DU POINT D'ORIGINE | NULLPUNKTVERSATZ |
| 14027 | ZERO POINT | ZERO (D'UNE ECHELLE), POINT ZERO | NULLPUNKT |
| 14028 | ZERO POSITION | POSITION DE ZERO | NULLSTELLUNG |
| 14029 | ZERO PRESSURE LINE | LIGNE DE NULLE PRESSION (DU DIAGRAMME D'INDICATEUR) | NULLINIE (INDIKATOR-DIAGRAMM) |
| 14030 | ZERO RESET | REMISE A ZERO | NULLRÜCKSTELLUNG |
| 14031 | ZERO SHIFT | DECALAGE DU POINT D'ORIGINE | NULLPUNKTVERSATZ |
| 14032 | ZERO SYNCHRONIZATION | REMISE A ZERO | NULLRÜCKSTELLUNG |
| 14033 | ZERO-SUPPRESSION | SUPPRESSION DES ZEROS | NULLUNTERDRÜCKUNG |
| 14034 | ZIGZAG RIVETED JOINT | RIVURE EN QUINCONCE | ZICKZACKNIETUNG, NIETUNG (VERSETZTE) |
| 14035 | ZINC | ZINC | ZINK |
| 14036 | ZINC ACETATE | ACETATE DE ZINC | ZINK (ESSIGSAURES), ZINKAZETAT |
| 14037 | ZINC CARBONATE | CARBONATE DE ZINC | ZINK (KOHLENSAURES), ZINKKARBONAT |
| 14038 | ZINC CHLORIDE | CHLORURE DE ZINC | ZINK (SALZSAURES), ZINKCHLORID, CHLORZINK |
| 14039 | ZINC CHROMATE | CHROMATE DE ZINC, JAUNE DE ZINC | ZINK (CHROMSAURES), ZINKCHROMAT, ZINKCHROMGELB |
| 14040 | ZINC CUTTINGS | ROGNURES DE ZINC | ZINKSPÄNE |
| 14041 | ZINC CYANIDE | CYANURE DE ZINC | ZYANZINK |
| 14042 | ZINC ORE | MINERAI DE ZINC | ZINKERZ |
| 14043 | ZINC OXIDE, ZINC WHITE | OXYDE DE ZINC, BLANC DE ZINC, BLANC DE NEIGE | ZINKOXYD, ZINKWEISS |
| 14044 | ZINC PLATING | ZINGAGE, GALVANISATION | VERZINKUNG |
| 14045 | ZINC SPRAYING | METALLISATION AU ZINC | SPRITZVERZINKEN |
| 14046 | ZINC SULPHATE, WHITE VITRIOL | SULFATE DE ZINC, VITRIOL BLANC, COUPEROSE BLANCHE | ZINKVITRIOL, VITRIOL (WEISSER), ZINKSCHWEFEL (SAURER), ZINKSULFAT |
| 14047 | ZINC TUBE | TUYAU EN ZINC | ZINKROHR |
| 14048 | ZINC WIRE | FIL DE ZINC | ZINKDRAHT |
| 14049 | ZIRCONIUM | ZIRCONIUM | ZIRKONIUM |
| 14050 | ZONE MELTING | FUSION PAR ZONE | ZONENSCHMELZEN |

| 14051 | **ZONE OF SPHERE** | ZONE SPHERIQUE, SEGMENT SPHERIQUE A DEUX BASES | KUGELSCHICHT, KUGELZONE |

# SUPLEMENTO ESPANHOL

1   CORRIENTE ALTERNA  *f*
2   PUESTO  *m* DE SOLDADURA CON CORRIENTE ALTERNA
3   CORRIENTE ALTERNA ALTA FRECUENCÍA  *f*
4   REDUCCIÓN  *f* DE TEMPLE
5   ABERRACIÓN (DE LA LUZ)  *f*
6   DESTRUCTIBILIDAD  *f*
7   CRECIMIENTO  *m* ANORMAL DE LOS CRISTALES
8   ACERO ANORMAL  *m*
9   HIERRO  *m* MALEABLE ANORMAL
10  ELIMINAR (O DESGASTAR AFILANDO), AMOLAR
11  MATERIA  *f* PULIMENTADORA
12  ENDEREZADOR (DE TUBOS) ABRAMSEN
13  ABRASIÓN  *f*
13  ELIMINACIÓN  *f* POR AFILADURA
14  DUREZA  *f* DE ABRASIÓN (DE AMOLADO)
15  MARCAS  *f* DEJADAS POR LA MUELA
16  PRUEBA  *f* DE DESGASTE
17  ABRASIVO  *m*
18  CINTA  *f* DE ESMERIL
18  CINTA  *f* ABRASIVA
19  PIEDRA  *f* DE AMOLAR, RUDLA  *f*
20  MUELA  *f* DE ESMERIL
21  GRANO  *m* ABRASIVO
22  MATERIA  *f* BRUÑIRA
23  GROSOR  *m* DE LOS GRANOS ABRASIVOS
24  PUNTAS  *f pl* ABRASIVAS
25  GRANALLA  *f*
26  DISCOS  *m pl* ABRASIVOS
26  MUELAS  *f pl*
27  ABSCISA  *f*
28  ALCOHOL ANHIDRO  *m*
28  ALCOHOL ABSOLUTO  *m*, ALCOHOL QUÍMICAMENTE PURO  *m*
29  ACOTACIÓN ABSOLUTA  *f*
30  HUMEDAD  *f* ABSOLUTA DEL AIRE
31  SISTEMA  *m* DE MEDIDA ABSOLUTA
32  MOVIMIENTO  *m* ABSOLUTO
33  PRESIÓN  *f* ABSOLUTA
34  PUNTO  *m* DE REFERENCIA ABSOLUTO
35  TEMPERATURA  *f* ABSOLUTA
36  CERO  *m* ABSOLUTO
37  ABSORBER
38  ABSORBIBLE
39  ABSORBENTE  *m*
40  ABSORBENTE  *m*
41  CAPACIDAD CALORÍFICA  *f*
42  PODER  *m* ABSORBENTE
42  POTENCIA  *f* ABSORBENTE
43  ABSORCIÓMETRO  *m*
44  ABSORCIÓN  *f*

45  BANDA  *f* DE ABSORCIÓN
46  COEFICIENTE APARENTE DE ABSORCIÓN  *m*
47  CONSTANTE DE ABSORCIÓN  *f*
48  DINAMÓMETRO  *m* DE ABSORCIÓN
49  BORDE  *m* DE ABSORCIÓN
50  LÍMITE  *m* DE ABSORCIÓN
51  ABSORCIÓN DEL CALOR  *f*
52  ABSORCIÓN DEL AGUA  *f*
53  RELACIÓN  *f* DE ABSORCIÓN
54  ESPECTRO  *m* DE ABSORCIÓN
55  DINAMÓMETRO  *m* DE ABSORCIÓN
55  DINAMÓMETRO  *m* DE FRENO
56  ABSORBENCIA  *f*
57  SOPORTE  *m*, APOYO  *m*
57  SÁLMER  *m*, SOPORTE  *m*, APOYO  *m*
57  APOYO  *m*, SOPORTE  *m*
57  SOPORTE  *m*
58  BRONCE  *m* AL ALUMINIO
59  PUESTO  *m* DE SOLDADURA CON CORRIENTES ALTERNA Y CONTINUA
60  MOVIMIENTO  *m* ACELERADO
61  BOMBA  *f* DE RECUPERACIÓN
62  ACELERACIÓN  *f*
63  ACELERACIÓN DE VELOCIDAD DE UN CUERPO QUE SE CAE  *f*
64  ACELERACIÓN DE LA GRAVEDAD  *f*
65  ACELERACIÓN DE LA GRAVEDAD  *f*
66  ACELERADOR  *m*
67  RECEPCIÓN  *f*
68  RECEPCIÓN  *f* (DE MÁQUINAS)
69  LÍMITE  *m* DE ACEPTACIÓN
70  CERTIFICADO DE RECEPCIÓN  *m* INSPECCIÓN
71  PRUEBA  *f* DE RECEPCIÓN
72  ACCESIBILIDAD  *f*
73  ACCESIBLE
74  ACCESORIOS  *m pl*
75  ACCIDENTE DE TRABAJO  *m*
76  ACUMULADOR  *m*
77  BATERÍA  *f* SECUNDARIA
78  CÉLULA  *f* (O ELEMENTO  *m*) DE ACUMULADOR
79  LOCOMOTORA  *f* ELÉCTRICA CON ACUMULADORES
80  METAL  *m* DE ACUMULADOR
81  PLACA  *f* DE ACUMULADOR
81  PLACA  *f* DE ACUMULADOR
82  PRECISIÓN  *f*
83  PRECISIÓN  *f* DE MECANIZACIÓN
84  HIDRURO  *m* DE ACETILO
84  ALDEHÍDO ACÉTICO  *m*
84  ÁCIDO ALDEHÍDICO  *m*
84  HIDRATO  *m* DE VINILO
84  ACETALDEHÍDO  *m*

| | | | | |
|---|---|---|---|---|
| 84 | ÓXIDO *m* DE ETILIDENO | 124 | ANTIÁCIDO ÁCIDORRESISTENTE *m* |
| 84 | ETANAL *m* | 125 | ALEACIONES ANTIÁCIDO *f pl*, ALEACIONES RESISTENTES AL ÁCIDO *f pl* |
| 85 | ACETATO *m* | 126 | CARBONATO ÁCIDO DE SODIO *m* |
| 86 | ÁCIDO ACÉTICO *m* | 126 | BICARBONATO *m* SÓDICO |
| 86 | VINAGRE *m* RADICAL | 127 | VAPORES *m pl* ÁCIDOS |
| 87 | ANHÍDRIDO ACÉTICO *m* | 128 | INATACABLE POR LOS ÁCIDOS |
| 88 | ACETATO DE ETILO *m* | 129 | ÁCIDO *m* AGRIO, ACETOSO |
| 88 | ETER ACÉTICO | 130 | ACIDIFICANTE |
| 89 | ACIDÍMETRO *m*, PESA-ÁCIDOS *m* | 131 | ACIDIMETRÍA *f* |
| 89 | ACIDÍMETRO, ACIDÓMETRO *m* | 132 | ÁCIDOS *m pl* |
| 90 | ACETONA *f* | 133 | ACIDULAR |
| 90 | DIMETILCETONA *f* | 134 | AGUA *f* ACIDULADA |
| 91 | ACETATO *m* | 135 | ACERACIÓN *f* |
| 91 | ACETATO DE CELULOSA, ACETIL-CELULOSA *m* | 136 | ACÚSTICA *f* |
| 92 | CLORURO DE ACETILO *m* | 137 | ACÚSTICA *f* |
| 93 | ACETILENO *m* | 138 | REVÉS (AL) *m*, COMTRAHÍLO (A) *m* |
| 94 | CORTE CON ACETILENO *m* | 139 | ACTÍNICO |
| 95 | LÁMPARA *f* DE ACETILENO | 140 | RAYOS *m* ACTÍNICOS |
| 96 | SOLDADURA *f* AL ACETILENO | 141 | ACTINIO *m* |
| 97 | HORNO *m* DE ACHESON | 142 | ACTINÓMETRO *m* |
| 98 | ACROMÁTICO | 143 | ACCIÓN DE UNA FUERZA *f* |
| 99 | ACROMATIZACIÓN *f* | 144 | ACTIVACIÓN *f* |
| 100 | ACROMATIZAR | 145 | ADICIÓN DE CARBONO *f* |
| 101 | ACROMATISMO | 146 | ACTIVADOR, ACTUADOR *m* |
| 102 | ACICULAR, ACUMÍNEO | 147 | ENERGÍA *f* DE ACTIVACIÓN |
| 103 | MARTENSITA *f* ACIDULAR | 148 | SUBSTANCIA *f* ACTIVADORA |
| 104 | ÁCIDO *m* AGRIO, ACETOSO | 149 | DEPÓSITO *m* ACTIVO |
| 105 | FUNDICIÓN *f* BRUTA BESSEMER | 150 | HIDRÓGENO *m* ATÓMICO |
| 106 | PROCEDIMIENTO BESSEMER CON CONVERTIDOR PROVISTO DE ÁCIDO | 151 | POTENCIA *f* EFECTIVA EN CABALLOS |
| 107 | ACERO BESSEMER *m* | 151 | POTENCIA *f* AL FRENO |
| 108 | SOLERA *f* ÁCIDA | 151 | CABALLO EFECTIVO *m* |
| 109 | FRAGILIDAD *f* AL DECAPADO | 152 | DIMENSIÓN *f* REAL |
| 110 | ESTAÑO *m* DE SOLDAR DE FUNDENTE ÁCIDO | 153 | VALOR *m* REAL |
| 111 | BAÑO *m* DE DECAPADO | 154 | ACUTÁNGULO *m* |
| 112 | DECAPADO *m* CON BAÑO ACIDULADO | 155 | ÁNGULO AGUDO *m* |
| 113 | ACERO ELÉCTRICO ÁCIDO *m* | 155 | ÁNGULO AGUDO *m* |
| 114 | FUNDENTE *m* ÁCIDO | 155 | ÁNGULO VIVO *m* |
| 115 | ELEMENTO *m* ACIDIFICADOR | 156 | BISECTRIZ *f* AGUDA |
| 116 | ACERO MARTIN AL PROCESO ÁCIDO *m* | 157 | TRIÁNGULO *m* ACUTÁNGULO |
| 117 | FUNDICIÓN *f* BESSEMER | 158 | BRILLO *m* DIAMANTINO |
| 118 | OXALATO *m* ÁCIDO DE POTASIO | 159 | LENGUAJE *m* DE PROGRAMACIÓN ADAPT |
| 119 | INCRUSTACIÓN *f* SARRO *m* | 160 | ADAPTADOR *m*, AJUSTADOR *m* |
| 119 | CRÉMOR *m* TÁRTARO | 161 | MANDO ADAPTIVO *m* |
| 119 | BITARTRATO *m* POTÁSICO | 162 | ADICIONAR, SUMAR |
| 119 | CREMOR *m* TÁRTARO | 162 | AUMENTAR, AÑADIR |
| 119 | CRISTALES *m pl* | 163 | ADICIONAR AGUA |
| 120 | PROCEDIMIENTO *m* ÁCIDO | 164 | ALTURA *f* DE LA CABEZA DE UN DIENTE |
| 121 | BOMBA *f* DE ÁCIDO | 164 | ALTURA *f* DEL FRENTE |
| 122 | REACCIÓN *f* ÁCIDA | 164 | ALTURA *f* DE DIENTE |
| 123 | REVESTIMIENTO *m* REFRACTARIO ÁCIDO | 165 | ÁNGULO DE CABEZA DE LA RUEDA CÓNICA *m* |

| | |
|---|---|
| 166 | CÍRCULO EXTERIOR *m*, CIRCUNFERENCIA DE DENTADURA (ENGRANAJES) *f* |
| 166 | CÍRCULO EXTERIOR *m* |
| 166 | CÍRCULO EXTERIOR *m* |
| 167 | CÍRCULO EXTERIOR *m* |
| 167 | FLANCO *m* DE SALIENTE |
| 168 | ADITIVO *m* |
| 168 | AGENTE *m* ADICIONAL |
| 169 | COADYUVANTE *m* |
| 169 | ADICIÓN *f* |
| 170 | PÉRDIDA *f* ADICIONAL |
| 172 | CONTROL DE ADHERENCIA *m* |
| 173 | ADHERENCIA *f* |
| 174 | ADHESIÓN *f* |
| 174 | ADHERENCIA *f* |
| 175 | ADHERENTE, ADHESIVO |
| 175 | ADHESIVO *m* |
| 176 | PODER *m* ADHERENTE |
| 177 | SUBSTANCIA *f* ADHESIVA |
| 178 | DATOS ADIABÁTICOS *m pl* |
| 179 | ADIABÁTICO *m* |
| 179 | LÍNEA *f* |
| 179 | CURVA ADIABÁTICA *f* |
| 180 | ÁNGULO ADYACENTE *m* |
| 181 | ADYACENTE, CONTIGUO *m* |
| 181 | CONTIGUO *m* |
| 182 | REGLAR, REGULAR, AJUSTAR |
| 183 | REGULABLE |
| 183 | AJUSTABLE, REGULABLE |
| 184 | ESCARIADOR DE MANO AJUSTABLE (EXTENSIBLE) *m* |
| 185 | CALZO DE NIVEL *m* |
| 185 | CALCE *m*, ESPESOR *m* |
| 185 | CALCE PARA RECUPERAR HOLGURA *m* |
| 185 | CALCE *m* |
| 185 | CLAVIJA DE APRIETE *f* |
| 186 | CALIBRE *m* MORDAZA GRADUABLE |
| 187 | FRENO *m* REGULABLE |
| 188 | ESCARIADOR CON DIENTES EXTENSIBLES *m* |
| 188 | ESCARIADOR DE CUCHILLAS GRADUABLES *m* |
| 189 | HILERAS *f pl* |
| 190 | REGLAJE *m* CON TORNILLO |
| 191 | TUERCA *f* DE AJUSTE (O DE REGULACIÓN) |
| 192 | TORNILLO *m* DE REGLAJE |
| 193 | TORNILLO *m* DE PRESIÓN |
| 194 | CASQUILLO *m* DE AJUSTE (DE REGULACIÓN) |
| 195 | REGLAJE *m* |
| 196 | TOBERA DE ESCAPE *f* |
| 196 | SURTIDOR *m* |
| 196 | BOQUILLA *f*, TOBERA *f* |
| 197 | BRONCE *m* DE CAÑONES |

| | |
|---|---|
| 198 | LATÓN *m* DE MARINA |
| 199 | LÍNEA *f* DE ADMISIÓN DEL VAPOR |
| 200 | CANAL *m* DE ADMISIÓN |
| 201 | VÁLVULA *f* DE ADMISIÓN |
| 202 | FIJAR POR ADSORCIÓN |
| 203 | ADSORCIÓN *f* |
| 204 | ADULTERAR |
| 204 | FALSIFICAR |
| 205 | FALSIFICACIÓN *f* |
| 205 | SOFISTICACIÓN *f* |
| 205 | FRAUDE *m* |
| 205 | ADULTERACIÓN *f* |
| 206 | AVANCE *m* |
| 207 | AZUELA *f* |
| 208 | AIREAR UNA ARENA |
| 209 | CÉLULA *f* DE AERACIÓN |
| 210 | VENTILACIÓN DEL AGUA *f* |
| 211 | VENTILADOR *m* |
| 212 | LÍNEA *f* AÉREA, TENDIDO *m* AÉREO |
| 213 | TRANSPORTADOR *m* AÉREO |
| 213 | TRANSPORTADOR *m* POR CABLE |
| 214 | AERODINÁMICO *m* |
| 215 | AERODINÁMICO *m* |
| 216 | BRONCE (DE) |
| 217 | AEROSTÁTICO *m* |
| 218 | AEROSTÁTICO *m* |
| 219 | ERRUGINOSO, HERRUMBROSO |
| 220 | CARDENILLO, VERDÍN *m* |
| 221 | REVENIDO *m* DEFORMACIÓN *f* POSTERIOR |
| 222 | ÁGATA *f* |
| 223 | ENDURECIMIENTO *m* POR ENVEJECIMIENTO |
| 224 | ENDURECIMIENTO *m* ESTRUCTURAL |
| 225 | ENVEJECIMIENTO *m* |
| 226 | ENVEJECIMIENTO *m* |
| 227 | AGREGADO *m*, CONJUNTO *m* |
| 228 | MATERIA *f* PARA MEZCLA |
| 229 | AGREGACIÓN *f*, AGREGADO *m* |
| 230 | TEMPERATURA *f* DE ENVEJECIMIENTO |
| 231 | ENVEJECIMIENTO *m* COMPLETO |
| 232 | ENVEJECIMIENTO *m* ESCALONADO |
| 233 | ENVEJECIMIENTO *m* NATURAL |
| 234 | ENVEJECIMIENTO *m* PROGRESIVO |
| 235 | ENVEJECIMIENTO *m* POR TRABAJO EN FRÍO |
| 236 | APARATO AGITADOR *m* |
| 237 | HUECO *m* DE AGITADOR |
| 238 | AGITADOR MECÁNICO *m* |
| 239 | BARNIZ *m* DEL JAPÓN |
| 240 | AIRE ATMOSFÉRICO *m* |
| 241 | CÁMARA DE VIENTO *f* |
| 242 | CHORRO *m* DE AIRE |
| 242 | SOPLADOR *m* |

| | |
|---|---|
| 243 | VIENTO DE LA MÁQUINA SOPLANTE  *m*, VIENTO INYECTADO  *m* |
| 244 | LIMPIEZA  *f* POR CHORRO DE AIRE |
| 245 | LADRILLO  *m* HUECO, RASILLA  *f* |
| 246 | CÁMARA DE AIRE  *f*, REGULADOR DE GOLPO DE ARIETE  *m* |
| 247 | CANALES DE VIENTO  *m pl* |
| 248 | CLASIFICACIÓN  *f* POR CORRIENTE GASEOSA |
| 249 | BOMBA  *f* DE AIRE |
| 249 | COMPRESOR DE AIRE  *m* |
| 250 | CLIMATIZADOR  *m* |
| 251 | MOTOR  *m* ENFRIADO POR EL AIRE |
| 252 | ENFRIAMIENTO  *m* EN EL AIRE |
| 253 | CORRIENTE DE AIRE  *f* |
| 254 | COLCHÓN DE AIRE  *m* |
| 254 | COLCHÓN  *m* |
| 254 | CAPA DE AIRE  *f* |
| 255 | AMORTIGUAMIENTO NEUMÁTICO  *m* |
| 256 | AMORTIGUADOR NEUMÁTICO  *m* |
| 256 | AMORTIGUADOR  *m* DE AIRE |
| 256 | COLCHÓN NEUMÁTICO  *m* |
| 257 | TIRO  *m* DE AIRE |
| 258 | MARTILLO  *m* PIQUETA (O.P.) |
| 259 | VÁLVULA  *f* DE AIRE |
| 260 | FILTRO  *m* DE AIRE |
| 261 | HORNO  *m* DE REVERBERO |
| 262 | INTERSTICIO  *m*, ABERTURA  *f* |
| 262 | ENTREHIERRO  *m* |
| 263 | ENTREHIERRO  *m* DE UN IMÁN |
| 264 | GAS  *m* AL AIRE |
| 265 | TERMÓMETRO  *m* DE GAS |
| 266 | CORRIENTE  *f* DE AIRE |
| 267 | TEMPLE  *m* AL AIRE |
| 268 | CALEFACCIÓN POR AIRE CALIENTE  *f* |
| 268 | CALENTAMIENTO DEL AIRE  *m* |
| 269 | ORIFICIO  *m* DE AIRE (RESPIRADERO) |
| 270 | TOMA  *f* DE AIRE |
| 271 | EYECTOR  *m* NEUMÁTICO |
| 272 | PISTOLA  *f* DE AIRE COMPRIMIDO |
| 273 | BOMBA  *f* DE AIRE COMPRIMIDO |
| 274 | COMPARTIMIENTO  *m* ESTANCO |
| 275 | TOBERA  *f* DE AIRE COMPRIMIDO |
| 276 | PISTOLA  *f* DE AIRE COMPRIMIDO |
| 277 | AIRE COMBURENTE  *m* |
| 277 | COMBURENTE  *m* |
| 278 | ESPACIO  *m* LIBRE |
| 278 | HUECO  *m* ENTRE LOS BARROTES DE UNA REJA |
| 279 | MANDRIL  *m* NEUMÁTICO |
| 280 | TEMPLE  *m* AL AIRE |
| 281 | TUBERÍA DE AIRE  *f* |
| 281 | TUBERÍA DE AIRE  *f* |

| | |
|---|---|
| 281 | DISTRIBUCIÓN  *f* DE AIRE |
| 282 | PISTÓN  *m* DE AIRE |
| 283 | CALIBRE  *m* NEUMÁTICO, CALIBRADOR  *m* NEUMÁTICO |
| 284 | BOMBA  *f* NEUMÁTICA |
| 284 | BOMBA  *f* DE AIRE |
| 284 | BOMBA  *f* DE VACÍO |
| 285 | TEMPLE  *m* AL AGUA |
| 286 | PISÓN  *m* NEUMÁTICO |
| 287 | RECALENTADOR  *m* DE AIRE |
| 288 | ESCAMA  *f* |
| 289 | TOMA  *f* DE AIRE |
| 290 | SEPARACIÓN  *f* NEUMÁTICA |
| 291 | POZO  *m* DE AERACIÓN |
| 292 | OBTURADOR  *m* DE AIRE |
| 293 | GRIFO  *m* DE AIRE |
| 294 | DEPÓSITO  *m* DE AIRE |
| 295 | SOLDADURA  *f* AEROACETILÉNICA |
| 296 | CONDENSADOR POR SUPERFICIE MEDIANTE AIRE  *m* |
| 297 | MADERA  *f* SECADA AL AIRE LIBRE |
| 298 | ACERO AUTOTEMPLABLE  *m* |
| 299 | MÁQUINA  *f* DE INYECCIÓN NEUMÁTICA |
| 300 | AFINO CON VIENTO  *m*, AFINO CON AIRE  *m* |
| 301 | AGLUTINANTE  *m* QUE SE ENDURECE AL AIRE |
| 302 | CEMENTO DE ENDURECIMIENTO AL AIRE  *m* |
| 303 | HERMÉTICO  *m* |
| 303 | ESTANCO AL AIRE, IMPERMEABLE AL AIRE, HERMÉTICO |
| 304 | ALABASTRO  *m* |
| 305 | APARATO DE ALARMA  *m*, DISPOSITIVO DE ALARMA  *m* |
| 306 | SEÑAL  *f* DE ALARMA |
| 307 | SILBATO  *m* AVISADOR |
| 307 | SILBATO  *m* DE ALARMA |
| 308 | ALBEDO  *m*, ALBEDO (COEFICIENTE DE REFLEXIÓN)  *m* |
| 309 | CABLE DE CABLEADO ALBERT  *m* |
| 310 | ALBÚMINA  *f* |
| 311 | PAPEL  *m* ALBÚMINA, PAPEL  *m* ALBUMIMADO |
| 312 | MOTOR  *m* DE ALCOHOL |
| 313 | ALCOHOL VÍNICO  *m* |
| 313 | ALCOHOL ETÍLICO  *m* |
| 313 | ALCOHOL ORDINARIO  *m* |
| 313 | HIDRATO  *m* DE ETILO |
| 314 | ALCOHÓLICO  *m* |
| 315 | SOLUCIÓN  *f* ALCOHÓLICA |
| 316 | ALCOHÓMETRO  *m*, ALCOHOLÍMETRO  *m*, ALCOHOLÓMETRO  *m* |
| 316 | ALCOHOLÍMETRO  *m*, AREÓMETRO  *m* |
| 317 | ALDEHÍDO  *m* |
| 318 | ALNUS GLUTINOSA |

| | |
|---|---|
| 318 | ALISO *m* |
| 319 | ALFÁMETRO *m* |
| 320 | ÁLGEBRA *f* |
| 321 | ALGEBRAICO, ALGÉBRICO |
| 322 | ECUACIÓN *f* ALGEBRAICA |
| 323 | AJUSTAR, CONTRAR, ALINEAR, NIVELAR |
| 324 | ALINEACIÓN *f*, LÍNEA DE FUGA *f* |
| 324 | LÍNEA *f* DE FUGA |
| 325 | ALINEACIÓN *f*, ALINEAMIENTO *m* |
| 326 | COMBINACIÓN ALIFÁTICA *f* |
| 327 | ALIZARINA *f* |
| 328 | ÁLCALI *m* |
| 329 | METALES *m pl* ALCALINOS |
| 330 | ALCALINIZAR, ALCALIZAR |
| 330 | HACER ALCALINO |
| 331 | ALCALÍMETRO *m* |
| 332 | ALCALIMÉTRICO *m* |
| 333 | ALCALIMETRÍA *f*, ALCALIMÉTRICO *m* |
| 334 | LIMPIEZA *f* ALCALINA |
| 335 | METALES *m pl* ALCALINO-TERROSOS |
| 336 | TIERRAS *f pl* ALCALINAS |
| 337 | REACCIÓN *f* ALCALINA |
| 338 | SAL *f* ALCALINA |
| 339 | SOLUCIÓN *f* ALCALINA |
| 340 | ALCALINIDAD *f* |
| 341 | ALCALOIDE *m*, ALCALOIDEO |
| 342 | PAPEL *m* DE ALHEÑA, PAPEL *m* DE ORCANETA |
| 342 | PAPEL *m* DE ORCANETINA |
| 343 | CABLE CONDUCTOR TODO-ALUMINIO *m* |
| 344 | FLOTACIÓN *f* |
| 345 | COMPLETAMENTE DE METALES FERROSOS |
| 346 | HIERRO *m* VIRGINAL |
| 347 | MUESTRA *f* DE METAL PURO |
| 348 | PIEL *f* DE COCODRILO |
| 349 | ALÓMERO *m* |
| 350 | ALOMERÍA *f* |
| 351 | ALOMORFISMO *m* |
| 352 | ALOMORFO *m* |
| 353 | TENSIÓN ADMISIBLE *f* |
| 354 | ALOTRIOMORFO *m* |
| 355 | TRANSFORMACIÓN *f* ALOTRÓPICA |
| 356 | ALOTRÓPICO *m* |
| 357 | ALOTROPÍA *f* |
| 357 | ISOMERÍA *f* |
| 358 | JUEGO *m*, TOLERANCIA *f* EN LA FABRICACIÓN |
| 358 | JUEGO *m* ENTRE EL MACHO Y EL MOLDE |
| 358 | TOLERANCIA *f* |
| 358 | SOBRE ESPESOR *m* DE MECANIZACIÓN |
| 359 | TOLERANCIA *f* ADMITIDA |
| 359 | TOLERANCIA *f* DE MECANIZACIÓN |

| | |
|---|---|
| 360 | ALEACIÓN *f* |
| 361 | ALEAR, LIGAR |
| 362 | BÁSCULA *f* PARA ALEACIONES |
| 363 | FUNDICIÓN *f* ALEADA |
| 364 | REVESTIMIENTO *m* DE ALEACIÓN |
| 365 | CONTAMINACIÓN DE UNA ALEACIÓN *f* |
| 366 | GALVANIZAR |
| 367 | POLVO *m* ALEADO |
| 368 | ACERO ALEADO (ESPECIAL, DE ALEACIÓN, DE LIGA) *m* |
| 369 | ANGULARES DE ALEACIÓN DE ACERO *m* |
| 370 | PALANQUILLAS *f pl* DE ACERO ALEADO (O ESPECIAL) |
| 371 | FLEJES *m pl* DE ACERO ALEADO |
| 372 | MOLDEADOS *m pl* DE ACERO DE ALEACIÓN |
| 373 | PLANOS *m pl* DE ACERO ALEADO |
| 374 | HEXÁGONOS *m* DE ALEACIÓN DE ACERO |
| 375 | BARRAS *f pl* OCTOGONALES DE ACERO ALEADO |
| 376 | ALAMBRE *m* HECHO DE ACERO ALEADO |
| 377 | REDONDOS *m pl* DE ACERO ALEADO |
| 378 | PLETINAS *f pl* DE ALEACIÓN DE ACERO |
| 379 | CUADRADOS DE ACERO ALEADO *m* |
| 380 | CHAPAS *f pl* FINAS DE ACERO ALEADO |
| 381 | SISTEMA *m* DE LAS ALEACIONES |
| 382 | ACERO POCO ALIADO *m* |
| 383 | ALEACIÓN RESISTENTE AL DESGASTE (A LA USURA) *f* |
| 384 | ALEACIÓN ANTIÁCIDO *f*, ALEACIÓN RESISTENTE AL ÁCIDO *f* |
| 385 | ALEACIÓN DE ANTIFRICCIÓN *f*, PATENTE *f* |
| 385 | ALEACIÓN PARA COJINETES *f* |
| 386 | ALEACIÓN DE SOLDADURA CON LATÓN O BRONCE *f* |
| 387 | ALEACIÓN INOXIDABLE *f* |
| 387 | ALEACIÓN INOXIDABLE *f* |
| 388 | ALEACIÓN PARA COLADA A PRESIÓN (O PARA FUNDICIÓN INYECTADA) *f* |
| 389 | ALEACIÓN FUSIBLE *f* |
| 390 | ALEACIÓN TERMORRESISTENTE E INOXIDABLE *f* |
| 391 | ALEACIÓN TERMORRESISTENTE *f* |
| 392 | ALEACIÓN MAGNÉTICA *f* |
| 393 | ALEACIÓN REFRACTARIA *f*, ALEACIÓN MUY TERMORRESISTENTE *f* |
| 394 | ADICIÓN *f* |
| 395 | ELEMENTOS *m pl* DE ALEACIÓN |
| 396 | ALEACIONES RESISTENTES A LA ABRASIÓN Y A LA CORROSIÓN *f pl* |
| 397 | AMALGAMA *f* |
| 398 | ALEACIÓN MAGNÉTICA 'ALNICO' *f* |
| 399 | LATÓN *m* ALFA |
| 400 | PARTÍCULA *f* ALFA |
| 401 | RADIADOR *m* ALFA |
| 402 | RAYOS *m* ALFA |

| | |
|---|---|
| 403 | LATÓN *m* ALFA-BETA |
| 404 | PAR *m* DE CONOS LISOS |
| 404 | CONO Y CONTRA-CONO |
| 405 | PRUEBA *f* POR INMERSIONES ALTERNADAS |
| 406 | CORRIENTE ALTERNA *f* |
| 407 | DINAMO *f*, GENERADOR *m* DE CORRIENTE ALTERNA |
| 407 | MÁQUINA *f* PARA CORRIENTE ALTERNA |
| 407 | ALTERNADOR *m* |
| 407 | GENERATRIZ *f* |
| 408 | ALTERNOMOTOR *m*, MOTOR DE CORRIENTE ALTERNA *m* |
| 408 | MOTOR *m* DE CORRIENTE ALTERNA |
| 409 | ALTERNATIVA *f* |
| 410 | VARIANTE *f* |
| 411 | ALTERNADOR *m* |
| 412 | ALÚMINA *f* |
| 413 | ALÚMINA *f* |
| 413 | ÓXIDO *m* DE ALUMINIO |
| 414 | ALUMINATO *m* |
| 415 | ALUMINÍFERO *m* |
| 416 | ALUMINIO *m* |
| 417 | ACETATO DE ALUMINIO *m* |
| 418 | ALEACIÓN DE BASE DE ALUMINIO *f* |
| 419 | LATÓN *m* DE ALUMINIO |
| 420 | BRONCE *m* AL ALUMINIO |
| 421 | CLORURO DE ALUMINIO *m* |
| 421 | CLORALUMINIO *m*, CLORURO DE ALUMINIO *m* |
| 422 | LIMA *f* DE ALUMINIO |
| 423 | ALÚMINA HIDRATADA *f* |
| 424 | ALUMINIO EN LINGOTE *m* |
| 425 | SILICATO *m* DE ALÚMINA |
| 426 | SULFATO *m* DE ALUMINIO |
| 427 | TUBO *m* DE ALUMINIO |
| 428 | ALAMBRE *m* DE ALUMINIO |
| 429 | ALUMINIACIÓN *f*, ALUMINIZACIÓN *f* |
| 430 | ALUMINO |
| 431 | ALUMINOTERMIA *f* |
| 432 | ALUMINIO *m* |
| 433 | ALEACIÓN DE ALUMINIO PLÁSTICA (O FORJABLE) *f* |
| 434 | CUPROALUMINIO *m* |
| 435 | ALEACIÓN DE ALUMINIO PARA COLADO (MOLDEADO, O MOLDEO) *f* |
| 436 | HOJA *f* DE ALUMINIO |
| 437 | ALEACIÓN DE ALUMINIO FORJABLE (O PLÁSTICA) *f* |
| 438 | ALÚMINA *f* |
| 439 | ALEACIÓN DE BASE DE ALUMINIO *f* |
| 440 | ALEACIÓN DE ALUMINIO BERILIO *f* |
| 441 | CHAPA *f* DE ACERO ALUMINADA |
| 442 | ACERO CALMADO AL ALUMINIO *m* |

| | |
|---|---|
| 443 | CEMENTO REFRACTARIO AL SILICATO DE ALUMINIO *m* |
| 444 | ALUMINIO *m* |
| 445 | AMALGAMA *f* |
| 446 | AMALGAMAR |
| 447 | AMALGAMACIÓN *f* |
| 448 | PROCEDIMIENTO *m* DE AMALGACIÓN |
| 449 | SUCESIVO *m*, ÁMBAR AMARILLO *m* |
| 449 | ÁMBAR AMARILLO *m* |
| 450 | AIRE AMBIENTE *m* |
| 451 | PASO *m* DEL SISTEMA SELLERS |
| 452 | CULOMBÍMETRO *m* |
| 452 | AMPERÍMETRO *m* |
| 453 | AMONIACO *m*, AMONÍACO *m* |
| 453 | GAS *m* AMONIACAL |
| 454 | AMONIACO *m*, AMONÍACO *m* |
| 455 | SOSA *f* AL AMONIACO |
| 455 | SOSA *f* SOLVAY |
| 455 | SAL *f* SOLVAY |
| 456 | AGUA *f* AMONIACAL DEL GAS |
| 457 | SOLUCIÓN *f* AMONIACAL |
| 458 | ACETATO DE AMONIO *m* |
| 459 | BICARBONATO *m* DE AMONIO |
| 460 | BISULFITO *m* DE AMONÍACO |
| 461 | CARBONATO DE AMONIO *m* |
| 461 | SAL *f* VOLÁTIL |
| 462 | SAL *f* AMONIACAL |
| 462 | CLORHIDRATO DE AMONÍACO *m* |
| 462 | CLORURO DE AMONIO *m* |
| 462 | HIDROCLORATO *m* |
| 462 | MURIATO *m* DE AMONIACO |
| 463 | FLUORURO *m* DE AMONIO |
| 464 | SULFIDRATO *m* DE AMONIO |
| 465 | NITRUM *m* FLAMMANS, NITRATO *m* DE AMONIO |
| 465 | NITRATO *m* DE AMONIO |
| 466 | NITRITO *m* DE AMONIO |
| 467 | OXALATO *m* DE AMONIACO |
| 468 | PERSULFATO *m* DE AMONÍACO |
| 469 | FOSFATO *m* DE AMONIO |
| 470 | CLORURO DOBLE DE ESTAÑO Y AMONIO *m* |
| 471 | SULFATO *m* DE AMONIO |
| 472 | SULFURO *m* DE AMONIO |
| 473 | TARTRATO *m* |
| 474 | MUNICIÓN *f* |
| 475 | AMORFO *m* |
| 476 | AZUFRE *m* AMORFO |
| 477 | CONTRACCIÓN *f* |
| 477 | COEFICIENTE DE RETRACCIÓN *m* |
| 478 | AMPERAJE *m* |
| 478 | INTENSIDAD *f* DE LA CORRIENTE |

| | |
|---|---|
| 478 | NÚMERO *m* DE AMPERIOS |
| 479 | AMPERIO *m* |
| 480 | AMPERIO-VUELTA *m* |
| 481 | AMPERIO-HORA *m* |
| 482 | AMPERIO-MINUTO *m* |
| 483 | AMPERIO-SEGUNDO *m* |
| 484 | ANFÓTERA |
| 485 | AMPLIFICADOR *m* |
| 486 | AMPLITUD *f* |
| 487 | ACETATO DE AMILO *m* |
| 487 | ACETATO *m* DE AMILO |
| 488 | ALCOHOL AMÍLICO *m* |
| 489 | ANAERÓBICO |
| 490 | ANALÓGICO |
| 491 | ANALIZAR |
| 492 | ANALIZADOR *m* |
| 493 | ANÁLISIS *m* |
| 494 | ANALÍTICO |
| 495 | QUÍMICA ANALÍTICA *f* |
| 496 | DETERMINACIÓN *f* ANALÍTICA |
| 497 | ANASTIGMAT, ANASTIGMÁTICO |
| 498 | ALEACIÓN PARA LA OSTEOPLÁSTICA *f* |
| 499 | ANCLAJE *m* |
| 500 | ANCLA *f* |
| 501 | BULÓN *m* DE ANCLAJE |
| 502 | CONTRAPLACA *f* (SELLADA EN EL SUELO) |
| 503 | ANEMÓMETRO *m* |
| 504 | ANEROIDE |
| 504 | BARÓMETRO *m* METÁLICO |
| 504 | BARÓMETRO *m* ANEROIDE |
| 505 | ÁNGULO *m* |
| 506 | ANGULAR *m* |
| 507 | ÁNGULO CENTRAL *m* |
| 508 | COJINETE *m* CON PLANO DE SEPARACIÓN INCLINADO |
| 509 | LLAVE TUBULAR CURVA *f* |
| 510 | MÉNSULA *f* DE FIJACIÓN, SOPORTE *m* EN ESCUADRA |
| 511 | GRIFO *m* DE ÁNGULO |
| 512 | BRIDA *f* DE HIERRO EN ÁNGULO |
| 513 | CALIBRE DE ÁNGULOS *m* |
| 514 | HIERRO *m* EN L |
| 514 | ESCUADRA *f*, HIERRO *m* ANGULAR |
| 514 | ANGULAR *m* |
| 514 | HIERRO *m* ANGULAR, CANTONERA *f* |
| 515 | ÁNGULO DE AVANCE *m* |
| 515 | ÁNGULO DE DECALADO HACIA ADELANTE *m* |
| 516 | ÁNGULO DE CHAFLÁN *m* |
| 517 | ÁNGULO DE CONTACTO *m* |
| 517 | |
| 518 | ÁNGULO DE DESVIACIÓN *m* |

| | |
|---|---|
| 519 | ÁNGULO DE FLEXIÓN *m* |
| 520 | ÁNGULO DE INCIDENCIA *m* |
| 521 | ÁNGULO DE INCLINACIÓN *m* |
| 522 | ÁNGULO DE RETARDO *m* |
| 522 | ÁNGULO DE DECALADO HACIA ATRÁS *m* |
| 523 | ÁNGULO DE DECALADO HACIA ATRÁS *m* |
| 524 | ÁNGULO DE DECALADO HACIA ADELANTE *m* |
| 525 | ÁNGULO DE REFLEXIÓN *m* |
| 526 | ÁNGULO DE REFRACCIÓN *m* |
| 527 | ÁNGULO DE ROZAMIENTO *m* |
| 528 | ÁNGULO DE ROTACIÓN *m* |
| 529 | ÁNGULO DE CALADO *m* |
| 530 | ÁNGULO DEL FILETEADO *m* |
| 531 | ÁNGULO DE LA HÉLICE *m* |
| 532 | ÁNGULO DE TORSIÓN *m* |
| 533 | ANGULAR *m* DE APOYO |
| 534 | VÁLVULA *f* EN ESCUADRA |
| 534 | GRIFO *m* EN ESCUADRA |
| 535 | TORNILLO *m* INCLINABLE |
| 536 | ANGSTRÖM *m*, ANGSTROEM *m* |
| 537 | ACELERACIÓN ANGULAR *f* |
| 538 | RODAMIENTO *m* DE BOLAS DE EMPUJE RADIAL Y AXIAL COMBINADOS |
| 538 | RODAMIENTO *m* DE BOLAS DE CARGAS RADIAL Y AXIAL COMBINADAS |
| 539 | CORTE ANGULAR *m* |
| 540 | FRESAS *f pl* CÓNICAS, FRESAS *f* DE AVELLANAR |
| 541 | DESPLAZAMIENTO *m* ANGULAR |
| 541 | DESPLAZAMIENTO *m* ANGULAR |
| 542 | CONTRACCIÓN *f* ANGULAR |
| 543 | FRESA *f* DE AVELLANAR |
| 543 | FRESA *f* ANGULAR |
| 544 | MOVIMIENTO *m* ANGULAR |
| 545 | ROSCA *f* TRIANGULAR |
| 546 | VELOCIDAD *f* ANGULAR |
| 547 | TORNILLO *m* DE ROSCA TRIANGULAR |
| 548 | ANHÍDRIDO *m* |
| 549 | ANHIDRITA *f*, SULFATO DE CALCIO ANHIDRO *m* |
| 549 | SULFATO *m* ANHIDRO |
| 550 | ANHIDRO *m*, ANHIDRA *f* |
| 551 | SAL *f* DE SOSA |
| 551 | CARBONATO SÓDICO ANHIDRO *m* |
| 552 | ANILINA *f* |
| 552 | FENILAMINA *f* |
| 553 | ACEITE DE ANILINA *m* |
| 554 | CARBÓN ANIMAL *m* |
| 555 | ACEITE *m* ANIMAL |
| 556 | ANION *m* |
| 557 | FLOTACIÓN *f* |
| 558 | ANISÓTROPO *m*, ANISÓTROPO *f* |

| | | | | |
|---|---|---|---|---|
| 559 | ANISOTROPÍA  f | | 602 | ELECTRODO  m  POSITIVO |
| 560 | RECOCER EL ACERO | | 603 | ANÓDICO  m,  ANÓDICA  f |
| 561 | ALAMBRE  m  RECOCIDO | | 604 | POLARIZACIÓN  f  ANÓDICA |
| 562 | RÉCOCIDO  m | | 605 | OXIDACIÓN  f  ANÓDICA, TRATAMIENTO  m  ANÓDICO |
| 563 | CAJA DE RECOCIDO  f | | 606 | ANOLITO  m |
| 564 | HORNO  m  DE RECOCIDO | | 606 | SOLUCIÓN  f  ANÓDICA |
| 564 | HORNO  m  DE RECOCIDO | | 607 | ANTRACENO  m |
| 564 | HORNO  m  DE RECOCER | | 608 | ACEITE  m  DE ANTRACENO |
| 565 | INSTALACIÓN  f  DE RECOCIDO | | 608 | ACEITE  m  ANTRACÉNICO |
| 566 | RECIPIENTE  m  PARA RECOCER | | 609 | ANTRACITA  f |
| 567 | CAJA DE RECOCIDO  f | | 609 | ANTRACITA  f |
| 568 | TRATAMIENTO  m  DE RECOCIDO | | 610 | CAÑÓN ANTIAÉREO  m |
| 569 | RESISTENCIA  f  AL ESTADO DE RECOCIDO | | 611 | ANTICÁTODO  m |
| 570 | BANDA  f  DE MACLAS | | 612 | ANTICONGELANTE  m |
| 571 | RECOCIDO  m  EN NEGRO | | 613 | CARBURANTE ANTIDEFLAGRANTE  m |
| 572 | RECOCIDO  m  AZUL | | 614 | ANTIMAGNÉTICO  m,  ANTIMAGNÉTICA  f |
| 573 | RECOCIDO  m  ROJO BLANCO | | 615 | COBERTOR  m |
| 574 | RECOCIDO  m  CONTINUO | | 616 | AGENTE ANTIPICADURAS  m |
| 575 | RECOCIDO  m  CON SOPLETE | | 617 | PROPIEDADES  f pl  ANTIFRICCIÓN |
| 576 | RECOCIDO  m  COMPLETO | | 618 | RODAMIENTO  m  DE RODILLOS |
| 577 | RECOCIDO  m  INTERMEDIO | | 618 | RODAMIENTO  m  DE BOLAS |
| 578 | RECOCIDO  m  INVERSO | | 619 | METAL ANTIFRICCIÓN  m |
| 579 | RECOCIDO  m  ISOTÉRMICO | | 619 | LIGA  f |
| 580 | RECOCIDO  m  SELECTIVO | | 619 | METAL  m  ANTIDESGASTE |
| 581 | RECOCIDO  m  DEL ACERO | | 620 | ANTILOGARITMO  m |
| 582 | RECOCIDO  m  PERIÓDICO | | 621 | PLOMO  m  ANTIMÓNICO |
| 583 | RECOCIDO  m  DE RELAJACIÓN | | 621 | PLOMO  m  FRÁGIL |
| 584 | RECOCIDO  m  REDUCTOR DE TENSIÓN | | 622 | ESTIBINA  f |
| 585 | EDIFICIO ANEJO (ANEXO, AUXILIAR)  m | | 623 | ANTIMONIO  m |
| 585 | EDIFICIO  m  ANEXO, EDIFICIO  m  AUXILIAR | | 624 | PENTACLORURO  m  DE ANTIMONIO |
| 586 | CAPA ANUAL  f | | 625 | PENTASULFURO  m  DE ANTIMONIO |
| 586 | ANILLO  m  ANUAL | | 625 | AZUFRE  m  DORADO DE ANTIMONIO |
| 586 | CÍRCULO ANUAL  m | | 625 | SULFURO  m  DORADO DE ANTIMONIO |
| 587 | SECCIÓN  f  ANULAR | | 626 | MANTEQUILLA  f  DE ANTIMONIO |
| 588 | ANULAR  m,  f | | 626 | TRICLORURO  m  DE ANTIMONIO |
| 589 | ANILLO  m | | 627 | TRISULFURO  m  DE ANTIMONIO |
| 589 | CORONA CIRCULAR  f,  ANILLO  m | | 627 | PROTOSULFURO  m |
| 590 | ÁNODO  m | | 628 | ANTIPÚTRIDO  m,  ANTIPÚTRIDA  f |
| 591 | PUNTA  f  DEL ÁNODO, PUNTA  f  ANÓDICA | | 628 | ANTISÉPTICO  m,  ANTISÉPTICA  f |
| 592 | PURIFICACIÓN  f  ANÓDICA | | 628 | ANTISÉPTICO  m,  ANTISÉPTICA  f |
| 593 | COBRE  m  ANÓDICO | | 629 | ANTIPÚTRIDO  m |
| 594 | COEFICIENTE DE CORROSIÓN ANÓDICA  m | | 629 | ANTISÉPTICO  m |
| 595 | CAÍDA ANÓDICA  f | | 629 | AGENTE ANTIPÚTRIDO  m |
| 596 | EFECTO  m  DE ÁNODO | | 630 | YUNQUE  m |
| 597 | RENDIMIENTO  m  ANÓDICO | | 631 | CORTADOR  m  DE YUNQUE |
| 598 | ÁNODO INSOLUBLE  m | | 631 | ROMPEDOR DE HIERRO  m |
| 599 | REVESTIMIENTO  m  (RECUBRIMIENTO) ANÓDICO | | 632 | CALZO  m |
| 599 | CAPA (DE PROTECCIÓN) ANÓDICA | | 632 | ESTACA  f |
| 600 | FANGO  m  ANÓDICO, LIMO  m  ANÓDICO | | 633 | BLOQUE  m  PORTAYUNQUE, YUNQUE  m  INFERIOR |
| 601 | DECAPADO  m  ANÓDICO | | 633 | BLOQUE PORTAYUNQUE  m |
| 602 | ÁNODO  m,  ELECTRODO POSITIVO  m | | | |

| | |
|---|---|
| 634 | APERIÓDICO *m*, APERIÓDICA *f* |
| 635 | INSTRUMENTO *m* APERIÓDICO |
| 636 | MOVIMIENTO *m* APERIÓDICO |
| 637 | APERIODICIDAD *f* |
| 638 | VÉRTICE *m*, ÁPICE *m*, ÁPEX *m* |
| 638 | VÉRTICE *m* |
| 639 | OBJETIVO APLANÉTICO *m* |
| 640 | APOCROMÁTICO *m*, APOCROMÁTICA *f* |
| 641 | APARATO *m*, INSTRUMENTO *m* |
| 642 | DENSIDAD *f* APARENTE |
| 643 | CONSTANTE DE RADIACIÓN APARENTE *f* |
| 644 | FORMACIÓN *f* DE GRIETAS |
| 645 | SOLICITANTE *m* DE PATENTE |
| 646 | SOLICITUD *f* (DE PATENTE) |
| 646 | SOLICITUD *f* DE PATENTE |
| 647 | APLICACIÓN *f* DE UNA FUERZA, ATAQUE *m* DE UNA FUERZA |
| 648 | QUÍMICA APLICADA *f* |
| 649 | INVESTIGACIÓN *f* APLICADA |
| 650 | APRETAR EL FRENO |
| 650 | APLICAR LOS FRENOS, FRENAR |
| 651 | SOLICITAR UNA PATENTE |
| 652 | APROXIMACIÓN *f* |
| 652 | CÁLCULO APROXIMADO *m* |
| 653 | VALOR *m* APROXIMADO |
| 654 | FÓRMULA *f* APROXIMADA |
| 654 | FÓRMULA *f* DE APROXIMACIÓN |
| 655 | TABLERO *m* |
| 656 | LENGUAJE *m* DE PROGRAMACIÓN APT |
| 657 | AGUA *f* FUERTE, ÁCIDO *m* NÍTRICO |
| 658 | AGUA *f* REGIA |
| 659 | ALCOHOL ACUOSO *m* |
| 660 | ÁLCALI VOLÁTIL *m*, AMONÍACO (O AMONIACO) *m* |
| 660 | AMONIACO *m*, AMONÍACO *m* |
| 660 | SOLUCIÓN *f* AMONIACAL |
| 661 | SOLUCIÓN *f* ACUOSA |
| 662 | EJE, ÁRBOL *m* |
| 663 | FRESAS *f pl* PROVISTAS DE ÁRBOL |
| 664 | ARCO *m* DE UNA CURVA |
| 665 | SOPLADURA *f* MAGNÉTICA AL ARCO |
| 666 | SOLDADURA *f* FUERTE AL ARCO |
| 667 | HORNO *m* ELÉCTRICO DE ARCO DIRECTO |
| 668 | HORNO *m* AL ARCO ELÉCTRICO |
| 669 | HORNO *m* AL ARCO INDIRECTO |
| 670 | HORNO *m* AL ARCO ELÉCTRICO CON ELECTRODOS DE CARBÓN |
| 671 | HORNO *m* ELÉCTRICO DE ARCO DIRECTO |
| 672 | LÁMPARA *f* DE ARCO CERRADO |
| 673 | LUZ *f* DEL ARCO VOLTAICO |
| 674 | ARCO *m* DE CÍRCULO |

| | |
|---|---|
| 674 | ARCO *m* DE CÍRCULO |
| 675 | ARCO *m* DE DEVANADO |
| 675 | CURVA DE CONTACTO *f* |
| 676 | TENSIÓN *f* (VOLTAJE) DEL ARCO |
| 677 | GOLPE DE SOLDADURA PUNTO DE PRINCIPIO DEL ARCO *m* |
| 678 | ESPESOR *m* DEL ARCO |
| 679 | TENSIÓN *f* DE SERVICIO DEL ARCO |
| 680 | MÁQUINA *f* DE SOLDADURA AL ARCO |
| 681 | SOLDADURA *f* AL ARCO ELÉCTRICO |
| 682 | SOLDADURA *f* POR CONTACTO |
| 683 | SOLDADURA *f* AL ARCO EN ATMÓSFERA INERTE |
| 684 | SOLDADURA *f* AL ARCO SUMERGIDO |
| 684 | PROCEDIMIENTO *m* 'UNIONMELT' |
| 685 | SOLDADURA *f* AL ARCO CON CORRIENTE ALTERNA |
| 686 | SOLDADURA *f* AL ARCO CON CORRIENTE CONTINUA |
| 687 | DOVELA *f* |
| 687 | DOVELA *f* |
| 688 | ARBOTANTE *m*, ESTRIBO *m*, PUNTAL *m* |
| 689 | BERBIQUÍ *m* HELICOIDAL |
| 690 | ESPIRAL *f* DE ARQUÍMEDES |
| 690 | ESPIRAL *f* DE ARQUÍMEDES |
| 691 | ARQUITECTO *m* |
| 692 | BRONCE *m* DE CONSTRUCCIÓN |
| 693 | DIBUJO *m* DE ARQUITECTURA |
| 694 | SUPERFICIE *f* |
| 695 | ÁREA DEL CÍRCULO *f* |
| 696 | SUPERFICIE *f* DE ENGRANAJE |
| 697 | ÁREA *f*, ESPACIO *m*, SECCIÓN *f*, SUPERFICIE *f* |
| 698 | COORDINADAS PLANAS *f pl* |
| 699 | MARGA *f* ARCILLOSA |
| 700 | ESQUISTO *m* ARCILLOSO |
| 701 | ARGÓN *m* |
| 702 | ARITMÉTICA *f* |
| 703 | MEDIA *f* ARITMÉTICA, TÉRMINO *m* MEDIO ARITMÉTICO |
| 704 | PROGRESIÓN *f* ARITMÉTICA |
| 705 | BRAZO *m* DE UN VOLANTE |
| 705 | BRAZO *m* DE UNA POLEA |
| 706 | BRAZO *m* DE PALANCA DE LA FUERZA |
| 707 | INDUCIDO *m* |
| 707 | INDUCIDO *m*, ROTOR *m* |
| 708 | CHAPA *f* PARA INDUCIDOS DE DINAMOS |
| 709 | MÁQUINA *f* BOBINADORA DE INDUCIDOS |
| 710 | ARMADURA *f* |
| 710 | ARMADURA *f* DE UN IMÁN |
| 710 | CONTACTO DE UN IMÁN *m* |
| 711 | HIERRO *m* ARMCO |
| 712 | PLANCHA *f* DE BLINDAJE |

| | | | |
|---|---|---|---|
| 713 | CABLE ARMADO *m* | 753 | ANILLO DE AMIANTO *m* |
| 714 | TUBO *m* FLEXIBLE *m* RODEADO DE ACERO | 754 | BANDA *f* DE AMIANTO (O ASBESTO) |
| 714 | TUBO *m* FLEXIBLE CON ARMADURA DE ALAMBRE | 755 | ASBESTO *m* |
| 715 | REVESTIMIENTO *m* DE UN CABLE | 755 | AMIANTO *m*, ASBESTO *m* |
| 715 | ARMADURA *f* (O PROTECCIÓN *f*) DE UN CABLE | 756 | TUBERÍA DE SUBIDA *f* |
| 716 | COMPUESTOS AROMÁTICOS *m pl* | 757 | RAMPA *f* |
| 717 | DISTRIBUCIÓN *f* DE LOS REMACHES | 758 | PORCENTAJE *m* DE CENIZAS |
| 718 | PUNTO *m* DE TRANSFORMACIÓN | 758 | PROPORCIÓN *f* DE CENIZAS |
| 719 | FLECHA *f* | 759 | CENICERO *m*, CENIZAL *m* |
| 720 | ARSEMIATO *m* | 760 | CENIZA *f* |
| 721 | ARSÉNICO *m* | 760 | CENIZAS *f pl* |
| 722 | ÁCIDO ARSÉNICO *m* | 761 | PIEDRA *f* DE TALLA, SILLAREJO |
| 723 | ANHÍDRIDO ARSÉNICO *m* | 762 | CONSTRUCCIÓN *f* DE PIEDRA DE SILLERÍA O CON SILLARES |
| 724 | TRICLORURO *m* DE ARSÉNICO | | |
| 725 | COBRE *m* ARSENICAL | 763 | ASFALTAR |
| 726 | ARSENIURO *m* | 763 | ASFALTAR |
| 727 | ANHÍDRIDO ARSENIOSO | 764 | MASTIC *m* DE ASFALTO |
| 727 | ANHÍDRIDO ARSENIOSO *m* | 765 | FIELTRO *m* ASFALTADO |
| 727 | ÁCIDO *m* AGRIO, ACETOSO | 766 | TUBO *m* PROTEGIDO CON CUBIERTA DE YUTE ASFALTADO |
| 728 | TRISULFURO *m* DE ARSÉNICO | | |
| 728 | OROPIMENTE *m*, SULFURO *m* NATURAL DE ARSÉNICO | 767 | ASFALTADO *m*, ASFALTAJE *m* |
| | | 768 | ASFALTO *m* |
| 729 | ARSENITO *m* | 768 | ASFALTO *m* SÓLIDO, BETÚN *m* SÓLIDO |
| 730 | HIDRÓGENO *m* ARSENIADO | 769 | ASPIRADOR *m* |
| 730 | HIDRÓGENO *m* ARSENIADO | 770 | NAVE *f* DE MONTAJE |
| 731 | ENVEJECIMIENTO *m* ARTIFICIAL | 771 | PASADOR *m* (O PERNO *m*, O BULÓN *m*) DE UNIÓN |
| 732 | COMBUSTIBLE ARTIFICIAL *m* | | |
| 733 | ILUMINACIÓN *f* ARTIFICIAL | 772 | PLANO *m* DE MONTAJE |
| 734 | LUZ *f* ARTIFICIAL | 773 | NAVE *f* DE MONTAJE |
| 735 | IMÁN ARTIFICIAL *m* | 773 | TALLER *m*, TALLER *m* DE CONSTRUCCIÓN DE MÁQUINAS |
| 736 | SEDA *f* ARTIFICIAL | | |
| 737 | PIEDRA *f* ARTIFICIAL | 774 | ASTATICO *m*, ASTÁTICA *f* |
| 738 | VENTILACIÓN *f* ARTIFICIAL | 775 | REGULADOR *m* ASTÁTICO |
| 739 | BRUTO *m* DE COLADA | 776 | ASTERISMO *m*, CONSTELACIÓN *f* |
| 740 | ESTADO *m* BRUTO | 777 | ELEMENTO *m* ASIMÉTRICO |
| 741 | ESTADO DE ENTREGA (EN) *m* | 778 | ASIMÉTRICO *m*, ASIMÉTRICA *f* |
| 742 | BRUTO *m* DE FORJA | 778 | DISIMÉTRICO |
| 743 | BRUTO *m* DE TEMPLE | 779 | DISIMETRÍA *f* |
| 744 | BRUTO *m* DE LAMINADO | 779 | ASIMETRÍA *f* |
| 745 | ESTADO DE SOLDADURA (EN) *m* | 780 | ASÍNTOTA *f* |
| 746 | AMIANTO *m*, ASBESTO *m* | 781 | ASINTÓTICO *m*, ASINTÓTICA *f* |
| 747 | CARTÓN DE ASBESTO *m* | 781 | ASINTÓTICO *m*, ASINTÓTICA *f* |
| 748 | LIENZO *m* DE AMIANTO | 782 | ASINCRONISMO *m* |
| 748 | TELA *f* DE AMIANTO | 783 | MOTOR *m* ASINCRÓNICO |
| 749 | CORDÓN *m* DE AMIANTO | 784 | ASÍNCRONO *m*, ASÍNCRONA *f* |
| 749 | FIBRA *f* DE AMIANTO | 785 | ATERMANEIDAD *f*, ATERMANIDAD *f* |
| 750 | FIELTRO *m* DE AMIANTO | 786 | ATÉRMANO *m*, ATÉRMANA *f* |
| 751 | CORDÓN DE AMIANTO *m* | 787 | ATMÓSFERA *f* |
| 751 | TRENZA *f* | 788 | ATMÓSFERA *f* |
| 751 | AMIANTO TRENZADO EN CUERDA *m* | 789 | ATMÓSFERA *f* ARTIFICIAL |
| 752 | PAPEL *m* DE AMIANTO | 790 | ATMÓSFERA *f* DE PROTECCIÓN |
| | | 791 | ATMÓSFERA *f* DE USO ESPECIAL |

385

| | | | |
|---|---|---|---|
| 792 | ACCIONES ATMOSFÉRICAS  *f pl* | 832 | CORTE  *m* AUTÓGENO |
| 793 | AGENTES ATMOSFÉRICOS  *m pl* | 833 | MÁQUINA  *f* PARA CORTE AUTÓGENO |
| 794 | PRESIÓN  *f* BAROMÉTRICA | 834 | SOLDADURA  *f* AUTÓGENA |
| 794 | PRESIÓN  *f* ATMOSFÉRICA | 834 | SOLDADURA  *f* AUTÓGENA |
| 794 | PRESIÓN  *f* DE X CM DE MERCURIO | 835 | SOLDADURA  *f* AUTÓGENA |
| 795 | CORROSIÓN ATMOSFÉRICA  *f* | 836 | ACELERACIÓN AUTOMÁTICA  *f* |
| 796 | ELECTRICIDAD  *f* ATMOSFÉRICA | 837 | AUTOMATICIDAD  *f*, AUTOMATIZACIÓN  *f*, AUTOMATISMO  *m* |
| 797 | VÁLVULA  *f* DE ESCAPE | 838 | ESTÁRTER  *m* AUTOMÁTICO |
| 798 | LÍNEA  *f* ATMOSFÉRICA | 839 | CICLO  *m* AUTOMÁTICO |
| 799 | MAZAROTA  *f* CON NÚCLEO ATMOSFÉRICO | 840 | TORNO  *m* DE CICLOS AUTOMÁTICOS |
| 800 | ÁTOMO  *m* | 841 | DESACELERACIÓN  *f* AUTOMÁTICA |
| 801 | SOLDADURA ARCATOM (AL ARCO PROTEGIDO CON HIDROGENO ATÓMICO) | 842 | PALANCA  *f* DE AVANCE AUTOMÁTICO |
| 802 | CALOR ATÓMICO  *m* | 843 | REGULADOR  *m* AUTOMÁTICO |
| 803 | NÚMERO  *m* ATÓMICO | 844 | ENCENDIDO AUTOMÁTICO  *m* |
| 804 | PLANO  *m* RETICULAR | 845 | GRIFO  *m* DE AISLAMIENTO |
| 805 | TEORÍA  *f* ATÓMICA | 846 | TORNO  *m* AUTOMÁTICO |
| 806 | VOLUMEN  *m* ATÓMICO | 847 | ESTABILIZADOR  *m* AUTOMÁTICO |
| 807 | PESO  *m* ATÓMICO | 848 | ENGRASE  *m* MECÁNICO |
| 808 | PULVERIZAR (UN LÍQUIDO) | 848 | ENGRASE  *m* AUTOMÁTICO |
| 809 | PULVERIZADOR  *m* | 849 | SOLDADURA  *f* AUTOMÁTICA |
| 809 | ATOMIZADOR  *m*, PULVERIZADOR  *m* | 850 | PROGRAMACIÓN  *f* AUTOMÁTICA |
| 810 | PULVERIZACIÓN  *f* DE UN LÍQUIDO | 851 | ENGRASADOR  *m* AUTOMÁTICO |
| 811 | PULVERIZACIÓN  *f* | 852 | VÁLVULA  *f* AUTOMÁTICA |
| 811 | ATOMIZACIÓN  *f*, PULVERIZACIÓN  *f* | 852 | VÁLVULA  *f* AUTOMÁTICA |
| 812 | ACCESORIO  *m* | 853 | MÁQUINA  *f* AUXILIAR |
| 812 | ACCESORIO  *m* | 854 | FUNCIÓN  *f* AUXILIAR |
| 813 | ATAQUE  *m*, CORROSIÓN  *f* | 855 | TEMPERATURA  *f* MEDIA |
| 814 | CONDUCCIÓN  *f*, OPERACIÓN  *f* | 856 | TIJERAS ARTICULADAS  *f pl* |
| 815 | ATRACCIÓN  *f* | 857 | HACHA  *f* |
| 816 | SEÑAL  *f* ACÚSTICA | ·858 | EJES  *m pl* QUE SE CORTAN A ÁNGULO RECTO |
| 817 | ALEACIÓN DE AUER  *f* | 859 | COMPONENTE AXIAL  *f* |
| 818 | TALADRO  *m* | 860 | DESPLAZAMIENTO  *m* PARALELO AL EJE |
| 819 | AUGITA  *f* | 860 | DESPLAZAMIENTO  *m* LONGITUDINAL |
| 820 | AUGITA-SIENITA  *f* | 860 | DESPLAZAMIENTO  *m* AXIAL |
| 821 | TRICLORURO  *m* DE ORO | 861 | BOMBA  *f* HELICOIDAL |
| 822 | AURÍFERO  *m*, AURÍFERA  *f* | 862 | TURBINA  *f* PARALELA |
| 823 | CLORURO DE ORO  *m* | 862 | TURBINA  *f* AXIAL |
| 824 | TEMPLE  *m* ESCALONADO BAINÍTICO | 863 | EJE  *m* DE SIMETRÍA DE LOS CRISTALES |
| 824 | TEMPLE  *m* POR ETAPAS | 864 | EJE  *m* DE COORDENADAS CARTESIANAS |
| 825 | AUSTENITA  *f* | 865 | EJE  *m* DE UN CRISTAL |
| 826 | ACERO AUSTENÍTICO  *m* | 866 | EJE  *m* DE UN TUBO |
| 827 | AUSTENITIZACIÓN  *f* | 867 | EJE  *m* DE OSCILACIÓN (O DE VIBRACIÓN) |
| 828 | (MOTOR DE) ARRANQUE  *m*, AUTOMÁTICO, ARRANCADOR  *m* AUTOMÁTICO | 868 | EJE  *m* DE ROTACIÓN |
| 829 | DIGESTOR  *m* | 869 | EJE  *m* DE SIMETRÍA |
| 829 | AUTOCLAVE  *m* | 870 | EJE  *m* DE SOLDADURA |
| 829 | MARMITA  *f* DE PAPIN | 871 | EJE  *m* DEL CORDEL (O DEL CORDÓN) DE SOLDADURA |
| 829 | MARMITA  *f* AUTOCLAVE | 872 | EJE  *m* DE LAS X |
| 830 | SUMISIÓN A UNA TENSIÓN PREVIA | 872 | EJE  *m* DE ABSCISAS |
| 831 | SOLDADURA  *f* AUTÓGENA | 873 | EJE  *m* DE ORDENADAS |

| | | | | |
|---|---|---|---|---|
| 873 | EJE *m* DE LAS Y | 910 | DESTOLONADO *m* |
| 874 | EJE *m* GEOMÉTRICO | 910 | DESTALONADO *m*, DESPOJAMIENTO *m* |
| 875 | EJE *m* O ÁRBOL *m* | 911 | CONTRA JUNTA *f* |
| 876 | COJINETE *m* DE EJE | 912 | ARENA *f* DE COBERTURA |
| 877 | CAJA *f* DE GRASA | 913 | TORNO DE DESPOJAR *m*, TORNO PARA DESTALONAR *m* |
| 877 | CAJA *f* DE EJE | | |
| 877 | COJINETE *m* DE EJE | 913 | TORNOS *m pl* DE DESNUDAR |
| 877 | CAJA *f* DE ENGRASE | 914 | JUEGO *m* ENTRE LOS DIENTES |
| 878 | TALADRADORA *f* PARA CAJA DE GRASA EJES | 915 | MECANISMO *m* DE REANUDACIÓN DE LOS JUEGOS, (REPOSICIÓN) |
| 879 | GRASA *f* PARA COCHE | | |
| 879 | GRASA *f* (PARA EJES) | 916 | JUEGO *m* INÚTIL |
| 880 | TORNO *m* PARA MANGUETA DE EJE | 916 | JUEGO *m* PERJUDICIAL, JUEGO *m* NOCIVO |
| 881 | TORNO *m* DE EJES DE RUEDAS | 916 | JUEGO *m* PERNICIOSO |
| 882 | MANGUETA *f* DE EJE | 917 | RESPALDO *m* |
| 883 | LLAVE DE EJE *f* | 918 | SOLDADURA *f* EN PASO DE PEREGRINO |
| 883 | LLAVE PARA EJE | 919 | RETROCESO *m* |
| 884 | EJE *m* | 919 | MOVIMIENTO *m* EN SENTIDO RETRÓGRADO |
| 885 | PERSPECTIVA *f* AXONOMÉTRICA | 919 | MOVIMIENTO *m* DE RETROCESO |
| 886 | AZURITA *f* | 920 | SOLDADURA *f* MAL HECHA |
| 887 | INSTITUTO *m* BRITÁNICO DE NORMALIZACIÓN | 920 | SOLDADURA *f* MAL HECHA |
| 888 | METAL *m* ANTIFRICCIÓN | 921 | DEFLECTOR *m* |
| 888 | METAL *m* BLANCO | 921 | DEFLECTOR *m* |
| 889 | METAL ANTI-FRICCIÓN | 921 | CHAPA *f* DEFLECTORA |
| 889 | METAL BABBITT *m* | 922 | DEFLECTOR *m*, PLACA DEFLECTORA *f* |
| 890 | DORSO *m*, ESPALDAS *f pl* | 923 | PROCEDIMIENTO *m* DE MOLDEADO POR MEDIO DEL SACO SACO DE CAUCHO |
| 891 | PORTEZUELA *f* TRASERA | | |
| 891 | PUERTA *f* | 924 | BAGAZO *m* |
| 891 | COMPUERTA *f* DE DESCARGA | 925 | BAINITA *f* |
| 892 | RETORNO *m* DE LA LLAMA | 926 | ARCILLA *f* CALCINADA |
| 893 | DESPEJAR | 927 | NÚCLEO *m* TRATADO |
| 893 | DESTALONAR, REBAJAR | 928 | SECADO *m* |
| 894 | MARCHA *f* EN CONTRAPRESIÓN | 929 | EQUILIBRIO *m* |
| 895 | VÁLVULA *f* DE CONTRAPRESIÓN | 930 | EQUILIBRAR, COMPENSAR, CONTRABALANCEAR |
| 896 | REFLEXIÓN *f* DE RETORNO | 930 | EQUILIBRAR |
| 897 | SIERRA *f* INVERTIDA | 930 | COMPENSAR |
| 898 | PUNTAL *m*, FRENO *m* | 931 | BALANZA *f*, BÁSCULA |
| 899 | LUNETA *f* TRASERA | 931 | BALANZA *f*, BÁSCULA |
| 900 | TERRAPLÉN *m* | 932 | ECONOMÍA *f* SANA |
| 900 | TERRAPLENADO *m* | 932 | ECONOMÍA *f* EN EQUILIBRÍO |
| 901 | SOLDADURA *f* EN PASO DE PEREGRINO | 933 | FILTROS *m pl* SIMÉTRICOS |
| 902 | CINTA-SOPORTE *f* | 934 | VÁLVULA *f* EQUILIBRADA |
| 902 | PLANO *m* SOPORTE | 934 | VÁLVULA *f* EQUILIBRADA |
| 903 | CILINDROS *m pl* DE SOPORTE | 935 | EQUILIBRADO *m*, BALANCE *m* |
| 904 | CORDÓN SOPORTE (AL REVÉS) *m* | 936 | DESCARGA *f* DE UNA VÁLVULA |
| 905 | FRESA *f* CON DIENTES LIBRES | 937 | MÁQUINA EQUILIBRADORA *f* |
| 905 | FRESA *f* DE PERFIL CONSTANTE | 938 | CILINDRO *m* DE EQUILIBADO |
| 905 | FRESA *f* CON DIENTES DESPEJADOS | 939 | CILINDRO *m* DE EQUILIBRADO |
| 906 | RETORNO *m* DE LLAMA | 940 | MÁQUINA DE EQUILIBRAR |
| 907 | SOLDADURA *f* A LA DERECHA | 941 | EQUILIBRIO *m* DE LAS MASAS |
| 908 | LUCES *f pl* DE RETROCESO | 942 | EQUILIBRACIÓN *f*, EQUILIBRADO *m*, COMPENSACIÓN *f* |
| 909 | METAL *m* SOPORTE | | |
| | | 942 | EQUILIBRACIÓN *f*, EQUILIBRADO *m* |

| | |
|---|---|
| 944 CORREA DE BALATA *f* | 977 SIERRA *f* DE CINTA |
| 945 BALA *f* | 978 SIERRA *f* DE CINTA |
| 946 RECOGEDORA *f* DE CASCABILLO | 978 SIERRA *f* DE HOJA SIN FIN |
| 947 CARRETILLA *f* | 979 ESTRUCTURA *f* ZONAL |
| 947 CARRETILLA *f* | 980 FLEJES *m pl* |
| 948 AGAVILLADORAS *f pl* MECANICAS DE TODA DENSIDAD | 980 TIRAS *f pl*, FLEJES *m pl*, BANDAS *f pl* |
| 949 VIGA *f* DE MADERA | 980 CINTAS *f pl* |
| 950 BOLA *f*, ESFERA *f* | 981 BARRA *f* |
| 951 MASA *f* DE ACERO, BLOQUE *m* DE ACERO | 982 MÁQUINA *f* PARA ESTIRAR LAS BARRAS Y LOS TUBOS |
| 951 BOLA *f* DE ACERO, MASA *f*, LINGOTE *m* DE ACERO | 983 TORNO *m* AUTOMÁTICO TRABAJANDO EN BARRA |
| 951 LINGOTE *m* FUNDICIÓN DE ACERO | 984 ACERO *m* EN BARRAS |
| 952 COJINETE *m* DE GORRÓN ESFÉRICO, O DE RÓTULA ESFÉRICA | 984 HIERRO *m* EN BARRAS, HIERRO *m* EN VARILLAS |
| 953 JUNTA *f* ESFÉRICA | 984 ACERO EN BARRAS *m* |
| 953 JUNTA *f* DE RÓTULA, JUNTA *f* ARTICULADA | 985 IMÁN RECTO *m* |
| 953 ARTICULACIÓN *f* | 985 IMÁN *m* RECTO |
| 954 RODAMIENTO *m* | 986 BARRA *f*, VIGUETA *f*, VIGA *f* |
| 954 RODAMIENTO *m* DE BOLAS | 986 VIGUETA *f* |
| 954 COJINETE *m* DE RODAMIENTO DE BOLAS | 987 ALAMBRE *f* ESPINOSO |
| 954 COJINETE DE BOLAS *m* | 987 ALAMBRE *m* DE ESPINO |
| 955 JAULA DE RODAMIENTO DE BOLAS *f* | 988 MÁQUINA *f* PARA ALAMBRE ESPINOSO |
| 956 PULIMENTO *m* CON BOLAS | 989 ELECTRODO *m* NO PROTEGIDO |
| 957 JAULA DE BOLAS *f* | 990 ALAMBRE *m* DESNUDO |
| 958 SUSPENSIÓN *f* DE RÓTULA | 991 BARCAZA *f*, GABARRA *f*, PINAZA *f* |
| 959 MOLINO *m* DE BOLAS | 991 EMBARCACIÓN *f*, PINAZA *f*, BARCAZA *f* |
| 960 MARTILLO *m* REDONDEADO | 992 BARIO *m* |
| 960 MARTILLO *m* DE BOCA BOMBEADA | 993 ACETATO DE BARIO *m* |
| 961 BOCA *f* REDONDA DE MARTILLO | 994 ALUMINATO DE BARITA *m* |
| 962 MARTILLO *m* DE BOCA REDONDA | 995 CARBURO DE BARIO *m* |
| 963 BOCA *f* ESFÉRICA DE MARTILLO | 996 CARBONATO DE BARIO *m* |
| 963 BOCA *f* DE MARTILLO BOMBEADA | 997 CLORURO DE BARIO *m* |
| 964 ARO *m* DE RODAMIENTO, ANILLO *m* DE BOLAS | 998 BIÓXIDO *m* DE BARIO |
| 964 ARO DE RODAMIENTO *m*, ANILLO DE BOLAS *m* | 999 FLUORURO *m* DE BARIO |
| 965 ANILLO DE RODADURA DE LAS BOLAS *m* | 1000 HIDRATO *m* DE BARIO |
| 966 COJINETE *m* A BOLAS | 1000 HIDRATO *m* DE BARITA |
| 967 DURÓMETRO A BOLA *m* | 1001 NITRATO *m* DE BARIO |
| 968 GRIFO *m* DE VÁLVULA ESFÉRICA (DE BOLA) | 1002 PLATINOCIANURO DE BARIO *m* |
| 968 VÁLVULA *f* DE NÚCLEO GIRATORIO | 1003 SULFATO *m* DE BARIO |
| 968 VÁLVULA *f* DE BOLA | 1003 BLANCO *m* DE BARITA |
| 968 VÁLVULA *f* DE BOLA | 1003 BLANCO *m* FIJO |
| 969 BALASTO *m* | 1004 SULFURO *m* DE BARIO |
| 970 VÁLVULA BALASTO *f* | 1005 CAPA INTERMEDIA DESCARBURADA *f* |
| 971 BALASTADO *m* | 1006 BARNIO *m*, FERMI *m* |
| 972 BAMBÚ *m* | 1006 UNIDAD *f* DE SUPERFICIE NUCLEAR |
| 973 ESTAÑO *m* DE BANCA | 1007 BARÓMETRO *m* REGISTRADOR |
| 974 BANDA *f*, CINTA *f* | 1008 BARÓMETRO *m* |
| 974 CINTA *f* | 1009 BAROMÉTRICO *m*, BAROMÉTRICA |
| 975 POLEA *f* DE CUERDA | 1010 CONDENSADOR BAROMÉTRICO *m* |
| 976 INDICADOR *m* DE TENSIÓN DE LA CINTA | 1011 BAROSCOPIO *m* |
| | 1012 PULIMENTO *m* EN TAMBOR |

| | |
|---|---|
| 1013 | MÁQUINA  f  DE ESCARIAR EN HUECO |
| 1014 | ACABADO  m  CON EL TAMBOR |
| 1015 | CILINDRO  m, CUERPO DE BOMBA |
| 1015 | CUERPO DE BOMBA  m |
| 1016 | GALVANOPLASTIA  f  AL TONEL |
| 1016 | REVESTIMIENTO  m  GALVÁNICO EN TAMBOR |
| 1017 | RODILLO  m  ABULTADO |
| 1018 | SERVOMOTOR  m  LANZADOR |
| 1018 | SERVOMOTOR  m  DE ARRANQUE |
| 1019 | AGUA  f  DE BARITA |
| 1020 | BARITA  f |
| 1020 | PROTÓXIDO  m  DE BARIO |
| 1021 | BARITITA  f, ESPATO  m  PESADO |
| 1021 | BARITINA  f |
| 1021 | ESPATO  m  PESADO |
| 1022 | BASALTO  m |
| 1023 | BASÁLTICO  m, BASÁLTICA  f |
| 1024 | BASE  f |
| 1025 | BASE  f |
| 1026 | BASE  f, PLACA  f  BASE (O DE FONDO) |
| 1026 | CARA  f  DE APOYO |
| 1026 | ZÓCALO  m |
| 1027 | BASE  f |
| 1028 | FONDO  m  DE ROSCA |
| 1028 | RAÍZ  f |
| 1028 | FONDO  m  DE ROSCA |
| 1029 | PLOMO  m  IMPURO |
| 1029 | PLOMO  m  SIN REFINAR |
| 1030 | CÍRCULO PRIMITIVO  m |
| 1030 | CÍRCULO BÁSICO  m |
| 1031 | METAL  m  NO PRECIOSO |
| 1032 | METAL  m  DE BASE |
| 1033 | BASE  f  DE UN LOGARITMO |
| 1034 | PATÍN  m  DE UN COJINETE |
| 1035 | BASAMENTO  m  DE UNA COLUMNA |
| 1036 | RAÍZ  f  DEL DIENTE |
| 1037 | ZÓCALO  m  DE FUNDICIÓN |
| 1037 | PLACA  f  DE FUNDACIÓN |
| 1037 | PLACA  f  DE BASE |
| 1037 | PLACA  f  DE FONDO |
| 1037 | PLACA  f  DE ASIENTO |
| 1038 | ELEMENTO  m  BÁSICO |
| 1039 | MUESTRA  f  DE METAL DE BASE |
| 1040 | PLACA  f  DE BASE |
| 1041 | PIE  m, PATA  f |
| 1041 | SOPORTE  m |
| 1042 | BÁSICO  m, BÁSICA |
| 1043 | PROCEDIMIENTO  m  THOMAS |
| 1043 | PROCEDIMIENTO  m  BÁSICO |
| 1044 | ACERO THOMAS  m |
| 1045 | SOLERA  f  Y ALIMENTACIÓN BÁSICAS |

| | |
|---|---|
| 1046 | FLUJO  m  BÁSICO |
| 1047 | ACERO MARTIN AL PROCESO BÁSICO  m |
| 1048 | ACERO DE SOLERA BÁSICA  m |
| 1048 | ACERO MARTIN |
| 1049 | FUNDICIÓN  f  THOMAS |
| 1050 | PROCEDIMIENTO  m  BÁSICO |
| 1051 | REFRACTARIOS BÁSICOS |
| 1052 | INVESTIGACIÓN  f  PURA |
| 1053 | CARA DE BASE  f |
| 1054 | ESCORIAS  f pl  BÁSICAS |
| 1055 | BASICIDAD  f |
| 1056 | LIBER  m |
| 1057 | LIMA  f  BASTARDA |
| 1058 | CORTE  m  LONGITUDINAL DE LA MADERA |
| 1058 | CORTA  f  GRANDE DE MADERA |
| 1058 | ASERRADO  m  A LO LARGO |
| 1058 | ASERRADO  m  PARALELO |
| 1059 | LOTE  m  DE COLADA |
| 1060 | HORNO  m  QUE CARGAR |
| 1060 | HORNO  m  NO CONTINUO |
| 1061 | RUEDA  f  DE TRINQUETE |
| 1062 | BAÑO  m |
| 1063 | GRIFO  m  DE BAÑERA |
| 1064 | CORRIENTE DEL BAÑO  f |
| 1065 | OBLICUIDAD  f |
| 1065 | INCLINACIÓN  f |
| 1066 | BATERÍA  f  DE ACUMULADORES |
| 1067 | CAJA  f  DE BATERÍA, VASO  m  DEL ACUMULADOR |
| 1068 | GRIFO  m  DE BATERÍA |
| 1069 | BATERÍA  f  DE CALDERAS |
| 1070 | EFECTO  m  BAUSCHINGER |
| 1071 | BAUXITA  f |
| 1072 | NAVE  f  (DE TALLER, DE MERCADO, ETC...) |
| 1073 | PROCEDIMIENTO  m  BAYER |
| 1074 | CIERRE  m  DE BAYONETA |
| 1074 | CIERRE  m  DE BAYONETA |
| 1074 | ACOPLAMIENTO  m |
| 1075 | TRABAJAR A LA TRACCIÓN |
| 1075 | TRABAJAR A LA COMPRESIÓN |
| 1076 | EQUILIBRARSE |
| 1077 | ENGRANARSE |
| 1077 | ENGRANARSE |
| 1078 | CIZALLAR, CORTAR |
| 1078 | ESTAR SOMETIDO A UN ESFUERZO CORTANTE |
| 1078 | TRABAJAR AL ESFUERZO CORTANTE |
| 1079 | MARCHAR CON PLENA CARGA, CON LA CARGA MÁXIMA |
| 1080 | MARCHAR CON CARGA COMPLETA |
| 1081 | MARCHAR DE VACÍO |
| 1082 | CORDÓN DE SOLDADURA  m |

| | |
|---|---|
| 1082 | CORDÓN *m* DE SOLDADURA, BORDÓN *m*, REFUERZO *m* |
| 1083 | BORDE *m* DOBLADO |
| 1083 | BORDE *m* REDONDEADO |
| 1084 | DOBLAR LOS BORDES |
| 1084 | DOBLAR LA BRIDA DE LOS TUBOS |
| 1084 | DOBLAR LOS BORDES |
| 1084 | DOBLAR LOS BORDES DE LAS CHAPAS |
| 1085 | SOLDADURA *f* LINEAL DE FRACCIÓN |
| 1086 | HIERRO *m* PARA CERCADO |
| 1087 | TUBO *m* DE COLLAR VUELTO |
| 1087 | TUBO *m* DE BORDE VUELTO |
| 1088 | REBORDE *m* |
| 1088 | DOBLEZ *f* |
| 1088 | DOBLAMIENTO *m* DE LA BRIDA DE LAS TUBOS |
| 1088 | DOBLAMIENTO *m*, DOBLEZ *f* PROYECCIÓN *f* |
| 1088 | DOBLAMIENTO *m* DE LOS BORDES DE LAS CHAPAS |
| 1089 | MÁQUINA *f* PARA HACER LAS PESTAÑAS |
| 1090 | PICO DE YUNQUE *m* |
| 1090 | BIGORNIA *f* DE YUNQUE, CUERNO *m* DE YUNQUE |
| 1091 | BIGORNIA *f*, PICO *m* |
| 1092 | CUBILETE *m*, VASO *m* DE PRECIPITACIÓN |
| 1093 | HAZ *m* ELECTRÓNICO |
| 1093 | HAZ *m* |
| 1093 | VIGUETA *f* |
| 1093 | VIGA *f* |
| 1094 | DISPOSITIVO *m* BIELA/MANIVELA |
| 1094 | MECANISMO *m* CON MANIVELA |
| 1095 | BALANZA *f* DE CRUZ |
| 1096 | COMPÁS DE VARA *m* |
| 1097 | VIGA *f* EMPOTRADA EN UN EXTREMO Y APOYADA EN EL OTRO |
| 1098 | VIGA *f* APOYADA EN SUS DOS EXTREMOS |
| 1099 | VIGA *f* |
| 1100 | COJINETE *m* |
| 1100 | COJINETE *m* |
| 1101 | SUPERFICIE *f* DE APOYO |
| 1102 | BOLA *f* PARA RODAMIENTOS |
| 1103 | SOPORTE DE COJINETE *m* |
| 1104 | TAPA DE COJINETE *f*, CUBIERTA DE PALIER *f* |
| 1105 | ROZAMIENTO *m* EN LOS COJINETES |
| 1106 | COMPOSICIÓN PARA COJINETE *f* |
| 1106 | METAL ANTIFRICCIÓN *m* |
| 1106 | METAL *m* PARA COJINETES |
| 1107 | SUPERFICIE *f* DE APOYO DE UN EJE |
| 1108 | AGUJAS PARA RODAMIENTOS *f pl* |
| 1109 | CHAPA *f* CONSTRUCCIÓN |
| 1110 | REACCIÓN *f* EN LOS APOYOS |
| 1110 | PRESIÓN *f* SOBRE LAS SUPERFICIES DE APOYO |
| 1111 | ANILLO DE RODADURA *m* |

| | |
|---|---|
| 1112 | RODILLO *m* PARA RODAMIENTOS |
| 1112 | RODILLO *m* |
| 1113 | CASCO DE COJINETE *m* |
| 1114 | RESORTE *m* DE SUSPENSIÓN |
| 1115 | SUPERFICIE *f* DE APOYO |
| 1115 | SUPERFICIE *f* DE APOYO |
| 1116 | SUPERFICIE *f* DE APOYO DE UN MUÑÓN |
| 1116 | SUPERFICIE *f* DE APOYO DE UNA MANIVELA |
| 1117 | RODAMIENTO *m* |
| 1117 | SOPORTE *m*, MANGA *f* DE EJE |
| 1118 | SOPORTE *m* (CONSTRUCCIÓN) |
| 1118 | APOYO *m*, SOPORTE *m*, COJINETE *m* |
| 1119 | BATIDERO *m*, BATIDO *m* |
| 1120 | BATIDO *m* DE METALES |
| 1121 | TERRAJA *f* PARA TUBOS |
| 1122 | CONCENTRARSE, CENTRARSE |
| 1123 | DESIMANTARSE, DESMAGNETIZARSE |
| 1124 | ELECTRIZARSE |
| 1125 | ALARGARSE, EXTENDERSE, DILATARSE |
| 1126 | IMANTARSE, MAGNETIZARSE |
| 1127 | PLACA *f* DE ASIENTO |
| 1127 | PLACA *f* DE APOYO |
| 1128 | SEBO *m* DE BUEY |
| 1129 | CERA DE ABEJAS *f* |
| 1130 | CAPA DE BEILBY *f* |
| 1131 | PALANCA *f* EN ESCUADRA, PALANCA *f* ACODADA |
| 1131 | PALANCA *f* DE SEÑAL ACÚSTICA |
| 1131 | PALANCA *f* ACODADA |
| 1132 | HORNO *m* DE CAMPANA |
| 1133 | CARTER DE EMBRAGUE *m* |
| 1134 | BRONCE *m* DE CAMPANAS, METAL *m* CAMPANIL |
| 1135 | HORNO *m* TIPO CAMPANA |
| 1136 | VÁLVULA *f* DE CORNOUAILLES |
| 1136 | VÁLVULA *f* DE CAMPANA |
| 1137 | TIMBRE *m* AVISADOR |
| 1137 | TIMBRE *m* |
| 1138 | GRIFO *m* DE FUELLE |
| 1139 | FUELLE *m* |
| 1139 | FUELLE *m* DE FORJA |
| 1140 | CORREA *f*, CINTA *f* |
| 1141 | CARGA POR TRANSPORTADOR DE CINTA *f* |
| 1142 | EMPALME *m* DE LAS CORREAS |
| 1142 | ACOPLAMIENTO *m* DE CORREAS, ENLACE *m* DE CORREAS |
| 1142 | EMPALMES *m pl* DE CORREA |
| 1143 | UTILLAJE *m* EN ESPINA, PARA CORREA DE TRANSMISIÓN |
| 1144 | TRANSMISIÓN *f* POR CORREAS |
| 1144 | DISPOSITIVO *m* POLEA Y CORREA |
| 1145 | MÁQUINA *f* DE ACCIONADO POR CORREA |

| | |
|---|---|
| 1146 | COLGADOR DE CORREOS  *m* |
| 1147 | POLEA  *f*  VOLANTE |
| 1147 | VOLANTE  *m*  POLEA |
| 1148 | HORNO  *m*  DE TRANSPORTADOR |
| 1149 | TRANSMISIÓN  *f*  DE ÁNGULO |
| 1150 | GUÍA  *f*  DE CORREA |
| 1151 | GRAPA  *f*  DE UNIÓN PARA CORREAS |
| 1151 | EMPALME  *m*  DE LAS CORREAS |
| 1151 | ACOPLAMIENTO  *m*  DE CORREAS |
| 1152 | POLEA  *f*  DE CORREA |
| 1153 | PERFORADOR  *m*  DE CORREAS, TENAZA  *f*  PERFORADORA DE CORREAS |
| 1154 | DISPOSITIVO DE CAMBIO DE SENTIDO DE MARCHA POR CORREA |
| 1155 | ROBLÓN  *m*  DE CORREAS |
| 1156 | PERNO  *m*  PARA CORREAS |
| 1157 | MECANISMO  *m*  DE DESEMBRAGUE DE LA CORREA |
| 1158 | PASO  *m*  DE LA CORREA DE UNA POLEA A OTRA |
| 1158 | DESPLAZAMIENTO  *m*  DE LA CORREA |
| 1159 | PORTACORREA  *m* |
| 1159 | MONTACORREA  *m* |
| 1159 | PASACORREA  *m* |
| 1160 | COLOCACIÓN  *f*  DE UNA CORREA |
| 1160 | MONTAJE  *m*  DE LA CORREA |
| 1161 | TENSOR  *m*  DE CORREAS |
| 1162 | TENSIÓN  *f*  DE LA CORREA |
| 1163 | CORREA MOTRIZ  *f* |
| 1163 | CORREA  *f*  MOTRIZ (DE MANDO) |
| 1164 | TRANSPORTADOR  *m*  DE CINTA |
| 1164 | TRANSPORTADOR  *m*  DE CORREA |
| 1164 | CINTA  *f*  TRANSPORTADORA |
| 1165 | CORREA  *f*  (ESPESOR DE UNA) |
| 1166 | CORREA DE X CAPAS  *f* |
| 1166 | CORREA DE X CAPAS  *f* |
| 1167 | BANCO  *m* |
| 1167 | BANCO  *m*  DE TRABAJO |
| 1168 | TALADRADORA  *f*  DE BANCO |
| 1169 | MOLDEO O MOLDEADO  *m*  EN MESA |
| 1170 | PRUEBA  *f*  EN BANCO |
| 1171 | TORNILLO  *m*  DE BANCO |
| 1172 | CODO  *m* |
| 1173 | ENCORVAR, ALABEAR, ARQUEAR, TORCER |
| 1173 | PLEGAR, DOBLAR |
| 1173 | CIMBRAR, CURVAR |
| 1174 | DOBLEGARSE |
| 1175 | CURVAR UN TUBO |
| 1175 | CURVAR UN TUBO, ACODAR UN TUBO |
| 1175 | CURVAR, ACODAR |
| 1176 | RADIO  *m*  DE CURVATURA |
| 1177 | PRUEBA  *f*  DE FLEXIÓN, PRUEBA  *f*  DE PLEGADO |

| | |
|---|---|
| 1178 | PRUEBA  *f*  DE FLEXIÓN DE LA CARA DE SOLDADURA |
| 1179 | PRUEBA  *f*  DE PLEGADO AL REVÉS |
| 1180 | CODO REDONDO  *m* |
| 1181 | MÁQUINA  *f*  PLEGADORA |
| 1182 | PLEGADO  *m* |
| 1182 | FLEXIÓN  *f* |
| 1182 | CURVADO  *m*, DOBLADO  *m* |
| 1182 | FLEXIÓN  *f* |
| 1183 | PESTAÑA  *f*  DE CINTRADO |
| 1184 | MÁQUINA  *f*  DE CURVAR, MÁQUINA  *f*  DE ENCORVAR |
| 1185 | MOMENTO  *m*  DE FLEXIÓN |
| 1185 | MOMENTO  *m*  FLECTOR |
| 1186 | CILINDRO  *m*  DE CINTRAR (DE CURVAR) |
| 1186 | CILINDRO  *m*  DE CINTRAR (DE CURVAR) |
| 1186 | MÁQUINA  *f*  DE ENROLLAR |
| 1187 | ESFUERZO  *m*  DE FLEXIÓN |
| 1188 | RESISTENCIA  *f*  AL PLEGADO |
| 1188 | RESISTENCIA  *f*  AL CIMBREO |
| 1189 | PRUEBA  *f*  DE PLEGADO |
| 1189 | PRUEBA  *f*  A LA FLEXIÓN |
| 1189 | PRUEBA  *f*  DE COMBADURA |
| 1190 | PRUEBA  *f*  DE FLEXIÓN POR CHOQUE EN BARRAS ENTALLADAS |
| 1190 | PRUEBA  *f*  DE FLEXÍON AL CHOQUE EN ENTALLADURA |
| 1191 | ESFUERZO  *m*  DE FLEXIÓN |
| 1191 | ESFUERZO  *m*  DE FLEXIÓN |
| 1191 | TRABAJO  *m*  A LA FLEXIÓN |
| 1192 | RESISTENCIA  *f*  A LA FLEXIÓN TRANSVERSAL |
| 1193 | TENSIÓN  *f*  DE FLEXIÓN |
| 1194 | CODO  *m*, TUBO ACODADO  *m* |
| 1194 | TUBO  *m*  CURVADO |
| 1194 | CUELLO DE CISNE  *m* |
| 1195 | LLAVE ACODADA  *f* |
| 1196 | MADERA  *f*  CURVADA, VARILLA  *f*  ELÁSTICA |
| 1197 | TORCIDO |
| 1198 | ESENCIA  *f*  DE ALMENDRAS AMARGAS, ALDEHIDO BENCÍLICO |
| 1198 | BENZALDEHÍDO  *m* |
| 1198 | ADEHÍDO BENCÍLICO  *m* |
| 1199 | BENCINA  *f* |
| 1199 | BENCENO  *m*, BENZOL  *m* |
| 1200 | ÁCIDO FENILSULFOROSO  *m* |
| 1200 | ÁCIDO BENCENO-SULFÓNICO  *m* |
| 1201 | BENCIDINA  *f* |
| 1202 | ÁCIDO BENZOICO  *m* |
| 1203 | BENJUÍ  *m* |
| 1204 | BENZOL  *m*, BENCENO  *m* |
| 1205 | BENZOFENONA  *f* |
| 1206 | AZUL  *m*  DE PRUSIA |

| | |
|---|---|
| 1206 | AZUL _m_ DE PRUSIA |
| 1207 | BERILIO _m_ |
| 1208 | BRONCE _m_ DE BERILIO |
| 1209 | CUPROBERILIO _m_, BRONCE _m_ AL BERILIO |
| 1210 | GLUCINIO _m_ |
| 1211 | SOBREALIMENTACIÓN _f_ DE AIRE BESSEMER |
| 1212 | CONVERTIDOR BESSEMER _m_ |
| 1213 | FUNDICIÓN BESSEMER _f_ |
| 1214 | PROCEDIMIENTO _m_ BESSEMER |
| 1215 | ACERO BESSEMER _m_ |
| 1216 | LATÓN _m_ BETA |
| 1217 | PARTÍCULA _f_ BETA |
| 1218 | RAYOS BETA |
| 1219 | ESTRUCTURA _f_ BETA |
| 1220 | PROCEDIMIENTO _m_ BETTS |
| 1221 | BISEL _m_, CHAFLÁN _m_ |
| 1221 | BISEL _m_, FONDO _m_ |
| 1222 | BISELAR, TALLAR EN BISEL |
| 1222 | CORTAR EN BISEL |
| 1222 | CORTAR EN BIÉS |
| 1223 | ÁNGULO _m_ DEL CHAFLÁN |
| 1223 | ÁNGULO DEL CHAFLÁN _m_ |
| 1224 | TRANSMISIÓN _f_ POR CONOS DE FRICCIÓN |
| 1225 | CONO DE FRICCIÓN _m_ |
| 1225 | RUEDA _f_ DE FRICCIÓN CÓNICA |
| 1226 | PIÑÓN _m_ CÓNICO |
| 1227 | ENGRANAJE _m_ DE ÁNGULO |
| 1227 | ENGRANAJE _m_ CÓNICO |
| 1228 | FALSA ESCUADRA _f_ |
| 1228 | FALSA ESCUADRA _f_ |
| 1228 | PANTÓMETRO _m_, GONIÓMETRO _m_, FALSA ESCUADRA _f_ |
| 1229 | RUEDA _f_ DE ÁNGULO |
| 1229 | RUEDA _f_ CÓNICA |
| 1230 | ACCIONAMIENTO POR ENGRANAJE CÓNICO _m_ |
| 1231 | BISELADO _m_ |
| 1231 | BISELADO _m_ |
| 1232 | COJINETE _m_ CÓNICO |
| 1233 | ELECTRODO _m_ BIPOLAR |
| 1234 | GRIFO _m_ DE BOCA CURVA |
| 1235 | GRIFO _m_ DE EXTRACCIÓN |
| 1236 | TRATAMIENTO _m_ CON BICROMATO |
| 1237 | LENTE AMB. BICÓNCAVO (A) |
| 1238 | LENTE AMB. BICONVEXO (A) |
| 1239 | CADENA DE BICICLETA _f_ |
| 1240 | SUSPENSIÓN _f_ BIFILAR |
| 1241 | ROBLONES _m pl_, REMACHES _m pl_ |
| 1242 | COJINETE DE CABEZA DE BIELA _m_ |
| 1243 | MADERO _m_, LEÑO _m_ |
| 1243 | PALANQUILLA _f_, TOCHO _m_ |
| 1243 | PALANQUILLA _f_, TOCHO _m_ |

| | |
|---|---|
| 1244 | SULFATO _m_ |
| 1244 | TIJERAS PARA PAQUETES Y PLETINAS _f pl_ |
| 1245 | LAMINADOR _m_ DE PAQUETES |
| 1246 | TIJERAS PARA PAQUETES _f pl_ |
| 1247 | ALEACIÓN BINARIA _f_ |
| 1248 | CÓDIGO BINARIO DECIMAL _m_ |
| 1249 | POSICIÓN _f_ BINARIA |
| 1249 | DIGITO _m_ BINARIO |
| 1250 | MALEABLE, DÚCTIL |
| 1250 | LUBRIFICANTE _m_ |
| 1251 | MÁQUINAS _f pl_ SEGADORAS Y MÁQUINAS _f pl_ AGAVILLADORAS |
| 1252 | ZUNCHO _m_ |
| 1253 | AGLOMERANTE _m_, AGLUTINANTE _m_ |
| 1253 | LEIN _m_ (GEOL.) CEMENTO |
| 1253 | AGLUTINANTE _m_ |
| 1253 | SUBSTANCIA _f_ AGLUTINANTE |
| 1253 | MATERIA _f_ AGLUTINANTE |
| 1254 | BORNE _m_ DE CONTACTO |
| 1255 | ALAMBRE _m_ (O HILO _m_) DE AMARRAR |
| 1256 | MICROSCOPIO _m_ BINOCULAR |
| 1257 | COEFICIENTE BINOMIAL _m_ |
| 1258 | LEY _f_ SINOMIAL |
| 1259 | ECUACIÓN _f_ BINOMIA |
| 1260 | SERIE _f_ BINOMIAL |
| 1261 | BIPLANO _m_ |
| 1262 | ECUACIÓN _f_ BICUADRADA, ECUACIÓN _f_ DE CUARTO GRADO |
| 1262 | ECUACIÓN _f_ DE CUARTO GRADO |
| 1262 | ECUACIÓN _f_ DE CUARTO GRADO |
| 1263 | MICROFISURA _f_ |
| 1264 | PERSPECTIVA _f_, VISTA _f_ EN PERSPECTIVA O CABALLERA |
| 1264 | VISTA _f_ A VUELO DE PÁJARO |
| 1265 | BIRREFRINGENTE _m_ |
| 1266 | BISECTAR |
| 1266 | COMPARTIR, PARTICIPAR, REPARTIR |
| 1266 | DIVIDIR EN DOS |
| 1267 | BISECCIÓN _f_ |
| 1268 | BISECTRIZ _f_ |
| 1269 | BISMUTO _m_ |
| 1270 | TRICLORURO _m_ DE BISMUTO |
| 1271 | NITRATO _m_ DE BISMUTO |
| 1271 | NITRATO _m_ DE BISMUTO |
| 1272 | ÓXIDO _m_ DE BISMUTO |
| 1273 | NITRATO _m_ DE BISMUTILO |
| 1274 | SOLDADURA _f_ AL BISMUTO |
| 1275 | BISMUTINA _f_ |
| 1276 | BIZCOCHO _m_ DE PORCELANA |
| 1277 | ÁNGULO DE CONTACTO _m_, ÁNGELO DE ATAQUE _m_ |

1278 AGARROTAMIENTO DE LA CUERDA EN LA RANURA *m*

1279 ENGRUMECIDO *m*

1279 GRANULACIÓN *f*

1280 BITUMEN *m*

1281 BITUMINOSO *m*, BITUMINOSA *f*

1282 HULLA *f* GRASA

1283 BARNIZ *m* AL ASFALTO

1283 BARNIZ *m* JAPÓN

1284 ALAMBRE *m* DE HIERRO RECOCIDO NEGRO

1285 CUERPO NEGRO *m*

1286 PERNO *m* EN BRUTO, PERNO *m* SIN MECANIZAR

1287 COBRE *m* NEGRO BRUTO

1288 CALENTADO AL ROJO NACIENTE

1289 CHAPAS *f pl* NEGRAS

1290 TUERCA *f* NEGRA, TUERCA EN BRUTO

1291 ACEITE *m* MINERAL OSCURO

1292 FUNDICIÓN *f* GRAFÍTICA

1293 PINO *m* NEGRO DE AUSTRIA

1294 CHAPA *f* NEGRA

1295 ROJO *m* NACIENTE

1296 CHAPA *f* NEGRA

1296 CHAPA *f* MATE

1296 HIERRO *m* NEGRO

1297 NEGRO *m* DE FUNDICIÓN

1298 TENAZAS *f pl* DE HERRERO

1298 TENAZAS *f pl*

1299 LÁMINA *f*, HOJA *f*, CUCHILLA *f*

1300 HOJA *f* TAJANTE, HOJA *f* CORTANTE, CUCHILLA *f*

1300 HOJA *f* DE UNA HERRAMIENTA CORTANTE

1301 LINGOTE *m*, TROZO *m*, CHATARRA *f*

1301 PIEZA *f* EN BRUTO

1301 PIEZA *f* EN BLANCO

1302 PERNO *m* NO ROSCADO

1303 EXTREMO *m* DE UN TUBO TAPADO

1304 BRIDA *f* CIEGA

1304 BRIDA *f* CIEGA, BRIDA *f* TAPADA

1304 BRIDA *f* CIEGA, BRIDA *f* TAPADA

1304 BRIDA *f* CIEGA, BRIDA *f* TAPADA

1305 SOPORTE *m* DE PIEZA A ESTAMPAR

1306 SEPARADOR SIN TALADRAR *m*

1307 TUERCA *f* EN BLANCO (A SOLDAR)

1308 TUERCA *f* SIN ROSCA

1309 CORTE *m*

1310 MATRIZADO *m* EN DISCO

1311 ALTO HORNO *m*

1312 ESCORIA *f* (DE ALTOS HORNOS)

1312 ESCORIA *f* DE LOS ALTOS HORNOS

1313 GAS *m* DE ALTO HORNO

1314 TUBERÍA DE AIRE O VIENTO *f*

1315 CORRIENTE DE AIRE FORZADO *f*

1315 VIENTO *m*

1316 LIMPIEZA *f* CON CHORRO DE ARENA

1317 CLORURO DE CAL *m*

1318 PURGADOR *m*

1319 TORNILLO *m* DE PURGA

1320 RESPIRADERO *m* AUTOMÁTICO

1321 MIGRACIÓN *f*

1321 SANGRÍA *f*

1321 DESATASCO *m*, DESAGÜE *m*

1322 CONTRACCIÓN *f* EN EL MOLDE

1323 DOSIFICAR

1323 MEZCLAR

1324 BLENDA *f*, ESMANIL *m*, METAL NEGRO *m*

1324 BLENDA *f*

1324 BLENDA *f*

1325 MEZCLADO

1325 MEZCLA *f* DE DIVERSAS FRACCIONES DE POLVO DE UNA MISMA SUBSTANCIA

1325 DOSIFICACIÓN *f*, MEZCLA *f*

1326 BRIDA *f* CIEGA, BRIDA *f* TAPADA

1326 TAPÓN *m* OBTURADOR

1327 PÚSTULA *f*

1327 AMPOLLA *f*

1328 BARRA *f* DE ACERO CEMENTADO

1329 COBRE *m* VESICULOSO

1330 SOPLADURAS *f*

1330 PÚSTULAS *f pl*

1330 AMPOLLAS *f pl*

1330 VENTEADURAS *f pl*

1331 ESPUMEO *m*

1331 HINCHAZÓN *f*

1332 BLOQUE *m*

1333 CAJA DE POLEA *f*

1334 FORMATO *m* BLOC DE DIRECCIONES

1335 FRENO *m* DE ZAPATA

1336 CADENA PLANA *f*

1337 SUPRESIÓN *f*

1337 SUPRESIÓN *f*

1339 ESTAÑO *m* EN LINGOTES

1340 CLISÉ TIPOGRÁFICO *m*

1341 PREFORMADO *m*

1341 ESBOZO *m*, BOSQUEJO *m*

1342 CONDENSADOR DE BLOQUEO *m*

1342 CONDENSADOR DE PARADA *m*

1343 DESBASTADOR *m*

1344 BLONDÍN *m*

1345 CHANGOTE (MET.)

1346 TOCHO *m* PRELAMINADO, LINGOTE *m* RECTANGULAR DE ACERO

1347 VELADO, TURBIO

| | | | |
|---|---|---|---|
| 1347 | CUCHARÓN *m* DE COLADA | 1381 | CARTÓN *m* |
| 1348 | LAMINADOR *m* PARA LINGOTES | 1382 | CLAVO PARA BUQUE *m*, ESTOPEROL *m* |
| 1348 | TREN *m* DESBASTADOR | 1383 | ASIENTO *m* SUSPENDIDO |
| 1349 | LINGOTES *m pl* GRUESOS, LUPIAS *f pl* | 1383 | BARQUILLA *f* |
| 1350 | CARPETA *f*, PAPEL *m* SECANTE | 1384 | BOBINA *f* |
| 1350 | PAPEL *m* SECANTE | 1385 | CUERPO *m* |
| 1351 | VENTEADURA *f* | 1385 | CARROCERÍA *f* |
| 1352 | FUNDIRSE (EN CORTO CIRCUITO) | 1386 | CUERPO EN REPOSO *m* |
| 1353 | VENTEADURA *f* | 1387 | TORNEADO *m* A PERFIL, REBAJAMIENTO *m* |
| 1353 | CUCHARA *f* DE RETIRAR | 1388 | ÁNGULO DE PROFUNDIDAD DEL DESTALONADO *m* |
| 1354 | DESPRENDIMIENTO *m*, DESPEGUE *m* | 1389 | COLOR OPACO *m* |
| 1355 | SOPLETE *m* | 1390 | LIMA *f* FRESA |
| 1356 | ANÁLISIS DE SOPLETE *m* | 1391 | MÁQUINA *f* DE ARQUEAR |
| 1357 | GRIFO *m* DE VACIADO | 1392 | CUERPO MÓVIL *m* |
| 1358 | VÁLVULA *f* DE VACIADO | 1392 | CUERPO EN MOVIMIENTO *m* |
| 1358 | VÁLVULA *f* DE EVACUACIÓN | 1393 | PROPIEDAD *f* CORRIENTE |
| 1358 | VÁLVULA *f* DE DESCARGA | 1393 | PROPIEDAD *f* DE CUBRIR DE UN COLOR |
| 1359 | VÁLVULA *f* DE EXTRACCIÓN | 1394 | NÚCLEO *m* DE UN TORNILLO |
| 1359 | GRIFO *m* DE EXTRACCIÓN | 1395 | CONSISTENCIA DE UN ACEITE *f*, DENSIDAD *f* |
| 1360 | VÁLVULA *f* DE ERUPCIÓN | 1396 | PRISMA *f* DE IGUAL RESISTENCIA |
| 1361 | SOPLADOR *m* | 1397 | ASIENTO *m* DE CUERPO DE VÁLVULA |
| 1361 | APARATO *m* SOPLANTE | 1398 | TALLER DE CHAPISTERÍA *m* |
| 1362 | VENTEADURAS *f pl* | 1398 | TALLER *m* DE CARROCERÍA |
| 1363 | MÁQUINA *f* SOPLADORA | 1399 | CENTRO CÚBICO *m* |
| 1364 | VACIADO *m* DE UNA CALDERA | 1400 | CRISTAL *m* BLANCO DE BOHEMIA |
| 1365 | VIDRIO *m* SOPLADO | 1401 | HERVIR |
| 1366 | METAL *m* PREAFINADO | 1401 | ESTAR EN EBULLICIÓN, HERVIR |
| 1367 | TUBERÍA DE AIRE O VIENTO *f* | 1402 | RELACIÓN *f* DE EVAPORACIÓN |
| 1368 | PAVONAR EL ACERO | 1403 | PRUEBA *f* DE PÉRDIDA TÉRMICA |
| 1369 | BAÑO *m* AZUL, BAÑO *m* DE CLORURO MERCÚRICO | 1404 | VAPOR *f* DE UN LÍQUIDO EN EBULLICIÓN |
| | | 1404 | VAPOR *m* DE EBULLICIÓN |
| 1369 | BAÑO *m* AZUL | 1405 | EVACUACIÓN *f* DEL VAPOR DE EBULLICIÓN |
| 1370 | CALOR *m* AZUL, CALOR *m* AL AZUL | 1406 | CALDERA *f* |
| 1371 | CALDEO AL AZUL *m* | 1407 | CUCÚRBITA *f* |
| 1372 | PRUEBA *f* DE RESISTENCIA AL CALOR AZUL | 1408 | MATERIA *f* CALORÍFUGA PARA CALDERAS |
| 1373 | REPRODUCCIÓN *f* AL FERROPRUSIATO EN AZUL SOBRE FONDO BLANCO | 1409 | TALADRADORA *f* DE CALDERAS |
| | | 1410 | EXPLOSIÓN *f* DE UNA CALDERA |
| 1374 | POLVO *m* DE CINC OXIDADO | 1411 | GUARNICIONES *f* DE CALDERAS |
| 1375 | REPRODUCCIÓN *f* AL FERROPRUSIATO EN BLANCO SOBRE FONDO AZUL | 1411 | ACCESORIOS PARA CALDERAS *m pl* |
| | | 1411 | APARATOS *m pl* ACCESORIOS (O AUXILIARES) |
| 1375 | FOTOCOPIA *f* AZUL, COPIA *f* HELIOCALCO, HELIOGRAFÍA *f* | 1412 | CONDUCTO INTERIOR DE CALDERA *m* |
| | | 1412 | TUBO *m* DE HOGAR |
| 1376 | SULFATO *m* DE COBRE, CALCAUTO *m*, CAPARROSA *f* AZUL | 1413 | NAVE *f* DE CALDERAS |
| | | 1413 | NAVE *f* DE CALDERAS |
| 1376 | VITRIOLO *m* AZUL | 1414 | INSPECCIÓN *f* DE LA CALDERA |
| 1376 | CAPARROSA AZUL *f*, SULFATO DE COBRE *m* | 1414 | INSPECCIÓN *f* DE LA CALDERA |
| 1377 | PAVONADO *m*, AZULADO *m* | 1415 | CALDERERO EN CHAPA *m* |
| 1378 | VELADO, TURBIO | 1415 | CALDERERO DE HIERRO *m* |
| 1378 | CUCHARÓN *m*, CAZO *m*, CACILLO *m* | 1416 | CHAPA *f* DE CALDERAS |
| 1379 | PLANCHA *f* DELGADA | 1417 | PRESIÓN *f* EN UNA CALDERA |
| 1380 | MARTINETE *m* DE PLANCHA | 1418 | SALA *f* DE CALDERAS |
| 1380 | MARTILLO PILÓN *m* CON PLANCHA | | |

| | |
|---|---|
| 1418 | SALA *f* DE CALDERAS |
| 1418 | SALA DE CALDERAS *f* |
| 1419 | CUERPO CILÍNDRICO DE CALDERA *m* |
| 1420 | TALLER *m* DE CALDERERÍA DE HIERRO |
| 1421 | PRUEBA *f* DE LA CALDERA A PRESIÓN |
| 1422 | TUBO *m* DE CALDERA |
| 1423 | CALDERERÍA DE HIERRO *f* |
| 1423 | CALDERERÍA *f* PESADA |
| 1424 | PUNTO *m* DE EBULLICIÓN |
| 1425 | EBULLICIÓN *f* (CON UN PUNTO ALTO DE) |
| 1426 | EBULLICIÓN *f* (CON UN PUNTO BAJO DE) |
| 1427 | TEMPERATURA *f* DE EBULLICIÓN |
| 1428 | AGUA *f* HIRVIENDO |
| 1429 | EBULLICIÓN *f* |
| 1430 | BOL *m*, CUBILETE *m*, ARCILLA *f* CALCAREOFERRUGINOSA |
| 1431 | BOLÓMETRO *m* |
| 1432 | CERROJO *m* |
| 1432 | PERNO *m*, BULÓN *m*, CERROJO *m*, PESTILLO *m* |
| 1433 | CÍRCULO DE LOS AGUJEROS PARA PERNOS *m* |
| 1434 | DIÁMETRO *m* DEL PERNO |
| 1435 | EMPERNAR |
| 1436 | CABEZA *f* DE UN TORNILLO |
| 1436 | CABEZA *f* DE UN REMACHE |
| 1437 | AGUJERO *m* DE ROBLÓN |
| 1438 | DIÁMETRO *m* DE PERFORACIÓN |
| 1439 | DIÁMETRO *m* DE TALADRADO |
| 1440 | DIÁMETRO *m* DEL AGUJERO DE PERNO |
| 1441 | TORNILLO *m* CON TUERCA, TORNILLO *m* CONTINUO |
| 1442 | JUNTA *f* POR TORNILLOS, ACOPLAMIENTO *m* POR TORNILLOS |
| 1442 | RACOR *m* DE TUERCAS |
| 1443 | JUNTA *f* POR TORNILLOS, ATORNILLADO *m* |
| 1443 | FABRICACIÓN *f* DE PERNOS |
| 1444 | APARATO DE CONSTRUCCIÓN *m* |
| 1445 | MORTERO *m* |
| 1445 | AGLUTINANTE *m* |
| 1446 | CABLES INYECTADOS *m pl* |
| 1447 | NEGRO *m* DE MARFIL |
| 1447 | NEGRO *m* ANIMAL |
| 1448 | HUESOS *m pl* PULVERIZADOS |
| 1448 | POLVO *m* DE HUESOS |
| 1449 | COLA FUERTE DE HUESOS |
| 1449 | OSEINA *f* |
| 1450 | ACEITE *m* DE PIE DE CARNERO |
| 1450 | ACEITE *m* DE PIE DE BUEY |
| 1451 | CAPÓ *m*, TAPA *f* |
| 1451 | CAPÓ MOTOR *m* |
| 1451 | TAPA *f* |
| 1452 | BRIDA *f* DE LA TAPA |

| | |
|---|---|
| 1453 | VARILLA *f* ROSCADA DE CAPÓ |
| 1454 | TAPA *f* |
| 1455 | CAMPANA *f* DE CHIMENEA, CAMPANA *f* DE ASPIRACIÓN DE HUMO |
| 1456 | |
| 1456 | SUPERCOMPRESOR *m* |
| 1456 | QUE AUMENTA LA TENSIÓN |
| 1456 | SUPERCOMPRESOR *m* |
| 1457 | SERVOFRENO *m* |
| 1458 | BAÚL *m* CAJA *f* |
| 1458 | BAÚL *m* |
| 1459 | BÓRAX *m* |
| 1459 | BORATO *m* DE SOSA ANHIDRA |
| 1459 | BÓRAX *m* |
| 1460 | CURVA LÍMITE *f* |
| 1461 | CALIBRADO DE CILINDRO *m* |
| 1461 | ALISADURA *f*, BARRENADO *m*, MANDRILADO *m* |
| 1462 | TORNEAR INTERIORMENTE, MANDRILAR, ESCARIAR, CALIBRAR |
| 1463 | AGUJERO *m* DE SONDEO |
| 1464 | DIÁMETRO *m* INTERIOR DE UN TUBO |
| 1465 | CAMISA DE CILINDRO *f* |
| 1466 | MANDRILAR, TORNEAR |
| 1467 | ÁCIDO BÓRICO *m* |
| 1468 | ALISADO *m*, CALIBRADO *m*, ALISAMIENTO *m* |
| 1468 | PERFORACIÓN *f* |
| 1468 | TALADRADO *m* |
| 1469 | VUELTA *f* EN EL AIRE EN PLATO HORIZONTAL |
| 1470 | BARRAS *f pl* DE TALADRAR |
| 1471 | MÁQUINA *f* DE ESCARIAR, MÁQUINA DE MANDRILAR |
| 1471 | PULIDORA *f*, MANDRINADORA *f*, TALADRADORA *f* |
| 1472 | MÁQUINA *f* TALADRADORA |
| 1473 | TORNEADO DE INTERIORES *m*, MANDRILADO *m* |
| 1474 | GAFAS *f pl* DE ESCARIADO |
| 1475 | PRUEBA *f* DE PERFORACIÓN |
| 1475 | ENSAYO *m* DE PERFORACIÓN |
| 1476 | VIRUTAS DE SONDEO *f pl* |
| 1477 | BORO *m* |
| 1478 | ALEACIÓN AL BORO *f* |
| 1479 | CARBURO DE BORO *m* |
| 1480 | BORT *m*, CARBONADO *m* |
| 1481 | CUBO *m* DE RUEDA |
| 1482 | CONFORMACIÓN *f* DE LAS PLANCHAS |
| 1483 | TAPÓN *m* |
| 1484 | CRISTAL *m* DE BOTELLAS |
| 1485 | CRIC *m* DE BOTELLA |
| 1486 | PLACA *f* DE FONDO |
| 1487 | CONCHA INFERIOR *f* |

| | | | | |
|---|---|---|---|---|
| 1487 | CASQUILLO *m* INFERIOR DEL COJINETE, SEMICOJINETE *m* INFERIOR | | 1522 | MÉNSULA *f* |
| 1488 | FUNDICIÓN EN FONDO *f* | | 1522 | VIGA *f*, CONSOLA *f* |
| 1489 | JUEGO *m* DEL FONDO DEL DIENTE | | 1523 | SOPORTE *m* CONSOLA |
| 1489 | JUEGO *m* A FONDO DE LOS DIENTES | | 1523 | SOPORTE *m* MURAL |
| 1490 | CANTONERA DE FONDO DE TANQUE *f* | | 1524 | AGUA *f* SALOBRE |
| 1491 | PUNTO *m* MUERTO BAJO | | 1525 | MÉTODO *m* DE BRAGG |
| 1492 | REBOSADERO *m* | | 1525 | LEY *f* DE BRAGG |
| 1493 | GRIFO *m* DE FONDO DE CUBA | | 1526 | GUARNICIÓN *f* CON TRENZA |
| 1494 | FONDO *m* DEL CILINDRO | | 1527 | CUERDA TRENZADA *f* |
| 1495 | TUBULADURA *f* DE FONDO | | 1528 | ALAMBRE *m* CON ENVOLTURA TRENZADA |
| 1496 | CUCHARA *f* DE COLAR POR EL FONDO | | 1529 | FRENO *m* |
| 1497 | ESTAMPA *f* DE MARTILLO, ESTAMPA *f* INFERIOR | | 1529 | PESTAÑA *f* DE CINTRADO |
| | | | 1530 | FRENAR |
| 1497 | MATRIZ *f* DE ABAJO | | 1531 | ZAPATA *f* DE FRENO |
| 1498 | VISTA *f* DE ABAJO ARRIBA | | 1532 | CILINDRO *m* DE FRENADO |
| 1498 | VISTA *f* POR DEBAJO | | 1532 | TAMBOR *m* |
| 1499 | TERRAJA *f* DE ACABADO | | 1533 | TAMBOR *m* DE FRENO |
| 1500 | CONTORNO DE GRANO *m* | | 1534 | DEPÓSITO *m* DE LÍQUIDO DE FRENO |
| 1500 | JUNTA F, UNIÓN F, JUNTURA F, ENLACE *m* | | 1535 | POTENCIA *f* AL FRENO |
| 1501 | MANÓMETRO *m* BOURDON | | 1536 | MORDAZA *f* DE FRENO |
| 1501 | MANÓMETRO *m* DE TUBO | | 1537 | PALANCA *f* DE FRENO |
| 1502 | BURNONITA *f* | | 1538 | GUARNICIÓN *f* DE FRENO |
| 1503 | COMPÁS DE ARCO *m* | | 1539 | MANDOS *m pl* DE FRENO |
| 1504 | ARCO *m*, ESTRIBO *m*, BASTIDOR *m* | | 1540 | POTENCIA *f* EFECTIVA |
| 1505 | SIERRA *f* DE CONTORNEAR | | 1540 | POTENCIA *f* AL FRENO |
| 1506 | FALTA *f* (EN LO LISO DE UNA SUPERFICIE) | | 1540 | POTENCIA *f* EFECTIVA |
| 1507 | BOJ *m* | | 1541 | ANILLO *m* DE FRENADO |
| 1508 | MOLDEO *m* EN CHASIS | | 1542 | SEGMENTO *m* DE FRENO |
| 1509 | CABEZA *f* DE BIELA DE CAJA CERRADA | | 1543 | ZAPATA *f* DE FRENO |
| 1510 | ACOPLADOR *m*, MANGUITO DE ACOPLAMIENTO *m* | | 1544 | CINTA *f* DE FRENO |
| 1511 | CHÁSIS-CAJA *m* | | 1544 | COLLARÍN DE FRENO *m* |
| 1512 | TUERCA *f* CIEGA | | 1544 | FRENO *m* DE CINTA |
| 1512 | TUERCA *f* TAPÓN | | 1545 | CIRCUITO DE FRENO *f*, SISTEMA DE FRENOS *m* |
| 1512 | TUERCA *f* TAPÓN, TUERCA DE CUBO | | 1546 | PRUEBA *f* AL FRENO |
| 1513 | CLAVIJA *f* DE CENTRADO | | 1547 | CONTRAPESO DEL FRENO *m* |
| 1514 | PISTÓN *m* VACIADO | | 1548 | POLEA *f* DE FRENO |
| 1515 | LLAVE TUBULAR *f* | | 1549 | FRENADO *m* |
| 1515 | LLAVE DE EXTREMOS *f* | | 1549 | PRESIÓN *f* DEL FRENO |
| 1515 | LLAVE DE EXTREMO *f* | | 1549 | MANIOBRA *f* DEL FRENO, FRENADO *m* |
| 1516 | REFUERZO *m* | | 1550 | ACCIÓN DEL FRENO *f* |
| 1516 | PUNTAL *m*, TORNAPUNTA *m* | | 1551 | POTENCIA *f* DE FRENADO |
| 1516 | TIRANTE *m* | | 1551 | FUERZA *f* FRENANTE |
| 1517 | COLOCAR PUNTALES, COLOCAR TORNAPUNTAS | | 1552 | RESISTENCIA *f* AL FRENADO |
| 1518 | BERBIQUÍ *m* CON TORNILLO DE PRESIÓN | | 1553 | PRENSA *f* BRINELL |
| 1519 | BERBIQUÍ | | 1554 | DERIVACIÓN *f* |
| 1520 | JABALCONES *m pl* | | 1554 | DERIVACIÓN *f*, CONEXIÓN *f*, EMPALME *m* |
| 1520 | TIRANTES *m pl* (DE UNA ESFERA) | | 1555 | RAMA *m* DE UNA CURVA |
| 1520 | CRUZETAS *f pl* DE ARMAZÓN | | 1556 | ENGANCHARSE, CONECTARSE |
| 1521 | INSTALACIÓN *f* DE TORNAPUNTAS, COLOCACIÓN *f* DE TORNAPUNTAS | | 1557 | TUBULADURA *f* DE EMPALME |
| | | | 1558 | TUBO *m* DE DERIVACIÓN |
| 1522 | SOPORTE *m* | | 1559 | RACOR *m* EN T |

| | |
|---|---|
| 1560 | PUNZÓN  *m* |
| 1560 | CIFRAS Y LETRAS EN CALIENTE / FRÍO  *f* |
| 1561 | PRUEBA  *f* DE RECALCAMIENTO |
| 1562 | COBRE  *m* AMARILLO, LATÓN  *m* |
| 1562 | LATÓN  *m* |
| 1563 | PALANQUILLA  *f* DE LATÓN |
| 1564 | BAÑO  *m* DE ABRILLANTAMIENTO |
| 1565 | SEGMENTO  *m* (O ANILLO  *m*) DE TENSIÓN (O DE FONDO) |
| 1566 | FUNDICIÓN  *f* DE COBRE |
| 1566 | GRIFERÍA  *f* |
| 1567 | CHAPEADO  *m* CON LATÓN |
| 1568 | ALAMBRE  *m* LAMINADO DE LATÓN |
| 1568 | ALAMBRE  *m* LAMINADO DE LATÓN |
| 1569 | CHAPA  *f* DE LATÓN |
| 1570 | TUBO  *m* DE LATÓN |
| 1571 | ALAMBRE  *m* DE LATÓN |
| 1571 | ALAMBRE  *m* DE LATÓN |
| 1572 | COJINETE EN CAJAS  *m* |
| 1572 | COJINETE DE DOS PIEZAS  *m* |
| 1573 | SOLDAR CON LATÓN |
| 1573 | SOLDAR FUERTE |
| 1574 | IMPLANTACIONES  *f* DE COBRE EN SOLDADURA |
| 1575 | COBRE  *m* DE SOLDADURA |
| 1576 | SOLDADURA  *f* FUERTE |
| 1576 | SOLDADURA  *f* A FUEGO, SOLDADURA CON LATÓN  *f* |
| 1576 | SOLDADURA  *f* CON LATÓN, SOLDADURA  *f* CON PLATA |
| 1576 | SOLDADURA  *f* |
| 1577 | HORNILLO  *m* PARA SOLDADURA FUERTE |
| 1578 | INSERCIONES  *f pl* DE SOLDADURA |
| 1579 | LARGURA  *f*, ANCHURA DEL DIENTE |
| 1580 | MACHACAR, MOLER |
| 1581 | PERTURBACIÓN  *f* DEL SERVICIO |
| 1581 | PERTURBACIÓN  *f* |
| 1581 | VIGA  *f* DE TEJADO, CABRIO  *m* |
| 1582 | TENSIÓN  *f* DE PERFORACIÓN |
| 1583 | ESCUADREO  *m*, DESBASTE  *m*, ESBOZO  *m* |
| 1584 | LARGURA  *f* DE RUPTURA |
| 1585 | CARGA DE ROTURA  *f* |
| 1586 | CARGA LÍMITE DE ELASTICIDAD  *f* |
| 1587 | RODAJE  *m* (DE UN COCHE) |
| 1588 | MACHAQUEO  *m* |
| 1589 | PERFORACIÓN  *f* |
| 1590 | PLASTRÓN  *m* |
| 1590 | PLASTRÓN  *m* DE CIGÜEÑAL |
| 1591 | RESPIRADERO  *m* |
| 1592 | DEPÓSITO  *m* TAMPÓN |
| 1593 | RESPIRACIÓN  *f* PURGADOR  *m* |
| 1593 | VÁLVULA  *f* DE SEGURIDAD |

| | |
|---|---|
| 1594 | PÉRDIDA  *f* POR PAUSAS, POR PAROS, POR DESCANSOS |
| 1595 | TUBO  *m* EN HORQUILLA |
| 1596 | LADRILLO  *m* |
| 1597 | CONSTRUIR, LABRAR |
| 1598 | TIERRA  *f* DE LADRILLOS |
| 1599 | CIMIENTOS  *m pl* DE MAMPOSTERÍA |
| 1599 | CIMIENTOS  *m pl* DE LADRILLO |
| 1600 | EMPOTRADO EN OBRA DE FÁBRICA |
| 1601 | ALBAÑILERÍA  *f*, MAMPOSTERÍA |
| 1602 | CONSTRUCCIÓN  *f* DE LADRILLOS |
| 1602 | TABIQUERÍA  *f*, FÁBRICA  *f* DE LADRILLO |
| 1603 | APONTAJE  *m*, ESTACADA  *f*, PONTÓN  *m* |
| 1604 | FORMACIÓN  *f* DE ENTIBACIÓN |
| 1604 | CORONACIÓN  *f* |
| 1605 | PASO  *m* DEL SISTEMA BRIGGS PARA TUBOS |
| 1606 | ALAMBRE  *m* RECOCIDO BLANCO |
| 1607 | TORNILLO  *m* TORNEADO |
| 1607 | PERNO  *m* ROSCADO |
| 1608 | BAÑO  *m* DE ABRILLANTADO |
| 1609 | SOLUCIÓN  *f* PARA ABRILLANTAR |
| 1610 | ALAMBRE  *m* DE HIERRO CLARO CRUDO |
| 1611 | SUPERFICIE  *f* METÁLICA PULIDA |
| 1612 | TUERCA  *f* PULIDA |
| 1613 | ROJO  *m* CLARO |
| 1613 | ROJO  *m* VIVO |
| 1614 | CALDEO AL ROJO CLARO  *m* |
| 1615 | AGENTE DE ABRILLANTADO  *m* |
| 1616 | BRILLO  *m* LUMINOSO |
| 1617 | AGUA  *f* SALADA |
| 1617 | SALMUERA  *f* |
| 1618 | PRUEBA  *f* POR LA BOLA DE BRINELL |
| 1618 | PRUEBA  *f* POR IMPRESIÓN DE BOLA |
| 1618 | ENSAYO  *m* DE DUREZA BRINELL |
| 1619 | DUREZA  *f* BRINELL |
| 1619 | CIFRA DE DUREZA BRINELL  *f* |
| 1620 | PRUEBA (DE DUREZA) BRINELL |
| 1621 | PUESTA  *f* A PUNTO DE UNA HERRAMIENTA |
| 1622 | BRIQUETA  *f* DE FERROALEACIÓN |
| 1623 | BRIQUETA  *f*, AGLOMERADO  *m* |
| 1623 | AGLOMERADO  *m* |
| 1624 | METAL  *m* BRITÁNICO |
| 1625 | CALORÍA INGLESA  *f* |
| 1626 | UNIDAD  *f* TÉRMICA INGLESA |
| 1627 | ROMPEDIZO  *m*, QUEBRADIZO  *m*, FRÁGIL  *m* |
| 1628 | FRAGILIDAD  *f* |
| 1628 | FALTA  *f* DE FLEXIBILIDAD |
| 1629 | FRAGILIDAD  *f* DEL HIERRO |
| 1630 | FRAGILIDAD  *f* POR DECAPADO |
| 1631 | FRAGILIDAD  *f* AL PAVÓN |
| 1632 | FRAGILIDAD  *f* A LA ENTALLADURA |

| | | | |
|---|---|---|---|
| 1633 | FRAGILIDAD *f* REOTRÓPICA | 1672 | FORMACIÓN *f* DE RECHUPES FORMACIÓN *f* DE BURBUJAS |
| 1634 | FRAGILIDAD *f* AL RECOCIDO | 1673 | PISTÓN *m* DE VÁLVULA |
| 1635 | AVELLANAR LOS AGUJEROS DE REMACHES | 1673 | PISTÓN *m* ELEVADOR |
| 1636 | ESCARIADOR *m*, DESBASTADOR *m* | 1674 | CUBO *m* |
| 1636 | ESCARIADOR *m*, TALADRO *m* | 1674 | CACILLO *m* |
| 1637 | BROCHADO *m*, ESCARIADO *m*, AVELLANADO *m* | 1675 | TRANSPORTADOR *m* DE CANGILÓNES |
| | | 1675 | TRANSPORTADOR *m* |
| 1638 | AVELLANADO DE LOS AGUJEROS DE REMACHES *m* | 1676 | ELEVADOR *m* DE CANGILONES |
| | | 1676 | NORIA *f* |
| 1639 | VIGA *f* DE ALAS ANCHAS | 1677 | PALETA *f* DE UNA RUEDA HIDRÁULICA |
| 1640 | HIERRO *m* T DE ALAS ANCHAS | 1677 | ÁLABE *m*, PALETA *f* |
| 1641 | VIGUETAS *f pl* DE ALAS ANCHAS | 1678 | ASIENTO *m* SILLÓN |
| 1642 | LAMINADOR *m* TRANSVERSAL | 1679 | CHAPA *f* EMBUTIDA |
| 1643 | CILINDROS *m pl* TRANSVERSALES | 1679 | CHAPA *f* ABOMBADA |
| 1644 | GRAVA *f* | 1680 | PLIEGUES *m pl* |
| 1644 | PIEDRAS *f pl* QUEBRANTADAS | 1681 | ONDULACIÓN *f* (DE LAS CHAPAS) |
| 1645 | BROMIRITA *f* | 1682 | RESISTENCIA *f* AL PANDEO |
| 1645 | BROMIRITA *f* | 1683 | RASTRILLOS *m pl* DE ATRESNALAR |
| 1645 | BROMURO *m* | 1684 | DISCO *m* PULIDOR DE CUERO |
| 1645 | BROMURO *m* | 1685 | PIEL *f* DE BÚFALO |
| 1645 | BROMURO *m* DE PLATA | 1685 | CUERO *m* ÁSPERO, BÚFALO *m* |
| 1645 | BROMURO *m* DE PLATA | 1686 | TOPE *m*, PARACHOQUES *m*, MÁQUINA *f* PULIDORA |
| 1646 | BROMATO *m* | | |
| 1647 | ÁCIDO BRÓMICO *m* | 1686 | TAMPÓN *m* |
| 1648 | BROMURO *m* | 1686 | PULIDOR *m* |
| 1649 | BROMO *m* | 1687 | BATERÍA *f* TAMPÓN |
| 1650 | BRONCE *m* | 1688 | RESORTE *m* AMORTIGUADOR DE CHOQUES |
| 1651 | BRONCEAR, PAVONAR | 1689 | MEMORIA *f* INTERMEDIA |
| 1652 | BRONCE *m* DE POLVO, POLVO *m* DE BRONCE | 1690 | SALES *m pl* DE PULIMENTO |
| 1652 | POLVO *m* DE BRONCE | 1691 | AMOLADURA *f*, AFILADURA *f* |
| 1653 | TUBO *m* DE BRONCE | 1692 | COMPOSICIÓN DE PULIDO CON MUELA *f* |
| 1654 | ALAMBRE *m* DE BRONCE | 1693 | DISCO *m* PULIDOR |
| 1655 | BRONCE *m* ACIDORRESISTENTE | 1694 | CONSTRUIR |
| 1656 | BRONCE *m* ALFA | 1695 | SOBRE ESPESOR *m* |
| 1657 | BRONCE *m* COMÚN | 1696 | PROCESO *m* DE RECARGA |
| 1657 | BRONCE *m* COMÚN | 1697 | PERPIAÑOS *m* |
| 1658 | SIMILOR *m*, LATÓN *m* ROJO | 1697 | PERPIAÑOS *m pl*, LADRILLO *m* DE ANCLA |
| 1659 | BRONCE *m* PARA FÁBRICA DE TORNILLOS | 1698 | CONTRATISTA *m* DE LA CONSTRUCCIÓN |
| 1660 | BRONCE *m* DE COJINETE, BRONCE *m* PLÁSTICO | 1699 | SOLAR *m* PARA LA EDIFICACIÓN |
| 1660 | BRONCE *m* PLÁSTICO, BRONCE *m* DE COJINETE | 1699 | SOLAR *m* PARA CONSTRUIR |
| 1661 | BRONCE *m* DE RESORTE | 1700 | PIEDRA *f* PROPIA PARA LA CONSTRUCCIÓN |
| 1662 | BRONCE *m* DE ADORNO | 1701 | ESPESAMIENTO *m*, ENSANCHE *m* |
| 1663 | BRONCE *m* DE ADORNO | 1702 | VIGA *f* EMPOTRADA |
| 1664 | BRONCEADO *m* | 1703 | VIGA *f* EMPOTRADA EN SUS DOS EXTREMOS |
| 1665 | LIGNITO *m* PERFECTO | 1704 | ELEMENTO *m* INCORPORADO DE ARMAZÓN |
| 1666 | AGLOMERADO DE LIGNITO *m* | 1705 | TRAÍDO, DEVUELTO, RELACIONADO |
| 1667 | ALQUITRÁN *m* DE LIGNITO | 1705 | ACUMULACIÓN *f* |
| 1668 | ACEITE *m* DE ALQUITRÁN DEL LIGNITO | 1706 | MANIVELA *f* EN VARIAS PIEZAS |
| 1669 | COBRE *m* DE ESCOBILLA | 1707 | VIRUTA ADHERENTE *f* |
| 1670 | BURBUJA *f* DE AIRE | 1708 | BRIDA *f* MÓVIL, BRIDA *f* SUELTA |
| 1671 | BURBUJA *f* DE GAS | | |

| | |
|---|---|
| 1709 | PISTÓN *m* DE DOS PIEZAS |
| 1710 | PLACA *f* MODELO |
| 1711 | BUZO *m* (DE TERMÓMETRO) |
| 1711 | BULBO *m* |
| 1712 | CANTONERA *f* CON BORDÓN |
| 1713 | ANGULAR CON NERVIO *m* |
| 1714 | HIERRO *m* PLANO CON BORDÓN |
| 1715 | RAÍLES *m* DE PESTAÑA |
| 1716 | HIERRO *m* DE BORDÓN |
| 1717 | AMPOLLA DEL TERMÓMETRO *f* |
| 1718 | PIPETA *f* DE CILINDRO |
| 1719 | HIERRO EN T CON BORDÓN |
| 1719 | HIERRO *m* EN H T CON BORDÓN |
| 1720 | CONVEXIDAD *f* |
| 1720 | ABOLLADURA *f*, ABOMBADO *m* |
| 1720 | BOMBEADO *m*, BOMBEO *m*, CONVEXIDAD *f* |
| 1720 | ABOMBADO *m*, VIENTRE *m*, ABOLLADURA *f* |
| 1720 | CRECIMIENTO *m* |
| 1721 | HINCHARSE, INFLARSE |
| 1722 | BOMBA *f*, BOMBEADO *m* |
| 1723 | ABOCARDADO *m*, ENSANCHAMIENTO *m*, ABOMBADO *m* |
| 1723 | AGRANDAMIENTO *m* |
| 1724 | DENSIDAD *f* EN EL LLENADO 37570 |
| 1725 | DENSIDAD *f* APARENTE |
| 1726 | TABIQUE *m* |
| 1727 | ESTIRADO *m* DESBASTADOR (O GRUESO) |
| 1728 | CUCHARA *f* DE GRÚA DE COLADA |
| 1729 | METAL *m* NOBLE EN BARRAS |
| 1730 | BARRA *f* DE METAL PRECIOSO |
| 1731 | MALACATE *m* |
| 1731 | CARRUSEL *m*, CADENA *f* DE TRANSPORTE EN CIRCUITO |
| 1732 | PISÓN *m* MECÁNICO |
| 1732 | PARACHOQUES *m*, PARAGOLPES *m* |
| 1733 | CRIBA *f* DE SACUDIDAS |
| 1734 | HERRAMIENTA *f* PARA AMARTILLADO A MANO |
| 1735 | PUENTE *m*, TERRERO *m* |
| 1736 | HAZ *m* (TUBOS O PERFILES) |
| 1737 | ATAR, ENFARDELAR, LIAR, LIGAR, AGAVILLAR, HACINAR |
| 1738 | ROLLO *m* DE FLEJE, BOBINA *f* DE FLEJE |
| 1739 | LITERA *f* |
| 1739 | ARMARIO-CAMA |
| 1740 | DEPÓSITO *m* |
| 1740 | CARBONERA *f* |
| 1741 | MECHERO *m* DE BUNSEN |
| 1741 | MECHERO *m* BUNSEN |
| 1742 | FLOTABILIDAD *f* |
| 1742 | EMPUJE *m* DE ABAJO ARRIBA |
| 1742 | FUERZA *f* ASCENSIONAL |

| | |
|---|---|
| 1743 | BURETA *f* |
| 1744 | EMPALMES *m pl* SUBTERRÁNEOS |
| 1745 | QUEMAR, ARDER, CALCINAR, COCER |
| 1746 | RECALENTAR |
| 1747 | COMBUSTIÓN NUCLEAR *f* |
| 1748 | LINGOTE *m* QUEMADO |
| 1749 | MECHERO *m*, QUEMADOR *m*, SOPLETE *m* |
| 1750 | QUEMADO *m* |
| 1751 | CALEFACCIÓN POR GAS *f* |
| 1752 | CALEFACCIÓN POR ACEITE PESADO *f* |
| 1752 | CALEFACCIÓN POR FUEL *f* |
| 1752 | CALEFACCIÓN POR NAFTA *f* |
| 1753 | CALEFACCIÓN POR CARBÓN PULVERIZADO *f* |
| 1754 | RECALENTAMIENTO *m* |
| 1755 | BRUÑIDO *m*, PULIMENTO *m*, PULIDO *m* |
| 1755 | BRUÑIDO *m*, PULIMENTO *m*, PULIDO *m* |
| 1755 | PULIDO *m* PERFECTO |
| 1756 | PULIR CON BRILLO |
| 1756 | BRUÑIR, PULIMENTAR, PULIR |
| 1756 | ABRILLANTAR |
| 1757 | BRUÑIDOR *m*, PULIDOR *m* |
| 1758 | BRUÑIDO *m*, PAVONADO *m* |
| 1758 | PULIMENTO *m* POR RODILLOS |
| 1759 | BOLAS *f pl* DE BRUÑIR |
| 1759 | BOLAS *f pl* DE PULIR |
| 1760 | LADRILLO *m* COCIDO |
| 1761 | DEPÓSITO *m* QUEMADO |
| 1762 | HIERRO *m* QUEMADO |
| 1763 | ACERO QUEMADO *m* |
| 1764 | REBABA *f* |
| 1764 | REBABA *f* |
| 1764 | REBABA *f*, GRIETA *f* DE PLIEGUE |
| 1764 | BARBA *f*, REBABA *f* |
| 1764 | REBABA *f* |
| 1765 | FRESA *f* DESBARBADORA |
| 1766 | DESBARBADURA *f* |
| 1767 | ESTALLIDO *m*, REVENTÓN *m* |
| 1768 | REVENTÓN *m* (DE UN TUBO) |
| 1768 | RUPTURA *f* DE UN TUBO |
| 1769 | ESTALLIDO *m* DE UN VOLANTE |
| 1769 | ESTALLIDO *m* DE UNA POLEA |
| 1770 | BARRA *f* COLECTORA, BARRA *f* DE ÓMNIBUS |
| 1770 | BARRA *f* COLECTORA, BARRA *f* ÓMNIBUS |
| 1770 | RAÍL *m* DE CONTACTO |
| 1771 | COJINETE DE UNA PIEZA *m* |
| 1772 | EMPAQUETADO *m*, EMPAQUETAMIENTO *m* |
| 1772 | PUESTA *f* EN MANOJOS |
| 1773 | SEMICOJINETE *m*, CASQUILLO *m* DE COJINETE |
| 1773 | MANGUITO *m* |
| 1773 | REDUCCIÓN *f* MACHO-HEMBRA |
| 1773 | CASQUILLO *m*, ANILLO *m* |

| | |
|---|---|
| 1774 | CONDUCTO ANULAR DE VIENTO CÁLIDO *m* |
| 1775 | BUTANO *m* |
| 1775 | HIDRURO *m* DE BUTILO |
| 1776 | JUNTA *f* DE CABEZA CON CABEZA |
| 1777 | JUNTA *f* EMPALMADA SOLDADA POR LOS DOS LADOS |
| 1778 | UNIÓN *f* EXTREMO CON EXTREMO |
| 1778 | UNIÓN *f*, JUNTA *f*, ENSAMBLADURA *f* |
| 1779 | JUNTA *f* EMPALMADA SOLDADA POR UN SOLO LADO |
| 1780 | CUERO *m* DE PRIMERA CALIDAD |
| 1781 | REMACHE *m* CON BANDA DE RECUBRIMIENTO |
| 1782 | JUNTA *f* DE ECLISAS |
| 1782 | EMPALME *m* (O UNIÓN *f*) POR (O CON) CUBREJUNTAS |
| 1783 | CUBREJUNTA *f* |
| 1783 | CUBREJUNTAS *m*, EDISA *f*, ESLABÓN *m* |
| 1784 | SOLDADURA *f* POR APROXIMACIÓN |
| 1784 | SOLDADURA *f* A TOPE |
| 1785 | SOLDAR POR CONTACTO |
| 1785 | SOLDAR POR ENCOLADO |
| 1786 | ESPESOR *m* DE UNA SOLDADURA A TOPE |
| 1787 | SOLDADURA *f* EN K SIN SEPARACIÓN |
| 1788 | SOLDADURA *f* DOBLE CERRADA |
| 1789 | SOLDADURA *f* EN MEDIA V SIN SEPARACIÓN |
| 1790 | JUNTA *f* DE SOLDADURA EN JUNTA CERRADA |
| 1791 | SOLDADURA *f* EN I SIN SEPARACIÓN DE LOS BORDES |
| 1792 | SOLDADURA *f* CÓNCAVA |
| 1793 | CHAFLÁN (SOLDADURA) EN K *m* |
| 1794 | SOLDADURA *f* POR CHISPORROTEO |
| 1795 | SOLDADURA *f* (ENSAMBLADO) EN T |
| 1796 | SOLDADURA *f* EN K CON SEPARACIÓN |
| 1797 | SOLDADURA *f* EN MEDIA V CON SEPARACIÓN |
| 1798 | SOLDADURA *f* EN J CON SEPARACIÓN |
| 1799 | SOLDADURA *f* A TOPE POR RESISTENCIA |
| 1800 | CHAFLÁN EN MEDIA V *m*, BISEL *m* |
| 1801 | SOLDADURA *f* (ENSAMBLADO) EN T |
| 1802 | SOLDADURA *f* POR ENCOLADO |
| 1802 | SOLDADURA *f* POR APROXIMACIÓN |
| 1803 | TUBO *m* SOLDADO A TOPE |
| 1804 | TUBO *m* DE CONTACTO |
| 1804 | TUBO *m* SOLDADO POR CONTACTO |
| 1805 | SOLDADURA *f* A TOPE (POR RESISTENCIA) |
| 1805 | SOLDADURA *f* POR APROXIMACIÓN |
| 1806 | SOLDADURA *f* A TOPE POR CHISPORROTEO |
| 1807 | SOLDADURA *f* A TOPE POR RESISTANCIA |
| 1809 | SOLDADURA *f* A TOPE |
| 1810 | ORIFICIOS *m pl* QUE SOLDAR (POR EL INTERIOR EN EL EXTREMO) |
| 1811 | VÁLVULA *f* DE MARIPOSA |
| 1812 | FONDO *m* CURVADO |

| | |
|---|---|
| 1813 | CABEZA *f* REDONDA DE UN TORNILLO |
| 1814 | ROSCA *f* TRAPEZOIDAL |
| 1815 | TORNILLO *m* DE ROSCA TRAPEZOIDAL |
| 1816 | BUTILENO *m* |
| 1817 | ÁCIDO BUTÍRICO *m* |
| 1818 | VOLVEDOR *m*, TUBERÍA *f* DE DERIVACIÓN |
| 1818 | TUBO DE DERIVACIÓN *m* |
| 1819 | VÁLVULA *f* DE DERIVACIÓN |
| 1820 | SUBPRODUCTO *m* |
| 1820 | PRODUCTO *m* SECUNDARIO |
| 1821 | DERIVACIÓN *f* |
| 1821 | DESVÍO *m*, DERIVACIÓN *f* |
| 1822 | LLAVE DE GANCHO *f* |
| 1823 | RESORTE *m* EN C |
| 1824 | CABINA *f* ADELANDADA |
| 1825 | CABLE ELÉCTRICO *m* |
| 1826 | FERROCARRIL FUNICULAR *m* |
| 1826 | FUNICULAR *m* |
| 1827 | TERMINAL DE CABLE *m* |
| 1828 | CABLEADO *m* |
| 1829 | CALABROTE *m* |
| 1830 | TELEGRAMA *m* |
| 1831 | CADMIO *m* |
| 1832 | CADMIADO *m* |
| 1833 | CESIO *m* |
| 1833 | CESIO *m* |
| 1834 | LINGOTE *m* A SU SALIDA |
| 1835 | HULLA *f* GRASA |
| 1836 | CALAMINA *f* |
| 1836 | ESMITSONITA *f* |
| 1837 | CONCRECIÓN CALCAREA *f* |
| 1838 | TOBA *f* CALCÁREA |
| 1839 | CALCINACIÓN *f* |
| 1839 | CALCINACIÓN *f* |
| 1840 | CALCINACIÓN DE LOS MINERALES *f* |
| 1841 | CALCINAR LOS MINERALES |
| 1842 | MAGNESIA *f* CALCINADA |
| 1843 | HORNO *m* DE CALCINACIÓN |
| 1844 | CALCITA *f* |
| 1845 | CALCITA *f* |
| 1845 | ESPATO *m* CALCÁREO |
| 1846 | CALCIO *m* |
| 1847 | BICARBONATO *m* DE CALCIO |
| 1848 | CARBURO *m* |
| 1848 | ACETILURO DE CALCIO *m* |
| 1849 | CARBONATO CÁLCICO *m* |
| 1850 | CLORURO DE CALCIO *m* |
| 1851 | CAL HIDRATADA *f* |
| 1851 | CAL MUERTA *f* |
| 1851 | HIDRATO *m* DE CAL |
| 1852 | MONOSULFURO *m* DE CALCIO |

| | |
|---|---|
| 1853 | OXALATO *m* DE CALCIO |
| 1854 | ÓXIDO *m* DE CALCIO |
| 1854 | CAL ANHÍDRA *f* |
| 1854 | CAL VIVA *f* |
| 1855 | FOSFATO *m* TRICÁLCICO |
| 1855 | FOSFATO *m* DE CALCIO |
| 1856 | SULFATO *m* D CALCIO |
| 1857 | CALCULAR, DISEÑAR |
| 1858 | VALOR *m* CALCULADO |
| 1858 | VALOR *m* TEÓRICO |
| 1859 | MÁQUINA *f* DE CALCULAR |
| 1859 | MÁQUINA *f* ARITMÉTICA |
| 1860 | CÁLCULO *m* CÓMPUTO *m* |
| 1861 | CALIBRAR |
| 1861 | CALIBRAR, AFORAR, CALCULAR LA CAPACIDAD |
| 1862 | CADENAS CALIBRADAS *f pl* |
| 1863 | CALIBRACIÓN *f* (DE UN DEPÓSITO) |
| 1864 | PRENSA *f* MECÁNICA DE CALIBRAR Y ESTAMPAR |
| 1865 | MÁQUINA *f* DE CALIBRAR |
| 1866 | RESORTE *m* CALIBRADO |
| 1867 | CALIBRADO *m*, VERIFICADOR DIMENSIONAL |
| 1867 | CALIBRADO *m*, CLASIFICACIÓN *f* |
| 1867 | CALIBRACIÓN *f* |
| 1868 | CONDENSADOR-PATRÓN *m* |
| 1869 | ERROR *m* DE CALIBRACIÓN |
| 1870 | COMPÁS *m* PARA CALIBRAR EL INTERIOR DE UN DIÁMETRO COMPÁS BAILARÍN *m* |
| 1871 | CALIBRE DE CORREDERA CON REGLA DE PROFUNDIDAD *m* |
| 1872 | MARTILLO *m* DE REBORDEAR |
| 1873 | COMPÁS DE GRUESOS *m* |
| 1874 | COMPÁS DE CALIBRE *m* |
| 1875 | MICRÓMETRO *m* |
| 1875 | MICRÓMETRO *m* |
| 1876 | ELECTRODO *m* DE CALOMEL |
| 1877 | CALORÍMETRO *m* |
| 1878 | CALORIMÉTRICO *m* |
| 1879 | CALORÍMETRO *m* DE COMBUSTIÓN |
| 1880 | ANÁLISIS CALORIMÉTRICO *m* |
| 1881 | CALORIMETRÍA *f* |
| 1882 | CALORIZACIÓN *f* |
| 1883 | LEVA *f*, EXCÉNTRICA *f* |
| 1883 | LEVA *f*, DEDO *m*, NARIE *f*, DIENTE *m* |
| 1884 | ALZADO DE LEVA *m* |
| 1885 | RODILLO *m* EMPUJADOR, RODILLO *m* PROPULSOR |
| 1886 | MECANISMO *m* DE LEVA |
| 1887 | PASADOR *m* DE LEVA |
| 1888 | ÁRBOL DE LEVA *m* |
| 1888 | ÁRBOL PORTALEVAS |
| 1889 | CONVEXIDAD DE LA CARROCERÍA *f* |

| | |
|---|---|
| 1889 | ARQUEO *m*, ÁNGULO DE CAÍDA *f* (CARROCERÍA) |
| 1889 | CARROZADO *m*, CAÍDA *f* |
| 1889 | BOMBEADO *m*, ARCO *m*, BÓVEDA *f*, ARQUEO *m* |
| 1890 | PELO *m* DE CAMELLO |
| 1890 | PELO *m* |
| 1891 | CORREA DE PELOS DE CAMELLO *f* |
| 1892 | BANDA *f* DE RECAUCHUTADO |
| 1893 | ALCANFOR *m* |
| 1894 | ACEITE *m* DE ALCANFOR |
| 1895 | RODILLO *m*, MOLETA *f* DE LEVA |
| 1895 | MOLETA *f* DE LA LEVA |
| 1896 | ÁRBOL DE LEVAS *m* |
| 1897 | TORNO *m* DE ÁRBOL DE LEVAS |
| 1898 | AMIANTO *m* (O FIBRA *f*) DEL CANADÁ |
| 1898 | AMIANTO *m*, ASBESTO *m* |
| 1899 | CANDELA *f* |
| 1899 | BUJÍA *f*, CANDELA *f* |
| 1900 | INTENSIDAD *f* EN BUJÍAS |
| 1901 | CARBÓN DE LLAMA LARGA *m* |
| 1902 | CHAFLÁN *m*, CANTO *m* |
| 1903 | LIMA *f* DE BISEL |
| 1903 | LIMA *f* DE BARRAS |
| 1904 | VIGA *f* EN VOLADIZO |
| 1904 | VIGA *f* EMPOTRADA POR UN EXTREMO |
| 1905 | VIGA *f* SIN ENTRELAZAR |
| 1905 | VIGA *f* EN VOLADIZO |
| 1906 | LONA *f* |
| 1907 | CORREA DE CÁÑAMO *f* |
| 1908 | TUBO *m* DE LONA DE CÁÑAMO |
| 1909 | ENLUCIR, REVOCAR, DAR UNA CAPA |
| 1910 | CAPERUZA *f*, TAPA *f*, TAPADERA *f* |
| 1910 | CAPERUZA *f*, TAPA *f*, TAPADERA *f* |
| 1910 | TAPÓN *m* |
| 1910 | CASQUETE *m* |
| 1911 | TAPA (DE UNA ESFERA) *f*, CASQUETA *m* |
| 1912 | CUBIERTA *f*, TAPA *f* |
| 1912 | TAPA DEL PALIER *f* |
| 1913 | TORNILLO *m* DE CABEZA |
| 1914 | APTO PARA SER COLADO |
| 1914 | QUE PUEDE COLARSE |
| 1915 | APTO PARA SER LAMINADO |
| 1916 | CONDENSADOR *m* |
| 1916 | CONDENSADOR (DE VAPOR) *m* |
| 1917 | CONTENIDO *m*, CAPACIDAD *f*, CABIDA *f* |
| 1917 | CAPACIDAD *f* (ELECTR.) |
| 1917 | CAPACIDAD *f*, POTENCIA *f* |
| 1917 | POTENCIA *f* |
| 1918 | RESISTENCIA *f* AL CHOQUE |
| 1918 | RESILIENCIA *f* |

| | |
|---|---|
| 1919 | FORMÓN *m*, ESCOPLO *m* |
| 1920 | CAPILARIDAD *f* |
| 1921 | TUBO *m* CAPILAR |
| 1922 | ASPIRACIÓN POR CAPILARIDAD *f* |
| 1923 | CONSTANTE CAPILAR *f* |
| 1924 | DEPRESIÓN *f* CAPILAR |
| 1925 | ASCENSIÓN *f*, SUBIDA *f*, ASCENSO *m* |
| 1925 | ELEVACIÓN *f* (O ASCENSIÓN *f*) CAPILAR |
| 1926 | CAPITAL DE COLUMNA *m* |
| 1927 | FORMACIÓN *f* DE UNA COSTRA, FORMACIÓN *f* DE CASCARILLA |
| 1928 | BANDAS *f pl* DE METAL DE RECUBRIMIENTO |
| 1929 | CABRESTANTE *m*, TORNO *m* ELEVADOR |
| 1930 | TORNILLO *m* DE PALANCA |
| 1930 | TORNILLO *m* DE HUSILLO |
| 1931 | TORNO *m* DE REVÓLVER |
| 1932 | VOLCADOR *m* DE VAGONETAS, BASCULADOR DE VAGONES *m* |
| 1933 | CARBURO *m* |
| 1934 | PRECIPITACIÓN *f* |
| 1935 | ESCARIADOR DE METAL DURA *m* |
| 1936 | BROCA *f* DE ATAQUE EN CARBURO |
| 1937 | HIDRATO *m* DE CARBONO |
| 1938 | ÁCIDO CARBÓLICO *m* |
| 1938 | ÁCIDO FÉNICO *m* |
| 1938 | FENOL *m* |
| 1939 | CARBOLINEO *m* |
| 1939 | CARBONILO *m* |
| 1940 | CARBONO *m* |
| 1941 | ARCO DE ELECTRODO DE CARBONO *m* |
| 1942 | CORTE POR ARCO AL CARBONO *m* |
| 1943 | SOLDADURA *f* AL ARCO ELECTRODO DE CARBONO |
| 1944 | ARCO *m* NO PROTEGIDO DE ELECTRODO DE CARBÓN |
| 1945 | ARCO PROTEGIDO DE ELECTRODO DE CARBÓN *m* |
| 1946 | ESCOBILLA *f* DE CARBÓN |
| 1947 | PROPORCIÓN *f* DE CARBONO |
| 1947 | CONTENIDO *m* EN CARBONO |
| 1947 | PROPORCIÓN *f* DE CARBONO |
| 1948 | GAS *m* CARBÓNICO |
| 1948 | ANHÍDRIDO CARBÓNICO *m* |
| 1949 | ÁCIDO CARBÓNICO *m* |
| 1950 | ELECTRODO *m* DE CARBONO |
| 1951 | LÁMPARA *f* DE FILAMENTO DE CARBÓN |
| 1952 | ÓXIDO *m* DE CARBONO |
| 1953 | REGENERACIÓN *f* DE PIEZAS DESCARBURIZADAS |
| 1953 | NUEVA CARBURACIÓN *f* |
| 1954 | ACERO AL CARBONO *m* |
| 1955 | TOCHOS *m pl* PRELAMINADOS DE ACERO AL CARBONO |
| 1956 | PLETINAS *f pl* DE ACERO AL CARBONO |
| 1957 | ACERO DURO DE ALTO CARBONO *m* |

| | |
|---|---|
| 1958 | ACERO DULCE (SUAVE) *m* |
| 1959 | ACERO SEMI-SUAVE *m* |
| 1960 | TECLARORURO *m* DE CARBONO |
| 1961 | EXENTO DE CARBONO, LIBRE DE CARBONO |
| 1962 | CARBONO COMBINADO *m* |
| 1963 | CARBONO DISUELTO *m* |
| 1964 | SULFURO *m* DE CARBONO |
| 1965 | CARBONO DE REVENIDO *m* |
| 1965 | PORCENTAJE *m* DE CARBÓN |
| 1966 | CARBONADO *m* |
| 1967 | DIAMANTE NEGRO *m* |
| 1968 | CARBONATO *m* |
| 1969 | CALIZA CARBONÍFERA *f* |
| 1970 | CARBONIZACIÓN *f* |
| 1971 | CARBONIZAR, HULLIFICAR |
| 1971 | CARBONAR |
| 1972 | CARBONITRURACIÓN *f* |
| 1973 | ATMÓSFERA *f* DE CARBONITRURACIÓN |
| 1974 | CARBONIZACIÓN *f* |
| 1975 | CARBONIZACIÓN *f* |
| 1975 | DESULFURACIÓN *f* |
| 1976 | CARBONILO *m* |
| 1977 | HIERRO *m* DE CARBONILO |
| 1978 | NÍQUEL *m* AL CARBONILO |
| 1979 | POLVO *m* DE CARBONILO |
| 1980 | SILICIURO *m* DE CARBONO |
| 1980 | CARBURO DE SILICIO *m* |
| 1980 | CARBORUNDO *m* |
| 1981 | DAMAJUANA *f*, GARRAFÓN *m* |
| 1981 | BOMBONA *f* |
| 1981 | DAMAJUANA *f*, BOMBONA *f* |
| 1982 | CARBURADOR *m* |
| 1983 | ALCOHOL CARBURADO *m* |
| 1984 | CARBURADOR *m* |
| 1985 | CARBURACIÓN DEL HIERRO *m* |
| 1986 | CARBURAR EL HIERRO |
| 1987 | CEMENTACIÓN VÍA EL CARBONO *f* |
| 1988 | CARBURANTES *m pl* |
| 1989 | CAJAS *f pl* DE CEMENTACIÓN |
| 1990 | LLAMA *f* CARBURANTE |
| 1991 | HORNO *m* DE CARBURIZACIÓN |
| 1992 | CEMENTACIÓN POR GAS *f* |
| 1993 | CEMENTACIÓN HOMOGÉNEA *f* |
| 1994 | BAÑO *m* DE CEMENTACIÓN |
| 1995 | CEMENTACIÓN SELECTIVA *f* |
| 1996 | CEMENTACIÓN EN CAJA *f* |
| 1997 | CARDÁN *m*, ACOPLAMIENTO *m* |
| 1998 | SUSPENSIÓN *f* DE CARDÁN |
| 1999 | TARJETA *f* |
| 1999 | CARTÓN LIGERO *m* |
| 2000 | DEFORMACIÓN *f* PRINCIPAL |

| | | | | |
|---|---|---|---|---|
| 2001 | CARDIOIDE  *f* | 2039 | FUNDICIÓN  *f* RESISTENTE A LA CORROSIÓN |
| 2002 | PAPEL  *m* CARMÍN | 2040 | FUNDICIÓN  *f* DÚCTIL |
| 2003 | CERA DE CARNAUBA  *f* | 2041 | FUNDICIÓN  *f* GRIS |
| 2004 | CICLO  *m* DE CARNOT | 2042 | FUNDICIÓN  *f* DE GRAN RESISTENCIA) |
| 2005 | CARPINTERO  *m* | 2043 | FUNDICIÓN  *f* MALEABLE |
| 2006 | CARPINTERÍA  *f* | 2044 | FUNDICIÓN  *f* MOTEADA |
| 2007 | MÁQUINA  *f* DE CEPILLAR CON MESA MÓVIL | 2045 | FUNDICIÓN  *f* DÚCTIL |
| 2008 | RESORTE  *m* DE COCHE | 2045 | FUNDICIÓN  *f* CON GRAFITO ESFEROIDAL |
| 2009 | BROCA  *f* CÓNICA, PERNO  *m* CÓNICO | 2046 | FUNDICIÓN  *f* PERLÍTICA |
| 2010 | EJE  *m* PORTANTE | 2047 | FUNDICIÓN  *f* MALEABLE PERLÍTICA |
| 2011 | CAPACIDAD DE CARGA  *f* | 2048 | FUNDICIÓN  *f* RESISTENTE AL DESGASTE |
| 2012 | VACIADOR  *m* DE CAJAS PARA SIN ELLAS LOGRAR EL MOLDE DE ARENA | 2049 | FUNDICIÓN  *f* BLANCA |
| | | 2050 | METAL  *m* COLADO |
| 2013 | CARRETILLA  *f*, CARRO  *m* | 2051 | CLAVO FUNDIDO  *m* |
| 2014 | COORDINADAS CARTESIANAS  *f pl* | 2052 | PLACA  *f* MODELO |
| 2015 | CARTUCHO  *m* | 2053 | ESTIRADO  *m* EN FRÍO DE TUBOS COLADOS SIN SOLDADURA |
| 2016 | LATÓN  *m* PARA CARTUCHERÍA | | |
| 2017 | VOLQUETE  *m* | 2054 | PROCEDENTE DE FUNDICIÓN |
| 2018 | CASCADA  *f* | 2054 | PROCEDENTE DE FUNDICIÓN |
| 2019 | SUPERFICIE  *f* | 2054 | PRODUCIDO EN LA COLADA |
| 2019 | CAPA SUPERFICIAL  *f* | 2055 | ACERO MOLDEADO  *m* |
| 2020 | PROFUNDIDAD  *f* DE LA CAPA CEMENTADA | 2055 | FUNDICIÓN  *f* DE ACERO |
| 2021 | CEMENTACIÓN  *f* | 2056 | CENTRO DE RUEDA DE ACERO FUNDIDO  *m* |
| 2021 | TEMPLE  *m* DE SUPERFICIE | 2057 | ACERO MOLDEADO AL CRISOL  *m* |
| 2022 | CEMENTO  *m* | 2058 | ESTRUCTURA  *f* DE LAS ALEACIONES |
| 2023 | CEMENTACIÓN PARCIAL  *f* | 2059 | DIENTE  *m* EN BRUTO DE FUNDICIÓN |
| 2023 | CEMENTACIÓN DE LA PIEZAS DE ACERO DULCE  *f* | 2060 | UNIÓN POR SOLDADURA DE PIEZAS FUNDIDAS  *f* |
| | | 2061 | CRECIMIENTO  *m* DE LA FUNDICIÓN |
| 2023 | TEMPLE  *m* EN SUPERFICIE | 2062 | CANALIZACIÓN DE FUNDICIÓN  *f* |
| 2024 | CEMENTOS  *m pl*, POLVOS  *m pl* | 2063 | BRIDA  *f* FUNDIDA INTEGRAL |
| 2024 | CARBURANTES  *m pl* | 2064 | COLABILIDAD  *f* |
| 2025 | CASEINA  *f* | 2065 | PRUEBA  *f* DE CAPACIDAD DE FUNDICIÓN |
| 2026 | CARTER  *m* | 2066 | AVANCE  *m* |
| 2027 | CALIBRE PARA TUBOS  *m* | 2067 | AVANCE (ÁNGULO DE)  *m* |
| 2028 | CASSETTE  *m*, CAJITA  *f*, CARRETE  *m* | 2068 | FUNDICIÓN  *f* (PRODUCTO) |
| 2029 | CASINOIDE  *f* | 2068 | COLADA  *f* |
| 2029 | LEMNISCATA  *f* | 2068 | COLADURA  *f* |
| 2029 | ELIPSE  *f* DE CASSINI, CASINOIDE  *f* | 2068 | MOLDEO  *m*, MOLDEADO  *m* |
| 2030 | FUNDIR, COLAR | 2069 | PIEZA  *f* MOLDEADA |
| 2030 | MOLDEAR | 2069 | LINGOTE  *m* |
| 2030 | FUNDIR | 2070 | FUSIÓN (OPERACIÓN)  *f* |
| 2031 | LATÓN  *m* COLADO | 2071 | NAVE  *f* DE COLADA |
| 2032 | REVESTIMIENTO  *m* FUNDIDO | 2071 | ÁREA DE COLADA  *f* |
| 2033 | AGUJERO  *m* PROCEDENTE DE FUNDICIÓN | 2072 | VAGONETA  *f* PARA CALDERO DE COLADA |
| 2034 | FUNDICIÓN  *f* (HIERRO COLADO) | 2073 | COBRE  *m* REFINADO |
| 2034 | ARRABIO  *m* - HIERRO COLADO  *m* | 2074 | FUNDICIÓN  *f* SIN TENSIONES INTERNAS |
| 2035 | TUBO  *m* DE FUNDICIÓN | 2075 | FUNDICIÓN  *f* SIN RECHUPES |
| 2036 | TERMITA  *f* DE FUNDICIÓN | 2076 | COLADA (LOTE DE ...)  *f* |
| 2037 | FUNDICIÓN  *f* ALEADA | 2077 | NAVE  *f* DE COLADA |
| 2038 | FUNDICIÓN  *f* TEMPLADA | 2078 | TENSIÓN  *f* DE VACIADO |
| 2038 | FUNDICIÓN  *f* EN COQUILLA | 2079 | PIEZA  *f* DE FUNDICIÓN |

| | |
|---|---|
| 2079 | PIEZA f DE FUNDICIÓN MOLDEADA |
| 2080 | PIEZAS f pl COLADAS (O DE MOLDE) |
| 2081 | TENSIÓN f DE COLADA |
| 2082 | PIEZAS f pl MOLDEADAS (O COLADAS) QUE RESISTEN A LA CORROSIÓN |
| 2083 | PIEZAS f pl MOLDEADAS EN FUNDICIÓN GRIS |
| 2084 | PIEZAS f pl MOLDEADAS RESISTIENDO A ELEVADAS TEMPERATURAS |
| 2085 | TUERCA f ALMADENADA, TUERCA DE CORONA |
| 2085 | TUERCA f ALMENADA, TUERCA DE CORONA |
| 2085 | TUERCA f CON REBORDE, TUERCA CON ANILLO |
| 2085 | TUERCA f ALMENADA, TUERCA DE CORONA |
| 2085 | TUERCA f DE CORONA, TUERCA CON ENTALLAS, TUERCA ALMADENADA |
| 2086 | ACEITE m DE RICINO |
| 2087 | MANGUITO m DE CENTRADO |
| 2088 | OJO m DE GATO |
| 2089 | CÁUSTICO POR REFLEXIÓN m |
| 2090 | CATÁLISIS f |
| 2091 | CATALIZADOR m |
| 2092 | CATALÍTICO m |
| 2093 | SALIENTE, RELIEVE m |
| 2094 | TRINQUETE DE PASADA m, FIADOR m |
| 2094 | PERRO m |
| 2094 | GATILLO m DEL TRINQUETE |
| 2094 | GATILLO m DEL TRINQUETE |
| 2095 | CADENETA (GEOM.) f |
| 2096 | CATETÓMETRO m |
| 2097 | CÁTODO m |
| 2098 | LIMPIEZA f CATÓDICA |
| 2099 | COBRE m ELECTROLÍTICO |
| 2100 | CAÍDA (DE TENSIÓN) CATÓDICA f, BAJA DE TENSIÓN |
| 2101 | RENDIMIENTO m CATÓDICO |
| 2102 | REVESTIMIENTO m CATÓDICO |
| 2103 | DECAPADO m CATÓDICO |
| 2104 | RAYOS m CATÓDICOS |
| 2105 | TUBO m CATÓDICO |
| 2105 | TUBO m DE RAYOS CATÓDICOS |
| 2106 | ELECTRODO m NEGATIVO |
| 2106 | CÁTODO m |
| 2107 | CORROSIÓN CATÓDICA f |
| 2108 | POLARIZACIÓN f CATÓDICA |
| 2109 | PROTECCIÓN f CATÓDICA |
| 2110 | GRABADO m CATÓDICO |
| 2111 | CATÓLITO m |
| 2112 | CATIÓN m |
| 2112 | ION m HIDRÓGENO |
| 2113 | RECALCAR, RETACAR, RETOCAR |
| 2114 | CORTAFRÍO m, TAJADERA f |
| 2115 | RECALCADURA f |
| 2116 | CÁUSTICO m |

| | |
|---|---|
| 2117 | BAÑO m DE HIDRÓXIDO DE SODIO |
| 2118 | FRAGILIDAD f CÁUSTICA |
| 2119 | LÍQUIDO m CAÚSTICO |
| 2120 | LEJÍA f |
| 2120 | SOLUCIÓN f DE SOSA CÁUSTICA |
| 2121 | SUPERFICIE f CÁUSTICA |
| 2122 | CAVETO m |
| 2122 | RANURA f |
| 2123 | CAVITACIÓN f |
| 2124 | CAVIDAD f POR CONTRACCIÓN |
| 2124 | CAPA DE AIRE f |
| 2125 | HUECO m, CAVIDAD f |
| 2125 | CAVIDAD f, HUECO m |
| 2125 | CAVIDAD f |
| 2126 | PILA f ELÉCTRICA |
| 2127 | CAVIDAD DE CELDA f |
| 2128 | CONSTANTE DE UNA CELDA ELECTROLÍTICA f |
| 2129 | RADIADOR m EN NIDO DE ABEJA |
| 2130 | CELULOIDE m |
| 2131 | CELULOSA f |
| 2132 | ACETATO DE CELULOSA m |
| 2133 | CEMENTO m |
| 2134 | RELLENAR CON MASILLA |
| 2134 | CIMENTAR (CUBRIR CON UNA CAPA DE CEMENTO) |
| 2134 | ACERAR |
| 2134 | CEMENTAR |
| 2134 | EMPLASTECER, ENMASILLAR |
| 2135 | HORMIGÓN m DE CEMENTO |
| 2136 | CEMENTO DE COBRE m |
| 2136 | COBRE m CEMENTADO |
| 2136 | COBRE m CEMENTADO |
| 2136 | COBRE m REGENERADO |
| 2137 | MORTERO m DE CEMENTO |
| 2138 | ACERO CEMENTADO m |
| 2138 | ACERO CEMENTADO m |
| 2138 | ACERO CEMENTADO m |
| 2139 | CEMENTO m |
| 2139 | AGENTE DE CARBURIZACIÓN (DE CEMENTACIÓN) m |
| 2139 | POLVO m CARBURANTE |
| 2140 | COLA PARA CORREAS f |
| 2141 | CEMENTACIÓN f |
| 2142 | CEMENTACIÓN (DE LAS BARRAS DE HIERRO) |
| 2142 | ACERACIÓN f |
| 2142 | ACERACIÓN f |
| 2143 | EMPALME m POR PEGADURA DE LAS CORREAS |
| 2144 | HERRAMIENTAS f pl CON INCLUSIONES DE CARBURO |
| 2145 | CORREA ENCOLADA f |
| 2146 | ENMASILLADO m, EMPLASTE |

| | | | |
|---|---|---|---|
| 2146 | CIMENTADO *m*, CIMENTACIÓN *f* (CUBRIR CON UNA CAPA DE CEMENTO) | 2186 | TERMÓMETRO *m* CENTÍGRADO |
| 2147 | CEMENTITA *f* | 2187 | CENTRADO *m* |
| 2148 | CENTRO *m* | 2188 | MÁQUINA *f* DE CENTRAR Y ENDEREZAR (O RECTIFICAR) |
| 2149 | PERNO *m* CAPUCHINO | 2189 | ACELERACIÓN CENTRÍPETA *f* |
| 2150 | TORNO *m* DE PUNTA | 2190 | FUERZA *f* CENTRÍPETA |
| 2151 | FIBRA *f* NEUTRA | 2191 | CENTRO DE SUPERFICIE *m* |
| 2151 | FIBRA *f* NEUTRA | 2192 | CERAMETAL *m* |
| 2152 | APOYO *m* CENTRAL, APOYO *m* MEDIANO | 2192 | MEZCLA *f* DE CARBUROS CEMENTADOS |
| 2153 | PEÓN *m* DE CENTRADO | 2193 | CERÁMICA *f* |
| 2154 | ANILLO *m* DE CENTRACIÓN | 2194 | CERESINA *f* |
| 2155 | RECTIFICADORA *f* PARA SUPERFICIES DE REVOLUCIÓN SIN CENTRO | 2194 | CERA MINERAL *f* |
| 2156 | RECTIFICACIÓN *f* SIN PUNTA(S) | 2195 | CERIO *m* |
| 2157 | ESCALA *f* DE CELSIO | 2196 | CERUSITA *f* |
| 2157 | ESCALA *f* CENTIGRADA | 2197 | CESIO *m* |
| 2158 | CENTÍMETRO *m* | 2198 | ÍNDICE *m* DE CETANO |
| 2159 | SISTEMA *m* C.G.G. | 2199 | CUCHILLA *f* DE CORTAR LA PAJA |
| 2159 | SISTEMA *m* CENTIMETRO-GRADO-SEGUNDO | 2200 | FATIGA *f* POR CONTACTOS DE ROCE |
| 2160 | CALEFACCIÓN CENTRAL *f* | 2201 | CADENA *f* |
| 2161 | CARGA CENTRAL *f* | 2202 | TAMBOR *m* PARA CADENA CABLE |
| 2162 | CENTRO *m* | 2202 | TAMBOR *m* DE CADENA |
| 2163 | CENTRAR | 2203 | FRENO *m* DE CADENA |
| 2164 | BROCA *f* PARA CENTRAR | 2204 | CARTER DE CADENAS *m*, CUBRECADENAS *m* |
| 2164 | BROCA *f* DE ESPIGA | 2205 | LÍNEA *f* DE UN TRAZO |
| 2164 | BROCA *f* DE TRES PUNTAS | 2206 | ACCIONAMIENTO POR CADENA *m* |
| 2164 | BROCA *f* DE CENTRO | 2207 | TRANSMISIÓN *f* POR CADENA |
| 2165 | DISTANCIA *f* ENTRE CENTROS | 2208 | ACCIONAMIENTO POR CADENA *m* |
| 2166 | INSTRUMENTO *m* PARA CENTRAR | 2209 | EMPARRILLADO DE CADENA |
| 2167 | CENTRO DE ARCO *m* | 2210 | SOLDADURA *f* DE ÁNGULO CON HILERAS ALTERNADAS SIMÉTRICAS |
| 2168 | CENTRO DE GRAVEDAD *m* | 2211 | ESLABÓN *m* DE CADENA |
| 2169 | CENTRO DE ROTACIÓN *m* | 2212 | ENGRASE *m* POR CADENA |
| 2170 | CENTRO DE OSCILACIÓN *m* | 2213 | APAREJO *m* DE CADENA |
| 2171 | CENTRO DEL REMACHE *m* | 2214 | ROBLÓN *m* DE CADENA |
| 2172 | PUNZÓN *m* DE CENTRADO | 2215 | REMACHE *m* CADENA |
| 2173 | BUSCACENTROS *m* | 2216 | SIERRA *f* DE CADENA |
| 2174 | MÁQUINA *f* PARA PASAR A LA MUELA SIN PUNTAS | 2217 | POLEA *f* DE CADENA |
| 2175 | FRENO *m* CENTRÍFUGO | 2217 | POLEA *f* DE CADENA |
| 2176 | FUNDICIÓN CENTRIFUGA *f* | 2217 | POLEA *f* DE CADENA |
| 2177 | ACOPLAMIENTO *m* CENTRÍFUGO | 2217 | RUEDA *f* MOTRIZ |
| 2178 | TURBOCOMPRESOR *m* | 2218 | TENSOR *m* DE CADENA |
| 2178 | COMPRESOR CENTRÍFUGO *m* | 2219 | TENSOR *m* DE CADENA |
| 2179 | VENTILADOR *m* DE FUERZA CENTRÍFUGA | 2220 | VOLANTE *m* DE CADENA ADAPTABLE |
| 2180 | FUERZA *f* CENTRÍFUGA | 2221 | SULFURO *m* EN CADENA |
| 2181 | REGULADOR *m* CENTRÍFUGO | 2222 | SERIE *f* DE OPERACIONES |
| 2182 | ENGRASADOR *m* CENTRÍFUGO | 2222 | GAMA *f* DE OPERACIONES |
| 2183 | MOMENTO *m* CENTRÍFUGO | 2223 | VOLANTE *m* DE CADENA |
| 2184 | BOMBA *f* CENTRÍFUGA | 2224 | GREDA *f* |
| 2185 | REGULADOR *m* DE WATT | 2225 | MARGA *f* CALCÁREA |
| 2185 | REGULADOR *m* DE BOLAS | 2226 | PULVERIZACIÓN *f* |
| 2185 | REGULADOR *m* DE FUERZA CENTRÍFUGA | 2226 | PULVERIZACIÓN *f* |

| | |
|---|---|
| 2227 | AGUA $f$ CALCÁREA, AGUA $f$ CALIZA |
| 2228 | ÁCIDO (SULFÚRICO) DE CÁMARA $m$ |
| 2229 | CAPILLA $f$ |
| 2229 | CÁMARA DE DISTRIBUCIÓN $f$ |
| 2229 | CAJA $f$ DE DISTRIBUCIÓN, UNIDAD $f$ DE DISTRIBUCIÓN |
| 2229 | CAJA $f$ DE VÁLVULAS |
| 2230 | BISELAR, ACHAFLANAR |
| 2230 | ACHAFLANAR, RECANTEAR |
| 2231 | CHAFLÁN $m$ |
| 2232 | MARTILLO BISELADO $m$ |
| 2233 | BISELADO $m$, ACHAFLANADO $m$ |
| 2234 | GAMUZA $f$ |
| 2234 | GAMUZA $f$ |
| 2235 | CHAMOTA $f$ |
| 2236 | CAMBIO DE DIRECCIÓN $m$ |
| 2237 | CAMBIO DE PRESIÓN $m$ |
| 2238 | CAMBIO DE ESTADO $m$ |
| 2239 | CAMBIO DE TEMPERATURA $m$ |
| 2240 | CAMBIO DE VOLUMEN $m$ |
| 2241 | INVERTIR, TRASTOCAR |
| 2241 | CONMUTAR |
| 2241 | INVERTIR LA CORRIENTE |
| 2242 | MECANISMO $m$ DE CAMBIO DE VELOCIDAD |
| 2243 | RUEDA $f$ DE REPUESTO |
| 2243 | RUEDA $f$ DE RECAMBIO |
| 2244 | CONMUTADOR $m$ |
| 2245 | CAMBIO DE MULTIPLICACIÓN $m$ |
| 2245 | CAMBIO DE VELOCIDAD $m$ |
| 2246 | INVERSIÓN DEL SENTIDO DE UNA CORRIENTE $f$ |
| 2246 | CONMUTACIÓN $f$ |
| 2247 | BARRACA $f$ DE VESTUARIO |
| 2248 | HIERRO $m$ EN U |
| 2248 | HIERRO $m$ EN U |
| 2248 | CANAL $m$ |
| 2249 | VIGUETA $f$ EN U |
| 2250 | HIERRO $m$ DE CAÑA, CANALES $m$ $pl$ EN U |
| 2250 | HIERRO $m$ EN U |
| 2250 | HIERRO $m$ EN E |
| 2251 | CANAL $m$ |
| 2251 | REGUERO $m$ CANAL $m$ |
| 2251 | CANALÓN, VERTEDERO $m$, CUNETA $f$ |
| 2252 | CHAPA $f$ ACANALADA |
| 2252 | CHAPA $f$ ESTRIADA |
| 2253 | SOPORTE $m$ DE ALMA, DE NÚCLEO |
| 2254 | PROCEDIMIENTO $m$ CHAPMAN |
| 2255 | CARÁCTER $m$ |
| 2256 | CARACTERÍSTICA $f$ |
| 2257 | CARACTERÍSTICA DE UN LOGARITMO $f$ |
| 2258 | FUNDICIÓN $f$ CON CARBÓN VEGETAL |
| 2259 | CARGA ELÉCTRICA $f$ |

| | |
|---|---|
| 2259 | CARGA $f$ |
| 2260 | CARGAR UN HORNO METALÚRGICO |
| 2261 | CARGAR UN ACUMULADOR |
| 2262 | CILINDRADA $f$ |
| 2263 | CARGA $f$ |
| 2263 | ALIMENTACIÓN $f$, CARGAMENTO $m$ |
| 2264 | CARGA DE UN HORNO METALÚRGICO $f$ |
| 2265 | CARGA DE UN ACUMULADOR $f$ |
| 2266 | CORRIENTE DE CARGA $f$ |
| 2267 | INDICADOR $m$ DE CARGA |
| 2268 | MÁQUINA $f$ PARA CARGAR LOS HORNOS |
| 2269 | CARGA $f$ |
| 2269 | LLENADO $m$ |
| 2270 | PRUEBA $f$ DE CHOQUE DE CHARPY (O EN BARRA ENTALLADA) |
| 2271 | PILÓN $m$ PÉNDULO DE CHARPY |
| 2272 | CALCINA $f$ |
| 2272 | CARBONIZADO $m$ |
| 2272 | CUERO $m$ TOSTADO (QUEMADO) |
| 2273 | ÁBACO $m$ |
| 2273 | CUADRO $m$ |
| 2274 | PEINE $m$ PARA LOS PASOS DE TORNILLO |
| 2275 | CHÁSIS $m$ |
| 2276 | MARCAS $f$ DE VIBRACIÓN |
| 2277 | VIBRACIONES $f$ $pl$ |
| 2277 | FUNCIONAMIENTO DESORDENADO DE LA VÁLVULA $m$ |
| 2278 | HENDIDURA $f$ |
| 2278 | GRIETA $f$, HENDIDURA $f$, FISURA $f$ |
| 2278 | GRIETA $f$, HENDIDURA $f$ |
| 2279 | VERIFICAR LAS MEDIDAS |
| 2280 | VERIFICACIÓN $f$ DE LA COMPOSICIÓN QUÍMICA |
| 2280 | CONTRA-ANÁLISIS $f$, ANÁLISIS DE CONTROL $m$ |
| 2280 | ANÁLISIS DE COMPROBACIÓN $m$ |
| 2281 | PERNO $m$ DE BLOQUEO |
| 2282 | MARCAS $f$ SUPERFICIALES EN FORMA DE V |
| 2283 | VÁLVULA DE RETENCIÓN $f$, VÁLVULA DE CHEQUE |
| 2284 | VÁLVULA DE RETENCIÓN $f$ |
| 2284 | VÁLVULA $f$ |
| 2285 | CHAPA $f$ ESTRIADA |
| 2285 | CHAPA $f$ GOFRADA |
| 2286 | FORMACIÓN $f$ DE RAJAS |
| 2286 | FORMACIÓN $f$ DE REDONDELES |
| 2287 | PARTE $f$ CENTRAL |
| 2288 | MUSELINA $f$ |
| 2289 | AGENTE DE QUELATO $m$ |
| 2290 | QUÍMICA $f$ |
| 2291 | PROCEDIMIENTO $m$ QUÍMICO |
| 2292 | AFINIDAD QUÍMICA $f$ |
| 2293 | ANÁLISIS QUÍMICO $m$ |

2294 BALANZA _f_ ANALÍTICA, BALANZA _f_ DE ANÁLISIS

2294 PESILLO _m_ PARA ANÁLISIS

2295 CARACTERÍSTICAS _f pl_, PROPIEDADES QUÍMICAS _f pl_

2295 PROPIEDADES _f pl_

2296 ALTERACIÓN QUÍMICA _f_

2296 TRANSFORMACIÓN _f_ QUÍMICA

2297 REVESTIMIENTO _m_ QUÍMICO

2298 COMPONENTE QUÍMICO _m_

2299 COMPOSICIÓN QUÍMICA _f_

2300 COMBINACIÓN QUÍMICA _f_

2301 CONSTITUCIÓN QUÍMICA _f_, COMPOSICIÓN QUÍMICA _f_

2302 CORROSIÓN QUÍMICA _f_

2303 FLUIDOS _m pl_ DE CORTE QUÍMICOS

2303 FLUIDOS _m pl_ DE CORTE SINTÉTICOS

2304 SOLDADURA _f_ POR IMMERSIÓN

2305 ENERGÍA _f_ QUÍMICA

2306 INGENIERO _m_ QUIMICO

2307 EQUILIBRIO _m_ QUÍMICO

2308 EQUIVALENTE QUÍMICO

2309 PROCEDIMIENTO _m_ DE ACABADO QUÍMICO DE SUPERFICIE

2310 FÓRMULA _f_ QUÍMICA

2311 PLOMO _m_ PURO

2312 REACCIÓN _f_ QUÍMICA

2313 ESTABILIDAD _f_ (QUÍMICA)

2314 PROCEDIMIENTOS _m pl_ QUÍMICOS DE TRATAMIENTOS DE SUPERFICIE

2315 SÍMBOLO (QUÍMICA)

2316 PASTA _f_ QUÍMICA DE MADERA, CELULOSA

2317 QUÍMICAMENTE COMBINADO _m_

2318 AGUA _f_ COMBINADA (QUÍMICAMENTE)

2318 AGUA _f_ DE CONSTITUCIÓN

2319 QUÍMICAMENTE PURO _m_

2320 PRODUCTOS _m pl_ QUÍMICOS

2321 QUÍMICO

2322 QUÍMICA _f_

2323 REACTOR _m_ DE RADIOQUÍMICA

2324 ESTAÑO _m_ QUÍMICAMENTE PURO

2325 CHAPA _f_ ESTRIADA

2326 COLOR CEREZA _m_

2326 ROJO _m_ CEREZA

2326 CALOR AL ROJO CEREZA _m_

2327 CALDEO _m_

2327 CALENTADO AL ROJO CEREZA

2328 MENUDOS _m pl_ DE CARBÓN

2328 GALLETILLA _f_

2328 GALLETILLA _f_ DE CARBÓN

2329 INGENIERO _m_ JEFE DE LA CONSTRUCCIÓN

2330 CALICHE _m_

2330 SALITRE, NITRO _m_

2330 NITRATO _m_ DE CHILE, CALICHE _m_, NITRATO _m_ DE SODIO

2330 NITRATO _m_ DE SODIO

2331 COQUILLA _f_

2332 TEMPLAR

2332 TEMPLAR (FUNDICIÓN)

2332 ENFRIAR

2333 HIERRO _m_ BRUTO COLADO EN COQUILLA

2334 FUNDIDO EN COQUILLA _m_

2334 FUNDICIÓN _f_ EN COQUILLA

2335 FUNDICIÓN _f_ EN COQUILLA

2336 FUNDICIÓN _f_ (ENDURECIDA)

2337 METAL _m_ FUNDIDO EN COQUILLA SIN DEFORMACIÓN

2338 TEMPLE _m_

2339 CHIMENEA _f_

2340 CAOLÍN _m_

2340 CAOLÍN _m_

2341 ESCRITURA _f_ CHINA

2342 SEBO _m_ VEGETAL DE CHINA

2343 VIRUTA _f_

2343 VIRUTA _f_

2344 ESCOPLEAR, CINCELAR, BURILAR

2345 ANÁLISIS DE VIRUTAS _m_

2346 VIRUTA _f_

2347 BURILADO _m_

2347 PICADO _m_ AL MARTILLO (CALDERAS)

2348 VIRUTAS DE METAL _f pl_

2349 FORMÓN _m_, CINCEL _m_

2349 BURIL _m_, ESCOPLO _m_, FORMÓN _m_

2350 SOLDADOR _m_ EN FORMA DE MARTILLO

2351 CLORATO _m_

2352 CLORURO _m_

2353 CLORURACIÓN _f_

2354 CLORO _m_

2355 ANHÍDRIDO HIPOCLOROSO _m_

2356 CLOROFORMO _m_

2357 ESTÁRTER _m_

2358 TAPONARSE

2358 OBSTRUIRSE, TAPARSE

2358 OBSTRUIRSE, ATRANCARSE, ATASCARSE

2359 DIFUSOR _m_ O BOQUILLA _f_ (O TOBERA _f_)

2360 SUPERFICIE _f_ FILTRANTE SATURADA

2361 TUBO _m_ TAPONADO

2361 TUBO _m_ ATASCADO

2362 OBSTRUCCIÓN _f_, ATASCO _m_

2362 OBSTRUCCIÓN _f_

2363 EBONITA _f_

2363 CAUCHO ENDURECIDO _m_

2364 CUERDA DE UN CÍRCULO _f_

2365 ESPESOR _m_ DEL DIENTE A LA CUERDA

| | | | | |
|---|---|---|---|---|
| 2366 | CROMATO *m* | 2405 | TOPE DEL PASADOR DEL PISTÓN *m* |
| 2367 | CROMATACIÓN *f* | 2406 | CIRCUITO ELÉCTRICO *m* |
| 2368 | CROMÁTICO *m* | 2407 | DISYUNTOR *m* |
| 2369 | ABERRACIÓN CROMÁTICA *f* | 2408 | REGISTRADOR *m* DE DIAGRAMA CIRCULAR |
| 2369 | ABERRACIÓN DE REFRANGIBILIDAD *f* | 2409 | CONO DE BASE CIRCULAR *m* |
| 2370 | ALUMBRE DE CROMO *m* | 2409 | CONO CIRCULAR *m* |
| 2371 | LADRILLO *m* DE CROMITA | 2410 | SECCIÓN *f* CIRCULAR |
| 2372 | VERDE ESMERALDA | 2411 | CILINDRO *m* DE BASE CIRCULAR |
| 2373 | CROMITA *f* | 2412 | MOLETA *f* (O PATÍN *m*) DE SOLDADURA |
| 2374 | ROJO *m* DE CROMO | 2413 | FUNCIÓN *f* CÍCLICA |
| 2375 | AMARILLO *m* CROMO | 2413 | FUNCIÓN *f* CIRCULAR |
| 2375 | CROMATO DE PLOMO *m* | 2414 | ESPEJO *m* REDONDO, CRISTAL *m* REDONDO |
| 2376 | ACERO CROMO-NÍQUEL *m* | 2414 | MIRILLA *f* REDONDA |
| 2377 | CUERO *m* CURTIDO AL CROMO | 2415 | RANURA *f* ANULAR |
| 2377 | CURTIR AL CROMO | 2415 | RANURA *f* CIRCULAR |
| 2378 | ACERO AL CROMO-WOLFRAMIO *m* | 2416 | INTERPOLACIÓN *f* CIRCULAR |
| 2379 | ÁCIDO CRÓMICO *m* | 2417 | CUCHILLO CIRCULAR *m* |
| 2380 | OXIDACIÓN *f* ANÓDICA POR EL ÁCIDO CRÓMICO | 2418 | TUBERÍA CIRCULAR *f* |
| 2381 | CLORURO CRÓMICO *m* | 2419 | MEDIDA *f* INTERCEPTADA DEL ARCO |
| 2381 | SESQUICLORURO *m* DE CROMO | 2420 | FRESADORA *f* CIRCULAR |
| 2382 | SESQUIÓXIDO *m* DE CROMO | 2421 | MOVIMIENTO *m* CIRCULAR |
| 2383 | ANHÍDRIDO CRÓMICO *m* | 2422 | PÉNDULO *m* CIRCULAR |
| 2384 | CROMITA *f* | 2423 | PASO *m* CIRCUNFERENCIAL |
| 2385 | CROMO *m* | 2424 | PLATILLOS *m pl* CIRCULARES |
| 2386 | ACERO AL NÍQUEL CROMO *m* | 2425 | CEPILLO *m* DE DISCO, CEPILLO *m* DE PULIR |
| 2387 | MATERIA *f* COLORANTE A BASE DE CROMO | 2426 | TRANSPORTADOR *m* DE CÍRCULO COMPLETO |
| 2388 | CROMADO ELECTROLÍTICO *m* | 2427 | SIERRA *f* CIRCULAR |
| 2389 | ACERO CROMADO *m* | 2427 | SIERRA *f* CIRCULAR |
| 2390 | CEMENTACIÓN POR EL CROMO *f* | 2428 | SIERRA *f* CIRCULAR |
| 2391 | CLORURO CROMOSO *m* | 2429 | CIZALLA CIRCULAR *f* |
| 2392 | CRISOLITO *m* | 2430 | NIVEL *m* ESFÉRICO |
| 2393 | MANDRIL *m*, PLATO *m* DE TORNO | 2431 | ESPESOR *m* CIRCULAR DEL DIENTE |
| 2393 | MANDRIL *m* DE TORNO | 2432 | CIRCULAR |
| 2394 | MORDAZA *f* SUAVE PARA CABEZALES | 2433 | CIRCULACIÓN *f* |
| 2395 | CORREDOR *m*, RAMPA *f* | 2434 | CIRCULACIÓN DE AGUA *f* |
| 2395 | CORREDERA *f* | 2435 | CÍRCULO CIRCONSCRITO *m* |
| 2395 | CANALÓN *m*, CONDUCTO *m* | 2435 | CÍRCULO CIRCUNSCRITO *m* |
| 2395 | CANALETA *f* | 2436 | POLÍGONO *m* CIRCUNSCRITO |
| 2395 | DESCARGA *f* | 2437 | CONTRACCIÓN *f* |
| 2396 | ENCENDEDOR DE CIGARROS *m* | 2437 | RETRACCIÓN *f* |
| 2397 | CENIZA *f* | 2437 | RETRACCIÓN *f* |
| 2397 | ESCORIA *f* | 2438 | CISÓIDE *m* |
| 2397 | CENIZA *f*, CERNADA *f* | 2439 | CISTERNA *f* |
| 2398 | ENFRIADOR *m* DE CENIZAS | 2440 | BARÓMETRO *m* DE CUBETAS |
| 2399 | AGUJERO *m* PARA LA ESCORIA | 2441 | ÁCIDO CÍTRICO *m* |
| 2400 | CINABRIO *m* | 2442 | ARQUITECTURA *f* |
| 2401 | CÍRCULO *m* | 2443 | INGENIERO *m* DE CONSTRUCCIONES CIVILES |
| 2402 | CÍRCULO DE ARCO *m* | 2443 | INGENIERO *m* CONSTRUCTOR |
| 2403 | CIZALLA CIRCULAR *f* | 2444 | INGENIERÍA *f* CIVIL |
| 2404 | CIRCUNFERENCIA *f*, CÍRCULO *m* | 2444 | OBRAS *f pl* PÚBLICAS |
| 2404 | PERIFERIA *f* DEL CÍRCULO | 2444 | CONSTRUCCIONES CIVILES *f pl* |

| | |
|---|---|
| 2445 | CHAPA  f  CONTRACHAPEADA |
| 2446 | ACERO CHAPADO  m |
| 2447 | FORRO  m, REVESTIMIENTO  m |
| 2447 | CHAPEADO  m |
| 2448 | COLLAR  m |
| 2449 | MANGUITO  m  DE COQUILLAS |
| 2449 | MANGUITO  m  CILÍNDRICO DE ACOPLAMIENTO |
| 2449 | MANGUITO  m  CON PERNOS EMPOTRADOS |
| 2450 | COLLAR  m  DE RETENCIÓN, GRAPA  f, ABRAZADERA |
| 2451 | CÁRCEL  f |
| 2451 | PRENSA  f  DE CARPINTERO |
| 2451 | PRENSA  f  DE COLLAR |
| 2452 | PRENSA  f  DE TORNILLO |
| 2452 | CÁRCEL  f |
| 2452 | CÁRCEL  f |
| 2453 | TORNILLO  m  DE FIJACIÓN |
| 2453 | TORNILLO  m |
| 2453 | TORNILLO  m  DE BLOQUEO |
| 2454 | CAJA DEL PORTAHERRAMIENTAS  f |
| 2455 | CLARIFICACIÓN  f |
| 2456 | CLARIFICAR |
| 2457 | CLAVO DE GANCHO  m, ESCARPIA  f |
| 2458 | CATEGORÍA DE HIERRO  f |
| 2458 | CLASE  f  DE HIERRO |
| 2459 | CATEGORÍA TIPO DE ACERO  f |
| 2460 | CLARIFICACIÓN  f |
| 2461 | EMBRAGUE (ACOPLAMIENTO) DE DIENTES  m |
| 2461 | ACOPLAMIENTO DE UÑAS (DE GARRAS)  m |
| 2461 | ACOPLAMIENTO  m  DE GARRAS |
| 2462 | MARTILLO  m  CON CODILLO PARTIDO, MARTILLO  m  DE OREJAS |
| 2462 | MARTILLO  m  DE DIENTE |
| 2463 | CODILLO  m  HENDIDO (MARTILLO) |
| 2463 | CODILLO  m  HENDIDO O DE OREJAS |
| 2464 | GRAPA  f, GARFIO  m |
| 2464 | DIENTE  m |
| 2465 | ARCILLA  f |
| 2466 | TERRENO  m  ARCILLOSO |
| 2467 | OCRE  m  AMARILLO |
| 2467 | LIMONITA  f  ARCILLOSA |
| 2468 | REBORDE  m  DE TIERRA ARCILLOSA (O DE TIERRA GRASA) |
| 2468 | ANILLO  m  DE ARCILLA |
| 2469 | DESBARBAR (O DESCORTEZAR) LAS PIEZAS COLADAS (O VACIADAS) |
| 2469 | DESBARBAR |
| 2469 | DESARENAR |
| 2470 | SUPERFICIE  f  METÁLICA DECAPADA |
| 2471 | PRODUCTO  m  DE LIMPIEZA |
| 2472 | LIMPIADOR  m  ALCALINO |
| 2473 | DISOLVENTE  m |

| | |
|---|---|
| 2474 | DESENGRASE  m, LIMPIEZA  f |
| 2474 | LIMPIEZA  f  DEL METAL |
| 2475 | PRODUCTOS  m pl  DE LIMPIEZA Y PULIMENTO |
| 2476 | BAÑO  m  DE DECAPADO INICIAL |
| 2477 | ACEITE  m  PARA LA LIMPIEZA |
| 2478 | DESARENADO  m |
| 2478 | DESBARBADURA  f |
| 2478 | DESBARBADO  m  (O DESCORTEZAMIENTO  m ) DE LAS PIEZAS COLADAS (O VACIADAS) |
| 2479 | IMAGEN  f  NETA, IMAGEN  f  CLARA |
| 2480 | ACEITE  m  MINERAL RUBIO |
| 2481 | VACÍO  m  LIBRE |
| 2482 | ESPACIO  m  NEUTRO |
| 2482 | ESPACIO  m  MUERTO |
| 2482 | ESPACIO  m  NOCIVO |
| 2483 | TOLERANCIA  f |
| 2483 | JUEGO  m  ENTRE EL MACHO Y EL MOLDE |
| 2483 | JUEGO  m, TOLERANCIA  f  DIMENSIONAL |
| 2484 | ÁNGULO DE REAFILADO  m, PENDIENTE MÁXIMA  f |
| 2485 | CORNAMUSA  f |
| 2486 | ROCA  f  HENDIBLE EN CAPAS |
| 2487 | LABRADO POR CAPAS  m, EXFOLIACIÓN  f |
| 2488 | PLAN  m  DE LABRADO POR ESTRATIFICACIÓN |
| 2489 | RECALCAR LOS REMACHES |
| 2489 | REMACHAR LA ESPIGA DEL ROBLÓN |
| 2490 | RECALCAMIENTO  m  DE LOS REMACHES |
| 2491 | ABRAZADERA  f, HORQUILLA  f |
| 2492 | CLAVIJA  f  CON CABEZA |
| 2493 | GATILLO  m  DEL TRINQUETE |
| 2494 | MECANISMO  m  DE DOBLE TRINQUETE |
| 2495 | RUEDA  f  DE TRINQUETE |
| 2496 | TRINQUETE  m |
| 2497 | FRESADO  m  ASPIRANDO |
| 2498 | COMPORTAMIENTO  m  EN CARRETERA EN CUESTA |
| 2499 | SUBIDA  f  DE LA CORREA |
| 2500 | ESCORIA  f |
| 2500 | FONDO  m  DE ESCORIA, CAGAFIERRO  m |
| 2501 | PROYECCIÓN  f  OBLICUA |
| 2502 | GRAPA  f |
| 2503 | POLEA  f  DE GARRAS |
| 2504 | DESBARBADURA  f |
| 2505 | LATÓN  m  DE RELOJERÍA |
| 2506 | EN EL SENTIDO DE LAS AGUJAS DE UN RELOJ |
| 2507 | ROTACIÓN  f  A LA DERECHA |
| 2508 | ENROLLADO  m  A LA DERECHA |
| 2508 | ENROLLADO A LA DERECHA |
| 2509 | MECANISMO  m  DE RELOJERÍA |
| 2510 | ENSUCIAMIENTO  m, ATASCAMIENTO  m |
| 2510 | COLMATADO  m, ENTARQUINAMIENTO  m |

| | |
|---|---|
| 2511 | HIERRO *m* DE GRANO FINO, HIERRO *m* DE FIBRA FINA |
| 2511 | HIERRO *m* DE GRANO FINO, HIERRO *m* DE FIBRA FINA |
| 2512 | TUBOS *m pl* EN CONTACTO |
| 2513 | CABLE CERRADO *m* |
| 2514 | ESTRUCTURA *f* COMPACTA (DE) |
| 2515 | CERRAR EL CIRCUITO ELÉCTRICO |
| 2516 | EJECUTAR UNA CABEZA DE REMACHE |
| 2516 | FORMAR LA CABEZA *f* DEL REMACHE *m* |
| 2516 | REMACHAR, ROBLONAR |
| 2517 | ESPUMA *f* CON CÉLULAS CERRADAS |
| 2518 | HIDROCARBUROS *m pl* DE SERIE AROMÁTICA |
| 2519 | UNIÓN *f* EN ÁNGULO |
| 2520 | CURVA CERRADA *f* |
| 2521 | ESTAMPAS *f pl* CERRADAS |
| 2522 | SOLDADURA *f* EN K SIN SEPARACIÓN |
| 2523 | SOLDADURA *f* DOBLE J CERRADA |
| 2524 | SOLDADURA *f* DE BORDE EN DOBLE U CERRADA |
| 2525 | SOLDADURA *f* DE BORDE EN DOBLE V SIN SEPARACIÓN |
| 2526 | RANURA CERRADA *f* |
| 2526 | RANURA ENCAJADA *f* |
| 2527 | RANURAS CERRADAS *f pl* |
| 2528 | SOLDADURA *f* EN MEDIA V SIN SEPARACIÓN |
| 2529 | SOLDADURA *f* EN J SIN SEPARACIÓN |
| 2530 | SOLDADURA *f* DE BORDE EN U CERRADA |
| 2531 | SOLDADURA *f* DE BORDE EN V SIN SEPARACIÓN |
| 2532 | SOLDADURA *f* EN I SIN SEPARACIÓN |
| 2533 | SISTEMA *m* DE CIRCUITO DE RETORNO |
| 2534 | MANÓMETRO *m* DE AIRE COMPRIMIDO |
| 2535 | PISTÓN *m* DE CIERRE DE MOLDE |
| 2536 | LÍNEA *f* DE CIERRE |
| 2537 | CIERRE *m* DE LA VÁLVULA |
| 2538 | MECHÓN *m* EN EL ORILLO DEL PAÑO |
| 2539 | RODILLOS *m pl* DE PULIMENTO DRAPEADOS |
| 2540 | TRATAMIENTO *m* CON CHORRO DE ARENA |
| 2541 | DISTURBIO *m* |
| 2541 | ENTURBIAMIENTO *m* |
| 2542 | MASA DE GUINIER PRESTON *f* |
| 2543 | LAMINADOR *m* DE SEIS CILINDROS |
| 2544 | ACOPLAMIENTO *m*, EMBRAGUE *m* |
| 2545 | GUARNICIÓN *f* DEL EMBRAGUE |
| 2546 | CARTER DE EMBRAGUE *m* |
| 2547 | PEDAL *m* DE EMBRAGUE |
| 2548 | DESEMBRAGUE *m*, DESACOPLAMIENTO *m* |
| 2549 | COJINETE *m* DE DESEMBRAGUE |
| 2550 | LAVAR (LOS MINERALES) |
| 2551 | LLAVE INGLESA *f* |
| 2552 | TORNILLO *m* PARA MADERA DE CABEZA CUADRADA |
| 2553 | PERNO *m* DE CARRETERÍA |
| 2553 | PERNO *m* DE CARROCERÍA, TORNILLO *m* DE FIJACIÓN |
| 2554 | CLAVOS DE CARROCERÍA *f* |
| 2555 | COAGULARSE |
| 2556 | COAGULACIÓN *f* |
| 2557 | COÁGULO *m* |
| 2558 | CARBÓN *m* |
| 2558 | CARBÓN FÓSIL *m* |
| 2558 | CARBÓN HULLA *m* |
| 2558 | HULLA *f* CARBÓN *m* DE PIEDRA |
| 2559 | TRITURADOR DE CARBÓN *m* |
| 2560 | AGLOMERADO DE HULLA *m* |
| 2561 | CARBONERA *f* |
| 2562 | REGIÓN *f* HULLERA |
| 2563 | POLVO *m* DE HULLA |
| 2564 | CALEFACCIÓN POR CARBÓN *f* |
| 2565 | HOGAR *m* DE CARBÓN |
| 2565 | HOGAR *m* DE HULLA |
| 2566 | HULLERA, MINA DE HULLA, CUENCA *f* HULLERA |
| 2566 | CARBONEO *m*, EXTRACCIÓN DE CARBÓN *f* |
| 2566 | MINA *f* DE HULLA |
| 2567 | MATERIA *f* COLORANTE DERIVADA DEL ALQUITRÁN DE HULLA |
| 2568 | ACEITE *m* DE ALQUITRÁN DE LA HULLA |
| 2569 | BREA *f* DE ALQUITRÁN DE HULLA |
| 2570 | ALQUITRÁN *m* DE GAS |
| 2570 | ALQUITRÁN *m* DE HULLA |
| 2570 | ALQUITRÁN *m* DE GAS |
| 2571 | COBRE *m* ELECTROLÍTICO COALESCIDO |
| 2572 | COALESCENCIA *f*, FUSIÓN *f* |
| 2573 | GRANO *m* GRUESO |
| 2574 | ARENA *f* DE GRANO GRUESO |
| 2575 | ROSCA *f* BASTA |
| 2576 | FILETEADO *m* GRUESO |
| 2577 | ACERO DE GRANO GRUESO *m* |
| 2578 | MALLAS ANCHAS (DE) *f pl* |
| 2579 | CABLE METÁLICO DE HILOS GRUESOS *m* |
| 2580 | POLVO *m* GRUESO |
| 2580 | POLVO *m* MOLIDO GROSERAMENTE |
| 2581 | CAPA DE LACA *f* |
| 2582 | MANO DE PINTURA AL ÓLEO *f* |
| 2583 | CAPA *f* DE PINTURA, MANO *f* DE PINTURA |
| 2583 | PINTURA *f* |
| 2584 | ELECTRODO *m* REVESTIDO |
| 2585 | PARTÍCULAS *f pl* RECUBIERTAS |
| 2586 | CHAPAS *f pl* RECUBIERTAS |
| 2587 | REVESTIMIENTO *m* |
| 2587 | REVESTIMIENTO *m* |
| 2588 | REVESTIMIENTO *m* ANÓDICO |
| 2589 | PRODUCTO *m* DE REVESTIMIENTO |
| 2590 | REVESTIMIENTO *m* |

| | |
|---|---|
| 2590 | RECUBRIMIENTO  *m* |
| 2590 | CAPAS  *f* |
| 2591 | CAPA DE CROMATO  *f* |
| 2592 | REVESTIMIENTOS  *m pl* POR TEMPLE |
| 2593 | REVESTIMIENTOS  *m pl* ELECTROLÍTICOS O GALVANOPLÁSTICOS |
| 2594 | REVESTIMIENTOS  *m pl* ESMALTADOS |
| 2595 | REVESTIMIENTO  *m* POR PINTURA |
| 2596 | REVESTIMIENTO  *m* METÁLICO |
| 2597 | REVESTIMIENTO  *m* NO METÁLICO |
| 2598 | REVESTIMIENTO  *m* DE ÓXIDO |
| 2599 | PINTURAS  *f pl* |
| 2600 | FOSFATACIÓN  *f* |
| 2601 | REVESTIMIENTO  *m* ANTIOXIDANTE |
| 2602 | REVESTIMIENTO  *m* DE ESTAÑO |
| 2603 | REVESTIMIENTO  *m* VÍTREO |
| 2604 | GALVANIZACIÓN  *f* CON CINC |
| 2605 | COAXIAL  *m* |
| 2606 | ALMENDRILLA  *f* (MIN.) |
| 2606 | GRUESOS  *m pl* DE CARBÓN |
| 2607 | COBALTO  *m* |
| 2608 | COBALTO-CARBONILO  *m* |
| 2609 | CLORURO DE COBALTO  *m* |
| 2610 | NITRATO  *m* DE COBALTO |
| 2611 | SESQUIÓXIDO  *m* DE COBALTO |
| 2612 | ACERO AL COBALTO  *m* |
| 2613 | ACERO AL COBALTO-CROMO  *m* |
| 2614 | COBALTINA  *f* |
| 2615 | SULFATO  *m* DE COBALTO |
| 2616 | TELARAÑA  *f* |
| 2617 | VÁLVULA  *f* |
| 2617 | VÁLVULA  *f* |
| 2617 | VÁLVULA COMPUERTA  *f* |
| 2617 | GRIFO  *m*, LLAVE  *f* |
| 2618 | LLAVE DE MANDO (PARA GRIFO DE CORREDERA) |
| 2619 | ONDULACIONES  *f pl* |
| 2620 | MANTECA  *f* DE COCO |
| 2620 | ACEITE  *m* DE COCO |
| 2621 | COEFICIENTE  *m*, FACTOR  *m* |
| 2622 | COEFICIENTE DE CONDUCTIBILIDAD CALÓRICA  *m* |
| 2623 | COEFICIENTE DE CONTRACCIÓN  *m* |
| 2624 | COEFICIENTE DE CORROSIÓN  *m* |
| 2625 | COEFICIENTE DE DILATACIÓN CÚBICA  *m* |
| 2626 | COEFICIENTE DE VERTIDO  *m* |
| 2627 | COEFICIENTE DE RESISTIVIDAD ELÉCTRICA  *m* |
| 2628 | COEFICIENTE DE DILATACIÓN  *m* |
| 2629 | COEFICIENTE DE ROZAMIENTO  *m* |
| 2630 | COEFICIENTE DE DILATACIÓN LINEAL  *m* |
| 2631 | COEFICIENTE DE PROPORCIONALIDAD  *m* |
| 2632 | COEFICIENTE DE RESISTENCIA  *m* |
| 2633 | COEFICIENTE DE RODAMIENTO  *m* |

| | |
|---|---|
| 2634 | COEFICIENTE DE DESLIZAMIENTO  *m* |
| 2635 | COEFICIENTE DE DILATACIÓN SUPERFICIAL  *m* |
| 2636 | COEFICIENTE DE DILATACIÓN  *m* |
| 2637 | COEFICIENTE DE EFECTO TERMOELÉCTRICO, PAR TERMOELÉCTRICO  *m* |
| 2638 | COEFICIENTE DE VELOCIDAD  *m* |
| 2639 | FUERZA  *f* COERCITIVA |
| 2640 | COERCITIVO  *m* |
| 2641 | FUERZA  *f* COERCITIVA |
| 2642 | LAMINADO  *m* DE LINGOTES |
| 2643 | COHERENCIA  *f* |
| 2644 | COHESIÓN  *f* |
| 2644 | FUERZA  *f* DE COHESIÓN |
| 2645 | RODILLO  *m* |
| 2645 | SERPENTÍN  *m* |
| 2645 | BOBINA  *f*, SERPENTÍN  *m*, RODILLO  *m* |
| 2646 | VUELTA  *f* DE ESPIRA |
| 2646 | ESPIRA  *f* |
| 2647 | RESORTE  *m* HELICOIDAL |
| 2648 | BOBINA  *f*, DEVANADO  *m* |
| 2649 | RESORTE  *m* DE FLEXIÓN ENROLLADO |
| 2650 | ENROLLADO  *m*, BOBINADO  *m* |
| 2651 | MATRIZADO  *m* EN PRENSA |
| 2651 | ESTAMPADO  *m* |
| 2651 | ACUÑACIÓN  *f* DE MONEDA |
| 2651 | CALIBRADO  *m*, TROQUELADO  *m*, ESTAMPACIÓN  *f* |
| 2652 | MATRIZ  *f* PARA ESTAMPADO |
| 2653 | PRENSA  *f* MONETARIA |
| 2654 | FIBRA  *f* DE COCO |
| 2654 | BORRA  *f* DE COCO, ESTOPA  *f* DE COCO |
| 2655 | COQUE  *m* |
| 2656 | DESULFURAR, COQUIFICAR |
| 2656 | TRANSFORMAR EN COQUE |
| 2657 | FUNDICIÓN  *f* CON COQUE (DE ALTO HORNO) |
| 2658 | ROMPEDOR DE CARBÓN  *m* |
| 2658 | TRITURADOR DE COQUE  *m* |
| 2659 | POLVO  *m* DE COQUE |
| 2659 | ESCARBILLA  *f* |
| 2659 | ESCARBILLOS  *m pl* (O GAUDINGA  *f*) DE COQUE |
| 2660 | FILTRO  *m* DE COQUE |
| 2661 | HORNO  *m* DE COQUE |
| 2662 | COQUE METALÚRGICO  *m* |
| 2662 | COQUE DE HORNO  *m* |
| 2663 | GAS  *m* DE HORNO DE COQUE |
| 2664 | FUNDICIÓN  *f* CON COQUE MADERA |
| 2665 | FÁBRICA  *f* DE CARBONIZACIÓN DE HULLA |
| 2666 | TRANSFORMACIÓN  *f* EN COQUE |
| 2666 | DESULFURACIÓN  *f* |
| 2666 | DESULFURACIÓN  *f* |
| 2667 | PRUEBA  *f* DE COMBADURA EN FRÍO |

| | |
|---|---|
| 2667 | PRUEBA *f* DE PLEGADO EN FRÍO |
| 2668 | PLEGADO *m* EN FRÍO, DOBLADO *m* EN FRÍO |
| 2668 | CURVADO EN FRÍO *m* |
| 2669 | FUNDICIÓN *f* AL AIRE FRÍO |
| 2670 | MÁQUINA *f* DE CÁMARA FRÍA |
| 2671 | FUNDICIÓN *f* EN CÁMARA FRÍA |
| 2672 | FORMÓN PARA FRÍO *m* |
| 2673 | ESTAMPADO *m* EN FRÍO |
| 2674 | GRIETA *f* (ROTURA *f*) EN FRÍO |
| 2675 | ESTIRADO EN FRÍO |
| 2676 | ESTIRADO *m* EN FRÍO |
| 2677 | ESTIRADO EN FRÍO |
| 2678 | TUBOS *m pl* ESTIRADOS EN FRÍO |
| 2679 | ACABADO *m* EN FRÍO |
| 2680 | DEFORMACIÓN *f* EN FRÍO |
| 2681 | FORJADO *m* EN FRÍO |
| 2682 | PERFIL *f* EN FRÍO |
| 2683 | GALVANIZACIÓN *f* EN FRÍO |
| 2684 | MARTILLAR |
| 2684 | AMARTILLAR EN FRÍO |
| 2685 | AMARTILLADO *m* EN FRÍO |
| 2685 | MARTILLADO *m* EN FRÍO |
| 2686 | HECHURA *f* DE LAS CABEZAS EN FRÍO |
| 2686 | BATIDO *m* EN FRÍO |
| 2687 | EXAMEN (INSPECCIÓN *f*) EN FRÍO |
| 2688 | SIERRA *f* EN FRÍO |
| 2689 | PENETRACIÓN *f* EN FRÍO |
| 2690 | PRENSADO *m* EN FRÍO |
| 2691 | ENDEREZAMIENTO *m* EN FRÍO |
| 2692 | REMACHAR, ROBLONAR EN FRÍO |
| 2693 | REMACHE *m* EN FRÍO |
| 2694 | LAMINAR EN FRÍO |
| 2695 | BARRAS *f pl* LAMINADAS EN FRÍO |
| 2696 | CHAPA *f* LAMINADA EN FRÍO |
| 2697 | ACERO TEMPLADO EN FRÍO *m* |
| 2698 | LAMINADO *m* EN FRÍO |
| 2699 | ASERRADO *m* EN FRÍO |
| 2700 | AISLACIÓN *f* DEL FRÍO |
| 2701 | CORTADURA *f* EN FRÍO |
| 2702 | HIERRO *m* QUEBRADIZO EN FRÍO |
| 2702 | HIERRO *m* AGRIO (O FRÁGIL) |
| 2703 | FRAGILIDAD *f* EN FRÍO |
| 2704 | FRAGILIDAD DEL HIERRO *f* |
| 2705 | UNIÓN *f* FRÍA, COSTURA *f* FRÍA |
| 2706 | GOTA *f* FRÍA |
| 2707 | DECAPADO *m* EN FRÍO |
| 2708 | TREN *m* LAMINADOR EN FRÍO |
| 2709 | PRUEBA *f* EN FRÍO |
| 2710 | TRATAMIENTO *m* DE LOS METALES EN FRÍO |
| 2711 | DESBARBADURA *f* EN FRÍO |
| 2712 | SOLDADURA *f* EN FRÍO |

| | |
|---|---|
| 2712 | SOLDADURA *f* EN FRÍO |
| 2713 | TRABAJO *m* EN FRÍO, MARTILLADO *m* EN FRÍO |
| 2713 | TRABAJO *m* EN FRÍO |
| 2713 | MECANIZACIÓN *f* EN FRÍO |
| 2714 | TUBO *m* ESTIRADO EN FRÍO |
| 2715 | ALAMBRE ESTIRADO EN FRÍO |
| 2716 | LAMINADO EN FRÍO |
| 2717 | FORMÓN PARA FRÍO *m* |
| 2718 | CAPACIDAD DE DESATASCAMIENTO *f* |
| 2719 | CAPOTA PLEGABLE *f* |
| 2720 | BRIDA *f* |
| 2720 | COLLAR *m* |
| 2721 | CALIBRE *m* ROSCADO HEMBRA |
| 2721 | ANILLO *m* DE CALIBRE |
| 2721 | COLLARÍN *m* DE CALIBRE, ANILLO *m* DE CALIBRE |
| 2721 | VENTANILLA *f* DE INSPECCIÓN, LUNETA *f* VERIFICADORA |
| 2722 | TEJUELO *m* ANULAR |
| 2723 | BRIDA *f* DEL COJINETE DE EMPUJE |
| 2724 | ARANDELA *f* DE UN ÁRBOL |
| 2724 | COLLAR *m* DE BASE |
| 2725 | TUBO *m* COLECTOR |
| 2726 | PLACAS *f pl* COLECTIVAS |
| 2727 | MANDRIL *m*, CABEZAL *m* |
| 2728 | CASQUILLO *m* (MANGUITO *m*) DE APRETADURA, DE FIJACIÓN |
| 2729 | MANDRIL *m* Y GARRAS PORTAFRESA |
| 2730 | COLIMAR |
| 2731 | COLIMACIÓN *f* |
| 2732 | COLIMADOR *m* |
| 2733 | COLODIÓN |
| 2734 | COLÓIDE *m* |
| 2735 | COLOIDAL |
| 2736 | PARTÍCULAS *f pl* COLOIDALES |
| 2737 | BREA *f* DE COLOFONIA |
| 2737 | COLOFONIA *f* |
| 2737 | PEZ *f* SECA |
| 2738 | METALOGRAFÍA *f* EN COLORES |
| 2739 | ESPECTROSCOPIA *f* CALORIMÉTRICA |
| 2740 | COLORACIÓN *f* |
| 2741 | COLOR (FÍSICA) |
| 2742 | LAVAR UN DIBUJO |
| 2743 | PINCEL *m* |
| 2744 | TEMPERATURA *f* DE FORJA |
| 2744 | CALOR DE FORJA *m* |
| 2745 | LÁPIZ *m* DE COLOR |
| 2745 | PASTEL *m* (PINTURA AL) |
| 2746 | CRISTAL *m* INCOLORO |
| 2747 | NIOBIO *m*, COLUMBIO *m* |
| 2748 | COLUMNA *f* |

| | | | | |
|---|---|---|---|---|
| 2748 | COLUMNA *f* | 2786 | TRITURACIÓN *m* MOLIENDA *f* |
| 2749 | CABEZA *f* DE POSTE | 2786 | PULVERIZACIÓN *f* |
| 2750 | COLUMNA LÍQUIDA *f* | 2787 | ALUMBRE POTÁSICO *m* |
| 2751 | COLUMNA BAROMÉTRICA *f* | 2787 | ALUMBRE ORDINARIO *m* |
| 2751 | COLUMNA DE MERCURIO *f* | 2788 | LOGARITMO *m* VULGAR |
| 2752 | COLUMNA DE AGUA *f* | 2788 | LOGARITMO *m* DECIMAL |
| 2753 | COLUMNA MONTANTE *f* | 2789 | DENOMINADOR *m* COMÚN |
| 2753 | TUBERÍA VERTICAL *f* | 2790 | CLORURO DE SODIO *m* |
| 2754 | ARMAZÓN DE POSTES *f* | 2790 | SAL *f* MARINA |
| 2755 | TALADRADORA *f* EN BASTIDOR O MONTANTE | 2790 | SAL *f* COMÚN |
| 2755 | PERFORADORA *f* DE COLUMNA | 2791 | COMPRIMIDO |
| 2756 | COLUMNA *f* CON LOS DOS EXTREMOS GUIADOS | 2791 | COMBUSTIBLE HECHO CON POLVO DE CARBÓN *m* |
| 2757 | CRISTAL *m* BASÁLTICO | 2792 | COQUE DENSO *m* |
| 2758 | ESTRUCTURA *f* BASÁLTICA | 2793 | COTAS DE EMPALME *f pl*, COTAS DE UNIÓN |
| 2759 | ARMAZÓN DE POSTES *f* | | *f pl* |
| 2760 | CALIBRE *m* DEL FILETEADO | 2794 | COMPARADOR *m* |
| 2761 | COMBINACIÓN *f* | 2795 | COMPARADORES *m pl* |
| 2762 | MOLDE *m* MÚLTIPLE | 2796 | CALCES DE COMPARACIÓN *m* |
| 2763 | BROCA *f* PARA CENTRAR | 2797 | MEDIDA *f* COMPARATIVA |
| 2764 | ALICATES *m* MOTORISTA | 2798 | CAJÓN *m*, CAJA *f* |
| 2765 | TOTALIZAR LOS DIAGRAMAS | 2798 | CASILLA *f* |
| 2765 | ORDENAR DIAGRAMAS SEGÚN EL MÉTODO DE | 2798 | COMPARTIMENTO |
| | RANKINE | 2799 | BRÚJULA *f* |
| 2766 | MÁQUINAS *f pl* SEGADORAS-TRILLADORAS, | 2800 | ROSA *f* DE LOS VIENTOS |
| | COSECHADORAS *f pl* | 2801 | CEPILLO *m* CIMBRADO |
| 2767 | CARBONO COMBINADO AL HIERRO *m* | 2802 | SERRUCHO *m* |
| 2768 | VENTILADOR *m* ASPIRANTE E IMPELENTE | 2803 | COMPÁS DE TIRALÍNEAS *m* |
| 2769 | TOBERA *f* CONVERGENTE | 2804 | COMPÁS PORTA-LAPIZ *m* |
| 2769 | TOBERA *f* | 2805 | COMPÁS DE RECAMBIOS *m* |
| 2769 | TOBERA CONVERGENTE *f* | 2806 | COMPATIBILIDAD *m* |
| 2770 | ORDENACIÓN *f* DE DIAGRAMAS SEGÚN EL MÉTODO | 2807 | COMPENSAR |
| | DE RANKINE | 2808 | COMPENSADOR *m* |
| 2771 | PROPORCIONES *f pl* DEFINIDAS | 2808 | PÉNDULO *m* COMPENSADOR |
| 2772 | COMBUSTIBLE *m* | 2808 | PÉNDULO *m* COMPENSADO |
| 2773 | COMBUSTIBILIDAD *f* | 2809 | COMPENSACIÓN *f* |
| 2774 | COMBUSTIÓN *f* | 2810 | COMPLEMENTO DE UN ÁNGULO *m* |
| 2775 | CARRERA DE COMBUSTIÓN *f* | 2811 | ÁNGULO COMPLEMENTARIO *m* |
| 2775 | CARRERA DE DESCARGA *f*, CARRERA DE | 2812 | COLOR COMPLEMENTARIO *m* |
| | EXPANSIÓN *f* | 2813 | NÚMERO *m* COMPLEJO |
| 2776 | CÁMARA DE COMBUSTIÓN *f* | 2814 | VARIABLE *f* COMPLEJA |
| 2777 | CÁMARA DE COMBUSTIÓN DE UN FUEGO *f* | 2815 | COMPONENTE *m* |
| 2778 | CÁMARA DE EXPLOSIONES DE UN MOTOR *f* | 2816 | FUERZA *f* COMPONENTE |
| 2779 | COMBUSTIÓN COMPLETA *f* | 2817 | COMPONENTE *f* |
| 2780 | ORDEN *f* | 2818 | MATRIZ *f* COMPUESTA |
| 2781 | RENDIMIENTO *m* INDUSTRIAL | 2819 | ELECTRODO *m* COMPUESTO |
| 2781 | RENDIMIENTO COMERCIAL | 2820 | NÚMERO *m* COMPUESTO |
| 2781 | RENDIMIENTO *m* ECONÓMICO | 2821 | DEPÓSITO *m* ELECTROLÍTICO EN VARIAS CAPAS |
| 2782 | RED *f* | 2822 | RESISTENCIA *f* COMPUESTA |
| 2783 | APLICACIÓN *f* INDUSTRIAL DE UNA INVENCIÓN | 2822 | RESISTENCIA *f* COMPLEJA |
| 2784 | VEHÍCULO *m* UTILITARIO | 2823 | COMPOSICIÓN *f* |
| 2785 | CINC *m* COMERCIAL | 2824 | LATÓN *m* ROJO |
| 2785 | CINC *m* BRUTO | | |

| | | | | |
|---|---|---|---|---|
| 2825 | COMPOSICIÓN DE LAS FUERZAS $f$ | | 2864 | TIEMPO $m$ DE COMPRESIÓN |
| 2826 | PLANO $m$ DE ENLACE (MACLA) | | 2865 | PRUEBA $f$ DE COMPRESIÓN |
| 2827 | PASTA $f$ PARA PULIR | | 2866 | MOTOR $m$ DIESEL |
| 2827 | COMPOSICIÓN QUÍMICA $f$ | | 2867 | SEGMENTO $m$ DE ESTANQUEIDAD |
| 2828 | COMPACTO COMPUESTO | | 2868 | FUERZA $f$ DE COMPRESIÓN |
| 2829 | MÁQUINA $f$ COMPOUND O COMPUESTA | | 2869 | TRABAJO $m$ A LA COMPRESIÓN |
| 2830 | MANOVACUÓMETRO $m$ | | 2869 | ESFUERZO $m$ DE COMPRESIÓN |
| 2831 | VIGA $f$ MIXTA O COMPUESTA | | 2870 | RESISTENCIA $f$ A LA COMPRESIÓN |
| 2832 | ACEITE $m$ MIXTO | | 2871 | TENSIÓN $f$ DE COMPRESIÓN |
| 2832 | ACEITE $m$ MINERAL COMPUESTO, ACEITE $m$ COMPOUND | | 2872 | PRUEBA $f$ A LA COMPRESIÓN |
| | | | 2873 | LÍMITE $m$ DE APLASTAMIENTO |
| 2833 | TORNILLO $m$ DIFERENCIAL | | 2874 | COMPRESOR $m$ |
| 2834 | RESORTE $m$ DE HOJAS SUPERPUESTAS | | 2875 | MANDO DIRECTO POR COMPUTADORA $m$ |
| 2834 | RESORTE $m$ DE VARIAS HOJAS | | 2876 | CONSUMO $m$ DE ENERGÍA DE FUERZA MOTRIZ |
| 2835 | MOTOR $m$ COMPOUND | | 2876 | CONSUMO DE ENERGÍA $m$ |
| 2836 | COMPRESOR COMPOUND $m$ | | 2877 | CÓNCAVO |
| 2836 | COMPRESOR ETAPA $m$ | | 2878 | SOLDADURA $f$ EN CAVETO |
| 2837 | COMPRIMIR | | 2878 | SOLDADURA $f$ DE ÁNGULO CÓNCAVA |
| 2838 | TENSAR UN MUELLE, COMPRIMIR UN MUELLE | | 2879 | ESPEJO $m$ CÓNCAVO |
| 2839 | AIRE COMPRIMIDO $m$ | | 2880 | CONCAVIDAD $f$ |
| 2840 | FRENO $m$ DE AIRE COMPRIMIDO | | 2881 | CONCENTRADO $m$ |
| 2841 | CILINDRO $m$ DE AIRE | | 2882 | CONCENTRAR, CONDENSAR |
| 2842 | MANDO NEUMÁTICO $m$ | | 2883 | SOLUCIÓN $f$ FUERTE |
| 2843 | AEROMOTOR, MOTOR ACCIONADO POR AIRE $m$ | | 2883 | SOLUCIÓN $f$ CONCENTRADA |
| 2843 | MOTOR $m$ DE AIRE COMPRIMIDO | | 2884 | ÁCIDO SULFÚRICO CONCENTRADO $m$ |
| 2844 | LOCOMOTORA $f$ POR AIRE COMPRIMIDO | | 2885 | CONCENTRACIÓN DE UNA SOLUCIÓN POR EVAPORACIÓN $f$, CONDENSACIÓN DE UNA SOLUCIÓN $f$ |
| 2845 | DISTRIBUCIÓN $f$ DE AIRE COMPRIMIDO | | | |
| 2845 | TUBERÍA $f$ | | 2886 | CONCENTRACIÓN $f$ |
| 2845 | TUBERÍAS $f$ $pl$ | | 2887 | PILA $f$ A DOS LÍQUIDOS |
| 2846 | PRUEBA $f$ CON AIRE COMPRIMIDO | | 2888 | CORROSIÓN DE LA PILA DE CONCENTRACIÓN $f$ |
| 2847 | GAS $m$ COMPRIMIDO | | 2889 | POLARIZACIÓN $f$ (DE UN ELECTRODO) POR CAÍDA DE CONCENTRACIÓN |
| 2848 | SOPLETE DE OXÍGENO COMPRIMIDO $m$ | | | |
| 2849 | ACERO COMPRIMIDO $m$ | | 2890 | CÍRCULOS CONCÉNTRICOS $m$ |
| 2850 | ÁRBOL DE ACERO COMPRIMIDO $m$ | | 2891 | CONCENTRICIDAD $f$ |
| 2851 | COMPRESIBILIDAD $f$ | | 2892 | CONCOIDE $m$ |
| 2852 | COMPRESIBILIDAD $f$ | | 2893 | FRACTURA CONCHOIDAL $f$ |
| 2853 | COMPRESIBLE | | 2894 | HORMIGÓN $m$ |
| 2854 | COMPRESIÓN $f$ | | 2895 | HORMIGONAR, VERTER EL HORMIGÓN |
| 2855 | BARRA $f$ CON COMPRESIÓN, BARRA $f$ COMPRIMIDA | | 2896 | MACIZO $f$ DE HORMIGÓN |
| | | | 2896 | CIMIENTOS $m$ $pl$ DE HORMIGÓN |
| 2856 | CÁMARA DE COMBUSTIÓN $f$ | | 2896 | FUNDACIÓN $f$, BASE $f$ |
| 2857 | LÍNEA $f$ DE COMPRESIÓN | | 2897 | CIZALLA PARA ARMADURA DE HORMIGÓN $f$ |
| 2858 | COMPRESIÓN DEL AIRE $f$ | | 2898 | TUBO $m$ DE CEMENTO |
| 2859 | PRESIÓN $f$ DE COMPRESIÓN | | 2899 | PRETENSADO $m$ DEL HORMIGÓN |
| 2860 | RELACIÓN $f$ DE COMPRESIÓN | | 2900 | LOSA $f$ DE HORMIGÓN (SOPORTE DE UN DEPÓSITO) |
| 2860 | RELACIÓN $f$ VOLUMÉTRICA | | | |
| 2860 | RELACIÓN $f$ DE COMPRESIÓN | | 2901 | OBRAS $f$ $pl$ DE HORMIGÓN |
| 2861 | SEGMENTO $m$ DE COMPRESIÓN | | 2902 | HORMIGONADO $m$ |
| 2862 | RESORTE $m$ DE COMPRESIÓN | | 2903 | FUERZAS $f$ $pl$ CONCURRENTES |
| 2863 | ESFUERZO $m$ DE COMPRESIÓN | | 2904 | CALENTAMIENTO ADICIONAL $m$ |
| 2864 | CARRERA DE COMPRESIÓN $f$ | | 2905 | CONDENSADO $m$ |

| | | |
|---|---|---|
| 2906 | CONDENSACIÓN  f | |
| 2907 | CONDENSARSE | |
| 2908 | CONDENSADOR (ELECTRICIDAD)  m | |
| 2908 | CONDENSADOR (QUÍMICA)  m | |
| 2908 | CONDENSADOR (ÓPTICA)  m | |
| 2909 | LENTE AMB. CONVERGENTE | |
| 2910 | LENTE AMB. CONVERGENTE | |
| 2910 | LENTE AMB. DE BORDE FINO, O DE BORDE DELGADO | |
| 2911 | MÁQUINA  f  CON CONDENSACIÓN | |
| 2912 | ELIMINACIÓN  f  DE LA CAPA SUPERFICIAL | |
| 2913 | CONDUCIR (LA ELECTRICIDAD, EL CALOR) | |
| 2914 | MEDIO CONDUCTOR  m | |
| 2915 | SALES  m pl  QUE AUMENTAN LA CONDUCTIBILIDAD DE UNA SOLUCIÓN | |
| 2916 | CONDUCCIÓN  f | |
| 2917 | CONDUCCIÓN DEL CALOR  f | |
| 2918 | CONDUCTOR (DE CALOR, DE CORRIENTE)  m | |
| 2919 | CONDUCTIVIDAD  f | |
| 2919 | CONDUCTIBILIDAD  f | |
| 2920 | CONDUCTIBILIDAD TÉRMICA CALORÍFICA  f | |
| 2921 | CONDUCTOR (ELECTRICIDAD)  m | |
| 2922 | CONDUCTOR DE CORRIENTE  m  CONDUCTOR ELÉCTRICO  m | |
| 2922 | ALAMBRE  m  (CONDUCTOR) ELÉCTRICO | |
| 2922 | HILO  m  CONDUCTOR | |
| 2923 | DARDO DE LA LLAMA | |
| 2924 | CONO (GEOMETRÍA)  m | |
| 2925 | CORREA TRAPEZOIDAL  f | |
| 2926 | FRENO  m  DE CONO | |
| 2927 | ACOPLAMIENTO  m  CON CONO | |
| 2928 | ACOPLAMIENTO POR CONO  m | |
| 2929 | SACADORES  m pl  DE CONOS | |
| 2930 | ACOPLAMIENTO  m  CON CONOS | |
| 2931 | ZUNCHO  m | |
| 2932 | CONO LUMINOSO  m | |
| 2933 | CONFOCAL  m | |
| 2934 | CONGLOMERADO  m | |
| 2935 | ROJO  m  CONGO | |
| 2936 | PAPEL  m  AL ROJO CONGO | |
| 2937 | CONGRUENCIA  f | |
| 2938 | FUSIÓN  f  CONGRUENTE | |
| 2939 | TRANSFORMACIÓN  f  CONGRUENTE | |
| 2940 | CÓNICO  m | |
| 2940 | SECCIÓN  f  CÓNICA | |
| 2941 | CONO DE GUÍA  m, RODILLO CÓNICO  m | |
| 2942 | RESORTE  m  CÓNICO | |
| 2943 | REGULADOR  m  CÓNICO | |
| 2944 | PISTÓN  m  CÓNICO | |
| 2945 | ANILLO  m  CÓNICO | |
| 2946 | ROBLÓN  m  DE CABEZA ACHAFLANADA | |
| 2946 | ROBLÓN  m  DE CABEZA CÓNICA | |
| 2947 | TECHO  m  CÓNICO | |
| 2948 | CONICIDAD  f | |
| 2949 | SUPERFICIE  f  LATERAL DE UN CONO | |
| 2950 | ELEMENTOS  m pl  DE REDUCCIÓN EN FORMA DE CONO TRUNCADO | |
| 2951 | VÁLVULA  f  DE ASIENTO CÓNICO | |
| 2952 | CONJUGADO  m | |
| 2953 | EJE  m  NO TRANSVERSO DE UNA HIPÉRBOLA | |
| 2954 | DIÁMETRO  m  CONJUGADO | |
| 2955 | ENLAZAR, CONECTAR | |
| 2955 | EMPALMAR, ENLAZAR, CONECTAR | |
| 2956 | AGRUPAR EN CANTIDAD | |
| 2956 | MONTAR EN PARALELO | |
| 2957 | MONTAR EN TENSION | |
| 2957 | REUNIR POR EMBUTIDO | |
| 2958 | ENLACE  m  (ELECTRICIDAD) | |
| 2959 | PERNO  m  DE UNIÓN | |
| 2960 | TUBO  m  DE COMUNICACIÓN | |
| 2960 | TUBO  m  DE EMPALME | |
| 2961 | ANILLO  m  DE UNIÓN | |
| 2962 | VÁSTAGO  m  DE ENLACE | |
| 2962 | BARRA  f  DE CONEXIÓN | |
| 2962 | TRIÁNGULO  m  DE ENLACE | |
| 2962 | BIELA  f | |
| 2963 | CABEZA  f  DE BIELA | |
| 2964 | PASARELA  f  DE ENLACE, PASARELA  f  DE COMUNICACIÓN | |
| 2965 | RACOR, EMPALME, ENLACE, MANGUITO  m | |
| 2966 | ENLACE  m  (ELECTRICIDAD) | |
| 2967 | CONSERVACIÓN DE LA ENERGÍA  f | |
| 2968 | CONSISTENCIA  f | |
| 2969 | CONSTANTE  f | |
| 2970 | GENERATRIZ  f  DE CORRIENTE CONTINUA PARA SOLDAR | |
| 2971 | VELOCIDAD  f  DE CORTE CONSTANTE | |
| 2972 | PRUEBA  f  DE FLEXIÓN CONSTANTE | |
| 2973 | FUERZA  f  CONSTANTE | |
| 2974 | PRUEBA  f  DE CARGA CONSTANTE | |
| 2975 | INTENSIDAD  f  DE LA GRAVEDAD | |
| 2976 | PRESIÓN  f  CONSTANTE | |
| 2977 | TEMPERATURA  f  CONSTANTE | |
| 2978 | TENSIÓN  f  CONSTANTE | |
| 2979 | FUENTE  f  DE CORRIENTE A TENSIÓN CONSTANTE (PARA SOLDADURA) | |
| 2980 | CONSTANTAN  m | |
| 2981 | CONSTITUYENTE  m, COMPONENTE  m | |
| 2981 | COMPONENTE  m | |
| 2982 | COMPONENTE DE UNA ALEACIÓN  m | |
| 2982 | CONSTITUYENTE  m, COMPONENTE  m | |
| 2982 | METAL  m  CONSTITUYENTE | |
| 2983 | COMPONENTE (QUÍMICA)  m | |

| | |
|---|---|
| 2984 | DIAGRAMA *m* DE LAS FASES |
| 2985 | MECANISMO *m* DE MANDO MECÁNICO |
| 2985 | MECANISMO *m* DE MANDO POSITIVO |
| 2986 | MONTAJE *m* |
| 2986 | CONSTRUCCIÓN *f* |
| 2987 | BARRACA *f* DE LA OBRA |
| 2988 | METALES *m pl* ORDINARIOS EN LA CONSTRUCCIÓN |
| 2989 | INGENIERO *m* ASESOR |
| 2990 | ELECTRODO *m* CONSUMIBLE |
| 2991 | JUNTA *f* FUSIBLE, EMPALME *m* FUSIBLE |
| 2992 | PESO *m* CONSUMIDO |
| 2993 | CONSUMO DE CORRIENTE *m* |
| 2994 | CONSUMO DE COMBUSTIBLE *m* |
| 2995 | CONSUMO *m*, GASTO *m* |
| 2995 | CONSUMO *m* (O GASTO *m*) DE VAPOR |
| 2996 | CONTACTO (GEN) *m* |
| 2996 | CONTACTO A LA MASA (ELECT) *m* |
| 2997 | ARCO DE CONTACTO *m* |
| 2998 | SUPERFICIE *f* DE CONTACTO |
| 2999 | LLANTA *f* DE CONTACTO |
| 3000 | GRANOS *m pl* DE CONTACTO (RUPTOR) |
| 3001 | ELECTRODO *m* DE CONTACTO |
| 3002 | CORROSIÓN POR CONTACTO *f* |
| 3003 | PLACA *f* DE CONTACTO |
| 3004 | DEPÓSITO *m* POR CONTACTO |
| 3005 | PUNTO *m* DE CONTACTO |
| 3006 | PUNTA *f* DE RECAMBIO |
| 3007 | POTENCIAL *m* DE CONTACTO |
| 3008 | RODILLO *m* DE CONTACTO |
| 3009 | PUNTO *m* DE CONTACTO |
| 3010 | RECIPIENTE *m* |
| 3011 | DOSIFICACIÓN *f*, CONTENIDO *m*, PROPORCIÓN *f* |
| 3011 | PROPORCIÓN *f* |
| 3011 | PROPORCIÓN *f* |
| 3012 | ENGRASE *m* CONTINUO |
| 3013 | PAPEL *m* CONTÍNUO |
| 3014 | CALCINACIÓN *f* CONTINUA |
| 3015 | TRANSMISIÓN *f* SOBRE POLEAS MÚLTIPLES |
| 3016 | SOLDADURA *f* CONTINUA |
| 3017 | CONTINUIDAD *f* |
| 3018 | VIGA *f* CONTINUA |
| 3019 | COLADA CONTINUA *f* |
| 3020 | ASCENSOR *m* CONTINUO |
| 3021 | MÁQUINA *f* PARA CORRIENTE CONTINUA |
| 3021 | GENERATRIZ *f* |
| 3021 | DINAMO *f*, GENERADOR *m* DE CORRIENTE CONTINUA |
| 3022 | MOTOR *m* DE CORRIENTE CONTINUA |
| 3023 | CORRIENTE CONTÍNUA *f* |

| | |
|---|---|
| 3024 | DESTILACIÓN *f* CONTINUA |
| 3025 | FUNCIÓN *f* CONTINUA |
| 3026 | HORNO *m* CONTINUO |
| 3027 | GALVANIZACIÓN *f* EN CONTINUO |
| 3028 | TEMPLE *m* CONTINUO EN CALIENTE |
| 3029 | COLADA CONTINUA *f* |
| 3030 | TREN *m* CONTINUO LAMINADOR |
| 3031 | MOVIMIENTO *m* CONTINUO |
| 3032 | MANDO CONTINUO *m* |
| 3033 | FASE *f* CONTINUA |
| 3033 | FASE *f* DISPERSIVA |
| 3034 | OPERACIONES *f pl* EN CADENA |
| 3034 | TRABAJO *m* EN CADENA |
| 3035 | LAMINADO *m* CONTINUO |
| 3036 | ESPECTRO *m* CONTINUO |
| 3037 | SOLDADURA *f* CONTINUA |
| 3038 | SERVICIO *m* CONTINUO |
| 3038 | FUNCIONAMIENTO *m* CONTINUO |
| 3039 | MANDO DE CONTORNO *m*, SISTEMA DE CONTROL DE CONTORNO *m* |
| 3040 | FRESADO *m* DE CONTORNOS, FRESADO DE PERFILES |
| 3041 | HECHURA *f* DEL MODELO |
| 3042 | ESTRECHADO |
| 3043 | CONTRACCIÓN *f* |
| 3043 | ESTRICCIÓN *f* |
| 3044 | CONTRACCIÓN DE LA VENA FLUIDO *f*, CONTRACCIÓN DEL CHORRO *f* |
| 3044 | CONTRACCIÓN *f* DE UNA VENA LÍQUIDA |
| 3045 | CONTRACCIÓN *f* |
| 3045 | ESTRICCIÓN *f* |
| 3045 | ESTRECHAMIENTO *m* |
| 3046 | CONTRACCIÓN DEL VÁSTAGO DEL REMACHE O ROBLÓN *f* |
| 3047 | REGLA *f* DE CONTRACCIÓN |
| 3048 | MANDO *m*, CONTROL *m* |
| 3048 | CONTROL *m* |
| 3049 | MANIOBRAR, ACCIONAR |
| 3049 | MANDAR, CONTROLAR |
| 3050 | BRAZO *m* DE SUSPENSIÓN |
| 3051 | CABLE DE MANDO *m* |
| 3052 | DISPOSITIVO *m* DE CONTROL |
| 3053 | CALIBRE *m* DE CONTROL |
| 3054 | CUADRO *m* DE MANDO |
| 3055 | HORNO *m* DE ATMÓSFERA CONTROLADA |
| 3056 | ENFRIAMIENTO *m* MANDADO |
| 3057 | ÓRGANO *m* DE MANDO |
| 3058 | ANGULAR DE SOPORTE *m*, CANTONERA *f* |
| 3058 | SOPORTE *m* ANGULAR |
| 3059 | CONVECCIÓN (CALOR IRRADIANTE) *f* |
| 3060 | CONVEXIÓN *f* |
| 3060 | CONVECCIÓN *f* |

| | | | |
|---|---|---|---|
| 3061 | FRESADO *m* CLÁSICO | 3094 | TORNO *m* DE ENFRIAMIENTO |
| 3062 | CONVERGER | 3095 | AGUA *f* DE REGRIGERACIÓN, AGUA DE ENFRIAMIENTO |
| 3063 | CONVERGENCIA *f* | | |
| 3064 | CONVERGENTE *m* | 3096 | VUELTA *f* A LA TEMPERATURA AMBIENTE |
| 3065 | SERIE *f* CONVERGENTE | 3097 | ACOTACIÓN ABSOLUTA *f* |
| 3066 | TOBERA CONVERGENTE *f* | 3098 | TALADRADORA-ESCARIADORA DE COORDENADAS |
| 3066 | TOBERA *f* CONVERGENTE | 3099 | POSICIÓN *f* POR COORDENADAS |
| 3067 | CONVERSIÓN *f* | 3100 | COORDENADAS *f pl* |
| 3067 | TRANSFORMACIÓN *f* | 3101 | COPAHÚ *m* |
| 3068 | TRANSFORMACIÓN *f* DEL HIERRO EN ACERO | 3101 | BÁLSAMO *m* DE COPAIBA |
| 3069 | MESA *f* DE TRANSFORMACIÓN | 3102 | GOMA COPAL *f* |
| 3069 | TABLA *f* DE CONVERSIÓN (DE REDUCCIÓN) | 3102 | GOMA COPAL |
| 3070 | TRANSFORMACIÓN *f* DE ENERGÍA | 3103 | BARNIZ *m* AL COPAL |
| 3071 | CONVERTIDOR *m* | 3104 | PARTE *f* DE ENCIMA |
| 3071 | CONMUTATRIZ *f* | 3105 | MODELO *m* EN DOS PARTES, MODELADO |
| 3072 | CONO *m* DEL CONVERTIDOR | 3106 | ALAMBRE *m* DE COBRE |
| 3073 | COCHE *m* DESCAPOTABLE | 3107 | GRUJIDO *m* |
| 3074 | HORNO *m* DE CEMENTACIÓN | 3108 | SIERRA *f* DE RECORTAR |
| 3075 | CAJA DE CEMENTACIÓN *f* | 3109 | PARACHISPAS *m* |
| 3076 | CONVEXO *m* | 3110 | COBRE *m* (COBRE ROJO) |
| 3077 | SOLDADURA *f* DE ÁNGULO CONVEXA | 3111 | ALEACIÓN DE BASE DE COBRE *f* |
| 3078 | ESPEJO *m* CONVEXO | 3112 | ÁNODO DE COBRE *m* |
| 3079 | RELACIÓN *f* DE CONVEXIDAD | 3113 | BARRA *f* DE COBRE |
| 3080 | TRANSPORTADOR *m* | 3114 | MONEDAS *f pl* DE COBRE, MONEDAS *f pl* DE BRONCE |
| 3080 | TRANSPORTADOR *m* | | |
| 3081 | ENFRIARSE | 3115 | CIANURO *m* DE COBRE |
| 3081 | REFRIGERAR | 3116 | ALAMBRE *m* DE COBRE PLANO |
| 3082 | TIEMPO *m* DE ENFRIAMIENTO | 3116 | ALAMBRE *m* PLANO DE COBRE |
| 3083 | REFRIGERANTE, ENFRIADOR *m* | 3117 | HOJA *f* DELGADA DE COBRE |
| 3083 | FLUIDO *m* DE ENFRIAMIENTO | 3118 | COBRE *m* VÍTREO (VIDRIOSO) |
| 3084 | PISTÓN *m* ENFRIADO | 3118 | COBRE *m* SULFURADO VIDRIOSO |
| 3085 | ENFRIAMIENTO *m* | 3118 | CALCOSINA *f* |
| 3085 | REFRIGERACIÓN | 3119 | MAZO *m* |
| 3086 | AGENTE DE REFRIGERACIÓN, AGENTE REFRIGERANTE *m* | 3119 | MACILLO *m* DE COBRE |
| | | 3120 | LINGOTE *m* DE COBRE |
| 3086 | AGENTE DE ENFRIAMIENTO *m* | 3121 | MATA *f* DE COBRE |
| 3087 | CURVA DE REFRIGERACIÓN *f*, CURVA DE ENFRIAMIENTO *f* | 3122 | MINERAL *m* DE COBRE |
| | | 3123 | PLACA *f* DE COBRE |
| 3088 | VENTILADOR *m* DE ENFRIAMIENTO | 3124 | ENCOBRAR, REVESTIR DE COBRE |
| 3089 | INSTALACIÓN *f* PARA ENFRIAMIENTO DE LAS AGUAS DE CONDENSACIÓN | 3125 | ENCOBRADO *m* |
| | | 3126 | COBRE *m* PIRITOSO, CALCOPIRITA *f* |
| 3089 | ENFRIADOR *m* PARA LAS AGUAS DE CONDENSACIÓN | 3126 | CALCOPIRITA *f* |
| | | 3126 | PIRITA *f* CUPROSA |
| 3090 | DEPÓSITO *m* ENFRIADOR | 3127 | CHAPA *f* DE COBRE |
| 3091 | ESFUERZOS *m pl* DE ENFRIAMIENTO | 3128 | GRANALLA *f* DE COBRE |
| 3092 | SUPERFICIE *f* DE ENFRIAMIENTO | 3129 | LINGOTE *m* PLANO DE COBRE |
| 3092 | SUPERFICIE *f* REFRIGERANTE | 3130 | ACERO AL COBRE *m* |
| 3092 | SUPERFICIE *f* DE REFRIGERACIÓN (DE ENFRIAMIENTO) | 3131 | LÁMINA *f* DE COBRE |
| | | 3131 | BANDA *f* DE COBRE |
| 3093 | CIRCUITO DE REFRIGERACIÓN *f*, SISTEMA DE REFRIGERACIÓN *m* | 3132 | TUBO *m* DE COBRE |
| | | 3133 | ALAMBRE *m* DE COBRE |
| 3093 | ENFRIAMIENTO *m* | | |

| | |
|---|---|
| 3134 | JUNTA *f* METALOPLÁSTICA |
| 3135 | CALDERERO DE COBRE *m* |
| 3136 | CALDERERÍA *f* |
| 3137 | COPPERWELD |
| 3138 | TORNO *m* DE COPIAR |
| 3138 | TORNO *m* DE REPRODUCIR |
| 3139 | MÁQUINA *f* DE REPRODUCIR |
| 3140 | REPISA *f* |
| 3141 | TRANSMISIÓN *f* CORREAS DE IMPULSIÓN |
| 3142 | NÚCLEO *m* MAGNÉTICO |
| 3142 | NÚCLEO *m* |
| 3142 | ALMA *f* |
| 3142 | MUESTRA *f* |
| 3143 | ARMADURA *f* DE HIERRO |
| 3144 | PUNTO *m* DE GUÍA DE LOS NÚCLEOS |
| 3145 | AGLOMERANTE *m* PARA LA FABRICACIÓN DE MACHOS |
| 3146 | MÁQUINA *f* PARA INSUFLAR LOS MACHOS |
| 3147 | CAJA *f* DE ALMAS, CAJA *f* DE MACHOS |
| 3148 | COQUILLA DE SECADO *f* |
| 3149 | ESCARIADOR *m* |
| 3150 | MÁQUINA *f* DE RECTIFICAR LOS MACHOS |
| 3151 | COLA DE NÚCLEOS *f* |
| 3152 | GANCHO DE NÚCLEOS |
| 3153 | MÁQUINA *f* DE VACIAR LA ARENA DEL MACHO, MÁQUINA *f* DE ELIMINAR LA BORRA |
| 3153 | MÁQUINA *f* DE EXTRAER LOS NÚCLEOS |
| 3154 | MÁQUINA *f* MOLDEADORA DE MACHOS |
| 3155 | NÚCLEO *m* DE UNA GUARNICIÓN |
| 3156 | NÚCLEO *m* DE LA SECCIÓN |
| 3157 | ACEITE *m* DE HUESOS DE FRUTAS |
| 3158 | ESTUFA *f* (DE MACHOS) |
| 3159 | JUNTA *f* DE INSERCIÓN |
| 3160 | SEGMENTO *m* DE CHAPA (DE INDUCIDO) |
| 3161 | SUPERFICIE *f* DE APOYO DE UN MODELO |
| 3162 | PUNZÓN *m*, MACHO *m* |
| 3162 | PUNZÓN *m* |
| 3163 | ARENA *f* PARA MACHOS |
| 3164 | NÚCLEO *m* FILTRO |
| 3165 | ESTRUCTURA *f* DEL CORAZÓN |
| 3166 | TIRO *m* DE AIRE DE LOS MACHOS |
| 3167 | ALMA DE UN CABLE *f* |
| 3168 | BARRA *f* DE MACHO FUSIBLE, BARRA *f* DE NOYO FUSIBLE |
| 3169 | CRISTAL *m* INHOMÓGENO |
| 3170 | HETEROGENEIDAD *f* |
| 3171 | LAVADO *m* PARA NÚCLEOS |
| 3172 | MICROSEGREGACIÓN *f* |
| 3172 | SEGREGACIÓN *f* |
| 3173 | CORCHO *m* |
| 3173 | TAPÓN *m* DE CORCHO |

| | |
|---|---|
| 3174 | LADRILLO *m* DE CORCHO |
| 3175 | TABLERO *m* DE CORCHO |
| 3176 | TAPÓN *m* DE CORCHO |
| 3177 | AVENTADORAS *f pl* CERNEDORAS CLASIFICADORAS |
| 3178 | MÁQUINA *f* DE HACER LOS AGUJEROS DE ÁNGULO |
| 3179 | JUNTA *f* EN ÁNGULO EXTERIOR |
| 3179 | JUNTA ANGULAR *f* |
| 3180 | COMPORTAMIENTO *m* EN CARRETERA EN CURVA |
| 3181 | CORRECCIÓN *f* |
| 3182 | CORROER |
| 3182 | ATACAR, CORROER |
| 3183 | CORROSIÓN *f* |
| 3184 | ACEROS CORROSIORRESISTENTES Y TERMORRESISTENTES *m pl* |
| 3185 | CORROSIÓN AGRIETANTE *f* |
| 3186 | FRAGILIDAD *f* POR CORROSIÓN |
| 3187 | FATIGA *f* POR CORROSIÓN |
| 3188 | LÍMITE *m* DE FATIGA POR CORROSIÓN |
| 3189 | PRODUCTO *m* ANTIOXIDANTE |
| 3190 | PICADURA *f* POR CORROSIÓN |
| 3191 | PROTECCIÓN *f* CONTRA LA CORROSIÓN |
| 3192 | DISOLVENTE *m* PARA CORROSIVOS |
| 3193 | VELOCIDAD *f* DE CORROSIÓN |
| 3194 | RESISTENCIA *f* A LA CORROSIÓN |
| 3195 | CORROSIÓN EN TENSIÓN *f* |
| 3196 | CORROSIVO *m*, MORDIENTE *m* |
| 3196 | MORDIENTE *m* |
| 3197 | SUBSTANCIA *f* CORROSIVA |
| 3197 | CORROSIVO *m* |
| 3197 | CORROSIVO *m* |
| 3198 | CHAPA *f* ONDULADA |
| 3199 | TUBO *m* PLEGADO |
| 3200 | REJILLA *f* ONDULADA |
| 3201 | CORINDÓN *m* |
| 3202 | COSECANTE *f* |
| 3203 | COSENO *m* |
| 3204 | GASTOS *m* DE MANUTENCIÓN |
| 3205 | GASTOS *m* DE EMBALAJE |
| 3206 | GASTOS *m* DE FUERZA MOTRIZ |
| 3207 | GASTOS *m* DE FABRICACIÓN |
| 3207 | GASTOS *m* DE PRODUCCIÓN |
| 3208 | GASTOS *m* DE REPARACIONES |
| 3209 | GASTOS *m* DE TRANSPORTES, GASTOS *m* POR PORTES |
| 3210 | PRECIO *m* DE COSTE |
| 3211 | COTANGENTE *f* |
| 3212 | PASADOR *m*, FIADOR *m* |
| 3212 | LLAVE *f* |
| 3212 | LLAVE *f* |
| 3213 | PASADOR DE RETENCIÓN *m* |

| | |
|---|---|
| 3214 | AGUJERO *m* DE PASADOR |
| 3215 | CLAVIJA DE CUÑA *f* |
| 3215 | CLAVIJA TRANSVERSAL *f* |
| 3215 | PASADOR DE UNIÓN *m*, BARRA CÓNICA DE ALINEACIÓN *f* |
| 3216 | SOPLETE DE CORTE *m* |
| 3217 | ALGODÓN *m* |
| 3218 | CORREA DE ALGODÓN *f* |
| 3219 | ALAMBRE *m* REVESTIDO |
| 3220 | TRENZA *f* DE ALGODÓN |
| 3221 | CABLE DE ALGODÓN *m* |
| 3222 | ACEITE *m* DE ALGODÓN |
| 3223 | ALGODÓN PARA LÍMPIAR *m* |
| 3224 | BARRERA *f* DE COTTRELL |
| 3225 | CULOMBIO *m* |
| 3226 | MÓDULO *m* DE RIGIDEZ, MÓDULO DE COULOMB |
| 3227 | VOLTÁMETRO *m* |
| 3228 | DINAMO *f* COMPOUND |
| 3229 | CONTADOR *m* |
| 3230 | CORRIENTE DE SENTIDO CONTRARIO *f* |
| 3230 | CONTRA-CORRIENTE *f* |
| 3231 | FUERZA *f* CONTRA-ELECTROMOTRIZ |
| 3232 | CONTRAPRESIÓN *f* |
| 3233 | ÁRBOL DE LA CONTRAMARCHA *m* |
| 3234 | BISELADO *m*, AVELLANADO *m* |
| 3234 | FRESADO *m* |
| 3235 | CIGÜEÑAL *m* DE CONTRAPESOS |
| 3236 | CONTRAESCARRIADO *m* |
| 3237 | SENTIDO OPUESTO A LAS AGUJAS DE UN RELOJ (EN) |
| 3238 | ROTACIÓN *f* A LA IZQUIERDA |
| 3239 | DE DERECHA A IZQUIERDA |
| 3239 | DE DERECHA A IZQUIERDA |
| 3239 | ENROLLADO A LA IZQUIERDA |
| 3240 | ÁRBOL INTERMEDIO *m*, ÁRBOL DE TRANSMISIÓN INTERMEDIA *m* |
| 3241 | ESCARIADOR *m* |
| 3242 | CONTRAESCARRIADO *m* |
| 3243 | MOVIMIENTO *m* EN SENTIDO CONTRARIO U OPUESTO |
| 3244 | TRANSMISIÓN *f* INTERMEDIA |
| 3244 | TRANSMISIÓN *f* DE MOVIMIENTO |
| 3245 | BROCA *f* DE FRESAR |
| 3245 | BROCA *f* DE AVELLANAR |
| 3245 | FRESA *f* PARA EL ALOJAMIENTO DE LA CABEZA DEL TORNILLO |
| 3246 | FRESAR EL AGUJERO PARA UN TORNILLO |
| 3246 | FRESAR EL AGUJERO PARA UN REMACHE |
| 3246 | RECUBRIR LA CABEZA DEL TORNILLO |
| 3246 | RECUBRIR LA CABEZA DEL REMACHE, EMPOTRADO *m* |
| 3247 | FRESADO *m* DE UN AGUJERO PARA TORNILLO |

| | |
|---|---|
| 3247 | FRESADO *m* DE ALOJAMIENTO DE UN REMACHE |
| 3248 | TORNILLO *m* DE CABEZA OCULTA |
| 3249 | ROBLÓN *m* DE CABEZA AVELLANADA ABOMBADA |
| 3250 | CABEZA *f* AVELLANADA |
| 3250 | CABEZA *f* OCULTA DE UN TORNILLO |
| 3251 | CONTRAPESO *m* |
| 3252 | PAR *m* |
| 3252 | PAR *m* |
| 3253 | ACOPLAR, APAREAR |
| 3254 | ACOPLAMIENTO *m*, ENMANGADO *m*, ENLACO *m* |
| 3254 | ACOPLAMIENTO *m* |
| 3254 | UNIÓN *f*, JUNTURA *f* |
| 3254 | ACOPLAMIENTO *m*, ACOPLE *m* |
| 3254 | RACOR, EMPALME, ENLACE, MANGUITO *m* |
| 3254 | ACOPLAMIENTO *m*, EMBRAGUE *m* |
| 3254 | ACOPLAMIENTO *m* |
| 3254 | ACOPLAMIENTO *m*, ENLACE *m*, EMPALME *m* |
| 3254 | ACOPLAMIENTO *m* |
| 3255 | BRIDA *f* DE ACOPLAMIENTO |
| 3255 | PLATILLO *m* DE ACOPLAMIENTO |
| 3256 | BIELA *f* DE ACOPLAMIENTO |
| 3257 | MANGUITO *m* DE ACOPLAMIENTO |
| 3258 | MANGUITO *m* |
| 3259 | HILADA *f* DE LADRILLOS |
| 3260 | VIROLA *f* DE UNA CALDERA |
| 3261 | COVARIACIÓN *f* |
| 3262 | TAPADERA *f* |
| 3263 | REVESTIR UN TUBO |
| 3263 | REVESTIR UN TUBO |
| 3264 | CAPA *f* DE ACABADO, ENLUCIDO *m* DE ACABADO |
| 3264 | VIDRIADO *m* |
| 3265 | COBETOR *m* |
| 3266 | TAPA DE GRIFO *f* |
| 3266 | COBERTURA DE UNA VÁLVULA *f* |
| 3267 | TAPADERA *f* |
| 3267 | PLACA *f* DE RECUBRIMIENTO |
| 3268 | CINTA *f* METÁLICA DE PROTECCIÓN |
| 3269 | TAPA *f* |
| 3270 | LEVA DE RANURA *f* |
| 3271 | ELECTRODO *m* REVESTIDO |
| 3272 | ALAMBRE *m* CUBIERTO |
| 3273 | PODER *m* DE CUBRIMIENTO |
| 3274 | REVESTIMIENTO *m* EXTERIOR |
| 3274 | CAMISA *f*, ENVOLTURA *f* |
| 3274 | REVESTIMIENTO *m*, CUBIERTA *f*, CAPA *f* |
| 3275 | CUERO *m* DE BUEY |
| 3275 | CUERO *m* DE VACA |
| 3276 | COBERTIZO *m* |
| 3277 | INSTALACIONES *f* DE ESTABLOS |

| | |
|---|---|
| 3278 | RUPTURA  *f* |
| 3278 | DESGARRADURA  *f* |
| 3278 | GRIETA  *f*, HENDIDURA  *f* |
| 3278 | HENDEDURA  *f* |
| 3278 | GRIETA  *f*, HENDIDURA  *f*, FISURA  *f* |
| 3278 | GRIETA  *f* |
| 3278 | FISURA  *f* |
| 3278 | FISURA  *f*, RANURA  *f* |
| 3278 | CORTE  *m* |
| 3279 | AGRIETARSE |
| 3280 | DETECTOR  *m* DE GRIETAS Y HENDIDURAS |
| 3281 | RAJA  *f* EN LOS BORDES |
| 3282 | FISURA  *f* DEL ACERO TEMPLADO |
| 3282 | RESQUEBRAJADURA  *f* |
| 3282 | GRIETA  *f* |
| 3283 | MICROFISURA  *f* |
| 3283 | GRIETA  *f* |
| 3284 | FISURACIÓN  *f* |
| 3284 | FISURACIÓN  *f* |
| 3284 | CRACKING  *m* |
| 3284 | CRACKING  *m* |
| 3285 | CRACKING  *m* |
| 3285 | DESTILACIÓN  *f* CON CRACKING |
| 3286 | RESQUEBRAJAMIENTO  *m* DE LOS AGUJEROS DE REMACHE |
| 3287 | TORNO  *m* DE CRÁCKING |
| 3288 | SOPORTE  *m* |
| 3288 | CUNA  *f*, SOPORTE  *m* |
| 3289 | OBRERO  *m* PROFESIONAL |
| 3289 | OBRERO  *m* EXPERIMENTADO, DUCHO EN SU TRABAJO |
| 3290 | GRÚA  *f* |
| 3291 | BRAZO  *m* DE GRÚA |
| 3292 | CUCHARA  *f* DE GRÚA DE COLADA |
| 3293 | RAÍL  *m* DE PUENTE GRÚA |
| 3294 | GRÚAS  *f* AGRÍCOLAS |
| 3295 | MANIVELA  *f* |
| 3296 | MANIVELA  *f* DE BRAZOS |
| 3297 | CUBO  *m* DE LA MANIVELA |
| 3298 | CÍRCULO DESCRITO POR LA MANIVELA  *m* |
| 3299 | CABEZA  *f* GRANDE DE BIELA |
| 3300 | EMPUÑADURA  *f* DE MANIVELA |
| 3300 | MANGUITO  *m* DE MANIVELA A BRAZO |
| 3301 | BRAZO  *m* DE MANIVELA |
| 3302 | BOTÓN  *m* DE MANIVELA |
| 3302 | BOTÓN  *m* DE MANIVELA |
| 3303 | COJINETE  *m* DEL CIGÜEÑAL, COJINETE  *m* PRINCIPAL |
| 3303 | COJINETE  *m* DEL ÁRBOL MANIVELA |
| 3303 | COJINETE  *m* DE ÁRBOL DE ASIENTO |
| 3304 | PLATO  *m* DE UN ÁRBOL ACODADO |

| | |
|---|---|
| 3305 | MANIVELA  *f* CON MANGUITO |
| 3306 | CARTER DEL MOTOR  *m* |
| 3307 | RESPIRADERO  *m* |
| 3308 | ACEITE DE PURGA  *m* (CARTER-MOTOR) |
| 3309 | CIGÜEÑAL  *m*, ÁRBOL  *m*, CIGÜEÑAL |
| 3309 | ÁRBOL ACODADO  *m* |
| 3309 | CIGÜEÑAL  *m*, ÁRBOL CIGÜEÑAL  *m*, ÁRBOL ACODADO  *m* |
| 3310 | (MOTOR DE) ARRANQUE  *m*, ARRANCADOR |
| 3311 | MUÑECA  *m* DE CIGÜEÑAL |
| 3311 | ESPIGA  *m* DE CIGÜEÑAL |
| 3312 | ANILLOS DE TORNEAR  *m pl* |
| 3313 | BERBIQUÍ  *m* |
| 3314 | COJINETE  *m* DEL CIGÜEÑAL |
| 3315 | PIÑÓN  *m* DE CIGÜEÑAL |
| 3316 | TORNO  *m* DE ÁRBOL ACODADO |
| 3317 | CRÁTER  *m* |
| 3318 | FISURA  *f* CAPILAR |
| 3318 | MICROGRIETA  *f* |
| 3319 | AGRIETADO  *m* SUPERFICIAL |
| 3320 | PLIEGUE  *m* |
| 3321 | MARTILLO  *m* DE BORDEAR |
| 3322 | REBORDE  *m* |
| 3323 | MÁQUINA  *f* DE RIBETEAR |
| 3324 | DEFORMACIÓN  *f* (METALES), FLUENCIA  *f* |
| 3325 | LÍMITE  *m* (CONVENCIONAL) DE FLUENCIA |
| 3326 | VELOCIDAD  *f* DE DEFORMACIÓN |
| 3327 | RESISTENCIA  *f* A LA DEFORMACIÓN EN UN PERIODE DETERMINADO |
| 3328 | RESISTENCIA  *f* A LA DEFORMACIÓN |
| 3329 | CONTRACCIÓN DE LA CORREA  *f* |
| 3330 | FLUENCIA  *f* DE UNA SOLUCIÓN |
| 3331 | CREOSOTA  *f* |
| 3332 | CREOSOTAJE  *m* |
| 3333 | VÉRTICE  *m* DE LA ROSCA |
| 3334 | CRESTA  *f* DE LA OLA |
| 3335 | JUEGO  *m* EN EL VÉRTICE |
| 3336 | PLISAR |
| 3336 | ONDULAR |
| 3337 | DEFORMACIÓN  *f* PERMANENTE |
| 3338 | CARGA DE RUPTURA AL PANDEO  *f* |
| 3339 | ESFUERZO  *m* DE FLEXIÓN POR COMPRESIÓN AXIAL, ESFUERZO  *m* DE PANDEO |
| 3339 | ESFUERZO DE FLEXIÓN POR COMPRESIÓN AXIAL, ESFUERZO  *m* DE PANDEO |
| 3340 | RESISTENCIA  *f* AL PANDEO |
| 3341 | TENSIÓN  *f* DE PANDEO |
| 3342 | ENSAYO  *m* DE PANDEO |
| 3343 | PANDEO  *m*, FLAMBEO  *m* |
| 3343 | PANDEO  *m*, FLAMBEO  *m* |
| 3344 | ENVEJECIMIENTO  *m* CRÍTICO |
| 3345 | ÁNGULO LÍMITE  *m* |

| | |
|---|---|
| 3346 HUMEDAD *f* CRÍTICA | 3387 CORREA INVERTIDA *f* |
| 3347 PUNTO *m* DE TRANSFORMACIÓN | 3388 CRUCETA *f* |
| 3347 PUNTO *m* CRÍTICO | 3388 ACODO *m* |
| 3348 PRESIÓN *f* CRÍTICA | 3389 EXTREMO *m* DE LA BIELA DEL LADO DE LA CRUCETA |
| 3349 ESTADO CRÍTICO | |
| 3350 DEFORMACIÓN *f* CRITICA | 3389 PIE *m* DE BIELA |
| 3351 TENSIÓN *f* CRÍTICA | 3390 COJINETE DE PIE DE BIELA *m* |
| 3352 TEMPERATURA *f* CRÍTICA | 3391 MUÑÓN *m* GIRATORIO PARA HORQUILLA |
| 3353 VELOCIDAD *f* CRÍTICA | 3391 MUÑÓN *m* GIRATORIO DE CRUCETA |
| 3354 VOLUMEN *m* CRÍTICO | 3391 MUÑÓN *m* GIRATORIO DE HORQUILLA |
| 3355 ROJO *m* DE INGLATERRA | 3392 LIMA *f* DE HOJA DE SAUCE |
| 3356 CAÍDA *f* | 3393 PUNTO *m* DE CRUCE |
| 3357 DESMOCHADO *m*, DESPUNTEO *m* | 3394 PALANCA *f* DE PIE DE CABRA |
| 3358 CIZALLA PARA RECORTES *f* | 3394 GRAN PALANCA *f* |
| 3359 CRUZ *f* | 3395 FLECHA *f* DE COTA |
| 3360 ESTRUCTURA DE CRUCETAS *f* | 3396 CONTORNO *m*, PERFIL *m* |
| 3361 TRAVESAÑO *m* | 3396 CÍRCULO DE CORONACIÓN *m* |
| 3362 VEHÍCULO *m* TODO TERRENO | 3396 CONVEXIDAD *f* |
| 3363 CORRIENTES CRUZADAS *f pl* | 3396 DOVELAJE *m* |
| 3364 BEDANO *m*, CINCEL *m* | 3397 CROWN-GLASS *m* |
| 3364 BURIL *m*, CINCEL *m* AGUDO, UÑETA *f*, GRADINA *f* | 3398 BOMBEO *m* DE LA LLANTA DE UNA POLEA |
| | 3399 CORONA DENTADA *f*, RUEDA DENTADA *f* |
| 3365 LLAVE *f* MAESTRA, LLAVÍN *m* | 3399 RUEDA *f* DE DIENTES PERPENDICULARES |
| 3365 TRONZONADOR *m* | 3400 POLEA *f* CONVEXA |
| 3365 SIERRA *f* DE TRONZONAR | 3401 CRISOL *m* (DE ALTO HORNO) |
| 3366 APLICACIÓN *f* DE PICADURAS CRUZADAS | 3402 HORNO *m* DE CRISOL |
| 3367 TRAVESAÑO *m* | 3402 HORNO *m* DE CRISOL |
| 3368 TUBO *m* EN CRUZ DE CUATRO PASOS | 3403 MANERAL *m* |
| 3369 CABRIO *m* TRANSVERSAL | 3404 PROCEDIMIENTO *m* EN CRISOL |
| 3370 PRENSA *f* DE COLADA | 3405 TENAZAS *f* DE CRISOL |
| 3371 SECCIÓN *f* EFICAZ | 3406 BRUTO *m*, SIN MECANIZAR |
| 3372 HIERRO *m* EN CRUZ | 3407 DEPÓSITO *m* DE PETRÓLEO BRUTO |
| 3373 PLANO *m* DE RUPTURA | 3408 BENCINA *f* BRUTA |
| 3373 SECCIÓN *f* DE RUPTURA | 3409 PLOMO *m* PARA CUBIERTAS |
| 3374 SECCIÓN *f* DE PASO | 3410 METAL *m* BRUTO |
| 3374 SECCIÓN *f* LIBRE | 3411 PETRÓLEO *m* BRUTO |
| 3375 SECCIÓN *f* SOMETIDA A UN ESFUERZO | 3412 PETRÓLEO *m* BRUTO |
| 3376 SECCIÓN *f* SOMETIDA A UN ESFUERZO | 3412 ACEITE *m* BRUTO DE PETRÓLEO |
| 3377 PERFIL *m* TRANSVERSAL | 3413 CAUCHO EN BRUTO *m* |
| 3377 SECCIÓN TRANSVERSAL *f* | 3413 CAUCHO *m* VIRGEN |
| 3378 SECCIÓN *f* TRANSVERSAL | 3414 ACERO BRUTO (EN BRUTO) *m* |
| 3379 CARRETILLA UNIVERSAL *f* | 3415 TREMENTINA *f* |
| 3380 DESVIACIÓN *f* DESVÍO *m* | 3416 AUTONOMÍA *f* |
| 3381 HIERRO *m* EN CRUZ | 3417 VELOCIDAD *f* DE CRUCERO |
| 3382 CORDÓN DE APLASTADO *m* | 3418 DESAGREGACIÓN *f* |
| 3383 RETICULO *m* | 3418 DESINTEGRACIÓN *f* DESMORONAMIENTO *m* |
| 3384 LAMINADO *m* TRANSVERSAL | 3419 TRITURADOR *m* |
| 3385 SOLDADURA *f* DE ALAMBRES EN CRUZ | 3419 MÁQUINA *f* DE QUEBRANTAR, MÁQUINA *f* QUEBRANTADORA |
| 3386 REGULADOR *m* FARCOT | |
| 3386 REGULADOR *m* DE BRAZOS CRUZADOS | 3419 MÁQUINA *f* DE APLASTAR O APLANAR |
| 3387 CORREA CRUZADA *f* | 3419 MÁQUINA *f* PARA TRITURAR |

| | |
|---|---|
| 3419 | MOLINO *m*, TRITURADOR *m*, MACHACADORA *f* |
| 3420 | APLASTAMIENTO *m* |
| 3421 | CORTEZA *f* |
| 3422 | CRIOHIDRATO *m* |
| 3423 | CRIOLITA *f* |
| 3424 | CRISTAL *m* |
| 3425 | ANÁLISIS (DETERMINACIÓN) DE LA ESTRUCTURA CRISTALINA *f* |
| 3426 | ALARGAMIENTO DE LOS CRISTALES *m* |
| 3427 | CARA *f* DE UN CRISTAL, CARA *f* CRISTALINA |
| 3427 | PLANO *m* DE CRISTAL |
| 3428 | CRISTAL *m* |
| 3429 | MANCHA *f* POR CRISTALES DE SULFURO DE COBRE |
| 3430 | ESTRUCTURA *f* CRISTALINA |
| 3431 | SISTEMA *m* DE LOS CRISTALES |
| 3432 | CRISTAL *m* OSCILANTE |
| 3433 | CRISTALINO *m* |
| 3434 | CONTEXTURA *f* CRISTALINA |
| 3435 | AZUFRE *m* CRISTALIZADO |
| 3436 | CRISTALIZABILIDAD *f* |
| 3437 | CRISTALIZABLE |
| 3438 | CRISTALIZACIÓN *f* |
| 3439 | CRISTALIZAR |
| 3440 | CRISTALIDAD *f* |
| 3441 | CRISTALOGRAMA *m* |
| 3441 | DIAGRAMA *m* DE DIFRACCIÓN DE RAYOS X |
| 3442 | CRISTALOGRAFÍA *f* |
| 3443 | CRISTALOIDE |
| 3444 | CUBICACIÓN *f* (EVALUACIÓN EN UNIDADES CÚBICAS) |
| 3445 | CUBO *m* |
| 3446 | CUBICAR |
| 3447 | RAÍZ *f* CÚBICA |
| 3448 | CILINDRADA *f* |
| 3449 | CENTÍMETRO CÚBICO *m* |
| 3450 | CRISTAL *m* CÚBICO |
| 3451 | DECÍMETRO *m* CÚBICO |
| 3452 | ECUACIÓN *f* CÚBICA, ECUACIÓN DE TERCER GRADO |
| 3452 | ECUACIÓN *f* DE TERCER GRADO |
| 3453 | PIE *m* CÚBICO (MEDIDA INGLESA) |
| 3454 | PULGADA *f* CÚBICA INGLESA |
| 3455 | METRO *m* CÚBICO |
| 3456 | MILÍMETRO *m* CÚBICO |
| 3457 | VIBROCULTORES *m pl* |
| 3457 | CULTIVADORES *m pl* |
| 3458 | CUERO *m* EMBUTIDO |
| 3459 | GUARNICIÓN *f* CON CUERO EMBUTIDO |
| 3460 | ACEBOLLADURA *f* |
| 3461 | ARANDELA *f* BELLEVILLE |
| 3462 | PROBADOR DE DUCTILIDAD *m* |

| | |
|---|---|
| 3463 | COPELACIÓN *f* |
| 3464 | CUBILOTE *m* |
| 3465 | REGULADOR *m* DE GASTO DE AIRE |
| 3466 | HORNO *m* A LA WILKINSON |
| 3466 | CUBILOTE *m* |
| 3467 | FUNDICIÓN *f* MALEABLE DE CUBILOTE |
| 3468 | METAL *m* DE CUBILOTE |
| 3469 | EMBUTIDO *m* EN CORTE DE ALAMBRES |
| 3469 | EMBUTIDO *m* PROFUNDO |
| 3470 | CARBONATO DE COBRE *m* |
| 3471 | ÓXIDO *m* CÚPRICO HIDRATADO |
| 3472 | NITRATO *m* DE COBRE |
| 3473 | NITRITO *m* DE COBRE |
| 3474 | ÓXIDO *m* CÚPRICO |
| 3475 | SULFATO *m* DE COBRE |
| 3476 | OXÍDULO *m* DE COBRE |
| 3477 | CUPRONÍQUEL *m* |
| 3478 | CLORURO CUPROSO *m* |
| 3479 | ÓXIDO *m* CUPROSO |
| 3480 | PESO *m* EN ORDEN DE MARCHA |
| 3481 | CURCUMINA *f*, AMARILLO *m* DE CÚRCUMA |
| 3482 | JABÓN *m* BLANCO ORDINARIO |
| 3483 | TOMA *f* |
| 3483 | ENDURECIMIENTO *m*, SOLIDIFICACIÓN *f* |
| 3484 | VULCANIZACIÓN *f* |
| 3484 | TOMA *f* (DEL CEMENTO) |
| 3485 | HERRAMIENTA *f* PARA CURVAR CHAPAS |
| 3486 | CORRIENTE *f* |
| 3487 | COORDINADAS CORRIENTES *f pl* |
| 3488 | DENSIDAD *f* DE CORRIENTE |
| 3489 | RENDIMIENTO *m* DE CORRIENTE |
| 3490 | INSTRUMENTO *m* PARA DETERMINAR LA VELOCIDAD DE UNA CORRIENTE |
| 3491 | REGULADOR *m* DE CORRIENTE |
| 3491 | REGULADOR *m* DE INTENSIDAD |
| 3492 | COLGADURAS *f pl*, CORTINAJES *m pl* |
| 3493 | CICLOIDE *f* ACORTADA |
| 3494 | ARCO *m*, CIMBRA *f* |
| 3494 | CURVATURA *f* |
| 3495 | CURVA DE UN DIAGRAMA *f* |
| 3496 | CURVA *f* |
| 3497 | BRAZO *m* PARABÓLICO DE UNA POLEA |
| 3498 | SUPERFICIE *f* CURVA |
| 3499 | CURVILÍNEO |
| 3500 | MOVIMIENTO *m* CURVILÍNEO |
| 3501 | CURVÍMETRO *m* |
| 3502 | PUNTO *m* DE RETORNO |
| 3503 | CORTE *m* |
| 3504 | CORTAR (GEOMETRÍA) |
| 3504 | LABRAR, CORTAR |
| 3505 | CORTAR CON PROCESO AUTÓGENO |

| | |
|---|---|
| 3505 | CORTAR AL SOPLETE |
| 3506 | CIZALLAR, CORTAR |
| 3507 | LABRAR LAS LIMAS |
| 3508 | RUEDA *f* DE DIENTES TALLADOS, ENGRANAJE *m* TALLADO |
| 3508 | RUEDA *f* DE DIENTES TALLADOS |
| 3509 | CORTAR EN LAS DIMENSIONES EXACTAS |
| 3510 | CORTAR |
| 3510 | CORTAR |
| 3510 | TRONZAR |
| 3511 | SACAR LOS REMACHES |
| 3511 | ESTAMPAR LOS ROBLONES |
| 3512 | FILETEAR, ATERRAJAR, CORTAR ROSCA |
| 3513 | CORTAR CHAPAS |
| 3514 | DIENTE *m* TALLADO |
| 3515 | CORTAR CON TAJADERA, TAJAR |
| 3515 | CORTAR |
| 3516 | DISYUNTOR *m* |
| 3517 | CORTE *m* DE SIERRA |
| 3518 | LABRA *f* DE UNA LIMA |
| 3518 | DENTADO *m* DE UNA LIMA |
| 3518 | DIENTES *m pl* DE UNA LIMA |
| 3519 | FRESA *f* |
| 3520 | ÁRBOL PORTACUCHILLA *m*, ÁRBOL PORTA-FRESAS *m* |
| 3521 | CORRECCIÓN DE ÚTIL *f* |
| 3522 | ENSILADORAS *f pl* |
| 3523 | CORTE *m* |
| 3523 | CORTE *m* |
| 3523 | LABRA *f* |
| 3523 | LABRA *f* |
| 3524 | ÁNGULO DE CORTE *m* |
| 3524 | ÁNGULO DE ATAQUE *m*, ÁNGULO DE CONTACTO *m* |
| 3525 | DISPOSITIVO *m* DE CORTE |
| 3526 | PROFUNDIDAD *f* DE CORTE |
| 3527 | PULIMENTO *m* DE LA SUPERFICIE |
| 3528 | FILO *m* PRINCIPAL, ARISTA CORTANTE *f* |
| 3528 | CORTE *m* DE UN ÚTIL |
| 3529 | LABRA *f* DE LIMAS |
| 3530 | FLUIDO *m* DE CORTE |
| 3531 | CABEZA *f* DE AVELLANADO (O DE CORTE) |
| 3532 | TENAZAS *f pl* CORTANTES |
| 3532 | PINZA *f* CORTANTE |
| 3533 | TRONZADO *m* |
| 3533 | TRONZADO *m* |
| 3533 | CORTE *m* |
| 3533 | CORTADURA *f*, CORTE *m* |
| 3534 | ACEITE *m* DE CORTE MECANIZADO |
| 3535 | ROSCADO *m*, FILETEADO *m*, ROSCA *f*, PASO *m* DE ROSCA |
| 3536 | CARRERA ÚTIL (DE UNA MÁQUINA-HERRAMIENTA) *f* |
| 3536 | CARRERA DE TRABAJO *f* |
| 3537 | SOPLETE *m* DE CORTE AUTÓGENO |
| 3538 | HERRAMIENTA *f* TAJANTE |
| 3538 | HERRAMIENTA *f* CORTANTE |
| 3538 | HERRAMIENTA *f* CON CORTE, HERRAMIENTA *f* TAJANTE |
| 3539 | SOPLETE *m* |
| 3540 | TORNO *m* DE ATERRAJAR |
| 3541 | TRONZADORA *f* |
| 3541 | MÁQUINA *f* DE TROCEAR O DE TRONZAR |
| 3542 | DISCO *m* DE CORTAR |
| 3542 | DISCO *m* DE CORTAR |
| 3543 | VIRUTAS *f pl* |
| 3544 | CIANATO *m* |
| 3545 | ÁCIDO CIÁNICO *m* |
| 3546 | EXTRACCIÓN *f* DEL ORO POR CIANURACIÓN |
| 3547 | CIANURO *m* |
| 3548 | PARTÍCULAS *f pl* DE METALES NOBLES, O DE METALES PRECIOSOS |
| 3549 | ENDURECIMIENTO *m* CON CIANURO |
| 3549 | CIRCULACIÓN AL CIANURO *f* |
| 3550 | HORNO *m* DE CIANURACIÓN |
| 3551 | CIANÓGENO *m* |
| 3552 | ÁCIDO CIANÚRICO *m* |
| 3553 | CICLO *m* |
| 3553 | CICLO *m* DE TRABAJO |
| 3554 | CICLO *m* DE OPERACIONES |
| 3555 | CURVA *m* CÍCLICA |
| 3556 | PERMUTACIÓN *f* CÍCLICA |
| 3557 | CICLOIDE *f* |
| 3558 | ENGRANAJE *m* CICLOIDAL, DENTADO *m* CICLOIDAL |
| 3559 | CONTADOR DE VENTANA *m* |
| 3559 | CONTADOR DE VENTANAS *m* |
| 3560 | CICLÓN *m* PULVERIZADOR |
| 3561 | CILINDRO *m* |
| 3562 | CUERPO *m* DE CILINDRO |
| 3563 | BROCA *f* DE CAÑÓN |
| 3564 | BLOQUE *m* MOTOR |
| 3565 | CALIBRE (DIÁMETRO INTERIOR) DEL CILINDRO *m* |
| 3566 | CILINDRADA *f* |
| 3567 | TAPADERA DEL CILÍNDRO *f* |
| 3567 | TAPADER DEL CILINDRO *f* |
| 3568 | MÁQUINA *f* DE RECTIFICAR EL INTERIOR DE LOS CILINDROS |
| 3569 | CULATA *f* |
| 3569 | CABEZA *f* DEL CILINDRO |
| 3570 | JUNTA *f* DE CULATA |
| 3571 | GUARNICIÓN *f* INTERIOR DEL CILINDRO |
| 3571 | CAMISA DEL CILINDRO *f* |

| | |
|---|---|
| 3572 | ACEITE *m* PARA CILINDROS |
| 3573 | REGISTRADOR *m* DE TAMBOR |
| 3574 | CABEZA *f* CILÍNDRICA DE UN TORNILLO |
| 3575 | GRIFO *m* DE BOTELLA (DE GAS COMPRIMIDO) |
| 3576 | TOBERA CILÍNDRICA *f* |
| 3577 | CILÍNDRICO *m* |
| 3578 | CALDERA CILÍNDRICA *f* |
| 3579 | TAMBOR *m* (O CILINDRO *m*) DE RANURAS |
| 3579 | TAMBOR *m* |
| 3580 | COORDINADAS CILÍNDRICAS *f pl* |
| 3581 | TAPÓN *m* Y MEDIA LUNA DE CALIBRE |
| 3581 | CALIBRE *m* Y ANILLO |
| 3581 | CALIBRE MACHO Y HEMBRA *m* |
| 3582 | CILINDRO *m* GRADUADO |
| 3583 | MÁQUINA *f* PARA RECTIFICAR PIEZAS CILINDRICAS |
| 3584 | GUÍA *f* CILÍNDRICA |
| 3585 | RESORTE *m* HELICOIDAL CILÍNDRICO |
| 3586 | TUBO *m* CILÍNDRICO |
| 3587 | CALIBRES MACHOS CILÍNDRICOS *m pl* |
| 3588 | ANILLO CILÍNDRICO *m* |
| 3588 | TORO *m* CIRCULAR |
| 3589 | RODILLO *m* CILÍNDRICO |
| 3590 | SUPERFICIE *f* LATERAL DE UN CILINDRO |
| 3591 | RUEDA *f* RECTA |
| 3591 | RUEDA *f* CILÍNDRICA |
| 3592 | DISTRIBUIDOR *m* CONCOIDEO |
| 3593 | TUBO *m* DE BAJADA |
| 3594 | SALARIO *m* |
| 3594 | PRECIO *m* POR DÍA |
| 3595 | MÁQUINAS *f pl* PARA LECHERÍAS |
| 3596 | PLACA *f* DE DAMA |
| 3597 | PRESA *f*, EMBALSE *m* ARTIFICIAL, PANTANO *m* |
| 3598 | RESINA *f* DAMMAR |
| 3598 | GOMA *f* DAMAR |
| 3599 | AIRE HÚMEDO *m* |
| 3600 | VIBRACIÓN *f* |
| 3601 | AMORTIGUADOR *m* |
| 3602 | AMORTIGUADOR *m* |
| 3602 | AMORTIGUADOR *m* |
| 3603 | REGISTRO *m* DE HUMOS |
| 3603 | REGISTRO *m* DE TIRO |
| 3604 | AMORTIGUACIÓN *f*, AMORTIGUAMIENTO *m* |
| 3604 | ATENUACIÓN *f*, AMORTIGUAMIENTO *m* |
| 3605 | CAPACIDAD DE AMORTIZACIÓN *f* |
| 3606 | AMORTIGUAMIENTO DE VIBRACIONES *m* |
| 3607 | HORNO *m* DE PRIMERA ALEACIÓN |
| 3608 | PELIGRO *m* DE INCENDIO |
| 3608 | PELIGRO DE INCENDIO *m* |
| 3608 | RIESGO *m* |

| | |
|---|---|
| 3609 | SECCIÓN *f* PELIGROSA |
| 3610 | CUADRO *m* DE INSTRUMENTOS |
| 3611 | AMORTIGUADOR *m* |
| 3611 | CATARATA *f* |
| 3612 | DATOS *m pl* |
| 3613 | COLECCIÓN *f* DE DATOS |
| 3614 | DOCUMENTACIÓN *f* TÉCNICA |
| 3615 | HOJAS *f pl* (O FICHAS *f pl*) TÉCNICAS |
| 3616 | FECHA *f* DEL REGISTRO DE SOLICITUD DE UNA PATENTE |
| 3616 | DÍA *m* |
| 3617 | DÍA *m* DE LA FIRMA DE LA PATENTE, FECHA *f* DE LA FIRMA |
| 3617 | FECHA *f* DE LA CONCESIÓN DE LA PATENTE |
| 3618 | PESCANTE *m* |
| 3619 | BRAZO *m* DE GRÚA |
| 3620 | TRABAJO *m* DE DÍA |
| 3621 | TRABAJO *m* POR DÍAS |
| 3622 | LUZ *f* DEL DÍA, LUZ *f* NATURAL |
| 3623 | DESGASIFICACIÓN *f* DEL AGUA |
| 3624 | EJE *m* FIJO |
| 3625 | ARISTA *f* TERMINAL |
| 3626 | PUNTO *m* MUERTO |
| 3627 | CONDUCTOR SIN TENSIÓN *m* |
| 3627 | CONDUCTOR SIN CORRIENTE *m* |
| 3628 | DECAPADO *m* APAGADO |
| 3629 | MARTINETE *m* |
| 3630 | AGUJERO *m* SIN SALIDA |
| 3630 | AGUJERO *m* CIEGO |
| 3631 | CARGA MUERTA *f* |
| 3632 | VÁLVULA *f* DE SEGURIDAD DE CARGA DIRECTA |
| 3633 | CARGA PERMANENTE *f* |
| 3634 | CALDEO POR ENCIMA DEL PUNTO DE FUSIÓN *m* |
| 3635 | PUNTO *m* MUERTO |
| 3636 | CALCINACIÓN *f* TOTAL |
| 3637 | PESO *m* PROPIO |
| 3637 | PESO *m* MUERTO |
| 3638 | FRENO *m* DE PALANCA Y CONTRAPESO |
| 3639 | MAGNESITA *f* MUERTA |
| 3640 | AMORTIGUAR UN GOLPE |
| 3641 | MATERIA *f* IMPERMEABLE AL SONIDO, MATERIA AISLANTE CONTRA EL RUIDO |
| 3641 | MATERIA *f* QUE ABSORBE EL RUIDO |
| 3642 | DESBARBADURA *f* |
| 3642 | DESBARBADURA *f* |
| 3643 | MÉTODO *m* DE DEBYE-SCHERRER |
| 3644 | DECÁGONO *m* |
| 3645 | DECAGRAMO *m* |
| 3646 | DECALESCENCIA *f* |
| 3647 | DECALITRO *m* |
| 3648 | DECÁMETRO *m* |

| | |
|---|---|
| 3649 | DECANTAR |
| 3650 | DECANTACIÓN  f |
| 3651 | DESCARBONATACIÓN  f |
| 3652 | DESCARBONIZAR |
| 3653 | DESCARBURACIÓN  f DEL HIERRO |
| 3654 | DESCARBURAR EL HIERRO |
| 3655 | DESCARBURACIÓN  f |
| 3656 | DECRECIMIENTO  m |
| 3657 | DECIGRAMO  m |
| 3658 | DECILITRO  m |
| 3659 | DECIMAL |
| 3660 | BÁSCULA  f, BALANZA  f DECIMAL |
| 3660 | BALANZA  f DECIMAL |
| 3660 | BALANZA  f DECIMAL |
| 3661 | CÓDIGO DECIMAL  m |
| 3662 | FRACCIÓN  f DECIMAL |
| 3663 | BUJÍA  f DECIMAL |
| 3664 | NÚMERO  m DECIMAL |
| 3665 | SISTEMA  m DECIMAL |
| 3666 | DECÍMETRO  m |
| 3667 | PUENTE  m |
| 3667 | TECHO  m |
| 3667 | VELA  f |
| 3668 | DECLINACIÓN  f MAGNÉTICA |
| 3669 | DECOCCIÓN  f |
| 3670 | TRADUCTOR  m DE CLAVE |
| 3671 | DESCOMPONIBLE |
| 3672 | DESCOMPONER |
| 3673 | DESCOMPONERSE |
| 3674 | DESCOMPOSICIÓN  f |
| 3675 | TENSIÓN  f DE DESCOMPOSICIÓN |
| 3676 | DESCOMPOSICIÓN  f DE LA LUZ |
| 3677 | PÉRDIDA DE VELOCIDAD  f |
| 3677 | DISMINUCIÓN  f |
| 3678 | REDUCIR LA VELOCIDAD |
| 3679 | VELOCIDAD  f DECRECIENTE |
| 3680 | VICIO  m DE MATERIA |
| 3681 | ALTURA  f DEL PIE |
| 3681 | ALTURA  f DEL FLANCO |
| 3681 | ALTURA  f DEL PIE DE DIENTE |
| 3682 | EXTRACCIÓN  f DEL POLVO, DESEMPOLVAMIENTO  m |
| 3683 | EMBUTIDO  m PROFUNDO |
| 3684 | PRUEBA  f DE CORROSIÓN PROFUNDA |
| 3685 | ATAQUE  m PROFUNDO |
| 3686 | TALADRO  m PARA PERFORACIÓN PROFUNDA |
| 3687 | MÁQUINA  f DE TALADRAR Y DE ESCARIAR LOS AGUJEROS PROFUNDOS |
| 3688 | FLEJES  m pl DE ACERO PARA EMBUTIDO PROFUNDO |
| 3689 | BOMBA  f PARA POZOS PROFUNDOS |
| 3690 | LATÓN  m DE CALIDAD PARA EMBUTIR |
| 3691 | DEFECTO  m, FALLA  f, IMPERFECCIÓN  f |
| 3692 | DEFECTO  m DEL MATERIAL |
| 3692 | VICIO  m |
| 3693 | VICIO  m DE CONSTRUCCIÓN |
| 3693 | DEFECTO  m DE CONSTRUCCIÓN |
| 3693 | DEFECTO  m DE FABRICACIÓN |
| 3694 | VICIO  m DE CONCEPCIÓN |
| 3695 | VICIO  m DE FUNCIONAMIENTO |
| 3696 | PIEZAS  f pl DEFECTUOSAS |
| 3696 | RESIDUOS  m DE FABRICACIÓN |
| 3697 | INTEGRAL  f DEFINIDA |
| 3698 | DEFORMACIÓN  f, FLEXIÓN  f |
| 3698 | FLEXIÓN  f |
| 3698 | FLEXIÓN  f, DEFORMACIÓN  f, FLECHA  f |
| 3699 | DESVIACIÓN  f DESVÍO  m |
| 3699 | DEFLEXIÓN  f, DESVIACIÓN  f, FLEXIÓN  f |
| 3699 | RECORRIDO  m (O DESVIACIÓN  f) DE LA AGUJA |
| 3700 | FLEXIÓN  f, DOBLAMIENTO  m |
| 3700 | FLEXIÓN  f TRANSVERSAL |
| 3701 | FLECHA  f, FLEXIÓN  f |
| 3702 | DEFLECTOR  m |
| 3703 | GRAFITO  m DESFLOCULADO |
| 3704 | ELIMINACIÓN  f DEL VAHO (DEL VAPOR) |
| 3705 | DEFORMABILIDAD  f |
| 3705 | CAPACIDAD DE DEFORMACIÓN  f |
| 3705 | PLASTICITA  f |
| 3706 | BANDA  f DE DEFORMACIÓN |
| 3707 | CAMBIO DE FORMA  m |
| 3707 | DEFORMACIÓN  f |
| 3708 | DESCONGELADOR  m |
| 3709 | ALEACIÓN DESGASIFICANTE  f |
| 3710 | DESGASIFICACIÓN  f, DESAIREACIÓN  f |
| 3711 | ADOBO  m PARA PIELES |
| 3711 | GRASA  f DE LOS CURTIDORES |
| 3712 | DESENGRASE  m |
| 3713 | COMPOSICIÓN DE DESENGRASE  f |
| 3714 | GRADO  m |
| 3715 | GRADO BAUMÉ |
| 3716 | GRADO CENTÍGRADO |
| 3717 | GRADO  m ENGLER |
| 3718 | GRADO  m FAHRENHEIT |
| 3719 | COEFICIENTE DE REGULARIDAD  m |
| 3719 | REGULARIDAD  f CÍCLICA |
| 3720 | GRADO  m DE DUREZA |
| 3721 | GRADO  m DE EXACTITUD, DE PRECISIÓN |
| 3721 | GRADO  m DE PRECISIÓN |
| 3722 | GRADO  m DE SATURACIÓN |
| 3723 | COEFICIENTE DE SENSIBILIDAD  m |
| 3724 | GRADO  m RÉAUMUR |
| 3725 | GRADO  m TWADDELL |

| | |
|---|---|
| 3726 | GRADOS *m pl* DE LIBERTAD |
| 3727 | DESHIDRATAR |
| 3727 | DESHIDRATARSE |
| 3728 | DESHIDRATACIÓN *f* |
| 3729 | DESIONIZACIÓN *f* |
| 3730 | RETRASO *m* |
| 3731 | RETRASO *m* EN LA ENTREGA |
| 3732 | CAER EN DELICUESCENCIA |
| 3733 | DELICUESCENCIA *f* |
| 3734 | DELICUESCENTE |
| 3735 | CESIÓN DE CALOR *f* |
| 3736 | TUBO *m* DE PRESIÓN |
| 3736 | TUBERÍAS *f pl* |
| 3736 | TUBO *m* DE EXPULSIÓN |
| 3736 | TUBULADURA *f* DE DERRAME |
| 3737 | CONDICIONES DE ENTREGA *f pl* |
| 3738 | TOBERA DIVERGENTE *f* |
| 3738 | TOBERA *f* DE EXPULSIÓN |
| 3738 | TOBERA *f* DIVERGENTE |
| 3739 | VÁLVULA *f* DE REPULSIÓN |
| 3739 | VÁLVULA DE DESCARGA *f* |
| 3740 | HIERRO *m* DELTA |
| 3741 | METAL *m* ALEACIÓN DELTA |
| 3742 | DESIMANTACIÓN *f* |
| 3743 | DESIMANTAR, DESMAGNETIZAR |
| 3744 | DESMAGNETIZADORES *m pl*, DESIMANTADORES *m pl* |
| 3745 | COMBUSTIBLE NECESARIO *m* |
| 3746 | FUERZA *f* NECESARIA |
| 3746 | POTENCIA *f* NECESARIA |
| 3746 | ENERGÍA *f* (NECESARIA) |
| 3747 | (AGENTE) DESNATURALIZANTE *m* |
| 3748 | DENDRITA *f* |
| 3749 | POLVO *m* DENTIFRICO |
| 3750 | ESTRUCTURA *f* DENDRÍTICA |
| 3751 | DESNIQUELADO *m* |
| 3752 | DENOMINADOR *m* |
| 3753 | DENSIFICACIÓN *f* |
| 3754 | MEDIO *m* DE HOMOGENEIZACIÓN |
| 3755 | DENSIMETRO *m* |
| 3756 | DENSIDAD *f* |
| 3757 | DENSIDAD *f* DE UN GAS |
| 3758 | DENSIDAD *f* DE UN LÍQUIDO |
| 3759 | RELACIÓN *f* DE DENSIDAD |
| 3760 | ABOLLADURA *f* |
| 3760 | ABOLLAMIENTO *m* |
| 3761 | DIENTE *m*, MUESCA, MORTAJA *f* |
| 3762 | DESOXIGENACIÓN *f* |
| 3762 | DESOXIDACIÓN *f* |
| 3763 | DESOXIDAR |
| 3763 | DESOXIGENAR |

| | |
|---|---|
| 3764 | COBRE *m* DESOXIDADO |
| 3765 | DESOXIDANTE |
| 3766 | DESOXIDACIÓN *f* |
| 3767 | REBAJA DE LA CONCENTRACIÓN *f* |
| 3768 | DESPOLARIZACIÓN *f* |
| 3769 | DESPOLARIZAR |
| 3770 | DESPOLARIZANTE, DESPOLARIZADOR |
| 3771 | DESPOLARIZACIÓN *f* |
| 3772 | DESPOLARIZANTE, DESPOLARIZADOR |
| 3772 | DESPOLARIZADOR, DESPOLARIZANTE |
| 3773 | SEDIMENTO *m* |
| 3774 | CORROSIÓN CAUSADA POR SEDIMENTACIÓN. *f* |
| 3775 | METAL *m* DE RECARGA, METAL *m* AÑADIDO O INCORPORADO |
| 3775 | METAL *m* DE APORTE, METAL *m* DE RECARGA |
| 3776 | METAL *m* FUNDIDO APLICADO |
| 3777 | RELACIÓN *f* DE DISTRIBUCIÓN DEL METAL |
| 3778 | DEPRESIÓN *f* |
| 3779 | PROFUNDIDAD *f* |
| 3780 | PERFORACIÓN *f* PROFUNDA |
| 3781 | CALIBRE DE PROFUNDIDAD *m* |
| 3781 | PIE *m* DE PROFUNDIDAD |
| 3782 | PROFUNDIDAD *f* DE CORTE |
| 3783 | PROFUNDIDAD *f* DEL CUELLO DE CISNE |
| 3784 | PROFUNDIDAD *f* DE LA ROSCA |
| 3785 | ALTURA *f* TOTAL DEL DIENTE |
| 3786 | DERIVADO |
| 3787 | BARCAZAS *f pl* DE TRANSPORTE |
| 3788 | GRÚA *f* DERRICK |
| 3788 | GRÚA *f* DE MÁSTIL |
| 3789 | DESACTIVACIÓN *f* |
| 3790 | BAÑO *m* DE DESCASCARILLADO (O DE DECAPADO) |
| 3791 | TUBERÍA DE BAJADA *f* |
| 3792 | PENDIENTE *f*, DECLIVE *m*, CUESTA *f* |
| 3792 | DECLIVIDAD *f*, DECLIVE *m*, PENDIENTE *f* |
| 3793 | ELIMINACIÓN *f* DE DEFECTOS SUPERFICIALES |
| 3794 | TRAZADO *m* |
| 3794 | PLANO *m* |
| 3794 | ESTUDIO *m*, DISEÑO *m* |
| 3794 | PROYECTO *m* |
| 3794 | CÁLCULO *m* DISEÑO *m* |
| 3794 | CONCEPCIÓN *f*, DISEÑO *m* |
| 3795 | CALCULAR, COMPUTAR |
| 3795 | DISEÑAR, ESTUDIAR |
| 3795 | TRAZAR |
| 3796 | OFICINA *f* TÉCNICA, OFICINA *f* DE ESTUDIOS |
| 3797 | CROQUIS *m* DE PRINCIPIO |
| 3798 | TEMPERATURA *f* DE CÁLCULO |
| 3798 | TEMPERATURA *f* DE ESTUDIO |
| 3799 | ESTUDIO *m* |

| | |
|---|---|
| 3800 | SECCIÓN  f  TÉCNICA, SALA  f  DE DIBUJO Y PROYECTOS |
| 3801 | DESARGENTAR, DESPLATAR, DESPLATEAR |
| 3802 | DESPLATE  m |
| 3803 | EVACUACIÓN  f  DE LA ESCORIA |
| 3804 | DESECADOR  m |
| 3805 | DESTILACIÓN  f  CON DESCOMPOSICIÓN |
| 3806 | ENSAYO  m  DESTRUCTIVO |
| 3807 | ELIMINACIÓN  f  DE LAS CAPAS SUPERFICIALES |
| 3808 | AMOVIBLE |
| 3809 | DIBUJO  m  DE DETALLE |
| 3810 | DETALLE  m  DE CONSTRUCCIÓN |
| 3811 | PIEZA  f  SUELTA |
| 3812 | PLANO  m  DETALLADO |
| 3813 | DETERGENTE |
| 3814 | DETERMINANTE |
| 3815 | DESARROLLAR |
| 3816 | DESARROLLABLE |
| 3817 | SUPERFICIE  f  DESARROLLABLE |
| 3817 | SUPERFICIE  f  DESARROLLABLE |
| 3818 | DESPRENDIMIENTO  m  DE GASES |
| 3819 | DESVIACIÓN  f, DESVÍO  m |
| 3819 | DESVIACIÓN  f, DESVÍO  m |
| 3820 | DISPOSITIVO  m, MECANISMO  m |
| 3821 | TOSTADOR  m |
| 3821 | BRASERO  m |
| 3822 | GANCHO  m  DE CADENA |
| 3823 | DESVITRIFICACIÓN  f |
| 3824 | PUNTO  m  DE CONDENSACIÓN |
| 3825 | DEXTRINA  f |
| 3826 | ÁCIDO TARTÁRICO DEXTRÓGIRO  m |
| 3827 | DEXTRÓGIRO |
| 3828 | DIABASA  f |
| 3829 | CÁUSTICA  f  POR REFRACCIÓN, DIACÁUSTICA  f |
| 3829 | CÁUSTICO POR REFRACCIÓN  m |
| 3830 | PROGRAMA  m  DIAGNÓSTICO |
| 3831 | DIAGONAL  f |
| 3831 | DIAGONAL |
| 3832 | PINZA  f  CORTANTE DIAGONAL |
| 3833 | ESCALA  f  TRANSVERSAL (UNIVERSAL) |
| 3834 | DIAGRAMA  m |
| 3834 | GRÁFICO  m |
| 3834 | ÁBACO  m |
| 3835 | DIAGRAMA  m  DE FUERZAS |
| 3836 | ESQUEMA  f |
| 3836 | CROQUIS  m  ESQUEMÁTICO |
| 3837 | ESFERA  f, DIAL  m |
| 3837 | INDICADOR  m |
| 3837 | DISCO  m |
| 3838 | COMPARADOR DE ESFERA PARA ESCARIADOS  m |
| 3839 | PRENSA  f  MECÁCINA CON PLATO REVOLVER |

| | |
|---|---|
| 3840 | INDICADOR  m  CON ESFERA |
| 3841 | ESCALA  f  ANULAR |
| 3842 | PALPADOR  m  CON ESFERA |
| 3843 | CRONOMETRIZADOR  m, RELOJ  m  REGULADOR |
| 3844 | DIALIZAR |
| 3845 | DIALIZADOR  m |
| 3846 | DIÁLISIS  f |
| 3847 | DIAMAGNÉTICO |
| 3848 | DIAMAGNETISMO  m |
| 3849 | DIÁMETRO  m |
| 3850 | DIÁMETRO  m  EN EL NÚCLEO DE UN TORNILLO |
| 3850 | DIÁMETRO  m  INTERIOR |
| 3850 | DIÁMETRO  m  EN EL NÚCLEO (DE UN TORNILLO) |
| 3850 | DIÁMETRO  m  PEQUEÑO DE LA ROSCA |
| 3851 | COMPLEMENTO DIAMETRAL  m |
| 3852 | DIÁMETRO  m  EXTERIOR |
| 3852 | DIÁMETRO  m  GRANDE DEL FILETEADO |
| 3853 | DIÁMETRO  m  (DEL CÍRCULO) DE PERFORACIÓN (DE TALADRO) |
| 3854 | DIÁMETRO  m  DE AGUJERO DE PERNO |
| 3855 | DIÁMETRO  m  DEL TALADRO |
| 3855 | TALADRADO  m, MANDRINADO  m, ESCARIADO  m, TORNEADO INTERIOR  m |
| 3856 | DIÁMETRO  m  DE UN ESLABÓN DE CADENA |
| 3857 | DIÁMETRO  m  DEL AGUJERO |
| 3858 | DIÁMETRO  m  DE UN TUBO |
| 3859 | DIÁMETRO  m  DEL REMACHE |
| 3860 | DIÁMETRO  m  DE UN ALAMBRE (DE UN HILO) |
| 3860 | ESPESOR  m  DE UN ALAMBRE |
| 3861 | MÓDULO  m  DE DENTADURA |
| 3861 | PASO  m  DIAMETRAL |
| 3861 | DIÁMETRO  m  PRIMITIVO |
| 3862 | DIAMANTE  m |
| 3863 | POLVO  m  DE DIAMANTE |
| 3863 | POLVO  m  DE DIAMANTE |
| 3864 | MUELA  f  DIAMANTE |
| 3865 | PRUEBA  f  DE DUREZA |
| 3866 | HERRAMIENTA  f  DIAMANTADA |
| 3867 | MUELA  f  DIAMANTADA |
| 3868 | DIAFANIDAD  f |
| 3869 | DIÁFANO |
| 3870 | DIAFRAGMA  m |
| 3870 | DIAFRAGMA  m |
| 3870 | MEMBRANA  f |
| 3871 | DIAFRAGMA  m |
| 3872 | GRIFO  m  REGULADOR DE MEMBRANA |
| 3872 | VÁLVULA  f  DE CONTROL |
| 3873 | MANÓMETRO  m  DE PLACA |
| 3874 | BOMBA  f  DE DIAFRAGMA |
| 3874 | BOMBA DE DIAFRAGMA  f |
| 3875 | RESORTE  m  DIAFRAGMA |

| | | | | |
|---|---|---|---|---|
| 3876 | GRIFO *m* DE MEMBRANA | | 3910 | GRAN CORONA *f* DE DIFERENCIAL |
| 3877 | DIAFRAGMAR | | 3911 | DINAMÓMETRO *m* DIFERENCIAL |
| 3878 | DIATERMANCIA *f* | | 3912 | ECUACIÓN *f* DIFERENCIAL |
| 3878 | DIATERMANCIA *f* | | 3913 | TREN *m* DIFERENCIAL |
| 3879 | DIATÉRMICO | | 3913 | MECANISMO *m* |
| 3879 | DIATÉRMANO | | 3913 | ENGRANAJE *m* DIFERENCIAL |
| 3880 | TIERRA *f* DE DIATOMEAS | | 3913 | MECANISMO *m* |
| 3881 | BIATÓMICO *m*, BIATÓMICA *f* | | 3913 | DIFERENCIAL *m* |
| 3881 | DIATÓMICO | | 3914 | TEMPLE *m* DIFERENCIAL |
| 3881 | BIVALENTE | | 3914 | TEMPLE *m* LOCALIZADO |
| 3882 | BIBÁSICO | | 3915 | CALENTAMIENTO SELECTIVO *m* |
| 3883 | HILERA *f*, TERRAJA *f* | | 3916 | COCIENTE *m* |
| 3883 | ESTAMPA *f*, TROQUEL *m* | | 3917 | RUEDA *f* DE DIFERENCIAL |
| 3883 | MATRIZ *f*, ESTAMPA *f* | | 3918 | SATÉLITE *m* DE DIFERENCIAL |
| 3883 | MATRIZ *f* | | 3919 | ANÁLISIS TÉRMICO SELECTIVO *m* |
| 3883 | MOLDE *m* | | 3920 | TERMÓMETRO *m* DIFERENCIAL |
| 3883 | MOLDE *m* METÁLICO | | 3921 | MANÓMETRO *m* DIFERENCIAL |
| 3884 | PORTAESTAMPA *m* | | 3922 | DIFERENCIAR |
| 3885 | PARTE *f* FIJA | | 3923 | DIFERENCIACIÓN *f* |
| 3885 | CUERPO DE LA ESTAMPA *m* | | 3924 | DIFRACCIÓN *f* |
| 3886 | COLADA A PRESIÓN *f* | | 3925 | RED *f* DE DIFRACCIÓN |
| 3887 | SUJETAMODELOS *m* | | 3926 | DIAGRAMA *m* DE DIFRACCIÓN RX |
| 3888 | MARCA *f* DE ESTAMPA | | 3927 | LUZ *f* DIFUSA |
| 3889 | METAL *m* PARA MATRICES | | 3928 | DIFUSOR *m* |
| 3890 | MONTURA *f* DE ESTAMPA CON GUÍA DE COLUMNAS | | 3929 | DIFUSIÓN *f* |
| | | | 3930 | REVESTIMIENTOS *m pl* DE DIFUSIÓN |
| 3891 | DESPLAZAMIENTO *m* DEL CUÑO | | 3931 | COEFICIENTE DE DIFUSIÓN *m* |
| 3892 | FRESADO *m* DE MATRICES | | 3932 | DIFUSIÓN *f* DE LOS GASES |
| 3893 | PUNZÓN *m* (DE INSPECCIÓN), CONTRASTE *m* | | 3933 | DIFUSIÓN *f* DE LA LUZ |
| 3894 | MARCADO *m* CON PUNZÓN DE LAS CHAPAS | | 3934 | ZONA *f* DE DIFUSIÓN |
| 3894 | MACA *f* O DEFECTO (EN LA CHAPA QUE MATRIZAR) | | 3935 | SUPERFICIE *f* DIFUSIBLE |
| | | | 3936 | DIFUSIBILIDAD *f* |
| 3894 | PUNZONADO *m* DE LAS CHAPAS | | 3937 | PONER A DIGERIR |
| 3895 | MONTURA *f* DE UNA HILERA CON COJINETES | | 3937 | HACER DIGERIR, DIGERIR |
| 3896 | COJINETE DE HILERA *m* | | 3938 | LAVADOR *m* |
| 3897 | MATRIZ *f* TROQUEL ESTAMPA DE HERRERO | | 3939 | DIGESTIÓN *f* |
| 3898 | NO CONDUCTOR | | 3940 | CIFRA *f* |
| 3898 | AISLANTE | | 3940 | POSICIÓN *f* |
| 3898 | DIELÉCTRICO | | 3941 | NUMÉRICO |
| 3899 | CONSTANTE DIELÉCTRICA *f* | | 3942 | INFORMACIÓN *f* DE ENTRADA NUMÉRICA |
| 3900 | RESISTENCIA *f* DIELÉCTRICA O DISRUPTIVA | | 3943 | CODIFICADOR NUMÉRICO *m* |
| 3901 | DIESEL | | 3944 | DIEDRO *m* |
| 3901 | MOTOR *m* DIESEL | | 3944 | ÁNGULO DIEDRO *m* |
| 3902 | DIFERENCIA *f* | | 3945 | LEVANTAMIENTO *m* DE TIERRA |
| 3903 | CALIBRE *m* DEL LÍMITE DE UNA TOLERANCIA | | 3946 | TERREROS *m* |
| 3904 | DIFERENCIA *f* DE TEMPERATURA | | 3947 | DILATABILIDAD *f* |
| 3905 | CALIBRE DE TOLERANCIA *m* | | 3948 | DILATABLE |
| 3906 | DIFERENCIAL *m* | | 3949 | DILATACIÓN *f* |
| 3907 | FRENO *m* DIFERENCIAL | | 3950 | DILATÓMETRO *m* |
| 3908 | CÁLCULO DIFERENCIAL *m* | | 3951 | DILUYENTE |
| 3909 | COEFICIENTE DIFERENCIAL *m* | | 3952 | DILUIR |

| | |
|---|---|
| 3952 | DILUIR UNA SOLUCIÓN |
| 3953 | SOLUCIÓN *f* DILUIDA |
| 3953 | SOLUCIÓN *f* DILUIDA |
| 3954 | DILUCIÓN *f* DE UNA SOLUCIÓN |
| 3955 | LUZ *f* DIFUSA |
| 3956 | COTA *f* |
| 3957 | LÍNEA *f* DE COTA |
| 3958 | ESTABILIDAD *f* DIMENSIONAL |
| 3959 | DIBUJO *m* CON DIMENSIONES |
| 3960 | DIMENSIONES *f pl*, MEDIDAS *f pl* |
| 3961 | PROYECCIÓN *f* DIMÉTRICA |
| 3962 | MANGUITO *m* DE REDUCCIÓN DE ESCARIADO |
| 3963 | INVERSOR *m*, FARO DE CRUCE |
| 3964 | DIODO *m* |
| 3965 | LÁMPARA *f* DE DIODO |
| 3966 | DIORITA *f* |
| 3967 | INMERSIÓN *f* |
| 3967 | BAÑO *m*, IMMERSIÓN *f* |
| 3968 | SUMERGIR, INMERGER, ZAMBULLIRSE |
| 3968 | INMERGER |
| 3969 | SOLDADURA *f* FUERTE POR INMERSIÓN |
| 3970 | APLICACIÓN *f* DE UN REVESTIMIENTO POR REMOJADO |
| 3971 | AGUJERO *m* DE MEDIDA |
| 3972 | AGUJERO *m* DE MEDIDA COMBINADO CON RESPIRADERO |
| 3973 | CUBA *f* DE INMERSIÓN |
| 3974 | DIFENILAMINA *f* |
| 3975 | INMERSIÓN *f* |
| 3975 | TEMPLE *m* |
| 3976 | CESTA DE INMERSIÓN *f* |
| 3977 | MÉTODO *m* AL TEMPLE |
| 3978 | TEMPLE *m* |
| 3978 | INMERSIÓN *f* |
| 3979 | INDICADOR *m* DEL NIVEL DE ACEITE |
| 3980 | ACCIÓN DIRECTA (DE) *f* |
| 3981 | MANDO DIRECTO POR COMPUTADORA *m* |
| 3982 | MÁQUINA *f* DE ACOPLAMIENTO DIRECTO |
| 3982 | MÁQUINA *f* DE ENMANGADO DIRECTO |
| 3983 | TOMA *f* DIRECTA |
| 3984 | EXTRUSIÓN *f* DIRECTA |
| 3985 | MANDO DIRECTO POR COMPUTADORA *m* |
| 3986 | PIE *m* DE REY CON ESFERA |
| 3987 | VÁLVULA *f* DE SEGURIDAD DE CARGA DIRECTA DE RESORTE |
| 3988 | CONDENSADOR POR MEZCLA *m* |
| 3989 | INTERMITENTES *m* |
| 3989 | LUCES *f pl* DE DIRECCIÓN |
| 3990 | DIRECCIÓN *f* DE UNA FUERZA |
| 3991 | DIRECCIÓN *f* DE MOVIMIENTO |
| 3992 | SENTIDO *m* DE ROTACIÓN |

| | |
|---|---|
| 3993 | DIRECCIÓN *f* DE LAS FIBRAS |
| 3994 | ORIENTACIÓN *f* DE LOS CRISTALES |
| 3995 | DIRECTOR *m* |
| 3995 | INTERPOLADOR |
| 3996 | DIRECTRIZ *f* |
| 3997 | TOMA *f* DE POLVO |
| 3998 | GRANOS *m pl* QUE CONTIENE LA FUNDICIÓN |
| 3999 | DESINTEGRAR |
| 3999 | DESAGREGAR |
| 4000 | DESAGREGACIÓN *f* |
| 4000 | DESINTEGRACIÓN *f*, DESAGREGACIÓN *f* |
| 4001 | FRENO *m* DE DISCO |
| 4002 | ACOPLAMIENTO *m* (O EMBRAGUE *m*) DE DISCO |
| 4003 | PLATILLO *m* MANIVELA |
| 4004 | VOLANTE *m* DE DISCO |
| 4004 | VOLANTE *m* EN DISCO |
| 4005 | TRANSMISIÓN *f* POR PLATOS |
| 4006 | PULIDORA *f* |
| 4007 | PULVERIZADORES *m pl* DE DISCOS |
| 4008 | PORTACHAPALETA *m* |
| 4009 | TUERCA *f* DE INMOVILIZACIÓN DE DISCO (DE VÁLVULA) |
| 4010 | PULIDORA *f* |
| 4011 | VÁLVULA *f* DE ASIENTO PLANO |
| 4011 | VÁLVULA *f* DE DISCO |
| 4012 | RUEDA *f* DE CENTRO LLENO |
| 4012 | RUEDA *f* DE DISCO |
| 4012 | RUEDA *f* DE DISCO |
| 4013 | DISCO *m* PLENO DE UN VOLANTE |
| 4013 | DISCO *m* DE RUEDA |
| 4014 | DISCO *m* (DE VÁLVULA) |
| 4015 | DISCO *m* |
| 4016 | VÁLVULA *f* (DE GRIFO O DE LLAVE) |
| 4017 | DESCARGA *f* |
| 4018 | DESCARGAR, VACIAR |
| 4018 | VACIAR |
| 4019 | DESCARGAR UN ACUMULADOR |
| 4020 | SECCIÓN *f* DEL ORIFICIO DE SALIDA |
| 4021 | ALTURA *f* DE LA IMPELENCIA DE UNA BOMBA |
| 4022 | TUBERÍA O TUBO DE DESCARGA |
| 4023 | VOLUMEN *m* QUE PASA A TRAVÉS DE UN ORIFICIO POR SEGUNDO |
| 4024 | VACIADO *m* |
| 4024 | DESCARGA *f*, VACIADO *m* |
| 4025 | DESCARGA *f* DE UN ACUMULADOR |
| 4026 | ALTERACIÓN DEL COLOR *f* |
| 4027 | DESMONTABLE |
| 4028 | DESCONEXIÓN *f* |
| 4029 | DISCRIMINANTE |
| 4030 | DESENGATILLAR, DESEMBRAGAR, DESENGANCHAR |
| 4030 | DESENGANCHAR, DESENGATILLAR, DESEMBRAGAR |

| | |
|---|---|
| 4031 | DESENGANCHE *m*, ESCAPE *m* DE UN RESORTE, DESENGATE *m* |
| 4031 | DESENGATE *m*, ESCAPE DE UN RESORTE |
| 4032 | ACOPLAMIENTO DE DESEMBRAGUE *m* |
| 4033 | ACOPLAMIENTO DE DESEMBRAGUE *m* |
| 4034 | MECANISMO *m* DE DESEMBRAGUE |
| 4034 | MECANISMO *m* DE EMBRAGUE |
| 4035 | PALANCA *f* DE DESEMBRAGUE |
| 4035 | PALANCA *f* DE DESCONEXIÓN |
| 4036 | CAJA *f* DE BOMBA |
| 4037 | RUEDA *f* DE DISCO ABOMBADA |
| 4038 | FONDO *m* EMBUTIDO |
| 4039 | TECHO *m* ABOMBADO |
| 4040 | BOMBEAMIENTO *m*, EMBUTIDO *m* |
| 4041 | ANTITARTAROSO *m* |
| 4041 | DESINCRUSTANTE |
| 4041 | DESINCRUSTANTE *m*, TARTRÍFUGO *m* |
| 4042 | DESINFECTANTE |
| 4043 | DESAGREGARSE |
| 4043 | DESAGREGARSE |
| 4044 | DESINTEGRACIÓN *f* |
| 4045 | TRITURADOR *m* |
| 4046 | ACOPLAMIENTO *m* DE DISCOS, EMBRAGUE *m* DE DISCOS |
| 4047 | DISLOCACIÓN *f* |
| 4048 | CALIBRE *m* DESMONTABLE |
| 4049 | FASE *f* DISPERSA |
| 4050 | AGENTE DE DISPERSIÓN *m* |
| 4050 | AGENTE *m* DE DISPERSIÓN |
| 4051 | DISPERSIÓN *f* |
| 4052 | DESPLAZABLE |
| 4053 | DESPLAZAMIENTO *m* |
| 4053 | VOLUMEN *m* DESPLAZADO |
| 4054 | DESPLAZAMIENTO *m* DE UN LÍQUIDO |
| 4055 | DESPLAZAMIENTO *m* DEL EJE, DESCENTRADO |
| 4056 | DISPOSICIÓN *f* |
| 4057 | RESISTENCIA *f* DISRUPTIVA |
| 4058 | DISOCIACIÓN *f* |
| 4059 | DISOLUCIÓN *f* |
| 4060 | DISOLUCIÓN *f* |
| 4061 | DISOLVERSE |
| 4061 | DISOLVER |
| 4061 | FUNDIR (QUIM.), DERRETIR |
| 4062 | PODER *m* DISOLVENTE |
| 4063 | DISTANCIA *f* |
| 4063 | DISTANCIA *f*, TRAYECTO *m* |
| 4063 | ESPACIO *m*, DISTANCIA *f* |
| 4063 | RECORRIDO *m*, TRAYECTO *m* |
| 4063 | TRAYECTO *m*, SEPARACIÓN *f* |
| 4064 | DISTANCIA *f* ENTRE LOS COJINETES |
| 4065 | DISTANCIA *f* ENTRE CENTROS, DISTANCIA *f* ENTRE EJES |
| 4065 | DISTANCIA *f* ENTRE EJES |
| 4065 | DISTANCIA *f* ENTRE PUNTAS |
| 4066 | DISTANCIA *f* DEL CENTRO DEL REMACHE AL BORDE DE LA CHAPA |
| 4067 | DISTANCIADOR *m*, SEPARADOR *m* |
| 4068 | DISTANCIADOR *m*, SEPARADOR *m* |
| 4068 | PIEZA *f* DE SEPARACIÓN |
| 4069 | TELETERMÓMETRO *m* |
| 4070 | DESTILAR |
| 4071 | DESTILACIÓN *f* (PRODUCTO) |
| 4071 | PRODUCTO *m* DE DESTILACIÓN |
| 4072 | DESTILACIÓN *f* (ACCIÓN) |
| 4073 | DESTILACIÓN *f* CON VAPOR DE AGUA |
| 4074 | DESTILACIÓN *f* DE LA HULLA |
| 4075 | DESTILACIÓN *f* EN EL VACÍO |
| 4075 | AISLADO |
| 4076 | AGUA *f* DESTILADA |
| 4077 | DISTORSIÓN *f* |
| 4077 | ABERRACIÓN *f*, DISTORSIÓN *f* |
| 4078 | CARGA DISTRIBUIDA *f* |
| 4079 | CONDUCTOR DE RED *m* |
| 4079 | CABLE DE DISTRIBUCIÓN *m* |
| 4080 | RED *f* DE DISTRIBUCIÓN ELÉCTRICA |
| 4080 | RED *f* DE CONDUCTORES ELÉCTRICOS |
| 4081 | REPARTICIÓN *f* DE UNA CARGA |
| 4082 | REPARTICIÓN *f* DE MASAS |
| 4083 | DISTRIBUCIÓN *f* DE LA TEMPERATURA |
| 4084 | DISTRIBUIDOR *m* |
| 4085 | BRAZO *m* DE ENCENDIDO |
| 4086 | DISTRIBUIDOR *m* |
| 4086 | DISTRIBUIDOR *m*, CAJA *f* DE DISTRIBUCIÓN |
| 4087 | DISTRIBUDORES *m pl* DE FERTILIZANTES |
| 4088 | MECANISMOS *m pl* DE ENGANCHE PARA REMOLQUES Y CAMIONES |
| 4089 | DISTRIBUIDORES *m pl* DE CAL |
| 4090 | ARADOS *m pl* DE SUBSUELO Y ARADOS *m pl* DE VERTEDERA |
| 4091 | DIVERGIR |
| 4092 | DIVERGENCIA *f* |
| 4093 | DIVERGENTE |
| 4094 | SERIE *f* DIVERGENTE |
| 4095 | LENTE AMB. DIVERGENTE |
| 4095 | LENTE AMB. DE BORDE ESPESO |
| 4096 | TOBERA DIVERGENTE |
| 4096 | TOBERA *f* DIVERGENTE |
| 4097 | DIVISOR *m* |
| 4098 | COJINETE *m* DE COQUILLAS |
| 4098 | COJINETE *m* EN DOS PARTES |
| 4099 | DIVIDENDO *m* |
| 4100 | DIVISOR *m* |

| | | | |
|---|---|---|---|
| 4100 | COMPÁS *m* | 4135 | DOBLE DECÍMETRO *m* |
| 4101 | COMPÁS RECTO DE PUNTAS *m* | 4136 | DOBLE DESCOMPOSICIÓN *f* |
| 4101 | COMPÁS DE PUNTAS FIJAS *m* | 4137 | CALIBRE *m* TAMPÓN DOBLE CON LIMITACIONES |
| 4102 | MÁQUINA *f* DE DIVIDIR O SECCIONAR | 4138 | ALIMENTACIÓN DOBLE *f* |
| 4103 | MÁQUINA *f* DE SECCIONAR LOS CÍRCULOS | 4139 | BRIDA *f* DOBLE |
| 4104 | MÁQUINA *f* DE DIVIDIR LAS LÍNEAS RECTAS | 4140 | MARTILLO *m* DE FORJA CON DOBLE CUERPO |
| 4105 | CABEZAL DIVISOR *m* | 4141 | JUNTA *f* SOLDADA CON DOBLE SOLAPA, JUNTA *f* SOLDADA CON DOBLE PESTAÑA |
| 4106 | PLATILLO *m* DIVISOR | | |
| 4107 | DIVISIÓN *f* | 4142 | DOBLE TREN *m* DE ENGRANAJES |
| 4108 | DIVISIÓN *f* DEL CÍRCULO | 4142 | DOBLE TREN *m* DE ENGRANAJES |
| 4109 | PLATO DIVISOR *m* | 4143 | RUEDA *f* DE ESPIGAS |
| 4109 | PLATILLO *m* DIVISOR | 4144 | DIENTE ANGULAR *m* |
| 4109 | PLATAFORMA *f* DE DIVIDIR | 4144 | DIENTE *m* DOBLE ANGULAR |
| 4109 | PLATILLO *m* DIVIDIDO | 4145 | INTEGRAL *f* DOBLE |
| 4110 | DIAFRAGMA *m* | 4146 | CEPILLO *m* DE DOBLE HOJA |
| 4110 | TABIQUE *m*, MURO DIVISORIO *m*, PARED *f* | 4147 | PALANCA DE DOS BRAZOS *f* |
| 4111 | DIVISOR *m* | 4147 | PALANCA *f* DOBLE |
| 4112 | DIDECAEDRO *m* | 4148 | CALIBRE *m* GAMA DE TOLERANCIAS |
| 4113 | ACOPLAMIENTO *m* DE GARRAS, EMBRAGUE *m* DENTADO | 4149 | MAMELÓN *m* DOBLE, DOBLE PEZÓN *m* |
| | | 4150 | MARCO DENTADO *m* |
| 4114 | DOLERITA *f* | 4150 | MARCO DE CREMALLERAS *m* |
| 4115 | CAZOLETA *f* | 4151 | DOBLE REFRACCIÓN *f* |
| 4116 | YUNQUE *m* PEQUEÑO | 4152 | REMACHE *m* DE DOS HILERAS |
| 4116 | MUELA *f* FLEXIBLE | 4152 | REMACHE *m* DOBLE |
| 4116 | DISCO *m* DE ORILLO DE TEJIDO | 4153 | SAL *f* DOBLE |
| 4116 | CARRO *m* | 4154 | GRIFO *m* DE VÁLVULA DOBLE |
| 4117 | DOLOMITA *f* | 4155 | REMACHE *m* CON DOS CORTES |
| 4117 | DOLOMÍA *f* | 4156 | ACERO *m* |
| 4118 | TUERCA *f* CIEGA | 4156 | ACERO *m* BATIDO DOS VECES |
| 4119 | LÁMPARA *f* DE TECHO | 4156 | ACERO *m* DOBLE REFINADO, ACERO BATIDO DOS VECES |
| 4120 | TECHO *m* ABOMBADO | | |
| 4121 | DEPÓSITO *m* DE TECHO ABOMBADO | 4157 | PRENSA *f* MECÁNICA DE ARCADA |
| 4122 | HIERROS *m pl* PARA BASTIDORES | 4158 | MANGUITO *m* PARA EMPALMAR DOS TUBOS CORTADOS |
| 4123 | CERRADURA *f* DE PORTEZUELA | | |
| 4124 | CHATARRAS *f pl* DE PROTECCIÓN PROPIA | 4159 | MONTANTE *m* GEMINADO |
| 4125 | TRAZO *m* PUNTEADO | 4159 | DOBLE MONTANTE *m* |
| 4125 | LÍNEA *f* DE PUNTOS | 4160 | BROCA *f* DE CORTANTES INVERTIDOS |
| 4125 | LÍNEA *f* DE PUNTOS | 4160 | BROCA *f* CON INVERSIÓN DE CORTES |
| 4126 | TIRALÍNEAS *m* DE PUNTEAR | 4161 | DEPÓSITO *m* DE DOBLE PARED |
| 4127 | POLEA *f* DE BRAZOS DOBLES | 4162 | OPÉRCULO *m* DOBLE |
| 4128 | CORREA DOBLE *f* | 4163 | DOBLE EFECTO *m* (DE) |
| 4129 | FRENO *m* DE DOS MORDAZAS | 4164 | PISTÓN *m* DE DOBLE EFECTO |
| 4129 | FRENO *m* DE DOS ZAPATAS | 4165 | MÁQUINA *f* DE DOBLE EFECTO |
| 4130 | REMACHE *m* CON DOS CUBREJUNTAS | 4166 | VÁLVULA *f* DE DOBLE ASIENTO |
| 4130 | REMACHE *m* CON DOBLE CUBREJUNTAS | 4167 | LLAVE DE HORQUILLA DOBLE *f* |
| 4131 | PALANCA *f* DE TRES BRAZOS | 4167 | LLAVE DE CALIBRE DOBLE *f* |
| 4132 | LABRA *f* CRUZADA | 4168 | MÁQUINA *f* CON DOBLE EXPANSIÓN |
| 4133 | LIMA *f* DE DOBLE TALLA | 4169 | MARTILLO *m* DE DOS BOCAS |
| 4133 | LIMA *f* DE TALLA CRUZADA | 4170 | DOBLE PARED *f* (DE) |
| 4134 | PICADURA *f* CRUZADA (DOBLE) DE UNA LIMA | 4171 | JUNTA *f* RECUBRIDORA SOLDADA POR LOS DOS LADOS |
| 4134 | LABRA *f* CRUZADA | | |
| | | 4172 | DIPOLO |

| | |
|---|---|
| 4173 | PRUEBA *f* DE PLEGADO |
| 4174 | PLATINA *f* |
| 4175 | ESPIGA *f* DE ABROCHADURA |
| 4175 | COLA *f* DE MILANO |
| 4175 | COLA *f* DE MILANO |
| 4176 | FRESAS *f pl* PARA HACER LA COLA DE MILANO |
| 4177 | COLA *f* DE MILANO |
| 4178 | ENSAMBLADURA EN COLA DE MILANO *f* |
| 4179 | MÁQUINA *f* PARA HACER LAS ESPIGAS COLA DE MILANO |
| 4180 | TARUGO *m*, ESPIGA *f* |
| 4180 | ESPIGA *f* DE MADERA |
| 4181 | ESPIGA *f* |
| 4182 | FRESADO *m* DESCENDIENDO |
| 4183 | TUBO *m* |
| 4183 | TUBO *m* DE BAJADA |
| 4184 | AGUA ABAJO, CORRIENTE ABAJO |
| 4184 | DETRÁS DE, AGUAS ABAJO |
| 4185 | TUBO *m* DE BAJADA |
| 4186 | EMBUDO *m* DE COLADA, BEBEDERO *m* |
| 4187 | CURSO *m* DESCENDENTE DEL ÉMBOLO (DEL PISTÓN), DESCENSO *m* (O BAJADA *f* ) DEL ÉMBOLO |
| 4187 | CARRERA DESCENDIENTE DEL ÉMBOLO *f* |
| 4188 | VERTEDERO *m* DE LOS PLATILLOS |
| 4189 | CARBURADOR INVERTIDO *m* |
| 4190 | SOLDADURA *f* EN POSICIÓN PLANA |
| 4191 | TIEMPO *m* MUERTO |
| 4192 | SOLDADURA *f* EN POSICIÓN VERTICAL DESCENDENTE |
| 4193 | MATRIZADO *m* POR DESCENSO ACCIONADO |
| 4194 | GAS *m* POBRE |
| 4195 | DIBUJAR |
| 4195 | TRAZAR |
| 4196 | TIRO *m* |
| 4196 | REBAJAMIENTO *m*, REDUCCIÓN *f* |
| 4196 | REDUCCIÓN *f* CONICIDAD |
| 4197 | ÁNGULO DE RETIRO *m* |
| 4198 | GABINETE *m* DE DIBUJO |
| 4199 | PARTE *f* DE DEBAJO (DEL MOLDE) |
| 4200 | COEFICIENTE DE CHORRO *m* |
| 4201 | SOLUCIÓN *f* ADHERENTE |
| 4202 | SOLUCIÓN *f* ARRASTRADA |
| 4203 | SANGRE *f* DE DRAGO |
| 4204 | PURGAR |
| 4204 | DESAGUAZAR, AVENAR, VACIAR |
| 4204 | VACIAR |
| 4204 | VACIAR |
| 4205 | GRIFO *m* PURGADOR |
| 4205 | GRIFO *m* DE VACIADO |
| 4206 | PURGA *f* |
| 4207 | TUBO *m* DE DESCARGA |

| | |
|---|---|
| 4207 | TUBO *m* DE EVACUACIÓN |
| 4207 | TUBO *m* DE SALIDA |
| 4207 | TUBO *m* DE DESAGÜE |
| 4208 | TAPÓN *m* DE VACIADO |
| 4209 | DESAGUAZAR EL SUELO (UNA TIERRA HÚMEDA) |
| 4210 | DRENAJE *m* |
| 4210 | DESECACIÓN *f*, DESECADO *m*, AGOTAMIENTO *m* |
| 4210 | DRENAJE *m* |
| 4211 | MANÓMETRO *m* PARA DETERMINACIONES ANEMOMÉTRICAS |
| 4212 | TIRO *m* DE UNA CHIMENEA |
| 4213 | DIBUJANTE, DELINEANTE |
| 4214 | MECÁNICO CONSTRUCTOR |
| 4215 | TIRAR |
| 4216 | BAJAR UNA VERTICAL |
| 4216 | BAJAR UNA PERPENDICULAR |
| 4217 | BARRA *f* DE ENGANCHE |
| 4217 | BARRA *f* DE ENGANCHE |
| 4218 | BANCO *m* DE ESTIRAR |
| 4219 | BATIR, MARTILLAR |
| 4220 | ESTIRAR (ALAMBRE), TREFILAR |
| 4220 | TREFILAR |
| 4221 | LLANA *f*, GARLOPA *f* |
| 4222 | AJUSTAR UNA RUEDA |
| 4222 | AJUSTAR UNA POLEA EN SU EJE |
| 4223 | HILERA *f* |
| 4223 | HILERA *f* DE TREFILAR |
| 4224 | ESTIRAR LOS TUBOS |
| 4225 | TRASIEGO, VACIADO *m* |
| 4226 | TUBULADURA *f* DE PURGA CON CUBETA PERIFÉRICA |
| 4227 | CAJÓN DE TRASIEGO *m* |
| 4228 | ESTIRABILIDAD *f* |
| 4229 | PLANO *m* |
| 4229 | DIBUJO *m*, PLANO *m* |
| 4230 | REVENIDO *m* |
| 4230 | HUECO *m* EN PIEZA COLADA |
| 4230 | ENFRIAMIENTO *m* LENTO |
| 4230 | TREFILADO *m* |
| 4230 | ESTIRADO *m*, ESTIRAMIENTO *m* |
| 4230 | ESTIRADO *m* EN FRÍO |
| 4230 | HILADO *m* |
| 4231 | TABLERO *m* DE DIBUJO |
| 4232 | LATÓN *m* DE ESTIRADO |
| 4233 | GRASA *f* DE ESTIRADO |
| 4234 | MATRIZ PARA ESTIRAR *f*, HILERA *f*, HERRAMIENTA PARA ESTIRAR *f* |
| 4234 | MATRIZ *f* QUE ESTIRAR |
| 4235 | BATIDO *m*, MARTILLADO |
| 4236 | OBJETOS *m pl* E INSTRUMENTOS *m pl* PARA DIBUJO |

| | | |
|---|---|---|
| 4236 | UTILLAJE | *m* PARA DELINEANTE |
| 4237 | MÁQUINA | *f* DE DESMOLDEAR |
| 4238 | OFICINA | *f* DE DIBUJO |
| 4239 | DISPOSITIVO | *m* QUE SE HA DE RETIRAR |
| 4240 | PAPEL | *m* DE DIBUJO |
| 4241 | TIRALÍNEAS | *m* |
| 4242 | CHINCHE | *f* |
| 4243 | MESA | *f* DE DIBUJO |
| 4243 | MESA | *f* DE DIBUJANTE |
| 4244 | HERRAMIENTA | *f* DE TREFILAR |
| 4244 | HERRAMIENTA | *f* DE ESTIRAR |
| 4245 | DIBUJO | *m* (REPRESENTACIÓN GRÁFICA) |

4246 DIBUJO *m* (ARTE DEL DIBUJANTE, DEL DELINEANTE)
4247 ESTIRADO
4248 BARRAS *f pl* DE ACERO ESTIRADAS
4249 HIERROS *m pl* DE MEDIA CAÑA TIRADOS
4250 CHAPAS *f pl* ESTIRADAS
4251 ACERO ESTIRADO *m*
4252 ALAMBRE *m* TREFILADO
4252 ALAMBRE *m* ESTIRADO, ALAMBRE *m* TREFILADO

4253 TRATAR MECÁNICAMENTE LOS MINERALES
4254 DESBARBADOR *m*, RECTIFICADOR *m*
4255 ARENA *f* SECA
4256 SECADERO *m*
4256 SECANTE *m*
4256 SECADERO *m*, ESTUFA *f*
4257 SECANTE *m*
4258 SECADEROS *m pl* DE GRANOS
4259 SECADEROS *m* DE FORRAJES
4260 MANDRIL *m*, HUSILLO *m*
4260 PÚA *f*, ESPIGA *f*
4261 PERNO *m* DE UNIÓN
4262 AGRANDAR (O ENSANCHAR) AGUJEROS CON EL MANDRIL
4262 MANDRILAR UN AGUJERO PARA REMATE
4263 BROCA *f*
4263 BROCA *f*, TALADRO *m*
4264 PERFORAR, TALADRAR, AGUJEREAR
4264 ATRAVESAR, PERFORAR, TALADRAR
4265 TRÉPANO, TALADRO *m*
4266 MANGUITO *m* ADAPTADOR DE BROCAS
4267 GÁLIBO *m* DE PERFORACIÓN
4267 CALIBRE DE TALADRO *m*
4268 GÁLIBOS *m* DE PERFORACIÓN
4269 DIÁMETRO *m* DE LA PUNTA DE LA BROCA
4270 ACEROS DE BARRENAS PARA PERFORACIONES *m pl*
4271 BROCA *f*
4271 BROCA *f*
4272 SEPARADOR TALADRADO *m*

4273 AGUJERO *m* RECTIFICADO
4273 AGUJERO *m* RECTIFICADO
4273 AGUJERO *m* PERFORADO
4274 CHAPA *f* DE AGUJEROS PERFORADOS
4275 AGUJERO *m* DE ROBLÓN PERFORADO
4275 PERFORADO (A)
4276 PERFORADOR *m*
4276 MECÁNICO *m* PERFORADOR, PERFORADOR MECÁNICO
4277 MANDRILADO *m*
4277 ATERRAJADO *m*
4277 TALADRADO *m*, BARRENADO *m*, MANDRILADO *m*
4278 CABEZAL *m* DE TALADRO
4279 ESCARIADOR *m*, MÁQUINA DE ESCARIAR *f*
4279 MÁQUINA *f* DE PERFORAR (O TALADRAR)
4279 MÁQUINA *f* DE PERFORAR
4279 PERFORADORA *f*
4279 TALADRADORA *f*, PERFORADORA *f*
4280 ACEITE *m* PARA TALADRAR
4281 AGUA *f* POTABLE, AGUA PARA BEBER
4281 AGUA *f* POTABLE
4282 GOTA *f*
4283 PARAGOTAS *m*, COLECTOR *m* DE ACEITE
4284 ENGRASE *m* POR CUENTAGOTAS
4285 GOTERA *f*
4286 PINZA *f* DE CHORRO DE AGUA, PINZA *f* DE MANGA
4287 ENGRASE *m* CUENTAGOTAS
4288 CUADRADO DE ARRASTRE *m*
4289 ACCIONAR
4289 ACCIONAR
4289 PONER EN MOVIMIENTO, HACER FUNCIONAR
4290 EJE *m* MOTOR
4291 ACCIONAR POR FRICCIÓN
4292 HINCAR (O CLAVAR) UN CLAVO
4293 METER UNA CUÑA, CLAVETEAR
4293 FORZAR UNA CLAVIJA EN SU RANURA
4294 TRANSMISIÓN *f*
4295 BOTAR UNA CHAVETA
4295 DESCALZAR
4296 EJE MOTRIZ *m*, ÁRBOL DE TRANSMISIÓN *m*
4297 MANDO *m*
4297 ACCIONAMIENTO *m*, PROPULSIÓN *f*
4298 POLEA *f* CONDUCIDA
4298 POLEA *f* RECEPTORA
4298 POLEA *f* CONDUCIDA
4298 POLEA *f* CONDUCIDA
4298 POLEA *f* CONDUCIDA
4299 ÁRBOL *m* CONDUCIDO
4299 ÁRBOL *m* RECEPTOR

| | | | | |
|---|---|---|---|
| 4299 | EJE GUIADO *m* | 4323 | ENGRASADOR *m* CUENTAGOTAS |
| 4300 | RUEDA GUIADA *f* | 4324 | PIEZA *f* MATRIZADA |
| 4300 | RUEDA *f* CONDUCIDA | 4325 | MARTINETE *m*, MARTILLO PILÓN *m* |
| 4300 | RUEDA *f* RECEPTORA | 4325 | MARTINETE *m* |
| 4301 | SALIENTE *m* | 4326 | MARTINETE *m* |
| 4301 | DISPOSITIVO *m* (O PERNO) DE ARRASTRE | 4326 | MARTILLO PILÓN *m*, MARTINETE |
| 4301 | UÑA *f* | 4327 | MARTINETE *m* DE CAÍDA LIBRE |
| 4301 | MANDRIL *m* DE ARRASTRE | 4327 | MARTINETE *m* |
| 4301 | ACCIONADOR *m*, DISPOSITIVO *m* DE ARRASTRE | 4328 | PRUEBA *f* DE FLEXIÓN POR CHOQUE |
| 4302 | PERMISO *m* DE CONDUCIR | 4328 | PRUEBA *f* DE FLEXIÓN AL CHOQUE EN BARRAS NO ENTALLADAS, ENSAYO *m* DE FLEXIÓN POR GOLPE |
| 4303 | ACCIONAMIENTO *m* | | |
| 4304 | ACCIONAMIENTO *m* POR FRICCIÓN | 4328 | PRUEBA *f* AL CHOQUE (DE CAÍDA) |
| 4305 | CADENA DE TRANSMISIÓN *f* | 4329 | PESO *m* DEL MARTINETE |
| 4306 | CADENA DE TRANSMISIÓN *f* | 4330 | ENSAYO *m* DE CAÍDA DE PESO |
| 4306 | CADENA MOTRIZ *f* | 4331 | ESCORIA *f*, GRASAS *f pl*, SUCIEDAD *f* |
| 4307 | AJUSTE *m*, MONTAJE *m*, AJUSTAMIENTO *m* | 4331 | RESIDUOS *m pl*, GRASAS *f pl* |
| 4307 | ACOPLAMIENTO *m* | 4332 | AGUJERO *m* DE SUCIEDAD |
| 4307 | MONTAJE *m* POR AJUSTE | 4333 | TAMBOR *m* |
| 4308 | FRASCO *m* SECADOR | 4333 | POLEA *f* TAMBOR |
| 4308 | FRASCO *m* SECADOR | 4334 | FRENO *m* DE TAMBOR |
| 4309 | ÓRGANO DE ACCIONAMIENTO *m*, MANDO *m* | 4335 | LIMPIEZA *f* EN TAMBOR |
| 4309 | ÓRGANO *m* DE MANDO, ÓRGANO DE ACCIONADO | 4336 | CUCHARA *f* TONEL |
| 4309 | MECANISMO *m* DE MANDO | 4337 | SIERRA *f* OSCILANTE |
| 4310 | EMPOTRAMIENTO *m* | 4338 | SECAR |
| 4310 | BLOQUEO DE UNA CHAVETA *m* | 4338 | DESECAR |
| 4311 | MECANISMO *m* DE ACCIONADO | 4339 | AIRE SECO *m* |
| 4312 | DESCALCE *m* | 4340 | BOMBA *f* DE AIRE SECO |
| 4313 | POLEA *f* CONDUCTORA | 4341 | ANÁLISIS POR VÍA SECA *m* |
| 4313 | POLEA *f* DE ATAQUE | 4342 | AGLUTINANTE *m* SECO |
| 4313 | POLEA *f* DE MANDO | 4343 | PILA *f* SECA |
| 4313 | POLEA *f* MOTRIZ | 4344 | ANTRACITA *f* DE LLAMA LARGA |
| 4313 | POLEA *f* CONDUCTORA | 4345 | COMPRESOR SECO *m* |
| 4314 | CABLE DE TRANSMISIÓN *m* | 4346 | DESTILACIÓN *f* SECA |
| 4314 | CABLE DE TRANSMISIÓN *m* | 4347 | ESTIRADO *m* BRILLANTE |
| 4315 | EJE DEL MOTOR *m*, ÁRBOL DEL MOTOR *m*, ÁRBOL MOTOR *m* | 4348 | CAMISA SECA *f* |
| | | 4349 | TERMOMETALURGIA *f* |
| 4315 | ÁRBOL DE MANDO *m* | 4350 | OXIDACIÓN *f* (O CORROSIÓN *f*) SECA |
| 4316 | PARTE *f* CONDUCTORA | 4351 | VAPOR *m* SECO |
| 4316 | RAMAL *m* TIRANTE, RAMAL *m* CONDUCTOR | 4352 | ESTABILIDAD *f* EN SECO |
| 4316 | RAMAL *m* TIRANTE, RAMAL *m* CONDUCTOR | 4353 | COLADA *f* EN ARENA SECA |
| 4316 | RAMAL *m* CONDUCTOR | 4353 | FUNDICIÓN EN ARENA SECA *f* |
| 4316 | CONDUCTOR *m* (DE UNA ACCIÓN) | 4354 | MOLDEADO *m* EN ARENA SECA |
| 4317 | BIELA *f* DE MANDO | 4354 | MOLDEADO *m* EN ARENA ESTUFADA |
| 4318 | RUEDA *f* LIBRE | 4354 | MOLDEADO *m* CALIENTE |
| 4318 | RUEDA *f* CONDUCTORA | 4355 | SECADERO *m* |
| 4318 | RUEDA *f* MOTRIZ | 4356 | SECADOR *m* |
| 4318 | RUEDA *f* DE MANDO | 4356 | APARATO *m* SECADOR |
| 4319 | ACCIONAMIENTO POR CORREA *m* | 4357 | ACEITE *m* SECATIVO |
| 4320 | CAER DE NUEVO (TRINQUETE) | 4358 | ESTUFA *f* |
| 4321 | CUENTAGOTAS *m* | 4359 | SECADO *m* |
| 4322 | LLANTA *f* DE BASE HUNDIDA | | |

| | |
|---|---|
| 4359 | DESECACIÓN  *f* |
| 4360 | CARBURADOR DE DOBLE CUERPO  *m* |
| 4361 | DÚCTIL |
| 4362 | FUNDICIÓN  *f* CON GRAFITO ESFEROIDAL |
| 4363 | DUCTILIDAD  *f* |
| 4364 | TURBA  *f* ATERRONADA |
| 4365 | ARISTA  *f* CORTANTE REBAJADA |
| 4366 | CROMADO MATE  *m* |
| 4367 | ROJO  *m* OSCURO |
| 4368 | CALDEO AL ROJO OSCURO  *m* |
| 4369 | EMPAÑAMIENTO  *m* |
| 4370 | MAQUETA  *f* |
| 4370 | PREMODELO  *m* |
| 4371 | PAQUETE  *m* PARA LAMINAR |
| 4372 | FUNCIONAR SIN OBJETO ÚTIL |
| 4372 | RANURA  *f* |
| 4373 | CILINDRO  *m* EN VACÍO |
| 4374 | PRUEBA  *f* DE RECALCAMIENTO (O DE APLASTAMIENTO) |
| 4375 | CAMIÓN VOLQUETE  *m* |
| 4376 | VERTIMIENTO  *m*, VERTIDO  *m* |
| 4377 | GRIETA  *f*, HENDIDURA  *f*, FISURA  *f* |
| 4378 | ALEACIÓN BINARIA  *f* |
| 4378 | ALEACIÓN DÚPLEX  *f* |
| 4379 | FRESADORA  *f* DUPLEX DE GRAN RENDIMIENTO |
| 4380 | PROCEDIMIENTO  *m* DUPLEX |
| 4381 | BOMBA  *f* DOBLE |
| 4382 | MÁQUINA  *f* DE SOLDADURA DOBLE PUNTO |
| 4383 | SEGUNDO VACIADO  *m* |
| 4384 | PRUEBA CONTRARIA  *f* |
| 4384 | PRUEBA CONTRARIA  *f* |
| 4385 | CONSERVABILIDAD  *f* |
| 4385 | DURABILIDAD  *f* |
| 4385 | ESTABILIDAD  *f* |
| 4386 | DURABLE |
| 4387 | DURALUMINIO  *m* |
| 4388 | COLADA TRANQUILA  *f* |
| 4389 | POLVO  *m* |
| 4390 | ASPIRADOR  *m* DE POLVO |
| 4391 | SEPARADORES  *m pl* DE POLVO |
| 4392 | CAPTACIÓN DEL GAS Y DESEMPOLVAMIENTO  *f* |
| 4393 | ABRIGO DEL POLVO (AL)  *m* |
| 4394 | ESPOLVOREADO  *m* CON SULFURO |
| 4395 | RÉGIMEN  *m* DE UTILIZACIÓN |
| 4396 | PARADA  *f* TEMPORIZADA |
| 4397 | COLORANTE  *m* |
| 4398 | TENSIÓN DINÁMICA  *f* |
| 4399 | DINÁMICO |
| 4400 | DINÁMICA  *f* |
| 4401 | DINAMITA  *f* |
| 4402 | DINAMO  *f* |

| | |
|---|---|
| 4403 | DINAMÓMETRO  *m* |
| 4404 | DINAMOMÉTRICO |
| 4405 | DINA  *f* |
| 4406 | DINODO  *m* |
| 4407 | DISPROSIO  *m* |
| 4408 | PLIEGUE  *m* |
| 4408 | PLIEGUE  *m*, DOBLEZ  *m* |
| 4409 | TIERRA  *f* |
| 4409 | MASA (TIERR)  *f* |
| 4410 | PONER EN TIERRA |
| 4410 | CONECTAR CON LA TIERRA (ELECTRICIDAD) |
| 4411 | CABLE DE TIERRA  *m* |
| 4412 | MATERIA  *f* COLORANTE MINERAL |
| 4413 | OZOQUERITA  *f* |
| 4413 | CERA FÓSIL  *f* |
| 4414 | EQUIPO  *m* PARA NIVELAR (MOVER) LA TIERRA |
| 4415 | CONTACTO A LA TIERRA  *m* |
| 4415 | TIERRA  *f* (ELECTRICIDAD) |
| 4416 | TUBO  *m* DE BARRO |
| 4416 | TUBO  *m* DE ARCILLA (O DE TIERRA) COCIDA |
| 4417 | PUESTA  *f* A TIERRA |
| 4418 | ABOLLONAMIENTO  *m* (O RESALTO  *m*) DE PUESTA A TIERRA |
| 4419 | BARRA  *f* DE TOMA DE TIERRA |
| 4420 | EXCAVACIONES  *f pl* |
| 4421 | FRACTURA TERROSA  *f* |
| 4422 | AGUA  *f* DE LABARRAQUE (SOLUCIÓN  *f* DE HIPOCLORITO SÓDICO) |
| 4423 | EBANO  *m* |
| 4424 | DESCENTRADO, EXCÉNTRICO |
| 4424 | EXCÉNTRICA  *f* |
| 4425 | EXCÉNTRICO |
| 4426 | CÍRCULOS EXCÉNTRICOS  *m* |
| 4427 | MECANISMO  *m* CON MANIVELA EXCÉNTRICA |
| 4428 | CARGA EXCÉNTRICA  *f* |
| 4429 | SEGMENTO  *m* DE PISTÓN EXCÉNTRICO |
| 4430 | PRENSA  *f* DE EXCÉNTRICA |
| 4431 | BIELA  *f* DE EXCÉNTRICA |
| 4431 | VÁSTAGO  *m* DE EXCÉNTRICA |
| 4432 | CABEZA  *f* DEL VÁSTAGO DE LA EXCÉNTRICA |
| 4433 | EXCÉNTRICA  *f* |
| 4433 | EXCÉNTRICO  *m* |
| 4434 | POLEA  *f* DE EXCÉNTRICA |
| 4434 | DISCO  *m* DE EXCÉNTRICA |
| 4435 | COLLAR DE EXCÉNTRICA  *m* |
| 4435 | MANGUITO  *m* EXCÉNTRICO |
| 4436 | EXCENTRICIDAD  *f* |
| 4437 | ECONOMIZADOR  *m* (DE CARBURANTE) |
| 4438 | CORRIENTE DE FOUCAULT  *f* |
| 4439 | FRENO  *m* DE CORRIENTES DE FOUCAULT |
| 4440 | CORRIENTE DE FOUCAULT  *f* |

4441 CANTO *m*, BORDE *m*
4441 REBORDE *m*
4441 ESPINA *f*, ARISTA *f*, ÁNGULO *m*, BORDE *m*, LIMA *f*
4441 ORILLA *f*, BORDE *m*
4442 LEVA *f*, EXCÉNTRICA *f*
4442 LEVA *f* DE DISCO CURVO
4443 DISLOCACIÓN *f* EN ESQUINA
4444 DISPOSITIVO *m* PARA MARCA LAS ORILLAS
4445 JUNTA *f* SOBRE CORTES
4446 FRESA *f* AXIAL
4447 BORDE *m*, O ARISTA *f*, DE UN ORIFICIO
4448 ARISTA DE RETROCESO *f*
4449 PREPARACIÓN *f* DE LOS BORDES
4450 MUELA *f* VERTICAL
4450 MOLINO *m* CON MUELAS VERTICALES
4451 MATRIZ *f* REDONDA Y DIVIDIDA CON JAULA VACIADORA
4452 RECHAZO *m*, IMPULSIÓN *f* BATIDO *m*
4453 MÁQUINAS *f pl* PLEGADORAS
4454 JAULA DE DESCARGA *f*
4455 RANURA DE PASO *f*
4455 PASADA *f* RIBETEADORA
4456 JAULA DE CILINDROS VERTICALES CILINDRO DE DESCARGA *f*
4457 CALOR ÚTIL *m*
4457 CALOR EFECTIVO *m*
4458 POTENCIA *f* AL FRENO
4458 POTENCIA *f* EFECTIVA
4459 PRESIÓN *f* REAL
4459 PRESIÓN *f* ABSOLUTA
4460 SECCIÓN *f* CARGADA
4461 EFERVESCENCIA *f*
4461 EBULLICIÓN *f*, EFERVESCENCIA *f*, FORMACIÓN *f* DE ESPUMA
4461 EFERVESCENCIA *f*
4462 ACERO EFERVESCENTE *m*
4462 ACERO EFERVESCENTE *m*
4463 RENDIMIENTO *m*
4463 EFECTO *m* ÚTIL
4464 EFLORESCENCIA *f*
4465 EFUSIÓN *f*
4466 EFUSIÓN *f* DE GASES
4467 CODO AL 1/2 *m*
4468 EXPULSAR, LANZAR
4468 DESMOLDEAR
4469 EYECTOR *m*
4470 CONDENSADOR *m* DE CHORRO (O DE EYECCIÓN)
4470 CONDENSADOR POR EYECCIÓN *m*
4471 DESHORNE *m* POR EXTRACTOR DE BRAZOS
4472 EYECTOR *m*
4472 ASPIRADOR *m*, EXPULSOR *m*

4473 ELÁSTICO
4474 EFECTO *m* POSTERIOR ELÁSTICO
4475 CONSTANTE DE ELASTICIDAD *f*
4476 MANGUITO *m* ELÁSTICO
4476 ACOPLAMIENTO ELÁSTICO *m*
4477 FLEXIÓN *f* ELÁSTICA
4478 DEFORMACIÓN *f* ELÁSTICA
4479 DIAFRAGMA *m* ELÁSTICO
4479 MEMBRANA *f*
4480 FUERZA *f* ELÁSTICA DE UN GAS
4481 LÍMITE *m* DE ELASTICIDAD
4481 LÍMITE *m* ELÁSTICO, LÍMITE DE LA ELASTICIDAD
4481 AMPERIO-HORA *m*
4482 JUNTA *f* PLÁSTICA
4482 GUARNICIÓN *f*
4483 MÓDULO *m* DE ELASTICIDAD
4484 SÓLIDO *m* ELÁSTICO
4485 DEFORMACIÓN *f* ELÁSTICA
4486 ARANDELA *f* ELÁSTICA
4487 ELASTICIDAD *f*
4488 ELASTICIDAD *f* DE COMPRESIÓN
4489 ELASTICIDAD *f* DE FLEXIÓN
4490 ELASTICIDAD *f* DE TORSIÓN
4491 ELASTICIDAD *f* DE TRACCIÓN
4492 DEPÓSITO *m* ELEVADO
4493 CODO *m*
4494 ARCO VOLTAICO *m*
4495 HORNO *m* AL ARCO
4496 SOLDADOR ELÉCTRICO *m*
4497 CALDERA ELÉCTRICA *f*
4498 SOLDADURA *f* ELÉCTRICA A FUEGO
4499 BOBINA *f*
4500 CORRIENTE ELÉCTRICA *f*
4501 DENSIDAD *f* ELÉCTRICA
4501 DENSIDAD *f* DE CORRIENTE
4502 DESCARGA *f* ELÉCTRICA
4503 MANDO ELÉCTRICO *m*
4504 CAMPO ELÉCTRICO *m*
4505 CAMPO ELÉCTRICO *m*
4506 INTENSIDAD *f* ELÉCTRICA DEL CAMPO
4507 HORNO *m* ELÉCTRICO
4508 RECOCIDO *m* EN EL HORNO ELÉCTRICO
4509 FUNDICIÓN *f* ELÉCTRICA
4510 FUNDICIÓN *f* EN HORNO ELÉCTRICO
4511 ACERO ELABORADO AL HORNO ELÉCTRICO *m*
4511 ACERO ELÉCTRICO *m*
4512 CENTRAL ELÉCTRICA *f*
4512 FÁBRICA *f* CENTRAL ELÉCTRICA
4513 CALEFACCIÓN ELÉCTRICA *f*, CALDEO ELÉCTRICO *m*

| | | | |
|---|---|---|---|
| 4514 | ENCENDIDO ELÉCTRICO *m* | 4551 | ELECTRICISTA *m* |
| 4515 | HORNO *m* ELÉCTRICO DE INDUCCIÓN | 4552 | ELECTRICIDAD *f* |
| 4516 | LÁMPARA *f* ELÉCTRICA | 4553 | CONTADOR DE LUZ *m* |
| 4517 | LUZ *f* ELÉCTRICA | 4554 | ELECTRIFICACIÓN *f* |
| 4518 | ALUMBRADO *m* ELÉCTRICO | 4555 | ELECTRIFICAR |
| 4519 | LÍNEA *f* DE ALUMBRADO | 4556 | BARRENO *m* ELÉCTRICO |
| 4520 | LOCOMOTORA *f* ELÉCTRICA | 4556 | BROCA *f* ELÉCTRICA |
| 4521 | LÍNEA *f* DE TRANSPORTE A LARGA DISTANCIA | 4557 | MOLDEO *m* ELÉCTRICO |
| 4522 | MÁQUINA *f* ELÉCTRICA | 4558 | AFINO ELECTROLÍTICO *m* |
| 4523 | CONDUCTO ELÉCTRICO *m* LÍNEA DE FLUIDO ELÉCTRICO *f* | 4559 | CORTE POR ELECTRO-EROSIÓN *m* |
| 4523 | LÍNEA *f* CONDUCTORA | 4560 | ELECTROQUÍMICO |
| 4523 | LÍNEA *f* | 4561 | ELECTROQUÍMICA *f* |
| 4524 | GRUPOS *m* ELECTRÓGENOS | 4562 | RECUBRIMIENTO *m* DE UN METAL POR VÍA ELECTROQUÍMICA |
| 4524 | MOTORES *m pl* ELÉCTRICOS | 4563 | ELECTRODINÁMICO |
| 4525 | CORRIENTE ELÉCTRICA ENERGIA *f* | 4564 | ELECTRODINAMÓMETRO *m* |
| 4526 | LÍNEA *f* DE TRANSPORTE DE ENERGÍA | 4565 | ELECTROEROSIÓN *f* |
| 4527 | REGULADOR *m* ELÉCTRICO | 4566 | ZINGAJE *m* ELECTROQUÍMICO ELECTROLÍTICO |
| 4528 | RESISTENCIA *f* ELÉCTRICA | 4567 | ELECTROIMÁN *m* |
| 4529 | SACUDIDA *f* ELÉCTRICA | 4568 | ELECTROSTÁTICO |
| 4529 | CHOQUE *m*, SACUDIDA *f* | 4569 | ELECTROTIPIA *f* |
| 4529 | CONMOCIÓN *f* | 4570 | ELECTROANÁLISIS *f* |
| 4530 | SOLDADOR *m* ELÉCTRICO | 4571 | EQUIVALENTE ELECTROMAGNÉTICO |
| 4531 | CHISPORROTEO *m* ELÉCTRICO | 4572 | RECTIFICADOR *m* ELECTROQUÍMICO |
| 4531 | ELECTROEROSIÓN *f* | 4573 | ELECTROQUÍMICA *f* |
| 4532 | ACERO AL HORNO ELÉCTRICO *m* | 4574 | ELECTRODO *m* |
| 4533 | SOLDADURA *f* (AL ARCO) ELÉCTRICA | 4575 | PORTAELECTRODO *m* |
| 4534 | ACUMULADOR ELÉCTRICO *m* | 4576 | METAL *m* DE ELECTRODO |
| 4534 | BATERÍA *f*, ACUMULADOR *m* | 4577 | POTENCIAL *m* DE ELECTRODO |
| 4534 | PILA *f* SECUNDARIA | 4578 | PUNTA *f* DEL ELECTRODO |
| 4535 | COMPARADOR ELÉCTRICO *m* | 4579 | PUNTA *f* DE ELECTRODO |
| 4536 | CONDUCTIBILIDAD ELÉCTRICA *f* | 4580 | DEPÓSITO *m* ELECTROLÍTICO |
| 4537 | CONDUCTOR ELÉCTRICO *m* | 4581 | DISOLUCIÓN *f* ELECTROLÍTICA |
| 4538 | METALES *m pl* UTILIZADOS COMO CONTACTO ELÉCTRICO | 4582 | EXTRACCIÓN *f* ELECTROLÍTICA |
| 4539 | ENERGÍA *f* (ELÉCTRICA) | 4583 | GALVANIZACIÓN *f* (CON CINC) ELECTROLÍTICA |
| 4539 | TRABAJO *m* ELÉCTRICO | 4584 | CALIBRE DE TOLERANCIAS *m* |
| 4540 | INGENIERO *m* ELECTRICISTA | 4585 | ELECTROLIZAR |
| 4541 | ELECTRICIDAD *f* INDUSTRIAL | 4586 | ELECTRÓLISIS *f* |
| 4542 | EQUIPO *m* ELÉCTRICO | 4587 | ELECTRÓLITO *m* |
| 4543 | MONTADOR *m* ELECTRICISTA | 4588 | CÉLULA (O CUBA) ELECTROLÍTICA *f* |
| 4544 | CHAPA *f* DE TRANSFORMADOR | 4589 | DECAPADO *m* (LIMPIEZA *f*) ELECTROLÍTICO |
| 4544 | CHAPA *f* ELÉCTRICA | 4590 | CONDENSADOR ELECTROLÍTICO *m* |
| 4545 | AISLACIÓN *f* ELÉCTRICA | 4591 | COBRE *m* ELECTROLÍTICO |
| 4546 | POTENCIA/ALIMENTACIÓN *f* | 4592 | DEPÓSITO *m* GALVANIZADO |
| 4547 | OSCILACIÓN *f* ELÉCTRICA | 4593 | DEPÓSITO *m* ELECTROLÍTICO |
| 4548 | RESISTIVIDAD *f* | 4593 | DEPÓSITO *m* ELECTROLÍTICO |
| 4548 | RESISTENCIA *f* ESPECÍFICA | 4594 | ANÁLISIS ELECTROLÍTICO *m* |
| 4549 | VÁLVULA *f* ELÉCTRICA | 4595 | DISOCIACIÓN *f* ELECTROLÍTICA |
| 4549 | VÁLVULA *f* ELÉCTRICA | 4596 | DESCOMPOSICIÓN *f* ELECTROLÍTICA |
| 4550 | FUNDICIÓN *f* ELÉCTRICA | 4596 | IONIZACIÓN *f* |
| | | 4597 | HORNO *m* DE CRISOL |

| | |
|---|---|
| 4598 | ORO *m* ELECTROLÍTICO |
| 4599 | MANGANESO *m* ELECTROLÍTICO |
| 4600 | NÍQUEL *m* ELECTROLÍTICO |
| 4601 | OXIDACIÓN *f* ELECTROLÍTICA |
| 4602 | SEPARACIÓN *f* ELECTROLÍTICA |
| 4603 | DECAPADO *m* ELECTROLÍTICO |
| 4604 | POLARIZACIÓN *f* ELECTROLÍTICA |
| 4605 | PULIMENTO *m* ELÉCTRICO |
| 4606 | RECTIFICADOR *m* (O DETECTOR) ELECTROLÍTICO |
| 4607 | REDUCCIÓN *f* ELECTROLÍTICA |
| 4607 | NEGATIVACIÓN *f* |
| 4608 | PLATA *f* ELECTROLÍTICA |
| 4609 | TENSIÓN *f* DE SOLUCIÓN ELECTROLÍTICA |
| 4610 | COBRE *m* ELECTROLÍTICO DE ÓXIDO CUPROSO |
| 4611 | ELECTROIMÁN *m* |
| 4612 | ELECTROMAGNÉTICO |
| 4613 | FRENO *m* ELECTROMAGNÉTICO |
| 4614 | APARATO *m* ELECTROMAGNÉTICO PARA ENSAYOS DE DUREZA |
| 4615 | INDUCCIÓN *f* MAGNETOELÉCTRICA |
| 4616 | DISPERSIÓN ELECTROMAGNÉTICA |
| 4617 | SOLDADURA *f* POR PERCUSIÓN ELECTROMAGNETICA |
| 4618 | SEPARACIÓN *f* ELECTROMAGNÉTICA |
| 4619 | SOLDADURA *f* POR INDUCCIÓN |
| 4620 | ELECTROMAGNETISMO *m* |
| 4621 | ELECTROMETALURGIA *f* |
| 4622 | F.E.M., FUERZA *f* ELECTROMOTRIZ |
| 4622 | FUERZA *f* ELECTROMOTRIZ |
| 4623 | ELECTROMOTOR *m* |
| 4623 | MOTOR *m* ELÉCTRICO |
| 4624 | ELECTRÓN *m* |
| 4625 | HAZ *m* DE ELECTRONES |
| 4626 | LENTE DE CONCENTRACIÓN DE LOS ELECTRONES |
| 4627 | SOLDADURA *f* POR BOMBARDEO ELECTRÓNICO |
| 4628 | CAÑÓN ELECTRÓNICO *m* |
| 4629 | MICROSCOPIO *m* ELECTRÓNICO |
| 4630 | SOLDADURA *f* POR HAZ DE ELECTRONES |
| 4631 | ELECTRONEGATIVO |
| 4632 | COMPARADOR ELECTRÓNICO *m* |
| 4633 | ENCENDIDO ELECTRÓNICO *m* |
| 4634 | RECTIFICADOR *m* ELECTRÓNICO |
| 4635 | REGULADOR *m* ELECTRÓNICO |
| 4636 | TUBOS *m pl* ELECTRÓNICOS |
| 4637 | ELECTRÓNICA *f* |
| 4638 | ELECTROÓSMOSIS *f* |
| 4639 | ELECTROFÓRESIS *f* |
| 4639 | CATAFORSIS *f* |
| 4640 | GALVANOPLASTIA *f* |
| 4640 | GALVANOPLASTIA *f* |
| 4640 | ELECTROQUÍMICA *f* |

| | |
|---|---|
| 4641 | ELECTROPOSITIVO |
| 4642 | FUERZA *f* ELECTROSTÁTICA |
| 4643 | GENERADOR *m* ELECTROSTÁTICO |
| 4644 | INDUCCIÓN *f* ELECTROSTÁTICA |
| 4645 | SOLDADURA *f* POR PERCUSIÓN CON CONDENSADOR |
| 4646 | SEPARACIÓN *f* ELECTROSTÁTICA |
| 4647 | ELECTROTÉCNICO |
| 4648 | ELECTROTÉCNICA *f* |
| 4649 | RENDIMIENTO *m* ELECTROTÉRMICO |
| 4650 | ELECTROTÉRMICA *f* |
| 4651 | GALVANOPLASTIA *f* |
| 4652 | EXTRACCIÓN *f* ELECTROLÍTICA |
| 4653 | ELECTRO *m* |
| 4653 | ELECTRO *m* |
| 4654 | ELEMENTO *m* |
| 4654 | CUERPO SIMPLE *m* |
| 4655 | ANÁLISIS ELEMENTAL *m* |
| 4656 | RESINA *f* ELEMÍ |
| 4656 | ELEMÍ *m* |
| 4657 | ELECTROANÁLISIS *f* |
| 4658 | TEMPERATURA *f* ELEVADA |
| 4659 | ELEVACIÓN *f* |
| 4659 | PROYECCIÓN *f* VERTICAL |
| 4660 | ASCENSOR *m* |
| 4661 | ELEVADORES *m pl* DE HENO Y DE PAJA |
| 4662 | ELIMINAR |
| 4663 | ELIMINAR |
| 4663 | ELIMINAR CALOR |
| 4664 | ELIMINACIÓN *f* |
| 4665 | EVACUACIÓN *f* DEL AIRE DE UN CONDUCTO |
| 4666 | SUBSTRACCIÓN *f* DEL CALOR |
| 4667 | ELIMINACIÓN *f* |
| 4667 | ELIMINACIÓN *f* |
| 4668 | ALEACIÓN *f* INVARIABLE |
| 4669 | ELIPSE *f* |
| 4669 | ÓVALO *m* |
| 4670 | ELIPSÓGRAFO *m* |
| 4671 | ELIPSOIDE *f* |
| 4672 | ELIPSOIDE *f* DE REVOLUCIÓN |
| 4672 | ELIPSOIDE *f* DE REVOLUCIÓN |
| 4673 | CABEZA *f* DE GOTA DE SEBO DE UN TORNILLO |
| 4674 | SECCIÓN *f* ELÍPTICA |
| 4675 | CILINDRO *m* ELÍPTICO |
| 4676 | INTEGRAL *f* ELÍPTICA |
| 4677 | RUEDA *f* ELÍPTICA |
| 4677 | ENGRANAJE *m* ELÍPTICO, RUEDA *f* ELÍPTICA |
| 4678 | ALAMBRE *m* OVAL |
| 4678 | HILO *m* (ELÍPTICO) |
| 4679 | ALARGAMIENTO *m* |
| 4680 | EXTENSIÓN *f* |

| | | | | |
|---|---|---|---|---|
| 4681 | ELUTRIACIÓN *f* | | 4718 | ASERRADO *m* VERTICAL |
| 4681 | LEVIGACIÓN *f* (QUIM.) | | 4718 | ASERRADO *m* DE TRAVÉS |
| 4681 | LAVADO *m* (DE LA ARENA) | | 4719 | MADERA *f* CORTADA A CONTRAHILO |
| 4681 | CLASIFICACIÓN *f* POR CORRIENTE GASEOSA | | 4720 | SOPORTE *m* DE EXTREMO |
| 4682 | EMPOTRAR EN EL HORMIGÓN | | 4721 | MUÑÓN *m* GIRATORIO FRONTAL |
| 4683 | GRADO *m* DE PENETRACIÓN, DE EMPOTRAMIENTO | | 4721 | MUÑÓN *m* GIRATORIO DE EXTREMO |
| | | | 4722 | FRESA *f* DE ALLANAR, FRESA *f* DE ALISAR |
| 4684 | RELIEVE *m*, REPUJADO *m* | | 4722 | FRESA *f* DE CORTE FRONTAL |
| 4685 | AUMENTO DE FRAGILIDAD *m* | | 4722 | FRESA *f* FRONTAL |
| 4685 | FRAGILIDAD *f* | | 4722 | FRESA *f* FRONTAL |
| 4686 | GERMEN *m* | | 4722 | FRESA *f* RADIAL |
| 4686 | EMBRIÓN *m* | | 4723 | FRESAS *f pl* EN EXTREMO |
| 4687 | FRENO *m* DE SOCORRO | | 4724 | FINAL *m* DE PROGRAMA |
| 4688 | ALUMBRADO *m* AUXILIAR, ALUMBRADO DE EMERGENCIA | | 4725 | FINAL *m* DE CINTA |
| | | | 4726 | SOPORTE DE EXTREMO *m* |
| 4688 | ALUMBRADO *m* AUXILIAR, ALUMBRADO DE EMERGENCIA | | 4727 | JUEGO *m* AXIAL |
| | | | 4728 | PARED *f* FRONTAL |
| 4689 | ALUMBRADO *m* AUXILIAR, ALUMBRADO DE EMERGENCIA | | 4729 | CARAS CENTRADAS (DE) *f* |
| 4690 | LÍNEA *f* DE SOCORRO | | 4730 | FINAL *m* DE BLOQUE |
| 4690 | LÍNEA DE EMERGENCIA *f* | | 4731 | FINAL *m* DE LÍNEA |
| 4691 | RAYO *m* EMERGENTE | | 4732 | CADENA SINFÍN *f* |
| 4692 | ESMERIL *m* | | 4733 | CABLE SINFIN *m* |
| 4693 | PAPEL *m* DE ESMERIL | | 4734 | EMPUJE *m* LONGITUDINAL |
| 4694 | PULIR CON ESMERIL | | 4734 | EMPUJE *m* AXIAL |
| 4695 | PULIMENTO *m* CON ESMERIL | | 4735 | JUEGO *m* LATERAL DE LOS ÁRBOLES |
| 4696 | PAPEL *m* DE ESMERIL | | 4736 | ENDÓSMOSIS |
| 4697 | POLVO *m* DE ESMERIL | | 4737 | ENDOTÉRMICO |
| 4698 | MUELA *f* DE ESMERIL | | 4738 | RESISTENCIA *f* |
| 4699 | ESMERIL *m* | | 4739 | FISURA *f* DE FATIGA/ DE RESISTENCIA |
| 4699 | CORINDÓN *m* | | 4740 | RUPTURA *f* DE FATIGA / DE CONSISTENCIA |
| 4700 | EMISIÓN *f* | | 4741 | LÍMITE *m* DE RESISTENCIA |
| 4701 | PODER *m* AMISIVO | | 4742 | RESISTENCIA *f* DE RUPTURA POR FRACCIÓN |
| 4702 | PODER *m* RADIANTE | | 4742 | RELACIÓN *f* : LÍMITE *f* DE FATIGA |
| 4703 | EMITIR RAYOS | | 4743 | PRUEBA *f* DE FATIGA / DE RESISTENCIA |
| 4704 | FÓRMULA *f* BRUTA | | 4744 | SUBSTANCIA *f* ACTIVADORA |
| 4705 | TUBULADURA *f* DE SALIDA/DE ASPIRACIÓN | | 4745 | ENERGÍA *f* |
| 4706 | ACEITE *m* EMULSIONADO | | 4746 | EFICACIA *f* ENERGÉTICA |
| 4707 | EMULSIONAR | | 4747 | CONSUMO *m* DE ENERGÍA |
| 4708 | EMULSIÓN *f* | | 4747 | TRABAJO *m* ABSORBIDO |
| 4709 | ESMALTE *m* | | 4747 | POTENCIA *f* RECOGIDA |
| 4710 | ESMALTAR | | 4747 | POTENCIA *f* ABSORBIDA |
| 4711 | PINTURA *f* AL BARNIZ | | 4748 | ENERGÍA *f* DE DESCARGA |
| 4712 | ESMALTADO *m* | | 4749 | ENGATILLAR, ENGANCHAR, EMBRAGAR |
| 4713 | ENANTIOTRÓPICO | | 4749 | ENGANCHAR, ENGATAR, ENCLAVAR |
| 4714 | VIGA *f* ENVUELTA | | 4750 | EMPLEAR, ADMITIR, COLOCAR |
| 4715 | MOTOR *m* BLINDADO O CON CORAZA | | 4750 | ENGRANAR |
| 4715 | MOTOR *m* CON CÁRTER | | 4751 | ENCLAVAMIENTO, ENGATILLADO *m* |
| 4716 | CODIFICACIÓN *f* | | 4751 | ENCLAVAMIENTO *m*, ENGATILLADO *m* |
| 4717 | VISTA *f* ANTERIOR POSTERIOR | | 4752 | ENGRANE *m* |
| 4718 | TRONZADO *m* DE LA MADERA | | 4753 | SALA *f* DE MÁQUINAS |
| 4718 | ASERRADO *m* A CONTRAHÍLO | | 4754 | SOPORTE *m* MOTOR |

| | |
|---|---|
| 4755 | ACEITE *m* PARA MAQUINARIA |
| 4756 | ÓRGANO *m* DE MÁQUINA |
| 4757 | SALA DE MÁQUINAS *f* |
| 4757 | SALA *f* DE MÁQUINAS |
| 4758 | ÁRBOL HORIZONTAL *m*, ÁRBOL MOTOR *m*, ARBOL DE IMPULSIÓN *m* |
| 4758 | ÁRBOL MOTOR *m* |
| 4759 | MÁQUINA *f* DE VAPOR SOBRECALENTADO |
| 4760 | FRENO-MOTOR *m* |
| 4761 | INGENIERO *m* |
| 4762 | INGENIERO *m* JEFE |
| 4763 | FUNDICIÓN *f* MECÁNICA |
| 4764 | TALLER DE CONSTRUCCIÓN MECÁNICA *m* |
| 4764 | TALLERES *m, pl* (ESTABLECIMIENTO) DE CONSTRUCCIÓN DE MAQUINARIA |
| 4764 | FÁBRICA *f* DE CONSTRUCCIÓN MECÁNICA |
| 4765 | MECÁNICO *m* (OFICIO) *m* |
| 4765 | CONDUCTOR DE MÁQUINA *m* |
| 4765 | MAQUINISTA AMB |
| 4766 | MOTORES *m pl* FIJOS Y MÓVILES |
| 4767 | COBRE *m* PARA GRABADO |
| 4768 | ENSANCHAMIENTO *m* DE UN TUBO |
| 4769 | AMPLIACIÓN DE UN DIBUJO |
| 4770 | VIENTO *m* RICO EN OXÍGENO |
| 4771 | AIRE FALSO (INFILTRADO, SECUNDARIO) *m* |
| 4771 | ENTRADA *f* DE AIRE |
| 4772 | INCLUSIÓN *f* DE ESCORIA |
| 4773 | ENTROPÍA *f* |
| 4774 | LADO DE INTRODUCCIÓN *m*, PARTE DE INTRODUCCIÓN *f* |
| 4774 | LADO DE ENTRADA *m*, PARTE DE ENTRADA *f* |
| 4775 | LÍNEA *f* DE RODILLOS DE TRAÍDA |
| 4776 | ENVOLVENTE *f* |
| 4777 | LUSTRE *m* |
| 4778 | TREN *m* EPICICLOIDAL |
| 4779 | EPICICLOIDE |
| 4780 | ENGRANAJE *m* EPICICLOIDAL, DENTADO *m* EPICICLOIDAL |
| 4780 | DENTADO *m* EPICICLOIDAL, ENGRANAJE *m* EPICICLOIDAL |
| 4781 | ANGULAR DE LADOS IGUALES *m* |
| 4782 | ECUACIÓN *f* |
| 4783 | ECUACIÓN *f* DE ESTADO |
| 4784 | CRISTALES *m pl* DE EJES IGUALES |
| 4785 | TRIÁNGULO *m* EQUILÁTERO |
| 4786 | EQUILIBRIO *m* |
| 4787 | CONSTANTE DE EQUILIBRIO *f* |
| 4788 | DIAGRAMA *m* DE EQUILIBRIO |
| 4789 | TENSIÓN *f* DE EQUILIBRIO |
| 4790 | TENSIÓN *f* DE EQUILIBRIO DE UNA REACCIÓN |
| 4791 | TEMPERATURA *f* DE EQUILIBRIO |
| 4792 | VALOR *m* DE EQUILIBRIO |

| | |
|---|---|
| 4793 | EQUILIBRIO *m* |
| 4794 | UTILLAJE *m* |
| 4795 | EQUIVALENCIA *f* |
| 4796 | EQUIVALENTE |
| 4797 | CONDUCTIBILIDAD EQUIVALENTE *f* |
| 4798 | RESISTIVIDAD *f* EQUIVALENTE |
| 4799 | RASPAR |
| 4799 | BORRAR |
| 4800 | RASPADOR *m* DE OFICINA, RASPADOR *m* DE DESPACHO |
| 4800 | RASPADOR *m* DE DELINEANTE |
| 4801 | GOMA *f* RASPADOR *m* |
| 4802 | RASPADO *m* |
| 4803 | RASPADO (RESULTADO) |
| 4804 | ERBIO *m* |
| 4805 | ERIGIR, PONER ENHIESTO, EDIFICAR |
| 4806 | LEVANTAR UNA PERPENDICULAR |
| 4806 | LEVANTAR UNA VERTICAL |
| 4807 | ASCIENDE SIMULTÁNEAMENTE O DE CONTINUO |
| 4808 | MONTAJE *m* |
| 4809 | MATERIAL *m* DE MONTAJE |
| 4810 | MATERIAL *m* DE MONTAJE |
| 4811 | TALLER *m* DE MONTAJE |
| 4812 | UTILLAJE *m* PARA MONTAJE |
| 4813 | MONTAJE *m* |
| 4814 | PLANO *m* DE MONTAJE |
| 4815 | MONTAJE *m* |
| 4816 | MONTADOR *m* |
| 4817 | UTILLAJE *m* DEL MONTADOR |
| 4818 | ERGIO *m* |
| 4818 | ERGIO *m* |
| 4819 | MÁQUINA *f* DE ENSAYOS DE EMBUTICIÓN DE ERICHSEN |
| 4820 | EROSIÓN *f* |
| 4820 | DESGASTE *m* |
| 4821 | ROCA *f* ERRÁTICA |
| 4822 | ERROR *m* |
| 4823 | CONTADOR DE ERRORES *m* |
| 4824 | ERROR *m* DE CÁLCULO |
| 4825 | ERROR *m* DE DISEÑO DEL CONSTRUCTOR |
| 4826 | ERROR *m* DE LECTURA |
| 4827 | ERROR *m* DE APRECIACIÓN |
| 4828 | ERROR *m* DE COLIMACIÓN |
| 4829 | ERROR *m* DE OBSERVACIÓN |
| 4830 | CONTADOR DE ERRORES *m* |
| 4831 | MALVARROSA *f* SOLUBLE |
| 4831 | ERITROSINA *f* |
| 4831 | ERITROSINA *f* |
| 4832 | ESCAPARSE |
| 4832 | ESCAPAR, ESCAPARSE, SALIR |
| 4833 | ESCAPE *m* DE VAPOR |

| | | | | |
|---|---|---|---|---|
| 4833 | ESCAPE *m* DE GAS | | 4866 | PÉRDIDA *f* POR EVAPORACIÓN |
| 4834 | CÍRCULO EXINSCRITO *m* | | 4867 | VAPORIZACIÓN *f* |
| 4835 | TAPA-ENTRADA *f*, GUARDAPOLVOS *m*, ESCUDETE *m* | | 4867 | EVAPORACIÓN *f* |
| 4835 | ARANDELA *f* PROTECTORA | | 4868 | CONDENSADOR DE EVAPORACIÓN *m* |
| 4836 | ACEITE *m* VOLÁTIL | | 4869 | APARATO *m* EVAPORADOR |
| 4836 | ACEITE *m* ESENCIAL | | 4870 | CAJA DEL CUERPO DE UN EVAPORADOR *f* |
| 4837 | ETER *m* COMPUESTO | | 4871 | ROTURA LISA *f* |
| 4838 | PRESUPUESTO *m*, ESTIMACIÓN DE LOS COSTES | | 4871 | ACEPILLADORA *f* |
| 4838 | PRESUPUESTO *m* | | 4872 | NÚMERO *m* PAR |
| 4839 | ATACAR AL ÁCIDO | | 4873 | EVOLUTA *f* |
| 4840 | BANDAS *f pl* REVELADAS POR ATAQUE QUÍMICO | | 4873 | EVOLUTA *f* |
| 4841 | GRIETAS *f pl* DE ATAQUE QUÍMICO | | 4874 | DESPRENDIMIENTO *m* DE CALOR |
| 4842 | FIGURAS *f pl* DE ATAQUE AL ÁCIDO | | 4875 | MEDICIÓN *f* PRECISA |
| 4843 | PICADURAS *f pl* A CAUSA DE LA CORROSIÓN | | 4875 | MEDICIÓN *f* EXACTA |
| 4844 | REACTIVO *m* | | 4876 | CONTROL *m* |
| 4845 | FIGURA *f* DE CORROSIÓN | | 4876 | EXAMEN *m* |
| 4846 | ATAQUE *m* AL ÁCIDO | | 4877 | INSPECCIÓN *f* CON TRÉPANO |
| 4846 | ATAQUE *m* CORROSIVO | | 4878 | EXCESO *m* |
| 4847 | REACTIVO *m* DE ATAQUE CON ÁCIDO | | 4879 | LIMITADOR *m* O REGULADOR *m* DE CAUDAL |
| 4847 | CÁUSTICO *m* CORROSIVO *m* | | 4880 | EXCESO *m* DE TRABAJO |
| 4847 | CÁUSTICO *m*, CORROSIVO *m* | | 4881 | SOBRETENSIÓN *f* |
| 4848 | ETANO *m* | | 4882 | LLAMA *f* REDUCTORA |
| 4848 | HIDRURO *m* DE ETILO | | 4883 | LLAMA OXIDANTE |
| 4848 | DIMETIL *m* | | 4884 | INTERCAMBIO *m* DE CALOR |
| 4849 | CLORURO DE ETILO *m* | | 4885 | EXCITACIÓN *f* |
| 4849 | CLORURO *m* ETÍLICO | | 4886 | ÁNODO DE EXCITACIÓN *m* |
| 4850 | ETER *m* NÍTRICO | | 4887 | EXCITAR |
| 4850 | ETER NÍTRICO | | 4888 | EXCITATRIZ *f*, EXCITADORA *f* |
| 4850 | NITRATO *m* DE ETILO | | 4889 | DESCASCADO *m*, EXFOLIACIÓN *f* |
| 4850 | NITRATO *m* DE ETILO | | 4889 | DESCONCHADO *m*, EXFOLIACIÓN *f* |
| 4851 | ETENO *m* | | 4890 | ESCAPE *m* (DE LOS GASES DE UN MOTOR) |
| 4851 | ETILENO *m* | | 4891 | GAS *m* DE ESCAPE |
| 4851 | GAS *m* OLEFIANTE | | 4892 | LÍNEA *f* DE ESCAPE DEL VAPOR |
| 4851 | HIDRÓGENO *m* BICARBONO | | 4893 | COLECTOR DE ESCAPE *m* |
| 4852 | EUDIÓMETRO *m* | | 4894 | TUBO *m* DE ESCAPE |
| 4853 | CLORURO CÚPRICO *m* | | 4894 | TUBULADURA *f* DE ESCAPE |
| 4854 | EUROPIO *m* | | 4895 | CONDUCTO *m* DE ESCAPE |
| 4855 | EUTÉCTICO | | 4896 | VAPOR *m* DE ESCAPE |
| 4856 | FUSIÓN *f* EUTÉCTICA | | 4897 | TUBO *m* DE ESCAPE DE VAPOR |
| 4857 | MEZCLA *f* EUTÉCTICA | | 4898 | CARRERA DE ESCAPE *f* |
| 4858 | TEMPERATURA *f* EUTÉCTICA | | 4899 | VÁLVULA *f* DE ESCAPE |
| 4859 | EUTECTOIDE | | 4899 | VÁLVULA *f* DE EMISIÓN |
| 4860 | REACCIÓN *f* EUTECTOIDE | | 4900 | EXTRACTOR *m* |
| 4861 | EVAPORABLE | | 4900 | EXHAUSTOR *m*, ASPIRADOR *m* |
| 4862 | EVAPORAR | | 4901 | EXOTÉRMICO |
| 4862 | EVAPORARSE | | 4902 | DILATARSE, EXPANSIONARSE |
| 4862 | VAPORIZAR | | 4903 | AGRANDAR UN TUBO CON EL MANDRIL, MANDRINAR UN TUBO |
| 4863 | EVAPORARSE AL AIRE LIBRE | | 4903 | MANDRILAR UN TUBO |
| 4864 | CÁPSULA *f* | | 4904 | METAL *m* DESPLEGADO |
| 4865 | TEMPERATURA *f* DE EVAPORACIÓN | | 4905 | TUBO *m* EXPANSIONADO |

| | |
|---|---|
| 4906 | MANDRILES *m* EXPANSIBLES |
| 4907 | MANDRIL *m* DE MONTAJE EXPANSIBLE |
| 4908 | CILINDRADO *m* DE TUBOS |
| 4908 | ENGARCE *m* DE TUBOS CON MANDRIL SEPARADOR |
| 4909 | POLEA *f* EXTENSIBLE |
| 4909 | POLEA *f* EXTENSIBLE |
| 4910 | RODILLO *m* TENSOR |
| 4911 | PRUEBA *f* DE MANDRINADO, PRUEBA DE ENSANCHAMIENTO |
| 4912 | AUMENTO *m* DE VOLUMEN |
| 4913 | TUBO *m* COMPENSADOR |
| 4913 | CODO *m* |
| 4913 | COMPENSADOR DE DILATACIÓN *m* |
| 4913 | COMPENSADOR *m* DE DILATACIÓN |
| 4913 | TUBO *m* COMPENSADOR DE DILATACIÓN |
| 4913 | CIMBRA DE DILATACIÓN *f* |
| 4914 | COEFICIENTE DE DILATACIÓN |
| 4915 | MANGUITO *m* DE DILATACIÓN |
| 4916 | CURVA DE EXPANSIÓN *f* |
| 4917 | ESCARIADOR DE MANO EXTENSIBLE *m* |
| 4918 | JUNTA *f* DE DILATACIÓN |
| 4919 | DILATACIÓN *f* DE UN METAL |
| 4920 | EXPANSIÓN *f* DE LOS GASES |
| 4921 | EXPANSIÓN *f* DEL VAPOR |
| 4921 | EXPANSIÓN *f* DE UN GAS |
| 4922 | PIEZA *f* DE COMPENSACIÓN |
| 4923 | ESCARIADOR AJUSTABLE *m*, ESCARIADOR EXTENSIBLE *m* |
| 4924 | MÁQUINA *f* CON EXPANSIÓN |
| 4924 | MÁQUINA *f* CON EXPANSIÓN |
| 4925 | TURBINA *f* DE EXPANSIÓN |
| 4926 | VÁLVULA *f* DE EXPANSIÓN |
| 4927 | ESPERANZA *f* MATEMÁTICA |
| 4928 | HACER ENSAYOS, HACER PRUEBAS |
| 4929 | DETERMINACIÓN *f* EXPERIMENTAL |
| 4930 | EXPERTO *m*, PERITO *m* |
| 4931 | APRECIACIÓN *f* PERICIAL |
| 4932 | EXPIRACIÓN *f* DE UNA PATENTE |
| 4933 | ESTALLAR |
| 4934 | VISTA *f* DISGREGADA |
| 4935 | EXPLOSIÓN *f* |
| 4936 | PRESIÓN *f* EXPLOSIVA |
| 4937 | EXPLOSIVO |
| 4938 | MEZCLA *f* DETONADORA |
| 4938 | MEZCLA *f* DETONANTE |
| 4938 | MEZCLA *f* EXPLOSIVA |
| 4939 | EXPOSITOR *m* |
| 4940 | EXPONENTE *m* DE ESCAPE |
| 4941 | LEY *f* EXPONENCIAL |
| 4942 | FUNCIÓN *f* EXPONENCIAL |
| 4943 | SERIE *f* EXPONENCIAL |
| 4944 | EXPOSICIÓN *f* |
| 4944 | TIEMPO *m* DE COLOCACIÓN |
| 4945 | ALARGADERA *f* DE MANGO |
| 4946 | EXTENSIÓN *f*, AMPLIACIÓN *f* |
| 4947 | ALARGADERA *f* |
| 4948 | DILATACIÓN *f* POR CALOR |
| 4949 | EXTENSÍMETRO *m* |
| 4950 | ÁNGULO EXTERNO *m* |
| 4951 | FRESA *f* DESBARBADORA HEMBRA |
| 4951 | FRESA *f* DE EXTERIOR PARA TUBOS |
| 4952 | PEINE *m* DE FILETEAR, DE ROSCAR |
| 4952 | PEINE *m* PARA EL EXTERIOR |
| 4953 | RECTIFICADORA *f* PARA SUPERFICIES DE REVOLUCIÓN EXTERIORES |
| 4954 | CARGA *f* |
| 4954 | FUERZA *f* EXTERIOR |
| 4954 | ESFUERZO *m* EXTERIOR, FUERZA *f* EXTERIOR, CARGA *f* |
| 4955 | CALIBRE *m* DE UN EXTERIOR |
| 4956 | ENGRANAJE *m* EXTERIOR |
| 4957 | RECTIFICACIÓN *f* EXTERIOR |
| 4958 | DIÁMETRO *m* EXTERIOR |
| 4959 | DENTADO *m* EXTERIOR |
| 4960 | ROSCA *f* EXTERIOR |
| 4961 | ROSCADO *m* EXTERIOR, ROSCA *f* EXTERIOR |
| 4962 | TRABAJO *m* EXTERIOR |
| 4963 | TUBO *m* DE ALETAS EXTERIORES |
| 4964 | EXTRACTO *m* |
| 4965 | LÍQUIDO *m* DE EXTRACCIÓN |
| 4966 | EXTRACCIÓN *f* DE LOS METALES |
| 4967 | EXTRACTOR *m* |
| 4968 | LEY *f* DE LOS VALORES EXTREMOS |
| 4969 | MOLDURAS *f pl* FILETEADAS |
| 4970 | EXTRUSIÓN *f* |
| 4970 | EXTRUSIÓN *f* |
| 4970 | HILADO *m* EN FRÍO |
| 4971 | TOCHO *m* PARA PRENSA DE ESTIRAR, TOCHO PARA EXTRUSIÓN |
| 4972 | PRENSA *f* DE ESTIRAR |
| 4973 | ARMELLA *f*, HEMBRILLA *f* |
| 4974 | GANCHO *m* DE OJETE |
| 4974 | GANCHO *m* DE OJETE |
| 4975 | OJO *m* DEL MARTILLO |
| 4976 | OJO *m* DE BIELA |
| 4977 | OCULAR *m* |
| 4977 | SISTEMA *m* OCULAR |
| 4978 | ESCARIADO DE UNA POLEA *m* |
| 4978 | ESCARIADO DE UNA RUEDA *m* |
| 4979 | MARTILLO ESTAMPA *m* |
| 4980 | OJETE *m* |

| | |
|---|---|
| 4980 | OJO *m* |
| 4981 | CORREA DE FIBRAS TEXTILES *f* |
| 4982 | RECIPIENTE (O DEPÓSITO) FORJADO (O TRABAJADO EN CALIENTE) *m* |
| 4983 | FABRICACIÓN *f*, CONFECCIÓN *f* |
| 4983 | MECANIZACIÓN *f* |
| 4984 | PLAN *m* DE EJECUCIÓN |
| 4985 | MONTAJE *m* DE MECANIZADO BASTIDOR MODELO |
| 4986 | NÚMERO *m* DE CONSTRUCCIÓN |
| 4987 | EXIGENCIAS *f pl* DE FABRICACIÓN |
| 4988 | TOLERANCIAS *f pl* DE MECANIZACIÓN |
| 4989 | CARA *f* |
| 4990 | ÁNGULO DEL CONO EXTERIOR *m* |
| 4991 | CÚBICO DE CARA CENTRAL |
| 4992 | FRESAS *f pl* CON DOS CORTES EN EXTREMO |
| 4993 | CABEZA *f* DE UN MARTILLO |
| 4993 | PLANCHA *f* DEL MARTILLO, CUERPO *m* DEL MARTILLO |
| 4994 | LADO *m* DE UNA TUERCA |
| 4995 | MESA *f* DE YUNQUE |
| 4996 | FRENTE *m* DE CAJA DE VÁLVULAS |
| 4997 | PERFIL *m* DE DIENTE, FLANCO *m* DE DIENTE |
| 4998 | SUPERFICIE *f* DE LA SOLDADURA |
| 4999 | PLACA *f* FRONTAL |
| 4999 | PLACA *f* CIRCULAR |
| 5000 | PANTALLA *f* DE SOLDADURA |
| 5001 | VUELTA *f* EN EL AIRE |
| 5002 | CARAS CENTRADAS (DE) *f* |
| 5003 | BRIDA *f* REVUELTA |
| 5004 | ADOQUÍN *m*, LADRILLO *m* DE PARAMENTO |
| 5004 | PIEDRA *f* DE SILLERÍA |
| 5005 | VUELTA *f* EN EL AIRE |
| 5006 | ARENA *f* DE CONTACTO |
| 5007 | SALIENTE *m* DE ENSAMBLADO RECTIFICADO (DE UNA PIEZA DE FUNDICIÓN) |
| 5008 | FACTOR |
| 5009 | FACTOR *m* DE SEGURIDAD |
| 5009 | COEFICIENTE DE SEGURIDAD *m* |
| 5010 | FÁBRICA *f* |
| 5011 | CALIBRE *m* DE REVISIÓN |
| 5012 | EDIFICIO *m* INDUSTRIAL |
| 5013 | FÁBRICA *f* |
| 5013 | FÁBRICA *f* |
| 5013 | FÁBRICA *f*, TALLER *m*, ESTABLECIMIENTO FABRIL |
| 5013 | MANUFACTURA *f* |
| 5014 | DESCOLORACIÓN *f*, DECOLORACIÓN *f* |
| 5015 | PAQUETE *m* DE HIERRO QUE SOLDAR |
| 5016 | CHATARRAS *f* EN PAQUETES |
| 5017 | PAQUETE *m* |
| 5017 | ESTUCHE *m* (METALURGIA) |

| | |
|---|---|
| 5018 | EMPAQUE *m*, EMPAQUETADO *m*, EMBALAJE *m* |
| 5019 | ESCALA *f* FAHRENHEIT |
| 5020 | TERMÓMETRO *m* FAHRENHEIT |
| 5021 | FALLO *m* DE UN MOTOR |
| 5022 | DESCENSO DE LA TEMPERATURA *m* |
| 5022 | CAÍDA *f* (O DESCENSO *m*) DE TEMPERATURA |
| 5023 | EXTREMO *m* LIBRE |
| 5023 | RAMAL *m* FIADOR DEL CABLE |
| 5023 | FIADOR *m* (DE UN POLIPASTO) |
| 5024 | CAÍDA LIBRE (DE) *f* |
| 5025 | TEMPERATURA *f* DESCENDENTE |
| 5026 | FALSO FONDO *m* |
| 5026 | DOBLE FONDO *m*, FALSO FONDO *m* |
| 5027 | FALSO NÚCLEO *m* |
| 5027 | NÚCLEO *m* EXTERIOR |
| 5028 | HAZ *m* DE CURVAS |
| 5029 | CORREA DE VENTILADOR *f* |
| 5030 | PALAS *f pl* DE VENTILADOR |
| 5031 | MOLINILLO *m* DINAMOMÉTRICO |
| 5031 | MOLINILLO *m* DE PALETAS |
| 5031 | FRENO *m* |
| 5032 | POLEA *f* DE VENTILADOR |
| 5033 | VENTILADOR *m* |
| 5034 | CONDUCTO DE UNIÓN *m* |
| 5035 | FARADIO *m* |
| 5036 | JAULA DE FARADAY *f*, PANTALLA ELÉCTRICA *f* |
| 5037 | ACOPLAMIENTO RÍGIDO *m* |
| 5037 | ACOPLAMIENTO FIJO *m* |
| 5038 | RALENTÍ *m* ACELERADO |
| 5039 | BRIDA *f* FIJA |
| 5040 | POLEA *f* FIJA |
| 5041 | FIJAR |
| 5042 | ÓRGANO *m* DE FIJACIÓN |
| 5043 | TORNILLO *m* O PERNO DE MONTAJE |
| 5043 | TORNILLO *m* O PERNO DE FIJACIÓN |
| 5044 | FIJACIÓN *f* |
| 5044 | FIJACIÓN *f* |
| 5045 | GRASA *f* |
| 5046 | CAL GRASA *f* |
| 5047 | FATIGA *f* |
| 5048 | FISURA *f* POR FATIGA |
| 5049 | PRUEBA *f* DE RESISTENCIA |
| 5049 | ENSAYO *m* DE RESISTENCIA A LOS CHOQUES REPETIDOS |
| 5050 | LÍMITE *m* DE RESISTENCIA O DE FATIGA |
| 5051 | FATIGA *f* (CANSANCIO *m*) DEL MATERIAL |
| 5052 | RESISTENCIA *f* A LA FATIGA |
| 5053 | LÍMITE *m* DE FATIGA |
| 5053 | RESISTENCIA *f* LÍMITE DE CONSISTENCIA |
| 5054 | PRUEBA *f* DE RESISTENCIA A LA FATIGA |

| | | | | |
|---|---|---|---|---|
| 5055 | ÁCIDO GRASO *m* | 5096 | ARANDELA *f* DE ALA |
| 5056 | DEFECTO *m* DE COLADA | 5097 | FERMENTO *m* |
| 5056 | DEFECTO *m* EN EL METAL FUNDIDO | 5098 | FERMENTACIÓN *f* |
| 5057 | DAÑADO, DETERIORADO, ESTROPEADO | 5099 | ACETATO FÉRRICO *m* |
| 5057 | DEFECTUOSO | 5100 | CLORURO FÉRRICO *m* |
| 5057 | DETERIORADO, ESTROPEADO | 5101 | PERÓXIDO *m* HIDRATADO DE HIERRO |
| 5058 | SUPERFICIE *f* DE NIVELACIÓN | 5102 | ÓXIDO *m* DE HIERRO |
| 5059 | LENG:UETA *f*, ENSAMBLADURA *f*, ESPIGA *f* | 5103 | SULFATO *m* FÉRRICO |
| 5060 | ALETA DE VÁLVULA *f* | 5104 | FERRITA *f* |
| 5061 | ESTRÍA *f* | 5105 | BANDA *f* DE FERRITA LIBRE, ZONA *f* DEFICIENTE EN PERLITA |
| 5062 | PERNO *m* CHATO, PERNO *m* DE PATILLA | 5106 | FERROALUMINIO *m* |
| 5063 | AVANCE *m*, ALIMENTACIÓN *f* | 5107 | FERROBORO *m* |
| 5063 | AVANCE *m* | 5108 | FERROCROMO *m* |
| 5064 | ALIMENTAR | 5109 | TUBO *m* DE CEMENTO ARMADO |
| 5065 | PALANCA *f* SELECTORA DE LOS AVANCES | 5110 | FERROMANGANESO *m* |
| 5066 | GRIFO *m* DE ALIMENTACIÓN | 5111 | FERROMOLIBDENO *m* |
| 5067 | MECANISMO *m* DE LOS AVANCES | 5112 | FERRONÍQUEL *m* |
| 5068 | AVANCE *m* DE UNA HERRAMIENTA | 5113 | FERROSILICIO *m* |
| 5069 | AVANCE *m* POR DIENTE | 5114 | FERROTITANIO *m* |
| 5070 | TUBO *m* DE ALIMENTACIÓN | 5115 | FERROTUNGSTENO *m* |
| 5071 | BOMBA *f* DE ALIMENTACIÓN | 5116 | FERROVANADIO *m* |
| 5072 | ALIMENTADOR AUTOMÁTICO *m* | 5117 | ALEACIONES *f pl* DE HIERRO |
| 5073 | PALANCA *f* DE INVERSIÓN DEL AVANCE | 5118 | FERROMAGNÉTICO |
| 5074 | CILINDRO *m* DE ALIMENTACIÓN | 5119 | PAPEL *m* AZUL PARA FOTOCALCO |
| 5074 | CILINDRO *m* DE ALIMENTACIÓN | 5119 | PAPEL *m* PRUSIATO |
| 5075 | TANQUE *m* (O CUBA *f*) DE ALIMENTACIÓN | 5119 | PAPEL *m* CIANOHIERRO |
| 5076 | VÁLVULA *f* DE ALIMENTACIÓN | 5119 | PAPEL *m* AL FERRO-PRUSIATO, PAPEL *m* CIANOGRÁFICO AZUL |
| 5077 | AGUA *f* DE ALIMENTACIÓN | 5119 | CIANOTIPO *m* |
| 5078 | RECALENTADOR *m* DE AGUA DE ALIMENTACIÓN | 5120 | ACETATO FERROSO *m* |
| 5079 | CORRECCIÓN DE VELOCIDAD DE AVANCE *f* | 5121 | CLORURO FERROSO *m* |
| 5080 | BUCLE *m* DE REACCIÓN | 5122 | MINERALES *m pl* DE MANGANESO FERROSO |
| 5081 | (CABLE) ALIMENTADOR *m* | 5123 | METALURGIA *f* DEL HIERRO |
| 5081 | CABLE PRINCIPAL *m* | 5124 | OXALATO *m* FERROSO |
| 5081 | ARTERIA *f*, CONDUCTO *m* | 5125 | ÓXIDO *m* FERROSO |
| 5082 | ALIMENTACIÓN *f* | 5125 | PROTÓXIDO *m* DE HIERRO |
| 5083 | ALIMENTADOR *m* | 5126 | CHATARRA *f* |
| 5084 | TUBULADURA *f* DE ALIMENTACIÓN | 5127 | FERRUGINOSO |
| 5085 | CÓDIGO DE VELOCIDAD DE AVANCE *m* | 5128 | VIROLA *f* |
| 5086 | CALIBRE DE ESPESORES *m* | 5129 | DESBARBADURA *f*, ELIMINACIÓN *f* DE LAS REBABAS |
| 5087 | FELDESPATO *m* | 5130 | TALLER *m* DE DESCOSTRADO |
| 5088 | LLANTA *f* DE UNA RUEDA | 5130 | TALLER *m* DE DESBARBADO |
| 5089 | FELDESPATO *m* | 5130 | TALLER *m* DE DESARENADO |
| 5090 | FIELTRO *m* | 5131 | FIBRA *f* |
| 5091 | CALIBRE *m* EXTERIOR | 5132 | EJE *m* DE FIBRA |
| 5092 | ROSCA *f* HEMBRA | 5133 | DIRECCIÓN *f* DE LAS FIBRAS |
| 5092 | FILETE *m*, ROSCA *f* | 5134 | ESFUERZO *m* EN LA FIBRA |
| 5092 | ROSCA *f* INTERIOR | 5135 | ESTRUCTURA *f* FIBROSA |
| 5093 | CUÑA *f* SUJETADORA DE LA CUCHILLA DEL CEPILLO | 5136 | FIBRA *f* |
| 5094 | CERCA *f*, CERCADO *m* | | |
| 5095 | ALA *f* | | |

| | | | |
|---|---|---|---|
| 5137 | FIBROSO | 5176 | TELA *f* FILTRANTE |
| 5138 | FRACTURA FIBROSA *f* | 5177 | PAPEL *m* FILTRO |
| 5139 | HIERRO *m* FIBROSO, NERVIO *m*, FIBRA *f* | 5178 | TANQUE *m* DE FILTRACIÓN |
| 5139 | HIERRO *m* FIBROSO, NERVIO *m* | 5179 | MATERIA *f* FILTRANTE |
| 5140 | MATERIA *f* FIBROSA | 5180 | FILTRO-PRENSA *m* |
| 5141 | CONTEXTURA *f* FIBROSA | 5181 | FILTRADO *m*, LÍQUIDO FILTRADO |
| 5142 | AFUSTE DE CAMPAÑA *m* | 5181 | LÍQUIDO *m* FILTRADO |
| 5143 | CAMPO VISUAL *m* | 5182 | FILTRACIÓN *f* |
| 5143 | CAMPO VISUAL *m* | 5182 | FILTRACIÓN *f* |
| 5144 | INTENSIDAD *f* DEL CAMPO | 5183 | ALERÓN *m*, ALÓN *m* |
| 5145 | JEFE DE OBRA *m* | 5183 | ALETA *f*, BARRETA *f* |
| 5146 | SOLDADURA *f* EJECUTADA EN LA OBRA | 5184 | REBABA *f* DE UNA PIEZA FUNDIDA |
| 5147 | RAÍZ *f* QUINTA | 5185 | PLANO *m* DEFINITIVO |
| 5148 | LIMA *f* | 5186 | TRANSMISIÓN *f* A LAS RUEDAS |
| 5149 | LIMAR | 5187 | POSICIÓN *f* FINAL |
| 5150 | CARDA *f* | 5188 | PRESIÓN *f* FINAL |
| 5150 | CEPILLO *m* PARA LIMAS, CARDA *f* LIMPIALIMAS | 5189 | PRODUCTO *m* FINAL |
| | | 5190 | ESTADO *m* FINAL |
| 5151 | TALLADOR *m* DE LIMAS | 5191 | TEMPERATURA *f* FINAL |
| 5152 | PRUEBA *f* DE DUREZA A LA LIMA | 5192 | VALOR *m* FINAL |
| 5153 | LIMADO *m* | 5193 | VELOCIDAD *f* FINAL |
| 5154 | MÁQUINA *f* DE LIMAR, MÁQUINA *f* LIMADORA | 5194 | RENDIMIENTO *m* FINAL |
| 5155 | LIMADURAS *f pl*, LIMALLA *f* | 5196 | MANDRINADORA DE PRECISIÓN *f*, TALADRADORA |
| 5156 | LLENAR | | DE PRECISIÓN *f* PULIDORA DE PRECISIÓN *f* |
| 5156 | CARGAR | 5197 | ESCARIADOR CON ESTRÍAS FINAS *m* |
| 5157 | CARGA QUÍMICA *f* | 5198 | ORO *m* FINO |
| 5158 | TAPÓN *m* DE CARGA, TAPÓN *m* DE LLENADO | 5199 | ARENA *f* DE GRANO FINO |
| 5159 | METAL *m* AÑADIDO EN SOLDADURA | 5200 | ESTRUCTURA *f* DE GRANOS FINOS |
| 5159 | ALEACIÓN ( *f* ) (METAL ( *m* ) DE APORTACIÓN (POR | 5201 | ROSCA *f* FINA |
| | SOLDADURA) | 5202 | PLATA *f* FINA |
| 5160 | GUÍA DE OBTURACIÓN *f* | 5203 | ESTRUCTURA *f* FINA (R.X.) |
| 5161 | MEDIACAÑA *f* | 5204 | ROSCA *f* FINA |
| 5162 | SOLDADURA *f* EN CAVETO | 5205 | ALAMBRE *m* FINO |
| 5162 | SOLDADURA *f* EN ÁNGULO | 5205 | ALAMBRE *m* DELGADO |
| 5163 | PÉRDIDA *f* POR REBOSAMIENTO | 5206 | MALLAS ESTRECHAS (DE) *f pl* |
| 5164 | MATERIA *f* PARA RELLENO | 5207 | CABLE METÁLICO DE HILOS FINOS *m* |
| 5165 | TORNILLO *m* DE CABEZA CILÍNDRICA | 5208 | FINURA *f* |
| 5166 | PELÍCULA *f* | 5209 | GRADO *m* DE PUREZA DE UNA ALEACIÓN |
| 5166 | PELÍCULA *f*, CAPA *f* | 5210 | ESTRUCTURA *f* FINA |
| 5166 | CAPA *f*, PELICULA *f* | 5211 | CUÑA *f*, CLAVIJA *f*, PASADOR *m* |
| 5167 | PELÍCULA *f* GRASA | 5211 | DEDO *m*, CLAVIJA *f* |
| 5167 | CAPA *f* DELGADA DE ACEITE DE ENGRASE | 5211 | VARILLA *f* |
| 5168 | PELÍCULA *f* DE ÓXIDO | 5212 | DEFORMACIONES *f pl* EN MEDIA LUNA DEL |
| 5169 | CAPA *f* ÍNFIMA DE AGUA, CAPA *f* TENUE DE | | CORDÓN DE SOLDADURA |
| | AGUA | 5213 | ACABADO *m* |
| 5170 | ESPESOR *m* DE PELÍCULA | 5213 | ACABADO *m*, ESTADO *m* DE SUPERFICIE |
| 5171 | PELÍCULA *f* | 5214 | ACABAR CON PERFECCIÓN |
| 5172 | FILTRO *m* | 5214 | ACABAR, TERMINAR, CONCLUIR |
| 5173 | FILTRAR | 5214 | RETOCAR |
| 5174 | COADYUVANTE DE FILTRACIÓN *m* | 5215 | LAMINADO *m* DE ACABADO |
| 5175 | CARTUCHO FILTRANTE *m* | 5216 | SOLDADURA *f* DE ACABADO |

| | |
|---|---|
| 5217 | CAPA SUPERFICIAL (DE PINTURA) f |
| 5218 | PRODUCTO m ACABADO |
| 5219 | JAULA DE ACABADO f |
| 5219 | MATRIZ f ACABADORA |
| 5220 | PERFECCIONAMIENTO m EN EL REMATADO |
| 5221 | TERRAJA f PARA ACABAR |
| 5222 | LAMINADOR m ACABADOR |
| 5223 | ACABADO m |
| 5224 | ACABADO m CON LA MUELA |
| 5225 | JAULA ACABADORES f |
| 5226 | ESCARIADOR DE ACABADO CÓNICO m |
| 5227 | TEMPERATURA f DE ACABADO |
| 5228 | HERRAMIENTA f DE ACABADO |
| 5229 | TREN m DE ACABADO |
| 5230 | ARANDELA f DECORATIVA |
| 5231 | FRACCIÓN f DECIMAL TERMINADA |
| 5232 | SERIE f FINITA |
| 5233 | RADIADOR m DE ALETAS |
| 5234 | TUBO m DE ALETAS |
| 5235 | CALENTAR |
| 5236 | ENCENDER EL HOGAR DE UNA CALDERA |
| 5237 | BARROTE m DE PARRILLA |
| 5238 | CAJA f DE FUEGO |
| 5239 | LADRILLO m REFRACTARIO |
| 5240 | HENDIDURA f EN CALIENTE |
| 5241 | TIERRA f REFRACTARIA |
| 5242 | PUERTA f |
| 5243 | DORADO m EN CALIENTE |
| 5244 | BOCA f DE INCENDIOS |
| 5245 | AFINO AL FUEGO m |
| 5246 | CAPA DE ÓXIDO DE COBRE f |
| 5247 | PUNTO m DE COMBUSTIÓN |
| 5247 | PUNTO m DE FUEGO (ACEITE) |
| 5248 | TUBO m DE HUMO |
| 5249 | CALDERA PIROTUBULAR f |
| 5249 | CALDERA PIROTUBULAR f |
| 5249 | CALDERA TUBULAR f |
| 5250 | COBRE m REFINADO AL FUEGO |
| 5251 | MAMPARA PIRORRESISTENTE f, TABIQUE ANTIFUEGO m |
| 5251 | TABLERO m DEL MOTOR |
| 5252 | LADRILLO m REFRACTARIO |
| 5253 | ARCILLA REFRACTARIA f |
| 5254 | LADRILLO m DE CLAMOTA |
| 5255 | CEMENTO REFRACTARIO m |
| 5256 | LOCOMOTORA f SIN HOGAR |
| 5257 | IGNÍFUGO |
| 5257 | REFRACTARIO |
| 5258 | LEÑA f |
| 5258 | LEÑA f |
| 5259 | CALEFACCIÓN f |

| | |
|---|---|
| 5260 | ORDEN f DE ENCENDIDO, ORDEN f DE EXPLOSIÓN |
| 5261 | APARATO m DE CALDEO |
| 5262 | CARGA f |
| 5262 | ALIMENTACIÓN DE UN HOGAR f |
| 5263 | ENCENDIDO DEL HOGAR DE UNA CALDERA m |
| 5264 | FORMÓN m, ESCOPLO-PUNZÓN m |
| 5265 | PRIMER FILTRO m |
| 5265 | FILTRO m PREVIO |
| 5266 | PRIMERA CABEZA f DE REMACHE |
| 5267 | CABEZA f DE DESTILACIÓN |
| 5268 | TERRAJA f DESBASTADORA |
| 5268 | TERRAJA f CÓNICA |
| 5269 | TORNILLO m DE BRIDA, BULÓN ·m DE VÍA |
| 5270 | ECLISAS f pl, PLANCHAS f pl DE EMPATE, BRIDAS f pl |
| 5271 | CAVIDAD EN V f |
| 5272 | VIENTRE DE PESCADO (CON) m |
| 5273 | RESQUEBRAJADURA f |
| 5274 | GRIETA f, RAJA f, RESQUEBRAJAMIENTO m |
| 5275 | ACOPLAMIENTO m, AJUSTE m |
| 5275 | MONTAJE m |
| 5275 | AJUSTE m, MONTAJE m, AJUSTAMIENTO m |
| 5276 | AJUSTAR, REGULAR |
| 5277 | ABOCAR (O ENCHUFAR) TUBOS |
| 5277 | ENCHUFAR TUBOS, EMPALMAR TUBOS |
| 5277 | ENCAJAR, AJUSTAR |
| 5278 | AJUSTADOR DE MÁQUINAS m |
| 5278 | CERRAJERO MECÁNICO m, MECÁNICO m |
| 5278 | AJUSTADOR m |
| 5279 | MARTILLO m DE AJUSTADOR |
| 5280 | AJUSTE m, MONTAJE m, AJUSTAMIENTO m |
| 5280 | RACOR, EMPALME, ENLACE, MANGUITO m |
| 5281 | ENCASTE m, ENCAJE m |
| 5281 | ENCAJE m, ENCASTE m |
| 5281 | ENCHUFE m DE TUBOS |
| 5282 | TALLER DE AJUSTE m |
| 5283 | PIEZAS f pl AUXILIARES, ACCESORIOS m pl |
| 5283 | ACCESORIOS m pl |
| 5284 | EMPOTRADO POR AMBOS EXTREMOS |
| 5285 | EMPOTRADO POR UN EXTREMO |
| 5286 | VIGA f EMPOTRADA |
| 5287 | POLEA f FIJA (DE UN APAREJO) |
| 5288 | FORMATO m DE BLOC FIJO |
| 5289 | CARBONO COMBINADO m |
| 5290 | CÍRCULO FIJO m |
| 5291 | GRÚA f FIJA |
| 5291 | GRÚA f ESTACIONARIA |
| 5292 | CICLO m FIJO |
| 5293 | CALIBRE FIJO m |
| 5294 | ACEITE m GRASO |

| | | | | |
|---|---|---|---|---|
| 5294 | ACEITE *m* FIJO | | 5337 | TUBULADURA *f* DE BRIDA |
| 5295 | PUNTO *m* FIJO | | 5337 | TUBULADURA *f* DE EMPALME |
| 5295 | APOYO FIJO *m* | | 5338 | ACOPLAMIENTO DE DISCOS EMPERNADOS *m* |
| 5296 | TECHO *m* FIJO | | 5338 | ACOPLAMIENTO POR MANGUITO DE PLATILLO *m* |
| 5297 | FORMATO *m* DE SECUENCIA FIJA | | 5339 | ORIFICIO *m* DE BRIDAS |
| 5298 | FRESADORA *f* FIJA DE BANCO | | 5340 | TUERCA *f* HEXAGONAL CON REBORDE |
| 5299 | MORDAZA *f* FIJA DE TORNILLO DE BANCO | | 5341 | TUBULADURA *f* DE BRIDA |
| 5300 | FIJACIÓN *f* DE UNA VARILLA DE ENSAYO | | 5343 | TUBO *m* DE BRIDAS |
| 5300 | EMPOTRAMIENTO *m* | | 5344 | JUNTA DE BRIDAS *f* |
| 5301 | MONTAJE *m* | | 5345 | REBORDEAMIENTO, EMBRIDAMIENTO *m* |
| 5302 | LOSA *f*, BALDOSA *f* | | 5346 | MÁQUINA *f* DE BORDEAR, MÁQUINA *f* DE EMBUTIR |
| 5303 | LAMINILLA *f*, COPO *m* | | 5346 | MÁQUINA *f* DE EMBUTIR |
| 5303 | LÁMINA *f* | | 5346 | MÁQUINA *f* DE PERFILAR EL BALASTO |
| 5304 | RESQUEBRAJADURA *f* | | 5346 | ENGASTADORA *f* |
| 5304 | GRIETA *f* DE TENSIÓN | | 5347 | PRUEBA *f* DE REBORDEADO |
| 5304 | FISURA *f* | | 5348 | FLANCO *m*, LADO *m* |
| 5305 | GRAFITO *m* LAMINAR | | 5349 | JUEGO *m* ENTRE LOS PUNTOS DE CONTACTO DE LOS DIENTES |
| 5306 | DESCASCADO *m* | | | |
| 5307 | SOPLETE *m* | | 5350 | FLANCO *m* DE LA ROSCA |
| 5308 | PUENTE *m* DE CALDEO | | 5351 | FLANCO *m* DEL DIENTE |
| 5309 | LIMPIAR CON MECHERO | | 5352 | FRANELA *f* |
| 5310 | DECAPADO *m* CON SOPLETE | | 5353 | VÁLVULA *f*, VÁLVULA DE CHAPELETA *f* |
| 5311 | SOPLETE DESOXIDADOR *m* | | 5353 | DISTRIBUIDOR *m* |
| 5312 | SOPLETE CORTADOR *m* | | 5353 | OBTURADOR *m* CON LEVANTADO ANGULAR |
| 5313 | DECAPADO *m* A LA LLAMA | | 5353 | VÁLVULA *f* DE RETENCIÓN |
| 5314 | CONTROLADOR DE LLAMA *m* | | 5353 | VÁLVULA *f* DE CHARNELA |
| 5315 | TEMPLE *m* CON SOPLETE | | 5354 | RUPTURA *f* DE LA CAPA DE ESCORIAS |
| 5316 | ENCENDIDO DE LLAMA *m* | | 5355 | HACHÓN *m* |
| 5317 | CHAPEADO *m* A LA LLAMA | | 5356 | ENSANCHAR, AGRANDAR |
| 5318 | CORTE CON LLAMA *m* | | 5356 | EXTENDERSE |
| 5319 | RECOCIDO *m* CON LLAMA | | 5356 | ENSANCHARSE |
| 5320 | ESPECTROSCOPIA *f* DE LA LLAMA | | 5357 | REBABA *f*, GRIETA *f* DE PLIEGUE |
| 5321 | PARALLAMAS *m* | | 5357 | REBABA *f* |
| 5322 | ANTIDEFLAGRANTE *m* | | 5358 | SOLDADURA *f* POR CHISPORROTÉO |
| 5323 | BRIDA *f*, | | 5359 | LANZAR LA LLAMA |
| 5323 | BRIDA *f* | | 5360 | ESTUFA *f* DE SECADO RÁPIDO |
| 5324 | REBORDEAR, PONER BRIDA | | 5361 | METALIZACIÓN *f* POR PULVERIZADOR, POR PISTOLA NEUMÁTICA |
| 5325 | ADAPTADOR (O RACOR) DE BRIDA *m* | | | |
| 5326 | DORSO *m* DE LA CARA DE BRIDA | | 5362 | CALENTAMIENTO *m* RÁPIDO |
| 5327 | CARA *f* DE BRIDA | | 5363 | PUNTO *m* DE INFLAMACIÓN |
| 5328 | AGUJEROS *m pl* DE BRIDA | | 5363 | PUNTO *m* DE LLAMA |
| 5329 | CUBO *m* DE BRIDA, BUJE *m* | | 5364 | DESBARBAR |
| 5330 | ALA (ACERO T) *f* | | 5364 | DESBARBAR |
| 5331 | ARO *m* DE UNA RUEDA | | 5365 | ENTRADA *f* DE LLAMA |
| 5332 | REBORDE *m* | | 5366 | INTERMITENTES *m* |
| 5332 | LATERAL *m* DE UNA POLEA | | 5367 | INCRUSTACIÓN *f* DE RESÍDUOS CARBONOSOS |
| 5333 | MÁQUINA *f* DE MANDRILAR LAS BRIDAS | | 5367 | ÁREA *f* DE ÓXIDO |
| 5334 | TORNO *m* DE BRIDAS | | 5368 | PUNTO *m* DE INFLAMABILIDAD |
| 5335 | SOLDADURA *f* SOBRE BORDES LEVANTADOS | | 5368 | PUNTO *m* DE COMBUSTION, DE INFLAMACIÓN |
| 5336 | POLEA *f* CON PESTAÑAS | | 5369 | BASTIDOR DE MOLDEO *m*, MOLDE *m* |
| 5336 | POLEA *f* DE DISCOS LATERALES | | | |

| | |
|---|---|
| 5370 FRASCO *m*, MATRAZ *m* | 5407 CABLE METÁLICO DE CABOS PLANOS *m* |
| 5371 RECOCIDO *m* EN CAJA | 5408 PULIMENTO *m* |
| 5372 PASADOR *m* DE CHASIS | 5408 PULIDO *m*, SATINADO *m*, BRUÑIDO *m*, ALISADO *m* |
| 5373 ARCO APAINELADO *m*, ARCO REBAJADO *m* | 5409 ENSAYO *m* DE MALEABILIDAD |
| 5374 BARRA *f* PLANA | 5410 MARTILLO PARA APLANAR *m* |
| 5375 HIERRO *m* PLANO | 5411 DEFECTO *m* |
| 5375 PLANOS *m pl*, LLANOS *m pl* | 5411 GRIETA INCIPIENTE *f* |
| 5375 HIERRO *m* PLANO | 5412 LINO *m* |
| 5375 HIERRO *m* EN BARRAS PLANAS | 5413 ESTOPA *f* DE LINO |
| 5376 HIERRO *m* PLANO CON BORDÓN | 5414 VUELTA DEL CUERO *f* |
| 5377 ESCOPLO *m* PLANO | 5415 FLEXIBILIDAD *f* |
| 5378 CURVA APLANADA *f* | 5415 FLEXIBILIDAD *f* |
| 5378 CURVA DE RADIO GRANDE *f* | 5416 FIJACIÓN *f* |
| 5379 RUEDA *f* DE DISCO PLANA | 5416 ENLACE *m*, UNIÓN *f*, EMPALME *m* |
| 5380 BROCA *f* DE LENGUA DE ASPID | 5416 JUNTA *f* FLEXIBLE |
| 5380 LENGUA *f* DE ASPID | 5417 ACOPLAMIENTO FLEXIBLE *m* |
| 5380 BROCA *f* PLANA | 5417 MANGUITO *m* FLEXIBLE |
| 5381 LIMA *f* PLANA | 5418 TUBO *m* DE JUNTA ESFÉRICA |
| 5382 BRIDA *f* PLANEADA | 5419 TUBO *m* METÁLICO FLEXIBLE |
| 5383 MOTOR *m* DE CUATRO CILINDROS OPUESTOS HORIZONTALES | 5420 TRANSMISIÓN *f* FLEXIBLE |
| 5384 CORREDERA *f* PLANA | 5420 ÁRBOL FLEXIBLE *m* |
| 5385 TORNILLO *m* DE CABEZA PLANA | 5421 TUBO *m* METÁLICO FLEXIBLE |
| 5386 TORNILLOS *m pl* DE CABEZA PLANA | 5422 FLEXIÓN |
| 5387 MEZCLADORA *f* DE SOLERA PLANA | 5423 RIGIDEZ *f* A LA FLEXIÓN |
| 5388 CLAVIJA PLANA *f* | 5424 RESISTENCIA *f* A LA FLEXIÓN |
| 5388 CLAVIJA COLOCADA EN PLANO *f* | 5425 TENSIÓN *f* DE FLEXIÓN |
| 5388 CLAVIJA PLANA *f* | 5426 FLEXIÓN *f*, FLECHA *f* |
| 5389 TRUNCAMIENTO *m* DE UN FILETE | 5426 DEFORMACIÓN *f* POR FLEXIÓN |
| 5390 LIMA *f* PLANA EN PUNTA | 5427 SILEX *m* PIRÓGENO |
| 5391 CILINDRO *m* LISO | 5427 FLINT |
| 5392 ACEROS LAMINADOS PLANOS *m pl* | 5427 PIEDRA *f* DE MECHERO |
| 5393 CABLE PLANO *m* | 5427 PIEDRA *f* DE FUSIL, PEDERNAL *m*, SILEX *m* |
| 5394 CABEZA *f* PLANA DE UN TORNILLO | 5428 FLINT-GLASS *m*, CRISTAL *m* DE ROCA |
| 5395 CHAPA *f* APLANADA | 5429 BÁSCULA *f* BINARIA |
| 5396 RESORTE *m* ESPIRAL | 5430 FLOTADOR *m* |
| 5397 CORREA DE TEJIDO TUBULAR *f* | 5431 CUBA *f* DE NIVEL CONSTANTE, CÁMARA *f* DE FLOTADOR |
| 5398 MOTOR *m* DE DOS CILINDROS OPUESTOS HORIZONTALES | 5432 PURGADOR *m* DE AGUA CONDENSADA DE FLOTADOR |
| 5399 ARANDELA *f* PLANA | 5433 GRIFO *m* DE FLOTADOR |
| 5400 CUÑA PLANA *f* | 5433 VÁLVULA *f* DE FLOTADOR |
| 5401 CORDÓN DE SOLDADURA PLANO *m* | 5434 MATIZADO *m* |
| 5402 ALAMBRE *m* PLANO | 5434 MANGUETAS *f pl* |
| 5402 ALAMBRE *m* PLANO | 5435 EJE *m* FLOTANTE |
| 5402 ALAMBRE *m* RECTANGULAR | 5436 CUERPO FLOTANTE *m* |
| 5403 PINZA *f* PLANA | 5437 MATRIZ *f* FLOTANTE |
| 5404 POLEA *f* CON LLANTA PLANA (O CILÍNDRICA) | 5438 MANDRIL *m* FLOTANTE |
| 5404 POLEA *f* DERECHA | 5439 DEPÓSITO *m* DE TECHO FLOTANTE |
| 5405 PLANEAR | 5440 CERO *m* FLOTANTE |
| 5406 APLASTADO *m*, APLASTADA *f*, ACHATADO *m*, ACHATADA *f* | 5441 FLOCULACIÓN *f* |

| | |
|---|---|
| 5442 | ENGRASE *m* A PRESIÓN CON CIRCULACIÓN CONTINUA |
| 5442 | ENGRASE *m* POR BOMBA Y CIRCULACIÓN DE ACEITE |
| 5443 | MANGUETAS *f pl* |
| 5443 | MATIZADO *m* |
| 5444 | TRANSMISIÓN *f* FIJADA EN EL SUELO |
| 5445 | MOLDEO *m* EN FOSO |
| 5445 | MOLDEADO *m* EN EL SUELO |
| 5446 | SUELO *m* DEL COCHE |
| 5447 | CHAPA *f* PARA REVESTIMIENTOS DE PISO |
| 5448 | COLUMNA DE MANIOBRA *f* |
| 5449 | ENTABLADO *m* |
| 5450 | SUELO *m*, REVESTIDO *m* DE SUELO |
| 5450 | SOLADO *m* |
| 5451 | ENTABLADO *m* |
| 5452 | FLOTACIÓN *f* |
| 5453 | POLVO *m* DE ESMERIL |
| 5454 | FLUJO *m*, CORRIENTE *f* |
| 5455 | GALGA DE FLUJO *f*, AFORADOR *m* |
| 5456 | LÍMITE *m* DE FLUJO (DE CIRCULACIÓN, DE DERRAME) |
| 5456 | LÍMITE *m* ELÁSTICO |
| 5457 | LÍNEA *f* DE CIRCULACIÓN |
| 5458 | CAUDALÍMETRO *m* |
| 5459 | CAUDAL *m* |
| 5459 | VELOCIDAD *f* DE DEFORMACIÓN |
| 5459 | TIEMPO *m* DE EVACUACIÓN |
| 5460 | ESFUERZO *m* DE FLUJO |
| 5461 | ESTRUCTURA *f* DEBIDA A LA DEFORMACIÓN PLÁSTICA |
| 5462 | VELOCIDAD *f* DE CIRCULACIÓN |
| 5463 | FLUIDEZ *f* |
| 5464 | AZUFRE *m* SUBLIMADO |
| 5464 | AZUFRE *m* SUBLIMADO |
| 5465 | FLUENCIA *f* DEL MATERIAL, SALIDA *f* DEL MATERIAL |
| 5466 | AGUA *f* CORRIENTE |
| 5467 | CONDUCTO *m* |
| 5468 | CALDERA DE QUEMADOR *f* |
| 5468 | CALDERA DE HORNO INTERNO *f*, CALDERA DE FUEGO INTERIOR *f* |
| 5469 | POLVO *m* DE CARBÓN |
| 5469 | POLVOS *m pl* DE GAS DE ALTO HORNO |
| 5469 | ESCARBILLAS *f pl* |
| 5470 | GAS *m* DE LA COMBUSTIÓN |
| 5470 | GAS *m* DEL HOGAR, GAS *m* DOMÉSTICO |
| 5471 | MUY MÓVIL |
| 5471 | MUY FLUIDO |
| 5472 | TRANSMISIÓN *f* HIDRÁULICA |
| 5473 | ROCE *m* INTERIOR DE LOS LÍQUIDOS |
| 5474 | FLUIDEZ *f* |

| | |
|---|---|
| 5475 | FUNDENTE *m* |
| 5476 | FLUORESCENCIA *f* |
| 5477 | PANTALLA *f* FLUORESCENTE |
| 5477 | PANTALLA *f* LUMINOSA |
| 5478 | FLUOR *m* |
| 5479 | FLUORURO *m* DE CALCIO |
| 5479 | FLUORURO *m* DE CALCIO |
| 5479 | FLUORINA *f* |
| 5479 | CAL FLUATADA *f* |
| 5479 | ESPATO *m* FLÚOR |
| 5480 | FARO *m* EMPOTRADO |
| 5481 | SOLDADURA *f* A TOPE SIN SOBREESPESOR |
| 5482 | AFLORADO |
| 5483 | ACANALADURA *f* |
| 5483 | GARGANTA *f* |
| 5484 | ACANALADO *m* ESTRIADO *m* |
| 5484 | ESTRÍA *f* |
| 5485 | ESCARIADOR CON ESTRÍAS *m*, escariador de RANURAS *m* |
| 5485 | ESCARIADOR ACANALADO *m*, ESCARIADOR CON ESTRÍAS *m* |
| 5486 | CILINDRO *m* RANURADO |
| 5486 | ESTRÍA *f* |
| 5487 | ESPECTRO *m* ACANALADO |
| 5488 | RUPTURA *f* POR FLEXIÓN |
| 5489 | FUNDENTE *m* |
| 5490 | FUNDENTE *m* PARA SOLDAR |
| 5491 | ACEITE *m* DERRETIDO |
| 5492 | ELECTRODO *m* REVESTIDO |
| 5493 | CENIZAS VOLANTES *f pl* |
| 5494 | HERRAMIENTA *f* DE TREPANAR, HERRAMIENTA *f* DE PERFORAR, TRÉPANO *m* |
| 5495 | CIZALLA DE VOLADIZO *f* |
| 5495 | CIZALLA DE VOLADIZO *f* |
| 5496 | VOLANTE *m* MOTOR |
| 5497 | VOLANTE *m* DE DOS SEGMENTOS |
| 5498 | FOSO *m* DEL VOLANTE |
| 5499 | ESPUMA *f* |
| 5500 | LONGITUD *f* FOCAL |
| 5500 | DISTANCIA *f* FOCAL |
| 5501 | PLANO *m* FOCAL |
| 5502 | FOCO (OPT. Y GEOM.) *m* |
| 5503 | DISTANCIA *f* FOCAL |
| 5504 | HAZ CONCENTRADO |
| 5504 | HAZ *m* FOCALIZADO |
| 5505 | PUESTA A PUNTO DE UN INSTRUMENTO DE ÓPTICA |
| 5506 | FARO *m* ANTINIEBLA |
| 5507 | ENSOMBRECIMIENTO *m*, OSCURECIMIENTO *m* |
| 5508 | HOJA *f*, CHAPA *f* |
| 5508 | PLANCHA *f* (O PLACA *f*) DE METAL |
| 5509 | HOJA *f* DELGADA DE METAL |

| | | |
|---|---|---|
| 5510 | REPLIEGUE *m* DE LAMINACIÓN |
| 5511 | REPLIEGUE *m* (TRABAJO DE LAS CHAPAS) |
| 5511 | PLIEGO *m* |
| 5512 | METRO *m* PLEGABLE |
| 5513 | FOLIUM *m* DE DESCARTES |
| 5514 | LUNETA *f* MÓVIL, LUNETA *f* DE SEGUIMIENTO |
| 5514 | LUNETA *f* MÓVIL |
| 5515 | ARISTA *f* DE SALIDA |
| 5516 | RAMAL *m* SUELTO |
| 5516 | RAMAL *m* SUELTO |
| 5516 | RAMAL *m* SUELTO |
| 5516 | RAMAL *m* CONDUCIDO |
| 5516 | RAMAL *m* SUELTO |
| 5517 | INDUSTRIA *f* DE LA ALIMENTACIÓN |
| 5518 | PIE *m* (MEDIDA INGLESA) |
| 5519 | FRENO DE PIE *m*, FRENO DE PEDAL *m* |
| 5519 | FRENO *m* DE PIE, FRENO *m* POR PEDAL |
| 5520 | TORNO *m* DE PEDAL |
| 5521 | PALANCA *f* DE PEDAL |
| 5522 | PIE-LIBRA (MEDIDA INGLESA DE PESO) *m* |
| 5523 | VÁLVULA DE FONDO *f* |
| 5523 | VÁLVULA DE FONDO *f* |
| 5523 | VÁLVULA FILTRO *f* |
| 5524 | COJINETE *m* VERTICAL |
| 5524 | COJINETE *m* DE PIE CON TEJUELO |
| 5525 | SEGADORAS *f pl* DE HIERBA |
| 5526 | DIAGRAMA *m* DE ESFUERZOS |
| 5526 | DIAGRAMA *m* DE FUERZAS |
| 5527 | ENMANGADO CON PRENSA *m* |
| 5527 | AJUSTE *m* (O ASIENTO *m*) PRENSADO |
| 5527 | MONTAJE *m* POR PRENSA, AJUSTE *m* |
| 5528 | FUERZA *f* DE UN MUELLE |
| 5529 | FUERZA *f* DE ATRACCIÓN |
| 5530 | FUERZA *f* REPULSIVA |
| 5531 | BOMBA *f* IMPELENTE |
| 5532 | FUERZA *f* |
| 5532 | ESFUERZO *m* |
| 5533 | TIRO *m* FORZADO |
| 5534 | CORRIENTE FUERZA *f* |
| 5535 | OSCILACIONES *f pl* FORZADAS |
| 5536 | TENACILLA *f* |
| 5537 | FUERZAS *f pl* EN DIRECCIÓN OPUESTA, FUERZAS *f* INVERSAS |
| 5538 | FUERZAS *f pl* EN LA MISMA DIRECCIÓN |
| 5539 | SOLDADURA *f* LLEVADA HACIA LA DERECHA |
| 5540 | PATENTE *f* EXTRANJERA |
| 5541 | CONTRAMAESTRE *m*, JEFE DE TALLER *m* |
| 5542 | FORJAR |
| 5543 | CARBÓN DE FORJA *m* |
| 5543 | HULLA *f* BLANDA |
| 5544 | FUNDICIÓN *f* AFINADA |

| | |
|---|---|
| 5545 | PRUEBA *f* DE FORJADO |
| 5546 | SOLDADURA *f* EN LA FORJA |
| 5547 | TALLER *m* DE FORJA |
| 5547 | FORJA *f* |
| 5548 | FRAGUA *f*, HERRERÍA *f* |
| 5548 | HERRERÍA *f* |
| 5548 | FUEGO *m* DE FORJA |
| 5549 | RACOR *m* DE ACERO FORJADO |
| 5550 | MANIVELA *f* FORJADA |
| 5550 | MANIVELA *f* ACODADA EN FORJA |
| 5550 | MANIVELA *f* VENIDA DE FORJA |
| 5551 | BARRA *f* DE OJALES |
| 5552 | FORJADO *m* DE UNA PIEZA EN LA MASA |
| 5553 | METALES *m* VIEJOS DE RECUPERACIÓN |
| 5553 | CHATARRA *f*, HIERRO VIEJO |
| 5553 | CHATARRA *f*, HIERRO VIEJO |
| 5554 | ACERO FORJADO *m* |
| 5555 | FORJADURA *f* |
| 5556 | PIEZA *f* DE FORJA |
| 5556 | PIEZA *f* TRABAJADA EN LA FORJA |
| 5556 | PIEZA *f* FORJADA |
| 5557 | FORJADO *m* |
| 5558 | LATÓN *m* DE FORJAR |
| 5559 | MARTILLO *m* DE FORJA |
| 5559 | MARTILLO *m* MECÁNICO |
| 5560 | TEMPERATURA *f* DE FORJA |
| 5561 | MÁQUINA *f* DE FORJAR |
| 5561 | MÁQUINA *f* DE RECALCAR |
| 5562 | PRENSA *f* DE FORJAR |
| 5563 | LAMINADOR *m* PARA FORJAR |
| 5564 | ESFUERZOS *m pl* DE FORJADO |
| 5565 | TEMPERATURA *f* DE FORJA |
| 5566 | HIERROS *m pl* FORJADOS |
| 5567 | HORQUETA *f* |
| 5567 | CARDÁN *m*, HORQUETA DE UNIÓN *f* |
| 5568 | HORQUILLA *f* |
| 5568 | PIE *m* DE LA BIELA CON HORQUILLA |
| 5569 | PALANCA *f* DE HORQUILLA |
| 5570 | MOLDE *m* |
| 5571 | FORMAR, DAR FORMA, LABRAR, TRABAJAR |
| 5571 | PERFILAR |
| 5572 | FACTOR *m* DE FORMA |
| 5573 | METANOL *m* |
| 5573 | ÓXIDO *m* DE METILENO |
| 5573 | FORMALDEHIDO *m* |
| 5573 | FORMOL *m* |
| 5573 | ALDEHÍDO METÍLICO *m* |
| 5573 | ALDEHÍDO FÓRMICO *m*, FORMOL *m* |
| 5574 | FORMATO *m* |
| 5575 | FORMACIÓN *f* DE MOHO |
| 5576 | TENSIÓN *f* DE FORMACIÓN |

| | | | |
|---|---|---|---|
| 5577 | FRESAS  *f pl*  MADRES | 5613 | NÚMERO  *m*  FRACCIONARIO |
| 5578 | ÁCIDO FÓRMICO  *m* | 5614 | TORNO  *m*  DE FRACCIONAMIENTO |
| 5579 | CURVADO  *m*, CONFORMACIÓN  *f* | 5615 | FRACCIONAR |
| 5579 | FORMACIÓN  *f* | 5616 | TEORÍA  *f*  DE LAS FRACTURAS |
| 5579 | MODELADO  *m* | 5617 | RUPTURA  *f* |
| 5580 | ESTAMPA  *f*  DE EMBUTIR | 5617 | FRACTURA  *f* |
| 5581 | HECHURA  *f*, AMOLDADO  *m* | 5618 | ESFUERZO  *m*  DE ROTURA (DE FRACTURA) |
| 5582 | FÓRMULA  *f* | 5619 | PRUEBA  *f*  DE ROTURA |
| 5583 | FÓRMULA  *f*  DE CONSTITUCIÓN | 5620 | FRACTURA  *f*, ROTURA  *f* |
| 5584 | AVANCE  *m*, MOVIMIENTO  *m*  DE AVANCE | 5620 | SECCIÓN  *f*  DE RUPTURA |
| 5584 | MOVIMIENTO  *m*  DE AVANCE | 5621 | FRÁGIL |
| 5585 | CARRERA  *f*  DIRECTA DEL PISTÓN | 5622 | FRAGILIDAD  *f* |
| 5585 | CARRERA DE IDA  *f* | 5623 | FRAGMENTACIÓN  *f*  DE GRANOS |
| 5585 | CARRERA ADELANTE  *f* | 5624 | ARMAZÓN  *f* |
| 5585 | CARRERA DIRECTA DEL ÉMBOLO  *f* | 5624 | BASTIDOR  *m* |
| 5585 | MARCHA  *f*  HACIA ADELANTE DEL PISTÓN | 5624 | CARCASA  *f*, ARMADURA  *f*, ARMAZÓN  *f*, CASCO  *m* (DE BUQUE) |
| 5586 | COMBUSTIBLE FÓSIL  *m* | | |
| 5587 | ESTORBARSE MUTUAMENTE | 5624 | MARCO  *m*, CUADRO  *m*, BASTIDOR  *m* |
| 5588 | ELECTRÓLITO  *m*  IMPURO | 5625 | LARGUERO  *m* |
| 5589 | MACIZO  *f*  DE CIMIENTOS | 5626 | BASTIDOR  *m*  DE UNA MÁQUINA |
| 5589 | CIMIENTOS  *m pl* | 5627 | LARGUERO  *m* |
| 5590 | BULÓN  *m*  DE FUNDACIÓN | 5628 | SIERRA  *f*  DE HENDER DE NUEVO |
| 5591 | OBRERO  *m*  FUNDIDOR | 5629 | MÁQUINA  *f*  ALTERNA PARA SERRAR |
| 5591 | FUNDIDOR  *m* | 5629 | SIERRA DE BASTIDOR (O DE BALLESTA)  *f*, SIERRA DE MANO  *f* |
| 5592 | FUNDICIÓN  *f*, FONDERÍA (TALLER DE) | | |
| 5592 | FUNDICIÓN  *f*  (ART) | 5629 | ASERRADORA  *f*  DE MOVIMIENTO ALTERNATIVO |
| 5592 | FUNDICIÓN  *f* | 5629 | SIERRA  *f*  DE BASTIDOR |
| 5593 | FUNDICIÓN  *f*, COLADA  *f* | 5630 | ARMADURA  *f* |
| 5594 | PREALEACIÓN  *f* | 5630 | ESTRUCTURA  *f*, ARMAZÓN  *f* |
| 5595 | COQUE DE CUBILOTE  *m* | 5631 | RAYAS  *f pl*  DE FRAUNHOFER |
| 5596 | FUNDICIÓN  *f*  GRIS | 5632 | CIANURO  *m*  LIBRE |
| 5596 | FUNDICIÓN  *f*  DE MOLDEO | 5633 | CAÍDA LIBRE  *f* |
| 5597 | FUNDICIONES  *f pl*  (INSTALACIONES  *f pl*) | 5634 | CORRIENTE LIBRE  *f* |
| 5598 | PUNTAS  *f pl*  PARA FUNDICIÓN | 5635 | SIN ÁCIDO, EXENTO DE ACIDO, LIBRE DE ÁCIDO |
| 5599 | SEDÁN  *m*  DE CUATRO PUERTAS | 5636 | EXENTO (O LIBRE) DE CENIZAS |
| 5600 | MOTOR  *m*  DE CUATRO TIEMPOS | 5637 | EXTRAER EL POLVO, DESEMPOLVAR |
| 5601 | PROPULSIÓN  *f*  CON 4 RUEDAS MOTRICES | 5638 | SIN ESCORIAS |
| 5602 | ASTROIDE  *f* | 5639 | ACERO MAQUINABLE RÁPIDO  *m* |
| 5603 | MOTOR  *m*  DE CUATRO TIEMPOS | 5640 | MAGNETISMO  *m*  LIBRE |
| 5604 | MANDRIL  *m*  DE CUATRO MORDAZAS INDEPENDIENTES | 5641 | ESCALERA  *f*  RECTA |
| | | 5642 | RESPIRADERO  *m*  LIBRE |
| 5605 | GRIFO  *m*  DE CUATRO PASOS | 5643 | OSCILACIÓN  *f*  LIBRE |
| 5606 | GRIFO  *m*  DE CUATRO PASOS | 5644 | RUEDA  *f*  LIBRE |
| 5607 | ALAMBRE  *m*  DE BRONCE FOSFOROSO | 5645 | LATÓN  *m*  DE FILETEADO |
| 5608 | CUARTA  *f*  POTENCIA | 5646 | ESCALERA  *f*  RECTA |
| 5609 | RAÍZ  *f*  BICUADRADA | 5647 | VIRGEN (MINERAL) |
| 5610 | MADERA  *f*  PODRIDA | 5647 | NATIVO  *m*, NATURAL  *m* |
| 5610 | MADERA  *f*  PODRIDA | 5647 | ESTADO NATIVO (O VIRGEN) (EN)  *m*, NATIVO (O VIRGEN) |
| 5611 | FRACCIÓN  *f*  DE DESTILACIÓN | | |
| 5612 | DESTILACION  *f*  FRACCIONADA | 5648 | DIBUJO  *m*  A MANO ALZADA |
| 5613 | FRACCIÓN  *f* | 5649 | SUSPENDIDO LIBREMENTE |

| | |
|---|---|
| 5650 | QUE REPOSA LIBREMENTE |
| 5651 | RUEDA *f* LIBRE |
| 5652 | MECANISMO *m* DE RUEDA LIBRE |
| 5653 | SOLIDIFICATIÓN *f* |
| 5654 | MEZCLA *f* REFRIGERANTE |
| 5655 | CONGELACIÓN DEL HORNO *f* |
| 5656 | PUNTO *m* DE CONGELACIÓN |
| 5656 | PUNTO *m* DE SOLIDIFICACIÓN |
| 5657 | ANTICONGELANTE *m* |
| 5658 | INTERVALO *m* DE SOLIDIFICACIÓN |
| 5658 | ZONA *f* DE SOLIDIFICACIÓN |
| 5659 | ESTEATITA *f* |
| 5659 | TALCO *m* |
| 5660 | PISTOLA *f* |
| 5660 | REGLA *f* CURVA |
| 5661 | FRECUENCIA *f* |
| 5662 | FRECUENCIA *f* EMPÍRICA |
| 5663 | AGUA *f* DULCE (O BLANDA) |
| 5664 | CALIZA DE AGUA DULCE *f* |
| 5664 | CALIZA BASTA *f* |
| 5665 | MÁQUINA *f* DE CONTORNEAR |
| 5665 | SIERRA *f* DE RECORTAR |
| 5665 | SALTADORA *f* |
| 5666 | CORROSIÓN POR ROCE *f* |
| 5667 | CORROSIÓN DE LAS CARAS EN CONTACTO *f* |
| 5667 | OXIDACIÓN *f* POR FROTAMIENTO |
| 5668 | FRICCIÓN *f* |
| 5668 | FROTAMIENTO *m*, ROCE *m*, FRICCIÓN *f* |
| 5669 | FRENO *m* DE FRICCIÓN |
| 5670 | COEFICIENTE DE ROCE *m* |
| 5671 | CONO DE FRICCIÓN *m* |
| 5672 | ACOPLAMIENTO *m* DE FRICCIÓN, EMBRAGUE DE FRICCIÓN |
| 5672 | ACOPLAMIENTO DE FRICCIÓN *m* |
| 5673 | PLATILLO *m* DE FRICCIÓN, DISCO *m* DE FRICCIÓN |
| 5674 | ENGRANAJE *m* DE FRICCIÓN |
| 5675 | TRINQUETE DE ROCE *m* |
| 5676 | MECANISMO *m* DE FRICCIÓN POR TRINQUETE, TRINQUETE *m* DE FRICCIÓN |
| 5677 | FROTAMIENTO *m* EN MARCHA |
| 5677 | FROTAMIENTO *m* DURANTE EL MOVIMIENTO |
| 5678 | FROTAMIENTO *m* AL PARTIR |
| 5678 | FROTAMIENTO *m* AL ARRANCAR |
| 5679 | RODILLO *m* DE FRICCIÓN |
| 5680 | ASERRADO *m* POR FRICCIÓN |
| 5681 | FRENO *m* DE CINTA |
| 5681 | FRENO *m* DE ENROLLAMIENTO |
| 5681 | FRENO *m* DE CINTA |
| 5681 | FRENO *m* DE COLLARÍN |
| 5682 | RUEDA *f* DE FRICCIÓN |

| | |
|---|---|
| 5683 | FUERZA *f* DE FROTAMIENTO, FUERZA *f* DE FRICCIÓN |
| 5684 | TRANSMISIÓN *f* POR FRICCIÓN |
| 5685 | PÉRDIDA *f* DEBIDA AL FROTAMIENTO |
| 5686 | RESISTENCIA *f* DE ROZAMIENTO |
| 5687 | SUPERFICIE *f* DE ROZAMIENTO |
| 5688 | SIN ROZAMIENTO |
| 5689 | LÍNEAS *f pl* DE LÍMITES |
| 5690 | SINTERIZACIÓN *f*, TOSTADO *m* |
| 5691 | EJE *m* DELANTERO |
| 5692 | TABLERO *m* |
| 5693 | TRAVESAÑO *m* DELANTERO |
| 5694 | VISTA *f* ANTERIOR |
| 5695 | CUBRETABLERO *m*, CAPÓ DEL SALPICADERO *m* |
| 5696 | GEOMETRÍA *f* DEL TREN DELANTERO |
| 5697 | VUELTA *f* FRONTAL (VUELTA EN EL AIRE) |
| 5698 | ÁNGULO MUERTO *m* |
| 5698 | ÁNGULO DE DESPRENDIMIENTO *m*, ÁNGULO DE ATAQUE *m* |
| 5699 | TRACCIÓN *f* DELANTERA |
| 5700 | ATRONADURA *f* DE LA MADERA |
| 5701 | CRISTAL *m* ESMERILADO |
| 5702 | ESCARCHADO *m* |
| 5703 | FORMACIÓN *f* DE ESPUMA |
| 5704 | LAVADORAS *f pl* Y ESCOGEDORAS *f pl* DE RAÍCES Y FRUTOS |
| 5705 | COMBUSTIBLE *m* |
| 5706 | PAÑOL *m* DE MAZUT, DE FUEL |
| 5707 | ECONOMÍA *f* (O AHORRO *m*) DE COMBUSTIBLE |
| 5708 | FILTRO *m* DE CUMBUSTIBLE |
| 5708 | FILTRO *m* DE COMBUSTIBLE |
| 5709 | GAS *m* PARA CALEFACCIÓN |
| 5709 | GAS *m* COMBUSTIBLE |
| 5710 | INDICADOR *m* DEL NIVEL DE GASOLINA |
| 5711 | BOMBA *f* DE INYECCIÓN |
| 5712 | CARTER DE BOMBA DE INYECCIÓN *m* |
| 5713 | BOMBA *f* DE ALIMENTACIÓN |
| 5714 | FUEL *m* |
| 5714 | ACEITE *m* PESADO (PARA FUERZA MOTRIZ) |
| 5714 | FUEL OIL *m* |
| 5715 | BOMBA *f* DE ALIMENTACIÓN |
| 5716 | DEPÓSITO *m* |
| 5716 | DEPÓSITO *m* DE GASOLINA |
| 5716 | DEPÓSITO *m* DE CARBURANTE |
| 5717 | CENTRO DE ROTACIÓN *m* |
| 5717 | PUNTO *m* DE ARTICULACIÓN |
| 5718 | TURBINA *f* DE ADMISIÓN TOTAL |
| 5719 | RECOCIDO *m* DE GRANO GRUESO |
| 5720 | JUNTA *f* SOLDADA CON SIMPLE SOLAPA, JUNTA *f* SOLDADA CON SIMPLE PESTAÑA |
| 5721 | ENDURECIMIENTO *m* COMPLETO |
| 5722 | PLENA CARGA *f* |

| | |
|---|---|
| 5723 | TAMAÑO NATURAL (DE), ESCALA NATURAL (A) |
| 5723 | TAMAÑO NATURAL (DE), ESCALA NATURAL (A) |
| 5724 | DIBUJO _m_ EN TAMAÑO NATURAL |
| 5724 | DIBUJO _m_ EN TAMAÑO NATURAL |
| 5725 | LÍNEA _f_ PLENA |
| 5726 | ESTAMPA _f_ DE DESBASTAR |
| 5726 | ESTAMPA _f_ DE ESTIRAR |
| 5727 | TIERRA _f_ DE BATÁN |
| 5728 | REDONDEAMIENTO _m_ |
| 5729 | DESTAJADOR _m_ REDONDO, COPADOR _m_, ALISADOR _m_, REDONDEADORA _f_ |
| 5730 | PRODUCTO _m_ ACABADO |
| 5730 | PIEZA _f_ ACABADA |
| 5730 | FABRICADO |
| 5731 | ÁCIDO FULMÍNICO _m_ |
| 5732 | HUMOS _m pl_, HUMAREDA _f_ |
| 5733 | ÁCIDO DE SAJONIA _m_ |
| 5733 | ÁCIDO DE NORDHAUSEN _m_ |
| 5733 | ÁCIDO SULFÚRICO FUMANTE _m_ |
| 5734 | FUNCIÓN _f_ (MATEM.) |
| 5735 | INVESTIGACIÓN _f_ FUNDAMENTAL |
| 5736 | VIBRACIÓN _f_ PROPIA |
| 5736 | VIBRACIÓN _f_ FUNDAMENTAL |
| 5737 | POLÍGONO _m_ FUNICULAR |
| 5737 | POLÍGONO _m_ ARTICULADO |
| 5738 | EMBUDO _m_ |
| 5739 | HORNO _m_ |
| 5739 | HORNO _m_ |
| 5740 | SOLDADURA _f_ CON HORNO |
| 5741 | CROMO PARA HORNO _m_ |
| 5742 | ENFRIAMIENTO _m_ DEL HORNO |
| 5743 | CANAL DE HUMO _m_ |
| 5744 | HOGAR _m_ DE GAS |
| 5745 | HOGAR _m_ DE ACEITE PESADO |
| 5745 | HOGAR _m_ DE PETRÓLEO |
| 5746 | HOGAR _m_ DE CARBÓN PULVERIZADO, HORNILLO _m_ DE CARBÓN EN POLVO |
| 5747 | HOGAR _m_ DE CALDERA |
| 5747 | HORNO _m_ DE CALDERA |
| 5748 | REVESTIMIENTO _m_ DEL HORNO |
| 5749 | CAMISA DEL HORNO _f_, ENVOLVENTE DEL HORNO _m_ |
| 5750 | MECANIZACIÓN _f_ ULTERIOR |
| 5751 | FUSIBLE _m_ |
| 5752 | PORTAFUSIBLES _m_ |
| 5753 | ELECTROCORINDÓN _m_ |
| 5754 | ACEITE _m_ DE PATATAS |
| 5755 | POSIBILIDAD _f_ |
| 5756 | FUSIBLE _m_ |
| 5756 | LICUABLE |
| 5757 | ALEACIÓN FUSIBLE _f_ |

| | |
|---|---|
| 5758 | FUSIBLE _m_ |
| 5758 | PLOMO _m_ FUSIBLE |
| 5758 | FUSIBLE _m_, PROTECTOR _m_ CORTACIRCUITOS |
| 5759 | PUNTO _m_ DE FUSIÓN |
| 5760 | FUSIÓN _f_ |
| 5761 | ZONA _f_ DE FUSIÓN |
| 5762 | SOLDADURA _f_ POR FUSIÓN |
| 5763 | ZONA _f_ DE FUSIÓN |
| 5764 | FUSIÓN _f_ ÍGNEA |
| 5764 | LICUEFACCIÓN _f_ |
| 5765 | GABRO _m_ |
| 5766 | DISPOSITIVO _m_ ACCESORIO |
| 5767 | GADOLINIO _m_ |
| 5768 | GÁLIBO _m_ |
| 5768 | CALIBRADOR _m_ |
| 5768 | INDICADOR _m_ |
| 5768 | CALIBRE _m_, INDICADOR _m_ |
| 5769 | CALIBRADORES _m pl_ |
| 5769 | CALIBRES _m pl_ DE CONTROL |
| 5769 | CALIBRES _m_, GALGOS _f_ |
| 5769 | CALIBRES _m pl_ |
| 5769 | GÁLIBOS _m_ |
| 5770 | CALIBRACIÓN _f_ DE UNA MEDIDA |
| 5771 | PRESIÓN _f_ MANOMÉTRICA |
| 5772 | GANCHO _m_ |
| 5772 | TIRADOR _m_ |
| 5772 | TIRANTE _m_ DE LEVANTAMIENTO |
| 5773 | GANANCIA _f_ |
| 5774 | REDUCCIÓN _f_ DE LOS EMPLAZAMIENTOS |
| 5775 | GALENA _f_ |
| 5775 | PLOMO _m_ SULFURADO |
| 5776 | PLATAFORMA _f_ |
| 5776 | PASARELA _f_ |
| 5777 | ÁCIDO GÁLICO _m_ |
| 5778 | GRIPAJE _m_ (GAL.) |
| 5778 | DESGASTE _m_ POR ROZAMIENTO |
| 5779 | GALIO _m_ |
| 5780 | ÁCIDO DIGÁLICO _m_ |
| 5780 | ÁCIDO TÁNICO _m_ |
| 5780 | TANINO _m_ |
| 5781 | GALÓN _m_ (MEDIDA INGLESA) |
| 5782 | PILA _f_ HIDROELÉCTRICA |
| 5782 | PILA _f_ GALVÁNICA |
| 5782 | PILA _f_ GALVÁNICA |
| 5782 | PAR ELECTROQUÍMICO _m_ |
| 5783 | CORROSIÓN GALVÁNICA _f_ |
| 5784 | GALVANIZAR CON CINC |
| 5784 | GALVANIZAR |
| 5785 | CHAPA _f_ GALVANIZADA |
| 5785 | CHAPA _f_ GALVANIZADA |
| 5786 | ALAMBRE _m_ GALVANIZADO |

| | |
|---|---|
| 5786 | ALAMBRE *m* GALVANIZADO |
| 5787 | GALVANIZACIÓN *f* CON CINC |
| 5787 | GALVANIZACIÓN *f* |
| 5788 | BANDAS *f pl* GALVANIZADAS |
| 5789 | GALVANIZACIÓN *f* CON CINC |
| 5789 | GALVANIZACIÓN *f* |
| 5790 | FRAGILIDAD *f* A LA GALVANIZACIÓN |
| 5791 | GALVANÓMETRO *m* |
| 5792 | GALVANOPLÁSTICO |
| 5793 | GOMA GUTA *f* |
| 5794 | FUNCIÓN *f* GAMMA |
| 5795 | HIERRO *m* GAMA |
| 5796 | RAYOS *m* GAMMA |
| 5797 | ESTRUCTURA *f* GAMMA |
| 5798 | GAMMAGRAFÍA *f* |
| 5799 | PERFORADORA *f* CON CABEZAS MÚLTIPLES, TALADRADORA *f* MÚLTIPLE, CON BROCAS MÚLTIPLES |
| 5800 | FRESADO *m* EN TREN |
| 5801 | PORTAÚTIL *m* PARA VARIOS ÚTILES |
| 5802 | GANGA *f* |
| 5802 | ROCA *f* MADRE |
| 5803 | GANISTER *m* |
| 5803 | LADRILLO *m* DINAS |
| 5804 | PUENTE GRÚA *m* DE OBRA/DE ESTACIÓN |
| 5805 | MEZCLA *f* DE GRANO SIN GRANOS INTERMEDIOS |
| 5806 | JUNTA *f* HENDIDA |
| 5806 | DIVERGENCIA *f* |
| 5807 | GRANATE *m* |
| 5808 | FLUIDO *m* GASEOSO |
| 5808 | GAS *m* |
| 5808 | CUERPO GASEOSO *m* |
| 5809 | ANÁLISIS DE GAS *m* |
| 5810 | SOLDADURA *f* CON SOPLETE |
| 5811 | QUEMADOR *m* DE GAS |
| 5811 | QUEMADOR *m* DE GAS |
| 5812 | CARBÓN DE RETORTA *m* |
| 5813 | HULLA *f* PARA GAS |
| 5814 | GRIFO *m* DE GAS |
| 5815 | CONSTANTE DE UN GAS *f* |
| 5816 | CORRIENTE GASEOSA *f* |
| 5817 | CORTE CON AUTÓGENA *f* |
| 5817 | CORTE CON SOPLETE *m* |
| 5817 | OXICORTE *m*, CORTE *m* AUTÓGENO |
| 5818 | CEMENTACIÓN NÍTRICA *f* |
| 5819 | MOTOR *m* DE GASOLINA |
| 5820 | HACHÓN *m* |
| 5821 | CONDUCTO DE GAS *m* |
| 5822 | ACANALADO *m* CON LLAMA |
| 5823 | ONDULACIONES *f pl* DEBIDAS AL GAS |
| 5824 | SOLDADOR *m* AL GAS |

| | |
|---|---|
| 5825 | VENTEADURA *f* |
| 5826 | LÁMPARA *f* DE GAS DE ALUMBRADO |
| 5827 | LUZ *f* DE GAS, LUZ *f* DE MECHERO DE GAS |
| 5828 | ALUMBRADO *m* POR GAS |
| 5829 | CONTADOR DE GAS *m* |
| 5830 | NITRURACIÓN *f* GASEOSA |
| 5831 | GAS-OIL *m* |
| 5832 | DECAPADO *m* CON GAS |
| 5833 | TUBO *m* DE GAS |
| 5834 | DISTRIBUCIÓN *f* DE GAS |
| 5834 | TUBERÍA DE GAS *f* |
| 5835 | PINZAS *f pl* PARA GAS |
| 5836 | VENTEADURA *f* |
| 5836 | INCLUSIÓN *f* DE GAS (O DE GASES) |
| 5837 | PRESIÓN *f* DEL GAS |
| 5838 | GENERADOR *m* POR GAS |
| 5838 | GASÓGENO *m* |
| 5839 | PURIFICACIÓN *f* DE LOS GASES |
| 5840 | TEMPLE *m* AL GAS |
| 5841 | CAPTACIÓN DE LOS GASES SIN COMBUSTIÓN *f* |
| 5842 | COLECTOR DE GAS *m* |
| 5843 | PASO *m* PARA TUBOS DE GAS |
| 5844 | TURBINA *f* DE GAS |
| 5845 | BOTELLA *f* PARA LAVADO DEL GAS, LAVADOR *m* DE GAS |
| 5845 | FRASCO *m* LAVADOR |
| 5846 | CALENTADOR DE AGUA DE GAS *m* |
| 5847 | SOLDADURA *f* AUTÓGENA |
| 5848 | FÁBRICA *f* DE GAS |
| 5849 | COQUE DE GAS *m* |
| 5849 | COQUE DE GAS *m* |
| 5850 | GENERATRIZ *f* DE GAS |
| 5851 | HORNO *m* DE CALDEO POR GAS |
| 5852 | SOLDADURA *f* AL ARCO BAJO PROTECCIÓN GASEOSA |
| 5853 | IMPERMEABLE A LOS GASES |
| 5854 | COMBUSTIBLE GASEOSO *m* |
| 5855 | INCLUSIÓN *f* GASEOSA |
| 5856 | MEZCLA *f* GASEOSA |
| 5857 | ESTADO *m* GASEOSO |
| 5858 | CORTE INICIAL *m* |
| 5859 | GASÓMETRO *m* |
| 5860 | GASIFICABLE |
| 5861 | GASIFICACIÓN *f* |
| 5862 | GASIFICAR |
| 5863 | JUNTA *f* DE HERMETICIDAD, JUNTA *f* DE ESTANQUEIDAD |
| 5863 | EMPALME *m* |
| 5863 | TRENZA *f* |
| 5864 | GASOLINA *f* |
| 5865 | GASIFICACIÓN *f* |

| | |
|---|---|
| 5866 | ENTRADA *f* DE COLADA |
| 5867 | VÁLVULA *f* DE COMPUERTA |
| 5867 | VÁLVULA *f* DE PASO |
| 5868 | MODELO *m* CON EMBUDOS, MODELADO |
| 5869 | AUMENTO *m* DE LA SECCIÓN TRANSVERSAL |
| 5870 | SISTEMA *m* DE COLADA Y DE ALIMENTACIÓN |
| 5871 | ANCHO *m* DE VÍA, ENTREVÍA *f* |
| 5871 | VERIFICADOR *m* (METROLOGÍA) |
| 5871 | CALIBRE *m*, GALGA *f* |
| 5871 | INSTRUMENTO *m* DE VERIFICACIÓN (DE CONTROL) |
| 5871 | VERIFICADOR *m* |
| 5872 | DESTARAR |
| 5872 | SELLAR, TIMBRAR |
| 5872 | CALIBRAR |
| 5873 | CALIBRES *m pl* |
| 5874 | CALIBRACIÓN *f* DE UNA MEDIDA |
| 5875 | GRIFO *m* DE AFORO |
| 5876 | FLOTADOR *m* (DE CALIBRACIÓN) |
| 5877 | CABEZA *f* DE MEDIDA |
| 5878 | LARGURA *f* DE REFERENCIA |
| 5879 | ÍNDICE *m*, SEÃNL *f* |
| 5880 | NÚMERO *m* DE CALIBRE DE UNA CHAPA |
| 5881 | NÚMERO *m* DE CALIBRE DE UN ALAMBRE |
| 5882 | PRESIÓN *f* RELATIVA |
| 5883 | TAPÓN *m* DE CALIBRE |
| 5884 | MONTAJE *m* DE CUÑAS CALIBRADORAS |
| 5885 | PLATAFORMA *f* CALIBRADORA |
| 5886 | DESTARA *f* |
| 5886 | TIMBRE *m* |
| 5886 | CALIBRACIÓN *f*, GRADUACIÓN *f* |
| 5886 | CALIBRACIÓN *f* |
| 5887 | ALUMBRADO *m* INTERIOR |
| 5887 | DISTRIBUCIÓN *f* GAUSSIANA |
| 5888 | GASA *f* |
| 5888 | TELA *f* METÁLICA |
| 5889 | PIÑÓN *m*, RUEDA *f* MOTRIZ |
| 5889 | ENGRANAJE *m* |
| 5890 | CAJA *f* DE VELOCIDADES |
| 5890 | CAJA DE CAMBIOS *f* |
| 5891 | MÁQUINA *f* PARA ENTALLAR LOS ENGRANAJES |
| 5891 | TALLADORA *f* DE ENGRANAJES |
| 5892 | ACCIONAMIENTO POR ENGRANAJE *m* |
| 5893 | MÁQUINA *f* DE ACCIONADO POR ENGRANAJE |
| 5894 | FRESADORA *f* PARA HACER LOS ENGRANAJES |
| 5895 | BOMBA *f* DE ENGRANAJE |
| 5896 | RELACIONES *f* ENTRE ENGRANAJES |
| 5897 | RELACIÓN *f* ENTRE ENGRANAJES |
| 5898 | FRESA *f* PARA HACER LOS ENGRANAJES |
| 5899 | PIE *m* DENTADO |

| | |
|---|---|
| 5900 | PIE *m* DE REY CON VERNIER PARA LOS DIENTES DE PIÑON |
| 5901 | TREN *m* DE ENGRANAJES |
| 5901 | JUEGO *m* DE ENGRANAJES |
| 5902 | BANCO *m* PARA VERIFICAR LOS ENGRANAJES |
| 5903 | RUEDA *f* DENTADA |
| 5903 | RUEDA *f* DENTADA |
| 5904 | ACERO PARA ENGRANAJES *m* |
| 5905 | BERBIQUÍ *m* DE ENGRANAJE |
| 5906 | VOLANTE *m* DENTADO |
| 5907 | ENGRANAJES *m pl* |
| 5907 | SERIE *f* DE ENGRANAJES |
| 5908 | TRANSMISIÓN *f* CON REDUCCIÓN DE LA VELOCIDAD |
| 5909 | MULTIPLICACIÓN *f* |
| 5910 | ENGRANE *m* (DE RUEDAS DENTADAS) |
| 5911 | CONTADOR GEIGER *m* |
| 5912 | GEL *m* |
| 5913 | GELATINA *f* PURA |
| 5914 | DISPOSICIÓN *f* GENERAL |
| 5914 | PLAN *m* DE DISPOSICIÓN |
| 5915 | DIRECTOR *m* DE FÁBRICA |
| 5916 | PRODUCIR (VAPOR, GAS) |
| 5917 | PRODUCIR UNA CORRIENTE ELÉCTRICA |
| 5918 | CONO COMPLEMENTARIO *m* |
| 5918 | CONO GENERADOR *m* |
| 5919 | FUNCIÓN *f* GENERATRIZ (DE MOMENTOS) |
| 5920 | INSTALACIÓN *f* GENERATRIZ DE CORRIENTE |
| 5921 | CÍRCULO MÓVIL *m* |
| 5921 | CÍRCULO RODANTE *m* |
| 5922 | PRODUCCIÓN *f* DE ENERGÍA |
| 5923 | GENERACIÓN *f* DE VAPOR |
| 5924 | GENERATRIZ *f* DE CORRIENTE |
| 5924 | DINAMO *f*, GENERADOR *m* DE CORRIENTE |
| 5925 | GENERATRIZ *f* (GEOM.) |
| 5926 | REPRESENTACIÓN *f* GEOMÉTRICA |
| 5927 | GEOMÉTRICO |
| 5928 | DIBUJO *m* GEOMÉTRICO |
| 5929 | MEDIA *f* GEOMÉTRICA, TÉRMINO *m* MEDIO GEOMÉTRICO |
| 5930 | PROGRESIÓN *f* GEOMÉTRICA |
| 5931 | GEOMETRÍA *f* |
| 5932 | METAL BLANCO *m*, PLATA *f* ALEMANA |
| 5932 | PLATA *f* ALEMANA, PACTUNG *m* |
| 5932 | METAL *m* BLANCO, ALPACA *f*, PLATA *f* NUEVA |
| 5932 | ARGENTÁN *m* |
| 5932 | METAL *m* BLANCO, PLATA *f* ALEMANA |
| 5933 | GERMANIO *m* |
| 5934 | GERMINACIÓN *f* |
| 5934 | FORMACIÓN *f* DE GÉRMENES |
| 5935 | CONDICIÓN CRÍTICA DE DEFORMACIÓN *f* |

| | |
|---|---|
| 5936 | GEYSER *m*, GÉISER *m* (SURTIDOR NATURAL) |
| 5937 | CONTRA-CHAVETA *f* |
| 5938 | CLAVIJA Y CONTRA-CLAVIJA *f* |
| 5939 | CLAVIJA DE GANCHO *f* |
| 5939 | CLAVIJA DE GANCHO *f* |
| 5939 | CLAVIJA DE GANCHO *f* |
| 5940 | CHAVETA *f* |
| 5941 | DORAR |
| 5942 | DORADO *m*, DORADURA *f* |
| 5943 | ALEACIÓN COBRE CINC *f* |
| 5944 | BARRENA *f* |
| 5944 | BARRENA *f* FINA |
| 5945 | CABRIA *f* |
| 5945 | CABRA DE TRÍPODE *f* |
| 5946 | VIGA *f* |
| 5947 | PLACA *f* DE ASIENTO DE VIGA |
| 5948 | SOLDADURA *f* FUERTE HORIZONTAL |
| 5949 | CEDER , DAR DE SÍ |
| 5950 | CEDER (GASTAR) CALOR |
| 5951 | CANTIDAD *f* CONOCIDA, DATO *m* |
| 5952 | ÁCIDO ACÉTICO CRISTALIZABLE *m* |
| 5953 | TAPA DE LA CAJA DE ESTOPA *f* |
| 5953 | PRENSAESTOPA *m* |
| 5954 | GRIFO *m* DE TAPONAMIENTO |
| 5955 | BRIDA *f* DEL CASQUETE |
| 5956 | VIDRIO, CRISTAL *m* |
| 5957 | PIEDRA *f* DE VIDRIO |
| 5958 | PAPEL *m* DE LIJA |
| 5959 | ELECTRODO *m* DE VIDRIO |
| 5960 | TUBO *m* CILÍNDRICO GRADUADO |
| 5961 | PAPEL *m* DE LIJA |
| 5962 | CRISTAL *m* MACHACADO |
| 5963 | PLACA *f* DE VIDRIO |
| 5964 | TEJA *f* DE VIDRIO |
| 5965 | TUBO *m* DE CRISTAL |
| 5966 | CRISTAL *m* HILADO |
| 5966 | LANA *f* DE VIDRIO |
| 5967 | SAL *f* DE GLAUBER |
| 5968 | VIDRIADO *m* |
| 5968 | VIDRIADO *m* |
| 5969 | ACRISTALAR |
| 5969 | LUSTRAR, ABRILLANTAR |
| 5970 | AZULEJO *m* |
| 5970 | LADRILLO *m* ESMALTADO |
| 5971 | MASILLA *f* DE LOS VIDRIEROS |
| 5972 | EMBOTAMIENTO *m*, BRUÑIMIENTO *m* |
| 5972 | ENCRISTALADO *m* |
| 5972 | VIDRIADO *m* |
| 5972 | VITRIFICADO *m*, GLASEADO *m* |
| 5973 | DESLIZAMIENTO *m* |
| 5974 | COEFICIENTE DE ELASTICIDAD DE CIZALLADURA *m* |
| 5974 | MÓDULO *m* DE ELASTICIDAD TRANSVERSAL |
| 5975 | PLANO *m* DE DESLIZAMIENTO |
| 5976 | CURVA *f* DE CORRIMIENTO |
| 5977 | GRIFO *m* DE VÁLVULA |
| 5977 | GRIFO *m* RECTO |
| 5978 | TORNILLO *m* ESFÉRICO |
| 5979 | POLVO *m* GLOBULAR |
| 5980 | CAJA *f* DE GUANTES, GUANTERA *f* |
| 5981 | CALOR |
| 5982 | CALENTAR AL ROJO |
| 5983 | INCANDESCENTE |
| 5984 | COLA *f* |
| 5985 | ENCOLAR, PEGAR |
| 5986 | JUNTA *f* PEGADA |
| 5987 | ENCOLADURA *f* |
| 5988 | GLICERINA *f* |
| 5989 | GNEIS *m* |
| 5990 | PROYECCÍONG GNOMÓNICA |
| 5991 | CALIBRE PASA-NO PASA *m* |
| 5992 | GAFAS *f pl* DE PROTECCIÓN |
| 5993 | ORO *m* |
| 5994 | BATIDERO *m* DE ORO |
| 5995 | BRONCE *m* DE ORO |
| 5996 | ORO *m* DE MONEDAS |
| 5997 | CIANURO *m* ÁURICO (O DE ORO) |
| 5998 | POLVO *m* DE ORO |
| 5999 | CHAPEADO, SOBREDORADO |
| 6000 | ORO *m* BATIDO |
| 6000 | HOJA *f* DE ORO |
| 6001 | LACA *f* DE BRONCE |
| 6002 | DORADURA *f*, DORADO *m* |
| 6003 | ORFEBRERÍA *f*, PLATERÍA *f* |
| 6004 | GONIÓMETRO *m* |
| 6005 | SOLDADURA *f* BIEN HECHA |
| 6006 | TEST *m* DE AJUSTE |
| 6007 | MONTACARGAS *m* |
| 6008 | SUPERFICIE *f* IRREGULAR DE LAS PIEZAS FUNDIDAS |
| 6009 | CUELLO DE CISNE *m* |
| 6010 | GUBIA *f* DE CARPINTERO |
| 6011 | TRABAJO *m* CON GUBIA |
| 6012 | MÁQUINA *f* DE CORTAR O RECORTAR |
| 6013 | REGULADOR *m* |
| 6014 | BRAZO *m* DEL REGULADOR |
| 6015 | BOLA *f* DEL REGULADOR |
| 6016 | CAJA DEL REGULADOR *f* |
| 6017 | MANGUITO *m* CASQUILLO *m* DEL REGULADOR |
| 6018 | EJE *m* DEL REGULADOR |
| 6018 | VARILLA *f* VERTICAL |

| | |
|---|---|
| 6019 | RESORTE *m* DE REGULADOR |
| 6020 | FRANQUICIA (DE DEMORA) *f* |
| 6021 | GRADO *m*, NIVEL *m* |
| 6021 | GRADO *m* |
| 6021 | NIVEL *m*, GRADUACIÓN *m* |
| 6022 | MATIZ *m* CALIDAD DEL ACERO, GRADUACIÓN *f* |
| 6023 | ANÁLISIS GRANULOMÉTRICO *m* |
| 6024 | VARIACIÓN *f* PROGRESIVA DE TEMPERATURA / DE VELOCIDAD |
| 6025 | GRADUAR |
| 6026 | CÍRCULO GRADUADO *m* |
| 6026 | CÍRCULO DIVIDIDO *m* |
| 6026 | LLANTA *f* |
| 6027 | ESFERA GRADUADA *f*, CUADRANTE GRADUADO *m* |
| 6028 | PIPETA *f* RECTA GRADUADA |
| 6029 | GRANO *m* (MEDIDA INGLESA) |
| 6030 | GRANO *m* |
| 6030 | CRISTAL *m* |
| 6031 | FIBRAS *f pl* (EN EL SENTIDO DE LAS) |
| 6032 | GRANULOMETRÍA *f* |
| 6033 | LÍMITE *m* DE LA SUPERFICIE DE GRANOS |
| 6034 | ELEVADORES-TRANSPORTADORES *m pl* DE GRANO |
| 6035 | ENGROSAMIENTO *m* DEL GRANO |
| 6035 | CRECIMIENTO *m* DE LOS GRANOS |
| 6036 | CHAPA *f* DE GRANO ORIENTADO |
| 6037 | AFINO DEL GRANO *m*, AFINACIÓN DEL GRANO *f* |
| 6038 | FLOR *f* DEL CUERO |
| 6038 | CARA PELO DEL CUERO *f* |
| 6038 | LADO PELO DEL CUERO *m* |
| 6039 | TAMAÑO *m* DEL GRANO |
| 6040 | GRANULOMETRÍA *f* |
| 6041 | ESTRUCTURA *f* DEL GRANO |
| 6042 | ESTAÑO *m* EN GRÁNULOS, GRANALLA *f* DE ESTAÑO |
| 6043 | GRANULACIÓN *f* |
| 6044 | MOLÉCULA-GRAMO *f* |
| 6045 | BAJA CALORÍA *f* |
| 6045 | CALORÍA GRAMO-GRADO *f* |
| 6046 | GRAMO *m* |
| 6047 | GRANITO *m* |
| 6048 | PLATINA *f* |
| 6049 | CONCESIÓN DE LA PATENTE *f* |
| 6049 | CONCESIÓN *f* DE PATENTE |
| 6050 | GRANULAR |
| 6051 | FRACTURA GRANULADA *f* |
| 6052 | ESTRUCTURA *f* GRANULAR |
| 6053 | CONTEXTURA *f* GRANULAR |
| 6054 | METAL *m* DE GRANALLA |
| 6055 | ESCORIA *f* GRANULADA |

| | |
|---|---|
| 6056 | POZO *m* DE GRANULACIÓN DE LA ESCORIA |
| 6057 | GRANULACIÓN *f* |
| 6058 | GLUCOSA *f* |
| 6058 | AZÚCAR *m* DE UVA |
| 6059 | CARBONO EN ESTADO GRAFITOIDE *m*, CARBONO GRAFÍTICO *m* |
| 6060 | CÁLCULO GRÁFICO *m* |
| 6060 | SOLUCIÓN *f* GRÁFICA |
| 6061 | GRAFOSTÁTICO |
| 6061 | ESTÁTICA *f* GRÁFICA |
| 6062 | GRAFITO *m* |
| 6063 | GRASA *f* MEJORADA |
| 6063 | GRASA *f* GRAFITADA |
| 6063 | ACEITE *m* GRAFITADO |
| 6063 | LUBRICANTE GRAFITADO |
| 6064 | CRISOL *m* DE GRAFITA |
| 6065 | PIRÓMETRO *m* DE GRAFITO |
| 6066 | GRAFILIZACIÓN *f* |
| 6067 | GRAFILIZANTE |
| 6068 | SUPERFICIE *f* DE REJILLA |
| 6069 | BARRAS *f pl* DE PARRILLAS |
| 6070 | PARRILLA *f* |
| 6071 | ENREJADO *m* |
| 6072 | AREÓMETRO *m* DE PESO CONSTANTE |
| 6073 | GRAVA *f*, GRAVILLA *f*, CASCAJO *m* |
| 6074 | FILTRO *m* DE GRAVA |
| 6075 | REJILLA *f* PARA CALIBRAR LA GRAVA |
| 6076 | TERRENO *m* GUIJOSO |
| 6077 | ANÁLISIS GRAVIMÉTRICA *f* |
| 6077 | GRAVIMETRÍA *f* |
| 6078 | GRAVEDAD *f* |
| 6078 | GRAVEDAD *f* |
| 6079 | COLADA A PRESIÓN POR GRAVEDAD *f* |
| 6080 | MARTINETE *m* |
| 6081 | TRAMO *m* AUTOMOTOR |
| 6081 | PLANO *m* INCLINADO |
| 6082 | TRANSPORTADOR *m* POR GRAVEDAD DE RODILLO |
| 6083 | CUERPO GRIS *m* |
| 6084 | ENGRASAR (UNTAR CON GRASA) |
| 6085 | CAJA *f* DE EJE, CAJA *f* DE GRASA |
| 6086 | ENGRASADOR *m* |
| 6087 | ENGRASE (UNTADO CON GRASA) *m* |
| 6087 | ENGRASE *m* CON SEBO |
| 6087 | ENGRASE *m* CON GRASA CONSISTENTE |
| 6088 | MATERIA AGLOMERADA *f* |
| 6089 | MALAQUITA *f* |
| 6090 | COMPACTO NO ACABADO |
| 6091 | RECOGEDORAS *f pl* DE FORRAJE |
| 6092 | ORO *m* VERDE |
| 6093 | VITRIOLO *m* VERDE |
| 6093 | CAPARROSA VERDE *f*, SULFATO DE HIERRO *m* |

| | |
|---|---|
| 6093 | SULFATO *m* DE HIERRO |
| 6093 | VITRIOLO *m* MARCIAL |
| 6094 | FUNDICIÓN *f* GRIS |
| 6095 | GRAUVACA (PETR.) *m* |
| 6096 | REJILLA *f* |
| 6096 | RED *f* ELÉCTRICA |
| 6096 | RED *f* DE ELECTRIFICACIÓN |
| 6097 | ACUMULADOR DE REJILLA *m* |
| 6098 | HIERRO *m* PARA BARRAS DE REJA |
| 6099 | CUADRÍCULA *f*, CUADRILLADO |
| 6100 | CORREDERA *f* DE REJILLA |
| 6101 | ENTABLADO *m*, ENTARIMADO *m*, SUELO *m* PAVIMENTADO |
| 6101 | ENJARETADO *m* |
| 6102 | ESCALONES *m* DE REJILLA METÁLICA |
| 6103 | MACHACAR, TRITURAR, PULVERIZAR, MOLAR |
| 6103 | REDUCIR EN POLVO |
| 6103 | PULVERIZAR |
| 6104 | ESMERILAR |
| 6105 | RECTIFICADOR *m* |
| 6105 | MÁQUINA DE AFILAR, RECTIFICADORA *f* |
| 6105 | AGUZADOR *m* |
| 6105 | VOLVER A MOLDEAR |
| 6106 | ABRASIÓN *f* |
| 6106 | RECTIFICACIÓN *f* |
| 6106 | RODAJE *m* |
| 6106 | TRITURACIÓN *f* FINA |
| 6106 | AFILADURA *f* CON MUELA |
| 6107 | SUBSTANCIA *f* DE DESGASTE |
| 6107 | MATERIA *f* PARA AFILAR |
| 6108 | PASTA *f* PARA ALISAR, PASTA DE ESMERIL |
| 6109 | ENFRIADOR *m* PARA MUELA |
| 6110 | POLVO *m* ABRASIVO |
| 6111 | RODAJE *m* CON ESMERIL |
| 6112 | LUBRIFICANTE *m* DE RODAJE |
| 6113 | MÁQUINA *f* PARA RECTIFICAR |
| 6113 | MÁQUINA *f* DE RECTIFICAR CON MUELA |
| 6113 | MÁQUINA *f* DE RECTIFICAR CON MUELA |
| 6113 | AMOLADORA *f* |
| 6114 | PLANO *m* PARA TRITURAR |
| 6115 | MUELA *f* |
| 6115 | RUEDA *f* DE MUELA |
| 6116 | MÁQUINA EQUILIBRADORA DE MUELAS *f* |
| 6117 | PULVERIZACIÓN *f* |
| 6117 | TRITURACIÓN *f* |
| 6117 | MOLIDO *m*, TRITURACIÓN *f* |
| 6118 | RUEDA *f* DE GRES |
| 6118 | MUELA *f* DE AFILAR |
| 6119 | PODER *m* DE OPACIDAD INSUFICIENTE |
| 6120 | MORDAZAS *f pl* |
| 6121 | MANDRIL *m* DE SUJECIÓN |

| | |
|---|---|
| 6122 | MORDAZA *f* (DE TORNO DE BANCO) |
| 6123 | ABRASIVO *m* |
| 6123 | GRANALLA *f* FINA |
| 6124 | GRANALLADO *m* (FINO) |
| 6125 | MORTERO *m* REFRACTARIO |
| 6125 | MORTERO REFRACTARIO *m* |
| 6126 | MORTERO REFRACTARIO *m* |
| 6127 | JUNTA *f* |
| 6127 | RANURA *f* |
| 6127 | RANURA *f* |
| 6128 | ACANALAR, HACER RANURAS |
| 6128 | ACANALAR, HACER RANURAS |
| 6129 | ÁNGULO DE LA CUÑA *m* |
| 6130 | BORDE *m* DE SOLDAR, BORDE *m* DE JUNTA |
| 6131 | RANURA *f* DE UNA POLEA |
| 6132 | RADIO *m* DE SEPARACIÓN ENTRE LOS BORDES |
| 6133 | SOLDADURA *f* DE BORDE |
| 6134 | LEVA DE RANURA *f* |
| 6135 | POLEA *f* DE GARGANTA |
| 6136 | CILINDRO *m* RANURADO |
| 6137 | ACANALADO *m* |
| 6137 | ACANALADO *m* |
| 6138 | MÁQUINA *f* DE ACANALAR |
| 6138 | MÁQUINA *f* DE ACANALAR |
| 6138 | MÁQUINA *f* DE RANURAR |
| 6139 | CEPILLO *m* PARA HEMBRAS |
| 6140 | POLEA *f* DE GARGANTA |
| 6141 | PESO *m* BRUTO |
| 6142 | SUPERFICIE *f* PULIDA |
| 6143 | ALTURA *f* LIBRE DESDE EL SUELO |
| 6144 | POLVO *m* DE CORCHO |
| 6144 | RECORTES *m pl* DE CORCHO |
| 6145 | CRISTAL *m* ESMERILADO (FOT) |
| 6145 | CRISTAL *m* ESMERILADO |
| 6146 | TAPÓN *m* ESMERILADO |
| 6147 | CAPA *f* SUBTERRÁNEA DE AGUA |
| 6147 | AGUAS *f pl* SUBTERRÁNEAS |
| 6148 | NIVEL *m* DEL AGUA SUBTERRÁNEA |
| 6149 | PUESTA *f* A TIERRA |
| 6150 | ACCIONAMIENTO POR GRUPOS *m* |
| 6151 | GRUPO *m* DE MÁQUINAS |
| 6152 | LECHADA *f* DE CEMENTO |
| 6152 | LECHADA *f* |
| 6153 | COLAR |
| 6153 | COLAR, RELLENAR, BATEAR |
| 6153 | EMPOTRAR CON CEMENTO |
| 6154 | LECHADO DEL CEMENTO *m* |
| 6155 | INFLACIÓN *f* |
| 6155 | CRECIMIENTO *m* |
| 6156 | TORNILLO *m* SIN CABEZA |
| 6157 | RED *f* PROTECTORA |

| | | |
|---|---|---|
| 6158 | EJE *m* DE PISTÓN |
| 6159 | PASADOR *m* DE LA ARTICULACIÓN DE LA HORQUILLA |
| 6160 | PLACA *f* DE GUARDA |
| 6160 | GUÍA *f* |
| 6160 | GUIADO *m* |
| 6160 | CORREDERA *f* |
| 6161 | RODILLO *m* GUIADOR |
| 6161 | RODILLO *m* GUÍA |
| 6161 | POLEA *f* DE TRANSMISIÓN |
| 6161 | POLEA *f* DE GUÍA |
| 6162 | RAÍL *m* DE GUÍA |
| 6163 | CASQUILLO *m* DE GUÍA |
| 6164 | VARILLA *f* DE GUÍA |
| 6164 | VARILLA *f* DE GUÍA |
| 6164 | BARRA *f* DE MANDO |
| 6165 | TUERCA *f* MATRIZ |
| 6166 | SUPERFICIE *f* DE GUÍA |
| 6167 | ÁLABE *m* DIRECTOR |
| 6167 | ÁLABE *m* FIJO DE UNA TURBINA |
| 6168 | SATÉLITE *m* |
| 6168 | CORONA DIRECTORA DE TURBINA *f*, ARO DIRECTOR *m*, ARO DE GUÍA DE TURBINA *m* |
| 6168 | CORONA FIJA *f* |
| 6169 | CORREDERA *f* DE CRUCETA |
| 6169 | GUÍA *f* DE LA CRUCETA |
| 6170 | TIJERAS DE GUILLOTINA *f pl* |
| 6171 | ZONA *f* DE GUINTER-PRESTON |
| 6172 | GOMA *f* ARÁBIGA |
| 6173 | GOMORRESINA *f* |
| 6174 | GOMA *f* ADRAGANTE |
| 6175 | AFUSTE *m* |
| 6176 | CELULOSA NITRADA *f* |
| 6176 | PIRÓXILO |
| 6176 | PIROXILINA *f* |
| 6176 | ALGODÓN PÓLVORA *m* |
| 6176 | XILOIDINA *f* |
| 6176 | NITROCELULOSA *f*, ALGODÓN PÓLVORA |
| 6176 | ALGODÓN PÓLVORA *m* |
| 6177 | BROCA *f* DE CAÑÓN |
| 6178 | BRONCE *m* DE CAÑÓN |
| 6179 | PINTURA *f* CON PISTOLA |
| 6180 | PISTOLA *f* PARA SOLDAR POR PUNTOS |
| 6181 | POLVO *m* NEGRO |
| 6182 | ESCUADRA *f* DE UNIÓN |
| 6183 | CORREA DE TUBULARES *f* |
| 6184 | GOMA *f* DE SUMATRA |
| 6184 | GOMA *f* GETTANIA |
| 6184 | GOMA *f* PLÁSTICA |
| 6185 | REGUERO *m*, CANAL *m* |
| 6185 | CANALÓN *m* DE DESAGÜE |

| | | |
|---|---|---|
| 6185 | REBOSADERO *m* |
| 6186 | TIRANTES *m pl* |
| 6187 | TIRANTE *m*, TENSOR *m*, VIENTO *m* |
| 6188 | VACIADO *m* EN ESCAYOLA |
| 6189 | MODELO *m* EN ESCAYOLA, MODELADO |
| 6190 | SULFATO *m* DE CALCIO |
| 6190 | PIEDRA *f* DE YESO, ESPEJUELO *m* |
| 6190 | ESCAYOLA *f*, YESO *m* DE VACIAR |
| 6191 | GIRÓSCOPO *m* |
| 6192 | ACCIÓN GIROSCÓPICA *f* |
| 6193 | MOVIMIENTO *m* GIROSCÓPICO |
| 6194 | HIERRO *m* EN DOBLE T |
| 6194 | HIERRO *m* EN I |
| 6195 | FRACTURA EN GAUCHO *f* |
| 6195 | FRACTURA ESTRIADA *f* |
| 6196 | SIERRA *f* DE METALES |
| 6197 | HOJA *f* PARA SIERRA DE METALES |
| 6198 | MÁQUINA *f* DE SERRAR ALTERNA |
| 6199 | HAFNIO *m* |
| 6200 | CORREA DE CRÍN *f* |
| 6200 | CORREA DE PELOS *f*, CORREA DE CRÍN *f* |
| 6201 | COMPÁS DE PRECISIÓN *m* |
| 6201 | COMPÁS DE PRECISIÓN *m* |
| 6202 | FISURA *f* CAPILAR |
| 6203 | FORMACIÓN *f* DE HALO |
| 6204 | HEMICÉLULA *f* |
| 6204 | SEMICÉLULA *f* |
| 6205 | MITAD *f* DEL ACOPLAMIENTO |
| 6206 | FRESAS *f pl* DE UN CORTE LATERAL |
| 6207 | CORREA SEMICRUZADA *f* |
| 6207 | CORREA TORCIDA *f* |
| 6208 | LIMA *f* DE MEDIA CAÑA |
| 6209 | PERFIL *m* DE MEDIACAÑA |
| 6210 | MADERA *f* SEMIRREDONDEADA |
| 6211 | CAPA DE SEMI-ESPESOR *f* |
| 6212 | RECTIFICACIÓN *f* SEMIONDA |
| 6213 | HALO *m*, AUREOLA *f*, RESPLANDOR *m* |
| 6214 | HALÓGENO *m* |
| 6215 | MARTILLO *m* |
| 6216 | MARTILLAR, AMARTILLAR |
| 6217 | VIRUTA *f* DE HIERRO |
| 6217 | BATIDURAS *f pl*, CASCARILLAS *f pl* |
| 6217 | MARTILLADURAS *f pl* |
| 6217 | ESCORIAS *f pl* DE FORJA |
| 6218 | SOLDADURA *f* EN LA FORJA |
| 6219 | MARTILLADO *m*, ENDURECIMIENTO *f* A MARTILLO |
| 6220 | AMARTILLADO |
| 6221 | METAL *m* AMARTILLADO |
| 6222 | ACERO PARA FORJA (FORJADO) *m* |
| 6223 | MARTILLEO *m* |

| | |
|---|---|
| 6224 GOLPE DE LA VÁLVULA *m* | 6265 HIERRO *m* PARA BARANDILLAS |
| 6225 HERRERO *m* A MANO | 6266 MONTANTE *m* DE BARANDILLA |
| 6226 AGUJA (DE MANÓMETRO) *f* | 6267 VOLANTE *m* A MANO |
| 6227 FRENO *m* DE MANO | 6268 TUERCA *f* DE VOLANTE |
| 6228 PULIMENTO *m* A MANO | 6269 MANEJABLE |
| 6229 CABRESTANTE *m* DE BRAZOS | 6270 COJINETE *m* COLGADO CERRADO |
| 6230 CARRETILLA *f* | 6271 COJINETE *m* COLGADO ABIERTO |
| 6231 MANIVELA *f* | 6272 PROCEDIMIENTO *m* HANSGIRG |
| 6232 CORTE MANUAL *m* | 6273 LADRILLO *m* DURO |
| 6233 MANDO MANUAL *m* | 6274 TEMPLE *m* PRODUCIDO POR ESTIRADO EN FRÍO |
| 6234 LIMA *f* DE MANO | 6275 GRASA *f* CONSISTENTE |
| 6235 MARTILLO *m* | 6276 PLOMO *m* ANTIMONIOSO |
| 6236 AGUJERO *m* DE MANO | 6276 PLOMO *m* ENDURECIDO, PLOMO *m* DURO |
| 6236 AGUJERO *m* DE BRAZO | 6276 METAL *m* BLANCO DURO |
| 6237 TRABAJO *m* MANUAL | 6277 METAL *m* DURO |
| 6238 CUCHARA *f* DE COLADA DE MANO | 6278 COLOCACIÓN *f* DE PLACAS DE CORTE METAL DURO |
| 6239 PALANCA *f* DE EMPUÑADURA | |
| 6240 TRABAJO *m* A MANO | 6279 SOLDADURA *f* FUERTE (COMPOSICIÓN FUSIBLE) |
| 6241 ACCIONADO A MANO (O MANUALMENTE) | 6279 AGITACIÓN *f* DEL BAÑO, BRACEADO *m* |
| 6242 PROGRAMACIÓN *f* MANUAL DE PIEZA | 6280 ACERO DURO *m* |
| 6243 ESCRITURA *f* RECTA | 6281 AGUA *f* CALCÁREA |
| 6243 ESCRITURA *f* PERPENDICULAR | 6281 AGUA *f* DURA (O CRUDA) |
| 6244 BOMBA *f* A MANO | 6282 MADERA *f* BRAVA, MADERA *f* DURA |
| 6244 BOMBA DE ACCIONAMIENTO A MANO *f* | 6282 MADERA *f* PESADA |
| 6245 HIERRO *m* DE BARANDILLA | 6283 GUARNICIONES *f* |
| 6246 PISÓN *m* DE MANO, RECALCADOR *m* | 6283 RECARGA *f* DURA |
| 6247 ESCARIADOR DE MANO *m*, PULIDOR A MANO *m* | 6284 ALEACIÓN DE RECARGUE DURO *f* |
| | 6285 TEMPLAR UN METAL |
| 6248 ROBLONADO *m* A MANO | 6286 ENDURECERSE (AL AIRE) |
| 6248 ROBLONADO *m* CON MARTILLO | 6286 ENDURECERSE, FRAGUARSE AL AIRE |
| 6249 SIERRA *f* DE MANO | 6286 SOLIDIFICARSE EN EL AIRE (CEMENTO) |
| 6250 CUCHARA *f* DE MANO CON MANGO | 6287 SOLIDIFICARSE EN EL AGUA (CEMENTO) |
| 6251 TIJERAS DE MANO *f pl* | 6287 FRAGUAR, SOLIDIFICARSE EN EL AGUA |
| 6252 PANTALLA *f*, MAMPARA *f*, ESCUDO *m* | 6287 ENDURECERSE (EN EL AGUA) |
| 6252 CARETA *f* | 6288 APTITUD *f* PARA EL TEMPLE |
| 6253 HERRAMIENTA *f* DE MANO | 6288 CAPACIDAD DE TEMPLE *f*, FACILIDAD DE TEMPLE *f* |
| 6254 TORNILLO *m* DE MANO | |
| 6255 VOLANTE *m* DE MANIOBRA | 6289 ACERO TEMPLADO *m* |
| 6256 TORNO *m* DE MANIVELA | 6290 ENDURECEDOR *m* (ALEACIÓN) |
| 6256 TORNO *m* A MANO | 6291 ENDURECIMIENTO *m*, TEMPLE *m* |
| 6257 TERRAJA *f* A MANO | 6291 TEMPLE *m* |
| 6258 BROCA DE MANO *f* | 6292 ENDURECIMIENTO *m*, SOLIDIFICACIÓN *f* |
| 6259 PRETIL *m*, ANTEPECHO *m* | 6292 SOLIDIFICACIÓN *f* |
| 6260 DESENTUMECIMIENTO *m* (PRECALENTAMIENTO *m* ANTES DE SOLDAR) | 6293 TEMPLE *m* DE METALES |
| | 6294 MEDIO *m* DE TEMPLE |
| 6261 FORJA *f* A MANO | 6295 ACEITE *m* DE TEMPLE |
| 6262 EMPUÑADURA *f*, MANEZUELA *f*, AGARRADOR *m* | 6296 FACULTAD *f* DE TOMAR BIEN EL TEMPLE |
| | 6297 DUREZA *f* |
| 6262 MANGO *m*, ASIDERO *m* | 6298 DUREZA *f* DEL AGUA |
| 6263 MANGO *m* DE UNA HERRAMIENTA | 6298 DUREZA *m* DEL AGUA |
| 6264 AGUJEROS *m pl* DE MANIPULACIÓN | 6299 GRADO *m* DE DUREZA DEL ACERO |

| | | | | |
|---|---|---|---|---|
| 6300 | PRUEBA *f* DE DUREZA | 6331 | CRISOL *m* |
| 6301 | MADERA *f* DE ÁRBOLES DE HOJA (O DE FRONDA) | 6331 | SOLERA *f* |
| 6302 | MOVIMIENTO *m* PENDULAR | 6332 | HORNO *m* DE CRISOL |
| 6303 | GRADAS *f* (CON CADENAS EN ZIG-ZAG EN LAS GRADAS FLEXIBLES) | 6333 | CALOR *m* |
| | | 6333 | COLADA *f* |
| 6304 | SOMBREAR | 6333 | PICADA *f* |
| 6305 | DESTRAL *m* | 6334 | CALENTAR, CALDEAR |
| 6305 | MACHETE *m* | 6334 | RECALENTAR |
| 6305 | HACHUELA *f* | 6335 | CAPACIDAD CALORÍFICA *f* |
| 6306 | TRAZOS *m* DE SOMBREAR (DELINEANTE) | 6336 | ACUMULADOR DE CALOR *m* |
| 6307 | GANCHOS *m pl* DE TRACCIÓN | 6337 | BALANCE *m* TÉRMICO |
| 6308 | PUNTO DE FUSIÓN ELEVADO (DE) *m* | 6337 | BALANCE *m* TÉRMICO |
| 6309 | GUINDALEZA *f*, CALABROTE *m*, ADRAL *m* | 6338 | CALENTAMIENTO *m* INTERNO |
| 6310 | DESCARGADOR *m* DE GARRAS | 6339 | CAPACIDAD CALORÍFICA *f* |
| 6311 | RASTRILLADORAS RECOGEDORAS *f pl* | 6340 | CONDUCTOR DE CALOR *m* |
| 6312 | RASTRILLOS *m pl* | 6341 | CONSTANTE CALORÍFICA *f* |
| 6313 | BRUMA *f* | 6342 | CAPACIDAD CALÓRICA *f* |
| 6314 | EXTREMIDAD *f*, EXTREMO *m* | 6343 | CALOR PRODUCIDO POR FRICCIÓN *m* |
| 6314 | FONDO *m* | 6344 | ENERGÍA *f* TÉRMICA |
| 6314 | PRESIÓN *f* (CALDERA) | 6344 | ENERGÍA *f* CALORÍFICA |
| 6315 | PÉRDIDA *f* DE CARGA, MERMA *f* | 6345 | MOTOR *m* TÉRMICO |
| 6316 | FONDO *m* DE UN TAMBOR | 6345 | MÁQUINA *f* |
| 6317 | CUERPO DEL MARTILLO *m* | 6346 | DIAGRAMA *m* DE ENTROPÍA |
| 6318 | NARIZ *f* DE PICAPORTE, TALÓN *m* DE CHAVETA | 6347 | EQUIVALENTE CALORÍFICO DEL TRABAJO |
| | | 6348 | NÚMERO *m* DE CALORÍAS QUE SE DESPRENDE EN UNA REACCIÓN |
| 6318 | PUNTA *f* DE UNA CLAVIJA | | |
| 6318 | TACÓN *m* DE UNA CHAVETA | 6348 | CALOR LIBERADO EN UNA REACCIÓN *m* |
| 6318 | CABEZA *f* DE UNA CHAVETA | 6349 | INTERCAMBIADOR *m* TÉRMICO |
| 6319 | CANAL *m* DE SUBIDA | 6349 | INTERCAMBIADOR *m* TÉRMICO |
| 6319 | CANAL DE ABASTECIMIENTO *m* | 6350 | TUBO *m* DE CAMBIADOR TÉRMICO |
| 6320 | CABECERA *f* | 6351 | CALENTAR AL CONTACTO DEL AIRE |
| 6321 | COLGANTE, PENDIENTE, SUSPENDIDO | 6351 | CALENTAR POR CONTACTO |
| 6321 | COJINETE *m* DE HORQUILLA | 6352 | MASA CALORÍFUGA *f* |
| 6321 | COJINETE *m* COLGADO, COJINETE *m* DE SUSPENSIÓN | 6352 | SUBSTANCIA *f* CALORÍFUGA |
| | | 6353 | PÉRDIDA *f* DE CALOR |
| 6322 | AGUA *f* ARRIBA | 6353 | PÉRDIDA *f* TÉRMICA |
| 6323 | CARGA DE AGUA *f* | 6354 | CALOR DE ABSORCIÓN *m* |
| 6324 | TIZÓN *m* | 6355 | CALOR DE CARBURACIÓN *m* |
| 6325 | CLAVERA *f* | 6356 | CALOR DE COMBUSTIÓN *m* |
| 6325 | CLAVERA *f* | 6357 | CALOR DE DESCOMPOSICIÓN *m* |
| 6325 | CLAVERA *f* | 6358 | CALOR DE DISOCIACIÓN *m* |
| 6325 | CLAVERA *f* | 6359 | CALOR DE EVAPORACIÓN *m* |
| 6325 | CLAVERA *f* | 6360 | CALOR DE FUSIÓN *m* |
| 6326 | PROYECCIÓN *f* | 6360 | TEMPERATURA *f* DE FUSIÓN |
| 6326 | FARO *m* | 6361 | CALOR DE OXIDACIÓN *m* |
| 6327 | FARO *m* | 6362 | CALOR DE REDUCCIÓN *m* |
| 6328 | CABEZAL *m* FIJO | 6363 | CALOR DE SUBLIMACIÓN *m* |
| 6328 | CABEZAL *m* DE TORNO | 6364 | CALOR DE TRANSFORMACIÓN *m* |
| 6329 | EXCÉNTRICA *f* | 6365 | CALOR LATENTE *m* |
| 6329 | EXCÉNTRICA *f* DE CORAZÓN, LEVA *f* DE CORAZÓN | 6366 | CALOR DE VAPORIZACIÓN *m* |
| 6330 | GUARDACABO OVALADO | 6367 | CALENTAR EN AMBIENTE CERRADO |

| | |
|---|---|
| 6368 | PENETRACIÓN *f* DEL CALOR |
| 6369 | RAYO *m* CALORÍFICO |
| 6370 | CALOR LIBERADO *m* |
| 6371 | COLORACIÓN TÉRMICA *f* |
| 6372 | TRANSFERENCIA *f* DE CALOR |
| 6372 | TRANSMISIÓN *f* |
| 6373 | COEFICIENTE DE CONDUCTIBILIDAD CALÓRICA *m* |
| 6374 | TRANSMISIÓN *f* DEL CALOR |
| 6374 | TRANSPORTE *m* DE CALOR |
| 6375 | TRATAMIENTO *m* TÉRMICO |
| 6376 | INSTALACIÓN *f* DE RECOCIDO |
| 6377 | TRATAMIENTO *m* TÉRMICO |
| 6378 | PODER *m* CALORÍFICO |
| 6379 | ONDA *f* CALORÍFICA |
| 6380 | ZONA *f* INFLUENCIADA POR EL CALOR |
| 6381 | PÉRDIDAS *f pl* TERMÓGENAS |
| 6382 | TIEMPO *m* DE CIRCULACIÓN DE CORRIENTE |
| 6382 | TIEMPO *m* DE SOLDADURA EFECTIVO |
| 6383 | ALEACIÓN PARA TEMPLE Y REVENIDO *f* |
| 6384 | PISTÓN *m* DE CALDEO |
| 6385 | RECALENTAR |
| 6386 | FILAMENTO *m* |
| 6387 | BUJÍA *f* INCANDESCENTE, BUJÍA *f* DE CALEFACCIÓN |
| 6388 | RESISTENCIA *f* DE BUJÍA DE PRECALDEO |
| 6389 | CONMUTADOR DE LAS BUJÍAS DE PRECALENTAMIENTO |
| 6390 | CALDEO *m*, CALEFACCIÓN *f* |
| 6390 | CALEFACCIÓN *f* CALDEO *m* |
| 6391 | SOPLETE DE CALDEO PREVIO *m* |
| 6392 | PODER *m* CALORÍFICO |
| 6392 | POTENCIA *f* CALORÍFICA |
| 6393 | AGUJERO *m* DE SOPLADURA |
| 6394 | INSTALACIÓN *f* DE CALEFACCIÓN CENTRAL |
| 6395 | CALEFACCIÓN DE LOS EDIFICIOS *f* |
| 6396 | TUBO *m* DE CALEFACCIÓN CENTRAL |
| 6397 | VAPOR *m* DE CALEFACCIÓN |
| 6398 | SUPERFICIE *f* DE CALDEO |
| 6399 | SOPLETE DE CALDEO *m* |
| 6400 | CALENTAMIENTO *m* DE LOS COJINETES |
| 6401 | CORRIENTE DE GRAN INTENSIDAD *f* |
| 6401 | CORRIENTE FUERTE *f* |
| 6402 | ENGRANAJE *m* DE FUERZA (MOTRIZ), RUEDA *f* DE FUERZA (MOTRIZ) |
| 6402 | ENGRANAJE *m* DE FUERZA (MOTRIZ), RUEDA *f* DE FUERZA (MOTRIZ) |
| 6403 | ACEITE *m* ESPECIAL |
| 6403 | ACEITE *m* ESPECIAL PARA VEHÍCULOS PESADOS (H.D.) |
| 6404 | FRESAS *f pl* SIMPLES PARA TRABAJOS DUROS |
| 6405 | CAMIÓN DE CARGA *m* |
| 6406 | PIEZA *f* DE FORJA PESADA |

| | |
|---|---|
| 6407 | METAL *m* PESADO |
| 6408 | MAZUT *m* |
| 6408 | ACEITE *m* PESADO |
| 6409 | CHAPA *f* FUERTE |
| 6410 | LAMINADOR *m* PARA CHAPAS GRUESAS |
| 6411 | PRENSA *f* PARA CHAPAS FUERTES |
| 6412 | MARCHA *f* PESADA |
| 6413 | PERFILES *m pl* PESADOS |
| 6414 | AGUA *f* PESADA |
| 6415 | HECTÓLITRO *m* |
| 6416 | HECTOVATIO *m* |
| 6417 | HECTOVATIO *m* HORA |
| 6418 | MÁQUINAS *f pl* PARA PODAR O IGUALAR LOS SETOS |
| 6419 | BUJÍA *f* HEFNER |
| 6419 | BUJÍA *f* HEFNER |
| 6420 | ALTURA *f* |
| 6421 | ALTURA *f* DE CAÍDA |
| 6422 | NIVEL *m* BAROMÉTRICO |
| 6423 | ALTURA *f* BAJO TRAVESAÑO |
| 6424 | SOPLETE *m* DE HELIO |
| 6425 | ENGRANAJE *m* HELICOIDAL |
| 6425 | RUEDA *f* HELICOIDAL |
| 6426 | MOVIMIENTO *m* HELICOIDAL |
| 6427 | RESORTE *m* HELICOIDAL |
| 6427 | RESORTE *m* HELICOIDAL |
| 6428 | HELICOIDE |
| 6428 | SUPERFICIE *f* HELICOIDAL |
| 6429 | HELIO *m* |
| 6430 | HÉLICE *f* |
| 6431 | ÁNGULO DE INCLINACIÓN *m*, ÁNGULO DE PASO *m* |
| 6432 | CASCO *m* |
| 6432 | CARETA *f* DE SOLDADOR |
| 6433 | MANGO *m* DE UN HACHA |
| 6434 | HEMATITES *f* |
| 6435 | FUNDICIÓN *f* DE HEMATITES |
| 6436 | CRISTAL *m* HEMIÉDRICO |
| 6437 | CRISTAL *m* HEMIMÓRFICO |
| 6438 | HEMISFERIO *m* |
| 6438 | SEMIESFERA *f*, HEMISFERIO *m* |
| 6439 | CÁÑAMO *m* |
| 6439 | ESTOPA *f* DE CÁÑAMO |
| 6440 | ALMA DE CÁÑAMO |
| 6441 | TRENZA *f* DE CÁÑAMO |
| 6442 | TRENZA *f* DE CÁÑAMO ENSEBADA |
| 6443 | CUERDA DE CÁÑAMO *f* |
| 6443 | CABLE DE CÁÑAMO *m* |
| 6444 | ESTOPA *f* DE CÁÑAMO |
| 6445 | GUARNICIÓN *f* DE CÁÑAMO |
| 6445 | GUARNICIÓN *f* CON CÁÑAMO |

| | |
|---|---|
| 6446 | ACEITE *m* DE CAÑAMONES |
| 6447 | CERRADO HERMÉTICAMENTE |
| 6447 | CERRADO |
| 6448 | ENGRANAJES *m pl* DE DIENTES ANGULARES |
| 6449 | TEJIDO *m* DE YUTE |
| 6449 | LONA *f* DE EMBALAJE |
| 6450 | IRRADIACIÓN *f* HETEROGÉNEA |
| 6451 | HETEROGÉNEO |
| 6452 | CONTEXTURA *f* HETEROGÉNEA |
| 6453 | HEXÁGONO *m* |
| 6454 | HIERRO *m* HEXAGONAL |
| 6455 | TUERCA *f* HEXAGONAL |
| 6456 | ESCUADRA *f* HEXAGONAL |
| 6457 | TORNILLO *m* |
| 6457 | TORNILLO *m* DE CABEZA HEXAGONAL |
| 6458 | ESTRUCTURA *f* EXAGONAL COMPACTA |
| 6459 | CRISTAL *m* HEXAGONAL |
| 6460 | PRISMA *f* EXAGONAL |
| 6461 | CABEZA *f* EXAGONAL DE UN TORNILLO |
| 6462 | ALAMBRE *m* (DE SECCIÓN) HEXAGONAL |
| 6463 | HEXAEDRO *m* |
| 6464 | IMPERFECCIONES *f* EN LA SUPERFICIE |
| 6465 | RUEDA *f* HIDRÁULICA DE ATAQUE FRONTAL |
| 6466 | MÁQUINA *f* DE GRAN RENDIMIENTO |
| 6466 | MÁQUINA *f* DE GRAN PRODUCCIÓN |
| 6467 | ALTA FRECUENCIA *f* |
| 6468 | CORRIENTE ALTA FRECUENCIA *f* |
| 6469 | HORNO *m* DE ALTA FRECUENCIA |
| 6470 | BROCA *f* EN HÉLICE APRETADA |
| 6471 | FRESAS *f pl* SIMPLES DE HÉLICE RÁPIDA |
| 6472 | PUNTOS *m pl* BRILLANTES |
| 6473 | FUERTE PRESIÓN *f* |
| 6473 | ALTA PRESIÓN *f* |
| 6474 | ACERO DE CORTE RÁPIDO *m* |
| 6475 | HERRAMIENTAS *f pl* DE ACERO DURO |
| 6476 | ALTA TEMPERATURA *f* |
| 6477 | VACIO *m* ACTIVADO |
| 6478 | ALTA TENSIÓN *f* |
| 6479 | ALTO VOLTAJE *m* |
| 6479 | ALTA TENSIÓN *f* |
| 6480 | LATÓN *m* DE CALIDAD |
| 6481 | ALEACIÓN DE ALTA DENSIDAD *f* |
| 6482 | METAL *m* DE ELEVADA DENSIDAD |
| 6483 | ALTO CONTENIDO (O GRADO) (DE) *m* |
| 6484 | COMBUSTIBLE DE EXCELENTE CALIDAD *m* |
| 6485 | MINERAL *m* DE ELEVADO PORCENTAJE |
| 6485 | MINERAL *m* RICO |
| 6486 | ACERO DE CALIDAD SUPERIOR *m* |
| 6486 | ACERO DE CALIDAD SUPERIOR *m* |
| 6487 | CALDERA DE ALTA PRESIÓN *f* |
| 6488 | CILINDRO *m* DE ALTA PRESIÓN |

| | |
|---|---|
| 6489 | CALEFACCIÓN POR AGUA CALIENTE ALTA PRESIÓN *f* |
| 6489 | SUBSTANCIA *f* MOLIDA FINAMENTE |
| 6490 | CANALIZACIÓN DE ALTA PRESIÓN *f* |
| 6491 | VAPOR *m* A ALTA PRESIÓN |
| 6492 | MÁQUINA *f* DE ALTA PRESIÓN |
| 6493 | CALEFACCIÓN POR VAPOR ALTA PRESIÓN *f* |
| 6494 | TURBINA *f* DE ALTA PRESIÓN |
| 6495 | PERFORADORA *f* A GRAN VELOCIDAD |
| 6496 | MÁQUINA *f* DE FUNCIONAMIENTO RÁPIDO |
| 6496 | MÁQUINA *f* DE GRAN VELOCIDAD |
| 6497 | ACERO RÁPIDO *m* |
| 6498 | OXIDACIÓN *f* A TEMPERATURA ELEVADA |
| 6499 | PRUEBA *f* A ALTA TEMPERATURA |
| 6500 | CORRIENTE ALTA TENSIÓN *f* |
| 6501 | LÍNEA *f* DE ALTA TENSIÓN |
| 6502 | MOTOR *m* DE ALTA TENSIÓN |
| 6503 | PELIGROSO *m* |
| 6503 | INFLAMABLE |
| 6504 | CONTRACCIÓN *f* CONTRARRESTADA |
| 6505 | BISAGRA *f* |
| 6505 | BISAGRA *f*, PALANCA *f* ARTICULADA, BRAZO *m* ARTICULADO |
| 6506 | PLEGADO *m* CHARNELA |
| 6507 | MONTANTE *m* DE PUERTA |
| 6508 | BISAGRA *f* (MACHO) |
| 6509 | PERNO *m* DE CHARNELA |
| 6509 | PERNO *m* DE CHARNELA |
| 6510 | TAPA DE BISAGRA *f* |
| 6511 | TORNILLO *m* DE BANCO ORDINARIO |
| 6511 | TORNILLO *m* DE BANCO ORDINARIO |
| 6511 | TORNILLO *m* ORDINARIO |
| 6512 | PLATO *m* DE HORNO |
| 6512 | FRESA *f* PARA ROSCAS DE TORNILLOS |
| 6513 | ACABADO *m* CON LA FRESA |
| 6514 | CORTE *m* A SACABOCADOS |
| 6515 | BINADORES *m* (ARRASTRADOS POR TRACTOR O MONTADOS EN ÉL) |
| 6516 | APAREJO *m*, POLEA *f* MÚLTIPLE |
| 6517 | ALZAR, ELEVAR |
| 6517 | LEVANTAMIENTO *m*, ALZADO *m*, LEVANTAR |
| 6518 | CADENA CABLE *f* |
| 6518 | CADENA DE ELEVACIÓN *f* |
| 6519 | MÁQUINA DE LEVAR *f*, APARATO DE ELEVACIÓN *m* |
| 6519 | APARATO (ELEVADOR) *m* |
| 6520 | CABLE DE ELEVACIÓN *m* |
| 6520 | CABLE DE EXTRACCIÓN *m* |
| 6521 | PARADA *f* FACULTATIVA |
| 6522 | CHAVETA *f* DE RETENCIÓN |
| 6523 | TIEMPO *m* DE MANTENIMIENTO DEL ESFUERZO |
| 6524 | AGUANTAR |

| | |
|---|---|
| 6524 | AGUANTAR (ROBLONADO) |
| 6524 | SOSTENER EL MONTÓN |
| 6525 | MECANISMO *m* DE RETENCIÓN EN POSICIÓN ABIERTA |
| 6526 | MANTENIMIENTO *m*, CONSERVACIÓN *f* |
| 6527 | HORNO *m* DE MANTENIMIENTO |
| 6528 | MANTENIMIENTO *m* DE TEMPERATURA |
| 6529 | TACO DE MANGO *m* |
| 6530 | AGUJERO *m* |
| 6530 | ORIFICIO *m* |
| 6530 | LAGUNA *f*, VACÍO *m*, FALLO *m* |
| 6531 | CALIBRE *m* DE CONTROL DE DIÁMETRO INTERIOR |
| 6532 | CALIBRE DE MATRIZ *m* |
| 6533 | TUERCA *f* (REDONDA) DE DOS O MÁS AGUJEROS |
| 6533 | TUERCA *f* ENTALLADA, TUERCA DE DOS O MÁS AGUJEROS |
| 6534 | EXPLORADOR *m* ELÉCTRICO |
| 6535 | ENSAYO *m* (O CONTROL *m*) CON ESCOBILLA ELÉCTRICA |
| 6536 | MERMAS *f*, FALTAS *f* (AFNOR) |
| 6536 | DÍAS *m pl* NO LABORABLES |
| 6537 | REDONDEADO *m* |
| 6537 | CUELLO DE EMPALME *m* |
| 6538 | CUERPO HUECO *m* |
| 6539 | PIEZA *f* DE MOLDEO EN HUECO |
| 6540 | CILINDRO *m* HUECO |
| 6541 | HIERRO *m* HUECO DE MEDIA CAÑA |
| 6542 | CLAVIJA VACIADA *f*, CLAVIJA HUECA *f* |
| 6542 | CLAVIJA HUECA *f* CLAVIJA DE FRICCIÓN *f* |
| 6542 | CLAVIJA HUECA *f* |
| 6543 | FONDO *m* DE LA ONDA |
| 6543 | VACÍO *m* ENTRE LAS ONDAS |
| 6544 | GOTERÓN *m*, CANALÓN *m* |
| 6545 | PUNZÓN *m* SACABOCADOS |
| 6545 | PUNZÓN *m* SACABOCADOS |
| 6546 | GUBIA *f* DE HERRERO |
| 6547 | EJE HUECO *m*, ÁRBOL HUECO *m* |
| 6548 | CAVIDAD *m* ENTRE DIENTES |
| 6548 | HUECO *m* ENTRE DOS DIENTES |
| 6549 | ESFERA *f* HUECA |
| 6550 | SECCIÓN *f* RECTANGULAR |
| 6550 | SECCIÓN *f* CON NERVIOS |
| 6551 | HOLMIO *m* |
| 6552 | CRISTAL *m* HOLOÉDRICO |
| 6553 | LEVANTAMIENTO *m*, ELEVACIÓN *f* |
| 6554 | CHATARRAS *f pl* DE PRODUCCIÓN PROPIA |
| 6555 | HOMOGÉNEO *m* |
| 6556 | UNIÓN *f* HOMOGÉNEA |
| 6557 | ECUACIÓN *f* HOMOGÉNEA |
| 6558 | SUBSTANCIA *f* HOMOGÉNEA |
| 6559 | IRRADIACIÓN *f* HOMOGÉNEA |
| 6560 | CONTEXTURA *f* HOMOGÉNEA |
| 6561 | HOMEGENEIZACIÓN *f* |
| 6562 | SERIE *f* HOMÓLOGA |
| 6563 | FUNDICIÓN *f* CON SOPLADO |
| 6564 | RODAJE *m* CON LÍQUIDO |
| 6564 | RECTIFICACIÓN *f* INTERIOR |
| 6565 | MÁQUINA *f* DE RODAR, DE ESMERILAR |
| 6566 | CAPÓ *m* |
| 6567 | CASCOS *m pl* DE ANIMALES ESCOFINADOS |
| 6568 | GANCHO *m* |
| 6569 | TORNILLO *m* DE GANCHO |
| 6570 | CADENA DE VAUCANSON *f* |
| 6571 | GANCHO *m* DE HERRERO |
| 6572 | MANGUITO *m* ARTICULADO UNIVERSAL |
| 6573 | ARTICULACIÓN CARDÁN *f* |
| 6573 | JUNTA *f* UNIVERSAL |
| 6573 | CARDÁN *m*, JUNTA DE CARDÁN *f*, ARTICULACIÓN DE CARDÁN |
| 6573 | BISAGRA UNIVERSAL *f* |
| 6573 | JUNTA *f* DE CARDÁN |
| 6574 | LEY *f* DE HOOKE |
| 6575 | CINTA *f* DE HIERRO |
| 6575 | HIERRO *m* EN CINTA, FLEJE *m* |
| 6576 | TENSIÓN CIRCULAR O PERIFÉRICA *f* |
| 6577 | TOLVA *f* |
| 6578 | HORIZONTAL |
| 6579 | CALDERA HORIZONTAL *f* |
| 6580 | DEPÓSITO *m* BALÓN |
| 6581 | PERFORADORA *f* HORIZONTAL |
| 6582 | MÁQUINA *f* HORIZONTAL |
| 6583 | SOLDADURA *f* EN ÁNGULO EN PLANO |
| 6584 | REJILLA *f* HORIZONTAL |
| 6585 | LÍNEA *f* HORIZONTAL |
| 6586 | APOYO *m* INTERMEDIARIO DE UN ÁRBOL |
| 6586 | SOPORTE *m* |
| 6587 | ÁRBOL HORIZONTAL *m* |
| 6588 | MÁQUINA *f* DE AMOLAR CON EJE HORIZONTAL |
| 6589 | FRESADORA *f* HORIZONTAL |
| 6590 | EMPUJE *m* HORIZONTAL |
| 6591 | SOLDADURA *f* EN CORNISA |
| 6592 | CLAXÓN *m* |
| 6592 | BRAZO *m* DEL ELECTRODO |
| 6592 | BOCINA *f* |
| 6593 | PLACA *f* DE GUARDA |
| 6594 | CENTRO DE COMPÁS *m* |
| 6595 | CUERNO RASPADO *m* |
| 6596 | DISTANCIA *f* ENTRE LOS BRAZOS |
| 6597 | EXTREMO *m* DEL SOPORTE |
| 6598 | ANFIBOLE |
| 6598 | HORNABLENDA *f* |
| 6599 | AMIANTO *m*, ASBESTO *m* |

| | |
|---|---|
| 6600 | ENTRADA  *f* EN FORMA DE CUERNO |
| 6601 | CLAVO PARA HERRADURA  *m* |
| 6602 | CABALLO VAPOR  *m* |
| 6603 | CABALLO HORA  *m* |
| 6604 | CRIN  *f* DE CABALLO |
| 6605 | HIERRO  *m* PARA HERRADURAS |
| 6606 | (IMÁN) EN HERRADURA |
| 6606 | IMÁN EN HERRADURA  *m* |
| 6607 | CALIBRE  *m* MORDAZA DE UNA RAMA PARA DIMENSIONES MÍNIMA Y MÁXIMA |
| 6608 | CALIBRE DE MORDAZA  *m* |
| 6609 | TUBO  *m* FLEXIBLE |
| 6610 | BRIDA DE APRIETE (PARA TUBO)  *f* |
| 6611 | BRIDA CON TORNILLO PARA LATIGUILLOS  *f* |
| 6612 | RACOR  *m* PARA TUBOS FLEXIBLES |
| 6613 | TUBULADURA  *f* FLEXIBLE DE PURGA |
| 6614 | TUBO  *m* FLEXIBLE |
| 6614 | TUBO  *m* FLEXIBLE, MANGA  *f* |
| 6615 | MOTOR  *m* DE AIRE CALIENTE |
| 6616 | CALEFACCIÓN POR AIRE CALIENTE  *f* |
| 6617 | ENFRIADERO  *m* |
| 6618 | PRUEBA  *f* DE PLEGADO EN CALIENTE |
| 6619 | PLEGADO  *m* EN CALIENTE, DOBLADO  *m* EN CALIENTE |
| 6619 | FLEXIÓN  *f* EN CALIENTE |
| 6620 | FUNDICIÓN  *f* AL AIRE CALIENTE |
| 6621 | RUPTURA  *f* EN CALIENTE |
| 6621 | HENDIDURA  *f* EN CALIENTE |
| 6622 | CORTE EN CALIENTE  *m* |
| 6623 | ESTIRADO EN CALIENTE |
| 6624 | ESTIRADO  *m* EN CALIENTE |
| 6624 | TREFILADO  *m* EN CALIENTE |
| 6625 | FRAGILIZACIÓN  *f* EN CALIENTE |
| 6626 | FORJADO  *m* EN CALIENTE |
| 6627 | MODELADO  *m* EN CALIENTE |
| 6627 | MOLDEADO  *m* EN CALIENTE |
| 6628 | GALVANIZACIÓN  *f* POR TEMPLE |
| 6629 | DUREZA  *f* EN CALIENTE |
| 6630 | SIERRA  *f* PARA METALES AL ROJO |
| 6630 | SIERRA  *f* EN CALIENTE |
| 6631 | METAL  *m* EN ESTADO DE FUSIÓN |
| 6631 | METAL  *m* EN FUSIÓN |
| 6632 | ESTAMPADO  *m* EN CALIENTE |
| 6633 | TEMPLE  *m* ESCALONADO |
| 6634 | REMACHAR, ROBLONAR EN CALIENTE |
| 6635 | REMACHE  *m* EN CALIENTE |
| 6636 | LAMINAR EN CALIENTE |
| 6637 | CHAPA  *f* LAMINADA EN CALIENTE |
| 6638 | LAMINADO  *m* EN CALIENTE |
| 6639 | AISLAMIENTO TÉRMICO  *m* |
| 6640 | CORTADURA  *f* EN CALIENTE |

| | |
|---|---|
| 6641 | FRAGILIDAD  *f* EN CALIENTE |
| 6642 | PUNTO  *m* CALIENTE |
| 6643 | ESTAMPADO  *m* EN CALIENTE |
| 6644 | SUPERFICIE  *f* MUY POROSA |
| 6645 | GRIETA  *f* DEBIDA A LA CONTRACCIÓN |
| 6646 | PRUEBA  *f* DE RESISTENCIA EN CALIENTE |
| 6647 | DESBARBADURA  *f* EN CALIENTE |
| 6648 | CALEFACCIÓN POR AGUA CALIENTE  *f* |
| 6649 | CAÑERÍA DE AGUA CALIENTE  *f* |
| 6650 | TRABAJO  *m* EN CALIENTE |
| 6650 | MECANIZACIÓN  *f* |
| 6651 | TUBERÍA DE AIRE O VIENTO CÁLIDO  *f* |
| 6652 | TUBO  *m* DE CÁTODO CALIENTE |
| 6653 | GALVANIZACIÓN  *f* EN CALIENTE |
| 6654 | TEMPERATURA  *f* SUPERFICIAL MÁXIMA |
| 6655 | ACABADO  *m* EN CALIENTE |
| 6656 | LAMINADO  *m* EN CALIENTE |
| 6657 | ASERRADO  *m* EN CALIENTE |
| 6658 | QUEBRADIZO EN CALIENTE  *m* |
| 6659 | PROCEDIMIENTO  *m* DE REVESTIMIENTO EN BAÑO CALIENTE |
| 6660 | ALOJAMIENTO  *m*, VIVIENDA  *f* |
| 6660 | CAJA  *f*, CARCASA  *f*, CÁRTER  *m* |
| 6661 | CUBO  *m* DE RUEDA |
| 6662 | EMBELLECEDOR  *m* DE RUEDA, TAPACUBOS  *m* DE RUEDA |
| 6663 | BRIDA  *f* DE CUBO |
| 6664 | HUMEDECEDOR, HUMECTATIVO |
| 6665 | ÁCIDO HÚMICO  *m* |
| 6666 | HUMEDAD  *f* DEL AIRE |
| 6666 | ESTADO  *m* HIGROMÉTRICO DEL AIRE |
| 6667 | HUMUS  *m*, MANTILLO  *m* |
| 6668 | QUINTAL  *m* (50 KGS APROXIMADAMENTE) |
| 6669 | SUSPENDIDO SOBRE UNA CUCHILLA |
| 6670 | BOMBEO  *m* |
| 6671 | OSCILACIONES  *f pl* DEL REGULADOR |
| 6672 | TOMA  *f* DE AGUA |
| 6672 | BOCA  *f* DE RIEGO |
| 6673 | HIDRATO  *m* |
| 6673 | HIDRÓXIDO  *m* |
| 6674 | HIDRATO  *m* |
| 6675 | AGUA  *f* DE HIDRATACIÓN |
| 6676 | HIDRÁULICA  *f* (CIENCIA) |
| 6677 | ACUMULADOR HIDRÁULICO  *m* |
| 6678 | AMORTIGUADOR DE LÍQUIDO  *m* |
| 6678 | FRENO  *m* HIDRÁULICO |
| 6678 | FRENO  *m* HIDRONEUMÁTICO |
| 6679 | MANDRILES  *m* HIDRÁULICOS |
| 6680 | COMPRESOR HIDRÁULICO  *m* |
| 6681 | ACOPLAMIENTO (EMBRAGUE) HIDRÁULICO  *m* |

| | |
|---|---|
| 6681 | ACOPLAMIENTO *m* (O EMBRAGUE *m*) HIDRÁULICO |
| 6682 | PRENSA *f* HIDRÁULICA DE EMBUTIR |
| 6683 | MANDO HIDRÁULICO *m* |
| 6684 | RENDIMIENTO *m* HIDRÁULICO |
| 6685 | CONSTRUCCIÓN HIDRÁULICA *f* |
| 6686 | TERRAPLÉN *m* HIDRÁULICO |
| 6687 | PRENSA *f* HIDRÁULICA DE MARTILLO PILÓN |
| 6687 | PRENSA *f* DE FORJAR HIDRÁULICA |
| 6688 | CRIC *m* HIDRÁULICO |
| 6689 | CAL HIDRÁULICA *f* |
| 6690 | MORTERO *m* HIDRÁULICO |
| 6691 | MOTOR *m* HIDRÁULICO |
| 6691 | MÁQUINA *f* HIFRÁULICA |
| 6692 | CENTRAL HIDRÁULICA *f* |
| 6692 | FÁBRICA *f* HIDRÁULICA |
| 6693 | PRENSA *f* HIDRÁULICA |
| 6694 | ARÍETE *m* HIDRÁULICO |
| 6695 | PRUEBA *f* HIDRÁULICA |
| 6696 | TURBINA *f* HIDRÁULICA |
| 6697 | VÁLVULA *f* DE MANDO HIDRÁULICO |
| 6698 | HIDRÁULICA |
| 6699 | PROCEDIMIENTO *m* A PARTIR DE LOS PRODUCTOS RESULTANTES DE LA DESCOMPOSOCIÓN DEL HIDRURO |
| 6700 | GENERATRIZ *f* HIDROELÉCTRICA |
| 6701 | FÁBRICA *f* HIDOELÉCTRICA |
| 6702 | CENTRIFUGAR, SECAR POR CENTRIFUGACIÓN |
| 6703 | SECADORA *f* CENTRÍFUGA |
| 6704 | ÁCIDO BROMHÍDRICO *m* |
| 6705 | HIDROCARBURO *m* |
| 6705 | HIDROCARBURO *m* |
| 6706 | ACIDO HIDROCLÓRICO *m* |
| 6706 | ÁCIDO CLORHÍDRICO *m* |
| 6706 | ESPÍRITU *m* DE SAL |
| 6706 | ÁCIDO *m* MURIÁTICO |
| 6707 | ÁCIDO CIANHÍDRICO *m* |
| 6707 | ÁCIDO PRÚSICO *m* |
| 6708 | HIDRODINÁMICO |
| 6709 | FRENO *m* HIDRÁULICO |
| 6710 | HIDRODINÁMICA *f* (CIENCIA) |
| 6711 | ÁCIDO FLUORHÍDRICO *m* |
| 6712 | HIDRÓGENO *m* |
| 6713 | FRAGILIDAD *f* AL DECAPADO |
| 6714 | LLAMA *f* DE HIDRÓGENO |
| 6715 | CONCENTRACIÓN DE LOS IONES DE HIDRÓGENO *f* |
| 6716 | BIÓXIDO DE HIDRÓGENO *m* |
| 6716 | AGUA *f* OXIGENADA |
| 6717 | HIDRÓGENO *m* SULFURADO |
| 6717 | HIDRÓGENO SULFURADO *m*, SULFURO DE HIDRÓGENO *m* |
| 6717 | GAS *m* HEDIONDO |
| 6718 | CORROSIÓN CON LIBERACIÓN DE HIDRÓGENO *f* |

| | |
|---|---|
| 6719 | HIDRÓLISIS *f* |
| 6720 | MECÁNICA *f* DE LOS CUERPOS LÍQUIDOS |
| 6721 | HIDROMETALURGIA *f* |
| 6722 | AREÓMETRO *m* |
| 6722 | ALCOHOLÍMETRO *m*, PESALICORES *m* |
| 6723 | AREÓMETRO *m* DE PESO VARIABLE |
| 6724 | HIDRÓFILO |
| 6725 | BALANZA *f* HIDROSTÁTICA |
| 6726 | PRESIÓN *f* HIDROSTÁTICA |
| 6727 | ENSAYO *m* HIDROSTÁTICO |
| 6728 | HIDROSTÁTICO |
| 6729 | HIGRÓMETRO *m* |
| 6730 | HIGROMÉTRICO |
| 6730 | AVIDO DE AGUA *m*, ÁVIDA DE AGUA *f* |
| 6731 | AGUA *f* HIGROSCÓPICA |
| 6732 | HIGROMETRICIDAD *f* |
| 6733 | HIPEREUTECTOIDE *m* |
| 6734 | HIPÉRBOLE *f* |
| 6735 | HIPERBÓLICO |
| 6736 | CILINDRO *m* HIPERBÓLICO |
| 6737 | FUNCIÓN *f* HIPERBÓLICA |
| 6738 | ESPIRAL *f* HIPERBÓLICA |
| 6739 | HIPERBOLOIDE DE UNA CAPA *m* |
| 6740 | HIPERBOLOIDE DE DOS CAPAS *m* |
| 6741 | HIPOEUTECTOIDE *m* |
| 6742 | ÁCIDO HIPOCLOROSO *m* |
| 6743 | HIPOCICLOIDE *m* |
| 6744 | DENTADO *m* EPICICLOIDAL |
| 6744 | ENGRANAJE HIPOCICLOIDAL, DENTADO *m* HIPOCICLOIDAL |
| 6745 | ENGRANAJES *m pl* HIPOIDES |
| 6746 | HIPOTENUSA *f* |
| 6747 | HISTÉRESIS *f* |
| 6748 | VIGUETA *f* EN I |
| 6749 | CALORÍMETRO DE HIELO *m* |
| 6750 | MÁQUINA *f* PARA HIELO |
| 6751 | CRISTAL *m* IDIOMÓRFICO |
| 6752 | MARCHA *f* DE VACÍO |
| 6753 | TIEMPO *m* MUERTO |
| 6754 | POLEA *f* LOCA |
| 6754 | RUEDA *f* INTERMEDIA |
| 6754 | RUEDA *f* DE TRANSPORTE |
| 6755 | RALENTI *m*, MARCHA *f* LENTA |
| 6756 | ÁRBOL INTERMEDIARIO *m*, CONTRAEJE *m* |
| 6756 | ÁRBOL INTERMEDIARIO *m*, CONTRAEJE *m* |
| 6757 | ENCENDER |
| 6757 | INFLAMARSE, ENCENDERSE |
| 6758 | DISTRIBUIDOR DEL ENCENDIDO *m* |
| 6759 | PUNTO *m* DE IGNICIÓN |
| 6759 | PUNTO *m* DE ENCENDIDO |
| 6760 | ENCENDIDO *m*, IGNICIÓN *f* |

| | |
|---|---|
| 6760 | IGNICIÓN *f* |
| 6760 | INFLAMACIÓN *f* |
| 6761 | BOBINA *f* DE ENCENDIDO |
| 6762 | DISTRIBUIDOR DEL ENCENDIDO *m* |
| 6762 | DISTRIBUIDOR *m* DE ENCENDIDO (DE IGNICIÓN) |
| 6763 | PÉRDIDAS *f pl* EN EL FUEGO |
| 6764 | PUNTO *m* DE INFLAMACIÓN |
| 6764 | PUNTO *m* DE LLAMA |
| 6765 | RESIDUO *m* DE CALCINACIÓN |
| 6765 | NO QUEMADOS |
| 6766 | CONTRACTADOR DE ENCENDIDO *m*, CONTACTO DE ENCENDIDO *m* |
| 6767 | TEMPERATURA *f* DE ENCENDIDO |
| 6767 | TEMPERATURA *f* DE IGNICIÓN (O DE INFLAMACIÓN) |
| 6768 | REGLAJE *m* DEL ENCENDIDO |
| 6769 | TESTIGO *m* DE ENCENDIDO |
| 6770 | ENCENDIDO (EN LOS MOTORES DE EXPLOSIÓN) *m* |
| 6771 | ILLINIO *m* |
| 6771 | PROMETEO *m* |
| 6772 | DISPOSITIVO DE ILUMINACIÓN *m* |
| 6773 | CUERPO ALUMBRADO *m*, CUERPO ILUMINADO *m* |
| 6774 | DISPOSITIVO *m* DE ALUMBRADO |
| 6775 | GAS *m* DE ALUMBRADO |
| 6775 | GAS *m* PARA LUZ |
| 6776 | PODER *m* LUMINOSO |
| 6777 | INTENSIDAD *f* DEL ALUMBRADO |
| 6778 | ILUSTRACIÓN *f* |
| 6778 | FIGURA *f*, ILUSTRACIÓN *f* |
| 6779 | IMAGEN *f* |
| 6780 | PUNTO *m* DE IMAGEN |
| 6781 | NÚMERO *m* IMAGINARIO |
| 6782 | MERMA *f*, (FALTA RESULTANTE EN EL VOLUMEN) |
| 6783 | IMPACTO *m* |
| 6784 | EXTRUSIÓN *f* POR CHOQUE |
| 6785 | RESISTENCIA *f* AL CHOQUE |
| 6785 | RESILIENCIA *f* |
| 6786 | PRUEBA *f* POR CHOQUE |
| 6786 | PRUEBA *f* DE RESISTENCIA AL CHOQUE |
| 6786 | PRUEBA *f* DE ROTURA AL CHOQUE |
| 6787 | PILÓN *m* PÉNDULO DE CHARPY |
| 6788 | RESILIENCIA *f* |
| 6789 | POLVO *m* IMPALPABLE |
| 6789 | SUBSTANCIA *f* EN POLVO FINO |
| 6790 | AFILAR UN INSTRUMENTO CORTANTE |
| 6790 | AFILAR, AMOLAR, RECTIFICAR |
| 6791 | APLICAR UNA CAPA PROTECTORA, APLICAR UNA CUBIERTA PROTECTORA |
| 6792 | APLICACIÓN *f* DE UNA CAPA PROTECTORA |
| 6793 | RECTIFICADO EN FINO *m* |
| 6794 | IMPEDANCIA *f* |

| | |
|---|---|
| 6794 | RESISTENCIA *f* APARENTE |
| 6795 | ROTOR *m* |
| 6795 | TURBINA *f* |
| 6795 | TURBINA *f* DE BOMBA CENTRÍFUGA |
| 6796 | IMPERMEABILIDAD *f* AL AGUA |
| 6797 | IMPERMEABILIDAD *f* |
| 6798 | IMPERMEABLE *m* (PRENDA DE VESTIR) |
| 6799 | CORROSIÓN BAJO LA EROSIÓN *f* |
| 6800 | IMPONDERABLE |
| 6801 | EMPOBRECIMIENTO *m*, AGOTAMIENTO *m* |
| 6802 | IMPREGNAR |
| 6802 | EMBEBER, EMPAPAR, IMPREGNAR |
| 6803 | TUBO *m* DE GAS DE PAPEL IMPREGNADO DE ASFALTO |
| 6804 | AGENTE DE IMPREGNACIÓN *m* |
| 6805 | IMPREGNACIÓN *f* |
| 6805 | IMBIBICIÓN *f*, IMPREGNACIÓN *f* |
| 6805 | INFILTRACIÓN *f* |
| 6806 | IMPRESIÓN *f* |
| 6807 | QUEBRADO *m* IMPROPIO |
| 6808 | RECTIFICAR EL ACERO CON UN REVENIDO |
| 6809 | MOVIMIENTO *m* MOTOR |
| 6809 | IMPULSIÓN *f* |
| 6810 | TURBINA *f* DE IMPULSIÓN |
| 6810 | TURBINA *f* DE LIBRE DESVIACIÓN |
| 6810 | TURBINA *f* DE ACCIÓN |
| 6811 | FUERZA *f* IMPULSIVA, FUERZA *f* DE EMPUJE |
| 6812 | CARGA PERIÓDICA |
| 6813 | IMPUREZAS *f pl* |
| 6813 | CUERPOS EXTRAÑOS *m pl* |
| 6813 | SUBSTANCIAS *f pl* ESTRAÑAS |
| 6814 | IMPUREZA *f* |
| 6815 | RAZÓN DIRECTA (EN) |
| 6816 | RAZÓN INVERSA (EN) |
| 6817 | EN FORMA DE VAPOR |
| 6818 | NO COMBINADO |
| 6818 | ESTADO LIBRE (EN) *m*, LIBRE |
| 6819 | ESTADO DE SERVICIO (EN) |
| 6820 | INACCESIBILIDAD *f* |
| 6821 | INACCESIBLE |
| 6822 | INCANDESCENCIA *f* |
| 6823 | CALOR BLANCO *m* |
| 6823 | INCANDESCENCIA *f*, CALOR *m* BLANCO |
| 6823 | CALOR *m* BLANCO, INCANDESCENCIA *f* |
| 6824 | CALDEO AL BLANCO *m* |
| 6824 | CALENTADO AL ROJO BLANCO |
| 6825 | LÁMPARA *f* DE INCANDESCENCIA |
| 6826 | LUZ *f* POR INCANDESCENCIA |
| 6827 | GAS *m* INCANDESCENTE |
| 6828 | LÁMPARA *f* DE INCANDESCENCIA |
| 6828 | LÁMPARA *f* DE GAS |

| | | | | |
|---|---|---|---|---|
| 6829 | LUZ  *f*  DEL GAS CON INCANDESCENCIA | | 6873 | CABALLO NOMINAL  *m* |
| 6830 | PULGADA  *f*  INGLESA | | 6874 | POTENCIA  *f*  INDICADA (O FISCAL) |
| 6831 | INCIDENCIA  *f* | | 6875 | POTENCIA  *f*  INDICADA |
| 6832 | RAYO  *m*  INCIDENTE | | 6876 | TRABAJO  *m*  INDICADO |
| 6833 | GRIETA INCIPIENTE  *f* | | 6877 | MICRÓMETRO  *m*  CON ESFERA |
| 6833 | FISURA INCIPIENTE  *f* | | 6878 | INDICADOR  *m*  DE PRESIÓN |
| 6834 | RANURA  *f*  (O FISURA) SUPERFICIAL | | 6879 | INDICADOR  *m* |
| 6835 | VOLCABLE | | 6879 | REACTIVO  *m*  INDICADOR |
| 6835 | INCLINABLE | | 6880 | PAPEL  *m*  DE INDICADOR |
| 6836 | INCLINACIÓN  *f* | | 6881 | DIAGRAMA  *m*  DE TRABAJO |
| 6836 | DECLIVE  *m* | | 6881 | DIAGRAMA  *m*  DEL INDICADOR |
| 6837 | REJILLA  *f*  INCLINADA | | 6882 | EQUILIBRIO  *m*  INDIFERENTE |
| 6838 | PLANO  *m*  INCLINADO | | 6883 | ACCIÓN INDIRECTA (DE)  *f* |
| 6839 | ACOPLAMIENTO  *m*  DE DENTADURA CÓNICA | | 6884 | EXTRUSIÓN  *f*  INDIRECTA |
| 6840 | INCLUSIÓN  *f* | | 6885 | INDIO  *m* |
| 6841 | INCLUSIÓN  *f*  MITIGADA | | 6886 | MANDO INDIVIDUAL  *m* |
| 6842 | INCOMBUSTIBILIDAD  *f* | | 6888 | INDUCIR |
| 6843 | INCOMBUSTIBLE | | 6889 | CORRIENTE DE INDUCCIÓN  *f* |
| 6844 | ALIMENTACIÓN DE LLEGADA  *f* | | 6890 | TIRO  *m*  INDUCIDO |
| 6845 | COMBUSTIÓN INCOMPLETA  *f* | | 6891 | INDUCTANCIA  *f* |
| 6846 | INCOMPRESIBILIDAD  *f* | | 6892 | INDUCCIÓN  *f* |
| 6847 | INCOMPRESIBLE | | 6893 | SOLDADURA  *f*  POR INDUCCIÓN |
| 6848 | AUMENTO  *m*  DE LA PRESIÓN | | 6894 | BOBINA  *f*  DE INDUCCIÓN |
| 6849 | AUMENTO DE VELOCIDAD  *m* | | 6895 | HORNO  *m*  DE INDUCCIÓN |
| 6850 | AUMENTO  *m*  DE LA RESISTENCIA | | 6896 | TEMPLE  *m*  POR INDUCCIÓN |
| 6851 | AUMENTAR LA VELOCIDAD | | 6897 | CALENTAMIENTO POR INDUCCIÓN  *m* |
| 6851 | ACELERAR | | 6898 | INDUCTOR  *m* |
| 6852 | VELOCIDAD  *f*  CRECIENTE | | 6899 | HUMOS  *m pl*  INDUSTRIALES, HUMAREDA  *f*  DE LAS INDUSTRIAS |
| 6853 | DEFORMACIÓN  *f*  PROGRESIVA | | | |
| 6854 | ACOTACIÓN RELATIVA  *f* | | 6900 | HORNO  *m*  INDUSTRIAL |
| 6855 | AUMENTO  *m*  DE PRESIÓN | | 6901 | ORGANIZACIÓN  *f*  DE LAS FÁBRICAS |
| 6856 | FORMACIÓN  *f*  DE INCRUSTACIONES | | 6902 | AGUAS  *f pl*  RESIDUALES |
| 6856 | FORMACIÓN  *f*  DE INCRUSTACIONES CALCÁREAS | | 6903 | INDUSTRIA  *f* |
| 6857 | INCUSTRADO | | 6904 | INELÁSTICO |
| 6857 | INCRUSTADO | | 6905 | GAS  *m*  DE PROTECCIÓN |
| 6858 | INTEGRAL  *f*  INDEFINIDA | | 6905 | GAS  *m*  INERTE |
| 6859 | IMPRESIÓN  *f*  DURA | | 6906 | SOLDADURA  *f*  T.I.G. (AL ARCO DE TUNGSTENO BAJO GAS INERTE) |
| 6860 | DUREZA  *f*  VICKERS | | | |
| 6861 | PRUEBA  *f*  DE DUREZA POR IMPRESIÓN DE BOLA | | 6907 | INERCIA  *f* |
| 6862 | DENTADO | | 6907 | FUERZA  *f* |
| 6863 | MÁQUINA  *f*  DE ACCIONADO INDEPENDIENTE | | 6907 | FUERZA  *f*  DE INERCIA |
| 6864 | ÍNDICE  *m*  (MAT) | | 6908 | FENECIMIENTO  *m*  PRECOZ |
| 6865 | MANIVELA  *f*  DE GRADUADO | | 6909 | SERIE  *f*  INFINITA |
| 6866 | ÍNDICE  *m*  DE REFRACCIÓN | | 6910 | INFINITAMENTE GRANDE |
| 6867 | SECTOR  *m*  GRADUADO | | 6911 | INFINITAMENTE PEQUEÑO |
| 6868 | INDICIO  *m* | | 6912 | CÁLCULO INFINITESIMAL  *m* |
| 6868 | AGUJA INDICADORA  *f* | | 6913 | INFLAMABILIDAD  *f* |
| 6869 | MECANISMO  *m*  DE INDEXACIÓN | | 6914 | INFLAMABLE |
| 6870 | PLATILLOS  *m pl*  DIVISORES | | 6915 | LLEGADA DE AGUA  *f* |
| 6871 | TINTA  *f*  DE CHINA | | 6915 | ENTRADA  *f*  DE AGUA |
| 6872 | RENDIMIENTO  *m*  INDICADO | | | |

6916 ATAQUE *m* A LOS DERECHOS DEL TITULAR DE LA PATENTE
6917 INFUSIBILIDAD *f*
6918 INFUSIBLE
6919 LINGOTE *m*
6920 CARRO PARA LINGOTES (TRANSPORTE DE LINGOTES) *m*
6921 HIERRO *m* FUNDIDO
6922 TORNO *m* DE LINGOTES
6923 LINGOTERA *f*, MOLDE *m*, COQUILLA *f*
6924 ACERO MOLDEADO *m*
6925 SEGREGACIÓN *f* MAYOR
6926 LIMITAR
6926 RETRASAR
6926 IMPEDIR
6927 INHIBIDOR *m*
6928 FRENADO *m* INICIAL
6929 PRESIÓN *f* INICIAL
6930 ESTADO *m* INICIAL
6931 TEMPERATURA *f* INICIAL
6932 VALOR *m* INICIAL
6933 VELOCIDAD *f* INICIAL
6934 PROYECTAR EN...
6934 INYECTAR
6935 INYECCIÓN *f*
6936 ORDEN *f* DE INYECCIÓN
6937 VÁLVULA *f* DE INJECCIÓN
6938 INYECTOR *m*
6938 INYECTOR *m*
6939 GOMA *f* PARA BORRAR TINTA
6940 PASAR A TINTA
6940 ENTINTAR, DAR TINTA
6941 DIBUJO *m* PASADO CON TINTA CHINA
6942 PASADA *f* A TINTA
6943 ENTRADA *f*
6943 ADMISIÓN, ENTRADA, TOMA *f*
6944 BORNE *m* DE ENTRADA
6945 COLECTOR DE ADMISIÓN *m*
6946 TUBULADURA *f* DE ENTRADA
6946 TUBULADURA *f* DE ENTRADA
6947 ORIFICIO *m* DE ADUCCIÓN
6947 ORIFICIO *m* DE LLEGADA
6947 ORIFICIO *m* DE INTRODUCCIÓN
6947 ORIFICIO *m* DE ADMISIÓN
6947 ORIFICIO *m* DE ENTRADA
6948 TUBULADURA *f* DE ADMISIÓN
6949 VÁLVULA *f* DE ADMISIÓN
6950 VELOCIDAD *f* A LA LLEGADA
6950 VELOCIDAD *f* DE LLEGADA
6950 VELOCIDAD *f* DE ENTRADA
6951 DARDO *m*
6952 DARDO *m* INTERIOR

6953 ANILLO *m* INTERIOR DEL COJINETE DE BOLAS
6954 SUPERFICIE *f* INTERIOR DE UN TUBO
6955 CÁMARA DE AIRE *f*
6956 INOCULACIÓN *f*
6957 MATERIA *f* INORGÁNICA
6958 QUÍMICA MINERAL O INORGÁNICA *f*
6959 INOXIDABLE
6960 SOPORTE *m* DE INFORMACIÓN DE ENTRADA
6961 CUADRILÁTERO *m* INSCRIBIBLE
6962 ÁNGULO INSCRITO *m*
6962 ÁNGULO INSCRITO *m*
6963 CÍRCULO INSCRITO *m*
6963 CÍRCULO INSCRITO *m*
6964 POLÍGONO *m* INSCRITO
6965 INSERCIÓN *f*
6965 INSERTO *m*
6965 PIEZA *f* INSERTA
6966 MATRIZ *f* AMOVIBLE
6967 COLOCAR LOS REMACHES
6968 VIGA *f* EMPOTRADA
6969 TUBULADURA *f* EMPOTRADA
6970 PIEZA *f* INCORPORADA, ADAPTADA
6971 FRESA *f* CON DIENTES FIJOS
6971 FRESA DE CUCHILLAS FIJAS *f*
6972 COLOCACIÓN *f* DE REMACHES
6973 CAUCHO ENTELADO *m*, GOMA PELO *f*
6974 LADO INTERIOR *m*
6975 COMPÁS *m* PARA CONTROL DEL DIÁMETRO INTERIOR
6975 COMPÁS PARA DIÁMETRO INTERIOR *m*
6976 MANIVELA *f* DE CIGÜEÑAL
6976 CODO DE UN ÁRBOL *m*
6977 DIÁMETRO *m* INTERIOR
6978 PASO *m* DE UNA CADENA
6979 CALIBRES MICROMÉTRICOS PARA INTERIORES *m pl*
6980 VÁLVULA *f* DE TORNILLO INTERIOR
6981 VÁSTAGO *m* DE TORNILLO INTERIOR
6982 ANCHURA *f* INTERIOR DE UN ESLABÓN
6983 INSOLUBILIDAD *f*
6984 INSOLUBLE
6985 INSPECCIÓN *f*
6986 LÍNEA *f* DE INSPECCIÓN
6987 CONTROL *m*
6988 INSTALACIÓN *f* INTERIOR
6989 CENTRO INSTANTÁNEO DE ROTACIÓN *m*
6990 VALOR *m* INSTANTÁNEO
6991 INSTRUCCIÓN *f*
6992 INSTRUCCIÓN *f*
6992 MODO *m* DE EMPLEO
6993 CUADRO *m* DE INSTRUMENTOS

| | |
|---|---|
| 6994 | AISLAR, AISLARSE |
| 6995 | DEPÓSITO *m* CALORÍFUGO |
| 6996 | ALAMBRE *m* AISLADO |
| 6997 | COMPUESTO AISLANTE *m* |
| 6998 | AISLANTE |
| 6998 | CALORÍFUGO *m*, MATERIAL AISLANTE *m* |
| 6998 | MATERIA *f* AISLANTE |
| 6999 | ACEITE *m* PARA AISLAR |
| 7000 | PODER *m* AISLANTE |
| 7001 | CINTA *f* AISLADORA |
| 7002 | TUBO *m* AISLADOR |
| 7003 | AISLACIÓN *f* TÉRMICA |
| 7003 | AISLAMIENTO *m* |
| 7003 | AISLACIÓN *f* |
| 7004 | AISLACIÓN *f* CONTRA EL RUIDO |
| 7004 | AISLACIÓN *f* CONTRA EL SONIDO |
| 7005 | RESISTENCIA *f* DE AISLAMIENTO |
| 7006 | AISLANTE |
| 7006 | AISLADOR *m* |
| 7007 | COLECTOR DE ADMISIÓN *m* |
| 7008 | TIEMPO *m* DE ADMISIÓN |
| 7009 | INTEGRAL |
| 7010 | VIGA *f* INCORPORADA |
| 7011 | CÁLCULO INTEGRAL *m* |
| 7012 | NÚMERO *m* ENTERO |
| 7013 | INTÉGRAFO *m* |
| 7014 | INTEGRAR |
| 7015 | INTEGRACIÓN *f* |
| 7016 | INTEGRADOR *m* |
| 7017 | PANTALLA *f* REFORZADORA |
| 7018 | INTENSIDAD *f* |
| 7019 | INTENSIDAD *f* LUMINOSA |
| 7019 | INTENSIDAD *f* DE RADIACIÓN |
| 7020 | REGULADOR *m* DE INTENSIDAD |
| 7021 | INTENSIDAD *f* DE UNA CORRIENTE |
| 7022 | INSERIR |
| 7022 | INTERCALAR |
| 7023 | INSERCIÓN *f* |
| 7023 | INTERCALACIÓN *f* |
| 7024 | INTERCEPTAR RAYOS |
| 7025 | INTERCAMBIABILIDAD *f* |
| 7026 | INTERCAMBIABLE |
| 7027 | RUEDAS *f pl* |
| 7027 | RUEDAS *f pl* DE CONJUNTO |
| 7028 | INTERCAMBIABILIDAD *f* DE FABRICACIÓN |
| 7029 | POROSIDAD *f* DE COMUNICACIÓN INTERNA |
| 7030 | CORROSIÓN INTERCRISTALINA *f* |
| 7030 | CORROSIÓN INTERGRANULAR *f* |
| 7031 | ATAQUE *f* INTERDENDRÍTICO |
| 7032 | DISTANCIA INTERFACES |
| 7033 | TENSIÓN *f* SUPERFICIAL |

| | |
|---|---|
| 7034 | ZONA *f* DE SUPERFICIE DE SEPARACIÓN |
| 7035 | INTERFERENCIA *f* |
| 7036 | BANDA *f* DE INTERFERENCIA |
| 7037 | COLOR DE INTERFERENCIA *m* |
| 7038 | COMPARADOR INTERFERENCIAL *m* |
| 7039 | FIGURA *f* DE INTERFERENCIA |
| 7040 | FRANJA *f* DE INTERFERENCIA |
| 7041 | CORROSIÓN INTERGRANULAR *f* |
| 7041 | CORROSIÓN INTERCRISTALINA *f* |
| 7042 | FRACTURA INTERGRANULAR *f* |
| 7043 | PRODUCTO *m* INTERMEDIO |
| 7044 | COJINETE *m* AUXILIAR |
| 7044 | COJINETE *m* SECUNDARIO, COJINETE *m* AUXILIAR |
| 7045 | TRANSMISIÓN *f* POR CORREA |
| 7046 | ENFRIADOR *m* INTERNO |
| 7047 | TENSOR *m* INTERMEDIO |
| 7048 | COJINETE *m* DEL ÁRBOL DE TRANSMISIÓN |
| 7049 | ÁRBOL INTERMEDIARIO *m*, EJE DE TRANSMISIÓN *m* |
| 7049 | ÁRBOL INTERMEDIARIO *m* |
| 7050 | SERIE *f* DE ENGRANAJES |
| 7050 | TRANSMISIÓN *f* POR ENGRANAJES |
| 7050 | ENGRANAJE *m* INTERMEDIO, CONTRAMARCHA *f* DE ENGRANAJES |
| 7051 | VALOR *m* INTERMEDIO |
| 7052 | COMPUESTO INTERMETÁLICO *m* |
| 7053 | MOVIMIENTO *m* INTERMITENTE |
| 7053 | MOVIMIENTO *m* DISCONTINUO |
| 7053 | MOVIMIENTO *m* SOFRENADO (DE SACUDIDAS) |
| 7054 | SOLDADURA *f* INTERMITENTE |
| 7055 | SOLDADURA *f* DISCONTINUA |
| 7056 | SERVICIO *m* INTERMITENTE |
| 7056 | FUNCIONAMIENTO *m* INTERMITENTE |
| 7057 | ÁNGULO INTERIOR *m* |
| 7057 | ÁNGULO INTERNO *m* |
| 7058 | ENGRANAJE *m* INTERIOR |
| 7059 | FRESA *f* DESBARBADORA MACHO |
| 7059 | FRESA *f* DE INTERIOR PARA TUBOS |
| 7060 | PEINE *m* DE ATERRAJAR |
| 7060 | PEINE *m* PARA EL INTERIOR |
| 7061 | MOTOR *m* DE EXPLOSIÓN |
| 7061 | MOTOR *m* DE COMBUSTIÓN INTERNA |
| 7062 | MOTOR *m* DE COMBUSTIÓN INTERNA |
| 7063 | DESPLAZAMIENTO *m* INTERNO |
| 7064 | FUERZA *f* INTERIOR |
| 7065 | FRICCIÓN *f* INTERNA |
| 7065 | ROCE *m* INTERNO |
| 7066 | CALIBRE *m* DE UN INTERIOR |
| 7067 | ENGRANAJES *m pl* INTERIORES |
| 7068 | MÁQUINA *f* PARA RECTIFICAR LAS SUPERFICIES INTERIORES |

| | |
|---|---|
| 7069 | RECTIFICACIÓN *f* INTERIOR |
| 7070 | CALOR INTERNO *m* |
| 7071 | DIÁMETRO *m* INTERIOR |
| 7072 | RESISTENCIA *f* INTERNA |
| 7073 | CAVIDAD *f* POR CONTRACCIÓN |
| 7073 | CAVIDAD *f* |
| 7074 | TENSIÓN *f* INTERNA |
| 7075 | TENSIÓNES *f pl* INTERNAS EN LA FUNDICIÓN |
| 7076 | CALIBRE *m* TAMPÓN CÓNICO |
| 7077 | DENTADO *m* INTERIOR |
| 7078 | ATERRAJADO *m* (INTERIOR) |
| 7078 | FILETEADO *m* INTERNO, ROSCA *f* INTERNA |
| 7079 | RUEDA *f* DE ENGRANAJE INTERIOR |
| 7080 | SOLDADURA *f* INTERIOR |
| 7081 | TRABAJO *m* INTERIOR |
| 7082 | TUBO *m* DE ALETAS INTERIORES |
| 7083 | FILETE *m* MÉTRICO INTERNACIONAL |
| 7084 | PASO *m* DEL SISTEMA INTERNACIONAL DE BASE MÉTRICA (S.I.) |
| 7085 | RECOCIDO *m* INTERMEDIO ENTRE DOS ESTIRADOS |
| 7086 | TEMPERATURA *f* DE LA PASADA INTERMEDIA |
| 7087 | DISTANCIA *f* RETICULAR |
| 7088 | INTERPOLAR |
| 7089 | INTERPOLACIÓN *f* |
| 7090 | INTERRUMPIR EL CIRCUITO ELÉCTRICO |
| 7090 | CORTAR LA CORRIENTE |
| 7091 | ENVEJECIMIENTO *m* INTERRUMPIDO |
| 7092 | INTERRUPCIÓN *f* DE SERVICIO |
| 7092 | INTERRUPCIÓN DE LA MARCHA *f* |
| 7092 | PARO *m*, DESEMPLEO *m*, |
| 7093 | INTERRUPCIÓN *f* DE PASO DE CORRIENTE ELÉCTRICA, CORTE *m* DE LA ELECTRICIDAD |
| 7094 | CORTARSE (GEOMETRÍA) |
| 7095 | PLANO *m* DE INTERSECCIÓN |
| 7096 | ÁRBOLES *m pl* CONCURRENTES |
| 7097 | RADIO *m* DE LOS NUDOS DE SOLDADURA |
| 7098 | JAULA MEDIA *f* |
| 7099 | AUTOCAR *m* |
| 7100 | REPOSO *m* |
| 7100 | PUESTA FUERA DE SERVICIO *f* |
| 7101 | INTERVALO *m*, ESPACIO *m* |
| 7102 | MEZCLA *f* ÍNTIMA |
| 7103 | RAYOS *m* INFRARROJOS |
| 7104 | INTENSIDAD *f* LUMINOSA POR UNIDAD DE SUPERFICIE |
| 7105 | INVAR *m*, ACERO AL NÍQUEL |
| 7105 | METAL INVAR *m*, ACERO *m* AL NÍQUEL |
| 7106 | INVARIANTE |
| 7107 | INVENCIÓN *f*, DESCUBRIMIENTO *m*, INVENTO *m* |
| 7108 | INVENTOR *m*, DESCUBRIDOR *m* |

| | |
|---|---|
| 7108 | AUTOR DE UNA INVENCIÓN *m* |
| 7109 | TEMPLE *m* INVERSO |
| 7110 | INVERSIÓN *f* (MAT.) |
| 7111 | GRIFO *m* DE CANILLA INVERTIDA |
| 7112 | HIERRO *m* PARA TABLEROS DE PUENTE |
| 7112 | HIERRO ZORÉ (S) |
| 7113 | SOLDADURA *f* EN EL TECHO |
| 7114 | EXAMEN *m* MICROSCÓPICO |
| 7115 | MOLDEO *m* A CERA PERDIDA |
| 7116 | MODELO *m* A LA CERA PERDIDA, MODELADO |
| 7117 | INVOLUTA *f* |
| 7118 | INVOLUTA *f* DEL CÍRCULO |
| 7119 | ENGRANAJE *m* DE EVOLVENTE |
| 7120 | IODO *m*, YODO *m* |
| 7121 | ION *m* |
| 7122 | CONCENTRACIÓN DE IONES *f* |
| 7123 | MIGRACIÓN *f* DE IONES |
| 7124 | IONIZACIÓN *f* |
| 7125 | CÁMARA DE IONIZACIÓN *f* |
| 7126 | CORRIENTE DE LA CÁMARA IONIZANTE *f* |
| 7127 | MÉTODO *m* DE IONIZACIÓN |
| 7128 | ZONA *f* IONIZADA |
| 7129 | IONÓGENO *m* |
| 7130 | DISOLVENTE *m* IONÓGENO |
| 7131 | IRIDIO *m* |
| 7132 | DIAFRAGMA *m* IRIS |
| 7133 | HIERRO *m* |
| 7134 | ACETATO DE HIERRO *m* |
| 7135 | ALUMBRE DE HIERRO *m*, HALOTRIQUITA *f* |
| 7136 | MÁQUINA *f* DE CIZALLAR HIERROS Y PERFILES |
| 7137 | ANGULARES DE HIERRO DE PAQUETES *m* |
| 7138 | CARBURO DE HIERRO *m* |
| 7139 | DIAGRAMA *m* HIERRO-CARBURO |
| 7140 | CARBONILO DE HIERRO *m* |
| 7141 | MASTIC *m* DE HIERRO |
| 7141 | MASTIC *m* PARA LA FUNDICIÓN |
| 7142 | FUNDICIÓN *f* DE HIERRO/ HIERRO *m* COLADO |
| 7143 | MINERAL *m* DE HIERRO |
| 7144 | ÓXIDO *m* DE HIERRO |
| 7145 | POLVO *m* DE HIERRO |
| 7146 | PIRITA *f* AMARILLA |
| 7146 | PIRITA *f* MARCIAL |
| 7147 | CABLE DE ALAMBRES *m* |
| 7148 | SESQUIÓXIDO *m* DE HIERRO |
| 7148 | COLCOTAR *m* |
| 7148 | ROJO *m* DE PULIR |
| 7148 | ROJO *m* INGLÉS |
| 7148 | ROJO *m* DE PRUSIA |
| 7148 | ÓXIDO *m* FÉRRICO |
| 7148 | PERÓXIDO *m* |
| 7149 | SILICATO *m* DE HIERRO |

| | | | |
|---|---|---|---|
| 7150 | TRAVIESA *f* DE HIERRO |
| 7151 | HIERRO *m* ESPONJOSO, HIERRO *m* POROSO |
| 7152 | CONSTRUCCIÓN METÁLICA *f* |
| 7152 | ESTRUCTURA METÁLICA *f* |
| 7153 | SULFURO *m* FERROSO/FÉRRICO |
| 7154 | DIENTE *m* DE HIERRO FUNDIDO |
| 7155 | ALAMBRE *m* DE HIERRO |
| 7156 | ALEACIÓN DE HIERRO *f* |
| 7157 | FUNDICIÓN *f* (HIERRO COLADO) |
| 7158 | PRENSADO *m* PROFUNDO |
| 7159 | HERRAJE *m* |
| 7160 | FORJA *f* (TALLER) |
| 7161 | IRRADIACIÓN *f* |
| 7162 | NÚMERO *m* IRRACIONAL O INCONMENSURABLE |
| 7163 | IRREGULAR |
| 7164 | POLÍGONO *m* IRREGULAR |
| 7165 | ACCIONAMIENTO *m* IRREGULAR |
| 7165 | MARCHA *f* IRREGULAR |
| 7166 | LÍNEA *f* QUEBRADA |
| 7167 | IRREGULARIDAD *f* DEL MOVIMIENTO |
| 7168 | IRREVERSIBILIDAD *f* |
| 7168 | NO REVERSIBILIDAD *f*, IRREVERSIBILIDAD *f* |
| 7169 | NO REVERSIBLE, IRREVERSIBLE |
| 7169 | IRREVERSIBLE |
| 7170 | CAMBIO IRREVERSIBLE *m* |
| 7171 | REACCIÓN *f* ELECTROLÍTICA IRREVERSIBLE |
| 7172 | MATERIAL *m* DE IRRIGACIÓN O DE RIEGO |
| 7173 | LÍNEA *f* ISENTRÓPICA |
| 7174 | COLA DE PESCADO *f*, COLAPEZ *f* |
| 7174 | ICTIOCOLA *f*, COLA *f* DE PESCADO |
| 7175 | PUNTO *m* ISOELÉCTRICO |
| 7176 | ISOBARA *f* |
| 7177 | CURVA DE ISOBARAS *f* |
| 7178 | ISOCRONISMO *m* |
| 7179 | ISÓCRONO |
| 7180 | REGULADOR *m* ISÓCRONO |
| 7181 | LÍNEA *f* ISOCLINA |
| 7182 | LÍNEA *f* ISODINÁMICA |
| 7182 | LÍNEA *f* ISODINÁMICA |
| 7183 | CARGA AISLADA *f* |
| 7184 | AISLACIÓN *f*, INCOMUNICACIÓN |
| 7185 | ISÓMERO *m* |
| 7186 | ISOMERÍA *f* |
| 7187 | ISOPLERA *f*, LÍNEA ISOMÉTRICA *f* |
| 7187 | LÍNEA *f* CURVA DE VOLUMEN CONSTANTE |
| 7188 | PROYECCIÓN *f* ISOMÉTRICA |
| 7189 | ISOMORFÍA *f* |
| 7190 | ISOMORFO |
| 7191 | ISOMORFISMO *m*, HOMOMORFISMO *m* |
| 7192 | TRIÁNGULO *m* ISÓSCELES |
| 7193 | LÍNEA *f* CURVA ISOMÉTRICA |

| | |
|---|---|
| 7194 | TRATAMIENTO *m* ISOTERMO |
| 7195 | TEMPLE *m* ISOTÉRMICO |
| 7196 | TRANSFORMACIÓN *f* ISOTERMA |
| 7197 | ISOTOPOS *m pl* (QUIM) |
| 7198 | ISOTROPO |
| 7199 | MARFIL *m* |
| 7200 | ENSAYO *m* DE IZOD |
| 7201 | GARLOPÍN *m*, LIMA *f* GRUESA, CINCEL *m* DE ALBAÑIL |
| 7202 | ÁRBOL INTERMEDIO *m* |
| 7203 | ZUNCHO *m* |
| 7204 | ENFRIAMIENTO *m* POR CAMISA DE AGUA |
| 7205 | VÁLVULA *f* CON ENVUELTA TERMÓGENA |
| 7206 | PATILLAS *f pl* DE LEVANTAMIENTO POR GATO, POR TORNILLO ELEVADOR |
| 7207 | ZAPATA *f* PARA DISPOSITIVO DE ELEVACIÓN |
| 7208 | MANDRIL *m* EXPANSIBLE JACOBS |
| 7209 | PERNO *m* DE ANCLAJE ESPINOSO |
| 7210 | ATASCARSE, AGARROTARSE |
| 7211 | MONTANTE *m* LATERAL DE ENTRADA, JAMBA *f* |
| 7212 | CONVERGENCIA *f* |
| 7212 | ATASCAMIENTO *m* |
| 7213 | CERA DEL JAPÓN *f* |
| 7214 | REVESTIMIENTO *m* CON BARNIZ FINO |
| 7215 | MÁQUINA *f* RÁPIDA DE MOLDEAR CON SACUDIDAS |
| 7216 | MORDAZA *f* DE LLAVE |
| 7216 | MORDAZA *f* DE UNA LLAVE |
| 7217 | CRISTAL *m* DE JENA |
| 7218 | SURTIDOR *m* |
| 7219 | PORTACHICLER *m* |
| 7220 | CONDENSADOR POR INYECCIÓN *m* |
| 7221 | CHORRO *m* LÍQUIDO |
| 7222 | ATRAVESADO *m* POR CHORRO DE FUEGO |
| 7223 | INYECTOR *m* |
| 7224 | GRÚA *f* DE PLUMA, GRÚA DE BRAZO |
| 7225 | LARGURA *f* DE LA FLECHA, (DE LA PLUMA, DEL BRAZO) |
| 7226 | BRAZO *m* PRINCIPAL DE UNA GRÚA |
| 7227 | DISPOSITIVO *m* DE SUJECIÓN (DE APRETADURA) |
| 7227 | DISPOSITIVO *m* DE FIJACIÓN |
| 7228 | MÁQUINA *f* PARA BURILAR |
| 7230 | FUNDICIÓN *f* CON MODELOS |
| 7231 | TRANSMISIÓN *f* CON SACUDIDAS |
| 7232 | MÁQUINAS *f pl* DE ACODAR |
| 7233 | CARPINTERO *m* |
| 7234 | BANCO *m* |
| 7234 | BANCO *m* DE CARPINTERO |
| 7235 | CARPINTERÍA *f* (TALLER) |
| 7236 | CARPINTERÍA *f* (ARTE) |
| 7237 | JUNTA *f* SOLDADA |
| 7238 | JUNTA *f* (PUNTO DE UNIÓN) |

| | |
|---|---|
| 7238 | ARTICULACIÓN  *f*, JUNTA  *f* |
| 7239 | FUNCIÓN  *f* DE REPARTO COMPUESTA |
| 7240 | GEOMETRÍA  *f* DE LA JUNTA |
| 7241 | JUNTA  *f* DE SEPARACIÓN DE UN COJINETE |
| 7242 | MUÑÓN  *m* GIRATORIO DE ARTICULACIÓN |
| 7243 | BRIDAR (O REBORDEAR) TUBOS |
| 7244 | EMPALMAR TUBOS |
| 7245 | GARLOPA  *f* |
| 7246 | MÁQUINA  *f* PARA HACER LAS JUNTAS |
| 7247 | JUNTA  *f* |
| 7247 | EMPAQUETADURA  *f*, ESTOPADA  *f*, JUNTA  *f* |
| 7247 | MATERIA  *f* PARA LAS JUNTAS |
| 7248 | EMPALME  *m* DE TUBOS |
| 7249 | PRUEBA  *f* DE SACUDIDAS Y TRAQUETEO |
| 7250 | MÁQUINA  *f* DE MOLDEAR CON SACUDIDAS |
| 7251 | MÁQUINA  *f* DE MOLDEAR CON SACUDIDAS Y CON PLACA REVERSIBLE |
| 7252 | MÁQUINA  *f* DE APRETADO POR SACUDIDA Y PRESIÓN SIN DESMOLDEO |
| 7253 | MÁQUINA  *f* DE MOLDEAR CON SACUDIDAS Y APRETADO COMBINADOS CON DESMOLDEO |
| 7254 | ENSAYO DE JOMINY |
| 7254 | PRUEBA  *f* DE REBOTE BRUSCO |
| 7255 | VOLTIO-CULOMBIO  *m* |
| 7255 | JULIO (FIS.)  *m* |
| 7256 | TRAMO  *m*, LUZ  *f* ALCANCE  *m* |
| 7256 | MUÑÓN  *m* GIRATORIO |
| 7257 | SUPERFICIE  *f* DE NIVEL |
| 7257 | COJINETE  *m* DE CARGA RADIAL/TRANSVERSAL |
| 7258 | ROZAMIENTO  *m* DE LOS MUÑONES |
| 7259 | PRESSIÓN/REACCIÓN  *f* SOBRE LOS MUÑONES |
| 7260 | ANDAMIO  *m* AÉREO, PUENTE  *m* VOLANTE |
| 7261 | TRANSPONTÍN  *m* |
| 7262 | PRUEBA  *f* DE RECALCAMIENTO (O DE APLASTAMIENTO) |
| 7263 | APLASTAR, RECALCAR |
| 7263 | BATIR, RECHAZAR, IMPULSAR |
| 7264 | CABLE VOLANTE  *m* |
| 7265 | RECHAZO  *m*, IMPULSIÓN  *f* BATIDO  *m* |
| 7265 | RECHAZO  *m*, IMPULSIÓN  *f* BATIDO  *m* |
| 7265 | RECALCAMIENTO  *m*, APLASTAMIENTO  *m* |
| 7266 | TAPADERA DEL CILINDRO  *f* |
| 7267 | CALIZA JURÁSICA  *f* |
| 7268 | YUTE  *m* |
| 7269 | COEFICIENTE CALÓRICO (O DE CONDUCTIBILIDAD TÉRMICA)  *m* |
| 7270 | HIERRO  *m* KAHLBAUM |
| 7271 | PROCEDIMIENTO  *m* HORNO KALDO |
| 7272 | CORTADORA DE NABAS  *f* |
| 7273 | LINGOTE  *m* PARA LA MECANIZACIÓN DE PROBETAS (EN FORMA DE QUILLA DE NAVÍO) |
| 7274 | ENTALLADURA  *f* |

| | |
|---|---|
| 7275 | KEROSENO  *m* |
| 7275 | ACEITE  *m* DE PETRÓLEO PARA LLAMA |
| 7275 | ACEITE  *m* PARA EL ALUMBRADO |
| 7275 | PETRÓLEO  *m* PARA LÁMPARAS |
| 7276 | CHAVETA  *f* |
| 7276 | CLAVIJA LONGITUDINAL  *f*, PASADOR  *m* |
| 7276 | CLAVIJA  *f* |
| 7277 | ENCHAVETAR, ENCLAVIJAR |
| 7277 | CALZAR |
| 7278 | BOTADOR  *m*, EXTRACTOR  *m* |
| 7279 | ENCHAVETAR, ENCLAVIJAR |
| 7279 | CALZAR EN ... |
| 7280 | GRAPA DE ENSAMBLADURA  *f* |
| 7281 | MÁQUINA  *f* DE FRESAR LAS RANURAS |
| 7282 | ALOJAMIENTO  *m* DE UNA CHAVETA |
| 7282 | RANURA  *f* |
| 7282 | RANURA  *f* |
| 7282 | RANURA  *f* PARA CHAVETA |
| 7282 | MORTAJA  *f* DE ESPIGA, DE CHAVETA |
| 7283 | CALIBRE  *m* PARA RANURA DE PASADOR |
| 7284 | LLAVE DE HORQUILLA  *f* |
| 7284 | LLAVE DE CALIBRE  *f* |
| 7285 | UNIÓN  *f* CON CHAVETA (TRANSVERSAL) |
| 7286 | TACÓN  *m* DE CHAVETA |
| 7287 | AGUJERO  *m* DE COLADA |
| 7288 | UNIÓN POR CLAVIJAS  *f* |
| 7289 | BRIDAS  *f pl* DE MORTAJADO |
| 7290 | REGLAS  *f pl* DE ESCOPLADURA, ENTALLADURA |
| 7291 | RANURA  *f* PARA CHAVETA |
| 7292 | KIESELGUR  *f*, HARINA  *f* FÓSIL DE INFUSORIOS |
| 7292 | SILICIO  *m* FARINÁCEO |
| 7292 | TIERRA  *f* DE INFUSORIOS |
| 7292 | TRÍPOLI  *m* SILÍCEO |
| 7292 | HARINA  *f* FÓSIL |
| 7292 | TIERRA  *f* PODRIDA |
| 7293 | AGUA  *f* PARA SOLDAR |
| 7293 | SOLUCIÓN  *f* DE CLORURO DE CINC |
| 7293 | LÍQUIDO  *m* DE DECAPADO |
| 7294 | ACERO CALMADO (REPOSADO, DESOXIDADO)  *m* |
| 7295 | HORNO  *m* DE CALCINACIÓN |
| 7296 | KILODINA  *f* |
| 7297 | KILÓGRAMO  *m* |
| 7298 | CALORÍA KILOGRAMO-GRADO  *f* |
| 7298 | GRAN CALORÍA  *f* |
| 7299 | KILOGRÁMETRO  *m* |
| 7300 | KILÓMETRO  *m* |
| 7301 | KILOVOLTIO  *m* |
| 7302 | KILOVOLTIO-AMPERIO  *m* |
| 7303 | KILOVATIO  *m* |
| 7304 | KILOVATIO-HORA  *m* |
| 7305 | CINEMÁTICO  *m* |

| | |
|---|---|
| 7306 | CINEMÁTICA *f* |
| 7307 | CINÉTICO *m* |
| 7308 | POTENCIA *f* |
| 7308 | FUERZA *f* VIVA |
| 7308 | ENERGÍA *f* ACTUAL (O CINÉTICA) |
| 7308 | ENERGÍA *f* CINÉTICA |
| 7309 | FROTAMIENTO *m* CINÉTICO |
| 7310 | CINÉTICA *f* |
| 7311 | PASADOR *m* GIRATORIO |
| 7311 | EJE *m* DE OSCILACIÓN |
| 7312 | ÁNGULO DE INCLINACIÓN LATERAL DEL PIVOTE |
| 7313 | NUDO *m* |
| 7313 | CASCO *m* |
| 7314 | BANDA *f* DE PLEGADO |
| 7316 | KIP 1.000 LIBRAS 453,59 KGS |
| 7317 | KISH *m* |
| 7318 | KLINGERITA *f* |
| 7319 | FRESADORA *f* CON CONSOLA Y COLUMNA |
| 7320 | CODO DE ESCUADRA *m* |
| 7321 | ESPALDÓN *m* |
| 7322 | MÁQUINA *f* DE FRESAR CON CONSOLA |
| 7323 | CUCHILLO *m* |
| 7324 | LIMA *f* CUCHILLO |
| 7325 | CUCHILLA *f* |
| 7325 | SOPORTE *m* DE CUCHILLA |
| 7326 | SUSPENSIÓN *f* DE CUCHILLA |
| 7327 | COLISIÓN *f*, CHOQUE *m* (DE NEUTRONES CON ÁTOMOS) |
| 7328 | EXTRACCIÓN *f* DE LA PIEZA DEL MOLDE, DESMOLDEO *m* |
| 7329 | DESMONTADO |
| 7329 | PIEZAS *f pl* SUELTAS (EN) |
| 7330 | GOLPETEO *m* |
| 7330 | DETONACIÓN *f* |
| 7331 | RUIDO *m* DE UNA BOMBA |
| 7332 | PUNZÓN *m*, TALADRO *m* |
| 7333 | BARRA *f* DE DESMOLDEO, PASADOR *m* EXTRACTOR |
| 7334 | REJILLA *f* DE DESMOLDEO |
| 7335 | CANTIDAD *f* CONOCIDA |
| 7336 | RÓTULA *f* |
| 7336 | CIERRE *m* CON ARTICULACIÓN |
| 7337 | MANDO POR TORNILLO MOLETEADO *m* |
| 7338 | MOLETRADO *m* |
| 7339 | CRIPTON (QUIM) *f* |
| 7340 | IMPREGNACIÓN *f* DE LA MADERA CON SUBLIMADO CORROSIVO, PROCEDIMIENTO DE KYAN |
| 7341 | PÉRDIDA *f* AL ROJO |
| 7341 | PÉRDIDA *f* EN EL FUEGO |
| 7342 | GAS *m* LICUADO, GAS LÍQUIDO |
| 7343 | FRÁGIL, CADUNO, INESTABLE (QUIM) |
| 7344 | LABORATORIO *m* |
| 7345 | JUEGO *m* DE LABORATORIO |
| 7346 | GASTOS *m*, COSTE *m* |
| 7346 | PRECIO *m* DE LA MANO DE OBRA |
| 7347 | GUARNICIÓN *f* |
| 7347 | JUNTA *f* DEFLECTORA |
| 7347 | JUNTA *f* DE LABERINTO |
| 7348 | UNIÓN *f* DE LAS CORREAS POR TIRAS DE CUERO |
| 7349 | MANGUITO *m* CON UNA TIRA DE CORREA |
| 7350 | CORREA COSIDA *f* |
| 7351 | ENCOLADURA *f*, ENCOLADO *m* |
| 7352 | HETEROGENEIDAD *f* DE UN MATERIAL |
| 7353 | BARNIZAR CON LACA |
| 7353 | BARNIZAR |
| 7354 | BARNIZ *m* AL ALCOHOL |
| 7354 | LACA *f* |
| 7355 | ÁCIDO LÁCTICO *m* |
| 7356 | CUCHARA *f* DE COLADA, CRISOL |
| 7357 | ADICIÓN EN LA CUCHARA *f* |
| 7358 | ANÁLISIS DE COLADA *m* |
| 7359 | LADRILLO *m* PARA CUCHARA |
| 7360 | SOLIDIFICACIÓN *f* DE LA MASA FUNDIDA EN LA BOLSA |
| 7361 | BUZA *f* |
| 7362 | COLADOR *m*, FUNDIDOR *m* |
| 7363 | BUZA *f* |
| 7364 | ÁCIDO TARTÁRICO LEVÓGIRO *m* |
| 7365 | LEVÓGIRO |
| 7366 | RETRASAR |
| 7367 | REVESTIMIENTO *m* CALORÍFUGO |
| 7368 | ATRASO *m* DE FASE, DESFASADO *m* HACIA ATRÁS |
| 7368 | ATRASO *m* DE FASE, DESPLAZAMIENTO *m* DE FASE HACIA ATRÁS |
| 7369 | RECUBRIMIENTO *m* DE TUBOS |
| 7369 | REVESTIMIENTO *m* DE TUBOS |
| 7370 | COBRE *m* DEL LAGO SUPERIOR |
| 7370 | COBRE *m* NATIVO |
| 7371 | LÁMINA *f*, LAMINILLA *f* |
| 7372 | LAMINAR |
| 7373 | ESTRUCTURA *f* LAMINAR |
| 7374 | CONTEXTURA *f* LAMINAR |
| 7375 | LAMINADO |
| 7376 | CORREA DE TIRAS DE CUERO TRABAJANDO EN CANTO *f* |
| 7377 | IMÁN DE LÁMINAS *m* |
| 7378 | ROTURA LAMINAR *f* |
| 7379 | METAL *m* ESTRATIFICADO |
| 7380 | RESORTE *m* RECTANGULAR DE HOJAS SUPERPUESTAS |
| 7381 | RESORTE *m* TRIANGULAR DE HOJAS SUPERPUESTAS |
| 7382 | DESDOBLE *m* DE LOS BORDES DE CHAPA |

| | |
|---|---|
| 7382 | ESTRATIFICACIÓN *f* |
| 7383 | FISURA *f* DE LAMINADO |
| 7384 | LÁMPARA *f* |
| 7385 | BOMBILLA *f*, AMPOLLA *f* |
| 7386 | NEGRO *m* DE HUMO |
| 7386 | NEGRO *m* DE SOMBREAR |
| 7387 | OXICORTE *m* |
| 7388 | APOYO *m* |
| 7389 | TORSIÓN *f* LANG |
| 7389 | CABLEADO *m* |
| 7390 | CABLE METÁLICO DE HILOS PARALELOS *m* |
| 7390 | CABLE DE CABLEADO LANG O ALBERT *m* |
| 7391 | LANOLINA *f* |
| 7392 | CASQUILLO *m* DE PRENSAESTOPA |
| 7392 | CAJA *f* DE VÁLVULA |
| 7393 | LINTERNA *f* |
| 7394 | LÁNTANO *m* |
| 7395 | REPLIEGUE *m* DE LAMINACIÓN |
| 7395 | REPLIEGUE *m* |
| 7396 | JUNTA *f* SOLAPADA, UNIÓN *f* A COLA DE MILANO |
| 7397 | JUNTA *f* A MEDIO HIERRO, JUNTA *f* DE RECUBRIMIENTO |
| 7397 | JUNTA *f* RECUBRIDORA |
| 7398 | PLETINA *f* GIRATORIA |
| 7399 | RECUBRIMIENTO *m* DEL DISTRIBUIDOR |
| 7400 | REMACHE *m* CON RECUBRIMIENTO |
| 7401 | SOLDADURA *f* CONTINUA POR RECUBRIMIENTO |
| 7402 | SOLDADURA *f* POR PUNTOS CON RECUBRIMIENTO |
| 7403 | SOLDADURA *f* POR RECUBRIMIENTO |
| 7404 | SOLDAR EN BISEL |
| 7405 | SOLDADURA *f* EN BISEL |
| 7405 | SOLDADURA *f* POR RECUBRIMIENTO |
| 7406 | TUBO *m* DE RECUBRIMIENTO |
| 7406 | TUBO *m* SOLDADO POR RECUBRIMIENTO |
| 7407 | RETOQUES *m* VISIBLES |
| 7407 | RODAJE *m* |
| 7408 | CADUCACIÓN *f* DE UNA PATENTE |
| 7409 | ACEITE *m* DE MANTECA DE CERDO |
| 7409 | ACEITE *m* DE GRASA |
| 7410 | MOTOR *m* DE GASOLINA CON GRAN POTENCIA |
| 7411 | GRAN DECLIVE *m* DEL CORTE EFECTIVO |
| 7412 | CALDERA GRAN CAPACIDAD *f* |
| 7413 | COLA *m* DE DESTILACIÓN |
| 7414 | PESTILLO *m*, FIADOR *m*, PASADOR *m*, PICAPORTE *m* |
| 7415 | CALOR LATENTE *m* |
| 7416 | CALOR LATENTE DE VAPORIZACIÓN *m* |
| 7417 | MAGNETISMO *m* LATENTE |
| 7418 | ALABEO *m* LATERAL |
| 7419 | DESVIACIÓN *f* (DESVÍO *m*) LATERAL |

| | |
|---|---|
| 7420 | DESPLAZAMIENTO *m* PERPENDICULAR AL EJE |
| 7420 | DESPLAZAMIENTO *m* LATERAL |
| 7421 | DILATACIÓN LATERAL |
| 7422 | PRESIÓN *f* LATERAL |
| 7423 | TRASLADO *m* LATERAL |
| 7424 | ESTRICCIÓN *f* |
| 7425 | LATEX *m* |
| 7426 | LATA *f* |
| 7427 | TORNO *m* |
| 7428 | TORNO *m* ACCIONADO POR TUERCA MATRIZ |
| 7429 | ENREJADO *m* METÁLICO |
| 7429 | RED *f* CRISTALINA |
| 7430 | CONSTANTES DE LA RED *f pl* |
| 7431 | VIGA *f* EN ENREJADO |
| 7432 | PLANO *m* RETICULAR |
| 7433 | ENREJADO *m* |
| 7434 | TEORÍA *f* DE LA DISTORSIÓN DE LA RED |
| 7435 | DIAGRAMA *m* DE LAUE |
| 7436 | CANAL DE COLADA *m* |
| 7437 | LAVA *f* |
| 7438 | MÉTODO *m* DE LAVADO |
| 7439 | MÁQUINAS *f pl* DE CORTAREL CÉSPED |
| 7440 | BARCAZAS *f pl* DE ASIENTO (O TENDIDO, O COLOCACIÓN) |
| 7441 | COLOCAR TUBOS |
| 7442 | CAPA *f*, ESTRATO *m* |
| 7443 | CORROSIÓN POR INFILTRACIÓN ESTRATIFICADA *f* |
| 7444 | ESTRATO *m* |
| 7445 | COMPARACIÓN DE DIMENSIONES *f* |
| 7446 | COLADA *f* (LAVADO CON AGUA Y LEJÍA) |
| 7447 | PLOMO *m* |
| 7448 | AVANZAR, ACELERAR, APRESURAR |
| 7449 | PAPEL *m* AL ACETATO DE PLOMO |
| 7450 | ACETATO DE PLOMO, SUBACETATO *m* |
| 7451 | ALEACIÓN DE BASE DE PLOMO *f* |
| 7452 | HAZ *m* DE ALAMBRES |
| 7453 | ALEACIÓN AL PLOMO *f* |
| 7454 | BAÑO *m* DE PLOMO |
| 7455 | ACUMULADOR DE PLOMO *m* |
| 7456 | BRONCE *m* PLOMOSO |
| 7457 | REPRODUCCIÓN *f* EN PLOMO FUNDIDO |
| 7458 | CLORURO DE PLOMO *m* |
| 7459 | ALAMBRE *m* CON CAPA DE PLOMO |
| 7460 | CHAPA *f* EMPLOMADA |
| 7461 | ÓXIDO *m* PARDO DE PLOMO, PERÓXIDO *m* DE PLOMO |
| 7461 | DIÓXIDO *m* DE PLOMO |
| 7462 | PLOMO *m* EN PLACAS |
| 7462 | CHAPA *f* DE PLOMO |
| 7463 | MACILLO *m* DE PLOMO |

| | |
|---|---|
| 7464 | JUNTA f DE ARANDELA DE PLOMO RECALCADA POR EL CANTO PARA CAÑERIAS |
| 7465 | MINERAL m DE PLOMO |
| 7466 | MATERIA f COLORANTE A BASE DE PLOMO |
| 7467 | DIBUJO m AL LÁPIZ |
| 7468 | TUBO m DE PLOMO |
| 7469 | TUBO m DE PLOMO ESTAÑADO INTERIORMENTE |
| 7470 | ANILLO m DE PLOMO |
| 7471 | TUERCA f MATRIZ |
| 7472 | GRANALLA f DE PLOMO |
| 7473 | SULFATO m DE PLOMO |
| 7474 | HIPOSULFITO m DE PLOMO |
| 7475 | SOLDADURA f CLARA |
| 7476 | SOLDADURA f DE PLOMO |
| 7477 | ALAMBRE m (O HILO m) DE PLOMO |
| 7478 | LÁPIZ m |
| 7479 | PRECINTADO, EMPLOMADO |
| 7480 | PRECINTO m DE PLOMO |
| 7481 | DIMENSIONES f pl PRINCIPALES |
| 7481 | DATOS m pl PRINCIPALES |
| 7482 | CAPATAZ m |
| 7483 | AVANCE m (O ADELANTO m) DE FASE |
| 7483 | AVANCE m DE FASE |
| 7484 | PLOMERÍA f |
| 7485 | RESORTE m DE HOJAS |
| 7486 | FUGA f POR LAS JUNTAS |
| 7487 | HUIR, PRODUCIRSE UNA FUGA f |
| 7488 | FUGA f, PÉRDIDA f |
| 7488 | EXUDACIÓN f |
| 7489 | REBABA f |
| 7490 | CORRIENTE DE FUGA f |
| 7490 | CORRIENTE DE DISPERSIÓN f |
| 7491 | ESTANQUEIDAD (FALTA DE) |
| 7491 | PERMEABLE |
| 7492 | FUGA f (DE GASES O LÍQUIDOS) |
| 7492 | PÉRDIDA POR FUGAS (DE UN LÍQUIDO) f |
| 7493 | PIERDE (QUE) |
| 7493 | HUYE (QUE) |
| 7494 | CUERO m |
| 7495 | CORREA DE CUERO f |
| 7496 | CORREA DE CUERO DE ESLABONES f |
| 7497 | RECORTES m pl DE CUERO |
| 7498 | DIAFRAGMA m DE CUERO |
| 7499 | TUBO m DE CUERO |
| 7500 | LINTERNA f PARA CORREAS |
| 7501 | MANGUITO m DE TIRAS DE CUERO |
| 7502 | GUARNICIÓN f CON CUERO |
| 7503 | CORREA DE CUERO f |
| 7504 | LEDEBURITA f |
| 7505 | SOTAVENTO m |
| 7506 | TORNILLO m A LA IZQUIERDA |
| 7507 | DESVIACIÓN f A LA IZQUIERDA |

| | |
|---|---|
| 7508 | PASO m A IZQUIERDA |
| 7509 | DENTADO m IZQUIERDO |
| 7510 | TORNILLO m A LA IZQUIERDA |
| 7511 | CABLE TORCIDO A IZQUIERDAS m |
| 7512 | LADO DE UN ÁNGULO m |
| 7513 | PIE m DE UN DIBUJO O PLANO, INSCRIPCIÓN f |
| 7514 | LEMNISCATA f |
| 7515 | RAYOS m DE LENARD |
| 7516 | LARGURA f |
| 7517 | LARGURA f DE ARCO |
| 7518 | LARGURA f LIBRE |
| 7519 | JUEGO m DEL PISTÓN, ESPACIO m MUERTO DEL PISTÓN |
| 7519 | CARRERA DEL PISTÓN O ÉMBOLO f |
| 7520 | LARGURA f DEL CORDÓN |
| 7521 | ALARGADERA f DE UN COMPÁS |
| 7522 | LENTE (AMB.) |
| 7523 | EFECTO m LEONARD |
| 7523 | VENTEADURA f |
| 7524 | INDICACIONES f DE UN DIBUJO |
| 7525 | NIVEL m |
| 7526 | INDICADOR m DE NIVEL |
| 7527 | SUPERFICIE f EQUIPOTENCIAL |
| 7528 | ACCIÓN f DE NIVELACIÓN |
| 7529 | TORNILLO m NIVELADOR |
| 7530 | PALANCA f |
| 7531 | BRAZO m DE PALANCA, BRAZO m MECÁNICO |
| 7532 | FRENO m DE PALANCA |
| 7533 | GATO m DE PALANCA |
| 7534 | PRENSA f DE PALANCA |
| 7535 | VÁLVULA f DE SEGURIDAD DE PALANCA Y CONTRAPESO |
| 7536 | LARGURA f DEL BRAZO DE LA PALANCA |
| 7536 | RELACIÓN f ENTRE LOS BRAZOS DE PALANCA |
| 7537 | LEVIGACIÓN f |
| 7537 | LEVIGACIONES f pl |
| 7538 | BAÑO m DE DESCOMPOSICIÓN DEL ELECTRÓLITO |
| 7539 | LICENCIA f DE EXPLOTACIÓN, AUTORIZACIÓN f DE EXPLOTAR |
| 7540 | CONCESIONARIO DE LICENCIA m |
| 7541 | DURACIÓN f |
| 7542 | ELEVAR (O LEVANTAR) UN PESO |
| 7542 | LEVANTAR |
| 7543 | VÁLVULA DE RETENCIÓN DE CHAPELETA f |
| 7544 | CARRERA DE VÁLVULA f |
| 7544 | LEVANTAMIENTO m DE LA VÁLVULA |
| 7545 | BOMBA f ELEVADORA |
| 7546 | CABLE DE ASCENSOR m |
| 7547 | VÁLVULA f DE RETENCIÓN |
| 7547 | VÁLVULA f DE RETENCIÓN |
| 7548 | TENAZAS f DE FUNDIDOR |

| | | | |
|---|---|---|---|
| 7549 | DESTEMPLEO *m* | 7587 | TOLERANCIA *f* LIMITE |
| 7550 | CILINDRO *m* DE ELEVACIÓN | 7588 | LÍMITE *m* ELÁSTICO |
| 7551 | ALTURA *f* DE LEVANTAMIENTO DE UNA GRÚA | 7589 | LÍMITE *m* DE ERRORES |
| 7552 | GANCHO *m* ELEVADOR | 7590 | LÍMITE *m* DE ELASTICIDAD PROPORCIONAL |
| 7553 | PALANCA *f* DE PURGA LIBRE | 7591 | LÍMITE *m* DE SATURACIÓN |
| 7554 | ELECTROIMÁN *m* DE ELEVACIÓN | 7592 | LÍMITE *m* DE TEMPERATURA |
| 7555 | PISTÓN *m* DE LEVANTAMIENTO | 7593 | PRESIÓN *f* LÍMITE |
| 7556 | TORNILLO *m* DE ELEVACIÓN | 7594 | VALOR *m* LÍMITE |
| 7557 | MORDAZA *f* (DE UN APARATO DE LEVANTAMIENTO) | 7595 | LÍMITES *m pl* DE TOLERANCIA |
| | | 7596 | LIMONITA *f* |
| 7558 | MUÑÓN *m* GIRATORIO CON GANCHO DE ELEVACIÓN | 7596 | HEMATITES *f* PARDA |
| 7559 | LEVANTAMIENTO *m* DE UN FARDO | 7597 | RAYA *f* |
| 7559 | SUBIDA *f* DE UNA CARGA | 7597 | LÍNEA *f* |
| 7560 | LUZ *f* | 7598 | REVESTIR, RECUBRIR |
| 7561 | SOLDADURA *f* EN CAVETO | 7598 | FORRAR, REVESTIR |
| 7561 | SOLDADURA *f* DE ÁNGULO CÓNCAVA | 7599 | FUENTE *f* LINEAL |
| 7562 | CARGA INFERIOR A LA NORMAL *f* | 7600 | INTEGRAL *f* LINEAL |
| 7562 | CARGA INCOMPLETA *f* | 7601 | LÍNEA *f* DE COLIMACIÓN, EJE *m* DE COLIMACIÓN |
| 7563 | CAMIONETA *f* | | |
| 7564 | ALEACIÓN LIGERA *f* | 7602 | LÍNEA *f* DE ENGRANAJE |
| 7564 | METAL *m* LIGERO | 7603 | LÍNEA *f* DE FUERZA, LÍNEA *f* DE ENERGÍA |
| 7565 | TORNO *m* PARA METALES LIGEROS | 7604 | LÍNEA *f* DE MARCADO AL GRAMIL |
| 7566 | FENÓMENO *m* LUMINOSO | 7605 | LÍNEA *f* DE INTERSECCIÓN |
| 7567 | MARCHA *f* SUAVE | 7606 | CARRIL *m*, FERROCARRIL *m*, VÍA FÉRREA *f* |
| 7568 | FUENTE *f* LUMINOSA | 7606 | VÍA *f* FÉRREA |
| 7569 | VELOCIDAD *f* DE LA LUZ | 7607 | HILERA *f* DE ÁRBOLES |
| 7570 | ACEITE *m* LIGERO | 7607 | LÍNEA *f* DE TRANSMISIÓN |
| 7571 | ONDA *f* LUMINOSA | 7608 | POSTE *m* DE LÍNEA ELÉCTRICA |
| 7572 | IMPERMEABLE A LA LUZ | 7609 | ACCIONAMIENTO POR ÁRBOL DE TRANSMISIÓN *m* |
| 7573 | COHETE *m* LUMINOSO | | |
| 7574 | ILUMINACIÓN *f* | 7610 | ESPECTRO *m* DISCONTINUO |
| 7574 | ALUMBRADO *m*, ILUMINACIÓN *f* | 7611 | ACELERACIÓN LINEAL *f* |
| 7575 | PARARRAYOS *m* | 7612 | ALARGAMIENTO *m* |
| 7576 | PARARRAYOS *m* | 7612 | DILATACIÓN *f* LINEAL |
| 7577 | LIGNINA *f* | 7613 | INTERPOLACIÓN *f* LINEAL |
| 7577 | LIGNINA *f* | 7614 | PERSPECTIVA *f* LINEAL |
| 7577 | LIGNINA *f* | 7615 | PASO *m* LINEAL |
| 7578 | LEÑOSO | 7616 | ECUACIÓN *f* DE PRIMER GRADO |
| 7578 | LIGNITO *m* | 7616 | ECUACIÓN *f* LINEAL, ECUACIÓN *f* DE PRIMER GRADO |
| 7579 | CERA DE PARAFINA *f* | | |
| 7579 | CERA DEL JAPÓN *f* | 7617 | VELOCIDAD *f* LINEAL |
| 7580 | LIGROÍNA *f*, ÉTER *m* DE PETRÓLEO | 7618 | CRISOL *m* ENLADRILLADO |
| 7580 | LIGROÍNA *f* | 7618 | CUCHARA *f* GUARNECIDA |
| 7581 | POLOS *m pl* SEMEJANTES | 7619 | LIENZO *m* |
| 7582 | CAL *f* | 7620 | GUARNICIÓN *f* |
| 7583 | REVESTIMIENTO *m* POR COMPOSICIÓN KB TI | 7620 | SEPARADOR *m* |
| 7584 | REVESTIMIENTO *m* BÁSICO | 7621 | HOJA DE ESPESOR *f* |
| 7585 | AGUA *f* DE CAL | 7621 | CHAPA *f* DE AJUSTE |
| 7586 | CALIZA *f* | 7622 | LÍNEAS *f pl* DE LUDERS |
| 7587 | LÍMITE *m* | 7623 | FORRO DE AISLAMIENTO TÉRMICO *m* |
| | | 7623 | FORRO *m*, CAMISA *f* |

| | | | | |
|---|---|---|---|---|
| 7623 | FORRO *m*, GUARNICIÓN *f*, CAMISA *f* | | 7657 | ESTADO *m* LÍQUIDO |
| 7623 | FORRO *m*, ENVOLTURA | | 7658 | CAJONES ESTANCOS *m pl* |
| 7623 | GUARNICIÓN *f*, FORRO *m* | | 7659 | TRANSFERENCIA *f* POR VENA LÍQUIDA |
| 7623 | REVESTIMIENTO *m* | | 7660 | LÍQUIDOS *m pl* |
| 7623 | REVESTIMIENTO *m* INTERIOR | | 7661 | LIQUIDUS *m* |
| 7623 | REVESTIMIENTO *m* | | 7661 | LÍNEA *f* DEL LIQUIDUS |
| 7624 | GUARNICIÓN *f* DE COJINETE | | 7662 | NOMENCLATURA *f* DE LAS PIEZAS |
| 7624 | GUARNICIÓN *f* DE METAL ANTIFRICCIÓN | | 7663 | LITARGIRIO *m* |
| 7624 | REVESTIMIENTO *m* DE ANTIFRICCIÓN | | 7663 | PROTÓXIDO *m* DE PLOMO |
| 7625 | CURSOR *m* | | 7664 | LITIO *m* |
| 7625 | GUÍA MÓVIL *f*, CURSOR *m* | | 7665 | CARBONATO DE LITIO *m* |
| 7625 | VIAJERO *m* | | 7666 | CLORURO DE LITIO *m* |
| 7626 | DISTRIBUCIÓN *f* POR CORREDERA | | 7667 | FLUORURO *m* DE LITIO |
| 7627 | ESLABÓN *m*, ANILLO DE CADENA | | 7668 | PAPEL *m* DE TORNASOL |
| 7627 | ESLABÓN *m* | | 7669 | LITRO *m* |
| 7627 | ESLABÓN *m* | | 7670 | CONDUCTOR ATRAVESADO POR UNA CORRIENTE *m* |
| 7627 | ESLABÓN DE UNA CADENA *m* | | | |
| 7628 | SISTEMA *m* ARTICULADO | | 7670 | ATRAVESADO POR UNA CORRIENTE |
| 7629 | ARTICULADO | | 7671 | CARGA VIVA *f* |
| 7630 | LINÓLEO *m* | | 7672 | CARGA VARIABLE *f* |
| 7631 | ACEITE *m* DE LINO, ACEITE *m* DE LINAZA | | 7672 | CARGA INTERMITENTE *f* |
| 7632 | PICO *m* DE COLADA | | 7673 | VAPOR *m* FRESCO |
| 7633 | BORDES *m pl* DE CORTES | | 7674 | HÍGADO *m* DE AZUFRE |
| 7634 | SUPERFICIE *f* DE LICUACIÓN | | 7675 | ESPESADO *m* |
| 7635 | LICUACIÓN *f* | | 7676 | LIXIVIAR |
| 7635 | SEGREGACIÓN *f* | | 7676 | ECHAR EN LEJÍA, LAVAR EN AGUA CON LEJÍA |
| 7636 | LICUEFACCIÓN *f* DE UN GAS | | 7677 | LIXIVIACIÓN *f* |
| 7637 | GAS *m* LÍQUIDO, GAS LICUADO | | 7677 | LIXIVIACIÓN (QUIM.) *f* |
| 7638 | GAS *m* DE PETRÓLEO LICUADO | | 7678 | DEPÓSITO *m* DE GNL |
| 7639 | LICUABLE | | 7679 | CARGA *f* |
| 7640 | LICUAR UN GAS | | 7679 | SOLICITACIONES *f pl* |
| 7641 | LÍQUIDO *m* | | 7679 | ESFUERZO *m* EXTERIOR, CARGA *f* |
| 7641 | FLUIDO *m* LÍQUIDO | | 7680 | CARGAR (RESISTENCIA DE LOS MATERIALES) |
| 7641 | FLUIDO *m* | | 7681 | FRENO *m* DE RETENCIÓN |
| 7641 | CUERPO LÍQUIDO *m* | | 7682 | CAPACIDAD DE CARGA *f* |
| 7642 | LÍQUIDO *m* | | 7683 | PLANO *m* DE CARGA |
| 7643 | AIRE LÍQUIDO *m* | | 7684 | REPARTICIÓN *f* DE CARGAS |
| 7644 | AMONIACO *m*, AMONÍACO *m* | | 7685 | CARGA SIN GOLPES *f* |
| 7645 | ÁCIDO CARBÓNICO LÍQUIDO *m* | | 7686 | MOTOR *m* BAJO TENSIÓN |
| 7645 | GAS *m* CARBÓNICO LICUADO | | 7687 | CARGADOR (O CARGADORA) PARA PASTO VERDE ( *m f* ) |
| 7646 | CEMENTACIÓN EN BAÑO *f* | | | |
| 7647 | CARGA LÍQUIDA *f* | | 7688 | CARGADORES DE SACOS Y REMOLACHAS *m* |
| 7648 | CONTRACCIÓN DE ENFRIAMIENTO *f* | | 7689 | CARGADORES DE ESTIÉRCOL *m* |
| 7649 | AMORTIGUAMIENTO POR LÍQUIDO *m* | | 7690 | MATERIA *f* DE CARGA |
| 7650 | COMBUSTIBLE LÍQUIDO *m* | | 7691 | TIERRA *f* ARCILLOSA |
| 7651 | TEMPLE *m* EN BAÑO DE SAL | | 7691 | ARCILLA *f*, GREDA *f*, TIERRA *f* DE MODELAR |
| 7652 | CARGA HIDROSTÁTICA *f* | | 7692 | ADOBE *m* |
| 7653 | RECTIFICACIÓN *f* AL CHORRO DE VAPOR | | 7692 | ADOBE *m* |
| 7654 | REGULADOR *m* DE NIVEL | | 7693 | MOLDE *m* DE ARCILLA DE MODELAR |
| 7655 | CONTROLADOR DE NIVEL *m*, AFORADOR *m* | | 7694 | PILA *f* LOCAL |
| 7656 | EXAMEN *m* POR RESUDACIÓN | | 7695 | CORROSIÓN LOCAL *f* |

| | |
|---|---|
| 7696 | CALDEO PARCIAL *m* |
| 7697 | TEMPLE *m* PARCIAL |
| 7698 | ESCLUSA *f*, COMPUERTA *f* |
| 7699 | BLOQUEAR |
| 7700 | BLOQUEAR UNA CHAVETA |
| 7700 | BLOQUEAR UNA TUERCA |
| 7701 | ÁNGULO DE VIRAJE *m* |
| 7702 | TUERCA *f* DE BLOQUEO |
| 7702 | TUERCA *f* DE SEGURIDAD |
| 7702 | CONTRATUERCA *f* |
| 7703 | ARANDELA *f* DE FRENO |
| 7703 | ARANDELA *f* DE AJUSTE |
| 7703 | ARANDELA *f* DE BLOQUEO |
| 7704 | BLOQUEO *m* DE CHAVETAS |
| 7704 | FIJACIÓN *f* DE UNA CUÑA DE APRIETE |
| 7705 | ENGANCHE *m*, ENGATILLADO *m*, MECANISMO *m* POR TRINQUETE |
| 7705 | DISPOSITIVO *m* DE BLOQUEO |
| 7706 | MANIJA *m* DE MANDO |
| 7707 | CONSOLIDACIÓN DE LOS PERNOS *f*, BLOQUEO *m* |
| 7707 | SEGURO *m* (O BLOQUEO *m*) DE LAS TUERCAS |
| 7707 | INMOVILIZACIÓN *f* DE TUERCAS Y PERNOS |
| 7708 | TORNILLO *m* DE BLOQUEO |
| 7709 | MECANISMO *m* DE PARADA O DE INMOVILIZACIÓN |
| 7710 | BLOQUEO *m* |
| 7711 | BLOCADO *m*, BLOQUEO *m* |
| 7711 | BLOCADO *m*, BLOQUEO *m* |
| 7712 | LOCOMOCIÓN *f* |
| 7713 | LOCOMOTORA *f* |
| 7714 | CALDERA TIPO LOCOMOTORA *f* |
| 7715 | LUGAR *m* GEOMÉTRICO |
| 7716 | LOESS *m* |
| 7717 | GRÁFICO *m*, DIAGRAMA *m* |
| 7717 | DIAGRAMA *m* |
| 7717 | PERFIL *m* |
| 7717 | ESTADO, APUNTE *m*, LISTA *f* LEVANTAMIENTO *m* |
| 7717 | SECCIÓN *f* |
| 7718 | LOGARITMO *m* |
| 7719 | SERIE *f* LOGARÍTMICA |
| 7720 | ESPIRAL *f* LOGARÍTMICA |
| 7721 | TABLA *f* DE LOGARITMOS |
| 7722 | ESTROFOIDE *f* |
| 7723 | ROLLIZOS *m pl* (MADERA), MADERA *f* EN ROLLO |
| 7724 | HULLA *f* DE LLAMA LARGA |
| 7725 | BARRA DE UÑA *f*, ESPEQUE *m*, PALANCA *f*, ALZAPRIMA *f* |
| 7726 | UNIÓN *f* POR MANGUITO Y TUERCA |
| 7727 | FABRICACIÓN *f* EN GRANDES SERIES |
| 7728 | RED *f* A GRAN DISTANCIA |

| | |
|---|---|
| 7729 | EFECTO *m* DE LÍNEA DE TRANSMISIÓN |
| 7730 | CADENA DE ESLABONES LARGOS *f* |
| 7731 | MÁQUINA *f* DE CARRERA LARGA |
| 7732 | MANIVELA *f* DE CARRERA LARGA |
| 7733 | EJE LONGITUDINAL |
| 7734 | TRAVIESA *f*, TRAVESAÑO *m* |
| 7735 | DUCTILIDAD *f* LONGITUDINAL |
| 7736 | PASO *m* DE REMACHE LONGITUDINAL |
| 7737 | SOLDADURA *f* LONGITUDINAL |
| 7738 | PERFIL *m* A LO LARGO |
| 7738 | CORTE LONGITUDINAL *m* |
| 7739 | OSCILACIÓN *f* LONGITUDINAL |
| 7740 | TUBO *m* CON NERVIOS LONGITUDINALES |
| 7740 | TUBO *m* DE NERVIOS LONGITUDINALES |
| 7741 | NODO *m* DE UNA CURVA |
| 7741 | LAZO *m*, LAZADA *f*, REVUELTA *f* (EN CARRETERAS) |
| 7742 | LAZO *m* DE UNA CUERDA |
| 7743 | ANILLA *f* DE DETENCIÓN, ANILLO *m* REGULADOR |
| 7743 | ANILLO *m* DESMONTABLE |
| 7743 | ARANDELA *f* CON PASADOR |
| 7744 | MODELO *m* DESMONTABLE, MODELADO |
| 7745 | PARTE *f* DESMONTABLE |
| 7746 | BRIDA *f* SUELTA |
| 7747 | POLEA *f* LOCA |
| 7748 | CAJA *f* (O CASQUILLO *m*) PARA POLEA LOCA (PARA MARCHA LIBRE) |
| 7749 | LOCO (SOBRE EL EJE) |
| 7750 | DESENCLAVIJAR, AFLOJAR UNA CHAVETA DE CUÑA |
| 7751 | DESENCLAVIJAMIENTO *m*, AFLOJAMIENTO *m* DE UNA CHAVETA DE CUÑA |
| 7751 | DESMONTAJE *m* (AFLOJAMIENTO *m*) DE UNA CHAVETA DE CUÑA |
| 7752 | CAMIÓN *m* |
| 7753 | CAMIÓN DE COSTADOS ARTICULADOS *m* |
| 7754 | PÉRDIDA *f* |
| 7755 | PÉRDIDA *f* DE FROTAMIENTO |
| 7756 | PÉRDIDA *f* POR FUGAS |
| 7757 | PÉRDIDA *f* POR CHOQUES |
| 7758 | PÉRDIDA *f* DE ENERGÍA |
| 7759 | MERMA *f* DE CARGA |
| 7760 | PÉRDIDA *f* DE CALOR, PÉRDIDA *f* CALORÍFICA |
| 7760 | PÉRDIDA *f* DE CALOR |
| 7761 | PÉRDIDA *f* EN EL FUEGO |
| 7762 | PÉRDIDA *f* DE POTENCIA, REDUCCIÓN *f* DE POTENCIA |
| 7763 | PÉRDIDA *f* DE PRESIÓN |
| 7764 | PÉRDIDA *f* DE PESO |
| 7765 | PÉRDIDA *f* DE TRABAJO |
| 7766 | LOTE *m* |
| 7767 | JUNTA *f* INFERIOR DE DÉBIL ORIENTÁCIÓN |

| | | | |
|---|---|---|---|
| 7768 | LATÓN *m* DE ALEACIÓN DÉBIL | 7807 | MECHA *f* DE ENGRASE |
| 7769 | RUEDA *f* DE COSTADO (HIDRÁULICA) | 7808 | LUBRIFICACIÓN *f* |
| 7770 | ACERO DULCE (SUAVE) *m* | 7808 | ENGRASE *m* |
| 7770 | ACERO DE BAJO CARBONO *m* | 7809 | ENGRASE *m* POR OLEOCOMPRESOR |
| 7771 | FRECUENCIA *f* BAJA | 7810 | CANAL *m* DE ENGRASE |
| 7772 | HORNO *m* DE INDUCCIÓN A BAJA FRECUENCIA | 7810 | PATA *f* DE ARAÑA, RANURA *f* DE ENGRASE |
| 7773 | ALEACIONES FUSIBLES *f pl* | 7811 | PERNO *m* DE ENGRASE (O DE LUBRIFICACIÓN) |
| 7774 | BAJA *f* PRESIÓN | 7812 | ÓRGANO *m* DE LUBRIFICACIÓN |
| 7775 | BAJA *f* TEMPERATURA | 7812 | ENGRASADOR *m* |
| 7776 | CARBONIZACIÓN INCOMPLETA *f* | 7812 | ENGRASE *m* |
| 7776 | CARBONIZACIÓN *f* INCOMPLETA, DESTILACIÓN *f* DE LOS COMBUSTIBLES A BAJA TEMPERATURA | 7813 | UNTUOSIDAD *f* DEL LUBRIFICANTE |
| 7777 | CORRIENTE BAJA TENSIÓN *f* | 7814 | ENGRASE *m* |
| 7778 | BAJA *f* TENSIÓN | 7815 | LÍNEAS *f pl* DE LUDERS |
| 7779 | METAL *m* LIGERO | 7815 | LÍNEAS *f pl* DE HARTMANN |
| 7780 | COMBUSTIBLE *m* DE MALA CALIDAD | 7816 | ASIENTO *m* |
| 7781 | MINERAL *m* POBRE | 7817 | OREJA *f*, FIJACIÓN *f*, PATA *f* |
| 7781 | MINERAL *m* DE BAJO PORCENTAJE | 7817 | OREJA *f* |
| 7782 | CALDERA BAJA PRESIÓN *f* | 7817 | PATA *f*, GRAPA *f*, PATILLA *f* |
| 7783 | CILINDRO *m* DE BAJA PRESIÓN | 7817 | OREJETA *f*, BRIDA *f* |
| 7784 | CALEFACCIÓN POR AGUA CALIENTE BAJA PRESIÓN *f* | 7818 | LUMEN *m* |
| 7785 | VAPOR *m* A ALTA PRESIÓN | 7819 | LUMINISCENCIA *f* |
| 7786 | MÁQUINA *f* DE PRESIÓN ORDINARIA | 7820 | LLAMA *f* REDUCTORA |
| 7787 | CALEFACCIÓN POR VAPOR BAJA PRESIÓN *f* | 7820 | LLAMA *f* LUMINOSA |
| 7788 | TURBINA *f* DE BAJA PRESIÓN | 7820 | LLAMA *f* LUMINOSA |
| 7789 | MÁQUINA *f* DE FUNCIONAMIENTO LENTO | 7821 | FLUJO *m* LUMINOSO |
| 7789 | MÁQUINA *f* DE PEQUEÑA VELOCIDAD | 7822 | INTENSIDAD *f* LUMINOSA |
| 7790 | ENSAMBLADURA A BAJA TEMPERATURA *f* | 7823 | PUNTO *m* LUMINOSO |
| 7791 | MOTOR *m* A BAJA TENSIÓN | 7824 | RAYO *m* LUMINOSO |
| 7792 | PASO *m* DEL SISTEMA LOWENHERZ | 7825 | VIBRACIÓN *f* LUMINOSA |
| 7793 | BAJAR UNA CARGA | 7826 | CARBÓN GRUESO *m* |
| 7794 | PUNZÓN *m* INFERIOR | 7827 | COMBUSTIBLE EN GRANDES TROZOS *m* |
| 7795 | BARANDILLA *f* INFERIOR | 7828 | NITRATO *m* DE PLATA |
| 7796 | GUÍA *f* DE LA CINTA INFERIOR | 7828 | NITRATO DE PLATA *m* |
| 7797 | BAJADA *f* DE UNA CARGA | 7828 | NITRATO *m* DE PLATA |
| 7798 | DESNIVELACIÓN *f*, DESNIVEL *m* | 7829 | LÚNULA *f* |
| 7798 | DESNIVELACIÓN *f*, DESNIVEL *m* | 7830 | BRILLO *m* |
| 7799 | REMACHE *m* EN ROMBO | 7831 | LUCHAR |
| 7800 | LUBRIFICANTE *m*, LUBRICANTE *m* | 7832 | ABRAZADERA *f*, BRIDA *f* (DE UN TUBO) |
| 7801 | LUBRIFICAR | 7833 | LUTECIO *m* |
| 7801 | ENGRASAR | 7834 | LUX *m* |
| 7802 | GRIFO *m* DE CANILLA LUBRIFICADA | 7835 | LEJÍA *f* |
| 7803 | LUBRIFICACIÓN *f* | 7836 | MACERAR |
| 7803 | ENGRASE *m* | 7837 | MACERACIÓN *f* |
| 7804 | GRASA *f* DE LUBRIFICACIÓN | 7838 | APTO PARA MECANIZACIÓN |
| 7805 | ACEITE *m* PARA ENGRASE | 7839 | MÁQUINA *f* DE TRABAJO |
| 7805 | ACEITE *m* LUBRIFICANTE, ACEITE *m* LUBRIFIANTE | 7839 | MÁQUINA *f* RECEPTORA |
| 7806 | CALIDAD *f* LUBRIFICANTE | 7840 | PERNO *m* EMBUTIDO, PERNO *m* PASADOR |
| 7806 | PODER *m* LUBRIFICANTE | 7840 | PERNO *m* EMBUTIDO, PERNO *m* PASADOR |
| | | 7841 | CLAVO TROQUELADO *m* |
| | | 7842 | CORTE *m* A MÁQUINA |
| | | 7843 | DIBUJO *m* DE MÁQUINAS |

| | |
|---|---|
| 7844 | ACABADO *m* CON MÁQUINA |
| 7845 | MÁQUINA *f* PARA ENSAYOS DE FLEXIÓN |
| 7846 | DINAMÓMETRO *m* |
| 7846 | DINAMÓMETRO *m* |
| 7846 | MÁQUINA *f* PARA ENSAYOS DE ROTURA POR TRACCIÓN |
| 7847 | FORJADO *m* A MÁQUINA |
| 7848 | MACIZO *m* BASE DE MÁQUINA |
| 7849 | RECTIFICACIÓN *f* CON MUELA EN MÁQUINA |
| 7850 | TRABAJO *m* A MÁQUINA |
| 7851 | MOLDEADO *m* MECÁNICO |
| 7852 | ÓRGANO *m* |
| 7852 | ÓRGANO *m* |
| 7852 | PIEZA *f* MECÁNICA |
| 7852 | PIEZA *f* DE MÁQUINA |
| 7852 | ELEMENTO *m* |
| 7853 | ESCARIADOR PARA MÁQUINA *m*, ESCARIADOR MECÁNICO *m* |
| 7854 | ROBLONADO *m* MECÁNICO |
| 7855 | SALA *f* DE MÁQUINAS |
| 7855 | SALA *f* DE MÁQUINAS |
| 7855 | TALLER DE MÁQUINAS *m* |
| 7856 | TALLER *m* DE MAQUINARIA |
| 7857 | ACERO DE UTENSILIOS *m* |
| 7858 | TERRAJA *f* A MÁQUINA |
| 7858 | ATERRAJADORA *f* |
| 7859 | MÁQUINA HERRAMIENTA *f* |
| 7860 | TRABAJO *m* MECÁNICO (TRABAJO HECHO A MÁQUINA) |
| 7861 | FÁBRICA *f* |
| 7862 | MAQUINARIA *f* |
| 7863 | FUNDICIÓN *f* MECÁNICA |
| 7864 | MECANIZACIÓN *f* |
| 7865 | SOBRE ESPESOR *m* DE MECANIZACIÓN |
| 7866 | GRADO *m* DE TRABAJO MECÁNICO |
| 7867 | ANCHURA *f* DE MECANIZADO |
| 7868 | OBRERO *m* MECÁNICO |
| 7868 | OBRERO *m*, OPERARIO *m* DE MÁQUINA HERRAMIENTA |
| 7869 | ESTRUCTURA *f* DE GRANOS GRUESOS |
| 7869 | MACROESTRUCTURA *f* |
| 7870 | MACROATAQUE POR ÁCIDO *m* |
| 7871 | MACROGRAFÍA *f* |
| 7872 | MACROSCÓPICO |
| 7873 | OBSERVACIÓN *f* MACROSCÓPICA A SIMPLE VISTA |
| 7874 | ESFUERZO *m* MACROSCÓPICO |
| 7875 | SECCIÓN *f* MACROSCÓPICA |
| 7876 | MACROSEGREGACIÓN *f* |
| 7877 | MAGNETOSCOPIA *f* |
| 7878 | MAGNALIO *m* |
| 7879 | MAGNESIA *f* |
| 7879 | ÓXIDO *m* DE MAGNESIO |

| | |
|---|---|
| 7880 | MAGNESITA *f*, ESPUMA DE MAR *f* |
| 7880 | GLOBERTITA *f* |
| 7881 | AGLOMERADO MAGNESIANO *m* |
| 7882 | MAGNESIO *m* |
| 7883 | BICARBONATO *m* DE MAGNESIO |
| 7884 | CARBONATO DE MAGNESIA *m* |
| 7885 | CLORURO DE MAGNESIO *m* |
| 7886 | FLUORURO *m* DE MAGNESIO |
| 7887 | HIDRATO *m* DE MAGNESIA |
| 7888 | SILICATO *m* DE MAGNESIO |
| 7889 | SAL *f* DE EPSON |
| 7889 | SAL *f* INGLESA |
| 7889 | SAL *f* DE SEDLITZ |
| 7889 | SULFATO *m* DE MAGNESIO |
| 7890 | ALEACIÓN DE BASE DE MAGNESIO *f* |
| 7891 | IMÁN *m* |
| 7892 | ACERO PARA IMANES *m* |
| 7893 | MAGNÉTICO |
| 7894 | ANÁLISIS MAGNÉTICO *m* |
| 7895 | ATRACCIÓN *f* MAGNÉTICA |
| 7896 | FRENO *m* MAGNÉTICO |
| 7897 | CALZOS MAGNÉTICOS DE FIJACIÓN *m* |
| 7898 | MANDRILES *m* MAGNÉTICOS |
| 7899 | DENSIDAD *f* MAGNÉTICA |
| 7900 | ENERGÍA *f* MAGNÉTICA |
| 7901 | CAMPO MAGNÉTICO *m* |
| 7902 | ESPECTRO *m* MAGNÉTICO |
| 7903 | FLUJO MAGNÉTICO |
| 7904 | FUERZA *f* MAGNÉTICA |
| 7905 | INDICADOR *m* MAGNÉTICO |
| 7906 | MAGNETIZACIÓN *f* |
| 7907 | PÉRDIDAS *f pl* DE MAGNETIZACIÓN |
| 7908 | INDUCCIÓN *f* MAGNÉTICA |
| 7909 | AGUJA IMANTADA *f* |
| 7910 | MAGNETOSCOPIA *f* |
| 7911 | PERMEABILIDAD *f* MAGNÉTICA |
| 7912 | PLATILLOS *m pl* MAGNÉTICOS |
| 7913 | POLO *m* MAGNÉTICO |
| 7914 | PIRITA *f* MAGNÉTICA |
| 7914 | PIROTINA *f* |
| 7915 | REPULSIÓN *f* MAGNÉTICA |
| 7916 | SATURACIÓN *f* MAGNÉTICA |
| 7917 | SEPARACIÓN *f* MAGNÉTICA |
| 7918 | SENSIBILIDAD *f* MAGNÉTICA |
| 7919 | CINTA *f* MAGNÉTICA |
| 7920 | PUNTO *m* DE CURIE |
| 7921 | MARTILLO *m* IMANTADO PARA GUARNICIONERO |
| 7922 | MAGNETIZABLE |
| 7923 | IMANTACIÓN *f*, IMANACIÓN *f* |
| 7924 | IMANTAR, IMANAR, MAGNETIZAR |
| 7925 | FUERZA *f* MAGNETIZANTE |

| | |
|---|---|
| 7926 | MAGNETISMO *m* |
| 7927 | MAGNETITA *f* |
| 7927 | HIERRO *m* MAGNÉTICO |
| 7927 | MINERAL *m* DE HIERRO MAGNÉTICO |
| 7928 | MAGNETIZACIÓN *f* |
| 7928 | MAGNETIZACIÓN *f* |
| 7929 | FUERZA *f* MAGNETOMOTRIZ ESPECÍFICA |
| 7930 | MÁQUINA *f* MAGNETOELÉCTRICA |
| 7930 | MAGNETO *m* |
| 7931 | EXAMEN *m* MAGNETOGRÁFICO |
| 7932 | FUERZA *f* MAGNETOMOTRIZ |
| 7933 | MAGNETOESTRICCIÓN *f* |
| 7934 | ACOPLAMIENTO *m* (O EMBRAGUE *m*) MAGNÉTICO |
| 7935 | AMPLIACIÓN *f*, AUMENTO *m* |
| 7935 | CRECIMIENTO *m* |
| 7936 | LUPA *f*, LENTE AMB. DE AUMENTO |
| 7936 | CRISTAL *m* DE AUMENTO |
| 7937 | PODER *m* DE AUMENTO |
| 7937 | AUMENTO *m* |
| 7938 | AUMENTO *m* DE UNA LENTE |
| 7939 | TAMAÑO *m* |
| 7939 | INTENSIDAD *f* DE UNA FUERZA |
| 7940 | RED *f* |
| 7940 | ALIMENTACIÓN *f*, SUMINISTRO *m* |
| 7941 | COJINETES *m pl* DEL CIGÜEÑAL |
| 7941 | COJINETE DE PALIER *m*, COJINETE LÍSO *m* |
| 7942 | SURTIDOR *m* PRINCIPAL |
| 7943 | ÁRBOL PRINCIPAL *m* |
| 7944 | ÁRBOL DE ACCIONAMIENTO *m*, ÁRBOL MOTOR *m* |
| 7944 | ÁRBOL DE TRANSMISIÓN *m* |
| 7944 | ÁRBOL DE TRANSMISIÓN *m* |
| 7944 | ÁRBOL MOTOR *m*, ÁRBOL DE MANDO *m*, ÁRBOL DE IMPULSIÓN *m* |
| 7944 | ÁRBOL DE TRANSMISIÓN *m* |
| 7944 | TRANSMISIÓN *f* PRINCIPAL |
| 7945 | GASTOS *m* DE ENTRETENIMIENTO, GASTOS *m* DE CONSERVACIÓN |
| 7946 | MANTENIMIENTO *m* |
| 7947 | EJE *m* MAYOR DE UNA ELIPSE |
| 7948 | MANUFACTURAR |
| 7948 | FABRICAR |
| 7949 | DISYUNTOR *m*, RUPTOR *m* |
| 7950 | ESTABLECER UN CONTACTO |
| 7950 | REALIZAR |
| 7951 | AFLORAMIENTO *m* |
| 7952 | MALEABILIZAR LA FUNDICIÓN |
| 7953 | HACER IMPERMEABLE, IMPERMEABILIZAR |
| 7953 | HACER ESTANCO |
| 7954 | RECALCADURA *f*, IMPERMEABILIZACIÓN *m* |
| 7955 | ROSCA *f* MACHO |

| | |
|---|---|
| 7955 | ROSCADO *m* EXTERIOR, ROSCA *f* EXTERIOR |
| 7956 | CALIBRE *m* TAMPÓN CÓNICO |
| 7957 | ENCAJE *m* MACHO-HEMBRA |
| 7958 | MALEABILIDAD *f* |
| 7958 | FORJABILIDAD *f* |
| 7959 | FUNDICIÓN *f* MALEABLE |
| 7960 | FORJABLE |
| 7960 | MALEABLE |
| 7961 | MALEABILIZACIÓN *f* |
| 7962 | MAZO *m* DE MADERA |
| 7963 | ABERTURA *f* |
| 7963 | AGUJERO *m* DE HOMBRE |
| 7963 | JUNTA *f* DE AUTOCLAVE |
| 7964 | CABEZAL *m* (DE TORNO) |
| 7964 | MANDRIL *m* DE REPOSICIÓN |
| 7964 | MANDRIL *m* DE MONTAJE |
| 7965 | PELOS *m pl* DE LAS CRINES |
| 7965 | CRIN *f* DE LA MELENA (DE CABALLO), CRINES *f pl* |
| 7966 | MANGANESO *m* |
| 7967 | BRONCE *m* MANGANÉSICO |
| 7967 | LATÓN *m* AL MANGANESO |
| 7968 | ACERO AL MANGANESO *m* |
| 7969 | ACERO CALMADO AL MANGANESO *m* |
| 7970 | SESQUIÓXIDO *m* DE MANGANESO |
| 7971 | MANGANESÍFERO |
| 7972 | CLORURO MANGANOSO *m* |
| 7973 | PROTÓXIDO *m* DE MAGNESIO |
| 7974 | SULFATO *m* MANGANOSO |
| 7975 | RUEDA *f* DENTADA INTERRUMPIDA |
| 7976 | AGUJERO *m* DE HOMBRE |
| 7977 | TAPA *f* DE AGUJERO DE INSPECCIÓN |
| 7978 | MANGUITO DE EMPALME DE AGUJERO DE HOMBRE O REGISTRO DE HOMBRE *m* |
| 7979 | COLECTOR *m* |
| 7980 | ABACÁ *m*, CÁÑAMO DE MANILA *m* |
| 7980 | CÁÑAMO DE MANILA *m* |
| 7980 | ANILLA *f* DE ENGANCHE |
| 7981 | CUERDA DE MANILA *f* |
| 7982 | VOLTEADOR *m* DE LINGOTES |
| 7982 | MÁQUINA *f* DE MANIPULACIÓN |
| 7983 | TUBO *m* MANNESMANN |
| 7984 | RENDIMIENTO *m* MANOMÉTRICO |
| 7985 | MANTISA *f* |
| 7986 | REVESTIMIENTO *m*, CAPA *f* |
| 7986 | FUNDA *f*, ENVOLTURA *f* |
| 7987 | INTRODUCCIÓN *f* MANUAL DE DATOS |
| 7988 | SOLDADURA *f* DEPOSITADA A MANO |
| 7989 | PRODUCTO *m* MANUFACTURADO |
| 7989 | FABRICACIÓN *f* |
| 7989 | CONSTRUCCIÓN *f* |

| | |
|---|---|
| 7990 | FABRICACIÓN *f* DE LOS AGLOMERADOS |
| 7990 | SINTERIZACIÓN *f*, AGLOMERACIÓN *f* |
| 7991 | CARBONIZACIÓN DE LA HULLA *f* |
| 7991 | FABRICACIÓN *f* DE COK |
| 7992 | FABRICANTE *m* |
| 7992 | CONSTRUCTOR *m* |
| 7992 | INDUSTRIAL |
| 7993 | INFORME *m* DESCRIPTIVO DEL FABRICANTE |
| 7994 | PROGRAMA *m* DE FABRICACIÓN |
| 7994 | GAMA *f* DE FABRICACIÓN |
| 7995 | ESPARCIDORAS *f pl* DE ABONO |
| 7996 | MANUSCRITO *m* (TAMBIÉN ES ADJETIVO) |
| 7997 | T.H. |
| 7997 | AGUJERO *m* DE HOMBRE |
| 7998 | MANGA *f* DE ABERTURA DE INSPECCIÓN O DE LIMPIEZA, BOCA DE ENTRADA A UNA CALDERA |
| 7998 | MANGUITO DE EMPALME DE AGUJERO DE HOMBRE O REGISTRO DE HOMBRE *m* |
| 7999 | PLUMA *f* DE DIBUJO |
| 8000 | ACERO AUTOTEMPLABLE (DE TEMPLE AL AIRE) *m* |
| 8001 | MÁRMOL (GEOL) *m* |
| 8002 | CHAPA *f* MARGINAL |
| 8003 | CALDERA MARINA *f* |
| 8004 | CADENAS DE MARINA *f pl* |
| 8005 | MÁQUINA *f* MARINA |
| 8005 | MOTOR *m* MARINO |
| 8006 | COLA *f* MARINA |
| 8007 | CABEZA *f* DE BIELA DE CAJA ABIERTA |
| 8008 | MARCAR |
| 8008 | MARCAR, SEÑALAR |
| 8009 | TRAZO *m* DE UNA ESCALA |
| 8010 | TRAZAR |
| 8010 | MARCAR |
| 8011 | MARCAR CON PUNZÓN UNA SEÑAL |
| 8011 | MARCAR POR MEDIO DE UN PUNZÓN |
| 8011 | PUNZONAR |
| 8012 | ÍNDICE *m*, SEÑAL *f* |
| 8013 | TRAZADOR, MECÁNICO |
| 8014 | PLOMO *m* DEL COMERCIO |
| 8014 | PLOMO *m* DULCE |
| 8015 | MARCADO *m* |
| 8015 | MARCACIÓN, INDICACIÓN, LOCALIZACIÓN |
| 8016 | CALIBRE DE TRAZADO *m* |
| 8016 | GRAMIL *m* DE PUNTA |
| 8017 | TRAZADO *m* |
| 8017 | TRAZADO *m* |
| 8018 | TRAZADO *m* DE CHAPAS |
| 8019 | MARGA *f* |
| 8020 | JABÓN *m* DE MARSELLA |
| 8021 | TEMPLE *m* EN BAÑO CALIENTE |

| | |
|---|---|
| 8021 | TEMPLE *m* MARTENSÍTICO |
| 8022 | MARTENSITA *f* |
| 8023 | ACERO M.S. *m* |
| 8024 | SOLDADURA *f* AL APLASTAMIENTO |
| 8025 | OBRA *f* DE CONSTRUCCIÓN |
| 8025 | OBRA *f* DE ALBAÑILERÍA, OBRA *f* DE MAMPOSTERÍA |
| 8026 | MASA (MEC.) *f* |
| 8027 | EFECTO *m* DE MASA |
| 8027 | SENSIBILIDAD *f* AL ESPESOR |
| 8028 | PRODUCCIÓN *f* |
| 8028 | FABRICACIÓN *f* |
| 8028 | CONSTRUCCIÓN *f* |
| 8028 | CONFECCIÓN *f*, CONSTRUCCIÓN EN SERIE *f* |
| 8028 | TRABAJO *m* EN GRAN SERIE |
| 8029 | ESPECTRÓMETRO *m* DE MASA |
| 8030 | COEFICIENTE DE ABSORCIÓN MÁSICA *m* |
| 8031 | GUILLOTINA *f*, MASICOTE |
| 8032 | MODELO *m* CONTRASTE |
| 8033 | PORTAESTAMPAS *m* |
| 8033 | PORTAPUNZONES *m* |
| 8034 | PIEZA *f* DE REFERENCIA |
| 8035 | CALIBRE *m* DE REFERENCIA |
| 8036 | JUEGO *m* DE MEDIDAS PARA EL CONTRASTE |
| 8037 | CILINDRO *m* DE MANDO |
| 8038 | MASILLA *f*, MASTIC *m*, MASTIQUE *m* |
| 8038 | MASILLA *f*, MÁSTIC *m*, MASTIQUE *m* |
| 8039 | MASTIC *m* EN GRANO |
| 8039 | MASTIC *m* EN GOTAS |
| 8040 | MASURIO *m* |
| 8040 | TECNECIO *m* |
| 8041 | ACEITE PESADO *m* |
| 8042 | SURTIR, ABASTECER |
| 8042 | AJUSTAR, EMBUTIR |
| 8043 | CARA *f* DE REFERENCIA |
| 8044 | PLACA *f* MODELO DOBLE CARA |
| 8045 | AJUSTAR O EMBUTIR EL REMACHE |
| 8046 | PRESIÓN EJERCIDA SOBRE LAS PLANCHAS *f* |
| 8047 | CEPILLO *m* DE TAPÓN |
| 8048 | AYUDA *f*, AUXILIO *m* |
| 8049 | GASTOS *m* DE CONSUMO |
| 8049 | GASTOS *m* DE MATERIAS, COSTE *m* DE MATERIAS PRIMAS |
| 8050 | MATERIAL *m* DE CONSTRUCCIÓN |
| 8051 | CAJA *f* DE COMPÁS (O DE CALIBRE) |
| 8051 | INSTRUMENTOS *m pl* DE MATEMÁTICAS |
| 8052 | BAREMO *m* |
| 8053 | MATEMÁTICO |
| 8054 | CONTRABRIDA *f* |
| 8055 | MATRIZ *f* |
| 8055 | MASA *f* PRINCIPAL |

| | |
|---|---|
| 8056 | LATÓN *m* DE BASE |
| 8057 | METAL *m* COMÚN |
| 8058 | MATA *f* |
| 8059 | BAÑO *m* DE BLANQUEO |
| 8059 | BAÑO *m* DE DECAPADO MATE |
| 8060 | SUPERFICIE *f* MATE |
| 8061 | MATERIAS *f pl* EN DISOLUCIÓN |
| 8062 | MATERIAS *f pl* EN SUSPENSIÓN |
| 8063 | TERMÓMETRO *m* DE MÁXIMA Y MÍNIMA |
| 8064 | FLECHA *f* MÁXIMA, FLEXIÓN *f* MÁXIMA |
| 8065 | CARGA MÁXIMA *f* |
| 8066 | POTENCIA *f* MÁXIMA |
| 8067 | VELOCIDAD *f* MÁXIMA |
| 8068 | TEMPERATURA *f* MÁXIMA |
| 8069 | VALOR *m* MÁXIMO |
| 8070 | PESO *m* MÁXIMO |
| 8071 | TEST *m* DE MCQUAID-EHN |
| 8072 | MEDIO *m* |
| 8073 | VALOR *m* MEDIO |
| 8074 | DESVÍO *m* MEDIO |
| 8075 | PRESIÓN *f* MEDIA |
| 8076 | CALOR ESPECÍFICO MEDIO *m* |
| 8077 | MEDIDA *f* |
| 8078 | MEDIR |
| 8079 | MEDIDA *f* DE CAPACIDAD, MEDIDA *f* DE ARQUEO (MAR.) |
| 8080 | MEDIDA *f* LINEAL |
| 8081 | MEDIDA *f* DE LA SUPERFICIE |
| 8082 | MEDIDA *f* DE VOLUMEN |
| 8083 | MEDIR LA POTENCIA DE LOS FRENOS O DEL FRENADO |
| 8084 | PLANIMETRAR |
| 8085 | REGLA *f* GRADUADA |
| 8086 | MEDIDA *f* DE LA TEMPERATURA |
| 8087 | PLANIMETRADO *m* |
| 8088 | MEDICIÓN *f* |
| 8089 | ERROR *m* DE MEDIDA |
| 8090 | INSTRUMENTO *m* DE MEDIDA |
| 8091 | PUNTO *m* DE MEDIDA |
| 8092 | RUEDA *f* DE AGRIMENSURA |
| 8092 | CINTA *f* |
| 8092 | METRO *m* DE CINTA |
| 8093 | MECÁNICO |
| 8094 | BENEFICIO *m* EN EL TRABAJO |
| 8094 | VENTAJA *f* DE TRABAJO |
| 8095 | MANDRILES *m* MECÁNICOS |
| 8096 | LIMPIEZA *f* MECÁNICA |
| 8097 | COMPARADOR MECÁNICO *m* |
| 8098 | TIRO *m* ARTIFICIAL |
| 8098 | TIRO *m* CON SOPLADURA |
| 8099 | DIBUJO *m* INDUSTRIAL |

| | |
|---|---|
| 8100 | RENDIMIENTO *m* MECÁNICO |
| 8100 | RENDIMIENTO *m* ORGÁNICO |
| 8101 | ENERGÍA *f* MECÁNICA |
| 8102 | INGENIERO *m* MECÁNICO |
| 8103 | CONSTRUCCIÓN *f* |
| 8103 | CONSTRUCCIÓN MECÁNICA *f* |
| 8103 | FABRICACIÓN *f* DE MAQUINARIA |
| 8104 | EQUIVALENTE MECÁNICO DEL CALOR |
| 8105 | ENGRASADOR *m* MOLLERUP |
| 8105 | ENGRASADOR A PRESIÓN MECÁNICO *m* |
| 8106 | MANUTENCIÓN *f* MECÁNICA, MANIPULACIÓN *f* |
| 8107 | METALURGIA *f* MECÁNICA |
| 8108 | CHAPEADO *m* MECÁNICO |
| 8109 | CARACTERÍSTICAS MECÁNICAS *f pl* |
| 8110 | HOGAR *m* AUTOMÁTICO |
| 8110 | CARGADOR *m* |
| 8111 | CALENTAMIENTO MECÁNICO *m* |
| 8112 | PRUEBAS *f pl* MECÁNICAS |
| 8113 | MACLA *f* DE DEFORMACIÓN |
| 8114 | VIBRACIÓN *f* MECÁNICA |
| 8115 | SOLDADURA *f* MECÁNICA (AUTOMÁTICA) |
| 8116 | PASTA *f* MECÁNICA DE MADERA, CELULOSA |
| 8117 | TRABAJO *m* MECÁNICO |
| 8117 | TRABAJO *m* MOTOR |
| 8118 | COMPARADOR ÓPTICO-MECÁNICO *m* |
| 8119 | MANDO MECÁNICO *m* |
| 8119 | ACCIONAMIENTO POR MOTOR *m* |
| 8120 | VÁLVULA *f* MANDADA |
| 8121 | MECÁNICA (FIS.) |
| 8122 | MECANISMO *m* |
| 8122 | MECANISMO *m* |
| 8123 | DIVISIÓN *f* DE UNA LÍNEA EN MEDIA Y EXTREMA RAZÓN |
| 8124 | LÍNEA *f* MEDIANERA |
| 8125 | ACEITE *m* MEDIO |
| 8126 | CALDERA DE MEDIO VOLUMEN *f* |
| 8127 | CALDERA DE MEDIA PRESIÓN *f* |
| 8128 | RADIO *m* POLAR |
| 8129 | MEGADINA *f* |
| 8130 | MEGAVOLTIO *m* |
| 8131 | MEGAERGIO *m* |
| 8132 | MEGAOHMIO *m*, MEGOHMIO *m* |
| 8133 | MELÁFIDO *m* (GEOL), MELAFIRIO *m* |
| 8134 | FUSIÓN *f* |
| 8134 | FUSIÓN *f* |
| 8135 | LICUAR |
| 8135 | FUNDIR |
| 8135 | PASAR A ESTADO LÍQUIDO |
| 8136 | FUSIÓN *f* |
| 8137 | BAÑO *m* DE FUSIÓN |
| 8138 | HORNO *m* DE FUSIÓN |

| | |
|---|---|
| 8139 | HIELO *m* QUE SE DERRITE |
| 8140 | PÉRDIDAS *f pl* DE FUSIÓN, MERMAS *f* DE FUSIÓN |
| 8141 | PUNTO *m* DE FUSIÓN |
| 8142 | CRISOL *m* |
| 8143 | INTERVALO *m* DE FUSIÓN |
| 8144 | VELOCIDAD *f* DE FUSIÓN |
| 8145 | ELEMENTO *m* |
| 8145 | ARMADURA *f*, ARMAZÓN *f* |
| 8146 | MEMORIA *f* |
| 8147 | MENISCO *m* CONVERGENTE |
| 8148 | HIERRO *m* COMERCIAL |
| 8149 | PERFILES *m pl* COMERCIALES |
| 8150 | BARÓMETRO *m* DE MERCURIO |
| 8151 | MANÓMETRO *m* DE MERCURIO |
| 8152 | TERMÓMETRO *m* DE MERCURIO |
| 8153 | SUBLIMADO *m* CORROSIVO |
| 8153 | DICLORURO *m* DE MERCURIO |
| 8153 | CLORURO MERCÚRICO *m* |
| 8154 | FULMINATO *m* DE MERCURIO |
| 8155 | YODURO *m* DE MERCURIO |
| 8156 | NITRATO *m* DE MERCURIO |
| 8156 | NITRATO *m* MERCÚRICO |
| 8157 | ÓXIDO *m* MERCÚRICO |
| 8157 | ÓXIDO *m* DE MERCURIO |
| 8158 | SULFATO *m* MERCÚRICO |
| 8159 | CALOMELANOS *m* |
| 8159 | CLORURO MERCUROSO *m* |
| 8159 | PROTOCLORURO *m* DE MERCURIO |
| 8160 | NITRATO *m* MERCURIOSO |
| 8160 | NITRATO *m* MERCURIOSO |
| 8161 | ÓXIDO *m* MERCURIOSO |
| 8161 | PROTÓXIDO *m* DE MERCURIO |
| 8162 | SULFATO *m* MERCÚRIOSO |
| 8163 | BOMBA *f* DE MERCURIO |
| 8164 | RECTIFICADOR *m* DE VAPOR DE MERCURIO |
| 8165 | CÉLULA (O CELDA) AL MERCURIO *f* |
| 8166 | CONTACTOR DE MERCURIO *m* |
| 8167 | LÁMPARA *f* DE VAPOR DE MERCURIO |
| 8168 | MERCURIO *m* |
| 8169 | REJILLA (DE UNA CRIBA) *f* |
| 8170 | REJILLA *f* (DE UN TAMIZ) |
| 8170 | REJILLA *f* DE UNA TELA METÁLICA |
| 8171 | EMBRAGADO, ACOPLADO |
| 8172 | METACENTRO *m* |
| 8173 | METAL *m* |
| 8174 | ARCO *m* METÁLICO |
| 8175 | CORTE POR ARCO METÁLICO *m* |
| 8176 | SOLDADURA *f* AL ARCO ELÉCTRICO |
| 8177 | CABLE DE FUNDA METÁLICA *m* |

| | |
|---|---|
| 8178 | MÁQUINA HERRAMIENTA *f* PARA TRABAJAR LOS METALES |
| 8178 | MÁQUINA *f* PARA METALES |
| 8179 | RELACIÓN *f* DE DISTRIBUCIÓN DEL METAL |
| 8180 | ELECTRODO METÁLICO |
| 8181 | LÁMPARA *f* DE FILAMENTO METÁLICO |
| 8182 | NIEBLA *f* METÁLICA |
| 8183 | BRONCE *m* DE ACUÑACIÓN, BRONCE *m* DE MONEDAS |
| 8184 | HOJA *f* METÁLICA |
| 8185 | METAL *m* PULVERIZADO |
| 8186 | SIERRA *f* DE METALES |
| 8186 | SIERRA *f* DE MONTURA METÁLICA |
| 8187 | TORNILLO *m* DE METALES |
| 8188 | ZAPATA *f* MAGNÉTICA |
| 8189 | REPUJADO *m* |
| 8189 | REPUJADO |
| 8189 | ESTAMPACIÓN *f* DE METALES, EMBUTIDO *m* |
| 8190 | METALIZACIÓN *f* |
| 8191 | TORNO *m* DE METALES |
| 8192 | MECANIZACIÓN *f* DE METALES |
| 8192 | TRABAJO *m* DE LOS METALES |
| 8193 | FRESA *f* AMORTAJADORA |
| 8193 | SIERRA *f* DE ESCOPLEAR |
| 8194 | REVESTIMIENTO *m* METÁLICO |
| 8195 | BRILLO *m* METÁLICO |
| 8196 | GUARNICIÓN *f* METÁLICA |
| 8197 | METALÍFERO |
| 8198 | MINA *f* METÁLICA |
| 8199 | PAPEL *m* METALIZADO |
| 8200 | REVESTIMIENTO *m* METALIZADO |
| 8201 | METALIZACIÓN *f* |
| 8202 | METALOGRÁFICO |
| 8203 | METALOGRAFÍA *f* |
| 8204 | ATAQUE *m* METALOGRÁFICO |
| 8205 | METALOIDE *m* |
| 8206 | METALÚRGICO |
| 8207 | HORNO *m* METALÚRGICO |
| 8208 | METALURGIA *f* |
| 8209 | METALURGIA *f* DEL HIERRO |
| 8209 | SIDERURGIA *f* |
| 8210 | ÁCIDO METAFOSFÓRICO *m* |
| 8211 | ÁCIDO METASILÍCICO *m* |
| 8212 | ESTADO *m* METAESTABLE |
| 8213 | AGUA *f* METEÓRICA |
| 8214 | CONTADOR *m* |
| 8215 | METANO *m* |
| 8215 | GAS *m* DE LOS PANTANOS |
| 8215 | PROTOCARBURO *m* DE HIDROCARBURO DE HIDRÓGENO |
| 8215 | HIDRURO *m* METÍLICO |

| | | | | |
|---|---|---|---|---|
| 8215 | METANO *m* | 8255 | TORNILLO *m* MICROMÉTRICO |
| 8216 | MÉTODO *m* | 8256 | CALIBRE *m* MICROMÉTRICO |
| 8217 | MODO *m* DE ATAQUE | 8257 | MICRÓN |
| 8218 | PROCEDIMIENTO *m* DE FABRICACIÓN | 8257 | MILÉSIMA *f* DE MILÍMETRO |
| 8219 | MÉTODO *m* DE MEDIDA | 8258 | MICROGRAFÍA *f* |
| 8220 | MÉTODO *m* DE TRABAJO, MÉTODO *m* DE LABOREO (MIN) | 8259 | MICROSCOPIO *m* |
| 8220 | MÉTODO *m* | 8260 | EXAMEN *m* MICROSCÓPICO |
| 8220 | MODO *m* OPERATORIO, MODO DE ACTUAR | 8261 | CORTE MICROGRÁFICO *m* |
| 8221 | CLORURO DE METILO *m* | 8262 | MICROESTRUCTURA |
| 8222 | ÓXIDO *m* DE METILO | 8263 | MICRÓTOMO *m* |
| 8222 | OXIDO *m* DE METILO, ETER METÍLICO | 8264 | MICROVOLTIO *m* |
| 8223 | HELIANTINA *f* | 8265 | POSICIÓN *f* MEDIA |
| 8223 | HELIANTINA *f* | 8265 | POSICIÓN *f* INTERMEDIA |
| 8224 | ALCOHOL DESNATURALIZADO *m*, ALCOHOL DE QUEMAR *m* | 8265 | POSICIÓN *f* INTERMEDIA |
| | | 8266 | LIMA *f* DE TALLA MEDIA |
| 8225 | METRO *m* (UNIDAD DE MEDIDA) | 8267 | FRAGMENTOS *m* MENUDOS |
| 8226 | METRO *m* RÍGIDO | 8268 | MIGRACIÓN *f*, EMIGRACIÓN *f* |
| 8226 | METRO *m* | 8269 | ABRASIVO DULCE *m* |
| 8226 | METRO *m* RECTO | 8270 | ACERO DULCE (SUAVE) *m* |
| 8227 | MEDIDA *f* MÉTRICA | 8271 | ENMOHECIMIENTO *m*, MOHO *m* |
| 8228 | MICRÓMETRO *m* MÉTRICO | 8272 | MILLA *f* (MEDIDA INGLESA DE LONGITUD) |
| 8229 | SISTEMA *m* MÉTRICO | 8273 | CRISTAL *m* OPACO |
| 8230 | CALIBRE *m* TAMPÓN DE CONO MÉTRICO | 8274 | LECHADA *f* DE CAL, ENLUCIDO *m* |
| 8231 | MICA *f* | 8275 | MÁQUINAS *f pl* PARA ORDEÑAR |
| 8232 | MICASQUISTO *m* | 8276 | FRESAR |
| 8233 | MICANITA *f* | 8277 | MOLETEAR UNA CABEZA DE TORNILLO |
| 8234 | MICROFISURAS *f* | 8278 | ACABADO *m* EN EL LAMINADOR |
| 8235 | SEGREGACIÓN *f* MENOR | 8279 | BATIDURAS *f pl* METÁLICAS |
| 8236 | CONTRAPUNTA MICROMÉTRICA *f* | 8279 | CASCARILLA *f* DE LAMINACIÓN |
| 8237 | MICROAMPERÍMETRO *m* | 8280 | TUERCA *f* MOLETEADA |
| 8238 | MICROAMPERÍO *m* | 8281 | CABEZA *f* ESTRIADA DE UN TORNILLO |
| 8239 | MICRODESTELLO *m* (TUBO DE RAYOS X) | 8282 | ÍNDICE *m* DE MILLER |
| 8240 | BARRA *f* DE ESCARIADO MICROMÉTRICO | 8283 | MILIAMPERIO/METRO *m* |
| 8241 | FOSFATO *m* DE AMONIO Y DE SODIO | 8284 | MILIAMPERIO *m* |
| 8241 | SAL *f* DE FÓSFORO | 8285 | MILÍGRAMO *m* |
| 8241 | SAL *f* MICROCÓSMICA | 8286 | MILÍMETRO *m* |
| 8242 | MICROFARADIO *m* | 8287 | MOLETEADO *m*, TRABAJO *m* CON LA MOLETA |
| 8243 | MICRIGRÁFICO | 8287 | MOLIDO *m*, TRITURACIÓN *f* |
| 8244 | MICROGRAFÍA *f* | 8287 | FRESADO *m* |
| 8245 | MICRODUREZA *f* | 8288 | MOLETEADO *m* DE UNA CABEZA DE TORNILLO |
| 8246 | PRUEBA *f* DE MICRODUREZA | 8289 | FRESA *f* |
| 8247 | MICROHMIO *m* | 8290 | PASADORES *m pl* DE FRESADO |
| 8248 | MICROPULGADA *f* | 8290 | MESAS *f pl* DE FIJACIÓN |
| 8249 | MICRÓMETRO *m* | 8291 | MÁQUINA *f* PARA FRESAR, MÁQUINA *f* FRESADORA |
| 8249 | MICRÓMETRO *m* | | |
| 8250 | PORTAMICRÓMETRO *m* | 8291 | FRESADORA *f* |
| 8251 | CALIBRES MICROMÉTRICOS *m pl* | 8292 | FRESADOR *m* |
| 8252 | MICRÓMETRO *m* DE PROFUNDIDAD | 8293 | TALLER DE FRESADO *m* |
| 8253 | ESCALA *f* CIRCULAR (ESFERA) MICROMÉTRICA | 8294 | MILIVOLTIO *m* |
| 8254 | OCULAR-MICRÓMETRO | 8295 | MOLINOS *m pl*, COMBINADO *m* DE MOLINOS |

8296 MOLINOS/ APLASTADORES *m pl*, QUEBRANTADORAS *f pl*
8297 MOLINOS/ TRITURADORES *m pl*
8298 MUELA *f* DE MOLINO
8299 PIEDRA *f* MOLEÑA
8299 PIEDRA *f* CONCHÍFERA
8300 MINA *f*
8301 MINERAL
8302 ÁCIDO MINERAL *m*
8303 YACIMIENTO *m* MINERO
8303 YACIMIENTO *m* MINERAL
8304 ACEITE *m* MINERAL
8305 MINERAL *m* POBRE DE HIERRO, MINERAL *m* COLÍTICO
8306 TEMPERATURA *f* MÍNIMA
8307 VALOR *m* MÍNIMO
8308 LÍMITE *m* ELÁSTICO MÍNIMO GARANTIZADO
8309 LONGITUD *f* MÍNIMA DE ONDA
8310 PESO *m* MÍNIMO
8311 EXPLOTACIÓN *f* MINERA
8311 INDUSTRIA *f* MINERA, LABOREO *m* DE MINAS
8312 INGENIERO *m* DE MINAS
8313 EJE *m* PEQUEÑO DE UNA ELIPSE
8314 DIÁMETRO *m* INTERIOR
8315 DETERMINANTE MENOR
8316 MINUENDO *m*
8317 GROSOR *m* MÍNIMO DEL GRANO
8318 CALEFACCIÓN POR VAPOR A PRESIÓN INFERIOR A LA PRESIÓN ATMOSFÉRICA *f*
8319 FUNCIÓN *f* AUXILIAR
8320 METAL *m* MISCH
8321 DESECHO *m*, PIEZA *f* NO LOGRADA
8321 DESHECHO, DESPERDICIO *m*
8322 PIEZA *f* FORJADA CON EXCESIVAS REBABAS
8323 ENGRANAJES *m pl* CONCURRENTES
8324 ENSAMBLADURA A INGLETE *f*, UNIÓN *f* A BISEL

8325 CARTABÓN *m* DE INGLETE
8326 INGLETE *m*
8327 MEZCLADO
8328 MEZCLAR
8328 AGITAR
8329 CRISTALES *m pl* MIXTOS
8330 TURBINA *f* MIXTA
8330 TURBINA *f* AMERICANA
8331 MEZCLADOR *m*
8332 MEZCLADORES *m pl*
8333 CUCHARA *f* MEZCLADORA
8334 MEZCLADOR *m*
8334 MEZCLADOR *m*, AMASADOR *m*
8335 GRIFO *m* MEZCLADOR
8336 MEZCLA *f* (QUÍMICA)
8336 MEZCLA *f* (ACCIÓN)

8337 MEZCLA *f* CARBURO
8338 MODULADOR *m*, MODEM
8338 MODEM *m*, MODULADOR *m*
8338 DESMODULADOR *m*
8339 MÓDULO *m*
8340 MEDIDA *f* DE ELASTICIDAD
8340 COEFICIENTE DE RESISTENCIA AL ALARGAMIENTO *m*
8341 MÓDULO *m* DE ELASTICIDAD
8342 MÓDULO *m* DE CORTE
8342 MÓDULO *m* DE DESLIZAMIENTO
8343 MÓDULO *m* DE RUPTURA
8344 ARADO *m* DE SUBSUELO
8344 ESCARIFICADOR *m*
8345 SUJECIÓN *f* DE MOHR
8346 ESCALA *f* (DE DUREZA) DE MOHS
8347 HUMECTAR, HUMEDECER, REMOJAR
8347 HUMECTAR
8348 HUMECTACIÓN *f*
8348 HUMECTACIÓN *f*, REMOJO *m*
8349 HIDRÓFUGO
8349 IMPERMEABLE A LA HUMEDAD
8350 CONDUCTANCIA MOL(ECUL)AR *f*
8351 RESISTENCIA *f* MOLECULAR
8352 MOLDE *m*
8353 CAVIDAD DEL MOLDE *f*
8354 CINCHA *f*, CINCHO *m* DE UNA RUEDA
8355 ENLUCIDO *m* DE LINGOTERAS
8356 PESO *m* DE CARGA
8357 SONDA *f* DE MOLDEADOR
8358 MÁQUINA *f* DE MOLDEAR
8359 ATRACCIÓN *f* MOLECULAR
8360 FUERZA *f* MOLECULAR
8361 ESTRUCTURA *f* MOLECULAR
8362 VOLUMEN *m* MOLECULAR
8363 PESO *m* MOLECULAR
8364 MOLÉCULA *f*
8365 METAL *m* EN FUSIÓN
8365 MATERIA *f* EN FUSIÓN
8366 MOLIBDENITA *f*
8367 MOLIBDENO *m*
8368 ACERO AL MOLIBDENO *m*
8369 ÁCIDO MOLÍBDICO *m*
8370 MOMENTO *m* DE UNA FUERZA
8371 MOMENTO *m* DE FROTACIÓN O DE ROCE
8372 MOMENTO *m* DE INERCIA
8373 MOMENTO *m* DE LA MAGNITUD DE MOVIMIENTO
8374 MOMENTO *m* DE RESISTENCIA
8374 PAR RESISTENTE *m*
8374 PAR REACCIÓN *m*
8375 MOMENTO *m* DE ESTABILIDAD

| | |
|---|---|
| 8376 | CANTIDAD *f* DE MOVIMIENTO |
| 8377 | MONOATÓMICO |
| 8377 | UNIVALENTE |
| 8378 | GAS *m* MOND |
| 8379 | METAL *m* MONEL |
| 8379 | MONEL *m*, ALEACIÓN DE NÍQUEL, HIERRO Y COBRE |
| 8380 | ENFRIADOR *m* DEL AGUJERO DE ESCORIA |
| 8381 | PARED *f* DE LA CAJA DE ENFRIAMIENTO |
| 8382 | PODER *m* EMISIVO MONOCROMÁTICO |
| 8383 | IRRADIACIÓN *f* MONOCROMÁTICA |
| 8384 | CRISTAL *m* MONOCLÍNICO |
| 8385 | GUARNICIÓN *f* MONOLÍTICA |
| 8386 | REACCIÓN *f* MONOTECTOIDE |
| 8387 | MONOTRON *m* |
| 8388 | MONOTRÓPICO *m*, MONOTROPE *m*, TRANSPOSICIÓN (QUIM) |
| 8389 | ELEVADOR *m* TUBULAR A PRESIÓN DE JUGOS (REFINERÍA AZUCARERA) |
| 8390 | FONDEADERO *m* |
| 8391 | MORDIENTE *m* |
| 8392 | CALIBRE *m* TAMPÓN DE CONO NORMAL (CONO MORSE) |
| 8393 | CALIBRE DE CONICIDAD NORMAL *m* |
| 8394 | MORTERO *m* (PARA CONSTRUCCIÓN) |
| 8395 | MORTERO *m* DE LABORATORIO (DE PORCELANA O ÁGATA) |
| 8396 | MORTERO *m*, ALMIREZ *m* (DE BRONCE) |
| 8397 | AFUSTE DE MORTERO *m* |
| 8398 | ESCOPLO *m* PUNZÓN *m* |
| 8399 | GRAMIL *m* DE ENSAMBLADO |
| 8400 | RUEDA *f* DE DIENTES DE MADERA |
| 8401 | MORTAJA *f*, MUESCA *f* |
| 8402 | MORTAJADORA *f* PARA MADERA |
| 8403 | ESTRUCTURA *f* MOSAICA |
| 8404 | GRANALLA *f* DE CINC |
| 8405 | AGUA *f* MADRE |
| 8405 | AGUA *f* MADRE (SALINAS *f pl*) |
| 8406 | MOVIMIENTO *m*, ACCIÓN *f*, ACTIVIDAD *f* |
| 8407 | MOVIMIENTO *m* DE TRANSLACIÓN |
| 8408 | AGENTE MOTRIZ, MATERIAL DE EXPLOTACIÓN *m* |
| 8409 | FUERZA *f* MOTRIZ |
| 8409 | POTENCIA *f* MOTRIZ |
| 8410 | AUTOBÚS *m* |
| 8411 | AUTOMÓVIL *m* |
| 8411 | AUTOMÓVIL *m* |
| 8411 | COCHE *m* AUTOMÓVIL |
| 8412 | AUTOCAR *m* |
| 8413 | MOTOR *m* GENERADOR, MOTOR-GENERADOR |
| 8413 | GRUPO *m* MOTOR-GENERADOR |
| 8414 | CAMIÓN AUTOMÓVIL *m* |
| 8414 | AUTOMÓVIL *m* INDUSTRIAL |

| | |
|---|---|
| 8415 | ACEITE *m* PARA MOTOR |
| 8416 | VÁLVULA *f* MOTORIZADA |
| 8417 | GRIFO *m* DE MOTOR |
| 8418 | (MOTOR DE) ARRANQUE *m*, ARRANCADOR *m* |
| 8419 | PUESTA *f* A PUNTO, AJUSTE |
| 8420 | FUNDICIÓN *f* MOTEADA |
| 8421 | LICUATURA *f*, LICUADO *m* |
| 8422 | LINGOTERA *f* |
| 8422 | CALIBRE PARA PERFILES *m* |
| 8423 | MOLDE *m* (FUND) |
| 8423 | TIERRA *f* VEGETAL |
| 8424 | MOLDEAR |
| 8425 | LADRILLO *m* PERFILADO |
| 8426 | HORMIGÓN *m* MOLDEADO |
| 8427 | MOLDEADOR *m* |
| 8427 | OBRERO *m* MOLDEADOR |
| 8428 | VACIADO *m* |
| 8429 | MÁQUINA *f* DE MOLDURAR, DE HACER MOLDURAS |
| 8429 | MÁQUINA *f* DE MOLDEAR |
| 8430 | ARENA *f* DE MOLDEADO |
| 8430 | ARENA *f* DE FUNDICIÓN |
| 8431 | HACER UN CALCO |
| 8432 | SUSPENDIDO SOBRE UN GORRÓN |
| 8432 | QUE REPOSA |
| 8433 | SOPLETE DE BOCA *m* |
| 8434 | EMBOCADURA *f* DE UN CEPILLO |
| 8435 | POLEA *f* MÓVIL (DE UN APAREJO) |
| 8436 | RODILLO *m* |
| 8437 | MORDAZA *f* MÓVIL DE TORNILLO DE BANCO |
| 8438 | MOVIMIENTO *m* |
| 8439 | SEGADORAS *f pl* ARRASTRADAS POR TRACTOR, MONTADAS Y SEMIMONTADAS |
| 8440 | EXTRACTO *m* MUCILAGINOSO |
| 8440 | MUCÍLAGO *m* |
| 8441 | BARRA *f* DE HIERRO BRUTO, TOCHO *m* LAMINADO |
| 8441 | HIERRO *m* PUDELADO EN BARRAS |
| 8442 | AGUJERO *m* DE VACIADO |
| 8443 | GUARDABARROS *m* |
| 8444 | LODO *m* |
| 8444 | FANGOS *m pl*, BARROS *m pl* |
| 8445 | FANGOSO *m*, FANGOSA *f* |
| 8446 | AGUA *f* LODOSA, AGUA FANGOSA |
| 8447 | HORNO *m* DE MUFLA |
| 8448 | SILENCIADOR *m* |
| 8448 | SILENCIADOR *m* |
| 8449 | MEZCLADORA *f* |
| 8450 | FROTADO *m* |
| 8451 | FROTADOR *m*, TRITURADOR *m* |
| 8452 | INYECTOR *m* DE AGUJEROS |
| 8453 | MOTOR *m* POLICILINDROS |

| | |
|---|---|
| 8454 | FRENO *m* DE DISCO |
| 8454 | FRENO *m* DE DISCO |
| 8455 | SOLDADURA *f* DE PASADAS MÚLTIPLES |
| 8456 | MÁQUINA *f* MÚLTIPLE |
| 8457 | MÁQUINA *f* DE PERFILAR CON RODILLOS MÚLTIPLES |
| 8458 | CABEZAL *m* DE TALADRADO MULTIBROCAS |
| 8459 | CABEZAL *m* MULTIBROCAS |
| 8460 | PERFORADORA *f* MULTIHUSILLO EN LÍNEA, CON HUSILLOS MÚLTIPLES |
| 8461 | PRENSAS *f pl* DE TRANSFERENCIA DE PUNZONES MÚLTIPLES |
| 8462 | CORRIENTE POLIFÁSICA *f* |
| 8463 | CORREA DE VARIOS ESPESORES *f* |
| 8463 | CORREA MÚLTIPLE *f* |
| 8464 | SOLDADURA *f* POR PUNTOS MÚLTIPLES |
| 8465 | INTEGRAL *f* MÚLTIPLE |
| 8466 | MOLDE *m* MÚLTIPLE |
| 8467 | GRIFO *m* DE DISTRIBUCIÓN |
| 8468 | SOLDADURA *f* POR RESALTES MÚLTIPLES |
| 8469 | TORNO *m* AUTOMÁTICO DE HUSILLOS MÚLTIPLES |
| 8470 | MÁQUINA *f* DE TALADRAR CON MANDRILES MÚLTIPLES |
| 8471 | FRESADORA *f* MÚLTIPLE |
| 8472 | SISTEMA *m* MÚLTIPLE |
| 8473 | TRANSMISIÓN *f* POR POLEAS DE GARGANTAS MÚLTIPLES |
| 8474 | TORNILLO *m* DE ROSCA MÚLTIPLE |
| 8475 | VÁLVULA *f* CON ETAPAS |
| 8476 | VÁLVULA *f* MÚLTIPLE |
| 8477 | MÁQUINA *f* CON MÚLTIPLE EXPANSIÓN |
| 8478 | CIGÜEÑAL *m* DE VARIOS CODOS |
| 8479 | MULTIPLICANDO *m* |
| 8480 | MULTIPLICACIÓN *f* |
| 8481 | REPRODUCCIÓN *f* |
| 8482 | MULTIPLICADOR *m* |
| 8483 | MULTIPLICAR |
| 8484 | REPRODUCIR |
| 8486 | METAL *m* MUNTZ |
| 8487 | CALCÁREA *f* DE MUSCHEL, CALCÁREA *f* CONCHÍFERA (MIN) |
| 8487 | CALIZA COQUILLAR *f* |
| 8488 | ESTADO *m* PASTOSO, FASE *f* PASTOSA |
| 8489 | INDUCCIÓN *f* MUTUA |
| 8490 | PUDINGA *f*, CONGLOMERADO *m* |
| 8491 | CLAVO *m* |
| 8492 | CLAVAR |
| 8493 | NAFTA *f* |
| 8494 | NAFTALINA *f* |
| 8494 | NAFTALENO *m* |
| 8495 | NAFTOL *m* |
| 8496 | FRESA *f* DE DISCO |

| | |
|---|---|
| 8497 | LIBERARSE (AL) (QUIM.) |
| 8497 | NACIENTE *m*, NATIVO (MINERAL) |
| 8498 | ALEACIÓN NATURAL *f* |
| 8499 | ABRASIVO NATURAL *m* |
| 8500 | ENVEJECIMIENTO *m* NATURAL |
| 8501 | TIRO *m* NATURAL |
| 8502 | EVAPORACIÓN *f* AL AIRE LIBRE |
| 8503 | COMBUSTIBLE NATURAL *m* |
| 8504 | GAS *m* NATURAL |
| 8505 | ILUMINACIÓN *f* NATURAL |
| 8506 | PIEDRA *f* IMÁN |
| 8506 | IMÁN NATURAL *m* |
| 8507 | PIEDRA *f* NATURAL |
| 8508 | VENTILACIÓN *f* NATURAL |
| 8509 | LOGARITMO *m* NATURAL |
| 8509 | LOGARITMO *m* HIPERBÓLICO |
| 8510 | CONSTRUCCIÓN NAVAL *f* |
| 8511 | LATÓN *m* NAVAL |
| 8511 | LATÓN *m* ALFA-BETA |
| 8512 | CUELLO *m* |
| 8512 | CUELLO *m* |
| 8513 | MUÑÓN *m* GIRATORIO INTERMEDIO |
| 8514 | TUBULADURA *f* DE COLLAR |
| 8515 | COLLARINO *m*, EJECUCIÓN *f* DE UNA GARGANTA |
| 8515 | ESTRICCIÓN *f* |
| 8516 | ESTRICCIÓN *f* |
| 8517 | PARTÍCULA *f* ACIDULAR |
| 8518 | RODAMIENTO *m* DE AGUJAS |
| 8519 | LIMA *f* AGUJA |
| 8520 | CUENCO *m* DE VIDRIO CON VARILLA |
| 8520 | ENGRASADOR *m* DE VÁSTAGO |
| 8520 | ENGRASADOR *m* DE AGUJA |
| 8521 | BRAZO *m* PORTAAGUJA DE UN COMPÁS |
| 8522 | PUNZÓN *m* |
| 8522 | GRIFO *m* DE AGUJA |
| 8523 | ACERO DE ESTRUCTURA ACICULAR *m* |
| 8524 | CLISÉ FOTOGRÁFICO *m*, NEGATIVO *m* |
| 8524 | PRUEBA *f* NEGATIVA |
| 8525 | ACELERACIÓN NEGATIVA *f* |
| 8526 | ELECTRICIDAD *f* NEGATIVA |
| 8527 | TEMPLA *m* NEGATIVO |
| 8528 | CALOR DE DESCOMPOSICIÓN *m* |
| 8529 | MATRIZ *f* NEGATIVA |
| 8530 | PLACA *f* NEGATIVA |
| 8531 | POLO *m* NEGATIVO |
| 8532 | SIGNO *m* NEGATIVO |
| 8533 | NEODIMIO *m* |
| 8534 | NEODIMIO *m* |
| 8535 | NEÓN *m* |
| 8536 | LÁMPARA *f* DE NEON |

| | |
|---|---|
| 8537 | ANÁLISIS NEFELOMÉTRICO *m* |
| 8538 | HAZ *m* DE TUBOS |
| 8539 | ESTRUCTURA *f* RETICULAR |
| 8540 | BANDAS *f pl* DE NEUMANN |
| 8541 | FIBRA *f* NEUTRA |
| 8542 | FIBRA *f* NEUTRA |
| 8543 | LLAMA NORMAL |
| 8543 | LLAMA *f* NEUTRA |
| 8544 | CAPA O ESTRATO DE LAS FIBRAS INVARIABLES *f* |
| 8545 | LÍNEA *f* NEUTRA |
| 8546 | SAL *f* NEUTRA |
| 8547 | ZONA *f* NEUTRA |
| 8548 | NEUTRALIZACIÓN *f* |
| 8549 | NEUTRALIZAR |
| 8550 | LINO *m* DE NUEVA ZELANDA |
| 8551 | COMPACTO TERMINADO *m* |
| 8552 | ROEDURA *f* |
| 8553 | ROEDERA *f* |
| 8554 | ENTALLAR, SANGRAR |
| 8554 | PRACTICAR UNA ENTALLADURA EN UNA PIEZA |
| 8554 | ENTALLAR, HACER UNA MUESCA |
| 8555 | PRUEBA *f* DE FLEXIÓN EN PIEZA ENTALLADA |
| 8556 | NÍQUEL *m* |
| 8557 | ALEACIÓN DE BASE DE NÍQUEL *f* |
| 8558 | SULFATO *m* DOBLE DE NÍQUEL Y AMONIACO |
| 8559 | LATÓN *m* AL NÍQUEL |
| 8560 | BRONCE *m* AL NÍQUEL |
| 8561 | CARBONILO DE NÍQUEL *m* |
| 8562 | CLORURO NIQUELOSO *m* |
| 8563 | MATA *f* DE NÍQUEL |
| 8564 | MINERAL *m* DE NÍQUEL |
| 8565 | PROTÓXIDO DE NÍQUEL |
| 8566 | NIQUELAR |
| 8567 | NIQUELADO *m* |
| 8567 | CHAPEADO *m* DE NÍQUEL |
| 8568 | GRANALLA *f* DE NÍQUEL |
| 8569 | ALPACA *f* |
| 8569 | NÍQUEL PLATA *m* |
| 8569 | METAL *m* BLANCO, ALPACA *f* |
| 8570 | ACERO AL NÍQUEL *m* |
| 8571 | SULFATO *m* DE NÍQUEL |
| 8572 | BRONCE *m* DE NÍQUEL Y ALUMINIO |
| 8573 | ACERO NIQUELADO *m* |
| 8574 | ÓXIDO *m* DE NÍQUEL |
| 8575 | TRABAJO *m* NOCTURNO |
| 8575 | TRABAJO *m* DE NOCHE |
| 8576 | NIOBIO *m*, COLUMBIO *m* |
| 8577 | ÁNGULO DE CONTACTO *m*, ÁNGULO DE ATAQUE *m* |
| 8578 | RACOR *m* MACHO |

| | |
|---|---|
| 8578 | MAMELÓN *m* |
| 8579 | NITRATO *m* |
| 8579 | NITRATO *m* |
| 8580 | AGUA *f* FUERTE, ÁCIDO *m* NÍTRICO |
| 8580 | ÁCIDO NÍTRICO *m* |
| 8580 | ÁCIDO NÍTRICO *m* |
| 8581 | BIÓXIDO DE NITRÓGENO *m*, NOTROSILO *m* |
| 8581 | ÓXIDO *m* NÍTRICO, ÓXIDO *m* AZOICO |
| 8582 | TEMPLE *m* POR NITRURACIÓN |
| 8583 | ATMÓSFERA DE NITRURACIÓN *f* |
| 8584 | HORNO *m* DE NITRURACIÓN |
| 8585 | ACERO NITRURADO *m* |
| 8586 | NITRITO *m* |
| 8586 | NITRITO *m* |
| 8587 | NITROBENCINA *f* |
| 8587 | NITROBENCENO *m* |
| 8587 | ESENCIA *f* DE MIRBANA, NITROBENCINA *f* |
| 8588 | NITRÓGENO *m* |
| 8588 | NITRÓGENO *m* |
| 8589 | NITRURACIÓN *f* |
| 8590 | ÁCIDO NÍTRICO ANHIDRO *m* |
| 8590 | ANHÍDRIDO NÍTRICO *m* |
| 8591 | PERÓXIDO DE NITRÓGENO *m* |
| 8591 | HIPOAZOIDE *m*, HIPONITROIDE *m* |
| 8591 | HIPOAZOICO *m*, HIPOMÍTRICO *m* |
| 8591 | PERÓXIDO *m* DE NITRÓGENO |
| 8591 | NITROXILO *m* |
| 8592 | ANHÍDRIDO NITROSO *m* |
| 8593 | NITROGLICERINA *f*, TRINITRINA *f* |
| 8593 | TRINITRINA *f* |
| 8594 | NITRÓMETRO *m* |
| 8595 | MEZCLA *f* SULFONÍTRICA |
| 8596 | ÁCIDO NITROSO *m* |
| 8597 | PROTÓXIDO *m* DE NITRÓGENO |
| 8597 | ÓXIDO *m* NITROSO |
| 8598 | MARCHA *f* DE VACÍO |
| 8599 | PÉRDIDA *f* EN VACÍO |
| 8600 | RESISTENCIA *f* EN LA MARCHA EN VACÍO |
| 8601 | TRABAJO *m* EN VACÍO |
| 8602 | METAL *m* NOBLE O PRECIOSO |
| 8603 | METAL *m* PRECIOSO |
| 8604 | CÍRCULO DE PUNTO NEUTRO *m* (CÁLCULO DE ARMAZONES DE RESISTENCIA A PRESIÓN) *m* |
| 8605 | NODO *m* DE OSCILACIÓN |
| 8605 | NODO *m* DE VIBRACIÓN |
| 8606 | NODULAR |
| 8606 | ESFEROIDAL |
| 8607 | FUNDICIÓN *f* NODULAR |
| 8608 | RUIDO *m* |
| 8609 | MARCHA *f* SILENCIOSA |
| 8610 | MARCHA *f* RUIDOSA |

| | | | |
|---|---|---|---|
| 8611 | DIÁMETRO *m* NOMINAL | 8655 | CARGA NORMAL *f* |
| 8612 | DIMENSIÓN *f* NOMINAL | 8656 | FOSFATO *m* DE MAGNESIA |
| 8613 | PRESIÓN *f* NOMINAL | 8657 | PRESIÓN *f* NORMAL |
| 8614 | TIMBRE *m* DE UN DEPÓSITO (A PRESIÓN) | 8658 | CAUDAL *m* NORMAL |
| 8615 | ORIFICIO *m* NOMINAL | 8659 | VOLTAJE *m* NORMAL |
| 8615 | DIMENSIÓN *f* (TAMAÑO *m*) NOMINAL | 8660 | SEGREGACIÓN *f* MAYOR |
| 8616 | VALOR *m* NOMINAL | 8661 | CARGA NORMAL *f* |
| 8617 | ÁBACO *m* | 8662 | NORMAL *f* DE UNA CURVA |
| 8618 | ELECTRODO *m* NO CONSUMIBLE | 8663 | VELOCIDAD *f* DE RÉGIMEN |
| 8619 | ALEACIÓN NO FERROSA *f* | 8663 | VELOCIDAD *f* NORMAL DE FUNCIONAMIENTO |
| 8620 | INCLUSIONES *f* NO METÁLICAS | 8663 | RÉGIMEN *m* DE VELOCIDAD |
| 8621 | INERTE | 8664 | RECOCIDO *m* PARA EMPLEO NORMAL |
| 8622 | ALEACIÓN NO REFRACTARIA *f* | 8665 | POLO *m* NORTE DE UN IMÁN |
| 8623 | VARILLA *f* FIJA | 8666 | PUNTA *f* DE UNA HERRAMIENTA |
| 8624 | VÁLVULA *f* DE VÁSTAGO FIJO | 8667 | PICO *m* |
| 8625 | CALIBRE (NO VARIABLE) *m* | 8667 | TACÓN *m* |
| 8626 | HULLA *f* SEMIGRASA | 8668 | ENTALLADURA *f*, CORTE *m* |
| 8627 | MÁQUINA *f* SIN CONDENSACIÓN | 8669 | FRAGILIDAD *f* A LA ENTALLADURA |
| 8627 | ESCAPE *m* LIBRE, ESCAPE ABIERTO | 8670 | SENSIBLIDAD *f* AL EFECTO DE ENTALLADURA |
| 8628 | AISLADOR TÉRMICO *m*, MATERIAL CALORÍFUGO *m* | 8671 | RESILIENCIA *f* |
| 8629 | MECANISMO *m* DE MANDO ELÁSTICO | 8671 | TENACIDAD *f* A LA ENTALLADURA |
| 8630 | ENSAYO *m* NO DESTRUCTIVO | 8672 | ENTALLADURA *f* |
| 8631 | NO FERROSO | 8672 | RANURA *f*, MUESCA *f* |
| 8632 | METAL *m* CON EXCLUSIÓN DEL HIERRO | 8672 | ENTALLE *m*, CORTE *m* |
| 8632 | METAL *m* CON EXCLUSIÓN DEL HIERRO | 8672 | MUESCA *f*, ENTALLADURA *f* |
| 8633 | VÁLVULA ANTIHIELO *f* | 8673 | PRUEBA *f* DE CHOQUE EN BARRA ENTALLADA |
| 8634 | INCONGELABILIDAD *f* | 8673 | PRUEBA *f* DE RESISTENCIA A LOS CHOQUES |
| 8635 | INCONGELABLE | 8674 | LINGOTE *m* ENTALLADO |
| 8636 | LLAMA *f* NO LUMINOSA, LLAMA *f* OXIDANTE | 8675 | BARRA *f* DE PRUEBA ENTALLADA |
| 8636 | LLAMA *f* INCOLORA | 8675 | BARRA *f* ENTALLADA |
| 8636 | LLAMA *f* NO LUMINOSA, LLAMA *f* OXIDANTE | 8676 | ENTALLADURA *f*, MORTAJADO *m* |
| 8637 | AMAGNÉTICO, ANTIMAGNÉTICO | 8677 | GRUJIDOR *m* |
| 8638 | ACERO NO MAGNÉTICO *m* | 8678 | MOLDE *m* DE ABAJO |
| 8639 | NO METÁLICO | 8679 | PATAS *f pl* DE UN MUEBLE |
| 8640 | METALOIDE *m* | 8679 | TUBULADURA *f* |
| 8641 | REVESTIMIENTO *m* NO METÁLICO | 8679 | LANZA *f*, TOBERA *f* |
| 8642 | MANDO ELÁSTICO *m* | 8679 | LANZA *f*, MANGA *f* |
| 8643 | SOLDADURA *f* POR FUSIÓN | 8680 | ALTURA *f* DE TOBERA |
| 8644 | ACERO INOXIDABLE *m* | 8681 | MÁQUINA *f* PARA TALADRAR LAS TOBERAS |
| 8645 | SISTEMA *m* ANTIDESLIZANTE | 8682 | PORTAINYECTOR *m* |
| 8646 | CABLE ANTIGIRATORIO *m* | 8683 | TUBULADURA *f* DE COLLAR |
| 8647 | MOVIMIENTO *m* SIN UNIFORMIDAD | 8684 | AGUJA DE INYECTOR *f* |
| 8648 | MOVIMIENTO *m* ACELERADO SIN UNIFORMIDAD | 8685 | TOBERA *f* |
| 8649 | MOVIMIENTO *m* RETARDADO SIN UNIFORMIDAD | 8685 | TOBERA *f*, HILERA *f* |
| 8650 | MOLDE *m* NO METÁLICO | 8686 | RESORTE *m* DE INYECTOR |
| 8651 | NUDO *m* CORREDIZO | 8687 | GERMINACIÓN *f* |
| 8652 | NORMAL *f* (GEOM.) | 8688 | GERMEN *m* (DE CRISTAL) |
| 8653 | ACELERACIÓN NORMAL *f* | 8688 | NÚCLEO CRISTALINO |
| 8654 | SECCIÓN *f* NORMAL | 8689 | NÚMERO *m* DE UN LOGARITMO |
| 8654 | SECCIÓN *f* RECTA | 8690 | NÚMERO *m* DE VUELTAS, NÚMERO *m* DE REVOLUCIONES |

| | |
|---|---|
| 8690 | REVOLUCIONES  *f pl* POR MINUTO |
| 8691 | NÚMERO  *m* DE DIENTES |
| 8692 | NÚMERO  *m* DE ROSCAS O DE PASOS DE ROSCA |
| 8693 | NUMERADOR  *m* |
| 8694 | SOLUCIÓN  *f* POR EL CÁLCULO |
| 8695 | SISTEMA  *m* DE MANDO NUMÉRICO |
| 8696 | DATOS  *m pl* NUMÉRICOS |
| 8697 | VALOR  *m* NUMÉRICO |
| 8698 | TUERCA  *f* |
| 8699 | TORNO  *m* DE ATERRAJAR TUERCAS |
| 8700 | TUERCA  *f* PRENSADA |
| 8701 | MECANISMO  *m* DE APRETADO DE LAS TUERCAS |
| 8701 | FRENO  *m* DE TUERCA |
| 8702 | NUTACIÓN  *f* |
| 8703 | JUNTA  *f* TÓRICA, JUNTA  *f* ABOCELADA |
| 8704 | CUERO  *m* CURTIDO CON CÁSCARA DE ROBLE |
| 8705 | OBELISCO  *m* |
| 8706 | PUNTO  *m* DE OBJETO |
| 8707 | ACCIÓN DE NULIDAD RELATIVA  *f* |
| 8708 | SISTEMA  *m* OBJETIVO |
| 8708 | OBJETIVO  *m* |
| 8708 | VIDRIO, CRISTAL  *m* |
| 8709 | CONO OBLICUO  *m* |
| 8710 | COORDINADAS OBLICUAS  *f pl* |
| 8711 | SECCIÓN  *f* OBLICUA |
| 8712 | CILINDRO  *m* OBLÍCUO |
| 8713 | PARALELEPÍPEDO  *m* OBLÍCUO |
| 8714 | MORTAJA  *f* DE EXTREMOS REDONDEADOS |
| 8714 | AGUJERO  *m* OBLONGO |
| 8715 | OBLONGO  *m* |
| 8716 | OBSIDIANA  *f* |
| 8717 | ÁNGULO OBTUSO  *m* |
| 8718 | TRIÁNGULO  *m* OBTUSÁNGULO |
| 8719 | OCLUSIÓN (QUIM) |
| 8720 | OCRE  *m* |
| 8720 | OCRE  *m*, LÁPIZ  *m* DE HEMATITES |
| 8720 | LÁPIZ  *m* ROJO |
| 8720 | SANGUINA  *f* |
| 8721 | OCTÓGONO  *m* |
| 8721 | OCTÁNGULO  *m* |
| 8722 | OCTAEDRO  *m* |
| 8723 | OCTANAJE |
| 8724 | OCTANTE  *m*, OCTAVA PARTE DE UN CÍRCULO |
| 8725 | NÚMERO  *m* IMPAR, NÚMERO  *m* NON |
| 8726 | ODONTÓGRAFO  *m* |
| 8727 | DIMENSIÓN  *f* (DE UNA) |
| 8728 | DIMENSIONES  *f pl* (EN TRES) |
| 8729 | DIMENSIONES  *f pl* (DE DOS) |
| 8730 | DESCENTRADO, DESPLAZADO |
| 8730 | DESCENTRADO |
| 8730 | DESCENTRADO |

| | |
|---|---|
| 8731 | DESCENTRADO |
| 8731 | FUERA DE EJE, DESCENTRADO |
| 8732 | COLADA PERDIDA  *f* |
| 8733 | FUNDICIÓN  *f* DE TRANSICIÓN |
| 8734 | INTERRUPCIÓN DE CORRIENTE  *f*, CORTE DE CORRIENTE  *m* |
| 8734 | TIEMPO  *m* DE REPOSO |
| 8735 | TRATAMIENTO  *m* INDIRECTO |
| 8736 | PUERTO  *m* DE DESCARA (DE NAVÍOS MERCANTES) |
| 8737 | DEFECTO  *m* DE ALINEACIÓN O DESNIVELACIÓN  *f* (DE UNA JUNTA SOLDADA) |
| 8738 | ALTA MAR (EN) |
| 8738 | MAR (EN) |
| 8739 | ACERO PARA PLATAFORMA DE SONDEO EN ALTA MAR  *m* |
| 8740 | PRUEBA  *f* OFICIAL |
| 8741 | ARCO EN ESCARPA  *m* |
| 8742 | OHMIO  *m* |
| 8743 | ACEITE  *m* |
| 8744 | ACEITAR |
| 8744 | ACEITES  *m pl* |
| 8745 | BAÑO  *m* DE ACEITE |
| 8746 | FILTRO  *m* DE AIRE CON BAÑO DE ACEITE |
| 8747 | INDICADOR  *m* CON RETORNO AL BAÑO DE ACEITE |
| 8748 | PAÑOLES  *m* DE COMBUSTIBLE |
| 8749 | ACEITERA  *f* |
| 8749 | ACEITERA  *f* |
| 8750 | SEGMENTO  *m* RASCADOR |
| 8751 | ENFRIADOR  *m* DE ACEITE |
| 8752 | ENFRIAMIENTO  *m* EN EL ACEITE |
| 8753 | ACEITERA  *f* |
| 8753 | ENGRASADOR  *m* |
| 8753 | ENGRASADOR  *m* |
| 8754 | COLCHÓN  *m* DE ACEITE, LECHO  *m* DE ACEITE |
| 8755 | FRENO  *m* DE ACEITE |
| 8755 | FRENO  *m* HIDRÁULICO |
| 8756 | MOTOR  *m* DE CARBURANTE |
| 8757 | FILTRO  *m* DE ACEITE |
| 8758 | GAS  *m* RICO |
| 8758 | GAS  *m* DE ACEITE |
| 8759 | CONDUCTO  *f* DE ENGRASE |
| 8760 | TEMPLE  *m* AL ACEITE |
| 8760 | TEMPLE  *m* DULCE |
| 8761 | AGUJERO  *m* ENGRASADOR |
| 8761 | ORIFICIO  *m* DE ENGRASE |
| 8762 | PERFORADOR  *m* EN CONDUCTO DE ACEITE |
| 8763 | TURBINA  *f* DE RETORNO DE ACEITE |
| 8764 | INDICADOR  *m* DEL NIVEL DE ACEITE |
| 8765 | AGUARRÁS  *m*, ACEITE  *m* (O ESENCIA) DE TREMENTINA |

| | |
|---|---|
| 8766 | PINTURA *f* AL ACEITE, PINTURA *f* AL ÓLEO |
| 8767 | CARTER DE ACEITE (INFERIOR) *m* |
| 8768 | INDICADOR *m* DE LA PRESIÓN DE ACEITE |
| 8769 | BOMBA *f* HIDRÁULICA |
| 8769 | BOMBA *f* DE ACEITE |
| 8769 | BOMBA *f* DE ENGRASE |
| 8770 | COLADOR *m* DE ACEITE |
| 8771 | MASILLA *f* CON ACEITE |
| 8772 | TEMPLE *m* AL ACEITE |
| 8773 | DEPÓSITO *m* DE ACEITE |
| 8774 | ANILLO *m* DE ENGRASE |
| 8775 | SEGMENTO *m* RASCADOR |
| 8776 | JUNTA *f* DE RETENCIÓN DE ACEITE |
| 8777 | EXTRACCIÓN *f* DEL ACEITE |
| 8778 | SEPARADOR *m* DE ACEITE |
| 8779 | SEPARADOR DE ACEITE PARA VAPOR |
| 8780 | ESQUISTO *m* BITUMINOSO |
| 8780 | NAFTOESQUISTO *m*, PIZARRA *f* BITUMINOSA |
| 8781 | PIEDRA *f* DE AFILAR CON ACEITE |
| 8782 | CARTER DE ACEITE (INFERIOR) *m* |
| 8783 | CONDUCCIÓN DE ACEITE *f* |
| 8784 | JERINGA *f* DE ACEITE |
| 8785 | MÁQUINA *f* PARA PROBAR LOS ACEITES |
| 8786 | ACEITE *m* DE LINAZA HERVIDO |
| 8786 | ACEITE *m* DE LINAZA PARA BARNIZ |
| 8786 | BARNIZ *m* AL ACEITE |
| 8787 | ÍNDICE *m* DE VISCOSIDAD |
| 8788 | PAPEL *m* ACEITADO |
| 8789 | PUNTO *m* QUE LUBRIFICAR |
| 8790 | ANILLO *m* DE LUBRICACIÓN |
| 8791 | ACEITADO *m* |
| 8791 | ACEITADO *m* |
| 8792 | INATACABLE POR EL ACEITE |
| 8793 | PROCEDIMIENTO *m* OLD |
| 8794 | JUNTA *f* OLDHAM |
| 8794 | JUNTA *f* DE DOBLE ROSCA |
| 8795 | ÁCIDO OLEICO *m* |
| 8796 | OLIVINA *f* |
| 8796 | PERIDOTO *m* MIN, OLIVINA *f* |
| 8797 | PRUEBA *f* DE EMBUTIDO ERICKSEN |
| 8798 | GASTOS *m* GENERALES |
| 8799 | TRATAMIENTO *m* DIRECTO |
| 8800 | MONTAJE *m* EN LA PROPIA OBRA (LUGAR DE TRABAJO) |
| 8801 | CALCÁREA *m* PISOLÍTICA |
| 8801 | CALIZA DOLÍTICA *f* |
| 8802 | OPACIDAD *f* |
| 8803 | OPACO |
| 8804 | CORREA RECTA *f*, CORREA ABIERTA *f* |
| 8804 | CORREA ABIERTA *f* |
| 8805 | EXCÉNTRICA *f* (O LEVA *f*) ABIERTA |

| | |
|---|---|
| 8806 | HIDROCARBUROS *m pl* DE SERIE GRASA |
| 8807 | CANAL ABIERTO *m* |
| 8807 | CANALIZACIÓN LIBRE *f* |
| 8808 | TENSIÓN *f* EN VACÍO |
| 8809 | SOLDADURA *f* DE ÁNGULO ABIERTA |
| 8810 | MATRIZ *f* ABIERTA |
| 8811 | SOLDADURA *f* EN K CON SEPARACIÓN |
| 8812 | SOLDADURA *f* DOBLE ABIERTA |
| 8813 | FUEGO *m* DIRECTO |
| 8814 | PRENSA *f* MECÁNICA DE BASTIDOR EN CUELLO DE CISNE |
| 8815 | HORNO *m* MARTÍN |
| 8816 | ACERO MARTIN |
| 8817 | SISTEMA *m* DE MANDO EN CIRCUITO ABIERTO |
| 8818 | MOTOR *m* ABIERTO, MOTOR *m* DESCUBIERTO |
| 8818 | MOTOR *m* NO PROTEGIDO |
| 8819 | HIERRO *m* DE GRANO GRUESO |
| 8820 | MOLDEO *m* DESCUBIERTO |
| 8821 | MÁQUINA *f* DE CEPILLAR ABIERTA POR EL LADO |
| 8821 | MÁQUINA *f* DE CEPILLAR CON UN SOLO MONTANTE |
| 8822 | SOLDADURA *f* EN MEDIA V CON SEPARACIÓN |
| 8823 | SOLDADURA *f* EN J CON SEPARACIÓN |
| 8824 | SOLDADURA *f* EN I CON SEPARACIÓN |
| 8825 | ACERO SEMICALMADO *m* |
| 8826 | ABRIR EL CIRCUITO ELÉCTRICO |
| 8827 | MANÓMETRO *m* DE AIRE LIBRE |
| 8828 | PRENSA *f* HIDRÁULICA DE CUELLO DE CISNE |
| 8828 | PRENSA *f* HIDRÁULICA DE CUELLO DE CISNE |
| 8829 | HORNO *m* MARTÍN |
| 8830 | PROCEDIMIENTO *m* SIEMENS-MARTÍN |
| 8831 | ABERTURA *f* |
| 8832 | APERTURA *f* DE LA VÁLVULA |
| 8833 | PALANCA *f* DE MANIOBRA |
| 8834 | CONDICIONES DE SERVICIO *f pl*, CONDICIONES DE OPERACIÓN *f pl* |
| 8835 | REGLAS *f pl* DE SERVICIO |
| 8835 | INSTRUCCIONES *f pl*, NORMAS *f pl* |
| 8836 | TEMPERATURA *f* DE SERVICIO |
| 8836 | TEMPERATURA *f* DE TRABAJO |
| 8837 | EXPLOTACIÓN *f* |
| 8837 | FUNCIONAMIENTO *m* (DE SERVICIO) |
| 8837 | SERVICIO *m* |
| 8838 | NÚMERO *m* DE LA OPERACIÓN EN CURSO |
| 8839 | PUESTO *m* DEL OBRERO |
| 8839 | PUESTO *m* |
| 8840 | ÓPTICA *f* |
| 8841 | EJE *m* ÓPTICO |
| 8842 | COMPARADOR ÓPTICO *m* |
| 8843 | PLANO *m* ÓPTICO |
| 8844 | INSTRUMENTO *m* DE ÓPTICA |

| | |
|---|---|
| 8845 | PIRÓMETRO *m* ÓPTICO |
| 8846 | PIROMETRÍA *f* ÓPTICA |
| 8847 | LECTORES *m pl* ÓPTICOS |
| 8848 | SISTEMA *m* ÓPTICO |
| 8849 | ÓPTICA *f* |
| 8850 | PARADA *f* FACULTATIVA |
| 8851 | EFECTO *m* DE MONDA DE NARANJA |
| 8852 | ORDEN *f* DE MAGNITUD |
| 8853 | ÓXIDO *m* DE ETILO |
| 8853 | ETER *m* ORDINARIO |
| 8853 | ETER SULFÚRICO |
| 8854 | MORTERO *m* DE CAL (QUE SE ENDURECE AL AIRE) |
| 8855 | CADENA CORRIENTE *f* |
| 8856 | ÁCIDO SULFÚRICO DEL COMERCIO *m* |
| 8857 | RÉGIMEN *m* |
| 8858 | ORDENADA *f* |
| 8859 | MINERAL *m* |
| 8860 | BRIQUETA *f* DE MINERAL |
| 8860 | BRIQUETA *f* DE MINERAL |
| 8861 | CONCENTRACIÓN *f* (O ENRIQUECIMIENTO *m*) DEL MINERAL |
| 8861 | TRATAMIENTO *m* MECÁNICO |
| 8861 | PREPARACIÓN *f* DE LOS MINERALES |
| 8862 | TUESTE *m* DEL MINERAL |
| 8863 | MINERALES *m pl* Y FUNDIENTES *m* |
| 8864 | ÁCIDO ORGÁNICO *m* |
| 8865 | QUÍMICA ORGÁNICA *f* |
| 8866 | MATERIA *f* ORGÁNICA |
| 8867 | ORIENTACIÓN *f* |
| 8868 | ORIGEN *m* DE LAS COORDENADAS |
| 8869 | TORNEADO *m* DE SUPERFICIES CON FIGURAS |
| 8870 | PROYECCIÓN *f* ORTOGONAL |
| 8871 | EJES *m pl* CRISTALINOS ORTOHEXAGONALES |
| 8872 | REPRESENTACIÓN *f* EXACTA |
| 8873 | ÁCIDO ORTOFOSFÓRICO *m* |
| 8874 | CRISTALES *m pl* ORTORRÓMBICOS |
| 8875 | ÁCIDO ORTOSILÍCICO *m* |
| 8876 | ÁCIDO TÚNGSTICO *m* |
| 8877 | OSCILAR |
| 8877 | VIBRAR |
| 8878 | LEVA OSCILANTE *f* |
| 8879 | MÉTODO *m* DE CRISTAL OSCILANTE |
| 8880 | MÁQUINA *f* CON CILINDRO OSCILANTE |
| 8881 | MOVIMIENTO *m* OSCILATORIO |
| 8882 | PISTÓN *m* OSCILANTE |
| 8883 | VIBRACIONES *f pl* DEBIDAS A LA RESONANCIA |
| 8884 | VIBRACIÓN *f* |
| 8884 | OSCILACIÓN *f* |
| 8885 | OSCILÓGRAFO *m* |
| 8886 | OSCILOSCOPIO *m* |

| | |
|---|---|
| 8887 | PLANO *m* OSCULADOR |
| 8888 | OSMIRIDIO *m* |
| 8889 | OSMIO *m* |
| 8890 | ÓSMOSIS *f* |
| 8891 | PRESIÓN *f* OSMÓTICA |
| 8892 | DESENGRANADO, DESACOPLADO |
| 8893 | DESCENTRADO |
| 8894 | DESREDONDEZ *f* |
| 8895 | FUERA DE ESCUADRA |
| 8896 | CAUDAL *m* |
| 8897 | ALUMBRADO *m* EXTERIOR |
| 8898 | ANILLO *m* EXTERIOR DEL COJINETE DE BOLAS |
| 8899 | SALIDA *f* DEL AGUA, DESAGÜE *m* |
| 8900 | SALIDA *f* |
| 8901 | TUBULADURA *f* DE SALIDA |
| 8902 | ORIFICIO *m* DE DESCARGA |
| 8902 | ORIFICIO *m* DE SALIDA |
| 8902 | ORIFICIO *m* DE ESCAPE |
| 8902 | ORIFICIO *m* DE SALIDA |
| 8903 | VELOCIDAD *f* DE CIRCULACIÓN |
| 8903 | VELOCIDAD *f* DE SALIDA |
| 8903 | VELOCIDAD *f* A LA SALIDA |
| 8904 | PRESA *f* DE SALIDA |
| 8905 | PLANO *m* DE CONJUNTO |
| 8905 | PLANO *m* DE CONJUNTO |
| 8905 | DIBUJO *m* LINEAL |
| 8905 | DIBUJO *m* LINEAL |
| 8906 | PERFIL *m* |
| 8906 | CONTORNO DE UNA LEVA *m* |
| 8907 | CONTORNO *m* |
| 8908 | CAUDAL *m* |
| 8909 | REGULADOR *m* DE POTENCIA |
| 8909 | REGULADOR *m* DE GASTO |
| 8910 | ÁRBOL SECUNDARIO *m*, ÁRBOL DE TRANSMISIÓN *m* |
| 8911 | LADO EXTERIOR *m* |
| 8912 | COMPÁS DE GRUESOS *m* COMPÁS DE EXTERIORES *m* |
| 8913 | DIÁMETRO *m* EXTERIOR |
| 8914 | VÁLVULA *f* DE TORNILLO EXTERIOR |
| 8915 | VÁSTAGO *m* DE TORNILLO EXTERIOR |
| 8916 | HIERRO *m* EN BARRAS PARA CLAVOS |
| 8916 | HIERRO *m* OVALADO |
| 8917 | SECCIÓN *f* OVAL |
| 8918 | BRIDA *f* OVALADA |
| 8919 | TORNO *m* PARA ÓVALOS |
| 8920 | HORNO *m* |
| 8921 | MULTIPLICADOR *m* DE VELOCIDAD |
| 8922 | DIMENSIONES *f pl* TOTALES |
| 8923 | SOBREENVEJECIMIENTO *m* |
| 8924 | ALTURA *f* DE CONSTRUCCIÓN |

| | |
|---|---|
| 8924 | ALTURA *f* TOTAL |
| 8925 | LARGURA *f* DE CONSTRUCCIÓN |
| 8925 | LARGURA *f* TOTAL |
| 8926 | ANCHURA *f* DE CONSTRUCCIÓN |
| 8926 | ANCHURA *f* TOTAL |
| 8927 | RENDIMIENTO *m* TOTAL |
| 8928 | SOBREPASAR |
| 8928 | PESAR MÁS QUE..., ULTRAPASAR |
| 8929 | VENCER UNA RESISTENCIA |
| 8930 | VELOCIDAD *f* MULTIPLICADA |
| 8931 | REBOSADERO *m* |
| 8931 | VERTEDERO *m*, ALIVIADERO *m*, REBOSADERO *m* |
| 8932 | REBOSADERO *m* |
| 8932 | TUBO *m* DE REBOSADERO |
| 8933 | VÁLVULA *f* DE REBOSADERO |
| 8934 | VOLADIZO, EN FALSO |
| 8935 | CILINDRO *m* SOBRESALIENTE (O EN VOLADIZO) |
| 8936 | VOLADIZO, EN FALSO |
| 8937 | REPASAR |
| 8937 | REVISAR |
| 8938 | CABLE AÉREO *m* |
| 8939 | ÁRBOL DE LEVAS EN CULATA *m*, ÁRBOL DE LEVAS EN CABEZA *m* |
| 8940 | TRANSMISIÓN *f* EN EL TECHO |
| 8941 | SOLDADURA *f* EN POSICIÓN TECHO |
| 8942 | PUENTE GRÚA *m* DE FÁBRICA |
| 8943 | VÁLVULAS *f pl* EN CABEZA |
| 8944 | SOLDADURA *f* EN EL TECHO |
| 8945 | ACERO SOBRECALENTADO *m* |
| 8946 | RECALENTIMIENTO *m* |
| 8947 | MANIVELA *f* FRONTAL |
| 8947 | MANIVELA *f* EN EXTREMO |
| 8947 | MANIVELA *f* EN SALEDIZO |
| 8948 | SUPERPOSICIÓN *f*, SOLAPE *m* |
| 8948 | RECUBRIMIENTO *m* |
| 8948 | REBASAMIENTO *m* |
| 8949 | REBABA *f* DE SOLDADURA |
| 8950 | SOLAPAR, CUBRIR |
| 8951 | SOLAPE *m*, RECUBRIMIENTO *m* |
| 8951 | RECUBRIMIENTO *m* |
| 8952 | RECUBIERTO |
| 8953 | SOBRECARGA *f* |
| 8954 | SOBRECARGAR |
| 8955 | SUPERPRESIÓN *f* |
| 8955 | PRESIÓN *f* SUPERIOR A LA PRESIÓN AUTORIZADA |
| 8956 | CONTRATOPE *m*, TOPE *m* DE PARACHOQUES |
| 8957 | ACOPLAMIENTO *m* (O EMBRAGUE) DE RUEDA LIBRE |
| 8958 | VIGILANTE *m* |
| 8959 | REBASAMIENTO *m* |

| | |
|---|---|
| 8960 | RUEDA *f* DE CANGILONES |
| 8960 | RUEDA *f* POR ENCIMA |
| 8960 | NORIA *f* |
| 8961 | AUMENTO *m* DE DIMENSIÓN |
| 8962 | SOBRECARGA *f* |
| 8962 | FATIGAR (O SOBRECARGAR) UN MATERIAL |
| 8963 | SOBRECARGA *f* |
| 8964 | HORAS *f* SUPLEMENTARIAS |
| 8965 | TRASTORNO *m* (CÁLCULO SOBRE SEÍSMOS) |
| 8966 | MOMENTO *m* DE LA INVERSIÓN |
| 8967 | SOBRETENSIÓN *f* |
| 8968 | OXALATO *m* |
| 8969 | ÁCIDO OXÁLICO *m* |
| 8970 | OXIDACIÓN *f* |
| 8971 | ÓXIDO *m* |
| 8972 | OXIDABLE |
| 8973 | OXIDARSE |
| 8973 | OXIDAR |
| 8974 | OXIDANTE *m* |
| 8975 | DARDO *m* DE SOPLETE |
| 8975 | LLAMA *f* OXIDANTE |
| 8976 | ELIMINACIÓN *f* DE LOS DEFECTOS SUPERFICIALES CON SOPLETE |
| 8977 | OXICORTE *m* |
| 8978 | SOLDADURA *f* AUTÓGENA POR PRESIÓN |
| 8979 | SOLDADURA *f* AUTÓGENA |
| 8979 | SOLDADURA *f* OXIACETILÉNICA |
| 8980 | OXÍGENO *m* |
| 8981 | LANZA *f* DE OXIGENO |
| 8982 | PROCEDIMIENTO *m* CON OXÍGENO |
| 8983 | COBRE *m* EXENTO DE OXÍGENO DE ALTA CONDUCTIVIDAD |
| 8984 | OXIGENACIÓN *f* |
| 8984 | OXIDACIÓN *f* |
| 8985 | GAS *m* OXHÍDRICO |
| 8986 | SOPLETE EXHÍDRICO *m* |
| 8987 | LUZ *f* OXHÍDRICA |
| 8987 | LUZ *f* DE DRUMMOND |
| 8988 | SOLDADURA *f* OXHÍDRICA |
| 8989 | OZONO *m* |
| 8990 | GUARNECER CON MATERIA DE JUNTAS |
| 8991 | EMBALAR |
| 8992 | CEMENTACIÓN CON POLVO *f* |
| 8993 | PELÍCULA *f* RÍGIDA |
| 8993 | PELÍCULA *f* RÍGIDA |
| 8993 | CLISÉ *m* |
| 8994 | LAMINADO *m* EN PAQUETE |
| 8995 | ACONDICIONAMIENTO *m*, ENVASE *m*, EMBALAJE *m* |
| 8996 | ACEITES *m pl* ACONDICIONADOS |
| 8997 | GRIFO *m* DE CANILLA |

| | |
|---|---|
| 8998 | GUARNICIÓN *f* DE JUNTA |
| 8998 | GUARNICIÓN *f* DE VÁLVULA |
| 8999 | REVESTIMIENTO *m* |
| 8999 | EMBALAJE *m* |
| 9000 | PRENSAESTOPAS *m* |
| 9001 | PRENSAESTOPAS *m*, EMPAQUETADURA *f* |
| 9002 | BRIDA *f* DEL PRENSAESTOPAS |
| 9003 | LISTA *f* DE BULTOS |
| 9004 | GUARNICIÓN *f*, EMPAQUETADURA *f* |
| 9004 | GUARNICIÓN *f* |
| 9005 | TUERCA DE PRENSAESTOPA, TUERCA DE EMPAQUETADURA |
| 9006 | PIEZA *f* DE AJUSTE |
| 9007 | ANILLO *m* DE JUNTA |
| 9007 | ANILLO *m* DE ESTANQUEIDAD |
| 9008 | PRENSAESTOPAS *m*, CAPA *f* DE EMPAQUETADURA |
| 9008 | PRENSAESTOPAS *m* |
| 9008 | PRENSAESTOPAS *m* |
| 9009 | JUNTA *f*, EMPAQUETADURA *f* |
| 9009 | GUARNICIÓN *f* |
| 9010 | GRIFO *m* SIN PRENSAESTOPA |
| 9011 | SOLERA *f* DE LOS ALTOS HORNOS |
| 9011 | SOLERA *f* DE ALTO HORNO |
| 9011 | RUGOSIDAD *f*, TAPÓN *m* |
| 9011 | BASE *f*, ZÓCALO *m*, ASIENTO *m* |
| 9011 | ALMOHADILLA *f* |
| 9012 | TUBULADURA *f* AUTOREFORZADA |
| 9013 | PINTURA *f* |
| 9014 | PINTAR *f* CON BROCHA |
| 9014 | PINTAR, APLICAR UNA MANO DE PINTURA |
| 9015 | COLOR *m*, PINTURA *f* |
| 9016 | TUBO *m* PROTEGIDO CON PINTURA |
| 9017 | ASIENTO *m* SUSPENDIDO PARA PINTOR |
| 9018 | PINTURA *f* |
| 9018 | PINTURA *f* CON BROCHA |
| 9019 | PINCEL *m* |
| 9019 | CEPILLO *m* |
| 9020 | PINTURA *f* CON PISTOLA PULVERIZADORA |
| 9021 | DEFECTOS *m pl* DE PINTURA |
| 9022 | COMPÁS *m* |
| 9023 | PALADIO *m* |
| 9024 | CHAPELETA DE VÁLVULA *f* |
| 9025 | CAMIONES PARA TRANSPORTAR BANDEJAS O PALETAS *m pl* |
| 9026 | PALETIZACIÓN *f* |
| 9027 | ACEITE *m* DE PALMA |
| 9028 | ÁCIDO PALMÍTICO *m* |
| 9029 | RECIPIENTE *m* LLANO |
| 9029 | CUBA *f* DE HORNO |
| 9030 | ROBLÓN *m* DE CABEZA TRONCOCÓNICA |

| | |
|---|---|
| 9031 | BOCA *f* DE MARTILLO |
| 9032 | PANEL *m* |
| 9032 | PLACA *f* |
| 9032 | TABLERO *m*, TABLA *f*, PLANCHA *f* |
| 9032 | MALLA *f* |
| 9033 | PANTÓGRAFO *m* |
| 9034 | POLEA *f* DE CARTÓN |
| 9035 | PASTA *f* DE PAPEL |
| 9036 | PASTA *f* DE PAPEL |
| 9036 | PAPEL *m* PODRIDO |
| 9037 | GOMA DE PARA *f* |
| 9038 | PARÁBOLA *f* |
| 9039 | CILINDRO *m* PARABÓLICO |
| 9040 | INTERPOLACIÓN *f* PARABÓLICA |
| 9041 | ESPEJO *m* PARABÓLICO |
| 9042 | PARABOLOIDE *m* DE REVOLUCIÓN |
| 9043 | PARAFINA *f* |
| 9044 | ACEITE *m* DE PARAFINA |
| 9044 | ACEITE *m* PESADO DE PARAFINA |
| 9045 | CERA DE PARAFINA *f* |
| 9046 | MOTOR *m* DE PETRÓLEO |
| 9047 | PARALAJE *m* |
| 9048 | ERROR *m* DE PARALAJE |
| 9049 | PARALELO |
| 9050 | PARALELO |
| 9051 | MONTAJE *m* |
| 9051 | MONTAJE *m* EN PARALELO |
| 9051 | MONTAJE *m* EN SUPERFICIE |
| 9051 | ACOPLAMIENTO EN CANTIDAD *m* |
| 9051 | AGRUPACIÓN *f* |
| 9052 | OPÉRCULO *m* PARALELO CON APRETADO POR MUELLE |
| 9053 | OPÉRCULO *m* PARALELO CON APRETADO MECÁNICO |
| 9054 | ENTRADA *f* EN PARALELO |
| 9055 | CORRIENTE DE FILETES PARALELOS *f* |
| 9056 | FUERZAS *f pl* PARALELAS |
| 9057 | PARALELÓGRAMA *m* ARTICULADO |
| 9058 | PROYECCIÓN *f* PARALELA |
| 9059 | REGLA *f* PARA TRAZAR PARALELAS |
| 9060 | VÁLVULA *f* DE ASIENTOS PARALELOS |
| 9061 | VÁLVULA *f* DE LIBRE DILATACIÓN |
| 9062 | VÁLVULA *f* DE BLOQUEO MECÁNICO |
| 9063 | ASIENTOS *m* PARALELOS |
| 9064 | ÁRBOLES *m pl* PARALELOS |
| 9065 | ROSCADO *m* CILÍNDRICO |
| 9066 | TORNILLO *m* PARALELO |
| 9067 | LIMA *f* ANCHA |
| 9067 | LIMA *f* PLANA DE MANO |
| 9068 | PARALELEPÍPEDO *m* |
| 9069 | PARALELISMO *m* |

| | | | |
|---|---|---|---|
| 9070 | PARALELÓGRAMA *m* | 9112 | PATENTE *f* DE INVENCIÓN |
| 9071 | PARALELÓGRAMA *m* DE LAS FUERZAS | 9113 | PATENTAR |
| 9072 | PARALELÓGRAMA *m* DE LAS VELOCIDADES | 9114 | AGENTE DE PATENTES DE INVENCIÓN *m* |
| 9073 | PARAMAGNÉTICO | 9115 | DERECHOS *m* DE PATENTE |
| 9074 | PARAMAGNETISMO *m* | 9116 | PATENTES *f pl* DE INVENCIÓN (LEY SOBRE LAS) |
| 9075 | PARÁMETRO *m* | 9117 | CUERO *m* CHAROLADO |
| 9075 | CARACTERÍSTICA *f* | 9118 | PLANEO *m* |
| 9076 | GALVANIZACIÓN *f* PARCIAL | 9119 | ESPECIALIDAD *f* FARMACÉUTICA |
| 9077 | PERGAMINO *m* | 9120 | PATENTES *f pl* DE INVENCIÓN (OFICINA DE LAS) |
| 9078 | PAPIRINA *f*, PERGAMINO *m* ARTIFICIAL | 9121 | DERECHOS *m pl* DE PATENTE |
| 9078 | PAPEL *m* PERGAMINO | 9122 | INVENTO *m* DIGNO DE PATENTE |
| 9078 | PERGAMINO *m* VEGETAL | 9122 | APTO PARA SER PATENTADO |
| 9079 | METAL *m* DE ORIGEN | 9123 | PATENTADO *m* |
| 9080 | FORMÓN DE CARPINTERO *m*, ESCOPLO *m* | 9124 | TEMPLE *m* DE LOS ALAMBRES DE ACERO |
| 9081 | CONTROL DE PARIDAD *m* | 9125 | CAMINO *m* SEGUIDO POR UN FLUIDO |
| 9082 | FRENO *m* DE MANO | 9126 | MICROBIO *m* PATÓGENO, BACTERIA *f* PATÓGENA |
| 9082 | FRENO *m* DE ESTACIONAMIENTO | | |
| 9083 | PIEZA *f* | 9127 | PÁTINA *f* |
| 9084 | PROGRAMACIÓN *f* DE PIEZA | 9128 | MODELO *m* |
| 9085 | TURBINA *f* DE ADMISIÓN PARCIAL | 9128 | GÁLIBO *m* |
| 9086 | ECUACIÓN *f* DIFERENCIAL PARCIAL | 9128 | DIAGRAMA *m* DE RX |
| 9087 | PRESIÓN *f* PARCIAL | 9129 | MODELO *m* PARA FUNDICIÓN, MODELADO |
| 9088 | PARTÍCULA *f* | 9130 | OBRERO *m* MODELADOR |
| 9089 | GROSOR *m* DE LA PARTÍCULA | 9131 | CARPINTERÍA *f* DE MODELOS (ARTE) |
| 9090 | COMPOSICIÓN GRANULOMÉTRICA *f* | 9132 | CARPINTERÍA *f* DE MODELOS (TALLER) |
| 9091 | PRECIPITACIÓN *f* | 9133 | MODELO *m* |
| 9092 | LUBRIFICANTE *m* PARA MOLDE | 9134 | SUPERFICIE *f* PICADA DE LA FUNDICIÓN |
| 9093 | LÍNEA *f* DE JUNTA | 9135 | MODELADO *m* |
| 9093 | PLANO *m* DE JUNTA | 9136 | PAVIMENTO *m* FIRME, SUELO |
| 9094 | ARENA *f* AISLADORA | 9136 | ENLOSADO *m* |
| 9095 | NOMENCLATURA *f* | 9137 | ADOQUÍN *m* |
| 9096 | OPERACIÓN *f* | 9138 | MECANISMO *m* DE TRINQUETE |
| 9096 | PASADA *f* | 9139 | CARGA ÚTIL *f* |
| 9096 | CAPA *f*, PASADA *f* | 9140 | GRANOS *m pl* PARA GASÓGENOS |
| 9097 | SECUENCIA *f* DE CALIBRES | 9141 | RECOGEDORAS *f* DE GUISANTES |
| 9098 | PASO *m* DEL CALOR | 9142 | MATRAZ *m* DE FONDO PLANO |
| 9099 | PASO *m* DE LA LUZ | 9143 | GRIS *m* PERLA, CENICIENTO |
| 9100 | ORIFICIO *m* DE PASO | 9144 | PERLITA *f*, MICROCONSTITUYENTE *m* DE ALEACIONES FERROSAS |
| 9101 | ASCENSOR *m*, MONTACARGAS *m* | | |
| 9102 | LUZ *f* PARA ADELANTAR | 9145 | ACERO PERLÍTICO *m* |
| 9103 | BAÑO *m* DE PASIVACIÓN | 9146 | PERLA *f* |
| 9104 | PELÍCULA *f* PASIVADORA | 9146 | BRILLO *m* ANACARADO |
| 9105 | PASIVACIÓN *f* | 9147 | TURBA *f* |
| 9106 | PASIVADOR *m* | 9148 | BRIQUETA *m* DE TURBA |
| 9107 | PASIVIDAD *f* | 9149 | AGLOMERADO DE TURBA *m* |
| 9108 | PASTA *f* PARA SOLDAR | 9150 | PLACA *f* DE TURBA |
| 9109 | REMIENDO *m* (RESULTADO) | 9151 | TURBA *f* PARA QUEMAR |
| 9109 | REMIENDO *m* | 9152 | GUIJARRO *m*, CANTO *m*, PIEDRA *f* |
| 9110 | REMENDAR | 9153 | NIDO *m* DE GUIJARROS |
| 9111 | REMIENDO *m* | 9154 | SOPORTE *m* DE ASIENTO EN EL SUELO |
| 9111 | REMIENDO *m* (ACCIÓN) | 9155 | CORTEZA *f* |

| | |
|---|---|
| 9156 | DESCORTEZADURA  *f*, DESPEGUE  *m* |
| 9156 | DESCASCADO  *m* |
| 9156 | DESCORTEZAMIENTO  *m*, DESCASCADO  *m* |
| 9157 | MARTILLEO  *m*, MARTILLEADO  *m*, AMARTILLADO  *m* |
| 9157 | INSTALACIÓN  *f* DE VIGAS SOPORTANDO LA CUBIERTA |
| 9158 | REGISTRO  *m* |
| 9159 | CLAVIJA  *f* |
| 9160 | BRAZO  *m* DEL TIRALÍNEAS DEL COMPÁS |
| 9161 | ESTILETE  *m* |
| 9161 | ESTILETE  *m* TRAZADOR |
| 9161 | PLUMA  *f* DE APARATO REGISTRADOR |
| 9161 | TRAZADOR  *m* |
| 9161 | ESTILETE  *m* (DE UN APARATO REGISTRADOR) |
| 9162 | HAZ  *m* LUMINOSO |
| 9162 | HAZ  *m* LUMINOSO |
| 9163 | GOMA  *f* PARA LÁPIZ, GOMA  *f* DE BORRAR |
| 9164 | HAZ  *m* DE RAYOS |
| 9165 | BRAZO  *m* DEL LAPICERO |
| 9165 | PORTALÁPIZ  *m* DE UN COMPÁS |
| 9166 | ASIENTO COLGANTE DE DOS PATAS  *m* |
| 9166 | SOPORTE EN U  *m* |
| 9167 | PÉNDULO  *m* |
| 9168 | REGULADOR  *m* PENDULO |
| 9169 | LÍQUIDO  *m* PENETRANTE |
| 9170 | PENETRACIÓN  *f* |
| 9171 | PENETRÓMETRO  *m* |
| 9172 | PENTÁGONO  *m* |
| 9173 | PRISMA  *f* PENTAGONAL |
| 9174 | PIRÁMIDE  *f* PENTAGONAL |
| 9175 | PENTAEDRO  *m* |
| 9176 | PENTANO  *m* NORMAL |
| 9177 | PENUMBRA  *f* |
| 9178 | POROSIDADES  *f* SUPERFICIALES |
| 9179 | VOLUMEN  *m* (PORCENTAJE DEL) |
| 9180 | PESO  *m* (PORCENTAJE DEL) |
| 9181 | AGUA  *f* DE INFILTRACIÓN |
| 9182 | PRENSA  *f* MECÁNICA PARA GOLPEAR |
| 9183 | SOLDADURA  *f* POR PERCUSIÓN |
| 9184 | COMBUSTIÓN PERFECTA  *f* |
| 9185 | GAS  *m* PERFECTO |
| 9186 | ABRIR AGUJEROS, AGUJEREAR |
| 9186 | PERFORAR, TALADRAR, BARRENAR |
| 9187 | SEPARADOR DE AGUJEROS  *m* |
| 9188 | POLEA  *f* DE LLANTA PERFORADA |
| 9189 | CHAPA  *f* PERFORADA |
| 9189 | CHAPA  *f* CON ABERTURAS |
| 9189 | CHAPA  *f* PERFORADA |
| 9190 | PERÍMETRO  *m* |
| 9191 | PERIÓDICO |

| | |
|---|---|
| 9192 | FRACCIÓN  *f* DECIMAL PERIÓDICA |
| 9193 | VIGILANCIA  *f* DE LAS CALDERAS |
| 9194 | MOVIMIENTO  *m* PERIÓDICO |
| 9195 | ENGRASE  *m* INTERMITENTE |
| 9196 | PERIODICIDAD  *f* |
| 9197 | RESISTENCIA  *f* SEGÚN LA TANGENTE |
| 9198 | VELOCIDAD  *f* PERIFÉRICA |
| 9198 | VELOCIDAD  *f* CIRCULAR |
| 9199 | REACCIÓN  *f* PERITÉCTICA |
| 9200 | FUNDICIÓN  *f* PERLÍTICA |
| 9201 | PERMALLOY  *m* |
| 9202 | DEFORMACIÓN  *f* PERMANENTE |
| 9203 | DUREZA  *f* PERMANENTE DEL AGUA |
| 9204 | IMÁN PERMANENTE  *m* |
| 9205 | PLATILLO  *m* DE IMANES PERMANENTES |
| 9206 | MAGNETISMO  *m* PERMANENTE |
| 9207 | COQUILLA  *f* |
| 9208 | FUNDIDO EN COQUILLA  *m* |
| 9209 | SERVICIO  *m* CONTINUO |
| 9210 | DEFORMACIÓN  *f* PERMANENTE |
| 9211 | PERMEABILIDAD  *f* |
| 9212 | PERMEABLE AL AIRE |
| 9213 | PERMEABLE |
| 9214 | PERMEÁMETRO  *m* |
| 9215 | CARGA ADMITIDA  *f* |
| 9216 | PERMUTACIÓN  *f* |
| 9217 | PERPENDICULAR |
| 9217 | VERTICAL  *f* |
| 9217 | PLOMO (A)  *m*, VERTICALMENTE |
| 9218 | LADO DEL ÁNGULO RECTO  *m* |
| 9219 | PERPENDICULARIDAD  *f* |
| 9219 | PERPENDICULARIDAD  *f*, APLOMO  *m* |
| 9220 | PERSPECTIVO  *m* |
| 9220 | PERSPECTIVA  *f* |
| 9221 | PISÓN  *m* DE MORTERO |
| 9222 | PETRÓLEO  *m* |
| 9222 | GASOLINA  *f*, BENCINA  *f* (DE PETRÓLEO) |
| 9222 | GASOLINA  *f* |
| 9222 | GASOLINA  *f* |
| 9222 | CARBURANTE  *m*, PETRÓLEO  *m* GASOLINA  *f* |
| 9223 | MOTOR  *m* DE BENCINA |
| 9224 | LÁMPARA  *f* DE GASOLINA, LÁMPARA  *f* DE PETRÓLEO |
| 9225 | LOCOMOTORA  *f* DE GASOLINA |
| 9225 | LOCOMOCIÓN  *f* CON BENCINA |
| 9226 | PETRÓLEO  *m* |
| 9227 | LÁMPARA  *f* DE PETRÓLEO |
| 9228 | GASOLINA  *f* |
| 9228 | ETER DE PETRÓLEO, GASOLINA  *f* |
| 9229 | PETRÓLEO  *m* |
| 9229 | ACEITE  *m* DE ROCA, PETRÓLEO  *m* |

| | |
|---|---|
| 9230 | ESTAÑO *m* DURO |
| 9230 | METAL *m* INGLÉS |
| 9231 | PH |
| 9232 | FASE *f* |
| 9233 | ÁNGULO DE FASE *m*, ÁNGULO DE DESFASE *m*, ÁNGULO DE DEFASAJE *m* |
| 9233 | ÁNGULO DE FASE *m*, ÁNGULO DE DESFASE *m*, ÁNGULO DE DEFASAJE *m* |
| 9234 | DESFASAMIENTO *m*, DESPLAZAMIENTO *m* DE FASES |
| 9234 | DESPLAZAMIENTO *m* DE FASE, DESFASADO *m*, DESFASAMIENTO *m* |
| 9235 | INDICADOR *m* DE FASES |
| 9236 | REGLA *f* DE FASES |
| 9237 | DESFASAMIENTO *m*, DESPLAZAMIENTO *m* DE FASE |
| 9238 | FENOLTALEÍNA *f* |
| 9238 | FTALEÍNA *f* DEL FENOL |
| 9239 | PAPEL *m* A LA FENOLFTALEÍNA |
| 9240 | FENÓMENO *m* |
| 9241 | HIERRO *m* EN FORMA DE CUADRANTE |
| 9242 | FONAUTÓGRAFO |
| 9243 | PERIDOTO *m*, CRISOLITA *f* |
| 9243 | OLIVINA *f* |
| 9244 | FOSFATO *m* |
| 9245 | CAPA DE FOSFATO *f* |
| 9246 | BRONCE *m* FOSFOROSO, BRONCE *m* FOSFORADO |
| 9247 | FOSFORESCENCIA *f* |
| 9248 | FOSFORESCENTE |
| 9249 | ANHÍDRIDO FOSFÓRICO *m* |
| 9250 | COBRE *m* FOSFOROSO |
| 9251 | SUBSTANCIAS *f pl* FOSFORESCENTES |
| 9252 | FÓSFORO *m* |
| 9253 | COBRE *m* FOSFOROSO |
| 9254 | PENTACLORURO *m* DE FÓSFORO |
| 9255 | TRIBROMURO *m* DE FÓSFORO |
| 9256 | TRICLORURO *m* DE FÓSFORO |
| 9257 | PAPEL *m* FOTOCALCO |
| 9258 | FOTODIODO *m* |
| 9259 | PILA *f* FOTOELÉCTRICA |
| 9260 | CÉLULA FOTOELÉCTRICA *f* |
| 9261 | CÉLULA FOTOCONDUCTORA *f* |
| 9262 | FOTOGRAFIAR |
| 9263 | FOTOGRAFÍA *f* |
| 9263 | REPRODUCCIÓN *f* FOTOGRÁFICA |
| 9264 | CÁMARA OSCURA *f* |
| 9265 | FOTOGRAFÍA *f* |
| 9266 | MACROFOTOGRAFÍA *f* |
| 9267 | FOTÓMETRO *m* |
| 9268 | BANCO *m* FOTOMÉTRICO |
| 9269 | FOTOMÉTRICO |
| 9270 | UNIDAD *f* FOTOMÉTRICA |

| | |
|---|---|
| 9270 | UNIDAD *f* DE LUZ |
| 9271 | FOTOMETRÍA *f* |
| 9272 | MICROFOTOGRAMA *m* |
| 9273 | CÉLULA FOTOEMISORA *f* |
| 9274 | FOTOMULTIPLICADOR *m* |
| 9275 | FOTÓN *m* |
| 9276 | FOTOCALCO *m* |
| 9276 | FOTOCOPIA *f* |
| 9277 | CÉLULA FOTOVOLTÁICA *f* |
| 9278 | FILITA *f* |
| 9279 | FÍSICA *f* (CIENCIA) |
| 9280 | CAMBIO FÍSICO *m* |
| 9280 | ALTERNACIÓN FÍSICA *f* |
| 9281 | QUÍMICA FÍSICA *f* |
| 9282 | METALURGIA *f* FÍSICA |
| 9283 | PROPIEDADES *f pl* FÍSICAS |
| 9284 | PRUEBA *f* FÍSICA, ENSAYO *m* FÍSICO |
| 9285 | FÍSICO |
| 9286 | QUÍMICA INDUSTRIAL O TECNOLÓGICA *f* |
| 9287 | CUERDA DE ACERO *f*, CUERDA PIANO *f* |
| 9287 | ALAMBRE *m* DE ACERO PARA CUERDAS DE PIANO |
| 9288 | DECAPADO *m* QUÍMICO |
| 9288 | DECAPADO *m* CON ÁCIDO |
| 9289 | BAÑO *m* DE DECAPADO, SOLUCIÓN *f* DE DECAPADO |
| 9289 | BAÑO *m* DE MORDENTACIÓN |
| 9290 | BAÑO *m* DE DECAPAJE ÁCIDO |
| 9290 | SOLUCIÓN *f* ÁCIDA |
| 9291 | ÁCIDO CARBAZÓTICO *m* |
| 9291 | ÁCIDO PÍCRICO *m* |
| 9292 | TROZO *m* DE TUBO |
| 9293 | PIEZA *f* QUE TRABAJAR, PIEZA *f* QUE MECANIZAR |
| 9293 | PIEZA *f* MECANIZADA |
| 9294 | TRABAJO *m* A DESTAJO |
| 9294 | TRABAJO *m* A DESTAJO |
| 9295 | SALARIO *m* A DESTAJO |
| 9295 | SALARIO *m* A DESTAJO |
| 9296 | MÁQUINA *f* PERFORADORA |
| 9297 | PIEZOELECTRICIDAD *f* |
| 9298 | LINGOTE *m* FUNDICIÓN |
| 9299 | FUNDICIÓN *f* BRUTA (EN LINGOTES) |
| 9299 | FUNDICIÓN *f* EN LINGOTES |
| 9300 | PIEL *f* DE CERDO |
| 9301 | GANCHO *m* DE COLA DE CERDO |
| 9302 | LINGOTE *m* FUNDICIÓN |
| 9303 | COLORANTE *m* |
| 9303 | COLOR *m*, COLORANTE *m* |
| 9303 | MATERIA *f* COLORANTE |
| 9304 | PILA *f* |

| | | | |
|---|---|---|---|
| 9305 | LOSA *f* SOPORTE / SOBRE PILOTES | 9340 | CAVIDAD *f* POR CONTRACCIÓN |
| 9306 | HINCADO *m* DE PILOTES | 9341 | CURVADO DE UN TUBO *m* |
| 9307 | APILAR (O AMONTONAR) LA MADERA | 9342 | TUBO *m* COLADO HORIZONTAL |
| 9308 | HORNO *m* DE RECALENTAR POR PAQUETES | 9343 | TUBO *m* COLADO VERTICAL |
| 9309 | APILAMIENTO *m* DE LA MADERA | 9344 | ABRAZADERA (PARA TUBO) *f* |
| 9310 | PASTILLADORA *f* | 9345 | ABRAZADERA DE TUBO *f* |
| 9310 | PRENSA *f* DE PASTILLAS | 9345 | BRIDA A SELLAR O EMPOTRAR *f* |
| 9311 | PILAR *m*, PILASTRA *f*, POSTE *m* | 9346 | SERPENTÍN *m* |
| 9312 | TALADRADORA *f* DE COLUMNA | 9347 | JUNTA *f* DE TUBOS, EMPALME *f* DE TUBOS |
| 9312 | PERFORADORA *f* DE COLUMNA | 9348 | CORTADOR DE TUBOS *m*, CORTATUBOS *m* |
| 9313 | CAJA DEL PALIER *f* | 9349 | MÁQUINA *f* PARA CORTAR LOS TUBOS |
| 9314 | GRANULACIÓN *f* SUPERFICIAL | 9350 | RACOR *m* PARA TUBOS |
| 9315 | PASADOR *m* | 9351 | BRIDA *f* DE TUBO |
| 9315 | PASADOR *m* AGUJA | 9351 | BRIDA *f* DE TUBO |
| 9315 | PASADOR *m* | 9352 | MÁQUINA *f* DE ENSANCHAR LOS TUBOS |
| 9315 | PIVOTE *m* | 9353 | RUPTURA *f* |
| 9315 | PIVOTE *m*, ESPIGA *f*, MUÑON *m*, CLAVIJA *f* | 9353 | ROTURA *f* DE UN TUBO |
| 9316 | BROCA *f* DE ESPIGA CILÍNDRICA | 9354 | GANCHO *m* PARA TUBOS |
| 9317 | CABEZA *f* DE ALFILER | 9355 | JUNTA *f* PARA CAÑERÍA, JUNTA *f* PARA TUBERÍA |
| 9318 | ARTICULACIÓN DE PASADOR *f* | | |
| 9319 | BOTÓN *m* DE MANIVELA, CUELLO *m* DE BIELA DEL CIGÜEÑAL | 9356 | COLOCACIÓN *f* DE TUBOS |
| | | 9357 | TUBERÍA *f* |
| 9319 | CABEZA *m* DE CIGÜEÑAL | 9357 | TUBO *m* DE CONDUCCIÓN |
| 9320 | BULÓN *m* DE UNA CADENA DE RODILLOS | 9357 | TUBERÍAS *f pl* |
| 9320 | ESPÁRRAGO *m* DE UNIÓN DE UNA CADENA DE RODILLOS | 9357 | TUBERÍAS *f pl* |
| | | 9358 | LAMINADOR *m* DE TUBOS |
| 9321 | ROBLONADO *m* CON ESPIGA | 9359 | NORMAS *m* PARA TUBERÍAS |
| 9321 | ROBLONADO *m* CON ROBLÓN SIN CABEZA | 9360 | PASO *m* PARA TUBOS |
| 9322 | LLAVE DE UÑAS EN EXTREMO *f* | 9361 | MÁQUINA *f* PARA ATERRAJAR Y ROSCAR LOS TUBOS |
| 9323 | PIVOTE *m* DE UN ENGRANAJE DE LINTERNA | | |
| 9324 | PIÑÓN *m* DE ENGRANAJES CÓNICOS | 9362 | TENAZAS *f pl* PARA TUBOS |
| 9325 | ENGRANAJE *m* DE LINTERNA | 9363 | TORNILLO *m* PARA TUBOS |
| 9325 | ENGRANAJE *m* DE LINTERNA | 9364 | TUBO *m* SOLDADO A LA AUTÓGENA |
| 9325 | ENGRANAJE *m* DE LINTERNA | 9365 | TUBOS *m pl* DE EMPALMES |
| 9326 | BOTADOR *m*, EXTRACTOR *m* | 9366 | MORDAZA *f* COCODRILO |
| 9327 | PINACOIDE *m* | 9366 | LLAVE DE TUBOS *f* |
| 9328 | TENAZAS *f pl* | 9366 | LLAVE DE TUBOS *f* |
| 9329 | REOSTRICCIÓN *f* | 9367 | TIERRA *f* DE TUBO |
| 9330 | LAMINADO *m* CON DÉBIL PRESIÓN (A PRESIÓN REDUCIDA) | 9368 | PIPETA *f* |
| | | 9369 | SIERRA *f* DE METALES CON MANGO DE PISTOLA |
| 9331 | DENDRITA *f* | 9370 | PISTÓN *m* |
| 9332 | AGUJERO *m* DE EJE O DE CHAVETA | 9371 | ACELERACIÓN DEL PISTÓN *f* |
| 9333 | PICADURA *f* | 9372 | VENTILADOR *m* DE PISTÓN |
| 9334 | PICADURAS *f pl* | 9373 | CUERPO DEL PISTÓN *m* |
| 9335 | PIÑÓN *m* | 9374 | COMPRESOR DE ÉMBOLO *m* |
| 9336 | ARRANCADOR *m* | 9375 | GUARNICIÓN *f* DEL PISTÓN |
| 9337 | PINTA *f* (MEDIDA INGLESA 47 CL.) | 9376 | PASADOR *m* DEL PISTÓN |
| 9338 | INYECTOR *m* DE TETÓN | 9377 | PRESIÓN *f* SOBRE EL ÉMBOLO |
| 9339 | TUBERÍA *f* | 9378 | BOMBA *f* DE ÉMBOLO |
| 9339 | TUBO *m* | 9379 | SEGMENTO *m* DE PISTÓN |
| 9339 | TUBO *m* | 9379 | SEGMENTO *m* DEL PISTÓN |

| | | | |
|---|---|---|---|
| 9380 | SEGMENTO *m* DE ÉMBOLO CON RANURA EN ANGULO RECTO | 9416 | PICADURAS *f pl* |
| 9381 | SEGMENTO *m* DE ÉMBOLO DE JUNTA EN BISEL | 9417 | PICADURA *f* DEL LAMINADO |
| 9382 | SEGMENTO *m* DE ÉMBOLO CON JUNTA SOLAPADA | 9418 | CORROSIÓN LOCALIZADA *f* |
| | | 9419 | PIVOTE *m* |
| 9383 | VÁSTAGO *m* DE ÉMBOLO | 9420 | PIVOTE *m* |
| 9384 | EXTREMIDAD *f*, EXTREMO *m* | 9420 | MUÑÓN *m* GIRATORIO |
| 9384 | COLA *f* DEL VÁSTAGO DEL ÉMBOLO | 9421 | MUÑÓN *m* GIRATORIO DE TOPE PARA TEJUELO |
| 9385 | GUÍA *f* DEL VÁSTAGO DE PISTÓN | 9421 | MUÑÓN *m* GIRATORIO DE APOYO |
| 9386 | GUARNICIÓN *f*, REVESTIMIENTO *m* | 9421 | PIVOTE *m* |
| 9386 | EMPAQUETADURA *f* DEL VÁSTAGO DEL ÉMBOLO | 9421 | PIVOTE *m* (DE ÁRBOL VERTICAL) |
| 9387 | VÁSTAGO *m* DE ÉMBOLO ATRAVESADOR | 9422 | PIVOTANTE |
| 9387 | VÁSTAGO *m* DEL ÉMBOLO BILATERAL | 9423 | LUGAR *m* DE INSTALACIÓN |
| 9388 | VELOCIDAD *f* DEL ÉMBOLO | 9423 | LUGAR *m* DE MONTAJE |
| 9389 | GOLPE DE PISTÓN *m* | 9423 | LUGAR *m* DE INSTALACIÓN |
| 9390 | DISTRIBUIDOR *m* CILÍNDRICO | 9424 | RODAMIENTO *m* LISO |
| 9390 | DISTRIBUIDOR *m* EQUILIBRADO | 9424 | SOPORTE *m* CON COJINETES LISOS |
| 9390 | DISTRIBUIDOR *m* DE ÉMBOLO | 9425 | MANDRIL *m* DE MONTAJE LISO, MANDRIL *m* DE AGUJERO SIMPLE |
| 9390 | PISTÓN *m* DISTRIBUIDOR | 9426 | DISTRIBUIDOR *m* PLANO |
| 9391 | PISTÓN *m* DE DOBLE VÁSTAGO | 9426 | PLANO *m* |
| 9391 | PISTÓN *m* DE DOBLE VÁSTAGO | 9427 | ACERO AL CARBONO *m* |
| 9392 | PISTÓN *m* CON VÁSTAGO ÚNICO | 9428 | TORNO *m* PARALELO |
| 9393 | PICADURA *f* | 9428 | TORNO *m* DE CILINDRAR |
| 9394 | COLADA EN FOSO *f* | 9429 | TORNILLO *m* SENCILLO |
| 9395 | MÁQUINA *f* DE CEPILLAR DE FOSO | 9430 | VISTA *f* DE CONJUNTO |
| 9396 | ARENA *f* DE CANTERA | 9430 | PLANO *m* |
| 9397 | AGUA *f* DE POZO DE MINA | 9430 | PLANO *m*, DIBUJO *m*, VISTA *f* DE CONJUNTO |
| 9398 | POZO *m* (DE MINA) | 9431 | CALIBRE HEMBRA LISO *m* |
| 9399 | PASO *m* DE UNA ROSCA | 9432 | CEPILLO *m* |
| 9400 | PEZ *f* | 9433 | PLANO *m* |
| 9401 | ÁNGULO PRIMITIVO *m* | 9434 | CEPILLAR |
| 9402 | RUEDA *f* | 9435 | CURVA PLANA *f* |
| 9402 | PIÑÓN *m* DE CADENA | 9436 | HIERRO *m* DEL CEPILLO |
| 9403 | CÍRCULO PRIMITIVO DE DENTADURA *m* | 9437 | ESPEJO *m* PLANO |
| 9404 | CÍRCULO PRIMITIVO *m* | 9438 | PLANO *m* DE PROYECCIÓN |
| 9404 | CIRCUNFERENCIA PRIMITIVA *f* | 9439 | PLANO *m* DE REFRACCIÓN |
| 9405 | LIGNITO *m* NEGRO | 9440 | PLANO *m* DE SIMETRÍA |
| 9406 | CONO PRIMITIVO *m* | 9441 | SUPERFICIE *f* PLANA |
| 9407 | DIÁMETRO *m* PRIMITIVO | 9442 | MÁQUINA *f* DE APLANAR Y PULIR |
| 9407 | DIÁMETRO *m* DE PASO DE ROSCA, DIÁMETRO PRIMITIVO | 9443 | ACEPILLADORA *f* |
| | | 9443 | ACEPILLADOR *m* |
| 9408 | PASO *m* DEL ENGRANAJE | 9443 | OBRERO *m* CEPILLADOR |
| 9409 | PASO *m* DE REMACHE | 9444 | PIÑÓN *m*, RUEDA *f* DENTADA |
| 9410 | PASO *m* DE TORNILLO | 9444 | RUEDA *f* PLANETARIA |
| 9410 | PASO *m* DE LA HÉLICE | 9444 | RUEDA *f* SATÉLITE |
| 9411 | PECBLENDA *f*, URANITA *f* | 9444 | SATÉLITE *m* |
| 9411 | URANITA *f*, ÓXIDO *m* NATURAL DE URANIO | 9445 | PLANETARIO *m* |
| 9412 | CADENA CALIBRADA *f* | 9446 | TREN *m* PLANETARIO |
| 9413 | MEOLLO *m* VEGETAL | 9446 | ENGRANAJE *m* (O TREN *m*) PLANETARIO |
| 9414 | PALANCA *f* DE MANDO | 9447 | MOVIMIENTO *m* PLANETARIO |
| 9415 | TUBO *m* DE PITOT | 9447 | SATÉLITE *m* |

| | |
|---|---|
| 9448 | PLANÍMETRO  *m* |
| 9449 | PLANIMETRÍA  *f* |
| 9450 | CEPILLADO  *m* |
| 9450 | CEPILLADURA  *f* |
| 9451 | MÁQUINA  *f* DE CEPILLAR |
| 9451 | APLANADORA, MÁQUINA CEPILLADORA  *f* |
| 9452 | MÁQUINA  *f* DE CEPILLAR |
| 9452 | ACEPILLADORA  *f* |
| 9453 | ACEPILLADORA  *f* FRESADORA |
| 9454 | PLANEO  *m* |
| 9455 | MARTILLO  *m* DE APLANAR |
| 9456 | LAMINADOR  *m* PARA PULIR |
| 9457 | TABLÓN  *m*, MADERO |
| 9457 | PLANCHA  *f* FUERTE |
| 9458 | LENTE AMB. PLANO-CÓNCAVO O PLANA-CÓNCAVA |
| 9459 | LENTE AMB. PLANO-CONVEXO O PLANA-CONVEXA |
| 9460 | FRESADORA  *f* CEPILLADORA |
| 9461 | INSTALACIÓN  *f* INDUSTRIAL (O DE FÁBRICA) |
| 9462 | RENTABILIDAD  *f* |
| 9462 | PROSPERIDAD  *f* ECONÓMICA DE UNA EMPRESA |
| 9463 | ENLUCIDO  *m*, REVOCO  *m* |
| 9464 | ENLUCIR, REVOCAR |
| 9465 | VACIADO  *m* EN ESCAYOLA, MOLDE  *m* DE ESCAYOLA |
| 9466 | YESO  *m*, ESCAYOLA  *f* |
| 9467 | CUERPO PLÁSTICO  *m* |
| 9468 | ALAMBRE  *m* (O HILO  *m*) CON FORRO DE PLÁSTICO |
| 9469 | DEFORMACIÓN  *f* PLÁSTICA |
| 9470 | ARCILLA PLÁSTICA  *f*, BARRO DE ALFAREROS  *m* |
| 9471 | DEFORMACIÓN  *f* PLÁSTICA |
| 9471 | DEFORMACIÓN  *f* PLÁSTICA |
| 9472 | CABLE AISLADO P.V.C.  *m* |
| 9473 | REFRACTARIO PLÁSTICO |
| 9474 | PLASTICIDAD  *f* |
| 9475 | PLASTIFICANTE |
| 9476 | MATERIAS  *f pl* PLÁSTICAS |
| 9477 | PLACA  *f*, PLANCHA  *f*, CHAPA  *f* |
| 9477 | CHAPA  *f* FUERTE |
| 9477 | CHAPA  *f* ESPESA |
| 9478 | CHAPA  *f* PARA EMBUTIDO |
| 9479 | CHAPEAR |
| 9480 | MÁQUINA  *f* DE CURVAR LAS CHAPAS |
| 9481 | PRENSA  *f* PLEGADORA |
| 9482 | LEVA DE PLATILLO  *f* |
| 9482 | LEVA DE DISCO  *f* |
| 9483 | BORDE  *m* DE CHAPA |
| 9484 | MÁQUINA  *f* DE ACHAFLANAR O BISELAR LAS CHAPAS |
| 9485 | MÁQUINA  *f* DE APLANAR LAS CHAPAS |
| 9486 | EMBRAGUE DE DISCOS  *m* |

| | |
|---|---|
| 9486 | ACOPLAMIENTO  *m* DE PLATOS, EMBRAGUE DE PLATOS |
| 9487 | CALIBRE DE UNA CHAPA  *m* |
| 9488 | VIGA  *f* COMPUESTA |
| 9489 | TENSOR  *m* DE VIGAS DE CHAPA |
| 9489 | TIRANTE  *m* |
| 9490 | VIGA  *f* COMPUESTA |
| 9491 | CRISTAL  *m* DE LUNAS |
| 9492 | HOJA  *f* (O LÁMINA  *f*) DE UN RESORTE (O DE UN MUELLE) |
| 9492 | HOJA  *f* DE BALLESTA |
| 9493 | RECORTE DE CHAPA  *m*, CHATARRA  *f* |
| 9494 | CIZALLA PARA CHAPA  *f* |
| 9495 | RESORTE  *m* DE LÁMINA |
| 9496 | DESBARBADURA  *f* DE CHAPA EN BISEL |
| 9497 | LEVAS DE DISCO  *f pl* |
| 9498 | PLAQUITA  *f* |
| 9499 | PLATINA  *f* DE FIJACIÓN |
| 9500 | CHAPAS  *f pl* (ORDEN DE COLOCACIÓN DE LAS) |
| 9501 | RECUBRIMIENTO  *m* DE CHAPAS |
| 9502 | PLATAFORMA  *f* |
| 9503 | CHAPEADO  *m* |
| 9503 | REVESTIMIENTO  *m* METÁLICO POR GALVANOPLASTIA |
| 9504 | PLANO  *m* DE LA CHAPISTERÍA |
| 9505 | CARRETILLA PARA COLGAR PIEZAS A TEMPLAR  *f* |
| 9506 | SALES  *m pl* PARA BAÑOS |
| 9507 | CLORURO PLATÍNICO  *m* |
| 9508 | ACERO PLATINITO (PLATINITA)  *m* |
| 9508 | PLATINITA  *f* (ALEACIÓN) |
| 9509 | CLORURO PLATINOSO  *m* |
| 9510 | PLATINO  *m* (METAL) |
| 9511 | NEGRO  *m* DE PLATINO |
| 9512 | CRISOL  *m* DE PLATINO |
| 9513 | ALAMBRE  *m* (O HILO  *m*) DE PLATINO |
| 9514 | ESPUMA  *f* DE PLATINO |
| 9515 | PLATINO  *m* IRIDIADO |
| 9516 | JUEGO  *m* EN EL MOVIMIENTO |
| 9516 | JUEGO  *m* DE MONTAJE |
| 9516 | JUEGO  *m* ÚTIL, JUEGO  *m* CONVENIENTE |
| 9516 | HOLGURA  *f* |
| 9517 | VENTILACIÓN  *f* POR IMPULSIÓN |
| 9518 | FLEXIBLE |
| 9519 | TRAZAR GRÁFICAMENTE |
| 9520 | TRAZAR UN DIAGRAMA |
| 9520 | LEVANTAR UN DIAGRAMA |
| 9521 | TRAZADO  *m* DE UN DIAGRAMA |
| 9522 | GUILLAME (CARP.)  *m*, CEPILLO  *m* PARA MOLDURAS |
| 9523 | ARADOS DE DISCOS (ARRASTRADOS O PORTADOS)  *m pl*, ESCARIFICADOR DE DISCOS  *m* |

| | |
|---|---|
| 9524 ARADOS MONTADOS *m pl* | 9560 PUNTO *m* EN EL ESPACIO |
| 9525 ARADOS ARRASTRADOS *m pl* | 9561 PUNTO *m* DE APLICACIÓN |
| 9526 ARADOS *m pl* | 9562 PUNTO *m* DE CONTACTO |
| 9526 ARADO *m* BRABANTE, BRABANTE *m* | 9562 PUNTO *m* DE TANGENCIA |
| 9527 ARADOS PARA ALOMAR *m pl* | 9563 PUNTO *m* DE RUPTURA |
| 9528 ACERO DE ARADO *m* | 9564 PUNTO *m* DE INFLEXIÓN |
| 9529 ENCHUFE *m* DE CORRIENTE | 9565 PUNTO *m* DE INTERSECCIÓN |
| 9529 TAPÓN *m*, OBTURADOR *m*, ENCHUFE *m* | 9565 PUNTO *m* DE CONCURSO |
| 9529 ENCHUFE *m* | 9565 PUNTO *m* DE ENCUENTRO |
| 9529 OBTURADOR *m* | 9566 PUNTO *m* DE REFERENCIA |
| 9530 GRIFO *m* DE LLAVE | 9567 PUNTO *m* DE APOYO |
| 9531 CALIBRE *m* | 9568 PUNTO *m* DE SUSPENSIÓN |
| 9532 MACHO *m* DE GRIFO, LLAVE *f* | 9569 CABEZA *f* DEL DIENTE |
| 9532 LLAVE DE GRIFO *f* | 9570 SUSPENSIÓN *f* DE GORRÓN |
| 9533 EJE CUADRADO (PARA LLAVE) *m* | 9571 BURIL *m* BISELADO |
| 9534 TERRAJA *f* CILINDRICA | 9572 MANDO PUNTO A PUNTO *m* |
| 9534 TERRAJA *f* DE ACABADO | 9573 SOLDADOR *m* DE PUNTA |
| 9535 GRIFO *m* DE CANILLA | 9574 CONTACTOS *m pl* |
| 9536 SOLDADURA *f* EN TAPÓN | 9575 ATIZAR |
| 9537 SOLDADURA *f* DE AGUJEROS DE ROBLONES | 9576 SOLDADURA *f* POR PUNTOS CON PISTOLA |
| 9538 PLOMADA *f* | 9576 SOLDADURA *f* CON PINZA |
| 9539 PLOMO *m*, FUSIBLE *m* | 9577 POLAR |
| 9539 PLOMADA *f* | 9578 COORDINADAS POLARES *f pl* |
| 9539 PERPENDÍCULO *m*, PLOMADA *f* | 9579 DISTANCIA *f* POLAR |
| 9540 NIVEL *m* DE HILO, NIVEL *m* DE PLOMADA | 9580 RADIO *m* POLAR |
| 9541 PLOMBAGINA *f* | 9581 TRIÁNGULO *m* POLAR |
| 9541 GRAFITO *m* | 9582 POLARIZACIÓN *f* |
| 9542 PLOMBAGINA *f* | 9583 MICROSCOPIO *m* POLARIZANTE |
| 9542 MINA *f* DE PLOMO | 9584 POLARISCOPIO *m* |
| 9543 COJINETE *m* DE PATÍN | 9585 LUZ *f* POLARIZADA |
| 9544 PUNZÓN *m* | 9586 POLARIZADOR *m* |
| 9545 PISTÓN *m* SUMERGIDO, PISTÓN *m* BUZO | 9586 PRISMA *f* POLARIZADOR |
| 9545 PISTÓN *m* BUZO | 9587 POLARIDAD *f* |
| 9546 BOMBA *f* DE ÉMBOLO DE SUMERSIÓN | 9588 INDICADOR *m* DE DIRECCIÓN DE LA CORRIENTE |
| 9547 RESORTE *m* DE ÉMBOLO CON CUBETA | 9589 POLARIZACIÓN *f* |
| 9548 RECHAZO *m* DE CRIBADO | 9590 POLAROGRAFÍA *f* |
| 9549 NEUMÁTICO *m* | 9591 POLO *m* (ELÉCTR.) |
| 9550 MANDRILES *m* NEUMÁTICOS | 9592 POLO *m* |
| 9551 MARTILLO *m* NEUMÁTICO (O.P.) | 9593 MASAS *f pl* POLARES |
| 9552 MARTINETE *m* | 9594 PAPEL *m* BUSCADOR DE POLOS |
| 9553 MARTILLO *m* NEUMÁTICO | 9594 PAPEL *m* POLO |
| 9553 MARTILLO *m* DE AIRE COMPRIMIDO | 9595 POLO *m* DE UN IMÁN |
| 9554 EYECTOR *m* NEUMÁTICO | 9596 FUERZA *f* POLAR |
| 9554 DESMOLDEO *m* | 9596 INTENSIDAD *f* DE POLO |
| 9554 DESMOLDEO *m* | 9597 TRABAJO *m* AL PANDEO |
| 9555 MARTILLO *m* MECÁNICO POR AIRE COMPRIMIDO | 9598 PULIR |
| 9555 MARTILLO *m* NEUMÁTICO PARA REMACHAR | 9599 PULIDO *m* (CAPAZ DE TOMAR UN) |
| 9556 HERRAMIENTA *f* NEUMÁTICA | 9599 PULIDO *m* (QUE TOMA BIEN EL) |
| 9557 VÁLVULA *f* DE MANDO NEUMÁTICO | 9599 PULIDO *m* (CAPAZ DE UN BUEN) |
| 9558 NEUMÁTICO *m* | 9600 PULIMENTO *m* |
| 9559 PUNTO *m* | 9601 ABRASIVO *m* |

| | |
|---|---|
| 9601 | MATERIA *f* ABRASIVA |
| 9601 | MATERIA *f* PARA PULIR, PARA PULIMENTAR |
| 9602 | TONEL *m* DE PULIR |
| 9603 | MÁQUINA *f* DE PULIR |
| 9604 | RUEDA *f* PULIDORA |
| 9604 | MUELA *f* |
| 9604 | MUELA *f* DE PULIR |
| 9605 | PULIMENTO *m* |
| 9606 | POLONIO *m* |
| 9607 | POLÍCROMO |
| 9608 | METAL *m* POLICRISTALINO |
| 9609 | POLÍGONO *m* |
| 9610 | POLÍGONO *m* DE FUERZAS |
| 9611 | LÍNEA *f* POLIGONAL |
| 9612 | POLIEDRO *m* |
| 9613 | POLÍMERO *m* |
| 9614 | POLIMERIZACIÓN *f* |
| 9615 | POLIMERIZARSE |
| 9616 | POLIMERÍA *f* |
| 9617 | POLIMORFISMO *m* |
| 9618 | CURVA POLITRÓPICA *f* |
| 9619 | PONDERABLE |
| 9620 | AGUJERO *m* DE HOMBRE |
| 9620 | AGUJERO *m* DE INSPECCIÓN DE UN CAJÓN |
| 9621 | ARTESÓN *m* (TEJADO DE) |
| 9622 | JAULA DESBROZADORA *f* |
| 9623 | CAL ANHÍDRA *f* |
| 9624 | ACEITE *m* DE CLAVEL |
| 9625 | PORCELANA *f* |
| 9626 | CRISOL *m* DE PORCELANA |
| 9627 | PORO *m* |
| 9628 | PORÓGENO |
| 9628 | PRODUCTO *m* FORMAND POROSIDADES |
| 9629 | POROSIDAD |
| 9629 | PICADO *m* PROVOCANDO POROSIDAD |
| 9630 | POROSO *m* |
| 9631 | TOBA *f* PORFÍRICA |
| 9632 | PÓRFIRO *m* |
| 9633 | ORIFICIO *m*, ABERTURA *f* |
| 9634 | ORIFICIO *m* DE PASO |
| 9635 | MÓVIL |
| 9635 | QUE RUEDA |
| 9636 | MÁQUINA *f* DE TALADRAR |
| 9636 | TALADRADORA *f* PORTÁTIL |
| 9637 | FORJA *f* VOLANTE |
| 9637 | FORJA *f* PORTÁTIL |
| 9638 | BOMBA *f* PORTÁTIL |
| 9639 | FERROCARRIL DE VÍA ESTRECHA *m* |
| 9639 | LÍNEA *f* DECAUVILLE |
| 9639 | VÍA *f* PORTÁTIL |
| 9639 | VÍA *f* DECAUVILLE |

| | |
|---|---|
| 9640 | LOCOMÓVIL |
| 9641 | PÓRTICO |
| 9641 | GRÚA *f* DE PÓRTICO |
| 9642 | FRESADORA *f* DE PÓRTICO |
| 9643 | TROZO *m* DE ÁRBOL |
| 9644 | CEMENTO PORTLAND *m* |
| 9645 | POSICIÓN *f* DE LA MANIVELA |
| 9646 | POSICIÓN *f* EN PUNTO MUERTO |
| 9647 | POSICIÓN *f* DE EQUILIBRIO |
| 9648 | POSICIÓN *f* DE REPOSO |
| 9649 | SENSOR DE POSICIÓN *m* |
| 9650 | MANDO DE POSICIONAMIENTO *m* |
| 9651 | TIEMPO *m* DE COLOCACIÓN |
| 9652 | ACELERACIÓN POSITIVA *f* |
| 9653 | BOMBA *f* VOLUMÉTRICA |
| 9654 | MANDO POSITIVO *m* |
| 9654 | MANDO MECÁNICO *m*, MANDO POSITIVO *m* |
| 9655 | ELECTRICIDAD *f* POSITIVA |
| 9656 | CALOR DE COMBINACIÓN *m* |
| 9656 | CALOR DE FORMACIÓN *m* |
| 9657 | CATIÓN *m* |
| 9658 | PLACA *f* POSITIVA |
| 9659 | POLO *m* POSITIVO |
| 9660 | LUZ *f* ANÓDICA |
| 9661 | SIGNO *m* POSITIVO |
| 9662 | ELECTRÓN POSITIVO |
| 9663 | COJINETE-CONSOLA *m* SOBRE COLUMNA |
| 9664 | BARRENAS *f pl* |
| 9665 | POSTPROCESOR *m* |
| 9666 | TRATAMIENTO *m* DE REPOSO DESPUÉS DE LA SOLDADURA |
| 9667 | RECOCIDO *m* REDUCTOR DE TENSIÓN |
| 9668 | POSTCALDEO *m* |
| 9669 | HORNO *m* DE CRISOL |
| 9670 | CEMENTACIÓN AL PRUSIATO AMARILLO *f* |
| 9670 | CEMENTACIÓN AL PRUSIATO POTÁSICO *f* |
| 9671 | SOLUCIÓN *f* DE POTASA CÁUSTICA |
| 9671 | LEJÍA *f* DE POTASA |
| 9672 | POTASIO *m* |
| 9673 | ACETATO DE POTASIO *m* |
| 9674 | ALUMINATO DE POTASIO *m* |
| 9675 | TÁRTARO *m* EMÉTICO |
| 9675 | TARTRATO *m* DE POTASA Y ANTIMONIO |
| 9675 | SARRO *m* ANTIMONIAL |
| 9676 | BICARBONATO *m* DE POTASA |
| 9677 | DICROMATO *m* POTÁSICO |
| 9678 | BROMURO *m* DE POTASIO |
| 9679 | CARBONATO POTÁSICO NEUTRO *m* |
| 9679 | POTASA *f* |
| 9680 | CLORATO POTÁSICO *m* |
| 9681 | CLORURO DE POTASIO *m* |

| | |
|---|---|
| 9682 | CROMATO NEUTRO DE POTASIO *m* |
| 9683 | CIANURO *m* DE POTASIO |
| 9684 | PRUSIATO *m* ROJO |
| 9684 | FERROCIANURO *m* DE POTASIO |
| 9685 | FERROCIANURO *m* DE POTASIO |
| 9685 | PRUSIATO *m* AMARILLO |
| 9685 | FERROCIANURO *m* DE POTASIO |
| 9686 | FLUORURO *m* DE POTASIO |
| 9687 | HIDRATO *m* DE POTASIO |
| 9687 | POTASA *f* CÁUSTICA |
| 9688 | CLORURO DE POTASA SOLUCIÓN DE *f* |
| 9689 | YODURO *m* DE POTASIO |
| 9690 | PAPEL *m* YODOALMIDONADO |
| 9691 | NITRITO *m* DE POTASA |
| 9691 | POTASA *f* NITROSA |
| 9691 | POTASA *f* NITROSA |
| 9691 | POTASA *f* NITROSA |
| 9692 | OXALATO *m* NEUTRO DE POTASIO |
| 9693 | PERCARBONATO *m* DE POTASA |
| 9694 | PERCLORATO *m* DE POTASA |
| 9695 | PERMANGANATO *m* DE POTASA |
| 9696 | FOSFATO *m* DE POTASIO |
| 9697 | POLISULFURO *m* DE POTASIO |
| 9698 | SILICATO *m* DE POTASA |
| 9699 | SULFATO *m* DE POTASA |
| 9700 | SULFURO *m* DE POTASA |
| 9701 | SULFOCIANURO *m* DE POTASIO |
| 9702 | APORCADOR *m* DE PATATAS |
| 9703 | LIMPIADORAS *f pl* DE PATATAS |
| 9704 | RECOGEDORAS *f* DE PATATAS |
| 9705 | PLANTADORAS *f pl* DE PATATAS |
| 9706 | CLASIFICADORAS *f pl* DE PATATAS |
| 9707 | ARRANCADORAS *f pl* DE PATATAS |
| 9708 | POTENCIAL *m* |
| 9709 | DIFERENCIA *f* DE POTENCIAL |
| 9709 | TENSIÓN *f* EN LOS ELECTRODOS |
| 9710 | ENERGÍA *f* POTENCIAL |
| 9710 | ENERGÍA *f* LATENTE |
| 9711 | POTENCIÓMETRO *m* |
| 9712 | APLASTAR, RECALCAR, TRITURAR |
| 9712 | TRITURAR, MACHACAR, DESMENUZAR |
| 9713 | ASFALTO *m* FUNDIDO |
| 9714 | HORMIGÓN *m* COLADO |
| 9715 | LECHADA *f*, COLADA *f* |
| 9716 | EMBUDO *m* DE COLADA |
| 9717 | SALIDA *f* EN LINGOTERA |
| 9718 | PRENSA *f* DE COMPRIMIR LOS POLVOS |
| 9719 | CORTE *m* CON POLVO |
| 9720 | METALURGIA *f* DE POLVOS |
| 9721 | MÉTODO *m* DE LOS POLVOS |
| 9722 | SOLDADURA *f* BAJO POLVO |

| | |
|---|---|
| 9723 | ASFALTO *m* PULVERULENTO |
| 9724 | LADRILLO *m* MACHACADO |
| 9725 | MAGNESIA *f* EN POLVO |
| 9726 | TURBA *f* MENUDA |
| 9726 | POLVO *m* DE TURBA |
| 9727 | POLVO *m* DE PÓMEZ |
| 9728 | PULVERULENTO *m* |
| 9729 | POTENCIA *f* (MATEMÁTICAS) |
| 9730 | POTENCIA *f* |
| 9730 | CAPACIDAD *f*, PODER *m* |
| 9730 | EFECTO *m* |
| 9731 | SERVOFRENO *m* |
| 9731 | FRENOS *m* ASISTIDOS |
| 9732 | TALADRO *m* |
| 9732 | PERFORADORA *f* ELÉCTRICA |
| 9733 | FUERZA *f* MOTRIZ |
| 9734 | MANDO MECÁNICO *m* |
| 9734 | ACCIONAMIENTO POR MOTOR *m* |
| 9735 | FACTOR *m* DE POTENCIA |
| 9736 | GAS *m* PARA ACCIONAR LOS MOTORES |
| 9737 | PRODUCCIÓN *f* DE ENERGÍA |
| 9738 | FUERZA *f* DEL HOMBRE |
| 9739 | INSTALACIÓN *f* PARA PRODUCCIÓN DE FUERZA MOTRIZ |
| 9740 | ROBLONADO *m* PARA CONSTRUCCIONES METÁLICAS |
| 9740 | REMACHE *m* DE ENSAMBLADO DE FUERZA |
| 9740 | REMACHE *m* DE FUERZA |
| 9741 | ASIENTO *m* DE REGLAJE AUTOMÁTICO |
| 9742 | FÁBRICA *f* DE FUERZA MOTRIZ |
| 9742 | ESTACIÓN *f* CENTRAL |
| 9742 | ESTACIÓN *f* GENERADORA |
| 9743 | SERVODIRECCIÓN *f* |
| 9743 | SERVODIRECCIÓN *f* |
| 9744 | DISTRIBUCIÓN *f* DE FUERZA MOTRIZ |
| 9745 | TOMA *f* DE FUERZA |
| 9746 | TRANSMISIÓN *f* DE POTENCIA |
| 9747 | SIERRA *f* MECÁNICA |
| 9747 | ASERRADERO *m* MECÁNICO |
| 9747 | MÁQUINA *f* DE SERRAR, MÁQUINA *f* ASERRADORA |
| 9748 | PUZOLANA *f* |
| 9748 | PUZOLANA *f* |
| 9749 | CEMENTO PUZÓLANICO *m* |
| 9750 | PRASEODIMIO *m* |
| 9751 | PREFILTRO *m* |
| 9752 | MECANIZACIÓN *f* PRERREGULADA |
| 9753 | PRECAUCIONES *f pl* |
| 9754 | PRECESIÓN *f* |
| 9755 | AFILADO DE PRECISIÓN *m* |
| 9756 | METAL *m* PRECIOSO |

505

9757 PRECIPITABLE
9758 PRECIPITANTE
9759 PRECIPITADO *m*
9760 PRECIPITARSE
9760 PRECIPITAR
9760 SEPARARSE
9761 PRECIPITACIÓN *f*
9762 ENDURECIMIENTO *m* POR PRECIPITACIÓN
9763 PRECISIÓN *f*
9764 BALANZA *f* DE PRECISIÓN
9765 MOLDEO *m* DE PRECISIÓN
9766 CALIBRE *m* DE PRECISIÓN
9767 REGLA *f* DIVIDIDA DE PRECISIÓN
9768 CALIBRE DE ALTURA DE PRECISIÓN *m*
9769 DIVISOR *m* DE PRECISIÓN
9770 MÁQUINA *f* DE PRECISIÓN
9771 ORIENTACIÓN *f* PREFERENCIAL
9772 PREFORMA *f*
9773 PREFORMADO *m*
9774 PRECALENTAR, CALENTAR PREVIAMENTE
9775 RECALENTAR
9776 PRECALDEO *m*
9776 CALENTAMIENTO PREVIO *m*
9776 EBULLICIÓN *f* PREVIA
9777 HORNO *m* PRECALENTADOR
9778 ENCENDIDO PREMATURO *m*, AVANCE DEL
      ENCENDIDO *m*
9779 PRUEBA *f* PRELIMINAR
9780 TRATAMIENTO *m* PREPARATORIO
9780 TRATAMIENTO *m* PRELIMINAR
9781 DISPOSITIVO *m* DE PRETENSADO
9782 PRECARGA *f*
9782 PRETENSADO *m*
9783 FORRO CUBIERTO PREVIAMENTE DE GRAVA
9784 PREPARACIÓN *f*
9784 PRODUCTO *m*
9785 PREPARACIÓN *f* DE UNA SOLUCIÓN
9786 FUNCIÓN *f* PREPARATORIA
9787 TRABAJOS *m pl* PRELIMINARES
9787 TRABAJOS *m pl* PREPARATORIOS
9787 OPERACIONES *f pl* PREPARATORIAS
9787 OPERACIONES *f pl* PRELIMINARES
9788 PREPARAR UNA SOLUCIÓN
9789 PRESELECCIÓN *f*
9790 CONSERVACIÓN DE LA MADERA *f*
9791 AGENTE DE CONSERVACIÓN *m*
9792 REVESTIMIENTOS *m pl* DE PROTECCIÓN
9793 CAPA PROTECTORA
9794 PRESINTERIZACIÓN *f*
9795 PRENSA *f*
9796 PISTOLAS *f pl* DE AIRE COMPRIMIDO

9797 BOTÓN *m* PULSADOR, PULSADOR *m*
9797 BOTÓN *m* PULSADOR, PULSADOR *m*
9797 BOTÓN *m* DE INTERRUPTOR
9797 PULSADOR *m*
9798 FORJADO *m* A PRENSA
9799 CALCINACIÓN *f* A PRESIÓN
9800 FORJAR A PRENSA
9801 PRESSPAHN *m*
9802 TABLERO *m* DE CORCHO AGLOMERADO
9803 COLLAR *m*, COLLARÍN *m*
9803 COLLAR *m*, COLLARÍN *m*
9804 TURBA *f* COMPRIMIDA
9805 POLEA *f* DE CHAPA EMBUTIDA
9806 PRENSADO *m*
9806 COMPRESIÓN *f*
9807 FORJADO *m* A PRENSA
9808 PRESIÓN *f*
9808 TENSIÓN *f*
9809 PRESIÓN *f* MANOMÉTRICA
9810 ÁNGULO DE ENGRANE DEL FLANCO DEL DIENTE *m*

9811 DEPRESIÓN *f*
9812 MOLDEADO *m* A PRESIÓN
9812 COLADA A PRESIÓN *f*
9813 CONTROLADOR DE PRESIÓN *m*, MANÓMETRO DE
      CONTROL *m*
9814 DIFERENCIA *f* DE PRESIÓN
9815 CAÍDA DE PRESIÓN *f*
9816 PRESIÓN *f* DEBIDA AL ROZAMIENTO
9817 VENTILADOR *m* DE IMPULSIÓN
9817 VENTILADOR *m* DE IMPULSIÓN
9818 ENGRASE *m* A PRESIÓN
9819 GASÓGENO *m* DE AIRE SOPLADO
9820 INDICADOR *m* DE PRESIÓN
9820 MANÓMETRO *m*
9821 MANÓMETRO *m*
9822 PRESIÓN *f* INTERIOR EN UNA CONDUCCIÓN
9823 CARGA DE FORJADO *f*
9824 ENGRASE *m* A PRESIÓN
9825 PRESIÓN *f* DE LA CORRIENTE
9826 PRESIÓN *f* SOBRE LAS ARISTAS
9827 CONDUCTO DE PRESIÓN *m*
9828 TIMBRE *m* DE UNA VÁLVULA
9828 TIMBRADO *m*
9829 DISPOSITIVO *m* DE CONTROL DE PRESIÓN
9830 ANILLO *m* DE PRESIÓN
9831 TORNILLO *m* DE PRESIÓN
9832 PRESIÓN *f* DE REGLAJE
9833 NIVEL *m* DE PRESIÓN
9834 CARRERA DE DESCARGA *f*
9835 MANOSTATO *m*

| | |
|---|---|
| 9836 PRUEBA *f* DE PRESIÓN | 9876 PRISMA *f* DE SECCIÓN OBLICUA |
| 9837 SOLDADURA *f* ALUMINOTÉRMICA | 9877 PLANO *m* PRISMÁTICO |
| 9838 SOLDADURA *f* RESISTENTE A LA PRESIÓN | 9878 ESPECTRO *m* PRODUCIDO POR PRISMA |
| 9839 RECIPIENTE (O DEPÓSITO) FORJADO A PRESIÓN *m* | 9879 PRISMÁTICO *m* |
| | 9880 PRISMOIDE *m* |
| 9839 RECIPIENTE *m* A PRESIÓN | 9881 FUNCIÓN *f* DE DISTRIBUCIÓN |
| 9840 CAÑERÍA DE AGUA A PRESIÓN *f* | 9882 PALPADOR *m* |
| 9840 CONDUCTO *m* DE AGUA FORZADA | 9883 PROCEDIMIENTO *m* |
| 9841 AGUA *f* A PRESIÓN | 9883 PROCESO *m* |
| 9842 SOLDADURA *f* POR PRESIÓN | 9884 RECOCIDO *m* INTERMEDIO DE MECANIZACIÓN |
| 9843 VÁLVULA *f* DE PRESIÓN DEPRESIÓN | 9885 MANUAL *m* DE FABRICACIÓN |
| 9844 PUNZÓN *m* DE TRAZAR | 9886 METALURGIA *f* DE EXTRACCIÓN |
| 9845 BATERÍA *f* DE PILAS, BATERÍA *f* PRIMARIA | 9887 PROCEDIMIENTO *m* DE MECANIZACIÓN |
| 9846 PILA *f* PRIMARIA | 9888 INDUSTRIA *f* DE TRANSFORMACIÓN |
| 9847 COLOR SENCILLO *m* | 9889 PROCESOR *m* |
| 9848 ELEMENTO *m* PROEUTÉCTICO | 9890 GAS *m* DE GASÓGENO |
| 9849 CRISTALIZACIÓN *f* PRIMARIA | 9891 PRODUCTO *m* (MATEMÁTICAS) |
| 9850 RELACIÓN *f* DE CORRIENTE PRIMARIA | 9892 PRODUCTO *m* |
| 9851 CARBÓN GRAFÍTICO *m* | 9893 PRODUCTO *m* DE COMBUSTIÓN |
| 9852 PRODUCTO *m* PRIMARIO | 9894 PRODUCCIÓN *f* DE CORRIENTE |
| 9853 METAL *m* NATIVO, METAL *m* VIRGEN | 9895 PRODUCCIÓN *f* DE FRÍO |
| 9854 RESISTENCIA *f* PRIMITIVA | 9896 PRODUCCIÓN *f* DE CALOR |
| 9855 APRESTO *m*, ACABADO *m* | 9897 PRODUCTIVIDAD *f* |
| 9856 CEBAR UNA BOMBA | 9898 PERFIL *m* |
| 9857 CAPA PRIMARIA *f* | 9898 PERFIL *m* |
| 9857 CAPA DE FONDO *f* | 9899 FRESA *f* DE FORMAR |
| 9858 GASTOS *m* DE PRIMERA INSTALACIÓN | 9899 FRESA *f* PERFILADA |
| 9859 MÁQUINA *f* MOTRIZ | 9900 FRESADORA *f* PARA COPIAR |
| 9859 TRACTOR *m* | 9900 FRESADORA *f* DESBASTADORA |
| 9859 MOTOR *m* | 9901 MÁQUINA *f* PARA TRABAJAR LA MADERA |
| 9860 NÚMERO *m* PRIMERO | 9902 PROGRAMA *m* |
| 9861 ALEACIÓN COBRE CINC *f* | 9903 PARADA *f* PROGRAMADA |
| 9862 PRODUCTOS *m pl* DE PRIMERA CALIDAD | 9904 PROGRAMACIÓN *f* |
| 9863 ARRASTRE *m* DEL AGUA POR EL VAPOR | 9905 AVANCE *m*, ACELERACIÓN *f* |
| 9864 PRIMERA CAPA *f* DE PINTURA | 9906 ENVEJECIMIENTO *m* PROGRESIVO |
| 9864 PINTURA *f* SUBYACENTE | 9907 CALIBRE *m* DE TOLERANCIAS ESCALONADAS |
| 9864 PRIMERA MANO *f* | 9908 SOLDADURA *f* POR INDUCCIÓN PROGRESIVA |
| 9865 TRANSLACIÓN *f* PRIMITIVA | 9909 PROYECTAR |
| 9866 EJE *m* PRINCIPAL | 9910 SALIENTE *m* |
| 9867 DINAMO *f* PRINCIPAL | 9911 CHAPA *f* EN RELIEVE |
| 9867 GENERATRIZ *f* | 9912 PROYECCIÓN *f* |
| 9868 SECCIÓN *f* PRINCIPAL | 9913 SALIENTE, RELIEVE *m* |
| 9869 TENSIÓN *f* PRINCIPAL | 9914 LENTE AMB. DIVERGENTE |
| 9870 IMPRESIÓN *f* DE PRUEBA, COPIA *f* | 9915 JUNTA *f* DE SOLDADURA POR REFUERZOS |
| 9870 COPIA (FOTOGRAFÍA) | 9916 SOLDADURA *f* POR RESALTES |
| 9871 CIRCUITO IMPRESO (C.I.) *m* | 9917 RESALTO *m* |
| 9872 QUE IMPRIME | 9917 SALIENTE, RELIEVE *m* |
| 9873 MÁQUINA *f* DE MOLETEAR LOS CILINDROS DE IMPRENTA | 9918 CICLOIDE *f* ALARGADA |
| | 9919 PROLONGACIÓN *f* DE VALIDEZ DE UNA PATENTE |
| 9874 CUADRO PARA FOTOCALCO *m* | 9920 FRENO *m* DINAMOMÉTRICO DE PRONY |
| 9875 PRISMA *f* | 9921 PRUEBA *f*, ENSAYO *m* |

| | |
|---|---|
| 9921 | PRUEBA *f*, ENSAYO *m* |
| 9922 | LÍMITE *m* ELÁSTICO CONVENCIONAL O APARENTE |
| 9923 | LÍMITE *m* DE ALARGAMIENTO |
| 9923 | LÍMITE *m* ELÁSTICO CONVENCIONAL |
| 9924 | ENSAYO *m* NO DESTRUCTIVO |
| 9925 | PUNTAL *m* DE REFUERZO |
| 9926 | PROPAGACIÓN *f* DE ONDAS |
| 9927 | PROPANO *m* |
| 9927 | HIDRURO *m* DE PROPILO |
| 9928 | PALA DE HÉLICE *f* |
| 9929 | VENTILADOR *m* DE HÉLICE |
| 9930 | ÁRBOL DE TRANSMISIÓN *m* |
| 9930 | ÁRBOL DE EXTREMIDAD *m*, ÁRBOL PORTAHÉLICE *m* |
| 9931 | HELICOMEZCLADOR *f* |
| 9932 | FRACCIÓN *f* PROPIA |
| 9932 | FRACCIÓN *f* PURA |
| 9933 | PROPORCIÓN (MATEMÁTICAS) |
| 9934 | PROPORCIÓN *f* |
| 9934 | DOSIFICACIÓN *f* DE LA MEZCLA |
| 9935 | PROPORCIONAL |
| 9936 | LÍMITE *m* PROPORCIONAL (DE ELASTICIDAD) |
| 9937 | COMPÁS DE REDUCCIÓN *m* |
| 9938 | PROPORCIONALIDAD *f* |
| 9939 | PROPILENO *m* |
| 9940 | PROTACTINIO *m* |
| 9941 | MOTOR *m* PROTEGIDO |
| 9942 | MANGUITO *m* PROTECTOR |
| 9943 | PROTECCIÓN *f* |
| 9944 | TAPA DE PROTECCIÓN *f* |
| 9945 | PROTECCIÓN *f* CONTRA LA OXIDACIÓN |
| 9946 | PROTECCIÓN *f* DE LA PROPIEDAD INDUSTRIAL |
| 9947 | ATMÓSFERA DE PROTECCIÓN *f* |
| 9948 | JAULA *f*, CAJA *f* PROTECTORA |
| 9948 | CAJA *f* DE PROTECCIÓN, ENVOLTURA *f* PROTECTORA |
| 9948 | SOBRE ESPESOR *m* |
| 9948 | CAJA *f* PROTECTORA, ENVOLTURA *f* PROTECTORA |
| 9949 | REVESTIMIENTO *m* PROTECTOR |
| 9950 | PELÍCULA PROTECTORA *f* |
| 9951 | ENREJADO *m* DE PROTECCIÓN |
| 9951 | ENREJADO *m* |
| 9952 | MATERIA *f* PROTECTORA |
| 9953 | PARED *f* PROTECTORA |
| 9954 | PROTÓN *m* |
| 9955 | PROTOTIPO *m* |
| 9956 | TRANSPORTADOR *m* |
| 9957 | REGULADOR *m* SEUDOESTÁTICO |
| 9958 | SISTEMA *m* CASI BINARIO |
| 9959 | CEMENTACIÓN BRILLANTE *f* |

| | |
|---|---|
| 9960 | PSICRÓMETRO *m* |
| 9961 | BAÑO *m* DE FUSIÓN |
| 9962 | HIERRO *m* PUDELADO |
| 9963 | ACERO PUDELADO *m* |
| 9964 | PUDELAR |
| 9965 | HORNO *m* DE PUDELADO |
| 9966 | MEZCLADORA *f* DE HORMIGÓN (O.P.), HORMIGONERA *f* |
| 9967 | TRACCIÓN *f* NORMALMENTE A LA DIRECCIÓN DE LAS FIBRAS |
| 9968 | TRACCIÓN *f* EN LA DIRECCIÓN DE LAS FIBRAS |
| 9969 | HACER CORRESPONDER LOS AGUJEROS DE REMACHES, AJUSTAR LOS AGUJEROS A LOS REMACHES |
| 9970 | TRACCÍON *f* |
| 9971 | POLEA *f* (APARATO ELEVADOR) |
| 9972 | MUFLA *f* |
| 9973 | MUFLAS *f* |
| 9973 | POLIPASTO *m*, CABRIA *f* |
| 9973 | POLEAS *f* DE APAREJO |
| 9974 | POLEA *f* DEFECTUOSA |
| 9975 | HORNO *m* CON POLEAS |
| 9976 | POLEA *f* DE BRAZOS PARABÓLICOS |
| 9976 | POLEA *f* DE BRAZOS CURVOS |
| 9977 | POLEA *f* DE BRAZOS RECTOS |
| 9978 | SOLDADURA *f* POR PULSACIÓN |
| 9979 | IMPULSIÓN *f* |
| 9980 | PULSÓMETRO *m* |
| 9981 | PULVERIZABLE |
| 9982 | PULVERIZAR |
| 9983 | PULVERIZADO |
| 9984 | POLVO *m* DE CARBÓN |
| 9984 | CARBÓN PULVERIZADO *m* |
| 9985 | PULVERIZACIÓN *f* |
| 9986 | PIEDRA *f* PÓMEZ |
| 9987 | APOMAZAR |
| 9988 | PÓMEZ *f* |
| 9988 | PIEDRA *f* PÓMEZ |
| 9989 | TOBA *f* DE NATURALEZA DE PÓMEZ |
| 9990 | APOMAZADO *m* |
| 9991 | BOMBA *f* |
| 9992 | CILINDRO *m* DE BOMBA |
| 9993 | INYECTOR *m* DE BOMBA |
| 9994 | ALENZA *f* CON VÁLVULA |
| 9995 | PISTÓN *m* DE BOMBA, ÉMBOLO *m* DE BOMBA |
| 9996 | BOMBAS *f pl* |
| 9997 | PUNZÓN *m* |
| 9997 | TALADRO *m* PARA CHAPA, BROCA *f* PARA CHAPA |
| 9998 | PUNZONAR, MARCAR CON PUNZÓN |
| 9998 | RECORTAR |

| | | | |
|---|---|---|---|
| 9999 | PUNZONAR | 10034 | DESEMBRAGAR, DESACOPLAR |
| 10000 | SACABOCADOS $m$ | 10034 | DESEMBRAGAR |
| 10000 | PINZAS $f$ $pl$ PUNZONADORAS, TENAZAS $f$ $pl$ SACABOCADOS | 10035 | PODREDUMBRE $f$ |
| 10001 | PERFORADORA $f$ | 10035 | PUTREFACCIÓN (ACCIÓN) $f$ |
| 10001 | PUNZONADORA $f$ | 10036 | PODRIRSE, PUDRIRSE |
| 10002 | TARJETA PERFORADA $f$ | 10036 | PODRIR, PUDRIR |
| 10003 | CHAPA $f$ DE AGUJEROS TALADRADOS | 10036 | FERMENTAR |
| 10004 | AGUJERO $m$ DE ROBLÓN TALADRADO | 10037 | MASILLA $f$ |
| 10005 | CINTA $f$ DE PAPEL PERFORADO | 10038 | PIRÁMIDE $f$ |
| 10006 | PUNZONADO $m$ | 10039 | DUREZA $f$ A LA PIRÁMIDE |
| 10006 | BARRENADO $m$ | 10040 | SISTEMA $m$ PIRAMIDAL |
| 10007 | PUNZONADORA-CIZALLADORA $f$ | 10041 | PIRIDINA $f$ |
| 10007 | MÁQUINA $f$ DE PUNZONAR Y DE CIZALLAR | 10042 | PIROELÉCTRICO $m$ |
| 10008 | PUNZONADO $m$ | 10043 | PIROELECTRICIDAD $f$ |
| 10009 | PUNZONADORA-RECORTADORA $f$ | 10044 | CONDUCTIVIDAD TERMOELÉCTRICA $f$ |
| 10009 | PUNZONADORA $f$, MÁQUINA $f$ PUNZONADORA | 10045 | ÁCIDO PIROGÁLICO $m$ |
| 10009 | MÁQUINA $f$ DE PUNZONAR | 10045 | PIROGALOL $m$ |
| 10010 | PRUEBA $f$ DE PERFORACIÓN | 10046 | ÁCIDO PIROLEÑOSO $m$ |
| 10010 | PRUEBA $f$ A LA FLEXIÓN | 10047 | PERÓXIDO $m$ DE MANGANESO |
| 10011 | UNIDAD $f$ DE PERFORACIÓN | 10047 | BIÓXIDO $m$ DE MANGANESO |
| 10012 | PUNZONADO $m$ | 10048 | PIROMETALURGIA $f$ |
| 10012 | RECORTE $m$ | 10049 | PIRÓMETRO $m$ |
| 10013 | PERFORACIÓN $f$ POR DESCARGA DISRUPTIVA | 10050 | CONO PIROMÉTRICO $m$ |
| 10014 | TORNO $m$ DE ENGRANAJE | 10051 | EQUIVALENTE DEL CONO PIROMÉTRICO |
| 10015 | CALIBRE $m$ DE RECEPCIÓN | 10052 | PIROMETRÍA $f$ |
| 10016 | INVESTIGACIÓN $f$ PURA | 10053 | ALEACIÓN PIROFÓRICA $f$ |
| 10017 | EFECTO $m$ DE LIMPIEZA | 10054 | ÁCIDO PIROFOSFÓRICO $m$ |
| 10018 | DEPURACIÓN $f$ DE LOS GASES, PURIFICACIÓN $f$ DE LOS GASES | 10055 | CUADRILÁTERO $m$ |
| 10019 | PURIFICACIÓN $f$ DEL AGUA | 10055 | PRISMA $f$ CUADRANGULAR |
| 10020 | PURGADOR $m$ | 10056 | CUADRANTE $m$ |
| 10020 | DEPURADOR $m$ | 10057 | ECUACIÓN $f$ DE SEGUNDO GRADO |
| 10021 | COMPRESIÓN EN EL SENTIDO DE LAS FIBRAS $f$ | 10057 | ECUACIÓN $f$ DE SEGUNDO GRADO |
| 10022 | COMPRESIÓN PERPENDICULAR AL SENTIDO DE LAS FIBRAS $f$ | 10058 | CUADRILÁTERO $m$ |
| 10023 | BANCO $m$ DE ESTIRAR | 10058 | CUADRÁNGULO $m$ |
| 10024 | HORNO $m$ CON SACUDIDAS | 10059 | MÁQUINA $f$ CON CUÁDRUPLE EXPANSIÓN |
| 10025 | AJUSTE $m$, MONTAJE $m$, AJUSTAMIENTO $m$ | 10060 | VÁLVULA $f$ DE CUÁDRUPLE ASIENTO |
| 10025 | MONTAJE $m$ FLOJO | 10061 | PENETRÓMETRO $m$ |
| 10025 | ACOPLAMIENTO $m$ | 10062 | ANÁLISIS CUALITATIVO $m$ |
| 10026 | VÁSTAGO $m$ DE BALANCÍN | 10063 | CONTROL DE CALIDAD $m$ |
| 10027 | SOLDADURA $f$ CON PINZA | 10064 | ANÁLISIS CUANTITATIVO $m$ |
| 10028 | COMPRESIÓN $f$ | 10064 | DOSIFICACIÓN $f$, ANÁLISIS CUANTITATIVA |
| 10029 | PULSADOR $m$ | 10065 | CANTIDAD $f$ |
| 10030 | HORNO $m$ CON DESCARGADOR DE COQUE | 10065 | TAMAÑO $m$ |
| 10031 | VÁSTAGO $m$ DE BALANCÍN | 10066 | CANTIDAD $f$ DE CALOR |
| 10032 | TENSAR UN RESORTE | 10067 | CANTIDAD $f$ DE ELECTRICIDAD |
| 10032 | CARGAR UN MUELLE | 10068 | CANTIDAD $f$ DE MOVIMIENTO |
| 10033 | EMBRAGAR, ACOPLAR | 10069 | CAUDAL $m$ |
| 10034 | DESENGRANAR, DESACOPLAR, DESENGANCHAR, | 10070 | CANTIDAD $f$ MEDIDA |
| | | 10071 | RENDIMIENTO $m$ CUÁNTICO |
| | | 10072 | LONGITUD $f$ CRÍTICA DE ONDAS |
| | | 10073 | CANTERA $f$ |

| | |
|---|---|
| 10074 | CODO REDONDO AL 1/4 *m* |
| 10074 | CODO REDONDO DE ÁNGULO RECTO *m* |
| 10075 | CORTE *m* RADIAL DE LA MADERA |
| 10075 | ASERRADO *m* POR IRRADIACIÓN |
| 10075 | ASERRADO *m* HOLANDÉS |
| 10076 | CUARTA *f* PARTE |
| 10076 | CUARTOS *m pl* DE LEÑA |
| 10077 | CUARZO *m* |
| 10078 | FILAMENTO DE CUARZO |
| 10079 | CRISTAL *m* DE CUARZO |
| 10080 | LÁMPARA *f* DE VAPOR DE MERCURIO EN CUARZO |
| 10081 | PÓRFIRO *m* CUARCÍFERO |
| 10082 | ARENA *f* CUARZOSA |
| 10082 | SILÍCEO |
| 10083 | CUARCITA *f* |
| 10084 | ALEACIÓN CUATERNARIA *f* |
| 10085 | ALEACIÓN CUATERNARIA EUTÉCTICA *f* |
| 10086 | CUATRIFOLIO *m* |
| 10087 | ENVEJECIMIENTO *m* POR ENFRIAMIENTO RÁPIDO |
| 10088 | FLEXIÓN EFECTUADA EN ACEROS TRATADOS CON TEMPLES (PRUEBA DE ...) |
| 10089 | ENDURECIMIENTO *m* POR TEMPLE |
| 10090 | CUBA *f* DE TEMPLE |
| 10091 | ENFRIAR BRUSCAMENTE EL ACERO |
| 10092 | TEMPLE *m* Y REVENIDO |
| 10093 | ACERO CALMADO Y TEMPLADO *m* |
| 10093 | ACERO TEMPLADO Y REVENIDO *m* |
| 10094 | TEMPLE *m* |
| 10095 | TEMPLE *m* Y REVENIDO |
| 10096 | MEDIO *m* DE ENDURECIMIENTO |
| 10097 | GRIETA *f* (DE TEMPLE) |
| 10097 | FISURA *f* DE TEMPLE |
| 10098 | MEDIO *m* DE TEMPLE |
| 10099 | ACEITE *m* DE TEMPLE |
| 10100 | ENFRIAMIENTO *m* BRUSCO DEL ACERO |
| 10101 | CUESTIONARIO *m* |
| 10102 | CURVA VIVA *f* |
| 10102 | CURVA DE PEQUEÑO RADIO *f* |
| 10102 | CURVA DE RADIO PEQUEÑO *f* |
| 10102 | CURVA DE RADIO PEQUEÑO *f* |
| 10103 | VÁLVULA *f* DE MANIOBRA RÁPIDA |
| 10104 | GRIFO *m* DE MANIOBRA RÁPIDA |
| 10105 | ROSCA *f* DE PASO ALARGADO |
| 10105 | ROSCA *f* DE PASO ALARGADO |
| 10106 | MECANISMO *m* PARA UN RÁPIDO RETORNO |
| 10106 | RETORNO *m* RÁPIDO |
| 10107 | CEMENTO DE FRAGUADO RÁPIDO *m* |
| 10108 | ADAPTADOR DE INTERCAMBIO RÁPIDO *m* |
| 10109 | COLADA TRANQUILA (PROCEDIMIENTO DURVILLE) *f* |

| | |
|---|---|
| 10110 | QUINIDRONA *f* (SEMICÉLULA A LA) |
| 10111 | QUINTAL *m* MÉTRICO |
| 10112 | ECUACIÓN *f* DE QUINTO GRADO |
| 10112 | ECUACIÓN *f* DE QUINTO GRADO |
| 10113 | CITAR |
| 10114 | COCIENTE *m* |
| 10115 | CEPILLO *m* DE INGLETE |
| 10116 | HURGÓN *m*, ATIZADERO *m* |
| 10117 | EMBALARSE, DISPARARSE, ACELERARSE ANORMALMENTE |
| 10117 | EMBALARSE, DISPARARSE, ACELERARSE ANORMALMENTE |
| 10118 | DISPARADA *f* DE UN MOTOR, ACELERACIÓN *f* EXAGERADA DE UN MOTOR |
| 10119 | CREMALLERA *f* |
| 10120 | CREMALLERA *f* Y PIÑÓN *m* |
| 10120 | ENGRANAJE *m* DE RUEDA DENTADA Y CREMALLERA |
| 10121 | GATO *m*, CRIC *m* |
| 10121 | ALZARUEDA *f* |
| 10122 | COMPÁS DE CREMALLERA *m* |
| 10123 | MECANISMO *m* DE INDEXACIÓN POR CREMALLERA |
| 10124 | VARILLA *f* DE CREMALLERA |
| 10125 | RADIAL |
| 10126 | NEUMÁTICO *m* DE ARMADURA RADIAL |
| 10127 | ACELERACIÓN CENTRÍFUGA *f* |
| 10128 | BRAZO *m* RADIAL |
| 10129 | MÁQUINA *f* RADIAL DE PERFORAR |
| 10130 | RODAMIENTO *m* DE PRESIÓN LATERAL |
| 10130 | RODAMIENTO *m* DE BOLAS DE CARGA RADIAL |
| 10131 | VIGA *f* RADIAL |
| 10132 | COMPONENTE RADIAL *f* |
| 10133 | DESPLAZAMIENTO *m* RADIAL |
| 10134 | TALADRADORA *f* RADIAL |
| 10135 | MOTOR *m* EN ESTRELLA, MOTOR *m* RADIAL |
| 10136 | TURBINA *f* RADIAL |
| 10137 | PROYECCIÓN *f* CENTRAL |
| 10138 | RADIÁN *m* |
| 10139 | ENERGÍA *f* IRRADIADA |
| 10140 | CALOR RADIANTE *m* |
| 10140 | CALOR RADIANTE *m* |
| 10141 | IRRADIAR |
| 10142 | SUPERFICIE *f* RADIANTE |
| 10143 | RADIACIÓN, IRRADIACIÓN *f* |
| 10143 | RADIACIÓN *f* |
| 10144 | CONSTANTE DE RADIACIÓN *f* |
| 10145 | PÉRDIDA *f* DE CALOR POR DIFUSIÓN |
| 10146 | IRRADIACIÓN *f* DEL CALOR |
| 10147 | IRRADIACIÓN *f* DE LA LUZ |
| 10148 | RADIADOR *m* |
| 10149 | RADIADOR *m* DE REFRIGERACIÓN |

| | |
|---|---|
| 10150 | RADIADOR  *m*  DE CALEFACCIÓN |
| 10151 | TAPÓN  *m*  DE RADIADOR |
| 10152 | CALANDRA DE RADIADOR  *f*, REJILLA DE RADIADOR  *f* |
| 10153 | GRIFO  *m*  DE RADIADOR |
| 10154 | RADICAL  *m* |
| 10155 | RADIOMETALOGRAFÍA  *f* |
| 10156 | ANTIPARÁSITO  *m* |
| 10157 | RADIOACTIVO |
| 10158 | SUBSTANCIAS  *f pl*  RADIOACTIVAS |
| 10159 | EMANACIÓN  *f* |
| 10159 | RADÓN  *m* |
| 10160 | RADIOACTIVIDAD  *f* |
| 10161 | RADIOGRAFÍA  *f* |
| 10162 | EXAMEN  *m*  RADIOGRÁFICO |
| 10163 | RADIOGRAFÍA  *f* |
| 10164 | RADIOGRAFÍA  *f* |
| 10165 | RADIO  *m* |
| 10166 | RADIO  *m* |
| 10167 | CANTONEADO  *m* |
| 10168 | RADIO  *m*  DE CURVATURA |
| 10169 | RADIO  *m*  DE GIRO |
| 10169 | RADIO  *m*  DE ROTACIÓN |
| 10170 | RADIO  *m*  VECTOR |
| 10171 | PICADURA  *f* |
| 10172 | PERNO  *m*  DE ANCLAJE |
| 10173 | DISCO  *m*  DE TRAPO (PARA PULIR) |
| 10174 | CILINDRO  *m*  DENTADO |
| 10175 | RAÍL, CARRIL  *m* |
| 10176 | MÁQUINA  *f*  PARA PERFORAR CARRILES Y ECLISAS |
| 10177 | PRODUCTOS  *m pl*  DE ACERO DE RAÍL |
| 10178 | MANCHAS  *f pl*  DE AGUA (DE LLUVIA) |
| 10179 | AGUA  *f*  PLUVIAL, AGUA DE LLUVIA |
| 10180 | ELEVAR A UNA POTENCIA |
| 10181 | CHAPA  *f*  GOTEADA |
| 10182 | RETENCIÓN  *f*  DE AGUA |
| 10183 | BRIDA  *f*  DE CARA ELEVADA (O ALZADA) |
| 10184 | PRUEBA  *f*  DE EMBUTIDO |
| 10185 | AUMENTO  *m*  DE VELOCIDAD |
| 10186 | ÁNGULO DE DESPRENDIMIENTO  *m*, ÁNGULO DE ATAQUE  *m* |
| 10187 | DENTADO  *m*  ALTERNADO |
| 10188 | PISTÓN  *m*  DE TORNILLO ELEVADOR |
| 10188 | TACO DE CORREDERA  *m* |
| 10189 | APISONAR |
| 10190 | FRESADORA  *f*  RADIAL DE CORREDERA |
| 10191 | GANCHO  *m*  DOBLE |
| 10191 | GANCHO  *m*  DOBLE |
| 10192 | RAMIO  *m* |
| 10192 | CHINA-GRASS |

| | |
|---|---|
| 10193 | HORMIGÓN  *m*  APISONADO |
| 10194 | AJUSTE  *m*, PRESIÓN  *f* |
| 10194 | PRESIÓN  *f* |
| 10195 | APISONAMIENTO  *m* |
| 10196 | PISTÓN  *m*  SUECO (RAMSBOTTOM) |
| 10196 | PISTÓN  *m*  RAMSBOTTOM |
| 10197 | ACEITE  *m*  RANCIO |
| 10198 | ACCESO DIRECTO  *m* |
| 10199 | ORIENTADO AL AZAR |
| 10200 | GAMA  *f* |
| 10201 | ALCANCE  *m*  (O CAMPO  *m*) DE MEDIDA DE UN INSTRUMENTO |
| 10202 | ALCANCE  *m*  DEL SONIDO |
| 10203 | DIAGRAMA  *m*  RANKINIZADO |
| 10203 | DIAGRAMA  *m*  TOTALIZADO |
| 10204 | ACEITE  *m*  DE COLZA |
| 10204 | ACEITE  *m*  DE COLZA |
| 10205 | COMBUSTIÓN VIVA  *f* |
| 10206 | BROCA  *f*  DE CORTE RÁPIDO |
| 10207 | ACERO RÁPIDO PARA HERRAMIENTAS  *m* |
| 10208 | AVANCE  *m*  RÁPIDO, AVANCE  *m*  BASTO |
| 10209 | ÁRBOL  *m*  DE GRAN VELOCIDAD |
| 10210 | TIERRAS  *f pl*  RARAS |
| 10211 | ENRARECIMIENTO  *m*  DE UN GAS |
| 10212 | ENRARECIMIENTO  *m*  DEL AIRE |
| 10213 | AIRE ENRARECIDO  *m* |
| 10214 | ENRARECER UN GAS |
| 10215 | ESCOFINA  *f* |
| 10216 | LIMA  *f*  DE COLA DE RATÓN |
| 10217 | FLOTADOR  *m*  DE ALMACENAJE Y DE ARRIBAJE |
| 10218 | TRINQUETE (MECANISMO PARA TRANSFORMAR UN MOVIMIENTO ALTERNO EN CONTINUO) |
| 10219 | CARRACA  *f* |
| 10219 | GARFIO  *m*  DE TRINQUETE |
| 10220 | EFECTO  *m*  DE ENGATILLAMIENTO |
| 10221 | MANGUITO  *m*  DE TRINQUETES |
| 10221 | ACOPLAMIENTO  *m*, EMBRAGUE  *m* |
| 10222 | CRIC  *m*  DE TRINQUETE |
| 10223 | PALANCA  *f*  DE TRINQUETE |
| 10224 | LLAVE DE TRINQUETE  *f* |
| 10225 | RUEDA  *f*  DE TRINQUETE |
| 10225 | RUEDA  *f*  DE TRINQUETE |
| 10225 | RUEDA  *f*  DE TRINQUETE |
| 10226 | VELOCIDAD  *f* |
| 10226 | TASA  *f*, TIPO  *m*, RELACIÓN  *f* |
| 10227 | VELOCIDAD  *f*  DE COMBUSTIÓN |
| 10228 | CAUDAL  *m*  DE UNA BOMBA |
| 10229 | VELOCIDAD  *f*  DE DEPÓSITO |
| 10230 | VELOCIDAD  *f*  DE PROPAGACIÓN DE LA LLAMA |
| 10231 | ELEVACIÓN  *f*  EN TEMPERATURA |
| 10232 | VELOCIDAD  *f*  DE CIRCULACIÓN DE ACEITE |

| | | |
|---|---|---|
| 10233 | POTENCIA *f* NOMINAL |
| 10233 | POTENCIA *f* FISCAL |
| 10234 | COCIENTE *m* |
| 10234 | RELACIÓN *f* |
| 10235 | NÚMERO COMENSURABLE *m* |
| 10235 | NÚMERO *m* RACIONAL |
| 10236 | JUNQUILLO *m*, BAGUETA *f* |
| 10236 | ROTA *f*, JUNCO *m* |
| 10237 | CUERO *m* EN BRUTO, CUERO VERDE |
| 10237 | CUERO *m* VERDE |
| 10238 | PIÑÓN *m* DE CUERO VERDE |
| 10239 | MATERIA *f* PRIMA |
| 10240 | AGUA *f* ORDINARIA |
| 10241 | IRRADIACIÓN *f* |
| 10242 | RADIOS *m* |
| 10243 | ÁNGULO ENTRANTE *m* |
| 10244 | VOLVER A MONTAR |
| 10245 | NUEVO MONTAJE *m* |
| 10246 | NUEVO EMPLEO *m* |
| 10246 | UTILIZAR DE NUEVO |
| 10247 | REACTANCIA *f* |
| 10248 | REACCIÓN *f* |
| 10248 | FUERZA *f* REACTIVA |
| 10249 | LÍMITE *m* DE REACCIÓN |
| 10250 | TURBINA *f* A PRESIÓN INTERIOR |
| 10250 | TURBINA *f* DE REACCIÓN |
| 10251 | REACTOR *m* |
| 10252 | LEER |
| 10253 | VISUALIZACIÓN *f* |
| 10254 | LECTURA *f* |
| 10255 | RETOCAR EL REGLAJE |
| 10256 | RETOQUE *m* DE REGLAJE |
| 10256 | REGLAJE *m* CONSECUTIVO |
| 10257 | REACTIVO *m* |
| 10258 | FOCO *m* REAL |
| 10259 | IMAGEN *f* REAL |
| 10260 | NÚMERO *m* REAL |
| 10261 | RESISTENCIA *f* EFECTIVA |
| 10262 | REJALGAR *m* |
| 10262 | DISULFURO *m* DE ARSÉNICO |
| 10263 | ALISADOR *m*, PULIDOR *m* |
| 10264 | PORTAMANDRILADOR *m* |
| 10265 | PUENTE *m* TRASERO (MOTOR) |
| 10265 | EJE *m* TRASERO (NO MOTOR) |
| 10266 | RETROVISOR *m* |
| 10267 | ESCALA *f* DE REAUMUR |
| 10268 | TERMÓMETRO *m* RÉAUMUR |
| 10269 | PLIEGUE *m*, REBAJO *m* |
| 10270 | RECTIFICACIÓN *f* DE DIÁMETRO INTERIOR |
| 10270 | RECTIFICAR CON LA MANDRILADORA |
| 10271 | RECTIFICACIÓN *f* CON MANDRILADORA |

| | | |
|---|---|---|
| 10271 | RECTIFICACIÓN *f* DE DIÁMETRO INTERIOR |
| 10272 | REBOTE, RECHAZO *m* |
| 10273 | SALTAR, REBOTAR |
| 10274 | RECALENTAMIENTO *m* |
| 10274 | DESPRENDIMIENTO *m* DE CALOR, RECALESCENCIA *f* |
| 10275 | NUEVA CARBURACIÓN *f* DEL HIERRO |
| 10276 | NUEVO CARBURANTE *m* |
| 10277 | RECIPIENTE *m* |
| 10277 | MATRAZ *m* |
| 10278 | ESTACIÓN *f* RECEPTORA |
| 10279 | CAVIDAD *f*, NICHO *m* |
| 10279 | HUECO *m* |
| 10280 | CANTIDAD *f* RECÍPROCA . |
| 10281 | RED *f* RECÍPROCA |
| 10282 | FRESADO *m* RECIPROCO |
| 10283 | MOVIMIENTO *m* DE VAIVÉN |
| 10283 | MOVIMIENTO *m* PENDULAR |
| 10283 | MOVIMIENTO *m* ALTERNO |
| 10284 | BOMBA *f* DE ÉMBOLO CON MOVIMIENTO RECTILÍNEO ALTERNATIVO |
| 10285 | MÁQUINA *f* DE PISTÓN |
| 10286 | GOLPE DE RETROCESO *m* |
| 10286 | CONTRAGOLPE *m* |
| 10287 | ARREGLO *m*, REVISIÓN *f* |
| 10288 | REGISTRAR |
| 10289 | REGISTRADOR *m* |
| 10289 | INSTRUMENTO *m* REGISTRADOR |
| 10290 | CILINDRO *m* (O TAMBOR *m*) REGISTRADOR |
| 10290 | TAMBOR *m* |
| 10291 | DINAMÓGRAFO *m* |
| 10292 | MANÓMETRO *m* REGISTRADOR |
| 10293 | TERMÓMETRO *m* REGISTRADOR |
| 10293 | TERMÓGRAFO *m* |
| 10294 | APARATO REGISTRADOR *m* |
| 10295 | RECUPERAR |
| 10296 | RECUPERACIÓN *m* |
| 10296 | RESTAURACIÓN *f* |
| 10297 | RECRISTALIZACIÓN |
| 10298 | TEMPERATURA *f* DE NUEVA CRISTALIZACIÓN |
| 10299 | RECTÁNGULO *m* |
| 10300 | MÁQUINA PARA BURILAR POR CHISPAS EN COORDENADAS RECTANGULARES |
| 10301 | COORDENADAS RECTANGULARES *f pl* |
| 10301 | COORDENADAS ORTOGONALES *f pl* |
| 10302 | SECCIÓN *f* RECTANGULAR |
| 10303 | CARGA RECTANGULAR *f* |
| 10304 | MALLA *f* RECTANGULAR |
| 10305 | PARALELEPÍPEDO *m* RECTÁNGULO |
| 10306 | RESORTE *m* RECTANGULAR DE LÁMINA PLANA |
| 10307 | RESORTE *m* DE LÁMINA RECTANGULAR DE PERFIL PARABÓLICO |

| | |
|---|---|
| 10308 | TRANSPORTADOR *m* EN FORMA DE ESCUADRA |
| 10309 | CABEZA *f* CUADRADA DE UN TORNILLO |
| 10310 | RECTÁNGULO *m* |
| 10311 | RECTIFICACIÓN *f* (QUÍMICA) |
| 10312 | ENDEREZAMIENTO *m* |
| 10312 | DESMODULACIÓN *f* |
| 10313 | ALCOHOL RECTIFICADO *m* |
| 10314 | RECTIFICADOR *m* DE CORRIENTE |
| 10315 | PLACA *f* DE RECTIFICADOR |
| 10316 | CÁTODO DE RECTIFICADOR *m* |
| 10317 | TUBO *m* RECTIFICADOR |
| 10318 | RECTIFICAR |
| 10319 | RECTILÍNEO |
| 10320 | MOVIMIENTO *m* RECTILÍNEO |
| 10321 | HORNO *m* DE REGENERACIÓN |
| 10322 | RECUPERADOR *m* |
| 10323 | AFILAR LAS LIMAS |
| 10324 | AFILADO *m* DE LIMAS |
| 10325 | LATÓN *m* ROJO |
| 10326 | SIMILOR *m*, LATÓN *m* ROJO |
| 10327 | HUMOS *m pl* ROJOS |
| 10328 | DUREZA *f* EN CALIENTE |
| 10329 | CALOR |
| 10329 | CALOR ROJO *m* |
| 10329 | ROJO *m* |
| 10330 | ROJO *m* AL FUEGO |
| 10330 | CALDEO AL ROJO *m* |
| 10331 | PRUEBA *f* DE RESISTENCIA AL CALOR ROJO |
| 10332 | MASTIC *m* ROJO |
| 10332 | MASTIC *m* AL MINIO |
| 10333 | MINIO *m* |
| 10333 | ÓXIDO *m* SALINO DE PLOMO |
| 10334 | FÓSFORO *m* ROJO |
| 10335 | HERRUMBRE *f*, ÓXIDO *m* |
| 10336 | GRÉS *m* ROJO |
| 10337 | QUEBRADIZO EN CALIENTE *m* |
| 10338 | HIERRO *m* QUEBRADIZO EN CALIENTE |
| 10338 | HIERRO *m* QUEBRADIZO EN CALIENTE (O AL ROJO) |
| 10338 | HIERRO *m* QUEBRADIZO AL ROJO |
| 10339 | FRAGILIDAD *f* EN CALIENTE |
| 10340 | RÚBRICA *f* |
| 10340 | TIERRA *f* ROJA |
| 10341 | CINC *m* REFUNDIDO |
| 10342 | REDUCIR (QUÍMICA) |
| 10343 | ESCALA *f* REDUCIDA |
| 10344 | TEMPERATURA *f* REDUCIDA |
| 10345 | REDUCTOR *m* |
| 10345 | REDUCTORA |
| 10346 | REDUCTOR *m* |
| 10346 | AGENTE DE REDUCCIÓN, DESOXIDANTE *m* |

| | |
|---|---|
| 10347 | ATMÓSFERA *f* REDUCTORA |
| 10348 | REDUCCIÓN *f* HEMBRA-HEMBRA |
| 10349 | LLAMA *f* REDUCTORA |
| 10350 | BRIDA *f* DE REDUCCIÓN |
| 10351 | MANGUITO *m* REDUCTOR |
| 10352 | TUBO *m* DE REDUCCIÓN |
| 10352 | RACOR *m* CÓNICO |
| 10353 | TREN *m* REDUCTOR |
| 10354 | TEMPERATURA *f* DE REDUCCIÓN |
| 10355 | VÁLVULA *f* DE REDUCCIÓN |
| 10355 | REDUCTOR *m* |
| 10355 | VÁLVULA DE REDUCCIÓN (DE REGULACIÓN) DE PRESIÓN |
| 10356 | REDUCCIÓN *f* (QUÍMICA) |
| 10357 | REDUCCIÓN *f* |
| 10358 | CONO REDUCTOR *m* |
| 10359 | HORNO *m* DE REDUCCIÓN |
| 10360 | RELACIÓN *f* DE REDUCCIÓN |
| 10361 | ESTRICCIÓN *f* |
| 10362 | REDUCCIÓN *f* DE LA SECCIÓN TRANSVERSAL |
| 10362 | DISMINUCIÓN *f* DE LA SECCIÓN TRANSVERSAL |
| 10363 | REDUCCIÓN *f* DE VELOCIDAD |
| 10364 | REDUNDANCIA *f* |
| 10365 | COMPARADOR DE HOJAS *m* |
| 10366 | CALIBRE *m* DE REFERENCIA |
| 10366 | TRANSPORTADOR *m* FIJO |
| 10367 | ÍNDICE *m* DE REPOSICIÓN |
| 10368 | PUNTO *m* DE REFERENCIA |
| 10369 | TEMPERATURA *f* DE REFERENCIA |
| 10370 | AFINAR, REFINAR, PURIFICAR |
| 10371 | AFINAR UN METAL |
| 10372 | REFINADO |
| 10372 | PURIFICADO |
| 10373 | ACEITE *m* DEPURADO |
| 10374 | PRODUCTO *m* DE REFINADO |
| 10375 | REFINERÍA *f* |
| 10376 | HACHÓN *m* DE REFINERÍA |
| 10377 | REFINADO *m* |
| 10377 | AFINO, AFINADO, REFINO *m*, AFINADURA *f* |
| 10378 | REFINADO *m* DE UN METAL |
| 10379 | HORNO *m* DE AFINO |
| 10380 | PROCEDIMIENTO *m* DE AFINADO |
| 10381 | TEMPERATURA *f* DE AFINADO |
| 10382 | REFLEJAR |
| 10382 | REFLEJAR |
| 10383 | LUZ *f* REFLEJADA |
| 10384 | RAYO *m* REFLEJADO |
| 10385 | SUPERFICIE *f* REFLECTANTE |
| 10386 | TELESCOPIO *m* |
| 10387 | REFLEXIÓN *f* |
| 10387 | DIFRACCIÓN *f*, REFLEXIÓN *f* |

| | |
|---|---|
| 10388 | RED $f$ DE REFLEXIÓN |
| 10389 | PÉRDIDA $f$ POR REFLEXIÓN |
| 10390 | REFLEXIÓN $f$ DE LA LUZ |
| 10391 | RELACIÓN $f$ DE REFLEXIÓN |
| 10392 | PODER $m$ REFLECTANTE |
| 10393 | PODER $m$ REFLECTANTE |
| 10394 | REFLECTOR $m$ |
| 10395 | INDICADOR $m$ POR REFRACCIÓN |
| 10396 | ESPEJO $m$ DE REFRACCIÓN |
| 10397 | RAYO $m$ REFRACTADO |
| 10397 | RAYO $m$ REFRACTADO |
| 10398 | LENTE AMB. DE ACERCAMIENTO, REFRACTO $m$, TELESCOPIO $m$ DE REFRACCIÓN |
| 10399 | REFRACCIÓN $f$ |
| 10400 | REFRACCIÓN $f$ DE LA LUZ |
| 10401 | REFRINGENTE |
| 10401 | MEDIO $m$ REFRACTIVO |
| 10402 | REFRINGENTE |
| 10403 | PODER $m$ REFRINGENTE |
| 10404 | REFRACTÓMETRO $m$ |
| 10405 | PROPIEDAD $f$ REFRACTARIA |
| 10406 | MORTERO REFRACTARIO $m$ |
| 10406 | MORTERO $m$ REFRACTARIO |
| 10407 | MÁQUINA $f$ DE FRÍO |
| 10407 | MÁQUINA $f$ FRIGORÍFICA |
| 10408 | INSTALACIÓN $f$ DE REFRIGERACIÓN |
| 10409 | REFRIGERADOR |
| 10409 | REFRIGERANTE, ENFRIADOR $m$ |
| 10410 | HORNO $m$ DE REGENERACIÓN |
| 10410 | HOGAR $m$ CON RECUPERACIÓN INTERMITENTE |
| 10411 | CALOR ENCERRADO $m$ |
| 10412 | RECUPERADOR $m$ |
| 10412 | REGENERADOR $m$ |
| 10412 | SISTEMA $m$ SIEMENS |
| 10413 | ANILLO $m$ CENTRADOR |
| 10414 | TORSIÓN $f$ ALTERNATIVA |
| 10414 | CABLEADO ALTERNATIVO $m$ |
| 10415 | CABLE METÁLICO DE TORSIÓN ALTERNATIVO $m$ |
| 10416 | POLÍGONO $m$ REGULAR |
| 10417 | REGULARIDAD $f$ DEL MOVIMIENTO |
| 10418 | DISPOSITIVO $m$ DE AJUSTE (DE GRADUACIÓN) |
| 10419 | REGLAJE $m$ DE LA PRESIÓN |
| 10420 | VÁLVULA DE REDUCCIÓN (DE REGULACIÓN) DE PRESIÓN |
| 10421 | REGULADOR $m$ DE VELOCIDAD |
| 10421 | MODERADOR $m$ |
| 10422 | METAL ANTI-FRICCIÓN |
| 10423 | RÉGULO $m$ DE ANTIMONIO |
| 10424 | RECALENTAR |
| 10425 | RECALENTAMIENTO $m$ |
| 10425 | RECALENTAMIENTO $m$ |

| | |
|---|---|
| 10426 | HORNO $m$ DE RECOCER |
| 10427 | REFUERZO $m$ DE LA SOLDADURA |
| 10428 | SOLDADURA $f$ DE REFUERZO |
| 10429 | REFUERZO $m$ |
| 10430 | CHAPA $f$ DE REVESTIMIENTO |
| 10430 | CHAPA $f$ DE REFUERZO |
| 10431 | RECHAZO $m$ DE RECEPCIÓN |
| 10431 | DESHECHO, DESPERDICIO $m$ |
| 10432 | HUMEDAD $f$ RELATIVA |
| 10433 | HUMEDAD $f$ RELATIVA DEL AIRE |
| 10433 | GRADO $m$ HIGROMÉTRICO DEL AIRE |
| 10434 | MOVIMIENTO $m$ RELATIVO |
| 10435 | RELAJACIÓN $f$, EXPANSIÓN $f$ |
| 10435 | RELAJACIÓN $f$ |
| 10436 | AFLOJAR UN FRENO |
| 10437 | GATILLO $m$ (LEVA $f$, DIENTE $m$) DE DISPARO |
| 10438 | PALANCA $f$ DE PUESTA EN MOVIMIENTO |
| 10439 | SEGURIDAD $f$ DE BUEN FUNCIONAMIENTO |
| 10439 | FIABILIDAD $f$ |
| 10439 | SEGURIDAD $f$ DE FUNCIONAMIENTO, SEGURIDAD $f$ DE SERVICIO |
| 10440 | FUNCIONAMIENTO $m$ SOBRE (DE) |
| 10441 | VÁLVULA DE DESCARGA $f$ VÁLVULA DE PURGA $f$ |
| 10441 | VÁLVULA $f$ DE DESCARGA |
| 10442 | ARCO $m$ DE ALIGERAMIENTO, ARCO DE DESCARGA $m$ |
| 10443 | TORNO $m$ DE AFINADO DE ÚTILES |
| 10444 | RELUCTANCIA $f$ |
| 10444 | RESISTENCIA $f$ MAGNÉTICA |
| 10445 | REMANENCIA $f$ |
| 10445 | IMANTACIÓN RESIDUAL $f$ |
| 10445 | IMANTACIÓN REMANENTE $f$ |
| 10445 | MAGNETISMO $m$ RESIDUAL |
| 10445 | MAGNETISMO $m$ REMANENTE |
| 10446 | REFUNDIR |
| 10447 | REFUNDICIÓN $f$ |
| 10448 | MANDO A DISTANCIA $m$, TELEMANDO $m$, CONTROL REMOTO $m$ |
| 10448 | TELEMANDO $m$ |
| 10449 | TELEAFOR $m$ |
| 10449 | AFORO $m$ A DISTANCIA, CALIBRADO $m$ A DISTANCIA, TELECALIBRADO |
| 10450 | MANIVELA $f$ AMOVIBLE |
| 10451 | DESMONTAJE $m$ Y NUEVO MONTAJE $m$ |
| 10452 | EVACUACIÓN $f$ DEL POLVO |
| 10453 | EVACUACIÓN $f$ DE LAS AGUAS RESIDUALES |
| 10454 | DESFERRIZACIÓN $f$ DEL AGUA, ELIMINACIÓN $f$ DEL HIERRO DEL AGUA |
| 10455 | EVACUAR LOS GASES |
| 10455 | DESGASIFICAR |
| 10456 | SOLUBILIZAR |

| | |
|---|---|
| 10457 | CAMBIAR UN ÓRGANO DE UNA MÁQUINA |
| 10458 | CAMBIO *m* DE UN ÓRGANO DE MÁQUINA |
| 10459 | REPARACIÓN *f* |
| 10460 | REPARAR |
| 10461 | TALLER *m* DE MANTENIMIENTO |
| 10461 | TALLER DE REPARACIONES *m* |
| 10462 | PRODUCCIÓN *f* |
| 10462 | FABRICACIÓN *f* |
| 10462 | TRABAJO EN SERIE *m*, SERIE *f* |
| 10462 | CONSTRUCCIÓN *f* |
| 10462 | TRABAJO *m* EN SERIE |
| 10463 | REEMPLAZAR |
| 10463 | RECAMBIAR |
| 10464 | RECAMBIO *m* DE UN ÓRGANO DE MÁQUINA |
| 10465 | REPRODUCCIÓN *f* |
| 10466 | MATERIALES *m* REFRACTARIOS |
| 10467 | REPRODUCCIÓN *f* (RESULTADO) |
| 10468 | REPULSIÓN *f* |
| 10469 | MAGNITUD *f* DESEADA |
| 10470 | NUEVA LAMINACIÓN *f* |
| 10471 | DEPÓSITO *m* |
| 10472 | ELASTICIDAD *f* RESIDUAL |
| 10473 | REMANENCIA *f* |
| 10474 | TENSIÓN RESIDUAL *f* |
| 10475 | RESIDUO *f* |
| 10476 | RESIDUO *m* DE LA COMBUSTIÓN |
| 10477 | RESILIENCIA *f* |
| 10477 | RESISTENCIA *f* VIVA |
| 10478 | RESINA *f* |
| 10479 | QUE ENCIERRA RESINA |
| 10480 | TRANSFORMACIÓN *f* EN RESINA |
| 10481 | TRANSFORMARSE EN RESINA |
| 10482 | MASTIC *m* DE RESINA |
| 10482 | MASTIC *m* RESINOSO |
| 10483 | MADERA *f* RESINOSA |
| 10484 | RESISTENCIA *f* |
| 10484 | FUERZA *f* RESISTENTE |
| 10485 | HORNO *m* AL ARCO CON RESISTENCIA |
| 10486 | ALEACIONES PARA RESISTENCIAS ELÉCTRICAS *f pl* |
| 10487 | SOLDADURA *f* POR RESISTENCIA |
| 10488 | SOLDADURA *f* A TOPE POR RESISTANCIA |
| 10489 | DIAGRAMA *m* DE RESISTENCIAS |
| 10490 | HORNO *m* ELÉCTRICO DE RESISTENCIA |
| 10491 | RESISTENCIA *f* DE UN CONDUCTOR |
| 10492 | RESISTENCIA *f* DEL AIRE |
| 10493 | SOLDADURA *f* POR PUNTOS POR RESISTENCIA |
| 10494 | VERIFICADOR *m* DE RESISTENCIA AL ESFUERZO |
| 10495 | PIRÓMETRO *m* ELÉCTRICO |
| 10495 | PIRÓMETRO *m* DE RESISTENCIA |
| 10496 | INATACABILIDAD *f* A LOS ÁCIDOS |

| | |
|---|---|
| 10497 | RESISTENCIA *f* AL MOVIMIENTO |
| 10497 | RESISTENCIA *f* PASIVA |
| 10498 | RESISTENCIA *f* AL DESLIZAMIENTO |
| 10499 | RESISTENCIA *f* AL DESGASTE |
| 10500 | SOLDADURA *f* POR RESISTENCIA |
| 10501 | HILO *m* PARA RESISTENCIAS ELÉCTRICAS |
| 10502 | RESISTENCIA *f* |
| 10503 | RESISTIVIDAD *f* |
| 10503 | RESISTENCIA *f* ESPECÍFICA ELÉCTRICA |
| 10504 | RESOLUCIÓN *f* |
| 10505 | DESCOMPOSICIÓN *f* DE FUERZAS |
| 10506 | RESONANCIA *f* |
| 10507 | CIZALLAMIENTO *m* |
| 10508 | PONER DE NUEVO EN MARCHA |
| 10509 | NUEVA PUESTA EN MARCHA *f* |
| 10510 | INHIBIDOR *m* |
| 10511 | RECTIFICACIÓN *f* |
| 10512 | RESULTADO *m* DE UNA PRUEBA |
| 10513 | RESULTANTE *f* |
| 10514 | TUERCA *f* DE RETENCIÓN |
| 10515 | ANILLO *m* DE RETENCIÓN |
| 10516 | VARILLA *f* DE RETENCIÓN |
| 10517 | RETRASO *m* EN LA EBULLICIÓN |
| 10518 | MOVIMIENTO *m* RETARDADO |
| 10519 | RETRASO *m* DEL CIERRE DE LA VÁLVULA |
| 10520 | ESTABILIZACIÓN *f* DE LA DUREZA |
| 10521 | RESISTENCIA *f* A LA DEFORMACIÓN |
| 10522 | PRUEBA CONTRARIA *f* |
| 10523 | RETORTA *f* |
| 10524 | HORNO *m* DE CONVERTIDOR |
| 10525 | RETORTA TUBULADA *f* |
| 10526 | RESORTE *m* ANTAGONISTA |
| 10527 | MONTAJE *m* ULTERIOR (MÁS ADELANTE) |
| 10528 | CONTRAMANUBRIO *m* |
| 10529 | CARRERA EN VACÍO *f* (DE UNA MÁQUINA-HERRAMIENTA) |
| 10530 | CARRERA DE RETROCESO *f* |
| 10530 | CARRERA DE RETROCESO DEL ÉMBOLO *f* |
| 10530 | MARCHA *f* HACIA ATRÁS DEL PISTÓN |
| 10530 | RETORNO *m* VUELTA *f* |
| 10531 | EMBELLECEDORES *m pl* |
| 10532 | HORNO *m* DE REVERBERO |
| 10533 | TIEMPO *m* DE INVERSIÓN |
| 10534 | INVERTIR EL SENTIDO DE LA MARCHA |
| 10535 | PRUEBA *f* DE FLEXIÓN INVERTIDA |
| 10536 | CONTRARREACCIÓN *f* |
| 10537 | REVERSIBILIDAD *f* |
| 10538 | REVERSIBILIDAD *f* |
| 10539 | CAMBIO REVERSIBLE *m* |
| 10540 | MOTOR *m* REVERSIBLE |
| 10541 | INVERSIÓN *f* DE LA MARCHA DE UNA MÁQUINA |

| | |
|---|---|
| 10542 | DISPOSITIVO *m* DE CAMBIO DE SENTIDO DE MARCHA DPOR TRANSMISIÓN |
| 10543 | MÁQUINA *f* DE VAPOR REVERSIBLE |
| 10544 | MECANISMO *m* DE CAMBIO DE MARCHA |
| 10545 | DISPOSITIVO *m* DE CAMBIO (INVERSIÓN) DE SENTIDO DE MARCHA POR ENGRANAJES *m pl* CÓNICOS |
| 10546 | DISPOSITIVO *m* DE CAMBIO DE SENTIDO DE MARCHA POR RUEDA DE FRICCIÓN |
| 10547 | DISPOSITIVO *m* DE CAMBIO DE MARCHA POR ENGRANAJES CILÍNDRICOS |
| 10548 | INVERSOR *m* DE MARCHA |
| 10549 | PALANCA *f* DE CAMBIO DE MARCHA |
| 10550 | ÁRBOL DE CAMBIO DE MARCHA *m* |
| 10550 | ÁRBOL DE CAMBIO DE MARCHA *m*, ÁRBOL DE INVERSIÓN DE MARCHA *m* |
| 10550 | ÁRBOL DE DISTRIBUCIÓN *m*, ÁRBOL DE MANDO *m* |
| 10551 | POLEA *f* DE TRANSMISIÓN |
| 10552 | INVERSIÓN *f* DE MOVIMIENTO |
| 10553 | VÁLVULA DE INVERSIÓN *f* VÁLVULA DE RENVÍO *f* |
| 10554 | REVERSIÓN *f* |
| 10555 | UNIÓN *f* DE LAS CORREAS CON REMACHES |
| 10556 | CUENTARREVOLUCIONES *m*, TACÓMETRO *m* |
| 10556 | CUENTARREVOLUCIONES *m*, TACÓMETRO *m* |
| 10556 | TAQUÍMETRO *m* |
| 10557 | TORNO *m* |
| 10557 | REVOLUCIÓN *f* |
| 10558 | RÉGIMEN *m* DE ROTACIÓN |
| 10558 | RÉGIMEN *m* |
| 10559 | REJILLA *f* ROTATIVA |
| 10559 | REJILLA *f* GIRATORIA |
| 10560 | CONTRAPUNTA GIRATORIA *f* |
| 10561 | MASA *f* EN ROTACIÓN |
| 10561 | MASA *f* GIRATORIA |
| 10562 | REOLOGÍA *f* |
| 10563 | REOSTATO *m* |
| 10564 | RODIO *m* |
| 10565 | CRISTAL *m* ROMBOÉDRICO |
| 10566 | ROMBOEDRO *m* |
| 10567 | ROMBOIDE *m* |
| 10568 | ROMBO *m* |
| 10568 | ROMBO *m* |
| 10569 | REFUERZO *m* |
| 10569 | NERVADURA *f* |
| 10570 | NERVADURA *f* DE UN TUBO, ESTRÍA *f* |
| 10571 | TUBOS *m pl* DE NERVIOS |
| 10571 | TUBO *m* DE ALETAS |
| 10571 | TUBO *m* DE ALETAS |
| 10572 | TAMIZ *m* |
| 10572 | CRIBA *f* |
| 10573 | MÁQUINA ALOMADORA : 2, 3 Y 4 HILERAS |

| | |
|---|---|
| 10574 | CHAPA *f* ESTRIADA |
| 10575 | LIMA *f* CURVA |
| 10576 | ESTRÍAS *f pl* |
| 10577 | ESCUADRA (DE), RECTO |
| 10577 | ÁNGULO RECTO *m* |
| 10578 | CONO RECTO *m* |
| 10578 | CONO *m* VERTICAL |
| 10579 | CILINDRO *m* RECTO |
| 10580 | TORNILLO *m* A LA DERECHA |
| 10581 | PARALELEPÍPEDO *m* RECTO |
| 10582 | TRIÁNGULO *m* RECTÁNGULO |
| 10583 | DESVIACIÓN *f* A LA DERECHA |
| 10584 | TORNILLO *m* A LA DERECHA |
| 10585 | ROSCA DERECHA |
| 10585 | PASO *m* A DERECHA |
| 10586 | DENTADO *m* DERECHO |
| 10587 | CABLE TORCIDO A DERECHAS *m* |
| 10588 | CUERPO RÍGIDO *m* |
| 10589 | ENLACE *m* RÍGIDO |
| 10589 | JUNTA *f* RÍGIDA |
| 10589 | FIJACIÓN *f* RÍGIDA |
| 10589 | JUNTA *f* RÍGIDA |
| 10590 | TALADRADORAS *f* RÍGIDAS |
| 10591 | RIGIDEZ, TENSIÓN *f* |
| 10591 | RIGIDEZ *f* |
| 10592 | LLANTA *f* |
| 10593 | LLANTA *f* DE VOLANTE |
| 10594 | CORONA *f* DE ENGRANAJE, CORONA DENTADA *f* |
| 10595 | LLANTA *f* DE UNA POLEA |
| 10596 | LLANTA DE UNA RUEDA *f*, CÍRCULO INTERIOR DE UNA RUEDA *f* |
| 10597 | RESPIRADERO *m* DE ESTANQUEIDAD |
| 10598 | ACERO EFERVESCENTE *m* |
| 10598 | ACERO SINTERIZADO *m* |
| 10599 | ACERO EFERVESCENTE *m* |
| 10599 | ACERO PARCIALMENTE REPESADO *m* |
| 10599 | ACERO ESPUMOSO *m* |
| 10600 | ARO *m* |
| 10600 | ANILLO *m* |
| 10601 | ENGRASE *m* POR ANILLO |
| 10602 | SOPORTE *m* CON ANILLO DE ENGRASE |
| 10603 | SEGMENTO *m* DE CORONA CIRCULAR |
| 10604 | JUNTA *f* ANULAR |
| 10605 | VÁLVULA *f* ANULAR |
| 10606 | PIVOTE *m* ANULAR |
| 10607 | LAVAR CON AGUA ABUNDANTE, LAVAR A TODA AGUA |
| 10607 | ACLARAR, ENJUAGAR |
| 10608 | ACLARADO *m*, ENJUAGADURA *f* |
| 10609 | SIERRA *f* A LO LARGO |
| 10610 | GUÍA *f* PARA SERRAR A LO LARGO |

| | |
|---|---|
| 10611 | ALTURA *f* DE ASCENSIÓN |
| 10611 | ALZA *f* |
| 10611 | LEVANTAMIENTO *m*, PROYECCIÓN *f* DE UN PLANO, RECORRIDO *m* O CARRERA DE VÁLVULA O PISTÓN |
| 10612 | AUMENTO *m* (O ELEVACIÓN *f*) DE LA TEMPERATURA |
| 10613 | COMBADURA *f*, ARQUEADO *m*, FLECHA *f* |
| 10613 | ASIENTO *m*, DEPRESIÓN *f*, DESLIZAMIENTO *m* |
| 10613 | FLECHA, SAGITA *f* |
| 10614 | COLUMNA MONTANTE *f* |
| 10614 | RESPIRADERO *m* |
| 10614 | CONTRAHUELLA *f* |
| 10615 | TUBO *m* VERTICAL |
| 10615 | TUBO *m* ELEVADOR |
| 10615 | TUBO *m* DE SUBIDA |
| 10615 | ASCENDENTE (TUBO) |
| 10616 | VARILLA *f* ASCENDENTE |
| 10617 | VÁLVULA *f* DE VÁSTAGO ASCENDENTE |
| 10618 | TEMPERATURA *f* CRECIENTE |
| 10619 | ARENA *f* DE RÍO |
| 10620 | AGUA *f* DE RÍO, AGUA FLUVIAL |
| 10620 | AGUA *f* FLUVIAL, AGUA DE RÍO |
| 10621 | REMACHE *m*, ROBLÓN *m* |
| 10622 | ROBLÓN *m* EN EL BORDE DE LA CHAPA |
| 10623 | HORNO *m* PARA CALENTAR LOS REMACHES |
| 10624 | CABEZA *f* DE ROBLÓN |
| 10625 | AGUJERO *m* EN LAS CHAPAS DE ENSAMBLADO |
| 10625 | AGUJERO *m* DE ROBLÓN |
| 10626 | ESTAMPA *f* DE ROBLONAR, CAZA *f* REMACHES |
| 10626 | ESTAMPA DE ROBLONAR *f* |
| 10627 | ACERO DE REMACHES *m* |
| 10628 | REMACHE *m*, ROBLADURA *f* |
| 10629 | ROBLONAR, REMACHAR |
| 10630 | TENAZAS *f pl* DE REMACHAR |
| 10631 | SOLDADURA *f* DE ROBLONES |
| 10632 | ROBLÓN *m* DE CABEZA CILÍNDRICA |
| 10633 | ROBLÓN *m* DE CABEZA DE GOTA DE SEBO |
| 10634 | ROBLÓN *m* DE CABEZA PLANA |
| 10635 | ROBLÓN *m* DE CABEZA IGUALADA |
| 10635 | ROBLÓN *m* DE CABEZA METIDA |
| 10635 | ROBLÓN *m* DE CABEZA PERDIDA |
| 10635 | ROBLÓN *m* DE CABEZA AVELLANADA |
| 10636 | ROBLÓN *m* DE CABEZA REDONDA |
| 10637 | ROBLÓN *m* DE CABEZA HEMISFÉRICA |
| 10638 | BRIDA *f* REMACHADA |
| 10639 | REMACHE *m*, ROBLADURA *f* |
| 10639 | CLAVADO *m*, UNIÓN POR CLAVO *f* |
| 10639 | JUNTA *f* ROBLONADA, UNIÓN *f* POR ROBLONADO |
| 10640 | TUBO *m* ROBLONADO |
| 10641 | OBRERO *m* REMACHADOR |
| 10641 | REMACHADOR *m* |
| 10642 | REMACHADORA *f* |
| 10642 | MÁQUINA *f* DE REMACHAR |
| 10643 | ROBLONADO *m*, REMACHADO *m* |
| 10644 | REMACHADORA *f* |
| 10644 | MARTILLO *m* DE REMACHAR |
| 10644 | MARTILLO *m* REMACHADOR |
| 10645 | MÁQUINA *f* DE ROBLAR |
| 10646 | ROBLONES *m pl*, REMACHES *m pl* |
| 10647 | GASOLINA *f* DE CARRETERA |
| 10648 | TOSTAR LOS MINERALES |
| 10649 | HORNO *m* DE TOSTACIÓN |
| 10650 | TUESTE *m* DE MINERALES |
| 10651 | ROCA *f* |
| 10652 | CRISTAL *m* DE ROCA |
| 10653 | SAL *f* GEMA |
| 10654 | BALANCÍN *m*, VOLTEADOR *m* |
| 10655 | REJILLA *f* CON SACUDIDAS |
| 10655 | ENREJILLADO *m* CON BARROTES MOVIBLES |
| 10655 | REJILLA *f* OSCILANTE |
| 10656 | PALANCA *f* OSCILANTE |
| 10657 | ÁRBOL OSCILANTE *m* |
| 10658 | CIZALLA BASCULANTE *f* |
| 10659 | PRUEBA *f* DE DUREZA ROCKWELL |
| 10660 | BARRA *f* |
| 10660 | BARRA *f*, BARROTE *m*, BARRETA *f* |
| 10660 | BARRA *f* |
| 10660 | VÁSTAGO *m*, VARILLA *f* |
| 10661 | CALIBRE DE DIÁMETRO *m* |
| 10662 | BRAZO *m* DE LA PUNTA DE HAZAR DEL PLANÍMETRO |
| 10663 | VÁSTAGO *m*, VARILLA *f* |
| 10663 | BARRA *f*, TIRANTE *m*, VARILLA *f* |
| 10663 | VARILLA *f* |
| 10664 | RADIOGRAFÍA *f* |
| 10665 | LAMINAR |
| 10665 | RODAR |
| 10666 | REDUCIR POR LAMINACIÓN |
| 10667 | PELÍCULA *f* EN CARRETE, EN BOBINA |
| 10668 | FORJADO *m* POR LAMINADO |
| 10668 | PERFILADURA *f* |
| 10669 | TREN *m* LAMINADOR |
| 10670 | TREN *m* LAMINADOR |
| 10671 | TAMBOR *m* |
| 10671 | RODILLO *m*, CILINDRO *m* TAMBOR *m* |
| 10671 | RODILLO *m* |
| 10671 | CILINDRO *m*, RODILLO *m* |
| 10672 | BRIDA *f* MANDRILADA |
| 10673 | SOBREDORADO |
| 10674 | CHAPA *f* LAMINADA |
| 10675 | PERFIL *m* DE LAMINACIÓN |

| | |
|---|---|
| 10676 | HIERRO _m_ LAMINADO |
| 10677 | TUBO _m_ LAMINADO |
| 10678 | ALAMBRE _m_ LAMINADO |
| 10679 | RODILLO _m_ |
| 10679 | RODILLO _m_ |
| 10680 | RODAMIENTO _m_ DE RODILLOS |
| 10680 | COJINETE _m_ DE RODILLOS |
| 10681 | RODAMIENTO _m_ DE RÓTULA SOBRE RODILLOS |
| 10682 | RODAMIENTO _m_ DE RODILLOS CILÍNDRICOS |
| 10683 | RODAMIENTO _m_ DE RODILLOS CÓNICOS |
| 10684 | CADENA DE RODILLOS _f_ |
| 10685 | ENDEREZADORA _f_ DE RODILLOS |
| 10686 | PALANCA _f_ RODADIZA |
| 10687 | MOLINO _m_ DE CÍLINDROS |
| 10688 | RODILLO _m_ DE UNA CADENA |
| 10689 | ANILLO DE RODADURA DE LOS RODILLOS _m_ |
| 10690 | SOPORTE _m_ DE RODILLOS |
| 10691 | COJINETE _m_ DE RODILLOS |
| 10692 | PULSADOR _m_ DE ROLDANA |
| 10693 | CALIBRE _m_ MORDAZA PARA FILETEADOS O ROSCADOS |
| 10694 | CUNA _f_ DE RODILLOS |
| 10695 | RODILLOS _m pl_ |
| 10695 | CANTOS RODADOS _m pl_ (QUE ALLANAR) |
| 10696 | LAMINADO _m_, LAMINACIÓN _f_ |
| 10696 | RODADURA _f_ |
| 10697 | CICLOIDE, RULETA _f_ |
| 10697 | CURVA RODANTE _f_ |
| 10698 | SENTIDO _m_ DE LAMINADO |
| 10699 | BRIDA _f_ DE MANDRILAR |
| 10700 | FRICCIÓN _f_ DE RODAMIENTO |
| 10701 | LAMINADOR _m_ |
| 10701 | TREN _m_ LAMINADOR |
| 10702 | MOVIMIENTO _m_ DE RODADURA |
| 10703 | RESISTENCIA _f_ A LA RODADURA |
| 10704 | JAULA DE CILINDROS _f_ |
| 10705 | SUPERFICIE _f_ DE RODADURA |
| 10706 | CARGA _f_ MÓVIL |
| 10706 | CARGA RODANTE _f_ |
| 10707 | CEMENTO ROMANO _m_ |
| 10708 | TECHO _m_ |
| 10709 | LÁMPARA _f_ DE TECHO |
| 10710 | AGUJERO _m_ DE HOMBRE DE TECHO |
| 10711 | TUBULADURA _f_ DE TECHO |
| 10712 | CARTÓN BITUMINOSO O ASFÁLTICO _m_ |
| 10713 | TEMPERATURA _f_ NORMAL DE LA SALA |
| 10713 | TEMPERATURA _f_ NORMAL |
| 10713 | TEMPERATURA _f_ AMBIENTE |
| 10714 | RAÍZ (METAMÁTICAS) |
| 10715 | CORTARRAÍCES _m_ |
| 10716 | ÁNGULO DE BASE (O DE PIE) DEL DIENTE _m_ |

| | |
|---|---|
| 10717 | CÍRCULO DE RAÍZ _m_ |
| 10718 | CONO DE FONDO _m_ |
| 10719 | DIÁMETRO _m_ DE PIE |
| 10720 | FLANCO _m_ DE BASE |
| 10720 | RAÍZ _f_ |
| 10721 | FLANCO _m_ DE RAÍZ |
| 10722 | ESCARIFICADOR _m_ |
| 10723 | CIRCUNFERENCIA DE VACIADO _f_ |
| 10723 | CÍRCULO DE FONDO _m_ |
| 10723 | CÍRCULO DE HUECO _m_ |
| 10723 | CÍRCULO DE FONDO _m_ |
| 10724 | PIE _m_ DE DIENTE |
| 10725 | PIE _m_ DEL DIENTE |
| 10726 | RAÍZ _f_ DE LA SOLDADURA |
| 10727 | ANCHURA _f_ DE LA SOLDADURA DE BASE |
| 10728 | RADIO _m_ DE SEPARACIÓN ENTRE LOS BORDES |
| 10729 | VENTILADOR _m_ SISTEMA ROOT |
| 10730 | CUERDA _f_ |
| 10730 | CABLE _m_, MAROMA _f_ |
| 10731 | MUFLA _f_ CORDAL |
| 10732 | FRENO _m_ DE CUERDA |
| 10733 | DIÁMETRO _m_ DE UN CABLE |
| 10734 | TRANSMISIÓN _f_ FUNICULAR |
| 10734 | TRANSMISIÓN _f_ POR CUERDAS CORREAS |
| 10734 | TRANSMISIÓN _f_ POR CABLES |
| 10735 | ACCIONAMIENTO POR CABLE _m_ |
| 10736 | MÁQUINA _f_ DE ACCIONADO POR CABLE |
| 10737 | TAMBOR _m_ DE ENROLLAMIENTO |
| 10738 | VOLANTE _m_ DE GARGANTAS |
| 10739 | CORCHA _f_ |
| 10739 | CABLEADO _m_ |
| 10740 | CORDÓN _m_ DE CABLE |
| 10741 | APAREJO _m_ DE CUERDA |
| 10742 | POLEA _f_ PARA CABLE DE TRANSMISIÓN |
| 10742 | POLEA _f_ DE CABLE |
| 10743 | HILO _m_ PARA CABLE |
| 10744 | HILO _m_ DE DEVANADERA |
| 10745 | CUERDAS _f_, CORDELERÍA _f_ |
| 10746 | ALCACHOFA _f_ DE REGADERA |
| 10747 | ESCARIADOR DE DIENTES FIJOS _m_, ESCARIADOR EXTENSIBLE _m_ |
| 10748 | COBRE _m_ ROSETA |
| 10749 | ACEITE _m_ DE RESINA |
| 10749 | ACEITE _m_ DE TREMENTINA |
| 10750 | ÁCIDO ROSÓLICO _m_ |
| 10751 | VENTILADOR _m_ DE PISTÓN ROTATIVO |
| 10752 | ENFRIAMIENTO _m_ CIRCULAR |
| 10753 | MOTOAGRARIOS _m_ CON FRESAS ROTATIVAS, MOTOCULTIVADORES |
| 10754 | MOTOR _m_ CON PISTONES ROTATIVOS |
| 10755 | LIMA _f_ ROTATIVA |

| | | | | |
|---|---|---|---|---|
| 10756 | PISTÓN *m* ROTATIVO | 10791 | HERRAMIENTA *f* DE DESBASTAR |
| 10757 | PRENSA *f* ROTATIVA | 10792 | RUGOSIDAD *f* |
| 10758 | BOMBA *f* ROTATIVA | 10792 | RUGOSIDAD *f* |
| 10758 | BOMBA *f* DE PALETAS ROTATIVAS | 10793 | REDONDEAR UNA ARISTA |
| 10758 | BOMBA *f* DE ROTOR | 10794 | CANTONERA *f* EN ÁNGULO REDONDEADO |
| 10759 | TIJERAS ROTATIVAS *f pl* | 10795 | HIERRO *m* REDONDO |
| 10760 | VÁLVULA *f* DE COMPUERTA GIRATORIA | 10796 | LIMA *f* REDONDA |
| 10760 | VÁLVULA *f* DE COMPUERTA GIRATORIA | 10797 | BRIDA *f* REDONDA |
| 10760 | GRIFO *m* DISTRIBUIDOR GIRATORIO | 10798 | MATRAZ *m* REDONDO, MATRAZ *m* DE CUELLO LARGO |
| 10760 | OBTURADOR *m* | | |
| 10760 | VÁLVULA *f* OSCILANTE | 10799 | LETRA *f* REDONDILLA |
| 10761 | MÁQUINA *f* ROTATIVA | 10800 | CEPILLO *m* REDONDO |
| 10762 | PLATILLO *m* GIRATORIO | 10801 | CABLE REDONDO *m* |
| 10763 | TORNEAR | 10802 | ROSCA *f* REDONDA |
| 10764 | ÁRBOL *m* GIRATORIO | 10803 | LEÑA *f* CORTA Y REDONDA |
| 10765 | ROTACIÓN *f* | 10803 | LEÑO *m* |
| 10766 | MOVIMIENTO *m* ROTATORIO | 10804 | ALAMBRE *m* REDONDO |
| 10766 | MOVIMIENTO *m* DE ROTACIÓN | 10805 | PINZA *f* REDONDA |
| 10767 | ROTOR *m* | 10806 | PLUMA *f* DE REDONDILLA |
| 10768 | MADERA *f* PUDRIDA | 10807 | TORNILLO *m* DE ROSCA REDONDA |
| 10769 | DESCOMPOSICIÓN *f* | 10808 | ARISTA *f* REDONDEADA |
| 10770 | CARIES *f*, LIZÓN *m* | 10809 | REDONDEADO *m* DEL FILETE |
| 10770 | PODREDUMBRE *f* DE LA MADERA | 10810 | ITINERARIO MARÍTIMO *m*, PERIPLO *m* |
| 10770 | NECROSIS *f* | 10810 | RECORRIDO *m*, CARRERA *f*, TRAYECTORIA *f* |
| 10771 | PERFORAR, TALADRAR, BARRENAR, AGUJEREAR | 10811 | PROGRAMA *m* DE COMPUTADOR |
| 10771 | PERFORAR PREVIAMENTE | 10812 | LÍNEA *f* |
| 10772 | CÁLCULO RÁPIDO APROXIMADO *m* | 10813 | LÍNEA *f* DE REMACHES |
| 10773 | RUEDA *f* DENTADA BRUTA DE FUNDICIÓN | 10813 | HILERA *f* DE REMACHES |
| 10773 | RUEDA *f* DE ENGRANAJE BRUTA | 10814 | REVOLUCIÓNES *f pl* POR MINUTO |
| 10773 | RUEDA *f* DENTADA Y FUNDIDA EN BRUTO | 10814 | REVOLUCIÓN *f* MINUTO |
| 10774 | LIMA *f* DE TALLA BASTA, LIMATÓN *m* | 10815 | ELIMINAR LA HERRUMBRE, DESOXIDAR |
| 10774 | LIMATÓN *m* | 10816 | CAUCHO *m*, GOMA *f* |
| 10774 | LIMA *f* FUERTE | 10817 | CORREA DE GOMA *f* |
| 10775 | DESBASTAR | 10817 | CORREA DE GOMA PELO *f* |
| 10775 | DESBASTAR | 10818 | TELA *f* ENCAUCHUTADA |
| 10776 | BRIDA *f* EN BRUTO | 10818 | TELA *f* CAUCHUTADA |
| 10777 | DESBASTE *m* CON MUELA | 10818 | LIENZO *m* CAUCHUTADO |
| 10778 | LAMINADO *m* BRUTO | 10819 | DIAFRAGMA *m* DE CAUCHO |
| 10779 | SUPERFICIE *f* RUGOSA | 10820 | JUNTA *f* DE ANILLO DE CAUCHO (ARANDELA DE CAUCHO) |
| 10780 | TUBO *m* RUGOSO | | |
| 10781 | PESO *m* BRUTO | 10821 | TUBO *m* (FLEXIBLE) DE CAUCHO |
| 10782 | AGUJERO *m* INICIAL | 10822 | CINTA *f* CAUCHUTADA |
| 10783 | HACER RUGOSO | 10823 | ARANDELA *f* DE CAUCHO |
| 10784 | SUPERFICIE *f* RUGOSA | 10823 | ANILLO *m* DE CAUCHO |
| 10785 | ESBOZO *m*, DESBASTE *m* | 10824 | TAPÓN *m* DE GOMA |
| 10786 | ESBOZO *m*, DESBASTE *m* | 10825 | GOMA *f* ELÁSTICA |
| 10786 | DESBASTE *m* | 10825 | CAUCHO *m*, GOMA *f* |
| 10787 | JAULA DESBASTADORES *f* | 10826 | ELIMINACIÓN *f* DE LA HERRUMBRE, DESOXIDACIÓN *f* |
| 10788 | TORNO *m* DE DESBASTAR | | |
| 10789 | TREN *m* DESBASTADOR | 10827 | MAMPUESTO *m* |
| 10790 | ESCARIADOR DE DESBASTADO CÓNICO *m* | 10828 | CONSTRUCCIÓN *f* DE MAMPOSTERÍA |

| | |
|---|---|
| 10829 | RUBIDIO  *m* |
| 10830 | BOBINA  *f*  DE RUHMKORFF |
| 10831 | REGLA  *f*  DE DIBUJANTE |
| 10832 | CAPA  *f*, MANO  *f* |
| 10832 | PASADA  *f* |
| 10833 | MARCHAR A GRAN VELOCIDAD |
| 10834 | MARCHAR A PEQUEÑA VELOCIDAD |
| 10835 | RODAR UN MOTOR |
| 10836 | REBABA  *f* |
| 10837 | FUNDIRSE (EL COJINETE SE FUNDE) |
| 10838 | TREN  *m*  DE RODILLOS DE SALIDA |
| 10839 | COLECTOR  *m* |
| 10840 | TORNEAR EN FALSA PASADA |
| 10841 | HULLA  *f*  BRUTA |
| 10841 | HULLA SIN CLASIFICAR |
| 10842 | CHAPA  *f*  TECNOLÓGICA |
| 10843 | DEPÓSITO  *m*  DE RECEPCIÓN |
| 10844 | CANAL DE COLADA  *m* |
| 10844 | RODILLO  *m*  DE RODAMIENTO |
| 10844 | COLADA  *f* |
| 10845 | COLADA  *f* |
| 10845 | SISTEMA  *m*  DE ALIMENTACIÓN (DEL MOLDE) |
| 10846 | MARCHA  *f*  ATRÁS |
| 10847 | ACOPLAMIENTO  *m*, ENCAJE  *m* |
| 10847 | MONTAJE  *m*  GIRATORIO |
| 10847 | AJUSTE  *m*, MONTAJE  *m*, AJUSTAMIENTO  *m* |
| 10848 | MARCHA  *f*  HACIA ADELANTE |
| 10849 | METRO  *m*  CORRIENTE |
| 10850 | MARCHA  *f*, FUNCIONAMIENTO  *m*  (DE UNA MÁQUINA, DE UN VEHICULO) |
| 10850 | MARCHA  *f*, VELOCIDAD DE UNA MÁQUINA  *f* |
| 10850 | FUNCIONAMIENTO  *m*  (DE MÁQUINA) |
| 10851 | RAMAL LIBRE DE UN APAREJO  *m* |
| 10851 | RAMAL  *m*  CORRIENTE |
| 10852 | TORNILLO  *m*  DE TRANSLACIÓN |
| 10853 | CARA INTERNA DE UNA CORREA  *f* |
| 10854 | RUEDA  *f*  PORTADORA |
| 10854 | RODILLO  *m*  DE RODAMIENTO (RUEDA PORTADORA) |
| 10855 | RODAJE  *m* |
| 10856 | REBABAS  *f pl* |
| 10857 | GUÍA  DE DESLIZAMIENTO (PARA ESCALERA MÓVIL DE TEJADO)  *f* |
| 10858 | FRACTURA  *f*, ROTURA  *f*, RUPTURA  *f*, ARRANCAMIENTO  *m* |
| 10858 | RUPTURA  *f* |
| 10858 | FRACTURA  *f*, ROTURA  *f* |
| 10859 | DESGARRARSE |
| 10860 | DISCO  *m*  DE ROTURA |
| 10860 | MEMBRANA  *f*  DE RUPTURA |
| 10861 | FRACTURA  *f*, ROTURA  *f*, RUPTURA  *f*, PLIEGUE  *m* |

| | |
|---|---|
| 10861 | RUPTURA  *f* |
| 10862 | ACEITE  *m*  DE PINO |
| 10863 | HERRUMBRE  *f*, ÓXIDO  *m* |
| 10864 | AHERRUMBRARSE, OXIDARSE |
| 10865 | FORMACIÓN  *f*  DE HERRUMBRE |
| 10866 | PRODUCTO  *m*  ANTIOXIDANTE |
| 10867 | JUNTA  *f*  DE FUNDICIÓN CON MASILLA |
| 10868 | PRESERVADOR  *m*  DE LA OXIDACIÓN |
| 10869 | PRESERVADOR  *m*  CONTRA LA OXIDACIÓN |
| 10869 | ANTIOXIDANTE  *m* |
| 10870 | PRODUCTO  *m*  ANTIOXIDANTE |
| 10871 | PROTECCIÓN  *f*  CONTRA LA OXIDACIÓN |
| 10872 | BAÑO  *m*  DE REMOCIÓN (O DE ELIMINACIÓN) DE LA HERRUMBRE |
| 10873 | HERRUMBRE  *f*, ÓXIDO  *m* |
| 10874 | RUTENIO  *m* |
| 10875 | FLEJE  *m*  INOXIDABLE |
| 10876 | PIEZA  *f*  DE APOYO, SOPORTE  *m*, ASIENTO  *m* |
| 10877 | ARMAZÓN  *f*, BASTIDOR  *m*, APOYO  *m* |
| 10878 | LIMA  *f*  DE LADOS LISOS |
| 10879 | CARGA DE SEGURIDAD  *f* |
| 10879 | CARGA PRÁCTICA  *f* |
| 10880 | ESFUERZO  *m*  ADMISIBLE |
| 10881 | APARATO DE PROTECCIÓN  *m* |
| 10881 | DISPOSITIVO  *m*  DE SEGURIDAD |
| 10881 | DISPOSITIVO  *m*  PROTECTOR |
| 10881 | DISPOSITIVO  *m*  DE SEGURIDAD |
| 10882 | CINTURÓN DE SEGURIDAD |
| 10883 | FRENO  *m*  DE SEGURIDAD |
| 10884 | MANGUITO  *m*  DE SEGURIDAD |
| 10885 | COEFICIENTE DE SEGURIDAD  *m* |
| 10886 | FUSIBLE  *m*  DE CORTACIRCUITOS, PLOMO  *m* |
| 10886 | CORTA CIRCUITO DE SEGURIDAD |
| 10886 | PLOMO  *m*  DE SEGURIDAD, DE PRECINTAR |
| 10886 | PLOMO  *m*  FUSIBLE, ALAMBRE  *m*  DE PLOMO |
| 10887 | DISCO  *m*  DE SEGURIDAD CONTRA ROTURA |
| 10888 | GANCHO  *m*  DE SEGURIDAD |
| 10889 | MEDIDAS  *f pl*  DE SEGURIDAD |
| 10890 | VÁLVULA  *f*  DE SEGURIDAD DE GRAN RECORRIDO |
| 10891 | VÁLVULA  *f*  DE SEGURIDAD |
| 10892 | DESCENTRADO  *m*, DOBLAMIENTO  *m* |
| 10892 | FLEXIÓN  *f* |
| 10892 | FLEXIÓN  *f* |
| 10892 | GOTEO  *m* |
| 10893 | DOBLEGARSE |
| 10894 | FLEXIÓN  *f* |
| 10895 | FLEXIONES  *f* |
| 10896 | ASBESTO  *m*, AMIANTO  *m* |
| 10897 | SALARIO  *m* |
| 10897 | ASIGNACIÓN  *f*, SUELDO  *m*, SALARIO  *m* |
| 10898 | INGENIERO  *m*  ENCARGADO DE LAS VENTAS |

| | |
|---|---|
| 10899 | ÁCIDO SALICÍLICO *m* |
| 10900 | ÁNGULO SALIENTE *m* |
| 10901 | AREÓMETRO *m* PARA SOLUCIONES SALINAS |
| 10902 | SEDÁN *m*, (COCHE *m* DE) CONDUCCIÓN INTERIOR |
| 10902 | BERLINA *f* |
| 10903 | SALITRE, NITRO *m* |
| 10903 | NITRATO *m* DE POTASIO |
| 10903 | NITRO *m* |
| 10903 | NITRATO *m* |
| 10904 | SAL *f* (QUÍMICA) |
| 10905 | BAÑO *m* DE SAL |
| 10906 | PROPORCIÓN *f* DE SAL |
| 10907 | SAL *f* DE ACEDERAS |
| 10908 | SOLUCIÓN *f* SALINA |
| 10909 | PRUEBA *f* DE PULVERIZACIÓN SALINA |
| 10910 | AGUA *f* SALINA |
| 10911 | SOLDADURA *f* |
| 10912 | HORNO *m* DE BAÑO DE SAL |
| 10913 | TEMPLA *m* EN BAÑO DE SAL |
| 10914 | SAMARIO *m* |
| 10915 | MUESTRA *f* |
| 10915 | MUESTRA *f*, ESPÉCIMEN *m* |
| 10916 | MUESTREO *m* |
| 10916 | TOMA *f* DE UNA MUESTRA |
| 10917 | ARENA *f* |
| 10918 | BAÑO *m* DE ARENA |
| 10919 | LIMPIAR CON CHORRO DE ARENA |
| 10920 | ARENADOR *m* |
| 10920 | MÁQUINA *f* DE CHORRO DE ARENA |
| 10921 | LIMPIEZA *f* CON CHORRO DE ARENA |
| 10922 | FUNDICIÓN EN ARENA *f* |
| 10923 | FILTRO *m* DE ARENA |
| 10924 | MOLDE *m* DE ARENA |
| 10925 | PAPEL *m* ESMERIL |
| 10926 | MÁQUINA *f* DE ALISAR CON PAPEL DE LIJA |
| 10927 | RESINA *f* |
| 10927 | SANDÁRACA *f* |
| 10928 | GRES *m*, ARENISCA *f* (GEOL.) |
| 10929 | LAMINADO *m* EN SANDWICH |
| 10929 | LAMINADO *m* ESTRATIFICADO |
| 10930 | TERRENO *m* ARENOSO |
| 10931 | EQUIPO *m* SANITARIO, INSTALACIONES *f pl* SANITARIAS |
| 10931 | INSTALACIONES *f* SANITARIAS |
| 10932 | SAPONIFICABLE |
| 10933 | SAPONIFICABLE |
| 10934 | SAPONIFICAR |
| 10935 | SAPONITA *f* |
| 10935 | PIEDRA *f* DE JABÓN, SAPONITA *f* |
| 10936 | ALBURA *f*, SÁMAGO *m* |

| | |
|---|---|
| 10937 | HIERRO *m* (BASTIDOR) DE CRISTALES |
| 10938 | ACABADO *m* SATINADO |
| 10939 | SATURAR |
| 10940 | HIDROCARBUROS *m pl* PARAFÍNICOS |
| 10940 | HIDROCARBUROS *m pl* SATURADOS |
| 10941 | SOLUCIÓN *f* SATURADA |
| 10942 | VAPOR *m* SATURANTE |
| 10942 | VAPOR *m* SATURADO |
| 10943 | SATURACIÓN *f* |
| 10944 | PRESIÓN *f* DE SATURACIÓN |
| 10945 | TEMPERATURA *f* DE SATURACIÓN |
| 10946 | SALSERILLA *f* |
| 10947 | ECONOMÍA *f* DE MANO DE OBRA |
| 10947 | ECONOMÍA *f* (O AHORRO *m*) DE TRABAJO |
| 10948 | ECONOMÍA *f* (O AHORRO *m*) DE FUERZA MOTRIZ |
| 10949 | ECONOMÍA *f* DE TIEMPO |
| 10949 | AHORRO *m* DE TIEMPO |
| 10950 | SIERRA *f* |
| 10951 | SERRAR, ASERRAR |
| 10952 | HOJA *f* DE SIERRA |
| 10953 | SERRÍN, ASERRÍN *m* |
| 10953 | ASERRIN *m* |
| 10954 | LIMA *f* PARA AFILAR LOS DIENTES DE SIERRA |
| 10955 | TORNILLO *m* PARA AFILAR SIERRAS |
| 10956 | ASERRADERO *m*, SERRERÍA *f* |
| 10957 | ÚTIL *m* PARA TRISCAR |
| 10957 | ÚTIL PARA TRISCAR UNA SIERRA |
| 10958 | TRISCADO *m* DE UNA SIERRA |
| 10958 | PUESTA *f* EN ESTADO DE LOS DIENTES DE UNA SIERRA |
| 10959 | DIENTE *m* DE SIERRA |
| 10960 | ACOPLAMIENTO *m* DE DIENTES DE SIERRA |
| 10961 | ASERRADO *m* |
| 10962 | MADERA *f* CORTADA |
| 10963 | SIERRAS *f pl* DE LEÑOS |
| 10964 | ESCAMA *f* |
| 10965 | ANDAMIAJE *m*, ANDAMIO *m* |
| 10966 | PRODUCTO *m* ESCALARIO |
| 10967 | ESCALARIO *m* |
| 10968 | ESCAMA *f* |
| 10968 | ESCALA *f* |
| 10969 | INCRUSTACIÓN *f* DE LAS CALDERAS |
| 10969 | INCRUSTACIONES *f* DE LAS CALDERAS |
| 10969 | CALIZA *f* |
| 10969 | DEPÓSITOS *m pl* CALCARIOS |
| 10970 | REPRODUCCIÓN *f* (EN AMPLIACIÓN) |
| 10971 | DESINCRUSTAR |
| 10971 | DESINCRUSTAR |
| 10972 | CRUZ *f* (O BRAZO *m*) DE BALANZA |
| 10973 | ESCALA *f* DE UN PLANO (DE UN DIBUJO) |

| | | | | |
|---|---|---|---|---|
| 10974 | ESCALA *f*, GAMA *f* (DE DUREZA) | | 11007 | CHATARRA *f* |
| 10974 | GAMA *f* DE DUREZA | | 11008 | RASPAR |
| 10975 | DESCASCARSE | | 11008 | RASPAR, RASCAR |
| 10976 | PLATILLO *m* DE BALANZA | | 11008 | LIMPIAR |
| 10977 | FOSO *m* DE BATIDURAS | | 11009 | RAEDERA *f* |
| 10978 | DESINCRUSTANTE PREVENTIVO | | 11009 | RASCADOR, RASPADOR *m* |
| 10978 | DESINCRUSTANTE | | 11009 | RASCADOR, RASPADOR *m* |
| 10978 | SUBSTANCIA *f* ANTIINCRUSTANTE | | 11009 | RASPADOR *m*, RASCADOR *m* |
| 10979 | DECAPADO *m* | | 11009 | RASPADOR *m* |
| 10980 | INOXIDABILIDAD *f* | | 11010 | TRANSPORTADOR *m* DE RASCADORES |
| 10981 | GRADUACIÓN *f* | | 11011 | EXPURGACIÓN *f*, LIMPIEZA *f* |
| 10981 | DIVISIÓN *f* | | 11011 | RASPADO *m* |
| 10981 | ESCALA *f* | | 11011 | RASPADO *m* |
| 10982 | ESCALA *f* | | 11012 | MÁQUINA *f* DE RASCAR O DE RAER |
| 10983 | DIBUJO *m* A ESCALA | | 11013 | GARRA *f* |
| 10984 | TRIÁNGULO *m* ESCALENO | | 11014 | CEPILLO *m* METÁLICO |
| 10985 | DESCASCADO *m* | | 11015 | RESISTENCIA *f* |
| 10986 | MARTILLO *m* PARA PICAR LAS CALDERAS | | 11016 | ACABADO *m* CON EL CEPILLO METÁLICO |
| 10986 | MARTILLO *m* DE DESBARBAR LA FUNDICIÓN, MARTILLO DESTAJADOR | | 11017 | PRUEBA *f* ESCLEROMÉTRICA |
| 10987 | DESINCRUSTACIÓN *f* | | 11018 | PANTALLA *f* |
| 10987 | DESINCRUSTACIÓN *f* | | 11018 | TAMIZ *m* |
| 10988 | DESCORTEZAMIENTO *m* | | 11019 | DIAFRAGMA *m* |
| 10989 | GRAFITO *m* EN COPOS | | 11020 | GRANULOMETRÍA *f* |
| 10990 | EXPLORAR, ANALIZAR | | 11021 | TORNILLO *m* |
| 10991 | ESCANDIO *m* | | 11021 | PERNO *m* ROSCADO |
| 10992 | EXPLORACIÓN *f* | | 11022 | ATORNILLAR |
| 10993 | REBAJAR METAL (AL SOPLETE) | | 11022 | APRETAR UN TORNILLO |
| 10994 | DIFUSIÓN *f* | | 11023 | BROCA *f* TORSADA, BROCA *f* AL ESTILO SUIZO |
| 10995 | ELIMINADOR *m* DE IMPUREZAS | | 11023 | BROCA *f* ESTIRIA O TORSADA |
| 10996 | VERDE DE SCHEELE | | 11024 | EJE *m* DE SIMETRÍA |
| 10996 | ARSENITO *m* DE COBRE | | 11025 | TAPÓN *m* ROSCADO |
| 10997 | TUNGSTATO NATURAL DE CALCIO *m* | | 11025 | TAPÓN *m* ROSCADO |
| 10997 | TUNGSTATO NATURAL DE CALCIO *m* | | 11025 | TAPÓN *m* ROSCADO |
| 10998 | BARNIZ *m* A LA GOMA LACA | | 11026 | MANGUITO *m* ROSCADO |
| 10999 | ESQUISTO *m* | | 11027 | TORNIQUETE *m* HIDRÁULICO (PARA MEDIR EL CAUDAL DE UNA CORRIENTE DE AGUA) |
| 11000 | VERDE DE SCHWEINFURT | | 11028 | ATERRAJADO *m*, CORTE *m* DE ROSCA |
| 11001 | DIRECCIÓN/ORGANIZACIÓN *f* CIENTÍFICA DE LOS TALLERES | | 11029 | TORNO *m* DE ROSCAR |
| 11002 | ESCLERÓMETRO *m* | | 11030 | TERRAJADO *m* DE UN FILETE |
| 11003 | DUREZA *f* AL ESCLERÓSCOPO, DUREZA SHORE | | 11030 | CORTE *m* DE ROSCA |
| 11004 | ESCORIFICACIÓN *f* | | 11031 | DISLOCACIÓN *f* EN TORNILLO (EN HÉLICE) |
| 11005 | DECAPAR, LIMPIAR, DESOXIDAR UN METAL | | 11032 | YUNQUE *m* CON SUFRIDERA DE REMACHAR |
| 11005 | DECAPAR | | 11032 | CAZAREMACHES *m* |
| 11005 | DESOXIDAR, DECAPAR | | 11033 | GRIFO *m* CON TORNILLO DE PRESIÓN |
| 11006 | DESOXIDACIÓN *f*, DECAPADO *m*, LIMPIA *f* | | 11034 | PALMER *m*, CALIBRADOR |
| 11006 | DECAPADO *m* | | 11035 | CRIC *m* |
| 11006 | DECAPADO *m* (LIMPIEZA *f*) DE UN METAL | | 11035 | GATO *m* DE TORNILLO |
| 11007 | RECORTES *m pl* DE HIERRO | | 11035 | GATO *m* DE TORNILLO |
| 11007 | CHATARRA *f* DE HIERRO | | 11036 | MÁQUINA *f* DE FRESAR LOS TORNILLOS |
| 11007 | CHATARRA *f* | | 11037 | ATORNILLAR EN |
| | | | 11037 | MONTAR POR TORNILLOS |

| | |
|---|---|
| 11038 | CALIBRE *m* DE LAS ROSCAS |
| 11039 | TERRAJA *f* EN FORMA DE PALETA |
| 11039 | TERRAJA *f* EN FORMA DE PALETA |
| 11040 | BALANCÍN *m* DE ROSCA, BALANCÍN *m* DE TORNILLO |
| 11040 | PRENSA *f* DE TORNILLO |
| 11041 | PROPULSOR *m* |
| 11041 | HÉLICE *f* PROPULSIVA |
| 11042 | BOMBA *f* HELICOIDAL |
| 11043 | TIRAFONDO *m* |
| 11044 | TERRAJA *f* |
| 11045 | PASO *m* DE TORNILLO |
| 11045 | ROSCADO *m*, ROSCA *f* |
| 11045 | FILETE *m*, PASO *m* DE ROSCA |
| 11046 | CORTAR ROSCA |
| 11047 | CUENTAHILOS *m* |
| 11048 | COMPARADOR MICROMÉTRICO PARA ROSCAS *m* |
| 11049 | CALIBRE *m* ROSCADO MACHO |
| 11049 | CALIBRE *m* DE DIÁMETRO INTERIOR |
| 11050 | CASQUILLO *m* ROSCADO DEL CALIBRE DE PUNTAS |
| 11051 | TORNILLO *m* DE CABEZA REDONDA |
| 11052 | LLAVE AJUSTABLE *f* |
| 11052 | LLAVE INGLESA *f* |
| 11053 | ORIFICIOS *m pl* ATERRAJADAOS (HEMBRAS) |
| 11054 | ORIFICIOS *m pl* ROSCADOS (MACHOS) |
| 11055 | BRIDA *f* DE ROSCAR |
| 11056 | AGUJERO *m* ROSCADO |
| 11056 | AGUJERO *m* ROSCADO |
| 11057 | HEMBRILLA *f* DE PUNTA ROSCADA |
| 11057 | GANCHO *m* DE TORNILLO (O DE ROSCADO) |
| 11058 | RACOR *m* ATORNILLADO |
| 11059 | TUBO *m* ROSCADO |
| 11059 | TUBO *m* ROSCADO |
| 11060 | TAPÓN *m* ROSCADO |
| 11060 | TAPÓN *m* ROSCADO |
| 11060 | TAPÓN *m* DE ROSCA |
| 11060 | TAPÓN *m* ROSCADO |
| 11061 | MANGUITO *m* ROSCADO |
| 11061 | MANGUITO *m* ATERRAJADO |
| 11061 | MANGUITO *m* HEMBRA |
| 11061 | RACOR *m* ROSCADO |
| 11062 | VARILLA *f* ROSCADA |
| 11063 | PLETINA *f* ATORNILLADA |
| 11064 | BRIDA *f* ROSCADA |
| 11065 | ATORNILLAMIENTO *m* |
| 11066 | ATERRAJADORA *f* |
| 11066 | MÁQUINA *f* DE ROSCAR |
| 11066 | MÁQUINA *f* DE ATERRAJAR |
| 11066 | MÁQUINA *f* DE ATORNILLAR |
| 11067 | MONTAJE *m* CON TORNILLOS |
| 11068 | PUNZÓN *m* |
| 11068 | PUNZÓN *m* |
| 11068 | PUNTA *f* DE TRAZAR |
| 11069 | GRAMIL *m* DE MÁRMOL |
| 11070 | NIVEL *m* DEL MAR |
| 11071 | ARENA *f* DE MAR |
| 11072 | AGUA *f* DE MAR |
| 11073 | CUBETA *f*, COLECTOR *m* |
| 11074 | CUBETA *f* DE PLATOS |
| 11075 | PLAQUETA *f* |
| 11076 | SOLDADURA *f* HERMÉTICA |
| 11077 | PRECINTAR |
| 11078 | JUNTA *f* PLÁSTICA DE ESTANQUEIDAD |
| 11078 | JUNTA *f* PLÁSTICA |
| 11079 | MONOBLOQUE *m* |
| 11079 | CABEZA *f* DE PROYECTOR |
| 11080 | TUBERÍA MARÍTIMA *f* |
| 11080 | CANALIZACIÓN MARINA *f* |
| 11081 | ESTANQUEIDAD *f*, IMPERMEABILIDAD *f* |
| 11082 | LÍQUIDO *m* OBTURADOR |
| 11083 | SOLDADURA *f* |
| 11084 | LÍNEA *f* DE LA UNIÓN DE LAS CHAPAS |
| 11085 | SOLDADURA *f* DE UN TUBO |
| 11086 | SOLDADURA *f* CONTINUA |
| 11086 | SOLDADURA *f* EN LÍNEA CONTINUA CON LA MOLETA |
| 11087 | MÁQUINA *f* PLEGADORA |
| 11088 | ENGASTADORA *f* |
| 11089 | TUBO *m* SIN SOLDADURA |
| 11090 | PALPADOR *m* |
| 11091 | PROYECTOR *m* DE LUZ |
| 11092 | GRIETA *f* DE ENVEJECIMIENTO |
| 11092 | AGRIETADO *m* ESTACIONAL |
| 11093 | CORROSIÓN INTERCRISTALINA DE LOS LATONES 70/ 30 *f* |
| 11094 | SECAR LA MADERA AL AIRE LIBRE |
| 11095 | DESECACIÓN *f* DE LA MADERA AL AIRE LIBRE |
| 11096 | CINTURÓN DE SEGURIDAD |
| 11097 | ASIENTO *m* DE VÁLVULA |
| 11098 | ASIENTO *m* |
| 11099 | SECANTE *f* |
| 11100 | LIMA *f* DE TALLA SEMIFINA |
| 11101 | SEGUNDO FILTRO *m* |
| 11102 | TERRAJA *f* INTERMEDIA |
| 11102 | TERRAJA *f* SEMICÓNICA |
| 11103 | COLOR COMPUESTO *m* |
| 11104 | FLUENCIA *f* SECUNDARIA |
| 11105 | TEMPLE *m* SECUNDARIO |
| 11106 | INCLUSIÓN *f* SECUNDARIA |
| 11107 | METAL *m* DE RECUPERACIÓN, CHATARRA *f* |
| 11108 | ESPECTRO *m* SECUNDARIO |

| | |
|---|---|
| 11109 | TENSIÓN SECUNDARIA  f |
| 11110 | CORRIENTE SECUNDARIA DE SOLDADURA  f |
| 11111 | SECCIÓN TRANSVERSAL  f |
| 11111 | SECCIÓN  f |
| 11112 | SECCIÓN DE UN DIBUJO  f |
| 11113 | OBJETO  m  QUE EXAMINAR CON EL MICROSCOPIO EN FORMA DE CORTE DELGADO |
| 11114 | PERFIL(ES)  m |
| 11115 | MÓDULO  m  DE INERCIA |
| 11116 | SECCIÓN (RECTA U OBLICUA) DE UNA VIGA |
| 11117 | ELEMENTO  m  DE UN RECIPIENTE A PRESIÓN |
| 11118 | SEGMENTO  m  DE RECTA |
| 11119 | PERFIL  m |
| 11119 | HIERRO  m  PERFILADO MODELADO |
| 11120 | SUPERFICIE  f |
| 11120 | ÁREA DE LA SECCIÓN  f |
| 11121 | SECCIÓN DE PASO DE UNA VÁLVULA  f |
| 11121 | SECCIÓN  f  DE PASO DE UNA VÁLVULA |
| 11122 | SECCIÓN  f |
| 11122 | CORTE  m, SECCIÓN  f |
| 11122 | SECCIÓN  f |
| 11123 | CALIBRE DE PERFILADO  m |
| 11124 | PROYECCIÓN  f  HORIZONTAL |
| 11124 | PLANO  m, PROYECCIÓN HORIZONTAL |
| 11125 | ACERO PERFILADO (TREFILADO)  m |
| 11126 | SECTOR  m  DE UN CÍRCULO |
| 11126 | SECTOR  m  CIRCULAR |
| 11127 | SECTOR  m  ESFÉRICO |
| 11128 | SEDÁN  m, BERLINA  f, CONDUCCIÓN  f  INTERIOR |
| 11129 | SEMBRADORA  f  AL VOLEO |
| 11130 | AGENTE DE PRECIPITACIÓN, PRECIPITANTE  m |
| 11131 | GOMA  f  LACA EN GRANOS |
| 11132 | MÁQUINAS  f  SEMBRADORAS |
| 11133 | TRASPLANTADORA  f |
| 11134 | CONO PIROMÉTRICO (DE SEGER)  m |
| 11134 | INDICADOR  m  FUSIBLE |
| 11134 | CONO  m  DE SEGER, CONO PIROMÉTRICO |
| 11135 | SEGMENTO  m |
| 11136 | SEGMENTO  m  DE CÍRCULO |
| 11137 | SEGMENTO  m  ESFÉRICO DE UNA BASE |
| 11137 | SEGMENTO ESFÉRICO  m |
| 11138 | VOLANTE  m  DE VARIOS SEGMENTOS |
| 11139 | CLASIFICACIÓN  f |
| 11139 | SEGREGACIÓN  f |
| 11140 | AGARROTARSE |
| 11141 | AGARROTAMIENTO  m |
| 11141 | AGARROTAMIENTO  m |
| 11142 | RECOCIDO  m  SELECTIVO |
| 11143 | CEMENTACIÓN SELECTIVA  f |
| 11144 | FLOTACIÓN  f  SELECTIVA |

| | |
|---|---|
| 11145 | TEMPLE  m  PARCIAL |
| 11146 | SELENIO  m |
| 11147 | CUERPO LUMINOSO  m |
| 11148 | AUTOMÁTICO  m, AUTOMÁTICA  f |
| 11149 | ACOPLAMIENTO AUTOMÁTICO  m |
| 11150 | COJINETE  m  AUTO-REGULADOR |
| 11151 | MÁQUINA  f  AISLADA |
| 11152 | MANDRILES  m  CON AUTOTRACCIÓN |
| 11153 | AUTOEXCITACIÓN  f |
| 11154 | ACERO DE TEMPLE AL AIRE  m |
| 11155 | SOLDADOR  m  DE CALENTAMIENTO  m  AUTOMÁTICO |
| 11156 | AUTOINDUCCIÓN  f, INDUCCIÓN  f  PROPIA |
| 11156 | INDUCCIÓN  f  PROPIA |
| 11156 | SELFINDUCCIÓN  f |
| 11157 | BLOQUEO  m  (DE) AUTOMÁTICO, AUTODETENCIÓN  f  (DE) |
| 11158 | COJINETE AUTOLUBRICANTE  m |
| 11159 | CONO AUTODESMONTABLE  m |
| 11160 | DEPÓSITO  m  DE TECHO CÓNICO AUTOSUSTENTADO |
| 11161 | ESTRUCTURA AUTOPORTANTE  f |
| 11162 | TORNILLO  m  ATERRAJADOR |
| 11163 | ARANDELA  f  AUTOROSCADA |
| 11164 | MANGUITO  m  DE ACOPLAMIENTO SELLERS |
| 11165 | HULLA  f  POBRE DE LLAMA CORTA |
| 11165 | HULLA  f  ANTRACITOSA |
| 11166 | SOLDADURA  f  SEMIAUTOMÁTICA AL ARCO |
| 11167 | SEMIEJE  m |
| 11168 | HULLA  f  POBRE |
| 11169 | SEMICIRCULAR |
| 11170 | SECCIÓN  f  SEMICIRCULAR |
| 11170 | SECCIÓN  f  DE MEDIACAÑA |
| 11171 | SEMIDIESEL |
| 11171 | MOTOR  m  SEMIDIESEL |
| 11172 | SEMIPERFORADORA  f  DE PRECISIÓN |
| 11173 | ACERO SEMICALMADO  m |
| 11174 | PRODUCTO  m  SEMIELABORADO |
| 11175 | MÁQUINA  f  DE VAPOR SEMIFIJA |
| 11176 | BOMBA  f  DE ÉMBOLO OSCILANTE |
| 11177 | FUNDICIÓN  f  ACERADA |
| 11178 | SEMIRREMOLQUE  m |
| 11179 | SEMICÍRCULO  m |
| 11180 | TRANSPORTADOR  m  EN SEMICÍRCULO |
| 11181 | LAMINADOR  m  SENDZIMIR |
| 11182 | SENTIDO  m  DE UNA FUERZA |
| 11183 | SENTIDO  m  DE MARCHA |
| 11183 | SENTIDO  m  DEL MOVIMIENTO |
| 11184 | CALOR SENSIBLE  m |
| 11185 | CLASIFICADORAS  f pl  ELECTRÓNICAS |
| 11186 | MÁQUINA  f  DE PERFORAR SENSIBLE |

| | |
|---|---|
| 11187 PLACA *f* SENSIBLE | 11220 PIEZA *f* DE ENCLAVIJAMIENTO |
| 11187 PLACA *f* FOTOGRÁFICA | 11220 PASADOR *m* DE RETENCIÓN |
| 11188 SENSIBILIDAD *f* DE UN INSTRUMENTO | 11221 VALOR *m* DE REGLAJE |
| 11189 SEPARAR (QUÍMICA) | 11222 TORNILLO *m* DE BLOQUEO DE ANILLO |
| 11190 INDEPENDIENTE | 11223 ESCUADRA *f* PARA DIBUJAR, CARTABÓN *m* |
| 11190 EXCITACIÓN *f* SEPARADA | 11224 TRISCAR UNA SIERRA |
| 11191 SEPARACIÓN *f* (QUÍMICA) | 11224 TRISCAR LOS DIENTES DE UNA SIERRA |
| 11192 SEPARACIÓN *f* DE UNA MEZCLA | 11225 CALIBRE *m* DE AJUSTADO |
| 11193 NÚMERO *m* DE SECUENCIA | 11226 TOMA *f* DEL CEMENTO |
| 11194 SECUENCIAL | 11227 DEPOSITARSE, SEDIMENTARSE |
| 11195 QUELATO *m* | 11228 DECANTACIÓN *f*, SEDIMENTACIÓN *f* |
| 11196 EN SERIE | 11228 SEDIMENTACIÓN *f* |
| 11197 NÚMERO *m* DE ORDEN DE LA FABRICACIÓN | 11229 DEPÓSITO *m* DE DECANTACIÓN |
| 11198 PRODUCCIÓN *f* EN SERIE | 11229 TANQUE *m* DE DECANTACIÓN, DE CLARIFICACIÓN |
| 11199 AGRUPACIÓN *f* | 11230 AGUAS *f pl* RESIDUALES, AGUAS NEGRAS, AGUAS |
| 11199 MONTAJE *m* | DE ALCANTARILLA |
| 11199 ACOPLAMIENTO EN TENSIÓN *m* | 11231 OJO *m* DEL HACHA |
| 11199 ACOPLAMIENTO EN SERIE *m* | 11232 ESLABONES *m pl* QUE MONTAR |
| 11200 SOLDADURA *f* POR PUNTOS EN SERIE POR | 11233 ARMELLAS *f*, GEMELOS *m pl* |
| RESISTENCIA | 11234 SOMBREAR |
| 11201 DINAMO *f* EN SERIE | 11235 DIBUJO *m* SOMBREADO |
| 11202 MOTOR *m* DE SERIE | 11236 SOMBRA *f* |
| 11203 SUCESIÓN *f* DE NUMEROS | 11237 SOMBREADO *m* |
| 11203 SERIE *f* | 11238 PROYECTOR *m* DE SOMBRA |
| 11203 PROGRESIÓN *f* | 11239 ÁRBOL *m*, EJE *m* |
| 11204 SERPENTINA *f* | 11240 ACOPLAMIENTO DE ÁRBOLES *m* |
| 11204 OFITA *f* | 11241 HORNO *m* DE CUBA |
| 11205 CRISOTILO *m* | 11241 HORNO *m* DE TÚNEL |
| 11206 CILINDRO *m* RANURADO | 11242 REGULADOR *m* PLAN |
| 11206 ESTRÍA *f* | 11242 REGULADOR *m* SOBRE EL ÁRBOL |
| 11207 ALBÚMINA DEL SUERO *f* | 11243 FUSTE *m* DE UNA COLUMNA |
| 11208 CONDICIONES DE USO *f pl* | 11244 MANGO *m* DE UN MARTILLO |
| 11209 REGLAMENTOS *m pl* DE FÁBRICA | 11245 MÁQUINA *f* PARA ENDEREZAR LOS ÁRBOLES |
| 11209 INSTRUCCIONES *f pl* RELATIVAS AL TRABAJO | 11246 TORNO *m* DE EJES |
| 11210 SERVOMECANISMO *m* | 11247 ÁRBOL *m* EN VELOCIDAD DE LOS DOS LADOS |
| 11211 SERVOMOTOR *m* | 11248 TRANSMISIÓN *f* |
| 11212 ACEITE *m* DE SÉSAMO | 11249 ÁRBOLES (PERPENDICULARES OBLICUOS) SITUADOS |
| 11213 SERIE *f* DE MÁQUINAS, JUEGO *m* DE PIEZAS | EN PLANOS DIFERENTES *m pl* |
| 11213 SERIE *f* | 11250 HENDIDURA *f* EN LA MADERA |
| 11213 SURTIDO *m*, JUEGO *m* | 11250 RAJADURA *f* |
| 11213 GRUPO *m* (DE MÁQUINAS ELÉCTRICAS) | 11250 GRIETA *f* DE LA MADERA |
| 11214 FRAGUAR | 11251 DESMOLDEO *m* |
| 11215 REVESTIR UNA CALDERA DE MAMPOSTERÍA | 11252 CRIBA *f* OSCILANTE |
| 11216 DESTARAR UNA VÁLVULA | 11253 TRANSPORTADOR *m* CON SACUDIDAS |
| 11217 CORTADURA *f* | 11253 TRANSPORTADOR *m* |
| 11218 MARTILLO *m* (HERRAMIENTA DE HERRERO) | 11254 AGITACIÓN DEL BAÑO *f*, BRACEADO *m* |
| 11219 JUEGO *m* DE PESOS, SERIE *f* DE PESOS | 11255 ALQUITRÁN *m* DE ESQUISTO |
| 11219 SERIE *f* | 11256 ACEITE *m* DE ESQUISTO |
| 11219 JUEGO *m* DE PESAS | 11257 COLA *f* |
| 11220 PRISIONERO *m* | 11257 VÁSTAGO *m*, VARILLA *f* |
| 11220 PASADOR *m* DE BLOQUEO | 11258 CUCHARA *f* DE COLADA CON ASA |

| | |
|---|---|
| 11259 | FRESA *f* DE ESPIGA |
| 11260 | ESPIGA *f* DE UN PERNO |
| 11260 | ESPIGA *f* DE UN TORNILLO |
| 11261 | CUERPO DE LA BIELA *m* |
| 11262 | CUERPO DE UNA CHAVETA *m* |
| 11262 | ESPIGA *f* DE UNA CHAVETA |
| 11263 | ESPIGA *f* DE ROBLÓN |
| 11263 | CUERPO DEL REMACHE *m* |
| 11263 | VÁSTAGO *m* DE REMACHE |
| 11264 | FORMA *f* |
| 11265 | PIEZA *f* MECANIZADA |
| 11266 | CHAPAS *f pl* RECORTADAS |
| 11267 | LIMADORA *f* |
| 11268 | HECHURA *f* |
| 11269 | LIMADORA *f* |
| 11270 | LIJA *f* |
| 11271 | CANTONERA *f* EN ÁNGULO VIVO |
| 11272 | ARISTA VIVA *f* |
| 11273 | AFILAR |
| 11273 | AGUZAR, AFILAR, AMOLAR |
| 11273 | AFILAR |
| 11273 | RECTIFICAR |
| 11273 | AFILAR, AGUZAR, AMOLAR |
| 11273 | AMOLAR, RECTIFICAR CON MUELA |
| 11274 | AFILADORA *f* |
| 11275 | AFILAMIENTO *m*, AGUZAMIENTO *m* |
| 11275 | AFILADO *m*, AFILADURA *f* |
| 11275 | RECTIFICACIÓN *f* |
| 11275 | RECTIFICACIÓN *f* CON MUELA |
| 11275 | AFILADURA *f*, AMOLADURA *f* |
| 11276 | CLARIDAD *f* DE UNA IMAGEN |
| 11277 | VIRUTAS DEL MANDRINADO *f pl*, LIMADURAS DEL ESCARIADOR *f pl* |
| 11278 | VIRUTAS *f pl* |
| 11279 | CIZALLA *f*, CIZALLAMIENTO *m* |
| 11279 | CIZALLAMIENTO *m* |
| 11280 | CIZALLAR, RECORTAR CON CIZALLA O CON TIJERAS |
| 11281 | ÁNGULO DE CIZALLAMIENTO *m* |
| 11282 | HOJA *f* DE UNA CIZALLA |
| 11283 | PASADOR *m* DE SEGURIDAD EN CORTE |
| 11284 | PLANO *m* DE CORTE |
| 11285 | RESISTENCIA *f* AL ESFUERZO CORTANTE |
| 11286 | TENSIÓN *f* DE CIZALLADURA |
| 11287 | PRUEBA *f* DE CORTE |
| 11288 | CIZALLAMIENTO *m* |
| 11288 | DESLIZAMIENTO *m* TRANSVERSAL |
| 11289 | IMBICICIÓN *f*, ABSORCIÓN *f* |
| 11290 | CIZALLAMIENTO *m* |
| 11290 | CIZALLAMIENTO *m* |
| '291 | FUERZA *f* DE CORTE |

| | |
|---|---|
| 11292 | CIZALLA MECÁNICA *f* |
| 11292 | CIZALLA MECÁNICA *f* |
| 11292 | MÁQUINA *f* DE CIZALLAR |
| 11293 | RUPTURA *f* DEL ROBLÓN POR CIZALLADURA |
| 11294 | PASADOR *m* DE SEGURIDAD EN CORTE |
| 11295 | ESFUERZO *m* DE CORTADURA |
| 11295 | ESFUERZO *m* DE CORTADURA (O DE CORTE) |
| 11295 | TRABAJO *m* AL ESFUERZO CORTANTE |
| 11296 | ESFUERZO *m* DE CORTADURA POR UNIDAD DE SECCIÓN, TENSIÓN TANGENCIAL |
| 11296 | ESFUERZO CORTANTE *m* |
| 11297 | TIJERAS *f pl* |
| 11297 | CIZALLA *f* |
| 11298 | CHAPA *f* |
| 11299 | ELECTRODO *m* BLINDADO |
| 11300 | ALAMBRE *m* FORRADO |
| 11301 | POLEA *f* |
| 11301 | POLEA *f* DE UN APAREJO |
| 11302 | COBERTIZO *m*, BARRACÓN *m*, TINGLADO *m* |
| 11302 | PARQUE *m* CUBIERTO, APARCAMIENTO *m* CUBIERTO |
| 11303 | CONCHA *f* |
| 11303 | CAPA *f*, CAMISA *f*, CUBIERTA *f* |
| 11303 | CAMISA *f*, ENVOLVENTE *m* |
| 11304 | CHAPA *f* FINA |
| 11305 | CHAPA *f* |
| 11306 | PLATINA *f* |
| 11306 | PLETINA *f* |
| 11307 | LATÓN *m* EN LÁMINAS |
| 11308 | COBRE *m* EN HOJAS |
| 11309 | CHAPA *f* DE HIERRO |
| 11310 | CAPÓ DE CHAPA *m*, TAPA DE CHAPA *f* |
| 11311 | CALIBRE *m* PARA EL ESPESOR DE LAS CHAPAS |
| 11312 | TUBO *m* DE CHAPA |
| 11313 | HOJA *f* DE CHAPA |
| 11314 | PLOMO *m* EN HOJAS |
| 11315 | PLACA *f* METALÚRGICA, PLANCHA METALÚRGICA |
| 11315 | CHAPA *f* |
| 11315 | HOJA *f* METÁLICA |
| 11316 | MÁQUINA *f* DE APLANAR Y ENDEREZAR LAS CHAPAS |
| 11317 | MÁQUINAS *f pl* PARA PERFORAR LAS CHAPAS |
| 11318 | MÁQUINAS *f pl* PARA APLANAR LAS CHAPAS |
| 11319 | MÁQUINA *f* DE ENTALLAR (O HACER MUESCAS) EN LAS CHAPAS |
| 11320 | MÁQUINAS *f pl* PARA TRABAJAR LA CHAPA |
| 11321 | TREN *m* DE CINTAS |
| 11322 | PLACA *f* DE FIELTRO |
| 11323 | MÁQUINA *f* DE CIZALLAR LOS METALES EN HOJAS O EN TIRAS |
| 11324 | TREN *m* LAMINADOR DE CHAPAS FINAS |
| 11325 | CHAPA *f* DE ACERO |

| | | | |
|---|---|---|---|
| 11326 | ESTAÑO *m* EN HOJAS | 11359 | PERCUSIÓN *f* |

11326 ESTAÑO *m* EN HOJAS
11327 HOJA *f* (O CHAPA) DE CINC
11327 CINC *m* EN HOJAS
11328 EXFOLIACIÓN *f*
11329 HOJA *f* DE CAUCHO (NEOPRENO)
11330 ENVOLTURA *f*
11331 LEVANTAMIENTO... DE TECHO FLOTANTE
11332 AGUJERO *m* DE HOMBRE LATERAL
11333 MOLDEO *m* EN COQUILLA
11334 CUERPO *m* DE UN GRIFO
11335 CHAPA *f* DE RECUBRIMIENTO
11336 ESCARIADOR HUECO DE DIENTES FIJOS *m*
11337 FRESAS *f pl* EN EXTREMO MANDRILADAS
11338 GOMA *f* LACA
11338 LACA *f* EN LÁMINAS, LACA *f* EN HOJUELAS
11338 LACA *f* EN PLACAS
11338 LACA *f* PLANA
11338 LACA *f* EN ESCAMAS
11339 DESCASCADO *m*
11340 PROTEGER POR EL CINC
11341 PROTECCIÓN *f* POR EL CINC
11342 PANTALLA *f* PROTECTORA, ESCUDO *m*
11342 DISPOSITIVO *m* DE PROTECCIÓN, ESCUDO *m*, BLINDAJE *m*
11343 CHAPA *f* DE REFUERZO
11343 CHAPA *f* DE BLINDAJE
11344 ELECTRODO *m* REVESTIDO
11345 SOLDADURA *f* AL ARCO METÁLICO BAJO GAS PROTECTOR
11346 PROTECCIÓN *f*
11346 PANTALLA *f*, PROTECCIÓN *f*
11347 JORNADA *f* DE TRABAJO, DÍA *m* LABORABLE
11348 EQUIPO *m* (O BRIGADA *f*) DE OBREROS
11349 DESPLAZAR LA CORREA
11350 TRABAJO *m* EN (DOS O TRES) TURNOS
11351 ARANDELA *f* DE ESPESOR
11352 ESPESOR *m*
11353 TREPIDACIÓN *f* OSCILANTE
11354 GUIJARROS *m pl* (GEOL.)
11355 AJUSTE *m*, PRESIÓN *f*
11355 COMPRESIÓN *f*
11355 APRETAMIENTO *m*
11356 CHAPA *f* (PARA CONSTRUCCIÓN) NAVAL
11357 MONTAR LA CORREA
11357 COLOCAR EN SU SITIO LA CORREA
11357 INSTALAR LA CORREA
11358 AMORTIGUADOR DE CHOQUES *m*
11359 SACUDIDA *f*
11359 GOLPE *m*
11359 GOLPE *m*, IMPACTO *m*, CHOQUE *m*
11359 CHOQUE *m*, ENCONTRONAZO *m*

11359 PERCUSIÓN *f*
11360 ZAPATA *f*
11361 PLAN *m* DE EJECUCIÓN (TALLER)
11362 SOLDADURA *f* EN EL TALLER
11363 DISEÑO *m* DE UNA PIEZA MECÁNICA
11364 TALLER *m*
11365 COLUMRA (PUNTAL VERTICAL) *f*
11366 ESCLERÓSCOPIO *m*
11366 ESCLOROSCOPIO *m*
11366 MEDIDOR *m* DE SALTOS
11367 PRUEBA *f* DE PERCUSIÓN CON LA BOLA (APARATO SHORE)
11368 HIERRO *m* QUEBRADIZO
11369 CORTO CIRCUITO *m*
11370 TRANSFERENCIA *f* POR CORTOCIRCUITO
11371 HULLA *f* DE LLAMA CORTA
11372 CORTO CIRCUITO *m*
11373 CADENA DE ESLABONES APRETADOS *f*
11373 CADENA DE ESLABONES CORTOS *f*
11374 MÁQUINA *f* DE CARRERA REDUCIDA
11375 MANIVELA *f* DE CARRERA CORTA
11376 ACORTAMIENTO *m*
11377 ACORTAMIENTO *m* DE UNA CORREA
11377 ACORTAMIENTO *m*
11378 FRAGILIDAD *f*
11379 GRANALLA *f*
11379 CHATARRA *f*
11380 GRANALLADO *m*
11381 DECAPADO *m* CON GRANALLA
11382 GRANALLADO *m* (GRUESO)
11383 ESPALDÓN *m*
11384 COLLAR *m* DE UN ÁRBOL
11384 ANILLO *m* FIJO DE UN ÁRBOL
11384 COLLARÍN DE UN EJE *m*
11385 PALA *f*
11386 PALEAR, TRABAJAR CON PALA
11387 GRIFO *m* DE DUCHA
11388 ENCOGERSE, ESTRECHARSE
11388 CONTRAERSE
11389 MONTAJE *m* POR PRENSA EN CALIENTE, AJUSTE *m* POR APRETADO EN CALIENTE
11389 ACOPLAMIENTO *m*
11390 ENMANGAR, FIJAR
11390 ZUNCHAR EN CALIENTE
11390 COLOCAR
11391 ZUNCHO *m* COLOCADO EN CALIENTE
11391 COLLAR A COLOCAR EN CALIENTE *m*
11391 ANILLO DE CIERRE *m*
11391 ANILLO *m* DE CIERRE
11392 CONTRACCIÓN *f*
11392 CONTRACCIÓN *f*

| | | | |
|---|---|---|---|
| 11393 | CAVIDAD  *f*  POR CONTRACCIÓN | 11423 | TAMIZAR |
| 11394 | REDUCCIÓN  *f*  POR CONTRACCIÓN | 11424 | TAMIZADO  *m* |
| 11395 | FISURA  *f*  DE RETRACCIÓN | 11424 | CRIBADO  *m* |
| 11396 | CONTRACCIÓN  *f*  DE LA MADERA | 11425 | ENGRASADOR  *m*  DE CAUDAL VISIBLE |
| 11397 | ESTRECHAMIENTO  *m* | 11426 | INDICADOR DE FLUJO  *m* |
| 11397 | RETRACCIÓN  *f* | 11427 | REGISTRO  *m* |
| 11397 | CONTRACCIÓN (DURANTE EL ENFRIAMIENTO)  *f* | 11428 | SOLDADURA  *f*  AL ARCO METÁLICO BAJO PROTECCIÓN DE GAS INERTE |
| 11398 | ZUNCHADO  *m*  EN CALIENTE, MONTAJE  *m*  EN CALIENTE | 11429 | SIGNO  *m* |
| 11398 | ZUNCHADO  *m* | 11430 | ENSILADORAS  *f pl* |
| 11399 | ARRUGAMIENTO  *m* | 11431 | SILENCIADOR  *m* |
| 11400 | CARA  *f*  LATERAL DE UNA RUEDA DE ENGRANAJE | 11431 | SILENCIADOR  *m* |
| 11400 | RESPALDO  *m*  (O ARO  *m* ) DE UNA RUEDA DE ENGRANAJE | 11432 | CADENA SILENCIOSA  *f* |
| 11401 | CALABROTE  *m*  FORMADO POR CUATRO GUINDALEZAS | 11433 | ENGATILLADO  *m*  SILENCIOSO |
| 11402 | RUEDA  *f*  DENTADA CON DISCOS LATERALES | 11434 | SILICIO  *m* |
| 11402 | RUEDA  *f*  DENTADA CON PESTAÑA | 11435 | BLOQUE  *m*  DE SÍLICE, LADRILLO  *m*  DE SÍLICE |
| 11403 | SHUNT  *m*  (DERIVACIÓN) | 11436 | SILICIO  *m* |
| 11403 | DERIVACIÓN  *f* | 11436 | SÍLICE  *f* , ÁCIDO SILÍCICO  *m* |
| 11404 | DINAMO  *f*  EN DERIVACIÓN | 11436 | ÁCIDO SILÍCICO  *m* |
| 11404 | DINAMO-SHUNT | 11437 | SILICATO  *m* |
| 11405 | MOTOR  *m*  EN DERIVACIÓN | 11438 | CINC  *m*  SILICATO |
| 11405 | MOTOR  *m*  EXCITADO EN DERIVACIÓN | 11439 | MARGA  *f*  SILICIOSA O SILÍCEA |
| 11406 | PONER UNA MÁQUINA FUERA DE SERVICIO | 11440 | SILICIO-ARRABIO ESPECULAR  *m* |
| 11407 | CERRAR LA INTRODUCCIÓN  *f* | 11441 | ÁCIDO FLUOSILÍCICO  *m* |
| 11407 | OBTURAR LA ADMISIÓN EN UNA TUBERÍA | 11442 | SILICIO  *m* |
| 11408 | GRIFO  *m*  DE RETENCIÓN | 11443 | LATÓN  *m*  SILICIOSO |
| 11409 | PAROS  *m pl* | 11444 | BRONCE  *m*  SILICIOSO, CUPROSILICIO  *m* |
| 11410 | PUESTA  *f*  FUERA DE SERVICIO DE UNA MÁQUINA | 11445 | CARBURO DE SILICIO  *m* |
| 11411 | RASTRILLOS  *m pl*  CON VERTIMIENTO LATERAL | 11446 | COBRE  *m*  SILICIOSO |
| 11412 | FRESA  *f*  EN DISCO | 11447 | ACERO AL SILICIO  *m* |
| 11413 | RAMAL  *m*  DE UNA CORREA | 11448 | CHAPA  *f*  ELÉCTRICA |
| 11413 | RAMAL  *m*  DE UNA CORREA | 11449 | ACERO AL SILICIO  *m* |
| 11414 | CARA DE UN POLÍGONO  *f* , LADO DE UN POLÍGONO  *m* | 11450 | ACERO MANGANOSILÍCEO, ACERO MANGANOSILICOSO  *m* |
| 11415 | MÁQUINA  *f*  DE CEPILLAR LATERALMENTE | 11451 | CALIZA SILÍCEA  *f* |
| 11416 | MALLA  *f*  DE UNA CADENA DE RODILLOS | 11452 | SEDA  *f* |
| 11416 | MORDAZA  *f*  DE UNA CADENA DE RODILLOS | 11453 | MATIZADO  *m* |
| 11417 | GUILLAME  *m* , DIMENSIONADO | 11454 | ROTURA SEDOSA  *f* |
| 11418 | ÁNGULO DE DESPRENDIMIENTO  *m* , ÁNGULO DE ATAQUE  *m* | 11455 | BRILLO  *m*  SEDOSO |
| 11419 | ONDULACIONES  *f pl* | 11456 | SILICONO  *m* |
| 11420 | VISTA  *f*  LATERAL | 11457 | ENCENEGAMIENTO  *m*  DE UN CONDUCTO |
| 11420 | PERFIL  *m*  (A LA DERECHA, A LA IZQUIERDA) | 11458 | PLATA  *f* , ARGENTO  *m* |
| 11421 | SIDEROSA  *f* | 11459 | ARGENTAR, PLATEAR |
| 11421 | HIERRO  *m*  ESPÁTICO | 11460 | SOLDADURA  *f*  CON ALEACIÓN DE PLATA |
| 11422 | TAMIZ  *m* | 11461 | CLORURO  *m*  DE PLATA |
| 11422 | CRIBA  *f* | 11461 | CLORURO DE PLATA  *m* |
| 11422 | CEDAZO, TAMIZ  *m* | 11462 | CIANURO  *m*  ARGÉNTICO (O DE PLATA) |
| 11423 | CERNER | 11463 | FULMINATO  *m*  DE PLATA |
| 11423 | CRIBAR | 11464 | IODURO  *m*  DE PLATA, YODURO DE PLATA |
| | | 11465 | AZOGADO DE ESPEJOS  *m* |
| | | 11466 | SOLDADURA  *f*  CON PLATA |

| | |
|---|---|
| 11466 | LAMINILLA *f* DE PLATA |
| 11467 | SULFATO *m* DE PLATA |
| 11468 | COBRE *m* ARGENTÍFERO |
| 11469 | PLATEADO *m* |
| 11470 | SIMILITUD *f* |
| 11471 | INTEGRAL *f* SINGULAR |
| 11472 | VÁSTAGO *m* |
| 11473 | ACERO AL CARBONO *m* |
| 11474 | QUE REPOSA LIBREMENTE SOBRE SUS DOS APOYOS |
| 11474 | SOSTENIDO LÍBREMENTE EN SUS DOS APOYOS |
| 11475 | SENO *m* |
| 11476 | CURVA SINUOSA *f* |
| 11477 | CORREA SENCILLA *f* |
| 11478 | REMACHE *m* CON CUBREJUNTAS SIMPLE |
| 11478 | REMACHE *m* CON UNA SOLA BANDA DE RECUBRIMIENTO |
| 11478 | REMACHE *m* CON CUBREJUNTAS SIMPLE |
| 11479 | COJINETE *m* DE EMPUJE DE UN SOLO APOYO |
| 11480 | MONOCRISTAL *m* |
| 11481 | ESCOFINA *f* |
| 11481 | LIMA *f* DE PICADURA SENCILLA |
| 11481 | LIMA *f* DE PICADURA SENCILLA |
| 11482 | LABRA *f* SIMPLE DE UNA LIMA |
| 11483 | FUERZA *f* ÚNICA |
| 11484 | PIEZA *f* SUELTA |
| 11485 | SOLDADURA *f* DE UNA PASADA |
| 11486 | MÁQUINA *f* PARA TRABAJOS ESPECIALES |
| 11487 | CLAVADO SIMPLE *m* |
| 11487 | REMACHE *m* DE UNA HILERA |
| 11487 | REMACHE *m* SIMPLE |
| 11487 | REMACHE *m* DE UNA HILERA |
| 11488 | GRIFO *m* DE VÁLVULA SIMPLE |
| 11489 | REMACHE *m* CON UN CORTE |
| 11490 | ACERO *m* |
| 11490 | ACERO *m* BATIDO UNA VEZ |
| 11490 | HIERRO *m* BATIDO, HIERRO FORJADO, HIERRO DULCE |
| 11491 | VÁLVULA *f* ÚNICA |
| 11492 | OPÉRCULO *m* SIMPLE |
| 11493 | SIMPLE EFECTO (DE) *m* |
| 11494 | PISTÓN *m* DE SIMPLE EFECTO |
| 11495 | MÁQUINA *f* DE SIMPLE EFECTO |
| 11496 | HERRAMIENTA *f* DE SIMPLE EFECTO |
| 11497 | VÁLVULA *f* DE ASIENTO SIMPLE |
| 11498 | MÁQUINA *f* MONOCILÍNDRICA |
| 11499 | LLAVE DE CALIBRE SENCILLO *f* |
| 11499 | LLAVE DE HORQUILLA SIMPLE *f* |
| 11500 | MÁQUINA *f* DE SIMPLE EXPANSIÓN |
| 11501 | CORRIENTE MONOFÁSICA *f* |
| 11502 | TORNILLO *m* DE UNA ROSCA |
| 11503 | CIGÜEÑAL DE UN SOLO CODO *m* |
| 11504 | JUNTA *f* RECUBRIDORA SOLDADA POR SU SOLO LADO |
| 11505 | CAVIDAD *f* POR CONTRACCIÓN |
| 11506 | MAZAROTA *f*, CABEZA *f* DE PIEZA DE FUNDICIÓN |
| 11507 | PENETRACIÓN *f* |
| 11508 | LAMINADOR *m* REDUCTOR |
| 11509 | AGLOMERARSE |
| 11509 | TOSTAR, CALCINAR, SINTERIZAR |
| 11510 | ALEACIÓN DE METAL DURO *f* |
| 11511 | CALCINACIÓN *f* |
| 11512 | HORNO *m* DE CALCINAR, HORNO *m* DE SINTERIZAR |
| 11513 | SINUSOIDE *f* |
| 11514 | SIFÓN *m* (DE MANÓMETRO) |
| 11515 | BARÓMETRO *m* DE SIFÓN |
| 11516 | ENGRASADOR *m* DE MECHA |
| 11517 | SIFÓN *m* |
| 11517 | SIFÓN *m* |
| 11518 | TROMPA *f* |
| 11518 | SIRENA *f* DE ALARMA |
| 11519 | BARRACA *f* DEL PERSONAL |
| 11520 | JEFE DE OBRA *m*, DIRECTOR DE LA OBRA *m* |
| 11521 | MAMPUESTO *m* |
| 11522 | GROSOR *m* DEL GRANO |
| 11523 | ANCHURA *f* DE LAS MALLAS |
| 11524 | CLASIFICACIÓN *f*, APARTADO *m* |
| 11524 | CALIBRADO *m*, DIMENSIONADO *m* |
| 11524 | ACABADO *m* DIMENSIONAL |
| 11525 | PRENSA *f* DE CALIBRAR |
| 11526 | MODELO *m* EN ESQUELETO, MODELADO |
| 11527 | FLEJE *m* PARA TUBOS |
| 11528 | CROQUIS *m* |
| 11529 | BOSQUEJAR |
| 11529 | BOSQUEJAR |
| 11530 | PAPEL *m* CUADRICULADO |
| 11531 | CHAPA *f* MARGINAL |
| 11532 | CROQUIS *m*, BOSQUEJO *m* |
| 11533 | ESBOZADO *m* |
| 11534 | RUEDA *f* HIPERBÓLICA, ENGRANAJE *m* DE DENTADO EN ESPIRAL |
| 11534 | ENGRANAJE *m* HIPERBÓLICO, RUEDA *f* HIPERBÓLICA |
| 11535 | SUPERFICIE *f* ALABEADA |
| 11536 | ESPUMADERA *f* |
| 11537 | CARENCIA *f*, DEFICIENCIA *f* |
| 11538 | COSTRA *f* DE LA FUNDICIÓN |
| 11539 | COLA DE PIELES *f* |
| 11540 | EMBALAJE *m* PELICULAR |
| 11541 | PASADA *f* DE ACABADO (LAMINACIÓN) |
| 11541 | PASADA *f* ACABADO |

| | |
|---|---|
| 11542 | PASADA *f* DE ACABADO |
| 11543 | PASADA *f* DE DESBASTE, DE APLANADO |
| 11543 | PASADA *f* DE ENDEREZADO |
| 11544 | PELÍCULA *f* |
| 11544 | CAPA SUPERFICIAL *f* |
| 11544 | COSTRA *f* DE LAMINADO |
| 11545 | FORMACIÓN *f* DE COSTRAS |
| 11546 | INTERRUPCIÓN *f* |
| 11546 | INSTRUCCIÓN *f* |
| 11547 | FALDA *f* |
| 11548 | FALDÓN *m* DE UN TAMPON |
| 11549 | FALDÓN *m* (DE UN DEPÓSITO) |
| 11550 | FONDO *m* DE CRISOL, DEFECTO *m* DE FABRICACIÓN, ERROR *m* DE TRABAJO |
| 11551 | LOSA *f* |
| 11551 | DESBASTE *m* PLANO, PLACA *f*, PLANCHA *f* |
| 11552 | DESBASTES *m pl* PLANOS (TREN DE LAMINAR) |
| 11553 | DESBASTES *m pl* PLANOS (CURVADO DE) |
| 11554 | TIJERAS PARA PAQUETES *f pl* |
| 11555 | LAMINADOR *m* PARA PAQUETES |
| 11556 | TRENES *m* DE LINGOTES APLASTADOS |
| 11557 | MENUDOS *m pl* DE HULLA, ALMENDRILLA *f* |
| 11557 | HULLA *f* MENUDA |
| 11558 | AFLOJAR UNA TUERCA |
| 11558 | AFLOJAR UN TORNILLO |
| 11559 | AFLOJARSE |
| 11560 | AFLOJAMIENTO *m*, DESAPRIETO *m* |
| 11560 | DESBLOQUEO *m* |
| 11561 | ESCORIA *f* |
| 11561 | ESCORIA *f* |
| 11562 | CONTENIENDO ESCORIAS |
| 11563 | PERPIAÑO *m* DE ESCORIA |
| 11564 | CEMENTO DE ESCORIAS *m* |
| 11564 | CEMENTO DE ESCORIAL *m* |
| 11565 | HORMIGÓN *m* DE ESCORIAS |
| 11565 | HORMIGÓN *m* DE ESCORIAS |
| 11566 | LANA *f* MINERAL, LANA *f* DE AMIANTO |
| 11567 | ESCORIA *f* ENCERRADA |
| 11568 | APAGAR LA CAL |
| 11569 | EXTINCIÓN *f* (O APAGAMIENTO *m*) DE LA CAL |
| 11569 | HIDRATACIÓN *f* DE LA CAL |
| 11570 | TRANSPORTADOR *m* DE TABLERO METÁLICO |
| 11570 | TRANSPORTADOR *m* DE PALETAS |
| 11571 | PIZARRA *f* |
| 11572 | MASA *m* |
| 11572 | MAZO *m* |
| 11573 | MARTILLO *m* DE HERRERO |
| 11573 | MARTILLO *m* DE HERRERO |
| 11574 | TRAVIESA *f* DE VÍA |
| 11575 | TIRAFONDOS *m pl* |
| 11576 | MANGA *f* |

| | |
|---|---|
| 11576 | MANGUITO *m*, VAINA *f* |
| 11576 | CASQUILLO *m*, MANGUITO *m*, FORRO *m* |
| 11577 | MANGUITO *m* CON ZUNCHOS |
| 11578 | REGULADOR *m* DE MANGUITO |
| 11578 | REGULADOR *m* DE MANGUITO |
| 11579 | VÁLVULA *f* DE CAMPANA INTERIOR |
| 11579 | VÁLVULA *f* CON MANGUITO |
| 11580 | ESBELTEZ *f*, FRAGILIDAD *f* |
| 11581 | ESBELTEZ *f* DE UNA VIGA |
| 11582 | RELACIÓN *f* DE LANZAMIENTO |
| 11583 | GRÚA *f* GIRATORIA |
| 11584 | TORNO *m* DE ATERRAJAR |
| 11585 | SUPERFICIE *f* DE DESLIZAMIENTO |
| 11585 | CORREDERA *f*, GUÍA *f* |
| 11585 | RESBALADERO *m* |
| 11586 | ESCURRIRSE, DESLIZARSE |
| 11586 | DESLIZAR |
| 11587 | PATÍN *m*, RESBALADERA *f* |
| 11587 | PATÍN *m*, ZAPATA *f* |
| 11587 | PATÍN *m* |
| 11588 | CORREDERA *f* |
| 11589 | LÁMINA *f* DE VIDRIO |
| 11590 | TORNO *m* DE CARRO |
| 11590 | TORNO *m* DE CILINDRAR |
| 11591 | REGLA *f* DE CÁLCULO |
| 11592 | DISTRIBUIDOR *m* |
| 11592 | VÁLVULA DE COMPUERTA *f* |
| 11592 | GRIFO *m*, LLAVE *f* |
| 11592 | DISTRIBUIDOR *m* |
| 11592 | OBTURADOR *m* DESLIZANTE O RESBALADIZO |
| 11593 | DIAGRAMA *m* DE DISTRIBUCIÓN |
| 11594 | DISTRIBUCIÓN *f* POR VÁLVULA DE CORREDERA |
| 11595 | DESLIZAMIENTO *m*, CORRIMIENTO *m* (DE TERRENO) |
| 11596 | SOPORTE *m* DESLIZANTE |
| 11597 | PIE *m* DE REY |
| 11598 | ENGRANAJE *m* DESLIZANTE |
| 11599 | MANGUITO *m* MÓVIL |
| 11599 | MANGUITO *m* DE EMBRAGUE |
| 11600 | ACOPLAMIENTO *m* |
| 11600 | AJUSTE *m* CORREDIZO (O DESLIZANTE), ASIENTO *m* DESLIZANTE |
| 11600 | AJUSTE *m* CORREDIZO, AJUSTE *m* HOLGADO |
| 11600 | MONTAJE *m* DESLIZANTE |
| 11600 | AJUSTE *m*, MONTAJE *m*, AJUSTAMIENTO *m* |
| 11601 | ROZAMIENTO *m* DE RESBALADURA |
| 11602 | ENGRANAJE *m* MÓVIL |
| 11603 | HORNO *m* CORREDIZO |
| 11604 | TAPA DE CORREDERA *f* |
| 11605 | MOVIMIENTO *m* DE DESLIZAMIENTO |
| 11606 | CUNA *f* DE DESLIZAMIENTO |

| | | |
|---|---|---|
| 11607 | ESCALA *f* MÓVIL | |
| 11608 | SUPERFICIE *f* DE DESLIZAMIENTO | |
| 11609 | CIENO *m* | |
| 11610 | ESLINGA *f* | |
| 11611 | RESBALADURA *f* | |
| 11612 | PATINAR, RESBALAR | |
| 11612 | PATINAR, RESBALAR | |
| 11613 | BANDAS *f pl* DE DESLIZAMIENTO | |
| 11614 | ACOPLAMIENTO *m* DE FRICCIÓN, EMBRAGUE *m* DE FRICCIÓN | |
| 11615 | GRIETA DE CLIVAJE | |
| 11616 | ENCOFADO DESLIZANTE (PARA HORMIGÓN) *m* | |
| 11617 | JUNTA *f* DESLIZANTE | |
| 11618 | COLECTOR *m* | |
| 11618 | ANILLO *m* COLECTOR | |
| 11619 | ACOPLAMIENTO *m* (O EMBRAGUE *m*) DESLIZANTE, ACOPLAMIENTO CON LIMITADOR DE PAR | |
| 11620 | RESBALAMIENTO *m* DE LA CORREA, DESLIZAMIENTO *m* | |
| 11620 | PATINAMIENTO *m* DE LA CORREA | |
| 11621 | PATINAJE *m* DE LAS RUEDAS | |
| 11622 | RAJAMIENTO *m* | |
| 11623 | LIMA *f* DE CORTE, LIMA *f* ESPADA | |
| 11624 | CORTEZA *f* | |
| 11625 | MINERAL *m* DE PLATA, MINERAL *m* ARGENTÍFERO | |
| 11626 | EMPUJES *m pl* | |
| 11627 | INCLINACIÓN *f*, DECLIVE *m* | |
| 11627 | RAMPA *f* | |
| 11627 | TALUD *m* | |
| 11628 | CRIBA *f* PARA LA ARENA | |
| 11628 | CRIBA *f* PARA TIERRA | |
| 11629 | RANURA *f*, FISURA *f* | |
| 11630 | MORTAJAR | |
| 11631 | CORREDERA Y MANUBRIO *f* | |
| 11631 | MANIVELA *f* DE CORREDERA | |
| 11632 | FRESAS *f pl* DE CUCHILLAS | |
| 11632 | FRESAS *f pl* PARA HACER RANURAS | |
| 11633 | CORREDERA *f* | |
| 11634 | FRESA *f* PARA ABRIR RANURAS | |
| 11635 | SOLDADURA *f* CON ENTALLADURA | |
| 11636 | SOLDADURA *f* DE ENTALLADURA | |
| 11637 | TORNILLO *m* DE CABEZA HENDIDA | |
| 11638 | PALANCA *f* DE CORREDERA | |
| 11639 | SEPARADOR DE RANURAS *m* | |
| 11640 | MORTAJADORAS *f pl* | |
| 11641 | MORTAJADO *m* | |
| 11642 | AMORTAJADORA *f*, MORTAJADORA *f* | |
| 11643 | MÁQUINA *f* DE AMORTAJAR, MÁQUINA *f* AMORTAJADORA | |
| 11643 | MORTAJADORA *f* | |

| | |
|---|---|
| 11644 | COMBUSTIÓN LENTA *f* |
| 11645 | REDUCIR LA MARCHA DE UNA MÁQUINA |
| 11646 | SURTIDOR *m* DE MARCHA LENTA |
| 11647 | ROSCA *f* DE PASO PEQUEÑO |
| 11648 | CEMENTO DE FRAGUADO LENTO *m* |
| 11649 | REDUCCIÓN *f* DE LA MARCHA |
| 11650 | ÁRBOL *m* DE PEQUEÑA VELOCIDAD |
| 11651 | PIEZA *f* BRUTA |
| 11652 | VÁLVULA *f* DE COMPUERTA |
| 11653 | GRIFO *m* VÁLVULA *f* DE COMPUERTA |
| 11654 | FANGO *m* |
| 11655 | BARRO *m* |
| 11656 | PROCEDIMIENTO *m* DE MOLDEADO INVERSO |
| 11657 | MENUDOS *m* DE COQUE |
| 11658 | MOTOR *m* DE GAS CON POCA POTENCIA |
| 11659 | SERRUCHO *m* |
| 11660 | QUINCALLA *f*, QUINCALLERÍA *f*, FERRETERÍA *f* |
| 11661 | MOTOR *m* DE REDUCIDA POTENCIA |
| 11662 | RUEDA *f* DE TRACCIÓN PARA CADENAS O CABLES |
| 11662 | POLEA *f* PARA CADENAS |
| 11663 | CALDERA BAJO VOLUMEN *f* |
| 11664 | TRATAR LOS MINERALES |
| 11665 | HORNO *m* DE FUNDIR |
| 11666 | FUSIÓN *f* |
| 11666 | TRATAMIENTO *m* DE LOS MINERALES |
| 11667 | HORNO *m* |
| 11667 | HORNO *m* DE FUSIÓN |
| 11668 | FÁBRICA *f* METALÚRGICA |
| 11669 | PIEZA *f* FORJADA A MANO |
| 11669 | FORJADO *m* A MANO |
| 11670 | PIEZA *f* FORJADA A MARTILLO |
| 11671 | HERRERO *m* |
| 11672 | HUMO *m* |
| 11673 | FUMÍVORO (A) |
| 11674 | CÁMARA *f* FUMÍVORA |
| 11675 | FORMACIÓN *f* DE HUMO |
| 11676 | PERJUICIO *m* A CAUSA DEL HUMO |
| 11678 | LLAMA *f* FULIGINOSA |
| 11679 | ALISAR, PULIR, PULIMENTAR, SATINAR, LUSTRAR |
| 11680 | LIMA *f* DE TALLA FINA |
| 11680 | LIMA *f* FINA |
| 11681 | MARCHA *f* REGULAR, MARCHA *f* NORMAL |
| 11682 | PERFECCIONAMIENTO *m*, ACABADO *m* PERFECTO DE UN TRABAJO |
| 11682 | ACABAMIENTO *m* |
| 11682 | ACABADO *m* |
| 11682 | TERMINACIÓN *f*, ACABADO |
| 11682 | RETOQUE *m* |
| 11683 | FRACTURA LIMPIA *f* |
| 11684 | TUBO *m* LISO |

| | | | | |
|---|---|---|---|---|
| 11685 | ARRANQUE *m* SUAVE | | 11724 | ÓXIDO *m* DE SODIO |
| 11685 | ARRANQUE *m* SUAVE (SIN SACUDIDAS) | | 11725 | NITRITO *m* DE SOSA |
| 11686 | BRUÑIDURA *f*, ALISADURA *f*, PULIMENTO *m* | | 11725 | SOSA *f* NITROSA |
| 11687 | CEPILLO *m* DE PULIR | | 11725 | SOSA *f* NITROSA |
| 11688 | ARDER SIN LLAMA, COQUIZAR A BAJA TEMPERATURA | | 11725 | SOSA *f* NITROSA |
| 11688 | ÍNCUBAR | | 11726 | OXALATO *m* DE SODIO |
| 11689 | DESBARBADURA *f* | | 11727 | BIÓXIDO *m* DE SODIO |
| 11689 | AMOLADURA *f* PARA RECTIFICAR O AFILAR | | 11728 | FOSFATO *m* DE SODIO |
| 11690 | INTERRUPTOR *m* DE ACCIÓN INSTANTÁNEA | | 11729 | TARTRATO *m* DE POTASA Y SOSA |
| 11691 | PORTAMOSQUETÓN *m* | | 11729 | SAL *f* DE SIEGNETTE |
| 11691 | MOSQUETÓN *m*, ENGANCHE *m*, ANILLO *m* PARA GANCHO | | 11730 | PIROFOSFATO *m* DE SOSA |
| | | | 11731 | SILICATO *m* DE SOSA |
| 11692 | ARANDELA *f* DE RETENCÍON, RETÉN *m* | | 11732 | ESTANNATO *m* DE SODIO |
| 11693 | CALIBRES DE MORDAZA *m pl* | | 11733 | SULFATO *m* NEUTRO DE SODIO |
| 11694 | RESPIRADERO *m* | | 11734 | SULFITO *m* DE SOSA |
| 11695 | CARGA DE NIEVE *f* | | 11735 | TANATO *m* DE SODIO |
| 11696 | CADENAS PARA LA NIEVE *f pl* | | 11736 | HIPOSULFITO *m* DE SODIO |
| 11697 | LIMPIEZA *f* POR INMERSIÓN | | 11737 | TUNGSTATO *m* DE SOSA |
| 11698 | HORNO *m* DE IGUALIZACIÓN | | 11738 | METAL *m* BLANDO |
| 11699 | FOSO *m* DE TEMPLAR | | 11738 | METAL *m* BLANDO |
| 11700 | TEMPERATURA *f* DE RECOCIDO | | 11739 | GUARNICIÓN *f* FLEXIBLE |
| 11701 | JABÓN *m* | | 11740 | JABÓN *m* VERDE |
| 11702 | AGUA *f* JABONOSA (O DE JABÓN) | | 11740 | JABÓN *m* BLANDO |
| 11702 | AGUA *f* JABONOSA, AGUA DE JABÓN | | 11740 | JABÓN *m* DE POTASA |
| 11703 | ESTEATITA *f* | | 11740 | JABÓN *m* NEGRO |
| 11703 | JABÓN *m* DE SASTRE | | 11741 | SOLDAR CON ESTAÑO |
| 11704 | ESCOPLO DE MANGUITO *m* | | 11742 | SOLDADURA *f* CON ESTAÑO |
| 11705 | MANGUITO *m* DE RACOR O DE EMPALME | | 11743 | SOLDADURA *f* CON ESTAÑO |
| 11706 | GRAPA DE EMPALME DE CABLES *f* | | 11744 | ACERO DULCE (SUAVE) *m* |
| 11707 | TUBO *m* PARA ENCAJAR | | 11745 | AGUA *f* DULCE, AGUA PURA |
| 11708 | EMPALME *m* DE AJUSTE CON SOLDADURA | | 11745 | AGUA *f* POCO CARGADA (DE SALES), AGUA DULCE |
| 11709 | LLAVE DE MANGUITO *f* | | | |
| 11710 | EXTREMO *m* HEMBRA DE UN TUBO | | 11746 | MADERA *f* BLANDA |
| 11711 | CRISTALES *m pl* DE SOSA | | 11746 | MADERA *f* BLANDA |
| 11712 | LEJÍA *f* DE SOSA | | 11746 | MADERA *f* BLANDA |
| 11713 | SOSA *f* | | 11747 | MARTILLO *m* DE CABEZA PLÁSTICA |
| 11713 | CARBONATO SÓDICO *m* | | 11748 | DESENDURECER EL AGUA, PURIFICAR EL AGUA POTABLE POR VÍA QUÍMICA |
| 11714 | SODIO *m* | | | |
| 11715 | ACETATO *m* SÓDICO | | 11748 | PURIFICAR LAS AGUAS DE ALIMENTACIÓN POR VÍA QUÍMICA |
| 11715 | ACETATO DE SODIO *m* | | | |
| 11716 | ALUMINATO DE SODIO *m* | | 11749 | ABLANDAMIENTO *m*, SUAVIZACIÓN *f* |
| 11717 | SULFATO *m* ÁCIDO DE SOSA | | 11750 | PUNTO *m* DE DESPLOME |
| 11718 | SULFITO *m* ÁCIDO | | 11751 | CONSISTENCIA *f* DEL SUELO |
| 11718 | BISULFITO *m* SÓDICO | | 11752 | ESTUDIO *m* DE SUELO (DE TERRENO) |
| 11719 | CITRATO DE SODIO *m* | | 11752 | ESTUDIO *m* DE TERRENO |
| 11720 | CIANURO *m* DE SODIO | | 11753 | ACEITE *m* SOLAR |
| 11721 | FLUORURO *m* DE SODIO | | 11754 | ESPECTRO *m* SOLAR |
| 11722 | SOSA *f* CÁUSTICA | | 11755 | ALEACIÓN FUSIBLE PARA SOLDAR O PARA SOLDAR CON LATÓN O BRONCE *f* |
| 11722 | HIDRATO *m* DE SODIO | | | |
| 11723 | RAYA *f* DEL SODIO | | 11755 | SOLDADURA *f* (COMPOSICIÓN FUSIBLE) |
| | | | 11756 | SOLDAR |

| | | |
|---|---|---|
| 11757 | FRAGILIDAD *f* POR PENETRACIÓN DE LA SOLDADURA | |
| 11758 | ARANDELA *f* SOLDADA | |
| 11758 | BRIDA *f* SOLDADA | |
| 11759 | UNIÓN POR SOLDADURA *f*, JUNTA *f* SOLDADA | |
| 11760 | TUBO *m* SOLDADO CON ALEACIÓN | |
| 11761 | SOLDADURA *f* (TRABAJO HECHO SOLDANDO CON INTERPOSICIÓN DE UNA ALEACIÓN) | |

11757 FRAGILIDAD *f* POR PENETRACIÓN DE LA SOLDADURA
11758 ARANDELA *f* SOLDADA
11758 BRIDA *f* SOLDADA
11759 UNIÓN POR SOLDADURA *f*, JUNTA *f* SOLDADA
11760 TUBO *m* SOLDADO CON ALEACIÓN
11761 SOLDADURA *f* (TRABAJO HECHO SOLDANDO CON INTERPOSICIÓN DE UNA ALEACIÓN)
11762 SOLDADURA *f*
11762 SOLDADURA *f*
11762 SOLDADURA *f* EN BAÑO DE SAL
11763 HORNO *m* DE SOLDAR
11764 HIERRO *m* SOLDADOR
11765 HIERRO *m* PARA SOLDAR
11766 LÁMPARA *f* DE SOLDAR, MECHERO *m* DE SOLDAR
11767 TENAZAS *f pl* DE SOLDAR
11767 PINZA *f* DE SOLDADOR
11768 SOLDADURA *f* CON SOPLETE
11769 SOLDADURA *f* CON SOLDADOR
11770 CUERO *m* FUERTE (PARA SUELAS)
11771 CAJA *f* DE UN CEPILLO
11772 PLACA *f* SOPORTE DE COJINETE
11773 SOLENOIDE *m*
11774 SOLENOIDE *m*
11774 GRIFO *m* ELECTROMAGNÉTICO
11774 VÁLVULA *f* ELECTROMAGNÉTICA
11774 VÁLVULA *f* ELECTROMAGNÉTICA
11775 CUERPO SÓLIDO *m*
11775 SÓLIDO *m*
11776 ÁNGULO SÓLIDO *m*
11777 COJINETE *m* CERRADO
11778 BARRA *f* TALADRADORA SÓLIDA
11779 CUBO *m* DE UNA SOLA PIEZA
11780 LADRILLO *m* MACIZO
11781 TERRAJA *f* REDONDA EN UN SOLO BLOQUE
11782 TUBO *m* ESTIRADO
11783 FRESAS *f pl* EN EXTREMO PLENAS
11784 VOLANTE *m* DE UNA SOLA PIEZA
11785 COMBUSTIBLE SÓLIDO *m*
11786 HIERRO *m* MACIZO DE MEDIA CAÑA
11787 CHORRO *m* DE SÓLIDOS
11788 COJINETE *m* DE UNA SOLA PIEZA
11789 MANDRIL *m* LISO
11790 CUERPO DE REVOLUCIÓN *m*
11791 PISTÓN *m* PLENO
11792 POLEA *f* DE UNA PIEZA
11793 ÁRBOL MACIZO *m*
11794 SOLUCIÓN *f* SÓLIDA
11795 ESTADO *m* SÓLIDO
11796 OPÉRCULO *m* MONOBLOQUE (ESQUINA), DISCO *m* DE CIERRE
11797 SOLIDIFICACIÓN *f*

11798 FRENTE *m* DE SOLIDIFICACIÓN
11798 FRENTE *m* DE CRISTALIZACIÓN
11799 SOLIDIFICACIÓN *f* DE UN LÍQUIDO
11800 PUNTO *m* DE SOLIDIFICACIÓN
11801 INTERVALO *m* DE SOLIDIFICACIÓN
11802 CONTRACCIÓN DE SOLIDIFICACIÓN *f*
11803 SOLIDIFICARSE POR ENFRIAMIENTO
11804 PUNTO *m* DE SOLIDIFICACIÓN
11804 PUNTO *m* DE TOMA
11805 SÓLIDOS *m pl*
11806 SOLUBILIDAD *f*
11807 SOLUBLE
11808 CRISTAL *m* LÍQUIDO
11808 VIDRIO *m* SOLUBLE
11809 SOLUBLE EN EL AGUA
11810 ACEITE *m* SOLUBLE
11811 SOLUCIÓN *f*
11812 RECOCIDO *m* DE PUESTA EN SOLUCIÓN
11813 RESOLVER
11813 DISOLVER
11814 DISOLVENTE
11814 DISOLVENTE *m*
11815 PRUEBA *f* ACÚSTICA
11816 HOLLÍN *m*
11817 MEZCLA *f* DE FERRITA Y CEMENTITA
11818 VIBRACIÓN *f* SONORA
11819 ONDA *f* SONORA
11820 MADERA *f* SANA
11821 HOMOGENEIDAD *f* DE UNA SOLDADURA
11822 PETRÓLEO *m* BRUTO SULFUROSO
11823 FUENTE *f* DE ELECTRICIDAD
11824 FUENTE *f* DE ENERGÍA
11825 FUENTE *f* DE ERRORES
11825 CAUSA DE ERROR *f*
11826 FUENTE *f* LUMINOSA
11827 POLO *m* SUR DE UN IMÁN
11828 RED *f* ESPACIAL
11829 ESPACIO *m* NECESARIO
11830 DESCASCADO *m*
11831 BRECHA *f*
11831 LUZ *f* (DISTANCIA ENTRE PUNTOS DE APOYO)
11832 OJO *m* PARA LA LLAVE
11833 LLAVE DE TUERCAS *f*
11834 PIEZA *f* DE RECAMBIO, PIEZA *f* DE REPUESTO
11834 PIEZA *f* INTERCAMBIABLE
11835 RUEDA *f* DE REPUESTO
11836 CHISPA *m*
11837 CORRECTOR DE AVANCE *m*
11838 BUJÍA *f* DE ENCENDIDO
11839 CASQUILLO *m* DE BUJÍA
11840 PRUEBA *f* CON CHISPA

| | |
|---|---|
| 11841 | BUJÍA  f  DE ENCENDIDO |
| 11842 | PERLA  f  DE SOLDADURA |
| 11842 | PROYECCIÓN  f |
| 11842 | SALPICADURA  f |
| 11843 | PÉRDIDAS  f pl  DE SALPICADURAS |
| 11844 | ESPÁTULA  f |
| 11845 | ESPECIALIDAD  f |
| 11845 | RAMO  m, RAMA  f |
| 11845 | ESPECIALIDAD  f, RAMO  m, CAMPO  m |
| 11846 | CHAPA  f  TRABAJADA POR ENCARGO |
| 11846 | CHAPA  f  PERFILADA |
| 11847 | ALAMBRE  m  PERFILADO |
| 11848 | ACERO ESPECIAL  m |
| 11849 | PRODUCTO  m  ESPECIAL |
| 11850 | DENSIDAD  f |
| 11850 | PESO  m  ESPECÍFICO |
| 11851 | PICNÓMETRO  m |
| 11852 | CALOR ESPECÍFICO  m |
| 11853 | PRESIÓN  f  EN KG POR UNIDAD DE SUPERFICIE |
| 11854 | VOLUMEN  m  ESPECÍFICO |
| 11855 | PLIEGO DE CONDICIONES  m, PLIEGO DE BASES  m |
| 11856 | DESCRIPCIÓN  f  DE UNA PATENTE |
| 11856 | MEMORIA  f  DESCRIPTIVA DE UNA PATENTE |
| 11857 | DIMENSIONES  f pl  NOMINALES |
| 11858 | MUESTRA  f  (DE METAL) |
| 11859 | COLORES DEL ESPECTRO  m |
| 11860 | ESPECTRÓGRAFO  m |
| 11861 | ANÁLISIS ESPECTRAL  m |
| 11862 | ESPECTROSCOPIO  m |
| 11862 | ESPECTRÓMETRO  m |
| 11863 | ESPECTRO  m |
| 11864 | ANÁLISIS ESPECTRAL  m |
| 11865 | HEMATITES  f  ROJA |
| 11865 | OLIGISTO  m |
| 11865 | HIERRO  m  ESPECULAR, FUNDICIÓN  f  MANGANESÍFERA |
| 11866 | SUPERFICIE  f  RELUCIENTE |
| 11867 | BRONCE  m  PARA ESPEJOS DE TELESCOPIOS |
| 11868 | VELOCIDAD  f |
| 11869 | TAQUÍMETRO  m |
| 11870 | VELOCIDAD  f  DE INFLAMACIÓN |
| 11871 | POLEA  f  ESCALONADA |
| 11871 | PERA  m  DE VELOCIDAD |
| 11871 | CONO DE TRANSMISIÓN  m |
| 11871 | CONO DE TRANSMISIÓN  m |
| 11871 | CONO DE TRANSMISIÓN  m |
| 11872 | REDUCTOR  m  DE VELOCIDAD |
| 11873 | REDUCTOR  m  DE VELOCIDAD |
| 11873 | ENGRANAJE  m  REDUCTOR DE VELOCIDAD |
| 11874 | REGULADOR  m  DE VELOCIDAD |

| | |
|---|---|
| 11875 | VELOCIDAD  f |
| 11876 | VELOCIDAD  f  DE ROTACIÓN |
| 11877 | INDICADOR DE VELOCIDAD  m, TAQUÍMETRO  m |
| 11878 | MATA  f  (MIN) |
| 11879 | CINC  m  (COMERCIAL) |
| 11880 | SOLDADURA  f  AMARILLA |
| 11881 | ACEITE  m  DE BLANCO DE BALLENA |
| 11882 | ESPERMA  f  DE BALLENA, ESPERMACETI  m |
| 11882 | CETINA  f, ESPERMA  f  DE BALLENA |
| 11883 | ESFERA  f |
| 11883 | ESFERA  f, GLOBO  m, FANAL  m |
| 11884 | ESFÉRICO |
| 11885 | ABERRACIÓN DE ESFERICIDAD  f |
| 11886 | HUSILLO  m  ESFÉRICO |
| 11887 | CASQUETE ESFÉRICO  m |
| 11888 | ESPEJO  m  ESFÉRICO |
| 11889 | MOVIMIENTO  m  ESFÉRICO |
| 11890 | COJINETE  m  DE EMPUJE DE BOLAS |
| 11891 | TRIÁNGULO  m  ESFÉRICO |
| 11892 | INGLETE  m  ESFÉRICO |
| 11893 | MUÑÓN  m  GIRATORIO |
| 11893 | PIVOTE  m  ESFÉRICO, MUÑEQUILLA  f |
| 11894 | FUNDICIÓN  f  DÚCTIL |
| 11894 | FUNDICIÓN  f  CON GRAFITO ESFEROIDAL |
| 11894 | FUNDICIÓN  f  NODULAR |
| 11895 | FUNDICIÓN  f  CON GRAFITO ESFEROIDAL |
| 11896 | GLOBULACIÓN  f |
| 11896 | HACERSE ESFEROIDAL |
| 11897 | ESFERÓMETRO  m |
| 11898 | ARRABIO  m  ESPECULAR |
| 11899 | ARRABIO  m  ESPECULAR |
| 11899 | ARRABIO  m  ESPECULAR |
| 11899 | FUNDICIÓN  f  ESPECULAR (SPIEGEL) |
| 11900 | JUNTA  f  CON MANGUITO, JUNTA  f  CONTRAPEADA |
| 11901 | EXTREMO  m  MACHO DE UN TUBO |
| 11902 | GANCHOS  m pl |
| 11903 | VENTEADURAS  f pl |
| 11904 | PÚA  f, MANDRIL  m, PUNZÓN  m, HUSILLO  m, EJE  m |
| 11904 | MANDRIL  m, CABEZAL  m |
| 11904 | MANDRIL  m, HUSILLO  m |
| 11905 | SOPORTE  m  DE UN MUÑÓN |
| 11905 | COJINETE  m  DEL HUSILLO |
| 11906 | PASADA  f  DE HUSILLO |
| 11907 | TUERCA  f  DE HUSILLO |
| 11908 | ACEITE  m  MINERAL PARA CABEZALES |
| 11909 | VELOCIDAD  f  DE HUSILLO |
| 11910 | SOPORTE  m  DE HUSO |
| 11911 | TORNO  m  DE REPUJAR Y ALISAR |
| 11912 | ESPIRAL  f |

| | |
|---|---|
| 11913 | LEVA DE ESPIRAL *f* |
| 11914 | TOBOGÁN *m* |
| 11915 | ESCARIADOR CON ESTRÍAS HELICOIDALES *m* |
| 11915 | ESCARIADOR CON RANURAS HELICOIDALES *m* |
| 11916 | PAR DE RUEDAS HELICOIDALES *m* |
| 11917 | FRESA *f* CON DENTADO HELICOIDAL |
| 11918 | ROBLONADO *m* EN ESPIRAL |
| 11919 | ESCALERA *f* HELICOIDAL |
| 11920 | TUBO *m* SOLDADO EN HÉLICE |
| 11920 | TUBO *m* SOLDADO EN ESPIRAL |
| 11921 | SOLDADURA *f* EN ESPIRAL |
| 11922 | TERMÓMETRO *m* DE ALCOHOL |
| 11923 | LÁMPARA *f* DE ALCOHOL |
| 11924 | CONO DEFLECTOR (EN DEPÓSITO) *m* |
| 11925 | ENGRASE *m* POR AGITACIÓN |
| 11926 | PANEL *m* PROTECTOR |
| 11927 | GUARDABARROS *m pl* |
| 11928 | ACEITE *m* VERTIDO |
| 11928 | ACEITE *m* PROYECTADO |
| 11929 | SALPICADURAS *f pl* DE METAL |
| 11930 | AYUSTE *m*, ENCOLCHADO *m* |
| 11931 | DESCOLCHAR (UNA CUERDA) |
| 11932 | ELEMENTOS *m pl* DE CUBREJUNTAS |
| 11933 | DESCOLCHADO *m* (DE CUERDA) |
| 11934 | DESCOLCHADO *m* (DE CUERDA) |
| 11935 | ÁRBOL ACANALADO *m*, ÁRBOL RANURADO *m* |
| 11936 | FRACTURA CEROIDE *f* |
| 11936 | (FRACTURA) ESCAMOSA |
| 11936 | (FRACTURA) ESCAMOSA *f* |
| 11937 | RANURA *f* |
| 11938 | CUBO *m* DE DOS PIEZAS |
| 11939 | ANILLO *m* DE RETENCIÓN PARTIDO |
| 11940 | PASADOR *m* HENDIDO |
| 11941 | VOLANTE *m* HENDIDO |
| 11942 | TUERCA *f* ENTALLADA |
| 11942 | TUERCA *f* ENTALLADA |
| 11943 | CLAVIJA *f* HENDIDA |
| 11944 | SEGMENTO *m* DE ÉMBOLO PARTIDO |
| 11945 | POLEA *f* ACANALADA |
| 11945 | POLEA *f* EN DOS PIEZAS |
| 11946 | ESCINDIR |
| 11946 | DESDOBLAR |
| 11947 | SEMICOJINETES *m pl* |
| 11948 | RESQUEBRAJAMIENTO *m* DE LA MADERA |
| 11949 | PRUEBA *f* DE RECALCAMIENTO |
| 11949 | PRUEBA *f* DE CORTE |
| 11950 | DESDOBLAMIENTO *m* |
| 11951 | RUEDA *f* DE RADIOS |
| 11952 | TRAPO PARA LIMPIAR *m* |
| 11952 | TRAPO PARA SECAR *m* |
| 11953 | VIRUTA *f* DE HIERRO |
| 11954 | PLOMO *m* ESPONJOSO |
| 11955 | ESPUMA *f* DE PLATINO |
| 11955 | ESPONJA *f* DE PLATINO |
| 11956 | AUTOINFLAMACIÓN *f* |
| 11956 | COMBUSTIÓN |
| 11956 | CONFLAGRACIÓN *f* ESPONTÁNEA |
| 11957 | BROCA *f* DE CUCHARA |
| 11957 | BROCA *f* DE CUCHARA |
| 11958 | PRUEBA *f* A LA GOTA |
| 11959 | SOLDADURA *f* POR PUNTOS |
| 11960 | ACABADO *m* PARCIAL |
| 11960 | MOTEADO |
| 11961 | FORMACIÓN *f* DE MANCHAS |
| 11962 | PISTOLA *f* DE PULVERIZACIÓN |
| 11962 | PISTOLA *f* DE PROYECCIÓN |
| 11963 | TOBERA *f* DE PULVERIZACIÓN |
| 11964 | TOBERA *f* DE PULVERIZACIÓN |
| 11965 | PINTURA *f* POR PULVERIZACIÓN CON PISTOLA NEUMÁTICA |
| 11966 | TEMPLE *m* POR PULVERIZACIÓN |
| 11967 | PULVERIZADOR *m* |
| 11968 | PULVERIZACIÓN *f* |
| 11968 | PROYECCIÓN *f* |
| 11969 | ESPOLVOREADORA *f pl* PORTÁTIL |
| 11970 | ESPOLVOREADORAS *f* SULFUROSAS |
| 11971 | ESPOLVOREADORAS *f pl* PULVERIZADORAS |
| 11972 | PROCEDIMIENTO *m* POR ASPERSIÓN |
| 11973 | SEPARADOR *m* |
| 11974 | RESORTE *m* |
| 11974 | RESORTE *m* ANTAGONISTA |
| 11975 | MÁQUINA *f* PARA ENSAYAR LOS MUELLES Y LOS ALAMBRES |
| 11976 | BALANZA *f* DE RESORTE |
| 11976 | BALANZA *f* DE MUELLE |
| 11977 | SUPRESIÓN *f* DEL HUMO |
| 11977 | HOJA *f* DE BALLESTA |
| 11978 | LATÓN *m* PARA MUELLES |
| 11979 | CASQUILLO *m* CON MUELLE |
| 11980 | CAJA *f* DE RESORTE |
| 11981 | FACTOR *m* DE VIBRACIÓN |
| 11982 | COMPRESOR DE ENGRASE *m* |
| 11983 | RESORTE *m* CARGADO |
| 11983 | RESORTE *m* TENSO |
| 11983 | RESORTE *m* ZUNCHADO |
| 11984 | REGULADOR *m* DE RESORTE |
| 11985 | VÁLVULA *f* DE SEGURIDAD DE PALANCA Y RESORTE |
| 11986 | VÁLVULA *f* DE SEGURIDAD DE RESORTE |
| 11987 | TRINQUETE DE FLEJE *m*, FIADOR *m* |
| 11988 | CAJA DE MUELLE *f* |
| 11989 | MANÓMETRO *m* DE MUELLE |

| | | | |
|---|---|---|---|
| 11989 | MANÓMETRO *m* METÁLICO | 12026 | PIRÁMIDE *f* CUADRANGULAR |
| 11990 | ANILLO ELÁSTICO *m*, CLIP *m* | 12027 | RAÍ *f* CUADRADA |
| 11990 | CÍRCULO ELÁSTICO *m* | 12028 | CABLE DE SECCIÓN CUADRADA *m* |
| 11991 | PLACA *f* DE MUELLE, PLACAS *f pl* GEMELAS DE MUELLE | 12029 | ÁRBOL DE SECCIÓN CUADRADA *m* |
| | | 12030 | ROSCA *f* PLANA (O RECTANGULAR) |
| 11992 | ACERO DE MUELLES *m* | 12031 | YARDA *f* CUADRADA |
| 11993 | RESORTE *m* DE FLEXIÓN | 12032 | SOLDADURA *f* SOBRE BORDES RECTOS |
| 11994 | RESORTE *m* DE TORSIÓN | 12033 | TORNILLO *m* DE CABEZA CUADRADA |
| 11995 | ARANDELA *f* GROWER | 12033 | TORNILLO *m* DE CABEZA CUADRADA |
| 11996 | AGUA *f* DE FUENTE (O DE MANANTIAL) | 12034 | TORNILLO *m* DE ROSCA CUADRADA |
| 11997 | ALAMBRE *m* PARA MUELLE | 12035 | MADERA *f* ENCUADRADA |
| 11998 | VÁLVULA *f* DE SEGURIDAD DE RESORTE | 12036 | CUADRATURA *f* |
| 11999 | RUPTURA *f* DE LAS CABEZAS DE ROBLÓN | 12037 | CIZALLA PARA DESPUNTAR *f* |
| 12000 | REGAR | 12038 | RETRASO *m* EN LA SOLDADURA |
| 12001 | PULVERIZACIÓN *f*, ASPERSIÓN *f* | 12039 | EXTRAER |
| 12002 | CADENA GALLE *f* | 12039 | EXPRESAR |
| 12003 | EMBUDO *m* DE COLADA, BEBEDERO *m* | 12040 | JAULA DE UN RODAMIENTO DE RODILLOS *f* |
| 12003 | EMBUDO *m*, BAJADA *f* DE COLADA | 12041 | ESTABILIDAD *f* |
| 12004 | CHORRO *m* DE COLADA, SANGRÍA DE HIERRO FUNDIDO | 12042 | ESTABILIZADOR *m* |
| | | 12043 | ESTABILIZACIÓN *f* |
| 12005 | CORDÓN *m*, MEOLLAR *m* | 12044 | RECOCIDO *m* REDUCTOR DE TENSIÓN |
| 12006 | MÁQUINAS *f pl* PARA ENTALLAR LOS ENGRANAJES RECTOS Y HELICOIDALES | 12045 | EQUILIBRIO *m* ESTABLE |
| | | 12046 | CHIMENEA *f* |
| 12007 | RUEDA *f* DE FRICCIÓN CILÍNDRICA | 12047 | PORTAOBJETO *m* |
| 12008 | ENGRANAJE *m* RECTO | 12048 | |
| 12008 | ENGRANAJE *m* RECTO | 12048 | ALTERNO *m* |
| 12009 | RUEDA *f* DENTADA RECTA | 12049 | SOLDADURA *f* DE ÁNGULO DISCONTINUA CON HILERAS ALTERNADAS |
| 12009 | RUEDA *f* DENTADA CILÍNDRICA | | |
| 12010 | ACCIONAMIENTO POR ENGRANAJE RECTO *m* | 12050 | AGUA *f* ESTANCADA (O MUERTA) |
| 12011 | POLIPASTO *m* RECTO DE ENGRANAJE | 12050 | AGUA *f* ESTANCADA (O MUERTA) |
| 12012 | RESPALDO *m*, TESTERA *f* | 12051 | ACERO CORROSIORRESISTENTE *m* |
| 12013 | CUADRADO *m* (SEGUNDA POTENCIA) | 12052 | ZANCA *f*, MADERO *m* EN QUE SE APOYAN LOS PELDAÑOS |
| 12013 | CUADRADO *m* (GEOM.) | | |
| 12014 | ESCUADRA *f* | 12053 | ESCALERA *f* |
| 12015 | HIERRO *m* CUADRADO | 12054 | ESTALAGMOMETRÍA *f* |
| 12016 | CENTÍMETRO CUADRADO *m* | 12055 | PISÓN *m* DE BOCARTE |
| 12017 | SECCIÓN *f* CUADRADA | 12056 | MATRIZAR, ESTAMPAR, TROQUELAR |
| 12018 | DECÍMETRO *m* CUADRADO | 12056 | ESTAMPAR |
| 12019 | LIMA CUADRADA *f* | 12056 | ESTAMPAR |
| 12019 | LIMA CUADRADA *f* CUADRADILLO *m* | 12057 | BOCARTE *m* |
| 12019 | CUADRADILLO *m* | 12057 | MOLINO *m* DE MAZAS |
| 12019 | LIMA *f* CUATRO CUARTOS | 12058 | CADENA ESTAMPADA *f*, CADENA TROQUELADA *f* |
| 12019 | LIMA *f* CUADRADA | | |
| 12019 | LIMA *f* CUATRO CUARTOS | 12059 | ESTAMPADO *m* |
| 12020 | PIE *m* CUADRADO (MEDIDA INGLESA) | 12059 | ESTAMPADO *m* |
| 12021 | PULGADA *f* CUADRADA INGLESA | 12059 | MATRIZADO *m*, ESTAMPADO *m* |
| 12022 | METRO *m* CUADRADO | 12060 | PRENSA *f* DE ESTAMPAR |
| 12023 | MILÍMETRO *m* CUADRADO | 12060 | ESTAMPADORA *f* |
| 12024 | TUERCA *f* CUADRADA | 12061 | PRUEBA *f* DE ESTAMPADO |
| 12025 | CUADRADO *m* | 12062 | MONTANTE *m* |
| 12026 | CUADRILÁTERO *m* | 12062 | APOYO *m*, POSTE *m*, PILAR *m*, COLUMNA *f* |

| | |
|---|---|
| 12063 | MONTANTE *m* |
| 12064 | ASIENTO EN EL SUELO *m* |
| 12065 | CÁMARA DE LAMINADOR *f* |
| 12066 | TUBO *m* DE TOMA DE AGUA |
| 12067 | PIEZÓMETRO *m* |
| 12068 | RESERVA (DE) |
| 12069 | COMPRESOR DE RESERVA *m* |
| 12070 | MÁQUINA *f* DE RESERVA |
| 12070 | MOTOR *m* DE RESERVA |
| 12071 | NORMA *f* |
| 12071 | ESTANDARD |
| 12071 | DIMENSIÓN *f* NORMAL (TIPO) |
| 12072 | PIE *m* CÚBICO NORMALIZADO |
| 12073 | MODELO *m* ESTANDARD, MODELO *m* NORMALIZADO |
| 12073 | DISEÑO NORMALIZADO O STANDARD *m* |
| 12074 | DESVÍO *m* TIPO, DESVÍO STANDARD |
| 12075 | SOLDADURA *f* DE ÁNGULO DE CORDÓN PLANO |
| 12076 | CALIBRE NORMAL *m* |
| 12076 | CALIBRE *m* STANDARD |
| 12077 | MEDIDA *f* PATRÓN, MEDIDA *f* STANDARD |
| 12077 | MEDIDA *f* DE CONTROL |
| 12077 | MEDIDA *f* CONTRASTE |
| 12078 | MONTANTE *m* DE UNA MÁQUINA |
| 12079 | AMPLITUD *f* DE COMPARACIÓN |
| 12080 | MANÓMETRO *m* SERVICIO CONTRASTE |
| 12081 | METRO *m* CONTRASTE |
| 12082 | CALIBRE NORMALIZADO (O STANDARD), MUESTRA *f* STANDARD |
| 12083 | PERFIL *m* NORMAL |
| 12084 | LICOR *m* NORMAL |
| 12084 | LICOR *m* GRADUADO |
| 12085 | TERMÓMETRO *m* PATRÓN |
| 12086 | TIPO *m* ESTANDARD |
| 12087 | CALIBRE *m* CON TAMPÓN NORMAL |
| 12088 | CALIBRE *m* DE MORDAZA NORMAL |
| 12089 | CALIBRADOR *m* BIRMINGHAM PARA ALAMBRES |
| 12089 | CALIBRE *m* INGLÉS |
| 12090 | UNIFICAR |
| 12090 | NORMALIZAR, ESTANDARDIZAR |
| 12090 | NORMALIZAR |
| 12091 | NORMALIZACIÓN *f* |
| 12091 | NORMALIZACIÓN *f* ESTANDARDIZACIÓN *f* |
| 12091 | UNIFICACIÓN *f* |
| 12092 | RAMAL *m* INMÓVIL (O FIJO) |
| 12092 | CORDÓN *m* FIJO DE UN POLIPASTO |
| 12093 | COLUMNA MONTANTE *f* |
| 12094 | PARADA DE UNA MÁQUINA *f* |
| 12095 | ESTANNATO *m* |
| 12096 | TETRACLORURO *m* |
| 12096 | DICLORURO *m* DE ESTAÑO |
| 12096 | CLORURO ESTÁNICO *m* |
| 12097 | ÁCIDO ESTÁNNICO *m* |
| 12098 | POLVO *m* DE ESTAÑO |
| 12098 | BIÓXIDO *m* DE ESTAÑO |
| 12098 | ÓXIDO *m* ESTÁNNICO |
| 12099 | ORO *m* MUSSIF, ORO *m* DE JUDEA, SULFURO *m* ESTÁNICO |
| 12099 | SULFURO *m* ESTÁNNICO |
| 12099 | DISULFURO *m* DE ESTAÑO |
| 12100 | PROTOCLORURO *m* DE ESTAÑO |
| 12100 | CLORURO ESTANOSO *m* |
| 12100 | SAL *f* DE ESTAÑO |
| 12101 | HIDRATO *m* ESTAÑOSO |
| 12102 | ÓXIDO *m* ESTANNOSO |
| 12103 | SULFURO *m* ESTAÑOSO |
| 12104 | GRAPA DE FONDO *f* |
| 12105 | GARFIO *m*, GRAPA *f* |
| 12105 | GRAPÓN *m* |
| 12106 | GRAPA *f* |
| 12107 | POLÍGONO *m* ESTRELLADO |
| 12108 | ATRONADO DE LA MADERA *m* |
| 12108 | ATRONADURA *f* |
| 12109 | RUEDA *f* ESTRELLADA |
| 12110 | SECCIÓN *f* ESTRELLADA |
| 12111 | ALMIDÓN *m* |
| 12111 | FÉCULA *f* |
| 12112 | ENGRUDO *m* |
| 12112 | PASTA *f* |
| 12112 | COLA DE ALMIDÓN *f*, ENGRUDO *m* |
| 12113 | ARRANCAR |
| 12114 | HACER QUE ARRANQUE UN MOTOR |
| 12114 | PONER EN MARCHA |
| 12114 | PONER EN MARCHA UNA MÁQUINA |
| 12114 | INSTALAR |
| 12115 | BOTÓN *m* MARCHA/PARADA |
| 12116 | (MOTOR DE) ARRANQUE *m*, ARRANCADOR *m* |
| 12117 | MANDO DEL ARRANQUE *m* |
| 12118 | ARRANQUE *m*, PUESTA *f* EN MARCHA |
| 12118 | PUESTA *f* EN MARCHA |
| 12118 | PUESTA *f* EN SERVICIO |
| 12119 | DISPOSITIVO DE PUESTA EN MARCHA *m* |
| 12120 | PALANCA *f* DE ARRANQUE |
| 12121 | MOTOR *m* DE ARRANQUE (POR REOSTATO O POR REACTANCIA) |
| 12122 | ARRANQUE *m* DE UN MOTOR |
| 12123 | PERÍODO *m* INICIAL O DE PUESTA EN MARCHA DE UNA FÁBRICA |
| 12124 | PUNTO *m* DE PARTIDA DE UN MOVIMIENTO |
| 12125 | HIPÓTESIS *f* DE BASE |
| 12126 | POSICIÓN *f* DE ARRANQUE |
| 12127 | BOTADOR *m*, EXTRACTOR *m* |

| | |
|---|---|
| 12128 | RESISTENCIA *f* AL ARRANQUE |
| 12129 | PAR DE ARRANQUE *m* |
| 12130 | PREPARACIÓN *f* |
| 12130 | PUESTA *f* EN MARCHA |
| 12130 | PUESTA *f* EN MARCHA DE UNA MÁQUINA |
| 12130 | ARRANQUE *m* DE UN MOTOR |
| 12131 | VÁLVULA *f* DE ARRANQUE |
| 12132 | ESTADO *m* DE EQUILIBRIO |
| 12133 | ESTÁTICO *m* |
| 12134 | FROTAMIENTO *m* ESTÁTICO |
| 12135 | REGULADOR *m* ESTÁTICO |
| 12136 | PRESIÓN *f* ESTÁTICA |
| 12137 | PRESIÓN *f* ESTÁTICA |
| 12138 | CARGA ESTÁTICA *f* |
| 12139 | MOMENTO *m* ESTÁTICO |
| 12140 | ESTÁTICA *f* |
| 12141 | FURGONETA *f*, CAMIONETA *f* |
| 12141 | COMERCIAL *m* |
| 12142 | HORNO *m* ESTACIONARIO FIJO |
| 12143 | CALDERA INDUSTRIAL *f* |
| 12144 | MÁQUINA *f* DE VAPOR FIJA |
| 12145 | ONDA *f* ESTACIONARIA |
| 12146 | ESTACIÓN *f* |
| 12147 | BRONCE *m* DE ARTE |
| 12147 | BRONCE *m* DE ARTE |
| 12148 | ENGRASADOR *m* |
| 12148 | ENGRASADOR *m* STAUFFER |
| 12149 | DUELA *f* |
| 12150 | SOSTENER |
| 12150 | APUNTALAR, REFORZAR, SOSTENER |
| 12150 | APUNTALAR |
| 12150 | APUNTALAR |
| 12151 | TIRANTE *m* |
| 12152 | REFUERZO *m* CON NERVADURAS |
| 12153 | APUNTALAMIENTO *m*, REFORZAMIENTO *m* |
| 12153 | APUNTALAMIENTO *m* |
| 12153 | APUNTALAMIENTO *m* |
| 12153 | APUNTALAMIENTO *m* |
| 12153 | SOSTENIMIENTO, SOSTÉN *m* |
| 12154 | LUNETA *f* FIJA |
| 12155 | VAPOR *m* |
| 12156 | ACUMULADOR DE VAPOR *m* |
| 12157 | BAÑO *m* DE VAPOR |
| 12158 | GENERADOR *m* DE VAPOR |
| 12158 | CALDERA DE VAPOR *f* |
| 12159 | FRENO *m* DE VAPOR |
| 12160 | CALORÍMETRO DE CONDENSACIÓN *m* |
| 12161 | SERPENTÍN *m* |
| 12162 | CILINDRO *m* DE VAPOR |
| 12163 | CÚPULA *f* DE TOMA DE VAPOR |
| 12164 | MÁQUINA *f* DE VAPOR |

| | |
|---|---|
| 12164 | MOTOR *m* DE VAPOR |
| 12165 | MÁQUINA *f* CON PLENA PRESIÓN |
| 12166 | MARTINETE *m*, MARTILLO PILÓN *m* |
| 12166 | MARTILLO *m* DE VAPOR |
| 12167 | CALEFACCIÓN POR VAPOR *f* |
| 12168 | CAMISA *f* |
| 12168 | CAMISA *f* DE VAPOR |
| 12169 | GENERADOR *m* POR VAPOR |
| 12170 | CHORRO *m* DE VAPOR |
| 12171 | INYECTOR *m* DE VAPOR |
| 12172 | EYECTOR *m*, SOPLADOR *m* |
| 12172 | SOPLADOR *m* DE VAPOR |
| 12173 | LOCOMOTORA *f* DE VAPOR |
| 12174 | CONTADOR DE VAPOR *m* |
| 12175 | TOBERA *f* DE VAPOR |
| 12176 | ABERTURA *f* (DE UN CILINDRO DE VAPOR), CONDUCTO *m* |
| 12177 | TUBO *m* DE VAPOR |
| 12177 | TUBO *m* DE VAPOR |
| 12178 | TUBERÍAS *f pl* |
| 12178 | TUBERÍA DE VAPOR *f* LÍNEA DE VAPOR *f* |
| 12178 | TUBERÍA *f*, CANALIZACIÓN *f* |
| 12179 | PISTÓN *m* DE VAPOR |
| 12180 | INSTALACIÓN *f* DE UNA MÁQUINA DE VAPOR |
| 12181 | PRESIÓN *f* DEL VAPOR |
| 12182 | PRUEBA *f* DE PRESIÓN A VAPOR DE LA CALDERA |
| 12182 | PRUEBA *f* DE LA CALDERA |
| 12183 | BOMBA *f* DE VAPOR |
| 12184 | SEPARADOR *m* DE VAPOR |
| 12185 | CÁMARA DE VAPOR DE UNA CALDERA *f* |
| 12186 | VÁLVULA *f* DE DETENCIÓN DE VAPOR |
| 12187 | VÁLVULA *f* DE TOMA DE VAPOR |
| 12187 | GRIFO *m* DE TOMA DE VAPOR |
| 12188 | PURGADOR *m* DE AGUA CONDENSADA |
| 12188 | SEPARADOR *m* DE AGUA |
| 12189 | TURBINA *f* DE VAPOR |
| 12190 | SILBATO *m* DE VAPOR |
| 12191 | GENERATRIZ *f* DE VAPOR |
| 12192 | VAPOR *m* DE AGUA |
| 12193 | HERMÉTICO (O IMPERMEABLE) AL VAPOR |
| 12194 | ÁCIDO ESTEÁRICO *m* |
| 12195 | ESTEARINA *f* |
| 12196 | ACERO *m* |
| 12197 | BANDA *f* DE ACERO, CINTA *f* DE ACERO |
| 12198 | HIERROS *m pl* PARA HORMIGÓN |
| 12199 | VIGA *f* DE HIERRO |
| 12200 | CINTA DE ACERO *f* |
| 12201 | CABLE DE ACERO *m* |
| 12201 | CABLE DE ACERO *m* |
| 12202 | ACERO COLADO (FUNDIDO) *m* |

| | |
|---|---|
| 12202 | ACERO MOLDEADO *m* |
| 12203 | CEMENTO ARMADO *m* |
| 12203 | HORMIGÓN *m* |
| 12204 | TUBO *m* DE ACERO (PARA GASES LICUADOS) |
| 12205 | ACERAR |
| 12206 | ACERACIÓN *f* |
| 12207 | FUNDICIÓN *f* DE ACERO, ACERÍA *f* |
| 12208 | ESTRUCTURA METÁLICA *f* |
| 12209 | ACERO SIN BURBUJAS *m* |
| 12210 | LINGOTE *m* DE ACERO |
| 12211 | FÁBRICA (FUNDICIÓN) DE ACERO *f* |
| 12212 | TUBO *m* DE ACERO |
| 12213 | CHAPA *f* DE ACERO |
| 12214 | ELABORACIÓN *f* DEL ACERO |
| 12215 | CABLE DE ACERO *m* |
| 12215 | CABLE DE ACERO *m* |
| 12216 | FLEJE *m* (CHAPA *f* FINA) |
| 12217 | TRENZADOS *m pl* DE ACERO PARA CABLES |
| 12218 | CONSTRUCCIÓN DE ACERO/ METÁLICA *f* |
| 12219 | TUBO *m* DE ACERO |
| 12220 | AROS *m pl* (O LLANTAS *f pl*) DE RUEDA |
| 12221 | ALAMBRE *m* DE ACERO |
| 12222 | ACERÍA *f* |
| 12223 | ACERO *m* |
| 12224 | ACERO EXTRA-DULCE *m* |
| 12224 | HIERRO *m* CON CALIDADES DE ACERO |
| 12225 | BÁSCULA *f* ROMANA |
| 12225 | BÁSCULA *f* ROMANA |
| 12226 | MANIOBRA *f* |
| 12226 | CONDUCCIÓN *f*, MANIOBRA *f* |
| 12227 | PALANCA *f* DE ATAQUE DE DIRECCIÓN |
| 12228 | COLUMNA DE DIRECCIÓN *f* |
| 12229 | CÁRTER *m* DE DIRECCIÓN |
| 12230 | SOPORTE *m* DE MANGUETA |
| 12231 | BARRA *f* DE ACOPLAMIENTO |
| 12232 | MANDOS *m pl* DE DIRECCIÓN |
| 12232 | MANDOS *m pl* (AUTOMÓVIL) |
| 12233 | VOLANTE *m* DE DIRECCIÓN |
| 12234 | ESTELITA *f* |
| 12235 | TERMÓMETRO *m* GRADUADO EN TUBO |
| 12236 | VÁSTAGO *m* DE VÁLVULA |
| 12236 | LLAVE *f* DE GRIFO |
| 12237 | VÁSTAGO *m*, VARILLA *f* |
| 12238 | CHAPA *f* DE ESTARCIR |
| 12239 | FASE *f*, GRADO *m* |
| 12239 | PASO *m* |
| 12239 | ESCALÓN *m*, PELDAÑO *m* |
| 12239 | ESCALÓN *m*, RETALLO *m*, GRADA (MIN) *f* |
| 12239 | ESCALÓN *m*, PELDAÑO *m*, GRADA *f* |
| 12240 | RECOCIDO *m* ESCALONADO |
| 12241 | COJINETE *m* DE SOPORTE, TEJUELO *m* |

| | |
|---|---|
| 12242 | TEMPLE *m* ESCALONADO |
| 12243 | TEMPLE *m* ESCALONADO MARTENSÍTICO |
| 12244 | TRANSFORMADOR *m* REDUCTOR DE POTENCIAL |
| 12244 | TRANSFORMADOR *m* DE DISMINUCIÓN DE VOLTAJE |
| 12245 | TRANSFORMADOR *m* AMPLIFICADOR DE POTENCIA |
| 12245 | TRANSFORMADOR *m* ELEVADOR DE VOLTAJE |
| 12246 | ESCALONADO |
| 12246 | ESCALONADO |
| 12246 | GRADERÍAS (A) *f pl*, ESCALONES (EN) *m pl* ESCALONADO *m* |
| 12247 | ENGRANAJE *m* DENTADO CRUZADO |
| 12247 | ENGRANAJE *m* DE DENTADO CRUZADO |
| 12248 | PARRILLA *f* ESCALONADA |
| 12248 | PARRILLA *f* ESCALONADA |
| 12249 | TEMPLE *m* ININTERRUMPIDO |
| 12250 | ESTEREOMÉTRICO |
| 12251 | ESTEREOMETRÍA *f* |
| 12252 | ESTERILIZACIÓN *f* DEL AGUA |
| 12253 | PLATA *f* A 92/5% |
| 12254 | GOMA *f* LACA EN RAMA |
| 12255 | AZUFRE *m* CILÍNDRICO |
| 12256 | ANGULO *m* DE REFUERZO |
| 12257 | PLACA *f* DE REFUERZO |
| 12257 | CHAPA *f* DE REFUERZO |
| 12258 | TENSIÓN *f* DE UNA CORREA |
| 12258 | TENSIÓN *f* DE UNA CUERDA |
| 12259 | ALAMBIQUE *m*, DESTILADOR *m* |
| 12259 | APARATO DE DESTILACIÓN *m*, DESTILADOR *m* |
| 12259 | DESTILADOR *m* |
| 12260 | AGITADOR, REVOLVEDOR *m* |
| 12260 | VARILLA *f* AGITADORA |
| 12261 | ESTRIBO *m* |
| 12261 | CERCO *m*, ESTRIBO *m* |
| 12262 | CUERPO *m* DE CEPILLO (CARP.) |
| 12263 | EXISTENCIAS *f pl*, STOCK *m* |
| 12263 | EXISTENCIAS, RESERVAS *f pl* |
| 12264 | TIJERAS DE BANCO *f pl.* |
| 12265 | DEPÓSITO *m* |
| 12265 | OBRA *f* |
| 12265 | APARCAMIENTO *m* SIN CUBRIR |
| 12266 | TERRAJA *f* DE COJINETES |
| 12267 | ESTOICOMÉTRICO |
| 12268 | ESTOICOMETRÍA *f* |
| 12269 | ALIMENTAR UN FUEGO, CARGAR UN HOGAR |
| 12269 | CARGAR UN FUERZO |
| 12270 | SALA DE CALDERAS *f* |
| 12271 | FOGONERO *m* |
| 12272 | FOGONERO *m* |
| 12273 | MACHACADORA DE MANDÍBULAS *f* |

12274 MASTIC *m* PARA PIEDRA
12275 REJILLA *f* PROTECTORA DE LAS PIEDRAS
12276 GRÉS *m* CERÁMICO
12277 TUBO *m* DE GRES
12278 TOPE *m*, LIMITADOR *m* DE CARRERA
12278 TOPE *m*, LIMITADOR *m* DE CARRERA
12278 TOPE *m*
12278 MANDRIL *m* LIMITADOR DE CARRERA
12278 TOPE *m*, LIMITADOR *m* DE CARRERA, PARADA *f*
12278 DISPOSITIVO *m* DE RETENIDA
12279 TAPONAR UNA FUGA
12280 PARAR UNA MÁQUINA
12281 GRIFO *m* DE RETENCIÓN
12282 VÁLVULA *f* DE DETENCIÓN
12283 CUENTASEGUNDOS *m*
12283 CRONÓMETRO CON STOP *m*
12284 TAPÓN *m* DE COLADA
12285 TAPÓN *m*
12286 PARADA DE UNA MÁQUINA *f*
12287 AISLACIÓN *f*, AISLAMIENTO *f* (DEL QUE SE AISLA)
12288 ALMACENAMIENTO *m*, ALMACENAJE *m*, ACUMULACIÓN *f*
12288 ALMACENADO *m*
12289 SOPORTE *m* DE INFORMACIÓN
12290 ACUMULACIÓN DE ENERGÍA *f*
12291 ACUMULACIÓN DE CALOR *f*
12292 DEPÓSITO *m* DE ALMACENAMIENTO
12293 DEPÓSITO *m*
12294 EXISTENCIAS, RESERVAS *f pl*
12294 ESTACIONAR
12294 DEPOSITAR, ALMACENAR
12294 ALMACENAR
12295 ACUMULAR (O ALMACENAR) ENERGÍA
12296 ACUMULAR (O ALMACENAR) ENERGÍA
12296 ACUMULAR EL CALOR
12297 ALMACÉN *m*
12298 ENCARGADO DE ALMACÉN *m*, ALMACENERO *m*, GUARDALMACÉN *m*
12298 MANUTENCIONARIO *m* (QUE TRASLADA DE UN LADO A OTRO)
12299 ALMACENAMIENTO *m*, ALMACENAJE *m*, ACUMULACIÓN *f*
12300 HORNO *m*
12300 HORNO *m*
12301 FRESADO *m* EN DUPLEX
12302 BRAZO *m* RECTO DE UNA POLEA
12303 REGLA *f* DE AFORO
12304 BROCA *f* CON ESTRÍAS RECTAS
12305 ESCARIADOR CON ESTRÍAS RECTAS *m*
12306 PALANCA *f* DERECHA

12307 FRESA *f* CON DENTADO RECTILÍNEO
12308 CABRIO *m* A LO LARGO
12308 MARTILLO *m* DE CALAFATE, MANDARRIA *f* (DE RETACAR)
12309 TUBO *m* RECTO
12310 LÍNEA *f* RECTA
12310 RECTA *f*
12311 DENTADO *m* DERECHO
12312 RESORTE *m* DE FLEXIÓN RECTO
12313 ACOPLAMIENTO *m* DE DENTADURA RECTA
12314 MANDO PARAXIAL *m*
12315 GUÍA *f* DEL MOVIMIENTO RECTILÍNEO
12316 PRENSA *f* MECÁNICA DE MONTANTE
12317 VÁLVULA *f* RECTA
12318 APLANAR, ENDEREZAR, CEPILLAR
12318 ENDEREZAR
12319 ENDEREZAMIENTO *m*
12319 DESBASTE *m*, ENDEREZAMIENTO *m*
12319 APLANAMIENTO *m*, ENDEREZAMIENTO *m*, DESBASTE *m*
12319 ENDEREZAMIENTO *m*, RECTIFICACIÓN *f*
12320 MÁQUINA *f* DE ENDEREZAR
12320 ENDEREZADERA *f*, MÁQUINA *f* DE ENDEREZAR CHAPA
12321 PLANO *m* PARA ENDEREZAR
12322 TENSIÓN *f*
12322 DEFORMACIÓN *f*, FORZAMIENTO *m*
12323 EJERCER UN ESFUERZO EN UN CUERPO
12323 SOMETER UN CUERPO A UNA CARGA
12324 ENVEJECIMIENTO *m* POR LOS ESFUERZOS
12325 EXTENSÓMETRO *m*
12326 ENDURECIMIENTO *m* (O TEMPLE *m*) DE DEFORMACIÓN
12327 ENVEJECIMIENTO *m* POR DEFORMACIÓN
12328 ENVEJECIMIENTO *m* POR DEFORMACIÓN
12329 VERIFICADOR *m* DE INCITACIÓN A LA RESISTENCIA
12330 VELOCIDAD *f* DE DEFORMACIÓN
12331 TRABAJO *m*
12331 ESFUERZO *m*
12331 CARGA *f*
12331 ACCIÓN DE UNA FUERZA EXTERIOR *f*
12331 SOLICITACIONES *f pl*
12332 ALCACHOFA *f*, COLADOR *m*
12332 CHUPETE *m*
12333 FILTRO *m*
12334 RODILLO *m* TENSOR
12334 RODILLO *m*
12334 RODILLO *m*
12334 POLEA *f* DE TENSIÓN
12334 TENSOR *m*
12334 TENSOR *m* DE POLEA

| | |
|---|---|
| 12335 | ESTAÑO *m* DE MALACA |
| 12336 | CABLE *m* TRENZADO |
| 12337 | TRENZAR |
| 12338 | CORDÓN DE UN CABLE *m* |
| 12339 | TRENZADO *m* DE UNA CUERDA |
| 12340 | TRENZADO *m* |
| 12341 | TRENZADORA *f* |
| 12342 | DISPOSITIVO *m* DE ESTRANGULAMIENTO |
| 12343 | FLEJE *m* |
| 12344 | FRENO *m* DE TORNILLO |
| 12345 | HORQUETA DE LA CABEZA DE BIELA *f*, HORQUILLA *f* |
| 12346 | HORQUILLA *f* GUIA DE CORREA |
| 12346 | HORQUILLA *f* DE DESEMBRAGUE |
| 12346 | HORQUILLA *f* |
| 12347 | GOZNE *m* |
| 12348 | FIBRA *f* DE PAJA |
| 12349 | CORRIENTE VAGABUNDA *f* |
| 12350 | CORROSIÓN POR CORRIENTE VAGABUNDA *f* |
| 12351 | LÍNEA *f* DE LA CORRIENTE, FILETE *m* DE CORRIENTE |
| 12351 | LÍNEA *f* AERODINÁMICA |
| 12352 | FUERZA *f* |
| 12352 | RESISTENCIA *f* |
| 12353 | RESISTENCIA *f* A LOS CHOQUES REPETIDOS |
| 12354 | GRADO *m* DE UNA SOLUCIÓN |
| 12355 | RESISTENCIA *f* DE MATERIALES |
| 12356 | PRUEBA *f* DE RESISTENCIA |
| 12357 | SOLDADURA *f* DE SOSTÉN |
| 12358 | REFORZAR |
| 12359 | REFUERZO *m* |
| 12359 | REFUERZO *m* |
| 12360 | CONCENTRACIÓN DE LA TENSIÓN *f* |
| 12361 | CORROSIÓN EN TENSIÓN *f* |
| 12362 | RECOCIDO *m* REDUCTOR DE TENSIÓN |
| 12363 | RECOCIDO *m* DE RELAJACIÓN |
| 12364 | FISURACIÓN *f* POR CORROSIÓN BAJO TENSIÓN |
| 12365 | CURVA ESFUERZO-DEFORMACIÓN *f* |
| 12366 | CURVA CARGA-ALARGAMIENTO *f* |
| 12366 | GRÁFICO *m* DE LA RESISTENCIA MECÁNICA |
| 12367 | CARGA *f* |
| 12367 | TENSIÓN *f*, ESFUERZO *m* |
| 12367 | TENSIÓN *f* |
| 12367 | ESFUERZO *m* UNITARIO, FATIGA *f* ESPECÍFICA |
| 12368 | SUPERFICIE *f* CARGADA |
| 12369 | SOGA *f*, LADO DEL SILLAR QUE QUEDA AL DESCUBIERTO |
| 12370 | TENSIÓN *f* DE ESTIRADO |
| 12371 | LÍNEAS *f pl* DE LUDERS |
| 12372 | MÁQUINA *f* PARA RECTIFICAR |
| 12372 | PULIDORA *f* |

| | |
|---|---|
| 12373 | ESFUERZO *m* DE TENSIÓN |
| 12374 | ALARGAMIENTO DE UN CABLE *m* |
| 12374 | ALARGAMIENTO DE UNA CORREA (O CINTA) *m* |
| 12375 | COOLPE *m* |
| 12376 | CORDÓN SOLDADO RECTILÍNEO *m* |
| 12377 | LIMO *m*, LÉGAMO *m*, ZANCA *f* DE ESCALERA |
| 12378 | FLEJE *m* |
| 12379 | DAÑAR LA ROSCA |
| 12380 | REGISTRADOR *m* DE DESENROLLADO CONTINUO |
| 12381 | DISOLVENTE *m* DE DECAPADO |
| 12382 | BAÑO *m* DE DECAPADO |
| 12383 | PUENTE *m* DE CORREDERA DESMOLDEADOR |
| 12384 | PEINE *m* |
| 12385 | ESTROBOSCOPIO *m* |
| 12386 | MÉTODO *m* ESTROBOSCÓPICO |
| 12387 | CARRERA *f*, RECORRIDO *m* |
| 12387 | TIEMPO *m* |
| 12388 | U *f* DE MONTAJE |
| 12389 | ESTRONCIO *m* |
| 12390 | FLUORURO *m* DE ESTRONCIO |
| 12391 | ELEMENTO *m* ESTRUCTURAL |
| 12392 | ACERO DE CONSTRUCCIÓN *m* |
| 12394 | ESTRUCTURA *f* |
| 12395 | ESTRUCTURA *f* |
| 12395 | CONTEXTURA *f* |
| 12395 | CONSTRUCCIÓN (EDIFICIO) *f* |
| 12395 | ESTRUCTURA *f* |
| 12396 | PUNTAL *m*, RIOSTRA *f*, TORNAPUNTA *f* |
| 12396 | PUNTAL |
| 12397 | ESPÁRRAGO *m* |
| 12398 | PERNO *m* DE VARILLA ROSCADA EN LOS DOS EXTREMOS |
| 12399 | PRISIONERO *m*, PRISIONERO *m* ROSCADO |
| 12399 | CLAVIJA *f* |
| 12399 | PRISIONERO *m* |
| 12400 | PISTOLA *f* PARA INCRUSTAR CLAVIJAS |
| 12401 | TORNO *m* DE ROBLONES |
| 12402 | TRAVESAÑO *m* DE UNA CADENA |
| 12402 | PUNTAL *m* |
| 12402 | TRAVESAÑO *m* DE UNA CADENA |
| 12403 | CADENA CABLE DE PUNTALES *f* |
| 12403 | CADENA DE PUNTALES *f* |
| 12403 | CADENA DE MALLAS APUNTALADAS *f* |
| 12404 | NEUMÁTICO *m* CON GRAPAS |
| 12404 | NEUMÁTICO *m* DE CLAVOS |
| 12405 | PRENSAESTOPAS *m*, EMPAQUETADURA *f* |
| 12405 | PRENSAESTOPA *m* |
| 12406 | GUARNICIÓN *f* DEL PRENSAESTOPAS, RELLENO *m* DEL PRENSAESTOPAS |
| 12406 | GUARNICIÓN *f* POR EMPAQUETADURA |
| 12407 | MÁQUINA *f* PARA EQUICORRIENTES |

| | |
|---|---|
| 12407 | MÁQUINA  f  EQUICORRIENTES |
| 12408 | JUNTA  f  INFERIOR |
| 12409 | SUBDIVISIÓN  f |
| 12410 | DIVISIÓN  f  DEL TRABAJO |
| 12411 | SUBLIMAR |
| 12412 | SUBLIMACIÓN  f |
| 12413 | SUMERGIR |
| 12414 | SOLDADURA  f  AL ARCO SUMERGIDO |
| 12415 | SUBPROGRAMA  m |
| 12416 | CAPA  f  INFERIOR (DE OXIDO) |
| 12417 | TRATAMIENTO  m  ULTERIOR |
| 12418 | DESPLOME, HUNDIMIENTO, ASENTAMIENTO  m |
| 12419 | MATERIA  f |
| 12419 | SUBSTANCIA  f |
| 12420 | SUCEDÁNEO  m |
| 12421 | SUBSTITUCIÓN (MATEMÁTICAS) |
| 12422 | METAL  m  NO PRECIOSO |
| 12423 | SUBESTRUCTURA  f |
| 12424 | SUBSTRAER |
| 12424 | RESTAR, CERCENAR |
| 12425 | SUBSTRACCIÓN  f |
| 12426 | NÚMERO  m  QUE RESTAR, CANTIDAD  f  QUE SUSTRAER |
| 12427 | ASPIRAR |
| 12428 | ASPIRACIÓN  f, INDUCCIÓN  f, SUCCIÓN  f |
| 12429 | VENTILADOR  m  ASPIRANTE |
| 12430 | GASÓGENO  m  DE ASPIRACIÓN |
| 12431 | REGULADOR  m  DE DEPRESIÓN |
| 12432 | ALTURA  f  DE ASPIRACIÓN DE UNA BOMBA |
| 12433 | TUBO  m  DE ASPIRACIÓN |
| 12434 | BOMBA  f  ASPIRANTE |
| 12435 | CARRERA DE ASPIRACIÓN  f |
| 12436 | VÁLVULA  f |
| 12436 | VÁLVULA DE ASPIRACIÓN  f |
| 12437 | VARIACIÓN  f  BRUSCA DE TEMPERATURA |
| 12438 | MÁQUINA  f  SEPARADORA PARA REMOLACHA AZUCARERA |
| 12439 | RECOGEDORAS  f  DE REMOLACHAS |
| 12440 | ARRANCADORAS  f pl  DE REMOLACHAS |
| 12441 | MÁQUINAS  f pl  PARA DESMOCHAR LA REMOLACHA |
| 12442 | FATIGA  f  POR EL SULFURO DE HIDRÓGENO |
| 12443 | CAPA DE ÓXIDO FERROSO  f |
| 12445 | SOSA  f  LEBLANC |
| 12446 | SULFURO  m |
| 12447 | SULFURO  m  DE HIERRO |
| 12448 | SULFITO  m |
| 12449 | AZUFRE  m |
| 12450 | ÓXIDO  m  SULFUROSO |
| 12450 | ANHÍDRIDO SULFUROSO  m |
| 12450 | ÁCIDO SULFUROSO  m |

| | |
|---|---|
| 12451 | CLORURO DE AZUFRE  m |
| 12452 | ANHÍDRIDO SULFÚRICO  m |
| 12453 | ÁCIDO VITRIÓLICO  m  ÁCIDO SULFÚRICO DE CÁMARA  m |
| 12453 | ÁCIDO SULFÚRICO  m |
| 12453 | ACEITE  m  DE VITRIOLO |
| 12453 | VITRIOLO  m |
| 12454 | SUMA  f |
| 12455 | VÉRTICE  m |
| 12455 | VÉRTICE  m  DE UNA ROSCA |
| 12456 | TREN  m  PLANETARIO |
| 12456 | MOVIMIENTO  m  CÓSMICO |
| 12457 | RUEDA  f  CENTRAL DE UN TREN PLANETARIO |
| 12458 | CLAVIJA SUMERGIDA  f, CHAVETA EMPOTRADA  f |
| 12459 | ALEACIÓN RESISTENTE A LAS ALTAS TEMPERATURAS  f |
| 12460 | RECALENTAMIENTO  m |
| 12461 | SUPERSATURACIÓN  f |
| 12462 | ACERO AFINO, ACERO AFINADO  m |
| 12463 | ENFRIAR POR DEBAJO DEL PUNTO DE CONGELACIÓN |
| 12463 | ENFRIAR POR DEBAJO DE LA TEMPERATURA DE CONDENSACIÓN |
| 12464 | LÍQUIDO  m  DE SOBREFUSIÓN |
| 12465 | SOBREFUSIÓN  f |
| 12465 | SOBRE ENFRIAMIENTO  m |
| 12466 | DILATACIÓN  f  SUPERFICIAL |
| 12467 | LIMA  f  DE TALLA MUY FINA |
| 12468 | RECALENTAR |
| 12469 | VAPOR  m  RECALENTADO |
| 12470 | AGUA  f  SOBRECALENTADA |
| 12471 | VAPOR  m  RECALENTADO |
| 12472 | RECALENTADOR  m |
| 12473 | RECALENTAMIENTO  m |
| 12473 | RECALENTAMIENTO  m |
| 12474 | VIGILAR |
| 12475 | SUPERESTRUCTURA  f |
| 12475 | SUPERESTRUCTURA  f |
| 12476 | SUPERPOSICIÓN  f  DE VIBRACIONES |
| 12477 | SUPERSATURAR |
| 12478 | SOLUCIÓN  f  SUPERSATURADA |
| 12479 | SUPERSATURACIÓN  f |
| 12480 | PRUEBA A LOS ULTRASONIDOS |
| 12481 | VIGILANCIA  f |
| 12482 | SUPLEMENTO  m  DE UN ÁNGULO |
| 12483 | ÁNGULO SUPLEMENTARIO  m |
| 12484 | CABLES DE ALIMENTACIÓN  m pl, CABLES DE LÍNEA  m pl |
| 12485 | SUMINISTRAR NUEVAS CALORÍAS |
| 12485 | SUMINISTRAR CALOR |
| 12486 | INTRODUCCIÓN  f  DE AIRE |
| 12486 | ADMISIÓN DE AIRE  f |

| | |
|---|---|
| 12487 | DISTRIBUCIÓN PÚBLICA DE ENERGÍA ELÉCTRICA |
| 12488 | SUMINISTRO *m* DE CALOR |
| 12489 | TUBO DE PASO DEL COMBUSTIBLE *m* |
| 12489 | TUBO *m* DE TRAÍDA DE AGUAS |
| 12489 | TUBO *m* DE ENTRADA |
| 12490 | SOPORTE *m* |
| 12490 | BASE *f*, ZÓCALO *m* |
| 12491 | APOYAR, BASAR |
| 12491 | SOPORTAR |
| 12491 | SOSTENER, SOPORTAR, SERVIR DE APOYO |
| 12492 | CORONA SOPORTE DE PLATÓ *f* |
| 12493 | MONTAJE *m* |
| 12493 | SOSTENIMIENTO, SOSTÉN *m* |
| 12494 | DATOS *m pl* JUSTIFICATIVOS |
| 12495 | CHAPA *f* SOPORTE |
| 12496 | SUPERFICIE *f* |
| 12497 | REFRENTAR |
| 12498 | RUGOSÍMETRO *m* REGISTRADOR |
| 12499 | CONDENSADOR POR SUPERFICIE *m* |
| 12500 | CONDICIÓN *f* DE SUPERFICIE, ESTADO *m* DE SUPERFICIE |
| 12501 | FISURA *f* SUPERFICIAL |
| 12501 | RESQUEBRAJADURA *f* SUPERFICIAL |
| 12502 | DEFECTO *m* SUPERFICIAL |
| 12503 | IRREGULARIDAD *f* DE LA SUPERFICIE |
| 12504 | ACABADO *m* DE SUPERFICIE |
| 12505 | MÁQUINA *f* PARA RECTIFICAR LAS SUPERFICIES PLANAS |
| 12506 | RECTIFICACIÓN *f* DE SUPERFICIE |
| 12507 | RECTIFICADORA *f* PAR SUPERFICIES PLANAS |
| 12508 | TEMPLE *m* SUPERFICIAL |
| 12509 | RUGOSÍMETRO *m* |
| 12510 | SUPERFICIE *f* DE CONTACTO |
| 12511 | SUPERFICIE *f* DE LA SECCIÓN |
| 12511 | SECCIÓN *f* |
| 12511 | ÁREA DE LA SECCIÓN TRANSVERSAL *f* |
| 12512 | SUPERFICIE *f* DE IMPRESIÓN |
| 12513 | SUPERFICIE *f* DE REVOLUCIÓN |
| 12514 | VÉRTICE *m* DEL DIENTE |
| 12515 | CEPILLADORA *f* |
| 12515 | MÁQUINA *f* DE DESBASTAR O DE ENDEREZAR |
| 12516 | MESA *f* RECTIFICADA |
| 12516 | PLANO *m* PARA ENDEREZAR |
| 12517 | PRESIÓN *f* SUPERFICIAL |
| 12518 | RUGOSIDAD *f* DE SUPERFICIE |
| 12519 | TENSIÓN *f* SUPERFICIAL |
| 12520 | AGUA *f* SUPERFICIAL |
| 12520 | AGUA *f* SUPERFICIAL |
| 12520 | AGUA *f* SUPERFICIAL (O DE FLOR DE TIERRA) |
| 12521 | SUPERFICIE *f* |
| 12522 | REFRENTADO *m* |

| | |
|---|---|
| 12522 | PASADA TRANSVERSAL *f* |
| 12523 | AGENTE DE TRATAMIENTO DE SUPERFICIE *m* |
| 12524 | TECHO *m* SUSPENDIDO |
| 12525 | DEPÓSITO *m* DE TECHO SUSPENDIDO |
| 12526 | SUSPENSIÓN *f* |
| 12527 | GANCHO *m* DE SUSPENSIÓN |
| 12528 | PUENTE *m* SUSPENDIDO |
| 12529 | ESCOBAZAMIENTO *m* |
| 12530 | ESTAMPAR |
| 12530 | ESTAMPAR EN CALIENTE |
| 12531 | ESTAMPA *f* |
| 12532 | ESTAMPADO *m* |
| 12532 | ESTAMPADO *m* |
| 12533 | MÁQUINA *f* DE ESTAMPAR |
| 12534 | ESTAMPADO *m* |
| 12534 | FORJADO *m* EN ESTAMPA |
| 12535 | CUELLO DE CISNE *m* |
| 12536 | VIRUTA *f* |
| 12537 | VOLTEADORA *f* DE HENO |
| 12538 | DESPLAZAMIENTO *m* LATERAL |
| 12538 | BALANCEO *m* |
| 12539 | BARRA *f* ESTABILIZADORA |
| 12540 | REZUMAMIENTO *m* |
| 12540 | EXUDACIÓN *f* |
| 12541 | RECOGEDORA *f* DE HENO |
| 12542 | CRECER, INFLAR |
| 12542 | INFLAR |
| 12543 | INFLACIÓN (POR LOS GASES DE FISIÓN) *f* |
| 12544 | HINCHAZÓN *f* DE LA MADERA |
| 12545 | VÁLVULA DE RETENCIÓN DE BATIENTE *f* |
| 12546 | JUNTA *f* ARTICULADA |
| 12547 | VARIACIÓN *f* (DIÁMETRO *m*) ADMISIBLE SOBRE EL BANCO |
| 12548 | OSCILACIÓN *f* DE UN PÉNDULO |
| 12549 | BRAZO *m* OSCILANTE |
| 12550 | PERFORADORA *f* CON BRAZO ARTICULADO |
| 12551 | CÁMARA DE TURBULENCIA *f* |
| 12552 | PASO *m* DEL SISTEMA THURY |
| 12553 | CONTACTOR ELÉCTRICO *m* |
| 12553 | INTERRUPTOR *m* DISYUNTOR *m* |
| 12553 | INTERRUPTOR-CONMUTADOR *m*, INTERRUPTOR *m* AUTOMÁTICO |
| 12553 | INTERRUPTOR *m* |
| 12554 | PONER FUERA DE CIRCUITO |
| 12555 | PONER EN CIRCUITO |
| 12556 | CAMBIO DE VÍA *m* |
| 12556 | CAMBIO DE AGUJA *m*, CAMBIO DE VÍA *m* |
| 12557 | CUADRO *m* DISTRIBUIDOR |
| 12557 | CUADRO *m* GENERAL |
| 12557 | CENTRALILLA *f* TELEFÓNICA |
| 12558 | DISTRIBUIDORES *m pl* ELÉCTRICOS |

| | |
|---|---|
| 12559 | PUESTA *f* FUERA DE CIRCUITO |
| 12560 | PUESTA *f* EN CIRCUITO |
| 12561 | GANCHO *m* MÓVIL |
| 12562 | TORNILLO *m* GIRATORIO |
| 12562 | TORNILLO *m* ORIENTABLE |
| 12563 | COJINETE DE RÓTULA *m* |
| 12563 | COJINETE *m* DE RÓTULA, COJINETE *m* DE ALINEACIÓN AUTOMÁTICA |
| 12564 | GANCHO *m* PIVOTANTE |
| 12565 | SIENTA *f* |
| 12566 | SIMÉTRICO *m* |
| 12567 | SIMETRÍA *f* |
| 12568 | SINCRÓNICO *m* |
| 12569 | SINCRONISMO *m* |
| 12570 | SÍNCRONO *m* |
| 12571 | MOTOR *m* SINCRÓNICO |
| 12572 | SÍNTESIS *f* |
| 12573 | SINTÉTICO |
| 12574 | SINTONÍA *f* |
| 12575 | SISTEMA *m* DE COORDENADAS |
| 12576 | SISTEMA *m* DE LENTES |
| 12577 | SISTEMA *m* DE CONJUNTO DE PALANCAS |
| 12578 | SISTEMA *m* DE MEDIDA |
| 12579 | RED *f* DE TUBERIAS |
| 12580 | SISTEMA *m* DE PESOS |
| 12581 | TE *f* DE DIBUJO |
| 12581 | ESCUADRA *f* DOBLE, ESCUADRA *f* EN T |
| 12582 | FRESAS *f pl* PARA ABRIR RANURAS EN T |
| 12583 | FORMATO *m* TABULAR |
| 12584 | MESA *f* |
| 12584 | ESTADO (SERIE DE NÚMEROS) |
| 12585 | RECORRIDO O DESPLAZAMIENTO TRANSVERSAL DE LA MESA *m* |
| 12586 | TAQUÍMETRO *m* REGISTRADOR |
| 12587 | TAQUÍMETRO *m* |
| 12587 | CUENTARREVOLUCIONES *m*, TACÓMETRO *m* |
| 12588 | TACHUELA *f* |
| 12588 | SIMIENTE *f* |
| 12589 | SOLDADURA *f* PROVISIONAL POR PUNTOS DE REFERENCIA |
| 12590 | SOLDADURA *f* PROVISIONAL POR PUNTOS |
| 12591 | EMPECINADO *m* |
| 12592 | PASADOR *m* (O PERNO *m*, O BULÓN *m*) DE UNIÓN PROVISIONAL |
| 12592 | PASADOR *m* (O PERNO *m*) DE UNIÓN PROVISIONAL DE LAS CHAPAS |
| 12593 | CHAPA *f* MUY FINA |
| 12594 | PELO *m* DE COLA DE CABALLO, CERDAS *f* |
| 12594 | CRIN *f* |
| 12595 | LUCES *f pl* TRASERAS |
| 12596 | CANAL *m* DE DESCENSO |
| 12596 | DESAGUADERO *m* |

| | |
|---|---|
| 12596 | CANAL DE DESCARGA *m* |
| 12597 | AGUA *f* (DE) ABAJO |
| 12598 | RESIDUOS *m pl* |
| 12599 | CABEZAL *m* MÓVIL |
| 12599 | CONTRAPUNTA *f*, CABEZA MÓVIL DE TORRETA *f* |
| 12600 | DESENSAMBAR, DESMONTAR, DESARMAR |
| 12600 | DESMONTAR |
| 12601 | RECIBIR UNA FUERZA |
| 12602 | TENSAR DE NUEVO UNA CORREA |
| 12603 | COMPENSAR LA HOLGURA DE UN COJINETE |
| 12603 | COMPENSACIÓN *f* DE JUEGO |
| 12603 | COMPENSAR EL DESGASTE |
| 12604 | DESENSAMBLADURA *f*, DESEMBLAJE *.m*, DESMONTAJE *m*, DESARME *m* |
| 12604 | DESMONTAJE *m* |
| 12605 | TENSIÓN DE UNA CORREA *f* |
| 12606 | RECTIFICACIÓN *f* DE ASIENTO (DE UN COJINETE) |
| 12606 | COMPENSACIÓN *f* DE JUEGO |
| 12607 | TALCO *m* EN POLVO |
| 12608 | TALCO *m* |
| 12608 | SÉBO *m* |
| 12610 | ASFALTO *m* COMPRIMIDO |
| 12611 | PISÓN *m* |
| 12611 | PISÓN *m* |
| 12611 | MAZO *m* |
| 12612 | CASCA *f* COMPRIMIDA |
| 12612 | CASCA *f* EN TERRONES |
| 12613 | MÁQUINA *f* TANDEM |
| 12614 | SEDA *f* |
| 12614 | MANGO *m* DE UNA HERRAMIENTA |
| 12615 | TANGENTE *f* |
| 12616 | TANGENTE *f* (GEOMETRÍA) |
| 12617 | TANGENTE *f* EN EL VÉRTICE |
| 12618 | CLAVIJA TANGENCIAL *f* |
| 12619 | TORNILLO *m* SIN FIN |
| 12620 | ACELERACIÓN TANGENCIAL *f* |
| 12621 | TURBINA *f* TANGENCIAL |
| 12622 | FUERZA *f* TANGENCIAL |
| 12623 | VELOCIDAD *f* TANGENCIAL |
| 12624 | ESFUERZO *m* TANGENCIAL |
| 12625 | DEPÓSITO *m* |
| 12626 | VAGÓN *m* DEPÓSITO |
| 12626 | VAGÓN *m* CISTERNA |
| 12627 | PARQUE *m* ALMACÉN DE HIDROCARBURO |
| 12628 | BASE DE DEPÓSITO *f* |
| 12629 | CUBA *f* DE RETENCIÓN DE UN DEPÓSITO |
| 12630 | ENVOLTURA *f* DEL DEPÓSITO |
| 12631 | DEPÓSITO *m* DE FONDO CÓNCAVO |
| 12632 | DEPÓSITO *m* DE FONDO CONVEXO |
| 12633 | TANATO *m* |

| | | | |
|---|---|---|---|
| 12634 | TÁNTALO *m* | 12671 | ADELGAZAMIENTO *m* DE UNA PIEZA |
| 12635 | CASCA *f* AGOTADA | 12672 | PULSADOR *m* |
| 12636 | ATERRAJAR | 12672 | EMPUJADOR *m* DE LEVA, IMPULSOR *m* |
| 12637 | AGUJERO *m* DE COLADA | 12673 | JUEGO *m* DE LAS VÁLVULAS |
| 12638 | TERRAJA *f* DE OJO CENTRAL | 12674 | RODILLO *m* DE LEVA |
| 12639 | TAPA *f* | 12675 | DESTAPADURA *f* |
| 12639 | GRIFO *m*, LLAVE *f* | 12675 | PERFORACIÓN *f*, TALADRADO *m*, HORADADO *m* |
| 12640 | TERRAJA *f* | | |
| 12641 | CINTA *f*, BANDA *f* | 12676 | APARATO DE ROSCAR *m* |
| 12641 | CINTA *f* | 12677 | ATERRAJADORA *f* |
| 12642 | VÁLVULA *f* DE RETENCIÓN | 12678 | ATERRAJADO *m* |
| 12643 | ENTRADA *f* DE DATOS POR CINTA | 12679 | ALQUITRÁN *m* |
| 12644 | MAGNETÓFONO *m*, REGISTRADOR *m* MAGNÉTICO | 12680 | ALQUITRANAR |
| | | 12681 | ACEITE *m* DE ALQUITRÁN |
| 12645 | SALIDA *f* DE COLADA (AGUJERO) | 12682 | ANTICÁTODO *m* |
| 12646 | CONICIDAD *f* | 12682 | BLANCO *m*, DIANA *f* |
| 12646 | ACHAFLANADO *m*, REBAJO *m* | 12682 | OBJETIVO *m* |
| 12647 | RACOR *m* CÓNICO | 12683 | SUPERFICIE *f* DEL BLANCO (OFRECIDA A LAS RADIACIONES) |
| 12648 | LIMA *f* PUNTIAGUDA | | |
| 12649 | AJUSTE *m* CÓNICO | 12684 | TUBO *m* DE RAYOS X |
| 12649 | AJUSTE *m* CÓNICO, ASIENTO *m* DEL CONO | 12685 | EMPAÑARSE |
| 12650 | ESCARIADOR DE MANO CÓNICO *m* | 12685 | OXIDARSE |
| 12651 | MANDRIL *m* CÓNICO | 12686 | CAMIÓN ENTOLDADO *m* |
| 12652 | MICRÓMETRO *m* DE CONICIDAD | 12687 | TUBO *m* PROTEGIDO CON ALQUITRÁN |
| 12652 | MICROPALPADOR *m* DE CONICIDAD | 12688 | CUERDA ALQUITRANADA *f* |
| 12653 | AJUSTE *m* DE CHAVETA | 12688 | CUERDA NEGRA *f* |
| 12654 | CONICIDAD DE UNA CHAVETA *f* | 12689 | ALQUITRANADO *m* |
| 12654 | PENDIENTE *f* DE UNA CLAVIJA | 12690 | ÁCIDO TARTÁRICO *m* |
| 12655 | PASADOR *m* CÓNICO | 12691 | TARTRATO *m* |
| 12656 | CALIBRE *m* TAMPÓN CÓNICO | 12692 | LEER |
| 12656 | CALIBRE MACHO CÓNICO *m* | 12693 | CUCHARA *f* TETERA |
| 12657 | CALIBRE *m* TAMPÓN CÓNICO CON TETÓN | 12694 | TÉCNICO |
| 12658 | ESCARIADOR CÓNICO *m* | 12695 | TÉCNICO |
| 12659 | CALIBRES HEMBRAS CÓNICOS *m pl* | 12696 | HENIFICADORAS *f pl* |
| 12660 | RODILLO *m* CÓNICO | 12697 | TE *f* |
| 12660 | RODILLO *m* CÓNICO | 12698 | HIERRO *m* EN T |
| 12661 | CABLE CÓNICO *m* | 12699 | TE *f* DE TRES DIRECCIONES |
| 12661 | CABLE DISMINUIDO *m* | 12700 | PERFIL *m* EN T |
| 12661 | CABLE DE SECCIÓN DECRECIENTE *m* | 12701 | TORNILLO *m* CON CABEZA DE MARTILLO |
| 12662 | VÁLVULA *f* DE ASIENTOS OBLICUOS | 12702 | UNIÓN *f* EN T |
| 12663 | ASIENTOS *m* OBLICUOS | 12703 | MOLDEADO *m* SALIDA EN LINGOTERA |
| 12664 | COLA *f* CÓNICA | 12703 | FUSIÓN *f*, COLADA *f* |
| 12665 | CLAVIJA CÓNICA *f* | 12704 | DENTADURA *f* |
| 12666 | ROSCADO *m* CÓNICO | 12705 | CABLE TELEDINÁMICO *m* |
| 12667 | MANDRIL *m* DE ESPIGA CÓNICA | 12706 | TRANSMISIÓN *f* POR CABLE TELEDINÁMICO |
| 12668 | TORNEADO *m* DE SUPERFICIES CÓNICAS | 12707 | TELÉGRAFO *m* |
| 12668 | TORNEADO *m* CÓNICO | 12708 | HILO *m* TELEGRÁFICO |
| 12668 | PASADA *f* | 12709 | TELEGRAFÍA *f* |
| 12669 | CONO LISO *m* | 12710 | TELÉFONO *m* |
| 12669 | POLEA *f* CÓNICA | 12711 | HILO *m* TELEFÓNICO |
| 12670 | BARRA *f* DE SECCÍON DECRECIENTE | 12712 | TELEFONÍA *f* |

| | |
|---|---|
| 12713 | CALIBRES TELESCÓPICOS *m pl* |
| 12714 | PIRÓMETRO *m* A DISTANCIA |
| 12715 | AGUJERO *m* TESTIGO |
| 12716 | TELURIO *m* |
| 12717 | DESTEMPLAR, RECOCER |
| 12717 | DULCIFICAR, SUAVIZAR, TEMPLAR, ABLANDAR, REBLANDECER |
| 12718 | DILUIR |
| 12718 | AMASAR, ARGAMASAR |
| 12718 | AMASAR, MEZCLAR (EL MORTERO DE CEMENTO) |
| 12719 | DESTEMPLAR, RECOCER |
| 12719 | RECOCER EL ACERO |
| 12720 | ENDEREZAMIENTO *m* |
| 12721 | TEMPERATURA *f* |
| 12722 | TERMOSTATO *m* |
| 12723 | CURVAS DE TEMPERATURA *f pl* |
| 12724 | CAÍDA DE TEMPERATURA *f*, DESCENSO DE TEMPERATURA *m* |
| 12725 | ESTADOS *m* DE TEMPERATURA |
| 12726 | INDICADOR *m* DE TEMPERATURA, TERMÓMETRO *m* |
| 12726 | TEMPERATURA *f* |
| 12727 | TEMPERATURA *f* DE INFLAMACIÓN |
| 12728 | TEMPERATURA *f* DEL AIRE |
| 12729 | TEMPERATURA *f* AMBIENTE |
| 12730 | GAMA *f* DE TEMPERATURA |
| 12731 | REVENIDO *m* |
| 12732 | TINTE *m* DE REVENIDO |
| 12732 | TINTE *m* DE RECOCIDO |
| 12732 | COLOR *m* |
| 12733 | REVENIDO *m* |
| 12733 | RECOCIDO *m* DEL ACERO |
| 12734 | GÁLIBO *m* |
| 12734 | PERFIL *m* |
| 12734 | MOLDE *m* DE CEMENTO |
| 12734 | PATRÓN *m*, PLANTILLA *f* |
| 12735 | DUREZA *f* TEMPORAL (O TRANSITORIA) DEL AGUA |
| 12736 | MEMORIA *f* TEMPORAL |
| 12737 | TENACIDAD *f* |
| 12738 | TENACIDAD *f* DE LOS BARROTES ENTALLADOS |
| 12739 | CABLES *m pl* |
| 12740 | ESPIGA *f* |
| 12741 | SIERRA *f* DE ESPIGAS |
| 12741 | SIERRA *f* DE ESPIGAS |
| 12741 | SIERRA *f* DE ENRASAR |
| 12742 | MÁQUINA *f* PARA HACER ESPIGAS |
| 12743 | MECÁNICO (ENSAYO) |
| 12744 | DEFORMACIÓN *f* POR TRACCIÓN |
| 12745 | FUERZA *f* DE TRACCIÓN |
| 12746 | CARACTERÍSTICAS MECÁNICAS *f pl* |
| 12747 | ESFUERZO *m* DE TRACCIÓN |

| | |
|---|---|
| 12747 | TRABAJO *m* A LA TRACCIÓN |
| 12748 | PRUEBA *f* DE TRACCIÓN |
| 12749 | CARGA DE ROTURA *f* |
| 12749 | RESISTENCIA *f* A LA TRACCIÓN |
| 12750 | TENSIÓN O FUERZA DE TRACCIÓN *f* |
| 12750 | TENSIÓN *f* DE TRACCIÓN |
| 12751 | PRUEBA *f* DE TRACCIÓN |
| 12752 | MÁQUINA *f* PARA ENSAYOS DE TRACCIÓN |
| 12753 | TENSIÓN *f* |
| 12754 | BARRA *f* ESTIRADA |
| 12755 | BOTÓN *m* DE TENSIÓN |
| 12756 | BASTIDOR PARA TENSAR *m* |
| 12756 | RAÍL *m* TENSOR |
| 12757 | ENERGÍA *f* DEL CHOQUE |
| 12758 | TORNILLO *m* DE TENSIÓN |
| 12759 | RESORTE *m* DE TRACCIÓN |
| 12760 | TERBIO *m* |
| 12761 | DURACIÓN *f* DE LA PATENTE |
| 12762 | BORNE *m* (O TERMINAL *m*) DE CONEXIÓN |
| 12762 | BORNA *f*, TERMINAL *m* |
| 12762 | TERMINAL *m* BORNE |
| 12763 | BORNE *m*, POLO *m*, LINDE *f* |
| 12764 | VOLTAJE *m* EN LOS BORNES |
| 12764 | TENSIÓN *f* |
| 12764 | VOLTAJE *m* EN LOS BORNES (EN LOS TERMINALES) |
| 12765 | TERMINALES *m*, BORNES *m* |
| 12766 | SISTEMA *m* TERNARIO |
| 12767 | TERRACOTA *f* |
| 12768 | TERRAZO *m* |
| 12769 | CHAPA *f* GOFRADA |
| 12770 | PRUEBA *f*, ENSAYO *m*, TEST *m* |
| 12770 | PRUEBA *f*, ENSAYO *m*, TEST *m* |
| 12771 | TORNO *m* DE PIEZAS DE ENSAYO |
| 12772 | BARRA *f* DE ENSAYO |
| 12772 | BARRA *f* DE ENSAYO |
| 12772 | BARRA *f* DE PRUEBA |
| 12773 | MESA *f* DE EXAMEN |
| 12773 | MESA *f* DE CONTROL |
| 12773 | BANCO *m* DE PRUEBAS |
| 12773 | PUESTO *m* DE PRUEBA |
| 12774 | PRUEBA *f* DE FLEXIÓN ALTERNADA |
| 12774 | PRUEBA *f* DE FLEXIÓN ALTERNADA |
| 12775 | CERTIFICADO DE PRUEBA *m* |
| 12776 | GRIFO *m* DE AFORO |
| 12777 | LINGOTE *m* PARA MECANIZAR PROBETAS |
| 12778 | PERFORACIÓN *f* DE ENSAYO, SONDEO *m* |
| 12778 | SONDEO *m* |
| 12779 | CALIBRE *m* DE COMPROBACIÓN |
| 12780 | PROBETA *f* |
| 12781 | CARGA DE PRUEBA *f* |

| | | | |
|---|---|---|---|
| 12782 | ENSAYO *m* DE MATERIALES |
| 12783 | PAPEL *m* REACTIVO |
| 12784 | MUESTRA *f* DE PRUEBA |
| 12785 | CLAVIJA *f* DE PRUEBAS |
| 12785 | TAMPÓN *m* |
| 12786 | PRESIÓN *f* DE PRUEBA |
| 12786 | PRESIÓN *f* DE PRUEBA |
| 12787 | BOMBA *f* DE PRUEBA |
| 12788 | PIEZA *f* DE PRUEBA, MUESTRA *f* DE PRUEBA |
| 12789 | MUESTRA *f* DE PRUEBA |
| 12790 | DEPÓSITO *m* DE AFORO |
| 12791 | PROBETA *f* |
| 12792 | PRUEBA *f*, EXPERIENCIA *f*, EXAMEN *m*, TEST *m* |
| 12792 | PRUEBA *f*, EXPERIENCIA *f*, ENSAYO *m* |
| 12792 | EXAMEN *m* |
| 12792 | EXPERIENCIA |
| 12793 | MÁQUINA *f* DE ENSAYAR |
| 12793 | INSTRUMENTO DE VERIFICACIÓN *m* |
| 12794 | PISTA *f* DE PRUEBAS |
| 12795 | CUADRÁTICO |
| 12796 | COBRE *m* GRIS |
| 12796 | PANABOSA *f*, SULFURO *m* NATURAL DE COBRE |
| 12797 | TETRAEDRO *m* |
| 12798 | TETRATÓMICO |
| 12798 | TETRAVALENTE |
| 12799 | FIBRA *f* TEXTIL |
| 12800 | CONTEXTURA *f* |
| 12800 | ESTRUCTURA *f* |
| 12801 | TALIO *m* |
| 12802 | MANUFACTURABLE |
| 12803 | CAPACIDAD TÉRMICA *f* |
| 12804 | CONDUCTIVIDAD TÉRMICA |
| 12805 | CONTRACCIÓN *f* TÉRMICA |
| 12806 | RENDIMIENTO *m* TÉRMICO |
| 12807 | FUERZA *f* ELECTROMOTRIZ TÉRMICA |
| 12808 | DILATACIÓN *f* TÉRMICA |
| 12809 | COEFICIENTE DE DILATACIÓN TÉRMICA *m* |
| 12810 | AISLACIÓN *f* TÉRMICA |
| 12811 | IRRADIACIÓN *f* DEL CALOR |
| 12812 | GOLPE O CHOQUE TÉRMICO *m* |
| 12813 | RESISTENCIA *f* A LAS VARIACIONES DE TEMPERATURA O AL CHOQUE TÉRMICO |
| 12814 | TENSIÓN *f* TÉRMICA |
| 12815 | TRATAMIENTO *m* TÉRMICO |
| 12816 | UNIDAD *f* TÉRMICA |
| 12816 | UNIDAD *f* DE CALOR |
| 12817 | THERMINOL *m* |
| 12818 | SOLDADURA *f* CON AÑADIDO DE HIERRO-TERMITA |
| 12818 | SOLDADURA *f* ALUMINOTÉRMICA |
| 12819 | SOLDADURA *f* POR ALUMINOTERMIA |

| | |
|---|---|
| 12820 | PILA *f* TÉRMICA |
| 12820 | PILA *f* TERMOELÉCTRICA |
| 12821 | PAR *m* TERMOELÉCTRICO |
| 12821 | TERMOPAR *m* |
| 12822 | TERMOQUÍMICA |
| 12823 | TERMOELÉCTRICO |
| 12824 | CORRIENTE TERMOELÉCTRICA *f* |
| 12825 | PIRÓMETRO *m* TERMOELÉCTRICO |
| 12826 | TERMOELECTRICIDAD *f* |
| 12827 | PAR *f* TERMOELÉCTRICO |
| 12827 | PAR TERMOELÉCTRICO *m* |
| 12828 | TERMODINÁMICA *f* |
| 12829 | TERMODINÁMICA *f* |
| 12830 | EFECTO *m* TERMOELÉCTRICO |
| 12831 | FUERZA *f* TERMOELÉCTRICA |
| 12832 | TERMÓGRAFO *m* |
| 12833 | TERMÓMETRO *m* |
| 12834 | INDICADOR *m* DE TEMPERATURA |
| 12835 | ESCALA *f* TERMOMÉTRICA |
| 12836 | PILA *f* TERMOELÉCTRICA |
| 12837 | TERMOSCOPIO *m* |
| 12838 | TERMOSTATO *m* |
| 12839 | PURGADOR *m* DE AGUA CONDENSADA DE DILATACIÓN |
| 12840 | REGULADOR *m* DE TEMPERATURA |
| 12841 | PARED *f* ESPESA (A) |
| 12842 | SUBSTANCIA *f* ESPESATIVA |
| 12843 | ESPESOR *m* |
| 12844 | ESPESOR *m* DE LA PARED (DEL METAL) DE UN TUBO |
| 12845 | ESPESOR *m* DE UNA CHAPA |
| 12846 | ESPESOR *m* DEL DIENTE |
| 12847 | MÁQUINA *f* DE CEPILLAR SACANDO LA MADERA DEL ESPESOR |
| 12848 | GUARDACABO *m* |
| 12849 | ALAMBRE *m* METÁLICO FINO |
| 12850 | CHAPA *f* FINA |
| 12851 | PARED *f* DELGADA (A) |
| 12852 | TIOSULFATO *m* |
| 12852 | HIPOSULFITO *m* |
| 12853 | ÁCIDO HIPOSULFUROSO *m* |
| 12853 | ÁCIDO TIOSULFÚRICO *m* |
| 12854 | TIXOTROPÍA *f* |
| 12855 | ACERO BÁSICO *m* |
| 12856 | TORIO *m* |
| 12857 | PASO *m* DE TORNILLO |
| 12857 | ROSCADO *m*, PASO DE ROSCA, ROSCA, FILETEADO |
| 12858 | JUEGO *m* A FONDO DE LA ROSCA |
| 12859 | TORNO *m* DE ROSCAR |
| 12860 | CALIBRES *m pl* PARA FILETEADOS (PARA PIEZAS ATERRAJADAS) |

| | | |
|---|---|---|
| 12861 | CALIBRE | *m* NORMAL DE TAMPÓN ROSCADO |
| 12862 | CALIBRES MACHOS PARA ROSCAS | *m pl* |
| 12863 | CALIBRE | *m* NORMAL DE ANILLO ROSCADO |
| 12864 | FONDO | *m* DE ROSCA |
| 12865 | GÁLIBO | *m* PARA HERRAMIENTAS DE ATERRAJAR |
| 12866 | BRIDA | *f* ROSCADA |
| 12867 | MANDRIL | *m* CON ESPIGA DE TORNILLO |
| 12868 | ATERRAJADO | *m*, ROSCADO *m* |
| 12868 | ATERRAJADO | *m* |
| 12869 | MÁQUINA | *f* DE ROSCAR |
| 12870 | LIMA | *f* TRIANGULAR |
| 12871 | VEHÍCULO | *m* DE TRES EJES |
| 12872 | CURVA DE TRES CENTROS | *f*, ARCO DE BÓVEDA *m* |
| 12873 | MÁQUINA | *f* DE TRES CILINDROS |
| 12874 | MANDRIL | *m* UNIVERSAL DE TRES MORDAZAS |
| 12875 | GENERATRIZ | *f* DE CORRIENTE TRIFÁSICA |
| 12876 | MOTOR | *m* TRIFÁSICO |
| 12876 | MOTOR | *m* DE CAMPO GIRATORIO |
| 12877 | CORRIENTE TRIFÁSICA | *f* |
| 12878 | CORREA TRIPLE | *f* |
| 12879 | TORNILLO | *m* DE TRES ROSCAS |
| 12880 | CIGÜEÑAL | *m* DE TRES CODOS |
| 12881 | GRIFO | *m* DE TRES PASOS |
| 12882 | GRIFO | *m* DE TRES PASOS |
| 12882 | VÁLVULA | *f* DE TRES PASOS |
| 12883 | MÉTODO | *m* LLAMADO DE TRES HILOS |
| 12884 | TRILLADORAS | *f pl* MECÁNICAS |
| 12885 | ESPESOR | *m* DE LA SOLDADURA |
| 12886 | ESPESOR | *m* DE UNA SOLDADURA EN ÁNGULO |
| 12887 | ANCHURA | *f* DE UNA SOLDADURA |
| 12888 | MARIPOSA | *f* DE GASES |
| 12888 | OBTURADOR | *m* DE GAS |
| 12889 | ESTRANGULAR | |
| 12890 | VÁLVULA | *f* MARIPOSA REGULADORA DEL GAS |
| 12890 | VÁLVULA | *f* DE MARIPOSA |
| 12890 | REGULADOR | *m* |
| 12891 | ESTRANGULACIÓN | *f* |
| 12892 | ENDURECIMIENTO | *m* COMPLETO (A FONDO) |
| 12893 | AGUJERO | *m* QUE ATRAVIESA LA PIEZA |
| 12894 | CARRERA DE LA EXCÉNTRICA | *f* |
| 12894 | CARRERA DE LA LEVA | *f* |
| 12895 | QUITAR LA CORREA | · |
| 12896 | HOJAS | *f pl* DE UNISERVICIO |
| 12897 | EMBRAGUE | *m* |
| 12898 | DESACOPLO | *m*, DESACOPLAMIENTO *m*, DESEMBRAGUE |
| 12898 | DESEMBRAGUE | *m*, DESACOPLO *m*, DESACOPLAMIENTO *m* |
| 12898 | DESEMBRAGUE | *m* |
| 12899 | ACCIÓN DE PROFUNDIDAD | *f* |

| | | |
|---|---|---|
| 12900 | COJINETE | *m* DE BOLAS PARA EMPUJE |
| 12901 | COJINETE | *m* A BOLAS |
| 12901 | RODAMIENTO | *m* DE BOLAS DE CARGA AXIAL |
| 12902 | COJINETE | *m* AXIAL |
| 12902 | COJINETE | *m* DE EMPUJE, RANGUA *f* |
| 12902 | COJINETE | *m* DE CARGA AXIAL |
| 12903 | COJINETE | *m* DE EMPUJE CON RANURAS |
| 12903 | COJINETE DE RANURAS | *m* |
| 12904 | COLLAR | *m* DE UN PIVOTE ACANALADO |
| 12904 | ANILLO | *m* DE AJUSTE |
| 12904 | PEINE | *m*, COLLARÍN *m* DE RETEN |
| 12904 | COLLARÍN | *m* |
| 12905 | QUICIONERA | *f* |
| 12905 | CASQUILLO | *m* DE CUBO DE RUEDA |
| 12906 | MUÑÓN | *m* GIRATORIO DE TOPE ACANALADO |
| 12906 | MUÑÓN | *m* GIRATORIO ACANALADO |
| 12907 | EMPUJE | *m* DE LAS TIERRAS |
| 12908 | EMPUJE | *m* EN EL VÉRTICE |
| 12909 | TORNILLO | *m* DE TOPE |
| 12910 | TULIO | *m* |
| 12911 | TUERCA | *f* MARIPOSA, TUERCA DE ALETAS, PALOMILLA |
| 12911 | TUERCA | *f* DE MARIPOSA, TUERCA DE ALETAS, PALOMILLA *f* |
| 12911 | TORNILLO | *m* VIOLÍN |
| 12912 | TORNILLO | *m* DE ALETAS |
| 12912 | TORNILLO | *m* DE OREJAS |
| 12913 | TIRISTOR | *m* |
| 12914 | ANCLAR | |
| 12914 | ENGANCHAR, COLGAR, AGARRAR | |
| 12915 | BARRA | *f* DE ACOPLAMIENTO |
| 12916 | BARRA | *f* DE ACOPLAMIENTO |
| 12917 | TIRANTE | *m* |
| 12918 | ANCLAJE | *m* |
| 12918 | ENGANCHE | *m* |
| 12919 | TIRANTES | *m* DE ESFERA |
| 12920 | ESTANCO, IMPERMEABLE, HERMÉTICO | |
| 12921 | JUNTA | *f* HERMÉTICA, JUNTA *f* ESTANCA |
| 12922 | ROBLÓN | *m* DE ESTANQUEIDAD |
| 12923 | CUERDA TENSADA | *f* |
| 12924 | APRETAR UNA CUÑA | |
| 12925 | APRETAR UN TORNILLO | |
| 12925 | APRETAR UNA TUERCA | |
| 12926 | APRETAR LA CAJA DE ESTOPA | |
| 12927 | APRETAR A FONDO UNA TUERCA | |
| 12927 | APRETAR A FONDO UNA TUERCA | |
| 12928 | AJUSTE | *f* DE UNA CUÑA |
| 12929 | AJUSTE | *m* CON CUÑA |
| 12930 | AJUSTE | *m* CON TUERCA |
| 12931 | PAR DE APRIETE | *m* |
| 12932 | ESTANQUEIDAD, IMPERMEABILIDAD | *f* |

| | |
|---|---|
| 12933 | BALDOSA  f  (CONSTR.), LADRILLO  m |
| 12934 | TEJA  f |
| 12935 | CUCHARA  f  DE COLADA CON VUELCO |
| 12936 | MOMENTO  m  BASCULANTE |
| 12937 | MADERA  f  DE CONSTRUCCIÓN |
| 12937 | MADERA  f  DE CONSTRUCCIÓN |
| 12938 | CORTE  m  RADIAL |
| 12939 | MADERA  f  A HILO |
| 12940 | MADERA  f  SIN NUDOS, MADERA  f  SIN DEFECTOS |
| 12941 | TRAVIESA  f  DE MADERA |
| 12942 | CONSTRUCCIÓN DE MADERA  f |
| 12942 | CARPINTERÍA  f, ESTRUCTURA DE MADERA  f |
| 12943 | TIEMPO  m |
| 12944 | CONSTANTE DE TIEMPO  f |
| 12945 | DURACIÓN  f  DE UNA OSCILACIÓN |
| 12946 | CONTADOR DE FICHAJES  m |
| 12946 | CUENTASEGUNDOS  m |
| 12946 | RELOJ DE PUNTEO  m |
| 12947 | CAJA DE DISTRIBUCIÓN  f |
| 12948 | CADENA DE DISTRIBUCIÓN  f |
| 12949 | PIÑÓN  m  DE DISTRIBUCIÓN |
| 12950 | CADENA DE DISTRIBUCIÓN  f |
| 12951 | MARCAS  f  DE FIJACIÓN |
| 12952 | CALADO DE LA DISTRIBUCIÓN  m |
| 12953 | ESTAÑO  m |
| 12954 | ESTAÑAR |
| 12955 | PAPEL  m  DE ESTAÑO, PLANCHA  f  DE ESTAÑO |
| 12955 | LAMINILLA  f  DE ESTAÑO, ESCAMAS  f pl  DE ESTAÑO |
| 12956 | MINERAL  m  DE ESTAÑO |
| 12957 | HOJALATA  f, CHAPA  f  BLANCA |
| 12957 | CHAPA  f  ESTAÑADA |
| 12958 | SOLDADURA  f  BLANDA |
| 12959 | CASITERICA  f |
| 12960 | TUBO  m  DE ESTAÑO |
| 12961 | BIDÓN  m |
| 12962 | ALAMBRE  m  (O HILO  m) ESTAÑADO |
| 12962 | ALAMBRE GALVANIZADO |
| 12963 | ESTAÑADO  m, ESTAÑADURA  f |
| 12964 | HOJALATERO  m |
| 12965 | LAVIS  m, DIBUJO A LA AGUADA |
| 12965 | DIBUJO  m  AL LAVADO |
| 12966 | BOQUILLA  f, EMBOCADURA  f, TOBERA  f |
| 12966 | BOQUILLA  f, DIFUSOR  m |
| 12967 | VEHÍCULO  m  DE VOLQUETE |
| 12968 | GRADUACIÓN  f |
| 12969 | PAPEL  m  JOSEPH, PAPEL  m  FILTRO BLANCO |
| 12969 | PAPEL  m  CEBOLLA |
| 12969 | PAPEL  m  DE SEDA |
| 12970 | TITANIO  m |

| | |
|---|---|
| 12971 | ANHÍDRIDO TITÁNICO  m |
| 12972 | ACERO AL TITANIO  m |
| 12973 | GRADUAR |
| 12974 | GRADUACIÓN  f |
| 12975 | REOSTRICCIÓN  f |
| 12976 | ABERTURA  f |
| 12977 | TOPE  m  PARA LOS PIES |
| 12978 | FRENO  m  DE PALANCA |
| 12979 | JUNTA  f  DE CODILLO |
| 12979 | PALANCA  f  DE ARTICULACIÓN, PALANCA  f  ACODADA |
| 12979 | PALANCA  f  ARTICULADA |
| 12980 | PRENSA  f  DE RÓTULA |
| 12981 | SUJETABARRAS  m |
| 12982 | TOLERANCIA  f |
| 12983 | TOLUENO  m |
| 12983 | TOLUOL  m |
| 12983 | METILBENCENO  m |
| 12983 | HIDRURO  m  DE CRESILO |
| 12983 | HIDRURO  m  DE BENCILO |
| 12984 | TUMBAGA  f  AMARILLA |
| 12985 | PALANCA  f  A TORNILLO |
| 12985 | PALANCA  f  DE TORNILLO |
| 12986 | TONELADA  f  (1000 KG) |
| 12987 | TENAZAS  f pl |
| 12987 | TENAZAS  f pl  (LAS), ALICATES  m pl  (LOS) |
| 12988 | MACHIHEMBRAR, ACOPLAR |
| 12988 | ACANALAR Y HACER LENGÜETAS |
| 12989 | LENG:UETA  f  Y RANURA  f, MACHIHEMBRADO  m |
| 12990 | ENCAJE  m  LENGÜETA-RANURA |
| 12991 | ENSAMBLADURA  f  DE RANURA Y LENGÜETA |
| 12991 | ENSAMBLADURA  f  DE RANURA Y LENGÜETA |
| 12992 | MÁQUINA  f  DE ACOPLAR, MÁQUINA  f  DE MACHIHEMBRAR |
| 12992 | MÁQUINA  f  PARA HACER RANURAS Y LENGÜETAS (MACHIHEMBRADO) |
| 12993 | CEPILLO  m  PARA MACHOS |
| 12994 | HERRAMIENTA  f |
| 12995 | CORTANTE |
| 12995 | ÁNGULO DE REAFILADO  m, PENDIENTE MÁXIMA  f |
| 12995 | ÁNGULO DE HERRAMIENTA  m |
| 12995 | ÁNGULO DE HERRAMIENTA  m |
| 12995 | ÁNGULO DE AFILADO  m |
| 12996 | BOLSA  f  DE HERRAMIENTAS |
| 12997 | CAJA  f  DE HERRAMIENTAS |
| 12998 | ARMARIO PARA HERRAMIENTAS  m |
| 12999 | TIEMPO  m  DE CAMBIO DE ÚTIL |
| 13000 | CAMBIADOR DE HERRAMIENTAS  m |
| 13001 | FUNCIÓN  f  DE HERRAMIENTA |
| 13002 | MÁQUINA  f  PARA AFILAR HERRAMIENTAS |

| | | | | | |
|---|---|---|---|---|---|
| 13002 | RECTIFICADOR *m* | | 13042 | SOPLETE *m* |
| 13003 | PORTAÚTIL *m* | | 13042 | SOPLETE *m* |
| 13004 | TORRETAS *f* POTAÚTILES | | 13043 | TORO *m* |
| 13005 | PORTAÚTILES *m* | | 13044 | FONDO TORICÓNICO |
| 13006 | HERRERIA *f* DE CORTE | | 13045 | FONDO *m* APAINELADO |
| 13006 | FABRICACIÓN *f* DE HERRAMIENTAS | | 13046 | TECHO *m* REBAJADO |
| 13007 | CORRECCIÓN DE POSICIÓN DE ÚTIL *f* | | 13047 | DEPÓSITO *m* DE TECHO REBAJADO |
| 13008 | TEMPLADOR *m* DE UTILLAJE | | 13048 | PAR MOTOR *m* |
| 13008 | OBRERO *m* TEMPLADOR | | 13048 | PAR *m* |
| 13009 | ACERO DE (PARA) HERRAMIENTAS *m* | | 13049 | LLAVE *f* CON DINAMÓMETRO DE TORSIÓN |
| 13010 | MONTANTE *m* PORTAHERRAMIENTA | | 13049 | LLAVE DINAMOMÉTRICA *f* |
| 13011 | HERRAMIENTA *f* CORTANTE, ELEMENTO *m* CORTANTE (DE UNA MAQUINA HERRAMIENTA) | | 13050 | PAR METRO *m* |
| | | | 13051 | TORSIÓN *f* |
| 13012 | PORTAÚTILES *m* | | 13052 | BALANZA *f* DE TORSIÓN, BALANZA *f* DE COULOMB |
| 13013 | BRIDAS *f pl* DE MECANIZACIÓN | | 13053 | BARRA *f* DE TORSIÓN |
| 13014 | MARTILLO *m* DEL ENCARGADO DEL UTILLAJE | | 13054 | TORSIÓN *f* |
| 13015 | UTILLAJE *m*, HERRAMENTAL *m* | | 13055 | FUERZA *f* DE TORSIÓN |
| 13016 | DIENTE *m* | | 13056 | ESFUERZO *m* DE TORSIÓN |
| 13017 | ALTURA *f* DE DIENTE | | 13056 | TRABAJO *m* A LA TORSIÓN |
| 13018 | FLANCO *m* DEL DIENTE | | 13057 | RESISTENCIA *f* A LA TORSIÓN |
| 13019 | PERFIL *m* DE UN DIENTE | | 13058 | TENSIÓN *f* DE TORSIÓN |
| 13020 | PERFIL *m* DE UN ENGRANAJE | | 13059 | PRUEBA *f* A LA TORSIÓN |
| 13021 | TRANSMISIÓN *f* POR ENGRANAJE (O POR RUEDAS DENTADAS) | | 13060 | REFLEXIÓN *f* TOTAL |
| | | | 13061 | ALTURA *f* DE ELEVACIÓN DE UNA BOMBA |
| 13022 | CREMALLERA *f* | | 13062 | CARGA TOTAL *f* |
| 13023 | CORONA DENTADA *f* | | 13063 | JUEGO *m* TOTAL PERDIDO |
| 13024 | SECTOR *m* DENTADO | | 13064 | CAUDAL *m* TOTAL |
| 13025 | ACCIONAMIENTO POR ENGRANAJES *m* | | 13065 | PRESIÓN *f* TOTAL |
| 13025 | ACCIONADO *m* POR RUEDA DENTADA | | 13066 | TOCAR (GEOMETRÍA) |
| 13026 | DENTADO *m* | | 13067 | TENAZ |
| 13027 | CEPILLO *m* DENTADO | | 13068 | HIERRO *m* TENAZ |
| 13028 | CANTONERA DE PARTE SUPERIOR (DE UN TANQUE O DEPÓSITO) *f* | | 13069 | COBRE *m* DE ÓXIDO CUPROSO |
| | | | 13070 | COBRE *m* REFINADO |
| 13029 | PLANO *m* DE MANTENIMIENTO, PLANO *m* SOSTÉN | | 13071 | RESILIENCIA *f* |
| | | | 13071 | TENACIDAD *f* |
| 13030 | CONCHA SUPERIOR *f* | | 13072 | TURMALINA *f* |
| 13030 | SEMICOJINETE SUPERIOR *m*, CONTRA-COJINETE *m* | | 13073 | ESTOPA *f* |
| | | | 13074 | BASURAS *f pl*, DESECHOS *m pl* |
| 13030 | CASQUILLO *m* SUPERIOR DEL COJINETE, SEMICOJINETE *m* SUPERIOR | | 13075 | AGUA *f* DE DISTRIBUCIÓN |
| | | | 13076 | TRAZADO *m* |
| 13031 | COLADA DIRECTA *f* | | 13077 | CALCAR |
| 13032 | PUNTO *m* MUERTO ALTO (P.M.A.) | | 13078 | CALCADOR *m* |
| 13033 | CONTRA-HIERRO *m* | | 13079 | PUNTA *f* TRAZADORA DEL PLANIMETRO |
| 13034 | SEGMENTO *m* DE FUEGO | | 13080 | FRESADORA *f* ACCIONADA POR DISPOSITIVO DE COPIA |
| 13035 | LISO, PLANO | | | |
| 13036 | ESTAMPA *f* DE YUNQUE, ESTAMPA *f* SUPERIOR | | 13081 | TRAQUITA *f* |
| 13036 | MATRIZ *f* DE ARRIBA | | 13082 | CALCO *m* |
| 13037 | VISTA *f* DE ARRIBA ABAJO | | 13082 | CALCADO *m* |
| 13038 | TOPACIO *m* | | 13082 | CALCO *m* |
| 13039 | TOPOQUÍMICA *f* | | 13083 | LIENZO *m* DE CALCAR |
| 13040 | PETRÓLEO *m* CRUDO | | | |
| 13041 | LIMA *f* OLIVA | | | |

| | | |
|---|---|---|
| 13084 | PAPEL *m* TRANSPARENTE |
| 13084 | PAPEL *m* DE CALCO |
| 13085 | PISTA *f* |
| 13085 | VÍA *f* |
| 13085 | CANAL *m* DE RODAMIENTO |
| 13086 | VERIFICACIÓN *f* DEL PARALELISMO |
| 13087 | GUÍA *f* DE CENTRADO |
| 13088 | TRACCIÓN *f* DE LOS VEHÍCULOS |
| 13089 | ESFUERZO *m* DE TRACCIÓN |
| 13090 | POTENCIA *f* DE ATRACCIÓN DE UN IMÁN |
| 13091 | TRACTOR *m* |
| 13092 | VEHÍCULO *m* ARTICULADO |
| 13093 | TRACTOR *m* AGRÍCOLA SEMIARRASTRADO |
| 13094 | TRACTOR *m* AGRÍCOLA ORUGA |
| 13095 | TRACTOR *m* AGRÍCOLA DE RUEDAS |
| 13096 | TRACTOR *m* HORTENSE |
| 13097 | TRACTOR *m* |
| 13098 | TRACTIVA |
| 13098 | RELATIVO A LA TRACCIÓN |
| 13099 | BALANZA *f* DEL COMERCIO EXTERIOR |
| 13100 | MARCA *f* DE FÁBRICAL |
| 13100 | MARCA *f* COMERCIA |
| 13101 | NO COMERCIAL *m* |
| 13102 | REMOLQUES *m pl* |
| 13103 | ACEITE *m* DE PESCADO |
| 13103 | ACEITE *m* DE BALLENA |
| 13104 | TRAYECTORIA *f* |
| 13105 | COMPÁS DE VARA *m* |
| 13106 | HIERRO *m* EN EL TRITURADOR |
| 13107 | ECUACIÓN *f* TRANSCENDENTE |
| 13108 | TRANSDUCTOR *m* |
| 13108 | TRANSDUCTOR *m* |
| 13109 | CALCOMANÍA *f* |
| 13110 | CUCHARA *f* TONEL |
| 13111 | TRANSMISIÓN *f* DEL CALOR |
| 13112 | TRANSFORMAR LA ENERGÍA |
| 13113 | ZONA *f* DE TRANSFORMACIÓN |
| 13114 | TEMPERATURA *f* DE TRANSFORMACIÓN |
| 13115 | TRANSFORMADOR *m* |
| 13115 | TRANSFORMADOR *m* DE POTENCIAL |
| 13116 | CHAPA *f* PARA TRANSFORMADORES |
| 13117 | ROTURA TRANSCRISTALINA *f* |
| 13118 | FLUENCIA *f* TRANSITORIA |
| 13119 | TRANSISTOR *m* |
| 13120 | RED *f* DE TRANSLACIÓN |
| 13121 | REDUCCIÓN *f* |
| 13121 | ELEMENTO *m* O PARTE *f* EN FORMA DE CONO TRUNCADO |
| 13122 | PUNTO *m* DE TRANSICIÓN |
| 13123 | DESPLAZAMIENTO *m*, TRASLADO *m* |
| 13123 | TRADUCCIÓN *f* |

| | |
|---|---|
| 13123 | TRANSLACIÓN *f* |
| 13124 | TRANSLUCIDEZ *f* |
| 13125 | TRANSLÚCIDO |
| 13126 | ÓRGANOS *m pl* DE TRANSMISIÓN |
| 13127 | DINAMÓMETRO *m* DE TRANSMISIÓN |
| 13128 | ENGRANAJE *m* DE TRANSMISIÓN, RUEDA *f* DE TRANSMISIÓN |
| 13129 | TRANSMISIÓN *f* DE ENERGÍA ELÉCTRICA |
| 13130 | TRANSMISIÓN *f* DE UN MOVIMIENTO |
| 13131 | TRANSMISIÓN *f* POR ENGRANAJES |
| 13132 | TRANSMISIÓN *f* POR PALANCA |
| 13133 | TRANSMISIÓN *f* DE ELECTRICIDAD |
| 13133 | TRANSPORTE *m* DE ENERGÍA ELÉCTRICA A GRAN DISTANCIA |
| 13134 | TRANSMISIÓN *f* DE POTENCIA |
| 13134 | TRANSPORTE *m* DE LA ENERGÍA |
| 13135 | TRANSPORTE *m* DE ENERGÍA A GRAN DISTANCIA |
| 13135 | DISTRIBUCIÓN *f* A DISTANCIA DE LA ENERGÍA |
| 13136 | TRANSMUTACIÓN *f* (QUIMICA) |
| 13137 | TRANSPARENCIA *f* |
| 13138 | TRANSPARENTE |
| 13139 | MEDIO *m* TRANSPARENTE |
| 13140 | TRANSPORTE *m* |
| 13141 | TRANSBORDADOR *m* |
| 13141 | PUENTE *m* TRANSBORDADOR |
| 13142 | EJE *m* TRANSVERSAL |
| 13143 | EJE *m* TRANSVERSO DE UNA HIPÉRBOLA |
| 13143 | EJE *m* FOCAL |
| 13144 | ELASTICIDAD *f* DE CORTE, ELASTICIDAD TRANSVERSAL |
| 13144 | ELASTICIDAD *f* TRANSVERSAL |
| 13145 | ROBLONES (DISTANCIA ENTRE ROBLONES) ENTRE CENTROS DE UNA LÍNEA A OTRA REMACHADOR *m pl* |
| 13146 | VIBRACIÓN *f* |
| 13146 | OSCILACIÓN *f* TRANSVERSAL |
| 13147 | TUBO *m* CON NERVIOS TRANSVERSALES |
| 13148 | TRAPECIO *m* |
| 13149 | TRAPEZOIDE *m* |
| 13150 | CARGA TRAPEZOIDAL *f* |
| 13151 | RESORTE *m* TRAPEZOIDAL |
| 13152 | TRASS *m* |
| 13153 | INDICADOR *m* DE APERTURA |
| 13154 | JUEGO *m* DE UNA VÁLVULA |
| 13155 | CARRETILLA DE PUENTE-GRÚA *f* |
| 13155 | CARRETILLA PORTA-APAREJO *f* |
| 13156 | PUENTE GRÚA *m* DE CORREDERA |
| 13157 | VIGA *f* DE PUENTE GRÚA |
| 13158 | TRANSLACIÓN *f* |
| 13159 | TUERCA *f* MÓVIL |
| 13160 | CURSOR *m* DE UNA BALANZA |

| | |
|---|---|
| 13161 | GRÚA *f* RODADIZA |
| 13161 | GRÚA *f* MÓVIL |
| 13162 | CALANDRAR |
| 13162 | TORNEAR UNA SUPERFICIE CILÍNDRICA *f* |
| 13163 | VOLANTE *m* DE TORNEADO |
| 13164 | PASADA LONGITUDINAL *f* |
| 13164 | PASADA EN UNA SUPERFICIE CILÍNDRICA *f* |
| 13164 | CILINDRADO *m* |
| 13165 | CRIC *m* DE CARRO |
| 13166 | TRAVERTINO *m* |
| 13167 | PLATILLO *m*, PLATO *m*, PLACA *f* |
| 13168 | TRAMPA *f* DE INSPECCIÓN CON TAPA |
| 13169 | DISTANCIA *f* ENTRE LOS PLATOS (ENTRE LAS PLACAS) |
| 13170 | CORONA SOPORTE DE PLATOS *f* |
| 13171 | TORNO *m* DE PLATOS |
| 13172 | SUPERFICIE *f* PERIFÉRICA DEL NEUMÁTICO |
| 13172 | MARCHA *f*, FUNCIONAMIENTO *m* |
| 13172 | CAPA *f* |
| 13173 | SUPERFICIE *f* DE RODADURA DE UNA RUEDA |
| 13174 | PEDAL *m* |
| 13175 | MALEABILIZACIÓN *f* DE LA FUNDICIÓN |
| 13176 | RUEDA *f* DE DIENTES DE DOBLE ÁNGULO |
| 13177 | REMACHE *m* TRIPLE DE TRIPLE HILERA |
| 13177 | REMACHE *m* DE TRES HILERAS |
| 13178 | REMACHE *m* CON TRES CORTES |
| 13179 | TARUGO DE MADERA *m*, ESPIGA DE MADERA *f* |
| 13180 | ENREJADO *m* |
| 13181 | TENDENCIA (CURVA) *f* |
| 13182 | MÁQUINA *f* DE TALADRAR (O PERFORAR) |
| 13183 | SECCIÓN *f* TRAPEZOIDAL |
| 13184 | MONTAJE *m* EN BLANCO |
| 13185 | TRIÁNGULO *m* |
| 13186 | TRIÁNGULO *m* DE FUERZAS |
| 13187 | COMPÁS DE TRES PUNTAS *m* |
| 13188 | SECCIÓN *f* TRIANGULAR |
| 13189 | LIMA *f* DE SECCIÓN TRIANGULAR |
| 13189 | LIMA *f* TRES CUARTOS |
| 13190 | CARGA TRIANGULAR *f* |
| 13191 | RESORTE *m* TRIANGULAR |
| 13192 | PRISMA *f* RECTANGULAR |
| 13193 | PIRÁMIDE *f* TRIANGULAR |
| 13194 | CABLE DE SECCIÓN TRIANGULAR *m* |
| 13195 | CABLE DE CABOS TRIANGULARES *m* |
| 13196 | ALAMBRE *m* (DE SECCIÓN) TRIANGULAR |
| 13197 | TRIVALENTE |
| 13197 | TRIATÓMICO |
| 13198 | TRIBÁSICO |
| 13199 | SISTEMA *m* TRICLÍNICO |
| 13200 | TRIGONOMÉTRICO *m* |
| 13201 | TRIGONOMETRÍA *f* |
| 13202 | TRIEDRO *m* |
| 13203 | COORDINADAS EN EL ESPACÍO *f pl* |
| 13204 | DESCARGAR, REBAJAR, CHIFLAR (LAS PIELES), ENGALANAR |
| 13204 | RECORTAR |
| 13205 | DESBARBAR UNA CHAPA |
| 13206 | DESBARBAR |
| 13206 | ELIMINAR (O QUITAR) LAS REBABAS, DESBARBAR |
| 13207 | ÓXIDO *m* SALINO DE MANGANESO |
| 13208 | PROYECCIÓN *f* TRIMÉTRICA |
| 13209 | RECORTADURA *f* |
| 13209 | CORTE *m*, ELIMINACIÓN DE LA REBABA *f* |
| 13209 | DESBARBADURA *f* |
| 13210 | DESBARBADURA *f* |
| 13210 | DESBARBADURA *f* |
| 13210 | DESBARBADURA *f* |
| 13210 | ELIMINACIÓN *f* DE LAS REBABAS |
| 13211 | PRENSA *f* DE DESBASTE |
| 13212 | ASFALTO *m* DE TRINIDAD |
| 13213 | ECUACIÓN *f* TRINOMIA |
| 13214 | GARRAS DE CONEXIÓN/DESCONEXIÓN *f* |
| 13215 | INTEGRAL *f* TRIPLE |
| 13216 | PUNTO *m* TRIPLE |
| 13217 | MÁQUINA *f* CON TRIPLE EXPANSIÓN |
| 13218 | CRIC *m* DE TRÍPODE |
| 13219 | TRIPODE *m* |
| 13220 | TRÍPOLI *m* |
| 13221 | DISCO *m* CON LEVAS |
| 13222 | TRITURAR |
| 13223 | TROCOIDE |
| 13224 | PÓRTICO DE RODAMIENTO |
| 13225 | TROLEBÚS *m* |
| 13226 | TROMEL *m* |
| 13227 | TROSTITA *f* |
| 13228 | ARTESA *f*, CUBA *f*, TINA *f*, BANDEJA *f* |
| 13228 | DEPÓSITO *m*, CUBA *f*, CISTERNA *f* |
| 13228 | CUBA *f*, TANQUE *m*, DEPÓSITO *m* |
| 13228 | ARTESA *f*, CUBA *f*, TINA *f* |
| 13229 | CABINA *f* DE CAMIÓN |
| 13230 | CARRETILLA (PARA MANIPULACIÓN TALLER Y ALMACÉN) *f* |
| 13231 | CARRETILLAS *f pl* |
| 13232 | ENDEREZAR, APLANAR |
| 13233 | APARATO PARA DIAMANTAR *m* |
| 13234 | ENDEREZAMIENTO *m*, APLANAMIENTO *m* |
| 13235 | CONO TRUNCADO *m* |
| 13235 | TRONCO *m* DE CONO |
| 13236 | RESORTE *m* TRONCOCÓNICO |
| 13237 | TRONCO *m* DE PARALELEPÍPEDO |
| 13238 | TRONCO *m* DE PIRÁMIDE |
| 13239 | COFRE *m* |

| | | |
|---|---|---|
| 13239 | BAÚL  *m*  CAJA  *f* | |
| 13240 | TAPA DEL POTAEQUIPAJES  *f* | |
| 13241 | PISTÓN  *m*  SIN VÁSTAGO | |
| 13242 | MUÑÓN  *m*  GIRATORIO COMO EJE DE ROTACIÓN | |
| 13242 | PIVOTE  *m*  DE GIRO | |
| 13243 | ARMADURA  *f*, CERCHA  *f* | |
| 13243 | TRAVESAÑO  *m* | |
| 13243 | ARMADURAS  *f* | |
| 13244 | ESTRUCTURA DE CERCHAS  *f* | |
| 13245 | ESCUADRA  *f*  CON ESPALDÓN | |
| 13246 | CÁMARA DE AIRE  *f* | |
| 13247 | CEPILLO  *m*  DE LIMPIAR TUBOS | |
| 13248 | CORTADOR DE TUBOS  *m*, CORTATUBOS  *m* | |
| 13249 | ESTIRADO  *m*  DE LOS TUBOS | |
| 13250 | MANDRIL  *m*  PARA ENSANCHAR LOS TUBOS | |
| 13251 | ENCENDIDO POR INCANDESCENCIA  *m* | |
| 13252 | TUBO  *m*  TRITURADOR | |
| 13253 | TUBO  *m*  DE FUERZA | |
| 13254 | PLACA  *f*  TUBULAR | |
| 13255 | TUBO  *m*  DEL TERMÓMETRO | |
| 13255 | TUBO  *m*  CAPILAR | |
| 13256 | TORNILLO  *m*  PARA TUBOS | |
| 13256 | TORNILLO  *m*  PARA TUBOS, TORNILLO  *m*  DE TUBERO | |
| 13257 | TUBO  *m* | |
| 13257 | TUBO  *m* | |
| 13258 | REFORZAMIENTO  *m*  TUBULAR, APUNTALAMIENTO  *m*  CON TUBOS | |
| 13258 | REFUERZO  *m*  EN TUBOS | |
| 13259 | NIVEL  *m*  DE BURBUJA | |
| 13260 | TOBA  *f* | |
| 13261 | TONEL  *m*  DE LIMPIEZA | |
| 13261 | TONEL  *m*  DE ACABADO | |
| 13261 | TAMBOR  *m*  DE LIMPIEZA | |
| 13262 | TUNGSTENO  *m* | |
| 13263 | BRONCE  *m*  DE TUNGSTENO | |
| 13264 | LÁMPARA  *f*  DE FILAMENTO DE TUNGSTENO | |
| 13265 | ACERO AL TUNGSTENO (WOLFRAMIO)  *m* | |
| 13266 | ANHÍDRIDO TÚNGSTICO  *m* | |
| 13267 | TURBINA  *f* | |
| 13268 | ÁLABES  *m pl*  DE TURBINAS | |
| 13269 | BOMBA  *f*  CENTRÍFUGA | |
| 13270 | TURBOVENTILADOR  *m* | |
| 13271 | TURBOGENERADOR  *m* | |
| 13272 | TURBOCOMPRESOR  *m* | |
| 13273 | TURBULENCIA  *f* | |
| 13274 | CORRIENTE TURBULENTA  *f* | |
| 13275 | PAPEL  *m*  DE CÚRCUMA | |
| 13276 | TORNEAR | |
| 13276 | TRABAJAR EN EL TORNO | |
| 13277 | TORNEAR SUPERFICIES ABOMBADAS | |

| | |
|---|---|
| 13278 | TORNO  *m*  DE UNA HÉLICE |
| 13279 | REVOLUCIÓN  *f* |
| 13280 | TORNEAR SUPERFICIES CON FIGURAS |
| 13281 | TORNEAR SUPERFICIES ESFÉRICAS |
| 13281 | TORNEAR CUERPOS REDONDOS |
| 13282 | TORNEAR SUPERFICIES OBLICUAS |
| 13283 | REMOVER CON LA PALA |
| 13284 | LLAVE EN MANO (NEGOCIO)  *f* |
| 13285 | TENSOR  *m*  DE TORNILLO |
| 13286 | TORNEAR |
| 13287 | TORNEADO  *m* |
| 13287 | TRABAJO  *m*  EN EL TORNO |
| 13288 | TORNEADO  *m*  DE SUPERFICIES ABOMBADAS |
| 13289 | TORNO  *m*  (MÁQUINA HERRAMIENTA) |
| 13290 | TALLER  *m*  DE TORNEAR |
| 13291 | TORNEADO  *m*  DE SUPERFICIES ESFÉRICAS |
| 13292 | HERRAMIENTA  *f*  PARA TORNO |
| 13293 | TORNEADURAS, VIRUTAS  *f pl* |
| 13294 | DESTORNILLADOR  *m* |
| 13295 | PLACA  *f*  GIRATORIA |
| 13296 | BARNIZ  *m*  A LA GASOLINA |
| 13297 | TORNO  *m*  REVÓLVER |
| 13298 | TORNO  *m*  DE UN HUSILLO AUTOMÁTICO CON TORRETA |
| 13299 | TOBERA  *f*  DE TRAÍDA DE AIRE A PRESIÓN |
| 13300 | MACLA  *f*  (DE CRISTALIZACIÓN) |
| 13301 | MOTOR  *m*  DE CILINDROS PAREADOS |
| 13302 | MACLADO  *m* |
| 13303 | CORCHAR LOS CABOS |
| 13303 | CABLEAR |
| 13304 | BROCA  *f*  HELICOIDAL |
| 13304 | BROCA  *f*  HELICOIDAL |
| 13304 | BROCA  *f*  AMERICANA |
| 13304 | BROCA  *f*  EN HÉLICE, BROCA  *f*  HELICOIDAL |
| 13305 | TORSIÓN  *f*  DE UNA CUERDA |
| 13305 | TORCIDO |
| 13306 | PRUEBA  *f*  DE TORSIÓN |
| 13307 | CURVA DE DOBLE CURVATURA  *f* |
| 13307 | CURVA EN EL ESPACIO  *f* |
| 13307 | CURVA EN EL ESPACIO  *f* |
| 13308 | MOMENTO  *m*  DE TORSIÓN |
| 13308 | MOMENTO  *m*  DE PAR |
| 13309 | RUPTURA  *f*  BRUSCA DEL CUERPO DE UN TORNILLO |
| 13310 | PRUEBA  *f*  SIMULTÁNEA DE TORSIÓN Y FLEXIÓN |
| 13311 | SISTEMA  *m*  DE PINTURA DE DOS COMPONENTES |
| 13312 | MOTOR  *m*  DE DOS TIEMPOS |
| 13313 | MÁQUINA  *f*  DE DOS CILINDROS |
| 13314 | CORRIENTE DIFÁSICA  *f* |
| 13315 | TORNILLO  *m*  DE DOBLE ROSCA |
| 13316 | ÁRBOL  *m*  CIGÜEÑAL DE CODO DOBLE |

| | |
|---|---|
| 13317 GRIFO *m* DE DOS PASOS | 13351 CORTE INFERIOR A LA COTA *m* |
| 13318 VÁLVULA *f* DE DOS PASOS | 13352 CORROSIÓN SUBYACENTE *f* |
| 13319 METAL *m* PROPIO PARA LA FABRICACIÓN DE LOS CARACTERES DE IMPRENTA | 13353 LÍNEA ELÉCTRICA SUBTERRÁNEA *f* |
| | 13353 LÍNEA *f* SUBTERRÁNEA |
| 13320 TIPO *m* | 13354 CANALIZACIÓN SUBTERRÁNEA *f* |
| 13321 TORNO *m* DE LLANTAS | 13354 CANALIZACIÓN *f* |
| 13322 NEUMÁTICO *m* | 13355 RUEDA *f* POR DEBAJO |
| 13322 BANDAJE *m* DE LA RUEDA | 13356 ANGULAR DE LADOS DESIGUALES *m* |
| 13323 CODO A 180 *m* | 13357 FRACTURA DESIGUAL *f* |
| 13323 CODO EN U *m* | 13358 INGLETE *m* CILINDRICO |
| 13324 COLLAR *m* DE TUBO, ABRAZADERA *f*, BRIDA *f* | 13359 TEMPLADO (NO) |
| | 13359 ENDURECIDO (NO-) |
| 13324 COLLAR DE TUBO *m*, CUELLO DE TUBO *m* | 13360 CORRIENTE DE MISMO SENTIDO *f* |
| 13325 TUBO *m* ACODADO DE DOS RAMAS COMUNICANTES ENTRE SÍ | 13361 ACELERACIÓN UNIFORME *f* |
| | 13362 MOVIMIENTO *m* UNIFORME |
| 13326 VACIADO *m* | 13363 VELOCIDAD *f* UNIFORME CONSTANTE |
| 13327 RESISTENCIA *f* | 13364 HOMOGENEIDAD *f* DE UN MATERIAL |
| 13327 RESISTENCIA *f* A LA RUPTURA | 13365 MOVIMIENTO *m* UNIFORMEMENTE ACELERADO |
| 13327 TENACIDAD *f* EXTREMA | 13366 CARGA UNIFORMEMENTE DISTRIBUIDA *f* |
| 13328 RESISTENCIA *f* AL ACORTAMIENTO | 13367 MOVIMIENTO *m* UNIFORMEMENTE RETARDADO |
| 13328 RESISTENCIA *f* A LA COMPRESIÓN | 13368 UNIÓN *f* |
| 13328 RESISTENCIA *f* AL APLASTAMIENTO | 13368 RACOR, EMPALME, ENLACE, MANGUITO *m* |
| 13329 | 13369 RACOR *m* DE UNIÓN |
| 13330 RESISTENCIA *f* AL DESLIZAMIENTO TRANSVERSAL | 13369 RACOR *m* TRES PIEZAS |
| 13330 RESISTENCIA *f* A LA RUPTURA TRANSVERSAL | 13369 UNIÓN *f* ROSCADA (DE TUBOS) |
| 13330 RESISTENCIA *f* AL ESFUERZO CORTANTE | 13370 DILATACIÓN *f* |
| 13331 RESISTENCIA *f* A LA EXTENSIÓN | 13371 CARGA POR UNIDAD DE SUPERFICIE *f* |
| 13331 RESISTENCIA *f* A LA TRACCIÓN | 13372 UNIDAD *f* DE SUPERFICIE |
| 13331 RESISTENCIA *f* AL ALARGAMIENTO | 13373 UNIDAD *f* DE LONGITUD |
| 13331 CARGA DE RUPTURA *f* | 13374 UNIDAD *f* DE MASA |
| 13332 RAYOS *m* ULTRAVIOLETAS | 13375 UNIDAD *f* DE MEDIDA |
| 13333 RAYOS *m* ULTRAVIOLETAS | 13376 UNIDAD *f* DE TIEMPO |
| 13334 AZUL *m* ULTRAMAR | 13377 UNIDAD *f* DE VOLUMEN |
| 13335 ULTRAMICROSCOPIO *m* | 13378 UNIDAD *f* DE PESO |
| 13336 EXAMEN *m* ULTRAMICROSCÓPICO | 13379 UNIDAD *f* DE TRABAJO |
| 13337 CONTROL POR ULTRASONIDOS *m* | 13380 VECTOR *m* UNITARIO |
| 13338 SOLDADURA *f* POR ULTRASONIDOS | 13381 CHÁSIS *m*, CAJA PORTANTE *f* |
| 13339 SOMBRA *f* ARROJADA | 13382 MANDRIL *m* UNIVERSAL |
| 13340 ALAMBRE *m* CLARO | 13383 MÁQUINA *f* UNIVERSAL PARA RECTIFICAR LAS SUPERFICIES DE REVOLUCIÓN |
| 13341 DESEQUILIBRIO *m* | |
| 13341 DESEQUILIBRIO | 13384 AFILADORA UNIVERSAL *f* |
| 13342 SIN FRAGILIDAD *f* | 13385 JUNTA *f* DE CARDÁN, JUNTA *f* UNIVERSAL |
| 13343 IRROMPIBLE | 13386 LAMINADOR *m* UNIVERSAL |
| 13344 NO QUEMADO | 13387 FRESADORA *f* UNIVERSAL |
| 13345 CARBONO NO COMBINADO AL HIERRO *m* | 13388 MÁQUINA *f* PARA ENSAYOS UNIVERSAL |
| 13346 VIBRACIÓN *f* NO AMORTIGUADA | 13389 TORNILLO *m* UNIVERSAL |
| 13347 SUBENFRIAMIENTO *m* | 13390 CABEZA *f* DE SOLDADURA UNIVERSAL |
| 13348 FALTA *f* DE MATERIA | 13391 CANTIDAD *f* DESCONOCIDA |
| 13349 DIMENSIÓN *f* INFERIOR A LAS PRESCRIPCIONES | 13391 DESCONOCIDA, INCÓGNITA *f* |
| 13350 FISURA *f* BAJO CORDÓN | 13392 POLOS *m pl* DIFERENTES |
| 13351 CANAL (SOLDADURA) *m* | 13392 POLOS *m pl* DE NOMBRE CONTRARIO |

| | |
|---|---|
| 13393 | HIDROCARBUROS *m pl* NO SATURADOS (LOS ETILÉNICOS Y LOS ACETILÉNICOS) |
| 13394 | SOLUCIÓN *f* NO SATURADA |
| 13395 | DESENROSCAR |
| 13395 | DESENROSCAR UN PERNO |
| 13396 | DESENROSCADO *m* |
| 13397 | SOLDADURA *f* AL ARCO METÁLICO SIN GAS PROTECTOR |
| 13398 | PEÓN *m*, OBRERO *m* SIN ESPECIALIDAD |
| 13398 | MANIOBRA *f* DE SERVICIO |
| 13399 | DESOLDAR |
| 13400 | DESOLDADURA *f* |
| 13401 | EQUILIBRIO *m* INSETABLE |
| 13402 | MANEJO *m* (DE DIFÍCIL), POCO MANEJABLE |
| 13403 | COMPENSACIÓN *f* DE JUEGO |
| 13404 | DESENROLLAR |
| 13405 | DESENROLLAMIENTO *m* |
| 13406 | CARRERA COMPLETA (IDA Y VUELTA) DEL ÉMBOLO *f* |
| 13407 | AGUA ARRIBA *f* |
| 13407 | AGUA ARRIBA *f* |
| 13408 | FRESADO *m* ASCENDIENDO |
| 13409 | CARRERA ASCENDENTE DEL ÉMBOLO *f* |
| 13409 | CARRERA ASCENDENTE *f* |
| 13409 | SUBIDA *f* DEL PISTÓN |
| 13410 | TIEMPO *m* ACTIVO |
| 13411 | PUNTO *m* MUERTO ALTO (P.M.A.) |
| 13412 | TALADRADORA *f* EN COLUMNA ESTANDARD |
| 13413 | SOLDADURA *f* A TOPE POR RESISTENCIA |
| 13414 | RECHAZO *m*, IMPULSIÓN *f* BATIDO *m* |
| 13415 | MÁQUINA *f* DE RECALCAR |
| 13416 | PRUEBA *f* DE RECALCAMIENTO |
| 13416 | PRUEBA *f* DE COMPRESIÓN |
| 13417 | BATIDO *m* CON CALDEO POR EFECTO JOULE |
| 13418 | CANAL *m* |
| 13419 | SOLDADURA *f* EN POSICIÓN VERTICAL ASCENDENTE |
| 13420 | URANIO *m* |
| 13421 | AUTOBÚS *m* |
| 13422 | SECCIÓN *f* ÚTIL |
| 13423 | DIÁMETRO ÚTIL |
| 13424 | LARGURA *f* ÚTIL |
| 13425 | CARGA ÚTIL *f* |
| 13426 | RESISTENCIA *f* ÚTIL |
| 13427 | ANCHURA *f* ÚTIL DE LAMINADO |
| 13428 | TRABAJO *m* ÚTIL |
| 13429 | UTILIZACIÓN *f* |
| 13430 | UTILIZAR |
| 13431 | CORREA TRAPEZOIDAL *f* |
| 13432 | GUBIA *f* TRIANGULAR |
| 13433 | INOCUPACIÓN *f*, VACANTE *f* |
| 13434 | PRESIÓN *f* |

| | |
|---|---|
| 13434 | DEPRESIÓN *f* ATMOSFÉRICA |
| 13434 | VACÍO |
| 13435 | CAJA *f* DE MARCHA EN VACÍO |
| 13436 | FRENO *m* POR DEPRESIÓN |
| 13436 | FRENO *m* POR VACÍO |
| 13437 | VÁLVULA *f* DE SUPRESIÓN DE VACÍO |
| 13438 | CAJA *f* DE MARCHA EN VACÍO |
| 13439 | MOLDEADO *m* EN EL VACÍO |
| 13440 | CÁMARA *f* DE VACÍO |
| 13440 | CÁMARA DE VACÍO *f* |
| 13441 | ATMÓSFERA *f* ENRARECIDA |
| 13442 | INDICADOR *m* DEL VACÍO |
| 13442 | VACUÓMETRO *m* |
| 13443 | TRATAMIENTO *m* TÉRMICO EN VACÍO |
| 13444 | FUSIÓN *f* EN EL VACÍO |
| 13445 | METALIZACIÓN *f* EN EL VACÍO |
| 13446 | METALURGIA *f* EN EL VACÍO |
| 13447 | REFINADO *m* EN EL VACÍO |
| 13448 | CALCINACIÓN *f* EN EL VACÍO |
| 13449 | CÁMARA DE VACÍO *f* |
| 13450 | VENTILACIÓN *f* POR ASPIRACIÓN |
| 13451 | DEPÓSITO *m* DE VACÍO |
| 13452 | VALENCIA *f* |
| 13453 | VÁLVULA *f* |
| 13453 | OBTURADOR *m* |
| 13453 | VÁLVULA *f* |
| 13453 | DISTRIBUIDOR *m* |
| 13453 | LÁMPARA *f*, TUBO *m* (ELECTRON.) |
| 13454 | CUERPO DE UNA VÁLVULA *m* |
| 13455 | GRIFO *m* CIERRE DE VÁLVULA |
| 13456 | CONTROL *m* DE VÁLVULA |
| 13457 | DIAGRAMA (DE ABERTURA Y DE CIERRE) DE UNA VÁLVULA |
| 13458 | EFECTO *m* DE VÁLVULA |
| 13459 | CHAPELETA DE VÁLVULA *f* |
| 13460 | DISTRIBUIDOR DE VAPOR *m* |
| 13460 | DISTRIBUCIÓN *f* POR VÁLVULAS |
| 13461 | TOPE *m* DE LA VÁLVULA |
| 13461 | LÍMITE *m* DE LA CARRERA DE LA VÁLVULA |
| 13462 | GUÍA *f* DE VÁLVULA |
| 13463 | CABEZA *f* DE UNA VÁLVULA |
| 13464 | TAPÓN *m* DE VÁLVULA |
| 13465 | PALANCA *f* DE VÁLVULA |
| 13466 | PULSADOR *m* DE VÁLVULA |
| 13467 | ENGRASADOR *m* DE VÁLVULA |
| 13468 | ASIENTO *m* DE VÁLVULA |
| 13469 | DESTARA *f* DE VÁLVULA |
| 13470 | RESORTE *m* DE VÁLVULA |
| 13471 | DISTRIBUCIÓN *f* |
| 13472 | VÁLVULA *f* |

| | |
|---|---|
| 13473 | CALIBRE DE AJUSTE DE VÁLVULA *m* |
| 13474 | FURGÓN *m* |
| 13475 | VANADIO *m* |
| 13476 | ACERO AL VANADIO *m* |
| 13477 | ALETAS DE REFRIGERACIÓN *f pl* |
| 13478 | BOMBA *f* DE PALETAS |
| 13479 | RUEDA *f* DE PALETAS, DE ALETAS |
| 13479 | RUEDA *f* DE PALETAS |
| 13480 | ÁLABE *m* DE UNA TURBINA |
| 13481 | TAPÓN *m* DE VAPOR |
| 13482 | RECUBRIMIENTO *m* POR DESCOMPOSICIÓN DE UN GAS |
| 13483 | VAPORIZACIÓN *f* |
| 13484 | VAPOR *m* |
| 13485 | ELIMINACIÓN *f* DEL VAPOR |
| 13485 | INSTALACIÓN *f* DE EVACUACIÓN |
| 13486 | DESENGRASE *m* CON VAPOR |
| 13487 | METALIZACIÓN *f* EN EL VACÍO |
| 13488 | VARIABLE *f* |
| 13489 | FORMATO *m* DE BLOC VARIABLE |
| 13490 | MOVIMIENTO *m* VARIADO |
| 13491 | PRESIÓN *f* VARIABLE |
| 13492 | CONJUNTO *m* DE MANDO DE VELOCIDAD VARIABLE |
| 13493 | VARIADOR *f* DE VELOCIDAD |
| 13494 | VARIABLE *f* |
| 13494 | VELOCIDAD *f* VARIABLE |
| 13495 | VARIACIÓN *f* |
| 13496 | VARIACIÓN *f* (MATEMÁTICAS) |
| 13497 | VARIACIONES *f pl* DE PRESIÓN |
| 13498 | VARIACIÓN *f* DE TEMPERATURA |
| 13499 | VARIACIONES *f pl* DE VELOCIDAD |
| 13499 | FLUCTUACIONES *f pl* DE VELOCIDAD |
| 13500 | VARIACIONES *f pl* DE NIVEL DE AGUA |
| 13501 | COBRE *m* EMPENACHADO (MULTICOLOR) |
| 13502 | GRÉS *m* ABIGARRADO |
| 13503 | CLASE *f* DE MADERA |
| 13503 | CLASE *f* DE MADERA |
| 13504 | BARNIZ *m* |
| 13505 | BARNIZADO *m* |
| 13506 | PAPEL *m* GOMA LACA |
| 13507 | ACELERACIÓN NO UNIFORME *f* |
| 13508 | GRASA *f* MINERAL |
| 13508 | COSMOLINA *f* |
| 13508 | VASELINA *f* |
| 13508 | PETROLEÍNA *f*, VASELINA *f*, GRASA MINERAL |
| 13508 | PETROLEÍNA *f* |
| 13508 | PIMELEÍNA *f*, PETROLEÍNA *f* |
| 13509 | PRODUCTO *m* VECTORIAL |
| 13510 | VECTOR *m* |
| 13511 | CORREA DE SECCIÓN TRIANGULAR *f* |

| | |
|---|---|
| 13511 | CORREA TRAPEZOIDAL *f* |
| 13512 | ACEITE *m* VEGETAL |
| 13513 | CURVA DE VELOCIDAD *f* |
| 13514 | DIAGRAMA *m* DE VELOCIDADES |
| 13515 | CARGA DE LA VELOCIDAD *f* |
| 13516 | VELOCIDAD *f* DE CORRIENTE |
| 13517 | VELOCIDAD *f* DE LA LUZ |
| 13518 | VELOCIDAD *f* DE PASO |
| 13519 | VELOCIDAD *f* DE PROPAGACIÓN |
| 13520 | VELOCIDAD *f* DEL SONIDO |
| 13521 | VELOCIDAD *f* DE TRANSFORMACIÓN |
| 13522 | RELACIÓN *f* DE VELOCIDADES |
| 13523 | FASE *f* DE VELOCIDAD |
| 13524 | CHAPA *f* |
| 13524 | CHAPA *f* DE MADERA |
| 13524 | CHAPEADO *m* |
| 13525 | MÁQUINA *f* PARA HACER LAS HOJAS DE CHAPADO |
| 13526 | SIERRA *f* DE ENCHAPADO |
| 13527 | TREMENTINA *f* DE VENECIA |
| 13528 | AGUJERO *m* DE AIRE |
| 13528 | RESPIRADERO *m*, VENTILACIÓN *f* |
| 13529 | MOTOR *m* BLINDADO VENTILADO |
| 13530 | VENTILACIÓN *f* |
| 13530 | TOMA DE AIRE, VENTILACIÓN, AIREACIÓN *f* |
| 13530 | VENTILACIÓN, AIREACIÓN, AERACIÓN *f* |
| 13531 | DEFLECTOR *m*, ABERTURA *f* DE VENTILACIÓN |
| 13532 | CONTADOR VENTURI *m* |
| 13532 | CONTADOR DE AGUA VENTURI *m* |
| 13532 | TUBO *m* DE INYECTOR |
| 13533 | VERDETE, CARDENILLO *m* |
| 13533 | CARDENILLO, VERDÍN *m* |
| 13533 | ACETATO DE COBRE *m* |
| 13534 | VERIFICACIÓN *f* |
| 13535 | BERMELLÓN *m* |
| 13535 | SULFURO *m* ROJO DE MERCURIO |
| 13536 | NONIO, VERNIER *m* |
| 13537 | PIE *m* |
| 13537 | PIED DE REY *m* |
| 13538 | CALIBRE DE CORREDERA DE PROFUNDIDAD *m* |
| 13539 | CALIBRE DE CORREDERA DE PROFUNDIDAD DE FIJACIÓN MICROMÉTRICA *m* |
| 13540 | MICRÓMETRO *m* CON VERNIER |
| 13541 | ESCALA *f* VERNIER |
| 13542 | FUNCIÓN *f* DE (EN) |
| 13543 | VÉRTICE *m* DE UN POLÍGONO |
| 13544 | CALDERA VERTICAL *f* |
| 13545 | TORNO *m* VERTICAL |
| 13546 | MÁQUINA *f* VERTICAL |
| 13547 | COLLAR PARA EJES VERTICALES *m* |
| 13547 | COJINETE *m* INTERMEDIO DEL ÁRBOL |

| | |
|---|---|
| 13548 | FRESADORA *f* VERTICAL |
| 13549 | CARRERA VERTICAL *f*, DESPLAZAMIENTO VERTICAL *m* |
| 13550 | ÁRBOL VERTICAL *m* |
| 13551 | VERTICAL |
| 13552 | MÁQUINA *f* DE PERFORAR VERTICAL |
| 13553 | VASOS *m pl* COMUNICANTES |
| 13554 | VIBRACIÓN *f* |
| 13555 | AMORTIGUADOR DE VIBRACIONES *m* |
| 13556 | VIBRACIÓN *f* DEBIDA A LOS ESFUERZOS DE FLEXIÓN |
| 13557 | VIBRACIÓN *f* DEBIDA A LOS ESFUERZOS DE TORSIÓN |
| 13558 | OSCILACIÓN *f* DE UN MUELLE |
| 13559 | TREPIDACIONES *f pl*, VIBRACIONES *f pl* |
| 13559 | VIBRACIONES *f pl* |
| 13559 | TREPIDACIONES *f pl* |
| 13560 | VIBRACIONES *f pl* |
| 13561 | TORNILLO *m* DE BANCO |
| 13562 | MORDAZA *f* ARTICULADA, MORDAZA *f* CON CHARNELA |
| 13563 | MORDAZA *f* DE TORNO (DE BANCO) |
| 13564 | MORDAZA *f* |
| 13564 | MORDAZA *f* DE TORNO (DE BANCO) |
| 13564 | MORDAZA *f* |
| 13565 | TENAZAS *f pl* ACHAFLANADAS |
| 13565 | MORDAZA *f* |
| 13566 | DUREZA *f* VICKERS |
| 13567 | VISTA *f* |
| 13568 | PANTALLA *f* DE PROYECCIÓN |
| 13569 | UNIDAD *f* VIOLLE (DE INTENSIDAD LUMÍNICA) |
| 13569 | ESTANDARD *m* VIOLLE |
| 13570 | METAL *m* VIRGEN |
| 13571 | FOCO *m* VIRTUAL IMAGINARIO |
| 13572 | IMAGEN *f* VIRTUAL |
| 13573 | VELOCIDAD *f* VIRTUAL |
| 13574 | VISCOSÍMETRO *m* |
| 13575 | VISCOSO |
| 13576 | VISCOSIDAD *f* |
| 13577 | VISCOSO |
| 13578 | FLUENCIA *f* VISCOSA |
| 13579 | TORNILLO *m* DE BANCO |
| 13580 | SEÑAL *f* ÓPTICA |
| 13581 | ÁNGULO ÓPTICO *m* |
| 13581 | ÁNGULO ÓPTICO *m* |
| 13582 | VÍTREO |
| 13583 | BRILLO *m* VÍTREO |
| 13584 | VITRIFICACIÓN *f* |
| 13585 | LAGUNA *f*, VACUIDAD *f*, HUECO *m*, VACANTE *f* |
| 13586 | PARTE *f* CONSTITUYENTE VOLÁTIL |
| 13587 | VOLATILIZACIÓN *f* |
| 13588 | VOLATILIZAR |
| 13589 | VOLATILIDAD *f* |
| 13590 | TOBA *f* VOLCÁNICA |
| 13591 | VOLTIO *m* |
| 13592 | VOLTIO-AMPERIO *m* |
| 13593 | VOLTAJE *m* |
| 13593 | NÚMERO *m* DE VOLTIOS |
| 13593 | TENSIÓN *f* DE CORRIENTE |
| 13594 | PÉRDIDA *f*, MERMA *f* |
| 13594 | CAÍDA DE POTENCIAL *f* |
| 13594 | CAÍDA DE TENSIÓN *f* |
| 13595 | REGULADOR *m* DE INTENSIDAD |
| 13595 | REGULADOR *m* DE CORRIENTE |
| 13595 | REGULADOR *m* DE TENSIÓN |
| 13596 | PILA *f* DE VOLTA |
| 13596 | PILA *f* VOLTAICA |
| 13597 | VOLTÍMETRO *m* |
| 13598 | VOLUMEN *m* |
| 13598 | VOLUMEN *m*, CUBICACIÓN *f* |
| 13599 | VOLUMEN *m* ENGENDRADO POR EL DESPLAZAMIENTO DEL ÉMBOLO |
| 13600 | REGULADOR *m* DE GASTO |
| 13601 | ANÁLISIS VOLUMÉTRICO *m* |
| 13602 | RENDIMIENTO *m* VOLUMÉTRICO |
| 13603 | DILATACIÓN *f* CÚBICA |
| 13604 | MEDIDOR *m* DE VOLUMEN |
| 13605 | RESORTE *m* CÓNICO DE SECCIÓN RECTANGULAR |
| 13605 | RESORTE *m* CÓNICO DE LÁMINA PLANA |
| 13606 | REMOLINO *m* |
| 13606 | REMOLINO *m* |
| 13607 | VULCANIZACIÓN *f* |
| 13608 | VULCANIZAR |
| 13609 | FIBRA *f* VULCANIZADA |
| 13609 | FIBRA *f* |
| 13610 | CAUCHO VULCANIZADO *m* |
| 13611 | FRACCIÓN *f* ORDINARIA |
| 13612 | GUATA *f* |
| 13613 | PAGO *m* |
| 13613 | PAGA *f* |
| 13613 | SALARIO *m* |
| 13614 | SONDADORA *f* SOBRE CAMIÓN |
| 13615 | DEROGACIÓN *f* |
| 13615 | RENUNCIA, RENUNCIACIÓN *f* |
| 13616 | PASARELA *f* |
| 13617 | HORNACINA *f* |
| 13618 | CONSOLA *f*, MÉNSULA *f* |
| 13618 | ASIENTO CONSOLA *m* |
| 13618 | CONSOLA *f* |
| 13619 | TRANSMISIÓN *f* FIJADA EN UN MURO |
| 13619 | TRANSMISIÓN *f* MURAL |
| 13620 | MÁQUINA *f* DE VAPOR MURAL |

| | | | | |
|---|---|---|---|---|
| 13621 | CONTRAPLACA *f* | 13660 | MARCA *f* INDICADORA DEL NIVEL DE AGUA |
| 13621 | PLACA *f* DE FIJACIÓN | 13661 | CONTADOR DE AGUA *m* |
| 13622 | CONTACTO DE CLAVIJA *m* | 13662 | AGUA *f* DE CONDENSACIÓN |
| 13623 | GRÚA *f* TIPO HORCA | 13663 | AGUA *f* DE CRISTALIZACIÓN |
| 13624 | PARED *f* DE UN AGUJERO | 13664 | PINTURA *f* AL AGUA, ACUARELA *f*, PINTURA *f* A LA AGUADA |
| 13625 | LIMA *f* DE ENTRADA | | |
| 13626 | ORDEN *f* DE FUNCIONAMIENTO | 13665 | TUBO *m* DE CONDUCCIÓN |
| 13627 | URDIMBRE DEL TEJIDO *f* | 13665 | TUBO *m* DE DISTRIBUCIÓN DE AGUA |
| 13628 | ALABEARSE, COMBARSE | 13666 | TUBERÍA *f*, CAÑERÍA *f* |
| 13628 | ABARQUILLARSE, ALABEARSE, COMBARSE | 13666 | DISTRIBUCIÓN *f* DE AGUA |
| 13628 | TORCER, LADEAR, ALABEAR | 13666 | TUBERÍA *f* |
| 13628 | VELARSE | 13667 | PISTÓN *m* DE MOTOR HIDRÁULICO |
| 13628 | DEFORMAR, DEFORMAR(SE), TORCER(SE) | 13667 | PISTÓN *m* DE AGUA |
| 13629 | TORCEDURA *f* | 13668 | FUERZA *f* HIDRÁULICA |
| 13629 | DEFORMACIÓN *f* POR ENROLLAMIENTO | 13669 | PRESIÓN *f* HIDRÁULICA |
| 13629 | DEFORMACIÓN *f* | 13669 | PRESIÓN *f* DE AGUA |
| 13630 | GRIFO *m* DE LAVABO | 13670 | MÁQUINA *f* DE COLUMNA DE AGUA |
| 13631 | ARANDELA *f* | 13671 | INATACABLE POR EL AGUA |
| 13632 | DESLAVADO *m* | 13671 | IMPERMEABLE |
| 13633 | MATRAZ *m* CON TAPÓN DE TUBO LAVADOR | 13672 | TEMPLE *m* AL AGUA |
| 13634 | GAS *m* PERDIDO | 13673 | TEMPLA *m* AL AGUA SEGUIDO DE REVENIDO |
| 13635 | CALOR PERDIDO *m* | 13674 | PRODUCTO *m* HIDRÓFUGO |
| 13636 | ACEITE *m* DE ESCURRIDO | 13675 | JUNTA *f* HIDRÁULICA |
| 13636 | EXCESO *m* DE ACEITE, ACEITE *m* EN EXCESO | 13676 | DEPURACIÓN QUÍMICA DEL AGUA POTABLE, DESENDURECIMIENTO *m* DEL AGUA |
| 13637 | RESÍDUOS *m pl.*, DESECHOS *m pl* | | |
| 13638 | PURIFICACIÓN *f* DE AGUAS RESIDUALES | 13677 | CÁMARA DE AGUA DE UNA CALDERA *f* |
| 13638 | DEPURACIÓN *f* | 13678 | ALIMENTACIÓN DE AGUA *f*, TRAÍDA DE AGUA *f* |
| 13639 | TORNO *m* DE RELOJERO | 13678 | DISTRIBUCIÓN *f* DE AGUA |
| 13640 | AGUA *f* | 13679 | DEPÓSITO *m* DE AGUA |
| 13641 | BAÑO *m* MARÍA | 13680 | DEPÓSITO *m*, TORRE DE AGUA *f* |
| 13642 | SUELO *m* ACUÍFERO | 13681 | TUBO *m* DE AGUA |
| 13643 | CALORÍMETRO DE AGUA *m* | 13682 | CALDERA DE SEGURIDAD *f* |
| 13644 | GRIFO *m* DE AGUA | 13682 | CALDERA ACUOTUBULAR *f* |
| 13645 | PROPORCIÓN *f* DE AGUA | 13682 | CALDERA MULTITUBULAR *f* |
| 13645 | PROPORCIÓN *f* DE AGUA | 13682 | CALDERA DE RÁPIDA VAPORIZACIÓN *f* |
| 13646 | ENFRIAMIENTO *m* EN EL AGUA | 13683 | ENFRIADO CON AGUA |
| 13647 | DECAPADO *m* CON AGUA | 13683 | ENFRIAMIENTO *m* DEL AGUA |
| 13648 | PELÍCULA *f* CONTRA EL AGUA | 13684 | CONDENSADOR POR SUPERFICIE MEDIANTE AGUA *m* |
| 13649 | AGUA *f* INDUSTRIAL | | |
| 13650 | AGUA *f* ASÉPTICA, AGUA ESTERILIZADA | 13685 | HIDRÓFUGO |
| 13650 | AGUA *f* ESTERILIZADA | 13686 | ESTANCO AL AGUA |
| 13651 | GAS *m* AL AGUA | 13687 | REGADERA *f*, REGADORA *f* |
| 13652 | INDICADOR *m* DE NIVEL | 13688 | ESTANCO AL AGUA, IMPERMEABLE AL AGUA |
| 13652 | NIVEL *m* DE AGUA | 13689 | IMPERMEABILIZAR |
| 13653 | GOLPE DE ARIETE *m* | 13690 | TELA *f* IMPERMEABLE |
| 13654 | TEMPLE *m* AL AGUA | 13691 | IMPERMEABILIZACIÓN *f* |
| 13555 | CAMISA DE AGUA *f* | 13692 | RECEPTOR *m* HIDRÁULICO |
| 13656 | CHORRO *m* DE AGUA | 13692 | RUEDA *f* |
| 13657 | INYECTOR *m* HIDRÁULICO | 13693 | INSTALACIÓN *f* DE DISTRIBUCIÓN DE AGUA |
| 13658 | INYECTOR *m* (O SOPLADOR) HIDRÁULICO | 13694 | VATIO *m* |
| 13659 | NIVEL *m* DE AGUA (ALTURA DE UN LÍQUIDO) | 13695 | VATIO-HORA *m* |

| | |
|---|---|
| 13696 | VATIO-MINUTO  m |
| 13697 | VATIO-SEGUNDO  m |
| 13698 | VATÍMETRO  m |
| 13699 | ONDA  f |
| 13700 | LONGITUD  f DE ONDA |
| 13701 | ONDULACIÓN  f |
| 13702 | CERA |
| 13703 | MODELO  m EN CERA, MODELADO |
| 13704 | HILO  m EMBEBIDO DE PEZ |
| 13705 | CORRIENTE DE BAJA INTENSIDAD  f |
| 13706 | SOLUCIÓN  f DÉBIL |
| 13707 | REDUCCIÓN DE LA SECCIÓN  f |
| 13708 | DEBILITAMIENTO DEL MATERIAL  m |
| 13709 | DESGASTE  m |
| 13710 | DESGASTE  m NORMAL |
| 13710 | DESGASTE  m, CONSUMO  m |
| 13711 | CUÑAS DE DESGASTE  f, ESPESOR DE DESGASTE  m |
| 13712 | DESGASTE  m POR ROZAMIENTO |
| 13713 | DESGASTARSE |
| 13714 | PRUEBA  f DE DESGASTE |
| 13715 | ENDURECIMIENTO  m DE DESGASTE |
| 13716 | CHAPA  f DE DESGASTE |
| 13717 | RESISTENCIA  f AL DESGASTE |
| 13718 | ACERO RESISTENTE AL DESGASTE  m |
| 13719 | OVALIZACIÓN  f DE UN COJINETE |
| 13720 | JUNTA  f SECUNDARIA DE HERMETICIDAD |
| 13721 | LADO DEL VIENTO  m, BARLOVENTO  m |
| 13722 | CAUCHO DE SELLADO  m, SELLO DE GOMA  m |
| 13723 | INALTERABLE |
| 13723 | INATACABLE POR LAS INTEMPERIES |
| 13724 | PASADA  f AMPLIA |
| 13725 | MOVIMIENTO  m ALTERNO |
| 13725 | VAIVÉN  m |
| 13726 | ALMA  f |
| 13727 | DEFORMACIÓN  f PERMANENTE DEL ALMA DE UNA VIGA |
| 13728 | PALA  f, PALETA  f |
| 13728 | BRAZO  m DE UN HIERRO EN ÁNGULO |
| 13729 | ALMA DE UNA VIGUETA  f |
| 13730 | ALMA DE UN HIERRO PERFILADO  f |
| 13731 | ESPESOR  m |
| 13731 | CALZO  m, ESPESOR  m |
| 13731 | ESPESOR  m, CALCE  m, CUÑA  f |
| 13731 | CUÑA  f |
| 13732 | RUEDA  f DE FRICCIÓN (CON LLANTA EN FORMA DE CUÑA) |
| 13733 | CUÑA DEL CEPILLO  f |
| 13734 | PRENSA  f DE CUÑA |
| 13735 | SECCIÓN  f CÓNICA |
| 13736 | TRANSMISIÓN  f POR RUEDAS DE LLANTA CUNEIFORME |

| | |
|---|---|
| 13736 | TRANSMISIÓN  f POR RUEDAS DE FRICCIÓN |
| 13737 | CUNEIFORME |
| 13738 | LADRILLO  m CINTRADO (O CIRCULAR) |
| 13739 | CUÑA  f |
| 13739 | CLAVIJA  f, PASADOR  m, CHAVETA  f |
| 13739 | CUÑA  f, CALZO  m |
| 13740 | SUJECIÓN  f, FIJACIÓN  f |
| 13740 | FIJACIÓN POR CLAVIJAS  f |
| 13741 | CORTADOR DE CARDOS Y HELECHOS  m |
| 13742 | ESCARDADORAS  f pl |
| 13743 | TRAMA  f |
| 13744 | PESAR |
| 13745 | PUENTE  m BASCULANTE |
| 13746 | PESADA  f |
| 13746 | PESADA  f, PESAJE  m |
| 13747 | PESO  m |
| 13748 | PESO  m POR METRO |
| 13749 | VÁLVULA  f DE SEGURIDAD DE CONTRAPESO |
| 13750 | RODILLO  m TENSOR LENIX |
| 13751 | PALANCA  f DE CONTRAPESO |
| 13752 | REGULADOR  m DE MASA CENTRAL |
| 13752 | REGULADOR  m PORTER |
| 13753 | ALIVIADERO  m, PRESA  f |
| 13753 | PRESA  f, DIQUE  m, BARRERA  f |
| 13754 | CRESTA  f DE VERTEDERO |
| 13755 | SOLDAR |
| 13756 | CORDÓN DE SOLDADURA  m |
| 13757 | SOLDADURA  f EN PASADAS SUPERPUESTAS |
| 13758 | SOLDAR A LA AUTÓGENA |
| 13759 | CORROSIÓN DE SOLDADURA  f |
| 13760 | DEFECTOS  m pl DE LA SOLDADURA |
| 13761 | METAL  m DEPOSITADO |
| 13762 | RECARGA  f DE UNA SOLDADURA |
| 13763 | METAL  m DE SOLDADURA |
| 13764 | PANTALLA  f PARA SOLDADURA, GAFAS  f pl PARA SOLDAR |
| 13765 | ACERO BATIDO  m |
| 13766 | HIERRO  m SOLDADO |
| 13767 | SOLDADURA  f |
| 13767 | SOLDADURA  f |
| 13767 | JUNTA  f SOLDADA |
| 13768 | CALIDAD  f DE SOLDABLE |
| 13769 | SOLDABLE |
| 13770 | CADENA DE MALLAS SOLDADAS  f |
| 13771 | ANILLO  m SOLDADO |
| 13772 | UNIÓN  f SOLDADA |
| 13773 | ARANDELA  f SOLDADA |
| 13773 | ARANDELA  f SOLDADA |
| 13774 | JUNTA  f SOLDADA |
| 13775 | TUBO  m SOLDADO |
| 13776 | JUNTA  f SOLDADA |

| | |
|---|---|
| 13776 | SOLDADURA *f* |
| 13777 | TUBO *m* SOLDADO |
| 13778 | SOLDADOR *m* |
| 13779 | SOLDADURA *f* |
| 13779 | SOLDADURA *f* |
| 13780 | INTENSIDAD *f* DE LA CORRIENTE PARA SOLDAR |
| 13781 | RACOR *m* PARA SOLDAR |
| 13782 | POSICIÓN *f* DE LA PISTOLA DE SOLDADURA |
| 13783 | CABEZA *f* DE SOLDADURA |
| 13784 | CALDA *f* DE LAVADO |
| 13784 | CALOR BLANCO DE SOLDADURA *m* |
| 13784 | CALOR DE SOLDADURA *m* |
| 13785 | GÁLIBO *m* DE SOLDADURA |
| 13786 | MÁQUINA *f* DE SOLDAR |
| 13787 | PARÁMETROS *m pl* DE SOLDADURA |
| 13788 | DURACIÓN *f* DEL CICLO DE SOLDADURA |
| 13789 | ELECTRODO *m* |
| 13789 | ALAMBRE *m* DE SOLDAR |
| 13790 | SUCESIÓN *m* DE LAS OPERACIONES DE SOLDADURA |
| 13791 | SÍMBOLOS *m pl* DE SOLDADURA |
| 13792 | PRUEBA *f* DE SOLDADURA |
| 13793 | ALAMBRE *m* DE SOLDAR |
| 13794 | BRIDA *f* DE CUELLO SOLDADA |
| 13795 | CONSTRUCCIÓN SOLDADA *f* |
| 13796 | AGUA *f* DE POZO |
| 13797 | MASTIC *m* DE LOS FONTANEROS |
| 13798 | POLIPASTO *m* DIFERENCIAL |
| 13798 | POLIPASTO *m* WESTON |
| 13799 | BOMBA *f* DE AIRE HÚMEDO |
| 13800 | ANÁLISIS POR VÍA HÚMEDA *f* |
| 13801 | COMPRESOR HÚMEDO *m* |
| 13802 | CORROSIÓN HÚMEDA *f* |
| 13803 | PASADA *f* HÚMEDA |
| 13804 | CAMISA HÚMEDA |
| 13805 | VAPOR *m* HÚMEDO |
| 13806 | HUMEDAD *f* DEL VAPOR |
| 13807 | HUMECTACIÓN *f* |
| 13808 | AGENTE HUMECTANTE, AGENTE HUMECTOR *m* |
| 13809 | PUENTE *m* DE WHEATSTONE |
| 13810 | RUEDA *f* |
| 13810 | VOLANTE *m* |
| 13811 | RADIOS *m* DE UNA RUEDA |
| 13812 | CARRETILLA *f*, VOLQUETE *m* |
| 13813 | ESPACIAMIENTO *m* DE LOS EJES |
| 13814 | CENTRO *m* DE RUEDA |
| 13815 | TAPACUBOS *m*, CUBRERRUEDAS *m* |
| 13815 | CAJA DE ENGRANAJES *f* |
| 13816 | TORNO *m* PARA RUEDAS |
| 13817 | TAMBOR *m* |
| 13817 | RUEDECILLA *f* DEL PLANÍMETRO |

| | |
|---|---|
| 13818 | LLANTA *f* DE UNA RUEDA |
| 13819 | DIENTE *m* DE RUEDA DENTADA (DE ENGRANAJE) |
| 13820 | ÁLABE *m* RECEPTOR |
| 13820 | ÁLABE *m* MÓVIL DE UNA TURBINA |
| 13821 | JUEGO *m* DE RUEDAS |
| 13822 | MÁQUINA *f* DE PERFILAR LAS LLANTAS DE RUEDAS |
| 13823 | RUEDA *f* DE UNA TURBINA |
| 13823 | CORONA MÓVIL *f* |
| 13824 | PIEDRA *f* DE AFILAR |
| 13824 | PIEDRA *f* DE AFILAR, PIEDRA *f* AMOLADORA |
| 13824 | PIEDRA *f* DE AMOLAR, PIEDRA *f* AFILADORA |
| 13825 | OSCILACIÓN *f* DE UNA CORREA, BAMBOLEO *m* DE UNA CORREA |
| 13825 | GOLPETEO *m* DE UNA CORREA |
| 13825 | SALTO *m* (O GOLPEO *m*) DE LA CORREA |
| 13826 | TERMÓMETRO *m* AGITADOR |
| 13827 | REMOLINO *m* |
| 13828 | HILO *m* (CRECIMIENTO EN FILAMENTO) |
| 13828 | HILO *m* MONOCRISTALINO *m* |
| 13829 | SILBATO *m* |
| 13830 | FUNDICIÓN *f* BLANCA |
| 13831 | ORO *m* BLANCO |
| 13832 | INCANDESCENCIA *f* |
| 13833 | MADERA *f* DE HOJALATA |
| 13833 | MADERA *f* DE HOJALATA |
| 13833 | MADERA *f* DE HOJALATA |
| 13834 | BLANCO *m* DE PLOMO |
| 13834 | CERUSA *f*, CERUCITA *f*, BLANCO *m* DE PLOMO |
| 13834 | BLANCO *m* DE CERUSA |
| 13834 | CERUSA *f*, ALBAYALDE *m* |
| 13835 | METAL *m* BLANCO DESFLOCULADO |
| 13836 | METAL *m* ANTIFRICCIÓN |
| 13836 | METAL *m* ALEACIÓN BLANCA |
| 13836 | METAL BLANCO *m* |
| 13837 | GUARNICIÓN *f* ANTIFRICCIÓN |
| 13838 | ACEITES *m pl* BLANCOS |
| 13839 | CUERDA SIN ALQUITRÁN *f* |
| 13840 | NEUMÁTICOS *m pl* CON FLANCOS BLANCOS |
| 13841 | BLANCO *m* DE ESPAÑA, BLANCO *m* DE PARÍS |
| 13841 | BLANCO *m* DE ESPAÑA |
| 13841 | BLANCO *m* DE PARÍS, BLANCO *m* DE ESPAÑA |
| 13842 | CARGA NEUTRA *f* |
| 13842 | CRETA *f*, TIZA *f* |
| 13842 | CAOLÍN (PARA LOS NEUMÁTICOS) |
| 13843 | MÁQUINA *f* DE MEDIR WHITWORTH |
| 13844 | PASO *m* INGLÉS |
| 13844 | PASO *m* WHITWORTH |
| 13845 | ALTURA *f* DE DIENTE |
| 13846 | MECHA *f* (DE LÁMPARA O DE ENGRASADOR) |
| 13847 | ENGRASE *m* POR MECHA |

| | |
|---|---|
| 13848 | FRESA *f* CILÍNDRICA |
| 13848 | FRESA *f* RECTILINEA |
| 13849 | VIGUETA *f* DE ALAS ANCHAS |
| 13850 | ANCHURA *f* |
| 13851 | TORNO *m* |
| 13852 | TORNOS *m pl* |
| 13853 | ENROLLAR, BOBINAR |
| 13854 | REBORDE *m* DE ESTANQUEIDAD |
| 13855 | MOLINO *m* DE VIENTO |
| 13855 | MOTOR *m* DE VIENTO |
| 13855 | MOTOR *m* EÓLICO NEUMÁTICO, DE VIENTO |
| 13856 | VIGA *f* TIRANTE |
| 13856 | VIGA *f* DE RIGIDEZ |
| 13857 | CARGA DEL VIENTO *f* |
| 13858 | EMPUJE *m* DEL VIENTO |
| 13858 | PRESIÓN *f* DEL VIENTO |
| 13859 | TURBINA *f* DE AIRE |
| 13860 | VELETA *f* |
| 13861 | RUEDA *f* ATMOSFÉRICA |
| 13862 | DEVANADO *m* |
| 13862 | ENROLLADO *m*, BOBINADO *m* |
| 13863 | TORNO *m* SIMPLE |
| 13864 | VENTANA *f* |
| 13865 | MARCO DE VENTANA *m* |
| 13866 | CRISTAL *m* DE VENTANAS |
| 13867 | MANIVELA *f* ELEVALUNAS |
| 13868 | CORREDERA *f* (DE VENTANA) |
| 13870 | LIMPIACRISTAL *m* |
| 13871 | LIMPIAPARABRISAS *m* |
| 13872 | PARABRISAS *m* |
| 13873 | JUEGO *m* |
| 13874 | ALETA *f* |
| 13875 | PLATAFORMA *f* EN SALEDIZO |
| 13876 | COMPÁS DE CUADRANTE *m* |
| 13877 | EXTRACCIÓN *f* DE LA HULLA |
| 13878 | LEVA *f* |
| 13879 | ANILLO *m* ESCURRIDOR |
| 13880 | ALAMBRE *m* (O HILO *m*) METÁLICO |
| 13881 | COLOCAR UN HILO CONDUCTOR |
| 13882 | ALAMBRE *m* EN VARILLA PARA TREFILADO |
| 13883 | MÁQUINA *f* PARA PLEGAR LOS ALAMBRES |
| 13884 | CEPILLO *m* DE ALAMBRE |
| 13884 | CEPILLO *m* DE ALAMBRE |
| 13885 | MÁQUINA *f* PARA HACER CADENAS DE ALAMBRE DE HIERRO |
| 13886 | TIJERA *f* |
| 13887 | HILERA *f* DE TREFILAR |
| 13888 | ESTIRADO *m* DE ALAMBRE |
| 13888 | TREFILERÍA *f* |
| 13889 | MÁQUINA *f* DE TREFILAR |
| 13890 | PARTÍCULAS *f pl* DE ACERO MUY MENUDAS, MORFIL (GAL) |
| 13891 | FORJADOR *m* DE CLAVOS |
| 13892 | CALIBRE *m* DE TREFILERÍA |
| 13892 | CALIBRE *m* PARA LOS ALAMBRES |
| 13893 | TELA *f* METÁLICA |
| 13893 | TELA *f* METÁLICA |
| 13894 | CRISTAL *m* ARMADO |
| 13894 | CRISTAL *m* ARMADO CON ALAMBRE |
| 13895 | PUNTA *f* DE PARÍS |
| 13896 | ENREJADO *m* METÁLICO |
| 13897 | MÁQUINA *f* PARA HACER REJILLAS |
| 13898 | CARRETE *m* PARA CABLE |
| 13898 | DEVANADERA *f* |
| 13899 | CABLE METÁLICO *m* |
| 13900 | VELOCIDAD *f* DEL HILO |
| 13901 | MÁQUINA *f* DE ENROLLAR LOS MUELLES HELICOIDALES |
| 13902 | TRENZADO *m* METÁLICO |
| 13903 | ENROLLADORA *f*, BOBINADORA *f* |
| 13903 | DESENROLLADORA DE ALAMBRE |
| 13904 | MÁQUINA *f* PARA TRABAJAR LOS ALAMBRES |
| 13905 | TREFILERÍA *f* (FÁBRICA) |
| 13906 | TREFILADO *m* |
| 13907 | TELEGRAFÍA *f* SIN FILOS |
| 13907 | RADIOTELEGRAFÍA *f* |
| 13908 | RADIOTELEFONÍA *f* |
| 13908 | TELEFONÍA *f* SIN FILOS |
| 13909 | COLOCACIÓN *f* DE UN HILO CONDUCTOR |
| 13910 | SUBSTRAER EL CALOR |
| 13911 | CARBONATO *m* NATURAL DE BARITA |
| 13911 | CARBONATO NATURAL DE BARITA *m* |
| 13912 | VOLFRAMIO *m* |
| 13913 | MADERA *f* |
| 13914 | CARBÓN DE MADERA *m* |
| 13915 | REVESTIMIENTO *m* DE MADERA |
| 13916 | POLVO *m* DE MADERA |
| 13917 | SIERRA *f* DE MADERA |
| 13918 | TORNILLO *m* METÁLICO PARA MADERA |
| 13919 | VIRUTAS (DE MADERA) *f pl* |
| 13920 | ALCOHOL METÍLICO, ALCOHOL *m* DE MADERA |
| 13920 | METILENO *m* |
| 13920 | ALCOHOL METÍLICO *m*, METANOL *m* |
| 13920 | HIDRATO *m* DE METILO |
| 13921 | ALQUITRÁN *m* DE MADERA, CREOSOTA *f* |
| 13921 | ALQUITRÁN *m* VEGETAL |
| 13922 | TORNO *m* DE MADERA |
| 13923 | VIRUTAS DE FIBRAS DE MADERA *f pl* |
| 13923 | LANA *f* DE MADERA |
| 13924 | TRABAJO *m* DE LA MADERA |

| | |
|---|---|
| 13925 | MÁQUINA HERRAMIENTA  *f*  PARA TRABAJAR LA MADERA |
| 13925 | MÁQUINA  *f*  PARA LA MADERA |
| 13926 | MALLETE  *m*, MALLETO  *m*, MAZO  *m* |
| 13927 | FORRO DE MADERA  *m* |
| 13927 | REVESTIMIENTO  *m*  DE MADERA |
| 13928 | TUBO  *m*  DE MADERA |
| 13929 | CHAVETA DE MEDIALUNA  *f* |
| 13929 | CLAVIJA SEMIREDONDA  *f*  CLAVIJA DE MEDIALUNA  *f* |
| 13929 | CLAVIJA DE DISCO  *f*, CLAVIJA DE MEDIALUNA  *f* |
| 13930 | FRESAS  *f pl*  DE RANURAR WOODRUFF |
| 13931 | MÁQUINAS  *f pl*  PARA MADERA |
| 13932 | LANA (DE GANADO OVINO)  *f* |
| 13933 | GRASA  *f* |
| 13934 | PALABRA  *f*, VOCABLO  *m* |
| 13935 | FORMATO  *m*  BLOC DE DIRECCIONES |
| 13936 | TRABAJO  *m* |
| 13937 | TRATAR |
| 13937 | TRABAJAR |
| 13937 | MECANIZAR |
| 13937 | LABRAR, LABORAR ESMERADAMENTE |
| 13938 | PONER EN EXPLOTACIÓN UN INVENTO |
| 13938 | EXPLOTAR UN INVENTO |
| 13939 | DISTRIBUCIÓN  *f*  DEL TRABAJO |
| 13940 | TRABAJO  *m*  EFECTUADO |
| 13941 | TRABAJO  *m*  DE COMPRESIÓN |
| 13942 | TRABAJO  *m*  DEL ROZAMIENTO |
| 13943 | TALLER  *m*, LUGAR DE TRABAJO  *m* |
| 13943 | LUGAR  *m*  DE TRABAJO |
| 13944 | TRABAJO  *m*  RESISTENTE |
| 13945 | MORDAZA  *f*  DE BLOQUEO |
| 13946 | APTO PARA MECANIZACIÓN |
| 13946 | FACILIDAD DEL TRABAJO, SUSCEPTIBILIDAD DE PODERSE TRABAJAR |
| 13947 | FÁCIL DE TRABAJAR |
| 13948 | EXPLOTACIÓN  *f*  DE UN INVENTO |
| 13949 | CONDICIONES DE SERVICIO  *f pl*, CONDICIONES DE TRABAJO  *f pl* |
| 13950 | GASTOS  *m*  DE EXPLOTACIÓN |
| 13951 | ALTURA  *f*  DE ACCIÓN |
| 13952 | PROFUNDIDAD  *f*  DE ENGRANAJE |
| 13953 | ÓRGANO  *m*  QUE TRABAJA |
| 13954 | CILINDRO  *m*  MOTOR |
| 13954 | CILINDRO  *m*  DE TRABAJO (MOTOR) |
| 13955 | CALIBRE  *m*  DE LA FABRICACIÓN |
| 13956 | CARGA ADMISIBLE  *f* |
| 13957 | PRESIÓN  *f*  DE SERVICIO |
| 13957 | PRESIÓN  *f*  DE RÉGIMEN |
| 13957 | TENSIÓN  *f*  DE SERVICIO |
| 13958 | TIPO  *m*  DE TRABAJO |
| 13959 | MECANIZACIÓN  *f* |

| | |
|---|---|
| 13959 | TRATAMIENTO  *m* |
| 13959 | TRABAJO  *m* |
| 13960 | OBRERO, TRABAJADOR  *m* |
| 13960 | OBRERO  *m* |
| 13961 | MANO  *f*  DE OBRA |
| 13962 | PERSONAL  *m*  OBRERO, PERSONAL  *m*  LABORAL |
| 13963 | DIRECCIÓN  *f*  DE LAS FÁBRICAS, DE LOS TALLERES, DEL TRABAJO |
| 13964 | JEFE DE FABRICACIÓN  *m*, DE SERVICIO, DE TALLER  *m* |
| 13965 | VÍA  *f*  FÉRREA DE TALLER |
| 13966 | EMPALME  *m*  DE VÍA INDUSTRIAL |
| 13967 | CALIBRE  *m*  DE LA PRODUCCIÓN |
| 13968 | TALLER  *m* |
| 13969 | TORNILLO  *m*  SIN FIN |
| 13970 | TORNILLO  *m*  TRANSPORTADOR |
| 13970 | TORNILLO  *m*  DE ARQUÍMEDES |
| 13970 | TRANSPORTADOR  *m*  DE HÉLICE |
| 13971 | FRESA  *f*  PARA ROSCAR |
| 13972 | FRESA  *f*  PARA HACER ENGRANAJES HELICOIDALES |
| 13973 | POLEA  *f*  DE TORNILLO TANGENTE |
| 13973 | POLEA  *f*  DE TORNILLO SIN FIN |
| 13974 | PAR DE RUEDA Y SINFÍN TANGENCIAL  *m* |
| 13974 | ENGRANAJE  *m*  DE TORNILLO SIN FIN |
| 13974 | MECANISMO  *m*  CON TORNILLO SIN FIN |
| 13975 | RUEDA  *f*  DE TORNILLO SIN FIN |
| 13976 | CARCOMIDO |
| 13977 | MADERA  *f*  CARCOMIDA |
| 13978 | SERPENTÍN  *m*  DE REFRIGERACIÓN |
| 13979 | TORNILLO  *m*  SIN FIN |
| 13980 | COJINETE DESGASTADO |
| 13980 | COJINETE DEFORMADO POR EL DESGASTE  *m* |
| 13981 | ROSCA  *f*  GASTADA |
| 13981 | ROSCA  *f*  GASTADA |
| 13982 | USO, EMPLEO  *m* |
| 13983 | CORREA TEJIDA  *f* |
| 13984 | PAPEL  *m*  DE EMBALAJE |
| 13985 | RIZADO  *m* |
| 13986 | ESPIGA  *f* |
| 13987 | LATÓN  *m*  EN BRUTO, LATÓN  *m*  BRUTO |
| 13988 | HIERRO  *m*  FORJADO |
| 13988 | HIERRO  *m* DULCE |
| 13989 | TUBO  *m*  DE HIERRO |
| 13990 | CLAVO FORJADO  *m* |
| 13991 | MOLIBDATO  *m*  NATURAL DE PLOMO |
| 13991 | MELINOSA  *f*  (GEOL), WULFENITA  *f* |
| 13992 | RED  *f*  WULFF (ESTEREOGRÁFICO) |
| 13992 | ÁBACO  *m* |
| 13993 | EXAMEN  *m*  RADIOGRÁFICO |
| 13994 | APARATO  *m*  RADIOGRÁFICO |

| | |
|---|---|
| 13995 | HAZ *m* DE RAYOS X |
| 13996 | RADIOCRISTALOGRAFÍA *f* |
| 13997 | DIAGRAMA *m* DE DIFRACCIÓN DE LOS RAYOS X |
| 13998 | CONTROL RADIOGRÁFICO *m* |
| 13999 | ANÁLISIS FLUORESCENTE *m* |
| 14000 | ESPECTRÓMETRO *m* DE RAYOS X |
| 14001 | ESPECTRO *m* DE LOS RAYOS X |
| 14002 | TUBO *m* DE RAYOS X |
| 14003 | RAYOS *m* X |
| 14004 | XENÓN *m* |
| 14005 | XEROGRAFÍA *f* |
| 14006 | XILOL |
| 14006 | XILENO *m* |
| 14007 | YARDA *f* |
| 14008 | LATÓN *m* |
| 14009 | FÓSFORO *m* BLANCO |
| 14010 | RENDIMIENTO *m* |
| 14011 | LÍMITE *m* ELÁSTICO |
| 14011 | LÍMITE *m* TARDÍO |
| 14011 | LÍMITE *m* DE PASO |
| 14012 | LÍMITE *m* ELÁSTICO |
| 14012 | LÍMITE *m* DE CORRIENTE |
| 14013 | LÍMITE *m* ELÁSTICO |
| 14014 | ARCADA *f*, BUCLE *m*, RIZO *m* |
| 14015 | TAPA DE ARCO *f* |
| 14016 | CASQUILLO *m* DE SOPORTE |
| 14017 | CULATA *f* DE UN IMÁN |
| 14018 | TUERCA *f* DE YUGO (O DE CABALLETE) |
| 14019 | ITERBIO *m* |
| 14020 | ITRIO *m* |
| 14021 | ZAMAK *m* |
| 14022 | BARNIZ *m* ZAPÓN |
| 14023 | HIERRO *m* EN Z |
| 14024 | DESVIACIÓN *f* (DESVÍO *m*) NULA |
| 14025 | LÍNEA *f* CERO |
| 14026 | DESPLAZAMIENTO *m* DEL PUNTO DE ORIGEN (DEL PUNTO CERO) |
| 14027 | PUNTO *m* CERO |
| 14027 | CERO *m* (DE UNA ESCALA) |
| 14028 | POSICIÓN *f* DE CERO |
| 14029 | LÍNEA *f* DE PRESIÓN NULA (DEL DIAGRAMA) |
| 14030 | PONER EN CERO |
| 14031 | DESPLAZAMIENTO *m* DEL PUNTO DE ORIGEN (DEL PUNTO CERO) |
| 14032 | PONER EN CERO |
| 14033 | SUPRESIÓN *f* DE LOS CEROS |
| 14034 | REMACHE *m* AL TRESBOLILLO |
| 14035 | CINC *m* |
| 14036 | ACETATO DE CINC *m* |
| 14037 | CARBONATO DE CINC *m* |
| 14038 | CLORURO DE CINC *m* |
| 14039 | CROMATO DE CINC *m* |
| 14039 | AMARILLO *m* DE CINC |
| 14040 | RECORTES *m pl* DE CINC |
| 14041 | CIANURO *m* DE CINC |
| 14042 | MINERAL *m* DE CINC |
| 14043 | BLANCO *m* DE CINC, ÓXIDO *m* DE CINC |
| 14043 | BLANCO *m* DE CINC |
| 14043 | ÓXIDO *m* DE CINC |
| 14044 | GALVANIZACIÓN *f* CON CINC |
| 14044 | GALVANIZACIÓN *f* |
| 14045 | METALIZACIÓN *f* AL CINC |
| 14046 | VITRIOLO *m* BLANCO |
| 14046 | SULFATO *m* DE CINC |
| 14046 | CAPARROSA BLANCA *f*, CAPARROSA DE CINC *f* |
| 14047 | TUBO *m* DE CINC |
| 14048 | ALAMBRE *m* (O HILO *m*) DE CINC |
| 14049 | ZIRCONIO *m* |
| 14050 | FUSIÓN *f* POR ZONA |
| 14051 | SEGMENTO *m* ESFÉRICO DE DOS BASES |
| 14051 | ZONA *f* ESFÉRICA |

# SEGUNDA PARTE

## ÍNDICE FRANCÊS
## ÍNDICE ALEMÃO
## ÍNDICE ESPANHOL

## ACC

A CONTREFIL 138
A-COUP 11359
A-H 481
ABACA 7980
ABAISSEMENT DE CONCENTRATION 3767
ABAISSEMENT DE LA TEMPERATURE 5022
ABAISSER UN FARDEAU 7793
ABAISSER UNE PERPENDICULAIRE 4216
ABAISSER UNE VERTICALE 4216
ABAQUE 13992
ABAQUE 8617
ABAQUE 2273
ABAQUE 3834
ABATTEURS POUR MOISSONNAGE 13869
ABATTRE UN ANGLE 2230
ABERRATION 4077
ABERRATION 5
ABERRATION CHROMATIQUE 2369
ABERRATION DE REFRANGIBILITE 2369
ABERRATION DE SPHERICITE 11885
ABIMER UN FILET 12379
ABOUCHER DES TUYAUX 5277
ABRASIF 6123
ABRASIF 17
ABRASIF 9601
ABRASIF DOUX 8269
ABRASIF NATUREL 8499
ABRASION 6106
ABRASION 13
ABRI DE LA POUSSIERE (A L') 4393
ABSCISSE 27
ABSORBABLE 38
ABSORBANT 39
ABSORBER 37
ABSORBEUR 40
ABSORPTIOMETRE 43
ABSORPTION 44
ABSORPTION D'EAU 52
ABSORPTION DE CHALEUR 51
ABSORPTIVITE 56
ACCELERATEUR 66
ACCELERATION 62
ACCELERATION ANGULAIRE 537
ACCELERATION AUTOMATIQUE 836
ACCELERATION CENTRIFUGE 10127
ACCELERATION CENTRIPETE 2189
ACCELERATION DE LA PESANTEUR 65
ACCELERATION DE LA PESANTEUR 64
ACCELERATION DE VITESSE D'UN CORPS TOMBANT 63
ACCELERATION DU PISTON 9371
ACCELERATION LINEAIRE 7611

ACCELERATION NEGATIVE 8525
ACCELERATION NON UNIFORME 13507
ACCELERATION NORMALE 8653
ACCELERATION POSITIVE 9652
ACCELERATION TANGENTIELLE 12620
ACCELERATION UNIFORME 13361
ACCELERER 6851
ACCES DIRECT 10198
ACCESSIBILITE 72
ACCESSIBLE 73
ACCESSOIRE 812
ACCESSOIRES 74
ACCESSOIRES 5283
ACCESSOIRES DE CHAUDIERES 1411
ACCIDENT DU TRAVAIL 75
ACCORD DU BREVET 6049
ACCOSTAGE DE TOLES 8046
ACCOSTER 8042
ACCOSTER DES TOLES (MONTAGE) 8045
ACCOUPLEMENT 3254
ACCOUPLEMENT 10221
ACCOUPLEMENT A DEBRAYAGE 4033
ACCOUPLEMENT A DENTS 2461
ACCOUPLEMENT A FRICTION 5672
ACCOUPLEMENT A GRIFFES 2461
ACCOUPLEMENT A MANCHON 1510
ACCOUPLEMENT A PLATEAUX BOULONNES 5338
ACCOUPLEMENT AUTOMATIQUE 11149
ACCOUPLEMENT D'ARBRES 11240
ACCOUPLEMENT DEBRAYAGE 4032
ACCOUPLEMENT ELASTIQUE 4476
ACCOUPLEMENT FIXE 5037
ACCOUPLEMENT FLEXIBLE 5417
ACCOUPLEMENT HYDRAULIQUE 6681
ACCOUPLEMENT PAR CONE 2928
ACCOUPLEMENT PAR MANCHON A PLATEAU 5338
ACCOUPLEMENT RIGIDE 5037
ACCOUPLER 3253
ACCROCHAGE 12918
ACCROCHER 12914
ACCROISSEMENT DE LA FRAGILITE 4685
ACCROISSEMENT DE VITESSE 6849
ACCUMULATEUR 76
ACCUMULATEUR A GRILLAGE 6097
ACCUMULATEUR AU PLOMB 7455
ACCUMULATEUR DE VAPEUR 12156
ACCUMULATEUR ELECTRIQUE 4534
ACCUMULATEUR HYDRAULIQUE 6677
ACCUMULATEUR THERMIQUE DE CHALEUR 6336
ACCUMULATION 1705
ACCUMULATION/EMMAGASINAGE D'ENERGIE 12290

**ACC** 566

ACCUMULATION/EMMAGASINAGE DE CHALEUR 12291
ACCUMULER LA CHALEUR 12296
ACETATE 91
ACETATE 85
ACETATE D'ALUMINIUM 417
ACETATE D'AMMONIUM 458
ACETATE D'AMYLE 487
ACETATE D'ETHYLE 88
ACETATE DE BARYUM 993
ACETATE DE CELLULOSE 2132
ACETATE DE CUIVRE 13533
ACETATE DE FER 7134
ACETATE DE PLOMB 7450
ACETATE DE POTASSE 9673
ACETATE DE SODIUM 11715
ACETATE DE SOUDE 11715
ACETATE DE ZINC 14036
ACETATE FERREUX 5120
ACETATE FERRIQUE 5099
ACETONE 90
ACETYLE DE CELLULOSE 91
ACETYLENE 93
ACETYLURE DE CALCIUM 1848
ACHEVEMENT 11682
ACHROMATIQUE 98
ACHROMATISATION 99
ACHROMATISER 100
ACHROMATISME 101
ACICULAIRE 102
ACIDE 727
ACIDE 129
ACIDE 12450
ACIDE ACETIQUE 86
ACIDE ACETIQUE CRISTALLISABLE 5952
ACIDE ALDEHYDIQUE 84
ACIDE ARSENIQUE 722
ACIDE AZOTEUX 8596
ACIDE AZOTIQUE 8580
ACIDE AZOTIQUE ANHYDRE 8590
ACIDE BENZOIQUE 1202
ACIDE BENZOSULFONIQUE 1200
ACIDE BORIQUE 1467
ACIDE BROMHYDRIQUE 6704
ACIDE BROMIQUE 1647
ACIDE BUTYRIQUE 1817
ACIDE CARBAZOTIQUE 9291
ACIDE CARBOLIQUE 1938
ACIDE CARBONIQUE 1949
ACIDE CARBONIQUE LIQUIDE 7645
ACIDE CHLORHYDRIQUE 6706
ACIDE CHROMIQUE 2379

ACIDE CITRIQUE 2441
ACIDE CYANHYDRIQUE 6707
ACIDE CYANIQUE 3545
ACIDE CYANURIQUE 3552
ACIDE DE NORDHAUSEN 5733
ACIDE DE SAXE 5733
ACIDE DES CHAMBRES 2228
ACIDE DIGALLIQUE 5780
ACIDE FLUORHYDRIQUE 6711
ACIDE FLUOSILICIQUE 11441
ACIDE FORMIQUE 5578
ACIDE FULMINIQUE 5731
ACIDE GALLIQUE 5777
ACIDE GRAS 5055
ACIDE HUMIQUE 6665
ACIDE HYDROCHLORIQUE 6706
ACIDE HYPOCHLOREUX 6742
ACIDE HYPOSULFUREUX 12853
ACIDE LACTIQUE 7355
ACIDE METAPHOSPHORIQUE 8210
ACIDE METASILICIQUE 8211
ACIDE MINERAL 8302
ACIDE MOLYBDIQUE 8369
ACIDE MURIATIQUE 6706
ACIDE NITRIQUE 8580
ACIDE OLEIQUE 8795
ACIDE ORGANIQUE 8864
ACIDE ORTHOPHOSPHORIQUE 8873
ACIDE ORTHOSILICIQUE 8875
ACIDE OXALIQUE 8969
ACIDE PALMITIQUE 9028
ACIDE PHENIQUE 1938
ACIDE PHENYLSULFUREUX 1200
ACIDE PICRIQUE 9291
ACIDE PRUSSIQUE 6707
ACIDE PYROGALLIQUE 10045
ACIDE PYROLIGNEUX 10046
ACIDE PYROPHOSPHORIQUE 10054
ACIDE ROSOLIQUE 10750
ACIDE SALICYLIQUE 10899
ACIDE SILICIQUE 11436
ACIDE STANNIQUE 12097
ACIDE STEARIQUE 12194
ACIDE SULFHYDRIQUE 6717
ACIDE SULFUREUX 104
ACIDE SULFURIQUE 12453
ACIDE SULFURIQUE COMMERCIAL 8856
ACIDE SULFURIQUE CONCENTRE 2884
ACIDE SULFURIQUE FUMANT 5733
ACIDE TANNIQUE 5780
ACIDE TARTARIQUE 12690

ACIDE TARTRIQUE DEXTROGYRE 3826
ACIDE TARTRIQUE LEVOGYRE 7364
ACIDE THIOSULFURIQUE 12853
ACIDE TUNGSTIQUE 8876
ACIDE VITRIOLIQUE 12453
ACIDES 132
ACIDIFIANT 130
ACIDIMETRE 89
ACIDIMETRIE 131
ACIDULER 133
ACIER 11490
ACIER 12223
ACIER 12196
ACIER 4156
ACIER A BAS CARBONE 8270
ACIER A CHARRUE 9528
ACIER A FAIBLE TENEUR EN CARBONE 7770
ACIER A GROS GRAIN 2577
ACIER A OUTILS 13009
ACIER A OUTILS 7857
ACIER A RESSORT 11992
ACIER A RIVETS 10627
ACIER A STRUCTURE ACICULAIRE 8523
ACIER ALLIE 368
ACIER ANORMAL 8
ACIER AU C. 9427
ACIER AU CARBONE 11473
ACIER AU CARBONE 1954
ACIER AU CHROME-TUNGSTENE 2378
ACIER AU COBALT 2612
ACIER AU COBALT-CHROME 2613
ACIER AU CUIVRE 3130
ACIER AU FOUR ELECTRIQUE 4532
ACIER AU MANGANESE 7968
ACIER AU MOLYBDENE 8368
ACIER AU NICKEL 8570
ACIER AU NICKEL-CHROME 2386
ACIER AU SILICIUM 11447
ACIER AU SILICIUM 11449
ACIER AU TITANE 12972
ACIER AU TUNGSTENE 13265
ACIER AU VANADIUM 13476
ACIER AUSTENITIQUE 826
ACIER AUTO-TREMPANT 298
ACIER AUTO-TREMPANT 11154
ACIER AUTOTREMPANT 8000
ACIER BATTU 6222
ACIER BESSEMER 107
ACIER BESSEMER 1215
ACIER BRULE 1763
ACIER BRUT 3414

ACIER CALME 7294
ACIER CALME A L'ALUMINIUM 442
ACIER CALME AU MANGANESE 7969
ACIER CALME ET TREMPE 10093
ACIER CEMENTE 2138
ACIER CHROME 2389
ACIER CHROME-NICKEL 2376
ACIER COMPRIME 2849
ACIER COULE 12202
ACIER DE CARBURATION 2138
ACIER DE CEMENTATION 2138
ACIER DE CONSTRUCTION 12392
ACIER DE DECOLLETAGE RAPIDE 5639
ACIER DE NITRURATION 8585
ACIER DE QUALITE SUPERIEURE 6486
ACIER DEMI-DOUX 1959
ACIER DOUX 1958
ACIER DOUX 7770
ACIER DOUX 11744
ACIER DOUX 8270
ACIER DUR 6280
ACIER DUR A HAUTE TENEUR EN CARBONE 1957
ACIER ECROUI 2697
ACIER EFFERVESCENT 10599
ACIER EFFERVESCENT 10598
ACIER EFFERVESCENT 4462
ACIER ELABORE AU FOUR ELECTRIQUE 4511
ACIER ELECTRIQUE 4511
ACIER ELECTRIQUE ACIDE 113
ACIER EN BARRES 984
ACIER ETIRE 4251
ACIER EXTRA-DOUX 12224
ACIER FAIBLEMENT ALLIE 382
ACIER FIN 12462
ACIER FONDU 6924
ACIER FONDU AU CREUSET 2057
ACIER FORGE 5554
ACIER FRETTE 10598
ACIER INOXYDABLE 12051
ACIER INOXYDABLE 8644
ACIER MANGANO-SILICEUX 11450
ACIER MARTIN 1048
ACIER MARTIN 8816
ACIER MARTIN PAR LE PROCEDE ACIDE 116
ACIER MARTIN PAR LE PROCEDE BASIQUE 1047
ACIER MOULE 12202
ACIER MOULE 2055
ACIER MOUSSEUX 10599
ACIER NICKELE 8573
ACIER NON CALME 4462
ACIER NON MAGNETIQUE 8638

**ACI** 568

ACIER PARTIELLEMENT DESOXYDE **10599**
ACIER PERLITIQUE **9145**
ACIER PLAQUE **2446**
ACIER PLATINITE **9508**
ACIER POUR AIMANTS **7892**
ACIER POUR ENGRENAGES **5904**
ACIER POUR PLATE-FORME DE FORAGE EN MER **8739**
ACIER PROFILE **11125**
ACIER PUDDLE **9963**
ACIER RAPIDE **6474**
ACIER RAPIDE **6497**
ACIER RAPIDE A OUTILS **10207**
ACIER RESISTANT A L'USURE **13718**
ACIER SANS SOUFFLURES **12209**
ACIER SEMI-CALME **8825**
ACIER SEMI-CALME **11173**
ACIER SIEMENS- MARTIN **8023**
ACIER SOUDE **13765**
ACIER SPECIAL **11848**
ACIER SUPERIEUR **6486**
ACIER SUR SOLE BASIQUE **1048**
ACIER SURCHAUFFE **8945**
ACIER THOMAS **1044**
ACIER THOMAS **12855**
ACIER TREMPE **6289**
ACIER TREMPE ET REVENU **10093**
ACIERAGE **12206**
ACIERAGE **135**
ACIERAGE **2142**
ACIERATION **2142**
ACIERER **12205**
ACIERER (MET.) **2134**
ACIERIE **12222**
ACIERIE **12211**
ACIERS DE TARIERES POUR FORAGES **4270**
ACIERS LAMINES PLATS **5392**
ACIERS RESISTANT A LA CORROSION ET A LA CHALEUR **3184**
ACOUSTIQUE **137**
ACOUSTIQUE **136**
ACTINIQUE **139**
ACTINIUM **141**
ACTINOMETRE **142**
ACTION D'OMBRER **11237**
ACTION D'UNE FORCE **143**
ACTION D'UNE FORCE EXTERIEURE **12331**
ACTION DE CROQUER **11533**
ACTION DE PARER **13209**
ACTION DE RETENDRE UNE COURROIE **12605**
ACTION DIRECTE (A) **3980**
ACTION DU FREIN **1550**

ACTION EN NULLITE RELATIVE A UN BREVET **8707**
ACTION EN PROFONDEUR **12899**
ACTION GYROSCOPIQUE **6192**
ACTION INDIRECTE (A) **6883**
ACTIONNER **4289**
ACTIONS ATMOSPHERIQUES **792**
ACTIVATEUR **146**
ACTIVATION **144**
ACUTANGLE **154**
ADAPTATEUR DE BRIDE **5325**
ADAPTEUR **160**
ADAPTEUR POUR ECHANGE RAPIDE **10108**
ADDITIF **168**
ADDITION **394**
ADDITION **169**
ADDITION DE CARBONE **145**
ADDITION EN POCHE **7357**
ADDITIONNER (MATH.) **162**
ADDITIONNER DE L'EAU **163**
ADENT **3761**
ADHERENCE **174**
ADHERENCE **173**
ADHERENT **175**
ADHESIF **175**
ADHESION **174**
ADIABATIQUE **178**
ADIABATIQUE **179**
ADJACENT **181**
ADJUVANT **169**
ADJUVANT DE FILTRATION **5174**
ADMISSION **6943**
ADMISSION D'AIR **12486**
ADOUCIR **12717**
ADOUCISSEMENT **11749**
ADRESSE **171**
ADSORBER **202**
ADSORPTION **203**
ADULTERATION **205**
ADULTERER **204**
AERAGE **13530**
AERATEUR **211**
AERATION **13530**
AERATION DE L'EAU **210**
AERER UN SABLE **208**
AERO-MOTEUR **2843**
AERODYNAMIQUE **215**
AERODYNAMIQUE **214**
AEROSTATIQUE **218**
AEROSTATIQUE **217**
AFFAIBLISSEMENT DE LA SECTION **13707**
AFFAIBLISSEMENT DU MATERIEL **13708**

569     **AIR**

AFFAIRE **7229**
AFFAISSEMENT **10613**
AFFAISSEMENT **12418**
AFFICHAGE **10253**
AFFILAGE **6793**
AFFILER **6790**
AFFINAGE **10377**
AFFINAGE AU FEU **5245**
AFFINAGE AU VENT **300**
AFFINAGE ELECTROLYTIQUE **4558**
AFFINEMENT DU GRAIN **6037**
AFFINER **10370**
AFFINER UN METAL **10371**
AFFINITE CHIMIQUE **2292**
AFFLEURE **5482**
AFFLEURER **7951**
AFFOLEMENT DE LA SOUPAPE **2277**
AFFOUILLEMENT **4889**
AFFUT **6175**
AFFUT DE CAMPAGNE **5142**
AFFUT DE MORTIER **8397**
AFFUTAGE **11275**
AFFUTAGE DE PRECISION **9755**
AFFUTER **11273**
AFFUTEUR **6105**
AFFUTEUSE **13002**
AFFUTEUSE **11274**
AFFUTEUSE UNIVERSELLE **13384**
AGATE **222**
AGENT ANTI-PIQURE **616**
AGENT ANTIPUTREFIANT **629**
AGENT D'IMPREGNATION **6804**
AGENT DE BREVETS D'INVENTION **9114**
AGENT DE BRILLANTAGE **1615**
AGENT DE CEMENTATION **2139**
AGENT DE CHELATION **2289**
AGENT DE CONSERVATION **9791**
AGENT DE DISPERSION **4050**
AGENT DE REFRIGERATION **3086**
AGENT DE TRAITEMENT DE SURFACE **12523**
AGENT FRIGORIFIQUE **3086**
AGENT MOTEUR **8408**
AGENT MOUILLANT **13808**
AGENT PRECIPITANT **11130**
AGENT REDUCTEUR **10346**
AGENTS ATMOSPHERIQUES **793**
AGGLOMERANT **1253**
AGGLOMERATION **7990**
AGGLOMERE **6088**
AGGLOMERE **2791**
AGGLOMERE **1623**

AGGLOMERE DE HOUILLE **2560**
AGGLOMERE DE LIGNITE **1666**
AGGLOMERE DE TOURBE **9149**
AGGLOMERE MAGNESIEN **7881**
AGGLUTINANT **1445**
AGITATEUR **12260**
AGITATEUR **236**
AGITATEUR MECANIQUE **238**
AGITATION DU BAIN **11254**
AGITER **8328**
AGRAFE DE JONCTION POUR CABLES **11706**
AGRAFE POUR COURROIES **1146**
AGRANDISSEMENT **7935**
AGRANDISSEMENT D'UN DESSIN **4769**
AGREGAT **227**
AGREGATION **229**
AIDE **8048**
AIGREUR DU FER **2704**
AIGUILLAGE **12556**
AIGUILLE (DE MANOMETRE) **6226**
AIGUILLE AIMANTEE **7909**
AIGUILLE D'INJECTEUR **8684**
AIGUILLE INDICATRICE **6868**
AIGUILLES POUR ROULEMENTS **1108**
AIGUISAGE **11275**
AIGUISER **11273**
AIGUISEUR **6105**
AILE **13728**
AILE **13874**
AILE **5095**
AILE (D'UN FER A T) **5330**
AILE D'UNE HELICE **9928**
AILERON **5183**
AILETTE **5183**
AILETTE DE LA SOUPAPE **5060**
AILETTES DE REFROIDISSEMENT **13477**
AIMANT **7891**
AIMANT A LAMES SUPERPOSEES **7377**
AIMANT ARTIFICIEL **735**
AIMANT EN FORME DE BARREAU **985**
AIMANT EN U **6606**
AIMANT NATUREL **8506**
AIMANT PERMANENT **9204**
AIMANTATION **7928**
AIMANTATION **7923**
AIMANTATION REMANENTE **10445**
AIMANTATION RESIDUELLE **10445**
AIMANTER **7924**
AIMANTER (S') **1126**
AIR AMBIANT **450**
AIR ATMOSPHERIQUE **240**

**AIR** 570

AIR COMBURANT 277
AIR COMPRIME 2839
AIR DE LA SOUFFLERIE 243
AIR HUMIDE 3599
AIR LIQUIDE 7643
AIR PARASITE 4771
AIR RAREFIE 10213
AIR SEC 4339
AIRE 697
AIRE DE L'OUVERTURE MASQUEE PAR LA SOUPAPE 11121
AIRE DE LA SECTION 11120
AIRE DE LA SECTION TRANSVERSALE 12511
AIRE DU CERCLE 695
AJOUTER 162
AJUSTABLE 183
AJUSTAGE 10847
AJUSTAGE 11600
AJUSTAGE 10025
AJUSTAGE 5275
AJUSTAGE 5280
AJUSTAGE 4307
AJUSTAGE A LA PRESSE 5527
AJUSTAGE CONIQUE 8679
AJUSTER 5276
AJUSTEUR 5278
AJUSTEUR-MECANICIEN 5278
AJUTAGE CONVERGENT 3066
AJUTAGE CONVERGENT 2769
AJUTAGE CYLINDRIQUE 3576
AJUTAGE D'ECOULEMENT 196
AJUTAGE DIVERGENT 3738
AJUTAGE DIVERGENT 4096
ALAMBIC 12259
ALBATRE 304
ALBEDO 308
ALBUMINE 310
ALBUMINE DU SERUM 11207
ALCALI 328
ALCALI VOLATIL 660
ALCALIMETRE 331
ALCALIMETRIE 333
ALCALIMETRIQUE 332
ALCALINISER 330
ALCALINITE 340
ALCALOIDE 341
ALCOOL ABSOLU 28
ALCOOL AMYLIQUE 488
ALCOOL ANHYDRE 28
ALCOOL AQUEUX 659
ALCOOL CARBURE 1983
ALCOOL DENATURE 8224

ALCOOL ETHYLIQUE 313
ALCOOL METHYLIQUE 13920
ALCOOL ORDINAIRE 313
ALCOOL RECTIFIE 10313
ALCOOL VINIQUE 313
ALCOOLIQUE 314
ALCOOMETRE 316
ALDEHYDE 317
ALDEHYDE ACETIQUE 84
ALDEHYDE BENZYLIQUE 1198
ALDEHYDE ETHYLIQUE 84
ALDEHYDE FORMIQUE 5573
ALDEHYDE METHYLIQUE 5573
ALESAGE 3855
ALESAGE 1461
ALESAGE 1468
ALESAGE AU TOUR 1473
ALESAGE D'UNE POULIE 4978
ALESAGE D'UNE ROUE 4978
ALESAGE DE CYLINDRE 1461
ALESAGE DES TROUS DE RIVET 1638
ALESAGE DU CYLINDRE 3565
ALESER 1462
ALESER AU TOUR 1466
ALESER LES TROUS DE RIVET 1635
ALESEUSE 4279
ALESEUSE 1471
ALESEUSE DE PRECISION 5196
ALESOIR 10263
ALESOIR 1636
ALESOIR A CANNELURES 5485
ALESOIR A FINES RAINURES 5197
ALESOIR A LAMES MOBILES 188
ALESOIR A MAIN 6247
ALESOIR A MAIN CONIQUE 12650
ALESOIR A MAIN EXPANSIBLE 4917
ALESOIR A MAIN REGLABLE 184
ALESOIR A MISE DE CARBURE 1935
ALESOIR A RAINURES 5485
ALESOIR A RAINURES DROITES 12305
ALESOIR A RAINURES HELICOIDALES 11915
ALESOIR A RAINURES TORSES 11915
ALESOIR CONIQUE 12658
ALESOIR DE MACHINE 7853
ALESOIR EBAUCHEUR CONIQUE 10790
ALESOIR EN BOUT 10747
ALESOIR EXPANSIBLE 4923
ALESOIR EXTENSIBLE 188
ALESOIR FINISSEUR CONIQUE 5226
ALESOIR/FRAISE CREUX 11336
ALESURES 11277

571           **ALL**

ALFAMETRE **319**
ALGEBRE **320**
ALGEBRIQUE **321**
ALIGNEMENT **325**
ALIGNEMENT **324**
ALIGNER **323**
ALIMENTATEUR AUTOMATIQUE **5072**
ALIMENTATION **5063**
ALIMENTATION **5082**
ALIMENTATION **2263**
ALIMENTATION **7940**
ALIMENTATION ARRIVEE **6844**
ALIMENTATION D'UN FOYER **5262**
ALIMENTATION DOUBLE **4138**
ALIMENTATION EN EAU **13678**
ALIMENTER **5064**
ALIMENTER UN FOYER **12269**
ALIZARINE **327**
ALLIAGE **360**
ALLIAGE **619**
ALLIAGE A BASE D'ALUMINIUM **439**
ALLIAGE A BASE D'ALUMINIUM **418**
ALLIAGE A BASE DE CUIVRE **3111**
ALLIAGE A BASE DE MAGNESIUM **7890**
ALLIAGE A BASE DE NICKEL **8557**
ALLIAGE A BASE DE PLOMB **7451**
ALLIAGE A HAUTE DENSITE **6481**
ALLIAGE ANTI-FRICTION **385**
ALLIAGE AU BORE **1478**
ALLIAGE AU PLOMB **7453**
ALLIAGE BINAIRE **4378**
ALLIAGE BINAIRE **1247**
ALLIAGE BLANC **13836**
ALLIAGE CUIVRE-ZINC **5943**
ALLIAGE CUIVRE-ZING **9861**
ALLIAGE D'ALUMINIUM FORGEABLE **433**
ALLIAGE D'ALUMINIUM POUR MOULAGE **435**
ALLIAGE D'ALUMINIUM-BERYLLIUM **440**
ALLIAGE D'ALUMUNIUM FORGEABLE **437**
ALLIAGE D'APPORT **5159**
ALLIAGE D'AUER **817**
ALLIAGE DE BRASAGE **386**
ALLIAGE DE FER **7156**
ALLIAGE DE RECHARGEMENT DUR **6284**
ALLIAGE DE TRAITEMENT **6383**
ALLIAGE DEGAZEUR **3709**
ALLIAGE DUPLEX **4378**
ALLIAGE DUR AUX CARBURES FRITTES **11510**
ALLIAGE FUSIBLE **5757**
ALLIAGE FUSIBLE **389**
ALLIAGE FUSIBLE POUR SOUDER OU BRASER **11755**

ALLIAGE HAUTE-TEMPERATURE **12459**
ALLIAGE INOXYDABLE **387**
ALLIAGE LEGER **7564**
ALLIAGE MAGNETIQUE **392**
ALLIAGE MAGNETIQUE 'ALNICO' **398**
ALLIAGE NATUREL **8498**
ALLIAGE NON REFRACTAIRE **8622**
ALLIAGE NON-FERREUX **8619**
ALLIAGE OSTEOPLASTIQUE **498**
ALLIAGE POUR COULEE SOUS PRESSION **388**
ALLIAGE POUR COUSSINET **1106**
ALLIAGE POUR COUSSINETS **385**
ALLIAGE PYROPHORIQUE **10053**
ALLIAGE QUATERNAIRE **10084**
ALLIAGE QUATERNAIRE EUTECTIQUE **10085**
ALLIAGE REFRACTAIRE **393**
ALLIAGE RESISTANT A L'USURE **383**
ALLIAGE RESISTANT A LA CHALEUR **391**
ALLIAGE RESISTANT A LA CHALEUR ET A LA CORROSION
   **390**
ALLIAGE RESISTANT A LA CORROSION **387**
ALLIAGE RESISTANT AUX ACIDES **384**
ALLIAGES FUSIBLES **7773**
ALLIAGES POUR RESISTANCES ELECTRIQUES **10486**
ALLIAGES RESISTANT AUX ACIDES **125**
ALLIAGES RESISTANTS A L'ABRASION ET A LA CORROSION
   **396**
ALLIER **361**
ALLOMERIE **350**
ALLOMERIQUE **349**
ALLOMORPHE **352**
ALLOMORPHIE **351**
ALLONGEMENT **4679**
ALLONGEMENT **4680**
ALLONGEMENT D'UN CABLE **12374**
ALLONGEMENT D'UNE COURROIE **12374**
ALLONGEMENT DES CRISTAUX **3426**
ALLONGEMENT LONGITUDINAL **7612**
ALLONGEMENT PROPORTIONNEL A LA LIMITE D'ELASTICITE
   **13329**
ALLONGEMENT RELATIF **13370**
ALLONGER (S') **1125**
ALLOTRIOMORPHE **354**
ALLOTROPIE **357**
ALLOTROPIQUE **356**
ALLUMAGE **6760**
ALLUMAGE (DANS LES MOTEURS A EXPLOSION) **6770**
ALLUMAGE A FLAMME **5316**
ALLUMAGE AUTOMATIQUE **844**
ALLUMAGE DU FOYER D'UNE CHAUDIERE **5263**
ALLUMAGE ELECTRIQUE **4514**

**ALL** 572

ALLUMAGE ELECTRONIQUE **4633**
ALLUMAGE PAR INCANDESCENCE **13251**
ALLUMAGE PREMATURE **9778**
ALLUME-CIGARETTE **2396**
ALLUMER **6757**
ALLUMER LE FOYER D'UNE CHAUDIERE **5236**
ALLUMEUR **6758**
ALLUMEUR **6762**
ALLURE (COURBE) **13181**
ALLURE D'UNE MACHINE **10850**
ALPACCA **8569**
ALPHABET A FRAPPER **1560**
ALTERATION CHIMIQUE **2296**
ALTERATION DE LA TEINTE **4026**
ALTERNATEUR **411**
ALTERNATEUR **407**
ALTERNATION PHYSIQUE **9280**
ALTERNATIVE **409**
ALTERNE **12048**
ALTERNO-MOTEUR **408**
ALUMINATE **414**
ALUMINATE DE BARYTE **994**
ALUMINATE DE POTASSIUM **9674**
ALUMINATE DE SODIUM **11716**
ALUMINATION **429**
ALUMINE **438**
ALUMINE **412**
ALUMINE **413**
ALUMINE HYDRATEE **423**
ALUMINIFERE **415**
ALUMINIUM **416**
ALUMINIUM **444**
ALUMINIUM **432**
ALUMINIUN EN LINGOT **424**
ALUMINO **430**
ALUMINOTHERMIE **431**
ALUN DE CHROME **2370**
ALUN DE FER **7135**
ALUN ORDINAIRE **2787**
ALUN POTASSIQUE **2787**
AMAGNETIQUE **8637**
AMALGAMATION **447**
AMALGAME **445**
AMALGAME **397**
AMALGAMER **446**
AMAS DE GUINIER-PRESTON **2542**
AMBRE JAUNE **449**
AME **3142**
AME **13726**
AME D'UN CABLE **3167**
AME D'UN FER PROFILE **13730**

AME D'UNE POUTRELLE **13729**
AME EN CHANVRE **6440**
AMENDE **5195**
AMENEE D'HUILE **8783**
AMIANTE **6599**
AMIANTE **1898**
AMIANTE **746**
AMIANTE **755**
AMIANTE TRESSE EN CORDELETTE **751**
AMIDON **12111**
AMMONIAC **454**
AMMONIAC **660**
AMMONIAQUE **453**
AMMONIAQUE **7644**
AMONT (D') **13407**
AMONT (EN) **13407**
AMORCAGE (DE COUPE) **5858**
AMORCE **1456**
AMORCE DE CRIQUE **6833**
AMORCE DE CRIQUE **5411**
AMORCE DE FISSURE **6833**
AMORCER AU MOYEN D'UN COUP DE POINTEAU **8011**
AMORCER UNE POMPE **9856**
AMORPHE **475**
AMORTIR UN CHOC **3640**
AMORTISSEMENT **3604**
AMORTISSEMENT DE VIBRATIONS **3606**
AMORTISSEMENT PAR LIQUIDE **7649**
AMORTISSEMENT PNEUMATIQUE **255**
AMORTISSEUR **3601**
AMORTISSEUR (ELECTR.) **3602**
AMORTISSEUR A LIQUIDE **6678**
AMORTISSEUR DE CHOCS **11358**
AMORTISSEUR DE VIBRATIONS **13555**
AMORTISSEUR PNEUMATIQUE **256**
AMOVIBLE **3808**
AMPERAGE **478**
AMPERE **479**
AMPERE-HEURE **481**
AMPERE-MINUTE **482**
AMPERE-SECONDE **483**
AMPERE-TOUR **480**
AMPEREMETRE **452**
AMPHIBOLE **6598**
AMPHOTERE **484**
AMPLIFICATEUR **485**
AMPLITUDE **486**
AMPOULE **7385**
AMPOULE DU THERMOMETRE **1717**
ANAEROBIQUE **489**
ANALOGIQUE **490**

573 ANG

ANALYSE **493**
ANALYSE (DETERMINATION) DE STRUCTURE CRISTALLINE **3425**
ANALYSE AU CHALUMEAU **1356**
ANALYSE CALORIMETRIQUE **1880**
ANALYSE CHIMIQUE **2293**
ANALYSE DE CONTROLE **2280**
ANALYSE DE COPEAUX **2345**
ANALYSE DE COULEE **7358**
ANALYSE DES GAZ **5809**
ANALYSE ELECTROLYTIQUE **4594**
ANALYSE ELEMENTAIRE **4655**
ANALYSE FLUORESCENTE **13999**
ANALYSE GRANULOMETRIQUE **6023**
ANALYSE GRANULOMETRIQUE **11020**
ANALYSE GRAVIMETRIQUE **6077**
ANALYSE MAGNETIQUE **7894**
ANALYSE NEPHELOMETRIQUE **8537**
ANALYSE PAR VOIE HUMIDE **13800**
ANALYSE PAR VOIE SECHE **4341**
ANALYSE PONDERALE **6077**
ANALYSE QUALITATIVE **10062**
ANALYSE QUANTITATIVE **10064**
ANALYSE SPECTRALE **11861**
ANALYSE SPECTRALE **11864**
ANALYSE THERMIQUE SELECTIVE **3919**
ANALYSE VOLUMETRIQUE **13601**
ANALYSER **491**
ANALYSEUR **492**
ANALYTIQUE **494**
ANASTIGMAT **497**
ANCRAGE **499**
ANCRAGE **12918**
ANCRE (CONSTR.) **500**
ANCRER **12914**
ANEMOMETRE **503**
ANEROIDE **504**
ANGLE (GEOM.) **505**
ANGLE ADJACENT **180**
ANGLE AIGU **155**
ANGLE AU CENTRE **507**
ANGLE COMPLEMENTAIRE **2811**
ANGLE D'AFFUTAGE **12995**
ANGLE D'ATTAQUE **8577**
ANGLE D'ATTAQUE **3524**
ANGLE D'ATTAQUE **1277**
ANGLE D'AVANCE **515**
ANGLE D'ENROULEMENT **517**
ANGLE D'INCIDENCE **520**
ANGLE D'INCIDENCE (D'UN OUTIL) **2484**
ANGLE D'INCLINAISON **521**

ANGLE D'INCLINATION DES PIVOTS **7312**
ANGLE D'OUVERTURE DE LA RAINURE **6129**
ANGLE DANS LE SEGMENT **6962**
ANGLE DE BRAQUAGE **7701**
ANGLE DE CALAGE **529**
ANGLE DE CARROSSAGE **1889**
ANGLE DE CISAILLEMENT **11281**
ANGLE DE COIN **12995**
ANGLE DE CONTACT **517**
ANGLE DE COUPE **10186**
ANGLE DE COUPE **3524**
ANGLE DE DECALAGE **9233**
ANGLE DE DECALAGE EN ARRIERE **522**
ANGLE DE DECALAGE EN AVANCE **515**
ANGLE DE DEGAGEMENT DU COPEAU **5698**
ANGLE DE DEPHASAGE **9233**
ANGLE DE DEPHASAGE EN ARRIERE **523**
ANGLE DE DEPHASAGE EN AVANCE **524**
ANGLE DE DEPOUILLE **5698**
ANGLE DE DETALONNAGE DU CORPS **1388**
ANGLE DE DEVIATION **518**
ANGLE DE FLEXION **519**
ANGLE DE FROTTEMENT **527**
ANGLE DE L'INCLINAISON DU FILET **531**
ANGLE DE L'OUTIL **12995**
ANGLE DE PENTE LATERALE **11418**
ANGLE DE PIED **10716**
ANGLE DE PRESSION **9810**
ANGLE DE REFLEXION **525**
ANGLE DE REFRACTION **526**
ANGLE DE RETARD **522**
ANGLE DE RETRAIT **4197**
ANGLE DE ROTATION **528**
ANGLE DE SAILLIE **165**
ANGLE DE TETE **4990**
ANGLE DE TORSION **532**
ANGLE DIEDRE **3944**
ANGLE DROIT **10577**
ANGLE DU CHANFREIN **1223**
ANGLE DU FILET **530**
ANGLE EXTERNE **4950**
ANGLE HELICOIDAL **6431**
ANGLE INSCRIT **6962**
ANGLE INTERIEUR **7057**
ANGLE INTERNE **7057**
ANGLE LIMITE **3345**
ANGLE OBTUS **8717**
ANGLE OPTIQUE **13581**
ANGLE POINTU **155**
ANGLE PRIMITIF **9401**
ANGLE RENTRANT **10243**

## ANG

574

ANGLE SAILLANT **10900**
ANGLE SOLIDE **11776**
ANGLE SUPPLEMENTAIRE **12483**
ANGLE TAILLANT **12995**
ANGLE VIF **155**
ANGLE VISUEL **13581**
ANGLOIR **1228**
ANGSTROM **536**
ANHYDRE **550**
ANHYDRIDE **8591**
ANHYDRIDE **11436**
ANHYDRIDE **548**
ANHYDRIDE ACETIQUE **87**
ANHYDRIDE ARSENIEUX **727**
ANHYDRIDE ARSENIQUE **723**
ANHYDRIDE AZOTEUX **8592**
ANHYDRIDE AZOTIQUE **8590**
ANHYDRIDE CARBONIQUE **1948**
ANHYDRIDE CHROMIQUE **2383**
ANHYDRIDE HYPOCHLOREUX **2355**
ANHYDRIDE PHOSPHORIQUE **9249**
ANHYDRIDE SULFUREUX **12450**
ANHYDRIDE SULFURIQUE **12452**
ANHYDRIDE TITANIQUE **12971**
ANHYDRIDE TUNGSTIQUE **13266**
ANHYDRIT **549**
ANILINE **552**
ANILINE DU COMMERCE **553**
ANION **556**
ANISOTROPE **558**
ANISOTROPIE **559**
ANNEAU **589**
ANNEAU **4234**
ANNEAU **7627**
ANNEAU **10600**
ANNEAU CYLINDRIQUE **3588**
ANNEAU D'AMIANTE **753**
ANNEAU DE ROULEMENT **964**
ANNEAU MIS A CHAUD **11391**
ANNEAUX A TOURILLONNER **3312**
ANNEXE D'UN BATIMENT **585**
ANNULAIRE **588**
ANODE **590**
ANODE **602**
ANODE D'EXCITATION **4886**
ANODE DE CUIVRE **3112**
ANODE INSOLUBLE **598**
ANODIQUE **603**
ANOLYTE **606**
ANSE DE PANIER **12872**
ANSPECT **7725**

ANTHRACENE **607**
ANTHRACITE **609**
ANTI CATHODE **611**
ANTI-ACIDE RESISTANT AUX ACIDES **124**
ANTI-GEL **5657**
ANTI-PARASITE **10156**
ANTI-ROUILLE **10869**
ANTI-TARTRE **4041**
ANTIBELIER **246**
ANTICATHODE **12682**
ANTIDEFLAGRANT **5322**
ANTIFRICTION **889**
ANTIFRICTION **619**
ANTIGEL **612**
ANTILOGARITHME **620**
ANTIMAGNETIQUE **614**
ANTIMOINE **623**
ANTIPUTRIDE **628**
ANTIPUTRIDE **629**
ANTISEPTIQUE **628**
ANTISEPTIQUE **629**
APERIODICITE **637**
APERIODIQUE **634**
APEX **638**
APLANAT **639**
APLATI **5406**
APLOMB **9219**
APLOMB **9539**
APLOMB (D') **9217**
APOCHROMATIQUE **640**
APPAREIL **641**
APPAREIL A BILLER **967**
APPAREIL A EQUILIBRER LES MEULES **6116**
APPAREIL A MORTAISER **11642**
APPAREIL A TARAUDER **12676**
APPAREIL CHAUDRONNE **4982**
APPAREIL CHAUDRONNE SOUS PRESSION **9839**
APPAREIL D'ALARME **305**
APPAREIL D'ALIMENTATION **5083**
APPAREIL D'ECLAIRAGE **6772**
APPAREIL D'EQUILIBRAGE **937**
APPAREIL D'ESSAI **12793**
APPAREIL D'ESSAI DE DUCTILITE **3462**
APPAREIL DE CONSTRUCTON **1444**
APPAREIL DE DISTILLATION **12259**
APPAREIL DE DISTRIBUTION A GLISSEMENT **11592**
APPAREIL DE DISTRIBUTION DE LA VAPEUR **13460**
APPAREIL DE GRAISSAGE SOUS PRESSION MECANIQUE
**8105**
APPAREIL DE LEVAGE **6519**
APPAREIL DE MANUTENTION **3080**

575 ARC

APPAREIL DE MISE EN MARCHE **12119**
APPAREIL DE PROTECTION **10881**
APPAREIL DISTILLATOIRE **12259**
APPAREIL DIVISEUR **4105**
APPAREIL ELECTRO MAGNETIQUE POUR ESSAI DE DURETE **4614**
APPAREIL ENREGISTREUR **10294**
APPAREIL EVAPORATEUR **4869**
APPAREIL POUR LES RUPTURES A LA TRACTION **7846**
APPAREIL RADIOGRAPHIQUE **13994**
APPAREIL SECHEUR **4356**
APPAREIL SHORE **11366**
APPAREIL SOUFFLANT **1361**
APPAREILS A DIAMANTER **13233**
APPAREILS ACCESSOIRES **1411**
APPAREILS DE DEPOUSSIERAGE **4391**
APPAREILS DE DISTRIBUTION (ELECTR.) **12558**
APPAUVRISSEMENT **6801**
APPLICATION D'UN REVETEMENT PAR TREMPAGE **3970**
APPLICATION D'UNE COUCHE PROTECTRICE **6792**
APPLICATION D'UNE FORCE **647**
APPLICATION EN PASSES CROISEES **3366**
APPLICATION INDUSTRIELLE D'UNE INVENTION **2783**
APPLIQUER UN FREIN **650**
APPLIQUER UNE COUCHE PROTECTRICE **6791**
APPOINTEMENTS **10897**
APPONTEMENT **1603**
APPRET **9855**
APPROXIMATION **652**
APPUI **12490**
APPUI **1118**
APPUI CALE **57**
APPUI FIXE **5295**
APPUI INTERMEDIAIRE D'UN ARBRE **6586**
APPUI MEDIAN **2152**
APPUIE-TETE **6320**
APPUYER **12491**
APTITUDE A LA TREMPE **6288**
APTITUDE AU DEBOURRAGE **2718**
ARBRE (MEC.) **11239**
ARBRE A CAME S **1888**
ARBRE A CAMES **1896**
ARBRE A CAMES EN TETE **8939**
ARBRE A GRANDE VITESSE **10209**
ARBRE A PETITE VITESSE **11650**
ARBRE A VILEBREQUIN **3309**
ARBRE CANNELE **11935**
ARBRE CARRE **12029**
ARBRE CONDUIT **4299**
ARBRE COUDE **3309**
ARBRE COUDE SIMPLE **11503**

ARBRE CREUX **6547**
ARBRE D'ATTAQUE **7944**
ARBRE D'ENTRAINEMENT **9930**
ARBRE D'HELICE **9930**
ARBRE DE CHANGEMENT DE MARCHE **10550**
ARBRE DE COMMANDE **4315**
ARBRE DE COUCHE **4758**
ARBRE DE DISTRIBUTION **10550**
ARBRE DE RELEVAGE **10550**
ARBRE DE RENVOI **6756**
ARBRE DE RENVOI **3233**
ARBRE DE RENVOI **3240**
ARBRE DE TRANSMISSION **4296**
ARBRE DE TRANSMISSION **7944**
ARBRE DEUXIEME MOTEUR **7944**
ARBRE EN ACIER COMPRIME **2850**
ARBRE EN PORTE-A-FAUX DES DEUX COTES **11247**
ARBRE FLEXIBLE **5420**
ARBRE HORIZONTAL **6587**
ARBRE INTERMEDIAIRE **6756**
ARBRE INTERMEDIAIRE **7202**
ARBRE INTERMEDIAIRE **7049**
ARBRE MENE **4299**
ARBRE MOTEUR **4315**
ARBRE OSCILLANT **10657**
ARBRE PLEIN **11793**
ARBRE PORTE-CAMES **1888**
ARBRE PORTE-FRAISE **3520**
ARBRE PREMIER MOTEUR **4758**
ARBRE PRIMAIRE OU PRINCIPAL **7943**
ARBRE PRINCIPAL **7944**
ARBRE RECEPTEUR **4299**
ARBRE ROTATIF **10764**
ARBRE SECOND MOTEUR **7944**
ARBRE SECONDAIRE **8910**
ARBRE SUCCIN **449**
ARBRE TROISIEME MOTEUR **7049**
ARBRE VERTICAL **13550**
ARBRE VILEBREQUIN A DEUX COUDES **13316**
ARBRE-MANIVELLE **3309**
ARBRES (PERPENDICULAIRES, OBLIQUES) SITUES DANS DES PLANS DIFFERENTS **11249**
ARBRES CONCOURANTS **7096**
ARBRES PARALLELES **9064**
ARC AVEC ELECTRODE DE CARBONE **1941**
ARC CIRCULAIRE **674**
ARC D'ENROULEMENT **675**
ARC D'UNE COURBE **664**
ARC DE CERCLE **674**
ARC DE CONTACT **2997**
ARC DE SOUTENEMENT **10442**

# ARC

ARC EN ANSE DE PANIER 5373
ARC EN DOS D'ANE 8741
ARC METALLIQUE 8174
ARC NON PROTEGE AVEC ELECTRODE AU CHARBON 1944
ARC PROTEGE AVEC ELECTRODE AU CHARBON 1945
ARC VOLTAIQUE 4494
ARC-BOUTANT 688
ARCADE 14014
ARCHET 1504
ARCHITECTE 691
ARCHITECTURE 2442
ARCOT 13987
ARDOISE 11571
AREOMETRE 6722
AREOMETRE A POIDS CONSTANT 6072
AREOMETRE A POIDS VARIABLE 6723
ARETE 4441
ARETE (DE SOUDURE) DUE AU REFOULEMENT 5357
ARETE ARRONDIE 10808
ARETE COUPANTE 3528
ARETE D'UN TROU 4447
ARETE DE REBROUSSEMENT 4448
ARETE DE SORTIE 5515
ARETE TERMINALE 3625
ARETE TRANCHANTE EMOUSSEE 4365
ARETE VIVE 11272
ARGENT 11458
ARGENT A 92/5% 12253
ARGENT ALLEMAND 5932
ARGENT BROMURE 1645
ARGENT CHLORURE 11461
ARGENT DE CHINE 5932
ARGENT ELECTROLYTIQUE 4608
ARGENT FIN 5202
ARGENT VERT 1645
ARGENTAL 5932
ARGENTAN 5932
ARGENTAN 8569
ARGENTER 11459
ARGENTURE 11469
ARGENTURE 11465
ARGILE 2465
ARGILE CALCINEE FONDUE 6125
ARGILE CUITE 926
ARGILE PLASTIQUE 9470
ARGILE REFRACTAIRE 5253
ARGILLITE 700
ARGON 701
ARITHMETIQUE 702
ARMATURE 5283
ARMATURE 707

ARMATURE 13243
ARMATURE D'UN AIMANT 710
ARMATURE D'UN CABLE 715
ARMATURE DE NOYAU 3143
ARMOIRE A OUTILS 12998
ARMURE 710
ARRACHEMENT 10858
ARRACHEMENTS 11626
ARRACHEUSES DE POMMES DE TERRE 9707
ARRACHEUSES DE TUBERCULES 9703
ARRET 12278
ARRET D'AXE DE PISTON 2405
ARRET D'UNE MACHINE 12286
ARRET D'UNE MACHINE (ETAT) 12094
ARRET D'UNE SOUPAPE 13461
ARRET D'USINE 7092
ARRET DE SERVICE 7100
ARRET DE SUSPENSION 6521
ARRET FACULTATIF 8850
ARRET PROGRAMME 9903
ARRET TEMPORISE 4396
ARRETE-FLAMMES 5321
ARRETE-PIEDS 12977
ARRETER UNE MACHINE 12280
ARRETS DE TRAVAIL 11409
ARRIVEE D'EAU 6915
ARRONDI 6537
ARRONDI DU FILET 10809
ARRONDIR UNE ARETE 10793
ARROSAGE 12001
ARROSER 12000
ARROSOIR 13687
ARSENIATE 720
ARSENIC 721
ARSENIQUE BLANC 727
ARSENITE 729
ARSENITE DE CUIVRE 10996
ARSENIURE 726
ARSENIURE D'HYDROGENE 730
ARTERE 5081
ARTICULATION 13242
ARTICULATION (MEC.) 7238
ARTICULATION A CARDAN 6573
ARTICULATION A TOURILLON 9318
ARTICULE 7629
ASBESTE 755
ASCENSEUR 9101
ASCENSEUR CONTINU 3020
ASCENSION 1925
ASCENSION D'UNE CHARGE 7559
ASEPTISANT 628

577 ATT

ASPERITE **9011**
ASPERITE **10792**
ASPHALTAGE **767**
ASPHALTE **768**
ASPHALTE COMPRIME **12610**
ASPHALTE COULE **9713**
ASPHALTE DE TRINIDAD **13212**
ASPHALTE EN POUDRE **9723**
ASPHALTER **763**
ASPIRATEUR **769**
ASPIRATEUR DE POUSSIERES **4390**
ASPIRATION **12428**
ASPIRATION PAR CAPILLARITE **1922**
ASPIRER **12427**
ASSECHEMENT **4210**
ASSEMBLAGE **3254**
ASSEMBLAGE **1778**
ASSEMBLAGE A BASSE TEMPERATURE **7790**
ASSEMBLAGE A BRIDES **5344**
ASSEMBLAGE A COUVRE-JOINTS **1782**
ASSEMBLAGE A ONGLET **8324**
ASSEMBLAGE A QUEUE D'ARONDE **4178**
ASSEMBLAGE EN ANGLE **2519**
ASSEMBLAGE EN T **12702**
ASSEMBLAGE PAR CLAVETTE **7285**
ASSEMBLAGE PAR RAINURE ET LANGUETTE **12991**
ASSEMBLAGE PAR RECOUVREMENT **7396**
ASSEMBLAGE PAR RECOUVREMENT **7397**
ASSEMBLAGE PAR RIVETS **10639**
ASSEMBLAGE PAR SOUDURE **11759**
ASSEMBLAGE PAR SOUDURE DE PIECES MOULEES **2060**
ASSEMBLAGE PAR VIS **1442**
ASSEMBLAGE RIGIDE **10589**
ASSEMBLER DES TUYAUX PAR EMBOITEMENT **5277**
ASSISE **9011**
ASSISE **2896**
ASSISE DE BRIQUES **3259**
ASSISE DE RESERVOIR **12628**
ASSOMBRISSEMENT **5507**
ASSORTIMENT **11219**
ASSORTIMENT (DE PIECES) **11213**
ASSORTIR **8042**
ASSUJETTISSEMENT **7711**
ASSURER LA CONCORDANCE DES TROUS DE RIVETS **9969**
ASTATIQUE **774**
ASTERISME **776**
ASTROIDE **5602**
ASYMETRIE **779**
ASYMETRIQUE **778**
ASYMPTOTE **780**
ASYMPTOTE **781**

ASYMPTOTIQUE **781**
ASYNCHRONE **784**
ASYNCHRONISME **782**
ATELIER **13968**
ATELIER **13943**
ATELIER **11364**
ATELIER **4764**
ATELIER **773**
ATELIER D'AJUSTAGE **5282**
ATELIER D'EBARBAGE **5130**
ATELIER D'ECROUTAGE **5130**
ATELIER D'ENTRETIEN **10461**
ATELIER DE CARROSSERIE **1398**
ATELIER DE CHAUDRONNERIE EN FER **1420**
ATELIER DE DESABLAGE **5130**
ATELIER DE FORGE **5547**
ATELIER DE FRAISAGE **8293**
ATELIER DE MACHINES **7855**
ATELIER DE MECANIQUE **7855**
ATELIER DE MECANIQUE **7856**
ATELIER DE MONTAGE **4811**
ATELIER DE REPARATION **10461**
ATELIER DE TOLERIE **1398**
ATELIER DE TOURNAGE **13290**
ATHERMANE **786**
ATHERMANEITE **785**
ATMOSPHERE **787**
ATMOSPHERE (UNITE DE PRESSION) **788**
ATMOSPHERE A USAGE SPECIAL **791**
ATMOSPHERE ARTIFICIELLE **789**
ATMOSPHERE DE CARBONITRURATION **1973**
ATMOSPHERE DE NITRURATION **8583**
ATMOSPHERE PROTECTRICE **9947**
ATMOSPHERE PROTECTRICE **790**
ATMOSPHERE RAREFIEE **13441**
ATMOSPHERE REDUCTRICE **10347**
ATOME **800**
ATOMISATION **811**
ATTACHE **7817**
ATTACHE **1522**
ATTACHE **2502**
ATTACHE DES COURROIES **1151**
ATTAQUE **813**
ATTAQUE **4297**
ATTAQUE **10845**
ATTAQUE (COR.) **4846**
ATTAQUE A L ACIDE **4846**
ATTAQUE DE COULEE **5866**
ATTAQUE EN CORNICHON **6600**
ATTAQUE INTERDENDRITIQUE **7031**
ATTAQUE MACROGRAPHIQUE **7870**

**ATT** 578

ATTAQUE METALLOGRAPHIQUE **8204**
ATTAQUE PROFONDE **3685**
ATTAQUER **3182**
ATTAQUER A L'ACIDE **4839**
ATTEINTE PORTEE AUX DROITS DU BREVETE **6916**
ATTENUATION **3604**
ATTIRAIL DE CHAUFFE **5261**
ATTRACTION **815**
ATTRACTION MAGNETIQUE **7895**
ATTRACTION MOLECULAIRE **8359**
AU LARGE **8738**
AUBE **1677**
AUBE D'UNE TURBINE **13480**
AUBE DIRECTRICE **6167**
AUBE FIXE D'UNE TURBINE **6167**
AUBE MOBILE D'UNE TURBINE **13820**
AUBE RECEPTRICE **13820**
AUBES DE TURBINES **13268**
AUBIER **10936**
AUGE **13228**
AUGITE **819**
AUGITE-SYENITE **820**
AUGMENTATION DE LA PRESSION **6848**
AUGMENTATION DE LA RESISTANCE **6850**
AUGMENTATION DE LA SECTION TRANSVERSALE **5869**
AUGMENTATION DE PRESSION **6855**
AUGMENTATION DE VITESSE **10185**
AUGMENTATION DE VOLUME **4912**
AUGMENTATION OU ELEVATION DE LA TEMPERATURE **10612**
AUGMENTER LA VITESSE **6851**
AULNE **318**
AUNE **318**
AURIFERE **822**
AUSSIERE **6309**
AUSTENITE **825**
AUSTENITISATION **827**
AUTEUR D'UNE INVENTION **7108**
AUTO **8411**
AUTO-EXCITATION **11153**
AUTO-INDUCTION **11156**
AUTO-INFLAMMATION **11956**
AUTOBUS **13421**
AUTOBUS **8410**
AUTOCAR **7099**
AUTOCAR **8412**
AUTOCLAVE **829**
AUTOMATICITE **837**
AUTOMATIQUE **11148**
AUTOMOBILE **8411**
AUTOMOBILE INDUSTRIELLE **8414**

AUTONOMIE **3416**
AUTOSOUDURE **834**
AUVENT **3276**
AUVENT **5695**
AVAL (EN) **4184**
AVAL (D') **4184**
AVANCE **5585**
AVANCE **206**
AVANCE **5063**
AVANCE D'UN OUTIL **5068**
AVANCE PAR DENT **5069**
AVANCE RAPIDE **10208**
AVANCEMENT **5584**
AVANCEMENT **9905**
AVANCER **7448**
AVANT-CLOU **5944**
AVANT-TROU **10782**
AVERTISSEUR SONORE **6592**
AVEUGLER UNE FUITE **12279**
AVIDE D'EAU **6730**
AVOYAGE D'UNE SCIE **10958**
AVOYER UNE SCIE **11224**
AXE **9315**
AXE **2151**
AXE **11904**
AXE **864**
AXE (DE PIVOT) **7311**
AXE D'ARTICULATION D'UNE FOURCHE **6159**
AXE D'OSCILLATION **867**
AXE D'UN CRISTAL **865**
AXE D'UN TUYAU **866**
AXE DE FIBRE **5132**
AXE DE PISTON **9376**
AXE DE PISTON **6158**
AXE DE PIVOTEMENT **7311**
AXE DE ROTATION **868**
AXE DE SOUDURE **870**
AXE DE SYMETRIE **11024**
AXE DE SYMETRIE **869**
AXE DE SYMETRIE DES CRISTAUX **863**
AXE DES ABCISSES **872**
AXE DES ORDONNEES **873**
AXE DES X **872**
AXE DES Y **873**
AXE DU CORDON DE SOUDURE **871**
AXE DU REGULATEUR **6018**
AXE FOCAL **13143**
AXE GEOMETRIQUE **874**
AXE LONGITUDINAL **7733**
AXE NEUTRE **8541**
AXE NON TRANSVERSE D'UNE HYPERBOLE **2953**

AXE OPTIQUE **8841**
AXE PRINCIPAL **9866**
AXE TRANSVERSAL **13142**
AXE TRANSVERSE D'UNE HYPERBOLE **13143**
AXES CRISTALLINS ORTHOHEXAGONAUX **8871**
AXES D'EQUERRE **858**
AZOTATE **1271**
AZOTATE **8579**
AZOTATE **4850**
AZOTATE D'ARGENT **7828**
AZOTATE DE BARYUM **1001**
AZOTATE DE BISMUTHYLE **1273**
AZOTATE DE COBALT **2610**
AZOTATE DE POTASSIUM **10903**
AZOTATE DE SODIUM **2330**
AZOTATE MERCUREUX **8160**
AZOTATE MERCURIQUE **8156**
AZOTE **8588**
AZOTITE **11725**
AZOTITE **9691**
AZOTITE **8586**
AZOTYLE **8591**
AZURITE **886**
BAC **13228**
BAC D'ALIMENTATION **5075**
BAC DE BATTERIE **1067**
BACHE **13228**
BAGASSE **924**
BAGUE **1773**
BAGUE **10600**
BAGUE **9379**
BAGUE AMOVIBLE **7743**
BAGUE COLLECTRICE **11618**
BAGUE CONIQUE **2945**
BAGUE D'ARRET **7743**
BAGUE D'ARRET **12904**
BAGUE D'ARRET EN DEUX PIECES **11939**
BAGUE D'ETANCHEITE **9007**
BAGUE D'EXCENTRIQUE **4435**
BAGUE DE BUTEE **12904**
BAGUE DE CALIBRE **2721**
BAGUE DE CENTRAGE **2154**
BAGUE DE CENTRAGE **10413**
BAGUE DE FOND **9000**
BAGUE DE FOND **1565**
BAGUE DE FREINAGE **1541**
BAGUE DE GARNITURE **9007**
BAGUE DE GRAISSAGE **8774**
BAGUE DE GRAISSAGE **8790**
BAGUE DE GUIDAGE **6163**
BAGUE DE PISTON A JOINT EN BISEAU **9381**

BAGUE DE PISTON AVEC FENTE D'EQUERRE **9380**
BAGUE DE PISTON AVEC JOINT (FENTE) A RECOUVREMENT **9382**
BAGUE DE PISTON FENDUE **11944**
BAGUE DE PRESSION **9830**
BAGUE DE RACCORD **2961**
BAGUE DE RETENUE **10515**
BAGUE DE ROULEMENT **964**
BAGUE DE SERRAGE **11391**
BAGUE EN CAOUTCHOUC **10823**
BAGUE EN PLOMB **7470**
BAGUE EN TERRE GLAISE **2468**
BAGUE EXTERIEURE D'UN ROULEMENT A BILLES **8898**
BAGUE INTERIEURE D'UN ROULEMENT A BILLES **6953**
BAGUE LARMIER **13879**
BAGUE PERIPHERIQUE **1232**
BAGUE SOUDEE **13771**
BAGUE TARAUDEE DU CALIBRE DE FILETAGE **11050**
BAGUETTE **10660**
BAGUETTE DE RETENUE **10516**
BAGUETTE EN VERRE **12260**
BAILLEMENT **5806**
BAIN **1062**
BAIN **3967**
BAIN BLEU **1369**
BAIN D'HUILE **8745**
BAIN D'HYDROXYDE DE SODIUM **2117**
BAIN DE BLANCHIMENT **8059**
BAIN DE BRILLANTAGE **1608**
BAIN DE BRILLANTAGE **1564**
BAIN DE BRILLANTAGE **1609**
BAIN DE CEMENTATION **1994**
BAIN DE CHLORURE DE MERCURE **1369**
BAIN DE DECALAMINAGE **3790**
BAIN DE DECAPAGE **9289**
BAIN DE DECAPAGE **111**
BAIN DE DECAPAGE **12382**
BAIN DE DECAPAGE A L'ACIDE **9290**
BAIN DE DECAPAGE MAT **8059**
BAIN DE DECAPAGE PRELIMINAIRE **2476**
BAIN DE DECOMPOSITION DE L ELECTROLYTE **7538**
BAIN DE DEROUILLAGE **10872**
BAIN DE FUSION **9961**
BAIN DE FUSION **8137**
BAIN DE MORDANCAGE **9289**
BAIN DE PASSIVATION **9103**
BAIN DE PLOMB **7454**
BAIN DE SABLE **10918**
BAIN DE SEL **10905**
BAIN DE TREMPE **10096**
BAIN DE TREMPE **6294**

# BAI 580

BAIN DE VAPEUR **12157**
BAIN-MARIE **13641**
BAINITE **925**
BAIONNETTE **1074**
BAISSE DE TEMPERATURE **5022**
BALAI AU CHARBON **1946**
BALAI ELECTRIQUE **6534**
BALANCE **931**
BALANCE **3660**
BALANCE A FLEAU **1095**
BALANCE A RESSORT **11976**
BALANCE D'ANALYSE **2294**
BALANCE DE PRECISION **9764**
BALANCE DE TORSION **13052**
BALANCE DU COMMERCE EXTERIEUR **13099**
BALANCE HYDROSTATIQUE **6725**
BALANCIER A VIS **11040**
BALATA **943**
BALAYAGE **10992**
BALAYER **10990**
BALLANT D'UNE COURROIE **13825**
BALLAST **969**
BALLASTAGE **971**
BALLE (DE MARCHANDISE) **945**
BALLON (CHIM.) **5370**
BALLON A FOND PLAT **9142**
BALLON ORDINAIRE **10798**
BALOURD **13341**
BAMBOU **972**
BAN DE TRACTION **7846**
BANC **1167**
BANC A RECTIFIER **12320**
BANC A TREFILER LES GROS FILS **1727**
BANC D'ESSAI **12773**
BANC D'ETIRAGE **10023**
BANC D'ETIRAGE **4218**
BANC DE CONTROLE **12773**
BANC DE MENUISIER **7234**
BANC PHOTOMETRIQUE **9268**
BANC POUR VERIFIER LES ENGRENAGES **5902**
BANC REFROIDISSEUR **6617**
BANDAGE DE ROUE **13322**
BANDAGES DE ROUE **12220**
BANDE **11983**
BANDE **974**
BANDE A JUMEAUX **570**
BANDE A TUBES **11527**
BANDE ARRASIVE **18**
BANDE D'ABSORPTION **45**
BANDE D'ACIER **12197**
BANDE D'AMIANTE **754**

BANDE D'INTERFERENCE **7036**
BANDE DE CUIVRE **3131**
BANDE DE DEFORMATION **3706**
BANDE DE FERRITE LIBRE **5105**
BANDE DE FREIN **1544**
BANDE DE PLIAGE **7314**
BANDE DE RECHAPAGE **1892**
BANDE DE RECOUVREMENT COUVRE-JOINT **1783**
BANDE DE ROULEMENT **13172**
BANDE MAGNETIQUE **7919**
BANDE PERFOREE **10005**
BANDELETTE **5375**
BANDER UN RESSORT **10032**
BANDES **980**
BANDES DE GLISSEMENT **11613**
BANDES DE METAL DE RECOUVREMENT **1928**
BANDES DE NEUMANN **8540**
BANDES GALVANISEES **5788**
BANDES NOIRES **1289**
BANDES REVELEES PAR ATTAQUE CHIMIQUE **4840**
BARAQUE DE CHANTIER **2987**
BARAQUE DE CHANTIER **11519**
BARAQUE DE VESTIAIRE **2247**
BARBE **1764**
BARBOTEUR POUR LAVAGES **5845**
BARBOTIN **2217**
BARBURE **1764**
BAREME **8052**
BARGE **991**
BARGES DE MANUTENTION **3787**
BARGES DE POSE **7440**
BARITEL **1731**
BARN **1006**
BAROMETRE **1008**
BAROMETRE A CUVETTE **2440**
BAROMETRE A MERCURE **8150**
BAROMETRE A SIPHON **11515**
BAROMETRE ANEROIDE **504**
BAROMETRE ENREGISTREUR **1007**
BAROMETRE METALLIQUE **504**
BAROMETRIQUE **1009**
BAROSCOPE **1011**
BARRAGE **13753**
BARRAGE D'UNE VALLEE **3597**
BARRAGE DE SORTIE **8904**
BARRE **10660**
BARRE **10663**
BARRE **981**
BARRE **986**
BARRE A NOYAU FUSIBLE **3168**
BARRE A OEILLETS **5551**

**581**        **BEC**

BARRE A SECTION DECROISSANTE **12670**
BARRE COLLECTRICE **1770**
BARRE D'ACCOUPLEMENT **12231**
BARRE D'ACCOUPLEMENT **12915**
BARRE D'ACCOUPLEMENT **12916**
BARRE D'ALESAGE MICROMETRIQUE **8240**
BARRE D'ALESAGE MONOPIECE **11778**
BARRE D'ATTELAGE **4217**
BARRE D'EXCENTRIQUE **4431**
BARRE DE CONNEXION **2962**
BARRE DE CONTACT **2999**
BARRE DE CUIVRE **3113**
BARRE DE DEVERSOIR **4185**
BARRE DE DEVERSOIR **3593**
BARRE DE FER BRUT **8441**
BARRE DE GUIDAGE **6164**
BARRE DE METAL NOBLE **1730**
BARRE DE PIQUAGE **7333**
BARRE DE TORSION **13053**
BARRE EN ACIER CEMENTE **1328**
BARRE OMNIBUS **1770**
BARRE PLATE **5374**
BARRE SOUMISE AUX ESSAIS **12772**
BARRE STABILISATRICE **12539**
BARRE TRAVAILLANT A LA COMPRESSION **2855**
BARRE TRAVAILLANT A LA TENSION **12754**
BARREAU **10660**
BARREAU AIMANTE **985**
BARREAU DE GRILLE **5237**
BARREAU ENTAILLE **8675**
BARREAU-EPROUVETTE **12772**
BARREAUX VERGES DE FER **984**
BARRES DE FORAGE **1470**
BARRES ETIREES **4248**
BARRES HUIT-PANS EN ACIER ALLIE **375**
BARRES LAMINEES A FROID **2695**
BARRES POUR GRILLAGES **6069**
BARRETTE **5211**
BARRIERE DE COTTRELL **3224**
BARYTE **1020**
BARYTINE **1021**
BARYTITE **1021**
BARYUM **992**
BASALTE **1022**
BASALTIQUE **1023**
BASCULANT **6835**
BASCULE **931**
BASCULE **3660**
BASCULE AU DIXIEME (AU 10) **3660**
BASCULE BINAIRE **5429**
BASCULE POUR ALLIAGE **362**

BASCULE ROMAINE **12225**
BASCULE ROMAINE (A CURSEUR) **12225**
BASCULEUR DE WAGONS **1932**
BASE **1027**
BASE **1026**
BASE (CHIM.) **1024**
BASE (D'UN SOLIDE) **1025**
BASE D'UN FILET **1028**
BASE D'UN LOGARITHME **1033**
BASICITE **1055**
BASIQUE **1042**
BASSE PRESSION **7774**
BASSE TEMPERATURE **7775**
BASSE TENSION **7778**
BASSIN A VIDE **13451**
BASSIN DE FILTRATION **5178**
BASSIN REFROIDISSANT **3090**
BATI D'UNE MACHINE **5626**
BATIMENT ANNEXE **585**
BATIMENT D'USINE **5012**
BATIMENT DE GENERATEUR **1413**
BATIMENT DES CHAUDIERES **1413**
BATIMENT DES MACHINES **4753**
BATITURE **8279**
BATTAGE DE PIEUX **9306**
BATTEMENT **1119**
BATTEMENT D'OR **5994**
BATTEMENT DES METAUX **1120**
BATTERIE **4534**
BATTERIE D'ACCUMULATEURS **77**
BATTERIE D'ACCUMULATEURS **1066**
BATTERIE DE CHAUDIERES **1069**
BATTERIE DE PILES **9845**
BATTERIE-TAMPON **1687**
BATTEUSES **12884**
BATTITURES **6217**
BATTRE EN FORME **1482**
BAUME DE COPAHU **3101**
BAUXITE **1071**
BAVURE **1764**
BAVURE **5357**
BAVURE **8948**
BAVURE **10836**
BAVURE (D'UNE PIECE MOULEE) **5184**
BAVURE (DE SOUDURE) **8949**
BEANT D'UN JOINT **5806**
BEC (D'UN OUTIL) **8666**
BEC A GAZ **5811**
BEC BUNSEN **1741**
BEC DE COULEE **7632**
BEC DE COULEE DE LA POCHE **7361**

# BEC

BEC DE LA POCHE DE COULEE **7363**
BEC DE PASSAGE DU LAITIER **2399**
BEC DE SOUFFLAGE **275**
BEC DU CONVERTISSEUR **3072**
BEC-D'ANE **3364**
BECHER **1092**
BEDANE **1919**
BEDANE **3364**
BEDANE DE MENUISIER **8398**
BELIER HYDRAULIQUE **6694**
BENEFICE DANS LE TRAVAIL **8094**
BENJOIN **1203**
BENZALDEHYDE **1198**
BENZENE **1199**
BENZIDINE **1201**
BENZINE **1199**
BENZOL **1204**
BENZOLINE **7580**
BENZOPHENONE **1205**
BERCEAU **3288**
BERCEAU **7816**
BERCEAU **10877**
BERCEAU A GALETS **10690**
BERCEAU A GALETS **10694**
BERCEAU A PATINS **11606**
BERLINE **11128**
BERLINE **10902**
BERLINE 4 PORTES **5599**
BERYLLIUM **1207**
BETON **2894**
BETON **12203**
BETON COULE DANS DES TROUS **9714**
BETON DAME **10193**
BETON DE CIMENT **2135**
BETON DE LAITIER **11565**
BETON DE MACHEFER **11565**
BETON MOULE **8426**
BETONNAGE **2902**
BETONNER **2895**
BEURRE D'ANTIMOINE LIQUIDE **626**
BEURRE DE COCO **2620**
BIAIS **1223**
BIAIS **1221**
BIATOMIQUE **3881**
BIBORATE DE SODIUM **1459**
BICARBONATE D'AMMONIUM **459**
BICARBONATE DE CALCIUM **1847**
BICARBONATE DE MAGNESIUM **7883**
BICARBONATE DE POTASSE **9676**
BICARBONATE DE SOUDE **126**
BICHLORURE D'ETAIN **12096**

BICHLORURE DE MERCURE **8153**
BICHROMATE DE POTASSIUM **9677**
BIDON (POUR HUILEESSENCEECT.) **12961**
BIEF D'AMONT **6319**
BIEF D'AVAL **12596**
BIELLE **2962**
BIELLE D'ACCOUPLEMENT **3256**
BIELLE DE COMMANDE **4317**
BIER **2251**
BIGORNE **1090**
BIGORNE **1091**
BILAN CALORIFIQUE **6337**
BILAN THERMIQUE **6337**
BILLAGE **1618**
BILLE **1243**
BILLE **950**
BILLE POUR ROULEMENTS **1102**
BILLES A POLIR **1759**
BILLES POUR BRUNISSAGE **1759**
BILLETTE **4371**
BILLETTE **1243**
BILLETTE DE LAITON **1563**
BILLETTES EN ACIER ALLIE **370**
BILLOT **633**
BIOXYDE D'AZOTE **8581**
BIOXYDE D'ETAIN **12098**
BIOXYDE D'HYDROGENE **6716**
BIOXYDE DE BARYUM **998**
BIOXYDE DE MANGANESE **10047**
BIOXYDE DE SODIUM **11727**
BIPLAN **1261**
BIREFRINGENT **1265**
BISCUIT **1276**
BISEAU **1221**
BISEAUTAGE **1231**
BISEAUTER **1222**
BISECTRICE AIGUE **156**
BISMUTH **1269**
BISMUTHINE **1275**
BISSECTER **1266**
BISSECTION **1267**
BISSECTRICE **1268**
BISULFITE D'AMMONIAQUE **460**
BISULFITE DE SODIUM **11718**
BISULFURE D'ARSENIC **10262**
BISULFURE D'ETAIN **12099**
BIT **1249**
BITARTRATE DE POTASSIUM **119**
BITORD **12005**
BITTERN **8405**
BITUME SOLIDE **768**

BITUMER **763**
BITUMINEUX **1281**
BLANC D'ARGENT **13834**
BLANC D'ESPAGNE **13841**
BLANC DE BALEINE **11882**
BLANC DE BARYTE **1003**
BLANC DE CERUSE **13834**
BLANC DE MEUDON **13841**
BLANC DE NEIGE **14043**
BLANC DE PLOMB **13834**
BLANC DE TROYES **13841**
BLANC DE ZINC **14043**
BLANC EBLOUISSANT **6823**
BLANC FIXE **1003**
BLANC INCANDESCENT **6823**
BLANC SOUDANT **13784**
BLENDE **1324**
BLEU **1375**
BLEU (CHAUDE) **1370**
BLEU DE BERLIN **1206**
BLEU DE CHYPRE **1376**
BLEU DE PRUSSE **1206**
BLEUIR L'ACIER **1368**
BLEUISSAGE **1377**
BLEUISSAGE **572**
BLOC (D'INFORMATIONS) **1332**
BLOC DE LA CROSSE **11587**
BLOC ERRATIQUE **4821**
BLOC OPTIQUE **11079**
BLOC-CYLINDRES **3564**
BLOCAGE **7704**
BLOCAGE **7711**
BLOCAGE AUTOMATIQUE (A) **11157**
BLOCAGE DES ECROUS **7707**
BLONDIN **1344**
BLOOM **1346**
BLOOMS EN ACIER AU CARBONE **1955**
BLOQUER UN ECROU **7700**
BLOQUER UNE CLAVETTE **7700**
BOBINAGE **2648**
BOBINAGE **13862**
BOBINE **2645**
BOBINE **4499**
BOBINE **1384**
BOBINE D'ALLUMAGE **6761**
BOBINE D'INDUCTION **6894**
BOBINE DE RUHMKORFF **10830**
BOCARD **12057**
BOIS **13913**
BOIS A BRULER **5258**
BOIS A COEUR POURRI **5610**

BOIS BLANC **11746**
BOIS BOUGE **1196**
BOIS CARIE **10768**
BOIS DE CHARPENTE **12937**
BOIS DE CHAUFFAGE **5258**
BOIS DE CONSTRUCTION **12937**
BOIS DE FER-BLANC **13833**
BOIS DE FIL **12939**
BOIS DE MAILLE **12938**
BOIS DE SABLE **13833**
BOIS DEBITE **10962**
BOIS DUR **6282**
BOIS EN GRUME **7723**
BOIS EN QUARTIERS **10076**
BOIS EN RONDINS **10803**
BOIS EQUARRI **12035**
BOIS FEUILLU **6301**
BOIS LEGER **11746**
BOIS LOURD **6282**
BOIS MI-PLAT **6210**
BOIS POUILLEUX **5610**
BOIS RESINEUX **10483**
BOIS SAIN **11820**
BOIS SANS NOEUDS **12940**
BOIS SECHE A L'AIR LIBRE **297**
BOIS TAILLE CONTRE LE FIL **4719**
BOIS TENDRE **11746**
BOIS VERMOULU **13977**
BOISSEAU D'UN ROBINET **11334**
BOISSEAU DE LA BOITE A ETOUPE **9008**
BOITE A BOURRAGE **9008**
BOITE A ETOUPE **12405**
BOITE A FEU **5238**
BOITE A FUSIBLES **5752**
BOITE A GANTS **5980**
BOITE A GARNITURES **9008**
BOITE A GRAISSE **6085**
BOITE A GRAISSE **877**
BOITE A HUILE **877**
BOITE A NOYAUX **3147**
BOITE A OUTILS **12997**
BOITE A RESSORT **11980**
BOITE A SOUPAPE **2229**
BOITE A VIDE **13435**
BOITE A VIDE **13438**
BOITE D'ESSIEU **877**
BOITE D'ESSIEU **876**
BOITE DE COMPAS **8051**
BOITE DE DISTRIBUTION **2229**
BOITE DE GRAISSAGE **877**
BOITE DE VITESSE **5890**

**BOI** 584

BOITE PROTECTRICE **9948**
BOITEMENT **7165**
BOITES DE CEMENTATION **1989**
BOITIER **6660**
BOITIER DE DIRECTION **12229**
BOITIER DE DISTRIBUTION **4086**
BOL **1430**
BOL DIARMENIE **8720**
BOLOMETRE **1431**
BOMBAGE **1889**
BOMBAGE **1723**
BOMBE **1720**
BOMBE **1722**
BOMBE CALORIMETRIQUE **1879**
BOMBEMENT **1720**
BOMBEMENT DE LA JANTE D'UNE POULIE **3398**
BOMBER **13628**
BONBONNE **1981**
BONDE DE FOND **1492**
BORATE DE SOUDE ANHYDRE **1459**
BORAX **1459**
BORD **4441**
BORD A SOUDER **6130**
BORD OU FLANC DE LA BANDE D'ABSORPTION **49**
BORD RABATTU **1083**
BORD TOMBE **1083**
BORDELAGE **1088**
BORE **1477**
BORNE **12763**
BORNE **12762**
BORNE D'ARRIVEE **6944**
BORNE DE RACCORDEMENT **12762**
BORNE DE RACCORDEMENT **1254**
BORT **1480**
BOSSAGE **1883**
BOSSAGE DE MISE A LA TERRE **4418**
BOSSE **1720**
BOSSE RENTRANTE **3760**
BOSSELAGE **4684**
BOTTE (DE TUBES OU PROFILES) **1736**
BOTTE DE FEUILLARD **1738**
BOTTELER **1737**
BOTTELEUSES MECANIQUES A TOUTE DENSITE **948**
BOUCHE D'ARROSAGE **6672**
BOUCHE D'EAU **6672**
BOUCHE D'INCENDIE **5244**
BOUCHER (SE) **2358**
BOUCHON **9529**
BOUCHON **3173**
BOUCHON **12285**
BOUCHON **1910**

BOUCHON **5758**
BOUCHON A L'EMERI **6146**
BOUCHON A VIS **11060**
BOUCHON DE CAOUTCHOUC **10824**
BOUCHON DE COULEE **12284**
BOUCHON DE JAUGE **5883**
BOUCHON DE LIEGE **3176**
BOUCHON DE RADIATEUR **10151**
BOUCHON DE REMPLISSAGE **5158**
BOUCHON DE VALVE **13464**
BOUCHON DE VAPEUR **13481**
BOUCHON DE VIDANGE **4208**
BOUCHON FEMELLE **11025**
BOUCHON FEMELLE **1910**
BOUCHON FILETE **11025**
BOUCHON FILETE **11060**
BOUCHON MALE **11060**
BOUCHON TARAUDE **11025**
BOUCHON VISSE **11060**
BOUCLE D'UNE CORDE **7742**
BOUCLE DE RETOUR **5080**
BOUCLIER **11342**
BOUDIN D'AMIANTE **749**
BOUDIN DE SOUDURE **1082**
BOUE **11609**
BOUE **8444**
BOUE **11655**
BOUE **11654**
BOUE D'ANODE **600**
BOUES **8444**
BOUEUX **8445**
BOUGIE **6419**
BOUGIE **1899**
BOUGIE D'ALLUMAGE **11841**
BOUGIE D'ALLUMAGE **11838**
BOUGIE DE PRECHAUFFAGE **6387**
BOUGIE DECIMALE **3663**
BOUILLIR **1401**
BOUILLONNEMENT **4461**
BOULE/SPHERE DU REGULATEUR **6015**
BOULON **1432**
BOULON A BASCULE **6509**
BOULON A CHARNIERE **6509**
BOULON A CROCHET **6569**
BOULON A ERGOT **5062**
BOULON A TETE A SIX PANS **6457**
BOULON A TETE CARREE **12033**
BOULON A TETE DE MARTEAU **12701**
BOULON A TIGE ENTIEREMENT FILETEE **12398**
BOULON A VIS **11021**
BOULON BRUT **1286**

BOULON D'ANCRAGE **501**
BOULON D'ASSEMBLAGE **771**
BOULON D'ASSEMBLAGE PROVISOIRE **12592**
BOULON D'ECLISSE **5269**
BOULON DE BLOCAGE **2281**
BOULON DE CARROSSERIE **2553**
BOULON DE CHARRONNAGE **2553**
BOULON DE FONDATION **5590**
BOULON DE LIAISON **2959**
BOULON DE SCELLEMENT **10172**
BOULON DE SCELLEMENT A BARBELURES **7209**
BOULON DECOLLETE **1607**
BOULON ETOQUIAU **2149**
BOULON FAIT A LA MACHINE **7840**
BOULON GRAISSEUR **7811**
BOULON LIBRE **1441**
BOULON MECANIQUE **7840**
BOULON NON FILETE **1302**
BOULON POUR COURROIES **1156**
BOULON PRISONNIER **12399**
BOULONNAGE **1443**
BOULONNER **1435**
BOULONNERIE **1443**
BOULONS A TETE PLATE **5386**
BOURNONITE **1502**
BOURRAGE **6445**
BOURRAGE **7247**
BOURRAGE **9004**
BOURRAGE **9009**
BOURRAGE DE TIGE DE PISTON **9386**
BOURRAGE PLASTIQUE ETANCHE **11078**
BOURRE DE COCO **2654**
BOURRELET D'ETANCHEITE **13854**
BOURRELET D'UNE ROUE **5331**
BOURRELET EN TERRE GLAISE **2468**
BOURRER **6153**
BOURSOUFLURES **1330**
BOUSSOLE **2799**
BOUT ANODIQUE **591**
BOUT D'ELECTRODE **4578**
BOUT DE TUBE FERME **1303**
BOUT FEMELLE D'UN TUYAU **11710**
BOUT MALE D'UN TUYAU **11901**
BOUTEROLLE A MAIN **10626**
BOUTEROLLE A MANCHE OU A OEIL **4979**
BOUTISSE **6324**
BOUTON D'INTERRUPTEUR **9797**
BOUTON DE MANIVELLE **3302**
BOUTON DE TENSION **12755**
BOUTON DE VILEBREQUIN **9319**
BOUTON ELECTRIQUE **9797**

BOUTON MARCHE/ARRET **12115**
BOUTON-POUSSOIR **9797**
BOUVET A FOURCHEMENT **8047**
BOUVET FEMELLE **6139**
BOUVET MALE **12993**
BOUVETAGE **12991**
BOUVETER **12988**
BOYAU **6614**
BRABANT (TRAINEES OU PORTEES) **9526**
BRACON (ELEMENT DE CHARPENTE METALLIQUE) **1516**
BRACONS DE CHARPENTE **1520**
BRAI GRAS NATUREL **1280**
BRAI LIQUIDE **2570**
BRAI SEC **2737**
BRAI SEC MINERAL **2569**
BRAISETTE **2659**
BRAME **11551**
BRAME (TRAIN A BRAMES) **11552**
BRAMES (CINTRAGE DES) **11553**
BRAN DE SCIE **10953**
BRANCARD **5625**
BRANCARD DE CREUSET **3403**
BRANCHE **11845**
BRANCHE D'UN FER CORNIERE **13728**
BRANCHE D'UNE COURBE **1555**
BRANCHE DE LA POINTE TRACANTE DU PLANIMETRE **10662**
BRANCHE PORTE-AIGUILLE D'UN COMPAS **8521**
BRANCHE PORTE-CRAYON **9165**
BRANCHE TIRE-LIGNE D'UN COMPAS **9160**
BRANCHEMENT **1554**
BRANCHEMENTS SOUTERRAINS **1744**
BRANCHER (SE) **1556**
BRAS D'ARTICULATION **6505**
BRAS D'UN VOLANT **705**
BRAS D'UNE POULIE **705**
BRAS DE L'ELECTRODE **6592**
BRAS DE LEVIER **7531**
BRAS DE LEVIER DE LA FORCE **706**
BRAS DE MANIVELLE **3301**
BRAS DE MANIVELLE **3296**
BRAS DE POTENCE **3619**
BRAS DE SUSPENSION **3050**
BRAS DROIT D'UNE POULIE **12302**
BRAS DYNAMOMETRIQUE **13049**
BRAS OSCILLANT **12549**
BRAS PARABOLIQUE D'UNE POULIE **3497**
BRAS RADIAL **10128**
BRAS/BRANCHE DE REGULATEUR **6014**
BRASAGE **11762**
BRASAGE **1576**

# BRA
586

BRASAGE AU BAIN SALIN **10911**
BRASAGE AU CHALUMEAU **5810**
BRASAGE AU FOUR **5740**
BRASAGE AU TREMPE BRASAGE PAR IMMERSION **2304**
BRASAGE DUR ELECTRIQUE **4498**
BRASAGE FORT A L'ARC **666**
BRASAGE PAR INDUCTION **6893**
BRASAGE PAR INDUCTION PROGRESSIVE **9908**
BRASAGE PAR RESISTANCE **10487**
BRASEMENT **1576**
BRASER **1573**
BRASERO **3821**
BRASSURE (D'UNE ROUE) **13814**
BRASURE **6279**
BRASURE **1576**
BRASURE A FROID **2705**
BRASURE A L'ALLIAGE D'ARGENT **11460**
BREAK **12141**
BREVET D'INVENTION **9112**
BREVET ETRANGER **5540**
BREVETE **9123**
BREVETER **9113**
BREVETS D'INVENTION (BUREAU DES) **9120**
BREVETS D'INVENTION (LOI SUR LES) **9116**
BRIDE **5323**
BRIDE **13773**
BRIDE **7817**
BRIDE A COLLET RABATTU **9803**
BRIDE A FACE SURELEVEE **10183**
BRIDE A MANDRINER **10699**
BRIDE A MOYEU **6663**
BRIDE A REDUCTION **10350**
BRIDE A SOUDER (EN BOUT A L'INTERIEUR) **13794**
BRIDE A VISSER **11055**
BRIDE ANGULAIRE **512**
BRIDE BRASEE **11758**
BRIDE BRUTE DE FONTE **10776**
BRIDE D'ACCOUPLEMENT **3255**
BRIDE DE CHAPEAU **1452**
BRIDE DE FOULOIR **5955**
BRIDE DE PRESSE-ETOUPE **9002**
BRIDE DE RECOUVREMENT **1304**
BRIDE DE TUBE **9351**
BRIDE FIXE **5039**
BRIDE FOLLE **7746**
BRIDE MANDRINEE **10672**
BRIDE OBTURATRICE **1304**
BRIDE OVALE **8918**
BRIDE PLATE **5382**
BRIDE PLEINE **1326**
BRIDE PLEINE **1304**

BRIDE RAPPORTEE **1708**
BRIDE RIVETEE **10638**
BRIDE RONDE **10797**
BRIDE RONDELLE DE TUBE **9351**
BRIDE TARAUDEE **12866**
BRIDE TARAUDEE **11064**
BRIDE TOURNANTE **7398**
BRIDE TOURNEE **5003**
BRIDE VENUE DE FONTE **2063**
BRIDE VISSEE **11063**
BRIDE-DIAMETRE DE PERCAGE **1439**
BRIDER DES TUYAUX **7243**
BRIDES D'USINAGE **13013**
BRIDES DE MORTAISAGE **7289**
BRILLANTER **1756**
BRIN CONDUCTEUR **4316**
BRIN CONDUIT **5516**
BRIN COURANT **10851**
BRIN D'UNE CHAINE SANS FIN **11413**
BRIN D'UNE COURROIE **11413**
BRIN DE CABLE **10740**
BRIN DORMANT **12092**
BRIN GARANT DU CABLE **5023**
BRIN LACHE **5516**
BRIN MENANT **4316**
BRIN MENE **5516**
BRIN MOTEUR **4316**
BRIN MOU **5516**
BRIN SORTANT (D UNE COURROIE SANS FIN) **5516**
BRIN TENDU (D'UNE COURROIE SANS FIN) **4316**
BRIQUE **1596**
BRIQUE ABRASIVE **19**
BRIQUE CIRCULAIRE, ARRONDIE, CINTREE **13738**
BRIQUE CREUSE **245**
BRIQUE CRUE **7692**
BRIQUE CUITE **1760**
BRIQUE DE CHROMITE **2371**
BRIQUE DE PAREMENT **5004**
BRIQUE DE POCHE **7359**
BRIQUE DINAS **5803**
BRIQUE DURE **6273**
BRIQUE DURE ET TRES CUITE **2500**
BRIQUE EMAILLEE **5970**
BRIQUE EN LIEGE **3174**
BRIQUE EN TOURBE **9148**
BRIQUE PILEE **9724**
BRIQUE PLEINE **11780**
BRIQUE PROFILEE **8425**
BRIQUE REFRACTAIRE **5239**
BRIQUE REFRACTAIRE **5252**
BRIQUE REFRACTAIRE ALUMINEUSE **5254**

| | |
|---|---|
| BRIQUE SECHEE A L'AIR **7692** | BRONZE DE RESSORT **1661** |
| BRIQUE SILICEUSE **11435** | BRONZE DES MONNAIES **8183** |
| BRIQUE VERNISSEE **5970** | BRONZE DU COMMERCE **1657** |
| BRIQUES CREUSES **1697** | BRONZE EN POUDRE **1652** |
| BRIQUETAGE **1602** | BRONZE ORNEMENTAL **1663** |
| BRIQUETTE **1623** | BRONZE PHOSPHOREUX **9246** |
| BRIQUETTE DE FERRO ALLIAGE **1622** | BRONZE PLASTIQUE **1660** |
| BRIQUETTE DE MINERAI **8860** | BRONZE POUR MIROIRS DE TELESCOPES **11867** |
| BRIS **10861** | BRONZE POUR VISSERIE **1659** |
| BRIS D'UN TUBE **9353** | BRONZE RESISTANT AUX ACIDES **1655** |
| BRISE **10397** | BRONZE SILICEUX **11444** |
| BROCHAGE **1637** | BRONZE STATUAIRE **12147** |
| BROCHE **11904** | BRONZE STATUAIRE **1662** |
| BROCHE **4260** | BRONZER **1651** |
| BROCHE **12985** | BROSSE **9019** |
| BROCHE (FRITTAGE) **3162** | BROSSE A LIMES **5150** |
| BROCHE CONIQUE **2009** | BROSSE CIRCULAIRE A POLIR **2425** |
| BROCHE D'ASSEMBLAGE **4261** | BROSSE EN FILS METALLIQUES **13884** |
| BROCHE POUR ASSEMBLAGE PROVISOIRE DES TOLES | BROSSE METALLIQUE **13884** |
| **12592** | BROSSE METALLIQUE **11014** |
| BROMARGURE **1645** | BROSSE RACLETTE POUR TUBES **13247** |
| BROMARGYRITE **1645** | BROUETTE **13812** |
| BROMATE **1646** | BROUILLARD METALLIQUE **8182** |
| BROME **1649** | BROYAGE **6117** |
| BROMITE **1645** | BROYAGE **8287** |
| BROMURE **1648** | BROYAGE FIN (FRITTAGE) **6106** |
| BROMURE DE POTASSIUM **9678** | BROYER **6103** |
| BROMYRITE **1645** | BROYEUR **3419** |
| BRONZAGE **1664** | BROYEUR A BOULETS **959** |
| BRONZE **1650** | BROYEUR A CYLINDRES **10687** |
| BRONZE **1658** | BRUIT **8608** |
| BRONZE (DE) **216** | BRULEMENT DU FER **1754** |
| BRONZE A CANON **6178** | BRULER **1745** |
| BRONZE ALPHA **1656** | BRULER LE FER **1746** |
| BRONZE ARCHITECTURAL **692** | BRULER SANS FLAMME **11688** |
| BRONZE AU BERYLLIUM **1208** | BRULEUR **1749** |
| BRONZE AU MANGANESE **7967** | BRULEUR A GAZ **5811** |
| BRONZE AU NICKEL **8560** | BRULEUR BUNSEN **1741** |
| BRONZE AU PLOMB **7456** | BRULURE **1750** |
| BRONZE AU TUNGSTENE **13263** | BRUNI **1755** |
| BRONZE AU ZING **10326** | BRUNIR **1756** |
| BRONZE D'ALUMINIUM **420** | BRUNISSAGE **1758** |
| BRONZE D'ALUMINIUM **58** | BRUNISSOIR **1757** |
| BRONZE D'ALUMINIUM CUPRO-ALUMINIUM **434** | BRUNISSURE **1755** |
| BRONZE D'ART **12147** | BRUT **3406** |
| BRONZE D'OR **5995** | BRUT DE COULEE **739** |
| BRONZE DE CANONS **197** | BRUT DE FORGE **742** |
| BRONZE DE CLOCHE **1134** | BRUT DE LAMINAGE **10778** |
| BRONZE DE COUSSINET **1660** | BRUT DE LAMINAGE **744** |
| BRONZE DE NICKEL ET ALUMINIUM **8572** | BRUT DE TREMPE **743** |
| BRONZE DE QUALITE COMMERCIALE **1657** | BUCHE **1243** |

**BUF** 588

BUEE 1404
BUFFLE 1685
BUIS 1507
BULBE 1711
BULLAGE 1672
BULLAGE 5703
BULLE D'AIR 1670
BULLE DE GAZ 1671
BUREAU D'ETUDE 3796
BUREAU D'ETUDES 3800
BUREAU DE DESSIN 4198
BUREAU DE DESSIN 4238
BURETTE 1743
BURETTE A HUILE 8749
BURETTE A PISTON 9994
BURETTE DE GRAISSAGE 8749
BURIN 5377
BURIN 2349
BURINAGE 2347
BURINER 2344
BUSE 12966
BUSE 8685
BUSE DE COUPE 3537
BUTANE 1775
BUTEE 57
BUTEE 12902
BUTEE 12278
BUTEE 898
BUTEE A BILLES 12901
BUTEE A BILLES 966
BUTEE A ROULEAUX (A GALETS) 10691
BUTEE D'UN ARBRE 11384
BUTEE D'UNE SOUPAPE 13461
BUTEE DE DEBRAYAGE 2549
BUTEE REGLABLE 187
BUTOIR 1686
BUTOIR 12278
BUTOIR DE PARE-CHOCS 8956
BUTTEUSES POUR POMMES DE TERRE 9702
BUTYLENE 1816
BUVARD 1350
BY-PASS 1821
BY-PASS 1818
CABESTAN 1929
CABESTAN A BRAS 6229
CABINE AVANCEE 1824
CABINE DE CAMION 13229
CABLAGE 7389
CABLAGE 1828
CABLAGE 10739
CABLAGE ALTERNATIF 10414

CABLE 10730
CABLE A CABLAGE ALBERT 309
CABLE A CABLAGE LANG OU ALBERT 7390
CABLE A GAINE METALLIQUE 8177
CABLE A SECTION CARREE 12028
CABLE A SECTION DECROISSANTE 12661
CABLE A SECTION TRIANGULAIRE 13194
CABLE A TORONS TRIANGULAIRES 13195
CABLE AERIEN 8938
CABLE ANTIGIRATOIRE 8646
CABLE ARME 713
CABLE CLOS 2513
CABLE CONDUCTEUR TOUT-ALUMINIUM 343
CABLE CONIQUE 12661
CABLE D'ASCENSEUR 7546
CABLE D'EXTRACTION 6520
CABLE DE CHANVRE 6443
CABLE DE COMMANDE 3051
CABLE DE DISTRIBUTION 4079
CABLE DE LEVAGE 6520
CABLE DE MASSE 4411
CABLE DE TRANSMISSION 4314
CABLE DIMINUE 12661
CABLE ELECTRIQUE 1825
CABLE EN ACIER 12215
CABLE EN ACIER 12201
CABLE EN COTON 3221
CABLE EN FILIN 12215
CABLE EN FILS DE FER 7147
CABLE EN GRELIN 12201
CABLE ISOLE AU P.V.C. 9472
CABLE METALLIQUE 13899
CABLE METALLIQUE A FILS PARALLELES 7390
CABLE METALLIQUE A TORONS MEPLATS 5407
CABLE METALLIQUE EN FILS FINS 5207
CABLE METALLIQUE EN GROS FILS 2579
CABLE METALLIQUE TORDU ALTERNATIF 10415
CABLE PLAT 5393
CABLE PRINCIPAL 5081
CABLE ROND 10801
CABLE SANS FIN 4733
CABLE TELEDYNAMIQUE 12705
CABLE TORDU A DROITE 10587
CABLE TORDU A GAUCHE 7511
CABLE VOLANT 7264
CABLER 13303
CABLES 12739
CABLES D'ALIMENTATION 12484
CABLES INJECTES 1446
CABROUET 947
CACHE-ENTREE 4835

CADMIAGE **1832**
CADMIUM **1831**
CADRAN DIVISE **3837**
CADRAN DU BOIS **12108**
CADRAN GRADUE **6027**
CADRANURE **12108**
CADRE **5624**
CADRE A CREMAILLERES **4150**
CADRE DENTE **4150**
CAESIUM **1833**
CAGE A BILLES **957**
CAGE A CYLINDRE VERTICAUX CYLINDRE DE REFOULEMENT **4456**
CAGE D'UN ROULEMENT A GALETS **12040**
CAGE DE CYLINDRES **10704**
CAGE DE FARADAY **5036**
CAGE DE LAMINOIR **12065**
CAGE DE ROULEMENT A BILLES **955**
CAGE DEGROSSISEURS **10787**
CAGE DEGROSSISSEUSE **9622**
CAGE FINISSEURS **5225**
CAGE FINISSEUSE **5219**
CAGE MEDIANE **7098**
CAGE PROTECTRICE **9948**
CAGE REFOULEUSE **4454**
CAHIER DES CHARGES **11855**
CAILLEBOTIS **6101**
CAILLOU **9152**
CAISSE DE CEMENTATION **3075**
CAISSE DE RECUIT **563**
CAISSE DE RECUIT **567**
CAISSE OU CORPS D'UN EVAPORATEUR **4870**
CAISSON **2798**
CAISSON (TOIT A...) **9621**
CAISSON DE SOUTIRAGE **4227**
CAISSONS ETANCHES **7658**
CALAGE **13740**
CALAGE D'UNE CLAVETTE **4310**
CALAGE DE LA DISTRIBUTION **12952**
CALAMINE **1836**
CALANDRE DE RADIATEUR **10152**
CALCAIRE **10969**
CALCAIRE **7586**
CALCAIRE CARBONIFERE **1969**
CALCAIRE COQUILLIER **8487**
CALCAIRE D'EAU DOUCE **5664**
CALCAIRE GROSSIER **5664**
CALCAIRE JURASSIQUE **7267**
CALCAIRE OOLITHIQUE **8801**
CALCAIRE PISOLITHIQUE **8801**
CALCAIRE SILICEUX **11451**

CALCINATION **1839**
CALCINATION DES MINERAIS **1840**
CALCINE **2272**
CALCINER LES MINERAIS **1841**
CALCITE **1845**
CALCITE **1844**
CALCIUM **1846**
CALCUL **1860**
CALCUL **3794**
CALCUL APPROXIMATIF **652**
CALCUL DIFFERENTIEL **3908**
CALCUL GRAPHIQUE **6060**
CALCUL INFINITESIMAL **6912**
CALCUL INTEGRAL **7011**
CALCUL RAPIDE APPROCHE **10772**
CALCULER **3795**
CALCULER **1857**
CALE **13731**
CALE **13739**
CALE D'EPAISSEUR **13731**
CALE D'EPAISSEUR **11352**
CALE DE RATTRAPAGE **185**
CALER **7277**
CALER SUR... **7279**
CALES D'USURE **13711**
CALES DE COMPARAISON **2796**
CALES MAGNETIQUES DE FIXATION **7897**
CALES-ETALONS **5873**
CALIBRAGE **2651**
CALIBRAGE **1867**
CALIBRAGE **11524**
CALIBRE **5871**
CALIBRE A COULISSE AVEC REGLE DE PROFONDEUR **1871**
CALIBRE A COULISSE DE PROFONDEUR **13538**
CALIBRE A COULISSE DE PROFONDEUR A FIXATION MICROMETRIQUE **13539**
CALIBRE A DEBIT **5455**
CALIBRE D'ALESAGE **10661**
CALIBRE D'ANGLES **513**
CALIBRE D'EPAISSEUR **5086**
CALIBRE D'UNE TOLE **9487**
CALIBRE DE CONICITE NORMAL **8393**
CALIBRE DE FILETAGE **11047**
CALIBRE DE HAUTEUR DE PRECISION **9768**
CALIBRE DE MATRICE **6532**
CALIBRE DE PERCAGE **4267**
CALIBRE DE PROFILAGE **11123**
CALIBRE DE PROFONDEUR **3781**
CALIBRE DE REGLAGE DE SOUPAPE **13473**
CALIBRE DE TOLERANCE **3905**
CALIBRE DE TRACAGE **8016**

# CAL

590

CALIBRE EN FER A CHEVAL **6608**
CALIBRE FEMELLE LISSE **9431**
CALIBRE FIXE **5293**
CALIBRE LIMITE (OU DE TOLERANCE) **4584**
CALIBRE MALE CONIQUE **12656**
CALIBRE MALE ET FEMELLE **3581**
CALIBRE NORMAL **12076**
CALIBRE PASSE-PASSE PAS **5991**
CALIBRE POUR PROFILS **8422**
CALIBRE POUR TUBES **2027**
CALIBRER **1861**
CALIBRES **5769**
CALIBRES FEMELLES CONIQUES **12659**
CALIBRES MALES CYLINDRIQUES **3587**
CALIBRES MALES POUR FILETAGES **12862**
CALIBRES MICROMETRIQUES **8251**
CALIBRES MICROMETRIQUES D'INTERIEUR **6979**
CALIBRES TELESCOPIQUES **12713**
CALIBRES-MACHOIRES **11693**
CALICHE **2330**
CALOMEL **8159**
CALORIE ANGLAISE **1625**
CALORIE GRAMME-DEGRE **6045**
CALORIE KILOGRAMME-DEGRE **7298**
CALORIFUGE **6998**
CALORIFUGE **8628**
CALORIFUGE **6352**
CALORIFUGEAGE **6639**
CALORIFUGEAGE **7623**
CALORIMETRE **1877**
CALORIMETRE A CONDENSATION **12160**
CALORIMETRE A EAU **13643**
CALORIMETRE A FUSION DE LA GLACE **6749**
CALORIMETRIE **1881**
CALORIMETRIQUE **1878**
CALORISATION **1882**
CALOTTE (D'UNE SPHERE) **1911**
CALOTTE SPHERIQUE **11887**
CALOTTE SPHERIQUE **11137**
CALQUAGE **13082**
CALQUE **13082**
CALQUER **13077**
CALQUEUR **13078**
CAMBOUIS **879**
CAMBOUIS **3308**
CAMBOUIS **6063**
CAMBRAGE **1889**
CAME **6329**
CAME **4442**
CAME **13878**
CAME A DISQUE **9482**

CAME A PLATEAU **9482**
CAME A PLATEAU COURBE **11913**
CAME A RAINURE **6134**
CAME A RAINURE **3270**
CAME EXCENTRIQUE BOSSE **1883**
CAME OSCILLANTE **8878**
CAMES-DISQUES **9497**
CAMION **7752**
CAMION A BENNE BASCULANTE **4375**
CAMION A RIDELLES **7753**
CAMION AUTOMOBILE **8414**
CAMION BACHE **12686**
CAMION POIDS LOURD **6405**
CAMIONNETTE **7563**
CAMIONS TRANSPALETTES **9025**
CAMPHRE **1893**
CANAL **2248**
CANAL D'ARRIVEE **6319**
CANAL DE COULEE **10844**
CANAL DE COULEE **7436**
CANAL DE DECHARGE **12596**
CANAL DE FUITE **12596**
CANAL DE TROP-PLEIN **6185**
CANAL DECOUVERT **8807**
CANALISATION **9339**
CANALISATION **13354**
CANALISATION **13666**
CANALISATION D'AIR **281**
CANALISATION DE SECOURS **4690**
CANALISATION DE VAPEUR **12178**
CANALISATION ELECTRIQUE **13353**
CANALISATION ELECTRIQUE **4523**
CANALISATION EN MER OUVERTE **11080**
CANAUX DE VENT **247**
CANIVEAU **2251**
CANIVEAU (SOUDURE) **13351**
CANNEL-COAL **1901**
CANNELE **5484**
CANNELURE **4372**
CANNELURE **7282**
CANNELURE **4455**
CANNELURE EMBOITEE **2526**
CANNELURE FERMEE **2526**
CANNELURES FERMEES **2527**
CANON A ELECTRONS **4628**
CANON ANTI-AERIEN **610**
CAOLIN **2340**
CAOUTCHOUC **10825**
CAOUTCHOUC **10816**
CAOUTCHOUC AVEC TOILE INTERCALEE **6973**
CAOUTCHOUC BRUT **3413**

CAOUTCHOUC D'ETANCHEITE **13722**
CAOUTCHOUC DE PARA **9037**
CAOUTCHOUC DURCI **2363**
CAOUTCHOUC VIERGE **3413**
CAOUTCHOUC VULCANISE **13610**
CAPACITE **1917**
CAPACITE (ELECTR.) **1917**
CAPACITE CALORIFIQUE **41**
CAPACITE CALORIFIQUE **6339**
CAPACITE CALORIFIQUE **6335**
CAPACITE CALORIQUE **6342**
CAPACITE D'AMORTISSEMENT **3605**
CAPACITE DE CHARGE **7682**
CAPACITE DE CHARGE **2011**
CAPACITE DE DEFORMATION **3705**
CAPACITE THERMIQUE **12803**
CAPILLARITE **1920**
CAPOT **1451**
CAPOT DE VOITURE **6566**
CAPOT EN TOLE **11310**
CAPOT-MOTEUR **1451**
CAPOTE PLIANTE **2719**
CAPSULE **4864**
CAPTAGE DES GAZ SANS COMBUSTION **5841**
CAPTAGE DU GAZ ET DEPOUSSIERAGE **4392**
CAPTEUR **13108**
CAPTEUR DE POSITION **9649**
CAPUCHON **1910**
CAR A LINGOTS (TRANSPORT DE LINGOT) **6920**
CARACTERE **2255**
CARACTERISTIQUE **9075**
CARACTERISTIQUE **2256**
CARACTERISTIQUE D'UN LOGARITHME **2257**
CARACTERISTIQUES CHIMIQUES **2295**
CARACTERISTIQUES MECANIQUES **12746**
CARACTERISTIQUES MECANIQUES **8109**
CARBOLINEUM **1939**
CARBONADO **1967**
CARBONATE **1968**
CARBONATE ACIDE DE SODIUM **126**
CARBONATE D'AMMONIUM **461**
CARBONATE DE BARYUM **996**
CARBONATE DE CHAUX **1849**
CARBONATE DE CUIVRE **3470**
CARBONATE DE LITHIUM **7665**
CARBONATE DE MAGNESIE **7884**
CARBONATE DE SODIUM **11713**
CARBONATE DE SOUDE ANHYDRE **551**
CARBONATE DE ZINC **14037**
CARBONATE NATUREL DE BARYTE **13911**
CARBONATE NEUTRE DE POTASSE **9679**

CARBONE **1966**
CARBONE **1940**
CARBONE A L'ETAT GRAPHITOIDE **6059**
CARBONE COMBINE **5289**
CARBONE COMBINE **1962**
CARBONE COMBINE AU FER **2767**
CARBONE DE REVENU **1965**
CARBONE DISSOUS **1963**
CARBONE NON COMBINE AU FER **13345**
CARBONISATION **1975**
CARBONISATION **1974**
CARBONISATION **1970**
CARBONISATION DE LA HOUILLE **7991**
CARBONISATION INCOMPLETE **7776**
CARBONISE **2272**
CARBONISER **1971**
CARBONITRURATION **1972**
CARBONYLE **1939**
CARBONYLE **1976**
CARBONYLE DE FER **7140**
CARBONYLE DE NICKEL **8561**
CARBORUNDUN **1980**
CARBURANT **9222**
CARBURANT ANTI-DETONNANT **613**
CARBURANTS **2024**
CARBURANTS **1988**
CARBURATEUR **1984**
CARBURATEUR **1982**
CARBURATEUR A DOUBLE CORPS **4360**
CARBURATEUR INVERSE **4189**
CARBURATION DU FER **1985**
CARBURE **1933**
CARBURE **1848**
CARBURE D'HYDROGENE **6705**
CARBURE DE BARYUM **995**
CARBURE DE BORE **1479**
CARBURE DE FER **7138**
CARBURE DE SILICIUM **11445**
CARBURE DE SILICUM **1980**
CARBURER LE FER **1986**
CARCASSE **5624**
CARDAN **6573**
CARDAN **5567**
CARDAN **1997**
CARDE **5150**
CARDIOIDE **2001**
CARIE **10770**
CARNEAU **5467**
CARNEAU **13418**
CARNEAU A GAZ **5821**
CARNEAU DE FUMEE **5743**

# CAR

592

CARNEAU DE RACCORDEMENT **5034**
CARNEAU INTERIEUR D'UNE CHAUDIERE **1412**
CAROTTE **3142**
CARRE **12025**
CARRE (DEUXIEME PUISSANCE) **12013**
CARRE (GEOM.) **12013**
CARRE (POUR CLEF) **9533**
CARRE D'ENTRAINEMENT **4288**
CARREAU **12019**
CARREAU (CONSTR.) **12933**
CARREE **12019**
CARRELET **12019**
CARRES EN ACIER ALLIE **379**
CARRIERE **10073**
CARROSSAGE **1889**
CARROSSERIE **1385**
CARROSSERIE PORTANTE **13381**
CARTE **1999**
CARTE PERFOREE **10002**
CARTER **2026**
CARTER D'EMBRAYAGE **2546**
CARTER D'EMBRAYAGE **1133**
CARTER D'ENGRENAGE **5890**
CARTER D'ENGRENAGES **13815**
CARTER D'HUILE (INFERIEUR) **8782**
CARTER D'HUILE (INFERIEUR) **8767**
CARTER DE CHAINES **2204**
CARTER DE DISTRIBUTION **12947**
CARTER DE POMPE D'INJECTION **5712**
CARTER DE REGULATEUR **6016**
CARTER-MOTEUR **3306**
CARTON **1381**
CARTON BITUME OU ASPHALTE **10712**
CARTON D'AMIANTE **747**
CARTON LEGER **1999**
CARTOUCHE **2015**
CARTOUCHE FILTRANTE **5175**
CASCADE **2018**
CASE **2798**
CASEINE **2025**
CASQUE **6432**
CASSANT **1627**
CASSANT A CHAUD **6658**
CASSANT A CHAUD **10337**
CASSE-COKE **2658**
CASSE-FER **631**
CASSETTE **2028**
CASSINOIDE **2029**
CASSITERITE **12959**
CASSURE **5620**
CASSURE **5617**

CASSURE CEROIDE **11936**
CASSURE CONCHOIDALE **2893**
CASSURE CROCHUE **6195**
CASSURE FIBREUSE **5138**
CASSURE GRENUE **6051**
CASSURE HACHEE **6195**
CASSURE INEGALE **13357**
CASSURE INTERGRANULAIRE **7042**
CASSURE LAMELLAIRE **7378**
CASSURE NETTE **11683**
CASSURE SOYEUSE **11454**
CASSURE TERREUSE **4421**
CASSURE TRANSCRISTALLINE **13117**
CASSURE UNIE **4871**
CATALYSE **2090**
CATALYSEUR **2091**
CATALYTIQUE **2092**
CATAPHORESE **4639**
CATARACTE **3611**
CATEGORIE DE FER **2458**
CATEGORIE SORTE D'ACIER **2459**
CATHETOMETRE **2096**
CATHODE **2097**
CATHODE **2106**
CATHODE DE REDRESSEUR **10316**
CATHOLYTE **2111**
CATION **2112**
CATION **9657**
CAUSE D'ERREUR **11825**
CAUSTIQUE **4847**
CAUSTIQUE (OPT.) **2116**
CAUSTIQUE PAR REFLEXION **2089**
CAUSTIQUE PAR REFRACTION **3829**
CAVALIER **1735**
CAVALIER **12106**
CAVALIER DE FOND **12104**
CAVALIERS **3946**
CAVET **2122**
CAVITATION **2123**
CAVITE **7073**
CAVITE **2125**
CAVITE DE CELLULE **2127**
CAVITE DU MOULE **8353**
CAVITE EN V **5271**
CEDER **5949**
CEINTURE DE SECURITE **11096**
CEINTURE DE SECURITE **10882**
CELLULE (OU CUVE) ELECTROLYTIQUE **4588**
CELLULE AU MERCURE **8165**
CELLULE PHOTO-CONDUCTRICE **9261**
CELLULE PHOTO-ELECTRIQUE **9260**

CELLULE PHOTO-EMISSIVE **9273**
CELLULE PHOTOVOLTAIQUE **9277**
CELLULOID **2130**
CELLULOSE **2131**
CELLULOSE NITREE **6176**
CEMENT **2022**
CEMENT **2139**
CEMENT DE CUIVRE **2136**
CEMENTATION **2021**
CEMENTATION **2141**
CEMENTATION (DES BARRES DE FER) **2142**
CEMENTATION A L'AZOTE **5818**
CEMENTATION A LA POUDRE **8992**
CEMENTATION AU PRUSSIATE DE POTASSE **9670**
CEMENTATION AU PRUSSIATE JAUNE **9670**
CEMENTATION BRILLANTE **9959**
CEMENTATION DES PIECES EN ACIER DOUX **2023**
CEMENTATION EN BAIN **7646**
CEMENTATION EN CAISSE **1996**
CEMENTATION HOMOGENE **1993**
CEMENTATION PAR GAZ **1992**
CEMENTATION PAR LE CARBONE **1987**
CEMENTATION PAR LE CHROME **2390**
CEMENTATION PARTIELLE **2023**
CEMENTATION SELECTIVE **1995**
CEMENTATION SELECTIVE **11143**
CEMENTER **2134**
CEMENTITE **2147**
CEMENTS **2024**
CENDRE **760**
CENDRE **2397**
CENDRES **760**
CENDRES VOLANTES **5493**
CENDRIER **759**
CENTIMETRE **2158**
CENTIMETRE CARRE **12016**
CENTIMETRE CUBE **3449**
CENTRAGE **2187**
CENTRALE ELECTRIQUE **4512**
CENTRALE HYDRAULIQUE **6692**
CENTRE **2148**
CENTRE **2162**
CENTRE A COMPAS **6594**
CENTRE CUBIQUE **1399**
CENTRE D'OSCILLATION **2170**
CENTRE DE COURBURE **2167**
CENTRE DE GRAVITE **2168**
CENTRE DE ROTATION **5717**
CENTRE DE ROTATION **2169**
CENTRE DE ROUE EN ACIER FONDU **2056**
CENTRE DE SURFACE **2191**

CENTRE DU RIVET **2171**
CENTRE INSTANTANE DE ROTATION **6989**
CENTRER **2163**
CERAMIQUE **2193**
CERCLE **2401**
CERCLE ANNUEL **586**
CERCLE CIRCONSCRIT **2435**
CERCLE DE BASE **1030**
CERCLE DE COURBURE **2402**
CERCLE DE CREUX **10723**
CERCLE DE FOND **10723**
CERCLE DE PIED **10717**
CERCLE DE PIED **10723**
CERCLE DE POINT NEUTRE (CALCUL DES CHARPENTES DE
  RESISTANCE SOUS PRESSION) **8604**
CERCLE DE TETE **3396**
CERCLE DE TETE **166**
CERCLE DE TETE **167**
CERCLE DECRIT PAR LA MANIVELLE **3298**
CERCLE DES TROUS DE BOULONS **1433**
CERCLE DIVISE **6026**
CERCLE ELASTIQUE **11990**
CERCLE EXINSCRIT **4834**
CERCLE EXTERIEUR **166**
CERCLE FIXE **5290**
CERCLE GRADUE **6026**
CERCLE INSCRIT **6963**
CERCLE MOBILE **5921**
CERCLE PRIMITIF **1030**
CERCLE PRIMITIF **9404**
CERCLE PRIMITIF DE DENTURE **9403**
CERCLE ROULANT **5921**
CERCLES CONCENTRIQUES **2890**
CERCLES EXCENTRIQUES **4426**
CERESINE **2194**
CERIUM **2195**
CERMET **2192**
CERTIFICAT D'EPREUVE **12775**
CERTIFICAT DE RECEPTION **70**
CERUSE **13834**
CERUSSITE **2196**
CESIUM **2197**
CESIUM **1833**
CESSION DE CHALEUR **3735**
CHABOTTE D'ENCLUME **633**
CHAINE **2201**
CHAINE A ETANCONS **12403**
CHAINE A MAILLES ETANCONNEES **12403**
CHAINE A MAILLES SOUDEES **13770**
CHAINE A MAILLONS COURTS **11373**
CHAINE A MAILLONS LONGS **7730**

# CHA

594

CHAINE A MAILLONS SERRES 11373
CHAINE A ROULEAUX 10684
CHAINE CALIBREE 9412
CHAINE D'UN TISSU 13627
CHAINE DE BICYCLETTE 1239
CHAINE DE DISTRIBUTION 12950
CHAINE DE DISTRIBUTION 12948
CHAINE DE LEVAGE 6518
CHAINE DE TRANSMISSION 4306
CHAINE DE TRANSMISSION 4305
CHAINE DE VAUCANSON 6570
CHAINE DECOUPEE 12058
CHAINE GALLE 12002
CHAINE MOTRICE 4306
CHAINE ORDINAIRE 8855
CHAINE PLATE 1336
CHAINE SANS FIN 4732
CHAINE SILENCIEUSE 11432
CHAINE-CABLE 6518
CHAINE-CABLE A ETAIS 12403
CHAINES CALIBREES 1862
CHAINES DE MARINE 8004
CHAINES DE NEIGE 11696
CHAINETTE (GEOM.) 2095
CHAINON 7627
CHAISE D'APPLIQUE 13618
CHAISE DE PALIER 1103
CHAISE EN BOUT 4726
CHAISE EN U 9166
CHAISE PENDANTE A DEUX JAMBES 9166
CHAISE SUR LE SOL 12064
CHAISE-CONSOLE 13618
CHALCOPYRITE 3126
CHALCOSINE 3118
CHALEUR 6333
CHALEUR ATOMIQUE 802
CHALEUR BLANCHE 6823
CHALEUR D'ABSORPTION 6354
CHALEUR D'EVAPORATION 6359
CHALEUR D'OXYDATION 6361
CHALEUR DE CARBURATION 6355
CHALEUR DE COMBINAISON 9656
CHALEUR DE COMBUSTION 6356
CHALEUR DE DECOMPOSITION 6357
CHALEUR DE DECOMPOSITION 8528
CHALEUR DE DISSOCIATION 6358
CHALEUR DE FORGE 2744
CHALEUR DE FORMATION 9656
CHALEUR DE FUSION 6360
CHALEUR DE REDUCTION 6362
CHALEUR DE SUBLIMATION 6363

CHALEUR DE TRANSFORMATION 6364
CHALEUR DE VAPORISATION 6366
CHALEUR DEGAGEE 6370
CHALEUR DEGAGEE DANS UNE REACTION 6348
CHALEUR EFFECTIVE 4457
CHALEUR EMMAGASINEE 10411
CHALEUR INTERNE 7070
CHALEUR LATENTE 7415
CHALEUR LATENTE 6365
CHALEUR LATENTE DE VAPORISATION 7416
CHALEUR PERDUE 13635
CHALEUR PRODUITE PAR FROTTEMENT 6343
CHALEUR RADIANTE 10140
CHALEUR RAYONNANTE 10140
CHALEUR ROUGE 10329
CHALEUR SENSIBLE 11184
CHALEUR SOUDANTE 13784
CHALEUR SPECIFIQUE 11852
CHALEUR SPECIFIQUE MOYENNE 8076
CHALEUR UTILE 4457
CHALUMEAU 1355
CHALUMEAU 3539
CHALUMEAU 13042
CHALUMEAU 5307
CHALUMEAU A BOUCHE 8433
CHALUMEAU A DECOUPER 3216
CHALUMEAU A OXYGENE COMPRIME 2848
CHALUMEAU COUPEUR 5312
CHALUMEAU DE CHAUFFAGE 6399
CHALUMEAU DE PRECHAUFFAGE 6391
CHALUMEAU DEROUILLEUR 5311
CHALUMEAU ELECTRIQUE 4496
CHALUMEAU OXYHYDRIQUE 8986
CHAMBRAGE 3236
CHAMBRAGE 3242
CHAMBRE A AIR 6955
CHAMBRE A AIR 13246
CHAMBRE A EAU D'UNE CHAUDIERE 13677
CHAMBRE A VIDE 13440
CHAMBRE A VIDE 13449
CHAMBRE D'EXPLOSIONS D'UN MOTEUR 2778
CHAMBRE D'IONISATION 7125
CHAMBRE DE COMBUSTION 2776
CHAMBRE DE COMBUSTION 2856
CHAMBRE DE COMBUSTION D'UN FOYER 2777
CHAMBRE DE DISTRIBUTION 2229
CHAMBRE DE TURBULENCE 12551
CHAMBRE DE VAPEUR D'UNE CHAUDIERE 12185
CHAMBRE DE VENT 241
CHAMBRE NOIRE 9264
CHAMOTTE 2235

| | |
|---|---|
| CHAMP DE VISION **5143** | CHAPITEAU D'UNE COLONNE **1926** |
| CHAMP ELECTRIQUE **4505** | CHARBON **2558** |
| CHAMP ELECTRIQUE **4504** | CHARBON ANIMAL **554** |
| CHAMP MAGNETIQUE **7901** | CHARBON DE BOIS **13914** |
| CHAMP VISUEL **5143** | CHARBON DE CORNUE **5812** |
| CHANCES D'INCENDIE **3608** | CHARBON DE FORGE **5543** |
| CHANDELLE **1899** | CHARBON DE TERRE **2558** |
| CHANDELLE (ETAI VERTICAL) **11365** | CHARBON FOSSILE **2558** |
| CHANFREIN **1902** | CHARBON GRAPHITIQUE **9851** |
| CHANFREIN **2231** | CHARBON GROS **7826** |
| CHANFREIN (SOUDURE) EN K **1793** | CHARBON PULVERISE **9984** |
| CHANFREIN D'ENTREE **516** | CHARBONNAGE **2566** |
| CHANFREIN EN DEMI-V **1800** | CHARBONNER **1971** |
| CHANFREINAGE **3234** | CHARGE **2259** |
| CHANFREINAGE **2233** | CHARGE **12367** |
| CHANFREINAGE **1231** | CHARGE **12331** |
| CHANFREINER **2230** | CHARGE **4954** |
| CHANGEMENT D'ETAT **2238** | CHARGE **7679** |
| CHANGEMENT D'ETAT NON REVERSIBLE **7170** | CHARGE ADMISE **9215** |
| CHANGEMENT D'ETAT PHYSIQUE **9280** | CHARGE ADMISSIBLE **13956** |
| CHANGEMENT D'ETAT REVERSIBLE **10539** | CHARGE CENTRALE **2161** |
| CHANGEMENT DE DIRECTION **2236** | CHARGE CHIMIQUE **5157** |
| CHANGEMENT DE FORME **3707** | CHARGE D'EAU **6323** |
| CHANGEMENT DE MULTIPLICATION **2245** | CHARGE D'ESSAI **12781** |
| CHANGEMENT DE PRESSION **2237** | CHARGE DE FORGEAGE **9823** |
| CHANGEMENT DE TEMPERATURE **2239** | CHARGE DE LA VITESSE **13515** |
| CHANGEMENT DE VITESSE **2245** | CHARGE DE NEIGE **11695** |
| CHANGEMENT DE VOIE **12556** | CHARGE DE RUPTURE **13331** |
| CHANGEMENT DE VOLUME **2240** | CHARGE DE RUPTURE **12749** |
| CHANGEMENT DU SENS D'UN COURANT **2246** | CHARGE DE RUPTURE **1585** |
| CHANGER LE SENS DU COURANT **2241** | CHARGE DE RUPTURE AU FLAMBAGE **3338** |
| CHANGEUR D'OUTILS **13000** | CHARGE DE SECURITE **10879** |
| CHANTIER **12265** | CHARGE DUE AU VENT **13857** |
| CHANTIER DE COULEE **2071** | CHARGE ELECTRIQUE **2259** |
| CHANTOURNAGE **10167** | CHARGE EXCENTRIQUE **4428** |
| CHANVRE **6439** | CHARGE HYDROSTATIQUE **7652** |
| CHANVRE DE MANILLE **7980** | CHARGE INCOMPLETE **7562** |
| CHAPE **13172** | CHARGE INFERIEURE A LA NORMALE **7562** |
| CHAPE **5567** | CHARGE INTERMITTENTE **7672** |
| CHAPE DE LA TETE DE BIELLE **12345** | CHARGE ISOLEE **7183** |
| CHAPE DE POULIE **1333** | CHARGE LIQUIDE **7647** |
| CHAPE DU BATTANT PORTE-OUTIL **2454** | CHARGE MAXIMUM **8065** |
| CHAPE-FOURCHETTE **5568** | CHARGE MOBILE **10706** |
| CHAPEAU **1910** | CHARGE MORTE **3631** |
| CHAPEAU **1454** | CHARGE NEUTRE **13842** |
| CHAPEAU **1451** | CHARGE NORMALE **8661** |
| CHAPEAU **1912** | CHARGE NORMALE **8655** |
| CHAPEAU A ARCADE **14015** | CHARGE PAR UNITE DE SURFACE **13371** |
| CHAPEAU DE LA BOITE A ETOUPE **5953** | CHARGE PERIODIQUE **6812** |
| CHAPEAU DE PALIER **1104** | CHARGE PERMANENTE **3633** |
| CHAPELLE **2229** | CHARGE PRATIQUE **10879** |

## CHA

596

CHARGE RECTANGULAIRE **10303**
CHARGE REPARTIE **4078**
CHARGE ROULANTE **10706**
CHARGE SANS CHOCS **7685**
CHARGE STATIQUE **12138**
CHARGE TOTALE **13062**
CHARGE TRAPEZOIDALE **13150**
CHARGE TRIANGULAIRE **13190**
CHARGE UNIFORMEMENT REPARTIE **13366**
CHARGE UTILE **9139**
CHARGE UTILE **13425**
CHARGE VARIABLE **7672**
CHARGE VIVE **7671**
CHARGE-LIMITE D'ELASTICITE **1586**
CHARGEMENT **2263**
CHARGEMENT **5262**
CHARGEMENT **2269**
CHARGEMENT D'UN ACCUMULATEUR **2265**
CHARGEMENT D'UN FOUR METALLURGIQUE **2264**
CHARGEMENT PAR CONVOYEUR A BANDE **1141**
CHARGER **5156**
CHARGER (RESISTANCE DES MATERIAUX) **7680**
CHARGER UN ACCUMULATEUR **2261**
CHARGER UN FOUR METALLURGIQUE **2260**
CHARGER UN FOYER **12269**
CHARGEUR **8110**
CHARGEUR (OU CHARGEUSE) POUR FOURRAGE VERT **7687**
CHARGEURS DE FUMIER **7689**
CHARGEURS DE SACS ET DE BETTERAVES **7688**
CHARIOT **4116**
CHARIOT (POUR MANUTENTION D'ATELIER ET MAGASIN) **13230**
CHARIOT D'ECRASEMENT **8436**
CHARIOT D'UN PONT-ROULANT **13155**
CHARIOT DE SUSPENSION POUR PIECES A TREMPER **9505**
CHARIOT PORTE-PALAN **13155**
CHARIOT TRANSVERSAL **3379**
CHARIOTAGE **12668**
CHARIOTAGE D'UNE SURFACE CYLINDRIQUE **13164**
CHARIOTAGE LONGITUDINAL **13164**
CHARIOTAGE TRANSVERSAL **12522**
CHARIOTER UNE SURFACE CYLINDRIQUE **13162**
CHARIOTS A BRAS **13231**
CHARNIERE **6505**
CHARNIERE (MALE) **6508**
CHARNIERE TYPE PENTURE **12347**
CHARNIERE UNIVERSELLE **6573**
CHARPENTE **5624**
CHARPENTE **12942**
CHARPENTE **5630**
CHARPENTE A CROISILLONS **3360**

CHARPENTE A FERMES **13244**
CHARPENTE A POTEAUX **2759**
CHARPENTE A POTEAUX **2754**
CHARPENTE AUTOPORTANTE **11161**
CHARPENTE METALLIQUE **12208**
CHARPENTE METALLIQUE **7152**
CHARPENTERIE **2006**
CHARPENTIER **2005**
CHARRETTE **2013**
CHARRETTE A BRAS **6230**
CHARRUES **9526**
CHARRUES A DISQUES (TRAINEES OU PORTEES) **9523**
CHARRUES BILLONEUSES **9527**
CHARRUES PORTEES **9524**
CHARRUES RIGOLEURSE **8344**
CHARRUES TRAINEES **9525**
CHASSE **9516**
CHASSE **2066**
CHASSE (ANGLE DE) **2067**
CHASSE (OUTIL DE FORGERON) **11218**
CHASSE A BISEAU **2232**
CHASSE A PARER **5410**
CHASSE-CLAVETTE **7278**
CHASSE-CLOU **12127**
CHASSE-GOUPILLE **9326**
CHASSE-POINTE **7332**
CHASSE-RIVET **10626**
CHASSER LES RIVETS **3511**
CHASSER UNE CLAVETTE **4295**
CHASSIS **5624**
CHASSIS **2275**
CHASSIS DE FENETRE **13865**
CHASSIS DE MOULAGE **5369**
CHASSIS POUR BLEUS **9874**
CHASSIS-CAISSON **1511**
CHASSIS-TENDEUR **12756**
CHATEAU D'EAU **13680**
CHAUDE **10329**
CHAUDE **5981**
CHAUDE ROUGE-CERISE **2326**
CHAUDE SUANTE **13784**
CHAUDIERE **1406**
CHAUDIERE A BASSE PRESSION **7782**
CHAUDIERE A FAIBLE VOLUME **11663**
CHAUDIERE A FOYER INTERIEUR **5468**
CHAUDIERE A GRAND VOLUME **7412**
CHAUDIERE A HAUTE PRESSION **6487**
CHAUDIERE A MOYEN VOLUME **8126**
CHAUDIERE A MOYENNE PRESSION **8127**
CHAUDIERE A TUBE FOYER **5468**
CHAUDIERE A TUBES D'EAU **13682**

597          **CHE**

CHAUDIERE A TUBES DE FUMEE **5249**
CHAUDIERE A VAPEUR **12158**
CHAUDIERE A VAPORISATION RAPIDE **13682**
CHAUDIERE CYLINDRIQUE **3578**
CHAUDIERE ELECTRIQUE **4497**
CHAUDIERE HORIZONTALE **6579**
CHAUDIERE IGNITUBULAIRE **5249**
CHAUDIERE INDUSTRIELLE **12143**
CHAUDIERE INEXPLOSIBLE **13682**
CHAUDIERE MARINE **8003**
CHAUDIERE MULTITUBULAIRE **13682**
CHAUDIERE TUBULAIRE **5249**
CHAUDIERE TYPE LOCOMOTIVE **7714**
CHAUDIERE VERTICALE **13544**
CHAUDRONNERIE **3136**
CHAUDRONNERIE EN FER **1423**
CHAUDRONNIER EN CUIVRE **3135**
CHAUDRONNIER EN FER **1415**
CHAUDRONNIER EN TOLE **1415**
CHAUFFAGE **6390**
CHAUFFAGE **5259**
CHAUFFAGE A AIR CHAUD **6616**
CHAUFFAGE A AIR CHAUD **268**
CHAUFFAGE A HUILE LOURDE **1752**
CHAUFFAGE AU CHARBON **2564**
CHAUFFAGE AU CHARBON PULVERISE **1753**
CHAUFFAGE AU GAZ **1751**
CHAUFFAGE AU NAPHTE **1752**
CHAUFFAGE AU PETROLE **1752**
CHAUFFAGE AU-DESSUS DU POINT DE FUSION **3634**
CHAUFFAGE CENTRAL **2160**
CHAUFFAGE DE L'AIR **268**
CHAUFFAGE DES BATIMENTS **6395**
CHAUFFAGE ELECTRIQUE **4513**
CHAUFFAGE MECANIQUE **8111**
CHAUFFAGE PAR INDUCTION **6897**
CHAUFFAGE PAR L'EAU CHAUDE **6648**
CHAUFFAGE PAR L'EAU CHAUDE A BASSE PRESSION **7784**
CHAUFFAGE PAR L'EAU CHAUDE A HAUTE PRESSION **6489**
CHAUFFAGE PAR LA VAPEUR **12167**
CHAUFFAGE PAR LA VAPEUR A BASSE PRESSION **7787**
CHAUFFAGE PAR LA VAPEUR A HAUTE PRESSION **6493**
CHAUFFAGE PAR LA VAPEUR A UNE PRESSION INFERIEURE
   A LA PRESSION ATMOSPHERIQUE **8318**
CHAUFFAGE PARTIEL **7696**
CHAUFFAGE PREALABLE **9776**
CHAUFFAGE SELECTIF **3915**
CHAUFFAGE SUPPLEMENTAIRE **2904**
CHAUFFE **2327**
CHAUFFE **6390**
CHAUFFE A BLANC **6824**

CHAUFFE AU BLEU **1371**
CHAUFFE AU ROUGE **10330**
CHAUFFE AU ROUGE CLAIR **1614**
CHAUFFE AU ROUGE SOMBRE **4368**
CHAUFFE EAU A GAZ **5846**
CHAUFFER **5235**
CHAUFFER AU CONTACT DE L'AIR **6351**
CHAUFFER EN PRESENCE **6351**
CHAUFFER EN VASE CLOS **6367**
CHAUFFER PREALABLEMENT **9774**
CHAUFFERIE **1418**
CHAUFFERIE **12270**
CHAUFFEUR **12272**
CHAUFFEUR **12271**
CHAUX **7582**
CHAUX ANHYDRE **1854**
CHAUX ETEINTE **1851**
CHAUX FLUATEE **5479**
CHAUX GRASSE **5046**
CHAUX HYDRATEE **1851**
CHAUX HYDRAULIQUE **6689**
CHAUX MAIGRE **9623**
CHAUX VIVE **1854**
CHEF D'EQUIPE **7482**
CHEF DE CHANTIER **5145**
CHEF DE CHANTIER **11520**
CHEF DE FABRICATION, DE SERVICE, D'ATELIER **13964**
CHELATION **11195**
CHEMIN **4063**
CHEMIN DE FER A VOIE ETROITE **9639**
CHEMIN DE FER FUNICULAIRE **1826**
CHEMIN DE ROULEMENT **1111**
CHEMIN DE ROULEMENT **7606**
CHEMIN DE ROULEMENT (POUR ECHELLE ROULANTE DE
   TOIT) **10857**
CHEMIN DE ROULEMENT DES BILLES **965**
CHEMIN DE ROULEMENT DES GALETS **10689**
CHEMINEE **2339**
CHEMISE **3274**
CHEMISE **12168**
CHEMISE **11303**
CHEMISE **7623**
CHEMISE D'EAU **13655**
CHEMISE DE CYLINDRE **1465**
CHEMISE DU CYLINDRE **3571**
CHEMISE DU FOUR **5749**
CHEMISE EN BOIS **13927**
CHEMISE HUMIDE **13804**
CHEMISE SECHE **4348**
CHEVAL EFFECTIF **151**
CHEVAL NOMINAL **6873**

# CHE

598

CHEVAL-HEURE **6603**
CHEVAL-VAPEUR **6602**
CHEVAUCHEMENT **8951**
CHEVAUCHER **8950**
CHEVILLE **9315**
CHEVILLE **4180**
CHEVILLE **7276**
CHEVILLE D'ASSEMBLAGE **3215**
CHEVILLE EN BOIS **13179**
CHEVRE A TROIS PIEDS **5945**
CHEVRON **4144**
CHICANE **921**
CHICANE **922**
CHIEN **2094**
CHIFFON A NETTOYER **11952**
CHIFFON D'ESSUYAGE **11952**
CHIFFRE **3940**
CHIFFRE DE DURETE BRINELL **1619**
CHIFFRES ET LETTRES A CHAUD/FROID **1560**
CHIGNOLE **9732**
CHIGNOLE **6258**
CHIMIE **2322**
CHIMIE ANALYTIQUE **495**
CHIMIE APPLIQUEE **648**
CHIMIE INDUSTRIELLE OU TECHNOLOGIQUE **9286**
CHIMIE MINERALE OU INORGANIQUE **6958**
CHIMIE ORGANIQUE **8865**
CHIMIE PHYSIQUE **9281**
CHIMIQUE **2290**
CHIMIQUEMENT COMBINE **2317**
CHIMIQUEMENT PUR **2319**
CHIMISTE **2321**
CHINA-GRASS **10192**
CHLORALUM **421**
CHLORATE **2351**
CHLORATE DE POTASSIUM **9680**
CHLORE **2354**
CHLORHYDRATE D'AMMONIAQUE **462**
CHLOROFORME **2356**
CHLORURATION **2353**
CHLORURE **2352**
CHLORURE CHROMEUX **2391**
CHLORURE CHROMIQUE **2381**
CHLORURE CUIVREUX **3478**
CHLORURE CUIVRIQUE **4853**
CHLORURE D'ACETYLE **92**
CHLORURE D'ALUMINIUM **421**
CHLORURE D'AMMONIUM **462**
CHLORURE D'ARGENT **11461**
CHLORURE D'ETHYLE **4849**
CHLORURE D'OR **823**

CHLORURE DE BARYUM **997**
CHLORURE DE CALCIUM **1850**
CHLORURE DE CHAUX **1317**
CHLORURE DE COBALT **2609**
CHLORURE DE LITHIUM **7666**
CHLORURE DE MAGNESIUM **7885**
CHLORURE DE METHYLE **8221**
CHLORURE DE PLOMB **7458**
CHLORURE DE POTASSE SOLUTION DE **9688**
CHLORURE DE POTASSIUM **9681**
CHLORURE DE SODIUM **2790**
CHLORURE DE SOUFRE **12451**
CHLORURE DE ZINC **14038**
CHLORURE DOUBLE D'ETAIN ET D'AMMONIUM **470**
CHLORURE FERREUX **5121**
CHLORURE FERRIQUE **5100**
CHLORURE MANGANEUX **7972**
CHLORURE MERCUREUX **8159**
CHLORURE MERCURIQUE **8153**
CHLORURE NICKELEUX **8562**
CHLORURE PLATINEUX **9509**
CHLORURE PLATINIQUE **9507**
CHLORURE STANNEUX **12100**
CHLORURE STANNIQUE **12096**
CHOC **11359**
CHOC **6783**
CHOC **4529**
CHOC DE LA SOUPAPE **6224**
CHOC EN ARRIERE **10286**
CHOC EN RETOUR **10286**
CHOC THERMIQUE **12812**
CHOMAGE **7092**
CHOMAGE MAT **4366**
CHROMAGE ELECTROLYTIQUE **2388**
CHROMATATION **2367**
CHROMATE **2366**
CHROMATE DE PLOMB **2375**
CHROMATE DE ZINC **14039**
CHROMATE NEUTRE DE POTASSIUM **9682**
CHROMATIQUE **2368**
CHROME **2385**
CHROME A FOUR **5741**
CHROMITE **2384**
CHROMITE **2373**
CHRONOMETRE A STOP **12283**
CHRYSOLITHE **2392**
CHRYSOTILE **11205**
CHUTE **3356**
CHUTE (DE TENSION) CATHODIQUE **2100**
CHUTE (RESTE) DE TOLE **9493**
CHUTE ANODIQUE **595**

CHUTE DE POTENTIEL **13594**
CHUTE DE PRESSION **9815**
CHUTE DE TEMPERATURE **12724**
CHUTE DE TENSION **13594**
CHUTE DE VITESSE **3677**
CHUTE LIBRE **5633**
CHUTE LIBRE (A) **5024**
CIBLE **12682**
CIMENT **2133**
CIMENT A PRISE LENTE **11648**
CIMENT A PRISE RAPIDE **10107**
CIMENT ARME **12203**
CIMENT DE LAITIER **11564**
CIMENT DE MACHEFER **11564**
CIMENT DE PORTLAND **9644**
CIMENT DURCISSANT A L'AIR **302**
CIMENT POUZZOLANIQUE **9749**
CIMENT REFRACTAIRE **5255**
CIMENT REFRACTAIRE AU SILICATE D'ALUMINIUM **443**
CIMENT ROMAIN **10707**
CIMENTATION (RECOUVREMENT D'UNE COUCHE DE CIMENT) **2146**
CIMENTER (COUVRIR D'UNE COUCHE DE CIMENT) **2134**
CINABRE **2400**
CINEMATIQUE **7305**
CINEMATIQUE **7306**
CINETIQUE **7307**
CINETIQUE **7310**
CINTRAGE **1182**
CINTRAGE **5579**
CINTRAGE A FROID **2668**
CINTRAGE D'UN TUBE **9341**
CINTRE **3494**
CINTRE DE DILATATION **4913**
CINTRER **1173**
CINTRER UN TUYAU **1175**
CIRCLIP **11990**
CIRCONFERENCE **2404**
CIRCONFERENCE CIRCONSCRITE **2435**
CIRCONFERENCE D'ECHANFREINEMENT **166**
CIRCONFERENCE D'EVIDEMENT **10723**
CIRCONFERENCE INSCRITE **6963**
CIRCONFERENCE PRIMITIVE **9404**
CIRCUIT DE FREINAGE **1545**
CIRCUIT DE REFROIDISSEMENT **3093**
CIRCUIT ELECTRIQUE **2406**
CIRCUIT IMPRIME (C.I.) **9871**
CIRCULATION **2433**
CIRCULATION AU CYANURE **3549**
CIRCULATION D'EAU **2434**
CIRCULER **2432**

CIRE **13702**
CIRE D'ABEILLES **1129**
CIRE DE CARNAUBA **2003**
CIRE DE LIGNITE **7579**
CIRE DE PARAFFINE **7579**
CIRE DE PARAFFINE **9045**
CIRE DU JAPON **7213**
CIRE FOSSILE **4413**
CIRE MINERALE **2194**
CISAILLAGE **11290**
CISAILLAGE **10507**
CISAILLE **11297**
CISAILLE **11279**
CISAILLE A DECOUPER LA CHUTE **3358**
CISAILLE A EBOUTER **12037**
CISAILLE A PORTE A FAUX **5495**
CISAILLE A TOLES **9494**
CISAILLE BASCULANTE **10658**
CISAILLE CIRCULAIRE **2403**
CISAILLE CIRCULAIRE **2429**
CISAILLE MECANIQUE **11292**
CISAILLE POUR FERS A BETON **2897**
CISAILLE VOLANTE **5495**
CISAILLEMENT **11290**
CISAILLEMENT **11288**
CISAILLEMENT **11279**
CISAILLER **1078**
CISAILLER (COUPER AVEC DES CISAILLES) **11280**
CISAILLES **11297**
CISAILLES A BRAMES **11554**
CISAILLES A GUILLOTINE **6170**
CISAILLES A MAIN **6251**
CISAILLES ARTICULEES **856**
CISAILLES D'ETABLI **12264**
CISAILLES POUR BILLETTES **1246**
CISAILLES POUR BILLETTES ET LARGETS **1244**
CISAILLES ROTATIVES **10759**
CISAILLEUSE **11292**
CISEAU **2349**
CISEAU A DOUILLE **11704**
CISEAU A FROID **2672**
CISEAU A FROID **2717**
CISEAU POUR MENUISIER **9080**
CISSOIDE **2438**
CITER **10113**
CITERNE **2439**
CITRATE DE SODIUM **11719**
CLAME D'ASSEMBLAGE **7280**
CLAMEAU **12105**
CLAPET **5353**
CLAPET **13453**

# CLA 600

CLAPET 970
CLAPET 2617
CLAPET (DE ROBINET) 4016
CLAPET ANTIGEL 8633
CLAPET D'ASPIRATION 12436
CLAPET D'UNE SOUPAPE 13459
CLAPET DE DECHARGE 10441
CLAPET DE FOND 5523
CLAPET DE PIED 5523
CLAPET DE REFOULEMENT 3739
CLAPET DE RETENUE 2284
CLAPET DE RETENUE 2283
CLAPET DE RETENUE A BATTANT 12545
CLAPET DE RETENUE A SOUPAPE 7543
CLAPET DE SOUPAPE 9024
CLAPET INVERSEUR 10553
CLAPET-CREPINE 5523
CLARIFICATION 2455
CLARIFIER 2456
CLASSEMENT 2460
CLAVETAGE 13740
CLAVETAGE 7288
CLAVETER 7279
CLAVETER 7277
CLAVETTE 7276
CLAVETTE 5211
CLAVETTE 13739
CLAVETTE A FRICTION 6542
CLAVETTE A MENTONNET 5939
CLAVETTE A MEPLAT 5388
CLAVETTE A TALON 5939
CLAVETTE A TETE 5939
CLAVETTE CONIQUE 12665
CLAVETTE CREUSE 6542
CLAVETTE D'ARRET 3213
CLAVETTE DE SERRAGE 185
CLAVETTE DEMI-RONDE 13929
CLAVETTE EN COIN 3215
CLAVETTE ET CONTRE-CLAVETTE 5938
CLAVETTE EVIDEE 6542
CLAVETTE LONGITUDINALE 7276
CLAVETTE NOYEE 12458
CLAVETTE PLATE 5388
CLAVETTE POSEE A PLAT 5388
CLAVETTE TANGENTIELLE 12618
CLAVETTE TRANSVERSALE 3215
CLAVETTE WOODRUFF 13929
CLAVETTE-CLEF 3212
CLAVETTE-DISQUE 13929
CLE 3212
CLE A DOUILLE 11709

CLE DYNAMOMETRIQUE 13049
CLE EN MAIN (AFFAIRE) 13284
CLEF 3212
CLEF A CLIQUET 10224
CLEF A CROCHET 1822
CLEF A DOUILLE 1515
CLEF A ECROUS 11833
CLEF A FOURCHE 7284
CLEF A FOURCHE DOUBLE 4167
CLEF A FOURCHE SIMPLE 11499
CLEF A GRIFFES EN BOUT 9322
CLEF A MOLETTE 2551
CLEF A TUBES 9366
CLEF AJUSTABLE 11052
CLEF ANGLAISE 11052
CLEF COUDEE 1195
CLEF CROCODILE 9366
CLEF D'ESSIEU 883
CLEF DE CALIBRE 7284
CLEF DE CALIBRE DOUBLE 4167
CLEF DE CALIBRE SIMPLE 11499
CLEF DE CHAPEAU 883
CLEF DE MANOEUVRE (POUR ROBINET A BOISSEAU) 2618
CLEF DE ROBINET 9532
CLEF EN BOUT 1515
CLEF TUBULAIRE 1515
CLEF TUBULAIRE COURBE 509
CLICHE PHOTOGRAPHIQUE 8524
CLICHE TYPOGRAPHIQUE 1340
CLIGNOTANTS 5366
CLIGNOTANTS 3989
CLIMATISEUR 250
CLINQUANT D'EPAISSEUR 7621
CLIQUET 2496
CLIQUET (MECANISME POUR TRANSFORMER UN MOUVEMENT ALTERNATIF EN MOUVEMENT CONTINU) 10218
CLIQUET A RESSORT 11987
CLIQUET D'ARRET 2094
CLIQUET DE FROTTEMENT 5675
CLIQUET POUR PERCER 10219
CLIVAGE 2487
CLOISON 4110
CLOISON 1726
CLOISON 3870
CLOISON PARE-FEU 5251
CLOQUAGE 1330
CLOTURE 5094
CLOU 8491
CLOU A BATEAU 1382
CLOU A CROCHET 2457
CLOU DECOUPE 7841

CLOU FONDU **2051**
CLOU FORGE **13990**
CLOU SEMENCE **12588**
CLOUER **8492**
CLOUERE **6325**
CLOUIERE **6325**
CLOUS DE CARROSSERIE **2554**
CLOUS DE FER A CHEVAL **6601**
CLOUTERE **6325**
CLOUTIERE **6325**
CLOUURE **10639**
CLOUURE SIMPLE **11487**
CLOUVIERE **6325**
COAGULATION **2556**
COAGULER (SE) **2555**
COAGULUM **2557**
COALESCENCE **2572**
COAXIAL **2605**
COBALT **2607**
COBALT-CARBONYLE **2608**
COBALTINE **2614**
CODAGE **4716**
CODE BINAIRE DECIMAL **1248**
CODE DE VITESSE D'AVANCE **5085**
CODE DECIMAL **3661**
CODEUR NUMERIQUE **3943**
COEFFICIENT **2621**
COEFFICIENT BINOMIAL **1257**
COEFFICIENT CALORIFIQUE (OU DE CONDUCTIVITE THERMIQUE) **7269**
COEFFICIENT D'ABSORPTION APPARENT **46**
COEFFICIENT D'ABSORPTION MASSIQUE **8030**
COEFFICIENT D'ECOULEMENT **2626**
COEFFICIENT D'EFFET THERMOELECTRIQUE COUPLE THERMOELECTRIQUE **2637**
COEFFICIENT D'ELASTICITE DE CISAILLEMENT **5974**
COEFFICIENT DE CONDUCTIBILITE CALORIFIQUE **6373**
COEFFICIENT DE CONDUCTIBILITE CALORIFIQUE **2622**
COEFFICIENT DE CONTRACTION **2623**
COEFFICIENT DE CORROSION **2624**
COEFFICIENT DE CORROSION ANODIQUE **594**
COEFFICIENT DE DIFFUSION **3931**
COEFFICIENT DE DILATATION **2628**
COEFFICIENT DE DILATATION **2636**
COEFFICIENT DE DILATATION CUBIQUE **2625**
COEFFICIENT DE DILATATION LINEAIRE **2630**
COEFFICIENT DE DILATATION SUPERFICIELLE **2635**
COEFFICIENT DE DILATATION THERMIQUE **12809**
COEFFICIENT DE DILATION **4914**
COEFFICIENT DE FROTTEMENT **2629**
COEFFICIENT DE FROTTEMENT **5670**

COEFFICIENT DE GLISSEMENT **2634**
COEFFICIENT DE PROPORTIONNALITE **2631**
COEFFICIENT DE REGULARITE **3719**
COEFFICIENT DE RESISTANCE **2632**
COEFFICIENT DE RESISTANCE A L'ALLONGEMENT **8340**
COEFFICIENT DE RESISTIVITE ELECTRIQUE **2627**
COEFFICIENT DE RETRAIT **477**
COEFFICIENT DE ROULEMENT **2633**
COEFFICIENT DE SECURITE **10885**
COEFFICIENT DE SECURITE **5009**
COEFFICIENT DE SENSIBILITE **3723**
COEFFICIENT DE TRAINEE **4200**
COEFFICIENT DE VITESSE **2638**
COEFFICIENT DIFFERENTIEL **3909**
COERCITIF **2640**
COFFRAGE GLISSANT (POUR BETON) **11616**
COFFRE **1458**
COFFRE **13239**
COGNEE **11572**
COGNEMENT **7330**
COHERENCE **2643**
COHESION **2644**
COIN **185**
COIN **13739**
COIN **13731**
COIN D'EPAISSEUR **185**
COIN DU RABOT **13733**
COIN PLAT **5400**
COIN POUR LE RATTRAPAGE DU JEU **185**
COINCEMENT **7212**
COINCEMENT DE LA CORDE DANS LA GORGE **1278**
COINCER (SE) **7210**
COKE **2655**
COKE D'USINE A GAZ **5849**
COKE DE CUBILOT **5595**
COKE DE FOUR **2662**
COKE DE GAZ **5849**
COKE DENSE **2792**
COKE METALLURGIQUE **2662**
COKEFACTION **2666**
COKEFACTION **1975**
COKEFICATION **2666**
COKEFIER **2656**
COL **8512**
COL DE CYGNE **1194**
COL DE CYGNE **6009**
COL DE CYGNE **12535**
COLCOTHAR **7148**
COLLAGE **7351**
COLLAGE **5987**
COLLE **5984**

# COL

COLLE A NOYAUX **3151**
COLLE D'AMIDON **12112**
COLLE DE POISSON **7174**
COLLE DES PEAUX **11539**
COLLE FORTE DES OS **1449**
COLLE POUR COURROIES **2140**
COLLECTEUR **11618**
COLLECTEUR **10839**
COLLECTEUR **7979**
COLLECTEUR D'ADMISSION **7007**
COLLECTEUR D'ADMISSION **6945**
COLLECTEUR D'ECHAPPEMENT **4893**
COLLECTEUR DE GAZ **5842**
COLLER **5985**
COLLERETTE **9803**
COLLET **12904**
COLLET D'UN ARBRE **11384**
COLLET DE T.H. **7998**
COLLET DE TROU D'HOMME **7978**
COLLIER **2448**
COLLIER **2720**
COLLIER A VIS POUR TUYAUX FLEXIBLES **6611**
COLLIER D'EXCENTRIQUE **4435**
COLLIER DE FIXATION (POUR TUBE) **9344**
COLLIER DE FREIN **1544**
COLLIER DE SERRAGE (POUR TUYAU) **6610**
COLLIER DE TUBE **13324**
COLLIER POSE A CHAUD **11391**
COLLIER POUR ARBRES VERTICAUX **13547**
COLLIER POUR SCELLEMENT DANS LES MURS **9345**
COLLIER POUR TUBES **9345**
COLLIMATER **2730**
COLLIMATEUR **2732**
COLLIMATION **2731**
COLLISION (DE NEUTRONS AVEC DES ATOMES) **7327**
COLLODION **2733**
COLLOIDAL **2735**
COLLOIDE **2734**
COLMATAGE **2510**
COLONNE **2748**
COLONNE BAROMETRIQUE **2751**
COLONNE D'EAU **2752**
COLONNE DE DIRECTION **12228**
COLONNE DE MANOEUVRE **5448**
COLONNE DE MERCURE **2751**
COLONNE LIQUIDE **2750**
COLONNE MONTANTE **2753**
COLONNE MONTANTE **12093**
COLONNE MONTANTE **10614**
COLONNE PERDUE **7620**
COLONNE PERDUE A FENTES **11639**

COLONNE PERDUE A TROUS **9187**
COLONNE PERDUE FORABLE **4272**
COLONNE PERDUE NON-PERFOREE **1306**
COLOPHANE **2737**
COLORANT **4397**
COLORANT **9303**
COLORATION **2740**
COLORATION THERMIQUE **6371**
COMBINAISON (MATH.) **2761**
COMBINAISON ALIPHATIQUE **326**
COMBINAISON CHIMIQUE **2300**
COMBURANT **277**
COMBUSTIBILITE **2773**
COMBUSTIBLE **2772**
COMBUSTIBLE **5705**
COMBUSTIBLE ARTIFICIEL **732**
COMBUSTIBLE DE TRES BONNE QUALITE **6484**
COMBUSTIBLE EN GROS MORCEAUX **7827**
COMBUSTIBLE FOSSILE **5586**
COMBUSTIBLE GAZEUX **5854**
COMBUSTIBLE LIQUIDE **7650**
COMBUSTIBLE NATUREL **8503**
COMBUSTIBLE NECESSAIRE **3745**
COMBUSTIBLE SOLIDE **11785**
COMBUSTION **2774**
COMBUSTION **11956**
COMBUSTION COMPLETE **2779**
COMBUSTION INCOMPLETE **6845**
COMBUSTION LENTE **11644**
COMBUSTION NUCLEAIRE **1747**
COMBUSTION PARFAITE **9184**
COMBUSTION VIVE **10205**
COMMAMDE ELECTRIQUE **4503**
COMMAMDE PAR VIS MOLETEE **7337**
COMMANDE **4297**
COMMANDE **3048**
COMMANDE **4309**
COMMANDE A DISTANCE **10448**
COMMANDE A LA MAIN **6233**
COMMANDE A LA MAIN (A) **6241**
COMMANDE ADAPTIVE **161**
COMMANDE CONTINUE **3032**
COMMANDE DE CONTOURNAGE **3039**
COMMANDE DE DEMARREUR **12117**
COMMANDE DE POSITIONNEMENT **9650**
COMMANDE DIRECTE PAR CALCULATEUR **3981**
COMMANDE DIRECTE PAR CALCULATEUR **3985**
COMMANDE DIRECTE PAR CALCULATEUR **2875**
COMMANDE ELASTIQUE **8642**
COMMANDE HYDRAULIQUE **6683**
COMMANDE INDIVIDUELLE **6886**

COMMANDE MECANIQUE **9734**
COMMANDE MECANIQUE **9654**
COMMANDE MECANIQUE **8119**
COMMANDE PAR ARBRE DE TRANSMISSION **7609**
COMMANDE PAR CABLE **10735**
COMMANDE PAR CHAINE **2206**
COMMANDE PAR CHAINE **2208**
COMMANDE PAR COURROIE **4319**
COMMANDE PAR ENGRENAGE **5892**
COMMANDE PAR ENGRENAGE CONIQUE **1230**
COMMANDE PAR ENGRENAGE DROIT **12010**
COMMANDE PAR ENGRENAGES **13025**
COMMANDE PAR GROUPES **6150**
COMMANDE PAR MOTEUR **8119**
COMMANDE PAR MOTEUR **9734**
COMMANDE PAR ROUE DENTEE **13025**
COMMANDE PARAXIALE **12314**
COMMANDE PNEUMATIQUE **2842**
COMMANDE POINT-A-POINT **9572**
COMMANDE POSITIVE **9654**
COMMANDER **3049**
COMMANDER **4289**
COMMERCIALE **12141**
COMMETTAGE **10739**
COMMETTRE LES TORONS **13303**
COMMOTION **4529**
COMMUTATEUR **2244**
COMMUTATEUR DES BOUGIES DE PRECHAUFFAGE **6389**
COMMUTATION **2246**
COMMUTATRICE **3071**
COMMUTER **2241**
COMPACT TERMINE **8551**
COMPARAISON DE DIMENSIONS **7445**
COMPARATEUR **2794**
COMPARATEUR A CADRAN POUR ALESAGES **3838**
COMPARATEUR A LAMES **10365**
COMPARATEUR ELECTRIQUE **4535**
COMPARATEUR ELECTRONIQUE **4632**
COMPARATEUR INTERFERENTIEL **7038**
COMPARATEUR MECANIQUE **8097**
COMPARATEUR MICROMETRIQUE POUR FILETAGES **11048**
COMPARATEUR OPTICO-MECANIQUE **8118**
COMPARATEUR OPTIQUE **8842**
COMPARATEURS **2795**
COMPARTIMENT **2798**
COMPARTIMENT MOTEUR **4757**
COMPAS **4100**
COMPAS **9022**
COMPAS A CHEVEU **6201**
COMPAS A COULISSE **13537**
COMPAS A CREMAILLERE **10122**

COMPAS A PIECES DE RECHANGE **2805**
COMPAS A POINTES SECHES **4101**
COMPAS A PORTE-CRAYON **2804**
COMPAS A QUART DE CERCLE **13876**
COMPAS A TIRE-LIGNE **2803**
COMPAS A TROIS BRANCHES **13187**
COMPAS A VERGE **13105**
COMPAS A VERGE **1096**
COMPAS D'EPAISSEUR **1873**
COMPAS D'EPAISSEUR **8912**
COMPAS DE CALIBRE **1874**
COMPAS DE DIAMETRE INTERIEUR **6975**
COMPAS DE PRECISION **6201**
COMPAS DE REDUCTION **9937**
COMPAS DROIT A POINTES **4101**
COMPAS-BALUSTRE **1503**
COMPATIBILITE **2806**
COMPENSATEUR **2808**
COMPENSATEUR DE DILATATION **4913**
COMPENSATION **2809**
COMPENSER **2807**
COMPENSER **930**
COMPENSER LE JEU D'UN COUSSINET **12603**
COMPLEMENT D'UN ANGLE **2810**
COMPLEMENT DIAMETRAL **3851**
COMPOSANT **2815**
COMPOSANT **2981**
COMPOSANT (CHIM.) **2983**
COMPOSANT D'UN ALLIAGE **2982**
COMPOSANTE **2817**
COMPOSANTE AXIALE **859**
COMPOSANTE RADIALE **10132**
COMPOSE INTERMETALLIQUE **7052**
COMPOSE ISOLANT **6997**
COMPOSES AROMATIQUES **716**
COMPOSITION **2823**
COMPOSITION CHIMIQUE **2299**
COMPOSITION CHIMIQUE **2827**
COMPOSITION DE DEGRAISSAGE **3713**
COMPOSITION DE POLISSAGE A LA MEULE **1692**
COMPOSITION DES FORCES **2825**
COMPOSITION GRANULOMETRIQUE **9090**
COMPOSITION POUR COUSSINET **1106**
COMPRESSEUR **2874**
COMPRESSEUR A GRAISSE **11982**
COMPRESSEUR A PISTON **9374**
COMPRESSEUR CENTRIFUGE **2178**
COMPRESSEUR COMPOUND **2836**
COMPRESSEUR D'AIR **249**
COMPRESSEUR DE RESERVE **12069**
COMPRESSEUR ETAGE **2836**

# COM

COMPRESSEUR HUMIDE **13801**
COMPRESSEUR HYDRAULIQUE **6680**
COMPRESSEUR SEC **4345**
COMPRESSIBILITE **2852**
COMPRESSIBILITE **2851**
COMPRESSIBLE **2853**
COMPRESSION **2854**
COMPRESSION **9806**
COMPRESSION **11355**
COMPRESSION **10028**
COMPRESSION DANS LA DIRECTION DES FIBRES **10021**
COMPRESSION DE L'AIR **2858**
COMPRESSION NORMALEMENT A LA DIRECTION DES FIBRES **10022**
COMPRIME **2791**
COMPRIMER **2837**
COMPRIMER UN RESSORT **2838**
COMPTE-GOUTTES **4321**
COMPTE-SECONDES **12946**
COMPTE-SECONDES **12283**
COMPTE-TOURS **12587**
COMPTE-TOURS **10556**
COMPTEUR **8214**
COMPTEUR **3229**
COMPTEUR A CHIFFRES **3559**
COMPTEUR A EAU **13661**
COMPTEUR A GAZ **5829**
COMPTEUR A POINTAGES **12946**
COMPTEUR D'EAU VENTURI **13532**
COMPTEUR D'ELECTRICITE **4553**
COMPTEUR D'ERREURS **4830**
COMPTEUR D'ERREURS **4823**
COMPTEUR DE TOURS **10556**
COMPTEUR DE VAPEUR **12174**
COMPTEUR DE VITESSE **11877**
COMPTEUR GEIGER **5911**
COMPTEUR VENTURI **13532**
COMPTEURS A FENETRES **3559**
CONCASSAGE **1588**
CONCASSAGE **2786**
CONCASSER **1580**
CONCASSEUR **4045**
CONCASSEUR **3419**
CONCASSEUR A CHARBON **2559**
CONCASSEUR A COKE **2658**
CONCASSEUR A MACHOIRES **12273**
CONCAVE **2877**
CONCAVITE **2880**
CONCENTRATION **2886**
CONCENTRATION D'IONS **7122**
CONCENTRATION D'UNE SOLUTION PAR EVAPORATION **2885**

CONCENTRATION DE LA CONTRAINTE **12360**
CONCENTRATION DES IONS HYDROGENE **6715**
CONCENTRE **2881**
CONCENTRER **2882**
CONCENTRER (SE) **1122**
CONCENTRICITE **2891**
CONCEPTION **3794**
CONCEPTION STANDARD **12073**
CONCESSIONNAIRE DE LICENCE **7540**
CONCHOIDE **2892**
CONCRETION CALCAIRE **1837**
CONDENSAT **2905**
CONDENSATEUR **1916**
CONDENSATEUR (ELECTR.) **2908**
CONDENSATEUR D'ARRET **1342**
CONDENSATEUR DE BLOCAGE **1342**
CONDENSATEUR ELECTROLYTIQUE **4590**
CONDENSATEUR-ETALON **1868**
CONDENSATION **2906**
CONDENSER (SE) **2907**
CONDENSEUR (CHIM.) **2908**
CONDENSEUR (DE VAPEUR) **1916**
CONDENSEUR (OPT.) **2908**
CONDENSEUR A EVAPORATION **4868**
CONDENSEUR BAROMETRIQUE **1010**
CONDENSEUR PAR EJECTION **4470**
CONDENSEUR PAR INJECTION **7220**
CONDENSEUR PAR MELANGE **3988**
CONDENSEUR PAR SURFACE **12499**
CONDENSEUR PAR SURFACE AU MOYEN DE L'AIR **296**
CONDENSEUR PAR SURFACE AU MOYEN DE L'EAU **13684**
CONDITION CRITIQUE DE DEFORMATION **5935**
CONDITIONNEMENT **8995**
CONDITIONS D'EMPLOI **11208**
CONDITIONS DE LIVRAISON **3737**
CONDITIONS DE SERVICE **8834**
CONDITIONS DE SERVICE **13949**
CONDUCTANCE MOL(ECUL)AIRE **8350**
CONDUCTEUR (DE LA CHALEUR DE L'ELECTRICITE) **2918**
CONDUCTEUR (ELECTR.) **2921**
CONDUCTEUR D'ELECRICITE **2922**
CONDUCTEUR DE LA CHALEUR **6340**
CONDUCTEUR DE MACHINE **4765**
CONDUCTEUR DE RESEAU **4079**
CONDUCTEUR ELECTRIQUE **4537**
CONDUCTEUR PARCOURU **7670**
CONDUCTEUR SANS COURANT **3627**
CONDUCTEUR SANS TENSION **3627**
CONDUCTIBILITE **2919**
CONDUCTIBILITE ELECTRIQUE **4536**
CONDUCTIBILITE EQUIVALENTE **4797**

| | |
|---|---|
| CONDUCTIBILITE THERMIQUE CALORIFIQUE **2920** | CONE GALOPIN **2941** |
| CONDUCTION **2916** | CONE GENERATEUR **5918** |
| CONDUCTION DE LA CHALEUR **2917** | CONE LISSE **12669** |
| CONDUCTIVITE **2919** | CONE LUMINEUX **2932** |
| CONDUCTIVITE THERMIQUE **12804** | CONE OBLIQUE **8709** |
| CONDUCTIVITE THERMO-ELECTRIQUE **10044** | CONE PRIMITIF **9406** |
| CONDUIRE (L'ELECTRICITELA CHALEUR) **2913** | CONE PYROMETRIQUE **10050** |
| CONDUIT ANNULAIRE DE VENT CHAUD **1774** | CONE PYROMETRIQUE (DE SEGER) **11134** |
| CONDUIT DE PRESSION **9827** | CONE TRONQUE **13235** |
| CONDUITE **12178** | CONE VERTICAL **10578** |
| CONDUITE **12226** | CONFECTION **8028** |
| CONDUITE **2845** | CONFECTION **10462** |
| CONDUITE **9357** | CONFOCAL **2933** |
| CONDUITE **13666** | CONGE **5161** |
| CONDUITE (D'UNE MACHINE) **814** | CONGE **8512** |
| CONDUITE ASCENDANTE **756** | CONGE DE RACCORDEMENT **6537** |
| CONDUITE CIRCULAIRE **2418** | CONGELATION DU FOUR **5655** |
| CONDUITE D'AIR **281** | CONGLOMERAT **2934** |
| CONDUITE D'ARRIVEE DU COMBUSTIBLE **12489** | CONGRUENCE **2937** |
| CONDUITE D'EAU CHAUDE **6649** | CONICITE **2948** |
| CONDUITE D'EAU FORCEE **9840** | CONICITE **12646** |
| CONDUITE D'EAU SOUS PRESSION **9840** | CONICITE D'UNE CLAVETTE **12654** |
| CONDUITE DE DERIVATION **1818** | CONIQUE **2940** |
| CONDUITE DE GAZ **5834** | CONJONCTEUR-DISJONCTEUR **7949** |
| CONDUITE DE REFOULEMENT **4022** | CONJUGUE **2952** |
| CONDUITE DE VENT **1314** | CONSERVABILITE **4385** |
| CONDUITE DE VENT **1367** | CONSERVATION DE L'ENERGIE **2967** |
| CONDUITE DE VENT CHAUD **6651** | CONSERVATION DU BOIS **9790** |
| CONDUITE DESCENDANTE **3791** | CONSISTANCE **2968** |
| CONDUITE EN FONTE **2062** | CONSISTANCE D'UNE HUILE **1395** |
| CONDUITE EN MER **11080** | CONSOLE **13618** |
| CONDUITE INTERIEURE **10902** | CONSOLE **1522** |
| CONDUITE LIBRE **8807** | CONSOLIDATION DES BOULONS **7707** |
| CONDUITE POUR HAUTE PRESSION **6490** | CONSOMMATION **13710** |
| CONDUITE SOUTERRAINE **13354** | CONSOMMATION **2995** |
| CONDUITE VERTICALE **2753** | CONSOMMATION D'ENERGIE **2876** |
| CONE (GEOM.) **2924** | CONSOMMATION DE COMBUSTIBLE **2994** |
| CONE A BASE CIRCULAIRE **2409** | CONSOMMATION DE COURANT **2993** |
| CONE A ETAGES **11871** | CONSTANTAN **2980** |
| CONE AUTO-DEMONTABLE **11159** | CONSTANTE **2969** |
| CONE CIRCULAIRE **2409** | CONSTANTE CALORIFIQUE **6341** |
| CONE COMPLEMENTAIRE **5918** | CONSTANTE CAPILLAIRE **1923** |
| CONE D'ATTAQUE **11871** | CONSTANTE D'ABSORPTION **47** |
| CONE DE DEFLECTION (DANS RESERVOIR) **11924** | CONSTANTE D'EQUILIBRE **4787** |
| CONE DE FRICTION **5671** | CONSTANTE D'UN GAZ **5815** |
| CONE DE FRICTION **1225** | CONSTANTE D'UNE CELLULE ELECTROLYTIQUE **2128** |
| CONE DE PIED **10718** | CONSTANTE DE RADIATION **10144** |
| CONE DE REDUCTION **10358** | CONSTANTE DE RADIATION APPARENTE **643** |
| CONE DE TRANSMISSION **11871** | CONSTANTE DE TEMPS **12944** |
| CONE DROIT **10578** | CONSTANTE DIELECTRIQUE **3899** |
| CONE ET CONTRE-CONE **404** | CONSTANTES D'ELASTICITE **4475** |

# CON 606

CONSTANTES DU RESEAU **7430**
CONSTITUANT **2982**
CONSTITUANT **2981**
CONSTITUANT CHIMIQUE **2298**
CONSTITUTION CHIMIQUE **2301**
CONSTRUCTEUR **7992**
CONSTRUCTION **8028**
CONSTRUCTION **2986**
CONSTRUCTION **7989**
CONSTRUCTION **8103**
CONSTRUCTION **10462**
CONSTRUCTION (EDIFICE) **12395**
CONSTRUCTION EN ACIER / METALLIQUE **12218**
CONSTRUCTION EN BOIS **12942**
CONSTRUCTION HYDRAULIQUE **6685**
CONSTRUCTION MECANIQUE **8103**
CONSTRUCTION METALLIQUE **7152**
CONSTRUCTION NAVALE **8510**
CONSTRUCTION SOUDEE **13795**
CONSTRUCTIONS CIVILES **2444**
CONSTRUIRE **1694**
CONTACT (GEN.) **2996**
CONTACT A FICHE **13622**
CONTACT A LA MASSE (ELECT.) **2996**
CONTACT A LA TERRE **4415**
CONTACT D'UN AIMANT **710**
CONTACTEUR A MERCURE **8166**
CONTACTEUR ELECTRIQUE **12553**
CONTACTS **9574**
CONTAMINATION D'UN ALLIAGE **365**
CONTENANCE **1917**
CONTENANT DES SCORIES **11562**
CONTIGU **181**
CONTINUITE **3017**
CONTOUR **8907**
CONTOUR D'UNE CAME **8906**
CONTOUR DE GRAIN **1500**
CONTRACTER (SE) **11388**
CONTRACTEUR D'ALLUMAGE **6766**
CONTRACTION **3045**
CONTRACTION **11392**
CONTRACTION (PENDANT LE REFROIDISSEMENT) **11397**
CONTRACTION DE LA COURROIE **3329**
CONTRACTION DE LA TIGE DU RIVET **3046**
CONTRACTION DE LA VEINE FLUIDE **3044**
CONTRACTION DE REFROIDISSEMENT **7648**
CONTRACTION DE SOLIDIFICATION **11802**
CONTRAINTE **12322**
CONTRAINTE **12367**
CONTRAINTE ADMISSIBLE **353**
CONTRAINTE CIRCONFERENTIELLE **6576**

CONTRAINTE DE CISAILLEMENT **11296**
CONTRAINTE DE TRACTION (FORCE) **12750**
CONTRAINTE DYNAMIQUE **4398**
CONTRAINTE RESIDUELLE **10474**
CONTRAINTE SECONDAIRE **11109**
CONTRE-ANALYSE **2280**
CONTRE-BALANCER **930**
CONTRE-BOUTEROLLE **4115**
CONTRE-BOUTEROLLE A MANCHE **6529**
CONTRE-CLAVETTE **5937**
CONTRE-COURANT **3230**
CONTRE-COUSSINET **13030**
CONTRE-ECROU **7702**
CONTRE-EPROUVETTE **4384**
CONTRE-ESSAI **4384**
CONTRE-ESSAI **10522**
CONTRE-FER **13033**
CONTRE-FICHE **3179**
CONTRE-JOINT **911**
CONTRE-MARCHE **10614**
CONTRE-POINTE **12599**
CONTRE-PRESSION **3232**
CONTRE-REACTION **10536**
CONTREBRIDE **8054**
CONTREFICHE **12396**
CONTREMAITRE **5541**
CONTREMANIVELLE **10528**
CONTREPLAQUE **13621**
CONTREPLAQUE (SCELLEE DANS LE SOL) **502**
CONTREPOIDS **3251**
CONTREPOIDS DU FREIN **1547**
CONTREPOINTE MICROMETRIQUE **8236**
CONTREPOINTE TOURNANTE **10560**
CONTROLE **3048**
CONTROLE **4876**
CONTROLE **6987**
CONTROLE AUX ULTRA-SONS **13337**
CONTROLE D'ADHERENCE **172**
CONTROLE DE PARITE **9081**
CONTROLE DE QUALITE **10063**
CONTROLE RADIOGRAPHIQUE **13998**
CONTROLEUR DE CIRCULATION **11426**
CONTROLEUR DE FLAMME **5314**
CONTROLEUR DE NIVEAU **7655**
CONTROLEUR DE PRESSION **9813**
CONVECTION **3060**
CONVECTION (CHALEUR RAYONNANTE) **3059**
CONVERGENCE **3063**
CONVERGENT **3064**
CONVERGENT (D'UNE TUYERE) **2769**
CONVERGER **3062**

CONVERSION **3067**
CONVERTISSEUR **3071**
CONVERTISSEUR BESSEMER **1212**
CONVEXE **3076**
CONVEXION **3060**
CONVEXITE **3396**
CONVEXITE **1720**
CONVOYEUR **1675**
COORDONNEES **3100**
COORDONNEES CARTESIENNES **2014**
COORDONNEES COURANTES **3487**
COORDONNEES CYLINDRIQUES **3580**
COORDONNEES DANS L'ESPACE **13203**
COORDONNEES OBLIQUES **8710**
COORDONNEES ORTHOGONALES **10301**
COORDONNEES PLANES **698**
COORDONNEES POLAIRES **9578**
COORDONNEES RECTANGULAIRES **10301**
COPAHU **3101**
COPAL **3102**
COPALE **3102**
COPEAU **2346**
COPEAU **2343**
COPEAU **12536**
COPEAU ADHERENT **1707**
COPEAU DE BURINAGE **2343**
COPEAUX **3543**
COPEAUX **11278**
COPEAUX (DE BOIS) **13919**
COPEAUX DE FIBRES DE BOIS **13923**
COPEAUX DE FORAGE **1476**
COPEAUX METALLIQUES **2348**
COPIE (PHOT.) **9870**
COPPERWELD **3137**
COQUE **7313**
COQUILLE **3883**
COQUILLE **2331**
COQUILLE **11303**
COQUILLE **9207**
COQUILLE DE COUSSINET **1113**
COQUILLE DE SECHAGE **3148**
COQUILLE INFERIEURE **1487**
COQUILLE SUPERIEURE **13030**
CORBEAU **3140**
CORBEILLE DE TREMPAGE **3976**
CORDAGE **10745**
CORDE **10730**
CORDE A PIANO **9287**
CORDE D'UN CERCLE **2364**
CORDE DE CHANVRE **6443**
CORDE EN MANILLE **7981**

CORDE GOUDRONNEE **12688**
CORDE NOIRE **12688**
CORDE NON GOUDRONNEE **13839**
CORDE TENDUE **12923**
CORDE TRESSEE **1527**
CORDE-COURROIE **4314**
CORDON D'AMIANTE **751**
CORDON D'ECRASEMENT **3382**
CORDON D'UN CABLE **12338**
CORDON DE SOUDURE **13756**
CORDON DE SOUDURE **1082**
CORDON DE SOUDURE PLAT **5401**
CORDON SOUDE RECTILIGNE **12376**
CORDON SUPPORT (A L'ENVERS) **904**
CORINDON **4699**
CORINDON **3201**
CORNE D'EMBOUTISSAGE **4408**
CORNE D'ENCLUME **1090**
CORNE RAPEE **6595**
CORNIERE **506**
CORNIERE **514**
CORNIERE A AILES EGALES **4781**
CORNIERE A AILES INEGALES **13356**
CORNIERE DE PIED DE BAC **1490**
CORNIERE DE TETE(D'UN RESERVOIR) **13028**
CORNIERE SUPPORT **3058**
CORNIERES A BOUDIN **1713**
CORNIERES DE FER AU PAQUET **7137**
CORNIERES EN ACIER ALLIE **369**
CORNUE **10523**
CORNUE TUBULEE **10525**
CORPS **1385**
CORPS AU REPOS **1386**
CORPS CREUX **6538**
CORPS CYLINDRIQUE D'UNE CHAUDIERE **1419**
CORPS D'UNE CLAVETTE **11262**
CORPS D'UNE SOUPAPE **13454**
CORPS DE L'ESTAMPE **3885**
CORPS DE LA BIELLE **11261**
CORPS DE POMPE **1015**
CORPS DE REVOLUTION **11790**
CORPS DU MARTEAU **6317**
CORPS DU PALIER **9313**
CORPS DU PISTON **9373**
CORPS DU RIVET **11263**
CORPS ECLAIRE **6773**
CORPS EN MOUVEMENT **1392**
CORPS ETRANGERS **6813**
CORPS FLOTTANT **5436**
CORPS GAZEUX **5808**
CORPS GRIS **6083**

# COR

608

CORPS LIQUIDE **7641**
CORPS LUMINEUX **11147**
CORPS MOBILE **1392**
CORPS NOIR **1285**
CORPS PLASTIQUE **9467**
CORPS RIGIDE **10588**
CORPS SIMPLE **4654**
CORPS SOLIDE **11775**
CORRECTEUR D'AVANCE **11837**
CORRECTION **3181**
CORRECTION D'OUTIL **3521**
CORRECTION DE POSITION D'OUTIL **13007**
CORRECTION DE VITESSE D'AVANCE **5079**
CORRIGER L'ACIER PAR UN REVENU **6808**
CORRODANT **3197**
CORRODER **3182**
CORROSIF **3197**
CORROSIF **3196**
CORROSIF **4847**
CORROSION **3183**
CORROSION ATMOSPHERIQUE **795**
CORROSION AVEC DEGAGEMENT D'HYDROGENE **6718**
CORROSION CATHODIQUE **2107**
CORROSION CHIMIQUE **2302**
CORROSION DE LA PILE DE CONCENTRATION **2888**
CORROSION DE SOUDURE **13759**
CORROSION DES FACES EN CONTACT **5667**
CORROSION DUE A DES DEPOTS **3774**
CORROSION FISSURANTE **3185**
CORROSION FISSURANTE **7041**
CORROSION GALVANIQUE **5783**
CORROSION HUMIDE **13802**
CORROSION INTERCRISTALLINE **7030**
CORROSION INTERCRISTALLINE **7041**
CORROSION INTERCRISTALLINE DES LAITONS 70/30 **11093**
CORROSION INTERGRANULAIRE **7030**
CORROSION LOCALE **7695**
CORROSION LOCALISEE **9418**
CORROSION PAR CONTACT **3002**
CORROSION PAR COURANT VAGABOND **12350**
CORROSION PAR FROTTEMENT **5666**
CORROSION PAR INFILTRATION STRATIFIEE **7443**
CORROSION SOUS EROSION **6799**
CORROSION SOUS TENSION **12361**
CORROSION SOUS TENSION **3195**
CORROSION SOUS-JACENTE **13352**
COSECANTE **3202**
COSINUS **3203**
COSMOLINE **13508**
COSSE **12848**
COSSE **1827**

COSSE OVALE **6330**
COSSES **12765**
COTANGENTE **3211**
COTATION ABSOLUE **3097**
COTATION ABSOLUE **29**
COTATION RELATIVE **6854**
COTE **3956**
COTE CHAIR DU CUIR **5414**
COTE D INTRODUCTION **4774**
COTE D'ENTREE **4774**
COTE D'UN ANGLE **7512**
COTE D'UN POLYGONE **11414**
COTE DE BASE **1053**
COTE DE L'ANGLE DROIT **9218**
COTE DU VENT **13721**
COTE EXTERIEUR **8911**
COTE FLEUR DU CUIR **6038**
COTE INTERIEUR **6974**
COTE INTERIEUR D'UNE COURROIE **10853**
COTE POIL DU CUIR **6038**
COTE SOUS LE VENT **7505**
COTES DE RACCORDEMENT **2793**
COTON **3217**
COTON A NETTOYER **3223**
COTONPOUDRE **6176**
COUCHE **5166**
COUCHE **7442**
COUCHE **254**
COUCHE **10832**
COUCHE **9096**
COUCHE (DE PROTECTION) ANODIQUE **599**
COUCHE ANNUELLE **586**
COUCHE D'AIR **2124**
COUCHE D'OXYDE DE CUIVRE **5246**
COUCHE D'OXYDE FERREUX **12443**
COUCHE DE BASE **9864**
COUCHE DE BEILBY **1130**
COUCHE DE CHROMATE **2591**
COUCHE DE COULEUR A L'HUILE **2582**
COUCHE DE DEMI-ATTENUATION **6211**
COUCHE DE FOND **9857**
COUCHE DE LAQUE **2581**
COUCHE DE PHOSPHATE **9245**
COUCHE DES FIBRES INVARIABLES **8544**
COUCHE INTERMEDIAIRE DECARBUREE **1005**
COUCHE PRIMAIRE **9857**
COUCHE PROTECTRICE **9793**
COUCHE PROTECTRICE **9950**
COUCHE SUPERFICIELLE **11544**
COUCHE SUPERFICIELLE **2019**
COUCHE SUPERFICIELLE (DE PEINTURE) **5217**

## 609 COU

COUCHES **2590**
COUCHETTE **1739**
COUDE **1194**
COUDE **1172**
COUDE **4913**
COUDE **4493**
COUDE A 180 **13323**
COUDE AU 1/2 **4467**
COUDE D'EQUERRE **7320**
COUDE D'UN ARBRE **6976**
COUDE EN U **13323**
COUDE ROND **1180**
COUDE ROND A ANGLE DROIT **10074**
COUDE ROND AU 1/4 **10074**
COUDER UN TUYAU **1175**
COULABILITE **2064**
COULAGE **2068**
COULAGE (D'UN LIQUIDE) **7492**
COULAGE DE CIMENT **6154**
COULEE **5592**
COULEE **8134**
COULEE **6333**
COULEE **12703**
COULEE **9715**
COULEE **10844**
COULEE **10845**
COULEE **2068**
COULEE (LOT DE...) **2076**
COULEE (OPERATION) **2070**
COULEE CENTRIFUGE **2176**
COULEE CONTINUE **3019**
COULEE CONTINUE **3029**
COULEE DIRECTE **13031**
COULEE EN COQUILLE **2334**
COULEE EN COQUILLE **9208**
COULEE EN FOSSE **9394**
COULEE EN SABLE **10922**
COULEE EN SABLE SEC **4353**
COULEE EN SOURCE **1488**
COULEE RATEE **8732**
COULEE SOUS PRESSION **9812**
COULEE SOUS PRESSION **3886**
COULEE SOUS PRESSION PAR GRAVITE **6079**
COULEE TRANQUILLE **4388**
COULEE TRANQUILLE (PROCEDE DURVILLE) **10109**
COULER **6153**
COULER **2030**
COULEUR **7362**
COULEUR **9303**
COULEUR **12732**
COULEUR **9015**

COULEUR (PHYS.) **2741**
COULEUR CERISE **2326**
COULEUR COMPLEMENTAIRE **2812**
COULEUR COMPOSEE **11103**
COULEUR D'INTERFERENCE **7037**
COULEUR OPAQUE **1389**
COULEUR SIMPLE **9847**
COULEURS SPECTRALES **11859**
COULIS **6152**
COULIS **10406**
COULIS REFRACTAIRE **6125**
COULIS REFRACTAIRE **6126**
COULISSE **11633**
COULISSE ET MANIVELLE **11631**
COULISSEAU **10188**
COULISSEAU **11585**
COULISSEAU D'OBTURATION **5160**
COULISSEAU MOBILE **7625**
COULISSER **11586**
COULOIR **2395**
COULOMB **3225**
COULOMBMETRE **452**
COULURE **7489**
COULURE POCHE **10892**
COULURES **10895**
COULURES **10856**
COUP **12375**
COUP DE BELIER **13653**
COUP DE PISTON **9389**
COUP DE SOUDURE POINT D'AMORCAGE DE L'ARC **677**
COUPAGE **3523**
COUPAGE A CHAUD **6622**
COUPAGE A L'ACETYLENE **94**
COUPAGE A L'ARC AU CARBONE **1942**
COUPAGE A L'ARC METALLIQUE **8175**
COUPAGE A L'AUTOGENE **5817**
COUPAGE A LA FLAMME **5318**
COUPAGE AU CHALUMEAU **5817**
COUPE **1309**
COUPE **9898**
COUPE **3503**
COUPE **11122**
COUPE **12511**
COUPE **7717**
COUPE **3523**
COUPE A LA MAIN **6232**
COUPE ANGULAIRE **539**
COUPE CHARDONS ET FOUGERES **13741**
COUPE D'UN DESSIN **11112**
COUPE INFERIEURE A LA COTE **13351**
COUPE LONGITUDINALE **7738**

# COU 610

COUPE MICROGRAPHIQUE **8261**
COUPE PAR ELECTRO-EROSION **4559**
COUPE TRANSVERSALE **3377**
COUPE TRANSVERSALE **11111**
COUPE-CIRCUIT DE SURETE **10886**
COUPE-FIL **13886**
COUPE-RACINES **10715**
COUPE-RAVES **7272**
COUPE-TUBE **13248**
COUPE-TUBES **9348**
COUPELLATION **3463**
COUPELLE DE RESSORT **11988**
COUPER (GEOM.) **3504**
COUPER (SE) (GEOM.) **7094**
COUPER AU TRANCHET **3515**
COUPER LE COURANT **7090**
COUPEROSE BLANCHE **14046**
COUPEROSE BLEUE **1376**
COUPEROSE VERTE **6093**
COUPLAGE **3254**
COUPLAGE EN QUANTITE **9051**
COUPLAGE EN SERIE **11199**
COUPLAGE EN TENSION **11199**
COUPLE **3252**
COUPLE **13048**
COUPLE DE DEMARRAGE **12129**
COUPLE DE ROUE ET VIS TANGENTE **13974**
COUPLE DE ROUES HELICOIDALES **11916**
COUPLE DE SERRAGE **12931**
COUPLE ELECTRO-CHIMIQUE **5782**
COUPLE METRE **13050**
COUPLE MOTEUR **13048**
COUPLE REACTION **8374**
COUPLE RESISTANT **8374**
COUPLE THERMO-ELECTRIQUE **12827**
COUPLE THERMOELECTRIQUE **12821**
COUPURE **3278**
COUPURE DE COURANT **8734**
COURANT **3486**
COURANT A BASSE TENSION **7777**
COURANT A FILETS PARALLELES **9055**
COURANT A HAUTE FREQUENCE **6468**
COURANT A HAUTE TENSION **6500**
COURANT ALTERNATIF **1**
COURANT ALTERNATIF **406**
COURANT ALTERNATIF HAUTE FREQUENCE **3**
COURANT CONTINU **3023**
COURANT D'AIR **253**
COURANT D'AIR FORCE **1315**
COURANT D'INDUCTION **6889**
COURANT D'UN PALAN **10851**

COURANT DE CHARGE **2266**
COURANT DE DISPERSION **7490**
COURANT DE FAIBLE INTENSITE **13705**
COURANT DE FOUCAULT **4438**
COURANT DE FUITE **7490**
COURANT DE GRANDE INTENSITE **6401**
COURANT DE LA CHAMBRE D'IONISATION **7126**
COURANT DIPHASE **13314**
COURANT DU BAIN **1064**
COURANT ELECTRIQUE **4500**
COURANT ELECTRIQUE ENERGIE **4525**
COURANT FORCE **5534**
COURANT FORT **6401**
COURANT GAZEUX **5816**
COURANT LIBRE **5634**
COURANT MONOPHASE **11501**
COURANT POLYPHASE **8462**
COURANT SECONDAIRE DE SOUDAGE **11110**
COURANT THERMOELECTRIQUE **12824**
COURANT TRIPHASE **12877**
COURANT TURBULENT **13274**
COURANT VAGABOND **12349**
COURANTS CROISES **3363**
COURANTS DE FOUCAULT **4440**
COURANTS DE MEME SENS **13360**
COURANTS DE SENS CONTRAIRE **3230**
COURBAGE **1182**
COURBE **3496**
COURBE A DOUBLE COURBURE **13307**
COURBE A FAIBLE RAYON **10102**
COURBE A GRAND RAYON **5378**
COURBE A PETIT RAYON **10102**
COURBE ADIABATIQUE **179**
COURBE APLATIE **5378**
COURBE CHARGE-ALLONGEMENT **12366**
COURBE D'UN DIAGRAMME **3495**
COURBE DANS L'ESPACE **13307**
COURBE DE CONTACT **675**
COURBE DE DETENTE **4916**
COURBE DE REFROIDISSEMENT **3087**
COURBE DE VITESSE **13513**
COURBE EFFORT-DEFORMATION **12365**
COURBE FERMEE **2520**
COURBE GAUCHE **13307**
COURBE ISOBARIQUE **7177**
COURBE LIMITE **1460**
COURBE PLANE **9435**
COURBE POLYTROPIQUE **9618**
COURBE RAIDE **10102**
COURBE ROULANTE **10697**
COURBE SINUEUSE **11476**

# 611 COU

COURBE VIVE **10102**
COURBER **1173**
COURBER UN TUYAU **1175**
COURBES DE TEMPERATURE **12723**
COURBURE **3494**
COURONNE CIRCULAIRE **589**
COURONNE D'UNE ROUE **10596**
COURONNE DE FIL **13898**
COURONNE DENTEE **3399**
COURONNE DENTEE **13023**
COURONNE DIRECTRICE D'UNE TURBINE **6168**
COURONNE FIXE **6168**
COURONNE MOBILE **13823**
COURONNE SUPPORT DE PLATEAU **12492**
COURONNE-SUPPORT DE PLATEAUX **13170**
COURONNEMENT **1604**
COURROIE **1140**
COURROIE (EPAISSEUR D'UNE) **1165**
COURROIE A PLUSIEURS EPAISSEURS **8463**
COURROIE A X PLIS **1166**
COURROIE COLLEE **2145**
COURROIE COUSUE **7350**
COURROIE CROISEE **3387**
COURROIE DE COMMANDE **1163**
COURROIE DE SECTION TRIANGULAIRE **13511**
COURROIE DE VENTILATEUR **5029**
COURROIE DEMI-CROISEE **6207**
COURROIE DOUBLE **4128**
COURROIE DROITE **8804**
COURROIE EN ACIER **12200**
COURROIE EN BALATA **944**
COURROIE EN BOYAUX **6183**
COURROIE EN CAOUTCHOUC **10817**
COURROIE EN CHANVRE **1907**
COURROIE EN COTON **3218**
COURROIE EN CRIN **6200**
COURROIE EN CUIR **7495**
COURROIE EN CUIR **7503**
COURROIE EN CUIR A MAILLONS **7496**
COURROIE EN FIBRES TEXTILES **4981**
COURROIE EN LANIERES DE CUIR TRAVAILLANT SUR CHAMP **7376**
COURROIE EN POILS **6200**
COURROIE EN POILS DE CHAMEAU **1891**
COURROIE EN TISSU CAOUTCHOUTE **10817**
COURROIE EN TISSU TUBULAIRE **5397**
COURROIE EN X EPAISSEURS **1166**
COURROIE MOTRICE **1163**
COURROIE MULTIPLE **8463**
COURROIE OUVERTE **8804**
COURROIE RENVERSEE **3387**

COURROIE SIMPLE **11477**
COURROIE TISSEE **13983**
COURROIE TORDUE **6207**
COURROIE TRAPEZOIDALE **13511**
COURROIE TRAPEZOIDALE **2925**
COURROIE TRAPEZOIDALE **13431**
COURROIE TRIPLE **12878**
COURSE **12387**
COURSE A VIDE (D'UNE MACHINE-OUTIL) **10529**
COURSE ALLER **5585**
COURSE ASCENDANTE **13409**
COURSE AVANT **5585**
COURSE COMPLETE (ALLER ET RETOUR) DU PISTON **13406**
COURSE D'ASPIRATION **12435**
COURSE D'ECHAPPEMENT **4898**
COURSE DE COMBUSTION **2775**
COURSE DE COMPRESSION **2864**
COURSE DE DETENTE **2775**
COURSE DE L'EXCENTRIQUE **12894**
COURSE DE LA CAME **12894**
COURSE DE REFOULEMENT **9834**
COURSE DE RETOUR **10530**
COURSE DE TRAVAIL **3536**
COURSE DESCENDANTE DU PISTON **4187**
COURSE DIRECTE DU PISTON **5585**
COURSE DU PISTON **7519**
COURSE MONTANTE DU PISTON **13409**
COURSE RETROGRADE DU PISTON **10530**
COURSE TRANSVERSALE DE LA TABLE **12585**
COURSE UTILE (D'UNE MACHINE-OUTIL) **3536**
COURSE VERTICALE **13549**
COURT-CIRCUIT **11372**
COURT-CIRCUIT **11369**
COUSSIN D'AIR **254**
COUSSIN PNEUMATIQUE **256**
COUSSINET **1100**
COUSSINET A BILLES **954**
COUSSINET A CANNELURES **12903**
COUSSINET A ROTULE **12563**
COUSSINET AUTO-GRAISSEUR **11158**
COUSSINET DE PALIER **7941**
COUSSINET DE PIED DE BIELLE **3390**
COUSSINET DE TETE DE BIELLE **1242**
COUSSINET EN COQUILLES **1572**
COUSSINET EN DEUX PIECES **1572**
COUSSINET EN UNE SEULE PIECE **1771**
COUSSINET OVALISE PAR L'USURE **13980**
COUSSINET USE **13980**
COUSSINETS DE FILIERE **3896**
COUTEAU **7325**
COUTEAU **7323**

# COU

612

COUTEAU CIRCULAIRE **2417**
COUVER **11688**
COUVERCLE **3269**
COUVERCLE **12639**
COUVERCLE A CHARNIERE **6510**
COUVERCLE A GLISSIERE **11604**
COUVERCLE D'UN ROBINET **3266**
COUVERCLE D'UNE SOUPAPE **3266**
COUVERCLE DU COFFRE **13240**
COUVERCLE DU CYLINDRE **3567**
COUVERCLE DU PALIER **1912**
COUVERCLE DU PISTON **7266**
COUVERCLE PROTECTEUR **9944**
COUVERTE **5968**
COUVERTE **615**
COUVERTURE DE SOL **5450**
COUVRE CULBUTEURS **3567**
COUVRE-OBJET **3265**
COUVRE-ROUES **13815**
COVARIANCE **3261**
CRABOTS ENCLENCHEURS/DECLENCHEURS **13214**
CRACHEMENT **11842**
CRACKING **3285**
CRAFE **2224**
CRAIE **13842**
CRAIE DE BRIANCON **11703**
CRAIE ROUGE **8720**
CRAMPON **12105**
CRAN **8672**
CRAPAUDINE **12241**
CRAPAUDINE **11905**
CRAPAUDINE A BILLES **11890**
CRAPAUDINE A PIVOT ANNULAIRE **2722**
CRAQUAGE OU CRACKING **3284**
CRAQUELURE SAISONNIERE **11092**
CRAQUELURE SUPERFICIELLE **3319**
CRASSE **4331**
CRATERE **3317**
CRAYON **7478**
CRAYON (D'UN APPAREIL ENREGISTREUR) **9161**
CRAYON DE COULEUR **2745**
CREMAILLERE **10119**
CREMAILLERE **13022**
CREMAILLERE ET PIGNON **10120**
CREME DE TARTRE **119**
CREOSOTAGE **3332**
CREOSOTE **3331**
CREPINE **12332**
CREPINE D'HUILE **8770**
CREPINE PREGRAVILLONNEE **9783**
CRETE D'UN DEVERSOIR **13754**

CRETE DE L'ONDE **3334**
CREUSAGE **11030**
CREUSEMENT D'UN FILET **11030**
CREUSER UN FILER **11046**
CREUSET **6331**
CREUSET **8142**
CREUSET (DE HAUT FOURNEAU) **3401**
CREUSET EN GRAPHITE **6064**
CREUSET EN PLATINE **9512**
CREUSET EN PORCELAINE **9626**
CREUX **2125**
CREUX DE LA DENT **6548**
CREUX DE LA SPHERE **13326**
CREUX ENTRE LES ONDES **6543**
CREUX SOUS LE PRIMITIF **3681**
CREVASSE **3278**
CRIBLAGE **11424**
CRIBLE **10572**
CRIBLE **11422**
CRIBLE A SECOUSSES **1733**
CRIBLE OSCILLANT **11252**
CRIBLE POUR LA TERRE **11628**
CRIBLE POUR LE SABLE **11628**
CRIBLER **11423**
CRIC **10121**
CRIC A LEVIER **7533**
CRIC A VIS **11035**
CRIC MECANIQUE **11035**
CRIN **12594**
CRIN DE CHEVAL **6604**
CRINS **7965**
CRIQUAGE **3284**
CRIQUE **3278**
CRIQUE **10097**
CRIQUE **2278**
CRIQUE A CHAUD **5240**
CRIQUE A CHAUD **6621**
CRIQUE DANS LE BOIS **11250**
CRIQUE DE CLIVAGE **11615**
CRIQUE DE RETRAIT **6645**
CRIQUE DE TENSION **5304**
CRIQUE DE VIEILLISSEMENT **11092**
CRIQUES D'ATTAQUE CHIMIQUE **4841**
CRISTAL **6030**
CRISTAL (MIN.) **3424**
CRISTAL (VERRE) **3428**
CRISTAL BASALTIQUE **2757**
CRISTAL CUBIQUE **3450**
CRISTAL DE ROCHE **10652**
CRISTAL HEMIEDRIQUE **6436**
CRISTAL HEMIMORPHE **6437**

CRISTAL HEXAGONAL **6459**
CRISTAL HOLOEDRE **6552**
CRISTAL IDIOMORPHE **6751**
CRISTAL INHOMOGENE **3169**
CRISTAL MONOCLINIQUE **8384**
CRISTAL OSCILLATEUR **3432**
CRISTAL RHOMBOEDRIQUE **10565**
CRISTALLIN **8688**
CRISTALLIN **3433**
CRISTALLISABILITE **3436**
CRISTALLISABLE **3437**
CRISTALLISATION **3438**
CRISTALLISATION PRIMAIRE **9849**
CRISTALLISER **3439**
CRISTALLITE **3440**
CRISTALLOGRAMME **3441**
CRISTALLOGRAPHIE **3442**
CRISTALLOIDE **3443**
CRISTAUX **119**
CRISTAUX DE SOUDE **11711**
CRISTAUX EQUIAXES **4784**
CRISTAUX MIXTES **8329**
CRISTAUX ORTHORHOMBIQUES **8874**
CROC **4974**
CROCHET **5772**
CROCHET **6568**
CROCHET A NOYAUX **3152**
CROCHET A OEIL **4974**
CROCHET A QUEUE DE COCHON **9301**
CROCHET A TETE DE BELIER **10191**
CROCHET A VIS **11057**
CROCHET D'ATTELAGE **4217**
CROCHET DE CHAINE **3822**
CROCHET DE LEVAGE **7552**
CROCHET DE SURETE **10888**
CROCHET DE SUSPENSION **12527**
CROCHET DOUBLE **10191**
CROCHET PIVOTANT **12564**
CROCHET POUR TUBES **9354**
CROCHETS **11902**
CROCHETS DE TRACTION **6307**
CROISILLONS DE CHARPENTE **1520**
CROISSANCE **6155**
CROISSANCE ANORMALE DES CRISTAUX **7**
CROISSANCE DES GRAINS **6035**
CROISSANT **7829**
CROIX **3359**
CROIX A QUATRE DIRECTIONS **3368**
CROQUER **11529**
CROQUIS **11532**
CROQUIS **11528**

CROQUIS DE PRINCIPE **3797**
CROQUIS SCHEMATIQUE **3836**
CROSSETTE **3388**
CROUTE **11624**
CROUTE **3421**
CROUTE **9155**
CROUTE DE LA FONTE **11538**
CROUTE DE LAMINAGE **11544**
CROWN-GLASS **3397**
CRUE **586**
CRYOHYDRATE **3422**
CRYOLITHE **3423**
CUBAGE **13598**
CUBAGE (EVALUATION EN UNITES CUBES) **3444**
CUBE (GEOM.) **3445**
CUBER **3446**
CUBILOT **3466**
CUBILOT **3464**
CUBIQUE A FACE CENTREE **4991**
CUCURBITE **1407**
CUIR **7494**
CUIR BRULE **2272**
CUIR BRUT **10237**
CUIR CHROME **2377**
CUIR DE BOEUF **3275**
CUIR DE VACHE **3275**
CUIR DU CROUPON **1780**
CUIR EMBOUTI **3458**
CUIR FORT **11770**
CUIR TANNE A L'ECORCE DE CHENE **8704**
CUIR VERNI **9117**
CUIR VERT **10237**
CUIVRAGE **3125**
CUIVRE (CUIVRE ROUGE) **3110**
CUIVRE A BALAI **1669**
CUIVRE A OXYDE CUIVREUX **13069**
CUIVRE A SOUFFLURES **1329**
CUIVRE AFFINE **2073**
CUIVRE AFFINE **13070**
CUIVRE AFFINE AU FEU **5250**
CUIVRE ANODIQUE **593**
CUIVRE ARGENTIFERE **11468**
CUIVRE ARSENICAL **725**
CUIVRE CEMENTATOIRE **2136**
CUIVRE DE BRASAGE **1575**
CUIVRE DE CEMENT **2136**
CUIVRE DESOXYDE **3764**
CUIVRE DU LAC SUPERIEUR **7370**
CUIVRE ELECTROLYTIQUE **2099**
CUIVRE ELECTROLYTIQUE **4591**
CUIVRE ELECTROLYTIQUE A OXYDE CUIVREUX **4610**

# CUI

614

CUIVRE ELECTROLYTIQUE COALESCE **2571**
CUIVRE EN FEUILLES **11308**
CUIVRE EXEMPT D'OXYGENE A HAUTE CONDUCTIVITE **8983**
CUIVRE GRIS **12796**
CUIVRE JAUNE **1562**
CUIVRE NATIF **7370**
CUIVRE NOIR BRUT **1287**
CUIVRE OXYDULE **3476**
CUIVRE PANACHE **13501**
CUIVRE PHOSPHOREUX **9250**
CUIVRE PHOSPHOREUX **9253**
CUIVRE POUR GRAVURE **4767**
CUIVRE PYRITEUX **3126**
CUIVRE REGENERE **2136**
CUIVRE ROSETTE **10748**
CUIVRE SILICEUX **11446**
CUIVRE SUFURE GRIS **3118**
CUIVRE VITREUX **3118**
CUIVRER **3124**
CULASSE **3569**
CULASSE D'UN AIMANT **14017**
CULBUTEUR **10654**
CULBUTEUR DE LINGOTS **7982**
CULEE **57**
CULOT D'UNE CRAPAUDINE **12905**
CULOT DE BOUGIE **11839**
CULOTTE **1595**
CULTIVATEURS **3457**
CUNEIFORME **13737**
CUPRO-BERYLLIUM **1209**
CUPRO-NICKEL **3477**
CURAGE **11011**
CURCUMINE **3481**
CURER **11008**
CURETTE **11009**
CURSEUR **7625**
CURSEUR D'UNE BALANCE **13160**
CURVILIGNE **3499**
CURVIMETRE **3501**
CUVE **13228**
CUVE **12046**
CUVE A NIVEAU CONSTANT **5431**
CUVE DE DECANTATION **11229**
CUVE DE FOUR **9029**
CUVE DE TREMPAGE **3973**
CUVE DE TREMPE **10090**
CUVETTE **11073**
CUVETTE D'EGOUTTAGE **4283**
CUVETTE DE PLATEAUX **11074**
CUVETTE DE RETENTION D'UN RESERVOIR **12629**
CYANATE **3544**

CYANOFERRURE DE POTASSIUM **9685**
CYANOGENE **3551**
CYANOTYPE **5119**
CYANURE **3547**
CYANURE D'ARGENT **11462**
CYANURE D'OR **5997**
CYANURE DE CUIVRE **3115**
CYANURE DE POTASSIUM **9683**
CYANURE DE SODIUM **11720**
CYANURE DE ZINC **14041**
CYANURE LIBRE **5632**
CYCLE **3554**
CYCLE **3553**
CYCLE AUTOMATIQUE **839**
CYCLE DE CARNOT **2004**
CYCLE DE TRAVAIL **3553**
CYCLE FIXE **5292**
CYCLIQUE **3555**
CYCLOIDE **3557**
CYCLOIDE RACCOURCIE **3493**
CYCLOIDE RALLONGEE **9918**
CYCLONE PULVERISATEUR **3560**
CYLINDRAGE **13164**
CYLINDRE **1015**
CYLINDRE **10671**
CYLINDRE (GEOM.) **3561**
CYLINDRE A AIR **2841**
CYLINDRE A BASE CIRCULAIRE **2411**
CYLINDRE A BASE ELLIPTIQUE **4675**
CYLINDRE A BASSE PRESSION **7783**
CYLINDRE A CINTRER **1186**
CYLINDRE A FREIN **1532**
CYLINDRE A HAUTE PRESSION **6488**
CYLINDRE A RAINURE **3579**
CYLINDRE A VAPEUR **12162**
CYLINDRE A VIDE **4373**
CYLINDRE CANNELE **5486**
CYLINDRE CANNELE **6136**
CYLINDRE CANNELE **11206**
CYLINDRE CREUX **6540**
CYLINDRE D'ALIMENTATION **5074**
CYLINDRE D'EQUILIBRAGE **938**
CYLINDRE D'EQUILIBRAGE **939**
CYLINDRE DE CINTRAGE **1186**
CYLINDRE DE LEVAGE **7550**
CYLINDRE DE POMPE **9992**
CYLINDRE DE TRAVAIL **13954**
CYLINDRE DROIT **10579**
CYLINDRE EN PORTE-A-FAUX **8935**
CYLINDRE ENTRAINEUR **5074**
CYLINDRE GRADUE **3582**

615 DEC

CYLINDRE HYPERBOLIQUE **6736**
CYLINDRE LISSE **5391**
CYLINDRE MOTEUR **13954**
CYLINDRE OBLIQUE **8712**
CYLINDRE PARABOLIQUE **9039**
CYLINDRE RUGUEUX **10174**
CYLINDRE TOURNANT D'UN ENREGISTREUR **10290**
CYLINDREE **2262**
CYLINDREE **3448**
CYLINDREE **3566**
CYLINDRER **13162**
CYLINDRES DE SUPPORT **903**
CYLINDRES TRANSVERSAUX **1643**
CYLINDRIQUE **3577**
DALLAGE **9136**
DALLE **11551**
DALLE **5302**
DALLE DE BETON (SUPPORT D'UN RESERVOIR) **2900**
DALLE SUPPORT / SUR PIEUX **9305**
DAMAGE **10195**
DAME **12611**
DAME-JEANNE **1981**
DAMER **10189**
DAMMAR **3598**
DAMPER **3602**
DANGER D'INCENDIE **3608**
DANGEREUX **6503**
DANS LE SENS DES AIGUILLES D'UNE MONTRE **2506**
DARD **6951**
DARD DE CHALUMEAU **8975**
DARD DE LA FLAMME **2923**
DARD INTERIEUR **6952**
DASHPOT **3611**
DASHPOT A AIR **256**
DATE DE L'ACCORD DU BREVET **3617**
DATE DU DEPOT DE LA DEMANDE DE BREVET **3616**
DEBIT **10069**
DEBIT **9730**
DEBIT **8908**
DEBIT **5459**
DEBIT **8896**
DEBIT A LA SCIE DE LONG **1058**
DEBIT AU COIN DU BOIS **10075**
DEBIT D'UNE POMPE **10228**
DEBIT NORMAL **8658**
DEBIT TOTAL **13064**
DEBITER AUX DIMENSIONS VOULUES **3509**
DEBITMETRE **5458**
DEBITMETRE **13604**
DEBLOCAGE **11560**
DEBOUCHAGE **12675**

DEBOURBAGE **7537**
DEBRAYAGE **4028**
DEBRAYAGE **12898**
DEBRAYAGE **2548**
DEBRAYER **10034**
DECAGONE **3644**
DECAGRAMME **3645**
DECALAGE **541**
DECALAGE (ACTION D'OTER LES CALES) **4312**
DECALAGE A DROITE **10583**
DECALAGE A GAUCHE **7507**
DECALAGE DE PHASE **9237**
DECALAGE DES PHASES **9234**
DECALAGE DU POINT D'ORIGINE **14026**
DECALAGE DU POINT D'ORIGINE **14031**
DECALAGE EN ARRIERE **7368**
DECALAGE EN AVANCE **7483**
DECALAMINAGE **10979**
DECALAMINAGE A L'EAU **13647**
DECALAMINAGE A LA FLAMME **5313**
DECALAMINAGE AU CHALUMEAU **5310**
DECALCOMANIE **13109**
DECALE **8731**
DECALE **8730**
DECALER **4295**
DECALESCENCE **3646**
DECALITRE **3647**
DECALQUE **13082**
DECAMETRE **3648**
DECANTATION **3650**
DECANTATION **4681**
DECANTATION **11228**
DECANTER **3649**
DECAPAGE **11006**
DECAPAGE A FROID **2707**
DECAPAGE A L'ACIDE **9288**
DECAPAGE ANODIQUE **601**
DECAPAGE AU BAIN ACIDULE **112**
DECAPAGE AU GAZ **5832**
DECAPAGE CATHODIQUE **2103**
DECAPAGE CHIMIQUE **9288**
DECAPAGE ELECTROLYTIQUE **4603**
DECAPAGE MAT **3628**
DECAPAGE PAR GRENAILLAGE **11381**
DECAPER **11005**
DECARBONISATION **3651**
DECARBONISER **3652**
DECARBURATION **3655**
DECARBURATION DU FER **3653**
DECARBURER LE FER **3654**
DECAUVILLE **9639**

# DEC

DECELERATION AUTOMATIQUE **841**
DECENTRE **8730**
DECHARGE **4024**
DECHARGE **4017**
DECHARGE **2395**
DECHARGE D'UN ACCUMULATEUR **4025**
DECHARGE ELECTRIQUE **4502**
DECHARGER **4018**
DECHARGER UN ACCUMULATEUR **4019**
DECHARGEURS A GRIFFES (MAT. ET GRUE) **6310**
DECHEANCE D'UN BREVET **7408**
DECHETS **13637**
DECHIRER (SE) **10859**
DECHIRURE **3278**
DECIGRAMME **3657**
DECILITRE **3658**
DECIMALE **3659**
DECIMETRE **3666**
DECIMETRE CARRE **12018**
DECIMETRE CUBE **3451**
DECLAVETAGE **7751**
DECLAVETER **7750**
DECLENCHEMENT **4031**
DECLENCHER **4030**
DECLINAISON MAGNETIQUE **3668**
DECLIQUETAGE **4031**
DECLIQUETER **4030**
DECLIVITE **3792**
DECOCHAGE **7328**
DECOCHAGE **9554**
DECOCTION **3669**
DECODEUR **3670**
DECOLLEMENT **1354**
DECOLLEMENT **9156**
DECOLLETAGE **3533**
DECOLLETER **3510**
DECOLORATION **5014**
DECOMPOSABLE **3671**
DECOMPOSER **3672**
DECOMPOSER (SE) **3673**
DECOMPOSITION **10769**
DECOMPOSITION (CHIM.) **3674**
DECOMPOSITION DE LA LUMIERE **3676**
DECOMPOSITION DES FORCES **10505**
DECOMPOSITION ELECTROLYTIQUE **4596**
DECOUPAGE **10012**
DECOUPAGE **3533**
DECOUPAGE A L'EMPORTE-PIECE **6514**
DECOUPAGE A LA MACHINE **7842**
DECOUPAGE A LA POUDRE **9719**
DECOUPAGE AUTOGENE **832**

DECOUPER **9998**
DECOUPER **3510**
DECOUPER A L'AUTOGENE **3505**
DECOUPER AU CHALUMEAU **3505**
DECOUPER DES TOLES **3513**
DECOUPOIR **6545**
DECRIQUER (AU CHALUMEAU) **10993**
DECROISSANCE **3656**
DEDOUBLEMENT **11950**
DEDOUBLER **11946**
DEFAILLANCE PRECOCE **6908**
DEFAUT **5411**
DEFAUT **3691**
DEFAUT D'ALIGNEMENT OU DENIVELLATION (D'UN JOINT SOUDE) **8737**
DEFAUT DE COULAGE **5056**
DEFAUT DE FABRICATION **3693**
DEFAUT DE MATIERE **3692**
DEFAUT DE SURFACE **12502**
DEFAUTS DE LA SOUDURE **13760**
DEFAUTS DE PEINTURE **9021**
DEFECTUEUX **5057**
DEFLECTEUR **921**
DEFLECTEUR **13531**
DEFLECTEUR **3702**
DEFLECTION **3699**
DEFONCEMENT **3760**
DEFORMABILITE **3705**
DEFORMATION **12322**
DEFORMATION **3707**
DEFORMATION **13629**
DEFORMATION (FLECHE) **3698**
DEFORMATION CRITIQUE **3350**
DEFORMATION ELASTIQUE **4485**
DEFORMATION ELASTIQUE **4478**
DEFORMATION EN GENOU **7315**
DEFORMATION PAR ENROULEMENT **13629**
DEFORMATION PAR FLEXION **5426**
DEFORMATION PAR TRACTION **12744**
DEFORMATION PERMANENTE **9202**
DEFORMATION PERMANENTE **9210**
DEFORMATION PERMANENTE **3337**
DEFORMATION PERMANENTE DE L'AME D'UNE POUTRE **13727**
DEFORMATION PLASTIQUE **9469**
DEFORMATION PLASTIQUE **9471**
DEFORMATION PRINCIPALE **2000**
DEFORMATION PROGRESSIVE **6853**
DEFORMATIONS EN DEMI-LUNE DU CORDON DE SOUDURE **5212**
DEFOURNEMENT PAR EXTRACTEUR A BRAS **4471**

617 DEN

DEGAGEMENT **910**
DEGAGEMENT DE CHALEUR **4874**
DEGAGEMENT DE CHALEUR **10274**
DEGAGEMENT DE GAZ **3818**
DEGAGER **893**
DEGAUCHIR **12318**
DEGAUCHISSAGE **12319**
DEGAUCHISSAGE A FROID **2691**
DEGAUCHISSEMENT **12319**
DEGAUCHISSEUSE **12515**
DEGAZAGE **3710**
DEGAZAGE DE L'EAU **3623**
DEGAZER **10455**
DEGIVREUR **3708**
DEGORGEMENT **1321**
DEGORGEMENT **5728**
DEGORGEOIR **5729**
DEGOULINAGE **10892**
DEGOURDISSAGE (PRECHAUFFAGE AVANT SOUDAGE) **6260**
DEGRAISSAGE **2474**
DEGRAISSAGE **3712**
DEGRAISSAGE A LA VAPEUR **13486**
DEGRAISSAGE D'UN METAL **11006**
DEGRAISSAGE ELECTROLYTIQUE **4589**
DEGRAISSER UN METAL **11005**
DEGRAISSEUR AU SOLVANT **2473**
DEGRAS **3711**
DEGRE **12239**
DEGRE **3714**
DEGRE **6021**
DEGRE BAUME **3715**
DEGRE CENTIGRADE **3716**
DEGRE D'ENCROUTEMENT **4683**
DEGRE D'EXACTITUDE **3721**
DEGRE D'USINAGE **7866**
DEGRE DE DURETE **3720**
DEGRE DE FIN D'UN ALLIAGE **5209**
DEGRE DE PRECISION **3721**
DEGRE DE SATURATION **3722**
DEGRE DE TREMPE DE L'ACIER **6299**
DEGRE ENGLER **3717**
DEGRE FAHRENHEIT **3718**
DEGRE HYDROTIMETRIQUE **6298**
DEGRE HYGROMETRIQUE DE L'AIR **10433**
DEGRE REAUMUR **3724**
DEGRE TWADDELL **3725**
DEGRES DE LIBERTE **3726**
DEGROSSIR **10775**
DEGROSSISSAGE **10786**
DEGROSSISSAGE A LA MEULE **10777**
DEJETER (SE) **13628**

DELARDAGE **12646**
DELARDAGE D'UNE TOLE **12671**
DELAVAGE **13632**
DELAYER **12718**
DELIQUESCENCE **3733**
DELIQUESCENT **3734**
DELIVRANCE D'UN BREVET **6049**
DEMAGNETISEURS **3744**
DEMANDE **646**
DEMANDER UN BREVET **651**
DEMANDEUR D'UN BREVET **645**
DEMARIEUSE POUR BETTERAVES A SUCRE **12438**
DEMARRAGE **12118**
DEMARRAGE D'UN MOTEUR **12122**
DEMARRAGE DOUX **11685**
DEMARRAGE SANS A-COUPS **11685**
DEMARRER **12113**
DEMARREUR **3310**
DEMARREUR **12116**
DEMARREUR **8418**
DEMARREUR AUTOMATIQUE **828**
DEMI-AXE **11167**
DEMI-CELLULE **6204**
DEMI-CERCLE **11179**
DEMI-CERCLE **12261**
DEMI-CIRCULAIRE **11169**
DEMI-COUSSINET INFERIEUR **1487**
DEMI-COUSSINET SUPERIEUR **13030**
DEMI-COUSSINETS **11947**
DEMI-MANCHON **6205**
DEMI-RONDS TREFILES **4249**
DEMI-SPHERE **6438**
DEMODULATEUR **8338**
DEMODULATION **10312**
DEMOISELLE **12611**
DEMONTABLE **4027**
DEMONTAGE **12604**
DEMONTAGE D'UNE CLAVETTE **7751**
DEMONTE **7329**
DEMONTER **12600**
DEMONTER UN BOULON **13395**
DEMOULAGE **9554**
DEMOULAGE **11251**
DEMOULER **4468**
DEMOULEUSE **4237**
DEMULTIPLICATION **5908**
DEMULTIPLICATION **10357**
DENATURANT **3747**
DENDRITE **3748**
DENDRITE **9331**
DENICKELAGE **3751**

# DEN

618

DENIVELLATION **7798**
DENIVELLEMENT **7798**
DENOMINATEUR **3752**
DENOMINATEUR COMMUN **2789**
DENSIFICATION **3753**
DENSIMETRE **3755**
DENSITE **3756**
DENSITE **11850**
DENSITE APPARENTE **642**
DENSITE APPARENTE **1725**
DENSITE AU REMPLISSAGE **1724**
DENSITE D'UN GAZ **3757**
DENSITE D'UN LIQUIDE **3758**
DENSITE DE COURANT **4501**
DENSITE DU COURANT **3488**
DENSITE ELECTRIQUE **4501**
DENSITE MAGNETIQUE **7899**
DENT **2464**
DENT **13016**
DENT A CHEVRON **4144**
DENT BRUTE DE FONTE **2059**
DENT D'ENGRENAGE **13819**
DENT DE SCIE **10959**
DENT EN FONTE **7154**
DENT TAILLEE **3514**
DENTELE **6862**
DENTS A FLANCS EPICYCLOIDAUX **4780**
DENTS A FLANCS HYPOCYCLOIDAUX **6744**
DENTS D'UNE LIME **3518**
DENTURE **13026**
DENTURE **12704**
DENTURE A PAS INCLINE A DROITE **10586**
DENTURE A PAS INCLINE A GAUCHE **7509**
DENTURE AVOYEE **10187**
DENTURE D'UNE LIME **3518**
DENTURE DROITE **12311**
DENTURE EXTERIEURE **4959**
DENTURE INTERIEURE **7077**
DEPASSEMENT **8959**
DEPASSEMENT **8948**
DEPENSE D'ENERGIE DE FORCE MOTRICE **2876**
DEPENSE DE VAPEUR **2995**
DEPENSER DE LA CHALEUR **5950**
DEPERDITION DE CHALEUR **7760**
DEPHASAGE **7368**
DEPHASAGE **7483**
DEPHASAGE **9234**
DEPLACABLE **4052**
DEPLACEMENT **13123**
DEPLACEMENT (CEN) **4053**
DEPLACEMENT ANGULAIRE **541**

DEPLACEMENT AXIAL **860**
DEPLACEMENT D'UN LIQUIDE **4054**
DEPLACEMENT DE L'ESTAMPE **3891**
DEPLACEMENT DE LA COURROIE **1158**
DEPLACEMENT INTERNE **7063**
DEPLACEMENT LATERAL **7420**
DEPLACEMENT LATERAL **12538**
DEPLACEMENT LONGITUDINAL **860**
DEPLACEMENT PARALLELE A L'AXE **860**
DEPLACEMENT PERPENDICULAIRE A L'AXE **7420**
DEPLACEMENT RADIAL **10133**
DEPLACER LA COURROIE **11349**
DEPOLARISANT **3770**
DEPOLARISANT **3772**
DEPOLARISATEUR **3772**
DEPOLARISATION **3768**
DEPOLARISATION **3771**
DEPOLARISER **3769**
DEPORT LATERAL **7423**
DEPOSE ET REMONTAGE **10451**
DEPOSER (SE) **11227**
DEPOSITION ELECTROLYTIQUE **4593**
DEPOT **12265**
DEPOT (ENDROIT) **12293**
DEPOT ACTIF **149**
DEPOT BRULE **1761**
DEPOT ELECTROLYTIQUE **4580**
DEPOT ELECTROLYTIQUE **4593**
DEPOT ELECTROLYTIQUE A PLUSIEURS COUCHES **2821**
DEPOT GALVANIQUE **4592**
DEPOT PAR CONTACT **3004**
DEPOTS CALCAIRES **10969**
DEPOUILLE **910**
DEPOUILLE **4196**
DEPOUILLER **893**
DEPOUSSIERAGE **3682**
DEPOUSSIERER **5637**
DEPRESSION **9811**
DEPRESSION **3778**
DEPRESSION ATMOSPHERIQUE **13434**
DEPRESSION CAPILLAIRE **1924**
DERANGEMENT DANS LE SERVICE **1581**
DERIVATION **1821**
DERIVATION **1554**
DERIVATION **11403**
DERIVE **3786**
DERIVER **3511**
DERNIERE FILIERE **5221**
DEROCHAGE **11006**
DEROCHER **11005**
DEROGATION **13615**

DET

DEROUILLEMENT **10826**
DEROUILLER **10815**
DEROULEMENT **13405**
DEROULER **13404**
DEROULEUSE DE FIL **13903**
DERRICK **3788**
DES DE FRAISAGE **8290**
DESABLAGE **2478**
DESABLER **2469**
DESACTIVATION **3789**
DESAGREGATION **4000**
DESAGREGER **3999**
DESAGREGER (SE) **4043**
DESAIMANTATION **3742**
DESAIMANTER **3743**
DESAIMANTER (SE) **1123**
DESARGENTAGE **3802**
DESARGENTER **3801**
DESASSEMBLAGE **12604**
DESASSEMBLER **12600**
DESAXAGE **4055**
DESAXE **8893**
DESAXE **8730**
DESCENDRE LA COURROIE **12895**
DESCENTE D'UN FARDEAU **7797**
DESCENTE DE COULEE **4186**
DESCENTE DE COULEE **12003**
DESCENTE DU PISTON **4187**
DESCRIPTION D'UN BREVET **11856**
DESEMBRAYAGE **12898**
DESEMBRAYER **10034**
DESEMBUAGE **3704**
DESENGRENAGE **12898**
DESENGRENE **8892**
DESENGRENER **10034**
DESEQUILIBRE **13341**
DESHUILEUR DE VAPEUR **8779**
DESHYDRATATION **3728**
DESHYDRATER **3727**
DESHYDRATER (SE) **3727**
DESINCRUSTANT CURATIF **4041**
DESINCRUSTANT PREVENTIF **10978**
DESINCRUSTATION **10987**
DESINCRUSTER **10971**
DESINFECTANT **4042**
DESINTEGRATION **4044**
DESINTEGRATION **3418**
DESINTEGRATION **4000**
DESINTEGRER **3999**
DESIONISATION **3729**
DESOXYDANT **3765**

DESOXYDATION **3766**
DESOXYDATION **3762**
DESOXYDER **3763**
DESOXYGENATION **3762**
DESOXYGENER **3763**
DESSECHAGE/DESSICCATION DES BOIS A L'AIR LIBRE **11095**
DESSECHER **4338**
DESSERRAGE **11560**
DESSERRER (SE) **11559**
DESSERRER UN ECROU **11558**
DESSERRER UN FREIN **10436**
DESSERRER UNE VIS **11558**
DESSICCATEUR **3804**
DESSICCATION **4359**
DESSIN **4229**
DESSIN **9430**
DESSIN (ART DU DESSINATEUR) **4246**
DESSIN (REPRESENTATION GRAPHIQUE) **4245**
DESSIN A L'ECHELLE **10983**
DESSIN A MAIN LEVEE **5648**
DESSIN AU CRAYON **7467**
DESSIN AU TRAIT **8905**
DESSIN COTE **3959**
DESSIN D'ARCHITECTURE **693**
DESSIN DE DETAIL **3809**
DESSIN DE MACHINE **7843**
DESSIN EN COUPE **11122**
DESSIN EN GRANDEUR NATURELLE **5724**
DESSIN GEOMETRIQUE **5928**
DESSIN INDUSTRIEL **8099**
DESSIN LAVE **12965**
DESSIN LINEAIRE **8905**
DESSIN NATURE **5724**
DESSIN OMBRE **11235**
DESSIN PASSE A L'ENCRE **6941**
DESSINATEUR **4213**
DESSINER **4195**
DESSINER A GRANDS TRAITS **11529**
DESSOUDAGE **13400**
DESSOUDER **13399**
DESSUS D'UN FILET **12455**
DESTRUCTIBILITE **6**
DETAIL DE CONSTRUCTION **3810**
DETALONNAGE **1387**
DETARTRAGE **10987**
DETARTRANT **10978**
DETARTRER **10971**
DETECTEUR DE CRIQUES ET FELURES **3280**
DETENDEUR **10420**
DETENDEUR **10355**

**DET** 620

DETENDRE (SE) **4902**
DETENTE **10435**
DETENTE D UN GAZ **4921**
DETENTE DE LA VAPEUR **4921**
DETENTE DES GAZ **4920**
DETERGENT **3813**
DETERIORE **5057**
DETERMINANT **3814**
DETERMINANT MINEUR **8315**
DETERMINATION ANALYTIQUE **496**
DETERMINATION EXPERIMENTALE **4929**
DETONATION **7330**
DETREMPAGE **7549**
DETREMPE DE L'ACIER **12733**
DETREMPER L'ACIER **12719**
DEVELOPPABLE **3817**
DEVELOPPABLE **3816**
DEVELOPPANTE **7117**
DEVELOPPANTE DU CERCLE **7118**
DEVELOPPEE **4873**
DEVELOPPER (GEOM.) **3815**
DEVERSEMENT **4376**
DEVERSER (SE) **13628**
DEVERSOIR **13753**
DEVERSOIR **8931**
DEVERSOIR DES PLATEAUX **4188**
DEVIATION **3819**
DEVIATION **3699**
DEVIATION **3380**
DEVIATION LATERALE **7419**
DEVIATION NULLE **14024**
DEVIDOIR **13898**
DEVIS **4838**
DEVISSAGE **13396**
DEVISSER **13395**
DEVITRIFICATION **3823**
DEXTRINE **3825**
DEXTROGYRE **3827**
DEXTRORSUM **2508**
DIABASE **3828**
DIABLE **947**
DIACAUSTIQUE **3829**
DIAGMAGNETISME **3848**
DIAGONAL **3831**
DIAGONALE **3831**
DIAGRAMME **3834**
DIAGRAMME **7717**
DIAGRAMME D'EQUILIBRE **4788**
DIAGRAMME D'INDICATEUR **6881**
DIAGRAMME D'OUVERTURE ET DE FERMETURE D'UNE
  SOUPAPE **13457**

DIAGRAMME DE DIFFRACTION A RAYONS X **3441**
DIAGRAMME DE DIFFRACTION DES RAYONS X. **13997**
DIAGRAMME DE DIFFRACTION RX **3926**
DIAGRAMME DE DISTRIBUTION **11593**
DIAGRAMME DE LAUE **7435**
DIAGRAMME DE PHASES **2984**
DIAGRAMME DE RX **9128**
DIAGRAMME DE TRAVAIL **6881**
DIAGRAMME DES EFFORTS **5526**
DIAGRAMME DES FORCES **5526**
DIAGRAMME DES FORCES **3835**
DIAGRAMME DES RESISTANCES **10489**
DIAGRAMME DES VITESSES **13514**
DIAGRAMME ENTROPIQUE **6346**
DIAGRAMME FER-CARBURE **7139**
DIAGRAMME RANKINISE **10203**
DIAGRAMME TOTALISE **10203**
DIALYSE **3846**
DIALYSER **3844**
DIALYSEUR **3845**
DIAMAGNETIQUE **3847**
DIAMANT **3862**
DIAMETRE **3849**
DIAMETRE (DU CERCLE) DE PERCAGE **3853**
DIAMETRE A FLANC DE FILET **9407**
DIAMETRE A FOND DE FILET **3850**
DIAMETRE ADMIS AU-DESSUS DU BANC **12547**
DIAMETRE CONJUGUE **2954**
DIAMETRE D'ALESAGE **3855**
DIAMETRE D'UN CABLE **10733**
DIAMETRE D'UN FIL **3860**
DIAMETRE D'UN TUYAU **3858**
DIAMETRE DE LA BARRE DE FER D'UN MAILLON **3856**
DIAMETRE DE LA POINTE DU FORET **4269**
DIAMETRE DE PERCAGE **1438**
DIAMETRE DE PIED **10719**
DIAMETRE DE TROU DE BOULON **3854**
DIAMETRE DU BOULON **1434**
DIAMETRE DU NOYAU **3850**
DIAMETRE DU RIVET **3859**
DIAMETRE DU TROU **3857**
DIAMETRE DU TROU DE BOULON **1440**
DIAMETRE EXTERIEUR **3852**
DIAMETRE EXTERIEUR **8913**
DIAMETRE EXTERIEUR **4958**
DIAMETRE INTERIEUR **8314**
DIAMETRE INTERIEUR **6977**
DIAMETRE INTERIEUR **7071**
DIAMETRE INTERIEUR **3850**
DIAMETRE INTERIEUR D'UN TUYAU **1464**
DIAMETRE NOMINAL **8611**

621 DIS

DIAMETRE PRIMITIF **9407**
DIAMETRE PRIMITIF **3861**
DIAMETRE UTILE **13423**
DIAPHANE **3869**
DIAPHANEITE **3868**
DIAPHRAGME **4110**
DIAPHRAGME **3870**
DIAPHRAGME (OPT.) **3871**
DIAPHRAGME ELASTIQUE **4479**
DIAPHRAGME EN CAOUTCHOUC **10819**
DIAPHRAGME EN CUIR **7498**
DIAPHRAGME IRIS **7132**
DIAPHRAGMER **3877**
DIATHERMANE **3879**
DIATHERMANEITE **3878**
DIATHERMANSIE **3878**
DIATHERMIQUE **3879**
DIATOMIQUE **3881**
DIBASIQUE **3882**
DIEDRE **3944**
DIELECTRIQUE **3898**
DIESEL **3901**
DIFFERENCE **3902**
DIFFERENCE DE POTENTIEL **9709**
DIFFERENCE DE POTENTIEL AUX BORNES **12764**
DIFFERENCE DE PRESSION **9814**
DIFFERENCE DE TEMPERATURE **3904**
DIFFERENCIATION **3923**
DIFFERENCIER **3922**
DIFFERENTIEL **3913**
DIFFERENTIEL **3906**
DIFFRACTION **3924**
DIFFRACTION **10387**
DIFFUSEUR **3928**
DIFFUSEUR OU BUSE **2359**
DIFFUSIBILITE **3936**
DIFFUSION **3929**
DIFFUSION **10994**
DIFFUSION DE LA LUMIERE **3933**
DIFFUSION DES GAZ **3932**
DIGESTEUR **829**
DIGESTION (CHIM.) **3939**
DILATABILITE **3947**
DILATABLE **3948**
DILATATION **3949**
DILATATION CUBIQUE **13603**
DILATATION D'UN METAL **4919**
DILATATION LATERALE **7421**
DILATATION LINEAIRE **7612**
DILATATION SOUS L'INFLUENCE DE LA CHALEUR **4948**
DILATATION SUPERFICIELLE **12466**

DILATATION THERMIQUE **12808**
DILATOMETRE **3950**
DILUANT **3951**
DILUER **3952**
DILUTION D'UNE SOLUTION **3954**
DIMENSION (A DEUX) **8729**
DIMENSION (A UNE) **8727**
DIMENSION INFERIEURE AUX PRESCRIPTIONS **13349**
DIMENSION NOMINALE **8612**
DIMENSION NOMINALE **8615**
DIMENSION NORMALE **12071**
DIMENSION REELLE **152**
DIMENSIONS **3960**
DIMENSIONS (A TROIS) **8728**
DIMENSIONS D'ENCOMBREMENT **7481**
DIMENSIONS HORS-TOUT **8922**
DIMENSIONS NOMINALES **11857**
DIMETHYLCETONE **90**
DIMETHYLE **4848**
DIMINUTION **3677**
DIMINUTION DE LA SECTION TRANSVERSALE **10362**
DIODE **3964**
DIORITE **3966**
DIOXYDE DE PLOMB **7461**
DIPHENYLAMINE **3974**
DIRECTEUR **3995**
DIRECTEUR D'USINE **5915**
DIRECTION ASSISTEE **9743**
DIRECTION D'UNE FORCE **3990**
DIRECTION DE MOUVEMENT **3991**
DIRECTION DES FIBRES **3993**
DIRECTION DES FIBRES **5133**
DIRECTION DES USINES, DES ATELIERS, DU TRAVAIL **13963**
DIRECTION/ORGANISATION SCIENTIFIQUE DES ATELIERS **11001**
DIRECTRICE **3996**
DISCRIMINANT **4029**
DISJONCTEUR **2407**
DISJONCTEUR **3516**
DISLOCATION **4047**
DISLOCATION-COIN **4443**
DISLOCATION-VIS (EN HELICE) **11031**
DISPERSANT **4050**
DISPERSEUR DE LIQUIDES **809**
DISPERSION **4051**
DISPERSION ELECTROMAGNETIQUE **4616**
DISPOSITIF **3820**
DISPOSITIF A RETIRER **4239**
DISPOSITIF ACCESSOIRE **5766**
DISPOSITIF BIELLE ET MANIVELLE **1094**

# DIS

622

DISPOSITIF D'ARRET **12278**
DISPOSITIF D'ECLAIRAGE **6774**
DISPOSITIF DE BLOCAGE **7705**
DISPOSITIF DE CHANGEMENT DE SENS DE MARCHE PAR COURROIE **1154**
DISPOSITIF DE CHANGEMENT DE SENS DE MARCHE PAR ENGRENAGE CONIQUE **10545**
DISPOSITIF DE CHANGEMENT DE SENS DE MARCHE PAR ENGRENAGE DROIT **10547**
DISPOSITIF DE CHANGEMENT DE SENS DE MARCHE PAR ROUE DE FRICTION **10546**
DISPOSITIF DE CHANGEMENT DE SENS DE MARCHE POUR TRANSMISSION **10542**
DISPOSITIF DE CONTROLE **3052**
DISPOSITIF DE CONTROLE DE PRESSION **9829**
DISPOSITIF DE COUPE **3525**
DISPOSITIF DE DEPART A FROID **12342**
DISPOSITIF DE FIXATION **7227**
DISPOSITIF DE PRECONTRAINTE **9781**
DISPOSITIF DE REGLAGE **10418**
DISPOSITIF DE REPERAGE DES RIVES **4444**
DISPOSITIF DE SECURITE **10881**
DISPOSITIF DE SERRAGE **7227**
DISPOSITIF DE SURETE **10881**
DISPOSITIF POULIE ET COURROIE **1144**
DISPOSITIF PROTECTEUR **10881**
DISPOSITION **4056**
DISPOSITION GENERALE **5914**
DISQUE **4015**
DISQUE **3837**
DISQUE (DE CLAPET) **4014**
DISQUE A CAMES **13221**
DISQUE A COUPER **3542**
DISQUE D' EXCENTRIQUE **4434**
DISQUE DE COUPER **3542**
DISQUE DE RUPTURE **10887**
DISQUE DE RUPTURE **10860**
DISQUE EN BUFFLE **1684**
DISQUE EN DRAP **10173**
DISQUE EN LISIERE DE TISSU **4116**
DISQUE POLISSEUR **1693**
DISQUE-SCIE **2427**
DISQUE-VOLANT **4004**
DISQUES ABRASIFS **26**
DISSOCIATION **4058**
DISSOCIATION ELECTROLYTIQUE **4595**
DISSOLUTION **4060**
DISSOLUTION (ACTION) (CHIM.) **4059**
DISSOLUTION ELECTROLYTIQUE **4581**
DISSOLVANT **11814**
DISSOUDRE **11813**
DISSOUDRE **4061**

DISSOUDRE (SE) **4061**
DISSYMETRIE **779**
DISSYMETRIQUE **778**
DISTANCE **4063**
DISTANCE D'AXE EN AXE **4065**
DISTANCE DE CENTRE A CENTRE DES RIVETS **9409**
DISTANCE DES RIVETS DE CENTRE A CENTRE EN LIGNE CONTINUE **7736**
DISTANCE DU CENTRE DU RIVET AU BORD DE LA TOLE **4066**
DISTANCE ENTRE LES BRAS **6596**
DISTANCE ENTRE POINTES **4065**
DISTANCE FOCALE **5500**
DISTANCE FOCALE **5503**
DISTANCE POLAIRE **9579**
DISTANCE RETICULAIRE **7087**
DISTILLATION **4071**
DISTILLATION (ACTION) **4072**
DISTILLATION A LA VAPEUR D'EAU **4073**
DISTILLATION AVEC CRACKING **3285**
DISTILLATION AVEC DECOMPOSITION **3805**
DISTILLATION CONTINUE **3024**
DISTILLATION DANS LE VIDE **4075**
DISTILLATION DE LA HOUILLE **4074**
DISTILLATION DES COMBUSTIBLES A BASSE TEMPERATURE **7776**
DISTILLATION FRACTIONNEE **5612**
DISTILLATION SECHE **4346**
DISTILLER **4070**
DISTORSION **4077**
DISTRIBUTEUR **4086**
DISTRIBUTEUR **13453**
DISTRIBUTEUR **4084**
DISTRIBUTEUR **5353**
DISTRIBUTEUR **11592**
DISTRIBUTEUR D'ALLUMAGE **6762**
DISTRIBUTEUR GLISSANT A ROBINET **10760**
DISTRIBUTEUR OSCILLANT **10760**
DISTRIBUTEURS D'ENGRAIS **4087**
DISTRIBUTEURS DE CHAUX **4089**
DISTRIBUTEURS VEHICULES POUR ATTACHEMENT **4088**
DISTRIBUTION **13471**
DISTRIBUTION A DISTANCE DE L'ENERGIE **13135**
DISTRIBUTION D'AIR **281**
DISTRIBUTION D'AIR COMPRIME **2845**
DISTRIBUTION D'EAU **13666**
DISTRIBUTION D'EAU **13678**
DISTRIBUTION DE FORCE MOTRICE **9744**
DISTRIBUTION DE GAZ **5834**
DISTRIBUTION DE LA TEMPERATURE **4083**
DISTRIBUTION DES RIVETS **717**

DISTRIBUTION GAUSSIENNE **5887**
DISTRIBUTION PAR COULISSE **7626**
DISTRIBUTION PAR SOUPAPE **13460**
DISTRIBUTION PAR TIROIR **11594**
DISTRIBUTION PUBLIQUE D'ENERGIE ELECTRIQUE **12487**
DIVALENT **3881**
DIVERGENCE **4092**
DIVERGENT **4093**
DIVERGER **4091**
DIVIDENDE **4099**
DIVISER (MATH.) **4097**
DIVISER EN DEUX **1266**
DIVISEUR **4111**
DIVISEUR **4100**
DIVISEUR DE PRECISION **9769**
DIVISEUR-AERATEUR **209**
DIVISION **10981**
DIVISION (MATH.) **4107**
DIVISION D'UNE LIGNE EN MOYENNE ET EXTREME RAISON **8123**
DIVISION DU CERCLE **4108**
DIVISION DU TRAVAIL **12410**
DODECAEDRE **4112**
DOIGT **5211**
DOIGT **4301**
DOIGT D'ALLUMEUR **4085**
DOIGT D'ENCLIQUETAGE **2493**
DOIGT D'ENCLIQUETAGE **2094**
DOIGT DE DECLENCHEMENT **10437**
DOIGT DE RETENUE **2094**
DOIGT INCLINE **1887**
DOLERITE **4114**
DOLOMIE **4117**
DOLOMITE **4117**
DOMAINE **11845**
DOMAINE DE TRANSFORMATION **13113**
DOME DE PRISE DE VAPEUR **12163**
DONNEE **5951**
DONNEES **3612**
DONNEES JUSTIFICATIVES **12494**
DONNEES NUMERIQUES **8696**
DONNEES PRINCIPALES **7481**
DONNER LA VOIE A UNE SCIE **11224**
DONNER LE FIL A UN INSTRUMENT TRANCHANT **6790**
DORAGE **6002**
DORER **5941**
DORMANT (DU CABLE D'UN PALAN) **12092**
DORURE **5942**
DORURE AU FEU **5243**
DOS **890**
DOS DE LA FACE DE BRIDE **5326**

DOSAGE **10064**
DOSAGE **1325**
DOSAGE **3011**
DOSAGE DU CARBONE **1947**
DOSAGE DU MELANGE **9934**
DOSER **1323**
DOSSIER **917**
DOSSIER **12012**
DOSSIER TECHNIQUE **3614**
DOUBLAGE **2447**
DOUBLAGE **7623**
DOUBLE **5999**
DOUBLE BRIDE **4139**
DOUBLE D'OR **10673**
DOUBLE DECIMETRE **4135**
DOUBLE DECOMPOSITION **4136**
DOUBLE EFFET (A) **4163**
DOUBLE FOND **5026**
DOUBLE HARNAIS **4142**
DOUBLE PAROI (A) **4170**
DOUBLE REFRACTION **4151**
DOUBLE TAILLE D'UNE LIME **4134**
DOUBLE TRAIN D'ENGRENAGES **4142**
DOUBLER **7598**
DOUBLET **4172**
DOUBLURE **7623**
DOUBLURE **11926**
DOUILLE **1773**
DOUILLE **11576**
DOUILLE A RESSORT **11979**
DOUILLE D'ARCADE **14016**
DOUILLE DE REGLAGE **194**
DOUILLE DE SERRAGE **2728**
DOUILLE POUR POULIE FOLLE **7748**
DOUILLE-FOULOIR (DE PRESSE-ETOUPE) **9001**
DOUVE **12149**
DRAINAGE **4210**
DRAINER **4204**
DRAINER UNE TERRE HUMIDE **4209**
DRAPERIES/COULURES EN FESTONS **3492**
DRESSAGE **12319**
DRESSAGE **12720**
DRESSAGE (ACTION DE RENDRE PLAN) **13234**
DRESSER (RENDRE PLAN) **13232**
DRESSEUSE A GALETS **10685**
DRILLE **689**
DROITE **12310**
DROITS DU BREVETE **9121**
DUCTILE **4361**
DUCTILITE **4363**
DUCTILITE LONGITUDINALE **7735**

# DUR

624

DUDGEONNAGE **4908**
DURABILITE **4385**
DURABLE **4386**
DURALUMIN **4387**
DURCI (NON-) **13359**
DURCIR **6286**
DURCIR **6287**
DURCISSEMENT **6291**
DURCISSEMENT **6292**
DURCISSEMENT **3483**
DURCISSEMENT A COEUR **5721**
DURCISSEMENT A COEUR **12892**
DURCISSEMENT PAR PRECIPITATION **9762**
DURCISSEMENT PAR TREMPE **10089**
DURCISSEMENT PAR VIEILLISSEMENT **223**
DURCISSEMENT STRUCTURAL **224**
DURCISSEUR (ALLIAGE) **6290**
DUREE **7541**
DUREE D'UNE OSCILLATION **12945**
DUREE DU BREVET **12761**
DUREE DU CYCLE DE SOUDAGE **13788**
DURETE **6297**
DURETE A CHAUD **6629**
DURETE A CHAUD **10328**
DURETE APRES REVENU **10520**
DURETE BRINELL **1619**
DURETE DE L'EAU **6298**
DURETE DE MEULAGE **14**
DURETE PERMANENTE DE L'EAU **9203**
DURETE SHORE **11003**
DURETE TEMPORAIRE DE L'EAU **12735**
DURETE VICKERS **13566**
DURETE VICKERS **6860**
DURETE VICKERS A LA PYRAMIDE **10039**
DURITE **6609**
DYNAMIQUE **4399**
DYNAMIQUE **4400**
DYNAMITE **4401**
DYNAMO **4402**
DYNAMO **5924**
DYNAMO **9867**
DYNAMO **407**
DYNAMO **3021**
DYNAMO COMPOUND **3228**
DYNAMO EN DERIVATION **11404**
DYNAMO EN SERIE **11201**
DYNAMO-SHUNT **11404**
DYNAMOGRAPHE **10291**
DYNAMOMETRE **7846**
DYNAMOMETRE **4403**
DYNAMOMETRE D'ABSORPTION **55**

DYNAMOMETRE D'ABSORPTION **48**
DYNAMOMETRE DE TRANSMISSION **13127**
DYNAMOMETRE DIFFERENTIEL **3911**
DYNAMOMETRE-FREIN **55**
DYNAMOMETRIQUE **4404**
DYNE **4405**
DYNE-CENTIMETRE **4818**
DYNODE **4406**
DYSPROSIUM **4407**
EAU **13640**
EAU A SOUDER **7293**
EAU ACIDULEE **134**
EAU AMMONIACALE DU GAZ **456**
EAU BOUEUSE **8446**
EAU BOUILLANTE **1428**
EAU CALCAIRE **2227**
EAU CALCAIRE **6281**
EAU CHIMIQUE **2318**
EAU COURANTE **5466**
EAU D'ALIMENTATION **5077**
EAU D'AMONT **6322**
EAU D'AVAL **12597**
EAU D'HYDRATATION **6675**
EAU D'INFILTRATION **9181**
EAU DE BARYTE **1019**
EAU DE BOISSON **4281**
EAU DE CHAUX **7585**
EAU DE CONDENSATION **13662**
EAU DE CONSTITUTION **2318**
EAU DE CRISTALLISATION **13663**
EAU DE DISTRIBUTION **13075**
EAU DE LABARRAQUE (SOLUTION DE CHLORURE DE SOUDE)
 **4422**
EAU DE MER **11072**
EAU DE PUITS **13796**
EAU DE PUITS DE MINE **9397**
EAU DE REFRIGERATION **3095**
EAU DE REFROIDISSEMENT **3095**
EAU DE RIVIERE **10620**
EAU DE SAVON **11702**
EAU DE SOURCE **11996**
EAU DE SURFACE **12520**
EAU DISTILLEE **4076**
EAU DORMANTE **12050**
EAU DOUCE **5663**
EAU DU JOUR **12520**
EAU DURE **6281**
EAU EXEMPTE DE MICROBES **13650**
EAU FLUVIALE **10620**
EAU FORTE **8580**
EAU FORTE **657**

625 ECH

EAU HYGROMETRIQUE **6731**
EAU INDUSTRIELLE **13649**
EAU LOURDE **6414**
EAU MERE **8405**
EAU METEORIQUE **8213**
EAU ORDINAIRE **10240**
EAU OXYGENEE **6716**
EAU PEU CHARGEE **11745**
EAU PLUVIALE **10179**
EAU POTABLE **4281**
EAU PURE **11745**
EAU REGALE **658**
EAU SALEE **1617**
EAU SALINE **10910**
EAU SAUMATRE **1524**
EAU SAVONNEUSE **11702**
EAU SOUS PRESSION **9841**
EAU STAGNANTE **12050**
EAU STERILISEE **13650**
EAU SUPERFICIELLE **12520**
EAU SURCHAUFFEE **12470**
EAUX D'EGOUTS **11230**
EAUX RESIDUAIRES **6902**
EAUX SOUTERRAINES **6147**
EBARBAGE **5129**
EBARBAGE **11689**
EBARBAGE **2504**
EBARBAGE **2478**
EBARBAGE **13209**
EBARBAGE **13210**
EBARBAGE **3642**
EBARBAGE A CHAUD **6647**
EBARBAGE A FROID **2711**
EBARBAGE DE TOLE EN BISEAU **9496**
EBARBE **1764**
EBARBEMENT **13210**
EBARBER **13206**
EBARBER **5364**
EBARBER **2469**
EBARBER UNE TOLE **13205**
EBARBEUR **4254**
EBARBURE **1764**
EBAUCHAGE **1341**
EBAUCHAGE **10786**
EBAUCHAGE **1583**
EBAUCHAGE **10785**
EBAUCHE **1301**
EBAUCHE **11651**
EBAUCHE A PLUSIEURS CONSTITUANTS **2828**
EBAUCHE DE COMPACT **6090**
EBAUCHE DE FORGEAGE PREALABLE **1343**

EBAUCHE POUR PRESSE A FILER **4971**
EBAUCHER **10775**
EBAUCHES **1349**
EBAVURAGE **3642**
EBAVURAGE **1766**
EBAVURAGE **13210**
EBAVURER **5364**
EBENE **4423**
EBONITE **2363**
EBOUTAGE **3357**
EBRANLEMENTS **13559**
EBULLITION BAS (A POINT D') **1426**
EBULLITION ELEVE (A POINT D') **1425**
EBULLITION PREABLE **9776**
EBULLITION PREALABLE **1429**
ECAILLAGE **10985**
ECAILLAGE **11830**
ECAILLAGE **5306**
ECAILLAGE **9156**
ECAILLAGE **11339**
ECAILLE **10968**
ECAILLE **10964**
ECAILLE **288**
ECAILLEMENT **4889**
ECAILLER (S') **10975**
ECAILLEUSE **11936**
ECART **3819**
ECART MOYEN **8074**
ECART TYPE **12074**
ECARTEMENT DE LA VOIE (CH. DE FER) **5871**
ECARTEMENT DES ESSIEUX **13813**
ECARTEMENT DES MAILLES **11523**
ECARTEMENT DES PALIERS **4064**
ECARTEMENT DES PLATEAUX **13169**
ECARTEUR **11973**
ECHAFAUDAGE **10965**
ECHAFAUDAGE VOLANT **7260**
ECHANCRURE **8672**
ECHANGE DE CHALEUR **4884**
ECHANGEUR DE CHALEUR **6349**
ECHANGEUR THERMIQUE **6349**
ECHANTILLON **10915**
ECHANTILLONNAGE **10916**
ECHAPPEMENT (DES GAZ D'UN MOTEUR) **4890**
ECHAPPEMENT DE GAZ **4833**
ECHAPPEMENT DE VAPEUR **4833**
ECHAPPEMENT LIBRE **8627**
ECHAPPER (S') **4832**
ECHAUFFEMENT DES COUSSINETS **6400**
ECHAUFFEMENT INTERNE **6338**
ECHAUFFEMENT RAPIDE **5362**

# ECH 626

ECHAUFFER **6334**
ECHELLE **10981**
ECHELLE **10974**
ECHELLE **10968**
ECHELLE (MOYEN DE COMPARAISON) **10982**
ECHELLE ANNULAIRE **3841**
ECHELLE CENTIGRADE **2157**
ECHELLE CIRCULAIRE MICROMETRIQUE **8253**
ECHELLE D'UN PLAN **10973**
ECHELLE DE CELSIUS **2157**
ECHELLE DE DURETE DE MOHS **8346**
ECHELLE DE PROPORTION **3833**
ECHELLE DE REAUMUR **10267**
ECHELLE FAHRENHEIT **5019**
ECHELLE MOBILE **11607**
ECHELLE REDUITE **10343**
ECHELLE THERMOMETRIQUE **12835**
ECHELLE VERNIER **13541**
ECHELONNE **12246**
ECLABOUSSURE **11842**
ECLABOUSSURES DE METAL **11929**
ECLAIRAGE **7574**
ECLAIRAGE ARTIFICIEL **733**
ECLAIRAGE AU GAZ **5828**
ECLAIRAGE DE SECOURS **4688**
ECLAIRAGE DE SECOURS **4689**
ECLAIRAGE ELECTRIQUE **4518**
ECLAIRAGE EXTERIEUR **8897**
ECLAIRAGE INTERIEUR **6887**
ECLAIRAGE NATUREL **8505**
ECLAIRAGE PROVISOIRE **4688**
ECLAT (MIN.) **7830**
ECLAT ADAMANTIN **158**
ECLAT LUMINEUX **1616**
ECLAT METALLIQUE **8195**
ECLAT NACRE **9146**
ECLAT SOYEUX **11455**
ECLAT VITREUX **13583**
ECLATEMENT **1767**
ECLATEMENT **1768**
ECLATEMENT D'UN VOLANT **1769**
ECLATEMENT D'UNE POULIE **1769**
ECLATEMENT DU BOIS **11948**
ECLISSE **1783**
ECLISSES **5270**
ECLUSE **7698**
ECOINE **11481**
ECONOMIE DANS LE TRAVAIL **10947**
ECONOMIE DE COMBUSTIBLE **5707**
ECONOMIE DE FORCE MOTRICE **10948**
ECONOMIE DE MAIN-D'OEUVRE **10947**

ECONOMIE DE TEMPS **10949**
ECONOMIE EN EQUILIBRE **932**
ECONOMIE SAINE **932**
ECONOMISEUR (DE CARBURANT) **4437**
ECOUANE **11481**
ECOUENNE **11481**
ECOULEMENT **4210**
ECOULEMENT **5454**
ECOULEMENT D'EAU **8899**
ECOULEMENT DU MATERIAU **5465**
ECOULER (S') **4832**
ECRAN **6252**
ECRAN **11018**
ECRAN **11346**
ECRAN (OPT.) **11019**
ECRAN DE PROJECTION **13568**
ECRAN DE PROTECTION **11342**
ECRAN DE SOUDAGE **5000**
ECRAN FLUORESCENT **5477**
ECRAN LUMINEUX **5477**
ECRAN RENFORCATEUR **7017**
ECRASEMENT **3420**
ECRASEMENT **7265**
ECRASEMENT DES RIVETS **2490**
ECRASER **9712**
ECRASER **7263**
ECRASER LES RIVETS **2489**
ECRITURE CHINOISE **2341**
ECRITURE DROITE **6243**
ECRITURE PERPENDICULAIRE **6243**
ECRITURE RONDE **10799**
ECROU **8698**
ECROU **11056**
ECROU A CHAPEAU **1512**
ECROU A CRENEAUX **2085**
ECROU A EMBASE **5342**
ECROU A ENCOCHES **6533**
ECROU A ENTAILLES **2085**
ECROU A FENETRES **2085**
ECROU A FENTE **11942**
ECROU A OREILLES **12911**
ECROU A RACCORD **11061**
ECROU A SIX PANS **6455**
ECROU A TROUS **6533**
ECROU BORGNE **4118**
ECROU BORGNE **1512**
ECROU BRUT DE FORGE **1290**
ECROU CARRE **12024**
ECROU CARRE A SOUDER **1307**
ECROU CRENELE **2085**
ECROU CREUX **1512**

| | |
|---|---|
| ECROU D'ARRET **10514** | EFFICACITE ENERGETIQUE **4746** |
| ECROU D'OPERCULE **11907** | EFFLORESCENCE **4464** |
| ECROU DE BLOCAGE **7702** | EFFORT **12331** |
| ECROU DE CLAPET **4009** | EFFORT **5532** |
| ECROU DE DOUILLE D'ARCADE **14018** | EFFORT ADMISSIBLE **10880** |
| ECROU DE PRESSE-ETOUPE **9005** | EFFORT D'INERTIE **6907** |
| ECROU DE RAPPEL **13369** | EFFORT DANS LA FIBRE **5134** |
| ECROU DE REGLAGE **191** | EFFORT DE CISAILLEMENT **11295** |
| ECROU DE SERRAGE **2453** | EFFORT DE CISAILLEMENT PAR UNITE DE SECTION **11296** |
| ECROU DE SURETE **7702** | EFFORT DE COMPRESSION **2863** |
| ECROU DE VOLANT **6268** | EFFORT DE COMPRESSION **2869** |
| ECROU DECOLLETE **1612** | EFFORT DE COMPRESSION PAR UNITE DE SECTION **2871** |
| ECROU EMBOUTI **8700** | EFFORT DE COMPRESSION SUR PIECES LONGUES **3339** |
| ECROU FENDU **11942** | EFFORT DE FLAMBAGE **3339** |
| ECROU HEXAGONAL (6-PANS) A EMBASE **5340** | EFFORT DE FLAMBAGE PAR UNITE DE SECTION **3341** |
| ECROU MOBILE **13159** | EFFORT DE FLEXION **1187** |
| ECROU MOLETE **8280** | EFFORT DE FLEXION **1191** |
| ECROU NON TARAUDE **1308** | EFFORT DE FLEXION PAR UNITE DE SECTION **1193** |
| ECROU PAPILLON **12911** | EFFORT DE FLUAGE **5460** |
| ECROUIR **2684** | EFFORT DE RUPTURE **5618** |
| ECROUIR **4219** | EFFORT DE TENSION **12373** |
| ECROUISSAGE **6219** | EFFORT DE TORSION **13056** |
| ECROUISSAGE **2685** | EFFORT DE TORSION PAR UNITE DE SECTION **13058** |
| ECROUISSAGE **13715** | EFFORT DE TRACTION **13089** |
| ECROUISSAGE **2713** | EFFORT DE TRACTION **12747** |
| ECROUISSAGE **4235** | EFFORT DE TRACTION PAR UNITE DE SECTION **12750** |
| ECROUISSAGE (DEFORMATION) **12326** | EFFORT EXTERIEUR **7679** |
| ECROUTAGE **10988** | EFFORT EXTERIEUR **4954** |
| ECROUTAGE **9156** | EFFORT INTERIEUR MOLECULAIRE **12367** |
| ECROUTAGE DES PIECES COULEES **2478** | EFFORT MACROSCOPIQUE **7874** |
| ECROUTER LES PIECES COULEES **2469** | EFFORT PAR UNITE DE SECTION **12367** |
| ECUME **4331** | EFFORT TANGENTIEL **12624** |
| ECUME DE GRAPHITE **7317** | EFFORT TANGENTIEL DU FREIN **1551** |
| ECUMOIRE **11536** | EFFORT TRANCHANT **11295** |
| EFFACER **4799** | EFFORT TRANSVERSAL **1191** |
| EFFERVESCENCE **4461** | EFFORTS DE REFROIDISSEMENT **3091** |
| EFFET **9730** | EFFORTS DUS AU FORGEAGE **5564** |
| EFFET BAUSCHINGER **1070** | EFFRITEMENT **3418** |
| EFFET D'ANODE **596** | EFFRITER (S') **4043** |
| EFFET D'EGALISATION **7528** | EFFUSION **4465** |
| EFFET DE CLIQUET **10220** | EFFUSION DES GAZ **4466** |
| EFFET DE LIGNE DE TRANSMISSION **7729** | EGRISE **3863** |
| EFFET DE MASSE **8027** | EJECTER **4468** |
| EFFET DE NETTOYAGE **10017** | EJECTEUR **12172** |
| EFFET DE PEAU D'ORANGE **8851** | EJECTEUR **4472** |
| EFFET DE PINCEMENT **9329** | EJECTEUR **4469** |
| EFFET DE SOUPAPE **13458** | EJECTEUR HYDRAULIQUE **13658** |
| EFFET LEONARD **7523** | EJECTEUR PNEUMATIQUE **271** |
| EFFET SIMPLE (A) **11493** | EJECTEUR PNEUMATIQUE **9554** |
| EFFET THERMOELECTRIQUE **12830** | EJECTO-CONDENSEUR **4470** |
| EFFET UTILE **4463** | ELABORATION DE L'ACIER **12214** |

**ELA** 628

ELANCEMENT **11580**
ELANCEMENT D'UNE POUTRE **11581**
ELARGIR **5356**
ELARGIR AU MANDRIN **4262**
ELARGIR UN TUBE AU MANDRIN **4903**
ELARGISSEMENT **1723**
ELASTICITE **4487**
ELASTICITE DE CISAILLEMENT **13144**
ELASTICITE DE COMPRESSION **4488**
ELASTICITE DE FLEXION **4489**
ELASTICITE DE SUITE **4474**
ELASTICITE DE TORSION **4490**
ELASTICITE DE TRACTION **4491**
ELASTICITE RESIDUELLE **10472**
ELASTICITE TRANSVERSALE **13144**
ELASTIQUE **4473**
ELECTRE **4653**
ELECTRICIEN **4551**
ELECTRICITE **4552**
ELECTRICITE ATMOSPHERIQUE **796**
ELECTRICITE INDUSTRIELLE **4541**
ELECTRICITE NEGATIVE **8526**
ELECTRICITE POSITIVE **9655**
ELECTRIFICATION **4554**
ELECTRIFIER **4555**
ELECTRISER (S') **1124**
ELECTRO-AIMANT **4567**
ELECTRO-AIMANT **4611**
ELECTRO-AIMANT PORTEUR **7554**
ELECTRO-CHIMIE **4573**
ELECTRO-CORINDON **5753**
ELECTRO-EROSION **4565**
ELECTRO-FORMAGE **4557**
ELECTRO-METALLURGIE **4621**
ELECTRO-OSMOSE **4638**
ELECTROANALYSE **4657**
ELECTROANALYSE **4570**
ELECTROCHIMIE **4640**
ELECTROCHIMIE **4561**
ELECTROCHIMIQUE **4560**
ELECTRODE **4574**
ELECTRODE **13789**
ELECTRODE A CONTACT **3001**
ELECTRODE AU CALOMEL **1876**
ELECTRODE BIPOLAIRE **1233**
ELECTRODE BLINDEE **11299**
ELECTRODE COMPOSITE **2819**
ELECTRODE DE CHARBON **1950**
ELECTRODE DE VERRE **5959**
ELECTRODE ENROBE **5492**
ELECTRODE ENROBEE **11344**

ELECTRODE ENROBEE **3271**
ELECTRODE ENROBEE **2584**
ELECTRODE FUSIBLE **2990**
ELECTRODE METALLIQUE **8180**
ELECTRODE NEGATIVE **2106**
ELECTRODE NON-CONSOMMABLE **8618**
ELECTRODE NUE **989**
ELECTRODE POSITIVE **602**
ELECTRODYNAMIQUE **4563**
ELECTRODYNAMOMETRE **4564**
ELECTROEROSION **4531**
ELECTROLYSE **4586**
ELECTROLYSER **4585**
ELECTROLYTE **4587**
ELECTROLYTE IMPUR **5588**
ELECTROMAGNETIQUE **4612**
ELECTROMAGNETISME **4620**
ELECTROMOTEUR **4623**
ELECTRON **4624**
ELECTRON POSITIF **9662**
ELECTRONEGATIF **4631**
ELECTRONIQUE **4637**
ELECTROPHORESE **4639**
ELECTROPOSITIF **4641**
ELECTROSTATIQUE **4568**
ELECTROTECHNIQUE **4648**
ELECTROTECHNIQUE **4647**
ELECTROTHERMIQUE **4650**
ELECTROTYPIE **4569**
ELECTRUM **4653**
ELEMENT **8145**
ELEMENT **4654**
ELEMENT **7852**
ELEMENT A DEUX LIQUIDES **2887**
ELEMENT ACIDIFICATEUR **115**
ELEMENT ASYMETRIQUE **777**
ELEMENT BASIQUE **1038**
ELEMENT D'ACCUMULATEUR **78**
ELEMENT D'ADDITION **168**
ELEMENT D'APPOINT **812**
ELEMENT D'UN RECIPIENT A PRESSION **11117**
ELEMENT DE CHARPENTE INCORPORE **1704**
ELEMENT DE PILE THERMOELECTRIQUE **12821**
ELEMENT GALVANIQUE **5782**
ELEMENT OU PARTIE TRONCONIQUE **13121**
ELEMENT PRO-EUTECTIQUE **9848**
ELEMENT RAIDISSEUR **12256**
ELEMENT REDRESSEUR **4549**
ELEMENT STRUCTURAL **12391**
ELEMENTS A COUVRE-JOINTS **11932**
ELEMENTS D'ADDITION **395**

EMM

ELEMENTS DE REDUCTION TRONCONIQUES **2950**
ELEMI **4656**
ELEVATEUR **4472**
ELEVATEUR (U.S. = ASCENSEUR) **4660**
ELEVATEUR A GODETS **1676**
ELEVATEURS DE FOIN ET DE PAILLE **4661**
ELEVATEURS DE GRAINS/AERO ENGRANGEURS **6034**
ELEVATION **4659**
ELEVATION CAPILLAIRE **1925**
ELEVER A UNE PUISSANCE **10180**
ELEVER UN FARDEAU **7542**
ELEVER UNE PERPENDICULAIRE **4806**
ELEVER UNE VERTICALE **4806**
ELIMINATEUR D'IMPURETES **10995**
ELIMINATION **4667**
ELIMINATION (MATH.) **4664**
ELIMINATION DES BUEES **13485**
ELIMINATION DES DEFAUTS DE SURFACE AU CHALUMEAU **8976**
ELIMINATION DES DEFAUTS SUPERFICIELS **3793**
ELIMINATION DU FER DE L'EAU **10454**
ELIMINER **4663**
ELIMINER (MATH.) **4662**
ELINGUE **11610**
ELINVAR **4668**
ELLIPSE **4669**
ELLIPSE DE CASSINI **2029**
ELLIPSOGRAPHE **4670**
ELLIPSOIDE **4671**
ELLIPSOIDE DE REVOLUTION **4672**
ELLIPSOIDE DE ROTATION **4672**
ELONGATION DE L'AIGUILLE **3699**
EMAIL **4709**
EMAILLAGE **4712**
EMAILLER **4710**
EMANATION **10159**
EMBALLAGE **8999**
EMBALLAGE MOULANT **11540**
EMBALLEMENT D'UN MOTEUR **10118**
EMBALLER **10117**
EMBALLER **8991**
EMBALLER (S') **10117**
EMBASE **1040**
EMBASE **2724**
EMBASE D'UN PIVOT CANNELE **12904**
EMBOITAGE **5281**
EMBOITEMENT **5281**
EMBOITEMENT DOUBLE (M ET F) **12990**
EMBOITEMENT SIMPLE (M ET F) **7957**
EMBOITER **5277**
EMBOUCHURE **12966**

EMBOUCHURE **196**
EMBOUCHURE CONVERGENTE **3066**
EMBOUCHURE DIVERGENTE **4096**
EMBOUTIR **5324**
EMBOUTISSAGE **5345**
EMBOUTISSAGE **8189**
EMBOUTISSAGE **4040**
EMBOUTISSAGE EN COUPE DE FILS **3469**
EMBOUTISSAGE PROFOND **3469**
EMBOUTISSAGE PROFOND **7158**
EMBOUTISSAGE PROFOND **3683**
EMBOUTISSEUSE **5346**
EMBRANCHEMENT INDUSTRIEL **13966**
EMBRAYAGE **12897**
EMBRAYAGE **2544**
EMBRAYAGE **3254**
EMBRAYAGE **2461**
EMBRAYAGE A CONE **2927**
EMBRAYAGE A CONES **2930**
EMBRAYAGE A DENTS DE SCIE **10960**
EMBRAYAGE A DENTURE CONIQUE **6839**
EMBRAYAGE A DENTURE DROITE **12313**
EMBRAYAGE A DISQUE **4002**
EMBRAYAGE A DISQUES **4046**
EMBRAYAGE A DISQUES **9486**
EMBRAYAGE A FRICTION **11614**
EMBRAYAGE A FRICTION **5672**
EMBRAYAGE A GRIFFES **4113**
EMBRAYAGE A LAMES **9486**
EMBRAYAGE A ROUE LIBRE **8957**
EMBRAYAGE CENTRIFUGE **2177**
EMBRAYAGE HYDRAULIQUE **6681**
EMBRAYAGE MAGNETIQUE **7934**
EMBRAYAGE PROGRESSIF A FRICTION **11619**
EMBRAYER **10033**
EMBRYON **4686**
EMBUS **11289**
EMERI **4692**
EMERI **4699**
EMERILLON **12561**
EMETTRE DES RAYONS **4703**
EMEULAGE **1691**
EMISSION **4700**
EMMAGANISER **12294**
EMMAGASINAGE **12288**
EMMAGASINAGE **12299**
EMMAGASINER DE L'ENERGIE **12295**
EMMAGASINER LA CHALEUR **12296**
EMMANCHEMENT **10847**
EMMANCHEMENT **11389**
EMMANCHEMENT **4307**

# EMM

## 630

EMMANCHEMENT **5275**
EMMANCHEMENT **1074**
EMMANCHEMENT **3254**
EMMANCHEMENT **11600**
EMMANCHEMENT **10025**
EMMANCHEMENT A CHAUD **11398**
EMMANCHEMENT A CONE **12649**
EMMANCHEMENT A LA PRESSE **5527**
EMMANCHEMENT CONIQUE **12649**
EMMANCHEMENT COULISSANT **11600**
EMMANCHEMENT DE TUBES **5281**
EMMANCHEMENT GRAS **11600**
EMMANCHER **11390**
EMOUDRE **11273**
EMOULAGE **11275**
EMOUSSAGE **5972**
EMPAQUETAGE **1772**
EMPECHER **6926**
EMPILAGE DU BOIS **9309**
EMPILER LE BOIS **9307**
EMPLACEMENT A BATIR **1699**
EMPOIS **12112**
EMPORTE-PIECE **10000**
EMPORTE-PIECE CYLINDRIQUE **6545**
EMPORTE-PIECE POUR COURROIE **1153**
EMPORTER SUR...(L') **8928**
EMPREINTE **10465**
EMPREINTE **6806**
EMPREINTE DE DURETE **6859**
EMULSEUR **273**
EMULSION **4708**
EMULSIONNER **4707**
ENANTIOTROPIQUE **4713**
ENCASTRE AUX DEUX EXTREMITES **5284**
ENCASTRE PAR UNE EXTREMITE **5285**
ENCASTREMENT **4310**
ENCASTREMENT **5300**
ENCASTRER DANS LE BETON **4682**
ENCEINTE A VIDE **13440**
ENCLANCHEMENT **4751**
ENCLENCHEMENT **4751**
ENCLENCHER **4749**
ENCLIQUETAGE **7705**
ENCLIQUETAGE A FROTTEMENT **5676**
ENCLIQUETAGE A ROCHET **9138**
ENCLIQUETAGE DOUBLE **2494**
ENCLIQUETAGE SILENCIEUX **11433**
ENCLIQUETER **4749**
ENCLUME **630**
ENCOCHAGE **8676**
ENCOCHE **8672**

ENCOMBREMENT **11829**
ENCRASSEMENT **2510**
ENCRE DE CHINE **6871**
ENCRER **6940**
ENDOMMAGE **5057**
ENDOSMOSE **4736**
ENDOTHERMIQUE **4737**
ENDUCTION **12529**
ENDUIRE **1909**
ENDUIRE **9014**
ENDUIRE (MACON.) **9464**
ENDUIT **2583**
ENDUIT (MACON.) **9463**
ENDUIT DE FINITION **3264**
ENDUIT POUR LINGOTIERES **8355**
ENDUIT POUR NOYAUX **3171**
ENDURANCE **4738**
ENDURCISSEMENT AU CYANURE **3549**
ENERGIE **3746**
ENERGIE **4747**
ENERGIE **4539**
ENERGIE **4745**
ENERGIE ACTUELLE **7308**
ENERGIE CALORIFIQUE **6344**
ENERGIE CHIMIQUE **2305**
ENERGIE CINETIQUE **7308**
ENERGIE D'ACTIVATION **147**
ENERGIE D'ECOULEMENT **4748**
ENERGIE DE RAYONNEMENT **10139**
ENERGIE DU CHOC **12757**
ENERGIE LATENTE **9710**
ENERGIE MAGNETIQUE **7900**
ENERGIE MECANIQUE **8101**
ENERGIE POTENTIELLE **9710**
ENERGIE THERMIQUE **6344**
ENFLAMMER (S') **6757**
ENFONCER UN CLOU **4292**
ENFONCER UN COIN **4293**
ENGAGE DANS UNE MACONNERIE **1600**
ENGAGER **4750**
ENGIN **6519**
ENGORGEMENT **2362**
ENGORGER (S') **2358**
ENGRENAGE **5889**
ENGRENAGE **13021**
ENGRENAGE A COIN **13736**
ENGRENAGE A DENTS RECROISEES **12247**
ENGRENAGE A DENTURE CROISEE **12247**
ENGRENAGE A DENTURE SPIRALE **11534**
ENGRENAGE A DEVELOPPANTE DE CERCLE **7119**
ENGRENAGE A DOUBLES CHEVRONS **13176**

| | |
|---|---|
| ENGRENAGE A FRICTION **5674** | ENREGISTREUR A TAMBOUR **3573** |
| ENGRENAGE A FUSEAUX **9325** | ENRICHISSEMENT DU MINERAI **8861** |
| ENGRENAGE A LANTERNE **9325** | ENROBAGE **8999** |
| ENGRENAGE A POINT **9325** | ENROBAGE **2587** |
| ENGRENAGE A VIS SANS FIN **13974** | ENROBAGE BASIQUE **7584** |
| ENGRENAGE BALADEUR **11598** | ENROULE A DROITE **3239** |
| ENGRENAGE BRUT DE FONTE **10773** | ENROULE A GAUCHE **3239** |
| ENGRENAGE CONIQUE **1227** | ENROULEMENT **2650** |
| ENGRENAGE CYCLOIDAL **3558** | ENROULEMENT **13862** |
| ENGRENAGE CYLINDRIQUE **12008** | ENROULER **13853** |
| ENGRENAGE D'ANGLE **1227** | ENROULEUR DE COURROIE LENIX LENEVEU **13750** |
| ENGRENAGE DE FORCE **6402** | ENROULEUSE **13903** |
| ENGRENAGE DE GRANDE FATIGUE **6402** | ENSEMBLE DE COMMANDE A VITESSE VARIABLE **13492** |
| ENGRENAGE DE TRANSMISSION **13128** | ENSILEUSES **11430** |
| ENGRENAGE DEMULTIPLICATEUR **11873** | ENSILEUSES **3522** |
| ENGRENAGE DIFFERENTIEL **3913** | ENTAILLE **8668** |
| ENGRENAGE DROIT **12008** | ENTAILLE **8672** |
| ENGRENAGE ELLIPTIQUE **4677** | ENTAILLER **8554** |
| ENGRENAGE EPICYCLIQUE **9446** | ENTARTRAGE **6856** |
| ENGRENAGE EPICYCLOIDAL **4780** | ENTARTRE **6857** |
| ENGRENAGE EXTERIEUR **4956** | ENTONNOIR **5738** |
| ENGRENAGE HELICOIDAL **6425** | ENTONNOIR **12003** |
| ENGRENAGE HYPERBOLOIDE **11534** | ENTONNOIR DE COULEE **9716** |
| ENGRENAGE HYPOCYCLOIDAL **6744** | ENTOURER UN TUYAU **3263** |
| ENGRENAGE INTERIEUR **7058** | ENTOURER UNE CHAUDIERE DE MACONNERIE **11215** |
| ENGRENAGE INTERMEDIAIRE **7050** | ENTRAINEMENT **4303** |
| ENGRENAGE PAR ROUE DENTEE ET CREMAILLERE **10120** | ENTRAINEMENT (PAR FROTTEMENT) **4304** |
| ENGRENAGE TAILLE **3508** | ENTRAINER PAR FROTTEMENT **4291** |
| ENGRENAGES **5907** | ENTRAINEUR **4301** |
| ENGRENAGES A CHEVRONS **6448** | ENTRAXE **4065** |
| ENGRENAGES CONCOURANTS **8323** | ENTRAXE **2165** |
| ENGRENAGES HYPOIDES **6745** | ENTREE **6943** |
| ENGRENAGES INTERIEURS **7067** | ENTREE D'EAU **6915** |
| ENGRENEMENT **4752** | ENTREE DES DONNEES PAR BANDE **12643** |
| ENGRENEMENT **5910** | ENTREE EN PARALLELE **9054** |
| ENGRENER **4750** | ENTREFER **262** |
| ENGRENER ENSEMBLE **1077** | ENTREFER D'UN AIMANT **263** |
| ENJOLIVEUR DE ROUE **6662** | ENTREPOSER **12294** |
| ENJOLIVEURS **10531** | ENTREPRENEUR DE BATIMENT **1698** |
| ENLEVEMENT **4667** | ENTRETIEN **7946** |
| ENLEVEMENT DE COUCHES SUPERFICIELLES **3807** | ENTRETOISAGE EN TUBES **13258** |
| ENLEVEMENT DE LA COUCHE SUPERFICIELLE **2912** | ENTRETOISE **12151** |
| ENLEVEMENT DES BAVURES **13210** | ENTRETOISE **4068** |
| ENLEVEMENT PAR EMOULAGE **13** | ENTRETOISE **4067** |
| ENLEVER (OU USER) EN EMOULANT **10** | ENTRETOISE **3388** |
| ENLEVER DE LA CHALEUR **4663** | ENTRETOISE **9489** |
| ENLEVER LES BAVURES **13206** | ENTRETOISE (CHARPENTE) **1516** |
| ENREGISTRER **10288** | ENTRETOISE D'UN CHAINON **12402** |
| ENREGISTREUR **10289** | ENTRETOISEMENT **12153** |
| ENREGISTREUR A DEROULEMENT CONTINU **12380** | ENTRETOISER **12150** |
| ENREGISTREUR A DIAGRAMME CIRCULAIRE **2408** | ENTROPIE **4773** |

# ENV

ENVASEMENT D'UNE CONDUITE **11457**
ENVELOPPE **11303**
ENVELOPPE **7986**
ENVELOPPE **3274**
ENVELOPPE (GEOM.) **4776**
ENVELOPPE DE TUYAUX **7369**
ENVELOPPE DE VAPEUR **12168**
ENVELOPPE PROTECTRICE **9948**
ENVELOPPER UN TUYAU **3263**
ENVOYER DE LA CHALEUR **12485**
EPAISSEUR **13731**
EPAISSEUR **12843**
EPAISSEUR A L'ARC **678**
EPAISSEUR CIRCULAIRE DE LA DENT **2431**
EPAISSEUR D'UN FIL **3860**
EPAISSEUR D'UNE SOUDURE BOUT A BOUT **1786**
EPAISSEUR D'UNE SOUDURE EN ANGLE **12886**
EPAISSEUR D'UNE TOLE **12845**
EPAISSEUR DE DENT A LA CORDE **2365**
EPAISSEUR DE FILM **5170**
EPAISSEUR DE LA DENT **12846**
EPAISSEUR DE LA PAROI (DU METAL) D'UN TUBE **12844**
EPAISSEUR DE LA SOUDURE **12885**
EPAISSISSEMENT **1701**
EPAISSISSEMENT (PEINTURE) **7675**
EPANDEURS DE FUMIER **7995**
EPANOUISSEMENT D'UN TUBE **4768**
EPAULEMENT **7321**
EPAULEMENT **11383**
EPAULEMENT D'UN ARBRE **11384**
EPAULEMENT D'UNE ROUE D'ENGRENAGE **11400**
EPICYCLOIDE **4779**
EPISSURE **11930**
EPISSURE (ACTION) **11934**
EPISSURE (RESULTAT) **11933**
EPISSURER **11931**
EPONGE DE FER **7151**
EPONGE DE PLATINE **11955**
EPREUVE **12792**
EPREUVE **9870**
EPREUVE **9921**
EPREUVE **12770**
EPREUVE A CHAUD DE LA CHAUDIERE **12182**
EPREUVE A L'AIR COMPRIME **2846**
EPREUVE DE PRESSION **9836**
EPREUVE DE RESISTANCE **12356**
EPREUVE HYDRAULIQUE **6695**
EPREUVE NEGATIVE **8524**
EPREUVE OFFICIELLE **8740**
EPROUVETTE **12784**
EPROUVETTE **12780**

EPROUVETTE **12772**
EPROUVETTE **12788**
EPROUVETTE (CHIM) **12791**
EPROUVETTE (MORCEAU D'ESSAI) **12789**
EPROUVETTE AVEC ENTAILLE **8675**
EPROUVETTE DE METAL **11858**
EPROUVETTE DE METAL DE BASE **1039**
EPROUVETTE DU METAL DEPOSE PUR **347**
EPURATEUR **10020**
EPURATION **13638**
EPURATION CHIMIQUE DES EAUX D'ALIMENTATION **13676**
EPURATION DES GAZ **5839**
EPURATION DES GAZ **10018**
EPURE D'UNE PIECE MECANIQUE **11363**
EPURE DE DISTRIBUTION **13456**
EPURER LES EAUX D'ALIMEMTATION PAR VOIE CHIMIQUE **11748**
EQUARRISSOIR **1636**
EQUATION **4782**
EQUATION ALGEBRIQUE **322**
EQUATION BICARREE **1262**
EQUATION BINOME **1259**
EQUATION BIQUADRATIQUE **1262**
EQUATION CUBIQUE **3452**
EQUATION D'ETAT **4783**
EQUATION DIFFERENTIELLE **3912**
EQUATION DIFFERENTIELLE PARTIELLE **9086**
EQUATION DU CINQUIEME DEGRE **10112**
EQUATION DU PREMIER DEGRE **7616**
EQUATION DU QUATRIEME DEGRE **1262**
EQUATION DU SECOND DEGRE **10057**
EQUATION DU TROISIEME DEGRE **3452**
EQUATION HOMOGENE **6557**
EQUATION LINEAIRE **7616**
EQUATION QUADRATIQUE **10057**
EQUATION QUINTIQUE **10112**
EQUATION TRANSCENDANTE **13107**
EQUATION TRINOME **13213**
EQUERRE **514**
EQUERRE **1131**
EQUERRE **12014**
EQUERRE (D') **10577**
EQUERRE A DESSIN **11223**
EQUERRE A EPAULEMENT A CHAPEAU **13245**
EQUERRE A ONGLET **8325**
EQUERRE A SIX PANS **6456**
EQUERRE A TRACER LES CENTRES **2173**
EQUERRE D'ABLOCAGE **533**
EQUERRE D'ASSEMBLAGE **510**
EQUERRE DOUBLE **12581**
EQUILIBRAGE **942**

## ESS

EQUILIBRAGE **935**
EQUILIBRAGE D'UNE SOUPAPE **936**
EQUILIBRAGE DES MASSES **941**
EQUILIBRATION **942**
EQUILIBRE **929**
EQUILIBRE **4793**
EQUILIBRE **4786**
EQUILIBRE CHIMIQUE **2307**
EQUILIBRE INDIFFERENT **6882**
EQUILIBRE INSTABLE **13401**
EQUILIBRE STABLE **12045**
EQUILIBRER **930**
EQUILIBRER (S') **1076**
EQUIPE D'OUVRIERS **11348**
EQUIPEMENT ELECTRIQUE **4542**
EQUIPEMENT POUR NIVELER LE SOL **4414**
EQUIPEMENT SANITAIRE **10931**
EQUIVALENCE **4795**
EQUIVALENT **4796**
EQUIVALENT CALORIFIQUE DU TRAVAIL **6347**
EQUIVALENT CHIMIQUE **2308**
EQUIVALENT DU CONE PYROMETRIQUE **10051**
EQUIVALENT ELECTROCHIMIQUE **4571**
EQUIVALENT MECANIQUE DE LA CHALEUR **8104**
ERBIUM **4804**
ERG **4818**
EROSION **4820**
ERREUR **4822**
ERREUR D'APPRECIATION **4827**
ERREUR D'ETALONNAGE **1869**
ERREUR D'OBSERVATION **4829**
ERREUR DE CALCUL **4824**
ERREUR DE COLLIMATION **4828**
ERREUR DE CONCEPTION DU CONSTRUCTEUR **4825**
ERREUR DE LECTURE **4826**
ERREUR DE MESURE **8089**
ERREUR PARALLACTIQUE **9048**
ERUGINEUX **219**
ERYTHROSINE **4831**
ESCALIER **12053**
ESCALIER DROIT **5641**
ESCALIER DROIT **5646**
ESCALIER HELICOIDAL **11919**
ESCARBILLE **2659**
ESCARBILLES **5469**
ESPACE CREUX **2125**
ESPACE MORT **2482**
ESPACE NEUTRE **2482**
ESPACE NUISIBLE **2482**
ESPACEMENT **4063**
ESPECE DE BOIS **13503**

ESPECE DE FER **2458**
ESPERANCE MATHEMATIQUE **4927**
ESPRIT DE BOIS **13920**
ESPRIT DE SEL **6706**
ESPRIT DE SEL DENATURE **7293**
ESQUILLEUSE **11936**
ESSAI **9921**
ESSAI **12792**
ESSAI **12770**
ESSAI (OU CONTROLE) AU BALAI ELECTRIQUE **6535**
ESSAI A FROID **2709**
ESSAI A HAUTE TEMPERATURE **6499**
ESSAI A L'ETINCELLE **11840**
ESSAI A LA COMPRESSION **2872**
ESSAI A LA FLEXION **1189**
ESSAI A LA GOUTTE **11958**
ESSAI A LA PERFORATION **10010**
ESSAI A LA TORSION **13059**
ESSAI A LA TRACTION **12751**
ESSAI ACOUSTIQUE **11815**
ESSAI AU BANC **1170**
ESSAI AU BROUILLARD SALIN **10909**
ESSAI AU FLAMBAGE **3342**
ESSAI AU FREIN **1546**
ESSAI AUX CHOCS REPETES **5049**
ESSAI AUX ULTRA-SONS **12480**
ESSAI BRINELL **1620**
ESSAI D'APLATISSEMENT **5409**
ESSAI D'ECRASEMENT **4374**
ESSAI D'ECRASEMENT **7262**
ESSAI D'ECRASEMENT **11949**
ESSAI D'ECRASEMENT **13416**
ESSAI D'ECRASEMENT SUR CYLINDRE DE BETON MASSIF **1561**
ESSAI D'EMBOUTISSAGE **10184**
ESSAI D'EMBOUTISSAGE ERICKSEN **8797**
ESSAI D'ENDURANCE **5049**
ESSAI D'ESTAMPAGE **12061**
ESSAI D'USURE **13714**
ESSAI DE CHARGE CONSTANTE **2974**
ESSAI DE CHOC (CHUTE) **4328**
ESSAI DE CHOC DE CHARPY (SUR EPROUVETTE ENTAILLEE) **2270**
ESSAI DE CHOC ET BALLOTTEMENT **7249**
ESSAI DE CHOC SUR BARREAU ENTAILLE **8673**
ESSAI DE CHOC SUR BARREAUX NON ENTAILLES **4328**
ESSAI DE CHOC SUR ENTAILLE **1190**
ESSAI DE CHUTE DE POIDS **4330**
ESSAI DE CINTRAGE **1189**
ESSAI DE CINTRAGE A FROID **2667**
ESSAI DE CISAILLEMENT **11949**

# ESS

634

ESSAI DE CISAILLEMENT **11287**
ESSAI DE COMPRESSION **2865**
ESSAI DE COMPRESSION **13416**
ESSAI DE COULABILITE **2065**
ESSAI DE DEPERDITION THERMIQUE **1403**
ESSAI DE DURETE **3865**
ESSAI DE DURETE **6300**
ESSAI DE DURETE A LA LIME **5152**
ESSAI DE DURETE PAR EMPREINTE DE BILLE **6861**
ESSAI DE DURETE ROCKWELL **10659**
ESSAI DE FATIGUE / D'ENDURANCE **4743**
ESSAI DE FLEXION ALTERNE **12774**
ESSAI DE FLEXION ALTERNEE **10535**
ESSAI DE FLEXION CONSTANTE **2972**
ESSAI DE FLEXION DE LA FACE DE LA SOUDURE **1178**
ESSAI DE FLEXION ESSAI DE PLIAGE **1177**
ESSAI DE FLEXION PAR CHOC **4328**
ESSAI DE FLEXION PAR CHOC SUR BARREAUX ENTAILLES **1190**
ESSAI DE FLEXION SUR EPROUVETTE ENTAILLEE **8555**
ESSAI DE FLEXION TOURNANTE **13310**
ESSAI DE FORAGE **1475**
ESSAI DE FORGEAGE **5545**
ESSAI DE LA CHAUDIERE **12182**
ESSAI DE LA CHAUDIERE SOUS PRESSION **1421**
ESSAI DE MACRO-ATTAQUE **3684**
ESSAI DE MANDRINAGE **4911**
ESSAI DE MICRODURETE **8246**
ESSAI DE PERCAGE **1475**
ESSAI DE PLIAGE **1189**
ESSAI DE PLIAGE **4173**
ESSAI DE PLIAGE A CHAUD **6618**
ESSAI DE PLIAGE A FROID **2667**
ESSAI DE PLIAGE A L'ENVERS **1179**
ESSAI DE POINCONNAGE **10010**
ESSAI DE RABATTEMENT **5347**
ESSAI DE REBONDISSEMENT BRUSQUE **7254**
ESSAI DE RECEPTION **71**
ESSAI DE RESILIENCE **8673**
ESSAI DE RESISTANCE A CHAUD **6646**
ESSAI DE RESISTANCE A LA FATIGUE **5054**
ESSAI DE RESISTANCE AU CHAUD BLEU **1372**
ESSAI DE RESISTANCE AU CHAUD ROUGE **10331**
ESSAI DE RESISTANCE AU CHOC **6786**
ESSAI DE RUPTURE **5619**
ESSAI DE RUPTURE AU CHOC **6786**
ESSAI DE SOUDABILITE **13792**
ESSAI DE TORSION **13306**
ESSAI DE TRACTION **12748**
ESSAI DES FILS AU PLIAGE **12774**
ESSAI DES MATERIAUX **12782**

ESSAI DESTRUCTIF **3806**
ESSAI HYDROSTATIQUE **6727**
ESSAI IZOD **7200**
ESSAI JOMINY **7254**
ESSAI NON DESTRUCTIF **9924**
ESSAI NON DESTRUCTIF **8630**
ESSAI PAR CHOC **6786**
ESSAI PAR EMPREINTE DE BILLE **1618**
ESSAI PAR IMMERSIONS ET EMERSIONS ALTERNEES **405**
ESSAI PAR LA BILLE DE BRINELL **1618**
ESSAI PAR REBONDISSEMENT DES BILLES (APPAREIL SHORE) **11367**
ESSAI PHYSIQUE **9284**
ESSAI PRELIMINAIRE **9779**
ESSAI SCLEROMETRIQUE **11017**
ESSAIS D'USURE **16**
ESSAIS MECANIQUES **8112**
ESSENCE **9222**
ESSENCE **5864**
ESSENCE CRAQUEE **10647**
ESSENCE D'AMANDES AMERES **1198**
ESSENCE DE BOIS **13503**
ESSENCE DE MIRBANE **8587**
ESSENCE DE POIRE **487**
ESSENCE DE TEREBENTHINE **8765**
ESSENCE DE TEREBENTHINE RUSSE **10862**
ESSENCE MINERALE **9222**
ESSENCE MINERALE BRUTE **3408**
ESSIEU **884**
ESSIEU ARRIERE (NON-MOTEUR) **10265**
ESSIEU AVANT **5691**
ESSIEU FIXE **3624**
ESSIEU MOTEUR **4290**
ESSIEU OU ARBRE **875**
ESSIEU PORTEUR **2010**
ESSIEU-FLOTTANT **5435**
ESSORER PAR FORCE CENTRIFUGE **6702**
ESSOREUSE CENTRIFUGE **6703**
ESSUIE-GLACE **13871**
ESTAMPAGE **12532**
ESTAMPAGE **12534**
ESTAMPAGE **2651**
ESTAMPAGE **12059**
ESTAMPAGE A CHAUD **6632**
ESTAMPAGE A FROID **2673**
ESTAMPE **3883**
ESTAMPE A DEGROSSIR **5726**
ESTAMPE A ETIRER **5726**
ESTAMPE D'EMBOUTISSAGE **5580**
ESTAMPER **12056**
ESTAMPER **12530**

| | |
|---|---|
| ESTAMPES FERMEES **2521** | ETANCHE A L'EAU **13688** |
| ESTAMPEUSE **12060** | ETANCHE A L'EAU **13686** |
| ESTIMATION **4838** | ETANCHE AUX GAZ **5853** |
| ETABLI **7234** | ETANCHEITE **12932** |
| ETABLI **1167** | ETANCHEITE **11081** |
| ETABLIR UN CONTACT **7950** | ETANCHEITE (MANQUE D') **7491** |
| ETABLISSEMENT DE CONSTRUCTON DE MACHINES **4764** | ETANCHEMENT **7954** |
| ETABLISSEMENT DE FABRICATION **5013** | ETANCHER **7953** |
| ETAGE DE PRESSION **9833** | ETANCON **12402** |
| ETAGE DE VITESSE **13523** | ETANCONNER **12150** |
| ETAI **12402** | ETAT BRUT **740** |
| ETAI **9925** | ETAT CRITIQUE **3349** |
| ETAIEMENT **12153** | ETAT D'EQUILIBRE **12132** |
| ETAIN **12953** | ETAT DE COLISAGE **9003** |
| ETAIN A SOUDER A FONDANT ACIDE **110** | ETAT DE LIVRAISON (A L') **741** |
| ETAIN CHIMIQUEMENT PUR **2324** | ETAT DE SERVICE (EN) **6819** |
| ETAIN DE BANCA **973** | ETAT DE SOUDAGE (A L') **745** |
| ETAIN DE MALACCA **12335** | ETAT DE SURFACE **12500** |
| ETAIN DUR **9230** | ETAT DE SURFACE **12504** |
| ETAIN EN FEUILLES **11326** | ETAT DE SURFACE **5213** |
| ETAIN EN GRENAILLES/EN GRAINS **6042** | ETAT DESCRIPTIF DU CONSTRUCTEUR **7993** |
| ETAIN EN SAUMONS **1339** | ETAT FINAL **5190** |
| ETALON **5768** | ETAT GAZEUX **5857** |
| ETALON **12077** | ETAT HYGROMETRIQUE DE L'AIR **6666** |
| ETALON **12076** | ETAT INITIAL **6930** |
| ETALON HEFNER **6419** | ETAT LIBRE (A L') **6818** |
| ETALON NORMALISE **12082** | ETAT LIQUIDE **7657** |
| ETALON PHOTOMETRIQUE **9270** | ETAT NATIF (A L') **5647** |
| ETALON VIOLLE **13569** | ETAT PATEUX **8488** |
| ETALONNAGE **5886** | ETAT SOLIDE **11795** |
| ETALONNAGE **1867** | ETAU **13579** |
| ETALONNAGE (D'UN RESERVOIR) **1863** | ETAU **13561** |
| ETALONNAGE D'UNE JAUGE **5770** | ETAU A CHANFREIN **13565** |
| ETALONNAGE D'UNE JAUGE **5874** | ETAU A MAIN **6254** |
| ETALONNEMENT **5886** | ETAU A PIED **6511** |
| ETALONNER **5872** | ETAU A SERRAGE PARALLELE **9066** |
| ETALONS **5769** | ETAU A TUBES **13256** |
| ETAMAGE **12963** | ETAU A TUBES **9363** |
| ETAMER **12954** | ETAU D'AFFUTAGE POUR SCIES **10955** |
| ETAMPAGE **12059** | ETAU D'ETABLI **1171** |
| ETAMPAGE A CHAUD **12534** | ETAU DE TUYAUTEUR **13256** |
| ETAMPAGE A CHAUD **6643** | ETAU DU NORD **6511** |
| ETAMPE **12531** | ETAU INCLINABLE **535** |
| ETAMPE **1497** | ETAU ORDINAIRE **6511** |
| ETAMPE **13036** | ETAU ORIENTABLE **12562** |
| ETAMPER **12056** | ETAU PIVOTANT **12562** |
| ETAMPER A CHAUD **12530** | ETAU SIMPLE **9429** |
| ETAMPEUSE **12060** | ETAU UNIVERSEL **13389** |
| ETANCHE **12920** | ETAU-LIMEUR **11269** |
| ETANCHE (A LA VAPEUR) **12193** | ETAUX-LIMEUR **11267** |
| ETANCHE A L'AIR **303** | ETAYAGE **12153** |

# ETA

636

ETAYEMENT **12153**
ETAYER **12150**
ETEINDRE LA CHAUX **11568**
ETENDRE UNE SOLUTION **3952**
ETENDUE DE L'ECHELLE D'UN INSTRUMENT **10201**
ETHANE **4848**
ETHENE **4851**
ETHER ACETIQUE **88**
ETHER AZOTIQUE **4850**
ETHER CHLORHYDRIQUE **4849**
ETHER COMPOSE **4837**
ETHER DE PETROLE **9228**
ETHER NITRIQUE **4850**
ETHER ORDINAIRE **8853**
ETHER OXYDE METHYLIQUE **8222**
ETHER SULFURIQUE **8853**
ETHYLAL **84**
ETHYLENE **4851**
ETINCELAGE ELECTRIQUE **4531**
ETINCELLE **11836**
ETIRABILITE **4228**
ETIRAGE **4230**
ETIRAGE A CHAUD **6624**
ETIRAGE A FROID **2676**
ETIRAGE A FROID **4230**
ETIRAGE A FROID DE TUBES COULES SANS SOUDURE **2053**
ETIRAGE BRILLANT **4347**
ETIRAGE DES TUBES **13249**
ETIRAGE EN FIL **13888**
ETIRE **4247**
ETIRE A FROID **2677**
ETIRER A CHAUD **6623**
ETIRER A FROID **2675**
ETIRER EN FIL **4220**
ETIRER LES TUBES **4224**
ETOFFE CAOUTCHOUTEE **10818**
ETOFFE FILTRANTE **5176**
ETOUPE **13073**
ETOUPE DE CHANVRE **6444**
ETOUPE DE LIN **5413**
ETRANGLEMENT **12891**
ETRANGLEMENT DE LA VEINE LIQUIDE **3044**
ETRANGLER **12889**
ETRE EN EBULLITION **1401**
ETRE SOUMIS A UN EFFORT DE CISAILLEMENT **1078**
ETRIER **2720**
ETRIER **12261**
ETRIER **13324**
ETRIER **2450**
ETUDE **3794**
ETUDE **3799**

ETUDE DE SOL **11752**
ETUDE DE TERRAIN **11752**
ETUDIER **3795**
ETUVE **3158**
ETUVE **4353**
ETUVE **4256**
ETUVE **4358**
ETUVE A SECHAGE RAPIDE **5360**
EUDIOMETRE **4852**
EUROPIUM **4854**
EUTECTIQUE **4855**
EUTECTOIDE **4859**
EVACUATION DE L'AIR D'UNE CONDUITE **4665**
EVACUATION DE LA VAPEUR D'EBULLITION **1405**
EVACUATION DES EAUX RESIDUAIRES **10453**
EVACUATION DES POUSSIERES **10452**
EVACUATION DU LAITIER **3803**
EVACUER LES GAZ **10455**
EVANT **10614**
EVAPORABLE **4861**
EVAPORATION **4867**
EVAPORATION A L'AIR LIBRE **8502**
EVAPORER **4862**
EVAPORER (S') **4862**
EVAPORER (S') A L'AIR LIBRE **4863**
EVENT **269**
EVENT **13528**
EVENT AUTOMATIQUE **1320**
EVENT D'ETANCHEITE **10597**
EVENT LIBRE **5642**
EVIDEMENT **8831**
EVIDEMENT **10279**
EVOLUTE **4873**
EXAMEN **4876**
EXAMEN **12792**
EXAMEN A FROID **2687**
EXAMEN A L'ULTRAMICROSCOPE **13336**
EXAMEN MAGNETOGRAPHIQUE **7931**
EXAMEN MICROSCOPIQUE **7114**
EXAMEN MICROSCOPIQUE **8260**
EXAMEN PAR RESSUAGE **7656**
EXAMEN RADIOGRAPHIQUE **10162**
EXAMEN RADIOGRAPHIQUE **13993**
EXCENTRATION **10892**
EXCENTRE **4424**
EXCENTRICITE **4436**
EXCENTRIQUE **4433**
EXCENTRIQUE **4425**
EXCENTRIQUE **4424**
EXCENTRIQUE A ONDES **4442**
EXCENTRIQUE CIRCULAIRE A COLLIER **4433**

EXCENTRIQUE EN COEUR **6329**
EXCENTRIQUE PLAN **8805**
EXCES **4878**
EXCES DE TRAVAIL **4880**
EXCITATION **4885**
EXCITATION SEPAREE **11190**
EXCITATRICE **4888**
EXCITER **4887**
EXECUTION D'UNE GORGE **8515**
EXEMPT D'ACIDE **5635**
EXEMPT DE CARBONE **1961**
EXEMPT DE CENDRES **5636**
EXERCER UN EFFORT SUR UN CORPS **12323**
EXFOLIATION **11328**
EXHAUSTEUR **4900**
EXIGENCES D'USINAGE **4987**
EXISTENCE **12263**
EXOTHERMIQUE **4901**
EXPERIENCE **12792**
EXPERT **4930**
EXPERTISE **4931**
EXPIRATION D'UN BREVET **4932**
EXPLOITATION **8837**
EXPLOITATION D'UNE INVENTION **13948**
EXPLOITATION MINIERE **8311**
EXPLOITER UNE INVENTION **13938**
EXPLOSER **4933**
EXPLOSIF **4937**
EXPLOSION **4935**
EXPLOSION D'UNE CHAUDIERE **1410**
EXPOSANT **4939**
EXPOSANT D'ECOULEMENT **4940**
EXPOSITION **4944**
EXPRESSION FRACTIONNAIRE **6807**
EXPRIMER **12039**
EXSUDATION **12540**
EXTENSION **4946**
EXTENSOMETRE **4949**
EXTENSOMETRE **12325**
EXTINCTION DE LA CHAUX **11569**
EXTRACTEUR **4900**
EXTRACTEUR (CHIM.) **4967**
EXTRACTEURS DE CONES **2929**
EXTRACTION DE L'HUILE **8777**
EXTRACTION DE L'OR PAR CYANURATION **3546**
EXTRACTION DE LA HOUILLE **13877**
EXTRACTION DES METAUX **4966**
EXTRACTION ELECTROLYTIQUE **4582**
EXTRACTION ELECTROLYTIQUE **4652**
EXTRAIRE **12039**
EXTRAIT **4964**

EXTRAIT MUCILAGINEUX **8440**
EXTREMITE **9384**
EXTREMITE **6314**
EXTREMITE DE LA BIELLE ARTICULEE AU PISTON **3389**
EXTREMITE DU BERCEAU **6597**
EXTREMITE LIBRE **5023**
EXTRUSION **4970**
EXTRUSION PAR CHOC **6784**
F E M **4622**
FABRICANT **7992**
FABRICATION **7989**
FABRICATION **8028**
FABRICATION **10462**
FABRICATION D'OUTILS A TAILLANTS **13006**
FABRICATION DES AGGLOMERES **7990**
FABRICATION DES MACHINES **8103**
FABRICATION DU COKE **7991**
FABRICATION EN GRANDES SERIES **7727**
FABRIQUE **5013**
FABRIQUE **5730**
FABRIQUER **7948**
FACE CRISTALLINE **3427**
FACE D'APPUI **1026**
FACE D'ATTAQUE **4989**
FACE D'UN TROU **13624**
FACE DE BRIDE **5327**
FACE DE LA DENT **4997**
FACE DE REFERENCE **8043**
FACES CENTREES (A) **5002**
FACES CENTREES (A) **4729**
FACILE A TRAVAILLER **13947**
FACILITE DU TRAVAIL **13946**
FACONNAGE **5581**
FACONNAGE **4983**
FACONNAGE **11268**
FACONNAGE A CHAUD **6627**
FACONNEMENT DES TETES A FROID **2686**
FACONNER **5571**
FACONNER UNE TETE DE RIVET **2516**
FACTEUR **5008**
FACTEUR DE FORME **5572**
FACTEUR DE PUISSANCE **9735**
FACTEUR DE SECURITE **5009**
FACTEUR DE VIBRATION **11981**
FACULTE DE PRENDRE BIEN LA TREMPE **6296**
FAIBLE FREQUENCE **7771**
FAIENCAGE **2286**
FAIRE CORRESPONDRE LES TROUS DE RIVETS **9969**
FAIRE DES ESSAIS **4928**
FAIRE DIGERER **3937**
FAIRE PRISE **6286**

## FAI

638

FAIRE PRISE 11214
FAIRE PRISE 6287
FAIRE REVENIR 12717
FAIRE REVENIR 12719
FAISCEAU 1093
FAISCEAU CONCENTRE 5504
FAISCEAU D'ELECTRONS 4625
FAISCEAU DE COURBES 5028
FAISCEAU DE FILS 7452
FAISCEAU DE RAYONS 9164
FAISCEAU DE RAYONS X 13995
FAISCEAU ELECTRONIQUE 1093
FAISCEAU FOCALISE 5504
FAISCEAU LUMINEUX 9162
FAISCEAU TUBULAIRE 8538
FALSIFICATION 205
FALSIFIER 204
FANEUSES 12696
FARAD 5035
FARINAGE 2226
FARINE FOSSILE 7292
FATIGUE 5047
FATIGUE D'UN MATERIEL 5051
FATIGUE PAR CONTACTS DE FROTTEMENT 2200
FATIGUE PAR CORROSION 3187
FATIGUE PAR L'HYDROGENE SULFURE 12442
FATIGUER UN MATERIEL 8962
FAUCHEUSES A FOURRAGES 5525
FAUCHEUSES A TRACTEUR-TRAINEES/MONTEES 8439
FAUSSE 1197
FAUSSE BRIDE 1304
FAUSSE EQUERRE 1228
FAUSSE GALENE 1324
FAUTE D'EXECUTION 3693
FAUX FOND 5026
FAUX NOYAU 5027
FAUX-ROND 8894
FECULE 12111
FEEDER 5081
FELDSPATH 5087
FELDSPATH 5089
FELURE 2278
FELURE A FROID 2674
FENDAGE 11622
FENDILLEMENT 5274
FENDILLEMENT DES TROUS DE RIVET 3286
FENDILLEMENT SUR LES BORDS 3281
FENDILLER (SE) 3279
FENETRE 13864
FENTE 11937
FENTE 11629

FENTE 3278
FENTE SUPERFICIELLE 6834
FER 7133
FER (MOULURE) A VITRAGES 10937
FER A BARREAUX DE GRILLE 6098
FER A BOUDIN 1716
FER A BOUDIN A PATIN 1719
FER A BRANCARDS 2250
FER A CHEVAL (EN) 6606
FER A GORGE 2248
FER A GRAIN FIN 2511
FER A GRAIN SERRE 2511
FER A GROS GRAIN 8819
FER A MAIN COURANTE 6265
FER A NERF 5139
FER A SOUDER 11765
FER A SOUDER 11764
FER A SOUDER A CHAUFFAGE AUTOMATIQUE 11155
FER A SOUDER A TETE CARREE 2350
FER A SOUDER AU GAZ 5824
FER A SOUDER DROIT 9573
FER A SOUDER ELECTRIQUE 4530
FER ACIEREUX 12224
FER AIGRE 2702
FER ARMCO 711
FER BRULE 1762
FER BRUT COULE EN COQUILLE 2333
FER CARRE 12015
FER CASSANT 11368
FER CASSANT A CHAUD 10338
FER CASSANT A FROID 2702
FER CAVALIER 6605
FER CORNIERE 514
FER CORNIERE A ANGLE ARRONDI 10794
FER CORNIERE A ANGLE VIF 11271
FER CORNIERE A BOUDIN 1712
FER CORROYE 11490
FER DANS LE BROYEUR 13106
FER DE CARBONYLE 1977
FER DE COULEUR 10338
FER DE MASSE 5553
FER DE RIBLONS 5553
FER DELTA 3740
FER DEMI-ROND CREUX 6541
FER DEMI-ROND PLEIN 11786
FER DOUBLE CORROYE 4156
FER DOUX 13988
FER DU RABOT 9436
FER EBAUCHE 8441
FER EN BANDES 5375
FER EN BARREAUX EN VERGES 984

| | |
|---|---|
| FER EN CROIX **3372** | FERMENTER **10036** |
| FER EN CROIX **3381** | FERMER L'INTRODUCTION **11407** |
| FER EN DOUBLE T **6194** | FERMER LE CIRCUIT ELECTRIQUE **2515** |
| FER EN E **2250** | FERMES **13243** |
| FER EN I **6194** | FERMETURE A BAIONNETTE **1074** |
| FER EN L **514** | FERMETURE A GRENOUILLERE **7336** |
| FER EN QUART DE ROND **9241** | FERMETURE DE LA SOUPAPE **2537** |
| FER EN T **12698** | FERMOIR **5264** |
| FER EN T A BOUDIN **1719** | FERRAILLE **5126** |
| FER EN T A LARGES AILES **1640** | FERRAILLE **11007** |
| FER EN U **2250** | FERRAILLES DE PROTECTION PROPRE **4124** |
| FER EN U **2248** | FERRICYANURE DE POTASSIUM **9684** |
| FER EN Z **14023** | FERRITE **5104** |
| FER FEUILLARD **6575** | FERRO-ALUMINIUM **5106** |
| FER FONDU **6921** | FERRO-BORE **5107** |
| FER FORGE **13988** | FERRO-CHROME **5108** |
| FER FORT **11490** | FERRO-MANGANESE **5110** |
| FER FORT SUPERIEUR **4156** | FERRO-MOLYBDENE **5111** |
| FER GAMMA **5795** | FERRO-NICKEL **5112** |
| FER HEXAGONAL **6454** | FERRO-SILICIUM **5113** |
| FER KAHLBAUM **7270** | FERRO-TITANE **5114** |
| FER LAMINE **10676** | FERRO-TUNGSTENE **5115** |
| FER LAMINE PROFILE **10675** | FERRO-VANADIUM **5116** |
| FER MAIN-COURANTE **6245** | FERROALLIAGES **5117** |
| FER MALLEABLE ANORMAL **9** | FERROCYANURE DE POTASSIUM **9685** |
| FER MARCHAND **8148** | FERROMAGNETIQUE **5118** |
| FER METIS **10338** | FERRUGINEUX **5127** |
| FER NERVEUX **5139** | FERRURE **7159** |
| FER NOIR **1296** | FERS A BETON **12198** |
| FER OLIVE **8916** | FERS D'HUISSERIE **4122** |
| FER OXYDULE **7927** | FERS FORGES **5566** |
| FER PLAT **5375** | FEU D'OXYDATION **8636** |
| FER PLAT A BOUDIN **1714** | FEU DE DEPASSEMENT **9102** |
| FER PLAT A BOUDIN **5376** | FEU DE FORGE **5548** |
| FER POUR CLOTURE **1086** | FEU DE REDUCTION **7820** |
| FER POUR TABLIERS DE PONT **7112** | FEU NU **8813** |
| FER PROFILE FACONNE **11119** | FEUILLARD **12378** |
| FER PUDDLE **9962** | FEUILLARD **12343** |
| FER ROND **10795** | FEUILLARD (TOLE MINCE) **12216** |
| FER SOUDE **13766** | FEUILLARD DE FER **6575** |
| FER SPATHIQUE **11421** | FEUILLARD INOX **10875** |
| FER SPECULAIRE **11865** | FEUILLARD-SUPPORT **902** |
| FER TENACE **13068** | FEUILLARDS **980** |
| FER VIRGINAL **346** | FEUILLARDS D'ACIER POUR EMBOUTISSAGE PROFOND **3688** |
| FER ZORES **7112** | FEUILLARDS EN ACIER ALLIE **371** |
| FER-BLANC **12957** | FEUILLE **5508** |
| FERAILLES DE PRODUCTION PROPRE **6554** | FEUILLE D'ALUMINIUM **436** |
| FERBLANTIER **12964** | FEUILLE D'ETAIN **12955** |
| FERME **6447** | FEUILLE D'OR **6000** |
| FERMENT **5097** | FEUILLE D'UN RESSORT **9492** |
| FERMENTATION **5098** | FEUILLE DE CAOUTCHOUC (NEOPRENE) **11329** |

# FEU

640

FEUILLE DE CLINQUANT **7621**
FEUILLE DE METAL **5508**
FEUILLE DE PLACAGE **13524**
FEUILLE DE PLOMB **7462**
FEUILLE DE TOLE **11313**
FEUILLE DE ZINC **11327**
FEUILLE METALLIQUE **8184**
FEUILLE METALLIQUE **11315**
FEUILLE MINCE DE CUIVRE **3117**
FEUILLE MINCE DE METAL **5509**
FEUILLERET **10115**
FEUILLET **13524**
FEUILLETAGE (DEDOUBLEMENT DES BORDS) DE TOLE **7382**
FEUILLURE **10269**
FEUTRE **5090**
FEUTRE ASPHALTE **765**
FEUTRE D'AMIANTE **750**
FEUX ARRIERE **12595**
FEUX DE DIRECTION **3989**
FEUX DE RECUL **908**
FIABILITE **10439**
FIBRE **13609**
FIBRE **5131**
FIBRE **5136**
FIBRE DE COCO **2654**
FIBRE DE PAILLE **12348**
FIBRE DU CANADA **1898**
FIBRE NEUTRE **8542**
FIBRE NEUTRE **2151**
FIBRE TEXTILE **12799**
FIBRE VULCANISEE **13609**
FIBRES (DANS LE SENS) **6031**
FIBREUX **5137**
FICHE D'ESSAI **12785**
FICHE DE PRISE DE COURANT **9529**
FICHES TECHNIQUES **3615**
FIDELITE DE SERVICE **10439**
FIGURE **6778**
FIGURE D'INTERFERENCE **7039**
FIGURE DE CORROSION **4845**
FIGURES D'ATTAQUE A L'ACIDE **4842**
FIL (BAGUETTE) A SOUDER **13793**
FIL (CROISSANCE EN FILAMENT) **13828**
FIL A PLOMB **9539**
FIL A SOUDER **13789**
FIL BARBELE **987**
FIL CLAIR **13340**
FIL CONDUCTEUR **2922**
FIL D'ACIER **12221**
FIL D'ACIER POUR CORDES A PIANO **9287**
FIL D'ALUMINIUM **428**

FIL D'AMIANTE **749**
FIL D'ARCHAL **1571**
FIL DE BRONZE **1654**
FIL DE BRONZE PHOSPHOREUX **5607**
FIL DE CARET **10744**
FIL DE CUIVRE **3133**
FIL DE CUIVRE **3106**
FIL DE CUIVRE PLAT **3116**
FIL DE FER **7155**
FIL DE FER CLAIR CRU **1610**
FIL DE FER RECUIT NOIR **1284**
FIL DE LAITON **1571**
FIL DE LIGATURE **1255**
FIL DE PLATINE **9513**
FIL DE PLOMB **7477**
FIL DE ZINC **14048**
FIL ELECTRIQUE **2922**
FIL ELLIPTIQUE **4678**
FIL EN VERGE POUR TREFILERIE **13882**
FIL ETAME **12962**
FIL ETIRE **4252**
FIL ETIRE A FROID **2715**
FIL FIN **5205**
FIL GAINE **11300**
FIL GAINE DE PLASTIQUE **9468**
FIL GALVANISE **5786**
FIL GALVANISE **12962**
FIL GUIPE **3219**
FIL HEXAGONAL **6462**
FIL ISOLE **6996**
FIL LAMINE **10678**
FIL LAMINE DE LAITON **1568**
FIL MACHINE DE LAITON **1568**
FIL MACHINE EN ACIER ALLIE **376**
FIL MEPLAT **5402**
FIL METALLIQUE **13880**
FIL METALLIQUE FIN **12849**
FIL MINCE **5205**
FIL MONOCRISTALLIN **13828**
FIL NU **990**
FIL OVALE **4678**
FIL PLAT **5402**
FIL PLAT EN CUIVRE **3116**
FIL PLOMBE **7459**
FIL POISSE **13704**
FIL POUR CABLE **10743**
FIL POUR RESISTANCES ELECTRIQUES **10501**
FIL POUR RESSORT **11997**
FIL PROFILE **11847**
FIL RECOUVERT **3272**
FIL RECTANGULAIRE **5402**

641  FIS

FIL RECUIT **561**
FIL RECUIT BLANC **1606**
FIL ROND **10804**
FIL TELEGRAPHIQUE **12708**
FIL TELEPHONIQUE **12711**
FIL TREFILE **4252**
FIL TRESSE **1528**
FIL TRIANGULAIRE **13196**
FIL ZINGUE **5786**
FILAGE **4970**
FILAGE **4230**
FILAGE A FROID **4970**
FILAGE AVEC REMONTEE DE MATIERES **6884**
FILAGE DIRECT **3984**
FILAMENT **6386**
FILAMENT DE QUARTZ **10078**
FILASSE DE CHANVRE **6439**
FILET **5092**
FILET **11045**
FILET (AGE) INTERIEUR **7078**
FILET A DROITE **10585**
FILET A GRAND DIAMETRE **2575**
FILET A PAS ALLONGE **10105**
FILET A PAS FIN **5201**
FILET A PAS RAPIDE **10105**
FILET A PETIT PAS **11647**
FILET CARRE **12030**
FILET EXTERIEUR **4960**
FILET FIN **5204**
FILET FLUIDE **12351**
FILET FOIRE **13981**
FILET JARETE **13981**
FILET METRIQUE INTERNATIONAL **7083**
FILET PROTECTEUR **6157**
FILET ROND **10802**
FILET TRAPEZOIDAL **1814**
FILET TRIANGULAIRE **545**
FILETAGE **12857**
FILETAGE **12868**
FILETAGE **11045**
FILETAGE **3535**
FILETAGE (OPERATION) **11028**
FILETAGE CONIQUE **12666**
FILETAGE CYLINDRIQUE **9065**
FILETAGE EXTERIEUR **7955**
FILETAGE EXTERIEUR **4961**
FILETAGE FEMELLE **5092**
FILETAGE INTERIEUR **5092**
FILETAGE MALE **7955**
FILETER **3512**
FILETEUSE **11066**

FILIERE **4223**
FILIERE **3883**
FILIERE A COUSSINETS **12266**
FILIERE A TREFILER **13887**
FILIERE A TRUELLE **11039**
FILIERE A TUBES **1121**
FILIERE DE TREFILAGE **4223**
FILIERE RONDE MONOBLOC **11781**
FILIERE SIMPLE **11039**
FILIERES **189**
FILM **5166**
FILM ANTI-MOUILLANT **13648**
FILM RIGIDE **8993**
FILTRAGE **5182**
FILTRAT **5181**
FILTRATION **5182**
FILTRE **5172**
FILTRE **12333**
FILTRE A AIR **260**
FILTRE A AIR A BAIN D'HUILE **8746**
FILTRE A CARBURANT **5708**
FILTRE A COKE **2660**
FILTRE A COMBUSTIBLE **5708**
FILTRE A GRAVIER **6074**
FILTRE A HUILE **8757**
FILTRE A SABLE **10923**
FILTRE PREPARATOIRE **5265**
FILTRE-PRESSE **5180**
FILTRER **5173**
FILTRES SYMETRIQUES **933**
FIN DE BANDE **4725**
FIN DE BLOC **4730**
FIN DE LIGNE **4731**
FIN DE PROGRAMME **4724**
FINESSE **5208**
FINI SATINE **10938**
FINIR **5214**
FINISSAGE **5223**
FINISSAGE **5213**
FINISSAGE **11682**
FINISSAGE A CHAUD **6655**
FINISSAGE A FROID **2679**
FINISSAGE A LA BROSSE METALLIQUE **11016**
FINISSAGE A LA MACHINE **7844**
FINISSAGE A LA MEULE **5224**
FINISSAGE AU LAMINOIR **8278**
FINISSAGE AU TONNEAU **1014**
FINISSAGE DIMENSIONNEL **11524**
FINITION **11682**
FINITION A LA FRAISE-MERE **6513**
FINITION PARTIELLE **11960**

FISSURAGE 3284
FISSURATION 3284
FISSURATION PAR CORROSION SOUS TENSION 12364
FISSURE 3278
FISSURE 2278
FISSURE 4377
FISSURE (MICROFISSURE) 3283
FISSURE CAPILLAIRE 3318
FISSURE CAPILLAIRE/MICROCRIQUE 6202
FISSURE CRIQUE DE LAMINAGE 7383
FISSURE DE FATIGUE / D'ENDURANCE 4739
FISSURE DE TREMPE 10097
FISSURE PAR FATIGUE 5048
FISSURE SOUS CORDON 13350
FISSURE SUPERFICIELLE 12501
FIXAGE 5044
FIXATION 5044
FIXATION 5416
FIXATION D'UN COIN DE SERRAGE 7704
FIXATION D'UNE EPROUVETTE 5300
FIXATION RIGIDE 10589
FIXER 5041
FLACON DESSECHANT 4308
FLACON LAVEUR 5845
FLACON SECHEUR 4308
FLAMBAGE 3343
FLAMBEMENT 3343
FLAMME CARBURANTE 1990
FLAMME D'HYDROGENE 6714
FLAMME ECLAIRANTE 7820
FLAMME FULIGINEUSE 11678
FLAMME INCOLORE 8636
FLAMME NEUTRE 8543
FLAMME NORMALE 8543
FLAMME OXYDANTE 8636
FLAMME OXYDANTE 8975
FLAMME OXYDANTE 4883
FLAMME REDUCTRICE 7820
FLAMME REDUCTRICE 4882
FLAMME REDUCTRICE 10349
FLANC 5348
FLANC DE BASE 10720
FLANC DE DENT 13018
FLANC DE LA DENT 5351
FLANC DE RACINE 10721
FLANC DE SAILLIE 167
FLANC DU FILET 5350
FLANELLE 5352
FLASQUE 5323
FLASQUE D'UN ARBRE COUDE 3304
FLASQUE D'UNE CHAINE A ROULEAUX 11416

FLEAU DE BALANCE 10972
FLECHE 5426
FLECHE 3698
FLECHE 10613
FLECHE 719
FLECHE (MEC.) 3701
FLECHE DE COTE 3395
FLECHE DE GRUE 3291
FLECHE MAXIMUM 8064
FLECHE PRINCIPALE D'UNE GRUE 7226
FLECHIR 1174
FLECHIR 10893
FLECHISSEMENT 10892
FLECHISSEMENT 10894
FLECHISSEMENT 3700
FLEUR DE SOUFRE 5464
FLEUR DU CUIR 6038
FLEURET ELECTRIQUE 4556
FLEXIBILITE 5415
FLEXIBLE 9518
FLEXION 5422
FLEXION 3698
FLEXION 1182
FLEXION A CHAUD 6619
FLEXION EFFECTUE SUR DES ACIERS TRAITES AVEC DES
    TREMPES (ESSAI DE...) 10088
FLEXION ELASTIQUE 4477
FLEXION TRANSVERSALE 3700
FLINT 5427
FLINT-GLASS 5428
FLOCON 5303
FLOCULATION 5441
FLOTTABILITE 1742
FLOTTATION 344
FLOTTATION 5452
FLOTTATION ANIONIQUE 557
FLOTTATION SELECTIVE 11144
FLOTTEMENT D'UNE COURROIE 13825
FLOTTEUR 5430
FLOTTEUR (DE JAUGE) 5876
FLOTTEUR DE STOCKAGE ET D'ACCOSTAGE 10217
FLUAGE (METAUX) 3324
FLUAGE A FROID 2680
FLUAGE PLASTIQUE 9471
FLUAGE SECONDAIRE 11104
FLUAGE TRANSITOIRE 13118
FLUAGE VISQUEUX 13578
FLUCTUATIONS DE VITESSE 13499
FLUIDE 7641
FLUIDE DE COUPE 3530
FLUIDE DE REFROIDISSEMENT 3083

643 FON

FLUIDE GAZEUX **5808**
FLUIDE LIQUIDE **7641**
FLUIDES DE COUPE CHIMIQUES **2303**
FLUIDES DE COUPE SYNTHETIQUES **2303**
FLUIDITE **5474**
FLUIDITE **5463**
FLUOR **5478**
FLUORESCENCE **5476**
FLUORINE **5479**
FLUORURE D'AMMONIUM **463**
FLUORURE DE BARYUM **999**
FLUORURE DE CALCIUM **5479**
FLUORURE DE LITHIUM **7667**
FLUORURE DE MAGNESIUM **7886**
FLUORURE DE POTASSIUM **9686**
FLUORURE DE SODIUM **11721**
FLUORURE DE STRONTIUM **12390**
FLUSSPATH **5479**
FLUX BASIQUE **1046**
FLUX LUMINEUX **7821**
FLUX MAGNETIQUE **7903**
FOIE DE SOUFRE **7674**
FOISONNER **12542**
FOLIUM DE DESCARTES **5513**
FONCTION (MATH.) **5734**
FONCTION AUXILIAIRE **8319**
FONCTION AUXILIAIRE **854**
FONCTION CIRCULAIRE **2413**
FONCTION CONTINUE **3025**
FONCTION CYCLIQUE **2413**
FONCTION DE (EN) **13542**
FONCTION DE DISTRIBUTION **9881**
FONCTION DE REPARTITION COMPOSEE **7239**
FONCTION EXPONENTIELLE **4942**
FONCTION GAMMA **5794**
FONCTION GENERATRICE (DES MOMENTS) **5919**
FONCTION HYPERBOLIQUE **6737**
FONCTION OUTIL **13001**
FONCTION PREPARATOIRE **9786**
FONCTIONNEMENT **10850**
FONCTIONNEMENT **8837**
FONCTIONNEMENT CONTINU **3038**
FONCTIONNEMENT INTERMITTENT **7056**
FONCTIONNEMENT SUR (DE) **10440**
FOND **6314**
FOND **1028**
FOND BOMBE **4036**
FOND D'UN BALLON **6316**
FOND DE FILET **12864**
FOND DE POCHE **1812**
FOND DU CYLINDRE **1494**

FOND EMBOUTI **4038**
FOND EN ANSE DE PANIER **13045**
FOND TORICONIQUE **13044**
FONDANT **5475**
FONDANT **5489**
FONDANT ACIDE **114**
FONDANT POUR SOUDER **5490**
FONDATION **5589**
FONDATION **2896**
FONDATION D'UNE MACHINE **7848**
FONDATION EN BRIQUES **1599**
FONDATION EN MACONNERIE **1599**
FONDERIE **5593**
FONDERIE **5592**
FONDERIE (ART) **5592**
FONDERIE D'ACIER **12207**
FONDERIE DE CUIVRE **1566**
FONDERIE DE FER/DE FONTE **7142**
FONDERIE SUR MODELES **7230**
FONDERIES (ETABLISSEMENT) **5597**
FONDEUR **5591**
FONDRE **8135**
FONDRE **2030**
FONDRE (CHIM.) **4061**
FONDRE (LE COUPE-CIRCUIT FOND) **1352**
FONDRE (LE COUSSINET FOND) **10837**
FONTE **2068**
FONTE **2034**
FONTE **7157**
FONTE (DURCIE) **2336**
FONTE A GRANDE RESISTANCE **2042**
FONTE A GRAPHITE SPEROIDAL **4362**
FONTE A GRAPHITE SPHEROIDAL **2045**
FONTE A GRAPHITE SPHEROIDAL **11895**
FONTE A GRAPHITE SPHEROIDAL **11894**
FONTE A L'AIR CHAUD **6620**
FONTE A L'AIR FROID **2669**
FONTE A SOUFFLURES **6563**
FONTE ACIEREE **11177**
FONTE ALLIEE **363**
FONTE ALLIEE **2037**
FONTE AU CHARBON DE BOIS **2258**
FONTE AU COKE (DE HAUT-FOURNEAU) **2657**
FONTE AU COKE BOIS **2664**
FONTE AU FOUR ELECTRIQUE **4510**
FONTE BESSEMER **1213**
FONTE BESSEMER **117**
FONTE BLANCHE **13830**
FONTE BLANCHE **2049**
FONTE BRUTE **9299**
FONTE BRUTE BESSEMER **105**

FONTE CRUE **9299**
FONTE D'ACIER **2055**
FONTE D'AFFINAGE **5544**
FONTE DE COQUILLE **2038**
FONTE DE FER **2034**
FONTE DE MOULAGE **5596**
FONTE DE TRANSITION **8733**
FONTE DUCTILE **11894**
FONTE DUCTILE **2045**
FONTE DUCTILE **2040**
FONTE ELECTRIQUE **4509**
FONTE ELECTRIQUE **4550**
FONTE EN CHAMBRE FROIDE **2671**
FONTE EN COQUILLE **2334**
FONTE EN COQUILLE **2335**
FONTE GRAPHITIQUE **1292**
FONTE GRISE **2041**
FONTE GRISE **5596**
FONTE GRISE **6094**
FONTE HEMATITE **6435**
FONTE MALLEABLE **7959**
FONTE MALLEABLE **2043**
FONTE MALLEABLE DE CUBILOT **3467**
FONTE MALLEABLE PERLITIQUE **2047**
FONTE MECANIQUE **7863**
FONTE MECANIQUE **4763**
FONTE NODULAIRE **8607**
FONTE NODULAIRE **11894**
FONTE PERLITIQUE **9200**
FONTE PERLITIQUE **2046**
FONTE RESISTANTE A L'USURE **2048**
FONTE RESISTANTE A LA CORROSION **2039**
FONTE SANS RETASSURES **2075**
FONTE SANS TENSIONS INTERNES **2074**
FONTE SPECULAIRE **11899**
FONTE THOMAS **1049**
FONTE TREMPEE **2038**
FONTE TRUITEE **2044**
FONTE TRUITEE **8420**
FORAGE **4277**
FORAGE **1468**
FORAGE D'ESSAI **12778**
FORAGE EN PROFONDEUR **3780**
FORCE **12352**
FORCE **6907**
FORCE **5532**
FORCE ASCENSIONNELLE **1742**
FORCE ATTRACTIVE **5529**
FORCE CENTRIFUGE **2180**
FORCE CENTRIPETE **2190**
FORCE COERCITIVE **2641**

FORCE COERCITIVE **2639**
FORCE COMPOSANTE **2816**
FORCE CONSTANTE **2973**
FORCE CONTRE-ELECTROMOTRICE **3231**
FORCE D'UN RESSORT **5528**
FORCE DE CISAILLEMENT **11291**
FORCE DE COHESION **2644**
FORCE DE COMPRESSION **2868**
FORCE DE L'HOMME **9738**
FORCE DE TORSION **13055**
FORCE DE TRACTION **12745**
FORCE DU FROTTEMENT **5683**
FORCE ELASTIQUE D'UN GAZ **4480**
FORCE ELECTROMOTRICE **4622**
FORCE ELECTROMOTRICE THERMIQUE **12807**
FORCE ELECTROSTATIQUE **4642**
FORCE EXTERIEUR **4954**
FORCE HYDRAULIQUE **13668**
FORCE IMPULSIVE **6811**
FORCE INTERIEURE **7064**
FORCE MAGNETIQUE **7904**
FORCE MAGNETISANTE **7925**
FORCE MAGNETOMOTRICE **7932**
FORCE MAGNETOMOTRICE SPECIFIQUE **7929**
FORCE MOLECULAIRE **8360**
FORCE MOTRICE **8409**
FORCE MOTRICE **9733**
FORCE NECESSAIRE **3746**
FORCE POLAIRE **9596**
FORCE REACTIVE **10248**
FORCE REPULSIVE **5530**
FORCE RESISTANCE **10484**
FORCE TANGENTIELLE **12622**
FORCE THERMOELECTRIQUE **12831**
FORCE UNIQUE **11483**
FORCE VIVE **7308**
FORCER UNE CLAVETTE DANS SA RAINURE **4293**
FORCES CONCOURANTES **2903**
FORCES DE MEME SENS **5538**
FORCES OPPOSEES EN DIRECTION **5537**
FORCES PARALLELES **9056**
FORE **4275**
FORER **4264**
FORER PREALABLEMENT **10771**
FORET **4271**
FORET **4263**
FORET A CANALISATION D'HUILE **8762**
FORET A CANON **6177**
FORET A CENTRE **2164**
FORET A CENTRER **2763**
FORET A COUTURE DROITE **12304**

**645**     **FOU**

FORET A CUILLER **11957**
FORET A FRAISER **3245**
FORET A HELICE **13304**
FORET A HELICE SERREE **6470**
FORET A LANGUE D'ASPIC **5380**
FORET A MISE EN CARBURE **1936**
FORET A TETON **2164**
FORET A TETON CYLINDRIQUE **9316**
FORET ALESEUR **3241**
FORET ALESEUR **3149**
FORET AMERICAIN **13304**
FORET CHAMPIGNON **3245**
FORET ELECTRIQUE **4556**
FORET HELICOIDAL **13304**
FORET HELICOIDE **13304**
FORET OU MECHE A CANON **3563**
FORET POUR PERCAGE PROFOND **3686**
FOREUR **4276**
FOREUSE **4279**
FOREUSE A COLONNE **9312**
FORGE **5548**
FORGE **5547**
FORGE (USINE) **7160**
FORGE A LA MAIN **6261**
FORGE D'UNE PIECE DANS LA MASSE **5552**
FORGE DE MARECHALE **5548**
FORGE PORTATIVE **9637**
FORGE VOLANTE **9637**
FORGEABILITE **7958**
FORGEABLE **7960**
FORGEAGE **5555**
FORGEAGE **5557**
FORGEAGE A CHAUD **6626**
FORGEAGE A FROID **2681**
FORGEAGE A LA MACHINE **7847**
FORGEAGE A LA MAIN **11669**
FORGEAGE A LA PRESSE **9807**
FORGEAGE A LA PRESSE **9798**
FORGEAGE PAR LAMINAGE **10668**
FORGER **5542**
FORGER A LA PRESSE **9800**
FORGERON **11671**
FORGERON A MAIN **6225**
FORMAGE **5579**
FORMAGE A CHAUD **6627**
FORMALDEHYDE **5573**
FORMAT **5574**
FORMAT A ADRESSES **13935**
FORMAT A ADRESSES DE BLOCS **1334**
FORMAT A BLOC FIXE **5288**
FORMAT A BLOC VARIABLE **13489**

FORMAT A SEQUENCE FIXE **5297**
FORMAT A TABULATION **12583**
FORMATION **5579**
FORMATION D'INCRUSTATIONS **6856**
FORMATION D'UNE CROUTE **1927**
FORMATION DE CIRQUES **2286**
FORMATION DE FISSURES **644**
FORMATION DE GERMES **5934**
FORMATION DE HALO **6203**
FORMATION DE LA FUMEE **11675**
FORMATION DE LA MOISISSURE **5575**
FORMATION DE PEAUX **11545**
FORMATION DE PONT **1604**
FORMATION DE ROUILLE **10865**
FORMATION DES TACHES **11961**
FORMATION DU MODELE **3041**
FORME **11264**
FORMENE **8215**
FORMER LA TETE DU RIVET **2516**
FORMOL **5573**
FORMULE **5582**
FORMULE APPROXIMATIVE **654**
FORMULE BRUTE **4704**
FORMULE CHIMIQUE **2310**
FORMULE D'APPROXIMATION **654**
FORMULE DE CONSTITUTION **5583**
FORTE PRESSION **6473**
FOSSE A BATTITURES **10977**
FOSSE DU VOLANT **5498**
FOUETTEMENT D'UNE COURROIE **13825**
FOULOIR A MAIN **6246**
FOULOIR PNEUMATIQUE **286**
FOUR **5739**
FOUR **8920**
FOUR **12300**
FOUR **11667**
FOUR A ARC **4495**
FOUR A ARC A RESISTANCE **10485**
FOUR A ARC ELECTRIQUE **668**
FOUR A ARC ELECTRIQUE A ELECTRODES DE CHARBON **670**
FOUR A ARC INDIRECT **669**
FOUR A ATMOSPHERE CONTROLEE **3055**
FOUR A BAIN DE SEL **10912**
FOUR A BANDE **1148**
FOUR A CHARGER **1060**
FOUR A CHARIOTER **11603**
FOUR A CHAUFFER LES RIVETS **10623**
FOUR A CLOCHE **1132**
FOUR A CLOCHE **1135**
FOUR A COKE **2661**

# FOU

646

FOUR A CORNUE **10524**
FOUR A CREUSET **9669**
FOUR A CREUSET **4597**
FOUR A CUVE **11241**
FOUR A CYANURATION **3550**
FOUR A FONDRE **11665**
FOUR A FRITTER **11512**
FOUR A HAUTE FREQUENCE **6469**
FOUR A INDUCTION **6895**
FOUR A INDUCTION A BASSE FREQUENCE **7772**
FOUR A MANCHE **11241**
FOUR A MOUFLE **8447**
FOUR A NITRURATION **8584**
FOUR A POULIES **9975**
FOUR A RECHAUFFER EN PAQUETS **9308**
FOUR A RECUIRE **564**
FOUR A RECUIRE **10426**
FOUR A REGENERATION **10321**
FOUR A REGENERATION **10410**
FOUR A REVERBERE **10532**
FOUR A SECOUSSES **10024**
FOUR A SOIE **6332**
FOUR A SOUDER **11763**
FOUR CHAUFFE AU GAZ **5851**
FOUR CONTINU **3026**
FOUR D'AFFINAGE **10379**
FOUR D'EGALISATION **11698**
FOUR D'HORLOGER **13639**
FOUR DE CALCINATION **1843**
FOUR DE CALCINATION **7295**
FOUR DE CARBURISATION **1991**
FOUR DE CEMENTATION **3074**
FOUR DE CHAUFFERIE **5747**
FOUR DE FUSION **8138**
FOUR DE GRILLAGE **10649**
FOUR DE MAINTIEN **6527**
FOUR DE PREMIER ALLIAGE **3607**
FOUR DE PUDDLAGE **9965**
FOUR DE RECUIT **564**
FOUR DE REVENU **564**
FOUR ELECTRIQUE **4507**
FOUR ELECTRIQUE A ARC DIRECT **671**
FOUR ELECTRIQUE A ARC DIRECT **667**
FOUR ELECTRIQUE A INDUCTION **4515**
FOUR ELECTRIQUE A RESISTANCE **10490**
FOUR INDUSTRIEL **6900**
FOUR MARTIN **8815**
FOUR MARTIN **8829**
FOUR METALLURGIQUE **8207**
FOUR NON CONTINU **1060**
FOUR POUSSANT **10030**

FOUR PRECHAUFFEUR **9777**
FOUR REDUCTEUR **10359**
FOUR REVERBERE **261**
FOUR STATIONNAIRE FIXE **12142**
FOURCHE DE DEBRAYAGE **12346**
FOURCHE GUIDE-COURROIE **12346**
FOURCHETTE **12346**
FOURGON **13474**
FOURNEAU **12300**
FOURNEAU **5739**
FOURNEAU A BRASER **1577**
FOURNEAU A CALEBASSE **3402**
FOURNEAU A CREUSET **3402**
FOURNEAU A LA WILKINSON **3466**
FOURNEAU D'ACHESON **97**
FOURNEAU DE FUSION **11667**
FOURNIR DE NOUVELLES CALORIES **12485**
FOURNITURE DE CHALEUR **12488**
FOURREAU **11576**
FOURRURE **7623**
FOURRURE DUN PALIER **7624**
FOURRURE EN BOIS **13927**
FOYER (OPT. ET GEOM.) **5502**
FOYER A CHARBON **2565**
FOYER A CHARBON PULVERISE **5746**
FOYER A GAZ **5744**
FOYER A HOUILLE **2565**
FOYER A HUILE LOURDE **5745**
FOYER A PETROLE **5745**
FOYER A RECUPERATION INTERMITTENTE **10410**
FOYER AUTOMATIQUE **8110**
FOYER DE CHAUDIERE **5747**
FOYER FIN (TUBE DE RAYONS X) **8239**
FOYER FUMIVORE **11674**
FOYER REEL **10258**
FOYER VIRTUEL IMAGINAIRE **13571**
FRACTION **5613**
FRACTION DE DISTILLATION **5611**
FRACTION DECIMALE **3662**
FRACTION DECIMALE PERIODIQUE **9192**
FRACTION DECIMALE TERMINEE **5231**
FRACTION ORDINAIRE **13611**
FRACTION PROPRE **9932**
FRACTIONNER **5615**
FRACTURE **10858**
FRAGILE **5621**
FRAGILISATION A CHAUD **6625**
FRAGILITE **4685**
FRAGILITE **5622**
FRAGILITE **11378**
FRAGILITE **1628**

FRAGILITE (NON-) 13342
FRAGILITE A CHAUD 10339
FRAGILITE A CHAUD 6641
FRAGILITE A FROID 2703
FRAGILITE AU BLEU 1631
FRAGILITE AU ZINGAGE 5790
FRAGILITE CAUSTIQUE 2118
FRAGILITE D'ENTAILLE 1632
FRAGILITE D'ENTAILLE 8669
FRAGILITE DE DECAPAGE 109
FRAGILITE DE DECAPAGE 6713
FRAGILITE DE REVENU 1634
FRAGILITE DU FER 1629
FRAGILITE PAR CORROSION 3186
FRAGILITE PAR DECAPAGE 1630
FRAGILITE PAR PENETRATION DE SOUDURE 11757
FRAGILITE RHEOTROPIQUE 1633
FRAGMENTATION DE GRAINS 5623
FRAGMENTS MENUS 8267
FRAIS 7346
FRAIS D'EMBALLAGE 3205
FRAIS D'ENTRETIEN 7945
FRAIS D'EXPLOITATON 13950
FRAIS DE CONSOMMATION 8049
FRAIS DE FABRICATION 3207
FRAIS DE FORCE MOTRICE 3206
FRAIS DE MANUTENTION 3204
FRAIS DE MATIERE 8049
FRAIS DE PREMIER ETABLISSEMENT 9858
FRAIS DE PRODUCTION 3207
FRAIS DE REPARATION 3208
FRAIS DE TRANSPORT 3209
FRAIS GENERAUX 8798
FRAISAGE 3234
FRAISAGE 8287
FRAISAGE CLASSIQUE 3061
FRAISAGE D'UN TROU DE RIVET 3247
FRAISAGE DES CONTOURS 3040
FRAISAGE DES MATRICES 3892
FRAISAGE EN AVALANT 2497
FRAISAGE EN DESCENDANT 4182
FRAISAGE EN DUPLEX 12301
FRAISAGE EN REMONTANT 13408
FRAISAGE EN TRAIN 5800
FRAISAGE RECIPROQUE 10282
FRAISE 8289
FRAISE 3519
FRAISE A DENTS DEGAGEES 905
FRAISE A DENTS DEPOUILLEES 905
FRAISE A DENTS RAPPORTEES 6971
FRAISE A DENTURE DROITE 12307

FRAISE A DENTURE HELICOIDALE 11917
FRAISE A DISQUE 8496
FRAISE A LAMES RAPPORTEES 6971
FRAISE A PROFIL CONSTANT 905
FRAISE A QUEUE 11259
FRAISE A SURFACER 4722
FRAISE A TAILLER LES ENGRENAGES 5898
FRAISE ANGULAIRE 543
FRAISE AXIALE 4446
FRAISE CONIQUE 543
FRAISE CYLINDRIQUE 13848
FRAISE D'EXTERIEUR POUR TUBES 4951
FRAISE D'INTERIEUR POUR TUBES 7059
FRAISE DE FACE 4722
FRAISE DE FORME 9899
FRAISE DISQUE 11412
FRAISE EBARBEUSE 1765
FRAISE EBARBEUSE FEMELLE 4951
FRAISE EBARBEUSE MALE 7059
FRAISE EN BOUT 4722
FRAISE FRONTALE 4722
FRAISE MERE 13971
FRAISE POUR LOGEMENT DE TETES DE VIS 3245
FRAISE POUR RAINURES 11634
FRAISE POUR TAILLER DES ENGRENAGES HELICOIDAUX 13972
FRAISE PROFILEE 9899
FRAISE RADIALE 4722
FRAISE RECTILIGNE 13848
FRAISE-MERE 6512
FRAISE-SCIE 8193
FRAISER 8276
FRAISER UN TROU DE RIVET 3246
FRAISER UN TROU DE VIS 3246
FRAISES A COUTEAUX 11632
FRAISES A DEUX TAILLES EN BOUT 4992
FRAISES A RAINURE WOODRUFF 13930
FRAISES A RAINURES 11632
FRAISES A UNE TAILLE LATERALE 6206
FRAISES ARBREES 663
FRAISES CONIQUES 540
FRAISES EN BOUT 4723
FRAISES EN BOUT ALESEES 11337
FRAISES EN BOUT PLEINES 11783
FRAISES POUR QUEUE D'ARONDE 4176
FRAISES POUR RAINURES EN T 12582
FRAISES SIMPLES POUR TRAVAUX LOURDS 6404
FRAISES SIMPLES A HELICE RAPIDE 6471
FRAISES-MERES 5577
FRAISEUR 8292
FRAISEUSE 8291

# FRA

648

FRAISEUSE A BANC FIXE **5298**

FRAISEUSE A COMMANDE PAR DISPOSITIF DE COPIAGE **13080**

FRAISEUSE A CONSOLE ET COLONNE **7319**

FRAISEUSE A COPIER **9900**

FRAISEUSE A PORTIQUE **9642**

FRAISEUSE A TAILLER LES ENGRENAGES **5894**

FRAISEUSE CIRCULAIRE **2420**

FRAISEUSE DUPLEX A GRAND RENDEMENT **4379**

FRAISEUSE HORIZONTALE **6589**

FRAISEUSE MULTIPLE **8471**

FRAISEUSE RADIALE A COULISSE **10190**

FRAISEUSE UNIVERSELLE **13387**

FRAISEUSE VERTICALE **13548**

FRAISEUSE-FACONNEUSE **9900**

FRAISEUSE-RABOTEUSE **9460**

FRAISSAGE D'UN TROU A VIS **3247**

FRANCHISE (DELAI AVANT) **6020**

FRANGE D'INTERFERENCE **7040**

FRAPPE-DEVANT **11573**

FRAPPEUR DE POINTES **13891**

FRAUDE **205**

FREIN **1529**

FREIN **5031**

FREIN A AIR COMPRIME **2840**

FREIN A BANDE **5681**

FREIN A CHAINE **2203**

FREIN A COLLIER **5681**

FREIN A CONE **2926**

FREIN A CORDE **10732**

FREIN A COURANTS DE FOUCAULT **4439**

FREIN A DEPRESSION **13436**

FREIN A DEUX MACHOIRES **4129**

FREIN A DEUX SABOTS **4129**

FREIN A DISQUE **8454**

FREIN A DISQUE **4001**

FREIN A ENROULEMENT **5681**

FREIN A FRICTION **5669**

FREIN A GENOUILLERE **12978**

FREIN A HUILE **8755**

FREIN A LAME **8454**

FREIN A LEVIER **7532**

FREIN A LEVIER ET CONTREPOIDS **3638**

FREIN A MAIN **6227**

FREIN A MAIN **9082**

FREIN A PEDALE **5519**

FREIN A PIED **5519**

FREIN A RUBAN **5681**

FREIN A SABOT **1335**

FREIN A TAMBOUR **4334**

FREIN A VAPEUR **12159**

FREIN A VIDE **13436**

FREIN A VIS **12344**

FREIN CENTRIFUGE **2175**

FREIN D'ECROU **8701**

FREIN DE RETENUE **7681**

FREIN DE SECOURS **4687**

FREIN DE SECURITE **10883**

FREIN DE STATIONNEMENT **9082**

FREIN DIFFERENTIEL **3907**

FREIN DYMAMOMETRIQUE DE PRONY **9920**

FREIN ELECTROMAGNETIQUE **4613**

FREIN HYDRAULIQUE **8755**

FREIN HYDRAULIQUE **6678**

FREIN HYDRAULIQUE **6709**

FREIN HYDROPNEUMATIQUE **6678**

FREIN MAGNETIQUE **7896**

FREIN-MOTEUR **4760**

FREINAGE **1549**

FREINAGE INITIAL **6928**

FREINER **1530**

FREINS ASSISTES **9731**

FREQUENCE **5661**

FREQUENCE EMPIRIQUE **5662**

FRETTAGE **11398**

FRETTE **7203**

FRETTE **2931**

FRETTE **1252**

FRETTE POSEE A CHAUD **11391**

FRETTER A CHAUD **11390**

FRICTION **5668**

FRICTION INTERNE **7065**

FRISAGE **13985**

FRITTAGE **5690**

FRITTAGE **11511**

FRITTAGE CONTINU **3014**

FRITTAGE SOUS PRESSION **9799**

FRITTAGE SOUS VIDE **13448**

FRITTER **11509**

FRONT DE CRISTALLISATION **11798**

FRONT DE SOLIDIFICATION **11798**

FROTTAGE **8450**

FROTTEMENT **5668**

FROTTEMENT AU DEMARRAGE **5678**

FROTTEMENT AU DEPART **5678**

FROTTEMENT CINETIQUE **7309**

FROTTEMENT DANS LES PALIERS **1105**

FROTTEMENT DE GLISSEMENT **11601**

FROTTEMENT DE ROULEMENT **10700**

FROTTEMENT DES TOURILLONS **7258**

FROTTEMENT EN MARCHE **5677**

FROTTEMENT INTERIEUR DES LIQUIDES **5473**

FROTTEMENT INTERNE **7065**
FROTTEMENT PENDANT LE MOUVEMENT **5677**
FROTTEMENT STATIQUE **12134**
FROTTEUR **8451**
FUEL **5714**
FUIR **7487**
FUIT (QUI) **7493**
FUITE **7488**
FUITE **7492**
FUITE AUX JOINTS **7486**
FULMICOTON **6176**
FULMINATE D'ARGENT **11463**
FULMINATE DE MERCURE **8154**
FUMEE **11672**
FUMEES **5732**
FUMEES INDUSTRIELLES **6899**
FUMEES ROUSSES **10327**
FUMIVORE **11673**
FUNICULAIRE **1826**
FUSEAU D'UN ENGRENAGE A LANTERNE **9323**
FUSEAU SPHERIQUE **11886**
FUSEE D'ESSIEU **882**
FUSEE ECLAIRANTE **7573**
FUSEES **5443**
FUSEES **5434**
FUSIBILITE **5755**
FUSIBLE **5751**
FUSIBLE **5758**
FUSIBLE **5756**
FUSIBLE DES COUPE-CIRCUIT **10886**
FUSION **11666**
FUSION **5760**
FUSION **8134**
FUSION **8136**
FUSION CONGRUENTE **2938**
FUSION EUTECTIQUE **4856**
FUSION IGNEE **5764**
FUSION PAR ZONE **14050**
FUSION SOUS VIDE **13444**
FUT D'UNE COLONNE **11243**
FUT DE CYLINDRE **3562**
FUT DE RABOT **12262**
FUT DU RIVET **11263**
GABARIT **9128**
GABARIT **12734**
GABARIT **5768**
GABARIT DE PERCAGE **4267**
GABARIT DE SOUDAGE **13785**
GABARIT POUR OUTILS A FILETER **12865**
GABARITS **5769**
GABARITS DE PERCAGE **4268**

GABBRO **5765**
GACHER **12718**
GADOLINIUM **5767**
GAILLETINS **2328**
GAILLETTE **2606**
GAILLETTERIE **2606**
GAIN **5773**
GAIN DE TEMPS **10949**
GAIN DE TRAVAIL **8094**
GAINE **7986**
GALBE **3396**
GALENE **5775**
GALET **1895**
GALET **10671**
GALET **12334**
GALET **10679**
GALET CONIQUE **12660**
GALET CYLINDRIQUE **3589**
GALET DE CONTACT **3008**
GALET DE FRICTION **5679**
GALET DE GUIDAGE **6161**
GALET DE POUSSOIR **1885**
GALET DE POUSSOIR **12674**
GALET DE ROULEMENT **10844**
GALET DE ROULEMENT **10854**
GALET POUR ROULEMENTS **1112**
GALET TENDEUR **4910**
GALET-GUIDE **6161**
GALETAGE **1758**
GALETS (GEOL.) **11354**
GALETS (POUR MISE SUR CHAMP) **10695**
GALETTE **9011**
GALLIUM **5779**
GALLON (MESURE ANGLAISE) **5781**
GALVANISATION **5787**
GALVANISATION **5789**
GALVANISATION **14044**
GALVANISATION (OU ZINGAGE) ELECTROLYTIQUE **4583**
GALVANISATION A CHAUD **6653**
GALVANISATION A FROID **2683**
GALVANISATION EN CONTINU **3027**
GALVANISATION PAR TREMPE **6628**
GALVANISATION PARTIELLE **9076**
GALVANISER **5784**
GALVANISER **366**
GALVANOMETRE **5791**
GALVANOPLASTIE **4640**
GALVANOPLASTIE **4651**
GALVANOPLASTIE AU TONNEAU **1016**
GALVANOPLASTIQUE **5792**
GALVANOSTEGIE **4640**

# GAM

650

GAMMA-GRAPHIE 5798
GAMME 10200
GAMME DE DURETE 10974
GAMME DE FABRICATION 7994
GAMME DE TEMPERATURE 12730
GAMME DES OPERATIONS 2222
GANGUE 5802
GANNISTER 5803
GARANT (D'UN PALAN) 5023
GARDE AU SOL 6143
GARDE-BOUE 11927
GARDE-CORPS 6259
GARNIR DE MATIERE DE JOINT 8990
GARNISSAGE 7623
GARNISSAGE DU FOUR 5748
GARNISSAGE REFRACTAIRE ACIDE 123
GARNITURE 9386
GARNITURE 7347
GARNITURE 9004
GARNITURE 4482
GARNITURE 7620
GARNITURE 9009
GARNITURE ANTI-FRICTION 13837
GARNITURE D'EMBRAYAGE 2545
GARNITURE DE BOITE A BOURRAGE 12406
GARNITURE DE FREIN 1538
GARNITURE DE JOINT 8998
GARNITURE DE METAL ANTIFRICTION 7624
GARNITURE DE PISTON 9375
GARNITURE DE PRESSE-ETOUPE 12406
GARNITURE DE SOUPAGE 8998
GARNITURE EN CHANVRE 6445
GARNITURE EN CUIR 7502
GARNITURE EN CUIR EMBOUTI 3459
GARNITURE EN TRESSE 1526
GARNITURE INTERIEURE DU CYLINDRE 3571
GARNITURE METALLIQUE 8196
GARNITURE MONOLITHIQUE 8385
GARNITURE SOUPLE 11739
GARNITURES 5283
GARNITURES DE CHAUDIERES 1411
GAUCHIR 13628
GAUCHISSEMENT 13629
GAUCHISSEMENT LATERAL 7418
GAZ 5808
GAZ A L'AIR 264
GAZ A L'EAU 13651
GAZ AMMONIAC 453
GAZ CARBONIQUE 1948
GAZ CARBONIQUE LIQUEFIE 7645
GAZ COMBUSTIBLE 5709

GAZ COMPRIME 2847
GAZ D'ECHAPPEMENT 4891
GAZ D'ECLAIRAGE 6775
GAZ D'HUILE 8758
GAZ DE CHAUFFAGE 5709
GAZ DE FOUR A COKE 2663
GAZ DE GAZOGENE 9890
GAZ DE HAUT FOURNEAU 1313
GAZ DE LA COMBUSTION 5470
GAZ DE PETROLE LIQUEFIE 7638
GAZ DE PROTECTION 6905
GAZ DES MARAIS 8215
GAZ DU FOYER 5470
GAZ INCANDESCENT 6827
GAZ INERTE 6905
GAZ LIQUEFIE 7342
GAZ LIQUEFIE 7637
GAZ LUMIERE 6775
GAZ MOND 8378
GAZ NATUREL 8504
GAZ OLEFIANT 4851
GAZ OXHYDRIQUE 8985
GAZ PARFAIT 9185
GAZ PAUVRE 4194
GAZ PERDU 13634
GAZ POUR ACTIONNER LES MOTEURS 9736
GAZ PUANT 6717
GAZ RICHE 8758
GAZE 5888
GAZE METALLIQUE 13893
GAZEIFIABLE 5860
GAZEIFICATION 5865
GAZEIFICATION 5861
GAZEIFIER 5862
GAZOGENE 5838
GAZOGENE A ASPIRATION 12430
GAZOGENE A VENT SOUFFLE 9819
GAZOLE 5831
GAZOLINE 9228
GAZOLINE 9222
GAZOMETRE 5859
GEL 5912
GELATINE PURE 5913
GELIVURE DU BOIS 5700
GENER MUTUELLEMENT (SE) 5587
GENERATEUR A GAZ 5838
GENERATEUR A VAPEUR 12169
GENERATEUR DE VAPEUR 12158
GENERATEUR ELECTROSTATIQUE 4643
GENERATION DE VAPEUR 5923
GENERATRICE 9867

651 GON

GENERATRICE **407**
GENERATRICE **3021**
GENERATRICE (GEOM.) **5925**
GENERATRICE A COURANT TRIPHASE **12875**
GENERATRICE A GAZ **5850**
GENERATRICE A VAPEUR **12191**
GENERATRICE DE COURANT **5924**
GENERATRICE DE SOUDAGE POUR COURANT CONSTANT **2970**
GENERATRICE HYDROELECTRIQUE **6700**
GENIE CIVIL **2444**
GENOU **953**
GENOUILLERE **12546**
GENOUILLERE **12979**
GEOMETRIE **5931**
GEOMETRIE DU JOINT **7240**
GEOMETRIE DU TRAIN AVANT **5696**
GEOMETRIQUE **5927**
GERCE **3282**
GERCE **11250**
GERCE **3278**
GERCURE **3282**
GERCURE **5304**
GERCURE **5273**
GERCURE DU BOIS **11250**
GERCURE SUPERFICIELLE **12501**
GERMANIUM **5933**
GERME **4686**
GERME (DE CRISTAL) **8688**
GERMINATION **8687**
GERMINATION **5934**
GEYSER (NATURE) **5936**
GIBET **5945**
GICLEUR **7218**
GICLEUR **196**
GICLEUR DE RALENTI **11646**
GICLEUR PRINCIPAL **7942**
GIFFARD **6938**
GIROUETTE **13860**
GISEMENT MINERAL **8303**
GITE MINIER **8303**
GIVRAGE **5702**
GLACAGE **5972**
GLACE A REFRACTION **10396**
GLACE DEPOLIE (PHOT.) **6145**
GLACE DU TIROIR **4996**
GLACE FONDANTE **8139**
GLACE RONDE **2414**
GLACER **5969**
GLACURE **5968**
GLACURE **3264**

GLACURE **5972**
GLAISE **7691**
GLISSEMENT **5973**
GLISSEMENT **11611**
GLISSEMENT **11595**
GLISSEMENT DE LA COURROIE **11620**
GLISSEMENT TRANSVERSAL **11288**
GLISSER **11586**
GLISSER **11612**
GLISSETTE **5976**
GLISSIERE **6160**
GLISSIERE **11588**
GLISSIERE **2395**
GLISSIERE (DE FENETRE) **13868**
GLISSIERE CYLINDRIQUE **3584**
GLISSIERE DE CROSSE **6169**
GLISSIERE PLATE **5384**
GLISSOIR **11587**
GLISSOIRE **11585**
GLOBE **11883**
GLOBERTITE **7880**
GLOBULISATION **11896**
GLU MARINE **8006**
GLUCINIUM **1210**
GLUCOSE **6058**
GLYCERINE **5988**
GNEISS **5989**
GODET **1674**
GODET (DU DESSINATEUR) **10946**
GODET DE GRAISSAGE **8753**
GODET EN VERRE A TIGE **8520**
GODET GRAISSEUR **8753**
GODET HUILEUR **8753**
GOMME A CRAYON **9163**
GOMME A ENCRE **6939**
GOMME ADRAGANTE **6174**
GOMME ARABIQUE **6172**
GOMME DAMMAR **3598**
GOMME DE SUMATRA **6184**
GOMME ELASTIQUE **10825**
GOMME GETTANIA **6184**
GOMME PLASTIQUE **6184**
GOMME-GRATTOIR **4801**
GOMME-GUTTE **5793**
GOMME-LAQUE **11338**
GOMME-LAQUE EN BRANCHES **12254**
GOMME-LAQUE EN GRAINS **11131**
GOMME-RESINE **6173**
GONFLEMENT **1720**
GONFLEMENT **6155**
GONFLEMENT **1331**

**GON** 652

GONFLEMENT (PAR LES GAZ DE FISSION) **12543**
GONFLEMENT DE LA FONTE **2061**
GONFLEMENT DU BOIS **12544**
GONFLER **12542**
GONFLER (SE) **1721**
GONIOMETRE **6004**
GORGE **6127**
GORGE **5483**
GORGE **2122**
GORGE D'UNE POULIE **6131**
GORGE DE ROULEMENT **13085**
GOUDRON **12679**
GOUDRON DE BOIS **13921**
GOUDRON DE GAZ **2570**
GOUDRON DE HOUILLE **2570**
GOUDRON DE LIGNITE **1667**
GOUDRON DE SCHISTE **11255**
GOUDRON VEGETAL **13921**
GOUDRONNAGE **12689**
GOUDRONNER **12680**
GOUGE DE FORGERON **6546**
GOUGE DE MENUISIER **6010**
GOUGE TRIANGULAIRE **13432**
GOUGEAGE **6011**
GOUJON **12399**
GOUJON **4181**
GOUJON **12397**
GOUJON AIGUILLE **9315**
GOUJON D'ASSEMBLAGE D'UNE CHAINE A ROULEAUX **9320**
GOUJON DE CENTRAGE **1513**
GOUJON EN BOIS **4180**
GOUJURE **5483**
GOULOTTE **2395**
GOUPILLE **9159**
GOUPILLE **9315**
GOUPILLE **13986**
GOUPILLE A TETE **2492**
GOUPILLE CONIQUE **12655**
GOUPILLE DE BLOCAGE **11220**
GOUPILLE DE CHASSIS **5372**
GOUPILLE DE CISAILLEMENT **11294**
GOUPILLE DE CISAILLEMENT **11283**
GOUPILLE DE CLAVETAGE **11220**
GOUPILLE DE RETENUE **11220**
GOUPILLE DE RETENUE **6522**
GOUPILLE FENDUE **11943**
GOUPILLE FENDUE **11940**
GOUSSET **6182**
GOUSSET **3058**
GOUTIERE A SECOUSSES **11253**
GOUTTE **4282**

GOUTTE FROIDE **2706**
GOUTTIERE **2395**
GOUTTIERE **6185**
GOUTTIERE **4285**
GRADE **6021**
GRADIN **12239**
GRADINS (EN) **12246**
GRADINS (A) **12246**
GRADUATION **10981**
GRADUER **6025**
GRAIN **12395**
GRAIN **12905**
GRAIN **6030**
GRAIN (MESURE ANGLAISE) **6029**
GRAIN ABRASIF **21**
GRAIN D'ORGE **9571**
GRAINS CONTENUS DANS LA FONTE **3998**
GRAINS DE CONTACT (RUPTEUR) **3000**
GRAINS POUR GAZOGENES **9140**
GRAISSAGE **7814**
GRAISSAGE **7803**
GRAISSAGE **7808**
GRAISSAGE **7812**
GRAISSAGE (ENDUCTION A LA GRAISSE) **6087**
GRAISSAGE A BAGUE **10601**
GRAISSAGE A CHAINETTE **2212**
GRAISSAGE A L'HUILE **8791**
GRAISSAGE A LA GRAISSE CONSISTANCE **6087**
GRAISSAGE A POMPE ET CIRCULATION D'HUILE **5442**
GRAISSAGE AU SUIF **6087**
GRAISSAGE AUTOMATIQUE **848**
GRAISSAGE COMPTE-GOUTTES **4287**
GRAISSAGE CONTINU **3012**
GRAISSAGE INTERMITTENT **9195**
GRAISSAGE MECANIQUE **848**
GRAISSAGE PAR BARBOTAGE **11925**
GRAISSAGE PAR COMPTE-GOUTTES **4284**
GRAISSAGE PAR MECHE **13847**
GRAISSAGE PAR OLEO-COMPRESSEUR **7809**
GRAISSAGE SOUS PRESSION **9818**
GRAISSAGE SOUS PRESSION **9824**
GRAISSAGE SOUS PRESSION A CIRCULATION CONTINUE **5442**
GRAISSE **5045**
GRAISSE AMELIOREE **6063**
GRAISSE CONSISTANTE **6275**
GRAISSE D'ETIRAGE **4233**
GRAISSE DE LUBRIFICATION **7804**
GRAISSE DE VOITURE **879**
GRAISSE DES TANNEURS **3711**
GRAISSE GRAPHITEE **6063**

GRAISSE MINERALE **13508**
GRAISSER **7801**
GRAISSER (ENDUIRE DE GRAISSE) **6084**
GRAISSER A L'HUILE **8744**
GRAISSEUR **6086**
GRAISSEUR **7812**
GRAISSEUR A DEBIT VISIBLE **11425**
GRAISSEUR A EPINGLETTE **8520**
GRAISSEUR A MECHE **11516**
GRAISSEUR A SOUPAPE **13467**
GRAISSEUR A TIGE **8520**
GRAISSEUR AUTOMATIQUE **851**
GRAISSEUR CENTRIFUGE **2182**
GRAISSEUR COMPTE-GOUTTES **4323**
GRAISSEUR MOLLERUP **8105**
GRAISSEUR STAUFFER **12148**
GRAMME **6046**
GRAND AXE D'UNE ELLIPSE **7947**
GRAND DEBIT DU BOIS **1058**
GRAND DIAMETRE DU FILET **3852**
GRAND LEVIER **3394**
GRANDE CALORIE **7298**
GRANDE COURONNE DE DIFFERENTIEL **3910**
GRANDE PENTE DE COUPE EFFECTIVE **7411**
GRANDES MAILLES (A) **2578**
GRANDEUR **7939**
GRANDEUR **10065**
GRANDEUR CHERCHEE **10469**
GRANDEUR D'EXECUTION (EN) **5723**
GRANDEUR DE COMPARAISON **12079**
GRANDEUR NATURELLE (EN) **5723**
GRANIT **6047**
GRANULAIRE **6050**
GRANULATION **1279**
GRANULATION **6057**
GRANULATION **6043**
GRANULATION SUPERFICIELLE **9314**
GRANULOMETRIE **6040**
GRANULOMETRIE **6032**
GRAPHIQUE **7717**
GRAPHIQUE **3834**
GRAPHIQUE DE LA RESISTANCE MECANIQUE **12366**
GRAPHITE **6062**
GRAPHITE **9541**
GRAPHITE DEFLOCULE **3703**
GRAPHITE EN PAILLETTES **10989**
GRAPHITE LAMELLAIRE **5305**
GRAPHITISANT **6067**
GRAPHITISATION **6066**
GRAPHOSTATIQUE **6061**
GRATTAGE **4802**

GRATTAGE **11011**
GRATTAGE (RESULTAT) **4803**
GRATTER **4799**
GRATTER **11008**
GRATTOIR **11009**
GRATTOIR DE BUREAU **4800**
GRATTOIR DE DESSINATEUR **4800**
GRAUWACKE **6095**
GRAVIER **6073**
GRAVITE **6078**
GRAVURE CATHODIQUE **2110**
GRELIN **1829**
GRELIN COMPOSE DE QUATRE AUSSIERES **11401**
GRENAILLAGE **11380**
GRENAILLAGE (FIN) **6124**
GRENAILLAGE (GROS) **11382**
GRENAILLE **25**
GRENAILLE **11379**
GRENAILLE DE CUIVRE **3128**
GRENAILLE DE NICKEL **8568**
GRENAILLE DE PLOMB **7472**
GRENAILLE DE ZINC **8404**
GRENAILLE FINE **6123**
GRENAT **5807**
GRES (GEOL.) **10928**
GRES BIGARRE **13502**
GRES CERAME **12276**
GRES ROUGE **10336**
GRESILLON DE COKE **11657**
GRIFFE **11013**
GRIFFE **2464**
GRIFFE DE FORGERON **6571**
GRIGNOTAGE **8552**
GRIGNOTEUSE **8553**
GRILLAGE **6071**
GRILLAGE **6096**
GRILLAGE **1839**
GRILLAGE DES MINERAIS **10650**
GRILLAGE DU MINERAI **8862**
GRILLAGE ONDULE **3200**
GRILLAGE TOTAL **3636**
GRILLE **6070**
GRILLE **6096**
GRILLE A BARREAUX MOBILES **10655**
GRILLE A CHAINE **2209**
GRILLE A ETAGES **12248**
GRILLE A GRADINS **12248**
GRILLE A GRAVIER **6075**
GRILLE A SECOUSSES **10655**
GRILLE DE DECOCHAGE **7334**
GRILLE HORIZONTALE **6584**

## GRI

| | |
|---|---|
| GRILLE INCLINEE **6837** | GUIDE A REFENDRE **10610** |
| GRILLE OSCILLANTE **10655** | GUIDE DE CENTRAGE **13087** |
| GRILLE ROTATIVE **10559** | GUIDE DE LA CROSSE **6169** |
| GRILLE TOURNANTE **10559** | GUIDE DE LA TIGE DU PISTON **9385** |
| GRILLER LES MINERAIS **10648** | GUIDE DE SOUPAPE **13462** |
| GRIMPEMENT D'UNE SOLUTION **3330** | GUIDE DU MOUVEMENT RECTILIGNE **12315** |
| GRIPPAGE **11141** | GUIDE-COURROIE **1150** |
| GRIPPAGE **5778** | GUIDE-RUBAN INFERIEUR **7796** |
| GRIPPEMENT **11141** | GUILLAUME **9522** |
| GRIPPER **11140** | GUILLAUME DE COTE **11417** |
| GROS FILET **2576** | GYPSE **6190** |
| GROS GRAIN **2573** | GYROSCOPE **6191** |
| GROSSE CHAUDRONNERIE **1423** | HACHE **857** |
| GROSSE POUDRE **2580** | HACHE PAILLES **2199** |
| GROSSE TETE DE BIELLE **3299** | HACHEREAU **6305** |
| GROSSEUR DE GRAIN MINIMALE **8317** | HACHERON **6305** |
| GROSSEUR DE LA PARTICULE **9089** | HACHETTE **6305** |
| GROSSEUR DES GRAINS D'ABRASIF **23** | HACHURE **6306** |
| GROSSEUR DU GRAIN **11522** | HACHURER **6304** |
| GROSSEUR DU GRAIN **6039** | HAFNIUM **6199** |
| GROSSISSEMENT **7937** | HALLE **1072** |
| GROSSISSEMENT **7935** | HALLE DE COULEE **2071** |
| GROSSISSEMENT D'UNE LENTILLE **7938** | HALLE DE COULEE **2077** |
| GROSSISSEMENT DU GRAIN **6035** | HALLE DE MONTAGE **770** |
| GROUPE (DE MACHINES ELECTRIQUES) **11213** | HALLE DE MONTAGE **773** |
| GROUPE DE MACHINES **6151** | HALO **6213** |
| GROUPE MOTEUR-GENERATEUR **8413** | HALOGENE **6214** |
| GROUPEMENT **9051** | HANGAR **11302** |
| GROUPEMENT **11199** | HAPPE **7548** |
| GROUPER EN QUANTITE **2956** | HARNAIS D'ENGRENAGES **7050** |
| GROUPER EN SERTIE **2957** | HARNAIS D'ENGRENAGES **5907** |
| GROUPES ELECTROGENES **4524** | HAUBAN **6187** |
| GRUE **3290** | HAUBANS DE SPHERE **12919** |
| GRUE A FLECHE **7224** | HAUSSE **10611** |
| GRUE A PORTIQUE **9641** | HAUT FOURNEAU **1311** |
| GRUE A POTENCE **13623** | HAUT VOLTAGE **6479** |
| GRUE DERRICK **3788** | HAUTE FREQUENCE **6467** |
| GRUE FIXE **5291** | HAUTE PERSSION **6473** |
| GRUE MOBILE **13161** | HAUTE TEMPERATURE **6476** |
| GRUE PIVOTANTE **11583** | HAUTE TENEUR (A) **6483** |
| GRUE ROULANTE **13161** | HAUTE TENSION **6478** |
| GRUE STATIONNAIRE **5291** | HAUTE TENSION **6479** |
| GRUES AGRICOLES **3294** | HAUTEUR **6420** |
| GRUGEAGE **3107** | HAUTEUR D'ACTION **13951** |
| GRUGEOIR **8677** | HAUTEUR D'ASCENSION **10611** |
| GRUMELAGE **1279** | HAUTEUR D'ASPIRATION D'UNE POMPE **12432** |
| GUEUSE **951** | HAUTEUR D'ELEVATION D'UNE POMPE **13061** |
| GUEUSE **9302** | HAUTEUR DE BUSE **8680** |
| GUEUSE **9298** | HAUTEUR DE CHUTE **6421** |
| GUIDAGE **6160** | HAUTEUR DE CONSTRUCTION **8924** |
| GUIDE **6160** | HAUTEUR DE DENT **13845** |

655 HUI

HAUTEUR DE DENT **13017**
HAUTEUR DE FACE **164**
HAUTEUR DE LA TETE D'UNE DENT **164**
HAUTEUR DE LEVAGE D'UNE GRUE **7551**
HAUTEUR DE REFOULEMENT D'UNE POMPE **4021**
HAUTEUR DU FLANC **3681**
HAUTEUR DU PIED DE DENT **3681**
HAUTEUR SOUS TRAVERSE **6423**
HAUTEUR TOTALE **8924**
HAUTEUR TOTALE DE LA DENT **3785**
HAYON **891**
HECTOLITRE **6415**
HECTOWATT **6416**
HECTOWATT-HEURE **6417**
HELIANTHINE **8223**
HELICE **6430**
HELICE PROPULSIVE **11041**
HELICO-MELANGEUR **9931**
HELICOIDE **6428**
HELIUM **6429**
HEMATITE **6434**
HEMATITE BRUNE **7596**
HEMATITE ROUGE **11865**
HEMICELLULE **6204**
HEMISPHERE **6438**
HERMETIQUE **303**
HERMETIQUEMENT CLOS **6447**
HERMINETTE **207**
HERSES (A CHAINEHERSES A ZIG-ZAGHERSES FLEXIBLE) **6303**
HETEROGENE **6451**
HETEROGENEITE **3170**
HEURES SUPPLEMENTAIRES **8964**
HEURT **11359**
HEXAEDRE **6463**
HEXAGONE **6453**
HEXAGONES EN ACIER ALLIE **374**
HOLMIUM **6551**
HOMOGENE **6555**
HOMOGENEISATION **6561**
HOMOGENEITE D'UN MATERIEL **13364**
HOMOGENEITE D'UNE SOUDURE **11821**
HONAGE AU JET DE VAPEUR **7653**
HORIZONTAL **6578**
HORLOGE POINCONNEUSE **12946**
HORNBLENDE **6598**
HORS D'AXE **8731**
HORS D'EQUERRE **8895**
HOTTE **1455**
HOUES (A TRACTEUR TRAINEE OU MONTEE) **6515**
HOUILLE **2558**

HOUILLE A COURTE FLAMME **11371**
HOUILLE A GAZ **5813**
HOUILLE A LONGUE FLAMME **7724**
HOUILLE ANTHRACITEUSE **11165**
HOUILLE COLLANTE **1835**
HOUILLE ECLATANTE **609**
HOUILLE GRASSE **1282**
HOUILLE MAIGRE **11168**
HOUILLE MAIGRE A COURTE FLAMME **11165**
HOUILLE MARECHALE **5543**
HOUILLE MENUE **11557**
HOUILLE NON COLLANTE **8626**
HOUILLE SECHE A LONGUE FLAMME **4344**
HOUILLE TOUT-VENANT **10841**
HOUILLERE **2566**
HUILAGE **8791**
HUILE **8743**
HUILE A ANTHRACENE **608**
HUILE A NOYAUX **3157**
HUILE ANIMALE **555**
HUILE BRUTE DE PETROLE **3412**
HUILE COMPOUND **2832**
HUILE D'ECLAIRAGE **7275**
HUILE D'EGOUTTAGE **13636**
HUILE D'OEILLETTE **9624**
HUILE DE BALEINE **13103**
HUILE DE BLANC DE BALEINE **11881**
HUILE DE CAMPHRE **1894**
HUILE DE CHENEVIS **6446**
HUILE DE COCO **2620**
HUILE DE COLZA **10204**
HUILE DE COTON **3222**
HUILE DE COUPE **3534**
HUILE DE FLUXAGE **5491**
HUILE DE GOUDRON **12681**
HUILE DE GOUDRON DE HOUILLE **2568**
HUILE DE GOUDRON DE LIGNITE **1668**
HUILE DE GRAISSAGE **7805**
HUILE DE GRAISSE **7409**
HUILE DE LIN **7631**
HUILE DE LIN A VERNIS **8786**
HUILE DE LIN BOUILLIE **8786**
HUILE DE NAVETTE **10204**
HUILE DE NETTOYAGE **2477**
HUILE DE PALME **9027**
HUILE DE PIED DE BOEUF **1450**
HUILE DE PIED DE MOUTON **1450**
HUILE DE PIERRE **9229**
HUILE DE PIN **10749**
HUILE DE POISSON **13103**
HUILE DE POMMES DE TERRE **5754**

# HUI

656

HUILE DE RESINE **10749**
HUILE DE RICIN **2086**
HUILE DE SAINDOUX **7409**
HUILE DE SCHISTE **11256**
HUILE DE SESAME **11212**
HUILE DE TREMPE **10099**
HUILE DE TREMPE **6295**
HUILE DE VITRIOL **12453**
HUILE EMULSIONNEE **4706**
HUILE EN EXCES **13636**
HUILE ENTHRACENIQUE **608**
HUILE EPUREE **10373**
HUILE ESSENTIELLE **4836**
HUILE FIXE **5294**
HUILE GRAPHITEE **6063**
HUILE GRASSE **5294**
HUILE H.D. **6403**
HUILE LAMPANTE DE PETROLE **7275**
HUILE LEGERE **7570**
HUILE LOURDE **6408**
HUILE LOURDE (POUR FORCE MOTRICE) **5714**
HUILE LOURDE DE PARAFFINE **9044**
HUILE LUBRIFIANTE **7805**
HUILE MINERALE **8304**
HUILE MINERALE BLONDE **2480**
HUILE MINERALE BRUNE **1291**
HUILE MINERALE POUR BROCHES **11908**
HUILE MIXTE **2832**
HUILE MOYENNE **8125**
HUILE PARAFFINE **9044**
HUILE POUR CYLINDRES **3572**
HUILE POUR FORER **4280**
HUILE POUR ISOLEMENT **6999**
HUILE POUR MACHINES **4755**
HUILE POUR MOTEUR **8415**
HUILE PROJETEE **11928**
HUILE RANCE **10197**
HUILE SICCATIVE **4357**
HUILE SOLAIRE **11753**
HUILE SOLUBLE **11810**
HUILE SPECIALE **6403**
HUILE VEGETALE **13512**
HUILE VERSEE **11928**
HUILE VOLATILE **4836**
HUILER **8744**
HUILES BLANCHES **13838**
HUILES CONDITIONNEES **8996**
HUMECTATION **13807**
HUMECTER **8347**
HUMIDIFIANT **6664**
HUMIDIFICATION **8348**

HUMIDITE ABSOLUE DE L'AIR **30**
HUMIDITE CRITIQUE **3346**
HUMIDITE DE L'AIR **6666**
HUMIDITE DE LA VAPEUR **13806**
HUMIDITE RELATIVE **10432**
HUMIDITE RELATIVE DE L'AIR **10433**
HUMUS **6667**
HYDRATATION DE LA CHAUX **11569**
HYDRATE **6674**
HYDRATE **6673**
HYDRATE D'ETHYLE **313**
HYDRATE DE BARYTE **1000**
HYDRATE DE BARYUM **1000**
HYDRATE DE CARBONE **1937**
HYDRATE DE CHAUX **1851**
HYDRATE DE MAGNESIE **7887**
HYDRATE DE METHYLE **13920**
HYDRATE DE POTASSIUM **9687**
HYDRATE DE SODIUM **11722**
HYDRATE DE VINYLE **84**
HYDRATE STANNEUX **12101**
HYDRAULIQUE **6676**
HYDRAULIQUE **6698**
HYDROCARBURE **6705**
HYDROCARBURES DE LA SERIE AROMATIQUE **2518**
HYDROCARBURES DE LA SERIE GRASSE **8806**
HYDROCARBURES NONSATURES (HYDROCARBURES
ETHYLENIQUESHYDROCARBURES ACETYLENIQUES) **13393**
HYDROCARBURES PARAFFINIQUES **10940**
HYDROCARBURES SATURES **10940**
HYDROCHLORATE **462**
HYDRODYNAMIQUE **6710**
HYDRODYNAMIQUE **6708**
HYDROFUGE **8349**
HYDROFUGE **13685**
HYDROGENE **6712**
HYDROGENE ARSENIE **730**
HYDROGENE ATOMIQUE **150**
HYDROGENE BICARBONE **4851**
HYDROGENE SULFURE **6717**
HYDROLYSE **6719**
HYDROMETALLURGIE **6721**
HYDROPHILE **6724**
HYDROSTATIQUE **6728**
HYDROXYDE **6673**
HYDRURE D'ACETYLE **84**
HYDRURE D'ETHYLE **4848**
HYDRURE DE BENZYLE **12983**
HYDRURE DE BUTYLE **1775**
HYDRURE DE CRESYLE **12983**
HYDRURE DE PROPYLE **9927**

657 IND

HYDRURE METHYLIQUE **8215**
HYGROMETRE **6729**
HYGROMETRICITE **6732**
HYGROMETRIQUE **6730**
HYPERBOLE **6734**
HYPERBOLIQUE **6735**
HYPERBOLOIDE A DEUX NAPPES **6740**
HYPERBOLOIDE A UNE NAPPE **6739**
HYPEREUTECTOIDE **6733**
HYPOAZOTIDE **8591**
HYPOAZOTIQUE **8591**
HYPOCYCLOIDE **6743**
HYPOEUTECTOIDE **6741**
HYPOSULFITE **12852**
HYPOSULFITE DE PLOMB **7474**
HYPOSULFITE DE SODIUM **11736**
HYPOTENUSE **6746**
HYPOTHESES DE BASE **12125**
HYSTERESIS **6747**
ICHTYOCOLLE **7174**
IGNIFUGE **5257**
IGNITION **6760**
ILLINIUM **6771**
ILLUMINATION **7574**
ILLUSTRATION **6778**
IMAGE **6779**
IMAGE NETTE **2479**
IMAGE REELLE **10259**
IMAGE VIRTUELLE **13572**
IMBIBER **6802**
IMBIBITION **6805**
IMBRULE **13344**
IMBRULES **6765**
IMCOMBUSTIBLE **6843**
IMMERGER **3968**
IMMERSION **3967**
IMMERSION **3975**
IMMERSION **3978**
IMMOBILISATION DES ECROUS ET BOULONS **7707**
IMPEDANCE **6794**
IMPERFECTIONS DE SURFACE **6464**
IMPERMEABILISATION **13691**
IMPERMEABILISER **13689**
IMPERMEABILITE **6797**
IMPERMEABILITE A L'EAU **6796**
IMPERMEABLE **13671**
IMPERMEABLE **6798**
IMPERMEABLE A L'HUMIDITE **8349**
IMPERMEABLE A LA LUMIERE **7572**
IMPONDERABLE **6800**
IMPREGNATION **6805**

IMPREGNATION DU BOIS AU SUBLIME CORROSIF PAR LE
   PROCEDE KYAN **7340**
IMPREGNER **6802**
IMPRIMANTE **9872**
IMPULSION **9979**
IMPULSION **6809**
IMPURETE **6814**
IMPURETES **6813**
INACCESSIBILITE **6820**
INACCESSIBLE **6821**
INALTERABLE **13723**
INATTAQUABILITE AUX ACIDES **10496**
INATTAQUABLE A L'EAU **13671**
INATTAQUABLE A L'HUILE **8792**
INATTAQUABLE AUX ACIDES **128**
INATTAQUABLE AUX INTEMPERIES **13723**
INCANDESCENCE **13832**
INCANDESCENCE **6822**
INCANDESCENT **5983**
INCASSABLE **13343**
INCIDENCE **6831**
INCLINABLE **6835**
INCLINAISON **6836**
INCLINAISON **11627**
INCLINAISON **1065**
INCLUSION **6840**
INCLUSION ALLONGEE **6841**
INCLUSION DE GAZ **5836**
INCLUSION DE SCORIE **4772**
INCLUSION GAZEUSE **5855**
INCLUSION SECONDAIRE **11106**
INCLUSIONS NON-METALLIQUES **8620**
INCOMBUSTIBILITE **6842**
INCOMPRESSIBILITE **6846**
INCOMPRESSIBLE **6847**
INCONGELABILITE **8634**
INCONGELABLE **8635**
INCONNUE **13391**
INCRUSTATION DE CALAMINE **5367**
INCRUSTATIONS DES CHAUDIERES **10969**
INCRUSTE **6857**
INDEPENDANTE **11190**
INDICATEUR **6879**
INDICATEUR **5768**
INDICATEUR **3837**
INDICATEUR A CADRAN **3840**
INDICATEUR A REFRACTION **10395**
INDICATEUR D'OUVERTURE **13153**
INDICATEUR DE CHARGE **2267**
INDICATEUR DE NIVEAU **13652**
INDICATEUR DE NIVEAU **7526**

## IND
658

INDICATEUR DE NIVEAU D'ESSENCE **5710**
INDICATEUR DE PHASES **9235**
INDICATEUR DE PRESSION **9820**
INDICATEUR DE PRESSION **6878**
INDICATEUR DE PRESSION D'HUILE **8768**
INDICATEUR DE TEMPERATURE **12834**
INDICATEUR DE TEMPERATURE **12726**
INDICATEUR DE TENSION DU RUBAN **976**
INDICATEUR DU SENS DE COURANT **9588**
INDICATEUR DU VIDE **13442**
INDICATIONS D'UN DESSIN **7524**
INDICE **6868**
INDICE (MATH.) **6864**
INDICE D'OCTANE **8723**
INDICE DE CETANE **2198**
INDICE DE RAPPEL **10367**
INDICE DE REFRACTION **6866**
INDICE DE VISCOSITE **8787**
INDICES DE MILLER **8282**
INDIUM **6885**
INDUCTANCE **6891**
INDUCTEUR **6898**
INDUCTION **6892**
INDUCTION ELECTROSIATIQUE **4644**
INDUCTION MAGNETIQUE **7908**
INDUCTION MAGNETOELECTRIQUE **4615**
INDUCTION MUTUELLE **8489**
INDUCTION PROPRE **11156**
INDUIRE **6888**
INDUIT **707**
INDUSTRIE **6903**
INDUSTRIE DE L'ALIMENTATION **5517**
INDUSTRIE DE TRANSFORMATION **9888**
INDUSTRIE MINIERE **8311**
INDUSTRIEL **7992**
INELASTIQUE **6904**
INERTE **8621**
INERTIE **6907**
INETANCHEITE **7491**
INFILTRATION **6805**
INFINIMENT GRAND **6910**
INFINIMENT PETIT **6911**
INFLAMMABILITE **6913**
INFLAMMABLE **6914**
INFLAMMABLE **6503**
INFLAMMATION **6760**
INFLAMMATION SPONTANEE **11956**
INFORMATION D'ENTREE NUMERIQUE **3942**
INFUSIBILITE **6917**
INFUSIBLE **6918**
INGENIEUR **4761**

INGENIEUR CHARGE DES VENTES **10898**
INGENIEUR DES CONSTRUCTIONS CIVILES **2443**
INGENIEUR DES MINES **8312**
INGENIEUR EN CHEF **4762**
INGENIEUR-CHIMISTE **2306**
INGENIEUR-CONSEIL **2989**
INGENIEUR-CONSTRUCTEUR **2443**
INGENIEUR-CONSTRUCTEUR EN CHEF **2329**
INGENIEUR-ELECTRICIEN **4540**
INGENIEUR-MECANICIEN **8102**
INHIBITEUR **6927**
INHIBITEUR **10510**
INHOMOGENEITE D'UN MATERIEL **7352**
INJECTER **6934**
INJECTEUR **6938**
INJECTEUR **7223**
INJECTEUR A TETON **9338**
INJECTEUR A TROUS **8452**
INJECTEUR DE POMPE **9993**
INJECTEUR DE VAPEUR **12171**
INJECTEUR HYDRAULIQUE **13657**
INJECTION **6935**
INOCULATION **6956**
INOXYDABILITE **10980**
INOXYDABLE **6959**
INSERER **7022**
INSERT **6965**
INSERTION **6965**
INSERTION **7023**
INSERTIONS DE BRASAGE **1578**
INSOLUBILITE **6983**
INSOLUBLE **6984**
INSPECTION **6985**
INSPECTION DE LA CHAUDIERE **1414**
INSPECTION PAR TREPANAGE **4877**
INSTALLATION D'EVACUATION **13485**
INSTALLATION DE CHAUFFAGE CENTRAL **6394**
INSTALLATION DE DISTRIBUTION D'EAU **13693**
INSTALLATION DE MACHINE A VAPEUR **12180**
INSTALLATION DE RECUIT **565**
INSTALLATION DE REFRIGERATION **10408**
INSTALLATION DE REVENU **6376**
INSTALLATION GENERATRICE DE COURANT **5920**
INSTALLATION INDUSTRIELLE OU USINE **9461**
INSTALLATION INTERIEURE **6988**
INSTALLATION POUR LA PRODUCTION DE FORCE MOTRICE **9739**
INSTALLATION POUR LE REFROIDISSEMENT DES EAUX DE CONDENSATION **3089**
INSTALLATIONS D'ETABLES **3277**
INSTALLATIONS SANITAIRES **10931**

ISO

INSTALLER LA COURROIE **11357**
INSTITUT BRITANNIQUE DE NORMALISATION **887**
INSTRUCTION **6992**
INSTRUCTION **6991**
INSTRUCTION DE SAUT **11546**
INSTRUCTIONS **8835**
INSTRUCTIONS RELATIVES AU TRAVAIL **11209**
INSTRUMENT A CENTRER **2166**
INSTRUMENT APERIODIQUE **635**
INSTRUMENT D'OPTIQUE **8844**
INSTRUMENT DE MESURE **8090**
INSTRUMENT DE VERIFICATION **5871**
INSTRUMENT ENREGISTREUR **10289**
INSTRUMENT POUR LA DETERMINATION DE LA VITESSE
  D'UN COURANT **3490**
INSTRUMENTS DE MATHEMATIQUES **8051**
INTEGRALE **7009**
INTEGRALE DEFINIE **3697**
INTEGRALE DOUBLE **4145**
INTEGRALE ELLIPTIQUE **4676**
INTEGRALE INDEFINIE **6858**
INTEGRALE LINEAIRE **7600**
INTEGRALE MULTIPLE **8465**
INTEGRALE SINGULIERE **11471**
INTEGRALE TRIPLE **13215**
INTEGRAPHE **7013**
INTEGRATEUR **7016**
INTEGRATION **7015**
INTEGRER **7014**
INTENSITE **7018**
INTENSITE D' ECLAIREMENT **6777**
INTENSITE D'UN COURANT **7021**
INTENSITE D'UNE FORCE **7939**
INTENSITE DE CHAMP **4506**
INTENSITE DE LA PESANTEUR **2975**
INTENSITE DE POLE **9596**
INTENSITE DE RADIATION **7019**
INTENSITE DU CHAMP **5144**
INTENSITE DU COURANT **478**
INTENSITE DU COURANT DE SOUDAGE **13780**
INTENSITE EN BOUGIES **1900**
INTENSITE LUMINEUSE **7822**
INTENSITE LUMINEUSE **7019**
INTENSITE LUMINEUSE PAR UNITE DE SURFACE **7104**
INTERCALATION **7023**
INTERCALER **7022**
INTERCEPTER DES RAYONS **7024**
INTERCHANGEABILITE **7025**
INTERCHANGEABILITE DE FABRICATION **7028**
INTERCHANGEABLE **7026**
INTERFACE **7032**

INTERFERENCE **7035**
INTERPOLATEUR **3995**
INTERPOLATION **7089**
INTERPOLATION CIRCULAIRE **2416**
INTERPOLATION LINEAIRE **7613**
INTERPOLATION PARABOLIQUE **9040**
INTERPOLER **7088**
INTERROMPRE LE CIRCUIT ELECTRIQUE **7090**
INTERRUPTEUR **12553**
INTERRUPTEUR A ACTION INSTANTANEE **11690**
INTERRUPTEUR-CONJONCTEUR **12553**
INTERRUPTEUR-DISJONCTEUR **12553**
INTERRUPTION **11546**
INTERRUPTION DE PASSAGE DU COURANT ELECTRIQUE
  **7093**
INTERRUPTION DE SERVICE **7092**
INTERSTICE **262**
INTERVALLE **7101**
INTERVALLE DE FUSION **8143**
INTERVALLE DE SOLIDIFICATION **11801**
INTERVALLE DE SOLIDIFICATION **5658**
INTERVALLE LIBRE **278**
INTRODUCTION D'AIR **12486**
INTRODUCTION MANUELLE DES DONNEES **7987**
INVAR **7105**
INVARIANT **7106**
INVENTEUR **7108**
INVENTION **7107**
INVENTION BREVETABLE **9122**
INVERSEUR DE MARCHE **10548**
INVERSEUR-PHARE-CODE **3963**
INVERSION (MATH.) **7110**
INVERSION DE MOUVEMENT **10552**
INVERTIR **2241**
IODE **7120**
IODURE D'ARGENT **11464**
IODURE DE MERCURE **8155**
IODURE DE POTASSIUM **9689**
ION **7121**
ION HYDROGENE **2112**
IONISATION **7124**
IONISATION **4596**
IONOGENE **7129**
IRIDIUM **7131**
IRRADIATION **7161**
IRRADIATION **10241**
IRREGULARITE DE SURFACE **12503**
IRREGULARITE DU MOUVEMENT **7167**
IRREGULIER **7163**
IRREVERSIBILITE **7168**
IRREVERSIBLE **7169**

## ISO

660

ISOBARE 7176
ISOCHRONE 7179
ISOCHRONISME 7178
ISOLANT 7006
ISOLANT 3898
ISOLANT 6998
ISOLATEUR 7006
ISOLATION 7003
ISOLATION 7184
ISOLATION 12287
ISOLATION A FROID 2700
ISOLATION CONTRE LE BRUIT 7004
ISOLATION CONTRE LE SON 7004
ISOLATION ELECTRIQUE 4545
ISOLATION THERMIQUE 7003
ISOLATION THERMIQUE 12810
ISOLEMENT 7003
ISOLER 6994
ISOMERE 7185
ISOMERIE 357
ISOMERIE 7186
ISOMORPHE 7190
ISOMORPHIE 7189
ISOMORPHISME 7191
ISOPLERE 7187
ISOTOPES 7197
ISOTROPE 7198
ITINERAIRE MARITIME 10810
IVOIRE 7199
JAMBE DE FORCE 12396
JANTE 10592
JANTE (COURONNE) D'UNE ROUE D'ENGRENAGE 10594
JANTE A BASE CREUSE 4322
JANTE D'UNE POULIE 10595
JANTE D'UNE ROUE 5088
JANTE DE ROUE 13818
JANTE DE VOLANT 10593
JAQUETTE 8354
JAUGE 5768
JAUGE 5871
JAUGE (NON- VARIABLE) 8625
JAUGE ANGLAISE 12089
JAUGE AVEC RENVOI A BAIN D'HUILE 8747
JAUGE D'AJUSTAGE 11225
JAUGE D'EXTERIEUR 5091
JAUGE D'EXTERIEUR 4955
JAUGE D'HUILE 8764
JAUGE D'HUILE 3979
JAUGE D'INTERIEUR 7066
JAUGE DE BIRMINGHAM POUR FILS METALLIQUES 12089
JAUGE DE CONTRAINTE (A FIL RESISTANT) 12329

JAUGE DE CONTRAINTE A RESISTANCE 10494
JAUGE DE CONTROLE 3053
JAUGE DE CONTROLE 12779
JAUGE DE FABRICATION 13967
JAUGE DE FABRICATION 13955
JAUGE DE FILETAGE 2760
JAUGE DE FILETAGE 11038
JAUGE DE PRECISION 9766
JAUGE DE RECEPTION 10015
JAUGE DE REFERENCE 10366
JAUGE DE REFERENCE 8035
JAUGE DE REVISION 5011
JAUGE DE TREFILERIE 13892
JAUGE DEMONTABLE 4048
JAUGE LIMITE DE TOLERANCE 3903
JAUGE MACHOIRE NORMALE 12088
JAUGE MAGNETIQUE 7905
JAUGE MICROMETRIQUE 8256
JAUGE NORMALE - TAMPON FILETE 12861
JAUGE NORMALE BAGUE FILETEE 12863
JAUGE PNEUMATIQUE 283
JAUGE POUR FILS METALLIQUES 13892
JAUGE POUR RAINURE DE CLAVETTE 7283
JAUGE POUR TOLES 11311
JAUGE TAMPON NORMALE 12087
JAUGE-FOURCHE A TOLERANCES 4148
JAUGE-MACHOIRE A UNE BRANCHE POUR COTES 'MINI' ET 'MAXI' 6607
JAUGE-MACHOIRE POUR FILETS 10693
JAUGE-MACHOIRE REGLABLE 186
JAUGE-TAMPON AU CONE METRIQUE 8230
JAUGE-TAMPON AU CONE MORSE 8392
JAUGE-TAMPON CONIQUE 7956
JAUGE-TAMPON CONIQUE 7076
JAUGE-TAMPON CONIQUE 12656
JAUGE-TAMPON CONIQUE AVEC TETON 12657
JAUGE-TAMPON DOUBLE A LIMITES 4137
JAUGEAGE 1867
JAUGEAGE A DISTANCE 10449
JAUGER 1861
JAUGES 5769
JAUGES POUR FILETAGES 12860
JAUNE DE CHROME 2375
JAUNE DE ZINC 14039
JET COMPACT 11787
JET D'AIR 242
JET D'EAU 13656
JET DE COULEE 12004
JET DE VAPEUR 12170
JET LIQUIDE 7221
JETER DE LA FLAMME 5359

661             **JOU**

JEU **11213**
JEU **13873**
JEU **358**
JEU **2483**
JEU (MOUVEMENT) **9516**
JEU A FOND DE FILET **12858**
JEU A FOND DES DENTS **1489**
JEU A LA CRETE **3335**
JEU AXIAL **4727**
JEU D'ENGRENAGES **5901**
JEU D'UNE SOUPAPE **13154**
JEU DE COIFFAGE **358**
JEU DE COIFFAGE **2483**
JEU DE LABORATOIRE **7345**
JEU DE MONTAGE **9516**
JEU DE POIDS **11219**
JEU DES SOUPAPES **12673**
JEU DU FOND DE LA DENT **1489**
JEU DU PISTON **7519**
JEU ENTRE DENTS **914**
JEU ENTRE LES POINTS DE CONTACT DES DENTS **5349**
JEU ETALON **8036**
JEU INUTILE **916**
JEU LATERAL DES ARBRES **4735**
JEU NUISIBLE **916**
JEU PERNICIEUX **916**
JEU TOTAL PERDU **13063**
JEU UTILE **9516**
JOINT **1500**
JOINT **5863**
JOINT **6127**
JOINT **7247**
JOINT (DE RETENUE) D'HUILE **8776**
JOINT (POINT DE JONCTION) **7238**
JOINT A BAGUE DE CAOUTCHOUC **10820**
JOINT A BAGUE DE PLOMB MATEE POUR TUYAUTERIES **7464**
JOINT A CARDAN **13385**
JOINT A CHICANE **7347**
JOINT A DOUBLE TOURNEVIS **8794**
JOINT A ECLISSES **1782**
JOINT A EMBOITEMENT **11900**
JOINT A INSERTION **3159**
JOINT A LABYRINTHE **7347**
JOINT A RECOUVREMENT **7397**
JOINT A RECOUVREMENT SOUDE D'UN SEUL COTE **11504**
JOINT A RECOUVREMENT SOUDE DES DEUX COTES **4171**
JOINT A ROTULE **953**
JOINT ABOUTE SOUDE D'UN SEUL COTE **1779**
JOINT ABOUTE SOUDE DES DEUX COTES **1777**
JOINT ANNULAIRE **10604**

JOINT AU MASTIC DE FONTE **10867**
JOINT AUTOCLAVE **7963**
JOINT BOUT A BOUT **1776**
JOINT COLLE **5986**
JOINT COULISSANT **11617**
JOINT D'ETANCHEITE **5863**
JOINT D'OLDHAM **8794**
JOINT DE CARDAN **6573**
JOINT DE CULASSE **3570**
JOINT DE DILATATION **4918**
JOINT DE SEPARATION D'UN PALIER **7241**
JOINT DE SOUDURE EN J FERMEE **1790**
JOINT DE SOUDURE PAR BOSSAGES **9915**
JOINT DE TUBES **9347**
JOINT EN ANGLE EXTERIEUR **3179**
JOINT ETANCHE **12921**
JOINT FUSIBLE **2991**
JOINT HYDRAULIQUE **13675**
JOINT METALLOPLASTIQUE **3134**
JOINT PLASTIQUE **4482**
JOINT PLASTIQUE **11078**
JOINT POUR TUYAUTERIE **9355**
JOINT RIGIDE **10589**
JOINT SECONDAIRE D'ETANCHEITE **13720**
JOINT SOUDE **13767**
JOINT SOUDE **13774**
JOINT SOUDE **13776**
JOINT SOUDE **7237**
JOINT SOUDE A DOUBLE CLIN **4141**
JOINT SOUDE A SIMPLE CLIN **5720**
JOINT SOUPLE **5416**
JOINT SPHERIQUE **953**
JOINT SUR TRANCHES **4445**
JOINT TORIQUE **8703**
JOINT UNIVERSEL **6573**
JONC D'ARRET **11692**
JONC DES INDES **10236**
JONCTION **3254**
JONCTION BOUT A BOUT **1778**
JONCTION DES COURROIES **1151**
JONCTION DES COURROIES PAR COLLAGE **2143**
JONCTION DES COURROIES PAR LANIERES EN CUIR **7348**
JONCTION DES COURROIES PAR RIVET **10555**
JONCTIONNEMENT DES COURROIES **1142**
JOUE D'UN RABOT **5093**
JOUE D'UNE CHAINE A ROULEAUX **11416**
JOUE D'UNE POULIE **5332**
JOUE D'UNE ROUE D'ENGRENAGE **11400**
JOUE DE CINTRAGE **1183**
JOUE DE CINTRAGE **1529**
JOUE DE CONTACT **3003**

## JOU

JOUE DU COUSSINET D'UNE BUTEE **2723**
JOULE **7255**
JOUR **3616**
JOUR DE LA SIGNATURE DU BREVET **3617**
JOURNEE DE TRAVAIL **11347**
JUMELLE **2491**
JUMELLE DE RESSORT **11991**
JUMELLES **11233**
JUPE **11547**
JUPE (D'UN RESERVOIR) **11549**
JUTE **7268**
KAOLIN **2340**
KAOLIN (POUR LES PNEUS) **13842**
KEROSENE **7275**
KIESEGUHR **7292**
KILODYNE **7296**
KILOGRAMME **7297**
KILOGRAMMETRE **7299**
KILOMETRE **7300**
KILOVOLT **7301**
KILOVOLT-AMPERE **7302**
KILOWATT **7303**
KILOWATT-HEURE **7304**
KIP = 1000 LIVRES = 453,59 KG **7316**
KLAXON **6592**
KLINGERITE **7318**
KRYPTON **7339**
LABILE **7343**
LABORATOIRE **7344**
LACET **7741**
LACUNE **6530**
LACUNE **13585**
LACUNE **13433**
LACUNES (AFNOR) **6536**
LAINE (DE MOUTON) **13932**
LAINE DE BOIS **13923**
LAINE DE VERRE **5966**
LAINE MINERALE **11566**
LAIT DE CHAUX **8274**
LAIT DE CIMENT **6152**
LAITIER **11561**
LAITIER **1312**
LAITIER **2397**
LAITIER GRANULE **6055**
LAITON **1562**
LAITON **14008**
LAITON A FORGER **5558**
LAITON A QUALITE D'EMBOUTISSAGE **3690**
LAITON ALPHA **399**
LAITON ALPHA-BETA **403**
LAITON ALPHA-BETA **8511**

LAITON AU MANGANESE **7967**
LAITON AU NICKEL **8559**
LAITON BETA **1216**
LAITON COULE **2031**
LAITON D'ALUMINIUM **419**
LAITON D'ETIRAGE **4232**
LAITON DE BASE **8056**
LAITON DE DECOLLETAGE **5645**
LAITON DE FAIBLE ALLIAGE **7768**
LAITON DE L'AMIRAUTE **8511**
LAITON DE MARINE **198**
LAITON DE QUALITE **6480**
LAITON DE RESSORT **11978**
LAITON EN FEUILLES **11307**
LAITON POUR CARTOUCHES **2016**
LAITON POUR HORLOGES **2505**
LAITON ROUGE **2824**
LAITON ROUGE **10325**
LAITON SILICEUX **11443**
LAMAGE **11960**
LAMBAGE (DE TOLES) **1681**
LAME **1299**
LAME D'ACCUMULATEUR **81**
LAME D'UN OUTIL TRANCHANT **1300**
LAME D'UN RESSORT **9492**
LAME D'UNE CISAILLE **11282**
LAME DE CUIVRE **3131**
LAME DE RESSORT **11977**
LAME DE SCIE **10952**
LAME DE VERRE **11589**
LAME POUR SCIE A METAUX **6197**
LAME TRANCHANTE **1300**
LAMELLAIRE **7372**
LAMELLE **7371**
LAMELLE **5303**
LAMINAGE **10696**
LAMINAGE A CHAUD **6656**
LAMINAGE A CHAUD **6638**
LAMINAGE A FAIBLE PRESSION **9330**
LAMINAGE A FROID **2698**
LAMINAGE CONTINU **3035**
LAMINAGE DE LINGOTS **2642**
LAMINAGE EN PAQUET **8994**
LAMINAGE EN SANDWICH **10929**
LAMINAGE FINISSEUR **5215**
LAMINAGE STRATIFIE **10929**
LAMINAGE TRANSVERSAL **3384**
LAMINE **7375**
LAMINE A FROID **2716**
LAMINER **10665**
LAMINER A CHAUD **6636**

# 663    LES

LAMINER A FROID **2694**
LAMINOIR **10701**
LAMINOIR A BILLETTES **1245**
LAMINOIR A BLOOMS **1348**
LAMINOIR A BRAMES **11555**
LAMINOIR A FORGER **5563**
LAMINOIR A POLIR **9456**
LAMINOIR A SIX CYLINDRES **2543**
LAMINOIR A TUBES **9358**
LAMINOIR FINISSEUR **5222**
LAMINOIR POUR TOLES FORTES **6410**
LAMINOIR REDUCTEUR **11508**
LAMINOIR SENDZIMIR **11181**
LAMINOIR TRANSVERSAL **1642**
LAMINOIR UNIVERSEL **13386**
LAMPE **13453**
LAMPE **7384**
LAMPE A ACETYLENE **95**
LAMPE A ALCOOL **11923**
LAMPE A ARC **672**
LAMPE A ESSENCE MINERALE **9224**
LAMPE A FILAMENT DE CARBONE **1951**
LAMPE A FILAMENT DE TUNGSTENE **13264**
LAMPE A FILAMENT METALLIQUE **8181**
LAMPE A GAZ **6828**
LAMPE A GAZ D'ECLAIRAGE **5826**
LAMPE A INCANDESCENCE **6828**
LAMPE A INCANDESCENCE **6825**
LAMPE A PETROLE **9227**
LAMPE A SOUDER **11766**
LAMPE A VAPEUR DE MERCURE **8167**
LAMPE A VAPEUR DE MERCURE EN QUARTZ **10080**
LAMPE AU NEON **8536**
LAMPE DIODE **3965**
LAMPE ELECTRIQUE **4516**
LANCE **8679**
LANCE A OXYGENE **8981**
LANCEMENT D'UN MOTEUR **12130**
LANCER UN MOTEUR **12114**
LANCEUR **9336**
LANGAGE DE PROGRAMMATION ADAPT **159**
LANGAGE DE PROGRAMMATION APT **656**
LANGUE D'ASPIC **5380**
LANGUETTE **5059**
LANGUETTE ET RAINURE **12989**
LANIERE POUR COURROIES **7500**
LANOLINE **7391**
LANTERNE **7393**
LANTERNE D'UNE VANNE **7392**
LANTERNE DE PRESSE-ETOUPE **7392**
LANTHANE **7394**

LAQUE **7354**
LAQUE DE BRONZE **6001**
LAQUE EN ECAILLES **11338**
LAQUE EN FEUILLES **11338**
LAQUE EN PLAQUES **11338**
LAQUE PLATE **11338**
LAQUER **7353**
LARDONS **5940**
LARGET **11306**
LARGETS EN ACIER ALLIE **378**
LARGETS EN ACIER AU CARBONE **1956**
LARGEUR **13850**
LARGEUR D'UNE SOUDURE **12887**
LARGEUR D'USINAGE **7867**
LARGEUR DE CONSTRUCTION **8926**
LARGEUR DE LA SOUDURE DE BASE **10727**
LARGEUR INTERIEURE D'UN MAILLON **6982**
LARGEUR TOTALE **8926**
LARGEUR UTILE DE LAMINAGE **13427**
LATEX **7425**
LATTE **7426**
LAVAGE (DU SABLE) **4681**
LAVE **7437**
LAVE-GLACE **13870**
LAVER (LES MINERAIS) **2550**
LAVER A GRANDE EAU **10607**
LAVER UN DESSIN **2742**
LAVEUSES ET TRIEURS DE RACINES ET DE FRUITS **5704**
LAVIS **12965**
LECTEURS OPTIQUES **8847**
LECTURE **10254**
LEDEBURITE **7504**
LEGENDE **7513**
LEIN (GEOL.): CIMENT **1253**
LEMNISCATE **2029**
LEMNISCATE **7514**
LENTILLE **7522**
LENTILLE A BORD EPAIS **4095**
LENTILLE A BORD MINCE **2910**
LENTILLE BICONCAVE **1237**
LENTILLE BICONVEXE **1238**
LENTILLE CONVERGENTE **2909**
LENTILLE CONVERGENTE **2910**
LENTILLE DE CONCENTRATION DES ELECTRONS **4626**
LENTILLE DE SOUDURE **13764**
LENTILLE DIVERGENTE **4095**
LENTILLE DIVERGENTE **9914**
LENTILLE PLAN-CONCAVE **9458**
LENTILLE PLAN-CONVEXE **9459**
LESSIVAGE **7677**
LESSIVAGE **7446**

# LES

664

LESSIVE 7835
LESSIVE 2120
LESSIVE DE POTASEE 9671
LESSIVE DE SOUDE 11712
LESSIVER 7676
LESSIVEUR 3938
LEVAGE 6553
LEVE-GLACE 13867
LEVE-ROUE 10121
LEVEE 10611
LEVEE DE CAME 1884
LEVEE DE LA SOUPAPE 7544
LEVEE DE TERRE 3945
LEVER 6517
LEVIER 7530
LEVIER A CLIQUET 10223
LEVIER A CONTREPOIDS 13751
LEVIER A COULISSE 11638
LEVIER A DEUX BRAS 4147
LEVIER A FOURCHE 5569
LEVIER A GENOUILLERE 12979
LEVIER A PEDALE 5521
LEVIER A POIGNEE 6239
LEVIER A SONNETTE 1131
LEVIER A TROIS BRAS 4131
LEVIER ARTICULE 12979
LEVIER COUDE 1131
LEVIER D'ATTAQUE DE DIRECTION 12227
LEVIER D'AVANCE AUTOMATIQUE 842
LEVIER D'INVERSION DE L'AVANCE 5073
LEVIER DE CHANGEMENT DE MARCHE 10549
LEVIER DE COMMANDE 9414
LEVIER DE DEBRAYAGE 4035
LEVIER DE DECLENCHEMENT 10438
LEVIER DE DEMARRAGE 12120
LEVIER DE DESEMBRAYAGE 4035
LEVIER DE FREIN 1537
LEVIER DE MANOEUVRE 8833
LEVIER DE PURGE LIBRE 7553
LEVIER DE SOUPAPE 13465
LEVIER DE VIS 12985
LEVIER DOUBLE 4147
LEVIER DROIT 12306
LEVIER OSCILLANT 10656
LEVIER ROULANT 10686
LEVIER SELECTEUR DES AVANCES 5065
LEVIGATION 4681
LEVIGATIONS 7537
LEVOGYRE 7365
LEVRES DE COUPES 7633
LIAISON 5416

LIAISON RIGIDE 10589
LIAISON SOUDEE 13772
LIAISONS DE COURROIE 1142
LIANT 1253
LIANT 1445
LIANT 1250
LIANT DE NOYAUTAGE 3145
LIANT DURCISSANT A L'AIR 301
LIANT SEC 4342
LIBER 1056
LIBERANT (SE) (CHIM.) 8497
LICENCE D'EXPLOITATION 7539
LIEGE 3173
LIEU D'ETABLISSEMENT 9423
LIEU D'INSTALLATION 9423
LIEU DE MONTAGE 9423
LIEU DE TRAVAIL 13943
LIEU GEOMETRIQUE 7715
LIGNE 7597
LIGNE 4523
LIGNE 10812
LIGNE 179
LIGNE A HAUTE TENSION 6501
LIGNE AERIENNE 212
LIGNE AERODYNAMIQUE 12351
LIGNE ATMOSPHERIQUE 798
LIGNE BRISEE 7166
LIGNE CONDUCTRICE 4523
LIGNE COURBE DE VOLUME CONSTANT 7187
LIGNE COURBE ISOTHERMIQUE 7193
LIGNE D'ADMISSION DE LA VAPEUR 199
LIGNE D'ARBRES 7607
LIGNE D'ECHAPPEMENT DE LA VAPEUR 4892
LIGNE D'ECLAIRAGE 4519
LIGNE D'ECOULEMENT 5457
LIGNE D'ENGRENEMENT 7602
LIGNE D'INSPECTION 6986
LIGNE D'INTERSECTION 7605
LIGNE DE COLLIMATION 7601
LIGNE DE COMPRESSION 2857
LIGNE DE COTE 3957
LIGNE DE FERMETURE 2536
LIGNE DE FORCE 7603
LIGNE DE FUITE 324
LIGNE DE JOINT 9093
LIGNE DE JONCTION DES TOLES 11084
LIGNE DE NULLE PRESSION (DU DIAGRAMME D'INDICATEUR) 14029
LIGNE DE RIVETS 10813
LIGNE DE ROULEAUX D'AMENEE 4775
LIGNE DE SECOURS 4690

665 LIM

LIGNE DE TRANSMISSION **7607**
LIGNE DE TRANSPORT A GRANDE DISTANCE **4521**
LIGNE DE TRANSPORT DE FORCE **4526**
LIGNE DE TRUSQUINAGE **7604**
LIGNE DROITE **12310**
LIGNE DU LIQUIDUS **7661**
LIGNE HORIZONTALE **6585**
LIGNE ISENTROPIQUE **7173**
LIGNE ISOCLINE **7181**
LIGNE ISODYNAME **7182**
LIGNE ISODYNAMIQUE **7182**
LIGNE NEUTRE **8545**
LIGNE PLEINE **5725**
LIGNE POINTILLEE **4125**
LIGNE POLYGONALE **9611**
LIGNE PONCTUEE **4125**
LIGNE SOUTERRAINE **13353**
LIGNE UN TRAIT **2205**
LIGNES D'HARTMANN **7815**
LIGNES DE LUDERS **7815**
LIGNES DE LUDERS **7622**
LIGNES DE LUDERS **12371**
LIGNES LIMITES **5689**
LIGNEUX **7578**
LIGNINE **7577**
LIGNITE **7578**
LIGNITE NOIR **9405**
LIGNITE PARFAIT **1665**
LIGNONE **7577**
LIGNOSE **7577**
LIGROINE **7580**
LIMAGE **5153**
LIMAILLE **5155**
LIMBE **6026**
LIME **5148**
LIME A ALUMINIUM **422**
LIME A BARRETTES **1903**
LIME A BISEAU **1903**
LIME A COTES LISSES **10878**
LIME A DOUBLE TAILLE **4133**
LIME A GROSSE TAILLE **10774**
LIME A LOSANGE **11623**
LIME A MAIN **6234**
LIME A SCIES **10954**
LIME A TAILLE BATARDE **1057**
LIME A TAILLE CROISEE **4133**
LIME A TAILLE DEMI-DOUCE **11100**
LIME A TAILLE DOUCE **11680**
LIME A TAILLE MOYENNE **8266**
LIME A TAILLE RUDE **10774**
LIME A TAILLE TRES DOUCE **12467**

LIME AIGUILLE **8519**
LIME CARREE **12019**
LIME D'ENTREE **13625**
LIME DEMI-RONDE **6208**
LIME FEUILLE DE SAUGE **3392**
LIME FINE **11680**
LIME FORTE **10774**
LIME LARGE **9067**
LIME OLIVE **13041**
LIME PLATE **5381**
LIME PLATE MAIN **9067**
LIME PLATE POINTUE **5390**
LIME POINTUE **12648**
LIME QUATRE-QUARTS **12019**
LIME QUEUE DE RAT **10216**
LIME RONDE **10796**
LIME ROTATIVE **10755**
LIME TIERS-POINT **13189**
LIME TIERS-POINT **12870**
LIME TROIS-QUARTS **13189**
LIME 4/4 **12019**
LIME-COUTEAU **7324**
LIME-FRAISE **1390**
LIMER **5149**
LIMITE **7587**
LIMITE (CONVENTIONNELLE) DE FLUAGE **3325**
LIMITE (D'ELASTICITE) PROPORTIONNELLE **9936**
LIMITE D'ABSORPTION **50**
LIMITE D'ACCEPTATION **69**
LIMITE D'ALLONGEMENT **9923**
LIMITE D'ECOULEMENT **5456**
LIMITE D'ECOULEMENT **14011**
LIMITE D'ECOULEMENT **14012**
LIMITE D'ECRASEMENT **2873**
LIMITE D'ELASTICITE **4481**
LIMITE D'ELASTICITE PROPORTIONNELLE **7590**
LIMITE D'ENDURANCE **4741**
LIMITE D'ENDURANCE OU DE FATIGUE **5050**
LIMITE D'ERREURS **7589**
LIMITE DE FATIGUE **5053**
LIMITE DE FATIGUE PAR CORROSION **3188**
LIMITE DE REACTION **10249**
LIMITE DE SATURATION **7591**
LIMITE DE TEMPERATURE **7592**
LIMITE ELASTIQUE **14011**
LIMITE ELASTIQUE **14012**
LIMITE ELASTIQUE **14013**
LIMITE ELASTIQUE **4481**
LIMITE ELASTIQUE **5456**
LIMITE ELASTIQUE **7588**
LIMITE ELASTIQUE CONVENTIONNELLE **9923**

# LIM

LIMITE ELASTIQUE CONVENTIONNELLE OU APPARENTE 9922
LIMITE ELASTIQUE MINIMALE GARANTIE 8308
LIMITE TARDIVE 14011
LIMITE/JOINT DE GRAIN 6033
LIMITER 6926
LIMITES DE TOLERANCE 7595
LIMITEUR OU REGULATEUR DE DEBIT 4879
LIMON 12377
LIMON 12052
LIMONITE 7596
LIMONITE ARGILEUSE 2467
LIMOUSINE 11521
LIN 5412
LIN DE LA NOUVELLE-ZELANDE 8550
LINGOT 6919
LINGOT 2069
LINGOT BRULE 1748
LINGOT D'ACIER 12210
LINGOT DE CUIVRE 3120
LINGOT DE DEPART 1834
LINGOT ENTAILLE 8674
LINGOT EPROUVETTE 12777
LINGOT PLAT DE CUIVRE 3129
LINGOT-EPROUVETTE (EN FORME DE QUILLE DE NAVIRE) 7273
LINGOTIERE 6923
LINGOTIERE 8422
LINOLEUM 7630
LIQUATION 7635
LIQUEFACTION 5764
LIQUEFACTION D'UN GAZ 7636
LIQUEFIABLE 7639
LIQUEFIABLE 5756
LIQUEFIER 8135
LIQUEFIER UN GAZ 7640
LIQUETURE 8421
LIQUEUR NORMALE 12084
LIQUEUR TITREE 12084
LIQUIDE 7642
LIQUIDE 7641
LIQUIDE CAUSTIQUE 2119
LIQUIDE D'EXTRACTION 4965
LIQUIDE DE DECAPAGE 7293
LIQUIDE FILTRE 5181
LIQUIDE OBTURATEUR 11082
LIQUIDE PENETRANT 9169
LIQUIDE SURFONDU 12464
LIQUIDES 7660
LIQUIDUS 7661
LIRE 12692

LIRE 10252
LISSAGE 11686
LISSAGE 5408
LISSE 13035
LISSER 11679
LIT-PLACARD 1739
LITHARGE 7663
LITHIUM 7664
LITRE 7669
LIVRE-PIED 5522
LIXIVIATION 7677
LIXIVIER 7676
LOCOMOBILE 9640
LOCOMOTION 7712
LOCOMOTION A BENZINE 9225
LOCOMOTIVE 7713
LOCOMOTIVE A AIR COMPRIME 2844
LOCOMOTIVE A ESSENCE 9225
LOCOMOTIVE A VAPEUR 12173
LOCOMOTIVE ELECTRIQUE 4520
LOCOMOTIVE ELECTRIQUE A ACCUMULATEURS 79
LOCOMOTIVE SANS FOYER 5256
LOESS 7716
LOGARITHME 7718
LOGARITHME DECIMAL 2788
LOGARITHME HYPERBOLIQUE 8509
LOGARITHME NATUREL 8509
LOGARITHME VULGAIRE 2788
LOGEMENT 6660
LOGEMENT D'UNE CLAVETTE 7282
LOI BINOMIALE 1258
LOI DE BRAGG 1525
LOI DE HOOKE 6574
LOI DES VALEURS EXTREMES 4968
LOI EXPONENTIELLE 4941
LONGERON 5627
LONGRINE 7734
LONGUE-VIS 7726
LONGUEUR 7516
LONGUEUR D'ARC 7517
LONGUEUR D'ONDE 13700
LONGUEUR D'ONDE MINIMALE 8309
LONGUEUR D'ONDES CRITIQUE 10072
LONGUEUR DE CONSTRUCTION 8925
LONGUEUR DE LA FLECHE 7225
LONGUEUR DE REFERENCE 5878
LONGUEUR DE RUPTURE 1584
LONGUEUR DU BRAS DE LEVIER 7536
LONGUEUR DU CORDON 7520
LONGUEUR FOCALE 5500
LONGUEUR LIBRE 7518

667 MAC

LONGUEUR TOTALE **8925**
LONGUEUR UTILE **13424**
LONGUEUR/LARGEUR DE LA DENT **1579**
LOPIN **1301**
LOQUET **7414**
LOSANGE **10568**
LOT **7766**
LOT DE COULEE **1059**
LOUCHE **1378**
LOUCHE **1347**
LOUCHISSEMENT **2541**
LOUP **10896**
LOUP **11550**
LOUPE **951**
LOUPE **7936**
LOUPE (MET.) **1345**
LUBRIFIANT **1250**
LUBRIFIANT **7800**
LUBRIFIANT DE MOULE **9092**
LUBRIFIANT DE RODAGE **6112**
LUBRIFICATION **7803**
LUBRIFICATION **7808**
LUBRIFIER **7801**
LUMEN **7818**
LUMIERE **7560**
LUMIERE (D'UN CYLINDRE A VAPEUR) **12176**
LUMIERE A INCANDESCENCE **6826**
LUMIERE ANODIQUE **9660**
LUMIERE ARTIFICIELLE **734**
LUMIERE D'ADMISSION **200**
LUMIERE D'ECHAPPEMENT **4895**
LUMIERE D'UN RABOT **8434**
LUMIERE DE DRUMMOND **8987**
LUMIERE DE L'ARC VOLTAIQUE **673**
LUMIERE DIFFUSE **3955**
LUMIERE DIFFUSE **3927**
LUMIERE DU GAZ **5827**
LUMIERE DU GAZ A INCANDESCENCE **6829**
LUMIERE DU JOUR **3622**
LUMIERE ELECTRIQUE **4517**
LUMIERE OXHYDRIQUE **8987**
LUMIERE POLARISEE **9585**
LUMIERE REFLECHIE **10383**
LUMINESCENCE **7819**
LUNETTE A SUIVRE **5514**
LUNETTE ARRIERE **899**
LUNETTE D'APPROCHE **10398**
LUNETTE DE CALIBRE **2721**
LUNETTE FIXE **12154**
LUNETTE MOBILE **5514**
LUNETTE VERIFICATRICE **2721**

LUNETTES D'ALESAGE **1474**
LUNETTES DE PROTECTION **5992**
LUT **8038**
LUTECIUM **7833**
LUTER **2134**
LUTTER **7831**
LUX **7834**
LYRE (D'UN TUYAU) **7832**
LYRE DE COMPENSATION **4913**
LYRE DE DILATATION **4913**
MACERATION **7837**
MACERER **7836**
MACHEFER (FOND) **2500**
MACHINE **6345**
MACHINE A ACCOUPLEMENT DIRECT **3982**
MACHINE A AFFUTER LES OUTILS **13002**
MACHINE A ALESER **1471**
MACHINE A ALESER EN CREUX **1013**
MACHINE A BOBINER LES INDUITS **709**
MACHINE A BOIS **13925**
MACHINE A BORDER **3323**
MACHINE A BOUVETER **12992**
MACHINE A BROYER **3419**
MACHINE A CALCULER **1859**
MACHINE A CALIBRER **1865**
MACHINE A CANNELER **6138**
MACHINE A CENTRER ET A DRESSER **2188**
MACHINE A CHAMBRE FROIDE **2670**
MACHINE A CHANFREINER LES TOLES **9484**
MACHINE A CHANTOURNER **5665**
MACHINE A CHARGER LES FOURS **2268**
MACHINE A CINTRER **1184**
MACHINE A CINTRER LES TOLES **9480**
MACHINE A CISAILLER **11292**
MACHINE A CISAILLER LES FERS ET PROFILES **7136**
MACHINE A CISAILLER LES METAUX EN FEUILLES OU EN BANDES **11323**
MACHINE A COLONNE D'EAU **13670**
MACHINE A COMMANDE INDEPENDANTE **6863**
MACHINE A COMMANDE PAR CABLE **10736**
MACHINE A COMMANDE PAR COURROIE **1145**
MACHINE A COMMANDE PAR ENGRENAGE **5893**
MACHINE A CONCASSER **3419**
MACHINE A COUPER LES TUBES **9349**
MACHINE A COURANT ALTERNATIF **407**
MACHINE A COURANT CONTINU **3021**
MACHINE A COURBER **1391**
MACHINE A CYLINDRE OSCILLANT **8880**
MACHINE A DEBOURRER **3153**
MACHINE A DECOUPER **6012**
MACHINE A DECOUPER AUTOGENE **833**

# MAC

668

MACHINE A DEGAUCHIR **12515**
MACHINE A DENOYAUTER **3153**
MACHINE A DETENTE **4924**
MACHINE A DEUX CYLINDRES **13313**
MACHINE A DIVISER **4102**
MACHINE A DIVISER LES CERCLES **4103**
MACHINE A DIVISER LES LIGNES DROITES **4104**
MACHINE A DOUBLE EFFET **4165**
MACHINE A DOUBLE EXPANSION **4168**
MACHINE A DRESSER **6113**
MACHINE A DRESSER **12372**
MACHINE A DRESSER ET A SURFACER **9442**
MACHINE A DRESSER LES ARBRES **11245**
MACHINE A ECRASER **3419**
MACHINE A ELARGIR LES TUBES **9352**
MACHINE A EMBOUTIR **5346**
MACHINE A ENROULER LES RESSORTS A BOUDIN **13901**
MACHINE A ENTAILLER LES TOLES **11319**
MACHINE A EQUICOURANT **12407**
MACHINE A EQUILIBRER **940**
MACHINE A ESSAYER **12793**
MACHINE A ESSAYER LES HUILES **8785**
MACHINE A ESSAYER LES RESSORTS ET LES FILS **11975**
MACHINE A ETIRER LES BARRES ET LES TUBES **982**
MACHINE A EXPANSION **4924**
MACHINE A FAIBLE COURSE **11374**
MACHINE A FAIRE LES BOURRELETS **1089**
MACHINE A FAIRE LES CHAINES EN FIL DE FER **13885**
MACHINE A FAIRE LES FEUILLES DE PLACAGE **13525**
MACHINE A FAIRE LES GRILLAGES **13897**
MACHINE A FAIRE LES JOINTS **7246**
MACHINE A FAIRE LES RAINURES ET LANGUETTES **12992**
MACHINE A FAIRE LES TENONS **12742**
MACHINE A FAIRE LES TENONS EN QUEUE D'ARONDE **4179**
MACHINE A FIL BARBELE **988**
MACHINE A FILETER **12869**
MACHINE A FILETER ET TARAUDER **11066**
MACHINE A FORER **13182**
MACHINE A FORER **4279**
MACHINE A FORER ET ALESER LES TROUS PROFONDS **3687**
MACHINE A FORGER **5561**
MACHINE A FRAISER **8291**
MACHINE A FRAISER A CONSOLE **7322**
MACHINE A FRAISER LES RAINURES **7281**
MACHINE A FRAISER LES VIS **11036**
MACHINE A FROID **10407**
MACHINE A GLACE **6750**
MACHINE A GRAND DEBIT **6466**
MACHINE A GRAND RENDEMENT **6466**

MACHINE A GRANDE COURSE **7731**
MACHINE A GRANDE VITESSE **6496**
MACHINE A GRATTER **11012**
MACHINE A HAUTE PRESSION **6492**
MACHINE A INJECTION PNEUMATIQUE **299**
MACHINE A LIMER **5154**
MACHINE A MANCHONNAGE DIRECT **3982**
MACHINE A MANDRINER LES BRIDES **5333**
MACHINE A MARCHE LENTE **7789**
MACHINE A MARCHE RAPIDE **6496**
MACHINE A MESURER WHITWORTH **13843**
MACHINE A METAUX **8178**
MACHINE A MEULER **6113**
MACHINE A MEULER A AXE HORIZONTAL **6588**
MACHINE A MEULER LES NOYAUX **3150**
MACHINE A MEULER SANS POINTES **2174**
MACHINE A MOLETER LES CYLINDRES D'IMPRIMERIE **9873**
MACHINE A MORTAISER **11643**
MACHINE A MOULER **8358**
MACHINE A MOULER **8429**
MACHINE A MOULER A SECOUSSES **7250**
MACHINE A MOULER A SECOUSSES AVEC PLAQUE REVERSIBLE **7251**
MACHINE A MOULER A SECOUSSES ET A SERRAGE COMBINES AVEC DEMOULAGE **7253**
MACHINE A MOULER LES NOYAUX **3154**
MACHINE A MOULER RAPIDE A SECOUSSES **7215**
MACHINE A MOULURER **8429**
MACHINE A MULTIPLE EXPANSION **8477**
MACHINE A PERCER **9636**
MACHINE A PERCER **4279**
MACHINE A PERCER A BROCHES MULTIPLES **8470**
MACHINE A PERCER LES TROUS A ANGLE **3178**
MACHINE A PERCER LES TUYERES **8681**
MACHINE A PERCER RADIALE **10129**
MACHINE A PERCER RAILS ET ECLISSES **10176**
MACHINE A PERCER SENSITIVE **11186**
MACHINE A PERCER VERTICALE **13552**
MACHINE A PETITE VITESSE **7789**
MACHINE A PISTON **10285**
MACHINE A PLANER ET DRESSER LES TOLES **11316**
MACHINE A PLANER LES TOLES **9485**
MACHINE A PLEINE PRESSION **12165**
MACHINE A PLIER LES FILS **13883**
MACHINE A POINCONNER **10009**
MACHINE A POINCONNER ET A CISAILLER **10007**
MACHINE A POINTER **7228**
MACHINE A POINTER PAR ETINCELAGE EN COORDONNEES RECTANGULAIRES **10300**
MACHINE A POLIR **9603**
MACHINE A PONCER AU PAPIER DE VERRE **10926**

MACHINE A PRESSION ORDINAIRE **7786**
MACHINE A PROFILER A GALETS MULTIPLES **8457**
MACHINE A PROFILER LES JANTES DE ROUES **13822**
MACHINE A QUADRUPLE EXPANSION **10059**
MACHINE A RABOTER **9451**
MACHINE A RABOTER **9452**
MACHINE A RABOTER A FOSSE **9395**
MACHINE A RABOTER A TABLE MOBILE **2007**
MACHINE A RABOTER A UN SEUL MONTANT **8821**
MACHINE A RABOTER LATERALE **11415**
MACHINE A RABOTER OUVERTE SUR LE COTE **8821**
MACHINE A RABOTER TIRANT LES BOIS D'EPAISSEUR **12847**
MACHINE A RAINER **6138**
MACHINE A RECTIFIER A LA MEULE **6113**
MACHINE A RECTIFIER L'INTERIEUR DES CYLINDRES **3568**
MACHINE A RECTIFIER LES PIECES CYLINDRIQUES **3583**
MACHINE A RECTIFIER LES SURFACES INTERIEURES **7068**
MACHINE A RECTIFIER LES SURFACES PLANES **12505**
MACHINE A REDRESSER **12320**
MACHINE A REFOULER **13415**
MACHINE A REFOULER **5561**
MACHINE A REPRODUIRE **3139**
MACHINE A RETREINDRE **12533**
MACHINE A RETROUSSER **5346**
MACHINE A RIVER **10645**
MACHINE A RIVETER **10642**
MACHINE A RODER **6565**
MACHINE A ROULER **1186**
MACHINE A SCIER **9747**
MACHINE A SCIER ALTERNATIVE **6198**
MACHINE A SERRAGE PAR SECOUSSE ET PRESSION SANS DEMOULAGE **7252**
MACHINE A SIMPLE EFFET **11495**
MACHINE A SIMPLE EXPANSION **11500**
MACHINE A SOUDER **13786**
MACHINE A SOUFFLER LES NOYAUX **3146**
MACHINE A TAILLER LES ENGRENAGES **5891**
MACHINE A TARAUDER ET FILETER LES TUBES **9361**
MACHINE A TRAVAILLER LES FILS METALLIQUES **13904**
MACHINE A TREFILER **13889**
MACHINE A TRIPLE EXPANSION **13217**
MACHINE A TROIS CYLINDRES **12873**
MACHINE A TRONCONNER **3541**
MACHINE A VAPEUR **12164**
MACHINE A VAPEUR DEMI-FIXE **11175**
MACHINE A VAPEUR FIXE **12144**
MACHINE A VAPEUR MURALE **13620**
MACHINE A VAPEUR REVERSIBLE **10543**
MACHINE A VAPEUR SURCHAUFFEE **4759**
MACHINE A VISSER **11066**

MACHINE ALTERNATIVE A SCIER **5629**
MACHINE ARITHMETIQUE **1859**
MACHINE AU JET DE SABLE **10920**
MACHINE AUXILIAIRE **853**
MACHINE AVEC CONDENSATION **2911**
MACHINE COMPOUND **2829**
MACHINE D'ESSAI D'EMBOUTISSAGE D'ERICHSEN **4819**
MACHINE D'ESSAI DE TRACTION **12752**
MACHINE D'ESSAIS UNIVERSELLE **13388**
MACHINE DE MANIPULATION **7982**
MACHINE DE PRECISION **9770**
MACHINE DE RESERVE **12070**
MACHINE DE SOUDAGE A L'ARC **680**
MACHINE DE SOUDAGE DOUBLE POINT **4382**
MACHINE DE TRAVAIL **7839**
MACHINE ELECTRIQUE **4522**
MACHINE FRIGORIFIQUE **10407**
MACHINE HORIZONTALE **6582**
MACHINE HYDRAULIQUE **6691**
MACHINE ISOLEE **11151**
MACHINE MAGNETO-ELECTRIQUE **7930**
MACHINE MARINE **8005**
MACHINE MONOCYLINDRIQUE **11498**
MACHINE MOTRICE **9859**
MACHINE MULTIPLE **8456**
MACHINE POUR ESSAIS DE FLEXION **7845**
MACHINE POUR TRAVAUX SPECIAUX **11486**
MACHINE RECEPTRICE **7839**
MACHINE ROTATIVE **10761**
MACHINE SANS CONDENSATION **8627**
MACHINE SOUFFLANTE **1363**
MACHINE STUMPF **12407**
MACHINE TANDEM **12613**
MACHINE UNIVERSELLE A RECTIFIER LES SURFACES DE REVOLUTION **13383**
MACHINE VERTICALE **13546**
MACHINE-OUTIL **7859**
MACHINE-OUTIL A TRAVAILLER LE BOIS **13925**
MACHINE-OUTIL A TRAVAILLER LES METAUX **8178**
MACHINERIE **7862**
MACHINES A BOIS **13931**
MACHINES A COUDER **7232**
MACHINES A ETETER LES BETTERAVES **12441**
MACHINES A PERFORER LES TOLES **11317**
MACHINES A PLANER LES TOLES **11318**
MACHINES A TAILLER LES ENGRENAGES DROITS ET HELICOIDAUX **12006**
MACHINES A TRAIRE **8275**
MACHINES A TRAVAILLER LA TOLE **11320**
MACHINES DE LAITERIE **3595**
MACHINES POUR COUPER LES HAIES **6418**

# MAC

MACHINISTE 4765
MACHOIRE 13564
MACHOIRE (D'ETAU) 6122
MACHOIRE DE BLOCAGE 13945
MACHOIRE DE CLEF 7216
MACHOIRE DE CROCODILE 9366
MACHOIRE DE FREIN 1536
MACHOIRE FIXE D'UN ETAU 5299
MACHOIRE MOBILE D'UN ETAU 8437
MACLAGE 13302
MACLE 13300
MACLE DE DEFORMATION 8113
MACONNER 1597
MACONNERIE 1601
MACONNERIE 8025
MACONNERIE EN BRIQUES 1602
MACONNERIE EN MOELLONS 10828
MACONNERIE EN PIERRES DE TAILLE 762
MACROGRAPHIE 7871
MACROPHOTOGRAPHIE 9266
MACROSCOPIQUE 7872
MACROSEGREGATION 7876
MACROSTRUCTURE 7869
MADRIER 9457
MAGASIN 12297
MAGASINAGE 12288
MAGASINIER 12298
MAGNALIUM 7878
MAGNESIE 7879
MAGNESIE CALCINEE 1842
MAGNESIE EN POUDRE 9725
MAGNESITE 7880
MAGNESITE MORTE 3639
MAGNESIUM 7882
MAGNETIQUE 7893
MAGNETISABLE 7922
MAGNETISATION 7928
MAGNETISATION 7906
MAGNETISME 7926
MAGNETISME LATENT 7417
MAGNETISME LIBRE 5640
MAGNETISME PERMANENT 9206
MAGNETISME REMANENT 10445
MAGNETISME RESIDUEL 10445
MAGNETITE 7927
MAGNETO 7930
MAGNETOPHONE 12644
MAGNETOSCOPIE 7877
MAGNETOSCOPIE 7910
MAGNETOSTRICTION 7933
MAILLE 9032

MAILLE (D'UN CRIBLE) 8169
MAILLE D'UN TAMIS 8170
MAILLE D'UNE CHAINE 7627
MAILLE D'UNE TOILE METALLIQUE 8170
MAILLE RECTANGULAIRE 10304
MAILLECHORT 8569
MAILLECHORT 5932
MAILLES SERREES (A) 5206
MAILLET 13926
MAILLET EN BOIS 7962
MAILLON 7627
MAILLON DE CHAINE 2211
MAIN-D'OEUVRE 13961
MAINTIEN 6526
MAINTIEN EN TEMPERATURE 6528
MAITRE A DANSER 6975
MAITRE A DANSER 1870
MAITRE-CYLINDRE 8037
MAL VENUE 8321
MALACHITE 6089
MALAXER (DU MORTIERDU CIMENT) 12718
MALAXEUR 8334
MALAXEUR 9966
MALAXEUR 8449
MALLE 13239
MALLE 1458
MALLEABILISATION 7961
MALLEABILISATION DE LA FONTE 13175
MALLEABILISER LA FONTE 7952
MALLEABILITE 7958
MALLEABLE 7960
MAMELON 8578
MAMELON A DEUX FILETS 4149
MANCHE 6262
MANCHE D'UN MARTEAU 11244
MANCHE D'UN OUTIL 6263
MANCHE D'UNE HACHE 6433
MANCHETTE 11576
MANCHETTE D'UN TAMPON 11548
MANCHON 3258
MANCHON 1773
MANCHON A BANDE DE COURROIE 7349
MANCHON A BOULONS NOYES 2449
MANCHON A CLIQUETS 10221
MANCHON A COQUILLES 2449
MANCHON A FRETTES 11577
MANCHON A LANIERES DE CUIR 7501
MANCHON A VIS 11026
MANCHON ARTICULE UNIVERSEL 6572
MANCHON D'ACCOUPLEMENT 3257
MANCHON D'ACCOUPLEMENT CYLINDRIQUE 2449

671 MAN

MANCHON D'ACCOUPLEMENT SELLERS **11164**
MANCHON D'EMBRAYAGE **11599**
MANCHON DE CENTRAGE **2087**
MANCHON DE DILATATION **4915**
MANCHON DE MANIVELLE A BRAS **3300**
MANCHON DE RACCORD **11705**
MANCHON DE REDUCTION D'ALESAGE **3962**
MANCHON DE SURETE **10884**
MANCHON DE T.H. COLLET DE T.H. **7998**
MANCHON ELASTIQUE **4476**
MANCHON FEMELLE **11061**
MANCHON FLEXIBLE **5417**
MANCHON MOBILE **11599**
MANCHON PORTE-MECHE **4266**
MANCHON POUR RACCORDER DEUX TUYAUX COUPES **4158**
MANCHON PROTECTEUR **9942**
MANCHON REDUCTEUR **10351**
MANCHON TARAUDE **11061**
MANCHON DOUILLE DU REGULATEUR **6017**
MANCHONNAGE **3254**
MANDRIN **2393**
MANDRIN **2727**
MANDRIN **4260**
MANDRIN **11904**
MANDRIN A ELARGIR LES TUBES **13250**
MANDRIN A QUATRE MORS INDEPENDANTS **5604**
MANDRIN A QUEUE CONIQUE **12667**
MANDRIN CONIQUE **12651**
MANDRIN DE MONTAGE **7964**
MANDRIN DE MONTAGE EXPANSIBLE **4907**
MANDRIN DE MONTAGE LISSE **9425**
MANDRIN DE REPRISE **7964**
MANDRIN DE SERRAGE **6121**
MANDRIN DE TOUR **2393**
MANDRIN ET PINCES PORTE-FRAISE **2729**
MANDRIN EXPANSIBLE JACOBS **7208**
MANDRIN FILETE **12867**
MANDRIN FLOTTANT **5438**
MANDRIN LISSE **11789**
MANDRIN PNEUMATIQUE **279**
MANDRIN UNIVERSEL **13382**
MANDRIN UNIVERSEL A TROIS MORS **12874**
MANDRINER UN TROU DE RIVET **4262**
MANDRINER UN TUBE **4903**
MANDRINS AUTO-ENTRAINEURS **11152**
MANDRINS EXPANSIBLES **4906**
MANDRINS HYDRAULIQUES **6679**
MANDRINS MAGNETIQUES **7898**
MANDRINS MECANIQUES **8095**
MANDRINS PNEUMATIQUES **9550**
MANEGE **1731**

MANETON **3302**
MANETON **3300**
MANETON **3311**
MANETON **9319**
MANETON DE VILEBREQUIN **3311**
MANETTE DE COMMANDE **7706**
MANGANESE **7966**
MANGANESE ELECTROLYTIQUE **4599**
MANGANESIFERE **7971**
MANIABLE **6269**
MANIABLE (PEU) **13402**
MANILLE **7980**
MANILLE D'ASSEMBLAGE **11232**
MANIVELLE **3295**
MANIVELLE A COULISSE **11631**
MANIVELLE A FAIBLE COURSE **11375**
MANIVELLE A GRANDE COURSE **7732**
MANIVELLE A MAIN **6231**
MANIVELLE A MANCHON **3305**
MANIVELLE AMOVIBLE **10450**
MANIVELLE COUDEE A LA FORGE **5550**
MANIVELLE D'INDEXAGE **6865**
MANIVELLE DU VILEBREQUIN **6976**
MANIVELLE EN BOUT **8947**
MANIVELLE EN PLUSIEURS PIECES **1706**
MANIVELLE EN PORTE-A-FAUX **8947**
MANIVELLE FORGEE **5550**
MANIVELLE FRONTALE **8947**
MANIVELLE VENUE DE FORGE **5550**
MANO-VACUOMETRE **2830**
MANOEUVRE **12226**
MANOEUVRE DE SERVICE **13398**
MANOEUVRE DU FREIN **1549**
MANOEUVRER **3049**
MANOMETRE **9820**
MANOMETRE **9821**
MANOMETRE A AIR COMPRIME **2534**
MANOMETRE A AIR LIBRE **8827**
MANOMETRE A MERCURE **8151**
MANOMETRE A PLAQUE **3873**
MANOMETRE A RESSORT **11989**
MANOMETRE A TUBE **1501**
MANOMETRE BOURDON **1501**
MANOMETRE DIFFERENTIEL **3921**
MANOMETRE ENREGISTREUR **10292**
MANOMETRE ETALON **12080**
MANOMETRE METALLIQUE **11989**
MANOMETRE POUR DETERMINATIONS ANEMOMETRIQUES
  **4211**
MANOSTAT **9835**
MANQUE **11537**

# MAN

672

MANQUE DE FUSION **6782**
MANQUE DE MATIERE **13348**
MANQUE DE PLANEITE **1506**
MANQUE DE SOUPLESSE **1628**
MANQUES (AFNOR) **6536**
MANTISSE **7985**
MANUEL DE FABRICATION **9885**
MANUFACTURABLE **12802**
MANUFACTURE **5013**
MANUFACTURER **7948**
MANUSCRIT **7996**
MANUTENTION MECANIQUE **8106**
MANUTENTIONNAIRE **12298**
MAQUETTE **4370**
MARBRE **12321**
MARBRE **6048**
MARBRE **6114**
MARBRE **8001**
MARBRE A DRESSER **12516**
MARCHE **10850**
MARCHE **12239**
MARCHE **13172**
MARCHE A VIDE **6752**
MARCHE A VIDE **8598**
MARCHE ARRIERE **10846**
MARCHE AVANT **10848**
MARCHE BRUYANTE **8610**
MARCHE DOUCE **7567**
MARCHE EN ARRIERE DU PISTON **10530**
MARCHE EN AVANT DU PISTON **5585**
MARCHE EN CONTRE-PRESSION **894**
MARCHE IRREGULIERE **7165**
MARCHE LOURDE **6412**
MARCHE REGULIERE **11681**
MARCHE SILENCIEUSE **8609**
MARCHER A CHARGE INCOMPLETE **1080**
MARCHER A GRANDE VITESSE **10833**
MARCHER A PETITE VITESSE **10834**
MARCHER A PLEINE CHARGE **1079**
MARCHER A VIDE **1081**
MARCHES EN CAILLEBOTIS **6102**
MARMITE AUTOCLAVE **829**
MARMITE DE PAPIN **829**
MARNE **8019**
MARNE ARGILEUSE **699**
MARNE CALCAIRE **2225**
MARNE SILICEUSE **11439**
MARQUAGE **8015**
MARQUAGE DES TOLES AU POINCON **3894**
MARQUE DE COMMERCE **13100**
MARQUE DE FABRIQUE **13100**

MARQUE DE L'ESTAMPE **3888**
MARQUE REPERE DE NIVEAU D'EAU **13660**
MARQUER **8008**
MARQUER **8010**
MARQUER UN REPERE AU POINTEAU **8011**
MARQUES DE MEULAGE **15**
MARQUES DE VIBRATION **2276**
MARQUES SUPERFICIELLES EN FORME DE V **2282**
MARTEAU **6215**
MARTEAU A AIR COMPRIME **9553**
MARTEAU A DENT **2462**
MARTEAU A DEUX TETES **4169**
MARTEAU A DEVANT **12308**
MARTEAU A EBARBER LA FONTE **10986**
MARTEAU A FRAPPER DEVANT **11573**
MARTEAU A MAIN **6235**
MARTEAU A MATER **1872**
MARTEAU A PANNE BOMBEE **960**
MARTEAU A PANNE FENDUE **2462**
MARTEAU A PANNE RONDE **962**
MARTEAU A PIQUER LES CHAUDIERES **10986**
MARTEAU A PLANER **9455**
MARTEAU A RIVER **10644**
MARTEAU A RIVER PNEUMATIQUE **9555**
MARTEAU A SUAGE **3321**
MARTEAU A TETE PLASTIQUE **11747**
MARTEAU A VAPEUR **12166**
MARTEAU ARRONDI **960**
MARTEAU D'AJUSTEUR **5279**
MARTEAU D'OUTILLEUR **13014**
MARTEAU DE FORGE **5559**
MARTEAU DE FORGE DOUBLE CORPS **4140**
MARTEAU DE TAPISSIER AIMANTE **7921**
MARTEAU MECANIQUE **5559**
MARTEAU MECANIQUE A AIR COMPRIME **9555**
MARTEAU PNEUMATIQUE **9551**
MARTEAU PNEUMATIQUE **9553**
MARTEAU-PELIN A PLANCHE **1380**
MARTEAU-PILON **4326**
MARTEAU-PILON **4325**
MARTEAU-PILON **4327**
MARTEAU-PILON **6080**
MARTEAU-PILON **9552**
MARTEAU-PILON **12166**
MARTEAU-PIQUEUR **258**
MARTEAU-RIVOIR **10644**
MARTELAGE **6223**
MARTELAGE **9157**
MARTELAGE A FROID **2685**
MARTELE **6220**
MARTELER **6216**

673 MAT

MARTELER A FROID **2684**
MARTELURES **6217**
MARTENSITE **8022**
MARTENSITE ACICULAIRE **103**
MASQUE **6252**
MASQUE DE SOUDAGE **6432**
MASSE **3119**
MASSE **11572**
MASSE **12611**
MASSE (MEC.) **8026**
MASSE (TERRE) **4409**
MASSE D'ACIER **951**
MASSE EN ROTATION **10561**
MASSE PRINCIPALE **8055**
MASSE TOURNANTE **10561**
MASSELOTTE **11506**
MASSELOTTE **3629**
MASSELOTTE A NOYAU ATMOSPHERIQUE **799**
MASSES POLAIRES **9593**
MASSETTE EN CUIVRE **3119**
MASSETTE EN PLOMB **7463**
MASSICOT **8031**
MASSIF DE FONDATION **5589**
MASSIF EN BETON **2896**
MASTIC **8038**
MASTIC **10037**
MASTIC A L'HUILE **8771**
MASTIC A LA RESINE **10482**
MASTIC A PIERRE **12274**
MASTIC AU MINIUM **10332**
MASTIC D'ASPHALTE **764**
MASTIC DE FER **7141**
MASTIC DES FONTAINIERS **13797**
MASTIC DES VITRIERS **5971**
MASTIC EN GRAINS **8039**
MASTIC EN LARMES **8039**
MASTIC POUR FONTE **7141**
MASTIC RESINEUX **10482**
MASTIC ROUGE **10332**
MASTICAGE **2146**
MASTIQUER **2134**
MASURIUM **8040**
MATAGE **2115**
MATELAS **254**
MATELAS D'HUILE **8754**
MATER **2113**
MATERIAUX REFRACTAIRES **10466**
MATERIEL D'IRRIGATION **7172**
MATERIEL DE CONSTRUCTION **8050**
MATERIEL DE MONTAGE **4810**
MATERIEL DE MONTAGE **4809**

MATHEMATIQUE **8053**
MATIERE **12419**
MATIERE A AIGUISER **6107**
MATIERE A POLIR **9601**
MATIERE A POLIR **11**
MATIERE A POLIR **22**
MATIERE ABRASIVE **9601**
MATIERE AGGLUTINANTE **1253**
MATIERE CALORIFUGE POUR CHAUDIERES **1408**
MATIERE CHARGEANTE **7690**
MATIERE COLORANTE **9303**
MATIERE COLORANTE A BASE DE CHROME **2387**
MATIERE COLORANTE A BASE DE PLOMB **7466**
MATIERE COLORANTE DERIVEE DU GOUDRON DE HOUILLE **2567**
MATIERE COLORANTE MINERALE **4412**
MATIERE DE MELANGE **228**
MATIERE DE REMPLISSAGE **5164**
MATIERE EN FUSION **8365**
MATIERE ETOUFFANT LE BRUIT **3641**
MATIERE FIBREUSE **5140**
MATIERE FILTRANTE **5179**
MATIERE IMPERMEABLE AU SON **3641**
MATIERE INORGANIQUE **6957**
MATIERE ISOLANTE **6998**
MATIERE ORGANIQUE **8866**
MATIERE POUR JOINT **7247**
MATIERE PREMIERE **10239**
MATIERE PROTECTRICE **9952**
MATIERES EN DISSOLUTION **8061**
MATIERES EN SUSPENSION **8062**
MATIERES PLASTIQUES **9476**
MATOIR **2114**
MATRAS **10277**
MATRICAGE **12059**
MATRICAGE **2651**
MATRICAGE **12532**
MATRICAGE (DEFAUT DE SURFACE DE TOLE) **3894**
MATRICE **3883**
MATRICE **8055**
MATRICE A DESCENTE COMMANDEE **4193**
MATRICE A DISQUE **1310**
MATRICE A ETIRER **4234**
MATRICE AMOVIBLE **6966**
MATRICE COMPOSITE **2818**
MATRICE D'ESTAMPAGE **2652**
MATRICE DE DESSOUS **1497**
MATRICE DE DESSUS **13036**
MATRICE ETAMPE ESTAMPE DE FORGERON **3897**
MATRICE FINISSEUSE **5219**
MATRICE FLOTTANTE **5437**

# MAT

674

MATRICE NEGATIVE **8529**
MATRICE OUVERTE **8810**
MATRICE RONDE ET DIVISEE CAGE REFOULEUSE **4451**
MATRICER **12056**
MATTE **11878**
MATTE **8058**
MATTE DE CUIVRE **3121**
MATTE DE NICKEL **8563**
MAUVAIS COMBUSTIBLE **7780**
MAZOUT **6408**
MAZOUT **8041**
MAZOUT **5714**
MECANICIEN **4765**
MECANICIEN-CONSTRUCTEUR **4214**
MECANIQUE **8121**
MECANIQUE **8093**
MECANIQUE (ESSAI) **12743**
MECANIQUE DES CORPS LIQUIDES **6720**
MECANISME **8122**
MECANISME **3913**
MECANISME A CAME **1886**
MECANISME A MANIVELLE **1094**
MECANISME A MANIVELLE EXCENTRIQUE **4427**
MECANISME A VIS SANS FIN **13974**
MECANISME D'ARRET **7709**
MECANISME D'ARRET DES ECROUS **8701**
MECANISME D'EMBRAYAGE **4034**
MECANISME D'INDEXAGE **6869**
MECANISME D'INDEXAGE POUR CREMAILLERE **10123**
MECANISME DE CHANGEMENT DE MARCHE **10544**
MECANISME DE CHANGEMENT DE VITESSE **2242**
MECANISME DE COMMANDE **4311**
MECANISME DE COMMANDE **4309**
MECANISME DE DEBRAYAGE **4034**
MECANISME DE DEBRAYAGE DE LA COURROIE **1157**
MECANISME DE REPRISE DES JEUX **915**
MECANISME DE RETENUE EN POSITION D'OUVERTURE **6525**
MECANISME DE ROUE LIBRE **5652**
MECANISME DES AVANCEMENTS **5067**
MECANISME POUR RETOUR RAPIDE **10106**
MECHE **11957**
MECHE **4271**
MECHE **4263**
MECHE (D'UNE LAMPED'UN GRAISSEUR) **13846**
MECHE A CENTRE **2164**
MECHE A COUPE RAPIDE **10206**
MECHE A COUTEAUX RENVERSES **4160**
MECHE A TROIS POINTES **2164**
MECHE DE GRAISSAGE **7807**
MECHE EN LISIERE DE DRAP **2538**
MECHE FACON SUISSE **11023**

MECHE PLATE **5380**
MECHE STYRIENNE **11023**
MECHE TORSE **4160**
MEDIANE **8124**
MEGADYNE **8129**
MEGAVOLT **8130**
MEGERG **8131**
MEGOHM **8132**
MELANGE **8327**
MELANGE **1325**
MELANGE (ACTION) **8336**
MELANGE (CHIMIQUE) **8336**
MELANGE CARBURE **8337**
MELANGE DE CARBURES FRITTES **2192**
MELANGE DE DIVERSES FRACTIONS DE POUDRES D'UNE
 MEME SUBSTANCE **1325**
MELANGE DE GRAIN SANS GRAINS INTERMEDIAIRES **5805**
MELANGE DETONANT **4938**
MELANGE EUTECTIQUE **4857**
MELANGE EXPLOSIF **4938**
MELANGE GAZEUX **5856**
MELANGE INTIME **7102**
MELANGE REFRIGERANT **5654**
MELANGE SULFONITRIQUE **8595**
MELANGE TONNANT **4938**
MELANGER **8328**
MELANGER **1323**
MELANGEUR **8334**
MELANGEUR **8331**
MELANGEUR A SOLE PLATE **5387**
MELANGEURS **8332**
MELAPHYRE **8133**
MELINOSE **13991**
MEMBRANE **3870**
MEMBRANE **4479**
MEMBRANE D'ECLATEMENT **10860**
MEMBRURE **8145**
MEMOIRE **8146**
MEMOIRE DESCRIPTIF DU BREVET **11856**
MEMOIRE INTERMEDIAIRE **1689**
MEMOIRE TEMPORAIRE **12736**
MENEUR **4316**
MENISQUE CONVERGENT **8147**
MENTONNET **12672**
MENTONNET D'UNE CLAVETTE **6318**
MENUISERIE **7236**
MENUISERIE (ATELIER) **7235**
MENUISERIE DE MODELES (ART) **9131**
MENUISERIE DE MODELES (ATELIER) **9132**
MENUISIER **7233**
MENUS DE HOUILLLE **11557**

675 MET

MER (EN) **8738**
MERCURE **8168**
MESURAGE **8088**
MESURAGE EXACT **4875**
MESURAGE PRECIS **4875**
MESURE **8077**
MESURE COMPARATIVE **2797**
MESURE DE CAPACITE **8079**
MESURE DE CONTROLE **12077**
MESURE DE L'ARC INTERCEPTE **2419**
MESURE DE L'ELASTICITE **8340**
MESURE DE LA TEMPERATURE **8086**
MESURE DE SURFACE **8081**
MESURE DE VOLUME **8082**
MESURE ETALON **12077**
MESURE LINEAIRE **8080**
MESURE METRIQUE **8227**
MESURER **8078**
MESURER LA PUISSANCE DES FREINS **8083**
MESURES DE SECURITE **10889**
METACENDRE **8172**
METAL **8173**
METAL **13836**
METAL A GRENAILLES **6054**
METAL A HAUTE DENSITE **6482**
METAL ALLIAGE DELTA **3741**
METAL ANGLAIS **9230**
METAL ANTI-FRICTION **13836**
METAL ANTIFRICTION **619**
METAL ANTIFRICTION **888**
METAL AUTRE QUE LE FER **8632**
METAL BLANC **888**
METAL BLANC DEFLOCULE **13835**
METAL BLANC DUR **6276**
METAL BRITANNIQUE **1624**
METAL BRUT **3410**
METAL CONSTITUANT **2982**
METAL COULE **2050**
METAL D'ACCUMULATEUR **80**
METAL D'APPORT **3775**
METAL D'APPORT **5159**
METAL DE BASE **8057**
METAL DE BASE **1032**
METAL DE BASE **12422**
METAL DE BASE **9079**
METAL DE CUBILOT **3468**
METAL DE L'ELECTRODE **4576**
METAL DE RECHARGE **3775**
METAL DE RECUPERATION **11107**
METAL DE SOUDURE **13763**
METAL DEPLOYE **4904**

METAL DEPOSE **13761**
METAL DUR **6277**
METAL EN ETAT DE FUSION **6631**
METAL EN FUSION **8365**
METAL EN FUSION **6631**
METAL FONDU APPLIQUE **3776**
METAL FONDU EN COQUILLE SANS DEFORMATION **2337**
METAL INVAR **7105**
METAL LEGER **7779**
METAL LEGER **7564**
METAL LOURD **6407**
METAL MARTELLE **6221**
METAL MONEL **8379**
METAL MOU **11738**
METAL MUNTZ **8486**
METAL NOBLE EN BARRES **1729**
METAL NOBLE OU PRECIEUX **8602**
METAL NON PRECIEUX **1031**
METAL POLYCRISTALLIN **9608**
METAL POUR COUSSINET **1106**
METAL POUR MATRICES **3889**
METAL PREAFFINE **1366**
METAL PRECIEUX **9756**
METAL PRECIEUX **8603**
METAL PROPRE A LA FABRICATION DES CARACTERES
  D'IMPRIMERIE **13319**
METAL PULVERISE **8185**
METAL STRATIFIE **7379**
METAL SUPPORT **909**
METAL TENDRE **11738**
METAL VIERGE **13570**
METAL VIERGE OU NAISSANT **9853**
METALLIFERE **8197**
METALLISATION **8201**
METALLISATION **8190**
METALLISATION AU PISTOLET **5361**
METALLISATION AU ZINC **14045**
METALLISATION SOUS VIDE **13445**
METALLISATION SOUS VIDE **13487**
METALLOGRAPHIE **8203**
METALLOGRAPHIE EN COULEURS **2738**
METALLOGRAPHIQUE **8202**
METALLOIDE **8640**
METALLOIDE **8205**
METALLURGIE **8208**
METALLURGIE D'EXTRACTION **9886**
METALLURGIE DES POUDRES **9720**
METALLURGIE DU FER **8209**
METALLURGIE DU FER **5123**
METALLURGIE MECANIQUE **8107**
METALLURGIE PHYSIQUE **9282**

# MET 676

METALLURGIE SOUS VIDE 13446
METALLURGIQUE 8206
METASTABLE 8212
METAUX ALCALIN-TERREUX 335
METAUX ALCALINS 329
METAUX DE CONSTRUCTION (ORDINAIRES) 2988
METAUX UTILISES COMME CONTACT ELECTRIQUE 4538
METHANAL 5573
METHANE 8215
METHODE 8216
METHODE 8220
METHODE AU TREMPE 3977
METHODE D'IONISATION 7127
METHODE DE BRAGG 1525
METHODE DE CRISTAL OSCILLANT 8879
METHODE DE DEBYE-SCHERRER 3643
METHODE DE LAVE 7438
METHODE DE MESURE 8219
METHODE DE TRAVAIL 8220
METHODE DES POUDRES 9721
METHODE DITE A TROIS FILS 12883
METHODE STROBOSCOPIQUE 12386
METHYLBENZENE 12983
METHYLENE 13920
METHYLORANGE 8223
METRE 8226
METRE (UNITE DE MESURE) 8225
METRE A RUBAN 8092
METRE CARRE 12022
METRE COURANT 10849
METRE CUBE 3455
METRE DROIT 8226
METRE ETALON 12081
METRE PLIANT 5512
METRE RIGIDE 8226
METTRE A DIGERER 3937
METTRE A LA TERRE 4410
METTRE DES CONTREFICHES 1517
METTRE EN CIRCUIT 12555
METTRE EN EXPLOITATION UNE INVENTION 13938
METTRE EN MARCHE 12114
METTRE EN MOUVEMENT 4289
METTRE EN PLACE LA COURROIE 11357
METTRE EN ROUTE UNE MACHINE 12114
METTRE EN TRAIN 12114
METTRE HORS CIRCUIT 12554
METTRE UNE MACHINE HORS SERVICE 11406
MEUBLE A POLIR 9604
MEULAGE 11275
MEULAGE 11689
MEULAGE 6106

MEULAGE A LA MACHINE 7849
MEULE 6115
MEULE 9604
MEULE D'AFFUTAGE 6118
MEULE D'EMERI 4698
MEULE D'EMERI 20
MEULE DE MOULIN 8298
MEULE DIAMANTEE 3867
MEULE EN GRES 6118
MEULE FLEXIBLE 4116
MEULE VERTICALE 4450
MEULE-DIAMANT 3864
MEULER 11273
MEULES 26
MEULEUSE 6113
MEULIERE 8299
MI-POSITION 8265
MICA 8231
MICANITE 8233
MICASCHISTE 8232
MICRO POUCE 8248
MICRO-PALPEUR DE CONICITE 12652
MICROAMPERE 8238
MICROAMPEREMETRE 8237
MICROBE PATHOGENE 9126
MICROCRIQUE 3318
MICRODURETE 8245
MICROFARAD 8242
MICROFISSURE 1263
MICROFISSURES 8234
MICROGRAPHIE 8244
MICROGRAPHIE 8258
MICROGRAPHIQUE 8243
MICROHM 8247
MICROMETRE 8249
MICROMETRE 1875
MICROMETRE A CADRAN 6877
MICROMETRE A VERNIER 13540
MICROMETRE DE CONICITE 12652
MICROMETRE DE PROFONDEUR 8252
MICROMETRE METRIQUE 8228
MICRON 8257
MICROPHOTOGRAMME 9272
MICROSCOPE 8259
MICROSCOPE BINOCULAIRE 1256
MICROSCOPE ELECTRONIQUE 4629
MICROSCOPE POLARISANT 9583
MICROSEGREGATION 3172
MICROSTRUCTURE 8262
MICROTOME 8263
MICROVOLT 8264

MIGRATION **8268**
MIGRATION **1321**
MIGRATION D'IONS **7123**
MILIEU CONDUCTEUR **2914**
MILIEU DE TREMPE **10098**
MILIEU REFRACTIF **10401**
MILIEU TRANSPARENT **13139**
MILLE (ANGLAIS) **8272**
MILLIAMPERE **8284**
MILLIAMPERE/METRE **8283**
MILLIEME DE MILLIMETRE **8257**
MILLIGRAMME **8285**
MILLIMETRE **8286**
MILLIMETRE CARRE **12023**
MILLIMETRE CUBE **3456**
MILLIVOLT **8294**
MINCE COUCHE D'HUILE DE GRAISSAGE **5167**
MINE **8300**
MINE DE HOUILLE **2566**
MINE DE PLOMB **9542**
MINE METALLIQUE **8198**
MINERAI **8859**
MINERAI BRIQUETTE **8860**
MINERAI D'ARGENT **11625**
MINERAI D'ETAIN **12956**
MINERAI DE BASSE TENEUR **7781**
MINERAI DE CUIVRE **3122**
MINERAI DE FER **7143**
MINERAI DE FER MAGNETIQUE **7927**
MINERAI DE HAUTE TENEUR **6485**
MINERAI DE NICKEL **8564**
MINERAI DE PLOMB **7465**
MINERAI DE ZINC **14042**
MINERAI PAUVRE **7781**
MINERAI RICHE **6485**
MINERAIS DE MANGANESE FERREUX **5122**
MINERAIS ET FONDANTS **8863**
MINERAL **8301**
MINETTE **8305**
MINIUM **10333**
MINUENDE **8316**
MINUTERIE **3843**
MIROIR CONCAVE **2879**
MIROIR CONVEXE **3078**
MIROIR PARABOLIQUE **9041**
MIROIR PLAN **9437**
MIROIR SPHERIQUE **11888**
MISCHMETAL **8320**
MISE A LA TERRE **6149**
MISE A LA TERRE **4417**
MISE AU POINT **8419**

MISE AU POINT D UN INSTRUMENT D OPTIQUE **5505**
MISE AU POINT D'UN OUTIL **1621**
MISE DE CONTREFICHES **1521**
MISE EN BOTTES **1772**
MISE EN CIRCUIT **12560**
MISE EN MARCHE **12130**
MISE EN MARCHE **12118**
MISE EN PLACE D'UNE COURROIE **1160**
MISE EN ROUTE D'UNE MACHINE **12130**
MISE EN SERVICE **12118**
MISE EN TRAIN **12130**
MISE EN VOIE DES DENTS D'UNE SCIE **10958**
MISE HORS CIRCUIT **12559**
MISE HORS SERVICE D'UNE MACHINE **11410**
MISES BRASEES **1574**
MITRAILLE **11379**
MITRAILLE **11007**
MITRAILLE **5553**
MITRAILLES PAQUETEES **5016**
MOBILE **9635**
MODE D'ATTAQUE **8217**
MODE D'EMPLOI **6992**
MODE OPERATOIRE **8220**
MODELAGE **9135**
MODELE **9133**
MODELE **9128**
MODELE A CIRE PERDUE **7116**
MODELE A ENTONNOIRS **5868**
MODELE DEMONTABLE **7744**
MODELE EN CIRE **13703**
MODELE EN DEUX **3105**
MODELE EN PLATRE **6189**
MODELE ETALON **8032**
MODELE POUR FONTE **9129**
MODELE SQUELETTE **11526**
MODELE STANDARD **12073**
MODEM **8338**
MODERATEUR **10421**
MODULATEUR **8338**
MODULE **8339**
MODULE D'ELASTICITE **8341**
MODULE D'ELASTICITE **4483**
MODULE D'ELASTICITE TRANVERSALE **5974**
MODULE D'INERTIE **11115**
MODULE DE CISAILLEMENT **8342**
MODULE DE COULOMB **3226**
MODULE DE DENTURE **3861**
MODULE DE GLISSEMENT **8342**
MODULE DE RUPTURE **8343**
MOELLE DU BOIS **9413**
MOELLON **10827**

**MOI** 678

MOELLON EN LAITIER **11563**
MOISISSURE **8271**
MOISSONNEUSES ET M. LIEUSES **1251**
MOISSONNEUSES-BATTEUSES **2766**
MOLECULE **8364**
MOLECULE-GRAMME **6044**
MOLETAGE **7338**
MOLETAGE **8287**
MOLETAGE D'UNE TETE DE VIS **8288**
MOLETTE (OU GALET) DE SOUDAGE **2412**
MOLETTE DE LA CAME **1895**
MOLETTER UNE TETE DE VIS **8277**
MOLYBDENE **8367**
MOLYBDENITE **8366**
MOMENT BASCULANT **12936**
MOMENT CENTRIFUGE **2183**
MOMENT D'INERTIE **8372**
MOMENT D'UNE FORCE **8370**
MOMENT DE FLEXION **1185**
MOMENT DE LA QUANTITE DE MOUVEMENT **8373**
MOMENT DE RENVERSEMENT **8966**
MOMENT DE STABILITE **8375**
MOMENT DU COUPLE **13308**
MOMENT DU FROTTEMENT **8371**
MOMENT FLECHISSANT **1185**
MOMENT RESISTANT **8374**
MOMENT STATIQUE **12139**
MOMENT TORDANT **13308**
MONEL **8379**
MONNAIES DE CUIVRE **3114**
MONNAYAGE **2651**
MONOATOMIQUE **8377**
MONOBLOC **11079**
MONOCRISTAL **11480**
MONOSULFURE DE CALCIUM **1852**
MONOTRON **8387**
MONOTROPE **8388**
MONTAGE **9051**
MONTAGE **11199**
MONTAGE **2986**
MONTAGE **5275**
MONTAGE **12493**
MONTAGE **5301**
MONTAGE **4815**
MONTAGE **4813**
MONTAGE **4808**
MONTAGE A BLANC **13184**
MONTAGE A LA PRESSE **5527**
MONTAGE A LA PRESSE A CHAUD **11389**
MONTAGE A VIS **11067**
MONTAGE BLOQUE **4307**

MONTAGE D'USINAGE BATI MANNEQUIN **4985**
MONTAGE DE CALES-ETALONS **5884**
MONTAGE DE LA COURROIE **1160**
MONTAGE EN PARALLELE **9051**
MONTAGE EN SURFACE **9051**
MONTAGE GLISSANT **11600**
MONTAGE LACHE **10025**
MONTAGE SUR CHANTIER **8800**
MONTAGE TOURNANT **10847**
MONTAGE ULTERIEUR **10527**
MONTANT **10615**
MONTANT **12063**
MONTANT **12062**
MONTANT D'UNE MACHINE **12078**
MONTANT DE GARDE-CORPS **6266**
MONTANT DE PORTE **6507**
MONTANT DOUBLE **4159**
MONTANT JUMELE **4159**
MONTANT LATERAL D'ENTREE **7211**
MONTANT PORTE-OUTIL **13010**
MONTE SIMULTANEMENT OU EN CONTINUITE **4807**
MONTE-CHARGE **6007**
MONTE-COURROIE **1159**
MONTE-JUS **8389**
MONTEE DE LA COURROIE **2499**
MONTEE DU PISTON **13409**
MONTEE EN TEMPERATURE **10231**
MONTER **4805**
MONTER **12491**
MONTER **6517**
MONTER A VIS **11037**
MONTER EN PARALLELE **2956**
MONTER EN TENSION **2957**
MONTER LA COURROIE **11357**
MONTER UN CALQUE **8431**
MONTEUR **4816**
MONTEUR-ELECTRICIEN **4543**
MONTRE DE SEGER **11134**
MONTRE FUSIBLE **11134**
MONTURE D'ESTAMPE A GUIDAGE A COLONNES **3890**
MONTURE D'UNE FILIERE A COUSSINETS **3895**
MORD D'UN ETAU **13564**
MORDACHE A CHARNIERE **13562**
MORDACHE D'UN ETAU **13563**
MORDACHES **6120**
MORDANT **8391**
MORDANT **3196**
MORFIL **13890**
MORS **13564**
MORS DOUX POUR MANDRINS **2394**
MORTAISAGE **11641**

MORTAISE **8401**
MORTAISE A CLAVETTE **7282**
MORTAISE A EXTREMITES ARRONDIES **8714**
MORTAISER **11630**
MORTAISEUSE **11643**
MORTAISEUSE A BOIS **8402**
MORTAISEUSES **11640**
MORTIER (A CONSTRUIRE) **8394**
MORTIER (VASE EN BRONZE) **8396**
MORTIER (VASE EN PORCELAINEEN AGATE) **8395**
MORTIER AERIEN **8854**
MORTIER DE CIMENT **2137**
MORTIER HYDRAULIQUE **6690**
MORTIER REFRACTAIRE **10406**
MOT **13934**
MOTEUR **9859**
MOTEUR A AIR CHAUD **6615**
MOTEUR A AIR COMPRIME **2843**
MOTEUR A ALCOOL **312**
MOTEUR A BASSE TENSION **7791**
MOTEUR A CARBURANT **8756**
MOTEUR A CARTER **4715**
MOTEUR A CHAMP TOURNANT **12876**
MOTEUR A COMBUSTION INTERNE **7061**
MOTEUR A COMBUSTION INTERNE **7062**
MOTEUR A COURANT ALTERNATIF **408**
MOTEUR A COURANT CONTINU **3022**
MOTEUR A CYLINDRES JUMELES **13301**
MOTEUR A DEUX TEMPS **13312**
MOTEUR A ESSENCE **5819**
MOTEUR A ESSENCE DE GRANDE PUISSANCE **7410**
MOTEUR A ESSENCE DE PETROLE **9223**
MOTEUR A EXPLOSIONS **7061**
MOTEUR A GAZ DE FAIBLE PUISSANCE **11658**
MOTEUR A HAUTE TENSION **6502**
MOTEUR A PETROLE **9046**
MOTEUR A PISTONS ROTATIFS **10754**
MOTEUR A QUATRE TEMPS **5603**
MOTEUR A QUATRE TEMPS **5600**
MOTEUR A VAPEUR **12164**
MOTEUR A VENT **13855**
MOTEUR A 2 CYLINDRES OPPOSES HORIZONTAUX **5398**
MOTEUR A 4 CYLINDRES OPPOSES HORIZONTAUX **5383**
MOTEUR ASYNCHRONE **783**
MOTEUR BLINDE OU CUIRASSE **4715**
MOTEUR BLINDE VENTILE **13529**
MOTEUR COMPOUND **2835**
MOTEUR DE DEMARRAGE **12121**
MOTEUR DE FAIBLE PUISSANCE **11661**
MOTEUR DE RESERVE **12070**
MOTEUR DIESEL **2866**

MOTEUR DIESEL **3901**
MOTEUR ELECTRIQUE **4623**
MOTEUR EN DERIVATION **11405**
MOTEUR EN ETOILE **10135**
MOTEUR EOLIEN PNEUMATIQUE **13855**
MOTEUR HYDRAULIQUE **6691**
MOTEUR MARIN **8005**
MOTEUR NON PROTEGE **8818**
MOTEUR OUVERT **8818**
MOTEUR POLYCYLINDRIQUE **8453**
MOTEUR PROTEGE **9941**
MOTEUR REFROIDI PAR AIR **251**
MOTEUR REVERSIBLE **10540**
MOTEUR SEMI-DIESEL **11171**
MOTEUR SOUS TENSION **7686**
MOTEUR SYNCHRONE **12571**
MOTEUR THERMIQUE **6345**
MOTEUR TRIPHASE **12876**
MOTEUR-GENERATEUR **8413**
MOTEUR-SERIE **11202**
MOTEUR-SHUNT **11405**
MOTEURS ELECTRIQUES **4524**
MOTEURS FIXES ET MOBILES **4766**
MOTOCULTEURS A FRAISES ROTATIVES **10753**
MOTTE DE TOURBE **9151**
MOUCHETTE **6544**
MOUFLE **9972**
MOUFLE A CORDE **10731**
MOUFLES **9973**
MOUILLAGE **8390**
MOUILLAGE **8348**
MOUILLER **8347**
MOULAGE **2068**
MOULAGE (REPRODUCTION A L'AIDE D'UN MOULE) **8428**
MOULAGE A CIRE PERDUE **7115**
MOULAGE A DECOUVERT **8820**
MOULAGE A LA TABLE **1169**
MOULAGE DE PRECISION **9765**
MOULAGE EN CHASSIS **1508**
MOULAGE EN COQUILLE **11333**
MOULAGE EN FOSSE **5445**
MOULAGE EN SABLE ETUVE **4354**
MOULAGE EN SABLE SEC **4354**
MOULAGE ETUVE **4354**
MOULAGE MECANIQUE **7851**
MOULAGE SORTIE EN LINGOTIERE **12703**
MOULAGE SOUS PRESSION **9812**
MOULAGE SOUS VIDE **13439**
MOULAGE SUR LE SOL **5445**
MOULAGES D'ACIER ALLIE **372**
MOULE **3883**

# MOU

MOULE 5570
MOULE 8352
MOULE (FOND.) 8423
MOULE A EMPREINTES MULTIPLES 2762
MOULE DE DESSOUS 8678
MOULE EN PLATRE 9465
MOULE EN PLATRE 6188
MOULE EN SABLE 10924
MOULE EN TERRE GLAISE 7693
MOULE METALLIQUE 3883
MOULE MULTIPLE 8466
MOULE NON-METALLIQUE 8650
MOULER 8424
MOULER 2030
MOULEUR 8427
MOULIN A BOCARDS 12057
MOULIN A MEULES VERTICALES 4450
MOULIN A VENT 13855
MOULINET A PALETTES 5031
MOULINET DYNAMOMETRIQUE 5031
MOULINET HYDRAULIQUE (POUR LA MESURE DE LA VITESSE D'ECOULEMENT D'UN COURANT D'EAU) 11027
MOULINS/APLATISSEURS 8296
MOULINS/BROYEUR 8297
MOULINS/COMBINE 8295
MOULURES FILEES 4969
MOUSQUETON 11691
MOUSSAGE 4461
MOUSSAGE 1331
MOUSSE 5499
MOUSSE A CELLULES FERMEES 2517
MOUSSE DE PLATINE 9514
MOUSSE DE PLATINE 11955
MOUSSELINE 2288
MOUTON 4325
MOUTON 4326
MOUTON A CHUTE LIBRE 4327
MOUTON A PLANCHE 1380
MOUTON-PENDULE CHARPY 2271
MOUTON-PENDULE DE CHARPY 6787
MOUVEMENT 8122
MOUVEMENT 3913
MOUVEMENT 12456
MOUVEMENT 8438
MOUVEMENT 8406
MOUVEMENT A COMMANDE ELASTIQUE 8629
MOUVEMENT A COMMANDE MECANIQUE 2985
MOUVEMENT A COMMANDE POSITIVE 2985
MOUVEMENT ABSOLU 32
MOUVEMENT ACCELERE 60
MOUVEMENT ALTERNATIF 10283

MOUVEMENT ALTERNATIF 13725
MOUVEMENT ANGULAIRE 544
MOUVEMENT APERIODIQUE 636
MOUVEMENT CIRCULAIRE 2421
MOUVEMENT CONTINU 3031
MOUVEMENT CURVILIGNE 3500
MOUVEMENT D'AVANCE 5584
MOUVEMENT D'HORLOGERIE 2509
MOUVEMENT DANS LE SENS RETROGRADE 919
MOUVEMENT DE GLISSEMENT 11605
MOUVEMENT DE RECUL 919
MOUVEMENT DE ROTATION 10766
MOUVEMENT DE ROULEMENT 10702
MOUVEMENT DE TRANSLATION 8407
MOUVEMENT DE VA-ET-VIENT 10283
MOUVEMENT DISCONTINU 7053
MOUVEMENT EN SENS CONTRAIRE 3243
MOUVEMENT GYROSCOPIQUE 6193
MOUVEMENT HELICOIDAL 6426
MOUVEMENT INTERMITTENT 7053
MOUVEMENT MOTEUR 6809
MOUVEMENT NON UNIFORME 8647
MOUVEMENT NON UNIFORMEMENT ACCELERE 8648
MOUVEMENT NON UNIFORMEMENT RETARDE 8649
MOUVEMENT OSCILLATOIRE 8881
MOUVEMENT PENDULAIRE 6302
MOUVEMENT PENDULAIRE 10283
MOUVEMENT PERIODIQUE 9194
MOUVEMENT PLANETAIRE 9447
MOUVEMENT RECTILIGNE 10320
MOUVEMENT RELATIF 10434
MOUVEMENT RETARDE 10518
MOUVEMENT ROTATOIRE 10766
MOUVEMENT SACCADE 7053
MOUVEMENT SPHERIQUE 11889
MOUVEMENT UNIFORME 13362
MOUVEMENT UNIFORMEMENT ACCELERE 13365
MOUVEMENT UNIFORMEMENT RETARDE 13367
MOUVEMENT VARIE 13490
MOYEN 8072
MOYEN D'HOMOGENEISATION 3754
MOYENNE ARITHMETIQUE 703
MOYENNE GEOMETRIQUE 5929
MOYEU 6661
MOYEU 1481
MOYEU D'UNE BRIDE 5329
MOYEU D'UNE SEULE PIECE 11779
MOYEU DE LA MANIVELLE 3297
MOYEU EN DEUX PIECES 11938
MUCILAGE 8440
MULTIPLICANDE 8479

# 681 NOM

MULTIPLICATEUR **8482**
MULTIPLICATEUR DE VITESSE **8921**
MULTIPLICATION **8480**
MULTIPLICATION **5909**
MULTIPLIER **8483**
MUNITION **474**
MURIATE D'AMMONIAQUE **462**
MUSCHELKALK **8487**
NACELLE **1383**
NACELLE DE PEINTRE **9017**
NAISSANT **8497**
NAPHTALENE **8494**
NAPHTALINE **8494**
NAPHTE **8493**
NAPHTOL **8495**
NAPHTOSCHISTE **8780**
NAPPE D'EAU SOUTERRAINE **6147**
NATIF **5647**
NECROSE **10770**
NEGATIVATION **4607**
NEODYME **8533**
NEODYMIUM **8534**
NEON **8535**
NERVURE **10569**
NERVURE D'UN TUBE **10570**
NETTETE D'UNE IMAGE **11276**
NETTOYAGE ALCALIN **334**
NETTOYAGE AU TAMBOUR **4335**
NETTOYAGE CATHODIQUE **2098**
NETTOYAGE DU METAL **2474**
NETTOYAGE MECANIQUE **8096**
NETTOYAGE PAR IMMERSION **11697**
NETTOYAGE PAR JETS D'AIR **244**
NETTOYANT ALCALIN **2472**
NETTOYER AU CHALUMEAU **5309**
NEUTRALISATION **8548**
NEUTRALISER **8549**
NEZ **8667**
NEZ D'UNE CLAVETTE **6318**
NICHE **10279**
NICHE **13617**
NICHE D'AGITATEUR **237**
NICKEL **8556**
NICKEL AU CARBONYLE **1978**
NICKEL ELECTROLYTIQUE **4600**
NICKELAGE **8567**
NICKELER **8566**
NIOBIUM **8576**
NIOBIUM **2747**
NITRATE **8579**
NITRATE **10903**

NITRATE D'AMMONIUM **465**
NITRATE D'ARGENT **7828**
NITRATE D'ETHYLE **4850**
NITRATE DE BISMUTH **1271**
NITRATE DE CUIVRE **3472**
NITRATE DE MERCURE **8156**
NITRATE DU CHILI **2330**
NITRATE MERCUREUX **8160**
NITRE **10903**
NITRITE **8586**
NITRITE D'AMMONIUM **466**
NITRITE DE CUIVRE **3473**
NITRITE DE POTASSE **9691**
NITRITE DE SOUDE **11725**
NITROBENZENE **8587**
NITROBENZINE **8587**
NITROCELLULOSE **6176**
NITROGENE **8588**
NITROGLYCERINE **8593**
NITROMETRE **8594**
NITRUM FLAMMANS **465**
NITRURATION **8589**
NITRURATION GAZEUSE **5830**
NIVEAU **6021**
NIVEAU **7525**
NIVEAU A BULLE D'AIR **13259**
NIVEAU A FIL **9540**
NIVEAU BAROMETRIQUE **6422**
NIVEAU D'EAU **13652**
NIVEAU D'EAU (HAUTEUR D'UN LIQUIDE) **13659**
NIVEAU DE L'EAU SOUTERRAINE **6148**
NIVEAU DE LA MER **11070**
NIVEAU SPHERIQUE **2430**
NODULAIRE **8606**
NOEUD **7313**
NOEUD COULANT **8651**
NOEUD D'OSCILLATION **8605**
NOEUD D'UNE COURBE **7741**
NOEUD DE VIBRATION **8605**
NOIR A NOIRCIR **7386**
NOIR ANIMAL **1447**
NOIR D'IVOIRE **1447**
NOIR DE FONDERIE **1297**
NOIR DE FUMEE **7386**
NOIR DE PLATINE **9511**
NOISETTES **2328**
NOIX D'ENTRAINEMENT POUR CHAINES-CABLES **11662**
NOIX DE ROBINET **9532**
NOIX POUR CHAINES **11662**
NOM COMMERCIAL **13101**
NOMBRE A SOUSTRAIRE **12426**

# NOM

682

NOMBRE ATOMIQUE **803**
NOMBRE COMMENSURABLE **10235**
NOMBRE COMPLEXE **2813**
NOMBRE COMPOSE **2820**
NOMBRE D'AMPERES **478**
NOMBRE D'UN LOGARITHME **8689**
NOMBRE DE CALORIES DEGAGEES DANS UNE REACTION **6348**
NOMBRE DE DENTS **8691**
NOMBRE DE FILETS **8692**
NOMBRE DE TOURS **8690**
NOMBRE DE VOLTS **13593**
NOMBRE DECIMAL **3664**
NOMBRE ENTIER **7012**
NOMBRE FRACTIONNAIRE **5613**
NOMBRE IMAGINAIRE **6781**
NOMBRE IMPAIR **8725**
NOMBRE IRRATIONNEL/INCOMMENSURABLE **7162**
NOMBRE PAIR **4872**
NOMBRE PREMIER **9860**
NOMBRE RATIONNEL **10235**
NOMBRE REEL **10260**
NOMENCLATURE **9095**
NOMENCLATURE DES PIECES **7662**
NON COMBINE **6818**
NON CONDUCTEUR **3898**
NON-FERREUX **8631**
NON-METALLIQUE **8639**
NON-REVERSIBILITE **7168**
NON-REVERSIBLE **7169**
NORIA **8960**
NORIA **1676**
NORMALE (GEOM.) **8652**
NORMALE D'UNE COURBE **8662**
NORMALISATION **12091**
NORMALISER **12090**
NORME **12071**
NOYAU **3142**
NOYAU D'UNE GARNITURE **3155**
NOYAU D'UNE VIS **1394**
NOYAU DE LA SECTION **3156**
NOYAU ETUVE **927**
NOYAU EXTERIEUR **5027**
NOYAU FILTRE **3164**
NOYAU MAGNETIQUE **3142**
NOYER UNE TETE DE RIVET **3246**
NOYER UNE TETE DE VIS **3246**
NUANCAGE **5434**
NUANCAGE **5443**
NUANCAGE **11453**
NUANCE/QUALITE DE L'ACIER **6022**

NUISANCE PAR LA FUMEE **11676**
NUMERATEUR **8693**
NUMERIQUE **3941**
NUMERO D'OPERATION EN COURS **8838**
NUMERO D'ORDRE DE LA FABRICATION **11197**
NUMERO DE CONSTRUCTION **4986**
NUMERO DE JAUGE D'UN FIL **5881**
NUMERO DE JAUGE D'UNE TOLE **5880**
NUMERO DE SEQUENCE **11193**
NUTATION **8702**
OBELISQUE **8705**
OBJECTIF **8708**
OBJECTIF **12682**
OBJET A EXAMINER AU MICROSCOPE SOUS FORME DE COUPE MINCE **11113**
OBLIQUITE **1065**
OBLONG **8715**
OBSERVATION MACROSCOPIQUE A L'OEIL NU **7873**
OBSIDIENNE **8716**
OBSTRUCTION **2362**
OBSTRUER (S') **2358**
OBTURATEUR **10760**
OBTURATEUR **9529**
OBTURATEUR **13453**
OBTURATEUR A LEVEE ANGULAIRE **5353**
OBTURATEUR GLISSANT **11592**
OBTURER L'ADMISSION DANS UNE TUYAUTERIE **11407**
OCCLUSION (CHIM.) **8719**
OCRE **8720**
OCRE JAUNE **2467**
OCTAEDRE **8722**
OCTANGLE **8721**
OCTANT **8724**
OCTOGONE **8721**
OCULAIRE **4977**
OCULAIRE-MICROMETRE **8254**
ODONTOGRAPHE **8726**
OEIL **4980**
OEIL D'UN MARTEAU **4975**
OEIL D'UNE HACHE **11231**
OEIL DE CHAT **2088**
OEIL DE LA BIELLE **4976**
OEILLET **4980**
OHM **8742**
OLIGISTE **11865**
OLIVES **8916**
OLIVINE **9243**
OLIVINE **8796**
OMBRE **11236**
OMBRE PORTEE **13339**
OMBRER **11234**

ONCTUOSITE DU LUBRIFIANT **7813**
ONDE **13699**
ONDE CALORIFIQUE **6379**
ONDE LUMINEUSE **7571**
ONDE SONORE **11819**
ONDE STATIONNAIRE **12145**
ONDULATION **13701**
ONDULATIONS **11419**
ONDULATIONS **2619**
ONDULATIONS DUES AU GAZ **5823**
ONDULER **3336**
ONGLET **8326**
ONGLET CYLINDRIQUE **13358**
ONGLET SPHERIQUE **11892**
OPACITE **8802**
OPAQUE **8803**
OPERATION **9096**
OPERATIONS A LA CHAINE **3034**
OPERATIONS PRELIMINAIRES **9787**
OPERATIONS PREPARATOIRES **9787**
OPERCULE DOUBLE **4162**
OPERCULE MONOBLOC (COIN) **11796**
OPERCULE PARALLELE A SERRAGE MECANIQUE **9053**
OPERCULE PARALLELE A SERRAGE PAR RESSORT **9052**
OPERCULE SIMPLE **11492**
OPHITE **11204**
OPTIQUE **8849**
OPTIQUE **8840**
OR **5993**
OR BATTU **6000**
OR BLANC **13831**
OR DE MONNAIE **5996**
OR ELECTROLYTIQUE **4598**
OR FIN **5198**
OR MUSIF **12099**
OR VERT **6092**
ORDONNEE **8858**
ORDRE **2780**
ORDRE D'ALLUMAGE **5260**
ORDRE D'INJECTION **6936**
ORDRE DE FONCTIONNEMENT **13626**
ORDRE DE GRANDEUR **8852**
ORDURES **13074**
OREILLE **7817**
ORFEVRERIE **6003**
ORGANE **7852**
ORGANE **7852**
ORGANE DE COMMANDE **3057**
ORGANE DE COMMANDE **4309**
ORGANE DE FIXATION **5042**
ORGANE DE LUBRIFICATION **7812**

ORGANE DE MACHINE **4756**
ORGANE TRAVAILLANT **13953**
ORGANES DE TRANSMISSION **13126**
ORGANISATION DES USINES **6901**
ORIENTATION **8867**
ORIENTATION DES CRISTAUX **3994**
ORIENTATION PREFERENTIELLE **9771**
ORIENTE AU HASARD **10199**
ORIFICE **9633**
ORIFICE **6530**
ORIFICE D'ADDUCTION **6947**
ORIFICE D'ADMISSION **6947**
ORIFICE D'ARRIVEE **6947**
ORIFICE D'ECHAPPEMENT **8902**
ORIFICE D'ECOULEMENT **8902**
ORIFICE D'ENTREE **6947**
ORIFICE D'INTRODUCTION **6947**
ORIFICE DE DECHARGE **8902**
ORIFICE DE GRAISSAGE **8761**
ORIFICE DE PASSAGE **9634**
ORIFICE DE PASSAGE **9100**
ORIFICE DE SORTIE **8902**
ORIFICE NOMINAL **8615**
ORIFICES A BRIDES **5339**
ORIFICES A SOUDER (EN BOUTA L'INTERIEUR) **1810**
ORIFICES FILETES (MALES) **11054**
ORIFICES TARAUDES (FEMELLES) **11053**
ORIGINE DES COORDONNEES **8868**
ORPIMENT **728**
OS PULVERISES **1448**
OSCILLATION **8884**
OSCILLATION D'UN PENDULE **12548**
OSCILLATION D'UN RESSORT **13558**
OSCILLATION ELECTRIQUE **4547**
OSCILLATION LIBRE **5643**
OSCILLATION LONGITUDINALE **7739**
OSCILLATION TRANSVERSALE **13146**
OSCILLATIONS DU REGULATEUR **6671**
OSCILLATIONS FORCEES **5535**
OSCILLER **8877**
OSCILLOGRAPHE **8885**
OSCILLOSCOPE **8886**
OSMIRIDIUM **8888**
OSMIUM **8889**
OSMOSE **8890**
OSSATURE **5630**
OSSEINE **1449**
OUATE **13612**
OUTIL **12994**
OUTIL A DEGROSSIR **10791**
OUTIL A ETIRER **4244**

# OUT

684

OUTIL A FINIR 5228
OUTIL A MAIN 6253
OUTIL A MAIN DE MARTELAGE 1734
OUTIL A SIMPLE EFFET 11496
OUTIL A TAILLANT 3538
OUTIL A TREFILER 4244
OUTIL A TREPANER 5494
OUTIL COUPANT 3538
OUTIL COUPANT (D'UNE MACHINE OUTIL) 13011
OUTIL DE ROULAGE 3485
OUTIL DE TOUR 13292
OUTIL DIAMANTE 3866
OUTIL PNEUMATIQUE 9556
OUTIL TRANCHANT 3538
OUTILLAGE 13015
OUTILLAGE 4794
OUTILLAGE DE MONTAGE 4812
OUTILLAGE DU DESSINATEUR 4236
OUTILLAGE DU MONTEUR 4817
OUTILLAGE EN ECHINE 1143
OUTILS A MISES EN CARBURE 2144
OUTILS EN ACIER RAPIDE 6475
OUTILS ET INSTRUMENTS DE DESSIN 4236
OUTREMER 13334
OUVERTURE 7963
OUVERTURE 12976
OUVERTURE DE CLEF 11832
OUVERTURE DE LA SOUPAPE 8832
OUVRAGE DE MACONNERIE 8025
OUVRAGER 13937
OUVRAGES EN BETON 2901
OUVRIER 13960
OUVRIER DE MACHINE -OUTIL 7868
OUVRIER EXPERIMENTE 3289
OUVRIER FONDEUR 5591
OUVRIER MECANICIEN 7868
OUVRIER MODELEUR 9130
OUVRIER MOULEUR 8427
OUVRIER NON SPECIALISE 13398
OUVRIER PROFESSIONNEL 3289
OUVRIER RABOTEUR 9443
OUVRIER RIVEUR 10641
OUVRIER TREMPEUR 13008
OUVRIR LE CIRCUIT ELECTRIQUE 8826
OVALE 4669
OVALISATION D'UN COUSSINET 13719
OXALATE 8968
OXALATE ACIDE DE POTASSIUM 118
OXALATE D'AMMONIAQUE 467
OXALATE DE CALCIUM 1853
OXALATE DE SODIUM 11726

OXALATE FERREUX 5124
OXALATE NEUTRE DE POTASSIUM 9692
OXIDATION ANODIQUE A L'ACIDE CHROMIQUE 2380
OXYCOUPAGE 5817
OXYCOUPAGE 8977
OXYCOUPAGE 7387
OXYDABLE 8972
OXYDANT 8974
OXYDATION 8970
OXYDATION 8984
OXYDATION (OU CORROSION) SECHE 4350
OXYDATION A TEMPERATURE ELEVEE 6498
OXYDATION ANODIQUE TRAITEMENT ANODIQUE 605
OXYDATION ELECTROLYTIQUE 4601
OXYDATION PAR FROTTEMENT 5667
OXYDE 8971
OXYDE AZOTEUX 8597
OXYDE AZOTIQUE 8581
OXYDE CUIVREUX 3479
OXYDE CUIVRIQUE 3474
OXYDE CUIVRIQUE HYDRATE 3471
OXYDE D'ALUMINIUM 413
OXYDE D'ETHYLE 8853
OXYDE D'ETHYLIDENE 84
OXYDE DE BISMUTH 1272
OXYDE DE CALCIUM 1854
OXYDE DE CARBONE 1952
OXYDE DE FER 5102
OXYDE DE FER 7144
OXYDE DE MAGNESIUM 7879
OXYDE DE MERCURE 8157
OXYDE DE METHYLE 8222
OXYDE DE METHYLENE 5573
OXYDE DE NICKEL 8574
OXYDE DE SODIUM 11724
OXYDE DE ZINC 14043
OXYDE FERREUX 5125
OXYDE FERRIQUE 7148
OXYDE MERCUREUX 8161
OXYDE MERCURIQUE 8157
OXYDE PUCE 7461
OXYDE SALIN DE MANGANESE 13207
OXYDE SALIN DE PLOMB 10333
OXYDE STANNEUX 12102
OXYDE STANNIQUE 12098
OXYDE SULFUREUX 12450
OXYDER 8973
OXYDER (S') 12685
OXYDER (S') 8973
OXYGENATION 8984
OXYGENE 8980

OZOKERITE **4413**
OZONE **8989**
PAIE **13613**
PAIEMENT **13613**
PAILLE **5056**
PAILLE **8279**
PAILLE **3283**
PAILLE DE FER **6217**
PAILLE DE FER **11953**
PAILLON D'ARGENT **11466**
PAILLON D'ETAIN **12955**
PAIRE **3252**
PAIRE DE CONES LISSES **404**
PALAN **6516**
PALAN **9973**
PALAN A CHAINE **2213**
PALAN A CORDE **10741**
PALAN A ENGRENAGE DROIT **12011**
PALAN A VIS SANS FIN **13973**
PALAN A VIS TANGENTE **13973**
PALAN DIFFERENTIEL **13798**
PALAN WESTON **13798**
PALES DE VENTILATEUR **5030**
PALETTE D'UNE ROUE HYDRAULIQUE **1677**
PALETTISATION **9026**
PALIER **9502**
PALIER **1117**
PALIER **1100**
PALIER **7388**
PALIER **12563**
PALIER A CHAISE SUR LE SOL **9154**
PALIER A CHARGE AXIALE **12902**
PALIER A CHARGE RADIALE/TRANSVERSALE **7257**
PALIER A COUSSINETS LISSES **9424**
PALIER A GALETS (A ROULEAUX) **10680**
PALIER A PATIN **9543**
PALIER A POTENCE **6321**
PALIER A ROULEMENT A BILLES **954**
PALIER A TOURILLON SPHERIQUE **952**
PALIER AUTO-REGULATEUR **11150**
PALIER AUXILIAIRE **7044**
PALIER AVEC PLAN DE SEPARATION INCLINE **508**
PALIER CONSOLE **1523**
PALIER COULISSANT **11596**
PALIER D'EXTREMITE **4720**
PALIER D'UN TOURILLON **11905**
PALIER DE BUTEE **12902**
PALIER DE BUTEE A BILLES **12900**
PALIER DE BUTEE A CANNELURES **12903**
PALIER DE BUTEE A UNE SEULE EMBASE **11479**
PALIER DE L'ARBRE DE COUCHE **3303**

PALIER DE L'ARBRE MANIVELLE **3303**
PALIER DE PIED; CRAPAUDINE **5524**
PALIER DE VILEBREQUIN **3314**
PALIER DE VILEBREQUIN **3303**
PALIER EN COQUILLES **4098**
PALIER EN DEUX PARTIES **4098**
PALIER EN UNE SEULE PIECE **11788**
PALIER FERME **11777**
PALIER GRAISSEUR A BAGUE **10602**
PALIER INTERMEDIAIRE **13547**
PALIER INTERMEDIAIRE **7048**
PALIER MURAL **1523**
PALIER PENDANT **6321**
PALIER PENDANT FERME **6270**
PALIER PENDANT OUVERT **6271**
PALIER SECONDAIRE **7044**
PALIER VERITICAL **5524**
PALIER-CONSOLE SUR COLONNE **9663**
PALIERS DE VILEBREQUIN **7941**
PALLADIUM **9023**
PALMER **11034**
PALMER **8249**
PALMER **1875**
PALPEUR **9882**
PALPEUR **11090**
PALPEUR A CADRAN **3842**
PAN D'UN ECROU **4994**
PANABASE **12796**
PANACHE **4777**
PAND D'UNE CLEF **7216**
PANNAGE **9157**
PANNE **1581**
PANNE A PIED DE BICHE **2463**
PANNE BOMBEE **963**
PANNE DU MARTEAU **9031**
PANNE EN LONG **12308**
PANNE EN TRAVERS **3369**
PANNE FENDUE **2463**
PANNE RONDE **961**
PANNE SPHERIQUE **963**
PANNEAU **9032**
PANNERESSE **12369**
PANTOGRAPHE **9033**
PAPIER A DESSIN **4240**
PAPIER A FILTRER **5177**
PAPIER A L'ACETATE DE PLOMB **7449**
PAPIER A LA PHENOIPHTALEINE **9239**
PAPIER ALBUMINE **311**
PAPIER AU FERRO-PRUSSIATE **5119**
PAPIER AU ROUGE CONGO **2936**
PAPIER BLEU POUR PHOTOCALQUE **5119**

**PAP** 686

PAPIER BUVARD **1350**
PAPIER CALQUE **13084**
PAPIER CARMIN **2002**
PAPIER CHERCHEUR DE POLES **9594**
PAPIER CONTINU **3013**
PAPIER CYANOFER **5119**
PAPIER D' EMERI **4696**
PAPIER D'AMIANTE **752**
PAPIER D'ANCHUSINE **342**
PAPIER D'EMBALLAGE **13984**
PAPIER D'INDICATEUR **6880**
PAPIER D'ORCANETINE **342**
PAPIER DE CURCUMA **13275**
PAPIER DE SOIE **12969**
PAPIER DE TOURNESOL **7668**
PAPIER DE VERRE **5961**
PAPIER GOMME/LAQUE **13506**
PAPIER HUILE **8788**
PAPIER IODOAMIDONNE **9690**
PAPIER JOSEPH **12969**
PAPIER MACHE **9036**
PAPIER METALLISE **8199**
PAPIER PELURE **12969**
PAPIER PHOTOCALQUE **9257**
PAPIER POLE **9594**
PAPIER POURRI **9036**
PAPIER PRUSSIATE **5119**
PAPIER QUADRILLE **11530**
PAPIER REACTIF **12783**
PAPIER SABLE **10925**
PAPIER TRANSPARENT **13084**
PAPIER-PARCHEMIN **9078**
PAPILLON **12888**
PAPILLON DE REGLAGE **12890**
PAPYRINE **9078**
PAQUET **5017**
PAQUET DE FER A SOUDER **5015**
PAQUETAGE **5018**
PARABOLE **9038**
PARABOLOIDE DE REVOLUTION **9042**
PARACHEVEMENT **11682**
PARACHEVEMENT **5220**
PARACHEVER **5214**
PARAFFINE **9043**
PARAFOUDRE **7575**
PARALLAXE **9047**
PARALLELE **9050**
PARALLELE **9049**
PARALLELEPIPEDE **9068**
PARALLELEPIPEDE DROIT **10581**
PARALLELEPIPEDE OBLIQUE **8713**

PARALLELEPIPEDE RECTANGLE **10305**
PARALLELISME **9069**
PARALLELOGRAMME **9070**
PARALLELOGRAMME ARTICULE **9057**
PARALLELOGRAMME DES FORCES **9071**
PARALLELOGRAMME DES VITESSES **9072**
PARAMAGNETIQUE **9073**
PARAMAGNETISME **9074**
PARAMETRE **9075**
PARAMETRES DE SOUDAGE **13787**
PARATONNERRE **7576**
PARC COUVERT **11302**
PARC DE STOCKAGE D'HYDROCARBURE **12627**
PARC NON COUVERT **12265**
PARCHEMIN **9077**
PARCHEMIN VEGETAL **9078**
PARCOURS **10810**
PARCOURS **4063**
PARE-BOUE **8443**
PARE-BRISE **13872**
PARE-CHOC **1732**
PARE-ETINCELLES **3109**
PARE-PIERRE **12275**
PARER **13204**
PAROI DE LA BOITE DE REFROIDISSEMENT **8381**
PAROI EPAISSE (A) **12841**
PAROI FRONTALE **4728**
PAROI MINCE (A) **12851**
PAROI PROTECTRICE **9953**
PARPAINGS **1697**
PART CENTRALE **2287**
PARTAGER **1266**
PARTICULE **9088**
PARTICULE ACICULAIRE **8517**
PARTICULE ALPHA **400**
PARTICULE BETA **1217**
PARTICULES COLLOIDALES **2736**
PARTICULES DE METAUX NOBLES **3548**
PARTICULES ENROBEES **2585**
PARTIE CONSTITUANTE VOLATILE **13586**
PARTIE DE DESSOUS (DE MOULE) **4199**
PARTIE DE DESSUS **3104**
PARTIE DEMONTABLE **7745**
PARTIE FIXE **3885**
PAS **12239**
PAS A DROITE **10585**
PAS A GAUCHE **7508**
PAS ANGLAIS **13844**
PAS CIRCONFERENTIEL **2423**
PAS D'UNE CHAINE **6978**
PAS DE FILETAGE **9399**

PAS DE L'ENGRENAGE **9408**
PAS DE L'HELICE **9410**
PAS DE VIS **9410**
PAS DE VIS **11045**
PAS DE VIS **12857**
PAS DIAMETRAL **3861**
PAS LINEAIRE **7615**
PAS POUR TUBES **9360**
PAS POUR TUBES A GAZ **5843**
PAS SYSTEME BRIGGS POUR TUBES **1605**
PAS SYSTEME INTERNATIONAL A BASE METRIQUE (S.I.) **7084**
PAS SYSTEME LOWENHERZ **7792**
PAS SYSTEME SELLERS **451**
PAS SYSTEME THURY **12552**
PAS WHITWORTH **13844**
PASSAGE A L'ENCRE **6942**
PASSAGE DE BROCHE **11906**
PASSAGE DE LA CHALEUR **9098**
PASSAGE DE LA COURROIE D'UNE POULIE SUR L'AUTRE **1158**
PASSAGE DE LA LUMIERE **9099**
PASSE **9096**
PASSE **10832**
PASSE A VIDE **4372**
PASSE DE DECALAMINAGE (LAMINAGE) **11541**
PASSE DE DEGAUCHISSAGE **11543**
PASSE DE DRESSAGE **11543**
PASSE DE FINISSAGE **11541**
PASSE DE FINISSAGE **11542**
PASSE HUMIDE **13803**
PASSE LARGE **13724**
PASSE REFOULEUSE **4455**
PASSE-COURROIE **1159**
PASSE-PARTOUT **3365**
PASSER A L'ENCRE **6940**
PASSER A L'ETAT LIQUIDE **8135**
PASSERELLE **5776**
PASSERELLE **13616**
PASSERELLE DE LIAISON **2964**
PASSIVANT **9106**
PASSIVATION **9105**
PASSIVITE **9107**
PASTEL **2745**
PASTILLEUSE **9310**
PATE **12112**
PATE A PAPIER **9035**
PATE A POLIR **2827**
PATE A SOUDER **9108**
PATE A SURFACER ET A RODER **6108**
PATE CHIMIQUE DE BOIS **2316**

PATE MECANIQUE DE BOIS **8116**
PATENTAGE **9124**
PATENTAGE A L'AIR **280**
PATIN **11587**
PATIN D'UN PALIER **1034**
PATINAGE DE LA COURROIE **11620**
PATINAGE DES ROUES **11621**
PATINE **9127**
PATINER **11612**
PATRON **12734**
PATTE **7817**
PATTE D'ARAIGNEE **7810**
PATTE D'ARAIGNEE **8759**
PATTES DE LEVAGE PAR VERINS **7206**
PAVE **9136**
PAVE (PIERRE) **9137**
PEAU D'ORANGE **6008**
PEAU D'ORANGE (AFNOR) **9134**
PEAU DE BUFFLE **1685**
PEAU DE CHAMOIS **2234**
PEAU DE CHIEN **11270**
PEAU DE CROCODILE **348**
PEAU DE NETTOYAGE **2234**
PEAU DE PORC **9300**
PECHBLENDE **9411**
PECHURANE **9411**
PEDALE **13174**
PEDALE D'EMBRAYAGE **2547**
PEIGNE **12384**
PEIGNE A FILETER **4952**
PEIGNE A TARAUDER **7060**
PEIGNE POUR L'EXTERIEUR **4952**
PEIGNE POUR L'INTERIEUR **7060**
PEIGNE POUR LES PAS DE VIS **2274**
PEINTURAGE **9018**
PEINTURE **9018**
PEINTURE **9013**
PEINTURE **2583**
PEINTURE A L'EAU **13664**
PEINTURE A L'HUILE **8766**
PEINTURE AU PISTOLET **9020**
PEINTURE AU PISTOLET **6179**
PEINTURE PAR PULVERISATION AU PISTOLET **11965**
PEINTURE SOUS-JACENTE **9864**
PEINTURE VERNISSANTE **4711**
PEINTURER **9014**
PEINTURES **2599**
PELLE **11385**
PELLETER **11386**
PELLICULE **5171**
PELLICULE **11544**

**PEL** 688

PELLICULE 5166
PELLICULE D'EAU 5169
PELLICULE D'OXYDE 5168
PELLICULE EN BOBINE 10667
PELLICULE GRASSE 5167
PELLICULE PASSIVANTE 9104
PELLICULE RIGIDE 8993
PENDANT 6321
PENDULE 9167
PENDULE CIRCULAIRE 2422
PENDULE COMPENSATEUR 2808
PENDULE COMPENSE 2808
PENETRATION 9170
PENETRATION 11507
PENETRATION A FROID 2689
PENETRATION DE LA CHALEUR 6368
PENETROMETRE 10061
PENETROMETRE 9171
PENICHE 991
PENOMBRE 9177
PENTACHLORURE D'ANTIMOINE 624
PENTACHLORURE DE PHOSPHORE 9254
PENTAEDRE 9175
PENTAGONE 9172
PENTANE NORMAL 9176
PENTASULFURE D'ANTIMOINE 625
PENTE 3792
PENTE 6836
PENTE 11627
PENTE D'UNE CLAVETTE 12654
PERCAGE 1468
PERCAGE 4277
PERCAGE 12675
PERCAGE 10006
PERCAGE PAR JET DE FLAMME 7222
PERCARBONATE DE POTASSE 9693
PERCEE 1589
PERCER 4264
PERCER 10771
PERCER DES TROUS 9186
PERCEUR -MECANICIEN 4276
PERCEUSE 9296
PERCEUSE 4279
PERCEUSE 1472
PERCEUSE A BRAS ARTICULE 12550
PERCEUSE A COLONNE 2755
PERCEUSE A COLONNE 9312
PERCEUSE A GRANDE VITESSE 6495
PERCEUSE A TETES MULTIPLES 5799
PERCEUSE D'ETABLI 1168
PERCEUSE DE CHAUDIERES 1409

PERCEUSE ELECTRIQUE 9732
PERCEUSE HORIZONTALE 6581
PERCEUSE MULTIBROCHE EN LIGNE 8460
PERCEUSE PORTATIVE 9636
PERCEUSE POUR BOITE D'ESSIEU 878
PERCEUSE RADIALE 10134
PERCEUSE SUR BATI OU MONTANT 2755
PERCEUSE SUR COLONNE STANDARD 13412
PERCEUSE-ALESEUSE A COORDONNEES 3098
PERCEUSES RIGIDES 10590
PERCHLORATE DE POTASSE 9694
PERCOIR POUR TOLE 9997
PERCUSSION 11359
PERD (QUI) 7493
PERFORATION PAR DECHARGE DISRUPTIVE 10013
PERFORER 9186
PERFOREUSE 10001
PERIDOT 9243
PERIDOT 8796
PERIMETRE 9190
PERIODE DE DEMARRAGE OU DE MISE EN MARCHE D'UNE USINE 12123
PERIODICITE 9196
PERIODIQUE 9191
PERIPHERIE DU CERCLE 2404
PERLASSE 9143
PERLE 9146
PERLE DE SOUDURE 11842
PERLITE 9144
PERMALLOY 9201
PERMANGANATE DE POTASSE 9695
PERMEABILITE 9211
PERMEABILITE MAGNETIQUE 7911
PERMEABLE 9213
PERMEABLE A L'AIR 9212
PERMEAMETRE 9214
PERMIS DE CONDUIRE 4302
PERMUTATION 9216
PERMUTATION CYCLIQUE 3556
PEROXYDE 7148
PEROXYDE D'AZOTE 8591
PEROXYDE DE MANGANESE 10047
PEROXYDE HYDRATE DE FER 5101
PERPENDICULAIRE 9217
PERPENDICULARITE 9219
PERSONNEL OUVRIER 13962
PERSPECTIF 9220
PERSPECTIVE 9220
PERSPECTIVE 1264
PERSPECTIVE AXONOMETRIQUE 885
PERSPECTIVE LINEAIRE 7614

689 PIE

PERSULFATE D'AMMONIAQUE **468**
PERTE **13594**
PERTE **7754**
PERTE A VIDE **8599**
PERTE ADDITIONNELLE **170**
PERTE AU FEU **7761**
PERTE AU FEU **7341**
PERTE AU ROUGE **7341**
PERTE D'ENERGIE **7758**
PERTE DE CHALEUR **6353**
PERTE DE CHALEUR **7760**
PERTE DE CHALEUR PAR RAYONNEMENT **10145**
PERTE DE CHARGE **6315**
PERTE DE CHARGE **7759**
PERTE DE FROTTEMENT **7755**
PERTE DE POIDS **7764**
PERTE DE PRESSION **7763**
PERTE DE PUISSANCE **7762**
PERTE DE TRAVAIL **7765**
PERTE DUE AU FROTTEMENT **5685**
PERTE PAR CHOCS **7757**
PERTE PAR EVAPORATION **4866**
PERTE PAR FUITES **7756**
PERTE PAR REFLEXION **10389**
PERTE PAR REMPLISSAGE **5163**
PERTE PAR RESPIRATION **1594**
PERTE THERMIQUE **6353**
PERTES AU FEU **6763**
PERTES DE FUSION **8140**
PERTES DE MAGNETISATION **7907**
PERTES PAR CRACHEMENT **11843**
PERTES THERMOGENES **6381**
PERTURBATION **1581**
PESAGE **13746**
PESANTEUR **6078**
PESE-ACIDES **89**
PESE-ALCOOLS **316**
PESE-LIQUEURS **6722**
PESE-SELS **10901**
PESEE **13746**
PESER **13744**
PESON A RESSORT **11976**
PETIT AXE D'UNE ELLIPSE **8313**
PETIT DIAMETRE DU FILET **3850**
PETIT METAL **8632**
PETITE CALORIE **6045**
PETREOLINE **13508**
PETROLE **9226**
PETROLE **9222**
PETROLE **9229**
PETROLE BRUT **3411**

PETROLE BRUT **3412**
PETROLE BRUT SULFUREUX **11822**
PETROLE BRUT TOPPE **13040**
PETROLE LAMPANT **7275**
PETROLEINE **13508**
PH. **9231**
PHARE **6326**
PHARE **6327**
PHARE DE BROUILLARD **5506**
PHARE ENCASTRE **5480**
PHASE **9232**
PHASE CONTINUE **3033**
PHASE DISPERSEE **4049**
PHASE DISPERSIVE **3033**
PHENOL **1938**
PHENOLPHTALEINE **9238**
PHENOMENE **9240**
PHENOMENE LUMINEUX **7566**
PHENYLAMINE **552**
PHONAUTOGRAPHE **9242**
PHOSPHATATION **2600**
PHOSPHATE **9244**
PHOSPHATE D'AMMONIUM **469**
PHOSPHATE DE CALCIUM **1855**
PHOSPHATE DE MAGNESIE **8656**
PHOSPHATE DE POTASSIUM **9696**
PHOSPHATE DE SODIUM **11728**
PHOSPHATE DE SODIUM ET D'AMMONIUM **8241**
PHOSPHATE TRICALCIQUE **1855**
PHOSPHORE **9252**
PHOSPHORE BLANC **14009**
PHOSPHORE ROUGE **10334**
PHOSPHORESCENCE **9247**
PHOSPHORESCENT **9248**
PHOTO-DIODE **9258**
PHOTOCALQUE **9276**
PHOTOCOPIE **9276**
PHOTOGRAPHIE **9263**
PHOTOGRAPHIE **9265**
PHOTOGRAPHIER **9262**
PHOTOMETRE **9267**
PHOTOMETRIE **9271**
PHOTOMETRIQUE **9269**
PHOTOMULTIPLICATEUR **9274**
PHOTON **9275**
PHTALEINE DU PHENOL **9238**
PHYLLITE **9278**
PHYSIQUE **9285**
PHYSIQUE **9279**
PIECE **9083**
PIECE A TRAVAILLER **9293**

**PIE** 690

PIECE BRUTE **1301**
PIECE D'AJUSTAGE **9006**
PIECE D'APPUI **10876**
PIECE D'ECARTEMENT **4068**
PIECE D'USINAGE **9293**
PIECE DE COMPENSATION **4922**
PIECE DE FONDERIE **2079**
PIECE DE FONTE MOULEE **2079**
PIECE DE FORGE **5556**
PIECE DE GROSSE FORGE **6406**
PIECE DE MACHINE **7852**
PIECE DE MOULAGE CREUSE **6539**
PIECE DE RECHANGE **11834**
PIECE DE REFERENCE **8034**
PIECE DETACHEE **3811**
PIECE DETACHEE **11484**
PIECE FACONNEE **11265**
PIECE FINIE **5730**
PIECE FORGEE **5556**
PIECE FORGEE A EBAVURAGE EXCESSIF **8322**
PIECE FORGEE A LA MAIN **11669**
PIECE FORGEE AU MARTEAU **11670**
PIECE INTERCHANGEABLE **11834**
PIECE MATRICEE **4324**
PIECE MECANIQUE **7852**
PIECE MOULEE **2069**
PIECE RAPPORTEE **6965**
PIECE RAPPORTEE **6970**
PIECE TRAVAILLEE A LA FORGE **5556**
PIECES COULEES (OU MOULEES) **2080**
PIECES DEFECTUEUSES **3696**
PIECES DETACHEES (EN) **7329**
PIECES MOULEES EN FONTE GRISE **2083**
PIECES MOULEES RESISTANTES AUX TEMPERATURES
ELEVEES **2084**
PIECES MOULEES(OU COULEES) RESISTANT A LA CORROSION
**2082**
PIED **1041**
PIED **13537**
PIED A COULISSE **11597**
PIED A COULISSE A CADRAN **3986**
PIED A COULISSE A VERNIER POUR DENTS DE PIGNON
**5900**
PIED A DENTURE **5899**
PIED A PROFONDEUR **3781**
PIED ANGLAIS **5518**
PIED CARRE ANGLAIS **12020**
PIED CUBE ANGLAIS **3453**
PIED CUBE NORMALISE **12072**
PIED DE BIELLE **3389**
PIED DE DENT **10724**

PIED DE LA BIELLE A FOURCHETTE **5568**
PIED DE LA DENT **10725**
PIEGE A CAILLOUX **9153**
PIERRAILLE **1644**
PIERRE A AFFILER **13824**
PIERRE A AFFUTER **13824**
PIERRE A AIGUISER **13824**
PIERRE A BATIR **1700**
PIERRE A BRIQUET **5427**
PIERRE A FUSIL **5427**
PIERRE A HUILE **8781**
PIERRE A PLATRE **6190**
PIERRE ARTIFICIELLE **737**
PIERRE D'AIMANT **8506**
PIERRE DE PAREMENT **5004**
PIERRE DE SAVON **10935**
PIERRE DE TAILLE **761**
PIERRE DE VERRE **5957**
PIERRE DE VIN **119**
PIERRE INFERNALE **7828**
PIERRE MEULIERE **8299**
PIERRE NATURELLE **8507**
PIERRE PONCE **9988**
PIERRE PONCE **9986**
PIERRES CONCASSEES **1644**
PIETEMENT **8679**
PIEZO-ELECTRICITE **9297**
PIEZOMETRE **12067**
PIGNON **5889**
PIGNON **9444**
PIGNON **9335**
PIGNON A FUSEAUX **9324**
PIGNON CONIQUE **1226**
PIGNON DE CHAINE **9402**
PIGNON DE DISTRIBUTION **12949**
PIGNON DE VILLEBREQUIN **3315**
PIGNON EN CUIR VERT **10238**
PILE **9304**
PILE DE VOLTA **13596**
PILE ELECTRIQUE **2126**
PILE GALVANIQUE **5782**
PILE HYDRO-ELECTRIQUE **5782**
PILE LOCALE **7694**
PILE PHOTO-ELECTRIQUE **9259**
PILE PRIMAIRE **9846**
PILE SECHE **4343**
PILE SECONDAIRE **4534**
PILE THERMIQUE **12820**
PILE THERMO-ELECTRIQUE **12836**
PILE THERMOELECTRIQUE **12820**
PILE VOLTAIQUE **13596**

691 PLA

PILER **9712**
PILETTE MECANIQUE **1732**
PILIER **9311**
PILON DE BOCARD **12055**
PILON DE MORTIER **9221**
PIMELEINE **13508**
PIN NOIR D'AUTRICHE **1293**
PINACOIDE **9327**
PINCE **3394**
PINCE (D'UN APPAREIL DE LEVAGE) **7557**
PINCE A CREUSET **3405**
PINCE A SOUDER **11767**
PINCE COUPANTE **3532**
PINCE COUPANTE DIAGONALE **3832**
PINCE DE FORGERON **1298**
PINCE DE JET D'EAU **4286**
PINCE DE MOHR **8345**
PINCE EMPORTE-PIECE **10000**
PINCE MOTORISTE **2764**
PINCE PLATE **5403**
PINCE RONDE **10805**
PINCEAU **9019**
PINCEAU **2743**
PINCEAU LUMINEUX **9162**
PINCEMENT **7212**
PINCEMENT **12975**
PINCES (S) **12987**
PINCES A GAZ **5835**
PINCES A TUBES **9362**
PINCETTE **5536**
PINT **9337**
PION DE CENTRAGE **2153**
PIPETTE **9368**
PIPETTE A CYLINDRE **1718**
PIPETTE DROITE GRADUEE **6028**
PIQUAGE **9629**
PIQUAGE AU MARTEAU **2347**
PIQUEE **6333**
PIQURE **9333**
PIQURE **9393**
PIQURE **10171**
PIQURE DE CORROSION **3190**
PIQURE DE LAMINAGE **9417**
PIQURES **9416**
PIQURES **9334**
PIQURES DE CORROSION **4843**
PISSETTE **13633**
PISTE **13085**
PISTE D'ESSAI **12794**
PISTOLET **5660**
PISTOLET A PROJETER **11962**

PISTOLET DE PULVERISATION **11962**
PISTOLET DE SOUDAGE PAR POINTS **6180**
PISTOLETS A GOUJONS **12400**
PISTON **9370**
PISTON A AIR **282**
PISTON A CLAPET **1673**
PISTON A CONTRE-TIGE **9391**
PISTON A DOUBLE EFFET **4164**
PISTON A DOUBLE TIGE **9391**
PISTON A EAU **13667**
PISTON A SIMPLE EFFET **11494**
PISTON A TIGE UNIQUE **9392**
PISTON A VAPEUR **12179**
PISTON CHAUFFE **6384**
PISTON CONIQUE **2944**
PISTON DE DEUX PIECES **1709**
PISTON DE FERMETURE DU MOULE **2535**
PISTON DE LEVAGE **7555**
PISTON DE MOTEUR HYDRAULIQUE **13667**
PISTON DE POMPE **9995**
PISTON DE VERIN **10188**
PISTON DISTRIBUTEUR **9390**
PISTON ELEVATOIRE **1673**
PISTON EVIDE **1514**
PISTON OSCILLANT **8882**
PISTON PLEIN **11791**
PISTON PLONGEUR **9545**
PISTON RAMSBOTTOM **10196**
PISTON REFROIDI **3084**
PISTON ROTATIF **10756**
PISTON SANS TIGE **13241**
PISTON SUEDOIS **10196**
PIT A TREMPER **11699**
PITON **4973**
PITON-VIS **11057**
PIVOT **9315**
PIVOT **9419**
PIVOT **9421**
PIVOT **9420**
PIVOT (D'UN ARBRE VERTICAL) **9421**
PIVOT ANNULAIRE **10606**
PIVOT D'UNE CHAINE A ROULEAU **9320**
PIVOT SPHERIQUE **11893**
PIVOTANT **9422**
PLACAGE **9503**
PLACAGE **13524**
PLACAGE **2447**
PLACAGE A LA FLAMME **5317**
PLACAGE AU LAITON **1567**
PLACAGE MECANIQUE **8108**
PLACE FOU (SUR L'ARBRE) **7749**

# PLA

692

PLAFONNIER 10709
PLAFONNIER 4119
PLAGE D'OXYDE 5367
PLAN 4229
PLAN 3794
PLAN 9433
PLAN 11124
PLAN 9426
PLAN 9430
PLAN AUTOMOTEUR 6081
PLAN D'ACCOLEMENT (MACLE) 2826
PLAN D'ENSEMBLE 8905
PLAN D'EXECUTION 4984
PLAN D'EXECUTION (ATELIER) 11361
PLAN D'INTERSECTION 7095
PLAN DE CHARGE 7683
PLAN DE CISAILLEMENT 11284
PLAN DE CLIVAGE 2488
PLAN DE CRISTAL 3427
PLAN DE DISPOSITION 5914
PLAN DE GLISSEMENT 5975
PLAN DE JOINT 9093
PLAN DE LA TOLERIE 9504
PLAN DE MASSE 8905
PLAN DE MONTAGE 4814
PLAN DE MONTAGE 772
PLAN DE PROJECTION 9438
PLAN DE REFRACTION 9439
PLAN DE RUPTURE 3373
PLAN DE SYMETRIE 9440
PLAN DEFINITIF 5185
PLAN DETAILLE 3812
PLAN FOCAL 5501
PLAN INCLINE 6081
PLAN INCLINE 6838
PLAN OPTIQUE 8843
PLAN OSCULATEUR 8887
PLAN PRISMATIQUE 9877
PLAN RETICULAIRE 804
PLAN RETICULAIRE 7432
PLANAGE 9118
PLANAGE 9454
PLANCHE 9032
PLANCHE A DESSIN 4231
PLANCHE DU MARTEAU 4993
PLANCHE FORTE 9457
PLANCHE MINCE 1379
PLANCHER COUVERTURE DE PLANCHER 5450
PLANCHER DE VOITURE 5446
PLANE 4221
PLANER 5405

PLANETAIRE 9445
PLANEUSE 9451
PLANEUSE 12372
PLANIMETRAGE 8087
PLANIMETRE 9448
PLANIMETRER 8084
PLANIMETRIE 9449
PLANTEUSES DE POMMES DE TERRE 9705
PLAQUAGE AU NICKEL 8567
PLAQUE 9477
PLAQUE 9032
PLAQUE CIRCULAIRE 4999
PLAQUE D'ACCUMULATEUR 81
PLAQUE D'ANCRAGE 13621
PLAQUE D'APPUI 1127
PLAQUE D'ASSISE 1037
PLAQUE DE BASE 1037
PLAQUE DE BLINDAGE 712
PLAQUE DE CONSCIENCE (DE VILLEBREQUIN) 1590
PLAQUE DE CUIVRE 3123
PLAQUE DE DAME 3596
PLAQUE DE FOND 1037
PLAQUE DE FOND 1486
PLAQUE DE FONDATION 1037
PLAQUE DE GARDE 6593
PLAQUE DE GARDE 6160
PLAQUE DE LIEGE 3175
PLAQUE DE LIEGE AGGLOMERE 9802
PLAQUE DE RECOUVREMENT 3267
PLAQUE DE REDRESSEUR 10315
PLAQUE DE RENFORT 12257
PLAQUE DE TOURBE 9150
PLAQUE DE VERRE 5963
PLAQUE EN FEUTRE 11322
PLAQUE FRONTALE 4999
PLAQUE METALLIQUE 11315
PLAQUE MODELE 1710
PLAQUE MODELE DOUBLE FACE 8044
PLAQUE NEGATIVE 8530
PLAQUE PHOTOGRAPHIQUE 11187
PLAQUE POSITIVE 9658
PLAQUE SENSIBLE 11187
PLAQUE TOURNANTE 13295
PLAQUE TUBULAIRE 13254
PLAQUE-MODELE 2052
PLAQUER 9479
PLAQUES COLLECTIVES 2726
PLAQUETTE 9498
PLAQUETTE 11075
PLAQUETTES UNISERVICE 12896
PLASTICITE 3705

**693** **POC**

PLASTICITE **9474**
PLASTIFIANT **9475**
PLASTRON **1590**
PLAT DE MAINTIEN **13029**
PLAT-SUPPORT **902**
PLATE **8993**
PLATE-FORME A DIVISER **4109**
PLATE-FORME EN PORTE-A-FAUX **13875**
PLATEAU **13167**
PLATEAU A AIMANTS PERMANENTS **9205**
PLATEAU A DIVISIONS **4109**
PLATEAU D'ACCOUPLEMENT **3255**
PLATEAU D'UNE BALANCE **10976**
PLATEAU DE DEMOTTAGE **2012**
PLATEAU DE FOUR **6512**
PLATEAU DE FRICTION **5673**
PLATEAU DIVISE **4109**
PLATEAU DIVISEUR **4109**
PLATEAU DIVISEUR **4106**
PLATEAU TOURNANT **10762**
PLATEAU-MANIVELLE **4003**
PLATEAUX CIRCULAIRES **2424**
PLATEAUX DIVISEURS **6870**
PLATEAUX MAGNETIQUES **7912**
PLATEFORME **5776**
PLATEFORME DE JAUGEAGE **5885**
PLATELAGE **6101**
PLATELAGE **5449**
PLATELAGE **5451**
PLATINE **11306**
PLATINE (METAL) **9510**
PLATINE (PETITE PLAQUE METALLIQUE) **4174**
PLATINE DE FIXATION **9499**
PLATINE IRIDIE **9515**
PLATINITE **9508**
PLATINOCYANURE DE BARYUM **1002**
PLATRE **9466**
PLATS **5375**
PLATS EN ACIER ALLIE **373**
PLEINE CHARGE **5722**
PLI **4408**
PLI **5511**
PLI **3320**
PLI CHARNIERE **6506**
PLIAGE **1182**
PLIAGE A CHAUD **6619**
PLIAGE A FROID **2668**
PLIER **1173**
PLIEUSE **1181**
PLIEUSE **11087**
PLIEUSES **4453**

PLIS **1680**
PLISSER **3336**
PLOMB **7447**
PLOMB **9539**
PLOMB (DU FIL A PLOMB) **9538**
PLOMB (SCEAU EN PLOMB) **7480**
PLOMB AIGRE **621**
PLOMB ANTIMONIAL **621**
PLOMB ANTIMONIEUX **6276**
PLOMB D'OEUVRE **3409**
PLOMB DE SURETE **10886**
PLOMB DOUX **8014**
PLOMB DURCI **6276**
PLOMB EN FEUILLES **7462**
PLOMB EN FEUILLES **11314**
PLOMB FUSIBLE **10886**
PLOMB FUSIBLE **5758**
PLOMB IMPUR **1029**
PLOMB MARCHAND **8014**
PLOMB NON RAFFINE **1029**
PLOMB PUR **2311**
PLOMB SPONGIEUX **11954**
PLOMB SULFURE **5775**
PLOMBAGINE **9542**
PLOMBAGINE **9541**
PLOMBE **7479**
PLOMBER (MARQUER D'UN SCEAU EN PLOMB) **11077**
PLOMBERIE **7484**
PLONGER **3968**
PLONGEUR **9545**
PLONGEUR (DE THERMOMETRE) **1711**
PLOT **3009**
PLUME **9161**
PLUME A DESSIN **7999**
PLUME DE RONDE **10806**
PNEU **13322**
PNEU A CARCASSE RADIALE **10126**
PNEU A CLOUS **12404**
PNEU A CRAMPONS **12404**
PNEUMATIQUE **9549**
PNEUMATIQUE **9558**
PNEUS A FLANCS BLANCS **13840**
POCHE A MAIN A MANCHE **6250**
POCHE A QUENOUILLE **1496**
POCHE BRIQUETEE **7618**
POCHE DE COULEE **7356**
POCHE DE COULEE A ANSE **11258**
POCHE DE COULEE A MAIN **6238**
POCHE DE COULEE A RENVERSEMENT **12935**
POCHE DE GRUE DE COULEE **1728**
POCHE DE GRUE DE COULEE **3292**

## POC

POCHE DE RETRAITE 1353
POCHE GARNIE 7618
POCHE MELANGEUSE 8333
POCHE THEIERE 12693
POCHE-TONNEAU 4336
POCHE-TONNEAU 13110
POCHOIR 12238
POIDS 13747
POIDS (POUR CENT DU) 9180
POIDS ATOMIQUE 807
POIDS AU METRE 13748
POIDS BRUT 10781
POIDS BRUT 6141
POIDS CONSOMME 2992
POIDS DE CHARGE 8356
POIDS DU MOUTON 4329
POIDS EN ORDRE DE MARCHE 3480
POIDS MAXIMUM 8070
POIDS MINIMUM 8310
POIDS MOLECULAIRE 8363
POIDS MORT 3637
POIDS PROPRE 3637
POIDS SPECIFIQUE 11850
POIGNEE 6262
POIL 1890
POILS DE CHAMEAU 1890
POILS DE LA CRINIERE 7965
POILS DE QUEUE DE CHEVAL 12594
POINCON 9544
POINCON 3162
POINCON 9997
POINCON (D'INSPECTION) 3893
POINCON DE TRACAGE 9844
POINCON INFERIEUR 7794
POINCONNAGE 10006
POINCONNAGE 10008
POINCONNAGE 10012
POINCONNAGE 3894
POINCONNER 9999
POINCONNER 9998
POINCONNEUSE 10001
POINCONNEUSE 10009
POINCONNEUSE-CISAILLE 10007
POINCONNEUSE-DECOUPEUSE 10009
POINT 9559
POINT A LUBRIFIER 8789
POINT CHAUD 6642
POINT CRITIQUE 3347
POINT D'AFFAISSEMENT 11750
POINT D'ALLUMAGE 6759
POINT D'APPLICATION 9561

POINT D'APPUI 9567
POINT D'ARTICULATION 5717
POINT D'EBULLITION 1424
POINT D'ECLAIR 5368
POINT D'IMAGE 6780
POINT D'INFLAMMABILITE 5368
POINT D'INFLAMMATION 5363
POINT D'INFLAMMATION 6764
POINT D'INFLAMMATION 6759
POINT D'INFLEXION 9564
POINT D'INTERSECTION 9565
POINT D'OBJET 8706
POINT DANS L'ESPACE 9560
POINT DE COMBUSTION 5247
POINT DE CONCOURS 9565
POINT DE CONDENSATION 3824
POINT DE CONGELATION 5656
POINT DE CONTACT 3005
POINT DE CONTACT 9562
POINT DE CROISEMENT 3393
POINT DE CURIE 7920
POINT DE DEPART D'UN MOUVEMENT 12124
POINT DE FEU (HUILE) 5247
POINT DE FLAMME 6764
POINT DE FLAMME 5363
POINT DE FUSION 5759
POINT DE FUSION 8141
POINT DE FUSION ELEVE (A) 6308
POINT DE GUIDAGE DES NOYAUX 3144
POINT DE MESURE 8091
POINT DE PRISE 11804
POINT DE REBROUSSEMENT 3502
POINT DE REFERENCE 10368
POINT DE REFERENCE ABSOLU 34
POINT DE RENCONTRE 9565
POINT DE REPERE 9566
POINT DE RUPTURE 9563
POINT DE SOLIDIFICATION 11804
POINT DE SOLIDIFICATION 11800
POINT DE SOLIDIFICATION 5656
POINT DE SUSPENSION 9568
POINT DE TANGENCE 9562
POINT DE TRANSFORMATION 718
POINT DE TRANSFORMATION 3347
POINT DE TRANSITION 13122
POINT FIXE 5295
POINT ISO-ELECTRIQUE 7175
POINT LUMINEUX 7823
POINT MORT 3635
POINT MORT 3626
POINT MORT BAS 1491

POINT MORT HAUT (P.M.H.) **13411**
POINT MORT HAUT (P.M.H) **13032**
POINT TRIPLE **13216**
POINT ZERO **14027**
POINTE A TRACER **11068**
POINTE DE L'ELECTRODE **4579**
POINTE DE PARIS **13895**
POINTE DE RECHANGE **3006**
POINTE TRACANTE DU PLANIMETRE **13079**
POINTEAU **8522**
POINTEAU DE CENTRAGE **2172**
POINTES ABRASIVES **24**
POINTES POUR FONDERIE **5598**
POINTS BRILLANTS **6472**
POIRE DE VITESSE **11871**
POISSAGE **12591**
POIX **9400**
POIX SECHE **2737**
POLAIRE **9577**
POLARISATION **9582**
POLARISATION **9589**
POLARISATION (D'UN ELECTRODE) PAR CHUTE DE
  CONCENTRATION **2889**
POLARISATION ANODIQUE **604**
POLARISATION CATHODIQUE **2108**
POLARISATION ELECTROLYTIQUE **4604**
POLARISCOPE **9584**
POLARISEUR **9586**
POLARITE **9587**
POLAROGRAPHIE **9590**
POLE **9592**
POLE (ELECTR.) **9591**
POLE D'UN AIMANT **9595**
POLE MAGNETIQUE **7913**
POLE NEGATIF **8531**
POLE NORD D'UN AIMANT **8665**
POLE POSITIF **9659**
POLE SUD D'UN AIMANT **11827**
POLES DE NOM CONTRAIRE **13392**
POLES DISSEMBLABLES **13392**
POLES SEMBLABLES **7581**
POLI (QUI PREND BIEN LE) **9599**
POLI (SUSCEPTIBLE D'UN BEAU) **9599**
POLI (SUSCEPTIBLE DE PRENDRE UN) **9599**
POLI PARFAIT **1755**
POLIR **9598**
POLIR A L'EMERI **4694**
POLIR BRILLANT **1756**
POLISSAGE **9600**
POLISSAGE **9605**
POLISSAGE **5408**

POLISSAGE A BILLES **956**
POLISSAGE A L'EMERI **4695**
POLISSAGE A LA MAIN **6228**
POLISSAGE AU TAMBOUR **1012**
POLISSAGE DE LA SURFACE **3527**
POLISSAGE ELECTROLYTIQUE **4605**
POLISSOIR **1686**
POLONIUM **9606**
POLYCHROME **9607**
POLYEDRE **9612**
POLYGONE **9609**
POLYGONE ARTICULE **5737**
POLYGONE CIRCONSCRIT **2436**
POLYGONE DES FORCES **9610**
POLYGONE ETOILE **12107**
POLYGONE FUNICULAIRE **5737**
POLYGONE INSCRIT **6964**
POLYGONE IRREGULIER **7164**
POLYGONE REGULIER **10416**
POLYMERE **9613**
POLYMERIE **9616**
POLYMERISATION **9614**
POLYMERISER (SE) **9615**
POLYMORPHISME **9617**
POLYSULFURE DE POTASSIUM **9697**
POMME D'ARROSOIR **10746**
POMPAGE **6670**
POMPE **9991**
POMPE A ACIDE **121**
POMPE A AIR **284**
POMPE A AIR HUMIDE **13799**
POMPE A AIR SEC **4340**
POMPE A BRAS **6244**
POMPE A DIAPHRAGME **3874**
POMPE A ENGRENAGE **5895**
POMPE A HUILE **8769**
POMPE A MAIN **6244**
POMPE A MENBRANE **3874**
POMPE A MERCURE **8163**
POMPE A PALETTES **13478**
POMPE A PALETTES ROTATIVES **10758**
POMPE A PISTON **9378**
POMPE A PISTON A MOUVEMENT RECTILIGNE ET
  ALTERNATIF **10284**
POMPE A PISTON OSCILLANT **11176**
POMPE A PISTON PLONGEUR **9546**
POMPE A ROTOR **10758**
POMPE A VAPEUR **12183**
POMPE A VIDE **284**
POMPE ASPIRANTE **12434**
POMPE CENTRIFUGE **13269**

**POM**

POMPE CENTRIFUGE **2184**
POMPE D'AIR **249**
POMPE D'ALIMENTATION **5715**
POMPE D'ALIMENTATION **5071**
POMPE D'ALIMENTATION **5713**
POMPE D'EPREUVE **12787**
POMPE D'INJECTION **5711**
POMPE DE GRAISSAGE **8769**
POMPE DE REPRISE **61**
POMPE DUPLEX **4381**
POMPE ELEVATOIRE **7545**
POMPE FOULANTE **5531**
POMPE HELICOIDALE **861**
POMPE HELICOIDALE **11042**
POMPE HYDRAULIQUE **8769**
POMPE PNEUMATIQUE **284**
POMPE PORTATIVE **9638**
POMPE POUR PUITS PROFONDS **3689**
POMPE ROTATIVE **10758**
POMPE VOLUMETRIQUE **9653**
POMPES **9996**
PONCAGE **9990**
PONCE **9988**
PONCER **9987**
PONCEUSE **4010**
PONCEUSE **4006**
PONDERABLE **9619**
PONT **3667**
PONT A BASCULE **13745**
PONT ARRIERE (MOTEUR) **10265**
PONT DE CHAUFFE **5308**
PONT DE WHEATSTONE **13809**
PONT ROULANT **13156**
PONT ROULANT DEMOULEUR **12383**
PONT SUSPENDU **12528**
PONT TRANSBORDEUR **13141**
PONT-ROULANT D'USINE **8942**
PONT-ROULANT DE CHANTIER/DE GARE **5804**
POQUETTE **1327**
PORCELAINE **9625**
PORE **9627**
POREUX **9630**
POROGENE **9628**
POROSITE **9629**
POROSITE A COMMUNICATION INTERNE **7029**
POROSITES SUPERFICIELLES **9178**
PORPHYRE **9632**
PORPHYRE QUARTZIFERE **10081**
PORT DE DECHARGEMENT (DE NAVIRES MARCHANDS) **8736**
PORTANCE DU SOL **11751**
PORTE **891**

PORTE A INCANDESCENCE **6824**
PORTE AU ROUGE CERISE **2327**
PORTE AU ROUGE NAISSANT **1288**
PORTE DU FOYER **5242**
PORTE OUTILS **13012**
PORTE-A-FAUX **8934**
PORTE-A-FAUX **8936**
PORTE-ALESOIRS **10264**
PORTE-CLAPET **4008**
PORTE-COURROIE **1159**
PORTE-CRAYON D'UN COMPAS **9165**
PORTE-ELECTRODE **4575**
PORTE-ESTAMPE **3884**
PORTE-ESTAMPES **8033**
PORTE-GICLEUR **7219**
PORTE-INJECTEUR **8682**
PORTE-MICROMETRE **8250**
PORTE-MOUSQUETON **11691**
PORTE-OBJET **12047**
PORTE-OUTIL **13003**
PORTE-OUTIL A PLUSIEURS OUTILS **5801**
PORTE-OUTILS **13005**
PORTE-POINCONS **8033**
PORTEE **7256**
PORTEE (DISTANCE ENTRE DEUX POINTS D'APPUI) **11831**
PORTEE D'ASSEMBLAGE DRESSEE (D'UNE PIECE DE FONDERIE) **5007**
PORTEE D'UN ARBRE **1107**
PORTEE D'UN MANETON **1116**
PORTEE DE MODELE **3161**
PORTEE DU SON **10202**
PORTER AU ROUGE **5982**
PORTES-BILLONNEUSES **10573**
PORTIERE ARRIERE **891**
PORTIQUE **9641**
PORTIQUE DE ROULEMENT **13224**
POSE D'UN FIL CONDUCTEUR **13909**
POSE DE PLAQUETTES DE COUPE METAL DUR **6278**
POSE DE TUBES **9356**
POSE DES RIVETS **6972**
POSER **11390**
POSER DES TUYAUX **7441**
POSER LES RIVETS **6967**
POSER UN FIL CONDUCTEUR **13881**
POSITION **3940**
POSITION AU POINT MORT **9646**
POSITION BINAIRE **1249**
POSITION D'EQUILIBRE **9647**
POSITION DE DEPART **12126**
POSITION DE LA MANIVELLE **9645**
POSITION DE MILIEU **8265**

POSITION DE REPOS **9648**
POSITION DE ZERO **14028**
POSITION DU PISTOLET DE SOUDAGE **13782**
POSITION FINALE **5187**
POSITION INTERMEDIAIRE **8265**
POST-PROCESSEUR **9665**
POSTCHAUFFAGE **9668**
POSTE **8839**
POSTE D'ESSAI **12773**
POSTE DE SOUDAGE A COURANT ALTERNATIF **2**
POSTE DE SOUDAGE A COURANTS ALTERNATIF ET CONTINU **59**
POSTE RECEPTEUR **10278**
POT A FEU **3821**
POT A RECUIRE **566**
POT D'ECHAPPEMENT **11431**
POT D'ECHAPPEMENT **8448**
POTASSE **9679**
POTASSE AZOTEUSE **9691**
POTASSE CAUSTIQUE **9687**
POTASSE NITREUSE **9691**
POTASSIUM **9672**
POTEAU **12062**
POTEAU **2748**
POTEAU AVEC LES DEUX EXTREMITES GUIDEES **2756**
POTEAU DE LIGNE ELECTRIQUE **7608**
POTEE D'EMERI **5453**
POTEE D'ETAIN **12098**
POTENCE **3618**
POTENTIEL **9708**
POTENTIEL D'ELECTRODE **4577**
POTENTIEL DE CONTACT **3007**
POTENTIOMETRE **9711**
POUCE ANGLAIS **6830**
POUCE CARRE ANGLAIS **12021**
POUCE CUBE ANGLAIS **3454**
POUDINGUE **8490**
POUDRAGE AU SULFURE **4394**
POUDRE ABRASIVE **6110**
POUDRE ALLIEE **367**
POUDRE CARBURANTE **2139**
POUDRE D'EMERI **4697**
POUDRE D'OS **1448**
POUDRE DE BOIS **13916**
POUDRE DE BRONZE **1652**
POUDRE DE CARBONYLE **1979**
POUDRE DE CHARBON **9984**
POUDRE DE DIAMANT **3863**
POUDRE DE FER **7145**
POUDRE DE LIEGE **6144**
POUDRE DE PONCE **9727**

POUDRE DE ZINC OXYDE **1374**
POUDRE DENTRIDIQUE **3749**
POUDRE GLOBULAIRE **5979**
POUDRE GROSSIEREMENT BROYEE **2580**
POUDRE IMPALPABLE **6789**
POUDRE NOIRE **6181**
POUDREUSES PORTATIVES **11969**
POUDREUSES PULVERISATEURS **11971**
POUDREUSES SOUFREUSES **11970**
POULIE **11301**
POULIE (APPAREIL DE LEVAGE) **9971**
POULIE A BRAS COURBES **9976**
POULIE A BRAS DROITS **9977**
POULIE A BRAS PARABOLIQUES **9976**
POULIE A BRASSURE DOUBLE **4127**
POULIE A CABLE **10742**
POULIE A CHAINE **2217**
POULIE A CORDE **975**
POULIE A COURROIE **1152**
POULIE A EMPREINTES **2217**
POULIE A EXPANSION **4909**
POULIE A GORGE **6140**
POULIE A GORGE **6135**
POULIE A GRIFFES **2503**
POULIE A JANTE PERFOREE **9188**
POULIE AVEC JOUES **5336**
POULIE AVEC REBORDS **5336**
POULIE BOMBEE **3400**
POULIE COMMANDEE **4298**
POULIE CONDUCTRICE **4313**
POULIE CONDUITE **4298**
POULIE CYLINDRIQUE **5404**
POULIE D' EXCENTRIQUE **4434**
POULIE D'ATTAQUE **4313**
POULIE DE COMMANDE **4313**
POULIE DE FREIN **1548**
POULIE DE RENVOI **6161**
POULIE DE RENVOI **10551**
POULIE DE TENSION **12334**
POULIE DE VENTILATEUR **5032**
POULIE DROITE **5404**
POULIE EN CARTON **9034**
POULIE EN DEUX PIECES **11945**
POULIE EN TOLE EMBOUTIE **9805**
POULIE EN UNE PIECE **11792**
POULIE ENTRAINEE **4298**
POULIE ETAGEE **11871**
POULIE EXTENSIBLE **4909**
POULIE FENDUE **11945**
POULIE FIXE **5040**
POULIE FIXE (D'UN PALAN) **5287**

# POU

698

POULIE FOLLE **6754**
POULIE FOLLE **7747**
POULIE MAL TOURNEE **9974**
POULIE MENANTE **4313**
POULIE MENEE **4298**
POULIE MOBILE (D'UN PALAN) **8435**
POULIE MOTRICE **4313**
POULIE POUR CABLE DE TRANSMISSION **10742**
POULIE RECEPTRICE **4298**
POULIE-CONE **12669**
POULIE-GUIDE **6161**
POULIE-TAMBOUR **4333**
POULIE-VOLANT **1147**
POULIES MOUFLEES **9973**
POUPEE (DE TOUR) **7964**
POUPEE (ELECTR.) **12762**
POUPEE DE PERCAGE **4278**
POUPEE DE TOUR **6328**
POUPEE FIXE **6328**
POUPEE MOBILE **12599**
POURCENTAGE DE CENDRES **758**
POURCENTAGE DE CHARBON **1965**
POURRIR **10036**
POURRITURE (ETAT) **10035**
POURRITURE DU BOIS **10770**
POUSEE DE BAS EN HAUT **1742**
POUSSEE AU SOMMET **12908**
POUSSEE AXIALE **4734**
POUSSEE DES TERRES **12907**
POUSSEE DU VENT **13858**
POUSSEE HORIZONTALE **6590**
POUSSEE LONGITUDINALE **4734**
POUSSIER DE COKE **2659**
POUSSIER DE HOUILLE **2563**
POUSSIER DE TOURBE **9726**
POUSSIERE **4389**
POUSSIERE D'OR **5998**
POUSSIERE DE GUEULARD **5469**
POUSSIERES DE GAZ DE HAUT FOURNEAU **5469**
POUSSOIR **10029**
POUSSOIR **9797**
POUSSOIR **12672**
POUSSOIR A GALET **10692**
POUSSOIR DE SOUPAPE **13466**
POUTRE **1099**
POUTRE **1093**
POUTRE **5946**
POUTRE A LARGES AILES **1639**
POUTRE AU VENT **13856**
POUTRE COMPOSEE **9488**
POUTRE COMPOSEE **9490**

POUTRE CONTINUE **3018**
POUTRE DE PONT ROULANT **13157**
POUTRE EN BOIS **949**
POUTRE EN FER **12199**
POUTRE EN PORTE-A-FAUX **1904**
POUTRE EN PORTE-A-FAUX **1905**
POUTRE EN TREILLIS **7431**
POUTRE ENCASTREE **6968**
POUTRE ENCASTREE **5286**
POUTRE ENCASTREE **1702**
POUTRE ENCASTREE A SES DEUX EXTREMITES **1703**
POUTRE ENCASTREE A UNE EXTREMITE **1904**
POUTRE ENCASTREE A UNE EXTREMITE ET REPOSANT A
  L'AUTRE SUR UN APPUI **1097**
POUTRE ENROBEE **4714**
POUTRE INCORPOREE **7010**
POUTRE MIXTE OU COMPOSEE **2831**
POUTRE NON ENTRETOISEE **1905**
POUTRE RAIDISSEUSE **13856**
POUTRE RAYONNANTE **10131**
POUTRE REPOSANT SOUTENUE LIBREMENT SUR DEUX APPUIS
  **1098**
POUTRELLE **1093**
POUTRELLE **986**
POUTRELLE A LARGES AILES **13849**
POUTRELLE EN I **6748**
POUTRELLE EN U **2249**
POUTRELLES A LARGES AILES **1641**
POUVOIR ABSORBANT **42**
POUVOIR ADHESIF **176**
POUVOIR CALORIFIQUE **6378**
POUVOIR CALORIFIQUE **6392**
POUVOIR COUVRANT **3273**
POUVOIR DISSOLVANT **4062**
POUVOIR ECLAIRANT **6776**
POUVOIR EMISSIF **4701**
POUVOIR EMISSIF MONOCHROMATIQUE **8382**
POUVOIR GROSSISSANT **7937**
POUVOIR ISOLANT **7000**
POUVOIR LUBRIFIANT **7806**
POUVOIR OPACIFIANT INSUFFISANT **6119**
POUVOIR RAYONNANT **4702**
POUVOIR REFLECHISSANT **10393**
POUVOIR REFLECHISSANT **10392**
POUVOIR REFRINGENT **10403**
POUZZOLANE **9748**
POZZOLANE **9748**
PRASEODYME **9750**
PRATIQUER UNE SAIGNEE DANS UNE PIECE **8554**
PRE-ALLIAGE **5594**
PRE-MODELE **4370**

PRECAUTIONS **9753**
PRECESSION **9754**
PRECHARGE **9782**
PRECHAUFFAGE **9776**
PRECIPITABLE **9757**
PRECIPITANT **9758**
PRECIPITATION **9761**
PRECIPITATION **9091**
PRECIPITATION DE CARBURE **1934**
PRECIPITE **9759**
PRECIPITER **9760**
PRECIPITER (SE) **9760**
PRECISION **9763**
PRECISION **82**
PRECISION D'USINAGE **83**
PRECONTRAINTE **9782**
PRECONTRAINTE DU BETON **2899**
PREFILTRE **9751**
PREFORMAGE **9773**
PREFORMAGE **1341**
PREFORME **9772**
PREFRITTAGE **9794**
PREMIER FILTRE **5265**
PREMIERE COUCHE DE PEINTURE **9864**
PREMIERE TETE DE RIVET **5266**
PREPARATION **9784**
PREPARATION D'UNE SOLUTION **9785**
PREPARATION DES BORDS **4449**
PREPARATION DES MINERAIS **8861**
PREPARER UNE SOLUTION **9788**
PRESELECTEUR **9789**
PRESERVANT DE LA ROUILLE **10868**
PRESERVATIF CONTRE LA ROUILLE **10869**
PRESSAGE **9806**
PRESSAGE A FROID **2690**
PRESSE **9795**
PRESSE A CALIBRER **11525**
PRESSE A COIN **13734**
PRESSE A COLLER **2451**
PRESSE A COMPRIMER LES POUDRES **9718**
PRESSE A EBARBER **13211**
PRESSE A EXCENTRIQUE **4430**
PRESSE A FILER **4972**
PRESSE A FORGER **5562**
PRESSE A FORGER HYDRAULIQUE **6687**
PRESSE A GENOUILLERES **12980**
PRESSE A LEVIER **7534**
PRESSE A PASTILLES **9310**
PRESSE A VIS **11040**
PRESSE A VIS **2452**
PRESSE BRINELL **1553**

PRESSE DE COULEE **3370**
PRESSE DE MENUISIER **2451**
PRESSE HYDRAULIQUE **6693**
PRESSE HYDRAULIQUE A COL DE CYGNE **8828**
PRESSE HYDRAULIQUE A EMBOUTIR **6682**
PRESSE HYDRAULIQUE A MARTEAU-PILON **6687**
PRESSE MECANIQUE A ARCADE **4157**
PRESSE MECANIQUE A BATI COL DE CYGNE **8814**
PRESSE MECANIQUE A CALIBRER ET A MATRICER **1864**
PRESSE MECANIQUE A FRAPPER **9182**
PRESSE MECANIQUE A MONTANT **12316**
PRESSE MECANIQUE A PLATEAU REVOLVER **3839**
PRESSE MONETAIRE **2653**
PRESSE PLIEUSE **9481**
PRESSE POUR TOLES FORTES **6411**
PRESSE ROTATIVE **10757**
PRESSE-ETOUPE **5953**
PRESSE-ETOUPE **12405**
PRESSES TRANSFERT A POINCONS MULTIPLES **8461**
PRESSION **13434**
PRESSION **9808**
PRESSION (CHAUD.) **6314**
PRESSION ABSOLUE **33**
PRESSION ABSOLUE **4459**
PRESSION ATMOSPHERIQUE **794**
PRESSION BAROMETRIQUE **794**
PRESSION CONSTANTE **2976**
PRESSION CRITIQUE **3348**
PRESSION D'EAU **13669**
PRESSION D'EPREUVE **12786**
PRESSION D'ESSAI **12786**
PRESSION DANS UNE CHAUDIERE **1417**
PRESSION DE COMPRESSION **2859**
PRESSION DE LA VAPEUR **12181**
PRESSION DE REGIME **13957**
PRESSION DE REGLAGE **9832**
PRESSION DE SATURATION **10944**
PRESSION DE SERVICE **13957**
PRESSION DE X CM DE MERCURE **794**
PRESSION DU COURANT **9825**
PRESSION DU GAZ **5837**
PRESSION DU VENT **13858**
PRESSION DUE AU FROTTEMENT **9816**
PRESSION EN KILOGRAMMES PAR UNITE DE SURFACE
 **11853**
PRESSION EXPLOSIVE **4936**
PRESSION FINALE **5188**
PRESSION HYDRAULIQUE **13669**
PRESSION HYDROSTATIQUE **6726**
PRESSION INITIALE **6929**
PRESSION INTERIEURE DANS UNE CONDUITE **9822**

# PRE 700

PRESSION LATERALE **7422**
PRESSION LIMITE **7593**
PRESSION MANOMETRIQUE **9809**
PRESSION MANOMETRIQUE **5771**
PRESSION MOYENNE **8075**
PRESSION NOMINALE **8613**
PRESSION NORMALE **8657**
PRESSION OSMOTIQUE **8891**
PRESSION PARTIELLE **9087**
PRESSION REELLE **4459**
PRESSION RELATIVE **5882**
PRESSION STATIQUE **12136**
PRESSION STATIQUE **12137**
PRESSION SUPERFICIELLE **12517**
PRESSION SUPERIEURE A LA PRESSION AUTORISEE **8955**
PRESSION SUR LE PISTON **9377**
PRESSION SUR LES ARETES **9826**
PRESSION SUR LES SURFACES D'APPUI **1110**
PRESSION TOTALE **13065**
PRESSION VARIABLE **13491**
PRESSION/REACTION SUR LES TOURILLONS **7259**
PRESSSPAHN **9801**
PRIMAGE (ENTRAINEMENT DE L'EAU PAR LA VAPEUR) **9863**
PRIMEROSE SOLUBLE **4831**
PRISE **3483**
PRISE (EN) **8171**
PRISE (DU CIMENT) **3484**
PRISE D'AIR **289**
PRISE D'AIR **270**
PRISE D'UN ECHANTILLON **10916**
PRISE DE FORCE **9745**
PRISE DE POUSSIERES **3997**
PRISE DIRECTE **3983**
PRISE DU CIMENT **11226**
PRISMATIQUE **9879**
PRISMATOIDE **9880**
PRISME **9875**
PRISME A SECTION OBLIQUE **9876**
PRISME D'EGALE RESISTANCE **1396**
PRISME HEXAGONAL **6460**
PRISME PENTAGONAL **9173**
PRISME POLARISATEUR **9586**
PRISME QUADRANGULAIRE **10055**
PRISME TRIANGULAIRE **13192**
PRISONNIER **12399**
PRISONNIER **11220**
PRIX A LA JOURNEE **3594**
PRIX DE MAIN-D'OEUVRE **7346**
PRIX DE REVIENT **3210**
PROCEDE **9883**

PROCEDE 'UNIONMELT' **684**
PROCEDE A L'OXYGENE **8982**
PROCEDE A PARTIR DES PRODUITS RESULTANT DE LA DECOMPOSITION DE L'HYDRURE. **6699**
PROCEDE ACIDE **120**
PROCEDE AU CREUSET **3404**
PROCEDE BASIQUE **1050**
PROCEDE BASIQUE **1043**
PROCEDE BAYER **1073**
PROCEDE BESSEMER **1214**
PROCEDE BESSEMER AU CONVERTISSEUR A GARNISSAGE ACIDE **106**
PROCEDE BETTS **1220**
PROCEDE CHAPMAN **2254**
PROCEDE CHIMIQUE **2291**
PROCEDE D'AFFINAGE **10380**
PROCEDE D'AMALGAMATION **448**
PROCEDE D'USINAGE **9887**
PROCEDE DE FABRICATION **8218**
PROCEDE DE FINITION CHIMIQUE DE SURFACE **2309**
PROCEDE DE MOULAGE AU MOYEN DU SAC EN CAOUTCHOUC **923**
PROCEDE DE MOULAGE INVERSE **11656**
PROCEDE DE REVETEMENT EN BAIN CHAUD **6659**
PROCEDE DUPLEX **4380**
PROCEDE FOUR KALDO **7271**
PROCEDE HANSGIRG **6272**
PROCEDE OLD **8793**
PROCEDE PAR ASPERSION **11972**
PROCEDE SIEMENS-MARTIN **8830**
PROCEDE THOMAS **1043**
PROCEDES CHIMIQUES DE TRAITEMENT DE SURFACE **2314**
PROCESSEUR **9889**
PROCESSUS **9883**
PROCESSUS DE RECHARGEMENT **1696**
PRODUCTION **10462**
PRODUCTION **8028**
PRODUCTION D'ENERGIE **5922**
PRODUCTION D'ENERGIE **9737**
PRODUCTION DE CHALEUR **9896**
PRODUCTION DE COURANT **9894**
PRODUCTION DU FROID **9895**
PRODUCTION EN SERIE **11198**
PRODUCTIVITE **9897**
PRODUIRE (DE LA VAPEURDES GAZ) **5916**
PRODUIRE UN COURANT ELECTRIQUE **5917**
PRODUIT **9892**
PRODUIT **9784**
PRODUIT (MATH.) **9891**
PRODUIT ANTI-ROUILLE **10870**
PRODUIT ANTI-ROUILLE **3189**

PRODUIT ANTI-ROUILLE **10866**
PRODUIT DE COMBUSTION **9893**
PRODUIT DE DISTILLATION **4071**
PRODUIT DE NETTOYAGE **2471**
PRODUIT DE RAFFINAGE **10374**
PRODUIT DE REVETEMENT **2589**
PRODUIT FINAL **5189**
PRODUIT FINI **5730**
PRODUIT FINI / PLAT / LONG **5218**
PRODUIT FORMANT DES POROSITES **9628**
PRODUIT HYDROFUGE **13674**
PRODUIT INTERMEDIAIRE **7043**
PRODUIT MANUFACTURE **7989**
PRODUIT PRIMAIRE **9852**
PRODUIT SCALAIRE **10966**
PRODUIT SECONDAIRE **1820**
PRODUIT SEMI-OUVRE **11174**
PRODUIT SPECIAL **11849**
PRODUIT VECTORIEL **13509**
PRODUITS CHIMIQUES **2320**
PRODUITS DE NETTOYAGE ET DE POLISSAGE **2475**
PRODUITS DE PREMIERE QUALITE **9862**
PRODUITS EN ACIER A RAIL **10177**
PROFIL **9898**
PROFIL **8906**
PROFIL **12734**
PROFIL **7717**
PROFIL (A DROITEA GAUCHE) **11420**
PROFIL D'UNE DENT **13019**
PROFIL DE DENTURE **13020**
PROFIL EN LONG **7738**
PROFIL NORMAL **12083**
PROFIL TRANSVERSAL **3377**
PROFILAGE **10668**
PROFILAGE A FROID **2682**
PROFILE **11119**
PROFILE EN T **12700**
PROFILE MI-ROND **6209**
PROFILE(S) **11114**
PROFILER **5571**
PROFILES LOURDS **6413**
PROFILES MARCHANDS **8149**
PROFONDEUR **3779**
PROFONDEUR D'ENGRENEMENT **13952**
PROFONDEUR DE COUPE **3782**
PROFONDEUR DE COUPE **3526**
PROFONDEUR DE LA COUCHE CEMENTEE **2020**
PROFONDEUR DU COL DE CYGNE **3783**
PROFONDEUR DU FILET **3784**
PROGRAMMATION **9904**
PROGRAMMATION AUTOMATIQUE **850**

PROGRAMMATION DE PIECE **9084**
PROGRAMMATION MANUELLE DE PIECE **6242**
PROGRAMME **9902**
PROGRAMME D'ORDINATEUR **10811**
PROGRAMME DE FABRICATION **7994**
PROGRAMME DIAGNOSTIQUE **3830**
PROGRESSION **11203**
PROGRESSION ARITHMETIQUE **704**
PROGRESSION GEOMETRIQUE **5930**
PROJECTEUR **6326**
PROJECTEUR D'OMBRE **11238**
PROJECTEUR DE LUMIERE **11091**
PROJECTION **11968**
PROJECTION **9912**
PROJECTION CENTRALE **10137**
PROJECTION DIMETRIQUE **3961**
PROJECTION GNOMOMIQUE **5990**
PROJECTION HORIZONTALE **11124**
PROJECTION ISOMETRIQUE **7188**
PROJECTION OBLIQUE **2501**
PROJECTION ORTHOGONALE **8870**
PROJECTION PARALLELE **9058**
PROJECTION TRIMETRIQUE **13208**
PROJECTION VERTICALE **4659**
PROJET **3794**
PROJETER **9909**
PROJETER DANS... **6934**
PROLONGATION DE DUREE D'UN BREVET **9919**
PROMETHEUM **6771**
PROPAGATION D'ONDES **9926**
PROPANE **9927**
PROPORTION **3011**
PROPORTION **9934**
PROPORTION (MATH.) **9933**
PROPORTION D'EAU **13645**
PROPORTION DE CARBONE **1947**
PROPORTIONNALITE **9938**
PROPORTIONNEL **9935**
PROPORTIONS DEFINIES **2771**
PROPRIETE COUVRANTE **1393**
PROPRIETE DE COUVRIR D'UNE COULEUR **1393**
PROPRIETE REFRACTAIRE **10405**
PROPRIETES ANTI-FRICTION **617**
PROPRIETES CHIMIQUES **2295**
PROPRIETES PHYSIQUES **9283**
PROPULSEUR **11041**
PROPULSION A 4 ROUES MOTRICES **5601**
PROPYLENE **9939**
PROSPERITE ECONOMIQUE D'UNE ENTREPRISE **9462**
PROTACTINIUM **9940**
PROTECTION **9943**

**PRO** 702

PROTECTION 11346
PROTECTION CATHODIQUE 2109
PROTECTION CONTRE LA CORROSION 3191
PROTECTION CONTRE LA ROUILLE 9945
PROTECTION CONTRE LA ROUILLE 10871
PROTECTION DE LA PROPRIETE INDUSTRIELLE 9946
PROTOCARBURE D'HYDROGENE 8215
PROTOCHLORURE D'ETAIN 12100
PROTOCHLORURE DE MERCURE 8159
PROTON 9954
PROTOSULFURE 627
PROTOTYPE 9955
PROTOXYDE D'AZOTE 8597
PROTOXYDE DE BARYUM 1020
PROTOXYDE DE FER 5125
PROTOXYDE DE MANGANESE 7973
PROTOXYDE DE MERCURE 8161
PROTOXYDE DE NICKEL 8565
PROTOXYDE DE PLOMB 7663
PRUSSIATE JAUNE 9685
PRUSSIATE ROUGE 9684
PSYCHROMETRE 9960
PUDDLER 9964
PUISSANCE 9730
PUISSANCE 7308
PUISSANCE 1917
PUISSANCE (MATH.) 9729
PUISSANCE ABSORBANTE 42
PUISSANCE ABSORBEE 4747
PUISSANCE AU FREIN 4458
PUISSANCE AU FREIN 1540
PUISSANCE AU FREIN 1535
PUISSANCE AU FREIN EN CHEVAUX 151
PUISSANCE CALORIFIQUE 6392
PUISSANCE DE FREINAGE 1551
PUISSANCE DE LEVAGE D'UN AIMANT 13090
PUISSANCE EFFECTIVE 1540
PUISSANCE EFFECTIVE 4458
PUISSANCE EFFECTIVE EN CHEVAUX 151
PUISSANCE FISCALE 10233
PUISSANCE INDIQUEE 6875
PUISSANCE INDIQUEE (OU FISCALE) 6874
PUISSANCE MAXIMUM 8066
PUISSANCE MOTRICE 8409
PUISSANCE NOMINALE 10233
PUISSANCE RECUEILLIE 4747
PUISSANCE REQUISE 3746
PUISSANCE/ALIMENTATION 4546
PUITS (D'UNE MINE) 9398
PUITS A GRANULATION DU LAITIER 6056
PUITS D'AERATION 291

PULSOMETRE 9980
PULVERISABLE 9981
PULVERISATEUR 11967
PULVERISATEUR 809
PULVERISATION 6117
PULVERISATION 811
PULVERISATION 2786
PULVERISATION 2226
PULVERISATION 11968
PULVERISATION 9985
PULVERISATION D'UN LIQUIDE 810
PULVERISE 9983
PULVERISER 9982
PULVERISER 6103
PULVERISER (UN LIQUIDE) 808
PULVERISEURS A DISQUES 4007
PULVERULENT 9728
PUNAISE 4242
PURE 9932
PURGE 4206
PURGER 4204
PURGEUR 10020
PURGEUR 1318
PURGEUR D'EAU CONDENSEE 12188
PURGEUR D'EAU CONDENSEE A DILATATION 12839
PURGEUR D'EAU CONDENSEE A FLOTTEUR 5432
PURIFICATION ANODIQUE 592
PURIFICATION DE L'EAU 10019
PURIFICATION DES EAUX RESIDUAIRES 13638
PURIFIE 10372
PURIFIER LES EAUX D'ALIMENTATION PAR VOIE CHIMIQUE 11748
PUSTULE 1327
PUSTULES 1330
PUTREFACTION (ACTION) 10035
PUTREFIER (SE) 10036
PYCNOMETRE 11851
PYRAMIDE 10038
PYRAMIDE PENTAGONALE 9174
PYRAMIDE QUADRANGULAIRE 12026
PYRAMIDE TRIANGULAIRE 13193
PYRIDINE 10041
PYRITE CUIVREUSE 3126
PYRITE JAUNE 7146
PYRITE MAGNETIQUE 7914
PYRITE MARTIALE 7146
PYROELECTRICITE 10043
PYROELECTRIQUE 10042
PYROGALLOL 10045
PYROMETALLURGIE 10048
PYROMETRE 10049

| | |
|---|---|
| PYROMETRE A DISTANCE **12714** | QUINTAL (50 KGS ENV.) **6668** |
| PYROMETRE A GRAPHITE **6065** | QUINTAL METRIQUE **10111** |
| PYROMETRE A RESISTANCE **10495** | QUOTIENT **10114** |
| PYROMETRE ELECTRIQUE **10495** | QUOTIENT **10234** |
| PYROMETRE OPTIQUE **8845** | QUOTIENT DIFFERENTIEL **3916** |
| PYROMETRE THERMOELECTRIQUE **12825** | RABATTEMENT **1088** |
| PYROMETRIE **10052** | RABATTEMENT DE LA COLLERETTE DES TUBES **1088** |
| PYROMETRIE OPTIQUE **8846** | RABATTRE LA COLLERETTE DES TUBES **1084** |
| PYROPHOSPHATE DE SOUDE **11730** | RABATTRE LES BORDS **1084** |
| PYROXYLE **6176** | RABBATRE L'EXCES DE LA TIGE DU RIVET **2489** |
| PYROXYLINE **6176** | RABOT **9432** |
| PYRRHOTINE **7914** | RABOT A CONTRE-FER **4146** |
| QUADRANGLE **10058** | RABOT A REPASSER **11687** |
| QUADRANT **10056** | RABOT CINTRE **2801** |
| QUADRATIQUE **12795** | RABOT DENTE A DENTS **13027** |
| QUADRATURE **12036** | RABOT ROND **10800** |
| QUADRILATERE **10058** | RABOTAGE **9450** |
| QUADRILATERE **10055** | RABOTEMENT **9450** |
| QUADRILATERE **12026** | RABOTER **9434** |
| QUADRILATERE INSCRIPTIBLE **6961** | RABOTEUR **9443** |
| QUADRILLAGE **6099** | RABOTEUSE **9452** |
| QUADRIVALENT **12798** | RABOTEUSE **4871** |
| QUALITE LUBRIFIANTE **7806** | RABOTEUSE **9443** |
| QUANTITE **10065** | RABOTEUSE-FRAISEUSE **9453** |
| QUANTITE CONNUE **7335** | RACCAGNAC **10219** |
| QUANTITE D'ELECTRICITE **10067** | RACCORD **5280** |
| QUANTITE DE CHALEUR **10066** | RACCORD **13368** |
| QUANTITE DE MOUVEMENT **10068** | RACCORD **3254** |
| QUANTITE DE MOUVEMENT **8376** | RACCORD **2965** |
| QUANTITE INCONNUE **13391** | RACCORD (ELECTR.) **2966** |
| QUANTITE MESUREE **10070** | RACCORD A ECROUS **1442** |
| QUANTITE RECIPROQUE **10280** | RACCORD A EMBOITEMENT POUR SOUDURE **11708** |
| QUARTIER **10076** | RACCORD A SOUDER **13781** |
| QUARTZ **10077** | RACCORD ACIER FORGE **5549** |
| QUARTZITE **10083** | RACCORD CONIQUE **12647** |
| QUATRE-FEUILLES **10086** | RACCORD CONIQUE **10352** |
| QUATRIEME PUISSANCE **5608** | RACCORD FILETE **11061** |
| QUESTIONNAIRE **10101** | RACCORD MALE **8578** |
| QUEUE **11257** | RACCORD POUR TUBES **9350** |
| QUEUE CONIQUE **12664** | RACCORD POUR TUYAUX FLEXIBLES **6612** |
| QUEUE D'ARONDE **4175** | RACCORD T **1559** |
| QUEUE D'ARONDE (A) **4177** | RACCORD TROIS PIECES **13369** |
| QUEUE D'HIRONDE **4175** | RACCORD VISSE **11058** |
| QUEUE D'UN OUTIL **12614** | RACCORD-UNION **13369** |
| QUEUE DE DISTILLATION **7413** | RACCORDEMENT (ELECTR.) **2958** |
| QUEUE DE LA TIGE DU PISTON **9384** | RACCORDEMENT DE TUYAUX **7248** |
| QUEUE DE ROBINET **12236** | RACCORDER **2955** |
| QUI PEUT SE COULER **1914** | RACCORDER DES TUYAUX **7244** |
| QUINCAILLERIE **11660** | RACCOURCISSEMENT **11376** |
| QUINCONE (EN) **12048** | RACCOURCISSEMENT D'UN CABLE **11377** |
| QUINHYDRONE (HEMI-CELLULE A LA) **10110** | RACCOURCISSEMENT D'UNE COURROIE **11377** |

# RAC

704

RACHETER L'USURE **12603**
RACINE **1028**
RACINE **10720**
RACINE (MATH.) **10714**
RACINE BIQUADRATIQUE **5609**
RACINE CARREE **12027**
RACINE CINQUIEME **5147**
RACINE CUBIQUE **3447**
RACINE DE LA DENT **1036**
RACINE DE LA SOUDURE **10726**
RACLAGE **11011**
RACLER **11008**
RACLETTE **11009**
RACLOIR **11009**
RADIAL **10125**
RADIAN **10138**
RADIATEUR **10148**
RADIATEUR A AILETTES **5233**
RADIATEUR ALPHA **401**
RADIATEUR DE CHAUFFAGE **10150**
RADIATEUR DE REFROIDISSEMENT **10149**
RADIATEUR NID D'ABEILLES **2129**
RADIATION **10143**
RADICAL **10154**
RADIO DES NOEUDS DE SOUDURE **7097**
RADIO-ACTIF **10157**
RADIO-ACTIVITE **10160**
RADIO-CRISTALLOGRAPHIE **13996**
RADIOGRAPHIE **10664**
RADIOGRAPHIE **10161**
RADIOGRAPHIE **10163**
RADIOLOGIE **10164**
RADIOMETALLOGRAPHIE **10155**
RADIOTELEGRAPHIE **13907**
RADIOTELEPHONIE **13908**
RADIUM **10165**
RADON **10159**
RAFFINAGE **10377**
RAFFINAGE D'UN METAL **10378**
RAFFINAGE SOUS VIDE **13447**
RAFFINE **10372**
RAFFINERIE **10375**
RAIDEUR **10591**
RAIDEUR D'UNE CORDE **12258**
RAIDEUR D'UNE COURROIE **12258**
RAIDISSEUR DE POUTRES EN TOLE **9489**
RAIDISSEUR INTERMEDIAIRE **7047**
RAIE **7597**
RAIE DU SODIUM **11723**
RAIES DE FRAUNHOFER **5631**
RAIL **10175**

RAIL DE CONTACT **1770**
RAIL DE PONT ROULANT **3293**
RAIL-GUIDE **6162**
RAIL-TENDEUR **12756**
RAILS A BOUDIN **1715**
RAINAGE **6137**
RAINER **6128**
RAINER ET LANGUETTER **12988**
RAINEUSE **6138**
RAINURAGE **6137**
RAINURAGE A LA FLAMME **5822**
RAINURE **6127**
RAINURE **7282**
RAINURE ANNULAIRE **2415**
RAINURE CIRCULAIRE **2415**
RAINURE DE CLAVETAGE **7282**
RAINURE DE CLAVETTE **7291**
RAINURER **6128**
RAISON DIRECTE (EN) **6815**
RAISON INVERSE (EN) **6816**
RALENTI **6755**
RALENTI ACCELERE **5038**
RALENTIR LA MARCHE D'UNE MACHINE **11645**
RALENTISSEMENT DE LA MARCHE **11649**
RALLONGE **4947**
RALLONGE D'UN COMPAS **7521**
RALLONGE DE MANCHE **4945**
RAMASSE FOIN **12541**
RAMASSE-BALLES **946**
RAMASSEUSES DE FOURRAGES **6091**
RAMIE **10192**
RAMPAGE **2437**
RAMPE **757**
RANG DE RIVETS **10813**
RANKINISATION DES DIAGRAMMES **2770**
RANKINISER **2765**
RAPE **10215**
RAPIECAGE **9109**
RAPIECAGE **9111**
RAPIECEMENT (ACTION) **9111**
RAPIECEMENT (RESULTAT) **9109**
RAPIECER **9110**
RAPPORT **10234**
RAPPORT : LIMITE DE FATIGUE **4742**
RAPPORT D'ABSORPTION **53**
RAPPORT D'ELANCEMENT **11582**
RAPPORT D'ENGRENAGE **5897**
RAPPORT DE COMPRESSION **2860**
RAPPORT DE CONVEXITE **3079**
RAPPORT DE DENSITE **3759**
RAPPORT DE DISTRIBUTION DU METAL **3777**

RAPPORT DE DISTRIBUTION DU METAL **8179**
RAPPORT DE REDUCTION **10360**
RAPPORT DE REFLEXION **10391**
RAPPORT DES BRAS DE LEVIER **7536**
RAPPORT DES VITESSES **13522**
RAPPORT VOLUMETRIQUE **2860**
RAPPORTE **1705**
RAPPORTEUR **9956**
RAPPORTEUR A FORME D'EQUERRE **10308**
RAPPORTEUR CERCLE ENTIER **2426**
RAPPORTEUR DEMI-CERCLE **11180**
RAPPORTEUR FIXE **10366**
RAPPORTS D'ENGRENAGES **5896**
RAREFACTION DE L'AIR **10212**
RAREFACTION D'UN GAZ **10211**
RAREFIER UN GAZ **10214**
RATE D'UN MOTEUR **5021**
RATEAUX **6312**
RATEAUX A DEVERSEMENT LATERAL **11411**
RATEAUX-AMMEULONNEURS **1683**
RATELEUSES RAMASSEUSES **6311**
RATTRAPAGE DE JEU **13403**
RATTRAPAGE DU JEU **12606**
RATTRAPER LE JEU D'EMBRAYAGE **12603**
RAYON **10166**
RAYON CALORIFIQUE **6369**
RAYON D'ECARTEMENT ENTRE LES BORDS **6132**
RAYON D'ECARTEMENT ENTRE LES BORDS **10728**
RAYON DE COURBURE **10168**
RAYON DE COURBURE **1176**
RAYON DE GIRATION **10169**
RAYON DE ROTATION **10169**
RAYON EMERGENT **4691**
RAYON INCIDENT **6832**
RAYON LUMINEUX **7824**
RAYON MEDULLAIRE **8128**
RAYON POLAIRE **9580**
RAYON REFLECHI **10384**
RAYON REFRACTE **10397**
RAYON VECTEUR **10170**
RAYONNEMENT **10143**
RAYONNEMENT DE LA CHALEUR **12811**
RAYONNEMENT DE LA CHALEUR **10146**
RAYONNEMENT HETEROGENE **6450**
RAYONNEMENT HOMOGENE **6559**
RAYONNEMENT IRRADIATION DE LA LUMIERE **10147**
RAYONNEMENT MONOCHROMATIQUE **8383**
RAYONNER **10141**
RAYONS **10242**
RAYONS ACTINIQUES **140**
RAYONS ALPHA **402**

RAYONS BETA **1218**
RAYONS CATHODIQUES **2104**
RAYONS D'UNE ROUE **13811**
RAYONS DE LENARD **7515**
RAYONS GAMMA **5796**
RAYONS INFRA-ROUGES **7103**
RAYONS ULTRA-ROUGES **13332**
RAYONS ULTRA-VIOLETS **13333**
RAYONS X **14003**
REA D'UN MOUFLE **11301**
REACTANCE **10247**
REACTEUR **10251**
REACTEUR DE RADIOCHIMIE **2323**
REACTIF **10257**
REACTIF **4844**
REACTIF D'ATTAQUE A L'ACIDE **4847**
REACTIF INDICATEUR **6879**
REACTION **10248**
REACTION ACIDE **122**
REACTION ALCALINE **337**
REACTION CHIMIQUE **2312**
REACTION DES APPUIS **1110**
REACTION ELECTROLYTIQUE IRREVERSIBLE **7171**
REACTION EUTECTOIDE **4860**
REACTION MONOTECTOIDE **8386**
REACTION PERITECTIQUE **9199**
REALESAGE **10271**
REALESER **10270**
REALGAR **10262**
REALISER **7950**
REBONDIMETRE **11366**
REBONDIR **10273**
REBONDISSEMENT **10272**
REBORD **4441**
REBORD **5332**
REBUT **8321**
REBUT **10431**
REBUTS DE FABRICATION **3696**
RECALAGE (D'UN COUSSINET) **12606**
RECALESCENCE **10274**
RECARBURANT **10276**
RECARBURATION **1953**
RECARBURATION DU FER **10275**
RECEPTEUR HYDRAULIQUE **13692**
RECEPTION **67**
RECEPTION (DE MACHINES) **68**
RECEVOIR UNE FORCE **12601**
RECHANGE D'UN ORGANE DE MACHINE **10464**
RECHANGER **10463**
RECHARGEMENT D'UNE SOUDURE **13762**
RECHARGEMENT DUR **6283**

**REC** 706

RECHAUFFAGE **10425**
RECHAUFFEMENT **10425**
RECHAUFFER **10424**
RECHAUFFER **6334**
RECHAUFFEUR **6385**
RECHAUFFEUR **9775**
RECHAUFFEUR D'AIR **287**
RECHAUFFEUR D'EAU D'ALIMENTATION **5078**
RECHERCHE APPLIQUEE **649**
RECHERCHE FONDAMENTALE **5735**
RECHERCHE PURE **1052**
RECHERCHE PURE **10016**
RECIPIENT **3010**
RECIPIENT (D'UNE CORNUE) **10277**
RECIPIENT PLAT **9029**
RECIPIENT SOUS PRESSION **9839**
RECOLTEUSES DE BETTERAVES **12439**
RECOLTEUSES DE POIS **9141**
RECOLTEUSES DE POMMES DE TERRE **9704**
RECOUVREMENT **8951**
RECOUVREMENT **8948**
RECOUVREMENT **2590**
RECOUVREMENT D'UN METAL PAR VOIE ELECTRO-CHIMIQUE **4562**
RECOUVREMENT DE TOLES **9501**
RECOUVREMENT DE TUYAUX **7369**
RECOUVREMENT DU TIROIR **7399**
RECOUVREMENT PAR DECOMPOSITION D'UN GAZ **13482**
RECRISTALLISATION **10297**
RECTANGLE **10299**
RECTANGLE **10310**
RECTIFICATION **11275**
RECTIFICATION **10511**
RECTIFICATION **6106**
RECTIFICATION (CHIM.) **10311**
RECTIFICATION A L'ALESOIR **10271**
RECTIFICATION DE SURFACE **12506**
RECTIFICATION DEMI-ONDE **6212**
RECTIFICATION EXTERIEURE **4957**
RECTIFICATION INTERIEURE **7069**
RECTIFICATION INTERIEURE **6564**
RECTIFICATION SANS POINTE(S) **2156**
RECTIFIER **11273**
RECTIFIER (CHIM.) **10318**
RECTIFIER AVEC L'ALESOIR **10270**
RECTIFIEUR **6105**
RECTIFIEUSE POUR SURFACE PLANES **12507**
RECTIFIEUSE POUR SURFACES DE REVOLUTION EXTERIEURES **4953**
RECTIFIEUSE POUR SURFACES DE REVOLUTION SANS CENTRE **2155**

RECTILIGNE **10319**
RECUEIL DE DONNEES **3613**
RECUIRE L'ACIER **560**
RECUIT **562**
RECUIT A GROSGRAIN **5719**
RECUIT A LA FLAMME **5319**
RECUIT AU CHALUMEAU **575**
RECUIT AU FOUR ELECTRIQUE **4508**
RECUIT BLANC **573**
RECUIT COMPLET **576**
RECUIT CONTINU **574**
RECUIT DE DETENTE **584**
RECUIT DE DETENTE **9667**
RECUIT DE DETENTE **12044**
RECUIT DE DETENTE **12362**
RECUIT DE L'ACIER **581**
RECUIT DE MISE EN SOLUTION **11812**
RECUIT DE NORMALISATION **8664**
RECUIT DE RELAXATION **583**
RECUIT DE RELAXATION **12363**
RECUIT ECHELONNE **12240**
RECUIT EN CAISSE **5371**
RECUIT EN NOIR **571**
RECUIT INTERMEDIAIRE **577**
RECUIT INTERMEDIAIRE D'USINAGE **9884**
RECUIT INTERMEDIAIRE ENTRE DEUX ETIRAGES **7085**
RECUIT INVERSE **578**
RECUIT ISOTHERMIQUE **579**
RECUIT PERIODIQUE **582**
RECUIT SELECTIF **580**
RECUIT SELECTIF **11142**
RECUL **919**
RECUPERATEUR **10412**
RECUPERATEUR **10322**
RECUPERATION **10296**
RECUPERER **10295**
REDONDANCE **10364**
REDRESSAGE **12319**
REDRESSEMENT **10312**
REDRESSER **12318**
REDRESSEUR (DE TUBES) ABRAMSEN **12**
REDRESSEUR (OU DETECTEUR) ELECTROLYTIQUE **4606**
REDRESSEUR A VAPEUR DE MERCURE **8164**
REDRESSEUR DE COURANT **10314**
REDRESSEUR ELECTROCHIMIQUE **4572**
REDRESSEUR ELECTRONIQUE **4634**
REDUCTEUR **10345**
REDUCTEUR **10346**
REDUCTEUR DE PRESSION **10355**
REDUCTEUR DE VITESSE **11872**
REDUCTEUR DE VITESSE **11873**

REDUCTION **13121**
REDUCTION (CHIM.) **10356**
REDUCTION CONICITE **4196**
REDUCTION DE LA SECTION TRANSVERSALE **10362**
REDUCTION DE TREMPE **4**
REDUCTION DE VITESSE **10363**
REDUCTION DES EMPLACEMENTS **5774**
REDUCTION ELECTROLYTIQUE **4607**
REDUCTION FEMELLE-FEMELLE **10348**
REDUCTION MALE-FEMELLE **1773**
REDUCTRICE **10345**
REDUIRE (CHIM.) **10342**
REDUIRE EN POUDRE **6103**
REDUIRE LA VITESSE **3678**
REDUIRE PAR LAMINAGE **10666**
REEMPLOI **10246**
REFLECHIR **10382**
REFLECTEUR **10394**
REFLETER **10382**
REFLEXION **10387**
REFLEXION DE LA LUMIERE **10390**
REFLEXION EN RETOUR **896**
REFLEXION TOTALE **13060**
REFONDRE **10446**
REFONTE **10447**
REFOULAGE **7265**
REFOULEMENT **7265**
REFOULEMENT **4452**
REFOULEMENT **13414**
REFOULEMENT A FROID **2686**
REFOULEMENT AVEC CHAUFFAGE PAR EFFET JOULE **13417**
REFOULER **7263**
REFRACTAIRE **5257**
REFRACTAIRE PLASTIQUE **9473**
REFRACTAIRES BASIQUES **1051**
REFRACTION **10399**
REFRACTION DE LA LUMIERE **10400**
REFRACTOMETRE **10404**
REFRIGERANT **10409**
REFRIGERANT **3083**
REFRIGERANT DE CENDRES **2398**
REFRIGERANT DE MEULAGE **6109**
REFRIGERANT POUR LES EAUX DE CONDENSATION **3089**
REFRIGERATEUR **10409**
REFRIGERATION **3085**
REFRIGERER **3081**
REFRINGENT **10402**
REFRINGENT **10401**
REFROIDI PAR L'EAU **13683**
REFROIDIR **2332**
REFROIDIR (SE) **3081**

REFROIDIR AU DESSOUS DU POINT DE CONGELATION **12463**
REFROIDIR AU-DESSOUS DE LA TEMPERATURE DE CONDENSATION **12463**
REFROIDIR BRUSQUEMENT L'ACIER **10091**
REFROIDISSEMENT **3093**
REFROIDISSEMENT **3085**
REFROIDISSEMENT (SOUS-) **13347**
REFROIDISSEMENT A L'AIR **252**
REFROIDISSEMENT A L'EAU **13646**
REFROIDISSEMENT A L'HUILE **8752**
REFROIDISSEMENT BRUSQUE DE L'ACIER **10100**
REFROIDISSEMENT COMMANDE **3056**
REFROIDISSEMENT D'EAU (A) **13683**
REFROIDISSEMENT DU FOUR **5742**
REFROIDISSEMENT LENT **4230**
REFROIDISSEMENT PAR CHEMISE D'EAU **7204**
REFROIDISSEUR CIRCULAIRE **10752**
REFROIDISSEUR D'HUILE **8751**
REFROIDISSEUR DU TROU DE LAITIER **8380**
REFROIDISSEUR INTERNE **7046**
REFUS DE CRIBLAGE **9548**
REFUS DE RECEPTION **10431**
REGARD **11427**
REGARD **9158**
REGENERATEUR **10412**
REGENERATION DES PIECES DECARBURISEES **1953**
REGIME **10558**
REGIME **8857**
REGIME D'UTILISATION **4395**
REGIME DE ROTATION **10558**
REGIME DE VITESSE **8663**
REGION HOUILLERE **2562**
REGISTRE DE FUMEE **3603**
REGISTRE DE TIRAGE **3603**
REGLABLE **183**
REGLAGE **195**
REGLAGE CONSECUTIF **10256**
REGLAGE DE L'ALLUMAGE **6768**
REGLAGE DE LA PRESSION **10419**
REGLAGE PAR VIS **190**
REGLE A CALCUL **11591**
REGLE A RETRAIT **3047**
REGLE A TRACER DES PARALLELES **9059**
REGLE COURBE **5660**
REGLE DE DESSINATEUR **10831**
REGLE DE JAUGE **12303**
REGLE DES PHASES **9236**
REGLE DIVISEE DE PRECISION **9767**
REGLE GRADUEE **8085**
REGLEMENTS D'USINE **11209**

**REG** 708

REGLER **182**
REGLES DE MORTAISAGE **7290**
REGLES DE SERVICE **8835**
REGULARITE CYCLIQUE **3719**
REGULARITE DU MOUVEMENT **10417**
REGULATEUR **6013**
REGULATEUR **12890**
REGULATEUR A BOULES **2185**
REGULATEUR A BRAS CROISES **3386**
REGULATEUR A DEPRESSION **12431**
REGULATEUR A DOUILLE **11578**
REGULATEUR A FORCE CENTRIFUGE **2185**
REGULATEUR A MANCHON **11578**
REGULATEUR A MASSE CENTRALE **13752**
REGULATEUR A RESSORT **11984**
REGULATEUR ASTATIQUE **775**
REGULATEUR AUTOMATIQUE **843**
REGULATEUR CENTRIFUGE **2181**
REGULATEUR CONIQUE **2943**
REGULATEUR D'INTENSITE **3491**
REGULATEUR D'INTENSITE **7020**
REGULATEUR D'INTENSITE **13595**
REGULATEUR DE COURANT **13595**
REGULATEUR DE COURANT **3491**
REGULATEUR DE DEBIT **13600**
REGULATEUR DE DEBIT **8909**
REGULATEUR DE DEBIT DE VENT **3465**
REGULATEUR DE NIVEAU **7654**
REGULATEUR DE PUISSANCE **8909**
REGULATEUR DE TEMPERATURE **12840**
REGULATEUR DE TENSION **13595**
REGULATEUR DE VITESSE **10421**
REGULATEUR DE VITESSE **11874**
REGULATEUR DE WATT **2185**
REGULATEUR ELECTRIQUE **4527**
REGULATEUR ELECTRONIQUE **4635**
REGULATEUR FARCOT **3386**
REGULATEUR ISOCHRONE **7180**
REGULATEUR PENDULE **9168**
REGULATEUR PLAN **11242**
REGULATEUR PORTER **13752**
REGULATEUR PSEUDO-ASTATIQUE **9957**
REGULATEUR STATIQUE **12135**
REGULATEUR SUR L'ARBRE **11242**
REGULE **10422**
REGULE **889**
REGULE D'ANTIMOINE **10423**
REHAUSSE ....DE TOIT FLOTTANT **11331**
RELAMINAGE **10470**
RELAXATION **10435**
RELEVE **7717**

RELEVER UN DIAGRAMME **9520**
RELEVES DE TEMPERATURE **12725**
RELIER (ELECTR.) **2955**
RELIER A LA TERRE (ELECTR.) **4410**
RELUCTANCE **10444**
REMANENCE **10445**
REMANENCE **10473**
REMBLAI **900**
REMBLAI HYDRAULIQUE **6686**
REMBLAYAGE **900**
REMETTRE EN MARCHE **10508**
REMISE A ZERO **14032**
REMISE A ZERO **14030**
REMISE EN ETAT **10287**
REMISE EN MARCHE **10509**
REMONTAGE **10245**
REMONTER **10244**
REMORQUES **13102**
REMOULEUR **6105**
REMOUS **13606**
REMPLACER **10463**
REMPLIR **5156**
REMPLISSAGE **2269**
REMUER A LA PELLE **13283**
RENDEMENT **14010**
RENDEMENT **4463**
RENDEMENT ANODIQUE **597**
RENDEMENT CATHODIQUE **2101**
RENDEMENT COMMERCIAL **2781**
RENDEMENT ECONOMIQUE **2781**
RENDEMENT ELECTROTHERMIQUE **4649**
RENDEMENT EN COURANT **3489**
RENDEMENT FINAL **5194**
RENDEMENT HYDRAULIQUE **6684**
RENDEMENT INDIQUE **6872**
RENDEMENT INDUSTRIEL **2781**
RENDEMENT MANOMETRIQUE **7984**
RENDEMENT MECANIQUE **8100**
RENDEMENT ORGANIQUE **8100**
RENDEMENT QUANTIQUE **10071**
RENDEMENT THERMIQUE **12806**
RENDEMENT TOTAL **8927**
RENDEMENT VOLUMETRIQUE **13602**
RENDRE ALCALIN **330**
RENDRE ETANCHE **7953**
RENDRE RUGUEUX **10783**
RENFERMANT DE LA RESINE **10479**
RENFORCEMENT **12359**
RENFORCEMENT DE LA SOUDURE **10427**
RENFORCEMENT EN TUBES **13258**
RENFORCEMENT PAR DES NERVURES **12152**

RENFORCER **12358**
RENFORT **10569**
RENFORT **10429**
RENFORT **1516**
RENFORT **12359**
RENIFLARD **1591**
RENIFLARD **3307**
RENIFLARD **11694**
RENONCIATION **13615**
RENOUVELER UN ORGANE DE MACHINE **10457**
RENOUVELLEMENT D'UN ORGANE DE MACHINE **10458**
RENTABILITE **9462**
RENTREE D'AIR **4771**
RENTREE DE FLAMME **5365**
RENVERSEMENT (CALCUL SOUS SEISMES) **8965**
RENVERSEMENT DE LA MARCHE D'UNE MACHINE **10541**
RENVERSER LE SENS DE LA MARCHE **10534**
RENVOI A COURROIE **7045**
RENVOI A ENGRENAGES **7050**
RENVOI A LA CHASSE **7231**
RENVOI D'ANGLE **1149**
RENVOI DE MOUVEMENT **3244**
RENVOI DE PLAFOND **8940**
RENVOI FIXE AU SOL **5444**
RENVOI FIXE CONTRE UN MUR **13619**
RENVOI MURAL **13619**
REPARATION **10459**
REPARER **10460**
REPARTITION D'UNE CHARGE **4081**
REPARTITION DES CHARGES **7684**
REPARTITION DES MASSES **4082**
REPARTITION DU TRAVAIL **13939**
REPASSER **11273**
REPERAGE **8015**
REPERAGE PAR COORDONNEES **3099**
REPERE **8012**
REPERE **5879**
REPERER **8008**
REPERER A L'AIDE D'UN POINTEAU **8011**
REPERES DE CALAGE **12951**
REPIQUEUSES **11133**
REPLI **7395**
REPLI (TRAVAIL DES TOLES) **5511**
REPLIURE DE LAMINAGE **7395**
REPLIURE DE LAMINAGE **5510**
REPOS **7100**
REPOSANT **8432**
REPOSANT LIBREMENT **5650**
REPOSANT LIBREMENT SUR DEUX APPUIS **11474**
REPOUSSAGE **8189**
REPOUSSE **8189**

REPRESENTATION CONFORME **8872**
REPRESENTATION GEOMETRIQUE **5926**
REPRISES VISIBLES **7407**
REPRODUCTION **8481**
REPRODUCTION (EN GRAND) **10970**
REPRODUCTION (RESULTAT) **10467**
REPRODUCTION AU FERRO-PRUSSIATE EN BLANC SUR FOND
    BLEU **1375**
REPRODUCTION AU FERROPRUSSIATE EN BLEU SUR FOND
    BLANC **1373**
REPRODUCTION EN PLOMB FONDU **7457**
REPRODUCTION PHOTOGRAPHIQUE **9263**
REPRODUIRE **8484**
REPULSION **10468**
REPULSION MAGNETIQUE **7915**
REQUETE DE BREVET **646**
RESEAU **7940**
RESEAU A GRANDE DISTANCE **7728**
RESEAU CRISTALLIN **7429**
RESEAU D'ELECTRIFICATION **6096**
RESEAU DE CONDUCTEURS ELECTRIQUES **4080**
RESEAU DE DIFFRACTION **3925**
RESEAU DE DISTRIBUTION ELECTRIQUE **4080**
RESEAU DE REFLEXION **10388**
RESEAU DE TRANSLATION **13120**
RESEAU DE TUYAUX **12579**
RESEAU DE WULFF (STEREOGRAPHIQUE) **13992**
RESEAU RECIPROQUE **10281**
RESEAU SPATIAL **11828**
RESERVE (DE) **12068**
RESERVOIR **10471**
RESERVOIR **12625**
RESERVOIR **1740**
RESERVOIR **5716**
RESERVOIR A AIR **294**
RESERVOIR A DOUBLE PAROI **4161**
RESERVOIR A EAU **13679**
RESERVOIR A FOND CONCAVE **12631**
RESERVOIR A FOND CONVEXE **12632**
RESERVOIR A PETROLE BRUT **3407**
RESERVOIR A TOIT BOMBE **4121**
RESERVOIR A TOIT CONIQUE AUTOPORTANT **11160**
RESERVOIR A TOIT FLOTTANT **5439**
RESERVOIR A TOIT SURBAISSE **13047**
RESERVOIR A TOIT SUSPENDU **12525**
RESERVOIR BALLON **6580**
RESERVOIR CALORIFUGE **6995**
RESERVOIR D'ESSENCE **5716**
RESERVOIR D'HUILE **8773**
RESERVOIR DE CARBURANT **5716**
RESERVOIR DE DECANTATION **11229**

# RES
710

RESERVOIR DE GNL **7678**
RESERVOIR DE JAUGEAGE **12790**
RESERVOIR DE LIQUIDE DE FREIN **1534**
RESERVOIR DE RECETTE **10843**
RESERVOIR SURELEVE **4492**
RESERVOIR TAMPON **1592**
RESERVOIRS DE STOCKAGE **12292**
RESIDU **10475**
RESIDU DE CALCINATION **6765**
RESIDU DE LA COMBUSTION **10476**
RESIDUS **12598**
RESILENCE **10477**
RESILIENCE **8671**
RESILIENCE **13071**
RESILIENCE **6785**
RESILIENCE **6788**
RESILIENCE **1918**
RESINE **10478**
RESINE DE VERNIS **10927**
RESINE ELEMI **4656**
RESINIFICATION **10480**
RESINIFIER (SE) **10481**
RESISTANCE **12352**
RESISTANCE **13327**
RESISTANCE **10484**
RESISTANCE **10502**
RESISTANCE A L'ABRASION **11015**
RESISTANCE A L'ALLONGEMENT **13331**
RESISTANCE A L'ECRASEMENT **13328**
RESISTANCE A L'ETAT DE RECUIT **569**
RESISTANCE A L'EXTENSION **13331**
RESISTANCE A L'USURE **13717**
RESISTANCE A L'USURE **10499**
RESISTANCE A LA COMPRESSION **2870**
RESISTANCE A LA COMPRESSION **13328**
RESISTANCE A LA CORROSION **3194**
RESISTANCE A LA DEFORMATION **10521**
RESISTANCE A LA FATIGUE **5052**
RESISTANCE A LA FLEXION **5424**
RESISTANCE A LA FLEXION TRANSVERSALE **1192**
RESISTANCE A LA RUPTURE **13327**
RESISTANCE A LA RUPTURE TRANSVERSALE **13330**
RESISTANCE A LA TORSION **13057**
RESISTANCE A LA TRACTION **12749**
RESISTANCE A LA TRACTION **13331**
RESISTANCE APPARENTE **6794**
RESISTANCE AU CHOC **6785**
RESISTANCE AU CHOC **1918**
RESISTANCE AU CINTRAGE **1188**
RESISTANCE AU CISAILLEMENT **13330**
RESISTANCE AU CISAILLEMENT **11285**

RESISTANCE AU DEMARRAGE **12128**
RESISTANCE AU FLAMBAGE **3340**
RESISTANCE AU FLAMBAGE **1682**
RESISTANCE AU FLUAGE **3328**
RESISTANCE AU FLUAGE POUR UNE DUREE FINIE **3327**
RESISTANCE AU FREINAGE **1552**
RESISTANCE AU GLISSEMENT **10498**
RESISTANCE AU GLISSEMENT TRANSVERSAL **13330**
RESISTANCE AU MOUVEMENT **10497**
RESISTANCE AU PLIAGE **1188**
RESISTANCE AU RACCOURCISSEMENT **13328**
RESISTANCE AU ROULEMENT **10703**
RESISTANCE AUX CHOCS REPETES **12353**
RESISTANCE AUX VARIATIONS DE TEMPERATURE OU AU CHOC THERMIQUE **12813**
RESISTANCE COMPLEXE **2822**
RESISTANCE COMPOSEE **2822**
RESISTANCE D'ISOLEMENT **7005**
RESISTANCE D'UN CONDUCTEUR **10491**
RESISTANCE DANS LA MARCHE A VIDE **8600**
RESISTANCE DE BOUGIE DE PRECHAUFFAGE **6388**
RESISTANCE DE L'AIR **10492**
RESISTANCE DE RUPTURE PAR FRACTION **4742**
RESISTANCE DES MATERIAUX **12355**
RESISTANCE DIELECTRIQUE OU DISRUPTIVE **3900**
RESISTANCE DISRUPTIVE **4057**
RESISTANCE DU FROTTEMENT **5686**
RESISTANCE EFFECTIVE **10261**
RESISTANCE ELECTRIQUE **4528**
RESISTANCE INTERNE **7072**
RESISTANCE MAGNETIQUE **10444**
RESISTANCE MOL(ECUL)AIRE **8351**
RESISTANCE PASSIVE **10497**
RESISTANCE PRIMITIVE **9854**
RESISTANCE SPECIFIQUE **4548**
RESISTANCE SPECIFIQUE ELECTRIQUE **10503**
RESISTANCE SUIVANT LA TANGENTE **9197**
RESISTANCE UTILE **13426**
RESISTANCE VIVE **10477**
RESISTANCE-LIMITE D'ENDURANCE **5053**
RESISTIVITE **10503**
RESISTIVITE **4548**
RESISTIVITE EQUIVALENTE **4798**
RESOLUTION **10504**
RESONANCE **10506**
RESOUDRE **11813**
RESPIRATION RENIFLARD **1593**
RESSAUT **9917**
RESSORT **11974**
RESSORT A BOUDIN **6427**
RESSORT A BOUDIN CYLINDRIQUE **3585**

# 711 REV

RESSORT A LAME **9495**
RESSORT A LAME RECTANGULAIRE A PROFIL PARABOLOIDE **10307**
RESSORT A LAMES **7485**
RESSORT A LAMES ETAGEES **2834**
RESSORT A PLUSIEURS LAMES **2834**
RESSORT AMORTISSEUR DES CHOCS **1688**
RESSORT ANTAGONISTE **11974**
RESSORT BANDE **12641**
RESSORT CHARGE **11983**
RESSORT CONIQUE **2942**
RESSORT CONIQUE A LAME PLATE **13605**
RESSORT CONIQUE A SECTION RECTANGULAIRE **13605**
RESSORT D'INJECTEUR **8686**
RESSORT DE COMPRESSION **2862**
RESSORT DE FLEXION **11993**
RESSORT DE FLEXION A ENROULEMENT **2649**
RESSORT DE FLEXION DROIT **12312**
RESSORT DE PISTON AVEC CUVETTE **9547**
RESSORT DE RAPPEL **10526**
RESSORT DE REGULATEUR **6019**
RESSORT DE SOUPAPE **13470**
RESSORT DE SUSPENSION **1114**
RESSORT DE TORSION **11994**
RESSORT DE TRACTION **12759**
RESSORT DE VOITURE **2008**
RESSORT DIAPHRAGME **3875**
RESSORT EN C **1823**
RESSORT EN HELICE **6427**
RESSORT HELICOIDAL **2647**
RESSORT RECTANGULAIRE A LAME PLATE **10306**
RESSORT RECTANGULAIRE A LAMES SUPERPOSEES **7380**
RESSORT SPIRALE **5396**
RESSORT TARE **1866**
RESSORT TENDU **11983**
RESSORT TRAPEZOIDAL **13151**
RESSORT TRIANGULAIRE **13191**
RESSORT TRIANGULAIRE A LAMES SUPERPOSEES **7381**
RESSORT TRONCONIQUE **13236**
RESTAURATION **10296**
RESULTANTE **10513**
RESULTAT D'UNE EPREUVE **10512**
RETAILLAGE DES LIMES **10324**
RETAILLER LES LIMES **10323**
RETARD **3730**
RETARD A L'EBULLITION **10517**
RETARD A LA FERMETURE DE LA SOUPAPE **10519**
RETARD DE LIVRAISON **3731**
RETARD DE SOUDAGE **12038**
RETARDER **7366**
RETARDER **6926**

RETASSEMENT **11394**
RETASSURE **11393**
RETASSURE **11505**
RETASSURE **2124**
RETASSURE **9340**
RETASSURE **7073**
RETENDRE UNE COURROIE **12602**
RETENUE D'EAU **10182**
RETICULE **3383**
RETIRURE **4230**
RETOMBER (CLIQUET) **4320**
RETOUCHE **11682**
RETOUCHE DE REGLAGE **10256**
RETOUCHER **5214**
RETOUCHER LE REGLAGE **10255**
RETOUR **10530**
RETOUR A LA TEMPERATURE AMBIANTE **3096**
RETOUR DE FLAMME **906**
RETOUR DE LA FLAMME **892**
RETOUR RAPIDE **10106**
RETRACTION **11397**
RETRACTION **2437**
RETRAIT **477**
RETRAIT **2437**
RETRAIT **3043**
RETRAIT **11392**
RETRAIT ANGULAIRE **542**
RETRAIT AU MOULE **1322**
RETRAIT CONTRARIE **6504**
RETRAIT DU BOIS **11396**
RETRAIT THERMIQUE **12805**
RETRANCHER **12424**
RETRECI **3042**
RETRECIR (SE) **11388**
RETRECISSEMENT **3045**
RETRECISSEMENT **11397**
RETROUSSEMENT DES BORDS DES TOLES **1088**
RETROUSSER LES BORDS DES TOLES **1084**
RETROVISEUR **10266**
REUNION **3254**
REUNION DE COURROIES **1151**
REUNION DES COURROIE ATTACHE DES COURROIES **1142**
REUTILISATION **10246**
REVENU **12733**
REVENU **12731**
REVENU **4230**
REVENU-FLUAGE POSTERIEUR **221**
REVERSIBILITE **10537**
REVERSIBLE **10538**
REVERSION **10554**
REVETEMENT **2590**

# REV

## 712

REVETEMENT **2587**
REVETEMENT **7623**
REVETEMENT (ENDUIT) ANODIQUE **599**
REVETEMENT ANODIQUE **2588**
REVETEMENT ANTI-ROUILLE **2601**
REVETEMENT AVEC VERNIS FIN **7214**
REVETEMENT CALORIFUGE **7367**
REVETEMENT CATHODIQUE **2102**
REVETEMENT CHIMIQUE **2297**
REVETEMENT D'ALLIAGE **364**
REVETEMENT D'ANTIFRICTION **7624**
REVETEMENT D'ETAIN **2602**
REVETEMENT D'OXYDE **2598**
REVETEMENT D'UN CABLE **715**
REVETEMENT EN BOIS **13915**
REVETEMENT EXTERIEUR **3274**
REVETEMENT FONDU **2032**
REVETEMENT GALVANIQUE AU TAMBOUR **1016**
REVETEMENT INTERIEUR **7623**
REVETEMENT METALLIQUE **8194**
REVETEMENT METALLIQUE **2596**
REVETEMENT METALLIQUE PAR GALVANOPLASTIE **9503**
REVETEMENT METALLISE **8200**
REVETEMENT NON-METALLIQUE **2597**
REVETEMENT NON-METALLIQUE **8641**
REVETEMENT PAR COMPOSITION KB TI **7583**
REVETEMENT PAR PEINTURE **2595**
REVETEMENT PROTECTEUR **9949**
REVETEMENT VITREUX **2603**
REVETEMENTS DE DIFFUSION **3930**
REVETEMENTS DE PROTECTION **9792**
REVETEMENTS ELECTROLYTIQUES OU GALVANOPLASTIQUES **2593**
REVETEMENTS EMAILLES **2594**
REVETEMENTS PAR TREMPE **2592**
REVETIR **7598**
REVISER **8937**
REVOIR **8937**
REVOLUTION **10557**
REVOLUTION DU FILET **13279**
REVOLUTIONS PAR MINUTE **10814**
RHEOLOGIE **10562**
RHEOSTAT **10563**
RHODIUM **10564**
RHOMBE **10568**
RHOMBOEDRE **10566**
RHOMBOIDE **10567**
RIBLONS DE FER **11007**
RIDAGE **11399**
RIFLARD **7201**
RIFLOIR **10575**

RIGIDITE **10591**
RIGIDITE A LA FLEXION **5423**
RIGOLE **6185**
RIGOLE **2251**
RIGOLE DE GRAISSAGE **7810**
RINCAGE **10608**
RINCER **10607**
RINGARD **10116**
RINGARDER **9575**
RISQUE D'INCENDIE **3608**
RIVE **4441**
RIVE CISAILLEE **3506**
RIVE DE TOLE **9483**
RIVER **2516**
RIVER A CHAUD **6634**
RIVER A FROID **2692**
RIVET **10621**
RIVET A TETE FRAISEE **10635**
RIVET A TETE AFFLEUREE **10635**
RIVET A TETE CHANFREINEE **2946**
RIVET A TETE CONIQUE **2946**
RIVET A TETE CYLINDRIQUE **10632**
RIVET A TETE FRAISEE AVEC BOMBE **3249**
RIVET A TETE GOUTTE DE SUIF **10633**
RIVET A TETE HEMISPHERIQUE **10637**
RIVET A TETE NOYEE **10635**
RIVET A TETE PERDUE **10635**
RIVET A TETE PLATE **10634**
RIVET A TETE RONDE **10636**
RIVET A TETE TRONCONIQUE **9030**
RIVET AU BORD DE LA TOLE **10622**
RIVET D'ETANCHEITE **12922**
RIVET DE CHAINE **2214**
RIVET POUR COURROIES **1155**
RIVETAGE **10643**
RIVETAGE A LA MAIN **6248**
RIVETAGE A RIVET SANS TETE **9321**
RIVETAGE A TIGE **9321**
RIVETAGE AU MARTEAU **6248**
RIVETAGE MECANIQUE **7854**
RIVETAGE POUR CONSTRUCTIONS METALLIQUES **9740**
RIVETE EN SPIRALE **11918**
RIVETER **10629**
RIVETS **10646**
RIVETS **1241**
RIVETS (DISTANCE DES) DE CENTRE A CENTRE D'UNE LIGNE A L'AUTRE **13145**
RIVEUR **10641**
RIVEUSE **10642**
RIVOIR **10644**
RIVURE **10628**

RIVURE **10639**
RIVURE A BANDE DE RECOUVREMENT **1781**
RIVURE A CHAUD **6635**
RIVURE A COUVRE-JOINT SIMPLE **11478**
RIVURE A DEUX COUPES **4155**
RIVURE A DEUX COUVRE-JOINTS **4130**
RIVURE A DEUX RANGS **4152**
RIVURE A DOUBLE COUVRE-JOINT **4130**
RIVURE A FROID **2693**
RIVURE A PLAT-JOINT **11478**
RIVURE A RECOUVREMENT **7400**
RIVURE A SIMPLE CLOUURE **11487**
RIVURE A TROIS COUPES **13178**
RIVURE A TROIS RANGS **13177**
RIVURE A UN RANG **11487**
RIVURE A UNE COUPE **11489**
RIVURE A UNE SEULE BANDE DE RECOUVREMENT **11478**
RIVURE D'ASSEMBLAGE DE FORCE **9740**
RIVURE DE FORCE **9740**
RIVURE DOUBLE **4152**
RIVURE EN CHAINE **2215**
RIVURE EN LOSANGE **7799**
RIVURE EN QUINCONCE **14034**
RIVURE SIMPLE **11487**
RIVURE TRIPLE A TRIPLE CLOUURE **13177**
ROBE **11330**
ROBE DU RESERVOIR **12630**
ROBINET **12639**
ROBINET **11592**
ROBINET **2617**
ROBINET A BEC COURBE **1234**
ROBINET A BOISSEAU **8997**
ROBINET A BOISSEAU **9535**
ROBINET A BOISSEAU LUBRIFIE **7802**
ROBINET A BOISSEAU RENVERSE **7111**
ROBINET A BOISSEAU SPHERIQUE (A BOULE) **968**
ROBINET A BOURRAGE **5954**
ROBINET A CLEF **9530**
ROBINET A DEUX VOIES **13317**
ROBINET A EAU **13644**
ROBINET A FLOTTEUR **5433**
ROBINET A GAZ **5814**
ROBINET A MANOEUVRE RAPIDE **10104**
ROBINET A MEMBRANE **3876**
ROBINET A MOTEUR **8417**
ROBINET A POINTEAU (A AIGUILLE) **8522**
ROBINET A QUATRE VOIES **5606**
ROBINET A QUATRE VOIES **5605**
ROBINET A SOUFFLET **1138**
ROBINET A SOUPAPE **5977**
ROBINET A SOUPAPE DOUBLE **4154**

ROBINET A SOUPAPE SIMPLE **11488**
ROBINET A TROIS VOIES **12881**
ROBINET A TROIS VOIES **12882**
ROBINET A VIS DE PRESSION **11033**
ROBINET D'AIR **293**
ROBINET D'ALIMENTATION **5066**
ROBINET D'ANGLE **511**
ROBINET D'ARRET **12281**
ROBINET D'ARRET **11408**
ROBINET D'EQUERRE **534**
ROBINET D'EXTRACTION **1359**
ROBINET D'ISOLEMENT **845**
ROBINET DE BAIGNOIRE **1063**
ROBINET DE BATTERIE **1068**
ROBINET DE BOUTEILLE (DE GAZ COMPRIME) **3575**
ROBINET DE DISTRIBUTEUR **8467**
ROBINET DE DOUCHE **11387**
ROBINET DE FOND DE CUVE **1493**
ROBINET DE JAUGE **12776**
ROBINET DE JAUGE **5875**
ROBINET DE LAVABO **13630**
ROBINET DE PRISE DE VAPEUR **12187**
ROBINET DE PUISAGE **1235**
ROBINET DE RADIATEUR **10153**
ROBINET DE VIDANGE **1357**
ROBINET DE VIDANGE **4205**
ROBINET DISTRIBUTEUR TOURNANT **10760**
ROBINET DROIT **5977**
ROBINET ELECTROMAGNETIQUE **11774**
ROBINET MELANGEUR **8335**
ROBINET PURGEUR **4205**
ROBINET REGULATEUR A MEMBRANE **3872**
ROBINET SANS PRESSE-ETOUPE **9010**
ROBINET-VALVE A SOUPAPE **13455**
ROBINET-VANNE **11653**
ROBINETTERIE **1566**
ROCHE **10651**
ROCHE CLIVABLE **2486**
ROCHE-MERE **5802**
ROCHET **10225**
ROCHET **1061**
RODAGE **6106**
RODAGE **10855**
RODAGE **7407**
RODAGE (D'UNE VOITURE) **1587**
RODAGE A L'EMERI **6111**
RODAGE AU LIQUIDE **6564**
RODER A L'EMERI **6104**
RODER UN MOTEUR **10835**
ROGNAGE **13209**
ROGNER **13204**

**ROG** 714

ROGNOIR **11009**
ROGNURES DE CUIR **7497**
ROGNURES DE FER **11007**
ROGNURES DE LIEGE **6144**
ROGNURES DE ZINC **14040**
RONCE ARTIFICIELLE **987**
RONDELLE **13631**
RONDELLE AUTOTARAUDEUSE **11163**
RONDELLE BELLEVILLE **3461**
RONDELLE BRASEE **11758**
RONDELLE D'AILE **5096**
RONDELLE D'EPAISSEUR **11351**
RONDELLE D'UN ARBRE **2724**
RONDELLE DE BLOCAGE **7703**
RONDELLE DE SERRAGE **7703**
RONDELLE DECORATIVE **5230**
RONDELLE ELASTIQUE **4486**
RONDELLE EN CAOUTCHOUC **10823**
RONDELLE FREIN **7703**
RONDELLE GOUPILLEE **7743**
RONDELLE GROWER **11995**
RONDELLE PLATE **5399**
RONDELLE PROTECTRICE **4835**
RONDELLE SOUDEE **13773**
RONDIN **10803**
RONDS EN ACIER ALLIE **377**
ROSE DES VENTS **2800**
ROTATION **10765**
ROTATION A DROITE **2507**
ROTATION A GAUCHE **3238**
ROTIN **10236**
ROTOR **10767**
ROTOR **6795**
ROTULE **7336**
ROUAGE **13821**
ROUE **13810**
ROUE **13692**
ROUE **9402**
ROUE A AUBES **13479**
ROUE A AUGETS **8960**
ROUE A CENTRE PLEIN **4012**
ROUE A CHEVRONS **4143**
ROUE A DENTS EN BOIS **8400**
ROUE A DENTS TAILLEES **3508**
ROUE A DENTURE BRUTE **10773**
ROUE A DENTURE INTERIEURE **7079**
ROUE A DISQUE **4012**
ROUE A EMPREINTES **2217**
ROUE A MEULER **6115**
ROUE A PALETTES, A AILETTES **13479**
ROUE A RAYONS **11951**

ROUE A ROCHET **10225**
ROUE A ROCHET **2495**
ROUE A VIS SANS FIN **13975**
ROUE A VOILE **4012**
ROUE A VOILE BOMBE **4037**
ROUE A VOILE DROIT **5379**
ROUE ATMOSPHERIQUE **13861**
ROUE CENTRALE D'UN TRAIN PLANETAIRE **12457**
ROUE CONDUCTRICE **4318**
ROUE CONDUITE **4300**
ROUE CONIQUE **1229**
ROUE CYLINDRIQUE **3591**
ROUE D'ANGLE **1229**
ROUE D'ENGRENAGE **5903**
ROUE D'ENGRENAGE AVEC JOUES **11402**
ROUE D'ENGRENAGE BRUTE DE FONDERIE **10773**
ROUE D'ENGRENAGE CYLINDRIQUE **12009**
ROUE D'ENGRENAGE DROITE **12009**
ROUE D'ENGRENAGE EPAULEE **11402**
ROUE D'UNE TURBINE **13823**
ROUE DE CHAMP **3399**
ROUE DE COMMANDE **4318**
ROUE DE COTE (HYDRAULIQUE) **7769**
ROUE DE DIFFERENTIEL **3917**
ROUE DE FRICTION **5682**
ROUE DE FRICTION (A JANTE EN FORME DE COIN) **13732**
ROUE DE FRICTION CONIQUE **1225**
ROUE DE FRICTION CYLINDRIQUE **12007**
ROUE DE POITRINE **6465**
ROUE DE RECHANGE **2243**
ROUE DE SECOURS **2243**
ROUE DE SECOURS **11835**
ROUE DE TRANSPORT **6754**
ROUE DENTEE **5903**
ROUE DENTEE A CLIQUET **10225**
ROUE DENTEE INTERROMPUE **7975**
ROUE DROITE **3591**
ROUE ELLIPTIQUE **4677**
ROUE ETOILEE **12109**
ROUE HELICOIDALE **6425**
ROUE INTERMEDIAIRE **6754**
ROUE LIBRE **5644**
ROUE LIBRE **5651**
ROUE MENANTE **4318**
ROUE MENEE **4300**
ROUE MOTRICE **4318**
ROUE PAR-DESSOUS **13355**
ROUE PAR-DESSUS **8960**
ROUE PLANETAIRE **9444**
ROUE POLISSEUSE **9604**
ROUE PORTEUSE **10854**

SAB

ROUE RECEPTRICE **4300**
ROUE SATELLITE **9444**
ROUES D'ASSORTIMENT **7027**
ROUES DE SERIE **7027**
ROUGE **10329**
ROUGE A POLIR **7148**
ROUGE ANGLAIS **7148**
ROUGE AU FEU **10330**
ROUGE CERISE **2326**
ROUGE CLAIR **1613**
ROUGE CONGO **2935**
ROUGE D'ANGLETERRE **3355**
ROUGE DE CHROME **2374**
ROUGE DE PRUSSE **7148**
ROUGE NAISSANT **1295**
ROUGE SOMBRE **4367**
ROUGE VIF **1613**
ROUILLE **10873**
ROUILLE **10335**
ROUILLE **10863**
ROUILLER (SE) **10864**
ROULANT **9635**
ROULEAU **12334**
ROULEAU **12334**
ROULEAU **10671**
ROULEAU **10679**
ROULEAU **2645**
ROULEAU **1112**
ROULEAU CONIQUE **12660**
ROULEAU D'UNE CHAINE **10688**
ROULEAU RENFLE **1017**
ROULEAUX **10695**
ROULEAUX DE POLISSAGE DRAPES **2539**
ROULEMENT **954**
ROULEMENT **10696**
ROULEMENT **1117**
ROULEMENT A AIGUILLES **8518**
ROULEMENT A BILLES **954**
ROULEMENT A BILLES **618**
ROULEMENT A BILLES A CHARGE AXIALE **12901**
ROULEMENT A BILLES A CHARGE RADIALE **10130**
ROULEMENT A BILLES A CHARGE RADIALE ET AXIALE
  COMBINEE **538**
ROULEMENT A BILLES A POUSSEE AXIALE ET LATERALE
  COMBINEE **538**
ROULEMENT A GALETS **618**
ROULEMENT A GALETS (A ROULEAUX) **10680**
ROULEMENT A GALETS CONIQUES **10683**
ROULEMENT A GALETS CYLINDRIQUES **10682**
ROULEMENT A POUSSEE LATERALE **10130**
ROULEMENT A ROTULE SUR ROULEAUX **10681**

ROULEMENT LISSE **9424**
ROULER **10665**
ROULETTE **10697**
ROULETTE D'ARPENTAGE **8092**
ROULETTE DU PLANIMETRE **13817**
ROULIS **12538**
ROULURE DU BOIS **3460**
RUBAN **12641**
RUBAN **974**
RUBAN **8092**
RUBAN CAOUTCHOUTE **10822**
RUBAN D'EMERI **18**
RUBAN DE FREIN **1544**
RUBAN ISOLANT **7001**
RUBAN METALLIQUE DE PROTECTION **3268**
RUBANS **980**
RUBIDIUM **10829**
RUBRIQUE **10340**
RUGOSIMETRE **12509**
RUGOSIMETRE ENREGISTREUR **12498**
RUGOSITE **10792**
RUGOSITE DE SURFACE **12518**
RUPTURE **5617**
RUPTURE **3278**
RUPTURE **10858**
RUPTURE **10861**
RUPTURE **9353**
RUPTURE A CHAUD **6621**
RUPTURE BRUSQUE DU CORPS D'UNE VIS **13309**
RUPTURE D'UN TUYAU **1768**
RUPTURE DE FATIGUE / D'ENDURANCE **4740**
RUPTURE DE LA COUCHE DE SCORIES **5354**
RUPTURE DES TETES DE RIVET **11999**
RUPTURE DU RIVET PAR CISAILLEMENT **11293**
RUPTURE PAR FLEXION **5488**
RUTHENIUM **10874**
S'AGGLOMERER **11509**
S'ELARGIR **5356**
S'ENGRENER **1077**
S'ETENDRE **5356**
SABLAGE **1316**
SABLAGE **10921**
SABLE **10917**
SABLE A GRAIN FIN **5199**
SABLE A GROS GRAIN **2574**
SABLE A NOYAUX **3163**
SABLE DE CARRIERE **9396**
SABLE DE CONTACT **5006**
SABLE DE COUVERTURE **912**
SABLE DE FONDERIE **8430**
SABLE DE MER **11071**

## SAB

716

SABLE DE MOULAGE **8430**
SABLE DE RIVIERE **10619**
SABLE ISOLANT **9094**
SABLE QUARTZEUX **10082**
SABLE SEC **4255**
SABLER **10919**
SABLEUSE **10920**
SABOT **11360**
SABOT DE FREIN **1543**
SABOT DE FREIN **1531**
SABOT MAGNETIQUE **8188**
SABOT POUR DISPOSITIF DE LEVAGE **7207**
SABOTS D'ANIMAUX RAPES **6567**
SAC A OUTILS **12996**
SAGETTE **10613**
SAIGNEE **7274**
SAIGNEE **1321**
SAIGNER **8554**
SAILLANT **9910**
SAILLANT **4301**
SAILLIE **9913**
SAILLIE **9917**
SAILLIE **2093**
SAILLIE SUR LE PRIMITIF **164**
SALAIRE **10897**
SALAIRE **3594**
SALAIRE **13613**
SALAIRE A LA TACHE **9295**
SALAIRE AUX PIECES **9295**
SALLE DE CHAUFFERIE **1418**
SALLE DES CHAUDIERES **1418**
SALLE DES MACHINES **4757**
SALLE DES MACHINES **7855**
SALPETRE **2330**
SALPETRE **10903**
SAMARIUM **10914**
SANDARAQUE **10927**
SANG-DRAGON **4203**
SANGUINE **8720**
SANS FROTTEMENT **5688**
SANS SCORIES **5638**
SAPONIFIABLE **10932**
SAPONIFICATION **10933**
SAPONIFIER **10934**
SAPONITE **10935**
SARCLEUSES **13742**
SAS **11422**
SAS A AIR **274**
SASSER **11423**
SATELLITE **9444**
SATELLITE **9447**

SATELLITE **6168**
SATELLITE DE DIFFERENTIEL **3918**
SATURATION **10943**
SATURATION MAGNETIQUE **7916**
SATURER **10939**
SAUMURE **1617**
SAUT DE BLOC **1337**
SAUTERELLE **1228**
SAUTEUSE **5665**
SAVON **11701**
SAVON BLANC ORDINAIRE **3482**
SAVON DE MARSEILLE **8020**
SAVON DE POTASSE **11740**
SAVON MOU **11740**
SAVON NOIR **11740**
SAVON VERT **11740**
SCALAIRE **10967**
SCANDIUM **10991**
SCELLER DE CIMENT **6153**
SCHEELIN CALCAIRE **10997**
SCHEELITE **10997**
SCHEMA **3836**
SCHISTE **10999**
SCHISTE BITUMINEUX **8780**
SCIAGE **10961**
SCIAGE A CHAUD **6657**
SCIAGE A FROID **2699**
SCIAGE CONTRE FIL **4718**
SCIAGE EN LONG **1058**
SCIAGE EN TRAVERS **4718**
SCIAGE HOLLANDAIS **10075**
SCIAGE PAR FRICTION **5680**
SCIAGE PAR RAYONNEMENT **10075**
SCIAGE PARALLELE **1058**
SCIAGE VERTICAL **4718**
SCIE **10950**
SCIE A ARASER **12741**
SCIE A BOIS **13917**
SCIE A CADRE **5629**
SCIE A CHAINETTE **2216**
SCIE A CHANTOURNER **1505**
SCIE A CHASSIS **5629**
SCIE A CHAUD **6630**
SCIE A CHEVILLES **12741**
SCIE A DECOUPER **5665**
SCIE A DOS **897**
SCIE A FROID **2688**
SCIE A GRUGER **3108**
SCIE A GUICHET **2802**
SCIE A LAME SANS FIN **978**
SCIE A MAIN **6249**

717     **SEG**

SCIE A METAUX **6196**
SCIE A METAUX **8186**
SCIE A METAUX A POIGNEE PISTOLET **9369**
SCIE A MONTURE METALLIQUE **8186**
SCIE A MORTAISER **8193**
SCIE A PLACAGE **13526**
SCIE A REFENDRE **5628**
SCIE A RUBAN **977**
SCIE A RUBAN **978**
SCIE A TENONS **12741**
SCIE A TRONCONNER **3365**
SCIE CIRCULAIRE **2427**
SCIE CIRCULAIRE **2428**
SCIE DE LONG **10609**
SCIE EGOINE **11659**
SCIE MECANIQUE **9747**
SCIE OSCILLANTE **4337**
SCIE PASSE-PARTOUT **3365**
SCIE POUR METAUX AU ROUGE **6630**
SCIER **10951**
SCIERIE (USINE) **10956**
SCIERIE A MOUVEMENT ALTERNATIF **5629**
SCIERIE MECANIQUE **9747**
SCIES A BUCHES **10963**
SCINDER **11946**
SCIURE DE BOIS **10953**
SCLEROMETRE **11002**
SCLEROSCOPE **11366**
SCORIE **11561**
SCORIE **2397**
SCORIE DES HAUTS-FOURNEAUX **1312**
SCORIE EMPRISONNEE **11567**
SCORIES BASIQUES **1054**
SCORIES DE FORGE **6217**
SCORIFICATION **11004**
SEAU **1674**
SECANTE **11099**
SECHAGE **928**
SECHAGE **4359**
SECHER **4338**
SECHER LES BOIS A L'AIR LIBRE **11094**
SECHEUR **4356**
SECHOIR **4355**
SECHOIR **4256**
SECHOIRS A FOURRAGES **4259**
SECHOIRS A GRAINS **4258**
SECOND FILTRE **11101**
SECOUSSE **11359**
SECOUSSE ELECTRIQUE **4529**
SECTEUR **2782**
SECTEUR CIRCULAIRE **11126**

SECTEUR D'UN CERCLE **11126**
SECTEUR DENTE **13024**
SECTEUR GRADUE **6867**
SECTEUR SPHERIQUE **11127**
SECTION **11111**
SECTION **11122**
SECTION (DROITE OU OBLIQUE) D'UNE POUTRE **11116**
SECTION A NERVURES **6550**
SECTION ANNULAIRE **587**
SECTION CARREE **12017**
SECTION CHARGEE **4460**
SECTION CIRCULAIRE **2410**
SECTION CONIQUE **2940**
SECTION CONIQUE **13735**
SECTION DANGEREUSE **3609**
SECTION DE L'ORIFICE D'ECOULEMENT **4020**
SECTION DE PASSAGE **3374**
SECTION DE PASSAGE D'UNE SOUPAPE **11121**
SECTION DE RUPTURE **3373**
SECTION DE RUPTURE **5620**
SECTION DROITE **8654**
SECTION EFFICACE **3371**
SECTION ELLIPTIQUE **4674**
SECTION ETOILEE **12110**
SECTION LIBRE **3374**
SECTION MACROSCOPIQUE **7875**
SECTION MI-RONDE **11170**
SECTION NORMALE **8654**
SECTION OBLIQUE **8711**
SECTION OVALE **8917**
SECTION PRINCIPALE **9868**
SECTION RECTANGULAIRE **10302**
SECTION RECTANGULAIRE CREUSE **6550**
SECTION SEMI-CIRCULAIRE **11170**
SECTION SOUMISE A UN EFFORT DE COMPRESSION **3375**
SECTION SOUMISE A UN EFFORT DE TRACTION **3376**
SECTION TRANSVERSALE **3378**
SECTION TRAPEZOIDALE **13183**
SECTION TRIANGULAIRE **13188**
SECTION UTILE **13422**
SECURITE DE BON FONCTIONNEMENT **10439**
SEDIMENT **3773**
SEDIMENTATION **11228**
SEGMENT **11135**
SEGMENT D'ANNEAU CIRCULAIRE **10603**
SEGMENT D'ETANCHEITE **2867**
SEGMENT D'UN CERCLE **11136**
SEGMENT D'UNE DROITE **11118**
SEGMENT DE COMPRESSION **2861**
SEGMENT DE FEU **13034**
SEGMENT DE FREIN **1542**

**SEG** 718

SEGMENT DE PISTON **9379**
SEGMENT DE PISTON EXCENTRE **4429**
SEGMENT DE TOLE (D'INDUIT) **3160**
SEGMENT RACLEUR **8750**
SEGMENT RACLEUR **8775**
SEGMENT SPHERIQUE A DEUX BASES **14051**
SEGMENT SPHERIQUE A UNE BASE **11137**
SEGREGATION **11139**
SEGREGATION **3172**
SEGREGATION **7635**
SEGREGATION MAJEURE **6925**
SEGREGATION MAJEURE **8660**
SEGREGATION MINEURE **8235**
SEL (CHIM.) **10904**
SEL ALCALIN **338**
SEL AMMONIAC **462**
SEL ANGLAIS **7889**
SEL COMMUN **2790**
SEL D'EPSOM **7889**
SEL D'ETAIN **12100**
SEL D'OSEILLE **10907**
SEL DE GLAUBER **5967**
SEL DE PHOSPHORE **8241**
SEL DE SEDLITZ **7889**
SEL DE SEIGNETTE **11729**
SEL DE SOUDE **551**
SEL DOUBLE **4153**
SEL GEMME **10653**
SEL MARIN **2790**
SEL MICROCOSMIQUE **8241**
SEL NEUTRE **8546**
SEL SOLVAY **455**
SEL VOLATIL D'ANGLETERRE **461**
SELENIUM **11146**
SELF-INDUCTION **11156**
SELS AUGMENTANT LA CONDUCTIBILITE D'UNE SOLUTION **2915**
SELS DE POLISSAGE **1690**
SELS POUR BAINS **9506**
SEMELLE **1127**
SEMELLE D'UN RABOT **11771**
SEMELLE D'UNE POUTRE **5947**
SEMELLE DE PALIER **11772**
SEMENCE **12588**
SEMI-DIESEL **11171**
SEMI-POINTEUSE **11172**
SEMI-REMORQUE **11178**
SEMOIRS A LA VOLEE **11129**
SEMOIRS POUR PORTES OUTILS **11132**
SENESTRORSUM **3239**
SENS D'UNE FORCE **11182**

SENS DE LA MARCHE **11183**
SENS DE LAMINAGE **10698**
SENS DE ROTATION **3992**
SENS DU MOUVEMENT **11183**
SENS INVERSE DES AIGUILLES D'UNE MONTRE (EN) **3237**
SENSIBILITE A L'EFFET D'ENTAILLE **8670**
SENSIBILITE A L'EPAISSEUR **8027**
SENSIBILITE D'UN INSTRUMENT **11188**
SEPARATEUR D'EAU **12188**
SEPARATEUR D'HUILE **8778**
SEPARATEUR DE VAPEUR **12184**
SEPARATION (CHIM.) **11191**
SEPARATION D'UN MELANGE **11192**
SEPARATION ELECTROLYTIQUE **4602**
SEPARATION ELECTROMAGNETIQUE **4618**
SEPARATION ELECTROSTATIQUE **4646**
SEPARATION MAGNETIQUE **7917**
SEPARATION PNEUMATIQUE **290**
SEPARER (CHIM.) **11189**
SEPARER (SE) **9760**
SEQUENCE DES CALIBRES **9097**
SEQUENTIEL **11194**
SERGENT **2452**
SERIE **11203**
SERIE **11213**
SERIE **11219**
SERIE (EN) **11196**
SERIE BINOMIALE **1260**
SERIE CONVERGENTE **3065**
SERIE DIVERGENTE **4094**
SERIE EXPONENTIELLE **4943**
SERIE FINIE **5232**
SERIE HOMOLOGUE **6562**
SERIE INFINIE **6909**
SERIE LOGARITHMIQUE **7719**
SERINGUE A HUILE **8784**
SERPENTIN **2645**
SERPENTIN **9346**
SERPENTIN CHAUFFE PAR LA VAPEUR **12161**
SERPENTIN DE REFROIDISSEMENT **13978**
SERPENTINE **11204**
SERRAGE **11355**
SERRAGE **10194**
SERRAGE D'UN COIN **12928**
SERRAGE DE CLAVETTE **12653**
SERRAGE DU FREIN **1549**
SERRAGE PAR COIN **12929**
SERRAGE PAR ECROUS **12930**
SERRE **10194**
SERRE-BARRES **12981**
SERRE-FLANS **3887**

## 719 SOL

SERRE-JOINTS **2451**
SERRE-JOINTS **2452**
SERRER A BLOC UN ECROU **12927**
SERRER A FOND UN ECROU **12927**
SERRER A VIS **11022**
SERRER LA BOITE A ETOUPE **12926**
SERRER LE FREIN **650**
SERRER UN COIN **12924**
SERRER UN ECROU **12925**
SERRER UNE POULIE SUR L'ARBRE **4222**
SERRER UNE ROUE **4222**
SERRER UNE VIS **12925**
SERRURE DE PORTIERE **4123**
SERTISSAGE DES TUYAUX AU DUDGEON **4908**
SERTISSEUSE **5346**
SERTISSEUSE **11088**
SERVICE **8837**
SERVICE CONTINU **3038**
SERVICE CONTINU **9209**
SERVICE INTERMITTENT **7056**
SERVO-DIRECTION **9743**
SERVO-FREIN **1457**
SERVO-FREINS **9731**
SERVO-MECANISME **11210**
SERVO-MOTEUR **11211**
SERVOMOTEUR DE DEMARRAGE **1018**
SERVOMOTEUR DE LANCEMENT **1018**
SESQUICHLORURE DE CHROME **2381**
SESQUIOXYDE DE CHROME **2382**
SESQUIOXYDE DE COBALT **2611**
SESQUIOXYDE DE FER **7148**
SESQUIOXYDE DE MANGANESE **7970**
SHERARDISATION **11341**
SHERARDISER **11340**
SHIMMY **11353**
SHUNT **11403**
SICCATIF **4257**
SICCATIF **4256**
SIDEROSE **11421**
SIDEROXYLE **13833**
SIDERURGIE **8209**
SIEGE **11098**
SIEGE A REGLAGE AUTOMATIQUE **9741**
SIEGE BAQUET **1678**
SIEGE DE CORPS DE VANNE **1397**
SIEGE DE SOUPAPE **11097**
SIEGE DE SOUPAPE **13468**
SIEGE SUSPENDU **1383**
SIEGES OBLIQUES **12663**
SIEGES PARALLELES **9063**
SIFFLET **13829**

SIFFLET A VAPEUR **12190**
SIFFLET AVERTISSEUR **307**
SIFFLET D'ALARME **307**
SIGNAL ACOUSTIQUE **816**
SIGNAL D'ALARME **306**
SIGNAL OPTIQUE **13580**
SIGNE **11429**
SIGNE NEGATIF **8532**
SIGNE POSITIF **9661**
SILENCIEUX **11431**
SILENCIEUX **8448**
SILEX PYROMAQUE **5427**
SILICATE **11437**
SILICATE D'ALUMINE **425**
SILICATE DE FER **7149**
SILICATE DE MAGNESIUM **7888**
SILICATE DE POTASSE **9698**
SILICATE DE SOUDE **11731**
SILICE **11436**
SILICE **11434**
SILICE FARINEUSE **7292**
SILICEUX **10082**
SILICIUM **11442**
SILICIURE DE CARBONE **1980**
SILICO-SPIEGEL **11440**
SILICONE **11456**
SIMILITUDE **11470**
SIMITHSONITE **1836**
SINISTRORSUM **3239**
SINUOIDE **11513**
SINUS **11475**
SIPHON **11517**
SIPHON (DE MANOMETRE) **11514**
SIRENE D'ALARME **11518**
SOCLE **1026**
SOCLE EN FONTE **1037**
SODIUM **11714**
SOIE **11452**
SOIE **12614**
SOIE ARTIFICIELLE **736**
SOL AQUIFERE **13642**
SOLE **6331**
SOLE ACIDE **108**
SOLE DE HAUT-FOURNEAU **9011**
SOLE ET GARNISSAGE BASIQUES **1045**
SOLENOIDE **11774**
SOLENOIDE **11773**
SOLIDE **11775**
SOLIDE ELASTIQUE **4484**
SOLIDIFICATION **6292**
SOLIDIFICATION **5653**

**SOL** 720

SOLIDIFICATION 11797
SOLIDIFICATION D'UN LIQUIDE 11799
SOLIDIFICATION DE LA MASSE FONDUE DANS LA POCHE 7360
SOLIDIFIER (SE) A L'AIR (CIMENT) 6286
SOLIDIFIER (SE) DANS L'EAU (CIMENT) 6287
SOLIDIFIER (SE) PAR REFROIDISSEMENT 11803
SOLIDUS 11805
SOLLICITATION 12331
SOLLICITATIONS 7679
SOLUBILISER 10456
SOLUBILITE 11806
SOLUBLE 11807
SOLUBLE DANS L'EAU 11809
SOLUTION 11811
SOLUTION ACIDE 9290
SOLUTION ADHERENTE 4201
SOLUTION ALCALINE 339
SOLUTION ALCOOLIQUE 315
SOLUTION AMMONIACALE 457
SOLUTION AMMONIACALE 660
SOLUTION ANODIQUE 606
SOLUTION AQUEUSE 661
SOLUTION CONCENTREE 2883
SOLUTION DE POTASSE CAUSTIQUE 9671
SOLUTION DE SOUDE CAUSTIQUE 2120
SOLUTION DILUEE 3953
SOLUTION ENTRAINEE 4202
SOLUTION ETENDUE 3953
SOLUTION FAIBLE 13706
SOLUTION FORTE 2883
SOLUTION GRAPHIQUE 6060
SOLUTION NON SATUREE 13394
SOLUTION PAR LE CALCUL 8694
SOLUTION SALINE 10908
SOLUTION SATUREE 10941
SOLUTION SOLIDE 11794
SOLUTION SURSATUREE 12478
SOLVANT 11814
SOLVANT IONOGENE 7130
SOLVANTS DE DECAPAGE 12381
SOLVANTS POUR CORROSIFS 3192
SOMME 12454
SOMMET 12455
SOMMET 638
SOMMET D'UN POLYGONE 13543
SOMMET DE LA DENT 12514
SOMMET DU FILET 3333
SONDAGE 12778
SONDE DE MOULEUR 8357
SONDEUSE SUR CAMION 13614

SONNERIE 1137
SOPHISTICATION 205
SORBITE 11817
SORTIE 8900
SORTIE DE COULEE (TROU) 12645
SORTIE EN LINGOTIERE 9717
SOUBASSEMENT D'UNE COLONNE 1035
SOUDABILITE 13768
SOUDABLE 13769
SOUDAGE 11762
SOUDAGE 13767
SOUDAGE 13779
SOUDAGE (A L'ARC) ELECTRIQUE 4533
SOUDAGE A DROITE 907
SOUDAGE A ENTAILLE 11636
SOUDAGE A FROID 2712
SOUDAGE A L'ACETYLENE 96
SOUDAGE A L'ARC A COURANT ALTERNATIF 685
SOUDAGE A L'ARC A COURANT CONTINU 686
SOUDAGE A L'ARC AVEC ELECTRODE AU CARBONE 1943
SOUDAGE A L'ARC ELECTRIQUE 8176
SOUDAGE A L'ARC EN ATMOSPHERE INERTE 683
SOUDAGE A L'ARC METALLIQUE SANS GAZ PROTECTEUR 13397
SOUDAGE A L'ARC METALLIQUE SOUS GAZ PROTECTEUR 11345
SOUDAGE A L'ARC METALLIQUE SOUS PROTECTION DE GAZ INERTE 11428
SOUDAGE A L'ARC SOUS PROTECTION GAZEUSE 5852
SOUDAGE A L'ARC SUBMERGE 12414
SOUDAGE A L'ARC SUBMERGE 684
SOUDAGE A LA CAROTTE 10027
SOUDAGE A LA CAROTTE 9576
SOUDAGE A LA FORGE 5546
SOUDAGE A LA FORGE 6218
SOUDAGE A PASSES MULTIPLES 8455
SOUDAGE AERO-ACETYLENIQUE 295
SOUDAGE ALUMINOTHERMIQUE PAR PRESSION 9837
SOUDAGE ARCATOM (A L'ARC PROTEGEA L'HYDROGENE ATOMIQUE) 801
SOUDAGE AU CONTACT 682
SOUDAGE AU PLAFOND 7113
SOUDAGE AUTOGENE 835
SOUDAGE AUTOGENE 8979
SOUDAGE AUTOGENE PAR PRESSION 8978
SOUDAGE AUTOMATIQUE 849
SOUDAGE BOUT A BOUT (PAR RESISTANCE) 1805
SOUDAGE CONTINU 3016
SOUDAGE CONTINU PAR RECOUVREMENT 7401
SOUDAGE DE FILS EN CROIX 3385
SOUDAGE DE PLOMB 7476
SOUDAGE DE RENFORCEMENT 10428

SOUDAGE DE TROUS DE RIVETS **9537**
SOUDAGE DES RIVETS **10631**
SOUDAGE EN ANGLE **5162**
SOUDAGE EN ATELIER **11362**
SOUDAGE EN BOUT PAR ETINCELAGE **1806**
SOUDAGE EN BOUT PAR RESISTANCE **1807**
SOUDAGE EN BOUT PAR RESISTANCE **10488**
SOUDAGE EN CONGE **5162**
SOUDAGE EN LIGNE CONTINUE A LA MOLETTE **11086**
SOUDAGE EN PAS DE PELERIN **918**
SOUDAGE EN SPIRALE **11921**
SOUDAGE ETANCHE **11076**
SOUDAGE INTERIEUR **7080**
SOUDAGE LONGITUDINAL **7737**
SOUDAGE MAL FAIT **920**
SOUDAGE MECANIQUE (AUTOMATIQUE) **8115**
SOUDAGE PAR ALUMINOTHERMIE **12819**
SOUDAGE PAR BOMBARDEMENT D'ELECTRONS **4630**
SOUDAGE PAR BOMBARDEMENT ELECTRONIQUE **4627**
SOUDAGE PAR BOSSAGES **9916**
SOUDAGE PAR BOSSAGES MULTIPLES **8468**
SOUDAGE PAR ETINCELAGE **5358**
SOUDAGE PAR FUSION **5762**
SOUDAGE PAR FUSION **8643**
SOUDAGE PAR INDUCTION **4619**
SOUDAGE PAR PERCUSSION A CONDENSATEUR **4645**
SOUDAGE PAR PERCUSSION ELECTROMAGNETIQUE **4617**
SOUDAGE PAR POINTS A RECOUVREMENT **7402**
SOUDAGE PAR POINTS AU PISTOLET **9576**
SOUDAGE PAR POINTS EN SERIE PAR RESISTANCE **11200**
SOUDAGE PAR POINTS MULTIPLES **8464**
SOUDAGE PAR POINTS PAR RESISTANCE **10493**
SOUDAGE PAR PRESSION **9842**
SOUDAGE PAR PULSATION **9978**
SOUDAGE PAR RAPPROCHEMENT **1805**
SOUDAGE PAR RECOUVREMENT **7403**
SOUDAGE PAR RESISTANCE **10500**
SOUDAGE PAR ULTRASONS **13338**
SOUDAGE PROVISOIRE PAR POINTS DE POINTAGE **12589**
SOUDAGE SEMI-AUTOMATIQUE A L'ARC **11166**
SOUDAGE SOUS POUDRE **9722**
SOUDAGE T.I.G (A L'ARC DE TUNGSTENE SOUS GAZ INERTE) **6906**
SOUDAGE TENDRE **12958**
SOUDAGE-FINITION **5216**
SOUDE **11713**
SOUDE A L'AMMONIAQUE **455**
SOUDE AZOTEUSE **11725**
SOUDE CAUSTIQUE **11722**
SOUDE LEBLANC **12445**
SOUDE NITREUSE **11725**

SOUDE SOLVAY **455**
SOUDER **11756**
SOUDER **13755**
SOUDER A L'AUTOGENE **13758**
SOUDER A L'ETAIN **11741**
SOUDER EN BISEAU **7404**
SOUDER FORT **1573**
SOUDER PAR CONTACT **1785**
SOUDER PAR ENCOLLAGE **1785**
SOUDEUR **13778**
SOUDURE **13776**
SOUDURE **13767**
SOUDURE **13779**
SOUDURE **11083**
SOUDURE **11762**
SOUDURE (ASSEMBLAGE) EN T **1801**
SOUDURE (ASSEMBLAGE) EN T **1795**
SOUDURE (COMPOSITION FUSIBLE) **11755**
SOUDURE (TRAVAIL FAIT EN SOUDANT AVEC INTERPOSITION D'UN ALLIAGE) **11761**
SOUDURE A ENTAILLE **11635**
SOUDURE A FROID **2712**
SOUDURE A L'ARC ELECTRIQUE **681**
SOUDURE A L'ARGENT **11466**
SOUDURE A L'ECRASEMENT **8024**
SOUDURE A L'ETAIN **11742**
SOUDURE A L'ETAIN **11743**
SOUDURE A PAS DE PELERIN **901**
SOUDURE ALUMINOTHERMIQUE **12818**
SOUDURE AU BISMUTH **1274**
SOUDURE AU CHALUMEAU **11768**
SOUDURE AU FER A SOUDER **11769**
SOUDURE AU PLAFOND **8944**
SOUDURE AUTOGENE **834**
SOUDURE AUTOGENE **831**
SOUDURE AUTOGENE **5847**
SOUDURE AVEC APPORT DE FER-THERMIT **12818**
SOUDURE BIEN FAITE **6005**
SOUDURE BOUT A BOUT **1784**
SOUDURE BOUT A BOUT **1809**
SOUDURE BOUT A BOUT PAR RESISTANCE **1799**
SOUDURE BOUT A BOUT PAR RESISTANCE **13413**
SOUDURE BOUT A BOUT SANS SUREPAISSEUR **5481**
SOUDURE CLAIRE **7475**
SOUDURE CONCAVE **1792**
SOUDURE CONTINE **11086**
SOUDURE CONTINUE **3037**
SOUDURE D'ANGLE A CORDON PLAT **12075**
SOUDURE D'ANGLE A RANGEES ALTERNEES SYMETRIQUES **2210**
SOUDURE D'ANGLE CONCAVE **7561**

**SOU** 722

SOUDURE D'ANGLE CONCAVE **2878**
SOUDURE D'ANGLE CONVEXE **3077**
SOUDURE D'ANGLE DISCONTINUE A RANGEES ALTERNEES **12049**
SOUDURE D'ANGLE OUVERTE **8809**
SOUDURE D'UN TUBE **11085**
SOUDURE DE BORD **6133**
SOUDURE DE BORD EN DOUBLE U FERMEE **2524**
SOUDURE DE BORD EN DOUBLE-V SANS ECARTEMENT **2525**
SOUDURE DE BORD EN U FERMEE **2530**
SOUDURE DE BORD EN V SANS ECARTEMENT **2531**
SOUDURE DEPOSEE A LA MAIN **7988**
SOUDURE DISCONTINUE **7055**
SOUDURE DOUBLE FERMEE **1788**
SOUDURE DOUBLE J FERMEE **2523**
SOUDURE DOUBLE OUVERTE **8812**
SOUDURE EN ANGLE A PLAT **6583**
SOUDURE EN BISEAU **7405**
SOUDURE EN BOUCHON **9536**
SOUDURE EN CONGE **7561**
SOUDURE EN CONGE **2878**
SOUDURE EN CORNICHE **6591**
SOUDURE EN DEMI-V AVEC ECARTEMENT **1797**
SOUDURE EN DEMI-V AVEC ECARTEMENT **8822**
SOUDURE EN DEMI-V SANS ECARTEMENT **1789**
SOUDURE EN DEMI-V SANS ECARTEMENT **2528**
SOUDURE EN I AVEC ECARTEMENT **8824**
SOUDURE EN I SANS ECARTEMENT **2532**
SOUDURE EN I SANS ECARTEMENT DES BORDS **1791**
SOUDURE EN J AVEC ECARTEMENT **1798**
SOUDURE EN J AVEC ECARTEMENT **8823**
SOUDURE EN J SANS ECARTEMENT **2529**
SOUDURE EN K AVEC ECARTEMENT **1796**
SOUDURE EN K AVEC ECARTEMENT **8811**
SOUDURE EN K SANS ECARTEMENT **1787**
SOUDURE EN K SANS ECARTEMENT **2522**
SOUDURE EN PASSES SUPERPOSEES **13757**
SOUDURE EN POSITION A PLAT **4190**
SOUDURE EN POSITION PLAFOND **8941**
SOUDURE EN POSITION VERTICALE DESCENDANTE **4192**
SOUDURE EN POSITON VERTICALE MONTANTE **13419**
SOUDURE EXECUTEE SUR CHANTIER **5146**
SOUDURE FORTE **1576**
SOUDURE FORTE (COMPOSITION FUSIBLE) **6279**
SOUDURE FORTE PAR IMMERSION **3969**
SOUDURE HORIZONTALE **5948**
SOUDURE INTERMITTENTE **7054**
SOUDURE JAUNE **11880**
SOUDURE LINEAIRE DE FRACTION **1085**
SOUDURE MAL FAITE **920**
SOUDURE MONOPASSE **11485**

SOUDURE OXHYDRIQUE **8988**
SOUDURE OXY-ACETYLENIQUE **8979**
SOUDURE PAR ENCOLLAGE **1802**
SOUDURE PAR ETINCELAGE **1794**
SOUDURE PAR PERCUSSION **9183**
SOUDURE PAR POINTS **11959**
SOUDURE PAR RAPPROCHEMENT **1784**
SOUDURE PAR RAPPROCHEMENT **1802**
SOUDURE PAR RECOUVREMENT **7405**
SOUDURE PORTANTE **12357**
SOUDURE POUSSEE VERS LA GAUCHE **5539**
SOUDURE PROVISOIRE PAR POINTS **12590**
SOUDURE RESISTANTE A LA PRESSION **9838**
SOUDURE SUR BORDS DROITS **12032**
SOUDURE SUR BORDS RELEVES **5335**
SOUFFLAGE MAGNETIQUE DE L'ARC **665**
SOUFFLERIE **1361**
SOUFFLERIE **242**
SOUFFLERIE DE VAPEUR **12172**
SOUFFLET **1139**
SOUFFLET DE FORGE **1139**
SOUFFLETTE **272**
SOUFFLETTE A AIR **276**
SOUFFLETTES **9796**
SOUFFLURE **7523**
SOUFFLURE **1353**
SOUFFLURE **1351**
SOUFFLURE **5825**
SOUFFLURE **5836**
SOUFFLURES **1362**
SOUFFLURES **1330**
SOUFFLURES **11903**
SOUFFRE DORE D'ANTIMOINE **625**
SOUFRE **12449**
SOUFRE AMORPHE **476**
SOUFRE CRISTALLISE **3435**
SOUFRE EN CANON **12255**
SOUFRE SUBLIME **5464**
SOULEVEMENT D'UN FARDEAU **7559**
SOULEVEMENT DE LA SOUPAPE **7544**
SOULEVER **7542**
SOULEVEUSES DE BETTERAVES **12440**
SOULEVEUSES DE RACINES **10722**
SOUMETTRE UN CORPS A UNE CHARGE **12323**
SOUMISSION A UNE PRE-TENSION **830**
SOUPAPE **13453**
SOUPAPE **13472**
SOUPAPE **2617**
SOUPAPE **2284**
SOUPAPE **12436**
SOUPAPE A AIR **259**

| | |
|---|---|
| SOUPAPE A BOULET **968** | SOUPAPE DE SURETE A RESSORT **11998** |
| SOUPAPE A CHARNIERE **5353** | SOUPAPE DE SURETE A RESSORT **11986** |
| SOUPAPE A CLAPET **5353** | SOUPAPE DE TROP PLEIN **8933** |
| SOUPAPE A CLAPET **7547** | SOUPAPE DE VIDANGE **1358** |
| SOUPAPE A CLOCHE **1136** | SOUPAPE DESMODROMIQUE **852** |
| SOUPAPE A CLOCHE INTERIEURE **11579** | SOUPAPE DROITE **12317** |
| SOUPAPE A COMMANDE HYDRAULIQUE **6697** | SOUPAPE ELECTROMAGNETIQUE **11774** |
| SOUPAPE A COMMANDE PNEUMATIQUE **9557** | SOUPAPE EQUILIBREE **934** |
| SOUPAPE A DEUX VOIES **13318** | SOUPAPE ETAGEE **8475** |
| SOUPAPE A DISQUE **4011** | SOUPAPE MULTIPLE **8476** |
| SOUPAPE A DOUBLE SIEGE **4166** | SOUPAPE PRESSION-DEPRESSION **9843** |
| SOUPAPE A FLOTTEUR **5433** | SOUPAPE UNIQUE **11491** |
| SOUPAPE A MANCHON **11579** | SOUPAPE-BILLE **968** |
| SOUPAPE A QUADRUPLE SIEGE **10060** | SOUPAPES EN TETE **8943** |
| SOUPAPE A SIEGE CONIQUE **2951** | SOUPLESSE **5415** |
| SOUPAPE A SIEGE PLAN **4011** | SOURCE D'ELECTRICITE **11823** |
| SOUPAPE A SIMPLE SIEGE **11497** | SOURCE D'ENERGIE **11824** |
| SOUPAPE A TROIS VOIES **12882** | SOURCE D'ERREURS **11825** |
| SOUPAPE ANNULAIRE **10605** | SOURCE DE COURANT A TENSION CONSTANTE (POUR SOUDAGE) **2979** |
| SOUPAPE AUTOMATIQUE **852** | |
| SOUPAPE CASSE-VIDE **13437** | SOURCE LINEAIRE **7599** |
| SOUPAPE CHAMPIGNON **7547** | SOURCE LUMINEUSE **7568** |
| SOUPAPE COMMANDEE **8120** | SOURCE LUMINEUSE **11826** |
| SOUPAPE D EMISSION **4899** | SOUS FORME DE VAPEUR **6817** |
| SOUPAPE D'ADMISSION **6949** | SOUS-COUCHE (D'OXYDE) **12416** |
| SOUPAPE D'ADMISSION **201** | SOUS-JOINT **12408** |
| SOUPAPE D'ALIMENTATION **5076** | SOUS-JOINT A FAIBLE DESORIENTATION **7767** |
| SOUPAPE D'ARRET **12282** | SOUS-LISSE **7795** |
| SOUPAPE D'ARRET DE VAPEUR **12186** | SOUS-PRODUIT **1820** |
| SOUPAPE D'ECHAPPEMENT **4899** | SOUS-PROGRAMME **12415** |
| SOUPAPE D'ECHAPPEMENT **797** | SOUS-SOLEUSES **8344** |
| SOUPAPE D'EQUERRE **534** | SOUS-SOLEUSES ET CHARRUES RIGOLEUSES **4090** |
| SOUPAPE D'EVACUATION **1358** | SOUS-STRUCTURE **12423** |
| SOUPAPE D'INJECTION **6937** | SOUSTRACTION **12425** |
| SOUPAPE DE CORNOUAILLES **1136** | SOUSTRACTION DE LA CHALEUR **4666** |
| SOUPAPE DE DECHARGE **1358** | SOUSTRAIRE **12424** |
| SOUPAPE DE DECHARGE **10441** | SOUSTRAIRE DE LA CHALEUR **13910** |
| SOUPAPE DE DERIVATION **1819** | SOUTE A CHARBON **2561** |
| SOUPAPE DE DETENTE **4926** | SOUTE A CHARBON **1740** |
| SOUPAPE DE PRISE DE VAPEUR **12187** | SOUTE A MAZOUT **5706** |
| SOUPAPE DE REDUCTION **10355** | SOUTENEMENT **12153** |
| SOUPAPE DE REFOULEMENT **3739** | SOUTENENENT **12493** |
| SOUPAPE DE SECURITE **1593** | SOUTENIR **12150** |
| SOUPAPE DE SURETE **10891** | SOUTENIR LE TAS **6524** |
| SOUPAPE DE SURETE A CHARGE DIRECTE **3632** | SOUTENU LIBREMENT SUR DEUX APPUIS **11474** |
| SOUPAPE DE SURETE A CHARGE DIRECTE A RESSORT **3987** | SOUTES A COMBUSTIBLE **8748** |
| | SOUTIRAGE-VIDANGE **4225** |
| SOUPAPE DE SURETE A CONTRE-POIDS **13749** | SPATH CALCAIRE **1845** |
| SOUPAPE DE SURETE A GRANDE LEVEE **10890** | SPATH FLUOR **5479** |
| SOUPAPE DE SURETE A LEVIER ET A RESSORT **11985** | SPATH PESANT **1021** |
| SOUPAPE DE SURETE A LEVIER ET CONTREPOIDS **7535** | SPATULE **11844** |

## SPE

724

SPECIALITE **11845**
SPECIALITE PHARMACEUTIQUE **9119**
SPECIMEN **10915**
SPECTRE **11863**
SPECTRE CANNELE **5487**
SPECTRE CONTINU **3036**
SPECTRE D'ABSORPTION **54**
SPECTRE DES RAYONS X **14001**
SPECTRE DISCONTINU **7610**
SPECTRE MAGNETIQUE **7902**
SPECTRE PRODUIT PAR PRISME **9878**
SPECTRE SECONDAIRE **11108**
SPECTRE SOLAIRE **11754**
SPECTROGRAPHE **11860**
SPECTROMETRE **11862**
SPECTROMETRE A RAYONS X **14000**
SPECTROMETRE DE MASSE **8029**
SPECTROSCOPE **11862**
SPECTROSCOPIE COLORIMETRIQUE **2739**
SPECTROSCOPIE DE LA FLAMME **5320**
SPERMACETI **11882**
SPHALERITE **1324**
SPHERE **11883**
SPHERE CREUSE **6549**
SPHERIQUE **11884**
SPHEROIDAL **8606**
SPHEROIDISATION **11896**
SPHEROMETRE **11897**
SPIEGEL **11898**
SPIEGEL **11899**
SPIEGELEISEN **11899**
SPIRALE **11912**
SPIRALE ARCHIMEDIENNE **690**
SPIRALE D'ARCHIMEDE **690**
SPIRALE HYPERBOLIQUE **6738**
SPIRALE LOGARITHMIQUE **7720**
SPIRE **2646**
STABILISATEUR **12042**
STABILISATEUR AUTOMATIQUE **847**
STABILISATION **12043**
STABILITE **12041**
STABILITE **4385**
STABILITE (CHIM.) **2313**
STABILITE A SEC **4352**
STABILITE DIMENSIONNELLE **3958**
STADE **12239**
STALAGMOMETRIE **12054**
STAND DE L'OUVRIER **8839**
STANDARD **12071**
STANDARD TELEPHONIQUE **12557**
STANDARDISATION **12091**

STANDARDISER **12090**
STANDARDS POUR TUYAUTERIES **9359**
STANNATE **12095**
STANNATE DE SODIUM **11732**
STARTER **2357**
STARTER AUTOMATIQUE **838**
STATION CENTRALE **9742**
STATION GENERATRICE **9742**
STATIONNER **12294**
STATIQUE **12133**
STATIQUE **12140**
STATIQUE GRAPHIQUE **6061**
STATOR **12146**
STAUFFER **12148**
STEARINE **12195**
STEATITE **11703**
STEATITE **5659**
STELLITE **12234**
STEREOMETRIE **12251**
STEREOMETRIQUE **12250**
STERILISATION DE L'EAU **12252**
STIBINE **622**
STOCK **12263**
STOCKER **12294**
STOECHIOMETRIE **12268**
STOECHIOMETRIQUE **12267**
STRAPONTIN **7261**
STRATE **7444**
STRATIFICATION **7382**
STRICTION **7424**
STRICTION **8515**
STRICTION **3043**
STRICTION **8516**
STRICTION **3045**
STRICTION **10361**
STRIE **5484**
STRIE **5486**
STRIE **11206**
STRIE **5061**
STRIES **10576**
STROBOSCOPE **12385**
STRONTIUM **12389**
STROPHOIDE **7722**
STRUCTURE **12394**
STRUCTURE **12395**
STRUCTURE **12800**
STRUCTURE A GRAINS FINS **5200**
STRUCTURE A GROS GRAINS **7869**
STRUCTURE BASALTIQUE **2758**
STRUCTURE BETA **1219**
STRUCTURE COMPACTE (A) **2514**

STRUCTURE CRISTALLINE 3430
STRUCTURE DENDRITIQUE 3750
STRUCTURE DES ALLIAGES 2058
STRUCTURE DU COEUR 3165
STRUCTURE DU GRAIN 6041
STRUCTURE DUE A LA DEFORMATION PLASTIQUE 5461
STRUCTURE FIBREUSE 5135
STRUCTURE FINE 5210
STRUCTURE FINE (R.X.) 5203
STRUCTURE GAMMA 5797
STRUCTURE GRANULAIRE 6052
STRUCTURE HEXAGONALE COMPACTE 6458
STRUCTURE LAMELLAIRE 7373
STRUCTURE MOLECULAIRE 8361
STRUCTURE MOSAIQUE 8403
STRUCTURE RETICULAIRE 8539
STRUCTURE ZONALE 979
STYLET 9161
STYLET TRACEUR 9161
SUAGE 3322
SUBDIVISION 12409
SUBLIMATION 12412
SUBLIME CORROSIF 8153
SUBLIMER 12411
SUBMERGER 12413
SUBSTANCE 12419
SUBSTANCE ACTIVATRICE 4744
SUBSTANCE ACTIVATRICE 148
SUBSTANCE ADHESIVE 177
SUBSTANCE AGGLUTINANTE 1253
SUBSTANCE ANTI-INCRUSTANTE 10978
SUBSTANCE CALORIFUGE 6352
SUBSTANCE CORROSIVE 3197
SUBSTANCE EN POUDRE FINE 6789
SUBSTANCE EPAISSISSANTE 12842
SUBSTANCE FINEMENT BROYEE 6789
SUBSTANCE HOMOGENE 6558
SUBSTANCE USANTE 6107
SUBSTANCES ETRANGERES 6813
SUBSTANCES PHOSPHORESCENTES 9251
SUBSTANCES RADIOACTIVES 10158
SUBSTITUTION (MATH.) 12421
SUCCEDANE 12420
SUCESSION DES OPERATIONS DE SOUDAGE 13790
SUCETTE 12332
SUCRE DE RAISIN 6058
SUIE 11816
SUIF 12609
SUIF DES BOEUFS 1128
SUIF VEGETAL DE CHINE 2342
SUINT 13933

SUINTEMENT 12540
SUINTEMENT 7488
SUITE 2222
SUITE 11203
SULFATE 12444
SULFATE ACIDE DE SOUDE 11717
SULFATE ANHYDRE DE CHAUX 549
SULFATE D'ALUMINIUM 426
SULFATE D'AMMONIUM 471
SULFATE D'ARGENT 11467
SULFATE DE BARYUM 1003
SULFATE DE CALCIUM 1856
SULFATE DE CALCIUM 6190
SULFATE DE COBALT 2615
SULFATE DE CUIVRE 3475
SULFATE DE FER 6093
SULFATE DE MAGNESIUM 7889
SULFATE DE NICKEL 8571
SULFATE DE PLOMB 7473
SULFATE DE POTASSE 9699
SULFATE DE ZINC 14046
SULFATE DOUBLE DE NICKEL ET D'AMMONIAQUE 8558
SULFATE FERRIQUE 5103
SULFATE MANGANEUX 7974
SULFATE MERCUREUX 8162
SULFATE MERCURIQUE 8158
SULFATE NEUTRE DE SODIUM 11733
SULFHYDRATE D'AMMONIUM 464
SULFITE 12448
SULFITE ACIDE 11718
SULFITE DE SOUDE 11734
SULFOCYANURE DE POTASSIUM 9701
SULFURE 12446
SULFURE D'AMMONIUM 472
SULFURE DE BARYUM 1004
SULFURE DE CARBONE 1964
SULFURE DE FER 12447
SULFURE DE POTASSE 9700
SULFURE DOREE 625
SULFURE EN CHAINE 2221
SULFURE FERREUX/FERRIQUE 7153
SULFURE ROUGE DE MERCURE 13535
SULFURE STANNEUX 12103
SULFURE STANNIQUE 12099
SUPER-RESEAU 12475
SUPERFICIE DE LA SOUDURE 4998
SUPERPOSITION DE VIBRATIONS 12476
SUPPLEMENT D'UN ANGLE 12482
SUPPORT 12490
SUPPORT 1041
SUPPORT 6586

# SUP

SUPPORT 57
SUPPORT 3288
SUPPORT 1522
SUPPORT (CONSTR.) 1118
SUPPORT A COUTEAU 7325
SUPPORT D'AME SUPPORT DE NOYAU 2253
SUPPORT D'INFORMATION 12289
SUPPORT D'INFORMATION D'ENTREE 6960
SUPPORT DE FUSEE 11910
SUPPORT DE FUSEE 12230
SUPPORT DE PIECE A ESTAMPER 1305
SUPPORT METALLIQUE DE NOYAU 662
SUPPORT MOTEUR 4754
SUPPORTER 12491
SUPPRESSION 1337
SUPPRESSION DE LA FUMEE 11677
SUPPRESSION DES ZEROS 14033
SURCHARGE 8963
SURCHARGE 8953
SURCHARGER 8954
SURCHARGER UN MATERIEL 8962
SURCHAUFFAGE 12473
SURCHAUFFAGE 12460
SURCHAUFFE 8946
SURCHAUFFE 12473
SURCHAUFFER 12468
SURCHAUFFEUR 12472
SURCOMPRESSEUR 1456
SURCOUCHE 8952
SURCROIT DE DIMENSION 8961
SUREPAISSEUR 8948
SUREPAISSEUR 1695
SUREPAISSEUR D'USINAGE 358
SUREPAISSEUR D'USINAGE 7865
SURFACAGE 12522
SURFACE 12521
SURFACE 12496
SURFACE 2019
SURFACE 694
SURFACE 11120
SURFACE CAUSTIQUE 2121
SURFACE CHARGEE 12368
SURFACE COURBE 3498
SURFACE D'AFFLEUREMENT 5058
SURFACE D'APPUI 1115
SURFACE D'ENGRENEMENT 696
SURFACE DE CHAUFFE 6398
SURFACE DE CONTACT 2998
SURFACE DE CONTACT 12510
SURFACE DE GLISSEMENT 11608
SURFACE DE GLISSEMENT 11585

SURFACE DE GRILLE 6068
SURFACE DE GUIDAGE 6166
SURFACE DE L'EMPREINTE 12512
SURFACE DE LA CIBLE (OFFERTE AUX RAYONNEMENTS) 12683
SURFACE DE LA COUPE 12511
SURFACE DE LIQUATION 7634
SURFACE DE NIVEAU 7527
SURFACE DE PORTEE D'UN TOURILLON 1116
SURFACE DE REFRIGERATION 3092
SURFACE DE REFROIDISSEMENT 3092
SURFACE DE REVOLUTION 12513
SURFACE DE ROULEMENT 10705
SURFACE DE ROULEMENT D'UNE ROUE 13173
SURFACE DEVALOPPABLE 3817
SURFACE DIFFUSIVE 3935
SURFACE EQUIPOTENTIELLE 7527
SURFACE FILTRANTE SATUREE 2360
SURFACE FROTTANTE 5687
SURFACE GAUCHE 11535
SURFACE HELICOIDALE 6428
SURFACE INTERIEURE D'UN TUYAU 6954
SURFACE LATERALE D'UN CONE 2949
SURFACE LATERALE D'UN CYLINDRE 3590
SURFACE MATE 8060
SURFACE METALLIQUE DECAPEE 2470
SURFACE METALLIQUE POLIE 1611
SURFACE MIROITANTE 11866
SURFACE PLANE 9441
SURFACE POLIE 6142
SURFACE PORTANTE 1101
SURFACE PORTANTE 1115
SURFACE RAYONNANTE 10142
SURFACE REFLECHISSANTE 10385
SURFACE REFROIDISSANTE 3092
SURFACE RUGUEUSE 10784
SURFACE RUGUEUSE 10779
SURFACE TRES POREUSE 6644
SURFACER 12497
SURFUSION 12465
SURMOULAGE 4383
SURPASSER 8928
SURPRESSEUR 1456
SURPRESSION 8955
SURREFROIDISSEMENT 12465
SURSATURATION 12461
SURSATURATION 12479
SURSATURER 12477
SURSOUFFLAGE BESSEMER 1211
SURSTRUCTURE 12475
SURVEILLANCE 12481

727 TAI

SURVEILLANCE DES CHAUDIERES 9193
SURVEILLANT 8958
SURVEILLER 12474
SURVIEILLISSEMENT 8923
SURVOLTAGE 4881
SURVOLTAGE 8967
SURVOLTEUR 1456
SUSCEPTIBILITE MAGNETIQUE 7918
SUSCEPTIBLE D'ETRE BREVETEE 9122
SUSCEPTIBLE D'ETRE COULE 1914
SUSCEPTIBLE D'ETRE LAMINE 1915
SUSPENDU LIBREMENT 5649
SUSPENDU SUR UN COUTEAU 6669
SUSPENDU SUR UN PIVOT 8432
SUSPENSION 12526
SUSPENSION A COUTEAU 7326
SUSPENSION A LA CARDAN 1998
SUSPENSION A PIVOT 9570
SUSPENSION A ROTULE 958
SUSPENSION BIFILAIRE 1240
SYENITE 12565
SYMBOLE (CHIM.) 2315
SYMBOLES DE SOUDAGE 13791
SYMETRIE 12567
SYMETRIQUE 12566
SYNCHRO 12568
SYNCHRONE 12570
SYNCHRONISME 12569
SYNTHESE 12572
SYNTHETIQUE 12573
SYNTONIE 12574
SYPHON 11517
SYSTEME A BOUCLE DE RETOUR 2533
SYSTEME ANTI-DERAPANT 8645
SYSTEME ARTICULE 7628
SYSTEME C.G.S. 2159
SYSTEME CENTIMETRE-GRAMME-SECONDE 2159
SYSTEME DE COMMANDE EN BOUCLE OUVERTE 8817
SYSTEME DE COMMANDE NUMERIQUE 8695
SYSTEME DE COORDONNEES 12575
SYSTEME DE COULEE ET D'ALIMENTATION 5870
SYSTEME DE LENTILLES 12576
SYSTEME DE MESURE 12578
SYSTEME DE MESURE ABSOLUE 31
SYSTEME DE PEINTURE A DEUX COMPOSANTS 13311
SYSTEME DE POIDS 12580
SYSTEME DECIMAL 3665
SYSTEME DES ALLIAGES 381
SYSTEME DES CRISTAUX 3431
SYSTEME ENSEMBLE DE LEVIERS 12577
SYSTEME METRIQUE 8229

SYSTEME MULTIPLE 8472
SYSTEME OBJECTIF 8708
SYSTEME OCULAIRE 4977
SYSTEME OPTIQUE 8848
SYSTEME PYRAMIDAL 10040
SYSTEME QUASI-BINAIRE 9958
SYSTEME SIEMENS 10412
SYSTEME TERNAIRE 12766
SYSTEME TRICLINIQUE 13199
T.H. 7997
TABLE 12584
TABLE A DESSIN 4243
TABLE D'ENCLUME 4995
TABLE D'EXAMEN 12773
TABLE DE CONVERSION 3069
TABLE DE DESSINATEUR 4243
TABLE DE TRANSFORMATION 3069
TABLE DES LOGARITHMES 7721
TABLE DRESSEE 12516
TABLEAU 2273
TABLEAU (SERIE DE NOMBRES) 12584
TABLEAU DE BORD 6993
TABLEAU DE BORD 3610
TABLEAU DE COMMANDE 3054
TABLEAU DISTRIBUTEUR 12557
TABLEAU GENERAL 12557
TABLES DE FIXATION 8290
TABLIER 5692
TABLIER 655
TABLIER DU MOTEUR 5251
TACHE DE NUIT 8575
TACHE PAR CRISTAUX DE SULFURE DE CUIVRE 3429
TACHES D'EAU (DE PLUIE) 10178
TACHYMETRE 10556
TACHYMETRE 11869
TACHYMETRE 12587
TACHYMETRE ENREGISTREUR 12586
TAILLAGE 3523
TAILLAGE DES LIMES 3529
TAILLANDERIE 13006
TAILLE 3523
TAILLE D'UNE LIME 3518
TAILLE CROISEE 4134
TAILLE CROISEE 4132
TAILLE SIMPLE D'UNE LIME 11482
TAILLER 3504
TAILLER EN BIAIS 1222
TAILLER EN SIFFLET 1222
TAILLER LES LIMES 3507
TAILLEUR DE LIMES 5151
TAILLEUSE D'ENGRENAGES 5891

# TAL

728

TALC **5659**
TALC **12608**
TALC EN POUDRE **12607**
TALON **8667**
TALON D'UNE CLAVETTE **6318**
TALON DE CLAVETTE **7286**
TALUS **11627**
TAMBOUR **10290**
TAMBOUR **10671**
TAMBOUR **4333**
TAMBOUR **13817**
TAMBOUR **1532**
TAMBOUR **3579**
TAMBOUR A CHAINE **2202**
TAMBOUR D'ENROULEMENT **10737**
TAMBOUR DE FREIN **1533**
TAMBOUR DE NETTOTAGE **13261**
TAMBOUR POUR CHAINE-CABLE **2202**
TAMIS **11018**
TAMIS **10572**
TAMIS **11422**
TAMISAGE **11424**
TAMISER **11423**
TAMPON **9529**
TAMPON **1686**
TAMPON **12785**
TAMPON **9011**
TAMPON **9531**
TAMPON **3267**
TAMPON (COUVERCLE D'UN TAMPON) **3262**
TAMPON A ECHELONS DE TOLERANCE **9907**
TAMPON BOUCHON **1483**
TAMPON D'ALESAGE **11049**
TAMPON DE CONTROLE D'ALESAGE **6531**
TAMPON DE TROU D'HOMME **7977**
TAMPON ET BAGUE **3581**
TAMPON ET LUNETTE DE CALIBRE **3581**
TAMPON FILETE **12367**
TAMPON FILETE FEMELLE **2721**
TAMPON FILETE MALE **11049**
TAMPON OBTURATEUR **1326**
TAMPONS DE CONTROLE **5769**
TAN COMPRIME **12612**
TAN EN MOTTES **12612**
TAN EPUISE **12635**
TANGENTE **12615**
TANGENTE (GEOM.) **12616**
TANGENTE AU SOMMET **12617**
TANNATE **12633**
TANNATE DE SODIUM **11735**
TANNE AU CHROME **2377**

TANNIN **5780**
TANTALE **12634**
TAPAGE D'UNE POMPE **7331**
TAPURE **5304**
TAPURE **3278**
TAPURE DE L'ACIER TREMPE **3282**
TAPURE DE RETRAIT **11395**
TAQUET **12278**
TAQUET **2485**
TAQUET **4301**
TAQUET DE MISE A LA TERRE **4419**
TARAGE **5886**
TARAGE DE SOUPAPE **13469**
TARARES CRIBLEURS T. TRIEURS **3177**
TARAUD **12640**
TARAUD **11044**
TARAUD A LA MACHINE **7858**
TARAUD A MAIN **6257**
TARAUD CONIQUE **5268**
TARAUD CYLINDRIQUE **9534**
TARAUD DEMI-CONIQUE **11102**
TARAUD EBAUCHEUR **5268**
TARAUD FINISSEUR **9534**
TARAUD FINISSEUR **1499**
TARAUD INTERMEDIAIRE **11102**
TARAUDAGE **4277**
TARAUDAGE **12868**
TARAUDAGE **12678**
TARAUDAGE (INTERIEUR) **7078**
TARAUDER **12636**
TARAUDEUSE **11066**
TARAUDEUSE **12677**
TARAUDEUSE **7858**
TARER **5872**
TARER UNE SOUPAPE **11216**
TARIERE **818**
TARTRATE **12691**
TARTRATE EMETIQUE **9675**
TARTRATE D'AMMONIAQUE **473**
TARTRATE DE POTASSE ET D'ANTIMOINE **9675**
TARTRATE DE POTASSE ET DE SOUDE **11729**
TARTRE **119**
TARTRE DES CHAUDIERES **10969**
TARTRE STIBIE **9675**
TARTRIFUGE **4041**
TAS **632**
TAS **4116**
TAS AVEC CONTRE-BOUTEROLLE **11032**
TASSEAU **632**
TASSEMENT **11355**
TAUX **10226**

**729** **TEN**

TAUX D'EVAPORATION **1402**
TAUX DE COMPRESSION **2860**
TAUX DE COURANT PRIMAIRE **9850**
TAUX DE TRAVAIL **13958**
TAXES DE BREVET **9115**
TE **12697**
TE A TROIS DIRECTIONS **12699**
TE DE DESSIN **12581**
TECHNETIUM **8040**
TECHNIQUE **12695**
TECHNIQUE **12694**
TEINTE DE RECUIT **12732**
TEINTE DE REVENU **12732**
TELE-THERMOMETRE **4069**
TELECOMMANDE **10448**
TELEGRAMME **1830**
TELEGRAPHE **12707**
TELEGRAPHIE **12709**
TELEGRAPHIE SANS FIL **13907**
TELEJAUGEAGE **10449**
TELEPHONE **12710**
TELEPHONIE **12712**
TELEPHONIE SANS FIL **13908**
TELESCOPE **10386**
TELLURE **12716**
TEMOIN D'ALLUMAGE **6769**
TEMPERATURE **12721**
TEMPERATURE ABAISSANTE **5025**
TEMPERATURE ABSOLUE **35**
TEMPERATURE AMBIANTE **12729**
TEMPERATURE AMBIANTE **10713**
TEMPERATURE CONSTANTE **2977**
TEMPERATURE CRITIQUE **3352**
TEMPERATURE CROISSANTE **10618**
TEMPERATURE D'AFFINAGE **10381**
TEMPERATURE D'ALLUMAGE **6767**
TEMPERATURE D'EBULLITION **1427**
TEMPERATURE D'EQUILIBRE **4791**
TEMPERATURE D'ETUDE **3798**
TEMPERATURE D'INFLAMMATION **12727**
TEMPERATURE D'INFLAMMATION **6767**
TEMPERATURE DE CALCUL **3798**
TEMPERATURE DE FINISSAGE **5227**
TEMPERATURE DE FORGEAGE **5565**
TEMPERATURE DE FORGEAGE **2744**
TEMPERATURE DE FORGEAGE **5560**
TEMPERATURE DE FUSION **6360**
TEMPERATURE DE L'AIR **12728**
TEMPERATURE DE LA PASSE INTERMEDIAIRE **7086**
TEMPERATURE DE RECRISTALLISATION **10298**
TEMPERATURE DE RECUIT **11700**

TEMPERATURE DE REDUCTION **10354**
TEMPERATURE DE REPERE **10369**
TEMPERATURE DE SATURATION **10945**
TEMPERATURE DE SERVICE **8836**
TEMPERATURE DE TRANSFORMATION **13114**
TEMPERATURE DE TRAVAIL **8836**
TEMPERATURE DE VAPORISATION **4865**
TEMPERATURE ELEVEE **4658**
TEMPERATURE EUTECTIQUE **4858**
TEMPERATURE FINALE **5191**
TEMPERATURE INITIALE **6931**
TEMPERATURE MAXIMUM **8068**
TEMPERATURE MINIMUM **8306**
TEMPERATURE MOYENNE **855**
TEMPERATURE NORMALE **10713**
TEMPERATURE ORDINAIRE DE LA SALLE **10713**
TEMPERATURE REDUITE **10344**
TEMPERATURE SUPERFICIELLE MAXIMALE **6654**
TEMPERATURES DE VIEILLISSEMENT **230**
TEMPS **12387**
TEMPS **12943**
TEMPS ACTIF **13410**
TEMPS D'ADMISSION **7008**
TEMPS D'ECOULEMENT **5459**
TEMPS D'ECOULEMENT DE COURANT **6382**
TEMPS D'INVERSION **10533**
TEMPS DE CHANGEMENT D'OUTIL **12999**
TEMPS DE COMPRESSION **2864**
TEMPS DE MAINTIEN DE L'EFFORT **6523**
TEMPS DE POSE **4944**
TEMPS DE POSITIONNEMENT **9651**
TEMPS DE REFROIDISSEMENT **3082**
TEMPS DE REPOS **8734**
TEMPS DE SOUDAGE EFFECTIF **6382**
TEMPS MORT **4191**
TEMPS MORT **6753**
TENACE **13067**
TENACITE **12737**
TENACITE **13071**
TENACITE A L'ENTAILLE **8671**
TENACITE DES BARREAUX ENTAILLES **12738**
TENACITE EXTREME **13327**
TENAILLE **9328**
TENAILLE **1298**
TENAILLE (S) **12987**
TENAILLE A CHANFREIN **13565**
TENAILLE A MORS COUPANTS **3532**
TENAILLE A RIVETS **10630**
TENAILLE A SOUDER **11767**
TENDEUR **12334**
TENDEUR A GALET **12334**

**TEN**

730

TENDEUR A VIS **13285**
TENDEUR DE CHAINE **2219**
TENDEUR DE CHAINE **2218**
TENDEUR DE COURROIES **1161**
TENDRE UN RESSORT **10032**
TENEUR **3011**
TENEUR EN CARBONE **1947**
TENEUR EN CENDRES **758**
TENEUR EN EAU **13645**
TENEUR EN SEL **10906**
TENIR (RIVETAGE) **6524**
TENIR LE COUP **6524**
TENON **12740**
TENON D'AGRAFAGE **4175**
TENSION **9808**
TENSION **12764**
TENSION **12753**
TENSION (VOLTAGE) DE L'ARC **676**
TENSION A VIDE **8808**
TENSION AUX ELECTRODES **9709**
TENSION CONSTANTE **2978.**
TENSION CRITIQUE **3351**
TENSION D'EQUILIBRE D'UNE ELECTRODE **4789**
TENSION D'EQUILIBRE D'UNE REACTION **4790**
TENSION D'ETIRAGE **12370**
TENSION DE CISAILLEMENT **11286**
TENSION DE CLAQUAGE **1582**
TENSION DE COULAGE **2078**
TENSION DE COULEE **2081**
TENSION DE DECOMPOSITION **3675**
TENSION DE FLEXION **5425**
TENSION DE FORMATION **5576**
TENSION DE LA COURROIE **1162**
TENSION DE SERVICE **13957**
TENSION DE SERVICE DE L'ARC **679**
TENSION DE SOLUTION ELECTROLYTIQUE **4609**
TENSION DU COURANT **13593**
TENSION INTERNE **7074**
TENSION PRINCIPALE **9869**
TENSION SUPERFICIELLE **7033**
TENSION SUPERFICIELLE **12519**
TENSION THERMIQUE **12814**
TENSIONS INTERNES DANS LA FONTE **7075**
TENUE DE ROUTE EN COTE **2498**
TENUE DE ROUTE EN VIRAGE **3180**
TERBIUM **12760**
TEREBENTHINE **3415**
TEREBENTHINE DE VENISE **13527**
TERNIR (SE) **12685**
TERNISSEMENT **4369**
TERRAIN A BATIR **1699**

TERRAIN ARGILEUX **2466**
TERRAIN GRAVELEUX **6076**
TERRAIN SABLEUX **10930**
TERRASSEMENTS **4420**
TERRAZZO **12768**
TERRE **4409**
TERRE (ELECTR.) **4415**
TERRE A BRIQUES **1598**
TERRE A FOULON **5727**
TERRE CUITE **12767**
TERRE D'INFUSOIRES **7292**
TERRE DE DIATOMEES **3880**
TERRE DE PIPE **9367**
TERRE GLAISE **7691**
TERRE POURRIE **7292**
TERRE REFRACTAIRE **5241**
TERRE RUBRIQUE **10340**
TERRE VEGETALE **8423**
TERRES ALCALINES **336**
TERRES RARES **10210**
TEST D'AJUSTEMENT **6006**
TEST DE MCQUAID-EHN **8071**
TETE A SIX PANS D'UNE VIS **6461**
TETE CARREE D'UNE VIS **10309**
TETE CYLINDRIQUE D'UNE VIS **3574**
TETE D'EPINGLE **9317**
TETE D'UN BOULON **1436**
TETE D'UN MARTEAU **4993**
TETE D'UNE CLAVETTE **6318**
TETE D'UNE SOUPAPE **13463**
TETE D'UNE VIS **1436**
TETE DE BIELLE **2963**
TETE DE BIELLE A CAGE FERMEE **1509**
TETE DE BIELLE A CAGE OUVERTE **8007**
TETE DE DISTILLATION **5267**
TETE DE FRAISAGE (OU DE COUPE) **3531**
TETE DE JAUGE **5877**
TETE DE LA DENT **9569**
TETE DE LA TIGE D'EXCENTRIQUE **4432**
TETE DE PERCAGE MULTIBROCHES **8458**
TETE DE POTEAU **2749**
TETE DE RIVET **10624**
TETE DE SOUDAGE **13783**
TETE DE SOUDAGE UNIVERSELLE **13390**
TETE DU CYLINDRE **3569**
TETE FRAISEE **3250**
TETE GOUTTE DE SUIF D'UNE VIS **4673**
TETE MOLETEE D'UNE VIS **8281**
TETE MULTI-BROCHES **8459**
TETE NOYEE D'UNE VIS **3250**
TETE PLATE D'UNE VIS **5394**

| | |
|---|---|
| TETE RONDE D'UNE VIS **1813** | THYRISTOR **12913** |
| TETES DE MOINEAU **2328** | TIGE **11257** |
| TETRACHLORURE **12096** | TIGE **10663** |
| TETRACHLORURE DE CARBONE **1960** | TIGE **10660** |
| TETRAEDRE **12797** | TIGE **12237** |
| TETRAIOD-FLUORESCEINE **4831** | TIGE A VIS EXTERIEURE **8915** |
| TETRATOMIQUE **12798** | TIGE A VIS INTERIEURE **6981** |
| TEXTURE **12800** | TIGE BILATERALE DE PISTON **9387** |
| TEXTURE **12395** | TIGE D'EXCENTRIQUE **4431** |
| TEXTURE CRISTALLINE **3434** | TIGE D'UN BOULON **11260** |
| TEXTURE FIBREUSE **5141** | TIGE D'UNE CLAVETTE **11262** |
| TEXTURE GRENUE **6053** | TIGE D'UNE VIS **11260** |
| TEXTURE HETEROGENE **6452** | TIGE DE CREMAILLERE **10124** |
| TEXTURE HOMOGENE **6560** | TIGE DE CULBUTEURS **10031** |
| TEXTURE LAMELLEUSE **7374** | TIGE DE GUIDAGE **6164** |
| THALLIUM **12801** | TIGE DE PISTON TRAVERSANTE **9387** |
| THEORIE ATOMIQUE **805** | TIGE DE PISTON UNILATERALE **11472** |
| THEORIE DE LA DISTORSION DU RESEAU **7434** | TIGE DE RACCORDEMENT **2962** |
| THEORIE DES CASSURES **5616** | TIGE DE SOUPAPE **12236** |
| THERMIT **12817** | TIGE DU CULBUTEUR **10026** |
| THERMITE DE FONTE **2036** | TIGE DU PISTON **9383** |
| THERMO-ELECTRICITE **12826** | TIGE DU RIVET **11263** |
| THERMO-ELECTRIQUE **12823** | TIGE DU THERMOMETRE **13255** |
| THERMOCHIMIE **12822** | TIGE FILETEE **11062** |
| THERMOCOUPLE **12827** | TIGE FILETEE DE CHAPEAU **1453** |
| THERMODYNAMIQUE **12828** | TIGE FIXE **8623** |
| THERMODYNAMIQUE **12829** | TIGE MONTANTE **10616** |
| THERMOGRAPHE **12832** | TIGE VERTICALE **6018** |
| THERMOGRAPHE **10293** | TIMBRAGE **9828** |
| THERMOMETALLURGIE **4349** | TIMBRE **5886** |
| THERMOMETRE **12726** | TIMBRE D'UN RESERVOIR (A. PRESSION) **8614** |
| THERMOMETRE **12833** | TIMBRE D'UNE SOUPAPE **9828** |
| THERMOMETRE A ALCOOL **11922** | TIMBRE-AVERTISSEUR **1137** |
| THERMOMETRE A GAZ **265** | TIMBRER **5872** |
| THERMOMETRE A MAXIMA ET MINIMA **8063** | TIMONERIE **12232** |
| THERMOMETRE A MERCURE **8152** | TIRAGE **4196** |
| THERMOMETRE CENTIGRADE **2186** | TIRAGE A SOUFFLERIE **8098** |
| THERMOMETRE DIFFERENTIEL **3920** | TIRAGE ARTIFICIEL **8098** |
| THERMOMETRE ENREGISTREUR **10293** | TIRAGE D'AIR **257** |
| THERMOMETRE ETALON **12085** | TIRAGE D'AIR DES NOYAUX **3166** |
| THERMOMETRE FAHRENHEIT **5020** | TIRAGE D'UNE CHEMINEE **4212** |
| THERMOMETRE GRADUE SUR TIGE **12235** | TIRAGE FORCE **5533** |
| THERMOMETRE REAUMUR **10268** | TIRAGE INDUIT **6890** |
| THERMOMETRE-FRONDE **13826** | TIRAGE NATUREL **8501** |
| THERMOSCOPE **12837** | TIRANT **12917** |
| THERMOSTAT **12838** | TIRANT D'ENLEVEMENT **5772** |
| THERMOSTAT **12722** | TIRANTS (DE SPHERE) **1520** |
| THIOSULFATE **12852** | TIRE-FOND **11043** |
| THIXOTROPIE **12854** | TIRE-LIGNE **4241** |
| THORIUM **12856** | TIRE-LIGNE A POINTILLER **4126** |
| THULIUM **12910** | TIREFONDS **11575** |

# TIR

732

TIRER **4215**
TIRETTE **5772**
TIROIR **11592**
TIROIR A COQUILLE **3592**
TIROIR A GRILLE **6100**
TIROIR A PISTON **9390**
TIROIR CYLINDRIQUE **9390**
TIROIR EQUILIBRE **9390**
TIROIR PLAT **9426**
TISSU CAOUTCHOUTE **10818**
TISSU D'AMIANTE **748**
TISSU IMPERMEABLE **13690**
TITANE **12970**
TITRAGE **12974**
TITRAGE **12968**
TITRE D'UNE SOLUTION **12354**
TITRER **12973**
TOBOGGAN **11914**
TOC D'ENTRAINEMENT **4301**
TOC LIMITANT LA COURSE **12278**
TOILE **7619**
TOILE A CALQUER **13083**
TOILE A VOILE **1906**
TOILE CAOUTCHOUTEE **10818**
TOILE D'AMIANTE **748**
TOILE D'ARAIGNEE **2616**
TOILE D'EMBALLAGE **6449**
TOILE D'UN VOLANT **4013**
TOILE D'UNE ROUE **4013**
TOILE DE JUTE **6449**
TOILE EMERI **4693**
TOILE METALLIQUE **5888**
TOILE METALLIQUE **13893**
TOILE TRANSPORTEUSE **1164**
TOILE VERREE **5958**
TOIT **3667**
TOIT **10708**
TOIT BOMBE **4120**
TOIT BOMBE **4039**
TOIT CONIQUE **2947**
TOIT FIXE **5296**
TOIT SURBAISSE **13046**
TOIT SUSPENDU **12524**
TOLE **11315**
TOLE **11298**
TOLE **11305**
TOLE (D'ACIER) ALUMINEE **441**
TOLE (POUR CONSTRUCTION) NAVALE **11356**
TOLE A GRAIN ORIENTE **6036**
TOLE A TROUS FORES **4274**
TOLE A TROUS POINCONNES **10003**

TOLE AJOUREE **9189**
TOLE BOMBEE **1679**
TOLE CANNELEE **2252**
TOLE D'ACIER **12213**
TOLE D'ACIER **11325**
TOLE D'USURE **13716**
TOLE DE BLINDAGE **11343**
TOLE DE CHAUDIERE **1416**
TOLE DE CONSTRUCTION **1109**
TOLE DE CUIVRE **3127**
TOLE DE FER **11309**
TOLE DE LAITON **1569**
TOLE DE RENFORT **10430**
TOLE DE RENFORT **12257**
TOLE DE RENFORT OU DOUBLANTE **11343**
TOLE DE ROBE **11335**
TOLE DE TRANSFORMATEUR **4544**
TOLE DECOUPEE A JOUR **9189**
TOLE DEFLECTRICE **921**
TOLE DOUBLANTE **10430**
TOLE DRESSEE **5395**
TOLE ELECTRIQUE **4544**
TOLE ELECTRIQUE **11448**
TOLE EMBOUTIE **1679**
TOLE EN SAILLIE **9911**
TOLE EPAISSE **9477**
TOLE ETAMEE **12957**
TOLE FACONNEE **11846**
TOLE FINE **11304**
TOLE FINE **12850**
TOLE FORTE **9477**
TOLE FORTE **6409**
TOLE GALVANISEE **5785**
TOLE GAUFREE **12769**
TOLE GAUFREE **2285**
TOLE LAMINEE **10674**
TOLE LAMINEE A CHAUD **6637**
TOLE LAMINEE A FROID **2696**
TOLE LARMEE **10181**
TOLE MARGINALE **11531**
TOLE MARGINALE **8002**
TOLE NOIRE **1294**
TOLE NOIRE **1296**
TOLE ONDULEE **3198**
TOLE PERFOREE **9189**
TOLE PLAQUEE **2445**
TOLE PLOMBEE **7460**
TOLE POUR EMBOUTISSAGE **9478**
TOLE POUR LES INDUITS DES DYNAMOS **708**
TOLE POUR REVETEMENT DE SOL **5447**
TOLE POUR TRANSFORMATEURS **13116**

TOLE PROFILEE **11846**
TOLE STRIEE **10574**
TOLE STRIEE **2325**
TOLE STRIEE **2285**
TOLE STRIEE **2252**
TOLE TECHNOLOGIQUE **10842**
TOLE TERNE **1296**
TOLE TRES MINCE **12593**
TOLE ZINGUEE **5785**
TOLE-SUPPORT **12495**
TOLERANCE **12982**
TOLERANCE **358**
TOLERANCE **2483**
TOLERANCE ADMISE **359**
TOLERANCE D'USINAGE **359**
TOLERANCE LIMITE **7587**
TOLERANCES D'USINAGE **4988**
TOLES (ORDRE DE MISE EN PLACE DES) **9500**
TOLES DECOUPEES **11266**
TOLES ENROBEES **2586**
TOLES ETIREES **4250**
TOLES MINCES EN ACIER ALLIE **380**
TOLUENE **12983**
TOLUOL **12983**
TOMBAC **12984**
TOMBAGE **1088**
TOMBER EN DELIQUESCENCE **3732**
TOMBER LES BORDS **1084**
TOMBERAUX **2017**
TONDEUSES A GAZON **7439**
TONNE (1000 KG) **12986**
TONNEAU A POLIR **9602**
TONNEAU DE FINISSAGE **13261**
TONNEAU DE NETTOYAGE **13261**
TOPAZE **13038**
TOPOCHIMIE **13039**
TORCHE **13042**
TORCHE A HELIUM **6424**
TORCHERE **5820**
TORCHERE **5355**
TORCHERE DE RAFFINERIE **10376**
TORE **13043**
TORE CIRCULAIRE **3588**
TORON **12336**
TORON D'UNE CORDE **12339**
TORON METALLIQUE **13902**
TORONNAGE **12340**
TORONNER **12337**
TORONNEUSE **12341**
TORONS EN ACIER POUR CABLES **12217**
TORS **13305**

TORSION **13054**
TORSION **13051**
TORSION ALTERNATIVE **10414**
TORSION D'UNE CORDE **13305**
TORSION LANG **7389**
TOTALISER LES DIAGRAMMES **2765**
TOUCHER (GEOM.) **13066**
TOUPIE **9901**
TOUR **10557**
TOUR **7427**
TOUR (MACHINE-OUTIL) **13289**
TOUR A ARBRE A CAMES **1897**
TOUR A ARBRE COUDE **3316**
TOUR A ARBRES **11246**
TOUR A BANDAGES **13321**
TOUR A BOIS **13922**
TOUR A BOULONS **12401**
TOUR A BRIDES **5334**
TOUR A CHARIOT **11590**
TOUR A CHARIOTER **11590**
TOUR A COMMANDES PAR VIS-MERE **7428**
TOUR A COPIER **3138**
TOUR A CYCLES AUTOMATIQUES **840**
TOUR A CYLINDRER **9428**
TOUR A DECOLLETER **11584**
TOUR A DECOLLETER **3540**
TOUR A DECOLLETER LES ECROUS **8699**
TOUR A DEGAGER **913**
TOUR A DEPOUILLER **913**
TOUR A DETALONNER **10443**
TOUR A EBAUCHER **10788**
TOUR A EPROUVETTES **12771**
TOUR A ESSIEUX **881**
TOUR A FILETER **12859**
TOUR A FILETER **11029**
TOUR A LINGOT **6922**
TOUR A METAUX **8191**
TOUR A OVALES **8919**
TOUR A PEDALE **5520**
TOUR A PLATEAUX **13171**
TOUR A POINTE **2150**
TOUR A REPOUSSER ET A LISSER **11911**
TOUR A REPRODUIRE **3138**
TOUR A REVOLVER **1931**
TOUR AUTOMATIQUE **846**
TOUR AUTOMATIQUE A BROCHES MULTIPLES **8469**
TOUR AUTOMATIQUE TRAVAILLANT EN BARRE **983**
TOUR D'UNE HELICE **13278**
TOUR DE CRAQUAGE **3287**
TOUR DE FRACTIONNEMENT **5614**
TOUR DE REFROIDISSEMENT **3094**

# TOU

734

TOUR DE REPRISE MULTIBROCHES **8485**
TOUR DE SPIRE **2646**
TOUR EN L'AIR **5005**
TOUR EN L'AIR **5001**
TOUR EN L'AIR A PLATEAU HORIZONTAL **1469**
TOUR FRONTAL (TOUR EN L'AIR) **5697**
TOUR MINUTE **10814**
TOUR MONOBROCHE AUTOMATIQUE A TOURELLE **13298**
TOUR PARALLELE **9428**
TOUR POUR FUSEE D'ESSIEU **880**
TOUR POUR METAUX LEGERS **7565**
TOUR POUR ROUES **13816**
TOUR REVOLVER **13297**
TOUR VERTICAL **13545**
TOURBE **9147**
TOURBE COMPRIMEE **9804**
TOURBE MENUE **9726**
TOURBE MOTTIERE **4364**
TOURBILLON **13606**
TOURBILLONNEMENT **13827**
TOURELLES PORTE-OUTILS **13004**
TOURIE **1981**
TOURILLON **7256**
TOURILLON **11893**
TOURILLON **9420**
TOURILLON A CANNELURES **12906**
TOURILLON A FOURCHETTE **3391**
TOURILLON CROCHET DE LEVAGE **7558**
TOURILLON D EXTREMITE **4721**
TOURILLON D'APPUI **9421**
TOURILLON D'ARTICULATION **7242**
TOURILLON DE BUTEE CANNELE **12906**
TOURILLON DE BUTEE POUR CRAPAUDINE **9421**
TOURILLON DE CROSSE **3391**
TOURILLON FRONTAL **4721**
TOURILLON INTERMEDIAIRE **8513**
TOURILLON SERVANT D'AXE DE ROTATION **13242**
TOURILLON-AXE POUR CHAPE-FOURCHETTE **3391**
TOURMALINE **13072**
TOURNAGE **13287**
TOURNAGE CONIQUE **12668**
TOURNAGE DES SURFACES BOMBEES **13288**
TOURNAGE DES SURFACES CONIQUES **12668**
TOURNAGE DES SURFACES FIGUREES **8869**
TOURNAGE DES SURFACES SPHERIQUES DES CORPS RONDS **13291**
TOURNE-A-GAUCHE **12638**
TOURNE-A-GAUCHE POUR AVOYER **10957**
TOURNE-A-GAUCHE POUR DONNER DU PAS/DE VOIE A UNE SCIE **10957**
TOURNER **10763**

TOURNER **13276**
TOURNER DES CORPS RONDS **13281**
TOURNER DES SURFACES BOMBEES **13277**
TOURNER DES SURFACES FIGUREES **13280**
TOURNER DES SURFACES OBLIQUES/RAMPANTES **13282**
TOURNER DES SURFACES SPHERIQUES **13281**
TOURNER FAUX-ROND **10840**
TOURNEUR **13286**
TOURNEVIS **13294**
TOURNURES **13293**
TOURS A LA MINUTE **8690**
TOUT EN METAUX FERREUX **345**
TOUT-VENANT **10841**
TRACAGE **8017**
TRACAGE DES TOLES **8018**
TRACE **8017**
TRACE **13076**
TRACE **3794**
TRACE D'UN DIAGRAMME **9521**
TRACER **8010**
TRACER **3795**
TRACER **4195**
TRACER GRAPHIQUEMENT **9519**
TRACER UN DIAGRAMME **9520**
TRACERET **11068**
TRACEUR **9161**
TRACEUR-MECANICIEN **8013**
TRACHYTE **13081**
TRACOIR **11068**
TRACTEUR **9859**
TRACTEUR **13097**
TRACTEUR **13091**
TRACTEUR AGRICOLE A CHENILLES **13094**
TRACTEUR AGRICOLE A ROUES **13095**
TRACTEUR AGRICOLE DEMI TRAC **13093**
TRACTEUR MARAICHERS **13096**
TRACTION **9970**
TRACTION AVANT **5699**
TRACTION DANS LA DIRECTION DES FIBRES **9968**
TRACTION DES VEHICULES **13088**
TRACTION NORMALEMENT A LA DIRECTION DES FIBRES **9967**
TRACTOIRE **13098**
TRACTRICE **13098**
TRADUCTION **13123**
TRAIN (DE LAMINOIRS) A TOLES FINES **11324**
TRAIN A BANDES **11321**
TRAIN BALADEUR **11602**
TRAIN CONTINU (DE LAMINOIR) **3030**
TRAIN D'ENGRENAGES **5901**
TRAIN DE LAMINAGE **10670**

735 TRA

TRAIN DE LAMINAGE A FROID **2708**
TRAIN DE LAMINOIR **10701**
TRAIN DE LAMINOIR **10669**
TRAIN DE ROULEAUX DE SORTIE **10838**
TRAIN DIFFERENTIEL **3913**
TRAIN EBAUCHEUR **1348**
TRAIN EBAUCHEUR **10789**
TRAIN EPICYCLOIDAL **4778**
TRAIN FINISSEUR **5229**
TRAIN PLANETAIRE **12456**
TRAIN PLANETAIRE **9446**
TRAIN REDUCTEUR **10353**
TRAIN(S) A BRAMES **11556**
TRAINEE D'AIR **266**
TRAIT D'UNE ECHELLE **8009**
TRAIT DE SCIE **3517**
TRAIT PONCTUE **4125**
TRAIT ZERO **14025**
TRAITEMENT **13959**
TRAITEMENT AU BICHROMATE **1236**
TRAITEMENT AU JET DE SABLE **2540**
TRAITEMENT DE DETENTE APRES SOUDAGE **9666**
TRAITEMENT DE RECUIT **568**
TRAITEMENT DES METAUX A FROID **2710**
TRAITEMENT DES MINERAIS **11666**
TRAITEMENT DIRECT **8799**
TRAITEMENT INDIRECT **8735**
TRAITEMENT ISOTHERME **7194**
TRAITEMENT MECANIQUE **8861**
TRAITEMENT PRELIMINAIRE **9780**
TRAITEMENT PREPARATOIRE **9780**
TRAITEMENT THERMIQUE **12815**
TRAITEMENT THERMIQUE **6375**
TRAITEMENT THERMIQUE **6377**
TRAITEMENT THERMIQUE SOUS VIDE **13443**
TRAITEMENT ULTERIEUR **12417**
TRAITER **13937**
TRAITER LES MINERAIS **11664**
TRAITER MECANIQUEMENT LES MINERAIS **4253**
TRAJECTOIRE **13104**
TRAJET SUIVI PAR UN FLUIDE **9125**
TRAJET, ECARTEMENT **4063**
TRAME **13743**
TRANCHANT **12995**
TRANCHANT D'UN OUTIL **3528**
TRANCHE **11217**
TRANCHE A CHAUD **6640**
TRANCHE A FROID **2701**
TRANCHER **3515**
TRANCHET D'ENCLUME **631**
TRANSBORDEUR **13141**

TRANSDUCTEUR **13108**
TRANSFERT DE CHALEUR **6372**
TRANSFERT PAR COURT-CIRCUIT **11370**
TRANSFERT PAR VEINE LIQUIDE **7659**
TRANSFORMATEUR **13115**
TRANSFORMATEUR AMPLIFICATEUR DE POTENTIEL **12245**
TRANSFORMATEUR DE POTENTIEL **13115**
TRANSFORMATEUR DEVOLTEUR **12244**
TRANSFORMATEUR REDUCTEUR DE POTENTIEL **12244**
TRANSFORMATEUR SURVOLTEUR **12245**
TRANSFORMATION **3067**
TRANSFORMATION ALLOTROPIQUE **355**
TRANSFORMATION CHIMIQUE **2296**
TRANSFORMATION CONGRUENTE **2939**
TRANSFORMATION D'ENERGIE **3070**
TRANSFORMATION DU FER EN ACIER **3068**
TRANSFORMATION EN COKE **2666**
TRANSFORMATION ISOTHERME **7196**
TRANSFORMER EN COKE **2656**
TRANSFORMER L'ENERGIE **13112**
TRANSISTOR **13119**
TRANSLATION **13158**
TRANSLATION **13123**
TRANSLATION PRIMITIVE **9865**
TRANSLUCIDE **13125**
TRANSLUCIDITE **13124**
TRANSMISSION **11248**
TRANSMISSION **6372**
TRANSMISSION **4294**
TRANSMISSION AUX ROUES **5186**
TRANSMISSION COURROIES DE CHASSE **3141**
TRANSMISSION D'ELECTRICITE **13133**
TRANSMISSION D'ENERGIE ELECTRIQUE **13129**
TRANSMISSION D'UN MOUVEMENT **13130**
TRANSMISSION DE CHALEUR **6374**
TRANSMISSION DE LA CHALEUR **13111**
TRANSMISSION DE PUISSANCE **13134**
TRANSMISSION DE PUISSANCE **9746**
TRANSMISSION FLEXIBLE **5420**
TRANSMISSION FUNICULAIRE **10734**
TRANSMISSION HYDRAULIQUE **5472**
TRANSMISSION INTERMEDIAIRE **3244**
TRANSMISSION PAR CABLE TELEDYNAMIQUE **12706**
TRANSMISSION PAR CABLES **10734**
TRANSMISSION PAR CHAINES **2207**
TRANSMISSION PAR CONES DE FRICTION **1224**
TRANSMISSION PAR CORDES COURROIES **10734**
TRANSMISSION PAR COURROIES **1144**
TRANSMISSION PAR ENGRENAGE **13131**
TRANSMISSION PAR FRICTION **5684**
TRANSMISSION PAR LEVIER **13132**

# TRA

736

TRANSMISSION PAR PLATEAUX **4005**
TRANSMISSION PAR POULIE A GORGES MULTIPLES **8473**
TRANSMISSION PAR ROUES DE FRICTION **13736**
TRANSMISSION PRINCIPALE **7944**
TRANSMISSION SUR POULIES MULTIPLES **3015**
TRANSMUTATION (CHIM.) **13136**
TRANSPARENCE **13137**
TRANSPARENT **13138**
TRANSPORT **13140**
TRANSPORT D'ENERGIE A GRANDE DISTANCE **13135**
TRANSPORT D'ENERGIE ELECTRIQUE A GRANDE DISTANCE **13133**
TRANSPORT DE CHALEUR **6374**
TRANSPORT DE L'ENERGIE **13134**
TRANSPORTEUR **3080**
TRANSPORTEUR **11253**
TRANSPORTEUR A COURROIE **1164**
TRANSPORTEUR A GODETS **1675**
TRANSPORTEUR A HELICE **13970**
TRANSPORTEUR A PALETTES **11570**
TRANSPORTEUR A RACLETTES **11010**
TRANSPORTEUR A TABLIER METALLIQUE **11570**
TRANSPORTEUR A TAPIS ROULANT **1164**
TRANSPORTEUR AERIEN **213**
TRANSPORTEUR PAR CABLE **213**
TRANSPORTEUR PAR GRAVITE A ROULEAUX **6082**
TRAPEZE **13148**
TRAPEZOIDE **13149**
TRAPPE DE VISITE DE PLATEAU **13168**
TRASS **13152**
TRAVAIL **13959**
TRAVAIL **12331**
TRAVAIL **13936**
TRAVAIL A CHAUD **6650**
TRAVAIL A FROID **2713**
TRAVAIL A LA CHAINE **3034**
TRAVAIL A LA COMPRESSION **2869**
TRAVAIL A LA FLEXION **1191**
TRAVAIL A LA JOURNEE **3621**
TRAVAIL A LA PERCHE **9597**
TRAVAIL A LA TACHE **9294**
TRAVAIL A LA TORSION **13056**
TRAVAIL A LA TRACTION **12747**
TRAVAIL A VIDE **8601**
TRAVAIL AU CISAILLEMENT **11295**
TRAVAIL AU TOUR **13287**
TRAVAIL AUX PIECES **9294**
TRAVAIL CONSOMME **4747**
TRAVAIL DE COMPRESSION **13941**
TRAVAIL DE JOUR **3620**
TRAVAIL DE NUIT **8575**

TRAVAIL DES METAUX **8192**
TRAVAIL DU BOIS **13924**
TRAVAIL DU FROTTEMENT **13942**
TRAVAIL EFFECTUE **13940**
TRAVAIL ELECTRIQUE **4539**
TRAVAIL EN (DEUX OU TROIS) EQUIPES **11350**
TRAVAIL EN GRANDE SERIE **8028**
TRAVAIL EN SERIE **10462**
TRAVAIL EXTERIEUR **4962**
TRAVAIL INDIQUE **6876**
TRAVAIL INTERIEUR **7081**
TRAVAIL MANUEL **6237**
TRAVAIL MECANIQUE **8117**
TRAVAIL MECANIQUE (TRAVAIL FAIT A LA MACHINE) **7860**
TRAVAIL MOTEUR **8117**
TRAVAIL RESISTANT **13944**
TRAVAIL UTILE **13428**
TRAVAILLE A LA MACHINE **7850**
TRAVAILLE A LA MAIN **6240**
TRAVAILLER **13937**
TRAVAILLER A LA COMPRESSION **1075**
TRAVAILLER A LA TRACTION **1075**
TRAVAILLER AU CISAILLEMENT **1078**
TRAVAILLER AU TOUR **13276**
TRAVAILLEUR **13960**
TRAVAUX PRELIMINAIRES **9787**
TRAVAUX PREPARATOIRES **9787**
TRAVAUX PUBLICS **2444**
TRAVERSE **3367**
TRAVERSE **3361**
TRAVERSE **13243**
TRAVERSE AVANT **5693**
TRAVERSE DE VOIE **11574**
TRAVERSE EN BOIS **12941**
TRAVERSE EN FER **7150**
TRAVERSE PAR UN COURANT **7670**
TRAVERTIN **13166**
TREBUCHET POUR ANALYSES **2294**
TREFILAGE **13906**
TREFILAGE **4230**
TREFILAGE A CHAUD **6624**
TREFILER **4220**
TREFILERIE **13888**
TREFILERIE (FABRIQUE) **13905**
TREILLAGE **13180**
TREILLAGE PROTECTEUR **9951**
TREILLIS **7433**
TREILLIS DE PROTECTION **9951**
TREILLIS METALLIQUE **7429**
TREILLIS METALLIQUE **13896**

TREMIE **6577**
TREMPABILITE **6288**
TREMPE **6291**
TREMPE **2338**
TREMPE **10094**
TREMPE **3975**
TREMPE **3978**
TREMPE (NON-) **13359**
TREMPE A L'AIR **285**
TREMPE A L'AIR **267**
TREMPE A L'EAU **13672**
TREMPE A L'EAU **13654**
TREMPE A L'EAU SUIVIE DE REVENU **13673**
TREMPE A L'HUILE **8772**
TREMPE A L'HUILE **8760**
TREMPE AU BAIN DE SEL **10913**
TREMPE AU CHALUMEAU **5315**
TREMPE AU GAZ **5840**
TREMPE CONTINUE A CHAUD **3028**
TREMPE DE SURFACE **2021**
TREMPE DES METAUX **6293**
TREMPE DIFFERENTIELLE **3914**
TREMPE DOUCE **8760**
TREMPE ECHELONNEE **6633**
TREMPE EN BAIN CHAUD **8021**
TREMPE EN BAIN DE SEL **7651**
TREMPE EN ETAPES **824**
TREMPE EN SURFACE **2023**
TREMPE ET REVENU **10095**
TREMPE ET REVENU **10092**
TREMPE ETAGEE **12242**
TREMPE ETAGEE BAINITIQUE **824**
TREMPE ETAGEE MARTENSITIQUE **12243**
TREMPE INTERROMPUE **12249**
TREMPE INVERSE **7109**
TREMPE ISOTHERME **7195**
TREMPE LOCALISEE **3914**
TREMPE MARTENSITIQUE **8021**
TREMPE NEGATIVE **8527**
TREMPE PAR INDUCTION **6896**
TREMPE PAR NITRURATION **8582**
TREMPE PAR PULVERISATION **11966**
TREMPE PARTIELLE **11145**
TREMPE PARTIELLE **7697**
TREMPE PRODUITE PAR ETIRAGE A FROID **6274**
TREMPE SECONDAIRE **11105**
TREMPE SUPERFICIELLE **12508**
TREMPER **2332**
TREMPER (FONTE) **2332**
TREMPER UN METAL **6285**
TREMPEUR D'OUTILLAGE **13008**

TREPAN **4265**
TREPIDATIONS **13559**
TREPIED **13219**
TRES FLUIDE **5471**
TRES MOBILE **5471**
TRESSE **5863**
TRESSE **751**
TRESSE DE CHANVRE SUIFFEE **6442**
TRESSE EN CHANVRE **6441**
TRESSE EN COTON **3220**
TREUIL **13851**
TREUIL A BRAS **6256**
TREUIL A ENGRENAGE **10014**
TREUIL A MANIVELLE **6256**
TREUIL SIMPLE **13863**
TREUILS **13852**
TRI **11139**
TRIAGE **11524**
TRIAGE PAR COURANT GAZEUX **248**
TRIAGE PAR COURANT GAZEUX **4681**
TRIANGLE **13185**
TRIANGLE ACUTANGLE **157**
TRIANGLE DE FORCES **13186**
TRIANGLE DE LIAISON **2962**
TRIANGLE EQUILATERAL **4785**
TRIANGLE ISOCELE **7192**
TRIANGLE OBTUSANGLE **8718**
TRIANGLE POLAIRE **9581**
TRIANGLE RECTANGLE **10582**
TRIANGLE SCALENE **10984**
TRIANGLE SPHERIQUE **11891**
TRIATOMIQUE **13197**
TRIBASIQUE **13198**
TRIBOMURE DE PHOSPHORE **9255**
TRICHLORURE D'ANTIMOINE **626**
TRICHLORURE D'ARSENIQUE **724**
TRICHLORURE D'OR **821**
TRICHLORURE DE BISMUTH **1270**
TRICHLORURE DE PHOSPHORE **9256**
TRIEDRE **13202**
TRIEURS DE POMMES DE TERRE **9706**
TRIEUSES ELECTRONIQUES **11185**
TRIGONOMETRIE **13201**
TRIGONOMETRIQUE **13200**
TRINGLE **10663**
TRINGLE DE GUIDAGE **6164**
TRINGLERIE DE DIRECTION **12232**
TRINGLERIE DE FREIN **1539**
TRINITRINE **8593**
TRIPOLI **13220**
TRIPOLI SILICEUX **7292**

# TRI

738

TRIRANTS **6186**
TRISULFURE D'ANTIMOINE **627**
TRISULFURE D'ARSENIC **728**
TRITURATION **6117**
TRITURER **13222**
TRIVALENT **13197**
TROCHOIDE **13223**
TROLLEYBUS **13225**
TROMMEL **13226**
TROMPE **11518**
TRONC DE CONE **13235**
TRONC DE PARALLELEPIPEDE **13237**
TRONC DE PYRAMIDE **13238**
TRONCATURE D'UN FILET **5389**
TRONCON D'ARBRE **9643**
TRONCON DE TUYAU **9292**
TRONCONNAGE **3533**
TRONCONNAGE DU BOIS **4718**
TRONCONNEMENT **3533**
TRONCONNER **3510**
TRONCONNEUSE **3541**
TROOSTITE **13227**
TROP PLEIN **8931**
TROP-PLEIN **8932**
TROU **6530**
TROU A CRASSE **4332**
TROU A MAIN **6236**
TROU ALESE **4273**
TROU BORGNE **3630**
TROU D'AIR **13528**
TROU D'AXE OU DE GOUPILLE **9332**
TROU D'HOMME **7976**
TROU D'HOMME **9620**
TROU D'HOMME **7963**
TROU D'HOMME **7997**
TROU D'HOMME DE ROBE **11332**
TROU D'HOMME DE TOIT **10710**
TROU DE BOULON **1437**
TROU DE BRAS **6236**
TROU DE COULEE **12637**
TROU DE COULEE **7287**
TROU DE GOUPILLE **3214**
TROU DE JAUGE **3971**
TROU DE JAUGE COMBINE AVEC EVENT **3972**
TROU DE RIVET **10625**
TROU DE RIVET PERCE **4275**
TROU DE RIVET POINCONNE **10004**
TROU DE SONDAGE **1463**
TROU DE SOUFFLAGE **6393**
TROU DE VIDANGE **8442**
TROU DE VISITE D'UN CAISSON **9620**

TROU DES TOLES A ASSEMBLER **10625**
TROU EN CUL DE SAC **3630**
TROU FILETE **11056**
TROU FORE **4273**
TROU GRAISSEUR **8761**
TROU OBLONG **8714**
TROU TEMOIN **12715**
TROU TRAVERSANT LA PIECE **12893**
TROU VENU DE FONTE **2033**
TROUBLE **2541**
TROUEE **11831**
TROUS DE BRIDE **5328**
TROUS DE MANIPULATION **6264**
TROUSSE (METALLURGIE) **5017**
TROUSSEAU **12734**
TRUSQUIN A MARBRE **11069**
TRUSQUIN A POINTE **8016**
TRUSQUIN D'ASSEMBLAGE **8399**
TUBE **9339**
TUBE **13257**
TUBE A AILERONS **10571**
TUBE A AILETTES **10571**
TUBE A AILETTES EXTERIEURES **4963**
TUBE A AILETTES INTERIEURES **7082**
TUBE A BORD RABATTU **1087**
TUBE A CATHODE CHAUDE **6652**
TUBE A COLLET RABATTU **1087**
TUBE A NERVURES LONGITUDINALES **7740**
TUBE A NERVURES TRANSVERSALES **13147**
TUBE A RACCORDS **9365**
TUBE A RAPPROCHEMENT **1804**
TUBE A RAYONS CATHODIQUES **2105**
TUBE A RAYONS X **14002**
TUBE A RAYONS-X **12684**
TUBE A RECOUVREMENT **7406**
TUBE BRASE **11760**
TUBE BROYEUR **13252**
TUBE CAPILLAIRE **13255**
TUBE CAPILLAIRE **1921**
TUBE CATHODIQUE **2105**
TUBE COMPENSATEUR **4913**
TUBE COUDE A DEUX BRANCHES COMMUNIQUANT ENTRE ELLES **13325**
TUBE COULE DEBOUT **9343**
TUBE COULE HORIZONTAL **9342**
TUBE CYLINDRIQUE GRADUE **5960**
TUBE D'ACIER **12212**
TUBE D'ACIER (POUR GAZ LIQUEFIES) **12204**
TUBE D'EAU **13681**
TUBE D'ECHANGEUR THERMIQUE **6350**
TUBE DE CHAUDIERE **1422**

TUBE DE DERIVATION **1558**
TUBE DE DESCENTE **4183**
TUBE DE FORCE **13253**
TUBE DE FUMEE **5248**
TUBE DE PITOT **9415**
TUBE DE REDUCTION **10352**
TUBE DE VAPEUR **12177**
TUBE DE VENTURI **13532**
TUBE DROIT **12309**
TUBE DUDGEONNE **4905**
TUBE EN ACIER **12219**
TUBE EN ALUMINIUM **427**
TUBE EN BRONZE **1653**
TUBE EN GRES **12277**
TUBE EN LAITON **1570**
TUBE EN VERRE **5965**
TUBE ETIRE **11782**
TUBE ETIRE A FROID **2714**
TUBE FILETE **11059**
TUBE FLEXIBLE **6614**
TUBE FLEXIBLE AVEC ARMATURE EN FIL DE FER **714**
TUBE FLEXIBLE CERCLE EN ACIER **714**
TUBE, FOYER **1412**
TUBE ISOLANT **7002**
TUBE LAMINE **10677**
TUBE LISSE **11684**
TUBE MANNESMANN **7983**
TUBE PLISSE **3199**
TUBE PROTEGE PAR GOUDRONNAGE **12687**
TUBE PROTEGE PAR UN RECOUVREMENT DE JUTE ASPHALTE **766**
TUBE PROTEGE PAR UNE PEINTURE **9016**
TUBE REDRESSEUR **10317**
TUBE RUGUEUX **10780**
TUBE SANS SOUDURE **11089**
TUBE SERVE **7740**
TUBE SOUDE **13775**
TUBE SOUDE **13777**
TUBE SOUDE A L'AUTOGENE **9364**
TUBE SOUDE BOUT A BOUT **1803**
TUBE SOUDE EN HELICE **11920**
TUBE SOUDE EN SPIRALE **11920**
TUBE SOUDE PAR RAPPROCHEMENT **1804**
TUBE SOUDE PAR RECOUVREMENT **7406**
TUBE TARAUDE **11059**
TUBES A NERVURES **10571**
TUBES ELECTRONIQUES **4636**
TUBES ETIRES A FROID **2678**
TUBES RAPPROCHES **2512**
TUBULURE **8679**
TUBULURE A BRIDE **5341**

TUBULURE A BRIDE **5337**
TUBULURE A COLLET **8683**
TUBULURE A COLLET **8514**
TUBULURE A COLLET DE RACCORDEMENT **5337**
TUBULURE AUTORENFORCEE **9012**
TUBULURE D ECHAPPEMENT **4894**
TUBULURE D'ADMISSION **6948**
TUBULURE D'ALIMENTATION **5084**
TUBULURE D'ARRIVEE **6946**
TUBULURE D'ENTREE **6946**
TUBULURE DE BRANCHEMENT **1557**
TUBULURE DE DEVERSEMENT **3736**
TUBULURE DE FOND **1495**
TUBULURE DE PURGE AVEC CUVETTE PERIPHERIQUE **4226**
TUBULURE DE SORTIE **8901**
TUBULURE DE SORTIE/D'ASPIRATION **4705**
TUBULURE DE TOIT **10711**
TUBULURE ENCASTREE **6969**
TUBULURE POUR PURGE SOUPLE **6613**
TUF **13260**
TUF CALCAIRE **1838**
TUF PONCEUX **9989**
TUF PORPHYRITIQUE **9631**
TUF VOLCANIQUE **13590**
TUILE **12934**
TUILE EN VERRE **5964**
TUNGSTATE DE SOUDE **11737**
TUNGSTENE **13262**
TURBINE **13267**
TURBINE **6795**
TURBINE A ACTION **6810**
TURBINE A ADMISSION PARTIELLE **9085**
TURBINE A ADMISSION TOTALE **5718**
TURBINE A AIR **13859**
TURBINE A BASSE PRESSION **7788**
TURBINE A DETENTE **4925**
TURBINE A GAZ **5844**
TURBINE A HAUTE PRESSION **6494**
TURBINE A IMPULSION **6810**
TURBINE A LIBRE DEVIATION **6810**
TURBINE A PRESSION INTERIEURE **10250**
TURBINE A REACTION **10250**
TURBINE A VAPEUR **12189**
TURBINE AMERICAINE **8330**
TURBINE AXIALE **862**
TURBINE DE POMPE CENTRIFUGE **6795**
TURBINE DE RETOUR D'HUILE **8763**
TURBINE HYDRAULIQUE **6696**
TURBINE MIXTE **8330**
TURBINE PARALLELE **862**
TURBINE RADIALE **10136**

# TUR

TURBINE TANGENTIELLE **12621**
TURBO-COMPRESSEUR **13272**
TURBO-COMPRESSEUR **2178**
TURBO-GENERATEUR **13271**
TURBO-VENTILATEUR **13270**
TURBULENCE **13273**
TURC **11032**
TUYAU **9339**
TUYAU **4183**
TUYAU **13257**
TUYAU (FLEXIBLE) DE CAOUTCHOUC **10821**
TUYAU A AILETTES **5234**
TUYAU A BRIDES **5343**
TUYAU A EMBOITEMENT **11707**
TUYAU A GAZ **5833**
TUYAU A GAZ EN PAPIER IMPREGNE DE BITUME **6803**
TUYAU A JOINT SPHERIQUE **5418**
TUYAU A PRESSION **3736**
TUYAU A VAPEUR **12177**
TUYAU ADDUCTEUR **12489**
TUYAU BOUCHE **2361**
TUYAU CINTRE **1194**
TUYAU COLLECTEUR **2725**
TUYAU CYLINDRIQUE **3586**
TUYAU D'ALIMENTATION **5070**
TUYAU D'AMENEE D'ARRIVEE **12489**
TUYAU D'ASCENSION **10615**
TUYAU D'ASPIRATION **12433**
TUYAU D'ECHAPPEMENT **4894**
TUYAU D'ECHAPPEMENT DE VAPEUR **4897**
TUYAU D'ECOULEMENT **4207**
TUYAU D'EVACUATION **4207**
TUYAU DE CHAUFFAGE CENTRAL **6396**
TUYAU DE COMMUNICATION **2960**
TUYAU DE CONDUITE **13665**
TUYAU DE CONDUITE **9357**
TUYAU DE DEBIT **4207**
TUYAU DE DECHARGE **4207**
TUYAU DE DISTRIBUTION D'EAU **13665**
TUYAU DE PRISE D'EAU **12066**
TUYAU DE RACCORDEMENT **2960**
TUYAU DE REFOULEMENT **3736**
TUYAU DE TROP-PLEIN **8932**
TUYAU ELEVATOIRE **10615**
TUYAU EM PLOMB ETAME A L'INTERIEUR **7469**
TUYAU EN BOIS **13928**
TUYAU EN CIMENT **2898**
TUYAU EN CIMENT ARME **5109**
TUYAU EN CUIR **7499**
TUYAU EN CUIVRE **3132**
TUYAU EN ETAIN **12960**

TUYAU EN FER **13989**
TUYAU EN FONTE **2035**
TUYAU EN PLOMB **7468**
TUYAU EN POTERIE **4416**
TUYAU EN TERRE CUITE **4416**
TUYAU EN TOILE DE CHANVRE **1908**
TUYAU EN TOLE **11312**
TUYAU EN ZINC **14047**
TUYAU ENGORGE **2361**
TUYAU METALLIQUE FLEXIBLE **5419**
TUYAU METALLIQUE FLEXIBLE **5421**
TUYAU RIVE **10640**
TUYAU VERTICAL **10615**
TUYAUTAGE **9357**
TUYAUTERIE **9357**
TUYAUTERIE **3736**
TUYAUTERIE **12178**
TUYAUTERIE **2845**
TUYERE **8685**
TUYERE A VAPEUR **12175**
TUYERE CONVERGENTE **2769**
TUYERE D'AMENEE DE L'AIR SOUS PRESSION **13299**
TUYERE DE PULVERISATION **11963**
TUYERE DE PULVERISATION **11964**
TUYERE DE REFOULEMENT **3738**
TUYERE DIVERGENTE **3738**
TYPE **13320**
TYPE STANDARD **12086**
U DE MONTAGE **12388**
ULTRAMICROSCOPE **13335**
UNIFICATION **12091**
UNIFIER **12090**
UNION **13368**
UNION HOMOGENE **6556**
UNITE DE CHALEUR **12816**
UNITE DE LONGUEUR **13373**
UNITE DE LUMIERE **9270**
UNITE DE MASSE **13374**
UNITE DE MESURE **13375**
UNITE DE POIDS **13378**
UNITE DE POINCONNAGE **10011**
UNITE DE SURFACE **13372**
UNITE DE SURFACE NUCLEAIRE **1006**
UNITE DE TEMPS **13376**
UNITE DE TRAVAIL D'ENERGIE **13379**
UNITE DE VOLUME **13377**
UNITE THERMIQUE **12816**
UNITE THERMIQUE ANGLAISE **1626**
UNIVALENT **8377**
URANIUM **13420**
USAGE **13982**

# 741 VAR

USER (S') **13713**
USINABILITE **13946**
USINABILITE **7838**
USINAGE **7864**
USINAGE **4983**
USINAGE **13959**
USINAGE A CHAUD **6650**
USINAGE A FROID **2713**
USINAGE DES METAUX **8192**
USINAGE PREREGLE **9752**
USINAGE ULTERIEUR **5750**
USINE **5010**
USINE **7861**
USINE **5013**
USINE A GAZ **5848**
USINE CENTRALE ELECTRIQUE **4512**
USINE DE CARBONISATION DE LA HOUILLE **2665**
USINE DE CONSTRUCTON MECANIQUE **4764**
USINE DE FORCE MOTRICE **9742**
USINE HYDRAULIQUE **6692**
USINE HYDROELECTRIQUE **6701**
USINE METALLURGIQUE **11668**
USINER **13937**
USURE **13709**
USURE **4820**
USURE NORMALE **13710**
USURE PAR FROTTEMENT **13712**
USURE PAR FROTTEMENT **5778**
UTILISATION **13429**
UTILISER **13430**
VA-ET-VIENT. **13725**
VACUOMETRE **13442**
VAINCRE UNE RESISTANCE **8929**
VALENCE **13452**
VALEUR APPROCHEE **653**
VALEUR CALCULEE **1858**
VALEUR D'EQUILIBRE **4792**
VALEUR DE REGLAGE **11221**
VALEUR FINALE **5192**
VALEUR INITIALE **6932**
VALEUR INSTANTANEE **6990**
VALEUR INTERMEDIAIRE **7051**
VALEUR LIMITE **7594**
VALEUR MAXIMUM **8069**
VALEUR MINIMUM **8307**
VALEUR MOYENNE **8073**
VALEUR NOMINALE **8616**
VALEUR NUMERIQUE **8697**
VALEUR REELLE **153**
VALEUR THEORIQUE **1858**
VALVE **13453**

VALVE A PAPILLON **12890**
VALVE DE CONTREPRESSION **895**
VALVE DE DEMARRAGE **12131**
VALVE ELECTRIQUE **4549**
VALVE ELECTROMAGNETIQUE **11774**
VALVE EQUILIBREE **934**
VALVE OSCILLANTE **10760**
VANADIUM **13475**
VANNE **5867**
VANNE **11652**
VANNE **2617**
VANNE A BLOCAGE MECANIQUE **9062**
VANNE A BOISSEAU SPHERIQUE **968**
VANNE A ENVELOPPE CHAUFFANTE **7205**
VANNE A LIBRE DILATATION **9061**
VANNE A MANOEUVRE RAPIDE **10103**
VANNE A PAPILLON **1811**
VANNE A PASSAGE DIRECT **5867**
VANNE A SIEGES OBLIQUES **12662**
VANNE A SIEGES PARALLELES **9060**
VANNE A TIGE FIXE **8624**
VANNE A TIGE MONTANTE **10617**
VANNE A VIS EXTERIEURE **8914**
VANNE A VIS INTERIEURE **6980**
VANNE D'ARRET **12642**
VANNE D'ERUPTION **1360**
VANNE D'EXTRACTION **1359**
VANNE DE CONTROLE **3872**
VANNE MOTORISEE **8416**
VAPEUR **13484**
VAPEUR **12155**
VAPEUR A BASSE PRESSION **7785**
VAPEUR A HAUTE PRESSION **6491**
VAPEUR D'EAU **12192**
VAPEUR D'EBULLITION **1404**
VAPEUR D'ECHAPPEMENT **4896**
VAPEUR DE CHAUFFAGE **6397**
VAPEUR FRAICHE **7673**
VAPEUR HUMIDE **13805**
VAPEUR SATURANTE **10942**
VAPEUR SATUREE **10942**
VAPEUR SECHE **4351**
VAPEUR SURCHAUFFEE **12469**
VAPEUR SURCHAUFFEE **12471**
VAPEURS ACIDES **127**
VAPORISATION **13483**
VAPORISATION **4867**
VAPORISER **4862**
VARIABLE **13488**
VARIABLE **13494**
VARIABLE COMPLEXE **2814**

# VAR

742

VARIANTE 410
VARIATEUR DE VITESSE 13493
VARIATION 13495
VARIATION (MATH.) 13496
VARIATION BRUSQUE DE TEMPERATURE 12437
VARIATION DE TEMPERATURE 13498
VARIATION PROGRESSIVE DE TEMPERATURE/DE VITESSE 6024
VARIATIONS DE NIVEAU D'EAU 13500
VARIATIONS DE PRESSION 13497
VARIATIONS DE VITESSE 13499
VARLOPE 7245
VASE CLOS 4075
VASELINE 13508
VASES COMMUNICANTS 13553
VECTEUR 13510
VECTEUR UNITAIRE 13380
VEHICULE A BENNE BASCULANTE 12967
VEHICULE A TROIS ESSIEUX 12871
VEHICULE ARTICULE 13092
VEHICULE TOUS TERRAINS 3362
VEHICULE UTILITAIRE 2784
VENT 1315
VENT ENRICHI D'OXYGENE 4770
VENTILATEUR 5033
VENTILATEUR A FORCE CENTRIFUGE 2179
VENTILATEUR A HELICE 9929
VENTILATEUR A PISTON 9372
VENTILATEUR A PISTON ROTATIF 10751
VENTILATEUR ASPIRANT 12429
VENTILATEUR ASPIRANT, ET SOUFFLANT 2768
VENTILATEUR DE REFROIDISSEMENT 3088
VENTILATEUR REFOULANT 9817
VENTILATEUR SOUFFLANT 9817
VENTILATEUR SYSTEME ROOT 10729
VENTILATION 13530
VENTILATION ARTIFICIELLE 738
VENTILATION NATURELLE 8508
VENTILATION PAR APPEL 13450
VENTILATION PAR PULSION 9517
VENTRE DE POISSON (A) 5272
VENU DE FONDERIE 2054
VENU DE FONTE 2054
VENUE A LA COULEE 2054
VERDET 13533
VERIFICATEUR (METR) 5871
VERIFICATION 13534
VERIFICATION DE LA COMPOSITION CHIMIQUE 2280
VERIFICATION DU PARALLELISME 13086
VERIFIER LES MESURES 2279
VERIN 11035

VERIN A BOUTEILLE 1485
VERIN A CHARIOT 13165
VERIN A CLIQUET 10222
VERIN A TREPIED 13218
VERIN HYDRAULIQUE 6688
VERMILLON 13535
VERMOULU 13976
VERNIER 13536
VERNIR 7353
VERNIS 13504
VERNIS A L'ALCOOL 7354
VERNIS A L'ESSENCE 13296
VERNIS A L'HUILE 8786
VERNIS A LA GOMME-LAQUE 10998
VERNIS AU BITUME 1283
VERNIS AU COPAL 3103
VERNIS DU JAPON 239
VERNIS JAPON 1283
VERNIS ZAPON 14022
VERNISSAGE 13505
VERRE 8708
VERRE 5956
VERRE A BOUTEILLES 1484
VERRE A FIL DE FER NOYE 13894
VERRE A GLACES 9491
VERRE A VITRES 13866
VERRE ARME 13894
VERRE BLANC DE BOHEME 1400
VERRE D'IENA 7217
VERRE DE QUARTZ 10079
VERRE DEPOLI 6145
VERRE DEPOLI 5701
VERRE FILE 5966
VERRE GROSSISSANT 7936
VERRE INCOLORE 2746
VERRE LIQUIDE 11808
VERRE OPAQUE 8273
VERRE PILE 5962
VERRE SOLUBLE 11808
VERRE SOUFFLE 1365
VERROU 1432
VERROUILLAGE 7710
VERROUILLER 7699
VERT DE SCHEELE 10996
VERT DE SCHWEINFURT 11000
VERT EMERAUDE 2372
VERT-DE-GRIS 220
VERT-DE-GRIS 13533
VERTICAL 13551
VERTICALE 9217
VIBRATION 8884

VIBRATION 13554
VIBRATION 13146
VIBRATION AMORTIE 3600
VIBRATION DUE A DES EFFORTS DE FLEXION 13556
VIBRATION DUE A DES EFFORTS DE TORSION 13557
VIBRATION FONDAMENTALE 5736
VIBRATION LUMINEUSE 7825
VIBRATION MECANIQUE 8114
VIBRATION NON AMORTIE 13346
VIBRATION PROPRE 5736
VIBRATION SONORE 11818
VIBRATIONS 2277
VIBRATIONS 13559
VIBRATIONS DE L'ETHER 13560
VIBRATIONS DUES A LA RESONANCE 8883
VIBRER 8877
VIBROCULTEURS 3457
VICE 3692
VICE DE CONCEPTION 3694
VICE DE CONSTRUCTION 3693
VICE DE FONCTIONNEMENT 3695
VICE DE MATIERE 3680
VIDANGE 4024
VIDANGE D'UNE CHAUDIERE 1364
VIDANGER 4204
VIDE 13434
VIDE ENTRE DEUX DENTS 6548
VIDE ENTRE LES BARREAUX DE LA GRILLE 278
VIDE ENTRE LES ONDES 6543
VIDE LIBRE 2481
VIDE POUSSE 6477
VIDER 4018
VIDER 4204
VIEILLISSEMENT 225
VIEILLISSEMENT ARTIFICIEL 226
VIEILLISSEMENT ARTIFICIEL 731
VIEILLISSEMENT COMPLET 231
VIEILLISSEMENT CRITIQUE 3344
VIEILLISSEMENT ECHELONNE 232
VIEILLISSEMENT INTERROMPU 7091
VIEILLISSEMENT NATUREL 233
VIEILLISSEMENT NATUREL 8500
VIEILLISSEMENT PAR DEFORMATION 12328
VIEILLISSEMENT PAR DEFORMATION 12327
VIEILLISSEMENT PAR LES EFFORTS 12324
VIEILLISSEMENT PAR REFROIDISSEMENT RAPIDE 10087
VIEILLISSEMENT PAR TRAVAIL A FROID 235
VIEILLISSEMENT PROGRESSIF 9906
VIEILLISSEMENT PROGRESSIF 234
VIERGE (MIN.) 5647
VILEBREQUIN 3313

VILEBREQUIN (OUTIL A PERCER) 1519
VILEBREQUIN A CONTREPOIDS 3235
VILEBREQUIN A ENGRENAGE 5905
VILEBREQUIN A PLUSIEURS COUDES 8478
VILEBREQUIN A TROIS COUDES 12880
VILEBREQUIN A VIS DE PRESSION 1518
VINAIGRE RADICAL 86
VIOLLE 13569
VIRE-ANDAINS 12537
VIROLE 5128
VIROLE D'UNE CHAUDIERE 3260
VIS 2453
VIS 6457
VIS 11021
VIS A BOIS A TETE CARREE 2552
VIS A BROCHE 1930
VIS A DEUX FILETS 13315
VIS A DROITE 10584
VIS A FILET CARRE 12034
VIS A FILET ROND 10807
VIS A FILET TRAPEZOIDAL 1815
VIS A FILET TRIANGULAIRE 547
VIS A GAUCHE 7510
VIS A LEVIER 1930
VIS A METAUX 8187
VIS A OREILLES 12912
VIS A PLUSIEURS FILETS 8474
VIS A TETE 1913
VIS A TETE CARREE 12033
VIS A TETE CYLINDRIQUE 5165
VIS A TETE FENDUE 11637
VIS A TETE NOYEE 3248
VIS A TETE PLATE 5385
VIS A TETE RONDE 11051
VIS A TROIS FILETS 12879
VIS A UN FILET 11502
VIS AILEE 12912
VIS AUTOTARAUDEUSE 11162
VIS D'ARCHIMEDE 13970
VIS D'ARRET 2453
VIS DE BLOCAGE 7708
VIS DE BUTEE 12909
VIS DE PRESSION 193
VIS DE PRESSION 9831
VIS DE PURGE 1319
VIS DE REGLAGE 192
VIS DE RELEVAGE 7556
VIS DE TENSION 12758
VIS DE TRANSLATION 10852
VIS DECOLLETEE 1607
VIS DIFFERENTIELLE 2833

# VIS

VIS EGALISATRICE **7529**
VIS FILETEE A DROITE **10580**
VIS FILETEE A GAUCHE **7506**
VIS GLOBIQUE **5978**
VIS MERE **7471**
VIS METALLIQUE A BOIS **13918**
VIS MICROMETRIQUE **8255**
VIS OU BOULON DE FIXATION **5043**
VIS OU BOULON DE MONTAGE **5043**
VIS POINTEAU POUR ARRET DE BAGUES **11222**
VIS SANS FIN **13979**
VIS SANS FIN **13969**
VIS SANS TETE **6156**
VIS TANGENTE **12619**
VIS TRANSPORTEUSE **13970**
VIS VIOLON **12911**
VIS-MERE **6165**
VISCOSE **13575**
VISCOSIMETRE **13574**
VISCOSITE **13576**
VISITE DE LA CHAUDIERE **1414**
VISQUEUX **13577**
VISSAGE **11065**
VISSER **11022**
VISSER SUR **11037**
VISUALISATION **10253**
VITESSE **11868**
VITESSE **10226**
VITESSE **11875**
VITESSE A L'ARRIVEE **6950**
VITESSE A LA SORTIE **8903**
VITESSE ANGULAIRE **546**
VITESSE CIRCONFERENTIELLE **9198**
VITESSE CRITIQUE **3353**
VITESSE CROISSANTE **6852**
VITESSE D'ARRIVEE **6950**
VITESSE D'ECOULEMENT **5462**
VITESSE D'ECOULEMENT **8903**
VITESSE D'ECOULEMENT D'HUILE **10232**
VITESSE D'ENTREE **6950**
VITESSE D'INFLAMMATION **11870**
VITESSE DE BROCHE **11909**
VITESSE DE COMBUSTION **10227**
VITESSE DE CORROSION **3193**
VITESSE DE COUPE CONSTANTE **2971**
VITESSE DE CROISIERE **3417**
VITESSE DE DEFORMATION **12330**
VITESSE DE DEPOT **10229**
VITESSE DE FLUAGE **3326**
VITESSE DE FLUAGE **5459**
VITESSE DE FUSION **8144**

VITESSE DE LA LUMIERE **7569**
VITESSE DE LA LUMIERE **13517**
VITESSE DE PASSAGE **13518**
VITESSE DE PROPAGATION **13519**
VITESSE DE PROPAGATION DE LA FLAMME **10230**
VITESSE DE REGIME **8663**
VITESSE DE ROTATION **11876**
VITESSE DE SORTIE **8903**
VITESSE DE TRANSFORMATION **13521**
VITESSE DECROISSANTE **3679**
VITESSE DU COURANT **13516**
VITESSE DU FIL **13900**
VITESSE DU PISTON **9388**
VITESSE DU SON **13520**
VITESSE FINALE **5193**
VITESSE INITIALE **6933**
VITESSE LINEAIRE **7617**
VITESSE MAXIMUM **8067**
VITESSE NORMALE DE FONCTIONNEMENT **8663**
VITESSE PERIPHERIQUE **9198**
VITESSE SURMULTIPLIEE **8930**
VITESSE TANGENTIELLE **12623**
VITESSE UNIFORME CONSTANTE **13363**
VITESSE VARIEE **13494**
VITESSE VIRTUELLE **13573**
VITRAGE **5972**
VITRER **5969**
VITREUX **13582**
VITRIFICATION **13584**
VITRIOL **12453**
VITRIOL BLANC **14046**
VITRIOL BLEU **1376**
VITRIOL MARTIAL **6093**
VITRIOL VERT **6093**
VOIE **13085**
VOIE DECAUVILLE **9639**
VOIE FERREE **7606**
VOIE FERREE D'ATELIER **13965**
VOIE PORTATIVE **9639**
VOILE **3667**
VOILE **1378**
VOILE **6313**
VOILE **1347**
VOILER (SE) **13628**
VOITURE AUTOMOBILE **8411**
VOITURE DECAPOTABLE **3073**
VOLANT **13810**
VOLANT A CHAINE **2223**
VOLANT A CHAINE ADAPTABLE **2220**
VOLANT A GORGES **10738**
VOLANT A MAIN **6267**

**745**  **ZON**

VOLANT D'UNE SEULE PIECE **11784**
VOLANT DE CHARIOTAGE **13163**
VOLANT DE DIRECTION **12233**
VOLANT DE MANOEUVRE **6255**
VOLANT DENTE **5906**
VOLANT EN DEUX SEGMENTS **5497**
VOLANT EN DISQUE **4004**
VOLANT EN PLUSIEURS SEGMENTS **11138**
VOLANT ENGRENAGE **5906**
VOLANT FENDU **11941**
VOLANT-MOTEUR **5496**
VOLANT-POULIE **1147**
VOLATILISATION **13587**
VOLATILISER **13588**
VOLATILITE **13589**
VOLET D'AIR **292**
VOLET DE GAZ **12888**
VOLT **13591**
VOLT-AMPERE **13592**
VOLT-COULOMB **7255**
VOLTAGE **13593**
VOLTAGE AUX BORNES **12764**
VOLTAGE NORMAL **8659**
VOLTAMETRE **3227**
VOLTMETRE **13597**
VOLUME **13598**
VOLUME (POUR CENT DU) **9179**
VOLUME ATOMIQUE **806**
VOLUME CRITIQUE **3354**
VOLUME DEPLACE (PHYS.) **4053**
VOLUME ENGENDRE PAR LE DEPLACEMENT DU PISTON **13599**
VOLUME MOLECULAIRE **8362**
VOLUME QUI PASSE AU TRAVERS D'UN ORIFICE PAR SECONDE **4023**
VOLUME SPECIFIQUE **11854**
VOUSSEAU **687**
VOUSSOIR **687**
VOUSSURE **3396**
VOYAGEUR **7625**
VOYANT ROND **2414**
VRILLE **5944**
VRILLES **9664**
VUE **13567**
VUE A VOL D'OISEAU **1264**
VUE D'ENSEMBLE **9430**
VUE DE BAS EN HAUT **1498**
VUE DE COTE **11420**
VUE DE FACE **5694**
VUE DE FACE POSTERIEURE **4717**
VUE DE HAUT EN BAS **13037**

VUE ECLATEE **4934**
VUE PAR-DESSOUS **1498**
VULCANISATION **3484**
VULCANISATION **13607**
VULCANISER **13608**
WAGON-CITERNE **12626**
WAGON-RESERVOIR **12626**
WAGONS CIGARES/POCHES **2072**
WATT **13694**
WATT-HEURE **13695**
WATT-MINUTE **13696**
WATT-SECONDE **13697**
WATTMETRE **13698**
WITHERITE **13911**
WOLFRAM **13912**
WULFENITE **13991**
XENON **14004**
XEROGRAPHIE **14005**
XYLENE **14006**
XYLOIDINE **6176**
XYLOL **14006**
YARD **14007**
YARD CARRE **12031**
YTTERBIUM **14019**
YTTRIUM **14020**
ZAMAK **14021**
ZERO (D'UNE ECHELLE) **14027**
ZERO ABSOLU **36**
ZERO FLOTTANT **5440**
ZINC **14035**
ZINC (COMMERCIAL) **11879**
ZINC BRUT **2785**
ZINC DU COMMERCE **2785**
ZINC EN FEUILLES **11327**
ZINC REFONDU **10341**
ZINC SILICATE **11438**
ZINGAGE **2604**
ZINGAGE **14044**
ZINGAGE **5787**
ZINGAGE **5789**
ZINGAGE ELECTROCHIMIQUE ELECTROLYTIQUE **4566**
ZINGUER **5784**
ZIRCONIUM **14049**
ZONE DE DIFFUSION **3934**
ZONE DE FUSION **5761**
ZONE DE FUSION **5763**
ZONE DE GUINIER-PRESTON **6171**
ZONE DE SOLIDIFICATION **5658**
ZONE DE SURFACE DE SEPARATION **7034**
ZONE INFLUENCEE PAR LA CHALEUR **6380**
ZONE IONISEE **7128**

# ZON

746

ZONE NEUTRE **8547**

ZONE SPHERIQUE **14051**

# DEUTSCHER INDEX

## ÍNDICE ALEMÃO

| | |
|---|---|
| ABAKUS (WULFFSCHER) **13992** | ABFALLENDE **3356** |
| ABBAUEN UND ERSETZEN **10451** | ABFALLSTOFFE **13637** |
| ABBEIZEN **11006** | ABFASEN **2230** |
| ABBEIZEN (EIN METALL) **11005** | ABFASEN **2233** |
| ABBILDUNG **6778** | ABFASUNG **2231** |
| ABBIMSEN **9990** | ABFLACHEN **5408** |
| ABBIMSEN **9987** | ABFLACHUNG DES GEWINDES **5389** |
| ABBINDEN **11214** | ABFLUCHTUNG **325** |
| ABBINDEN DES ZEMENTS **11226** | ABFLUSS **8900** |
| ABBLASEHAHN **1357** | ABFLUSS **8899** |
| ABBLASEN EINES KESSELS **1364** | ABFLUSSGESCHWINDIGKEIT **8903** |
| ABBLASEN MIT PRESSLUFT **244** | ABFLUSSMENGE **4023** |
| ABBLASEVENTIL **1358** | ABFLUSSROHR **4207** |
| ABBLASHAHN **272** | ABFORMEN **8428** |
| ABBLÄTTERN **10975** | ABFORMEN **8424** |
| ABBLÄTTERN **9156** | ABGAS **13634** |
| ABBLÄTTERUNG **11830** | ABGEFLACHT **5406** |
| ABBLÄTTERUNG **5306** | ABGENUTZT **13982** |
| ABBLÄTTERUNG **11328** | ABGEPLATTET **5406** |
| ABBLÄTTERUNG **11339** | ABGERUNDET **10794** |
| ABBLÄTTERUNG **10985** | ABGESCHRECKTEN ZUSTAND (IM) **743** |
| ABBLÄTTERUNG **4889** | ABGESTUFT **12246** |
| ABBLENDEN **3877** | ABGIESSEN **3649** |
| ABBRAND **1747** | ABGIESSEN **3650** |
| ABBRANDVERLUST **7761** | ABGRATEN **1766** |
| ABBRENNSCHWEISSEN **5358** | ABGRATEN **3642** |
| ABBRENNSTUMPFSCHWEISSEN **1806** | ABGRATEN **13209** |
| ABBRENNSTUMPFSCHWEISSUNG **1794** | ABGRATEN **13206** |
| ABDAMPF **4896** | ABGRATEN **13210** |
| ABDAMPF-ENTÖLER **8779** | ABGRATEN (EIN BLECH) **13205** |
| ABDAMPFROHR **4897** | ABGRATPRESSE **13211** |
| ABDAMPFSCHALE **4864** | ABGUSS **9717** |
| ABDAMPFVORRICHTUNG **4869** | ABGUSS **12703** |
| ABDECKLEISTEN **1928** | ABHANG **11627** |
| ABDECKMITTEL **615** | ABHÄNGIGKEIT VON (IN) **13542** |
| ABDECKPLATTE **3267** | ABHEBEFORMMASCHINE **4237** |
| ABDECKUNG **12287** | ABKANTEN **2233** |
| ABDICHTEN **7954** | ABKANTEN **12671** |
| ABDICHTEN **7953** | ABKANTEN **12646** |
| ABDICHTEN **7831** | ABKANTEN **2230** |
| ABDICHTUNG **11081** | ABKANTMASCHINEN **4453** |
| ABDREHEN **13164** | ABKLÄREN **3650** |
| ABDREHEN **13162** | ABKLÄREN **3649** |
| ABDRUCK **10465** | ABKLOPPEN **2347** |
| ABDRÜCKSCHRAUBE **7556** | ABKOCHUNG **3669** |
| ABERRATION (CHROMATISCHE) **2369** | ABKREIDEN **2226** |
| ABERRATION (SPHÄRISCHE) **11885** | ABKÜHLEN **3085** |
| ABERRATION DES LICHTES **5** | ABKÜHLEN **2332** |
| ABFALL **12536** | ABKÜHLEN (SICH) **3081** |
| ABFÄLLE **13637** | ABKÜHLUNG MIT WASSERMANTEL **7204** |
| ABFALLEISEN **5553** | ABKÜHLUNGSKURVE **3087** |

**ABK**         750

ABKÜHLUNGSSCHRUMPFUNG 7648
ABKÜHLUNGSSPANNUNGEN 3091
ABKÜHLUNGSZEIT 3082
ABLAGERUNG 2510
ABLAGERUNG 11228
ABLAGERUNG (GEOL.) 3773
ABLÄNGEN 3509
ABLASSEN 4230
ABLASSHAHN 1318
ABLASSHAHN 4205
ABLASSROHRLEITUNG 4022
ABLASSSCHLAUCH-STUTZEN 6613
ABLASSSCHRAUBE 4208
ABLASSVENTIL 4205
ABLASSVENTIL 1358
ABLAUF EINES PATENTES 4932
ABLAUFKANAL 12596
ABLEITBLECH 921
ABLEITBLECH 3702
ABLEITUNG VON WÄRME 4666
ABLEITUNGSROHR 4207
ABLENKKEGEL 11924
ABLENKPLATTE 11926
ABLENKUNG (PHYS.) 3819
ABLENKUNG (SEITLICHE) 7419
ABLESEFEHLER 4826
ABLESEGERÄTE (OPTISCHE) 8847
ABLESEN 10254
ABLESEN 12692
ABLESUNG 10254
ABLÖSEN 9156
ABLÖSUNG 1354
ABMASS 358
ABMESSEN 8078
ABMESSUNGEN 3960
ABNAHME 3656
ABNAHME 67
ABNAHME (VON MASCHINEN) 68
ABNAHMEBESCHEINIGUNG 70
ABNAHMEGRENZE 69
ABNAHMELEHRE 10015
ABNAHMEPRÜFUNG 71
ABNAHMEVERSUCH 71
ABNAHMEVERWEIGERUNG 10431
ABNEHMBAR 3808
ABNIETEN 3511
ABNÜTZEN (SICH) 13713
ABNÜTZUNG 13709
ABNÜTZUNG (NATÜRLICHE) 13710
ABPLATTEN 5408
ABRAMSEN-ROHRRICHTMASCHINE 12

ABRÄNDERN 2230
ABREISSEN DER NIETKÖPFE 11999
ABRICHT- U. FLÄCHENSCHLEIFMASCHINE 9442
ABRICHTAPPARATE 13233
ABRICHTEN 13232
ABRICHTEN 13234
ABRICHTHOBELMASCHINE 12515
ABRICHTPLATTE 6048
ABRIEB 13712
ABRIEB 13
ABRUNDEN 10793
ABRUNDUNG DES GEWINDES 10809
ABRUNDUNGSBOGEN 6537
ABRUNDUNGSHALBMESSER 10168
ABSANDEN 10919
ABSANDEN 10921
ABSATZ 12239
ABSATZ 11383
ABSATZMUFFE 3962
ABSATZSTELLEN 5367
ABSAUGER 4900
ABSCHALTEN (ELEKTR.) 12554
ABSCHALTEN (ELEKTR.) 12559
ABSCHALTEN EINE ROHRLEITUNG 11407
ABSCHEIDEN 11191
ABSCHEIDEN (CHEM.) 11189
ABSCHEIDEN (SICH) 9760
ABSCHEIDUNG 11191
ABSCHEIDUNG (ELEKTROLYTICHE) 4593
ABSCHEIDUNG (ELEKTROLYTISCHE) 4580
ABSCHEIDUNGSGESCHWINDGKEIT 10229
ABSCHERBOLZEN 11294
ABSCHEREN 11280
ABSCHEREN 11290
ABSCHEREN DES NIETES 11293
ABSCHERSTIFT 11283
ABSCHERUNG 11295
ABSCHLÄMMEN 7537
ABSCHLAMMVENTIL 1359
ABSCHLEIFEN 13
ABSCHLEIFEN 10
ABSCHLEIFEN 5972
ABSCHLEIFVERSUCH 16
ABSCHMELZVERBINDUNGSRING 2991
ABSCHMIRGELN 4694
ABSCHMIRGELN 4695
ABSCHNEIDEN (MIT DER SCHERE) 11280
ABSCHRÄGEN 1231
ABSCHRÄGEN 1222
ABSCHRÄGUNG 1221
ABSCHRÄGUNG 1902

ABSCHRÄGUNG **2233**
ABSCHRÄGUNG **1231**
ABSCHRÄGUNGSWINKEL **1223**
ABSCHRÄGWINKEL **516**
ABSCHRAUBEN **13396**
ABSCHRAUBEN **13395**
ABSCHRECKALTERUNG **10087**
ABSCHRECKBEHÄLTER **10090**
ABSCHRECKBIEGEPROBE **10088**
ABSCHRECKEN **2338**
ABSCHRECKEN **2332**
ABSCHRECKEN (FONTE) **10094**
ABSCHRECKEN (ÖRTLICH BEGRENZTES) **3914**
ABSCHRECKEN DES STAHLES **10100**
ABSCHRECKHÄRTUNG **10089**
ABSCHRECKHÄRTUNG **2338**
ABSCHRECKMITTEL **10098**
ABSCHROT **631**
ABSCHROTEN **3515**
ABSCHRÖTER **631**
ABSEHLINIE **7601**
ABSENKUNG DES WASSERSPIEGELS **7798**
ABSETZEN **11228**
ABSETZEN (SICH) **11227**
ABSIEBEN **11423**
ABSORBATOR **40**
ABSORBER **40**
ABSORBIERBAR **38**
ABSORBIERBARKEIT **42**
ABSORBIEREN **37**
ABSORPTIOMETER **43**
ABSORPTION **44**
ABSORPTIONSDYNAMOMETER **48**
ABSORPTIONSDYNAMOMETER **55**
ABSORPTIONSFÄHIGKEIT **42**
ABSORPTIONSGRENZE **50**
ABSORPTIONSKANTE **49**
ABSORPTIONSKOEFFIZIENT **46**
ABSORPTIONSKONSTANTE **47**
ABSORPTIONSMITTEL **39**
ABSORPTIONSSPEKTRUM **54**
ABSORPTIONSSTREIFEN **45**
ABSORPTIONSVERHÄLTNIS **53**
ABSORPTIONSVERMÖGEN **42**
ABSORPTIONSVERMÖGEN **56**
ABSORPTIONSWÄRME **6354**
ABSPANNTRANSFORMATOR **12244**
ABSPERREN (EINE ROHRLEITUNG) **11407**
ABSPERRHAHN **11408**
ABSPERRHAHN **12281**
ABSPERRSCHIEBER **12642**

ABSPERRSCHIEBER **11653**
ABSPERRSCHIEBER **5867**
ABSPERRSCHIEBER MIT AUSSENSPINDEL **8914**
ABSPERRSCHIEBER MIT INNENLIEGENDEM SPINDELGEWINDE **6980**
ABSPERRSCHIEBER MIT INNENSPINDEL **6980**
ABSPERRSCHIEBER MIT NICHTSTEIGENDER SPINDEL **8624**
ABSPERRSCHIEBER MIT STEIGENDER SPINDEL **10617**
ABSPERRSTÜCK **9529**
ABSPERRUNGSSTÖSSEL **5160**
ABSPERRVENTIL **5977**
ABSPERRVENTIL **12282**
ABSPERRVENTIL FÜR GASFLASCHEN **3575**
ABSPRINGEN DER NIETKÖPFE **11999**
ABSTAND **4063**
ABSTAND (LICHTER) **2481**
ABSTAND DER NIETE VOM BLECHRAND **4066**
ABSTANDHALTER **4068**
ABSTANDHALTER **11973**
ABSTANDHÜLSE **4068**
ABSTANDHÜLSE **4067**
ABSTECHBANK **3540**
ABSTECHDREHMASCHINE **11584**
ABSTECHE **12675**
ABSTECHEN **3533**
ABSTECHEN **3510**
ABSTECHMASCHINE **3541**
ABSTEIFEN **12153**
ABSTEIFEN **12150**
ABSTEIFUNG **12153**
ABSTELLEN (EINE MASCHINE) **12280**
ABSTELLEN EINER MASCHINE **12286**
ABSTELLHAHN **11408**
ABSTELLHEBEL **4035**
ABSTICH **6333**
ABSTICHLOCH **12637**
ABSTICHLOCH **12645**
ABSTICHRINNE **7436**
ABSTICHVERSCHLUSS-STOPFEN **12284**
ABSTIMMUNG **12574**
ABSTOSSUNG **10468**
ABSTOSSUNG (MAGNETISCHE) **7915**
ABSTOSSUNGSKRAFT **5530**
ABSTREIFPLATTE **12384**
ABSTREIFPLATTE **6160**
ABSTREIFSCHMIERUNG **10601**
ABSTRÖMGESCHWINDIGKEIT **8903**
ABSTUMPFEN **8549**
ABSTUMPFUNG **8548**
ABSUD **3669**
ABSZISSE **27**

# ABT

752

ABSZISSENACHSE **872**
ABTAST-UND-SORTIERMASCHINEN **11185**
ABTASTEN **10990**
ABTEIL **2798**
ABTEILUNG **2798**
ABTÖTENDES MITTEL **629**
ABTRENNUNG **7184**
ABTRIEBSWELLE **8910**
ABTRIEBSWELLE **7943**
ABWÄLZ-FRÄSEN **6513**
ABWALZFRÄSEN **6512**
ABWÄRME **13635**
ABWÄRTSSCHWEISSUNG **4192**
ABWÄRTSTRANSFORMATOR **12244**
ABWÄSSER VON STÄDTEN **11230**
ABWÄSSERBESEITIGUNG **10453**
ABWÄSSERREINIGUNG **13638**
ABWEICHUNG **13615**
ABWEICHUNG **3819**
ABWEICHUNG **4077**
ABWEICHUNG (CHROMATISCHE) **2369**
ABWEICHUNG (DURCHSCHNITTLICHE) **8074**
ABWEICHUNG (SPHÄRISCHE) **11885**
ABWEICHUNG DER MAGNETNADEL **3668**
ABWEICHUNG DES LICHTES **5**
ABWERFEN (DEN RIEMEN) **12895**
ABWICKELBAR (GEOM.) **3816**
ABWICKELN **13404**
ABWICKELN **13405**
ABWICKELN (GEOM.) **3815**
ABWIEGEN **13744**
ABWINDEN **13404**
ABWINDEN **13405**
ABWÜRGEN (EINER SCHRAUBE) **13309**
ABZIEHBILD **13109**
ABZIEHEN **12424**
ABZIEHEN **12425**
ABZIEHEN **6790**
ABZIEHEN **6793**
ABZIEHSTEIN **13824**
ABZUG (PHOT.) **9870**
ABZUGSMANTELMATRIZE **4193**
ABZWEIG **1558**
ABZWEIGEN **1556**
ABZWEIGROHR **9365**
ABZWEIGROHR **1558**
ABZWEIGSTUTZEN **1557**
ACHAT **222**
ACHESON-OFEN **97**
ACHROMASIE **101**
ACHROMATISCH **98**

ACHROMATISIEREN **100**
ACHROMATISIEREN **99**
ACHROMATISMUS **101**
ACHSABSTAND **2165**
ACHSABSTAND **4065**
ACHSBÜCHSE **877**
ACHSBÜCHSE **6085**
ACHSDRUCK **1100**
ACHSE **875**
ACHSE **11239**
ACHSE **2151**
ACHSE **874**
ACHSE **884**
ACHSE (FESTSTEHENDE) **3624**
ACHSE (KLEINE) EINER ELLIPSE **8313**
ACHSE (NEUTRALE) **8541**
ACHSE (OPTISCHE) **8841**
ACHSEN (SICH RECHTWINKLIG SCHNEIDENDE) **858**
ACHSENDREHBANK **881**
ACHSENGABEL **6593**
ACHSENKREUZ **12575**
ACHSENREGLER **11242**
ACHSENVERSCHIEBUNG **4055**
ACHSKAPPENSCHLÜSSEL **883**
ACHSLAGER **877**
ACHSLAGER **876**
ACHSLAGERBOHRMASCHINE **878**
ACHSSCHENKEL **12230**
ACHSSCHENKEL **882**
ACHSSCHENKELBOLZEN **7311**
ACHSSCHENKELDREHBANK **880**
ACHSSTAND **13813**
ACHTECK **8721**
ACHTELKREIS **8724**
ACHTELKRÜMMER **4467**
ACHTELWINKELMASS **8325**
ACHTFLACH **8722**
ACHTFLÄCHNER **8722**
ACHTKANTEISEN AUS LEGIERTEN STÄHLEN **375**
ACIDISCH **129**
ACKERKRÄNE **3294**
ACKERRADSCHLEPPER **13095**
ACKERSCHIENEN **13012**
ACKERWAGEN **2017**
ACKERWALZEN **10695**
ACKERWINDEN **13852**
ADAPT-PROGRAMMIERSPRACHE **159**
ADAPTOR **160**
ADDIEREN **162**
ADDITION **169**
ADER **3142**

| | |
|---|---|
| ADHÄSIONSKRAFT **174** | ALBEDO **308** |
| ADIABATE **179** | ALBERTSCHLAG **7389** |
| ADIABATISCH **178** | ALBUMIN **310** |
| ADJUSTIEREN **195** | ALBUMINPAPIER **311** |
| ADJUSTIEREN **182** | ALDEHYD **84** |
| ADJUSTIERSCHRAUBE **192** | ALDEHYD **317** |
| ADMIRALITÄTSMETALL **198** | ALFAMETER **319** |
| ADRESSE **171** | ALGEBRA **320** |
| ADSORBIEREN **202** | ALGEBRAISCH **321** |
| ADSORPTION **203** | ALITIERTES (STAHL-)BLECH **441** |
| AEQUIVALENT **4796** | ALIZARIN **327** |
| AERODYNAMIK **215** | ALKALI **328** |
| AERODYNAMISCH **214** | ALKALILAUGE **339** |
| AEROMECHANIK **9558** | ALKALIMETALLE **329** |
| AEROSTATIK **218** | ALKALIMETER **331** |
| AEROSTATISCH **217** | ALKALIMETRIE **333** |
| AFFINIEREN **10377** | ALKALIMETRISCH **332** |
| AFFINITÄT (CHEMISCHE) **2292** | ALKALINITÄT **340** |
| AGGREGAT **227** | ALKALISALZ **338** |
| AGGREGAT-ZUSTAND (FLÜSSIGER) **7657** | ALKALISCH MACHEN **330** |
| AGGREGAT-ZUSTAND (GASFÖRMIGER) **5857** | ALKALISCHE BESCHAFFENHEIT **340** |
| ÄHNLICHKEIT (GEOM.) **11470** | ALKALISIEREN **330** |
| AILANTHUSBAUM **239** | ALKALOID **341** |
| AKKORDARBEIT **9294** | ALKANNAROTPAPIER **342** |
| AKKORDLOHN **9295** | ALKOHOL **313** |
| AKKUMULATOR **4534** | ALKOHOL (ABSOLUTER) **28** |
| AKKUMULATOR **76** | ALKOHOL (KARBURIERTER) **1983** |
| AKKUMULATOR (HYDRAULISCHER) **6677** | ALKOHOL (REKTIFIZIERTER) **10313** |
| AKKUMULATOR ENTLADEN (EINEN) **4019** | ALKOHOL (VERGÄLLTER) **8224** |
| AKKUMULATORENBATTERIE **77** | ALKOHOL (WASSERFREIER) **28** |
| AKKUMULATORENLOKOMOTIVE **79** | ALKOHOL (WÄSSERIGER) **659** |
| AKKUMULATORENMETALL **80** | ALKOHOLFIRNIS **7354** |
| AKKUMULATORPLATTE **81** | ALKOHOLISCH **314** |
| AKKUMULATORZELLE **78** | ALKOHOLMETER **316** |
| AKTINISCH **139** | ALKOHOLTHERMOMETER **11922** |
| AKTINIUM **141** | ALLOMER **349** |
| AKTINOMETER **142** | ALLOMERISMUS **350** |
| AKTIONSTURBINE **6810** | ALLOMORPH **352** |
| AKTIVATOR **146** | ALLOMORPHIE **351** |
| AKTIVATOR **148** | ALLOTRIOMORPH **354** |
| AKTIVIERUNG **144** | ALLOTROP **356** |
| AKTIVIERUNGSENERGIE **147** | ALLOTROPIE **357** |
| AKTIVIERUNGSMITTEL **148** | ALLSTROMSCHWEISSMASCHINE **59** |
| AKUSTIK **137** | ALNICO **398** |
| AKUSTISCH **136** | ALPAKA **8569** |
| ALABASTER **304** | ALPHA-BETA-MESSING **403** |
| ALARMPFEIFE **307** | ALPHA-BRONZE **1656** |
| ALARMSIGNAL **306** | ALPHA-MESSING **399** |
| ALARMVORRICHTUNG **305** | ALPHA-STRAHLENQUELLE **401** |
| ALARMZEICHEN **306** | ALPHA-STRAHLER **401** |
| ALAUN **2787** | ALPHA-STRAHLUNG **402** |

**ALT** 754

ALPHA-TEILCHEN **400**
ALTEISEN **11007**
ALTERNATIVE **409**
ALTERNATOR **407**
ALTERSRISS **11092**
ALTERUNG **225**
ALTERUNG (KRITISCHE) **3344**
ALTERUNG (KÜNSTLICHE) **226**
ALTERUNG (KÜNSTLICHE) **731**
ALTERUNG (NATÜRLICHE) **233**
ALTERUNG (NATÜRLICHE) **8500**
ALTERUNG (PROGRESSIVE) **234**
ALTERUNG (STUFENWEISE) **232**
ALTERUNG (UNTERBROCHENE) **7091**
ALTERUNG (VOLLSTÄNDIGE) **231**
ALTERUNG DURCH KALTBEARBEITUNG **235**
ALTERUNGSBEREICH **230**
ALUMINAT **414**
ALUMINISIEREN **429**
ALUMINIUM **416**
ALUMINIUM **432**
ALUMINIUM **444**
ALUMINIUM-BERYLLIUM-LEGIERUNG **440**
ALUMINIUM-SCHMIEDE-LEGIERUNG **437**
ALUMINIUMAZETAT **417**
ALUMINIUMBRONZE **420**
ALUMINIUMBRONZE **434**
ALUMINIUMCHLORID **421**
ALUMINIUMDRAHT **428**
ALUMINIUMEISEN **5106**
ALUMINIUMFEILE **422**
ALUMINIUMFOLIE **436**
ALUMINIUMHALTIG **415**
ALUMINIUMHYDROXYD **423**
ALUMINIUMLEGIERUNG **418**
ALUMINIUMMESSING **419**
ALUMINIUMOXYD **413**
ALUMINIUMOXYD **412**
ALUMINIUMROHBLOCK **424**
ALUMINIUMROHR **427**
ALUMINIUMSILIKAT **425**
ALUMINO **430**
ALUMINOTHERMIE **431**
ALUMINOTHERMISCHE SCHWEISSUNG **12818**
ALUMINUIMSULFAT **426**
AMALGAM **397**
AMALGAM **445**
AMALGAMATION **447**
AMALGAMIEREN **447**
AMALGAMIEREN **446**
AMALGAMIERUNG **447**

AMALGAMIERUNGSVERFAHREN **448**
AMBOSS **630**
AMBOSSBAHN **4995**
AMBOSSHORN **1090**
AMBOSSSTOCK **633**
AMBOSSSTÖCKEL **632**
AMBOSSUNTERSATZ **633**
AMEISENSÄURE **5578**
AMIANT **755**
AMIDOBENZOL **552**
AMMONIAK **7644**
AMMONIAK **454**
AMMONIAK (DOPPELTKOHLENSAURES) **459**
AMMONIAK (ESSIGSAURES) **458**
AMMONIAK (KOHLENSAURES) **461**
AMMONIAK (OXALSAURES) **467**
AMMONIAK (PHOSPHORSAURES) **469**
AMMONIAK (SALPETERSAURES) **465**
AMMONIAK (SALPETRIGSAURES) **466**
AMMONIAK (SAURES) **460**
AMMONIAK (SCHWEFELSAURES) **471**
AMMONIAK (SCHWEFLIGSAURES) **460**
AMMONIAK (ÜBERSCHWEFELSAURES) **468**
AMMONIAK (WEINSAURES) **473**
AMMONIAKFLÜSSIGKEIT **660**
AMMONIAKGAS **453**
AMMONIAKSALPETER **465**
AMMONIAKSODA **455**
AMMONIAKWASSER **456**
AMMONIUMAZETAT **458**
AMMONIUMBIKARBONAT **459**
AMMONIUMBISULFIT **460**
AMMONIUMCHLORID **462**
AMMONIUMFLUORID **463**
AMMONIUMHYDROSULFID **464**
AMMONIUMKARBONAT **461**
AMMONIUMNITRAT **465**
AMMONIUMNITRIT **466**
AMMONIUMOXALAT **467**
AMMONIUMPERSULFAT **468**
AMMONIUMPHOSPHAT **469**
AMMONIUMSULFAT **471**
AMMONIUMSULFHYDRAT **464**
AMMONIUMSULFID **472**
AMMONIUMTARTRAT **473**
AMMONIUMZINNCHLORID **470**
AMORPH **475**
AMORPHER PHOSPHOR **10334**
AMPERE **479**
AMPEREMETER **452**
AMPEREMINUTE **482**

AMPERESEKUNDE 483
AMPERESTUNDE 481
AMPEREWINDUNG 480
AMPEREZAHL 478
AMPHOTER 484
AMPLITUDE 486
AMYLALKOHOL 488
AMYLAZETAT 487
AMYLOXYDHYDRAT 488
ANAEROB 489
ANALOG 490
ANALYSATOR 492
ANALYSE 493
ANALYSE (CHEMISCHE) 2293
ANALYSE (ELEKTROLYTISCHE) 4570
ANALYSE (KOLORIMETRISCHE) 2739
ANALYSE (MAGNETISCHE) 7894
ANALYSE (QUALITATIVE) 10062
ANALYSE (QUANTITATIVE) 10064
ANALYSE (SELEKTIVE THERMISCHE) 3919
ANALYSE AUF NASSEM WEGE 13800
ANALYSE AUF TROCKENEM WEGE 4341
ANALYSENWAAGE 2294
ANALYSIEREN 491
ANALYTISCH 494
ANASTIGMAT 497
ANBAU 585
ANBRUCH 6834
ÄNDERUNG (ALLMÄHLICHE DER TEMPERATUR) 6024
ÄNDERUNG (PLÖTZLICHE) DER TEMPERATUR 12437
ÄNDERUNG DER GESCHWIDIGKEIT 6024
ANDREISSSCHABLONE 8016
ANEMOMETER 503
ANEROID BAROMETER 504
ANFANGSDRUCK 6929
ANFANGSGESCHWINDIGKEIT 6933
ANFANGSKRIECHEN 6928
ANFANGSLAGE 12126
ANFANGSPUNKT DER KOORDINATEN 8868
ANFANGSSTELLUNG 12126
ANFANGSTEMPERATUR 6931
ANFANGSWERT 6932
ANFANGSZUSTAND 6930
ANFEUCHTEN 8348
ANFEUCHTEN 8347
ANFEUERN (EINEN KESSEL) 5236
ANFEUERN EINES KESSELS 5263
ANFRESSEN 3182
ANFRESSUNG 5778
ANFRESSUNG 3183
ANFÜHREN 10113

ANGEL 9419
ANGEL EINES WERKZEUGS 12614
ANGENÄHERTER WERT 653
ANGESCHRIEBENER KREIS 4834
ANGETRIEBENE SCHEIBE 4298
ANGREIFEN 647
ANGREIFEN 3182
ANGREIFLÖCHER 6264
ANGRENZEND 181
ANGRIFF 813
ANGRIFF (INTERDENDRITISCHER) 7031
ANGRIFF EINER KRAFT 647
ANGRIFFSPUNKT 9561
ANGSTRÖM 536
ANGUSS 10845
ANGUSS 12004
ANHAFTEN 8042
ANHALTEN (EINE MASCHINE) 12280
ANHALTEN EINER MASCHINE 12286
ANHALTSPUNKTE 12125
ANHÄNGER 13102
ANHÄNGEVORRICHTUNGEN FÜR WAGEN 4088
ANHEIZEN 5236
ANHEIZEN EINES KESSELS 5263
ANHYDRID 548
ANHYDRIT 549
ANILIN 552
ANILINÖL 553
ANION 556
ANISOTROP 558
ANISOTROPIE 559
ANKER 5590
ANKER 500
ANKER EINER GLEICHSTROMMASCHINE 707
ANKER EINES MAGNETEN 710
ANKERBLECH 708
ANKERBOLZEN 5590
ANKERDRAHT 6187
ANKERPLATTE 13621
ANKERPLATTE (IM FUNDAMENT) 502
ANKERPLATZ 8390
ANKERROSETTE 13621
ANKERSCHNITT 3160
ANKERSCHRAUBE 5590
ANKERSCHRAUBE 501
ANKERSEILE 6186
ANKERUNG 499
ANKERWICKELMASCHINE 709
ANKERZUGSEILE 12919
ANKERZUGSTANGE 12919
ANKOMMENDER STROM 6844

## ANK

756

ANKÖRNEN 8011
ANKÖRNER 2172
ANKREIS 4834
ANLAGE (ELEKTRISCHE) 4542
ANLAGEFLÄCHE 5058
ANLAGEKOSTEN 9858
ANLAGEN 9461
ANLASS 12731
ANLASSEN 12733
ANLASSEN 12717
ANLASSEN (DEN STAHL) 12719
ANLASSEN (EINE MASCHINE) 12114
ANLASSEN (EINER MASCHINE) 12130
ANLASSER 12116
ANLASSER 3310
ANLASSER 9336
ANLASSER (ELEKTR.) 8418
ANLASSFARBE 12732
ANLASSHÄRTE 10520
ANLASSHEBEL 12120
ANLASSMASCHINE 1018
ANLASSMOTOR 12121
ANLASSPRÖDIGKEIT 1634
ANLASSSCHALTER 12117
ANLASSVENTIL 12131
ANLASSVORRICHTUNG 12119
ANLASSWIDERSTAND 12128
ANLAUF 12118
ANLAUF (STOSSFREIER) 11685
ANLAUF EINER MASCHINE 12122
ANLAUF EINER WELLE 11384
ANLAUFEN 12685
ANLAUFEN (EINER MASCHINE) 12122
ANLAUFEN (MASCHINE) 12113
ANLAUFEN LASSEN (EINE MASCHINE) 12114
ANLAUFFARBE 12732
ANLAUFPERIODE 12123
ANLAUFWIDERSTAND 12128
ANLEGEMASSSTAB 4135
ANLENKBOLZEN 13986
ANLIEGEND 181
ANLÜFTHEBEL 7553
ANMACHEN (MÖRTELZEMENT) 12718
ANMELDUNGSDATUM EINER ERFINDUNG 3616
ANNÄHERUNGSRECHNUNG 652
ANODE 590
ANODE 602
ANODE (UNLÖSLICHE) 598
ANODENBEIZUNG 601
ANODENBRENNFLECK 591
ANODENEFFEKT 596

ANODENFALL 595
ANODENFLÜSSIGKEIT 606
ANODENKUPFER 593
ANODENPOLARISATION 604
ANODENRÜCKSTAND 600
ANODENSCHLAMM 600
ANODENSTRAHLUNG 9660
ANODENWIRKUNGSGRAD 597
ANODISCH 603
ANOLYT 606
ANORDNUNG 4056
ANORGANISCHER STOFF 6957
ANPASSEN 5276
ANPRALL DES VENTILS 6224
ANREICHERN 2882
ANREICHERN (SICH) 1122
ANREICHERUNG 2886
ANREISSEN 8010
ANREISSEN 8017
ANREISSER 8013
ANREISSNADEL 11068
ANREISSPLATTE 12516
ANREISSSPITZE 11068
ANRISS 6833
ANRISS 5411
ANRISS 6834
ANRÜHREN (MÖRTELZEMENT) 12718
ANSÄTZE 7407
ANSATZFEILE 10878
ANSATZROHR 196
ANSÄUERN 133
ANSAUG-ROHR 6945
ANSAUGEN 12427
ANSAUGEN 12428
ANSAUGLEITUNG 7007
ANSAUGUNG 12428
ANSCHAFFUNGSKOSTEN 9858
ANSCHLAG 2485
ANSCHLAG 12278
ANSCHLAG EINES HOBELS 5093
ANSCHLAGBOLZEN 13214
ANSCHLAGVORRICHTUNG 12278
ANSCHLAGWINKEL 13245
ANSCHLIESSEN (ELEKTR.) 2955
ANSCHLIESSEN (ELEKTR.) 2958
ANSCHLUSS 5280
ANSCHLUSS (ELEKTR.) 2966
ANSCHLUSSGLEIS 13966
ANSCHLUSSKLEMME 1254
ANSCHLUSSMASSE 2793
ANSCHLUSSPOL 12763

ANSCHLUSSROHR **2960**
ANSCHLUSSSTUTZEN **1557**
ANSCHMIEGUNGSWINKEL **517**
ANSCHNITTSYSTEM **5870**
ANSCHRAUBEN **11065**
ANSCHRAUBEN **11022**
ANSCHÜTTEN **971**
ANSETZEN **1621**
ANSETZEN (EINE LÖSUNG) **9788**
ANSETZEN EINER LÖSUNG **9785**
ANSETZEN VON SCHMUTZ **2510**
ANSICHT **13567**
ANSICHT (EXPLODIERTE) **4934**
ANSTÄHLEN **12205**
ANSTÄHLEN **12206**
ANSTAUUNG **10182**
ANSTELLEN EINES WERKZEUGES **1621**
ANSTELLUNGSWINKEL **2484**
ANSTIEG **757**
ANSTIEG (MECH.) **10611**
ANSTOSS **7327**
ANSTOSSEND **181**
ANSTREICHEN **12529**
ANSTREICHEN **9018**
ANSTREICHEN **9014**
ANSTRICH **9013**
ANSTRICH **9018**
ANSTRICHFARBE **9015**
ANSTRICHGONDEL **9017**
ANSTRICHMÄNGEL **9021**
ANSTRICHMITTEL **2589**
ANTHRAZEN **607**
ANTHRAZENÖL **608**
ANTHRAZIT **609**
ANTIFRIKTIONSMETALL **619**
ANTIFRIKTIONSWIRKUNG **617**
ANTIKATHODE **12682**
ANTIKATHODE **611**
ANTILOGARITHMUS **620**
ANTIMAGNETISCH **614**
ANTIMON **623**
ANTIMONBLEI **6276**
ANTIMONBLEI **621**
ANTIMONBUTTER **626**
ANTIMONCHLORÜR **626**
ANTIMONGLANZ **622**
ANTIMONIT **622**
ANTIMONPENTACHLORID **624**
ANTIMONPENTASULFID **625**
ANTIMONREGULUS **10423**
ANTIMONSULFÜR **627**

ANTIMONSUPERCHLORID **624**
ANTIMONTRICHLORID **626**
ANTIMONTRISULFID **627**
ANTISEPTIKUM **629**
ANTISEPTISCH **628**
ANTISEPTISCHES MITTEL **629**
ANTREIBEN **4289**
ANTREIBEN **4297**
ANTRIEB **4303**
ANTRIEB **4297**
ANTRIEB (ELEKTRISCHER) **4503**
ANTRIEB (HYDRAULISCHER) **6683**
ANTRIEB (KRAFTSCHLÜSSIGER) **8642**
ANTRIEB (MASCHINELLER) **9734**
ANTRIEB (MECHANISCHER) **9734**
ANTRIEB (ZWANGSLÄUFIGER) **9654**
ANTRIEB EINER KRAFT **6809**
ANTRIEB MIT DRUCKLUFT **2842**
ANTRIEB VON HAND **6233**
ANTRIEBART **8217**
ANTRIEBMACHINE **9859**
ANTRIEBMECHANISMUS **4309**
ANTRIEBSCHEIBE **4313**
ANTRIEBSCHRAUBE **11041**
ANTRIEBSEIL **4314**
ANTRIEBSELEMENTE **13126**
ANTRIEBSPINDEL **4317**
ANTRIEBSWELLE **4296**
ANTRIEBVORRICHTUNG **4309**
ANTRIEBWELLE **4315**
ANWÄRMBRENNER **6399**
ANWÄRMBRENNER **6391**
ANWÄRMEN **6260**
ANWÄRMER **6385**
ANWÄRMHITZE (KURZE) **5362**
ANWEISUNG **6991**
ANZAPFUNGSTANK **4227**
ANZEICHNEN **8015**
ANZEICHNEN **8008**
ANZEIGE **10253**
ANZEIGE (DIGITALE) **8696**
ANZEIGEBEREICH EINES INSTRUMENTS **10201**
ANZEIGEEINRICHTUNG **12715**
ANZEIGEVORRICHTUNG **13153**
ANZIEHEN (DIE STOPFBÜCHSE) **12926**
ANZIEHEN (EINE SCHRAUBE) **12925**
ANZIEHEN (EINEN KEIL) **12924**
ANZIEHEN (ZEMENT) **11214**
ANZIEHEN EINES KEILES **12928**
ANZIEHUNG **815**
ANZIEHUNG (MAGNETISCHE) **7895**

# ANZ

758

ANZIEHUNG (MOLEKULARE) 8359
ANZIEHUNGSKRAFT 5529
ANZUG 12654
ANZUG 4196
ANZUG EINES KEILES 12928
ANZUGMOMENT 12129
ANZUGSDREHMOMENT 12931
ANZÜNDEN 6757
APERIODISCH 634
APERIODIZITÄT 637
APFELSINEN(SCHALEN-)EFFEKT 6008
APFELSINEN-(SCHALEN-)EFFEKT 9134
APLANAT 639
APOCHROMATISCH 640
APPARAT 641
APPARAT (PHOTOGRAPHISCHER) 9264
APPELSINENSCHALENEFFEKT 8851
APSPERRSCHIEBER MIT AUSSENLIEBGENDEM
  SPINDELGEWINDE 8914
APT-PROGRAMMIERSPRACHE 656
AQUA FORTIS 8580
ÄQUIVALENT (CHEMISCHES) 2308
ÄQUIVALENT (ELEKTROCHEMISCHES) 4571
ÄQUIVALENTE LEITFÄHIGKEIT 4797
ÄQUIVALENTE WIDERSTANDSFÄHIGKEIT 4798
ÄQUIVALENTGEWICHT 2308
ARÄOMETER 6722
ARBEIT 4747
ARBEIT 13936
ARBEIT 13961
ARBEIT 7229
ARBEIT (ABGEGEBENE) 13940
ARBEIT (GELEISTETE) 13940
ARBEIT (INDIZIERTE) 6876
ARBEIT (INNERE) 7081
ARBEIT (MECHANISCHE) 8117
ARBEIT (NUTZBARE) 13428
ARBEITEN (SELBSTTÄTIGES) 837
ARBEITER 13960
ARBEITER (UNGELERNTER) 13398
ARBEITERSCHAFT 13962
ARBEITSABLAUF (SELBSTTÄTIGER) 839
ARBEITSAUFWAND 2876
ARBEITSBREITE 7867
ARBEITSDIAGRAMM 6881
ARBEITSDRUCK 4459
ARBEITSEINHEIT 13379
ARBEITSERSPARNIS 10947
ARBEITSFORTSCHRITT 9905
ARBEITSGANG 3536
ARBEITSGANG 9096

ARBEITSGANG 2222
ARBEITSGERÜST 10965
ARBEITSGEWINN 8094
ARBEITSKOSTEN 7346
ARBEITSLEHRE 13967
ARBEITSLEHRE 13955
ARBEITSLEISTE 5007
ARBEITSLEISTUNG 14010
ARBEITSLEISTUNG 9730
ARBEITSLOHN 13613
ARBEITSMASCHINE 7839
ARBEITSMETHODE 8220
ARBEITSPAUSE 7100
ARBEITSPLATZ 8839
ARBEITSPROZESS 9887
ARBEITSRAD 13128
ARBEITSRAUM 13943
ARBEITSSTAND 8839
ARBEITSSTÜCK 9293
ARBEITTAKT 12387
ARBEITTEILUNG 12410
ARBEITSTEMPERATUR 8836
ARBEITSVERFAHREN 8220
ARBEITSVERLUST 7765
ARBEITSVERMÖGEN 4745
ARBEITSVERMÖGEN (MECHANISCHES) 8101
ARBEITSVERTEILUNG 13939
ARBEITSVORGANG 9887
ARBEITSWEISE 8220
ARBEITSZEICHNUNG 11363
ARBEITSZEIT 13410
ARBEITSZYLINDER 13954
ARBEITSZYLINDER 10188
ARCHITEKT 691
ARCHITEKTUR 2442
ARGENTAN 5932
ARGENTAN 8569
ARGILLIT 700
ARGON 701
ARITHMETIK 702
ARM (EINER RIEMENSCHEIBE) 705
ARM (EINES SCHWUNGRADES) 705
ARMABSTAND 6596
ARMATUR 5283
ARMATUR EINES KABELS 715
ARMATUREN 5283
ARMAUSWURF 4471
ARMCO-LISEN 711
ARMFEILE 10774
ARRETIERUNG 7705
ARSEN 721

ARSENDISULFID **10262**
ARSENIAT **720**
ARSENID **726**
ARSENIGS ÄUREANHYDRID **727**
ARSENIGSÄURESALZ **729**
ARSENIK (GELBES) **728**
ARSENIK (WEISSER) **727**
ARSENIT **729**
ARSENKUPFER **725**
ARSENMETALL **726**
ARSENPENTOXYD **723**
ARSENSÄURE **722**
ARSENSÄUREANHYDRID **723**
ARSENSÄURESALZ **720**
ARSENSULFÜR **10262**
ARSENSUPERSULFÜR **728**
ARSENTRICHLORID **724**
ARSENTRIOXYD **727**
ARSENTRISULFID **728**
ARSENWASSERSTOFF **730**
ASBEST **746**
ASBEST **755**
ASBESTFILZ **750**
ASBESTGEWEBE **748**
ASBESTPAPIER **752**
ASBESTPAPPE **747**
ASBESTRING **753**
ASBESTSCHNUR **749**
ASBESTSTREIFEN **754**
ASBESTZOPF **751**
ASCHE **2397**
ASCHE **760**
ASCHE (KLEINE) **11904**
ASCHEFREI **5636**
ASCHENFALL **759**
ASCHENGEHALT **758**
ASCHENKÜHLER **2398**
ASCHENRAUM **759**
ASPHALT **768**
ASPHALT-GOUDRON **1280**
ASPHALT-TEER **1280**
ASPHALTFILZ **765**
ASPHALTIEREN **763**
ASPHALTIEREN **767**
ASPHALTIERTES ROHR **766**
ASPHALTLACK **1283**
ASPHALTMASTIX **764**
ASPHALTROHR **6803**
ASPHALTSTEINPULVER **9723**
ASPIRATIONSVENTILATION **13450**
ASPIRATOR **769**

AST **1555**
ASTATISCH **774**
ASTERISMUS **776**
ASTROIDE **5602**
ASYMMETRIE **779**
ASYMMETRISCH **778**
ASYMPTOTE **780**
ASYMPTOTISCH **781**
ASYNCHRON **784**
ASYNCHRONISMUS **782**
ASYNCHRONMOTOR **783**
ÄTHAN **4848**
ÄTHANDISÄURE **8969**
ÄTHER **8853**
ATHERMAN **786**
ÄTHERSCHWINGUNGEN **13560**
ÄTHYLALDEHYD **84**
ÄTHYLALKOHOL **313**
ÄTHYLÄTHER **8853**
ÄTHYLAZETAT **88**
ÄTHYLCHLORID **4849**
ÄTHYLEN **4851**
ÄTHYLNITRAT **4850**
ÄTHYLWASSERSTOFF **4848**
ATLASGLANZ **11455**
ATMOSPHÄRE **787**
ATMOSPHÄRE (MASSEINHEIT) **788**
ATMOSPHÄRE (PRÄPARIERTE) **789**
ATMOSPHÄRE (VERDÜNNTE) **13441**
ATMOSPHÄRILIEN **793**
ATMUNGSVERLUST **1594**
ATOM **800**
ATOMGEWICHT **807**
ATOMTHEORIE **805**
ATOMVOLUMEN **806**
ATOMWÄRME **802**
ATOMZAHL **803**
ÄTZALKALISCHE LÖSUNG **9671**
ÄTZAMMONIAK **660**
ÄTZBARYT **1000**
ÄTZE **657**
ÄTZEN **4839**
ÄTZEN **4846**
ÄTZEN (KATHODISCHES) **2110**
ÄTZEND **3196**
ÄTZFIGUR **4845**
ÄTZFIGUREN **4842**
ÄTZFLÜSSIGKEIT **4847**
ÄTZGRÜBCHEN **9416**
ÄTZKALI **9687**
ÄTZKALILAUGE **9671**

# ATZ

ÄTZKALK **1854**
ÄTZLAUGE **2119**
ÄTZMITTEL **3197**
ÄTZMITTEL **4847**
ÄTZMITTEL **4844**
ÄTZNATRON **11722**
ÄTZNATRONLAUGE **2120**
ÄTZRISSE **4841**
ÄTZUNG **4846**
ÄTZUNG HERVORTRETENDE BÄNDER (DURCH) **4840**
AUER METALL **817**
AUFBAU **3794**
AUFBAU **4813**
AUFBAU (CHEMISCHER) **2301**
AUFBAUSCHNEIDE **1707**
AUFBEREITETE ÖLE **8996**
AUFBEREITUNG VON ERZEN **8861**
AUFBLÄHEN **1331**
AUFBRAUSEN **4461**
AUFBRECHEN DER SCHLACKENSCHICHT **5354**
AUFBRINGEMITTEL **5490**
AUFBRINGEN EINER SCHUTZSCHICHT **6792**
AUFDORNEN (EIN ROHR) **4903**
AUFDORNPROBE **10010**
AUFFANGSCHALE **4283**
AUFFLAMMEN **5359**
AUFGENIETETER FLANSCH **10638**
AUFGENOMMENE LEISTUNG **4747**
AUFGESCHWEISSTER BUND **13771**
AUFGEWANDTE ENERGIE **4747**
AUFHÄNGEHAKEN **12527**
AUFHÄNGEPUNKT **9568**
AUFHÄNGUNG **12526**
AUFHÄNGUNG (BIFILARE) **1240**
AUFHÄNGUNG (KARDANISCHE) **1998**
AUFHEBEN (SICH) **1076**
AUFKEILEN **7279**
AUFKEILWINKEL **529**
AUFKLAPPBARER DECKEL **6510**
AUFKOHLEN **1987**
AUFKOHLUNG **1953**
AUFKOHLUNG (SELEKTIVE) **11143**
AUFKOHLUNGSMITTEL **1988**
AUFKOHLUNGSMITTEL **2024**
AUFLAGE (MEHRSCHICHT-ELEKTROLYTISCHE) **2821**
AUFLAGEFLÄCHE **1115**
AUFLAGEFLÄCHE **1101**
AUFLAGEPRESSUNG **1110**
AUFLAGER **1118**
AUFLAGERDRUCK **1110**
AUFLAGERFLÄCHE EINES ZAPFENS **1116**

AUFLAGERPLATTE (BAUW.) **1127**
AUFLAST **7679**
AUFLEGEN DES RIEMENS **1160**
AUFLOCKERN **3999**
AUFLOCKERN (DEN SAND) **208**
AUFLOCKERUNG **4000**
AUFLÖSEN (CHEM.) **4059**
AUFLÖSEN (MATH.) **11813**
AUFLÖSEN (SICH) (CHEM.) **4061**
AUFLÖSUNG **11811**
AUFLÖSUNG **4060**
AUFLÖSUNG **10504**
AUFLÖSUNG (ELEKTROLYSTISCHE) **4581**
AUFLÖSUNGSVERMÖGEN **4062**
AUFMASS **1695**
AUFNAHME **4747**
AUFNAHME **4944**
AUFNAHMEDORN **7964**
AUFNAHMEFÄHIGKEIT **1917**
AUFNEHMEN **37**
AUFNEHMEN (EINE KRAFT) **12601**
AUFPLATZEN EINES ROHRES **1768**
AUFPRALLAFLÄCHE **12683**
AUFPRALLKORROSION **6799**
AUFPRESSEN (EIN RAD) **4222**
AUFPRESSEN (EINE RIEMENSCHEIBE) **4222**
AUFQUELLEN **12542**
AUFQUELLUNG **8440**
AUFRAUHEN **10783**
AUFRECHT **13551**
AUFREIBEN DER NIETLÖCHER **1638**
AUFREIBER **1636**
AUFREISSEN **10859**
AUFREISSEN (DIE NIETL:OCHER) **1635**
AUFRISS **4659**
AUFROLLEN **2650**
AUFSATZ **1454**
AUFSATZ FÜR SCHWIMMDACH **11331**
AUFSATZBUCHSE **14016**
AUFSATZRING **7392**
AUFSATZSPITZE **3006**
AUFSAUGEFÄHIGKEIT **42**
AUFSAUGEN **44**
AUFSAUGEN **37**
AUFSAUGUNG **44**
AUFSCHLAG **12375**
AUFSCHLIESSEN **3999**
AUFSCHLIESSUNG **4000**
AUFSCHRAUBEN **11037**
AUFSCHRAUBEN **11067**
AUFSCHRAUBEN **13396**

AUS

AUFSCHRAUBEN **13395**
AUFSCHRUMPFEN **11390**
AUFSCHRUMPFEN **11398**
AUFSEHER **8958**
AUFSICHT **12481**
AUFSICHTSBILD **13037**
AUFSPANNPLATTE **9499**
AUFSPANNVORRICHTUNG **5301**
AUFSPEICHERN **12294**
AUFSPEICHERN **12299**
AUFSPEICHERUNG VON ENERGIE **12290**
AUFSPEICHREUNG VON VÄRME **12291**
AUFSTAPELN (HOLZ) **9307**
AUFSTAPELN DES HOLZES **9309**
AUFSTECKFRÄSER **663**
AUFSTECKREIBAHLE **11336**
AUFSTECKSCHLÜSSEL **509**
AUFSTELLEN **4805**
AUFSTELLER **4816**
AUFSTELLUNG **4808**
AUFSTELLUNGSORT **9423**
AUFTRAG **2587**
AUFTRAGEN EINER SCHUTZSCHICHT **6792**
AUFTRAGSCHWEISSUNG **13762**
AUFTRAGSMETALL **3775**
AUFTRAGSPROZESS **1696**
AUFTRAGSSCHWEISSZUSATZ **8952**
AUFTREIBEN (EIN ROHR) **4903**
AUFTREIBEPROBE **4911**
AUFTRIEB **1742**
AUFWACHSEN **12543**
AUFWALLEN **4461**
AUFWÄRTSSCHWEISSUNG **13419**
AUFWÄRTSTRANSFORMATOR **12245**
AUFWEITEN **5356**
AUFWEITEN (EIN ROHR) **4903**
AUFWEITEPROBE **4911**
AUFWEITUNG **1723**
AUFWICKELN **13862**
AUFWICKELN **13853**
AUFWINDEN **6517**
AUFWINDEN **13853**
AUFWINDEN **6553**
AUFWINDEN **13862**
AUFWÖLBUNG **1723**
AUFWULSTUNG **1723**
AUFZEICHNEN **9519**
AUFZEICHNEN **10288**
AUFZEICHNEN EINES DIAGRAMMES **9521**
AUFZIEHEN **7549**
AUFZIEHEN (EIN RAD) **4222**

AUFZIEHEN (EINE RIEMENSCHEIBE) **4222**
AUFZUG **9101**
AUFZUG **6007**
AUFZUGSEIL **7546**
AUGE **4980**
AUGE (ANGEGOSSENES) **7817**
AUGE EINES HAMMERS **4975**
AUGENLAGER **11788**
AUGENSTAB (GESCHMIEDETER) **5551**
AUGIT **819**
AUGITSYENIT **820**
AURICHLORID **821**
AURIPIGMENT **728**
AUROCHLORID **823**
AUS DEM GROBEN **10786**
AUSBALANCIEREN **930**
AUSBALANCIERUNG **942**
AUSBAUCHEN (SICH) **1721**
AUSBAUCHUNG **1723**
AUSBAUCHUNG **1720**
AUSBESSERN **10460**
AUSBESSERUNG **10459**
AUSBESSERUNGSKOSTEN **3208**
AUSBEULEN **5405**
AUSBEULUNG **1720**
AUSBLASEHAHN **1357**
AUSBLASEVENTIL **1358**
AUSBLÜHUNG **4464**
AUSBLUTEN **1321**
AUSBOHREN **1468**
AUSBOHREN **1462**
AUSBOHRMASCHINE **1471**
AUSBREITEPROBE **5409**
AUSDEHNEN (SICH) **4902**
AUSDEHNUNG **4679**
AUSDEHNUNG (LINEAIRE) **7612**
AUSDEHNUNG (RÄUMLICHE) **13603**
AUSDEHNUNG DURCH WÄRME **4948**
AUSDEHNUNG VON DAMPF ODER GAS **4921**
AUSDEHNUNGSFÄHIG **3948**
AUSDEHNUNGSFÄHIGKEIT **3947**
AUSDEHNUNGSFUGE **4918**
AUSDEHNUNGSHUB **2775**
AUSDEHNUNGSKOEFFIZIENT **2636**
AUSDEHNUNGSKOEFFIZIENT **4914**
AUSDEHNUNGSKUPPLUNG **4915**
AUSDEHNUNGSKUPPLUNG **11617**
AUSDEHNUNGSSTÜCK **4922**
AUSDEHNUNGSZAHL **2628**
AUSDREHEN **1473**
AUSDREHEN **1466**

**AUS** 762

AUSDREHWINKEL 3781
AUSEINANDERLAUFEN 4091
AUSEINANDERLAUFEND 4093
AUSEINANDERNEHMBAR 4027
AUSEINANDERNEHMEN 12604
AUSEINANDERNEHMEN 12600
AUSFÄLLBAR 9757
AUSFÄLLEN 9761
AUSFÄLLEN 9760
AUSFLOCKUNG 5441
AUSFLUSS 4466
AUSFLUSSDÜSE 196
AUSFLUSSEXPONENT 4940
AUSFLUSSGESCHWINDIGKEIT 8903
AUSFLUSSMENGE 4023
AUSFLUSSMÜNDUNG 8902
AUSFLUSSÖFFNUNG 8902
AUSFLUSSQUERSCHNITT 4020
AUSFLUSSSTUTZEN 196
AUSFLUSSSTUTZEN (SICH ERWEITERNDER) 4096
AUSFLUSSSTUTZEN (SICH VERENGERNDER) 3066
AUSFLUSSZAHL 2626
AUSFÜHRUNG 13961
AUSFÜHRUNGSFORM 13320
AUSFÜHRUNGSZEICHNUNG 4984
AÜSFÜHRUNGSZEICHNUNG 3812
AUSFÜLLMASSE 5164
AUSFÜTTERN 7598
AUSFÜTTERN 7623
AUSFÜTTERUNG 7623
AUSGANG 8900
AUSGANGS-ROHRSTUTZEN 4705
AUSGANGSBLOCK 1834
AUSGANGSLAGE 12126
AUSGANGSPUNKT EINER BEWEGUNG 12124
AUSGANGSSTOFF 9852
AUSGANGSTEMPERATUR 6931
AUSGEBAUCHT 1722
AUSGELAUFENES LAGER 10837
AUSGESCHMOLZENES 10837
AUSGEZACKT 6862
AUSGLEICH 2809
AUSGLEICH 929
AUSGLEICHEN 930
AUSGLEICHEN 2807
AUSGLEICHFUGE 4918
AUSGLEICHGEWICHT 3251
AUSGLEICHOFEN 11698
AUSGLEICHROHR 4913
AUSGLEICHSKEGELRAD 3918
AUSGLEICHUNG 2809

AUSGLEICHUNG 942
AUSGLEICHZYLINDER 939
AUSGLEICHZYLINDER 938
AUSGLÜHEN 581
AUSGLÜHEN 562
AUSGLÜHEN (SELEKTIVES) 11142
AUSGLÜHEN (VOLLSTÄNDIGES) 576
AUSHÄRTEN 3483
AUSHÄRTUNG 6291
AUSHÄRTUNG 223
AUSHAUEN 2347
AUSHAUMASCHINE 8553
AUSHEBEBAND 5772
AUSHILFSMASCHINE 12070
AUSKEHLEN 10167
AUSKEHLUNG 5483
AUSKLEIDEN 7623
AUSKLEIDEN 7598
AUSKLEIDUNG 7623
AUSKLINKEN 4031
AUSKLINKEN 4030
AUSKLINKEN 3107
AUSKLINKMASCHINE 8677
AUSKRAGUNG 9917
AUSKRATZEN 4799
AUSKUPPELN 10034
AUSKUPPELN 12898
AUSKUPPLUNG 12898
AUSLADUNG 9917
AUSLADUNG 9913
AUSLADUNGSTIEFE 3783
AUSLANDSPATENT 5540
AUSLASS 4890
AUSLASSKOHLENSTOFF 1965
AUSLASSÖFFNUNG 8902
AUSLASSSCHLITZ 4895
AUSLASSSTUTZEN 8901
AUSLASSVENTIL 4899
AUSLASTUNGSGRAD 4395
AUSLAUFBLECH 10842
AUSLAUFHAHN 1357
AUSLAUFROLLGANG 10838
AUSLAUFVENTIL 1235
AUSLAUGEFLÜSSIGKEIT 4965
AUSLAUGEN 7677
AUSLAUGEN 7676
AUSLAUGER 4967
AUSLAUGUNG 7677
AUSLAUGUNG 7446
AUSLEEREN 7328
AUSLEERROST 7334

AUSLEGERARM 10128
AUSLEGERKRAN 7224
AUSLERGERLÄNGE 7225
AUSLÖSCHEBEL 10438
AUSLÖSEDAUMEN 10437
AUSLÖSEFINGER 10437
AUSLÖSER 2407
AUSLÖSUNGSKUPPLUNG 4032
AUSMASSE 3960
AUSMESSEN 8078
AUSNÜTZEN 13430
AUSNUTZEN (EINE ERFINDUNG) 13938
AUSNUTZUNG 13429
AUSNUTZUNG EINER ERFINDUNG 13948
AUSPRESSEN 12039
AUSPUFF 4890
AUSPUFFDAMPFMASCHINE 8627
AUSPUFFGAS 4891
AUSPUFFGERÄUSCHDÄMPFER 8448
AUSPUFFHUB 4898
AUSPUFFROHR 4894
AUSPUFFSAMMELROHR 4893
AUSPUFFTOPF 11431
AUSPUFFTOPF 8448
AUSPUFFVENTIL 797
AUSRADIEREN 4799
AUSRECHNEN 3795
AUSREIBER 1636
AUSRICHTEN 324
AUSRICHTEN 12319
AUSRICHTEN 323
AUSRICHTEN 12318
AUSRÜCKBARE KUPPLUNG 4033
AUSRÜCKEN 2548
AUSRÜCKEN 10034
AUSRÜCKEN 12898
AUSRÜCKHEBEL 4035
AUSRÜCKMUFFE 11599
AUSRÜCKUNG 4028
AUSRÜCKUNG 12898
AUSRÜCKVORRICHTUNG 4034
AUSRUNDUNG 6537
AUSRÜSTUNG 5283
AUSSCHALTEN 12559
AUSSCHALTEN 12898
AUSSCHALTEN 10034
AUSSCHALTEN (EINE ROHRLEITUNG) 11407
AUSSCHALTEN (ELEKTR.) 12554
AUSSCHALTER 2407
AUSSCHALTER (ELEKT.) 12553
AUSSCHALTUNG 12898

AUSSCHEIDEN (SICH) 9760
AUSSCHEIDUNG 9761
AUSSCHEIDUNGSHÄRTUNG 9762
AUSSCHLAG 486
AUSSCHLAGBILDUNG 11961
AUSSCHLAGEISEN 6545
AUSSCHLAGEN 9554
AUSSCHLAGEN 11251
AUSSCHLAGEN 7328
AUSSCHLAGPUNZE 6545
AUSSCHLAGROST 7334
AUSSCHLAGRÜTTLER 3153
AUSSCHLAGSTAHL 6545
AUSSCHLAGWINKEL 518
AUSSCHLEUDERN 6702
AUSSCHMELZMODELL 7116
AUSSCHNEIDEN 10012
AUSSCHNEIDEN 9998
AUSSCHNITT 11135
AUSSCHNITT 5866
AUSSCHUSS 3696
AUSSCHUSSWARE 3696
AUSSCHWIMMEN 5443
AUSSCHWIMMEN 5434
AUSSCHWITZUNG 12540
AUSSEN-RUNDSCHLEIF-MASCHINE 4953
AUSSEN-RUNDSCHLEIF-MASCHINE (SPITZENLOSE) 2155
AUSSENBELEUCHTUNG 8897
AUSSENDURCHMESSER 8913
AUSSENGETRIEBE 4956
AUSSENGEWINDE 4960
AUSSENGEWINDE 4961
AUSSENGEWINDE 7955
AUSSENGEWINDESCHNEIDEN 3512
AUSSENGEWINDESCHNEIDMASCHINE 12869
AUSSENHANDELSBILANZ 13099
AUSSENLEHRE 5091
AUSSENLEHRE 4955
AUSSENLUFT 450
AUSSENMASSE 8922
AUSSENPUTZ 3264
AUSSENRING EINES KUGELLAGERS 8898
AUSSENSCHLIFF 4957
AUSSENSEITE 8911
AUSSENSTRÄHLER 4952
AUSSENTASTER 8912
AUSSENVERZAHNUNG 4959
AUSSENWINKEL 4950
AUSSER BETRIEB SETZEN (EINE MASCHINE) 11406
AUSSER EINGRIFF 8892
AUSSERACHSIG 8893

# AUS

**764**

AUSSERBETRIEBSETZUNG EINER MASCHINE **11410**
ÄUSSERE ARBEIT **4962**
ÄUSSERE ERREGUNG **11190**
ÄUSSERE KRAFT **4954**
ÄUSSERER RING **8898**
AUSSERMITTIG **4424**
AUSSETZEN DER SÄGEZÄHNE **10958**
AUSSONDERUNG **11139**
AUSSPARUNG **8831**
AUSSPARUNG **10279**
AUSSTANZEN **10006**
AUSSTEIFEN **12150**
AUSSTELLFENSTER **13531**
AUSSTOSSEN **4468**
AUSSTOSSFÄHIGKEIT **2718**
AUSSTRAHLEN **4703**
AUSSTRAHLUNG **10143**
AUSSTRAHLUNGSSTÄRKE **7019**
AUSSTRAHLUNGSVERMÖGEN **4701**
AUSSTRÖMEN **4832**
AUSSTRÖMEN VON DAMPF **4833**
AUSSTRÖMLINIE **4892**
AUSSTRÖMUNG **4465**
AUSSTRÖMUNGSENERGIE **4748**
AUSTAUSCH EINES MASCHINENTEILS **10464**
AUSTAUSCHBAR **7026**
AUSTAUSCHBARKEIT **7025**
AUSTAUSCHBARKEIT **7028**
AUSTAUSCHEN **10463**
AUSTEMPERUNG **824**
AUSTENIT **825**
AUSTENITISIERUNG **827**
AUSTRAG **4202**
AUSTREIBEN (EINEN KEIL) **4295**
AUSTREIBEN EINES KEILS **4312**
AUSTRITTGESCHWINDIGKEIT **8903**
AUSTRITTKANTE **5515**
AUSTROCKNEN DES HOLZES **11095**
AUSWAHL **10916**
AUSWALZEN **10696**
AUSWALZEN **10665**
AUSWALZEN **10666**
AUSWALZEN **5215**
AUSWECHSELBAR **7026**
AUSWECHSELBARKEIT **7025**
AUSWECHSELN **10463**
AUSWECHSLUNG EINES MASCHINENTEILS **10464**
AUSWERFEN **4468**
AUSWERFER **4469**
AUSWERFER **9554**
AUSWERFER (PNEUMATISCHER) **271**

AUSWITTERUNG **4464**
AUSWUCHTEN **930**
AUSWUCHTMASCHINE **940**
AUSWUCHTMASCHINE **937**
AUSWUCHTUNG **942**
AUSWURFKEGEL **3928**
AUSZIEHEN (MIT TUSCHE) **6940**
AUSZIEHEN (ZU DRAHT) **4220**
AUSZIEHEN MIT TUSCHE **6942**
AUSZIEHTUSCHE **6871**
AUSZIEHVORRICHTUNG **4239**
AUSZIEHWINKEL **4197**
AUSZUG **4964**
AUTO **8411**
AUTOGEN-PRESS-SCHWEISSEN **8978**
AUTOGEN-SCHWEISSUNG **831**
AUTOGENE FORMGEBUNG **5318**
AUTOGENE OBERFLÄCHENHÄRTUNG **5315**
AUTOGENE RILLUNG **5822**
AUTOGENES BRENNSCHNEIDEN **8976**
AUTOGENSCHNEIDEN **3505**
AUTOGENSCHWEISSEN **13758**
AUTOGENSCHWEISSEN **8979**
AUTOGENSCHWEISSEN **835**
AUTOKLAV **829**
AUTOMAT **846**
AUTOMATENMESSING **5645**
AUTOMATENSCHWEISSEN **849**
AUTOMATENSTAHL **5639**
AUTOMATISCH **11148**
AUTOMOBIL **8411**
AUTOSTARTER **828**
AXIALDRUCK **4734**
AXIALFRÄSER **4446**
AXIALGEBLÄSE **9929**
AXIALKOMPONENTE **859**
AXIALKUGELLAGER **12900**
AXIALLAGER **12902**
AXIALSCHUB **4734**
AXIALTURBINE **862**
AXT **857**
AZETALDEHYD **84**
AZETAT **85**
AZETON **90**
AZETYLCHLORID **92**
AZETYLEN **93**
AZETYLEN-LUFTSCHWEISSEN **295**
AZETYLEN-SAUERSTOFF BRENNSCHNEIDEVERFAHREN **8977**
AZETYLENGASSCHWEISSUNG **96**
AZETYLENLAMPE **95**
AZETYLENSCHNEIDVERFAHREN **94**

| | |
|---|---|
| AZETYLZELLULOSE **91** | BANDSCHARNIER **12347** |
| AZETYLZELLULOSE **2132** | BANDSCHREIBER **12380** |
| AZIDIMETRIE **131** | BANDSEIL **5393** |
| AZURBLAU **13334** | BANDSPANNUNGSANZEIGER **976** |
| BACKEN EINES SCHRAUBENSCHLÜSSELS **7216** | BANDSPEKTRUM **5487** |
| BACKEN EINES SCHRAUBSTOCKS **13564** | BANDSTAHL **12216** |
| BACKENFUTTER EINES SCHRAUBSTOCKS **13563** | BANDSTAHL **902** |
| BACKSTEIN **1596** | BANDSTAHL (WARMGEWALZTER) **371** |
| BAD **1062** | BANDTRANSPORTEUR **1164** |
| BAD **3967** | BANK **1167** |
| BAD (ELEKTROLYTISCHES) **4588** | BANK (OPTISCHE) **9268** |
| BADSTROM **1064** | BANKAZINN **973** |
| BADZEMENTIEREN **7646** | BANKBOHRMASCHINE **1168** |
| BADZUSATZ **168** | BANKFORMUNG **1169** |
| BADZUSÄTZE **9506** | BANKHAMMER **6235** |
| BAGASSE **924** | BANKMEISSEL **2717** |
| BAGGER **4414** | BANKSCHRAUBSTOCK **1171** |
| BAHN **13104** | BÄR **11550** |
| BAHN (ABSCHÜSSIGE) **2395** | BARETTFEILE **1903** |
| BAHN EINES HAMMERS **4993** | BARIUM **992** |
| BAHNSTEUERUNG **3039** | BARIUM (KOHLENSAURES) **996** |
| BAINITE **925** | BARIUM (SCHWEFELSAURES) **1003** |
| BAJONETTVERSCHLUSS **1074** | BARIUMALUMINAT **994** |
| BALANCIEREN **935** | BARIUMAZETAT (ESSIGSAURES) **993** |
| BALATA **943** | BARIUMCHLORID **997** |
| BALATAHARZ **943** | BARIUMDIOXYD **998** |
| BALATARIEMEN **944** | BARIUMHYDROXYD **1000** |
| BALKEN (EINGEBAUTER) **7010** | BARIUMHYPEROXYD **998** |
| BALKEN (HÖLZERNER) **949** | BARIUMKARBID **995** |
| BALKENWAAGE **1095** | BARIUMKARBONAT **996** |
| BALKENWERK **5630** | BARIUMMONOXYD **1020** |
| BALLEN **945** | BARIUMNITRAT **1001** |
| BALLENKARREN **947** | BARIUMOXYDHYDRAT **1000** |
| BALLHAMMER **2232** | BARIUMPLATINZYANÜR **1002** |
| BALLIGDREHEN **13288** | BARIUMSULFAT **1003** |
| BALLIGDREHEN **13277** | BARIUMSULFID **1004** |
| BALLIGKEIT **1506** | BARIUMSUPEROXYD **998** |
| BALLIGKEIT **3396** | BARN **1006** |
| BALLON **1981** | BAROGRAPH **1007** |
| BAMBUSROHR **972** | BAROMETER **1008** |
| BAND **12641** | BAROMETERSTAND **6422** |
| BAND **974** | BAROMETRISCH **1009** |
| BANDBREMSE **5681** | BAROSKOP **1011** |
| BANDEISEN **6575** | BART **1764** |
| BÄNDER **980** | BARUIMFLUORID **999** |
| BANDKETTE **12058** | BARYT **993** |
| BANDKUPPKLUNG **7349** | BARYT **1020** |
| BANDMASS **8092** | BARYT (KAUSTISCHER) **1000** |
| BANDNIETUNG **1781** | BARYT (KOHLENSAURER) **13911** |
| BANDSÄGE **978** | BARYT (SALPETERSAURER) **1001** |
| BANDSÄGEMASCHINE **977** | BARYT (SCHWEFELSAURER) **1021** |

# BAR

766

BARYTHYDRAT **1000**
BARYTWASSER **1019**
BARYTWEISS **1003**
BASALT **1022**
BASALTTUFF **1023**
BASE **1026**
BASE (CHEM.) **1024**
BASIS (GEOM.) **1027**
BASIS EINES GEWINDES **1028**
BASIS EINES LOGARITHMUS **1033**
BASISCH **1042**
BASIZITÄT **1055**
BASIZITÄT **340**
BAST **1056**
BASTARDFEILE **1057**
BATTERIE **1066**
BATTERIE **4534**
BATTERIE (GALVANISCHE) **9845**
BATTERIEKASTEN **1067**
BATTERIESCHALTER **1068**
BAU **12395**
BAUART **13320**
BAUART **3794**
BAUBREITE **8926**
BAUBRONZE **692**
BAUCHSÄGE **3365**
BAUEN **1694**
BAUGERÜST **10965**
BAUGLIED **8145**
BAUGRUND **1699**
BAUHÖHE **8924**
BAUHOLZ **12937**
BAUINGENIEUR **2443**
BAUINGENIEURWESEN **2444**
BAULÄNGE **8925**
BAULÄNGE EINES KETTENGLIEDES **6978**
BAULEITER **5145**
BAUMATERIAL **8050**
BAUMETALLE (GEWÖHNLICHE) **2988**
BAUMWOLLE **3217**
BAUMWOLLRIEMEN **3218**
BAUMWOLLSAMENÖL **3222**
BAUMWOLLSEIL **3221**
BAUMWOLLZOPF **3220**
BAUSCHINGER-EFFEKT **1070**
BAUSTAHL **12392**
BAUSTAHL **12393**
BAUSTAHLBLECH **1109**
BAUSTEIN **1700**
BAUSTEINE **1697**
BAUSTELLENBARACKE **2987**

BAUSTELLENBUDE **11519**
BAUSTELLENLEITER **11520**
BAUSTELLENMONTAGE **8800**
BAUSTELLENSCHWEISSNAHT **5146**
BAUSTOFF **8050**
BAUTEIL (EINGEBAUTES) **1704**
BAUUNTERNEHMER **1698**
BAUWERK **12395**
BAUXIT **1071**
BAUZEICHNUNG **693**
BAYER-VERFAHREN **1073**
BEANSPRUCHEN (EINEN KÖRPER) **12323**
BEANSPRUCHT WERDEN (AUF DRUCK) **1075**
BEANSPRUCHT WERDEN (AUF ZUG) **1075**
BEANSPRUCHUNG **12331**
BEANSPRUCHUNG **12367**
BEANSPRUCHUNG **7679**
BEANSPRUCHUNG (DYNAMISCHE) **4398**
BEANSPRUCHUNG (KRITISCHE) **3351**
BEANSPRUCHUNG (MAKROSKOPISCHE) **7874**
BEANSPRUCHUNG (ZULÄSSIGE) **9215**
BEANSPRUCHUNG (ZULÄSSIGE) **10880**
BEANSPRUCHUNG (ZULÄSSIGE) **353**
BEANSPRUCHUNG AUF BIEGUNG **1191**
BEANSPRUCHUNG AUF DRUCK **2869**
BEANSPRUCHUNG AUF KNICKUNG **3339**
BEANSPRUCHUNG AUF SCHUB **11295**
BEANSPRUCHUNG AUF ZUG **12747**
BEARBEITBAR **13947**
BEARBEITBARKEIT **7838**
BEARBEITBARKEIT **13946**
BEARBEITEN **13937**
BEARBEITEN **13959**
BEARBEITEN MIT SANDSTRAHL **10921**
BEARBEITET **7861**
BEARBEITUNG **7864**
BEARBEITUNG **10786**
BEARBEITUNG **13959**
BEARBEITUNG (VOREINGESTELLTE) **9752**
BEARBEITUNG AUS DEM ROHEN **10786**
BEARBEITUNGSFÄHIG **13947**
BEARBEITUNGSFLANSCHE **13013**
BEARBEITUNGSSTUFE **7866**
BEARBEITUNGSZUGABE **7865**
BEARBEITUNGSZUGABE **358**
BEAUFSICHTIGEN **12474**
BEAUFSICHTIGUNG **12481**
BECHERGLAS **1092**
BECHERKABEL **1675**
BECHERKETTE **1675**
BECHERWERK **1676**

BECKEN DES ABSTELLTISCHES **11074**
BEDAMPFEN (METALLDAMPF) **13487**
BEDEUTUNG **8852**
BEDIENUNG **814**
BEDIENUNGSBÜHNE **5776**
BEDIENUNGSGANG **13616**
BEDIENUNGSTAFEL **3054**
BEDIENUNGSVORSCHRIFTEN **8835**
BEFEHL **2780**
BEFEHL **6991**
BEFESTIGEN **5041**
BEFESTIGUNG **5044**
BEFESTIGUNGSELEMENT **5042**
BEFESTIGUNGSKEIL **5211**
BEFESTIGUNGSSCHRAUBE **5043**
BEFESTIGUNGSWINKEL **3058**
BEFESTIGUNSFLACHEISEN **13029**
BEFEUCHTER **6664**
BEFÖRDERUNG **8106**
BEFÖRDERUNG **13140**
BEFÖRDERUNGSKOSTEN **3209**
BEGRENZUNGSKURVE EINES EXZENTERS **8906**
BEHÄLTER **12625**
BEHÄLTER **3010**
BEHÄLTER **12632**
BEHÄLTER **12631**
BEHÄLTER (TIEFGEZOGENER) **4982**
BEHÄLTER (UNTER DRUCK TIEFGEZOGENER) **9839**
BEHÄLTERMANTEL **12630**
BEHANDLUNG (ISOTHERMISCHE) **7194**
BEHARRUNGSVERMÖGEN **6907**
BEIDERSEITIG EINGESPANNT **5284**
BEIDERSEITIG EINGESPANNTER TRÄGER **1703**
BEIDERSEITIG GESCHWEISSTE ÜBERLAPPUNGSVERBINDUNG **4171**
BEIFLAMME **4777**
BEIL **6305**
BEILAGE **5937**
BEILAGEBLECH **7621**
BEILBY-SCHICHT **1130**
BEILEGESCHEIBE **11352**
BEIMENGEN **162**
BEIMENGUNGEN **6813**
BEIMISCHEN **162**
BEINSCHWARZ **1447**
BEISSZANGE **3532**
BEIWERT **2621**
BEIZBAD **12382**
BEIZBAD **9289**
BEIZBEHANDLUNG (SAURE) **112**
BEIZE **8391**

BEIZEN **9288**
BEIZEN **11006**
BEIZLÖSUNG **9289**
BEIZLÖSUNG **9290**
BEIZMITTEL **12381**
BEIZSPRÖDIGKEIT **109**
BEIZSPRÖDIGKEIT **6713**
BEIZUNG (ELEKTROLYTISCHE) **4603**
BEIZUNGSVERSPRÖDIGKEIT **1630**
BELAGBLECH FÜR FUSSBÖDEN **5447**
BELAGEISEN **7112**
BELAGKORROSION **3774**
BELASTBARKEIT IM GEBRAUCH **13958**
BELASTEN **7680**
BELASTUNG **7679**
BELASTUNG (AUSSERMITTIGE) **4428**
BELASTUNG (EXZENTRISCHE) **4428**
BELASTUNG (HYDROSTATISCHE) **7652**
BELASTUNG (INTERMITTIERENDE) **7672**
BELASTUNG (PULSIEREND) **6812**
BELASTUNG (RUHENDE) **3633**
BELASTUNG (STÄNDIGE) **3633**
BELASTUNG (STATISCHE) **12138**
BELASTUNG (STETIGE) **3633**
BELASTUNG (STOSSFREIE) **7685**
BELASTUNG (STOSSWEISE) **6812**
BELASTUNG (UNSTETE) **7672**
BELASTUNG (VOLLE) **5722**
BELASTUNG (WECHSELNDE) **7672**
BELASTUNG (ZENTRALE) **2161**
BELASTUNG (ZENTRISCHE) **2161**
BELASTUNG (ZULÄSSIGE) **13956**
BELASTUNG MITTIGE **2161**
BELASTUNGSDIAGRAMM **7683**
BELASTUNGSFLÄCHE **12368**
BELASTUNGSGEWICHT **3251**
BELASTUNGSGEWICHT **8356**
BELEUCHTETER KÖRPER **6773**
BELEUCHTUNG **6777**
BELEUCHTUNG **7574**
BELEUCHTUNG (ELEKTRISCHE) **4518**
BELEUCHTUNG (KÜNSTLICHE) **733**
BELEUCHTUNG (NATÜRLICHE) **8505**
BELEUCHTUNGSKÖRPER **6772**
BELEUCHTUNGSSTÄRKE **6777**
BELEUCHTUNGSVORRICHTUNG **6774**
BELICHTUNG **4944**
BELLEVILLE FEDER **3461**
BELÜFTUNG DES WASSERS **210**
BELÜFTUNGSELEMENT **209**
BENETZEN **12000**

## BEN

BENETZEN 12001
BENETZUNGSMITTEL 13808
BENZALDEHYD 1198
BENZIDIN 1201
BENZIN 5864
BENZIN 9222
BENZINLAMPE 9224
BENZINLOKOMOTIVE 9225
BENZINMOTOR 9223
BENZOEHARZ 1203
BENZOESÄURE 1202
BENZOL 1199
BENZOLSULFOSÄURE 1200
BENZOPHENOL 1938
BENZOPHENON 1205
BENZOYLWASSERSTOFF 1198
BENZYLWASSERSTOFF 12983
BEOBACHTUNG 7114
BEOBACHTUNG (MAKROSKOPISCHE) 7873
BEOBACHTUNG (ULTRAMIKROSKOPISCHE) 13336
BEOBACHTUNGSFEHLER 4829
BEOBACHTUNGSÖFFNUNG 12715
BEPLATTEN 9479
BEPLATTUNG 9503
BERECHNEN 1857
BERECHNUNG 1860
BEREICH 10200
BERGBAU 8311
BERGBLAU 886
BERGE 12598
BERGINGENIEUR 8312
BERGKRISTALL 10652
BERGTALG 4413
BERGWACHS 4413
BERGWERK 8300
BERGWERKSWASSER 9397
BERGZINNOBER 2400
BERICHT (TECHNISCHER) 3614
BERICHTIGUNG 3181
BERNSTEIN 449
BERSTEN 4933
BERSTEN 4935
BERSTEN 1410
BERSTEN (EINER SCHEIBE) 1769
BERUHIGTER STAHL 7294
BERUHIGUNG VON SCHWINGUNGEN 3606
BERÜHREN (GEOM.) 13066
BERÜHRUNGSFLÄCHE 1026
BERÜHRUNGSFLÄCHE 12510
BERÜHRUNGSKORROSION 3002
BERÜHRUNGSLINIE 12616

BERÜHRUNGSPUNKT 9562
BERÜHRUNGSPUNKT 3005
BERÜHRUNGSSTELLE 9562
BERYLLIUM 1210
BERYLLIUM 1207
BERYLLIUMBRONZE 1209
BERYLLIUMBRONZE 1208
BESCHICHTUNG 2590
BESCHICKEN (EINE FEUERUNG) 12269
BESCHICKEN (EINEN METALLURGISCHEN OFFEN) 2260
BESCHICKUNG 2263
BESCHICKUNG (ELEKTR.) 2259
BESCHICKUNG EINER FEUERUNG 5262
BESCHICKUNG EINES METALLURGISCHEN OFENS 2264
BESCHLAG 7159
BESCHLÄGE 7159
BESCHLÄGE FÜR TÜREN UND FENSTER 4122
BESCHLEUNIGER 148
BESCHLEUNIGER 66
BESCHLEUNIGUNG 62
BESCHLEUNIGUNG (AUTOMATISCHE) 836
BESCHLEUNIGUNG (GLEICHBLEIBENDE) 13361
BESCHLEUNIGUNG (LINEARE) 7611
BESCHLEUNIGUNG (NEGATIVE) 8525
BESCHLEUNIGUNG (POSITIVE) 9652
BESCHLEUNIGUNG (UNGLEICHFÖRMIGE) 13507
BESCHNEIDEN 13204
BESCHNEIDEN 13209
BESCHRIFTUNG EINER ZEICHNUNG 7524
BESCHWEREISEN 8356
BESCHWERUNGSMITTEL 7690
BESEITIGUNG 4667
BESEITIGUNG DER OBERFLÄCHENSCHICHT 2912
BESPRENGEN 12001
BESPRENGEN 12000
BESSEMER-BIRNE 1212
BESSEMER-KONVERTER 1212
BESSEMER-NACHBLASEN 1211
BESSEMER-OFEN 1212
BESSEMER-ROHEISEN 117
BESSEMER-ROHEISEN 1213
BESSEMER-ROHEISEN 105
BESSEMER-STAHL 1215
BESSEMER-STAHL 107
BESSEMER-VERFAHREN 1214
BESSEMER-VERFAHREN 106
BESTÄNDIGKEIT 10502
BESTÄNDIGKEIT 10484
BESTÄNDIGKEIT (CHEM.) 2313
BESTANDTEIL 2298
BESTANDTEIL 2983

BESTANDTEIL (ARBEITENDER) **13953**
BESTANDTEIL (FLÜCHTIGER) **13586**
BESTANDTEIL EINER LEGIERUNG **2982**
BESTIMMUNG (ANALYTISCHE) **496**
BESTIMMUNG (ELEKTROLYTISCHE) **4594**
BESTIMMUNG (EXPERIMENTELLE) **4929**
BESTIMMUNG (GRAVIMETRISCHE) **6077**
BESTIMMUNG (KALORIMETRISCHE) **1880**
BESTRAHLUNG **7161**
BESTRAHLUNG **10241**
BETAMESSING **1216**
BETASTRAHLEN **1218**
BETASTRUKTUR **1219**
BETATEILCHEN **1217**
BETON **2894**
BETON (ARMIERTER) **12203**
BETON (BEWEHRTER) **12203**
BETON-(DECKEN-)PLATTE **2900**
BETONARBEITEN **2901**
BETONEISEN **12198**
BETONEISENSCHERE **2897**
BETONFUNDAMENT **2896**
BETONIEREN **2895**
BETONIEREN **2902**
BETONROHR **2898**
BETONVORSPANNUNG **2899**
BETRIEB **8837**
BETRIEB (AUSSETZENDER) **7056**
BETRIEB (INTERMITTIERENDER) **7056**
BETRIEB (UNUNTERBROCHENER) **3038**
BETRIEBFOLGE **13626**
BETRIEBSBEDINGUNGEN **11208**
BETRIEBSBELASTUNG **10879**
BETRIEBSDRUCK **13957**
BETRIEBSFÄHIG **6819**
BETRIEBSFÄHIGEM ZUSTAND (IN) **6819**
BETRIEBSFÜHRER **13964**
BETRIEBSFÜHRUNG **13963**
BETRIEBSFÜHRUNG (WISSENCHAFTLICHE) **11001**
BETRIEBSGESCHWINDIGKEIT **8663**
BETRIEBSKOSTEN **13950**
BETRIEBSKRAFT **8409**
BETRIEBSLEITER **13964**
BETRIEBSPAUSE **7100**
BETRIEBSSICHER **10440**
BETRIEBSSICHERHEIT **10439**
BETRIEBSSPANNUNG (ELEKTR.) **8659**
BETRIEBSSTOFF **8408**
BETRIEBSSTÖRUNG **1581**
BETRIEBSTEMPERATUR **8836**
BETRIEBSUNFALL **75**

BETRIEBSUNTERBRECHUNG **7092**
BETRIEBSVERHÄLTNISSE **13949**
BETRIEBSVERHÄLTNISSE **8834**
BETRIEBSVORSCHRIFTEN **11209**
BETRIEBSWASSER **13649**
BETRIEBSZUSTAND (NORMALER) **8857**
BETTS-VERFAHREN **1220**
BEUGUNG **3924**
BEUGUNGSGITTER **3925**
BEULE **1720**
BEWÄSSERUNGSANLAGEN **7172**
BEWEGUNG **8438**
BEWEGUNG **8406**
BEWEGUNG (ABSOLUTE) **32**
BEWEGUNG (APERIODISCHE) **636**
BEWEGUNG (AUSSETZENDE) **7053**
BEWEGUNG (BESCHLEUNIGTE) **60**
BEWEGUNG (DREHENDE) **10766**
BEWEGUNG (FORTSCHREITENDE) **8407**
BEWEGUNG (GEGENLÄUFIGE) **3243**
BEWEGUNG (GEGENSEITIGE) **10434**
BEWEGUNG (GERADLINIGE) **10320**
BEWEGUNG (GLEICHFÖRMIGE) **13362**
BEWEGUNG (GLEICHMÄSSIG BESCHLEUNIGTE) **13365**
BEWEGUNG (GLEICHMÄSSIG VERZÖGERTE) **13367**
BEWEGUNG (GLEITENDE) **11605**
BEWEGUNG (HIN-UND HERGEHENDE) **13725**
BEWEGUNG (HIN-UND HERGEHENDE) **10283**
BEWEGUNG (INTERMITTIERENDE) **7053**
BEWEGUNG (KRAFTSCHLÜSSIGE) **8629**
BEWEGUNG (KREISFÖRMIGE) **2421**
BEWEGUNG (KRUMMLINIGE) **3500**
BEWEGUNG (PERIODISCHE) **9194**
BEWEGUNG (RELATIVE) **10434**
BEWEGUNG (ROLLENDE) **10702**
BEWEGUNG (RÜCKLÄUFIGE) **919**
BEWEGUNG (RUCKWEISE) **7053**
BEWEGUNG (SCHWINGENDE) **8881**
BEWEGUNG (SENKRECHTE) **13549**
BEWEGUNG (SPHÄRISCHE) **11889**
BEWEGUNG (STETIGE) **3031**
BEWEGUNG (STOSSWEISE) **7053**
BEWEGUNG (UNGLEICHFÖRMIG BESCHLEUNIGTE) **8648**
BEWEGUNG (UNGLEICHFÖRMIG VERZÖGERTE) **8649**
BEWEGUNG (UNGLEICHFÖRMIGE) **8647**
BEWEGUNG (UNTERBROCHENE) **7053**
BEWEGUNG (VARIABLE) **13490**
BEWEGUNG (VERÄNDERLICHE) **13490**
BEWEGUNG (VERZÖGERTE) **10518**
BEWEGUNG (ZWANGSLÄUFIGE) **2985**
BEWEGUNG AUF EINER SCHRAUBENLINIE **6426**

# BEW 770

BEWEGUNGSGRÖSSE 10068
BEWEGUNGSGRÖSSE 8376
BEWEGUNGSLEHRE 7310
BEWEGUNGSRICHTUNG 3991
BEWEGUNGSSCHRAUBE 10852
BEWEGUNGSSINN 11183
BEWEGUNGSÜBERTRAGUNG 13130
BEWEGUNGSUMKEHR 10552
BEWEGUNGSWIDERSTAND 10497
BEWEHRUNG 715
BEWERBER UM EIN PATENT 645
BEZUGSFORMSTÜCK 8034
BEZUGSGERÄTESATZ 8036
BEZUGSGRÖSSE 12079
BEZUGSKANTE 8043
BEZUGSLÄNGE 5878
BEZUGSMASSSYSTEM 29
BEZUGSMASSSYSTEM 3097
BEZUGSPUNKT 10368
BEZUGSPUNKT 9566
BEZUGSPUNKT (ABSOLUTER) 34
BEZUGSTEMPERATUR 10369
BEZUGSZEICHEN 10367
BIBGUNG 3698
BICHROMATBEHANDLUNG 1236
BIEGBAR 9518
BIEGBARKEIT 5415
BIEGEBACKE 1183
BIEGEBACKE 1529
BIEGEBEANSPRUCHUNG 1191
BIEGEBEANSPRUCHUNG 1187
BIEGEBRUCH 5488
BIEGEFEDER 11993
BIEGEFEDER (GERADE) 12312
BIEGEFEDER (GEWUNDENE) 2649
BIEGEFESTIGKEIT 1192
BIEGEFESTIGKEIT 1188
BIEGEFESTIGKET 5424
BIEGEGLIED 1181
BIEGEHALBMESSER 10168
BIEGEMASCHINE 1184
BIEGEMASCHINE (FÜR VERSUCHE) 7845
BIEGEMOMENT 1185
BIEGEN 1182
BIEGEN 1173
BIEGEN (EIN ROHR) 1175
BIEGEN EINES ROHRES 9341
BIEGEPRESSE 1184
BIEGEPRESSE (FÜR VERSUCHE) 7845
BIEGEPROBE 1189
BIEGEPROBE 1177

BIEGEPROBE AN DER OBERFLÄCHE DER SCHWEISSTELLE 1178
BIEGERADIUS 1176
BIEGESPANNUNG 1193
BIEGESPANNUNG 5425
BIEGESTEIFIGKEIT 5423
BIEGEVERSUCH 1189
BIEGEVERSUCH MIT DER WURZEL IN DER ZUGZONE 1179
BIEGEWALZE 1186
BIEGEWALZWERK 1186
BIEGEWINKEL 519
BIEGSAM 9518
BIEGSAMKEIT 5415
BIEGUNG 3700
BIEGUNG 1182
BIEGUNG 5422
BIEGUNG 5426
BIEGUNGSELASTIZITÄT 4489
BIEGUNGSFEDER 11993
BIEGUNGSMOMENT 1185
BIEGUNGSSCHWINGUNG 13556
BIEGUNGSWALZE 1186
BIENENWACHS 1129
BILD (OPT.) 6779
BILD (REELLES) 10259
BILD (SCHARFES) 2479
BILD (VIRTUELLES) 13572
BILD (WIRKLICHES) 10259
BILDHAVERBRONZE 1662
BILDPUNKT 6780
BILDSAMKEIT 9474
BILDSCHÄRFE 11276
BILDUNGSWÄRME 9656
BIMETALLLEGIERUNG 4378
BIMS 9988
BIMSEN 9990
BIMSSAND 9727
BIMSSTEIN 9988
BIMSSTEINTUFF 9989
BINÄR-DEZIMALCODE 1248
BINÄRSTELLE 1249
BINÄRZEICHEN 1249
BINDEDRAHT 1255
BINDEFEHLER 6782
BINDEFEHLER 7351
BINDEMITTEL 1250
BINDEMITTEL 1445
BINDEMITTEL 1253
BINDEMITTEL (LUFTHÄRTENDES) 301
BINDER (BAUW.) 6324
BINDERIEMEN 7500

| | |
|---|---|
| BINDERMASCHINEN ALLER ARTEN **948** | BLÄTTRIGE STRUKTUR **7373** |
| BINOMIALKOEFFIZIENT **1257** | BLATTZINN **12955** |
| BINOMIALREIHE **1260** | BLAU (BERLINER) **1206** |
| BINOMIALVERTEILUNG **1258** | BLAUBRENNE **1369** |
| BIRNE **7385** | BLAUBRÜCHIGKEIT **1631** |
| BISEKTRIX (SPITZE) **156** | BLAUBRUCHPROBE **1372** |
| BISKUIT **1276** | BLAUDRUCKPAPIER **5119** |
| BISKUITGUT **1276** | BLAUGLÜHEN **572** |
| BISMUTIN **1275** | BLAUGLUT **1370** |
| BIT **1249** | BLAUPAUSE **1375** |
| BITTERMANDELÖL **1198** | BLAUSÄURE **6707** |
| BITTERSALZ **7889** | BLAUSAURES KALI **9683** |
| BITTERSPAT **7880** | BLAUSTICHIGES EOSIN **4831** |
| BITUMEN **1280** | BLAUUNG **1377** |
| BITUMENHALTIG **1281** | BLAUWARM **1371** |
| BITUMINÖS **1281** | BLECH **11315** |
| BLANK SCHLEIFEN **9598** | BLECH **11298** |
| BLANKBEIZEN **11005** | BLECH **11305** |
| BLANKBEIZEN **11006** | BLECH (EIN) ENTGRATEN **13205** |
| BLANKE STELLE **6536** | BLECH (GALVANISIERTES) **5785** |
| BLANKETT **1301** | BLECH (GELOCHTES) **9189** |
| BLANKGLÜHDRAHT **1606** | BLECH (GERICHTETES) **5395** |
| BLANKGLÜHEN **573** | BLECH (GERIFFELTES) **2325** |
| BLANKSCHLEIFEN **9605** | BLECH (GERIPPTES) **2325** |
| BLASE **1353** | BLECH (GEWALZTES) **10674** |
| BLASE **1351** | BLECH (GLATTES) **1296** |
| BLASEBALG **1139** | BLECH (KALTGEWALZTES) **2696** |
| BLASEBALGHAHN **1138** | BLECH (KORNORIENTIERTES) **6036** |
| BLASEN **1330** | BLECH (PERFORIERTES) **9189** |
| BLASEN **11903** | BLECH (PLATTIERTES) **2445** |
| BLASEN **1362** | BLECH (SCHWARZES) **1294** |
| BLASENBILDUNG **1330** | BLECH (VERBLEITES) **7460** |
| BLASENBILDUNG **2437** | BLECH (VERZINKTES) **5785** |
| BLASENBILDUNG **1672** | BLECH (WARMGEWALZTES) **6637** |
| BLASENDER LÜFTER **9817** | BLECH (ZUGESCHNITTENES) **11266** |
| BLASENSTAHL **2138** | BLECH MIT GEBOHRTEN LÖCHERN **4274** |
| BLASFORM **13299** | BLECH MIT GESTANZTEN LÖCHERN **10003** |
| BLASIGE STELLE IM GUSS **1353** | BLECH- ODER BANDMETALLSCHERMASCHINE **11323** |
| BLASLOCH **6393** | BLECHABFALL **9493** |
| BLASLÖTROHR **8433** | BLECHABKANTPRESSE **9481** |
| BLASWIRKUNG (MAGNETISCHE) **665** | BLECHANHAFTUNG **8046** |
| BLATT **1299** | BLECHANREISSEN **8018** |
| BLATT (DESCARTESSCHES) **5513** | BLECHBEARBEITUNGSMASCHINEN **11320** |
| BLÄTTERMAGNET **7377** | BLECHBIEGEMASCHINE **9480** |
| BLATTFEDER **7485** | BLECHDICKE **9487** |
| BLATTFEDER **9495** | BLECHDICKE **12845** |
| BLATTFEDERWERK **2834** | BLECHE (GESTRECKTE) **4250** |
| BLATTGOLD **6000** | BLECHE (UMHÜLLTE) **2586** |
| BLATTGOLDSCHLÄGEREI **5994** | BLECHE ANEINANDERLEGEN **8045** |
| BLATTKOHLSCHNEIDER **7272** | BLECHE AUS LEGIERTEN STÄHLEN **380** |
| BLATTMETALL **5509** | BLECHEINLEGEFOLGE **9500** |

**BLE** 772

BLECHKANNE 12961
BLECHKANTE 9483
BLECHKANTENABSCHRÄGUNG 9496
BLECHKANTENHOBELMASCHINE 9484
BLECHKONSTRUKTIONSZEICHNUNG 9504
BLECHLEHRE 11311
BLECHMANTEL 11310
BLECHNUMMER 5880
BLECHPERFORIERMASCHINEN 11317
BLECHPLANIERMASCHINEN 11318
BLECHRAND 9483
BLECHRAND 4441
BLECHRICHTMASCHINE 9485
BLECHRICHTMASCHINE 11316
BLECHRITZMASCHINE 11319
BLECHROHR 11312
BLECHSCHERE 9494
BLECHSCHERMASCHINE 9494
BLECHSCHUTZ 655
BLECHSTÄRKE 12845
BLECHSTREIFENWALZWERK 11321
BLECHTAFEL 11313
BLECHTRÄGER 9490
BLECHWALZSTRASSE 11324
BLEI 7447
BLEI (BASISCH) 13834
BLEI (CHROMSAURES) 2375
BLEI (KOHLENSAURES) 13834
BLEI (REINES) 2311
BLEI (SCHWEFESAURES) 7473
BLEI (UNREINLICHES) 1029
BLEI (UNTERSCHWEFLIGSAURES) 7474
BLEI UNRAFFINIERTES) 1029
BLEI-ZINNLOT 7475
BLEIABGUSS 7457
BLEIAKKUMULATOR 7455
BLEIAZETAT 7450
BLEIBAD 7454
BLEIBENDE HÄRTE DES WASSERS 9203
BLEIBLECH 11314
BLEIBRONZE 7456
BLEICHERDE 5727
BLEICHKALK 1317
BLEICHLORID 7458
BLEICHPULVER 1317
BLEICHROMAT 2375
BLEIDICHTUNG FÜR ROHRE 7464
BLEIDIOXYD 7461
BLEIDRAHT 7477
BLEIERZ 7465
BLEIESSIGSÄURE 7450

BLEIFARBE 7466
BLEIFOLIE 7462
BLEIGELB 8031
BLEIGLANZ 5775
BLEIGLÄTTE 7663
BLEIHAMMER 7463
BLEIKARBONAT 2196
BLEILEGIERUNG 7451
BLEILEGIERUNG 7453
BLEILOT 9540
BLEIMENNIGE 10333
BLEIOXYD 7663
BLEIOXYD (GELBES) 8031
BLEIPEROXYD 7461
BLEIRING 7470
BLEIROHR 7468
BLEISCHROT 7472
BLEISCHWAMM 11954
BLEISCHWEISSEN 7476
BLEISPAT 2196
BLEISTIFT 7478
BLEISTIFTEINSATZ FÜR ZIRKEL 9165
BLEISTIFTGUMMI 9163
BLEISTIFTZEICHNUNG 7467
BLEISTIFTZIRKEL 2804
BLEISULFAT 7473
BLEISUPEROXYD 7461
BLEITHIOSULFAT 7474
BLEIVERARBEITUNG 7484
BLEIWAAGE 9540
BLEIWEISS 13834
BLEIZUCKER 7450
BLEIZUCKERPAPIER 7449
BLENDE 3871
BLENDE 1324
BLENDUNG 1325
BLINDAUFKOHLEN 9959
BLINDBODEN 5026
BLINDFLANSCH 1304
BLINDFLANSCH 1326
BLINDKALIBER 4372
BLINDLOCH 3630
BLINDSTICH 4372
BLINDWALZE 4373
BLINDWERDEN 5507
BLINDWIDERSTAND 10247
BLINKLEUCHTE 5366
BLINKLICHTER 3989
BLITZABLEITER 7576
BLITZSCHUTZVORRICHTUNG 7575
BLITZTROCKNER 5360

| | |
|---|---|
| BLOCK **6919** | BOHR-LÜNETTEN **1474** |
| BLOCK **1332** | BOHRBRETT **1590** |
| BLOCK ERRATISCHER **4821** | BOHRDURCHMESSER **1439** |
| BLOCKDREHBANK **6922** | BOHREN **4277** |
| BLÖCKE AUS KOHLENSTOFFSTAHL **1955** | BOHREN **4264** |
| BLOCKENDE **4730** | BOHREN **1468** |
| BLOCKFORM **6923** | BOHREN (EINES GEWINDES) **12678** |
| BLOCKKETTE **1336** | BOHREN (GEWINDE) **12636** |
| BLOCKSEIGERUNG **8660** | BOHRER **4271** |
| BLOCKSEIGERUNG **6925** | BOHRER **4263** |
| BLOCKWAGEN **6920** | BOHRER (ARBEITER) **4276** |
| BLOCKWALZEN **2642** | BOHRER (GERADEGENUTETER) **12304** |
| BLOCKZINN **1339** | BOHRER (HARTMETALLBESTÜCKTER) **1936** |
| BLUTALBUMIN **11207** | BOHRERLEHRE **4267** |
| BOCK **12490** | BOHRERSPITZENDURCHMESSER **4269** |
| BOCKKRAN **5804** | BOHRFUTTER **4266** |
| BOCKLAGER **9154** | BOHRHAMMER **258** |
| BOCKWINDE **13851** | BOHRKERN **3142** |
| BODEN (FALSCHER) **5026** | BOHRKNARRE **10219** |
| BODEN (FLACHGEWÖLBTER) **13045** | BOHRKÖPFE (MEHRSPINDLIGE) **8458** |
| BODEN (GEWÖLBTER) **4036** | BOHRKRONE **4265** |
| BODEN (WASSERFÜHRENDER) **13642** | BOHRKURBEL **1518** |
| BODEN ENTWÄSSERN **4209** | BOHRLEHRE **4267** |
| BODENABLAUF **1492** | BOHRLOCH **4273** |
| BODENBEARBEITUNGSGERÄTE **3457** | BOHRLOCH (IM GESTEIN) **1463** |
| BODENBELAG **5451** | BOHRMASCHINE **1471** |
| BODENBLECH **5446** | BOHRMASCHINE **4279** |
| BODENBRETT **5446** | BOHRMASCHINE (FAHRBARE) (TRAGBARE) **9636** |
| BODENDÜSE **1495** | BOHRMASCHINE (LIEGENDE) **6581** |
| BODENFREIHEIT **6143** | BOHRMASCHINE (MEHRSPINDLIGE) **8470** |
| BODENLÄNGSTRÄGER **5625** | BOHRMASCHINE (STEHENDE) **13552** |
| BODENPLATTE **5449** | BOHRMASCHINEN FÜR MASTEN **9664** |
| BODENSATZ **9759** | BOHRÖL **4280** |
| BODENSTEIN (BASISCHER) UND FUTTER (BASISCHES) **1045** | BOHRRATSCHE **10219** |
| BODENUNTERSUCHUNG **11752** | BOHRSPÄNE **1476** |
| BODENVENTIL **1493** | BOHRSPÄNE **11277** |
| BODENVENTIL **5523** | BOHRSPINDELSTOCK **4278** |
| BOGEN **664** | BOHRSTÄHLE FÜR GESTEINS-BOHRUNGEN **4270** |
| BOGENDACH **4039** | BOHRSTANGE **4265** |
| BOGENHÖHE **10613** | BOHRSTANGE (EINTEILIGE) **11778** |
| BOGENLAMPE **672** | BOHRSTANGEN **1470** |
| BOGENLÄNGE **7517** | BOHRTURM PONTON **3787** |
| BOGENLICHT **673** | BOHRUNG **3855** |
| BOGENMASS **2419** | BOHRUNG **4277** |
| BOGENROHR **1180** | BOHRUNG **6530** |
| BOGENSÄGE **8186** | BOHRUNG **1461** |
| BOGENSÄGE **3108** | BOHRUNG EINER RIEMENSCHEIBE **4978** |
| BOGENSTÜCK **1180** | BOHRUNG EINES RADES **4978** |
| BOGENZIRKEL **13876** | BOHRUNGSDURCHMESSER **3855** |
| BOGENZIRKEL MIT GEZAHNTEM BOGEN **10122** | BOHRUNGSLEHRE **6531** |
| BOHLE **9457** | BOHRUNGSMESSGERÄT MIT SKALA **3838** |

## BOH

774

BOHRUNGSSTEUERVORRICHTUNG 4268
BOHRVERSUCH 1475
BOHRWAGEN 13614
BOHRWERK 1472
BOHRWINDE 1519
BOILER (WAAGERECHTER) 6580
BOLOMETER 1431
BOLUS 1430
BOLZEN 4180
BOLZEN 9315
BOLZEN 9320
BOLZEN 1432
BOLZEN (ROHER) 1286
BOLZEN EINER SCHRAUBE 11260
BOLZEN OHNE GEWINDE 1302
BOLZENBOHRUNGSDURCHMESSER 1440
BOLZENDREHBANK 12401
BOLZENDURCHMESSER 1434
BOLZENGELENK 9318
BOLZENGEWINDE 7955
BOLZENZAPFEN 12397
BOMBE (KALORIMETRISCHE) 1879
BOMBENKALORIMETER 1879
BOMBIERUNG 1889
BOR 1477
BORAX 1459
BORAXSÄURE 1467
BORBOHRER 5944
BÖRDEL 1083
BÖRDELBLECH 9478
BÖRDELFLANSCH 9803
BÖRDELMASCHINE 5346
BÖRDELN 1088
BÖRDELNAHT 5335
BÖRDELPROBE 5347
BÖRDELROHR 1087
BORDSCHEIBE EINER RIEMENSCHEIBE 5332
BORDSCHEIBE EINES ZAHNRADES 11400
BOREISEN 5107
BORKARBID 1479
BORLEGIERUNG 1478
BORSÄURE 1467
BORSTE 5273
BORT 1480
BÖSCHUNG 11627
BOTTICH 13228
BOURNONIT 1502
BRACKWASSER 1524
BRAMME 11551
BRAMME (BRAMMENSTRASSE) 11552
BRAMMEN-STRASSE 11556

BRAMMENBIEGEN 11553
BRAMMENSCHERE 11554
BRAMMENWALZWERK 11555
BRANDLACKIEREN 7214
BRANDRISS 5240
BRAUCHWASSER 13649
BRAUNEISENERZ 7596
BRAUNEISENSTEIN 7596
BRAUNEISENSTEIN (TONIGER) 2467
BRAUNKOHLE 1665
BRAUNKOHLENBENZIN 11753
BRAUNKOHLENBRIKETT 1666
BRAUNKOHLENTEER 1667
BRAUNKOHLENTEERÖL 1668
BRÄUNUNG 1758
BRAUSE 10746
BRAUSEVENTIL 11387
BRAUSTEIN 10047
BRECHEN 10861
BRECHMASCHINE 3419
BRECHSICHERUNG 10887
BRECHSTANGE 3394
BRECHSTANGE 7333
BRECHUNG 3924
BRECHUNG DES LICHTES 10400
BRECHUNGSEBENE 9439
BRECHUNGSEXPONENT 6866
BRECHUNGSINDEX 6866
BRECHUNGSWINKEL 526
BRECHUNGSZAHL 6866
BRECHWEINSTEIN 9675
BREITE 13850
BREITFLANSCHTRÄGER 13849
BREITFLANSCHTRÄGER 1639
BREITFLANSCHTRÄGER 1641
BREMSBACKE 1542
BREMSBACKE 1543
BREMSBACKE 1536
BREMSBAND 1544
BREMSBELAG 1538
BREMSBERG 6081
BREMSDYNAMOMETER 55
BREMSE 1529
BREMSE (ELEKTRISCHE) 4613
BREMSE (ELEKTROMAGNETISCHE) 4613
BREMSE (MAGNETISCHE) 7896
BREMSE ANZIEHEN (EINE) 650
BREMSEN 1549
BREMSEN 1530
BREMSFLÜSSIGKEITSBEHÄLTER 1534
BREMSGESTÄNGE 1539

## 775 BRU

BREMSGEWICHT **1547**
BREMSHEBEL **1537**
BREMSKLOTZ **1543**
BREMSKLOTZ **1531**
BREMSKRAFT **1551**
BREMSKREIS **1545**
BREMSLEISTUNG **1535**
BREMSLEISTUNG **1540**
BREMSLEISTUNG **4458**
BREMSPFERDESTÄRKE (EFFEKTIVE) **151**
BREMSRING **1541**
BREMSSCHEIBE **1548**
BREMSTROMMEL **1532**
BREMSTROMMEL **1533**
BREMSVERSUCH **1546**
BREMSWIDERSTAND **1552**
BREMSWIRKUNG **1550**
BREMSZYLINDER **1532**
BRENNBAR **2772**
BRENNBARKEIT **2773**
BRENNEBENE **5501**
BRENNEN **1745**
BRENNER **1749**
BRENNER **13042**
BRENNER **2848**
BRENNFLÄCHE **2121**
BRENNGAS **5709**
BRENNGESCHWINDIGKEIT **10227**
BRENNHÄRTEN **5315**
BRENNHOLZ **5258**
BRENNKEGEL **11134**
BRENNLINIE **2116**
BRENNLINIE DURCH REFLEXION **2089**
BRENNLINIE DURCH REFRAKTION **3829**
BRENNMITTEL **5705**
BRENNOFEN **7295**
BRENNPUNKT **5502**
BRENNPUNKT (EINES ÖLES) **5247**
BRENNPUNKT (REELLER) **10258**
BRENNPUNKT (SCHEINBARER) **13571**
BRENNPUNKT (VIRTUELLER) **13571**
BRENNPUNKT (WIRKLICHER) **10258**
BRENNPUNKTABSTAND **5503**
BRENNPUTZEN **5309**
BRENNPUTZEN (FLÄMMEN) **8976**
BRENNSCHNEIDEN **7387**
BRENNSCHNEIDEN **5817**
BRENNSTOFF **5705**
BRENNSTOFF (FESTER) **11785**
BRENNSTOFF (FLÜSSIGER) **7650**
BRENNSTOFF (FOSSILER) **5586**

BRENNSTOFF (GASFÖRMIGER) **5854**
BRENNSTOFF (HOCHWERTIGER) **6484**
BRENNSTOFF (KÜNSTLICHER) **732**
BRENNSTOFF (NATÜRIICHER) **8503**
BRENNSTOFF (STÜCKIGER) **7827**
BRENNSTOFF MINDERWERTIGER **7780**
BRENNSTOFFBEDARF **3745**
BRENNSTOFFERSPARNIS **5707**
BRENNSTOFFVERBRAUCH **2994**
BRENNSTOFFZUFÜHRUNG **5082**
BRENNWEITE **5503**
BRENNWEITE **5500**
BRENZESSIGGEIST **90**
BRETT **1379**
BRETTFALLHAMMER **1380**
BRETTSÄGE **10609**
BRIGGS'SCHES GEWINDE **1605**
BRIKETT **1623**
BRIKETTIERTES ERZ **8860**
BRIKETTIERUNG **7990**
BRILLE (FESTSTEHENDE) **12154**
BRILLE (LAUFENDE) **5514**
BRINELL-HÄRTEPRÜFER **1553**
BRINELL-PRESSE **1553**
BRINELL'SCHER **1620**
BRINELLHÄRTE **1619**
BRINELLPROBE **1618**
BRITANNIAMETALL **1624**
BROM **1649**
BROMARGYRIT **1645**
BROMAT **1646**
BROMID **1648**
BROMIT **1645**
BROMKALIUM **9678**
BROMMETALL **1648**
BROMSÄURE **1647**
BROMSILBER **1645**
BROMWASSERSTOFFSÄURE **6704**
BRONZE **1650**
BRONZE (SÄUREBESTÄNDIGE) **1655**
BRONZEDRAHT **1654**
BRONZELACK **6001**
BRONZEN **216**
BRONZEPULVER **1652**
BRONZEROHR **1653**
BRONZIEREN **1651**
BRONZIEREN **1664**
BRUCH **5620**
BRUCH **10861**
BRUCH **10858**
BRUCH **3278**

# BRU

776

BRUCH **5613**
BRUCH **5617**
BRUCH (BLÄTTRIGER) **7378**
BRUCH (EBENER) **4871**
BRUCH (ECHTER) **9932**
BRUCH (ERDIGER) **4421**
BRUCH (FASERIGER) **5138**
BRUCH (GEMEINER) **13611**
BRUCH (GLATTER) **11683**
BRUCH (GRIESIGER) **6051**
BRUCH (HAKIGER) **6195**
BRUCH (KÖRNIGER) **6051**
BRUCH (MUSCHELIGER) **2893**
BRUCH (SEHNIGER) **5138**
BRUCH (SEIDIGER) **11454**
BRUCH (SPLITTRIGER) **11936**
BRUCH (TRANSKRISTALLINER) **13117**
BRUCH (UNEBENER) **13357**
BRUCH (UNECHTER) **6807**
BRUCH (ZACKIGER) **6195**
BRUCHBELASTUNG **1586**
BRUCHBELASTUNG **13331**
BRUCHDEHNUNG **13329**
BRUCHFESTIGKEIT **13327**
BRUCHFESTIGKEIT **13331**
BRUCHFLÄCHE **5620**
BRUCHFLÄCHE (MUSCHELIGE) **2893**
BRUCHGRENZE **4481**
BRÜCHIG **1627**
BRÜCHIGKEIT **11378**
BRÜCHIGWERDEN **4685**
BRUCHLAST **1585**
BRUCHLAST **12749**
BRUCHLAST **13331**
BRUCHMODUL **8343**
BRUCHPROBE **5619**
BRUCHQUERSCHNITT **3373**
BRUCHSCHEIBE **10860**
BRUCHSPANNUNG **5618**
BRUCHSTEIN **10827**
BRUCHSTEINMAUERWERK **10828**
BRUCHSTELLE **9563**
BRUCHTHEORIE **5616**
BRÜCKE WHEATSTONESCHE **13809**
BRÜCKENBILDUNG **1604**
BRÜCKENKRAN **13141**
BRÜCKENVIERECK **13809**
BRÜCKENWAAGE **13745**
BRÜNIERUNG **1758**
BRUNNENMACHERKITT **13797**
BRUNNENWASSER **13796**

BRUST EINER WELLE **11384**
BRUSTBRETT **1590**
BRUSTLEIER **1519**
BRUSTRAD **6465**
BRUSTSCHEIBE **1590**
BRUSTWINKEL **10186**
BRUSTWINKEL **5698**
BRUTTOGEWICHT **6141**
BRUTTOGEWICHT **10781**
BUCHSBAUM **1507**
BÜCHSE **1771**
BÜCHSE EINER ROLLENKETTE **10688**
BÜCHSENMUTTER **1512**
BUCKELPLATTE **1679**
BUCKELSCHWEISSEN **9916**
BUCKELSCHWEISSNAHT **9915**
BÜFFELLEDER **1685**
BUFFER **1686**
BÜGEL **2450**
BÜGEL **2720**
BÜGEL **12261**
BÜGEL **14014**
BÜGELAUFSATZ **14015**
BÜGELFEDER **1823**
BÜGELMESSSCHRAUBE **8249**
BÜGELSÄGE **6196**
BÜGELSÄGE **8186**
BÜGELSÄGEMASCHINE **6198**
BÜGELSCHRAUBE **13324**
BÜGELVERSCHRAUBUNG **14018**
BÜHNE **9502**
BÜHNE **5776**
BUND **2645**
BUND VON BANDEISEN **1738**
BÜNDEL **1093**
BÜNDELN **1737**
BUNDGESPÄRRE **13244**
BÜNDIG **5482**
BÜNDIG MACHEN **7951**
BUNDMUTTER **5342**
BUNDRING **2724**
BUNKER **1740**
BUNSENBRENNER **1741**
BUNTKUPFERERZ **13501**
BUNTSANDSTEIN **13502**
BÜRETTE **1743**
BÜRSTENKUPFERBLECH **1669**
BÜRSTENSCHEIBE **2425**
BUTAN **1775**
BUTTERSÄURE **1817**
BUTYLEN **1816**

| | |
|---|---|
| CANNELKOHLE **1901** | CHLORKOBALT **2609** |
| CANTONSPHOSPHOR **1852** | CHLORMAGNESIUM **7885** |
| CARBONADO **1967** | CHLORMANGAN **7972** |
| CARNAUBAWACHS **2003** | CHLORMETALL **2352** |
| CASSIOPEIUM **7833** | CHLORMETHYL **8221** |
| CELESIUSTHERMOMETER **2186** | CHLORMONOXYD **2355** |
| CELSIUSGRAD **3716** | CHLORNATRIUM **2790** |
| CELSIUSSKALA **2157** | CHLORNICKEL **8562** |
| CER **2195** | CHLOROFORM **2356** |
| CERMET **2192** | CHLORPLATIN **9507** |
| CESIUM **2197** | CHLORSAURES KALI **9680** |
| CETANZAHL **2198** | CHLORSÄURESALZ **2351** |
| CHALKOPYRIT **3126** | CHLORSCHWEFEL **12451** |
| CHAPMAN-VERFAHREN **2254** | CHLORSILBER **11461** |
| CHARAKTERISTIK **2256** | CHLORWASSERSTOFFÄTHER **4849** |
| CHARGENOFEN **1060** | CHLORWASSERSTOFFSÄURE **6706** |
| CHARPY SCHLAGPROBE **2270** | CHLORWISMUT **1270** |
| CHARPY-PRÜFMASCHINE **6787** | CHLORZINK **14038** |
| CHEFKONSTRUKTEUR **2329** | CHROM **2385** |
| CHELATBILDUNG **11195** | CHROM-WOLFRAMSTAHL **2378** |
| CHELATBILDUNGSMITTEL **2289** | CHROMALAUN **2370** |
| CHEMIE **2322** | CHROMAT **2366** |
| CHEMIE (ANALYTISCHE) **495** | CHROMATIEREN **2367** |
| CHEMIE (ANGEWANDTE) **648** | CHROMATISCH **2368** |
| CHEMIE (ANORGANISCHE) **6958** | CHROMATSCHICHT **2591** |
| CHEMIE (ORGANISCHE) **8865** | CHROMCHLORID **2381** |
| CHEMIE (PHYSIKALISCHE) **9281** | CHROMCHLORÜR **2391** |
| CHEMIE (TECHNISCHE) **9286** | CHROMEISEN **5108** |
| CHEMIKALIEN **2320** | CHROMEISENSTEIN **2384** |
| CHEMIKER **2321** | CHROMEISENSTEIN **2373** |
| CHEMISCH **2290** | CHROMERZMÖRTEL **5741** |
| CHEMISCH GEBUNDEN **2317** | CHROMERZSTEIN **2371** |
| CHEMISCH REIN **2319** | CHROMFARBE **2387** |
| CHILISALPETER **2330** | CHROMGELB **2375** |
| CHINESISCHER TALG **2342** | CHROMGRÜN **2372** |
| CHINHYDRONELEKTRODE **10110** | CHROMIT **2384** |
| CHLOR **2354** | CHROMIT **2373** |
| CHLORALUMINIUM **421** | CHROMITSTEIN **2371** |
| CHLORAMMONIUM **462** | CHROMNICKELSTAHL **2386** |
| CHLORANTIMON **626** | CHROMNICKELSTAHL **2376** |
| CHLORARSEN **724** | CHROMOXYD **2382** |
| CHLORAT **2351** | CHROMROT **2374** |
| CHLORÄTHYL **4849** | CHROMSÄURE **2379** |
| CHLORBARIUM **997** | CHROMSÄUREANHYDRID **2383** |
| CHLORBLEI **7458** | CHROMSÄURESALZ **2366** |
| CHLORGOLD **821** | CHROMSTAHL **2389** |
| CHLORID **2352** | CHROMTRIOXYD **2383** |
| CHLORIERUNG **2353** | CHRYSOLITH **2392** |
| CHLORKALIUM **9681** | CLUSTER **2542** |
| CHLORKALK **1317** | CODIERER **3943** |
| CHLORKALZIUM **1850** | COMPOUNDDYNAMO **3228** |

# COM 778

COMPOUNDMASCHINE **2829**
COMPOUNDMOTOR **2835**
COMPOUNDÖL **2832**
COMPOUNDVERDICHTER **2836**
CONSUTRODE **2990**
COPPERWELD **3137**
COTTONÖL **3222**
COTTRELL-SCHRANKE **3224**
COULOMB **3225**
COULOMETER **3227**
CRACKINGDESTILLATION **3285**
CROWNGLAS **3397**
CUPROOXYD ELEKTROLYT (KUPFER ENTHALTENDES) **4610**
CURIEPUNKT **7920**
CYANID **3547**
CYANIDLAUGEREI **3546**
CYANIDLAUGUNGSVERFAHREN **3546**
D-SCHIEBER **3592**
DACH **10708**
DACH **3667**
DACH (FLACHEWÖLBTES) **13046**
DACH-MANNLOCH **10710**
DACHPAPPE **10712**
DÄCHSEL **207**
DACHSTUTZEN **10711**
DACHZIEGEL **12934**
DAMMARHARZ **3598**
DAMMERDE **8423**
DAMPF **13484**
DAMPF **12155**
DAMPF (GESÄTTIGTER) **10942**
DAMPF (ÜBERHITZTER) **12469**
DAMPF (ÜBERHITZTER) **12471**
DAMPF VON NIEDRIGER SPANNUNG **7785**
DAMPFABLEITUNGSROHR **4897**
DAMPFABSCHEIDER **12184**
DAMPFABSPERRVENTIL **12186**
DAMPFAUSLASSROHR **4897**
DAMPFAUSSTRÖMLINIE **4892**
DAMPFBAD **12157**
DAMPFBLASENBILDUNG **13481**
DAMPFBREMSE **12159**
DAMPFDICHT **12193**
DAMPFDOM **12163**
DAMPFDRUCK **12181**
DAMPFDRUCKPROBE **12182**
DAMPFDRUCKPUMPE **9980**
DAMPFDÜSE **12175**
DAMPFDYNAMO **12191**
DAMPFEINSTRÖMLINIE **199**
DÄMPFEN (EINEN STOSS) **3640**

DAMPFENTNAHMEVENTIL **12187**
DÄMPFER **11358**
DÄMPFER **3601**
DÄMPFER **3602**
DAMPFERZEUGER **12169**
DAMPFERZEUGUNG **5923**
DAMPFFASS **829**
DAMPFFÖRMIG **6817**
DAMPFHAMMER **12166**
DAMPFHEIZUNG **12167**
DAMPFKALORIMETER **12160**
DAMPFKANAL **12176**
DAMPFKESSEL **12158**
DAMPFKESSEL (ELEKTRISCH GEHEIZTER) **4497**
DAMPFKESSELROHR **1422**
DAMPFKESSELÜBERWACHUNG **9193**
DAMPFKOCHTOPF **829**
DAMPFKOCHTOPF **3938**
DAMPFKOLBEN **12179**
DAMPFKRAFTANLAGE **12180**
DAMPFKRAFTMASCHINE **12164**
DAMPFLEITUNG **12178**
DAMPFLEITUNGSROHR **12177**
DAMPFLOKOMOTIVE **12173**
DAMPFMANTEL **12168**
DAMPFMASCHINE (DOPPELTWIRKENDE) **4165**
DAMPFMASCHINE (EINFACHWIRKENDE) **11495**
DAMPFMASCHINE (FESTSTEHENDE) **12144**
DAMPFMASCHINE (ORTSFESTE) **12144**
DAMPFMASCHINE (STATIONÄRE) **12144**
DAMPFMASCHINE MIT SCHWINGENDEM ZYLINDER **8880**
DAMPFMASCHINE MIT UMKEHRUNG **10543**
DAMPFMASCHINE MIT UMLAUFENDEM KOLBEN **10761**
DAMPFMASCHINEN-ZYLINDER **12162**
DAMPFMASCHINENANLAGE **12180**
DAMPFMETALLISIEREN **13482**
DAMPFNÄSSE **13806**
DAMPFPFEIFE **12190**
DAMPFPUMPE **12183**
DAMPFRAUM EINES KESSELS **12185**
DAMPFSAMMLER **12163**
DAMPFSCHLANGE **12161**
DAMPFSPANNUNG **12181**
DAMPFSPEICHER **12156**
DAMPFSTRAHL **12170**
DAMPFSTRAHLGEBLÄSE **12172**
DAMPFSTRAHLLUFTPUMPE **12171**
DAMPFTROCKENER **12184**
DAMPFTROCKNER **4351**
DAMPFTURBINE **12189**
DAMPFÜBERHITZER **12472**

DÄMPFUNG **3606**
DÄMPFUNG **3604**
DÄMPFUNG (INNERE) **7065**
DÄMPFUNGSFÄHIGKEIT **3605**
DÄMPFUNGSVERMÖGEN **3605**
DÄMPFUNGVORRICHTUNG (HYDRODYNAMISCHE) **6709**
DAMPFVERBRAUCH **2995**
DAMPFVERBRAUCHMESSER **12174**
DAMPFWEG **12176**
DARMSAITENRIEMEN **6183**
DARSTELLUNG (GEOMETRISCHE) **5926**
DATEN **3612**
DATEN **8696**
DATEN (NUMERISCH EINGEGEBENE) **3942**
DATENEINGABE (MANUELLE) **7987**
DATENREGISTER **3613**
DATENTRÄGER **12289**
DATENWORT **13934**
DAUBE **12149**
DAUER EINES PATENTRECHTES **12761**
DAUERBELASTUNG **3633**
DAUERBETRIEB **3038**
DAUERBETRIEB **9209**
DAUERBRUCH **4740**
DAUERFESTIGKEIT **5052**
DAUERFESTIGKEIT **4741**
DAUERFESTIGKEITSVERHÄLTNIS **4742**
DAUERFORM **9207**
DAUERGRENZE **5050**
DAUERHAFT **4386**
DAUERHAFTIGKEIT **4385**
DAUERHAFTIGKEIT **4738**
DAUERLASTPRÜFUNG **2974**
DAUERMAGNET **9204**
DAUERMAGNET-SPANNPLATTE **9205**
DAUERRISS **4739**
DAUERSCHWINGFESTIGKEIT **5053**
DAUERSPANNUNG **2978**
DAUERSTANDGRENZE **3325**
DAUERVERSUCH **5049**
DAUERVERSUCH **4743**
DAUMEN **1883**
DAUMENKRAFT **6688**
DAUMENSCHEIBE **13221**
DAUMENWELLE **1888**
DÄUMLING **13878**
DEBYE-SCHERRER METHODE **3643**
DECHSEL **207**
DECKANSTRICH **5217**
DECKE **3667**
DECKEL **13033**

DECKEL **3269**
DECKEL **3266**
DECKEL **1910**
DECKELBILDUNG **1927**
DECKELFLANSCH **1304**
DECKELMANSCHETTE **11548**
DECKENLAGER **6321**
DECKENLEUCHTE **4119**
DECKENLEUCHTE **10709**
DECKENVORGELEGE **8940**
DECKFÄHIGKEIT **3273**
DECKFARBE **1389**
DECKGLAS **3265**
DECKKRAFT EINER FARBE **1393**
DECKLACK **13505**
DECKPLATTE **13033**
DECKPLATTE **3267**
DECKRING **1232**
DECKSCHICHT **9950**
DEFEKT **5411**
DEFORMATIONSBAND **3706**
DEGRAS **3711**
DEHNBAR **4361**
DEHNBARKEIT **4363**
DEHNGRENZE **9923**
DEHNUNG **3949**
DEHNUNG **4946**
DEHNUNG **4679**
DEHNUNG (RELATIVE) **13370**
DEHNUNGSDICHTUNG **4918**
DEHNUNGSFUGE **4918**
DEHNUNGSKURVE **12365**
DEHNUNGSMESSER **4949**
DEHNUNGSMESSER **12325**
DEHNUNGSMESSSTREIFE **12329**
DEHNUNGSROHR **4913**
DEICH **3945**
DEKAGRAMM **3645**
DEKALESZENZ **3646**
DEKALITER **3647**
DEKAMETER **3648**
DEKANTIEREN **3649**
DEKANTIEREN **3650**
DEKAPIERBAD **111**
DEKAPIEREN **11005**
DEKAPIEREN **9288**
DEKAPIEREN EINES METALLES **11006**
DEKLINATION **3668**
DEKODIERER **3670**
DEKUPIEREN **8552**
DEKUPIERMASCHINE **6012**

# DEL

DELIQUESZENZ **3733**
DELIQUESZIEREN **3732**
DELTA-EISEN **3740**
DELTAMETALL **3741**
DEMIJOHN **1981**
DEMODULATION **10312**
DEMODULATOR **8338**
DEMONTAGE **12604**
DEMONTIEREN **12600**
DENATURIERTER SPIRITUS **8224**
DENATURIERUNGSMITTEL **3747**
DENDRIT **3748**
DENDRIT **9331**
DENSIMETER **3755**
DEPOLARISATION **3771**
DEPOLARISATION **3768**
DEPOLARISATOR **3772**
DEPOLARISATOR **3770**
DEPOLARISIEREN **3769**
DERIVAT **3786**
DERRICKKRAN **3788**
DESINFEKTIONSMITTEL **4042**
DESINTEGRATOR **4045**
DESOXYDATION **3762**
DESOXYDATION **3766**
DESOXYDATIONSMITTEL **3765**
DESOXYDIEREN **3763**
DESTILLAT **4071**
DESTILLATION **4072**
DESTILLATION (FRAKTIONIERTE) **5612**
DESTILLATION (STETIGE) **3024**
DESTILLATION (STUFENWEISE) **5612**
DESTILLATION (TROCKENE) **4346**
DESTILLATION (UNTERBROCHENE) **5612**
DESTILLATION IM VAKUUM **4075**
DESTILLATION MIT WASSERDAMPF **4073**
DESTILLATIONSERZEUGNIS **4071**
DESTILLIERBLASE **1407**
DESTILLIEREN **4070**
DESTILLIEREN (STUFENWEISE) **5615**
DESTILLIERKOLBEN **10523**
DESTILLIERVORRICHTUNG **12259**
DESTRUKTIVE DESTILLATION **3805**
DETAILZEICHNUNG **3809**
DETERMINANTE **3814**
DEUTSCHES GASÖL **1668**
DEXTRIN **3825**
DEXTROSE **6058**
DEZENTRIERT **8893**
DEZIGRAMM **3657**
DEZILITER **3658**

DEZIMALBRUCH **3662**
DEZIMALBRUCH (ENDLICHER) **5231**
DEZIMALBRUCH (PERIODISCHER) **9192**
DEZIMALE **3659**
DEZIMALKERZE **3663**
DEZIMALKODE **3661**
DEZIMALSTELLE **3659**
DEZIMALSYSTEM **3665**
DEZIMALWAAGE **3660**
DEZIMALZAHL **3664**
DEZIMETER **3666**
DIABAS **3828**
DIAGNOSEPROGRAMM **3830**
DIAGONAL **3831**
DIAGONALE **3831**
DIAGRAMM **7717**
DIAGRAMM **3834**
DIAGRAMM (RANKINISIERTES) **10203**
DIAGRAMM AUFZEICHNEN (EIN) **9520**
DIAGRAMME RANKINISIEREN **2765**
DIAGRAMMKURVE **3495**
DIAGRAMMLINIE **3495**
DIAKAUSTISCHE LINIE **3829**
DIALYSATOR **3845**
DIALYSE **3846**
DIALYSIEREN **3844**
DIAMAGNETISCH **3847**
DIAMAGNETISMUS **3848**
DIAMANT **3862**
DIAMANT (SCHWARZER) **1967**
DIAMANTGLANZ **158**
DIAMANTHÄRTEPROBE **3865**
DIAMANTSCHLEIFSCHEIBE **3867**
DIAMANTSCHLEIFSCHEIBE **3864**
DIAMANTSTAUB **3863**
DIAMANTWERKZEUG **3866**
DIANTHIN **4831**
DIAPHAN **3869**
DIAPHANITÄT **3868**
DIAPHRAGMA **3870**
DIAPHRAGMA **3871**
DIATHERMAN **3879**
DIATHERMANITÄT **3878**
DIATHERMANSIE **3878**
DIATOMEENERDE **7292**
DIATOMEENERDE **3880**
DICHT **12920**
DICHTE **3756**
DICHTE (ELEKTRISCHE) **4501**
DICHTE (MAGNETISCHE) **7899**
DICHTEN **7954**

DICHTEVERHÄLNIS **3759**
DICHTFLANSCH **5863**
DICHTGEPACKT **2514**
DICHTHALTEN **12932**
DICHTHALTEND **12920**
DICHTHEIT **6797**
DICHTIGKEIT **12932**
DICHTPLÄTTCHEN **11075**
DICHTSCHEIBE **4014**
DICHTSCHLIESSEND **12920**
DICHTSCHWEISSEN **11076**
DICHTUNG **8998**
DICHTUNG **5863**
DICHTUNG **9009**
DICHTUNG MIT GUMMIRING **10820**
DICHTUNGSBÜCHSE **9001**
DICHTUNGSMASSE **10037**
DICHTUNGSMATERIAL **7247**
DICHTUNGSMITTEL **7247**
DICHTUNGSNIETUNG **12922**
DICHTUNGSRING **9007**
DICHTUNGSSTOFF **7247**
DICHTUNGSSTREIFEN **13722**
DICHTUNGSZOPF **5863**
DICKE **12843**
DICKE DER ZEMENTIERSCHICHT **2020**
DICKENHOBELMASCHINE **12847**
DICKENVERGLEICHER **2796**
DICKENWACHSTUM **3851**
DICKFLÜSSIG **13577**
DICKFLÜSSIGKEIT **13576**
DICKWANDIG **12841**
DICKZIRKEL **8912**
DIELEKTRIKUM **3898**
DIELEKTRISCH **3898**
DIELEKTRIZITÄTSKONSTANTE **3899**
DIELENSÄGE **10609**
DIESELMASCHINE **3901**
DIESELMOTOR **3901**
DIFFENRENZLEHRE **3905**
DIFFERENFIALGETRIEBE **3913**
DIFFERENTIAL **3906**
DIFFERENTIALANTRIEBS-KEGELRAD **3910**
DIFFERENTIALBREMSE **3907**
DIFFERENTIALDYNAMOMETER **3911**
DIFFERENTIALFLASCHENZUG **13798**
DIFFERENTIALGLEICHUNG **3912**
DIFFERENTIALKOEFFIZIENT **3909**
DIFFERENTIALMANOMETER **3921**
DIFFERENTIALQUOTIENT **3916**
DIFFERENTIALRECHUNG **3908**

DIFFERENTIALSCHRAUBE **2833**
DIFFERENTIALTHERMOMETER **3920**
DIFFERENTIATION (MATH.) **3923**
DIFFERENZ (MATH.) **3902**
DIFFERENZIEREN (MATH.) **3922**
DIFFRAKTION **3924**
DIFFUSER **3928**
DIFFUSION **3929**
DIFFUSION DES LICHTES **3933**
DIFFUSION VON GASEN **3932**
DIFFUSIONGEBIET **3934**
DIFFUSIONSKOEFFIZIENT **3931**
DIFFUSIONSÜBERZÜGE **3930**
DIFFUSIONSVERMÖGEN **3936**
DIGERIEREN **3939**
DIGERIEREN **3937**
DIGESTION **3939**
DIGESTOR **829**
DIGITAL **3941**
DILATATION **3949**
DILATOMETER **3950**
DIMENSIONEN **3960**
DIMETHYL **4848**
DIMETHYLKETON **90**
DINASSTEIN **11435**
DIODE **3964**
DIORIT **3966**
DIOXYBERNSTEINSÄURE **12690**
DIPHENYLAMIN **3974**
DIREKT WIRKEND **3980**
DIREKTRIX **3996**
DISKRIMINANTE **4029**
DISLOKATION **4047**
DISPERGIERUNGSMITTEL **4050**
DISPERSION **4051**
DISPERSIONSMITTEL **4050**
DISPERSIONSPHASE **4049**
DISPOSITIONSZEICHNUNG **5914**
DISSOZIATION **4058**
DISSOZIATION (ELEKTROLYTISCHE) **4596**
DISSOZIATION (ELEKTROLYTISCHE) **4595**
DISSOZIATIONSWÄRME **6358**
DISTANZ **4063**
DISTANZBOLZEN **12151**
DISTANZSTÜCK **4068**
DIVERGENT **4093**
DIVERGENZ **4092**
DIVERGIEREN **4091**
DIVIDEND **4099**
DIVIDIEREN **4097**
DIVISION **4107**

# DOC

782

DIVISOR **4111**
DOCHT **13846**
DOCHTÖLER **11516**
DOCHTSCHMIERUNG **13847**
DODBKAEDER **4112**
DOLERIT **4114**
DOLOMIT **4117**
DOPPEL-J-NAHT MIT LUFTSPALT **8812**
DOPPEL-J-NAHT OHNE LUFTSPALT **2523**
DOPPEL-T-EISEN **6194**
DOPPEL-U-FUGENNAHT OHNE LUFTSPALT **2524**
DOPPELBACKENBREMSE **4129**
DOPPELBODEN **5026**
DOPPELBRECHEND **1265**
DOPPELBRECHUNG **4151**
DOPPELDECKER **1261**
DOPPELFLANSCH **4139**
DOPPELGÄRBSTAHL **4156**
DOPPELGETRIEBE **4142**
DOPPELHAKEN **10191**
DOPPELHE **4147**
DOPPELHOBEL **4146**
DOPPELINTEGRAL **4145**
DOPPELKALIBER **3905**
DOPPELKEHLNAHT **4141**
DOPPELKEIL **5938**
DOPPELKLINKENGETRIEBE **2494**
DOPPELKLOTZBREMSE **4129**
DOPPELKOPFSCHIENEN **1715**
DOPPELKRÜMMER **13323**
DOPPELLASCHENNIETUNG **4130**
DOPPELMUFFE **4158**
DOPPELNAHT OHNE LUFTSPALT **1788**
DOPPELNIPPEL **4149**
DOPPELPFEILZAHNRAD **13176**
DOPPELPUNKTSCHWEISSMASCHINE **4382**
DOPPELRIEMEN **4128**
DOPPELSALZ **4153**
DOPPELSAÜLESCHMIEDEHAMMER **4140**
DOPPELSCHLUSSDYNAMO **3228**
DOPPELSCHLÜSSEL **4167**
DOPPELSCHLUSSMOTOR **2835**
DOPPELSCHNITTFEILE **4133**
DOPPELSITZVENTIL **4154**
DOPPELSITZVENTIL **4166**
DOPPELSTÄNDER **4159**
DOPPELSTÄNDER PRESSE (MECHANISCHE) **4157**
DOPPELT GEKRÖPFTE KURBELWELLE **13316**
DOPPELT KOHLENSAURES KALI **9676**
DOPPELTCHROMSAURES KALI **9677**
DOPPELTER ANSCHLAGWINKEL **12581**

DOPPELTKOHLENSÄURE MAGNESIA **7883**
DOPPELTWIRKEND **4163**
DOPPELVERGASER **4360**
DOPPELWANDIG **4170**
DOPPELWANDIGER **4161**
DOPPELWINKELZAHNRAD **13176**
DOPPELZENTNER **10111**
DÖPPER **10626**
DOPPLUNG **7382**
DORN **7964**
DORN **11904**
DORN **3162**
DORN **4260**
DORN (FESTER) **9425**
DORN (FESTER) **11789**
DOSENBAROMETER **504**
DOSENLIBELLE **2430**
DOUBLE **5999**
DOUBLET **4172**
DOWSONGAS **4194**
DRACHENBLUT **4203**
DRAHT **13880**
DRAHT (BLANKER) **13340**
DRAHT (BLANKER) **990**
DRAHT (DREIKANTIGER) **13196**
DRAHT (EIRUNDER) **4678**
DRAHT (ELLIPTISCHER) **4678**
DRAHT (FEINER) **12849**
DRAHT (FEINGEZOGNER) **12849**
DRAHT (GALVANISIERTER) **5786**
DRAHT (GEFLOCHTENER) **1528**
DRAHT (GEGLÜHTER) **561**
DRAHT (GEWALZTER) **10678**
DRAHT (GEZOGENER) **4252**
DRAHT (HARTGEZOGENER) **13340**
DRAHT (ISOLIERTER) **6996**
DRAHT (KALTGEZOGENER) **2715**
DRAHT (KUNSTSTOFFUMKLEIDETER) **9468**
DRAHT (NACKTER) **990**
DRAHT (NICHT ISOLIERTER ELEKTR.) **990**
DRAHT (OVALER) **4678**
DRAHT (RECHTECKIGER) **5402**
DRAHT (RUNDER) **10804**
DRAHT (UMHÜLLTER) **11300**
DRAHT (UMKLÖPPELTER) **1528**
DRAHT (UMMANTELTER) **3272**
DRAHT (UNGEGLÜHTER) **13340**
DRAHT (VERBLEITER) **7459**
DRAHT (VERZINKTER) **5786**
DRAHT (VERZINNTER) **12962**
DRAHT UMFLOCHTENER **1528**

DRAHTABSPULER **13898**
DRAHTABSPULGESCHWINDIGKEIT **13900**
DRAHTAUF-U.ABWICKELMASCHINE **13903**
DRAHTBARREN **13882**
DRAHTBIEGEMASCHINE **13883**
DRAHTBÜRSTE **13884**
DRAHTFEDERNWINDEMASCHINE **13901**
DRAHTFLECHTMASCHINEN **13897**
DRAHTGAZE **13893**
DRAHTGEFLECHT **13896**
DRAHTGEWEBE **13893**
DRAHTGEWEBE **5888**
DRAHTGLAS **13894**
DRAHTHASPEL **13898**
DRAHTKETTENMASCHINE **13885**
DRAHTKLAMMER **12104**
DRAHTLEHRE **13892**
DRAHTLEHRE (ENGLISCHE) (B. W. G.) **12089**
DRAHTLITZE **13902**
DRAHTNAGEL **13895**
DRAHTNETZ **13896**
DRAHTNUMMER **5881**
DRAHTÖSE **12106**
DRAHTSCHNEIDER **13886**
DRAHTSEIL **13899**
DRAHTSEIL (FLACHLITZIGES) **5407**
DRAHTSEIL IM GLEICHSCHLAG **309**
DRAHTSEIL NACH ALBERTSCHLAG **7390**
DRAHTSEILBAHN **213**
DRAHTSEILHERSTELLUNGSMASCHINE **12341**
DRAHTSTÄRKE **3860**
DRAHTSTIFT **13895**
DRAHTSTIFTSCHLAGMASCHINE **13891**
DRAHTVERARBEITUNGSMASCHINE **13904**
DRAHTZANGE (FLACHE) **5403**
DRAHTZANGE (RUNDE) **10805**
DRAHTZIEHBANK **4218**
DRAHTZIEHEISEN **4223**
DRAHTZIEHEN **4230**
DRAHTZIEHEN **13888**
DRAHTZIEHEN **13906**
DRAHTZIEHEN **4220**
DRAHTZIEHEREI **13905**
DRAHTZIEHMASCHINE **13889**
DRAHTZIEHSTEIN **13887**
DRAHTZIEHSTEIN **189**
DRAHTZWICKZANGE **3532**
DRALL EINES SEILES **13305**
DRAUFSICHTSBILD **13037**
DREHACHSE **868**
DREHAUTOMAT **846**

DREHBANK **13289**
DREHBANK **7427**
DREHBANK (SELBSTTÄTIGE) **846**
DREHBANKFUTTER **2393**
DREHBAR **9422**
DREHBEANSPRUCHUNG **13056**
DREHBESCHLEUNIGUNG **537**
DREHBEWEGUNG **10766**
DREHEN (AUF DER DREHBANK) **13276**
DREHEN (AUF DER DREHBANK) **13287**
DREHEN (KEGELIG) **13282**
DREHEN (KONISCH) **13282**
DREHEN (SICH) **10763**
DREHENDE WELLE (SICH) **10764**
DREHER **13286**
DREHEREI **13290**
DREHFEILE **10755**
DREHFUTTER-BACKEN **2394**
DREHGESCHWINDIGKEIT **11876**
DREHKOLBEN **10756**
DREHKOLBENPUMPE **10758**
DREHKRAN **11583**
DREHLING **7393**
DREHMASCHINE **1018**
DREHMASCHINE MIT AUTOMATISCHEN ARBEITSABLÄUFEN
**840**
DREHMASCHINE MIT FRONTBEDIENUNG **5697**
DREHMELDER **12568**
DREHMOMENT **13048**
DREHMOMENT **13308**
DREHMOMENTMESSER **13050**
DREHMOMENTSCHRAUBENSCHLÜSSEL **13049**
DREHPUNKT **2169**
DREHPUNKT **5717**
DREHRICHTUNG **3992**
DREHROST **10559**
DREHSCHEIBE **13295**
DREHSCHIEBER **10760**
DREHSCHWINGUNG **13557**
DREHSINN **3992**
DREHSPÄNE **13293**
DREHSPANNUNG **13058**
DREHSTAB **13053**
DREHSTABSTABILISATOR **12539**
DREHSTAHL **13292**
DREHSTICHEL **13292**
DREHSTROM **12877**
DREHSTROMDYNAMO **12875**
DREHSTROMMASCHINE **12875**
DREHSTROMMOTOR **12876**
DREHSTUHL **13639**

**DRE** 784

DREHTISCH 10762
DREHUNG 10765
DREHUNG 13054
DREHUNGSELLIPSOID 4672
DREHUNGSFEDER 11994
DREHUNGSFESTIGKEIT 13057
DREHUNGSFLÄCHE 12513
DREHUNGSHALBMESSER 10169
DREHUNGSKÖRPER 11790
DREHUNGSPARABOLOID 9042
DREHUNGSWINKEL 528
DREHZAHL 8690
DREHZAHL 10814
DREHZAHL 10558
DREHZAHLMESSER 10556
DREHZAHLREGLER 11874
DREHZAHLREGLER 13493
DREHZAHLREGLER 6013
DREHZAPFEN 13242
DREHZAPFEN 7256
DREIATOMIG 13197
DREIBACKENFUTTER 12874
DREIBASISCH 13198
DREIBEIN 5945
DREIDIMENSIONAL 8728
DREIECK 11223
DREIECK (GEOM.) 13185
DREIECK (GLEICHSCHENKLIGES) 7192
DREIECK (GLEICHSEITIGES) 4785
DREIECK (RECHTWINKLIGES) 10582
DREIECK (SPHÄRISCHES) 11891
DREIECK (SPITZWINKLIGES) 157
DREIECK (STUMPFWINKLIGES) 8718
DREIECK (UNGLEICHSEITIGES) 10984
DREIECKFEDER 13191
DREIECKFEDER (GESCHICHTETE) 7381
DREIECKGEWINDE 545
DREIECKLAST 13190
DREIFACH-SCHWEFELANTIMON 627
DREIFACHEXPANSIONSMASCHINE 13217
DREIFADENMETHODE 12883
DREIFLACH 13202
DREIFUSSWINDE 13218
DREIKANT 13202
DREIKANTFEILE 13189
DREIKANTLITZENSEIL 13195
DREIKANTSEIL 13194
DREIPHASENDYNAMO 12875
DREIPHASENMOTOR 12876
DREIPHASENSTROM 12877
DREISCHENKELZIRKEL 13187

DREISTOFFSYSTEM 12766
DREIWEGESTÜCK 12699
DREIWEGEVENTIL 12882
DREIWEGHAHN 12881
DREIWEGSCHIEBER 3592
DREIWERTIG 13197
DREIZYLINDERMASCHINE 12873
DRESCHMASCHINEN 12884
DRESSIEREN 12720
DRESSIEREN 12319
DRESSIEREN 9157
DRILLBOHRER 689
DRILLBRETT 1590
DRILLUNG 532
DRITTE POTENZ 3445
DRITTE WURZEL 3447
DROSSELKLAPPE 2357
DROSSELKLAPPE 1811
DROSSELKLAPPE 12890
DROSSELKLAPPE 12888
DROSSELN 12889
DROSSELN 12891
DROSSELUNG 12891
DRUCK 10028
DRUCK 6314
DRUCK 9808
DRUCK (ABSOLUTER) 4459
DRUCK (ABSOLUTER) 33
DRUCK (ATMOSPHÄRISCHER) 794
DRUCK (GLEICHBLEIBENDER) 2976
DRUCK (HOHER) 6473
DRUCK (HYDROSTATISCHER) 6726
DRUCK (HYDROSTATISCHER) 7652
DRUCK (INNERER) 9822
DRUCK (KONSTANTER) 2976
DRUCK (KRITISCHER) 3348
DRUCK (MANOMETRISCHER) 5771
DRUCK (MITTLERER) 8075
DRUCK (NIEDERER) 7774
DRUCK (OSMOTISCHER) 8891
DRUCK (RUHENDER) 12137
DRUCK (SEITLICHER) 7422
DRUCK (SPEZIFISCHER) 11853
DRUCK (STATISCHER) 12137
DRUCK (STATISCHER) 12136
DRUCK (VERÄNDERLICHER) 13491
DRUCK (ZULÄSSIGER) 9828
DRUCK PARALLEL ZUR FASER 10021
DRUCK SENKRECHT ZUR FASER 10022
DRUCK-UND PLANIERMASCHINE 11911
DRUCKABFALL 9815

DRUCKÄNDERUNG 2237
DRUCKANSTIEG 6848
DRUCKBACKEN EINER SCHERE 11282
DRUCKBEANSPRUCHUNG 2863
DRUCKBEANSPRUCHUNG 2869
DRUCKBEGRENZUNGSVENTIL 10441
DRUCKBELASTUNG 9823
DRUCKDÜSE 3738
DRUCKELASTIZITÄT 4488
DRÜCKEN 8189
DRUCKER 9872
DRUCKFEDER 2862
DRUCKFESTIGKEIT 2870
DRUCKFESTIGKEIT 13328
DRUCKGASGENERATOR 9819
DRUCKGEFÄSS 9839
DRUCKGIESSVERFAHREN 3886
DRUCKGUSS 3886
DRUCKGUSS 9812
DRUCKGUSSLEGIERUNG 388
DRUCKHÖHE (HÖHE DER FLÜSSIGKEITSSÄULE) 6323
DRUCKHÖHE EINER PUMPE 4021
DRUCKHUB 9834
DRUCKKESSEL 829
DRUCKKLAPPE 3739
DRUCKKNOPF 9797
DRUCKKRAFT 2868
DRUCKLAGER 12902
DRUCKLEITUNG 3736
DRUCKLUFT 2839
DRUCKLUFTANTRIEB 2842
DRUCKLUFTBEHÄLTERGLIED 11117
DRUCKLUFTBREMSE 2840
DRUCKLÜFTER 9817
DRUCKLUFTFUTTER 279
DRUCKLUFTHAMMER 9551
DRUCKLUFTHAMMER 9553
DRUCKLUFTLEITUNG 2845
DRUCKLUFTLOKOMOTIVE 2844
DRUCKLUFTMOTOR 2843
DRUCKLUFTNIETHAMMER 9555
DRUCKLUFTNIETHAMMER 12400
DRUCKLUFTPROBE 2846
DRUCKLUFTPUMPE 273
DRUCKLÜFTUNG 9517
DRUCKLUFTZYLINDER 2841
DRUCKMESSER 9820
DRUCKMESSER 9821
DRUCKMINDERER 10355
DRUCKMINDERER 10420
DRUCKMINDERUNGSVENTIL 10355

DRUCKMINDERVENTIL 10355
DRUCKPROBE 9836
DRUCKPROBE 2865
DRUCKPUMPE 5531
DRUCKQUERSCHNITT 3375
DRUCKREGLER 9813
DRUCKREGLER 9829
DRUCKREGLER 10355
DRUCKREGLUNG 10419
DRUCKRING 9830
DRUCKRING 12904
DRUCKROHRLEITUNG 3736
DRUCKROHRLEITUNG 9827
DRUCKSCHALTER 9835
DRUCKSCHMIERUNG 9824
DRUCKSCHMIERUNG 9818
DRUCKSCHRAUBE 9831
DRUCKSCHRAUBE 193
DRUCKSCHWANKUNG 13497
DRUCKSINTERN 9799
DRUCKSPANNUNG 2871
DRUCKSTAB 2855
DRUCKSTEIGERUNG 6848
DRUCKSTOCK 1340
DRUCKSTUFE 9833
DRUCKTURBINE 6810
DRUCKUNTERSCHIED 9814
DRUCKVENTIL 3739
DRUCKVERLUST 6315
DRUCKVERLUST 7759
DRUCKVERLUST 7763
DRUCKVERSUCH 2872
DRUCKVOLUMENDIAGRAMM 6881
DRUCKWALZENRÄNDELMASCHINE 9873
DRUCKWASSER 9841
DRUCKWASSERANTRIEB 6683
DRUCKWASSERLEITUNG 9840
DRUCKWASSERPRESSE 6693
DRUCKWASSERPROBE 6695
DRUCKWASSERSCHMIEDEPRESSE 6687
DRUCKWASSERSPEICHER 6677
DRUCKZUG 5533
DRUCKZUNAHME 6848
DRUMMONDSCHES LICHT 8987
DÜBEL 7276
DÜBEL 12397
DÜBEL 4180
DUBLEE 5999
DUBLETT 4172
DUKTILITÄT 4363
DUKTILITÄTSPRÜFMASCHINE 3462

**DUN** 786

DÜNENSAND 11071
DÜNGERAUSBREITEMASCHINEN 7995
DÜNGERLADER 7689
DÜNGERSTREUER 4087
DUNKELROTGLÜHEND 4368
DUNKELROTGLUT 4367
DUNKELSCHALTER 3963
DÜNNFLÜSSIG 5471
DÜNNFLÜSSIGKEIT 5474
DÜNNSCHLIFF 11113
DÜNNWANDIG 12851
DUNST 1404
DUPLEXPUMPE 4381
DUPLEXVERFAHREN 4380
DURALUMIN 4387
DURCHBIEGEN (SICH) 1174
DURCHBIEGUNG 5426
DURCHBIEGUNG 3700
DURCHBIEGUNG 3698
DURCHBIEGUNG (BLEIBENDE) EINES TRÄGERSTEGS 13727
DURCHBIEGUNG (ELASTISCHE) 4477
DURCHBIEGUNG (GRÖSSTE) 8064
DURCHBIEGUNG (MASS) 3701
DURCHBIEGUNGS PRÜFUNG (KONSTANTE) 2972
DURCHBRENNEN (SICHERUNG) 1352
DURCHBRUCH 1589
DURCHBRUCHSPANNUNG 1582
DURCHDRINGLICHKEIT 9211
DURCHDRINGUNG 9170
DURCHFEDERUNG 4477
DURCHFLUSSANZEIGER 11426
DURCHFLUSSGESCHWINDIGKEIT 13518
DURCHFLUSSGRÖSSE 5459
DURCHFLUSSMENGE 10069
DURCHFLUSSMESSER 5455
DURCHFLUSSMESSER 5458
DURCHFLUSSÖFFNUNG 9100
DURCHFLUSSQUERSCHNITT 3374
DURCHGANGSHAHN 12281
DURCHGANGSÖFFNUNG 9100
DURCHGANGSQUERSCHNITT 3374
DURCHGANGSVENTIL 12317
DURCHGANGSVENTIL 5977
DURCHGANGSVENTIL 5867
DURCHGANGSWEITE 9634
DURCHGEHEN (MASCHINE) 10117
DURCHGEHEN EINER MASCHINE 10118
DURCHHANG 10894
DURCHHÄNGEN 10893
DURCHHÄNGEN 10892
DURCHHÄRTUNG 12892

DURCHHÄRTUNG 5721
DURCHLÄSSIG 9213
DURCHLÄSSIG FÜR WÄRMESTRAHLEN 3879
DURCHLÄSSIGKEIT 9211
DURCHLÄSSIGKEIT (MAGNETISCHE) 7911
DURCHLÄSSIGKEIT FÜR WÄRMESTRAHLEN 3878
DURCHLASSÖFFNUNG 9100
DURCHLAUF 5181
DURCHLAUFBANDGLÜHEN 574
DURCHLAUFERHITZER 5846
DURCHLAUFOFEN 3026
DURCHLAUFSCHWEISSEN 3016
DURCHLOCHEN 9186
DURCHMESSER 3849
DURCHMESSER (ÄUSSERER) 4958
DURCHMESSER (INNERER) 7071
DURCHMESSER (KONJUGIERTER) 2954
DURCHMESSER (ZUGEORDNETER) 2954
DURCHMESSER DES TEILKREISES 3861
DURCHMESSERTEILUNG 3861
DURCHMISCHEN 7102
DURCHPAUSEN 13077
DURCHPAUSEN 13082
DURCHSCHEINEND 13125
DURCHSCHLAG 7332
DURCHSCHLAG 9997
DURCHSCHLAG (ELEKTR.) 10013
DURCHSCHLAGEN 1321
DURCHSCHLAGSFESTIGKEIT 3900
DURCHSCHLAGSFESTIGKEIT 4057
DURCHSCHNEIDEN (GEOM.) 3504
DURCHSCHNITT NACH A-B 11112
DURCHSCHNITTLICHE DICHTE 642
DURCHSCHNITTSTEMPERATUR 855
DURCHSCHNITTSWERT 8073
DURCHSICHTIG 13138
DURCHSICHTIGKEIT 13137
DURCHSIEBEN 11423
DURCHSTECKSCHRAUBE 1441
DURCHSTOSSOFEN 10030
DURCHTRÄNKEN 6805
DURCHTRÄNKEN 6802
DURCHTREIBER 4261
DURCHTRITTSQUERSCHNITT 3374
DURCHWÄRMETEMPERATUR 11700
DURCHWEICHUNGSGRUBE 11699
DURCHWURFSIEB 11628
DUSCHVENTIL 11387
DÜSE 8679
DÜSE 7218
DÜSE 12966

| | |
|---|---|
| DÜSE EINES GEBLÄSES **8685** | EDELMETALL **8603** |
| DÜSENBOHRMASCHINE **8681** | EDELMETALL **8602** |
| DÜSENFEDER **8686** | EDELMETALLBAR **1730** |
| DÜSENHALTER **8682** | EDELMETALLBARREN **1729** |
| DÜSENHÖHE **8680** | EDELMETALLTEILCHEN **3548** |
| DÜSENNADEL **8684** | EDELROST **220** |
| DÜSENTRÄGER **7219** | EDELROST **9127** |
| DYN **4405** | EDELSTAHL **12462** |
| DYNAMIK **4400** | EFEUBLATTKURVE **2438** |
| DYNAMISCH **4399** | EFFEKT **9730** |
| DYNAMIT **4401** | EFFEKT-KOEFFIZIENT (THERMOELEKTRISCHER) **2637** |
| DYNAMO (IN SERIE GESCHALTETER) **11201** | EFFLORESZENZ **4464** |
| DYNAMOBLECH **708** | EFFUSION **4465** |
| DYNAMOELEKTRISCHE MASCHINE **5924** | EFFUSION VON GASEN **4466** |
| DYNAMOGRAPH **10291** | EGALISIERBANK **9428** |
| DYNAMOMASCHINE **5924** | EGALISIEREN **13164** |
| DYNAMOMETER **4403** | EGALISIEREN **13162** |
| DYNAMOMETER MIT SCHREIBVORRICHTUNG **10291** | EGGEN (GLEIDEREGGENZIGZAGEGGEN) **6303** |
| DYNAMOMETRISCH **4404** | EICHEN **5872** |
| DYNE **4405** | EICHEN **5886** |
| DYNODE **4406** | EICHFEHLER **1869** |
| DYSPROSIUM **4407** | EICHKONDENSATOR **1868** |
| E-EISEN **2250** | EICHMASS **5768** |
| EAU DE JAVEL **9688** | EICHMASS **12076** |
| EAU DE LABARRAQUE | EICHUNG **5886** |
| (NATRIUMHYPOCHLORITLÖSUNGCHLORSODALÖSUNG) **4422** | EICHUNG **1867** |
| EBENE (GEOM.) **9433** | EICHUNG (EINES BEHÄLTERS) **1863** |
| EBENE (PRISMATISCHE) **9877** | EIGENERREGUNG **11153** |
| EBENE (SCHIEFE) **6838** | EIGENFEDERUNG **4487** |
| EBENENWINKEL **3944** | EIGENGEWICHT **3637** |
| EBENES VENTIL **4011** | EIGENLAST **3637** |
| EBENHOLZ **4423** | EIGENSCHAFTEN (MECHANISCHE) **8109** |
| EBONIT **2363** | EIGENSCHAFTEN (PHYSIKALISCHE) **9283** |
| ECKBLECH **6182** | EIGENSCHWINGUNG **5736** |
| ECKBOHRMASCHINE **3178** | EIGENSPANNUNG **10474** |
| ECKBOHRWINDE **5905** | EIMER **1674** |
| ECKE **4408** | EIN-UND AUSRÜCKKUPPLUNG **4033** |
| ECKE (EINSPRINGENDE) **10243** | EINATOMIG **8377** |
| ECKE EINES POLYGONS **13543** | EINBAUTRÄGER **1702** |
| ECKEN **7212** | EINBAUTRÄGER **6968** |
| ECKEN **7210** | EINBETONIEREN **4682** |
| ECKENBOHRER **5905** | EINBETONIERTER TRÄGER **4714** |
| ECKENLINIE **3831** | EINBEULUNG **3760** |
| ECKNAHTVERBINDUNG MIT LUFTSPALT **8809** | EINBEULVERSUCH **8797** |
| ECKNAHTVERBINDUNG OHNE LUFTSPALT **2522** | EINBRANDKERBEN **13351** |
| ECKVENTIL **534** | EINBRENNHÄRTUNG **9670** |
| ECKVERBAND **2519** | EINDAMPFEN EINER LÖSUNG **2885** |
| ECKVERBAND **4445** | EINDIMENSIONAL **8727** |
| ECKWINKEL **510** | EINDRINGUNGSGRAD **4683** |
| EDELGAS **6905** | EINDRUCK **6806** |
| EDELMETALL **9756** | EINDRUCKFLÄCHE **12512** |

**EIN** 788

EINDRUCKVERSUCH 1618
EINFACH GEKRÖPFTE KURBELWELLE 11503
EINFACH-CHLORZINN 12100
EINFACHCHLOREISEN 5121
EINFACHER HIEB EINER FEILE 11482
EINFACHEXPANSIONSMASCHINE 11500
EINFACHRIEMEN 11477
EINFACHWIRKEND 11493
EINFAHRZEIT 10855
EINFAHRZEIT 1587
EINFALLEN (KLINKE) 4320
EINFALLWINKEL 520
EINFASSUNG 11547
EINFETTEN 6084
EINFETTEN 6087
EINFLUSSÖFFNUNG 6947
EINFRESSEN 11141
EINFRESSEN (SICH) 11140
EINFRIEREN DES OFENS 5655
EINFÜGESCHWEISSFITTING 11708
EINFÜLLVERSCHLUSS 5158
EINGABEDATENTRÄGER 6960
EINGABEFORMAT (FESTES) 5288
EINGABEFORMAT IN ADRESSSCHREIBWEISE 13935
EINGABEFORMAT IN FESTER WORTFOLGESCHREIBWEISE ·
  5297
EINGABEFORMAT IN TABULATOR-SCHREIBWEISE 12583
EINGABEFORMAT IN VARIABLER SATZSCHREIBWEISE
  13489
EINGANG 6943
EINGANGS-ROHRSTUTZEN 6946
EINGANGSKLEMME 6944
EINGEMAUERT 1600
EINGESCHLEPPTE LOSÜNG 4201
EINGESCHNÜRT 3042
EINGESCHRIEBENER KREIS 6963
EINGESCHRIEBENES MASS 3956
EINGESPANNTER TRÄGER 5286
EINGREIFEN 4750
EINGRIFF 5910
EINGRIFF 4752
EINGRIFF (IM) 8171
EINGRIFF BRINGEN IN 10033
EINGRIFF STEHEN (IM) 1077
EINGRIFFSBOGEN 675
EINGRIFFSFLÄCHE 696
EINGRIFFSLINIE 7602
EINGRIFFSTIEFE 13951
EINGRIFFSTIEFE 13952
EINGRIFFSWINKEL 9810
EINGUSSKANAL 4186

EINGUSSTRICHTER 12003
EINHALSUNG 8516
EINHÄNGEGESTELL 9505
EINHEIT PHOTOMETRISCHE 9270
EINHEITSGEWICHT 11850
EINHEITSVEKTOR 13380
EINHÜLLENDE 4776
EINKAPSELUNG 2026
EINKERBBIEGEPROBE 1190
EINKERBEN 8554
EINKERBUNG 8672
EINKLINKEN 4749
EINKLINKEN 4751
EINKRIECHEN DES RIEMENS 3329
EINKRISTALL 11480
EINKUPPELN 10033
EINKUPPELN 12897
EINKUPPLUNG 12897
EINLAGE 6965
EINLAGE 11352
EINLAGE EINER PACKUNG 3155
EINLAGERN 12299
EINLAGERN 12294
EINLAGERUNG 12288
EINLASS 6943
EINLASSEN (EINEN SCHRAUBENKOPF) 3246
EINLASSEN (EINES NIETKOPFES, EINES SCHRAUBENKOPFES)
  3247
EINLASSHUB 7008
EINLASSÖFFNUNG 6947
EINLASSSCHLITZ 200
EINLASSVENTIL 6949
EINLASSVENTIL 201
EINLAUF 4186
EINLAUFEN LASSEN (EINE MASCHINE) 10835
EINLEGESTREIFEN 7620
EINLIEGENDER KREIS 6963
EINMITTELN 2187
EINMITTELN 2163
EINPASSEN 5280
EINPASSEN 5276
EINPHASENSTROM 11501
EINPILASTERHOBELMASCHINE 8821
EINPRÄGUNG 6806
EINRAMMEN 9306
EINREICHUNG EINES PATENTGESUCHES 646
EINREISSEN 10859
EINRICHTUNG (SANITÄRE) 10931
EINRINGDRUCKLAGER 11479
EINRÜCKEN 12897
EINRÜCKEN 10033

EINRÜCKUNG **12897**
EINRÜCKVORRICHTUNG **4034**
EINSATZ (FLÜSSIGER) **7647**
EINSATZBAD **1994**
EINSATZFUTTER **10358**
EINSATZGELENK **6966**
EINSATZHÄRTEN **2141**
EINSATZHÄRTUNG **2023**
EINSATZHÄRTUNG **2021**
EINSATZHÄRTUNG **1987**
EINSATZKASTEN **1989**
EINSATZMATRIZE **6966**
EINSATZMITTEL **1988**
EINSATZMITTEL **2024**
EINSATZOFEN **1060**
EINSATZPULVER **2022**
EINSATZSTAHL **2138**
EINSATZSTÜCK **6965**
EINSATZZIRKEL **2805**
EINSATZZYLINDER **3571**
EINSAUGUNG **11289**
EINSCHALTEN **7088**
EINSCHALTEN **7023**
EINSCHALTEN **7022**
EINSCHALTEN **12897**
EINSCHALTEN **10033**
EINSCHALTEN (ELEKTR.) **12560**
EINSCHALTEN (ELEKTR.) **12555**
EINSCHALTER **12553**
EINSCHALTUNG **7089**
EINSCHALTUNG **12897**
EINSCHEIBENKOLBEN **11791**
EINSCHIEBEN **7023**
EINSCHIEBEN **7022**
EINSCHLAG EINES GEWEBES **13743**
EINSCHLAGEN (EINEN NAGEL) **4292**
EINSCHLAGWINKEL **7701**
EINSCHLEIFEN **6104**
EINSCHLEIFEN **6111**
EINSCHLIESSUNGSGRAD **4683**
EINSCHLUSS **6840**
EINSCHLUSS (SEKUNDÄRER) **11106**
EINSCHLÜSSE (NICHTMETALLISCHE) **8620**
EINSCHMELZEN **10446**
EINSCHMELZEN **10447**
EINSCHMIRGEIN **6111**
EINSCHMIRGELN **6104**
EINSCHNÜRUNG **5728**
EINSCHNÜRUNG **3045**
EINSCHNÜRUNG **3044**
EINSCHNÜRUNG **8515**

EINSCHNÜRUNG **10361**
EINSCHNÜRUNGSEFFEKT **9329**
EINSCHRUMPFEN **11397**
EINSCHRUMPFEN **11388**
EINSCHWEISSENDEN **1810**
EINSCHWEISSFLANSCH **13794**
EINSEITIG EINGESPANNT **5285**
EINSEITIG GESCHWEISSTE ÜBERLAPPUNGSVERBINDUNG
    **11504**
EINSEITIGE GRENZRACHENLEHRE MIT ZWEI MESSSTELLEN
    FÜR 'GUT' UND 'AUSSCHUSSSEITE' **6607**
EINSEITIGE LASCHENNIETUNG **11478**
EINSEMENNIGE **7148**
EINSETZEN **2021**
EINSETZEN DER NIETEN **6972**
EINSINKEN **11507**
EINSINKEN **12418**
EINSITZIGES VENTIL **11497**
EINSITZVENTIL **11497**
EINSITZVENTIL **11488**
EINSPANNEN EINES PROBESTABES **5300**
EINSPANNVORRICHTUNG **7227**
EINSPINDEL-AUTOMAT MIT REVOLVERKOPF **13298**
EINSPRENGEN **12001**
EINSPRENGEN **12000**
EINSPRITZDÜSE **6938**
EINSPRITZEN **6935**
EINSPRITZEN **6934**
EINSPRITZFOLGE **6936**
EINSPRITZKONDENSATOR **7220**
EINSPRITZPUMPE **5711**
EINSPRITZPUMPEN-GEHÄUSE **5712**
EINSPRITZROHR **9993**
EINSPRITZUNG **6935**
EINSPRITZVENTIL **6937**
EINSPRUCH GEGEN EIN PATENT **8707**
EINSTÄNDERHOBELMASCHINE **8821**
EINSTÄNDERPRESSE (HYDRAULISCHE) **8828**
EINSTÄNDERPRESSE (MECHANISCHE) **8814**
EINSTAUBEN MIT SCHWEFEL **4394**
EINSTECKKURBEL **10450**
EINSTECKSEITE **4774**
EINSTEIGELOCH **7976**
EINSTELLEN **195**
EINSTELLEN **182**
EINSTELLEN **5505**
EINSTELLEN **2730**
EINSTELLHÜLSE **194**
EINSTELLLEHRE **11225**
EINSTELLLEHRE **5086**
EINSTELLSCHRAUBE **192**

**EIN** 790

EINSTELLUNG 195
EINSTELLUNG EINES OPTISCHEN INSTRUMENTS 5505
EINSTELLUNGSANGELPUNKTE 12951
EINSTRAHLUNG 6831
EINSTREICHFEILE 11623
EINSTRÖMLINIE 199
EINTAUCH-VERFAHREN (KONTINUIERLICHES) 3028
EINTAUCHEN 3978
EINTAUCHEN 3968
EINTAUCHREINIGUNG 11697
EINTAUCHVERFAHREN 3977
EINTRAG 4201
EINTREIBDORN 4260
EINTREIBEN (EINEN KEIL) 4293
EINTREIBEN (EINEN NAGEL) 4292
EINTREIBEN EINES KEILS 4310
EINTRITTGESCHWINDIGKEIT 6950
EINTRITTSEITE 4774
EINWALZEN VON ROHREN 4908
EINWERTIG 8377
EINWICKELPAPIER 13984
EINWIRKUNG (CHEMISCHE) 2312
EINWIRKUNG (EINER KRAFT) 143
EINZELANTRIEB 6886
EINZELKEHLNAHT 5720
EINZELKRAFT 11483
EINZELLAST 7183
EINZELLOS 1059
EINZELTEIL 11484
EINZELTEIL 3811
EINZELZEICHNUNG 3809
EINZIEHEN DER NIETEN 6972
EINZYLINDERMASCHINE 11498
EIS SCHMELZENDES 8139
EISBLUMENBILDUNG 5702
EISEN 7133
EISEN (BRÜCHIGES) 11368
EISEN (DAS) KOHLEN 1986
EISEN (DAS) ÜBERHITZEN 1746
EISEN (KALTBRÜCHIGES) 2702
EISEN (KLEINLUCKIGES) 2511
EISEN (NICHT-ROSTENDES) 12051
EISEN (OXALSAURES) 5124
EISEN (ROTBRÜCHIGES) 10338
EISEN (SEHNIGES) 5139
EISEN (SPRÖDES) 11368
EISEN (STAHLARTIGES) 12224
EISEN (VERBRANNTES) 1762
EISEN IM BRECHGUT 13106
EISEN- UND FORMSTAHLSCHEREN 7136
EISEN-KOHLENSTOFF-DIAGRAMM 7139

EISEN-STAHLUMWANDLUG 3068
EISENALAUN 7135
EISENAZETAT 7134
EISENBAHNRADREIFEN 12220
EISENBAHNSCHWELLE 11574
EISENBAU 7152
EISENBESCHLAG 7159
EISENBETON 12203
EISENBLAUPAPIER 5119
EISENBLECH 11309
EISENBLECHE (VERZINKTE) 5788
EISENCHLORID 5100
EISENCHLORÜR 5121
EISENDRAHT 7155
EISENDRAHT (BLANKGEZOGENER) 1610
EISENDRAHT (SCHWARZGEGLÜHTER) 1284
EISENDRAHTSEIL 7147
EISENERZ 7143
EISENGIESSEREI 7142
EISENGLANZ 11865
EISENHALTIG 5127
EISENHALTIGES MANGANERZ 5122
EISENHOLZ 13833
EISENHÜTTE 7160
EISENHÜTTENWESEN 8209
EISENHYDROXYD 5101
EISENKARBID 7138
EISENKARBONYL 7140
EISENKIES 7146
EISENKITT 7141
EISENKONSTRUKTION 12208
EISENKONSTRUKTION 7152
EISENLEGIERUNG 7156
EISENLEGIERUNGEN 5117
EISENMANGAN 5110
EISENOXALAT 5124
EISENOXYD 5102
EISENOXYD 7144
EISENOXYD (ESSIGSAURES) 5099
EISENOXYDHYDRAT 5101
EISENOXYDSCHICHT 12443
EISENOXYDUL 5125
EISENOXYDULOXYD 7927
EISENOXYDULSUFAT 6093
EISENPULVER 7145
EISENSCHROTT 5126
EISENSCHWAMM 7151
EISENSCHWELLE 7150
EISENSESQUIOXYD 7148
EISENSILIKAT 7149
EISENSORTE 2458

EISENSPALT 262
EISENSPAT 11421
EISENSULFID 12447
EISENSULFID 7153
EISENTRÄGER 12199
EISENVITRIOL 6093
EISENWERK 7160
EISENZAHN 7154
EISENZYANPAPIER 5119
EISESSIG 5952
EISKALORIMETER 6749
EISKLUFT 5700
EISMASCHINE 6750
EISTEIN 3423
EIWEISS 310
EIWEISSPAPIER 311
EJEKTOR 4469
EJEKTOR 4472
EKONOMISER 4437
ELASTISCH 4473
ELASTIZITÄT 4487
ELASTIZITÄTSGRENZE 4481
ELASTIZITÄTSGRENZE 14013
ELASTIZITÄTSGRENZE 7588
ELASTIZITÄTSMASS 8340
ELASTIZITÄTSMODUL 8340
ELASTIZITÄTSMODUL 4483
ELASTIZITÄTSMODUL 8341
ELECTROLYTREINIGUNGSBAD 7538
ELEKTRIFIZIEREN 4555
ELEKTRIFIZIERUNG 4554
ELEKTRISCH WERDEN 1124
ELEKTRISCHE ZENTRALE 4512
ELEKTRISCHEN STROM ERZEUGEN 5917
ELEKTRISCHEN STROM UNTERBRECHEN (DEN) 7090
ELEKTRISCHER SAMMLER 4534
ELEKTRIZITÄT 4552
ELEKTRIZITÄT (ATMOSPHÄRISCHE) 796
ELEKTRIZITÄT (NEGATIVE) 8526
ELEKTRIZITÄT (POSITIVE) 9655
ELEKTRIZITÄTSMENGE 10067
ELEKTRIZITÄTSVERSORGUNG 12487
ELEKTRIZITÄTSWERK 4512
ELEKTRIZITÄTSZÄHLER 4553
ELEKTRO-OSMOSIS 4638
ELEKTROANALYSE 4657
ELEKTROANALYSE 4570
ELEKTROBLECH 4544
ELEKTROBLECH 11448
ELEKTROBOHRMASCHINE 4556
ELEKTROCHEMIE 4573

ELEKTROCHEMIE 4561
ELEKTROCHEMISCH 4560
ELEKTRODAMPFKESSEL 4497
ELEKTRODE 4574
ELEKTRODE (BLECHUMHÜLLTE) 11299
ELEKTRODE (DICKUMHÜLLTE) 11344
ELEKTRODE (NACKTE) 989
ELEKTRODE (NEGATIVE) 2106
ELEKTRODE (NICHTSCHMELZENDE) 8618
ELEKTRODE (POSITIVE) 602
ELEKTRODE (SCHMELZBARE) 2990
ELEKTRODE (UMHÜLLTE) 2584
ELEKTRODE (UMMANTELTE) 5492
ELEKTRODE (ZWEIPOLIGE) 1233
ELEKTRODENARBEITSFLÄCHE 4579
ELEKTRODENARM 6592
ELEKTRODENARMAUSLADUNG 12885
ELEKTRODENHALTER 4575
ELEKTRODENMETALL 4576
ELEKTRODENPOTENTIAL 4577
ELEKTRODENREST 4578
ELEKTRODENROLLE 2412
ELEKTRODENSPANNUNG 9709
ELEKTRODENSPITZE 4579
ELEKTRODENZANGE 4575
ELEKTRODYNAMISCH 4563
ELEKTRODYNAMOMETER 4564
ELEKTROEROSION 4565
ELEKTROGRENZLEHRE 4584
ELEKTROGUSSEISEN 4510
ELEKTROGUSSEISEN 4509
ELEKTROHARTLÖTEN 4498
ELEKTROINGENIEUR 4540
ELEKTROINGENIEURWESEN 4541
ELEKTROKUNSTKORUND 5753
ELEKTROLICHTBOGENOFEN 4495
ELEKTROLYSE 4586
ELEKTROLYSEUR 4588
ELEKTROLYSIEREN 4585
ELEKTROLYT 4587
ELEKTROLYT (VERBRAUCHTER) 5588
ELEKTROLYTGLEICHRICHTER 4606
ELEKTROLYTGOLD 4598
ELEKTROLYTKONDENSATOR 4590
ELEKTROLYTKUPFER 4591
ELEKTROLYTKUPFER 2099
ELEKTROLYTNICKEL 4600
ELEKTROLYTSILBER 4608
ELEKTROLYTZELLENKONSTANTE 2128
ELEKTROMAGNET 4567
ELEKTROMAGNET 4611

# ELE

792

ELEKTROMAGNETISCH **4612**
ELEKTROMAGNETISMUS **4620**
ELEKTROMETALLURGIE **4621**
ELEKTROMONTEUR **4543**
ELEKTROMOTOR **4623**
ELEKTROMOTOREN **4524**
ELEKTRON **4624**
ELEKTRONEGATIV **4631**
ELEKTRONENBÜNDEL **1093**
ELEKTRONENKANONE **4628**
ELEKTRONENMIKROSKOP **4629**
ELEKTRONENRÖHREN **4636**
ELEKTRONENSTRAHL **4625**
ELEKTRONENSTRAHLEN **2104**
ELEKTRONENSTRAHLER **4628**
ELEKTRONENSTRAHLKONZENTRATIONS-LINSE **4626**
ELEKTRONENSTRAHLRÖHRE **2105**
ELEKTRONENSTRAHLSCHWEISSEN **4627**
ELEKTRONENSTRAHLSCHWEISSEN **4630**
ELEKTRONIK **4637**
ELEKTRONIKZÜNDUNG **4633**
ELEKTROOFEN **4507**
ELEKTROPHORESE **4639**
ELEKTROPLATTIERUNG **4640**
ELEKTROPLATTIERUNG **2593**
ELEKTROPOLIEREN **4605**
ELEKTROPOSITIV **4641**
ELEKTROROHEISEN **4550**
ELEKTROSCHWEISSEN **4533**
ELEKTROSTAHL **4511**
ELEKTROSTAHL **4532**
ELEKTROSTAHL (SAURER) **113**
ELEKTROSTAHLOFEN **4507**
ELEKTROSTATISCH **4568**
ELEKTROSTAUCHVERFAHREN **13417**
ELEKTROTECHNIK **4648**
ELEKTROTECHNIKER **4551**
ELEKTROTECHNISCH **4647**
ELEKTROTHERMIE **4650**
ELEKTROTYPIE **4569**
ELEKTROWÄRMELEHRE **4650**
ELEKTRUM **4653**
ELEMENT **8145**
ELEMENT **4654**
ELEMENT (ASYMMETRISCHES) **777**
ELEMENT (BASENBILDENDES) **1038**
ELEMENT (CHEMISCHES) **4654**
ELEMENT (GALVANISCHES) **5782**
ELEMENTARANALYSE **4655**
ELEMENTARBESTANDTEIL **2981**
ELEMENTHOHLRAUM **2127**

ELEMENTUMWANDLUNG **13136**
ELEMIHARZ **4656**
ELEVATOR (U.S. = AUFZUGLIFT) **4660**
ELFENBEIN **7199**
ELIMINATION (MATH.) **4664**
ELIMINIEREN (MATH.) **4662**
ELINVARLEGIERUNG **4668**
ELLIPSE **4669**
ELLIPSE **2029**
ELLIPSENRAD **4677**
ELLIPSENZIRKEL **4670**
ELLIPSOGRAPH **4670**
ELLIPSOID **4671**
ELLIPSOID **8715**
ELOXIEREN **605**
EMAIL **4709**
EMAILFARBE **4711**
EMAILLE **4709**
EMAILLEÜBERZUG **2594**
EMAILLIEREN **4712**
EMAILLIEREN **4710**
EMAILLIERUNG **4712**
EMANATION DES RADIUMS **10159**
EMISSION **4700**
EMISSIONSPHOTOZELLE **9273**
EMISSIONSVERMÖGEN **4701**
EMISSIONSVERMÖGEN (MONOCHROMATISCHES) **8382**
EMK **4622**
EMMISSIONSFLÄCHE **10142**
EMPFANGSTANK **10843**
EMPFINDLICHKEIT EINES INSTRUMENTS **11188**
EMPFINDLICHKEITSGRAD **3723**
EMPIRISCHE FORMEL **4704**
EMULGIEREN **4707**
EMULSION **4708**
EMULSIONSÖL **4706**
ENANTIOTROPISCH **4713**
ENDAUSBEUTE **5194**
ENDDRUCK **5188**
ENDERZEUGNIS **5189**
ENDGESCHWINDIGKEIT **5193**
ENDKURBEL **8947**
ENDLAGE **5187**
ENDMARKE **5879**
ENDOSMOSE **4736**
ENDOTHERM **4737**
ENDOTHERMISCH **4737**
ENDPRODUKT **5189**
ENDSTEIN **5221**
ENDSTELLUNG **5187**
ENDTEMPERATUR **5191**

ENDWERT **5192**
ENDZUSTAND **5190**
ENERGIE **4745**
ENERGIE (CHEMISCHE) **2305**
ENERGIE (ELEKTRISCHE) **4539**
ENERGIE (KINETISCHE) **7308**
ENERGIE (MAGNETISCHE) **7900**
ENERGIE (MECHANISCHE) **8101**
ENERGIE (POTENTIELLE) **9710**
ENERGIE (STATISCHE) **9710**
ENERGIE (STRAHLENDE) **10139**
ENERGIE AUFSPEICHERN **12295**
ENERGIE DER BEWEGUNG **7308**
ENERGIE DYNAMISCHE **7308**
ENERGIE UMWANDELN **13112**
ENERGIEEINHEIT **13379**
ENERGIEERZEUGUNG **5922**
ENERGIEQUELLE **11824**
ENERGIETRANSPORT **13134**
ENERGIEUMWANDLUNG **3070**
ENERGIEVERBRAUCH **2876**
ENERGIEVERLUST **7758**
ENGLERGRAD **3717**
ENGLISCHROT **7148**
ENGMASCHIG **5206**
ENTAKTIVIERUNG **3789**
ENTDUNSTUNGSANLAGE **13485**
ENTEISENUNG DES WASSERS **10454**
ENTFERNEN **4667**
ENTFERNUNG **4667**
ENTFERNUNG DER OBERFLÄCHENFEHLER **3793**
ENTFETTEN IM TRIDAMPF **13486**
ENTFETTUNG **2474**
ENTFETTUNG **3712**
ENTFETTUNGSMITTEL **3713**
ENTFLAMMBAR **6914**
ENTFLAMMBARKEIT **6913**
ENTFLAMMUNG **6760**
ENTFROSTER **3708**
ENTGASUNG **3710**
ENTGASUNG DER KOHLE **4074**
ENTGASUNGSLEGIERUNG **3709**
ENTGEGENGESETZT DEM UHRZEIGERSINN **3237**
ENTGLASUNG **3823**
ENTGRATEN **2504**
ENTGRATEN **5364**
ENTGRATEN **5129**
ENTGRATEN **1766**
ENTGRATUNG **2504**
ENTHÄRTEN DES WASSERS **13676**
ENTHÄRTUNG **11749**

ENTIONISIERUNG **3729**
ENTKEIMUNG DES WASSERS **12252**
ENTKOHLEN **3652**
ENTKOHLEN **3651**
ENTKOHLEN (EISEN) **3654**
ENTKOHLEN DES EISENS **3653**
ENTKOHLUNG **3651**
ENTKOHLUNG **3655**
ENTKUPPELN **12898**
ENTKUPPELN **10034**
ENTKUPPLUNG **12898**
ENTLADEHAFEN **8736**
ENTLADESTATION **8736**
ENTLADUNG **4017**
ENTLADUNG (ELEKTRISCHE) **4502**
ENTLADUNG EINES AKKUMULATORS **4025**
ENTLASTUNG EINES VENTILS **936**
ENTLASTUNGSVENTIL **1819**
ENTLEEREN **4018**
ENTLEERUNG **4024**
ENTLEERUNGSROHR **4206**
ENTLEERUNGSSTUTZEN MIT UMFANGSWANNE **4226**
ENTLÜFTER **13528**
ENTLÜFTER **211**
ENTLÜFTERROHR **1591**
ENTLÜFTUNG **3166**
ENTLÜFTUNG DES WASSERS **3623**
ENTLÜFTUNG EINER ROHRLEITUNG **4665**
ENTLÜFTUNGSNUT **266**
ENTLÜFTUNGSRILLE **266**
ENTLÜFTUNGSSCHRAUBE **1319**
ENTLÜFTUNGSVENTIL **259**
ENTMAGNETISIEREN **3743**
ENTMAGNETISIEREN **3742**
ENTMAGNETISIERUNGSAPPARATE **3744**
ENTMISCHUNG **3172**
ENTMISCHUNG **11192**
ENTNAHME **4225**
ENTNAHME EINER PROBE **10916**
ENTNEBELUNG **3704**
ENTNEBELUNGSANLAGE **13485**
ENTNICKELUNG **3751**
ENTNIETEN **3511**
ENTÖLER **8778**
ENTÖLUNG **8777**
ENTROPIE **4773**
ENTROPIEDIAGRAMM **6346**
ENTROSTEN **10826**
ENTROSTEN **10815**
ENTROSTUNG SBRENNER **5311**
ENTROSTUNGSBAD **10872**

**ENT**　794

ENTSILBERN 3801
ENTSILBERUNG 3802
ENTSPANNUNG 10435
ENTSPANNUNGSGLÜHEN 12363
ENTSTAUBEN 10452
ENTSTAUBEN 5637
ENTSTAUBEN 3682
ENTSTAUBUNG 10452
ENTSTAUBUNGSAPPARATE 4391
ENTWÄSSERN 4204
ENTWÄSSERN 4210
ENTWÄSSERUNGSGERÄTE UND GRABENPFLÜGE 4090
ENTWÄSSERUNGSTOPF 12188
ENTWEICHEN 4832
ENTWEICHEN 4833
ENTWERFEN 3795
ENTWERFEN 3799
ENTWICKELN 3794
ENTWURF 3794
ENTWURFSMANGEL 3694
ENTWURFSZEICHNUNG 3797
ENTWURFZEICHNUNG 11528
ENTZÜNDBAR 6914
ENTZÜNDBARKEIT 6913
ENTZÜNDEN 6757
ENTZUNDERN 11006
ENTZUNDERN 11005
ENTZUNDERUNG 10979
ENTZUNDERUNG (THERMISCHE) 5313
ENTZUNDERUNGSBAD 3790
ENTZÜNDUNG 6760
ENTZÜNDUNGSGESCHWINDIGKEIT 11870
ENTZÜNDUNGSPUNKT 6764
ENTZÜNDUNGSTEMPERATUR 6767
ENTZÜNDUNGSTEMPERATUR 12727
ENVELOPPE 4776
EPIZYKELVORGELEGE 4778
EPIZYKLOIDE 4779
EPIZYKLOIDENVERZAHNUNG 4780
EPSOMER SALZ 7889
EQUIPOTENTIALFLÄCHE 7527
ERBAUUNG 2986
ERBIUM 4804
ERBSENSCHNEIDER 9141
ERBSKOHLE 9140
ERDALKALIEN 336
ERDALKALIMETALLE 335
ERDARBEITEN 4420
ERDAUFSCHÜTTUNG 3946
ERDBAUTEN 4420
ERDDRUCK 12907

ERDE 4409
ERDE 4415
ERDEN 4410
ERDEN (ALKALISCHE) 336
ERDEN (SELTENE) 10210
ERDFARBE 4412
ERDGAS 8504
ERDKONTAKT 4418
ERDLEITUNG 4415
ERDÖL 9226
ERDÖL 9229
ERDÖL (SCHWEFELHALTIGES) 11822
ERDPECH 768
ERDRAMMER 12611
ERDSCHLUSS 4415
ERDSIEB 11628
ERDUNG 4417
ERDUNG 6149
ERDUNG 5589
ERDUNG 4415
ERDUNGSKLEMME 4419
ERDWACHS 4413
ERFAHRUNGSFORMEL 4704
ERFINDER 7108
ERFINDUNG 7107
ERFINDUNG (PATENTFÄHIGE) 9122
ERFINDUNG (SCHUTZFÄHIGE) 9122
ERFINDUNGSPATENT 9112
ERG 4818
ERGÄNZUNGSFARBE 2812
ERGÄNZUNGSKEGEL 5918
ERHALTUNG DER ENERGIE 2967
ERHÄRTEN 6292
ERHÄRTEN (AN DER LUFT) (ZEMENT) 6286
ERHÄRTUNG (MÖRTELZEMENT) 6292
ERHEBEN (IN EINE POTENZ) 10180
ERHITZEN 6390
ERHITZEN 6334
ERHITZEN (UNTER LUFTABSCHLUSS) 6367
ERHITZER 6385
ERICHSEN-TIEFZIEHVERSUCH 8797
ERICHSEN-TIEFZIEHVERSUCHSMASCHINE 4819
ERLE 318
ERLÖSCHEN EINES PATENTES 7408
ERMÜDUNG 5047
ERMÜDUNG DES MATERIALS 5051
ERMÜDUNG DURCH SCHWEFELWASSERSTOFF 12442
ERMÜDUNGSRISS 5048
ERMÜDUNGSRISS 4739
ERMÜDUNGSVERSUCH 4743
ERMÜDUNGSVERSUCH 5054

ERNEUERUNG EINES MASCHINENTEILS **10458**
ERNTEMASCHINEN FÜR HACKFRÜCHTE **10722**
EROSION **4820**
ERREGEN **4887**
ERREGERANODE **4886**
ERREGERMASCHINE **4888**
ERREGERWICKLUNG **6898**
ERREGUNG (PHYS.) **4885**
ERSATZ **12420**
ERSATZRAD **11835**
ERSATZRAD **2243**
ERSATZSTOFF **12420**
ERSATZTEIL **11834**
ERSCHÜTTERUNGEN **13559**
ERSTARREN **11797**
ERSTARREN **11803**
ERSTARRUNG **5653**
ERSTARRUNG **11797**
ERSTARRUNG DER SCHMELZE IN DER PFANNE **7360**
ERSTARRUNG EINER FLÜSSIGKEIT **11799**
ERSTARRUNGS-BEREICH **5658**
ERSTARRUNGS-INTERVALL **5658**
ERSTARRUNGSBEREICH **11801**
ERSTARRUNGSFRONT **11798**
ERSTARRUNGSPUNKT **5656**
ERSTARRUNGSPUNKT **11800**
ERSTARRUNGSPUNKT **11804**
ERSTARRUNGSSCHWINDUNG **11802**
ERSTFARBE **9847**
ERTEILUNG EINES PATENTS **6049**
ERTRAGSFÄHIGKEIT **9897**
ERUPTIONSABSPERRVORRICHTUNG **1360**
ERWÄRMEN **6334**
ERWÄRMEN **6390**
ERWÄRMUNG **6390**
ERWARTUNGSWERT **4927**
ERWEICHUNGSPUNKT **11750**
ERWEITERN (SICH) **5356**
ERWEITERTER TEIL (EINES ROHRES) **4768**
ERWEITERUNG **4768**
ERYTHROSIN **4831**
ERZ **8859**
ERZ (ARMES) **7781**
ERZ (REICHES) **6485**
ERZ UND SCHMELZMITTEL **8863**
ERZANREICHERUNG **8861**
ERZBERGWERK **8198**
ERZBRIKETT **8860**
ERZE AUFBEREITEN **4253**
ERZE GLÜHEN **1841**
ERZE RÖSTEN **10648**

ERZEUGEN **7948**
ERZEUGEN (DAMPF, GAS) **5916**
ERZEUGENDE **5925**
ERZEUGENDE FUNKTION **5919**
ERZEUGER **7992**
ERZEUGNIS **7989**
ERZEUGNIS **9892**
ERZEUGUNG **4983**
ERZGRUBE **8198**
ERZPRESSSTEIN **8860**
ERZRÖSTEN **8862**
ERZZIEGEL **8860**
ESELRÜCKENBOGEN **8741**
ESSE **2339**
ESSENKLAPPE **3603**
ESSIGGEIST **90**
ESSIGSÄURE **86**
ESSIGSÄUREANHYDRID **87**
ESSIGSÄUREÄTHER **88**
ESSIGSÄUREÄTHYLESTER **88**
ESSIGSAURES EISEN **7134**
ESSIGSAURES EISENOXYDUL **5120**
ESSIGSAURES KALI **9673**
ESSIGSAURES SALZ **85**
ESTER **4837**
ETAGENVENTIL **8475**
EUDIOMETER **4852**
EUROPIUM **4854**
EUTEKTIKUM **4855**
EUTEKTISCH **4855**
EUTEKTOID **4859**
EUTEKTOIDE REAKTION **4860**
EVOLUTE **4873**
EVOLVENTE **7117**
EVOLVENTENVERZAHNUNG **7119**
EXHAUSTOR **4900**
EXOTHERM **4901**
EXOTHERMISCH **4901**
EXPANDIEREN **4902**
EXPANSION **4921**
EXPANSIONSDAMPFMASCHINE **4924**
EXPANSIONSHUB **2775**
EXPANSIONSKURVE **4916**
EXPANSIONSREIBAHLE **188**
EXPANSIONSRIEMENSCHEIBE **4909**
EXPANSIONSTURBINE **4925**
EXPANSIONSVENTIL **4926**
EXPERIMENT **12792**
EXPERIMENTIEREN **4928**
EXPLODIEREN **4933**
EXPLOSION **4935**

# EXP

796

EXPLOSION EINER SCHEIBE **1769**
EXPLOSION EINES KESSELS **1410**
EXPLOSION EINES SCHWUNGRADES **1769**
EXPLOSIONSDRUCK **4936**
EXPLOSIV **4937**
EXPLOSIVSTOFF **4937**
EXPONENT **4939**
EXPONENTIALFUNKTION **4942**
EXPONENTIALREIHE **4943**
EXPONENTIALVERTEILUNG **4941**
EXSIKKATOR **3804**
EXTRAKT **4964**
EXTRAKTION (ELEKTROLYTISCHE) **4582**
EXTRAKTION (ELEKTROLYTISCHE) **4652**
EXTRAKTIONSAPPARAT **4967**
EXTRAKTIONSMETALLURGIE **9886**
EXZENTER **4433**
EXZENTER **4425**
EXZENTER (GESCHLOSSENES) **3270**
EXZENTER (OFFENES) **8805**
EXZENTER (UNRUNDE SCHEIBEHUBSCHEIBE) **1883**
EXZENTERBÜGEL **4435**
EXZENTERHUB **12894**
EXZENTERPRESSE **4430**
EXZENTERRING **4435**
EXZENTERROLLE **1895**
EXZENTERSCHEIBE **4434**
EXZENTERSTANGE **4431**
EXZENTERSTANGENKOPF **4432**
EXZENTERTRIEBWERK **1886**
EXZENTRISCH **4424**
EXZENTRISCH **8730**
EXZENTRIZITÄT **4436**
FABRIK **5013**
FABRIKABWÄSSER **6902**
FABRIKANSCHLUSSGLEIS **13966**
FABRIKANT **7992**
FABRIKAT **7989**
FABRIKATION **7989**
FABRIKATIONSFEHLER **3693**
FABRIKATIONSGANG **2222**
FABRIKATIONSLÄNGE **8925**
FABRIKATIONSVERFAHREN **8218**
FABRIKAUFSEHER **8958**
FABRIKBAHN **13965**
FABRIKDIREKTOR **5915**
FABRIKGEBÄUDE **5012**
FABRIKMARKE **13100**
FABRIKNUMMER **11197**
FABRIKNUMMER **4986**
FABRIKORGANISATION **6901**

FABRIZIEREN **7948**
FACH **2798**
FACHGEBIET **11845**
FACHWERK **7433**
FACHWERKTRÄGER **7431**
FACKEL **13042**
FACKEL **5355**
FADENKREUZ **3383**
FADENKRISTALL **13828**
FADENZIEHEN **2616**
FAHLERZ **12796**
FAHRARM DES PLANIMETERS **10662**
FAHRBAR **9635**
FAHRBARER KRAN **13161**
FAHRBEREICH **3416**
FAHRBEWEGUNG **13158**
FAHRENHEITGRAD **3718**
FAHRENHEITSKALA **5019**
FAHRENHEITTHERMOMETER **5020**
FAHRFLÄCHE-LAUFBAHN **10857**
FAHRGESTELL **5624**
FAHRGESTELL **2275**
FAHRRADKETTE **1239**
FAHRSCHIENE **10175**
FAHRSTIFT DES PLANIMETERS **13079**
FAHRSTRAHL **10170**
FAHRT **10810**
FAHRTRICHTUNGSANZEIGER **3989**
FAKTOR (MATH.) **5008**
FALLBESCHLEUNIGUNG **63**
FALLE **7414**
FÄLLEN **9761**
FÄLLEN (EIN LOT) **4216**
FALLENDGIESSEN **13031**
FALLGEWICHT **4329**
FALLHAMMER **4326**
FALLHAMMER **4327**
FALLHAMMER **4325**
FALLHÖHE **6421**
FALLKLINKE **7414**
FÄLLMITTEL **9758**
FÄLLMITTEL **11130**
FALLROHR **4185**
FALLROHR **4183**
FALLROHR **3593**
FALLROHR UNTER SCHEIBEN **4188**
FALLSTROMVERGASER **4189**
FÄLLUNG (ELEKTROLYTISCHE) **4593**
FALLVERSUCH **4328**
FALLWERK **4326**
FALSCHLUFT **4771**

**FED**

FÄLSCHUNG 205
FALTE 3320
FALTE 4408
FALTEN 1680
FALTEN VERFORMEN 3336
FALTENBALG 1139
FALTENBILDUNG 13985
FALTMASSSTAB 5512
FALTVERSUCH 4173
FALZ (BAUWESEN) 10269
FALZ (BLECHBEARBEITUNG) 5511
FALZBIEGEMASCHINE 11087
FALZHOBEL 10115
FALZMASCHINE 11088
FANGELEKTRODE 12682
FARAD 5035
FARADAYSCHER KÄFIG 5036
FARBANSTRICH 2583
FARBAUFTRAG 2599
FARBE 9303
FARBE (DECKENDE) 1389
FARBE (PHYS.) 2741
FARBMETALLOGRAPHIE 2738
FARBSPRITZVERFAHREN 6179
FARBSTIFT 2745
FARBSTOFF 4397
FARBSTOFF 9303
FARBÜBERZUG 2583
FÄRBUNG 2740
FASER 5136
FASER 5131
FASER (NEUTRALE) 8542
FASER (PARALLEL ZUR) 6031
FASERACHSE 5132
FASERIG 5137
FASERN (IN DER RICHTUNG) 6031
FASERRICHTUNG 5133
FASERRICHTUNG 3993
FASERSCHICHT (NEUTRALE) 8544
FASERSPANNUNG 5134
FASERSTOFF 5140
FASERSTOFFRIEMEN 4981
FASERSTRUKTUR 5135
FASSFLÄCHENKORROSION 5667
FASSONDRAHT 11847
FASSONDREHBANK 3138
FASSONEISEN 11119
FASSONFRÄSER 9899
FASSONROHR 9350
FASSPOLIEREN 1012
FASSUNGSVERMÖGEN 1917

FAULEN 10036
FÄULNIS 10035
FÄULNIS 10769
FÄULNIS DES HOLZES 10770
FÄULNIS ÜBERGEHEN (IN) 10036
FÄULNISVERHINDERNDES MITTEL 629
FÄULNISWIDRIG 628
FAUSTHAMMER 6235
FAUSTLEIER 1519
FAUSTSCHERE 856
FEDER 5059
FEDER 11974
FEDER (EINE) ZUSAMMENDRÜCKEN 2838
FEDER (GESCHICHTETE) 2834
FEDER (GESPANNTE) 11983
FEDER (ZUSAMMENGESETZTE) 2834
FEDER SPANNEN (EINE) 10032
FEDER UND NUT 12990
FEDER UND NUT 12989
FEDER-UND DRAHT-PRÜFMASCHINE 11975
FEDERBAROMETER 504
FEDERBLATT 11977
FEDERBLATT 9492
FEDERBOLZEN 2149
FEDERBRONZE 1661
FEDERDRAHT 11997
FEDERGEHÄNGE 11233
FEDERHARZ 10825
FEDERHOBEL 12993
FEDERKEIL 5059
FEDERKLINKE 11987
FEDERKRAFT 4487
FEDERKRAFTREGLER 11984
FEDERLASCHE 11991
FEDERMANOMETER 11989
FEDERMEMBRAN 4479
FEDERMESSING 11978
FEDERND 4473
FEDERPLATTE 11988
FEDERPUFFER 11980
FEDERRING 11990
FEDERRING 11995
FEDERRING 4486
FEDERROHR 4913
FEDERSCHMIERBÜCHSE 11982
FEDERSICHERHEITSVENTIL 11998
FEDERSTAHL 11992
FEDERTELLER 11988
FEDERWAAGE 11976
FEDERWAAGE 4403
FEDERWIRKUNG 4487

## FED

FEDERZANGE **5536**
FEDERZINKENEGGEN **3457**
FEDERZIRKEL **1503**
FEHLER **5411**
FEHLER **3692**
FEHLER **4822**
FEHLER **3691**
FEHLERFREIHEIT DER SCHWEISSNAHT **11821**
FEHLERGRENZE **7589**
FEHLERHAFTE STELLE IM MATERIAL **3692**
FEHLERHAFTER BETRIEB **3695**
FEHLERQUELLE **11825**
FEHLERSUCHPROGRAMM **3830**
FEHLERZÄHLER **4830**
FEHLERZÄHLER **4823**
FEHLSCHMELZE **8732**
FEHLSTELLE **13585**
FEILE **5148**
FEILE (DREIKANTIGE) **12870**
FEILE (EINHIEBIGE) **11481**
FEILE MIT ZWEI RUNDEN KANTEN **13041**
FEILE ZWEIHIEBIGE **4133**
FEILEN **5153**
FEILEN **5149**
FEILEN AUFHAUEN **10323**
FEILEN HAUEN **3507**
FEILENAUFHAUEN **10324**
FEILENBÜRSTE **5150**
FEILENHÄRTEPROBE **5152**
FEILENHAUEN **3529**
FEILENHAUER **5151**
FEILENHIEB **3518**
FEILICHT **5155**
FEILKLOBEN **6254**
FEILMASCHINE **5154**
FEILMASCHINE **11269**
FEILSPÄNE **12536**
FEILSPÄNE **5155**
FEILSPÄNKURVEN **7902**
FEINBLECH **11304**
FEINBLECH **12850**
FEINBLECH (SEHR DÜNNES) **12593**
FEINBOHRMASCHINE **5196**
FEINDRAHT **12849**
FEINDRAHT **5205**
FEINES GEWINDE **5201**
FEINFILTER **11101**
FEINGEFÜGE **8262**
FEINGEHALT **5209**
FEINGEWINDE **5201**
FEINGEWINDE **5204**

FEINGOLD **5198**
FEINHEIT **5208**
FEINHIEBFEILE **11680**
FEINKOHLE **11557**
FEINKORNEISEN **2511**
FEINMASCHIG **5206**
FEINMESSUNG **4875**
FEINPAPPE **1999**
FEINSCHLEIFMASCHINE **6113**
FEINSCHLICHTFEILE **12467**
FEINSILBER **5202**
FEINSTMAHLUNG **9985**
FEINSTRUKTUR **5203**
FEINSTRUKTUR **5210**
FEINVERKLEINERUNG **6106**
FEINWAAGE **9764**
FEINZERKLEINERUNG **2786**
FEINZINKLEGIERUNG **14021**
FELD (ELECTRISCHES) **4504**
FELD (ELEKTRISCHES) **4505**
FELD (MAGNETISCHES) **7901**
FELDBAHN **9639**
FELDDICHTE **5144**
FELDINTENSITÄT **5144**
FELDLAFETTE **5142**
FELDSCHMIEDE **9637**
FELDSPAT **5087**
FELDSPAT **5089**
FELDSTÄRKE **4506**
FELDSTÄRKE **5144**
FELGE **5088**
FELS (SERPENTIN) **11204**
FENSTER **13864**
FENSTERDICHTUNGSCHNUR **13854**
FENSTERFÜHRUNG **13868**
FENSTERGLAS **13866**
FENSTERKURBEL **13867**
FENSTERÖFFNUNG **12887**
FENSTERRAHMEN **13865**
FERMENTATION **5098**
FERNEICHUNG **10449**
FERNKRAFTÜBERTRAGUNG (ELEKTRISCHE) **13133**
FERNLEITUNG (ELEKTRISCHE) **4521**
FERNLEITUNG VON ENERGIE **13135**
FERNLEITUNGSNETZ **7728**
FERNMESSUNG **10449**
FERNROHR **10398**
FERNROHRLEITUNG (EINGEERDETE) **1744**
FERNSPRECHER **12710**
FERNSPRECHERDRAHT **12711**
FERNSPRECHWESEN **12712**

# FEU

799

FERNSTEUERUNG **10448**
FERNTHERMOMETER **12714**
FERNTHERMOMETER **4069**
FERNTRIEB **12706**
FERNTRIEBSEIL **12705**
FERNÜBERTRAGUNG VON ELEKTRISCHER ENERGIE **13133**
FERRIAZETAT **5099**
FERRICHLORID **5100**
FERRIFERROZYANID **1206**
FERRIHYDRAT **5101**
FERRIHYDROXYD **5101**
FERRISULFAT **5103**
FERRIT **5104**
FERRITBAND (FREIES) **5105**
FERRIZYANKALIUM **9684**
FERROALUMINIUM **5106**
FERROAZETAT **5120**
FERROBOR **5107**
FERROCHLORID **5121**
FERROCHROM **5108**
FERROLEGIERUNGSBRIKETT **1622**
FERROMAGNETISCH **5118**
FERROMANGAN **5110**
FERROMOLYBDÄN **5111**
FERRONICKEL **5112**
FERROOXALAT **5124**
FERROOXYD **5125**
FERROSILIZIUM **5113**
FERROSULFAT **6093**
FERROTITAN **5114**
FERROVANADIUM **5116**
FERROWOLFRAM **5115**
FERROZYANKALIUM **9685**
FERTIGBEARBEITUNG **11682**
FERTIGBEARBEITUNG **5220**
FERTIGBEARBEITUNG (MASCHINELLE) **7844**
FERTIGER PRESSLING **8551**
FERTIGERZEUGNIS **5218**
FERTIGERZEUGNIS **5730**
FERTIGGERÜST **5219**
FERTIGGESENK **5219**
FERTIGSCHLEIFEN **5224**
FERTIGSCHNEIDER **1499**
FERTIGSCHWEISSEN **5216**
FERTIGSTRASSE **5229**
FERTIGUNGSARBEIT **5223**
FERTIGUNGSBEREICH **7994**
FERTIGUNGSPROGRAMM **7994**
FERTIGUNGSTEMPERATUR **5227**
FERTIGUNGSUMFANG **7994**
FERTIGWALZE **5225**

FERTIGWALZEN **5215**
FERTIGWALZWERK **5222**
FEST ANZIEHEN (EINE SCHRAUBE) **12927**
FESTBETTFRÄSMASCHINE **5298**
FESTDACH **5296**
FESTER AGGREGAT-ZUSTAND **11795**
FESTER STEMPELTEIL **3885**
FESTER ZYKLUS **5292**
FESTFRESSEN **11141**
FESTIGKEIT **12352**
FESTIGKEIT **10484**
FESTIGKEIT (ZUSAMMENGESETZTE) **2822**
FESTIGKEIT DES MATERIALS **12355**
FESTIGKEITS-PRÜFMASCHINE **12793**
FESTIGKEITSEIGENSCHAFTEN **12746**
FESTIGKEITSGUSS **2042**
FESTIGKEITSPRÜFUNG **12356**
FESTKÖRPER **11775**
FESTPUNKT **5295**
FESTSCHEIBE **5040**
FESTSCHRAUBEN **11065**
FESTSCHRAUBEN **11022**
FESTSPANNEINRICHTUNG **13945**
FESTSTAMPFEN **10189**
FESTSTAMPFEN **10195**
FESTSTELLBREMSE **9082**
FESTSTELLBREMSE **9082**
FESTSTELLHEBEL **7706**
FESTSTELLSCHRAUBE **11222**
FESTSTELLVORRICHTUNG **7705**
FESTSTOFF (ELASTISCHER) **4484**
FESTWERT **2969**
FETT (CHEM.) **5045**
FETT (KONSISTENTES) **6275**
FETTGAS **8758**
FETTKALK **5046**
FETTKOHLE **1282**
FETTLÖSUNGSMITTEL **2473**
FETTSÄURE **5055**
FETTSCHMIERUNG **6087**
FEUCHTE LUFT **3599**
FEUCHTEN **13807**
FEUCHTIGKEIT (ABSOLUTE) DER LUFT **30**
FEUCHTIGKEIT (HYGROSKOPISCHE) **6731**
FEUCHTIGKEIT (KRITISCHE) **3346**
FEUCHTIGKEIT (RELATIVE) **10432**
FEUCHTIGKEITSGEHALT **30**
FEUCHTIGKEITSGRAD **10433**
FEUCHTIGKEITSKORROSION **13802**
FEUCHTIGKEITSMESSER **6729**
FEUERBESTÄNDIG **5257**

## FEU

800

FEUERBESTÄNDIGKEIT **10405**
FEUERBRÜCKE **5308**
FEUERBÜCHSE **5238**
FEUERFEST **5257**
FEUERFESTERZIEGEL **5252**
FEUERFESTIGKEIT **10405**
FEUERGASE **5470**
FEUERGEFÄHRLICH **6503**
FEUERKANAL **5743**
FEUERLOSE LOKOMOTIVE **5256**
FEUERN **5259**
FEUERN **5235**
FEUERRAUM **12270**
FEUERROST **6070**
FEUERSGEFAHR **3608**
FEUERSICHER **5257**
FEUERSTEIN **5427**
FEUERTAUCHVERZINKEN **6653**
FEUERTON **5253**
FEUERTOPF **3821**
FEUERTÜR **5242**
FEUERUNG FÜR RAUCHFREIE VERBRENNUNG **11674**
FEUERUNGSANLAGE **5747**
FEUERUNGSGERÄT **5261**
FEUERVERGOLDUNG **5243**
FEUERVERZINKUNG **6628**
FEUERVERZINKUNG **5787**
FEUERZIEGEL **5252**
FEUERZUG **5743**
FIBER **13609**
FILM **11544**
FILM **5166**
FILM ROLLEN **10667**
FILMDICKE **5170**
FILTER **5172**
FILTER **12333**
FILTER (SYMMETRISCHE) **933**
FILTERBECKEN **5178**
FILTEREINSATZ **5175**
FILTERFLÄCHE (ÜBERSÄTTIGTE) **2360**
FILTERHILFSSTOFF **5174**
FILTERN **5182**
FILTERN **5173**
FILTERPAPIER **5177**
FILTERPRESSE **5180**
FILTERSIEB **5175**
FILTERSTOFF **5179**
FILTERTUCH **5176**
FILTRAT **5181**
FILTRATION **5182**
FILTRIEREN **5182**

FILTRIEREN **5173**
FILTRIERMATERIAL **5179**
FILTRIERPAPIER **5177**
FILZ **5090**
FILZPLATTE **11322**
FINDLING **4821**
FINGERFRÄSER **11259**
FINNE **9031**
FINNE (GESPALTENE) **2463**
FINSPANNBACKEN **6120**
FIRNIS **13504**
FISCHBAUCHFÖRMIG **5272**
FISCHHAUT **11270**
FISCHLEIM **7174**
FISCHÖL **13103**
FISCHTRAN **13103**
FIXPUNKT **5295**
FLACHDRAHT **5402**
FLÄCHE **694**
FLÄCHE **12521**
FLÄCHE **12496**
FLÄCHE (ABWICKELBARE) **3817**
FLÄCHE (EBENE) **9441**
FLÄCHE (GEKRÜMMTE) **3498**
FLÄCHE (GERAUHTE) **10784**
FLÄCHE (KRUMME) **3498**
FLÄCHE (LICHTZERSTREUENDE) **3935**
FLÄCHE (RAUHE) **10779**
FLÄCHE (REFLEKTIERENDE) **10385**
FLÄCHE (SPIEGELNDE) **11866**
FLÄCHE (STRAHLENDE) **10142**
FLÄCHE (TRAGENDE) **1115**
FLÄCHE (ZURÜCKSTRAHLENDE) **10385**
FLACHE KURVE **5378**
FLACHEISEN **5375**
FLACHEISEN AUS LEGIERTEN STÄHLEN **373**
FLÄCHENAUSDEHNUNG **12466**
FLÄCHENAUSDEHNUNGSZAHL **2635**
FLÄCHENDRUCK **1110**
FLÄCHENEINHEIT **13372**
FLÄCHENEINHEITSLAST **13371**
FLÄCHENHAMMER **4169**
FLÄCHENHELLIGKEIT **7104**
FLÄCHENINHALT **697**
FLÄCHENMASS **8081**
FLÄCHENMITTELPUNKT **2191**
FLÄCHENSCHLEIFEN **12506**
FLÄCHENSCHLEIFMASCHINE **12505**
FLÄCHENSCHLEIFMASCHINE **12507**
FLÄCHENZENTRIERT **5002**
FLÄCHENZENTRIERT **4729**

801 **FLA**

FLACHFEILE **5390**
FLACHFEILE **5381**
FLACHFÜHRUNG **5384**
FLACHGÄNGIGE SCHRAUBE **12034**
FLACHGEWINDE **12030**
FLACHHAMMER **5410**
FLACHHERDMISCHER **5387**
FLACHKABBER (GESCHLOSSENES) **2526**
FLACHKEHLNAHT **12075**
FLACHKEIL **5388**
FLACHKEIL **5400**
FLACHMEISSEL **2672**
FLACHMEISSEL **5377**
FLACHNAHT **5481**
FLACHREGLER **11242**
FLACHS **5412**
FLACHSCHEIBE **5399**
FLACHSCHIEBER **9426**
FLACHSEIL **5393**
FLACHSTAB **5374**
FLACHSTAHL **5392**
FLACHSWERG **5413**
FLACHWALZE **5391**
FLACHWULSTEISEN **5376**
FLACHWULSTEISEN **1714**
FLACHZANGE **5403**
FLADERSCHNITT **1058**
FLAK-GESCHÜTZ **610**
FLAMME (AUFKOHLENDE) **1990**
FLAMME (KARBURIERENDE) **1990**
FLAMME (LEUCHTENDE) **7820**
FLAMME (NICHTLEUCHTENDE) **8636**
FLAMME (OXIDIERENDE) **8975**
FLAMME (REDUZIERENDE) **10349**
FLAMME (RUSSENDE) **11678**
FLÄMMEN **10993**
FLAMMEN-LÖSCHER **5321**
FLAMMENDER SALPETER **465**
FLAMMENENTZUNDERUNG **5310**
FLAMMENKEGEL **2923**
FLAMMENKEGEL (INNERER) **6952**
FLAMMENLÖTUNG **11768**
FLAMMENRÜCKSCHLAG **906**
FLAMMENRÜCKSCHLAG **5365**
FLAMMENSICHER **5322**
FLAMMENSPEKTROSKOPIE **5320**
FLAMMENWÄCHTER **5314**
FLAMMENZÜNDUNG **5316**
FLÄMMHOBELN **6011**
FLAMMLÖTEN **5810**
FLAMMOFEN **261**

FLAMMOFEN **10532**
FLAMMPLATTIERUNG **5317**
FLAMMPUNKT **6764**
FLAMMPUNKT **5368**
FLAMMPUNKT **5363**
FLAMMPUTZEN **5309**
FLAMMROHR **1412**
FLAMMROHRKESSEL **5468**
FLANELL **5352**
FLANGEABDECKUNG **3267**
FLANKE **5348**
FLANKE EINES GEWINDES **5350**
FLANKENDURCHMESSER **9407**
FLANKENKEHLNAHT **12702**
FLANKENSPIEL (ZAHNRÄDERN) **5349**
FLANKENSPIELRAUM **914**
FLANKENWINKEL DES GEWINDES **530**
FLANSCH **5323**
FLANSCH (ANGEGOSSENER) **2063**
FLANSCH (AUFGELÖTETER) **11758**
FLANSCH (AUFGESCHRAUBTER) **11063**
FLANSCH (AUFGESCHWEISSTER) **13773**
FLANSCH (AUFGEWALZTER) **10672**
FLANSCH (BEARBEITETER) **5003**
FLANSCH (FESTER) **5039**
FLANSCH (GLATTER) **5382**
FLANSCH (LOSER) **7746**
FLANSCH (OVALER) **8918**
FLANSCH (ROHER) **10776**
FLANSCH (RUNDER) **10797**
FLANSCH (ÜBERHÖHTER) **10183**
FLANSCH (UNBEARBEITETER) **10776**
FLANSCH EINES EISENS **5330**
FLANSCH EINES ROHRES **9351**
FLANSCHANPASSSTÜCK **5325**
FLANSCHBOHRUNGEN **5328**
FLANSCHENANSCHLUSS **5339**
FLANSCHENAUFWALZMASCHINE **5333**
FLANSCHENDECKEL **1304**
FLANSCHENDREHBANK **5334**
FLANSCHENKUPPLUNG **5338**
FLANSCHENROHR **5343**
FLANSCHENVERBINDUNG **5344**
FLANSCHENVERSCHRAUBUNG **5344**
FLANSCHFLÄCHE **5327**
FLANSCHNABE **5329**
FLANSCHRING **1708**
FLANSCHROHRSTUTZEN **8683**
FLANSCHRÜCKFLÄCHE **5326**
FLANSCHSTUTZEN **5337**
FLANSCHWULSTEISEN **1719**

# FLA

802

FLASCHE 1333
FLASCHE (FESTE) 5287
FLASCHE (LOSE) 8435
FLASCHENGLAS 1484
FLASCHENSCHRAUBSTOCK 6511
FLASCHENWINDE 1485
FLASCHENZUG 9973
FLASCHENZUG 9972
FLATTERN 11353
FLATTERN 2277
FLATTERN DES RIEMENS 13825
FLECHTWERK 13180
FLEISCHSEITE DES LEDERS 5414
FLICKEN 9109
FLICKEN 9110
FLICKEN 9111
FLICKMASSE 5803
FLIEGEND ANGEORDNETE KURBEL 8947
FLIEGEND GELAGERT 8936
FLIEHKRAFT 2180
FLIEHKRAFTBESCHLEUNIGUNG 10127
FLIEHKRAFTKUPPLUNG 2177
FLIEHKRAFTREGLER 2185
FLIEHKRAFTREGLER 2181
FLIESE 12933
FLIESSARBEIT 3034
FLIESSEN 5454
FLIESSEN 13578
FLIESSEN (PLASTISCHES) 9471
FLIESSEN DES MATERIALS 5465
FLIESSFÄHIGKEIT 5463
FLIESSFIGUREN 12371
FLIESSGESCHWINDIGKEIT 5459
FLIESSGRENZE 5456
FLIESSGRENZE 14012
FLIESSGRENZE 14011
FLIESSKUNDE 10562
FLIESSLINIE 5457
FLIESSMARK 5457
FLIESSPAPIER 1350
FLIESSPRESSE 4972
FLIESSPRESSEN 4970
FLIESSSCHEIDE 8547
FLIESSTEXTUR 5461
FLIESSVERMÖGEN 2064
FLIESSZEIT 5459
FLINT 5427
FLINTGLAS 5428
FLOCKE 5303
FLOCKEN VON WEISSMETALL 13835
FLOCKENGRAPHIT 5305

FLOCKENGRAPHIT 3703
FLOTATION 5452
FLOTATION (ANIONISCHE) 557
FLÜCHTIGKEIT 13589
FLUCHTLINIE 324
FLUCHTLINIENTAFEL 8617
FLUCHTSCHLEUSE 8904
FLUGASCHE 5493
FLÜGEL EINES VENTILS 5060
FLÜGELBREMSE 5031
FLÜGELGEBLÄSE 10751
FLÜGELMUTTER 12911
FLÜGELPUMPE 13478
FLÜGELPUMPE 11176
FLÜGELRAD 13479
FLÜGELSCHRAUBE 12912
FLUOBARIUM 999
FLUOR 5478
FLUORAMMONIUM 463
FLUORESZENZ 5476
FLUORESZENZSCHIRM 5477
FLUORKALIUM 9686
FLUORKALZIUM 5479
FLUORMAGNESIUM 7886
FLUORNATRIUM 11721
FLUORWASSERSTOFFSÄURE 6711
FLURSÄULE 5448
FLUSS (BASISCHER) 1046
FLUSSEISEN 6921
FLUSSEISEN 11744
FLÜSSIG 7642
FLÜSSIGGAS 7342
FLÜSSIGGAS 7638
FLÜSSIGKEIT 7641
FLÜSSIGKEITEN 7660
FLÜSSIGKEITSBREMSE 6678
FLÜSSIGKEITSDÄMPFUNG 7649
FLÜSSIGKEITSDICHTE 3758
FLÜSSIGKEITSDRUCK 6726
FLÜSSIGKEITSGRAD 5474
FLÜSSIGKEITSREIBUNG 5473
FLÜSSIGKEITSSÄULE 2750
FLÜSSIGKEITSSTRAHL 7221
FLUSSMITTEL 5475
FLUSSMITTEL 5489
FLUSSMITTEL (SAURES) 114
FLUSSSAND 10619
FLUSSSÄURE 6711
FLUSSSPAT 5479
FLUSSSPATSÄURE 6711
FLUSSSTAHL 6924

FLUSSSTAHL **11744**
FLUSSTAHL **1958**
FLUSSWASSER **10620**
FOKUS **5502**
FOKUSSIEREN **5505**
FOLIE **5508**
FOLIE **5509**
FOLIUM (KARTESISCHES) **5513**
FÖRDERBAND **1164**
FÖRDERBANDBELADUNG **1141**
FÖRDERBANDOFEN **1148**
FÖRDEREINRICHTUNG **3080**
FÖRDERGURT **1164**
FÖRDERHÖHE EINER PUMPE **13061**
FÖRDERHÖHE EINES KRANS **7551**
FÖRDERKARREN **13230**
FÖRDERKETTE **1675**
FÖRDERKOHLE **10841**
FÖRDERKOSTEN **3204**
FÖRDERMENGE **10228**
FÖRDERPUMPE **5713**
FÖRDERRINNE **2395**
FÖRDERSCHNECKE **13970**
FÖRDERSEIL **6520**
FÖRDERUNG **8106**
FÖRDERUNGSANLAGE (HEU UND STROH) **4661**
FORM **3883**
FORM **5570**
FORM **8352**
FORM **11264**
FORM (NICHT-METALLISCHE) **8650**
FORM GEBEN **5571**
FORMALDEHYD **5573**
FORMALIN **5573**
FORMÄNDERUNG **3707**
FORMÄNDERUNG (BLEIBENDE) **3337**
FORMÄNDERUNG (BLEIBENDE) **9210**
FORMÄNDERUNG (ELASTISCHE) **10477**
FORMÄNDERUNG (ELASTISCHE) **4485**
FORMÄNDERUNG (ELASTISCHE) **4478**
FORMÄNDERUNGSVERMÖGEN **3705**
FORMAT **5574**
FORMBESTÄNDIGKEIT **3958**
FORMBESTÄNDIGKEIT **10521**
FORMBLECH **11846**
FORMDRAHT **11847**
FORMDREHBANK **3138**
FORMEISEN **11119**
FORMEL **5582**
FORMEL (CHEMISCHE) **2310**
FORMEN **8428**

FORMEN **5571**
FORMEN **5581**
FORMEN NACH DEM GUSSTÜCK **4383**
FORMENHOHLRAUM **8353**
FORMENTON **9470**
FORMER **8427**
FORMERSTIFTE **5598**
FORMFAKTOR **5572**
FORMFRÄSER **9899**
FORMFRÄSER **5577**
FORMFRÄSMASCHINE **9900**
FORMGEBUNG **11268**
FORMGEBUNG **5581**
FORMGEBUNG **5579**
FORMIERUNG **5579**
FORMIERUNGSSPANNUNG **5576**
FORMKALIBER **8422**
FORMKASTEN **5369**
FORMKASTENSTIFT **5372**
FORMMASCHINE **8358**
FORMMASCHINE **8429**
FORMOBERTEIL **3104**
FORMOL **5573**
FORMSAND **8430**
FORMSCHLICHTE **8355**
FORMSCHWÄRZE **1297**
FORMSTAHL **11114**
FORMSTEIN **8425**
FORMSTÜCK **11265**
FORMSTÜCK FÜR ROHRLEITUNGEN **9350**
FORMUNG AUF DEM BODEN **5445**
FORMUNTERTEIL **4199**
FORMVERSATZ **1322**
FORMYLSÄURE **5578**
FORSCHUNG (ANGEWANDTE) **649**
FORTBEWEGUNG **7712**
FORTFÜRHRUNG DER WARME **3060**
FORTPFLANZUNG VON WELLEN **9926**
FORTPFLANZUNGSGESCHWINDIGKEIT **13519**
FORTRÜCKUNG (ALLG.) **4053**
FOTODIODE **9258**
FOUCAULTSCHE STRÖME **4440**
FOURDRINIERDRAHT **5607**
FRACHT **3209**
FRACHTKOSTEN **3209**
FRAGEBOGEN **10101**
FRAKTION (EINER DESTILLATION) **5611**
FRAKTIONIEREN **5615**
FRAKTIONIERTURM **5614**
FRAKTIONIERTURM **13171**
FRAKTOGRAPHIE **5616**

**FRA** 804

FRÄSE 8289
FRÄSEN 8276
FRÄSEN 8287
FRÄSEN (GEGENLÄUFIGES) 3061
FRÄSEN (GLEICHLÄUFIGES) 2497
FRÄSER 3519
FRÄSER 8289
FRÄSER (ARBEITER) 8292
FRÄSER (EINFACHER) FÜR SCHWERE SCHNITTE 6404
FRÄSER FÜR WOODRUFFKEILE 13930
FRÄSER MIT EINGESETZTEN ZÄHNEN 6971
FRÄSER MIT GERADEN SCHNEIDEN 12307
FRÄSER MIT HINTERDREHTEN ZÄHNEN 905
FRÄSER MIT SCHRAUBENFÖRMIGEN SCHNEIDEN 11917
FRÄSEREI 8293
FRÄSERSPINDEL 3520
FRÄSKOPF 3531
FRÄSMASCHINE 8291
FRÄSMASCHINE (FÜHLERGESTEUERTE) 13080
FRÄSMASCHINE (HORIZONTALE) 6589
FRÄSMASCHINE (STEHENDE) 13548
FRÄSMASCHINE (WAAGERECHTE) 6589
FRÄSMASCHINE MIT MEHREREN SPINDELN 8471
FRÄSMASCHINE VERTIKALE 13548
FRÄSSTIFTE 8290
FRÄSVORRICHTUNG 1390
FRAUNHOFERSCHE LINIEN 5631
FREI AUFGEHÄNGT 5649
FREI AUFLIEGEND 11474
FREI AUFLIEGEND 5650
FREI GELAGERT 5650
FREIES FEUER 8813
FREIFALL 5633
FREIFALLEND 5024
FREIFALLHAMMER 6080
FREIFORMSCHMIEDESTÜCK 11670
FREIHANDZEICHNUNG 5648
FREIHÄNGEND 8936
FREIHEITSGRADE 3726
FREILÄNGE 7518
FREILAUF 5651
FREILAUFKUPPLUNG 10221
FREILAUFKUPPLUNG 8957
FREILAUFMECHANISMUS 5652
FREILAUFRAD 5644
FREILEITUNG 212
FREISCHWEBEND 8936
FREISCHWEBENDER KOLBEN 9391
FREITRÄGER 1905
FREITRÄGER 1904
FREIWERDEND (CHEM.) 8497

FREMDERREGUNG 11190
FREMDSTOFFE 6813
FREQUENZ 5661
FRESSEN 5778
FRESSEN 11141
FRESSEN 11140
FRIKTIONSSCHEIBE 5673
FRISCHDAMPF 7673
FRISCHEISEN 346
FRISCHEREIÖFEN 3607
FRISCHOFEN 10379
FRISCHUNGSTEMPERATUR 10381
FRISCHVERFAHREN 10380
FRONT FÜHRERHAUS 1824
FROSCHLAGER 11788
FROSCHPERSPEKTIVE 1498
FROSTBESTÄNDIG 8635
FROSTBESTÄNDIGKEIT 8634
FROSTRISS DES HOLZES 5700
FROSTSCHUTZMITTEL 612
FROSTSCHUTZMITTEL 5657
FROSTSCHUTZVENTIL 8633
FRÜHEINSTELLUNG 206
FRÜHZÜNDUNG 9778
FUCHS (EINER FEUERUNGSANLAGE) 13418
FUCHSSCHWANZ 11659
FUGE 11083
FUGE 7238
FUGE 6127
FUGE (DICHTE) 12921
FUGEINLAGE 7621
FÜGEMASCHINE 7246
FUGENFLANKE 6130
FUGENNAHT 6133
FUGENÖFFNUNGSWINKEL 6129
FUGENRADIUS 6132
FUGENRADIUS 10728
FÜHLER 11090
FÜHLER 1711
FÜHRERHAUS 13229
FÜHRERSCHEIN 4302
FÜHRUNG 6160
FÜHRUNGSARM 6505
FÜHRUNGSBAHN 6166
FÜHRUNGSLEISTE 5060
FÜHRUNGSRING 6163
FÜHRUNGSRIPPE 5060
FÜHRUNGSROLLE 6161
FÜHRUNGSSCHIENE 6162
FÜHRUNGSSCHUH 11587
FÜHRUNGSSTANGE 6164

805 GAN

FÜHRUNGSSTIFT **1513**
FÜLLDICHTE **1724**
FÜLLEN **5156**
FÜLLEN **2269**
FULLERERDE **5727**
FÜLLHAHN **5066**
FÜLLMETALL **5159**
FÜLLSAND **912**
FÜLLSTOFF **5157**
FÜLLSTOFF **5164**
FÜLLSTOFF (BAUW.) **228**
FÜLLTRICHTER **6577**
FÜLLUNG **2269**
FÜLLVERLUST **5163**
FUNDAMENT **5589**
FUNDAMENT EINER MASCHINE **7848**
FUNDAMENTALSCHWINGUNG **5736**
FUNDAMENTANKER **501**
FUNDAMENTBOLZEN **5590**
FUNDAMENTPLATTE **2900**
FUNDAMENTSCHRAUBE **5590**
FUNDIERUNG **5589**
FÜNFECK **9172**
FÜNFFACH-SCHWEFELANTIMON **625**
FÜNFFLACH **9175**
FÜNFFLÄCHNER **9175**
FUNKE **11836**
FUNKENEROSION **4531**
FUNKENEROSIONS-LEHRENBOHR-MASCHINE (IN RECHTECKIGEN KOORDINATEN ARBEITEND) **10300**
FUNKENEROSIONSCHNITT **4559**
FUNKENFÄNGER **3109**
FUNKENPROBE **11840**
FUNKTION (MATH.) **5734**
FUNKTION (STETIGE) **3025**
FURCHENZIEHER (2-3-UND 4-REIHIG) **10573**
FURNIERHOBELMASCHINE **13525**
FURNIERHOLZ **13524**
FURNIERSÄGE **13526**
FUSELÖL **5754**
FUSS (ENGLISCHER) **5518**
FUSS EINER SÄULE **1035**
FUSSBODEN (BELAG) **5450**
FUSSBODENBELAG **5450**
FUSSBODENBELAGBLECH **5447**
FUSSBODENPLATTE **5302**
FUSSBODENVORGELEGE **5444**
FUSSBREMSE **5519**
FUSSGESTELL **1041**
FUSSHEBEL **5521**
FUSSKREIS **10717**

FUSSKREIS **10723**
FUSSLAGER **5524**
FUSSLEISTE **12977**
FUSSPFUND **5522**
FUSSSCHRAUBE **7529**
FUSSTRITTDREHBANK **5520**
FUSSVENTIL **5523**
FUSSVENTIL **5523**
FUTTER **7623**
FUTTER **10614**
FUTTER (HYDRAULISCHE) **6679**
FUTTER (MECHANISCHES) **8095**
FUTTER (PNEUMATISCHE) **9550**
FUTTER (SELBSTTÄTIGE) **11152**
FÜTTERN **7623**
G.C.S.-SYSTEM **2159**
GABBRO **5765**
GABELBOLZEN **2492**
GABELGELENK **5567**
GABELGIESSPFANNE **11258**
GABELHEUWENDER **12696**
GABELROHR **1595**
GABELSCHLÜSSEL **9322**
GABELZAPFEN **6159**
GADOLINIUM **5767**
GALENIT **5775**
GALLESCHE KETTE **12002**
GALLIUM **5779**
GALLONE **5781**
GALLUSGERBSÄURE **5780**
GALLUSSÄURE **5777**
GALMEI (EDLER) **1836**
GALVANISCHER UEBERZUG **9503**
GALVANISIEREN **366**
GALVANISIEREN **5789**
GALVANISIERUNG **4562**
GALVANOMETER **5791**
GALVANOPLASTIK **4557**
GALVANOPLASTISCH **5792**
GALVANOSTEGIE **4640**
GAMMA-EISEN **5795**
GAMMA-FUNKTION **5794**
GAMMA-STRAHLEN **5796**
GAMMA-STRAHLENBILD **5798**
GAMMA-STRUKTUR **5797**
GANG (DIREKTER) **3983**
GANG (GERÄUSCHLOSER) **8609**
GANG (GERÄUSCHVOLLER) **8610**
GANG (HARTER) **6412**
GANG (LEICHTER) **7567**
GANG (RUHIGER) **11681**

## GAN

806

GANG (SCHWERER) **6412**
GANG (STOSSENDER) **6412**
GANG (STOSSFREIER) **7567**
GANG (TOTER) **13873**
GANG (TOTER) **916**
GANG (UNRUHIGER) **7165**
GANG (WEICHER) **7567**
GANG EINER MASCHINE **10850**
GANG EINES GEWINDES **13279**
GANG SETZEN (WIEDER IN) **10508**
GANGART **5802**
GANGGESTEIN **5802**
GANGHÖHE EINER SCHRAUBE **9410**
GANGMINERAL **5802**
GANGSPILL **6229**
GANGTIEFE EINER SCHRAUBE **3784**
GANGZAHL EINES GEWINDES **8692**
GANISTER **5803**
GANZ-ALUMINIUMLEITER **343**
GANZEISEN **345**
GANZFABRIKAT **5730**
GANZHOLZ **7723**
GÄRBSTAHL **11490**
GÄRFUTTERZUBEREITUNGSMASCHINEN **11430**
GARNITUR **11213**
GARSCHAUMGRAPHIT **7317**
GÄRSTOFF **5097**
GÄRTNEREI- **13096**
GÄRUNG **5098**
GÄRUNGSSTOFF **5097**
GAS **5808**
GAS (GLÜHENDES) **6827**
GAS (KOMPRIMIERTES) **2847**
GAS (VERDICHTETES) **2847**
GAS (VERFLÜSSIGTES) **7637**
GAS (VOLLKOMMENES) **9185**
GAS VERFLÜSSIGEN (EIN) **7640**
GASABZUG **5821**
GASABZUG OHNE VERBRENNUNG MIT WIEDERGEWINNUNG **5841**
GASABZUG UND STAUBABSAUGUNG **4392**
GASANALYSE **5809**
GASANSTALT **5848**
GASÄTHER **9228**
GASBEHÄLTER **5859**
GASBEIZUNG **5832**
GASBELEUCHTUNG **5828**
GASBLASE **7523**
GASBLASE **1353**
GASBLASE **1671**
GASBLASE **5836**

GASBLASE **5825**
GASBRENNER **5811**
GASDICHT **5853**
GASDICHTE **3757**
GASDRUCK **5837**
GASDYNAMO **5850**
GASE ABFÜHREN **10455**
GASEINSCHLUSS **5836**
GASEINSCHLUSS **1353**
GASEINSCHLUSS **5855**
GASEINSCHLUSS **5825**
GASENTWICKLUNG **3818**
GASERZEUGER **5838**
GASEXPANSION **4920**
GASFABRIK **5848**
GASFACKEL **5820**
GASFANG **5842**
GASFEUERUNG **1751**
GASFEUERUNG **5744**
GASFÖRMIGER KÖRPER **5808**
GASGEMISCH **5856**
GASGENERATOR **5838**
GASGLOCKE **5859**
GASGLÜHLICHT **6829**
GASGLÜHLICHTLAMPE **6828**
GASHAHN **5814**
GASHÄRTUNG **5840**
GASKOHLE **5813**
GASKOHLE (ECHTE) **1901**
GASKOKS **5849**
GASKONSTANTE **5815**
GASKRAFTMASCHINE **5819**
GASLAMPE **5826**
GASLEITUNG **5834**
GASLICHT **5827**
GASLÖTEN **5810**
GASLÖTKOLBEN **5824**
GASMESSER **5829**
GASMOTOR **5819**
GASNITRIEREN **5830**
GASÖL **5831**
GASOLIN **9228**
GASOMETER **5859**
GASPORE **9629**
GASPRÜFER **4852**
GASREINIGUNG **5839**
GASREINIGUNG **10018**
GASRILLEN **5823**
GASROHR **5833**
GASROHRGEWINDE **5843**
GASROHRZANGE **5835**

807 GEL

GASSCHWEISSEN **5847**
GASSTROM **5816**
GASTEER **2570**
GASTHERMOMETER **265**
GASTURBINE **5844**
GASUHR **5829**
GASWASCHFLASCHE **5845**
GASWASSER **456**
GASWERK **5848**
GATTERSÄGE **5629**
GATTERSTAB (UNTERER) **7796**
GAUSS'SCHE VERTEILUNG **5887**
GAVALNOPLASTIK **4651**
GAZE **5888**
GEBLÄSE **242**
GEBLÄSE **1361**
GEBLÄSEDÜSE **8685**
GEBLÄSEMASCHINE **1363**
GEBLÄSEWIND **243**
GEBLÄSEWIND **1315**
GEBRAUCHSANWEISUNG **6992**
GEBÜNDELTER STRAHL **5504**
GEBUNDENER KOHLENSTOFF **5289**
GEDIEGEN (MIN.) **5647**
GEDRÜCKTER STAB **2855**
GEFÄLLE (NEIGUNG) **3792**
GEFÄSSBAROMETER **2440**
GEFÄSSE (KOMMUNIZIERENDE) **13553**
GEFÄSSMANOMETER **8827**
GEFLANSCHTE ENDEN **5339**
GEFLECHTÜBERZUG **1526**
GEFRIERPUNKT **5656**
GEFÜGE **12395**
GEFÜGE **12394**
GEFÜGE **12800**
GEFÜGE (BLÄTTRIGES) **7374**
GEFÜGE (FASERIGES) **5141**
GEFÜGE (FEINKÖRNIGES) **5200**
GEFÜGE (GLEICHARTIGES) **6560**
GEFÜGE (HETEROGENES) **6452**
GEFÜGE (HOMOGENES) **6560**
GEFÜGE (INHOMOGENES) **6452**
GEFÜGE (KÖRNIGES) **6053**
GEFÜGE (KRISTALLINISCHES) **3434**
GEFÜGE (UNGLEICHARTIGES) **6452**
GEFÜGE DER LEGIERUNGEN **2058**
GEFÜHLSBOHRMASCHINE **11186**
GEGEN DEN STROM **13407**
GEGEN-EMK **3231**
GEGENBEWEGUNG **3243**
GEGENDRUCK **3232**

GEGENDRUCKBETRIEB **894**
GEGENDRUCKSCHRAUBE **12909**
GEGENDRUCKVENTIL **895**
GEGENDRUCKVENTIL **5523**
GEGENEINANDER VERSETZT **12048**
GEGENFEDER **11974**
GEGENFLANSCH **8054**
GEGENGEWICHT **3251**
GEGENHALTEN **6524**
GEGENHALTER **4115**
GEGENHALTER **1305**
GEGENHALTER **898**
GEGENKEIL **5937**
GEGENKOPPLUNG **10536**
GEGENKRAFT **10248**
GEGENKURBEL **10528**
GEGENLOGARITHMUS **620**
GEGENMUTTER **7702**
GEGENPROE **4384**
GEGENSCHRAUBE **2281**
GEGENSCHRITTSCHWEISSEN **918**
GEGENSTOSS **1918**
GEGENSTREBE **3179**
GEGENSTROM **3230**
GEGENSTROMMESSER IN ÖLBAD **8747**
GEGENWELLE **3233**
GEGOSSEN (IN EINEM STÜCK) **2054**
GEHALT **3011**
GEHALT **10897**
GEHÄMMERT **6220**
GEHÄUSE **1385**
GEHÄUSE **6660**
GEHÄUSE **227**
GEHÄUSE (EINES MASCHINENTEILS) **2026**
GEHÄUSE EINES HAHNES **11334**
GEHÄUSE EINES SCHIEBERS **2229**
GEHÄUSE EINES VENTILS **2229**
GEHRDREIECK **8325**
GEHRFUGE **8324**
GEHRMASS **8325**
GEHRSTOSS **8324**
GEHRUNG **8326**
GEIGER-ZÄHLER **5911**
GEISER **5936**
GEISSFUSS (STEMMEISEN) **13432**
GEKRÄTZ **4331**
GEL **5912**
GELAGERT (AUF EINE SCHNEIDE) **6669**
GELAGERT (AUF EINER SPITZE) **8432**
GELAGERT (AUF ZAPFEN) **9422**
GELÄNDER-EISEN **1086**

# GEL
808

GELÄNDEREISEN **6265**
GELÄNDERSTÜTZE **6266**
GELÄNDEWAGEN **3362**
GELATINE **5913**
GELBBLEIERZ **13991**
GELBBRENNE **1608**
GELBBRENNSÄURE **657**
GELBES BLUTLAUGENSALZ **9685**
GELBES CHROMKALI **9682**
GELBES CHROMSAURES KALI **9682**
GELBES ZYANEISENKALIUM **9685**
GELBGUSS **1562**
GELBKUPFER **1562**
GELBÖL **1668**
GELDSTRAFE **5195**
GELENK (MECH.) **7238**
GELENKBAND **6505**
GELENKBOLZEN **7242**
GELENKIG VERBUNDEN **7629**
GELENKKETTE **12002**
GELENKMASSSTAB **5512**
GELENKPUNKT **5717**
GELENKROHR **5418**
GELENKSPINDELBOHRMASCHINE **12550**
GELENKSTEIN **7625**
GELENKSYSTEM **7628**
GELENKZAPFEN **7242**
GELERNTER ARBEITER **3289**
GEMISCH **8327**
GEMISCH (BRENNBARES) **4938**
GEMISCH (ENTZÜNDLICHES) **4938**
GEMISCH (ZÜNDFÄHIGES) **4938**
GENAUIGKEIT **9763**
GENAUIGKEIT **82**
GENAUIGKEIT DER AUSFÜHRUNG **83**
GENAUIGKEITSGRAD **3721**
GENAUIGKEITSTEILGERÄT **9769**
GENEHMIGUNGSDRUCK **8614**
GENERALNENNER **2789**
GENERATOR (ELEKTRISCHER) **5924**
GENERATOR (ELEKTROSTATISCHER) **4643**
GENERATORGAS **9890**
GENERATRIX **5925**
GENIETETES ROHR **10640**
GEOMETRIE **5931**
GEOMETRISCH **5927**
GEPULVERT **9983**
GERADE **12310**
GERADE LINIE **12310**
GERADER SETZHAMMER **5410**
GERADERICHTEN **12319**

GERADERICHTEN **12318**
GERADFÜHRUNG **12315**
GERADFÜHRUNG (DAMPFM.) **6169**
GERADLINIG **10319**
GERADLINIGE LÄNGSTEIGUNG **7615**
GERADVERZAHNUNG **12311**
GERADVERZAHNUNGSKUPPLUNG **12313**
GERÄT **641**
GERÄUSCH **8608**
GERBSTOFF **5780**
GERIEFT **5484**
GERIFFELT **5484**
GERINNE **2251**
GERINNEN **2556**
GERINNEN **2555**
GERINNSEL **2557**
GERIPPE **5624**
GERIPPE (SELBSTTRAGENDES) **11161**
GERMANIUM **5933**
GERÖLLE **11354**
GERÜST **10965**
GERÜST **5624**
GERÜST (SELBSTTRAGENDES) **11161**
GERÜSTKRAN **5804**
GESAMTBELASTUNG **13062**
GESAMTDRUCK **13065**
GESAMTLÄNGE **8925**
GESAMTLEISTUNG **13064**
GESAMTTOTGANG **13063**
GESAMTWIRKUNGSGRAD **8927**
GESCHÄFT **7229**
GESCHICHTET **7375**
GESCHIEBE **11354**
GESCHMIEDET (AUS DEM VOLLEN) **5552**
GESCHRECKT **4247**
GESCHÜTZBRONZE **6178**
GESCHÜTZBRONZE **197**
GESCHÜTZTER MOTOR **9941**
GESCHWINDIGKEIT **10226**
GESCHWINDIGKEIT **11875**
GESCHWINDIGKEIT **11868**
GESCHWINDIGKEIT (ABNEHMENDE) **3679**
GESCHWINDIGKEIT (KONSTANTE) **13363**
GESCHWINDIGKEIT (KRITISCHE) **3353**
GESCHWINDIGKEIT (LINEARE) **7617**
GESCHWINDIGKEIT (TANGENTIALE) **12623**
GESCHWINDIGKEIT (UNVERÄNDERLICHE) **13363**
GESCHWINDIGKEIT (VERÄNDERLICHE) **13494**
GESCHWINDIGKEIT (VIRTUELLE) **13573**
GESCHWINDIGKEIT (ZUNEHMENDE) **6852**
GESCHWINDIGKEIT ERHÖHEN **6851**

GESCHWINDIGKEIT STEIGERN **6851**
GESCHWINDIGKEIT VERRINGERN **3678**
GESCHWINDIGKEITSABNAHME **3677**
GESCHWINDIGKEITSÄNDERUNG **2245**
GESCHWINDIGKEITSDIAGRAMM **13514**
GESCHWINDIGKEITSERHÖHUNG **10185**
GESCHWINDIGKEITSHÖHE **13515**
GESCHWINDIGKEITSIKURVE **13513**
GESCHWINDIGKEITSMESSER **11877**
GESCHWINDIGKEITSMESSER **11869**
GESCHWINDIGKEITSPARALLELOGRAMM **9072**
GESCHWINDIGKEITSREGLER **11872**
GESCHWINDIGKEITSREGLER **11874**
GESCHWINDIGKEITSSCHREIBER **12586**
GESCHWINDIGKEITSSCHWANKUNGEN **13499**
GESCHWINDIGKEITSSTUFE **13523**
GESCHWINDIGKEITSVERMINDERUNG **10363**
GESCHWINDIGKEITSZAHL **2638**
GESCHWINDIGKEITVERMINDERN **3678**
GESCHWINDIGKEITZUNAHME **6849**
GESENK **3897**
GESENK (OFFENES) **8810**
GESENK (ZWEITEILIGES) **2818**
GESENKFRÄSEN **3892**
GESENKKLOTZ **12531**
GESENKMETALL **3889**
GESENKPLATTE **12531**
GESENKSCHMIEDEN **12532**
GESENKSCHMIEDEN **12534**
GESENKSCHMIEDEN **12059**
GESENKSCHMIEDEN **3894**
GESENKSCHMIEDESTÜCK **4324**
GESENKSTOCK **12531**
GESETZ (BRAGGSCHES) **1525**
GESETZ VON BRAGG **1525**
GESICHTSFELD **5143**
GESICHTSSCHUTZMASKE **5000**
GESICHTSWINKEL **13581**
GESIMSHOBEL **9522**
GESPERRE **7709**
GESPINSTFASER **12799**
GESTALTUNG **3794**
GESTÄNGE **12577**
GESTEHUNGSKOSTEN **3207**
GESTEHUNGSPREIS **3210**
GESTEIN **10651**
GESTEIN (SPALTBARES) **2486**
GESTELL **5624**
GESTELL **12490**
GESTELLSÄGE **9747**
GESTÜTZT (BEIDERSEITIG) **11474**

GETREIDEFÖRDERER UND HEBER **6034**
GETREIDETROCKNER **4258**
GETRIEBE **8122**
GETRIEBE MIT AUSSENVERZAHNUNG **4956**
GETRIEBE MIT INNENVERZAHNUNG **7058**
GETRIEBELEHRE **7306**
GETRIEBENE SCHEIBE **4298**
GEWALZTEN ZUSTAND (IM) **744**
GEWÄSSERTES NATRIUMKARBONAT **11711**
GEWEBE (WASSERDICHTES) **13690**
GEWICHT **13747**
GEWICHT (SPEZIFISCHES) **11850**
GEWICHT (SPEZIFISCHES) **3756**
GEWICHT (TOTES) **3637**
GEWICHT (VERBRAUCHTES) **2992**
GEWICHTSANALYSE **6077**
GEWICHTSARÄOMETER **6723**
GEWICHTSATZ **11219**
GEWICHTSEINHEIT **13378**
GEWICHTSFALLVERSUCH **4330**
GEWICHTSHEBEL **13751**
GEWICHTSHEBELBREMSE **3638**
GEWICHTSPROZENT **9180**
GEWICHTSREGLER **13752**
GEWICHTSSCHALE **10976**
GEWICHTSSICHERHEITSVENTIL **13749**
GEWICHTSSYSTEM **12580**
GEWICHTSTEIL **9180**
GEWICHTSVERLUST **7764**
GEWINDE **11045**
GEWINDE **12857**
GEWINDE (AUSGELEIERTES) **13981**
GEWINDE (FLACHES) **12030**
GEWINDE (FLACHGÄNGIGES) **12030**
GEWINDE (GROBES) **2575**
GEWINDE (HALBIERTES) **1814**
GEWINDE (INTERNATIONALES METRISCHES) **7083**
GEWINDE (KONISCHES) **12666**
GEWINDE (LINKSGÄNGIGES) **7508**
GEWINDE (METRISCHESINTERNATIONALES) **7084**
GEWINDE (RECHTSÄNGIGES) **10585**
GEWINDE (RUNDES) **10802**
GEWINDE (SCHARFES) **545**
GEWINDE (SCHARFGÄNGIGES) **545**
GEWINDE (WHITWORTHSCHES) **13844**
GEWINDE (ZYLINDRISCHES) **9065**
GEWINDE LEHREN **12860**
GEWINDE MIT SCHWACHER STEIGUNG **11647**
GEWINDE MIT STARKER STEIGUNG **10105**
GEWINDE SCHNEIDEN **11046**
GEWINDEBASIS **1028**

# GEW

810

GEWINDEBOHREN 12678
GEWINDEBOHRER 11044
GEWINDEBOHRER 12640
GEWINDEBOLZEN 12398
GEWINDEDORN 12867
GEWINDEDREHBANK 12859
GEWINDEDREHBANK 11029
GEWINDEDURCHMESSER (ÄUSSERER) 3852
GEWINDEEISEN 11039
GEWINDEFLANSCH 11064
GEWINDEFLANSCH 12866
GEWINDEFLANSCH 11055
GEWINDEFRÄSMASCHINE 11036
GEWINDEGANG 13279
GEWINDEGANGZAHL 8692
GEWINDEGRUND 1028
GEWINDEKERN 12864
GEWINDEKLUPPE 1121
GEWINDEKONTROLLEHRE 2760
GEWINDEKONTROLLEHRE 11038
GEWINDEKOPF 12455
GEWINDEKUPPLUNG 11026
GEWINDELEHRDORN 12862
GEWINDELEHRDORN 11049
GEWINDELEHRE 11047
GEWINDELEHRMUTTER 11050
GEWINDELOCH 11056
GEWINDEMITTELSCHNEIDER 11102
GEWINDEMUFFE 11061
GEWINDENACHSCHNEIDER 9534
GEWINDEPFROPFEN 11060
GEWINDEROHR 11059
GEWINDESCHNEID-KLUPPE 12266
GEWINDESCHNEIDBACKEN 3896
GEWINDESCHNEIDEN 11030
GEWINDESCHNEIDEN 12868
GEWINDESCHNEIDKOPF (RUNDER) 11781
GEWINDESCHNEIDMASCHINE 11066
GEWINDESCHNEIDVORRICHTUNG 12676
GEWINDESPINDEL 11062
GEWINDESPITZE 12455
GEWINDESPITZE 3333
GEWINDESTAHL 2274
GEWINDESTAHLLEHRE 12865
GEWINDESTEIGUNG 9399
GEWINDESTIFT 6156
GEWINDESTRÄHLER 2274
GEWINDETIEFE 3784
GEWINDEVORSCHNEIDER 5268
GEWINDEWEITEN 11054
GEWINN AN ARBEIT 8094

GEWINNUNG DER KOHLE 13877
GEWINNUNG VON METALLEN 4966
GEWÖLBESTEIN 687
GEWUNDENE KURVE 13307
GEZÄHNELT 6862
GEZAHNTER SEKTOR 13024
GICHT 2076
GICHT 1059
GICHTGAS 1313
GICHTSTAUB 5469
GICHTSTAUBSAMMLER 4390
GIESSBAR 1914
GIESSEN 9715
GIESSEN 5592
GIESSEN 2068
GIESSEN 2030
GIESSEN 2070
GIESSEN 12703
GIESSEN (KONTINUIERLICHES) 3019
GIESSEN (STEIGENDES) 1488
GIESSEN (WIRBELFREIES) 4388
GIESSEN (WIRBELFREIES) (DURVILLE-VERFAHREN) 10109
GIESSEN MIT VERLORENER GIESSFORM 7115
GIESSER 5591
GIESSEREI 5592
GIESSEREI 5593
GIESSEREI 5597
GIESSEREI 2071
GIESSEREIKOKS 2662
GIESSEREIKOKS 5595
GIESSEREIROHEISEN 5596
GIESSHALLE 2071
GIESSHALLE 2077
GIESSHAUS 5597
GIESSKANNE 13687
GIESSKOPF 11506
GIESSKUNST 5592
GIESSPFANNE 7356
GIESSPFANNE (GEMAUERTE) 7618
GIESSPFANNENWAGEN 2072
GIESSRAHMEN 8354
GIESSTRICHTER 9716
GIESSTROMMEL 4336
GIPS 6190
GIPS (GEBRANNTER) 9466
GIPSFORM 6188
GIPSFORM 9465
GIPSMODELL 6189
GITTER 7429
GITTER 6096
GITTER 6071

811 GLE

GITTER (REZIPROKES) 10281
GITTERAKKUMULATOR 6097
GITTEREBENE 804
GITTERKONSTANTE 9075
GITTERKONSTANTE 7430
GITTERPAPIER 11530
GITTERROST 6101
GITTERROSTSTUFEN 6102
GITTERSCHIEBER 6100
GITTERTRÄGER 7431
GITTERVERZERRUNGSTHEORIE 7434
GLANZ (METALLISCHER) 8195
GLANZ (MIN.) 7830
GLANZ (VERLIEREN DEN) 12685
GLANZ SCHLEIFEN 9598
GLÄNZBAD (CHEMISCHES) 1564
GLANZBRENNE 1609
GLANZDECKEL 9801
GLANZKOBALT 2614
GLANZLEDER 9117
GLANZLICHTER 6472
GLANZMITTEL 1615
GLANZPAPPE 9801
GLANZPUNKTE 6472
GLANZSCHLEIFEN 9605
GLANZVERLUST 4369
GLANZZIEHEN 4347
GLANZZUSATZ 1615
GLAS 5956
GLAS 11589
GLAS (BÖHMISCHES) 1400
GLAS (FARBLOSES) 2746
GLAS (GEBLASENES) 1365
GLAS (NICHT SPLITTERNDES) 13894
GLAS-HALBZELLE 5959
GLASBAUSTEIN 5957
GLASERKITT 5971
GLASFLUSS 4709
GLASGLANZ 13583
GLASIEREN 5972
GLASIEREN 5969
GLASIG 13582
GLASKOLBEN 5370
GLASLEINWAND 5958
GLASMEHL 5962
GLASPAPIER 5961
GLASPLATTE 5963
GLASRÖHRE 5965
GLASSCHEIBE 5963
GLASTAFEL 5963
GLASUR 5972

GLASUR 5968
GLASURSTEIN 5970
GLASWOLLE 5966
GLASZIEGEL 5964
GLÄTTEN 5408
GLÄTTEN 11686
GLÄTTEN 11679
GLÄTTEN 9157
GLÄTTEN 9454
GLATTWALZEN 10695
GLÄTTWALZWERK 9456
GLÄTTZAHN 1757
GLAUBERSALZ 5967
GLEICHACHSIG 2605
GLEICHFÖRMIGKEIT DER BEWEGUNG 10417
GLEICHFÖRMIGKEIT DES MATERIALS 13364
GLEICHFÖRMIGKEITSGRAD 3719
GLEICHGEWICHT 4793
GLEICHGEWICHT 4786
GLEICHGEWICHT (INDIFFERENTES) 6882
GLEICHGEWICHT (LABILES) 13401
GLEICHGEWICHT (STABILES) 12045
GLEICHGEWICHT SEIN (MIT) 1076
GLEICHGEWICHTSDIAGRAMM 4788
GLEICHGEWICHTSKONSTANTE 4787
GLEICHGEWICHTSLAGE 9647
GLEICHGEWICHTSLIEHRE 12140
GLEICHGEWICHTSPOTENTIAL EINER ELEKTRODE 4789
GLEICHGEWICHTSTEMPERATUR 4791
GLEICHGEWICHTSWERT 4792
GLEICHGEWICHTSZUSTAND 12132
GLEICHGEWISCHT (CHEMISCHES) 2307
GLEICHLÄUFIGES FRÄSEN 13408
GLEICHLÄUFIGES FRÄSEN 4182
GLEICHMASSGRENZE 7590
GLEICHMÄSSIG 6555
GLEICHRICHTER 10314
GLEICHRICHTER (ELEKTROCHEMISCHER) 4572
GLEICHRICHTER (ELEKTRONISCHER) 4634
GLEICHRICHTERANODE 10315
GLEICHRICHTERKATODE 10316
GLEICHRICHTERRÖHRE 10317
GLEICHRICHTUNG 10312
GLEICHSCHLAGRAHTSEIL 7390
GLEICHSTROM 3023
GLEICHSTROM (VON FLÜSSIGKEITEN) 13360
GLEICHSTROM-LICHTBOGENSCHWEISSEN 686
GLEICHSTROMDAMPFMASCHINE 12407
GLEICHSTROMDYNAMO 3021
GLEICHSTROMGENERATOR 3021
GLEICHSTROMMASCHINE 3021

## GLE

812

GLEICHSTROMMOTOR **3022**
GLEICHUNG **4782**
GLEICHUNG (ALGEBRAISCHE) **322**
GLEICHUNG (BINOMISCHE) **1259**
GLEICHUNG (BIQUADRATISCHE) **1262**
GLEICHUNG (DREIGLIEDRIGE) **13213**
GLEICHUNG (HOMOGENE) **6557**
GLEICHUNG (KUBISCHE) **3452**
GLEICHUNG (LINEARE) **7616**
GLEICHUNG (QUADRATISCHE) **10057**
GLEICHUNG (TRANSZENDENTE) **13107**
GLEICHUNG (TRINOMISCHE) **13213**
GLEICHUNG (ZWEIGLIEDRIGE) **1259**
GLEICHUNG DRITTEN GRADES **3452**
GLEICHUNG ERSTEN GRADES **7616**
GLEICHUNG FÜNFTEN GRADES **10112**
GLEICHUNG VIERTEN GRADES **1262**
GLEICHUNG ZWEITEN GRADES **10057**
GLEICHWERTIG **4796**
GLEICHWERTIGKEIT **4795**
GLEICHZEITIG UND FORTLAUFEND MONTIERT **4807**
GLEIS **7606**
GLEISHAMMER **4326**
GLEISSEILBAHN **1826**
GLEISWAAGE **13745**
GLEIT **5973**
GLEITBAHN **6160**
GLEITBAHN **11588**
GLEITBAHN (DAMPFM.) **6169**
GLEITBEWEGUNG **11605**
GLEITEBENE **5975**
GLEITEN **11595**
GLEITEN **11586**
GLEITEN **11612**
GLEITEN DES RIEMENS **11620**
GLEITFLÄCHE **11585**
GLEITFLÄCHE **11588**
GLEITFLÄCHE **11608**
GLEITKLOTZ DES KREUZKOPFES **11587**
GLEITKURVE **5976**
GLEITLAGER **9424**
GLEITLAGER **11596**
GLEITLINIEN **11613**
GLEITMASS **5974**
GLEITMODUL **8342**
GLEITMODUL **5974**
GLEITSCHIENE **6162**
GLEITSCHIENE (DAMPFM.) **6169**
GLEITSCHLUPF **11620**
GLEITSCHUH **11587**
GLEITSCHUTZDIFFERENTIAL **8645**

GLEITSCHUTZREIFEN **12404**
GLEITSITZ **11600**
GLEITSTÜCK **11585**
GLEITUNG **11611**
GLEITUNG **11288**
GLEITVERSCHALUNG **11616**
GLEITWIDERSTAND **10498**
GLIEDER (VORGESPANNTE) **1446**
GLIEDERBREITE EINER KETTE **6982**
GLIEDERKETTE **8855**
GLIEDERLÄNGE **6978**
GLIEDERMASSSTAB **5512**
GLIEDERRIEMEN AUS LEDER **7496**
GLIMMEN (KATHODISCHES) **2110**
GLIMMER **8231**
GLIMMESCHIEFER **8232**
GLOBOIDSCHNECKE **5978**
GLOBOIDSCHRAUBE **5978**
GLOCKENBRONZE **1134**
GLOCKENMETALL **1134**
GLOCKENSPEISE **1134**
GLOCKENVENTIL **1136**
GLÜHANLAGE **565**
GLÜHANLASSSCHALTER **6389**
GLÜHBEHANDLUNG **6377**
GLÜHDRAHT **6386**
GLÜHEN **5982**
GLÜHEN **562**
GLÜHEN **1840**
GLÜHEN **568**
GLÜHEN (ENTSPANNENDES) **583**
GLÜHEN (SPANNUNGSFREIES) **584**
GLÜHEN (SPANNUNGSFREIES) **12044**
GLÜHEN IN DEM ELEKTROOFEN **4508**
GLÜHEN ZWISCHEN ZWEI ZÜGEN **7085**
GLÜHEND **5983**
GLÜHFADENPYROMETRIE **8846**
GLÜHFARBE **2744**
GLÜHFESTIGKEIT **569**
GLÜHFRISCHEN **562**
GLÜHFRISCHEN **13175**
GLÜHFRISCHEN (INVERSES) **578**
GLÜHHITZE **5981**
GLÜHKATODENRÖHRE **6652**
GLÜHKERZE **6387**
GLÜHKERZENWIDERSTAND **6388**
GLÜHKISTE **3075**
GLÜHKISTE **567**
GLÜHKISTE **563**
GLÜHLAMPE **6825**
GLÜHLICHT **6826**

GLÜHOFEN 564
GLÜHROHRZÜNDUNG 13251
GLÜHRÜCKSTAND 6765
GLÜHSPAN 6217
GLÜHTOPF 566
GLÜHUNG 6822
GLÜHUNG (ISOTHERME) 579
GLÜHVERLUST 6763
GLÜHVERLUST 7341
GLUKOSE 6058
GLYKOSE 6058
GLYZERIN 5988
GNEIS 5989
GOLD 5993
GOLD (ABESSINISCHES) 58
GOLD (GRÜNES) 6092
GOLDBRONZE 5995
GOLDCHLORID 821
GOLDCHLORÜR 823
GOLDDUBLEE 10673
GOLDHALTIG 822
GOLDMONOCHLORID 823
GOLDPLATTIERUNG 6002
GOLDSCHMIEDEKUNST 6003
GOLDSCHWEFEL 625
GOLDSTAUB 5998
GOLDTRICHLORID 821
GOLDZYANID 5997
GONIOMETER 6004
GÖPEL 1731
GÖTTERBAUM 239
GRABENPFLÜGE 8344
GRAD 6021
GRAD 3714
GRAD BAUME 3715
GRAD CELSIUS 3716
GRAD FAHRENHEIT 3718
GRAD REAUMUR 3724
GRAD TWADDELL 3725
GRADBOGEN 9956
GRADEINTEILUNG 10981
GRADEINTEILUNG VERSEHEN (MIT) 6025
GRADSTRICH 8009
GRADUIEREN 6025
GRAIN 6029
GRAMM 6046
GRAMM-ZENTIMETER-SEKUNDE-SYSTEM 2159
GRAMMKALORIE 6045
GRAMMOL 6044
GRAMMOLEKÜL 6044
GRANALIE 25

GRANALIEN 6054
GRANALIEN BLASEN 11382
GRANALIENZINN 6042
GRANAT 5807
GRANIT 6047
GRANULAT 11379
GRANULIERGRUBE 6056
GRANULIERTES ZINN 6042
GRANULIERUNG 6057
GRAPHIT 9541
GRAPHIT 6062
GRAPHIT 9542
GRAPHIT (AUSGEFLOCKTER) 3703
GRAPHITIERUNG 6066
GRAPHITIERUNGSMITTEL 6067
GRAPHITKOHLE 9851
GRAPHITÖL 6063
GRAPHITPYROMETER 6065
GRAPHITSCHMIERE 6063
GRAPHITTIEGEL 6064
GRASTROCKNER 4259
GRAT 5357
GRAT 1764
GRAT 10836
GRAUGUSS 6094
GRAUGUSS 2034
GRAUGUSS 2041
GRAUGUSSSTÜCKE 2083
GRAUSPIESSGLANZERZ 622
GRAUSTRAHLER 6083
GRAUWACKE 6095
GRAVIERKUPFER 4767
GRAVIMETER 6722
GRAVITATION 6078
GRAVITATIONSKONSTANTE 2975
GREIFBOGEN 2997
GREIFERSCHEIBE 2503
GREIFOBERFLÄCHE 2998
GREIFWINKEL 517
GREIFWINKEL 1277
GREIFWINKEL 8577
GREIFZIRKEL 1870
GREIFZIRKEL 1874
GRENZ-RACHENLEHRE (DOPPELSEITIGE) 4148
GRENZ-RACHENLEHRE (EINSTELLBARE) 186
GRENZDRUCK 7593
GRENZEN 7595
GRENZGEWINDERACHENLEHRE MIT MESSROLLEN 10693
GRENZKURVE 1460
GRENZLEHRDORN 4137
GRENZLEHRDORN 9907

# GRE 814

GRENZLEHRE 3905
GRENZLINIEN 5689
GRENZMASS 7587
GRENZWELLENLÄNGE 8309
GRENZWELLENLÄNGE 10072
GRENZWERT 7594
GRENZWERTVERTEILUNG 4968
GRENZWINKEL (OPT.) 3345
GRENZZUSTAND 3349
GRIFF EINES WERKZEUGS 6263
GRIFFKURBEL 6231
GRIT 6123
GROBBLECH 9477
GROBBLECH 6409
GROBBLECHPRESSE 6411
GROBEN BEARBEITEN (AUS DEM) 10775
GROBFEILE 10774
GROBGEFÜGE 7869
GROBGEWINDE 2575
GROBGEWINDE 2576
GROBKALK 5664
GROBKOHLE 7826
GROBKORN 2573
GROBKORNEISEN 8819
GROBMASCHIG 2578
GROBMÖRTEL 2894
GROBSCHMIED 11671
GROBWALZWERK 6410
GROBZUG 1727
GRÖNTARNSPAT 3423
GRÖSSE (BEKANNTE) 7335
GRÖSSE (GEGEBENE) 5951
GRÖSSE (GESUCHTE) 10469
GRÖSSE (MATH.) 10065
GRÖSSE (UNBEKANNTE) 13391
GRÖSSE (WIRKLICHE) 152
GROSSE ACHSE EINER ELLIPSE 7947
GRÖSSE EINER KRAFT 7939
GRÖSSENORDNUNG 8852
GRÖSSENVERHÄLTNIS 10982
GROSSGASMASCHINE 7410
GROSSLUCKIGES EISEN 8819
GROSSSERIENANFERTIGUNG 7727
GRÖSSTWERT 8069
GROSSWASSERRAUMKESSEL 7412
GRÜBCHEN 9393
GRUBE 8300
GRUBENGAS 8215
GRUBENGUSS 9394
GRUBENHOBELMASCHINE 9395
GRUBENKLEIN (MITTELGROSSES) 8267

GRUBENSAND 9396
GRUBENSCHACHT 9398
GRUBENWASSER 9397
GRÜN (SCHEELESCHES) 10996
GRUND 1028
GRUNDANSTRICH 9864
GRUNDBELASTUNG 8655
GRUNDBÜCHSE 1565
GRUNDFARBE 9847
GRUNDFLÄCHE 1025
GRUNDIERLACK 9855
GRUNDIERUNG 9864
GRUNDKEGEL 9406
GRUNDKREIS 1030
GRUNDLAGENFORSCHUNG 5735
GRUNDLAGENFORSCHUNG 1052
GRUNDLAGENFORSCHUNG 10016
GRUNDLAGER 7941
GRUNDLAST 8655
GRUNDLINIE 1027
GRUNDMASS 1053
GRUNDMASSE 8055
GRUNDMESSING 8056
GRUNDMETALL 8057
GRUNDMETALL 1032
GRUNDMETALL 9079
GRUNDMETALLPROBESTÜCK 1039
GRUNDPLATTE 1026
GRUNDPLATTE 1127
GRUNDPLATTE 1486
GRUNDPLATTE EINER MASCHINE 1037
GRUNDRING 9000
GRUNDRISS 11124
GRUNDRISS 5914
GRUNDSCHICHT 9857
GRUNDSCHWINGUNG 5736
GRUNDSTOFF 9852
GRUNDSTOFF 4654
GRUNDSTOFF (HOMOGENER) 6558
GRUNDWASSER 6147
GRUNDWASSERSPIEGEL 6148
GRUNDWERKSTOFF 909
GRUNDZAHL 9860
GRUNDZAHL 1033
GRÜNFUTTERLADER 7687
GRÜNFUTTERLADER 6091
GRÜNLING 6090
GRÜNSANDBINDER 1445
GRÜNSPAN 220
GRÜNSPAN 219
GRÜNSPAN 13533

815 HAF

GRÜNSPANÄHNLICH **219**
GRÜNSTEIN **3828**
GRUPPENANTRIEB **6150**
GRUPPENVENTIL **8476**
GRUPPIERUNG DER NIETE **717**
GRUSKOHLE **11557**
GUINIER-PRESTON ZONE **6171**
GUMMI **10816**
GUMMI (ARABISCHES) **6172**
GUMMI MIT GEWEBEEINLAGE **6973**
GUMMI- (ODER NEOPREN-) ISOLIERUNG **11329**
GUMMIGUTT **5793**
GUMMIHARZ **6173**
GUMMIISOLIER BAND **10822**
GUMMILACK **12254**
GUMMIMEMBRAN **10819**
GUMMIPFROPFEN **10824**
GUMMIRIEMEN **10817**
GUMMIRING **10823**
GUMMIRINGDICHTUNG **10820**
GUMMISACKVERFAHREN **923**
GUMMISCHLAUCH **10821**
GUMMISTOFF **10818**
GUMMITRAGANT **6174**
GURTFÖRDERER **1164**
GUSS **2068**
GUSS **9715**
GUSS **2034**
GUSS (BLASIGER) **6563**
GUSS (LUNKERFREIER) **2075**
GUSS (SCHMIEDBARER) **7959**
GUSS (SPANNUNGSFREIER) **2074**
GUSS FÜR DEN MASCHINENBAU **4763**
GUSSALUMINIUM **435**
GUSSASPHALT **9713**
GUSSBETON **8426**
GUSSBLASE **1353**
GUSSEISEN **2034**
GUSSEISEN **9299**
GUSSEISEN **7157**
GUSSEISEN (KORROSIONSBESTÄNDIGES) **2039**
GUSSEISEN (LEGIERTES) **363**
GUSSEISEN (LEGIERTES) **2037**
GUSSEISEN (MELIERTES) **2044**
GUSSEISEN (PERLITISCHES) **2046**
GUSSEISEN (VERSCHLEISSFESTES) **2048**
GUSSEISEN (WEISSES) **2049**
GUSSEISEN MIT KUGELGRAPHIT **2045**
GUSSEISEN MIT KUGELGRAPHIT **11895**
GUSSEISEN MIT KUGELGRAPHIT **11894**
GUSSEISEN MIT KUGELGRAPHIT **2040**

GUSSEISEN MIT LAMELLENGRAPHIT **2041**
GUSSEISEN MIT STAHLZUSATZ **11177**
GUSSEISEN-ROHRLEITUNG **2062**
GUSSEISENQUELLUNG **2061**
GUSSEISENROHR **2035**
GUSSEISENTHERMIT **2036**
GUSSFEHLER **5056**
GUSSFORM **8422**
GUSSFORM (GIESS.) **8423**
GUSSHAUT **11538**
GUSSKUPFER **2073**
GUSSMESSING **2031**
GUSSMETALL **2050**
GUSSMODELL **9129**
GUSSNAHT **5184**
GUSSPLATTIERUNG **2032**
GUSSPUTZER **4254**
GUSSPUTZEREI **5130**
GUSSPUTZHAMMER **10986**
GUSSRINNE **10844**
GUSSSPANNUNG **7075**
GUSSSPANNUNG **2081**
GUSSSPANNUNG **2078**
GUSSSTAHL **2057**
GUSSSTÜCK **2069**
GUSSSTÜCK **2079**
GUSSSTÜCKE (HITZEBESTÄNDIGE) **2084**
GUSSTÜCKE **2080**
GUSSTÜCKE (KORROSIONSBESTÄNDIGE) **2082**
GUSSTÜCKENZUSAMMENSCHWEISSEN **2060**
GUSSWERK **5593**
GUSSZAPFEN **12004**
GUT-UND-AUSSCHUSS-GRENZLEHRE **5991**
GUTACHTEN **4931**
GUTACHTER **4930**
GÜTEPRÜFUNG **10063**
GÜTEVERHÄLTNIS **4463**
GUTTAPERCHA **6184**
H.D. ÖL **6403**
HAARRIEMEN **6200**
HAARRISS **6202**
HAARRISS **4377**
HAARRISS **3318**
HAARROHR **1921**
HAARRÖHRCHENWIRKUNG **1920**
HAARSEITE **6038**
HAARZIRKEL **6201**
HACKFRÄSEN UND BODENFRÄSEN **10753**
HAFNIUM **6199**
HAFT- **175**
HAFTEND **175**

# HAF

**816**

HAFTFÄHIGKEITSVERSUCH 172
HAFTFESTIGKEIT 173
HAFTREIBUNG 12134
HAFTREIBUNG 5678
HAFTVERMÖGEN 176
HAHN 2617
HAHN 12639
HAHN (SELBSTDICHTENDER) 7111
HAHN MIT ABLAUF 1234
HAHN MIT GEHÄUSESCHMIERUNG 7802
HAHNGEHÄUSE 11334
HAHNKEGEL 9532
HAHNKÜKEN 9532
HAHNREIBER 9532
HAHNSCHLÜSSEL 9532
HAHNSCHLÜSSEL 2618
HAHNVENTIL 9535
HAHNVENTIL 8997
HAHNVENTIL (GEÖLTES) 7802
HAHNWIRBEL 9532
HAKEN 6568
HAKENKETTE 6570
HAKENNAGEL 2457
HAKENNÄGEL 11902
HAKENSCHLÜSSEL 1822
HAKENSCHRAUBE 6569
HALB-V-HAHT MIT LUFTSPALT 8822
HALB-V-NAHT 1800
HALB-V-NAHT MIT LUFTSPALT 1797
HALB-V-NAHT OHNE LUFTSPALT 2528
HALB-V-NAHT OHNE LUFTSPALT 1789
HALBACHSE (GEOM.) 11167
HALBDIESELMOTOR 11171
HALBFABRIKAT 11174
HALBHOLZ 6210
HALBIEREN (MATH.) 1267
HALBIEREN (MATH.) 1266
HALBIERUNGSLINIE EINES WINKELS 1268
HALBKREIS 11179
HALBKREISFÖRMIG 11169
HALBKREISTRANSPORTEUR 11180
HALBKREUZRIEMENTRIEB 6207
HALBKUGEL 6438
HALBLEHRENBOHRMASCHINE 11172
HALBMESSER 10166
HALBMONDFÖRMIGE SCHWEISSNAHT-VERZERRUNGEN 5212
HALBRAUPENSCHLEPPER 13093
HALBRUNDEISEN (HOHLES) 6541
HALBRUNDEISEN (VOLLES) 11786
HALBRUNDER MEISSEL 6546
HALBRUNDFEILE 6208

HALBRUNDPROFILEISEN 6209
HALBRUNDSTAHL (GEZOGENER) 4249
HALBSCHATTEN 9177
HALBSCHLICHTFEILE 11100
HALBVERSENKNIET 3249
HALBWASSERGAS 4194
HALBWELLENGLEICHRICHTEN 6212
HALBWERTSCHICHT 6211
HALBZELLE 6204
HALBZEUG 11174
HALLE 1072
HALO 6213
HALOGEN 6214
HALS 8512
HALSLAGER EINER LIEGENDEN WELLE 6586
HALSLAGER EINER STEHENDEN WELLE 13547
HALSSTUTZEN 8514
HALSZAPFEN 8513
HALT (WAHLWEISER) 8850
HALT (WAHLWEISER) 6521
HALTBARKEIT 4385
HALTEPUNKT 3347
HALTER 12490
HALTERUNG 1522
HALTESEILE 6186
HALTESTEIN 9159
HALTESTIFT 9159
HALTESTIFT 11220
HALTESTREIFEN 10516
HALTEZEIT 6528
HÄMATIT 11865
HÄMATIT 6434
HÄMATITROHEISEN 6435
HAMMER 6215
HAMMER MIT GESPALTENER FINNE 2462
HAMMER MIT KUGELFINNE 960
HAMMER MIT KUGELFINNE 962
HAMMER MIT ZWEI BAHNEN 4169
HAMMERBAHN 4993
HÄMMERBAR 7960
HÄMMERBARKEIT 7958
HAMMERFINNE 9031
HAMMERKOPF 6317
HAMMERKOPFSCHRAUBE 12701
HAMMERLÖTKOLBEN 2350
HAMMERMÜHLEN 8297
HÄMMERN 9157
HÄMMERN 6223
HÄMMERN 6216
HAMMERPINNE 9031
HAMMERSCHLAG 6217

817            **HAR**

HAMMERSCHWEISSEN **6218**
HAMMERSTAHL **6222**
HAMMERSTIEL **11244**
HANBREIBAHLE **6247**
HAND (NACHSTELLBARE) **4917**
HAND ANGETRIEBEN **6241**
HAND-STOSSELEKTRODENSCHWEISSEN **10027**
HAND-TEILEPROGRAMM **6242**
HANDANTRIEB **6233**
HANDARBEIT **6237**
HANDBETRIEB **6233**
HANDBETRIEB (FÜR) **6241**
HANDBOHRMASCHINE **6258**
HANDBOHRMASCHINE (ELEKTRISCHE) **9732**
HANDBREMSE **9082**
HANDBREMSE **6227**
HANDELSBEZEICHNUNG **13101**
HANDELSEISEN **8148**
HANDELSGÜTEBRONZE **1657**
HANDELSPROFILE **8149**
HANDELSSCHWEFELSÄURE **8856**
HANDELSÜBLICHE BEZEICHNUNG **13101**
HANDELSZINK **2785**
HANDELSZINK **11879**
HANDFEILE **6234**
HANDGEARBEITET **6240**
HANDGEFERTIGT **6240**
HANDGESCHMIEDET **6261**
HANDGEWINDEBOHRER **6257**
HANDGLANZSCHLEIFEN **6228**
HANDGRIFF **6262**
HANDHABE **6262**
HANDHAMMER **6235**
HANDHEBEL **6239**
HANDKARREN **6230**
HANDKARREN **13231**
HANDKLOBEN **6254**
HANDKURBEL **6231**
HANDLAUF **13035**
HANDLÄUFEREISEN **6265**
HANDLEISTE **13035**
HANDLEISTENEISEN **6245**
HANDLEISTENEISEN **6265**
HANDLICH **6269**
HANDLOCH **6236**
HANDNIETUNG **6248**
HANDPFANNE **6238**
HANDPUMPE **6244**
HANDRAD **6267**
HANDRAD **13810**
HANDRAD **6255**

HANDRADMUTTER **6268**
HANDREIBAHLE (EINSTELLBARE) **184**
HANDSÄGE **6249**
HANDSCHERE **6251**
HANDSCHIRM **6252**
HANDSCHMIEDEN **11669**
HANDSCHNEIDEN **6232**
HANDSCHUHKASTEN **5980**
HANDSTAMPFER **6246**
HANDSTICHTORF **4364**
HANDWERKZEUG **13015**
HANDWERKZEUG **6253**
HANDWINDE **6256**
HANDZEICHNUNG **5648**
HANF **6439**
HANFDICHTUNG **6445**
HANFLIDERUNG **6445**
HANFÖL **6446**
HANFPACKUNG **6445**
HANFRIEMEN **1907**
HANFSCHLAUCH **1908**
HANFSEELE **6440**
HANFSEIL **6443**
HANFWERG **6444**
HANFZOPF **6441**
HANFZOPF (GEFETTETER) **6442**
HÄNGEBOCK **9166**
HÄNGEBRÜCKE **12528**
HÄNGEDACHTANK **12525**
HÄNGEDECKE **12524**
HÄNGELAGER **6321**
HÄNGELAGER (GESCHLOSSENES) **6270**
HÄNGELAGER (OFFENES) **6271**
HÄNGENBLEIBEN **7210**
HÄNGESITZ **1383**
HARDENIT **8022**
HÄRTBARKEIT **6288**
HÄRTBARKEIT EINES METALLES **6296**
HARTBLEI **6276**
HARTBRANDSTEIN **6273**
HÄRTE **6297**
HÄRTE BEI HOCHTEMPERATUR **6629**
HÄRTE DES WASSERS **6298**
HÄRTE DES WASSERS **9203**
HÄRTE DES WASSERS (SCHWINDENDE) **12735**
HÄRTE DES WASSERS (TEMPORÄRE) **12735**
HÄRTE DES WASSERS (VORÜBERGEHENDE) **12735**
HÄRTE-EINDRUCK **6859**
HÄRTEBAD **10096**
HÄRTEGRAD **3720**
HÄRTEGRAD DES STAHLES **6299**

# HAR

818

HÄRTEMASS 3720
HÄRTEN 6219
HÄRTEN (GEBROCHENES) 12249
HÄRTEN (PARTIELLES) 7697
HÄRTEN UND ANLASSEN 10092
HÄRTEN VON METALLEN 6293
HÄRTEÖL 6295
HÄRTEÖL 10099
HÄRTEPROBE 6300
HÄRTEPRÜFER 11366
HÄRTEPRÜFER (ELEKTROMAGNETISCHER) 4614
HÄRTEPRÜFUNG 6300
HÄRTEPULVER 2139
HÄRTERISS 3282
HÄRTERISS 10097
HARTES HOLZ 6282
HÄRTESKALA 10974
HÄRTESKALA (MOHSCHE) 8346
HÄRTESTUFE 3720
HARTGUMMI 2363
HARTGUSS 2335
HARTGUSS 2038
HARTGUSS (UMGEKEHRTER) 7109
HARTHOLZ 6301
HARTHOLZ 6282
HARTLOT 6279
HARTLÖTEN 1576
HARTLÖTEN 1573
HARTLÖTKUPFER 1575
HARTLÖTLEGIERUNG 386
HARTLÖTOFEN 1577
HARTLÖTUNG 1576
HARTLÖTUNGSEINLAGEN 1578
HARTMETALL 6277
HARTMETALL-AUFTRAGSCHWEISSUNG 6283
HARTMETALL-AUFTRAGSLEGIERUNG 6284
HARTMETALLBESTÜCKUNG 6278
HARTMETALLLEGIERUNG 11510
HARTMETALLSCHNEIDWERKZEUG 2144
HARTPARAFFIN 9045
HARTSTAHL 1957
HARTSTAHL 6280
HÄRTUNG 6291
HÄRTUNG (ISOTHERMISCHE) 7195
HÄRTUNGSBAD 6294
HÄRTUNGSFLÜSSIGKEIT 6294
HÄRTUNGSGRAD BEIM KALTZIEHEN 6274
HÄRTUNGSMINDERUNG 4
HÄRTUNGSMITTEL 6290
HARTZINN 9230
HARZ 10478

HARZHALTIG 10479
HARZKITT 10482
HARZÖL 10749
HASPEL 13863
HAUBE 3276
HAUBE 1451
HAUBE 6566
HAUBE EINES SCHIEBERS 3266
HAUBE EINES VENTILS 3266
HAUBENFLANSCH 1452
HAUBENGEWINDEBOLZEN 1453
HAUBENOFEN 1132
HAUBENOFEN 1135
HAUCHBILDUNG 1347
HAUEN (DURCH TRAKTOREN ANGETRIEBEN) 6515
HÄUFEPFLÜGE 9527
HÄUFIGKEITSFUNKTION 5662
HAUPTABMESSUNGEN 7481
HAUPTACHSE 9866
HAUPTACHSE DER HYPERBEL 13143
HAUPTAUSLEGER 7226
HAUPTDÜSE 7942
HAUPTDYNAMO 9867
HAUPTLAGER 7941
HAUPTLAGER 3303
HAUPTLEITUNG (ELEKTR.) 5081
HAUPTMASCHINE 9867
HAUPTMASSE 7481
HAUPTNENNER 2789
HAUPTSCHLUSSDYNAMO 11201
HAUPTSCHLUSSMOTOR 11202
HAUPTSCHNITT 9868
HAUPTSPANNUNG 9869
HAUPTSPEISELEITUNG 7940
HAUPTVERFORMUNG 2000
HAUPTWELLE 7943
HAUPTWELLE 7944
HAUPTZYLINDER 8037
HAUSENBLASE 7174
HAUSTEIN 761
HAUT 5171
HAUT-LEIM 11539
HAUTBILDUNG 11545
HAUTPACKUNG 11540
HAUTRISS 12501
HÄUTUNG 4889
HEAV DUTY ÖL 6403
HEBEBAUM 7725
HEBEBOCK 5945
HEBEBOCK (HYDRAULISCHER) 6688
HEBEDAUMEN 13878

819                                                                                         **HER**

HEBEHAKEN 7558
HEBEKOLBEN 7555
HEBEL 7530
HEBEL (BELASTETER) 13751
HEBEL (DOPPELARMIGER) 4147
HEBEL (DREIARMIGER) 4131
HEBEL (GEGABELTER) 5569
HEBEL (GERADARMIGER) 12306
HEBEL (ZWEIARMIGER) 4147
HEBELADE 7533
HEBELARM 7531
HEBELARM 706
HEBELBREMSE 7532
HEBELPRESSE 7534
HEBELÜBERSETZUNG 13132
HEBELÜBERSETZUNG (VERHÄLTNIS) 7536
HEBELWERK 12577
HEBEMASCHINE 6519
HEBEMASCHINEN (SÄCKEBÜNDEL UND ZUCKE PRÜBEN) 7688
HEBEN (EINE LAST) 7542
HEBEN EINER LAST 7559
HEBER 11517
HEBERBAROMETER 11515
HEBERMANOMETER 2534
HEBESTUTZEN 7206
HEBEZEUG 6519
HEBEZEUG 6516
HEBLING 12672
HECKENSCHNEIDER 6418
HECTOWATTSTUNDE 6417
HEFNERKERZE 6419
HEFT EINES WERKZEUGES 6263
HEFTKURBEL 3305
HEFTNIET 12592
HEFTNIETUNG 12922
HEFTSCHWEISSEN 12590
HEFTSCHWEISSEN 12589
HEFTSTIFT 4242
HEFTZWEKE 4242
HEISSDAMPF 12471
HEISSDAMPFMASCHINE 4759
HEISSFERTIGPUTZEN 6647
HEISSINDLEITUNG 1774
HEISSLAUFEN 6334
HEISSLAUFEN DER LAGER 6400
HEISSLUFTMASCHINE 6615
HEISSSÄGE 6630
HEISSWASSERHEIZUNG 6489
HEISSWINDLEITUNG 6651
HEIZDAMPF 6397

HEIZELEMENT 10150
HEIZEN 5259
HEIZEN 5235
HEIZER 12271
HEIZER 12272
HEIZFLÄCHE 6398
HEIZGAS 5709
HEIZKANAL 5743
HEIZKÖRPER 10150
HEIZMANTELSCHIEBER 7205
HEIZÖL 5714
HEIZRAUM 12270
HEIZRÖHRENKESSEL 5249
HEIZSCHLANGE 12161
HEIZSTOFF 5705
HEIZTÜR 5242
HEIZUNG 5259
HEIZUNG (ELEKTRISCHE) 4513
HEIZUNG (ZUSÄTZLICHE) 2904
HEIZUNG VON GEBÄUDEN 6395
HEIZUNGS-REGULIERVENTIL 10153
HEIZUNGSANLAGE 6394
HEIZUNGSROHR 6396
HEIZWERT 6378
HEIZWERT 6392
HEKTOLITER 6415
HEKTOWATT 6416
HELIANTHIN 8223
HELIARC-BRENNER 6424
HELIUM 6429
HELLIGKEIT 1616
HELLIGKEITSMESSER 9267
HELLROTGLÜHEND 1614
HELLROTGLUT 1613
HELM EINER AXT 6433
HELM EINES BEILES 6433
HELMLOCH EINER AXT 11231
HEMIEDERKRISTALL 6436
HEMMEN 6926
HEMMSTOFF 6927
HERABSETZUNG DER GESCHWINDIGKEIT 10363
HERAUSGESCHLEPPTE LÖSUNG 4202
HERD 6331
HERD 3401
HERDGLÜHOFEN 10532
HERDGUSS 8820
HERDOFEN 6332
HERDSCHLACKE 2500
HERDWANNE 9029
HERMETISCH VERSCHLOSSEN 6447
HERSTELLEN 7948

**HER** 820

HERSTELLER 7992
HERSTELLERBESCHREIBUNG 7993
HERSTELLUNG 4983
HERSTELLUNG 7989
HERSTELLUNGSFEHLER 3693
HERSTELLUNGSHANDBUCH 9885
HERSTELLUNGSKOSTEN 3207
HERSTELLUNGSVERFAHREN 8218
HERUNTERWALZEN 2691
HERZEXZENTER 6329
HERZKAUSCHE 6330
HERZKURVE 2001
HERZSCHEIBE 6329
HETEROGEN 6451
HETEROGENE STRAHLUNG 6450
HEUBÜNDLER 946
HEUGABELN UND GREIFER 6310
HEUMÄHDRESCHBINDER 6311
HEURAFFER 12541
HEURECHEN 6312
HEXAEDER 6463
HEXAGONAL-DICHTGEPACKTE STRUKTUR 6458
HEXAGONALER KRISTALL 6459
HIEB EINER FEILE 3518
HILFS- 12068
HILFSARBEITER 8048
HILFSBELEUCHTUNG 4688
HILFSFUNKTION 854
HILFSFUNKTION 8319
HILFSKOMPRESSOR 12069
HILFSMASCHINE 853
HILFSMOTOR 11211
HILFSVENTIL 1819
HILFSVERDICHTER 12069
HILFSWELLE 7049
HIN- UND HERBIEGEPROBE 12774
HIN-UND HERBIEGEVERSUCH 10535
HINDERN 6926
HINDERN (SICH BEI DER BEWEGUNG GEGENSEITIG) 5587
HINTERACHSE 10265
HINTERACHSWELLENRAD 3917
HINTERDREHBANK 10443
HINTERDREHBANK 913
HINTERDREHEN 910
HINTERDREHEN 893
HINTEREINANDERSCHALTUNG 11199
HINTERFRÄSEN 1387
HINTERFRÄSWINKEL 1388
HINTERFÜLLUNG 900
HINTERTÜR 891
HINZUFÜGEN 169

HIRNHOLZ 4719
HIRNSCHNITT 4718
HIRSCHHORNSALZ 461
HITZE 6333
HITZEMESSER 10049
HOBEL 9432
HOBEL-UND FRÄSMASCHINE 9453
HOBELBANK 7234
HOBELEISEN 9436
HOBELKASTEN 12262
HOBELKEIL 13733
HOBELMASCHINE 9452
HOBELMASCHINE 9443
HOBELMASCHINE 9451
HOBELMESSER 9436
HOBELN 9434
HOBELN 9450
HOBELSPÄNE 13919
HOBELSTAHL 9436
HOBELSTICHEL 9436
HOBLER 9443
HOCH GESPANNTER DAMPF 6491
HOCHBAU 2442
HOCHBEHÄLTER 4492
HOCHDRUCK 6473
HOCHDRUCKDAMPF 6491
HOCHDRUCKDAMPFHEIZUNG 6493
HOCHDRUCKDAMPFMASCHINE 6492
HOCHDRUCKKESSEL 6487
HOCHDRUCKLEITUNG 6490
HOCHDRUCKTURBINE 6494
HOCHDRUCKWASSERHEIZUNG 6489
HOCHDRUCKZYLINDER 6488
HOCHFREQUENZ 6467
HOCHFREQUENZOFEN 6469
HOCHFREQUENZSTROM 6468
HOCHGLANZ 1755
HOCHGLANZPOLIEREN 1758
HOCHGLANZPOLIEREN 1756
HOCHGLÜHEN 5719
HOCHHUBSICHERHEITSVENTIL 10890
HOCHKANTRIEMEN 7376
HOCHLEISTUNGSDUPLEXFRÄSMASCHINE 4379
HOCHLEISTUNGSMASCHINE 6466
HOCHOFEN 1311
HOCHOFEN-ROHEISEN 2657
HOCHOFENBODEN 9011
HOCHOFENGAS 1313
HOCHOFENSCHLACKE 1312
HOCHPROZENTIG 6483
HOCHRESERVOIR 4492

| | |
|---|---|
| HOCHSCHMELZEND **6308** | HOLZ (LUFTTROCKENES) **297** |
| HOCHSPANNUNG **6478** | HOLZ (MORSCHES) **10768** |
| HOCHSPANNUNGSLEITUNG **6501** | HOLZ (ROTFAULES) **5610** |
| HOCHSPANNUNGSMOTOR **6502** | HOLZ (WURMSTICHIGES) **13977** |
| HOCHSPANNUNGSSTROM **6500** | HOLZ AN DER LUFT TROCKNEN **11094** |
| HOCHSPANNUUG (ELEKT.) **6479** | HOLZ AUSTROCKNEN **11094** |
| HÖCHSTBELASTUNG **8065** | HOLZALKOHOL **13920** |
| HÖCHSTGESCHWINDIGKEIT **8067** | HOLZART **13503** |
| HÖCHSTGEWICHT **8070** | HOLZÄTHER. METHYLOXYD **8222** |
| HÖCHSTLEISTUNG **8066** | HOLZBAU **12942** |
| HÖCHSTTEMPERATUR **8068** | HOLZBEARBEITUNG **13924** |
| HÖCHSTWERT **8069** | HOLZBEARBEITUNGSMASCHINE **13925** |
| HOCHVAKUUM **6477** | HOLZBEARBEITUNGSMASCHINEN **13931** |
| HOCHWINDEN **6517** | HOLZDREHBANK **13922** |
| HOCHWINDEN **6553** | HOLZEISENRAD **8400** |
| HÖHE **6420** | HOLZESSIG **10046** |
| HÖHE UNTER QUERBALKEN **6423** | HOLZFRÄSMASCHINE **9901** |
| HOHLBOHRMASCHINE **13182** | HOLZFUTTER **13927** |
| HOHLBOHRMASCHINE **1013** | HOLZGEIST **13920** |
| HOHLEISEN **6010** | HOLZHAMMER **7962** |
| HOHLGUSS **6539** | HOLZHAMMER **13926** |
| HOHLKEHLE **5161** | HOLZKOHLE **13914** |
| HOHLKEHLE **2122** | HOLZKOHLENROHEISEN **2258** |
| HOHLKEHLNAHT **2878** | HOLZKONSTRUKTION **12942** |
| HOHLKEHLNAHT **7561** | HOLZLATTE **7426** |
| HOHLKEIL **6542** | HOLZMEHL **13916** |
| HOHLKOLBEN **1514** | HOLZNAGEL **13179** |
| HOHLKÖRPER **6538** | HOLZNAPHTA **13920** |
| HOHLKUGELWALZE **6549** | HOLZROHR **13928** |
| HOHLLINSE **4095** | HOLZRÖHRE **13928** |
| HOHLMASS **8079** | HOLZSÄGE **13917** |
| HOHLNAHT (KONCAVE) **1792** | HOLZSÄURE **10046** |
| HOHLRAUM **2125** | HOLZSCHEIT **1243** |
| HOHLRAUMBILDUNG **2123** | HOLZSCHLIFF **8116** |
| HOHLSCHLEIFMASCHINE **7068** | HOLZSCHRAUBE **13918** |
| HOHLSOGBILDUNG **2123** | HOLZSCHWELLE **12941** |
| HOHLSPIEGEL **2879** | HOLZSPIRITUS **13920** |
| HOHLWÖLBUNG **2880** | HOLZSTOFF **8116** |
| HOHLZAHNRAD **7079** | HOLZTEER **13921** |
| HOHLZIEGEL **245** | HOLZVERKLEIDUNG **13915** |
| HOHLZIRKEL **6975** | HOLZVERSCHALUNG **13915** |
| HOHLZYLINDER **6540** | HOLZWOLLE **13923** |
| HÖLLENSTEIN **7828** | HOLZZELLSTOFF **2316** |
| HOLMIUM **6551** | HOMOGEN **6555** |
| HOLOEDERKRISTALL **6552** | HOMOGENISIERUNG **6561** |
| HOLZ **13913** | HOMOGENISIERUNGSMITTEL **3754** |
| HOLZ (ASTFREIES) **12940** | HOMÖOMORPHIE **7191** |
| HOLZ (GEBOGENES) **1196** | HONEN **6564** |
| HOLZ (GELAGERTES) **297** | HOOKESCHER SCHLÜSSEL **6573** |
| HOLZ (GESUNDES) **11820** | HOOKESCHES GESETZ **6574** |
| HOLZ (KERNFAULES) **5610** | HÖRBARES ZEICHEN **816** |

**HOR**

HORIZONTAL **6578**
HORIZONTALBOHRMASCHINE **6581**
HORIZONTALE **6585**
HORIZONTALKEHLNAHTSCHWEISSEN **6583**
HORIZONTALPROJEKTION **11124**
HORIZONTALSCHUB **6590**
HORN **6592**
HORNBLENDE **6598**
HORNBLENDEASBEST **6599**
HORNEINGUSS **6600**
HORNSPÄNE **6595**
HORNZULAUF **6600**
HÖRSIGNAL **816**
HOSENROHR **1595**
HUB **12387**
HUB **7519**
HUB EINES KOLBENS **9389**
HUBBEGRENZER **12278**
HUBBEGRENZER EINES VENTILS **13461**
HUBHÖHE **7551**
HUBHÖHE EINES KOLBENS **7519**
HUBKETTE **6518**
HUBKOLBEN **7555**
HUBLÄNGE **7519**
HUBMAGNET **7554**
HUBPUMPE **7545**
HUBVENTIL **7547**
HUBVOLUMEN **13599**
HUBZYLINDER **7550**
HUFEISENMAGNET **6606**
HUFMEHL **6567**
HUFNÄGEL **6601**
HUFSTABEISEN **6605**
HÜLLKURVE **4776**
HÜLSE **1773**
HÜLSE **11576**
HÜLSE **11303**
HÜLSENKEGEL **2931**
HÜLSENKEIL **2931**
HÜLSENKUPPLUNG **11577**
HÜLSENSCHLÜSSEL **509**
HUMUS **6667**
HUMUSSÄURE **6665**
HUPE **6592**
HUTMUTTER **4118**
HÜTTENBLEI **8014**
HÜTTENKOKS **2662**
HÜTTENMÄNNISCH **8206**
HÜTTENSCHROTT **4124**
HÜTTENSCHROTT **6554**
HÜTTENWERK **11668**

HÜTTENWESEN **8208**
HÜTTENZINK **2785**
HYBRID-VERFAHREN **6699**
HYDRANT **6672**
HYDRANTENSTANDROHR **12066**
HYDRAT **6673**
HYDRATWASSER **6675**
HYDRATWASSER ENTZIEHEN (DAS) **3727**
HYDRATWASSER VERLIEREN (DAS) **3727**
HYDRAULIK **6698**
HYDRAULIKPUMPE **8769**
HYDRAULISCH **6676**
HYDRAULISCHE ÜBERTRAGUNG **5472**
HYDRODYNAMIK **6710**
HYDRODYNAMISCH **6708**
HYDROKARBÜR **6705**
HYDROLYSE **6719**
HYDROMECHANIK **6720**
HYDROMETALLURGIE **6721**
HYDROMETRISCHER FLÜGEL **11027**
HYDROPHIL **6724**
HYDROPHOBIERUNGSFILM **13648**
HYDROSTATIK **6728**
HYDROXYD **6673**
HYGROMETER **6729**
HYGROSKOPISCH **6730**
HYGROSKOPISCHE EIGENSCHAFT **6732**
HYGROSKOPIZITÄT **6732**
HYPERBEL **6734**
HYPERBELFUNKTION **6737**
HYPERBELRAD **11534**
HYPERBOLISCH **6735**
HYPERBOLOID (EINSCHALIGES) **6739**
HYPERBOLOID (ZWEISCHALIGES) **6740**
HYPERBOLOIDRAD **11534**
HYPERMANGANSAURES KALI **9695**
HYPOIDGETRIEBE **6745**
HYPOSULFIT **12852**
HYPOTENUSE **6746**
HYPOZYKLOIDE **6743**
HYPOZYKLOIDE (VIERSPITZIGE) **5602**
HYPOZYKLOIDENVERZAHNUNG **6744**
HYSTERESE **6747**
HYSTERESIS **6747**
I-EISEN **6194**
I-NAHT MIT LUFTSPALT **8824**
I-NAHT OHNE LUFTSPALT **2532**
I-NAHTVERBINDUNG (I-STOSS) OHNE LUFTSPALT **1791**
I-STUMPFNAHT **12032**
I-TRÄGER **6748**
ICHTERSCHEINUNG **7566**

IMMERSION **3975**
IMPEDANZ **6794**
IMPFUNG **6956**
IMPRÄGNIEREN **6802**
IMPRÄGNIEREN **6805**
IMPRÄGNIERUNGSMITTEL **6804**
IMPULS **6809**
IMPULS **9979**
IN GANG SETZEN (EINE MASCHINE) **12114**
INAKTIVES GAS **6905**
INANSPRUCHNAHME **12331**
INBETRIEBSETZUNG **12118**
INCHROMIEREN **2390**
INDEX (MATH.) **6864**
INDEXHANDKURBEL **6865**
INDEXSCHALTEINRICHTUNG **6869**
INDIFFERENTES GAS **6905**
INDIKATOR (CHEM.) **6879**
INDIKATOR (DAMPFM.) **6878**
INDIKATORDIAGRAMM **6881**
INDIKATORPAPIER **6880**
INDIREKT WIRKEND **6883**
INDIUM **6885**
INDIZES (MILLERSCHE) **8282**
INDUKTANZ **6891**
INDUKTION **6892**
INDUKTION (ELEKTROMAGNETISCHE) **4615**
INDUKTION (ELEKTROSTATISCHE) **4644**
INDUKTION (GEGENSEITIGE) **8489**
INDUKTION (MAGNETISCHE) **7908**
INDUKTION (REMANENTE) **10473**
INDUKTION (WECHSELSEITIGE) **8489**
INDUKTIONSHARTLÖTEN **6893**
INDUKTIONSHÄRTUNG **6896**
INDUKTIONSHEIZUNG **6897**
INDUKTIONSOFEN **6895**
INDUKTIONSOFEN **4515**
INDUKTIONSSCHWEISSEN **4619**
INDUKTIONSSTROM **6889**
INDUSTRIE **6903**
INDUSTRIEABWÄSSER **6902**
INDUSTRIEGLEIS **13966**
INDUSTRIELLE RAUCHGASE **6899**
INDUSTRIEOFEN **6900**
INDUZIEREN **6888**
INEINANDERGREIFEN **5910**
INEINANDERGREIFEN **1077**
INEINANDERSTECKEN VON ROHREN **5281**
INERT **8621**
INFINITESIMALRECHNUNG **6912**
INFLEXIONSPUNKT (GEOM.) **9564**

INFUSORIENERDE **7292**
INGANGSETZEN EINER MASCHINE **12130**
INGENIEUR **4761**
INGENIEUR (BERATENDER) **2989**
INGENIEURCHEMIKER **2306**
INHABER EINES PATENTS **9123**
INHALT EINER FLÄCHE **697**
INHALTSBERECHNUNG EINES KÖRPERS **3444**
INHIBITOR **6927**
INJEKTOR **6938**
INKREIS **6963**
INNENBELEUCHTUNG **6887**
INNENBOLZEN EINER ROLLENKETTE **9320**
INNENDURCHMESSER **6977**
INNENGETRIEBE **7058**
INNENGETRIEBE **7067**
INNENGEWINDE **5092**
INNENGEWINDE **7078**
INNENGEWINDE **12868**
INNENGEWINDESCHNEIDMASCHINE **12677**
INNENKONUS **6951**
INNENLENKER **11128**
INNENLENKER **10902**
INNENLUNKER **7073**
INNENRING **6953**
INNENSCHLEIFMASCHINE **7068**
INNENSCHLIFF **7069**
INNENSCHWEISSEN **7080**
INNENSEITE **6974**
INNENSTEUERLIMOUSINE **10902**
INNENSTRÄHLER **7060**
INNENTASTER **6975**
INNENTASTER (MIKROMETRISCHER) **6979**
INNENVERZAHNUNG **7077**
INNENWANDUNG EINES ROHRES **6954**
INNENWINKEL **7057**
INNERE **6978**
INNERE LICHTE EINER KETTE **6982**
INNERER GEWINDEDURCHMESSER **3850**
INNERWANDUNGSMANNLOCH **11332**
INNIGES MISCHEN **7102**
INRICHTUNGBRINGEN **324**
INSPEKTION **6985**
INSTALLATION **6988**
INSTANDHALTUNG **7946**
INSTANDHALTUNGSKOSTEN **7945**
INSTRUMENT (APERIODISCHES) **635**
INSTRUMENT (GEDÄMPFTES) **635**
INSTRUMENT (OPTISCHES) **8844**
INSTRUMENTENBRETT **3610**
INSTRUMENTENBRETT **6993**

# INT

824

INTEGRAL **7009**
INTEGRAL (BESTIMMTES) **3697**
INTEGRAL (DREIFACHES) **13215**
INTEGRAL (ELLIPTISCHES) **4676**
INTEGRAL (MEHRFACHES) **8465**
INTEGRAL (SINGULÄRES) **11471**
INTEGRAL (UNBESTIMMTES) **6858**
INTEGRAL (VIELFACHES) **8465**
INTEGRALRECHNUNG **7011**
INTEGRAPH **7013**
INTEGRATION **7015**
INTEGRATOR **7016**
INTEGRIEREN **7014**
INTENSITÄT **7018**
INTENSITÄT EINER KRAFT **7939**
INTERFERENZ **7035**
INTERFERENZFARBE **7037**
INTERFERENZFIGUR **7039**
INTERFERENZKOMPARATOR **7038**
INTERFERENZSTREIFEN **7036**
INTERFERENZSTREIFEN **7040**
INTERMETALLISCHE VERBINDUNG **7052**
INTERPOLATION **7089**
INTERPOLATION (LINEAIRE) **7613**
INTERPOLATION (ZIRKULARE) **2416**
INTERPOLATOR **3995**
INTERPOLIEREN **7088**
INTERVALL **7101**
INVAR **7105**
INVARIANTE **7106**
INVERSION **7110**
INVESTMENTGUSS **7115**
INVOLUTE **7117**
ION **7121**
IONENKONZENTRATION **7122**
IONENWANDERUNG **7123**
·IONISATION **7124**
IONISATION **4596**
IONISATIONSKAMMER **7125**
IONISATIONSMETHODE **7127**
IONISIERUNG **7124**
IONOGEN **7129**
IRIDIUM **7131**
IRISBLENDE **7132**
IRRSTROMKORROSION **12350**
ISENTROPE **7173**
ISOBARE **7176**
ISOBARE **7177**
ISOCHRON **7179**
ISOCHRONISMUS **7178**
ISOKLINE **7181**

ISOLATION **4545**
ISOLATOR **7006**
ISOLIERBAND **7001**
ISOLIEREN **7003**
ISOLIEREN **6994**
ISOLIEREND GEGEN WÄRME **8628**
ISOLIERFESTIGKEIT **7005**
ISOLIERKÖRPER **7006**
ISOLIERMASSE **6997**
ISOLIERMATERIAL **6998**
ISOLIERMITTEL **6998**
ISOLIERÖL **6999**
ISOLIERROHR **7002**
ISOLIERSTOFF **6998**
ISOLIERUNG **7003**
ISOLIERUNG **7184**
ISOLIERUNG **4545**
ISOLIERUNG (THERMISCHE) **12810**
ISOLIERUNG GEGEN SCHALL **7004**
ISOLIERVERMÖGEN **7000**
ISOMER **7185**
ISOMERIE **7186**
ISOMERISMUS **357**
ISOMERISMUS **7186**
ISOMORPH **7190**
ISOMORPHIE **7189**
ISOMORPHISMUS **7191**
ISOMORPHISMUS **7189**
ISOPLERE **7187**
ISOTHERME **7193**
ISOTOPEN **7197**
ISOTROP **7198**
ISOZYKLISCHE KOHLENWASSERSTOFFE **2518**
ISTWERT **153**
IZOD-PROBE **7200**
J-NAHT MIT LUFTSPALT **8823**
J-NAHT MIT LUFTSPALT **1798**
J-NAHT OHNE LUFTSPALT **2529**
J-NAHTVERBINDUNG **1790**
JACOBS-SPREIZZANGENFUTTER **7208**
JAHRESRING **586**
JÄTMASCHINEN UND ACKERFRÄSEN **13742**
JAVELLESCHE LAUGE **9688**
JENAER GLAS **7217**
JOCH EINES MAGNETEN **14017**
JOD **7120**
JODEOSIN **4831**
JODINROT **8155**
JODKALIUM **9689**
JODKALIUMSTÄRKEPAPIER **9690**
JODSILBER **11464**

JODZINNOBER **8155**
JOMINY-PROBE **7254**
JOULE **7255**
JURAKALK **7267**
JUSTIEREN **5280**
JUSTIEREN **5276**
JUTE **7268**
K-NAHT **1793**
K-NAHT MIT LUFTSPALT **8811**
K-NAHT MIT LUFTSPALT **1796**
K-NAHT OHNE LUFTSPALT **1787**
KABBER **2526**
KABEL **13899**
KABEL **1829**
KABEL (KUNSTSTOFFISOLIERTES) **9472**
KABEL MIT METALLMANTEL **8177**
KABELARMATUR **715**
KABELBÜNDEL **7452**
KABELKRAN **1344**
KABELVERSEILUNG **1828**
KABRIOLETT **3073**
KADMIEREN **1832**
KADMIUM **1831**
KÄFIG EINES KUGELLAGERS **957**
KÄFIG EINES ROLLENLAGERS **12040**
KAHLBAUM-EISEN **7270**
KALAMIN **1836**
KALDOVERFAHREN **7271**
KALI (OXALSAURES) **118**
KALI (SAURES) **118**
KALIALAUN **2787**
KALIBER **1873**
KALIBER (METR) **5871**
KALIBER UND KALIBERRING **3581**
KALIBERFOLGE **9097**
KALIBERRING **2721**
KALIBERSTOPFEN **5883**
KALIBRIER-UND GESENKSCHMIEDE-PRESSE **1864**
KALIBRIEREN **2651**
KALIBRIEREN **1861**
KALIBRIEREN **1867**
KALIBRIERMASCHINE **1865**
KALIBRIERPRESSE **11525**
KALIBRIERTE FEDER **1866**
KALIBRIERUNG **1867**
KALIBRIERUNG **11524**
KALICHROMALAUN **2370**
KALIHYDRAT **9687**
KALIKALKGLAS **1400**
KALILAUGE **9671**
KALINATRON (WEINSAURES) **11729**

KALISALPETER **10903**
KALIUM **9672**
KALIUMALUMINAT **9674**
KALIUMALUMINIUMSULFAT **2787**
KALIUMAZETAT **9673**
KALIUMBICHROMAT **9677**
KALIUMBIKARBONAT **9676**
KALIUMBIOXALAT **118**
KALIUMBITARTRAT **119**
KALIUMBROMID **9678**
KALIUMCHLORAT **9680**
KALIUMCHLORID **9681**
KALIUMDICHROMAT **9677**
KALIUMEISENZYANID **9684**
KALIUMEISENZYANÜR **9685**
KALIUMFLUORID **9686**
KALIUMHYDROKARBONAT **9676**
KALIUMHYDROXYD **9687**
KALIUMHYPOCHLORITLÖSUNG **9688**
KALIUMJODID **9689**
KALIUMKARBONAT **9679**
KALIUMNATRIUMTARTRAT **11729**
KALIUMNITRAT **10903**
KALIUMNITRIT **9691**
KALIUMOXYDHYDRAT **9687**
KALIUMPERCHLORAT **9694**
KALIUMPERKARBONAT **9693**
KALIUMPERMANGANAT **9695**
KALIUMPHOSPHAT **9696**
KALIUMPOLYSULFID **9697**
KALIUMRHODANID **9701**
KALIUMSILIKAT **9698**
KALIUMSULFAT **9699**
KALIUMSULFOZYANAT **9701**
KALIUMZYANID **9683**
KALIWASSERGLAS **9698**
KALK **7582**
KALK (FETTER) **5046**
KALK (GEBRANNTER) **1854**
KALK (GELÖSCHTER) **1851**
KALK (HYDRAULISCHER) **6689**
KALK (KOHLENSAURER) **1849**
KALK (MAGERER) **9623**
KALK (OXALSAURER) **1853**
KALK (PHOSPHORSAURER) **1855**
KALK (WASSERFREIER SCHWEFELSAURER) **549**
KALK LÖSCHEN **11568**
KALKBASISCHE UMHÜLLUNG **7584**
KALKDINAS **5803**
KALKHYDRAT **1851**
KALKLICHT **8987**

# KAL

826

KALKMERGEL 2225
KALKMILCH 8274
KALKMÖRTEL 8854
KALKSINTER 1837
KALKSPAT 1845
KALKSTEIN 7586
KALKSTREUER 4089
KALKTUFF 1838
KALKWASSER 7585
KALOMEL 8159
KALOMELELEKTRODE 1876
KALORIE (ENGLISCHE) 1625
KALORIMETER 1877
KALORIMETRIE 1881
KALORIMETRISCH 1878
KALORISCHES ARBEITSÄQUIVALENT 6347
KALORISIERUNG 1882
KALOTTE 11137
KALT GEZOGEN 2677
KALT-ODER WARM-AUSHÄRTUNG 224
KALTABGRATEN 2711
KALTABSPRITZEN 2707
KALTANKÖPFEN 2686
KALTBEARBEITUNG 2713
KALTBEHANDLUNG 2710
KALTBIEGEPROBE 2667
KALTBIEGUNG 2668
KALTBRÜCHIGKEIT 2703
KALTBRÜCHIGKEIT DES EISENS 2704
KALTDURCHBOHRUNG 2689
KÄLTEBESTÄNDIG 8635
KÄLTEERZEUGUNG 9895
KÄLTEISOLIERUNGSMITTEL 2700
KÄLTEMASCHINE 10407
KÄLTEMISCHUNG 5654
KÄLTEMITTEL 3086
KÄLTESCHUTZ 7003
KALTFLIESSEN 2680
KALTFORMUNG 2682
KALTGEWALZT 2716
KALTGEWALZTER STABSTAHL 2695
KALTGUSS 2706
KALTHÄMMERN 2684
KALTHÄMMERN 2685
KALTHÄRTUNG 12326
KALTHÄRTUNG 13715
KALTKAMMER- DRUCKGIESSEN 2671
KALTKAMMER-DRUCKGIESSMASCHINE 2670
KALTLÖTSTELLE 2705
KALTMEISSEL 2717
KALTNACHPRESSEN 2679

KALTNACHWALZUNG 9330
KALTNIETEN 2693
KALTNIETEN 2692
KALTPRESSEN 2673
KALTPRESSEN 2690
KALTPROFILIEREN 2682
KALTPRÜFUNG 2687
KALTRECKEN 830
KALTRISS 2674
KALTSÄGE 2688
KALTSÄGEN 2699
KALTSCHMIEDEN 2681
KALTSCHROTMEISSEL 2701
KALTSCHWEISSE 2705
KALTSCHWEISSEN 2712
KALTSPRITZEN 4970
KALTSTAUCHEN 2686
KALTSTICH 11541
KALTVERFORMUNG 2713
KALTVERSUCH 2709
KALTWALZEN 2698
KALTWALZEN 2694
KALTWALZWERK 2708
KALTZIEHEN 2676
KALTZIEHEN 2675
KALTZIEHEN VON NAHTLOSGEGOSSENEN RÖHREN 2053
KALZINIEREN 1841
KALZINIEREN 1839
KALZINIEREN VON ERZEN 1840
KALZINIEROFEN 1843
KALZINIERUNG 1839
KALZIT 1844
KALZIT 1845
KALZIUM 1846
KALZIUM (DOPPELTKOHLENSAURES) 1847
KALZIUM (KOHLENSAURES) 1849
KALZIUMBIKARBONAT 1847
KALZIUMCHLORID 1850
KALZIUMFLUORID 5479
KALZIUMHYDROXYD 1851
KALZIUMKARBID 1848
KALZIUMKARBONAT 1849
KALZIUMOXALAT 1853
KALZIUMOXYD 1854
KALZIUMPHOSPHAT 1855
KALZIUMSULFAT 6190
KALZIUMSULFAT 1856
KALZIUMSULFID 1852
KAMELHAAR 1890
KAMELHAARRIEMEN 1891
KAMERA 9264

KAMIN **2339**
KAMINZUG **4212**
KAMM **12904**
KÄMMEN VON ZAHNRÄDERN **5910**
KAMMER **2776**
KAMMEROFEN **10524**
KAMMERSÄURE **2228**
KAMMERSTROM (IONISATION) **7126**
KAMMLAGER **12903**
KAMMZAHNRAD **8400**
KAMMZAPFEN **12906**
KAMPFER **1893**
KAMPFERÖL **1894**
KANADAFASER **1898**
KANAL **2248**
KANALBLECH **2252**
KANISTER **12961**
KANNELKOHLE **1901**
KANONENBOHRER **3563**
KANONENBOHRER **6177**
KANONENGUT **6178**
KANONENMETALL **6178**
KANTE **4441**
KANTE (ABGEFASTE) **2231**
KANTE (ABGERUNDETE) **10808**
KANTE (GESCHNITTENE) **3506**
KANTE (SCHARFE) **11272**
KANTE RUNDEN (EINE) **10793**
KANTENABSCHRÄGWINKEL **1223**
KANTENDETEKTIONSVORRICHTUNG **4444**
KANTENPRESSUNG **9826**
KANTENRISS **3281**
KANTENVORBEREITUNG **4449**
KANTHOLZ **12035**
KANTVORRICHTUNG **7982**
KAOLIN **2340**
KAPAZITÄT **1917**
KAPAZITÄT (ELEKTR.) **1917**
KAPILLARDEPRESSION **1924**
KAPILLARELEVATION **1925**
KAPILLARITÄT **1920**
KAPILLARKONSTANTE **1923**
KAPILLARROHR **1921**
KAPILLARWIRKUNG **1922**
KAPITÄL EINER SÄULE **1926**
KAPPE **1910**
KAPPE EINES HOBELEISENS **13033**
KAPPENKOPF EINER SCHUBSTANGE **12345**
KAPPENMUTTER **1512**
KAPSELGEBLÄSE **10751**
KAPSELGUSS **2335**

KAPSELPUMPE **10758**
KARABINERHAKEN **11691**
KARBID **1933**
KARBID **1848**
KARBIDAUSSCHEIDUNG **1934**
KARBINOL **13920**
KARBOLINEUM **1939**
KARBOLSÄURE **1938**
KARBONAT **1967**
KARBONAT **1968**
KARBONISATION **1970**
KARBONISIEREN **1971**
KARBONISIERUNG **1974**
KARBONISIERUNGSWÄRME **6355**
KARBONITRIEREN **1972**
KARBONITRIERUNGSATMOSPHÄRE **1973**
KARBONYL **1976**
KARBONYLEISEN **1977**
KARBONYLNICKEL **1978**
KARBONYLPULVER **1979**
KARBORUND **1980**
KARBORUNDUM **1980**
KARBURATOR **1984**
KARBURIEROFEN **1991**
KARDANGELENK **6573**
KARDANGELENK **13385**
KARDANISCHES GELENK **6573**
KARDANKUPPLUNG **1997**
KARDIOIDE **2001**
KARENZZEIT **6020**
KARMINPAPIER **2002**
KAROSSERIE **1385**
KAROSSERIE (SELBSTTRAGENDE) **13381**
KAROSSERIENAGEL **2554**
KAROSSERIEWERKSTATT **1398**
KARRE **2013**
KARREN **2013**
KARREN UND BREITSÄMASCHINEN **11129**
KARTOFFELERNTEMASCHINEN **9704**
KARTOFFELLEGEMASCHINEN **9705**
KARTOFFELPFLÜGE **9707**
KARTOFFELRODER **9703**
KARTOFFELSORTIERMASCHINEN **9706**
KARTOFFELZUCKER **6058**
KARTON **1999**
KARUSSELLDREHBANK **1469**
KARUSSELLDREHMASCHINE **13545**
KARUSSELLPRESSE **10757**
KASEIN **2025**
KASKADE **2018**
KASSETTE **2028**

# KAS

828

KASSITERIT 12959
KASTEN 2798
KASTENGLÜHEN 5371
KASTENGUSS 1508
KASTENKABBER 2526
KASTENRAHMEN 1511
KASTENZEMENTIERUNG 1996
KASTORÖL 2086
KATAKAUSTISCHE LINIE 2089
KATALYSATOR 2091
KATALYSE 2090
KATALYTISCH 2092
KATAPHORESE 4639
KATARAKT 3611
KATHETE 9218
KATHETOMETER 2096
KATHODE 2106
KATHODENNICKEL 4600
KATION 2112
KATION 9657
KATODE 2097
KATODENBEIZUNG 2103
KATODENPOLARISATION 2108
KATODENSPANNUNGSABFALL 2100
KATODENSTRAHLEN 2104
KATODENSTRAHLRÖHRE 2105
KATODENWIRKUNGSGRAD 2101
KATODISCHE REINIGUNG 2098
KATOLYT 2111
KATZENAUGE 2088
KAUFBLEI 8014
KAUSCHE 12848
KAUSTISCHE SODA 11722
KAUTSCHUK 10825
KAUTSCHUK (VULKANISIERTER) 13610
KAUTSCHUKSTOPFEN 10824
KAVITATION 2123
KB-TI-MISCHTYP-ÜBERZUG 7583
KEGEL 2924
KEGEL 4016
KEGEL (ABGESTUMPFTER) 13235
KEGEL (GERADER) 10578
KEGEL (SCHIEFER) 8709
KEGEL (SELBSTLÖSENDER) 11159
KEGELAUSZIEHER 2929
KEGELBREMSE 2926
KEGELDACH 2947
KEGELFEDER 2942
KEGELFEDER MIT RECHTECKIGEM QUERSCHNITT 13605
KEGELFORM 2948
KEGELFRÄSER 543

KEGELHAHN 9530
KEGELHALTERUNG 4008
KEGELHANDREIBAHLE 12650
KEGELIGDREHEN 12668
KEGELKUPPLUNG 2927
KEGELKUPPLUNG 2928
KEGELKUPPLUNG 6839
KEGELLEHRDORN 12656
KEGELLEHRDORN 7956
KEGELLEHRDORN 7076
KEGELLEHRDORN MIT MITNEHMER-LAPPEN 12657
KEGELLEHRHÜLSE (METRISCHE) 8230
KEGELLEHRHÜLSEN 12659
KEGELMUTTER 4009
KEGELPENDELREGLER 2943
KEGELRAD 1226
KEGELRAD 1229
KEGELRADANTRIEB 1230
KEGELRÄDERWENDEGETRIEBE 10545
KEGELRADGETRIEBE 1227
KEGELRADPAAR MIT ÜBERSETZUNGS-VERHÄLTNIS 1:1 8323
KEGELREIBAHLE 12658
KEGELREIBUNGSKUPPLUNG 2930
KEGELROLLE 12660
KEGELSCHAFT 12664
KEGELSCHAFTSPANNDORN 12667
KEGELSCHEIBE 12669
KEGELSCHLICHTBOHRER 5226
KEGELSCHNITT 2940
KEGELSENKKOPF 13044
KEGELSITZ 12649
KEGELSITZVENTIL 2951
KEGELSPINDEL 2009
KEGELSTIFT 12655
KEGELSTUMPF 13235
KEGELSTUMPFFEDER 13236
KEGELTROMMEL 2941
KEGELTROMMEL 12669
KEGELWALZE 12660
KEHLE 8512
KEHLHOBEL 10800
KEHLMASCHINE 8429
KEHLNAHT (UNTERBROCHENE VERSETZTE) 12049
KEHLNAHTDICKE 12886
KEHLNÄHTE (SYMMETRISCH VERSETZTE) 2210
KEHLNAHTSCHWEISSEN 5162
KEHRGETRIEBE 10544
KEHRPFLÜGE UND ANHANGEPFLÜGE 9526
KEIL 13731
KEIL 13739
KEIL 7276

KEIL **5211**
KEIL (EINTEILIGER) **11492**
KEIL (MASSIVER) **11796**
KEIL (VERSENKTER) **12458**
KEIL LÖSEN (EINEN) **7750**
KEILANSTELLUNG **12653**
KEILBEILAGE **5937**
KEILBOLZEN **11262**
KEILFÖRMIG **13737**
KEILLOCH **3214**
KEILLOCH EINES HOBELS **8434**
KEILNASE **6318**
KEILNASE **7286**
KEILNUT **7282**
KEILNUT **7291**
KEILNUTENFLANSCHEN **7289**
KEILNUTENFRÄSMASCHINE **7281**
KEILNUTENSCHABLONE **7283**
KEILNUTENSCHABLONE **7290**
KEILPRESSE **13734**
KEILRAD **13732**
KEILRÄDERGETRIEBE **13736**
KEILRIEMEN **2925**
KEILRIEMEN **13431**
KEILRIEMEN **13511**
KEILRILLE **7282**
KEILRING **2945**
KEILSCHIEBER **12662**
KEILSICHERUNG **7704**
KEILSTEIN **13738**
KEILTREIBER **7278**
KEILVERBINDUNG **7285**
KEILVERBINDUNG **7288**
KEILVERSPANNUNG **12929**
KEILWELLE **11935**
KEIM **8688**
KEIM **4686**
KEIMBILDUNG **5934**
KEIMBILDUNG **8687**
KENNBLATT (TECHNISCHES) **3615**
KENNELKOHLE **1901**
KENNLINIE **2256**
KENNWERT **9075**
KENNZAHL **2621**
KENNZIFFER EINES LOGARITHMUS **2257**
KERAMIK **2193**
KERBBIEGEVERSUCH **8555**
KERBE **8672**
KERBE **8668**
KERBEMPFINDLICHKEIT **8670**
KERBEN **8554**

KERBEN **8676**
KERBSCHLAGPROBE **1190**
KERBSCHLAGPROBE **8673**
KERBSCHLAGVERSUCH **2270**
KERBSCHLAGZÄHIGKEIT **6788**
KERBSCHLAGZÄHIGKEIT **8671**
KERBSPRÖDIGKEIT **8669**
KERBSPRÖDIGKEIT **1632**
KERBZÄHIGKEIT **8671**
KERBZÄHIGKEIT **12738**
KERN **13726**
KERN **3162**
KERN **8688**
KERN **3142**
KERN EINER SCHRAUBE **1394**
KERN EINES QUERSCHNITTES **3156**
KERNBILDUNG **8687**
KERNBINDER **3145**
KERNBLASMASCHINE **3146**
KERNDURCHMESSER **8314**
KERNDURCHMESSER **10719**
KERNDURCHMESSER EINER SCHRAUBE **3850**
KERNFORMMASCHINE **3154**
KERNFÜHRUNGSBLOCK **3144**
KERNGEFÜGE **3165**
KERNHAKEN **3152**
KERNKASTEN **3147**
KERNKLEBEMITTEL **3151**
KERNLEDER **1780**
KERNMARKE **3161**
KERNÖL **3157**
KERNSAND **3163**
KERNSCHÄLE DES HOLZES **3460**
KERNSCHLEIFMASCHINE **3150**
KERNSEIFE **3482**
KERNSTANGE **3143**
KERNSTÜCK **5027**
KERNSTÜTZE **2253**
KERNTROCKENOFEN **3158**
KERRSCHLAGZÄHIGKEIT **10477**
KERZE **1899**
KERZE (INTERNATIONALE) **3663**
KERZENSTÄRKE **1900**
KESSEL (LIEGENDER) **6579**
KESSEL (STEHENDER) **13544**
KESSEL EINMAUERN (EINEN) **11215**
KESSELABDECKUNGSMATERIAL **1408**
KESSELARMATUR **1411**
KESSELAUSRÜSTUNG **1411**
KESSELBATTERIE **1069**
KESSELBLECH **1416**

# KES 830

KESSELBODEN (GEWÖLBTER) **4038**
KESSELBODENWINKELEISEN **1490**
KESSELBOHRMASCHINE **1409**
KESSELDRUCK **1417**
KESSELDRUCKPROBE **1421**
KESSELEXPLOSION **1410**
KESSELFABRIK **1423**
KESSELHAUS **1413**
KESSELISOLIERMATERIAL **1408**
KESSELKONTROLLE **9193**
KESSELMANTEL **1419**
KESSELRAUM **1418**
KESSELROHR **1422**
KESSELSCHLACKE; KLINKER **2500**
KESSELSCHMIED **1415**
KESSELSCHMIEDE **1420**
KESSELSCHUSS **3260**
KESSELSTEIN **10969**
KESSELSTEIN ENTFERNEN **10971**
KESSELSTEINENTFERNUNG **10987**
KESSELSTEINHAMMER **10986**
KESSELSTEINLÖSUNGSMITTEL **4041**
KESSELSTEINVERHÜTUNGSMITTEL **10978**
KESSELTROMMELBODEN **6316**
KESSELUNTERSUCHUNG **1414**
KESSELWAGEN **12626**
KESSELWÄRTER **12272**
KESSELZUBEHÖR **1411**
KETTE **2201**
KETTE (ADJUSTIERTE) **9412**
KETTE (ENDLOSE) **4732**
KETTE (GERÄUSCHLOSE) **11432**
KETTE (GESCHWEISSTE) **13770**
KETTE (KALIBRIERTE) **9412**
KETTE (KURZGLIEDRIGE) **11373**
KETTE (LANGGLIEDRIGE) **7730**
KETTE EINES GEWEBES **13627**
KETTEN (KALIBRIERTE) **1862**
KETTENANTRIEB **2206**
KETTENBAND **7496**
KETTENBOLZEN **9320**
KETTENBREMSE **2203**
KETTENEISENSTÄRKE **3856**
KETTENFLASCHENZUG **2213**
KETTENGLIED **2211**
KETTENGLIED **7627**
KETTENKÄSTEN **2204**
KETTENLINIE **2095**
KETTENMASSSYSTEM **6854**
KETTENNIET **2214**
KETTENNIETUNG **2215**

KETTENNUSS **11662**
KETTENRAD **2223**
KETTENRADANTRIEB **2208**
KETTENRADSCHIEBER **2220**
KETTENROLLE **2217**
KETTENROST **2209**
KETTENSÄGE **2216**
KETTENSCHMIERUNG **2212**
KETTENSPANNER **2219**
KETTENSPANNER **2218**
KETTENSTEG **12402**
KETTENTEILUNG **6978**
KETTENTRIEB **2207**
KETTENTROMMEL **2202**
KETTENZAHNRAD **9402**
KIELBLOCK **7273**
KIELKLOTZ **7273**
KIENÖL **10862**
KIENRUSS **7386**
KIES **6073**
KIESBODEN **6076**
KIESELERDE **11436**
KIESELERDE **11434**
KIESELFLUORWASSERSTOFFSÄURE **11441**
KIESELFLUSSSÄURE **11441**
KIESELGALMEI **11438**
KIESELGUR **7292**
KIESELGUR **3880**
KIESELKALK **11451**
KIESELSÄURE **11436**
KIESELSÄUREANHYDRID **11436**
KIESELSAURES KALIUM **9698**
KIESELSAURES NATRIUM **11731**
KIESELSAURES SALZ **11437**
KIESELSTEIN **9152**
KIESELZINKERZ **11438**
KIESFILTER **6074**
KIESROST **6075**
KILO **7297**
KILODYN **7296**
KILOGRAMM **7297**
KILOGRAMMETER **7299**
KILOGRAMMLKALORIE **7298**
KILOMETER **7300**
KILOVOLT **7301**
KILOVOLTAMPERE **7302**
KILOWATT **7303**
KILOWATTSTUNDE **7304**
KINEMATIK **7306**
KINEMATISCH **7305**
KINETIK **7310**

831           **KNA**

KINETISCH **7307**
KINKE **7313**
KIP = 1000 PFD = 453,59 KG **7316**
KIPPBAR **6835**
KIPPEN **4376**
KIPPER **1932**
KIPPER **4375**
KIPPER **12967**
KIPPFANNE **12935**
KIPPHEBEL **10654**
KIPPMOMENT **8966**
KIPPMOMENT **12936**
KIPPSCHALTUNG (BI-STABILE) **5429**
KIPPSCHERE **10658**
KIRSCHROTGLÜHEND **2327**
KIRSCHROTGLUT **2326**
KISTENZEMENTIERUNG **1996**
KITT **10037**
KITT **8038**
KITTEN **2146**
KLAFFEN EINER FUGE **5806**
KLAMMER **2502**
KLAMMER **12105**
KLAMMERHAKEN **12105**
KLAPPDECKEL **6510**
KLAPPE **5353**
KLAPPE **2617**
KLAPPENVENTIL **5353**
KLAPPERN DES VENTILS **2277**
KLAPPMASSSTAB **5512**
KLAPPSCHRAUBE **6509**
KLAPPSITZ **7261**
KLAPPVERDECK **2719**
KLÄRBOTTICH **11229**
KLÄREN **2456**
KLÄREN **2455**
KLÄRGEFÄSS **11229**
KLASSIERUNG **2460**
KLAUE **2464**
KLAUE EINES HAMMERS **2463**
KLAUENFETT **1450**
KLAUENHAMMER **2462**
KLAUENKUPPLUNG **2461**
KLAUENKUPPLUNG **4113**
KLAUENMEHL **6567**
KLAUENÖL ; KNOCHENÖL **1450**
KLAVIERSAITENDRAHT **9287**
KLEBÄTHER **2733**
KLEBEMITTEL **177**
KLEBRIG **13577**
KLEBRIGKEIT **12591**

KLEBSTOFF **177**
KLEESALZ **10907**
KLEESÄURE **8969**
KLEINEISENWAREN **11660**
KLEINGASMASCHINE **11658**
KLEINLASTWAGEN **7563**
KLEINMOTOR **11661**
KLEINSCHLAG **1644**
KLEINSTWERT **8307**
KLEINWASSERRAUMKESSEL **11663**
KLEISTER **12112**
KLEMMBACKE **5675**
KLEMMBACKENSCHALTGETRIEBE **5676**
KLEMME (ELEKTR.) **12762**
KLEMMEN **12765**
KLEMMEN **7212**
KLEMMEN (SICH) **7210**
KLEMMEN DES SEILES IN DER RILLE **1278**
KLEMMENSPANNUNG **12764**
KLEMMGESPERRE **5676**
KLEMMKLINKE **5675**
KLEMMKUPPLUNG **11164**
KLEMMNABE **11938**
KLEMMRING **11939**
KLEMMSCHELLE **2720**
KLEMMSCHRAUBE **2453**
KLEMPNER **12964**
KLETTERN DES RIEMENS **2499**
KLIMAANLAGE **250**
KLINGE **1299**
KLINGE EINES SCHNEIDWERKZEUGS **1300**
KLINGELVORRICHTUNG **1137**
KLINGERIT **7318**
KLINGWERK **1061**
KLINKE **6608**
KLINKEN **9138**
KLINKENGETRIEBE **9138**
KLINKENHEBEL **10223**
KLINKENRAD **10225**
KLISCHEE **1340**
KLOBEN **1333**
KLOBENZUG **9973**
KLOBSÄGE **13526**
KLOPFEN **7330**
KLOPFEN (IN DIE FORM) **1482**
KLOPPERBODEN **4038**
KLOTZBREMSE **1335**
KLUPPE **12266**
KLUPPENHALTER **3895**
KNABBERN **8552**
KNAGGE **2485**

# KNA

832

KNAGGE 1883
KNAGGENSCHEIBE 13221
KNALL 7330
KNALLGAS 8985
KNALLGASGEBLÄSE 8986
KNALLQUECKSILBER 8154
KNALLSÄURE 5731
KNALLSILBER 11463
KNARRE 10218
KNARRENSCHRAUBENSCHLÜSSEL 10224
KNEBELSCHRAUBE 1930
KNEIFZANGE 3532
KNEIPZANGE 3532
KNETALUMINIUM-LEGIERUNG 433
KNICK 7313
KNICKBAND 7314
KNICKBEANSPRUCHUNG 3339
KNICKBELASTUNG 3338
KNICKEN 3343
KNICKFESTIGKEIT 3340
KNICKFESTIGKEIT 1682
KNICKLAST 3338
KNICKSPANNUNG 3341
KNICKUNG 3343
KNICKUNG 1681
KNICKUNG 7315
KNICKVERSUCH 3342
KNIEHEBEL 12979
KNIEHEBELBREMSE 12978
KNIEHEBELPRESSE 12980
KNIEHEBELVERBINDUNG 12979
KNIEHEBELVERCHLUSS 7336
KNIEROHR 7320
KNIESTÜCK 12546
KNIESTÜCK 7320
KNIESTÜCK 4493
KNOCHENGELENK 7336
KNOCHENKOHLE 554
KNOCHENLEIM 1449
KNOCHENMEHL 1448
KNOCHENSÄURE 8873
KNODIG 8606
KNOLLIG 8606
KNÜPPEL 1243
KNÜPPEL AUS LEGIERTEN STÄHLEN 370
KNÜPPEL U. PLATINENSCHERE 1244
KNÜPPELSCHERE 1246
KNÜPPELWALZWERK 1245
KOAGULIEREN 2556
KOAGULIEREN 2555
KOAGULUM 2557

KOALESZENZ 2572
KOALESZIERTES ELEKTROLYTKUPFER 2571
KOAXIAL 2605
KOBALT 2607
KOBALT (SALPETERSAURER) 2610
KOBALT-CHROMSTAHL 2613
KOBALT-KARBONYL 2608
KOBALTCHLORÜR 2609
KOBALTGLANZ 2614
KOBALTNITRAT 2610
KOBALTOCHLORID 2609
KOBALTOSULFAT 2615
KOBALTOXYD 2611
KOBALTOXYDUL (SCHWEFELSAURES) 2615
KOBALTOXYDULSULFAT 2615
KOBALTSTAHL 2612
KOBALTVITRIOL 2615
KOCHEN 1401
KOCHEN 1429
KOCHER 1406
KOCHKESSEL 1406
KOCHSALZ 2790
KODIERUNG 4716
KOEFFIZIENT 2621
KOERZITIV 2640
KOERZITIVEFELD 2639
KOERZITIVKRAFT 2641
KOERZITIVKRAFT 2639
KOFFERRAUM 1458
KOFFERRAUM 13239
KOFFERRAUMDECKEL 13240
KOHÄRENZ 2644
KOHÄSION 2644
KOHÄSTONSKRAFT 2644
KOHLE 2558
KOHLE (ANTHRAZITISCHE) 11165
KOHLE (BACKENDE) 1835
KOHLE (KURZFLAMMIGE) 11371
KOHLE (LANGFLAMMIGE) 7724
KOHLE (MAGERE) 11168
KOHLE (NICHTBACKENDE) 8626
KOHLE (TROCKNE) 4344
KOHLE(LICHTBOGEN)SCHWEISSEN 1943
KOHLEBÜRSTE 1946
KOHLEELEKTRODEN-LICHTBOGENOFEN 670
KOHLEFADENGLÜHLAMPE 1951
KOHLEHYDRAT 1937
KOHLELEKTRODE 1950
KOHLELICHTBOGEN 1941
KOHLELICHTBOGENSCHNEIDEN 1942
KOHLENBERGWERK 2566

KOHLENBRECHER **2559**
KOHLENBUNKER **2561**
KOHLENBUNKER **1740**
KOHLENDIOXYD **1948**
KOHLENDISULFID **1964**
KOHLENFEUERUNG **2564**
KOHLENFEUERUNG (ANLAGE) **2565**
KOHLENGEBIET **2562**
KOHLENGRUBE **2566**
KOHLENGRUS **11557**
KOHLENKALK **1969**
KOHLENMONOXYD **1952**
KOHLENOXYDNICKEL **8561**
KOHLENSÄURE **1948**
KOHLENSÄURE **1949**
KOHLENSÄURE (FLÜSSIGE) **7645**
KOHLENSAURES KALI **9679**
KOHLENSAURES KALI **9676**
KOHLENSCHLACKE **2500**
KOHLENSTAUB **9984**
KOHLENSTAUBFEUERUNG **5746**
KOHLENSTAUBFEUERUNG **1753**
KOHLENSTOFF **1940**
KOHLENSTOFF (CHEMISCH GEBUNDENER IM EISEN) **2767**
KOHLENSTOFF (GEBUNDENER) **1962**
KOHLENSTOFF (GELÖSTER) **1963**
KOHLENSTOFF (GRAPHITISCHER) **6059**
KOHLENSTOFFARTIG KOHLENSTOFFHALTIG **1966**
KOHLENSTOFFGEHALT **1947**
KOHLENSTOFFGEHALT **1965**
KOHLENSTOFFREI **1961**
KOHLENSTOFFSTAHL **1954**
KOHLENSTOFFSTAHL **11473**
KOHLENSTOFFZUGABE **145**
KOHLENWASSERSTOFF **6705**
KOHLENWASSERSTOFFE (GESÄTTIGTE) **10940**
KOHLENWASSERSTOFFE (UNGESÄTTIGTE) **13393**
KOHLENWASSERSTOFFE DER FETTREIHE **8806**
KOHLENWASSERSTOFFE DER KARBOREIHE **2518**
KOHLENZECHE **2566**
KOHLUNG DES EISENS **1985**
KOKEREI **7991**
KOKEREI **2665**
KOKEREIGAS **2663**
KOKILLE **2331**
KOKILLE **3883**
KOKILLE **11303**
KOKILLE **9207**
KOKILLENAUSTRITT **9717**
KOKILLENGUSS **9208**
KOKILLENGUSS **2334**

KOKILLENGUSS **2335**
KOKILLENGUSS **2038**
KOKOSFASER **2654**
KOKOSFETT **2620**
KOKOSNUSSÖL **2620**
KOKOSTALG **2620**
KOKS **2655**
KOKS (KOMPAKTER) **2792**
KOKSABRIEB **2659**
KOKSBRECHER **2658**
KOKSBRENNEREI **7991**
KOKSFABRIKATION **7991**
KOKSFILTER **2660**
KOKSKLEIN **11657**
KOKSLÖSCHE **2659**
KOKSOFEN **2661**
KOKSOFENGAS **2663**
KOKSROHEISEN **2664**
KOLBEN **5370**
KOLBEN (AUFLIEGENDER) **9392**
KOLBEN (DOPPELTWIRKENDER) **4164**
KOLBEN (GEHEIZTER) **6384**
KOLBEN (GEKÜHLTER) **3084**
KOLBEN (GETEILTER) **1709**
KOLBEN (KONISCHER) **2944**
KOLBEN (MASCHINENB.) **9370**
KOLBEN (SCHWEBENDERVON DER STANGE GETRAGENER) **9391**
KOLBEN (SCHWINGENDER) **8882**
KOLBEN (VON DER ZYLINDERWAND GETRAGENER) **9392**
KOLBEN EINFACHWIRKENDER **11494**
KOLBENAUFGANG **13409**
KOLBENBESCHLEUNIGUNG **9371**
KOLBENBEWEGUNG **9389**
KOLBENBOLZEN **9376**
KOLBENBOLZEN **6158**
KOLBENDAMPFMASCHINE **10285**
KOLBENDECKEL **7266**
KOLBENDICHTUNG **9375**
KOLBENDRUCK **9377**
KOLBENFEDER MIT TELLER **9547**
KOLBENGESCHWINDIGKEIT **9388**
KOLBENHINGANG **5585**
KOLBENHUB **9389**
KOLBENHUB **7519**
KOLBENKÖRPER **9373**
KOLBENLÖTUNG **11769**
KOLBENNIEDERGANG **4187**
KOLBENPUMPE **9378**
KOLBENPUMPE **10284**
KOLBENRING **9379**

# KOL

834

KOLBENRING 2861
KOLBENRING (EXZENTRISCHER) 4429
KOLBENRING (GESCHLITZTER) 11944
KOLBENRING (GESPALTENER) 11944
KOLBENRING MIT SCHRÄGER STOSSFUGE 9381
KOLBENRING MIT SENKRECHTER STOSSFUGE 9380
KOLBENRING MIT TREPPENSTOSS 9382
KOLBENRING MIT ÜBERLAPPTER STOSSFUGE 9382
KOLBENRÜCKGANG 10530
KOLBENRÜCKKEHR 10530
KOLBENSCHIEBER 9390
KOLBENSPIEL 13406
KOLBENSTANGE 2962
KOLBENSTANGE 9383
KOLBENSTANGE (DURCHGEHENDE) 9387
KOLBENSTANGE (DURCHLAUFENDE) 9387
KOLBENSTANGE (EINSEITIGE) 11472
KOLBENSTANGENENDE 9384
KOLBENSTANGENFÜHRUNG 9385
KOLBENSTANGENLAGER 1100
KOLBENSTANGENPACKUNG 9386
KOLBENVERDICHTER 9374
KOLBENWEG 7519
KOLGENGEBLÄSE 9372
KOLKOTHAR 7148
KOLLEKTOR 11618
KOLLERGANG 4450
KOLLERN 8450
KOLLIDIEREN 5587
KOLLIMATION 2731
KOLLIMATIONSFEHLER 4828
KOLLIMATIONSLINIE 7601
KOLLIMATOR 2732
KOLLISPEZIFIKATION 9003
KOLLODIUM 2733
KOLLOID 2734
KOLLOIDAL 2735
KOLLOIDTEILCHEN 2736
KOLOPHONIUM 2737
KOMBINATION (MATH.) 2761
KOMBINATIONS-KRAFTWAGEN 12141
KOMBIWAGEN 12141
KOMMANDO 2780
KOMPARATOR 2794
KOMPASS 2799
KOMPENSATION 2809
KOMPENSATIONSPENDEL 2808
KOMPENSATIONSROHR 4913
KOMPENSIEREN 2807
KOMPENSIERUNG 2809
KOMPLEMENT EINES WINKELS 2810

KOMPLEMENTÄRFARBE 2812
KOMPLEMENTWINKEL 2811
KOMPLEXE VERÄNDERLICHE 2814
KOMPONENTE 2815
KOMPONENTE 2817
KOMPONENTE (CHEM.) 2983
KOMPONENTE (CHEMISCHE) 2298
KOMPOSITION 2823
KOMPOUNDSCHNITT 2762
KOMPRESSIBILITÄT 2852
KOMPRESSION 2854
KOMPRESSIONSDRUCK 2859
KOMPRESSIONSLINIE 2857
KOMPRESSIONSRING 2861
KOMPRESSIONSRING (OBERER) 13034
KOMPRESSOR 2874
KOMPRIMIERBAR 2853
KOMPRIMIEREN 2837
KONCHOIDE 2892
KONDENSAT 13662
KONDENSAT 2905
KONDENSATION 2906
KONDENSATIONSDAMPFMASCHINE 2911
KONDENSATIONSWASSERABLEITER 12188
KONDENSATOR 1916
KONDENSATOR (BAROMETRISCHER) 1010
KONDENSATOR (CHEM.) 2908
KONDENSATOR (ELEKTR.) 2908
KONDENSATORSTOSSENTLADUNGS-SCHWEISSEN 4645
KONDENSIEREN (SICH) 2907
KONDENSOR (OPT.) 2908
KONDENSTOPF 12188
KONDENSTOPF (THERMOSTATISCHER) 12839
KONDENSWASSER 13662
KONDENSWASSERABSCHEIDER 12188
KONFOKAL 2933
KONGLOMERAT 2934
KONGOPAPIER 2936
KONGOROT 2935
KONGRUENZ (GEOM.) 2937
KÖNIGSGELB 8031
KÖNIGSWASSER 658
KÖNIGSWELLE 13550
KONISCHDREHEN 12668
KONIZITÄT 12646
KONIZITÄTSMIKROMETER 12652
KONJUGIERT (MATH.) 2952
KONKAV 2877
KONKAVSPIEGEL 2879
KONSERVIERUNG DES HOLZES 9790
KONSERVIERUNGSMITTEL 9791

| | |
|---|---|
| KONSISTENZ **2968** | KONUS (GEOM.) **2924** |
| KONSISTENZ EINES ÖLES **1395** | KONUS EINES HAHNES **9532** |
| KONSOL-UND SÄULENFRÄSMASCHINE **7319** | KONUSDORN **12651** |
| KONSOLE **1522** | KONUSSTIFT **2009** |
| KONSOLE **3140** | KONVEKTION **3059** |
| KONSOLFRÄSMASCHINE **7322** | KONVEKTION DER WÄRME **3060** |
| KONSOLLAGER **1523** | KONVERGENT **3064** |
| KONSTANTAN **2980** | KONVERGENZ **3063** |
| KONSTANTE **2969** | KONVERGIEREN **3062** |
| KONSTANTSPANNUNGSSTROMQUELLE **2979** | KONVERTERBIRNE **3071** |
| KONSTITUTION (CHEMISCHE) **2301** | KONVERTERHUT **3072** |
| KONSTITUTIONSFORMEL **5583** | KONVEX **3076** |
| KONSTITUTIONSWASSER **2318** | KONVEXITÄTSVERHÄLTNIS WÖLBUNGSVERHÄLTNIS **3079** |
| KONSTRUIEREN **3795** | KONVEXSPIEGEL **3078** |
| KONSTRUIEREN **3799** | KONVEYOR **1675** |
| KONSTRUKTEUR **4214** | KONZENTRAT **2881** |
| KONSTRUKTION **2986** | KONZENTRATION **2886** |
| KONSTRUKTION **3799** | KONZENTRATIONS POLARISATION (EINER ELEKTRODE) **2889** |
| KONSTRUKTION **13320** | KONZENTRATIONSELEMENT **2887** |
| KONSTRUKTION **12395** | KONZENTRATIONSELEMENT-KORROSION **2888** |
| KONSTRUKTION (SELBSTTRAGENDE) **11161** | KONZENTRATIONSHERABSETZUNG **3767** |
| KONSTRUKTIONSBÜRO **3800** | KONZENTRIZITÄT **2891** |
| KONSTRUKTIONSBÜRO **3796** | KONZEPTION **3794** |
| KONSTRUKTIONSEINZELHEIT **3810** | KOORDINATE (KARTESISCHE) **2014** |
| KONSTRUKTIONSFEHLER **4825** | KOORDINATEN **3100** |
| KONSTRUKTIONSINGENIEUR **4214** | KOORDINATEN (LAUFENDE) **3487** |
| KONSTRUKTIONSSTAHL **12393** | KOORDINATEN (RECHTWINKLIGE) **10301** |
| KONTAKT (ELEKTR.) BERÜHRUNG (ALLG.) **2996** | KOORDINATEN (SCHIEFWINKLIGE) **8710** |
| KONTAKT HERSTELLEN (EINEN) **7950** | KOORDINATEN-BOHR-U. AUSBOHR-MASCHINE **3098** |
| KONTAKT SCHWEISSEN **682** | KOORDINATEN-EBENE **698** |
| KONTAKTBACKE **2999** | KOORDINATENACHSE **864** |
| KONTAKTBLOCK **3003** | KOORDINATENANFANG **8868** |
| KONTAKTELEKTRODE **3001** | KOORDINATENSYSTEM **3099** |
| KONTAKTKNOPF **9797** | KOORDINATENSYSTEM **12575** |
| KONTAKTMETALLE (ELEKTRISCHE) **4538** | KOPAIVABALSAM **3101** |
| KONTAKTPLATTIERUNG **3004** | KOPAL **3102** |
| KONTAKTPOTENTIAL **3007** | KOPALLACK **3103** |
| KONTAKTROLLE **3008** | KOPF **12455** |
| KONTAKTSTÜCKE **9574** | KOPF **6314** |
| KONTAKTUNTERBRECHER **3000** | KOPF (VERLORENER) **3629** |
| KONTERMUTTER **7702** | KOPF EINER SCHRAUBE **1436** |
| KONTINUITÄT **3017** | KOPF EINES HAMMERS **6317** |
| KONTRAKTION **10361** | KOPFDREHBANK **5005** |
| KONTRAKTION **3045** | KOPFDREHBANK **5001** |
| KONTRAKTION EINES FLÜSSIGKEITSSTRAHLES **3044** | KOPFFLANKE **167** |
| KONTRAKTIONSZAHL **2623** | KOPFKEGELWINKEL **4990** |
| KONTROLL **3048** | KOPFKREIS **167** |
| KONTROLLANALYSE **2280** | KOPFKREIS **166** |
| KONTROLLMANOMETER **12080** | KOPFLEHNE **6320** |
| KONTROLLSTEMPEL **3893** | KOPFPLATTE **3388** |
| KONTUR **8907** | KOPFSCHERE **12037** |

# KOP

836

KOPFSCHRAUBE 1913
KOPFSPIEL EINES ZAHNRADES 1489
KOPFWAND 4728
KOPFWINKEL 165
KOPIE 10467
KOPIERDREHBANK 3138
KOPIERDREHMASCHINE 3138
KOPIERFRÄSMASCHINE 9900
KOPIERMASCHINE 3139
KOPIERMODELL 8034
KORBBOGEN 5373
KORBBOGENBODEN 13045
KORBBOGENKOPF 4673
KORBBOGENLINIE 12872
KORBFLASCHE 1981
KORDELGEWINDE 10802
KORDELUNG 7338
KORDIEREN EINES SCHRAUBENKOPFES 8288
KORK 3173
KORK 3176
KORKKLEIN 6144
KORKMEHL 6144
KORKPLATTE 3175
KORKPLATTE (GEPRESSTE) 9802
KORKSCHROT 6144
KORKSTEIN 3174
KORKSTOPFEN 3176
KORN 6030
KORNBINDUNG 1279
KÖRNER 2172
KÖRNER 6054
KÖRNER 9844
KÖRNERLACK 11131
KÖRNERSPITZE (MIKROMETRISCHE EINSTELLBARE) 8236
KORNGEMISCH OHNE MITTELKORN 5805
KORNGRENZE 6033
KORNGRENZENBRUCH 7030
KORNGRENZENBRUCH 7042
KORNGRÖSSE 6039
KORNGRÖSSE 11522
KORNGRÖSSENVERTEILUNG 6040
KORNGRÖSSENVERTEILUNG 9090
KÖRNIG 6050
KORNSTRUKTUR 6041
KÖRNUNG 6043
KÖRNUNG 6057
KÖRNUNG 6032
KÖRNUNG 6040
KORNVERFEINERUNG 6037
KORNVERSTÜCKELUNG 5623
KORNVERTEILUNGSBESTIMMUNG 6023

KORNWASCHSTUM 6035
KÖRPER 1385
KÖRPER (BEWEGTER) 1392
KÖRPER (BILDSAMER) 9467
KÖRPER (FESTER) 11775
KÖRPER (FLÜSSIGER) 7641
KÖRPER (FORMBARER) 9467
KÖRPER (PLASTISCHER) 9467
KÖRPER (RUHENDER) 1386
KÖRPER (SCHWARZER) 1285
KÖRPER (SCHWIMMENDER) 5436
KÖRPER (SELBSTLEUCHTENDER) 11147
KÖRPER (STARRER) 10588
KÖRPER VON GLEICHEM WIDERSTAND 1396
KÖRPERINHALT (DEN) BERECHNEN 3446
KÖRPERINHALTSBERECHNUNG 3444
KÖRPERMASS 8082
KORROSION 3183
KORROSION (ATMOSPHÄRISCHE) 795
KORROSION (CHEMISCHE) 2302
KORROSION (GALVANISCHE) 5783
KORROSION (INTERKRISTALLINE) 7030
KORROSION (INTERKRISTALLINE) 7041
KORROSION (KATHODISCHE) 2107
KORROSION DER SCHWEISSNAHT 13759
KORROSION UNTER WASSERSTOFFENTWICKLUNG 6718
KORROSIONSBESTÄNDIGKEIT 3194
KORROSIONSERMÜDUNG 3187
KORROSIONSERMÜDUNGSGRENZE 3188
KORROSIONSGESCHWINDIGKEIT 3193
KORROSIONSKOEFFIZIENT 2624
KORROSIONSKOEFFIZIENT (ANODISCHE) 594
KORROSIONSNARBE 3190
KORROSIONSRISSBILDUNG DURCH LATENTE SPANNUNGEN 12364
KORROSIONSSCHUTZ 3191
KORROSIONSSCHUTZ (GALVANISCHER) 2109
KORROSIONSSPRÖDIGKEIT 3186
KORROSIONSVERHÜTUNG 3191
KORUND 4699
KORUND 3201
KOSEKANTE 3202
KOSINUS 3203
KOSTENANSCHLAG 4838
KOTANGENTE 3211
KOTFLÜGEL 5095
KOTFLÜGEL 13874
KOTFLÜGELSCHEIBE 5096
KRACKEN 3284
KRACKTURM 3287
KRACKUNG 3285

| | |
|---|---|
| KRACKVERFAHREN 3285 | KRAFTSTOFFLUFTGEMISCH 8337 |
| KRAFT 5532 | KRAFTSTOFFPUMPE 5715 |
| KRAFT 9730 | KRAFTSTOFFSPARER 4437 |
| KRAFT 12352 | KRAFTSTOFFSTANDMESSER 5710 |
| KRAFT (ELEKTROMOTORISCHE) 4622 | KRAFTERZEUGUNG 9737 |
| KRAFT (ELEKTROSTATISCHE) 4642 | KRAFTÜBERTRAGUNG 9746 |
| KRAFT (GEGENELEKTROMOTORISCHE) 3231 | KRAFTÜBERTRAGUNG 13134 |
| KRAFT (GLEICHBLEIBENDE) 2973 | KRAFTÜBERTRAGUNG 4294 |
| KRAFT (INNERE) 7064 | KRAFTÜBERTRAGUNG (ELEKTRISCHE) 13129 |
| KRAFT (KONTINUIERLICHE) 2973 | KRAFTÜBERTRAGUNG DURCH HEBEL 13132 |
| KRAFT (MAGNETISCHE) 7904 | KRAFTÜBERTRAGUNG DURCH RÄDER 13131 |
| KRAFT (MAGNETISIERENDE) 7925 | KRAFTVERBRAUCH 2876 |
| KRAFT (MAGNETOMOTORISCHE) 7932 | KRAFTVERLUST 7758 |
| KRÄFT (PARALLELE) 9056 | KRAFTVERSORGUNG 9744 |
| KRAFT (THERMOELEKTRISCHE) 12831 | KRAFTWAGEN 8411 |
| KRAFT (THERMOELEKTROMOTORISCHE) 12807 | KRAFTWERK 9742 |
| KRAFTANLAGE 9739 | KRAFTWIRKUNG 143 |
| KRAFTANTRIEB 9733 | KRAFTWIRKUNGSFIGUR 4845 |
| KRAFTARM 706 | KRAFTZAHNRAD 6402 |
| KRAFTAUFWAND 2876 | KRAFTZENTRALE 9742 |
| KRAFTBEDARF 3746 | KRAGSTÜCK 3140 |
| KRAFTBEDARFSKOSTEN 3206 | KRAMPE 12105 |
| KRÄFTE (ENTGEGENGESETZT GERICHTETE) 5537 | KRAMPE 12106 |
| KRÄFTE (GLEICHGERICHTETE) 5538 | KRAN 3290 |
| KRÄFTE MIT GEMEINSAMEM ANGRIFFSPUNKT 2903 | KRAN (STANDFESTER) (ORTSFESTER) 5291 |
| KRAFTECK 9610 | KRANAUSLEGER 3291 |
| KRÄFTEDREIECK 13186 | KRANGIESSPFANNE 3292 |
| KRÄFTEPARALLELOGRAMM 9071 | KRANGIESSPFANNE 1728 |
| KRÄFTEPLAN 3835 | KRANKHEITSERREGER 9126 |
| KRÄFTEPLAN 5526 | KRANKHEITSKEIM 9126 |
| KRÄFTEPOLYGON 9610 | KRANPFANNE 1728 |
| KRAFTERSPARNIS 10948 | KRANSÄGE 10609 |
| KRAFTGAS 4194 | KRANSCHIENE 3293 |
| KRAFTGAS 9736 | KRANZ 3396 |
| KRAFTLEITUNG (ELEKTRISCHE) 4526 | KRANZ EINER RIEMENSCHEIBE 10595 |
| KRAFTLINIE 7603 | KRANZ EINES ZAHNRADES 10594 |
| KRAFTLINIENBILD 7902 | KRATER 3317 |
| KRAFTLINIENFLUSS 7903 | KRATERBILDUNG 9334 |
| KRAFTLINIENSTROM 7903 | KRATZBÜRSTE 11014 |
| KRAFTMACHINE 9859 | KRÄTZE 4331 |
| KRAFTMESSER 4403 | KRATZEN 11011 |
| KRAFTNIETUNG 9740 | KRATZER 11010 |
| KRAFTRICHTUNG 3990 | KRATZFESTIGKEIT 11015 |
| KRAFTRÖHRE 13253 | KRÄUSELN 11399 |
| KRAFTSINN 11182 | KRAUSKOPF 3245 |
| KRAFTSPIRITUS 1983 | KREIDE 13842 |
| KRAFTSTATION 9742 | KREIDE 2224 |
| KRAFTSTOFF 9222 | KREIS 2401 |
| KRAFTSTOFF (KLOPFFESTER) 613 | KREIS 2404 |
| KRAFTSTOFFBEHÄLTER 5716 | KREIS (FESTER) 5290 |
| KRAFTSTOFFILTER 5708 | KREIS (UMGESCHRIEBENER) 2435 |

# KRE 838

KREIS (UMLIEGENDER) 2435
KREISABSCHNITT 11136
KREISAUSSCHNITT 11126
KREISBLATTSCHREIBER 2408
KREISBOGEN 674
KREISBOGENSICHEL 7829
KREISE (EXZENTRISCHE) 4426
KREISE (KONZENTRISCHE) 2890
KREISEL 6191
KREISELBEWEGUNG 6193
KREISELFRÄSER 9901
KREISELGEBLÄSE 13270
KREISELPUMPE 2184
KREISELVERSICHTER 2178
KREISELWIRKUNG 6192
KREISEVOLVENTE 7118
KREISEXZENTER 4433
KREISFLÄCHE 695
KREISFRÄSMASCHINE 2420
KREISFREQUENZ 546
KREISFUNKTION 2413
KREISINHALT 695
KREISKEGEL 2409
KREISKOLBENPUMPE 10758
KREISLAUFGLÜHUNG 582
KREISLINIE 2404
KREISMESSER 2417
KREISPENDEL 2422
KREISPROZESS 3554
KREISPROZESS (CARNOTSCHER) 2004
KREISRING 589
KREISSÄGE 2427
KREISSÄGEMASCHINE 2428
KREISSCHERE 2429
KREISSCHERE 2403
KREISSEGMENT 11136
KREISSEHNE 2421
KREISSEHNE 2364
KREISSEILTRIEB 3015
KREISSEKTOR 11126
KREISSICHELSTÜCK 7829
KREISTEILMASCHINE 4103
KREISTEILUNG 4108
KREISUMFANG 2404
KREISVIERECK 6961
KREISZYLINDER 2411
KREMPE 1083
KREMPEN 1084
KREMPEN 1088
KREMPMASCHINE 5346
KREOSOT 3331

KREOSOTIEREN 3332
KREOSOTÖL 3331
KREUZAUFTRAGUNG 3366
KREUZDRAHTSCHWEISSEN 3385
KREUZEISEN 3372
KREUZGELENK 6573
KREUZGESCHLAGENES DRAHTSEIL 10415
KREUZHAMMER 12308
KREUZHIEB 4134
KREUZHIEB 4132
KREUZHOLZ 10076
KREUZKOPF 3388
KREUZKOPFENDE DER SCHUBSTANGE 3389
KREUZKOPFZAPFEN 3391
KREUZKOPFZAPFENLAGER 3390
KREUZMEISSEL 3364
KREUZMEISSEL 1919
KREUZPROFILEISEN 3381
KREUZROHR 3368
KREUZSCHEIBENKUPPLUNG 8794
KREUZSCHLAG 12308
KREUZSCHLAG 10414
KREUZSTREBEN 1520
KREUZSTREBENTRAGWERK 3360
KREUZSTROM 3363
KREUZSTÜCK 3368
KREUZSTÜCK 3359
KREUZTRIEB 3387
KREUZUNGSPUNKT 3393
KREUZWINKEL 12581
KRIECHEN 9471
KRIECHEN 3324
KRIECHEN 3330
KRIECHGESCHWINDIGKEIT 3326
KRIECHGRENZE (KONVENTIONELLE) 3325
KRISTALL 3424
KRISTALL 6030
KRISTALL (HEMIMORPHER) 6437
KRISTALL (IDIOMORFER) 6751
KRISTALL (INHOMOGENER) 3169
KRISTALL (ISOMETRISCHER) 3450
KRISTALL (KUBISCHER) 3450
KRISTALL (MONOKLINER) 8384
KRISTALL (REGULÄRER) 3450
KRISTALL (RHOMBOEDRISHER) 10565
KRISTALLACHSE 865
KRISTALLACHSEN (ORTHOHEXAGONALE) 8871
KRISTALLBILDUNG 3438
KRISTALLDEHNUNG 3426
KRISTALLE (GLEICHGERICTETE) 4784
KRISTALLE (ORTHORHOMBISCHE) 8874

KRISTALLELEKTRIZITÄT **10043**
KRISTALLFLÄCHE **3427**
KRISTALLGLAS **3428**
KRISTALLINISCH **3433**
KRISTALLISATION **3438**
KRISTALLISATION (PRIMÄRE) **9849**
KRISTALLISATIONSFRONT **11798**
KRISTALLISIERBAR **3437**
KRISTALLISIERBARKEIT **3436**
KRISTALLISIEREN **3439**
KRISTALLISIERTE SODA **11711**
KRISTALLIT **3440**
KRISTALLKERN **8688**
KRISTALLOGRAFIE **3442**
KRISTALLOGRAMM **3441**
KRISTALLOID **3443**
KRISTALLORIENTIERUNG **3994**
KRISTALLSODA **11711**
KRISTALLSTRUKTUR **3430**
KRISTALLSTRUKTUR-ANALYSE **3425**
KRISTALLSYMMETRIEACHSE **863**
KRISTALLSYSTEM **3431**
KRISTALLSYSTEM (TRIKLINE) **13199**
KRISTALLWACHSTUM (ABNORMALES) **7**
KRISTALLWASSER **13663**
KROKODILNARBUNG **348**
KRONENKREIS **166**
KRONENMUTTER **2085**
KRONENVENTIL **1136**
KRONGLAS **3397**
KRONGRENZE **1500**
KRONRAD **3399**
KROPFEISEN **3822**
KRÖPFMASCHINEN **7232**
KRÖPFUNG **7321**
KRÖPFUNG DER WELLE **6976**
KRUMMACHSE **6976**
KRUMMAXT **207**
KRUMME LINIE **3496**
KRÜMMER **1180**
KRUMMLINIG **3499**
KRÜMMUNG **3494**
KRÜMMUNGSHALBMESSER **10168**
KRÜMMUNGSKREIS **2402**
KRÜMMUNGSMESSER **11897**
KRÜMMUNGSMITTELPUNKT **2167**
KRUMMZAPFEN **9319**
KRUMMZIEHEN **13629**
KRUSTENBILDUNG; KESSELSTEINBILDUNG **6856**
KRYOHYDRAT **3422**
KRYOLITH **3423**

KRYPTON **7339**
KUBATUR **3444**
KÜBELSITZ **1678**
KUBIEREN **3446**
KUBIKDEZIMETER **3451**
KUBIKFUSS (ENGLISCHER) **3453**
KUBIKFUSS (GENORMTER) **12072**
KUBIKMETER **3455**
KUBIKMILLIMETER **3456**
KUBIKWURZEL **3447**
KUBIKZENTIMETER **3449**
KUBIKZOLL (ENGLISCHER) **3454**
KUBISCH-FLÄCHEN-ZENTRIERT **4991**
KUBISCHRAUMZENTRIERT **1399**
KUBUS **3445**
KUGEL **950**
KUGEL (GEOM.) **11883**
KUGEL EINES KUGELLAGERS **1102**
KUGELARM **6014**
KUGELAUSSCHNITT **11127**
KUGELBAHN **965**
KUGELBEWEGUNG **11889**
KUGELBILDUNG **11896**
KUGELDREHEN **13291**
KUGELDREIECK **11891**
KUGELDRUCK- UND TRAGLAGER **538**
KUGELDRUCKHÄRTE **1619**
KUGELDRUCKHÄRTEPRÜFUNG **6861**
KUGELDRUCKLAGER **12901**
KUGELDRUCKLAGER **966**
KUGELDRUCKPRÜFAPPARAT **967**
KUGELDRUCKVERSUCH **1620**
KUGELDRUCKVERSUCH NACH BRINELL **1618**
KUGELFALLHÄRTE **11003**
KUGELFALLPROBE NACH SHORE **11367**
KUGELFINNE **963**
KUGELFINNE **961**
KUGELFÖRMIG **11884**
KUGELGELENK **953**
KUGELGELENKAUFHÄNGUNG **958**
KUGELGRAPHIT-GUSSEISEN **4362**
KUGELGRAPHITGUSSEISEN **8607**
KUGELHAHN **2617**
KUGELHAHN **968**
KUGELHAUBE **1911**
KUGELHAUBE **11137**
KUGELIG **11884**
KUGELIG **8606**
KUGELIG DREHEN **13281**
KUGELKÄFIG **957**
KUGELKALOTTE **1911**

# KUG

840

KUGELKAPPE 1911
KUGELKEIL 11892
KUGELLAGER 954
KUGELLAGERSCHALE 955
KUGELMÜHLE 959
KUGELPOLIEREN 956
KUGELQUERDRUCKLAGER 10130
KUGELRING 964
KUGELSCHALE 11137
KUGELSCHALE 1911
KUGELSCHALE 11887
KUGELSCHALENLAGER 12563
KUGELSCHICHT 14051
KUGELSCHULTERLAGER 538
KUGELSEKTOR 11127
KUGELSPIEGEL 11888
KUGELSPUR (EINES LAGERS) 965
KUGELSPURLAGER 11890
KUGELSPURLAGER 12901
KUGELSTRAHLEN 11381
KUGELSTÜTZLAGER 12901
KUGELVENTIL 968
KUGELVENTIL 5977
KUGELWEISE GESCHLAGENES SEIL 11401
KUGELWINKEL 11886
KUGELZAPFEN 11893
KUGELZAPFENLAGER 952
KUGELZONE 14051
KUGELZWEIECK 11886
KÜHLANLAGE 10408
KÜHLBETT 6617
KÜHLEN 3085
KÜHLER 10409
KÜHLER 10148
KÜHLER (FÜR MOTOREN) 10149
KÜHLERRIPPE 13477
KÜHLERSPRITZBLECH 11927
KÜHLERVERKLEIDUNG 10152
KÜHLERVERSCHRAUBUNG 10151
KÜHLFLÄCHE 3092
KÜHLKASTEN 8380
KÜHLKASTENKOPFWAND 8381
KÜHLKÖRPER (EINGEGOSSENER) 7046
KÜHLLUFTGEBLASE 3088
KÜHLLUFTREGLER 12838
KÜHLMANTEL 13655
KÜHLMITTEL 3083
KÜHLMITTEL 3086
KÜHLSCHLANGE 13978
KÜHLSYSTEM 3093
KÜHLTEICH 3090

KÜHLTURM 3094
KÜHLUNG 3085
KÜHLUNG 3093
KÜHLUNG (GESTEUERTE) 3056
KÜHLWASSER 3095
KUHSTALL-AUSSTATTUNGEN 3277
KÜKEN 9532
KÜKEN 9529
KULISSE 11633
KULISSENHEBEL 11638
KULISSENSTEIN 7625
KULISSENSTEUERUNG 7626
KULISSENZAHNSTANGE 4150
KÜMPELARBEIT 4040
KÜMPELMASCHINE 5346
KÜMPELN 5345
KÜMPELN 5324
KUNDENGIESSEREI 7230
KUNSTBRONZE 12147
KUNSTSEIDE 736
KUNSTSTEIN 737
KUNSTSTOFF-DICHTPACKUNG 11078
KUNSTSTOFFBAHNHAMMER 11747
KUNSTSTOFFE 9476
KUNSTSTOFFPLATTE 9032
KUPELLATION 3463
KUPFER 3110
KUPFER (CUPRIOXYD-ENTHALTENDES) 13069
KUPFER (DESOXYDIERTES) 3764
KUPFER (GEDIEGENES) 7370
KUPFER (HAMMERGARE) 13070
KUPFER (KOHLENSAURES) 3470
KUPFER (RAFFINIERTES) 13070
KUPFER (SALPETERSAURES) 3472
KUPFER (SALPETRIGSAURES) 3473
KUPFER (SCHWEFELSAURES) 3475
KUPFER (SILBERHALTIGES) 11468
KUPFER (THERMISCH VEREDELTES) 5250
KUPFER (THERMISCH VERGÜTETES) 5250
KUPFER VON LAKE-SUPERIOR-ERZEN 7370
KUPFERANODE 3112
KUPFERASBESTDICHTUNG 3134
KUPFERAZETAT 13533
KUPFERBARREN 3120
KUPFERBLECH 11308
KUPFERBLECH 3127
KUPFERBLOCK 3120
KUPFERCHLORID 4853
KUPFERCHLORÜR 3478
KUPFERDRAHT 3133
KUPFERDRAHT 3106

**841** **KUR**

KUPFERERZ 3122
KUPFERFLACHBLOCK 3129
KUPFERFLACHDRAHT 3116
KUPFERFLACHPROFIL 902
KUPFERFOLIE 3117
KUPFERGLANZ 3118
KUPFERHAMMER 3119
KUPFERHYDROXYD 3471
KUPFERKARBONAT 3470
KUPFERKIES 3126
KUPFERLASUR 886
KUPFERLECH 3121
KUPFERLEGIERUNG 3111
KUPFERMÜNZEN 3114
KUPFERNICKEL 3477
KUPFERNITRAT 3472
KUPFERNITRIT 3473
KUPFEROXIDSCHICHT 5246
KUPFEROXYD 3474
KUPFEROXYDHYDRAT 3471
KUPFEROXYDUL 3479
KUPFERPLATTE 3123
KUPFERROHR 3132
KUPFERSCHMIED 3135
KUPFERSCHMIEDEN 3136
KUPFERSCHROT 3128
KUPFERSTAB 3113
KUPFERSTAHL 3130
KUPFERSTEIN 3121
KUPFERSTREIFEN 3131
KUPFERSULFAT 3475
KUPFERVITRIOL 1376
KUPFERZINKLEGIERUNG 5943
KUPFERZINKLEGIERUNG 9861
KUPFERZYANID 3115
KUPOL.. 3464
KUPOLOFEN 3466
KUPOLOFENABSTICH 12675
KUPOLOFENKOKS 5595
KUPOLOFENMETALL 3468
KUPOLOFENTEMPERGUSS 3467
KUPPELDACH 4120
KUPPELN 3254
KUPPELN 3253
KUPPELOFEN 3466
KUPPELSCHEIBE 6205
KUPPELSTANGE 3256
KUPPLUNG 3254
KUPPLUNG 2544
KUPPLUNG 11240
KUPPLUNG 12603

KUPPLUNG (BEWEGLICHE) 5417
KUPPLUNG (ELASTISCHE) 4476
KUPPLUNG (ELASTISCHE) 5417
KUPPLUNG (FESTE) 5037
KUPPLUNG (HYDRAULISCHE) 6681
KUPPLUNG (LÄNGSBEWEGLICHE) 4915
KUPPLUNG (MAGNETISCHE) 7934
KUPPLUNG (NACHGIEBIGE) 5417
KUPPLUNG (SELBSTEINRÜCKENDE) 11149
KUPPLUNGSBELAG 2545
KUPPLUNGSDRUCKLAGER 2549
KUPPLUNGSFUSSHEBEL 2547
KUPPLUNGSGEHÄUSE 1133
KUPPLUNGSGEHÄUSE 2546
KUPPLUNGSHÄLFTE 6205
KUPPLUNGSKLAUE 2464
KUPPLUNGSMUFFE 3257
KUPPLUNGSSCHEIBE 3255
KUPPLUNSFLANSCH 3255
KUPPUNG (ELEKTROMAGNETISCHE) 7934
KUPRIHYDROXYD 3471
KUPRINITRAT 3472
KUPROCHLORID 3478
KUPRONITRAT 3473
KURBEL 3295
KURBEL (GEBAUTE) 1706
KURBEL (GEKRÖPFTE) 6976
KURBEL (GESCHMIEDETE) 5550
KURBEL (KURZHÜBIGE) 11375
KURBEL (LANGHÜBIGE) 7732
KURBEL (ZUSAMMENGEBAUTE) 1706
KURBELARM 3296
KURBELARM 3301
KURBELAUGE 3297
KURBELENDE DER SCHUBSTANGE 3299
KURBELGEHÄUSE 3306
KURBELGEHÄUSE-ENTLÜFTUNG 3307
KURBELGEHÄUSE-UNTERTEIL 8782
KURBELGEHÄUSE-UNTERTEIL 8767
KURBELGETRIEBE 1094
KURBELGRIFF 3300
KURBELKREIS 3298
KURBELNABE 3297
KURBELSCHEIBE 4003
KURBELSCHLEIFE 11631
KURBELSTELLUNG 9645
KURBELTRIEB (EXZENTRISCHER) 4427
KURBELTRIEB (GESCHRÄNKTER) 4427
KURBELWANGE 3304
KURBELWELLE 3313
KURBELWELLE 3309

# KUR

842

KURBELWELLE (DREIFACH GEKRÖPFTE) **12880**
KURBELWELLE (MEHRFACH GEKRÖPFTE) **8478**
KURBELWELLE MIT GEGENGEWICHT **3235**
KURBELWELLENDREHBANK **3316**
KURBELWELLENLAGER **3303**
KURBELWELLENLAGER **3314**
KURBELWELLENZAHNRAD **3315**
KURBELWELLENZAPFEN **3311**
KURBELZAPFEN **3302**
KURBELZAPFENLAGER **1242**
KURKUMAGELB **3481**
KURKUMAPAPIER **13275**
KURKUMIN **3481**
KURVE **3496**
KURVE (CASSINISCHE) **2029**
KURVE (EBENE) **9435**
KURVE (GESCHLOSSENE) **2520**
KURVE (ISODYNAME) **7182**
KURVE (ISODYNAMISCHE) **7182**
KURVE (POLYTROPISCHE) **9618**
KURVE (STEILE) **10102**
KURVE (ZYKLISCHE) **3555**
KURVE DOPPELTER KRÜMMUNG **13307**
KURVENFESTIGKEIT **3180**
KURVENLINEAL **5660**
KURVENSCHAR **5028**
KURVENSCHEIBE **4442**
KURVENSCHIENE **5660**
KURVENTRIEB **1886**
KURVIMETER **3501**
KURZSCHLUSS **11372**
KURZSCHLUSS **11369**
KURZSCHLUSSÜBERTRAGUNG **11370**
KÜRZUNG EINES RIEMENS **11377**
KÜRZUNG EINES SEILES **11377**
KÜSTENNAHE..... **8738**
KYANISIEREN DES HOLZES **7340**
L-EISEN **514**
LABARRAQUESCHE LAUGE **4422**
LABIL **7343**
LABORATORIUM **7344**
LABORGERÄTESATZ **7345**
LABYRINTHDICHTUNG **7347**
LACK (ALKOHOLISCHER) **7354**
LACK IN KÖRNERN **11131**
LACK IN STANGENFORM **12254**
LACKANSTRICH **2581**
LACKIEREN **7353**
LACKIERUNG **2581**
LACKMUSPAPIER **7668**
LACKÜBERZUG **2595**

LADEFÄHIGKEIT **9139**
LADEKONTROLLAMPE **2267**
LADEN (EINEN AKKHUMULATOR) **2261**
LADEN EINES AKKUMULATORS **2265**
LADESTROM **2266**
LADUNG **2262**
LADUNG **7679**
LADUNG (ELEKTR.) **2259**
LAFETTE **6175**
LAGE **9096**
LAGE **10832**
LAGE **7382**
LAGE **7442**
LAGEFLÄCHE **1101**
LAGENRISS **7383**
LAGENSICHERUNG **7711**
LAGEPLAN **9430**
LAGER **12263**
LAGER **1100**
LAGER **6660**
LAGER **1118**
LAGER **12297**
LAGER **12292**
LAGER **1117**
LAGER (AUSGELAUFENES) **13980**
LAGER (EINTEILIGES) **11788**
LAGER (EINTEILIGES) **11777**
LAGER (GESCHLOSSENES) **11788**
LAGER (GETEILTES) **4098**
LAGER (SCHIEF GESCHNITTENES) **508**
LAGER (SCHRÄG) **508**
LAGER (SELBSTSCHMIERENDES) **11158**
LAGER (SICH SELBSTEINSTELLENDES **11150**
LAGER (UNRUNDGEWORDENES) **13980**
LAGER-WEISSMETAL **889**
LAGERBESTAND **12263**
LAGERBOCK **12064**
LAGERBOCK **1103**
LAGERBRONZE **1660**
LAGERBÜCHSE **1771**
LAGERBÜCHSE **1773**
LAGERDECKEL **1104**
LAGERDECKEL **5323**
LAGERDECKEL **1912**
LAGERENTFERNUNG **4064**
LAGERFUGE **7241**
LAGERFUSS **1034**
LAGERFUTTER **7624**
LAGERHALS EINER WELLE **1107**
LAGERHAUS **12297**
LAGERHÜLSE **1771**

843           LAS

LAGERKÖRPER **9313**
LAGERLEGIERUNG **385**
LAGERMETALL **10422**
LAGERMETALL **1106**
LAGERN **12491**
LAGERN **12493**
LAGERPLATZ **12265**
LAGERRAUM **12293**
LAGERREIBUNG **1105**
LAGERSCHALE **1113**
LAGERSCHALE **1100**
LAGERSCHALE **1773**
LAGERSCHALE (GETEILTE) **1572**
LAGERSCHALE (OBERE) **13030**
LAGERSCHALE (UNGETEILTE) **1771**
LAGERSCHALE (UNTERE) **1487**
LAGERSCHUPPEN **11302**
LAGERSTÄTTE EINES MINERALS **8303**
LAGERSTUHL **12064**
LAGERUNG **12493**
LAGERUNG **12299**
LAGERUNG **1118**
LAGERVERWALTER **12298**
LAGERVORRAT **12263**
LAMELLAR **7372**
LAMELLE **7371**
LAMELLE **5303**
LAMELLENBREMSE **8454**
LAMELLENKUPPLUNG **9486**
LAMELLENKUPPLUNG **4002**
LAMELLENKUPPLUNG **4046**
LAMELLENMAGNET **7377**
LAMELLENVERGLEICHSMESSER **10365**
LAMELLIERT **7375**
LAMINÄRE STRÖMUNG **13578**
LAMPE **7385**
LAMPE **7384**
LAMPE (ELEKTRISCHE) **4516**
LANDDAMPFKESSEL **12143**
LANGDREHEN **13164**
LANGDREHEN **13162**
LÄNGE **7516**
LÄNGE (NUTZBARE) **13424**
LÄNGEN (SICH) **1125**
LÄNGENAUSDEHNUNGSZAHL **2630**
LÄNGENEINHEIT **13373**
LÄNGENHOLZ **12939**
LÄNGENMASS **8080**
LÄNGENPROFIL **7738**
LÄNGENSÄGE **10609**
LÄNGENTEILMASCHINE **4104**

LÄNGESCHWINGUNG **7739**
LANGFRÄSMASCHINE IN HOBELMASCHINENFORM **9460**
LANGGESTRECKETER EINSCHLUSS **6841**
LANGHOBEL **7245**
LANGHOLZ **12939**
LANGLEITUNGSEFFEKT **7729**
LANGLOCH **8714**
LANGLOCHFRÄSMASCHINE **7281**
LANGNIPPEL **7726**
LÄNGSABBLATTERUNG **348**
LÄNGSACHSE **7733**
LANGSÄGEFÜHRUNG **10610**
LANGSAMES ABKÜHLEN **4230**
LANGSAMLAUFEN **10834**
LÄNGSDEHNUNG **4680**
LANGSDEHNUNG **7612**
LÄNGSDRUCKLAGER **12902**
LÄNGSDUKTILITÄT **7735**
LÄNGSFEDER **5059**
LÄNGSFINNE **12308**
LÄNGSKEIL **7276**
LÄNGSNAHTSCHWEISSEN **7737**
LÄNGSNASE **5059**
LÄNGSNIETTEILUNG **7736**
LÄNGSRIEGEL **7734**
LÄNGSSCHNITT **7738**
LÄNGSSCHUB **4734**
LÄNGSVERSCHIEBUNG **860**
LÄNGUNG EINES RIEMENS **12374**
LÄNGUNG EINES SEILES **12374**
LANOLIN **7391**
LANTHAN **7394**
LÄPPEN **7407**
LÄRCHENTERPENTIN **13527**
LARDÖL **7409**
LASCHE **1783**
LASCHE EINER ROLLENKETTE **11416**
LASCHENBOLZEN **5269**
LASCHENKETTE **12002**
LASCHENNIETUNG **1781**
LASCHENNIETUNG (DOPPELSEITIGE) **4130**
LASCHENNIETUNG (ZWEISEITIGE) **4130**
LASCHENVERBINDUNGEN **11932**
LAST **7679**
LAST (BEWEGLICHE) **7671**
LAST (BEWEGLICHE) **10706**
LAST (ELEKTRISCHE) **4546**
LAST (FAHRENDE) **10706**
LAST (GLEICHMÄSSIG VERTEILTE) **13366**
LAST (TOTE) **3631**
LAST (TOTE) **3633**

# LAS

844

LAST (VERTEILTE) **4078**
LAST (WANDERNDE) **10706**
LAST SENKEN (EINE) **7793**
LASTAUTO **8414**
LASTDRUCKBREMSE **7681**
LASTENAUFZUG **6007**
LASTENHEFT **11855**
LASTHAKEN **7552**
LASTKAHN **991**
LASTKETTE **6518**
LASTKRAFTWAGEN **7753**
LASTKRAFTWAGEN **8414**
LASTKRAFTWAGEN (DREIACHSIG) **12871**
LASTKRAFTWAGEN MIT PLANE UND SPRIEGEL **12686**
LASTMAGNET **7554**
LASTSCHEIBE **5040**
LASTVERTEILUNG **4081**
LASTVERTEILUNG **7684**
LASTWAGEN **7752**
LASTZANGE **7557**
LASURBLAU **13334**
LATERNE **7393**
LATERNE EINES SCHIEBERS **7392**
LATEX **7425**
LAUBSÄGE **5665**
LAUF **13181**
LAUFBÜCHSE (NASSE) **13804**
LAUFBÜCHSE (TROCKENE) **4348**
LAUFENDES BAND **1164**
LAUFENDES TRUMM EINES FLASCHENZUGES **10851**
LÄUFER **10767**
LÄUFER **10856**
LÄUFER (BAUW.) **12369**
LÄUFER EINER WAAGE **13160**
LAUFFLÄCHE **1116**
LAUFFLÄCHE EINES RADES **13173**
LAUFGEWICHT **13160**
LAUFGEWICHTSWAAGE **12225**
LAUFKATZE **13155**
LAUFKRAN **13156**
LAUFKRAN **8942**
LAUFKRANTRÄGER **13157**
LAUFRAD **10854**
LAUFRAD **6795**
LAUFRAD EINER TURBINE **13823**
LAUFRADSCHAUFEL EINER TURBINE **13820**
LAUFRILLE **13085**
LAUFRING **964**
LAUFRING **1111**
LAUFROLLE **10844**
LAUFSCHIENE **3293**

LAUFSEITE EINES RIEMENS **10853**
LAUFSITZ **10847**
LAUFSTEG **13616**
LAUGE **7835**
LAUGENSPRÖDIGKEIT **2118**
LÄUTERN **10370**
LÄUTERN **10377**
LÄUTWERK **1137**
LAVA **7437**
LAVE-VERFAHREN **7438**
LEBENDIGE KRAFT **7308**
LEBENSDAUER **7541**
LEBENSMITTELINDUSTRIE **5517**
LEBLANC-SODA **12445**
LECH **11878**
LECH **8058**
LECK **7486**
LECK **7488**
LECK SEIN **7487**
LECKEN **7487**
LECKEN **7492**
LECKSTELLE **7489**
LEDEBURIT **7504**
LEDER **7494**
LEDER (CHROMGARES) **2377**
LEDER (GERÖSTETES) **2272**
LEDERABFÄLLE **7497**
LEDERDICHTUNG **7502**
LEDERGLIEDERRIEMEN **7496**
LEDERHOCKANTRIEMEN **7376**
LEDERLASCHENKUPPLUNG **7501**
LEDERLEIM **11539**
LEDERLEIM **2140**
LEDERMANSCHETTE **3458**
LEDERMEMBRAN **7498**
LEDERPACKUNG **7502**
LEDERPOLIERSCHEIBE **1684**
LEDERRIEMEN **7503**
LEDERRIEMEN **7495**
LEDERRIEMENKUPPLUNG **7349**
LEDERSCHLAUCH **7499**
LEDERSTULP **3458**
LEDERSTULPDICHTUNG **3459**
LEERGANG (EINER WERKZEUGMASCHINE) **10529**
LEERLAUF **8598**
LEERLAUF **6752**
LEERLAUF **6755**
LEERLAUF (ERHÖHTER) **5038**
LEERLAUF (SCHNELLER) **5038**
LEERLAUFARBEIT **8601**
LEERLAUFBÜCHSE **7748**

## LEI

LEERLAUFDÜSE 11646
LEERLAUFEN 1081
LEERLAUFSPANNUNG 8808
LEERLAUFVERLUST 8599
LEERLAUFWIDERSTAND 8600
LEERLAUFZET 6753
LEERRAUM 13326
LEERSCHEIBE 7747
LEERSTELLE 13433
LEERZEIT 6753
LEESEITE 7505
LEGENDE 7513
LEGIEREN 361
LEGIERT 379
LEGIERT 371
LEGIERUNG 360
LEGIERUNG (BINÄRE) 1247
LEGIERUNG (FEUERFISTE) 393
LEGIERUNG (HITZE-UND KORROSIONSBESTÄNDIGE) 390
LEGIERUNG (HITZEBESTÄNDIGE) 391
LEGIERUNG (KORROSIONSBESTÄNDIGE) 387
LEGIERUNG (LEICHT SCHMELZBARE) 5757
LEGIERUNG (MAGNETISCHE) 392
LEGIERUNG (NATÜRLICHE) 8498
LEGIERUNG (NICHT-FEUERFESTE) 8622
LEGIERUNG (QUATERNÄRE EUTEKTISCHE) 10085
LEGIERUNG (QUATERNÄRE) 10084
LEGIERUNG (SÄUREBESTÄNDIGE) 384
LEGIERUNG (VERSCHLEISSFESTE) 383
LEGIERUNG GROSSER DICHTE 6481
LEGIERUNG MIT ALUMINIUM ALS GRUNDMETALL 439
LEGIERUNGEN (ABRIED-UND KORROSIONFESTE) 396
LEGIERUNGEN (NIEDRIG SCHMELZENDE) 7773
LEGIERUNGSABSCHEIDUNG 364
LEGIERUNGSKONTAMINATIONVERSEUCHUNG 365
LEGIERUNGSSYSTEM 381
LEGIERUNGSÜBERZUG 364
LEGIERWAAGSCHALE 362
LEHM 2465
LEHM 7691
LEHMBODEN 2466
LEHMFORM 7693
LEHMMÜHLE 9966
LEHMPATZEN 7692
LEHMSTEIN 7692
LEHRBOLZEN 3581
LEHRDORN 9531
LEHRDORN UND LOCHLEHRE 3581
LEHRE 5768
LEHRE 5769
LEHRE 5871

LEHRE (MIKROMETRISCHE) 8251
LEHRE (UNVERSTELLBARE) 8625
LEHRE (ZUSAMMENSTELLBARE) 4048
LEHRENBOHRMASCHINE 7228
LEHRGERÄT 3053
LEHRRING (NORMALE) 9431
LEHRSTÜCKE 5873
LEHRSTÜCKENMONTAGE 5884
LEICHTES KOHLENWASSERSTOFFGAS 8215
LEICHTFLÜSSIG 5471
LEICHTFLÜSSIGKEIT 5474
LEICHTMETALL 7564
LEICHTMETALL 7779
LEICHTMETALLDREHBANK 7565
LEICHTÖL 7570
LEICHTSIEDEND 1426
LEIM 5984
LEIMEN 5987
LEIMEN 5985
LEIMVERBAND 5986
LEIMZWINGE 2451
LEINEN 7619
LEINÖL 7631
LEINÖLFIRNIS 8786
LEINWAND 7619
LEISTEN 5940
LEISTENHOBEL 6544
LEISTUNG 5459
LEISTUNG 4463
LEISTUNG 9730
LEISTUNG 8908
LEISTUNG 8896
LEISTUNG (ABGEGEBENE) 13940
LEISTUNG (INDIZIERTE) 6875
LEISTUNG (TATSÄCHLICHE) 4458
LEISTUNG ABBREMSEN (DIE) 8083
LEISTUNGSFAKTOR 9735
LEISTUNGSFAKTORMESSER 9235
LEISTUNGSGEWICHT (FAHRFERTIG) 3480
LEISTUNGSMESSER 4403
LEISTUNGSREGLER 8909
LEISTUNGSVERLUST 7762
LEITBLECH 921
LEITBLECH 922
LEITEN (ELEKTRIZITÄTWÄRME) 2913
LEITEND (WÄRMEELEKTRIZITÄT) 2918
LEITER (ELEKTR.) 2921
LEITER (ELEKTRISCHER) 4537
LEITER (SPANNUNGSLOSER) 3627
LEITER (STROMLOSER) 3627
LEITER (UNTER SPANNUNG STEHENDER) 7670

# LEI

LEITFÄHIGKEIT **2919**
LEITFÄHIGKEIT (ELEKTRISCHE) **4536**
LEITFÄHIGKEIT (THERMO-ELEKTRISCHE) **10044**
LEITFÄHIGKEITSMOLARE **8350**
LEITKUPFER OHNE SAUERSTOFF **8983**
LEITLINIE **3996**
LEITRAD **6168**
LEITRAD EINER TURBINE **6168**
LEITROLLE **6161**
LEITSALZE **2915**
LEITSCHAUFEL EINER TURBINE **6167**
LEITSPINDEL **7471**
LEITSPINDEL **6165**
LEITSPINDELDREHBANK **7428**
LEITSTRAHL **10170**
LEITUNG **9339**
LEITUNG (ELEKTRISCHE) **4523**
LEITUNG (FALLENDE) **3791**
LEITUNG (UNTERIRDISCHE) **13353**
LEITUNGSDRAHT **2922**
LEITUNGSDRUCK **9822**
LEITUNGSKABEL **1825**
LEITUNGSKANAL **8807**
LEITUNGSMAST **7608**
LEITUNGSNETZ **4080**
LEITUNGSSCHUH **1827**
LEITUNGSWASSER **13075**
LEITUNGSWIDERSTAND (ELEKTR.) **10491**
LEITWIDERSTAND (SPEZIFISCHER) **10503**
LEMNISKATE **7514**
LENARD-STRAHLEN **7515**
LENKGESTÄNGE **12232**
LENKGETRIEBE **12229**
LENKRAD **12233**
LENKSÄULE **12228**
LENKSTOCKHEBEL **9414**
LENKSTOCKHEBEL **12227**
LEONARD-EFFEKT **7523**
LESEN **10252**
LEUCHTBOMBE **7573**
LEUCHTDICHTE **7104**
LEUCHTGAS **6775**
LEUCHTGASLAMPE **5826**
LEUCHTKRAFT **6776**
LEUCHTÖL **7275**
LEUCHTPETROLEUM **7275**
LEUCHTSCHIRM **13568**
LEUCHTSCHIRM **5477**
LIBELLE **13259**
LICHBOGEN(ELEKTRO)OFEN **4495**
LICHSTÄRKE **7822**

LICHT **7560**
LICHT (DIFFUSES) **3927**
LICHT (ELEKTRISCHES) **4517**
LICHT (KÜNSTLICHES) **734**
LICHT (POLARISIERTES) **9585**
LICHT (REFLEKTIERTES) **10383**
LICHT (ZERSTREUTES) **3927**
LICHT (ZURÜCKGEWORFENES) **10383**
LICHT BOGEN-WIDERSTANDSOFEN **10485**
LICHTBILD **9263**
LICHTBOGEN (ELEKTR.) **4494**
LICHTBOGEN-ARBEITSSPANNUNG **679**
LICHTBOGEN-HARTLÖTEN **666**
LICHTBOGEN-SCHWEISSEN (TEILAUTOMATISCHES) **11166**
LICHTBOGEN-SCHWEISSMASCHINE **680**
LICHTBOGENOFEN **668**
LICHTBOGENOFEN (DIREKTER) **671**
LICHTBOGENOFEN (DIREKTER) **667**
LICHTBOGENOFEN (INDIREKTER) **669**
LICHTBOGENSCHWEISSEN **683**
LICHTBOGENSCHWEISSEN **682**
LICHTBOGENSCHWEISSEN MIT WECHSELSTROM **685**
LICHTBOGENSCHWEISSUNG **681**
LICHTBOGENSPANNUNG **676**
LICHTBRECHEND **10402**
LICHTBRECHUNG **10400**
LICHTBRECHUNGSVERMÖGEN **10403**
LICHTDICHT **7572**
LICHTDURCHGANG **9099**
LICHTDURCHLÄSSIG **3869**
LICHTDURCHLÄSSIGKEIT **3868**
LICHTE WEITE EINES ROHRES **1464**
LICHTEINHEIT **9270**
LICHTGESCHWINDIGKEIT **7569**
LICHTGESCHWINDIGKEIT **13517**
LICHTHOFBILDUNG **6203**
LICHTINTENSITÄT **7822**
LICHTISTÄRKEMESSUNG **9271**
LICHTKEGEL **2932**
LICHTLEITUNG (ELEKTRISCHE) **4519**
LICHTMASCHINE **4402**
LICHTMASCHINE **5924**
LICHTPAUSAPPARAT **9874**
LICHTPAUSE **9276**
LICHTPAUSE (NEGATIVE) **1375**
LICHTPAUSE (POSITIVE) **1373**
LICHTPAUSPAPIER **9257**
LICHTPHÄNOMEN **7566**
LICHTQUELLE **7568**
LICHTQUELLE **11826**
LICHTSCHWINGUNG **7825**

| | |
|---|---|
| LICHTSPIEGEL **10394** | LINKSVERSCHIEBUNG **7507** |
| LICHTSTÄRKEMESSER **9267** | LINKSWEINSÄURE **7364** |
| LICHTSTRAHL **7824** | LINOLEUM **7630** |
| LICHTSTRAHLENBÜNDEL **9162** | LINSE **7522** |
| LICHTSTRAHLUNG **10147** | LINSE (BIKONKAVE) **1237** |
| LICHTSTROM **7821** | LINSE (BIKONVEXE) **1238** |
| LICHTUNDURCHLÄSSIG **7572** | LINSE (KOKAVE) **4095** |
| LICHTWELLE **7571** | LINSE (KONKAVKONVEXE) **8147** |
| LIDERN **8990** | LINSE (KONVEXE) **2910** |
| LIDERUNG **9009** | LINSE (PLANKONKAVE) **9458** |
| LIDERUNGSRING **9007** | LINSE (PLANKONVEXE) **9459** |
| LIEFERMENGE EINER PUMPE **10228** | LINSENSYSTEM **12576** |
| LIEFERUNGSBEDINGUNGEN **3737** | LIQUIDUSLINIE **7661** |
| LIEFERUNGSVERZUG **3731** | LITER **7669** |
| LIEFERWAGEN **13474** | LITHIUM **7664** |
| LIEFERWALZE **5074** | LITHIUMCHLORID **7666** |
| LIEFERZUSTAND (IM) **741** | LITHIUMKARBONAT **7665** |
| LIEGEND **6578** | LITHLUMFLUORID **7667** |
| LIEGENDE FRÄSMASCHINE **6589** | LITZE **12336** |
| LIGNIN **7577** | LITZE EINES SEILES **12339** |
| LIGNIT **7578** | LIZENZ (PATENTRECHTLICHE) **7539** |
| LIGROIN **7580** | LIZENZINHABER **7540** |
| LIMBUS **6026** | LOCH **6530** |
| LIMONIT **7596** | LOCH (BLINDES) **3630** |
| LIMOUSINE **11521** | LOCH (DURCHGEHENDES) **12893** |
| LINEAL **10831** | LOCH (GEBOHRTES) **4273** |
| LINEARZEICHNUNG **8905** | LOCH (GEGOSSENES) **2033** |
| LINER (GESCHLITZER) **11639** | LOCH (NICHT DURCHGEHENDES) **3630** |
| LINER (KIESBEDECKTER) **9783** | LOCH (VORGEBOHRTES) **10782** |
| LINIE **7597** | LOCHBEITEL **8398** |
| LINIE (ATMOSPHÄRISCHE) **798** | LOCHEISEN **6545** |
| LINIE (AUSGEZOGENE) **5725** | LOCHEISENHOHLRÄUME **6514** |
| LINIE (GEBROCHENE) **7166** | LOCHEN **10008** |
| LINIE (GESTRICHELTE) **4125** | LOCHEN **10006** |
| LINIE (PUNKTIERTE) **4125** | LOCHEN **9999** |
| LINIE (STRICHPUNKTIERTE) **2205** | LOCHER **9997** |
| LINIE GLEICHEN DRUCKES **7177** | LÖCHER STANZEN **9999** |
| LINIE GLEICHEN RAUMINHALTES **7187** | LOCHFRASS **9418** |
| LINIEN (LÜDERSCHE) **7815** | LOCHKANTE **4447** |
| LINIEN (NEUMANNSCHE) **8540** | LOCHKARTE **10002** |
| LINIENENDE **4731** | LOCHKREIS **1433** |
| LINIENINTEGRAL **7600** | LOCHKREISDURCHMESSER **3853** |
| LINIENNETZ (QUADRATISCHES) **6099** | LOCHKREUZDURCHMESSER **1438** |
| LINIENSPEKTRUM **7610** | LOCHLEHRE **6608** |
| LINKSDREHEND **7365** | LOCHLEHRE **7066** |
| LINKSDREHEND **3237** | LOCHLEIBUNG **13624** |
| LINKSDREHUNG **3238** | LOCHLINER **9187** |
| LINKSGEWICKELT **3239** | LOCHMASCHINE **10009** |
| LINKSGEWINDE **7508** | LOCHMASCHINE **9296** |
| LINKSGEWUNDEN **3239** | LOCHMASCHINE MIT SCHERE **10007** |
| LINKSSCHWEISSUNG **5539** | LOCHMUTTER **6533** |

# LOC

848

LOCHNAHTSCHWEISSUNG 9536
LOCHPLATTE 12531
LOCHPRESS 10001
LOCHRAND 4447
LOCHRINGÖFFNUNG 6532
LOCHSÄGE 2802
LOCHSTAHL 6545
LOCHSTANZE 10009
LOCHSTANZE 10001
LOCHSTEIN 245
LOCHSTEMPEL 9997
LOCHSTREIFEN 10005
LOCHSTREIFENEINGABE 12643
LOCHSTREIFENENDE 4725
LOCHTASTER 6975
LOCHVERSUCH 10010
LOCHWAND 13624
LOCHWEITE 3857
LOCHWINKEL 3781
LOCHZANGE 10000
LOCHZIEGEL 245
LOCHZIRKEL 6975
LOCKER WERDEN 11559
LOCKERN (SICH) 11559
LOCKERUNG 11560
LOCKERWERDEN 11560
LÖFFELBOHRER 11957
LOGARITHMENTAFEL 7721
LOGARITHMUS 7718
LOGARITHMUS (BRIGG'SSCHER) 2788
LOGARITHMUS (GEMEINER) 2788
LOGARITHMUS (HYPERBOLISCHER) 8509
LOGARITHMUS (NATÜRLICHER) 8509
LOHE (VERBRAUCHTE) 12635
LOHGARES 8704
LOHKÄSE 12612
LOHKUCHEN 12612
LOHN 13613
LOHNARBEIT 3621
LOHNSKALA (GLEITENDE) 11607
LOKALANGRIFF 7695
LOKALELEMENT 7694
LOKALHEIZUNG 7696
LOKALKORROSION 7695
LOKOMOBILE 9640
LOKOMOBILE (FESTSTEHENDE) 11175
LOKOMOBILE (ORTSFESTE) 11175
LOKOMOBILE (STATIONÄRE) 11175
LOKOMOTIVE 7713
LOKOMOTIVE (ELEKTRISCHE) 4520
LOKOMOTIVKESSEL 7714

LOS 7766
LÖSBARE KUPPLUNG 4033
LÖSCHE 2659
LÖSCHEN DES KALKES 11569
LÖSCHPAPIER 1350
LOSE AUFGESETZT (AUF DIE WELLE) 7749
LÖSEN 4059
LÖSEN (EINE BREMSE) 10436
LÖSEN (SICH) 4061
LÖSEN EINES KEILS 7751
LOSKEILEN 7750
LOSKUPPELN 10034
LÖSLICH 11807
LÖSLICH MACHEN 10456
LÖSLICHKEIT 11806
LOSLÖTEN 13399
LOSLÖTEN 13400
LÖSS 7716
LOSSCHEIBE 7747
LOSSCHRAUBEN 13396
LOSSCHRAUBEN 13395
LÖSUNG 11811
LÖSUNG (ALKOHOLISCHE) 315
LÖSUNG (AMMONIAKALISCHE) 457
LÖSUNG (ANGEREICHERTE) 2883
LÖSUNG (FESTE) 11794
LÖSUNG (GESÄTTIGTE) 10941
LÖSUNG (KONZENTRIERTE) 2883
LÖSUNG (RECHNERISCHE) 8694
LÖSUNG (SCHWACHE) 13706
LÖSUNG (ÜBERSÄTTIGTE) 12478
LÖSUNG (UNGESÄTTIGTE) 13394
LÖSUNG (WÄSSRIGE) 661
LÖSUNG (ZAHLENMÄSSIGE) 8694
LÖSUNG (ZEICHNERISCHE) 6060
LÖSUNG EINES KEILS 7751
LÖSUNGSBREMSE 3638
LÖSUNGSGLÜHEN 11812
LÖSUNGSMITTEL 11814
LÖSUNGSMITTEL (IONISIERENDES) 7130
LÖSUNGSMITTEL FÜR KORROSION 3192
LÖSUNGSSPANNUNG 4609
LÖSUNGSSTOFFE 8061
LÖSUNGSVERMÖGEN 4062
LOT 9539
LOT 11755
LOT 9217
LOT (SAURES) 110
LÖTAUFBRINGEMITTEL 5490
LÖTBRENNER FÜR VERDICHTETEN SAUERSTOFF 2848
LÖTEISEN 11765

LÖTEN 11756
LÖTEN 11762
LÖTFLUSSMITTEL 5490
LÖTKOLBEN 11765
LÖTKOLBEN 11764
LÖTKOLBEN (ELEKTRISCHER) 4530
LÖTKOLBEN MIT SELBSTBEHEIZUNG 11155
LÖTLAMPE 11766
LÖTMITTEL 11755
LÖTOFEN 11763
LÖTPASTE 9108
LOTRECHTE 9217
LÖTROHR 1355
LÖTROHR (ELEKTRISCHES) 4496
LÖTROHR MIT MUNDSTÜCK 8433
LÖTROHRPROBE 1356
LÖTSTELLE 11761
LÖTUNG 11762
LÖTVERBINDUNG 11759
LÖTWASSER 7293
LÖTZANGE 11767
LÖTZINN 11742
LÖWENHERZGEWINDE 7792
LUBRIZITÄT 7813
LÜCKE 13433
LÜCKENSUCHGERÄT 6534
LÜDERSFLIESSFIGUREN 7622
LUDERSLINIEN 12371
LUFT 243
LUFT (ATMOSPHÄRISCHE) 240
LUFT (FLÜSSIGE) 7643
LUFT (KOMPRIMIERTE) 2839
LUFT (TROCKNE) 4339
LUFT (VERDICHTETE) 2839
LUFT (VERDÜNNTE) 10213
LUFTABSTAND 262
LUFTABZUG (AUTOMATISCHER) 1320
LUFTABZUG (FREIER) 5642
LUFTANSAUGEVENTIL 11694
LUFTBEWEGUNGSLEHRE 215
LUFTBLASE 1670
LUFTDÄMPFUNG 255
LUFTDICHT 303
LUFTDICHT 6447
LUFTDRUCK 794
LUFTDRUCKBREMSE 2840
LUFTDRUCKLEHRE 218
LUFTDRUCKPUMPE 273
LUFTDURCHLÄSSIG 9212
LUFTEINLASS 289
LUFTEINLASS 270

LUFTEINSPRITZUNGMASCHINE 299
LUFTELEKTRIZITÄT 796
LÜFTER 5033
LUFTERHITZER 287
LUFTFEUCHTIGKEIT 6666
LUFTFILTER 260
LUFTGAS 264
LUFTHAHN 293
LUFTHAMMER 9553
LUFTHÄRTUNG 285
LUFTHÄRTUNG 267
LUFTHEIZUNG 268
LUFTHEIZUNG 6616
LUFTKABEL 8938
LUFTKAMMER 246
LUFTKAPPENVERSTELLUNG (AUTOMATISCHE) 838
LUFTKISSEN 254
LUFTKOLBEN 282
LUFTKOMPRESSOR 249
LUFTKÜHLUNG 252
LUFTLEEREMESSER 13442
LUFTLEERER 13434
LUFTLEITUNG 212
LUFTLEITUNG 281
LUFTLOCH 269
LUFTMÖRTEL 8854
LUFTMOTOR 6615
LUFTPATENTIEREN 280
LUFTPISTOLE 276
LUFTPOLSTER 254
LUFTPUFFER 256
LUFTPUMPE 284
LUFTPUMPE (NASSE) 13799
LUFTPUMPE (TROCKNE) 4340
LUFTREIBUNG 10492
LUFTSAUGEBREMSE 13436
LUFTSCHACHT 291
LUFTSCHICHT 2124
LUFTSCHIEBER 3603
LUFTSCHLAUCH 6955
LUFTSCHLEUSE 274
LUFTSEILBAHN 213
LUFTSPALT 262
LUFTSPALT EINES MAGNETEN 263
LUFTSTECHEN 3166
LUFTSTOSS 242
LUFTSTRAHL 242
LUFTSTRECKE 262
LUFTSTROM 253
LUFTSTROMREGLER 3465
LUFTTEMPERATUR 12728

**LUF** 850

LUFTTHERMOMETER 265
LUFTTRICHTER 2359
LÜFTUNG 13530
LÜFTUNG (KÜNSTLICHE) 738
LÜFTUNG (NATÜRLICHE) 8508
LÜFTUNGSBREMSE 3638
LÜFTUNGSÖFFNUNG 13528
LUFTVENTIL 259
LUFTVENTIL 276
LUFTVERDICHTER 249
LUFTVERDICHTUNG 2858
LUFTVERDÜNNUNG 10212
LUFTWIDERSTAND 10492
LUFTZIEGEL 7692
LUFTZUFUHR 12486
LUFTZUG 257
LUFTZWISCHENRAUM 262
LUMEN 7818
LUMINESZENZ 7819
LUNGER 9340
LUNKER 9340
LUNKER 11505
LUNKER 11393
LUNKER 2124
LUNKER 1362
LUPE 7936
LUPPE 1345
LUPPEN 1349
LUTETIUM 7833
LUTTE 247
LUVSEITE 13721
LUX 7834
LYRA 4913
MADENSCHRAUBE 6156
MAGAZIN 12297
MAGERES GAS 9890
MAGERKALK 9623
MAGNALIUM 7878
MAGNESIA 7879
MAGNESIA (GEBRANNTE) 1842
MAGNESIA (GEMAHLENE) 9725
MAGNESIA-KIESELSÄURE 7888
MAGNESIA-SCHWEFELSÄURE 7889
MAGNESIAKOHLENSÄURE 7884
MAGNESIT 7880
MAGNESIT (TOTGEBRANNTER) 3639
MAGNESITSTEIN 7881
MAGNESIUM 7882
MAGNESIUMBIKARBONAT 7883
MAGNESIUMCHLORID 7885
MAGNESIUMFLUORID 7886

MAGNESIUMHYDROXYD 7887
MAGNESIUMKARBONAT 7884
MAGNESIUMLEGIERUNG 7890
MAGNESIUMOXYD 7879
MAGNESIUMPHOSPHAT 8656
MAGNESIUMSILIKAT 7888
MAGNESIUMSULFAT (ENGLISCHES) 7889
MAGNET 7891
MAGNET (KÜNSTLICHER) 735
MAGNET (NATÜRLICHER) 8506
MAGNET-PLANSCHEIBEN 7912
MAGNETANKER 710
MAGNETBAND 7919
MAGNETBREMSKLOTZ 8188
MAGNETEISENERZ 7927
MAGNETEISENSTEIN 7927
MAGNETFUTTER 7898
MAGNETHAMMER 7921
MAGNETISCH 7893
MAGNETISCH WERDEN 1126
MAGNETISCH. EISENOXYD 7927
MAGNETISCHE STRÖMUNG 7903
MAGNETISCHER KRAFTFLUSS 7903
MAGNETISCHES MAGAZIN 7377
MAGNETISIERBAR 7922
MAGNETISIEREN 7924
MAGNETISIEREN 7923
MAGNETISIERUNG 7928
MAGNETISIERUNG 7923
MAGNETISIERUNG 7906
MAGNETISIERUNGSKOEFFIZIENT 7918
MAGNETISIERUNGSVERLUSTE 7907
MAGNETISM 7926
MAGNETISMUS 7926
MAGNETISMUS (FREIER) 5640
MAGNETISMUS (GEBUNDENER) 7417
MAGNETISMUS (PERMANENTER) 9206
MAGNETISMUS (REMANENTER) 10445
MAGNETIT 7927
MAGNETKIES 7914
MAGNETNADEL 7909
MAGNETOMOTORISCHE KRAFT 7929
MAGNETOSKOPIE 7910
MAGNETOSTRIKTION 7933
MAGNETPOL 7913
MAGNETPOL 9595
MAGNETPULVER-PRÜFVERFAHREN 7877
MAGNETSPANNFUTTER 7897
MAGNETSTAHL 7892
MAGNETSTEIN 7927
MAGNETVENTIL 11774

851 MAS

MÄHBINDER UND ERNTEMASCHINEN **1251**
MÄHDRESCHER UND ZUSÄTZLICHE ANLAGE **2766**
MÄHHÄCKSLER **5525**
MAHLEN **6103**
MAHLEN **8287**
MAHLEN **6106**
MAHLEN **6117**
MAHLSTEIN **8298**
MÄHMASCHINEN (DURCH TRAKTOREN ANGETRIEBEN) UND HALBSATTELMÄHMASCHINEN **8439**
MÄHNENHAAR **7965**
MAKROÄTZUNG **7870**
MAKROGRAPHIE **7871**
MAKROPHOTOGRAPHIE **9266**
MAKROSEIGERUNG **7876**
MAKROSKOPISCH **7872**
MALACHIT **6089**
MALAKKAZINN **12335**
MALPINSEL **9019**
MANGAN **7966**
MANGAN (ELEKTROLYTISCHES) **4599**
MANGAN-SESQUIOXYD **7970**
MANGANBRONZE **7967**
MANGANCHLORÜR **7972**
MANGANDIOXYD **10047**
MANGANEISEN **5110**
MANGANHALTIG **7971**
MANGANHYPEROXYD **10047**
MANGANMONOXYD **7973**
MANGANOCHLORID **7972**
MANGANOSULFAT **7974**
MANGANOXYDUL **7973**
MANGANOXYDULOXYD **13207**
MANGANSTAHL **7968**
MANGANSUPEROXYD **10047**
MÄNGEL **11537**
MANGELRAD **7975**
MANILAHANF **7980**
MANILAHANFSEIL **7981**
MANNESMANNROHR **7983**
MANNLOCH **7963**
MANNLOCH **7997**
MANNLOCHDECKEL **7977**
MANNLOCHRING **7978**
MANNLOCHRING **7998**
MANO-VAKUUMMETER **2830**
MANOMETER **9820**
MANOMETER **9821**
MANOMETER (REGISTRIERENDES) **10292**
MANOSTAT **9835**
MANSCHETTE **11576**

MANSCHETTENDICHTUNG **3459**
MANTEL **11303**
MANTEL **7986**
MANTELBLECH **11335**
MANTELELEKTRODE **3271**
MANTELELEKTRODE **2584**
MANTELENDE EINES ROHRES **11901**
MANTELFLÄCHE EINES KEGELS **2949**
MANTELFLÄCHE EINES ZYLINDERS **3590**
MANTELFRÄSER **13848**
MANTELROHR **7469**
MANTISSE **7985**
MANUSKRIPT **7996**
MARINEKOLBEN **2944**
MARINEKOPF **8007**
MARINELEIM **8006**
MARK DES HOLZES **9413**
MARKIEREN **8008**
MARKIEREN **8015**
MARKSTRAHL **8128**
MARMOR **8001**
MARSEILLER SEIFE **8020**
MARTENSIT **8022**
MARTENSIT **8000**
MARTENSIT (NADELFÖRMIGER) **103**
MARTENSITHÄRTUNG (GESTAFFELTE) **12243**
MARTIN-STAHL **8816**
MASCHE **8169**
MASCHENGRÖSSE **8170**
MASCHENWEITE **11523**
MASCHINABSCHNEIDEN **7842**
MASCHINE **9859**
MASCHINE **7839**
MASCHINE (DIREKTGEKUPPELTE) **3982**
MASCHINE (ELEKTRISCHE) **4522**
MASCHINE (FREISTEHENDE) **11151**
MASCHINE (KURZHÜBIGE) **11374**
MASCHINE (LANGHÜBIGE) **7731**
MASCHINE (LANGSAMLAUFENDE) **7789**
MASCHINE (LIEGENDE) **6582**
MASCHINE (MAGNETELEKTRISCHE) **7930**
MASCHINE (STEHENDE) **13546**
MASCHINE FÜR RIEMENANTRIEB **1145**
MASCHINE FÜR SEILANTRIEB **10736**
MASCHINE FÜR SONDERZWECKE **11486**
MASCHINE MIT EINZELANTRIEB **6863**
MASCHINE MIT ZAHNRADANTRIEB **5893**
MASCHINELL **7850**
MASCHINELL ANGETRIEBEN **8119**
MASCHINEN FÜR MAULWURFSDRÄNUNG **8344**
MASCHINEN HERGESTELLT (MIT) **7850**

**MAS** 852

MASCHINEN ZUM AUFZIEHEN DES HEUES IN SCHWADEN 13869
MASCHINEN ZUM BEDECKEN DER KARTOFFELPFLANZEN 9702
MASCHINENAGGREGAT **6151**
MASCHINENANTRIEB **9734**
MASCHINENARBEIT **7860**
MASCHINENARBEITER **7868**
MASCHINENBAU **8103**
MASCHINENBAUANSTALT **4764**
MASCHINENBAUINGENIEUR **8102**
MASCHINENBETRIEB **9734**
MASCHINENBETRIEB (FÜR) **8119**
MASCHINENBRONZE **12984**
MASCHINENEINRICHTUNG **7862**
MASCHINENFABRIK **4764**
MASCHINENFORMUNG **7851**
MASCHINENFÜHRER **4765**
MASCHINENFUNDAMENT **7848**
MASCHINENGEBÄUDE **4753**
MASCHINENGEWINDEBOHRER **7858**
MASCHINENGUSS **4763**
MASCHINENGUSS **7863**
MASCHINENHALLE **7855**
MASCHINENHALLE **4757**
MASCHINENHAUS **4753**
MASCHINENNIETUNG **7854**
MASCHINENÖL **4755**
MASCHINENRAHMEN **5626**
MASCHINENRAUM **4757**
MASCHINENREIBAHLE **7853**
MASCHINENSÄGE **9747**
MASCHINENSATZ **6151**
MASCHINENSÄTZE **4524**
MASCHINENSCHERE **11292**
MASCHINENSCHLEIFEN **7849**
MASCHINENSCHLOSSER **5278**
MASCHINENSCHMIEDEN **7847**
MASCHINENSCHRAUBE **7840**
MASCHINENSCHWEISSEN **8115**
MASCHINENSTÄNDER **12078**
MASCHINENTEIL **7852**
MASCHINENTEIL ERNEUERN (EINEN) **10457**
MASCHINENTORF **9804**
MASCHINENWÄRTER **4765**
MASCHINENWELLE **4758**
MASCHINENWERKSTATT **7855**
MASCHINENWERKSTATT **7856**
MASCHINENZEICHNUNG **7843**
MASCHINIST **4765**
MASKENFORMEN **11333**

MASS **8077**
MASS (METRISCHES) **8227**
MASSABFERTIGUNG **11524**
MASSANALYSE (VOLUMETRISCHE) **13601**
MASSBEZEICHNUNG **3956**
MASSE **3960**
MASSE **4409**
MASSE **2827**
MASSE **8026**
MASSE (AUFGESCHÜTTETE) **969**
MASSEINHEIT **13375**
MASSEKABEL **4411**
MASSEKERN **3142**
MASSEL **9302**
MASSENABSORPTIONSKOEFFIZIENT **8030**
MASSENAUSGLEICH **941**
MASSENEFFEKT **8027**
MASSENEINHEIT **13374**
MASSENFABRIKATION **8028**
MASSENHERSTELLUNG **8028**
MASSENMITTELPUNKT **2168**
MASSENSPEKTROMETER **8029**
MASSENVERTEILUNG **4082**
MASSFLÜSSIGKEIT **12084**
MASSICOT **8031**
MASSLINIE **3957**
MASSPFEIL **3395**
MASSSCHLEIFEN **9755**
MASSSTAB **8085**
MASSSTAB **10982**
MASSSTAB **10968**
MASSSTAB (IN NATÜRLICHEM) **5723**
MASSSTAB (IN VERGRÖSSERTEM) **10970**
MASSSTAB (IN VERJÜNGTEM) **10343**
MASSSTAB EINER ZEICHNUNG **10973**
MASSSTÄBLICH VERGRÖSSERT **10970**
MASSSTÄBLICH VERKLEINERT **10343**
MASSSYSTEM **12578**
MASSSYSTEM (ABSOLUTES) **2159**
MASSZAHL **3956**
MASSZEICHNUNG **3959**
MASTIX **8039**
MASURIUM **8040**
MASUT **6408**
MASUT **8041**
MATERIAL **8050**
MATERIAL (PORENERZEUGENDES) **9628**
MATERIAL ÜBERANSTRENGEN (EIN) **8962**
MATERIALFEHLER **3680**
MATERIALFEHLER **3692**
MATERIALFESTIGKEIT **12355**

MATERIALKOSTEN **8049**
MATERIALPRÜFUNG **12782**
MATERIE **12419**
MATHEMATIK **8053**
MATRIZE **8055**
MATRIZE **3883**
MATRIZENSPUR **3888**
MATTBEIZEN **3628**
MATTBRENNE **8059**
MATTBRENNEN **3628**
MATTGESCHLIFFEN **10938**
MATTGLAS **5701**
MATTIEREN **12685**
MATTSCHEIBE **6145**
MATTVERCHROMUNG **4366**
MAUERANKER **500**
MAUERKASTEN **13617**
MAUERN **1601**
MAUERN **1597**
MAUERPLATTE **13621**
MAUERSTEIN **1596**
MAUERVERBAND **1444**
MAUERWERK **8025**
MAUERZIEGEL **1596**
MAULRINGSCHLÜSSEL **2764**
MAXIMALE OBERFLÄCHENTEMPERATUR **6654**
MAXIMALGEWICHT **8070**
MAXIMALTEMPERATUR **8068**
MAXIMALWERT **8069**
MAXIMUM-UND MINIMUM-THERMOMETER **8063**
MAZERATION **7837**
MAZERIEREN **7836**
MCQUAID-EHN-PRÜFUNG **8071**
MECHANIK **8121**
MECHANIK DER LUFT **9558**
MECHANISCH **8093**
MECHANISCH **8119**
MECHANISCH **7850**
MECHANISCHE WÄRMELEHRE **12829**
MECHANISMUS **8122**
MEDAILLENBRONZE **8183**
MEDIANE **8124**
MEDIUM (DURCHSICHTIGES) **13139**
MEDIUM (LEITENDES) **2914**
MEDIUM (STRAHLENBRECHENDES) **10401**
MEERESHÖHE **11070**
MEERESSAND **11071**
MEERESSPIEGEL **11070**
MEERWASSER **11072**
MEGADYN **8129**
MEGAVOLT **8130**

MEGERG **8131**
MEGOHM **8132**
MEHRARBEIT **4880**
MEHRFACHBUCKELSCHWEISSEN **8468**
MEHRFACHEXPANSIONSMASCHINE **8477**
MEHRFACHFORM **8466**
MEHRFACHRIEMEN **8463**
MEHRFACHSYSTEM **8472**
MEHRLAGENSCHWEISSEN **8455**
MEHRLAGENSCHWEISSUNG **13757**
MEHRLOCHDÜSE **8452**
MEHRPHASENSTROM **8462**
MEHRROLLENPROFILIERMASCHINE **8457**
MEHRSCHICHTMETALL **7379**
MEHRSPINDEL-BOHRMASCHINE **5799**
MEHRSPINDELAUTOMAT **8469**
MEHRSPINDELBOHRKOPF **8459**
MEHRSPINDLIGE BOHRMASCHINE IN REIHENANORDNUNG
    **8460**
MEHRSTOFFPRESSLING **2828**
MEHRWEGEVENTIL **8467**
MEHRZWECKMACHINE **8456**
MEHRZYLINDERMASCHINE **8453**
MEILE (ENGLISCHE) **8272**
MEISSEL **2349**
MEISSELKLAPPENHALTER **2454**
MEISSELN **2344**
MEISSELN **2347**
MEISSELSATZ **5801**
MEISSELSPAN **2343**
MEISSELWINKEL **12995**
MEISTER **5541**
MELAPHYR **8133**
MELDEVORRICHTUNG **305**
MEMBRAN **3870**
MEMBRAN-REGELVENTIL **3872**
MEMBRAN-VENTIL **3876**
MEMBRANFEDER **3875**
MEMBRANPUMPE **3874**
MEMBRANPUMPE **61**
MEMBRANVENTIL **13453**
MENGENBESTIMMUNG **10064**
MENGENMESSER **5458**
MENGENMESSER **13604**
MENGENREGLER **13600**
MENGENVERHÄLTNIS **3011**
MENNIGEKITT **10332**
MENSCHENKRAFT **9738**
MERGEL **8019**
MERGEL (KIESELIGER) **11439**
MERKURBLENDE **2400**

**MER** 854

MERKURICHLORID **8153**
MERKURIJODID **8155**
MERKURINITRAT **8156**
MERKURIOXYD **8157**
MERKURISULFAT **8158**
MERKUROCHLORID **8159**
MERKURONITRAT **8160**
MERKUROOXYD **8161**
MERKUROSULFAT **8162**
MERKZEICHEN **8012**
MESSBAND **8092**
MESSBEREICH **10201**
MESSBRÜCHIGKEIT **6641**
MESSDORN (ZYLINDRISCHER) **3587**
MESSEN **8088**
MESSEN **8078**
MESSER **7323**
MESSER (MAGNETISCHER) **7905**
MESSER (PNEUMATISCHER) **283**
MESSERDRUCK **5771**
MESSERFEILE **7324**
MESSERKOPF **6971**
MESSFEHLER **8089**
MESSFÜHLER **9882**
MESSGERÄT **8090**
MESSGERÄT **5768**
MESSGRÖSSE **10070**
MESSING **14008**
MESSING **1562**
MESSING (HOCHWERTIGES) **6480**
MESSING (NIEDRIGLEGIERTES) **7768**
MESSINGBLECH **11307**
MESSINGBLECH **1569**
MESSINGDRAHT **1571**
MESSINGGIESSEREI **1566**
MESSINGKNÜPPEL **1563**
MESSINGLOT **11880**
MESSINGROHR **1570**
MESSINGWALZDRAHT **1568**
MESSINSTRUMENT **8090**
MESSMASCHINE VON WHITWORTH **13843**
MESSPIPETTE **6028**
MESSPUNKT **8091**
MESSRAD **3501**
MESSROLLE DES PLANIMETERS **13817**
MESSSTAB **8085**
MESSSTAB-UND LUFTLOCH **3972**
MESSSTABLOCH **3971**
MESSUHR **3842**
MESSUNG **8088**
MESSVERFAHREN **8219**

MESSWERTERFASSUNG (ABSOLUTE) **31**
MESSZYLINDER **3582**
MESSZYLINDER **5960**
METAKIESELSÄURE **8211**
METALFOLIE **5508**
METALL **8173**
METALL (GEDIEGENES) **9853**
METALL (GEDIEGENES) **13570**
METALL (GEHÄMMERTES) **6221**
METALL (POLYKRISTALLINES) **9617**
METALL (UNEDLES) **1031**
METALL (VERFORMUNGSFREIESIN METALLFORM GEGOSSENES **2337**
METALL EDLES **8603**
METALL GROSSER DICHTE **6482**
METALL HÄRTEN (EIN) **6285**
METALL IM SCHMELZZUSTAND **6631**
METALL VEREDELN (EIN) **10371**
METALL-AUFSPRITZEN **8201**
METALL-KERAMIKMISCHUNG (GESINTERTE) **2192**
METALL-LICHTBOGEN **8174**
METALL-LICHTBOGEN-SCHWEISSEN MIT UMHÜLLTER ELEKTRODE **11345**
METALL-LICHTBOGENSCHNEIDEN **8175**
METALL-LICHTBOGENSCHWEISSEN **8176**
METALL-LICHTBOGENSCHWEISSEN OHNE SCHUTZGAS **13397**
METALLAUSDEHNUNG **4919**
METALLBAROMETER **504**
METALLBEARBEITUNG **8192**
METALLBEARBEITUNGSMASCHINE **8178**
METALLBLOCK **6919**
METALLBÜRSTEN-FERTIGBEARBEITUNG **11016**
METALLDRAHTLAMPE **8181**
METALLDREHBANK **8191**
METALLDRÜCKEN **8189**
METALLDRÜCKEREI **8189**
METALLELEKTRODE **8180**
METALLFADENLAMPE **8181**
METALLFLÄCHE (BLANKE) **1611**
METALLFOLIE **8184**
METALLGLANZ **8195**
METALLHALTIG **8197**
METALLHÄMMERN **1120**
METALLIDERUNG **8196**
METALLKERNSTÜTZE **662**
METALLNEBEL **8182**
METALLOGRAPHIE **8203**
METALLOGRAPHISCH **8202**
METALLOGRAPHISCHE ÄTZUNG **8204**
METALLOID **8205**
METALLOID **8640**

| | |
|---|---|
| METALLPACKUNG **8196** | MIKROFARAD **8242** |
| METALLPACKUNG (NACHGIEBIGE) **4482** | MIKROGEFÜGE **8262** |
| METALLPULVER **8185** | MIKROGRAPHISCH **8243** |
| METALLPULVERPRESSE **9718** | MIKROHÄRTE **8245** |
| METALLREINIGUNG **2474** | MIKROHÄRTEPRÜFUNG **8246** |
| METALLSÄGE **8186** | MIKROHM **8247** |
| METALLSÄGEBLATT **6197** | MIKROMETER (METRISCHER) **8228** |
| METALLSANDSTRAHLUNG **6124** | MIKROMETERHALTER **8250** |
| METALLSCHLAUCH **5421** | MIKROMETERLEHRE **1875** |
| METALLSCHLAUCH **5419** | MIKROMETERRUNDSKALA **8253** |
| METALLSCHRAUBE **8187** | MIKROMETERSCHRAUBE **8255** |
| METALLSPÄNE **2348** | MIKROMETERSCHRAUBE **13540** |
| METALLSPRITZEN **8190** | MIKROMETRISCHER SCHRAUBENGEWINDE-KOMPARATOR **11048** |
| METALLSPRITZEN **5361** | |
| METALLSULFITFLECK **3429** | MIKROMILLIMETER **8257** |
| METALLTROPFEN **11929** | MIKROPHOTOGRAMM **8258** |
| METALLÜBERGANG (FLÜSSIGER) **7659** | MIKROPHOTOGRAMM **9272** |
| METALLÜBERZUG **2596** | MIKRORISS **1263** |
| METALLÜBERZUG **8194** | MIKRORISSE **8234** |
| METALLURGIE **8208** | MIKROSCHLIFF **8261** |
| METALLURGIE (MECHANISCHE) **8107** | MIKROSEIGERUNG **8235** |
| METALLURGIE (PHYSIKALISCHE) **9282** | MIKROSEIGERUNG **3172** |
| METALLURGIE DES EISENS **5123** | MIKROSKOP **8259** |
| METALLURGISCH **8206** | MIKROSKOP (BINOKULARES) **1256** |
| METAPHOSPHORSÄURE **8210** | MIKROTOM **8263** |
| METASTABIL **8212** | MIKROVOLT **8264** |
| METAZENTRUM **8172** | MILCHGLAS **8273** |
| METAZINNSÄURE **12101** | MILCHSÄURE **7355** |
| METEORISCHES WASSER **8213** | MILLIAMPERE **8284** |
| METER **8225** | MILLIAMPEREMETER **8283** |
| METER (LAUFENDES) **10849** | MILLIGRAMM **8285** |
| METERGEWICHT **13748** | MILLIMETER **8286** |
| METERKILOGRAMM **7299** | MILLIMETERTASTER **8256** |
| METERMASS **8226** | MILLIONSTEL ZOLL **8248** |
| METERMASSSTAB **8226** | MILLIVOLT **8294** |
| METERZENTNER **10111** | MILROMETER **8249** |
| METHAN **8215** | MINDESTGEWICHT **8310** |
| METHANOL **13920** | MINDESTSTRECKGRENZE **8308** |
| METHYLALKOHOL **13920** | MINDESTWERT **8307** |
| METHYLÄTHER **8222** | MINERAL **8301** |
| METHYLBENZOL **12983** | MINERALFARBE **4412** |
| METHYLCHLORID **8221** | MINERALFETT **13508** |
| METHYLENHYDRAT **8222** | MINERALGRÜN **10996** |
| METHYLORANGE **8223** | MINERALÖL **8304** |
| METRISCHER ZENTNER **10111** | MINERALÖL (GEREINIGTES) **2480** |
| MIKANIT **8233** | MINERALÖL (RAFFINNIERTES) **2480** |
| MIKROAMPERE **8238** | MINERALÖL (UNGEREINIGTES) **1291** |
| MIKROAMPEREMETER **8237** | MINERALSÄURE **8302** |
| MIKROAUFNAHME **8244** | MINERALSÄURE **9203** |
| MIKROBOHRWERKZEUG **8240** | MINERALWEISS **1003** |
| MIKROBRUCH **1263** | MINETTE **8305** |

## MIN

MINIMALGEWICHT **8310**
MINIMALTEMPERATUR **8306**
MINIMALWERT **8307**
MINIUMKITT **10332**
MINUEND **8316**
MINUSKORNGRÖSSE **8317**
MINUSPLATTE **8530**
MINUSZEICHEN **8532**
MIRBANÖL **8587**
MISCHBATTERIE FÜR BADEWANNEN **1063**
MISCHDÜSE **2769**
MISCHEN **8328**
MISCHEN **1323**
MISCHEN **8336**
MISCHEN **1325**
MISCHER **8331**
MISCHERPFANNE **8333**
MISCHFARBE **11103**
MISCHGAS **4194**
MISCHKOLLERGANG **8451**
MISCHKOLLERGANG **8449**
MISCHKONDENSATOR **3988**
MISCHKRISTALL **11794**
MISCHKRISTALLE **8329**
MISCHMASCHINE **8334**
MISCHMETALL **8320**
MISCHMETALL **817**
MISCHÖL **2832**
MISCHSÄURE **8595**
MISCHTROMMEL **8331**
MISCHUNG **8336**
MISCHUNG **8327**
MISCHUNG **1325**
MISCHUNG EUTEKTISCHE **4857**
MISCHUNGSVERHÄLTNIS **9934**
MISCHVENTIL **8335**
MITNEHMEN (DURCH REIBUNG) **4304**
MITNEHMER **4301**
MITNEHMERSTANGENEINSATZ **4288**
MITREISSEN VON WASSER IM DAMPF **9863**
MITSCHWINGEN **10506**
MITTEL **8072**
MITTEL (ARITHMETISCHES) **703**
MITTEL (GEOMETRISCHES) **5929**
MITTEL (WASSERABWEISENDES) **13674**
MITTEL-(WALZ-)GERÜST **7098**
MITTELAUFLAGER **2152**
MITTELDRUCKKESSEL **8127**
MITTELHIEBFEILE **8266**
MITTELKRAFT **10513**
MITTELLAGE **8265**

MITTELLINIE **8124**
MITTELLINIE **2151**
MITTELLINIE **874**
MITTELÖL **8125**
MITTELPUNKT **2148**
MITTELPUNKT (GEOM.) **2162**
MITTELPUNKTSUCHER **2173**
MITTELSTANGE **7795**
MITTELSTELLUNG **8265**
MITTELWASSERRAUMKESSEL **8126**
MITTELWERT **8073**
MITTEN **2163**
MITTENKURBEL **6976**
MITTNEHMER **1883**
MITVERÄNDERUNG **3261**
MKG **7299**
MODELL **9133**
MODELL **13320**
MODELL **9128**
MODELL (ZELEGBARES) **7744**
MODELL (ZWEITEILIGES) **3105**
MODELL MIT EINGUSSTRICHTERN **5868**
MODELLFORMUNG **3041**
MODELLGUSSPLATTE **2052**
MODELLHERSTELLUNG **9135**
MODELLPLATTE **1710**
MODELLPLATTE (ZWEISEITIGE) **8044**
MODELLSAND **5006**
MODELLSCHREINER **9130**
MODELLTISCHLER **9130**
MODELLTISCHLEREI (HERSTELLUNG VON MODELLEN) **9131**
MODELLTISCHLEREI (WERKSTÄTTE) **9132**
MODEM **8338**
MODUL **8339**
MODULATOR **8338**
MOHNÖL **9624**
MOL **6044**
MOLEKEL **8364**
MOLEKÜL **8364**
MOLEKULARGEWICHT **8363**
MOLEKULARKRAFT **8360**
MOLEKULARVOLUMEN **8362**
MOLEKÜLSTRUKTUR **8361**
MOLKEREIMASCHINEN UND ZUSATZGERÄTE **3595**
MOLKMASCHINEN **8275**
MOLYBDÄN **8367**
MOLYBDÄNBLEISPAT **13991**
MOLYBDÄNEISEN **5111**
MOLYBDÄNGLANZ **8366**
MOLYBDÄNSÄURE **8369**
MOLYBDÄNSTAHL **8368**

857     **MUT**

MOMENT (STATISCHES) **12139**
MOMENT EINER KRAFT **8370**
MOMENTANKRAFT **6811**
MOMENTANWERT **6990**
MOMENTANZENTRUM **6989**
MÖNCH **9997**
MÖNCHSKOLBEN **9545**
MONDGAS **8378**
MONELMETALL **8379**
MONOCHLORÄTHAN **4849**
MONOTEKTOIDE REAKTION **8386**
MONOTRON **8387**
MONOTROP **8388**
MONOXYBENZOL **1938**
MONTAGE **4808**
MONTAGE **4815**
MONTAGE **4813**
MONTAGEAUSRÜSTUNG **4810**
MONTAGEGESTELL **4116**
MONTAGEHALLE **773**
MONTAGEHALLE **4811**
MONTAGEHALLE **770**
MONTAGEMATERIAL **4809**
MONTAGEWERKZEUG **4812**
MONTAGEWERKZEUG **4817**
MONTAGEZEICHNUNG **772**
MONTAGEZEICHNUNG **4814**
MONTANWACHS **7579**
MONTEJUS **8389**
MONTEUR **4816**
MONTIEREN **4805**
MONTIERHAMMER **5279**
MONTIERWERKSTATT **4811**
MOORINGSYSTEM (DREHBARES) **10217**
MORSEKEGELLEHRDORN **8392**
MORSEKEGELLEHRE **8393**
MÖRSER **8396**
MÖRSERKEULE **9221**
MÖRSERLAFETTE **8397**
MÖRTEL **8394**
MÖRTEL (ALUMINIUM-SILIKAT-FEUERFESTER) **443**
MÖRTEL (FEUERFESTER) **10406**
MÖRTEL (HYDRAULISCHER) **6690**
MOSAIKSTRUKTUR **8403**
MOTOR **9859**
MOTOR (BELASTETER) **7686**
MOTOR (GEKAPSELTER) **4715**
MOTOR (GESCHLOSSENER) **4715**
MOTOR (HYDRAULISCHER) **6691**
MOTOR (LUFTGEKÜHLTER) **251**
MOTOR (UMKEHRBARER) **10540**

MOTOR (VENTILIERTER) **13529**
MOTOR-BREMSE **4760**
MOTORAUFHÄNGUNG **4754**
MOTOREINSTELLUNG **8419**
MOTOREN (BENZINKEROSIN UND DIESEL) **4766**
MOTORENSPIRITUS **1983**
MOTORGENERATOR **8413**
MOTORHAUBE **1451**
MOTORÖL **8415**
MOTORRAUM **4757**
MOTORSCHIEBER **8416**
MOTORVENTIL **8417**
MUFFE **3258**
MUFFE **11548**
MUFFE **11705**
MUFFE **3257**
MUFFE (KONISCHE) **12647**
MUFFELOFEN **8447**
MUFFENANSCHLUSS **11053**
MUFFENENDE EINES ROHRES **11710**
MUFFENKUPPLUNG **1510**
MUFFENREGLER **11578**
MUFFENROHR **11707**
MUFFENVERBINDUNG **11900**
MÜHLEN (KOMBINIERT) **8295**
MÜHLSTEIN **8298**
MÜHLSTEIN (GEOL.) **8299**
MÜLL **13074**
MULL **2288**
MULTIPLIKAND **8479**
MULTIPLIKATION **8480**
MULTIPLIKATOR **8482**
MULTIPLIZIEREN **8483**
MUNDSTÜCK **12966**
MUNDSTÜCK **196**
MUNITION **474**
MUNTZMETALL **8486**
MÜNZEN **2651**
MÜNZENBRONZE **8183**
MÜNZGOLD **5996**
MUSCHELKALK **8487**
MUSCHELLINIE **2892**
MUSCHELSCHIEBER **3592**
MUSIVGOLD **12099**
MUSTER **10915**
MUSTER **9128**
MUSTERMODELL **8032**
MUTTER **8698**
MUTTER (AUFGESCHNITTENE) **11942**
MUTTER (BEARBEITETE) **1612**
MUTTER (BLANKE) **1612**

# MUT

858

MUTTER (GEDRÜCKTE) 8700
MUTTER (GEPRESSTE) 8700
MUTTER (GERÄNDELTE) 8280
MUTTER (GESCHLITZTE) 11942
MUTTER (GESCHLOSSENE) 1512
MUTTER (GETEILTE) 11942
MUTTER (ROHE) 1290
MUTTER (SCHWARZE) 1290
MUTTER (UNBEARBEITETE) 1290
MUTTER OHNE GEWINDE 1308
MUTTERAUTOMAT 8699
MUTTERGEWINDE 5092
MUTTERLAUGE 8405
MUTTERRAD 13975
MUTTERSCHLÜSSEL 11833
MUTTERSCHRAUBE 1441
MUTTERWERKSTOFF 9079
NABE 1481
NABE 6661
NABE (GESCHLITZTE) 11938
NABE (GETEILTE) 11938
NABE (UNGETEILTE) 11779
NABENFLANSCH 6663
NACHARBEITEN 11682
NACHAUSRÜSTUNG 10527
NACHBEARBEITEN 5214
NACHBEARBEITUNG 11682
NACHBEHANDLUNG 12417
NACHBOHREN 10270
NACHBOHREN 10271
NACHDREHMASCHINE (MEHRSPINDLIGE) 8485
NACHEILEN 7366
NACHEILWINKEL 522
NACHFLIESSEN 221
NACHGEBEN 5949
NACHGLÜHEN 221
NACHHALTEZEIT 6523
NACHLASSEN (DEN STAHL) 12719
NACHLASSEN DES STAHLES 12733
NACHLAUF 2066
NACHLAUF (WINKEL) 2067
NACHLAUF DER DESTILLATION 7413
NACHMESSEN 2279
NACHRICHTEN 10511
NACHSCHÄRFEN 6790
NACHSCHÄRFEN 6793
NACHSEHEN 8937
NACHSPANNEN (EINEN RIEMEN) 12602
NACHSPANNEN EINES RIEMENS 12605
NACHSPANNVORRICHTUNG 13285
NACHSTELLBAR 183

NACHSTELLEN 13403
NACHSTELLEN 10255
NACHSTELLEN 10256
NACHSTELLEN EIN LAGER 12603
NACHSTELLEN EINER KUPPLUNG 12606
NACHSTELLEN EINES LAGERS 12606
NACHSTELLKEIL 185
NACHSTELLMUTTER 191
NACHSTELLUNG 10256
NACHTSCHICHT 8575
NACHWALZEN 10470
NACHWÄRMEN 10425
NACHWÄRMEN 9668
NACHWÄRMOFEN 10426
NACHWIRKUNG (ELASTISCHE) 10472
NACHWIRKUNG (ELASTISCHE) 4474
NADEL- (KRISTALL-)FÖRMIG 102
NADELEINSATZ FÜR ZIRKEL 8521
NADELFEILE 8519
NADELHOLZ 10483
NADELIG 102
NADELLAGER 8518
NADELÖLER 8520
NADELSTAPEL 9317
NADELSTRUKTUR (MIT) 102
NADELVENTIL 8522
NAGEL 8491
NAGEL (GEGOSSENER) 2051
NAGEL (GESCHMIEDETER) 13990
NAGEL (GESCHNITTENER) 7841
NAGELBOHRER 5944
NAGELEISEN 6325
NAGELFLUH 8490
NAGELN 8492
NAGELTREIBER 12127
NAGELZANGE 9328
NÄHERUNGSFORMEL 654
NÄHERUNGSWERT 653
NÄHRIEMEN 7500
NÄHRMITTEL- UND BETONMISCHMASCHINEN 8332
NAHT 11083
NAHT (DRUCKFESTE) 9838
NAHT (DURCHLAUFENDE) 3037
NAHT (HANDGESCHWEISSTE) 7988
NAHT (TRAGENDE) 12357
NAHT (ÜBERLAPPTE) 7403
NAHT (UNTERBROCHENE) 7054
NAHT (UNTERBROCHENE) 7055
NAHT EINES ROHRES 11085
NAHTACHSE 870
NAHTFEHLER 13760

NAHTSCHWEISSUNG **11086**
NAHTÜBERHÖHUNG **8948**
NAHTWURZEL **10726**
NAPHTHA **8493**
NAPHTHALIN **8494**
NAPHTHOL (A-NAPHTHOLSS-NAPHTHOL) **8495**
NAPHTHYLWASSERSTOFF **8494**
NARBENSEITE DES LEDERS **6038**
NASE **2093**
NASE **8667**
NASENBILDUNG **10892**
NASENKEIL **5939**
NASENSCHRAUBE **5062**
NASSDAMPF **13805**
NASSZUG **13803**
NATRIUM **11726**
NATRIUM **11714**
NATRIUM (ESSIGSAURES) **11715**
NATRIUM (GERBSAURES) **11735**
NATRIUM (OXALSAURES) **11726**
NATRIUM (SALPETRIGSAURES) **11725**
NATRIUM (SAURES) **11717**
NATRIUM (SCHWEFELSAURES) **11717**
NATRIUM (WOLFRAMSAURES) **11737**
NATRIUM (ZINNSAURES) **11732**
NATRIUMALUMINAT **11716**
NATRIUMAMMONIUMPHOSPHAT **8241**
NATRIUMAZETAT **11715**
NATRIUMBIBORAT **1459**
NATRIUMBIKARBONAT **126**
NATRIUMBISULFAT **11717**
NATRIUMBISULFIT **11718**
NATRIUMCHLORID **2790**
NATRIUMHYDROXYD **11722**
NATRIUMHYDROXYDBAD **2117**
NATRIUMHYPOSULFIT **11736**
NATRIUMKARBONAT **11713**
NATRIUMKARBONAT (WASSERFREIES) **551**
NATRIUMLINIE **11723**
NATRIUMNITRAT **2330**
NATRIUMNITRIT **11725**
NATRIUMOXALAT **11726**
NATRIUMOXYD **11724**
NATRIUMOXYDHYDRAT **11722**
NATRIUMPEROXYD **11727**
NATRIUMPHOSPHAT **11728**
NATRIUMPYROPHOSPHAT **11730**
NATRIUMSILIKAT **11731**
NATRIUMSTANNAT **11732**
NATRIUMSULFAT **11733**
NATRIUMSULFIT **11734**

NATRIUMSUPEROXYD **11727**
NATRIUMTANNAT **11735**
NATRIUMTHIOSULFAT **11736**
NATRIUMWOLFRAMAT **11737**
NATRIUMZITRAT **11719**
NATRIUMZYANID **11720**
NATRON **11724**
NATRON (BORSAURES) **1459**
NATRON (DOPPELTKOHLENSAURES) **126**
NATRON (DOPPELTSCHWEFLIGSAURES) **11718**
NATRON (PHOSPHORSAURES) **11728**
NATRON (SCHWEFELSAURES) **11733**
NATRON (SCHWEFLIGSAURES) **11734**
NATRON (SCHWEFLIGSAURES) **11718**
NATRON (UNTERSCHWEFLIGSAURES) **11736**
NATRON (ZITRONENSAURES) **11719**
NATRONHYDRAT **11722**
NATRONLAUGE **2120**
NATRONSALPETER **2330**
NATRONWASSERGLAS **11731**
NATRONWEINSTEIN **11729**
NATURBIMSSTEIN **9986**
NATURGAS **8504**
NATÜRLICHER GRÖSSE (IN) **5723**
NATURSTEIN **8507**
NEBELLAMPE **5506**
NEBENACHSE DER HYPERBEL **2953**
NEBENEINANDERSCHALTUNG **9051**
NEBENERZEUGNIS **1820**
NEBENGESTEIN **5802**
NEBENLAGER **7044**
NEBENPRODUKT **1820**
NEBENSCHLUSS **1818**
NEBENSCHLUSS **1821**
NEBENSCHLUSS **11403**
NEBENSCHLUSSDYNAMO **11404**
NEBENSCHLUSSMOTOR **11405**
NEBENSPANNUNG **11109**
NEBENSPEKTRUM **11108**
NEBENWINKEL **180**
NEGATIV (PHOTOGRAPHISCHES) **8524**
NEGATIVE **8529**
NEGATIVE HÄRTUNG **8527**
NEGATIVELEKTRISCH **4631**
NEIGUNG **6836**
NEIGUNG **1065**
NEIGUNG **11627**
NEIGUNG EINES KEILS **12654**
NEIGUNGSWINKEL **521**
NENNABMESSUNG **8612**
NENNDRUCK (ND) **8613**

**NEN**

860

NENNDURCHMESSER **8611**
NENNER **3752**
NENNER (GEMEINSCHAFTLICHER) **2789**
NENNLEISTUNG **8658**
NENNMASS **8615**
NENNMASS **11857**
NENNSPANNUNG **8659**
NENNWEITE (NW) **8615**
NENNWERT **8616**
NEODYM **8534**
NEODYM **8533**
NEON **8535**
NEONLAMPE **8536**
NETZANSCHLUSS **2782**
NETZEBENE **804**
NETZEBENE **7432**
NETZEBENEN-ABSTAND **7087**
NETZGEFÜGE **8539**
NETZPAPIER **11530**
NETZSTRUKTUR **8539**
NEUGELB **8031**
NEUSEELANDHANF **8550**
NEUSILBER **8569**
NEUSILBER **5932**
NEUTRALE FASER **2151**
NEUTRALES KALIUMCHROMAT **9682**
NEUTRALES KALIUMOXALAT **9692**
NEUTRALISATION **8548**
NEUTRALISIEREN **8549**
NEUWEISS **1003**
NICHT BRENNBAR **6843**
NICHT OXYDIERBAR **6959**
NICHT RECHTWINKELIG **8895**
NICHT SPIEGELGLEICH **778**
NICHT UMKEHRBAR **7169**
NICHT ZUSAMMENDRÜCKBAR **6847**
NICHT-METALLISCH **8639**
NICHTEISEN- **8631**
NICHTEISENLEGIERUNG **8619**
NICHTEISENMATALL **8632**
NICHTLEITEND **3898**
NICHTLEITER **3898**
NICHTUMKEHRBARKEIT **7168**
NICKEL **8556**
NICKELALUMINIUMBRONZE **8572**
NICKELAMMONIUMSULFAT **8558**
NICKELBRONZE **8560**
NICKELCHLORÜR **8562**
NICKELEISEN **5112**
NICKELERZ **8564**
NICKELKARBONYL **8561**

NICKELKOHLENOXYD **8561**
NICKELLEGIERUNG **8557**
NICKELMESSING **8559**
NICKELOXYD **8574**
NICKELOXYDUL **8565**
NICKELPLATTIERUNG **8567**
NICKELSCHROT **8568**
NICKELSTAHL **8570**
NICKELSTEIN **8563**
NICKELSULFAT **8571**
NICKELVITRIOL **8571**
NIEDERDRUCK **7774**
NIEDERDRUCKDAMPF **7785**
NIEDERDRUCKDAMPFHEIZUNG **7787**
NIEDERDRUCKDAMPFMASCHINE **7786**
NIEDERDRUCKKESSEL **7782**
NIEDERDRUCKTURBINE **7788**
NIEDERDRUCKWASSERHEIZUNG **7784**
NIEDERDRUCKZYLINDER **7783**
NIEDERFREQUENZ **7771**
NIEDERFREQUENZOFEN **7772**
NIEDERHALTER **3887**
NIEDERSCHLAG **9759**
NIEDERSCHLAG **9761**
NIEDERSCHLAG (ANGEBRANNTER) **1761**
NIEDERSCHLAG (GALVANISCHER) **4592**
NIEDERSCHLAG (RADIOAKTIVER) **149**
NIEDERSCHLAGEN **2907**
NIEDERSCHLAGSVERTEILUNGSVERHÄLTNIS **3777**
NIEDERSCHLAGSVERTEILUNGSVERHÄLTNIS **8179**
NIEDERSCHLAGWASSER **8213**
NIEDERSCHLAGWASSER **13662**
NIEDERSCHRAUBHAHN **11033**
NIEDERSPANNUNG (EL.) **7778**
NIEDERSPANNUNGSMOTOR **7791**
NIEDERSPANNUNGSSTROM **7777**
NIEDRIG GESPANNTER DAMPF **7785**
NIEDRIGGESPANNTER STROM **7777**
NIEDRIGTEMPERATURVERBINDUNG **7790**
NIET **10621**
NIET MIT BÜNDIGEM KOPF **10635**
NIET MIT DREIECKPROFILKOPF **2946**
NIET MIT FLACHEM KOPF **10634**
NIET MIT GEHÄMMERTEM KOPF **2946**
NIET MIT HALBRUNDKOPF **10636**
NIET MIT HALBVERSENKTEM KOPF **3249**
NIET MIT KORBBOGENKOPF **10633**
NIET MIT RUNDKOPF **10637**
NIET MIT SCHELLKOPF **10637**
NIET MIT TRAPEZPROFILKOPF **9030**
NIET MIT VERSENKTEM KOPF **10635**

NIET MIT ZYLINDRISCHEM KOPF **10632**
NIETBOLZEN **11263**
NIETE **10646**
NIETE (DIE) HERAUSSCHLAGEN **3511**
NIETE STAUCHEN **2489**
NIETEISEN **10627**
NIETEN **10643**
NIETEN EINSETZEN (DIE) **6967**
NIETEN EINZIEHEN (DIE) **6967**
NIETER **10641**
NIETFLANSCH **10638**
NIETHAMMER **10644**
NIETKOPF **10624**
NIETLOCH **10625**
NIETLOCH (GELOCHTES) **10004**
NIETLOCH (GESTANZTES) **10004**
NIETLOCH AUFDORNEN (EIN) **4262**
NIETLOCH GEBOHRTES **4275**
NIETLÖCHER AUFEINANDERPASSEN (DIE) **9969**
NIETLOCHSCHWEISSEN **9537**
NIETMASCHINE **10645**
NIETMASCHINE **10642**
NIETMITTE **2171**
NIETNAHT **11084**
NIETPFANNE **4115**
NIETREIHE **10813**
NIETSCHAFT **11263**
NIETSCHWEISSEN **10631**
NIETSTÄRKE **3859**
NIETTEILUNG **9409**
NIETUNG **10639**
NIETUNG **10643**
NIETUNG (DOPPELTE) **4152**
NIETUNG (DREIREIHIGE) **13177**
NIETUNG (DREISCHNITTIGE) **13178**
NIETUNG (EINFACHE) **11487**
NIETUNG (EINREIHIGE) **11487**
NIETUNG (EINSCHNITTIGE) **11489**
NIETUNG (VERJÜNGTE) **7799**
NIETUNG (VERSETZTE) **14034**
NIETUNG (ZWEIREIHIGE) **4152**
NIETUNG (ZWEISCHNITTIGE) **4155**
NIETVERBINDUNG **10639**
NIETVERTEILUNG **717**
NIETWÄRMEOFEN **10623**
NIETWINDE **11032**
NIETZANGE **10630**
NIGGERÖL **3222**
NIOB **2747**
NIOBIUM **8576**
NIPPEL **8578**

NIROSTAHL **12051**
NISCHE **10279**
NITRAT **8579**
NITRIERATMOSPHÄRE **8583**
NITRIERHÄRTUNG **8582**
NITRIEROFEN **8584**
NITRIERSÄURE **8595**
NITRIERSTAHL **8585**
NITRIERUNG **8589**
NITRIT **8586**
NITROBENZOL **8587**
NITROGLYZERIN **8593**
NITROMETER **8594**
NITROZELLULOSE **6176**
NITROZEMENTIERUNG **5818**
NIVEAU **13259**
NIVEAU (HÖHENLAGE) **7525**
NIVEAU REGLER **7654**
NIVEAUFLÄCHE **7527**
NIVEAUSCHWANKUNGEN **13500**
NIVEAUSTANDSREGLER **7655**
NIVELLIERSCHRAUBE **7529**
NOCKE **1883**
NOCKEN **1883**
NOCKENANLAUFSCHRÄGER **1887**
NOCKENHUB **1884**
NOCKENROLLE **1895**
NOCKENSCHEIBE **13221**
NOCKENWELLE **1896**
NOCKENWELLE (OBENLIEGENDE) **8939**
NOCKENWELLENDREHBANK **1897**
NODULAR **8606**
NONIUS **13536**
NORDHÄUSER VITRIOLÖL **5733**
NORDPOL EINES MAGNETEN **8665**
NORM **12071**
NORMAL (GEOM.) **8652**
NORMAL LEHRDORN **12087**
NORMALBESCHLEUNIGUNG **8653**
NORMALDRUCK **8657**
NORMALE **12071**
NORMALE EINER KURVE **8662**
NORMALFLAMME **8543**
NORMALGEWINDE (SCHWEIZER) **12552**
NORMALGEWINDELEHRDORN **12861**
NORMALGEWINDELEHRRING **12863**
NORMALGLÜHEN **8664**
NORMALISIEREN **12090**
NORMALISIEREN DES STAHLS **581**
NORMALISIERUNG **12091**
NORMALKRÜMMER **10074**

## NOR

NORMALLEHRE 12076
NORMALLEISTUNG 8658
NORMALLÖSUNG 12084
NORMALMASS 12077
NORMALMASSSTAB 12081
NORMALMODELL 12086
NORMALPROFIL 12083
NORMALRACHENLEHRE 12088
NORMALSCHNITT 8654
NORMALSPANNUNG 8661
NORMALTHERMOMETER 12085
NORMEN 12090
NORMENINSTITUT (ENGLISCHES) 887
NORMKERZE 3663
NORMPROBE 12082
NORMUNG 12091
NOTBELEUCHTUNG 4688
NOTBELEUCHTUNG 4689
NOTBREMSE 4687
NOTLEITUNG (ELEKTR.) 4690
NULLACHSE 8541
NULLEITUNG 8545
NULLINIE 8541
NULLINIE (INDIKATOR-DIAGRAMM) 14029
NULLMARKE 14025
NULLPUNKT 14027
NULLPUNKT (ABSOLUTER) 36
NULLPUNKT (BELIEBIGER) 5440
NULLPUNKT DER KOORDINATEN 8868
NULLPUNKTABWEICHUNG 14024
NULLPUNKTVERSATZ 14031
NULLPUNKTVERSATZ 14026
NULLRÜCKSTELLUNG 14032
NULLRÜCKSTELLUNG 14030
NULLSCHICHT 8544
NULLSTELLUNG 14028
NULLSTRICH 14025
NULLUNTERDRÜCKUNG 14033
NUMERISCH 3941
NUMERUS EINES LOGARITHMUS 8689
NUMMER DES ARBEITSGANGES 8838
NUSSKOHLE 2328
NUT 6127
NUT (MIT EINER) VERSEHEN 6128
NUT UND FEDER VERSEHEN (MIT) 12988
NUTATION 8702
NUTEN 6128
NUTEN 6137
NUTEN STOSSEN 11630
NUTENFRÄSER 11634
NUTENFRÄSER 11632

NUTENFRÄSMASCHINE 7281
NUTENSCHEIBE 6134
NUTENSCHLÜSSEL 1822
NUTENSTOSSEN 11641
NUTENTROMMEL 3579
NUTHOBEL 6139
NUTKEIL 12458
NUTSTOSSMASCHINE 11643
NUTZARBEIT 13428
NUTZBAR MACHEN 13430
NUTZBARMACHUNG 13429
NUTZDURCHMESSER 13423
NUTZEFFEKT 4463
NUTZFAHRZEUG 2784
NUTZHOLZ 12937
NUTZLÄNGE 13424
NUTZLAST 13425
NUTZLEISTUNG 4458
NUTZWÄRME 4457
NUTZWASSER 13649
NUTZWIDERSTAND 13426
O-RING 8703
OBELISK 8705
OBERFLÄCHE 12521
OBERFLÄCHE 2019
OBERFLÄCHE (AUSGESEIGERTE) 7634
OBERFLÄCHE (GLANZLOSE) 8060
OBERFLÄCHE (METALLREINE) 2470
OBERFLÄCHE (SAUGENDE) 6644
OBERFLÄCHEN-BEHANDLUNGSVERFAHREN (CHEMISCHES)
  2314
OBERFLÄCHEN-U. EINSCHLEIFMASSE 6108
OBERFLÄCHENARTUNG 2021
OBERFLÄCHENBEHANDLUNGSMITTEL 12523
OBERFLÄCHENBESCHAFFENHEIT 12500
OBERFLÄCHENBESCHAFFENHEIT 12504
OBERFLÄCHENBESCHAFFENHEIT 5213
OBERFLÄCHENDRUCK 12517
OBERFLÄCHENENDBEARBEITUNG (CHEMISCHE) 2309
OBERFLÄCHENFEHLER 12502
OBERFLÄCHENGLÄTTUNG 3807
OBERFLÄCHENGLÜHUNG 575
OBERFLÄCHENHAARRISSE 3319
OBERFLÄCHENHÄRTUNG 2023
OBERFLÄCHENHÄRTUNG 12508
OBERFLÄCHENKONDENSATOR 12499
OBERFLÄCHENKONDENSATOR MIT LUFTKÜHLUNG 296
OBERFLÄCHENKONDENSATOR MIT WASSERKÜHLUNG 13684
OBERFLÄCHENPOLIERUNG 3527
OBERFLÄCHENPORE 1351
OBERFLÄCHENPOREN 9178

OLF

| | |
|---|---|
| OBERFLÄCHENPRÜFGERÄT **12498** | ÖFFNUNG **6530** |
| OBERFLÄCHENPRÜFGERÄT **12509** | ÖFFNUNG **9633** |
| OBERFLÄCHENRAUHIGKEIT **12518** | ÖFFNUNG **13528** |
| OBERFLÄCHENRISS **12501** | OHM **8742** |
| OBERFLÄCHENSCHICHT **2019** | ÖHR EINES HAMMERS **4975** |
| OBERFLÄCHENSPANNUNG **7033** | OKKLUSION (CHEM.) **8719** |
| OBERFLÄCHENSPANNUNG **12519** | OKTAEDER **8722** |
| OBERFLÄCHENUNEBENHEIT **12503** | OKTANT **8724** |
| OBERFLÄCHENWASSER **12520** | OKTANZAHL **8723** |
| OBERGESENK **13036** | OKULAR **4977** |
| OBERINGENIEUR **4762** | OKULARMIKROMETER **8254** |
| OBERIRDISCHE LEITUNG **212** | ÖL **8743** |
| OBERSCHALE **13030** | ÖL (ABLAUFENDES) **13636** |
| OBERSCHLÄCHTIGES WASSERRAD **8960** | ÖL (FETTES) **5294** |
| OBERSEE KUPFER **7370** | ÖL (FLÜCHTIGES) **4836** |
| OBERWASSER **6322** | ÖL (GELÄUTERTES) **10373** |
| OBERWASSERKANAL **6319** | ÖL (RAFFINIERTES) **10373** |
| OBERWINKELEISEN **13028** | ÖL (RANZIGES) **10197** |
| OBJEKTIV **8708** | ÖL (ROSTLÖSENDES) **9169** |
| OBJEKTPUNKT **8706** | ÖL (TIERISCHES) **555** |
| OBJEKTTISCH **12047** | ÖL (TROCKNENDES) **4357** |
| OBJEKTTRÄGER **11589** | ÖL (VEGETABILISCHES) **13512** |
| OBSIDIAN **8716** | ÖL (VERSPRITZTES) **11928** |
| OBUS **13225** | ÖL (WASSERLÖSLICHES) **11810** |
| OCKER **8720** | ÖL-ABSTREIFRING **13879** |
| ODONTOGRAPH **8726** | ÖLABSCHEIDER **8779** |
| OFEN **8920** | ÖLABSCHEIDER **8778** |
| OFEN **5739** | ÖLABSCHEIDUNG **8777** |
| OFEN **12300** | ÖLABSTREIFRING **8775** |
| OFEN (ELEKTRISCHER) **4507** | ÖLABSTREIFRING **8750** |
| OFEN (FESTSTEGENDER) **12142** | ÖLBAD **8745** |
| OFEN (GASGEHEIZTER) **5851** | ÖLBADLUFTFILTER **8746** |
| OFEN (KONTINUIERLICHER) **3026** | ÖLBILDENDES GAS **4851** |
| OFEN (METALLURGISCHER) **8207** | ÖLBREMSE **8755** |
| OFENBESCHICKUNGSMASCHINE **2268** | ÖLBUNKER **8748** |
| OFENFUTTER **5748** | ÖLBUNKER **5706** |
| OFENFUTTER (BASISCHES) **1051** | OLD VERFAHREN (OXYGENE-LINZ-DONAWITZ) **8793** |
| OFENFUTTER (MONOLITHISCHES) **8385** | OLDHAMKUPPLUNG **8794** |
| OFENFUTTER (SAURES) **123** | ÖLDRUCKMESSER **8768** |
| OFENHARTLÖTEN **5740** | ÖLDURCHLÄSSIGKEITSMASS **10232** |
| OFENKÜHLUNG **5742** | OLEINSÄURE **8795** |
| OFENMANTEL **5749** | ÖLEN **8791** |
| OFENPLATTE **6512** | ÖLEN **8744** |
| OFENSAU **10896** | OLEUM **5733** |
| OFF-LINE-BETRIEB **8735** | ÖLFÄNGER **4283** |
| OFF-SHORE **8738** | ÖLFANGRING **8776** |
| OFFENE LEHRE **6608** | ÖLFARBE **8766** |
| OFFENER MOTOR **8818** | ÖLFARBENANSTRICH **2582** |
| OFFENER SCHUBSTANGENKOPF **8007** | ÖLFEST **8792** |
| OFFENESFEUER **8813** | ÖLFEUERUNG **1752** |
| OFFENHALTUNGSVORRICHTUNG **6525** | ÖLFEUERUNG **5745** |

**OLF** 864

ÖLFILTER **8757**
ÖLFLÜGELRAD **8763**
ÖLGAS **8758**
ÖLHÄRTUNG **8760**
ÖLHÄRTUNG **8772**
OLIVIN **8796**
ÖLKANNE **8749**
ÖLKITT **8771**
ÖLKÜHLER **8751**
ÖLKÜHLUNG **8752**
ÖLMASCHINE **8756**
ÖLMESSSTAB **3979**
ÖLMESSSTAB **8764**
ÖLNUT **8759**
ÖLPAPIER **8788**
ÖLPOLSTER (DÄMPFUNG) **8754**
ÖLPRÜFMASCHINE **8785**
ÖLPUFFER **8755**
ÖLPUMPE **8769**
ÖLPUMPENSIEB **8770**
ÖLRING **8774**
ÖLSÄURE **8795**
ÖLSCHALE **4283**
ÖLSCHIEFER **8780**
ÖLSCHIFF **4283**
ÖLSCHMIERUNG **8791**
ÖLSPEICHER **8773**
ÖLSPRITZE **8784**
ÖLSTEIN **8781**
ÖLSÜSS **5988**
ÖLTROPFAPPARAT **4323**
ÖLVASE **8753**
ÖLVISKOSITÄTSINDEX **8787**
ÖLWANNE **8782**
ÖLZUFÜHRUNG **8783**
ON-LINE-BETRIEB **8799**
OOLITHKALK **8801**
OPERMENT **728**
OPTIK **8849**
OPTISCH **8840**
ORANGENSCHALENEFFEKT **8851**
ORDINATE **8858**
ORDINATENACHSE **873**
ORIENTIERUNG **8867**
ORIENTIERUNG (VORZUGSWEISE) **9771**
ORIGINALGRÖSSE (IN) **5723**
ORT (GEOMETRISCHER) **7715**
ÖRTERSÄGE **5628**
ORTHOKIESELSÄURE **8875**
ORTHOPHOSPHORSÄURE **8873**
ORTSVERÄNDERUNG **7712**

ÖSE **4980**
ÖSE EINES HAMMERS **4975**
ÖSENHAKEN **4974**
ÖSENSCHRAUBE **4973**
OSMIRIDIUM **8888**
OSMIUM **8889**
OSMOSE **8890**
OSTEOPLASTIKLEGIERUNG **498**
OSZILLATION **8884**
OSZILLIEREN **8877**
OSZILLIERENDE DAMPFMASCHINE **8880**
OSZILLOGRAPH **8885**
OSZILLOSKOP **8886**
OVALDREHBANK **8919**
OVALEISEN **8916**
OXALAT **8968**
OXALSÄURE **8969**
OXALSAURES KALI **9692**
OXALSAURES SALZ **8968**
OXYD **8971**
OXYDATION **8970**
OXYDATION (CHROMSAURE ANODISCHE) **2380**
OXYDATION (ELEKTROCHEMISCHE) **4601**
OXYDATION (ODER KORROSION) (TROCKENE) **4350**
OXYDATION BEI HOCHTEMPERATUR **6498**
OXYDATIONSFLAMME **4883**
OXYDATIONSMITTEL **8974**
OXYDATIONSWÄRME **6361**
OXYDBELAG **2598**
OXYDHAUT **5168**
OXYDIERBAR **8972**
OXYDIEREN **8984**
OXYDIEREN **8973**
OXYDIERUNG **8970**
OXYDUL **5124**
OZOKERIT **4413**
OZON **8989**
OZOZEROTIN **2194**
P-DIAMIDODIPHENYL **1201**
PAAR **3252**
PACKEN **8990**
PACKFONG **5932**
PACKHAHN **5954**
PACKHAHN **8997**
PACKLEINWAND **6449**
PACKMATERIAL **9004**
PACKPAPIER **13984**
PACKUNG **9009**
PACKUNG **8998**
PACKUNG (METALLISCHE) **8196**
PACKUNG (WEICHE) **11739**

PACKUNG MIT EINLAGE 3159
PACKUNGSRAUM 9008
PACKUNGSRING 9007
PACKUNGSZOPF 5863
PAKET 5017
PAKETIEREN 5018
PAKETIEREN 1772
PAKETIERSCHROTT 5016
PAKETWALZEN 8994
PAKETWÄRMOFEN 9308
PALETTEN-HUBLASTWAGEN 9025
PALETTIEREN 9026
PALLADIUM 9023
PALMBUTTER 9027
PALMFETT 9027
PALMITINSÄURE 9028
PALMÖL 9027
PANNE 1581
PANTOGRAPH 9033
PANZERBLECH 11343
PANZERKABEL 713
PANZERPLATTE 712
PAPIER (ENDLOSES) 3013
PAPIER (GEFIRNISSTES) 13506
PAPIER (KARIERTES) 11530
PAPIER (LACKIERTES) 13506
PAPIER (METALLISIERTES) 8199
PAPIERMACHE 9036
PAPIERRIEMENSCHEIBE 9034
PAPIERROHR 6803
PAPIERSTOFF 9035
PAPIERZEUG 9035
PAPINSCHER TOPF 829
PAPPDECKEL 1381
PAPPE 1381
PARABEL 9038
PARABELINTERPOLATION 9040
PARABOLSPIEGEL 9041
PARAFFIN 9043
PARAFFINGASÖL 1668
PARAFFINÖL 9044
PARAGUMMI 9037
PARAKAUTSCHUK 9037
PARALLAXE 9047
PARALLAXENFEHLER 9048
PARALLEL 9050
PARALLELANZEIGE 9054
PARALLELDREHBANK 9428
PARALLELDREHEN 13164
PARALLELDREHEN 13162
PARALLELE 9049

PARALLELENDMASS 5769
PARALLELEPIPED 9068
PARALLELEPIPED (ABGESTUMPFTES) 13237
PARALLELEPIPED (GERADES) 10581
PARALLELEPIPED (NORMALES) 10581
PARALLELEPIPED (RECHTWINKLIGES) 10305
PARALLELEPIPED (SCHIEFES) 8713
PARALLELHAMMER 4326
PARALLELITÄT 9069
PARALLELLINEAL 9059
PARALLELMASS 8016
PARALLELNIETUNG 2215
PARALLELOGRAMM 9070
PARALLELOGRAMM DER GESCHWINDIGKEITEN 9072
PARALLELOGRAMM DER KRÄFTE 9071
PARALLELOGRAMMGETRIEBE 9057
PARALLELPROJEKTION 9058
PARALLELPROJEKTION (KLINOGRAPHISCHE) 2501
PARALLELPROJEKTION (ORTHOGONALE) 8870
PARALLELPROJEKTION (ORTHOGRAPHISCHE) 8870
PARALLELPROJEKTION (RECHTWINKLIGE) 8870
PARALLELPROJEKTION (SCHIEFE) 2501
PARALLELREISSER 8016
PARALLELREISSLINIE 7604
PARALLELSCHALTUNG 9051
PARALLELSCHIEBER 9060
PARALLELSCHIEBER (SELBSTDICHTENDER) 9061
PARALLELSCHIEBER MIT FEDERVERSCHLUSS 9052
PARALLELSCHIEBER MIT MECHANISCHEM VERSCHLUSS 9053
PARALLELSCHRAUBSTOCK 9066
PARALLELSTRÖMUNG 9055
PARALLELVERSCHIEBUNG 13123
PARAMAGNETISCH 9073
PARAMAGNETISMUS 9074
PARAMETER 9075
PARAPHOSPHORSÄURE 10054
PARISER STIFT 13895
PARITÄTSPRÜFUNG 9081
PARTIALTURBINE 9085
PARTIELLE DIFFERENTIALGLEICHUNG 9086
PASSBLECH 7621
PASSBOLZEN 4181
PASSFLÄCHE 5058
PASSFLÄCHENKORROSION 5666
PASSIG DREHEN 13280
PASSIGDREHEN 8869
PASSIVIERBAD 9103
PASSIVIERUNG 9105
PASSIVIERUNGSMITTEL 9106
PASSIVIERUNGSSCHICHT 9104
PASSIVITÄT 9107

# PAS

866

PASSSTIFT **4181**
PASSSTÜCK **160**
PASSSTÜCK **9006**
PASSUNG **5275**
PASSUNGSPRÜFUNG **6006**
PATENT **9112**
PATENT ANMELDEN (EIN) **651**
PATENT-PFLUGSTAHL **9528**
PATENTABLAUF **4932**
PATENTAMT **9120**
PATENTANMELDER **645**
PATENTANMELDUNG **646**
PATENTANWALT **9114**
PATENTBESCHREIBUNG **11856**
PATENTBEWERBER **645**
PATENTEINSPRUCH **8707**
PATENTERTEILUNG **6049**
PATENTGEBÜHREN **9115**
PATENTGESETZ **9116**
PATENTGESUCH EINREICHEN (EIN) **651**
PATENTIEREN **9124**
PATENTIEREN **9113**
PATENTINHABER **9123**
PATENTRECHTE **9121**
PATENTRECHTLICH SCHÜTZEN **9113**
PATENTSCHRIFT **11856**
PATENTVERLÄGERUNG **9919**
PATENTVERLETZUNG **6916**
PATERNOSTERAUFZUG **3020**
PATERNOSTERWERK **1676**
PATINA **220**
PATINA **9127**
PATRONE **2015**
PATRONENMESSING **2016**
PAUSE **13082**
PAUSE AUFZIEHEN (EINE) **8431**
PAUSEN **13082**
PAUSEN **13077**
PAUSER **13078**
PAUSLEINWAND **13083**
PAUSPAPIER **13084**
PECH **9400**
PECHBLENDE **9411**
PECHDRAHT **13704**
PECHGARN **13704**
PECHKOHLE **9405**
PEILBÜHNE **5885**
PEILEICHUNG **5874**
PEILEICHUNG **5770**
PEILKOPF **5877**
PEITSCHEN DES RIEMENS **13825**

PELIT **2465**
PENDEL **9167**
PENDELARM **6014**
PENDELDORN **5438**
PENDELFRÄSER **10282**
PENDELFUTTER **5438**
PENDELHAMMER **6787**
PENDELHAMMER FÜR SCHLAGVERSUCHE **2271**
PENDELN **6670**
PENDELRAUPE **13724**
PENDELREGLER **9168**
PENDELSCHWINGUNG **12548**
PENETROMETER **9171**
PENTAEDER **9175**
PENTAN (NORMALES) **9176**
PENTHYLALKOHOL **488**
PERFORIERBARES VERLORENES ROHR **4272**
PERFORIEREN **9186**
PERGAMENT **9077**
PERGAMENT (VEGETABILISCHES) **9078**
PERGAMENTPAPIER **9078**
PERIODE **3553**
PERIODENZAHL **5661**
PERIODISCH **9191**
PERIODIZITÄT **9196**
PERIPHERIE **2404**
PERIPHERIEWINKEL **6962**
PERLASCHE **9143**
PERLEN **2437**
PERLIT **9144**
PERLITGUSS **9200**
PERLKOHLE **9140**
PERLMUTTERGLANZ **9146**
PERMALLOY **9201**
PERMANENTE HÄRTE DES WASSERS **9203**
PERMANENTWEISS **1003**
PERMEABILITÄT **9211**
PERMEABILITÄT (MAGNETISCHE) **7911**
PERMEAMETER **9214**
PERMUTATION **9216**
PERSONENAUFZUG **9101**
PERSPEKTIVE **9220**
PERSPEKTIVE (AXONOMETRISCHE) **885**
PERSPEKTIVE (LINEARE) **7614**
PERSPEKTIVE (MATHEMATISCHE) **7614**
PERSPEKTIVISCH **9220**
PERUSALPETER **2330**
PETROLEUM **9229**
PETROLEUM **9226**
PETROLEUMBENZIN **9222**
PETROLEUMLAMPE **9227**

PETROLEUMMOTOR **9046**
PETROLIEUMÄTHER **9228**
PEWTER **9230**
PFAHLEINTREIBEN **9306**
PFAHLKAPPE **9305**
PFANNE **7356**
PFANNENANALYSE **7358**
PFANNENAUSGUSS **7361**
PFANNENAUSGUSS **7363**
PFANNENAUSGUSS **7632**
PFANNENBÄR **1812**
PFANNENFÜHRER **7362**
PFANNENSAURE **2884**
PFANNENSTEIN **7359**
PFANNENZIEGEL **7359**
PFANNENZUSATZ **7357**
PFEIFE **13829**
PFEIFENERDE **9367**
PFEIFENTON **9367**
PFEILER **9311**
PFEILER **2748**
PFEILHÖHE **10613**
PFEILRAD **4143**
PFEILZAHN **4144**
PFEILZAHNRÄDER **6448**
PFERDEHAAR **6604**
PFERDEKRAFT **6602**
PFERDESTÄRKE **6602**
PFERDESTÄRKE (ANGEGEBENE) **6874**
PFERDESTÄRKE (GEBREMSTE) **151**
PFERDESTÄRKE (INDIZIERTE) **6873**
PFERDESTÄRKE (NUTZBARE) **151**
PFERDESTÄRKE-STUNDE **6603**
PFLANZENÖL **13512**
PFLASTER **9136**
PFLASTERSTEIN **9137**
PFLASTERUNG **9136**
PFLOCK **9529**
PFLÜGE (DURCH TRAKTOREN ANGETRIEBENE) **9525**
PFOSTEN **12062**
PFROPFEN **9529**
PFROPFEN **3176**
PH-WERT **9231**
PHASE **9232**
PHASE (DISPERSIVE) **3033**
PHASE (KONTINUIERLICHE) **3033**
PHASENGESETZ **9236**
PHASENINDIKATOR **9235**
PHASENMESSER **9235**
PHASENNACHEILUNG **7368**
PHASENNACHEILWINKEL **523**

PHASENUMWANDLUNG **355**
PHASENVERSCHIEBUNG **9234**
PHASENVERSCHIEBUNG **9237**
PHASENVERSCHIEBUNGSWINKEL **9233**
PHASENVOREILUNG **7483**
PHASENVOREILWINKEL **524**
PHENOL **1938**
PHENOLPHTALEIN **9238**
PHENOLPHTALEINPAPIER **9239**
PHENYLALKOHOL **1938**
PHENYLAMIN **552**
PHENYLSÄURE **1938**
PHONAUTOGRAPH **9242**
PHONOLITH **9243**
PHOSPHAT **9244**
PHOSPHATISIERUNG **2600**
PHOSPHATÜBERZUG **9245**
PHOSPHOR **9252**
PHOSPHOR (GELBWEISSER) **14009**
PHOSPHOR (KRISTALLINISCHER) **14009**
PHOSPHORBROMÜR **9255**
PHOSPHORBRONZE **9246**
PHOSPHORCHLORÜR **9256**
PHOSPHORESZENZ **9247**
PHOSPHORESZIEREND **9248**
PHOSPHORKUPFER **9253**
PHOSPHORKUPFER **9250**
PHOSPHORPENTACHLORID **9254**
PHOSPHORPENTOXYD **9249**
PHOSPHORSALZ **8241**
PHOSPHORSÄURE **8873**
PHOSPHORSAURE MAGNESIA **8656**
PHOSPHORSÄUREANHYDRID **9249**
PHOSPHORSAURES KALI **9696**
PHOSPHORSAURES SALZ **9244**
PHOSPHORSUPERCHLORID **9254**
PHOSPHORTRIBROMID **9255**
PHOSPHORTRICHLORID **9256**
PHOTOGRAPHIE **9263**
PHOTOGRAPHIE **9265**
PHOTOGRAPHIEREN **9265**
PHOTOGRAPHIEREN **9262**
PHOTOGRAPHISCH AUFNEHMEN **9262**
PHOTOMETER **9267**
PHOTOMETERBANK **9268**
PHOTOMETRIE **9271**
PHOTOMETRISCH **9269**
PHOTON **9275**
PHOTOVERVIELFACHER **9274**
PHOTOWIDERSTAND **9261**
PHOTOZELLE (LICHTELEKTRISCHE) **9260**

**PHY** 868

PHYLLIT **9278**
PHYSIK **9285**
PHYSIKALISCH **9279**
PICKELBILDUNG **9314**
PIEZOELEKTRIZITÄT **9297**
PIEZOMETER **12067**
PIKIERMASCHINEN UND SISALPFLANZMASCHINEN **11133**
PIKRINSÄURE **9291**
PILGERSCHRITTSCHWEISSVERFAHREN **901**
PINAKOID **9327**
PINCHEFFEKT **9329**
PINKSALZ **470**
PINNE EINES HAMMERS **9031**
PINSEL **2743**
PINT **9337**
PINZETTE **5536**
PIPETTE **9368**
PISTOLENGRIFFMETALLSÄGE **9369**
PITOTROHR **9415**
PLANDREHBANK **5001**
PLANDREHBANK **5005**
PLANDREHBANK MIT WAAGERECHTER PLANSCHEIBE **1469**
PLANDREHEN **12497**
PLANDREHEN **12522**
PLANETARISCH **9445**
PLANETENBEWEGUNG **9447**
PLANETENGETRIEBE **12456**
PLANETENGETRIEBE **9446**
PLANETENRAD **9444**
PLANFILM **8993**
PLANFLÄCHE (OPTISCHE) **8843**
PLANFRÄSER **4446**
PLANIEREN **9454**
PLANIERHAMMER **9455**
PLANIERKOLBEN **4116**
PLANIMETER **9448**
PLANIMETRIE **9449**
PLANIMETRIEREN **8084**
PLANIMETRIERUNG **8087**
PLANROST **6584**
PLANSCHEIBE **4999**
PLANSCHEIBENGETRIEBE **4005**
PLANSCHEIBENKUPPLUNG **9486**
PLANSCHLEIFEN **12506**
PLANSCHLEIFMASCHINE **12505**
PLANUNG **3794**
PLASTIZITÄT **9474**
PLASTMASSE (FEUERFESTE) **9473**
PLASTSTAMPFER (MECHANISCHER) **1732**
PLATIN **9510**
PLATIN-IRIDIUM **9515**

PLATINCHLORID **9507**
PLATINCHLORÜR **9509**
PLATINDRAHT **9513**
PLATINE **11306**
PLATINE **4174**
PLATINEINHEIT (DER LICHTSTÄRKE) **13569**
PLATINEN AUS LEGIERTEN STÄHLEN **1956**
PLATINEN AUS LEGIERTEN STÄHLEN **378**
PLATINENSCHNITT **1310**
PLATINID **9508**
PLATINMOHR **9511**
PLATINMOHR **9514**
PLATINSCHWAMM **11955**
PLATINSCHWARZ **9511**
PLATINTETRACHLORID **9507**
PLATINTHERMOMETER **10495**
PLATINTIEGEL **9512**
PLÄTTCHEN **9498**
PLATTE **11551**
PLATTE **9477**
PLATTE (LICHTEMPFINDLICHE) **11187**
PLATTE (NEGATIVE) **8530**
PLATTE (PHOTOGRAPHISCHE) **11187**
PLATTE (POSITIVE) **9658**
PLATTENABDICHTUNGSSCHALE **11073**
PLATTENFEDERMANOMETER **3873**
PLATTENFÖRDERER **11570**
PLATTENÜBERLAPPUNG **9501**
PLATTENVENTIL **4011**
PLATTFORM (AUSKRAGENDE) **13875**
PLATTIEREN **9503**
PLATTIEREN **9479**
PLATTIERUNG **2447**
PLATTIERUNG (MECHANISCHE) **8108**
PLATZBEDARF **11829**
PLATZEN **1767**
PLATZERSPARNIS **5774**
PLEUELKOPF **2963**
PLEUELSTANGE **2962**
PLOMBE **7480**
PLOMBE (MIT EINER) VERSEHEN **11077**
PLOMBIEREN **11077**
PLUMBAGO **9542**
PLUNGER **9545**
PLUNGERPUMPE **9546**
PLUNSCHEPUMPE **9546**
PLUNSCHER **9545**
PLUSPLATTE **9658**
PLUSZEICHEN **9661**
PNEUMATISCH **9549**
POCHSTEMPEL **12055**

POCHWERK **12057**
POL (ELEKTRISCHER) **9591**
POL (GEOM.) **9592**
POL (NEGATIVER) **8531**
POL (POSITIVER) **9659**
POL EINES MAGNETEN **9595**
POLABSTAND **9579**
POLARDREIECK **9581**
POLARE **9577**
POLARISATION **9582**
POLARISATION **9589**
POLARISATION (ELEKTROLYTISCHE) **4604**
POLARISATIONSAPPARAT **9584**
POLARISATIONSMIKROSKOP **9583**
POLARISATIONSPRISMA **9586**
POLARISATOR **9586**
POLARISKOP **9584**
POLARITÄT **9587**
POLARKOORDINATEN **9578**
POLAROGRAPHIE **9590**
POLE (GLEICHNAMIGE) **7581**
POLE (UNGLEICHNAMIGE) **13392**
POLEN **9597**
POLGEHÄUSE **5624**
POLIERBAR **9599**
POLIEREISEN **1757**
POLIEREN **9598**
POLIEREN **9605**
POLIEREN **9600**
POLIEREN (ELEKTROLYTISCHES) **4605**
POLIERFASS **9602**
POLIERKUGELN **1759**
POLIERMASCHINE **1686**
POLIERMASCHINE **9603**
POLIERMITTEL **11**
POLIERMITTEL **22**
POLIERMITTEL **9601**
POLIERPASTE **2827**
POLIERROLLEN (STOFFBEKLEIDETE) **2539**
POLIERROT **7148**
POLIERSCHEIBE **9604**
POLIERSCHEIBE **1693**
POLIERSCHIEFER **13220**
POLIERSTAHL **1757**
POLIERSTICH **11541**
POLIERSTICH **11542**
POLIERSTOCK **632**
POLIERTONNE **9602**
POLIERTROMMEL **9602**
POLONIUM **9606**
POLSCHUHEN **9593**

POLSTÄRKE **9596**
POLSTRAHL **9580**
POLSUCHPAPIER **9594**
POLYEDER **9612**
POLYGON **9609**
POLYGON (EINGESCHRIEBENES) **6964**
POLYGON (IRREGULÄRES) **7164**
POLYGON (REGELMÄSSIGES) **10416**
POLYGON (REGULÄRES) **10416**
POLYGON (UMSCHRIEBENES) **2436**
POLYGON (UNREGELMÄSSIGES) **7164**
POLYGONSEITE **11414**
POLYGONZUG **9611**
POLYKRISTALLINES METALL **9608**
POLYMER **9613**
POLYMEREKÖRPER **9613**
POLYMERIE **9616**
POLYMERISATION **9614**
POLYMERISIEREN (SICH) **9615**
POLYSULFID DES KALIUMS **9697**
POLYTROPE **9618**
PONTONSMANNLOCH **9620**
PORE **9627**
PORENVERMUTTUNGSMITTEL **616**
PORIG **9630**
PORIGKEIT **9629**
PORÖS **9630**
POROSITÄT **9629**
PORPHYR **9632**
PORPHYRTUFF **9631**
PORTALFRÄSWERKE **9642**
PORTALKRAN **13224**
PORTALKRAN **9641**
PORTLANDZEMENT **9644**
PORZELLAN **9625**
PORZELLANERDE **2340**
PORZELLANTIEGEL **9626**
PORZELLANTON **2340**
POSITIONIERZEIT **9651**
POSITIONSSTEUERUNG **9650**
POSITIVELEKTRISCH **4641**
POSITRON **9662**
POST-PROZESSOR **9665**
POTENTIAL **9708**
POTENTIALDIFFERENZ **9709**
POTENTIALGEFÄLLE **13594**
POTENTIOMETER **9711**
POTENZ (MATH.) **9729**
POTENZ (VIERTE) **5608**
POTENZIEREN **10180**
POTTASCHE **9679**

**PRA** 870

POTTASCHE (GEREINIGTE) **9143**
PRÄGEN **12056**
PRÄGEN **12059**
PRÄGEN **2651**
PRÄGEPOLIEREN **1758**
PRÄGEPRESSE **2653**
PRÄGEPRESSE **12060**
PRÄGEPROBE **12061**
PRÄGESTEMPEL **2652**
PRÄGESTEMPEL **3883**
PRÄGESTEMPEL **5580**
PRÄGUNG **3894**
PRÄGWERK **12060**
PRÄPARAT **9784**
PRÄPARIERSALZ **11732**
PRASEODYM **9750**
PRÄZESSION **9754**
PRÄZIPITAT **9759**
PRÄZISIONSGUSS **9765**
PRÄZISIONSHÖHENMESSER **9768**
PRÄZISIONSLEHRE **9766**
PRÄZISIONSMASCHINE **9770**
PRÄZISIONSMASSSTAB **9767**
PRÄZISIONSSCHLEIFMASCHINE **6113**
PRÄZISIONSWAAGE **9764**
PRESSASBEST **747**
PRESSBACKEN **6120**
PRESSBLOCK (IN DER STRANGPRESSE) **4371**
PRESSE **9795**
PRESSE (GERADSEITIGE MECHANISCHE) **12316**
PRESSE (HYDRAULISCHE) **6693**
PRESSEN **9806**
PRESSEN (MIT DER SCHMIEDEPRESSE) **9800**
PRESSEN (MIT DER SCHMIEDEPRESSE) **9807**
PRESSKÖRPER **6088**
PRESSKÖRPER **2791**
PRESSLING **1623**
PRESSLING **6088**
PRESSLING **2791**
PRESSLUFT **2839**
PRESSLUFT-AUSWURFVORRICHTUNGEN **9796**
PRESSLUFTDÜSE **275**
PRESSLUFTHAMMER **9553**
PRESSLUFTLEITUNG **2845**
PRESSLUFTLOKOMOTIVE **2844**
PRESSLUFTMOTOR **2843**
PRESSLUFTNIETHAMMER **9555**
PRESSLUFTSTAMPFER **286**
PRESSLUFTVENTIL **9557**
PRESSLUFTWERKZEUG **9556**
PRESSMITTEL **1250**

PRESSRING **3883**
PRESSSCHMIEDEN **9798**
PRESSSCHMIERUNG **9818**
PRESSSCHWEISSEN **9842**
PRESSSCHWEISSEN (ALUMINOTHERMISCHES) **9837**
PRESSSITZ **5527**
PRESSSPAN **9801**
PRESSSTAHL **2849**
PRESSTORF **9804**
PRESSZUSATZ **1250**
PREUSSISCHBLAU **1206**
PRIMÄRELEMENT **9846**
PRIMÄRSTROMVERHÄLTNIS **9850**
PRIMITIVE TRANSLATION **9865**
PRIMZAHL **9860**
PRISMA **9875**
PRISMA (DREISEITIGES) **13192**
PRISMA (FÜNFSEITIGES) **9173**
PRISMA (SCHIEF ABGESCHNITTENES) **9876**
PRISMA (SECHSSEITIGES) **6460**
PRISMATISCH **9879**
PRISMATOID **9880**
PRISMENHAMMER **4326**
PRISMENSPEKTRUM **9878**
PROBE **12770**
PROBE **10915**
PROBE **11858**
PROBE (HYDRAULISCHE) **6695**
PROBE (HYDROTATISCHE) **6727**
PROBE(STÜCK) **12788**
PROBEBELASTUNG **12781**
PROBEBLOCK **12777**
PROBEDRUCK **12786**
PROBEENTNAHME **10916**
PROBEFAHRBAHN **12794**
PROBENEHMEN **10916**
PROBESTAB **12772**
PROBESTAB MIT EINKERBUNG **8675**
PROBESTABDREHBANK **12771**
PROBESTÜCK **12784**
PROBESTÜCK **10915**
PROBESTÜCK **12789**
PROBIERGLAS **12780**
PROBIERHAHN **12776**
PROBIERHAHN **5875**
PROBIERSTAND **12773**
PROBIERVENTIL **5875**
PRODUKT **9892**
PRODUKT (MATH.) **9891**
PRODUKT (SKALARES) **10966**
PRODUKT (VEKTORISCHES) **13509**

| | |
|---|---|
| PRODUKTE (ERSTKLASSIGE) 9862 | PRÜFSTAND 12773 |
| PRODUKTIONSKOSTEN 3207 | PRÜFSTANDVERSUCH 1170 |
| PRODUKTIVITÄT 9897 | PRÜFSTEMPEL 3893 |
| PROFIL 9898 | PRÜFSTÖPSEL 12785 |
| PROFILDRAHT 11847 | PRÜFSTRASSE 6986 |
| PROFILE 6413 | PRÜFSTÜCK 12784 |
| PROFILEISEN 11119 | PRÜFSTÜCK 1039 |
| PROFILFRÄSER 9899 | PRÜFTANK 12790 |
| PROFILFRÄSMASCHINE 9900 | PRÜFUNG 13534 |
| PROFILKALIBER 11123 | PRÜFUNG 12770 |
| PROFILSTAHL 11125 | PRÜFUNG 6987 |
| PROFILWALZE 6136 | PRÜFUNG (AKUSTISCHE) 11815 |
| PROFILWALZEN 10668 | PRÜFUNG (AMTLICHE) 8740 |
| PROGRAMM 9902 | PRÜFUNG (MAGNETOGRAPHISCHE) 7931 |
| PROGRAMMENDE 4724 | PRÜFUNG (MECHANISCHE) 8112 |
| PROGRAMMIEREN 9904 | PRÜFUNG (PHYSIKALISCHE) 9284 |
| PROGRAMMIEREN (MASCHINELLES) 850 | PRÜFUNG (ZERSTÖRENDE) 3806 |
| PROGRAMMIERTER HALT 9903 | PRÜFUNG (ZERSTÖRUNGSFREIE) 8630 |
| PROGRESSIVE ALTERUNG 9906 | PRÜFUNG BEI HOCHTEMPERATUR 6499 |
| PROGRESSIVINDUKTIONSSCHWEISSEN 9908 | PRÜFUNG DES MATERIALS 12782 |
| PROJEKTION 9912 | PRÜFUNG MIT DEM LÜCKENSUCHGERÄT 6535 |
| PROJEKTION (DIMETRISCHE) 3961 | PRÜFUNGSANALYSE 2280 |
| PROJEKTION (GNOMONISCHE) 5990 | PRÜFUNGSERGEBNIS 10512 |
| PROJEKTION (ISOMETRISCHE) 7188 | PRÜFUNGSRESULTAT 10512 |
| PROJEKTION (TRIMETRISCHE) 13208 | PRÜFUNGSZEUGNIS 12775 |
| PROJEKTIONSEBENE 9438 | PSE 151 |
| PROJEKTIV 9914 | PSI 6873 |
| PROJIZIEREN 9909 | PSYCHROMETER 9960 |
| PROMETHIUM 6771 | PUDDELEISEN 9962 |
| PROPAN 9927 | PUDDELLUPPE 1345 |
| PROPELLER 11041 | PUDDELN 9964 |
| PROPORTION 9933 | PUDDELOFEN 9965 |
| PROPORTIONAL 9935 | PUDDELROHEISEN 5544 |
| PROPORTIONALITÄT 9938 | PUDDELSTAHL 9963 |
| PROPORTIONALITÄTSFAKTOR 2631 | PUFFER 1686 |
| PROPORTIONALITÄTSGRENZE 9936 | PUFFER-SPEICHER 1689 |
| PROPORTIONALITÄTSGRENZE 7590 | PUFFERBATTERIE 1687 |
| PROPORTIONALZIRKEL 9937 | PUFFERFEDER 1688 |
| PROPYLEN 9939 | PUFFERSPEICHER 12736 |
| PROTAKTINIUM 9940 | PUFFERVORRICHTUNG 3611 |
| PROTON 9954 | PULSATIONSSCHWEISSVERFAHREN 9978 |
| PROZESS 2291 | PULSIONSVENTILATION 9517 |
| PROZESSOR 9889 | PULSOMETER 9980 |
| PRÜFDEHNGRENZE 9922 | PULVER (DENDRITISCHES) 3749 |
| PRÜFDRUCK 12786 | PULVER (FEINGEMAHLENES) 6789 |
| PRÜFGLAS 12780 | PULVER (GROBGEMAHLENES) 2580 |
| PRÜFHAHN 12776 | PULVER (KUGELIGES) 5979 |
| PRÜFLEHRE 12779 | PULVER (LEGIERTES) 367 |
| PRÜFLEHRE 8035 | PULVERBRENNSCHNEIDEN 9719 |
| PRÜFLEHRE 10366 | PULVERFORM (IN) 9728 |
| PRÜFPUMPE 12787 | PULVERFÖRMIG 9728 |

**PUL** 872

PULVERIG **9728**
PULVERISIERBAR **9981**
PULVERISIEREN **9982**
PULVERISIERT **9983**
PULVERISIERUNG **9985**
PULVERMETALLURGIE **9720**
PULVERMETHODE **9721**
PULVERMETHODE **3643**
PULVERMISCHUNG **8336**
PULVERSPRITZSCHWEISSEN **9722**
PULVERZEMENTIEREN **8992**
PUMPANLAGEN **9996**
PUMPE **9991**
PUMPE (TRAGBARE) **9638**
PUMPE ANHEBEN LASSEN (EINE) **9856**
PUMPE ANSAUGEN (EINE) **9856**
PUMPE MIT GERADLINIG HIN-UND HERGEHENDEM KOLBEN **10284**
PUMPE MIT SCHWINGENDEM ODER OSZILLIERENDEM KOLBEN **11176**
PUMPENELEMENT **9995**
PUMPENZYLINDER **1015**
PUMPZYLINDER **9992**
PUNKT **9559**
PUNKT (ISOELEKTRISCHER) **7175**
PUNKT (KRITISCHER) **3347**
PUNKT (LEUCHTENDER) **7823**
PUNKTIERFEDER **4126**
PUNKTSCHWEISSEN MIT HANDBETÄTIGTER SCHWEISSENELEKTRODE **9576**
PUNKTSCHWEISSUNG **11959**
PUNKTSCHWEISSUNG **11959**
PUNKTSTEUERUNG **9572**
PUTZ **9463**
PUTZBÜRSTE **11014**
PUTZEN **11689**
PUTZEN **5129**
PUTZEN (GUSSSTÜCKE) **2469**
PUTZEN DER GUSSSTÜCKE **2478**
PUTZEREI **5130**
PUTZLAPPEN **11952**
PUTZLEDER **2234**
PUTZÖL **2477**
PUTZTROMMEL **13261**
PUTZTUCH **11952**
PUTZWOLLE **3223**
PUZZOLANERDE **9748**
PUZZOLANZEMENT **9749**
PV-DIAGRAMM **6881**
PYKNOMETER **11851**
PYRAMIDE **10038**

PYRAMIDE (ABGESTUMPFTE) **13238**
PYRAMIDE (DREISEITIGE) **13193**
PYRAMIDE (FÜNFSEITIGE) **9174**
PYRAMIDE (VIERSEITIGE) **12026**
PYRAMIDENSTUMPF **13238**
PYRAMIDENSYSTEM **10040**
PYRIDIN **10041**
PYRIT **7146**
PYROELEKTRISCH **10042**
PYROELEKTRIZITÄT **10043**
PYROGALLOL **10045**
PYROGALLUSSÄURE **10045**
PYROLUSIT **10047**
PYROMETALLURGIE **10048**
PYROMETALLURGIE **4349**
PYROMETER **10049**
PYROMETER (OPTISCHES) **8845**
PYROMETER (THERMOELEKTRISCHES) **12825**
PYROMETERKEGEL **10050**
PYROMETERKEGEL-FALLPUNKT **10051**
PYROMETRIE **10052**
PYROPHOSPHORSÄURE **10054**
PYROPHOSPHORSAURES NATRON **11730**
PYROXYLIN **6176**
PYRRHOTIN **7914**
QUADER **761**
QUADERMAUERWERK **762**
QUADRANT **10056**
QUADRANTEISEN **9241**
QUADRAT (GEOM.) **12013**
QUADRATDEZIMETER **12018**
QUADRATEISEN **12015**
QUADRATFUSS (ENGLISCHER) **12020**
QUADRATMETER **12022**
QUADRATMILLIMETER **12023**
QUADRATSEIL **12028**
QUADRATUR **12036**
QUADRATWURZEL **12027**
QUADRATYARD (ENGLISCHES) **12031**
QUADRATZENTIMETER **12016**
QUADRATZOLL (ENGLISCHER) **12021**
QUALIMETER **10061**
QUALITÄTSGUSS **2042**
QUALITÄTSKONTROLLE **10063**
QUANTENAUSBEUTE **10071**
QUARZ **10077**
QUARZFADEN **10078**
QUARZGLAS **10079**
QUARZIT **10083**
QUARZPORPHYR **10081**
QUARZQUECKSILBERLAMPE **10080**

873 RAD

QUARZSAND **10082**
QUECKSILBER **8168**
QUECKSILBER-SCHALTER **8166**
QUECKSILBERBAROMETER **8150**
QUECKSILBERCHLORID **8153**
QUECKSILBERCHLORIDBAD **1369**
QUECKSILBERCHLORÜR **8159**
QUECKSILBERDAMPF-GLEICHRICHTER **8164**
QUECKSILBERDAMPFLAMPE **8167**
QUECKSILBERJODID **8155**
QUECKSILBERLUFTPUMPE **8163**
QUECKSILBERMANOMETER **8151**
QUECKSILBEROXYD **8157**
QUECKSILBEROXYD (SALPETERSAURES) **8156**
QUECKSILBEROXYDNITRAT **8156**
QUECKSILBEROXYDSULFAT **8158**
QUECKSILBEROXYDUL **8161**
QUECKSILBEROXYDUL (SALPETERSAURES) **8160**
QUECKSILBEROXYDULNITRAT **8160**
QUECKSILBEROXYDULSULFAT **8162**
QUECKSILBERSÄULE **2751**
QUECKSILBERTHERMOMETER **8152**
QUECKSILBERZELLE **8165**
QUELLEN DES HOLZES **12544**
QUELLWASSER **11996**
QUER ZUR FASERRICHTUNG **138**
QUERACHSE **13142**
QUERAUSBAUCHUNG **7421**
QUERBALKEN **3361**
QUERDEHNUNG **7421**
QUERDRUCKLAGER **7257**
QUERFINNE **3369**
QUERGLEITUNG **3380**
QUERHAUPT **3388**
QUERKEIL **3215**
QUERKONSOLE **4726**
QUERKONTRAKTION **7424**
QUERKRAFT **11291**
QUERNIETTEILUNG **13145**
QUERPROFIL **3377**
QUERRIEGEL **1432**
QUERRIEGEL **3361**
QUERRISS **3281**
QUERSÄGE **3365**
QUERSCHLITTEN **3379**
QUERSCHNITT **3378**
QUERSCHNITT **11111**
QUERSCHNITT (DREIECKIGER) **13188**
QUERSCHNITT (EIRUNDER) **8917**
QUERSCHNITT (ELLIPTISCHER) **4674**
QUERSCHNITT (GEDRÜCKTER) **3375**

QUERSCHNITT (GEFÄHRLICHER) **3609**
QUERSCHNITT (GEZOGENER) **3376**
QUERSCHNITT (HALBRUNDER) **11170**
QUERSCHNITT (HOHLRECHTECKIGER) **6550**
QUERSCHNITT (KEILFÖRMIGER) **13735**
QUERSCHNITT (KREISFÖRMIGER) **2410**
QUERSCHNITT (KREISRINGFÖRMIGER) **587**
QUERSCHNITT (MAKROSKOPISCHER) **7875**
QUERSCHNITT (NUTZBARER) **13422**
QUERSCHNITT (OVALER) **8917**
QUERSCHNITT (QUADRATISCHER) **12017**
QUERSCHNITT (RECHTECKIGER) **10302**
QUERSCHNITT (RINGFÖRMIGER) **587**
QUERSCHNITT (STERNFÖRMIGER) **12110**
QUERSCHNITT (TRAPEZF:ORMIGER) **13183**
QUERSCHNITT (WIRKSAMER) **4460**
QUERSCHNITT DES HOLZES **4718**
QUERSCHNITTFLÄCHE **11120**
QUERSCHNITTSVERGRÖSSERUNG **5869**
QUERSCHNITTSVERMINDERUNG **10362**
QUERSCHWINGUNG **13146**
QUERTRÄGER **3367**
QUERVERSCHIEBUNG **7420**
QUERVERSTREBUNG **1516**
QUERWALZEN **1643**
QUERWALZEN **3384**
QUERWALZWERK **1642**
QUERWAND **5692**
QUETSCH-UND SCHROTMÜHLEN **8296**
QUETSCHGRENZE **2873**
QUETSCHHAHN **8345**
QUOTIENT **10114**
RACHENLEHRE **11693**
RACHENLEHRE **6608**
RAD **13810**
RAD (ANGETRIEBENES) **4300**
RAD (KONISCHES) **1229**
RAD (ZYLINDRISCHES) **3591**
RAD(NABEN)KAPPE **6662**
RADACHSE **884**
RADANTRIEB **5186**
RADARM **13811**
RADAUSFLUCHTUNGSKONTROLLE **13086**
RÄDELERZ **1502**
RÄDER (AUSTAUSCHBARE) **7027**
RÄDERANTRIEB **13025**
RÄDERBOHRER **5905**
RÄDERDREHBANK **13816**
RÄDERFRÄSMASCHINE **5894**
RÄDERGETRIEBE **5907**
RÄDERGETRIEBE **13021**

**RAD** 874

RÄDERGETRIEBE (ZUSAMMENGESETZTES) **5901**
RÄDERGRUPPE **5901**
RÄDERKASTEN **5890**
RÄDERÜBERSETZUNG **13131**
RÄDERÜBERSETZUNG (VERHÄLTNIS) **5897**
RÄDERVORGELEGE **7050**
RÄDERWERK **13821**
RÄDERWINDE **10014**
RADFELGE **13818**
RADFELGE **5088**
RADIAL **10125**
RADIALBOHRMASCHINE **10134**
RADIALBOHRMASCHINE **10129**
RADIALE VERSCHIEBUNG **10133**
RADIALFRÄSER **4722**
RADIALKOMPONENTE **10132**
RADIALKUGELLAGER **10130**
RADIALREIFEN **10126**
RADIALSCHNITT DES HOLZES **10075**
RADIALTRÄGER **10131**
RADIALTURBINE **10136**
RADIAN **10138**
RADIATION **10143**
RADIATOR **10150**
RADIEREN **4799**
RADIEREN **4802**
RADIERGUMMI **4801**
RADIERMESSER **4800**
RADIERSTELLE **4803**
RADIKAL (CHEM.) **10154**
RADIOAKTIV **10157**
RADIOAKTIVITÄT **10160**
RADIOCHEMIEREAKTOR **2323**
RADIOEMPFÄNGER **10278**
RADIOGRAMM EINER SCHWEISSNAHT **7097**
RADIOGRAPHIE **10163**
RADIOLOGIE **10164**
RADIUM **10165**
RADIUS **10166**
RADIUSVEKTOR **10170**
RADKRANZ **10596**
RADKRANZ **10592**
RADKRANZPROFILIERMASCHINE **13822**
RADLINIE **3557**
RADMUTTERSCHLÜSSEL **883**
RADREIFEN **13322**
RADREIFENDREHBANK **13321**
RADSCHEIBE **4013**
RADSPEICHE **13811**
RADSTAND **13813**
RADSTERN **13814**

RADSTURZ **1889**
RADVERDECK **13815**
RADZAHN **13819**
RAFFINADEKUPFER **13070**
RAFFINAT **10374**
RAFFINERIE **10375**
RAFFINERIEFACKEL **10376**
RAFFINIEREN **10370**
RAFFINIEREN **10377**
RAFFINIERT **10372**
RAHMEN **3837**
RAHMEN **5624**
RAHMENBLECHSCHERE **6170**
RAHMENFÜLLUNG **9032**
RAHMENHAMMER **4326**
RAHMENLÄNGSTRÄGER **5627**
RAHMENWERK **5630**
RAMIE **10192**
RAMIEFASER **10192**
RAMSBOTTOMKOLBEN **10196**
RAND **4441**
RANDABSTAND DER NIETE **4066**
RANDBLECH **11531**
RANDBLECH **8002**
RÄNDELMUTTER **8280**
RÄNDELN **8287**
RÄNDELN EINES SCHRAUBENKOPFES **8288**
RÄNDELSCHRAUBENANTRIEB **7337**
RÄNDELUNG **7338**
RANDENTFERNUNG **4066**
RANDLUFTÖFFNUNG **10597**
RANDNIET **10622**
RANDSCHICHT **11544**
RANDSTAHL **10598**
RANKINISIEREN VON DIAGRAMMEN **2770**
RASCHER RÜCKLAUF **10106**
RASENEISENERZ **7596**
RASENMÄHER **7439**
RASPEL **10215**
RAST **8672**
RASUR **4803**
RATIONELLE FORMEL **5583**
RATSCHE **10218**
RÄTSCHE **10218**
RATTENSCHWANZ **10216**
RATTERMARKEN **2276**
RAUCH **11672**
RAUCH (BRAUNER) **10327**
RAUCHBELÄSTIGUNG **11676**
RAUCHBILDUNG **11675**
RAUCHENTWICKLUNG **11675**

875  **RED**

RAUCHFANG **1455**
RAUCHFANG **5467**
RAUCHGASE **5470**
RAUCHGASE **5732**
RAUCHGASVORWÄRMER **4437**
RAUCHKANAL **5467**
RAUCHROHR **5248**
RAUCHRÖHRENKESSEL **5249**
RAUCHSCHIEBER **3603**
RAUCHVERHÜTUNG **11677**
RAUCHVERZEHREND **11673**
RAUHBANK **7245**
RAUHIGKEIT **9011**
RAUHIGKEIT **10792**
RAUM **13434**
RAUM **2798**
RAUM (SCHÄDLICHER) **2482**
RAUM (TOTER) **2482**
RAUMAUSDEHNUNG **13603**
RAUMAUSDEHNUNGSZAHL **2625**
RAUMBEANSPRUCHUNG **11829**
RAUMBEDARF **11829**
RAUMEINHEIT **13377**
RÄUMEN **1637**
RÄUMER **1636**
RAUMERSPARNIS **5774**
RAUMGITTER **11828**
RAUMINHALT **13598**
RAUMINHALTSBERECHNUNG **3444**
RAUMKOORDINATEN **13203**
RAUMKURVE **13307**
RÄUMLICHE KURVE **13307**
RÄUMMASCHINE (SENKRECHTE) **10190**
RAUMPROZENT **9179**
RAUMPUNKT **9560**
RAUMTEIL **9179**
RAUMTEMPERATUR **10713**
RAUPE (FLACHE) **5401**
RAUPENSCHLEPPER **13094**
RAUSCHGELB **728**
RAUSCHROT **10262**
RAUTE **10568**
RAUTENFLÄCHNER **10566**
REAGENS **10257**
REAGENZGLAS **12791**
REAGENZGLAS **12780**
REAGENZPAPIER **12783**
REAKTANZ **10247**
REAKTION **10248**
REAKTION (ALKALISCHE) **337**
REAKTION (BASISCHE) **337**

REAKTION (CHEMISCHE) **2312**
REAKTION (IRREVERSIBEL ELEKTROLYTISCHE) **7171**
REAKTION (PERITEKTISCHE) **9199**
REAKTION (SAURE) **122**
REAKTIONSENERGIE **2305**
REAKTIONSGRENZE **10249**
REAKTIONSTURBINE **10250**
REAKTOR (KERN) **10251**
REALGAR **10262**
REAUMURGRAD **3724**
REAUMURSKALA **10267**
REAUMURTHERMOMETER **10268**
RECHENFEHLER **4824**
RECHENMASCHINE **1859**
RECHENSCHIEBER **11591**
RECHENTABELLE **8052**
RECHENTAFEL **8052**
RECHNERPROGRAMM **10811**
RECHNERSTEUERUNG (DIREKTE) **3981**
RECHNERSTEUERUNG (DIREKTE) **2875**
RECHNERSTEURUNG (DIREKTE) **3985**
RECHTECK **10299**
RECHTECKFEDER **10306**
RECHTECKFEDER (GESCHICHTETE) **7380**
RECHTECKFEDER (ZUGESCHÄRFTE) **10307**
RECHTECKGEWINDE **12030**
RECHTECKLAST **10303**
RECHTECKMASCHE **10304**
RECHTKANT **10305**
RECHTSDREHEND **3827**
RECHTSDREHEND **2506**
RECHTSDREHUNG **2507**
RECHTSGEWICKELT **2508**
RECHTSGEWINDE **10585**
RECHTSGEWUNDEN **2508**
RECHTSSCHWEISSUNG **907**
RECHTSVERSCHIEBUNG **10583**
RECHTSWEINSÄURE **3826**
RECHTWINKLIG **10310**
RECKALTERUNG **12324**
RECKEN **4235**
RECKEN **4219**
RECKSPANNUNG **12370**
REDUKTION (CHEM.) **10356**
REDUKTION (ELEKTROLYTISCHE) **4607**
REDUKTIONS... **10345**
REDUKTIONSATMOSPHÄRE **10347**
REDUKTIONSFLAMME **4882**
REDUKTIONSFLANSCH **10350**
REDUKTIONSGETRIEBE **11873**
REDUKTIONSMITTEL **10346**

# RED 876

REDUKTIONSMUFFE **3962**
REDUKTIONSROHR **10352**
REDUKTIONSTEMPERATUR **10354**
REDUKTIONSWÄRME **6362**
REDUKTIONSZIRKEL **9937**
REDUNDANZ **10364**
REDUZIER... **10345**
REDUZIER-ELEMENTE (KEGELSTUMPFE) **2950**
REDUZIERANSCHLUSS **13121**
REDUZIEREN (CHEM.) **10342**
REDUZIEREND **10345**
REDUZIERMASCHINE **12533**
REDUZIERMUFFE **10348**
REDUZIERNIPPEL **10351**
REDUZIEROFEN **10359**
REDUZIERSTÜCK **1773**
REDUZIERVENTIL **10355**
REDUZIERWALZSTRASSE **10353**
REDUZIERWALZWERK **11508**
REFBUNGSKUPPLUNG **5672**
REFLEKTIEREN **10382**
REFLEKTION **10387**
REFLEKTOR **10394**
REFLEXION **10387**
REFLEXION (TOTALE) **13060**
REFLEXION DES LICHTES **10390**
REFLEXIONS-WASSERSTANDSANZEIGER **10395**
REFLEXIONSGITTER **10388**
REFLEXIONSGLAS **10396**
REFLEXIONSVERHÄLTNIS **10391**
REFLEXIONSVERLUST **10389**
REFLEXIONSVERMÖGEN **10393**
REFLEXIONSVERMÖGEN **10392**
REFLEXIONSWINKEL **525**
REFRAKTION **10400**
REFRAKTIONSVERMÖGEN **10403**
REFRAKTOMETER **10404**
REGELABWEICHUNG **3819**
REGELANTRIEBSTEUERUNG **13492**
REGELDRUCK **9832**
REGELLEISTUNG **8658**
REGELLOS ORIENTIERT **10199**
REGELN **182**
REGELUNG **195**
REGELVENTIL **12890**
REGELVORRICHTUNG **10418**
REGELVORRICHTUNG **3052**
REGELWIDERSTAND **10563**
REGENERATIVFEUERUNG **10410**
REGENERATOR **10412**
REGENRINNENZANGE **4286**

REGENWASSER **10179**
REGENWASSERFLECKEN **10178**
REGISTRIEREN **10288**
REGISTRIERENDES INSTRUMENT **10289**
REGISTRIERTROMMEL **10290**
REGISTRIERVORRICHTUNG **10294**
REGISTRIERWALZE **10290**
REGLER **10421**
REGLER (ASTATISCHER) **775**
REGLER (ELEKTRISCHER) **4527**
REGLER (ELEKTRONISCHER) **4635**
REGLER (ISOCHRONER) **7180**
REGLER (PSEUDOASTATISCHER) **9957**
REGLER (SELBSTTÄTIGER) **843**
REGLER (STATISCHER) **12135**
REGLER MIT GEKREUZTEN STANGEN **3386**
REGLERARM **6014**
REGLERFEDER **6019**
REGLERGEHÄUSE **6016**
REGLERHÜLSE **6017**
REGLERKUGEL **6015**
REGLERMUFFE **6017**
REGLERSPINDEL **6018**
REGLERWELLE **6018**
REGULATOR **10421**
REGULIEREN **182**
REGULIERUNG **195**
REGULIERWIDERSTAND **10563**
REIBAHLE **10263**
REIBAHLE **1636**
REIBAHLE (GENUTETE) **5485**
REIBAHLE (GERADEGENUTETE) **12305**
REIBAHLE (GERIFFELTE) **5197**
REIBAHLE (HARTMETALLBESTÜCKTE) **1935**
REIBAHLE (KEGELIGE) **12658**
REIBAHLE (KONISCHE) **12658**
REIBAHLE (NACHSTELLBARE) **4923**
REIBAHLE (VERSTELLBARE) **188**
REIBAHLENHALTER **10264**
REIBER **9532**
REIBER **9221**
REIBGETRIEBE **5674**
REIBKEGELGETRIEBE **1224**
REIBKEGELRAD **1225**
REIBRAD **5682**
REIBRAD (ZYLINDRISCHES) **12007**
REIBRÄDERWENDEGETRIEBE **10546**
REIBROLLE **5679**
REIBSCHALE **8395**
REIBSCHEIBE **5673**
REIBUNG **5668**

REIBUNG (GLEITENDE) **11601**
REIBUNG (INNERE) **7065**
REIBUNG (INNERE) **5473**
REIBUNG (MAGNETISCHE) **6747**
REIBUNG (ROLLENDE) **10700**
REIBUNG (RUHENDE) **5678**
REIBUNG DER BEWEGUNG **5677**
REIBUNG DER RUHE **5678**
REIBUNG MITNEHMEN (DURCH) **4291**
REIBUNGERMÜDUNG **2200**
REIBUNGSARBEIT **13942**
REIBUNGSBREMSE **5669**
REIBUNGSDRUCK **9816**
REIBUNGSFLÄCHE **5687**
REIBUNGSGESPERRE **5676**
REIBUNGSGETRIEBE **5684**
REIBUNGSGRENZE **7309**
REIBUNGSKEGEL **5671**
REIBUNGSKLINKE **5675**
REIBUNGSKOEFFIZIENT **2629**
REIBUNGSKOEFFIZIENT FÜR GLEITENDE REIBUNG **2634**
REIBUNGSKOEFFIZIENT FÜR ROLLENDE REIBUNG **2633**
REIBUNGSKRAFT **5683**
REIBUNGSKUPPLUNG **11614**
REIBUNGSLOS **5688**
REIBUNGSMOMENT **8371**
REIBUNGSOXYDATION **5666**
REIBUNGSOXYDATION **5667**
REIBUNGSSÄGEN **5680**
REIBUNGSSCHALTWERK **5676**
REIBUNGSVERLUST **5685**
REIBUNGSVERLUST **7755**
REIBUNGSWÄRME **6343**
REIBUNGSWIDERSTAND **5686**
REIBUNGSWINKEL **527**
REIBUNGSZAHL **5670**
REICHGAS **8758**
REICHWEITE DES SCHALLES **10202**
REIFENLAUFFLÄCHE **13172**
REIFENSCHLAUCH **13246**
REIFKLOBEN **13565**
REIHE **11203**
REIHE (ARITHMETISCHE) **704**
REIHE (BINOMISCHE) **1260**
REIHE (DIVERGENTE) **4094**
REIHE (ENDLICHE) **5232**
REIHE (GEOMETRISCHE) **5930**
REIHE (HOMOLOGE) (CHEM.) **6562**
REIHE (KONVERGENTE) **3065**
REIHE (LOGARITHMISCHE) **7719**
REIHE (UNENDLICHE) **6909**

REIHENANFERTIGUNG **10462**
REIHENSCHALTUNG **11199**
REIHENSCHLUSSDYNAMO **11201**
REIHENSCHLUSSMOTOR **11202**
REINGEHALT EINER LEGIERUNG **5209**
REINIGEN **10370**
REINIGEN **10377**
REINIGER **10020**
REINIGER (ALKALISCHER) **2472**
REINIGUNG (ALKALISCHE) **334**
REINIGUNG (ANODISCHE) **592**
REINIGUNG (ELEKTROLYTISCHE) **4589**
REINIGUNG (MECHANISCHE) **8096**
REINIGUNG DES WASSERS **10019**
REINIGUNGS- UND POLIERMITTEL **2475**
REINIGUNGS- UND SCHNEIDEMASCHINEN FÜR WURZELN UND RÜBEN **10715**
REINIGUNGSMITTEL **10995**
REINIGUNGSMITTEL **2473**
REINIGUNGSMITTEL **2471**
REINIGUNGSMITTEL **3813**
REINIGUNGSTROMMEL **13261**
REINIGUNGSWIRKUNG **10017**
REISEGESCHWINDIGKEIT **3417**
REISEOMNIBUS **8412**
REISSBRETT **4231**
REISSEN **10859**
REISSEN DES HOLZES **11948**
REISSFEDER **4241**
REISSLÄNGE **1584**
REISSMASS **8016**
REISSMODELL **8016**
REISSNADEL **11068**
REISSNAGEL **4242**
REISSSCHIENE **12581**
REISSZEUG **8051**
REISSZWECKE **4242**
REITSTOCK **6328**
REITSTOCK **12599**
REITSTOCKSPITZE (UMLAUFENDE) **10560**
REKALESZENZ **10274**
REKRISTALLISATION **10297**
REKRISTALLISATIONSTEMPERATUR **10298**
REKTIFIKATION (CHEM.) **10311**
REKTIFIZIEREN (CHEM.) **10318**
REKUPERATIVOFEN **10321**
REKUPERATIVOFEN **10410**
REKUPERATOR **10322**
RELATIVE FEUCHTIGKEIT DER LUFT **10433**
RELIEFARBEIT **4684**
RELUKTANZ **10444**

**REP** 878

REMANENZ 10445
REPARATUR 10459
REPARATURKOSTEN 3208
REPARATURWERKSTÄTTE 10461
REPARIEREN 10460
REPRODUKTION 10467
REPRODUZIEREN 8484
REPRODUZIEREN 8481
RESERVE- 12068
RESERVEMASCHINE 12070
RESERVERAD 11835
RESERVERAD 2243
RESILIENZ 13071
RESONANZ 10506
RESONANZSCHWINGUNG 8883
RESULTANTE 10513
RESULTIERENDE 10513
RESULTIERENDER WIRKUNGSGRAD 8927
RETORTE 10523
RETORTE (TUBULIERTE) 10525
RETORTENGRAPHIT 5812
RETORTENKOHLE 5812
RETORTENOFEN 10524
RETORTENVORLAGE 10277
REVERBERIEROFEN 10532
REVERSIERDAMPFMASCHINE 10543
REVISION 6985
REVISIONSLEHRE 5011
REVOLVERDREHBANK 1931
REVOLVERDREHMASCHINE 13297
REVOLVERPRESSEN (MECHANISCHE) 3839
RHEOLOGIE 10562
RHEOSTAT 10563
RHEOTROPE SPRÖDIGKEIT 1633
RHODANKALIUM 9701
RHODIUM 10564
RHOMBOEDER 10566
RHOMBOID 10567
RHOMBUS 10568
RICHTEN 12318
RICHTEN 13234
RICHTEN 12319
RICHTEN 2730
RICHTHAKEN 6571
RICHTHORN 6571
RICHTLINEAL 12303
RICHTMASCHINE 12320
RICHTPLATTE 12321
RICHTPLATTE 12516
RICHTSCHIENE 12303
RICHTSTICH 11543

RICHTUNG (SENKRECHTE) 9219
RICHTUNG EINER KRAFT 3990
RICHTUNGSÄNDERUNG 2236
RICHTUNGSPFEIL 719
RICHTUNGSWECHSEL 2236
RIEFIG 5484
RIEGEL 1432
RIEMEN 1140
RIEMEN 1163
RIEMEN (DREIFACHER) 12878
RIEMEN (GELEIMTER) 2145
RIEMEN (GENÄHTER) 7350
RIEMEN (GEWEBTER) 13983
RIEMEN (X-FACHER) 1166
RIEMEN AUFLEGEN (DEN) 11357
RIEMEN AUS WIRBELBAHNEN 1143
RIEMEN AUS X LAGEN 1166
RIEMEN SCHALTEN (DEN) 11349
RIEMEN VERSCHIEBEN (DEN) 11349
RIEMENANTRIEB 1144
RIEMENANTRIEB 4319
RIEMENAUFLEGER 1159
RIEMENAUSRÜCKER 1157
RIEMENBETRIEB 4319
RIEMENFÜHRER 1150
RIEMENGABEL 12346
RIEMENKEGEL 12669
RIEMENKEGELTRIEB 404
RIEMENKLAMMER 1146
RIEMENKONOID 12669
RIEMENKONUS 12669
RIEMENKUPPLUNG 7349
RIEMENLOCHZANGE 1153
RIEMENNIET 1155
RIEMENS (SCHICHT EINES) 1165
RIEMENSCHALTER 1157
RIEMENSCHALTUNG 1158
RIEMENSCHEIBE 1152
RIEMENSCHEIBE 11793
RIEMENSCHEIBE (BALLIGE) 3400
RIEMENSCHEIBE (DURCHLOCHTE) 9188
RIEMENSCHEIBE (FESTE) 5040
RIEMENSCHEIBE (GERADE) 5404
RIEMENSCHEIBE (GETEILTE) 11945
RIEMENSCHEIBE (GEWÖLBTE) 3400
RIEMENSCHEIBE (LOSE) 7747
RIEMENSCHEIBE (UNGETEILTE) (GANZE) 11792
RIEMENSCHEIBE AUS GEPRESSTEM BLECH 9805
RIEMENSCHEIBE AUS PAPIER 9034
RIEMENSCHEIBE MIT BORD SCHEIBE 5336
RIEMENSCHEIBE MIT DOPPELSPEICHEN 4127

**ROH**     879

RIEMENSCHEIBE MIT DURCHLOCHTEM KRANZ **9188**
RIEMENSCHEIBE MIT GERADEN ARMEN **9977**
RIEMENSCHEIBE MIT GESCHWEIFTEN ARMEN **9976**
RIEMENSCHEIBENDREHBANK **9975**
RIEMENSCHEIBENSCHWUNGRAD **1147**
RIEMENSCHLOSS **1146**
RIEMENSCHRAUBE **1156**
RIEMENSPANNER **1161**
RIEMENSPANNUNG **1162**
RIEMENTRIEB **1144**
RIEMENTRIEB (GEKREUZTER) **3387**
RIEMENTRIEB (GESCHRÄNKTER) **3387**
RIEMENTRIEB (HALBGESCHRÄNSKTER) **6207**
RIEMENTRIEB (OFFENER) **8804**
RIEMENTROMMEL **4333**
RIEMENVERBINDER **1146**
RIEMENVERBINDUNG **1151**
RIEMENVERBINDUNG **1142**
RIEMENVERBINDUNG (GELEIMTE) **2143**
RIEMENVERBINDUNG (GENÄHTE) **7348**
RIEMENVERBINDUNG (GENIETETE) **10555**
RIEMENVERSCHIEBUNG **1158**
RIEMENVORGELEGE **7045**
RIEMENWENDEGETRIEBE **1154**
RIFFEL **10576**
RIFFELBLECH **10574**
RIFFELBLECH **2285**
RIFFELBLECH **2325**
RIFFELFEILE **10575**
RIFFELMASCHINE **6138**
RIFFELWALZE **5486**
RIFFELWALZE **11206**
RILLE **6127**
RILLENEISEN **2248**
RILLENRAD **13732**
RILLENSCHEIBE **6140**
RINDLEDER **3275**
RINDSTALG **1128**
RING **12904**
RING **10600**
RING (INNERER) EINES KUGELLAGERS **6953**
RING (ZYLINDRISCHER) **3588**
RINGBOLZEN **4973**
RINGDICHTUNG **10604**
RINGFLÄCHE EINES KAMMLAGERS **2723**
RINGFÖRMIG **588**
RINGKEIL **2931**
RINGKLUFT **3460**
RINGKÖRPER (GEOM.) **13043**
RINGLEITUNG **2418**
RINGLEITUNG **1774**

RINGNUT **2415**
RINGSCHMIERLAGER **10602**
RINGSCHMIERUNG **10601**
RINGSKALA **3841**
RINGSKALA-ANZEIGER **3840**
RINGSPURLAGER **2722**
RINGSPURZAPFEN **10606**
RINGSTÜCK **10603**
RINGVENTIL **10605**
RINNE **6127**
RINNE **6185**
RINNE **2251**
RINNEN **7492**
RINNEN **7487**
RIPPE **10569**
RIPPE **5183**
RIPPENROHR **5234**
RIPPENROHR **10571**
RIPPENROHR MIT AUSSENRIPPEN **4963**
RIPPENROHR MIT INNENRIPPEN **7082**
RIPPENROHR MIT LÄNGSRIPPEN **7740**
RIPPENROHR MIT QUERRIPPEN **13147**
RIPPENROHRKÜHLER **5233**
RIPPENVERSTEIFUNG **12152**
RISS **3284**
RISS **3278**
RISS **2278**
RISS **3283**
RISS IM HOLZ **11250**
RISS- UND FEHLERDETEKTOR **3280**
RISSBILDUNG **3284**
RISSBILDUNG **2286**
RISSBILDUNG **644**
RISSIG WERDEN **3279**
RISSIGWERDEN DER NIETLÖCHER **3286**
RITZ **11013**
RITZEL **9336**
RITZEL **9335**
RITZHÄRTEPRÜFER **11002**
RITZVERSUCH **11017**
RIZINUSÖL **2086**
ROCHELLESALZ **11729**
ROCKWELL-HÄRTEPRÜFUNG **10659**
ROENTGENBILD **10664**
ROENTGENBILD **10161**
ROENTGENMETALLOGRAPHIE **10155**
ROENTGENRÖHRE **12684**
ROENTGENUNTERSUCHUNG **10162**
ROGENSTEIN **8801**
ROH **740**
ROHANILIN **553**

**ROH** 880

ROHBEARBEITUNG 10785
ROHBENZIN 3408
ROHBENZOL 1204
ROHBLOCK 6919
ROHEISEN 9299
ROHEISEN (BASISCHES) 1049
ROHEISEN (GRAUES) 6094
ROHEISEN (GRAUES) 5596
ROHEISEN (HALBIERTES) 8420
ROHEISEN (HARTGEGOSSEN) 2336
ROHEISEN (HEISS ERBLASENES) 6620
ROHEISEN (KALT ERBLASENES) 2669
ROHEISEN (MELIERTES) 8420
ROHEISEN (SCHWARZES) 1292
ROHEISEN (WEISSES) 13830
ROHEISEN IN KOKILLENGUSS 2333
ROHEISENMASSEL 9298
ROHEN BEARBEITEN (AUS DEM) 10775
ROHERDÖL 3411
ROHERDÖL 3406
ROHGEGOSSEN 739
ROHGESCHMIEDET 742
ROHGEWICHT 10781
ROHGUMMI 3413
ROHGUSS 9299
ROHHAUT 10237
ROHHAUTRITZEL 10238
ROHKUPFER 1287
ROHKUPFER (KUPFERBLASIGES) 1329
ROHLAUFSTREIFEN 1892
ROHLING 1301
ROHLING 11651
ROHLINGE 1349
ROHMATERIAL 10239
ROHMESSING 13987
ROHÖL 3412
ROHÖLTANK 3407
ROHPETROLEUM 3412
ROHR 9339
ROHR 13257
ROHR (ANGESTRICHENES) 9016
ROHR (AUTOGEN GESCHWEISSTES) 9364
ROHR (EINGEWALZTES) 4905
ROHR (GEKRÖPFTES) 12535
ROHR (GEKRÜMMTES) 1194
ROHR (GELÖTETES) 11760
ROHR (GERADES) 12309
ROHR (GERIPPTES) 10571
ROHR (GESCHWEISSTES) 13775
ROHR (GESCHWEISSTES) 13777
ROHR (GESTRICHENES) 9016

ROHR (GETEERTES) 12687
ROHR (GEWALZTES) 10677
ROHR (GEZOGENES) 11782
ROHR (GLATTES) 11684
ROHR (GUSSEISERNES) 2035
ROHR (KALTGEZOGENES) 2714
ROHR (LIEGEND GEGOSSENES) 9342
ROHR (NAHTLOSES) 11089
ROHR (NICHTGELOCHTES) 1306
ROHR (RAUHES) 10780
ROHR (SCHMIEDEEISERNES) 13989
ROHR (SPANISCHES) 10236
ROHR (SPIRALGESCHWEISSTES) 11920
ROHR (STEHEND GEGOSSENES) 9343
ROHR (STUMPFGESCHWEISSTES) 1804
ROHR (ÜBERLAPPT GESCHWEISSTES) 7406
ROHR (VERLORENES) 1306
ROHR (VERLORENES) 7620
ROHR (VERSTOPFTES) 2361
ROHR (ZYLINDRISCHES) 3586
ROHR-ODER FORMSTAHLBÜNDEL 1736
ROHRABSCHNEIDEMASCHINE 9349
ROHRABSCHNEIDER 9348
ROHRABSCHNEIDER 13248
ROHRACHSE 866
ROHRANSATZ 1557
ROHRANSCHLUSS 1554
ROHRAUFWEITEDORN 13250
ROHRBOGEN 7832
ROHRBOGEN 1172
ROHRBOGENAUSGLEICHER 4913
ROHRBRUCH 9353
ROHRBRUCHVENTIL 845
ROHRBÜNDEL 8538
ROHRDICHTUNG 9355
ROHRDURCHMESSER 3858
RÖHRE 13453
RÖHRE 13257
RÖHRE (KALTGEZOGENE) 2678
ROHRE DURCH FLANSCHEN VERBINDEN 7243
ROHRE INEINANDERSTECKEN 5277
ROHRE MIT OFFENER NAHT 2512
ROHRE VERBINDEN 7244
ROHRE VERLEGEN 7441
ROHRE ZIEHEN 4224
RÖHREN (KOMMUNIZIERENDE) 13325
RÖHRENBÜNDEL 8538
ROHRENDE (BLINDES) 1303
RÖHRENFAHRT 9357
RÖHRENFEDERMANOMETER 1501
RÖHRENLIBELLE 13259

**881**            **RON**

RÖHRENSTREIFEN **11527**
RÖHRENTOUR **9357**
RÖHRENWALZWERK **9358**
ROHRFLANSCH **9351**
ROHRFORMSTÜCK **9350**
ROHRFRÄSER **1765**
ROHRFRÄSER ZUM AUSSENFRÄSEN **4951**
ROHRFRÄSER ZUM INNENFRÄSEN **7059**
ROHRGEWINDE **9360**
ROHRGEWINDE-SCHNEIDEMASCHINE **9361**
ROHRHAKEN **9354**
ROHRKALIBER **2027**
ROHRKOLBEN **9545**
ROHRKONTROLLE DURCH TRENNUNG **4877**
ROHRKRÜMMER **1180**
ROHRLEITUNG **9357**
ROHRLEITUNG (UNTERIRDISCHE) **13354**
ROHRMEISSEL **11704**
ROHRMUFFE **11705**
ROHRMÜHLE **13252**
ROHRNAHT **11085**
ROHRNETZ **12579**
ROHRNORMALIEN **9359**
ROHRPLATTE **13254**
ROHRREINIGER **13247**
ROHRRIPPE **10570**
ROHRSCHELLE **13324**
ROHRSCHELLE **9345**
ROHRSCHELLE **9344**
ROHRSCHLANGE **9346**
ROHRSCHLANGE **2645**
ROHRSCHLÜSSEL **9366**
ROHRSCHRAUBSTOCK **9363**
ROHRSCHRAUBSTOCK **13256**
ROHRSTRANG **9357**
ROHRSTRECKE **9357**
ROHRSTÜCK **9292**
ROHRSTUTZEN **5341**
ROHRSTUTZEN **1557**
ROHRSTUTZEN (EINGELASSENER) **6969**
ROHRSTUTZEN (SELBSTVERSTEIFTER) **9012**
ROHRVENTIL **11579**
ROHRVERBINDUNG **9347**
ROHRVERBINDUNG (STUMPFGESCHWEISSTE) **1803**
ROHRVERKLEIDUNG **7369**
ROHRVERSCHRAUBUNG **13369**
ROHRWEITE **1464**
ROHRWEITEMASCHINE **9352**
ROHRZANGE **9362**
ROHSCHIENE **8441**
ROHSTAHL **3414**

ROHSTAHLBLOCK **12210**
ROHSTEIN **11878**
ROHSTOFF **10239**
ROHWASSER **10240**
ROHZINK **2785**
ROLLBAHN **6082**
ROLLBAHN (FÜR ROLLEITER) **10857**
ROLLBANDMASS **8092**
ROLLBEWEGUNG **10702**
ROLLBÖCKE **13231**
ROLLE **2645**
ROLLE **8435**
ROLLE **10671**
ROLLE **10679**
ROLLE **5287**
ROLLE (ALS HEBEZEUG) **9971**
ROLLE (TONNENFÖRMIGE) **1017**
ROLLE EINES FLASCHENZUGS **11301**
ROLLE EINES ROLLENLAGERS **1112**
ROLLEN **10665**
ROLLEN **10696**
ROLLEN **10695**
ROLLEN(NAHT)SCHWEISSEN **11086**
ROLLENBAHN (EINES LAGERS) **10689**
ROLLENBOHRER **1504**
ROLLENDER KREIS **5921**
ROLLENFÖRDERER **6082**
ROLLENKÄFIG **12040**
ROLLENKETTE **10684**
ROLLENKLOBEN **1333**
ROLLENLAGER **10680**
ROLLENLAGER MIT KEGELROLLEN **10683**
ROLLENLAGER MIT TONNENFÖRMIGEN ROLLEN **10681**
ROLLENLAGER MIT ZYLINDRISCHEN ROLLEN **10682**
ROLLENLAGERNADELN **1108**
ROLLENQUETSCHNAHT **8024**
ROLLENRICHTMASCHINE **10685**
ROLLENSPURLAGER **10691**
ROLLENSTÖSSEL **10692**
ROLLENTRANSPORTEUR **6082**
ROLLENTROMMELSATTEL **10690**
ROLLENZUG **9973**
ROLLGABELSCHLÜSSEL **2551**
ROLLGANG **6082**
ROLLKREIS **5921**
ROLLKURVE **10697**
ROLLQUESTSCHE **4450**
ROLLWERKZEUG **3485**
ROLLWIDERSTAND **10703**
ROMANZEMENT **10707**
RÖNTGEN-FLUORESZENZ-ANALYSE **13999**

# RON

882

RÖNTGEN-REFLEXE 3926
RÖNTGENANALYSE 13993
RÖNTGENAPPARAT 13994
RÖNTGENBEUGUNGSBILD 3441
RÖNTGENBEUGUNGSDIAGRAMM 13997
RÖNTGENBILD ODER DIAGRAM 9128
RÖNTGENKRISTALLOGRAPHIE 13996
RÖNTGENPHOTOGRAPHIE 10163
RÖNTGENRÖHRE 14002
RÖNTGENSPEKTROMETER 14000
RÖNTGENSPEKTRUM 14001
RÖNTGENSTRAHLEN 14003
RÖNTGENSTRAHLENBÜNDEL 13995
RÖNTGENUNTERSUCHUNG 13998
ROOTGEBLÄSE 10729
ROSETTENKUPFER 10748
ROSOLSÄURE 10750
ROSSHAAR 6604
ROSSWERK 1731
ROST 10863
ROST 6096
ROST (EISENOXYD) 10335
ROSTBILDUNG 10865
ROSTDICHTUNG 10867
ROSTEN 10865
RÖSTEN VON ERZEN 10650
ROSTFLÄCHE 6068
ROSTFUGE 278
ROSTIG 10873
ROSTKITT 7141
RÖSTOFEN 10649
ROSTSCHIEBER 6100
ROSTSCHUTZ 10871
ROSTSCHUTZ 9945
ROSTSCHUTZMITTEL 10870
ROSTSCHUTZMITTEL 10869
ROSTSCHUTZMITTEL 10866
ROSTSCHUTZMITTEL 3189
ROSTSCHUTZMITTEL 2601
ROSTSPALT 278
ROSTSTAB 5237
ROSTSTABEISEN 6098
ROSTSTÄHLE 6069
RÖSTUNG 1839
ROSTVERHÜTEND 10868
ROT (PARISER) 3355
ROTATION 10765
ROTATIONSDAMPFMASCHINE 10761
ROTATIONSELLIPSOID 4672
ROTATIONSFLÄCHE 12513
ROTATIONSKÖRPER 11790

ROTATIONSPARABOLOID 9042
ROTATIONSPUMPE 10758
ROTBRUCHPROBE 10331
ROTEISENERZ 11865
ROTEISENSTEIN 11865
RÖTEL 10340
ROTER ARSENIK 10262
ROTER PHOSPHOR 10334
ROTES BLEIOXYD 10333
ROTES BLUTLAUGENSALZ 9684
ROTES CHROMKALI 9677
ROTES CHROMSALZ 9677
ROTES CHROMSAURES KALI 9677
ROTES JODQUECKSILBER 8155
ROTES MANGANOXYD 13207
ROTES PRÄZIPITAT 8157
ROTES SCHWEFELARSEN 10262
ROTES ZYANEISENKALIUM 9684
ROTGARES LEDER 8704
ROTGLÜHEND 10330
ROTGLUT 10329
ROTGUSS 10326
ROTGUSS 1658
ROTGUSS 12984
ROTIEREN 10763
ROTIERENDE DAMPFMASCHINE 10761
ROTIERENDE WELLE 10764
ROTKUPFERERZ 3476
ROTMESSING 10325
ROTMESSING 12984
ROTMESSING 2824
ROTMETALL 12984
ROTÖL 1668
ROTOR 10767
ROTORPLATTE 3160
ROTOXID 8157
ROTWARM 10330
RUBIDIUM 10829
RÜBÖL 10204
RÜCKANSICHT 4717
RÜCKAUFNAHME LAUEDIAGRAMM 7435
RÜCKBILDUNG 10554
RÜCKBLICKSPIEGEL 10266
RÜCKBOGEN 13323
RÜCKEN 890
RÜCKENLEHNE 917
RÜCKENSÄGE 897
RÜCKENSTÄUBER UND RÜCKENSPRITZGRERÄTE 11969
RÜCKENWINKEL 2484
RÜCKFENSTER 899
RÜCKFLUSSVENTIL MIT KLAPPE 12545

| | |
|---|---|
| RÜCKFÜHRKREIS **5080** | RUNDFÜHRUNG **3584** |
| RÜCKFÜHRUNGSREGELSYSTEM **2533** | RUNDGÄNGIGE SCHRAUBE **10807** |
| RÜCKGEWINNUNG **10296** | RUNDGESENK **4451** |
| RÜCKKEHRKANTE **4448** | RUNDHOLZ **10803** |
| RÜCKKOHLUNG DES EISENS **10275** | RUNDKOLBEN **10798** |
| RÜCKKOHLUNGSMITTEL **10276** | RUNDKOPFSCHRAUBE **11051** |
| RÜCKKÜHLANLAGE **3089** | RUNDMASCHINE **1391** |
| RÜCKKÜHLUNG ZU UMGEBUNGSTEMPERATUR **3096** | RUNDMASCHINE **1186** |
| RÜCKLICHT **908** | RUNDNAHTSCHWEISSUNG **5948** |
| RÜCKOHLUNG **1953** | RUNDSCHLEIFMASCHINE **3583** |
| RÜCKPRALL **10272** | RUNDSCHRAUBENKOPF **1813** |
| RÜCKSCHAGVENTIL **7543** | RUNDSCHRIFT **10799** |
| RÜCKSCHLAG **10286** | RUNDSCHRIFTFEDER **10806** |
| RÜCKSCHLAG **906** | RUNDSEIL **10801** |
| RÜCKSCHLAGKLAPPE **2284** | RUNDSTAB **10795** |
| RÜCKSCHLAGKLAPPE **2283** | RUNDTISCHE **2424** |
| RÜCKSCHLAGKLAPPE **12545** | RUNDZANGE **10805** |
| RÜCKSCHLAGKLAPPE **7543** | RUSS **11816** |
| RÜCKSCHLAGVENTIL **13437** | RUTHENIUM **10874** |
| RÜCKSCHLAGVENTIL **2284** | RUTSCHE **2395** |
| RÜCKSPRUNG **10272** | RUTSCHEN DES RIEMENS **11620** |
| RÜCKSTAND **10475** | RUTSCHKUPPLUNG **11619** |
| RÜCKSTAND (MAGNETISCHER) **10445** | RÜTTELFORM-MASCHINE **7250** |
| RÜCKSTÄNDE **12598** | RÜTTELFORMMASCHINE **7215** |
| RÜCKSTOSS **10286** | RÜTTELPRESS-FORMMASCHINE OHNE ENTFORMUNG **7252** |
| RÜCKSTRAHLUNG **10390** | RÜTTELPRESSFORMMASCHINE **7253** |
| RÜCKSTRAHLUNG **896** | S-BOGEN **6009** |
| RÜCKSTRAHLUNGSVERMÖGEN **10392** | S-I-GEWINDE **7084** |
| RÜCKSTROMSCHALTELEMENT **7949** | S-ROHR **12535** |
| RÜCKWÄRTSBEWEGUNG **919** | S-STÜCK **12535** |
| RÜCKWÄRTSFLIESSPRESSEN **6884** | SAATGUT UND GETREIDEREINIGUNGS-MASCHINEN **3177** |
| RÜCKWÄRTSGANG **10846** | SACHVERSTÄNDIGER **4930** |
| RÜCKWIRKUNG **10248** | SACKKARREN **947** |
| RÜCKZIEHFEDER **10526** | SAFTHEBER **8389** |
| RÜCKZUGFEDER **10526** | SÄGE **10950** |
| RÜCKZÜNDUNG **906** | SÄGEBLATT **10952** |
| RUHELAGE **9648** | SÄGEEINSCHNITT **3517** |
| RUHMKORFF-INDUKTOR **10830** | SÄGEFEILE **10954** |
| RÜHRAPPARAT **236** | SÄGEFEILKLUPPE **10955** |
| RÜHREN **11254** | SÄGEMEHL **10953** |
| RÜHREN **8328** | SÄGEN **10961** |
| RÜHRER **236** | SÄGEN **10951** |
| RÜHRSTAB **12260** | SÄGEN UND SÄGEBÄNKE **10963** |
| RÜHRWERK **238** | SÄGESCHNITT **3517** |
| RÜHRWERK **236** | SÄGESCHNITTFUGE **3517** |
| RÜHRWERKNISCHE **237** | SÄGESPÄNE **10953** |
| RUNDDRAHT **10804** | SÄGEVERZAHNUNG (GESCHRÄNKTE) **10187** |
| RUNDEISEN **10795** | SÄGEWERK **10956** |
| RUNDEISEN AUS LEGIERTEN STÄHLEN **377** | SÄGEZAHN **10959** |
| RUNDFEILE **10796** | SÄGEZÄHNE AUSSETZEN (DIE) **11224** |
| RUNDFRÄSMASCHINE **2420** | SÄGEZÄHNE SCHRÄNKEN **11224** |

**SAI** 884

SÄGEZAHNKUPPLUNG 10960
SAIGERUNG 7635
SALINOMETER 10901
SALIZYLSÄURE 10899
SALMIAK 462
SALMIAKGEIST 660
SALMIAKSPIRITUS 660
SALPETER 10903
SALPETERGAS 8581
SALPETERSALZSÄURE 658
SALPETERSÄURE 8580
SALPETERSÄUREÄTHER 4850
SALPETERSAURES KALI 10903
SALPETERSAURES NATRON 2330
SALPETERSAURES SALZ 8579
SALPETERSSÄUREANHYDRID 8590
SALPETRIGSÄUREANHYDRID 8592
SALPETRIGSAURES KALI 9691
SALPETRIGSAURES SALZ 8586
SALZ (ALKALISCHES) 338
SALZ (CHEM.) 10904
SALZ (GERBSAURES) 12633
SALZ (KOHLENSAURES) 1968
SALZ (NEUTRALES) 8546
SALZ (UNTERSCHWEFLIGSAURES) 12852
SALZÄTHER 4849
SALZBAD 10905
SALZBADHÄRTUNG 10913
SALZBADHÄRTUNG 7651
SALZBADLÖTEN 10911
SALZBADOFEN 10912
SALZBILDNER 6214
SALZGEHALT 10906
SALZKRUSTE 3421
SALZLÖSUNG 10908
SALZSÄURE 6706
SALZSOLE 1617
SALZSPINDEL 10901
SALZSPRÜHNEBELPRÜFUNG 10909
SALZWAAGE 10901
SALZWASSER 10910
SAMARIUM 10914
SÄMASCHINEN 11132
SÄMISCHLEDER 2234
SAMMELBEHÄLTER 10471
SAMMELBEHÄLTER 12292
SAMMELLEITUNG 7979
SAMMELLINSE 2910
SAMMELLINSE 2909
SAMMELPLATTEN 2726
SAMMELROHR 2725

SAMMELSCHIENE 1770
SAMMLER 76
SAMMLERBATTERIE 77
SAMMLERLOKOMOTIVE 79
SAND 10917
SAND (FEINKÖRNIGER) 5199
SAND (GROBKÖRNIGER) 2574
SAND (TROCKENER) 4255
SANDARAK 10927
SANDBAD 10918
SANDBODEN 10930
SANDEINSCHLUSS IM GUSS 3998
SANDFILTER 10923
SANDFORM 10924
SANDFORMMASCHINE 8429
SANDGUSS 10922
SANDHAKEN 5772
SANDKOHLE 4344
SANDPAPIER 10925
SANDPAPIERMASCHINE 10926
SANDSCHLEUDER 209
SANDSIEB 11628
SANDSTEIN 10928
SANDSTEIN (ROTER) 10336
SANDSTRAHL BEARBEITEN (MIT) 10919
SANDSTRAHLEN 1316
SANDSTRAHLGEBLÄSE 10920
SANDTRAHLUNG 10921
SANDWICHWALZEN 10929
SAPONIT 10935
SATTDAMPF 10942
SATTEL 10876
SATTELBEFESTIGUNG 3288
SATTELENDE 6597
SATTELHALTER 10877
SATTELSCHLEPPER 11178
SATTELZUG 13092
SÄTTIGEN 10939
SÄTTIGUNG 10943
SÄTTIGUNG (MAGNETISCHE) 7916
SÄTTIGUNGSGRAD 3722
SÄTTIGUNGSGRENZE 7591
SÄTTIGUNGSTEMPERATUR 10945
SÄTTINGUNGSDRUCK 10944
SATZ 10226
SATZ 11213
SATZ 1332
SATZ 1059
SATZADRESSEEINGABEFORMAT 1334
SATZFRÄSER 5800
SATZNUMMER 11193

| | |
|---|---|
| SATZRÄDER **7027** | SÄURE (ORGANISCHE) **8864** |
| SATZUNTERDRÜCKUNG **1337** | SÄURE (SALPETRIGE) **8596** |
| SAUERKLEESALZ **10907** | SÄURE (SCHWEFLIGE) **12450** |
| SAUERKLEESÄURE **8969** | SÄURE (UNTERCHLORIGE) **6742** |
| SAUERSTOFF **8980** | SÄUREÄTHER **4837** |
| SAUERSTOFF ENTZIEHEN (DEN) **3763** | SÄUREBESTÄNDIG **124** |
| SAUERSTOFF-AZETYLEN **8979** | SÄUREBESTÄNDIG **128** |
| SAUERSTOFF-WASSERSTOFF-SCHWEISSUNG **8988** | SÄUREBESTÄNDIGKEIT **10496** |
| SAUERSTOFFENTZIEHUNG **3762** | SÄUREBILDEND **130** |
| SAUERSTOFFGEBLÄSE **8986** | SÄUREBILDNER **115** |
| SAUERSTOFFION **556** | SÄUREDÄMPFE **127** |
| SAUERSTOFFLANZE **8981** | SÄUREFEST **128** |
| SAUERSTOFFSCHNEID-MASCHINE (AUTOGENE) **833** | SÄUREFEST **124** |
| SAUERSTOFFVERFAHREN **8982** | SÄUREFESTE LEGIERUNGEN **125** |
| SAUG- UND DRUCKLÜFTER **2768** | SÄUREFESTIGKEIT **10496** |
| SAUG- UND DRUCKVENTILATOR **2768** | SÄUREFREI **5635** |
| SAUG-DRUCKVENTIL **9843** | SÄUREGEHALTSBESTIMMUNG **131** |
| SAUGEN **12428** | SÄUREMESSER **89** |
| SAUGENDER LÜFTER **12429** | SÄUREN **132** |
| SAUGGAS **4194** | SÄUREPUMPE **121** |
| SAUGGASGENERATOR **12430** | SAUSCHWANZHAKEN **9301** |
| SAUGHEBER **11517** | SCHABEMASCHINE **11012** |
| SAUGHÖHE EINER PUMPE **12432** | SCHABEN **11008** |
| SAUGHUB **12435** | SCHABEN **11011** |
| SAUGHUB **7008** | SCHABER **11009** |
| SAUGKLAPPE **12436** | SCHABLONE **9128** |
| SAUGKOPF **12332** | SCHABLONE **12238** |
| SAUGKORB **12332** | SCHABLONE **12734** |
| SAUGLEITUNG **12433** | SCHABLONE (FIXE) **5293** |
| SAUGLEITUNG **6948** | SCHABLONENDREHBANK **3138** |
| SAUGLÜFTER **12429** | SCHACHT **9398** |
| SAUGLÜFTUNG **13450** | SCHACHT **12046** |
| SAUGPUMPE **12434** | SCHACHTHYDRANT **6672** |
| SAUGROHR **12433** | SCHACHTOFEN **11241** |
| SAUGROHR **6945** | SCHADHAFT **5057** |
| SAUGSIEB **12332** | SCHÄDLICHER WIDERSTAND **10497** |
| SAUGTRICHTER **9340** | SCHAFT **12237** |
| SAUGVENTIL **12436** | SCHAFT **11260** |
| SAUGZUG **6890** | SCHAFT **11257** |
| SÄULE **2748** | SCHAFT DER SCHUBSTANGE **11261** |
| SÄULE (VOLTASCHE) **13596** | SCHAFTFRÄSER **11259** |
| SÄULEFÜHRUNGSGESTELL **3890** | SCHAFTFRÄSER **11783** |
| SÄULENBOHRMASCHINE **9312** | SCHAFTFRÄSER **4723** |
| SÄULENFUSS **1035** | SCHAFWOLLE **13932** |
| SÄULENGERÜST **2759** | SCHAKE **7627** |
| SÄULENKAPITÄL **1926** | SCHÄKEL **11232** |
| SÄULENKOPF **2749** | SCHÄKEL **2491** |
| SÄULENLAGER **9663** | SCHAKENKETTE **8855** |
| SÄULENSTAMM **11243** | SCHALE **11303** |
| SÄURE **104** | SCHALE **9029** |
| SÄURE (ARSENIGE) **727** | SCHALE **9155** |

# SCH                                        886

SCHALE 2331
SCHALE 11624
SCHÄLEN 9156
SCHALENGUSS 2334
SCHALENGUSS 2335
SCHALENHARTGUSS 2038
SCHALENKUPPLUNG 2449
SCHALENLAGER (GETEILTES) 11947
SCHALLDÄMPFENDES MITTEL 3641
SCHALLDÄMPFER 11431
SCHALLDÄMPFER 8448
SCHALLDICHTER STOFF 3641
SCHALLEHRE 137
SCHALLGESCHWINDIGKEIT 13520
SCHALLSCHWINGUNG 11818
SCHALLWELLE 11819
SCHALTANLAGE 12558
SCHALTBRETT 12557
SCHALTDRAHT 7264
SCHALTEN HINTEREINANDER 2957
SCHALTEN IN REIHE 2957
SCHALTEN NEBENEINANDER 2956
SCHALTEN PARALLEL 2956
SCHALTER 12553
SCHALTGETRIEBE 9138
SCHALTGETRIEBE 5890
SCHALTHEBEL 10223
SCHALTKLINKE 2493
SCHALTLINKE 2496
SCHALTMASCHINE 1018
SCHALTMECHANISMUS 9138
SCHALTRAD 10225
SCHALTSCHÜTZ 3516
SCHALTTAFEL 12557
SCHALTUNG (GEDRÜCKTE) 9871
SCHALTWERK 9138
SCHÄLUNG 10988
SCHAMOTTE 5241
SCHAMOTTE 2235
SCHAMOTTE (GEMAHLENE) 6125
SCHAMOTTEMEHL 9724
SCHAMOTTEMÖRTEL 6126
SCHAMOTTEMÖRTEL 5255
SCHAMOTTESTEIN 5254
SCHAMOTTESTEIN 5239
SCHAR VON KURVEN 5028
SCHARF ANZIEHEN (EINE SCHRAUBE) 12927
SCHÄRFEN 11275
SCHÄRFEN 11273
SCHÄRFMASCHINE 11274
SCHÄRFMASCHINE 13002

SCHÄRFMITTEL 6107
SCHARFSCHLEIFEN 11273
SCHARFSCHLEIFEN 11275
SCHARNIER 6505
SCHARNIERHEBEL 6506
SCHARNIERSCHRAUBE 6509
SCHARNIERSTIFT 6508
SCHARNIERZIRKEL (GERADER) 4101
SCHARPFLÜGE UND SCHLEPPERPFLÜGE 9524
SCHATTENAUFNAHMEAPPARAT 11238
SCHATTIEREN 11234
SCHATTIEREN 11237
SCHATTIERUNG 11236
SCHÄTZUNGSFEHLER 4827
SCHAUBILD 3834
SCHAUFEL 11385
SCHAUFEL EINER TURBINE 13480
SCHAUFEL EINES WASSERRADES 1677
SCHAUFELN 11386
SCHAUFELVERDICHTER 2178
SCHAUGLAS 11427
SCHAUGLAS (RUNDES) 2414
SCHAULINIE 3495
SCHAULOCH 11427
SCHAULOCH 9158
SCHAUM 4331
SCHAUM 5499
SCHAUMBILDUNG 5703
SCHÄUMEN 4461
SCHAUMLÖFFEL 11536
SCHAUMSTOFF (GESCHLOSSENZELLIGER) 2517
SCHAUÖFFNUNG 11427
SCHAUÖLER 11425
SCHEELIT 10997
SCHEELSÄURE 8876
SCHEIBE 4015
SCHEIBE (GEWUNDENE) 11913
SCHEIBE (KRUMME) 11913
SCHEIBE (SELBSTSCHNEIDENDE) 11163
SCHEIBENARM (GERADER) 12302
SCHEIBENARM (GESCHWUNGENER) 3497
SCHEIBENBOLZEN 5386
SCHEIBENBREMSE 4001
SCHEIBENDREHBANK 5001
SCHEIBENEGGEN 4007
SCHEIBENEXZENTER 9482
SCHEIBENFEDER 13929
SCHEIBENFRÄSER 11412
SCHEIBENFRÄSER 8496
SCHEIBENFRÄSER MIT EINSEITIGER STIRNVERZAHNUNG
   6206

SCH

SCHEIBENFRÄSERPAAR **12301**
SCHEIBENKOLBEN **11791**
SCHEIBENKRANZ **10595**
SCHEIBENKUPPLUNG **5338**
SCHEIBENKURBEL **4433**
SCHEIBENLAGER **12903**
SCHEIBENMESSER **2417**
SCHEIBENPFLÜGE UND ANBAUPFLÜGE **9523**
SCHEIBENRAD **4012**
SCHEIBENRAD (GERADES) **5379**
SCHEIBENRAD (GEWÖLBTES) **4037**
SCHEIBENVENTIL **4011**
SCHEIBENWASCHER **13870**
SCHEIBENWISCHER **13871**
SCHEIBENWÖLBUNG **3398**
SCHEIBENZAPFEN **12906**
SCHEIDEWAND **3870**
SCHEIDEWAND **4110**
SCHEIDEWASSER **8580**
SCHEIDUNG **9091**
SCHEIDUNG (ELEKTROLYTISCHE) **4602**
SCHEIDUNG (ELEKTROMAGNETISCHE) **4618**
SCHEINBILD **13572**
SCHEINDICHTE **1725**
SCHEINDICHTE **642**
SCHEINWERFER **11091**
SCHEINWERFER **6326**
SCHEINWERFER **6327**
SCHEINWERFER (EINGELASSENER) **5480**
SCHEINWIDERSTAND **6794**
SCHEIT **1243**
SCHEITEL **638**
SCHEITELDRUCK **12908**
SCHEITELTANGENTE **12617**
SCHELF.... **8738**
SCHELLACK **11338**
SCHELLACKFIRNIS **10998**
SCHELLACKPAPIER **13506**
SCHELLEISEN **10626**
SCHELLHAMMER **4979**
SCHENKEL EINES TAUES **12338**
SCHENKEL EINES WINKELEISENS **13728**
SCHENKEL EINES WINKELS **7512**
SCHERBACKEN **11282**
SCHERBEANSPRUCHUNG **11295**
SCHERBLATT **11282**
SCHERE **11297**
SCHERE **1333**
SCHERE **11279**
SCHERE (FLIEGENDE) **5495**
SCHERE (ROTIERENDE) **10759**

SCHERFESTIGKEIT **11285**
SCHERFESTIGKEIT **13330**
SCHERFLÄCHE **11284**
SCHERKLINGE **11282**
SCHERKRAFT **11291**
SCHERMESSER **11282**
SCHERSPANNUNG **11296**
SCHERUNG **11290**
SCHERVERSUCH **11287**
SCHERVERSUCH **11949**
SCHERWINKEL **11281**
SCHEUERTROMMEL **9602**
SCHICHT **5166**
SCHICHT **2590**
SCHICHT **7442**
SCHICHT (ARBEITERGRUPPE) **11348**
SCHICHT (ARBEITSZEIT) **11347**
SCHICHT (DÜNNE) **5171**
SCHICHTARBEIT **11350**
SCHICHTENRISS **7383**
SCHICHTENSTRÖMUNG **9055**
SCHICHTFLÄCHE **7527**
SCHICHTKORROSION **7443**
SCHICHTLINIE **7444**
SCHICHTUNG **7382**
SCHIEBEDECKEL **11604**
SCHIEBEKLINKE **2496**
SCHIEBELEHRE **13541**
SCHIEBER **11592**
SCHIEBER MIT MECHANISCHER ABSPERRUNG **9062**
SCHIEBERÄDERGETRIEBE **11598**
SCHIEBERDIAGRAMM **11593**
SCHIEBERSPIEGEL **4996**
SCHIEBERSTEUERUNG **11594**
SCHIEBESITZ **10025**
SCHIEBLEHRE **13537**
SCHIEBUNG **11288**
SCHIEFER (BAUW.) **11571**
SCHIEFER (GEOL.) **10999**
SCHIEFERBRUCH **11615**
SCHIEFERÖL **11256**
SCHIEFERTEER **11255**
SCHIEMANNSGARN **12005**
SCHIENE **10175**
SCHIENEN- U. LASCHENBOHRMASCHINE **10176**
SCHIENENSCHRAUBE **11043**
SCHIENENSCHRAUBEN **11575**
SCHIENENSTAHL (UMGEWALZTER) **10177**
SCHIESSBAUMWOLLE **6176**
SCHIESSPULVER **6181**
SCHIFFBAU **8510**

**SCH** 888

SCHIFFHOBEL 2801
SCHIFFSBLECH 11356
SCHIFFSKESSEL 8003
SCHIFFSKETTEN 8004
SCHIFFSKOPF 8007
SCHIFFSMASCHINE 8005
SCHIFFSNAGEL 1382
SCHIFFSPECH 9400
SCHIMMEL 8271
SCHIMMELBILDUNG 5575
SCHIPPE 11385
SCHIRM 11346
SCHIRM 11018
SCHIRM (OPT.) 11019
SCHLABBERVENTIL 8933
SCHLACKE 11561
SCHLACKE 2397
SCHLACKE (EINGESCHLOSSENE) 11567
SCHLACKE (EINGEWALZTE) 11567
SCHLACKE (GEKÖRNTE) 6055
SCHLACKE (GRANULIERTE) 6055
SCHLACKENABZUG 3803
SCHLACKENBETON 11565
SCHLACKENBLECH 3596
SCHLACKENEINSCHLUSS 4772
SCHLACKENFORM 2399
SCHLACKENFORMKÜHLER 8380
SCHLACKENFREI 5638
SCHLACKENHALTIG 11562
SCHLACKENKRANZBILDUNG 1604
SCHLACKENLOCH 2399
SCHLACKENLOCH 4332
SCHLACKENSTEIN 11563
SCHLACKENWOLLE 11566
SCHLACKENZEMENT 11564
SCHLACKENZUSCHLAG 5475
SCHLAFKOJE 1739
SCHLAG 12375
SCHLAG 6783
SCHLAG (ELEKTRISCHER) 4529
SCHLAGBIEGEPROBE 4328
SCHLAGBIEGEPROBE MIT EINGEKERBTEN PROBESTÜCKEN 1190
SCHLÄGEL 7962
SCHLAGEN 6224
SCHLAGEN DER PUMPE 7331
SCHLAGEN DES RIEMENS 13825
SCHLAGFESTIGKEIT 6785
SCHLAGFLIESSPRESSEN 6784
SCHLAGFRÄSER 5494
SCHLAGLOT 6279

SCHLAGNIETHAMMER 9555
SCHLAGPRESSE (MECHANISCHE) 9182
SCHLAGSCHATTEN 13339
SCHLAGSCHWEISSEN 9183
SCHLAGSCHWEISSEN (ELEKTROMAGNETISCHES) 4617
SCHLAGSTÄRKE 12757
SCHLAGSTÖCKCHEN 632
SCHLAGVERSUCH 6786
SCHLAGVERSUCH 4328
SCHLAMM 11609
SCHLAMM 8444
SCHLAMM 11655
SCHLAMM 11654
SCHLÄMMEN 4681
SCHLÄMMEN 2550
SCHLAMMHAHN 1357
SCHLAMMIG 8445
SCHLÄMMKREIDE 13841
SCHLAMMLOCH 8442
SCHLÄMMUNG 4681
SCHLAMMVENTIL 1358
SCHLANGENBOHRER 4160
SCHLANGENROST 3200
SCHLANKHEIT 11580
SCHLANKHEIT (EINES TRÄGERS) 11581
SCHLANKHEITSGRAD 11582
SCHLAUCH 9339
SCHLAUCH 6614
SCHLAUCH (GEPANZERTER) 714
SCHLAUCHGEWEBERIEMEN 5397
SCHLAUCHKLAMMER 6611
SCHLAUCHKLEMME 6611
SCHLAUCHKUPPLUNG 6612
SCHLAUCHSCHELLE 6611
SCHLAUCHSCHELLE 6610
SCHLAUFE 8651
SCHLECHTAUSGELAUFEN 8321
SCHLEIERBILDUNG 2541
SCHLEIERBILDUNG 1347
SCHLEIERBILDUNG 6313
SCHLEIFBAND 18
SCHLEIFE 11633
SCHLEIFE EINER KURVE 7741
SCHLEIFEN 11275
SCHLEIFEN 6106
SCHLEIFEN 9605
SCHLEIFEN (SPITZENLOSES) 2156
SCHLEIFENKURVE 7514
SCHLEIFER 6105
SCHLEIFGRAT 13890
SCHLEIFHÄRTE 14

SCHLEIFKOLBEN **9392**
SCHLEIFKORN **21**
SCHLEIFKÖRPER **26**
SCHLEIFKÜHLMITTEL **6109**
SCHLEIFMASCHINE (SPITZENLOSE) **2174**
SCHLEIFMASCHINE (ZUM PUTZEN UND SCHLICHTEN) **6113**
SCHLEIFMATERIALKORNGRÖSSE **23**
SCHLEIFMITTEL **22**
SCHLEIFMITTEL **17**
SCHLEIFMITTEL **6107**
SCHLEIFMITTEL **9601**
SCHLEIFMITTEL (MILDES) **8269**
SCHLEIFMITTEL (NATÜRLICHES) **8499**
SCHLEIFPLATTE **6114**
SCHLEIFPULVER **6110**
SCHLEIFRING **11618**
SCHLEIFSCHEIBE **6118**
SCHLEIFSCHEIBE **6115**
SCHLEIFSCHEIBE **4010**
SCHLEIFSCHEIBE **4006**
SCHLEIFSCHEIBEN-AUSGLEICHAPPARATE **6116**
SCHLEIFSCHMIERSTOFF **6112**
SCHLEIFSCHMIRGELSCHEIBE **20**
SCHLEIFSCHMIRGELSCHEIBEN **26**
SCHLEIFSPITZEN **24**
SCHLEIFSPUREN **15**
SCHLEIFSTEIN **19**
SCHLEIFSTEIN **13824**
SCHLEIFSTEIN **6118**
SCHLEIMHARZ **6173**
SCHLEPPER **11010**
SCHLEPPER **13097**
SCHLEPPKETTE **11010**
SCHLEPPKURVE **13098**
SCHLEPPSEIL **11010**
SCHLEUDER **6703**
SCHLEUDERBREMSE **2175**
SCHLEUDERGEBLÄSE **2179**
SCHLEUDERGUSS **2176**
SCHLEUDERMÜHLE **4045**
SCHLEUDERPUMPE **2184**
SCHLEUDERSTRAHLEN **6124**
SCHLEUDERTHERMOMETER **13826**
SCHLEUSE **7698**
SCHLICHTE **3171**
SCHLICHTEN **11682**
SCHLICHTEN **5214**
SCHLICHTFEILE **11680**
SCHLICHTHAMMER **9455**
SCHLICHTHAMMER **1734**
SCHLICHTHOBEL **11687**

SCHLICHTSTAHL **5228**
SCHLIERE **5061**
SCHLIESSKOFF (DEN) BILDEN **2516**
SCHLIESSKOLBEN (FORM) **2535**
SCHLIESSKOPF **10628**
SCHLIFF **6106**
SCHLIFF FÜR MIKROSKOPIE **11113**
SCHLIFFFLÄCHE **6142**
SCHLINGE **11610**
SCHLITTEN **10188**
SCHLITTEN MIT GLEITPLATTEN **11606**
SCHLITTEN MIT ROLLEN **10694**
SCHLITTENKREUZBEWEGUNGS-HANDRAD **13163**
SCHLITTENLAGER **11596**
SCHLITTENWINDE **13165**
SCHLITZHEBEL **11638**
SCHLITZMUTTER **11942**
SCHLITZNAHT **11635**
SCHLITZSÄGE **8193**
SCHLITZSCHRAUBE **11637**
SCHLITZSCHWEISSEN **11636**
SCHLITZTROMMEL **3579**
SCHLOSSER **5278**
SCHLOSSERWERKSTATT **5282**
SCHLOSSSCHRAUBE **2553**
SCHLOT **2339**
SCHLUBKLINKE **2496**
SCHLÜPFEN **11612**
SCHLÜPFEN DER RÄDER **11621**
SCHLÜPFEN DES RIEMENS **11620**
SCHLÜPFRIGKEIT EINES SCHMIERSTOFFES **7813**
SCHLÜSSEL **9532**
SCHLÜSSEL (GEKRÖPFTER) **509**
SCHLÜSSELFEILE **13625**
SCHLÜSSELFERTIG **13284**
SCHLÜSSELLOCHDECKEL **4835**
SCHLÜSSELLOCH **7287**
SCHLÜSSELWEITE **11832**
SCHLUSSLATERNE **12595**
SCHLUSSLINIE **2536**
SCHMALZÖL **7409**
SCHMEIZTIEGEL **3401**
SCHMELZ **4709**
SCHMELZBAD **8137**
SCHMELZBAR **5756**
SCHMELZBARKEIT **5755**
SCHMELZBEREICH **5761**
SCHMELZBEREICH **8143**
SCHMELZE **2076**
SCHMELZE **6333**
SCHMELZE **8134**

# SCH

890

SCHMELZE 8365
SCHMELZEN 5764
SCHMELZEN 8135
SCHMELZEN 5760
SCHMELZEN 8136
SCHMELZEN 11666
SCHMELZEN (KONGRUENTES) 2938
SCHMELZFARBE 4711
SCHMELZFUSS 8365
SCHMELZGESCHWINDIGKEIT 8144
SCHMELZKEGEL 11134
SCHMELZKEGEL 10050
SCHMELZKOKS 2662
SCHMELZLEGIERUNG 5757
SCHMELZLEGIERUNG 389
SCHMELZOFEN 11665
SCHMELZOFEN 11667
SCHMELZOFEN 8138
SCHMELZPFROPFEN 5758
SCHMELZPUNKT 8141
SCHMELZPUNKT 5759
SCHMELZSCHWEISSEN 5762
SCHMELZSCHWEISSEN 8643
SCHMELZTAUCHVERFAHREN 6659
SCHMELZTIEGELZANGE 3405
SCHMELZTOPF 8142
SCHMELZUNG 5764
SCHMELZUNG (EUTEKTISCHE) 4856
SCHMELZVERLUSTE 8140
SCHMELZWÄRME 6360
SCHMELZZONE 5763
SCHMIED 11671
SCHMIEDBAR 7960
SCHMIEDBARKEIT 7958
SCHMIEDBARMACHEN 7961
SCHMIEDE 5547
SCHMIEDEEISEN 13988
SCHMIEDEEISEN (ANORMALES) 9
SCHMIEDEESSE 5548
SCHMIEDEFEUER 5548
SCHMIEDEHAMMER 6235
SCHMIEDEHAMMER 11572
SCHMIEDEHAMMER 9552
SCHMIEDEHAMMER (MECHANISCHER) 5559
SCHMIEDEHERD 5548
SCHMIEDEISEN (PERLITISCHES) 2047
SCHMIEDEKOHLE 5543
SCHMIEDEMASCHINE 5561
SCHMIEDEMESSING 5558
SCHMIEDEMESSING 8486
SCHMIEDEN 5542

SCHMIEDEN 5555
SCHMIEDEN 5557
SCHMIEDEN (IM GESENK) 12530
SCHMIEDEPRESSE 5562
SCHMIEDEPRESSE (HYDRAULISCHE) 6687
SCHMIEDEPROBE 5545
SCHMIEDESCHWEISSUNG 5546
SCHMIEDESINTER 6217
SCHMIEDESPANNUNG 5564
SCHMIEDESTAHL 5554
SCHMIEDESTAHLANSCHLUSS 5549
SCHMIEDESTÜCK 5556
SCHMIEDESTÜCK (SCHWERES) 6406
SCHMIEDESTÜCK (ÜBERENTGRATETES) 8322
SCHMIEDESTÜCKE 5566
SCHMIEDETEMPERATUR 5560
SCHMIEDETEMPERATUR 5565
SCHMIEDEWALZWERK 5563
SCHMIEDEWERKSTATT 5547
SCHMIEDEZANGE 1298
SCHMIEGE 1228
SCHMIEGSAM-STRECKBAR 4361
SCHMIEGUNGSEBENE 8887
SCHMIERBOHRER 8762
SCHMIERBOHRUNG 8761
SCHMIERBÜCHSE 8753
SCHMIERBÜCHSE 6085
SCHMIERDOCHT 7807
SCHMIERE (ALTE) 3308
SCHMIEREN 7808
SCHMIEREN 7801
SCHMIERFETT 7804
SCHMIERGEFÄSS 7812
SCHMIERGEFÄSS (UMLAUFENDES) 2182
SCHMIERKANNE 8749
SCHMIERKELCH 8753
SCHMIERLOCH 8761
SCHMIERMATERIAL 7800
SCHMIERMITTEL 7800
SCHMIERNAPF 8753
SCHMIERNIPPEL 6086
SCHMIERNUT 7810
SCHMIERÖL 7805
SCHMIERÖLPUMPE 8769
SCHMIERPRESSE 8105
SCHMIERRING 8790
SCHMIERRING 8774
SCHMIERSCHICHT 5167
SCHMIERSCHRAUBE 7811
SCHMIERSEIFE 11740
SCHMIERSTELLE 8789

891 SCH

SCHMIERSTOFF **7800**
SCHMIERUNG **7808**
SCHMIERUNG **7803**
SCHMIERUNG **7814**
SCHMIERUNG (BESTÄNDIGE) **3012**
SCHMIERUNG (SELBSTTÄTIGE) **848**
SCHMIERUNG (UNTERBROCHENE) **9195**
SCHMIERVORRICHTUNG **7812**
SCHMIERVORRICHTUNG (SELBSTTÄTIGE) **851**
SCHMIERWERT **7806**
SCHMIRGEL **4692**
SCHMIRGEL **4699**
SCHMIRGEL (GESCHLÄMMTER) **5453**
SCHMIRGELLEINEN **4693**
SCHMIRGELLEINWAND **4693**
SCHMIRGELN **4695**
SCHMIRGELPAPIER **4696**
SCHMIRGELPULVER **4697**
SCHMIRGELSCHEIBE **4698**
SCHMUTZANHAFTUNG **3997**
SCHMUTZFÄNGER **12333**
SCHMUTZFÄNGER **8443**
SCHNAPPSCHALTER **11690**
SCHNARCHVENTIL **11694**
SCHNECKE **6430**
SCHNECKE **13979**
SCHNECKE **13970**
SCHNECKE **13969**
SCHNECKENBOHRER **11023**
SCHNECKENFEDER **5396**
SCHNECKENFLASCHENZUG **13973**
SCHNECKENFRÄSER **13972**
SCHNECKENFRÄSER **13971**
SCHNECKENGEBLÄSE **9929**
SCHNECKENRAD **13975**
SCHNECKENRADGETRIEBE **13974**
SCHNEEKETTEN **11696**
SCHNEELAST **11695**
SCHNEEWEISS **1003**
SCHNEIBRENNERDÜSE **3537**
SCHNEIDBACKEN **3896**
SCHNEIDBRENNER **3216**
SCHNEIDBRENNER **3539**
SCHNEIDBRENNER **5307**
SCHNEIDBRENNER (AUTOGEN) **5312**
SCHNEIDE **3528**
SCHNEIDE (STUMPFE) **4365**
SCHNEIDEARBEIT **1309**
SCHNEIDEINSATZ **3525**
SCHNEIDEISEN **11039**
SCHNEIDEN **9998**

SCHNEIDEN **3523**
SCHNEIDEN **10012**
SCHNEIDEN **3504**
SCHNEIDEN **11290**
SCHNEIDEN (AUTOGENES) **832**
SCHNEIDEN (BLECHE) **3513**
SCHNEIDEN (INNENGEWINDE) **12636**
SCHNEIDEN (SICH) (GEOM.) **7094**
SCHNEIDEN EINES AUSSENGEWINDES **3535**
SCHNEIDEN EINES GEWINDES **11030**
SCHNEIDEN EINES INNENGEWINDES **12678**
SCHNEIDENAUFHÄNGUNG **7326**
SCHNEIDENDE WELLEN (SICH) **7096**
SCHNEIDENLAGER **7325**
SCHNEIDFLÜSSIGKEIT **3530**
SCHNEIDFLÜSSIGKEITEN (CHEMISCHE) **2303**
SCHNEIDKANTE EINES WERKZEUGS **3528**
SCHNEIDKLINGE **11039**
SCHNEIDKLUPPE **12266**
SCHNEIDLIPPEN **7633**
SCHNEIDMASCHINE **833**
SCHNEIDÖL **3534**
SCHNEIDSCHEIBE **3542**
SCHNEIDSTAHL **13011**
SCHNEIDWERKZEUG **3538**
SCHNEIDWERKZEUGE AUS SCHNELLSTAHL **6475**
SCHNEIDWINKEL **3524**
SCHNELLARBEITSSTAHL **6497**
SCHNELLAUFEN **10833**
SCHNELLAUFENDE MASCHINE **6496**
SCHNELLÄUFER **6496**
SCHNELLBOHRER **10206**
SCHNELLBOHRMASCHINE **6495**
SCHNELLDREHSTAHL **6497**
SCHNELLDREHSTAHL **6474**
SCHNELLGANG **10208**
SCHNELLGANG **8930**
SCHNELLÖFFNUNGS-SCHIEBER **10103**
SCHNELLOT **11742**
SCHNELLRÜCKLAUFGETRIEBE **10106**
SCHNELLSCHLUSSVENTIL **10104**
SCHNELLTROCKNER **5360**
SCHNELLWAAGE **12225**
SCHNELLWECHSELEINRICHTUNG **10108**
SCHNITT **9898**
SCHNITT **11112**
SCHNITT **3503**
SCHNITT (GOLDENER) **8123**
SCHNITT (SCHIEFER) **8711**
SCHNITTEBENE **7095**
SCHNITTFLÄCHE **12511**

# SCH 892

SCHNITTFUGE **7274**
SCHNITTFUGE EINER SÄGE **3517**
SCHNITTGANG (EINER WERKZEUGSMASCHINE) **3536**
SCHNITTGESCHWINDIGKEIT (KONSTANTE) **2971**
SCHNITTHOLZ **10962**
SCHNITTIEFE **3782**
SCHNITTIEFE **3526**
SCHNITTLINIE **7605**
SCHNITTNAGEL **7841**
SCHNITTPUNKT **9565**
SCHNITTSCHRAUBE **6156**
SCHNITTZEICHNUNG **11122**
SCHNITZMESSER **4221**
SCHNÜFFELVENTIL **1593**
SCHNÜFFELVENTIL **11694**
SCHNÜFFLER **11694**
SCHNURSCHEIBE **975**
SCHNURTRIEB **3141**
SCHOBERRECHEN **1683**
SCHOPFEN **3357**
SCHOPFSCHERE **3358**
SCHÖPFWERK **1676**
SCHOPPENDE **3356**
SCHORNSTEIN **2339**
SCHORNSTEINKLAPPE **3603**
SCHORNSTEINZUG **4212**
SCHOTT **1726**
SCHOTTER **1644**
SCHRAFFIEREN **6304**
SCHRAFFIERUNG **6306**
SCHRAFFUR **6306**
SCHRÄGE **4196**
SCHRÄGE **1065**
SCHRÄGER SETZHAMMER **2232**
SCHRÄGLAGER **508**
SCHRÄGMASS **1228**
SCHRÄGMESSER **1228**
SCHRÄGROST. SCHÜTTROST **6837**
SCHRÄGWINKEL **1228**
SCHRÄGZAHNRAD **6425**
SCHRÄNKEISEN **10957**
SCHRÄNKEN **10958**
SCHRAUBE **11021**
SCHRAUBE (DOPPELGÄNGIGE) **13315**
SCHRAUBE (DREIGÄNGIE) **12879**
SCHRAUBE (DURCHGEHENDE) **1441**
SCHRAUBE (EINGÄNGIGE) **11502**
SCHRAUBE (LINKSGÄNGIGE) **7506**
SCHRAUBE (LINKSGÄNGIGE) **7510**
SCHRAUBE (MEHRGÄNGIGE) **8474**
SCHRAUBE (RECHTSGÄNGIGE) **10584**

SCHRAUBE (RECHTSGÄNGIGE) **10580**
SCHRAUBE (SCHARFGÄNGIGE) **547**
SCHRAUBE (SCHWARZE) **1286**
SCHRAUBE (SELBSTSCHNEIDENDE) **11162**
SCHRAUBE (UNBEARBEITETE) **1286**
SCHRAUBE (ZWEIGÄNGIGE) **13315**
SCHRAUBE LOCKERN (EINE) **11558**
SCHRAUBE MIT DREIECKGEWINDE **547**
SCHRAUBE MIT FLACHGEWINDE **12034**
SCHRAUBE MIT RUNDGEWINDE **10807**
SCHRAUBE MIT TRAPEZGEWINDE **1815**
SCHRAUBE MIT ZYLINDERKOPF **11051**
SCHRAUBE OHNE ENDE **13979**
SCHRAUBE UND MUTTER **1432**
SCHRAUBENBEWEGUNG **6426**
SCHRAUBENBLECH **11039**
SCHRAUBENBOLZEN **11260**
SCHRAUBENBOLZEN (BEARBEITETER) **1607**
SCHRAUBENBOLZEN (BLANKER) **1607**
SCHRAUBENBREMSE **12344**
SCHRAUBENBRONZE **1659**
SCHRAUBENFEDER **2647**
SCHRAUBENFEDER **6427**
SCHRAUBENFEDER (KEGELIGE) **2942**
SCHRAUBENFEDER (ZYLINDRISCHE) **3585**
SCHRAUBENFLÄCHE **6428**
SCHRAUBENFLASCHENZUG **13973**
SCHRAUBENFLÜGEL **9928**
SCHRAUBENGEBLÄSE **9929**
SCHRAUBENGEWINDE **11045**
SCHRAUBENHAKEN **11057**
SCHRAUBENHEBEL **12985**
SCHRAUBENHEBER **11035**
SCHRAUBENKERN **1394**
SCHRAUBENKOPF **1436**
SCHRAUBENKOPF (FLACHER) **5394**
SCHRAUBENKOPF (GERÄNDELTER) **8281**
SCHRAUBENKOPF KORDIEREN (EINEN) **8277**
SCHRAUBENKOPF RÄNDELN (EINEN) **8277**
SCHRAUBENKOPFFEILE **11623**
SCHRAUBENKREIS **1433**
SCHRAUBENKUPPLUNG **11026**
SCHRAUBENLINIE **6430**
SCHRAUBENLOCH **1437**
SCHRAUBENLOCHDURCHMESSER **3854**
SCHRAUBENMUTTER **8698**
SCHRAUBENPRESSE **11040**
SCHRAUBENPUMPE **11042**
SCHRAUBENPUMPE **861**
SCHRAUBENRAD **6425**
SCHRAUBENRADGETRIEBE **11916**

## SCH

SCHRAUBENSCHAFT **11260**
SCHRAUBENSCHLOSS **13285**
SCHRAUBENSCHLÜSSEL **11833**
SCHRAUBENSCHLÜSSEL (DOPPELMÄULIGER) **4167**
SCHRAUBENSCHLÜSSEL (EINFACHER) **11499**
SCHRAUBENSCHLÜSSEL (EINMÄULIGER) **11499**
SCHRAUBENSCHLÜSSEL (ENGLISCHER) **11052**
SCHRAUBENSCHLÜSSEL (GEWÖHNLICHER) **7284**
SCHRAUBENSCHLÜSSEL (VERSTELLBARER) **11052**
SCHRAUBENSCHLÜSSEL MIT SCHRÄGEM MAUL **1195**
SCHRAUBENSCHLÜSSELWEITE **11832**
SCHRAUBENSCHNEIDEN **11028**
SCHRAUBENSCHNEIDMASCHINE **11066**
SCHRAUBENSICHERUNG **7707**
SCHRAUBENSICHERUNGSVORRICHTUNG **8701**
SCHRAUBENSPINDEL **11062**
SCHRAUBENVERBINDUNG **1442**
SCHRAUBENVERSETZUNG **11031**
SCHRAUBENVERSPANNUNG **12930**
SCHRAUBENWELLE **9930**
SCHRAUBENWINDE **11035**
SCHRAUBENWINDE MIT RATSCHE **10222**
SCHRAUBENZIEHER **13294**
SCHRAUBGETRIEBE **13974**
SCHRAUBKAPPE **11025**
SCHRAUBLEHRE **11034**
SCHRAUBMUFFE **11061**
SCHRAUBSTAHL **2274**
SCHRAUBSTOCK **13579**
SCHRAUBSTOCK **13561**
SCHRAUBSTOCK (EINFACHER) **9429**
SCHRAUBSTOCK (SCHWENKBARER) **12562**
SCHRAUBSTOCKBACKE **6122**
SCHRAUBSTOCKBACKEN (BEWEGLICHER) **8437**
SCHRAUBSTOCKBACKEN (FESTER) **5299**
SCHRAUBVERBINDUNG **11058**
SCHRAUBVERSHLUSS **11025**
SCHRAUBZWINGE **2452**
SCHREIBER **10289**
SCHREIBSTIFT (EINER REGISTRIERVORRICHTUNG) **9161**
SCHREIBVORRICHTUNG **10294**
SCHREIBWERK **10294**
SCHREIBZEUG **10294**
SCHREINER **7233**
SCHREINEREI **7235**
SCHREINEREI (HANDWERK) **7236**
SCHRIFT (CHINESISCHE) **2341**
SCHRIFTMETALL **13319**
SCHRIFTSTEMPEL **1560**
SCHRITT **12239**
SCHROBHOBEL **7201**

SCHROPPHOBEL **7201**
SCHROT **7472**
SCHROT **11379**
SCHROTHOBEL **7201**
SCHROTMEISSEL **11217**
SCHROTSÄGE **3365**
SCHROTSTRAHLPUTZEN **11380**
SCHROTT **11007**
SCHRUMPFEN **11397**
SCHRUMPFEN DES NIETSCHAFTES **3046**
SCHRUMPFMASS **477**
SCHRUMPFRING **11391**
SCHRUMPFRING **1252**
SCHRUMPFRING **7203**
SCHRUMPFSITZ **11389**
SCHRUMPFUNG **11392**
SCHRUMPFUNG **3043**
SCHRUPPARBEIT **10786**
SCHRUPPDREHBANK **10788**
SCHRUPPEN **10786**
SCHRUPPEN **10775**
SCHRUPPHOBEL **7201**
SCHRUPPSTAHL **10791**
SCHUB **11279**
SCHUB (FESTIGKEITSL.) **11288**
SCHUBBEANSPRUCHTWERDEN **1078**
SCHUBBEANSPRUCHUNG **11295**
SCHUBELASTIZITÄT **13144**
SCHUBELASTIZITÄTSMODUL **8342**
SCHUBELASTIZITÄTSMODUL **5974**
SCHUBFALLE **2496**
SCHUBFESTIGKEIT **13330**
SCHUBKARREN **13812**
SCHUBKRAFT **11291**
SCHUBLEHRE **11597**
SCHUBLEHRE **13537**
SCHUBLEHRE MIT DIREKTER ABLESUNG **3986**
SCHUBLEHRE MIT TIEFENMASSSTAB **1871**
SCHUBMODUL **3226**
SCHUBSPANNUNG **5460**
SCHUBSPANNUNG **11296**
SCHUBSTANGE **2962**
SCHUBSTANGENAUGE **4976**
SCHUBSTANGENGABEL **5568**
SCHUBSTANGENKOPF **2963**
SCHUBSTANGENKOPF (GEGABELTER) **5568**
SCHUBSTANGENKOPF (GESCHLOSSENER) **1509**
SCHUBVERFORMUNG **11286**
SCHUBWINKEL **3781**
SCHUH **11360**
SCHUH **11587**

# SCH

894

SCHUH FÜR HEBEVORRICHTUNG 7207
SCHULTER 11383
SCHULTER EINER WELLE 11384
SCHUPPE 10964
SCHUPPE 10968
SCHUPPE 288
SCHUPPEN 11302
SCHUPPENGRAPHIT 10989
SCHUPPENGRAPHIT 5305
SCHÜREISEN 10116
SCHÜREN 9575
SCHURFHOBEL 7201
SCHÜRFHOBEL 7201
SCHÜRFRAUPE 4414
SCHÜRZE 11549
SCHUSS EINES GEWEBES 13743
SCHUSS EINES KESSELS 3260
SCHUSTERPECH 9400
SCHÜTTBETON 9714
SCHÜTTELRINNE 11253
SCHÜTTELROST 10655
SCHÜTTELSIEB 11252
SCHÜTTRUMPF 6577
SCHÜTTUNG 971
SCHÜTTUNG 969
SCHÜTZ 11652
SCHUTZ 9943
SCHUTZ (KATHODISCHER) 2109
SCHUTZ DES GEWERBLICHEN EIGENTUMS 9946
SCHUTZANSTRICH 9793
SCHUTZATMOSPHÄRE 9947
SCHUTZATMOSPHÄRE 790
SCHUTZBLECH 11343
SCHUTZBRILLEN 5992
SCHUTZDECKEL 9944
SCHÜTZE 11652
SCHUTZGAS 6905
SCHUTZGAS-LICHTBOGEN-SCHWEISSEN (ATOMARES) 801
SCHUTZGAS-LICHTBOGENSCHWEISSEN 5852
SCHUTZGAS-SCHWEISSEN 683
SCHUTZGASLICHTBOGEN 1945
SCHUTZGASOFEN 3055
SCHUTZGEHÄUSE 9948
SCHUTZGITTER 9951
SCHUTZHAUBE 6432
SCHUTZHÜLLE 9949
SCHUTZKAPPE 9944
SCHUTZMARKE 13100
SCHUTZMASSE 6997
SCHUTZMUFFE 9942
SCHUTZNETZ 6157

SCHUTZRAHMEN 8354
SCHUTZSCHICHT 9793
SCHUTZSCHICHT (EINE) AUFTRAGEN 6791
SCHUTZSCHICHT AUFBRINGEN 6791
SCHUTZSCHILD 11342
SCHUTZSTOFF 9952
SCHUTZSTREIFEN AUS METALL 3268
SCHUTZÜBERZUG 9793
SCHUTZÜBERZÜGE 9792
SCHUTZVORRICHTUNG 10881
SCHUTZVORRICHTUNG 11346
SCHUTZVORRICHTUNG 11342
SCHUTZWAND 9953
SCHWABBEL 2538
SCHWABBELMITTEL 1692
SCHWABBELN 1691
SCHWABBELSALZE 1690
SCHWABBELSCHEIBE 1693
SCHWABBELSCHEIBE 4116
SCHWABBELSCHEIBE 10173
SCHWACHGAS 9890
SCHWACHSTROM 13705
SCHWÄCHUNG 13707
SCHWÄCHUNG DES MATERIALS 13708
SCHWADENMÄHER 11411
SCHWADENWENDER 12537
SCHWALBENSCHWANZ 4175
SCHWALBENSCHWANZFÖRMIG 4177
SCHWALBENSCHWANZFRÄSER 4176
SCHWALBENSCHWANZVERBINDUNG 4178
SCHWAMMEISEN 11953
SCHWANENSALZ 11729
SCHWANKUNG 13495
SCHWANKUNGEN DES WASSERSTANDES 13500
SCHWANZENDE EINES ROHRES 11901
SCHWARZBLECH 1296
SCHWARZBLECHE 1289
SCHWARZGLÜHEN 571
SCHWARZKIEFER 1293
SCHWARZKUPFER 1287
SCHWARZROTGLÜHEND 1288
SCHWARZROTGLUT 1295
SCHWEBEACHSE 5435
SCHWEBEMANTELMATRIZE 5437
SCHWEBESTOFFE 8062
SCHWEBUNG 1119
SCHWEDISCHER KOLBEN 10196
SCHWEDISCHGRÜN 10996
SCHWEFEL 12449
SCHWEFEL (AMORPHER) 476
SCHWEFEL (KRISTALLINISCHER) 3435

SCH

SCHWEFELALKOHOL **1964**
SCHWEFELAMMONIUM **472**
SCHWEFELÄTHER **8853**
SCHWEFELBARIUM **1004**
SCHWEFELBESTÄUBUNG **4394**
SCHWEFELBLEI **5775**
SCHWEFELBLUMEN **5464**
SCHWEFELBLÜTE **5464**
SCHWEFELCHLORÜR **12451**
SCHWEFELDIOXYD **12450**
SCHWEFELKALIUM **9700**
SCHWEFELKALZIUM (EINFACH) **1852**
SCHWEFELKIES **7146**
SCHWEFELKOHLENSTOFF **1964**
SCHWEFELLEBER **7674**
SCHWEFELMONOCHLORID **12451**
SCHWEFELSÄURE **12453**
SCHWEFELSÄURE (KONZENTRIERTE) **2884**
SCHWEFELSÄURE (RAUCHENDE) **5733**
SCHWEFELSÄURE (ROHE) **8856**
SCHWEFELSÄUREANHYDRID **12452**
SCHWEFELSAURER KALK **6190**
SCHWEFELSAURES CHROMOXYDKALL **2370**
SCHWEFELSAURES EISENOXYDUL **6093**
SCHWEFELSAURES KALI **9699**
SCHWEFELSAURES NICKELOXYDUL **8571**
SCHWEFELSAURES NICKELOXYDULAMMONIAK **8558**
SCHWEFELSAURES SILBER **11467**
SCHWEFELSTANGEN **12255**
SCHWEFELTRIOXYD **12452**
SCHWEFELWASSERSTOFF **6717**
SCHWEFELZYANKALIUM **9701**
SCHWEFLIGSÄUREANHYDRID **12450**
SCHWEIFHAAR **12594**
SCHWEIFSÄGE **1505**
SCHWEINFURTERGRÜN **11000**
SCHWEINSLEDER **9300**
SCHWEISS- UND BELEUCHTUNGSANLAGEN **4524**
SCHWEISSBAD **9961**
SCHWEISSBAR **13769**
SCHWEISSBARKEIT **13768**
SCHWEISSBRENNER **5307**
SCHWEISSDRAHT **13789**
SCHWEISSDRAHT **13793**
SCHWEISSDRAHT **8180**
SCHWEISSEISEN **13766**
SCHWEISSELEKTRODE **13789**
SCHWEISSEN **13779**
SCHWEISSEN **13755**
SCHWEISSEN (ELEKTRISCHES) **4533**
SCHWEISSEN (SPIRALFÖRMIGES) **11921**

SCHWEISSEN (WAAGERECHTES) **6591**
SCHWEISSEN MIT VERDECKTEN LICHTBOGEN **684**
SCHWEISSER **13778**
SCHWEISSFEHLER **13760**
SCHWEISSFITTING **13781**
SCHWEISSFOLGE **13790**
SCHWEISSGENERATOR FÜR KONSTANTEN STROM **2970**
SCHWEISSGUT **13763**
SCHWEISSGUT **13761**
SCHWEISSGUT (EINGEBRACHTES) **3776**
SCHWEISSGUT (REINES) **347**
SCHWEISSHITZE **13784**
SCHWEISSKONSTRUKTION **13795**
SCHWEISSKOPF **13783**
SCHWEISSLINSE **13764**
SCHWEISSMASCHINE **13786**
SCHWEISSNAHT **13776**
SCHWEISSNAHT (EINLAGIGE) **11485**
SCHWEISSNAHT (LEICHTE) **1792**
SCHWEISSNAHTLÄNGE **7520**
SCHWEISSNAHTOBERFLÄCHE **4998**
SCHWEISSNAHTSINNBILDER **13791**
SCHWEISSNAHTÜBERHÖHUNG **10427**
SCHWEISSPAKET **5015**
SCHWEISSPAKET **5017**
SCHWEISSPARAMETER **13787**
SCHWEISSPERLE **11842**
SCHWEISSRAUPE **13756**
SCHWEISSRAUPE **1082**
SCHWEISSRAUPENACHSE **871**
SCHWEISSRIPPE **5357**
SCHWEISSROLLE **2412**
SCHWEISSSPIELZEIT **13788**
SCHWEISSSTAB **13793**
SCHWEISSSTAHL **13765**
SCHWEISSSTROMSTÄRKE **13780**
SCHWEISSUNG **13767**
SCHWEISSUNG **13779**
SCHWEISSUNG (AUTOGENE) **834**
SCHWEISSUNG (ELEKTRISCHE) **4533**
SCHWEISSUNG (HYDROOXYGENE) **8988**
SCHWEISSUNG (STUMPFE) **1802**
SCHWEISSUNG (WAAGERECHTE) **4190**
SCHWEISSVERBINDUG (SCHLECHTE) **920**
SCHWEISSVERBINDUNG **13767**
SCHWEISSVERBINDUNG **7237**
SCHWEISSVERBINDUNG **13774**
SCHWEISSVERBINDUNG **13772**
SCHWEISSVERBINDUNG (GUTE) **6005**
SCHWEISSVERBINDUNG (ÜBERLAPPTE) **7405**
SCHWEISSVERSUCH **13792**

**SCH** 896

SCHWEISSVERZÖGERUNGSZEIT 12038
SCHWEISSVORRICHTUNG 13785
SCHWEISSWÄRME 13784
SCHWEISSZUSTAND (IM) 745
SCHWELEN 7776
SCHWELEN 11688
SCHWELEREI 7776
SCHWELLE 11574
SCHWELLENSCHRAUBE 11043
SCHWELLFESTIGKEITSVERHÄLTNIS 4742
SCHWELLUNG 12543
SCHWENKARM 12549
SCHWENKFENSTER 13531
SCHWENKKRAN 3618
SCHWENKKRAN 11583
SCHWENKKRANARM 3619
SCHWENKZAPFEN 13242
SCHWERARBEITSSITZ 9017
SCHWERE 6413
SCHWERE 6078
SCHWEREBESCHLEUNIGUNG 64
SCHWEREBESCHLEUNIGUNG 65
SCHWERERDE 1020
SCHWERES KOHLENWASSERSTOFFGAS 4851
SCHWERFLÜSSIG 13577
SCHWERKRAFT 6078
SCHWERKRAFTDRUCKGUSS 6079
SCHWERKRAFTLASTWAGEN 6405
SCHWERLINIE 8124
SCHWERMETALL 6407
SCHWERÖL 6408
SCHWERÖL 5714
SCHWERPUNKT 2168
SCHWERPUNKTACHSE 869
SCHWERSIEDEND 1425
SCHWERSPAT 1021
SCHWERTFEILE 11623
SCHWERWASSER 6414
SCHWIMMAUFBEREITUNG 5452
SCHWIMMAUFBEREITUNG (ANIONISCHE) 557
SCHWIMMAUFBEREITUNG (SELEKTIVE) 11144
SCHWIMMBRÜCKENDACH 9621
SCHWIMMDACHTANK 5439
SCHWIMMER 5876
SCHWIMMER 5430
SCHWIMMERHAHN 5433
SCHWIMMERKAMMER 5431
SCHWIMMERKONDENSTOPF 5432
SCHWIMMERNADELVENTIL 8522
SCHWIMMERVENTIL 5433
SCHWIMMFÄHIGKEIT 1742

SCHWIMMVERFAHREN 344
SCHWIMMWAAGE 6722
SCHWINDEN 11388
SCHWINDEN 11392
SCHWINDEN 11397
SCHWINDEN DES HOLZES 11396
SCHWINDEN EINES METALLS BEIM ERSTARREN 11394
SCHWINDMASS 477
SCHWINDMASSSTAB 3047
SCHWINDRING 11391
SCHWINDUNG 11392
SCHWINDUNG 4230
SCHWINDUNG (BEHINDERTE) 6504
SCHWINDUNGSRISS 6645
SCHWINDUNGSRISS 11395
SCHWINGARM 3050
SCHWINGBEWEGUNG 8881
SCHWINGE 11633
SCHWINGE 11253
SCHWINGEN 8877
SCHWINGENDE WELLE 10657
SCHWINGGEWICHT 6015
SCHWINGHEBEL 10656
SCHWINGKOLBEN 8882
SCHWINGKRISTALLMETHODE 8879
SCHWINGNOCKEN 8878
SCHWINGPLATTE 3870
SCHWINGQUARZ 3432
SCHWINGUNG 8884
SCHWINGUNG 13554
SCHWINGUNG (ELEKTRISCHE) 4547
SCHWINGUNG (ERZWUNGENE) 5535
SCHWINGUNG (FREIE) 5643
SCHWINGUNG (GEDÄMPFTE) 3600
SCHWINGUNG (MECHANISCHE) 8114
SCHWINGUNG (UNGEDÄMPFTE) 13346
SCHWINGUNG EINER FEDER 13558
SCHWINGUNGSACHSE 867
SCHWINGUNGSDÄMPFER 3602
SCHWINGUNGSDÄMPFER 13555
SCHWINGUNGSDAUER 12945
SCHWINGUNGSFAKTOR 11981
SCHWINGUNGSFESTIGKEIT 12353
SCHWINGUNGSKNOTEN 8605
SCHWINGUNGSMITTELPUNKT 2170
SCHWINGUNGSWEITE 486
SCHWINGUNGZ HARMONISCHE BEWEGUNG 6302
SCHWUNGKUGEL 6015
SCHWUNGMASSE 10561
SCHWUNGMOMENT 8373
SCHWUNGRAD 5496

897     **SEI**

SCHWUNGRAD (EINTEILIGES) **11784**
SCHWUNGRAD (GESPRENGTES) **11941**
SCHWUNGRAD (GEZAHNTES) **5906**
SCHWUNGRAD (MEHRSTELLIGES) **11138**
SCHWUNGRAD (VERZAHNTES) **5906**
SCHWUNGRAD (ZWEITEILIGES) **5497**
SCHWUNGRADGRUBE **5498**
SCHWUNGRADKRANZ **10593**
SCHWUNGSCHEIBE **4004**
SCHWUNGSZAHL **8341**
SEALED-BEAM SCHEINMERFER **11079**
SECHSECK **6453**
SECHSFLACH **6463**
SECHSFLÄCHNER **6463**
SECHSKANTBUNDMUTTER **5340**
SECHSKANTDRAHT **6462**
SECHSKANTE **6456**
SECHSKANTEISEN **6454**
SECHSKANTEISEN AUS LEGIERTEN STÄHLEN **374**
SECHSKANTMUTTER **6455**
SECHSKANTSCHRAUBE **6457**
SECHSKANTSCHRAUBENKOPF **6461**
SECHSKANTWINKEL **6456**
SECHSROLLENWALZWERK **2543**
SEDLITZERSALZ **7889**
SEEBECK-EFFEKT **12830**
SEEHÖHE **11070**
SEELE **3142**
SEELE EINES SEILES **3167**
SEEROHRLEITUNG **11080**
SEESAND **11071**
SEEWASSER **11072**
SEEWEG **10810**
SEGELTUCH **1906**
SEGERKEGEL **10050**
SEGERKEGEL **11134**
SEGMENTKEIL **13929**
SEHFELD **5143**
SEHNENPOLYGON **6964**
SEHNENSCHNITT **1058**
SEIDE **11452**
SEIDENGLANZ **11455**
SEIDENPAPIER **12969**
SEIFE **11701**
SEIFENBILDUNG **10933**
SEIFENLAUGE **11702**
SEIFENLÖSUNG **11702**
SEIFENSTEIN **10935**
SEIFENWASSER **11702**
SEIGERUNG **7635**
SEIGERUNG **3172**

SEIGERUNGSPRÜFUNG **7656**
SEIGNETTESALZ **11729**
SEIHER **12332**
SEIL **10730**
SEIL (DRALLFREIES) **8646**
SEIL (ENDLOSES) **4733**
SEIL (FEINDRÄHTIGES) **5207**
SEIL (GEFLOCHTENES) **1527**
SEIL (GESPANNTES) **12923**
SEIL (GETEERTES) **12688**
SEIL (GROBDRÄHTIGES) **2579**
SEIL (LINKSGESCHLAGENES) **7511**
SEIL (RECHTSGESCHLAGENES) **10587**
SEIL (TROSSWEISE GESCHLAGENES) **6309**
SEIL (UNGESTEURTES) **13839**
SEIL (VERJÜNGTES) **12661**
SEIL (VERSCHLOSSENES) **2513**
SEIL (VOLLSCHLÄCHTIGES) **2513**
SEILANTRIEB **10735**
SEILBAHN **1826**
SEILBREMSE **10732**
SEILDICKE **10733**
SEILDRAHT **10743**
SEILDURCHMESSER **10733**
SEILECK **5737**
SEILFADEN **10744**
SEILFERNTRIEB **12706**
SEILFLASCHENZUG **10741**
SEILFÖRDERER **11010**
SEILGARN **10744**
SEILKAUSCHE **12848**
SEILLITZE **12339**
SEILPOLYGON **5737**
SEILROLLE **10742**
SEILSCHEIBE **10742**
SEILSCHEIBE **6135**
SEILSCHEIBENRILLE **6131**
SEILSCHEIBENSCHWUNGRAD **10738**
SEILSCHLAG **10739**
SEILSCHLINGE **7742**
SEILSCHLOSS **11706**
SEILSPLISS **11933**
SEILSTÄRKE **10733**
SEILSTRAHL **9580**
SEILSTRANG **10740**
SEILTRIEB **10734**
SEILTRIEB (MEHRFACHER) **8473**
SEILTROMMEL **10737**
SEILVERSPLEISSUNG **11934**
SEILZUG **5737**
SEITE EINES POLYGONS **11414**

## SEI

898

SEITENANSICHT 9898
SEITENANSICHT 11420
SEITENDRUCK 7422
SEITENFLÄCHE EINER MUTTER 4994
SEITENHALBIERENDE 8124
SEITENHOBELMASCHINE 11415
SEITENKRAFT 2817
SEITENLASCHE 11416
SEITENNEIGUNG 12538
SEITENSCHEIBE EINES ZAHNRADES 11400
SEITENSCHNEIDER 3832
SEITLICH VERSCHOBEN 8731
SEKANTE 11099
SEKUNDÄRE HÄRTUNG 11105
SEKUNDÄRELEMENT 4534
SEKUNDÄRES KRIECHEN 11104
SEKUNDÄRSCHWEISSSTROM 11110
SELBSTAUFZEICHNENDES INSTRUMENT 10289
SELBSTENTZÜNDUNG 11956
SELBSTENTZÜNDUNGSMOTOR 2866
SELBSTERREGUNG 11153
SELBSTHÄRTERSTAHL 298
SELBSTHÄRTESTAHL 11154
SELBSTHEMMEND 11157
SELBSTINDUKTION 11156
SELBSTINDUKTIONSSPULE 6894
SELBSTINDUKTIONSWIDERSTAND 6891
SELBSTKOSTEN 3207
SELBSTKOSTENPREIS 3210
SELBSTÖLER 851
SELBSTSCHLUSSVENTIL 845
SELBSTSCHREIBER 10289
SELBSTSPANNENDER KOLBENRING 11990
SELBSTSPANNER 11990
SELBSTSPERREND 11157
SELBSTSTABILISIERUNGSSYSTEM 847
SELBSTTÄTIG 11148
SELBSTTÄTIGE MECHANISCHE ROSTBESCHICKUNG 8111
SELBSTTÄTIGKEIT 837
SELBSTTRAGENDER KOLBEN 9392
SELBSTWÄRMENDER LÖTKOLBEN 11155
SELBSTZÜNDUNG 844
SELEKTIVE ERHITZUNG 3915
SELEKTIVES FRISCHGLÜHEN 580
SELEN 11146
SELLERSGEWINDE 451
SELLERSKUPPLUNG 11164
SELLERSLAGER 12563
SELSTTÄTIGE MECHANISCHE
  ROSTBESCHICKUNGSVORRICHTUNG 8110
SENDZIMIRWALZWERK 11181

SENKEL 9539
SENKELBIRNE 9538
SENKELGEWICHT 9538
SENKEN EINER LAST 7797
SENKKASTEN (FLÜSSIGKEITSDICHTER) 7658
SENKLOT 9539
SENKNIET 10635
SENKRECHT ZUR FASER 138
SENKRECHTE 9217
SENKRECHTE ERRICHTEN (EINE) 4806
SENKRECHTE SCHWEISSUNG 13419
SENKRECHTER ODER SCHRÄGER ABSCHNITT EINES BALKENS
  11116
SENKRECHTFRÄSMASCHINE 13548
SENKRECHTSTOSSMASCHINEN 11640
SENKSCHRAUBE 5385
SENKSCHRAUBE 3248
SENKSPERRBREMSE 7681
SENKUNG 7798
SENKWAAGE 6722
SEQUENTIELL 11194
SERIEN- 11196
SERIENBAU 10462
SERIENDYNAMO 11201
SERIENFABRIKATION 10462
SERIENMOTOR 11202
SERIENPRODUKTION 11198
SERIENPUNKTNAHT 11200
SERIENSCHALTUNG 11199
SERPENTINASBEST 11205
SERVO-BREMSE 1457
SERVO-STEUERUNG 11210
SERVOBREMSEN 9731
SERVOLENKUNG 9743
SERVOMOTOR 11211
SESAMÖL 11212
SETZEISEN 10626
SETZHAMMER 11218
SETZHAMMER (RUNDER) 5729
SETZKEIL 3213
SETZKOPF 5266
SETZMEISSEL 11217
SHAPINGMASCHINE 11269
SHERARDISIEREN 11341
SHERARDISIEREN 11340
SHOREHÄRTE 11003
SICHERHEITSBREMSE 10883
SICHERHEITSFAKTOR 10885
SICHERHEITSFAKTOR 5009
SICHERHEITSGRAD 5009
SICHERHEITSGURT 10882

## SIN

SICHERHEITSHAKEN **10888**
SICHERHEITSKOEFFIZIENT **5009**
SICHERHEITSKUPPLUNG **10884**
SICHERHEITSMEMBRANE **10860**
SICHERHEITSMUTTER **7702**
SICHERHEITSVENTIL **10891**
SICHERHEITSVENTIL **1593**
SICHERHEITSVENTIL (FEDERBELASTETES) **11986**
SICHERHEITSVENTIL MIT FEDERBELASTUNG **11998**
SICHERHEITSVENTIL MIT GEWICHTSBELASTUNG **13749**
SICHERHEITSVORRICHTUNG **10881**
SICHERHEITSVORSCHRIFTEN **10889**
SICHERHEITSZUGABE **5009**
SICHERN (EINE MUTTER) **7700**
SICHERN (EINEN KEIL) **7700**
SICHERUNG **5751**
SICHERUNG (ELEKTR.) **10886**
SICHERUNG GEGEN VERSCHIEBEN **7711**
SICHERUNG VON SCHRAUBEN **7707**
SICHERUNGSKASTEN **5752**
SICHERUNGSRING F. KOLBENBOLZEN **2405**
SICHERUNGSSCHEIBE **7703**
SICHERUNGSSCHRAUBE **7708**
SICHERUNGSSCHRAUBENMUTTER **10514**
SICHTSIGNAL **13580**
SICKENHAMMER **3321**
SICKENMASCHINE **3323**
SICKENSTOCK **3322**
SICKERWASSER **9181**
SIDERIT **11421**
SIEB **10572**
SIEB **11422**
SIEB **11018**
SIEBANALYSE **11020**
SIEBEN **11424**
SIEBEN **11423**
SIEBKERN **3164**
SIEBMASCHE **8169**
SIEBRÜCKSTAND **9548**
SIEDEDAMPF **1404**
SIEDEDAMPFABLASSDÜSE **1405**
SIEDEHITZE **1427**
SIEDEN **1429**
SIEDEN **1401**
SIEDEPUNKT **1424**
SIEDESALZ **2790**
SIEDETEMPERATUR **1427**
SIEDEVERZUG **10517**
SIEKENSTOCK **3322**
SIEMENS MARTINSTAHL (SAURER) **116**
SIEMENS-MARTIN-OFEN **8829**

SIEMENS-MARTIN-OFEN **8815**
SIEMENS-MARTIN-STAHL **8816**
SIEMENS-MARTIN-STAHL (BASISCHER) **1048**
SIEMENS-MARTINS-VERFAHREN **8830**
SIEMENS-MARTINSTAHL **8023**
SIEMENSMARTINSTAHL (BASISCHER) **1047**
SIGMA-SCHWEISSEN **11428**
SIGNAL (AKUSTISCHES) **816**
SIGNAL (OPTISCHES) **13580**
SIGNALPFEIFE **307**
SIKKATIV **4256**
SIKKATIV **4257**
SILBER **11458**
SILBER (92/5% FEIN) **12253**
SILBERBROMID **1645**
SILBERCHLORID **11461**
SILBERERZ **11625**
SILBERHARTLÖTEN **11460**
SILBERJODID **11464**
SILBERNITRAT **7828**
SILBERSCHLAGLOT **11466**
SILBERSULFAT **11467**
SILBERZYANID **11462**
SILIERMASCHINEN **3522**
SILIKASTEIN **11435**
SILIKAT **11437**
SILIKON **11456**
SILIKOSPIEGEL **11440**
SILIZIUM **11442**
SILIZIUM-MANGANSTAHL **11450**
SILIZIUMBRONZE **11444**
SILIZIUMDIOXYD **11434**
SILIZIUMDIOXYD **11436**
SILIZIUMEISEN **5113**
SILIZIUMKARBID **1980**
SILIZIUMKARBID **11445**
SILIZIUMKUPFER **11446**
SILIZIUMMANGANEISEN **11440**
SILIZIUMMESSING **11443**
SILIZIUMSTAHL **11449**
SILIZIUMSTAHL **11447**
SIMSHOBEL **9522**
SINKSTOFFE **8062**
SINN EINER KRAFT **11182**
SINTERGRUBE **10977**
SINTERKOHLE **4344**
SINTERN **11511**
SINTERN (KONTINUIERLICHES) **3014**
SINTEROFEN **11512**
SINTERSTAHL **10599**
SINTERSTAHL **10598**

# SIN
900

SINTERUNG 13584
SINTERUNG 5690
SINTERUNG 11511
SINUS 11475
SINUS-SCHRAUBSTROCK 535
SINUSKURVE 11476
SINUSOIDE 11513
SINUSSCHWINGUNG 6302
SIPHON 11517
SIPHONPFANNE 12693
SIRENE 11518
SITUATIONSPLAN 9430
SITZ 11098
SITZ (ANGEGOSSENER) 7816
SITZ (SELBSTEINSTELLENDER) 9741
SITZE (PARALLELE) 9063
SITZE (SCHRÄGE) 12663
SITZFLÄCHE 11098
SITZGURT 11096
SITZRÜCKENLEHNE 12012
SKALA 10981
SKALAR 10967
SKALENARÄOMETER 6072
SKALENSCHEIBE 6027
SKALENSCHEIBENMIKROMETER 6877
SKANDIUM 10991
SKELETT-MODELL 11526
SKINPACKUNG 11540
SKIZZE 11532
SKIZZE 11528
SKIZZIEREN 11533
SKIZZIEREN 11529
SKLEROMETER 11002
SKLEROSKOP NACH SHORE 11366
SMITHSONI 1836
SODA 11713
SODA (GEGLÜHTE) (KALZINIERTE) 551
SODALAUGE 11712
SODASALZ (KALZINIERTES) 551
SODASTANNAT 11732
SOHLE 2900
SOHLE (SAURE) 108
SOHLE AUF PFÄHLEN 9305
SOHLE EINES HOBELS 11771
SOHLLEDER 11770
SOHLPLATTE (FÜR LAGER) 11772
SOLARÖL 11753
SOLE 1617
SOLENOID 11773
SOLIDUS 11805
SOLIDUSLINIE 11805

SOLLDURCHMESSER 8611
SOLLWERT 11221
SOLLWERT 1858
SOLVAYSODA 455
SOLWAAGE 10901
SONDE 9882
SONDERERREGUNG 11190
SONDERERZEUGNIS 11849
SONDERGEBIET 11845
SONDERMESSING (SEEWASSERFESTES) 8511
SONDERSTAHL 11848
SONDERSTAHL 368
SONDERZWECKATMOSPHÄRE 791
SONNENRAD 12457
SONNENSPEKTRUM 11754
SORBIT 11817
SORTIER-UND WASCHMASCHINEN FÜR FRÜCHTE UND GEMÜSE 5704
SORTIERUNG 11524
SPACHTEL 11844
SPALT 11629
SPALT 11937
SPALTE 3278
SPALTEN 11622
SPALTEN (CHEM.) 11946
SPALTEN (CHEM.) 11950
SPALTFLÄCHE 2488
SPALTFLÄCHE 2487
SPALTKORROSION 3185
SPALTQUERSCHNITT EINES VENTILS 11121
SPALTROHR 2732
SPALTSÄGE 10609
SPALTSCHIEBER 6100
SPALTUNG 2487
SPALTUNG 4058
SPALTUNGSDESTILLATION 3805
SPAN 2346
SPAN 2343
SPAN 12536
SPANANALYSE 2345
SPÄNE 3543
SPÄNE 11278
SPANHOBELMASCHINE 13525
SPANNBACKE 6121
SPANNDORN 2727
SPANNDRAHT 6187
SPANNFINGER 7280
SPANNFUTTER 2393
SPANNHÜLSE 2931
SPANNKEIL 185
SPANNKLUPPE 13562

SPANNKRAFT 12373
SPANNKRAFT EINER FEDER 5528
SPANNKRAFT EINES GASES 4480
SPANNMASCHINE 12372
SPANNRING 11990
SPANNROLLE 12334
SPANNROLLE 1161
SPANNROLLE 4910
SPANNROLLE NACH LENIX 13750
SPANNSÄGE 5628
SPANNSCHELLE 2448
SPANNSCHLITTEN 12756
SPANNSCHLOSS 13285
SPANNSCHRAUBE 2453
SPANNTISCHE 8290
SPANNUNG 12367
SPANNUNG 9808
SPANNUNG 13593
SPANNUNG 12322
SPANNUNG 9708
SPANNUNG 12753
SPANNUNG (INNERE) 7074
SPANNUNG (KRITISCHE) 3350
SPANNUNG (ZULÄSSIGE) 9215
SPANNUNGS-DEHNUNGSKURVE 12366
SPANNUNGSABFALL 13594
SPANNUNGSABFALL AN DER ANODE 595
SPANNUNGSDIAGRAMM 6881
SPANNUNGSDIAGRAMM 12366
SPANNUNGSFELD 4505
SPANNUNGSFLÄCHE 12368
SPANNUNGSFREIGLÜHEN 12362
SPANNUNGSGEFÄLLE 13594
SPANNUNGSKALTRISS 2674
SPANNUNGSKONZENTRATION 12360
SPANNUNGSKORROSION 3195
SPANNUNGSKORROSION 12361
SPANNUNGSMESSER 13597
SPANNUNGSREGLER 13595
SPANNUNGSREGULATOR 13595
SPANNUNGSRISS 5304
SPANNUNGSRISSKORROSION 11093
SPANNUNGSUNTERSCHIED 9709
SPANNUNGSVERLUST 13594
SPANNUNGSZEIGER 13597
SPANNUNGSZUSTAND (KRITISCHER) 5935
SPANNUT 5483
SPANNVORRICHTUNG 3370
SPANNVORRICHTUNG 13285
SPANNWAGEN 12756
SPANNWEITE 11831

SPANWINKEL 11418
SPANWINKEL 10186
SPARBEIZE 10510
SPATEISENSTEIN 11421
SPECKÖL 7409
SPECKSTEIN 11703
SPECKSTEIN 5659
SPEICHENRAD 11951
SPEICHER 76
SPEICHER 8146
SPEICHER 12297
SPEICHERUNG 1705
SPEICHERUNG 12290
SPEICHERWÄRME 10411
SPEISEBEHÄLTER 5075
SPEISEDÜSE 5084
SPEISEHAHN 5066
SPEISELEITUNG 5070
SPEISELEITUNG 5081
SPEISELEITUNG 12484
SPEISEN 5064
SPEISEPUMPE 5071
SPEISEREGLER 5072
SPEISEROHR 5070
SPEISEVENTIL 5076
SPEISEVORRICHTUNG 5083
SPEISEWALZE 5074
SPEISEWASSER 5077
SPEISEWASSER-VORWÄRMER 5078
SPEISUNG 5063
SPEKTRALANALYSE 11861
SPEKTRALANALYSE 11864
SPEKTRALAPPARAT 11862
SPEKTRALFARBEN 11859
SPEKTROGRAPH 11860
SPEKTROGRAPH 11862
SPEKTROMETER 11862
SPEKTROSKOP 11862
SPEKTRUM 11863
SPEKTRUM (KONTINUIERLICHES) 3036
SPENGLER 12964
SPERRAD 10225
SPERRAD 2495
SPERRADHEBEL 10223
SPERRE 7705
SPERREN 7699
SPERRFLÜSSIGKEIT 11082
SPERRHAKEN 2094
SPERRHORN 1091
SPERRING 5128
SPERRKEGEL 2094

# SPE
902

SPERRKLINKE **2094**
SPERRKLINKEEFFEKT **10220**
SPERRKONDENSATOR **1342**
SPERRSCHICHTPHOTOZELLE **9277**
SPERRWERK **7709**
SPEZIALARTIKEL **11849**
SPEZIALGEBIET **11845**
SPEZIALITÄT (PHARMAZEUTISCHE) **9119**
SPEZIALMASCHINE **11486**
SPHALERIT **1324**
SPHÄRISCH **11884**
SPHÄROMETER **11897**
SPIEGEL (EBENER) **9437**
SPIEGEL (ERHABENER) **3078**
SPIEGEL (SPHÄRISCHER) **11888**
SPIEGELBRONZE **11867**
SPIEGELEISEN **11899**
SPIEGELEISEN **11898**
SPIEGELFERNROHR **10386**
SPIEGELGLAS **9491**
SPIEGELGLEICH **12566**
SPIEGELHOLZ **12938**
SPIEGELKLUFT DES HOLZES **12108**
SPIEGELMETALL **11867**
SPIEGELSCHNITT **10075**
SPIEL **2483**
SPIEL **358**
SPIEL (RAUM) **9516**
SPIEL (SEITLICHES) DER WELLE **4735**
SPIELRAUM **359**
SPIELRAUM **358**
SPIELRAUM (AXIALER) **4727**
SPIELRAUM DER KERNMARKE **2483**
SPIELVERRINGERUNGSEINRICHTUNG **915**
SPIESSGLANZ **623**
SPILL **1929**
SPINDEL **11062**
SPINDEL **11904**
SPINDEL **12236**
SPINDEL **12237**
SPINDEL (NICHTSTEIGENDE) **8623**
SPINDEL (STEIGENDE) **10616**
SPINDEL MIT AUSSENLIEGENDEM GEWINDE **8915**
SPINDEL MIT INNENLIEGENDEM GEWINDE **6981**
SPINDEL-DURCHLASS **11906**
SPINDELBREMSE **12344**
SPINDELDREHZAHLEN **11909**
SPINDELHALTER **11910**
SPINDELÖL **11908**
SPINDELPRESSE **11040**
SPINDELSTOCK **6328**

SPINDELVERSCHRAUBUNG **11907**
SPINNFASER **12799**
SPIRALBOHRER **13304**
SPIRALBOHRER MIT GROSSEM DRALLWINKEL **6470**
SPIRALE **11912**
SPIRALE (HYPERBOLISCHE) **6738**
SPIRALE (LOGARITHMISCHE) **7720**
SPIRALE ARCHIMEDISCHE **690**
SPIRALFEDER **5396**
SPIRALFÖRMIG GENIETET **11918**
SPIRALFRÄSER **11917**
SPIRALFRÄSER MIT GROSSEM DRALLWINKEL **6471**
SPIRALGENUTETE REIBAHLE **11915**
SPIRALMISCHER **9931**
SPIRALRUTSCHE **11914**
SPIRALSEIL **10415**
SPIRALSENKER **3149**
SPIRALZAHNSTIRNRAD **6425**
SPIRITUS **313**
SPIRITUSBRENNER **11923**
SPIRITUSFIRNIS **7354**
SPIRITUSLACK **7354**
SPIRITUSLAMPE **11923**
SPIRITUSMOTOR **312**
SPITZBOHRER **5380**
SPITZE (GEOM.) **638**
SPITZE EINER KURVE **3502**
SPITZE EINES GEWINDES **12455**
SPITZEN (AUFGELÖTETE) **1574**
SPITZENAUFHÄNGUNG **9570**
SPITZENBELASTUNG **8065**
SPITZENDE EINES ROHRES **11901**
SPITZENDREHBANK **2150**
SPITZENLAST **8065**
SPITZENSPIEL **3335**
SPITZENSPIEL IM GEWINDE **12858**
SPITZENWEITE **4065**
SPITZFEILE **12648**
SPITZLÖTKOLBEN **9573**
SPITZSÄGE **2802**
SPITZSÄULE **8705**
SPITZSTAHL **9571**
SPITZSTAHL **3866**
SPITZWINKLIG **154**
SPITZZIRKEL **4101**
SPLEISS **11930**
SPLEISSEN **11934**
SPLEISSEN (EIN SEIL) **11931**
SPLESSGLANZBUTTER **626**
SPLINT **11940**
SPLINT **3213**

SPLINT **11943**
SPLINT **10936**
SPLINTHOLZ **10936**
SPLINTLOCH **9333**
SPLINTLOCH **9332**
SPLINTTREIBER **9326**
SPLISS **11933**
SPLISSEN **11934**
SPLISSEN (EIN SEIL) **11931**
SPREIZBARE DORNE **4906**
SPREIZDORN **4907**
SPREIZRING **11990**
SPRENGRING **10515**
SPRENGRING **11692**
SPRENGSTOFF **4937**
SPRINGENDES ZÄHLWERK **3559**
SPRINGSCHALTER **11690**
SPRITZDUSE ZERSTÄUBER **11967**
SPRITZEN **11968**
SPRITZEN **11842**
SPRITZER **11967**
SPRITZFLASCHE **13633**
SPRITZLACKIEREN **9020**
SPRITZLACKIERUNG **11965**
SPRITZPISTOLE **11962**
SPRITZVERFAHREN **11972**
SPRITZVERLUSTE **11843**
SPRITZVERZINKEN **14045**
SPRITZWAND **5251**
SPRITZWASSERSCHUTZ **13720**
SPRÖDE **1627**
SPRÖDIGKEIT **1628**
SPRÖDIGKEIT **4685**
SPRÖDIGKEIT DES EISENS **1629**
SPRÖDIGWERDEN **4685**
SPROSSENEISEN **10937**
SPRÜHDÜSE **11964**
SPRÜHHÄRTUNG **11966**
SPRUNG **3278**
SPRUNG-BILDUNG **5274**
SPRUNGBILDUNG **2286**
SPRUNGGERÜST **7260**
SPULE **1384**
SPULE **2645**
SPULE **4499**
SPÜLEN **10607**
SPÜLEN **10608**
SPULENWICKLUNG **2648**
SPÜLSCHMIERUNG **5442**
SPÜLVERSATZ **6686**
SPUND **12989**

SPUNDEN **12988**
SPUNDEN **12991**
SPUNDHOBEL **8047**
SPUNDMASCHINE **12992**
SPUR **13085**
SPUR **13076**
SPURKRANZ EINES DRUCKLAGERS **12904**
SPURKRANZ EINES RADES **5331**
SPURLAGER **12241**
SPURLAGER **5524**
SPURPFANNE **12905**
SPURPLATTE **12905**
SPURRING **12904**
SPURSTANGE **12231**
SPURSTANGE **12915**
SPURSTANGE **12916**
SPURWEITE **13085**
SPURWEITE (EISENBAHN) **5871**
SPURZAPFEN **9421**
SS-STAHL **8000**
STAB **10660**
STAB **981**
STAB (EINES FACHWERKES) **986**
STAB (GEZOGENER) **12754**
STAB MIT SCHMELZKERN **3168**
STABEISEN **984**
STABILISATOR **12042**
STABILISIERUNG **12043**
STABILITÄT **12041**
STABILITÄTSMOMENT **8375**
STABMAGNET **985**
STABSTAHL (GEZOGENER) **4248**
STABTHERMOMETER **12235**
STACHELDRAHT **987**
STACHELDRAHTMASCHINE **988**
STADTBUS **13421**
STADTOMNIBUS **8410**
STAHL **9427**
STAHL **13292**
STAHL **13011**
STAHL **12196**
STAHL **12223**
STAHL (ALUMINIUM-BERUHIGTER) **442**
STAHL (ANORMALER) **8**
STAHL (AUSHÄRTENDER) **8000**
STAHL (AUSTENITISCHER) **826**
STAHL (BERUHIGTER UND GEHÄRTETER) **10093**
STAHL (BLASENFREIER) **12209**
STAHL (DEN) BLAU ANLAUFENLASSEN **1368**
STAHL (GEHÄRTETER) **6289**
STAHL (GESCHMIEDETER) **5554**

# STA 904

STAHL (GEZOGENER) 4251
STAHL (GROBKÖRNIGER) 2577
STAHL (HALBBERUHIGTER) 11173
STAHL (HALBHARTER) 1959
STAHL (HARTER) 6280
STAHL (HOCHWERTIGER) 6486
STAHL (KALTGERECKTER) 2697
STAHL (KOHLENSTOFFARMER) 8270
STAHL (KOHLENSTOFFARMER) 7770
STAHL (KOHLENSTOFFEICHER) 1957
STAHL (KOMPRIMIERTER) 2849
STAHL (LEGIERTER) 368
STAHL (NATURHARTER) 8000
STAHL (NICHTROSTENDER) 8644
STAHL (NICKELPLATTIERTER) 8573
STAHL (NIEDRIGLEGIERTER) 382
STAHL (PERLITISCHER) 9145
STAHL (PLATTIERTER) 2446
STAHL (ROSTFREIER) 12051
STAHL (ÜBERHITZTER) 8945
STAHL (UNBERUHIGTER) 4462
STAHL (UNBERUHIGTER) 10598
STAHL (UNLEGIERTER) 1954
STAHL (UNMAGNETISIERBARER) 8638
STAHL (UNVOLLSTÄNDIG DESOXYDIERTER) 8825
STAHL (VERBRANNTER) 1763
STAHL (VERGÜTETER) 10093
STAHL (VERSCHLEISSFESTER) 13718
STAHL (WEICHER) 11744
STAHL (WEICHER) 8270
STAHL (WEICHER) 7770
STAHL (WEICHER) 1958
STAHL (ZWEIMAL GEGÄRBTER) 4156
STAHL ABSCHRECKEN (DEN) 10091
STAHL AUSGLÜHEN 560
STAHL FÜR KÜSTENNAHE ÖLBOHRUNG 8739
STAHL MIT MANGAN (BERUHIGTER) 7969
STAHL MIT NADELIGER STRUKTUR 8523
STAHL NORMALISIEREN 560
STAHL VERGÜTEN (DEN) 6808
STAHLBAND 12197
STAHLBAND 12343
STAHLBAND (ROSTFREIES) 10875
STAHLBANDRIEMEN 12200
STAHLBARREN 12210
STAHLBAU 12218
STAHLBILDUNG 145
STAHLBLECH 12213
STAHLBLECH 11325
STAHLBLOCK 12210
STAHLDEUL 951

STAHLDRAHT 12221
STAHLDRAHTSEIL 12215
STÄHLE (KORROSIONS-UND WÄRMEBESTÄNDIGE) 3184
STÄHLEN 12205
STÄHLEN 12206
STAHLERZEUGUNG 12214
STAHLFLASCHE 12204
STAHLFORMGUSS 12202
STAHLFORMGUSS AUS LEGIERTEN STÄHLEN 372
STAHLGERIPPE 12208
STAHLGERÜST 12218
STAHLGIESSEREI 12207
STAHLGUSS 2055
STAHLGUSSRADSTERN 2056
STAHLHALTER 13010
STAHLHALTER 13005
STAHLHALTER-REVOLVERKÖPFE 13004
STAHLKABEL 12201
STAHLKONSTRUKTION 12218
STAHLKONSTRUKTION 12208
STAHLLINEAL MIT TEILUNG 4100
STAHLLITZEN 12217
STAHLROHR 12219
STAHLROHR 12212
STAHLSANDBLASEN 11380
STAHLSORTE 2459
STAHLSORTE 6022
STAHLSPITZE 8666
STAHLUNG 135
STAHLWERK 12222
STAHLWERKE 12211
STAHLWERKSKOKILLE 6923
STALAGMOMETRIE 12054
STAMM EINER SÄULE 11243
STAMPFASPHALT 12610
STAMPFBETON 10193
STAMPFEN 10194
STAMPFEN 10195
STAMPFWERK 12057
STANDARDABWEICHUNG 12074
STANDARDKERZE 3663
STANDARDMODELL 12073
STÄNDER 12490
STÄNDER 12146
STÄNDER 12062
STÄNDER 13219
STÄNDERBOHRMASCHINE 13412
STÄNDERBOHRMASCHINE 2755
STÄNDERTRAGWERK 2754
STANDFESTIGKEIT 2643
STANDFESTIGKEIT 12041

905 STE

STANDGUSS **6079**
STANDPEILER **7526**
STANDROHR **12066**
STANDROHR **12093**
STANDROHR **12067**
STANDSICHERHEIT **12041**
STANDVENTIL **13630**
STANGE **10663**
STANGE **10660**
STANGE EINES SCHIEBERS **12236**
STANGE EINES VENTILS **12236**
STANGEN-SPANNZANGEN **12981**
STANGEN-UND ROHRZIEHMASCHINE **982**
STANGENDICHTUNG **9386**
STANGENDRAHT **13882**
STANGENDREHAUTOMAT **983**
STANGENLACK **12254**
STANGENSCHWEFEL **12255**
STANGENZIRKEL **1096**
STANGENZIRKEL **13105**
STANNAT **12095**
STANNICHLORID **12096**
STANNIOL **12955**
STANNOCHLORID **12100**
STANNOOXYD **12102**
STANZE **12060**
STANZE **10009**
STANZE (AUSSCHNEIDEMASCHINE) **10009**
STANZEINHEIT **10011**
STANZEN **10012**
STANZEN **10006**
STANZEN **9998**
STANZEN **12059**
STANZEN **12056**
STANZEN VON LÖCHERN **10008**
STANZPROBE **12061**
STAPEL **9304**
STÄRKE **12843**
STÄRKE **12111**
STÄRKEGUMMI **3825**
STÄRKEKLEISTER **12112**
STÄRKEZUCKER **6058**
STARKSTROM **6401**
STARKWANDIG **12841**
STARRBOHRMASCHINEN **10590**
STARRFETT **6275**
STARRSCHMIERE **6275**
STARRSCHMIERUNG **6087**
START/STOP DRUCKKNOPF **12115**
STARTERKLAPPE **292**
STARTERKLAPPE **12342**

STATIK **12140**
STATIK (GRAPHISCHE) **6061**
STATISCH **12133**
STATISCHES GLEICHGEWICHTSPOTENTIAL EINER REAKTION **4790**
STATIV **13219**
STATOR (ELEKTR.) **12146**
STATUENBRONZE **12147**
STAU **10182**
STAUANLAGE **13753**
STAUB **4389**
STAUBDICHT **4393**
STAUBFÄNGER **4390**
STAUBKOHLE **2563**
STAUCHALTERUNG **12324**
STAUCHEN **4452**
STAUCHEN **13414**
STAUCHEN DER NIETE **2490**
STAUCHGERÜST **4451**
STAUCHGERÜST **4454**
STAUCHGRAT **5357**
STAUCHKALIBER **4455**
STAUCHMASCHINE **13415**
STAUCHMASCHINE **5561**
STAUCHSCHLITTEN **8436**
STAUCHSTICH **4455**
STAUCHSTREIFEN **3382**
STAUCHUNG **3420**
STAUCHVERSUCH **11949**
STAUCHVERSUCH **4374**
STAUCHVERSUCH **13416**
STAUCHVERSUCH **7262**
STAUCHWALZE **4456**
STAUFFERBÜCHSE **12148**
STAUHÖHE **13515**
STEARIN **12195**
STEARINÖL **8795**
STEARINSÄURE **12194**
STEATIT **11703**
STECHBEITEL **9080**
STECHEN **8515**
STECHKARREN **947**
STECHUHR **12946**
STECKKONTAKT **13622**
STECKSCHLÜSSEL **1515**
STECKSCHLÜSSEL **11709**
STEG **13729**
STEG **13726**
STEG EINER KETTE **12402**
STEG EINES FORMEISENS **13730**
STEGFLANKE **10721**

# STE

STEGKETTE 12403
STEHBOCK 12064
STEHBOLZEN 12151
STEHEND 13551
STEHKOLBEN 9142
STEHLAGER 9543
STEIFE 9925
STEIFHEIT EINES RIEMENS 12258
STEIFIGKEIT 10591
STEIFIGKEIT EINES SEILES 12258
STEIGDRUCK 6855
STEIGENDE LEITUNG 756
STEIGER 269
STEIGERUNG DER GESCHWINDIGKEIT 10185
STEIGERUNG DER REAKTIONSFÄHIGKEIT 144
STEIGHÖHE (MECH.) 10611
STEIGLEITUNG 10614
STEIGLEITUNG 2753
STEIGROHR 10615
STEIGTRICHTER 10614
STEIGUNG 12654
STEIGUNG 757
STEIGUNGSWINKEL 6431
STEIGUNGSWINKEL EINER SCHRAUBE 531
STEIGVERMÖGEN 2498
STEILSCHRIFT 6243
STEIN 8058
STEIN (FEUERFESTER) 5239
STEIN (KÜNSTLICHER) 737
STEIN (NATÜRLICHER) 8507
STEINBRECHER 12273
STEINBRECHMASCHINE 12273
STEINBRUCH 10073
STEINFÄNGER 9153
STEINKITT 12274
STEINKOHLE 2558
STEINKOHLENBENZIN 1199
STEINKOHLENBRIKETT 2560
STEINKOHLENKREOSOT 1938
STEINKOHLENTEER 2570
STEINKOHLENTEERKAMPFER 8494
STEINKOHLENTEERÖL 2568
STEINKOHLENTEERPECH 2569
STEINMÖRTEL 2894
STEINÖL 9229
STEINSALZ 10653
STEINSCHLAG 1644
STEINSCHLAGGITTER 12275
STEINSCHRAUBE 10172
STEINSCHRAUBE MIT AUFGEHAUENEN KANTEN 7209
STEINZEUG 12276

STEINZEUGROHR 12277
STEKENHAMMER 3321
STELLE 3940
STELLE (HEISSE) 6642
STELLE (WARME) 6642
STELLHEBEL 7706
STELLIT 12234
STELLIT (RÖMISCHE) 12225
STELLKEIL 185
STELLMUTTER 7702
STELLMUTTER 191
STELLÖL 5491
STELLRING 7743
STELLRING 12904
STELLRING (ZWEITEILIGER) 11939
STELLSCHRAUBE 192
STELLSCHRAUBE 11222
STELLSPINDEL 6522
STELLUNG 9219
STELLUNG (LAGE) DER SCHWEISSPISTOLE 13782
STELLWINKEL 1228
STEMMASCHINE 8402
STEMMBEITEL 5264
STEMMEISEN 5264
STEMMEISSEL 2114
STEMMHAMMER 1872
STEMPEL 1560
STEMPEL 9997
STEMPEL 9544
STEMPEL 12055
STEMPEL (GESCHLOSSENE) 2521
STEMPELBLOCK 3884
STEMPELHALTER 8033
STEMPELHAMMER 4326
STEMPELVERSCHIEBUNG 3891
STENGELGEFÜGE 2758
STENGELKRISTALL 2757
STEREOMETRIE 12251
STEREOMETRISCH 12250
STERNKURVE 5602
STERNMOTOR 10135
STERNPOLYGON 12107
STERNRAD 12109
STETIGBAHNSTEUERUNG 3032
STETIGER VERLAUF 3017
STETIGKEIT 3017
STEUERDIREKTOR 3995
STEUERGEHÄUSE 12947
STEUERHEBEL 8833
STEUERKETTE 8817
STEUERKETTE 12948

STEUERKETTE **12950**
STEUERLEISTUNG **10233**
STEUERN **3049**
STEUERRAD **12233**
STEUERSCHEIBEN **9497**
STEUERSEIL **3051**
STEUERUNG **3057**
STEUERUNG **3048**
STEUERUNG **12226**
STEUERUNG **13471**
STEUERUNG (ADAPTIVE) **161**
STEUERUNG (DAMPFM.) **13460**
STEUERUNGS-SYSTEM (NUMERISCHES) **8695**
STEUERUNGSEINSTELLUNG **12952**
STEUERWELLE **10550**
STEUERWELLE **4315**
STICH **10613**
STICHEL **13011**
STICHFLAMME **8975**
STICHFOLGE **9097**
STICHHÖHE **10613**
STICHLOCH **12645**
STICHLOCH **7287**
STICHMASS **10661**
STICHSÄGE **2802**
STICKOXYD **8581**
STICKSTOFF **8588**
STICKSTOFF MONOXYD **8581**
STICKSTOFFDIOXYD **8591**
STICKSTOFFOXYDUL **8597**
STICKSTOFFPENTOXYD **8590**
STICKSTOFFPEROXYD **8591**
STICKSTOFFSÄURE **8580**
STICKSTOFFSESQUIOXYD **8592**
STICKSTOFFTETROXYD **8591**
STICKSTOFFTRIOXYD **8592**
STIEL EINES HAMMERS **11244**
STIELPFANNE **6250**
STIFT **12397**
STIFT **9315**
STIFT (KONISCHER) **12655**
STIFTLOCH **9332**
STIFTNIETUNG **9321**
STIFTÖLER **8520**
STIFTRAD **9324**
STIFTSCHLÜSSEL **9322**
STIFTSCHRAUBE **12399**
STIFTSCHRAUBE **11220**
STIFTSCHRAUBE **12397**
STILL SETZEN **11406**
STILLEGUNG **11409**

STILLSETZEN EINER MASCHINE **11410**
STILLSTAND EINER MASCHINE **12094**
STILLSTANDZEIT **4191**
STIRNABSCHRECKPROBE **7254**
STIRNFLÄCHE **4989**
STIRNFRÄSER **4722**
STIRNFRÄSER **4992**
STIRNKURBEL **8947**
STIRNLAGER **4720**
STIRNRAD **12009**
STIRNRADANTRIEB **12010**
STIRNRÄDERGETRIEBE **12008**
STIRNRÄDERWENDEGETRIEBE **10547**
STIRNRADFLASCHENZUG **12011**
STIRNSENKUNG **11960**
STIRNWAND **4728**
STIRNZAPFEN **4721**
STÖCHIOMETRIE **12268**
STÖCHIOMETRISCH **12267**
STÖCKEL **632**
STOCKFLECKEN **4843**
STOCKGETRIEBE **9325**
STOCKLACK **12254**
STOCKPUNKT **11804**
STOCKSCHERE **12264**
STOCKTHERMOMETER **12235**
STOFF **12419**
STOFF (ORGANISCHER) **8866**
STOFFE (FEUERFESTE) **10466**
STOFFMANGEL **13348**
STOPFBÜCHSE **12405**
STOPFBÜCHSE **9001**
STOPFBÜCHSE **5953**
STOPFBÜCHSENBRILLE **9002**
STOPFBÜCHSENFLANSCH **5955**
STOPFBÜCHSENHAHN **5954**
STOPFBÜCHSENMUTTER **9005**
STOPFBÜCHSENPACKUNG **12406**
STOPFBÜCHSGEHÄUSE **9008**
STOPFBÜCHSRAUM **12405**
STOPFBÜCHSTOPF **9008**
STOPFEN **9529**
STOPFEN **12285**
STOPFEN **9011**
STOPFEN **1483**
STOPFENHAHN **8997**
STOPFENPFANNE **1496**
STOPFENSTECKER **9529**
STOPPUHR **12283**
STÖPSEL **12285**
STÖPSEL **12639**

# STO 908

STÖPSEL (EINGESCHLIFFENER) 6146
STÖPSELKONTAKT 13622
STORCHSCHNABEL 9033
STÖRSCHUTZ 10156
STÖRUNG 1581
STOSS 6783
STOSS 7238
STOSS (MECH.) 11359
STOSS (MIT LASCHE) 1782
STOSS AUF GEHRUNG 8324
STOSS-UND RÜTTELPRÜFUNG 7249
STOSSAPPARATE 11642
STOSSDÄMPFER 11358
STOSSEISEN 7333
STÖSSEL 12674
STÖSSEL 9221
STÖSSEL 10188
STÖSSEL 1885
STÖSSEL 12672
STÖSSELKOPFSTAHLHALTER 13003
STÖSSELSPIEL 12673
STÖSSELSTANGE 10031
STOSSEN 11630
STOSSEN 11641
STOSSFÄNGER 1732
STOSSFESTIGKEIT 1918
STOSSFESTIGKEIT 6785
STOSSHEBER 6694
STOSSKRAFT 6811
STOSSLASCHE 1783
STOSSLASCHENTEIL 11932
STOSSMASCHINE 11643
STOSSNAHT 1784
STOSSOFEN 10030
STOSSOFEN 10024
STOSSPLATTE 1783
STOSSPUNKTER 6180
STOSSSIEB 1733
STOSSSTANGENHORN 8956
STOSSSTELLE 7238
STOSSTANGE 10026
STOSSVERBINDUNG 1778
STOSSVERBINDUNG 1776
STOSSVERLUST 7757
STOSSVERSUCH 6786
STOSSVORRICHTUNG 10029
STRAHL (AUFTREFFENDER) 6832
STRAHL (AUSTRETENDER) 4691
STRAHL (EINFALLENDER) 6832
STRAHL (GEBROCHENER) 10397
STRAHL (REFLEKTIERTER) 10384

STRAHL (ZUSAMMENHALTENDER) 11787
STRAHL (ZUÜCKGEWORFENER) 10384
STRAHLDÜSENBOHREN 7222
STRAHLEN 10141
STRAHLEN 10242
STRAHLEN (ARTINISCHE) 140
STRAHLEN (INFRAROTE) 7103
STRAHLEN (ULTRAROTE) 13332
STRAHLEN (ULTRAVIOLETTE) 13333
STRAHLEN AUFFANGEN 7024
STRAHLEN AUSSENDEN 4703
STRAHLENBRECHUNG 10399
STRAHLENBÜNDEL 9164
STRAHLENEMISSION 10143
STRAHLENKUNDE 10164
STRAHLENMESSER 142
STRAHLENMESSER 1431
STRAHLENRISS 12108
STRÄHLER 2274
STRAHLHONVERFAHREN 7653
STRAHLKONDENSATOR 4470
STRAHLPUMPE 7223
STRAHLROHR 8679
STRAHLSANDBLASEN 2540
STRAHLUNG (HOMOGENE) 6559
STRAHLUNG (MONOCHROMATISCHE) 8383
STRAHLUNGSINTENSITÄT 7019
STRAHLUNGSKONSTANTE 10144
STRAHLUNGSKONSTANTE (SCHEINBARE) 643
STRAHLUNGSVERMÖGEN 4702
STRAHLUNGSWÄRME 10140
STRAHLUNGSWÄRMEVERLUST 10145
STRANG EINES TAUES 12338
STRANGGIESSEN 3029
STRANGPRESSEN 4970
STRANGPRESSENROHLING 4971
STRASSENÖL 10647
STREBE 12396
STREBE 1516
STREBEBOGEN 688
STRECKBAR 4361
STRECKBARKEIT 4363
STRECKDRAHT 4252
STRECKE (GEOM.) 11118
STRECKEN (EISEN) 4219
STRECKEN DES EISENS 4235
STRECKENSTEUERUNG 12314
STRECKFESTIGKEIT 14012
STRECKGESENK 5726
STRECKGRENZE 14012
STRECKGRENZE 14011

909 STU

STRECKGRENZE 14013
STRECKMETALL 4904
STRECKPROBE 5409
STRECKRICHTEN 9118
STREICHMASS 8016
STREICHMASS (STEHENDES) 11069
STREICHMODELL 8016
STREIFEN 12378
STREIFEN 11613
STREIFEN 980
STREIFIGKEIT 11453
STRENGFLÜSSIG 13577
STRENGLOT 6279
STREUDÜSE 11963
STREULICHT 3955
STREUSAND 9094
STREUSTROM 7490
STREUSTROM 12349
STREUUNG 10994
STREUUNG 3933
STREUUNG (ELEKTROMAGNETISCHE) 4616
STRICHFOKUS 7599
STRICHNAHT 1085
STRICHRAUPE 12376
STRICHZEICHNUNG 8905
STRIPPERKRAN 12383
STROBOSKOP 12385
STROBOSKOPISCHE METHODE 12386
STROHFASER 12348
STROHFEILE 10774
STROHHÄCKSLER 2199
STROM 3486
STROM (ELEKTRISCHER) 4525
STROM (ELEKTRISCHER) 4500
STROM (HOCHGESPANNTER) 6500
STROM (INDUZIERTER) 6889
STROM (MIT DEM) 4184
STROMABWÄRTS 4184
STROMAUFWÄRTS 13407
STROMAUSBEUTE 3489
STROMBEGRENZUNGSVENTIL 4879
STROMDICHTE 3488
STROMDICHTE 4501
STROMERZEUGER 5924
STROMERZEUGUNG 9894
STROMERZEUGUNGSANLAGE 5920
STROMFÜHRENDER LEITER 7670
STROMKREIS 2406
STROMKREIS (DEN) SCHLIESSEN 2515
STROMKREIS ÖFFNEN (DEN) 8826
STROMLEITUNGSNETZ 4080

STROMLIEFERUNG 12487
STROMLINIE 12351
STROMMESSER 452
STROMPAUSE 8734
STROMQUELLE 11823
STROMREGLER 3491
STROMRICHTUNGSANZEIGER 9588
STROMSCHIENE 1770
STROMSTÄRKE 7021
STROMSTÄRKE 478
STROMSTÄRKEREGLER 7020
STROMUMFORMER 3071
STRÖMUNG (AUFGEZWUNGENE) 5534
STRÖMUNG (FREIE) 5634
STRÖMUNG (GEORDNETE) 9055
STRÖMUNG (LAMINARE) 9055
STRÖMUNG (TURBULENTE) 13274
STRÖMUNG (UNGEORDNETE) 13274
STRÖMUNG (WIRBELIGE) 13274
STRÖMUNGSDRUCK 9825
STRÖMUNGSGESCHWINDIGKEIT 13516
STRÖMUNGSGESCHWINDIGKEIT 5462
STRÖMUNGSMESSER 3490
STRÖMUNGSWEG 9125
STROMUNTERBRECHUNG 7093
STROMVERBRAUCH 2993
STROMVERSORGUNG 12487
STROMVERSORGUNGSNETZ 6096
STROMVERTEILUNGSNETZ 4080
STROMZÄHLER 4553
STROMZEIGER 452
STROMZEIT 6382
STRONTIUM 12389
STRONTIUMFLUORID 12390
STROPHOIDE 7722
STRUKTUR 12395
STRUKTUR 12394
STRUKTUR 12800
STRUKTUR (DENDRITISCHE) 3750
STRUKTUR (KÖRNIGE) 6052
STRUKTURELEMENT 12391
STÜCK 4067
STÜCK (EINGESETZTES) 6970
STÜCKARBEIT 9294
STÜCKKOHLE 7826
STÜCKLISTE 7662
STÜCKLOHN 9295
STÜCKZEICHNUNG 3809
STUFE 6021
STUFE 12239
STUFE 11383

**STU** 910

STUFE 13172
STUFEN... 12246
STUFENFÖRMIG 12246
STUFENGLÜHEN 12240
STUFENHÄRTUNG 12242
STUFENHÄRTUNG 6633
STUFENPRESSEN (MECHANISCHE) 8461
STUFENRAD 12247
STUFENROST 12248
STUFENSCHEIBE 11871
STUFENVENTIL 8475
STUFENVERDICHTER 2836
STUFENVERSETZUNG 4443
STUMMES GESPERRE 11433
STUMPF 1776
STUMPF-(SCHWEISS-)NAHT 1784
STUMPFFEILE 9067
STUMPFNAHT 1809
STUMPFNAHTDICKE 1786
STUMPFSCHWEISSEN 1785
STUMPFSCHWEISSEN 1805
STUMPFSTOSS (BEIDERSEITIG GESCHWEISSTER) 1777
STUMPFSTOSS (EINSEITIG GESCHWEISSTER) 1779
STUMPFSTOSSVERBINDUNG 1776
STURZ 7312
STURZ (WINKEL) 1889
STURZBLECH 11304
STÜRZGUSSVERFAHREN 11656
STÜTZBLECH 12495
STÜTZBOGEN 10442
STÜTZDRUCK, LAGERDRUCK 1110
STÜTZE 1522
STÜTZE 9925
STÜTZE 11365
STÜTZE 12490
STÜTZEN 12493
STUTZEN 8679
STÜTZEN 12491
STUTZEN 1557
STÜTZGESTELL 10877
STÜTZKUGELLAGER 12901
STÜTZLAGER 5524
STÜTZPUNKT 9567
STÜTZRAUPE 904
STÜTZRING 911
STÜTZRING 12492
STÜTZWALZEN 903
STÜTZWEITE 11831
STÜTZZAPFEN 9421
SUBLIMAT 8153
SUBLIMATION 12412

SUBLIMATIONSWÄRME 6363
SUBLIMIEREN 12411
SUBSTANZ 12419
SUBSTANZ (AKTIVIERENDE) 4744
SUBSTANZEN (RADIOAKTIVE) 10158
SUBSTANZEN (SELBSTLEUCHTENDE) 9251
SUBSTITUTION (MATH.) 12421
SUBSTRAT 12422
SUBSTRUKTUR 12423
SUBTRAHEND 12426
SUBTRAHIEREN 12424
SUBTRAKTION 12425
SÜDPOL EINES MAGNETEN 11827
SULFAT 12444
SULFATSODA 12445
SULFID 12446
SULFID (KETTENFÖRMIGES) 2221
SULFIT 12448
SULFURAURAT 625
SUMMATION 169
SUMME 12454
SUMMIEREN 162
SUMPFAGS 8215
SUMPFERZ 7596
SUPERLEGIERUNG 12459
SUPPLEMENT EINES WINKELS 12482
SUPPLEMENTWINKEL 12483
SUPPORTDREHBANK 11590
SÜSSWASSER 5663
SUSZEPTIBILITÄT (MAGNETISCHE) 7918
SYENIT 12565
SYMBOL (CHEMISCHES) 2315
SYMMETRIBACHSE 869
SYMMETRIE 12567
SYMMETRIEACHSE 11024
SYMMETRIEEBENE 9440
SYMMETRISCH 12566
SYNCHRON 12570
SYNCHRONISMUS 12569
SYNCHRONMOTOR 12571
SYNGONIE 3431
SYNTHESE 12572
SYNTHETISCH 12573
SYNTONIE 12574
SYSTEM (METRISCHES) 8229
SYSTEM (OPTISCHES) 8848
SYSTEM (QUASIBINÄRES) 9958
T-EISEN 12698
T-EISEN (BREITFÜSSIGES) 1640
T-MUFFE 12702
T-NAHT 1795

T-NAHT **1801**
T-SPANN-NUTEN FRÄSER **12582**
T-STÜCK **12699**
T-STUCK **1559**
T-TRÄGER **12700**
T-VERSCHRAUBUNG **1559**
T-WULST **1719**
TABELLE **2273**
TABELLE **12584**
TABLETT **13167**
TABLETTABSTAND **13169**
TABLETTENMANNLOCH **13168**
TABLETTENMASCHINE **9310**
TABLETTRINGHALTER **13170**
TACHOGRAPH **12586**
TACHOMETER **12587**
TACHOMETER **11869**
TAFEL **12584**
TAFEL **9032**
TAG DER ANMELDUNG **3616**
TAG DER ERTEILUNG EINES PATENTES **3617**
TAGELOHN **3594**
TAGESLICHT **3622**
TAGSCHICHT **3620**
TAGWASSER **12520**
TALG **12609**
TALK **12608**
TALKPULVER **12607**
TALKSPAT **7880**
TALKUM **12607**
TALKUM **5659**
TALSPERRE **3597**
TANDEMDAMPFMASCHINE **12613**
TANGENS **12615**
TANGENTE **12616**
TANGENTE **12615**
TANGENTENPOLYGON **2436**
TANGENTENSCHRAUBE **12619**
TANGENTIALBESCHLEUNIGUNG **12620**
TANGENTIALKEIL **12618**
TANGENTIALKRAFT **12622**
TANGENTIALSPANNUNG **12624**
TANGENTIALTURBINE **12621**
TANGENTIATLSCHNITT DES HOLZES **1058**
TANK **4161**
TANK **12625**
TANK **3973**
TANK (WÄRMEISOLIERTER) **6995**
TANK FÜR FLÜSSIGES ERDGAS **7678**
TANK MIT GEWÖLBTEM DECKEL **4121**
TANK MIT KONKAVEM BODEN **12631**

TANK MIT KONVEXEM BODEN **12632**
TANK MIT SELBSTTRAGENDEM KONUSDACH **11160**
TANKBODEN **6314**
TANKGRUBE **12629**
TANKLAGER **12627**
TANKUNTERBAU **12628**
TANKWALL **1735**
TANKZUGANGSLEITER **5646**
TANNAT **12633**
TANNENBAUMKRISTALL **3748**
TANNIN **5780**
TANTAL **12634**
TANZEN DES REGLERS **6671**
TANZMEISTER **6975**
TARIEREN **11216**
TARTRAT **12691**
TASTER **1874**
TASTERLEHRE **6608**
TASTZIRKEL **1874**
TAU **1829**
TAUCHAUFTRAG **3970**
TAUCHBADSCHMIERUNG **11925**
TAUCHBEHÄLTER **3973**
TAUCHEN **3975**
TAUCHHARTLÖTUNG **3969**
TAUCHKOLBEN **9545**
TAUCHKOLBENPUMPE **9546**
TAUCHKORB **3976**
TAUCHLÖTEN **2304**
TAUCHROHR **1711**
TAUCHSCHMIERUNG **11925**
TAUCHÜBERZUG **2592**
TAUKLOBEN **10731**
TAUMELSÄGE **4337**
TAUPUNKT **3824**
TECHNETIUM **8040**
TECHNIK **12695**
TECHNISCH **12694**
TEER **12679**
TEEREN **12689**
TEEREN **12680**
TEERFARBSTOFF **2567**
TEERÖL **12681**
TEERPAPPE **10712**
TEESTÜCK **12697**
TEIGZUSTAND **8488**
TEIL **9083**
TEIL (LOSER) **7745**
TEIL (ZENTRALER) **2287**
TEILCHEN **9088**
TEILCHEN (NADELFÖRMIGES) **8517**

# TEI 912

TEILCHEN (UMHÜLLTE) **2585**
TEILCHENGRÖSSE **9089**
TEILDRUCK **9087**
TEILEN **4097**
TEILEPROGRAMM **9084**
TEILFERTIGUNG **11960**
TEILFUGE **7241**
TEILFUGE **3888**
TEILGERÄT **4100**
TEILHÄRTUNG **11145**
TEILKEGELWINKEL **9401**
TEILKRAFT **2816**
TEILKRAFT **2817**
TEILKREIS **6026**
TEILKREIS **2423**
TEILKREIS **9404**
TEILKREISDURCHMESSER **9407**
TEILLISTE **9095**
TEILMASCHINE **4102**
TEILMONTAGE-WERKSTATT **5282**
TEILPLATTE **6867**
TEILSCHEIBE **4109**
TEILSCHEIBE **4106**
TEILSCHEIBE **4105**
TEILSCHEIBEN **6870**
TEILSTRICH **8009**
TEILUNG **10981**
TEILUNG **9399**
TEILUNG **4107**
TELEGRAMM **1830**
TELEGRAPH **12707**
TELEGRAPHENDRAHT **12708**
TELEGRAPHIE **12709**
TELEGRAPHIE (DRAHTLOSE) **13907**
TELEPHON **12710**
TELEPHONDRAHT **12711**
TELEPHONIE **12712**
TELEPHONIE (DRAHTLOSE) **13908**
TELESKOP **10386**
TELESKOPLEHRE **12713**
TELESKOPSTEIL **4945**
TELLER (EINES VENTILS) **13463**
TELLERKOLBEN **11791**
TELLERVENTIL **4011**
TELLUR **12716**
TEMPERATUR **12721**
TEMPERATUR (ABNEHMENDE) **5025**
TEMPERATUR (ABSOLUTE) **35**
TEMPERATUR (DER UMGEBENDEN LUFT) **12729**
TEMPERATUR (ERHÖHTE) **4658**
TEMPERATUR (EUTEKTISCHE) **4858**

TEMPERATUR (FALLENDE) **5025**
TEMPERATUR (GERECHNETE) **3798**
TEMPERATUR (GLEICHBLEIBENDE) **2977**
TEMPERATUR (HERABGESETZTE) **10344**
TEMPERATUR (HOHE) **6476**
TEMPERATUR (KONSTANTE) **2977**
TEMPERATUR (KRITISCHE) **3352**
TEMPERATUR (MITTLERE) **855**
TEMPERATUR (NIEDRIGE) **7775**
TEMPERATUR (SINKENDE) **5025**
TEMPERATUR (STEIGENDE) **10618**
TEMPERATUR (TIEFE) **7775**
TEMPERATUR (TIEFSTE) **8306**
TEMPERATUR (ZUNEHMENDE) **10618**
TEMPERATUR-REGELVENTIL **12840**
TEMPERATURABNAHME **5022**
TEMPERATURÄNDERUNG **2239**
TEMPERATURANSTIEG **10231**
TEMPERATURANSTIEG **10612**
TEMPERATURBEREICH **12730**
TEMPERATURDIAGRAMME **12725**
TEMPERATURERHÖHUNG **10612**
TEMPERATURERNIEDRIGUNG **5022**
TEMPERATURFUGE **4918**
TEMPERATURGEFÄLLE **12724**
TEMPERATURGRENZE **7592**
TEMPERATURKURVEN **12723**
TEMPERATURMESSUNG **8086**
TEMPERATURREGLER **12840**
TEMPERATURRÜCKGANG **5022**
TEMPERATURSCHOCK **12812**
TEMPERATURSCHWANKUNG **13498**
TEMPERATURSKALA **12835**
TEMPERATURSTEIGERUNG **10612**
TEMPERATURUNTERSCHIED **3904**
TEMPERATURVERTEILUNG **4083**
TEMPERATURWECHSEL **2239**
TEMPERATURWECHSELBESTÄNDIGKEIT **12813**
TEMPERATURZUNAHME **10612**
TEMPERGUSS **12959**
TEMPERGUSS **2043**
TEMPERKOHLE **13345**
TEMPERKOHLEABSCHEIDUNG **6066**
TEMPERN **4230**
TEMPERN **562**
TEMPERN **568**
TEMPERN **12717**
TEMPERN **13175**
TEMPERN **7952**
TEMPERSTAHLGUSS **7959**
TERBIUM **12760**

TERPENTIN **3415**
TERPENTIN (VENEZIANER) **13527**
TERPENTINÖL **8765**
TERPENTINÖLLACK **13296**
TERRAKOTTA **12767**
TERRAZZO **12768**
TETRACHLORKOHLENSTOFF **1960**
TETRAEDER **12797**
TETRAGONAL **12795**
TETRAJODFLUORESZEIN **4831**
TEXEL **207**
TEXTILFASER **12799**
TEXTILRIEMEN **4981**
THALLIUM **12801**
THERMISCHE ERWEICHUNG **5319**
THERMISCHER WIRKUNGSGRAD **12806**
THERMIT **12817**
THERMIT-VERFAHREN **431**
THERMITPRESSSCHWEISSEN **9837**
THERMITSCHWEISSUNG **12818**
THERMITSCHWEISSUNG **12819**
THERMOCHEMIE **12822**
THERMODYNAMIK **12829**
THERMODYNAMISCH **12828**
THERMOELEKTRISCH **12823**
THERMOELEKTRISCHER STROM **12824**
THERMOELEKTRIZITÄT **12826**
THERMOELEMENT **12827**
THERMOELEMENT **12821**
THERMOGRAPH **10293**
THERMOMETER **12833**
THERMOMETER **12726**
THERMOMETER (ACHTZIGTEILIGES) **10268**
THERMOMETER (AUFZEICHNENDES) **10293**
THERMOMETER (HUNDERTTEILIGES) **2186**
THERMOMETER REGISTRIERENDES **10293**
THERMOMETER SCHREIBENDES **10293**
THERMOMETEREINTEILUNG **12835**
THERMOMETERKUGEL **1717**
THERMOMETERRÖHRE **13255**
THERMOMETERSKALA **12835**
THERMOSÄULE **12820**
THERMOSÄULE **12836**
THERMOSKOP **12837**
THERMOSTAT **12838**
THERMOSTAT **12722**
THERMOSTROM **12824**
THIOSCHWEFELSÄURE **12853**
THIOSULFAT **12852**
THIXOTROPIE **12854**
THOMAS-VERFAHREN **1043**

THOMASROHEISEN **1049**
THOMASSCHLACKE **1054**
THOMASSTAHL **1044**
THOMASSTAHL **12855**
THORIUM **12856**
THULIUM **12910**
THYRISTOR **12913**
TIEFBAU **2444**
TIEFBEHÄLTER **13047**
TIEFBEIZEN **3685**
TIEFBEIZPROBE **3684**
TIEFBETTFELGE **4322**
TIEFBOHRUNG **3780**
TIEFBRUNNENPUMPE **3689**
TIEFE **3779**
TIEFENLEHRE **3781**
TIEFENLEHRE **13538**
TIEFENLEHRE MIT MIKROMETERSCHRAUBE **13539**
TIEFENMASS **8357**
TIEFENMASS **3781**
TIEFENMIKROMETER **8252**
TIEFENSTREUUNG **12899**
TIEFLOCH-BOHRMASCHINE **3687**
TIEFLOCHBOHRER **3686**
TIEFZIEHBANDSTAHL **3688**
TIEFZIEHEN **3683**
TIEFZIEHEN **7158**
TIEFZIEHEN **3469**
TIEFZIEHQUALITÄTSMESSING **3690**
TIEGEL **3401**
TIEGELGUSSSSTAHL **3410**
TIEGELGUSSSTAHL **2057**
TIEGELOFEN **4597**
TIEGELOFEN **3402**
TIEGELSCHERE **3403**
TIEGELSCHMELZOFEN **9669**
TIEGELSCHMELZVERFAHREN **3404**
TIEGELZANGE **7548**
TIEGELZANGE **3405**
TINTENEINSATZ **9160**
TINTENGUMMI **6939**
TISCH-QUERBEWEGUNG **12585**
TISCHBOHRMASCHINE **1168**
TISCHHOBELMASCHINE **2007**
TISCHHOBELMASCHINE (EINSEITIG OFFENE) **8821**
TISCHLER **7233**
TISCHLEREI **7236**
TISCHLEREI (WERKSTÄTTE) **7235**
TISCHLERSÄGE **5628**
TITAN **12970**
TITANDIOXYD **12971**

# TIT

914

TITANEISEN **5114**
TITANSÄUREANHYDRID **12971**
TITANSTAHL **12972**
TITER EINER LÖSUNG **12354**
TITERFLÜSSIGKEIT **12084**
TITRATION **12968**
TITRIEREN **12968**
TITRIEREN **12973**
TITRIERTE LÖSUNG **12084**
TITRIERUNG **12968**
TITRIERUNG **12974**
TOBOGGAN **11914**
TOLERANZ **12982**
TOLERANZ **359**
TOLERANZ **2483**
TOLERANZ **358**
TOLERANZGRENZE **7595**
TOLERANZKALIBER **3905**
TOLERANZLEHRE **3905**
TOLERANZLEHRE **3903**
TOLUOL **12983**
TOMBAK **12984**
TON **2465**
TON (FEUERFESTER) **5241**
TON (GEBRANNTER) **926**
TON (GEBRANNTER) **6125**
TONBANDGERÄT **12644**
TONEISENSTEIN **2467**
TONERDE **413**
TONERDE **412**
TONERDE **438**
TONERDE (ESSIGSAURE) **417**
TONERDE (KIESELSAURE) **425**
TONERDE (SCHWEFELSAURE) **426**
TONERDEHYDRAT **423**
TONERDENATRON **11716**
TONERDESILIKAT **425**
TONMERGEL **699**
TONNE (1000 KG) **12986**
TONNENLAGER **10681**
TONRING **2468**
TONROHR **4416**
TONSCHIEFER **700**
TOPAS **13038**
TOPOCHEMIE **13039**
TOPPRÜCKSTAND **13040**
TORF **9147**
TORFBRIKETT **9149**
TORFKUCHEN **9151**
TORFMEHL **9726**
TORFMULL **9726**

TORFPLATTE **9150**
TORFSODE **9151**
TORFSTEIN **9148**
TORSION **13054**
TORSION **13051**
TORSION **13056**
TORSIONSELASTIZITÄT **4490**
TORSIONSFEDER **11994**
TORSIONSFESTIGKEIT **13057**
TORSIONSKRAFT **13055**
TORSIONSSCHWINGUNG **13557**
TORSIONSSPANNUNG **13058**
TORSIONSWAAGE **13052**
TORSONSBEANSPRUCHUNG **13056**
TORUSRING **8703**
TOTALRÖSTUNG **3636**
TOTER PUNKT **3626**
TOTLAGEKREIS **8604**
TOTPUNKT **3625**
TOTPUNKT **3626**
TOTPUNKT **3635**
TOTPUNKT (OBERER) **13411**
TOTPUNKT (OBERER) **13032**
TOTPUNKT (UNTER) **1491**
TOTPUNKTLAGE **9646**
TOTPUNKTSTELLUNG **9646**
TOTRAUM **2482**
TOTWASSER **12050**
TOUR **10557**
TOURENZAHL **10814**
TOURENZAHL **8690**
TOURENZÄHLER **10556**
TRACHYT **13081**
TRAFOBLECH **3160**
TRAGACHSE **2010**
TRAGANT **6174**
TRAGANTGUMMI **6174**
TRAGBALKEN **13243**
TRAGBELAG **9011**
TRÄGER **12490**
TRÄGER **5946**
TRÄGER **1522**
TRÄGER **1093**
TRÄGER (BAUW.) **1099**
TRÄGER (BEIDERSEITS EINGESPANNTER) **2756**
TRÄGER (DURCHGEHENDER) **3018**
TRÄGER (DURCHLAUFENDER) **3018**
TRÄGER (EINGESPANNTER) **10131**
TRÄGER (EINSEITIG EINGESPANNTER) **1097**
TRÄGER (EISERNER) **12199**
TRÄGER (FREI AUFLIEGENDER) **1098**

915 TRE

TRÄGER (HALBEINGESPANNTER) 1097
TRÄGERFUSSPLATTE 5947
TRAGFÄHIGKEIT 7682
TRAGFÄHIGKEIT 2011
TRAGFÄHIGKEIT DES BODENS 11751
TRAGFÄHIGKEIT DES BODENS 11752
TRAGFEDER 1114
TRAGFLÄCHE 1115
TRAGGESTELL 4116
TRÄGHEIT 6907
TRÄGHEITSHALBMESSER 10169
TRÄGHEITSKRAFT 6907
TRÄGHEITSMOMENT 8372
TRAGKRAFT 13090
TRAGLAGER 7257
TRAGMAGNET 7554
TRAGSCHERE 3403
TRAGSTANGE 11365
TRAGSTÜTZE 1522
TRAGWEITE 11831
TRAGZAPFEN 7256
TRAINEUR 1164
TRAJEKTORIE 13104
TRAKTION 13088
TRAKTOR 13097
TRAKTOR 9859
TRAKTOREN (GÄRTNEREI-) 13096
TRAKTRIX 13098
TRAN 13103
TRÄNENBLECH 10181
TRÄNKEN 6805
TRÄNKUNG 6805
TRÄNKUNGSMITTEL 6804
TRANSDUCER 13108
TRANSDUKTOR 13108
TRANSFORMATIONSGESCHWINDIGKEIT 13521
TRANSFORMATOR 13115
TRANSFORMATORBLECH 13116
TRANSFORMATORENBLECH 4544
TRANSISTOR 13119
TRANSLATION 13123
TRANSLATIONSBEWEGUNG 8407
TRANSLATIONSGITTER 13120
TRANSMISSION 11248
TRANSMISSIONSANTRIEB 7609
TRANSMISSIONSDYNAMOMETER 13127
TRANSMISSIONSSEIL 4314
TRANSMISSIONSWELLE 7944
TRANSPARENT 13125
TRANSPARENZ 13124
TRANSPORT 13140

TRANSPORT IM WERK 8106
TRANSPORTBAND 1164
TRANSPORTEUR 9956
TRANSPORTKARREN 13230
TRANSPORTKOSTEN 3209
TRANSPORTPFANNE 13110
TRANSPORTRAD 6754
TRANSPORTROHR 10839
TRANSPORTSCHNECKE 13970
TRANSVERSALE 8124
TRANSVERSALKRAFT 11291
TRANSVERSALMASSSTAB 3833
TRAPEZ 13148
TRAPEZFEDER 13151
TRAPEZFÖRMIGES GEWINDE 1814
TRAPEZGEWINDE 1814
TRAPEZLAST 13150
TRAPEZOID 13149
TRASS 13152
TRAUBENZUCKER 6058
TRAVERTIN 13166
TRECKSÄGE 3365
TREFFPUNKT 9565
TREIBACHSE 4290
TREIBENDE SCHEIBE 4313
TREIBENDES RAD 4318
TREIBKEIL 2485
TREIBKEIL 12665
TREIBKETTE 4306
TREIBMITTEL 8408
TREIBÖL 5714
TREIBPROBE 10184
TREIBRIEMEN 1163
TREIBSCHRAUBE 11041
TREIBSEIL 4314
TREIBSITZ 4307
TREIBSTANGE 2962
TREIBSTOFFSYSTEM 9339
TREIBWELLE 9930
TRENNLINIE 9093
TRENNMITTEL 9092
TRENNSCHEIBE 3542
TRENNUNG (ELEKTROSTATISCHE) 4646
TRENNUNG (MAGNETISCHE) 7917
TRENNUNGSFLÄCHENGEBIET 7034
TRENNUNGSFUGE EINES LAGERS 7241
TRENNUNGSWAND 4110
TRENNUNGSWÄRME 8528
TRENNWAND 1726
TREPPE 12053
TREPPE (GERADE) 5641

**TRE**

916

TREPPENABSATZ 9502
TREPPENABSATZ 7388
TREPPENFÖRMIG 12246
TREPPENGELÄNDER 6259
TREPPENPFOSTEN 12063
TREPPENROST 12248
TREPPENWANGE 12377
TREPPENWANGE 12052
TRETSCHEMEL 13174
TRICHTER 5738
TRICHTERKOLBEN 2944
TRIEB 4309
TRIEBKETTE 4306
TRIEBKETTE 4305
TRIEBKRAFT 8409
TRIEBRAD 4318
TRIEBSTOCK 9323
TRIEBSTOCKGETRIEBE 9325
TRIEBSTOCKRAD 9324
TRIEBWEK 8122
TRIEBWELLE 4315
TRIEBWERK 4311
TRIEBWERK 4756
TRIEBWERKSEIL 4314
TRIEBWERKSRAD 13128
TRIEBWERKSWELLE 7944
TRIEDER 13202
TRIGONOMETRIE 13201
TRIGONOMETRISCH 13200
TRINIDADASPHALT 13212
TRINITROPHENOL 9291
TRINKWASSER 4281
TRIOXYBENZOESÄURE 5777
TRIPEL 13220
TRIPELPUNKT 13216
TRITT 13174
TRITTHEBEL 5521
TRIZYANSÄURE 3552
TROCHOIDE 13223
TROCKENBINDER 4342
TROCKENELEMENT 4343
TROCKENFESTIGKEIT 4352
TROCKENFLASCHE 4308
TROCKENGLAS 4308
TROCKENGUSS 4353
TROCKENKAMMER 4356
TROCKENKASTEN 4358
TROCKENKERN 927
TROCKENLEGUNG 4210
TROCKENOFEN 4358
TROCKENÖL 4357

TROCKENPLATTE 2012
TROCKENSANDBINDER 3145
TROCKENSANDFORMEN 4354
TROCKENSCHALE 3148
TROCKENSCHLEUDER 6703
TROCKENSCHRANK 4256
TROCKENSCHRANK 4358
TROCKENSTOFF 4257
TROCKENVORRICHTUNG 4355
TROCKNEN 4359
TROCKNEN 4338
TROCKNEN DES HOLZES AN DER LUFT 11095
TROCKNER 4355
TROCKNUNG 928
TROG 13228
TROGBLECH 1679
TROMMEL 4333
TROMMEL 10290
TROMMELBREMSE 4334
TROMMELGALVANISIERUNG 1016
TROMMELN 1014
TROMMELN 4335
TROMMELPFANNE 4336
TROMMELSCHREIBER 3573
TROMMELSIEB 13226
TROOSTIT 13227
TROPFBAR 7642
TROPFEN 7492
TROPFEN 4282
TROPFEN 7487
TROPFFLASCHE 4321
TROPFÖL 13636
TROPFÖLER 4323
TROPFÖLSCHMIERUNG 4287
TROPFPROBE 11958
TROPFRINNE 4285
TROPFSCHALE 4283
TROPFSCHMIERUNG 4284
TRÜBUNG 2541
TRÜBUNGSANALYSE 8537
TRUMM (AUFLAUFENDES) 4316
TRUMM (EINES FLASCHENZUGS) 12092
TRUMM (FESTES) 12092
TRUMM (FREIES) 5023
TRUMM (GEZOGENES) 5516
TRUMM (LOSESABLAUFENDES) TRUMM 5516
TRUMM (RÜCKLAUFENDES) 5516
TRUMM (STEHENDES) 12092
TRUMM (ZIEHENDES) 4316
TRUMM EINES KETTENTRIEBS 11413
TRUMM EINES RIEMENS 11413

917 UBE

TRUNKKOLBEN **13241**
TS-DIAGRAMM **6346**
TUCHSCHEIBE **10173**
TUFF **13260**
TUFF (VULKANISCHER) **13590**
TUFFSTEIN **1838**
TUNGSTEINSÄURE **8876**
TÜPPELUNG **8421**
TURBINE **13267**
TURBINE (GEMISCHTE) **8330**
TURBINENRAD **13823**
TURBINENSCHAUFELN **13268**
TURBODYNAMO **13271**
TURBOGEBLÄSE **13270**
TURBOGENERATOR **13271**
TURBOKOMPRESSOR **2178**
TURBOKOMPRESSOR **13272**
TURBOPUMPE **13269**
TURBULENZ **13273**
TURMALIN **13072**
TÜRPFOSTEN **6507**
TÜRSCHLOSS **4123**
TÜRSTEIN **7211**
TUSCHE **6871**
TUSCHEINSATZ FÜR ZIRKEL **9160**
TUSCHNAPF **10946**
TUSCHPINSEL **2743**
TUSCHSCHALE **10946**
TUSCHZEICHNUNG **12965**
TYP **13320**
U-EISEN **2248**
U-EISEN **2250**
U-FUGENNAHT OHNE LUFTSPALT **2530**
U-MONTAGETEIL **12388**
U-ROHR **13323**
U-TRÄGER **2249**
U/MIN **10814**
ÜBERALTERUNG **8923**
ÜBERBEANSPRUCHUNG **8963**
ÜBERBELASTEN **8954**
ÜBERBELASTUNG **8953**
ÜBERBLATTUNGSNIETUNG **7400**
ÜBERCHLORSAURES KALI **9694**
ÜBERDECKUNG DES SCHIEBERS **7399**
ÜBERDICKE **1695**
ÜBERDREHEN (EIN GEWINDE) **12379**
ÜBERDRUCK **9809**
ÜBERDRUCK **5882**
ÜBERDRUCK **8955**
ÜBERDRUCKTURBINE **10250**
ÜBERDRUCKVENTIL **10441**

ÜBEREINANDERGREIFEN **8950**
ÜBEREINANDERGREIFEN **8951**
ÜBEREINANDERLIEGEN **8950**
ÜBEREINANDERSTEHEN **8950**
ÜBEREUTEKTOID **6733**
ÜBERFAHREN **8959**
ÜBERFALL **8931**
ÜBERFALLKANTE **13754**
ÜBERFALLROHR **8932**
ÜBERFLÜSSIGE ZUTAT **5766**
ÜBERGANG (KONGRUENTER) **2939**
ÜBERGANGSFLANSCH **10350**
ÜBERGANGSMUFFE **3962**
ÜBERGANGSPUNKT **13122**
ÜBERGANGSROHEISEN **8733**
ÜBERGANGSROHR **10352**
ÜBERGLASUNG **2603**
ÜBERGRÖSSE **8961**
ÜBERHANG **8934**
ÜBERHÄNGEND **8936**
ÜBERHITZEN **12473**
ÜBERHITZEN **12468**
ÜBERHITZER **12472**
UBERHITZUNG **8946**
ÜBERHITZUNG **12460**
ÜBERHITZUNG **1754**
ÜBERHOLEN **8937**
ÜBERHOLUNGSLEUCHTE **9102**
ÜBERKOHLENSAURES KALIUM **9693**
ÜBERKOPFSCHWEISSEN **7113**
ÜBERKOPFSCHWEISSNAHT **8944**
ÜBERKOPFSCHWEISSUNG **8941**
ÜBERKRAGUNG **9913**
ÜBERKRIECHEN EINER LÖSUNG **3330**
ÜBERLADUNG **8953**
ÜBERLAGERUNG **8948**
ÜBERLAGERUNG **8952**
ÜBERLAGERUNG VON SCHWINGUNGEN **12476**
ÜBERLANDBUS **7099**
ÜBERLAPPEN **8951**
ÜBERLAPPNAHTSCHWEISSEN **7401**
ÜBERLAPPT SCHWEISSEN **7404**
ÜBERLAPPTE SCHWEISSUNG **7405**
ÜBERLAPPTER STOSS **7396**
ÜBERLAPPTER STOSS **7397**
ÜBERLAPPUNG **7396**
ÜBERLAPPUNG **8949**
ÜBERLAPPUNG **8948**
ÜBERLAPPUNG **8951**
ÜBERLAPPUNG DES SCHIEBERS **7399**
ÜBERLAPPUNGSFLANSCH **7398**

# UBE 918

ÜBERLAPPUNGSNIETUNG **7400**
ÜBERLAPPUNGSPUNKTNAHT **7402**
ÜBERLAPPUNGSSCHWEISSUNG **7405**
ÜBERLAPPUNGSVERBINDUNG **7397**
ÜBERLASCHTER STOSS **1782**
ÜBERLASCHUNG **1782**
ÜBERLAST **8953**
ÜBERLASTUNG **8963**
ÜBERLAUFROHR **8932**
ÜBERLAUFROHR **6185**
ÜBERMANGANSAURES **9695**
ÜBERMASS **8961**
ÜBERNORMALDRUCK **8955**
ÜBERPRÜFUNG **4876**
ÜBERSÄTTIGEN **12477**
ÜBERSÄTTIGUNG **12461**
ÜBERSÄTTIGUNG **12479**
ÜBERSCHIEBER **4158**
ÜBERSCHIEBMUFFE **4158**
ÜBERSCHLÄGIGE RECHNUNG **10772**
ÜBERSCHLAGSRECHNUNG **10772**
ÜBERSCHMELZEN **12465**
ÜBERSCHMELZEN **3634**
ÜBERSCHMOLZENE FLÜSSKIGKEIT **12464**
ÜBERSCHUSS **4878**
ÜBERSETZUNG **13123**
ÜBERSETZUNG **5909**
ÜBERSETZUNGSGETRIEBE **8921**
ÜBERSETZUNGSVERHÄLTNIS **13522**
ÜBERSETZUNGSVERHÄLTNIS **5896**
ÜBERSICHTSPLAN **9430**
ÜBERSPANNUNG **8967**
ÜBERSPANNUNG (ELEKTR.) **4881**
ÜBERSPRINGUNSBEFEHL **11546**
ÜBERSTEHEND **8936**
ÜBERSTRÖMVENTIL **8933**
ÜBERSTRUKTUR **12475**
ÜBERSTUNDEN **8964**
ÜBERTRAGUNG **2916**
ÜBERTRAGUNG EINER BEWEGUNG **13130**
ÜBERTRAGUNG VON ELEKTRISCHER ENERGIE **13133**
ÜBERTRAGUNGSRAD **6754**
ÜBERTRAGUNGSWELLE **7049**
ÜBERVERDICHTER **1456**
ÜBERWACHEN **12474**
ÜBERWACHUNG **12481**
ÜBERWALZUNGSFEHLER **7395**
ÜBERWALZUNGSFEHLER **5510**
ÜBERWIEGEN **8928**
ÜBERWURFFLANSCH **7746**
ÜBERWURFFLANSCH **1452**

ÜBERWURFMUTTER **1512**
ÜBERZIEHEN **1909**
ÜBERZUG **2590**
ÜBERZUG **2587**
ÜBERZUG (ANODISCHER) **2588**
ÜBERZUG (ANODISCHER) **599**
ÜBERZUG (CHEMISCHER) **2297**
ÜBERZUG (KATODISCHER) **2102**
ÜBERZUG (METALLBEDAMPFTER) **8200**
ÜBERZUG (METALLISCHER) **8194**
ÜBERZUG (NICHT-METALLISCHER) **8641**
ÜBERZUG (NICHTMETALLISCHE) **2597**
ÜBERZUG (TEILWEISER) **9076**
ÜBERZUG IN FÄSSER (GALVANISCHER) **1016**
ÜBERZUGSLACK **13505**
UHRENMESSING **2505**
UHRWERK **2509**
UHRZEIGERSINN (IM) **2506**
ULTRAMARIN **13334**
ULTRAMIKROSKOP **13335**
ULTRASCHALLPRÜFUNG **13337**
ULTRASCHALLPRÜFUNG **12480**
ULTRASCHALLSCHWEISSEN **13338**
ULTRASCHALLUNTERSUCHUNG **13337**
UMBIEGBAR **6835**
UMBÖRDELN **1084**
UMBÖRDELN **1088**
UMBÖRDELUNG **1088**
UMDREHUNG **10765**
UMDREHUNG **10557**
UMDREHUNGEN PRO MINUTE **10814**
UMDREHUNGSACHSE **868**
UMDREHUNGSELLIPSOID **4672**
UMDREHUNGSFLÄCHE **12513**
UMDREHUNGSGESCHWINDIGKEIT **11876**
UMDREHUNGSKÖRPER **11790**
UMDREHUNGSPARABOLOID **9042**
UMDREHUNGSZAHL **8690**
UMFANG (GEOM.) **9190**
UMFANGSGESCHWINDIGKEIT **9198**
UMFANGSKRAFT **12622**
UMFANGSSPANNUNG **6576**
UMFANGSTEILUNG **2423**
UMFANGSWIDERSTAND **9197**
UMFORMER **3071**
UMFÜHRUNG **1818**
UMFÜHRUNGSVENTIL **1819**
UMGEBUNGSTEMPERATUR **12729**
UMGEHUNG **1821**
UMGEHUNGSVENTIL **1819**
UMHÜLLEN (EIN ROHR) **3263**

# UNG

UMHÜLLEN VON ROHREN 7369
UMHÜLLUNG 8999
UMHÜLLUNG 3274
UMHÜLLUNG 2587
UMHÜLLUNGSKURVE 4776
UMKEHRBAR 10538
UMKEHRBARKEIT 10537
UMKEHRDAMPFMASCHINE 10543
UMKEHREN (DIE BEWEGUNG) 10534
UMKEHRUNG 8965
UMKEHRUNG 7110
UMKEHRUNG EINER BEWEGUNG 10552
UMKEHRVORGELEGE 10542
UMKIPPBAR 6835
UMKLEIDEBUDE 2247
UMKREIS 2435
UMLAUF 10557
UMLAUF 2433
UMLAUFBEWEGUNG 10557
UMLAUFEN 10763
UMLAUFEN 2432
UMLAUFENDE WELLE 10764
UMLAUFGESCHWINDIGKEIT 11876
UMLAUFGETRIEBE 12456
UMLAUFKÜHLER 10752
UMLAUFMOTOR 10754
UMLAUFSCHMIERUNG 5442
UMLAUFVENTIL 1819
UMLAUFVORGELEGE 4778
UMLAUFZAHL 8690
UMLAUFZÄHLER 10556
UMLENKKONUS 11924
UMLENKSCHEIBE 10551
UMRECHNUNG 3067
UMRECHNUNGSTAFEL 3069
UMRISS 8907
UMRISSFRÄSEN 3040
UMRISSLINIE 8907
UMROLL-RÜTTELFORM MASCHINE 7251
UMSCHALTEN (ELEKTR.) 2246
UMSCHALTEN (ELEKTR.) 2241
UMSCHALTER (ELEKTR.) 2244
UMSCHALTVENTIL 10553
UMSCHAUFELN 13283
UMSCHLINGUNGSBOGEN 675
UMSCHLINGUNGSWINKEL 517
UMSCHMELZEN 10447
UMSCHMELZEN 10446
UMSCHMELZMETALL 11107
UMSETZUNG 13123
UMSETZUNG (CHEMISCHE) 4136

UMSPANNER 13115
UMSPANNUNGSBOGEN 675
UMSPONNENER DRAHT 3219
UMSTELLVENTIL 12882
UMSTELLZEIT 10533
UMSTEUERGETRIEBE 10548
UMSTEUERHEBEL 10549
UMSTEUERN 10534
UMSTEUERUNG 10543
UMSTEUERUNG EINER MASCHINE 10541
UMSTEUERWELLE 10550
UMSTÜRZEN 8965
UMWANDLER 13115
UMWANDLUNG 13136
UMWANDLUNG (CHEMISCHE) 2296
UMWANDLUNG (ISOTHERMISCHE) 7196
UMWANDLUNG (PHYSISCHE) 9280
UMWANDLUNG VON ENERGIE 3070
UMWANDLUNGSBEREICH 13113
UMWANDLUNGSPUNKT 3347
UMWANDLUNGSPUNKT 718
UMWANDLUNGSTEMPERATUR 13114
UMWANDLUNGSWÄRME 6364
UMWICKLUNG 13629
UNBALANZ 13341
UNBEKANNTE 13391
UNBELASTET 1081
UNDICHT 7493
UNDICHTE STELLE 7486
UNDICHTHEIT 7491
UNDICHTIGKEIT 7486
UNDICHTIGKEIT 7491
UNDICHTIGKEITSVERLUST 7756
UNDURCHLÄSSIG 6798
UNDURCHLÄSSIG FÜR WÄRMESTRAHLEN 786
UNDURCHLÄSSIGKEIT 6797
UNDURCHLÄSSIGKEIT FÜR WÄRMESTRAHLEN 785
UNDURCHSICHTIG 8803
UNDURCHSICHTIGKEIT 8802
UNEBENHEITEN 6464
UNELASTISCH 6904
UNEMPFLINDLICHKEITSGRAD 3723
UNENDLICH GROSS 6910
UNENDLICH KLEIN 6911
UNFALL 75
UNGEBUNDEN 6818
UNGEHÄRTET 13359
UNGENÜGENDE DECKKRAFT 6119
UNGESCHÜTZTER KOHLELICHTBOGEN 1944
UNGLEICHARTIGKEIT 3170
UNGLEICHFÖRMIGKEIT DER BEWEGUNG 7167

## UNG

920

UNGLEICHFÖRMIGKEIT DES MATERIALS 7352
UNGLEICHFÖRMIGKEITSGRAD 3719
UNGLEICHGEWICHT 13341
UNHANDLICH 13402
UNIVERSAL-GELENKKUPPLUNG 6572
UNIVERSAL-RUNDSCHLEIFMASCHINE 13383
UNIVERSALEISEN 5375
UNIVERSALFRÄSMASCHINE 13387
UNIVERSALFUTTER 13382
UNIVERSALGELENK 6573
UNIVERSALPRÜFMASCHINE 13388
UNIVERSALSCHLEIFMASCHINE 13384
UNIVERSALSCHRAUBENSCHLÜSSEL 11052
UNIVERSALSCHRAUBSTOCK 13389
UNIVERSALSCHWEISSKOPF 13390
UNIVERSALSTAHLWALZWERK 13386
UNKOMPRIMIERBAR 6847
UNKOSTEN (ALLGEMEINE) 8798
UNKRAUTDISTEL-UND FARNKRAUTSCHNEIDER 13741
UNLÖSLICH 6984
UNLÖSLICHKEIT 6983
UNMAGNETISCH 8637
UNMAGNETISCH WERDEN 1123
UNMITTELBAR WIRKEND 3980
UNORGANISCHER STOFF 6957
UNREGELMÄSSIG 7163
UNREINHEIT 6814
UNREINIGKEITEN 6813
UNRUND DREHEN 13280
UNRUND LAUFEN 10840
UNRUNDDREHEN 8869
UNRUNDE RIEMENSCHEIBE 9974
UNRUNDE SCHEIBE 4442
UNRUNDHEIT 8894
UNRUNDWERDEN EINES LAGERS 13719
UNSCHLITT 12609
UNSCHMELZBAR 6918
UNSCHMELZBARKEIT 6917
UNSTETIGKEIT 11546
UNSYMMETRIE 13341
UNSYMMETRISCH 778
UNTER LUFTZUTRITT ERHITZEN 6351
UNTERBAU 1026
UNTERBAU 5589
UNTERBELASTET LAUFEN 1080
UNTERBELASTUNG 7562
UNTERBRECHERKONTAKT 3009
UNTERBRECHUNG DES ELEKTRISCHEN STROMES 7093
UNTERCHLORIGSÄUREANHYDRID 2355
UNTERDETERMINANTE 8315
UNTERDRUCK 9811

UNTERDRUCK 13434
UNTERDRUCK 3778
UNTERDRUCKBREMSE 13436
UNTERDRUCKMESSER 13442
UNTERDRUCKREGLER 12431
UNTEREUTEKTOID 6741
UNTERFLURHYDRANT 5244
UNTERGESENK 1497
UNTERGESTELL MIT GLEITSCHUH 11606
UNTERHALTUNG 7946
UNTERHALTUNGSKOSTEN 7945
UNTERKASTEN 8678
UNTERKÜHLEN 12465
UNTERKÜHLEN 12463
UNTERKÜHLTE FLÜSSIGKEIT 12464
UNTERKÜHLUNG 13347
UNTERLAGE 12490
UNTERLAGE 12416
UNTERLAGEN 12494
UNTERLAGKEIL 13731
UNTERLAGSCHEIBE 13631
UNTERLAGSCHEIBE (FERERNDE) 7703
UNTERLAST 7562
UNTERLAUFHAHN 1234
UNTERLEGBLECH 11351
UNTERLEGRING (FEDERNDER) 4486
UNTERMASS 477
UNTERMASS 13349
UNTERNAHTRISS 13350
UNTEROXYDSCHICHT 12416
UNTERPLATTE 1040
UNTERPROGRAMM 12415
UNTERPULVER-SCHWEISSEN 684
UNTERPULVERSCHWEISSEN 12414
UNTERROSTUNG 13352
UNTERSALPETERSÄURE 8591
UNTERSATZ 12490
UNTERSCHALE 1487
UNTERSCHICHT 9857
UNTERSCHNITT 13351
UNTERSCHWEFLIGE SÄURE 12853
UNTERSETZUNG 10357
UNTERSETZUNG 5908
UNTERSETZUNGSVERHÄLTNIS 10360
UNTERSTEMPEL 7794
UNTERSTÜTZUNGSPUNKT 9567
UNTERSUCHUNG (MAKROSKOPISCHE) 7873
UNTERSUCHUNG (MIKROSKOPISCHE) 7114
UNTERSUCHUNG (MIKROSKOPISCHE) 8260
UNTERSUCHUNG (ULTRAMIKROSKOPISCHE) 13336
UNTERTAUCHEN 12413

| | |
|---|---|
| UNTERTEILUNG 12409 | VAUCANSONSCHE KETTE 6570 |
| UNTERVERBINOUNG 12408 | VEBRENNUNGSRÜCKSTAND 10476 |
| UNTERWASSER 12597 | VEKTOR 13510 |
| UNTERWASSERKANAL 12596 | VEKTORPRODUKT 13509 |
| UNVERBRANNT 13344 | VENTIL 13453 |
| UNVERBRENNBAR 6843 | VENTIL 970 |
| UNVERBRENNBARKEIT 6842 | VENTIL 2617 |
| UNVERBRENNLICH 6843 | VENTIL (AUSBALANCIERTES) 934 |
| UNVERBRENNLICHKEIT 6842 | VENTIL (DOPPELSITZIGES) 4166 |
| UNWÄGBAR 6800 | VENTIL (EINFACHES) 11491 |
| UNZERBRECHLICH 13343 | VENTIL (ELEKTRISCHES) 4549 |
| UNZERBRECHLICHKEIT 13342 | VENTIL (ENTLASTETES) 934 |
| UNZUGÄNGLICH 6821 | VENTIL (GESTEUERTES) 8120 |
| UNZUGÄNGLICHKEIT 6820 | VENTIL (HYDRAULISCH BETÄTIGTES) 6697 |
| UNZUSAMMENDDRÜCKBARKEIT 6846 | VENTIL (MEHRFACHES) 8476 |
| UNZUSAMMENDRÜCKBAR 6847 | VENTIL (MEHRSTÖCKIGES) 8475 |
| URAN 13420 | VENTIL (PNEUMATISCH GESTEUERTES) 9557 |
| URMUSTER 9955 | VENTIL (SELBSTTÄTIGES) 852 |
| URSPRUNG DER KOORDINATEN 8868 | VENTIL (STOPFBÜCHSLOSES) 9010 |
| URSPRUNGSFESTIGKEIT 9854 | VENTIL (UNGESTEUERTES) 852 |
| URTONSCHIEFER 9278 | VENTIL (VIERSITZIGES) 10060 |
| V-FUGENNAHT OHNE LUFTSPALT 2531 | VENTIL MIT FALTENBALG-ABDICHTUNG 1138 |
| V-LUNKER 5271 | VENTIL MIT HEBELFEDERBELASTUNG 11985 |
| VAKUMMETALLISIERUNG 13445 | VENTIL MIT HEBELGEWICHTSBELASTUNG 7535 |
| VAKUUM 13434 | VENTIL MIT UNMITTELBARER FEDERBELASTUNG 3987 |
| VAKUUM WÄRMEBEHANDLUNG 13443 | VENTIL MIT UNMITTELBARER GEWICHTSBELASTUNG 3632 |
| VAKUUMBREMSE 13436 | VENTILATION 13530 |
| VAKUUMDESTILLATION 4075 | VENTILATOR 5033 |
| VAKUUMFORMEN 13439 | VENTILATOR 12429 |
| VAKUUMGEHÄUSE 13438 | VENTILATOR 9817 |
| VAKUUMHEIZUNG 8318 | VENTILATORFLÜGELBLATT 5030 |
| VAKUUMKAMMER 13440 | VENTILATORRIEMEN 5029 |
| VAKUUMKAMMER 13449 | VENTILATORRIEMENSCHEIBE 5032 |
| VAKUUMKASTEN 13435 | VENTILAUSSCHLAG 7544 |
| VAKUUMKESSEL 13451 | VENTILDIAGRAMM 13457 |
| VAKUUMMETALLURGIE 13446 | VENTILE (HÄNGENDE) 8943 |
| VAKUUMMETER 13442 | VENTILEINSTELLUNGTARIEREN 13469 |
| VAKUUMPUMPE 284 | VENTILERÖFFNUNG 8832 |
| VAKUUMRAFFINIERUNG 13447 | VENTILFÄNGER 13461 |
| VAKUUMSCHMELZEN 13444 | VENTILFEDER 13470 |
| VAKUUMSINTERUNG 13448 | VENTILFÜHRUNG 13462 |
| VALENZ 13452 | VENTILHAHN 13455 |
| VANADIN 13475 | VENTILHEBEL 13465 |
| VANADIUM 13475 | VENTILHUB 7544 |
| VANADIUMEISEN 5116 | VENTILKAMMER 2229 |
| VANADIUMSTAHL 13476 | VENTILKASTEN 2229 |
| VARIABLE 13488 | VENTILKLAPPE 9024 |
| VARIANTE 410 | VENTILKLAPPE 13459 |
| VARIATION (MATH.) 13496 | VENTILKOLBEN 1673 |
| VASELIN 13508 | VENTILKÖRPER 13454 |
| VATERGEWINDE 7955 | VENTILKÖRPERSITZ 1397 |

## VEN

922

VENTILLEHRE 13473
VENTILÖLER 13467
VENTILÖLKANNE 9994
VENTILRÖHRE 13472
VENTILSCHLAG 6224
VENTILSCHLUSS 2537
VENTILSCHLUSS (VERSPÄTETER) 10519
VENTILSITZ 11097
VENTILSITZ 13468
VENTILSPIEL 13154
VENTILSTEUERUNG 13456
VENTILSTEUERUNG 13460
VENTILSTEUERUNGS-ZAHNRAD 12949
VENTILSTÖSSEL 13466
VENTILTELLER 13463
VENTILVERSCHRAUBUNG 13464
VENTILWIRKUNG 13458
VENTURIMESSER 13532
VENTURIROHR 13532
VERALUMINIEREN 429
VERÄNDERLICHE 13488
VERÄNDERUNG (CHEMISCHE) 2296
VERÄNDERUNG (PHYSIKALISCHE) 9280
VERÄNDERUNG DES WASSERSPIEGELS 13500
VERANKERN 12918
VERANKERN 12914
VERANKERUNG 1520
VERANKERUNG 12918
VERANKERUNGSDRAHT 6187
VERARBEITBAR 12802
VERARBEITUNGSANFORDERUNGEN 4987
VERARBEITUNGSTOLERANZEN 4988
VERARMUNG 6801
VERBAND 1444
VERBINDEN 3254
VERBINDEN DER RIEMENENDEN 1142
VERBINDEN VON ROHREN 7248
VERBINDUNG 6609
VERBINDUNG 3254
VERBINDUNG 2965
VERBINDUNG (ALIPHATISHE) 326
VERBINDUNG (CHEMISCHE) 2300
VERBINDUNG (CHEMISCHE) 2827
VERBINDUNG (HOMOGENE) 6556
VERBINDUNG (NACHGIEBIGE) 5416
VERBINDUNG (STARRE) 10589
VERBINDUNGEN (AROMATISCHE) 716
VERBINDUNGSBOLZEN 771
VERBINDUNGSGEOMETRIE 7240
VERBINDUNGSGEWICHT 2771
VERBINDUNGSKANAL 5034

VERBINDUNGSLASCHEN 5270
VERBINDUNGSROHR 2960
VERBINDUNGSSCHRAUBE 771
VERBINDUNGSSCHRAUBE 2959
VERBINDUNGSSTANGE 2962
VERBINDUNGSSTEG 2964
VERBLASSEN 5014
VERBLEIT 7479
VERBLENDER 5004
VERBLENDSTEIN 5004
VERBLOCKUNGSKONDENSATOR 1342
VERBOGEN 1197
VERBOLZEN 1435
VERBOLZUNG 1443
VERBRANNTER BLOCK 1748
VERBRENNEN 1745
VERBRENNEN 1750
VERBRENNEN (DAS) 1746
VERBRENNEN DES EISENS 1754
VERBRENNLICHKEIT 2773
VERBRENNUNG 2774
VERBRENNUNG (LANGSAME) 11644
VERBRENNUNG (LEBHAFTE) 10205
VERBRENNUNG (UNVOLLKOMMENE) 6845
VERBRENNUNG (VOLLSTÄNDIGE) 2779
VERBRENNUNGSDRUCK 4936
VERBRENNUNGSERZEUGNIS 9893
VERBRENNUNGSGASE 5470
VERBRENNUNGSLUFT 277
VERBRENNUNGSMOTOR 7061
VERBRENNUNGSMOTOR 7062
VERBRENNUNGSPRODUKT 9893
VERBRENNUNGSRAUM 2776
VERBRENNUNGSRAUM 2856
VERBRENNUNGSRAUM EINER FEUERUNG 2777
VERBRENNUNGSRAUM EINES MOTORS 2778
VERBRENNUNGSWÄRME 6356
VERBUNDDAMPFMASCHINE 2829
VERBUNDDYNAMO 3228
VERBUNDELEKTRODE 2819
VERBUNDMOTOR 2835
VERBUNDPOROSITÄT 7029
VERBUNDTRÄGER 9488
VERBUNDTRÄGER 2831
VERBUNDVERDICHTER 2836
VERCHROMUNG (ELEKTROLYTISCHE) 2388
VERDAMPFBAR 4861
VERDAMPFEN 4867
VERDAMPFEN 4862
VERDAMPFEN 13483
VERDAMPFER 4869

| | |
|---|---|
| VERDAMPFERKÖRPER **4870** | VEREDELUNG EINES METALLS **10378** |
| VERDAMPFUNGSKONDENSATOR **4868** | VEREDLUNGSINDUSTRIE **9888** |
| VERDAMPFUNGSTEMPERATUR **4865** | VERENGERUNG **3045** |
| VERDAMPFUNGSVERLUST **4866** | VERENGT **3042** |
| VERDAMPFUNGSWÄRME **6366** | VERFAHREN **9883** |
| VERDAMPFUNGSWÄRME **6359** | VERFAHREN **8216** |
| VERDAMPFUNGSWÄRME (LATENTE) **7416** | VERFAHREN (BASISCHES) **1050** |
| VERDICHTBARKEIT **2851** | VERFAHREN (HANSGIRGSCHE) **6272** |
| VERDICHTEN **2837** | VERFAHREN (SAURES) **120** |
| VERDICHTER **2874** | VERFÄLSCHEN **204** |
| VERDICHTER (HYDRAULISCHER) **6680** | VERFÄLSCHUNG **205** |
| VERDICHTER (NASSER) **13801** | VERFÄRBUNG **4026** |
| VERDICHTER (TROCKENER) **4345** | VERFESTIGUNG **6850** |
| VERDICHTERRAD **6795** | VERFEUERN GASFÖRMIGER BRENNSTOFFE **1751** |
| VERDICHTUNG **11355** | VERFEUERN VON KOHLEN **2564** |
| VERDICHTUNG **2854** | VERFEUERN VON KOHLENSTAUB **1753** |
| VERDICHTUNG **3753** | VERFEUERN VON ÖL **1752** |
| VERDICHTUNGSARBEIT **13941** | VERFLÜCHTIGEN **13588** |
| VERDICHTUNGSHUB **2864** | VERFLÜCHTIGUNG **13587** |
| VERDICHTUNGSRING **2867** | VERFLÜSSIGBAR **7639** |
| VERDICHTUNGSVERHÄLTNIS **2860** | VERFLÜSSIGER **2908** |
| VERDICKER **12842** | VERFLÜSSIGUNG EINES GASES **7636** |
| VERDICKUNG **7675** | VERFORMBARKEIT **3705** |
| VERDICKUNG (FASERIGE) **10745** | VERFORMUNG **3698** |
| VERDRÄNGERPUMPE **9653** | VERFORMUNG **4077** |
| VERDRÄNGUNG EINER FLÜSSIGKEIT **4054** | VERFORMUNG **12322** |
| VERDREHUNG **13054** | VERFORMUNG (BLEIBENDE) **9202** |
| VERDREHUNGSBEANSPRUCHUNG **13056** | VERFORMUNG (PLASTISCHE) **9469** |
| VERDREHUNGSFESTIGKEIT **13057** | VERFORMUNG (STUFENLOSE) **6853** |
| VERDREHUNGSPROBE **13306** | VERFORMUNGGESCHWINDIGKEIT **12330** |
| VERDREHUNGSSCHWINGUNG **13557** | VERFORMUNGSALTERUNG **12328** |
| VERDREHUNGSVERSUCH **13059** | VERFORMUNGSALTERUNG **12327** |
| VERDREHUNGSWAAGE **13052** | VERFORMUNGSBAND **3706** |
| VERDREHUNGSWINKEL **532** | VERGÄLLUNGSMITTEL **3747** |
| VERDRILLUNG **13054** | VERGASBAR **5860** |
| VERDÜNNEN (EIN GAS) **10214** | VERGASEN **5862** |
| VERDÜNNEN (EINE LÖSUNG) **3952** | VERGASER **1984** |
| VERDÜNNEN EINER LÖSUNG **3954** | VERGASER **1982** |
| VERDÜNNTE LÖSUNG **3953** | VERGASUNG **5861** |
| VERDÜNNUNG EINER LÖSUNG **3954** | VERGASUNG **5865** |
| VERDÜNNUNG EINES GASES **10211** | VERGIESSBARKEIT **2064** |
| VERDÜNNUNGSMITTEL **3951** | VERGIESSBARKEITSVERSUCH **2065** |
| VERDUNSTEN **4863** | VERGIESSEN **2030** |
| VERDUNSTUNG **8502** | VERGIESSEN **2068** |
| VERDUNSTUNGSHÖHE **1402** | VERGIESSEN (MIT MÖRTELZEMENT) **6153** |
| VERDUNSTUNGSKONDENSATOR **4868** | VERGIESSEN (MIT ZEMENTMÖRTEL) **6154** |
| VERDUNSTUNGSWÄRME **6366** | VERGLASEN **5969** |
| VERDUNSTUNGSWÄRME **6359** | VERGLASEN **5972** |
| VEREDELUNG **10377** | VERGLASUNG **13584** |
| VEREDELUNG (ELEKTROLYTISCHE) **4558** | VERGLEICH VON ABMESSUNGEN **7445** |
| VEREDELUNG (THERMISCHE) **5245** | VERGLEICHER **2795** |

**VER** 924

VERGLEICHER (ELEKTRISCHER) **4535**
VERGLEICHER (ELEKTRONISCHER) **4632**
VERGLEICHER (MECHANISCHER) **8097**
VERGLEICHER (OPTISCH-MECHANISCHER) **8118**
VERGLEICHER (OPTISCHER) **8842**
VERGLEICHSMESSUNG **2797**
VERGOLDEN **5942**
VERGOLDEN **5941**
VERGOLDUNG **5942**
VERGRÖSSERUNG (OPT.) **7935**
VERGRÖSSERUNG EINER LINSE **7938**
VERGRÖSSERUNG EINER ZEICHNUNG **4769**
VERGRÖSSERUNGSGLAS **7936**
VERGRÖSSERUNGSKRAFT **7937**
VERGÜTEANLAGE **6376**
VERGÜTUNG **6375**
VERGÜTUNG **10092**
VERGÜTUNG **10095**
VERGÜTUNG (ELEKTROLYTISCHE) **4558**
VERGÜTUNG (THERMISCHE) **5245**
VERGÜTUNG BEI NORMALER TEMPERATUR **223**
VERGÜTUNGSLEGIERUNG **6383**
VERHALTEN (CHEMISCHES) **2295**
VERHÄLTNIS **10234**
VERHÄLTNIS **9933**
VERHÄLTNIS **10226**
VERHÄLTNIS (IN DIREKTEM) **6815**
VERHÄLTNIS (IN GERADEM) **6815**
VERHÄLTNIS (IN UMGEKEHRTEM) **6816**
VERHÄLTNISGLEICH **9935**
VERHÄLTNISGLEICHUNG **9933**
VERHÄLTNISMÄSSIG **9935**
VERHÄLTNISZÄHNEZAHL **3861**
VERHARZEN **10481**
VERHARZEN **10480**
VERHARZUNG **10480**
VERHÜTTEN **11664**
VERHÜTTUNG **11666**
VERIEGEIN **7710**
VERJÜNGTER STAB **12670**
VERJÜNGUNGSROHR **10352**
VERKAUFSINGENIEUR **10898**
VERKEHRSLAST **10706**
VERKEILEN **13740**
VERKEILEN **7277**
VERKEILUNG **13740**
VERKITTEN **2134**
VERKITTEN MIT ZEMENT **2146**
VERKLEIDEN **7369**
VERKLEIDEN (EIN ROHR) **3263**
VERKLEIDUNG **3274**

VERKLEINERUNGSGLAS **4095**
VERKOHLEN **1971**
VERKOHLUNG **1974**
VERKOHLUNG **1975**
VERKOHLUNG **1970**
VERKOKEN **2656**
VERKOKUNG **1975**
VERKOKUNG **2666**
VERKOKUNGSANSTALT **2665**
VERKRUSTET **6857**
VERKUPFERN **3124**
VERKUPFERUNG **3125**
VERKÜRZEN **11376**
VERKÜRZUNG **11376**
VERLADEBRÜCKE **13141**
VERLÄNGERUNG EINES PATENTES **9919**
VERLÄNGERUNGSSTÜCK FÜR ZIRKEL **7521**
VERLÄNGERUNGSTAB **4947**
VERLANGSAMEN (DEN GANG EINER MASCHINE) **11645**
VERLANGSAMEN DES GANGES **11649**
VERLAUF **13181**
VERLAUFEFFEKT **7528**
VERLEGEN (EINEN LEITUNGSDRAHT) **13881**
VERLEGEN VON ROHREN **9356**
VERLEGESCHIFF **7440**
VERLEGUNG EINES LEITUNGSDRAHTES **13909**
VERLETZUNG EINES PATENTES **6916**
VERLITZEN **12337**
VERLITZEN **12340**
VERLUST **7754**
VERLUST (ZUSÄTZLICHER) **170**
VERLUSTSTROM **7490**
VERLUSTWIDERSTAND **10497**
VERMESSINGUNG **1567**
VERMILLON **13535**
VERNICKELN **8566**
VERNICKELUNG **8567**
VERNIER **13536**
VERNIETEN **10643**
VERNIETEN **10629**
VERPACKEN **8991**
VERPACKEN **8990**
VERPACKUNG **8995**
VERPACKUNG **8999**
VERPACKUNGSKOSTEN **3205**
VERPUFFUNGSDRUCK **4936**
VERPULVERUNG **2226**
VERPUTZ **9463**
VERPUTZEN (BAUW.) **9464**
VERPUTZEN MIT ZEMENT **2134**
VERPUTZEN MIT ZEMENT **2146**

VERRIEGELN **7699**
VERRIEGELUNG **7710**
VERROSTEN **10865**
VERROSTEN **10864**
VERROSTET **10873**
VERROTTUNG **3183**
VERSAGEN EINES MOTORS **5021**
VERSAND **13140**
VERSANDKOSTEN **3209**
VERSCHIEBBAR **4052**
VERSCHIEBBARE KUPPLUNG **4033**
VERSCHIEBBARE KUPPLUNGSMUFFE **11599**
VERSCHIEBUNG **4053**
VERSCHIEBUNG (AXIALE) **860**
VERSCHIEBUNG (INNERE) **7063**
VERSCHIEBUNG (SEITLICHE) **7423**
VERSCHIEBUNGSTRUKTUR **5461**
VERSCHLACKUNG **11004**
VERSCHLAMMEN EINER ROHRLEITUNG **11457**
VERSCHLEISS **13710**
VERSCHLEISS **13709**
VERSCHLEISS **4820**
VERSCHLEISSBLECH **13716**
VERSCHLEISSEN **13713**
VERSCHLEISSFESTIGKEIT **13717**
VERSCHLEISSFESTIGKEIT **10499**
VERSCHLEISSPLATTEN **13711**
VERSCHLEISSPRÜFUNG **13714**
VERSCHLEISSWIDERSTAND **10499**
VERSCHLUSS (EINES MANNLOCHS) **3262**
VERSCHLUSSDECKEL **1910**
VERSCHLUSSKAPPE **11025**
VERSCHLUSSNIETUNG **12922**
VERSCHLUSSPFROPFEN **11060**
VERSCHLUSSSCHRAUBE **11060**
VERSCHLUSSSTÜCK **9529**
VERSCHMUTZEN **2510**
VERSCHNEIDEN **1325**
VERSCHOBEN **8730**
VERSCHRAUBEN **11022**
VERSCHRAUBEN **11065**
VERSCHRAUBUNG **11058**
VERSCHRAUBUNG **13368**
VERSCHRAUBUNG **3254**
VERSCHWÄCHUNG DES QUERSCHNITTS **13707**
VERSEIFBAR **10932**
VERSEIFEN **10934**
VERSEIFUNG **10933**
VERSEILEN **10739**
VERSEILEN **13303**
VERSENKBOHRER **3245**

VERSENKEN **3236**
VERSENKEN **3242**
VERSENKEN **3234**
VERSENKEN (EINEN NIETKOPF) **3246**
VERSENKEN (EINEN SCHRAUBENKOPF) **3246**
VERSENKEN (EINES SCHRAUBENKOPFES) **3247**
VERSENKEN (EINLASSEN EINES NIETKOPFES) **3247**
VERSENKER **10747**
VERSENKER **3245**
VERSENKTER SCHRAUBENKOPF **3250**
VERSENKTES NIET **10635**
VERSETZEN (MIT WASSER) **163**
VERSETZUNG **4047**
VERSETZUNG **8737**
VERSETZUNG **9216**
VERSICKERUNG **7488**
VERSILBERN **11469**
VERSILBERN **11459**
VERSILBERUNG **11469**
VERSILBERUNG **11465**
VERSINKUNG (GALVANISCHE) **4583**
VERSPÄTUNG **3730**
VERSPRÖDUNG BEIM VERZINKEN **5790**
VERSPRÖDUNG DURCH EINDRINGEN VON LOT **11757**
VERSPRÖDUNG. **4685**
VERSTAHLEN **135**
VERSTÄHLEN **12206**
VERSTÄHLEN **12205**
VERSTÄRKER **485**
VERSTÄRKERFOLIE **7017**
VERSTÄRKUNG **5773**
VERSTÄRKUNG **1701**
VERSTÄRKUNG **10429**
VERSTÄRKUNGSBLECH **11343**
VERSTÄRKUNGSBLECH **10430**
VERSTÄRKUNGSRIPPE EINES ROHRES **10570**
VERSTÄRKUNGSSCHWEISSNAHT **10428**
VERSTEIFEN **12359**
VERSTEIFEN **12358**
VERSTEIFTER WALZTRÄGER **2831**
VERSTEIFTES ZAHNRAD **11402**
VERSTEIFUNG **10569**
VERSTEIFUNG **12359**
VERSTEIFUNGSBALKEN **13856**
VERSTEIFUNGSBLECH **9489**
VERSTEIFUNGSELEMENT **12256**
VERSTEIFUNGSPLATTE **12257**
VERSTEIFUNGSROHR **13258**
VERSTELLBAR **183**
VERSTELLUNG DURCH SCHRAUBE **190**
VERSTEMMEN **2113**

# VER
926

VERSTEMMEN 2115
VERSTEMMUNG 2115
VERSTOPFEN 2362
VERSTOPFEN (EINE UNDICHTE STELLE) 12279
VERSTOPFEN (SICH) 2358
VERSTOPFUNG 2362
VERSTOPFUNG 8719
VERSTREBEN 1521
VERSTREBEN 1517
VERSTREBUNG 1516
VERSUCH 12792
VERSUCH 12770
VERSUCH 9921
VERSUCH (ZERSTÖRUNGSFREIER) 9924
VERSUCHE MACHEN 4928
VERSUCHSBOHRUNG 12778
VERSUCHSERGEBNIS 10512
VERSUCHSMONTAGE 13184
VERSUCHSSTÜCK 12789
VERSUCHSTAND 12773
VERTAUSCHUNG 9216
VERTAUSCHUNG (ZYKLISCHE) 3556
VERTEILER 4084
VERTEILERKASTEN 4086
VERTEILERKOPF 4086
VERTEILERLÄUFER 4085
VERTEILGESENK 4451
VERTEILUNG (MEHRDIMENSIONALE) 7239
VERTEILUNGSLEITUNG 4079
VERTEILUNGSWAND 922
VERTIKAL 13551
VERTIKALBOHRMASCHINE 13552
VERTIKALE 9217
VERTIKALGERÜST 4456
VERTIKALHOBELMASCHINE 11643
VERTIKALPROJEKTION 4659
VERTRÄGLICHKEIT (GEGENSEITIGE) 2806
VERUNREINIGUNGEN 6813
VERVIELFACHEN 8480
VERVIELFACHEN 8483
VERVIELFÄLTIGEN 8484
VERVIELFÄLTIGEN 8481
VERVIELFÄLTIGUNG 10467
VERWACHSUNG 2572
VERWANDLUNG IN STAHL 145
VERWANDTSCHAFT 2292
VERWEILZEIT 4396
VERWERFUNG (SEITLICHE) 7418
VERWERTEN 13430
VERWERTUNG 13429
VERWERTUNG (GEWERBLICHE) EINER ERFINDUNG 2783

VERWINDEPROBE 13310
VERZAHNMASCHINEN FÜR STIRN- U. SCHRÄGVERZAHNUNGEN 12006
VERZAHNTER SEKTOR 13024
VERZAHNUNG 13026
VERZAHNUNG 12704
VERZAHNUNG (LINKSSTEIGENDE) 7509
VERZAHNUNG (RECHTSSTEIGENDE) 10586
VERZERRUNG 4077
VERZERRUNGSZWILLINGSKRISTALL 8113
VERZICHT 13615
VERZIEHEN 13629
VERZIEHEN (SEITLICHES) 7418
VERZIEHEN (SICH) 13628
VERZINKEN 5789
VERZINKEN 5784
VERZINKEN (KONTINUIERLICHES) 3027
VERZINKUNG 14044
VERZINKUNG 2604
VERZINKUNG (ELEKTROLYTISCHE) 2683
VERZINKUNG (ELEKTROLYTISCHE) 4566
VERZINKUNG (HEISSE) 5787
VERZINKUNG (KALTE) 4566
VERZINKUNG GALVANISCHE 4566
VERZINNEN 12954
VERZINNEN 12963
VERZINNUNG 12963
VERZÖGERN 6926
VERZÖGERUNG 8525
VERZÖGERUNG (AUTOMATISCHE) 841
VERZÖGERUNGSWINKEL 522
VIBROGRAPH 9242
VICKERS-PYRAMIDHÄRTE 10039
VICKERSHÄRTE 13566
VICKERSHÄRTE 6860
VIELECK 9609
VIELFARBIG 9607
VIELFLACH 9612
VIELPUNKTSCHWEISSEN 8464
VIELRINNDRUCKLAGER 12903
VIER-ZYLINDER-BOXER-MOTOR 5383
VIERATOMIG 12798
VIERBACKENFUTTER 5604
VIERBLATT 10086
VIERECK 10058
VIERFACHEXPANSIONSMASCHINE 10059
VIERFLACH 12797
VIERFLÄCHNER 12797
VIERKANT 9533
VIERKANT 12025
VIERKANTEISEN 12015

VIERKANTFEILE **12019**
VIERKANTMUTTER **12024**
VIERKANTMUTTER (SCHWEISSBARE) **1307**
VIERKANTSCHRAUBE **12033**
VIERKANTSCHRAUBENKOPF **10309**
VIERKANTSEIL **12028**
VIERKANTSTAHL **379**
VIERKANTWELLE **12029**
VIERRADANTRIEB **5601**
VIERSEITIGES PRISMA **10055**
VIERTAKTMOTOR **5600**
VIERTAKTMOTOR **5603**
VIERTELHOLZ **10076**
VIERTELKREIS **10056**
VIERTÜRIGE LIMOUSINE **5599**
VIERWEGESTÜCK **3368**
VIERWEGHAHN **5605**
VIERWEGVENTIL **5606**
VIERWERTIG **12798**
VISIERSCHEIBE **6145**
VISKOS **13577**
VISKOSE **13575**
VISKOSIMETER **13574**
VISKOSITÄT **13576**
VITRIOL (BLAUER) **1376**
VITRIOL (GRÜNES) **6093**
VITRIOL (WEISSER) **14046**
VOGELPERSPEKTIVE **1264**
VOGELZUNGE **3392**
VOLLAST-EINSTELLSCHRAUBE **187**
VOLLBELASTET LAUFEN **1079**
VOLLDRUCKDAMPFMASCHINE **12165**
VOLLDRUCKLINIE **199**
VOLLKEHLNAHT **3077**
VOLLKOMMENE VERBRENNUNG **9184**
VOLLKREISTRANSPORTEUR **2426**
VOLLPIPETTE **1718**
VOLLSCHEIBE **5040**
VOLLSTEIN **11780**
VOLLTURBINE **5718**
VOLLZIEGEL **11780**
VOLT **13591**
VOLT-AMPERE **13592**
VOLTAMETER **3227**
VOLTMETER **13597**
VOLTZAHL **13593**
VOLUMEN **13598**
VOLUMEN (KRITISCHES) **3354**
VOLUMEN (SPEZIFISCHES) **11854**
VOLUMEN (VERDRÄNGTES) (PHYS.) **4053**
VOLUMEN-AUFNAHME **4912**

VOLUMENÄNDERUNG **2240**
VOLUMENELASTIZITÄT **2852**
VOLUMPROZENT **9179**
VON GASEN **4833**
VOR-EUTEKTISCHER BESTANDTEIL **9848**
VOR-UND RÜCKSPRUNG **7957**
VORANSCHLAG **4838**
VORARBEIT **1583**
VORARBEITEN **9787**
VORARBEITER **7482**
VORBEARBEITEN **10775**
VORBEARBEITUNG **10786**
VORBEHANDLUNG **9780**
VORBELASTUNG **9782**
VORBLECH **11306**
VORBLOCK **1346**
VORBLOCKWALZWERK **1348**
VORBOHREN **10771**
VORBRENNE **2476**
VORDERACHSE **5691**
VORDERACHSGEOMETRIE **5696**
VORDERANSICHT **5694**
VORDERQUERTRÄGER **5693**
VORDERRADANTRIEB **5699**
VOREILEN **7448**
VOREILWINKEL **515**
VORFEILE **1057**
VORFILTER **5265**
VORFILTER **9751**
VORFORMLING **9772**
VORFORMUNG **9773**
VORFORMUNG **1341**
VORFRÄSEN **5858**
VORGANG **9883**
VORGANG **9240**
VORGANG (CHEMISCHER) **2291**
VORGEKERBTER BLOCK **8674**
VORGELEGE **3244**
VORGELEGEWELLE **3240**
VORGELEGEWELLE **3233**
VORGELEGEWELLE **6756**
VORGEWALZT **10778**
VORGEWALZTER BLOCK **1346**
VORHALTEN **6524**
VORHALTER **4115**
VORHALTHAMMER **6529**
VORHÄNGEBILDUNG **3492**
VORHÄNGEBILDUNG **10895**
VORKRAGUNG **9917**
VORLAGE **10277**
VORLAUF (DER DESTILLATION) **5267**

# VOR 928

VORLÄUFIGES FLIESSEN 13118
VORLEGIERUNG 5594
VORMETALL 1366
VORMODELL 4370
VORREIBAHLE (KONISCHE) 10790
VORREISSEN 8010
VORREISSEN 8017
VORREISSER 11068
VORREISSER (ARBEITER) 8013
VORRICHTUNG 3820
VORSCHLAGHAMMER 11573
VORSCHLEIFEN 10777
VORSCHMIEDEGESENK 1343
VORSCHUB 5063
VORSCHUB EINES WERKZEUGS 5068
VORSCHUB JE ZAHN 5069
VORSCHUBGESCHWINDIGKEITSKORREKTUR 5079
VORSCHUBHEBEL (SELBSTTÄTIGER) 842
VORSCHUBMECHANISMUS 5067
VORSCHUBUMSTEUERHEBEL 5073
VORSCHUBWÄHLHEBEL 5065
VORSCHUBZAHL 5085
VORSCHWEISSBUND 13771
VORSCHWEISSENDEN 1810
VORSCHWEISSFLANSCH 13794
VORSCHWEISSFLANSCH 13773
VORSICHTSMASSREGEIN 9753
VORSINTERN 9794
VORSINTERUNG 9794
VORSPANNEN 830
VORSPANNUNG 9782
VORSPANNUNGSKABEL 12739
VORSPANNVORRICHTUNG 9781
VORSPRINGEND 9910
VORSPRINGENDE ECKE 10900
VORSPRINGENDES BLECH 9911
VORSPRUNG 9913
VORSPUR 12975
VORSPUR (NEGATIVE) 12976
VORSTECKER 3212
VORSTECKKEIL 3212
VORSTECKSTIFT 3212
VORSTEHEND 9910
VORSTRASSE 10789
VORSTRECKGERÜST 9622
VORVERSUCH 9779
VORWÄHLER 9789
VORWALZE 10787
VORWALZEN 1583
VORWALZWERK 1348
VORWÄRMEN 6260

VORWÄRMEN 9774
VORWÄRMEN 9776
VORWÄRMER 9775
VORWÄRMOFEN 9777
VORWÄRTSBEWEGUNG 5584
VORWÄRTSFLIESSPRESSEN 3984
VORWÄRTSGANG 10848
VORZEICHEN 11429
VORZEICHEN (NEGATIVES) 8532
VORZEICHEN (POSITIVES) 9661
VULKANFIBER 13609
VULKANISIEREN 13608
VULKANISIEREN 13607
VULKANISIEREN 3484
VULKANIT 2363
WAAGE 931
WAAGE (CHEMISCHE) 2294
WAAGE (HYDROSTATISCHE) 6725
WAAGEBALKEN 10972
WAAGERECHTE 6585
WAAGERECHTSPINDELSCHLEIFBOCK 6588
WAAGERECHTSTOSSMASCHINEN 11267
WAAGRECHT 6578
WAAGRECHTSTOSSMASCHINE 11269
WAAGSCHALE 10976
WACHS 13702
WACHS (JAPANISCHES) 7213
WACHSAUSSCHMELZGUSS 9765
WACHSEN 6155
WACHSMODELL 13703
WACHSTUM 6155
WAFFELBLECH 12769
WÄGBAR 9619
WÄGEN 13744
WÄGEN 13746
WAGENFEDER 2008
WAGENFETT 879
WAGENHEBER 11035
WAGENKIPPER 1932
WAGENSCHMIERE 879
WAGENSCHRAUBE 2552
WAGENWINDE 10121
WÄGUNG 13746
WAHRSCHEINLICHKEITSVERTEILUNG 9881
WALKERDE 5727
WALLPLATTE 3596
WALRAT 11882
WALRATÖL 11881
WALZBAR 1915
WALZBLEI 11314
WALZDRAHT 10678

929 WAR

WALZDRAHT AUS LEGIERTEN STÄHLEN **376**
WALZE **10671**
WALZE (GEOM.) **3561**
WALZE (GERIFFELTE) **6136**
WALZE (RAUHE) **10174**
WALZE EINER REGISTRIERVORRICHTUNG **10290**
WALZEISEN **10676**
WALZEN **10665**
WALZEN **10696**
WALZEN (KONTINUIERLICHES) **3035**
WALZENBIEGEMASCHINE **1186**
WALZENFRÄSER **13848**
WALZENKESSEL **3578**
WALZENLAGER **10680**
WALZENMÜHLE **10687**
WALZENPUMPE **10758**
WALZENSPURLAGER **10691**
WALZENSTIRNFRÄSER **11337**
WALZENSTRASSE **10669**
WALZENSTRASSE **10701**
WALZENSTRASSE **10670**
WALZFERTIGUNG **8278**
WÄLZFLÄCHE **10705**
WALZFLANSCH **10672**
WALZFLANSCH **10699**
WALZGERÜST **10704**
WALZGERÜST **12065**
WALZGOLD **10673**
WALZHAUT **11544**
WÄLZHEBEL **10686**
WÄLZKREIS **5921**
WÄLZLAGER **618**
WALZNARBE **10171**
WALZNARBE **9417**
WALZNUTEN (GESCHLOSSENE) **2527**
WALZNUTZBREITE **13427**
WALZPROFIL **10675**
WALZRICHTUNG **10698**
WALZSCHMIEDEN **10668**
WALZSPLITTER **7383**
WALZSPLITTER **11626**
WALZSTRASSE (KONTINUIERLICHE) **3030**
WALZSTRECKE **10701**
WALZWERK **10701**
WALZZUNDER **8279**
WANDARM **13618**
WANDBETT **13621**
WANDBOHRMASCHINE **13620**
WANDDAMPFMASCHINE **13620**
WANDDICKE EINES ROHRES **12844**
WANDDREHKRAN **13623**

WANDERMUTTER **13159**
WANDERUNG **8268**
WANDHOBEL **11417**
WANDKONSOLE **13618**
WANDLAGER **1523**
WANDLAGERSTUHL **13618**
WANDPLATTE **13621**
WANDSTÄRKE EINES ROHRES **12844**
WANDUNG **11330**
WANDVORGELEGE **13619**
WANGENHOBEL **11417**
WANZE **1327**
WARENAUFZUG **6007**
WARENZEICHEN **13100**
WARM AUFZIEHEN **11390**
WARMAUFZIEHEN **11398**
WARMBADHÄRTUNG **8021**
WARMBEARBEITUNG **6650**
WARMBEHANDLUNG **6377**
WARMBIEGEPROBE **6618**
WARMBIEGUNG **6619**
WARMBRUCH **6621**
WARMBRÜCHIG **6658**
WARMBRÜCHIG **10337**
WARMBRÜCHIGKEIT **6641**
WARMBRÜCHIGKEIT **10339**
WÄRME **6333**
WÄRME (FREIGEWORDENE) **6370**
WÄRME (FÜHLBARE) **11184**
WÄRME (INNERE) **7070**
WÄRME (LATENTE) **7415**
WÄRME (LATENTE) **6365**
WÄRME (MITTLERE SPEZIFISCHE) **8076**
WÄRME (SPEZIFISCHE) **11852**
WÄRME (STRAHLENDE) **10140**
WÄRME ABFÜHREN **4663**
WÄRME ABGEBEN **5950**
WÄRME AUFSPEICHERN **12296**
WÄRME ENTZIEHEN **13910**
WÄRME ZUFÜHREN **12485**
WÄRMEABFUHR **3735**
WÄRMEABGABE **3735**
WÄRMEABLEITUNG **4666**
WÄRMEAKKUMULATOR **6336**
WÄRMEÄQUIVALENT (MECHANISCHES) **8104**
WÄRMEAUFNAHME **51**
WÄRMEAUFNAHMEFÄHIGKEIT **6335**
WÄRMEAUFNAHMEFÄHIGKET **41**
WÄRMEAUFSPEICHERUNG **12291**
WÄRMEAUSDEHNUNG **12808**
WÄRMEAUSDEHNUNG **4948**

# WAR

930

WÄRMEAUSDEHNUNGSKOEFFIZIENT **12809**
WÄRMEAUSTAUSCH **4884**
WÄRMEAUSTAUSCHER **6349**
WÄRMEBEHANDLUNG **12815**
WÄRMEBEHANDLUNG **6375**
WÄRMEBEHANDLUNG NACH DEM SCHWEISSEN **9667**
WÄRMEBILANZ **6337**
WÄRMEDÄMMUNG **6639**
WÄRMEDIAGRAMM **6346**
WÄRMEEINDRINGTIEFE **6368**
WÄRMEEINFLUSSZONE **6380**
WÄRMEEINHEIT **12816**
WÄRMEEINHEIT (BRITISCHE) **1626**
WÄRMEENERGIE **6344**
WÄRMEENTWICKLUNG **4874**
WÄRMEENTWICKLUNG **6338**
WÄRMEENTWICKLUNG **10274**
WÄRMEERZEUGENDE VERLUSTE **6381**
WÄRMEERZEUGUNG **9896**
WÄRMEGEBEND **4901**
WÄRMEGEFÄLLE **12724**
WÄRMEGRAD **12721**
WÄRMEINHALT **6342**
WÄRMEISOLIERUNGSBEKLEIDUNG **7623**
WÄRMEKAPAZITÄT **12803**
WÄRMEKAPAZITÄT **6339**
WÄRMEKAPAZITÄT **6335**
WÄRMEKONSTANTE **6341**
WÄRMEKRAFTMASCHINE **6345**
WÄRMELEITER **6340**
WÄRMELEITFÄHIGKEIT **2920**
WÄRMELEITFÄHIGKEIT **12804**
WÄRMELEITUNG **2917**
WÄRMELEITVERMÖGEN **2920**
WÄRMELEITZAHL **2622**
WÄRMELEITZAHL **7269**
WÄRMEMENGE **10066**
WÄRMEMESSER **12833**
WÄRMENACHBEHANDLUNG **9666**
WÄRMESCHREIBER **12832**
WÄRMESCHUTZ **7367**
WÄRMESCHUTZ **7003**
WÄRMESCHUTZ- **8628**
WÄRMESCHUTZMITTEL **6352**
WÄRMESCHUTZSTOFF **6352**
WÄRMESCHWANKUNG **13498**
WÄRMESCHWINDUNG **12805**
WÄRMESPANNUNG **12814**
WÄRMESPEICHER **10412**
WÄRMESPEICHER **6336**
WÄRMESTOSS **12812**

WÄRMESTRAHL **6369**
WÄRMESTRAHLUNG **12811**
WÄRMESTRAHLUNG **10146**
WÄRMETAUSCHERROHR **6350**
WÄRMETÖNUNG **6348**
WÄRMETÖNUNG **6371**
WÄRMEÜBERGANG **6372**
WÄRMEÜBERGANG **9098**
WÄRMEÜBERGANG **6374**
WÄRMEÜBERGANGSZAHL **6373**
WÄRMEÜBERTRAGUNG **6372**
WÄRMEÜBERTRAGUNG **6374**
WÄRMEÜBERTRAGUNG **13111**
WÄRMEVERLUST **6353**
WÄRMEVERLUST **7760**
WÄRMEVERLUSTPRÜFUNG **1403**
WÄRMEVERZEHREND **4737**
WÄRMEWELLE **6379**
WÄRMEWERT DER ARBEITSEINHEIT **6347**
WÄRMEWIRKUNGSGRAD **12806**
WÄRMEZUFUHR **12488**
WARMFORMUMG **6627**
WARMGESENKDRÜCKEN **6643**
WARMHALTEN **6526**
WARMHALTEOFEN **6527**
WARMHÄRTE **10328**
WARMLAGER **6617**
WARMLAUFEN **6334**
WARMLAUFEN **6400**
WARMNIETEN **6635**
WARMNIETEN **6634**
WARMPRESSEN **6632**
WARMRISS **6621**
WARMRISS **6645**
WARMRISS **5240**
WARMSÄGE **6630**
WARMSÄGEN **6657**
WARMSCHMIEDEN **6626**
WARMSCHNEIDEN **6622**
WARMSCHROTMEISSEL **6640**
WARMSITZ **11389**
WARMVERGÜTUNG **6655**
WARMVERSPRÖDUNG **6625**
WARMVERSUCH **6646**
WARMWALZEN **6638**
WARMWALZEN **6636**
WARMWALZEN **6656**
WARMWASSERHEIZUNG **7784**
WARMWASSERLEITUNG **6649**
WARMZIEHEN **6624**
WARMZIEHEN **6623**

WARNPFEIFE 307
WARNZEICHEN 306
WARTUNG 814
WARTUNG 7946
WARZENBLECH 12769
WASCHEN 13632
WASCHLEDER 2234
WASSER 13640
WASSER (ANGESÄUERTES) 134
WASSER (DESTILLIERTES) 4076
WASSER (FLIESSENDES) 5466
WASSER (GEBUNDENES) 2318
WASSER (HARTES) 6281
WASSER (HYGROSKOPISCHES) 6731
WASSER (KALKHALTIGES) 6281
WASSER (KALKHALTIGES) 2227
WASSER (KEIMFREIES) 13650
WASSER (KOCHENDES) 1428
WASSER (SALZHALTIGES) 10910
WASSER (SCHLAMMIGES) 8446
WASSER (SIEDENDES) 1428
WASSER (STAGNIERENDES) 12050
WASSER (STEHENDES) 12050
WASSER (STRÖMENDES) 5466
WASSER (TOTES) 12050
WASSER (ÜBERHITZTES) 12470
WASSER ENTHÄRTEN 11748
WASSER ERHÄRTEN (IM) (ZEMENT) 6287
WASSERABFLUSS 8899
WASSERABSCHEIDER 12188
WASSERABWEISEND 8349
WASSERABWEISEND 13685
WASSERANZIEHEND 6730
WASSERAUFNAHME 52
WASSERAUFSAUGEND 6730
WASSERBAD (CHEM.) 13641
WASSERBAU 6685
WASSERBEHÄLTER 13679
WASSERBESTÄNDIG 13671
WASSERDAMPF 12192
WASSERDICHT 13686
WASSERDICHT 13688
WASSERDICHT MACHEN 13689
WASSERDICHTMACHEN 13691
WASSERDRUCK 13669
WASSERDRUCKPROBE 6695
WASSERDYNAMO 6700
WASSERENTHÄRTUNG 13676
WASSERENTZIEHUNG (CHEM.) 3728
WASSERENTZUNDERUNG 13647
WASSERFARBE 13664

WASSERFEST 13671
WASSERFREI (CHEM.) 550
WASSERFREIE SCHWEFELSÄURE 12452
WASSERFREIES KALZIUMSULFAT 549
WASSERGAS 13651
WASSERGEHALT 13645
WASSERGEKÜHLT 13683
WASSERGIER 6732
WASSERGIERIG 6730
WASSERGLAS 11808
WASSERHAHN 13644
WASSERHALTIG 6674
WASSERHÄRTUNG 13654
WASSERHÄRTUNG 13672
WASSERHAUT 5169
WASSERHEIZUNG 6648
WASSERKALK 6689
WASSERKALORIMETER 13643
WASSERKOLBEN 13667
WASSERKRAFT 13668
WASSERKRAFTANLAGE 6692
WASSERKRAFTMASCHINE 6691
WASSERKÜHLUNG 13646
WASSERLEITUNG 13666
WASSERLEITUNGSROHR 13665
WASSERLÖSLICH 11809
WASSERMANTEL 13655
WASSERMESSER 13661
WASSERMESSER (VENTURISCHER) 13532
WASSERMESSFLÜGEL 11027
WASSERMESSSCHRAUBE 11027
WASSERMÖRTEL 6690
WASSERMOTOR 6691
WASSERRAD 13692
WASSERRAD (MITTELSCHLÄCHTIGES) 7769
WASSERRAD (RÜCKENSCHLÄCHTIGES) 6465
WASSERRAD (UNTERSCHLÄCHTIGES) 13355
WASSERRAUM EINES KESSELS 13677
WASSERREINIGUNG 10019
WASSERROHR (DAMPFKESSEL) 13681
WASSERRÖHRENKESSEL 13682
WASSERSACKROHR 11514
WASSERSAMMLER 12188
WASSERSÄULE 2752
WASSERSÄULENMASCHINE 13670
WASSERSÄULENVERDICHTER 13801
WASSERSCHLAG 13653
WASSERSPIEGEL 13659
WASSERSTAND 13652
WASSERSTAND 13659
WASSERSTANDMARKE 13660

# WAS

932

WASSERSTANDSANZEIGER **13652**
WASSERSTANDSGLAS **13652**
WASSERSTOFF **6712**
WASSERSTOFF (ATOMARER) **150**
WASSERSTOFFFLAMME **6714**
WASSERSTOFFION **2112**
WASSERSTOFFIONENKONZENTRATION **6715**
WASSERSTOFFSULFID **6717**
WASSERSTOFFSUPEROXYD **6716**
WASSERSTRAHL **13656**
WASSERSTRAHLGEBLÄSE **13658**
WASSERSTRAHLLUFTPUMPE **13657**
WASSERTHERMOMETER **12834**
WASSERTURBINE **6696**
WASSERTURM **13680**
WASSERUHR **13661**
WASSERUMLAUF **2434**
WASSERUNDURCHLÄSSIGKEIT **6796**
WASSERVERGÜTEN **13673**
WASSERVERSCHLUSS **13675**
WASSERVERSORGUNG **13678**
WASSERVERSORGUNGSANLAGE **13693**
WASSERWAAGE **13259**
WASSERWERK **13693**
WASSERZIRKULATION **2434**
WASSERZUFLUSS **6915**
WATT **13694**
WATTE **13612**
WATTMETER **13698**
WATTMINUTE **13696**
WATTSEKUNDE **13697**
WATTSTUNDE **13695**
WECHSELGETRIEBE **2242**
WECHSELRAD **2243**
WECHSELSTROM **1**
WECHSELSTROM **406**
WECHSELSTROM (HOCHFREQUENZER) **3**
WECHSELSTROMDYNAMO **407**
WECHSELSTROMGENERATOR **407**
WECHSELSTROMGENERATOR **411**
WECHSELSTROMMASCHINE **407**
WECHSELSTROMMOTOR **408**
WECHSELSTROMSCHWEISSMASCHINE **2**
WECHSELTAUCHVERSUCH-PRÜFUNG **405**
WECHSELVENTIL **12882**
WECHSELZERSETZUNG **4136**
WEG (MECH.); ENTFERNUNG **4063**
WEGBEDINGUNG **9786**
WEGMESSGERÄT **9649**
WEGRADIEREN **4799**
WEGWERFPLATTEN **12896**

WEHR **13753**
WEHRKANTE **13754**
WEHRKRONE **13754**
WEICH LÖTEN **11741**
WEICHBLEI **8014**
WEICHE **12556**
WEICHES HOLZ **11746**
WEICHES WASSER **11745**
WEICHGUMMI **13610**
WEICHGUSS **7959**
WEICHHOLZ **11746**
WEICHKAUTSCHUK **13610**
WEICHLOT **11742**
WEICHLÖTEN **11743**
WEICHLÖTEN **12958**
WEICHMACHER **9475**
WEICHMETALL **11738**
WEINGEIST **8224**
WEINGEIST **313**
WEINGEISTFIRNIS **7354**
WEINGEISTLAK **7354**
WEINGEISTTHERMOMETER **11922**
WEINSÄURE **12690**
WEINSAURES ANTIMONOXYDKALI **9675**
WEINSAURES KALI **119**
WEINSAURES SALZ **12691**
WEINSTEIN (SAURER) **119**
WEINSTEINSÄURE **12690**
WEISSANLAUFEN **1378**
WEISSBLECH **12957**
WEISSBLEIERZ **2196**
WEISSES MINERALÖL **13838**
WEISSGLÜHEND **6824**
WEISSGLUT **6823**
WEISSGLUT **13832**
WEISSGOLD **13831**
WEISSKUPFER **5932**
WEISSLOT **11742**
WEISSMETALL **13836**
WEISSMETALL **888**
WEISSMETALL (HARTES) **6276**
WEISSMETALLAUSGUSS **13837**
WEISSPAUSE **1373**
WEISSWANDREIFEN **13840**
WEITERSPANNWINKEL **7411**
WEITERVERARBEITUNG **5750**
WEITMASCHIG **2578**
WELLBLECH **3198**
WELLE **875**
WELLE **9315**
WELLE (ANGETRIEBENE) **4299**

933 WHI

WELLE (BIEGSAME) **5420**
WELLE (DREIKURBELIGE) **12880**
WELLE (EINKURBELIGE) **11503**
WELLE (GEKRÖPFTE) **3309**
WELLE (HOHLE) **6547**
WELLE (KOMPRIMIERTE) **2850**
WELLE (LANGSAMLAUFENDE) **11650**
WELLE (LIEGENDE) **6587**
WELLE (MASCHB.) **11239**
WELLE (MASSIVE) **11793**
WELLE (MEHRKURBELIGE) **8478**
WELLE (PHYS.) **13699**
WELLE (SCHNELLAUFENDE) **10209**
WELLE (SENKRECHTE) **13550**
WELLE (STEHENDE) **13550**
WELLE (STEHENDE) (PHYS.) **12145**
WELLE (TREIBENDE) **4315**
WELLE (VOLLE) **11793**
WELLE MIT ÜBERSTEHENDEN ENDEN **11247**
WELLEN (GESCHRÄNKTE) **11249**
WELLEN (PARALLELE) **9064**
WELLEN (SICH KREUZENDE) **11249**
WELLENANTRIEB **7609**
WELLENBAND **11863**
WELLENBERG **3334**
WELLENBUND **2724**
WELLENDREHBANK **13289**
WELLENDREHBANK **11246**
WELLENHALS **8513**
WELLENKUPPLUNG **11240**
WELLENLAGER **1117**
WELLENLÄNGE **13700**
WELLENLEITUNG **11248**
WELLENRICHTMASCHINE **11245**
WELLENSTRANG **7607**
WELLENSTÜCK **9643**
WELLENTAL **6543**
WELLENZAPFEN **9420**
WELLIGGRAT **2619**
WELLIGKEIT **13701**
WELLIGKEIT **11419**
WELLROHR **3199**
WENDEEISEN **12638**
WENDEGETRIEBE **10544**
WENDELRUTSCHE **11914**
WENDELTREPPE **11919**
WENDEPLATTE **8044**
WENDEPUNKT **9564**
WENDERAD **7975**
WENDESCHLÜSSEL **1195**
WERFEN **13629**

WERFEN (SICH) **13628**
WERG **13073**
WERK **5010**
WERKBANK **1167**
WERKBANKBOHRMASCHINE **1168**
WERKBLEL **3409**
WERKE **9461**
WERKFÜHRER **5541**
WERKHOLZ **12937**
WERKMEISTER **5541**
WERKSGERÄT **4794**
WERKSTATT **11364**
WERKSTATT **13968**
WERKSTATTABNAHMELEHRE **5011**
WERKSTÄTTE **13968**
WERKSTATTSCHWEISSEN **11362**
WERKSTATTZEICHNUNG **11361**
WERKSTEIN **761**
WERKSTOFFPRÜFUNG **12782**
WERKSTÜCK **9293**
WERKSTÜCKAUFNAHME **4985**
WERKZEICHNUNG **11363**
WERKZEUG **12994**
WERKZEUG (EINFACHWIRKENDES) **11496**
WERKZEUGAUSRÜSTUNG **13015**
WERKZEUGBAUHAMMER **13014**
WERKZEUGBEFEHL **13001**
WERKZEUGFABRIKATION **13006**
WERKZEUGKOFFER **12997**
WERKZEUGKORREKTUR **3521**
WERKZEUGMASCHINE **7859**
WERKZEUGSCHLEIFMASCHINE **13002**
WERKZEUGSCHLOSSER **13008**
WERKZEUGSCHNELLSTAHL **10207**
WERKZEUGSCHRANK **12998**
WERKZEUGSTAHL **13009**
WERKZEUGSTAHL **7857**
WERKZEUGTASCHE **12996**
WERKZEUGVERSATZ **13007**
WERKZEUGWECHSELVORRICHTUNG **13000**
WERKZEUGWECHSELZEIT **12999**
WERT (ERRECHNETER) **1858**
WERT (MITTLERER) **8073**
WERT (RECHNERISCHER) **1858**
WERT (REZIPROKER) **10280**
WERTIGKEIT **13452**
WETTERBESTÄNDIG **13723**
WETTERFANG **247**
WETTERFEST **13723**
WETTERLEITUNG **247**
WETTERLUTTE **247**

# WIC

934

WHISKER-WACHSTUM 13828
WICKELDRAHT 1255
WICKLUNG 13862
WIDDER (HYDRAULISCHER) 6694
WIDDERKOPF 10191
WIDDERSTOSS 13653
WIDERLAGER 57
WIDERSTAND 10484
WIDERSTAND (ELEKTRISCHER) 4528
WIDERSTAND (INNERER) 7072
WIDERSTAND (MAGNETISCHER) 10444
WIDERSTAND (SCHEINBARER) 6794
WIDERSTAND (SPEZIFISCHER) 4548
WIDERSTAND ÜBERWINDEN (EINEN) 8929
WIDERSTANDS-BEIWERT (ELEKTRISCHER) 2627
WIDERSTANDSARBEIT 13944
WIDERSTANDSBEIWERT (LUFT) 4200
WIDERSTANDSDEHNUNGSMESSTREIFEN 10494
WIDERSTANDSDIAGRAMM 10489
WIDERSTANDSDRAHT 10501
WIDERSTANDSFÄHIGKEIT 10502
WIDERSTANDSFÄHIGKEIT 4548
WIDERSTANDSFÄHIGKEIT 1918
WIDERSTANDSHARTLÖTEN 10487
WIDERSTANDSKRAFT 10484
WIDERSTANDSMOLARE 8351
WIDERSTANDSMOMENT 8374
WIDERSTANDSMOMENT 11115
WIDERSTANDSOFEN (ELEKTRISCHER) 10490
WIDERSTANDSPUNKTSCHWEISSEN 10493
WIDERSTANDSPYROMETER 10495
WIDERSTANDSREGLER 10563
WIDERSTANDSSCHWEISSEN 10500
WIDERSTANDSSCHWEISSUNG 10500
WIDERSTANDSSTUMPFNAHT 1799
WIDERSTANDSSTUMPFSCHWEISSEN 1807
WIDERSTANDSSTUMPFSCHWEISSEN 13413
WIDERSTANDSSTUMPFSCHWEISSUNG 10488
WIDERSTANDSTHERMOMETER 10495
WIDERSTANDSVERLUST 7759
WIDERSTANDSVERMÖGEN 10502
WIDERSTANDSZAHL 2632
WIDERTANDSLEGIERUNGEN 10486
WIEDERERHITZEN 10424
WIEDERERHITZEN 10425
WIEDERGEWINNEN 10295
WIEDERGEWINNUNG 10296
WIEDERHERSTELLUNGSKOSTEN 3208
WIEDERHOLUNGSVERSUCH 10522
WIEDERINGANGSETZEN 10509
WIEDERINSTANDSETZEN 10460

WIEDERINSTANDSETZUNG 10459
WIEDERINSTANDSETZUNG 10287
WIEDERVERWENDUNG 10246
WIEDERVERWERTUNG 10246
WIEDERVERWERTUNG 10296
WIEDERZUSAMMENSETZEN 10244
WIEDERZUSAMMENSETZUNG 10245
WIEGEN 13746
WIND 1315
WIND 243
WIND (SAUERSTOFFANGEREICHERTER) 4770
WINDBELASTUNG 13857
WINDDRUCK 13858
WINDE 13851
WINDE 11035
WINDEISEN 12638
WINDFAHNE 13860
WINDFANG 3276
WINDFLÜGEL 5033
WINDFORM 13299
WINDFRISCHEN 300
WINDKAMMER 241
WINDKANÄLE 247
WINDKESSEL 294
WINDKRAFTMASCHINE 13855
WINDLAUF 5695
WINDLEITUNG 1367
WINDLEITUNG 1314
WINDMESSER 503
WINDMOTOR 13855
WINDRAD 13861
WINDRING 1774
WINDROSE 2800
WINDSCHIEFE FLÄCHE 11535
WINDSCHUTZSCHEIBE 13872
WINDSICHTUNG 290
WINDSICHTUNG 248
WINDTURBINE 13859
WINDUNG EINER SCHRAUBENLINIE 13278
WINDUNG EINER SPIRALE 2646
WINKEL 11223
WINKEL 12014
WINKEL (EINSPRINGENDER) 10243
WINKEL (GEOM.) 505
WINKEL (KÖRPERLICHER) 11776
WINKEL (RECHTER) 10577
WINKEL (SPITZER) 155
WINKEL (STUMPFER) 8717
WINKELARM 4726
WINKELBESCHLEUNIGUNG 537
WINKELBEWEGUNG 544

WINKELEISEN **514**
WINKELEISEN **506**
WINKELEISEN (GLEICHSCHENKLIGES) **4781**
WINKELEISEN (INNEN SCHARF) **11271**
WINKELEISEN (INNEN VOLL) **10794**
WINKELEISEN (UNGLEICHSCHENKLIGES) **13356**
WINKELEISEN AUS PAKETEISEN **7137**
WINKELFLANSCH **512**
WINKELFRÄSER **540**
WINKELFRÄSER **543**
WINKELGESCHWINDIGKEIT **546**
WINKELHAHN **511**
WINKELHAKEN **12014**
WINKELHALBIERENDE **1268**
WINKELHEBEL **1131**
WINKELKONSOLE **4726**
WINKELLEHRE **513**
WINKELMASS **12014**
WINKELMESSER **9956**
WINKELMESSER **6004**
WINKELPLATTE **533**
WINKELPROFIL **506**
WINKELRAD **1229**
WINKELRAD **4143**
WINKELRÄDERGETRIEBE **1227**
WINKELRECHT **8652**
WINKELRIEMENGETRIEBE **1149**
WINKELSCHNITT **539**
WINKELSCHRUMPFUNG **542**
WINKELSTAHL (LEGIERTER) **369**
WINKELSTOSSVERBINDUNG **3179**
WINKELTRANSPORTEUR **10308**
WINKELTREUE KONFORME ABBILDUNG **8872**
WINKELVERSCHIEBUNG **541**
WINKELWULSTEISEN **1713**
WINKELWULSTEISEN **1712**
WINKELZAHN **4144**
WIPPE **11253**
WIRBEL **9532**
WIRBEL (EINER KETTE) **12561**
WIRBEL (EINES HAKENS) **12561**
WIRBEL (PHYS.) **13606**
WIRBELHAKEN **12564**
WIRBELKAMMER **12551**
WIRBELSTROM **4438**
WIRBELSTROMBREMSE **4439**
WIRBELSTRÖME **4440**
WIRBELUNG **13827**
WIRKLICHLEISTUNG **1540**
WIRKUNGSGRAD **4463**
WIRKUNGSGRAD (ELEKTROTHERMISCHER) **4649**

WIRKUNGSGRAD (ENERGETISCHER) **4746**
WIRKUNGSGRAD (HYDRAULISCHER) **6684**
WIRKUNGSGRAD (INDIZIERTER) **6872**
WIRKUNGSGRAD (KOMMERZIELLER) **2781**
WIRKUNGSGRAD (MANOMETRISCHER) **7984**
WIRKUNGSGRAD (MECHANISCHER) **8100**
WIRKUNGSGRAD (RÄUMLICHER) **13602**
WIRKUNGSGRAD (VOLUMETRISCHER) **13602**
WIRKUNGSGRAD (WIRTSCHAFTLICHER) **2781**
WIRKUNGSQUERSCHNITT **3371**
WIRKWIDERSTAND **10261**
WIRSTSCHAFT (GESUNDE) **932**
WIRTSCHAFTLICHKEIT EINES BETRIEBES **9462**
WIRTSCHAFTSWASSER **13649**
WISMUT **1269**
WISMUT (SALPETERSAURES) **1271**
WISMUTSESQUIOXYD **1272**
WISMUTCHLORID **1270**
WISMUTGLANZ **1275**
WISMUTLOT **1274**
WISMUTNITRAT **1271**
WISMUTNITRAT (BASISCHES) **1273**
WISMUTSUBNITRAT **1273**
WITHERIT **13911**
WITTERUNGSEINFLÜSSE **792**
WÖLBHALBMESSER **10168**
WÖLBKEHLNAHT **3077**
WÖLBUNG **3396**
WÖLBUNG **2619**
WÖLBUNG **1720**
WÖLBUNG **1889**
WÖLBUNG EINER RIEMENSCHEIBE **3398**
WOLFRAM **13262**
WOLFRAM-INERTGAS-SCHWEISSEN **6906**
WOLFRAMBRONZE **13263**
WOLFRAMDRAHTLAMPE **13264**
WOLFRAMEISEN **5115**
WOLFRAMIT **13912**
WOLFRAMSÄURE **8876**
WOLFRAMSÄUREANHYDRID **13266**
WOLFRAMSTAHL **13265**
WOLFRAMTRIOXYD **13266**
WOLLFETT **13933**
WOODRUFFKEIL **13929**
WUCHT **7308**
WÜHLGRUBBER **3457**
WULFENIT **13991**
WULST **1082**
WULSTEISEN **1716**
WULSTMASCHINE **1089**
WULSTWINKEL **1712**

# WUR
936

WÜRFEL **3445**
WÜRFELKOHLE **2606**
WURFGITTER **11628**
WÜRGELPUMPE **10758**
WURM **13979**
WURMGETRIEBE **13974**
WURMSCHRAUBE **6156**
WURMSTICHIG **13976**
WURZEL (BIQUADRATISCHE) **5609**
WURZEL (FÜNFTE) **5147**
WURZEL (MATH.) **10714**
WURZEL (VIERTE) **5609**
WURZEL (ZWEITE) **12027**
WURZELFLANKE **10720**
WURZELKREIS **10723**
WURZELSEITIGE GEGENNAHT **904**
WURZELSPALT **10727**
X-ACHSE **872**
X-FUGENNAHT OHNE LUFTSPALT **2525**
XENON **14004**
XEROGRAPHIE **14005**
XYLOL **14006**
Y-ACHSE **873**
YARD **14007**
YTTERBIUM **14019**
YTTRIUM **14020**
Z-EISEN **14023**
ZACKIG **6862**
ZÄH **13067**
ZÄHES EISEN **13068**
ZÄHFLÜSSIG **13577**
ZÄHFLÜSSIGKEIT **13576**
ZÄHIGKEIT **13576**
ZÄHIGKEIT **13071**
ZÄHIGKEIT **12737**
ZÄHIGKEITSMESSER **13574**
ZÄHIGKEITSREIBUNG **5473**
ZAHL **3940**
ZAHL (GANZE) **7012**
ZAHL (GEBROCHENE) **5613**
ZAHL (GERADE) **4872**
ZAHL (IMAGINÄRE) **6781**
ZAHL (IRRATIONALE) **7162**
ZAHL (IRRATIONALE) **10260**
ZAHL (KOMPLEXE) **2813**
ZAHL (NATÜRLICHE) **7012**
ZAHL (RATIONALE) **10235**
ZAHL (UNGERADE) **8725**
ZAHL (ZUSAMMENGESETZTE) **2820**
ZAHLENWERT **8697**
ZÄHLER **3229**

ZÄHLER (FLÜSSIGKEITS-) **8214**
ZÄHLER (MATH.) **8693**
ZÄHLVORRICHTUNG **3229**
ZÄHLWERK MIT SPRINGENDEN ZAHLEN **3559**
ZAHN **13016**
ZAHN (BEARBEITETER) **3514**
ZAHN (UNBEARBEITETER) **2059**
ZAHN UND EINZAHNUNG **3761**
ZAHNBOGEN **13024**
ZAHNBREITE **1579**
ZAHNDICKE **12846**
ZÄHNEZAHL **8691**
ZAHNFLANKE **13018**
ZAHNFLANKE (ÜBER DEM TEILKREIS) **4997**
ZAHNFLANKE (UNTER DEM TEILKREIS) **5351**
ZAHNFLANKENZIRKEL **8726**
ZAHNFORM **13019**
ZAHNFUSS **10725**
ZAHNFUSSHÖHE **3681**
ZAHNFUSSKEGEL **10718**
ZAHNFUSSLÄNGE **3681**
ZAHNFUSSWINKEL **10716**
ZAHNGESPERRE **9138**
ZAHNHOBEL **13027**
ZAHNHÖHE **13017**
ZAHNHÖHE **12846**
ZAHNHÖHE **13845**
ZAHNKETTE **11432**
ZAHNKOPF **9569**
ZAHNKOPFLÄNGE **164**
ZAHNKRANZ **10594**
ZAHNKRANZ **13023**
ZAHNKRONE **9569**
ZAHNKUPPLUNG **2461**
ZAHNLÄNGE **3785**
ZAHNLÜCKE **6548**
ZAHNMESS-SCHIEBLEHRE **5899**
ZAHNPROFIL **13019**
ZAHNPROFIL **13020**
ZAHNRAD **5903**
ZAHNRAD **5889**
ZAHNRAD (BEARBEITETES) **3508**
ZAHNRAD (GESCHNITTENES) **3508**
ZAHNRAD (KLEINERES) **9335**
ZAHNRAD (ROH GEGOSSENES) **10773**
ZAHNRAD MIT BORDSCHEIBEN **11402**
ZAHNRAD-NONIUSSCHUBLEHRE **5900**
ZAHNRADANTRIEB **13025**
ZAHNRADANTRIEB **5892**
ZAHNRÄDERPRÜFMASCHINE **5902**
ZAHNRADFRÄSER **5898**

937 ZEI

ZAHNRADGETRIEBE **5907**
ZAHNRADGETRIEBE **13021**
ZAHNRADPUMPE **5895**
ZAHNRADSATZ (VERSCHIEBBARER) **11602**
ZAHNRADSCHNEIDEMASCHINE **5891**
ZAHNRADSTAHL **5904**
ZAHNRADVORGELEGE **7050**
ZAHNRÜCKEN **12514**
ZAHNSCHEITEL **12514**
ZAHNSEKTOR **13024**
ZAHNSTANGE **13022**
ZAHNSTANGE **10124**
ZAHNSTANGE **10119**
ZAHNSTANGENGETRIEBE **10120**
ZAHNSTANGENSCHIEBER **1359**
ZAHNSTANGENTEILVORRICHTUNG **10123**
ZAHNSTANGENWINDE **10121**
ZAHNSTÄRKE **2365**
ZAHNSTÄRKE **12846**
ZAHNSTÄRKE (IM ROLLKREIS) **678**
ZAHNSTÄRKE IM ROLLKREIS **2431**
ZAHNTEILKREIS **9403**
ZAHNTEILUNG **9408**
ZAHNTEILUNG **2423**
ZAHNTIEFE **13845**
ZAHNTRIEB **13021**
ZAHNWURZEL **1036**
ZAHNWURZEL **10724**
ZANGE **12987**
ZANGENFUTTER **2728**
ZANGENFUTTER **2729**
ZANGENSPANNFUTTER **11979**
ZAPFEN **9420**
ZAPFEN **9419**
ZAPFEN **9315**
ZAPFEN **7256**
ZAPFEN (TISCHLEREI) **12740**
ZAPFENBOHRER **9316**
ZAPFENDREHRINGE **3312**
ZAPFENDRUCK **7259**
ZAPFENDÜSE **9338**
ZAPFENFUGE **7231**
ZAPFENGELENK **9318**
ZAPFENLAGER **11905**
ZAPFENLAGER **1117**
ZAPFENLAUFFLÄCHE **1116**
ZAPFENLOCH **8401**
ZAPFENREIBUNG **7258**
ZAPFENSÄGE **12741**
ZAPFENSCHNEIDMASCHINE **12742**
ZAPFENSTREICHMASS **8399**

ZAPFENZAHNRAD **9324**
ZAPFHAHN **1234**
ZAPFWELLE **9745**
ZAPONLACK **14022**
ZÄSIUM **1833**
ZÄSIUM **2197**
ZAUM (PRONYSCHER) **9920**
ZAUN **5094**
ZECHE **8300**
ZECHENKOKS **2662**
ZEHNECK **3644**
ZEICHEN **3940**
ZEICHEN **2255**
ZEICHEN **8012**
ZEICHEN (CHEMISCHES) **2315**
ZEICHEN (SICHTBARES) **13580**
ZEICHENBRETT **4231**
ZEICHENBÜRO **4238**
ZEICHENBÜRO **4198**
ZEICHENFEDER **7999**
ZEICHENGERÄT **4236**
ZEICHENLEINWAND **13083**
ZEICHENPAPIER **4240**
ZEICHENSAAL **4238**
ZEICHENSTIFT **7478**
ZEICHENTISCH **4243**
ZEICHENUTENSILIEN **4236**
ZEICHNEN **4195**
ZEICHNEN **4246**
ZEICHNER **4213**
ZEICHNUNG **4229**
ZEICHNUNG **4245**
ZEICHNUNG (AUSGEZOGENE) **6941**
ZEICHNUNG (EINE) ANLEGEN **2742**
ZEICHNUNG (EINE) AUSTUSCHEN **2742**
ZEICHNUNG (ENDGÜLTIGE) **5185**
ZEICHNUNG (GEOMETRISCHE) **5928**
ZEICHNUNG (GETUSCHTE) **12965**
ZEICHNUNG (MASSSTÄBLICHE) **10983**
ZEICHNUNG (SCHATTIERTE) **11235**
ZEICHNUNG (SCHEMATISCHE) **3836**
ZEICHNUNG (TECHNISCHE) **8099**
ZEICHNUNG IN NATÜRLICHER GRÖSSE **5724**
ZEICHNUNG MIT EINGESCHRIEBENEN MASSEN **3959**
ZEICHNUNGSMASSSTAB **10973**
ZEIGER **13153**
ZEIGER **6226**
ZEIGER (EINES INSTRUMENTS) **6868**
ZEIGERAUSSCHLAG **3699**
ZEIGERWERK **3843**
ZEILE **10812**

# ZEI 938

ZEILENSTRUKTUR 979
ZEIT 12943
ZEIT DER ANFANGSAUSFÄLLE 6908
ZEITEINHEIT 13376
ZEITERSPARNIS 10949
ZEITKONSTANTE 12944
ZEITREGLER 3611
ZEITSTANDFESTIGKEIT 3328
ZEITSTANDFESTIGKEIT 3327
ZEITSTRECKE 7101
ZELLE (ELEKTR.) 2126
ZELLE (GALVANISCHE) 5782
ZELLE (PHOTOELEKTRISCHE) 9259
ZELLENKÜHLER 2129
ZELLHORN 2130
ZELLSTOFF 2131
ZELLULOID 2130
ZELLULOSE 2131
ZELLULOSEAZETAT 2132
ZELLULOSEAZETAT 91
ZELLULOSENITRAT 6176
ZEMENT 2133
ZEMENT (LANGSAM BINDENDER) 11648
ZEMENT (LUFTHÄRTENDER) 302
ZEMENT (SCHNELL BINDENDER) 10107
ZEMENTATION 2142
ZEMENTATION IN GASATMOSPHÄRE 1992
ZEMENTAUSHÄRTUNG 3484
ZEMENTBETON 2135
ZEMENTIEREN 2142
ZEMENTIEREN 2134
ZEMENTIEREN 2146
ZEMENTIEREN 2141
ZEMENTIEREN (MIT KOHLENSTOFF) 1987
ZEMENTIERKISTE 3075
ZEMENTIEROFEN 3074
ZEMENTIERUNG 2141
ZEMENTIERUNG (GLEICHARTIGE) 1993
ZEMENTIERUNG (SELEKTIVE) 1995
ZEMENTIT 2147
ZEMENTKUPFER 2136
ZEMENTMILCH 6152
ZEMENTMÖRTEL 2137
ZEMENTROHR 2898
ZEMENTROHR MIT EISENEINLAGE 5109
ZEMENTSTAHL 2138
ZEMENTSTAHLHERSTELLUNG 2142
ZEMENTSTAHLSTAB 1328
ZENTIMETER 2158
ZENTIMETER-GRAMM-SEKUNDE-SYSTEM 2159
ZENTNER (50 KGS ENV.) 6668

ZENTRALE (HYDROELKTRISCHE) 6701
ZENTRALE (WASSERELEKTRISCHE) 6701
ZENTRALHEIZUNG 2160
ZENTRALLINIE 874
ZENTRALPROJEKTION 10137
ZENTRALSCHMIERUNG 7809
ZENTRIER-U. PLANDREHMASCHINE 2188
ZENTRIERBOHRER (KOMBINIERTER) 2763
ZENTRIEREN 2187
ZENTRIEREN 2163
ZENTRIERFÜHRUNG 13087
ZENTRIERLEISTE 10413
ZENTRIERRING 10413
ZENTRIERRING 2087
ZENTRIERRING 2154
ZENTRIERSTIFT 2153
ZENTRIERSTIFT 1513
ZENTRIERVORRICHTUNG 2166
ZENTRIERWINKEL 2173
ZENTRIFUGALBREMSE 2175
ZENTRIFUGALKRAFT 2180
ZENTRIFUGALMOMENT 2183
ZENTRIFUGALÖLER 2182
ZENTRIFUGALPUMPE 13269
ZENTRIFUGALPUMPE 10758
ZENTRIFUGALPUMPE 2184
ZENTRIFUGALREGLER 2185
ZENTRIFUGE 6703
ZENTRIFUGGALGEBLÄSE 2179
ZENTRIFUGIEREN 6702
ZENTRIPETALBESCHLEUNIGUNG 2189
ZENTRIPETALKRAFT 2190
ZENTRIWINKEL 507
ZENTRUMBOHRER 2164
ZENTRUMSCHEIBE (FÜR ZIRKEL) 6594
ZER 2195
ZERBRECHLICH 5621
ZERBRECHLICHKEIT 5622
ZERBRECHLICHKEIT 1628
ZERBRÖCKLUNG 4044
ZERESIN 2194
ZERFALL 3418
ZERFALLEN 4044
ZERFALLEN 4043
ZERFLIESSEN 3732
ZERFLIESSEND 3734
ZERFLIESSLICH 3734
ZERFLIESSLICHKEIT 3733
ZERIUM 2195
ZERKLEINERN 1588
ZERKLEINERN 1580

## 939 ZIN

ZERKLEINERUNG **1588**
ZERKLEINERUNGSMASCHINE **3419**
ZERKNALL **4935**
ZERKNALLEN **4933**
ZERLEGBAR **3671**
ZERLEGBAR **4027**
ZERLEGEN **12604**
ZERLEGEN **12600**
ZERLEGEN (CHEM.) **3672**
ZERLEGT **7329**
ZERLEGUNG **12604**
ZERLEGUNG (CHEM.) **3674**
ZERLEGUNG DES LICHTS **3676**
ZERLEGUNG VON KRÄFTEN **10505**
ZERREIBEN **13222**
ZERREISS(PRÜF)MASCHINE **12752**
ZERREISSFESTIGKEIT **4057**
ZERREISSMASCHINE **7846**
ZERREISSVERSUCH **12751**
ZERSETZBAR **3671**
ZERSETZEN (SICH) **3673**
ZERSETZLICHKEIT **6**
ZERSETZUNG **3674**
ZERSETZUNG **10769**
ZERSETZUNGSDESTILLATION **3805**
ZERSETZUNGSPANNUNG **3675**
ZERSETZUNGSWÄRME **6357**
ZERSTÄUBEN **4043**
ZERSTÄUBEN (EINE FLÜSSIGKEIT) **808**
ZERSTÄUBEN EINER FLÜSSIGKEIT **810**
ZERSTÄUBER **809**
ZERSTÄUBER **272**
ZERSTÄUBUNG **3418**
ZERSTÄUBUNG **811**
ZERSTÄUBUNGS-UND SPRITZMASCHINEN (FRÜCHTE UND HOPFEN) **11970**
ZERSTÄUBUNGS-UND SPRITZMASCHINEN (GRAS UND GETREIDE) **11971**
ZERSTOSSEN **9712**
ZERSTREUUNG **4051**
ZERSTREUUNGSLINSE **4095**
ZERUSSIT **2196**
ZEUGSCHMIED **13008**
ZICKZACKNIETUNG **14034**
ZIEGEL **12934**
ZIEGEL (GEBRANNTER) **1760**
ZIEGELERDE **1598**
ZIEGELMAUERWERK **1602**
ZIEGELMEHL **9724**
ZIEGELSTEIN **1596**
ZIEGELSTEINFUNDAMENT **1599**

ZIEGESTEINSCHICHT **3259**
ZIEHBANK **4218**
ZIEHBANK **10023**
ZIEHBAR **4361**
ZIEHBARKEIT **4228**
ZIEHBARKEIT **4363**
ZIEHEISEN **4223**
ZIEHEN **4230**
ZIEHEN **4970**
ZIEHEN **4215**
ZIEHEN VON DRAHT **13888**
ZIEHEN VON ROHREN **13249**
ZIEHFEDER **4241**
ZIEHFEDEREINSATZ **9160**
ZIEHFEDERZIRKEL **2803**
ZIEHFETT **4233**
ZIEHKLINGE **4221**
ZIEHMESSER **4221**
ZIEHMESSING **4232**
ZIEHPRESSE (HYDRAULISCHE) **6682**
ZIEHRING **4234**
ZIEHSCHLEIF- U. LÄPPMASCHINE **6565**
ZIEHSCHLEIFEN **6564**
ZIEHSPUREN (V-FÖRMIGE) **2282**
ZIEHWERKZEUG **4234**
ZIEHWERKZEUG **4244**
ZIEL **12682**
ZIELLINIE **7601**
ZIERBRONZE **1663**
ZIERLEISTEN **10531**
ZIERLEISTEN (STRANGGEPRESSTE) **4969**
ZIERRING **5230**
ZIFFERBLATT **3837**
ZIGARETTENANZÜNDER **2396**
ZIMMEREI **2006**
ZIMMERMANN **2005**
ZIMMERMANNBOHRER **818**
ZIMMERWÄRME **10713**
ZINK **14035**
ZINK (CHROMSAURES) **14039**
ZINK (ESSIGSAURES) **14036**
ZINK (KOHLENSAURES) **14037**
ZINK (SALZSAURES) **14038**
ZINK (UMGESCHMOLZENES) **10341**
ZINKAZETAT **14036**
ZINKBLECH **11327**
ZINKBLENDE **1324**
ZINKCHLORID **14038**
ZINKCHROMAT **14039**
ZINKCHROMGELB **14039**
ZINKDRAHT **14048**

**ZIN.** 940

ZINKENSCHNEIDMASCHINE **4179**
ZINKERZ **14042**
ZINKGRIES **8404**
ZINKKARBONAT **14037**
ZINKOXYD **14043**
ZINKROHR **14047**
ZINKSCHWEFEL (SAURER) **14046**
ZINKSPÄNE **14040**
ZINKSPAT **1836**
ZINKSTAUB **1374**
ZINKSULFAT **14046**
ZINKVITRIOL **14046**
ZINKWEISS **14043**
ZINN **12953**
ZINN (CHEMISCH REINES) **2324**
ZINN IN KÖRNERN **6042**
ZINNABARIT **2400**
ZINNASCHE **12098**
ZINNBLECH **11326**
ZINNBRONZE **9246**
ZINNCHLORÜR **12100**
ZINNDICHLORID **12100**
ZINNDIOXYD **12098**
ZINNDISULFID **12099**
ZINNERZ **12956**
ZINNFOLIE **12955**
ZINNHYDROXYD **12097**
ZINNLOT **11742**
ZINNMONOSULFID **12103**
ZINNOBER **13535**
ZINNOBER **2400**
ZINNOBERROT **13535**
ZINNOXYDHYDRAT **12097**
ZINNOXYDNATRON **11732**
ZINNOXYDUL **12102**
ZINNROHR **12960**
ZINNSALZ **12100**
ZINNSÄURE **12097**
ZINNSÄUREANHYDRID **12098**
ZINNSÄURESALZ **12095**
ZINNSODA **11732**
ZINNSTEIN **12959**
ZINNSULFÜR **12103**
ZINNTETRACHLORID **12096**
ZINNÜBERZUG **2602**
ZIRKEL **9022**
ZIRKEL (DREISPITZIGER) **13187**
ZIRKELVERLÄNGERUNG **7521**
ZIRKONIUM **14049**
ZIRKULATION **2433**
ZIRKULATIONSSCHMIERUNG **5442**

ZIRKULATIONSVENTIL **1819**
ZIRKULIEREN **2432**
ZISSOIDE **2438**
ZISTERNE **2439**
ZISTERNENWAGEN **12626**
ZITIEREN **10113**
ZITRONENSÄURE **2441**
ZOLL (ENGLISCHER) **6830**
ZOLLSTOCK **5512**
ZONE (IONISIERTE) **7128**
ZONENABTASTEN **10992**
ZONENSCHMELZEN **14050**
ZOPF FÜR PACKUNGEN **5863**
ZOPFENDE EINES ROHRES **11901**
ZORESEISEN **7112**
ZUBEHÖR **5283**
ZUBEHÖR **74**
ZUBEHÖRTEILE **74**
ZUCKERRÜBENHEBER UND PFLÜGE **12440**
ZUCKERRÜBENKÖPFER **12441**
ZUCKERRÜBENLICHTMASCHINEN **12438**
ZUCKERRÜBENVOLLERNTEGERÄTE **12439**
ZUFAHRT **1603**
ZUFLUSS **6915**
ZUFLUSS **6943**
ZUFLUSSGESCHWINDIGKEIT **6950**
ZUFLUSSROHR **12489**
ZUFUHR (DOPPELTE) **4138**
ZUFUHRROLLGANG **4775**
ZUFÜHRUNG **5063**
ZUFÜHRWALZE **5074**
ZUG **257**
ZUG **4196**
ZUG **12743**
ZUG **9973**
ZUG (KÜNSTLICHER) **8098**
ZUG (MECH.) **9970**
ZUG (NATÜRLICHER) **8501**
ZUG (PARALLEL ZUR FASER) **9968**
ZUG (SENKRECHT ZUR FASER) **9967**
ZUG EINER KURVE **1555**
ZUG EINES SCHORNSTEINS **4212**
ZUGÄNGLICH **73**
ZUGÄNGLICHKEIT **72**
ZUGANKER **12917**
ZUGBEANSPRUCHUNG **12747**
ZUGBOLZEN **12755**
ZUGEBAUT **1705**
ZUGEFÜHRTE LEISTUNG **4747**
ZUGELASSENER DREHDURCHMESSER ÜBER BETT **12547**
ZUGELASTIZITÄT **4491**

941 ZUS

ZUGFEDER **12759**
ZUGFESTIGKEIT **12749**
ZUGFESTIGKEIT **13331**
ZUGFÖRDERUNG **13088**
ZUGHAKEN **4217**
ZUGHAKEN **6307**
ZUGKNOTEN **8651**
ZUGKRAFT (EINES TRAKTORS) **13089**
ZUGKRAFT (FESTIGKEITSL.) **12745**
ZUGKRAFT EINES MAGNETEN **13090**
ZUGMASCHINE **13097**
ZUGMASCHINE **13091**
ZUGMESSER (FÜR SCHORNSTEINE UND GEBLÄSE) **4211**
ZUGNAHT **1085**
ZUGQUERSCHNITT **3376**
ZUGREGLER **3603**
ZUGRIFF (DIREKTER) **10198**
ZUGSCHRAUBE **12758**
ZUGSPANNUNG **12747**
ZUGSPANNUNG **12750**
ZUGSPINDELDREHMASCHINE **11603**
ZUGSTAB **12754**
ZUGSTANGE **12917**
ZUGSTANGE **4217**
ZUGTRUMM (EINES FLASCHENZUGS) **5023**
ZUGVERFORMUNG **12744**
ZUGVERSUCH **12748**
ZUGVERSUCH **12751**
ZUGWAGEN **13097**
ZULÄSSIGE ABWEICHUNG **359**
ZULAUFLEITUNG **12489**
ZULEITUNGSKANAL **6319**
ZULEITUNGSROHR **12489**
ZÜNDER **6758**
ZUNDER **6217**
ZUNDERBESTÄNDIGKEIT **10980**
ZUNDERFLECK **5367**
ZÜNDFÄHIGKEIT **6913**
ZÜNDFOLGE **5260**
ZÜNDGESCHWINDIGKEIT **10230**
ZÜNDGESCHWINDIGKEIT **11870**
ZÜNDKERZE **11841**
ZÜNDKERZE **11838**
ZÜNDKERZENGEHÄUSE **11839**
ZÜNDLEGIERUNG **10053**
ZÜNDPUNKT **6759**
ZÜNDSCHALTER **6766**
ZÜNDSPULE **6761**
ZÜNDSTELLE **677**
ZÜNDTEMPERATUR **12727**
ZÜNDUNG **6770**

ZÜNDUNG **6760**
ZÜNDUNG (ELEKTRISCHE) **4514**
ZÜNDUNGPRÜFLAMPE **6769**
ZÜNDVERSTELLUNG **11837**
ZÜNDVERTEILER **6762**
ZÜNDVORRICHTUNG **6758**
ZÜNDZEITVERSTELLUNG **6768**
ZURICHTEN **10786**
ZURICHTEN **10775**
ZURÜCKGEWINNEN **10295**
ZURÜCKGEWINNUNG **10296**
ZURÜCKPRALLEN **10273**
ZURÜCKSCHLAGEN DER FLAMME **892**
ZURÜCKSPRINGEN **10273**
ZURÜCKSTRAHLEN **10382**
ZÜRÜCKWEISUNG **10431**
ZURÜCKWERFEN **10382**
ZUSAMMENBALLUNG **2572**
ZUSAMMENBAUEN **4805**
ZUSAMMENDRÜCKBAR **2853**
ZUSAMMENDRÜCKBARKEIT **2852**
ZUSAMMENDRÜCKEN **10028**
ZUSAMMENGEGOSSEN **2054**
ZUSAMMENGESETZTER ÄTHER **4837**
ZUSAMMENLAUFEN **3062**
ZUSAMMENLAUFEND **3064**
ZUSAMMENPASSEN **8042**
ZUSAMMENSCHRAUBEN **11022**
ZUSAMMENSCHRAUBEN **11065**
ZUSAMMENSCHWEISSEN **13755**
ZUSAMMENSETZUNG **2823**
ZUSAMMENSETZUNG **229**
ZUSAMMENSETZUNG (CHEMISCHE) **2299**
ZUSAMMENSETZUNG VON KRÄFTEN **2825**
ZUSAMMENSINTERN **11509**
ZUSAMMENSTAUCHEN **7265**
ZUSAMMENSTAUCHEN **7263**
ZUSAMMENZÄHLEN **169**
ZUSAMMENZÄHLEN **162**
ZUSAMMENZIEHEN **3046**
ZUSATZ **169**
ZUSATZ **394**
ZUSATZDYNAMO **1456**
ZUSATZEINRICHTUNG **812**
ZUSATZELEMENT **168**
ZUSATZELEMENTE **395**
ZUSATZMASCHINE **1456**
ZUSATZVENTIL **1819**
ZUSATZVERLUST **170**
ZUSATZWERKSTOFF **5159**
ZUSCHÄRFUNGSWINKEL **12995**

**ZUS** 942

ZUSCHIEBUNG 5063
ZUSCHLAG 5489
ZUSCHLÄGER 6225
ZUSCHLAGHAMMER 11573
ZUSCHLAGSTOFF 228
ZUSCHNEIDEN 10507
ZUSETZEN (WASSER) 163
ZUSTAND (FESTER) 11795
ZUSTAND (IN FREIEM) (CHEM.) 6818
ZUSTAND (IN UNGEBUNDENEM) 6818
ZUSTAND (KRITISCHER) 3349
ZUSTANDSÄNDERUNG 2238
ZUSTANDSÄNDERUNG (NICHTUMKEHRBARE) 7170
ZUSTANDSÄNDERUNG (UMKEHRBARE) 10539
ZUSTANDSDIAGRAMM 2984
ZUSTANDSGLEICHUNG 4783
ZUSTRÖMGESCHWINDIGKEIT 6950
ZUVERLÄSSIGKEIT 10439
ZWECKE (NAGEL) 12588
ZWEIATOMIG 3881
ZWEIBASISCH 3882
ZWEIDIMENSIONAL 8729
ZWEIELEKTRODENLAMPE 3965
ZWEIFACH-CHLORZINN 12096
ZWEIFACH-EXPANSIONSMASCHINE 4168
ZWEIFACHER HIEB EINER FELLE 4134
ZWEIFACHJODQUECKSILBER 8155
ZWEIFACHKOHLENSÄURE 7883
ZWEIG 1555
ZWEIKNOPFNIETSTIFTE 1241
ZWEIKOMPONENTENLACK 13311
ZWEIKURBELIGE WELLE 13316
ZWEIPHASENSTROM 13314
ZWEITAKTMOTOR 13312
ZWEITE POTENZ 12013
ZWEITEILIGER KEIL 4162
ZWEITEILIGER KOLBEN 1709
ZWEITES KRIECHSTADIUM 11104
ZWEITFARBE 11103
ZWEIWEGEHAHN 13317
ZWEIWEGEVENTIL 13318
ZWEIWERTIG 3881
ZWEIZYLINDER-BOXER-MOTOR 5398
ZWEIZYLINDERDAMPFMASCHINE 13313
ZWICKEL 6182
ZWICKZANGE 3532
ZWIESELKALIBER 3905
ZWILLING 13300
ZWILLINGSBAND 570
ZWILLINGSBILDUNG 13302
ZWILLINGSFLÄCHE 2826

ZWILLINGSMASCHINE 13301
ZWINGE 5128
ZWISCHENBODEN 5026
ZWISCHENERZEUGNIS 7043
ZWISCHENFLÄCHE 7032
ZWISCHENGLÜHEN 577
ZWISCHENGLÜHUNG 9884
ZWISCHENKEIL 13731
ZWISCHENLAGE 7621
ZWISCHENLAGENTEMPERATUR 7086
ZWISCHENLAGERBEHÄLTER 1592
ZWISCHENLAGESCHEIBE 11352
ZWISCHENPLATTE 4174
ZWISCHENPODEST 7048
ZWISCHENPRODUKT 7043
ZWISCHENRING 2961
ZWISCHENRING 7392
ZWISCHENSCHICHT (ENTKOHLTE) 1005
ZWISCHENSTUFENGEFÜGE 925
ZWISCHENSTUFENHÄRTUNG 824
ZWISCHENSTUFENVERGÜTUNG 824
ZWISCHENTRÄGER 7047
ZWISCHENTRIEBRAD 6754
ZWISCHENWAND 4110
ZWISCHENWELLE 7049
ZWISCHENWELLE 7202
ZWISCHENWERT 7051
ZWISCHENZEIT 7101
ZWÖLFFLACH 4112
ZWÖLFFLÄCHERN 4112
ZYAN 3551
ZYANAT 3544
ZYANGOLD 5997
ZYANID 3547
ZYANID (FREIES) 5632
ZYANIDVERFAHRENOFEN 3550
ZYANKALI 9683
ZYANKUPFER 3115
ZYANMETALL 3547
ZYANNATRIUM 11720
ZYANSALZBARHÄRTUNG 3549
ZYANSÄURE 3545
ZYANSÄURESALZ 3544
ZYANSILBER 11462
ZYANURSÄURE 3552
ZYANWASSERSTOFF 6707
ZYANWASSERSTOFFSÄURE 6707
ZYANZINK 14041
ZYCLUS 3553
ZYKLOIDE 3557
ZYKLOIDE (GEDEHNTE) 9918

| | |
|---|---|
| ZYKLOIDE (VERKÜRZTE) **3493** | ZYLINDERFUTTER **3571** |
| ZYKLOIDE (VERLÄNGERTE) **9918** | ZYLINDERHUF **13358** |
| ZYKLOIDENVERZAHNUNG **3558** | ZYLINDERINHALT **3566** |
| ZYKLON **3560** | ZYLINDERINHALT **2262** |
| ZYLINDER **13954** | ZYLINDERINHALT **3448** |
| ZYLINDER **3561** | ZYLINDERKKOPFDECKEL **3567** |
| ZYLINDER **10671** | ZYLINDERKOORDINATEN **3580** |
| ZYLINDER **1461** | ZYLINDERKOPF **3569** |
| ZYLINDER (ELLIPTISCHER) **4675** | ZYLINDERKOPFDICHTUNG **3570** |
| ZYLINDER (FREIHÄNGENDER) **8935** | ZYLINDERLAUFBÜCHSE **3562** |
| ZYLINDER (FREITRAGENDER) **8935** | ZYLINDERLAUFBÜCHSE **3571** |
| ZYLINDER (GERADER) **10579** | ZYLINDERLAUFBÜCHSE **1465** |
| ZYLINDER (HYPERBOLISCHER) **6736** | ZYLINDERMASS **10661** |
| ZYLINDER (PARABOLISCHER) **9039** | ZYLINDERÖL **3572** |
| ZYLINDER (SCHIEFER) **8712** | ZYLINDERROLLE **3589** |
| ZYLINDER (SCHWEBENDER) **8935** | ZYLINDERSCHLEIFMASCHINE **3568** |
| ZYLINDER EINER DAMPFMASCHINE **12162** | ZYLINDERSCHRAUBE **5165** |
| ZYLINDERBLOCK **3564** | ZYLINDERSCHRAUBE **13979** |
| ZYLINDERBODEN **1494** | ZYLINDERSENKER **3241** |
| ZYLINDERBOHRUNG **3565** | ZYLINDERSPALTVERSUCH **1561** |
| ZYLINDERDECKEL **3567** | ZYLINDRISCH **3577** |
| ZYLINDEREINSATZ **3571** | ZYLINDRISCHER AUSFLUSSSTUTZEN **3576** |
| ZYLINDERFRÄSER **13848** | ZYLINDRISCHER SCHRAUBENKOPF **3574** |

# ÍNDICE ESPAÑOL

# ÍNDICE ESPANHOL

947 ACC

ABACÁ *m* **7980**
ÁBACO *m* **8617**
ÁBACO *m* **3834**
ÁBACO *m* **2273**
ÁBACO *m* **13992**
ABARQUILLARSE **13628**
ABASTECER **8042**
ABERRACIÓN *f* **4077**
ABERRACIÓN CROMÁTICA *f* **2369**
ABERRACIÓN DE ESFERICIDAD *f* **11885**
ABERRACIÓN (DE LA LUZ) *f* **5**
ABERRACIÓN DE REFRANGIBILIDAD *f* **2369**
ABERTURA *f* **262**
ABERTURA *f* **9633**
ABERTURA *f* **7963**
ABERTURA *f* **8831**
ABERTURA *f* **12976**
ABERTURA *f* (DE UN CILINDRO DE VAPOR) **12176**
ABERTURA *f* DE VENTILACIÓN **13531**
ABLANDAMIENTO *m* **11749**
ABLANDAR **12717**
ABOCAR (O ENCHUFAR) TUBOS **5277**
ABOCARDADO *m* **1723**
ABOLLADURA *f* **1720**
ABOLLADURA *f* **1720**
ABOLLADURA *f* **3760**
ABOLLAMIENTO *m* **3760**
ABOLLONAMIENTO *m* (O RESALTO *m*) DE PUESTA A
  TIERRA **4418**
ABOMBADO *m* **1720**
ABOMBADO *m* **1720**
ABOMBADO *m* **1723**
ABRASIÓN *f* **13**
ABRASIÓN *f* **6106**
ABRASIVO *m* **6123**
ABRASIVO *m* **17**
ABRASIVO *m* **9601**
ABRASIVO DULCE *m* **8269**
ABRASIVO NATURAL *m* **8499**
ABRAZADERA *f* **7832**
ABRAZADERA *f* **13324**
ABRAZADERA *f* **2491**
ABRAZADERA **2450**
ABRAZADERA DE TUBO *f* **9345**
ABRAZADERA (PARA TUBO) *f* **9344**
ABRIGO DEL POLVO (AL) *m* **4393**
ABRILLANTAR **5969**

ABRILLANTAR **1756**
ABRIR AGUJEROS **9186**
ABRIR EL CIRCUITO ELÉCTRICO **8826**
ABSCISA *f* **27**
ABSORBENCIA *f* **56**
ABSORBENTE *m* **40**
ABSORBENTE *m* **39**
ABSORBER **37**
ABSORBIBLE **38**
ABSORCIÓMETRO *m* **43**
ABSORCIÓN *f* **44**
ABSORCIÓN *f* **11289**
ABSORCIÓN DEL AGUA *f* **52**
ABSORCIÓN DEL CALOR *f* **51**
ACABADO *m* **5213**
ACABADO *m* **5223**
ACABADO *m* **5213**
ACABADO *m* **9855**
ACABADO **11682**
ACABADO *m* **11682**
ACABADO *m* CON EL CEPILLO METÁLICO **11016**
ACABADO *m* CON EL TAMBOR **1014**
ACABADO *m* CON LA FRESA **6513**
ACABADO *m* CON LA MUELA **5224**
ACABADO *m* CON MÁQUINA **7844**
ACABADO *m* DE SUPERFICIE **12504**
ACABADO *m* DIMENSIONAL **11524**
ACABADO *m* EN CALIENTE **6655**
ACABADO *m* EN EL LAMINADOR **8278**
ACABADO *m* EN FRÍO **2679**
ACABADO *m* PARCIAL **11960**
ACABADO *m* PERFECTO DE UN TRABAJO **11682**
ACABADO *m* SATINADO **10938**
ACABAMIENTO *m* **11682**
ACABAR **5214**
ACABAR CON PERFECCIÓN **5214**
ACANALADO *m* **6137**
ACANALADO *m* **6137**
ACANALADO *m* CON LLAMA **5822**
ACANALADO *m* ESTRIADO *m* **5484**
ACANALADURA *f* **5483**
ACANALAR **6128**
ACANALAR **6128**
ACANALAR Y HACER LENGÜETAS **12988**
ACCESIBILIDAD *f* **72**
ACCESIBLE **73**
ACCESO DIRECTO *m* **10198**
ACCESORIO *m* **812**
ACCESORIO *m* **812**
ACCESORIOS *m pl* **74**

**ACC** 948

ACCESORIOS  *m pl* **5283**
ACCESORIOS  *m pl* **5283**
ACCESORIOS PARA CALDERAS  *m pl* **1411**
ACCIDENTE DE TRABAJO  *m* **75**
ACCIÓN  *f* **8406**
ACCIÓN  *f* DE NIVELACIÓN **7528**
ACCIÓN DE NULIDAD RELATIVA  *f* **8707**
ACCIÓN DE PROFUNDIDAD  *f* **12899**
ACCIÓN DE UNA FUERZA  *f* **143**
ACCIÓN DE UNA FUERZA EXTERIOR  *f* **12331**
ACCIÓN DEL FRENO  *f* **1550**
ACCIÓN DIRECTA (DE)  *f* **3980**
ACCIÓN GIROSCÓPICA  *f* **6192**
ACCIÓN INDIRECTA (DE)  *f* **6883**
ACCIONADO  *m* POR RUEDA DENTADA **13025**
ACCIONADO A MANO (O MANUALMENTE) **6241**
ACCIONADOR  *m* **4301**
ACCIONAMIENTO  *m* **4297**
ACCIONAMIENTO  *m* **4303**
ACCIONAMIENTO  *m* IRREGULAR **7165**
ACCIONAMIENTO  *m* POR FRICCIÓN **4304**
ACCIONAMIENTO POR ÁRBOL DE TRANSMISIÓN  *m* **7609**
ACCIONAMIENTO POR CABLE  *m* **10735**
ACCIONAMIENTO POR CADENA  *m* **2206**
ACCIONAMIENTO POR CADENA  *m* **2208**
ACCIONAMIENTO POR CORREA  *m* **4319**
ACCIONAMIENTO POR ENGRANAJE  *m* **5892**
ACCIONAMIENTO POR ENGRANAJE CÓNICO  *m* **1230**
ACCIONAMIENTO POR ENGRANAJE RECTO  *m* **12010**
ACCIONAMIENTO POR ENGRANAJES  *m* **13025**
ACCIONAMIENTO POR GRUPOS  *m* **6150**
ACCIONAMIENTO POR MOTOR  *m* **8119**
ACCIONAMIENTO POR MOTOR  *m* **9734**
ACCIONAR **4289**
ACCIONAR **4289**
ACCIONAR **3049**
ACCIONAR POR FRICCIÓN **4291**
ACCIONES ATMOSFÉRICAS  *f pl* **792**
ACEBOLLADURA  *f* **3460**
ACEITADO  *m* **8791**
ACEITADO  *m* **8791**
ACEITAR **8744**
ACEITE  *m* **8743**
ACEITE  *m* ANIMAL **555**
ACEITE  *m* ANTRACÉNICO **608**
ACEITE  *m* BRUTO DE PETRÓLEO **3412**
ACEITE  *m* COMPOUND **2832**
ACEITE  *m* DE ALCANFOR **1894**
ACEITE  *m* DE ALGODÓN **3222**
ACEITE  *m* DE ALQUITRÁN **12681**

ACEITE  *m* DE ALQUITRÁN DE LA HULLA **2568**
ACEITE  *m* DE ALQUITRÁN DEL LIGNITO **1668**
ACEITE  *m* DE ANTRACENO **608**
ACEITE  *m* DE BALLENA **13103**
ACEITE  *m* DE BLANCO DE BALLENA **11881**
ACEITE  *m* DE CAÑAMONES **6446**
ACEITE  *m* DE CLAVEL **9624**
ACEITE  *m* DE COCO **2620**
ACEITE  *m* DE COLZA **10204**
ACEITE  *m* DE COLZA **10204**
ACEITE  *m* DE CORTE MECANIZADO **3534**
ACEITE  *m* DE ESCURRIDO **13636**
ACEITE  *m* DE ESQUISTO **11256**
ACEITE  *m* DE GRASA **7409**
ACEITE  *m* DE HUESOS DE FRUTAS **3157**
ACEITE  *m* DE LINAZA **7631**
ACEITE  *m* DE LINAZA HERVIDO **8786**
ACEITE  *m* DE LINAZA PARA BARNIZ **8786**
ACEITE  *m* DE LINO **7631**
ACEITE  *m* DE MANTECA DE CERDO **7409**
ACEITE  *m* DE PALMA **9027**
ACEITE  *m* DE PARAFINA **9044**
ACEITE  *m* DE PATATAS **5754**
ACEITE  *m* DE PESCADO **13103**
ACEITE  *m* DE PETRÓLEO PARA LLAMA **7275**
ACEITE  *m* DE PIE DE BUEY **1450**
ACEITE  *m* DE PIE DE CARNERO **1450**
ACEITE  *m* DE PINO **10862**
ACEITE  *m* DE RESINA **10749**
ACEITE  *m* DE RICINO **2086**
ACEITE  *m* DE ROCA **9229**
ACEITE  *m* DE SÉSAMO **11212**
ACEITE  *m* DE TEMPLE **10099**
ACEITE  *m* DE TEMPLE **6295**
ACEITE  *m* DE TREMENTINA **10749**
ACEITE  *m* DE VITRIOLO **12453**
ACEITE  *m* DEPURADO **10373**
ACEITE  *m* DERRETIDO **5491**
ACEITE  *m* EMULSIONADO **4706**
ACEITE  *m* EN EXCESO **13636**
ACEITE  *m* ESENCIAL **4836**
ACEITE  *m* ESPECIAL **6403**
ACEITE  *m* ESPECIAL PARA VEHÍCULOS PESADOS (H.D.) **6403**
ACEITE  *m* FIJO **5294**
ACEITE  *m* GRAFITADO **6063**
ACEITE  *m* GRASO **5294**
ACEITE  *m* LIGERO **7570**
ACEITE  *m* LUBRIFIANTE **7805**
ACEITE  *m* LUBRIFICANTE **7805**

ACEITE *m* MEDIO **8125**
ACEITE *m* MINERAL **8304**
ACEITE *m* MINERAL COMPUESTO **2832**
ACEITE *m* MINERAL OSCURO **1291**
ACEITE *m* MINERAL PARA CABEZALES **11908**
ACEITE *m* MINERAL RUBIO **2480**
ACEITE *m* MIXTO **2832**
ACEITE *m* (O ESENCIA) DE TREMENTINA **8765**
ACEITE *m* PARA AISLAR **6999**
ACEITE *m* PARA CILINDROS **3572**
ACEITE *m* PARA EL ALUMBRADO **7275**
ACEITE *m* PARA ENGRASE **7805**
ACEITE *m* PARA LA LIMPIEZA **2477**
ACEITE *m* PARA MAQUINARIA **4755**
ACEITE *m* PARA MOTOR **8415**
ACEITE *m* PARA TALADRAR **4280**
ACEITE *m* PESADO **6408**
ACEITE *m* PESADO DE PARAFINA **9044**
ACEITE *m* PESADO (PARA FUERZA MOTRIZ) **5714**
ACEITE *m* PROYECTADO **11928**
ACEITE *m* RANCIO **10197**
ACEITE *m* SECATIVO **4357**
ACEITE *m* SOLAR **11753**
ACEITE *m* SOLUBLE **11810**
ACEITE *m* VEGETAL **13512**
ACEITE *m* VERTIDO **11928**
ACEITE *m* VOLÁTIL **4836**
ACEITE DE ANILINA *m* **553**
ACEITE DE PURGA *m* (CARTER-MOTOR) **3308**
ACEITE PESADO *m* **8041**
ACEITERA *f* **8753**
ACEITERA *f* **8749**
ACEITERA *f* **8749**
ACEITES *m pl* **8744**
ACEITES *m pl* ACONDICIONADOS **8996**
ACEITES *m pl* BLANCOS **13838**
ACELERACIÓN *f* **9905**
ACELERACIÓN *f* **62**
ACELERACIÓN *f* EXAGERADA DE UN MOTOR **10118**
ACELERACIÓN ANGULAR *f* **537**
ACELERACIÓN AUTOMÁTICA *f* **836**
ACELERACIÓN CENTRÍFUGA *f* **10127**
ACELERACIÓN CENTRÍPETA *f* **2189**
ACELERACIÓN DE LA GRAVEDAD *f* **64**
ACELERACIÓN DE LA GRAVEDAD *f* **65**
ACELERACIÓN DE VELOCIDAD DE UN CUERPO QUE SE CAE *f* **63**
ACELERACIÓN DEL PISTÓN *f* **9371**
ACELERACIÓN LINEAL *f* **7611**
ACELERACIÓN NEGATIVA *f* **8525**

ACELERACIÓN NO UNIFORME *f* **13507**
ACELERACIÓN NORMAL *f* **8653**
ACELERACIÓN POSITIVA *f* **9652**
ACELERACIÓN TANGENCIAL *f* **12620**
ACELERACIÓN UNIFORME *f* **13361**
ACELERADOR *m* **66**
ACELERAR **7448**
ACELERAR **6851**
ACELERARSE ANORMALMENTE **10117**
ACELERARSE ANORMALMENTE **10117**
ACEPILLADOR *m* **9443**
ACEPILLADORA *f* **9443**
ACEPILLADORA *f* **9452**
ACEPILLADORA *f* **4871**
ACEPILLADORA *f* FRESADORA **9453**
ACERACIÓN *f* **12206**
ACERACIÓN *f* **135**
ACERACIÓN *f* **2142**
ACERACIÓN *f* **2142**
ACERAR **2134**
ACERAR **12205**
ACERÍA *f* **12207**
ACERÍA *f* **12222**
ACERO *m* **12223**
ACERO *m* **12196**
ACERO *m* **11490**
ACERO *m* **4156**
ACERO *m* AL NÍQUEL **7105**
ACERO *m* BATIDO DOS VECES **4156**
ACERO *m* BATIDO UNA VEZ **11490**
ACERO *m* DOBLE REFINADO **4156**
ACERO *m* EN BARRAS **984**
ACERO AFINADO *m* **12462**
ACERO AFINO **12462**
ACERO AL CARBONO *m* **11473**
ACERO AL CARBONO *m* **9427**
ACERO AL CARBONO *m* **1954**
ACERO AL COBALTO *m* **2612**
ACERO AL COBALTO-CROMO *m* **2613**
ACERO AL COBRE *m* **3130**
ACERO AL CROMO-WOLFRAMIO *m* **2378**
ACERO AL HORNO ELÉCTRICO *m* **4532**
ACERO AL MANGANESO *m* **7968**
ACERO AL MOLIBDENO *m* **8368**
ACERO AL NÍQUEL *m* **8570**
ACERO AL NÍQUEL **7105**
ACERO AL NÍQUEL CROMO *m* **2386**
ACERO AL SILICIO *m* **11447**
ACERO AL SILICIO *m* **11449**
ACERO AL TITANIO *m* **12972**

**ACE** 950

ACERO AL TUNGSTENO (WOLFRAMIO) *m* **13265**
ACERO AL VANADIO *m* **13476**
ACERO ALEADO (ESPECIALDE ALEACIÓNDE LIGA) *m* **368**
ACERO ANORMAL *m* **8**
ACERO AUSTENÍTICO *m* **826**
ACERO AUTOTEMPLABLE *m* **298**
ACERO AUTOTEMPLABLE (DE TEMPLE AL AIRE) *m* **8000**
ACERO BÁSICO *m* **12855**
ACERO BATIDO *m* **13765**
ACERO BATIDO DOS VECES **4156**
ACERO BESSEMER *m* **107**
ACERO BESSEMER *m* **1215**
ACERO BRUTO (EN BRUTO) *m* **3414**
ACERO CALMADO AL ALUMINIO *m* **442**
ACERO CALMADO AL MANGANESO *m* **7969**
ACERO CALMADO (REPOSADODESOXIDADO) *m* **7294**
ACERO CALMADO Y TEMPLADO *m* **10093**
ACERO CEMENTADO *m* **2138**
ACERO CEMENTADO *m* **2138**
ACERO CEMENTADO *m* **2138**
ACERO CHAPADO *m* **2446**
ACERO COLADO (FUNDIDO) *m* **12202**
ACERO COMPRIMIDO *m* **2849**
ACERO CORROSIORRESISTENTE *m* **12051**
ACERO CROMADO *m* **2389**
ACERO CROMO-NÍQUEL *m* **2376**
ACERO DE ARADO *m* **9528**
ACERO DE BAJO CARBONO *m* **7770**
ACERO DE CALIDAD SUPERIOR *m* **6486**
ACERO DE CALIDAD SUPERIOR *m* **6486**
ACERO DE CONSTRUCCIÓN *m* **12392**
ACERO DE CORTE RÁPIDO *m* **6474**
ACERO DE ESTRUCTURA ACICULAR *m* **8523**
ACERO DE GRANO GRUESO *m* **2577**
ACERO DE MUELLES *m* **11992**
ACERO DE (PARA) HERRAMIENTAS *m* **13009**
ACERO DE REMACHES *m* **10627**
ACERO DE SOLERA BÁSICA *m* **1048**
ACERO DE TEMPLE AL AIRE *m* **11154**
ACERO DE UTENSILIOS *m* **7857**
ACERO DULCE (SUAVE) *m* **8270**
ACERO DULCE (SUAVE) *m* **7770**
ACERO DULCE (SUAVE) *m* **11744**
ACERO DULCE (SUAVE) *m* **1958**
ACERO DURO *m* **6280**
ACERO DURO DE ALTO CARBONO *m* **1957**
ACERO EFERVESCENTE *m* **4462**
ACERO EFERVESCENTE *m* **4462**
ACERO EFERVESCENTE *m* **10598**
ACERO EFERVESCENTE *m* **10599**

ACERO ELABORADO AL HORNO ELÉCTRICO *m* **4511**
ACERO ELÉCTRICO *m* **4511**
ACERO ELÉCTRICO ÁCIDO *m* **113**
ACERO EN BARRAS *m* **984**
ACERO ESPECIAL *m* **11848**
ACERO ESPUMOSO *m* **10599**
ACERO ESTIRADO *m* **4251**
ACERO EXTRA-DULCE *m* **12224**
ACERO FORJADO *m* **5554**
ACERO INOXIDABLE *m* **8644**
ACERO MANGANOSILÍCEO **11450**
ACERO MANGANOSILICOSO *m* **11450**
ACERO MAQUINABLE RÁPIDO *m* **5639**
ACERO MARTIN **1048**
ACERO MARTIN **8816**
ACERO MARTIN AL PROCESO ÁCIDO *m* **116**
ACERO MARTIN AL PROCESO BÁSICO *m* **1047**
ACERO MOLDEADO *m* **2055**
ACERO MOLDEADO *m* **6924**
ACERO MOLDEADO *m* **12202**
ACERO MOLDEADO AL CRISOL *m* **2057**
ACERO M.S. *m* **8023**
ACERO NIQUELADO *m* **8573**
ACERO NITRURADO *m* **8585**
ACERO NO MAGNÉTICO *m* **8638**
ACERO PARA ENGRANAJES *m* **5904**
ACERO PARA FORJA (FORJADO) *m* **6222**
ACERO PARA IMANES *m* **7892**
ACERO PARA PLATAFORMA DE SONDEO EN ALTA MAR *m* **8739**
ACERO PARCIALMENTE REPESADO *m* **10599**
ACERO PERFILADO (TREFILADO) *m* **11125**
ACERO PERLÍTICO *m* **9145**
ACERO PLATINITO (PLATINITA) *m* **9508**
ACERO POCO ALIADO *m* **382**
ACERO PUDELADO *m* **9963**
ACERO QUEMADO *m* **1763**
ACERO RÁPIDO *m* **6497**
ACERO RÁPIDO PARA HERRAMIENTAS *m* **10207**
ACERO RESISTENTE AL DESGASTE *m* **13718**
ACERO SEMI-SUAVE *m* **1959**
ACERO SEMICALMADO *m* **11173**
ACERO SEMICALMADO *m* **8825**
ACERO SIN BURBUJAS *m* **12209**
ACERO SINTERIZADO *m* **10598**
ACERO SOBRECALENTADO *m* **8945**
ACERO TEMPLADO *m* **6289**
ACERO TEMPLADO EN FRÍO *m* **2697**
ACERO TEMPLADO Y REVENIDO *m* **10093**
ACERO THOMAS *m* **1044**

ACEROS CORROSIORRESISTENTES Y TERMORRESISTENTES *m pl* **3184**
ACEROS DE BARRENAS PARA PERFORACIONES *m pl* **4270**
ACEROS LAMINADOS PLANOS *m pl* **5392**
ACETALDEHÍDO *m* **84**
ACETATO *m* **85**
ACETATO *m* **91**
ACETATO *m* DE AMILO **487**
ACETATO *m* SÓDICO **11715**
ACETATO DE ALUMINIO *m* **417**
ACETATO DE AMILO *m* **487**
ACETATO DE AMONIO *m* **458**
ACETATO DE BARIO *m* **993**
ACETATO DE CELULOSA *m* **2132**
ACETATO DE CELULOSA **91**
ACETATO DE CINC *m* **14036**
ACETATO DE COBRE *m* **13533**
ACETATO DE ETILO *m* **88**
ACETATO DE HIERRO *m* **7134**
ACETATO DE PLOMO **7450**
ACETATO DE POTASIO *m* **9673**
ACETATO DE SODIO *m* **11715**
ACETATO FÉRRICO *m* **5099**
ACETATO FERROSO *m* **5120**
ACETIL-CELULOSA *m* **91**
ACETILENO *m* **93**
ACETILURO DE CALCIO *m* **1848**
ACETONA *f* **90**
ACETOSO **129**
ACETOSO **104**
ACETOSO **727**
ACHAFLANADO *m* **2233**
ACHAFLANADO *m* **12646**
ACHAFLANAR **2230**
ACHAFLANAR **2230**
ACHATADA *f* **5406**
ACHATADO *m* **5406**
ACICULAR **102**
ACIDIFICANTE **130**
ACIDIMETRÍA *f* **131**
ACIDÍMETRO *m* **89**
ACIDÍMETRO **89**
ÁCIDO *m* AGRIO **129**
ÁCIDO *m* AGRIO **104**
ÁCIDO *m* AGRIO **727**
ÁCIDO *m* MURIÁTICO **6706**
ÁCIDO *m* NÍTRICO **657**
ÁCIDO *m* NÍTRICO **8580**
ÁCIDO ACÉTICO *m* **86**
ÁCIDO ACÉTICO CRISTALIZABLE *m* **5952**

ÁCIDO ALDEHÍDICO *m* **84**
ÁCIDO ARSÉNICO *m* **722**
ÁCIDO BENCENO-SULFÓNICO *m* **1200**
ÁCIDO BENZOICO *m* **1202**
ÁCIDO BÓRICO *m* **1467**
ÁCIDO BROMHÍDRICO *m* **6704**
ÁCIDO BRÓMICO *m* **1647**
ÁCIDO BUTÍRICO *m* **1817**
ÁCIDO CARBAZÓTICO *m* **9291**
ÁCIDO CARBÓLICO *m* **1938**
ÁCIDO CARBÓNICO *m* **1949**
ÁCIDO CARBÓNICO LÍQUIDO *m* **7645**
ÁCIDO CIANHÍDRICO *m* **6707**
ÁCIDO CIÁNICO *m* **3545**
ÁCIDO CIANÚRICO *m* **3552**
ÁCIDO CÍTRICO *m* **2441**
ÁCIDO CLORHÍDRICO *m* **6706**
ÁCIDO CRÓMICO *m* **2379**
ÁCIDO DE NORDHAUSEN *m* **5733**
ÁCIDO DE SAJONIA *m* **5733**
ÁCIDO DIGÁLICO *m* **5780**
ÁCIDO ESTÁNNICO *m* **12097**
ÁCIDO ESTEÁRICO *m* **12194**
ÁCIDO FÉNICO *m* **1938**
ÁCIDO FENILSULFOROSO *m* **1200**
ÁCIDO FLUORHÍDRICO *m* **6711**
ÁCIDO FLUOSILÍCICO *m* **11441**
ÁCIDO FÓRMICO *m* **5578**
ÁCIDO FULMÍNICO *m* **5731**
ÁCIDO GÁLICO *m* **5777**
ÁCIDO GRASO *m* **5055**
ÁCIDO HIDROCLÓRICO *m* **6706**
ÁCIDO HIPOCLOROSO *m* **6742**
ÁCIDO HIPOSULFUROSO *m* **12853**
ÁCIDO HÚMICO *m* **6665**
ÁCIDO LÁCTICO *m* **7355**
ÁCIDO METAFOSFÓRICO *m* **8210**
ÁCIDO METASILÍCICO *m* **8211**
ÁCIDO MINERAL *m* **8302**
ÁCIDO MOLÍBDICO *m* **8369**
ÁCIDO NÍTRICO *m* **8580**
ÁCIDO NÍTRICO *m* **8580**
ÁCIDO NÍTRICO ANHIDRO *m* **8590**
ÁCIDO NITROSO *m* **8596**
ÁCIDO OLEICO *m* **8795**
ÁCIDO ORGÁNICO *m* **8864**
ÁCIDO ORTOFOSFÓRICO *m* **8873**
ÁCIDO ORTOSILÍCICO *m* **8875**
ÁCIDO OXÁLICO *m* **8969**
ÁCIDO PALMÍTICO *m* **9028**

**ACI** 952

ÁCIDO PÍCRICO *m* **9291**
ÁCIDO PIROFOSFÓRICO *m* **10054**
ÁCIDO PIROGÁLICO *m* **10045**
ÁCIDO PIROLEÑOSO *m* **10046**
ÁCIDO PRÚSICO *m* **6707**
ÁCIDO ROSÓLICO *m* **10750**
ÁCIDO SALICÍLICO *m* **10899**
ÁCIDO SILÍCICO *m* **11436**
ÁCIDO SILÍCICO *m* **11436**
ÁCIDO SULFÚRICO *m* **12453**
ÁCIDO SULFÚRICO CONCENTRADO *m* **2884**
ÁCIDO (SULFÚRICO) DE CÁMARA *m* **2228**
ÁCIDO SULFÚRICO DEL COMERCIO *m* **8856**
ÁCIDO SULFÚRICO FUMANTE *m* **5733**
ÁCIDO SULFUROSO *m* **12450**
ÁCIDO TÁNICO *m* **5780**
ÁCIDO TARTÁRICO *m* **12690**
ÁCIDO TARTÁRICO DEXTRÓGIRO *m* **3826**
ÁCIDO TARTÁRICO LEVÓGIRO *m* **7364**
ÁCIDO TIOSULFÚRICO *m* **12853**
ÁCIDO TÚNGSTICO *m* **8876**
ÁCIDO VITRIÓLICO *m* ÁCIDO SULFÚRICO DE CÁMARA *m* **12453**
ACIDÓMETRO *m* **89**
ÁCIDOS *m pl* **132**
ACIDULAR **133**
ACLARADO *m* **10608**
ACLARAR **10607**
ACODAR **1175**
ACODAR UN TUBO **1175**
ACODO *m* **3388**
ACONDICIONAMIENTO *m* **8995**
ACOPLADO **8171**
ACOPLADOR *m* **1510**
ACOPLAMIENTO *m* **5275**
ACOPLAMIENTO **2544**
ACOPLAMIENTO **4307**
ACOPLAMIENTO **3254**
ACOPLAMIENTO **3254**
ACOPLAMIENTO **3254**
ACOPLAMIENTO **3254**
ACOPLAMIENTO **3254**
ACOPLAMIENTO **3254**
ACOPLAMIENTO **3254**
ACOPLAMIENTO *m* **1997**
ACOPLAMIENTO *m* **1074**
ACOPLAMIENTO *m* **11600**
ACOPLAMIENTO *m* **10221**
ACOPLAMIENTO *m* **10025**
ACOPLAMIENTO *m* **10847**

ACOPLAMIENTO *m* **11389**
ACOPLAMIENTO *m* CENTRÍFUGO **2177**
ACOPLAMIENTO *m* CON CONO **2927**
ACOPLAMIENTO *m* CON CONOS **2930**
ACOPLAMIENTO *m* DE CORREAS **1151**
ACOPLAMIENTO *m* DE CORREAS **1142**
ACOPLAMIENTO *m* DE DENTADURA CÓNICA **6839**
ACOPLAMIENTO *m* DE DENTADURA RECTA **12313**
ACOPLAMIENTO *m* DE DIENTES DE SIERRA **10960**
ACOPLAMIENTO *m* DE DISCOS **4046**
ACOPLAMIENTO *m* DE FRICCIÓN **5672**
ACOPLAMIENTO *m* DE FRICCIÓN **11614**
ACOPLAMIENTO *m* DE GARRAS **4113**
ACOPLAMIENTO *m* DE GARRAS **2461**
ACOPLAMIENTO *m* DE PLATOS **9486**
ACOPLAMIENTO *m* (O EMBRAGUE *m*) DE DISCO **4002**
ACOPLAMIENTO *m* (O EMBRAGUE *m*) DESLIZANTE **11619**
ACOPLAMIENTO *m* (O EMBRAGUE *m*) HIDRÁULICO **6681**
ACOPLAMIENTO *m* (O EMBRAGUE *m*) MAGNÉTICO **7934**
ACOPLAMIENTO *m* (O EMBRAGUE) DE RUEDA LIBRE **8957**
ACOPLAMIENTO *m* POR TORNILLOS **1442**
ACOPLAMIENTO AUTOMÁTICO *m* **11149**
ACOPLAMIENTO CON LIMITADOR DE PAR **11619**
ACOPLAMIENTO DE ÁRBOLES *m* **11240**
ACOPLAMIENTO DE DESEMBRAGUE *m* **4032**
ACOPLAMIENTO DE DESEMBRAGUE *m* **4033**
ACOPLAMIENTO DE DISCOS EMPERNADOS *m* **5338**
ACOPLAMIENTO DE FRICCIÓN *m* **5672**
ACOPLAMIENTO DE UÑAS (DE GARRAS) *m* **2461**
ACOPLAMIENTO ELÁSTICO *m* **4476**
ACOPLAMIENTO (EMBRAGUE) HIDRÁULICO *m* **6681**
ACOPLAMIENTO EN CANTIDAD *m* **9051**
ACOPLAMIENTO EN SERIE *m* **11199**
ACOPLAMIENTO EN TENSIÓN *m* **11199**
ACOPLAMIENTO FIJO *m* **5037**
ACOPLAMIENTO FLEXIBLE *m* **5417**
ACOPLAMIENTO POR CONO *m* **2928**
ACOPLAMIENTO POR MANGUITO DE PLATILLO *m* **5338**
ACOPLAMIENTO RÍGIDO *m* **5037**
ACOPLAR **3253**
ACOPLAR **10033**
ACOPLAR **12988**
ACOPLE *m* **3254**
ACORTAMIENTO *m* **11376**
ACORTAMIENTO *m* **11377**
ACORTAMIENTO *m* DE UNA CORREA **11377**
ACOTACIÓN ABSOLUTA *f* **3097**
ACOTACIÓN ABSOLUTA *f* **29**
ACOTACIÓN RELATIVA *f* **6854**

ACRISTALAR **5969**
ACROMÁTICO **98**
ACROMATISMO **101**
ACROMATIZACIÓN *f* **99**
ACROMATIZAR **100**
ACTÍNICO **139**
ACTINIO *m* **141**
ACTINÓMETRO *m* **142**
ACTIVACIÓN *f* **144**
ACTIVADOR **146**
ACTIVIDAD *f* **8406**
ACTUADOR *m* **146**
ACUARELA *f* **13664**
ACUMÍNEO **102**
ACUMULACIÓN *f* **1705**
ACUMULACIÓN *f* **12299**
ACUMULACIÓN *f* **12288**
ACUMULACIÓN DE CALOR *f* **12291**
ACUMULACIÓN DE ENERGÍA *f* **12290**
ACUMULADOR *m* **76**
ACUMULADOR *m* **4534**
ACUMULADOR DE CALOR *m* **6336**
ACUMULADOR DE PLOMO *m* **7455**
ACUMULADOR DE REJILLA *m* **6097**
ACUMULADOR DE VAPOR *m* **12156**
ACUMULADOR ELÉCTRICO *m* **4534**
ACUMULADOR HIDRÁULICO *m* **6677**
ACUMULAR EL CALOR **12296**
ACUMULAR (O ALMACENAR) ENERGÍA **12296**
ACUMULAR (O ALMACENAR) ENERGÍA **12295**
ACUÑACIÓN *f* DE MONEDA **2651**
ACÚSTICA *f* **137**
ACÚSTICA *f* **136**
ACUTÁNGULO *m* **154**
ADAPTADA **6970**
ADAPTADOR *m* **160**
ADAPTADOR DE INTERCAMBIO RÁPIDO *m* **10108**
ADAPTADOR (O RACOR) DE BRIDA *m* **5325**
ADEHÍDO BENCÍLICO *m* **1198**
ADELGAZAMIENTO *m* DE UNA PIEZA **12671**
ADHERENCIA *f* **174**
ADHERENCIA *f* **173**
ADHERENTE **175**
ADHESIÓN *f* **174**
ADHESIVO **175**
ADHESIVO *m* **175**
ADIABÁTICO *m* **179**
ADICIÓN *f* **169**
ADICIÓN *f* **394**
ADICIÓN DE CARBONO *f* **145**

ADICIÓN EN LA CUCHARA *f* **7357**
ADICIONAR **162**
ADICIONAR AGUA **163**
ADITIVO *m* **168**
ADMISIÓN **6943**
ADMISIÓN DE AIRE *f* **12486**
ADMITIR **4750**
ADOBE *m* **7692**
ADOBE *m* **7692**
ADOBO *m* PARA PIELES **3711**
ADOQUÍN *m* **5004**
ADOQUÍN *m* **9137**
ADRAL *m* **6309**
ADSORCIÓN *f* **203**
ADULTERACIÓN *f* **205**
ADULTERAR **204**
ADYACENTE **181**
AERACIÓN *f* **13530**
AERODINÁMICO *m* **214**
AERODINÁMICO *m* **215**
AEROMOTOR **2843**
AEROSTÁTICO *m* **218**
AEROSTÁTICO *m* **217**
AFILADO *m* **11275**
AFILADO *m* DE LIMAS **10324**
AFILADO DE PRECISIÓN *m* **9755**
AFILADORA *f* **11274**
AFILADORA UNIVERSAL *f* **13384**
AFILADURA *f* **11275**
AFILADURA *f* **11275**
AFILADURA *f* **1691**
AFILADURA *f* CON MUELA **6106**
AFILAMIENTO *m* **11275**
AFILAR **11273**
AFILAR **11273**
AFILAR **11273**
AFILAR **11273**
AFILAR **6790**
AFILAR LAS LIMAS **10323**
AFILAR UN INSTRUMENTO CORTANTE **6790**
AFINACIÓN DEL GRANO *f* **6037**
AFINADO **10377**
AFINADURA *f* **10377**
AFINAR **10370**
AFINAR UN METAL **10371**
AFINIDAD QUÍMICA *f* **2292**
AFINO **10377**
AFINO AL FUEGO *m* **5245**
AFINO CON AIRE *m* **300**
AFINO CON VIENTO *m* **300**

**AFI** 954

AFINO DEL GRANO *m* **6037**
AFINO ELECTROLÍTICO *m* **4558**
AFLOJAMIENTO *m* **11560**
AFLOJAMIENTO *m* DE UNA CHAVETA DE CUÑA **7751**
AFLOJAR UN FRENO **10436**
AFLOJAR UN TORNILLO **11558**
AFLOJAR UNA CHAVETA DE CUÑA **7750**
AFLOJAR UNA TUERCA **11558**
AFLOJARSE **11559**
AFLORADO **5482**
AFLORAMIENTO *m* **7951**
AFORADOR *m* **7655**
AFORADOR *m* **5455**
AFORAR **1861**
AFORO *m* A DISTANCIA **10449**
AFUSTE *m* **6175**
AFUSTE DE CAMPAÑA *m* **5142**
AFUSTE DE MORTERO *m* **8397**
AGARRADOR *m* **6262**
AGARRAR **12914**
AGARROTAMIENTO *m* **11141**
AGARROTAMIENTO *m* **11141**
AGARROTAMIENTO DE LA CUERDA EN LA RANURA *m* **1278**
AGARROTARSE **11140**
AGARROTARSE **7210**
ÁGATA *f* **222**
AGAVILLADORAS *f pl* MECANICAS DE TODA DENSIDAD **948**
AGAVILLAR **1737**
AGENTE *m* ADICIONAL **168**
AGENTE *m* DE DISPERSIÓN **4050**
AGENTE ANTIPICADURAS *m* **616**
AGENTE ANTIPÚTRIDO *m* **629**
AGENTE DE ABRILLANTADO *m* **1615**
AGENTE DE CARBURIZACIÓN (DE CEMENTACIÓN) *m* **2139**
AGENTE DE CONSERVACIÓN *m* **9791**
AGENTE DE DISPERSIÓN *m* **4050**
AGENTE DE ENFRIAMIENTO *m* **3086**
AGENTE DE IMPREGNACIÓN *m* **6804**
AGENTE DE PATENTES DE INVENCIÓN *m* **9114**
AGENTE DE PRECIPITACIÓN **11130**
AGENTE DE QUELATO *m* **2289**
AGENTE DE REDUCCIÓN **10346**
AGENTE DE REFRIGERACIÓN **3086**
AGENTE DE TRATAMIENTO DE SUPERFICIE *m* **12523**
(AGENTE) DESNATURALIZANTE *m* **3747**
AGENTE HUMECTANTE **13808**
AGENTE HUMECTOR *m* **13808**
AGENTE MOTRIZ **8408**
AGENTE REFRIGERANTE *m* **3086**

AGENTES ATMOSFÉRICOS *m pl* **793**
AGITACIÓN *f* DEL BAÑO **6279**
AGITACIÓN DEL BAÑO *f* **11254**
AGITADOR **12260**
AGITADOR MECÁNICO *m* **238**
AGITAR **8328**
AGLOMERACIÓN *f* **7990**
AGLOMERADO *m* **1623**
AGLOMERADO *m* **1623**
AGLOMERADO DE HULLA *m* **2560**
AGLOMERADO DE LIGNITO *m* **1666**
AGLOMERADO DE TURBA *m* **9149**
AGLOMERADO MAGNESIANO *m* **7881**
AGLOMERANTE *m* **1253**
AGLOMERANTE *m* PARA LA FABRICACIÓN DE MACHOS **3145**
AGLOMERARSE **11509**
AGLUTINANTE *m* **1253**
AGLUTINANTE *m* **1253**
AGLUTINANTE *m* **1445**
AGLUTINANTE *m* QUE SE ENDURECE AL AIRE **301**
AGLUTINANTE *m* SECO **4342**
AGOTAMIENTO *m* **4210**
AGOTAMIENTO *m* **6801**
AGRANDAMIENTO *m* **1723**
AGRANDAR **5356**
AGRANDAR (O ENSANCHAR) AGUJEROS CON EL MANDRIL **4262**
AGRANDAR UN TUBO CON EL MANDRIL **4903**
AGREGACIÓN *f* **229**
AGREGADO *m* **227**
AGREGADO *m* **229**
AGRIETADO *m* ESTACIONAL **11092**
AGRIETADO *m* SUPERFICIAL **3319**
AGRIETARSE **3279**
AGRUPACIÓN *f* **11199**
AGRUPACIÓN *f* **9051**
AGRUPAR EN CANTIDAD **2956**
AGUA *f* **13640**
AGUA *f* A PRESIÓN **9841**
AGUA *f* ACIDULADA **134**
AGUA *f* AMONIACAL DEL GAS **456**
AGUA *f* ARRIBA **6322**
AGUA *f* ASÉPTICA **13650**
AGUA *f* CALCÁREA **6281**
AGUA *f* CALCÁREA **2227**
AGUA *f* CALIZA **2227**
AGUA *f* COMBINADA (QUÍMICAMENTE) **2318**
AGUA *f* CORRIENTE **5466**
AGUA *f* (DE) ABAJO **12597**
AGUA *f* DE ALIMENTACIÓN **5077**

| | |
|---|---|
| AGUA *f* DE BARITA **1019** | AGUA *f* SUPERFICIAL (O DE FLOR DE TIERRA) **12520** |
| AGUA *f* DE CAL **7585** | AGUA ABAJO **4184** |
| AGUA *f* DE CONDENSACIÓN **13662** | AGUA ARRIBA *f* **13407** |
| AGUA *f* DE CONSTITUCIÓN **2318** | AGUA ARRIBA *f* **13407** |
| AGUA *f* DE CRISTALIZACIÓN **13663** | AGUA DE ENFRIAMIENTO **3095** |
| AGUA *f* DE DISTRIBUCIÓN **13075** | AGUA DE JABÓN **11702** |
| AGUA *f* DE FUENTE (O DE MANANTIAL) **11996** | AGUA DE LLUVIA **10179** |
| AGUA *f* DE HIDRATACIÓN **6675** | AGUA DE RÍO **10620** |
| AGUA *f* DE INFILTRACIÓN **9181** | AGUA DULCE **11745** |
| AGUA *f* DE LABARRAQUE (SOLUCIÓN *f* DE HIPOCLORITO SÓDICO) **4422** | AGUA ESTERILIZADA **13650** |
| AGUA *f* DE MAR **11072** | AGUA FANGOSA **8446** |
| AGUA *f* DE POZO **13796** | AGUA FLUVIAL **10620** |
| AGUA *f* DE POZO DE MINA **9397** | AGUA PARA BEBER **4281** |
| AGUA *f* DE REGRIGERACIÓN **3095** | AGUA PURA **11745** |
| AGUA *f* DE RÍO **10620** | AGUANTAR **6524** |
| AGUA *f* DESTILADA **4076** | AGUANTAR (ROBLONADO) **6524** |
| AGUA *f* DULCE **11745** | AGUARRÁS *m* **8765** |
| AGUA *f* DULCE (O BLANDA) **5663** | AGUAS *f pl* RESIDUALES **6902** |
| AGUA *f* DURA (O CRUDA) **6281** | AGUAS *f pl* RESIDUALES **11230** |
| AGUA *f* ESTANCADA (O MUERTA) **12050** | AGUAS *f pl* SUBTERRÁNEAS **6147** |
| AGUA *f* ESTANCADA (O MUERTA) **12050** | AGUAS ABAJO **4184** |
| AGUA *f* ESTERILIZADA **13650** | AGUAS DE ALCANTARILLA **11230** |
| AGUA *f* FLUVÌAL **10620** | AGUAS NEGRAS **11230** |
| AGUA *f* FUERTE **8580** | AGUJA DE INYECTOR *f* **8684** |
| AGUA *f* FUERTE **657** | AGUJA (DE MANÓMETRO) *f* **6226** |
| AGUA *f* HIGROSCÓPICA **6731** | AGUJA IMANTADA *f* **7909** |
| AGUA *f* HIRVIENDO **1428** | AGUJA INDICADORA *f* **6868** |
| AGUA *f* INDUSTRIAL **13649** | AGUJAS PARA RODAMIENTOS *f pl* **1108** |
| AGUA *f* JABONOSA **11702** | AGUJEREAR **4264** |
| AGUA *f* JABONOSA (O DE JABÓN) **11702** | AGUJEREAR **10771** |
| AGUA *f* LODOSA **8446** | AGUJEREAR **9186** |
| AGUA *f* MADRE **8405** | AGUJERO *m* **6530** |
| AGUA *f* MADRE (SALINAS *f pl*) **8405** | AGUJERO *m* CIEGO **3630** |
| AGUA *f* METEÓRICA **8213** | AGUJERO *m* DE AIRE **13528** |
| AGUA *f* ORDINARIA **10240** | AGUJERO *m* DE BRAZO **6236** |
| AGUA *f* OXIGENADA **6716** | AGUJERO *m* DE COLADA **12637** |
| AGUA *f* PARA SOLDAR **7293** | AGUJERO *m* DE COLADA **7287** |
| AGUA *f* PESADA **6414** | AGUJERO *m* DE EJE O DE CHAVETA **9332** |
| AGUA *f* PLUVIAL **10179** | AGUJERO *m* DE HOMBRE **9620** |
| AGUA *f* POCO CARGADA (DE SALES) **11745** | AGUJERO *m* DE HOMBRE **7963** |
| AGUA *f* POTABLE **4281** | AGUJERO *m* DE HOMBRE **7976** |
| AGUA *f* POTABLE **4281** | AGUJERO *m* DE HOMBRE **7997** |
| AGUA *f* REGIA **658** | AGUJERO *m* DE HOMBRE DE TECHO **10710** |
| AGUA *f* SALADA **1617** | AGUJERO *m* DE HOMBRE LATERAL **11332** |
| AGUA *f* SALINA **10910** | AGUJERO *m* DE INSPECCIÓN DE UN CAJÓN **9620** |
| AGUA *f* SALOBRE **1524** | AGUJERO *m* DE MANO **6236** |
| AGUA *f* SOBRECALENTADA **12470** | AGUJERO *m* DE MEDIDA **3971** |
| AGUA *f* SUPERFICIAL **12520** | AGUJERO *m* DE MEDIDA COMBINADO CON RESPIRADERO **3972** |
| AGUA *f* SUPERFICIAL **12520** | AGUJERO *m* DE PASADOR **3214** |

# AGU

956

AGUJERO *m* DE ROBLÓN **1437**
AGUJERO *m* DE ROBLÓN **10625**
AGUJERO *m* DE ROBLÓN PERFORADO **4275**
AGUJERO *m* DE ROBLÓN TALADRADO **10004**
AGUJERO *m* DE SONDEO **1463**
AGUJERO *m* DE SOPLADURA **6393**
AGUJERO *m* DE SUCIEDAD **4332**
AGUJERO *m* DE VACIADO **8442**
AGUJERO *m* EN LAS CHAPAS DE ENSAMBLADO **10625**
AGUJERO *m* ENGRASADOR **8761**
AGUJERO *m* INICIAL **10782**
AGUJERO *m* OBLONGO **8714**
AGUJERO *m* PARA LA ESCORIA **2399**
AGUJERO *m* PERFORADO **4273**
AGUJERO *m* PROCEDENTE DE FUNDICIÓN **2033**
AGUJERO *m* QUE ATRAVIESA LA PIEZA **12893**
AGUJERO *m* RECTIFICADO **4273**
AGUJERO *m* RECTIFICADO **4273**
AGUJERO *m* ROSCADO **11056**
AGUJERO *m* ROSCADO **11056**
AGUJERO *m* SIN SALIDA **3630**
AGUJERO *m* TESTIGO **12715**
AGUJEROS *m pl* DE BRIDA **5328**
AGUJEROS *m pl* DE MANIPULACIÓN **6264**
AGUZADOR *m* **6105**
AGUZAMIENTO *m* **11275**
AGUZAR **11273**
AGUZAR **11273**
AHERRUMBRARSE **10864**
AHORRO *m* DE TIEMPO **10949**
AIRE AMBIENTE *m* **450**
AIRE ATMOSFÉRICO *m* **240**
AIRE COMBURENTE *m* **277**
AIRE COMPRIMIDO *m* **2839**
AIRE ENRARECIDO *m* **10213**
AIRE FALSO (INFILTRADOSECUNDARIO) *m* **4771**
AIRE HÚMEDO *m* **3599**
AIRE LÍQUIDO *m* **7643**
AIRE SECO *m* **4339**
AIREACIÓN *f* **13530**
AIREACIÓN **13530**
AIREAR UNA ARENA **208**
AISLACIÓN *f* **12287**
AISLACIÓN *f* **7184**
AISLACIÓN *f* **7003**
AISLACIÓN *f* CONTRA EL RUIDO **7004**
AISLACIÓN *f* CONTRA EL SONIDO **7004**
AISLACIÓN *f* DEL FRÍO **2700**
AISLACIÓN *f* ELÉCTRICA **4545**
AISLACIÓN *f* TÉRMICA **7003**

AISLACIÓN *f* TÉRMICA **12810**
AISLADO **4075**
AISLADOR *m* **7006**
AISLADOR TÉRMICO *m* **8628**
AISLAMIENTO *m* **7003**
AISLAMIENTO *f* (DEL QUE SE AISLA) **12287**
AISLAMIENTO TÉRMICO *m* **6639**
AISLANTE **3898**
AISLANTE **6998**
AISLANTE **7006**
AISLAR **6994**
AISLARSE **6994**
AJUSTABLE **183**
AJUSTADOR *m* **160**
AJUSTADOR *m* **5278**
AJUSTADOR DE MÁQUINAS *m* **5278**
AJUSTAMIENTO *m* **5280**
AJUSTAMIENTO *m* **5275**
AJUSTAMIENTO *m* **4307**
AJUSTAMIENTO *m* **10025**
AJUSTAMIENTO *m* **10847**
AJUSTAMIENTO *m* **11600**
AJUSTAR **8042**
AJUSTAR **182**
AJUSTAR **323**
AJUSTAR **5276**
AJUSTAR **5277**
AJUSTAR LOS AGUJEROS A LOS REMACHES **9969**
AJUSTAR O EMBUTIR EL REMACHE **8045**
AJUSTAR UNA POLEA EN SU EJE **4222**
AJUSTAR UNA RUEDA **4222**
AJUSTE *m* **4307**
AJUSTE *m* **5280**
AJUSTE *m* **5527**
AJUSTE *m* **5275**
AJUSTE *m* **5275**
AJUSTE *m* **11600**
AJUSTE *m* **10025**
AJUSTE *m* **10194**
AJUSTE *m* **10847**
AJUSTE *m* **11355**
AJUSTE **8419**
AJUSTE *m* CON CUÑA **12929**
AJUSTE *m* CON TUERCA **12930**
AJUSTE *m* CÓNICO **12649**
AJUSTE *m* CÓNICO **12649**
AJUSTE *m* CORREDIZO **11600**
AJUSTE *m* CORREDIZO (O DESLIZANTE) **11600**
AJUSTE *m* DE CHAVETA **12653**
AJUSTE *f* DE UNA CUÑA **12928**

957 ALC

AJUSTE *m* HOLGADO **11600**
AJUSTE *m* (O ASIENTO *m*) PRENSADO **5527**
AJUSTE *m* POR APRETADO EN CALIENTE **11389**
ALA *f* **5095**
ALA (ACERO T) *f* **5330**
ALABASTRO *m* **304**
ÁLABE *m* **1677**
ÁLABE *m* DE UNA TURBINA **13480**
ÁLABE *m* DIRECTOR **6167**
ÁLABE *m* FIJO DE UNA TURBINA **6167**
ÁLABE *m* MÓVIL DE UNA TURBINA **13820**
ÁLABE *m* RECEPTOR **13820**
ALABEAR **1173**
ALABEAR **13628**
ALABEARSE **13628**
ALABEARSE **13628**
ALABEO *m* LATERAL **7418**
ÁLABES *m pl* DE TURBINAS **13268**
ALAMBIQUE *m* **12259**
ALAMBRE *m* AISLADO **6996**
ALAMBRE *m* CLARO **13340**
ALAMBRE *m* CON CAPA DE PLOMO **7459**
ALAMBRE *m* CON ENVOLTURA TRENZADA **1528**
ALAMBRE *m* (CONDUCTOR) ELÉCTRICO **2922**
ALAMBRE *m* CUBIERTO **3272**
ALAMBRE *m* DE ACERO **12221**
ALAMBRE *m* DE ACERO PARA CUERDAS DE PIANO **9287**
ALAMBRE *m* DE ALUMINIO **428**
ALAMBRE *m* DE BRONCE **1654**
ALAMBRE *m* DE BRONCE FOSFOROSO **5607**
ALAMBRE *m* DE COBRE **3133**
ALAMBRE *m* DE COBRE **3106**
ALAMBRE *m* DE COBRE PLANO **3116**
ALAMBRE *m* DE ESPINO **987**
ALAMBRE *m* DE HIERRO **7155**
ALAMBRE *m* DE HIERRO CLARO CRUDO **1610**
ALAMBRE *m* DE HIERRO RECOCIDO NEGRO **1284**
ALAMBRE *m* DE LATÓN **1571**
ALAMBRE *m* DE LATÓN **1571**
ALAMBRE *m* DE PLOMO **10886**
ALAMBRE *m* (DE SECCIÓN) HEXAGONAL **6462**
ALAMBRE *m* (DE SECCIÓN) TRIANGULAR **13196**
ALAMBRE *m* DE SOLDAR **13789**
ALAMBRE *m* DE SOLDAR **13793**
ALAMBRE *m* DELGADO **5205**
ALAMBRE *m* DESNUDO **990**
ALAMBRE *m* EN VARILLA PARA TREFILADO **13882**
ALAMBRE *f* ESPINOSO **987**
ALAMBRE *m* ESTIRADO **4252**
ALAMBRE *m* FINO **5205**

ALAMBRE *m* FORRADO **11300**
ALAMBRE *m* GALVANIZADO **5786**
ALAMBRE *m* GALVANIZADO **5786**
ALAMBRE *m* HECHO DE ACERO ALEADO **376**
ALAMBRE *m* LAMINADO **10678**
ALAMBRE *m* LAMINADO DE LATÓN **1568**
ALAMBRE *m* LAMINADO DE LATÓN **1568**
ALAMBRE *m* METÁLICO FINO **12849**
ALAMBRE *m* (O HILO *m*) CON FORRO DE PLÁSTICO **9468**
ALAMBRE *m* (O HILO *m*) DE AMARRAR **1255**
ALAMBRE *m* (O HILO *m*) DE CINC **14048**
ALAMBRE *m* (O HILO *m*) DE PLATINO **9513**
ALAMBRE *m* (O HILO *m*) DE PLOMO **7477**
ALAMBRE *m* (O HILO *m*) ESTAÑADO **12962**
ALAMBRE *m* (O HILO *m*) METÁLICO **13880**
ALAMBRE *m* OVAL **4678**
ALAMBRE *m* PARA MUELLE **11997**
ALAMBRE *m* PERFILADO **11847**
ALAMBRE *m* PLANO **5402**
ALAMBRE *m* PLANO **5402**
ALAMBRE *m* PLANO DE COBRE **3116**
ALAMBRE *m* RECOCIDO **561**
ALAMBRE *m* RECOCIDO BLANCO **1606**
ALAMBRE *m* RECTANGULAR **5402**
ALAMBRE *m* REDONDO **10804**
ALAMBRE *m* REVESTIDO **3219**
ALAMBRE *m* TREFILADO **4252**
ALAMBRE *m* TREFILADO **4252**
ALAMBRE ESTIRADO EN FRÍO **2715**
ALAMBRE GALVANIZADO **12962**
ALARGADERA *f* **4947**
ALARGADERA *f* DE MANGO **4945**
ALARGADERA *f* DE UN COMPÁS **7521**
ALARGAMIENTO *m* **7612**
ALARGAMIENTO *m* **4679**
ALARGAMIENTO DE LOS CRISTALES *m* **3426**
ALARGAMIENTO DE UN CABLE *m* **12374**
ALARGAMIENTO DE UNA CORREA (O CINTA) *m* **12374**
ALARGARSE **1125**
ALBAÑILERÍA *f* **1601**
ALBAYALDE *m* **13834**
ALBEDO *m* **308**
ALBEDO (COEFICIENTE DE REFLEXIÓN) *m* **308**
ALBÚMINA *f* **310**
ALBÚMINA DEL SUERO *f* **11207**
ALBURA *f* **10936**
ALCACHOFA *f* **12332**
ALCACHOFA *f* DE REGADERA **10746**
ÁLCALI *m* **328**

**ALC** 958

ÁLCALI VOLÁTIL *m* **660**
ALCALIMETRÍA *f* **333**
ALCALIMÉTRICO *m* **333**
ALCALIMÉTRICO *m* **332**
ALCALÍMETRO *m* **331**
ALCALINIDAD *f* **340**
ALCALINIZAR **330**
ALCALIZAR **330**
ALCALOIDE *m* **341**
ALCALOIDEO **341**
ALCANCE *m* DEL SONIDO **10202**
ALCANCE *m* (O CAMPO *m*) DE MEDIDA DE UN INSTRUMENTO **10201**
ALCANFOR *m* **1893**
ALCOHOL *m* DE MADERA **13920**
ALCOHOL ABSOLUTO *m* **28**
ALCOHOL ACUOSO *m* **659**
ALCOHOL AMÍLICO *m* **488**
ALCOHOL ANHIDRO *m* **28**
ALCOHOL CARBURADO *m* **1983**
ALCOHOL DE QUEMAR *m* **8224**
ALCOHOL DESNATURALIZADO *m* **8224**
ALCOHOL ETÍLICO *m* **313**
ALCOHOL METÍLICO **13920**
ALCOHOL METÍLICO *m* **13920**
ALCOHOL ORDINARIO *m* **313**
ALCOHOL QUÍMICAMENTE PURO *m* **28**
ALCOHOL RECTIFICADO *m* **10313**
ALCOHOL VÍNICO *m* **313**
ALCOHÓLICO *m* **314**
ALCOHOLÍMETRO *m* **316**
ALCOHOLÍMETRO *m* **316**
ALCOHOLÍMETRO *m* **6722**
ALCOHOLÓMETRO *m* **316**
ALCOHÓMETRO *m* **316**
ALDEHÍDO *m* **317**
ALDEHÍDO ACÉTICO *m* **84**
ALDEHIDO BENCÍLICO **1198**
ALDEHÍDO FÓRMICO *m* **5573**
ALDEHÍDO METÍLICO *m* **5573**
ALEACIÓN *f* **360**
ALEACIÓN *f* INVARIABLE **4668**
ALEACIÓN ( *f* ) (METAL ( *m* ) DE APORTACIÓN (POR SOLDADURA) **5159**
ALEACIÓN AL BORO *f* **1478**
ALEACIÓN AL PLOMO *f* **7453**
ALEACIÓN ANTIÁCIDO *f* **384**
ALEACIÓN BINARIA *f* **1247**
ALEACIÓN BINARIA *f* **4378**
ALEACIÓN COBRE CINC *f* **5943**
ALEACIÓN COBRE CINC *f* **9861**

ALEACIÓN CUATERNARIA *f* **10084**
ALEACIÓN CUATERNARIA EUTÉCTICA *f* **10085**
ALEACIÓN DE ALTA DENSIDAD *f* **6481**
ALEACIÓN DE ALUMINIO BERILIO *f* **440**
ALEACIÓN DE ALUMINIO FORJABLE (O PLÁSTICA) *f* **437**
ALEACIÓN DE ALUMINIO PARA COLADO (MOLDEADOO MOLDEO) *f* **435**
ALEACIÓN DE ALUMINIO PLÁSTICA (O FORJABLE) *f* **433**
ALEACIÓN DE ANTIFRICCIÓN *f* **385**
ALEACIÓN DE AUER *f* **817**
ALEACIÓN DE BASE DE ALUMINIO *f* **418**
ALEACIÓN DE BASE DE ALUMINIO *f* **439**
ALEACIÓN DE BASE DE COBRE *f* **3111**
ALEACIÓN DE BASE DE MAGNESIO *f* **7890**
ALEACIÓN DE BASE DE NÍQUEL *f* **8557**
ALEACIÓN DE BASE DE PLOMO *f* **7451**
ALEACIÓN DE HIERRO *f* **7156**
ALEACIÓN DE METAL DURO *f* **11510**
ALEACIÓN DE NÍQUEL **8379**
ALEACIÓN DE RECARGUE DURO *f* **6284**
ALEACIÓN DE SOLDADURA CON LATÓN O BRONCE *f* **386**
ALEACIÓN DESGASIFICANTE *f* **3709**
ALEACIÓN DÚPLEX *f* **4378**
ALEACIÓN FUSIBLE *f* **5757**
ALEACIÓN FUSIBLE *f* **389**
ALEACJÓN FUSIBLE PARA SOLDAR O PARA SOLDAR CON LATÓN O BRONCE *f* **11755**
ALEACIÓN INOXIDABLE *f* **387**
ALEACIÓN INOXIDABLE *f* **387**
ALEACIÓN LIGERA *f* **7564**
ALEACIÓN MAGNÉTICA *f* **392**
ALEACIÓN MAGNÉTICA 'ALNICO' *f* **398**
ALEACIÓN MUY TERMORRESISTENTE *f* **393**
ALEACIÓN NATURAL *f* **8498**
ALEACIÓN NO FERROSA *f* **8619**
ALEACIÓN NO REFRACTARIA *f* **8622**
ALEACIÓN PARA COJINETES *f* **385**
ALEACIÓN PARA COLADA A PRESIÓN (O PARA FUNDICIÓN INYECTADA) *f* **388**
ALEACIÓN PARA LA OSTEOPLÁSTICA *f* **498**
ALEACIÓN PARA TEMPLE Y REVENIDO *f* **6383**
ALEACIÓN PIROFÓRICA *f* **10053**
ALEACIÓN REFRACTARIA *f* **393**
ALEACIÓN RESISTENTE A LAS ALTAS TEMPERATURAS *f* **12459**
ALEACIÓN RESISTENTE AL ÁCIDO *f* **384**
ALEACIÓN RESISTENTE AL DESGASTE (A LA USURA) *f* **383**
ALEACIÓN TERMORRESISTENTE *f* **391**
ALEACIÓN TERMORRESISTENTE E INOXIDABLE *f* **390**
ALEACIONES *f pl* DE HIERRO **5117**

959 ALT

ALEACIONES ANTIÁCIDO  f pl **125**
ALEACIONES FUSIBLES  f pl **7773**
ALEACIONES PARA RESISTENCIAS ELÉCTRICAS  f pl **10486**
ALEACIONES RESISTENTES A LA ABRASIÓN Y A LA CORROSIÓN  f pl **396**
ALEACIONES RESISTENTES AL ÁCIDO  f pl **125**
ALEAR **361**
ALENZA  f CON VÁLVULA **9994**
ALERÓN  m **5183**
ALETA  f **5183**
ALETA  f **13874**
ALETA DE VÁLVULA  f **5060**
ALETAS DE REFRIGERACIÓN  f pl **13477**
ALFÁMETRO  m **319**
ÁLGEBRA  f **320**
ALGEBRAICO **321**
ALGÉBRICO **321**
ALGODÓN  m **3217**
ALGODÓN PARA LÍMPIAR  m **3223**
ALGODÓN PÓLVORA  m **6176**
ALGODÓN PÓLVORA **6176**
ALGODÓN PÓLVORA **6176**
ALICATES  m pl (LOS) **12987**
ALICATES  m MOTORISTA **2764**
ALIMENTACIÓN  f **2263**
ALIMENTACIÓN  f **5063**
ALIMENTACIÓN  f **5082**
ALIMENTACIÓN  f **7940**
ALIMENTACIÓN DE AGUA  f **13678**
ALIMENTACIÓN DE LLEGADA  f **6844**
ALIMENTACIÓN DE UN HOGAR  f **5262**
ALIMENTACIÓN DOBLE  f **4138**
ALIMENTADOR  m **5083**
ALIMENTADOR AUTOMÁTICO  m **5072**
ALIMENTAR **5064**
ALIMENTAR UN FUEGO **12269**
ALINEACIÓN  f **324**
ALINEACIÓN  f **325**
ALINEAMIENTO  m **325**
ALINEAR **323**
ALISADO  m **1468**
ALISADO  m **5408**
ALISADOR  m **5729**
ALISADOR  m **10263**
ALISADURA  f **11686**
ALISADURA  f **1461**
ALISAMIENTO  m **1468**
ALISAR **11679**
ALISO  m **318**
ALIVIADERO  m **8931**

ALIVIADERO  m **13753**
ALIZARINA  f **327**
ALMA ·f **3142**
ALMA  f **13726**
ALMA DE CÁÑAMO  f **6440**
ALMA DE UN CABLE  f **3167**
ALMA DE UN HIERRO PERFILADO  f **13730**
ALMA DE UNA VIGUETA  f **13729**
ALMACÉN  m **12297**
ALMACENADO  m **12288**
ALMACENAJE  m **12288**
ALMACENAJE  m **12299**
ALMACENAMIENTO  m **12288**
ALMACENAMIENTO  m **12299**
ALMACENAR **12294**
ALMACENAR **12294**
ALMACENERO  m **12298**
ALMENDRILLA  f **11557**
ALMENDRILLA  f (MIN.) **2606**
ALMIDÓN  m **12111**
ALMIREZ  m (DE BRONCE) **8396**
ALMOHADILLA  f **9011**
ALNUS GLUTINOSA **318**
ALOJAMIENTO  m **6660**
ALOJAMIENTO  m DE UNA CHAVETA **7282**
ALOMERÍA  f **350**
ALÓMERO  m **349**
ALOMORFISMO  m **351**
ALOMORFO  m **352**
ALÓN  m **5183**
ALOTRIOMORFO  m **354**
ALOTROPÍA  f **357**
ALOTRÓPICO  m **356**
ALPACA  f **5932**
ALPACA  f **8569**
ALPACA  f **8569**
ALQUITRÁN  m **12679**
ALQUITRÁN  m DE ESQUISTO **11255**
ALQUITRÁN  m DE GAS **2570**
ALQUITRÁN  m DE GAS **2570**
ALQUITRÁN  m DE HULLA **2570**
ALQUITRÁN  m DE LIGNITO **1667**
ALQUITRÁN  m DE MADERA **13921**
ALQUITRÁN  m VEGETAL **13921**
ALQUITRANADO  m **12689**
ALQUITRANAR **12680**
ALTA FRECUENCIA  f **6467**
ALTA MAR (EN) **8738**
ALTA PRESIÓN  f **6473**
ALTA TEMPERATURA  f **6476**

**ALT** 960

ALTA TENSIÓN  f **6478**
ALTA TENSIÓN  f **6479**
ALTERACIÓN DEL COLOR  f **4026**
ALTERACIÓN QUÍMICA  f **2296**
ALTERNACIÓN FÍSICA  f **9280**
ALTERNADOR  m **407**
ALTERNADOR  m **411**
ALTERNATIVA  f **409**
ALTERNO  m **12048**
ALTERNOMOTOR  m **408**
ALTO CONTENIDO (O GRADO) (DE)  m **6483**
ALTO HORNO  m **1311**
ALTO VOLTAJE  m **6479**
ALTURA  f **6420**
ALTURA  f BAJO TRAVESAÑO **6423**
ALTURA  f DE ACCIÓN **13951**
ALTURA  f DE ASCENSIÓN **10611**
ALTURA  f DE ASPIRACIÓN DE UNA BOMBA **12432**
ALTURA  f DE CAÍDA **6421**
ALTURA  f DE CONSTRUCCIÓN **8924**
ALTURA  f DE DIENTE **13017**
ALTURA  f DE DIENTE **164**
ALTURA  f DE DIENTE **13845**
ALTURA  f DE ELEVACIÓN DE UNA BOMBA **13061**
ALTURA  f DE LA CABEZA DE UN DIENTE **164**
ALTURA  f DE LA IMPELENCIA DE UNA BOMBA **4021**
ALTURA  f DE LEVANTAMIENTO DE UNA GRÚA **7551**
ALTURA  f DE TOBERA **8680**
ALTURA  f DEL FLANCO **3681**
ALTURA  f DEL FRENTE **164**
ALTURA  f DEL PIE **3681**
ALTURA  f DEL PIE DE DIENTE **3681**
ALTURA  f LIBRE DESDE EL SUELO **6143**
ALTURA  f TOTAL **8924**
ALTURA  f TOTAL DEL DIENTE **3785**
ALUMBRADO  m **7574**
ALUMBRADO  m AUXILIAR **4689**
ALUMBRADO  m AUXILIAR **4688**
ALUMBRADO  m AUXILIAR **4688**
ALUMBRADO  m ELÉCTRICO **4518**
ALUMBRADO  m EXTERIOR **8897**
ALUMBRADO  m INTERIOR **5887**
ALUMBRADO  m POR GAS **5828**
ALUMBRADO DE EMERGENCIA **4688**
ALUMBRADO DE EMERGENCIA **4688**
ALUMBRADO DE EMERGENCIA **4689**
ALUMBRE DE CROMO  m **2370**
ALUMBRE DE HIERRO  m **7135**
ALUMBRE ORDINARIO  m **2787**
ALUMBRE POTÁSICO  m **2787**

ALÚMINA  f **438**
ALÚMINA  f **412**
ALÚMINA  f **413**
ALÚMINA HIDRATADA  f **423**
ALUMINATO  m **414**
ALUMINATO DE BARITA  m **994**
ALUMINATO DE POTASIO  m **9674**
ALUMINATO DE SODIO  m **11716**
ALUMINIACIÓN  f **429**
ALUMINÍFERO  m **415**
ALUMINIO  m **432**
ALUMINIO  m **444**
ALUMINIO  m **416**
ALUMINIO EN LINGOTE  m **424**
ALUMINIZACIÓN  f **429**
ALUMINO **430**
ALUMINOTERMIA  f **431**
ALZA  f **10611**
ALZADO  m **6517**
ALZADO DE LEVA  m **1884**
ALZAPRIMA  f **7725**
ALZAR **6517**
ALZARUEDA  m **10121**
AMAGNÉTICO **8637**
AMALGAMA  f **445**
AMALGAMA  f **397**
AMALGAMACIÓN  f **447**
AMALGAMAR **446**
AMARILLO  m CROMO **2375**
AMARILLO  m DE CINC **14039**
AMARILLO  m DE CÚRCUMA **3481**
AMARTILLADO **6220**
AMARTILLADO  m **9157**
AMARTILLADO  m EN FRÍO **2685**
AMARTILLAR **6216**
AMARTILLAR EN FRÍO **2684**
AMASADOR  m **8334**
AMASAR **12718**
AMASAR **12718**
ÁMBAR AMARILLO  m **449**
ÁMBAR AMARILLO  m **449**
AMIANTO  m **746**
AMIANTO  m **755**
AMIANTO  m **1898**
AMIANTO  m **6599**
AMIANTO  m **10896**
AMIANTO  m (O FIBRA  f) DEL CANADÁ **1898**
AMIANTO TRENZADO EN CUERDA  m **751**
AMOLADORA  f **6113**
AMOLADURA  f **1691**

## 961      ANC

AMOLADURA  *f* **11275**
AMOLADURA  *f* PARA RECTIFICAR O AFILAR **11689**
AMOLAR **6790**
AMOLAR **11273**
AMOLAR **11273**
AMOLAR **11273**
AMOLAR **10**
AMOLDADO  *m* **5581**
AMONÍACO  *m* **453**
AMONIACO  *m* **454**
AMONÍACO  *m* **454**
AMONIACO  *m* **453**
AMONIACO  *m* **660**
AMONÍACO  *m* **660**
AMONIACO  *m* **7644**
AMONÍACO  *m* **7644**
AMONÍACO (O AMONIACO)  *m* **660**
AMORFO  *m* **475**
AMORTAJADORA  *f* **11642**
AMORTIGUACIÓN  *f* **3604**
AMORTIGUADOR  *m* **3611**
AMORTIGUADOR  *m* **3602**
AMORTIGUADOR  *m* **3601**
AMORTIGUADOR  *m* **3602**
AMORTIGUADOR  *m* DE AIRE **256**
AMORTIGUADOR DE CHOQUES  *m* **11358**
AMORTIGUADOR DE LÍQUIDO  *m* **6678**
AMORTIGUADOR DE VIBRACIONES  *m* **13555**
AMORTIGUADOR NEUMÁTICO  *m* **256**
AMORTIGUAMIENTO  *m* **3604**
AMORTIGUAMIENTO  *m* **3604**
AMORTIGUAMIENTO DE VIBRACIONES  *m* **3606**
AMORTIGUAMIENTO NEUMÁTICO  *m* **255**
AMORTIGUAMIENTO POR LÍQUIDO  *m* **7649**
AMORTIGUAR UN GOLPE **3640**
AMOVIBLE **3808**
AMPERAJE  *m* **478**
AMPERÍMETRO  *m* **452**
AMPERIO  *m* **479**
AMPERIO-HORA  *m* **481**
AMPERIO-HORA  *m* **4481**
AMPERIO-MINUTO  *m* **482**
AMPERIO-SEGUNDO  *m* **483**
AMPERIO-VUELTA  *m* **480**
AMPLIACIÓN  *f* **4946**
AMPLIACIÓN  *f* **7935**
AMPLIACIÓN DE UN DIBUJO **4769**
AMPLIFICADOR  *m* **485**
AMPLITUD  *f* **486**
AMPLITUD  *f* DE COMPARACIÓN **12079**

AMPOLLA  *f* **7385**
AMPOLLA  *f* **1327**
AMPOLLA DEL TERMÓMETRO  *f* **1717**
AMPOLLAS  *f pl* **1330**
AÑADIR **162**
ANAERÓBICO **489**
ANÁLISIS  *m* **493** .
ANÁLISIS CALORIMÉTRICO  *m* **1880**
ANÁLISIS CUALITATIVO  *m* **10062**
ANÁLISIS CUANTITATIVA **10064**
ANÁLISIS CUANTITATIVO  *m* **10064**
ANÁLISIS DE COLADA  *m* **7358**
ANÁLISIS DE COMPROBACIÓN  *m* **2280**
ANÁLISIS DE CONTROL  *m* **2280**
ANÁLISIS DE GAS  *m* **5809**
ANÁLISIS DE SOPLETE  *m* **1356**
ANÁLISIS DE VIRUTAS  *m* **2345**
ANÁLISIS (DETERMINACIÓN) DE LA ESTRUCTURA
   CRISTALINA  *f* **3425**
ANÁLISIS ELECTROLÍTICO  *m* **4594**
ANÁLISIS ELEMENTAL  *m* **4655**
ANÁLISIS ESPECTRAL  *m* **11861**
ANÁLISIS ESPECTRAL  *m* **11864**
ANÁLISIS FLUORESCENTE  *m* **13999**
ANÁLISIS GRANULOMÉTRICO  *m* **6023**
ANÁLISIS GRAVIMÉTRICA  *f* **6077**
ANÁLISIS MAGNÉTICO  *m* **7894**
ANÁLISIS NEFELOMÉTRICO  *m* **8537**
ANÁLISIS POR VÍA HÚMEDA  *f* **13800**
ANÁLISIS POR VÍA SECA  *f* **4341**
ANÁLISIS QUÍMICO  *m* **2293**
ANÁLISIS TÉRMICO SELECTIVO  *m* **3919**
ANÁLISIS VOLUMÉTRICO  *m* **13601**
ANALÍTICO **494**
ANALIZADOR  *m* **492**
ANALIZAR **491**
ANALIZAR **10990**
ANALÓGICO **490**
ANASTIGMAT **497**
ANASTIGMÁTICO **497**
ANCHO  *m* DE VÍA **5871**
ANCHURA  *f* **13850**
ANCHURA  *f* DE CONSTRUCCIÓN **8926**
ANCHURA  *f* DE LA SOLDADURA DE BASE **10727**
ANCHURA  *f* DE LAS MALLAS **11523**
ANCHURA  *f* DE MECANIZADO **7867**
ANCHURA  *f* DE UNA SOLDADURA **12887**
ANCHURA  *f* INTERIOR DE UN ESLABÓN **6982**
ANCHURA  *f* TOTAL **8926**
ANCHURA  *f* ÚTIL DE LAMINADO **13427**

**ANC** 962

ANCHURA DEL DIENTE **1579**
ANCLA *f* **500**
ANCLAJE *m* **499**
ANCLAJE *m* **12918**
ANCLAR **12914**
ANDAMIAJE *m* **10965**
ANDAMIO *m* **10965**
ANDAMIO *m* AÉREO **7260**
ANEMÓMETRO *m* **503**
ANEROIDE **504**
ANFIBOLE **6598**
ANFÓTERA **484**
ÁNGELO DE ATAQUE *m* **1277**
ANGSTROEM *m* **536**
ANGSTRÖM *m* **536**
ANGULAR *m* **514**
ANGULAR *m* **506**
ANGULAR *m* DE APOYO **533**
ANGULAR CON NERVIO *m* **1713**
ANGULAR DE LADOS DESIGUALES *m* **13356**
ANGULAR DE LADOS IGUALES *m* **4781**
ANGULAR DE SOPORTE *m* **3058**
ANGULARES DE ALEACIÓN DE ACERO *m* **369**
ANGULARES DE HIERRO DE PAQUETES *m* **7137**
ÁNGULO *m* **505**
ÁNGULO *m* **4441**
ANGULO *m* DE REFUERZO **12256**
ÁNGULO *m* DEL CHAFLÁN **1223**
ÁNGULO ADYACENTE *m* **180**
ÁNGULO AGUDO *m* **155**
ÁNGULO AGUDO *m* **155**
ÁNGULO CENTRAL *m* **507**
ÁNGULO COMPLEMENTARIO *m* **2811**
ÁNGULO DE AFILADO *m* **12995**
ÁNGULO DE ATAQUE *m* **10186**
ÁNGULO DE ATAQUE *m* **8577**
ÁNGULO DE ATAQUE *m* **11418**
ÁNGULO DE ATAQUE *m* **3524**
ÁNGULO DE ATAQUE *m* **5698**
ÁNGULO DE AVANCE *m* **515**
ÁNGULO DE BASE (O DE PIE) DEL DIENTE *m* **10716**
ÁNGULO DE CABEZA DE LA RUEDA CÓNICA *m* **165**
ÁNGULO DE CAÍDA *f* (CARROCERÍA) **1889**
ÁNGULO DE CALADO *m* **529**
ÁNGULO DE CHAFLÁN *m* **516**
ÁNGULO DE CIZALLAMIENTO *m* **11281**
ÁNGULO DE CONTACTO *m* **8577**
ÁNGULO DE CONTACTO *m* **517**
ÁNGULO DE CONTACTO *m* **1277**
ÁNGULO DE CONTACTO *m* **3524**

ÁNGULO DE CORTE *m* **3524**
ÁNGULO DE DECALADO HACIA ADELANTE *m* **524**
ÁNGULO DE DECALADO HACIA ADELANTE *m* **515**
ÁNGULO DE DECALADO HACIA ATRÁS *m* **523**
ÁNGULO DE DECALADO HACIA ATRÁS *m* **522**
ÁNGULO DE DEFASAJE *m* **9233**
ÁNGULO DE DEFASAJE *m* **9233**
ÁNGULO DE DESFASE *m* **9233**
ÁNGULO DE DESFASE *m* **9233**
ÁNGULO DE DESPRENDIMIENTO *m* **10186**
ÁNGULO DE DESPRENDIMIENTO *m* **11418**
ÁNGULO DE DESPRENDIMIENTO *m* **5698**
ÁNGULO DE DESVIACIÓN *m* **518**
ÁNGULO DE ENGRANE DEL FLANCO DEL DIENTE *m* **9810**
ÁNGULO DE FASE *m* **9233**
ÁNGULO DE FASE *m* **9233**
ÁNGULO DE FLEXIÓN *m* **519**
ÁNGULO DE HERRAMIENTA *m* **12995**
ÁNGULO DE HERRAMIENTA *m* **12995**
ÁNGULO DE INCIDENCIA *m* **520**
ÁNGULO DE INCLINACIÓN *m* **521**
ÁNGULO DE INCLINACIÓN *m* **6431**
ÁNGULO DE INCLINACIÓN LATERAL DEL PIVOTE **7312**
ÁNGULO DE LA CUÑA *m* **6129**
ÁNGULO DE LA HÉLICE *m* **531**
ÁNGULO DE PASO *m* **6431**
ÁNGULO DE PROFUNDIDAD DEL DESTALONADO *m* **1388**
ÁNGULO DE REAFILADO *m* **2484**
ÁNGULO DE REAFILADO *m* **12995**
ÁNGULO DE REFLEXIÓN *m* **525**
ÁNGULO DE REFRACCIÓN *m* **526**
ÁNGULO DE RETARDO *m* **522**
ÁNGULO DE RETIRO *m* **4197**
ÁNGULO DE ROTACIÓN *m* **528**
ÁNGULO DE ROZAMIENTO *m* **527**
ÁNGULO DE TORSIÓN *m* **532**
ÁNGULO DE VIRAJE *m* **7701**
ÁNGULO DEL CHAFLÁN *m* **1223**
ÁNGULO DEL CONO EXTERIOR *m* **4990**
ÁNGULO DEL FILETEADO *m* **530**
ÁNGULO DIEDRO *m* **3944**
ÁNGULO ENTRANTE *m* **10243**
ÁNGULO EXTERNO *m* **4950**
ÁNGULO INSCRITO *m* **6962**
ÁNGULO INSCRITO *m* **6962**
ÁNGULO INTERIOR *m* **7057**
ÁNGULO INTERNO *m* **7057**
ÁNGULO LÍMITE *m* **3345**
ÁNGULO MUERTO *m* **5698**
ÁNGULO OBTUSO *m* **8717**

963          **ANT**

ÁNGULO ÓPTICO  *m* **13581**
ÁNGULO ÓPTICO  *m* **13581**
ÁNGULO PRIMITIVO  *m* **9401**
ÁNGULO RECTO  *m* **10577**
ÁNGULO SALIENTE  *m* **10900**
ÁNGULO SÓLIDO  *m* **11776**
ÁNGULO SUPLEMENTARIO  *m* **12483**
ÁNGULO VIVO  *m* **155**
ANHIDRA  *f* **550**
ANHÍDRIDO  *m* **548**
ANHÍDRIDO ACÉTICO  *m* **87**
ANHÍDRIDO ARSÉNICO  *m* **723**
ANHÍDRIDO ARSENIOSO **727**
ANHÍDRIDO ARSENIOSO  *m* **727**
ANHÍDRIDO CARBÓNICO  *m* **1948**
ANHÍDRIDO CRÓMICO  *m* **2383**
ANHÍDRIDO FOSFÓRICO  *m* **9249**
ANHÍDRIDO HIPOCLOROSO  *m* **2355**
ANHÍDRIDO NÍTRICO  *m* **8590**
ANHÍDRIDO NITROSO  *m* **8592**
ANHÍDRIDO SULFÚRICO  *m* **12452**
ANHÍDRIDO SULFUROSO  *m* **12450**
ANHÍDRIDO TITÁNICO  *m* **12971**
ANHÍDRIDO TÚNGSTICO  *m* **13266**
ANHIDRITA  *f* **549**
ANHIDRO  *m* **550**
ANILINA  *f* **552**
ANILLA  *f* DE DETENCIÓN **7743**
ANILLA  *f* DE ENGANCHE **7980**
ANILLO  *m* **10600**
ANILLO  *m* **589**
ANILLO  *m* **589**
ANILLO  *m* **1773**
ANILLO  *m* ANUAL **586**
ANILLO  *m* CENTRADOR **10413**
ANILLO  *m* COLECTOR **11618**
ANILLO  *m* CÓNICO **2945**
ANILLO  *m* DE AJUSTE **12904**
ANILLO  *m* DE ARCILLA **2468**
ANILLO  *m* DE BOLAS **964**
ANILLO  *m* DE CALIBRE **2721**
ANILLO  *m* DE CALIBRE **2721**
ANILLO  *m* DE CAUCHO **10823**
ANILLO  *m* DE CENTRACIÓN **2154**
ANILLO  *m* DE CIERRE **11391**
ANILLO  *m* DE ENGRASE **8774**
ANILLO  *m* DE ESTANQUEIDAD **9007**
ANILLO  *m* DE FRENADO **1541**
ANILLO  *m* DE JUNTA **9007**
ANILLO  *m* DE LUBRICACIÓN **8790**

ANILLO  *m* DE PLOMO **7470**
ANILLO  *m* DE PRESIÓN **9830**
ANILLO  *m* DE RETENCIÓN **10515**
ANILLO  *m* DE RETENCIÓN PARTIDO **11939**
ANILLO  *m* DE UNIÓN **2961**
ANILLO  *m* DESMONTABLE **7743**
ANILLO  *m* ESCURRIDOR **13879**
ANILLO  *m* EXTERIOR DEL COJINETE DE BOLAS **8898**
ANILLO  *m* FIJO DE UN ÁRBOL **11384**
ANILLO  *m* INTERIOR DEL COJINETE DE BOLAS **6953**
ANILLO  *m* PARA GANCHO **11691**
ANILLO  *m* REGULADOR **7743**
ANILLO  *m* SOLDADO **13771**
ANILLO CILÍNDRICO  *m* **3588**
ANILLO DE AMIANTO  *m* **753**
ANILLO DE BOLAS  *m* **964**
ANILLO DE CADENA **7627**
ANILLO DE CIERRE  *m* **11391**
ANILLO DE RODADURA  *m* **1111**
ANILLO DE RODADURA DE LAS BOLAS  *m* **965**
ANILLO DE RODADURA DE LOS RODILLOS  *m* **10689**
ANILLO ELÁSTICO  *m* **11990**
ANILLOS DE TORNEAR  *m pl* **3312**
ANION  *m* **556**
ANISOTROPÍA  *f* **559**
ANISÓTROPO  *m* **558**
ANISÓTROPO  *f* **558**
ANÓDICA  *f* **603**
ANÓDICO  *m* **603**
ÁNODO  *m* **602**
ÁNODO  *m* **590**
ÁNODO DE COBRE  *m* **3112**
ÁNODO DE EXCITACIÓN  *m* **4886**
ÁNODO INSOLUBLE  *m* **598**
ANOLITO  *m* **606**
ANTEPECHO  *m* **6259**
ANTIÁCIDO ÁCIDORRESISTENTE  *m* **124**
ANTICÁTODO  *m* **611**
ANTICÁTODO  *m* **12682**
ANTICONGELANTE  *m* **612**
ANTICONGELANTE  *m* **5657**
ANTIDEFLAGRANTE  *m* **5322**
ANTILOGARITMO  *m* **620**
ANTIMAGNÉTICA  *f* **614**
ANTIMAGNÉTICO  *m* **614**
ANTIMAGNÉTICO **8637**
ANTIMONIO  *m* **623**
ANTIOXIDANTE  *m* **10869**
ANTIPARÁSITO  *m* **10156**
ANTIPÚTRIDA  *f* **628**

# ANT

964

ANTIPÚTRIDO *m* **629**
ANTIPÚTRIDO *m* **628**
ANTISÉPTICA *f* **628**
ANTISÉPTICA *f* **628**
ANTISÉPTICO *m* **629**
ANTISÉPTICO *m* **628**
ANTISÉPTICO *m* **628**
ANTITARTAROSO *m* **4041**
ANTRACENO *m* **607**
ANTRACITA *f* **609**
ANTRACITA *f* **609**
ANTRACITA *f* DE LLAMA LARGA **4344**
ANULAR *m* **588**
APAGAR LA CAL **11568**
APARATO *m* **641**
APARATO *m* DE CALDEO **5261**
APARATO *m* ELECTROMAGNÉTICO PARA ENSAYOS DE DUREZA **4614**
APARATO *m* EVAPORADOR **4869**
APARATO *m* RADIOGRÁFICO **13994**
APARATO *m* SECADOR **4356**
APARATO *m* SOPLANTE **1361**
APARATO AGITADOR *m* **236**
APARATO DE ALARMA *m* **305**
APARATO DE CONSTRUCCIÓN *m* **1444**
APARATO DE DESTILACIÓN *m* **12259**
APARATO DE ELEVACIÓN *m* **6519**
APARATO DE PROTECCIÓN *m* **10881**
APARATO DE ROSCAR *m* **12676**
APARATO (ELEVADOR) *m* **6519**
APARATO PARA DIAMANTAR *m* **13233**
APARATO REGISTRADOR *m* **10294**
APARATOS *m pl* ACCESORIOS (O AUXILIARES) **1411**
APARCAMIENTO *m* CUBIERTO **11302**
APARCAMIENTO *m* SIN CUBRIR **12265**
APAREAR **3253**
APAREJO *m* **6516**
APAREJO *m* DE CADENA **2213**
APAREJO *m* DE CUERDA **10741**
APARTADO *m* **11524**
APERIÓDICA *f* **634**
APERIODICIDAD *f* **637**
APERIÓDICO *m* **634**
APERTURA *f* DE LA VÁLVULA **8832**
ÁPEX *m* **638**
ÁPICE *m* **638**
APILAMIENTO *m* DE LA MADERA **9309**
APILAR (O AMONTONAR) LA MADERA **9307**
APISONAMIENTO *m* **10195**
APISONAR **10189**

APLANADORA **9451**
APLANAMIENTO *m* **13234**
APLANAMIENTO *m* **12319**
APLANAR **12318**
APLANAR **13232**
APLASTADA *f* **5406**
APLASTADO *m* **5406**
APLASTAMIENTO *m* **3420**
APLASTAMIENTO *m* **7265**
APLASTAR **7263**
APLASTAR **9712**
APLICACIÓN *f* DE PICADURAS CRUZADAS **3366**
APLICACIÓN *f* DE UN REVESTIMIENTO POR REMOJADO **3970**
APLICACIÓN *f* DE UNA CAPA PROTECTORA **6792**
APLICACIÓN *f* DE UNA FUERZA **647**
APLICACIÓN *f* INDUSTRIAL DE UNA INVENCIÓN **2783**
APLICAR LOS FRENOS **650**
APLICAR UNA CAPA PROTECTORA **6791**
APLICAR UNA CUBIERTA PROTECTORA **6791**
APLICAR UNA MANO DE PINTURA **9014**
APLOMO *m* **9219**
APOCROMÁTICA *f* **640**
APOCROMÁTICO *m* **640**
APOMAZADO *m* **9990**
APOMAZAR **9987**
APONTAJE *m* **1603**
APORCADOR *m* DE PATATAS **9702**
APOYAR **12491**
APOYO *m* **7388**
APOYO *m* **10877**
APOYO *m* **12062**
APOYO *m* **1118**
APOYO *m* **57**
APOYO *m* **57**
APOYO *m* **57**
APOYO *m* CENTRAL **2152**
APOYO *m* INTERMEDIARIO DE UN ÁRBOL **6586**
APOYO *m* MEDIANO **2152**
APOYO FIJO *m* **5295**
APRECIACIÓN *f* PERICIAL **4931**
APRESTO *m* **9855**
APRESURAR **7448**
APRETAMIENTO *m* **11355**
APRETAR A FONDO UNA TUERCA **12927**
APRETAR A FONDO UNA TUERCA **12927**
APRETAR EL FRENO **650**
APRETAR LA CAJA DE ESTOPA **12926**
APRETAR UN TORNILLO **12925**
APRETAR UN TORNILLO **11022**

965 ARB

APRETAR UNA CUÑA **12924**
APRETAR UNA TUERCA **12925**
APROXIMACIÓN *f* **652**
APTITUD *f* PARA EL TEMPLE **6288**
APTO PARA MECANIZACIÓN **7838**
APTO PARA MECANIZACIÓN **13946**
APTO PARA SER COLADO **1914**
APTO PARA SER LAMINADO **1915**
APTO PARA SER PATENTADO **9122**
APUNTALAMIENTO *m* **12153**
APUNTALAMIENTO *m* **12153**
APUNTALAMIENTO *m* **12153**
APUNTALAMIENTO *m* **12153**
APUNTALAMIENTO *m* CON TUBOS **13258**
APUNTALAR **12150**
APUNTALAR **12150**
APUNTALAR **12150**
APUNTE *m* **7717**
ARADO *m* BRABANTE **9526**
ARADO *m* DE SUBSUELO **8344**
ARADOS *m pl* **9526**
ARADOS *m pl* DE SUBSUELO Y ARADOS *m pl* DE VERTEDERA **4090**
ARADOS ARRASTRADOS *m pl* **9525**
ARADOS DE DISCOS (ARRASTRADOS O PORTADOS) *m pl* **9523**
ARADOS MONTADOS *m pl* **9524**
ARADOS PARA ALOMAR *m pl* **9527**
ARANDELA *f* **13631**
ARANDELA *f* AUTOROSCADA **11163**
ARANDELA *f* BELLEVILLE **3461**
ARANDELA *f* CON PASADOR **7743**
ARANDELA *f* DE AJUSTE **7703**
ARANDELA *f* DE ALA **5096**
ARANDELA *f* DE BLOQUEO **7703**
ARANDELA *f* DE CAUCHO **10823**
ARANDELA *f* DE ESPESOR **11351**
ARANDELA *f* DE FRENO **7703**
ARANDELA *f* DE RETENCÍON **11692**
ARANDELA *f* DE UN ÁRBOL **2724**
ARANDELA *f* DECORATIVA **5230**
ARANDELA *f* ELÁSTICA **4486**
ARANDELA *f* GROWER **11995**
ARANDELA *f* PLANA **5399**
ARANDELA *f* PROTECTORA **4835**
ARANDELA *f* SOLDADA **11758**
ARANDELA *f* SOLDADA **13773**
ARANDELA *f* SOLDADA **13773**
ÁRBOL *m* **11239**
ÁRBOL *m* **662**
ÁRBOL *m* **3309**

ÁRBOL *m* CIGÜEÑAL DE CODO DOBLE **13316**
ÁRBOL *m* CONDUCIDO **4299**
ÁRBOL *m* DE GRAN VELOCIDAD **10209**
ÁRBOL *m* DE PEQUEÑA VELOCIDAD **11650**
ÁRBOL *m* EN VELOCIDAD DE LOS DOS LADOS **11247**
ÁRBOL *m* GIRATORIO **10764**
ÁRBOL *m* RECEPTOR **4299**
ÁRBOL ACANALADO *m* **11935**
ÁRBOL ACODADO *m* **3309**
ÁRBOL ACODADO *m* **3309**
ÁRBOL CIGÜEÑAL *m* **3309**
ÁRBOL DE ACCIONAMIENTO *m* **7944**
ÁRBOL DE ACERO COMPRIMIDO *m* **2850**
ÁRBOL DE CAMBIO DE MARCHA *m* **10550**
ÁRBOL DE CAMBIO DE MARCHA *m* **10550**
ÁRBOL DE DISTRIBUCIÓN *m* **10550**
ÁRBOL DE EXTREMIDAD *m* **9930**
ÁRBOL DE IMPULSIÓN *m* **7944**
ÁRBOL DE IMPULSIÓN *m* **4758**
ÁRBOL DE INVERSIÓN DE MARCHA *m* **10550**
ÁRBOL DE LA CONTRAMARCHA *m* **3233**
ÁRBOL DE LEVA *m* **1888**
ÁRBOL DE LEVAS *m* **1896**
ÁRBOL DE LEVAS EN CABEZA *m* **8939**
ÁRBOL DE LEVAS EN CULATA *m* **8939**
ÁRBOL DE MANDO *m* **7944**
ÁRBOL DE MANDO *m* **10550**
ÁRBOL DE MANDO *m* **4315**
ÁRBOL DE SECCIÓN CUADRADA *m* **12029**
ÁRBOL DE TRANSMISIÓN *m* **7944**
ÁRBOL DE TRANSMISIÓN *m* **7944**
ÁRBOL DE TRANSMISIÓN *m* **7944**
ÁRBOL DE TRANSMISIÓN *m* **8910**
ÁRBOL DE TRANSMISIÓN *m* **9930**
ÁRBOL DE TRANSMISIÓN *m* **4296**
ÁRBOL DE TRANSMISIÓN INTERMEDIA *m* **3240**
ÁRBOL DEL MOTOR *m* **4315**
ÁRBOL FLEXIBLE *m* **5420**
ÁRBOL HORIZONTAL *m* **6587**
ÁRBOL HORIZONTAL *m* **4758**
ÁRBOL HUECO *m* **6547**
ÁRBOL INTERMEDIARIO *m* **7049**
ÁRBOL INTERMEDIARIO *m* **7049**
ÁRBOL INTERMEDIARIO *m* **6756**
ÁRBOL INTERMEDIARIO *m* **6756**
ÁRBOL INTERMEDIO *m* **7202**
ÁRBOL INTERMEDIO *m* **3240**
ÁRBOL MACIZO *m* **11793**
ÁRBOL MOTOR *m* **7944**
ÁRBOL MOTOR *m* **7944**

**ARB** 966

ÁRBOL MOTOR  *m* **4315**
ÁRBOL MOTOR  *m* **4758**
ÁRBOL MOTOR  *m* **4758**
ÁRBOL OSCILANTE  *m* **10657**
ÁRBOL PORTA-FRESAS  *m* **3520**
ÁRBOL PORTACUCHILLA  *m* **3520**
ÁRBOL PORTAHÉLICE  *m* **9930**
ÁRBOL PORTALEVAS **1888**
ÁRBOL PRINCIPAL  *m* **7943**
ÁRBOL RANURADO  *m* **11935**
ÁRBOL SECUNDARIO  *m* **8910**
ÁRBOL VERTICAL  *m* **13550**
ÁRBOLES  *m pl* CONCURRENTES **7096**
ÁRBOLES  *m pl* PARALELOS **9064**
ÁRBOLES (PERPENDICULARES OBLICUOS) SITUADOS EN PLANOS DIFERENTES  *m pl* **11249**
ARBOTANTE  *m* **688**
ARCADA  *f* **14014**
ARCILLA  *f* **2465**
ARCILLA  *f* **7691**
ARCILLA  *f* CALCAREOFERRUGINOSA **1430**
ARCILLA  *f* CALCINADA **926**
ARCILLA PLÁSTICA  *f* **9470**
ARCILLA REFRACTARIA  *f* **5253**
ARCO  *m* **3494**
ARCO  *m* **1889**
ARCO  *m* **1504**
ARCO  *m* DE ALIGERAMIENTO **10442**
ARCO  *m* DE CÍRCULO **674**
ARCO  *m* DE CÍRCULO **674**
ARCO  *m* DE DEVANADO **675**
ARCO  *m* DE UNA CURVA **664**
ARCO  *m* METÁLICO **8174**
ARCO  *m* NO PROTEGIDO DE ELECTRODO DE CARBÓN **1944**
ARCO APAINELADO  *m* **5373**
ARCO DE BÓVEDA  *m* **12872**
ARCO DE CONTACTO  *m* **2997**
ARCO DE DESCARGA  *m* **10442**
ARCO DE ELECTRODO DE CARBONO  *m* **1941**
ARCO EN ESCARPA  *m* **8741**
ARCO PROTEGIDO DE ELECTRODO DE CARBÓN  *m* **1945**
ARCO REBAJADO  *m* **5373**
ARCO VOLTAICO  *m* **4494**
ARDER **1745**
ARDER SIN LLAMA **11688**
ÁREA  *f* **697**
ÁREA  *f* DE ÓXIDO **5367**
ÁREA DE COLADA  *f* **2071**
ÁREA DE LA SECCIÓN  *f* **11120**
ÁREA DE LA SECCIÓN TRANSVERSAL  *f* **12511**

ÁREA DEL CÍRCULO  *f* **695**
ARENA  *f* **10917**
ARENA  *f* AISLADORA **9094**
ARENA  *f* CUARZOSA **10082**
ARENA  *f* DE CANTERA **9396**
ARENA  *f* DE COBERTURA **912**
ARENA  *f* DE CONTACTO **5006**
ARENA  *f* DE FUNDICIÓN **8430**
ARENA  *f* DE GRANO FINO **5199**
ARENA  *f* DE GRANO GRUESO **2574**
ARENA  *f* DE MAR **11071**
ARENA  *f* DE MOLDEADO **8430**
ARENA  *f* DE RÍO **10619**
ARENA  *f* PARA MACHOS **3163**
ARENA  *f* SECA **4255**
ARENADOR  *m* **10920**
ARENISCA  *f* (GEOL.) **10928**
AREÓMETRO  *m* **316**
AREÓMETRO  *m* **6722**
AREÓMETRO  *m* DE PESO CONSTANTE **6072**
AREÓMETRO  *m* DE PESO VARIABLE **6723**
AREÓMETRO  *m* PARA SOLUCIONES SALINAS **10901**
ARGAMASAR **12718**
ARGENTÁN  *m* **5932**
ARGENTAR **11459**
ARGENTO  *m* **11458**
ARGÓN  *m* **701**
ARÍETE  *m* HIDRÁULICO **6694**
ARISTA  *f* **4441**
ARISTA  *f* CORTANTE REBAJADA **4365**
ARISTA  *f* DE SALIDA **5515**
ARISTA  *f* REDONDEADA **10808**
ARISTA  *f* TERMINAL **3625**
ARISTA CORTANTE  *f* **3528**
ARISTA DE RETROCESO  *f* **4448**
ARISTA VIVA  *f* **11272**
ARITMÉTICA  *f* **702**
ARMADURA  *f* **710**
ARMADURA  *f* **5630**
ARMADURA  *f* **5624**
ARMADURA  *f* **8145**
ARMADURA  *f* **13243**
ARMADURA  *f* DE HIERRO **3143**
ARMADURA  *f* DE UN IMÁN **710**
ARMADURA  *f* (O PROTECCIÓN  *f*) DE UN CABLE **715**
ARMADURAS  *f* **13243**
ARMARIO PARA HERRAMIENTAS  *m* **12998**
ARMARIO-CAMA **1739**
ARMAZÓN  *f* **5624**
ARMAZÓN  *f* **5624**

967 ASI

ARMAZÓN *f* **5630**
ARMAZÓN *f* **10877**
ARMAZÓN *f* **8145**
ARMAZÓN DE POSTES *f* **2754**
ARMAZÓN DE POSTES *f* **2759**
ARMELLA *f* **4973**
ARMELLAS *f* **11233**
ARO *m* **10600**
ARO *m* DE RODAMIENTO **964**
ARO *m* DE UNA RUEDA **5331**
ARO DE GUÍA DE TURBINA *m* **6168**
ARO DE RODAMIENTO *m* **964**
ARO DIRECTOR *m* **6168**
AROS *m pl* (O LLANTAS *f pl*) DE RUEDA **12220**
ARQUEADO *m* **10613**
ARQUEAR **1173**
ARQUEO *m* **1889**
ARQUEO *m* **1889**
ARQUITECTO *m* **691**
ARQUITECTURA *f* **2442**
ARRABIO *m* - HIERRO COLADO *m* **2034**
ARRABIO *m* ESPECULAR **11898**
ARRABIO *m* ESPECULAR **11899**
ARRABIO *m* ESPECULAR **11899**
ARRANCADOR *m* **8418**
ARRANCADOR *m* **9336**
ARRANCADOR *m* **12116**
ARRANCADOR **3310**
ARRANCADOR *m* AUTOMÁTICO **828**
ARRANCADORAS *f pl* DE PATATAS **9707**
ARRANCADORAS *f pl* DE REMOLACHAS **12440**
ARRANCAMIENTO *m* **10858**
ARRANCAR **12113**
ARRANQUE *m* **12118**
ARRANQUE *m* DE UN MOTOR **12130**
ARRANQUE *m* DE UN MOTOR **12122**
ARRANQUE *m* SUAVE **11685**
ARRANQUE *m* SUAVE (SIN SACUDIDAS) **11685**
ARRASTRE *m* DEL AGUA POR EL VAPOR **9863**
ARREGLO *m* **10287**
ARRUGAMIENTO *m* **11399**
ARSEMIATO *m* **720**
ARSÉNICO *m* **721**
ARSENITO *m* **729**
ARSENITO *m* DE COBRE **10996**
ARSENIURO *m* **726**
ARTERIA *f* **5081**
ARTESA *f* **13228**
ARTESA *f* **13228**
ARTESÓN *m* (TEJADO DE) **9621**

ARTICULACIÓN *f* **7238**
ARTICULACIÓN *f* **953**
ARTICULACIÓN CARDÁN *f* **6573**
ARTICULACIÓN DE CARDÁN **6573**
ARTICULACIÓN DE PASADOR *f* **9318**
ARTICULADO **7629**
ASBESTO *m* **10896**
ASBESTO *m* **6599**
ASBESTO *m* **1898**
ASBESTO *m* **755**
ASBESTO *m* **746**
ASBESTO *m* **755**
ASCENDENTE (TUBO) **10615**
ASCENSIÓN *f* **1925**
ASCENSO *m* **1925**
ASCENSOR *m* **4660**
ASCENSOR *m* **9101**
ASCENSOR *m* CONTINUO **3020**
ASCIENDE SIMULTÁNEAMENTE O DE CONTINUO **4807**
ASENTAMIENTO *m* **12418**
ASERRADERO *m* **10956**
ASERRADERO *m* MECÁNICO **9747**
ASERRADO *m* **10961**
ASERRADO *m* A CONTRAHÍLO **4718**
ASERRADO *m* A LO LARGO **1058**
ASERRADO *m* DE TRAVÉS **4718**
ASERRADO *m* EN CALIENTE **6657**
ASERRADO *m* EN FRÍO **2699**
ASERRADO *m* HOLANDÉS **10075**
ASERRADO *m* PARALELO **1058**
ASERRADO *m* POR FRICCIÓN **5680**
ASERRADO *m* POR IRRADIACIÓN **10075**
ASERRADO *m* VERTICAL **4718**
ASERRADORA *f* DE MOVIMIENTO ALTERNATIVO **5629**
ASERRAR **10951**
ASERRIN *m* **10953**
ASERRÍN *m* **10953**
ASFALTADO *m* **767**
ASFALTAJE *m* **767**
ASFALTAR **763**
ASFALTAR **763**
ASFALTO *m* **768**
ASFALTO *m* COMPRIMIDO **12610**
ASFALTO *m* DE TRINIDAD **13212**
ASFALTO *m* FUNDIDO **9713**
ASFALTO *m* PULVERULENTO **9723**
ASFALTO *m* SÓLIDO **768**
ASIDERO *m* **6262**
ASIENTO *m* **10613**
ASIENTO *m* **11098**

# ASI

968

ASIENTO *m* **10876**
ASIENTO *m* **9011**
ASIENTO *m* **7816**
ASIENTO *m* DE CUERPO DE VÁLVULA **1397**
ASIENTO *m* DE REGLAJE AUTOMÁTICO **9741**
ASIENTO *m* DE VÁLVULA **11097**
ASIENTO *m* DE VÁLVULA **13468**
ASIENTO *m* DEL CONO **12649**
ASIENTO *m* DESLIZANTE **11600**
ASIENTO *m* SILLÓN **1678**
ASIENTO *m* SUSPENDIDO **1383**
ASIENTO *m* SUSPENDIDO PARA PINTOR **9017**
ASIENTO COLGANTE DE DOS PATAS *m* **9166**
ASIENTO CONSOLA *m* **13618**
ASIENTO EN EL SUELO *m* **12064**
ASIENTOS *m* OBLICUOS **12663**
ASIENTOS *m* PARALELOS **9063**
ASIGNACIÓN *f* **10897**
ASIMETRÍA *f* **779**
ASIMÉTRICA *f* **778**
ASIMÉTRICO *m* **778**
ASÍNCRONA *f* **784**
ASINCRONISMO *m* **782**
ASÍNCRONO *m* **784**
ASÍNTOTA *f* **780**
ASINTÓTICA *f* **781**
ASINTÓTICA *f* **781**
ASINTÓTICO *m* **781**
ASINTÓTICO *m* **781**
ASPERSIÓN *f* **12001**
ASPIRACIÓN *f* **12428**
ASPIRACIÓN POR CAPILARIDAD *f* **1922**
ASPIRADOR *m* **769**
ASPIRADOR *m* **4472**
ASPIRADOR *m* **4900**
ASPIRADOR *m* DE POLVO **4390**
ASPIRAR **12427**
ASTÁTICA *f* **774**
ASTATICO *m* **774**
ASTERISMO *m* **776**
ASTROIDE *f* **5602**
ATACAR **3182**
ATACAR AL ÁCIDO **4839**
ATAQUE *m* **813**
ATAQUE *m* A LOS DERECHOS DEL TITULAR DE LA PATENTE **6916**
ATAQUE *m* AL ÁCIDO **4846**
ATAQUE *m* CORROSIVO **4846**
ATAQUE *m* DE UNA FUERZA **647**
ATAQUE *f* INTERDENDRÍTICO **7031**

ATAQUE *m* METALOGRÁFICO **8204**
ATAQUE *m* PROFUNDO **3685**
ATAR **1737**
ATASCAMIENTO *m* **2510**
ATASCAMIENTO *m* **7212**
ATASCARSE **7210**
ATASCARSE **2358**
ATASCO *m* **2362**
ATENUACIÓN *f* **3604**
ATÉRMANA *f* **786**
ATERMANEIDAD *f* **785**
ATERMANIDAD *f* **785**
ATÉRMANO *m* **786**
ATERRAJADO *m* **4277**
ATERRAJADO *m* **11028**
ATERRAJADO *m* **12678**
ATERRAJADO *m* **12868**
ATERRAJADO *m* **12868**
ATERRAJADO *m* (INTERIOR) **7078**
ATERRAJADORA *f* **11066**
ATERRAJADORA *f* **12677**
ATERRAJADORA *f* **7858**
ATERRAJAR **12636**
ATERRAJAR **3512**
ATIZADERO *m* **10116**
ATIZAR **9575**
ATMÓSFERA *f* **788**
ATMÓSFERA *f* **787**
ATMÓSFERA *f* ARTIFICIAL **789**
ATMÓSFERA *f* DE CARBONITRURACIÓN **1973**
ATMÓSFERA *f* DE PROTECCIÓN **790**
ATMÓSFERA *f* DE USO ESPECIAL **791**
ATMÓSFERA *f* ENRARECIDA **13441**
ATMÓSFERA *f* REDUCTORA **10347**
ATMÓSFERA DE NITRURACIÓN *f* **8583**
ATMÓSFERA DE PROTECCIÓN *f* **9947**
ATOMIZACIÓN *f* **811**
ATOMIZADOR *m* **809**
ÁTOMO *m* **800**
ATORNILLADO *m* **1443**
ATORNILLAMIENTO *m* **11065**
ATORNILLAR **11022**
ATORNILLAR EN **11037**
ATRACCIÓN *f* **815**
ATRACCIÓN *f* MAGNÉTICA **7895**
ATRACCIÓN *f* MOLECULAR **8359**
ATRANCARSE **2358**
ATRASO *m* DE FASE **7368**
ATRASO *m* DE FASE **7368**
ATRAVESADO *m* POR CHORRO DE FUEGO **7222**

969 BAJ

ATRAVESADO POR UNA CORRIENTE **7670**
ATRAVESAR **4264**
ATRONADO DE LA MADERA *m* **12108**
ATRONADURA *f* **12108**
ATRONADURA *f* DE LA MADERA **5700**
AUGITA *f* **819**
AUGITA-SIENITA *f* **820**
AUMENTAR **162**
AUMENTAR LA VELOCIDAD **6851**
AUMENTO *m* **7937**
AUMENTO *m* **7935**
AUMENTO *m* DE DIMENSIÓN **8961**
AUMENTO *m* DE LA PRESIÓN **6848**
AUMENTO *m* DE LA RESISTENCIA **6850**
AUMENTO *m* DE LA SECCIÓN TRANSVERSAL **5869**
AUMENTO *m* DE PRESIÓN **6855**
AUMENTO *m* DE UNA LENTE **7938**
AUMENTO *m* DE VELOCIDAD **10185**
AUMENTO *m* DE VOLUMEN **4912**
AUMENTO *m* (O ELEVACIÓN *f*) DE LA TEMPERATURA **10612**
AUMENTO DE FRAGILIDAD *m* **4685**
AUMENTO DE VELOCIDAD *m* **6849**
AUREOLA *f* **6213**
AURÍFERA *f* **822**
AURÍFERO *m* **822**
AUSTENITA *f* **825**
AUSTENITIZACIÓN *f* **827**
AUTOBÚS *m* **8410**
AUTOBÚS *m* **13421**
AUTOCAR *m* **8412**
AUTOCAR *m* **7099**
AUTOCLAVE *m* **829**
AUTODETENCIÓN *f* (DE) **11157**
AUTOEXCITACIÓN *f* **11153**
AUTOINDUCCIÓN *f* **11156**
AUTOINFLAMACIÓN *f* **11956**
AUTOMÁTICA *f* **11148**
AUTOMATICIDAD *f* **837**
AUTOMÁTICO *m* **11148**
AUTOMATISMO *m* **837**
AUTOMATIZACIÓN *f* **837**
AUTOMÓVIL *m* **8411**
AUTOMÓVIL *m* **8411**
AUTOMÓVIL *m* INDUSTRIAL **8414**
AUTONOMÍA *f* **3416**
AUTOR DE UNA INVENCIÓN *m* **7108**
AUTORIZACIÓN *f* DE EXPLOTAR **7539**
AUXILIO *m* **8048**
AVANCE *m* **9905**

AVANCE *m* **5584**
AVANCE *m* **5063**
AVANCE *m* **5063**
AVANCE *m* **2066**
AVANCE *m* **206**
AVANCE *m* BASTO **10208**
AVANCE *m* DE FASE **7483**
AVANCE *m* DE UNA HERRAMIENTA **5068**
AVANCE *m* (O ADELANTO *m*) DE FASE **7483**
AVANCE *m* POR DIENTE **5069**
AVANCE *m* RÁPIDO **10208**
AVANCE (ÁNGULO DE) *m* **2067**
AVANCE DEL ENCENDIDO *m* **9778**
AVANZAR **7448**
AVELLANADO *m* **1637**
AVELLANADO *m* **3234**
AVELLANADO DE LOS AGUJEROS DE REMACHES *m* **1638**
AVELLANAR LOS AGUJEROS DE REMACHES **1635**
AVENAR **4204**
AVENTADORAS *f pl* CERNEDORAS CLASIFICADORAS **3177**
AVIDA DE AGUA *f* **6730**
AVIDO DE AGUA *m* **6730**
AYUDA *f* **8048**
AYUSTE *m* **11930**
AZOGADO DE ESPEJOS *m* **11465**
AZÚCAR *m* DE UVA **6058**
AZUELA *f* **207**
AZUFRE *m* **12449**
AZUFRE *m* AMORFO **476**
AZUFRE *m* CILÍNDRICO **12255**
AZUFRE *m* CRISTALIZADO **3435**
AZUFRE *m* DORADO DE ANTIMONIO **625**
AZUFRE *m* SUBLIMADO **5464**
AZUFRE *m* SUBLIMADO **5464**
AZUL *m* DE PRUSIA **1206**
AZUL *m* DE PRUSIA **1206**
AZUL *m* ULTRAMAR **13334**
AZULADO *m* **1377**
AZULEJO *m* **5970**
AZURITA *f* **886**
BACTERIA *f* PATÓGENA **9126**
BAGAZO *m* **924**
BAGUETA *f* **10236**
BAINITA *f* **925**
BAJA *f* PRESIÓN **7774**
BAJA *f* TEMPERATURA **7775**
BAJA *f* TENSIÓN **7778**
BAJA CALORÍA *f* **6045**
BAJA DE TENSIÓN **2100**
BAJADA *f* DE COLADA **12003**

**BAJ** 970

BAJADA *f* DE UNA CARGA **7797**
BAJAR UNA CARGA **7793**
BAJAR UNA PERPENDICULAR **4216**
BAJAR UNA VERTICAL **4216**
BALA *f* **945**
BALANCE *m* **935**
BALANCE *m* TÉRMICO **6337**
BALANCE *m* TÉRMICO **6337**
BALANCEO *m* **12538**
BALANCÍN *m* **10654**
BALANCÍN *m* DE ROSCA **11040**
BALANCÍN *m* DE TORNILLO **11040**
BALANZA *f* **931**
BALANZA *f* **931**
BALANZA *f* ANALÍTICA **2294**
BALANZA *f* DE ANÁLISIS **2294**
BALANZA *f* DE COULOMB **13052**
BALANZA *f* DE CRUZ **1095**
BALANZA *f* DE MUELLE **11976**
BALANZA *f* DE PRECISIÓN **9764**
BALANZA *f* DE RESORTE **11976**
BALANZA *f* DE TORSIÓN **13052**
BALANZA *f* DECIMAL **3660**
BALANZA *f* DECIMAL **3660**
BALANZA *f* DECIMAL **3660**
BALANZA *f* DEL COMERCIO EXTERIOR **13099**
BALANZA *f* HIDROSTÁTICA **6725**
BALASTADO *m* **971**
BALASTO *m* **969**
BALDOSA *f* **5302**
BALDOSA *f* (CONSTR.) **12933**
BÁLSAMO *m* DE COPAIBA **3101**
BAMBOLEO *m* DE UNA CORREA **13825**
BAMBÚ *m* **972**
BANCO *m* **1167**
BANCO *m* **7234**
BANCO *m* DE CARPINTERO **7234**
BANCO *m* DE ESTIRAR **10023**
BANCO *m* DE ESTIRAR **4218**
BANCO *m* DE PRUEBAS **12773**
BANCO *m* DE TRABAJO **1167**
BANCO *m* FOTOMÉTRICO **9268**
BANCO *m* PARA VERIFICAR LOS ENGRANAJES **5902**
BANDA *f* **974**
BANDA *f* **12641**
BANDA *f* DE ABSORCIÓN **45**
BANDA *f* DE ACERO **12197**
BANDA *f* DE AMIANTO (O ASBESTO) **754**
BANDA *f* DE COBRE **3131**
BANDA *f* DE DEFORMACIÓN **3706**

BANDA *f* DE FERRITA LIBRE **5105**
BANDA *f* DE INTERFERENCIA **7036**
BANDA *f* DE MACLAS **570**
BANDA *f* DE PLEGADO **7314**
BANDA *f* DE RECAUCHUTADO **1892**
BANDAJE *m* DE LA RUEDA **13322**
BANDAS *f pl* **980**
BANDAS *f pl* DE DESLIZAMIENTO **11613**
BANDAS *f pl* DE METAL DE RECUBRIMIENTO **1928**
BANDAS *f pl* DE NEUMANN **8540**
BANDAS *f pl* GALVANIZADAS **5788**
BANDAS *f pl* REVELADAS POR ATAQUE QUÍMICO **4840**
BANDEJA *f* **13228**
BAÑO *m* **3967**
BAÑO *m* **1062**
BAÑO *m* AZUL **1369**
BAÑO *m* AZUL **1369**
BAÑO *m* DE ABRILLANTADO **1608**
BAÑO *m* DE ABRILLANTAMIENTO **1564**
BAÑO *m* DE ACEITE **8745**
BAÑO *m* DE ARENA **10918**
BAÑO *m* DE BLANQUEO **8059**
BAÑO *m* DE CEMENTACIÓN **1994**
BAÑO *m* DE CLORURO MERCÚRICO **1369**
BAÑO *m* DE DECAPADO **111**
BAÑO *m* DE DECAPADO **12382**
BAÑO *m* DE DECAPADO **9289**
BAÑO *m* DE DECAPADO INICIAL **2476**
BAÑO *m* DE DECAPADO MATE **8059**
BAÑO *m* DE DECAPAJE ÁCIDO **9290**
BAÑO *m* DE DESCASCARILLADO (O DE DECAPADO) **3790**
BAÑO *m* DE DESCOMPOSICIÓN DEL ELECTRÓLITO **7538**
BAÑO *m* DE FUSIÓN **8137**
BAÑO *m* DE FUSIÓN **9961**
BAÑO *m* DE HIDRÓXIDO DE SODIO **2117**
BAÑO *m* DE MORDENTACIÓN **9289**
BAÑO *m* DE PASIVACIÓN **9103**
BAÑO *m* DE PLOMO **7454**
BAÑO *m* DE REMOCIÓN (O DE ELIMINACIÓN) DE LA HERRUMBRE **10872**
BAÑO *m* DE SAL **10905**
BAÑO *m* DE VAPOR **12157**
BAÑO *m* MARÍA **13641**
BARANDILLA *f* INFERIOR **7795**
BARBA *f* **1764**
BARCAZA *f* **991**
BARCAZA *f* **991**
BARCAZAS *f pl* DE ASIENTO (O TENDIDOO COLOCACIÓN) **7440**
BARCAZAS *f pl* DE TRANSPORTE **3787**
BAREMO *m* **8052**

971  BAS

BARIO *m* **992**
BARITA *f* **1020**
BARITINA *f* **1021**
BARITITA *f* **1021**
BARLOVENTO *m* **13721**
BARNIO *m* **1006**
BARNIZ *m* **13504**
BARNIZ *m* A LA GASOLINA **13296**
BARNIZ *m* A LA GOMA LACA **10998**
BARNIZ *m* AL ACEITE **8786**
BARNIZ *m* AL ALCOHOL **7354**
BARNIZ *m* AL ASFALTO **1283**
BARNIZ *m* AL COPAL **3103**
BARNIZ *m* DEL JAPÓN **239**
BARNIZ *m* JAPÓN **1283**
BARNIZ *m* ZAPÓN **14022**
BARNIZADO *m* **13505**
BARNIZAR **7353**
BARNIZAR CON LACA **7353**
BAROMÉTRICA **1009**
BAROMÉTRICO *m* **1009**
BARÓMETRO *m* **1008**
BARÓMETRO *m* ANEROIDE **504**
BARÓMETRO *m* DE CUBETAS **2440**
BARÓMETRO *m* DE MERCURIO **8150**
BARÓMETRO *m* DE SIFÓN **11515**
BARÓMETRO *m* METÁLICO **504**
BARÓMETRO *m* REGISTRADOR **1007**
BAROSCOPIO *m* **1011**
BARQUILLA *f* **1383**
BARRA *f* **986**
BARRA *f* **981**
BARRA *f* **10660**
BARRA *f* **10663**
BARRA *f* **10660**
BARRA *f* **10660**
BARRA *f* COLECTORA **1770**
BARRA *f* COLECTORA **1770**
BARRA *f* COMPRIMIDA **2855**
BARRA *f* CON COMPRESIÓN **2855**
BARRA *f* DE ACERO CEMENTADO **1328**
BARRA *f* DE ACOPLAMIENTO **12231**
BARRA *f* DE ACOPLAMIENTO **12916**
BARRA *f* DE ACOPLAMIENTO **12915**
BARRA *f* DE COBRE **3113**
BARRA *f* DE CONEXIÓN **2962**
BARRA *f* DE DESMOLDEO **7333**
BARRA *f* DE ENGANCHE **4217**
BARRA *f* DE ENGANCHE **4217**
BARRA *f* DE ENSAYO **12772**

BARRA *f* DE ENSAYO **12772**
BARRA *f* DE ESCARIADO MICROMÉTRICO **8240**
BARRA *f* DE HIERRO BRUTO **8441**
BARRA *f* DE MACHO FUSIBLE **3168**
BARRA *f* DE MANDO **6164**
BARRA *f* DE METAL PRECIOSO **1730**
BARRA *f* DE NOYO FUSIBLE **3168**
BARRA *f* DE OJALES **5551**
BARRA *f* DE ÓMNIBUS **1770**
BARRA *f* DE PRUEBA **12772**
BARRA *f* DE PRUEBA ENTALLADA **8675**
BARRA *f* DE SECCÍON DECRECIENTE **12670**
BARRA *f* DE TOMA DE TIERRA **4419**
BARRA *f* DE TORSIÓN **13053**
BARRA *f* ENTALLADA **8675**
BARRA *f* ESTABILIZADORA **12539**
BARRA *f* ESTIRADA **12754**
BARRA *f* ÓMNIBUS **1770**
BARRA *f* PLANA **5374**
BARRA *f* TALADRADORA SÓLIDA **11778**
BARRA CÓNICA DE ALINEACIÓN *f* **3215**
BARRA DE UÑA *f* **7725**
BARRACA *f* DE LA OBRA **2987**
BARRACA *f* DE VESTUARIO **2247**
BARRACA *f* DEL PERSONAL **11519**
BARRACÓN *m* **11302**
BARRAS *f pl* DE ACERO ESTIRADAS **4248**
BARRAS *f pl* DE PARRILLAS **6069**
BARRAS *f pl* DE TALADRAR **1470**
BARRAS *f pl* LAMINADAS EN FRÍO **2695**
BARRAS *f pl* OCTOGONALES DE ACERO ALEADO **375**
BARRENA *f* **5944**
BARRENA *f* FINA **5944**
BARRENADO *m* **4277**
BARRENADO *m* **1461**
BARRENADO *m* **10006**
BARRENAR **9186**
BARRENAR **10771**
BARRENAS *f pl* **9664**
BARRENO *m* ELÉCTRICO **4556**
BARRERA *f* **13753**
BARRERA *f* DE COTTRELL **3224**
BARRETA *f* **5183**
BARRETA *f* **10660**
BARRO *m* **11655**
BARRO DE ALFAREROS *m* **9470**
BARROS *m pl* **8444**
BARROTE *m* **10660**
BARROTE *m* DE PARRILLA **5237**
BASÁLTICA *f* **1023**

# BAS

972

BASÁLTICO *m* 1023
BASALTO *m* 1022
BASAMENTO *m* DE UNA COLUMNA 1035
BASAR 12491
BÁSCULA 931
BÁSCULA 931
BÁSCULA *f* 3660
BÁSCULA *f* BINARIA 5429
BÁSCULA *f* PARA ALEACIONES 362
BÁSCULA *f* ROMANA 12225
BÁSCULA *f* ROMANA 12225
BASCULADOR DE VAGONES *m* 1932
BASE *f* 1027
BASE *f* 1026
BASE *f* 1025
BASE *f* 1024
BASE *f* 2896
BASE *f* 12490
BASE *f* 9011
BASE *f* DE UN LOGARITMO 1033
BASE DE DEPÓSITO *f* 12628
BÁSICA 1042
BASICIDAD *f* 1055
BÁSICO *m* 1042
BASTIDOR *m* 1504
BASTIDOR *m* 5624
BASTIDOR *m* 5624
BASTIDOR *m* 10877
BASTIDOR *m* DE UNA MÁQUINA 5626
BASTIDOR DE MOLDEO *m* 5369
BASTIDOR PARA TENSAR *m* 12756
BASURAS *f pl* 13074
BATEAR 6153
BATERÍA *f* 4534
BATERÍA *f* DE ACUMULADORES 1066
BATERÍA *f* DE CALDERAS 1069
BATERÍA *f* DE PILAS 9845
BATERÍA *f* PRIMARIA 9845
BATERÍA *f* SECUNDARIA 77
BATERÍA *f* TAMPÓN 1687
BATIDERO *m* 1119
BATIDERO *m* DE ORO 5994
BATIDO *m* 4235
BATIDO *m* 1119
BATIDO *m* CON CALDEO POR EFECTO JOULE 13417
BATIDO *m* DE METALES 1120
BATIDO *m* EN FRÍO 2686
BATIDURAS *f pl* 6217
BATIDURAS *f pl* METÁLICAS 8279
BATIR 7263

BATIR 4219
BAÚL *m* 1458
BAÚL *m* CAJA *f* 1458
BAÚL *m* CAJA *f* 13239
BAUXITA *f* 1071
BEBEDERO *m* 4186
BEBEDERO *m* 12003
BEDANO *m* 3364
BENCENO *m* 1199
BENCENO *m* 1204
BENCIDINA *f* 1201
BENCINA *f* 1199
BENCINA *f* BRUTA 3408
BENCINA *f* (DE PETRÓLEO) 9222
BENEFICIO *m* EN EL TRABAJO 8094
BENJUÍ *m* 1203
BENZALDEHÍDO *m* 1198
BENZOFENONA *f* 1205
BENZOL *m* 1204
BENZOL *m* 1199
BERBIQUÍ 1519
BERBIQUÍ *m* 3313
BERBIQUÍ *m* CON TORNILLO DE PRESIÓN 1518
BERBIQUÍ *m* DE ENGRANAJE 5905
BERBIQUÍ *m* HELICOIDAL 689
BERILIO *m* 1207
BERLINA *f* 10902
BERLINA *f* 11128
BERMELLÓN *m* 13535
BETÚN *m* SÓLIDO 768
BIATÓMICA *f* 3881
BIATÓMICO *m* 3881
BIBÁSICO 3882
BICARBONATO *m* DE AMONIO 459
BICARBONATO *m* DE CALCIO 1847
BICARBONATO *m* DE MAGNESIO 7883
BICARBONATO *m* DE POTASA 9676
BICARBONATO *m* SÓDICO 126
BIDÓN *m* 12961
BIELA *f* 2962
BIELA *f* DE ACOPLAMIENTO 3256
BIELA *f* DE EXCÉNTRICA 4431
BIELA *f* DE MANDO 4317
BIGORNIA *f* 1091
BIGORNIA *f* DE YUNQUE 1090
BINADORES *m* (ARRASTRADOS POR TRACTOR O MONTADOS EN ÉL) 6515
BIÓXIDO *m* DE BARIO 998
BIÓXIDO *m* DE ESTAÑO 12098
BIÓXIDO *m* DE MANGANESO 10047

BIÓXIDO *m* DE SODIO **11727**
BIÓXIDO DE HIDRÓGENO *m* **6716**
BIÓXIDO DE NITRÓGENO *m* **8581**
BIPLANO *m* **1261**
BIRREFRINGENTE *m* **1265**
BISAGRA *f* **6505**
BISAGRA *f* **6505**
BISAGRA *f* (MACHO) **6508**
BISAGRA UNIVERSAL *f* **6573**
BISECCIÓN *f* **1267**
BISECTAR **1266**
BISECTRIZ *f* **1268**
BISECTRIZ *f* AGUDA **156**
BISEL *m* **1800**
BISEL *m* **1221**
BISEL *m* **1221**
BISELADO *m* **1231**
BISELADO *m* **1231**
BISELADO *m* **2233**
BISELADO *m* **3234**
BISELAR **2230**
BISELAR **1222**
BISMUTINA *f* **1275**
BISMUTO *m* **1269**
BISULFITO *m* DE AMONÍACO **460**
BISULFITO *m* SÓDICO **11718**
BITARTRATO *m* POTÁSICO **119**
BITUMEN *m* **1280**
BITUMINOSA *f* **1281**
BITUMINOSO *m* **1281**
BIVALENTE **3881**
BIZCOCHO *m* DE PORCELANA **1276**
BLANCO *m* **12682**
BLANCO *m* DE BARITA **1003**
BLANCO *m* DE CERUSA **13834**
BLANCO *m* DE CINC **14043**
BLANCO *m* DE CINC **14043**
BLANCO *m* DE ESPAÑA **13841**
BLANCO *m* DE ESPAÑA **13841**
BLANCO *m* DE ESPAÑA **13841**
BLANCO *m* DE PARÍS **13841**
BLANCO *m* DE PARÍS **13841**
BLANCO *m* DE PLOMO **13834**
BLANCO *m* DE PLOMO **13834**
BLANCO *m* FIJO **1003**
BLENDA *f* **1324**
BLENDA *f* **1324**
BLENDA *f* **1324**
BLINDAJE *m* **11342**
BLOCADO *m* **7711**

BLOCADO *m* **7711**
BLONDÍN *m* **1344**
BLOQUE *m* **1332**
BLOQUE *m* DE ACERO **951**
BLOQUE *m* DE SÍLICE **11435**
BLOQUE *m* MOTOR **3564**
BLOQUE *m* PORTAYUNQUE **633**
BLOQUE PORTAYUNQUE *m* **633**
BLOQUEAR **7699**
BLOQUEAR UNA CHAVETA **7700**
BLOQUEAR UNA TUERCA **7700**
BLOQUEO *m* **7711**
BLOQUEO *m* **7711**
BLOQUEO *m* **7707**
BLOQUEO *m* **7710**
BLOQUEO *m* (DE) AUTOMÁTICO **11157**
BLOQUEO *m* DE CHAVETAS **7704**
BLOQUEO DE UNA CHAVETA *m* **4310**
BOBINA *f* **4499**
BOBINA *f* **1384**
BOBINA *f* **2648**
BOBINA *f* **2645**
BOBINA *f* DE ENCENDIDO **6761**
BOBINA *f* DE FLEJE **1738**
BOBINA *f* DE INDUCCIÓN **6894**
BOBINA *f* DE RUHMKORFF **10830**
BOBINADO *m* **2650**
BOBINADO *m* **13862**
BOBINADORA *f* **13903**
BOBINAR **13853**
BOCA *f* DE INCENDIOS **5244**
BOCA *f* DE MARTILLO **9031**
BOCA *f* DE MARTILLO BOMBEADA **963**
BOCA *f* DE RIEGO **6672**
BOCA *f* ESFÉRICA DE MARTILLO **963**
BOCA *f* REDONDA DE MARTILLO **961**
BOCA DE ENTRADA A UNA CALDERA **7998**
BOCARTE *m* **12057**
BOCINA *f* **6592**
BOJ *m* **1507**
BOL *m* **1430**
BOLA *f* **950**
BOLA *f* DE ACERO **951**
BOLA *f* DEL REGULADOR **6015**
BOLA *f* PARA RODAMIENTOS **1102**
BOLAS *f pl* DE BRUÑIR **1759**
BOLAS *f pl* DE PULIR **1759**
BOLÓMETRO *m* **1431**
BOLSA *f* DE HERRAMIENTAS **12996**
BOMBA *f* **9991**

# BOM

974

BOMBA  f 1722
BOMBA  f A MANO 6244
BOMBA  f ASPIRANTE 12434
BOMBA  f CENTRÍFUGA 13269
BOMBA  f CENTRÍFUGA 2184
BOMBA  f DE ACEITE 8769
BOMBA  f DE ÁCIDO 121
BOMBA  f DE AIRE 284
BOMBA  f DE AIRE 249
BOMBA  f DE AIRE COMPRIMIDO 273
BOMBA  f DE AIRE HÚMEDO 13799
BOMBA  f DE AIRE SECO 4340
BOMBA  f DE ALIMENTACIÓN 5715
BOMBA  f DE ALIMENTACIÓN 5713
BOMBA  f DE ALIMENTACIÓN 5071
BOMBA  f DE DIAFRAGMA 3874
BOMBA  f DE ÉMBOLO 9378
BOMBA  f DE ÉMBOLO CON MOVIMIENTO RECTILÍNEO ALTERNATIVO 10284
BOMBA  f DE ÉMBOLO DE SUMERSIÓN 9546
BOMBA  f DE ÉMBOLO OSCILANTE 11176
BOMBA  f DE ENGRANAJE 5895
BOMBA  f DE ENGRASE 8769
BOMBA  f DE INYECCIÓN 5711
BOMBA  f DE MERCURIO 8163
BOMBA  f DE PALETAS 13478
BOMBA  f DE PALETAS ROTATIVAS 10758
BOMBA  f DE PRUEBA 12787
BOMBA  f DE RECUPERACIÓN 61
BOMBA  f DE ROTOR 10758
BOMBA  f DE VACÍO 284
BOMBA  f DE VAPOR 12183
BOMBA  f DOBLE 4381
BOMBA  f ELEVADORA 7548
BOMBA  f HELICOIDAL 11042
BOMBA  f HELICOIDAL 861
BOMBA  f HIDRÁULICA 8769
BOMBA  f IMPELENTE 5531
BOMBA  f NEUMÁTICA 284
BOMBA  f PARA POZOS PROFUNDOS 3689
BOMBA  f PORTÁTIL 9638
BOMBA  f ROTATIVA 10758
BOMBA  f VOLUMÉTRICA 9653
BOMBA DE ACCIONAMIENTO A MANO  f 6244
BOMBA DE DIAFRAGMA  f 3874
BOMBAS  f pl 9996
BOMBEADO  m 1720
BOMBEADO  m 1722
BOMBEADO  m 1889
BOMBEAMIENTO  m 4040

BOMBEO  m 6670
BOMBEO  m 1720
BOMBEO  m DE LA LLANTA DE UNA POLEA 3398
BOMBILLA  f 7385
BOMBONA  f 1981
BOMBONA  f 1981
BOQUILLA  f 196
BOQUILLA  f 12966
BOQUILLA  f 12966
BORATO  m DE SOSA ANHIDRA 1459
BÓRAX  m 1459
BÓRAX  m 1459
BORDE  m 4441
BORDE  m 4441
BORDE  m 4441
BORDE  m 4447
BORDE  m DE ABSORCIÓN 49
BORDE  m DE CHAPA 9483
BORDE  m DE JUNTA 6130
BORDE  m DE SOLDAR 6130
BORDE  m DOBLADO 1083
BORDE  m REDONDEADO 1083
BORDES  m pl DE CORTES 7633
BORDÓN  m 1082
BORNA  f 12762
BORNE  m 12763
BORNE  m DE CONTACTO 1254
BORNE  m DE ENTRADA 6944
BORNE  m (O TERMINAL  m) DE CONEXIÓN 12762
BORNES  m 12765
BORO  m 1477
BORRA  f DE COCO 2654
BORRAR 4799
BORT  m 1480
BOSQUEJAR 11529
BOSQUEJAR 11529
BOSQUEJO  m 11532
BOSQUEJO  m 1341
BOTADOR  m 9326
BOTADOR  m 7278
BOTADOR  m 12127
BOTAR UNA CHAVETA 4295
BOTELLA  f PARA LAVADO DEL GAS 5845
BOTÓN  m DE INTERRUPTOR 9797
BOTÓN  m DE MANIVELA 9319
BOTÓN  m DE MANIVELA 3302
BOTÓN  m DE MANIVELA 3302
BOTÓN  m DE TENSIÓN 12755
BOTÓN  m MARCHA/PARADA 12115
BOTÓN  m PULSADOR 9797

BOTÓN *m* PULSADOR **9797**
BÓVEDA *f* **1889**
BRABANTE *m* **9526**
BRACEADO *m* **11254**
BRACEADO *m* **6279**
BRASERO *m* **3821**
BRAZO *m* ARTICULADO **6505**
BRAZO *m* DE ENCENDIDO **4085**
BRAZO *m* DE GRÚA **3291**
BRAZO *m* DE GRÚA **3619**
BRAZO *m* DE LA PUNTA DE HAZAR DEL PLANÍMETRO **10662**
BRAZO *m* DE MANIVELA **3301**
BRAZO *m* DE PALANCA **7531**
BRAZO *m* DE PALANCA DE LA FUERZA **706**
BRAZO *m* DE SUSPENSIÓN **3050**
BRAZO *m* DE UN HIERRO EN ÁNGULO **13728**
BRAZO *m* DE UN VOLANTE **705**
BRAZO *m* DE UNA POLEA **705**
BRAZO *m* DEL ELECTRODO **6592**
BRAZO *m* DEL LAPICERO **9165**
BRAZO *m* DEL REGULADOR **6014**
BRAZO *m* DEL TIRALÍNEAS DEL COMPÁS **9160**
BRAZO *m* MECÁNICO **7531**
BRAZO *m* OSCILANTE **12549**
BRAZO *m* PARABÓLICO DE UNA POLEA **3497**
BRAZO *m* PORTAAGUJA DE UN COMPÁS **8521**
BRAZO *m* PRINCIPAL DE UNA GRÚA **7226**
BRAZO *m* RADIAL **10128**
BRAZO *m* RECTO DE UNA POLEA **12302**
BREA *f* DE ALQUITRÁN DE HULLA **2569**
BREA *f* DE COLOFONIA **2737**
BRECHA *f* **11831**
BRIDA *f* **13324**
BRIDA *f* **7817**
BRIDA *f* **2720**
BRIDA *f* **5323**
BRIDA *f* **5323**
BRIDA *f* CIEGA **1326**
BRIDA *f* CIEGA **1304**
BRIDA *f* CIEGA **1304**
BRIDA *f* CIEGA **1304**
BRIDA *f* CIEGA **1304**
BRIDA *f* DE ACOPLAMIENTO **3255**
BRIDA *f* DE CARA ELEVADA (O ALZADA) **10183**
BRIDA *f* DE CUBO **6663**
BRIDA *f* DE CUELLO SOLDADA **13794**
BRIDA *f* DE HIERRO EN ÁNGULO **512**
BRIDA *f* DE LA TAPA **1452**
BRIDA *f* DE MANDRILAR **10699**

BRIDA *f* DE REDUCCIÓN **10350**
BRIDA *f* DE ROSCAR **11055**
BRIDA *f* DE TUBO **9351**
BRIDA *f* DE TUBO **9351**
BRIDA *f* (DE UN TUBO) **7832**
BRIDA *f* DEL CASQUETE **5955**
BRIDA *f* DEL COJINETE DE EMPUJE **2723**
BRIDA *f* DEL PRENSAESTOPAS **9002**
BRIDA *f* DOBLE **4139**
BRIDA *f* EN BRUTO **10776**
BRIDA *f* FIJA **5039**
BRIDA *f* FUNDIDA INTEGRAL **2063**
BRIDA *f* MANDRILADA **10672**
BRIDA *f* MÓVIL **1708**
BRIDA *f* OVALADA **8918**
BRIDA *f* PLANEADA **5382**
BRIDA *f* REDONDA **10797**
BRIDA *f* REMACHADA **10638**
BRIDA *f* REVUELTA **5003**
BRIDA *f* ROSCADA **11064**
BRIDA *f* ROSCADA **12866**
BRIDA *f* SOLDADA **11758**
BRIDA *f* SUELTA **7746**
BRIDA *f* SUELTA **1708**
BRIDA *f* TAPADA **1326**
BRIDA *f* TAPADA **1304**
BRIDA *f* TAPADA **1304**
BRIDA *f* TAPADA **1304**
BRIDA A SELLAR O EMPOTRAR *f* **9345**
BRIDA CON TORNILLO PARA LATIGUILLOS *f* **6611**
BRIDA DE APRIETE (PARA TUBO) *f* **6610**
BRIDAR (O REBORDEAR) TUBOS **7243**
BRIDAS *f pl* **5270**
BRIDAS *f pl* DE MECANIZACIÓN **13013**
BRIDAS *f pl* DE MORTAJADO **7289**
BRILLO *m* **7830**
BRILLO *m* ANACARADO **9146**
BRILLO *m* DIAMANTINO **158**
BRILLO *m* LUMINOSO **1616**
BRILLO *m* METÁLICO **8195**
BRILLO *m* SEDOSO **11455**
BRILLO *m* VÍTREO **13583**
BRIQUETA *f* **1623**
BRIQUETA *f* DE FERROALEACIÓN **1622**
BRIQUETA *f* DE MINERAL **8860**
BRIQUETA *f* DE MINERAL **8860**
BRIQUETA *m* DE TURBA **9148**
BROCA *f* **4271**
BROCA *f* **4271**
BROCA *f* **4263**

# BRO

976

BROCA  *f* **4263**
BROCA  *f* AL ESTILO SUIZO **11023**
BROCA  *f* AMERICANA **13304**
BROCA  *f* CON ESTRÍAS RECTAS **12304**
BROCA  *f* CON INVERSIÓN DE CORTES **4160**
BROCA  *f* CÓNICA **2009**
BROCA  *f* DE ATAQUE EN CARBURO **1936**
BROCA  *f* DE AVELLANAR **3245**
BROCA  *f* DE CAÑON **3563**
BROCA  *f* DE CAÑON **6177**
BROCA  *f* DE CENTRO **2164**
BROCA  *f* DE CORTANTES INVERTIDOS **4160**
BROCA  *f* DE CORTE RÁPIDO **10206**
BROCA  *f* DE CUCHARA **11957**
BROCA  *f* DE CUCHARA **11957**
BROCA  *f* DE ESPIGA **2164**
BROCA  *f* DE ESPIGA CILÍNDRICA **9316**
BROCA  *f* DE FRESAR **3245**
BROCA  *f* DE LENGUA DE ASPID **5380**
BROCA  *f* DE TRES PUNTAS **2164**
BROCA  *f* ELÉCTRICA **4556**
BROCA  *f* EN HÉLICE **13304**
BROCA  *f* EN HÉLICE APRETADA **6470**
BROCA  *f* ESTIRIA O TORSADA **11023**
BROCA  *f* HELICOIDAL **13304**
BROCA  *f* HELICOIDAL **13304**
BROCA  *f* HELICOIDAL **13304**
BROCA  *f* PARA CENTRAR **2164**
BROCA  *f* PARA CENTRAR **2763**
BROCA  *f* PARA CHAPA **9997**
BROCA  *f* PLANA **5380**
BROCA  *f* TORSADA **11023**
BROCA DE MANO  *f* **6258**
BROCHADO  *m* **1637**
BROMATO  *m* **1646**
BROMIRITA  *f* **1645**
BROMIRITA  *f* **1645**
BROMO  *m* **1649**
BROMURO  *m* **1645**
BROMURO  *m* **1648**
BROMURO  *m* **1645**
BROMURO  *m* DE PLATA **1645**
BROMURO  *m* DE PLATA **1645**
BROMURO  *m* DE POTASIO **9678**
BRONCE  *m* **1650**
BRONCE  *m* ACIDORRESISTENTE **1655**
BRONCE  *m* AL ALUMINIO **58**
BRONCE  *m* AL ALUMINIO **420**
BRONCE  *m* AL BERILIO **1209**
BRONCE  *m* AL NÍQUEL **8560**

BRONCE  *m* ALFA **1656**
BRONCE  *m* COMÚN **1657**
BRONCE  *m* COMÚN **1657**
BRONCE  *m* DE ACUÑACIÓN **8183**
BRONCE  *m* DE ADORNO **1662**
BRONCE  *m* DE ADORNO **1663**
BRONCE  *m* DE ARTE **12147**
BRONCE  *m* DE ARTE **12147**
BRONCE  *m* DE BERILIO **1208**
BRONCE  *m* DE CAMPANAS **1134**
BRONCE  *m* DE CAÑÓN **6178**
BRONCE  *m* DE CAÑONES **197**
BRONCE  *m* DE COJINETE **1660**
BRONCE  *m* DE COJINETE **1660**
BRONCE  *m* DE CONSTRUCCIÓN **692**
BRONCE  *m* DE MONEDAS **8183**
BRONCE  *m* DE NÍQUEL Y ALUMINIO **8572**
BRONCE  *m* DE ORO **5995**
BRONCE  *m* DE POLVO **1652**
BRONCE  *m* DE RESORTE **1661**
BRONCE  *m* DE TUNGSTENO **13263**
BRONCE  *m* FOSFORADO **9246**
BRONCE  *m* FOSFOROSO **9246**
BRONCE  *m* MANGANÉSICO **7967**
BRONCE  *m* PARA ESPEJOS DE TELESCOPIOS **11867**
BRONCE  *m* PARA FÁBRICA DE TORNILLOS **1659**
BRONCE  *m* PLÁSTICO **1660**
BRONCE  *m* PLÁSTICO **1660**
BRONCE  *m* PLOMOSO **7456**
BRONCE  *m* SILICIOSO **11444**
BRONCE (DE) **216**
BRONCEADO  *m* **1664**
BRONCEAR **1651**
BRÚJULA  *f* **2799**
BRUMA  *f* **6313**
BRUÑIDO  *m* **5408**
BRUÑIDO  *m* **1758**
BRUÑIDO  *m* **1755**
BRUÑIDO  *m* **1755**
BRUÑIDOR  *m* **1757**
BRUÑIDURA  *f* **11686**
BRUÑIMIENTO  *m* **5972**
BRUÑIR **1756**
BRUTO  *m* **3406**
BRUTO  *m* DE COLADA **739**
BRUTO  *m* DE FORJA **742**
BRUTO  *m* DE LAMINADO **744**
BRUTO  *m* DE TEMPLE **743**
BUCLE  *m* **14014**
BUCLE  *m* DE REACCIÓN **5080**

BÚFALO *m* **1685**
BUJE *m* **5329**
BUJÍA *f* **1899**
BUJÍA *f* DE CALEFACCIÓN **6387**
BUJÍA *f* DE ENCENDIDO **11841**
BUJÍA *f* DE ENCENDIDO **11838**
BUJÍA *f* DECIMAL **3663**
BUJÍA *f* HEFNER **6419**
BUJÍA *f* HEFNER **6419**
BUJÍA *f* INCANDESCENTE **6387**
BULBO *m* **1711**
BULÓN *m* **1432**
BULÓN *m* DE ANCLAJE **501**
BULÓN *m* DE FUNDACIÓN **5590**
BULÓN *m* DE UNA CADENA DE RODILLOS **9320**
BULÓN *m* DE VÍA **5269**
BURBUJA *f* DE AIRE **1670**
BURBUJA *f* DE GAS **1671**
BURETA *f* **1743**
BURIL *m* **3364**
BURIL *m* **2349**
BURIL *m* BISELADO **9571**
BURILADO *m* **2347**
BURILAR **2344**
BURNONITA *f* **1502**
BUSCACENTROS *m* **2173**
BUTANO *m* **1775**
BUTILENO *m* **1816**
BUZA *f* **7363**
BUZA *f* **7361**
BUZO *m* (DE TERMÓMETRO) **1711**
CABALLO EFECTIVO *m* **151**
CABALLO HORA *m* **6603**
CABALLO NOMINAL *m* **6873**
CABALLO VAPOR *m* **6602**
CABECERA *f* **6320**
CABEZA *f* AVELLANADA **3250**
CABEZA *f* CILÍNDRICA DE UN TORNILLO **3574**
CABEZA *f* CUADRADA DE UN TORNILLO **10309**
CABEZA *f* DE ALFILER **9317**
CABEZA *f* DE AVELLANADO (O DE CORTE) **3531**
CABEZA *f* DE BIELA **2963**
CABEZA *f* DE BIELA DE CAJA ABIERTA **8007**
CABEZA *f* DE BIELA DE CAJA CERRADA **1509**
CABEZA *m* DE CIGÜEÑAL **9319**
CABEZA *f* DE DESTILACIÓN **5267**
CABEZA *f* DE GOTA DE SEBO DE UN TORNILLO **4673**
CABEZA *f* DE MEDIDA **5877**
CABEZA *f* DE PIEZA DE FUNDICIÓN **11506**
CABEZA *f* DE POSTE **2749**

CABEZA *f* DE PROYECTOR **11079**
CABEZA *f* DE ROBLÓN **10624**
CABEZA *f* DE SOLDADURA **13783**
CABEZA *f* DE SOLDADURA UNIVERSAL **13390**
CABEZA *f* DE UN MARTILLO **4993**
CABEZA *f* DE UN REMACHE **1436**
CABEZA *f* DE UN TORNILLO **1436**
CABEZA *f* DE UNA CHAVETA **6318**
CABEZA *f* DE UNA VÁLVULA **13463**
CABEZA *f* DEL CILINDRO **3569**
CABEZA *f* DEL DIENTE **9569**
CABEZA *f* DEL VÁSTAGO DE LA EXCÉNTRICA **4432**
CABEZA *f* ESTRIADA DE UN TORNILLO **8281**
CABEZA *f* EXAGONAL DE UN TORNILLO **6461**
CABEZA *f* GRANDE DE BIELA **3299**
CABEZA *f* OCULTA DE UN TORNILLO **3250**
CABEZA *f* PLANA DE UN TORNILLO **5394**
CABEZA *f* REDONDA DE UN TORNILLO **1813**
CABEZA MÓVIL DE TORRETA *f* **12599**
CABEZAL *m* **11904**
CABEZAL *m* **2727**
CABEZAL *m* DE TALADRADO MULTIBROCAS **8458**
CABEZAL *m* DE TALADRO **4278**
CABEZAL *m* DE TORNO **6328**
CABEZAL *m* (DE TORNO) **7964**
CABEZAL *m* FIJO **6328**
CABEZAL *m* MÓVIL **12599**
CABEZAL *m* MULTIBROCAS **8459**
CABEZAL DIVISOR *m* **4105**
CABIDA *f* **1917**
CABINA *f* ADELANTADA **1824**
CABINA *f* DE CAMIÓN **13229**
CABLE *m* **10730**
CABLE *m* TRENZADO **12336**
CABLE AÉREO **8938**
CABLE AISLADO P.V.C. *m* **9472**
(CABLE) ALIMENTADOR *m* **5081**
CABLE ANTIGIRATORIO *m* **8646**
CABLE ARMADO *m* **713**
CABLE CERRADO *m* **2513**
CABLE CONDUCTOR TODO-ALUMINIO *m* **343**
CABLE CÓNICO *m* **12661**
CABLE DE ACERO *m* **12215**
CABLE DE ACERO *m* **12201**
CABLE DE ACERO *m* **12201**
CABLE DE ACERO *m* **12215**
CABLE DE ALAMBRES *m* **7147**
CABLE DE ALGODÓN *m* **3221**
CABLE DE ASCENSOR *m* **7546**
CABLE DE CABLEADO ALBERT *m* **309**

**CAB** 978

CABLE DE CABLEADO LANG O ALBERT  *m* **7390**
CABLE DE CABOS TRIANGULARES  *m* **13195**
CABLE DE CÁÑAMO  *m* **6443**
CABLE DE DISTRIBUCIÓN  *m* **4079**
CABLE DE ELEVACIÓN  *m* **6520**
CABLE DE EXTRACCIÓN  *m* **6520**
CABLE DE FUNDA METÁLICA  *m* **8177**
CABLE DE MANDO  *m* **3051**
CABLE DE SECCIÓN CUADRADA  *m* **12028**
CABLE DE SECCIÓN DECRECIENTE  *m* **12661**
CABLE DE SECCIÓN TRIANGULAR  *m* **13194**
CABLE DE TIERRA  *m* **4411**
CABLE DE TRANSMISIÓN  *m* **4314**
CABLE DE TRANSMISIÓN  *m* **4314**
CABLE DISMINUIDO  *m* **12661**
CABLE ELÉCTRICO  *m* **1825**
CABLE METÁLICO  *m* **13899**
CABLE METÁLICO DE CABOS PLANOS  *m* **5407**
CABLE METÁLICO DE HILOS FINOS  *m* **5207**
CABLE METÁLICO DE HILOS GRUESOS  *m* **2579**
CABLE METÁLICO DE HILOS PARALELOS  *m* **7390**
CABLE METÁLICO DE TORSIÓN ALTERNATIVO  *m* **10415**
CABLE PLANO  *m* **5393**
CABLE PRINCIPAL  *m* **5081**
CABLE REDONDO  *m* **10801**
CABLE SINFIN  *m* **4733**
CABLE TELEDINÁMICO  *m* **12705**
CABLE TORCIDO A DERECHAS  *m* **10587**
CABLE TORCIDO A IZQUIERDAS  *m* **7511**
CABLE VOLANTE  *m* **7264**
CABLEADO  *m* **7389**
CABLEADO  *m* **10739**
CABLEADO  *m* **1828**
CABLEADO ALTERNATIVO  *m* **10414**
CABLEAR **13303**
CABLES  *m pl* **12739**
CABLES DE ALIMENTACIÓN  *m pl* **12484**
CABLES DE LÍNEA  *m pl* **12484**
CABLES INYECTADOS  *m pl* **1446**
CABRA DE TRÍPODE  *f* **5945**
CABRESTANTE  *m* **1929**
CABRESTANTE  *m* DE BRAZOS **6229**
CABRIA  *f* **5945**
CABRIA  *f* **9973**
CABRIO  *m* **1581**
CABRIO  *m* A LO LARGO **12308**
CABRIO  *m* TRANSVERSAL **3369**
CACILLO  *m* **1674**
CACILLO  *m* **1378**
CADENA  *f* **2201**

CADENA  *f* DE TRANSPORTE EN CIRCUITO **1731**
CADENA CABLE  *f* **6518**
CADENA CABLE DE PUNTALES  *f* **12403**
CADENA CALIBRADA  *f* **9412**
CADENA CORRIENTE  *f* **8855**
CADENA DE BICICLETA  *f* **1239**
CADENA DE DISTRIBUCIÓN  *f* **12950**
CADENA DE DISTRIBUCIÓN  *f* **12948**
CADENA DE ELEVACIÓN  *f* **6518**
CADENA DE ESLABONES APRETADOS  *f* **11373**
CADENA DE ESLABONES CORTOS  *f* **11373**
CADENA DE ESLABONES LARGOS  *f* **7730**
CADENA DE MALLAS APUNTALADAS  *f* **12403**
CADENA DE MALLAS SOLDADAS  *f* **13770**
CADENA DE PUNTALES  *f* **12403**
CADENA DE RODILLOS  *f* **10684**
CADENA DE TRANSMISIÓN  *f* **4306**
CADENA DE TRANSMISIÓN  *f* **4305**
CADENA DE VAUCANSON  *f* **6570**
CADENA ESTAMPADA  *f* **12058**
CADENA GALLE  *f* **12002**
CADENA MOTRIZ  *f* **4306**
CADENA PLANA  *f* **1336**
CADENA SILENCIOSA  *f* **11432**
CADENA SINFÍN  *f* **4732**
CADENA TROQUELADA  *f* **12058**
CADENAS CALIBRADAS  *f pl* **1862**
CADENAS DE MARINA  *f pl* **8004**
CADENAS PARA LA NIEVE  *f pl* **11696**
CADENETA (GEOM.)  *f* **2095**
CADMIADO  *m* **1832**
CADMIO  *m* **1831**
CADUCACIÓN  *f* DE UNA PATENTE **7408**
CADUNO **7343**
CAER DE NUEVO (TRINQUETE) **4320**
CAER EN DELICUESCENCIA **3732**
CAGAFIERRO  *m* **2500**
CAÍDA  *f* **3356**
CAÍDA  *f* **1889**
CAÍDA  *f* (O DESCENSO  *m*) DE TEMPERATURA **5022**
CAÍDA ANÓDICA  *f* **595**
CAÍDA DE POTENCIAL  *f* **13594**
CAÍDA DE PRESIÓN  *f* **9815**
CAÍDA DE TEMPERATURA  *f* **12724**
CAÍDA DE TENSIÓN  *f* **13594**
CAÍDA (DE TENSIÓN) CATÓDICA  *f* **2100**
CAÍDA LIBRE  *f* **5633**
CAÍDA LIBRE (DE)  *f* **5024**
CAJA  *f* **6660**
CAJA  *f* **2798**

CAL

| | |
|---|---|
| CAJA  *f*  DE ALMAS **3147** | CAL HIDRATADA  *f*  **1851** |
| CAJA  *f*  DE BATERÍA **1067** | CAL HIDRÁULICA  *f*  **6689** |
| CAJA  *f*  DE BOMBA **4036** | CAL MUERTA  *f*  **1851** |
| CAJA  *f*  DE COMPÁS (O DE CALIBRE) **8051** | CAL VIVA  *f*  **1854** |
| CAJA  *f*  DE DISTRIBUCIÓN **4086** | CALABROTE  *m*  **1829** |
| CAJA  *f*  DE DISTRIBUCIÓN **2229** | CALABROTE  *m*  **6309** |
| CAJA  *f*  DE EJE **6085** | CALABROTE  *m*  FORMADO POR CUATRO GUINDALEZAS **11401** |
| CAJA  *f*  DE EJE **877** | |
| CAJA  *f*  DE ENGRASE **877** | CALADO DE LA DISTRIBUCIÓN  *m*  **12952** |
| CAJA  *f*  DE FUEGO **5238** | CALAMINA  *f*  **1836** |
| CAJA  *f*  DE GRASA **6085** | CALANDRA DE RADIADOR  *f*  **10152** |
| CAJA  *f*  DE GRASA **877** | CALANDRAR **13162** |
| CAJA  *f*  DE GUANTES **5980** | CALCADO  *m*  **13082** |
| CAJA  *f*  DE HERRAMIENTAS **12997** | CALCADOR  *m*  **13078** |
| CAJA  *f*  DE MACHOS **3147** | CALCAR **13077** |
| CAJA  *f*  DE MARCHA EN VACÍO **13435** | CALCÁREA  *f*  CONCHÍFERA (MIN) **8487** |
| CAJA  *f*  DE MARCHA EN VACÍO **13438** | CALCÁREA  *f*  DE MUSCHEL **8487** |
| CAJA  *f*  DE PROTECCIÓN **9948** | CALCÁREA  *m*  PISOLÍTICA **8801** |
| CAJA  *f*  DE RESORTE **11980** | CALCAUTO  *m*  **1376** |
| CAJA  *f*  DE UN CEPILLO **11771** | CALCE  *m*  **185** |
| CAJA  *f*  DE VÁLVULA **7392** | CALCE  *m*  **185** |
| CAJA  *f*  DE VÁLVULAS **2229** | CALCE  *m*  **13731** |
| CAJA  *f*  DE VELOCIDADES **5890** | CALCE PARA RECUPERAR HOLGURA  *m*  **185** |
| CAJA  *f*  (O CASQUILLO  *m* ) PARA POLEA LOCA (PARA MARCHA LIBRE) **7748** | CALCES DE COMPARACIÓN  *m*  **2796** |
| | CALCINA  *f*  **2272** |
| CAJA  *f*  PROTECTORA **9948** | CALCINACIÓN  *f*  **1839** |
| CAJA  *f*  PROTECTORA **9948** | CALCINACIÓN  *f*  **1839** |
| CAJA DE CAMBIOS  *f*  **5890** | CALCINACIÓN  *f*  **11511** |
| CAJA DE CEMENTACIÓN  *f*  **3075** | CALCINACIÓN  *f*  A PRESIÓN **9799** |
| CAJA DE DISTRIBUCIÓN  *f*  **12947** | CALCINACIÓN  *f*  CONTINUA **3014** |
| CAJA DE ENGRANAJES  *f*  **13815** | CALCINACIÓN  *f*  EN EL VACÍO **13448** |
| CAJA DE MUELLE  *f*  **11988** | CALCINACIÓN  *f*  TOTAL **3636** |
| CAJA DE POLEA  *f*  **1333** | CALCINACIÓN DE LOS MINERALES  *f*  **1840** |
| CAJA DE RECOCIDO  *f*  **563** | CALCINAR **1745** |
| CAJA DE RECOCIDO  *f*  **567** | CALCINAR **11509** |
| CAJA DEL CUERPO DE UN EVAPORADOR  *f*  **4870** | CALCINAR LOS MINERALES **1841** |
| CAJA DEL PALIER  *f*  **9313** | CALCIO  *m*  **1846** |
| CAJA DEL PORTAHERRAMIENTAS  *f*  **2454** | CALCITA  *f*  **1845** |
| CAJA DEL REGULADOR  *f*  **6016** | CALCITA  *f*  **1844** |
| CAJA PORTANTE  *f*  **13381** | CALCO  *m*  **13082** |
| CAJAS  *f pl*  DE CEMENTACIÓN **1989** | CALCO  *m*  **13082** |
| CAJITA  *f*  **2028** | CALCOMANÍA  *f*  **13109** |
| CAJÓN  *m*  **2798** | CALCOPIRITA  *f*  **3126** |
| CAJÓN DE TRASIEGO  *m*  **4227** | CALCOPIRITA  *f*  **3126** |
| CAJONES ESTANCOS  *m pl*  **7658** | CALCOSINA  *f*  **3118** |
| CAL  *f*  **7582** | CALCULAR **3795** |
| CAL ANHÍDRA  *f*  **9623** | CALCULAR **1857** |
| CAL ANHÍDRA  *f*  **1854** | CALCULAR LA CAPACIDAD **1861** |
| CAL FLUATADA  *f*  **5479** | CÁLCULO  *m*  CÓMPUTO  *m*  **1860** |
| CAL GRASA  *f*  **5046** | CÁLCULO  *m*  DISEÑO  *m*  **3794** |

**CAL**

CÁLCULO APROXIMADO  *m* **652**
CÁLCULO DIFERENCIAL  *m* **3908**
CÁLCULO GRÁFICO  *m* **6060**
CÁLCULO INFINITESIMAL  *m* **6912**
CÁLCULO INTEGRAL  *m* **7011**
CÁLCULO RÁPIDO APROXIMADO  *m* **10772**
CALDA  *f* DE LAVADO **13784**
CALDEAR **6334**
CALDEO  *m* **6390**
CALDEO  *m* **2327**
CALDEO AL AZUL  *m* **1371**
CALDEO AL BLANCO  *m* **6824**
CALDEO AL ROJO  *m* **10330**
CALDEO AL ROJO CLARO  *m* **1614**
CALDEO AL ROJO OSCURO  *m* **4368**
CALDEO ELÉCTRICO  *m* **4513**
CALDEO PARCIAL  *m* **7696**
CALDEO POR ENCIMA DEL PUNTO DE FUSIÓN  *m* **3634**
CALDERA  *f* **1406**
CALDERA ACUOTUBULAR  *f* **13682**
CALDERA BAJA PRESIÓN  *f* **7782**
CALDERA BAJO VOLUMEN  *f* **11663**
CALDERA CILÍNDRICA  *f* **3578**
CALDERA DE ALTA PRESIÓN  *f* **6487**
CALDERA DE FUEGO INTERIOR  *f* **5468**
CALDERA DE HORNO INTERNO  *f* **5468**
CALDERA DE MEDIA PRESIÓN  *f* **8127**
CALDERA DE MEDIO VOLUMEN  *f* **8126**
CALDERA DE QUEMADOR  *f* **5468**
CALDERA DE RÁPIDA VAPORIZACIÓN  *f* **13682**
CALDERA DE SEGURIDAD  *f* **13682**
CALDERA DE VAPOR  *f* **12158**
CALDERA ELÉCTRICA  *f* **4497**
CALDERA GRAN CAPACIDAD  *f* **7412**
CALDERA HORIZONTAL  *f* **6579**
CALDERA INDUSTRIAL  *f* **12143**
CALDERA MARINA  *f* **8003**
CALDERA MULTITUBULAR  *f* **13682**
CALDERA PIROTUBULAR  *f* **5249**
CALDERA PIROTUBULAR  *f* **5249**
CALDERA TIPO LOCOMOTORA  *f* **7714**
CALDERA TUBULAR  *f* **5249**
CALDERA VERTICAL  *f* **13544**
CALDERERÍA  *f* **3136**
CALDERERÍA  *f* PESADA **1423**
CALDERERÍA DE HIERRO  *f* **1423**
CALDERERO DE COBRE  *m* **3135**
CALDERERO DE HIERRO  *m* **1415**
CALDERERO EN CHAPA  *m* **1415**
CALEFACCIÓN  *f* **5259**

CALEFACCIÓN  *f* **6390**
CALEFACCIÓN  *f* CALDEO  *m* **6390**
CALEFACCIÓN CENTRAL  *f* **2160**
CALEFACCIÓN DE LOS EDIFICIOS  *f* **6395**
CALEFACCIÓN ELÉCTRICA  *f* **4513**
CALEFACCIÓN POR ACEITE PESADO  *f* **1752**
CALEFACCIÓN POR AGUA CALIENTE  *f* **6648**
CALEFACCIÓN POR AGUA CALIENTE ALTA PRESIÓN  *f* **6489**
CALEFACCIÓN POR AGUA CALIENTE BAJA PRESIÓN  *f* **7784**
CALEFACCIÓN POR AIRE CALIENTE  *f* **6616**
CALEFACCIÓN POR AIRE CALIENTE  *f* **268**
CALEFACCIÓN POR CARBÓN  *f* **2564**
CALEFACCIÓN POR CARBÓN PULVERIZADO  *f* **1753**
CALEFACCIÓN POR FUEL  *f* **1752**
CALEFACCIÓN POR GAS  *f* **1751**
CALEFACCIÓN POR NAFTA  *f* **1752**
CALEFACCIÓN POR VAPOR  *f* **12167**
CALEFACCIÓN POR VAPOR A PRESIÓN INFERIOR A LA PRESIÓN ATMOSFÉRICA  *f* **8318**
CALEFACCIÓN POR VAPOR ALTA PRESIÓN  *f* **6493**
CALEFACCIÓN POR VAPOR BAJA PRESIÓN  *f* **7787**
CALENTADO AL ROJO BLANCO **6824**
CALENTADO AL ROJO CEREZA **2327**
CALENTADO AL ROJO NACIENTE **1288**
CALENTADOR DE AGUA DE GAS  *m* **5846**
CALENTAMIENTO  *m* DE LOS COJINETES **6400**
CALENTAMIENTO  *m* INTERNO **6338**
CALENTAMIENTO  *m* RÁPIDO **5362**
CALENTAMIENTO ADICIONAL  *m* **2904**
CALENTAMIENTO DEL AIRE  *m* **268**
CALENTAMIENTO MECÁNICO  *m* **8111**
CALENTAMIENTO POR INDUCCIÓN  *m* **6897**
CALENTAMIENTO PREVIO  *m* **9776**
CALENTAMIENTO SELECTIVO  *m* **3915**
CALENTAR **5235**
CALENTAR **6334**
CALENTAR AL CONTACTO DEL AIRE **6351**
CALENTAR AL ROJO **5982**
CALENTAR EN AMBIENTE CERRADO **6367**
CALENTAR POR CONTACTO **6351**
CALENTAR PREVIAMENTE **9774**
CALIBRACIÓN  *f* **5886**
CALIBRACIÓN  *f* **5886**
CALIBRACIÓN  *f* **1867**
CALIBRACIÓN  *f* (DE UN DEPÓSITO) **1863**
CALIBRACIÓN  *f* DE UNA MEDIDA **5874**
CALIBRACIÓN  *f* DE UNA MEDIDA **5770**
CALIBRADO  *m* **2651**
CALIBRADO  *m* **1867**

CALIBRADO *m* **1867**
CALIBRADO *m* **1468**
CALIBRADO *m* **11524**
CALIBRADO *m* A DISTANCIA **10449**
CALIBRADO DE CILINDRO *m* **1461**
CALIBRADOR *m* **5768**
CALIBRADOR **11034**
CALIBRADOR *m* BIRMINGHAM PARA ALAMBRES **12089**
CALIBRADOR *m* NEUMÁTICO **283**
CALIBRADORES *m pl* **5769**
CALIBRAR **5872**
CALIBRAR **1861**
CALIBRAR **1861**
CALIBRAR **1462**
CALIBRE *m* **5871**
CALIBRE *m* **5768**
CALIBRE *m* **9531**
CALIBRE *m* CON TAMPÓN NORMAL **12087**
CALIBRE *m* DE AJUSTADO **11225**
CALIBRE *m* DE COMPROBACIÓN **12779**
CALIBRE *m* DE CONTROL **3053**
CALIBRE *m* DE CONTROL DE DIÁMETRO INTERIOR **6531**
CALIBRE *m* DE DIÁMETRO INTERIOR **11049**
CALIBRE *m* DE LA FABRICACIÓN **13955**
CALIBRE *m* DE LA PRODUCCIÓN **13967**
CALIBRE *m* DE LAS ROSCAS **11038**
CALIBRE *m* DE MORDAZA NORMAL **12088**
CALIBRE *m* DE PRECISIÓN **9766**
CALIBRE *m* DE RECEPCIÓN **10015**
CALIBRE *m* DE REFERENCIA **10366**
CALIBRE *m* DE REFERENCIA **8035**
CALIBRE *m* DE REVISIÓN **5011**
CALIBRE *m* DE TOLERANCIAS ESCALONADAS **9907**
CALIBRE *m* DE TREFILERÍA **13892**
CALIBRE *m* DE UN EXTERIOR **4955**
CALIBRE *m* DE UN INTERIOR **7066**
CALIBRE *m* DEL FILETEADO **2760**
CALIBRE *m* DEL LÍMITE DE UNA TOLERANCIA **3903**
CALIBRE *m* DESMONTABLE **4048**
CALIBRE *m* EXTERIOR **5091**
CALIBRE *m* GAMA DE TOLERANCIAS **4148**
CALIBRE *m* INGLÉS **12089**
CALIBRE *m* MICROMÉTRICO **8256**
CALIBRE *m* MORDAZA DE UNA RAMA PARA DIMENSIONES MÍNIMA Y MÁXIMA **6607**
CALIBRE *m* MORDAZA GRADUABLE **186**
CALIBRE *m* MORDAZA PARA FILETEADOS O ROSCADOS **10693**
CALIBRE *m* NEUMÁTICO **283**
CALIBRE *m* NORMAL DE ANILLO ROSCADO **12863**
CALIBRE *m* NORMAL DE TAMPÓN ROSCADO **12861**

CALIBRE *m* PARA EL ESPESOR DE LAS CHAPAS **11311**
CALIBRE *m* PARA LOS ALAMBRES **13892**
CALIBRE *m* PARA RANURA DE PASADOR **7283**
CALIBRE *m* ROSCADO HEMBRA **2721**
CALIBRE *m* ROSCADO MACHO **11049**
CALIBRE *m* STANDARD **12076**
CALIBRE *m* TAMPÓN CÓNICO **12656**
CALIBRE *m* TAMPÓN CÓNICO **7076**
CALIBRE *m* TAMPÓN CÓNICO **7956**
CALIBRE *m* TAMPÓN CÓNICO CON TETÓN **12657**
CALIBRE *m* TAMPÓN DE CONO MÉTRICO **8230**
CALIBRE *m* TAMPÓN DE CONO NORMAL (CONO MORSE) **8392**
CALIBRE *m* TAMPÓN DOBLE CON LIMITACIONES **4137**
CALIBRE *m* Y ANILLO **3581**
CALIBRE DE AJUSTE DE VÁLVULA *m* **13473**
CALIBRE DE ALTURA DE PRECISIÓN *m* **9768**
CALIBRE DE ÁNGULOS *m* **513**
CALIBRE DE CONICIDAD NORMAL *m* **8393**
CALIBRE DE CORREDERA CON REGLA DE PROFUNDIDAD *m* **1871**
CALIBRE DE CORREDERA DE PROFUNDIDAD *m* **13538**
CALIBRE DE CORREDERA DE PROFUNDIDAD DE FIJACIÓN MICROMÉTRICA *m* **13539**
CALIBRE DE DIÁMETRO *m* **10661**
CALIBRE DE ESPESORES *m* **5086**
CALIBRE DE MATRIZ *m* **6532**
CALIBRE DE MORDAZA *m* **6608**
CALIBRE DE PERFILADO *m* **11123**
CALIBRE DE PROFUNDIDAD *m* **3781**
CALIBRE DE TALADRO *m* **4267**
CALIBRE DE TOLERANCIA *m* **3905**
CALIBRE DE TOLERANCIAS *m* **4584**
CALIBRE DE TRAZADO *m* **8016**
CALIBRE DE UNA CHAPA *m* **9487**
CALIBRE (DIÁMETRO INTERIOR) DEL CILINDRO *m* **3565**
CALIBRE FIJO *m* **5293**
CALIBRE HEMBRA LISO *m* **9431**
CALIBRE MACHO CÓNICO *m* **12656**
CALIBRE MACHO Y HEMBRA *m* **3581**
CALIBRE (NO VARIABLE) *m* **8625**
CALIBRE NORMAL *m* **12076**
CALIBRE NORMALIZADO (O STANDARD) **12082**
CALIBRE PARA PERFILES *m* **8422**
CALIBRE PARA TUBOS *m* **2027**
CALIBRE PASA-NO PASA *m* **5991**
CALIBRES *m pl* **5873**
CALIBRES *m pl* **5769**
CALIBRES *m* **5769**
CALIBRES *m pl* DE CONTROL **5769**

**CAL** 982

CALIBRES *m pl* PARA FILETEADOS (PARA PIEZAS ATERRAJADAS) **12860**
CALIBRES DE MORDAZA *m pl* **11693**
CALIBRES HEMBRAS CÓNICOS *m pl* **12659**
CALIBRES MACHOS CILÍNDRICOS *m pl* **3587**
CALIBRES MACHOS PARA ROSCAS *m pl* **12862**
CALIBRES MICROMÉTRICOS *m pl* **8251**
CALIBRES MICROMÉTRICOS PARA INTERIORES *m pl* **6979**
CALIBRES TELESCÓPICOS *m pl* **12713**
CALICHE *m* **2330**
CALICHE *m* **2330**
CALIDAD *f* DE SOLDABLE **13768**
CALIDAD *f* LUBRIFICANTE **7806**
CALIZA *f* **7586**
CALIZA *f* **10969**
CALIZA BASTA *f* **5664**
CALIZA CARBONÍFERA *f* **1969**
CALIZA COQUILLAR *f* **8487**
CALIZA DE AGUA DULCE *f* **5664**
CALIZA DOLÍTICA *f* **8801**
CALIZA JURÁSICA *f* **7267**
CALIZA SILÍCEA *f* **11451**
CALOMELANOS *m* **8159**
CALOR **10329**
CALOR **5981**
CALOR *m* **6333**
CALOR *m* AL AZUL **1370**
CALOR *m* AZUL **1370**
CALOR *m* BLANCO **6823**
CALOR *m* BLANCO **6823**
CALOR AL ROJO CEREZA *m* **2326**
CALOR ATÓMICO *m* **802**
CALOR BLANCO *m* **6823**
CALOR BLANCO DE SOLDADURA *m* **13784**
CALOR DE ABSORCIÓN *m* **6354**
CALOR DE CARBURACIÓN *m* **6355**
CALOR DE COMBINACIÓN *m* **9656**
CALOR DE COMBUSTIÓN *m* **6356**
CALOR DE DESCOMPOSICIÓN *m* **6357**
CALOR DE DESCOMPOSICIÓN *m* **8528**
CALOR DE DISOCIACIÓN *m* **6358**
CALOR DE EVAPORACIÓN *m* **6359**
CALOR DE FORJA *m* **2744**
CALOR DE FORMACIÓN *m* **9656**
CALOR DE FUSIÓN *m* **6360**
CALOR DE OXIDACIÓN *m* **6361**
CALOR DE REDUCCIÓN *m* **6362**
CALOR DE SOLDADURA *m* **13784**
CALOR DE SUBLIMACIÓN *m* **6363**
CALOR DE TRANSFORMACIÓN *m* **6364**

CALOR DE VAPORIZACIÓN *m* **6366**
CALOR EFECTIVO *m* **4457**
CALOR ENCERRADO *m* **10411**
CALOR ESPECÍFICO *m* **11852**
CALOR ESPECÍFICO MEDIO *m* **8076**
CALOR INTERNO *m* **7070**
CALOR LATENTE *m* **7415**
CALOR LATENTE *m* **6365**
CALOR LATENTE DE VAPORIZACIÓN *m* **7416**
CALOR LIBERADO *m* **6370**
CALOR LIBERADO EN UNA REACCIÓN *m* **6348**
CALOR PERDIDO *m* **13635**
CALOR PRODUCIDO POR FRICCIÓN *m* **6343**
CALOR RADIANTE *m* **10140**
CALOR RADIANTE *m* **10140**
CALOR ROJO *m* **10329**
CALOR SENSIBLE *m* **11184**
CALOR ÚTIL *m* **4457**
CALORÍA GRAMO-GRADO *f* **6045**
CALORÍA INGLESA *f* **1625**
CALORÍA KILOGRAMO-GRADO *f* **7298**
CALORÍFUGO *m* **6998**
CALORIMETRÍA *f* **1881**
CALORIMÉTRICO *m* **1878**
CALORÍMETRO *m* **1877**
CALORÍMETRO *m* DE COMBUSTIÓN **1879**
CALORÍMETRO DE AGUA *m* **13643**
CALORÍMETRO DE CONDENSACIÓN *m* **12160**
CALORÍMETRO DE HIELO *m* **6749**
CALORIZACIÓN *f* **1882**
CALZAR **7277**
CALZAR EN ... **7279**
CALZO *m* **632**
CALZO *m* **13739**
CALZO *m* **13731**
CALZO DE NIVEL *m* **185**
CALZOS MAGNÉTICOS DE FIJACIÓN *m* **7897**
CÁMARA *f* DE FLOTADOR **5431**
CÁMARA *f* DE VACÍO **13440**
CÁMARA *f* FUMÍVORA **11674**
CÁMARA DE AGUA DE UNA CALDERA *f* **13677**
CÁMARA DE AIRE *f* **13246**
CÁMARA DE AIRE *f* **6955**
CÁMARA DE AIRE *f* **246**
CÁMARA DE COMBUSTIÓN *f* **2776**
CÁMARA DE COMBUSTIÓN *f* **2856**
CÁMARA DE COMBUSTIÓN DE UN FUEGO *f* **2777**
CÁMARA DE DISTRIBUCIÓN *f* **2229**
CÁMARA DE EXPLOSIONES DE UN MOTOR *f* **2778**
CÁMARA DE IONIZACIÓN *f* **7125**

| | |
|---|---|
| CÁMARA DE LAMINADOR  f 12065 | CAMPO  m 11845 |
| CÁMARA DE TURBULENCIA  f 12551 | CAMPO ELÉCTRICO  m 4505 |
| CÁMARA DE VACÍO  f 13440 | CAMPO ELÉCTRICO  m 4504 |
| CÁMARA DE VACÍO  f 13449 | CAMPO MAGNÉTICO  m 7901 |
| CÁMARA DE VAPOR DE UNA CALDERA  f 12185 | CAMPO VISUAL  m 5143 |
| CÁMARA DE VIENTO  f 241 | CAMPO VISUAL  m 5143 |
| CÁMARA OSCURA  f 9264 | CANAL  m 6185 |
| CAMBIADOR DE HERRAMIENTAS  m 13000 | CANAL  m 2248 |
| CAMBIAR UN ÓRGANO DE UNA MÁQUINA 10457 | CANAL  m 2251 |
| CAMBIO  m DE UN ÓRGANO DE MÁQUINA 10458 | CANAL  m 13418 |
| CAMBIO DE AGUJA  m 12556 | CANAL  m DE ADMISIÓN 200 |
| CAMBIO DE DIRECCIÓN  m 2236 | CANAL  m DE DESCENSO 12596 |
| CAMBIO DE ESTADO  m 2238 | CANAL  m DE ENGRASE 7810 |
| CAMBIO DE FORMA  m 3707 | CANAL  m DE RODAMIENTO 13085 |
| CAMBIO DE MULTIPLICACIÓN  m 2245 | CANAL  m DE SUBIDA 6319 |
| CAMBIO DE PRESIÓN  m 2237 | CANAL ABIERTO  m 8807 |
| CAMBIO DE TEMPERATURA  m 2239 | CANAL DE ABASTECIMIENTO  m 6319 |
| CAMBIO DE VELOCIDAD  m 2245 | CANAL DE COLADA  m 7436 |
| CAMBIO DE VÍA  m 12556 | CANAL DE COLADA  m 10844 |
| CAMBIO DE VÍA  m 12556 | CANAL DE DESCARGA  m 12596 |
| CAMBIO DE VOLUMEN  m 2240 | CANAL DE HUMO  m 5743 |
| CAMBIO FÍSICO  m 9280 | CANAL (SOLDADURA)  m 13351 |
| CAMBIO IRREVERSIBLE  m 7170 | CANALES  m pl EN U 2250 |
| CAMBIO REVERSIBLE  m 10539 | CANALES DE VIENTO  m pl 247 |
| CAMINO  m SEGUIDO POR UN FLUIDO 9125 | CANALETA  f 2395 |
| CAMIÓN  m 7752 | CANALIZACIÓN  f 13354 |
| CAMIÓN AUTOMÓVIL  m 8414 | CANALIZACIÓN  f 12178 |
| CAMIÓN DE CARGA  m 6405 | CANALIZACIÓN DE ALTA PRESIÓN  f 6490 |
| CAMIÓN DE COSTADOS ARTICULADOS  m 7753 | CANALIZACIÓN DE FUNDICIÓN  f 2062 |
| CAMIÓN ENTOLDADO  m 12686 | CANALIZACIÓN LIBRE  f 8807 |
| CAMIÓN VOLQUETE  m 4375 | CANALIZACIÓN MARINA  f 11080 |
| CAMIONES PARA TRANSPORTAR BANDEJAS O PALETAS  m pl 9025 | CANALIZACIÓN SUBTERRÁNEA  f 13354 |
| CAMIONETA  f 7563 | CANALÓN  m 2395 |
| CAMIONETA  f 12141 | CANALÓN 2251 |
| CAMISA  f 11303 | CANALÓN  m 6544 |
| CAMISA  f 7623 | CANALÓN  m DE DESAGÜE 6185 |
| CAMISA  f 12168 | CÁÑAMO  m 6439 |
| CAMISA  f 11303 | CÁÑAMO DE MANILA  m 7980 |
| CAMISA  f 7623 | CÁÑAMO DE MANILA  m 7980 |
| CAMISA  f 3274 | CANDELA  f 1899 |
| CAMISA  f DE VAPOR 12168 | CANDELA  f 1899 |
| CAMISA DE AGUA  f 13655 | CAÑERÍA  f 13666 |
| CAMISA DE CILINDRO  f 1465 | CAÑERÍA DE AGUA A PRESIÓN  f 9840 |
| CAMISA DEL CILINDRO  f 3571 | CAÑERÍA DE AGUA CALIENTE  f 6649 |
| CAMISA DEL HORNO  f 5749 | CAÑÓN ANTIAÉREO  m 610 |
| CAMISA HÚMEDA 13804 | CAÑÓN ELECTRÓNICO  m 4628 |
| CAMISA SECA  f 4348 | CANTERA  f 10073 |
| CAMPANA  f DE ASPIRACIÓN DE HUMO 1455 | CANTIDAD  f 10065 |
| CAMPANA  f DE CHIMENEA 1455 | CANTIDAD  f CONOCIDA 7335 |
| | CANTIDAD  f CONOCIDA 5951 |

# CAN

984

CANTIDAD  *f* DE CALOR **10066**
CANTIDAD  *f* DE ELECTRICIDAD **10067**
CANTIDAD  *f* DE MOVIMIENTO **10068**
CANTIDAD  *f* DE MOVIMIENTO **8376**
CANTIDAD  *f* DESCONOCIDA **13391**
CANTIDAD  *f* MEDIDA **10070**
CANTIDAD  *f* QUE SUSTRAER **12426**
CANTIDAD  *f* RECÍPROCA **10280**
CANTO  *m* **9152**
CANTO  *m* **4441**
CANTO  *m* **1902**
CANTONEADO  *m* **10167**
CANTONERA  *f* **514**
CANTONERA  *f* **3058**
CANTONERA  *f* CON BORDÓN **1712**
CANTONERA  *f* EN ÁNGULO REDONDEADO **10794**
CANTONERA  *f* EN ÁNGULO VIVO **11271**
CANTONERA DE FONDO DE TANQUE  *f* **1490**
CANTONERA DE PARTE SUPERIOR (DE UN TANQUE O DEPÓSITO)  *f* **13028**
CANTOS RODADOS  *m pl* (QUE ALLANAR) **10695**
CAOLÍN  *m* **2340**
CAOLÍN  *m* **2340**
CAOLÍN (PARA LOS NEUMÁTICOS) **13842**
CAPA  *f* **3274**
CAPA  *f* **5166**
CAPA  *f* **5166**
CAPA  *f* **7986**
CAPA  *f* **13172**
CAPA  *f* **11303**
CAPA  *f* **10832**
CAPA  *f* **7442**
CAPA  *f* **9096**
CAPA  *f* DE ACABADO **3264**
CAPA  *f* DE EMPAQUETADURA **9008**
CAPA  *f* DE PINTURA **2583**
CAPA  *f* DELGADA DE ACEITE DE ENGRASE **5167**
CAPA  *f* INFERIOR (DE OXIDO) **12416**
CAPA  *f* ÍNFIMA DE AGUA **5169**
CAPA  *f* SUBTERRÁNEA DE AGUA **6147**
CAPA  *f* TENUE DE AGUA **5169**
CAPA ANUAL  *f* **586**
CAPA DE AIRE  *f* **254**
CAPA DE AIRE  *f* **2124**
CAPA DE BEILBY  *f* **1130**
CAPA DE CROMATO  *f* **2591**
CAPA DE FONDO  *f* **9857**
CAPA DE FOSFATO  *f* **9245**
CAPA DE LACA  *f* **2581**
CAPA DE ÓXIDO DE COBRE  *f* **5246**

CAPA DE ÓXIDO FERROSO  *f* **12443**
CAPA (DE PROTECCIÓN) ANÓDICA **599**
CAPA DE SEMI-ESPESOR  *f* **6211**
CAPA INTERMEDIA DESCARBURADA  *f* **1005**
CAPA O ESTRATO DE LAS FIBRAS INVARIABLES  *f* **8544**
CAPA PRIMARIA  *f* **9857**
CAPA PROTECTORA **9793**
CAPA SUPERFICIAL  *f* **11544**
CAPA SUPERFICIAL  *f* **2019**
CAPA SUPERFICIAL (DE PINTURA)  *f* **5217**
CAPACIDAD  *f* **1917**
CAPACIDAD  *f* **1917**
CAPACIDAD  *f* **9730**
CAPACIDAD  *f* (ELECTR.) **1917**
CAPACIDAD CALÓRICA  *f* **6342**
CAPACIDAD CALORÍFICA  *f* **6335**
CAPACIDAD CALORÍFICA  *f* **6339**
CAPACIDAD CALORÍFICA  *f* **41**
CAPACIDAD DE AMORTIZACIÓN  *f* **3605**
CAPACIDAD DE CARGA  *f* **2011**
CAPACIDAD DE CARGA  *f* **7682**
CAPACIDAD DE DEFORMACIÓN  *f* **3705**
CAPACIDAD DE DESATASCAMIENTO  *f* **2718**
CAPACIDAD DE TEMPLE  *f* **6288**
CAPACIDAD TÉRMICA  *f* **12803**
CAPARROSA  *f* AZUL **1376**
CAPARROSA AZUL  *f* **1376**
CAPARROSA BLANCA  *f* **14046**
CAPARROSA DE CINC  *f* **14046**
CAPARROSA VERDE  *f* **6093**
CAPAS  *f* **2590**
CAPATAZ  *m* **7482**
CAPERUZA  *f* **1910**
CAPERUZA  *f* **1910**
CAPILARIDAD  *f* **1920**
CAPILLA  *f* **2229**
CAPITAL DE COLUMNA  *m* **1926**
CAPÓ  *m* **1451**
CAPÓ  *m* **6566**
CAPÓ DE CHAPA  *m* **11310**
CAPÓ DEL SALPICADERO  *m* **5695**
CAPÓ MOTOR  *m* **1451**
CAPOTA PLEGABLE  *f* **2719**
CÁPSULA  *f* **4864**
CAPTACIÓN DE LOS GASES SIN COMBUSTIÓN  *f* **5841**
CAPTACIÓN DEL GAS Y DESEMPOLVAMIENTO  *f* **4392**
CARA  *f* **4989**
CARA  *f* CRISTALINA **3427**
CARA  *f* DE APOYO **1026**
CARA  *f* DE BRIDA **5327**

CARA *f* DE REFERENCIA **8043**
CARA *f* DE UN CRISTAL **3427**
CARA *f* LATERAL DE UNA RUEDA DE ENGRANAJE **11400**
CARA DE BASE *f* **1053**
CARA DE UN POLÍGONO *f* **11414**
CARA INTERNA DE UNA CORREA *f* **10853**
CARA PELO DEL CUERO *f* **6038**
CARÁCTER *m* **2255**
CARACTERÍSTICA *f* **2256**
CARACTERÍSTICA *f* **9075**
CARACTERÍSTICA DE UN LOGARITMO *f* **2257**
CARACTERÍSTICAS *f pl* **2295**
CARACTERÍSTICAS MECÁNICAS *f pl* **8109**
CARACTERÍSTICAS MECÁNICAS *f pl* **12746**
CARAS CENTRADAS (DE) *f* **5002**
CARAS CENTRADAS (DE) *f* **4729**
CARBOLINEO *m* **1939**
CARBÓN *m* **2558**
CARBÓN ANIMAL *m* **554**
CARBÓN DE FORJA *m* **5543**
CARBÓN DE LLAMA LARGA *m* **1901**
CARBÓN DE MADERA *m* **13914**
CARBÓN DE RETORTA *m* **5812**
CARBÓN FÓSIL *m* **2558**
CARBÓN GRAFÍTICO *m* **9851**
CARBÓN GRUESO *m* **7826**
CARBÓN HULLA *m* **2558**
CARBÓN PULVERIZADO *m* **9984**
CARBONADO *m* **1480**
CARBONADO *m* **1966**
CARBONAR **1971**
CARBONATO *m* **1968**
CARBONATO *m* NATURAL DE BARITA **13911**
CARBONATO ÁCIDO DE SODIO *m* **126**
CARBONATO CÁLCICO *m* **1849**
CARBONATO DE AMONIO *m* **461**
CARBONATO DE BARIO *m* **996**
CARBONATO DE CINC *m* **14037**
CARBONATO DE COBRE *m* **3470**
CARBONATO DE LITIO *m* **7665**
CARBONATO DE MAGNESIA *m* **7884**
CARBONATO NATURAL DE BARITA *m* **13911**
CARBONATO POTÁSICO NEUTRO *m* **9679**
CARBONATO SÓDICO *m* **11713**
CARBONATO SÓDICO ANHIDRO *m* **551**
CARBONEO *m* **2566**
CARBONERA *f* **2561**
CARBONERA *f* **1740**
CARBONILO *m* **1939**
CARBONILO *m* **1976**

CARBONILO DE HIERRO *m* **7140**
CARBONILO DE NÍQUEL *m* **8561**
CARBONITRURACIÓN *f* **1972**
CARBONIZACIÓN *f* **1970**
CARBONIZACIÓN *f* **1974**
CARBONIZACIÓN *f* **1975**
CARBONIZACIÓN *f* INCOMPLETA **7776**
CARBONIZACIÓN DE LA HULLA *f* **7991**
CARBONIZACIÓN INCOMPLETA *f* **7776**
CARBONIZADO *m* **2272**
CARBONIZAR **1971**
CARBONO *m* **1940**
CARBONO COMBINADO *m* **1962**
CARBONO COMBINADO *m* **5289**
CARBONO COMBINADO AL HIERRO *m* **2767**
CARBONO DE REVENIDO *m* **1965**
CARBONO DISUELTO *m* **1963**
CARBONO EN ESTADO GRAFITOIDE *m* **6059**
CARBONO GRAFÍTICO *m* **6059**
CARBONO NO COMBINADO AL HIERRO *m* **13345**
CARBORUNDO *m* **1980**
CARBURACIÓN DEL HIERRO *m* **1985**
CARBURADOR *m* **1982**
CARBURADOR *m* **1984**
CARBURADOR DE DOBLE CUERPO *m* **4360**
CARBURADOR INVERTIDO *m* **4189**
CARBURANTE *m* **9222**
CARBURANTE ANTIDEFLAGRANTE *m* **613**
CARBURANTES *m pl* **1988**
CARBURANTES *m pl* **2024**
CARBURAR EL HIERRO **1986**
CARBURO *m* **1933**
CARBURO *m* **1848**
CARBURO DE BARIO *m* **995**
CARBURO DE BORO *m* **1479**
CARBURO DE HIERRO *m* **7138**
CARBURO DE SILICIO *m* **11445**
CARBURO DE SILICIO *m* **1980**
CARCASA *f* **6660**
CARCASA *f* **5624**
CÁRCEL *f* **2452**
CÁRCEL *f* **2451**
CÁRCEL *f* **2452**
CARCOMIDO **13976**
CARDA *f* **5150**
CARDA *f* LIMPIALIMAS **5150**
CARDÁN *m* **6573**
CARDÁN *m* **5567**
CARDÁN *m* **1997**
CARDENILLO **220**

# CAR

CARDENILLO 13533
CARDENILLO *m* 13533
CARDIOIDE *f* 2001
CARENCIA *f* 11537
CARETA *f* 6252
CARETA *f* DE SOLDADOR 6432
CARGA *f* 5262
CARGA *f* 4954
CARGA *f* 4954
CARGA *f* 2269
CARGA *f* 2259
CARGA *f* 2263
CARGA *f* 12367
CARGA *f* 12331
CARGA *f* 7679
CARGA *f* 7679
CARGA *f* MÓVIL 10706
CARGA ADMISIBLE *f* 13956
CARGA ADMITIDA *f* 9215
CARGA AISLADA *f* 7183
CARGA CENTRAL *f* 2161
CARGA DE AGUA *f* 6323
CARGA DE FORJADO *f* 9823
CARGA DE LA VELOCIDAD *f* 13515
CARGA DE NIEVE *f* 11695
CARGA DE PRUEBA *f* 12781
CARGA DE ROTURA *f* 12749
CARGA DE ROTURA *f* 1585
CARGA DE RUPTURA *f* 13331
CARGA DE RUPTURA AL PANDEO *f* 3338
CARGA DE SEGURIDAD *f* 10879
CARGA DE UN ACUMULADOR *f* 2265
CARGA DE UN HORNO METALÚRGICO *f* 2264
CARGA DEL VIENTO *f* 13857
CARGA DISTRIBUIDA *f* 4078
CARGA ELÉCTRICA *f* 2259
CARGA ESTÁTICA *f* 12138
CARGA EXCÉNTRICA *f* 4428
CARGA HIDROSTÁTICA *f* 7652
CARGA INCOMPLETA *f* 7562
CARGA INFERIOR A LA NORMAL *f* 7562
CARGA INTERMITENTE *f* 7672
CARGA LÍMITE DE ELASTICIDAD *f* 1586
CARGA LÍQUIDA *f* 7647
CARGA MÁXIMA *f* 8065
CARGA MUERTA *f* 3631
CARGA NEUTRA *f* 13842
CARGA NORMAL *f* 8661
CARGA NORMAL *f* 8655
CARGA PERIÓDICA 6812

CARGA PERMANENTE *f* 3633
CARGA POR TRANSPORTADOR DE CINTA *f* 1141
CARGA POR UNIDAD DE SUPERFICIE *f* 13371
CARGA PRÁCTICA *f* 10879
CARGA QUÍMICA *f* 5157
CARGA RECTANGULAR *f* 10303
CARGA RODANTE *f* 10706
CARGA SIN GOLPES *f* 7685
CARGA TOTAL *f* 13062
CARGA TRAPEZOIDAL *f* 13150
CARGA TRIANGULAR *f* 13190
CARGA UNIFORMEMENTE DISTRIBUIDA *f* 13366
CARGA ÚTIL *f* 13425
CARGA ÚTIL *f* 9139
CARGA VARIABLE *f* 7672
CARGA VIVA *f* 7671
CARGADOR *m* 8110
CARGADOR (O CARGADORA) PARA PASTO VERDE ( *m* *f* )
  7687
CARGADORES DE ESTIÉRCOL *m* 7689
CARGADORES DE SACOS Y REMOLACHAS *m* 7688
CARGAMENTO *m* 2263
CARGAR 5156
CARGAR (RESISTENCIA DE LOS MATERIALES) 7680
CARGAR UN ACUMULADOR 2261
CARGAR UN FUERZO 12269
CARGAR UN HOGAR 12269
CARGAR UN HORNO METALÚRGICO 2260
CARGAR UN MUELLE 10032
CARIES *f* 10770
CARPETA *f* 1350
CARPINTERÍA *f* 2006
CARPINTERÍA *f* 12942
CARPINTERÍA *f* (ARTE) 7236
CARPINTERÍA *f* DE MODELOS (ARTE) 9131
CARPINTERÍA *f* DE MODELOS (TALLER) 9132
CARPINTERÍA *f* (TALLER) 7235
CARPINTERO *m* 7233
CARPINTERO *m* 2005
CARRACA *f* 10219
CARRERA *f* 10810
CARRERA *f* 12387
CARRERA *f* DIRECTA DEL PISTÓN 5585
CARRERA ADELANTE *f* 5585
CARRERA ASCENDENTE *f* 13409
CARRERA ASCENDENTE DEL ÉMBOLO *f* 13409
CARRERA COMPLETA (IDA Y VUELTA) DEL ÉMBOLO *f*
  13406
CARRERA DE ASPIRACIÓN *f* 12435
CARRERA DE COMBUSTIÓN *f* 2775
CARRERA DE COMPRESIÓN *f* 2864

CAT

CARRERA DE DESCARGA *f* **2775**
CARRERA DE DESCARGA *f* **9834**
CARRERA DE ESCAPE *f* **4898**
CARRERA DE EXPANSIÓN *f* **2775**
CARRERA DE IDA *f* **5585**
CARRERA DE LA EXCÉNTRICA *f* **12894**
CARRERA DE LA LEVA *f* **12894**
CARRERA DE RETROCESO *f* **10530**
CARRERA DE RETROCESO DEL ÉMBOLO *f* **10530**
CARRERA DE TRABAJO *f* **3536**
CARRERA DE VÁLVULA *f* **7544**
CARRERA DEL PISTÓN O ÉMBOLO *f* **7519**
CARRERA DESCENDENTE DEL ÉMBOLO *f* **4187**
CARRERA DIRECTA DEL ÉMBOLO *f* **5585**
CARRERA EN VACÍO *f* (DE UNA MÁQUINA-HERRAMIENTA) **10529**
CARRERA ÚTIL (DE UNA MÁQUINA-HERRAMIENTA) *f* **3536**
CARRERA VERTICAL *f* **13549**
CARRETE *m* **2028**
CARRETE *m* PARA CABLE **13898**
CARRETILLA *f* **13812**
CARRETILLA *f* **2013**
CARRETILLA *f* **947**
CARRETILLA *f* **947**
CARRETILLA *f* **6230**
CARRETILLA DE PUENTE-GRÚA *f* **13155**
CARRETILLA PARA COLGAR PIEZAS A TEMPLAR *f* **9505**
CARRETILLA (PARA MANIPULACIÓN TALLER Y ALMACÉN) *f* **13230**
CARRETILLA PORTA-APAREJO *f* **13155**
CARRETILLA UNIVERSAL *f* **3379**
CARRETILLAS *f pl* **13231**
CARRIL *m* **7606**
CARRIL *m* **10175**
CARRO *m* **4116**
CARRO *m* **2013**
CARRO PARA LINGOTES (TRANSPORTE DE LINGOTES) *m* **6920**
CARROCERÍA *f* **1385**
CARROZADO *m* **1889**
CARRUSEL *m* **1731**
CARTABÓN *m* **11223**
CARTABÓN *m* DE INGLETE **8325**
CARTER *m* **2026**
CÁRTER *m* **6660**
CÁRTER *m* DE DIRECCIÓN **12229**
CARTER DE ACEITE (INFERIOR) *m* **8782**
CARTER DE ACEITE (INFERIOR) *m* **8767**
CARTER DE BOMBA DE INYECCIÓN *m* **5712**
CARTER DE CADENAS *m* **2204**
CARTER DE EMBRAGUE *m* **2546**

CARTER DE EMBRAGUE *m* **1133**
CARTER DEL MOTOR *m* **3306**
CARTÓN *m* **1381**
CARTÓN BITUMINOSO O ASFÁLTICO *m* **10712**
CARTÓN DE ASBESTO *m* **747**
CARTÓN LIGERO *m* **1999**
CARTUCHO *m* **2015**
CARTUCHO FILTRANTE *m* **5175**
CASCA *f* AGOTADA **12635**
CASCA *f* COMPRIMIDA **12612**
CASCA *f* EN TERRONES **12612**
CASCADA *f* **2018**
CASCAJO *m* **6073**
CASCARILLA *f* DE LAMINACIÓN **8279**
CASCARILLAS *f pl* **6217**
CASCO *m* **6432**
CASCO *m* **7313**
CASCO *m* (DE BUQUE) **5624**
CASCO DE COJINETE *m* **1113**
CASCOS *m pl* DE ANIMALES ESCOFINADOS **6567**
CASEINA *f* **2025**
CASILLA *f* **2798**
CASINOIDE *f* **2029**
CASINOIDE *f* **2029**
CASITERICA *f* **12959**
CASQUETA *f* **1911**
CASQUETE *m* **1910**
CASQUETE ESFÉRICO *m* **11887**
CASQUILLO *m* **11576**
CASQUILLO *m* **1773**
CASQUILLO *m* CON MUELLE **11979**
CASQUILLO *m* DE AJUSTE (DE REGULACIÓN) **194**
CASQUILLO *m* DE BUJÍA **11839**
CASQUILLO *m* DE COJINETE **1773**
CASQUILLO *m* DE CUBO DE RUEDA **12905**
CASQUILLO *m* DE GUÍA **6163**
CASQUILLO *m* DE PRENSAESTOPA **7392**
CASQUILLO *m* DE SOPORTE **14016**
CASQUILLO *m* INFERIOR DEL COJINETE **1487**
CASQUILLO *m* (MANGUITO *m*) DE APRETADURA **2728**
CASQUILLO *m* ROSCADO DEL CALIBRE DE PUNTAS **11050**
CASQUILLO *m* SUPERIOR DEL COJINETE **13030**
CASSETTE *m* **2028**
CATAFORSIS *f* **4639**
CATÁLISIS *f* **2090**
CATALÍTICO *m* **2092**
CATALIZADOR *m* **2091**
CATARATA *f* **3611**
CATEGORÍA DE HIERRO *f* **2458**

**CAT** 988

CATEGORÍA TIPO DE ACERO *f* **2459**
CATETÓMETRO *m* **2096**
CATIÓN *m* **2112**
CATIÓN *m* **9657**
CÁTODO *m* **2106**
CÁTODO *m* **2097**
CÁTODO DE RECTIFICADOR *m* **10316**
CATÓLITO **2111**
CAUCHO *m* **10816**
CAUCHO *m* **10825**
CAUCHO *m* VIRGEN **3413**
CAUCHO DE SELLADO *m* **13722**
CAUCHO EN BRUTO *m* **3413**
CAUCHO ENDURECIDO *m* **2363**
CAUCHO ENTELADO *m* **6973**
CAUCHO VULCANIZADO *m* **13610**
CAUDAL *m* **10069**
CAUDAL *m* **8896**
CAUDAL *m* **8908**
CAUDAL *m* **5459**
CAUDAL *m* DE UNA BOMBA **10228**
CAUDAL *m* NORMAL **8658**
CAUDAL *m* TOTAL **13064**
CAUDALÍMETRO *m* **5458**
CAUSA DE ERROR *f* **11825**
CÁUSTICA *f* POR REFRACCIÓN **3829**
CÁUSTICO *m* **2116**
CÁUSTICO *m* **4847**
CÁUSTICO *m* CORROSIVO *m* **4847**
CÁUSTICO POR REFLEXIÓN *m* **2089**
CÁUSTICO POR REFRACCIÓN *m* **3829**
CAVETO *m* **2122**
CAVIDAD *f* **2125**
CAVIDAD *f* **2125**
CAVIDAD *f* **2125**
CAVIDAD *f* **10279**
CAVIDAD *f* **7073**
CAVIDAD *f* ENTRE DIENTES **6548**
CAVIDAD *f* POR CONTRACCIÓN **2124**
CAVIDAD *f* POR CONTRACCIÓN **11505**
CAVIDAD *f* POR CONTRACCIÓN **9340**
CAVIDAD *f* POR CONTRACCIÓN **11393**
CAVIDAD *f* POR CONTRACCIÓN **7073**
CAVIDAD DE CELDA *f* **2127**
CAVIDAD DEL MOLDE *f* **8353**
CAVIDAD EN V *f* **5271**
CAVITACIÓN *f* **2123**
CAZA *f* REMACHES **10626**
CAZAREMACHES *m* **11032**
CAZO *m* **1378**

CAZOLETA *f* **4115**
CEBAR UNA BOMBA **9856**
CEDAZO **11422**
CEDER **5949**
CEDER (GASTAR) CALOR **5950**
CÉLULA *f* DE AERACIÓN **209**
CÉLULA *f* (O ELEMENTO *m*) DE ACUMULADOR **78**
CÉLULA FOTOCONDUCTORA *f* **9261**
CÉLULA FOTOELÉCTRICA *f* **9260**
CÉLULA FOTOEMISORA *f* **9273**
CÉLULA FOTOVOLTÁICA *f* **9277**
CÉLULA (O CELDA) AL MERCURIO *f* **8165**
CÉLULA (O CUBA) ELECTROLÍTICA *f* **4588**
CELULOIDE *m* **2130**
CELULOSA *f* **2131**
CELULOSA **2316**
CELULOSA **8116**
CELULOSA NITRADA *f* **6176**
CEMENTACIÓN *f* **2141**
CEMENTACIÓN *f* **2021**
CEMENTACIÓN AL PRUSIATO AMARILLO *f* **9670**
CEMENTACIÓN AL PRUSIATO POTÁSICO *f* **9670**
CEMENTACIÓN BRILLANTE *f* **9959**
CEMENTACIÓN CON POLVO *f* **8992**
CEMENTACIÓN DE LA PIEZAS DE ACERO DULCE *f* **2023**
CEMENTACIÓN (DE LAS BARRAS DE HIERRO) **2142**
CEMENTACIÓN EN BAÑO *f* **7646**
CEMENTACIÓN EN CAJA *f* **1996**
CEMENTACIÓN HOMOGÉNEA *f* **1993**
CEMENTACIÓN NÍTRICA *f* **5818**
CEMENTACIÓN PARCIAL *f* **2023**
CEMENTACIÓN POR EL CROMO *f* **2390**
CEMENTACIÓN POR GAS *f* **1992**
CEMENTACIÓN SELECTIVA *f* **1995**
CEMENTACIÓN SELECTIVA *f* **11143**
CEMENTACIÓN VÍA EL CARBONO *f* **1987**
CEMENTAR **2134**
CEMENTITA *f* **2147**
CEMENTO *m* **2133**
CEMENTO *m* **2139**
CEMENTO *m* **2022**
CEMENTO ARMADO *m* **12203**
CEMENTO DE COBRE *m* **2136**
CEMENTO DE ENDURECIMIENTO AL AIRE *m* **302**
CEMENTO DE ESCORIAL *m* **11564**
CEMENTO DE ESCORIAS *m* **11564**
CEMENTO DE FRAGUADO LENTO *m* **11648**
CEMENTO DE FRAGUADO RÁPIDO *m* **10107**
CEMENTO PORTLAND *m* **9644**
CEMENTO PUZÓLANICO *m* **9749**

CEMENTO REFRACTARIO *m* **5255**
CEMENTO REFRACTARIO AL SILICATO DE ALUMINIO *m* **443**
CEMENTO ROMANO *m* **10707**
CEMENTOS *m pl* **2024**
CENICERO *m* **759**
CENICIENTO **9143**
CENIZA *f* **760**
CENIZA *f* **2397**
CENIZA *f* **2397**
CENIZAL *m* **759**
CENIZAS *f pl* **760**
CENIZAS VOLANTES *f pl* **5493**
CENTÍMETRO *m* **2158**
CENTÍMETRO CUADRADO *m* **12016**
CENTÍMETRO CÚBICO *m* **3449**
CENTRADO *m* **2187**
CENTRAL ELÉCTRICA *f* **4512**
CENTRAL HIDRÁULICA *f* **6692**
CENTRALILLA *f* TELEFÓNICA **12557**
CENTRAR **2163**
CENTRARSE **1122**
CENTRIFUGAR **6702**
CENTRO *m* **2148**
CENTRO *m* **2162**
CENTRO *m* DE RUEDA **13814**
CENTRO CÚBICO *m* **1399**
CENTRO DE ARCO *m* **2167**
CENTRO DE COMPÁS *m* **6594**
CENTRO DE GRAVEDAD *m* **2168**
CENTRO DE OSCILACIÓN *m* **2170**
CENTRO DE ROTACIÓN *m* **2169**
CENTRO DE ROTACIÓN *m* **5717**
CENTRO DE RUEDA DE ACERO FUNDIDO *m* **2056**
CENTRO DE SUPERFICIE *m* **2191**
CENTRO DEL REMACHE *m* **2171**
CENTRO INSTANTÁNEO DE ROTACIÓN *m* **6989**
CEPILLADO *m* **9450**
CEPILLADORA *f* **12515**
CEPILLADURA *f* **9450**
CEPILLAR **9434**
CEPILLAR **12318**
CEPILLO *m* **9019**
CEPILLO *m* **9432**
CEPILLO *m* CIMBRADO **2801**
CEPILLO *m* DE ALAMBRE **13884**
CEPILLO *m* DE ALAMBRE **13884**
CEPILLO *m* DE DISCO **2425**
CEPILLO *m* DE DOBLE HOJA **4146**
CEPILLO *m* DE INGLETE **10115**

CEPILLO *m* DE LIMPIAR TUBOS **13247**
CEPILLO *m* DE PULIR **11687**
CEPILLO *m* DE PULIR **2425**
CEPILLO *m* DE TAPÓN **8047**
CEPILLO *m* DENTADO **13027**
CEPILLO *m* METÁLICO **11014**
CEPILLO *m* PARA HEMBRAS **6139**
CEPILLO *m* PARA LIMAS **5150**
CEPILLO *m* PARA MACHOS **12993**
CEPILLO *m* PARA MOLDURAS **9522**
CEPILLO *m* REDONDO **10800**
CERA **13702**
CERA DE ABEJAS *f* **1129**
CERA DE CARNAUBA *f* **2003**
CERA DE PARAFINA *f* **7579**
CERA DE PARAFINA *f* **9045**
CERA DEL JAPÓN *f* **7213**
CERA DEL JAPÓN *f* **7579**
CERA FÓSIL *f* **4413**
CERA MINERAL *f* **2194**
CERAMETAL *m* **2192**
CERÁMICA *f* **2193**
CERCA *f* **5094**
CERCADO *m* **5094**
CERCENAR **12424**
CERCHA *f* **13243**
CERCO *m* **12261**
CERDAS *f* **12594**
CERESINA *f* **2194**
CERIO *m* **2195**
CERNADA *f* **2397**
CERNER **11423**
CERO *m* ABSOLUTO **36**
CERO *m* (DE UNA ESCALA) **14027**
CERO *m* FLOTANTE **5440**
CERRADO **6447**
CERRADO HERMÉTICAMENTE **6447**
CERRADURA *f* DE PORTEZUELA **4123**
CERRAJERO MECÁNICO *m* **5278**
CERRAR EL CIRCUITO ELÉCTRICO **2515**
CERRAR LA INTRODUCCIÓN *f* **11407**
CERROJO *m* **1432**
CERROJO *m* **1432**
CERTIFICADO DE PRUEBA *m* **12775**
CERTIFICADO DE RECEPCIÓN *m* INSPECCIÓN **70**
CERUCITA *f* **13834**
CERUSA *f* **13834**
CERUSA *f* **13834**
CERUSITA *f* **2196**
CESIO *m* **2197**

**CES** 990

CESIO  *m* **1833**
CESIO  *m* **1833**
CESIÓN DE CALOR  *f* **3735**
CESTA DE INMERSIÓN  *f* **3976**
CETINA  *f* **11882**
CHAFLÁN  *m* **2231**
CHAFLÁN  *m* **1902**
CHAFLÁN  *m* **1221**
CHAFLÁN EN MEDIA V  *m* **1800**
CHAFLÁN (SOLDADURA) EN K  *m* **1793**
CHAMOTA  *f* **2235**
CHANGOTE (MET.) **1345**
CHAPA  *f* **5508**
CHAPA  *f* **13524**
CHAPA  *f* **11298**
CHAPA  *f* **11315**
CHAPA  *f* **11305**
CHAPA  *f* **9477**
CHAPA  *f* ABOMBADA **1679**
CHAPA  *f* ACANALADA **2252**
CHAPA  *f* APLANADA **5395**
CHAPA  *f* BLANCA **12957**
CHAPA  *f* CON ABERTURAS **9189**
CHAPA  *f* CONSTRUCCIÓN **1109**
CHAPA  *f* CONTRACHAPEADA **2445**
CHAPA  *f* DE ACERO **11325**
CHAPA  *f* DE ACERO **12213**
CHAPA  *f* DE ACERO ALUMINADA **441**
CHAPA  *f* DE AGUJEROS PERFORADOS **4274**
CHAPA  *f* DE AGUJEROS TALADRADOS **10003**
CHAPA  *f* DE AJUSTE **7621**
CHAPA  *f* DE BLINDAJE **11343**
CHAPA  *f* DE CALDERAS **1416**
CHAPA  *f* DE COBRE **3127**
CHAPA  *f* DE DESGASTE **13716**
CHAPA  *f* DE ESTARCIR **12238**
CHAPA  *f* DE GRANO ORIENTADO **6036**
CHAPA  *f* DE HIERRO **11309**
CHAPA  *f* DE LATÓN **1569**
CHAPA  *f* DE MADERA **13524**
CHAPA  *f* DE PLOMO **7462**
CHAPA  *f* DE RECUBRIMIENTO **11335**
CHAPA  *f* DE REFUERZO **11343**
CHAPA  *f* DE REFUERZO **10430**
CHAPA  *f* DE REFUERZO **12257**
CHAPA  *f* DE REVESTIMIENTO **10430**
CHAPA  *f* DE TRANSFORMADOR **4544**
CHAPA  *f* DEFLECTORA **921**
CHAPA  *f* ELÉCTRICA **4544**
CHAPA  *f* ELÉCTRICA **11448**

CHAPA  *f* EMBUTIDA **1679**
CHAPA  *f* EMPLOMADA **7460**
CHAPA  *f* EN RELIEVE **9911**
CHAPA  *f* ESPESA **9477**
CHAPA  *f* ESTAÑADA **12957**
CHAPA  *f* ESTRIADA **10574**
CHAPA  *f* ESTRIADA **2252**
CHAPA  *f* ESTRIADA **2325**
CHAPA  *f* ESTRIADA **2285**
CHAPA  *f* FINA **11304**
CHAPA  *f* FINA **12850**
CHAPA  *f* FUERTE **9477**
CHAPA  *f* FUERTE **6409**
CHAPA  *f* GALVANIZADA **5785**
CHAPA  *f* GALVANIZADA **5785**
CHAPA  *f* GOFRADA **2285**
CHAPA  *f* GOFRADA **12769**
CHAPA  *f* GOTEADA **10181**
CHAPA  *f* LAMINADA **10674**
CHAPA  *f* LAMINADA EN CALIENTE **6637**
CHAPA  *f* LAMINADA EN FRÍO **2696**
CHAPA  *f* MARGINAL **8002**
CHAPA  *f* MARGINAL **11531**
CHAPA  *f* MATE **1296**
CHAPA  *f* MUY FINA **12593**
CHAPA  *f* NEGRA **1296**
CHAPA  *f* NEGRA **1294**
CHAPA  *f* ONDULADA **3198**
CHAPA  *f* (PARA CONSTRUCCIÓN) NAVAL **11356**
CHAPA  *f* PARA EMBUTIDO **9478**
CHAPA  *f* PARA INDUCIDOS DE DINAMOS **708**
CHAPA  *f* PARA REVESTIMIENTOS DE PISO **5447**
CHAPA  *f* PARA TRANSFORMADORES **13116**
CHAPA  *f* PERFILADA **11846**
CHAPA  *f* PERFORADA **9189**
CHAPA  *f* PERFORADA **9189**
CHAPA  *f* SOPORTE **12495**
CHAPA  *f* TECNOLÓGICA **10842**
CHAPA  *f* TRABAJADA POR ENCARGO **11846**
CHAPAS  *f pl* ESTIRADAS **4250**
CHAPAS  *f pl* FINAS DE ACERO ALEADO **380**
CHAPAS  *f pl* NEGRAS **1289**
CHAPAS  *f pl* (ORDEN DE COLOCACIÓN DE LAS) **9500**
CHAPAS  *f pl* RECORTADAS **11266**
CHAPAS  *f pl* RECUBIERTAS **2586**
CHAPEADO  *m* **2447**
CHAPEADO **5999**
CHAPEADO  *m* **9503**
CHAPEADO  *m* **13524**
CHAPEADO  *m* A LA LLAMA **5317**

| | | |
|---|---|---|
| CHAPEADO *m* CON LATÓN **1567** | CIANURO *m* ARGÉNTICO (O DE PLATA) **11462** | |
| CHAPEADO *m* DE NÍQUEL **8567** | CIANURO *m* ÁURICO (O DE ORO) **5997** | |
| CHAPEADO *m* MECÁNICO **8108** | CIANURO *m* DE CINC **14041** | |
| CHAPEAR **9479** | CIANURO *m* DE COBRE **3115** | |
| CHAPELETA DE VÁLVULA *f* **13459** | CIANURO *m* DE POTASIO **9683** | |
| CHAPELETA DE VÁLVULA *f* **9024** | CIANURO *m* DE SODIO **11720** | |
| CHÁSIS *m* **13381** | CIANURO *m* LIBRE **5632** | |
| CHÁSIS *m* **2275** | CICLO *m* **3553** | |
| CHÁSIS-CAJA *m* **1511** | CICLO *m* AUTOMÁTICO **839** | |
| CHATARRA *f* **1301** | CICLO *m* DE CARNOT **2004** | |
| CHATARRA *f* **5553** | CICLO *m* DE OPERACIONES **3554** | |
| CHATARRA *f* **5553** | CICLO *m* DE TRABAJO **3553** | |
| CHATARRA *f* **5126** | CICLO *m* FIJO **5292** | |
| CHATARRA *f* **9493** | CICLOIDE *f* **3557** | |
| CHATARRA *f* **11379** | CICLOIDE **10697** | |
| CHATARRA *f* **11007** | CICLOIDE *f* ACORTADA **3493** | |
| CHATARRA *f* **11007** | CICLOIDE *f* ALARGADA **9918** | |
| CHATARRA *f* **11107** | CICLÓN *m* PULVERIZADOR **3560** | |
| CHATARRA *f* DE HIERRO **11007** | CIENO *m* **11609** | |
| CHATARRAS *f pl* DE PRODUCCIÓN PROPIA **6554** | CIERRE *m* CON ARTICULACIÓN **7336** | |
| CHATARRAS *f pl* DE PROTECCIÓN PROPIA **4124** | CIERRE *m* DE BAYONETA **1074** | |
| CHATARRAS *f* EN PAQUETES **5016** | CIERRE *m* DE BAYONETA **1074** | |
| CHAVETA *f* **5940** | CIERRE *m* DE LA VÁLVULA **2537** | |
| CHAVETA *f* **7276** | CIFRA *f* **3940** | |
| CHAVETA *f* **13739** | CIFRA DE DUREZA BRINELL *f* **1619** | |
| CHAVETA *f* DE RETENCIÓN **6522** | CIFRAS Y LETRAS EN CALIENTE / FRÍO *f* **1560** | |
| CHAVETA DE MEDIALUNA *f* **13929** | CIGÜEÑAL *m* **3309** | |
| CHAVETA EMPOTRADA *f* **12458** | CIGÜEÑAL *m* **3309** | |
| CHIFLAR (LAS PIELES) **13204** | CIGÜEÑAL **3309** | |
| CHIMENEA *f* **12046** | CIGÜEÑAL *m* DE CONTRAPESOS **3235** | |
| CHIMENEA *f* **2339** | CIGÜEÑAL *m* DE TRES CODOS **12880** | |
| CHINA-GRASS **10192** | CIGÜEÑAL *m* DE VARIOS CODOS **8478** | |
| CHINCHE *f* **4242** | CIGÜEÑAL DE UN SOLO CODO *m* **11503** | |
| CHISPA *m* **11836** | CILINDRADA *f* **3448** | |
| CHISPORROTEO *m* ELÉCTRICO **4531** | CILINDRADA *f* **3566** | |
| CHOQUE *m* **4529** | CILINDRADA *f* **2262** | |
| CHOQUE *m* **11359** | CILINDRADO *m* **13164** | |
| CHOQUE *m* **11359** | CILINDRADO *m* DE TUBOS **4908** | |
| CHOQUE *m* (DE NEUTRONES CON ÁTOMOS) **7327** | CILÍNDRICO *m* **3577** | |
| CHORRO *m* DE AGUA **13656** | CILINDRO *m* **3561** | |
| CHORRO *m* DE AIRE **242** | CILINDRO *m* **1015** | |
| CHORRO *m* DE COLADA **12004** | CILINDRO *m* **10671** | |
| CHORRO *m* DE SÓLIDOS **11787** | CILINDRO *m* DE AIRE **2841** | |
| CHORRO *m* DE VAPOR **12170** | CILINDRO *m* DE ALIMENTACIÓN **5074** | |
| CHORRO *m* LÍQUIDO **7221** | CILINDRO *m* DE ALIMENTACIÓN **5074** | |
| CHUPETE *m* **12332** | CILINDRO *m* DE ALTA PRESIÓN **6488** | |
| CIANATO *m* **3544** | CILINDRO *m* DE BAJA PRESIÓN **7783** | |
| CIANÓGENO *m* **3551** | CILINDRO *m* DE BASE CIRCULAR **2411** | |
| CIANOTIPO *m* **5119** | CILINDRO *m* DE BOMBA **9992** | |
| CIANURO *m* **3547** | CILINDRO *m* DE CINTRAR (DE CURVAR) **1186** | |

**CIL** 992

CILINDRO *m* DE CINTRAR (DE CURVAR) **1186**
CILINDRO *m* DE ELEVACIÓN **7550**
CILINDRO *m* DE EQUILIBADO **938**
CILINDRO *m* DE EQUILIBRADO **939**
CILINDRO *m* DE FRENADO **1532**
CILINDRO *m* DE MANDO **8037**
CILINDRO *m* DE TRABAJO (MOTOR) **13954**
CILINDRO *m* DE VAPOR **12162**
CILINDRO *f* DENTADO **10174**
CILINDRO *m* ELÍPTICO **4675**
CILINDRO *m* EN VACÍO **4373**
CILINDRO *m* GRADUADO **3582**
CILINDRO *m* HIPERBÓLICO **6736**
CILINDRO *m* HUECO **6540**
CILINDRO *m* LISO **5391**
CILINDRO *m* MOTOR **13954**
CILINDRO *m* (O TAMBOR *m*) REGISTRADOR **10290**
CILINDRO *m* OBLÍCUO **8712**
CILINDRO *m* PARABÓLICO **9039**
CILINDRO *m* RANURADO **11206**
CILINDRO *m* RANURADO **5486**
CILINDRO *m* RANURADO **6136**
CILINDRO *m* RECTO **10579**
CILINDRO *m* SOBRESALIENTE (O EN VOLADIZO) **8935**
CILINDRO *m* TAMBOR *m* **10671**
CILINDROS *m pl* DE SOPORTE **903**
CILINDROS *m pl* TRANSVERSALES **1643**
CIMBRA *f* **3494**
CIMBRA DE DILATACIÓN *f* **4913**
CIMBRAR **1173**
CIMENTACIÓN *f* (CUBRIR CON UNA CAPA DE CEMENTO) **2146**
CIMENTADO *m* **2146**
CIMENTAR (CUBRIR CON UNA CAPA DE CEMENTO) **2134**
CIMIENTOS *m pl* **5589**
CIMIENTOS *m pl* DE HORMIGÓN **2896**
CIMIENTOS *m pl* DE LADRILLO **1599**
CIMIENTOS *m pl* DE MAMPOSTERÍA **1599**
CINABRIO *m* **2400**
CINC *m* **14035**
CINC *m* BRUTO **2785**
CINC *m* COMERCIAL **2785**
CINC *m* (COMERCIAL) **11879**
CINC *m* EN HOJAS **11327**
CINC *m* REFUNDIDO **10341**
CINC *m* SILICATO **11438**
CINCEL *m* **2349**
CINCEL *m* **3364**
CINCEL *m* AGUDO **3364**
CINCEL *m* DE ALBAÑIL **7201**

CINCELAR **2344**
CINCHA *f* **8354**
CINCHO *m* DE UNA RUEDA **8354**
CINEMÁTICA *f* **7306**
CINEMÁTICO *m* **7305**
CINÉTICA *f* **7310**
CINÉTICO *m* **7307**
CINTA *f* **8092**
CINTA *f* **12641**
CINTA *f* **12641**
CINTA *f* **1140**
CINTA *f* **974**
CINTA *f* **974**
CINTA *f* ABRASIVA **18**
CINTA *f* AISLADORA **7001**
CINTA *f* CAUCHUTADA **10822**
CINTA *f* DE ACERO **12197**
CINTA *f* DE ESMERIL **18**
CINTA *f* DE FRENO **1544**
CINTA *f* DE HIERRO **6575**
CINTA *f* DE PAPEL PERFORADO **10005**
CINTA *f* MAGNÉTICA **7919**
CINTA *f* METÁLICA DE PROTECCIÓN **3268**
CINTA *f* TRANSPORTADORA **1164**
CINTA DE ACERO *f* **12200**
CINTA-SOPORTE *f* **902**
CINTAS *f pl* **980**
CINTURÓN DE SEGURIDAD **10882**
CINTURÓN DE SEGURIDAD **11096**
CIRCUITO DE FRENO *f* **1545**
CIRCUITO DE REFRIGERACIÓN *f* **3093**
CIRCUITO ELÉCTRICO *m* **2406**
CIRCUITO IMPRESO (C.I.) *m* **9871**
CIRCULACIÓN *f* **2433**
CIRCULACIÓN AL CIANURO *f* **3549**
CIRCULACIÓN DE AGUA *f* **2434**
CIRCULAR **2432**
CÍRCULO *m* **2401**
CÍRCULO *m* **2404**
CÍRCULO ANUAL *m* **586**
CÍRCULO BÁSICO *m* **1030**
CÍRCULO CIRCONSCRITO *m* **2435**
CÍRCULO CIRCUNSCRITO *m* **2435**
CÍRCULO DE ARCO *m* **2402**
CÍRCULO DE CORONACIÓN *m* **3396**
CÍRCULO DE FONDO *m* **10723**
CÍRCULO DE FONDO *m* **10723**
CÍRCULO DE HUECO *m* **10723**
CÍRCULO DE LOS AGUJEROS PARA PERNOS *m* **1433**

CÍRCULO DE PUNTO NEUTRO  m (CÁLCULO DE ARMAZONES DE RESISTENCIA A PRESIÓN)  m **8604**
CÍRCULO DE RAÍZ  m **10717**
CÍRCULO DESCRITO POR LA MANIVELA  m **3298**
CÍRCULO DIVIDIDO  m **6026**
CÍRCULO ELÁSTICO  m **11990**
CÍRCULO EXINSCRITO  m **4834**
CÍRCULO EXTERIOR  m **167**
CÍRCULO EXTERIOR  m **166**
CÍRCULO EXTERIOR  m **166**
CÍRCULO EXTERIOR  m **166**
CÍRCULO FIJO  m **5290**
CÍRCULO GRADUADO  m **6026**
CÍRCULO INSCRITO  m **6963**
CÍRCULO INSCRITO  m **6963**
CÍRCULO INTERIOR DE UNA RUEDA  f **10596**
CÍRCULO MÓVIL  m **5921**
CÍRCULO PRIMITIVO  m **1030**
CÍRCULO PRIMITIVO  m **9404**
CÍRCULO PRIMITIVO DE DENTADURA  m **9403**
CÍRCULO RODANTE  m **5921**
CÍRCULOS CONCÉNTRICOS  m **2890**
CÍRCULOS EXCÉNTRICOS  m **4426**
CIRCUNFERENCIA  f **2404**
CIRCUNFERENCIA DE DENTADURA (ENGRANAJES)  f **166**
CIRCUNFERENCIA DE VACIADO  f **10723**
CIRCUNFERENCIA PRIMITIVA  f **9404**
CISOIDE  m **2438**
CISTERNA  f **2439**
CISTERNA  f **13228**
CITAR **10113**
CITRATO DE SODIO  m **11719**
CIZALLA  f **11279**
CIZALLA  f **11297**
CIZALLA BASCULANTE  f **10658**
CIZALLA CIRCULAR  f **2429**
CIZALLA CIRCULAR  f **2403**
CIZALLA DE VOLADIZO  f **5495**
CIZALLA DE VOLADIZO  f **5495**
CIZALLA MECÁNICA  f **11292**
CIZALLA MECÁNICA  f **11292**
CIZALLA PARA ARMADURA DE HORMIGÓN  f **2897**
CIZALLA PARA CHAPA  f **9494**
CIZALLA PARA DESPUNTAR  f **12037**
CIZALLA PARA RECORTES  f **3358**
CIZALLAMIENTO  m **10507**
CIZALLAMIENTO  m **11279**
CIZALLAMIENTO  m **11290**
CIZALLAMIENTO  m **11290**
CIZALLAMIENTO  m **11279**

CIZALLAMIENTO  m **11288**
CIZALLAR **11280**
CIZALLAR **3506**
CIZALLAR **1078**
CLARIDAD  f DE UNA IMAGEN **11276**
CLARIFICACIÓN  f **2460**
CLARIFICACIÓN  f **2455**
CLARIFICAR **2456**
CLASE  f DE HIERRO **2458**
CLASE  f DE MADERA **13503**
CLASE  f DE MADERA **13503**
CLASIFICACIÓN  f **11524**
CLASIFICACIÓN  f **11139**
CLASIFICACIÓN  f **1867**
CLASIFICACIÓN  f POR CORRIENTE GASEOSA **248**
CLASIFICACIÓN  f POR CORRIENTE GASEOSA **4681**
CLASIFICADORAS  f pl DE PATATAS **9706**
CLASIFICADORAS  f pl ELECTRÓNICAS **11185**
CLAVADO  m **10639**
CLAVADO SIMPLE  m **11487**
CLAVAR **8492**
CLAVERA  f **6325**
CLAVERA  f **6325**
CLAVERA  f **6325**
CLAVERA  f **6325**
CLAVERA  f **6325**
CLAVETEAR **4293**
CLAVIJA  f **5211**
CLAVIJA  f **5211**
CLAVIJA  f **9159**
CLAVIJA  f **12399**
CLAVIJA  f **7276**
CLAVIJA  f **9315**
CLAVIJA  f **13739**
CLAVIJA  f CON CABEZA **2492**
CLAVIJA  f DE CENTRADO **1513**
CLAVIJA  f DE PRUEBAS **12785**
CLAVIJA  f HENDIDA **11943**
CLAVIJA COLOCADA EN PLANO  f **5388**
CLAVIJA CÓNICA  f **12665**
CLAVIJA DE APRIETE  f **185**
CLAVIJA DE CUÑA  f **3215**
CLAVIJA DE DISCO  f **13929**
CLAVIJA DE GANCHO  f **5939**
CLAVIJA DE GANCHO  f **5939**
CLAVIJA DE GANCHO  f **5939**
CLAVIJA DE MEDIALUNA  f **13929**
CLAVIJA HUECA  f **6542**
CLAVIJA HUECA  f **6542**
CLAVIJA HUECA  f CLAVIJA DE FRICCIÓN  f **6542**

# CLA

994

CLAVIJA LONGITUDINAL  *f* **7276**
CLAVIJA PLANA  *f* **5388**
CLAVIJA PLANA  *f* **5388**
CLAVIJA SEMIREDONDA  *f* CLAVIJA DE MEDIALUNA  *f* **13929**
CLAVIJA SUMERGIDA  *f* **12458**
CLAVIJA TANGENCIAL  *f* **12618**
CLAVIJA TRANSVERSAL  *f* **3215**
CLAVIJA VACIADA  *f* **6542**
CLAVIJA Y CONTRA-CLAVIJA  *f* **5938**
CLAVO  *m* **8491**
CLAVO DE GANCHO  *m* **2457**
CLAVO FORJADO  *m* **13990**
CLAVO FUNDIDO  *m* **2051**
CLAVO PARA BUQUE  *m* **1382**
CLAVO PARA HERRADURA  *m* **6601**
CLAVO TROQUELADO  *m* **7841**
CLAVOS DE CARROCERÍA  *f* **2554**
CLAXÓN  *m* **6592**
CLIMATIZADOR  *m* **250**
CLIP  *m* **11990**
CLISÉ  *m* **8993**
CLISÉ FOTOGRÁFICO  *m* **8524**
CLISÉ TIPOGRÁFICO  *m* **1340**
CLORALUMINIO  *m* **421**
CLORATO  *m* **2351**
CLORATO POTÁSICO  *m* **9680**
CLORHIDRATO DE AMONÍACO  *m* **462**
CLORO  *m* **2354**
CLOROFORMO  *m* **2356**
CLORURACIÓN  *f* **2353**
CLORURO  *m* **2352**
CLORURO  *m* DE PLATA **11461**
CLORURO  *m* ETÍLICO **4849**
CLORURO CRÓMICO  *m* **2381**
CLORURO CROMOSO  *m* **2391**
CLORURO CÚPRICO  *m* **4853**
CLORURO CUPROSO  *m* **3478**
CLORURO DE ACETILO  *m* **92**
CLORURO DE ALUMINIO  *m* **421**
CLORURO DE ALUMINIO  *m* **421**
CLORURO DE AMONIO  *m* **462**
CLORURO DE AZUFRE  *m* **12451**
CLORURO DE BARIO  *m* **997**
CLORURO DE CAL  *m* **1317**
CLORURO DE CALCIO  *m* **1850**
CLORURO DE CINC  *m* **14038**
CLORURO DE COBALTO  *m* **2609**
CLORURO DE ETILO  *m* **4849**
CLORURO DE LITIO  *m* **7666**

CLORURO DE MAGNESIO  *m* **7885**
CLORURO DE METILO  *m* **8221**
CLORURO DE ORO  *m* **823**
CLORURO DE PLATA  *m* **11461**
CLORURO DE PLOMO  *m* **7458**
CLORURO DE POTASA SOLUCIÓN DE  *f* **9688**
CLORURO DE POTASIO  *m* **9681**
CLORURO DE SODIO  *m* **2790**
CLORURO DOBLE DE ESTAÑO Y AMONIO  *m* **470**
CLORURO ESTÁNICO  *m* **12096**
CLORURO ESTANOSO  *m* **12100**
CLORURO FÉRRICO  *m* **5100**
CLORURO FERROSO  *m* **5121**
CLORURO MANGANOSO  *m* **7972**
CLORURO MERCÚRICO  *m* **8153**
CLORURO MERCUROSO  *m* **8159**
CLORURO NIQUELOSO  *m* **8562**
CLORURO PLATÍNICO  *m* **9507**
CLORURO PLATINOSO  *m* **9509**
COADYUVANTE  *m* **169**
COADYUVANTE DE FILTRACIÓN  *m* **5174**
COAGULACIÓN  *f* **2556**
COAGULARSE  **2555**
COÁGULO  *m* **2557**
COALESCENCIA  *f* **2572**
COAXIAL  *m* **2605**
COBALTINA  *f* **2614**
COBALTO  *m* **2607**
COBALTO-CARBONILO  *m* **2608**
COBERTIZO  *m* **3276**
COBERTIZO  *m* **11302**
COBERTOR  *m* **615**
COBERTURA DE UNA VÁLVULA  *f* **3266**
COBETOR  *m* **3265**
COBRE  *m* AMARILLO **1562**
COBRE  *m* ANÓDICO **593**
COBRE  *m* ARGENTÍFERO **11468**
COBRE  *m* ARSENICAL **725**
COBRE  *m* CEMENTADO **2136**
COBRE  *m* CEMENTADO **2136**
COBRE  *m* (COBRE ROJO) **3110**
COBRE  *m* DE ESCOBILLA **1669**
COBRE  *m* DE ÓXIDO CUPROSO **13069**
COBRE  *m* DE SOLDADURA **1575**
COBRE  *m* DEL LAGO SUPERIOR **7370**
COBRE  *m* DESOXIDADO **3764**
COBRE  *m* ELECTROLÍTICO **4591**
COBRE  *m* ELECTROLÍTICO **2099**
COBRE  *m* ELECTROLÍTICO COALESCIDO **2571**
COBRE  *m* ELECTROLÍTICO DE ÓXIDO CUPROSO **4610**

COBRE *m* EMPENACHADO (MULTICOLOR) **13501**
COBRE *m* EN HOJAS **11308**
COBRE *m* EXENTO DE OXÍGENO DE ALTA CONDUCTIVIDAD **8983**
COBRE *m* FOSFOROSO **9253**
COBRE *m* FOSFOROSO **9250**
COBRE *m* GRIS **12796**
COBRE *m* NATIVO **7370**
COBRE *m* NEGRO BRUTO **1287**
COBRE *m* PARA GRABADO **4767**
COBRE *m* PIRITOSO **3126**
COBRE *m* REFINADO **2073**
COBRE *m* REFINADO **13070**
COBRE *m* REFINADO AL FUEGO **5250**
COBRE *m* REGENERADO **2136**
COBRE *m* ROSETA **10748**
COBRE *m* SILICIOSO **11446**
COBRE *m* SULFURADO VIDRIOSO **3118**
COBRE *m* VESICULOSO **1329**
COBRE *m* VÍTREO (VIDRIOSO) **3118**
COCER **1745**
COCHE *m* AUTOMÓVIL **8411**
(COCHE *m* DE) CONDUCCIÓN INTERIOR **10902**
COCHE *m* DESCAPOTABLE **3073**
COCIENTE *m* **3916**
COCIENTE *m* **10234**
COCIENTE *m* **10114**
CODIFICACIÓN *f* **4716**
CODIFICADOR NUMÉRICO *m* **3943**
CÓDIGO BINARIO DECIMAL *m* **1248**
CÓDIGO DE VELOCIDAD DE AVANCE *m* **5085**
CÓDIGO DECIMAL *m* **3661**
CODILLO *m* HENDIDO (MARTILLO) **2463**
CODILLO *m* HENDIDO O DE OREJAS **2463**
CODO *m* **1194**
CODO *m* **1172**
CODO *m* **4913**
CODO *m* **4493**
CODO A 180 *m* **13323**
CODO AL 1/2 *m* **4467**
CODO DE ESCUADRA *m* **7320**
CODO DE UN ÁRBOL *m* **6976**
CODO EN U *m* **13323**
CODO REDONDO *m* **1180**
CODO REDONDO AL 1/4 *m* **10074**
CODO REDONDO DE ÁNGULO RECTO *m* **10074**
COEFICIENTE *m* **2621**
COEFICIENTE APARENTE DE ABSORCIÓN *m* **46**
COEFICIENTE BINOMIAL *m* **1257**
COEFICIENTE CALÓRICO (O DE CONDUCTIBILIDAD TÉRMICA) *m* **7269**

COEFICIENTE DE ABSORCIÓN MÁSICA *m* **8030**
COEFICIENTE DE CHORRO *m* **4200**
COEFICIENTE DE CONDUCTIBILIDAD CALÓRICA *m* **2622**
COEFICIENTE DE CONDUCTIBILIDAD CALÓRICA *m* **6373**
COEFICIENTE DE CONTRACCIÓN *m* **2623**
COEFICIENTE DE CORROSIÓN *m* **2624**
COEFICIENTE DE CORROSIÓN ANÓDICA *m* **594**
COEFICIENTE DE DESLIZAMIENTO *m* **2634**
COEFICIENTE DE DIFUSIÓN *m* **3931**
COEFICIENTE DE DILATACIÓN *m* **2636**
COEFICIENTE DE DILATACIÓN *m* **2628**
COEFICIENTE DE DILATACIÓN **4914**
COEFICIENTE DE DILATACIÓN CÚBICA *m* **2625**
COEFICIENTE DE DILATACIÓN LINEAL *m* **2630**
COEFICIENTE DE DILATACIÓN SUPERFICIAL *m* **2635**
COEFICIENTE DE DILATACIÓN TÉRMICA *m* **12809**
COEFICIENTE DE EFECTO TERMOELÉCTRICO **2637**
COEFICIENTE DE ELASTICIDAD DE CIZALLADURA *m* **5974**
COEFICIENTE DE PROPORCIONALIDAD *m* **2631**
COEFICIENTE DE REGULARIDAD *m* **3719**
COEFICIENTE DE RESISTENCIA *m* **2632**
COEFICIENTE DE RESISTENCIA AL ALARGAMIENTO *m* **8340**
COEFICIENTE DE RESISTIVIDAD ELÉCTRICA *m* **2627**
COEFICIENTE DE RETRACCIÓN *m* **477**
COEFICIENTE DE ROCE *m* **5670**
COEFICIENTE DE RODAMIENTO *m* **2633**
COEFICIENTE DE ROZAMIENTO *m* **2629**
COEFICIENTE DE SEGURIDAD *m* **5009**
COEFICIENTE DE SEGURIDAD *m* **10885**
COEFICIENTE DE SENSIBILIDAD *m* **3723**
COEFICIENTE DE VELOCIDAD *m* **2638**
COEFICIENTE DE VERTIDO *m* **2626**
COEFICIENTE DIFERENCIAL *m* **3909**
COERCITIVO *m* **2640**
COFRE *m* **13239**
COHERENCIA *f* **2643**
COHESIÓN *f* **2644**
COHETE *m* LUMINOSO **7573**
COJINETE *m* **1118**
COJINETE *m* **1100**
COJINETE *m* **1100**
COJINETE *m* A BOLAS **966**
COJINETE *m* A BOLAS **12901**
COJINETE *m* AUTO-REGULADOR **11150**
COJINETE *m* AUXILIAR **7044**
COJINETE *m* AUXILIAR **7044**
COJINETE *m* AXIAL **12902**
COJINETE *m* CERRADO **11777**
COJINETE *m* COLGADO **6321**

**COJ** 996

COJINETE  *m*  COLGADO ABIERTO **6271**
COJINETE  *m*  COLGADO CERRADO **6270**
COJINETE  *m*  CON PLANO DE SEPARACIÓN INCLINADO **508**
COJINETE  *m*  CÓNICO **1232**
COJINETE  *m*  DE ALINEACIÓN AUTOMÁTICA **12563**
COJINETE  *m*  DE ÁRBOL DE ASIENTO **3303**
COJINETE  *m*  DE BOLAS PARA EMPUJE **12900**
COJINETE  *m*  DE CARGA AXIAL **12902**
COJINETE  *m*  DE CARGA RADIAL/TRANSVERSAL **7257**
COJINETE  *m*  DE COQUILLAS **4098**
COJINETE  *m*  DE DESEMBRAGUE **2549**
COJINETE  *m*  DE EJE **876**
COJINETE  *m*  DE EJE **877**
COJINETE  *m*  DE EMPUJE **12902**
COJINETE  *m*  DE EMPUJE CON RANURAS **12903**
COJINETE  *m*  DE EMPUJE DE BOLAS **11890**
COJINETE  *m*  DE EMPUJE DE UN SOLO APOYO **11479**
COJINETE  *m*  DE GORRÓN ESFÉRICO **952**
COJINETE  *m*  DE HORQUILLA **6321**
COJINETE  *m*  DE PATÍN **9543**
COJINETE  *m*  DE PIE CON TEJUELO **5524**
COJINETE  *m*  DE RODAMIENTO DE BOLAS **954**
COJINETE  *m*  DE RODILLOS **10691**
COJINETE  *m*  DE RODILLOS **10680**
COJINETE  *m*  DE RÓTULA **12563**
COJINETE  *m*  DE SOPORTE **12241**
COJINETE  *m*  DE SUSPENSIÓN **6321**
COJINETE  *m*  DE UNA SOLA PIEZA **11788**
COJINETE  *m*  DEL ÁRBOL DE TRANSMISIÓN **7048**
COJINETE  *m*  DEL ÁRBOL MANIVELA **3303**
COJINETE  *m*  DEL CIGÜEÑAL **3303**
COJINETE  *m*  DEL CIGÜEÑAL **3314**
COJINETE  *m*  DEL HUSILLO **11905**
COJINETE  *m*  EN DOS PARTES **4098**
COJINETE  *m*  INTERMEDIO DEL ÁRBOL **13547**
COJINETE  *m*  PRINCIPAL **3303**
COJINETE  *m*  SECUNDARIO **7044**
COJINETE  *m*  VERTICAL **5524**
COJINETE AUTOLUBRICANTE  *m*  **11158**
COJINETE DE BOLAS  *m*  **954**
COJINETE DE CABEZA DE BIELA  *m*  **1242**
COJINETE DE DOS PIEZAS  *m*  **1572**
COJINETE DE HILERA  *m*  **3896**
COJINETE DE PALIER  *m*  **7941**
COJINETE DE PIE DE BIELA  *m*  **3390**
COJINETE DE RANURAS  *m*  **12903**
COJINETE DE RÓTULA  *m*  **12563**
COJINETE DE UNA PIEZA  *m*  **1771**
COJINETE DEFORMADO POR EL DESGASTE  *m*  **13980**

COJINETE DESGASTADO  *m*  **13980**
COJINETE EN CAJAS  *m*  **1572**
COJINETE LÍSO  *m*  **7941**
COJINETE-CONSOLA  *m*  SOBRE COLUMNA **9663**
COJINETES  *m pl*  DEL CIGÜEÑAL **7941**
COLA  *f*  **11257**
COLA  *f*  **5984**
COLA  *f*  CÓNICA **12664**
COLA  *m*  DE DESTILACIÓN **7413**
COLA  *f*  DE MILANO **4175**
COLA  *f*  DE MILANO **4175**
COLA  *f*  DE MILANO **4177**
COLA  *f*  DE PESCADO **7174**
COLA  *f*  DEL VÁSTAGO DEL ÉMBOLO **9384**
COLA  *f*  MARINA **8006**
COLA DE ALMIDÓN  *f*  **12112**
COLA DE NÚCLEOS  *f*  **3151**
COLA DE PESCADO  *f*  **7174**
COLA DE PIELES  *f*  **11539**
COLA FUERTE DE HUESOS **1449**
COLA PARA CORREAS  *f*  **2140**
COLABILIDAD  *f*  **2064**
COLADA  *f*  **2068**
COLADA  *f*  **5593**
COLADA  *f*  **6333**
COLADA  *f*  **12703**
COLADA  *f*  **9715**
COLADA  *f*  **10845**
COLADA  *f*  **10844**
COLADA  *f*  EN ARENA SECA **4353**
COLADA  *f*  (LAVADO CON AGUA Y LEJÍA) **7446**
COLADA A PRESIÓN  *f*  **9812**
COLADA A PRESIÓN  *f*  **3886**
COLADA A PRESIÓN POR GRAVEDAD  *f*  **6079**
COLADA CONTINUA  *f*  **3029**
COLADA CONTINUA  *f*  **3019**
COLADA DIRECTA  *f*  **13031**
COLADA EN FOSO  *f*  **9394**
COLADA (LOTE DE ...)  *f*  **2076**
COLADA PERDIDA  *f*  **8732**
COLADA TRANQUILA  *f*  **4388**
COLADA TRANQUILA (PROCEDIMIENTO DURVILLE)  *f*  **10109**
COLADOR  *m*  **12332**
COLADOR  *m*  **7362**
COLADOR  *m*  DE ACEITE **8770**
COLADURA  *f*  **2068**
COLAPEZ  *f*  **7174**
COLAR **2030**
COLAR **6153**
COLAR **6153**

COLCHÓN *m* **254**
COLCHÓN *m* DE ACEITE **8754**
COLCHÓN DE AIRE *m* **254**
COLCHÓN NEUMÁTICO *m* **256**
COLCOTAR *m* **7148**
COLECCIÓN *f* DE DATOS **3613**
COLECTOR *m* **10839**
COLECTOR *m* **11618**
COLECTOR *m* **7979**
COLECTOR *m* **11073**
COLECTOR *m* DE ACEITE **4283**
COLECTOR DE ADMISIÓN *m* **6945**
COLECTOR DE ADMISIÓN *m* **7007**
COLECTOR DE ESCAPE *m* **4893**
COLECTOR DE GAS *m* **5842**
COLGADOR DE CORREOS *m* **1146**
COLGADURAS *f pl* **3492**
COLGANTE **6321**
COLGAR **12914**
COLIMACIÓN *f* **2731**
COLIMADOR *m* **2732**
COLIMAR **2730**
COLISIÓN *f* **7327**
COLLAR *m* **9803**
COLLAR *m* **9803**
COLLAR *m* **2720**
COLLAR *m* **2448**
COLLAR *m* DE BASE **2724**
COLLAR *m* DE RETENCIÓN **2450**
COLLAR *m* DE TUBO **13324**
COLLAR *m* DE UN ÁRBOL **11384**
COLLAR *m* DE UN PIVOTE ACANALADO **12904**
COLLAR A COLOCAR EN CALIENTE *m* **11391**
COLLAR DE EXCÉNTRICA *m* **4435**
COLLAR DE TUBO *m* **13324**
COLLAR PARA EJES VERTICALES *m* **13547**
COLLARÍN *m* **12904**
COLLARÍN *m* **9803**
COLLARÍN *m* **9803**
COLLARÍN *m* DE CALIBRE **2721**
COLLARÍN *m* DE RETEN **12904**
COLLARÍN DE FRENO *m* **1544**
COLLARÍN DE UN EJE *m* **11384**
COLLARINO *m* **8515**
COLMATADO *m* **2510**
COLOCACIÓN *f* DE PLACAS DE CORTE METAL DURO **6278**
COLOCACIÓN *f* DE REMACHES **6972**
COLOCACIÓN *f* DE TORNAPUNTAS **1521**
COLOCACIÓN *f* DE TUBOS **9356**
COLOCACIÓN *f* DE UN HILO CONDUCTOR **13909**

COLOCACIÓN *f* DE UNA CORREA **1160**
COLOCAR **4750**
COLOCAR **11390**
COLOCAR EN SU SITIO LA CORREA **11357**
COLOCAR LOS REMACHES **6967**
COLOCAR PUNTALES **1517**
COLOCAR TORNAPUNTAS **1517**
COLOCAR TUBOS **7441**
COLOCAR UN HILO CONDUCTOR **13881**
COLODIÓN **2733**
COLOFONIA *f* **2737**
COLOIDAL **2735**
COLÓIDE *m* **2734**
COLOR *m* **12732**
COLOR *m* **9303**
COLOR *m* **9015**
COLOR CEREZA *m* **2326**
COLOR COMPLEMENTARIO *m* **2812**
COLOR COMPUESTO *m* **11103**
COLOR DE INTERFERENCIA *m* **7037**
COLOR (FÍSICA) **2741**
COLOR OPACO *m* **1389**
COLOR SENCILLO *m* **9847**
COLORACIÓN *f* **2740**
COLORACIÓN TÉRMICA *f* **6371**
COLORANTE *m* **4397**
COLORANTE *m* **9303**
COLORANTE *m* **9303**
COLORES DEL ESPECTRO *m* **11859**
COLUMBIO *m* **8576**
COLUMBIO *m* **2747**
COLUMNA *f* **2748**
COLUMNA *f* **2748**
COLUMNA *f* **12062**
COLUMNA *f* CON LOS DOS EXTREMOS GUIADOS **2756**
COLUMNA BAROMÉTRICA *f* **2751**
COLUMNA DE AGUA *f* **2752**
COLUMNA DE DIRECCIÓN *f* **12228**
COLUMNA DE MANIOBRA *f* **5448**
COLUMNA DE MERCURIO *f* **2751**
COLUMNA LÍQUIDA *f* **2750**
COLUMNA MONTANTE *f* **2753**
COLUMNA MONTANTE *f* **12093**
COLUMNA MONTANTE *f* **10614**
COLUMRA (PUNTAL VERTICAL) *f* **11365**
COMBADURA *f* **10613**
COMBARSE **13628**
COMBARSE **13628**
COMBINACIÓN *f* **2761**
COMBINACIÓN ALIFÁTICA *f* **326**

## COM

998

COMBINACIÓN QUÍMICA  f 2300
COMBINADO  m DE MOLINOS 8295
COMBURENTE  m 277
COMBUSTIBILIDAD  f 2773
COMBUSTIBLE  m 2772
COMBUSTIBLE  m 5705
COMBUSTIBLE  m DE MALA CALIDAD 7780
COMBUSTIBLE ARTIFICIAL  m 732
COMBUSTIBLE DE EXCELENTE CALIDAD  m 6484
COMBUSTIBLE EN GRANDES TROZOS  m 7827
COMBUSTIBLE FÓSIL  m 5586
COMBUSTIBLE GASEOSO  m 5854
COMBUSTIBLE HECHO CON POLVO DE CARBÓN  m 2791
COMBUSTIBLE LÍQUIDO  m 7650
COMBUSTIBLE NATURAL  m 8503
COMBUSTIBLE NECESARIO  m 3745
COMBUSTIBLE SÓLIDO  m 11785
COMBUSTIÓN 11956
COMBUSTIÓN  f 2774
COMBUSTIÓN COMPLETA  f 2779
COMBUSTIÓN INCOMPLETA  f 6845
COMBUSTIÓN LENTA  f 11644
COMBUSTIÓN NUCLEAR  f 1747
COMBUSTIÓN PERFECTA  f 9184
COMBUSTIÓN VIVA  f 10205
COMERCIAL  m 12141
COMPACTO COMPUESTO 2828
COMPACTO NO ACABADO 6090
COMPACTO TERMINADO  m 8551
COMPARACIÓN DE DIMENSIONES  f 7445
COMPARADOR  m 2794
COMPARADOR DE ESFERA PARA ESCARIADOS  m 3838
COMPARADOR DE HOJAS  m 10365
COMPARADOR ELÉCTRICO  m 4535
COMPARADOR ELECTRÓNICO  m 4632
COMPARADOR INTERFERENCIAL  m 7038
COMPARADOR MECÁNICO  m 8097
COMPARADOR MICROMÉTRICO PARA ROSCAS  m 11048
COMPARADOR ÓPTICO  m 8842
COMPARADOR ÓPTICO-MECÁNICO  m 8118
COMPARADORES  m pl 2795
COMPARTIMENTO 2798
COMPARTIMIENTO  m ESTANCO 274
COMPARTIR 1266
COMPÁS  m 4100
COMPÁS  m 9022
COMPÁS  m PARA CALIBRAR EL INTERIOR DE UN
DIÁMETRO COMPÁS BAILARÍN  m 1870
COMPÁS  m PARA CONTROL DEL DIÁMETRO INTERIOR
6975
COMPÁS DE ARCO  m 1503

COMPÁS DE CALIBRE  m 1874
COMPÁS DE CREMALLERA  m 10122
COMPÁS DE CUADRANTE  m 13876
COMPÁS DE GRUESOS  m 1873
COMPÁS DE GRUESOS  m COMPÁS DE EXTERIORES  m
8912
COMPÁS DE PRECISIÓN  m 6201
COMPÁS DE PRECISIÓN  m 6201
COMPÁS DE PUNTAS FIJAS  m 4101
COMPÁS DE RECAMBIOS  m 2805
COMPÁS DE REDUCCIÓN  m 9937
COMPÁS DE TIRALÍNEAS  m 2803
COMPÁS DE TRES PUNTAS  m 13187
COMPÁS DE VARA  m 13105
COMPÁS DE VARA  m 1096
COMPÁS PARA DIÁMETRO INTERIOR  m 6975
COMPÁS PORTA-LAPIZ  m 2804
COMPÁS RECTO DE PUNTAS  m 4101
COMPATIBILIDAD  m 2806
COMPENSACIÓN  f 2809
COMPENSACIÓN  f 942
COMPENSACIÓN  f DE JUEGO 13403
COMPENSACIÓN  f DE JUEGO 12606
COMPENSACIÓN  f DE JUEGO 12603
COMPENSADOR  m 2808
COMPENSADOR  m DE DILATACIÓN 4913
COMPENSADOR DE DILATACIÓN  m 4913
COMPENSAR 930
COMPENSAR 930
COMPENSAR 2807
COMPENSAR EL DESGASTE 12603
COMPENSAR LA HOLGURA DE UN COJINETE 12603
COMPLEMENTO DE UN ÁNGULO  m 2810
COMPLEMENTO DIAMETRAL  m 3851
COMPLETAMENTE DE METALES FERROSOS 345
COMPONENTE  m 2981
COMPONENTE  m 2981
COMPONENTE  m 2982
COMPONENTE  f 2817
COMPONENTE  m 2815
COMPONENTE AXIAL  f 859
COMPONENTE DE UNA ALEACIÓN  m 2982
COMPONENTE (QUÍMICA)  m 2983
COMPONENTE QUÍMICO  m 2298
COMPONENTE RADIAL  f 10132
COMPORTAMIENTO  m EN CARRETERA EN CUESTA 2498
COMPORTAMIENTO  m EN CARRETERA EN CURVA 3180
COMPOSICIÓN  f 2823
COMPOSICIÓN DE DESENGRASE  f 3713
COMPOSICIÓN DE LAS FUERZAS  f 2825

COMPOSICIÓN DE PULIDO CON MUELA *f* **1692**
COMPOSICIÓN GRANULOMÉTRICA *f* **9090**
COMPOSICIÓN PARA COJINETE *f* **1106**
COMPOSICIÓN QUÍMICA *f* **2827**
COMPOSICIÓN QUÍMICA *f* **2299**
COMPOSICIÓN QUÍMICA *f* **2301**
COMPRESIBILIDAD *f* **2851**
COMPRESIBILIDAD *f* **2852**
COMPRESIBLE **2853**
COMPRESIÓN *f* **2854**
COMPRESIÓN *f* **9806**
COMPRESIÓN *f* **11355**
COMPRESIÓN *f* **10028**
COMPRESIÓN DEL AIRE *f* **2858**
COMPRESIÓN EN EL SENTIDO DE LAS FIBRAS *f* **10021**
COMPRESIÓN PERPENDICULAR AL SENTIDO DE LAS FIBRAS *f* **10022**
COMPRESOR *m* **2874**
COMPRESOR CENTRÍFUGO *m* **2178**
COMPRESOR COMPOUND *m* **2836**
COMPRESOR DE AIRE *m* **249**
COMPRESOR DE ÉMBOLO *m* **9374**
COMPRESOR DE ENGRASE *m* **11982**
COMPRESOR DE RESERVA *m* **12069**
COMPRESOR ETAPA *m* **2836**
COMPRESOR HIDRÁULICO *m* **6680**
COMPRESOR HÚMEDO *m* **13801**
COMPRESOR SECO *m* **4345**
COMPRIMIDO **2791**
COMPRIMIR **2837**
COMPRIMIR UN MUELLE **2838**
COMPUERTA *f* **7698**
COMPUERTA *f* DE DESCARGA **891**
COMPUESTO AISLANTE *m* **6997**
COMPUESTO INTERMETÁLICO *m* **7052**
COMPUESTOS AROMÁTICOS *m pl* **716**
COMPUTAR **3795**
COMTRAHÍLO (A) *m* **138**
CON BROCAS MÚLTIPLES **5799**
CON HUSILLOS MÚLTIPLES **8460**
CON LA CARGA MÁXIMA **1079**
CONCAVIDAD *f* **2880**
CÓNCAVO **2877**
CONCENTRACIÓN *f* **2886**
CONCENTRACIÓN *f* (O ENRIQUECIMIENTO *m*) DEL MINERAL **8861**
CONCENTRACIÓN DE IONES *f* **7122**
CONCENTRACIÓN DE LA TENSIÓN *f* **12360**
CONCENTRACIÓN DE LOS IONES DE HIDRÓGENO *f* **6715**
CONCENTRACIÓN DE UNA SOLUCIÓN POR EVAPORACIÓN *f* **2885**

CONCENTRADO *m* **2881**
CONCENTRAR **2882**
CONCENTRARSE **1122**
CONCENTRICIDAD *f* **2891**
CONCEPCIÓN *f* **3794**
CONCESIÓN *f* DE PATENTE **6049**
CONCESIÓN DE LA PATENTE *f* **6049**
CONCESIONARIO DE LICENCIA *m* **7540**
CONCHA *f* **11303**
CONCHA INFERIOR *f* **1487**
CONCHA SUPERIOR *f* **13030**
CONCLUIR **5214**
CONCOIDE *m* **2892**
CONCRECIÓN CALCAREA *f* **1837**
CONDENSACIÓN *f* **2906**
CONDENSACIÓN DE UNA SOLUCIÓN *f* **2885**
CONDENSADO *m* **2905**
CONDENSADOR *m* **1916**
CONDENSADOR *m* DE CHORRO (O DE EYECCIÓN) **4470**
CONDENSADOR BAROMÉTRICO *m* **1010**
CONDENSADOR DE BLOQUEO *m* **1342**
CONDENSADOR DE EVAPORACIÓN *m* **4868**
CONDENSADOR DE PARADA *m* **1342**
CONDENSADOR (DE VAPOR) *m* **1916**
CONDENSADOR (ELECTRICIDAD) *m* **2908**
CONDENSADOR ELECTROLÍTICO *m* **4590**
CONDENSADOR (ÓPTICA) *m* **2908**
CONDENSADOR POR EYECCIÓN *m* **4470**
CONDENSADOR POR INYECCIÓN *m* **7220**
CONDENSADOR POR MEZCLA *m* **3988**
CONDENSADOR POR SUPERFICIE *m* **12499**
CONDENSADOR POR SUPERFICIE MEDIANTE AGUA *m* **13684**
CONDENSADOR POR SUPERFICIE MEDIANTE AIRE *m* **296**
CONDENSADOR (QUÍMICA) *m* **2908**
CONDENSADOR-PATRÓN *m* **1868**
CONDENSAR **2882**
CONDENSARSE **2907**
CONDICIÓN *f* DE SUPERFICIE **12500**
CONDICIÓN CRÍTICA DE DEFORMACIÓN *f* **5935**
CONDICIONES DE ENTREGA *f pl* **3737**
CONDICIONES DE OPERACIÓN *f pl* **8834**
CONDICIONES DE SERVICIO *f pl* **8834**
CONDICIONES DE SERVICIO *f pl* **13949**
CONDICIONES DE TRABAJO *f pl* **13949**
CONDICIONES DE USO *f pl* **11208**
CONDUCCIÓN *f* **12226**
CONDUCCIÓN *f* **2916**
CONDUCCIÓN *f* **814**
CONDUCCIÓN *f* INTERIOR **11128**

# CON                                          1000

CONDUCCIÓN DE ACEITE  *f* **8783**
CONDUCCIÓN DEL CALOR  *f* **2917**
CONDUCIR (LA ELECTRICIDADEL CALOR) **2913**
CONDUCTANCIA MOL(ECUL)AR  *f* **8350**
CONDUCTIBILIDAD  *f* **2919**
CONDUCTIBILIDAD ELÉCTRICA  *f* **4536**
CONDUCTIBILIDAD EQUIVALENTE  *f* **4797**
CONDUCTIBILIDAD TÉRMICA CALORÍFICA  *f* **2920**
CONDUCTIVIDAD  *f* **2919**
CONDUCTIVIDAD TÉRMICA **12804**
CONDUCTIVIDAD TERMOELÉCTRICA  *f* **10044**
CONDUCTO  *m* **12176**
CONDUCTO  *m* **2395**
CONDUCTO  *m* **5081**
CONDUCTO  *m* **5467**
CONDUCTO  *m* DE AGUA FORZADA **9840**
CONDUCTO  *f* DE ENGRASE **8759**
CONDUCTO  *m* DE ESCAPE **4895**
CONDUCTO ANULAR DE VIENTO CÁLIDO  *m* **1774**
CONDUCTO DE GAS  *m* **5821**
CONDUCTO DE PRESIÓN  *m* **9827**
CONDUCTO DE UNIÓN  *m* **5034**
CONDUCTO ELÉCTRICO  *m* LÍNEA DE FLUIDO ELÉCTRICO  *f*  **4523**
CONDUCTO INTERIOR DE CALDERA  *m* **1412**
CONDUCTOR  *m* (DE UNA ACCIÓN) **4316**
CONDUCTOR ATRAVESADO POR UNA CORRIENTE  *m* **7670**
CONDUCTOR DE CALOR  *m* **6340**
CONDUCTOR (DE CALORDE CORRIENTE)  *m* **2918**
CONDUCTOR DE CORRIENTE  *m* CONDUCTOR ELÉCTRICO  *m* **2922**
CONDUCTOR DE MÁQUINA  *m* **4765**
CONDUCTOR DE RED  *m* **4079**
CONDUCTOR (ELECTRICIDAD)  *m* **2921**
CONDUCTOR ELÉCTRICO  *m* **4537**
CONDUCTOR SIN CORRIENTE  *m* **3627**
CONDUCTOR SIN TENSIÓN  *m* **3627**
CONECTAR **2955**
CONECTAR **2955**
CONECTAR CON LA TIERRA (ELECTRICIDAD) **4410**
CONECTARSE **1556**
CONEXIÓN  *f* **1554**
CONFECCIÓN  *f* **4983**
CONFECCIÓN  *f* **8028**
CONFLAGRACIÓN  *f* ESPONTÁNEA **11956**
CONFOCAL  *m* **2933**
CONFORMACIÓN  *f* **5579**
CONFORMACIÓN  *f* DE LAS PLANCHAS **1482**
CONGELACIÓN DEL HORNO  *f* **5655**
CONGLOMERADO  *m* **2934**
CONGLOMERADO  *m* **8490**

CONGRUENCIA  *f* **2937**
CONICIDAD  *f* **2948**
CONICIDAD  *f* **12646**
CONICIDAD DE UNA CHAVETA  *f* **12654**
CÓNICO  *m* **2940**
CONJUGADO  *m* **2952**
CONJUNTO  *m* **227**
CONJUNTO  *m* DE MANDO DE VELOCIDAD VARIABLE **13492**
CONMOCIÓN  *f* **4529**
CONMUTACIÓN  *f* **2246**
CONMUTADOR  *m* **2244**
CONMUTADOR DE LAS BUJÍAS DE PRECALENTAMIENTO **6389**
CONMUTAR **2241**
CONMUTATRIZ  *f* **3071**
CONO  *m* DE SEGER **11134**
CONO  *m* DEL CONVERTIDOR **3072**
CONO  *m* VERTICAL **10578**
CONO AUTODESMONTABLE  *m* **11159**
CONO CIRCULAR  *m* **2409**
CONO COMPLEMENTARIO  *m* **5918**
CONO DE BASE CIRCULAR  *m* **2409**
CONO DE FONDO  *m* **10718**
CONO DE FRICCIÓN  *m* **1225**
CONO DE FRICCIÓN  *m* **5671**
CONO DE GUÍA  *m* **2941**
CONO DE TRANSMISIÓN  *m* **11871**
CONO DE TRANSMISIÓN  *m* **11871**
CONO DE TRANSMISIÓN  *m* **11871**
CONO DEFLECTOR (EN DEPÓSITO)  *m* **11924**
CONO GENERADOR  *m* **5918**
CONO (GEOMETRÍA)  *m* **2924**
CONO LISO  *m* **12669**
CONO LUMINOSO  *m* **2932**
CONO OBLICUO  *m* **8709**
CONO PIROMÉTRICO **11134**
CONO PIROMÉTRICO  *m* **10050**
CONO PIROMÉTRICO (DE SEGER)  *m* **11134**
CONO PRIMITIVO  *m* **9406**
CONO RECTO  *m* **10578**
CONO REDUCTOR  *m* **10358**
CONO TRUNCADO  *m* **13235**
CONO Y CONTRA-CONO **404**
CONSERVABILIDAD  *f* **4385**
CONSERVACIÓN  *f* **6526**
CONSERVACIÓN DE LA ENERGÍA  *f* **2967**
CONSERVACIÓN DE LA MADERA  *f* **9790**
CONSISTENCIA  *f* **2968**
CONSISTENCIA  *f* DEL SUELO **11751**
CONSISTENCIA DE UN ACEITE  *f* **1395**

CONSOLA  f **1522**
CONSOLA  f **13618**
CONSOLA  f **13618**
CONSOLIDACIÓN DE LOS PERNOS  f **7707**
CONSTANTAN  m **2980**
CONSTANTE  f **2969**
CONSTANTE CALORÍFICA  f **6341**
CONSTANTE CAPILAR  f **1923**
CONSTANTE DE ABSORCIÓN  f **47**
CONSTANTE DE ELASTICIDAD  f **4475**
CONSTANTE DE EQUILIBRIO  f **4787**
CONSTANTE DE RADIACIÓN  f **10144**
CONSTANTE DE RADIACIÓN APARENTE  f **643**
CONSTANTE DE TIEMPO  f **12944**
CONSTANTE DE UN GAS  f **5815**
CONSTANTE DE UNA CELDA ELECTROLÍTICA  f **2128**
CONSTANTE DIELÉCTRICA  f **3899**
CONSTANTES DE LA RED  f pl **7430**
CONSTELACIÓN  f **776**
CONSTITUCIÓN QUÍMICA  f **2301**
CONSTITUYENTE  m **2981**
CONSTITUYENTE  m **2982**
CONSTRUCCIÓN  f **2986**
CONSTRUCCIÓN  f **8103**
CONSTRUCCIÓN  f **8028**
CONSTRUCCIÓN  f **7989**
CONSTRUCCIÓN  f **10462**
CONSTRUCCIÓN  f DE LADRILLOS **1602**
CONSTRUCCIÓN  f DE MAMPOSTERÍA **10828**
CONSTRUCCIÓN  f DE PIEDRA DE SILLERÍA O CON SILLARES **762**
CONSTRUCCIÓN DE ACERO/ METÁLICA  f **12218**
CONSTRUCCIÓN DE MADERA  f **12942**
CONSTRUCCIÓN (EDIFICIO)  f **12395**
CONSTRUCCIÓN EN SERIE  f **8028**
CONSTRUCCIÓN HIDRÁULICA  f **6685**
CONSTRUCCIÓN MECÁNICA  f **8103**
CONSTRUCCIÓN METÁLICA  f **7152**
CONSTRUCCIÓN NAVAL  f **8510**
CONSTRUCCIÓN SOLDADA  f **13795**
CONSTRUCCIONES CIVILES  f pl **2444**
CONSTRUCTOR  m **7992**
CONSTRUIR **1597**
CONSTRUIR **1694**
CONSUMO  m **2995**
CONSUMO  m **13710**
CONSUMO  m DE ENERGÍA **4747**
CONSUMO  m DE ENERGÍA DE FUERZA MOTRIZ **2876**
CONSUMO  m (O GASTO  m) DE VAPOR **2995**
CONSUMO DE COMBUSTIBLE  m **2994**

CONSUMO DE CORRIENTE  m **2993**
CONSUMO DE ENERGÍA  m **2876**
CONTACTO A LA MASA (ELECT)  m **2996**
CONTACTO A LA TIERRA  m **4415**
CONTACTO DE CLAVIJA  m **13622**
CONTACTO DE ENCENDIDO  m **6766**
CONTACTO DE UN IMÁN  m **710**
CONTACTO (GEN)  m **2996**
CONTACTOR DE MERCURIO  m **8166**
CONTACTOR ELÉCTRICO  m **12553**
CONTACTOS  m pl **9574**
CONTADOR  m **8214**
CONTADOR  m **3229**
CONTADOR DE AGUA  m **13661**
CONTADOR DE AGUA VENTURI  m **13532**
CONTADOR DE ERRORES  m **4823**
CONTADOR DE ERRORES  m **4830**
CONTADOR DE FICHAJES  m **12946**
CONTADOR DE GAS  m **5829**
CONTADOR DE LUZ  m **4553**
CONTADOR DE VAPOR  m **12174**
CONTADOR DE VENTANA  m **3559**
CONTADOR DE VENTANAS  m **3559**
CONTADOR GEIGER  m **5911**
CONTADOR VENTURI  m **13532**
CONTAMINACIÓN DE UNA ALEACIÓN  f **365**
CONTENIDO  m **1917**
CONTENIDO  m **3011**
CONTENIDO  m EN CARBONO **1947**
CONTENIENDO ESCORIAS **11562**
CONTEXTURA  f **12800**
CONTEXTURA  f **12395**
CONTEXTURA  f CRISTALINA **3434**
CONTEXTURA  f FIBROSA **5141**
CONTEXTURA  f GRANULAR **6053**
CONTEXTURA  f HETEROGÉNEA **6452**
CONTEXTURA  f HOMOGÉNEA **6560**
CONTEXTURA  f LAMINAR **7374**
CONTIGUO  m **181**
CONTIGUO  m **181**
CONTINUIDAD  f **3017**
CONTORNO  m **3396**
CONTORNO  m **8907**
CONTORNO DE GRANO  m **1500**
CONTORNO DE UNA LEVA  m **8906**
CONTRA JUNTA  f **911**
CONTRA-ANÁLISIS  f **2280**
CONTRA-CHAVETA  f **5937**
CONTRA-COJINETE  m **13030**
CONTRA-CORRIENTE  f **3230**

**CON** 1002

CONTRA-HIERRO *m* **13033**
CONTRABALANCEAR **930**
CONTRABRIDA *f* **8054**
CONTRACCIÓN *f* **11392**
CONTRACCIÓN *f* **11392**
CONTRACCIÓN *f* **477**
CONTRACCIÓN *f* **3043**
CONTRACCIÓN *f* **3045**
CONTRACCIÓN *f* **2437**
CONTRACCIÓN *f* ANGULAR **542**
CONTRACCIÓN *f* CONTRARRESTADA **6504**
CONTRACCIÓN *f* DE LA MADERA **11396**
CONTRACCIÓN *f* DE UNA VENA LÍQUIDA **3044**
CONTRACCIÓN *f* EN EL MOLDE **1322**
CONTRACCIÓN *f* TÉRMICA **12805**
CONTRACCIÓN DE ENFRIAMIENTO *f* **7648**
CONTRACCIÓN DE LA CORREA *f* **3329**
CONTRACCIÓN DE LA VENA FLUIDO *f* **3044**
CONTRACCIÓN DE SOLIDIFICACIÓN *f* **11802**
CONTRACCIÓN DEL CHORRO *f* **3044**
CONTRACCIÓN DEL VÁSTAGO DEL REMACHE O ROBLÓN *f* **3046**
CONTRACCIÓN (DURANTE EL ENFRIAMIENTO) *f* **11397**
CONTRACTADOR DE ENCENDIDO *m* **6766**
CONTRAEJE *m* **6756**
CONTRAEJE *m* **6756**
CONTRAERSE **11388**
CONTRAESCARRIADO *m* **3242**
CONTRAESCARRIADO *m* **3236**
CONTRAGOLPE *m* **10286**
CONTRAHUELLA *f* **10614**
CONTRAMAESTRE *m* **5541**
CONTRAMANUBRIO *m* **10528**
CONTRAMARCHA *f* DE ENGRANAJES **7050**
CONTRAPESO *m* **3251**
CONTRAPESO DEL FRENO *m* **1547**
CONTRAPLACA *f* **13621**
CONTRAPLACA *f* (SELLADA EN EL SUELO) **502**
CONTRAPRESIÓN *f* **3232**
CONTRAPUNTA *f* **12599**
CONTRAPUNTA GIRATORIA *f* **10560**
CONTRAPUNTA MICROMÉTRICA *f* **8236**
CONTRAR **323**
CONTRARREACCIÓN *f* **10536**
CONTRASTE *m* **3893**
CONTRATISTA *m* DE LA CONSTRUCCIÓN **1698**
CONTRATOPE *m* **8956**
CONTRATUERCA *f* **7702**
CONTROL *m* **6987**
CONTROL *m* **4876**

CONTROL *m* **3048**
CONTROL *m* **3048**
CONTROL *m* DE VÁLVULA **13456**
CONTROL DE ADHERENCIA *m* **172**
CONTROL DE CALIDAD *m* **10063**
CONTROL DE PARIDAD *m* **9081**
CONTROL POR ULTRASONIDOS *m* **13337**
CONTROL RADIOGRÁFICO *m* **13998**
CONTROL REMOTO *m* **10448**
CONTROLADOR DE LLAMA *m* **5314**
CONTROLADOR DE NIVEL *m* **7655**
CONTROLADOR DE PRESIÓN *m* **9813**
CONTROLAR **3049**
CONVECCIÓN *f* **3060**
CONVECCIÓN (CALOR IRRADIANTE) *f* **3059**
CONVERGENCIA *f* **3063**
CONVERGENCIA *f* **7212**
CONVERGENTE *m* **3064**
CONVERGER **3062**
CONVERSIÓN *f* **3067**
CONVERTIDOR *m* **3071**
CONVERTIDOR BESSEMER *m* **1212**
CONVEXIDAD *f* **1720**
CONVEXIDAD *f* **1720**
CONVEXIDAD *f* **3396**
CONVEXIDAD DE LA CARROCERÍA *f* **1889**
CONVEXIÓN *f* **3060**
CONVEXO *m* **3076**
COOLPE *m* **12375**
COORDINADAS *f pl* **3100**
COORDINADAS CARTESIANAS *f pl* **2014**
COORDINADAS CILÍNDRICAS *f pl* **3580**
COORDINADAS CORRIENTES *f pl* **3487**
COORDINADAS EN EL ESPACÍO *f pl* **13203**
COORDINADAS OBLICUAS *f pl* **8710**
COORDINADAS ORTOGONALES *f pl* **10301**
COORDINADAS PLANAS *f pl* **698**
COORDINADAS POLARES *f pl* **9578**
COORDINADAS RECTANGULARES *f pl* **10301**
COPADOR *m* **5729**
COPAHÚ *m* **3101**
COPELACIÓN *f* **3463**
COPIA *f* **9870**
COPIA *f* HELIOCALCO **1375**
COPIA (FOTOGRAFÍA) **9870**
COPO *m* **5303**
COPPERWELD **3137**
COQUE *m* **2655**
COQUE DE CUBILOTE *m* **5595**
COQUE DE GAS *m* **5849**

COQUE DE GAS  *m* **5849**
COQUE DE HORNO  *m* **2662**
COQUE DENSO  *m* **2792**
COQUE METALÚRGICO  *m* **2662**
COQUIFICAR **2656**
COQUILLA  *f* **2331**
COQUILLA  *f* **9207**
COQUILLA  *f* **6923**
COQUILLA DE SECADO  *f* **3148**
COQUIZAR A BAJA TEMPERATURA **11688**
CORCHA  *f* **10739**
CORCHAR LOS CABOS **13303**
CORCHO  *m* **3173**
CORDELERÍA  *f* **10745**
CORDÓN  *m* **12005**
CORDÓN  *m* DE AMIANTO **749**
CORDÓN  *m* DE CABLE **10740**
CORDÓN  *m* DE SOLDADURA **1082**
CORDÓN  *m* FIJO DE UN POLIPASTO **12092**
CORDÓN DE AMIANTO  *m* **751**
CORDÓN DE APLASTADO  *m* **3382**
CORDÓN DE SOLDADURA  *m* **1082**
CORDÓN DE SOLDADURA  *m* **13756**
CORDÓN DE SOLDADURA PLANO  *m* **5401**
CORDÓN DE UN CABLE  *m* **12338**
CORDÓN SOLDADO RECTILÍNEO  *m* **12376**
CORDÓN SOPORTE (AL REVÉS)  *m* **904**
CORINDÓN  *m* **3201**
CORINDÓN  *m* **4699**
CORNAMUSA  *f* **2485**
CORONA  *f* DE ENGRANAJE **10594**
CORONA CIRCULAR  *f* **589**
CORONA DENTADA  *f* **3399**
CORONA DENTADA  *f* **10594**
CORONA DENTADA  *f* **13023**
CORONA DIRECTORA DE TURBINA  *f* **6168**
CORONA FIJA  *f* **6168**
CORONA MÓVIL  *f* **13823**
CORONA SOPORTE DE PLATÓ  *f* **12492**
CORONA SOPORTE DE PLATÓS  *f* **13170**
CORONACIÓN  *f* **1604**
CORREA  *f* **1140**
CORREA  *f* (ESPESOR DE UNA) **1165**
CORREA  *f* MOTRIZ (DE MANDO) **1163**
CORREA ABIERTA  *f* **8804**
CORREA ABIERTA  *f* **8804**
CORREA COSIDA  *f* **7350**
CORREA CRUZADA  *f* **3387**
CORREA DE ALGODÓN  *f* **3218**
CORREA DE BALATA  *f* **944**

CORREA DE CÁÑAMO  *f* **1907**
CORREA DE CRÍN  *f* **6200**
CORREA DE CRÍN  *f* **6200**
CORREA DE CUERO  *f* **7495**
CORREA DE CUERO  *f* **7503**
CORREA DE CUERO DE ESLABONES  *f* **7496**
CORREA DE FIBRAS TEXTILES  *f* **4981**
CORREA DE GOMA  *f* **10817**
CORREA DE GOMA PELO  *f* **10817**
CORREA DE PELOS  *f* **6200**
CORREA DE PELOS DE CAMELLO  *f* **1891**
CORREA DE SECCIÓN TRIANGULAR  *f* **13511**
CORREA DE TEJIDO TUBULAR  *f* **5397**
CORREA DE TIRAS DE CUERO TRABAJANDO EN CANTO  *f*
   **7376**
CORREA DE TUBULARES  *f* **6183**
CORREA DE VARIOS ESPESORES  *f* **8463**
CORREA DE VENTILADOR  *f* **5029**
CORREA DE X CAPAS  *f* **1166**
CORREA DE X CAPAS  *f* **1166**
CORREA DOBLE  *f* **4128**
CORREA ENCOLADA  *f* **2145**
CORREA INVERTIDA  *f* **3387**
CORREA MOTRIZ  *f* **1163**
CORREA MÚLTIPLE  *f* **8463**
CORREA RECTA  *f* **8804**
CORREA SEMICRUZADA  *f* **6207**
CORREA SENCILLA  *f* **11477**
CORREA TEJIDA  *f* **13983**
CORREA TORCIDA  *f* **6207**
CORREA TRAPEZOIDAL  *f* **2925**
CORREA TRAPEZOIDAL  *f* **13511**
CORREA TRAPEZOIDAL  *f* **13431**
CORREA TRIPLE  *f* **12878**
CORRECCIÓN  *f* **3181**
CORRECCIÓN DE POSICIÓN DE ÚTIL  *f* **13007**
CORRECCIÓN DE ÚTIL  *f* **3521**
CORRECCIÓN DE VELOCIDAD DE AVANCE  *f* **5079**
CORRECTOR DE AVANCE  *m* **11837**
CORREDERA  *f* **11588**
CORREDERA  *f* **11633**
CORREDERA  *f* **11585**
CORREDERA  *f* **6160**
CORREDERA  *f* **2395**
CORREDERA  *f* DE CRUCETA **6169**
CORREDERA  *f* DE REJILLA **6100**
CORREDERA  *f* (DE VENTANA) **13868**
CORREDERA  *f* PLANA **5384**
CORREDERA Y MANUBRIO  *f* **11631**
CORREDOR  *m* **2395**

**COR** 1004

CORRIENTE  f 3486
CORRIENTE  f 5454
CORRIENTE  f DE AIRE 266
CORRIENTE ABAJO 4184
CORRIENTE ALTA FRECUENCIA  f 6468
CORRIENTE ALTA TENSIÓN  f 6500
CORRIENTE ALTERNA  f 406
CORRIENTE ALTERNA  f 1
CORRIENTE ALTERNA ALTA FRECUENCÍA  f 3
CORRIENTE BAJA TENSIÓN  f 7777
CORRIENTE CONTÍNUA  f 3023
CORRIENTE DE AIRE  f 253
CORRIENTE DE AIRE FORZADO  f 1315
CORRIENTE DE BAJA INTENSIDAD  f 13705
CORRIENTE DE CARGA  f 2266
CORRIENTE DE DISPERSIÓN  f 7490
CORRIENTE DE FILETES PARALELOS  f 9055
CORRIENTE DE FOUCAULT  f 4438
CORRIENTE DE FOUCAULT  f 4440
CORRIENTE DE FUGA  f 7490
CORRIENTE DE GRAN INTENSIDAD  f 6401
CORRIENTE DE INDUCCIÓN  f 6889
CORRIENTE DE LA CÁMARA IONIZANTE  f 7126
CORRIENTE DE MISMO SENTIDO  f 13360
CORRIENTE DE SENTIDO CONTRARIO  f 3230
CORRIENTE DEL BAÑO  f 1064
CORRIENTE DIFÁSICA  f 13314
CORRIENTE ELÉCTRICA  f 4500
CORRIENTE ELÉCTRICA ENERGIA  f 4525
CORRIENTE FUERTE  f 6401
CORRIENTE FUERZA  f 5534
CORRIENTE GASEOSA  f 5816
CORRIENTE LIBRE  f 5634
CORRIENTE MONOFÁSICA  f 11501
CORRIENTE POLIFÁSICA  f 8462
CORRIENTE SECUNDARIA DE SOLDADURA  f 11110
CORRIENTE TERMOELÉCTRICA  f 12824
CORRIENTE TRIFÁSICA  f 12877
CORRIENTE TURBULENTA  f 13274
CORRIENTE VAGABUNDA  f 12349
CORRIENTES CRUZADAS  f pl 3363
CORRIMIENTO  m (DE TERRENO) 11595
CORROER 3182
CORROER 3182
CORROSIÓN  f 3183
CORROSIÓN  f 813
CORROSIÓN AGRIETANTE  f 3185
CORROSIÓN ATMOSFÉRICA  f 795
CORROSIÓN BAJO LA EROSIÓN  f 6799
CORROSIÓN CATÓDICA  f 2107

CORROSIÓN CAUSADA POR SEDIMENTACIÓN  f 3774
CORROSIÓN CON LIBERACIÓN DE HIDRÓGENO  f 6718
CORROSIÓN DE LA PILA DE CONCENTRACIÓN  f 2888
CORROSIÓN DE LAS CARAS EN CONTACTO  f 5667
CORROSIÓN DE SOLDADURA  f 13759
CORROSIÓN EN TENSIÓN  f 3195
CORROSIÓN EN TENSIÓN  f 12361
CORROSIÓN GALVÁNICA  f 5783
CORROSIÓN HÚMEDA  f 13802
CORROSIÓN INTERCRISTALINA  f 7030
CORROSIÓN INTERCRISTALINA  f 7041
CORROSIÓN INTERCRISTALINA DE LOS LATONES 70/30  f 11093
CORROSIÓN INTERGRANULAR  f 7041
CORROSIÓN INTERGRANULAR  f 7030
CORROSIÓN LOCAL  f 7695
CORROSIÓN LOCALIZADA  f 9418
CORROSIÓN POR CONTACTO  f 3002
CORROSIÓN POR CORRIENTE VAGABUNDA  f 12350
CORROSIÓN POR INFILTRACIÓN ESTRATIFICADA  f 7443
CORROSIÓN POR ROCE  f 5666
CORROSIÓN QUÍMICA  f 2302
CORROSIÓN SUBYACENTE  f 13352
CORROSIVO  m 3196
CORROSIVO  m 3197
CORROSIVO  m 3197
CORROSIVO  m 4847
CORTA  f GRANDE DE MADERA 1058
CORTA CIRCUITO DE SEGURIDAD 10886
CORTADOR  m DE YUNQUE 631
CORTADOR DE CARDOS Y HELECHOS  m 13741
CORTADOR DE TUBOS  m 9348
CORTADOR DE TUBOS  m 13248
CORTADORA DE NABAS  f 7272
CORTADURA  f 11217
CORTADURA  f 3533
CORTADURA  f EN CALIENTE 6640
CORTADURA  f EN FRÍO 2701
CORTAFRÍO  m 2114
CORTANTE 12995
CORTAR 1078
CORTAR 3510
CORTAR 3506
CORTAR 3504
CORTAR 3510
CORTAR 3815
CORTAR AL SOPLETE 3505
CORTAR CHAPAS 3513
CORTAR CON PROCESO AUTÓGENO 3505
CORTAR CON TAJADERA 3515

CORTAR EN BIÉS **1222**
CORTAR EN BISEL **1222**
CORTAR EN LAS DIMENSIONES EXACTAS **3509**
CORTAR (GEOMETRÍA) **3504**
CORTAR LA CORRIENTE **7090**
CORTAR ROSCA **11046**
CORTAR ROSCA **3512**
CORTARRAÍCES *m* **10715**
CORTARSE (GEOMETRÍA) **7094**
CORTATUBOS *m* **13248**
CORTATUBOS *m* **9348**
CORTE *m* **8668**
CORTE *m* **13209**
CORTE *m* **11122**
CORTE *m* **8672**
CORTE *m* **3523**
CORTE *m* **3523**
CORTE *m* **3533**
CORTE *m* **3533**
CORTE *m* **3503**
CORTE *m* **3278**
CORTE *m* **1309**
CORTE *m* A MÁQUINA **7842**
CORTE *m* A SACABOCADOS **6514**
CORTE *m* AUTÓGENO **5817**
CORTE *m* AUTÓGENO **832**
CORTE *m* CON POLVO **9719**
CORTE *m* DE LA ELECTRICIDAD **7093**
CORTE *m* DE ROSCA **11028**
CORTE *m* DE ROSCA **11030**
CORTE *m* DE SIERRA **3517**
CORTE *m* DE UN ÚTIL **3528**
CORTE *m* LONGITUDINAL DE LA MADERA **1058**
CORTE *m* RADIAL **12938**
CORTE *m* RADIAL DE LA MADERA **10075**
CORTE ANGULAR *m* **539**
CORTE CON ACETILENO *m* **94**
CORTE CON AUTÓGENA *m* **5817**
CORTE CON LLAMA *m* **5318**
CORTE CON SOPLETE *m* **5817**
CORTE DE CORRIENTE *m* **8734**
CORTE EN CALÍENTE *m* **6622**
CORTE INFERIOR A LA COTA *m* **13351**
CORTE INICIAL *m* **5858**
CORTE LONGITUDINAL *m* **7738**
CORTE MANUAL *m* **6232**
CORTE MICROGRÁFICO *m* **8261**
CORTE POR ARCO AL CARBONO *m* **1942**
CORTE POR ARCO METÁLICO *m* **8175**
CORTE POR ELECTRO-EROSIÓN *m* **4559**

CORTEZA *f* **3421**
CORTEZA *f* **9155**
CORTEZA *f* **11624**
CORTINAJES *m pl* **3492**
CORTO CIRCUITO *m* **11372**
CORTO CIRCUITO *m* **11369**
COSECANTE *f* **3202**
COSECHADORAS *f pl* **2766**
COSENO *m* **3203**
COSMOLINA *f* **13508**
COSTE *m* **7346**
COSTE *m* DE MATERIAS PRIMAS **8049**
COSTRA *f* DE LA FUNDICIÓN **11538**
COSTRA *f* DE LAMINADO **11544**
COSTURA *f* FRÍA **2705**
COTA *f* **3956**
COTANGENTE *f* **3211**
COTAS DE EMPALME *f pl* **2793**
COTAS DE UNIÓN *f pl* **2793**
COVARIACIÓN *f* **3261**
CRACKING *m* **3284**
CRACKING *m* **3285**
CRACKING *m* **3284**
CRÁTER *m* **3317**
CRECER **12542**
CRECIMIENTO *m* **7935**
CRECIMIENTO *m* **1720**
CRECIMIENTO *m* **6155**
CRECIMIENTO *m* ANORMAL DE LOS CRISTALES 7
CRECIMIENTO *m* DE LA FUNDICIÓN **2061**
CRECIMIENTO *m* DE LOS GRANOS **6035**
CREMALLERA *f* **10119**
CREMALLERA *f* **13022**
CREMALLERA *f* Y PIÑÓN *m* **10120**
CRÉMOR *m* TÁRTARO **119**
CREMOR *m* TÁRTARO **119**
CREOSOTA *f* **3331**
CREOSOTA *f* **13921**
CREOSOTAJE *m* **3332**
CRESTA *f* DE LA OLA **3334**
CRESTA *f* DE VERTEDERO **13754**
CRETA *f* **13842**
CRIBA *f* **10572**
CRIBA *f* **11422**
CRIBA *f* DE SACUDIDAS **1733**
CRIBA *f* OSCILANTE **11252**
CRIBA *f* PARA LA ARENA **11628**
CRIBA *f* PARA TIERRA **11628**
CRIBADO *m* **11424**
CRIBAR **11423**

**CRI** 1006

CRIC *m* 11035
CRIC *m* 10121
CRIC *m* DE BOTELLA 1485
CRIC *m* DE CARRO 13165
CRIC *m* DE TRINQUETE 10222
CRIC *m* DE TRÍPODE 13218
CRIC *m* HIDRÁULICO 6688
CRIN *f* 12594
CRIN *f* DE CABALLO 6604
CRIN *f* DE LA MELENA (DE CABALLO) 7965
CRINES *f pl* 7965
CRIOHIDRATO *m* 3422
CRIOLITA *f* 3423
CRIPTON (QUIM) *f* 7339
CRISOL 7356
CRISOL *m* 8142
CRISOL *m* 6331
CRISOL *m* (DE ALTO HORNO) 3401
CRISOL *m* DE GRAFITA 6064
CRISOL *m* DE PLATINO 9512
CRISOL *m* DE PORCELANA 9626
CRISOL *m* ENLADRILLADO 7618
CRISOLITA *f* 9243
CRISOLITO *m* 2392
CRISOTILO *m* 11205
CRISTAL *m* 8708
CRISTAL *m* 3428
CRISTAL *m* 3424
CRISTAL *m* 6030
CRISTAL *m* 5956
CRISTAL *m* ARMADO 13894
CRISTAL *m* ARMADO CON ALAMBRE 13894
CRISTAL *m* BASÁLTICO 2757
CRISTAL *m* BLANCO DE BOHEMIA 1400
CRISTAL *m* CÚBICO 3450
CRISTAL *m* DE AUMENTO 7936
CRISTAL *m* DE BOTELLAS 1484
CRISTAL *m* DE CUARZO 10079
CRISTAL *m* DE JENA 7217
CRISTAL *m* DE LUNAS 9491
CRISTAL *m* DE ROCA 10652
CRISTAL *m* DE ROCA 5428
CRISTAL *m* DE VENTANAS 13866
CRISTAL *m* ESMERILADO 5701
CRISTAL *m* ESMERILADO 6145
CRISTAL *m* ESMERILADO (FOT) 6145
CRISTAL *m* HEMIÉDRICO 6436
CRISTAL *m* HEMIMÓRFICO 6437
CRISTAL *m* HEXAGONAL 6459
CRISTAL *m* HILADO 5966

CRISTAL *m* HOLOÉDRICO 6552
CRISTAL *m* IDIOMÓRFICO 6751
CRISTAL *m* INCOLORO 2746
CRISTAL *m* INHOMÓGENO 3169
CRISTAL *m* LÍQUIDO 11808
CRISTAL *m* MACHACADO 5962
CRISTAL *m* MONOCLÍNICO 8384
CRISTAL *m* OPACO 8273
CRISTAL *m* OSCILANTE 3432
CRISTAL *m* REDONDO 2414
CRISTAL *m* ROMBOÉDRICO 10565
CRISTALES *m pl* 119
CRISTALES *m pl* DE EJES IGUALES 4784
CRISTALES *m pl* DE SOSA 11711
CRISTALES *m pl* MIXTOS 8329
CRISTALES *m pl* ORTORRÓMBICOS 8874
CRISTALIDAD *f* 3440
CRISTALINO *m* 3433
CRISTALIZABILIDAD *f* 3436
CRISTALIZABLE 3437
CRISTALIZACIÓN *f* 3438
CRISTALIZACIÓN *f* PRIMARIA 9849
CRISTALIZAR 3439
CRISTALOGRAFÍA *f* 3442
CRISTALOGRAMA *m* 3441
CRISTALOIDE 3443
CROMADO ELECTROLÍTICO *m* 2388
CROMADO MATE *m* 4366
CROMATACIÓN *f* 2367
CROMÁTICO *m* 2368
CROMATO *m* 2366
CROMATO DE CINC *m* 14039
CROMATO DE PLOMO *m* 2375
CROMATO NEUTRO DE POTASIO *m* 9682
CROMITA *f* 2384
CROMITA *f* 2373
CROMO *m* 2385
CROMO PARA HORNO *m* 5741
CRONOMETRIZADOR *m* 3843
CRONÓMETRO CON STOP *m* 12283
CROQUIS *m* 11532
CROQUIS *m* 11528
CROQUIS *m* DE PRINCIPIO 3797
CROQUIS *m* ESQUEMÁTICO 3836
CROWN-GLASS *m* 3397
CRUCETA *f* 3388
CRUZ *f* 3359
CRUZ *f* (O BRAZO *m*) DE BALANZA 10972
CRUZETAS *f pl* DE ARMAZÓN 1520
CUADRADILLO *m* 12019

| | |
|---|---|
| CUADRADO *m* **12025** | CUBILETE *m* **1092** |
| CUADRADO *m* (GEOM.) **12013** | CUBILETE *m* **1430** |
| CUADRADO *m* (SEGUNDA POTENCIA) **12013** | CUBILOTE *m* **3464** |
| CUADRADO DE ARRASTRE *m* **4288** | CUBILOTE *m* **3466** |
| CUADRADOS DE ACERO ALEADO *m* **379** | CUBO *m* **3445** |
| CUADRÁNGULO *m* **10058** | CUBO *m* **1674** |
| CUADRANTE *m* **10056** | CUBO *m* DE BRIDA **5329** |
| CUADRANTE GRADUADO *m* **6027** | CUBO *m* DE DOS PIEZAS **11938** |
| CUADRÁTICO **12795** | CUBO *m* DE LA MANIVELA **3297** |
| CUADRATURA *f* **12036** | CUBO *m* DE RUEDA **1481** |
| CUADRÍCULA *f* **6099** | CUBO *m* DE RUEDA **6661** |
| CUADRILÁTERO *m* **12026** | CUBO *m* DE UNA SOLA PIEZA **11779** |
| CUADRILÁTERO *m* **10058** | CUBRECADENAS *m* **2204** |
| CUADRILÁTERO *m* **10055** | CUBREJUNTA *f* **1783** |
| CUADRILÁTERO *m* INSCRIBIBLE **6961** | CUBREJUNTAS *m* **1783** |
| CUADRILLADO **6099** | CUBRERRUEDAS *m* **13815** |
| CUADRO *m* **5624** | CUBRETABLERO *m* **5695** |
| CUADRO *m* **2273** | CUBRIR **8950** |
| CUADRO *m* DE INSTRUMENTOS **3610** | CUCHARA *f* DE COLADA **7356** |
| CUADRO *m* DE INSTRUMENTOS **6993** | CUCHARA *f* DE COLADA CON ASA **11258** |
| CUADRO *m* DE MANDO **3054** | CUCHARA *f* DE COLADA CON VUELCO **12935** |
| CUADRO *m* DISTRIBUIDOR **12557** | CUCHARA *f* DE COLADA DE MANO **6238** |
| CUADRO *m* GENERAL **12557** | CUCHARA *f* DE COLAR POR EL FONDO **1496** |
| CUADRO PARA FOTOCALCO *m* **9874** | CUCHARA *f* DE GRÚA DE COLADA **1728** |
| CUARCITA *f* **10083** | CUCHARA *f* DE GRÚA DE COLADA **3292** |
| CUARTA *f* PARTE **10076** | CUCHARA *f* DE MANO CON MANGO **6250** |
| CUARTA *f* POTENCIA **5608** | CUCHARA *f* DE RETIRAR **1353** |
| CUARTOS *m pl* DE LEÑA **10076** | CUCHARA *f* GUARNECIDA **7618** |
| CUARZO *m* **10077** | CUCHARA *f* MEZCLADORA **8333** |
| CUATRIFOLIO *m* **10086** | CUCHARA *f* TETERA **12693** |
| CUBA *f* **13228** | CUCHARA *f* TONEL **13110** |
| CUBA *f* **13228** | CUCHARA *f* TONEL **4336** |
| CUBA *f* **13228** | CUCHARÓN *m* **1378** |
| CUBA *f* **13228** | CUCHARÓN *m* DE COLADA **1347** |
| CUBA *f* DE HORNO **9029** | CUCHILLA *f* **1299** |
| CUBA *f* DE INMERSIÓN **3973** | CUCHILLA *f* **1300** |
| CUBA *f* DE NIVEL CONSTANTE **5431** | CUCHILLA *f* **7325** |
| CUBA *f* DE RETENCIÓN DE UN DEPÓSITO **12629** | CUCHILLA *f* DE CORTAR LA PAJA **2199** |
| CUBA *f* DE TEMPLE **10090** | CUCHILLO *m* **7323** |
| CUBETA *f* **11073** | CUCHILLO CIRCULAR *m* **2417** |
| CUBETA *f* DE PLATOS **11074** | CUCÚRBITA *f* **1407** |
| CUBICACIÓN *f* **13598** | CUELLO *m* **8512** |
| CUBICACIÓN *f* (EVALUACIÓN EN UNIDADES CÚBICAS) **3444** | CUELLO *m* **8512** |
| CUBICAR **3446** | CUELLO *m* DE BIELA DEL CIGÜEÑAL **9319** |
| CÚBICO DE CARA CENTRAL **4991** | CUELLO DE CISNE *m* **12535** |
| CUBIERTA *f* **1912** | CUELLO DE CISNE *m* **1194** |
| CUBIERTA *f* **3274** | CUELLO DE CISNE *m* **6009** |
| CUBIERTA *f* **11303** | CUELLO DE EMPALME *m* **6537** |
| CUBIERTA DE PALIER *f* **1104** | CUELLO DE TUBO *m* **13324** |
| | CUENCA *f* HULLERA **2566** |

# CUE

1008

CUENCO *m* DE VIDRIO CON VARILLA **8520**
CUENTAGOTAS *m* **4321**
CUENTAHILOS *m* **11047**
CUENTARREVOLUCIONES *m* **10556**
CUENTARREVOLUCIONES *m* **10556**
CUENTARREVOLUCIONES *m* **12587**
CUENTASEGUNDOS *m* **12283**
CUENTASEGUNDOS *m* **12946**
CUERDA *f* **10730**
CUERDA ALQUITRANADA *f* **12688**
CUERDA DE ACERO *f* **9287**
CUERDA DE CÁÑAMO *f* **6443**
CUERDA DE MANILLA *f* **7981**
CUERDA DE UN CÍRCULO *f* **2364**
CUERDA NEGRA *f* **12688**
CUERDA PIANO *f* **9287**
CUERDA SIN ALQUITRÁN *f* **13839**
CUERDA TENSADA *f* **12923**
CUERDA TRENZADA *f* **1527**
CUERDAS *f* **10745**
CUERNO *m* DE YUNQUE **1090**
CUERNO RASPADO *m* **6595**
CUERO *m* **7494**
CUERO *m* ÁSPERO **1685**
CUERO *m* CHAROLADO **9117**
CUERO *m* CURTIDO AL CROMO **2377**
CUERO *m* CURTIDO CON CÁSCARA DE ROBLE **8704**
CUERO *m* DE BUEY **3275**
CUERO *m* DE PRIMERA CALIDAD **1780**
CUERO *m* DE VACA **3275**
CUERO *m* EMBUTIDO **3458**
CUERO *m* EN BRUTO **10237**
CUERO *m* FUERTE (PARA SUELAS) **11770**
CUERO *m* TOSTADO (QUEMADO) **2272**
CUERO *m* VERDE **10237**
CUERO VERDE **10237**
CUERPO *m* **1385**
CUERPO *m* DE CEPILLO (CARP.) **12262**
CUERPO *m* DE CILINDRO **3562**
CUERPO *m* DE UN GRIFO **11334**
CUERPO *m* DEL MARTILLO **4993**
CUERPO ALUMBRADO *m* **6773**
CUERPO CILÍNDRICO DE CALDERA *m* **1419**
CUERPO DE BOMBA **1015**
CUERPO DE BOMBA *m* **1015**
CUERPO DE LA BIELA *m* **11261**
CUERPO DE LA ESTAMPA *m* **3885**
CUERPO DE REVOLUCIÓN *m* **11790**
CUERPO DE UNA CHAVETA *m* **11262**
CUERPO DE UNA VÁLVULA *m* **13454**

CUERPO DEL MARTILLO *m* **6317**
CUERPO DEL PISTÓN *m* **9373**
CUERPO DEL REMACHE *m* **11263**
CUERPO EN MOVIMIENTO *m* **1392**
CUERPO EN REPOSO *m* **1386**
CUERPO FLOTANTE *m* **5436**
CUERPO GASEOSO *m* **5808**
CUERPO GRIS *m* **6083**
CUERPO HUECO *m* **6538**
CUERPO ILUMINADO *m* **6773**
CUERPO LÍQUIDO *m* **7641**
CUERPO LUMINOSO *m* **11147**
CUERPO MÓVIL *m* **1392**
CUERPO NEGRO *m* **1285**
CUERPO PLÁSTICO *m* **9467**
CUERPO RÍGIDO *m* **10588**
CUERPO SIMPLE *m* **4654**
CUERPO SÓLIDO *m* **11775**
CUERPOS EXTRAÑOS *m pl* **6813**
CUESTA *f* **3792**
CUESTIONARIO *m* **10101**
CULATA *f* **3569**
CULATA *f* DE UN IMÁN **14017**
CULOMBÍMETRO *m* **452**
CULOMBIO *m* **3225**
CULTIVADORES *m pl* **3457**
CUNA *f* **3288**
CUÑA *f* **5211**
CUÑA *f* **13739**
CUÑA *f* **13731**
CUÑA *f* **13731**
CUÑA *f* **13739**
CUNA *f* DE DESLIZAMIENTO **11606**
CUNA *f* DE RODILLOS **10694**
CUÑA *f* SUJETADORA DE LA CUCHILLA DEL CEPILLO **5093**
CUÑA DEL CEPILLO *f* **13733**
CUÑA PLANA *f* **5400**
CUÑAS DE DESGASTE *f* **13711**
CUNEIFORME **13737**
CUNETA *f* **2251**
CUPROALUMINIO *m* **434**
CUPROBERILIO *m* **1209**
CUPRONÍQUEL *m* **3477**
CUPROSILICIO *m* **11444**
CÚPULA *f* DE TOMA DE VAPOR **12163**
CURCUMINA *f* **3481**
CURSO *m* DESCENDENTE DEL ÉMBOLO (DEL PISTÓN) **4187**
CURSOR *m* **7625**
CURSOR *m* **7625**

1009        **DEC**

CURSOR *m* DE UNA BALANZA **13160**
CURTIR AL CROMO **2377**
CURVA *f* **3496**
CURVA *m* CÍCLICA **3555**
CURVA *f* DE CORRIMIENTO **5976**
CURVA ADIABÁTICA *f* **179**
CURVA APLANADA *f* **5378**
CURVA CARGA-ALARGAMIENTO *f* **12366**
CURVA CERRADA *f* **2520**
CURVA DE CONTACTO *f* **675**
CURVA DE DOBLE CURVATURA *f* **13307**
CURVA DE ENFRIAMIENTO *f* **3087**
CURVA DE EXPANSIÓN *f* **4916**
CURVA DE ISOBARAS *f* **7177**
CURVA DE PEQUEÑO RADIO *f* **10102**
CURVA DE RADIO GRANDE *f* **5378**
CURVA DE RADIO PEQUEÑO *f* **10102**
CURVA DE RADIO PEQUEÑO *f* **10102**
CURVA DE REFRIGERACIÓN *f* **3087**
CURVA DE TRES CENTROS *f* **12872**
CURVA DE UN DIAGRAMA *f* **3495**
CURVA DE VELOCIDAD *f* **13513**
CURVA EN EL ESPACIO *f* **13307**
CURVA EN EL ESPACIO *f* **13307**
CURVA ESFUERZO-DEFORMACIÓN *f* **12365**
CURVA LÍMITE *f* **1460**
CURVA PLANA *f* **9435**
CURVA POLITRÓPICA *f* **9618**
CURVA RODANTE *f* **10697**
CURVA SINUOSA *f* **11476**
CURVA VIVA *f* **10102**
CURVADO *m* **1182**
CURVADO *m* **5579**
CURVADO DE UN TUBO *m* **9341**
CURVADO EN FRÍO *m* **2668**
CURVAR **1173**
CURVAR **1175**
CURVAR UN TUBO **1175**
CURVAR UN TUBO **1175**
CURVAS DE TEMPERATURA *f pl* **12723**
CURVATURA *f* **3494**
CURVILÍNEO **3499**
CURVÍMETRO *m* **3501**
DAMAJUANA *f* **1981**
DAMAJUANA *f* **1981**
DAÑADO **5057**
DAÑAR LA ROSCA **12379**
DAR DE SÍ **5949**
DAR FORMA **5571**
DAR TINTA **6940**

DAR UNA CAPA **1909**
DARDO *m* **6951**
DARDO *m* DE SOPLETE **8975**
DARDO *m* INTERIOR **6952**
DARDO DE LA LLAMA **2923**
DATO *m* **5951**
DATOS *m pl* **3612**
DATOS *m pl* JUSTIFICATIVOS **12494**
DATOS *m pl* NUMÉRICOS **8696**
DATOS *m pl* PRINCIPALES **7481**
DATOS ADIABÁTICOS *m pl* **178**
DE ALETAS **13479**
DE APLANADO **11543**
DE CHAVETA **7282**
DE CLARIFICACIÓN **11229**
DE DERECHA A IZQUIERDA **3239**
DE DERECHA A IZQUIERDA **3239**
DE EMPOTRAMIENTO **4683**
DE ESMERILAR **6565**
DE FIJACIÓN **2728**
DE FUEL **5706**
DE HACER MOLDURAS **8429**
DE INFLAMACIÓN **5368**
(DE LA PLUMADEL BRAZO) **7225**
DE LOS TALLERES **13963**
DE NÚCLEO **2253**
DE PRECINTAR **10886**
DE PRECISIÓN **3721**
DE ROSCAR **4952**
DE SERVICIO **13964**
DE TALLER *m* **13964**
DE UN ORIFICIO **4447**
DE VIENTO **13855**
DEBILITAMIENTO DEL MATERIAL *m* **13708**
DECÁGONO *m* **3644**
DECAGRAMO *m* **3645**
DECALESCENCIA *f* **3646**
DECALITRO *m* **3647**
DECÁMETRO *m* **3648**
DECANTACIÓN *f* **3650**
DECANTACIÓN *f* **11228**
DECANTAR **3649**
DECAPADO *m* **10979**
DECAPADO *m* **11006**
DECAPADO *m* **11006**
DECAPADO *m* A LA LLAMA **5313**
DECAPADO *m* ANÓDICO **601**
DECAPADO *m* APAGADO **3628**
DECAPADO *m* CATÓDICO **2103**
DECAPADO *m* CON ÁCIDO **9288**

# DEC

1010

DECAPADO *m* CON AGUA **13647**
DECAPADO *m* CON BAÑO ACIDULADO **112**
DECAPADO *m* CON GAS **5832**
DECAPADO *m* CON GRANALLA **11381**
DECAPADO *m* CON SOPLETE **5310**
DECAPADO *m* ELECTROLÍTICO **4603**
DECAPADO *m* EN FRÍO **2707**
DECAPADO *m* (LIMPIEZA *f*) DE UN METAL **11006**
DECAPADO *m* (LIMPIEZA *f*) ELECTROLÍTICO **4589**
DECAPADO *m* QUÍMICO **9288**
DECAPAR **11005**
DECAPAR **11005**
DECAPAR **11005**
DECIGRAMO *m* **3657**
DECILITRO *m* **3658**
DECIMAL **3659**
DECÍMETRO *m* **3666**
DECÍMETRO *m* CUADRADO **12018**
DECÍMETRO *m* CÚBICO **3451**
DECLINACIÓN *f* MAGNÉTICA **3668**
DECLIVE *m* **3792**
DECLIVE *m* **3792**
DECLIVE *m* **11627**
DECLIVE *m* **6836**
DECLIVIDAD *f* **3792**
DECOCCIÓN *f* **3669**
DECOLORACIÓN *f* **5014**
DECRECIMIENTO *m* **3656**
DEDO *m* **1883**
DEDO *m* **5211**
DEFECTO *m* **5411**
DEFECTO *m* **3691**
DEFECTO *m* DE ALINEACIÓN O DESNIVELACIÓN *f* (DE UNA JUNTA SOLDADA) **8737**
DEFECTO *m* DE COLADA **5056**
DEFECTO *m* DE CONSTRUCCIÓN **3693**
DEFECTO *m* DE FABRICACIÓN **3693**
DEFECTO *m* DE FABRICACIÓN **11550**
DEFECTO *m* DEL MATERIAL **3692**
DEFECTO *m* EN EL METAL FUNDIDO **5056**
DEFECTO *m* SUPERFICIAL **12502**
DEFECTOS *m pl* DE LA SOLDADURA **13760**
DEFECTOS *m pl* DE PINTURA **9021**
DEFECTUOSO **5057**
DEFICIENCIA *f* **11537**
DEFLECTOR *m* **13531**
DEFLECTOR *m* **921**
DEFLECTOR *m* **921**
DEFLECTOR *m* **922**
DEFLECTOR *m* **3702**

DEFLEXIÓN *f* **3699**
DEFORMABILIDAD *f* **3705**
DEFORMACIÓN *f* **3698**
DEFORMACIÓN *f* **3698**
DEFORMACIÓN *f* **3707**
DEFORMACIÓN *f* **13629**
DEFORMACIÓN *f* **12322**
DEFORMACIÓN *f* CRITICA **3350**
DEFORMACIÓN *f* ELÁSTICA **4478**
DEFORMACIÓN *f* ELÁSTICA **4485**
DEFORMACIÓN *f* EN FRÍO **2680**
DEFORMACIÓN *f* (METALES) **3324**
DEFORMACIÓN *f* PERMANENTE **3337**
DEFORMACIÓN *f* PERMANENTE **9202**
DEFORMACIÓN *f* PERMANENTE **9210**
DEFORMACIÓN *f* PERMANENTE DEL ALMA DE UNA VIGA **13727**
DEFORMACIÓN *f* PLÁSTICA **9471**
DEFORMACIÓN *f* PLÁSTICA **9471**
DEFORMACIÓN *f* PLÁSTICA **9469**
DEFORMACIÓN *f* POR ENROLLAMIENTO **13629**
DEFORMACIÓN *f* POR FLEXIÓN **5426**
DEFORMACIÓN *f* POR TRACCIÓN **12744**
DEFORMACIÓN *f* PRINCIPAL **2000**
DEFORMACIÓN *f* PROGRESIVA **6853**
DEFORMACIONES *f pl* EN MEDIA LUNA DEL CORDÓN DE SOLDADURA **5212**
DEFORMAR **13628**
DEFORMAR(SE) **13628**
DEL TRABAJO **13963**
DELICUESCENCIA *f* **3733**
DELICUESCENTE **3734**
DELINEANTE **4213**
DENDRITA *f* **3748**
DENDRITA *f* **9331**
DENOMINADOR *m* **3752**
DENOMINADOR *m* COMÚN **2789**
DENSIDAD *f* **3756**
DENSIDAD *f* **1395**
DENSIDAD *f* **11850**
DENSIDAD *f* APARENTE **642**
DENSIDAD *f* APARENTE **1725**
DENSIDAD *f* DE CORRIENTE **4501**
DENSIDAD *f* DE CORRIENTE **3488**
DENSIDAD *f* DE UN GAS **3757**
DENSIDAD *f* DE UN LÍQUIDO **3758**
DENSIDAD *f* ELÉCTRICA **4501**
DENSIDAD *f* EN EL LLENADO 37570 **1724**
DENSIDAD *f* MAGNÉTICA **7899**
DENSIFICACIÓN *f* **3753**
DENSIMETRO *m* **3755**

DENTADO **6862**
DENTADO *m* **13026**
DENTADO *m* ALTERNADO **10187**
DENTADO *m* CICLOIDAL **3558**
DENTADO *m* DE UNA LIMA **3518**
DENTADO *m* DERECHO **10586**
DENTADO *m* DERECHO **12311**
DENTADO *m* EPICICLOIDAL **4780**
DENTADO *m* EPICICLOIDAL **4780**
DENTADO *m* EPICICLOIDAL **6744**
DENTADO *m* EXTERIOR **4959**
DENTADO *m* HIPOCICLOIDAL **6744**
DENTADO *m* INTERIOR **7077**
DENTADO *m* IZQUIERDO **7509**
DENTADURA *f* **12704**
DEPOSITAR **12294**
DEPOSITARSE **11227**
DEPÓSITO *m* **10471**
DEPÓSITO *m* **12265**
DEPÓSITO *m* **12293**
DEPÓSITO *m* **12625**
DEPÓSITO *m* **13228**
DEPÓSITO *m* **13228**
DEPÓSITO *m* **13680**
DEPÓSITO *m* **5716**
DEPÓSITO *m* **1740**
DEPÓSITO *m* DE RECEPCIÓN **10843**
DEPÓSITO *m* ACTIVO **149**
DEPÓSITO *m* BALÓN **6580**
DEPÓSITO *m* CALORÍFUGO **6995**
DEPÓSITO *m* DE ACEITE **8773**
DEPÓSITO *m* DE AFORO **12790**
DEPÓSITO *m* DE AGUA **13679**
DEPÓSITO *m* DE AIRE **294**
DEPÓSITO *m* DE ALMACENAMIENTO **12292**
DEPÓSITO *m* DE CARBURANTE **5716**
DEPÓSITO *m* DE DECANTACIÓN **11229**
DEPÓSITO *m* DE DOBLE PARED **4161**
DEPÓSITO *m* DE FONDO CÓNCAVO **12631**
DEPÓSITO *m* DE FONDO CONVEXO **12632**
DEPÓSITO *m* DE GASOLINA **5716**
DEPÓSITO *m* DE GNL **7678**
DEPÓSITO *m* DE LÍQUIDO DE FRENO **1534**
DEPÓSITO *m* DE PETRÓLEO BRUTO **3407**
DEPÓSITO *m* DE TECHO ABOMBADO **4121**
DEPÓSITO *m* DE TECHO CÓNICO AUTOSUSTENTADO **11160**
DEPÓSITO *m* DE TECHO FLOTANTE **5439**
DEPÓSITO *m* DE TECHO REBAJADO **13047**
DEPÓSITO *m* DE TECHO SUSPENDIDO **12525**

DEPÓSITO *m* DE VACÍO **13451**
DEPÓSITO *m* ELECTROLÍTICO **4580**
DEPÓSITO *m* ELECTROLÍTICO **4593**
DEPÓSITO *m* ELECTROLÍTICO **4593**
DEPÓSITO *m* ELECTROLÍTICO EN VARIAS CAPAS **2821**
DEPÓSITO *m* ELEVADO **4492**
DEPÓSITO *m* ENFRIADOR **3090**
DEPÓSITO *m* GALVANIZADO **4592**
DEPÓSITO *m* POR CONTACTO **3004**
DEPÓSITO *m* QUEMADO **1761**
DEPÓSITO *m* TAMPÓN **1592**
DEPÓSITOS *m pl* CALCARIOS **10969**
DEPRESIÓN *f* **9811**
DEPRESIÓN *f* **10613**
DEPRESIÓN *f* **3778**
DEPRESIÓN *f* ATMOSFÉRICA **13434**
DEPRESIÓN *f* CAPILAR **1924**
DEPURACIÓN *f* **13638**
DEPURACIÓN *f* DE LOS GASES **10018**
DEPURACIÓN QUÍMICA DEL AGUA POTABLE **13676**
DEPURADOR *m* **10020**
DERECHOS *m* DE PATENTE **9115**
DERECHOS *m pl* DE PATENTE **9121**
DERIVACIÓN *f* **11403**
DERIVACIÓN *f* **1821**
DERIVACIÓN *f* **1821**
DERIVACIÓN *f* **1554**
DERIVACIÓN *f* **1554**
DERIVADO **3786**
DEROGACIÓN *f* **13615**
DERRETIR **4061**
DESACELERACIÓN *f* AUTOMÁTICA **841**
DESACOPLADO **8892**
DESACOPLAMIENTO *m* **12898**
DESACOPLAMIENTO *m* **12898**
DESACOPLAMIENTO *m* **2548**
DESACOPLAR **10034**
DESACOPLAR **10034**
DESACOPLO *m* **12898**
DESACOPLO *m* **12898**
DESACTIVACIÓN *f* **3789**
DESAGREGACIÓN *f* **4000**
DESAGREGACIÓN *f* **4000**
DESAGREGACIÓN *f* **3418**
DESAGREGAR **3999**
DESAGREGARSE **4043**
DESAGREGARSE **4043**
DESAGUADERO *m* **12596**
DESAGUAZAR **4204**
DESAGUAZAR EL SUELO (UNA TIERRA HÚMEDA) **4209**

**DES** 1012

DESAGÜE  *m* 1321
DESAGÜE  *m* 8899
DESAIREACIÓN  *f* 3710
DESAPRIETO  *m* 11560
DESARENADO  *m* 2478
DESARENAR 2469
DESARGENTAR 3801
DESARMAR 12600
DESARME  *m* 12604
DESARROLLABLE 3816
DESARROLLAR 3815
DESATASCO  *m* 1321
DESBARBADO  *m* (O DESCORTEZAMIENTO  *m* ) DE LAS
  PIEZAS COLADAS (O VACIADAS) 2478
DESBARBADOR  *m* 4254
DESBARBADURA  *f* 5129
DESBARBADURA  *f* 1766
DESBARBADURA  *f* 3642
DESBARBADURA  *f* 3642
DESBARBADURA  *f* 2478
DESBARBADURA  *f* 2504
DESBARBADURA  *f* 13210
DESBARBADURA  *f* 13210
DESBARBADURA  *f* 13209
DESBARBADURA  *f* 13210
DESBARBADURA  *f* 11689
DESBARBADURA  *f* DE CHAPA EN BISEL 9496
DESBARBADURA  *f* EN CALIENTE 6647
DESBARBADURA  *f* EN FRÍO 2711
DESBARBAR 2469
DESBARBAR 5364
DESBARBAR 5364
DESBARBAR 13206
DESBARBAR 13206
DESBARBAR (O DESCORTEZAR) LAS PIEZAS COLADAS (O
  VACIADAS) 2469
DESBARBAR UNA CHAPA 13205
DESBASTADOR  *m* 1636
DESBASTADOR  *m* 1343
DESBASTAR 10775
DESBASTAR 10775
DESBASTE  *m* 10785
DESBASTE  *m* 10786
DESBASTE  *m* 10786
DESBASTE  *m* 12319
DESBASTE  *m* 12319
DESBASTE  *m* 1583
DESBASTE  *m* CON MUELA 10777
DESBASTE  *m* PLANO 11551
DESBASTES  *m pl* PLANOS (CURVADO DE) 11553
DESBASTES  *m pl* PLANOS (TREN DE LAMINAR) 11552

DESBLOQUEO  *m* 11560
DESCALCE  *m* 4312
DESCALZAR 4295
DESCARBONATACIÓN  *f* 3651
DESCARBONIZAR 3652
DESCARBURACIÓN  *f* 3655
DESCARBURACIÓN  *f* DEL HIERRO 3653
DESCARBURAR EL HIERRO 3654
DESCARGA  *f* 2395
DESCARGA  *f* 4024
DESCARGA  *f* 4017
DESCARGA  *f* DE UN ACUMULADOR 4025
DESCARGA  *f* DE UNA VÁLVULA 936
DESCARGA  *f* ELÉCTRICA 4502
DESCARGADOR  *m* DE GARRAS 6310
DESCARGAR 4018
DESCARGAR 13204
DESCARGAR UN ACUMULADOR 4019
DESCASCADO  *m* 5306
DESCASCADO  *m* 4889
DESCASCADO  *m* 11830
DESCASCADO  *m* 10985
DESCASCADO  *m* 11339
DESCASCADO  *m* 9156
DESCASCADO  *m* 9156
DESCASCARSE 10975
DESCENSO  *m* (O BAJADA  *f* ) DEL ÉMBOLO 4187
DESCENSO DE LA TEMPERATURA  *m* 5022
DESCENSO DE TEMPERATURA  *m* 12724
DESCENTRADO 8893
DESCENTRADO 8731
DESCENTRADO 8730
DESCENTRADO 8731
DESCENTRADO 8730
DESCENTRADO 8730
DESCENTRADO  *m* 10892
DESCENTRADO 4055
DESCENTRADO 4424
DESCOLCHADO  *m* (DE CUERDA) 11934
DESCOLCHADO  *m* (DE CUERDA) 11933
DESCOLCHAR (UNA CUERDA) 11931
DESCOLORACIÓN  *f* 5014
DESCOMPONER 3672
DESCOMPONERSE 3673
DESCOMPONIBLE 3671
DESCOMPOSICIÓN  *f* 3674
DESCOMPOSICIÓN  *f* 10769
DESCOMPOSICIÓN  *f* DE FUERZAS 10505
DESCOMPOSICIÓN  *f* DE LA LUZ 3676
DESCOMPOSICIÓN  *f* ELECTROLÍTICA 4596

DES

DESCONCHADO *m* **4889**
DESCONEXIÓN *f* **4028**
DESCONGELADOR *m* **3708**
DESCONOCIDA **13391**
DESCORTEZADURA *f* **9156**
DESCORTEZAMIENTO *m* **9156**
DESCORTEZAMIENTO *m* **10988**
DESCRIPCIÓN *f* DE UNA PATENTE **11856**
DESCUBRIDOR *m* **7108**
DESCUBRIMIENTO *m* **7107**
DESDOBLAMIENTO *m* **11950**
DESDOBLAR **11946**
DESDOBLE *m* DE LOS BORDES DE CHAPA **7382**
DESECACIÓN *f* **4210**
DESECACIÓN *f* **4359**
DESECACIÓN *f* DE LA MADERA AL AIRE LIBRE **11095**
DESECADO *m* **4210**
DESECADOR *m* **3804**
DESECAR **4338**
DESECHO *m* **8321**
DESECHOS *m pl* **13074**
DESECHOS *m pl* **13637**
DESEMBLAJE *m* **12604**
DESEMBRAGAR **10034**
DESEMBRAGAR **10034**
DESEMBRAGAR **4030**
DESEMBRAGAR **4030**
DESEMBRAGUE *m* **2548**
DESEMBRAGUE **12898**
DESEMBRAGUE *m* **12898**
DESEMBRAGUE *m* **12898**
DESEMPLEO *m* **7092**
DESEMPOLVAMIENTO *m* **3682**
DESEMPOLVAR **5637**
DESENCLAVIJAMIENTO *m* **7751**
DESENCLAVIJAR **7750**
DESENDURECER EL AGUA **11748**
DESENDURECIMIENTO *m* DEL AGUA **13676**
DESENGANCHAR **10034**
DESENGANCHAR **4030**
DESENGANCHAR **4030**
DESENGANCHE *m* **4031**
DESENGATE *m* **4031**
DESENGATE *m* **4031**
DESENGATILLAR **4030**
DESENGATILLAR **4030**
DESENGRANADO **8892**
DESENGRANAR **10034**
DESENGRASE *m* **2474**
DESENGRASE *m* **3712**

DESENGRASE *m* CON VAPOR **13486**
DESENROLLADORA DE ALAMBRE **13903**
DESENROLLAMIENTO *m* **13405**
DESENROLLAR **13404**
DESENROSCADO *m* **13396**
DESENROSCAR **13395**
DESENROSCAR UN PERNO **13395**
DESENSAMBAR **12600**
DESENSAMBLADURA *f* **12604**
DESENTUMECIMIENTO *m* (PRECALENTAMIENTO *m* ANTES DE SOLDAR) **6260**
DESEQUILIBRIO *m* **13341**
DESEQUILIBRIO **13341**
DESFASADO *m* **9234**
DESFASADO *m* HACIA ATRÁS **7368**
DESFASAMIENTO *m* **9234**
DESFASAMIENTO *m* **9234**
DESFASAMIENTO *m* **9237**
DESFERRIZACIÓN *f* DEL AGUA **10454**
DESGARRADURA *f* **3278**
DESGARRARSE **10859**
DESGASIFICACIÓN *f* **3710**
DESGASIFICACIÓN *f* DEL AGUA **3623**
DESGASIFICAR **10455**
DESGASTARSE **13713**
DESGASTE *m* **13709**
DESGASTE *m* **13710**
DESGASTE *m* **4820**
DESGASTE *m* NORMAL **13710**
DESGASTE *m* POR ROZAMIENTO **13712**
DESGASTE *m* POR ROZAMIENTO **5778**
DESHECHO **10431**
DESHECHO **8321**
DESHIDRATACIÓN *f* **3728**
DESHIDRATAR **3727**
DESHIDRATARSE **3727**
DESHORNE *m* POR EXTRACTOR DE BRAZOS **4471**
DESIMANTACIÓN *f* **3742**
DESIMANTADORES *m pl* **3744**
DESIMANTAR **3743**
DESIMANTARSE **1123**
DESINCRUSTACIÓN *f* **10987**
DESINCRUSTACIÓN *f* **10987**
DESINCRUSTANTE **10978**
DESINCRUSTANTE *m* **4041**
DESINCRUSTANTE **4041**
DESINCRUSTANTE PREVENTIVO **10978**
DESINCRUSTAR **10971**
DESINCRUSTAR **10971**
DESINFECTANTE **4042**

# DES

1014

DESINTEGRACIÓN  f 4044
DESINTEGRACIÓN  f 4000
DESINTEGRACIÓN  f DESMORONAMIENTO  m 3418
DESINTEGRAR 3999
DESIONIZACIÓN  f 3729
DESLAVADO  m 13632
DESLIZAMIENTO  m 11620
DESLIZAMIENTO  m 11595
DESLIZAMIENTO  m 10613
DESLIZAMIENTO  m 5973
DESLIZAMIENTO  m TRANSVERSAL 11288
DESLIZAR 11586
DESLIZARSE 11586
DESMAGNETIZADORES  m pl 3744
DESMAGNETIZAR 3743
DESMAGNETIZARSE 1123
DESMENUZAR 9712
DESMOCHADO  m 3357
DESMODULACIÓN  f 10312
DESMODULADOR  m 8338
DESMOLDEAR 4468
DESMOLDEO  m 7328
DESMOLDEO  m 11251
DESMOLDEO  m 9554
DESMOLDEO  m 9554
DESMONTABLE 4027
DESMONTADO 7329
DESMONTAJE  m 12604
DESMONTAJE  m 12604
DESMONTAJE  m (AFLOJAMIENTO  m) DE UNA CHAVETA
  DE CUÑA 7751
DESMONTAJE  m Y NUEVO MONTAJE  m 10451
DESMONTAR 12600
DESMONTAR 12600
DESNIQUELADO  m 3751
DESNIVEL  m 7798
DESNIVEL  m 7798
DESNIVELACIÓN  f 7798
DESNIVELACIÓN  f 7798
DESOLDADURA  f 13400
DESOLDAR 13399
DESOXIDACIÓN  f 10826
DESOXIDACIÓN  f 11006
DESOXIDACIÓN  f 3762
DESOXIDACIÓN  f 3766
DESOXIDANTE 3765
DESOXIDANTE  m 10346
DESOXIDAR 11005
DESOXIDAR 10815
DESOXIDAR 3763

DESOXIDAR UN METAL 11005
DESOXIGENACIÓN  f 3762
DESOXIGENAR 3763
DESPEGUE  m 1354
DESPEGUE  m 9156
DESPEJAR 893
DESPERDICIO  m 10431
DESPERDICIO  m 8321
DESPLATAR 3801
DESPLATE  m 3802
DESPLATEAR 3801
DESPLAZABLE 4052
DESPLAZADO 8730
DESPLAZAMIENTO  m 13123
DESPLAZAMIENTO  m 4053
DESPLAZAMIENTO  m ANGULAR 541
DESPLAZAMIENTO  m ANGULAR 541
DESPLAZAMIENTO  m AXIAL 860
DESPLAZAMIENTO  m DE FASE 9237
DESPLAZAMIENTO  m DE FASE 9234
DESPLAZAMIENTO  m DE FASE HACIA ATRÁS 7368
DESPLAZAMIENTO  m DE FASES 9234
DESPLAZAMIENTO  m DE LA CORREA 1158
DESPLAZAMIENTO  m DE UN LÍQUIDO 4054
DESPLAZAMIENTO  m DEL CUÑO 3891
DESPLAZAMIENTO  m DEL EJE 4055
DESPLAZAMIENTO  m DEL PUNTO DE ORIGEN (DEL PUNTO
  CERO) 14026
DESPLAZAMIENTO  m DEL PUNTO DE ORIGEN (DEL PUNTO
  CERO) 14031
DESPLAZAMIENTO  m INTERNO 7063
DESPLAZAMIENTO  m LATERAL 7420
DESPLAZAMIENTO  m LATERAL 12538
DESPLAZAMIENTO  m LONGITUDINAL 860
DESPLAZAMIENTO  m PARALELO AL EJE 860
DESPLAZAMIENTO  m PERPENDICULAR AL EJE 7420
DESPLAZAMIENTO  m RADIAL 10133
DESPLAZAMIENTO VERTICAL  m 13549
DESPLAZAR LA CORREA 11349
DESPLOME 12418
DESPOJAMIENTO  m 910
DESPOLARIZACIÓN  f 3771
DESPOLARIZACIÓN  f 3768
DESPOLARIZADOR 3772
DESPOLARIZADOR 3770
DESPOLARIZADOR 3772
DESPOLARIZANTE 3772
DESPOLARIZANTE 3772
DESPOLARIZANTE 3770
DESPOLARIZAR 3769
DESPRENDIMIENTO  m 1354

DESPRENDIMIENTO *m* DE CALOR **4874**
DESPRENDIMIENTO *m* DE CALOR **10274**
DESPRENDIMIENTO *m* DE GASES **3818**
DESPUNTEO *m* **3357**
DESREDONDEZ *f* **8894**
DESTAJADOR *m* REDONDO **5729**
DESTALONADO *m* **910**
DESTALONAR **893**
DESTAPADURA *f* **12675**
DESTARA *f* **5886**
DESTARA *f* DE VÁLVULA **13469**
DESTARAR **5872**
DESTARAR UNA VÁLVULA **11216**
DESTEMPLAR **12717**
DESTEMPLAR **12719**
DESTEMPLEO *m* **7549**
DESTILACIÓN *f* (ACCIÓN) **4072**
DESTILACIÓN *f* CON CRACKING **3285**
DESTILACIÓN *f* CON DESCOMPOSICIÓN **3805**
DESTILACIÓN *f* CON VAPOR DE AGUA **4073**
DESTILACIÓN *f* CONTINUA **3024**
DESTILACIÓN *f* DE LA HULLA **4074**
DESTILACIÓN *f* DE LOS COMBUSTIBLES A BAJA
   TEMPERATURA **7776**
DESTILACIÓN *f* EN EL VACÍO **4075**
DESTILACION *f* FRACCIONADA **5612**
DESTILACIÓN *f* (PRODUCTO) **4071**
DESTILACIÓN *f* SECA **4346**
DESTILADOR *m* **12259**
DESTILADOR *m* **12259**
DESTILADOR *m* **12259**
DESTILAR **4070**
DESTOLONADO *m* **910**
DESTORNILLADOR *m* **13294**
DESTRAL *m* **6305**
DESTRUCTIBILIDAD *f* **6**
DESULFURACIÓN *f* **1975**
DESULFURACIÓN *f* **2666**
DESULFURACIÓN *f* **2666**
DESULFURAR **2656**
DESVIACIÓN *f* **3699**
DESVIACIÓN *f* **3819**
DESVIACIÓN *f* **3819**
DESVIACIÓN *f* A LA DERECHA **10583**
DESVIACIÓN *f* A LA IZQUIERDA **7507**
DESVIACIÓN *f* DESVÍO *m* **3699**
DESVIACIÓN *f* DESVÍO *m* **3380**
DESVIACIÓN *f* (DESVÍO *m*) LATERAL **7419**
DESVIACIÓN *f* (DESVÍO *m*) NULA **14024**
DESVÍO *m* **3819**

DESVÍO *m* **3819**
DESVÍO *m* **1821**
DESVÍO *m* MEDIO **8074**
DESVÍO *m* TIPO **12074**
DESVÍO STANDARD **12074**
DESVITRIFICACIÓN *f* **3823**
DETALLE *m* DE CONSTRUCCIÓN **3810**
DETECTOR *m* DE GRIETAS Y HENDIDURAS **3280**
DETERGENTE **3813**
DETERIORADO **5057**
DETERIORADO **5057**
DETERMINACIÓN *f* ANALÍTICA **496**
DETERMINACIÓN *f* EXPERIMENTAL **4929**
DETERMINANTE **3814**
DETERMINANTE MENOR **8315**
DETONACIÓN *f* **7330**
DETRÁS DE **4184**
DEVANADERA *f* **13898**
DEVANADO *m* **13862**
DEVANADO *m* **2648**
DEVUELTO **1705**
DEXTRINA *f* **3825**
DEXTRÓGIRO **3827**
DÍA *m* **3616**
DÍA *m* DE LA FIRMA DE LA PATENTE **3617**
DÍA *m* LABORABLE **11347**
DIABASA *f* **3828**
DIACÁUSTICA *f* **3829**
DIAFANIDAD *f* **3868**
DIÁFANO **3869**
DIAFRAGMA *m* **3870**
DIAFRAGMA *m* **3871**
DIAFRAGMA *m* **3870**
DIAFRAGMA *m* **4110**
DIAFRAGMA *m* **11019**
DIAFRAGMA *m* DE CAUCHO **10819**
DIAFRAGMA *m* DE CUERO **7498**
DIAFRAGMA *m* ELÁSTICO **4479**
DIAFRAGMA *m* IRIS **7132**
DIAFRAGMAR **3877**
DIAGONAL **3831**
DIAGONAL *f* **3831**
DIAGRAMA *m* **3834**
DIAGRAMA *m* **7717**
DIAGRAMA *m* **7717**
DIAGRAMA *m* DE DIFRACCIÓN DE LOS RAYOS X **13997**
DIAGRAMA *m* DE DIFRACCIÓN DE RAYOS X **3441**
DIAGRAMA *m* DE DIFRACCIÓN RX **3926**
DIAGRAMA *m* DE DISTRIBUCIÓN **11593**
DIAGRAMA *m* DE ENTROPÍA **6346**

**DIA** 1016

DIAGRAMA *m* DE EQUILIBRIO **4788**
DIAGRAMA *m* DE ESFUERZOS **5526**
DIAGRAMA *m* DE FUERZAS **5526**
DIAGRAMA *m* DE FUERZAS **3835**
DIAGRAMA *m* DE LAS FASES **2984**
DIAGRAMA *m* DE LAUE **7435**
DIAGRAMA *m* DE RESISTENCIAS **10489**
DIAGRAMA *m* DE RX **9128**
DIAGRAMA *m* DE TRABAJO **6881**
DIAGRAMA *m* DE VELOCIDADES **13514**
DIAGRAMA *m* DEL INDICADOR **6881**
DIAGRAMA *m* HIERRO-CARBURO **7139**
DIAGRAMA *m* RANKINIZADO **10203**
DIAGRAMA *m* TOTALIZADO **10203**
DIAGRAMA (DE ABERTURA Y DE CIERRE) DE UNA VÁLVULA **13457**
DIAL *m* **3837**
DIÁLISIS *f* **3846**
DIALIZADOR *m* **3845**
DIALIZAR **3844**
DIAMAGNÉTICO **3847**
DIAMAGNETISMO *m* **3848**
DIAMANTE *m* **3862**
DIAMANTE NEGRO *m* **1967**
DIÁMETRO *m* **3849**
DIÁMETRO *m* CONJUGADO **2954**
DIÁMETRO *m* DE AGUJERO DE PERNO **3854**
DIÁMETRO *m* DE LA PUNTA DE LA BROCA **4269**
DIÁMETRO *m* DE PASO DE ROSCA **9407**
DIÁMETRO *m* DE PERFORACIÓN **1438**
DIÁMETRO *m* DE PIE **10719**
DIÁMETRO *m* DE TALADRADO **1439**
DIÁMETRO *m* DE UN ALAMBRE (DE UN HILO) **3860**
DIÁMETRO *m* DE UN CABLE **10733**
DIÁMETRO *m* DE UN ESLABÓN DE CADENA **3856**
DIÁMETRO *m* DE UN TUBO **3858**
DIÁMETRO *m* DEL AGUJERO **3857**
DIÁMETRO *m* DEL AGUJERO DE PERNO **1440**
DIÁMETRO *m* (DEL CÍRCULO) DE PERFORACIÓN (DE TALADRO) **3853**
DIÁMETRO *m* DEL PERNO **1434**
DIÁMETRO *m* DEL REMACHE **3859**
DIÁMETRO *m* DEL TALADRO **3855**
DIÁMETRO *m* EN EL NÚCLEO (DE UN TORNILLO) **3850**
DIÁMETRO *m* EN EL NÚCLEO DE UN TORNILLO **3850**
DIÁMETRO *m* EXTERIOR **3852**
DIÁMETRO *m* EXTERIOR **4958**
DIÁMETRO *m* EXTERIOR **8913**
DIÁMETRO *m* GRANDE DEL FILETEADO **3852**
DIÁMETRO *m* INTERIOR **3850**
DIÁMETRO *m* INTERIOR **8314**

DIÁMETRO *m* INTERIOR **7071**
DIÁMETRO *m* INTERIOR **6977**
DIÁMETRO *m* INTERIOR DE UN TUBO **1464**
DIÁMETRO *m* NOMINAL **8611**
DIÁMETRO *m* PEQUEÑO DE LA ROSCA **3850**
DIÁMETRO *m* PRIMITIVO **3861**
DIÁMETRO *m* PRIMITIVO **9407**
DIÁMETRO PRIMITIVO **9407**
DIÁMETRO ÚTIL **13423**
DIANA *f* **12682**
DÍAS *m pl* NO LABORABLES **6536**
DIATERMANCIA *f* **3878**
DIATERMANCIA *f* **3878**
DIATÉRMANO **3879**
DIATÉRMICO **3879**
DIATÓMICO **3881**
DIBUJANTE **4213**
DIBUJAR **4195**
DIBUJO *m* **4229**
DIBUJO *m* **9430**
DIBUJO *m* A ESCALA **10983**
DIBUJO *m* A MANO ALZADA **5648**
DIBUJO *m* AL LÁPIZ **7467**
DIBUJO *m* AL LAVADO **12965**
DIBUJO *m* (ARTE DEL DIBUJANTEDEL DELINEANTE) **4246**
DIBUJO *m* CON DIMENSIONES **3959**
DIBUJO *m* DE ARQUITECTURA **693**
DIBUJO *m* DE DETALLE **3809**
DIBUJO *m* DE MÁQUINAS **7843**
DIBUJO *m* EN TAMAÑO NATURAL **5724**
DIBUJO *m* EN TAMAÑO NATURAL **5724**
DIBUJO *m* GEOMÉTRICO **5928**
DIBUJO *m* INDUSTRIAL **8099**
DIBUJO *m* LINEAL **8905**
DIBUJO *m* LINEAL **8905**
DIBUJO *m* PASADO CON TINTA CHINA **6941**
DIBUJO *m* (REPRESENTACIÓN GRÁFICA) **4245**
DIBUJO *m* SOMBREADO **11235**
DIBUJO A LA AGUADA **12965**
DICLORURO *m* DE ESTAÑO **12096**
DICLORURO *m* DE MERCURIO **8153**
DICROMATO *m* POTÁSICO **9677**
DIDECAEDRO *m* **4112**
DIEDRO *m* **3944**
DIELÉCTRICO **3898**
DIENTE *m* **3761**
DIENTE *m* **2464**
DIENTE *m* **1883**
DIENTE *m* **13016**
DIENTE *m* DE HIERRO FUNDIDO **7154**

DIENTE *m* DE RUEDA DENTADA (DE ENGRANAJE) **13819**
DIENTE *m* DE SIERRA **10959**
DIENTE *m* DOBLE ANGULAR **4144**
DIENTE *m* EN BRUTO DE FUNDICIÓN **2059**
DIENTE *m* TALLADO **3514**
DIENTE ANGULAR *m* **4144**
DIENTES *m pl* DE UNA LIMA **3518**
DIESEL **3901**
DIFENILAMINA *f* **3974**
DIFERENCIA *f* **3902**
DIFERENCIA *f* DE POTENCIAL **9709**
DIFERENCIA *f* DE PRESIÓN **9814**
DIFERENCIA *f* DE TEMPERATURA **3904**
DIFERENCIACIÓN *f* **3923**
DIFERENCIAL *m* **3913**
DIFERENCIAL *m* **3906**
DIFERENCIAR **3922**
DIFRACCIÓN *f* **3924**
DIFRACCIÓN *f* **10387**
DIFUSIBILIDAD *f* **3936**
DIFUSIÓN *f* **3929**
DIFUSIÓN *f* **10994**
DIFUSIÓN *f* DE LA LUZ **3933**
DIFUSIÓN *f* DE LOS GASES **3932**
DIFUSOR *m* **3928**
DIFUSOR *m* **12966**
DIFUSOR *m* O BOQUILLA *f* (O TOBERA *f*) **2359**
DIGERIR **3937**
DIGESTIÓN *f* **3939**
DIGESTOR *m* **829**
DIGITO *m* BINARIO **1249**
DILATABILIDAD *f* **3947**
DILATABLE **3948**
DILATACIÓN *f* **3949**
DILATACIÓN *f* **13370**
DILATACIÓN *f* CÚBICA **13603**
DILATACIÓN *f* DE UN METAL **4919**
DILATACIÓN *f* LINEAL **7612**
DILATACIÓN *f* POR CALOR **4948**
DILATACIÓN *f* SUPERFICIAL **12466**
DILATACIÓN *f* TÉRMICA **12808**
DILATACIÓN LATERAL **7421**
DILATARSE **4902**
DILATARSE **1125**
DILATÓMETRO *m* **3950**
DILUCIÓN *f* DE UNA SOLUCIÓN **3954**
DILUIR **3952**
DILUIR **12718**
DILUIR UNA SOLUCIÓN **3952**
DILUYENTE **3951**

DIMENSIÓN *f* (DE UNA) **8727**
DIMENSIÓN *f* INFERIOR A LAS PRESCRIPCIONES **13349**
DIMENSIÓN *f* NOMINAL **8612**
DIMENSIÓN *f* NORMAL (TIPO) **12071**
DIMENSIÓN *f* REAL **152**
DIMENSIÓN *f* (TAMAÑO *m*) NOMINAL **8615**
DIMENSIONADO **11417**
DIMENSIONADO *m* **11524**
DIMENSIONES *f pl* **3960**
DIMENSIONES *f pl* (DE DOS) **8729**
DIMENSIONES *f pl* (EN TRES) **8728**
DIMENSIONES *f pl* NOMINALES **11857**
DIMENSIONES *f pl* PRINCIPALES **7481**
DIMENSIONES *f pl* TOTALES **8922**
DIMETIL *m* **4848**
DIMETILCETONA *f* **90**
DINA *f* **4405**
DINÁMICA *f* **4400**
DINÁMICO **4399**
DINAMITA *f* **4401**
DINAMO *f* **5924**
DINAMO *f* **407**
DINAMO *f* **4402**
DINAMO *f* **3021**
DINAMO *f* COMPOUND **3228**
DINAMO *f* EN DERIVACIÓN **11404**
DINAMO *f* EN SERIE **11201**
DINAMO *f* PRINCIPAL **9867**
DINAMO-SHUNT **11404**
DINAMÓGRAFO *m* **10291**
DINAMOMÉTRICO **4404**
DINAMÓMETRO *m* **4403**
DINAMÓMETRO *m* **7846**
DINAMÓMETRO *m* **7846**
DINAMÓMETRO *m* DE ABSORCIÓN **55**
DINAMÓMETRO *m* DE ABSORCIÓN **48**
DINAMÓMETRO *m* DE FRENO **55**
DINAMÓMETRO *m* DE TRANSMISIÓN **13127**
DINAMÓMETRO *m* DIFERENCIAL **3911**
DINODO *m* **4406**
DIODO *m* **3964**
DIORITA *f* **3966**
DIÓXIDO *m* DE PLOMO **7461**
DIPOLO **4172**
DIQUE *m* **13753**
DIRECCIÓN *f* DE LAS FÁBRICAS **13963**
DIRECCIÓN *f* DE LAS FIBRAS **3993**
DIRECCIÓN *f* DE LAS FIBRAS **5133**
DIRECCIÓN *f* DE MOVIMIENTO **3991**
DIRECCIÓN *f* DE UNA FUERZA **3990**

**DIR** 1018

DIRECCIÓN/ORGANIZACIÓN *f* CIENTÍFICA DE LOS TALLERES 11001
DIRECTOR *m* 3995
DIRECTOR *m* DE FÁBRICA 5915
DIRECTOR DE LA OBRA *m* 11520
DIRECTRIZ *f* 3996
DISCO *m* 3837
DISCO *m* 4015
DISCO *m* CON LEVAS 13221
DISCO *m* DE CIERRE 11796
DISCO *m* DE CORTAR 3542
DISCO *m* DE CORTAR 3542
DISCO *m* DE EXCÉNTRICA 4434
DISCO *m* DE FRICCIÓN 5673
DISCO *m* DE ORILLO DE TEJIDO 4116
DISCO *m* DE ROTURA 10860
DISCO *m* DE RUEDA 4013
DISCO *m* DE SEGURIDAD CONTRA ROTURA 10887
DISCO *m* DE TRAPO (PARA PULIR) 10173
DISCO *m* (DE VÁLVULA) 4014
DISCO *m* PLENO DE UN VOLANTE 4013
DISCO *m* PULIDOR 1693
DISCO *m* PULIDOR DE CUERO 1684
DISCOS *m pl* ABRASIVOS 26
DISCRIMINANTE 4029
DISEÑAR 3795
DISEÑAR 1857
DISEÑO *m* 3794
DISEÑO *m* 3794
DISEÑO *m* DE UNA PIEZA MECÁNICA 11363
DISEÑO NORMALIZADO O STANDARD *m* 12073
DISIMETRÍA *f* 779
DISIMÉTRICO 778
DISLOCACIÓN *f* 4047
DISLOCACIÓN *f* EN ESQUINA 4443
DISLOCACIÓN *f* EN TORNILLO (EN HÉLICE) 11031
DISMINUCIÓN *f* 3677
DISMINUCIÓN *f* DE LA SECCIÓN TRANSVERSAL 10362
DISOCIACIÓN *f* 4058
DISOCIACIÓN *f* ELECTROLÍTICA 4595
DISOLUCIÓN *f* 4059
DISOLUCIÓN *f* 4060
DISOLUCIÓN *f* ELECTROLÍTICA 4581
DISOLVENTE *m* 2473
DISOLVENTE *m* 11814
DISOLVENTE 11814
DISOLVENTE *m* DE DECAPADO 12381
DISOLVENTE *m* IONÓGENO 7130
DISOLVENTE *m* PARA CORROSIVOS 3192
DISOLVER 4061

DISOLVER 11813
DISOLVERSE 4061
DISPARADA *f* DE UN MOTOR 10118
DISPARARSE 10117
DISPARARSE 10117
DISPERSIÓN *f* 4051
DISPERSIÓN ELECTROMAGNÉTICA 4616
DISPOSICIÓN *f* 4056
DISPOSICIÓN *f* GENERAL 5914
DISPOSITIVO *m* 3820
DISPOSITIVO *m* ACCESORIO 5766
DISPOSITIVO *m* BIELA/MANIVELA 1094
DISPOSITIVO *m* DE AJUSTE (DE GRADUACIÓN) 10418
DISPOSITIVO *m* DE ALUMBRADO 6774
DISPOSITIVO *m* DE ARRASTRE 4301
DISPOSITIVO *m* DE BLOQUEO 7705
DISPOSITIVO *m* DE CAMBIO DE MARCHA POR ENGRANAJES CILÍNDRICOS 10547
DISPOSITIVO *m* DE CAMBIO DE SENTIDO DE MARCHA DPOR TRANSMISIÓN 10542
DISPOSITIVO *m* DE CAMBIO DE SENTIDO DE MARCHA POR RUEDA DE FRICCIÓN 10546
DISPOSITIVO *m* DE CAMBIO (INVERSIÓN) DE SENTIDO DE MARCHA POR ENGRANAJES *m pl* CÓNICOS 10545
DISPOSITIVO *m* DE CONTROL 3052
DISPOSITIVO *m* DE CONTROL DE PRESIÓN 9829
DISPOSITIVO *m* DE CORTE 3525
DISPOSITIVO *m* DE ESTRANGULAMIENTO 12342
DISPOSITIVO *m* DE FIJACIÓN 7227
DISPOSITIVO *m* DE PRETENSADO 9781
DISPOSITIVO *m* DE PROTECCIÓN 11342
DISPOSITIVO *m* DE RETENIDA 12278
DISPOSITIVO *m* DE SEGURIDAD 10881
DISPOSITIVO *m* DE SEGURIDAD 10881
DISPOSITIVO *m* DE SUJECIÓN (DE APRETADURA) 7227
DISPOSITIVO *m* (O PERNO) DE ARRASTRE 4301
DISPOSITIVO *m* PARA MARCA LAS ORILLAS 4444
DISPOSITIVO *m* POLEA Y CORREA 1144
DISPOSITIVO *m* PROTECTOR 10881
DISPOSITIVO *m* QUE SE HA DE RETIRAR 4239
DISPOSITIVO DE ALARMA *m* 305
DISPOSITIVO DE CAMBIO DE SENTIDO DE MARCHA POR CORREA 1154
DISPOSITIVO DE ILUMINACIÓN *m* 6772
DISPOSITIVO DE PUESTA EN MARCHA *m* 12119
DISPROSIO *m* 4407
DISTANCIA *f* 4063
DISTANCIA *f* 4063
DISTANCIA *f* 4063
DISTANCIA *f* DEL CENTRO DEL REMACHE AL BORDE DE LA CHAPA 4066
DISTANCIA *f* ENTRE CENTROS 4065

## 1019 DOB

DISTANCIA *f* ENTRE CENTROS **2165**
DISTANCIA *f* ENTRE EJES **4065**
DISTANCIA *f* ENTRE EJES **4065**
DISTANCIA *f* ENTRE LOS BRAZOS **6596**
DISTANCIA *f* ENTRE LOS COJINETES **4064**
DISTANCIA *f* ENTRE LOS PLATOS (ENTRE LAS PLACAS) **13169**
DISTANCIA *f* ENTRE PUNTAS **4065**
DISTANCIA *f* FOCAL **5503**
DISTANCIA *f* FOCAL **5500**
DISTANCIA *f* POLAR **9579**
DISTANCIA *f* RETICULAR **7087**
DISTANCIA INTERFACES **7032**
DISTANCIADOR *m* **4068**
DISTANCIADOR *m* **4067**
DISTORSIÓN *f* **4077**
DISTORSIÓN *f* **4077**
DISTRIBUCIÓN *f* **13471**
DISTRIBUCIÓN *f* A DISTANCIA DE LA ENERGÍA **13135**
DISTRIBUCIÓN *f* DE AGUA **13678**
DISTRIBUCIÓN *f* DE AGUA **13666**
DISTRIBUCIÓN *f* DE AIRE **281**
DISTRIBUCIÓN *f* DE AIRE COMPRIMIDO **2845**
DISTRIBUCIÓN *f* DE FUERZA MOTRIZ **9744**
DISTRIBUCIÓN *f* DE GAS **5834**
DISTRIBUCIÓN *f* DE LA TEMPERATURA **4083**
DISTRIBUCIÓN *f* DE LOS REMACHES **717**
DISTRIBUCIÓN *f* DEL TRABAJO **13939**
DISTRIBUCIÓN *f* GAUSSIANA **5887**
DISTRIBUCIÓN *f* POR CORREDERA **7626**
DISTRIBUCIÓN *f* POR VÁLVULA DE CORREDERA **11594**
DISTRIBUCIÓN *f* POR VÁLVULAS **13460**
DISTRIBUCIÓN PÚBLICA DE ENERGÍA ELÉCTRICA **12487**
DISTRIBUDORES *m pl* DE FERTILIZANTES **4087**
DISTRIBUIDOR *m* **4084**
DISTRIBUIDOR *m* **4086**
DISTRIBUIDOR *m* **4086**
DISTRIBUIDOR *m* **5353**
DISTRIBUIDOR *m* **11592**
DISTRIBUIDOR *m* **11592**
DISTRIBUIDOR *m* **13453**
DISTRIBUIDOR *m* CILÍNDRICO **9390**
DISTRIBUIDOR *m* CONCOIDEO **3592**
DISTRIBUIDOR *m* DE ÉMBOLO **9390**
DISTRIBUIDOR *m* DE ENCENDIDO (DE IGNICIÓN) **6762**
DISTRIBUIDOR *m* EQUILIBRADO **9390**
DISTRIBUIDOR *m* PLANO **9426**
DISTRIBUIDOR DE VAPOR *m* **13460**
DISTRIBUIDOR DEL ENCENDIDO *m* **6758**
DISTRIBUIDOR DEL ENCENDIDO *m* **6762**

DISTRIBUIDORES *m pl* DE CAL **4089**
DISTRIBUIDORES *m pl* ELÉCTRICOS **12558**
DISTURBIO *m* **2541**
DISULFURO *m* DE ARSÉNICO **10262**
DISULFURO *m* DE ESTAÑO **12099**
DISYUNTOR *m* **7949**
DISYUNTOR *m* **2407**
DISYUNTOR *m* **3516**
DIVERGENCIA *f* **4092**
DIVERGENCIA *f* **5806**
DIVERGENTE **4093**
DIVERGIR **4091**
DIVIDENDO *m* **4099**
DIVIDIR EN DOS **1266**
DIVISIÓN *f* **4107**
DIVISIÓN *f* **10981**
DIVISIÓN *f* DE UNA LÍNEA EN MEDIA Y EXTREMA RAZÓN **8123**
DIVISIÓN *f* DEL CÍRCULO **4108**
DIVISIÓN *f* DEL TRABAJO **12410**
DIVISOR *m* **4111**
DIVISOR *m* **4100**
DIVISOR *m* **4097**
DIVISOR *m* DE PRECISIÓN **9769**
DOBLADO *m* **1182**
DOBLADO *m* EN CALIENTE **6619**
DOBLADO *m* EN FRÍO **2668**
DOBLAMIENTO *m* **3700**
DOBLAMIENTO *m* **1088**
DOBLAMIENTO *m* **10892**
DOBLAMIENTO *m* DE LA BRIDA DE LAS TUBOS **1088**
DOBLAMIENTO *m* DE LOS BORDES DE LAS CHAPAS **1088**
DOBLAR **1173**
DOBLAR LA BRIDA DE LOS TUBOS **1084**
DOBLAR LOS BORDES **1084**
DOBLAR LOS BORDES **1084**
DOBLAR LOS BORDES DE LAS CHAPAS **1084**
DOBLE DECÍMETRO *m* **4135**
DOBLE DESCOMPOSICIÓN *f* **4136**
DOBLE EFECTO *m* (DE) **4163**
DOBLE FONDO *m* **5026**
DOBLE MONTANTE *m* **4159**
DOBLE PARED *f* (DE) **4170**
DOBLE PEZÓN *m* **4149**
DOBLE REFRACCIÓN *f* **4151**
DOBLE TREN *m* DE ENGRANAJES **4142**
DOBLE TREN *m* DE ENGRANAJES **4142**
DOBLEGARSE **1174**
DOBLEGARSE **10893**
DOBLEZ *f* **1088**

**DOB** 1020

DOBLEZ *m* **4408**
DOBLEZ *f* PROYECCIÓN *f* **1088**
DOCUMENTACIÓN *f* TÉCNICA **3614**
DOLERITA *f* **4114**
DOLOMÍA *f* **4117**
DOLOMITA *f* **4117**
DORADO *m* **6002**
DORADO *m* **5942**
DORADO *m* EN CALIENTE **5243**
DORADURA *f* **6002**
DORADURA *f* **5942**
DORAR **5941**
DORSO *m* **890**
DORSO *m* DE LA CARA DE BRIDA **5326**
DOSIFICACIÓN *f* **3011**
DOSIFICACIÓN *f* **1325**
DOSIFICACIÓN *f* **10064**
DOSIFICACIÓN *f* DE LA MEZCLA **9934**
DOSIFICAR **1323**
DOVELA *f* **687**
DOVELA *f* **687**
DOVELAJE *m* **3396**
DRENAJE *m* **4210**
DRENAJE *m* **4210**
DUCHO EN SU TRABAJO **3289**
DÚCTIL **4361**
DÚCTIL **1250**
DUCTILIDAD *f* **4363**
DUCTILIDAD *f* LONGITUDINAL **7735**
DUELA *f* **12149**
DULCIFICAR **12717**
DURABILIDAD *f* **4385**
DURABLE **4386**
DURACIÓN *f* **7541**
DURACIÓN *f* DE LA PATENTE **12761**
DURACIÓN *f* DE UNA OSCILACIÓN **12945**
DURACIÓN *f* DEL CICLO DE SOLDADURA **13788**
DURALUMINIO *m* **4387**
DUREZA *f* **6297**
DUREZA *f* A LA PIRÁMIDE **10039**
DUREZA *f* AL ESCLERÓSCOPO **11003**
DUREZA *f* BRINELL **1619**
DUREZA *f* DE ABRASIÓN (DE AMOLADO) **14**
DUREZA *f* DEL AGUA **6298**
DUREZA *m* DEL AGUA **6298**
DUREZA *f* EN CALIENTE **6629**
DUREZA *f* EN CALIENTE **10328**
DUREZA *f* PERMANENTE DEL AGUA **9203**
DUREZA *f* TEMPORAL (O TRANSITORIA) DEL AGUA **12735**

DUREZA *f* VICKERS **13566**
DUREZA *f* VICKERS **6860**
DUREZA SHORE **11003**
DURÓMETRO A BOLA *m* **967**
EBANO *m* **4423**
EBONITA *f* **2363**
EBULLICIÓN *f* **4461**
EBULLICIÓN *f* **1429**
EBULLICIÓN *f* (CON UN PUNTO ALTO DE) **1425**
EBULLICIÓN *f* (CON UN PUNTO BAJO DE) **1426**
EBULLICIÓN *f* PREVIA **9776**
ECHAR EN LEJÍA **7676**
ECLISAS *f pl* **5270**
ECONOMÍA *f* DE MANO DE OBRA **10947**
ECONOMÍA *f* DE TIEMPO **10949**
ECONOMÍA *f* EN EQUILIBRÍO **932**
ECONOMÍA *f* (O AHORRO *m*) DE COMBUSTIBLE **5707**
ECONOMÍA *f* (O AHORRO *m*) DE FUERZA MOTRIZ **10948**
ECONOMÍA *f* (O AHORRO *m*) DE TRABAJO **10947**
ECONOMÍA *f* SANA **932**
ECONOMIZADOR *m* (DE CARBURANTE) **4437**
ECUACIÓN *f* **4782**
ECUACIÓN *f* ALGEBRAICA **322**
ECUACIÓN *f* BICUADRADA **1262**
ECUACIÓN *f* BINOMIA **1259**
ECUACIÓN *f* CÚBICA **3452**
ECUACIÓN *f* DE CUARTO GRADO **1262**
ECUACIÓN *f* DE CUARTO GRADO **1262**
ECUACIÓN *f* DE CUARTO GRADO **1262**
ECUACIÓN *f* DE ESTADO **4783**
ECUACIÓN *f* DE PRIMER GRADO **7616**
ECUACIÓN *f* DE PRIMER GRADO **7616**
ECUACIÓN *f* DE QUINTO GRADO **10112**
ECUACIÓN *f* DE QUINTO GRADO **10112**
ECUACIÓN *f* DE SEGUNDO GRADO **10057**
ECUACIÓN *f* DE SEGUNDO GRADO **10057**
ECUACIÓN *f* DE TERCER GRADO **3452**
ECUACIÓN *f* DIFERENCIAL **3912**
ECUACIÓN *f* DIFERENCIAL PARCIAL **9086**
ECUACIÓN *f* HOMOGÉNEA **6557**
ECUACIÓN *f* LINEAL **7616**
ECUACIÓN *f* TRANSCENDENTE **13107**
ECUACIÓN *f* TRINOMIA **13213**
ECUACIÓN DE TERCER GRADO **3452**
EDIFICAR **4805**
EDIFICIO *m* ANEXO **585**
EDIFICIO *m* AUXILIAR **585**
EDIFICIO *m* INDUSTRIAL **5012**
EDIFICIO ANEJO (ANEXOAUXILIAR) *m* **585**

1021           **ELE**

EDISA  *f* **1783**
EFECTO  *m* **9730**
EFECTO  *m* BAUSCHINGER **1070**
EFECTO  *m* DE ÁNODO **596**
EFECTO  *m* DE ENGATILLAMIENTO **10220**
EFECTO  *m* DE LIMPIEZA **10017**
EFECTO  *m* DE LÍNEA DE TRANSMISIÓN **7729**
EFECTO  *m* DE MASA **8027**
EFECTO  *m* DE MONDA DE NARANJA **8851**
EFECTO  *m* DE VÁLVULA **13458**
EFECTO  *m* LEONARD **7523**
EFECTO  *m* POSTERIOR ELÁSTICO **4474**
EFECTO  *m* TERMOELÉCTRICO **12830**
EFECTO  *m* ÚTIL **4463**
EFERVESCENCIA  *f* **4461**
EFERVESCENCIA  *f* **4461**
EFERVESCENCIA  *f* **4461**
EFICACIA  *f* ENERGÉTICA **4746**
EFLORESCENCIA  *f* **4464**
EFUSIÓN  *f* **4465**
EFUSIÓN  *f* DE GASES **4466**
EJE **662**
EJE  *m* **884**
EJE  *m* **11904**
EJE  *m* **11239**
EJE  *m* DE ABSCISAS **872**
EJE  *m* DE COLIMACIÓN **7601**
EJE  *m* DE COORDENADAS CARTESIANAS **864**
EJE  *m* DE FIBRA **5132**
EJE  *m* DE LAS X **872**
EJE  *m* DE LAS Y **873**
EJE  *m* DE ORDENADAS **873**
EJE  *m* DE OSCILACIÓN **7311**
EJE  *m* DE OSCILACIÓN (O DE VIBRACIÓN) **867**
EJE  *m* DE PISTÓN **6158**
EJE  *m* DE ROTACIÓN **868**
EJE  *m* DE SIMETRÍA **869**
EJE  *m* DE SIMETRÍA **11024**
EJE  *m* DE SIMETRÍA DE LOS CRISTALES **863**
EJE  *m* DE SOLDADURA **870**
EJE  *m* DE UN CRISTAL **865**
EJE  *m* DE UN TUBO **866**
EJE  *m* DEL CORDEL (O DEL CORDÓN) DE SOLDADURA
  **871**
EJE  *m* DEL REGULADOR **6018**
EJE  *m* DELANTERO **5691**
EJE  *m* FIJO **3624**
EJE  *m* FLOTANTE **5435**
EJE  *m* FOCAL **13143**
EJE  *m* GEOMÉTRICO **874**

EJE  *m* MAYOR DE UNA ELIPSE **7947**
EJE  *m* MOTOR **4290**
EJE  *m* NO TRANSVERSO DE UNA HIPÉRBOLA **2953**
EJE  *m* O ÁRBOL  *m* **875**
EJE  *m* ÓPTICO **8841**
EJE  *m* PEQUEÑO DE UNA ELIPSE **8313**
EJE  *m* PORTANTE **2010**
EJE  *m* PRINCIPAL **9866**
EJE  *m* TRANSVERSAL **13142**
EJE  *m* TRANSVERSO DE UNA HIPÉRBOLA **13143**
EJE  *m* TRASERO (NO MOTOR) **10265**
EJE CUADRADO (PARA LLAVE)  *m* **9533**
EJE DE TRANSMISIÓN  *m* **7049**
EJE DEL MOTOR  *m* **4315**
EJE GUIADO  *m* **4299**
EJE HUECO  *m* **6547**
EJE LONGITUDINAL  *m* **7733**
EJE MOTRIZ  *m* **4296**
EJECUCIÓN  *f* DE UNA GARGANTA **8515**
EJECUTAR UNA CABEZA DE REMACHE **2516**
EJERCER UN ESFUERZO EN UN CUERPO **12323**
EJES  *m pl* CRISTALINOS ORTOHEXAGONALES **8871**
EJES  *m pl* QUE SE CORTAN A ÁNGULO RECTO **858**
ELABORACIÓN  *f* DEL ACERO **12214**
ELASTICIDAD  *f* **4487**
ELASTICIDAD  *f* DE COMPRESIÓN **4488**
ELASTICIDAD  *f* DE CORTE **13144**
ELASTICIDAD  *f* DE FLEXIÓN **4489**
ELASTICIDAD  *f* DE TORSIÓN **4490**
ELASTICIDAD  *f* DE TRACCIÓN **4491**
ELASTICIDAD  *f* RESIDUAL **10472**
ELASTICIDAD  *f* TRANSVERSAL **13144**
ELASTICIDAD TRANSVERSAL **13144**
ELÁSTICO **4473**
ELECTRICIDAD  *f* **4552**
ELECTRICIDAD  *f* ATMOSFÉRICA **796**
ELECTRICIDAD  *f* INDUSTRIAL **4541**
ELECTRICIDAD  *f* NEGATIVA **8526**
ELECTRICIDAD  *f* POSITIVA **9655**
ELECTRICISTA  *m* **4551**
ELECTRIFICACIÓN  *f* **4554**
ELECTRIFICAR **4555**
ELECTRIZARSE **1124**
ELECTRO  *m* **4653**
ELECTRO  *m* **4653**
ELECTROANÁLISIS  *f* **4657**
ELECTROANÁLISIS  *f* **4570**
ELECTROCORINDÓN  *m* **5753**
ELECTRODINÁMICO **4563**
ELECTRODINAMÓMETRO  *m* **4564**

**ELE** 1022

ELECTRODO *m* **4574**
ELECTRODO *m* **13789**
ELECTRODO *m* BIPOLAR **1233**
ELECTRODO *m* BLINDADO **11299**
ELECTRODO *m* COMPUESTO **2819**
ELECTRODO *m* CONSUMIBLE **2990**
ELECTRODO *m* DE CALOMEL **1876**
ELECTRODO *m* DE CARBONO **1950**
ELECTRODO *m* DE CONTACTO **3001**
ELECTRODO *m* DE VIDRIO **5959**
ELECTRODO *m* NEGATIVO **2106**
ELECTRODO *m* NO CONSUMIBLE **8618**
ELECTRODO *m* NO PROTEGIDO **989**
ELECTRODO *m* POSITIVO **602**
ELECTRODO *m* REVESTIDO **3271**
ELECTRODO *m* REVESTIDO **2584**
ELECTRODO *m* REVESTIDO **5492**
ELECTRODO *m* REVESTIDO **11344**
ELECTRODO METÁLICO **8180**
ELECTRODO POSITIVO *m* **602**
ELECTROEROSIÓN *f* **4531**
ELECTROEROSIÓN *f* **4565**
ELECTROFÓRESIS *f* **4639**
ELECTROIMÁN *m* **4611**
ELECTROIMÁN *m* **4567**
ELECTROIMÁN *m* DE ELEVACIÓN **7554**
ELECTRÓLISIS *f* **4586**
ELECTRÓLITO *m* **4587**
ELECTRÓLITO *m* IMPURO **5588**
ELECTROLIZAR **4585**
ELECTROMAGNÉTICO **4612**
ELECTROMAGNETISMO *m* **4620**
ELECTROMETALURGIA *f* **4621**
ELECTROMOTOR *m* **4623**
ELECTRÓN *m* **4624**
ELECTRÓN POSITIVO **9662**
ELECTRONEGATIVO **4631**
ELECTRÓNICA *f* **4637**
ELECTROÓSMOSIS *f* **4638**
ELECTROPOSITIVO **4641**
ELECTROQUÍMICA *f* **4640**
ELECTROQUÍMICA *f* **4573**
ELECTROQUÍMICA *f* **4561**
ELECTROQUÍMICO **4560**
ELECTROSTÁTICO **4568**
ELECTROTÉCNICA *f* **4648**
ELECTROTÉCNICO **4647**
ELECTROTÉRMICA *f* **4650**
ELECTROTIPIA *f* **4569**
ELEMENTO *m* **4654**

ELEMENTO *m* **8145**
ELEMENTO *m* **7852**
ELEMENTO *m* ACIDIFICADOR **115**
ELEMENTO *m* ASIMÉTRICO **777**
ELEMENTO *m* BÁSICO **1038**
ELEMENTO *m* CORTANTE (DE UNA MÁQUINA HERRAMIENTA) **13011**
ELEMENTO *m* DE UN RECIPIENTE A PRESIÓN **11117**
ELEMENTO *m* ESTRUCTURAL **12391**
ELEMENTO *m* INCORPORADO DE ARMAZÓN **1704**
ELEMENTO *m* O PARTE *f* EN FORMA DE CONO TRUNCADO **13121**
ELEMENTO *m* PROEUTÉCTICO **9848**
ELEMENTOS *m pl* DE ALEACIÓN **395**
ELEMENTOS *m pl* DE CUBREJUNTAS **11932**
ELEMENTOS *m pl* DE REDUCCIÓN EN FORMA DE CONO TRUNCADO **2950**
ELEMÍ *m* **4656**
ELEVACIÓN *f* **4659**
ELEVACIÓN *f* **6553**
ELEVACIÓN *f* EN TEMPERATURA **10231**
ELEVACIÓN *f* (O ASCENSIÓN *f*) CAPILAR **1925**
ELEVADOR *m* DE CANGILONES **1676**
ELEVADOR *m* TUBULAR A PRESIÓN DE JUGOS (REFINERÍA AZUCARERA) **8389**
ELEVADORES *m pl* DE HENO Y DE PAJA **4661**
ELEVADORES-TRANSPORTADORES *m pl* DE GRANO **6034**
ELEVAR **6517**
ELEVAR A UNA POTENCIA **10180**
ELEVAR (O LEVANTAR) UN PESO **7542**
ELIMINACIÓN *f* **4667**
ELIMINACIÓN *f* **4667**
ELIMINACIÓN *f* **4664**
ELIMINACIÓN *f* DE DEFECTOS SUPERFICIALES **3793**
ELIMINACIÓN *f* DE LA CAPA SUPERFICIAL **2912**
ELIMINACIÓN *f* DE LA HERRUMBRE **10826**
ELIMINACIÓN *f* DE LAS CAPAS SUPERFICIALES **3807**
ELIMINACIÓN *f* DE LAS REBABAS **5129**
ELIMINACIÓN *f* DE LAS REBABAS **13210**
ELIMINACIÓN *f* DE LOS DEFECTOS SUPERFICIALES CON SOPLETE **8976**
ELIMINACIÓN *f* DEL HIERRO DEL AGUA **10454**
ELIMINACIÓN *f* DEL VAHO (DEL VAPOR) **3704**
ELIMINACIÓN *f* DEL VAPOR **13485**
ELIMINACIÓN *f* POR AFILADURA **13**
ELIMINACIÓN DE LA REBABA *f* **13209**
ELIMINADOR *m* DE IMPUREZAS **10995**
ELIMINAR **4662**
ELIMINAR **4663**
ELIMINAR CALOR **4663**
ELIMINAR LA HERRUMBRE **10815**

## 1023 EMP

ELIMINAR (O DESGASTAR AFILANDO) **10**
ELIMINAR (O QUITAR) LAS REBABAS **13206**
ELIPSE *f* **4669**
ELIPSE *f* DE CASSINI **2029**
ELIPSÓGRAFO *m* **4670**
ELIPSOIDE *f* **4671**
ELIPSOIDE *f* DE REVOLUCIÓN **4672**
ELIPSOIDE *f* DE REVOLUCIÓN **4672**
ELUTRIACIÓN *f* **4681**
EMANACIÓN *f* **10159**
EMBALAJE *m* **8999**
EMBALAJE *m* **8995**
EMBALAJE *m* **5018**
EMBALAJE *m* PELICULAR **11540**
EMBALAR **8991**
EMBALARSE **10117**
EMBALARSE **10117**
EMBALSE *m* ARTIFICIAL **3597**
EMBARCACIÓN *f* **991**
EMBEBER **6802**
EMBELLECEDOR *m* DE RUEDA **6662**
EMBELLECEDORES *m pl* **10531**
EMBOCADURA *f* **12966**
EMBOCADURA *f* DE UN CEPILLO **8434**
ÉMBOLO *m* DE BOMBA **9995**
EMBOTAMIENTO *m* **5972**
EMBRAGADO **8171**
EMBRAGAR **10033**
EMBRAGAR **4749**
EMBRAGUE *m* **3254**
EMBRAGUE *m* **2544**
EMBRAGUE *m* **10221**
EMBRAGUE *m* **12897**
EMBRAGUE *m* DE DISCOS **4046**
EMBRAGUE *m* DE FRICCIÓN **11614**
EMBRAGUE *m* DENTADO **4113**
EMBRAGUE (ACOPLAMIENTO) DE DIENTES *m* **2461**
EMBRAGUE DE DISCOS *m* **9486**
EMBRAGUE DE FRICCIÓN **5672**
EMBRAGUE DE PLATOS **9486**
EMBRIDAMIENTO *m* **5345**
EMBRIÓN *m* **4686**
EMBUDO *m* **5738**
EMBUDO *m* **12003**
EMBUDO *m* DE COLADA **12003**
EMBUDO *m* DE COLADA **9716**
EMBUDO *m* DE COLADA **4186**
EMBUTIDO *m* **4040**
EMBUTIDO *m* **8189**
EMBUTIDO *m* EN CORTE DE ALAMBRES **3469**

EMBUTIDO *m* PROFUNDO **3469**
EMBUTIDO *m* PROFUNDO **3683**
EMBUTIR **8042**
EMIGRACIÓN *f* **8268**
EMISIÓN *f* **4700**
EMITIR RAYOS **4703**
EMPALMAR **2955**
EMPALMAR TUBOS **5277**
EMPALMAR TUBOS **7244**
EMPALME **13368**
EMPALME *m* **1554**
EMPALME **2965**
EMPALME **3254**
EMPALME *m* **3254**
EMPALME **5280**
EMPALME *m* **5863**
EMPALME *m* **5416**
EMPALME *m* DE AJUSTE CON SOLDADURA **11708**
EMPALME *m* DE LAS CORREAS **1151**
EMPALME *m* DE LAS CORREAS **1142**
EMPALME *f* DE TUBOS **9347**
EMPALME *m* DE TUBOS **7248**
EMPALME *m* DE VÍA INDUSTRIAL **13966**
EMPALME *m* FUSIBLE **2991**
EMPALME *m* (O UNIÓN *f*) POR (O CON) CUBREJUNTAS **1782**
EMPALME *m* POR PEGADURA DE LAS CORREAS **2143**
EMPALMES *m pl* DE CORREA **1142**
EMPALMES *m pl* SUBTERRÁNEOS **1744**
EMPAÑAMIENTO *m* **4369**
EMPAÑARSE **12685**
EMPAPAR **6802**
EMPAQUE *m* **5018**
EMPAQUETADO *m* **5018**
EMPAQUETADO *m* **1772**
EMPAQUETADURA *f* **7247**
EMPAQUETADURA *f* **9009**
EMPAQUETADURA *f* **9004**
EMPAQUETADURA *f* **9001**
EMPAQUETADURA *f* **12405**
EMPAQUETADURA *f* DEL VÁSTAGO DEL ÉMBOLO **9386**
EMPAQUETAMIENTO *m* **1772**
EMPARRILLADO DE CADENA **2209**
EMPECINADO *m* **12591**
EMPERNAR **1435**
EMPLASTE **2146**
EMPLASTECER **2134**
EMPLEAR **4750**
EMPLEO *m* **13982**
EMPLOMADO **7479**

**EMP** 1024

EMPOBRECIMIENTO  *m*  **6801**
EMPOTRADO  *m*  **3246**
EMPOTRADO EN OBRA DE FÁBRICA **1600**
EMPOTRADO POR AMBOS EXTREMOS **5284**
EMPOTRADO POR UN EXTREMO **5285**
EMPOTRAMIENTO  *m*  **5300**
EMPOTRAMIENTO  *m*  **4310**
EMPOTRAR CON CEMENTO **6153**
EMPOTRAR EN EL HORMIGÓN **4682**
EMPUJADOR  *m*  DE LEVA **12672**
EMPUJE  *m*  LONGITUDINAL **4734**
EMPUJE  *m*  AXIAL **4734**
EMPUJE  *m*  DE ABAJO ARRIBA **1742**
EMPUJE  *m*  DE LAS TIERRAS **12907**
EMPUJE  *m*  DEL VIENTO **13858**
EMPUJE  *m*  EN EL VÉRTICE **12908**
EMPUJE  *m*  HORIZONTAL **6590**
EMPUJES  *m pl*  **11626**
EMPUÑADURA  *f*  **6262**
EMPUÑADURA  *f*  DE MANIVELA **3300**
EMULSIÓN  *f*  **4708**
EMULSIONAR **4707**
EN BOBINA **10667**
EN EL SENTIDO DE LAS AGUJAS DE UN RELOJ **2506**
EN FALSO **8934**
EN FALSO **8936**
EN FORMA DE VAPOR **6817**
EN SERIE **11196**
ENANTIOTRÓPICO **4713**
ENCAJAR **5277**
ENCAJE  *m*  **5281**
ENCAJE  *m*  **5281**
ENCAJE  *m*  **10847**
ENCAJE  *m*  LENGÜETA-RANURA **12990**
ENCAJE  *m*  MACHO-HEMBRA **7957**
ENCARGADO DE ALMACÉN  *m*  **12298**
ENCASTE  *m*  **5281**
ENCASTE  *m*  **5281**
ENCENDEDOR DE CIGARROS  *m*  **2396**
ENCENDER **6757**
ENCENDER EL HOGAR DE UNA CALDERA **5236**
ENCENDERSE **6757**
ENCENDIDO  *m*  **6760**
ENCENDIDO AUTOMÁTICO  *m*  **844**
ENCENDIDO DE LLAMA  *m*  **5316**
ENCENDIDO DEL HOGAR DE UNA CALDERA  *m*  **5263**
ENCENDIDO ELÉCTRICO  *m*  **4514**
ENCENDIDO ELECTRÓNICO  *m*  **4633**
ENCENDIDO (EN LOS MOTORES DE EXPLOSIÓN)  *m*  **6770**
ENCENDIDO POR INCANDESCENCIA  *m*  **13251**

ENCENDIDO PREMATURO  *m*  **9778**
ENCENEGAMIENTO  *m*  DE UN CONDUCTO **11457**
ENCHAVETAR **7277**
ENCHAVETAR **7279**
ENCHUFAR TUBOS **5277**
ENCHUFE  *m*  **9529**
ENCHUFE  *m*  **9529**
ENCHUFE  *m*  DE CORRIENTE **9529**
ENCHUFE  *m*  DE TUBOS **5281**
ENCLAVAMIENTO  *m*  **4751**
ENCLAVAMIENTO **4751**
ENCLAVAR **4749**
ENCLAVIJAR **7279**
ENCLAVIJAR **7277**
ENCOBRADO  *m*  **3125**
ENCOBRAR **3124**
ENCOFADO DESLIZANTE (PARA HORMIGÓN)  *m*  **11616**
ENCOGERSE **11388**
ENCOLADO  *m*  **7351**
ENCOLADURA  *f*  **7351**
ENCOLADURA  *f*  **5987**
ENCOLAR **5985**
ENCOLCHADO  *m*  **11930**
ENCONTRONAZO  *m*  **11359**
ENCORVAR **1173**
ENCRISTALADO  *m*  **5972**
ENDEREZADERA  *f*  **12320**
ENDEREZADOR (DE TUBOS) ABRAMSEN **12**
ENDEREZADORA  *f*  DE RODILLOS **10685**
ENDEREZAMIENTO  *m*  **10312**
ENDEREZAMIENTO  *m*  **12319**
ENDEREZAMIENTO  *m*  **12319**
ENDEREZAMIENTO  *m*  **12319**
ENDEREZAMIENTO  *m*  **12319**
ENDEREZAMIENTO  *m*  **12720**
ENDEREZAMIENTO  *m*  **13234**
ENDEREZAMIENTO  *m*  EN FRÍO **2691**
ENDEREZAR **13232**
ENDEREZAR **12318**
ENDEREZAR **12318**
ENDÓSMOSIS **4736**
ENDOTÉRMICO **4737**
ENDURECEDOR  *m*  (ALEACIÓN) **6290**
ENDURECERSE **6286**
ENDURECERSE (AL AIRE) **6286**
ENDURECERSE (EN EL AGUA) **6287**
ENDURECIDO (NO-) **13359**
ENDURECIMIENTO  *m*  **6291**
ENDURECIMIENTO  *m*  **6292**
ENDURECIMIENTO  *m*  **3483**

ENDURECIMIENTO  *f* A MARTILLO **6219**
ENDURECIMIENTO  *m* COMPLETO **5721**
ENDURECIMIENTO  *m* COMPLETO (A FONDO) **12892**
ENDURECIMIENTO  *m* CON CIANURO **3549**
ENDURECIMIENTO  *m* DE DESGASTE **13715**
ENDURECIMIENTO  *m* ESTRUCTURAL **224**
ENDURECIMIENTO  *m* (O TEMPLE  *m*) DE DEFORMACIÓN **12326**
ENDURECIMIENTO  *m* POR ENVEJECIMIENTO **223**
ENDURECIMIENTO  *m* POR PRECIPITACIÓN **9762**
ENDURECIMIENTO  *m* POR TEMPLE **10089**
ENERGÍA  *f* **4745**
ENERGÍA  *f* ACTUAL (O CINÉTICA) **7308**
ENERGÍA  *f* CALORÍFICA **6344**
ENERGÍA  *f* CINÉTICA **7308**
ENERGÍA  *f* DE ACTIVACIÓN **147**
ENERGÍA  *f* DE DESCARGA **4748**
ENERGÍA  *f* DEL CHOQUE **12757**
ENERGÍA  *f* (ELÉCTRICA) **4539**
ENERGÍA  *f* IRRADIADA **10139**
ENERGÍA  *f* LATENTE **9710**
ENERGÍA  *f* MAGNÉTICA **7900**
ENERGÍA  *f* MECÁNICA **8101**
ENERGÍA  *f* (NECESARIA) **3746**
ENERGÍA  *f* POTENCIAL **9710**
ENERGÍA  *f* QUÍMICA **2305**
ENERGÍA  *f* TÉRMICA **6344**
ENFARDELAR **1737**
ENFRIADERO  *m* **6617**
ENFRIADO CON AGUA **13683**
ENFRIADOR  *m* **10409**
ENFRIADOR  *m* **3083**
ENFRIADOR  *m* DE ACEITE **8751**
ENFRIADOR  *m* DE CENIZAS **2398**
ENFRIADOR  *m* DEL AGUJERO DE ESCORIA **8380**
ENFRIADOR  *m* INTERNO **7046**
ENFRIADOR  *m* PARA LAS AGUAS DE CONDENSACIÓN **3089**
ENFRIADOR  *m* PARA MUELA **6109**
ENFRIAMIENTO  *m* **3093**
ENFRIAMIENTO  *m* **3085**
ENFRIAMIENTO  *m* BRUSCO DEL ACERO **10100**
ENFRIAMIENTO  *m* CIRCULAR **10752**
ENFRIAMIENTO  *m* DEL HORNO **5742**
ENFRIAMIENTO  *m* DEL AGUA **13683**
ENFRIAMIENTO  *m* EN EL ACEITE **8752**
ENFRIAMIENTO  *m* EN EL AGUA **13646**
ENFRIAMIENTO  *m* EN EL AIRE **252**
ENFRIAMIENTO  *m* LENTO **4230**
ENFRIAMIENTO  *m* MANDADO **3056**
ENFRIAMIENTO  *m* POR CAMISA DE AGUA **7204**

ENFRIAR **2332**
ENFRIAR BRUSCAMENTE EL ACERO **10091**
ENFRIAR POR DEBAJO DE LA TEMPERATURA DE CONDENSACIÓN **12463**
ENFRIAR POR DEBAJO DEL PUNTO DE CONGELACIÓN **12463**
ENFRIARSE **3081**
ENGALANAR **13204**
ENGANCHAR **12914**
ENGANCHAR **4749**
ENGANCHAR **4749**
ENGANCHARSE **1556**
ENGANCHE  *m* **11691**
ENGANCHE  *m* **12918**
ENGANCHE  *m* **7705**
ENGARCE  *m* DE TUBOS CON MANDRIL SEPARADOR **4908**
ENGASTADORA  *f* **5346**
ENGASTADORA  *f* **11088**
ENGATAR **4749**
ENGATILLADO  *m* **4751**
ENGATILLADO  *m* **4751**
ENGATILLADO  *m* **7705**
ENGATILLADO  *m* SILENCIOSO **11433**
ENGATILLAR **4749**
ENGRANAJE  *m* **5889**
ENGRANAJE  *m* CICLOIDAL **3558**
ENGRANAJE  *m* CÓNICO **1227**
ENGRANAJE  *m* DE ÁNGULO **1227**
ENGRANAJE  *m* DE DENTADO CRUZADO **12247**
ENGRANAJE  *m* DE DENTADO EN ESPIRAL **11534**
ENGRANAJE  *m* DE EVOLVENTE **7119**
ENGRANAJE  *m* DE FRICCIÓN **5674**
ENGRANAJE  *m* DE FUERZA (MOTRIZ) **6402**
ENGRANAJE  *m* DE FUERZA (MOTRIZ) **6402**
ENGRANAJE  *m* DE LINTERNA **9325**
ENGRANAJE  *m* DE LINTERNA **9325**
ENGRANAJE  *m* DE LINTERNA **9325**
ENGRANAJE  *m* DE RUEDA DENTADA Y CREMALLERA **10120**
ENGRANAJE  *m* DE TORNILLO SIN FIN **13974**
ENGRANAJE  *m* DE TRANSMISIÓN **13128**
ENGRANAJE  *m* DENTADO CRUZADO **12247**
ENGRANAJE  *m* DESLIZANTE **11598**
ENGRANAJE  *m* DIFERENCIAL **3913**
ENGRANAJE  *m* ELÍPTICO **4677**
ENGRANAJE  *m* EPICICLOIDAL **4780**
ENGRANAJE  *m* EPICICLOIDAL **4780**
ENGRANAJE  *m* EXTERIOR **4956**
ENGRANAJE  *m* HELICOIDAL **6425**
ENGRANAJE  *m* HIPERBÓLICO **11534**
ENGRANAJE  *m* INTERIOR **7058**

**ENG** 1026

ENGRANAJE *m* INTERMEDIO **7050**
ENGRANAJE *m* MÓVIL **11602**
ENGRANAJE *m* (O TREN *m*) PLANETARIO **9446**
ENGRANAJE *m* RECTO **12008**
ENGRANAJE *m* RECTO **12008**
ENGRANAJE *m* REDUCTOR DE VELOCIDAD **11873**
ENGRANAJE *m* TALLADO **3508**
ENGRANAJE HIPOCICLOIDAL **6744**
ENGRANAJES *m pl* **5907**
ENGRANAJES *m pl* CONCURRENTES **8323**
ENGRANAJES *m pl* DE DIENTES ANGULARES **6448**
ENGRANAJES *m pl* HIPOIDES **6745**
ENGRANAJES *m pl* INTERIORES **7067**
ENGRANAR **4750**
ENGRANARSE **1077**
ENGRANARSE **1077**
ENGRANE *m* **4752**
ENGRANE *m* (DE RUEDAS DENTADAS) **5910**
ENGRASADOR *m* **6086**
ENGRASADOR *m* **8753**
ENGRASADOR *m* **8753**
ENGRASADOR *m* **7812**
ENGRASADOR *m* **12148**
ENGRASADOR *m* AUTOMÁTICO **851**
ENGRASADOR *m* CENTRÍFUGO **2182**
ENGRASADOR *m* CUENTAGOTAS **4323**
ENGRASADOR *m* DE AGUJA **8520**
ENGRASADOR *m* DE CAUDAL VISIBLE **11425**
ENGRASADOR *m* DE MECHA **11516**
ENGRASADOR *m* DE VÁLVULA **13467**
ENGRASADOR *m* DE VÁSTAGO **8520**
ENGRASADOR *m* MOLLERUP **8105**
ENGRASADOR *m* STAUFFER **12148**
ENGRASADOR A PRESIÓN MECÁNICO *m* **8105**
ENGRASAR **7801**
ENGRASAR (UNTAR CON GRASA) **6084**
ENGRASE *m* **7803**
ENGRASE *m* **7808**
ENGRASE *m* **7814**
ENGRASE *m* **7812**
ENGRASE *m* A PRESIÓN **9818**
ENGRASE *m* A PRESIÓN **9824**
ENGRASE *m* A PRESIÓN CON CIRCULACIÓN CONTINUA **5442**
ENGRASE *m* AUTOMÁTICO **848**
ENGRASE *m* CON GRASA CONSISTENTE **6087**
ENGRASE *m* CON SEBO **6087**
ENGRASE *m* CONTINUO **3012**
ENGRASE *m* CUENTAGOTAS **4287**
ENGRASE *m* INTERMITENTE **9195**

ENGRASE *m* MECÁNICO **848**
ENGRASE *m* POR AGITACIÓN **11925**
ENGRASE *m* POR ANILLO **10601**
ENGRASE *m* POR BOMBA Y CIRCULACIÓN DE ACEITE **5442**
ENGRASE *m* POR CADENA **2212**
ENGRASE *m* POR CUENTAGOTAS **4284**
ENGRASE *m* POR MECHA **13847**
ENGRASE *m* POR OLEOCOMPRESOR **7809**
ENGRASE (UNTADO CON GRASA) *m* **6087**
ENGROSAMIENTO *m* DEL GRANO **6035**
ENGRUDO *m* **12112**
ENGRUDO *m* **12112**
ENGRUMECIDO *m* **1279**
ENJARETADO *m* **6101**
ENJUAGADURA *f* **10608**
ENJUAGAR **10607**
ENLACE **13368**
ENLACE **3254**
ENLACE *m* **1500**
ENLACE **5280**
ENLACE *m* **5416**
ENLACE *m* **3254**
ENLACE **2965**
ENLACE *m* DE CORREAS **1142**
ENLACE *m* (ELECTRICIDAD) **2966**
ENLACE *m* (ELECTRICIDAD) **2958**
ENLACE *m* RÍGIDO **10589**
ENLACO *m* **3254**
ENLAZAR **2955**
ENLAZAR **2955**
ENLOSADO *m* **9136**
ENLUCIDO *m* **9463**
ENLUCIDO *m* **8274**
ENLUCIDO *m* DE ACABADO **3264**
ENLUCIDO *m* DE LINGOTERAS **8355**
ENLUCIR **9464**
ENLUCIR **1909**
ENMANGADO *m* **3254**
ENMANGADO CON PRENSA *m* **5527**
ENMANGAR **11390**
ENMASILLADO *m* **2146**
ENMASILLAR **2134**
ENMOHECIMIENTO *m* **8271**
ENRARECER UN GAS **10214**
ENRARECIMIENTO *m* DE UN GAS **10211**
ENRARECIMIENTO *m* DEL AIRE **10212**
ENREJADO *m* **13180**
ENREJADO *m* **7433**
ENREJADO *m* **9951**

## ENV

ENREJADO *m* **6071**
ENREJADO *m* DE PROTECCIÓN **9951**
ENREJADO *m* METÁLICO **7429**
ENREJADO *m* METÁLICO **13896**
ENREJILLADO *m* CON BARROTES MOVIBLES **10655**
ENROLLADO *m* **13862**
ENROLLADO *m* **2650**
ENROLLADO *m* A LA DERECHA **2508**
ENROLLADO A LA DERECHA **2508**
ENROLLADO A LA IZQUIERDA **3239**
ENROLLADORA *f* **13903**
ENROLLAR **13853**
ENSAMBLADURA *f* **1778**
ENSAMBLADURA *f* **5059**
ENSAMBLADURA *f* DE RANURA Y LENGÜETA **12991**
ENSAMBLADURA *f* DE RANURA Y LENGÜETA **12991**
ENSAMBLADURA A BAJA TEMPERATURA *f* **7790**
ENSAMBLADURA A INGLETE *f* **8324**
ENSAMBLADURA EN COLA DE MILANO *f* **4178**
ENSANCHAMIENTO *m* **1723**
ENSANCHAMIENTO *m* DE UN TUBO **4768**
ENSANCHAR **5356**
ENSANCHARSE **5356**
ENSANCHE *m* **1701**
ENSAYO *m* **9921**
ENSAYO *m* **9921**
ENSAYO *m* **12770**
ENSAYO *m* **12792**
ENSAYO *m* **12770**
ENSAYO *m* DE CAÍDA DE PESO **4330**
ENSAYO *m* DE DUREZA BRINELL **1618**
ENSAYO *m* DE FLEXIÓN POR GOLPE **4328**
ENSAYO *m* DE IZOD **7200**
ENSAYO *m* DE MALEABILIDAD **5409**
ENSAYO *m* DE MATERIALES **12782**
ENSAYO *m* DE PANDEO **3342**
ENSAYO *m* DE PERFORACIÓN **1475**
ENSAYO *m* DE RESISTENCIA A LOS CHOQUES REPETIDOS **5049**
ENSAYO *m* DESTRUCTIVO **3806**
ENSAYO *m* FÍSICO **9284**
ENSAYO *m* HIDROSTÁTICO **6727**
ENSAYO *m* NO DESTRUCTIVO **9924**
ENSAYO *m* NO DESTRUCTIVO **8630**
ENSAYO *m* (O CONTROL *m*) CON ESCOBILLA ELÉCTRICA **6535**
ENSAYO DE JOMINY **7254**
ENSILADORAS *f pl* **11430**
ENSILADORAS *f pl* **3522**
ENSOMBRECIMIENTO *m* **5507**
ENSUCIAMIENTO *m* **2510**

ENTABLADO *m* **5449**
ENTABLADO *m* **5451**
ENTABLADO *m* **6101**
ENTALLADURA *f* **7274**
ENTALLADURA **7290**
ENTALLADURA *f* **8668**
ENTALLADURA *f* **8672**
ENTALLADURA *f* **8676**
ENTALLADURA *f* **8672**
ENTALLAR **8554**
ENTALLAR **8554**
ENTALLE *m* **8672**
ENTARIMADO *m* **6101**
ENTARQUINAMIENTO *m* **2510**
ENTINTAR **6940**
ENTRADA *f* **6943**
ENTRADA **6943**
ENTRADA *f* DE AGUA **6915**
ENTRADA *f* DE AIRE **4771**
ENTRADA *f* DE COLADA **5866**
ENTRADA *f* DE DATOS POR CINTA **12643**
ENTRADA *f* DE LLAMA **5365**
ENTRADA *f* EN FORMA DE CUERNO **6600**
ENTRADA *f* EN PARALELO **9054**
ENTREHIERRO *m* **262**
ENTREHIERRO *m* DE UN IMÁN **263**
ENTREVÍA *f* **5871**
ENTROPÍA *f* **4773**
ENTURBIAMIENTO *m* **2541**
ENVASE *m* **8995**
ENVEJECIMIENTO *m* **226**
ENVEJECIMIENTO *m* **225**
ENVEJECIMIENTO *m* ARTIFICIAL **731**
ENVEJECIMIENTO *m* COMPLETO **231**
ENVEJECIMIENTO *m* CRÍTICO **3344**
ENVEJECIMIENTO *m* ESCALONADO **232**
ENVEJECIMIENTO *m* INTERRUMPIDO **7091**
ENVEJECIMIENTO *m* NATURAL **8500**
ENVEJECIMIENTO *m* NATURAL **233**
ENVEJECIMIENTO *m* POR DEFORMACIÓN **12328**
ENVEJECIMIENTO *m* POR DEFORMACIÓN **12327**
ENVEJECIMIENTO *m* POR ENFRIAMIENTO RÁPIDO **10087**
ENVEJECIMIENTO *m* POR LOS ESFUERZOS **12324**
ENVEJECIMIENTO *m* POR TRABAJO EN FRÍO **235**
ENVEJECIMIENTO *m* PROGRESIVO **234**
ENVEJECIMIENTO *m* PROGRESIVO **9906**
ENVOLTURA *f* **11330**
ENVOLTURA *f* **7986**
ENVOLTURA **7623**
ENVOLTURA *f* **3274**

**ENV** 1028

ENVOLTURA  *f*  DEL DEPÓSITO **12630**
ENVOLTURA  *f*  PROTECTORA **9948**
ENVOLTURA  *f*  PROTECTORA **9948**
ENVOLVENTE  *m* **11303**
ENVOLVENTE  *f* **4776**
ENVOLVENTE DEL HORNO  *m* **5749**
EPICICLOIDE **4779**
EQUILIBRACIÓN  *f* **942**
EQUILIBRACIÓN  *f* **942**
EQUILIBRADO  *m* **942**
EQUILIBRADO  *m* **942**
EQUILIBRADO  *m* **935**
EQUILIBRAR **930**
EQUILIBRAR **930**
EQUILIBRARSE **1076**
EQUILIBRIO  *m* **929**
EQUILIBRIO  *m* **4793**
EQUILIBRIO  *m* **4786**
EQUILIBRIO  *m*  DE LAS MASAS **941**
EQUILIBRIO  *m*  ESTABLE **12045**
EQUILIBRIO  *m*  INDIFERENTE **6882**
EQUILIBRIO  *m*  INSETABLE **13401**
EQUILIBRIO  *m*  QUÍMICO **2307**
EQUIPO  *m*  ELÉCTRICO **4542**
EQUIPO  *m*  (O BRIGADA  *f*) DE OBREROS **11348**
EQUIPO  *m*  PARA NIVELAR (MOVER) LA TIERRA **4414**
EQUIPO  *m*  SANITARIO **10931**
EQUIVALENCIA  *f* **4795**
EQUIVALENTE **4796**
EQUIVALENTE CALORÍFICO DEL TRABAJO **6347**
EQUIVALENTE DEL CONO PIROMÉTRICO **10051**
EQUIVALENTE ELECTROMAGNÉTICO **4571**
EQUIVALENTE MECÁNICO DEL CALOR **8104**
EQUIVALENTE QUÍMICO **2308**
ERBIO  *m* **4804**
ERGIO  *m* **4818**
ERGIO  *m* **4818**
ERIGIR **4805**
ERITROSINA  *f* **4831**
ERITROSINA  *f* **4831**
EROSIÓN  *f* **4820**
ERROR  *m* **4822**
ERROR  *m*  DE APRECIACIÓN **4827**
ERROR  *m*  DE CÁLCULO **4824**
ERROR  *m*  DE CALIBRACIÓN **1869**
ERROR  *m*  DE COLIMACIÓN **4828**
ERROR  *m*  DE DISEÑO DEL CONSTRUCTOR **4825**
ERROR  *m*  DE LECTURA **4826**
ERROR  *m*  DE MEDIDA **8089**
ERROR  *m*  DE OBSERVACIÓN **4829**

ERROR  *m*  DE PARALAJE **9048**
ERROR  *m*  DE TRABAJO **11550**
ERRUGINOSO **219**
ESBELTEZ  *f* **11580**
ESBELTEZ  *f*  DE UNA VIGA **11581**
ESBOZADO  *m* **11533**
ESBOZO  *m* **10786**
ESBOZO  *m* **10785**
ESBOZO  *m* **1341**
ESBOZO  *m* **1583**
ESCALA  *f* **10968**
ESCALA  *f* **10981**
ESCALA  *f* **10982**
ESCALA  *f* **10974**
ESCALA  *f*  ANULAR **3841**
ESCALA  *f*  CENTIGRADA **2157**
ESCALA  *f*  CIRCULAR (ESFERA) MICROMÉTRICA **8253**
ESCALA  *f*  DE CELSIO **2157**
ESCALA  *f*  (DE DUREZA) DE MOHS **8346**
ESCALA  *f*  DE REAUMUR **10267**
ESCALA  *f*  DE UN PLANO (DE UN DIBUJO) **10973**
ESCALA  *f*  FAHRENHEIT **5019**
ESCALA  *f*  MÓVIL **11607**
ESCALA  *f*  REDUCIDA **10343**
ESCALA  *f*  TERMOMÉTRICA **12835**
ESCALA  *f*  TRANSVERSAL (UNIVERSAL) **3833**
ESCALA  *f*  VERNIER **13541**
ESCALA NATURAL (A) **5723**
ESCALA NATURAL (A) **5723**
ESCALARIO  *m* **10967**
ESCALERA  *f* **12053**
ESCALERA  *f*  HELICOIDAL **11919**
ESCALERA  *f*  RECTA **5646**
ESCALERA  *f*  RECTA **5641**
ESCALÓN  *m* **12239**
ESCALÓN  *m* **12239**
ESCALÓN  *m* **12239**
ESCALONADO **12246**
ESCALONADO **12246**
ESCALONES  *m*  DE REJILLA METÁLICA **6102**
ESCALONES (EN)  *m pl/*ESCALONADO  *m* **12246**
ESCAMA  *f* **10968**
ESCAMA  *f* **10964**
ESCAMA  *f* **288**
ESCAMAS  *f pl*  DE ESTAÑO **12955**
ESCANDIO  *m* **10991**
ESCAPAR **4832**
ESCAPARSE **4832**
ESCAPARSE **4832**
ESCAPE  *m*  DE GAS **4833**

ESE

ESCAPE *m* (DE LOS GASES DE UN MOTOR) **4890**
ESCAPE *m* DE UN RESORTE **4031**
ESCAPE *m* DE VAPOR **4833**
ESCAPE *m* LIBRE **8627**
ESCAPE ABIERTO **8627**
ESCAPE DE UN RESORTE **4031**
ESCARBILLA *f* **2659**
ESCARBILLAS *f pl* **5469**
ESCARBILLOS *m pl* (O GAUDINGA *f*) DE COQUE **2659**
ESCARCHADO *m* **5702**
ESCARDADORAS *f pl* **13742**
ESCARIADO *m* **1637**
ESCARIADO *m* **3855**
ESCARIADO DE UNA POLEA *m* **4978**
ESCARIADO DE UNA RUEDA *m* **4978**
ESCARIADOR *m* **1636**
ESCARIADOR *m* **1636**
ESCARIADOR *m* **4279**
ESCARIADOR *m* **3241**
ESCARIADOR *m* **3149**
ESCARIADOR ACANALADO *m* **5485**
ESCARIADOR AJUSTABLE *m* **4923**
ESCARIADOR CON DIENTES EXTENSIBLES *m* **188**
ESCARIADOR CON ESTRÍAS *m* **5485**
ESCARIADOR CON ESTRÍAS *m* **5485**
ESCARIADOR CON ESTRÍAS FINAS *m* **5197**
ESCARIADOR CON ESTRÍAS HELICOIDALES *m* **11915**
ESCARIADOR CON ESTRÍAS RECTAS *m* **12305**
ESCARIADOR CON RANURAS HELICOIDALES *m* **11915**
ESCARIADOR CÓNICO *m* **12658**
ESCARIADOR DE ACABADO CÓNICO *m* **5226**
ESCARIADOR DE CUCHILLAS GRADUABLES *m* **188**
ESCARIADOR DE DESBASTADO CÓNICO *m* **10790**
ESCARIADOR DE DIENTES FIJOS *m* **10747**
ESCARIADOR DE MANO *m* **6247**
ESCARIADOR DE MANO AJUSTABLE (EXTENSIBLE) *m* **184**
ESCARIADOR DE MANO CÓNICO *m* **12650**
ESCARIADOR DE MANO EXTENSIBLE *m* **4917**
ESCARIADOR DE METAL DURA *m* **1935**
ESCARIADOR DE RANURAS *m* **5485**
ESCARIADOR EXTENSIBLE *m* **4923**
ESCARIADOR EXTENSIBLE *m* **10747**
ESCARIADOR HUECO DE DIENTES FIJOS *m* **11336**
ESCARIADOR MECÁNICO *m* **7853**
ESCARIADOR PARA MÁQUINA *m* **7853**
ESCARIAR **1462**
ESCARIFICADOR *m* **8344**
ESCARIFICADOR *m* **10722**
ESCARIFICADOR DE DISCOS *m* **9523**
ESCARPIA *f* **2457**

ESCAYOLA *f* **6190**
ESCAYOLA *f* **9466**
ESCINDIR **11946**
ESCLERÓMETRO *m* **11002**
ESCLERÓSCOPIO *m* **11366**
ESCLOROSCOPIO *m* **11366**
ESCLUSA *f* **7698**
ESCOBAZAMIENTO *m* **12529**
ESCOBILLA *f* DE CARBÓN **1946**
ESCOFINA *f* **11481**
ESCOFINA *f* **10215**
ESCOPLEAR **2344**
ESCOPLO *m* **2349**
ESCOPLO *m* **1919**
ESCOPLO *m* **9080**
ESCOPLO *m* PLANO **5377**
ESCOPLO *m* PUNZÓN *m* **8398**
ESCOPLO DE MANGUITO *m* **11704**
ESCOPLO-PUNZÓN *m* **5264**
ESCORIA *f* **2397**
ESCORIA *f* **2500**
ESCORIA *f* **4331**
ESCORIA *f* **11561**
ESCORIA *f* **11561**
ESCORIA *f* (DE ALTOS HORNOS) **1312**
ESCORIA *f* DE LOS ALTOS HORNOS **1312**
ESCORIA *f* ENCERRADA **11567**
ESCORIA *f* GRANULADA **6055**
ESCORIAS *f pl* BÁSICAS **1054**
ESCORIAS *f pl* DE FORJA **6217**
ESCORIFICACIÓN *f* **11004**
ESCRITURA *f* CHINA **2341**
ESCRITURA *f* PERPENDICULAR **6243**
ESCRITURA *f* RECTA **6243**
ESCUADRA *f* **514**
ESCUADRA *f* **12014**
ESCUADRA *f* CON ESPALDÓN **13245**
ESCUADRA *f* DE UNIÓN **6182**
ESCUADRA *f* DOBLE **12581**
ESCUADRA *f* EN T **12581**
ESCUADRA *f* HEXAGONAL **6456**
ESCUADRA *f* PARA DIBUJAR **11223**
ESCUADRA (DE) **10577**
ESCUADREO *m* **1583**
ESCUDETE *m* **4835**
ESCUDO *m* **6252**
ESCUDO *m* **11342**
ESCUDO *m* **11342**
ESCURRIRSE **11586**
ESENCIA *f* DE ALMENDRAS AMARGAS **1198**

# ESE
1030

ESENCIA  *f* DE MIRBANA **8587**
ESFERA  *f* **11883**
ESFERA  *f* **11883**
ESFERA  *f* **950**
ESFERA  *f* **3837**
ESFERA  *f* HUECA **6549**
ESFERA GRADUADA  *f* **6027**
ESFÉRICO **11884**
ESFEROIDAL **8606**
ESFERÓMETRO  *m* **11897**
ESFUERZO  *m* **12367**
ESFUERZO  *m* **12331**
ESFUERZO  *m* **5532**
ESFUERZO  *m* ADMISIBLE **10880**
ESFUERZO  *m* DE COMPRESIÓN **2863**
ESFUERZO  *m* DE COMPRESIÓN **2869**
ESFUERZO  *m* DE CORTADURA **11295**
ESFUERZO  *m* DE CORTADURA (O DE CORTE) **11295**
ESFUERZO  *m* DE CORTADURA POR UNIDAD DE SECCIÓN **11296**
ESFUERZO  *m* DE FLEXIÓN **1191**
ESFUERZO  *m* DE FLEXIÓN **1187**
ESFUERZO  *m* DE FLEXIÓN **1191**
ESFUERZO  *m* DE FLEXIÓN POR COMPRESIÓN AXIAL **3339**
ESFUERZO  *m* DE FLUJO **5460**
ESFUERZO  *m* DE PANDEO **3339**
ESFUERZO  *m* DE PANDEO **3339**
ESFUERZO  *m* DE ROTURA (DE FRACTURA) **5618**
ESFUERZO  *m* DE TENSIÓN **12373**
ESFUERZO  *m* DE TORSIÓN **13056**
ESFUERZO  *m* DE TRACCIÓN **13089**
ESFUERZO  *m* DE TRACCIÓN **12747**
ESFUERZO  *m* EN LA FIBRA **5134**
ESFUERZO  *m* EXTERIOR **4954**
ESFUERZO  *m* EXTERIOR **7679**
ESFUERZO  *m* MACROSCÓPICO **7874**
ESFUERZO  *m* TANGENCIAL **12624**
ESFUERZO  *m* UNITARIO **12367**
ESFUERZO CORTANTE  *m* **11296**
ESFUERZO DE FLEXIÓN POR COMPRESIÓN AXIAL **3339**
ESFUERZOS  *m pl* DE ENFRIAMIENTO **3091**
ESFUERZOS  *m pl* DE FORJADO **5564**
ESLABÓN  *m* **1783**
ESLABÓN  *m* **7627**
ESLABÓN  *m* **7627**
ESLABÓN  *m* **7627**
ESLABÓN  *m* DE CADENA **2211**
ESLABÓN DE UNA CADENA  *m* **7627**
ESLABONES  *m pl* QUE MONTAR **11232**
ESLINGA  *f* **11610**

ESMALTADO  *m* **4712**
ESMALTAR **4710**
ESMALTE  *m* **4709**
ESMANIL  *m* **1324**
ESMERIL  *m* **4692**
ESMERIL  *m* **4699**
ESMERILAR **6104**
ESMITSONITA  *f* **1836**
ESPACIAMENTO  *m* DE LOS EJES **13813**
ESPACIO  *m* **697**
ESPACIO  *m* **4063**
ESPACIO  *m* **7101**
ESPACIO  *m* LIBRE **278**
ESPACIO  *m* MUERTO **2482**
ESPACIO  *m* MUERTO DEL PISTÓN **7519**
ESPACIO  *m* NECESARIO **11829**
ESPACIO  *m* NEUTRO **2482**
ESPACIO  *m* NOCIVO **2482**
ESPALDAS  *f pl* **890**
ESPALDÓN  *m* **11383**
ESPALDÓN  *m* **7321**
ESPARCIDORAS  *f pl* DE ABONO **7995**
ESPÁRRAGO  *m* **12397**
ESPÁRRAGO  *m* DE UNIÓN DE UNA CADENA DE RODILLOS **9320**
ESPATO  *m* CALCÁREO **1845**
ESPATO  *m* FLÚOR **5479**
ESPATO  *m* PESADO **1021**
ESPATO  *m* PESADO **1021**
ESPÁTULA  *f* **11844**
ESPECIALIDAD  *f* **11845**
ESPECIALIDAD  *f* **11845**
ESPECIALIDAD  *f* FARMACÉUTICA **9119**
ESPÉCIMEN  *m* **10915**
ESPECTRO  *m* **11863**
ESPECTRO  *m* ACANALADO **5487**
ESPECTRO  *m* CONTINUO **3036**
ESPECTRO  *m* DE ABSORCIÓN **54**
ESPECTRO  *m* DE LOS RAYOS X **14001**
ESPECTRO  *m* DISCONTINUO **7610**
ESPECTRO  *m* MAGNÉTICO **7902**
ESPECTRO  *m* PRODUCIDO POR PRISMA **9878**
ESPECTRO  *m* SECUNDARIO **11108**
ESPECTRO  *m* SOLAR **11754**
ESPECTRÓGRAFO  *m* **11860**
ESPECTRÓMETRO  *m* **11862**
ESPECTRÓMETRO  *m* DE MASA **8029**
ESPECTRÓMETRO  *m* DE RAYOS X **14000**
ESPECTROSCOPIA  *f* CALORIMÉTRICA **2739**
ESPECTROSCOPIA  *f* DE LA LLAMA **5320**

1031 EST

ESPECTROSCOPIO  *m* **11862**
ESPEJO  *m* CÓNCAVO **2879**
ESPEJO  *m* CONVEXO **3078**
ESPEJO  *m* DE REFRACCIÓN **10396**
ESPEJO  *m* ESFÉRICO **11888**
ESPEJO  *m* PARABÓLICO **9041**
ESPEJO  *m* PLANO **9437**
ESPEJO  *m* REDONDO **2414**
ESPEJUELO  *m* **6190**
ESPEQUE  *m* **7725**
ESPERANZA  *f* MATEMÁTICA **4927**
ESPERMA  *f* DE BALLENA **11882**
ESPERMA  *f* DE BALLENA **11882**
ESPERMACETI  *m* **11882**
ESPESADO  *m* **7675**
ESPESAMIENTO  *m* **1701**
ESPESOR  *m* **185**
ESPESOR  *m* **11352**
ESPESOR  *m* **12843**
ESPESOR  *m* **13731**
ESPESOR  *m* **13731**
ESPESOR  *m* **13731**
ESPESOR  *m* CIRCULAR DEL DIENTE **2431**
ESPESOR  *m* DE LA PARED (DEL METAL) DE UN TUBO **12844**
ESPESOR  *m* DE LA SOLDADURA **12885**
ESPESOR  *m* DE PELÍCULA **5170**
ESPESOR  *m* DE UN ALAMBRE **3860**
ESPESOR  *m* DE UNA CHAPA **12845**
ESPESOR  *m* DE UNA SOLDADURA A TOPE **1786**
ESPESOR  *m* DE UNA SOLDADURA EN ÁNGULO **12886**
ESPESOR  *m* DEL ARCO **678**
ESPESOR  *m* DEL DIENTE **12846**
ESPESOR  *m* DEL DIENTE A LA CUERDA **2365**
ESPESOR DE DESGASTE  *m* **13711**
ESPIGA  *f* **13986**
ESPIGA  *f* **4260**
ESPIGA  *f* **4181**
ESPIGA  *f* **4180**
ESPIGA  *f* **5059**
ESPIGA  *f* **12740**
ESPIGA  *f* **9315**
ESPIGA  *f* DE ABROCHADURA **4175**
ESPIGA  *m* DE CIGÜEÑAL **3311**
ESPIGA  *f* DE MADERA **4180**
ESPIGA  *f* DE ROBLÓN **11263**
ESPIGA  *f* DE UN PERNO **11260**
ESPIGA  *f* DE UN TORNILLO **11260**
ESPIGA  *f* DE UNA CHAVETA **11262**
ESPIGA DE MADERA  *f* **13179**

ESPINA  *f* **4441**
ESPIRA  *f* **2646**
ESPIRAL  *f* **11912**
ESPIRAL  *f* DE ARQUÍMEDES **690**
ESPIRAL  *f* DE ARQUÍMEDES **690**
ESPIRAL  *f* HIPERBÓLICA **6738**
ESPIRAL  *f* LOGARÍTMICA **7720**
ESPÍRITU  *m* DE SAL **6706**
ESPOLVOREADO  *m* CON SULFURO **4394**
ESPOLVOREADORA  *f pl* PORTÁTIL **11969**
ESPOLVOREADORAS  *f pl* PULVERIZADORAS **11971**
ESPOLVOREADORAS  *f* SULFUROSAS **11970**
ESPONJA  *f* DE PLATINO **11955**
ESPUMA  *f* **5499**
ESPUMA  *f* CON CÉLULAS CERRADAS **2517**
ESPUMA  *f* DE PLATINO **11955**
ESPUMA  *f* DE PLATINO **9514**
ESPUMA DE MAR  *f* **7880**
ESPUMADERA  *f* **11536**
ESPUMEO  *m* **1331**
ESQUEMA  *f* **3836**
ESQUISTO  *m* **10999**
ESQUISTO  *m* ARCILLOSO **700**
ESQUISTO  *m* BITUMINOSO **8780**
ESTABILIDAD  *f* **12041**
ESTABILIDAD  *f* **4385**
ESTABILIDAD  *f* DIMENSIONAL **3958**
ESTABILIDAD  *f* EN SECO **4352**
ESTABILIDAD  *f* (QUÍMICA) **2313**
ESTABILIZACIÓN  *f* **12043**
ESTABILIZACIÓN  *f* DE LA DUREZA **10520**
ESTABILIZADOR  *m* **12042**
ESTABILIZADOR  *m* AUTOMÁTICO **847**
ESTABLECER UN CONTACTO **7950**
ESTABLECIMIENTO FABRIL **5013**
ESTACA  *f* **632**
ESTACADA  *f* **1603**
ESTACIÓN  *f* **12146**
ESTACIÓN  *f* CENTRAL **9742**
ESTACIÓN  *f* GENERADORA **9742**
ESTACIÓN  *f* RECEPTORA **10278**
ESTACIONAR **12294**
ESTADO **7717**
ESTADO  *m* BRUTO **740**
ESTADO  *m* DE EQUILIBRIO **12132**
ESTADO  *m* DE SUPERFICIE **12500**
ESTADO  *m* DE SUPERFICIE **5213**
ESTADO  *m* FINAL **5190**
ESTADO  *m* GASEOSO **5857**
ESTADO  *m* HIGROMÉTRICO DEL AIRE **6666**

# EST

1032

ESTADO *m* INICIAL **6930**
ESTADO *m* LÍQUIDO **7657**
ESTADO *m* METAESTABLE **8212**
ESTADO *m* PASTOSO **8488**
ESTADO *m* SÓLIDO **11795**
ESTADO CRÍTICO **3349**
ESTADO DE ENTREGA (EN) *m* **741**
ESTADO DE SERVICIO (EN) **6819**
ESTADO DE SOLDADURA (EN) *m* **745**
ESTADO LIBRE (EN) *m* **6818**
ESTADO NATIVO (O VIRGEN) (EN) *m* **5647**
ESTADO (SERIE DE NÚMEROS) **12584**
ESTADOS *m* DE TEMPERATURA **12725**
ESTALAGMOMETRÍA *f* **12054**
ESTALLAR **4933**
ESTALLIDO *m* **1767**
ESTALLIDO *m* DE UN VOLANTE **1769**
ESTALLIDO *m* DE UNA POLEA **1769**
ESTAMPA *f* **3883**
ESTAMPA *f* **3883**
ESTAMPA *f* **12531**
ESTAMPA *f* DE DESBASTAR **5726**
ESTAMPA *f* DE EMBUTIR **5580**
ESTAMPA *f* DE ESTIRAR **5726**
ESTAMPA *f* DE MARTILLO **1497**
ESTAMPA *f* DE ROBLONAR **10626**
ESTAMPA *f* DE YUNQUE **13036**
ESTAMPA *f* INFERIOR **1497**
ESTAMPA *f* SUPERIOR **13036**
ESTAMPA DE ROBLONAR *f* **10626**
ESTAMPACIÓN *f* **2651**
ESTAMPACIÓN *f* DE METALES **8189**
ESTAMPADO *m* **12059**
ESTAMPADO *m* **12059**
ESTAMPADO *m* **12059**
ESTAMPADO *m* **12534**
ESTAMPADO *m* **12532**
ESTAMPADO *m* **12532**
ESTAMPADO *m* **2651**
ESTAMPADO *m* EN CALIENTE **6632**
ESTAMPADO *m* EN CALIENTE **6643**
ESTAMPADO *m* EN FRÍO **2673**
ESTAMPADORA *f* **12060**
ESTAMPAR **12056**
ESTAMPAR **12056**
ESTAMPAR **12056**
ESTAMPAR **12530**
ESTAMPAR EN CALIENTE **12530**
ESTAMPAR LOS ROBLONES **3511**
ESTAMPAS *f pl* CERRADAS **2521**

ESTAÑADO *m* **12963**
ESTAÑADURA *f* **12963**
ESTAÑAR **12954**
ESTANCO **12920**
ESTANCO AL AGUA **13688**
ESTANCO AL AGUA **13686**
ESTANCO AL AIRE **303**
ESTANDARD **12071**
ESTANDARD *m* VIOLLE **13569**
ESTANDARDIZAR **12090**
ESTANNATO *m* **12095**
ESTANNATO *m* DE SODIO **11732**
ESTAÑO *m* **12953**
ESTAÑO *m* DE BANCA **973**
ESTAÑO *m* DE MALACA **12335**
ESTAÑO *m* DE SOLDAR DE FUNDENTE ÁCIDO **110**
ESTAÑO *m* DURO **9230**
ESTAÑO *m* EN GRÁNULOS **6042**
ESTAÑO *m* EN HOJAS **11326**
ESTAÑO *m* EN LINGOTES **1339**
ESTAÑO *m* QUÍMICAMENTE PURO **2324**
ESTANQUEIDAD *f* **11081**
ESTANQUEIDAD **12932**
ESTANQUEIDAD (FALTA DE) **7491**
ESTAR EN EBULLICIÓN **1401**
ESTAR SOMETIDO A UN ESFUERZO CORTANTE **1078**
ESTÁRTER *m* **2357**
ESTÁRTER *m* AUTOMÁTICO **838**
ESTÁTICA *f* **12140**
ESTÁTICA *f* GRÁFICA **6061**
ESTÁTICO *m* **12133**
ESTEARINA *f* **12195**
ESTEATITA *f* **11703**
ESTEATITA *f* **5659**
ESTELITA *f* **12234**
ESTEREOMETRÍA *f* **12251**
ESTEREOMÉTRICO **12250**
ESTERILIZACIÓN *f* DEL AGUA **12252**
ESTIBINA *f* **622**
ESTILETE *m* **9161**
ESTILETE *m* (DE UN APARATO REGISTRADOR) **9161**
ESTILETE *m* TRAZADOR **9161**
ESTIMACIÓN DE LOS COSTES **4838**
ESTIRABILIDAD *f* **4228**
ESTIRADO *m* **4230**
ESTIRADO **4247**
ESTIRADO *m* BRILLANTE **4347**
ESTIRADO *m* DE ALAMBRE **13888**
ESTIRADO *m* DE LOS TUBOS **13249**
ESTIRADO *m* DESBASTADOR (O GRUESO) **1727**

ESTIRADO *m* EN CALIENTE **6624**
ESTIRADO *m* EN FRÍO **4230**
ESTIRADO *m* EN FRÍO **2676**
ESTIRADO *m* EN FRÍO DE TUBOS COLADOS SIN SOLDADURA **2053**
ESTIRADO EN CALIENTE **6623**
ESTIRADO EN FRÍO **2675**
ESTIRADO EN FRÍO **2677**
ESTIRAMIENTO *m* **4230**
ESTIRAR (ALAMBRE) **4220**
ESTIRAR LOS TUBOS **4224**
ESTOICOMETRÍA *f* **12268**
ESTOICOMÉTRICO **12267**
ESTOPA *f* **13073**
ESTOPA *f* DE CÁÑAMO **6444**
ESTOPA *f* DE CÁÑAMO **6439**
ESTOPA *f* DE COCO **2654**
ESTOPA *f* DE LINO **5413**
ESTOPADA *f* **7247**
ESTOPEROL *m* **1382**
ESTORBARSE MUTUAMENTE **5587**
ESTRANGULACIÓN *f* **12891**
ESTRANGULAR **12889**
ESTRATIFICACIÓN *f* **7382**
ESTRATO *m* **7444**
ESTRATO *m* **7442**
ESTRECHADO **3042**
ESTRECHAMIENTO *m* **3045**
ESTRECHAMIENTO *m* **11397**
ESTRECHARSE **11388**
ESTRÍA *f* **11206**
ESTRÍA *f* **10570**
ESTRÍA *f* **5486**
ESTRÍA *f* **5484**
ESTRÍA *f* **5061**
ESTRÍAS *f pl* **10576**
ESTRIBO *m* **12261**
ESTRIBO *m* **12261**
ESTRIBO *m* **688**
ESTRIBO *m* **1504**
ESTRICCIÓN *f* **3045**
ESTRICCIÓN *f* **3043**
ESTRICCIÓN *f* **7424**
ESTRICCIÓN *f* **8515**
ESTRICCIÓN *f* **8516**
ESTRICCIÓN *f* **10361**
ESTROBOSCOPIO *m* **12385**
ESTROFOIDE *f* **7722**
ESTRONCIO *m* **12389**
ESTROPEADO **5057**

ESTROPEADO **5057**
ESTRUCTURA *f* **5630**
ESTRUCTURA *f* **12394**
ESTRUCTURA *f* **12395**
ESTRUCTURA *f* **12395**
ESTRUCTURA *f* **12800**
ESTRUCTURA *f* BASÁLTICA **2758**
ESTRUCTURA *f* BETA **1219**
ESTRUCTURA *f* COMPACTA (DE) **2514**
ESTRUCTURA *f* CRISTALINA **3430**
ESTRUCTURA *f* DE GRANOS FINOS **5200**
ESTRUCTURA *f* DE GRANOS GRUESOS **7869**
ESTRUCTURA *f* DE LAS ALEACIONES **2058**
ESTRUCTURA *f* DEBIDA A LA DEFORMACIÓN PLÁSTICA **5461**
ESTRUCTURA *f* DEL CORAZÓN **3165**
ESTRUCTURA *f* DEL GRANO **6041**
ESTRUCTURA *f* DENDRÍTICA **3750**
ESTRUCTURA *f* EXAGONAL COMPACTA **6458**
ESTRUCTURA *f* FIBROSA **5135**
ESTRUCTURA *f* FINA **5210**
ESTRUCTURA *f* FINA (R.X.) **5203**
ESTRUCTURA *f* GAMMA **5797**
ESTRUCTURA *f* GRANULAR **6052**
ESTRUCTURA *f* LAMINAR **7373**
ESTRUCTURA *f* MOLECULAR **8361**
ESTRUCTURA *f* MOSAICA **8403**
ESTRUCTURA *f* RETICULAR **8539**
ESTRUCTURA *f* ZONAL **979**
ESTRUCTURA AUTOPORTANTE *f* **11161**
ESTRUCTURA DE CERCHAS *f* **13244**
ESTRUCTURA DE CRUCETAS *f* **3360**
ESTRUCTURA DE MADERA *f* **12942**
ESTRUCTURA METÁLICA *f* **12208**
ESTRUCTURA METÁLICA *f* **7152**
ESTUCHE *m* (METALURGIA) **5017**
ESTUDIAR **3795**
ESTUDIO *m* **3799**
ESTUDIO *m* **3794**
ESTUDIO *m* DE SUELO (DE TERRENO) **11752**
ESTUDIO *m* DE TERRENO **11752**
ESTUFA *f* **4358**
ESTUFA *f* **4256**
ESTUFA *f* (DE MACHOS) **3158**
ESTUFA *f* DE SECADO RÁPIDO **5360**
ETANAL *m* **84**
ETANO *m* **4848**
ETENO *m* **4851**
ETER *m* COMPUESTO **4837**
ÉTER *m* DE PETRÓLEO **7580**

**ETE** 1034

ETER *m* NÍTRICO **4850**
ETER *m* ORDINARIO **8853**
ETER ACÉTICO **88**
ETER DE PETRÓLEO **9228**
ETER METÍLICO **8222**
ETER NÍTRICO **4850**
ETER SULFÚRICO **8853**
ETILENO *m* **4851**
EUDIÓMETRO *m* **4852**
EUROPIO *m* **4854**
EUTÉCTICO **4855**
EUTECTOIDE **4859**
EVACUACIÓN *f* DE LA ESCORIA **3803**
EVACUACIÓN *f* DE LAS AGUAS RESIDUALES **10453**
EVACUACIÓN *f* DEL AIRE DE UN CONDUCTO **4665**
EVACUACIÓN *f* DEL POLVO **10452**
EVACUACIÓN *f* DEL VAPOR DE EBULLICIÓN **1405**
EVACUAR LOS GASES **10455**
EVAPORABLE **4861**
EVAPORACIÓN *f* **4867**
EVAPORACIÓN *f* AL AIRE LIBRE **8502**
EVAPORAR **4862**
EVAPORARSE **4862**
EVAPORARSE AL AIRE LIBRE **4863**
EVOLUTA *f* **4873**
EVOLUTA *f* **4873**
EXAMEN *m* **4876**
EXAMEN *m* **12792**
EXAMEN *m* **12792**
EXAMEN *m* MAGNETOGRÁFICO **7931**
EXAMEN *m* MICROSCÓPICO **8260**
EXAMEN *m* MICROSCÓPICO **7114**
EXAMEN *m* POR RESUDACIÓN **7656**
EXAMEN *m* RADIOGRÁFICO **10162**
EXAMEN *m* RADIOGRÁFICO **13993**
EXAMEN *m* ULTRAMICROSCÓPICO **13336**
EXAMEN (INSPECCIÓN *f*) EN FRÍO **2687**
EXCAVACIONES *f pl* **4420**
EXCÉNTRICA *f* **1883**
EXCÉNTRICA *f* **6329**
EXCÉNTRICA *f* **4433**
EXCÉNTRICA *f* **4442**
EXCÉNTRICA *f* **4424**
EXCÉNTRICA *f* DE CORAZÓN **6329**
EXCÉNTRICA *f* (O LEVA *f*) ABIERTA **8805**
EXCENTRICIDAD *f* **4436**
EXCÉNTRICO **4424**
EXCÉNTRICO **4425**
EXCÉNTRICO *m* **4433**
EXCESO *m* **4878**

EXCESO *m* DE ACEITE **13636**
EXCESO *m* DE TRABAJO **4880**
EXCITACIÓN *f* **4885**
EXCITACIÓN *f* SEPARADA **11190**
EXCITADORA *f* **4888**
EXCITAR **4887**
EXCITATRIZ *f* **4888**
EXENTO DE ACIDO **5635**
EXENTO DE CARBONO **1961**
EXENTO (O LIBRE) DE CENIZAS **5636**
EXFOLIACIÓN *f* **4889**
EXFOLIACIÓN *f* **4889**
EXFOLIACIÓN *f* **2487**
EXFOLICACIÓN *f* **11328**
EXHAUSTOR *m* **4900**
EXIGENCIAS *f pl* DE FABRICACIÓN **4987**
EXISTENCIAS *f pl* **12263**
EXISTENCIAS **12294**
EXISTENCIAS **12263**
EXOTÉRMICO **4901**
EXPANSIÓN *f* **10435** EXPANSIONARSE **4902**
EXPANSIÓN *f* DE LOS GASES **4920**
EXPANSIÓN *f* DE UN GAS **4921**
EXPANSIÓN *f* DEL VAPOR **4921**
EXPERIENCIA **12792**
EXPERIENCIA *f* **12792**
EXPERIENCIA *f* **12792**
EXPERTO *m* **4930**
EXPIRACIÓN *f* DE UNA PATENTE **4932**
EXPLORACIÓN *f* **10992**
EXPLORADOR *m* ELÉCTRICO **6534**
EXPLORAR **10990**
EXPLOSIÓN *f* **4935**
EXPLOSIÓN *f* DE UNA CALDERA **1410**
EXPLOSIVO **4937**
EXPLOTACIÓN *f* **8837**
EXPLOTACIÓN *f* DE UN INVENTO **13948**
EXPLOTACIÓN *f* MINERA **8311**
EXPLOTAR UN INVENTO **13938**
EXPONENTE *m* DE ESCAPE **4940**
EXPOSICIÓN *f* **4944**
EXPOSITOR *m* **4939**
EXPRESAR **12039**
EXPULSAR **4468**
EXPULSOR *m* **4472**
EXPURGACIÓN *f* **11011**
EXTENDERSE **1125**
EXTENDERSE **5356**
EXTENSÍMETRO *m* **4949**
EXTENSIÓN *f* **4946**

1035     **FAL**

EXTENSÍON *f* **4680**

EXTENSÓMETRO *m* **12325**

EXTINCIÓN *f* (O APAGAMIENTO *m*) DE LA CAL **11569**

EXTRACCIÓN *f* DE LA HULLA **13877**

EXTRACCIÓN *f* DE LA PIEZA DEL MOLDE **7328**

EXTRACCIÓN *f* DE LOS METALES **4966**

EXTRACCIÓN *f* DEL ACEITE **8777**

EXTRACCIÓN *f* DEL ORO POR CIANURACIÓN **3546**

EXTRACCIÓN *f* DEL POLVO **3682**

EXTRACCIÓN *f* ELECTROLÍTICA **4582**

EXTRACCIÓN *f* ELECTROLÍTICA **4652**

EXTRACCIÓN DE CARBÓN *f* **2566**

EXTRACTO *m* **4964**

EXTRACTO *m* MUCILAGINOSO **8440**

EXTRACTOR *m* **9326**

EXTRACTOR *m* **12127**

EXTRACTOR *m* **7278**

EXTRACTOR *m* **4967**

EXTRACTOR *m* **4900**

EXTRAER **12039**

EXTRAER EL POLVO **5637**

EXTREMIDAD *f* **6314**

EXTREMIDAD *f* **9384**

EXTREMO *m* **9384**

EXTREMO *m* **6314**

EXTREMO *m* DE LA BIELA DEL LADO DE LA CRUCETA **3389**

EXTREMO *m* DE UN TUBO TAPADO **1303**

EXTREMO *m* DEL SOPORTE **6597**

EXTREMO *m* HEMBRA DE UN TUBO **11710**

EXTREMO *m* LIBRE **5023**

EXTREMO *m* MACHO DE UN TUBO **11901**

EXTRUSIÓN *f* **4970**

EXTRUSIÓN *f* **4970**

EXTRUSIÓN *f* DIRECTA **3984**

EXTRUSIÓN *f* INDIRECTA **6884**

EXTRUSIÓN *f* POR CHOQUE **6784**

EXUDACIÓN *f* **7488**

EXUDACIÓN *f* **12540**

EYECTOR *m* **12172**

EYECTOR *m* **4472**

EYECTOR *m* **4469**

EYECTOR *m* NEUMÁTICO **271**

EYECTOR *m* NEUMÁTICO **9554**

FÁBRICA *f* **7861**

FÁBRICA *f* **5013**

FÁBRICA *f* **5013**

FÁBRICA *f* **5010**

FÁBRICA *f* **5013**

FÁBRICA *f* CENTRAL ELÉCTRICA **4512**

FÁBRICA *f* DE CARBONIZACIÓN DE HULLA **2665**

FÁBRICA *f* DE CONSTRUCCIÓN MECÁNICA **4764**

FÁBRICA *f* DE FUERZA MOTRIZ **9742**

FÁBRICA *f* DE GAS **5848**

FÁBRICA *f* DE LADRILLO **1602**

FÁBRICA *f* HIDOELÉCTRICA **6701**

FÁBRICA *f* HIDRÁULICA **6692**

FÁBRICA *f* METALÚRGICA **11668**

FÁBRICA (FUNDICIÓN) DE ACERO *f* **12211**

FABRICACIÓN *f* **7989**

FABRICACIÓN *f* **8028**

FABRICACIÓN *f* **10462**

FABRICACIÓN *f* **4983**

FABRICACIÓN *f* DE COK **7991**

FABRICACIÓN *f* DE HERRAMIENTAS **13006**

FABRICACIÓN *f* DE LOS AGLOMERADOS **7990**

FABRICACIÓN *f* DE MAQUINARIA **8103**

FABRICACIÓN *f* DE PERNOS **1443**

FABRICACIÓN *f* EN GRANDES SERIES **7727**

FABRICADO **5730**

FABRICANTE *m* **7992**

FABRICAR **7948**

FÁCIL DE TRABAJAR **13947**

FACILIDAD DE TEMPLE *f* **6288**

FACILIDAD DEL TRABAJO **13946**

FACTOR **5008**

FACTOR *m* **2621**

FACTOR *m* DE FORMA **5572**

FACTOR *m* DE POTENCIA **9735**

FACTOR *m* DE SEGURIDAD **5009**

FACTOR *m* DE VIBRACIÓN **11981**

FACULTAD *f* DE TOMAR BIEN EL TEMPLE **6296**

FALDA *f* **11547**

FALDÓN *m* (DE UN DEPÓSITO) **11549**

FALDÓN *m* DE UN TAMPON **11548**

FALLA *f* **3691**

FALLO *m* **6530**

FALLO *m* DE UN MOTOR **5021**

FALSA ESCUADRA *f* **1228**

FALSA ESCUADRA *f* **1228**

FALSA ESCUADRA *f* **1228**

FALSIFICACIÓN *f* **205**

FALSIFICAR **204**

FALSO FONDO *m* **5026**

FALSO FONDO *m* **5026**

FALSO NÚCLEO *m* **5027**

FALTA *f* DE FLEXIBILIDAD **1628**

FALTA *f* DE MATERIA **13348**

FALTA *f* (EN LO LISO DE UNA SUPERFICIE) **1506**

(FALTA RESULTANTE EN EL VOLUMEN) **6782**

**FAL** 1036

FALTAS  *f*  (AFNOR) **6536**
FANAL  *m*  **11883**
FANGO  *m*  **11654**
FANGO  *m*  ANÓDICO **600**
FANGOS  *m pl*  **8444**
FANGOSA  *f*  **8445**
FANGOSO  *m*  **8445**
FARADIO  *m*  **5035**
FARO  *m*  **6327**
FARO  *m*  **6326**
FARO  *m*  ANTINIEBLA **5506**
FARO  *m*  EMPOTRADO **5480**
FARO DE CRUCE **3963**
FASE  *f*  **9232**
FASE  *f*  **12239**
FASE  *f*  CONTINUA **3033**
FASE  *f*  DE VELOCIDAD **13523**
FASE  *f*  DISPERSA **4049**
FASE  *f*  DISPERSIVA **3033**
FASE  *f*  PASTOSA **8488**
FATIGA  *f*  **5047**
FATIGA  *f*  (CANSANCIO  *m* ) DEL MATERIAL **5051**
FATIGA  *f*  ESPECÍFICA **12367**
FATIGA  *f*  POR CONTACTOS DE ROCE **2200**
FATIGA  *f*  POR CORROSIÓN **3187**
FATIGA  *f*  POR EL SULFURO DE HIDRÓGENO **12442**
FATIGAR (O SOBRECARGAR) UN MATERIAL **8962**
FECHA  *f*  DE LA CONCESIÓN DE LA PATENTE **3617**
FECHA  *f*  DE LA FIRMA **3617**
FECHA  *f*  DEL REGISTRO DE SOLICITUD DE UNA PATENTE **3616**
FÉCULA  *f*  **12111**
FELDESPATO  *m*  **5087**
FELDESPATO  *m*  **5089**
F.E.M. **4622**
FENECIMIENTO  *m*  PRECOZ **6908**
FENILAMINA  *f*  **552**
FENOL  *m*  **1938**
FENOLTALEÍNA  *f*  **9238**
FENÓMENO  *m*  **9240**
FENÓMENO  *m*  LUMINOSO **7566**
FERMENTACIÓN  *f*  **5098**
FERMENTAR **10036**
FERMENTO  *m*  **5097**
FERMI  *m*  **1006**
FERRETERÍA  *f*  **11660**
FERRITA  *f*  **5104**
FERROALUMINIO  *m*  **5106**
FERROBORO  *m*  **5107**
FERROCARRIL  *m*  **7606**

FERROCARRIL DE VÍA ESTRECHA  *m*  **9639**
FERROCARRIL FUNICULAR  *m*  **1826**
FERROCIANURO  *m*  DE POTASIO **9685**
FERROCIANURO  *m*  DE POTASIO **9685**
FERROCIANURO  *m*  DE POTASIO **9684**
FERROCROMO  *m*  **5108**
FERROMAGNÉTICO **5118**
FERROMANGANESO  *m*  **5110**
FERROMOLIBDENO  *m*  **5111**
FERRONÍQUEL  *m*  **5112**
FERROSILICIO  *m*  **5113**
FERROTITANIO  *m*  **5114**
FERROTUNGSTENO  *m*  **5115**
FERROVANADIO  *m*  **5116**
FERRUGINOSO **5127**
FIABILIDAD  *f*  **10439**
FIADOR  *m*  **11987**
FIADOR  *m*  **7414**
FIADOR  *m*  **3212**
FIADOR  *m*  **2094**
FIADOR  *m*  (DE UN POLIPASTO) **5023**
FIBRA  *f*  **5139**
FIBRA  *f*  **5136**
FIBRA  *f*  **5131**
FIBRA  *f*  **13609**
FIBRA  *f*  DE AMIANTO **749**
FIBRA  *f*  DE COCO **2654**
FIBRA  *f*  DE PAJA **12348**
FIBRA  *f*  NEUTRA **8541**
FIBRA  *f*  NEUTRA **8542**
FIBRA  *f*  NEUTRA **2151**
FIBRA  *f*  NEUTRA **2151**
FIBRA  *f*  TEXTIL **12799**
FIBRA  *f*  VULCANIZADA **13609**
FIBRAS  *f pl*  (EN EL SENTIDO DE LAS) **6031**
FIBROSO **5137**
FIELTRO  *m*  **5090**
FIELTRO  *m*  ASFALTADO **765**
FIELTRO  *m*  DE AMIANTO **750**
FIGURA  *f*  **6778**
FIGURA  *f*  DE CORROSIÓN **4845**
FIGURA  *f*  DE INTERFERENCIA **7039**
FIGURAS  *f pl*  DE ATAQUE AL ÁCIDO **4842**
FIJACIÓN  *f*  **5044**
FIJACIÓN  *f*  **5044**
FIJACIÓN  *f*  **5416**
FIJACIÓN  *f*  **7817**
FIJACIÓN  *f*  **13740**
FIJACIÓN  *f*  DE UNA CUÑA DE APRIETE **7704**
FIJACIÓN  *f*  DE UNA VARILLA DE ENSAYO **5300**

FIJACIÓN *f* RÍGIDA **10589**
FIJACIÓN POR CLAVIJAS *f* **13740**
FIJAR **11390**
FIJAR **5041**
FIJAR POR ADSORCIÓN **202**
FILAMENTO *m* **6386**
FILAMENTO DE CUARZO **10078**
FILETE *m* **11045**
FILETE *m* **5092**
FILETE *m* DE CORRIENTE **12351**
FILETE *m* MÉTRICO INTERNACIONAL **7083**
FILETEADO **12857**
FILETEADO *m* **3535**
FILETEADO *m* GRUESO **2576**
FILETEADO *m* INTERNO **7078**
FILETEAR **3512**
FILITA *f* **9278**
FILO *m* PRINCIPAL **3528**
FILTRACIÓN *f* **5182**
FILTRACIÓN *f* **5182**
FILTRADO *m* **5181**
FILTRAR **5173**
FILTRO *m* **5172**
FILTRO *m* **12333**
FILTRO *m* DE ACEITE **8757**
FILTRO *m* DE AIRE **260**
FILTRO *m* DE AIRE CON BAÑO DE ACEITE **8746**
FILTRO *m* DE ARENA **10923**
FILTRO *m* DE COMBUSTIBLE **5708**
FILTRO *m* DE COQUE **2660**
FILTRO *m* DE CUMBUSTIBLE **5708**
FILTRO *m* DE GRAVA **6074**
FILTRO *m* PREVIO **5265**
FILTRO-PRENSA *m* **5180**
FILTROS *m pl* SIMÉTRICOS **933**
FINAL *m* DE BLOQUE **4730**
FINAL *m* DE CINTA **4725**
FINAL *m* DE LÍNEA **4731**
FINAL *m* DE PROGRAMA **4724**
FINURA *f* **5208**
FÍSICA *f* (CIENCIA) **9279**
FÍSICO **9285**
FISURA *f* **11629**
FISURA *f* **5304**
FISURA *f* **4377**
FISURA *f* **3278**
FISURA *f* **3278**
FISURA *f* **3278**
FISURA *f* **2278**
FISURA *f* BAJO CORDÓN **13350**

FISURA *f* CAPILAR **3318**
FISURA *f* CAPILAR **6202**
FISURA *f* DE FATIGA/ DE RESISTENCIA **4739**
FISURA *f* DE LAMINADO **7383**
FISURA *f* DE RETRACCIÓN **11395**
FISURA *f* DE TEMPLE **10097**
FISURA *f* DEL ACERO TEMPLADO **3282**
FISURA *f* POR FATIGA **5048**
FISURA *f* SUPERFICIAL **12501**
FISURA INCIPIENTE *f* **6833**
FISURACIÓN *f* **3284**
FISURACIÓN *f* **3284**
FISURACIÓN *f* POR CORROSIÓN BAJO TENSIÓN **12364**
FLAMBEO *m* **3343**
FLAMBEO *m* **3343**
FLANCO *m* **5348**
FLANCO *m* DE BASE **10720**
FLANCO *m* DE DIENTE **4997**
FLANCO *m* DE LA ROSCA **5350**
FLANCO *m* DE RAÍZ **10721**
FLANCO *m* DE SALIENTE **167**
FLANCO *m* DEL DIENTE **5351**
FLANCO *m* DEL DIENTE **13018**
FLECHA *f* **10613**
FLECHA **10613**
FLECHA *f* **3701**
FLECHA *f* **719**
FLECHA *f* **5426**
FLECHA *f* **3698**
FLECHA *f* DE COTA **3395**
FLECHA *f* MÁXIMA **8064**
FLEJE *m* **12378**
FLEJE *m* **12343**
FLEJE *m* **6575**
FLEJE *m* (CHAPA *f* FINA) **12216**
FLEJE *m* INOXIDABLE **10875**
FLEJE *m* PARA TUBOS **11527**
FLEJES *m pl* **980**
FLEJES *m pl* **980**
FLEJES *m pl* DE ACERO ALEADO **371**
FLEJES *m pl* DE ACERO PARA EMBUTIDO PROFUNDO **3688**
FLEXIBILIDAD *f* **5415**
FLEXIBILIDAD *f* **5415**
FLEXIBLE **9518**
FLEXIÓN *f* **10894**
FLEXIÓN *f* **10892**
FLEXIÓN *f* **10892**
FLEXIÓN *f* **1182**
FLEXIÓN *f* **3698**

**FLE** 1038

FLEXIÓN **5422**
FLEXIÓN *f* **1182**
FLEXIÓN *f* **3698**
FLEXIÓN *f* **3700**
FLEXIÓN *f* **3698**
FLEXIÓN *f* **3699**
FLEXIÓN *f* **3701**
FLEXIÓN *f* **5426**
FLEXIÓN *f* ELÁSTICA **4477**
FLEXIÓN *f* EN CALIENTE **6619**
FLEXIÓN *f* MÁXIMA **8064**
FLEXIÓN *f* TRANSVERSAL **3700**
FLEXIÓN EFECTUADA EN ACEROS TRATADOS CON TEMPLES (PRUEBA DE ...) **10088**
FLEXIONES *f* **10895**
FLINT **5427**
FLINT-GLASS *m* **5428**
FLOCULACIÓN *f* **5441**
FLOR *f* DEL CUERO **6038**
FLOTABILIDAD *f* **1742**
FLOTACIÓN *f* **344**
FLOTACIÓN *f* **557**
FLOTACIÓN *f* **5452**
FLOTACIÓN *f* SELECTIVA **11144**
FLOTADOR *m* **5430**
FLOTADOR *m* DE ALMACENAJE Y DE ARRIBAJE **10217**
FLOTADOR *m* (DE CALIBRACIÓN) **5876**
FLUCTUACIONES *f pl* DE VELOCIDAD **13499**
FLUENCIA *f* **3324**
FLUENCIA *f* DE UNA SOLUCIÓN **3330**
FLUENCIA *f* DEL MATERIAL **5465**
FLUENCIA *f* SECUNDARIA **11104**
FLUENCIA *f* TRANSITORIA **13118**
FLUENCIA *f* VISCOSA **13578**
FLUIDEZ *f* **5474**
FLUIDEZ *f* **5463**
FLUIDO *m* **7641**
FLUIDO *m* DE CORTE **3530**
FLUIDO *m* DE ENFRIAMIENTO **3083**
FLUIDO *m* GASEOSO **5808**
FLUIDO *m* LÍQUIDO **7641**
FLUIDOS *m pl* DE CORTE QUÍMICOS **2303**
FLUIDOS *m pl* DE CORTE SINTÉTICOS **2303**
FLUJO *m* **5454**
FLUJO *m* BÁSICO **1046**
FLUJO *m* LUMINOSO **7821**
FLUJO MAGNÉTICO **7903**
FLUOR *m* **5478**
FLUORESCENCIA *f* **5476**
FLUORINA *f* **5479**

FLUORURO *m* DE AMONIO **463**
FLUORURO *m* DE BARIO **999**
FLUORURO *m* DE CALCIO **5479**
FLUORURO *m* DE CALCIO **5479**
FLUORURO *m* DE ESTRONCIO **12390**
FLUORURO *m* DE LITIO **7667**
FLUORURO *m* DE MAGNESIO **7886**
FLUORURO *m* DE POTASIO **9686**
FLUORURO *m* DE SODIO **11721**
FOCO *m* REAL **10258**
FOCO *m* VIRTUAL IMAGINARIO **13571**
FOCO (OPT. Y GEOM.) *m* **5502**
FOGONERO *m* **12272**
FOGONERO *m* **12271**
FOLIUM *m* DE DESCARTES **5513**
FONAUTÓGRAFO **9242**
FONDEADERO *m* **8390**
FONDERÍA (TALLER DE) **5592**
FONDO *m* **6314**
FONDO *m* **1221**
FONDO *m* APAINELADO **13045**
FONDO *m* CURVADO **1812**
FONDO *m* DE CRISOL **11550**
FONDO *m* DE ESCORIA **2500**
FONDO *m* DE LA ONDA **6543**
FONDO *m* DE ROSCA **1028**
FONDO *m* DE ROSCA **1028**
FONDO *m* DE ROSCA **12864**
FONDO *m* DE UN TAMBOR **6316**
FONDO *m* DEL CILINDRO **1494**
FONDO *m* EMBUTIDO **4038**
FONDO TORICÓNICO **13044**
FORJA *f* **5547**
FORJA *f* A MANO **6261**
FORJA *f* PORTÁTIL **9637**
FORJA *f* (TALLER) **7160**
FORJA *f* VOLANTE **9637**
FORJABILIDAD *f* **7958**
FORJABLE **7960**
FORJADO *m* **5557**
FORJADO *m* A MANO **11669**
FORJADO *m* A MÁQUINA **7847**
FORJADO *m* A PRENSA **9798**
FORJADO *m* A PRENSA **9807**
FORJADO *m* DE UNA PIEZA EN LA MASA **5552**
FORJADO *m* EN CALIENTE **6626**
FORJADO *m* EN ESTAMPA **12534**
FORJADO *m* EN FRÍO **2681**
FORJADO *m* POR LAMINADO **10668**
FORJADOR *m* DE CLAVOS **13891**

FORJADURA  *f* **5555**
FORJAR **5542**
FORJAR A PRENSA **9800**
FORMA  *f* **11264**
FORMACIÓN  *f* **5579**
FORMACIÓN  *f* DE CASCARILLA **1927**
FORMACIÓN  *f* DE COSTRAS **11545**
FORMACIÓN  *f* DE ENTIBACIÓN **1604**
FORMACIÓN  *f* DE ESPUMA **4461**
FORMACIÓN  *f* DE ESPUMA **5703**
FORMACIÓN  *f* DE GÉRMENES **5934**
FORMACIÓN  *f* DE GRIETAS **644**
FORMACIÓN  *f* DE HALO **6203**
FORMACIÓN  *f* DE HERRUMBRE **10865**
FORMACIÓN  *f* DE HUMO **11675**
FORMACIÓN  *f* DE INCRUSTACIONES **6856**
FORMACIÓN  *f* DE INCRUSTACIONES CALCÁREAS **6856**
FORMACIÓN  *f* DE MANCHAS **11961**
FORMACIÓN  *f* DE MOHO **5575**
FORMACIÓN  *f* DE RAJAS **2286**
FORMACIÓN  *f* DE RECHUPES FORMACIÓN  *f* DE BURBUJAS **1672**
FORMACIÓN  *f* DE REDONDELES **2286**
FORMACIÓN  *f* DE UNA COSTRA **1927**
FORMALDEHIDO  *m* **5573**
FORMAR **5571**
FORMAR LA CABEZA  *f* DEL REMACHE  *m* **2516**
FORMATO  *m* **5574**
FORMATO  *m* BLOC DE DIRECCIONES **1334**
FORMATO  *m* BLOC DE DIRECCIONES **13935**
FORMATO  *m* DE BLOC FIJO **5288**
FORMATO  *m* DE BLOC VARIABLE **13489**
FORMATO  *m* DE SECUENCIA FIJA **5297**
FORMATO  *m* TABULAR **12583**
FORMOL  *m* **5573**
FORMOL  *m* **5573**
FORMÓN  *m* **2349**
FORMÓN  *m* **1919**
FORMÓN  *m* **5264**
FORMÓN  *m* **2349**
FORMÓN DE CARPINTERO  *m* **9080**
FORMÓN PARA FRÍO  *m* **2717**
FORMÓN PARA FRÍO  *m* **2672**
FÓRMULA  *f* **5582**
FÓRMULA  *f* APROXIMADA **654**
FÓRMULA  *f* BRUTA **4704**
FÓRMULA  *f* DE APROXIMACIÓN **654**
FÓRMULA  *f* DE CONSTITUCIÓN **5583**
FÓRMULA  *f* QUÍMICA **2310**
FORRAR **7598**

FORRO  *m* **7623**
FORRO  *m* **7623**
FORRO  *m* **7623**
FORRO  *m* **7623**
FORRO  *m* **11576**
FORRO  *m* **2447**
FORRO CUBIERTO PREVIAMENTE DE GRAVA **9783**
FORRO DE AISLAMIENTO TÉRMICO  *m* **7623**
FORRO DE MADERA  *m* **13927**
FORZAMIENTO  *m* **12322**
FORZAR UNA CLAVIJA EN SU RANURA **4293**
FOSFATACIÓN  *f* **2600**
FOSFATO  *m* **9244**
FOSFATO  *m* DE AMONIO **469**
FOSFATO  *m* DE AMONIO Y DE SODIO **8241**
FOSFATO  *m* DE CALCIO **1855**
FOSFATO  *m* DE MAGNESIA **8656**
FOSFATO  *m* DE POTASIO **9696**
FOSFATO  *m* DE SODIO **11728**
FOSFATO  *m* TRICÁLCICO **1855**
FOSFORESCENCIA  *f* **9247**
FOSFORESCENTE **9248**
FÓSFORO  *m* **9252**
FÓSFORO  *m* BLANCO **14009**
FÓSFORO  *m* ROJO **10334**
FOSO  *m* DE BATIDURAS **10977**
FOSO  *m* DE TEMPLAR **11699**
FOSO  *m* DEL VOLANTE **5498**
FOTOCALCO  *m* **9276**
FOTOCOPIA  *f* **9276**
FOTOCOPIA  *f* AZUL **1375**
FOTODIODO  *m* **9258**
FOTOGRAFÍA  *f* **9265**
FOTOGRAFÍA  *f* **9263**
FOTOGRAFIAR **9262**
FOTOMETRÍA  *f* **9271**
FOTOMÉTRICO **9269**
FOTÓMETRO  *m* **9267**
FOTOMULTIPLICADOR  *m* **9274**
FOTÓN  *m* **9275**
FRACCIÓN  *f* **5613**
FRACCIÓN  *f* DE DESTILACIÓN **5611**
FRACCIÓN  *f* DECIMAL **3662**
FRACCIÓN  *f* DECIMAL PERIÓDICA **9192**
FRACCIÓN  *f* DECIMAL TERMINADA **5231**
FRACCIÓN  *f* ORDINARIA **13611**
FRACCIÓN  *f* PROPIA **9932**
FRACCIÓN  *f* PURA **9932**
FRACCIONAR **5615**
FRACTURA  *f* **5617**

# FRA

1040

FRACTURA *f* **5620**
FRACTURA *f* **10861**
FRACTURA *f* **10858**
FRACTURA *f* **10858**
FRACTURA CEROIDE *f* **11936**
FRACTURA CONCHOIDAL *f* **2893**
FRACTURA DESIGUAL *f* **13357**
FRACTURA EN GAUCHO *f* **6195**
(FRACTURA) ESCAMOSA **11936**
(FRACTURA) ESCAMOSA *f* **11936**
FRACTURA ESTRIADA *f* **6195**
FRACTURA FIBROSA *f* **5138**
FRACTURA GRANULADA *f* **6051**
FRACTURA INTERGRANULAR *f* **7042**
FRACTURA LIMPIA *f* **11683**
FRACTURA TERROSA *f* **4421**
FRÁGIL *m* **1627**
FRÁGIL **5621**
FRÁGIL **7343**
FRAGILIDAD *f* **11378**
FRAGILIDAD *f* **11580**
FRAGILIDAD *f* **5622**
FRAGILIDAD *f* **4685**
FRAGILIDAD *f* **1628**
FRAGILIDAD *f* A LA ENTALLADURA **1632**
FRAGILIDAD *f* A LA ENTALLADURA **8669**
FRAGILIDAD *f* A LA GALVANIZACIÓN **5790**
FRAGILIDAD *f* AL DECAPADO **6713**
FRAGILIDAD *f* AL DECAPADO **109**
FRAGILIDAD *f* AL PAVÓN **1631**
FRAGILIDAD *f* AL RECOCIDO **1634**
FRAGILIDAD *f* CÁUSTICA **2118**
FRAGILIDAD *f* DEL HIERRO **1629**
FRAGILIDAD *f* EN CALIENTE **6641**
FRAGILIDAD *f* EN CALIENTE **10339**
FRAGILIDAD *f* EN FRÍO **2703**
FRAGILIDAD *f* POR CORROSIÓN **3186**
FRAGILIDAD *f* POR DECAPADO **1630**
FRAGILIDAD *f* POR PENETRACIÓN DE LA SOLDADURA **11757**
FRAGILIDAD *f* REOTRÓPICA **1633**
FRAGILIDAD DEL HIERRO *f* **2704**
FRAGILIZACIÓN *f* EN CALIENTE **6625**
FRAGMENTACIÓN *f* DE GRANOS **5623**
FRAGMENTOS *m* MENUDOS **8267**
FRAGUA *f* **5548**
FRAGUAR **6287**
FRAGUAR **11214**
FRAGUARSE AL AIRE **6286**
FRANELA *f* **5352**

FRANJA *f* DE INTERFERENCIA **7040**
FRANQUICIA (DE DEMORA) *f* **6020**
FRASCO *m* **5370**
FRASCO *m* LAVADOR **5845**
FRASCO *m* SECADOR **4308**
FRASCO *m* SECADOR **4308**
FRAUDE *m* **205**
FRECUENCIA *f* **5661**
FRECUENCIA *f* BAJA **7771**
FRECUENCIA *f* EMPÍRICA **5662**
FRENADO *m* **1549**
FRENADO *m* **1549**
FRENADO *m* INICIAL **6928**
FRENAR **1530**
FRENAR **650**
FRENO *m* **898**
FRENO *m* **1529**
FRENO *m* **5031**
FRENO *m* CENTRÍFUGO **2175**
FRENO *m* DE ACEITE **8755**
FRENO *m* DE AIRE COMPRIMIDO **2840**
FRENO *m* DE CADENA **2203**
FRENO *m* DE CINTA **5681**
FRENO *m* DE CINTA **5681**
FRENO *m* DE CINTA **1544**
FRENO *m* DE COLLARÍN **5681**
FRENO *m* DE CONO **2926**
FRENO *m* DE CORRIENTES DE FOUCAULT **4439**
FRENO *m* DE CUERDA **10732**
FRENO *m* DE DISCO **8454**
FRENO *m* DE DISCO **8454**
FRENO *m* DE DISCO **4001**
FRENO *m* DE DOS MORDAZAS **4129**
FRENO *m* DE DOS ZAPATAS **4129**
FRENO *m* DE ENROLLAMIENTO **5681**
FRENO *m* DE ESTACIONAMIENTO **9082**
FRENO *m* DE FRICCIÓN **5669**
FRENO *m* DE MANO **6227**
FRENO *m* DE MANO **9082**
FRENO *m* DE PALANCA **7532**
FRENO *m* DE PALANCA **12978**
FRENO *m* DE PALANCA Y CONTRAPESO **3638**
FRENO *m* DE PIE **5519**
FRENO *m* DE RETENCIÓN **7681**
FRENO *m* DE SEGURIDAD **10883**
FRENO *m* DE SOCORRO **4687**
FRENO *m* DE TAMBOR **4334**
FRENO *m* DE TORNILLO **12344**
FRENO *m* DE TUERCA **8701**
FRENO *m* DE VAPOR **12159**

**FRE**

FRENO *m* DE ZAPATA **1335**
FRENO *m* DIFERENCIAL **3907**
FRENO *m* DINAMOMÉTRICO DE PRONY **9920**
FRENO *m* ELECTROMAGNÉTICO **4613**
FRENO *m* HIDRÁULICO **6678**
FRENO *m* HIDRÁULICO **6709**
FRENO *m* HIDRÁULICO **8755**
FRENO *m* HIDRONEUMÁTICO **6678**
FRENO *m* MAGNÉTICO **7896**
FRENO *m* POR DEPRESIÓN **13436**
FRENO *m* POR PEDAL **5519**
FRENO *m* POR VACÍO **13436**
FRENO *m* REGULABLE **187**
FRENO DE PEDAL *m* **5519**
FRENO DE PIE *m* **5519**
FRENO-MOTOR *m* **4760**
FRENOS *m* ASISTIDOS **9731**
FRENTE *m* DE CAJA DE VÁLVULAS **4996**
FRENTE *m* DE CRISTALIZACIÓN **11798**
FRENTE *m* DE SOLIDIFICACIÓN **11798**
FRESA *f* **8289**
FRESA *f* **3519**
FRESA *f* AMORTAJADORA **8193**
FRESA *f* ANGULAR **543**
FRESA *f* AXIAL **4446**
FRESA *f* CILÍNDRICA **13848**
FRESA *f* CON DENTADO HELICOIDAL **11917**
FRESA *f* CON DENTADO RECTILINEO **12307**
FRESA *f* CON DIENTES DESPEJADOS **905**
FRESA *f* CON DIENTES FIJOS **6971**
FRESA *f* CON DIENTES LIBRES **905**
FRESA *f* DE ALISAR **4722**
FRESA *f* DE ALLANAR **4722**
FRESA *f* DE AVELLANAR **543**
FRESA *f* DE CORTE FRONTAL **4722**
FRESA *f* DE DISCO **8496**
FRESA *f* DE ESPIGA **11259**
FRESA *f* DE EXTERIOR PARA TUBOS **4951**
FRESA *f* DE FORMAR **9899**
FRESA *f* DE INTERIOR PARA TUBOS **7059**
FRESA *f* DE PERFIL CONSTANTE **905**
FRESA *f* DESBARBADORA **1765**
FRESA *f* DESBARBADORA HEMBRA **4951**
FRESA *f* DESBARBADORA MACHO **7059**
FRESA *f* EN DISCO **11412**
FRESA *f* FRONTAL **4722**
FRESA *f* FRONTAL **4722**
FRESA *f* PARA ABRIR RANURAS **11634**
FRESA *f* PARA EL ALOJAMIENTO DE LA CABEZA DEL TORNILLO **3245**

FRESA *f* PARA HACER ENGRANAJES HELICOIDALES **13972**
FRESA *f* PARA HACER LOS ENGRANAJES **5898**
FRESA *f* PARA ROSCAR **13971**
FRESA *f* PARA ROSCAS DE TORNILLOS **6512**
FRESA *f* PERFILADA **9899**
FRESA *f* RADIAL **4722**
FRESA *f* RECTILINEA **13848**
FRESA DE CUCHILLAS FIJAS *f* **6971**
FRESADO *m* **8287**
FRESADO *m* **3234**
FRESADO *m* ASCENDIENDO **13408**
FRESADO *m* ASPIRANDO **2497**
FRESADO *m* CLÁSICO **3061**
FRESADO *m* DE ALOJAMIENTO DE UN REMACHE **3247**
FRESADO *m* DE CONTORNOS **3040**
FRESADO *m* DE MATRICES **3892**
FRESADO *m* DE UN AGUJERO PARA TORNILLO **3247**
FRESADO *m* DESCENDIENDO **4182**
FRESADO *m* EN DUPLEX **12301**
FRESADO *m* EN TREN **5800**
FRESADO *m* RECIPROCO **10282**
FRESADO DE PERFILES **3040**
FRESADOR *m* **8292**
FRESADORA *f* **8291**
FRESADORA *f* ACCIONADA POR DISPOSITIVO DE COPIA **13080**
FRESADORA *f* CEPILLADORA **9460**
FRESADORA *f* CIRCULAR **2420**
FRESADORA *f* CON CONSOLA Y COLUMNA **7319**
FRESADORA *f* DE PÓRTICO **9642**
FRESADORA *f* DESBASTADORA **9900**
FRESADORA *f* DUPLEX DE GRAN RENDIMIENTO **4379**
FRESADORA *f* FIJA DE BANCO **5298**
FRESADORA *f* HORIZONTAL **6589**
FRESADORA *f* MÚLTIPLE **8471**
FRESADORA *f* PARA COPIAR **9900**
FRESADORA *f* PARA HACER LOS ENGRANAJES **5894**
FRESADORA *f* RADIAL DE CORREDERA **10190**
FRESADORA *f* UNIVERSAL **13387**
FRESADORA *f* VERTICAL **13548**
FRESAR **8276**
FRESAR EL AGUJERO PARA UN REMACHE **3246**
FRESAR EL AGUJERO PARA UN TORNILLO **3246**
FRESAS *f pl* CON DOS CORTES EN EXTREMO **4992**
FRESAS *f* CÓNICAS **540**
FRESAS *f* DE AVELLANAR **540**
FRESAS *f pl* DE CUCHILLAS **11632**
FRESAS *f pl* DE RANURAR WOODRUFF **13930**
FRESAS *f pl* DE UN CORTE LATERAL **6206**
FRESAS *f pl* EN EXTREMO **4723**

**FRE** 1042

FRESAS *f pl* EN EXTREMO MANDRILADAS **11337**
FRESAS *f pl* EN EXTREMO PLENAS **11783**
FRESAS *f pl* MADRES **5577**
FRESAS *f pl* PARA ABRIR RANURAS EN T **12582**
FRESAS *f pl* PARA HACER LA COLA DE MILANO **4176**
FRESAS *f pl* PARA HACER RANURAS **11632**
FRESAS *f pl* PROVISTAS DE ÁRBOL **663**
FRESAS *f pl* SIMPLES DE HÉLICE RÁPIDA **6471**
FRESAS *f pl* SIMPLES PARA TRABAJOS DUROS **6404**
FRICCIÓN *f* **5668**
FRICCIÓN *f* **5668**
FRICCIÓN *f* DE RODAMIENTO **10700**
FRICCIÓN *f* INTERNA **7065**
FROTADO *m* **8450**
FROTADOR *m* **8451**
FROTAMIENTO *m* **5668**
FROTAMIENTO *m* AL ARRANCAR **5678**
FROTAMIENTO *m* AL PARTIR **5678**
FROTAMIENTO *m* CINÉTICO **7309**
FROTAMIENTO *m* DURANTE EL MOVIMIENTO **5677**
FROTAMIENTO *m* EN MARCHA **5677**
FROTAMIENTO *m* ESTÁTICO **12134**
FTALEÍNA *f* DEL FENOL **9238**
FUEGO *m* DE FORJA **5548**
FUEGO *m* DIRECTO **8813**
FUEL *m* **5714**
FUEL OIL *m* **5714**
FUELLE *m* **1139**
FUELLE *m* DE FORJA **1139**
FUENTE *f* DE CORRIENTE A TENSIÓN CONSTANTE (PARA SOLDADURA) **2979**
FUENTE *f* DE ELECTRICIDAD **11823**
FUENTE *f* DE ENERGÍA **11824**
FUENTE *f* DE ERRORES **11825**
FUENTE *f* LINEAL **7599**
FUENTE *f* LUMINOSA **7568**
FUENTE *f* LUMINOSA **11826**
FUERA DE EJE **8731**
FUERA DE ESCUADRA **8895**
FUERTE PRESIÓN *f* **6473**
FUERZA *f* **5532**
FUERZA *f* **6907**
FUERZA *f* **12352**
FUERZA *f* ASCENSIONAL **1742**
FUERZA *f* CENTRÍFUGA **2180**
FUERZA *f* CENTRÍPETA **2190**
FUERZA *f* COERCITIVA **2639**
FUERZA *f* COERCITIVA **2641**
FUERZA *f* COMPONENTE **2816**
FUERZA *f* CONSTANTE **2973**

FUERZA *f* CONTRA-ELECTROMOTRIZ **3231**
FUERZA *f* DE ATRACCIÓN **5529**
FUERZA *f* DE COHESIÓN **2644**
FUERZA *f* DE COMPRESIÓN **2868**
FUERZA *f* DE CORTE **11291**
FUERZA *f* DE EMPUJE **6811**
FUERZA *f* DE FRICCIÓN **5683**
FUERZA *f* DE FROTAMIENTO **5683**
FUERZA *f* DE INERCIA **6907**
FUERZA *f* DE TORSIÓN **13055**
FUERZA *f* DE TRACCIÓN **12745**
FUERZA *f* DE UN MUELLE **5528**
FUERZA *f* DEL HOMBRE **9738**
FUERZA *f* ELÁSTICA DE UN GAS **4480**
FUERZA *f* ELECTROMOTRIZ **4622**
FUERZA *f* ELECTROMOTRIZ **4622**
FUERZA *f* ELECTROMOTRIZ TÉRMICA **12807**
FUERZA *f* ELECTROSTÁTICA **4642**
FUERZA *f* EXTERIOR **4954**
FUERZA *f* EXTERIOR **4954**
FUERZA *f* FRENANTE **1551**
FUERZA *f* HIDRÁULICA **13668**
FUERZA *f* IMPULSIVA **6811**
FUERZA *f* INTERIOR **7064**
FUERZA *f* MAGNÉTICA **7904**
FUERZA *f* MAGNETIZANTE **7925**
FUERZA *f* MAGNETOMOTRIZ **7932**
FUERZA *f* MAGNETOMOTRIZ ESPECÍFICA **7929**
FUERZA *f* MOLECULAR **8360**
FUERZA *f* MOTRIZ **8409**
FUERZA *f* MOTRIZ **9733**
FUERZA *f* NECESARIA **3746**
FUERZA *f* POLAR **9596**
FUERZA *f* REACTIVA **10248**
FUERZA *f* REPULSIVA **5530**
FUERZA *f* RESISTENTE **10484**
FUERZA *f* TANGENCIAL **12622**
FUERZA *f* TERMOELÉCTRICA **12831**
FUERZA *f* ÚNICA **11483**
FUERZA *f* VIVA **7308**
FUERZAS *f pl* CONCURRENTES **2903**
FUERZAS *f pl* EN DIRECCIÓN OPUESTA **5537**
FUERZAS *f pl* EN LA MISMA DIRECCIÓN **5538**
FUERZAS *f* INVERSAS **5537**
FUERZAS *f pl* PARALELAS **9056**
FUGA *f* **7488**
FUGA *f* (DE GASES O LÍQUIDOS) **7492**
FUGA *f* POR LAS JUNTAS **7486**
FULMINATO *m* DE MERCURIO **8154**
FULMINATO *m* DE PLATA **11463**

FUMÍVORO (A) **11673**
FUNCIÓN *f* AUXILIAR **8319**
FUNCIÓN *f* AUXILIAR **854**
FUNCIÓN *f* CÍCLICA **2413**
FUNCIÓN *f* CIRCULAR **2413**
FUNCIÓN *f* CONTINUA **3025**
FUNCIÓN *f* DE DISTRIBUCIÓN **9881**
FUNCIÓN *f* DE (EN) **13542**
FUNCIÓN *f* DE HERRAMIENTA **13001**
FUNCIÓN *f* DE REPARTO COMPUESTA **7239**
FUNCIÓN *f* EXPONENCIAL **4942**
FUNCIÓN *f* GAMMA **5794**
FUNCIÓN *f* GENERATRIZ (DE MOMENTOS) **5919**
FUNCIÓN *f* HIPERBÓLICA **6737**
FUNCIÓN *f* (MATEM.) **5734**
FUNCIÓN *f* PREPARATORIA **9786**
FUNCIONAMIENTO *m* **13172**
FUNCIONAMIENTO *m* CONTINUO **3038**
FUNCIONAMIENTO *m* (DE MÁQUINA) **10850**
FUNCIONAMIENTO *m* (DE SERVICIO) **8837**
FUNCIONAMIENTO *m* (DE UNA MÁQUINA DE UN VEHÍCULO) **10850**
FUNCIONAMIENTO *m* INTERMITENTE **7056**
FUNCIONAMIENTO *m* SOBRE (DE) **10440**
FUNCIONAMIENTO DESORDENADO DE LA VÁLVULA *m* **2277**
FUNCIONAR SIN OBJETO ÚTIL **4372**
FUNDA *f* **7986**
FUNDACIÓN *f* **2896**
FUNDENTE *m* **5489**
FUNDENTE *m* **5475**
FUNDENTE *m* ÁCIDO **114**
FUNDENTE *m* PARA SOLDAR **5490**
FUNDICIÓN *f* **5592**
FUNDICIÓN *f* **5592**
FUNDICIÓN *f* **5593**
FUNDICIÓN *f* ACERADA **11177**
FUNDICIÓN *f* AFINADA **5544**
FUNDICIÓN *f* AL AIRE CALIENTE **6620**
FUNDICIÓN *f* AL AIRE FRÍO **2669**
FUNDICIÓN *f* ALEADA **363**
FUNDICIÓN *f* ALEADA **2037**
FUNDICIÓN *f* (ART) **5592**
FUNDICIÓN *f* BESSEMER **117**
FUNDICIÓN *f* BLANCA **2049**
FUNDICIÓN *f* BLANCA **13830**
FUNDICIÓN *f* BRUTA BESSEMER **105**
FUNDICIÓN *f* BRUTA (EN LINGOTES) **9299**
FUNDICIÓN *f* CON CARBÓN VEGETAL **2258**
FUNDICIÓN *f* CON COQUE (DE ALTO HORNO) **2657**
FUNDICIÓN *f* CON COQUE MADERA **2664**

FUNDICIÓN *f* CON GRAFITO ESFEROIDAL **4362**
FUNDICIÓN *f* CON GRAFITO ESFEROIDAL **2045**
FUNDICIÓN *f* CON GRAFITO ESFEROIDAL **11894**
FUNDICIÓN *f* CON GRAFITO ESFEROIDAL **11895**
FUNDICIÓN *f* CON MODELOS **7230**
FUNDICIÓN *f* CON SOPLADO **6563**
FUNDICIÓN *f* DE ACERO **2055**
FUNDICIÓN *f* DE ACERO **12207**
FUNDICIÓN *f* DE COBRE **1566**
FUNDICIÓN *f* DE GRAN RESISTENCIA) **2042**
FUNDICIÓN *f* DE HEMATITES **6435**
FUNDICIÓN *f* DE HIERRO/ HIERRO *m* COLADO **7142**
FUNDICIÓN *f* DE MOLDEO **5596**
FUNDICIÓN *f* DE TRANSICIÓN **8733**
FUNDICIÓN *f* DÚCTIL **11894**
FUNDICIÓN *f* DÚCTIL **2045**
FUNDICIÓN *f* DÚCTIL **2040**
FUNDICIÓN *f* ELÉCTRICA **4509**
FUNDICIÓN *f* ELÉCTRICA **4550**
FUNDICIÓN *f* EN CÁMARA FRÍA **2671**
FUNDICIÓN *f* EN COQUILLA **2334**
FUNDICIÓN *f* EN COQUILLA **2335**
FUNDICIÓN *f* EN COQUILLA **2038**
FUNDICIÓN *f* EN HORNO ELÉCTRICO **4510**
FUNDICIÓN *f* EN LINGOTES **9299**
FUNDICIÓN *f* (ENDURECIDA) **2336**
FUNDICIÓN *f* ESPECULAR (SPIEGEL) **11899**
FUNDICIÓN *f* GRAFÍTICA **1292**
FUNDICIÓN *f* GRIS **2041**
FUNDICIÓN *f* GRIS **6094**
FUNDICIÓN *f* GRIS **5596**
FUNDICIÓN *f* (HIERRO COLADO) **2034**
FUNDICIÓN *f* (HIERRO COLADO) **7157**
FUNDICIÓN *f* MALEABLE **7959**
FUNDICIÓN *f* MALEABLE **2043**
FUNDICIÓN *f* MALEABLE DE CUBILOTE **3467**
FUNDICIÓN *f* MALEABLE PERLÍTICA **2047**
FUNDICIÓN *f* MANGANESÍFERA **11865**
FUNDICIÓN *f* MECÁNICA **7863**
FUNDICIÓN *f* MECÁNICA **4763**
FUNDICIÓN *f* MOTEADA **2044**
FUNDICIÓN *f* MOTEADA **8420**
FUNDICIÓN *f* NODULAR **8607**
FUNDICIÓN *f* NODULAR **11894**
FUNDICIÓN *f* PERLÍTICA **9200**
FUNDICIÓN *f* PERLÍTICA **2046**
FUNDICIÓN *f* (PRODUCTO) **2068**
FUNDICIÓN *f* RESISTENTE A LA CORROSIÓN **2039**
FUNDICIÓN *f* RESISTENTE AL DESGASTE **2048**
FUNDICIÓN *f* SIN RECHUPES **2075**

**FUN** 1044

FUNDICIÓN *f* SIN TENSIONES INTERNAS **2074**
FUNDICIÓN *f* TEMPLADA **2038**
FUNDICIÓN *f* THOMAS **1049**
FUNDICIÓN BESSEMER *f* **1213**
FUNDICIÓN CENTRIFUGA *f* **2176**
FUNDICIÓN EN ARENA *f* **10922**
FUNDICIÓN EN ARENA SECA *f* **4353**
FUNDICIÓN EN FONDO *f* **1488**
FUNDICIONES *f pl* (INSTALACIONES *f pl*) **5597**
FUNDIDO EN COQUILLA *m* **2334**
FUNDIDO EN COQUILLA *m* **9208**
FUNDIDOR *m* **7362**
FUNDIDOR *m* **5591**
FUNDIR **2030**
FUNDIR **2030**
FUNDIR **8135**
FUNDIR (QUIM.) **4061**
FUNDIRSE (EL COJINETE SE FUNDE) **10837**
FUNDIRSE (EN CORTO CIRCUITO) **1352**
FUNICULAR *m* **1826**
FURGÓN *m* **13474**
FURGONETA *f* **12141**
FUSIBLE *m* **9539**
FUSIBLE *m* **5758**
FUSIBLE *m* **5758**
FUSIBLE *m* **5756**
FUSIBLE *m* **5751**
FUSIBLE *m* DE CORTACIRCUITOS **10886**
FUSIÓN *f* **8136**
FUSIÓN *f* **8134**
FUSIÓN *f* **8134**
FUSIÓN *f* **11666**
FUSIÓN *f* **12703**
FUSIÓN *f* **5760**
FUSIÓN *f* **2572**
FUSIÓN *f* CONGRUENTE **2938**
FUSIÓN *f* EN EL VACÍO **13444**
FUSIÓN *f* EUTÉCTICA **4856**
FUSIÓN *f* ÍGNEA **5764**
FUSIÓN *f* POR ZONA **14050**
FUSIÓN (OPERACIÓN) *f* **2070**
FUSTE *m* DE UNA COLUMNA **11243**
GABARRA *f* **991**
GABINETE *m* DE DIBUJO **4198**
GABRO *m* **5765**
GADOLINIO *m* **5767**
GAFAS *f pl* DE ESCARIADO **1474**
GAFAS *f pl* DE PROTECCIÓN **5992**
GAFAS *f pl* PARA SOLDAR **13764**
GALENA *f* **5775**

GALGA *f* **5871**
GALGA DE FLUJO *f* **5455**
GALGOS *f* **5769**
GÁLIBO *m* **5768**
GÁLIBO *m* **9128**
GÁLIBO *m* **12734**
GÁLIBO *m* DE PERFORACIÓN **4267**
GÁLIBO *m* DE SOLDADURA **13785**
GÁLIBO *m* PARA HERRAMIENTAS DE ATERRAJAR **12865**
GÁLIBOS *m* **5769**
GÁLIBOS *m* DE PERFORACIÓN **4268**
GALIO *m* **5779**
GALLETILLA *f* **2328**
GALLETILLA *f* DE CARBÓN **2328**
GALÓN *m* (MEDIDA INGLESA) **5781**
GALVANIZACIÓN *f* **5787**
GALVANIZACIÓN *f* **5789**
GALVANIZACIÓN *f* **14044**
GALVANIZACIÓN *f* CON CINC **14044**
GALVANIZACIÓN *f* CON CINC **5787**
GALVANIZACIÓN *f* CON CINC **5789**
GALVANIZACIÓN *f* CON CINC **2604**
GALVANIZACIÓN *f* (CON CINC) ELECTROLÍTICA **4583**
GALVANIZACIÓN *f* EN CALIENTE **6653**
GALVANIZACIÓN *f* EN CONTINUO **3027**
GALVANIZACIÓN *f* EN FRÍO **2683**
GALVANIZACIÓN *f* PARCIAL **9076**
GALVANIZACIÓN *f* POR TEMPLE **6628**
GALVANIZAR **5784**
GALVANIZAR **366**
GALVANIZAR CON CINC **5784**
GALVANÓMETRO *m* **5791**
GALVANOPLASTIA *f* **4651**
GALVANOPLASTIA *f* **4640**
GALVANOPLASTIA *f* **4640**
GALVANOPLASTIA *f* AL TONEL **1016**
GALVANOPLÁSTICO **5792**
GAMA *f* **10200**
GAMA *f* (DE DUREZA) **10974**
GAMA *f* DE DUREZA **10974**
GAMA *f* DE FABRICACIÓN **7994**
GAMA *f* DE OPERACIONES **2222**
GAMA *f* DE TEMPERATURA **12730**
GAMMAGRAFÍA *f* **5798**
GAMUZA *f* **2234**
GAMUZA *f* **2234**
GANANCIA *f* **5773**
GANCHO *m* **5772**
GANCHO *m* **6568**
GANCHO *m* DE CADENA **3822**

**1045**         **GAS**

GANCHO *m* DE COLA DE CERDO **9301**
GANCHO *m* DE HERRERO **6571**
GANCHO *m* DE OJETE **4974**
GANCHO *m* DE OJETE **4974**
GANCHO *m* DE SEGURIDAD **10888**
GANCHO *m* DE SUSPENSIÓN **12527**
GANCHO *m* DE TORNILLO (O DE ROSCADO) **11057**
GANCHO *m* DOBLE **10191**
GANCHO *m* DOBLE **10191**
GANCHO *m* ELEVADOR **7552**
GANCHO *m* MÓVIL **12561**
GANCHO *m* PARA TUBOS **9354**
GANCHO *m* PIVOTANTE **12564**
GANCHO DE NÚCLEOS **3152**
GANCHOS *m pl* **11902**
GANCHOS *m pl* DE TRACCIÓN **6307**
GANGA *f* **5802**
GANISTER *m* **5803**
GARFIO *m* **2464**
GARFIO *m* **12105**
GARFIO *m* DE TRINQUETE **10219**
GARGANTA *f* **5483**
GARLOPA *f* **4221**
GARLOPA *f* **7245**
GARLOPÍN *m* **7201**
GARRA *f* **11013**
GARRAFÓN *m* **1981**
GARRAS DE CONEXIÓN/DESCONEXIÓN *f* **13214**
GAS *m* **5808**
GAS *m* AL AGUA **13651**
GAS *m* AL AIRE **264**
GAS *m* AMONIACAL **453**
GAS *m* CARBÓNICO **1948**
GAS *m* CARBÓNICO LICUADO **7645**
GAS *m* COMBUSTIBLE **5709**
GAS *m* COMPRIMIDO **2847**
GAS *m* DE ACEITE **8758**
GAS *m* DE ALTO HORNO **1313**
GAS *m* DE ALUMBRADO **6775**
GAS *m* DE ESCAPE **4891**
GAS *m* DE GASÓGENO **9890**
GAS *m* DE HORNO DE COQUE **2663**
GAS *m* DE LA COMBUSTIÓN **5470**
GAS *m* DE LOS PANTANOS **8215**
GAS *m* DE PETRÓLEO LICUADO **7638**
GAS *m* DE PROTECCIÓN **6905**
GAS *m* DEL HOGAR **5470**
GAS *m* DOMÉSTICO **5470**
GAS *m* HEDIONDO **6717**
GAS *m* INCANDESCENTE **6827**

GAS *m* INERTE **6905**
GAS *m* LICUADO **7342**
GAS *m* LÍQUIDO **7637**
GAS *m* MOND **8378**
GAS *m* NATURAL **8504**
GAS *m* OLEFIANTE **4851**
GAS *m* OXHÍDRICO **8985**
GAS *m* PARA ACCIONAR LOS MOTORES **9736**
GAS *m* PARA CALEFACCIÓN **5709**
GAS *m* PARA LUZ **6775**
GAS *m* PERDIDO **13634**
GAS *m* PERFECTO **9185**
GAS *m* POBRE **4194**
GAS *m* RICO **8758**
GAS LICUADO **7637**
GAS LÍQUIDO **7342**
GAS-OIL *m* **5831**
GASA *f* **5888**
GASIFICABLE **5860**
GASIFICACIÓN *f* **5865**
GASIFICACIÓN *f* **5861**
GASIFICAR **5862**
GASÓGENO *m* **5838**
GASÓGENO *m* DE AIRE SOPLADO **9819**
GASÓGENO *m* DE ASPIRACIÓN **12430**
GASOLINA *f* **9222**
GASOLINA *f* **9222**
GASOLINA *f* **9222**
GASOLINA *f* **9228**
GASOLINA *f* **9228**
GASOLINA *f* **5864**
GASOLINA *f* DE CARRETERA **10647**
GASÓMETRO *m* **5859**
GASTO *m* **2995**
GASTOS *m* **7346**
GASTOS *m* DE CONSERVACIÓN **7945**
GASTOS *m* DE CONSUMO **8049**
GASTOS *m* DE EMBALAJE **3205**
GASTOS *m* DE ENTRETENIMIENTO **7945**
GASTOS *m* DE EXPLOTACIÓN **13950**
GASTOS *m* DE FABRICACIÓN **3207**
GASTOS *m* DE FUERZA MOTRIZ **3206**
GASTOS *m* DE MANUTENCIÓN **3204**
GASTOS *m* DE MATERIAS **8049**
GASTOS *m* DE PRIMERA INSTALACIÓN **9858**
GASTOS *m* DE PRODUCCIÓN **3207**
GASTOS *m* DE REPARACIONES **3208**
GASTOS *m* DE TRANSPORTES **3209**
GASTOS *m* GENERALES **8798**
GASTOS *m* POR PORTES **3209**

**GAT** 1046

GATILLO *m* DEL TRINQUETE **2493**
GATILLO *m* DEL TRINQUETE **2094**
GATILLO *m* DEL TRINQUETE **2094**
GATILLO *m* (LEVA *f*DIENTE *m*) DE DISPARO **10437**
GATO *m* **10121**
GATO *m* DE PALANCA **7533**
GATO *m* DE TORNILLO **11035**
GATO *m* DE TORNILLO **11035**
GÉISER *m* (SURTIDOR NATURAL) **5936**
GEL *m* **5912**
GELATINA *f* PURA **5913**
GEMELOS *m pl* **11233**
GENERACIÓN *f* DE VAPOR **5923**
GENERADOR *m* DE CORRIENTE **5924**
GENERADOR *m* DE CORRIENTE ALTERNA **407**
GENERADOR *m* DE CORRIENTE CONTINUA **3021**
GENERADOR *m* DE VAPOR **12158**
GENERADOR *m* ELECTROSTÁTICO **4643**
GENERADOR *m* POR GAS **5838**
GENERADOR *m* POR VAPOR **12169**
GENERATRIZ *f* **9867**
GENERATRIZ *f* **407**
GENERATRIZ *f* **3021**
GENERATRIZ *f* DE CORRIENTE **5924**
GENERATRIZ *f* DE CORRIENTE CONTINUA PARA SOLDAR **2970**
GENERATRIZ *f* DE CORRIENTE TRIFÁSICA **12875**
GENERATRIZ *f* DE GAS **5850**
GENERATRIZ *f* DE VAPOR **12191**
GENERATRIZ *f* (GEOM.) **5925**
GENERATRIZ *f* HIDROELÉCTRICA **6700**
GEOMETRÍA *f* **5931**
GEOMETRÍA *f* DE LA JUNTA **7240**
GEOMETRÍA *f* DEL TREN DELANTERO **5696**
GEOMÉTRICO **5927**
GERMANIO *m* **5933**
GERMEN *m* **4686**
GERMEN *m* (DE CRISTAL) **8688**
GERMINACIÓN *f* **8687**
GERMINACIÓN *f* **5934**
GEYSER *m* **5936**
GIRÓSCOPO *m* **6191**
GLASEADO *m* **5972**
GLICERINA *f* **5988**
GLOBERTITA *f* **7880**
GLOBO *m* **11883**
GLOBULACIÓN *f* **11896**
GLUCINIO *m* **1210**
GLUCOSA *f* **6058**
GNEIS *m* **5989**

GOLPE *m* **11359**
GOLPE *m* **11359**
GOLPE DE ARIETE *m* **13653**
GOLPE DE LA VÁLVULA *m* **6224**
GOLPE DE PISTÓN *m* **9389**
GOLPE DE RETROCESO *m* **10286**
GOLPE DE SOLDADURA PUNTO DE PRINCIPIO DEL ARCO *m* **677**
GOLPE O CHOQUE TÉRMICO *m* **12812**
GOLPETEO *m* **7330**
GOLPETEO *m* DE UNA CORREA **13825**
GOMA *f* **10816**
GOMA *f* **10825**
GOMA *f* ADRAGANTE **6174**
GOMA *f* ARÁBIGA **6172**
GOMA *f* DAMAR **3598**
GOMA *f* DE BORRAR **9163**
GOMA *f* DE SUMATRA **6184**
GOMA *f* ELÁSTICA **10825**
GOMA *f* GETTANIA **6184**
GOMA *f* LACA **11338**
GOMA *f* LACA EN GRANOS **11131**
GOMA *f* LACA EN RAMA **12254**
GOMA *f* PARA BORRAR TINTA **6939**
GOMA *f* PARA LÁPIZ **9163**
GOMA *f* PLÁSTICA **6184**
GOMA *f* RASPADOR *m* **4801**
GOMA COPAL *f* **3102**
GOMA COPAL **3102**
GOMA DE PARA *f* **9037**
GOMA GUTA *f* **5793**
GOMA PELO *f* **6973**
GOMORRESINA *f* **6173**
GONIÓMETRO *m* **6004**
GONIÓMETRO *m* **1228**
GOTA *f* **4282**
GOTA *f* FRÍA **2706**
GOTEO *m* **10892**
GOTERA *f* **4285**
GOTERÓN *m* **6544**
GOZNE *m* **12347**
GRABADO *m* CATÓDICO **2110**
GRADA *f* **12239**
GRADA (MIN) *f* **12239**
GRADAS *f* (CON CADENAS EN ZIG-ZAG EN LAS GRADAS FLEXIBLES) **6303**
GRADERÍAS (A) *f pl* **12246**
GRADINA *f* **3364**
GRADO *m* **3714**
GRADO *m* **6021**
GRADO *m* **6021**

GRADO *m* 12239
GRADO *m* DE DUREZA 3720
GRADO *m* DE DUREZA DEL ACERO 6299
GRADO *m* DE EXACTITUD 3721
GRADO *m* DE PENETRACIÓN 4683
GRADO *m* DE PRECISIÓN 3721
GRADO *m* DE PUREZA DE UNA ALEACIÓN 5209
GRADO *m* DE SATURACIÓN 3722
GRADO *m* DE TRABAJO MECÁNICO 7866
GRADO *m* DE UNA SOLUCIÓN 12354
GRADO *m* ENGLER 3717
GRADO *m* FAHRENHEIT 3718
GRADO *m* HIGROMÉTRICO DEL AIRE 10433
GRADO *m* RÉAUMUR 3724
GRADO *m* TWADDELL 3725
GRADO BAUMÉ 3715
GRADO CENTÍGRADO 3716
GRADOS *m pl* DE LIBERTAD 3726
GRADUACIÓN *f* 6022
GRADUACIÓN *m* 6021
GRADUACIÓN *f* 5886
GRADUACIÓN *f* 10981
GRADUACIÓN *f* 12974
GRADUACIÓN *f* 12968
GRADUAR 12973
GRADUAR 6025
GRÁFICO *m* 3834
GRÁFICO *m* 7717
GRÁFICO *m* DE LA RESISTENCIA MECÁNICA 12366
GRAFILIZACIÓN *f* 6066
GRAFILIZANTE 6067
GRAFITO *m* 6062
GRAFITO *m* 9541
GRAFITO *m* DESFLOCULADO 3703
GRAFITO *m* EN COPOS 10989
GRAFITO *m* LAMINAR 5305
GRAFOSTÁTICO 6061
GRAMIL *m* DE ENSAMBLADO 8399
GRAMIL *m* DE MÁRMOL 11069
GRAMIL *m* DE PUNTA 8016
GRAMO *m* 6046
GRAN CALORÍA *f* 7298
GRAN CORONA *f* DE DIFERENCIAL 3910
GRAN DECLIVE *m* DEL CORTE EFECTIVO 7411
GRAN PALANCA *f* 3394
GRANALLA *f* 25
GRANALLA *f* 11379
GRANALLA *f* DE CINC 8404
GRANALLA *f* DE COBRE 3128
GRANALLA *f* DE ESTAÑO 6042

GRANALLA *f* DE NÍQUEL 8568
GRANALLA *f* DE PLOMO 7472
GRANALLA *f* FINA 6123
GRANALLADO *m* 11380
GRANALLADO *m* (FINO) 6124
GRANALLADO *m* (GRUESO) 11382
GRANATE *m* 5807
GRANITO *m* 6047
GRANO *m* 6030
GRANO *m* ABRASIVO 21
GRANO *m* GRUESO 2573
GRANO *m* (MEDIDA INGLESA) 6029
GRANOS *m pl* DE CONTACTO (RUPTOR) 3000
GRANOS *m pl* PARA GASÓGENOS 9140
GRANOS *m pl* QUE CONTIENE LA FUNDICIÓN 3998
GRANULACIÓN *f* 1279
GRANULACIÓN *f* 6043
GRANULACIÓN *f* 6057
GRANULACIÓN *f* SUPERFICIAL 9314
GRANULAR 6050
GRANULOMETRÍA *f* 6032
GRANULOMETRÍA *f* 6040
GRANULOMETRÍA *f* 11020
GRAPA *f* 12105
GRAPA *f* 12106
GRAPA *f* 7817
GRAPA *f* 2464
GRAPA *f* 2502
GRAPA *f* 2450
GRAPA *f* DE UNIÓN PARA CORREAS 1151
GRAPA DE EMPALME DE CABLES *f* 11706
GRAPA DE ENSAMBLADURA *f* 7280
GRAPA DE FONDO *f* 12104
GRAPÓN *m* 12105
GRASA *f* 5045
GRASA *f* 13933
GRASA *f* CONSISTENTE 6275
GRASA *f* DE ESTIRADO 4233
GRASA *f* DE LOS CURTIDORES 3711
GRASA *f* DE LUBRIFICACIÓN 7804
GRASA *f* GRAFITADA 6063
GRASA *f* MEJORADA 6063
GRASA *f* MINERAL 13508
GRASA *f* PARA COCHE 879
GRASA *f* (PARA EJES) 879
GRASA MINERAL 13508
GRASAS *f pl* 4331
GRASAS *f pl* 4331
GRAUVACA (PETR.) *m* 6095
GRAVA *f* 6073

# GRA

1048

GRAVA f 1644
GRAVEDAD f 6078
GRAVEDAD f 6078
GRAVILLA f 6073
GRAVIMETRÍA f 6077
GREDA f 2224
GREDA f 7691
GRES m 10928
GRÉS m ABIGARRADO 13502
GRÉS m CERÁMICO 12276
GRÉS m ROJO 10336
GRIETA f 3278
GRIETA f 4377
GRIETA f 2278
GRIETA f 2278
GRIETA f 3278
GRIETA f 3282
GRIETA f 3278
GRIETA f 3283
GRIETA f 5274
GRIETA f DE ENVEJECIMIENTO 11092
GRIETA f DE LA MADERA 11250
GRIETA f DE PLIEGUE 5357
GRIETA f DE PLIEGUE 1764
GRIETA f (DE TEMPLE) 10097
GRIETA f DE TENSIÓN 5304
GRIETA f DEBIDA A LA CONTRACCIÓN 6645
GRIETA f (ROTURA f) EN FRÍO 2674
GRIETA DE CLIVAJE 11615
GRIETA INCIPIENTE f 6833
GRIETA INCIPIENTE f 5411
GRIETAS f pl DE ATAQUE QUÍMICO 4841
GRIFERÍA f 1566
GRIFO m 2617
GRIFO m 11592
GRIFO m 12639
GRIFO m CIERRE DE VÁLVULA 13455
GRIFO m CON TORNILLO DE PRESIÓN 11033
GRIFO m DE AFORO 12776
GRIFO m DE AFORO 5875
GRIFO m DE AGUA 13644
GRIFO m DE AGUJA 8522
GRIFO m DE AIRE 293
GRIFO m DE AISLAMIENTO 845
GRIFO m DE ALIMENTACIÓN 5066
GRIFO m DE ÁNGULO 511
GRIFO m DE BAÑERA 1063
GRIFO m DE BATERÍA 1068
GRIFO m DE BOCA CURVA 1234
GRIFO m DE BOTELLA (DE GAS COMPRIMIDO) 3575

GRIFO m DE CANILLA 8997
GRIFO m DE CANILLA 9535
GRIFO m DE CANILLA INVERTIDA 7111
GRIFO m DE CANILLA LUBRIFICADA 7802
GRIFO m DE CUATRO PASOS 5606
GRIFO m DE CUATRO PASOS 5605
GRIFO m DE DISTRIBUCIÓN 8467
GRIFO m DE DOS PASOS 13317
GRIFO m DE DUCHA 11387
GRIFO m DE EXTRACCIÓN 1235
GRIFO m DE EXTRACCIÓN 1359
GRIFO m DE FLOTADOR 5433
GRIFO m DE FONDO DE CUBA 1493
GRIFO m DE FUELLE 1138
GRIFO m DE GAS 5814
GRIFO m DE LAVABO 13630
GRIFO m DE LLAVE 9530
GRIFO m DE MANIOBRA RÁPIDA 10104
GRIFO m DE MEMBRANA 3876
GRIFO m DE MOTOR 8417
GRIFO m DE RADIADOR 10153
GRIFO m DE RETENCIÓN 11408
GRIFO m DE RETENCIÓN 12281
GRIFO m DE TAPONAMIENTO 5954
GRIFO m DE TOMA DE VAPOR 12187
GRIFO m DE TRES PASOS 12882
GRIFO m DE TRES PASOS 12881
GRIFO m DE VACIADO 1357
GRIFO m DE VACIADO 4205
GRIFO m DE VÁLVULA 5977
GRIFO m DE VÁLVULA DOBLE 4154
GRIFO m DE VÁLVULA ESFÉRICA (DE BOLA) 968
GRIFO m DE VÁLVULA SIMPLE 11488
GRIFO m DISTRIBUIDOR GIRATORIO 10760
GRIFO m ELECTROMAGNÉTICO 11774
GRIFO m EN ESCUADRA 534
GRIFO m MEZCLADOR 8335
GRIFO m PURGADOR 4205
GRIFO m RECTO 5977
GRIFO m REGULADOR DE MEMBRANA 3872
GRIFO m SIN PRENSAESTOPA 9010
GRIFO m VÁLVULA f DE COMPUERTA 11653
GRIPAJE m (GAL.) 5778
GRIS m PERLA 9143
GROSOR m DE LA PARTÍCULA 9089
GROSOR m DE LOS GRANOS ABRASIVOS 23
GROSOR m DEL GRANO 11522
GROSOR m MINIMO DEL GRANO 8317
GRÚA f 3290
GRÚA f DE MÁSTIL 3788

1049 HAC

GRÚA  f  DE PLUMA **7224**
GRÚA  f  DE PÓRTICO **9641**
GRÚA  f  DERRICK **3788**
GRÚA  f  ESTACIONARIA **5291**
GRÚA  f  FIJA **5291**
GRÚA  f  GIRATORIA **11583**
GRÚA  f  MÓVIL **13161**
GRÚA  f  RODADIZA **13161**
GRÚA  f  TIPO HORCA **13623**
GRÚA DE BRAZO **7224**
GRÚAS  m pl  AGRÍCOLAS **3294**
GRUESOS  m pl  DE CARBÓN **2606**
GRUJIDO  m  **3107**
GRUJIDOR  m  **8677**
GRUPO  m  DE MÁQUINAS **6151**
GRUPO  m  (DE MÁQUINAS ELÉCTRICAS) **11213**
GRUPO  m  MOTOR-GENERADOR **8413**
GRUPOS  m  ELECTRÓGENOS **4524**
GUANTERA  f  **5980**
GUARDABARROS  m  **8443**
GUARDABARROS  m pl  **11927**
GUARDACABO  m  **12848**
GUARDACABO OVALADO **6330**
GUARDALMACÉN  m  **12298**
GUARDAPOLVOS  m  **4835**
GUARNECER CON MATERIA DE JUNTAS **8990**
GUARNICIÓN  f  **7620**
GUARNICIÓN  f  **7347**
GUARNICIÓN  f  **9004**
GUARNICIÓN  f  **9009**
GUARNICIÓN  f  **9004**
GUARNICIÓN  f  **7623**
GUARNICIÓN  f  **7623**
GUARNICIÓN  f  **9386**
GUARNICIÓN  f  **4482**
GUARNICIÓN  f  ANTIFRICCIÓN **13837**
GUARNICIÓN  f  CON CÁÑAMO **6445**
GUARNICIÓN  f  CON CUERO **7502**
GUARNICIÓN  f  CON CUERO EMBUTIDO **3459**
GUARNICIÓN  f  CON TRENZA **1526**
GUARNICIÓN  f  DE CÁÑAMO **6445**
GUARNICIÓN  f  DE COJINETE **7624**
GUARNICIÓN  f  DE FRENO **1538**
GUARNICIÓN  f  DE JUNTA **8998**
GUARNICIÓN  f  DE METAL ANTIFRICCIÓN **7624**
GUARNICIÓN  f  DE VÁLVULA **8998**
GUARNICIÓN  f  DEL EMBRAGUE **2545**
GUARNICIÓN  f  DEL PISTÓN **9375**
GUARNICIÓN  f  DEL PRENSAESTOPAS **12406**
GUARNICIÓN  f  FLEXIBLE **11739**

GUARNICIÓN  f  INTERIOR DEL CILINDRO **3571**
GUARNICIÓN  f  METÁLICA **8196**
GUARNICIÓN  f  MONOLÍTICA **8385**
GUARNICIÓN  f  POR EMPAQUETADURA **12406**
GUARNICIONES  f  **6283**
GUARNICIONES  f  DE CALDERAS **1411**
GUATA  f  **13612**
GUBIA  f  DE CARPINTERO **6010**
GUBIA  f  DE HERRERO **6546**
GUBIA  f  TRIANGULAR **13432**
GUÍA  f  **11585**
GUÍA  f  **6160**
GUÍA  f  CILÍNDRICA **3584**
GUÍA  f  DE CENTRADO **13087**
GUÍA  f  DE CORREA **1150**
GUÍA  f  DE LA CINTA INFERIOR **7796**
GUÍA  f  DE LA CRUCETA **6169**
GUÍA  f  DE VÁLVULA **13462**
GUÍA  f  DEL MOVIMIENTO RECTILÍNEO **12315**
GUÍA  f  DEL VÁSTAGO DE PISTÓN **9385**
GUÍA  f  PARA SERRAR A LO LARGO **10610**
GUÍA DE DESLIZAMIENTO (PARA ESCALERA MÓVIL DE TEJADO)  f  **10857**
GUÍA DE OBTURACIÓN  f  **5160**
GUÍA MÓVIL  f  **7625**
GUIADO  m  **6160**
GUIJARRO  m  **9152**
GUIJARROS  m pl  (GEOL.) **11354**
GUILLAME  m  **11417**
GUILLAME (CARP.)  m  **9522**
GUILLOTINA  f  **8031**
GUINDALEZA  f  **6309**
HACER ALCALINO **330**
HACER CORRESPONDER LOS AGUJEROS DE REMACHES **9969**
HACER DIGERIR **3937**
HACER ENSAYOS **4928**
HACER ESTANCO **7953**
HACER FUNCIONAR **4289**
HACER IMPERMEABLE **7953**
HACER PRUEBAS **4928**
HACER QUE ARRANQUE UN MOTOR **12114**
HACER RANURAS **6128**
HACER RANURAS **6128**
HACER RUGOSO **10783**
HACER UN CALCO **8431**
HACER UNA MUESCA **8554**
HACERSE ESFEROIDAL **11896**
HACHA  f  **857**
HACHÓN  m  **5820**
HACHÓN  m  **5355**

**HAC** 1050

HACHÓN *m* DE REFINERÍA **10376**
HACHUELA *f* **6305**
HACINAR **1737**
HAFNIO *m* **6199**
HALO *m* **6213**
HALÓGENO *m* **6214**
HALOTRIQUITA *f* **7135**
HARINA *f* FÓSIL **7292**
HARINA *f* FÓSIL DE INFUSORIOS **7292**
HAZ *m* **1093**
HAZ *m* DE ALAMBRES **7452**
HAZ *m* DE CURVAS **5028**
HAZ *m* DE ELECTRONES **4625**
HAZ *m* DE RAYOS **9164**
HAZ *m* DE RAYOS X **13995**
HAZ *m* DE TUBOS **8538**
HAZ *m* ELECTRÓNICO **1093**
HAZ *m* FOCALIZADO **5504**
HAZ *m* LUMINOSO **9162**
HAZ *m* LUMINOSO **9162**
HAZ *m* (TUBOS O PERFILES) **1736**
HAZ CONCENTRADO **5504**
HECHURA *f* **5581**
HECHURA *f* **11268**
HECHURA *f* DE LAS CABEZAS EN FRÍO **2686**
HECHURA *f* DEL MODELO **3041**
HECTÓLITRO *m* **6415**
HECTOVATIO *m* **6416**
HECTOVATIO *m* HORA **6417**
HELIANTINA *f* **8223**
HELIANTINA *f* **8223**
HÉLICE *f* **6430**
HÉLICE *f* PROPULSIVA **11041**
HELICOIDE **6428**
HELICOMEZCLADOR *f* **9931**
HELIO *m* **6429**
HELIOGRAFÍA *f* **1375**
HEMATITES *f* **6434**
HEMATITES *f* PARDA **7596**
HEMATITES *f* ROJA **11865**
HEMBRILLA *f* **4973**
HEMBRILLA *f* DE PUNTA ROSCADA **11057**
HEMICÉLULA *f* **6204**
HEMISFERIO *m* **6438**
HEMISFERIO *m* **6438**
HENDEDURA *f* **3278**
HENDIDURA *f* **4377**
HENDIDURA *f* **2278**
HENDIDURA *f* **2278**
HENDIDURA *f* **2278**

HENDIDURA *f* **3278**
HENDIDURA *f* **3278**
HENDIDURA *f* EN CALIENTE **6621**
HENDIDURA *f* EN CALIENTE **5240**
HENDIDURA *f* EN LA MADERA **11250**
HENIFICADORAS *f pl* **12696**
HERMÉTICO **12920**
HERMÉTICO *m* **303**
HERMÉTICO **303**
HERMÉTICO (O IMPERMEABLE) AL VAPOR **12193**
HERRAJE *m* **7159**
HERRAMENTAL *m* **13015**
HERRAMIENTA *f* **12994**
HERRAMIENTA *f* CON CORTE **3538**
HERRAMIENTA *f* CORTANTE **3538**
HERRAMIENTA *f* CORTANTE **13011**
HERRAMIENTA *f* DE ACABADO **5228**
HERRAMIENTA *f* DE DESBASTAR **10791**
HERRAMIENTA *f* DE ESTIRAR **4244**
HERRAMIENTA *f* DE MANO **6253**
HERRAMIENTA *f* DE PERFORAR **5494**
HERRAMIENTA *f* DE SIMPLE EFECTO **11496**
HERRAMIENTA *f* DE TREFILAR **4244**
HERRAMIENTA *f* DE TREPANAR **5494**
HERRAMIENTA *f* DIAMANTADA **3866**
HERRAMIENTA *f* NEUMÁTICA **9556**
HERRAMIENTA *f* PARA AMARTILLADO A MANO **1734**
HERRAMIENTA *f* PARA CURVAR CHAPAS **3485**
HERRAMIENTA *f* PARA TORNO **13292**
HERRAMIENTA *f* TAJANTE **3538**
HERRAMIENTA *f* TAJANTE **3538**
HERRAMIENTA PARA ESTIRAR *f* **4234**
HERRAMIENTAS *f pl* CON INCLUSIONES DE CARBURO **2144**
HERRAMIENTAS *f pl* DE ACERO DURO **6475**
HERRERÍA *f* **5548**
HERRERÍA *f* **5548**
HERRERIA *f* DE CORTE **13006**
HERRERO *m* **11671**
HERRERO *m* A MANO **6225**
HERRUMBRE *f* **10335**
HERRUMBRE *f* **10873**
HERRUMBRE *f* **10863**
HERRUMBROSO **219**
HERVIR **1401**
HERVIR **1401**
HETEROGENEIDAD *f* **3170**
HETEROGENEIDAD *f* DE UN MATERIAL **7352**
HETEROGÉNEO **6451**
HEXAEDRO *m* **6463**

HEXÁGONO *m* **6453**
HEXÁGONOS *m* DE ALEACIÓN DE ACERO **374**
HIDRATACIÓN *f* DE LA CAL **11569**
HIDRATO *m* **6673**
HIDRATO *m* **6674**
HIDRATO *m* DE BARIO **1000**
HIDRATO *m* DE BARITA **1000**
HIDRATO *m* DE CAL **1851**
HIDRATO *m* DE CARBONO **1937**
HIDRATO *m* DE ETILO **313**
HIDRATO *m* DE MAGNESIA **7887**
HIDRATO *m* DE METILO **13920**
HIDRATO *m* DE POTASIO **9687**
HIDRATO *m* DE SODIO **11722**
HIDRATO *m* DE VINILO **84**
HIDRATO *m* ESTAÑOSO **12101**
HIDRÁULICA **6698**
HIDRÁULICA *f* (CIENCIA) **6676**
HIDROCARBURO *m* **6705**
HIDROCARBURO *m* **6705**
HIDROCARBUROS *m pl* DE SERIE AROMÁTICA **2518**
HIDROCARBUROS *m pl* DE SERIE GRASA **8806**
HIDROCARBUROS *m pl* NO SATURADOS (LOS ETILÉNICOS Y LOS ACETILÉNICOS) **13393**
HIDROCARBUROS *m pl* PARAFÍNICOS **10940**
HIDROCARBUROS *m pl* SATURADOS **10940**
HIDROCLORATO *m* **462**
HIDRODINÁMICA *f* (CIENCIA) **6710**
HIDRODINÁMICO **6708**
HIDRÓFILO **6724**
HIDRÓFUGO **8349**
HIDRÓFUGO **13685**
HIDRÓGENO *m* **6712**
HIDRÓGENO *m* ARSENIADO **730**
HIDRÓGENO *m* ARSENIADO **730**
HIDRÓGENO *m* ATÓMICO **150**
HIDRÓGENO *m* BICARBONO **4851**
HIDRÓGENO *m* SULFURADO **6717**
HIDRÓGENO SULFURADO *m* **6717**
HIDRÓLISIS *f* **6719**
HIDROMETALURGIA *f* **6721**
HIDROSTÁTICO **6728**
HIDRÓXIDO *m* **6673**
HIDRURO *m* DE ACETILO **84**
HIDRURO *m* DE BENCILO **12983**
HIDRURO *m* DE BUTILO **1775**
HIDRURO *m* DE CRESILO **12983**
HIDRURO *m* DE ETILO **4848**
HIDRURO *m* DE PROPILO **9927**
HIDRURO *m* METÁLICO **8215**

HIELO *m* QUE SE DERRITE **8139**
HIERRO *m* **7133**
HIERRO *m* AGRIO (O FRÁGIL) **2702**
HIERRO *m* ANGULAR **514**
HIERRO *m* ANGULAR **514**
HIERRO *m* ARMCO **711**
HIERRO *m* (BASTIDOR) DE CRISTALES **10937**
HIERRO *m* BATIDO **11490**
HIERRO *m* BRUTO COLADO EN COQUILLA **2333**
HIERRO *m* COMERCIAL **8148**
HIERRO *m* CON CALIDADES DE ACERO **12224**
HIERRO *m* CUADRADO **12015**
HIERRO *m* DE BARANDILLA **6245**
HIERRO *m* DE BORDÓN **1716**
HIERRO *m* DE CAÑA **2250**
HIERRO *m* DE CARBONILO **1977**
HIERRO *m* DE FIBRA FINA **2511**
HIERRO *m* DE FIBRA FINA **2511**
HIERRO *m* DE GRANO FINO **2511**
HIERRO *m* DE GRANO FINO **2511**
HIERRO *m* DE GRANO GRUESO **8819**
HIERRO *m* DEL CEPILLO **9436**
HIERRO *m* DELTA **3740**
HIERRO *m* DULCE **13988**
HIERRO *m* EN BARRAS **984**
HIERRO *m* EN BARRAS PARA CLAVOS **8916**
HIERRO *m* EN BARRAS PLANAS **5375**
HIERRO *m* EN CINTA **6575**
HIERRO *m* EN CRUZ **3381**
HIERRO *m* EN CRUZ **3372**
HIERRO *m* EN DOBLE T **6194**
HIERRO *m* EN E **2250**
HIERRO *m* EN EL TRITURADOR **13106**
HIERRO *m* EN FORMA DE CUADRANTE **9241**
HIERRO *m* EN H T CON BORDÓN **1719**
HIERRO *m* EN I **6194**
HIERRO *m* EN L **514**
HIERRO *m* EN T **12698**
HIERRO *m* EN U **2250**
HIERRO *m* EN U **2248**
HIERRO *m* EN U **2248**
HIERRO *m* EN VARILLAS **984**
HIERRO *m* EN Z **14023**
HIERRO *m* ESPÁTICO **11421**
HIERRO *m* ESPECULAR **11865**
HIERRO *m* ESPONJOSO **7151**
HIERRO *m* FIBROSO **5139**
HIERRO *m* FIBROSO **5139**
HIERRO *m* FORJADO **13988**
HIERRO *m* FUNDIDO **6921**

**HIE** 1052

HIERRO *m* GAMA **5795**
HIERRO *m* HEXAGONAL **6454**
HIERRO *m* HUECO DE MEDIA CAÑA **6541**
HIERRO *m* KAHLBAUM **7270**
HIERRO *m* LAMINADO **10676**
HIERRO *m* MACIZO DE MEDIA CAÑA **11786**
HIERRO *m* MAGNÉTICO **7927**
HIERRO *m* MALEABLE ANORMAL **9**
HIERRO *m* NEGRO **1296**
HIERRO *m* OVALADO **8916**
HIERRO *m* PARA BARANDILLAS **6265**
HIERRO *m* PARA BARRAS DE REJA **6098**
HIERRO *m* PARA CERCADO **1086**
HIERRO *m* PARA HERRADURAS **6605**
HIERRO *m* PARA SOLDAR **11765**
HIERRO *m* PARA TABLEROS DE PUENTE **7112**
HIERRO *m* PERFILADO MODELADO **11119**
HIERRO *m* PLANO **5375**
HIERRO *m* PLANO **5375**
HIERRO *m* PLANO CON BORDÓN **5376**
HIERRO *m* PLANO CON BORDÓN **1714**
HIERRO *m* POROSO **7151**
HIERRO *m* PUDELADO **9962**
HIERRO *m* PUDELADO EN BARRAS **8441**
HIERRO *m* QUEBRADIZO **11368**
HIERRO *m* QUEBRADIZO AL ROJO **10338**
HIERRO *m* QUEBRADIZO EN CALIENTE **10338**
HIERRO *m* QUEBRADIZO EN CALIENTE (O AL ROJO) **10338**
HIERRO *m* QUEBRADIZO EN FRÍO **2702**
HIERRO *m* QUEMADO **1762**
HIERRO *m* REDONDO **10795**
HIERRO *m* SOLDADO **13766**
HIERRO *m* SOLDADOR **11764**
HIERRO *m* T DE ALAS ANCHAS **1640**
HIERRO *m* TENAZ **13068**
HIERRO *m* VIRGINAL **346**
HIERRO DULCE **11490**
HIERRO EN T CON BORDÓN **1719**
HIERRO FORJADO **11490**
HIERRO VIEJO **5553**
HIERRO VIEJO **5553**
HIERRO Y COBRE **8379**
HIERRO ZORÉ (S) **7112**
HIERROS *m pl* DE MEDIA CAÑA TIRADOS **4249**
HIERROS *m pl* FORJADOS **5566**
HIERROS *m pl* PARA BASTIDORES **4122**
HIERROS *m pl* PARA HORMIGÓN **12198**
HÍGADO *m* DE AZUFRE **7674**
HIGROMETRICIDAD *f* **6732**

HIGROMÉTRICO **6730**
HIGRÓMETRO *m* **6729**
HILADA *f* DE LADRILLOS **3259**
HILADO *m* **4230**
HILADO *m* EN FRÍO **4970**
HILERA *f* **4223**
HILERA *f* **4234**
HILERA *f* **3883**
HILERA *f* **8685**
HILERA *f* DE ÁRBOLES **7607**
HILERA *f* DE REMACHES **10813**
HILERA *f* DE TREFILAR **4223**
HILERA *f* DE TREFILAR **13887**
HILERAS *f pl* **189**
HILO *m* CONDUCTOR **2922**
HILO *m* (CRECIMIENTO EN FILAMENTO) **13828**
HILO *m* DE DEVANADERA **10744**
HILO *m* (ELÍPTICO) **4678**
HILO *m* EMBEBIDO DE PEZ **13704**
HILO *m* MONOCRISTALINO *m* **13828**
HILO *m* PARA CABLE **10743**
HILO *m* PARA RESISTENCIAS ELÉCTRICAS **10501**
HILO *m* TELEFÓNICO **12711**
HILO *m* TELEGRÁFICO **12708**
HINCADO *m* DE PILOTES **9306**
HINCAR (O CLAVAR) UN CLAVO **4292**
HINCHARSE **1721**
HINCHAZÓN *f* **1331**
HINCHAZÓN *f* DE LA MADERA **12544**
HIPÉRBOLE *f* **6734**
HIPERBÓLICO **6735**
HIPERBOLOIDE DE DOS CAPAS *m* **6740**
HIPERBOLOIDE DE UNA CAPA *m* **6739**
HIPEREUTECTOIDE *m* **6733**
HIPOAZOICO *m* **8591**
HIPOAZOIDE *m* **8591**
HIPOCICLOIDE *m* **6743**
HIPOEUTECTOIDE *m* **6741**
HIPOMÍTRICO *m* **8591**
HIPONITROIDE *m* **8591**
HIPOSULFITO *m* **12852**
HIPOSULFITO *m* DE PLOMO **7474**
HIPOSULFITO *m* DE SODIO **11736**
HIPOTENUSA *f* **6746**
HIPÓTESIS *f* DE BASE **12125**
HISTÉRESIS *f* **6747**
HOGAR *m* AUTOMÁTICO **8110**
HOGAR *m* CON RECUPERACIÓN INTERMITENTE **10410**
HOGAR *m* DE ACEITE PESADO **5745**
HOGAR *m* DE CALDERA **5747**

1053         **HOR**

HOGAR  *m*  DE CARBÓN **2565**
HOGAR  *m*  DE CARBÓN PULVERIZADO **5746**
HOGAR  *m*  DE GAS **5744**
HOGAR  *m*  DE HULLA **2565**
HOGAR  *m*  DE PETRÓLEO **5745**
HOJA  *f* **5508**
HOJA  *f* **1299**
HOJA  *f*  CORTANTE **1300**
HOJA  *f*  DE ALUMINIO **436**
HOJA  *f*  DE BALLESTA **9492**
HOJA  *f*  DE BALLESTA **11977**
HOJA  *f*  DE CAUCHO (NEOPRENO) **11329**
HOJA  *f*  DE CHAPA **11313**
HOJA  *f*  DE ORO **6000**
HOJA  *f*  DE SIERRA **10952**
HOJA  *f*  DE UNA CIZALLA **11282**
HOJA  *f*  DE UNA HERRAMIENTA CORTANTE **1300**
HOJA  *f*  DELGADA DE COBRE **3117**
HOJA  *f*  DELGADA DE METAL **5509**
HOJA  *f*  METÁLICA **11315**
HOJA  *f*  METÁLICA **8184**
HOJA  *f*  (O CHAPA) DE CINC **11327**
HOJA  *f*  (O LÁMINA  *f*) DE UN RESORTE (O DE UN MUELLE) **9492**
HOJA  *f*  PARA SIERRA DE METALES **6197**
HOJA  *f*  TAJANTE **1300**
HOJA DE ESPESOR  *f* **7621**
HOJALATA  *f* **12957**
HOJALATERO  *m* **12964**
HOJAS  *f pl*  DE UNISERVICIO **12896**
HOJAS  *f pl*  (O FICHAS  *f pl*) TÉCNICAS **3615**
HOLGURA  *f* **9516**
HOLLÍN  *m* **11816**
HOLMIO  *m* **6551**
HOMEGENEIZACIÓN  *f* **6561**
HOMOGENEIDAD  *f*  DE UN MATERIAL **13364**
HOMOGENEIDAD  *f*  DE UNA SOLDADURA **11821**
HOMOGÉNEO  *m* **6555**
HOMOMORFISMO  *m* **7191**
HORADADO  *m* **12675**
HORAS  *f*  SUPLEMENTARIAS **8964**
HORIZONTAL **6578**
HORMIGÓN  *m* **2894**
HORMIGÓN  *m* **12203**
HORMIGÓN  *m*  APISONADO **10193**
HORMIGÓN  *m*  COLADO **9714**
HORMIGÓN  *m*  DE CEMENTO **2135**
HORMIGÓN  *m*  DE ESCORIAS **11565**
HORMIGÓN  *m*  DE ESCORIAS **11565**
HORMIGÓN  *m*  MOLDEADO **8426**

HORMIGONADO  *m* **2902**
HORMIGONAR **2895**
HORMIGONERA  *f* **9966**
HORNABLENDA  *f* **6598**
HORNACINA  *f* **13617**
HORNILLO  *m*  DE CARBÓN EN POLVO **5746**
HORNILLO  *m*  PARA SOLDADURA FUERTE **1577**
HORNO  *m* **5739**
HORNO  *m* **5739**
HORNO  *m* **12300**
HORNO  *m* **12300**
HORNO  *m* **11667**
HORNO  *m* **8920**
HORNO  *m*  A LA WILKINSON **3466**
HORNO  *m*  AL ARCO **4495**
HORNO  *m*  AL ARCO CON RESISTENCIA **10485**
HORNO  *m*  AL ARCO ELÉCTRICO **668**
HORNO  *m*  AL ARCO ELÉCTRICO CON ELECTRODOS DE CARBÓN **.670**
HORNO  *m*  AL ARCO INDIRECTO **669**
HORNO  *m*  CON DESCARGADOR DE COQUE **10030**
HORNO  *m*  CON POLEAS **9975**
HORNO  *m*  CON SACUDIDAS **10024**
HORNO  *m*  CONTINUO **3026**
HORNO  *m*  CORREDIZO **11603**
HORNO  *m*  DE ACHESON **97**
HORNO  *m*  DE AFINO **10379**
HORNO  *m*  DE ALTA FRECUENCIA **6469**
HORNO  *m*  DE ATMÓSFERA CONTROLADA **3055**
HORNO  *m*  DE BAÑO DE SAL **10912**
HORNO  *m*  DE CALCINACIÓN **7295**
HORNO  *m*  DE CALCINACIÓN **1843**
HORNO  *m*  DE CALCINAR **11512**
HORNO  *m*  DE CALDEO POR GAS **5851**
HORNO  *m*  DE CALDERA **5747**
HORNO  *m*  DE CAMPANA **1132**
HORNO  *m*  DE CARBURIZACIÓN **1991**
HORNO  *m*  DE CEMENTACIÓN **3074**
HORNO  *m*  DE CIANURACIÓN **3550**
HORNO  *m*  DE CONVERTIDOR **10524**
HORNO  *m*  DE COQUE **2661**
HORNO  *m*  DE CRISOL **3402**
HORNO  *m*  DE CRISOL **3402**
HORNO  *m*  DE CRISOL **4597**
HORNO  *m*  DE CRISOL **6332**
HORNO  *m*  DE CRISOL **9669**
HORNO  *m*  DE CUBA **11241**
HORNO  *m*  DE FUNDIR **11665**
HORNO  *m*  DE FUSIÓN **11667**
HORNO  *m*  DE FUSIÓN **8138**

**HOR** 1054

HORNO *m* DE IGUALIZACIÓN **11698**
HORNO *m* DE INDUCCIÓN **6895**
HORNO *m* DE INDUCCIÓN A BAJA FRECUENCIA **7772**
HORNO *m* DE MANTENIMIENTO **6527**
HORNO *m* DE MUFLA **8447**
HORNO *m* DE NITRURACIÓN **8584**
HORNO *m* DE PRIMERA ALEACIÓN **3607**
HORNO *m* DE PUDELADO **9965**
HORNO *m* DE RECALENTAR POR PAQUETES **9308**
HORNO *m* DE RECOCER **10426**
HORNO *m* DE RECOCER **564**
HORNO *m* DE RECOCIDO **564**
HORNO *m* DE RECOCIDO **564**
HORNO *m* DE REDUCCIÓN **10359**
HORNO *m* DE REGENERACIÓN **10321**
HORNO *m* DE REGENERACIÓN **10410**
HORNO *m* DE REVERBERO **10532**
HORNO *m* DE REVERBERO **261**
HORNO *m* DE SINTERIZAR **11512**
HORNO *m* DE SOLDAR **11763**
HORNO *m* DE TOSTACIÓN **10649**
HORNO *m* DE TRANSPORTADOR **1148**
HORNO *m* DE TÚNEL **11241**
HORNO *m* ELÉCTRICO **4507**
HORNO *m* ELÉCTRICO DE ARCO DIRECTO **667**
HORNO *m* ELÉCTRICO DE ARCO DIRECTO **671**
HORNO *m* ELÉCTRICO DE INDUCCIÓN **4515**
HORNO *m* ELÉCTRICO DE RESISTENCIA **10490**
HORNO *m* ESTACIONARIO FIJO **12142**
HORNO *m* INDUSTRIAL **6900**
HORNO *m* MARTÍN **8829**
HORNO *m* MARTÍN **8815**
HORNO *m* METALÚRGICO **8207**
HORNO *m* NO CONTINUO **1060**
HORNO *m* PARA CALENTAR LOS REMACHES **10623**
HORNO *m* PRECALENTADOR **9777**
HORNO *m* QUE CARGAR **1060**
HORNO *m* TIPO CAMPANA **1135**
HORQUETA *f* **5567**
HORQUETA DE LA CABEZA DE BIELA *f* **12345**
HORQUETA DE UNIÓN *f* **5567**
HORQUILLA *f* **5568**
HORQUILLA *f* **2491**
HORQUILLA *f* **12346**
HORQUILLA *f* **12345**
HORQUILLA *f* DE DESEMBRAGUE **12346**
HORQUILLA *f* GUIA DE CORREA **12346**
HUECO *m* **13585**
HUECO *m* **10279**
HUECO *m* **2125**

HUECO *m* **2125**
HUECO *m* DE AGITADOR **237**
HUECO *m* EN PIEZA COLADA **4230**
HUECO *m* ENTRE DOS DIENTES **6548**
HUECO *m* ENTRE LOS BARROTES DE UNA REJA **278**
HUESOS *m pl* PULVERIZADOS **1448**
HUIR **7487**
HULLA *f* ANTRACITOSA **11165**
HULLA *f* BLANDA **5543**
HULLA *f* BRUTA **10841**
HULLA *f* CARBÓN *m* DE PIEDRA **2558**
HULLA *f* DE LLAMA CORTA **11371**
HULLA *f* DE LLAMA LARGA **7724**
HULLA *f* GRASA **1282**
HULLA *f* GRASA **1835**
HULLA *f* MENUDA **11557**
HULLA *f* PARA GAS **5813**
HULLA *f* POBRE **11168**
HULLA *f* POBRE DE LLAMA CORTA **11165**
HULLA *f* SEMIGRASA **8626**
HULLA SIN CLASIFICAR **10841**
HULLERA **2566**
HULLIFICAR **1971**
HUMAREDA *f* **5732**
HUMAREDA *f* DE LAS INDUSTRIAS **6899**
HUMECTACIÓN *f* **8348**
HUMECTACIÓN *f* **8348**
HUMECTACIÓN *f* **13807**
HUMECTAR **8347**
HUMECTAR **8347**
HUMECTATIVO **6664**
HUMEDAD *f* ABSOLUTA DEL AIRE **30**
HUMEDAD *f* CRÍTICA **3346**
HUMEDAD *f* DEL AIRE **6666**
HUMEDAD *f* DEL VAPOR **13806**
HUMEDAD *f* RELATIVA **10432**
HUMEDAD *f* RELATIVA DEL AIRE **10433**
HUMEDECEDOR **6664**
HUMEDECER **8347**
HUMO *m* **11672**
HUMOS *m pl* **5732**
HUMOS *m pl* INDUSTRIALES **6899**
HUMOS *m pl* ROJOS **10327**
HUMUS *m* **6667**
HUNDIMIENTO **12418**
HURGÓN *m* **10116**
HUSILLO *m* **11904**
HUSILLO *m* **11904**
HUSILLO *m* **4260**
HUSILLO *m* ESFÉRICO **11886**

HUYE (QUE) **7493**
ICTIOCOLA *f* **7174**
IGNICIÓN *f* **6760**
IGNICIÓN *f* **6760**
IGNÍFUGO **5257**
ILLINIO *m* **6771**
ILUMINACIÓN *f* **7574**
ILUMINACIÓN *f* **7574**
ILUMINACIÓN *f* ARTIFICIAL **733**
ILUMINACIÓN *f* NATURAL **8505**
ILUSTRACIÓN *f* **6778**
ILUSTRACIÓN *f* **6778**
IMAGEN *f* **6779**
IMAGEN *f* CLARA **2479**
IMAGEN *f* NETA **2479**
IMAGEN *f* REAL **10259**
IMAGEN *f* VIRTUAL **13572**
IMÁN *m* **7891**
IMÁN *m* RECTO **985**
IMÁN ARTIFICIAL *m* **735**
IMÁN DE LÁMINAS *m* **7377**
IMÁN EN HERRADURA *m* **6606**
(IMÁN) EN HERRADURA **6606**
IMÁN NATURAL *m* **8506**
IMÁN PERMANENTE *m* **9204**
IMÁN RECTO *m* **985**
IMANACIÓN *f* **7923**
IMANAR **7924**
IMANTACIÓN *f* **7923**
IMANTACIÓN REMANENTE *f* **10445**
IMANTACIÓN RESIDUAL *f* **10445**
IMANTAR **7924**
IMANTARSE **1126**
IMBIBICIÓN *f* **6805**
IMBICICIÓN *f* **11289**
IMMERSIÓN *f* **3967**
IMPACTO *m* **6783**
IMPACTO *m* **11359**
IMPEDANCIA *f* **6794**
IMPEDIR **6926**
IMPERFECCIÓN *f* **3691**
IMPERFECCIONES *f* EN LA SUPERFICIE **6464**
IMPERMEABILIDAD *f* **12932**
IMPERMEABILIDAD *f* **11081**
IMPERMEABILIDAD *f* **6797**
IMPERMEABILIDAD *f* AL AGUA **6796**
IMPERMEABILIZACIÓN *m* **7954**
IMPERMEABILIZACIÓN *f* **13691**
IMPERMEABILIZAR **13689**
IMPERMEABILIZAR **7953**

IMPERMEABLE **13671**
IMPERMEABLE **12920**
IMPERMEABLE *m* (PRENDA DE VESTIR) **6798**
IMPERMEABLE A LA HUMEDAD **8349**
IMPERMEABLE A LA LUZ **7572**
IMPERMEABLE A LOS GASES **5853**
IMPERMEABLE AL AGUA **13688**
IMPERMEABLE AL AIRE **303**
IMPLANTACIONES *f* DE COBRE EN SOLDADURA **1574**
IMPONDERABLE **6800**
IMPREGNACIÓN *f* **6805**
IMPREGNACIÓN *f* **6805**
IMPREGNACIÓN *f* DE LA MADERA CON SUBLIMADO
  CORROSIVO **7340**
IMPREGNAR **6802**
IMPREGNAR **6802**
IMPRESIÓN *f* **6806**
IMPRESIÓN *f* DE PRUEBA **9870**
IMPRESIÓN *f* DURA **6859**
IMPULSAR **7263**
IMPULSIÓN *f* **6809**
IMPULSIÓN *f* **9979**
IMPULSIÓN *f* BATIDO *m* **13414**
IMPULSIÓN *f* BATIDO *m* **7265**
IMPULSIÓN *f* BATIDO *m* **7265**
IMPULSIÓN *f* BATIDO *m* **4452**
IMPULSOR *m* **12672**
IMPUREZA *f* **6814**
IMPUREZAS *f pl* **6813**
INACCESIBILIDAD *f* **6820**
INACCESIBLE **6821**
INALTERABLE **13723**
INATACABILIDAD *f* A LOS ÁCIDOS **10496**
INATACABLE POR EL ACEITE **8792**
INATACABLE POR EL AGUA **13671**
INATACABLE POR LAS INTEMPERIES **13723**
INATACABLE POR LOS ÁCIDOS **128**
INCANDESCENCIA *f* **13832**
INCANDESCENCIA *f* **6822**
INCANDESCENCIA *f* **6823**
INCANDESCENCIA *f* **6823**
INCANDESCENTE **5983**
INCIDENCIA *f* **6831**
INCLINABLE **6835**
INCLINACIÓN *f* **6836**
INCLINACIÓN *f* **11627**
INCLINACIÓN *f* **1065**
INCLUSIÓN *f* **6840**
INCLUSIÓN *f* DE ESCORIA **4772**
INCLUSIÓN *f* DE GAS (O DE GASES) **5836**

**INC** 1056

INCLUSIÓN f GASEOSA **5855**
INCLUSIÓN f MITIGADA **6841**
INCLUSIÓN f SECUNDARIA **11106**
INCLUSIONES f NO METÁLICAS **8620**
INCÓGNITA f **13391**
INCOMBUSTIBILIDAD f **6842**
INCOMBUSTIBLE **6843**
INCOMPRESIBILIDAD f **6846**
INCOMPRESIBLE **6847**
INCOMUNICACIÓN **7184**
INCONGELABILIDAD f **8634**
INCONGELABLE **8635**
INCRUSTACIÓN f DE LAS CALDERAS **10969**
INCRUSTACIÓN f DE RESÍDUOS CARBONOSOS **5367**
INCRUSTACIÓN f SARRO m **119**
INCRUSTACIONES f DE LAS CALDERAS **10969**
INCRUSTADO **6857**
ÍNCUBAR **11688**
INCUSTRADO **6857**
INDEPENDIENTE **11190**
INDICACIÓN **8015**
INDICACIONES f DE UN DIBUJO **7524**
INDICADOR m **6879**
INDICADOR m **3837**
INDICADOR m **5768**
INDICADOR m **5768**
INDICADOR m CON ESFERA **3840**
INDICADOR m CON RETORNO AL BAÑO DE ACEITE **8747**
INDICADOR m DE APERTURA **13153**
INDICADOR m DE CARGA **2267**
INDICADOR m DE DIRECCIÓN DE LA CORRIENTE **9588**
INDICADOR m DE FASES **9235**
INDICADOR m DE LA PRESIÓN DE ACEITE **8768**
INDICADOR m DE NIVEL **7526**
INDICADOR m DE NIVEL **13652**
INDICADOR m DE PRESIÓN **9820**
INDICADOR m DE PRESIÓN **6878**
INDICADOR m DE TEMPERATURA **12834**
INDICADOR m DE TEMPERATURA **12726**
INDICADOR m DE TENSIÓN DE LA CINTA **976**
INDICADOR m DEL NIVEL DE ACEITE **3979**
INDICADOR m DEL NIVEL DE ACEITE **8764**
INDICADOR m DEL NIVEL DE GASOLINA **5710**
INDICADOR m DEL VACÍO **13442**
INDICADOR m FUSIBLE **11134**
INDICADOR m MAGNÉTICO **7905**
INDICADOR m POR REFRACCIÓN **10395**
INDICADOR DE FLUJO m **11426**
INDICADOR DE VELOCIDAD m **11877**
ÍNDICE m **8012**

ÍNDICE m **5879**
ÍNDICE m DE CETANO **2198**
ÍNDICE m DE MILLER **8282**
ÍNDICE m DE REFRACCIÓN **6866**
ÍNDICE m DE REPOSICIÓN **10367**
ÍNDICE m DE VISCOSIDAD **8787**
ÍNDICE m (MAT) **6864**
INDICIO m **6868**
INDIO m **6885**
INDUCCIÓN f **6892**
INDUCCIÓN f **12428**
INDUCCIÓN f ELECTROSTÁTICA **4644**
INDUCCIÓN f MAGNÉTICA **7908**
INDUCCIÓN f MAGNETOELÉCTRICA **4615**
INDUCCIÓN f MUTUA **8489**
INDUCCIÓN f PROPIA **11156**
INDUCCIÓN f PROPIA **11156**
INDUCIDO m **707**
INDUCIDO m **707**
INDUCIR **6888**
INDUCTANCIA f **6891**
INDUCTOR m **6898**
INDUSTRIA f **6903**
INDUSTRIA f DE LA ALIMENTACIÓN **5517**
INDUSTRIA f DE TRANSFORMACIÓN **9888**
INDUSTRIA f MINERA **8311**
INDUSTRIAL **7992**
INELÁSTICO **6904**
INERCIA f **6907**
INERTE **8621**
INESTABLE (QUIM) **7343**
INFILTRACIÓN f **6805**
INFINITAMENTE GRANDE **6910**
INFINITAMENTE PEQUEÑO **6911**
INFLACIÓN f **6155**
INFLACIÓN (POR LOS GASES DE FISIÓN) f **12543**
INFLAMABILIDAD f **6913**
INFLAMABLE **6914**
INFLAMABLE **6503**
INFLAMACIÓN f **6760**
INFLAMARSE **6757**
INFLAR **12542**
INFLAR **12542**
INFLARSE **1721**
INFORMACIÓN f DE ENTRADA NUMÉRICA **3942**
INFORME m DESCRIPTIVO DEL FABRICANTE **7993**
INFUSIBILIDAD f **6917**
INFUSIBLE **6918**
INGENIERÍA f CIVIL **2444**
INGENIERO m **4761**

INGENIERO *m* ASESOR **2989**
INGENIERO *m* CONSTRUCTOR **2443**
INGENIERO *m* DE CONSTRUCCIONES CIVILES **2443**
INGENIERO *m* DE MINAS **8312**
INGENIERO *m* ELECTRICISTA **4540**
INGENIERO *m* ENCARGADO DE LAS VENTAS **10898**
INGENIERO *m* JEFE **4762**
INGENIERO *m* JEFE DE LA CONSTRUCCIÓN **2329**
INGENIERO *m* MECÁNICO **8102**
INGENIERO *m* QUIMICO **2306**
INGLETE *m* **8326**
INGLETE *m* CILINDRICO **13358**
INGLETE *m* ESFÉRICO **11892**
INHIBIDOR *m* **10510**
INHIBIDOR *m* **6927**
INMERGER **3968**
INMERGER **3968**
INMERSIÓN *f* **3967**
INMERSIÓN *f* **3975**
INMERSIÓN *f* **3978**
INMOVILIZACIÓN *f* DE TUERCAS Y PERNOS **7707**
INOCULACIÓN *f* **6956**
INOCUPACIÓN *f* **13433**
INOXIDABILIDAD *f* **10980**
INOXIDABLE **6959**
INSCRIPCIÓN *f* **7513**
INSERCIÓN *f* **7023**
INSERCIÓN *f* **6965**
INSERCIONES *f pl* DE SOLDADURA **1578**
INSERIR **7022**
INSERTO *m* **6965**
INSOLUBILIDAD *f* **6983**
INSOLUBLE **6984**
INSPECCIÓN *f* **6985**
INSPECCIÓN *f* CON TRÉPANO **4877**
INSPECCIÓN *f* DE LA CALDERA **1414**
INSPECCIÓN *f* DE LA CALDERA **1414**
INSTALACIÓN *f* DE CALEFACCIÓN CENTRAL **6394**
INSTALACIÓN *f* DE DISTRIBUCIÓN DE AGUA **13693**
INSTALACIÓN *f* DE EVACUACIÓN **13485**
INSTALACIÓN *f* DE RECOCIDO **6376**
INSTALACIÓN *f* DE RECOCIDO **565**
INSTALACIÓN *f* DE REFRIGERACIÓN **10408**
INSTALACIÓN *f* DE TORNAPUNTAS **1521**
INSTALACIÓN *f* DE UNA MÁQUINA DE VAPOR **12180**
INSTALACIÓN *f* DE VIGAS SOPORTANDO LA CUBIERTA **9157**
INSTALACIÓN *f* GENERATRIZ DE CORRIENTE **5920**
INSTALACIÓN *f* INDUSTRIAL (O DE FÁBRICA) **9461**
INSTALACIÓN *f* INTERIOR **6988**

INSTALACIÓN *f* PARA ENFRIAMIENTO DE LAS AGUAS DE CONDENSACIÓN **3089**
INSTALACIÓN *f* PARA PRODUCCIÓN DE FUERZA MOTRIZ **9739**
INSTALACIONES *f* DE ESTABLOS **3277**
INSTALACIONES *f pl* SANITARIAS **10931**
INSTALACIONES *f* SANITARIAS **10931**
INSTALAR **12114**
INSTALAR LA CORREA **11357**
INSTITUTO *m* BRITÁNICO DE NORMALIZACIÓN **887**
INSTRUCCIÓN *f* **6991**
INSTRUCCIÓN *f* **6992**
INSTRUCCIÓN *f* **11546**
INSTRUCCIONES *f pl* **8835**
INSTRUCCIONES *f pl* RELATIVAS AL TRABAJO **11209**
INSTRUMENTO *m* **641**
INSTRUMENTO *m* APERIÓDICO **635**
INSTRUMENTO *m* DE MEDIDA **8090**
INSTRUMENTO *m* DE ÓPTICA **8844**
INSTRUMENTO *m* DE VERIFICACIÓN (DE CONTROL) **5871**
INSTRUMENTO *m* PARA CENTRAR **2166**
INSTRUMENTO *m* PARA DETERMINAR LA VELOCIDAD DE UNA CORRIENTE **3490**
INSTRUMENTO *m* REGISTRADOR **10289**
INSTRUMENTO DE VERIFICACIÓN *m* **12793**
INSTRUMENTOS *m pl* DE MATEMÁTICAS **8051**
INTEGRACIÓN *f* **7015**
INTEGRADOR *m* **7016**
INTÉGRAFO *m* **7013**
INTEGRAL **7009**
INTEGRAL *f* DEFINIDA **3697**
INTEGRAL *f* DOBLE **4145**
INTEGRAL *f* ELÍPTICA **4676**
INTEGRAL *f* INDEFINIDA **6858**
INTEGRAL *f* LINEAL **7600**
INTEGRAL *f* MÚLTIPLE **8465**
INTEGRAL *f* SINGULAR **11471**
INTEGRAL *f* TRIPLE **13215**
INTEGRAR **7014**
INTENSIDAD *f* **7018**
INTENSIDAD *f* DE LA CORRIENTE **478**
INTENSIDAD *f* DE LA CORRIENTE PARA SOLDAR **13780**
INTENSIDAD *f* DE LA GRAVEDAD **2975**
INTENSIDAD *f* DE POLO **9596**
INTENSIDAD *f* DE RADIACIÓN **7019**
INTENSIDAD *f* DE UNA CORRIENTE **7021**
INTENSIDAD *f* DE UNA FUERZA **7939**
INTENSIDAD *f* DEL ALUMBRADO **6777**
INTENSIDAD *f* DEL CAMPO **5144**
INTENSIDAD *f* ELÉCTRICA DEL CAMPO **4506**
INTENSIDAD *f* EN BUJÍAS **1900**

**INT** 1058

INTENSIDAD *f* LUMINOSA **7822**
INTENSIDAD *f* LUMINOSA **7019**
INTENSIDAD *f* LUMINOSA POR UNIDAD DE SUPERFICIE **7104**
INTERCALACIÓN *f* **7023**
INTERCALAR **7022**
INTERCAMBIABILIDAD *f* **7025**
INTERCAMBIABILIDAD *f* DE FABRICACIÓN **7028**
INTERCAMBIABLE **7026**
INTERCAMBIADOR *m* TÉRMICO **6349**
INTERCAMBIADOR *m* TÉRMICO **6349**
INTERCAMBIO *m* DE CALOR **4884**
INTERCEPTAR RAYOS **7024**
INTERFERENCIA *f* **7035**
INTERMITENTES *m* **5366**
INTERMITENTES *m* **3989**
INTERPOLACIÓN *f* **7089**
INTERPOLACIÓN *f* CIRCULAR **2416**
INTERPOLACIÓN *f* LINEAL **7613**
INTERPOLACIÓN *f* PARABÓLICA **9040**
INTERPOLADOR **3995**
INTERPOLAR **7088**
INTERRUMPIR EL CIRCUITO ELÉCTRICO **7090**
INTERRUPCIÓN *f* **11546**
INTERRUPCIÓN *f* DE PASO DE CORRIENTE ELÉCTRICA **7093**
INTERRUPCIÓN *f* DE SERVICIO **7092**
INTERRUPCIÓN DE CORRIENTE *f* **8734**
INTERRUPCIÓN DE LA MARCHA *f* **7092**
INTERRUPTOR *m* **12553**
INTERRUPTOR *m* AUTOMÁTICO **12553**
INTERRUPTOR *m* DE ACCIÓN INSTANTÁNEA **11690**
INTERRUPTOR *m* DISYUNTOR *m* **12553**
INTERRUPTOR-CONMUTADOR *m* **12553**
INTERSTICIO *m* **262**
INTERVALO *m* **7101**
INTERVALO *m* DE FUSIÓN **8143**
INTERVALO *m* DE SOLIDIFICACIÓN **11801**
INTERVALO *m* DE SOLIDIFICACIÓN **5658**
INTRODUCCIÓN *f* DE AIRE **12486**
INTRODUCCIÓN *f* MANUAL DE DATOS **7987**
INVAR *m* **7105**
INVARIANTE **7106**
INVENCIÓN *f* **7107**
INVENTO *m* **7107**
INVENTO *m* DIGNO DE PATENTE **9122**
INVENTOR *m* **7108**
INVERSIÓN *f* DE LA MARCHA DE UNA MÁQUINA **10541**
INVERSIÓN *f* DE MOVIMIENTO **10552**
INVERSIÓN *f* (MAT.) **7110**
INVERSIÓN DEL SENTIDO DE UNA CORRIENTE *f* **2246**

INVERSOR *m* **3963**
INVERSOR *m* DE MARCHA **10548**
INVERTIR **2241**
INVERTIR EL SENTIDO DE LA MARCHA **10534**
INVERTIR LA CORRIENTE **2241**
INVESTIGACIÓN *f* APLICADA **649**
INVESTIGACIÓN *f* FUNDAMENTAL **5735**
INVESTIGACIÓN *f* PURA **1052**
INVESTIGACIÓN *f* PURA **10016**
INVOLUTA *f* **7117**
INVOLUTA *f* DEL CÍRCULO **7118**
INYECCIÓN *f* **6935**
INYECTAR **6934**
INYECTOR *m* **6938**
INYECTOR *m* **6938**
INYECTOR *m* **7223**
INYECTOR *m* DE AGUJEROS **8452**
INYECTOR *m* DE BOMBA **9993**
INYECTOR *m* DE TETÓN **9338**
INYECTOR *m* DE VAPOR **12171**
INYECTOR *m* HIDRÁULICO **13657**
INYECTOR *m* (O SOPLADOR) HIDRÁULICO **13658**
IODO *m* **7120**
IODURO *m* DE PLATA **11464**
ION *m* **7121**
ION *m* HIDRÓGENO **2112**
IONIZACIÓN *f* **4596**
IONIZACIÓN *f* **7124**
IONÓGENO *m* **7129**
IRIDIO *m* **7131**
IRRADIACIÓN *f* **7161**
IRRADIACIÓN *f* **10143**
IRRADIACIÓN *f* **10241**
IRRADIACIÓN *f* DE LA LUZ **10147**
IRRADIACIÓN *f* DEL CALOR **10146**
IRRADIACIÓN *f* DEL CALOR **12811**
IRRADIACIÓN *f* HETEROGÉNEA **6450**
IRRADIACIÓN *f* HOMOGÉNEA **6559**
IRRADIACIÓN *f* MONOCROMÁTICA **8383**
IRRADIAR **10141**
IRREGULAR **7163**
IRREGULARIDAD *f* DE LA SUPERFICIE **12503**
IRREGULARIDAD *f* DEL MOVIMIENTO **7167**
IRREVERSIBILIDAD *f* **7168**
IRREVERSIBILIDAD *f* **7168**
IRREVERSIBLE **7169**
IRREVERSIBLE **7169**
IRROMPIBLE **13343**
ISOBARA *f* **7176**
ISOCRONISMO *m* **7178**

| | | |
|---|---|---|
| ISÓCRONO **7179** | JUEGO | *m* CONVENIENTE **9516** |
| ISOMERÍA *f* **7186** | JUEGO | *m* DE ENGRANAJES **5901** |
| ISOMERÍA *f* **357** | JUEGO | *m* DE LABORATORIO **7345** |
| ISÓMERO *m* **7185** | JUEGO | *m* DE LAS VÁLVULAS **12673** |
| ISOMORFÍA *f* **7189** | JUEGO | *m* DE MEDIDAS PARA EL CONTRASTE **8036** |
| ISOMORFISMO *m* **7191** | JUEGO | *m* DE MONTAJE **9516** |
| ISOMORFO **7190** | JUEGO | *m* DE PESAS **11219** |
| ISOPLERA *f* **7187** | JUEGO | *m* DE PESOS **11219** |
| ISOTOPOS *m pl* (QUIM) **7197** | JUEGO | *m* DE PIEZAS **11213** |
| ISOTROPO **7198** | JUEGO | *m* DE RUEDAS **13821** |
| ITERBIO *m* **14019** | JUEGO | *m* DE UNA VÁLVULA **13154** |
| ITINERARIO MARÍTIMO *m* **10810** | JUEGO | *m* DEL FONDO DEL DIENTE **1489** |
| ITRIO *m* **14020** | JUEGO | *m* DEL PISTÓN **7519** |
| JABALCONES *m pl* **1520** | JUEGO | *m* EN EL MOVIMIENTO **9516** |
| JABÓN *m* **11701** | JUEGO | *m* EN EL VÉRTICE **3335** |
| JABÓN *m* BLANCO ORDINARIO **3482** | JUEGO | *m* ENTRE EL MACHO Y EL MOLDE **2483** |
| JABÓN *m* BLANDO **11740** | JUEGO | *m* ENTRE EL MACHO Y EL MOLDE **358** |
| JABÓN *m* DE MARSELLA **8020** | JUEGO | *m* ENTRE LOS DIENTES **914** |
| JABÓN *m* DE POTASA **11740** | JUEGO | *m* ENTRE LOS PUNTOS DE CONTACTO DE LOS DIENTES **5349** |
| JABÓN *m* DE SASTRE **11703** | JUEGO | *m* INÚTIL **916** |
| JABÓN *m* NEGRO **11740** | JUEGO | *m* LATERAL DE LOS ÁRBOLES **4735** |
| JABÓN *m* VERDE **11740** | JUEGO | *m* NOCIVO **916** |
| JAMBA *f* **7211** | JUEGO | *m* PERJUDICIAL **916** |
| JAULA *f* **9948** | JUEGO | *m* PERNICIOSO **916** |
| JAULA ACABADORES *f* **5225** | JUEGO | *m* TOTAL PERDIDO **13063** |
| JAULA DE ACABADO *f* **5219** | JUEGO | *m* ÚTIL **9516** |
| JAULA DE BOLAS *f* **957** | JULIO (FIS.) | *m* **7255** |
| JAULA DE CILINDROS *f* **10704** | JUNCO | *m* **10236** |
| JAULA DE CILINDROS VERTICALES CILINDRO DE DESCARGA *f* **4456** | JUNQUILLO | *m* **10236** |
| JAULA DE DESCARGA *f* **4454** | JUNTA | *f* **7247** |
| JAULA DE FARADAY *f* **5036** | JUNTA | *f* **7247** |
| JAULA DE RODAMIENTO DE BOLAS *f* **955** | JUNTA | *f* **7238** |
| JAULA DE UN RODAMIENTO DE RODILLOS *f* **12040** | JUNTA | *f* **9009** |
| JAULA DESBASTADORES *f* **10787** | JUNTA | *f* **1778** |
| JAULA DESBROZADORA *f* **9622** | JUNTA | *f* **6127** |
| JAULA MEDIA *f* **7098** | JUNTA | *f* A MEDIO HIERRO **7397** |
| JEFE DE FABRICACIÓN *m* **13964** | JUNTA | *f* ABOCELADA **8703** |
| JEFE DE OBRA *m* **11520** | JUNTA | *f* ANULAR **10604** |
| JEFE DE OBRA *m* **5145** | JUNTA | *f* ARTICULADA **12546** |
| JEFE DE TALLER *m* **5541** | JUNTA | *f* ARTICULADA **953** |
| JERINGA *f* DE ACEITE **8784** | JUNTA | *f* CON MANGUITO **11900** |
| JORNADA *f* DE TRABAJO **11347** | JUNTA | *f* CONTRAPEADA **11900** |
| JUEGO *m* **11213** | JUNTA | *f* DE ANILLO DE CAUCHO (ARANDELA DE CAUCHO) **10820** |
| JUEGO *m* **2483** | JUNTA | *f* DE ARANDELA DE PLOMO RECALCADA POR EL CANTO PARA CAÑERIAS **7464** |
| JUEGO *m* **358** | JUNTA | *f* DE AUTOCLAVE **7963** |
| JUEGO *m* **13873** | JUNTA | *f* DE CABEZA CON CABEZA **1776** |
| JUEGO *m* A FONDO DE LA ROSCA **12858** | JUNTA | *f* DE CARDÁN **6573** |
| JUEGO *m* A FONDO DE LOS DIENTES **1489** | JUNTA | *f* DE CARDÁN **13385** |
| JUEGO *m* AXIAL **4727** | | |

**JUN** 1060

JUNTA *f* DE CODILLO **12979**
JUNTA *f* DE CULATA **3570**
JUNTA *f* DE DILATACIÓN **4918**
JUNTA *f* DE DOBLE ROSCA **8794**
JUNTA *f* DE ECLISAS **1782**
JUNTA *f* DE ESTANQUEIDAD **5863**
JUNTA *f* DE FUNDICIÓN CON MASILLA **10867**
JUNTA *f* DE HERMETICIDAD **5863**
JUNTA *f* DE INSERCIÓN **3159**
JUNTA *f* DE LABERINTO **7347**
JUNTA *f* DE RECUBRIMIENTO **7397**
JUNTA *f* DE RETENCIÓN DE ACEITE **8776**
JUNTA *f* DE RÓTULA **953**
JUNTA *f* DE SEPARACIÓN DE UN COJINETE **7241**
JUNTA *f* DE SOLDADURA EN JUNTA CERRADA **1790**
JUNTA *f* DE SOLDADURA POR REFUERZOS **9915**
JUNTA *f* DE TUBOS **9347**
JUNTA *f* DEFLECTORA **7347**
JUNTA *f* DESLIZANTE **11617**
JUNTA *f* EMPALMADA SOLDADA POR LOS DOS LADOS **1777**
JUNTA *f* EMPALMADA SOLDADA POR UN SOLO LADO **1779**
JUNTA *f* EN ÁNGULO EXTERIOR **3179**
JUNTA *f* ESFÉRICA **953**
JUNTA *f* ESTANCA **12921**
JUNTA *f* FLEXIBLE **5416**
JUNTA *f* FUSIBLE **2991**
JUNTA *f* HENDIDA **5806**
JUNTA *f* HERMÉTICA **12921**
JUNTA *f* HIDRÁULICA **13675**
JUNTA *f* INFERIOR **12408**
JUNTA *f* INFERIOR DE DÉBIL ORIENTÁCIÓN **7767**
JUNTA *f* METALOPLÁSTICA **3134**
JUNTA *f* OLDHAM **8794**
JUNTA *f* PARA CAÑERÍA **9355**
JUNTA *f* PARA TUBERÍA **9355**
JUNTA *f* PEGADA **5986**
JUNTA *f* PLÁSTICA **4482**
JUNTA *f* PLÁSTICA **11078**
JUNTA *f* PLÁSTICA DE ESTANQUEIDAD **11078**
JUNTA *f* POR TORNILLOS **1443**
JUNTA *f* POR TORNILLOS **1442**
JUNTA *f* (PUNTO DE UNIÓN) **7238**
JUNTA *f* RECUBRIDORA **7397**
JUNTA *f* RECUBRIDORA SOLDADA POR LOS DOS LADOS **4171**
JUNTA *f* RECUBRIDORA SOLDADA POR SU SOLO LADO **11504**
JUNTA *f* RÍGIDA **10589**
JUNTA *f* RÍGIDA **10589**

JUNTA *f* ROBLONADA **10639**
JUNTA *f* SECUNDARIA DE HERMETICIDAD **13720**
JUNTA *f* SOBRE CORTES **4445**
JUNTA *f* SOLAPADA **7396**
JUNTA *f* SOLDADA **7237**
JUNTA *f* SOLDADA **11759**
JUNTA *f* SOLDADA **13776**
JUNTA *f* SOLDADA **13774**
JUNTA *f* SOLDADA **13767**
JUNTA *f* SOLDADA CON DOBLE PESTAÑA **4141**
JUNTA *f* SOLDADA CON DOBLE SOLAPA **4141**
JUNTA *f* SOLDADA CON SIMPLE PESTAÑA **5720**
JUNTA *f* SOLDADA CON SIMPLE SOLAPA **5720**
JUNTA *f* TÓRICA **8703**
JUNTA *f* UNIVERSAL **13385**
JUNTA *f* UNIVERSAL **6573**
JUNTA ANGULAR *f* **3179**
JUNTA DE BRIDAS *f* **5344**
JUNTA DE CARDÁN *f* **6573**
JUNTA F **1500**
JUNTURA *f* **3254**
JUNTURA F **1500**
KEROSENO *m* **7275**
KIESELGUR *f* **7292**
KILODINA *f* **7296**
KILOGRÁMETRO *m* **7299**
KILÓGRAMO *m* **7297**
KILÓMETRO *m* **7300**
KILOVATIO *m* **7303**
KILOVATIO-HORA *m* **7304**
KILOVOLTIO *m* **7301**
KILOVOLTIO-AMPERIO *m* **7302**
KIP = 1.000 LIBRAS = 453 **7316**
KISH *m* **7317**
KLINGERITA *f* **7318**
LABORAR ESMERADAMENTE **13937**
LABORATORIO *m* **7344**
LABOREO *m* DE MINAS **8311**
LABRA *f* **3523**
LABRA *f* **3523**
LABRA *f* CRUZADA **4132**
LABRA *f* CRUZADA **4134**
LABRA *f* DE LIMAS **3529**
LABRA *f* DE UNA LIMA **3518**
LABRA *f* SIMPLE DE UNA LIMA **11482**
LABRADO POR CAPAS *m* **2487**
LABRAR **5571**
LABRAR **1597**
LABRAR **3504**
LABRAR **13937**

LABRAR LAS LIMAS **3507**
LACA *f* **7354**
LACA *f* DE BRONCE **6001**
LACA *f* EN ESCAMAS **11338**
LACA *f* EN HOJUELAS **11338**
LACA *f* EN LÁMINAS **11338**
LACA *f* EN PLACAS **11338**
LACA *f* PLANA **11338**
LADEAR **13628**
LADO *m* **5348**
LADO *m* DE UNA TUERCA **4994**
LADO DE ENTRADA *m* **4774**
LADO DE INTRODUCCIÓN *m* **4774**
LADO DE UN ÁNGULO *m* **7512**
LADO DE UN POLÍGONO *m* **11414**
LADO DEL ÁNGULO RECTO *m* **9218**
LADO DEL SILLAR QUE QUEDA AL DESCUBIERTO **12369**
LADO DEL VIENTO *m* **13721**
LADO EXTERIOR *m* **8911**
LADO INTERIOR *m* **6974**
LADO PELO DEL CUERO *m* **6038**
LADRILLO *m* **1596**
LADRILLO *m* **12933**
LADRILLO *m* CINTRADO (O CIRCULAR) **13738**
LADRILLO *m* COCIDO **1760**
LADRILLO *m* DE ANCLA **1697**
LADRILLO *m* DE CLAMOTA **5254**
LADRILLO *m* DE CORCHO **3174**
LADRILLO *m* DE CROMITA **2371**
LADRILLO *m* DE PARAMENTO **5004**
LADRILLO *m* DE SÍLICE **11435**
LADRILLO *m* DINAS **5803**
LADRILLO *m* DURO **6273**
LADRILLO *m* ESMALTADO **5970**
LADRILLO *m* HUECO **245**
LADRILLO *m* MACHACADO **9724**
LADRILLO *m* MACIZO **11780**
LADRILLO *m* PARA CUCHARA **7359**
LADRILLO *m* PERFILADO **8425**
LADRILLO *m* REFRACTARIO **5239**
LADRILLO *m* REFRACTARIO **5252**
LAGUNA *f* **6530**
LAGUNA *f* **13585**
LÁMINA *f* **7371**
LÁMINA *f* **5303**
LÁMINA *f* **1299**
LÁMINA *f* DE COBRE **3131**
LÁMINA *f* DE VIDRIO **11589**
LAMINACIÓN *f* **10696**
LAMINADO *m* **10696**

LAMINADO **7375**
LAMINADO *m* BRUTO **10778**
LAMINADO *m* CON DÉBIL PRESIÓN (A PRESIÓN REDUCIDA) **9330**
LAMINADO *m* CONTINUO **3035**
LAMINADO *m* DE ACABADO **5215**
LAMINADO *m* DE LINGOTES **2642**
LAMINADO *m* EN CALIENTE **6656**
LAMINADO *m* EN CALIENTE **6638**
LAMINADO *m* EN FRÍO **2698**
LAMINADO *m* EN PAQUETE **8994**
LAMINADO *m* EN SANDWICH **10929**
LAMINADO *m* ESTRATIFICADO **10929**
LAMINADO *m* TRANSVERSAL **3384**
LAMINADO EN FRÍO **2716**
LAMINADOR *m* **10701**
LAMINADOR *m* ACABADOR **5222**
LAMINADOR *m* DE PAQUETES **1245**
LAMINADOR *m* DE SEIS CILINDROS **2543**
LAMINADOR *m* DE TUBOS **9358**
LAMINADOR *m* PARA CHAPAS GRUESAS **6410**
LAMINADOR *m* PARA FORJAR **5563**
LAMINADOR *m* PARA LINGOTES **1348**
LAMINADOR *m* PARA PAQUETES **11555**
LAMINADOR *m* PARA PULIR **9456**
LAMINADOR *m* REDUCTOR **11508**
LAMINADOR *m* SENDZIMIR **11181**
LAMINADOR *m* TRANSVERSAL **1642**
LAMINADOR *m* UNIVERSAL **13386**
LAMINAR **7372**
LAMINAR **10665**
LAMINAR EN CALIENTE **6636**
LAMINAR EN FRÍO **2694**
LAMINILLA *f* **5303**
LAMINILLA *f* **7371**
LAMINILLA *f* DE ESTAÑO **12955**
LAMINILLA *f* DE PLATA **11466**
LÁMPARA *f* **13453**
LÁMPARA *f* **7384**
LÁMPARA *f* DE ACETILENO **95**
LÁMPARA *f* DE ALCOHOL **11923**
LÁMPARA *f* DE ARCO CERRADO **672**
LÁMPARA *f* DE DIODO **3965**
LÁMPARA *f* DE FILAMENTO DE CARBÓN **1951**
LÁMPARA *f* DE FILAMENTO DE TUNGSTENO **13264**
LÁMPARA *f* DE FILAMENTO METÁLICO **8181**
LÁMPARA *f* DE GAS **6828**
LÁMPARA *f* DE GAS DE ALUMBRADO **5826**
LÁMPARA *f* DE GASOLINA **9224**
LÁMPARA *f* DE INCANDESCENCIA **6828**

# LAM

1062

LÁMPARA  f  DE INCANDESCENCIA **6825**
LÁMPARA  f  DE NEON **8536**
LÁMPARA  f  DE PETRÓLEO **9227**
LÁMPARA  f  DE PETRÓLEO **9224**
LÁMPARA  f  DE SOLDAR **11766**
LÁMPARA  f  DE TECHO **10709**
LÁMPARA  f  DE TECHO **4119**
LÁMPARA  f  DE VAPOR DE MERCURIO **8167**
LÁMPARA  f  DE VAPOR DE MERCURIO EN CUARZO **10080**
LÁMPARA  f  ELÉCTRICA **4516**
LANA  f  DE AMIANTO **11566**
LANA  f  DE MADERA **13923**
LANA  f  DE VIDRIO **5966**
LANA  f  MINERAL **11566**
LANA (DE GANADO OVINO)  f  **13932**
LANOLINA  f  **7391**
LÁNTANO  m  **7394**
LANZA  f  **8679**
LANZA  f  **8679**
LANZA  f  DE OXIGENO **8981**
LANZAR **4468**
LANZAR LA LLAMA **5359**
LÁPIZ  m  **7478**
LÁPIZ  m  DE COLOR **2745**
LÁPIZ  m  DE HEMATITES **8720**
LÁPIZ  m  ROJO **8720**
LARGUERO  m  **5627**
LARGUERO  m  **5625**
LARGURA  f  **1579**
LARGURA  f  **7516**
LARGURA  f  DE ARCO **7517**
LARGURA  f  DE CONSTRUCCIÓN **8925**
LARGURA  f  DE LA FLECHA **7225**
LARGURA  f  DE REFERENCIA **5878**
LARGURA  f  DE RUPTURA **1584**
LARGURA  f  DEL BRAZO DE LA PALANCA **7536**
LARGURA  f  DEL CORDÓN **7520**
LARGURA  f  LIBRE **7518**
LARGURA  f  TOTAL **8925**
LARGURA  f  ÚTIL **13424**
LATA  f  **7426**
LATERAL  m  DE UNA POLEA **5332**
LATEX  m  **7425**
LATÓN  m  **1562**
LATÓN  m  **1562**
LATÓN  m  **14008**
LATÓN  m  AL MANGANESO **7967**
LATÓN  m  AL NÍQUEL **8559**
LATÓN  m  ALFA **399**
LATÓN  m  ALFA-BETA **403**

LATÓN  m  ALFA-BETA **8511**
LATÓN  m  BETA **1216**
LATÓN  m  BRUTO **13987**
LATÓN  m  COLADO **2031**
LATÓN  m  DE ALEACIÓN DÉBIL **7768**
LATÓN  m  DE ALUMINIO **419**
LATÓN  m  DE BASE **8056**
LATÓN  m  DE CALIDAD **6480**
LATÓN  m  DE CALIDAD PARA EMBUTIR **3690**
LATÓN  m  DE ESTIRADO **4232**
LATÓN  m  DE FILETEADO **5645**
LATÓN  m  DE FORJAR **5558**
LATÓN  m  DE MARINA **198**
LATÓN  m  DE RELOJERÍA **2505**
LATÓN  m  EN BRUTO **13987**
LATÓN  m  EN LÁMINAS **11307**
LATÓN  m  NAVAL **8511**
LATÓN  m  PARA CARTUCHERÍA **2016**
LATÓN  m  PARA MUELLES **11978**
LATÓN  m  ROJO **10326**
LATÓN  m  ROJO **10325**
LATÓN  m  ROJO **1658**
LATÓN  m  ROJO **2824**
LATÓN  m  SILICIOSO **11443**
LAVA  f  **7437**
LAVADO  m  (DE LA ARENA) **4681**
LAVADO  m  PARA NÚCLEOS **3171**
LAVADOR  m  **3938**
LAVADOR  m  DE GAS **5845**
LAVADORAS  f pl  Y ESCOGEDORAS  f pl  DE RAÍCES Y FRUTOS **5704**
LAVAR A TODA AGUA **10607**
LAVAR CON AGUA ABUNDANTE **10607**
LAVAR EN AGUA CON LEJÍA **7676**
LAVAR (LOS MINERALES) **2550**
LAVAR UN DIBUJO **2742**
LAVIS  m  **12965**
LAZADA  f  **7741**
LAZO  m  **7741**
LAZO  m  DE UNA CUERDA **7742**
LECHADA  f  **9715**
LECHADA  f  **6152**
LECHADA  f  DE CAL **8274**
LECHADA  f  DE CEMENTO **6152**
LECHADO DEL CEMENTO  m  **6154**
LECHO  m  DE ACEITE **8754**
LECTORES  m pl  ÓPTICOS **8847**
LECTURA  f  **10254**
LEDEBURITA  f  **7504**
LEER **12692**

LIG

LEER **10252**
LÉGAMO *m* **12377**
LEIN *m* (GEOL.) CEMENTO **1253**
LEJÍA *f* **2120**
LEJÍA *f* **7835**
LEJÍA *f* DE POTASA **9671**
LEJÍA *f* DE SOSA **11712**
LEMNISCATA *f* **7514**
LEMNISCATA *f* **2029**
LEÑA *f* **5258**
LEÑA *f* **5258**
LEÑA *f* CORTA Y REDONDA **10803**
LENGUA *f* DE ASPID **5380**
LENGUAJE *m* DE PROGRAMACIÓN ADAPT **159**
LENGUAJE *m* DE PROGRAMACIÓN APT **656**
LENG:UETA *f* **5059**
LENG:UETA *f* Y RANURA *f* **12989**
LEÑO *m* **10803**
LEÑO *m* **1243**
LEÑOSO **7578**
LENTE (AMB.) **7522**
LENTE AMB. BICÓNCAVO (A) **1237**
LENTE AMB. BICONVEXO (A) **1238**
LENTE AMB. CONVERGENTE **2909**
LENTE AMB. CONVERGENTE **2910**
LENTE AMB. DE ACERCAMIENTO **10398**
LENTE AMB. DE AUMENTO **7936**
LENTE AMB. DE BORDE ESPESO **4095**
LENTE AMB. DE BORDE FINO **2910**
LENTE AMB. DIVERGENTE **4095**
LENTE AMB. DIVERGENTE **9914**
LENTE AMB. PLANO-CÓNCAVO O PLANA-CÓNCAVA **9458**
LENTE AMB. PLANO-CONVEXO O PLANA-CONVEXA **9459**
LENTE DE CONCENTRACIÓN DE LOS ELECTRONES **4626**
LETRA *f* REDONDILLA **10799**
LEVA *f* **1883**
LEVA *f* **1883**
LEVA *f* **4442**
LEVA *f* **13878**
LEVA *f* DE CORAZÓN **6329**
LEVA *f* DE DISCO CURVO **4442**
LEVA DE DISCO *f* **9482**
LEVA DE ESPIRAL *f* **11913**
LEVA DE PLATILLO *f* **9482**
LEVA DE RANURA *f* **3270**
LEVA DE RANURA *f* **6134**
LEVA OSCILANTE *f* **8878**
LEVANTAMIENTO *m* **10611**
LEVANTAMIENTO *m* **6517**
LEVANTAMIENTO *m* **6553**

LEVANTAMIENTO *m* DE LA VÁLVULA **7544**
LEVANTAMIENTO *m* DE TIERRA **3945**
LEVANTAMIENTO *m* DE UN FARDO **7559**
LEVANTAMIENTO... DE TECHO FLOTANTE **11331**
LEVANTAR **7542**
LEVANTAR **6517**
LEVANTAR UN DIAGRAMA **9520**
LEVANTAR UNA PERPENDICULAR **4806**
LEVANTAR UNA VERTICAL **4806**
LEVAS DE DISCO *f pl* **9497**
LEVIGACIÓN *f* **7537**
LEVIGACIÓN *f* (QUIM.) **4681**
LEVIGACIONES *f pl* **7537**
LEVÓGIRO **7365**
LEY *f* DE BRAGG **1525**
LEY *f* DE HOOKE **6574**
LEY *f* DE LOS VALORES EXTREMOS **4968**
LEY *f* EXPONENCIAL **4941**
LEY *f* SINOMIAL **1258**
LIAR **1737**
LIBER *m* **1056**
LIBERARSE (AL) (QUIM.) **8497**
LIBRE **6818**
LIBRE DE ÁCIDO **5635**
LIBRE DE CARBONO **1961**
LICENCIA *f* DE EXPLOTACIÓN **7539**
LICOR *m* GRADUADO **12084**
LICOR *m* NORMAL **12084**
LICUABLE **7639**
LICUABLE **5756**
LICUACIÓN *f* **7635**
LICUADO *m* **8421**
LICUAR **8135**
LICUAR UN GAS **7640**
LICUATURA *f* **8421**
LICUEFACCIÓN *f* **5764**
LICUEFACCIÓN *f* DE UN GAS **7636**
LIENZO *m* **7619**
LIENZO *m* CAUCHUTADO **10818**
LIENZO *m* DE AMIANTO **748**
LIENZO *m* DE CALCAR **13083**
LIGA *f* **619**
LIGAR **361**
LIGAR **1737**
LIGNINA *f* **7577**
LIGNINA *f* **7577**
LIGNINA *f* **7577**
LIGNITO *m* **7578**
LIGNITO *m* NEGRO **9405**
LIGNITO *m* PERFECTO **1665**

**LIG**  1064

LIGROÍNA  *f* **7580**
LIGROÍNA  *f* **7580**
LIJA  *f* **11270**
LIMA  *f* **4441**
LIMA  *f* **5148**
LIMA  *f* AGUJA **8519**
LIMA  *f* ANCHA **9067**
LIMA  *f* BASTARDA **1057**
LIMA  *f* CUADRADA **12019**
LIMA  *f* CUATRO CUARTOS **12019**
LIMA  *f* CUATRO CUARTOS **12019**
LIMA  *f* CUCHILLO **7324**
LIMA  *f* CURVA **10575**
LIMA  *f* DE ALUMINIO **422**
LIMA  *f* DE BARRAS **1903**
LIMA  *f* DE BISEL **1903**
LIMA  *f* DE COLA DE RATÓN **10216**
LIMA  *f* DE CORTE **11623**
LIMA  *f* DE DOBLE TALLA **4133**
LIMA  *f* DE ENTRADA **13625**
LIMA  *f* DE HOJA DE SAUCE **3392**
LIMA  *f* DE LADOS LISOS **10878**
LIMA  *f* DE MANO **6234**
LIMA  *f* DE MEDIA CAÑA **6208**
LIMA  *f* DE PICADURA SENCILLA **11481**
LIMA  *f* DE PICADURA SENCILLA **11481**
LIMA  *f* DE SECCIÓN TRIANGULAR **13189**
LIMA  *f* DE TALLA BASTA **10774**
LIMA  *f* DE TALLA CRUZADA **4133**
LIMA  *f* DE TALLA FINA **11680**
LIMA  *f* DE TALLA MEDIA **8266**
LIMA  *f* DE TALLA MUY FINA **12467**
LIMA  *f* DE TALLA SEMIFINA **11100**
LIMA  *f* ESPADA **11623**
LIMA  *f* FINA **11680**
LIMA  *f* FRESA **1390**
LIMA  *f* FUERTE **10774**
LIMA  *f* GRUESA **7201**
LIMA  *f* OLIVA **13041**
LIMA  *f* PARA AFILAR LOS DIENTES DE SIERRA **10954**
LIMA  *f* PLANA **5381**
LIMA  *f* PLANA DE MANO **9067**
LIMA  *f* PLANA EN PUNTA **5390**
LIMA  *f* PUNTIAGUDA **12648**
LIMA  *f* REDONDA **10796**
LIMA  *f* ROTATIVA **10755**
LIMA  *f* TRES CUARTOS **13189**
LIMA  *f* TRIANGULAR **12870**
LIMA CUADRADA  *f* **12019**
LIMA CUADRADA  *f* CUADRADILLO  *m* **12019**

LIMADO  *m* **5153**
LIMADORA  *f* **11269**
LIMADORA  *f* **11267**
LIMADURAS  *f pl* **5155**
LIMADURAS DEL ESCARIADOR  *f pl* **11277**
LIMALLA  *f* **5155**
LIMAR **5149**
LIMATÓN  *m* **10774**
LIMATÓN  *m* **10774**
LIMITADOR  *m* DE CARRERA **12278**
LIMITADOR  *m* DE CARRERA **12278**
LIMITADOR  *m* DE CARRERA **12278**
LIMITADOR  *m* O REGULADOR  *m* DE CAUDAL **4879**
LIMITAR **6926**
LÍMITE  *m* **7587**
LÍMITE  *m* (CONVENCIONAL) DE FLUENCIA **3325**
LÍMITE  *m* DE ABSORCIÓN **50**
LÍMITE  *m* DE ACEPTACIÓN **69**
LÍMITE  *m* DE ALARGAMIENTO **9923**
LÍMITE  *m* DE APLASTAMIENTO **2873**
LÍMITE  *m* DE CORRIENTE **14012**
LÍMITE  *m* DE ELASTICIDAD **4481**
LÍMITE  *m* DE ELASTICIDAD PROPORCIONAL **7590**
LÍMITE  *m* DE ERRORES **7589**
LÍMITE  *m* DE FATIGA **5053**
LÍMITE  *m* DE FATIGA POR CORROSIÓN **3188**
LÍMITE  *m* DE FLUJO (DE CIRCULACIÓNDE DERRAME) **5456**
LÍMITE  *m* DE LA CARRERA DE LA VÁLVULA **13461**
LÍMITE  *m* DE LA SUPERFICIE DE GRANOS **6033**
LÍMITE  *m* DE PASO **14011**
LÍMITE  *m* DE REACCIÓN **10249**
LÍMITE  *m* DE RESISTENCIA **4741**
LÍMITE  *m* DE RESISTENCIA O DE FATIGA **5050**
LÍMITE  *m* DE SATURACIÓN **7591**
LÍMITE  *m* DE TEMPERATURA **7592**
LÍMITE  *m* ELÁSTICO **7588**
LÍMITE  *m* ELÁSTICO **5456**
LÍMITE  *m* ELÁSTICO **4481**
LÍMITE  *m* ELÁSTICO **14012**
LÍMITE  *m* ELÁSTICO **14013**
LÍMITE  *m* ELÁSTICO **14011**
LÍMITE  *m* ELÁSTICO CONVENCIONAL **9923**
LÍMITE  *m* ELÁSTICO CONVENCIONAL O APARENTE **9922**
LÍMITE  *m* ELÁSTICO MÍNIMO GARANTIZADO **8308**
LÍMITE  *m* PROPORCIONAL (DE ELASTICIDAD) **9936**
LÍMITE  *m* TARDÍO **14011**
LÍMITE DE LA ELASTICIDAD **4481**
LÍMITES  *m pl* DE TOLERANCIA **7595**
LIMO  *m* **12377**

1065     **LIN**

LIMO *m* ANÓDICO **600**
LIMONITA *f* **7596**
LIMONITA *f* ARCILLOSA **2467**
LIMPIA *f* **11006**
LIMPIACRISTAL *m* **13870**
LIMPIADOR *m* ALCALINO **2472**
LIMPIADORAS *f pl* DE PATATAS **9703**
LIMPIAPARABRISAS *m* **13871**
LIMPIAR **11005**
LIMPIAR **11008**
LIMPIAR CON CHORRO DE ARENA **10919**
LIMPIAR CON MECHERO **5309**
LIMPIEZA *f* **2474**
LIMPIEZA *f* **11011**
LIMPIEZA *f* ALCALINA **334**
LIMPIEZA *f* CATÓDICA **2098**
LIMPIEZA *f* CON CHORRO DE ARENA **1316**
LIMPIEZA *f* CON CHORRO DE ARENA **10921**
LIMPIEZA *f* DEL METAL **2474**
LIMPIEZA *f* EN TAMBOR **4335**
LIMPIEZA *f* MECÁNICA **8096**
LIMPIEZA *f* POR CHORRO DE AIRE **244**
LIMPIEZA *f* POR INMERSIÓN **11697**
LINDE *f* **12763**
LÍNEA *f* **10812**
LÍNEA *f* **7597**
LÍNEA *f* **179**
LÍNEA *f* **4523**
LÍNEA *f* AÉREA **212**
LÍNEA *f* AERODINÁMICA **12351**
LÍNEA *f* ATMOSFÉRICA **798**
LÍNEA *f* CERO **14025**
LÍNEA *f* CONDUCTORA **4523**
LÍNEA *f* CURVA DE VOLUMEN CONSTANTE **7187**
LÍNEA *f* CURVA ISOMÉTRICA **7193**
LÍNEA *f* DE ADMISIÓN DEL VAPOR **199**
LÍNEA *f* DE ALTA TENSIÓN **6501**
LÍNEA *f* DE ALUMBRADO **4519**
LÍNEA *f* DE CIERRE **2536**
LÍNEA *f* DE CIRCULACIÓN **5457**
LÍNEA *f* DE COLIMACIÓN **7601**
LÍNEA *f* DE COMPRESIÓN **2857**
LÍNEA *f* DE COTA **3957**
LÍNEA *f* DE ENERGÍA **7603**
LÍNEA *f* DE ENGRANAJE **7602**
LÍNEA *f* DE ESCAPE DEL VAPOR **4892**
LÍNEA *f* DE FUERZA **7603**
LÍNEA *f* DE FUGA **324**
LÍNEA *f* DE INSPECCIÓN **6986**
LÍNEA *f* DE INTERSECCIÓN **7605**

LÍNEA *f* DE JUNTA **9093**
LÍNEA *f* DE LA CORRIENTE **12351**
LÍNEA *f* DE LA UNIÓN DE LAS CHAPAS **11084**
LÍNEA *f* DE MARCADO AL GRAMIL **7604**
LÍNEA *f* DE PRESIÓN NULA (DEL DIAGRAMA) **14029**
LÍNEA *f* DE PUNTOS **4125**
LÍNEA *f* DE PUNTOS **4125**
LÍNEA *f* DE REMACHES **10813**
LÍNEA *f* DE RODILLOS DE TRAÍDA **4775**
LÍNEA *f* DE SOCORRO **4690**
LÍNEA *f* DE TRANSMISIÓN **7607**
LÍNEA *f* DE TRANSPORTE A LARGA DISTANCIA **4521**
LÍNEA *f* DE TRANSPORTE DE ENERGÍA **4526**
LÍNEA *f* DE UN TRAZO **2205**
LÍNEA *f* DECAUVILLE **9639**
LÍNEA *f* DEL LIQUIDUS **7661**
LÍNEA *f* HORIZONTAL **6585**
LÍNEA *f* ISENTRÓPICA **7173**
LÍNEA *f* ISOCLINA **7181**
LÍNEA *f* ISODINÁMICA **7182**
LÍNEA *f* ISODINÁMICA **7182**
LÍNEA *f* MEDIANERA **8124**
LÍNEA *f* NEUTRA **8545**
LÍNEA *f* PLENA **5725**
LÍNEA *f* POLIGONAL **9611**
LÍNEA *f* QUEBRADA **7166**
LÍNEA *f* RECTA **12310**
LÍNEA *f* SUBTERRÁNEA **13353**
LÍNEA DE EMERGENCIA *f* **4690**
LÍNEA DE FUGA *f* **324**
LÍNEA ELÉCTRICA SUBTERRÁNEA *f* **13353**
LÍNEA ISOMÉTRICA *f* **7187**
LÍNEAS *f pl* DE HARTMANN **7815**
LÍNEAS *f pl* DE LÍMITES **5689**
LÍNEAS *f pl* DE LUDERS **7815**
LÍNEAS *f pl* DE LUDERS **7622**
LÍNEAS *f pl* DE LUDERS **12371**
LINGOTE *m* **6919**
LINGOTE *m* **1301**
LINGOTE *m* **2069**
LINGOTE *m* A SU SALIDA **1834**
LINGOTE *m* DE ACERO **951**
LINGOTE *m* DE ACERO **12210**
LINGOTE *m* DE COBRE **3120**
LINGOTE *m* ENTALLADO **8674**
LINGOTE *m* FUNDICIÓN **9298**
LINGOTE *m* FUNDICIÓN **9302**
LINGOTE *m* FUNDICIÓN DE ACERO **951**
LINGOTE *m* PARA LA MECANIZACIÓN DE PROBETAS (EN FORMA DE QUILLA DE NAVÍO) **7273**

**LIN** 1066

LINGOTE  *m*  PARA MECANIZAR PROBETAS **12777**
LINGOTE  *m*  PLANO DE COBRE **3129**
LINGOTE  *m*  QUEMADO **1748**
LINGOTE  *m*  RECTANGULAR DE ACERO **1346**
LINGOTERA  *f*  **6923**
LINGOTERA  *f*  **8422**
LINGOTES  *m pl*  GRUESOS **1349**
LINO  *m*  **5412**
LINO  *m*  DE NUEVA ZELANDA **8550**
LINÓLEO  *m*  **7630**
LINTERNA  *f*  **7393**
LINTERNA  *f*  PARA CORREAS **7500**
LÍQUIDO  *m*  **7642**
LÍQUIDO  *m*  **7641**
LÍQUIDO  *m*  CAÚSTICO **2119**
LÍQUIDO  *m*  DE DECAPADO **7293**
LÍQUIDO  *m*  DE EXTRACCIÓN **4965**
LÍQUIDO  *m*  DE SOBREFUSIÓN **12464**
LÍQUIDO  *m*  FILTRADO **5181**
LÍQUIDO  *m*  OBTURADOR **11082**
LÍQUIDO  *m*  PENETRANTE **9169**
LÍQUIDO FILTRADO **5181**
LÍQUIDOS  *m pl*  **7660**
LIQUIDUS  *m*  **7661**
LISO **13035**
LISTA  *f*  DE BULTOS **9003**
LISTA  *f*  LEVANTAMIENTO  *m*  **7717**
LITARGIRIO  *m*  **7663**
LITERA  *f*  **1739**
LITIO  *m*  **7664**
LITRO  *m*  **7669**
LIXIVIACIÓN  *f*  **7677**
LIXIVIACIÓN (QUIM.)  *f*  **7677**
LIXIVIAR **7676**
LIZÓN  *m*  **10770**
LLAMA  *f*  CARBURANTE **1990**
LLAMA  *f*  DE HIDRÓGENO **6714**
LLAMA  *f*  FULIGINOSA **11678**
LLAMA  *f*  INCOLORA **8636**
LLAMA  *f*  LUMINOSA **7820**
LLAMA  *f*  LUMINOSA **7820**
LLAMA  *f*  NEUTRA **8543**
LLAMA  *f*  NO LUMINOSA **8636**
LLAMA  *f*  NO LUMINOSA **8636**
LLAMA  *f*  OXIDANTE **8636**
LLAMA  *f*  OXIDANTE **8636**
LLAMA  *f*  OXIDANTE **8975**
LLAMA  *f*  REDUCTORA **7820**
LLAMA  *f*  REDUCTORA **10349**
LLAMA  *f*  REDUCTORA **4882**

LLAMA NORMAL **8543**
LLAMA OXIDANTE **4883**
LLANA  *f*  **4221**
LLANOS  *m pl*  **5375**
LLANTA  *f*  **6026**
LLANTA  *f*  **10592**
LLANTA  *f*  DE BASE HUNDIDA **4322**
LLANTA  *f*  DE CONTACTO **2999**
LLANTA  *f*  DE UNA POLEA **10595**
LLANTA  *f*  DE UNA RUEDA **5088**
LLANTA  *f*  DE UNA RUEDA **13818**
LLANTA  *f*  DE VOLANTE **10593**
LLANTA DE UNA RUEDA  *f*  **10596**
LLAVE  *f*  **9532**
LLAVE  *f*  **11592**
LLAVE  *f*  **12639**
LLAVE  *f*  **3212**
LLAVE  *f*  **3212**
LLAVE  *f*  **2617**
LLAVE  *f*  CON DINAMÓMETRO DE TORSIÓN **13049**
LLAVE  *f*  DE GRIFO **12236**
LLAVE  *f*  MAESTRA **3365**
LLAVE ACODADA  *f*  **1195**
LLAVE AJUSTABLE  *f*  **11052**
LLAVE DE CALIBRE  *f*  **7284**
LLAVE DE CALIBRE DOBLE  *f*  **4167**
LLAVE DE CALIBRE SENCILLO  *f*  **11499**
LLAVE DE EJE  *f*  **883**
LLAVE DE EXTREMO  *f*  **1515**
LLAVE DE EXTREMOS  *f*  **1515**
LLAVE DE GANCHO  *f*  **1822**
LLAVE DE GRIFO  *f*  **9532**
LLAVE DE HORQUILLA  *f*  **7284**
LLAVE DE HORQUILLA DOBLE  *f*  **4167**
LLAVE DE HORQUILLA SIMPLE  *f*  **11499**
LLAVE DE MANDO (PARA GRIFO DE CORREDERA) **2618**
LLAVE DE MANGUITO  *f*  **11709**
LLAVE DE TRINQUETE  *f*  **10224**
LLAVE DE TUBOS  *f*  **9366**
LLAVE DE TUBOS  *f*  **9366**
LLAVE DE TUERCAS  *f*  **11833**
LLAVE DE UÑAS EN EXTREMO  *f*  **9322**
LLAVE DINAMOMÉTRICA  *f*  **13049**
LLAVE EN MANO (NEGOCIO)  *f*  **13284**
LLAVE INGLESA  *f*  **11052**
LLAVE INGLESA  *f*  **2551**
LLAVE PARA EJE **883**
LLAVE TUBULAR  *f*  **1515**
LLAVE TUBULAR CURVA  *f*  **509**
LLAVÍN  *m*  **3365**

# 1067  MAC

LLEGADA DE AGUA  *f* **6915**
LLENADO  *m* **2269**
LLENAR **5156**
LOCALIZACIÓN **8015**
LOCO (SOBRE EL EJE) **7749**
LOCOMOCIÓN  *f* **7712**
LOCOMOCIÓN  *f* CON BENCINA **9225**
LOCOMOTORA  *f* **7713**
LOCOMOTORA  *f* DE GASOLINA **9225**
LOCOMOTORA  *f* DE VAPOR **12173**
LOCOMOTORA  *f* ELÉCTRICA **4520**
LOCOMOTORA  *f* ELÉCTRICA CON ACUMULADORES **79**
LOCOMOTORA  *f* POR AIRE COMPRIMIDO **2844**
LOCOMOTORA  *f* SIN HOGAR **5256**
LOCOMÓVIL **9640**
LODO  *m* **8444**
LOESS  *m* **7716**
LOGARITMO  *m* **7718**
LOGARITMO  *m* DECIMAL **2788**
LOGARITMO  *m* HIPERBÓLICO **8509**
LOGARITMO  *m* NATURAL **8509**
LOGARITMO  *m* VULGAR **2788**
LONA  *f* **1906**
LONA  *f* DE EMBALAJE **6449**
LONGITUD  *f* CRÍTICA DE ONDAS **10072**
LONGITUD  *f* DE ONDA **13700**
LONGITUD  *f* FOCAL **5500**
LONGITUD  *f* MÍNIMA DE ONDA **8309**
LOSA  *f* **11551**
LOSA  *f* **5302**
LOSA  *f* DE HORMIGÓN (SOPORTE DE UN DEPÓSITO) **2900**
LOSA  *f* SOPORTE / SOBRE PILOTES **9305**
LOTE  *m* **7766**
LOTE  *m* DE COLADA **1059**
LUBRICANTE  *m* **7800**
LUBRICANTE GRAFITADO **6063**
LUBRIFICACIÓN  *f* **7803**
LUBRIFICACIÓN  *f* **7808**
LUBRIFICANTE  *m* **7800**
LUBRIFICANTE  *m* **1250**
LUBRIFICANTE  *m* DE RODAJE **6112**
LUBRIFICANTE  *m* PARA MOLDE **9092**
LUBRIFICAR **7801**
LUCES  *f pl* DE DIRECCIÓN **3989**
LUCES  *f pl* DE RETROCESO **908**
LUCES  *f pl* TRASERAS **12595**
LUCHAR **7831**
LUGAR  *m* DE INSTALACIÓN **9423**
LUGAR  *m* DE INSTALACIÓN **9423**
LUGAR  *m* DE MONTAJE **9423**

LUGAR  *m* DE TRABAJO **13943**
LUGAR  *m* GEOMÉTRICO **7715**
LUGAR DE TRABAJO  *m* **13943**
LUMEN  *m* **7818**
LUMINISCENCIA  *f* **7819**
LUNETA  *f* DE SEGUIMIENTO **5514**
LUNETA  *f* FIJA **12154**
LUNETA  *f* MÓVIL **5514**
LUNETA  *f* MÓVIL **5514**
LUNETA  *f* TRASERA **899**
LUNETA  *f* VERIFICADORA **2721**
LÚNULA  *f* **7829**
LUPA  *f* **7936**
LUPIAS  *f pl* **1349**
LUSTRAR **5969**
LUSTRAR **11679**
LUSTRE  *m* **4777**
LUTECIO  *m* **7833**
LUX  *m* **7834**
LUZ  *f* **7560**
LUZ  *f* ALCANCE  *m* **7256**
LUZ  *f* ANÓDICA **9660**
LUZ  *f* ARTIFICIAL **734**
LUZ  *f* DE DRUMMOND **8987**
LUZ  *f* DE GAS **5827**
LUZ  *f* DE MECHERO DE GAS **5827**
LUZ  *f* DEL ARCO VOLTAICO **673**
LUZ  *f* DEL DÍA **3622**
LUZ  *f* DEL GAS CON INCANDESCENCIA **6829**
LUZ  *f* DIFUSA **3927**
LUZ  *f* DIFUSA **3955**
LUZ  *f* (DISTANCIA ENTRE PUNTOS DE APOYO) **11831**
LUZ  *f* ELÉCTRICA **4517**
LUZ  *f* NATURAL **3622**
LUZ  *f* OXHÍDRICA **8987**
LUZ  *f* PARA ADELANTAR **9102**
LUZ  *f* POLARIZADA **9585**
LUZ  *f* POR INCANDESCENCIA **6826**
LUZ  *f* REFLEJADA **10383**
MACA  *f* O DEFECTO (EN LA CHAPA QUE MATRIZAR) **3894**
MACERACIÓN  *f* **7837**
MACERAR **7836**
MACHACADORA  *f* **3419**
MACHACADORA DE MANDÍBULAS  *f* **12273**
MACHACAR **9712**
MACHACAR **1580**
MACHACAR **6103**
MACHAQUEO  *m* **1588**
MACHETE  *m* **6305**

# MAC

MACHIHEMBRADO *m* **12989**
MACHIHEMBRAR **12988**
MACHO *m* **3162**
MACHO *m* DE GRIFO **9532**
MACILLO *m* DE COBRE **3119**
MACILLO *m* DE PLOMO **7463**
MACIZO *m* BASE DE MÁQUINA **7848**
MACIZO *f* DE CIMIENTOS **5589**
MACIZO *f* DE HORMIGÓN **2896**
MACLA *f* (DE CRISTALIZACIÓN) **13300**
MACLA *f* DE DEFORMACIÓN **8113**
MACLADO *m* **13302**
MACROATAQUE POR ÁCIDO *m* **7870**
MACROESTRUCTURA *f* **7869**
MACROFOTOGRAFÍA *f* **9266**
MACROGRAFÍA *f* **7871**
MACROSCÓPICO **7872**
MACROSEGREGACIÓN *f* **7876**
MADERA *f* **13913**
MADERA *f* A HILO **12939**
MADERA *f* BLANDA **11746**
MADERA *f* BLANDA **11746**
MADERA *f* BLANDA **11746**
MADERA *f* BRAVA **6282**
MADERA *f* CARCOMIDA **13977**
MADERA *f* CORTADA **10962**
MADERA *f* CORTADA A CONTRAHILO **4719**
MADERA *f* CURVADA **1196**
MADERA *f* DE ÁRBOLES DE HOJA (O DE FRONDA) **6301**
MADERA *f* DE CONSTRUCCIÓN **12937**
MADERA *f* DE CONSTRUCCIÓN **12937**
MADERA *f* DE HOJALATA **13833**
MADERA *f* DE HOJALATA **13833**
MADERA *f* DE HOJALATA **13833**
MADERA *f* DURA **6282**
MADERA *f* EN ROLLO **7723**
MADERA *f* ENCUADRADA **12035**
MADERA *f* PESADA **6282**
MADERA *f* PODRIDA **5610**
MADERA *f* PODRIDA **5610**
MADERA *f* PUDRIDA **10768**
MADERA *f* RESINOSA **10483**
MADERA *f* SANA **11820**
MADERA *f* SECADA AL AIRE LIBRE **297**
MADERA *f* SEMIRREDONDEADA **6210**
MADERA *f* SIN DEFECTOS **12940**
MADERA *f* SIN NUDOS **12940**
MADERO **9457**
MADERO *m* **1243**
MADERO *m* EN QUE SE APOYAN LOS PELDAÑOS **12052**

MAGNALIO *m* **7878**
MAGNESIA *f* **7879**
MAGNESIA *f* CALCINADA **1842**
MAGNESIA *f* EN POLVO **9725**
MAGNESIO *m* **7882**
MAGNESITA *f* **7880**
MAGNESITA *f* MUERTA **3639**
MAGNÉTICO **7893**
MAGNETISMO *m* **7926**
MAGNETISMO *m* LATENTE **7417**
MAGNETISMO *m* LIBRE **5640**
MAGNETISMO *m* PERMANENTE **9206**
MAGNETISMO *m* REMANENTE **10445**
MAGNETISMO *m* RESIDUAL **10445**
MAGNETITA *f* **7927**
MAGNETIZABLE **7922**
MAGNETIZACIÓN *f* **7928**
MAGNETIZACIÓN *f* **7928**
MAGNETIZACIÓN *f* **7906**
MAGNETIZAR **7924**
MAGNETIZARSE **1126**
MAGNETO *m* **7930**
MAGNETOESTRICCIÓN *f* **7933**
MAGNETÓFONO *m* **12644**
MAGNETOSCOPIA *f* **7910**
MAGNETOSCOPIA *f* **7877**
MAGNITUD *f* DESEADA **10469**
MALACATE *m* **1731**
MALAQUITA *f* **6089**
MALEABILIDAD *f* **7958**
MALEABILIZACIÓN *f* **7961**
MALEABILIZACIÓN *f* DE LA FUNDICIÓN **13175**
MALEABILIZAR LA FUNDICIÓN **7952**
MALEABLE **7960**
MALEABLE **1250**
MALLA *f* **9032**
MALLA *f* DE UNA CADENA DE RODILLOS **11416**
MALLA *f* RECTANGULAR **10304**
MALLAS ANCHAS (DE) *f pl* **2578**
MALLAS ESTRECHAS (DE) *f pl* **5206**
MALLETE *m* **13926**
MALLETO *m* **13926**
MALVARROSA *f* SOLUBLE **4831**
MAMELÓN *m* **8578**
MAMELÓN *m* DOBLE **4149**
MAMPARA *f* **6252**
MAMPARA PIRORRESISTENTE *f* **5251**
MAMPOSTERÍA **1601**
MAMPUESTO *m* **11521**
MAMPUESTO *m* **10827**

# 1069  MAN

MANCHA  f POR CRISTALES DE SULFURO DE COBRE **3429**
MANCHAS  f pl DE AGUA (DE LLUVIA) **10178**
MANDAR **3049**
MANDARRIA  f (DE RETACAR) **12308**
MANDO  m **3048**
MANDO  m **4309**
MANDO  m **4297**
MANDO A DISTANCIA  m **10448**
MANDO ADAPTIVO  m **161**
MANDO CONTINUO  m **3032**
MANDO DE CONTORNO  m **3039**
MANDO DE POSICIONAMIENTO  m **9650**
MANDO DEL ARRANQUE  m **12117**
MANDO DIRECTO POR COMPUTADORA  m **2875**
MANDO DIRECTO POR COMPUTADORA  m **3981**
MANDO DIRECTO POR COMPUTADORA  m **3985**
MANDO ELÁSTICO  m **8642**
MANDO ELÉCTRICO  m **4503**
MANDO HIDRÁULICO  m **6683**
MANDO INDIVIDUAL  m **6886**
MANDO MANUAL  m **6233**
MANDO MECÁNICO  m **8119**
MANDO MECÁNICO  m **9654**
MANDO MECÁNICO  m **9734**
MANDO NEUMÁTICO  m **2842**
MANDO PARAXIAL  m **12314**
MANDO POR TORNILLO MOLETEADO  m **7337**
MANDO POSITIVO  m **9654**
MANDO POSITIVO  m **9654**
MANDO PUNTO A PUNTO  m **9572**
MANDOS  m pl (AUTOMÓVIL) **12232**
MANDOS  m pl DE DIRECCIÓN **12232**
MANDOS  m pl DE FRENO **1539**
MANDRIL  m **2727**
MANDRIL  m **2393**
MANDRIL  m **4260**
MANDRIL  m **11904**
MANDRIL  m **11904**
MANDRIL  m **11904**
MANDRIL  m CON ESPIGA DE TORNILLO **12867**
MANDRIL  m CÓNICO **12651**
MANDRIL  m DE AGUJERO SIMPLE **9425**
MANDRIL  m DE ARRASTRE **4301**
MANDRIL  m DE CUATRO MORDAZAS INDEPENDIENTES **5604**
MANDRIL  m DE ESPIGA CÓNICA **12667**
MANDRIL  m DE MONTAJE **7964**
MANDRIL  m DE MONTAJE EXPANSIBLE **4907**
MANDRIL  m DE MONTAJE LISO **9425**
MANDRIL  m DE REPOSICIÓN **7964**

MANDRIL  m DE SUJECIÓN **6121**
MANDRIL  m DE TORNO **2393**
MANDRIL  m EXPANSIBLE JACOBS **7208**
MANDRIL  m FLOTANTE **5438**
MANDRIL  m LIMITADOR DE CARRERA **12278**
MANDRIL  m LISO **11789**
MANDRIL  m NEUMÁTICO **279**
MANDRIL  m PARA ENSANCHAR LOS TUBOS **13250**
MANDRIL  m UNIVERSAL **13382**
MANDRIL  m UNIVERSAL DE TRES MORDAZAS **12874**
MANDRIL  m Y GARRAS PORTAFRESA **2729**
MANDRILADO  m **4277**
MANDRILADO  m **4277**
MANDRILADO  m **1473**
MANDRILADO  m **1461**
MANDRILAR **1462**
MANDRILAR **1466**
MANDRILAR UN AGUJERO PARA REMATE **4262**
MANDRILAR UN TUBO **4903**
MANDRILES  m CON AUTOTRACCIÓN **11152**
MANDRILES  m EXPANSIBLES **4906**
MANDRILES  m HIDRÁULICOS **6679**
MANDRILES  m MAGNÉTICOS **7898**
MANDRILES  m MECÁNICOS **8095**
MANDRILES  m NEUMÁTICOS **9550**
MANDRINADO  m **3855**
MANDRINADORA  f **1471**
MANDRINADORA DE PRECISIÓN  f **5196**
MANDRINAR UN TUBO **4903**
MANEJABLE **6269**
MANEJO  m (DE DIFÍCIL) **13402**
MANERAL  m **3403**
MANEZUELA  f **6262**
MANGA  f **6614**
MANGA  f **11576**
MANGA  f **8679**
MANGA  f DE ABERTURA DE INSPECCIÓN O DE LIMPIEZA **7998**
MANGA  f DE EJE **1117**
MANGANESÍFERO **7971**
MANGANESO  m **7966**
MANGANESO  m ELECTROLÍTICO **4599**
MANGO  m **6262**
MANGO  m DE UN HACHA **6433**
MANGO  m DE UN MARTILLO **11244**
MANGO  m DE UNA HERRAMIENTA **12614**
MANGO  m DE UNA HERRAMIENTA **6263**
MANGUETA  f DE EJE **882**
MANGUETAS  f pl **5443**
MANGUETAS  f pl **5434**

**MAN** 1070

MANGUITO *m* **3258**
MANGUITO *m* **1773**
MANGUITO *m* **5280**
MANGUITO *m* **3254**
MANGUITO *m* **2965**
MANGUITO *m* **13368**
MANGUITO *m* **11576**
MANGUITO *m* **11576**
MANGUITO *m* ADAPTADOR DE BROCAS **4266**
MANGUITO *m* ARTICULADO UNIVERSAL **6572**
MANGUITO *m* ATERRAJADO **11061**
MANGUITO *m* CASQUILLO *m* DEL REGULADOR **6017**
MANGUITO *m* CILÍNDRICO DE ACOPLAMIENTO **2449**
MANGUITO *m* CON PERNOS EMPOTRADOS **2449**
MANGUITO *m* CON UNA TIRA DE CORREA **7349**
MANGUITO *m* CON ZUNCHOS **11577**
MANGUITO *m* DE ACOPLAMIENTO **3257**
MANGUITO *m* DE ACOPLAMIENTO SELLERS **11164**
MANGUITO *m* DE CENTRADO **2087**
MANGUITO *m* DE COQUILLAS **2449**
MANGUITO *m* DE DILATACIÓN **4915**
MANGUITO *m* DE EMBRAGUE **11599**
MANGUITO *m* DE MANIVELA A BRAZO **3300**
MANGUITO *m* DE RACOR O DE EMPALME **11705**
MANGUITO *m* DE REDUCCIÓN DE ESCARIADO **3962**
MANGUITO *m* DE SEGURIDAD **10884**
MANGUITO *m* DE TIRAS DE CUERO **7501**
MANGUITO *m* DE TRINQUETES **10221**
MANGUITO *m* ELÁSTICO **4476**
MANGUITO *m* EXCÉNTRICO **4435**
MANGUITO *m* FLEXIBLE **5417**
MANGUITO *m* HEMBRA **11061**
MANGUITO *m* MÓVIL **11599**
MANGUITO *m* PARA EMPALMAR DOS TUBOS CORTADOS **4158**
MANGUITO *m* PROTECTOR **9942**
MANGUITO *m* REDUCTOR **10351**
MANGUITO *m* ROSCADO **11061**
MANGUITO *m* ROSCADO **11026**
MANGUITO DE ACOPLAMIENTO *m* **1510**
MANGUITO DE EMPALME DE AGUJERO DE HOMBRE O REGISTRO DE HOMBRE *m* **7978**
MANGUITO DE EMPALME DE AGUJERO DE HOMBRE O REGISTRO DE HOMBRE *m* **7998**
MANIJA *m* DE MANDO **7706**
MANIOBRA *f* **12226**
MANIOBRA *f* **12226**
MANIOBRA *f* DE SERVICIO **13398**
MANIOBRA *f* DEL FRENO **1549**
MANIOBRAR **3049**
MANIPULACIÓN *f* **8106**

MANIVELA *f* **3295**
MANIVELA *f* **6231**
MANIVELA *f* ACODADA EN FORJA **5550**
MANIVELA *f* AMOVIBLE **10450**
MANIVELA *f* CON MANGUITO **3305**
MANIVELA *f* DE BRAZOS **3296**
MANIVELA *f* DE CARRERA CORTA **11375**
MANIVELA *f* DE CARRERA LARGA **7732**
MANIVELA *f* DE CIGÜEÑAL **6976**
MANIVELA *f* DE CORREDERA **11631**
MANIVELA *f* DE GRADUADO **6865**
MANIVELA *f* ELEVALUNAS **13867**
MANIVELA *f* EN EXTREMO **8947**
MANIVELA *f* EN SALEDIZO **8947**
MANIVELA *f* EN VARIAS PIEZAS **1706**
MANIVELA *f* FORJADA **5550**
MANIVELA *f* FRONTAL **8947**
MANIVELA *f* VENIDA DE FORJA **5550**
MANO *f* **10832**
MANO *f* DE OBRA **13961**
MANO *f* DE PINTURA **2583**
MANO DE PINTURA AL ÓLEO *f* **2582**
MANÓMETRO *m* **9821**
MANÓMETRO *m* **9820**
MANÓMETRO *m* BOURDON **1501**
MANÓMETRO *m* DE AIRE COMPRIMIDO **2534**
MANÓMETRO *m* DE AIRE LIBRE **8827**
MANÓMETRO *m* DE MERCURIO **8151**
MANÓMETRO *m* DE MUELLE **11989**
MANÓMETRO *m* DE PLACA **3873**
MANÓMETRO *m* DE TUBO **1501**
MANÓMETRO *m* DIFERENCIAL **3921**
MANÓMETRO *m* METÁLICO **11989**
MANÓMETRO *m* PARA DETERMINACIONES ANEMOMÉTRICAS **4211**
MANÓMETRO *m* REGISTRADOR **10292**
MANÓMETRO *m* SERVICIO CONTRASTE **12080**
MANÓMETRO DE CONTROL *m* **9813**
MANOSTATO *m* **9835**
MANOVACUÓMETRO *m* **2830**
MANTECA *f* DE COCO **2620**
MANTENIMIENTO *m* **6526**
MANTENIMIENTO *m* **7946**
MANTENIMIENTO *m* DE TEMPERATURA **6528**
MANTEQUILLA *f* DE ANTIMONIO **626**
MANTILLO *m* **6667**
MANTISA *f* **7985**
MANUAL *m* DE FABRICACIÓN **9885**
MANUFACTURA *f* **5013**
MANUFACTURABLE **12802**

**1071**  **MAQ**

MANUFACTURAR **7948**

MANUSCRITO  *m*  (TAMBIÉN ES ADJETIVO) **7996**

MANUTENCIÓN  *f*  MECÁNICA **8106**

MANUTENCIONARIO  *m*  (QUE TRASLADA DE UN LADO A OTRO) **12298**

MAQUETA  *f*  **4370**

MÁQUINA  *f*  **6345**

MÁQUINA  *f*  AISLADA **11151**

MÁQUINA  *f*  ALTERNA PARA SERRAR **5629**

MÁQUINA  *f*  AMORTAJADORA **11643**

MÁQUINA  *f*  ARITMÉTICA **1859**

MÁQUINA  *f*  ASERRADORA **9747**

MÁQUINA  *f*  AUXILIAR **853**

MÁQUINA  *f*  BOBINADORA DE INDUCIDOS **709**

MÁQUINA  *f*  COMPOUND O COMPUESTA **2829**

MÁQUINA  *f*  CON CILINDRO OSCILANTE **8880**

MÁQUINA  *f*  CON CONDENSACIÓN **2911**

MÁQUINA  *f*  CON CUÁDRUPLE EXPANSIÓN **10059**

MÁQUINA  *f*  CON DOBLE EXPANSIÓN **4168**

MÁQUINA  *f*  CON EXPANSIÓN **4924**

MÁQUINA  *f*  CON EXPANSIÓN **4924**

MÁQUINA  *f*  CON MÚLTIPLE EXPANSIÓN **8477**

MÁQUINA  *f*  CON PLENA PRESIÓN **12165**

MÁQUINA  *f*  CON TRIPLE EXPANSIÓN **13217**

MÁQUINA  *f*  DE ACANALAR **6138**

MÁQUINA  *f*  DE ACANALAR **6138**

MÁQUINA  *f*  DE ACCIONADO INDEPENDIENTE **6863**

MÁQUINA  *f*  DE ACCIONADO POR CABLE **10736**

MÁQUINA  *f*  DE ACCIONADO POR CORREA **1145**

MÁQUINA  *f*  DE ACCIONADO POR ENGRANAJE **5893**

MÁQUINA  *f*  DE ACHAFLANAR O BISELAR LAS CHAPAS **9484**

MÁQUINA  *f*  DE ACOPLAMIENTO DIRECTO **3982**

MÁQUINA  *f*  DE ACOPLAR **12992**

MÁQUINA  *f*  DE ALISAR CON PAPEL DE LIJA **10926**

MÁQUINA  *f*  DE ALTA PRESIÓN **6492**

MÁQUINA  *f*  DE AMOLAR CON EJE HORIZONTAL **6588**

MÁQUINA  *f*  DE AMORTAJAR **11643**

MÁQUINA  *f*  DE APLANAR LAS CHAPAS **9485**

MÁQUINA  *f*  DE APLANAR Y ENDEREZAR LAS CHAPAS **11316**

MÁQUINA  *f*  DE APLANAR Y PULIR **9442**

MÁQUINA  *f*  DE APLASTAR O APLANAR **3419**

MÁQUINA  *f*  DE APRETADO POR SACUDIDA Y PRESIÓN SIN DESMOLDEO **7252**

MÁQUINA  *f*  DE ARQUEAR **1391**

MÁQUINA  *f*  DE ATERRAJAR **11066**

MÁQUINA  *f*  DE ATORNILLAR **11066**

MÁQUINA  *f*  DE BORDEAR **5346**

MÁQUINA  *f*  DE CALCULAR **1859**

MÁQUINA  *f*  DE CALIBRAR **1865**

MÁQUINA  *f*  DE CÁMARA FRÍA **2670**

MÁQUINA  *f*  DE CARRERA LARGA **7731**

MÁQUINA  *f*  DE CARRERA REDUCIDA **11374**

MÁQUINA  *f*  DE CENTRAR Y ENDEREZAR (O RECTIFICAR) **2188**

MÁQUINA  *f*  DE CEPILLAR **9452**

MÁQUINA  *f*  DE CEPILLAR **9451**

MÁQUINA  *f*  DE CEPILLAR ABIERTA POR EL LADO **8821**

MÁQUINA  *f*  DE CEPILLAR CON MESA MÓVIL **2007**

MÁQUINA  *f*  DE CEPILLAR CON UN SOLO MONTANTE **8821**

MÁQUINA  *f*  DE CEPILLAR DE FOSO **9395**

MÁQUINA  *f*  DE CEPILLAR LATERALMENTE **11415**

MÁQUINA  *f*  DE CEPILLAR SACANDO LA MADERA DEL ESPESOR **12847**

MÁQUINA  *f*  DE CHORRO DE ARENA **10920**

MÁQUINA  *f*  DE CIZALLAR **11292**

MÁQUINA  *f*  DE CIZALLAR HIERROS Y PERFILES **7136**

MÁQUINA  *f*  DE CIZALLAR LOS METALES EN HOJAS O EN TIRAS **11323**

MÁQUINA  *f*  DE COLUMNA DE AGUA **13670**

MÁQUINA  *f*  DE CONTORNEAR **5665**

MÁQUINA  *f*  DE CORTAR O RECORTAR **6012**

MÁQUINA  *f*  DE CURVAR **1184**

MÁQUINA  *f*  DE CURVAR LAS CHAPAS **9480**

MÁQUINA  *f*  DE DESBASTAR O DE ENDEREZAR **12515**

MÁQUINA  *f*  DE DESMOLDEAR **4237**

MÁQUINA  *f*  DE DIVIDIR LAS LÍNEAS RECTAS **4104**

MÁQUINA  *f*  DE DIVIDIR O SECCIONAR **4102**

MÁQUINA  *f*  DE DOBLE EFECTO **4165**

MÁQUINA  *f*  DE DOS CILINDROS **13313**

MÁQUINA  *f*  DE ELIMINAR LA BORRA **3153**

MÁQUINA  *f*  DE EMBUTIR **5346**

MÁQUINA  *f*  DE EMBUTIR **5346**

MÁQUINA  *f*  DE ENCORVAR **1184**

MÁQUINA  *f*  DE ENDEREZAR **12320**

MÁQUINA  *f*  DE ENDEREZAR CHAPA **12320**

MÁQUINA  *f*  DE ENMANGADO DIRECTO **3982**

MÁQUINA  *f*  DE ENROLLAR **1186**

MÁQUINA  *f*  DE ENROLLAR LOS MUELLES HELICOIDALES **13901**

MÁQUINA  *f*  DE ENSANCHAR LOS TUBOS **9352**

MÁQUINA  *f*  DE ENSAYAR **12793**

MÁQUINA  *f*  DE ENSAYOS DE EMBUTICIÓN DE ERICHSEN **4819**

MÁQUINA  *f*  DE ENTALLAR (O HACER MUESCAS) EN LAS CHAPAS **11319**

MÁQUINA  *f*  DE ESCARIAR **1471**

MÁQUINA  *f*  DE ESCARIAR EN HUECO **1013**

MÁQUINA  *f*  DE ESTAMPAR **12533**

MÁQUINA  *f*  DE EXTRAER LOS NÚCLEOS **3153**

MÁQUINA  *f*  DE FORJAR **5561**

MÁQUINA  *f*  DE FRESAR CON CONSOLA **7322**

**MAQ** 1072

MÁQUINA  ƒ DE FRESAR LAS RANURAS **7281**
MÁQUINA  ƒ DE FRESAR LOS TORNILLOS **11036**
MÁQUINA  ƒ DE FRÍO **10407**
MÁQUINA  ƒ DE FUNCIONAMIENTO LENTO **7789**
MÁQUINA  ƒ DE FUNCIONAMIENTO RÁPIDO **6496**
MÁQUINA  ƒ DE GRAN PRODUCCIÓN **6466**
MÁQUINA  ƒ DE GRAN RENDIMIENTO **6466**
MÁQUINA  ƒ DE GRAN VELOCIDAD **6496**
MÁQUINA  ƒ DE HACER LOS AGUJEROS DE ÁNGULO **3178**
MÁQUINA  ƒ DE INYECCIÓN NEUMÁTICA **299**
MÁQUINA  ƒ DE LIMAR **5154**
MÁQUINA  ƒ DE MACHIHEMBRAR **12992**
MÁQUINA  ƒ DE MANDRILAR LAS BRIDAS **5333**
MÁQUINA  ƒ DE MANIPULACIÓN **7982**
MÁQUINA  ƒ DE MEDIR WHITWORTH **13843**
MÁQUINA  ƒ DE MOLDEAR **8429**
MÁQUINA  ƒ DE MOLDEAR **8358**
MÁQUINA  ƒ DE MOLDEAR CON SACUDIDAS **7250**
MÁQUINA  ƒ DE MOLDEAR CON SACUDIDAS Y APRETADO COMBINADOS CON DESMOLDEO **7253**
MÁQUINA  ƒ DE MOLDEAR CON SACUDIDAS Y CON PLACA REVERSIBLE **7251**
MÁQUINA  ƒ DE MOLDURAR **8429**
MÁQUINA  ƒ DE MOLETEAR LOS CILINDROS DE IMPRENTA **9873**
MÁQUINA  ƒ DE PEQUEÑA VELOCIDAD **7789**
MÁQUINA  ƒ DE PERFILAR CON RODILLOS MÚLTIPLES **8457**
MÁQUINA  ƒ DE PERFILAR EL BALASTO **5346**
MÁQUINA  ƒ DE PERFILAR LAS LLANTAS DE RUEDAS **13822**
MÁQUINA  ƒ DE PERFORAR **4279**
MÁQUINA  ƒ DE PERFORAR (O TALADRAR) **4279**
MÁQUINA  ƒ DE PERFORAR SENSIBLE **11186**
MÁQUINA  ƒ DE PERFORAR VERTICAL **13552**
MÁQUINA  ƒ DE PISTÓN **10285**
MÁQUINA  ƒ DE PRECISIÓN **9770**
MÁQUINA  ƒ DE PRESIÓN ORDINARIA **7786**
MÁQUINA  ƒ DE PULIR **9603**
MÁQUINA  ƒ DE PUNZONAR **10009**
MÁQUINA  ƒ DE PUNZONAR Y DE CIZALLAR **10007**
MÁQUINA  ƒ DE QUEBRANTAR **3419**
MÁQUINA  ƒ DE RANURAR **6138**
MÁQUINA  ƒ DE RASCAR O DE RAER **11012**
MÁQUINA  ƒ DE RECALCAR **13415**
MÁQUINA  ƒ DE RECALCAR **5561**
MÁQUINA  ƒ DE RECTIFICAR CON MUELA **6113**
MÁQUINA  ƒ DE RECTIFICAR CON MUELA **6113**
MÁQUINA  ƒ DE RECTIFICAR EL INTERIOR DE LOS CILINDROS **3568**
MÁQUINA  ƒ DE RECTIFICAR LOS MACHOS **3150**
MÁQUINA  ƒ DE REMACHAR **10642**

MÁQUINA  ƒ DE REPRODUCIR **3139**
MÁQUINA  ƒ DE RESERVA **12070**
MÁQUINA  ƒ DE RIBETEAR **3323**
MÁQUINA  ƒ DE ROBLAR **10645**
MÁQUINA  ƒ DE RODAR **6565**
MÁQUINA  ƒ DE ROSCAR **11066**
MÁQUINA  ƒ DE ROSCAR **12869**
MÁQUINA  ƒ DE SECCIONAR LOS CÍRCULOS **4103**
MÁQUINA  ƒ DE SERRAR **9747**
MÁQUINA  ƒ DE SERRAR ALTERNA **6198**
MÁQUINA  ƒ DE SIMPLE EFECTO **11495**
MÁQUINA  ƒ DE SIMPLE EXPANSIÓN **11500**
MÁQUINA  ƒ DE SOLDADURA AL ARCO **680**
MÁQUINA  ƒ DE SOLDADURA DOBLE PUNTO **4382**
MÁQUINA  ƒ DE SOLDAR **13786**
MÁQUINA  ƒ DE TALADRAR **9636**
MÁQUINA  ƒ DE TALADRAR CON MANDRILES MÚLTIPLES **8470**
MÁQUINA  ƒ DE TALADRAR (O PERFORAR) **13182**
MÁQUINA  ƒ DE TALADRAR Y DE ESCARIAR LOS AGUJEROS PROFUNDOS **3687**
MÁQUINA  ƒ DE TRABAJO **7839**
MÁQUINA  ƒ DE TREFILAR **13889**
MÁQUINA  ƒ DE TRES CILINDROS **12873**
MÁQUINA  ƒ DE TROCEAR O DE TRONZAR **3541**
MÁQUINA  ƒ DE VACIAR LA ARENA DEL MACHO **3153**
MÁQUINA  ƒ DE VAPOR **12164**
MÁQUINA  ƒ DE VAPOR FIJA **12144**
MÁQUINA  ƒ DE VAPOR MURAL **13620**
MÁQUINA  ƒ DE VAPOR REVERSIBLE **10543**
MÁQUINA  ƒ DE VAPOR SEMIFIJA **11175**
MÁQUINA  ƒ DE VAPOR SOBRECALENTADO **4759**
MÁQUINA  ƒ ELÉCTRICA **4522**
MÁQUINA  ƒ EQUICORRIENTES **12407**
MÁQUINA  ƒ FRESADORA **8291**
MÁQUINA  ƒ FRIGORÍFICA **10407**
MÁQUINA  ƒ HIFRÁULICA **6691**
MÁQUINA  ƒ HORIZONTAL **6582**
MÁQUINA  ƒ LIMADORA **5154**
MÁQUINA  ƒ MAGNETOELÉCTRICA **7930**
MÁQUINA  ƒ MARINA **8005**
MÁQUINA  ƒ MOLDEADORA DE MACHOS **3154**
MÁQUINA  ƒ MONOCILÍNDRICA **11498**
MÁQUINA  ƒ MOTRIZ **9859**
MÁQUINA  ƒ MÚLTIPLE **8456**
MÁQUINA  ƒ PARA AFILAR HERRAMIENTAS **13002**
MÁQUINA  ƒ PARA ALAMBRE ESPINOSO **988**
MÁQUINA  ƒ PARA ATERRAJAR Y ROSCAR LOS TUBOS **9361**
MÁQUINA  ƒ PARA BURILAR **7228**
MÁQUINA  ƒ PARA CARGAR LOS HORNOS **2268**

1073 **MAQ**

MÁQUINA *f* PARA CORRIENTE ALTERNA **407**

MÁQUINA *f* PARA CORRIENTE CONTINUA **3021**

MÁQUINA *f* PARA CORTAR LOS TUBOS **9349**

MÁQUINA *f* PARA CORTE AUTÓGENO **833**

MÁQUINA *f* PARA ENDEREZAR LOS ÁRBOLES **11245**

MÁQUINA *f* PARA ENSAYAR LOS MUELLES Y LOS ALAMBRES **11975**

MÁQUINA *f* PARA ENSAYOS DE FLEXIÓN **7845**

MÁQUINA *f* PARA ENSAYOS DE ROTURA POR TRACCIÓN **7846**

MÁQUINA *f* PARA ENSAYOS DE TRACCIÓN **12752**

MÁQUINA *f* PARA ENSAYOS UNIVERSAL **13388**

MÁQUINA *f* PARA ENTALLAR LOS ENGRANAJES **5891**

MÁQUINA *f* PARA EQUICORRIENTES **12407**

MÁQUINA *f* PARA ESTIRAR LAS BARRAS Y LOS TUBOS **982**

MÁQUINA *f* PARA FRESAR **8291**

MÁQUINA *f* PARA HACER CADENAS DE ALAMBRE DE HIERRO **13885**

MÁQUINA *f* PARA HACER ESPIGAS **12742**

MÁQUINA *f* PARA HACER LAS ESPIGAS COLA DE MILANO **4179**

MÁQUINA *f* PARA HACER LAS HOJAS DE CHAPADO **13525**

MÁQUINA *f* PARA HACER LAS JUNTAS **7246**

MÁQUINA *f* PARA HACER LAS PESTAÑAS **1089**

MÁQUINA *f* PARA HACER RANURAS Y LENGÜETAS (MACHIHEMBRADO) **12992**

MÁQUINA *f* PARA HACER REJILLAS **13897**

MÁQUINA *f* PARA HIELO **6750**

MÁQUINA *f* PARA INSUFLAR LOS MACHOS **3146**

MÁQUINA *f* PARA LA MADERA **13925**

MÁQUINA *f* PARA METALES **8178**

MÁQUINA *f* PARA PASAR A LA MUELA SIN PUNTAS **2174**

MÁQUINA *f* PARA PERFORAR CARRILES Y ECLISAS **10176**

MÁQUINA *f* PARA PLEGAR LOS ALAMBRES **13883**

MÁQUINA *f* PARA PROBAR LOS ACEITES **8785**

MÁQUINA *f* PARA RECTIFICAR **12372**

MÁQUINA *f* PARA RECTIFICAR **6113**

MÁQUINA *f* PARA RECTIFICAR LAS SUPERFICIES INTERIORES **7068**

MÁQUINA *f* PARA RECTIFICAR LAS SUPERFICIES PLANAS **12505**

MÁQUINA *f* PARA RECTIFICAR PIEZAS CILINDRICAS **3583**

MÁQUINA *f* PARA TALADRAR LAS TOBERAS **8681**

MÁQUINA *f* PARA TRABAJAR LA MADERA **9901**

MÁQUINA *f* PARA TRABAJAR LOS ALAMBRES **13904**

MÁQUINA *f* PARA TRABAJOS ESPECIALES **11486**

MÁQUINA *f* PARA TRITURAR **3419**

MÁQUINA *f* PERFORADORA **9296**

MÁQUINA *f* PLEGADORA **11087**

MÁQUINA *f* PLEGADORA **1181**

MÁQUINA *f* PULIDORA **1686**

MÁQUINA *f* PUNZONADORA **10009**

MÁQUINA *f* QUEBRANTADORA **3419**

MÁQUINA *f* RADIAL DE PERFORAR **10129**

MÁQUINA *f* RÁPIDA DE MOLDEAR CON SACUDIDAS **7215**

MÁQUINA *f* RECEPTORA **7839**

MÁQUINA *f* ROTATIVA **10761**

MÁQUINA *f* SEPARADORA PARA REMOLACHA AZUCARERA **12438**

MÁQUINA *f* SIN CONDENSACIÓN **8627**

MÁQUINA *f* SOPLADORA **1363**

MÁQUINA *f* TALADRADORA **1472**

MÁQUINA *f* TANDEM **12613**

MÁQUINA *f* UNIVERSAL PARA RECTIFICAR LAS SUPERFICIES DE REVOLUCIÓN **13383**

MÁQUINA *f* VERTICAL **13546**

MÁQUINA ALOMADORA : 2 **10573**

MÁQUINA CEPILLADORA *f* **9451**

MÁQUINA DE AFILAR **6105**

MÁQUINA DE EQUILIBRAR **940**

MÁQUINA DE ESCARIAR *f* **4279**

MÁQUINA DE LEVAR *f* **6519**

MÁQUINA DE MANDRILAR **1471**

MÁQUINA EQUILIBRADORA *f* **937**

MÁQUINA EQUILIBRADORA DE MUELAS *f* **6116**

MÁQUINA HERRAMIENTA *f* **7859**

MÁQUINA HERRAMIENTA *f* PARA TRABAJAR LA MADERA **13925**

MÁQUINA HERRAMIENTA *f* PARA TRABAJAR LOS METALES **8178**

MÁQUINA PARA BURILAR POR CHISPAS EN COORDINADAS RECTANGULARES **10300**

MAQUINARIA *f* **7862**

MÁQUINAS *f pl* DE ACODAR **7232**

MÁQUINAS *f pl* DE CORTAREL CÉSPED **7439**

MÁQUINAS *f pl* PARA APLANAR LAS CHAPAS **11318**

MÁQUINAS *f pl* PARA DESMOCHAR LA REMOLACHA **12441**

MÁQUINAS *f pl* PARA ENTALLAR LOS ENGRANAJES RECTOS Y HELICOIDALES **12006**

MÁQUINAS *f pl* PARA LECHERÍAS **3595**

MÁQUINAS *f pl* PARA MADERA **13931**

MÁQUINAS *f pl* PARA ORDEÑAR **8275**

MÁQUINAS *f pl* PARA PERFORAR LAS CHAPAS **11317**

MÁQUINAS *f pl* PARA PODAR O IGUALAR LOS SETOS **6418**

MÁQUINAS *f pl* PARA TRABAJAR LA CHAPA **11320**

MÁQUINAS *f pl* PLEGADORAS **4453**

MÁQUINAS *f pl* SEGADORAS Y MÁQUINAS *f pl* AGAVILLADORAS **1251**

MÁQUINAS *f pl* SEGADORAS-TRILLADORAS **2766**

# MAQ

MÁQUINAS  *f*  SEMBRADORAS **11132**
MAQUINISTA AMB **4765**
MAR (EN) **8738**
MARCA  *f*  COMERCIA **13100**
MARCA  *f*  DE ESTAMPA **3888**
MARCA  *f*  DE FÁBRICAL **13100**
MARCA  *f*  INDICADORA DEL NIVEL DE AGUA **13660**
MARCACIÓN **8015**
MARCADO  *m*  **8015**
MARCADO  *m*  CON PUNZÓN DE LAS CHAPAS **3894**
MARCAR **8010**
MARCAR **8008**
MARCAR **8008**
MARCAR CON PUNZÓN **9998**
MARCAR CON PUNZÓN UNA SEÑAL **8011**
MARCAR POR MEDIO DE UN PUNZÓN **8011**
MARCAS  *f*  DE FIJACIÓN **12951**
MARCAS  *f*  DE VIBRACIÓN **2276**
MARCAS  *f*  DEJADAS POR LA MUELA **15**
MARCAS  *f*  SUPERFICIALES EN FORMA DE V **2282**
MARCHA  *f*  **13172**
MARCHA  *f*  **10850**
MARCHA  *f*  **10850**
MARCHA  *f*  ATRÁS **10846**
MARCHA  *f*  DE VACÍO **8598**
MARCHA  *f*  DE VACÍO **6752**
MARCHA  *f*  EN CONTRAPRESIÓN **894**
MARCHA  *f*  HACIA ADELANTE **10848**
MARCHA  *f*  HACIA ADELANTE DEL PISTÓN **5585**
MARCHA  *f*  HACIA ATRÁS DEL PISTÓN **10530**
MARCHA  *f*  IRREGULAR **7165**
MARCHA  *f*  LENTA **6755**
MARCHA  *f*  NORMAL **11681**
MARCHA  *f*  PESADA **6412**
MARCHA  *f*  REGULAR **11681**
MARCHA  *f*  RUIDOSA **8610**
MARCHA  *f*  SILENCIOSA **8609**
MARCHA  *f*  SUAVE **7567**
MARCHAR A GRAN VELOCIDAD **10833**
MARCHAR A PEQUEÑA VELOCIDAD **10834**
MARCHAR CON CARGA COMPLETA **1080**
MARCHAR CON PLENA CARGA **1079**
MARCHAR DE VACÍO **1081**
MARCO  *m*  **5624**
MARCO DE CREMALLERAS  *m*  **4150**
MARCO DE VENTANA  *m*  **13865**
MARCO DENTADO  *m*  **4150**
MARFIL  *m*  **7199**
MARGA  *f*  **8019**
MARGA  *f*  ARCILLOSA **699**

MARGA  *f*  CALCÁREA **2225**
MARGA  *f*  SILICIOSA O SILÍCEA **11439**
MARIPOSA  *f*  DE GASES **12888**
MARMITA  *f*  AUTOCLAVE **829**
MARMITA  *f*  DE PAPIN **829**
MÁRMOL (GEOL)  *m*  **8001**
MAROMA  *f*  **10730**
MARTENSITA  *f*  **8022**
MARTENSITA  *f*  ACIDULAR **103**
MARTILLADO  *m*  **6219**
MARTILLADO **4235**
MARTILLADO  *m*  EN FRÍO **2713**
MARTILLADO  *m*  EN FRÍO **2685**
MARTILLADURAS  *f pl*  **6217**
MARTILLAR **6216**
MARTILLAR **2684**
MARTILLAR **4219**
MARTILLEADO  *m*  **9157**
MARTILLEO  *m*  **9157**
MARTILLEO  *m*  **6223**
MARTILLO  *m*  **6215**
MARTILLO  *m*  **6235**
MARTILLO  *m*  CON CODILLO PARTIDO **2462**
MARTILLO  *m*  DE AIRE COMPRIMIDO **9553**
MARTILLO  *m*  DE AJUSTADOR **5279**
MARTILLO  *m*  DE APLANAR **9455**
MARTILLO  *m*  DE BOCA BOMBEADA **960**
MARTILLO  *m*  DE BOCA REDONDA **962**
MARTILLO  *m*  DE BORDEAR **3321**
MARTILLO  *m*  DE CABEZA PLÁSTICA **11747**
MARTILLO  *m*  DE CALAFATE **12308**
MARTILLO  *m*  DE DESBARBAR LA FUNDICIÓN **10986**
MARTILLO  *m*  DE DIENTE **2462**
MARTILLO  *m*  DE DOS BOCAS **4169**
MARTILLO  *m*  DE FORJA **5559**
MARTILLO  *m*  DE FORJA CON DOBLE CUERPO **4140**
MARTILLO  *m*  DE HERRERO **11573**
MARTILLO  *m*  DE HERRERO **11573**
MARTILLO  *m*  DE OREJAS **2462**
MARTILLO  *m*  DE REBORDEAR **1872**
MARTILLO  *m*  DE REMACHAR **10644**
MARTILLO  *m*  DE VAPOR **12166**
MARTILLO  *m*  DEL ENCARGADO DEL UTILLAJE **13014**
MARTILLO  *m*  (HERRAMIENTA DE HERRERO) **11218**
MARTILLO  *m*  IMANTADO PARA GUARNICIONERO **7921**
MARTILLO  *m*  MECÁNICO **5559**
MARTILLO  *m*  MECÁNICO POR AIRE COMPRIMIDO **9555**
MARTILLO  *m*  NEUMÁTICO **9553**
MARTILLO  *m*  NEUMÁTICO (O.P.) **9551**
MARTILLO  *m*  NEUMÁTICO PARA REMACHAR **9555**

MARTILLO *m* PARA PICAR LAS CALDERAS **10986**
MARTILLO *m* PIQUETA (O.P.) **258**
MARTILLO *m* REDONDEADO **960**
MARTILLO *m* REMACHADOR **10644**
MARTILLO BISELADO *m* **2232**
MARTILLO DESTAJADOR **10986**
MARTILLO ESTAMPA *m* **4979**
MARTILLO PARA APLANAR *m* **5410**
MARTILLO PILÓN *m* **4325**
MARTILLO PILÓN *m* **4326**
MARTILLO PILÓN *m* **12166**
MARTILLO PILÓN *m* CON PLANCHA **1380**
MARTINETE *m* **6080**
MARTINETE *m* **4325**
MARTINETE *m* **4326**
MARTINETE *m* **4325**
MARTINETE *m* **4327**
MARTINETE **4326**
MARTINETE *m* **3629**
MARTINETE *m* **12166**
MARTINETE *m* **9552**
MARTINETE *m* DE CAÍDA LIBRE **4327**
MARTINETE *m* DE PLANCHA **1380**
MASA *f* **951**
MASA *m* **11572**
MASA *f* DE ACERO **951**
MASA *f* EN ROTACIÓN **10561**
MASA *f* GIRATORIA **10561**
MASA *f* PRINCIPAL **8055**
MASA CALORÍFUGA *f* **6352**
MASA DE GUINIER PRESTON *f* **2542**
MASA (MEC.) *f* **8026**
MASA (TIERR) *f* **4409**
MASAS *f pl* POLARES **9593**
MASICOTE **8031**
MASILLA *f* **8038**
MASILLA *f* **8038**
MASILLA *f* **10037**
MASILLA *f* CON ACEITE **8771**
MASILLA *f* DE LOS VIDRIEROS **5971**
MASTIC *m* **8038**
MÁSTIC *m* **8038**
MASTIC *m* AL MINIO **10332**
MASTIC *m* DE ASFALTO **764**
MASTIC *m* DE HIERRO **7141**
MASTIC *m* DE LOS FONTANEROS **13797**
MASTIC *m* DE RESINA **10482**
MASTIC *m* EN GOTAS **8039**
MASTIC *m* EN GRANO **8039**
MASTIC *m* PARA LA FUNDICIÓN **7141**

MASTIC *m* PARA PIEDRA **12274**
MASTIC *m* RESINOSO **10482**
MASTIC *m* ROJO **10332**
MASTIQUE *m* **8038**
MASTIQUE *m* **8038**
MASURIO *m* **8040**
MATA *f* **8058**
MATA *f* DE COBRE **3121**
MATA *f* DE NÍQUEL **8563**
MATA *f* (MIN) **11878**
MATEMÁTICO **8053**
MATERIA *f* **12419**
MATERIA *f* ABRASIVA **9601**
MATERIA *f* AGLUTINANTE **1253**
MATERIA *f* AISLANTE **6998**
MATERIA *f* BRUÑIRA **22**
MATERIA *f* CALORÍFUGA PARA CALDERAS **1408**
MATERIA *f* COLORANTE **9303**
MATERIA *f* COLORANTE A BASE DE CROMO **2387**
MATERIA *f* COLORANTE A BASE DE PLOMO **7466**
MATERIA *f* COLORANTE DERIVADA DEL ALQUITRÁN DE HULLA **2567**
MATERIA *f* COLORANTE MINERAL **4412**
MATERIA *f* DE CARGA **7690**
MATERIA *f* EN FUSIÓN **8365**
MATERIA *f* FIBROSA **5140**
MATERIA *f* FILTRANTE **5179**
MATERIA *f* IMPERMEABLE AL SONIDO **3641**
MATERIA *f* INORGÁNICA **6957**
MATERIA *f* ORGÁNICA **8866**
MATERIA *f* PARA AFILAR **6107**
MATERIA *f* PARA LAS JUNTAS **7247**
MATERIA *f* PARA MEZCLA **228**
MATERIA *f* PARA PULIR **9601**
MATERIA *f* PARA RELLENO **5164**
MATERIA *f* PRIMA **10239**
MATERIA *f* PROTECTORA **9952**
MATERIA *f* PULIMENTADORA **11**
MATERIA *f* QUE ABSORBE EL RUIDO **3641**
MATERIA AGLOMERADA *f* **6088**
MATERIA AISLANTE CONTRA EL RUIDO **3641**
MATERIAL *m* DE CONSTRUCCIÓN **8050**
MATERIAL *m* DE IRRIGACIÓN O DE RIEGO **7172**
MATERIAL *m* DE MONTAJE **4809**
MATERIAL *m* DE MONTAJE **4810**
MATERIAL AISLANTE *m* **6998**
MATERIAL CALORÍFUGO *m* **8628**
MATERIAL DE EXPLOTACIÓN *m* **8408**
MATERIALES *m* REFRACTARIOS **10466**
MATERIAS *f pl* EN DISOLUCIÓN **8061**

**MAT**

1076

MATERIAS *f pl* EN SUSPENSIÓN **8062**
MATERIAS *f pl* PLÁSTICAS **9476**
MATIZ *m* CALIDAD DEL ACERO **6022**
MATIZADO *m* **5443**
MATIZADO *m* **5434**
MATIZADO *m* **11453**
MATRAZ *m* **10277**
MATRAZ *m* **5370**
MATRAZ *m* CON TAPÓN DE TUBO LAVADOR **13633**
MATRAZ *m* DE CUELLO LARGO **10798**
MATRAZ *m* DE FONDO PLANO **9142**
MATRAZ *m* REDONDO **10798**
MATRIZ *f* **8055**
MATRIZ *f* **3883**
MATRIZ *f* **3883**
MATRIZ *f* ABIERTA **8810**
MATRIZ *f* ACABADORA **5219**
MATRIZ *f* AMOVIBLE **6966**
MATRIZ *f* COMPUESTA **2818**
MATRIZ *f* DE ABAJO **1497**
MATRIZ *f* DE ARRIBA **13036**
MATRIZ *f* FLOTANTE **5437**
MATRIZ *f* NEGATIVA **8529**
MATRIZ *f* PARA ESTAMPADO **2652**
MATRIZ *f* QUE ESTIRAR **4234**
MATRIZ *f* REDONDA Y DIVIDIDA CON JAULA VACIADORA **4451**
MATRIZ *f* TROQUEL ESTAMPA DE HERRERO **3897**
MATRIZ PARA ESTIRAR *f* **4234**
MATRIZADO *m* **12059**
MATRIZADO *m* EN DISCO **1310**
MATRIZADO *m* EN PRENSA **2651**
MATRIZADO *m* POR DESCENSO ACCIONADO **4193**
MATRIZAR **12056**
MAZAROTA *f* **11506**
MAZAROTA *f* CON NÚCLEO ATMOSFÉRICO **799**
MAZO *m* **3119**
MAZO *m* **11572**
MAZO *m* **12611**
MAZO *m* **13926**
MAZO *m* DE MADERA **7962**
MAZUT *m* **6408**
MECÁNICA *f* DE LOS CUERPOS LÍQUIDOS **6720**
MECÁNICA (FIS.) **8121**
MECÁNICO **8093**
MECÁNICO **8013**
MECÁNICO *m* **5278**
MECÁNICO *m* (OFICIO) *m* **4765**
MECÁNICO *m* PERFORADOR **4276**
MECÁNICO CONSTRUCTOR **4214**

MECÁNICO (ENSAYO) **12743**
MECANISMO *m* **8122**
MECANISMO *m* **8122**
MECANISMO *m* **3913**
MECANISMO *m* **3913**
MECANISMO *m* **3820**
MECANISMO *m* CON MANIVELA **1094**
MECANISMO *m* CON MANIVELA EXCÉNTRICA **4427**
MECANISMO *m* CON TORNILLO SIN FIN **13974**
MECANISMO *m* DE ACCIONADO **4311**
MECANISMO *m* DE APRETADO DE LAS TUERCAS **8701**
MECANISMO *m* DE CAMBIO DE MARCHA **10544**
MECANISMO *m* DE CAMBIO DE VELOCIDAD **2242**
MECANISMO *m* DE DESEMBRAGUE **4034**
MECANISMO *m* DE DESEMBRAGUE DE LA CORREA **1157**
MECANISMO *m* DE DOBLE TRINQUETE **2494**
MECANISMO *m* DE EMBRAGUE **4034**
MECANISMO *m* DE FRICCIÓN POR TRINQUETE **5676**
MECANISMO *m* DE INDEXACIÓN **6869**
MECANISMO *m* DE INDEXACIÓN POR CREMALLERA **10123**
MECANISMO *m* DE LEVA **1886**
MECANISMO *m* DE LOS AVANCES **5067**
MECANISMO *m* DE MANDO **4309**
MECANISMO *m* DE MANDO ELÁSTICO **8629**
MECANISMO *m* DE MANDO MECÁNICO **2985**
MECANISMO *m* DE MANDO POSITIVO **2985**
MECANISMO *m* DE PARADA O DE INMOVILIZACIÓN **7709**
MECANISMO *m* DE REANUDACIÓN DE LOS JUEGOS **915**
MECANISMO *m* DE RELOJERÍA **2509**
MECANISMO *m* DE RETENCIÓN EN POSICIÓN ABIERTA **6525**
MECANISMO *m* DE RUEDA LIBRE **5652**
MECANISMO *m* DE TRINQUETE **9138**
MECANISMO *m* PARA UN RÁPIDO RETORNO **10106**
MECANISMO *m* POR TRINQUETE **7705**
MECANISMOS *m pl* DE ENGANCHE PARA REMOLQUES Y CAMIONES **4088**
MECANIZACIÓN *f* **4983**
MECANIZACIÓN *f* **6650**
MECANIZACIÓN *f* **7864**
MECANIZACIÓN *f* **13959**
MECANIZACIÓN *f* DE METALES **8192**
MECANIZACIÓN *f* EN FRÍO **2713**
MECANIZACIÓN *f* PRERREGULADA **9752**
MECANIZACIÓN *f* ULTERIOR **5750**
MECANIZAR **13937**
MECHA *f* DE ENGRASE **7807**
MECHA *f* (DE LÁMPARA O DE ENGRASADOR) **13846**
MECHERO *m* **1749**
MECHERO *m* BUNSEN **1741**

MET

MECHERO *m* DE BUNSEN **1741**
MECHERO *m* DE SOLDAR **11766**
MECHÓN *m* EN EL ORILLO DEL PAÑO **2538**
MEDIA *f* ARITMÉTICA **703**
MEDIA *f* GEOMÉTRICA **5929**
MEDIACAÑA *f* **5161**
MEDICIÓN *f* **8088**
MEDICIÓN *f* EXACTA **4875**
MEDICIÓN *f* PRECISA **4875**
MEDIDA *f* **8077**
MEDIDA *f* COMPARATIVA **2797**
MEDIDA *f* CONTRASTE **12077**
MEDIDA *f* DE ARQUEO (MAR.) **8079**
MEDIDA *f* DE CAPACIDAD **8079**
MEDIDA *f* DE CONTROL **12077**
MEDIDA *f* DE ELASTICIDAD **8340**
MEDIDA *f* DE LA SUPERFICIE **8081**
MEDIDA *f* DE LA TEMPERATURA **8086**
MEDIDA *f* DE VOLUMEN **8082**
MEDIDA *f* INTERCEPTADA DEL ARCO **2419**
MEDIDA *f* LINEAL **8080**
MEDIDA *f* MÉTRICA **8227**
MEDIDA *f* PATRÓN **12077**
MEDIDA *f* STANDARD **12077**
MEDIDAS *f pl* **3960**
MEDIDAS *f pl* DE SEGURIDAD **10889**
MEDIDOR *m* DE SALTOS **11366**
MEDIDOR *m* DE VOLUMEN **13604**
MEDIO *m* **8072**
MEDIO *m* DE ENDURECIMIENTO **10096**
MEDIO *m* DE HOMOGENEIZACIÓN **3754**
MEDIO *m* DE TEMPLE **6294**
MEDIO *m* DE TEMPLE **10098**
MEDIO *m* REFRACTIVO **10401**
MEDIO *m* TRANSPARENTE **13139**
MEDIO CONDUCTOR *m* **2914**
MEDIR **8078**
MEDIR LA POTENCIA DE LOS FRENOS O DEL FRENADO **8083**
MEGADINA *f* **8129**
MEGAERGIO *m* **8131**
MEGAOHMIO *m* **8132**
MEGAVOLTIO *m* **8130**
MEGOHMIO *m* **8132**
MELÁFIDO *m* (GEOL) **8133**
MELAFIRIO *m* **8133**
MELINOSA *f* (GEOL) **13991**
MEMBRANA *f* **3870**
MEMBRANA *f* **4479**
MEMBRANA *f* DE RUPTURA **10860**

MEMORIA *f* **8146**
MEMORIA *f* DESCRIPTIVA DE UNA PATENTE **11856**
MEMORIA *f* INTERMEDIA **1689**
MEMORIA *f* TEMPORAL **12736**
MENISCO *m* CONVERGENTE **8147**
MÉNSULA *f* **13618**
MÉNSULA *f* **1522**
MÉNSULA *f* DE FIJACIÓN **510**
MENUDOS *m pl* DE CARBÓN **2328**
MENUDOS *m* DE COQUE **11657**
MENUDOS *m pl* DE HULLA **11557**
MEOLLAR *m* **12005**
MEOLLO *m* VEGETAL **9413**
MERCURIO *m* **8168**
MERMA *f* **13594**
MERMA *f* **6315**
MERMA *f* **6782**
MERMA *f* DE CARGA **7759**
MERMAS *f* **6536**
MERMAS *f* DE FUSION **8140**
MESA *f* **12584**
MESA *f* DE CONTROL **12773**
MESA *f* DE DIBUJANTE **4243**
MESA *f* DE DIBUJO **4243**
MESA *f* DE EXAMEN **12773**
MESA *f* DE TRANSFORMACIÓN **3069**
MESA *f* DE YUNQUE **4995**
MESA *f* RECTIFICADA **12516**
MESAS *f pl* DE FIJACIÓN **8290**
METACENTRO *m* **8172**
METAL *m* **8173**
METAL *m* ALEACIÓN BLANCA **13836**
METAL *m* ALEACIÓN DELTA **3741**
METAL *m* AMARTILLADO **6221**
METAL *m* AÑADIDO EN SOLDADURA **5159**
METAL *m* AÑADIDO O INCORPORADO **3775**
METAL *m* ANTIDESGASTE **619**
METAL *m* ANTIFRICCIÓN **888**
METAL *m* ANTIFRICCIÓN **13836**
METAL *m* BLANCO **888**
METAL *m* BLANCO **5932**
METAL *m* BLANCO **5932**
METAL *m* BLANCO **8569**
METAL *m* BLANCO DESFLOCULADO **13835**
METAL *m* BLANCO DURO **6276**
METAL *m* BLANDO **11738**
METAL *m* BLANDO **11738**
METAL *m* BRITÁNICO **1624**
METAL *m* BRUTO **3410**
METAL *m* CAMPANIL **1134**

# MET

1078

METAL *m* COLADO **2050**
METAL *m* COMÚN **8057**
METAL *m* CON EXCLUSIÓN DEL HIERRO **8632**
METAL *m* CON EXCLUSIÓN DEL HIERRO **8632**
METAL *m* CONSTITUYENTE **2982**
METAL *m* DE ACUMULADOR **80**
METAL *m* DE APORTE **3775**
METAL *m* DE BASE **1032**
METAL *m* DE CUBILOTE **3468**
METAL *m* DE ELECTRODO **4576**
METAL *m* DE ELEVADA DENSIDAD **6482**
METAL *m* DE GRANALLA **6054**
METAL *m* DE ORIGEN **9079**
METAL *m* DE RECARGA **3775**
METAL *m* DE RECARGA **3775**
METAL *m* DE RECUPERACIÓN **11107**
METAL *m* DE SOLDADURA **13763**
METAL *m* DEPOSITADO **13761**
METAL *m* DESPLEGADO **4904**
METAL *m* DURO **6277**
METAL *m* EN ESTADO DE FUSIÓN **6631**
METAL *m* EN FUSIÓN **6631**
METAL *m* EN FUSIÓN **8365**
METAL *m* ESTRATIFICADO **7379**
METAL *m* FUNDIDO APLICADO **3776**
METAL *m* FUNDIDO EN COQUILLA SIN DEFORMACIÓN **2337**
METAL *m* INGLÉS **9230**
METAL *m* LIGERO **7564**
METAL *m* LIGERO **7779**
METAL *m* MISCH **8320**
METAL *m* MONEL **8379**
METAL *m* MUNTZ **8486**
METAL *m* NATIVO **9853**
METAL *m* NO PRECIOSO **12422**
METAL *m* NO PRECIOSO **1031**
METAL *m* NOBLE EN BARRAS **1729**
METAL *m* NOBLE O PRECIOSO **8602**
METAL *m* PARA COJINETES **1106**
METAL *m* PARA MATRICES **3889**
METAL *m* PESADO **6407**
METAL *m* POLICRISTALINO **9608**
METAL *m* PREAFINADO **1366**
METAL *m* PRECIOSO **9756**
METAL *m* PRECIOSO **8603**
METAL *m* PROPIO PARA LA FABRICACIÓN DE LOS CARACTERES DE IMPRENTA **13319**
METAL *m* PULVERIZADO **8185**
METAL *m* SOPORTE **909**
METAL *m* VIRGEN **9853**
METAL *m* VIRGEN **13570**

METAL ANTI-FRICCIÓN **10422**
METAL ANTI-FRICCIÓN **889**
METAL ANTIFRICCIÓN *m* **1106**
METAL ANTIFRICCIÓN *m* **619**
METAL BABBITT *m* **889**
METAL BLANCO *m* **5932**
METAL BLANCO *m* **13836**
METAL INVAR *m* **7105**
METAL NEGRO *m* **1324**
METALES *m pl* ALCALINO-TERROSOS **335**
METALES *m pl* ALCALINOS **329**
METALES *m pl* ORDINARIOS EN LA CONSTRUCCIÓN **2988**
METALES *m pl* UTILIZADOS COMO CONTACTO ELÉCTRICO **4538**
METALES *m* VIEJOS DE RECUPERACIÓN **5553**
METALÍFERO **8197**
METALIZACIÓN *f* **8201**
METALIZACIÓN *f* **8190**
METALIZACIÓN *f* AL CINC **14045**
METALIZACIÓN *f* EN EL VACÍO **13487**
METALIZACIÓN *f* EN EL VACÍO **13445**
METALIZACIÓN *f* POR PULVERIZADOR **5361**
METALOGRAFÍA *f* **8203**
METALOGRAFÍA *f* EN COLORES **2738**
METALOGRÁFICO **8202**
METALOIDE *m* **8205**
METALOIDE *m* **8640**
METALURGIA *f* **8208**
METALURGIA *f* DE EXTRACCIÓN **9886**
METALURGIA *f* DE POLVOS **9720**
METALURGIA *f* DEL HIERRO **8209**
METALURGIA *f* DEL HIERRO **5123**
METALURGIA *f* EN EL VACÍO **13446**
METALURGIA *f* FÍSICA **9282**
METALURGIA *f* MECÁNICA **8107**
METALÚRGICO **8206**
METANO *m* **8215**
METANO *m* **8215**
METANOL *m* **5573**
METANOL *m* **13920**
METER UNA CUÑA **4293**
METILBENCENO *m* **12983**
METILENO *m* **13920**
MÉTODO *m* **8216**
MÉTODO *m* **8220**
MÉTODO *m* AL TEMPLE **3977**
MÉTODO *m* DE BRAGG **1525**
MÉTODO *m* DE CRISTAL OSCILANTE **8879**
MÉTODO *m* DE DEBYE-SCHERRER **3643**
MÉTODO *m* DE IONIZACIÓN **7127**

MÉTODO *m* DE LABOREO (MIN) **8220**
MÉTODO *m* DE LAVADO **7438**
MÉTODO *m* DE LOS POLVOS **9721**
MÉTODO *m* DE MEDIDA **8219**
MÉTODO *m* DE TRABAJO **8220**
MÉTODO *m* ESTROBOSCÓPICO **12386**
MÉTODO *m* LLAMADO DE TRES HILOS **12883**
METRO *m* **8226**
METRO *m* CONTRASTE **12081**
METRO *m* CORRIENTE **10849**
METRO *m* CUADRADO **12022**
METRO *m* CÚBICO **3455**
METRO *m* DE CINTA **8092**
METRO *m* PLEGABLE **5512**
METRO *m* RECTO **8226**
METRO *m* RÍGIDO **8226**
METRO *m* (UNIDAD DE MEDIDA) **8225**
MEZCLA *f* **1325**
MEZCLA *f* (ACCIÓN) **8336**
MEZCLA *f* CARBURO **8337**
MEZCLA *f* DE CARBUROS CEMENTADOS **2192**
MEZCLA *f* DE DIVERSAS FRACCIONES DE POLVO DE UNA MISMA SUBSTANCIA **1325**
MEZCLA *f* DE FERRITA Y CEMENTITA **11817**
MEZCLA *f* DE GRANO SIN GRANOS INTERMEDIOS **5805**
MEZCLA *f* DETONADORA **4938**
MEZCLA *f* DETONANTE **4938**
MEZCLA *f* EUTÉCTICA **4857**
MEZCLA *f* EXPLOSIVA **4938**
MEZCLA *f* GASEOSA **5856**
MEZCLA *f* ÍNTIMA **7102**
MEZCLA *f* (QUÍMICA) **8336**
MEZCLA *f* REFRIGERANTE **5654**
MEZCLA *f* SULFONÍTRICA **8595**
MEZCLADO **8327**
MEZCLADO **1325**
MEZCLADOR *m* **8334**
MEZCLADOR *m* **8331**
MEZCLADOR *m* **8334**
MEZCLADORA *f* **8449**
MEZCLADORA *f* DE HORMIGÓN (O.P.) **9966**
MEZCLADORA *f* DE SOLERA PLANA **5387**
MEZCLADORES *m pl* **8332**
MEZCLAR **8328**
MEZCLAR **1323**
MEZCLAR (EL MORTERO DE CEMENTO) **12718**
MICA *f* **8231**
MICANITA *f* **8233**
MICASQUISTO *m* **8232**
MICRIGRÁFICO **8243**

MICROAMPERÍMETRO *m* **8237**
MICROAMPERÍO *m* **8238**
MICROBIO *m* PATÓGENO **9126**
MICROCONSTITUYENTE *m* DE ALEACIONES FERROSAS **9144**
MICRODESTELLO *m* (TUBO DE RAYOS X) **8239**
MICRODUREZA *f* **8245**
MICROESTRUCTURA **8262**
MICROFARADIO *m* **8242**
MICROFISURA *f* **1263**
MICROFISURA *f* **3283**
MICROFISURAS *f* **8234**
MICROFOTOGRAMA *m* **9272**
MICROGRAFÍA *f* **8244**
MICROGRAFÍA *f* **8258**
MICROGRIETA *f* **3318**
MICROHMIO *m* **8247**
MICRÓMETRO *m* **8249**
MICRÓMETRO *m* **8249**
MICRÓMETRO *m* **1875**
MICRÓMETRO *m* **1875**
MICRÓMETRO *m* CON ESFERA **6877**
MICRÓMETRO *m* CON VERNIER **13540**
MICRÓMETRO *m* DE CONICIDAD **12652**
MICRÓMETRO *m* DE PROFUNDIDAD **8252**
MICRÓMETRO *m* MÉTRICO **8228**
MICRÓN **8257**
MICROPALPADOR *m* DE CONICIDAD **12652**
MICROPULGADA *f* **8248**
MICROSCOPIO *m* **8259**
MICROSCOPIO *m* BINOCULAR **1256**
MICROSCOPIO *m* ELECTRÓNICO **4629**
MICROSCOPIO *m* POLARIZANTE **9583**
MICROSEGREGACIÓN *f* **3172**
MICRÓTOMO *m* **8263**
MICROVOLTIO *m* **8264**
MIGRACIÓN *f* **8268**
MIGRACIÓN *f* **1321**
MIGRACIÓN *f* DE IONES **7123**
MILÉSIMA *f* DE MILÍMETRO **8257**
MILIAMPERIO *m* **8284**
MILIAMPERIO/METRO *m* **8283**
MILÍGRAMO *m* **8285**
MILÍMETRO *m* **8286**
MILÍMETRO *m* CUADRADO **12023**
MILÍMETRO *m* CÚBICO **3456**
MILIVOLTIO *m* **8294**
MILLA *f* (MEDIDA INGLESA DE LONGITUD) **8272**
MINA *f* **8300**
MINA *f* DE HULLA **2566**

**MIN** 1080

MINA *f* DE PLOMO **9542**
MINA *f* METÁLICA **8198**
MINA DE HULLA **2566**
MINERAL **8301**
MINERAL *m* **8859**
MINERAL *m* ARGENTÍFERO **11625**
MINERAL *m* COLÍTICO **8305**
MINERAL *m* DE BAJO PORCENTAJE **7781**
MINERAL *m* DE CINC **14042**
MINERAL *m* DE COBRE **3122**
MINERAL *m* DE ELEVADO PORCENTAJE **6485**
MINERAL *m* DE ESTAÑO **12956**
MINERAL *m* DE HIERRO **7143**
MINERAL *m* DE HIERRO MAGNÉTICO **7927**
MINERAL *m* DE NÍQUEL **8564**
MINERAL *m* DE PLATA **11625**
MINERAL *m* DE PLOMO **7465**
MINERAL *m* POBRE **7781**
MINERAL *m* POBRE DE HIERRO **8305**
MINERAL *m* RICO **6485**
MINERALES *m pl* DE MANGANESO FERROSO **5122**
MINERALES *m pl* Y FUNDIENTES *m* **8863**
MINIO *m* **10333**
MINUENDO *m* **8316**
MIRILLA *f* REDONDA **2414**
MITAD *f* DEL ACOPLAMIENTO **6205**
MODELADO **6189**
MODELADO **5868**
MODELADO *m* **5579**
MODELADO **3105**
MODELADO **7116**
MODELADO **9129**
MODELADO *m* **9135**
MODELADO **7744**
MODELADO **11526**
MODELADO **13703**
MODELADO *m* EN CALIENTE **6627**
MODELO *m* **9128**
MODELO *m* **9133**
MODELO *m* A LA CERA PERDIDA **7116**
MODELO *m* CON EMBUDOS **5868**
MODELO *m* CONTRASTE **8032**
MODELO *m* DESMONTABLE **7744**
MODELO *m* EN CERA **13703**
MODELO *m* EN DOS PARTES **3105**
MODELO *m* EN ESCAYOLA **6189**
MODELO *m* EN ESQUELETO **11526**
MODELO *m* ESTANDARD **12073**
MODELO *m* NORMALIZADO **12073**
MODELO *m* PARA FUNDICIÓN **9129**

MODEM **8338**
MODEM *m* **8338**
MODERADOR *m* **10421**
MODO *m* DE ATAQUE **8217**
MODO *m* DE EMPLEO **6992**
MODO *m* OPERATORIO **8220**
MODO DE ACTUAR **8220**
MODULADOR *m* **8338**
MODULADOR *m* **8338**
MÓDULO *m* **8339**
MÓDULO *m* DE CORTE **8342**
MÓDULO *m* DE DENTADURA **3861**
MÓDULO *m* DE DESLIZAMIENTO **8342**
MÓDULO *m* DE ELASTICIDAD **8341**
MÓDULO *m* DE ELASTICIDAD **4483**
MÓDULO *m* DE ELASTICIDAD TRANSVERSAL **5974**
MÓDULO *m* DE INERCIA **11115**
MÓDULO *m* DE RIGIDEZ **3226**
MÓDULO *m* DE RUPTURA **8343**
MÓDULO DE COULOMB **3226**
MOHO *m* **8271**
MOLAR **6103**
MOLDE *m* **5369**
MOLDE *m* **5570**
MOLDE *m* **3883**
MOLDE *m* **8352**
MOLDE *m* **6923**
MOLDE *m* DE ABAJO **8678**
MOLDE *m* DE ARCILLA DE MODELAR **7693**
MOLDE *m* DE ARENA **10924**
MOLDE *m* DE CEMENTO **12734**
MOLDE *m* DE ESCAYOLA **9465**
MOLDE *m* (FUND) **8423**
MOLDE *m* METÁLICO **3883**
MOLDE *m* MÚLTIPLE **2762**
MOLDE *m* MÚLTIPLE **8466**
MOLDE *m* NO METÁLICO **8650**
MOLDEADO *m* **2068**
MOLDEADO *m* A PRESIÓN **9812**
MOLDEADO *m* CALIENTE **4354**
MOLDEADO *m* EN ARENA ESTUFADA **4354**
MOLDEADO *m* EN ARENA SECA **4354**
MOLDEADO *m* EN CALIENTE **6627**
MOLDEADO *m* EN EL SUELO **5445**
MOLDEADO *m* EN EL VACÍO **13439**
MOLDEADO *m* MECÁNICO **7851**
MOLDEADO *m* SALIDA EN LINGOTERA **12703**
MOLDEADOR *m* **8427**
MOLDEADOS *m pl* DE ACERO DE ALEACIÓN **372**
MOLDEAR **2030**

## MON

MOLDEAR **8424**
MOLDEO *m* **2068**
MOLDEO *m* A CERA PERDIDA **7115**
MOLDEO *m* DE PRECISIÓN **9765**
MOLDEO *m* DESCUBIERTO **8820**
MOLDEO *m* ELÉCTRICO **4557**
MOLDEO *m* EN CHASIS **1508**
MOLDEO *m* EN COQUILLA **11333**
MOLDEO *m* EN FOSO **5445**
MOLDEO O MOLDEADO *m* EN MESA **1169**
MOLDURAS *f pl* FILETEADAS **4969**
MOLÉCULA *f* **8364**
MOLÉCULA-GRAMO *f* **6044**
MOLER **1580**
MOLETA *f* DE LA LEVA **1895**
MOLETA *f* DE LEVA **1895**
MOLETA *f* (O PATÍN *m*) DE SOLDADURA **2412**
MOLETEADO *m* **8287**
MOLETEADO *m* DE UNA CABEZA DE TORNILLO **8288**
MOLETEAR UNA CABEZA DE TORNILLO **8277**
MOLETRADO *m* **7338**
MOLIBDATO *m* NATURAL DE PLOMO **13991**
MOLIBDENITA *f* **8366**
MOLIBDENO *m* **8367**
MOLIDO *m* **8287**
MOLIDO *m* **6117**
MOLINILLO *m* DE PALETAS **5031**
MOLINILLO *m* DINAMOMÉTRICO **5031**
MOLINO *m* **3419**
MOLINO *m* CON MUELAS VERTICALES **4450**
MOLINO *m* DE BOLAS **959**
MOLINO *m* DE CÍLINDROS **10687**
MOLINO *m* DE MAZAS **12057**
MOLINO *m* DE VIENTO **13855**
MOLINOS *m pl* **8295**
MOLINOS/APLASTADORES *m pl* **8296**
MOLINOS/TRITURADORES *m pl* **8297**
MOMENTO *m* BASCULANTE **12936**
MOMENTO *m* CENTRÍFUGO **2183**
MOMENTO *m* DE ESTABILIDAD **8375**
MOMENTO *m* DE FLEXIÓN **1185**
MOMENTO *m* DE FROTACIÓN O DE ROCE **8371**
MOMENTO *m* DE INERCIA **8372**
MOMENTO *m* DE LA INVERSIÓN **8966**
MOMENTO *m* DE LA MAGNITUD DE MOVIMIENTO **8373**
MOMENTO *m* DE PAR **13308**
MOMENTO *m* DE RESISTENCIA **8374**
MOMENTO *m* DE TORSIÓN **13308**
MOMENTO *m* DE UNA FUERZA **8370**
MOMENTO *m* ESTÁTICO **12139**

MOMENTO *m* FLECTOR **1185**
MONEDAS *f pl* DE BRONCE **3114**
MONEDAS *f pl* DE COBRE **3114**
MONEL *m* **8379**
MONOATÓMICO **8377**
MONOBLOQUE *m* **11079**
MONOCRISTAL *m* **11480**
MONOSULFURO *m* DE CALCIO **1852**
MONOTRON *m* **8387**
MONOTROPE *m* **8388**
MONOTRÓPICO *m* **8388**
MONTACARGAS *m* **9101**
MONTACARGAS *m* **6007**
MONTACORREA *m* **1159**
MONTADAS Y SEMIMONTADAS **8439**
MONTADOR *m* **4816**
MONTADOR *m* ELECTRICISTA **4543**
MONTAJE *m* **5280**
MONTAJE *m* **5301**
MONTAJE *m* **5275**
MONTAJE *m* **5275**
MONTAJE *m* **4808**
MONTAJE *m* **4815**
MONTAJE *m* **4813**
MONTAJE *m* **2986**
MONTAJE *m* **4307**
MONTAJE *m* **11199**
MONTAJE *m* **11600**
MONTAJE *m* **9051**
MONTAJE *m* **10847**
MONTAJE *m* **10025**
MONTAJE *m* **12493**
MONTAJE *m* CON TORNILLOS **11067**
MONTAJE *m* DE CUÑAS CALIBRADORAS **5884**
MONTAJE *m* DE LA CORREA **1160**
MONTAJE *m* DE MECANIZADO BASTIDOR MODELO **4985**
MONTAJE *m* DESLIZANTE **11600**
MONTAJE *m* EN BLANCO **13184**
MONTAJE *m* EN CALIENTE **11398**
MONTAJE *m* EN LA PROPIA OBRA (LUGAR DE TRABAJO) **8800**
MONTAJE *m* EN PARALELO **9051**
MONTAJE *m* EN SUPERFICIE **9051**
MONTAJE *m* FLOJO **10025**
MONTAJE *m* GIRATORIO **10847**
MONTAJE *m* POR AJUSTE **4307**
MONTAJE *m* POR PRENSA **5527**
MONTAJE *m* POR PRENSA EN CALIENTE **11389**
MONTAJE *m* ULTERIOR (MÁS ADELANTE) **10527**
MONTANTE *m* **12062**

# MON

1082

MONTANTE *m* 12063
MONTANTE *m* DE BARANDILLA 6266
MONTANTE *m* DE PUERTA 6507
MONTANTE *m* DE UNA MÁQUINA 12078
MONTANTE *m* GEMINADO 4159
MONTANTE *m* LATERAL DE ENTRADA 7211
MONTANTE *m* PORTAHERRAMIENTA 13010
MONTAR EN PARALELO 2956
MONTAR EN TENSION 2957
MONTAR LA CORREA 11357
MONTAR POR TORNILLOS 11037
MONTURA *f* DE ESTAMPA CON GUÍA DE COLUMNAS 3890
MONTURA *f* DE UNA HILERA CON COJINETES 3895
MORDAZA *f* 13565
MORDAZA *f* 13564
MORDAZA *f* 13564
MORDAZA *f* ARTICULADA 13562
MORDAZA *f* COCODRILO 9366
MORDAZA *f* CON CHARNELA 13562
MORDAZA *f* DE BLOQUEO 13945
MORDAZA *f* DE FRENO 1536
MORDAZA *f* DE LLAVE 7216
MORDAZA *f* DE TORNO (DE BANCO) 13563
MORDAZA *f* DE TORNO (DE BANCO) 13564
MORDAZA *f* (DE TORNO DE BANCO) 6122
MORDAZA *f* (DE UN APARATO DE LEVANTAMIENTO) 7557
MORDAZA *f* DE UNA CADENA DE RODILLOS 11416
MORDAZA *f* DE UNA LLAVE 7216
MORDAZA *f* FIJA DE TORNILLO DE BANCO 5299
MORDAZA *f* MÓVIL DE TORNILLO DE BANCO 8437
MORDAZA *f* SUAVE PARA CABEZALES 2394
MORDAZAS *f pl* 6120
MORDIENTE *m* 3196
MORDIENTE *m* 3196
MORDIENTE *m* 8391
MORFIL (GAL) 13890
MORTAJA *f* 8401
MORTAJA *f* 3761
MORTAJA *f* DE ESPIGA 7282
MORTAJA *f* DE EXTREMOS REDONDEADOS 8714
MORTAJADO *m* 8676
MORTAJADO *m* 11641
MORTAJADORA *f* 11643
MORTAJADORA *f* 11642
MORTAJADORA *f* PARA MADERA 8402
MORTAJADORAS *f pl* 11640
MORTAJAR 11630
MORTERO *m* 8396
MORTERO *m* 1445
MORTERO *m* DE CAL (QUE SE ENDURECE AL AIRE) 8854

MORTERO *m* DE CEMENTO 2137
MORTERO *m* DE LABORATORIO (DE PORCELANA O ÁGATA) 8395
MORTERO *m* HIDRÁULICO 6690
MORTERO *m* (PARA CONSTRUCCIÓN) 8394
MORTERO *m* REFRACTARIO 10406
MORTERO *m* REFRACTARIO 6125
MORTERO REFRACTARIO *m* 6126
MORTERO REFRACTARIO *m* 6125
MORTERO REFRACTARIO *m* 10406
MOSQUETÓN *m* 11691
MOTEADO 11960
MOTOAGRARIOS *m* CON FRESAS ROTATIVAS 10753
MOTOCULTIVADORES 10753
MOTOR *m* 9859
MOTOR *m* A BAJA TENSIÓN 7791
MOTOR *m* ABIERTO 8818
MOTOR *m* ASINCRÓNICO 783
MOTOR *m* BAJO TENSIÓN 7686
MOTOR *m* BLINDADO O CON CORAZA 4715
MOTOR *m* BLINDADO VENTILADO 13529
MOTOR *m* COMPOUND 2835
MOTOR *m* CON CÁRTER 4715
MOTOR *m* CON PISTONES ROTATIVOS 10754
MOTOR *m* DE AIRE CALIENTE 6615
MOTOR *m* DE AIRE COMPRIMIDO 2843
MOTOR *m* DE ALCOHOL 312
MOTOR *m* DE ALTA TENSIÓN 6502
MOTOR *m* DE ARRANQUE (POR REOSTATO O POR REACTANCIA) 12121
MOTOR *m* DE BENCINA 9223
MOTOR *m* DE CAMPO GIRATORIO 12876
MOTOR *m* DE CARBURANTE 8756
MOTOR *m* DE CILINDROS PAREADOS 13301
MOTOR *m* DE COMBUSTIÓN INTERNA 7061
MOTOR *m* DE COMBUSTIÓN INTERNA 7062
MOTOR *m* DE CORRIENTE ALTERNA 408
MOTOR *m* DE CORRIENTE CONTINUA 3022
MOTOR *m* DE CUATRO CILINDROS OPUESTOS HORIZONTALES 5383
MOTOR *m* DE CUATRO TIEMPOS 5600
MOTOR *m* DE CUATRO TIEMPOS 5603
MOTOR *m* DE DOS CILINDROS OPUESTOS HORIZONTALES 5398
MOTOR *m* DE DOS TIEMPOS 13312
MOTOR *m* DE EXPLOSIÓN 7061
MOTOR *m* DE GAS CON POCA POTENCIA 11658
MOTOR *m* DE GASOLINA 5819
MOTOR *m* DE GASOLINA CON GRAN POTENCIA 7410
MOTOR *m* DE PETRÓLEO 9046
MOTOR *m* DE REDUCIDA POTENCIA 11661

1083           **MUE**

MOTOR *m* DE RESERVA **12070**
MOTOR · *m* DE SERIE **11202**
MOTOR *m* DE VAPOR **12164**
MOTOR *m* DE VIENTO **13855**
MOTOR *m* DESCUBIERTO **8818**
MOTOR *m* DIESEL **3901**
MOTOR *m* DIESEL **2866**
MOTOR *m* ELÉCTRICO **4623**
MOTOR *m* EN DERIVACIÓN **11405**
MOTOR *m* EN ESTRELLA **10135**
MOTOR *m* ENFRIADO POR EL AIRE **251**
MOTOR *m* EÓLICO NEUMÁTICO **13855**
MOTOR *m* EXCITADO EN DERIVACIÓN **11405**
MOTOR *m* GENERADOR **8413**
MOTOR *m* HIDRÁULICO **6691**
MOTOR *m* MARINO **8005**
MOTOR *m* NO PROTEGIDO **8818**
MOTOR *m* POLICILINDROS **8453**
MOTOR *m* PROTEGIDO **9941**
MOTOR *m* RADIAL **10135**
MOTOR *m* REVERSIBLE **10540**
MOTOR *m* SEMIDIESEL **11171**
MOTOR *m* SINCRÓNICO **12571**
MOTOR *m* TÉRMICO **6345**
MOTOR *m* TRIFÁSICO **12876**
MOTOR ACCIONADO POR AIRE *m* **2843**
(MOTOR DE) ARRANQUE *m* **3310**
(MOTOR DE) ARRANQUE *m* **12116**
(MOTOR DE) ARRANQUE *m* **8418**
(MOTOR DE) ARRANQUE *m* AUTOMÁTICO **828**
MOTOR DE CORRIENTE ALTERNA *m* **408**
MOTOR-GENERADOR **8413**
MOTORES *m pl* ELÉCTRICOS **4524**
MOTORES *m pl* FIJOS Y MÓVILES **4766**
MÓVIL **9635**
MOVIMIENTO *m* **8406**
MOVIMIENTO *m* **8438**
MOVIMIENTO *m* ABSOLUTO **32**
MOVIMIENTO *m* ACELERADO **60**
MOVIMIENTO *m* ACELERADO SIN UNIFORMIDAD **8648**
MOVIMIENTO *m* ALTERNO **10283**
MOVIMIENTO *m* ALTERNO **13725**
MOVIMIENTO *m* ANGULAR **544**
MOVIMIENTO *m* APERIÓDICO **636**
MOVIMIENTO *m* CIRCULAR **2421**
MOVIMIENTO *m* CONTINUO **3031**
MOVIMIENTO *m* CÓSMICO **12456**
MOVIMIENTO *m* CURVILÍNEO **3500**
MOVIMIENTO *m* DE AVANCE **5584**
MOVIMIENTO *m* DE AVANCE **5584**

MOVIMIENTO *m* DE DESLIZAMIENTO **11605**
MOVIMIENTO *m* DE RETROCESO **919**
MOVIMIENTO *m* DE RODADURA **10702**
MOVIMIENTO *m* DE ROTACIÓN **10766**
MOVIMIENTO *m* DE TRANSLACIÓN **8407**
MOVIMIENTO *m* DE VAIVÉN **10283**
MOVIMIENTO *m* DISCONTINUO **7053**
MOVIMIENTO *m* EN SENTIDO CONTRARIO U OPUESTO **3243**
MOVIMIENTO *m* EN SENTIDO RETRÓGRADO **919**
MOVIMIENTO *m* ESFÉRICO **11889**
MOVIMIENTO *m* GIROSCÓPICO **6193**
MOVIMIENTO *m* HELICOIDAL **6426**
MOVIMIENTO *m* INTERMITENTE **7053**
MOVIMIENTO *m* MOTOR **6809**
MOVIMIENTO *m* OSCILATORIO **8881**
MOVIMIENTO *m* PENDULAR **10283**
MOVIMIENTO *m* PENDULAR **6302**
MOVIMIENTO *m* PERIÓDICO **9194**
MOVIMIENTO *m* PLANETARIO **9447**
MOVIMIENTO *m* RECTILÍNEO **10320**
MOVIMIENTO *m* RELATIVO **10434**
MOVIMIENTO *m* RETARDADO **10518**
MOVIMIENTO *m* RETARDADO SIN UNIFORMIDAD **8649**
MOVIMIENTO *m* ROTATORIO **10766**
MOVIMIENTO *m* SIN UNIFORMIDAD **8647**
MOVIMIENTO *m* SOFRENADO (DE SACUDIDAS) **7053**
MOVIMIENTO *m* UNIFORME **13362**
MOVIMIENTO *m* UNIFORMEMENTE ACELERADO **13365**
MOVIMIENTO *m* UNIFORMEMENTE RETARDADO **13367**
MOVIMIENTO *m* VARIADO **13490**
MUCÍLAGO *m* **8440**
MUELA *f* **9604**
MUELA *f* **6115**
MUELA *f* DE AFILAR **6118**
MUELA *f* DE ESMERIL **4698**
MUELA *f* DE ESMERIL **20**
MUELA *f* DE MOLINO **8298**
MUELA *f* DE PULIR **9604**
MUELA *f* DIAMANTADA **3867**
MUELA *f* DIAMANTE **3864**
MUELA *f* FLEXIBLE **4116**
MUELA *f* VERTICAL **4450**
MUELAS *f pl* **26**
MUESCA **3761**
MUESCA *f* **8401**
MUESCA *f* **8672**
MUESCA *f* **8672**
MUESTRA *f* **10915**
MUESTRA *f* **10915**

# MUE

1084

MUESTRA *f* 3142
MUESTRA *f* (DE METAL) 11858
MUESTRA *f* DE METAL DE BASE 1039
MUESTRA *f* DE METAL PURO 347
MUESTRA *f* DE PRUEBA 12784
MUESTRA *f* DE PRUEBA 12789
MUESTRA *f* DE PRUEBA 12788
MUESTRA *f* STANDARD 12082
MUESTREO *m* 10916
MUFLA *f* 9972
MUFLA *f* CORDAL 10731
MUFLAS *f* 9973
MULTIPLICACIÓN *f* 8480
MULTIPLICACIÓN *f* 5909
MULTIPLICADOR *m* 8482
MULTIPLICADOR *m* DE VELOCIDAD 8921
MULTIPLICANDO *m* 8479
MULTIPLICAR 8483
MUÑECA *m* DE CIGÜEÑAL 3311
MUÑEQUILLA *f* 11893
MUNICIÓN *f* 474
MUÑON *m* 9315
MUÑON *m* GIRATORIO 7256
MUÑON *m* GIRATORIO 11893
MUÑON *m* GIRATORIO 9420
MUÑON *m* GIRATORIO ACANALADO 12906
MUÑON *m* GIRATORIO COMO EJE DE ROTACIÓN 13242
MUÑON *m* GIRATORIO CON GANCHO DE ELEVACIÓN 7558
MUÑON *m* GIRATORIO DE APOYO 9421
MUÑON *m* GIRATORIO DE ARTICULACIÓN 7242
MUÑON *m* GIRATORIO DE CRUCETA 3391
MUÑON *m* GIRATORIO DE EXTREMO 4721
MUÑON *m* GIRATORIO DE HORQUILLA 3391
MUÑON *m* GIRATORIO DE TOPE ACANALADO 12906
MUÑON *m* GIRATORIO DE TOPE PARA TEJUELO 9421
MUÑON *m* GIRATORIO FRONTAL 4721
MUÑON *m* GIRATORIO INTERMEDIO 8513
MUÑON *m* GIRATORIO PARA HORQUILLA 3391
MURIATO *m* DE AMONIACO 462
MURO DIVISORIO *m* 4110
MUSELINA *f* 2288
MUY FLUIDO 5471
MUY MÓVIL 5471
NACIENTE *m* 8497
NAFTA *f* 8493
NAFTALENO *m* 8494
NAFTALINA *f* 8494
NAFTOESQUISTO *m* 8780
NAFTOL *m* 8495

NARIE *f* 1883
NARIZ *f* DE PICAPORTE 6318
NATIVO *m* 5647
NATIVO (MINERAL) 8497
NATIVO (O VIRGEN) 5647
NATURAL *m* 5647
NAVE *f* DE CALDERAS 1413
NAVE *f* DE CALDERAS 1413
NAVE *f* DE COLADA 2071
NAVE *f* DE COLADA 2077
NAVE *f* DE MONTAJE 773
NAVE *f* DE MONTAJE 770
NAVE *f* (DE TALLERDE MERCADOETC...) 1072
NECROSIS *f* 10770
NEGATIVACIÓN *f* 4607
NEGATIVO *m* 8524
NEGRO *m* ANIMAL 1447
NEGRO *m* DE FUNDICIÓN 1297
NEGRO *m* DE HUMO 7386
NEGRO *m* DE MARFIL 1447
NEGRO *m* DE PLATINO 9511
NEGRO *m* DE SOMBREAR 7386
NEODIMIO *m* 8533
NEODIMIO *m* 8534
NEÓN *m* 8535
NERVADURA *f* 10569
NERVADURA *f* DE UN TUBO 10570
NERVIO *m* 5139
NERVIO *m* 5139
NEUMÁTICO *m* 9558
NEUMÁTICO *m* 9549
NEUMÁTICO *m* 13322
NEUMÁTICO *m* CON GRAPAS 12404
NEUMÁTICO *m* DE ARMADURA RADIAL 10126
NEUMÁTICO *m* DE CLAVOS 12404
NEUMÁTICOS *m pl* CON FLANCOS BLANCOS 13840
NEUTRALIZACIÓN *f* 8548
NEUTRALIZAR 8549
NICHO *m* 10279
NIDO *m* DE GUIJARROS 9153
NIEBLA *f* METÁLICA 8182
NIOBIO *m* 8576
NIOBIO *m* 2747
NÍQUEL *m* 8556
NÍQUEL *m* AL CARBONILO 1978
NÍQUEL *m* ELECTROLÍTICO 4600
NÍQUEL PLATA *m* 8569
NIQUELADO *m* 8567
NIQUELAR 8566
NITRATO *m* 8579

NUC

NITRATO  *m* **8579**
NITRATO  *m* **10903**
NITRATO  *m* DE AMONIO **465**
NITRATO  *m* DE AMONIO **465**
NITRATO  *m* DE BARIO **1001**
NITRATO  *m* DE BISMUTILO **1273**
NITRATO  *m* DE BISMUTO **1271**
NITRATO  *m* DE BISMUTO **1271**
NITRATO  *m* DE CHILE **2330**
NITRATO  *m* DE COBALTO **2610**
NITRATO  *m* DE COBRE **3472**
NITRATO  *m* DE ETILO **4850**
NITRATO  *m* DE ETILO **4850**
NITRATO  *m* DE MERCURIO **8156**
NITRATO  *m* DE PLATA **7828**
NITRATO  *m* DE PLATA **7828**
NITRATO  *m* DE POTASIO **10903**
NITRATO  *m* DE SODIO **2330**
NITRATO  *m* DE SODIO **2330**
NITRATO  *m* MERCÚRICO **8156**
NITRATO  *m* MERCURIOSO **8160**
NITRATO  *m* MERCURIOSO **8160**
NITRATO DE PLATA  *m* **7828**
NITRITO  *m* **8586**
NITRITO  *m* **8586**
NITRITO  *m* DE AMONIO **466**
NITRITO  *m* DE COBRE **3473**
NITRITO  *m* DE POTASA **9691**
NITRITO  *m* DE SOSA **11725**
NITRO  *m* **10903**
NITRO  *m* **10903**
NITRO  *m* **2330**
NITROBENCENO  *m* **8587**
NITROBENCINA  *f* **8587**
NITROBENCINA  *f* **8587**
NITROCELULOSA  *f* **6176**
NITRÓGENO  *m* **8588**
NITRÓGENO  *m* **8588**
NITROGLICERINA  *f* **8593**
NITRÓMETRO  *m* **8594**
NITROXILO  *m* **8591**
NITRUM  *m* FLAMMANS **465**
NITRURACIÓN  *f* **8589**
NITRURACIÓN  *f* GASEOSA **5830**
NIVEL  *m* **6021**
NIVEL  *m* **6021**
NIVEL  *m* **7525**
NIVEL  *m* BAROMÉTRICO **6422**
NIVEL  *m* DE AGUA **13652**
NIVEL  *m* DE AGUA (ALTURA DE UN LÍQUIDO) **13659**

NIVEL  *m* DE BURBUJA **13259**
NIVEL  *m* DE HILO **9540**
NIVEL  *m* DE PLOMADA **9540**
NIVEL  *m* DE PRESIÓN **9833**
NIVEL  *m* DEL AGUA SUBTERRÁNEA **6148**
NIVEL  *m* DEL MAR **11070**
NIVEL  *m* ESFÉRICO **2430**
NIVELAR **323**

NO COMBINADO **6818**

NO COMERCIAL  *m* **13101**

NO CONDUCTOR **3898**

NO FERROSO **8631**

NO METÁLICO **8639**

NO QUEMADO **13344**

NO QUEMADOS **6765**

NO REVERSIBILIDAD  *f* **7168**

NO REVERSIBLE **7169**
NODO  *m* DE OSCILACIÓN **8605**
NODO  *m* DE UNA CURVA **7741**
NODO  *m* DE VIBRACIÓN **8605**
NODULAR **8606**
NOMENCLATURA  *f* **9095**
NOMENCLATURA  *f* DE LAS PIEZAS **7662**
NONIO **13536**
NORIA  *f* **8960**
NORIA  *f* **1676**
NORMA  *f* **12071**
NORMAL  *f* DE UNA CURVA **8662**
NORMAL  *f* (GEOM.) **8652**
NORMALIZACIÓN  *f* **12091**
NORMALIZACIÓN  *f* ESTANDARDIZACIÓN  *f* **12091**
NORMALIZAR **12090**
NORMALIZAR **12090**
NORMAS  *f pl* **8835**
NORMAS  *m* PARA TUBERÍAS **9359**
NOTROSILO  *m* **8581**
NÚCLEO  *m* **3142**
NÚCLEO  *m* DE LA SECCIÓN **3156**
NÚCLEO  *m* DE UN TORNILLO **1394**
NÚCLEO  *m* DE UNA GUARNICIÓN **3155**
NÚCLEO  *m* EXTERIOR **5027**

# NUC

1086

NÚCLEO *m* FILTRO **3164**
NÚCLEO *m* MAGNÉTICO **3142**
NÚCLEO *m* TRATADO **927**
NÚCLEO CRISTALINO **8688**
NUDO *m* **7313**
NUDO *m* CORREDIZO **8651**
NUEVA CARBURACIÓN *f* **1953**
NUEVA CARBURACIÓN *f* DEL HIERRO **10275**
NUEVA LAMINACIÓN *f* **10470**
NUEVA PUESTA EN MARCHA *f* **10509**
NUEVO CARBURANTE *m* **10276**
NUEVO EMPLEO *m* **10246**
NUEVO MONTAJE *m* **10245**
NUMERADOR *m* **8693**
NUMÉRICO **3941**
NÚMERO *m* ATÓMICO **803**
NÚMERO *m* COMPLEJO **2813**
NÚMERO *m* COMPUESTO **2820**
NÚMERO *m* DE AMPERIOS **478**
NÚMERO *m* DE CALIBRE DE UN ALAMBRE **5881**
NÚMERO *m* DE CALIBRE DE UNA CHAPA **5880**
NÚMERO *m* DE CALORÍAS QUE SE DESPRENDE EN UNA REACCIÓN **6348**
NÚMERO *m* DE CONSTRUCCIÓN **4986**
NÚMERO *m* DE DIENTES **8691**
NÚMERO *m* DE LA OPERACIÓN EN CURSO **8838**
NÚMERO *m* DE ORDEN DE LA FABRICACIÓN **11197**
NÚMERO *m* DE REVOLUCIONES **8690**
NÚMERO *m* DE ROSCAS O DE PASOS DE ROSCA **8692**
NÚMERO *m* DE SECUENCIA **11193**
NÚMERO *m* DE UN LOGARITMO **8689**
NÚMERO *m* DE VOLTIOS **13593**
NÚMERO *m* DE VUELTAS **8690**
NÚMERO *m* DECIMAL **3664**
NÚMERO *m* ENTERO **7012**
NÚMERO *m* FRACCIONARIO **5613**
NÚMERO *m* IMAGINARIO **6781**
NÚMERO *m* IMPAR **8725**
NÚMERO *m* IRRACIONAL O INCONMENSURABLE **7162**
NÚMERO *m* NON **8725**
NÚMERO *m* PAR **4872**
NÚMERO *m* PRIMERO **9860**
NÚMERO *m* QUE RESTAR **12426**
NÚMERO *m* RACIONAL **10235**
NÚMERO *m* REAL **10260**
NÚMERO COMENSURABLE *m* **10235**
NUTACIÓN *f* **8702**
O ARISTA *f* **4447**
O DE BORDE DELGADO **2910**
O DE METALES PRECIOSOS **3548**

O DE RÓTULA ESFÉRICA **952**
OBELISCO *m* **8705**
OBJETIVO *m* **8708**
OBJETIVO *m* **12682**
OBJETIVO APLANÉTICO *m* **639**
OBJETO *m* QUE EXAMINAR CON EL MICROSCOPIO EN FORMA DE CORTE DELGADO **11113**
OBJETOS *m pl* E INSTRUMENTOS *m pl* PARA DIBUJO **4236**
OBLICUIDAD *f* **1065**
OBLONGO *m* **8715**
OBRA *f* **12265**
OBRA *f* DE ALBAÑILERÍA **8025**
OBRA *f* DE CONSTRUCCIÓN **8025**
OBRA *f* DE MAMPOSTERÍA **8025**
OBRAS *f pl* DE HORMIGÓN **2901**
OBRAS *f pl* PÚBLICAS **2444**
OBRERO *m* **7868**
OBRERO **13960**
OBRERO *m* **13960**
OBRERO *m* CEPILLADOR **9443**
OBRERO *m* EXPERIMENTADO **3289**
OBRERO *m* FUNDIDOR **5591**
OBRERO *m* MECÁNICO **7868**
OBRERO *m* MODELADOR **9130**
OBRERO *m* MOLDEADOR **8427**
OBRERO *m* PROFESIONAL **3289**
OBRERO *m* REMACHADOR **10641**
OBRERO *m* SIN ESPECIALIDAD **13398**
OBRERO *m* TEMPLADOR **13008**
OBSERVACIÓN *f* MACROSCÓPICA A SIMPLE VISTA **7873**
OBSIDIANA *f* **8716**
OBSTRUCCIÓN *f* **2362**
OBSTRUCCIÓN *f* **2362**
OBSTRUIRSE **2358**
OBSTRUIRSE **2358**
OBTURADOR *m* **10760**
OBTURADOR *m* **9529**
OBTURADOR *m* **9529**
OBTURADOR *m* **13453**
OBTURADOR *m* CON LEVANTADO ANGULAR **5353**
OBTURADOR *m* DE AIRE **292**
OBTURADOR *m* DE GAS **12888**
OBTURADOR *m* DESLIZANTE O RESBALADIZO **11592**
OBTURAR LA ADMISIÓN EN UNA TUBERÍA **11407**
OCLUSIÓN (QUIM) **8719**
OCRE *m* **8720**
OCRE *m* **8720**
OCRE *m* AMARILLO **2467**
OCTAEDRO *m* **8722**
OCTANAJE **8723**

OCTÁNGULO  m 8721
OCTANTE  m 8724
OCTAVA PARTE DE UN CÍRCULO 8724
OCTÓGONO  m 8721
OCULAR  m 4977
OCULAR-MICRÓMETRO 8254
ODONTÓGRAFO  m 8726
OFICINA  f DE DIBUJO 4238
OFICINA  f DE ESTUDIOS 3796
OFICINA  f TÉCNICA 3796
OFITA  f 11204
OHMIO  m 8742
OJETE  m 4980
OJO  m 4980
OJO  m DE BIELA 4976
OJO  m DE GATO 2088
OJO  m DEL HACHA 11231
OJO  m DEL MARTILLO 4975
OJO  m PARA LA LLAVE 11832
OLIGISTO  m 11865
OLIVINA  f 8796
OLIVINA  f 8796
OLIVINA  f 9243
ONDA  f 13699
ONDA  f CALORÍFICA 6379
ONDA  f ESTACIONARIA 12145
ONDA  f LUMINOSA 7571
ONDA  f SONORA 11819
ONDULACIÓN  f 13701
ONDULACIÓN  f (DE LAS CHAPAS) 1681
ONDULACIONES  f pl 2619
ONDULACIONES  f pl 11419
ONDULACIONES  f pl DEBIDAS AL GAS 5823
ONDULAR 3336
OPACIDAD  f 8802
OPACO 8803
OPERACIÓN  f 9096
OPERACIÓN  f 814
OPERACIONES  f pl EN CADENA 3034
OPERACIONES  f pl PRELIMINARES 9787
OPERACIONES  f pl PREPARATORIAS 9787
OPERARIO  m DE MÁQUINA HERRAMIENTA 7868
OPÉRCULO  m DOBLE 4162
OPÉRCULO  m MONOBLOQUE (ESQUINA) 11796
OPÉRCULO  m PARALELO CON APRETADO MECÁNICO
   9053
OPÉRCULO  m PARALELO CON APRETADO POR MUELLE
   9052
OPÉRCULO  m SIMPLE 11492
ÓPTICA  f 8849
ÓPTICA  f 8840

ORDEN  f 2780
ORDEN  f DE ENCENDIDO 5260
ORDEN  f DE EXPLOSIÓN 5260
ORDEN  f DE FUNCIONAMIENTO 13626
ORDEN  f DE INYECCIÓN 6936
ORDEN  f DE MAGNITUD 8852
ORDENACIÓN  f DE DIAGRAMAS SEGÚN EL MÉTODO DE
   RANKINE 2770
ORDENADA  f 8858
ORDENAR DIAGRAMAS SEGÚN EL MÉTODO DE RANKINE
   2765
OREJA  f 7817
OREJA  f 7817
OREJETA  f 7817
ORFEBRERÍA  f 6003
ORGANIZACIÓN  f DE LAS FÁBRICAS 6901
ÓRGANO  m 7852
ÓRGANO  m 7852
ÓRGANO  m DE FIJACIÓN 5042
ÓRGANO  m DE LUBRIFICACIÓN 7812
ÓRGANO  m DE MANDO 3057
ÓRGANO  m DE MANDO 4309
ÓRGANO  m DE MÁQUINA 4756
ÓRGANO  m QUE TRABAJA 13953
ÓRGANO DE ACCIONADO 4309
ÓRGANO DE ACCIONAMIENTO  m 4309
ÓRGANOS  m pl DE TRANSMISIÓN 13126
ORIENTACIÓN  f 8867
ORIENTACIÓN  f DE LOS CRISTALES 3994
ORIENTACIÓN  f PREFERENCIAL 9771
ORIENTADO AL AZAR 10199
ORIFICIO  m 9633
ORIFICIO  m 6530
ORIFICIO  m DE ADMISIÓN 6947
ORIFICIO  m DE ADUCCIÓN 6947
ORIFICIO  m DE AIRE (RESPIRADERO) 269
ORIFICIO  m DE BRIDAS 5339
ORIFICIO  m DE DESCARGA 8902
ORIFICIO  m DE ENGRASE 8761
ORIFICIO  m DE ENTRADA 6947
ORIFICIO  m DE ESCAPE 8902
ORIFICIO  m DE INTRODUCCIÓN 6947
ORIFICIO  m DE LLEGADA 6947
ORIFICIO  m DE PASO 9100
ORIFICIO  m DE PASO 9634
ORIFICIO  m DE SALIDA 8902
ORIFICIO  m DE SALIDA 8902
ORIFICIO  m NOMINAL 8615
ORIFICIOS  m pl ATERRAJADAOS (HEMBRAS) 11053
ORIFICIOS  m pl QUE SOLDAR (POR EL INTERIOR EN EL
   EXTREMO) 1810

# ORI

1088

ORIFICIOS  *m pl* ROSCADOS (MACHOS) **11054**
ORIGEN  *m* DE LAS COORDENADAS **8868**
ORILLA  *f* **4441**
ORO  *m* **5993**
ORO  *m* BATIDO **6000**
ORO  *m* BLANCO **13831**
ORO  *m* DE JUDEA **12099**
ORO  *m* DE MONEDAS **5996**
ORO  *m* ELECTROLÍTICO **4598**
ORO  *m* FINO **5198**
ORO  *m* MUSSIF **12099**
ORO  *m* VERDE **6092**
OROPIMENTE  *m* **728**
OSCILACIÓN  *f* **8884**
OSCILACIÓN  *f* DE UN MUELLE **13558**
OSCILACIÓN  *f* DE UN PÉNDULO **12548**
OSCILACIÓN  *f* DE UNA CORREA **13825**
OSCILACIÓN  *f* ELÉCTRICA **4547**
OSCILACIÓN  *f* LIBRE **5643**
OSCILACIÓN  *f* LONGITUDINAL **7739**
OSCILACIÓN  *f* TRANSVERSAL **13146**
OSCILACIONES  *f pl* DEL REGULADOR **6671**
OSCILACIONES  *f pl* FORZADAS **5535**
OSCILAR **8877**
OSCILÓGRAFO  *m* **8885**
OSCILOSCOPIO  *m* **8886**
OSCURECIMIENTO  *m* **5507**
OSEINA  *f* **1449**
OSMIO  *m* **8889**
OSMIRIDIO  *m* **8888**
ÓSMOSIS  *f* **8890**
OVALIZACIÓN  *f* DE UN COJINETE **13719**
ÓVALO  *m* **4669**
OXALATO  *m* **8968**
OXALATO  *m* ÁCIDO DE POTASIO **118**
OXALATO  *m* DE AMONIACO **467**
OXALATO  *m* DE CALCIO **1853**
OXALATO  *m* DE SODIO **11726**
OXALATO  *m* FERROSO **5124**
OXALATO  *m* NEUTRO DE POTASIO **9692**
OXICORTE  *m* **8977**
OXICORTE  *m* **7387**
OXICORTE  *m* **5817**
OXIDABLE **8972**
OXIDACIÓN  *f* **8970**
OXIDACIÓN  *f* **8984**
OXIDACIÓN  *f* A TEMPERATURA ELEVADA **6498**
OXIDACIÓN  *f* ANÓDICA **605**
OXIDACIÓN  *f* ANÓDICA POR EL ÁCIDO CRÓMICO **2380**
OXIDACIÓN  *f* ELECTROLÍTICA **4601**

OXIDACIÓN  *f* (O CORROSIÓN  *f*) SECA **4350**
OXIDACIÓN  *f* POR FROTAMIENTO **5667**
OXIDANTE  *m* **8974**
OXIDAR **8973**
OXIDARSE **12685**
OXIDARSE **10864**
OXIDARSE **8973**
ÓXIDO  *m* **8971**
ÓXIDO  *m* **10863**
ÓXIDO  *m* **10873**
ÓXIDO  *m* **10335**
ÓXIDO  *m* AZOICO **8581**
ÓXIDO  *m* CÚPRICO **3474**
ÓXIDO  *m* CÚPRICO HIDRATADO **3471**
ÓXIDO  *m* CUPROSO **3479**
ÓXIDO  *m* DE ALUMINIO **413**
ÓXIDO  *m* DE BISMUTO **1272**
ÓXIDO  *m* DE CALCIO **1854**
ÓXIDO  *m* DE CARBONO **1952**
ÓXIDO  *m* DE CINC **14043**
ÓXIDO  *m* DE CINC **14043**
ÓXIDO  *m* DE ETILIDENO **84**
ÓXIDO  *m* DE ETILO **8853**
ÓXIDO  *m* DE HIERRO **7144**
ÓXIDO  *m* DE HIERRO **5102**
ÓXIDO  *m* DE MAGNESIO **7879**
ÓXIDO  *m* DE MERCURIO **8157**
ÓXIDO  *m* DE METILENO **5573**
ÓXIDO  *m* DE METILO **8222**
ÓXIDO  *m* DE METILO **8222**
ÓXIDO  *m* DE NÍQUEL **8574**
ÓXIDO  *m* DE SODIO **11724**
ÓXIDO  *m* ESTÁNNICO **12098**
ÓXIDO  *m* ESTANNOSO **12102**
ÓXIDO  *m* FÉRRICO **7148**
ÓXIDO  *m* FERROSO **5125**
ÓXIDO  *m* MERCÚRICO **8157**
ÓXIDO  *m* MERCURIOSO **8161**
ÓXIDO  *m* NATURAL DE URANIO **9411**
ÓXIDO  *m* NÍTRICO **8581**
ÓXIDO  *m* NITROSO **8597**
ÓXIDO  *m* PARDO DE PLOMO **7461**
ÓXIDO  *m* SALINO DE MANGANESO **13207**
ÓXIDO  *m* SALINO DE PLOMO **10333**
ÓXIDO  *m* SULFUROSO **12450**
OXÍDULO  *m* DE COBRE **3476**
OXIGENACIÓN  *f* **8984**
OXÍGENO  *m* **8980**
OZONO  *m* **8989**
OZOQUERITA  *f* **4413**

**1089**             **PAP**

PACTUNG *m* **5932**
PAGA *f* **13613**
PAGO *m* **13613**
PALA *f* **11385**
PALA *f* **13728**
PALA DE HÉLICE *f* **9928**
PALABRA *f* **13934**
PALADIO *m* **9023**
PALANCA *f* **7725**
PALANCA *f* **7530**
PALANCA *f* A TORNILLO **12985**
PALANCA *f* ACODADA **12979**
PALANCA *f* ACODADA **1131**
PALANCA *f* ACODADA **1131**
PALANCA *f* ARTICULADA **6505**
PALANCA *f* ARTICULADA **12979**
PALANCA *f* DE ARRANQUE **12120**
PALANCA *f* DE ARTICULACIÓN **12979**
PALANCA *f* DE ATAQUE DE DIRECCIÓN **12227**
PALANCA *f* DE AVANCE AUTOMÁTICO **842**
PALANCA *f* DE CAMBIO DE MARCHA **10549**
PALANCA *f* DE CONTRAPESO **13751**
PALANCA *f* DE CORREDERA **11638**
PALANCA *f* DE DESCONEXIÓN **4035**
PALANCA *f* DE DESEMBRAGUE **4035**
PALANCA *f* DE EMPUÑADURA **6239**
PALANCA *f* DE FRENO **1537**
PALANCA *f* DE HORQUILLA **5569**
PALANCA *f* DE INVERSIÓN DEL AVANCE **5073**
PALANCA *f* DE MANDO **9414**
PALANCA *f* DE MANIOBRA **8833**
PALANCA *f* DE PEDAL **5521**
PALANCA *f* DE PIE DE CABRA **3394**
PALANCA *f* DE PUESTA EN MOVIMIENTO **10438**
PALANCA *f* DE PURGA LIBRE **7553**
PALANCA *f* DE SEÑAL ACÚSTICA **1131**
PALANCA *f* DE TORNILLO **12985**
PALANCA *f* DE TRES BRAZOS **4131**
PALANCA *f* DE TRINQUETE **10223**
PALANCA *f* DE VÁLVULA **13465**
PALANCA *f* DERECHA **12306**
PALANCA *f* DOBLE **4147**
PALANCA *f* EN ESCUADRA **1131**
PALANCA *f* OSCILANTE **10656**
PALANCA *f* RODADIZA **10686**
PALANCA *f* SELECTORA DE LOS AVANCES **5065**
PALANCA DE DOS BRAZOS *f* **4147**
PALANQUILLA *f* **1243**
PALANQUILLA *f* **1243**
PALANQUILLA *f* DE LATÓN **1563**

PALANQUILLAS *f pl* DE ACERO ALEADO (O ESPECIAL) **370**
PALAS *f pl* DE VENTILADOR **5030**
PALEAR **11386**
PALETA *f* **1677**
PALETA *f* **13728**
PALETA *f* DE UNA RUEDA HIDRÁULICA **1677**
PALETIZACIÓN *f* **9026**
PALMER *m* **11034**
PALOMILLA **12911**
PALOMILLA *f* **12911**
PALPADOR *m* **11090**
PALPADOR *m* **9882**
PALPADOR *m* CON ESFERA **3842**
PANABOSA *f* **12796**
PANDEO *m* **3343**
PANDEO *m* **3343**
PANEL *m* **9032**
PANEL *m* PROTECTOR **11926**
PAÑOL *m* DE MAZUT **5706**
PAÑOLES *m* DE COMBUSTIBLE **8748**
PANTALLA *f* **11018**
PANTALLA *f* **11346**
PANTALLA *f* **6252**
PANTALLA *f* DE PROYECCIÓN **13568**
PANTALLA *f* DE SOLDADURA **5000**
PANTALLA *f* FLUORESCENTE **5477**
PANTALLA *f* LUMINOSA **5477**
PANTALLA *f* PARA SOLDADURA **13764**
PANTALLA *f* PROTECTORA **11342**
PANTALLA *f* REFORZADORA **7017**
PANTALLA ELÉCTRICA *f* **5036**
PANTANO *m* **3597**
PANTÓGRAFO *m* **9033**
PANTÓMETRO *m* **1228**
PAPEL *m* A LA FENOLFTALEÍNA **9239**
PAPEL *m* ACEITADO **8788**
PAPEL *m* AL ACETATO DE PLOMO **7449**
PAPEL *m* AL FERRO-PRUSIATO **5119**
PAPEL *m* AL ROJO CONGO **2936**
PAPEL *m* ALBUMIMADO **311**
PAPEL *m* ALBÚMINA **311**
PAPEL *m* AZUL PARA FOTOCALCO **5119**
PAPEL *m* BUSCADOR DE POLOS **9594**
PAPEL *m* CARMÍN **2002**
PAPEL *m* CEBOLLA **12969**
PAPEL *m* CIANOGRÁFICO AZUL **5119**
PAPEL *m* CIANOHIERRO **5119**
PAPEL *m* CONTÍNUO **3013**
PAPEL *m* CUADRICULADO **11530**

**PAP** 1090

PAPEL *m* DE ALHEÑA **342**
PAPEL *m* DE AMIANTO **752**
PAPEL *m* DE CALCO **13084**
PAPEL *m* DE CÚRCUMA **13275**
PAPEL *m* DE DIBUJO **4240**
PAPEL *m* DE EMBALAJE **13984**
PAPEL *m* DE ESMERIL **4696**
PAPEL *m* DE ESMERIL **4693**
PAPEL *m* DE ESTAÑO **12955**
PAPEL *m* DE INDICADOR **6880**
PAPEL *m* DE LIJA **5961**
PAPEL *m* DE LIJA **5958**
PAPEL *m* DE ORCANETA **342**
PAPEL *m* DE ORCANETINA **342**
PAPEL *m* DE SEDA **12969**
PAPEL *m* DE TORNASOL **7668**
PAPEL *m* ESMERIL **10925**
PAPEL *m* FILTRO **5177**
PAPEL *m* FILTRO BLANCO **12969**
PAPEL *m* FOTOCALCO **9257**
PAPEL *m* GOMA LACA **13506**
PAPEL *m* JOSEPH **12969**
PAPEL *m* METALIZADO **8199**
PAPEL *m* PERGAMINO **9078**
PAPEL *m* PODRIDO **9036**
PAPEL *m* POLO **9594**
PAPEL *m* PRUSIATO **5119**
PAPEL *m* REACTIVO **12783**
PAPEL *m* SECANTE **1350**
PAPEL *m* SECANTE **1350**
PAPEL *m* TRANSPARENTE **13084**
PAPEL *m* YODOALMIDONADO **9690**
PAPIRINA *f* **9078**
PAQUETE *m* **5017**
PAQUETE *m* DE HIERRO QUE SOLDAR **5015**
PAQUETE *m* PARA LAMINAR **4371**
PAR *m* **3252**
PAR *m* **3252**
PAR *m* **13048**
PAR *m* DE CONOS LISOS **404**
PAR *m* TERMOELÉCTRICO **12821**
PAR *f* TERMOELÉCTRICO **12827**
PAR DE APRIETE *m* **12931**
PAR DE ARRANQUE *m* **12129**
PAR DE RUEDA Y SINFÍN TANGENCÍAL *m* **13974**
PAR DE RUEDAS HELICOIDALES *m* **11916**
PAR ELECTROQUÍMICO *m* **5782**
PAR METRO *m* **13050**
PAR MOTOR *m* **13048**
PAR REACCIÓN *m* **8374**

PAR RESISTENTE *m* **8374**
PAR TERMOELÉCTRICO *m* **12827**
PAR TERMOELÉCTRICO *m* **2637**
PARA CORREA DE TRANSMISIÓN **1143**
PARA PULIMENTAR **9601**
PARÁBOLA *f* **9038**
PARABOLOIDE *m* DE REVOLUCIÓN **9042**
PARABRISAS *m* **13872**
PARACHISPAS *m* **3109**
PARACHOQUES *m* **1686**
PARACHOQUES *m* **1732**
PARADA *f* **12278**
PARADA *f* FACULTATIVA **8850**
PARADA *f* FACULTATIVA **6521**
PARADA *f* PROGRAMADA **9903**
PARADA *f* TEMPORIZADA **4396**
PARADA DE UNA MÁQUINA *f* **12286**
PARADA DE UNA MÁQUINA *f* **12094**
PARAFINA *f* **9043**
PARAGOLPES *m* **1732**
PARAGOTAS *m* **4283**
PARALAJE *m* **9047**
PARALELEPÍPEDO *m* **9068**
PARALELEPÍPEDO *m* OBLÍCUO **8713**
PARALELEPÍPEDO *m* RECTÁNGULO **10305**
PARALELEPÍPEDO *m* RECTO **10581**
PARALELISMO *m* **9069**
PARALELO **9050**
PARALELO **9049**
PARALELÓGRAMA *m* **9070**
PARALELÓGRAMA *m* ARTICULADO **9057**
PARALELÓGRAMA *m* DE LAS FUERZAS **9071**
PARALELÓGRAMA *m* DE LAS VELOCIDADES **9072**
PARALLAMAS *m* **5321**
PARAMAGNÉTICO **9073**
PARAMAGNETISMO *m* **9074**
PARÁMETRO *m* **9075**
PARÁMETROS *m pl* DE SOLDADURA **13787**
PARAR UNA MÁQUINA **12280**
PARARRAYOS *m* **7575**
PARARRAYOS *m* **7576**
PARED *f* **4110**
PARED *f* DE LA CAJA DE ENFRIAMIENTO **8381**
PARED *f* DE UN AGUJERO **13624**
PARED *f* DELGADA (A) **12851**
PARED *f* ESPESA (A) **12841**
PARED *f* FRONTAL **4728**
PARED *f* PROTECTORA **9953**
PARO *m* **7092**
PAROS *m pl* **11409**

PAS

PARQUE *m* ALMACÉN DE HIDROCARBURO **12627**
PARQUE *m* CUBIERTO **11302**
PARRILLA *f* **6070**
PARRILLA *f* ESCALONADA **12248**
PARRILLA *f* ESCALONADA **12248**
PARTE *f* CENTRAL **2287**
PARTE *f* CONDUCTORA **4316**
PARTE *f* CONSTITUYENTE VOLÁTIL **13586**
PARTE *f* DE DEBAJO (DEL MOLDE) **4199**
PARTE *f* DE ENCIMA **3104**
PARTE *f* DESMONTABLE **7745**
PARTE *f* FIJA **3885**
PARTE DE ENTRADA *f* **4774**
PARTE DE INTRODUCCIÓN *f* **4774**
PARTICIPAR **1266**
PARTÍCULA *f* **9088**
PARTÍCULA *f* ACIDULAR **8517**
PARTÍCULA *f* ALFA **400**
PARTÍCULA *f* BETA **1217**
PARTÍCULAS *f pl* COLOIDALES **2736**
PARTÍCULAS *f pl* DE ACERO MUY MENUDAS **13890**
PARTÍCULAS *f pl* DE METALES NOBLES **3548**
PARTÍCULAS *f pl* RECUBIERTAS **2585**
PASACORREA *m* **1159**
PASADA *f* **10832**
PASADA *f* **12668**
PASADA *f* **9096**
PASADA *f* **9096**
PASADA *f* A TINTA **6942**
PASADA *f* ACABADO **11541**
PASADA *f* AMPLIA **13724**
PASADA *f* DE ACABADO **11542**
PASADA *f* DE ACABADO (LAMINACIÓN) **11541**
PASADA *f* DE DESBASTE **11543**
PASADA *f* DE ENDEREZADO **11543**
PASADA *f* DE HUSILLO **11906**
PASADA *f* HÚMEDA **13803**
PASADA *f* RIBETEADORA **4455**
PASADA EN UNA SUPERFICIE CILÍNDRICA *f* **13164**
PASADA LONGITUDINAL *f* **13164**
PASADA TRANSVERSAL *f* **12522**
PASADOR *m* **9315**
PASADOR *m* **9315**
PASADOR *m* **7414**
PASADOR *m* **7276**
PASADOR *m* **3212**
PASADOR *m* **5211**
PASADOR *m* **13739**
PASADOR *m* AGUJA **9315**
PASADOR *m* CÓNICO **12655**

PASADOR *m* DE BLOQUEO **11220**
PASADOR *m* DE CHASIS **5372**
PASADOR *m* DE LA ARTICULACIÓN DE LA HORQUILLA **6159**
PASADOR *m* DE LEVA **1887**
PASADOR *m* DE RETENCIÓN **11220**
PASADOR *m* DE SEGURIDAD EN CORTE **11283**
PASADOR *m* DE SEGURIDAD EN CORTE **11294**
PASADOR *m* DEL PISTÓN **9376**
PASADOR *m* EXTRACTOR **7333**
PASADOR *m* GIRATORIO **7311**
PASADOR *m* HENDIDO **11940**
PASADOR *m* (O PERNO *m*) DE UNIÓN PROVISIONAL DE LAS CHAPAS **12592**
PASADOR *m* (O PERNO *m* O BULÓN *m*) DE UNIÓN **771**
PASADOR *m* (O PERNO *m* O BULÓN *m*) DE UNIÓN PROVISIONAL **12592**
PASADOR DE RETENCIÓN *m* **3213**
PASADOR DE UNIÓN *m* **3215**
PASADORES *m pl* DE FRESADO **8290**
PASAR A ESTADO LÍQUIDO **8135**
PASAR A TINTA **6940**
PASARELA *f* **13616**
PASARELA *f* **5776**
PASARELA *f* DE COMUNICACIÓN **2964**
PASARELA *f* DE ENLACE **2964**
PASIVACIÓN *f* **9105**
PASIVADOR *m* **9106**
PASIVIDAD *f* **9107**
PASO *m* **12239**
PASO *m* A DERECHA **10585**
PASO *m* A IZQUIERDA **7508**
PASO *m* CIRCUNFERENCIAL **2423**
PASO *m* DE LA CORREA DE UNA POLEA A OTRA **1158**
PASO *m* DE LA HÉLICE **9410**
PASO *m* DE LA LUZ **9099**
PASO *m* DE REMACHE **9409**
PASO *m* DE REMACHE LONGITUDINAL **7736**
PASO *m* DE ROSCA **11045**
PASO *m* DE ROSCA **3535**
PASO *m* DE TORNILLO **11045**
PASO *m* DE TORNILLO **9410**
PASO *m* DE TORNILLO **12857**
PASO *m* DE UNA CADENA **6978**
PASO *m* DE UNA ROSCA **9399**
PASO *m* DEL CALOR **9098**
PASO *m* DEL ENGRANAJE **9408**
PASO *m* DEL SISTEMA BRIGGS PARA TUBOS **1605**
PASO *m* DEL SISTEMA INTERNACIONAL DE BASE MÉTRICA (S.I.) **7084**
PASO *m* DEL SISTEMA LOWENHERZ **7792**

**PAS** 1092

PASO *m* DEL SISTEMA SELLERS **451**
PASO *m* DEL SISTEMA THURY **12552**
PASO *m* DIAMETRAL **3861**
PASO *m* INGLÉS **13844**
PASO *m* LINEAL **7615**
PASO *m* PARA TUBOS **9360**
PASO *m* PARA TUBOS DE GAS **5843**
PASO *m* WHITWORTH **13844**
PASO DE ROSCA **12857**
PASTA *f* **12112**
PASTA *f* DE PAPEL **9035**
PASTA *f* DE PAPEL **9036**
PASTA *f* MECÁNICA DE MADERA **8116**
PASTA *f* PARA ALISAR **6108**
PASTA *f* PARA PULIR **2827**
PASTA *f* PARA SOLDAR **9108**
PASTA *f* QUÍMICA DE MADERA **2316**
PASTA DE ESMERIL **6108**
PASTEL *m* (PINTURA AL) **2745**
PASTILLADORA *f* **9310**
PATA *f* **7817**
PATA *f* **7817**
PATA *f* **1041**
PATA *f* DE ARAÑA **7810**
PATAS *f pl* DE UN MUEBLE **8679**
PATENTADO *m* **9123**
PATENTAR **9113**
PATENTE *f* **385**
PATENTE *f* DE INVENCIÓN **9112**
PATENTE *f* EXTRANJERA **5540**
PATENTES *f pl* DE INVENCIÓN (LEY SOBRE LAS) **9116**
PATENTES *f pl* DE INVENCIÓN (OFICINA DE LAS) **9120**
PATILLA *f* **7817**
PATILLAS *f pl* DE LEVANTAMIENTO POR GATO **7206**
PATÍN *m* **11587**
PATÍN *m* **11587**
PATÍN *m* **11587**
PATÍN *m* DE UN COJINETE **1034**
PÁTINA *f* **9127**
PATINAJE *m* DE LAS RUEDAS **11621**
PATINAMIENTO *m* DE LA CORREA **11620**
PATINAR **11612**
PATINAR **11612**
PATRÓN *m* **12734**
PAVIMENTO *m* FIRME **9136**
PAVONADO *m* **1377**
PAVONADO *m* **1758**
PAVONAR **1651**
PAVONAR EL ACERO **1368**
PECBLENDA *f* **9411**

PEDAL *m* **13174**
PEDAL *m* DE EMBRAGUE **2547**
PEDERNAL *m* **5427**
PEGAR **5985**
PEINE *m* **12904**
PEINE *m* **12384**
PEINE *m* DE ATERRAJAR **7060**
PEINE *m* DE FILETEAR **4952**
PEINE *m* PARA EL EXTERIOR **4952**
PEINE *m* PARA EL INTERIOR **7060**
PEINE *m* PARA LOS PASOS DE TORNILLO **2274**
PELDAÑO *m* **12239**
PELDAÑO *m* **12239**
PELÍCULA *f* **11544**
PELÍCULA *f* **5166**
PELICULA *f* **5166**
PELÍCULA *f* **5171**
PELÍCULA *f* **5166**
PELÍCULA *f* CONTRA EL AGUA **13648**
PELÍCULA *f* DE ÓXIDO **5168**
PELÍCULA *f* EN CARRETE **10667**
PELÍCULA *f* GRASA **5167**
PELÍCULA *f* PASIVADORA **9104**
PELÍCULA *f* RÍGIDA **8993**
PELÍCULA *f* RÍGIDA **8993**
PELÍCULA PROTECTORA *f* **9950**
PELIGRO *m* DE INCENDIO **3608**
PELIGRO DE INCENDIO *m* **3608**
PELIGROSO *m* **6503**
PELO *m* **1890**
PELO *m* DE CAMELLO **1890**
PELO *m* DE COLA DE CABALLO **12594**
PELOS *m pl* DE LAS CRINES **7965**
PENDIENTE *f* **3792**
PENDIENTE *f* **3792**
PENDIENTE **6321**
PENDIENTE *f* DE UNA CLAVIJA **12654**
PENDIENTE MÁXIMA *f* **12995**
PENDIENTE MÁXIMA *f* **2484**
PÉNDULO *m* **9167**
PÉNDULO *m* CIRCULAR **2422**
PÉNDULO *m* COMPENSADO **2808**
PÉNDULO *m* COMPENSADOR **2808**
PENETRACIÓN *f* **9170**
PENETRACIÓN *f* **11507**
PENETRACIÓN *f* DEL CALOR **6368**
PENETRACIÓN *f* EN FRÍO **2689**
PENETRÓMETRO *m* **9171**
PENETRÓMETRO *m* **10061**
PENTACLORURO *m* DE ANTIMONIO **624**

## PER

PENTACLORURO *m* DE FÓSFORO **9254**
PENTAEDRO *m* **9175**
PENTÁGONO *m* **9172**
PENTANO *m* NORMAL **9176**
PENTASULFURO *m* DE ANTIMONIO **625**
PENUMBRA *f* **9177**
PEÓN *m* **13398**
PEÓN *m* DE CENTRADO **2153**
PERA *m* DE VELOCIDAD **11871**
PERCARBONATO *m* DE POTASA **9693**
PERCLORATO *m* DE POTASA **9694**
PERCUSIÓN *f* **11359**
PÉRDIDA *f* **7488**
PÉRDIDA *f* **7754**
PÉRDIDA *f* **13594**
PÉRDIDA *f* ADICIONAL **170**
PÉRDIDA *f* AL ROJO **7341**
PÉRDIDA *f* CALORÍFICA **7760**
PÉRDIDA *f* DE CALOR **7760**
PÉRDIDA *f* DE CALOR **7760**
PÉRDIDA *f* DE CALOR **6353**
PÉRDIDA *f* DE CALOR POR DIFUSIÓN **10145**
PÉRDIDA *f* DE CARGA **6315**
PÉRDIDA *f* DE ENERGÍA **7758**
PÉRDIDA *f* DE FROTAMIENTO **7755**
PÉRDIDA *f* DE PESO **7764**
PÉRDIDA *f* DE POTENCIA **7762**
PÉRDIDA *f* DE PRESIÓN **7763**
PÉRDIDA *f* DE TRABAJO **7765**
PÉRDIDA *f* DEBIDA AL FROTAMIENTO **5685**
PÉRDIDA *f* EN EL FUEGO **7761**
PÉRDIDA *f* EN EL FUEGO **7341**
PÉRDIDA *f* EN VACÍO **8599**
PÉRDIDA *f* POR CHOQUES **7757**
PÉRDIDA *f* POR EVAPORACIÓN **4866**
PÉRDIDA *f* POR FUGAS **7756**
PÉRDIDA *f* POR PAUSAS **1594**
PÉRDIDA *f* POR REBOSAMIENTO **5163**
PÉRDIDA *f* POR REFLEXIÓN **10389**
PÉRDIDA *f* TÉRMICA **6353**
PÉRDIDA DE VELOCIDAD *f* **3677**
PÉRDIDA POR FUGAS (DE UN LÍQUIDO) *f* **7492**
PÉRDIDAS *f pl* DE FUSIÓN **8140**
PÉRDIDAS *f pl* DE MAGNETIZACIÓN **7907**
PÉRDIDAS *f pl* DE SALPICADURAS **11843**
PÉRDIDAS *f pl* EN EL FUEGO **6763**
PÉRDIDAS *f pl* TERMÓGENAS **6381**
PERFECCIONAMIENTO *m* **11682**
PERFECCIONAMIENTO *m* EN EL REMATADO **5220**
PERFIL *m* **3396**

PERFIL *m* **9898**
PERFIL *m* **7717**
PERFIL *m* **12734**
PERFIL *m* **9898**
PERFIL *m* **11119**
PERFIL *m* **8906**
PERFIL *m* (A LA DERECHAA LA IZQUIERDA) **11420**
PERFIL *m* A LO LARGO **7738**
PERFIL *m* DE DIENTE **4997**
PERFIL *m* DE LAMINACIÓN **10675**
PERFIL *m* DE MEDIACAÑA **6209**
PERFIL *m* DE UN DIENTE **13019**
PERFIL *m* DE UN ENGRANAJE **13020**
PERFIL *f* EN FRÍO **2682**
PERFIL *m* EN T **12700**
PERFIL *m* NORMAL **12083**
PERFIL *m* TRANSVERSAL **3377**
PERFILADURA *f* **10668**
PERFILAR **5571**
PERFIL(ES) *m* **11114**
PERFILES *m pl* COMERCIALES **8149**
PERFILES *m pl* PESADOS **6413**
PERFORACIÓN *f* **1589**
PERFORACIÓN *f* **1468**
PERFORACIÓN *f* **12675**
PERFORACIÓN *f* DE ENSAYO **12778**
PERFORACIÓN *f* POR DESCARGA DISRUPTIVA **10013**
PERFORACIÓN *f* PROFUNDA **3780**
PERFORADO (A) **4275**
PERFORADOR *m* **4276**
PERFORADOR *m* DE CORREAS **1153**
PERFORADOR *m* EN CONDUCTO DE ACEITE **8762**
PERFORADOR MECÁNICO **4276**
PERFORADORA **4279**
PERFORADORA *f* **4279**
PERFORADORA *f* **10001**
PERFORADORA *f* A GRAN VELOCIDAD **6495**
PERFORADORA *f* CON BRAZO ARTICULADO **12550**
PERFORADORA *f* CON CABEZAS MÚLTIPLES **5799**
PERFORADORA *f* DE COLUMNA **2755**
PERFORADORA *f* DE COLUMNA **9312**
PERFORADORA *f* ELÉCTRICA **9732**
PERFORADORA *f* HORIZONTAL **6581**
PERFORADORA *f* MULTIHUSILLO EN LÍNEA **8460**
PERFORAR **9186**
PERFORAR **10771**
PERFORAR **4264**
PERFORAR **4264**
PERFORAR PREVIAMENTE **10771**
PERGAMINO *m* **9077**

**PER** 1094

PERGAMINO  *m*  ARTIFICIAL **9078**
PERGAMINO  *m*  VEGETAL **9078**
PERIDOTO  *m*  **9243**
PERIDOTO  *m*  MIN **8796**
PERIFERIA  *f*  DEL CÍRCULO **2404**
PERÍMETRO  *m*  **9190**
PERIODICIDAD  *f*  **9196**
PERIÓDICO **9191**
PERÍODO  *m*  INICIAL O DE PUESTA EN MARCHA DE UNA FÁBRICA **12123**
PERIPLO  *m*  **10810**
PERITO  *m*  **4930**
PERJUICIO  *m*  A CAUSA DEL HUMO **11676**
PERLA  *f*  **9146**
PERLA  *f*  DE SOLDADURA **11842**
PERLITA  *f*  **9144**
PERMALLOY  *m*  **9201**
PERMANGANATO  *m*  DE POTASA **9695**
PERMEABILIDAD  *f*  **9211**
PERMEABILIDAD  *f*  MAGNÉTICA **7911**
PERMEABLE **7491**
PERMEABLE **9213**
PERMEABLE AL AIRE **9212**
PERMEÁMETRO  *m*  **9214**
PERMISO  *m*  DE CONDUCIR **4302**
PERMUTACIÓN  *f*  **9216**
PERMUTACIÓN  *f*  CÍCLICA **3556**
PERNO  *m*  **1432**
PERNO  *m*  CAPUCHINO **2149**
PERNO  *m*  CHATO **5062**
PERNO  *m*  CÓNICO **2009**
PERNO  *m*  DE ANCLAJE **10172**
PERNO  *m*  DE ANCLAJE ESPINOSO **7209**
PERNO  *m*  DE BLOQUEO **2281**
PERNO  *m*  DE CARRETERÍA **2553**
PERNO  *m*  DE CARROCERÍA **2553**
PERNO  *m*  DE CHARNELA **6509**
PERNO  *m*  DE CHARNELA **6509**
PERNO  *m*  DE ENGRASE (O DE LUBRIFICACIÓN) **7811**
PERNO  *m*  DE PATILLA **5062**
PERNO  *m*  DE UNIÓN **2959**
PERNO  *m*  DE UNIÓN **4261**
PERNO  *m*  DE VARILLA ROSCADA EN LOS DOS EXTREMOS **12398**
PERNO  *m*  EMBUTIDO **7840**
PERNO  *m*  EMBUTIDO **7840**
PERNO  *m*  EN BRUTO **1286**
PERNO  *m*  NO ROSCADO **1302**
PERNO  *m*  PARA CORREAS **1156**
PERNO  *m*  PASADOR **7840**
PERNO  *m*  PASADOR **7840**

PERNO  *m*  ROSCADO **11021**
PERNO  *m*  ROSCADO **1607**
PERNO  *m*  SIN MECANIZAR **1286**
PERÓXIDO  *m*  **7148**
PERÓXIDO  *m*  DE MANGANESO **10047**
PERÓXIDO  *m*  DE NITRÓGENO **8591**
PERÓXIDO  *m*  DE PLOMO **7461**
PERÓXIDO  *m*  HIDRATADO DE HIERRO **5101**
PERÓXIDO DE NITRÓGENO  *m*  **8591**
PERPENDICULAR **9217**
PERPENDICULARIDAD  *f*  **9219**
PERPENDICULARIDAD  *f*  **9219**
PERPENDÍCULO  *m*  **9539**
PERPIAÑO  *m*  DE ESCORIA **11563**
PERPIAÑOS  *m*  **1697**
PERPIAÑOS  *m pl*  **1697**
PERRO  *m*  **2094**
PERSONAL  *m*  LABORAL **13962**
PERSONAL  *m*  OBRERO **13962**
PERSPECTIVA  *f*  **1264**
PERSPECTIVA  *f*  **9220**
PERSPECTIVA  *f*  AXONOMÉTRICA **885**
PERSPECTIVA  *f*  LINEAL **7614**
PERSPECTIVO  *m*  **9220**
PERSULFATO  *m*  DE AMONÍACO **468**
PERTURBACIÓN  *f*  **1581**
PERTURBACIÓN  *f*  DEL SERVICIO **1581**
PESA-ÁCIDOS  *m*  **89**
PESADA  *f*  **13746**
PESADA  *f*  **13746**
PESAJE  *m*  **13746**
PESALICORES  *m*  **6722**
PESAR **13744**
PESAR MÁS QUE... **8928**
PESCANTE  *m*  **3618**
PESILLO  *m*  PARA ANÁLISIS **2294**
PESO  *m*  **13747**
PESO  *m*  ATÓMICO **807**
PESO  *m*  BRUTO **6141**
PESO  *m*  BRUTO **10781**
PESO  *m*  CONSUMIDO **2992**
PESO  *m*  DE CARGA **8356**
PESO  *m*  DEL MARTINETE **4329**
PESO  *m*  EN ORDEN DE MARCHA **3480**
PESO  *m*  ESPECÍFICO **11850**
PESO  *m*  MÁXIMO **8070**
PESO  *m*  MÍNIMO **8310**
PESO  *m*  MOLECULAR **8363**
PESO  *m*  MUERTO **3637**
PESO  *m*  POR METRO **13748**

PESO *m* (PORCENTAJE DEL) **9180**
PESO *m* PROPIO **3637**
PESTAÑA *f* DE CINTRADO **1183**
PESTAÑA *f* DE CINTRADO **1529**
PESTILLO *m* **1432**
PESTILLO *m* **7414**
PETROLEÍNA *f* **13508**
PETROLEÍNA *f* **13508**
PETROLEÍNA *f* **13508**
PETRÓLEO *m* **9226**
PETRÓLEO **9229**
PETRÓLEO *m* **9222**
PETRÓLEO *m* **9229**
PETRÓLEO *m* BRUTO **3411**
PETRÓLEO *m* BRUTO **3412**
PETRÓLEO *m* BRUTO SULFUROSO **11822**
PETRÓLEO *m* CRUDO **13040**
PETRÓLEO *m* GASOLINA *f* **9222**
PETRÓLEO *m* PARA LÁMPARAS **7275**
PEZ *f* **9400**
PEZ *f* SECA **2737**
PH **9231**
PICADA *f* **6333**
PICADO *m* AL MARTILLO (CALDERAS) **2347**
PICADO *m* PROVOCANDO POROSIDAD **9629**
PICADURA *f* **9393**
PICADURA *f* **9333**
PICADURA *f* **10171**
PICADURA *f* CRUZADA (DOBLE) DE UNA LIMA **4134**
PICADURA *f* DEL LAMINADO **9417**
PICADURA *f* POR CORROSIÓN **3190**
PICADURAS *f pl* **9334**
PICADURAS *f pl* **9416**
PICADURAS *f pl* A CAUSA DE LA CORROSIÓN **4843**
PICAPORTE *m* **7414**
PICNÓMETRO *m* **11851**
PICO *m* **8667**
PICO *m* **1091**
PICO *m* DE COLADA **7632**
PICO DE YUNQUE *m* **1090**
PIE *m* **1041**
PIE *m* **13537**
PIE *m* CUADRADO (MEDIDA INGLESA) **12020**
PIE *m* CÚBICO (MEDIDA INGLESA) **3453**
PIE *m* CÚBICO NORMALIZADO **12072**
PIE *m* DE BIELA **3389**
PIE *m* DE DIENTE **10724**
PIE *m* DE LA BIELA CON HORQUILLA **5568**
PIE *m* DE PROFUNDIDAD **3781**
PIE *m* DE REY **11597**

PIE *m* DE REY CON ESFERA **3986**
PIE *m* DE REY CON VERNIER PARA LOS DIENTES DE PIÑON **5900**
PIE *m* DE UN DIBUJO O PLANO **7513**
PIE *m* DEL DIENTE **10725**
PIE *m* DENTADO **5899**
PIE *m* (MEDIDA INGLESA) **5518**
PIE-LIBRA (MEDIDA INGLESA DE PESO) *m* **5522**
PIED DE REY *m* **13537**
PIEDRA *f* **9152**
PIEDRA *f* AFILADORA **13824**
PIEDRA *f* AMOLADORA **13824**
PIEDRA *f* ARTIFICIAL **737**
PIEDRA *f* CONCHÍFERA **8299**
PIEDRA *f* DE AFILAR **13824**
PIEDRA *f* DE AFILAR **13824**
PIEDRA *f* DE AFILAR CON ACEITE **8781**
PIEDRA *f* DE AMOLAR **13824**
PIEDRA *f* DE AMOLAR **19**
PIEDRA *f* DE FUSIL **5427**
PIEDRA *f* DE JABÓN **10935**
PIEDRA *f* DE MECHERO **5427**
PIEDRA *f* DE SILLERÍA **5004**
PIEDRA *f* DE TALLA **761**
PIEDRA *f* DE VIDRIO **5957**
PIEDRA *f* DE YESO **6190**
PIEDRA *f* IMÁN **8506**
PIEDRA *f* MOLEÑA **8299**
PIEDRA *f* NATURAL **8507**
PIEDRA *f* PÓMEZ **9988**
PIEDRA *f* PÓMEZ **9986**
PIEDRA *f* PROPIA PARA LA CONSTRUCCIÓN **1700**
PIEDRAS *f pl* QUEBRANTADAS **1644**
PIEL *f* DE BÚFALO **1685**
PIEL *f* DE CERDO **9300**
PIEL *f* DE COCODRILO **348**
PIERDE (QUE) **7493**
PIEZA *f* **9083**
PIEZA *f* ACABADA **5730**
PIEZA *f* BRUTA **11651**
PIEZA *f* DE AJUSTE **9006**
PIEZA *f* DE APOYO **10876**
PIEZA *f* DE COMPENSACIÓN **4922**
PIEZA *f* DE ENCLAVIJAMIENTO **11220**
PIEZA *f* DE FORJA **5556**
PIEZA *f* DE FORJA PESADA **6406**
PIEZA *f* DE FUNDICIÓN **2079**
PIEZA *f* DE FUNDICIÓN MOLDEADA **2079**
PIEZA *f* DE MÁQUINA **7852**
PIEZA *f* DE MOLDEO EN HUECO **6539**

**PIE** 1096

PIEZA *f* DE PRUEBA **12788**
PIEZA *f* DE RECAMBIO **11834**
PIEZA *f* DE REFERENCIA **8034**
PIEZA *f* DE REPUESTO **11834**
PIEZA *f* DE SEPARACIÓN **4068**
PIEZA *f* EN BLANCO **1301**
PIEZA *f* EN BRUTO **1301**
PIEZA *f* FORJADA **5556**
PIEZA *f* FORJADA A MANO **11669**
PIEZA *f* FORJADA A MARTILLO **11670**
PIEZA *f* FORJADA CON EXCESIVAS REBABAS **8322**
PIEZA *f* INCORPORADA **6970**
PIEZA *f* INSERTA **6965**
PIEZA *f* INTERCAMBIABLE **11834**
PIEZA *f* MATRIZADA **4324**
PIEZA *f* MECÁNICA **7852**
PIEZA *f* MECANIZADA **11265**
PIEZA *f* MECANIZADA **9293**
PIEZA *f* MOLDEADA **2069**
PIEZA *f* NO LOGRADA **8321**
PIEZA *f* QUE MECANIZAR **9293**
PIEZA *f* QUE TRABAJAR **9293**
PIEZA *f* SUELTA **11484**
PIEZA *f* SUELTA **3811**
PIEZA *f* TRABAJADA EN LA FORJA **5556**
PIEZAS *f pl* AUXILIARES **5283**
PIEZAS *f pl* COLADAS (O DE MOLDE) **2080**
PIEZAS *f pl* DEFECTUOSAS **3696**
PIEZAS *f pl* MOLDEADAS EN FUNDICIÓN GRIS **2083**
PIEZAS *f pl* MOLDEADAS (O COLADAS) QUE RESISTEN A LA CORROSIÓN **2082**
PIEZAS *f pl* MOLDEADAS RESISTIENDO A ELEVADAS TEMPERATURAS **2084**
PIEZAS *f pl* SUELTAS (EN) **7329**
PIEZOELECTRICIDAD *f* **9297**
PIEZÓMETRO *m* **12067**
PILA *f* **9304**
PILA *f* A DOS LÍQUIDOS **2887**
PILA *f* DE VOLTA **13596**
PILA *f* ELÉCTRICA **2126**
PILA *f* FOTOELÉCTRICA **9259**
PILA *f* GALVÁNICA **5782**
PILA *f* GALVÁNICA **5782**
PILA *f* HIDROELÉCTRICA **5782**
PILA *f* LOCAL **7694**
PILA *f* PRIMARIA **9846**
PILA *f* SECA **4343**
PILA *f* SECUNDARIA **4534**
PILA *f* TÉRMICA **12820**
PILA *f* TERMOELÉCTRICA **12836**
PILA *f* TERMOELÉCTRICA **12820**

PILA *f* VOLTAICA **13596**
PILAR *m* **12062**
PILAR *m* **9311**
PILASTRA *f* **9311**
PILÓN *m* PÉNDULO DE CHARPY **6787**
PILÓN *m* PÉNDULO DE CHARPY **2271**
PIMELEÍNA *f* **13508**
PINACOIDE *m* **9327**
PINAZA *f* **991**
PINAZA *f* **991**
PINCEL *m* **2743**
PINCEL *m* **9019**
PINO *m* NEGRO DE AUSTRIA **1293**
PIÑÓN *m* **5889**
PIÑÓN *m* **9335**
PIÑÓN *m* **9444**
PIÑÓN *m* CÓNICO **1226**
PIÑÓN *m* DE CADENA **9402**
PIÑÓN *m* DE CIGÜEÑAL **3315**
PIÑÓN *m* DE CUERO VERDE **10238**
PIÑÓN *m* DE DISTRIBUCIÓN **12949**
PIÑÓN *m* DE ENGRANAJES CÓNICOS **9324**
PINTA *f* (MEDIDA INGLESA = 47 CL.) **9337**
PINTAR **9014**
PINTAR *f* CON BROCHA **9014**
PINTURA *f* **9013**
PINTURA *f* **9015**
PINTURA *f* **9018**
PINTURA *f* **2583**
PINTURA *f* A LA AGUADA **13664**
PINTURA *f* AL ACEITE **8766**
PINTURA *f* AL AGUA **13664**
PINTURA *f* AL BARNIZ **4711**
PINTURA *f* AL ÓLEO **8766**
PINTURA *f* CON BROCHA **9018**
PINTURA *f* CON PISTOLA **6179**
PINTURA *f* CON PISTOLA PULVERIZADORA **9020**
PINTURA *f* POR PULVERIZACIÓN CON PISTOLA NEUMÁTICA **11965**
PINTURA *f* SUBYACENTE **9864**
PINTURAS *f pl* **2599**
PINZA *f* CORTANTE **3532**
PINZA *f* CORTANTE DIAGONAL **3832**
PINZA *f* DE CHORRO DE AGUA **4286**
PINZA *f* DE MANGA **4286**
PINZA *f* DE SOLDADOR **11767**
PINZA *f* PLANA **5403**
PINZA *f* REDONDA **10805**
PINZAS *f pl* PARA GAS **5835**
PINZAS *f pl* PUNZONADORAS **10000**

1097        **PLA**

PIPETA   *f* **9368**
PIPETA   *f* DE CILINDRO **1718**
PIPETA   *f* RECTA GRADUADA **6028**
PIRÁMIDE   *f* **10038**
PIRÁMIDE   *f* CUADRANGULAR **12026**
PIRÁMIDE   *f* PENTAGONAL **9174**
PIRÁMIDE   *f* TRIANGULAR **13193**
PIRIDINA   *f* **10041**
PIRITA   *f* AMARILLA **7146**
PIRITA   *f* CUPROSA **3126**
PIRITA   *f* MAGNÉTICA **7914**
PIRITA   *f* MARCIAL **7146**
PIROELECTRICIDAD   *f* **10043**
PIROELÉCTRICO   *m* **10042**
PIROFOSFATO   *m* DE SOSA **11730**
PIROGALOL   *m* **10045**
PIROMETALURGIA   *f* **10048**
PIROMETRÍA   *f* **10052**
PIROMETRÍA   *f* ÓPTICA **8846**
PIRÓMETRO   *m* **10049**
PIRÓMETRO   *m* A DISTANCIA **12714**
PIRÓMETRO   *m* DE GRAFITO **6065**
PIRÓMETRO   *m* DE RESISTENCIA **10495**
PIRÓMETRO   *m* ELÉCTRICO **10495**
PIRÓMETRO   *m* ÓPTICO **8845**
PIRÓMETRO   *m* TERMOELÉCTRICO **12825**
PIROTINA   *f* **7914**
PIROXILINA   *f* **6176**
PIRÓXILO **6176**
PISÓN   *m* **12611**
PISÓN   *m* **12611**
PISÓN   *m* DE BOCARTE **12055**
PISÓN   *m* DE MANO **6246**
PISÓN   *m* DE MORTERO **9221**
PISÓN   *m* MECÁNICO **1732**
PISÓN   *m* NEUMÁTICO **286**
PISTA   *f* **13085**
PISTA   *f* DE PRUEBAS **12794**
PISTOLA   *f* **5660**
PISTOLA   *f* DE AIRE COMPRIMIDO **272**
PISTOLA   *f* DE AIRE COMPRIMIDO **276**
PISTOLA   *f* DE PROYECCIÓN **11962**
PISTOLA   *f* DE PULVERIZACIÓN **11962**
PISTOLA   *f* PARA INCRUSTAR CLAVIJAS **12400**
PISTOLA   *f* PARA SOLDAR POR PUNTOS **6180**
PISTOLAS   *f pl* DE AIRE COMPRIMIDO **9796**
PISTÓN   *m* **9370**
PISTÓN   *m* BUZO **9545**
PISTÓN   *m* BUZO **9545**
PISTÓN   *m* CON VÁSTAGO ÚNICO **9392**

PISTÓN   *m* CÓNICO **2944**
PISTÓN   *m* DE AGUA **13667**
PISTÓN   *m* DE AIRE **282**
PISTÓN   *m* DE BOMBA **9995**
PISTÓN   *m* DE CALDEO **6384**
PISTÓN   *m* DE CIERRE DE MOLDE **2535**
PISTÓN   *m* DE DOBLE EFECTO **4164**
PISTÓN   *m* DE DOBLE VÁSTAGO **9391**
PISTÓN   *m* DE DOBLE VÁSTAGO **9391**
PISTÓN   *m* DE DOS PIEZAS **1709**
PISTÓN   *m* DE LEVANTAMIENTO **7555**
PISTÓN   *m* DE MOTOR HIDRÁULICO **13667**
PISTÓN   *m* DE SIMPLE EFECTO **11494**
PISTÓN   *m* DE TORNILLO ELEVADOR **10188**
PISTÓN   *m* DE VÁLVULA **1673**
PISTÓN   *m* DE VAPOR **12179**
PISTÓN   *m* DISTRIBUIDOR **9390**
PISTÓN   *m* ELEVADOR **1673**
PISTÓN   *m* ENFRIADO **3084**
PISTÓN   *m* OSCILANTE **8882**
PISTÓN   *m* PLENO **11791**
PISTÓN   *m* RAMSBOTTOM **10196**
PISTÓN   *m* ROTATIVO **10756**
PISTÓN   *m* SIN VÁSTAGO **13241**
PISTÓN   *m* SUECO (RAMSBOTTOM) **10196**
PISTÓN   *m* SUMERGIDO **9545**
PISTÓN   *m* VACIADO **1514**
PIVOTANTE **9422**
PIVOTE   *m* **9421**
PIVOTE   *m* **9420**
PIVOTE   *m* **9419**
PIVOTE   *m* **9315**
PIVOTE   *m* **9315**
PIVOTE   *m* ANULAR **10606**
PIVOTE   *m* (DE ÁRBOL VERTICAL) **9421**
PIVOTE   *m* DE GIRO **13242**
PIVOTE   *m* DE UN ENGRANAJE DE LINTERNA **9323**
PIVOTE   *m* ESFÉRICO **11893**
PIZARRA   *f* **11571**
PIZARRA   *f* BITUMINOSA **8780**
PLACA   *f* **9477**
PLACA   *f* **11551**
PLACA   *f* **13167**
PLACA   *f* **9032**
PLACA   *f* BASE (O DE FONDO) **1026**
PLACA   *f* CIRCULAR **4999**
PLACA   *f* DE ACUMULADOR **81**
PLACA   *f* DE ACUMULADOR **81**
PLACA   *f* DE APOYO **1127**
PLACA   *f* DE ASIENTO **1127**

**PLA** 1098

PLACA *f* DE ASIENTO 1037
PLACA *f* DE ASIENTO DE VIGA 5947
PLACA *f* DE BASE 1037
PLACA *f* DE BASE 1040
PLACA *f* DE COBRE 3123
PLACA *f* DE CONTACTO 3003
PLACA *f* DE DAMA 3596
PLACA *f* DE FIELTRO 11322
PLACA *f* DE FIJACIÓN 13621
PLACA *f* DE FONDO 1037
PLACA *f* DE FONDO 1486
PLACA *f* DE FUNDACIÓN 1037
PLACA *f* DE GUARDA 6593
PLACA *f* DE GUARDA 6160
PLACA *f* DE MUELLE 11991
PLACA *f* DE RECTIFICADOR 10315
PLACA *f* DE RECUBRIMIENTO 3267
PLACA *f* DE REFUERZO 12257
PLACA *f* DE TURBA 9150
PLACA *f* DE VIDRIO 5963
PLACA *f* FOTOGRÁFICA 11187
PLACA *f* FRONTAL 4999
PLACA *f* GIRATORIA 13295
PLACA *f* METALÚRGICA 11315
PLACA *f* MODELO 1710
PLACA *f* MODELO 2052
PLACA *f* MODELO DOBLE CARA 8044
PLACA *f* NEGATIVA 8530
PLACA *f* POSITIVA 9658
PLACA *f* SENSIBLE 11187
PLACA *f* SOPORTE DE COJINETE 11772
PLACA *f* TUBULAR 13254
PLACA DEFLECTORA *f* 922
PLACAS *f pl* COLECTIVAS 2726
PLACAS *f pl* GEMELAS DE MUELLE 11991
PLAN *m* DE DISPOSICIÓN 5914
PLAN *m* DE EJECUCIÓN 4984
PLAN *m* DE EJECUCIÓN (TALLER) 11361
PLAN *m* DE LABRADO POR ESTRATIFICACIÓN 2488
PLANCHA *f* 9032
PLANCHA *f* 11551
PLANCHA *f* 9477
PLANCHA *f* DE BLINDAJE 712
PLANCHA *f* DE ESTAÑO 12955
PLANCHA *f* DEL MARTILLO 4993
PLANCHA *f* DELGADA 1379
PLANCHA *f* FUERTE 9457
PLANCHA *f* (O PLACA *f*) DE METAL 5508
PLANCHA METALÚRGICA 11315
PLANCHAS *f pl* DE EMPATE 5270

PLANEAR 5405
PLANEO *m* 9454
PLANEO *m* 9118
PLANETARIO *m* 9445
PLANIMETRADO *m* 8087
PLANIMETRAR 8084
PLANIMETRÍA *f* 9449
PLANÍMETRO *m* 9448
PLANO *m* 9430
PLANO *m* 9430
PLANO *m* 9426
PLANO *m* 9433
PLANO *m* 11124
PLANO 13035
PLANO *m* 4229
PLANO *m* 4229
PLANO *m* 3794
PLANO *m* DE CARGA 7683
PLANO *m* DE CONJUNTO 8905
PLANO *m* DE CONJUNTO 8905
PLANO *m* DE CORTE 11284
PLANO *m* DE CRISTAL 3427
PLANO *m* DE DESLIZAMIENTO 5975
PLANO *m* DE ENLACE (MACLA) 2826
PLANO *m* DE INTERSECCIÓN 7095
PLANO *m* DE JUNTA 9093
PLANO *m* DE LA CHAPISTERÍA 9504
PLANO *m* DE MANTENIMIENTO 13029
PLANO *m* DE MONTAJE 772
PLANO *m* DE MONTAJE 4814
PLANO *m* DE PROYECCIÓN 9438
PLANO *m* DE REFRACCIÓN 9439
PLANO *m* DE RUPTURA 3373
PLANO *m* DE SIMETRÍA 9440
PLANO *m* DEFINITIVO 5185
PLANO *m* DETALLADO 3812
PLANO *m* FOCAL 5501
PLANO *m* INCLINADO 6081
PLANO *m* INCLINADO 6838
PLANO *m* ÓPTICO 8843
PLANO *m* OSCULADOR 8887
PLANO *m* PARA ENDEREZAR 12321
PLANO *m* PARA ENDEREZAR 12516
PLANO *m* PARA TRITURAR 6114
PLANO *m* PRISMÁTICO 9877
PLANO *m* RETICULAR 7432
PLANO *m* RETICULAR 804
PLANO *m* SOPORTE 902
PLANO *m* SOSTÉN 13029
PLANOS *m pl* 5375

1099         **PLO**

PLANOS *m pl* DE ACERO ALEADO **373**
PLANTADORAS *f pl* DE PATATAS **9705**
PLANTILLA *f* **12734**
PLAQUETA *f* **11075**
PLAQUITA *f* **9498**
PLASTICIDAD *f* **9474**
PLASTICITA *f* **3705**
PLASTIFICANTE **9475**
PLASTRÓN *m* **1590**
PLASTRÓN *m* DE CIGÜEÑAL **1590**
PLATA *f* **11458**
PLATA *f* A 92/5% **12253**
PLATA *f* ALEMANA **5932**
PLATA *f* ALEMANA **5932**
PLATA *f* ALEMANA **5932**
PLATA *f* ELECTROLÍTICA **4608**
PLATA *f* FINA **5202**
PLATA *f* NUEVA **5932**
PLATAFORMA *f* **5776**
PLATAFORMA *f* **9502**
PLATAFORMA *f* CALIBRADORA **5885**
PLATAFORMA *f* DE DIVIDIR **4109**
PLATAFORMA *f* EN SALEDIZO **13875**
PLATEADO *m* **11469**
PLATEAR **11459**
PLATERÍA *f* **6003**
PLATILLO *m* **13167**
PLATILLO *m* DE ACOPLAMIENTO **3255**
PLATILLO *m* DE BALANZA **10976**
PLATILLO *m* DE FRICCIÓN **5673**
PLATILLO *m* DE IMANES PERMANENTES **9205**
PLATILLO *m* DIVIDIDO **4109**
PLATILLO *m* DIVISOR **4106**
PLATILLO *m* DIVISOR **4109**
PLATILLO *m* GIRATORIO **10762**
PLATILLO *m* MANIVELA **4003**
PLATILLOS *m pl* CIRCULARES **2424**
PLATILLOS *m pl* DIVISORES **6870**
PLATILLOS *m pl* MAGNÉTICOS **7912**
PLATINA *f* **11306**
PLATINA *f* **4174**
PLATINA *f* **6048**
PLATINA *f* DE FIJACIÓN **9499**
PLATINITA *f* (ALEACIÓN) **9508**
PLATINO *m* IRIDIADO **9515**
PLATINO *m* (METAL) **9510**
PLATINOCIANURO DE BARIO *m* **1002**
PLATO *m* **13167**
PLATO *m* DE HORNO **6512**
PLATO *m* DE TORNO **2393**

PLATO *m* DE UN ÁRBOL ACODADO **3304**
PLATO DIVISOR *m* **4109**
PLEGADO *m* **1182**
PLEGADO *m* CHARNELA **6506**
PLEGADO *m* EN CALIENTE **6619**
PLEGADO *m* EN FRÍO **2668**
PLEGAR **1173**
PLENA CARGA *f* **5722**
PLETINA *f* **11306**
PLETINA *f* ATORNILLADA **11063**
PLETINA *f* GIRATORIA **7398**
PLETINAS *f pl* DE ACERO AL CARBONO **1956**
PLETINAS *f pl* DE ALEACIÓN DE ACERO **378**
PLIEGO *m* **5511**
PLIEGO DE BASES *m* **11855**
PLIEGO DE CONDICIONES *m* **11855**
PLIEGUE *m* **10861**
PLIEGUE *m* **10269**
PLIEGUE *m* **3320**
PLIEGUE *m* **4408**
PLIEGUE *m* **4408**
PLIEGUES *m pl* **1680**
PLISAR **3336**
PLOMADA *f* **9539**
PLOMADA *f* **9538**
PLOMADA *f* **9539**
PLOMBAGINA *f* **9542**
PLOMBAGINA *f* **9541**
PLOMERÍA *f* **7484**
PLOMO *m* **7447**
PLOMO *m* **9539**
PLOMO *m* **10886**
PLOMO *m* ANTIMÓNICO **621**
PLOMO *m* ANTIMONIOSO **6276**
PLOMO *m* DE SEGURIDAD **10886**
PLOMO *m* DEL COMERCIO **8014**
PLOMO *m* DULCE **8014**
PLOMO *m* DURO **6276**
PLOMO *m* EN HOJAS **11314**
PLOMO *m* EN PLACAS **7462**
PLOMO *m* ENDURECIDO **6276**
PLOMO *m* ESPONJOSO **11954**
PLOMO *m* FRÁGIL **621**
PLOMO *m* FUSIBLE **5758**
PLOMO *m* FUSIBLE **10886**
PLOMO *m* IMPURO **1029**
PLOMO *m* PARA CUBIERTAS **3409**
PLOMO *m* PURO **2311**
PLOMO *m* SIN REFINAR **1029**
PLOMO *m* SULFURADO **5775**

**PLO** 1100

PLOMO (A) *m* **9217**
PLUMA *f* DE APARATO REGISTRADOR **9161**
PLUMA *f* DE DIBUJO **7999**
PLUMA *f* DE REDONDILLA **10806**
POCO MANEJABLE **13402**
PODER *m* **9730**
PODER *m* ABSORBENTE **42**
PODER *m* ADHERENTE **176**
PODER *m* AISLANTE **7000**
PODER *m* AMISIVO **4701**
PODER *m* CALORÍFICO **6392**
PODER *m* CALORÍFICO **6378**
PODER *m* DE AUMENTO **7937**
PODER *m* DE CUBRIMIENTO **3273**
PODER *m* DE OPACIDAD INSUFICIENTE **6119**
PODER *m* DISOLVENTE **4062**
PODER *m* EMISIVO MONOCROMÁTICO **8382**
PODER *m* LUBRIFICANTE **7806**
PODER *m* LUMINOSO **6776**
PODER *m* RADIANTE **4702**
PODER *m* REFLECTANTE **10393**
PODER *m* REFLECTANTE **10392**
PODER *m* REFRINGENTE **10403**
PODREDUMBRE *f* **10035**
PODREDUMBRE *f* DE LA MADERA **10770**
PODRIR **10036**
PODRIRSE **10036**
POLAR **9577**
POLARIDAD *f* **9587**
POLARISCOPIO *m* **9584**
POLARIZACIÓN *f* **9589**
POLARIZACIÓN *f* **9582**
POLARIZACIÓN *f* ANÓDICA **604**
POLARIZACIÓN *f* CATÓDICA **2108**
POLARIZACIÓN *f* (DE UN ELECTRODO) POR CAÍDA DE CONCENTRACIÓN **2889**
POLARIZACIÓN *f* ELECTROLÍTICA **4604**
POLARIZADOR *m* **9586**
POLAROGRAFÍA *f* **9590**
POLEA *f* **11301**
POLEA *f* ACANALADA **11945**
POLEA *f* (APARATO ELEVADOR) **9971**
POLEA *f* CON LLANTA PLANA (O CILÍNDRICA) **5404**
POLEA *f* CON PESTAÑAS **5336**
POLEA *f* CONDUCIDA **4298**
POLEA *f* CONDUCIDA **4298**
POLEA *f* CONDUCIDA **4298**
POLEA *f* CONDUCIDA **4298**
POLEA *f* CONDUCTORA **4313**
POLEA *f* CONDUCTORA **4313**

POLEA *f* CÓNICA **12669**
POLEA *f* CONVEXA **3400**
POLEA *f* DE ATAQUE **4313**
POLEA *f* DE BRAZOS CURVOS **9976**
POLEA *f* DE BRAZOS DOBLES **4127**
POLEA *f* DE BRAZOS PARABÓLICOS **9976**
POLEA *f* DE BRAZOS RECTOS **9977**
POLEA *f* DE CABLE **10742**
POLEA *f* DE CADENA **2217**
POLEA *f* DE CADENA **2217**
POLEA *f* DE CADENA **2217**
POLEA *f* DE CARTÓN **9034**
POLEA *f* DE CHAPA EMBUTIDA **9805**
POLEA *f* DE CORREA **1152**
POLEA *f* DE CUERDA **975**
POLEA *f* DE DISCOS LATERALES **5336**
POLEA *f* DE EXCÉNTRICA **4434**
POLEA *f* DE FRENO **1548**
POLEA *f* DE GARGANTA **6140**
POLEA *f* DE GARGANTA **6135**
POLEA *f* DE GARRAS **2503**
POLEA *f* DE GUÍA **6161**
POLEA *f* DE LLANTA PERFORADA **9188**
POLEA *f* DE MANDO **4313**
POLEA *f* DE TENSIÓN **12334**
POLEA *f* DE TORNILLO SIN FIN **13973**
POLEA *f* DE TORNILLO TANGENTE **13973**
POLEA *f* DE TRANSMISIÓN **10551**
POLEA *f* DE TRANSMISIÓN **6161**
POLEA *f* DE UN APAREJO **11301**
POLEA *f* DE UNA PIEZA **11792**
POLEA *f* DE VENTILADOR **5032**
POLEA *f* DEFECTUOSA **9974**
POLEA *f* DERECHA **5404**
POLEA *f* EN DOS PIEZAS **11945**
POLEA *f* ESCALONADA **11871**
POLEA *f* EXTENSIBLE **4909**
POLEA *f* EXTENSIBLE **4909**
POLEA *f* FIJA **5040**
POLEA *f* FIJA (DE UN APAREJO) **5287**
POLEA *f* LOCA **6754**
POLEA *f* LOCA **7747**
POLEA *f* MOTRIZ **4313**
POLEA *f* MÓVIL (DE UN APAREJO) **8435**
POLEA *f* MÚLTIPLE **6516**
POLEA *f* PARA CABLE DE TRANSMISIÓN **10742**
POLEA *f* PARA CADENAS **11662**
POLEA *f* RECEPTORA **4298**
POLEA *f* TAMBOR **4333**
POLEA *f* VOLANTE **1147**

POLEAS *f* DE APAREJO **9973**
POLÍCROMO **9607**
POLIEDRO *m* **9612**
POLÍGONO *m* **9609**
POLÍGONO *m* ARTICULADO **5737**
POLÍGONO *m* CIRCUNSCRITO **2436**
POLÍGONO *m* DE FUERZAS **9610**
POLÍGONO *m* ESTRELLADO **12107**
POLÍGONO *m* FUNICULAR **5737**
POLÍGONO *m* INSCRITO **6964**
POLÍGONO *m* IRREGULAR **7164**
POLÍGONO *m* REGULAR **10416**
POLIMERÍA *f* **9616**
POLIMERIZACIÓN *f* **9614**
POLIMERIZARSE **9615**
POLÍMERO *m* **9613**
POLIMORFISMO *m* **9617**
POLIPASTO *m* **9973**
POLIPASTO *m* DIFERENCIAL **13798**
POLIPASTO *m* RECTO DE ENGRANAJE **12011**
POLIPASTO *m* WESTON **13798**
POLISULFURO *m* DE POTASIO **9697**
POLO *m* **9592**
POLO *m* **12763**
POLO *m* DE UN IMÁN **9595**
POLO *m* (ELÉCTR.) **9591**
POLO *m* MAGNÉTICO **7913**
POLO *m* NEGATIVO **8531**
POLO *m* NORTE DE UN IMÁN **8665**
POLO *m* POSITIVO **9659**
POLO *m* SUR DE UN IMÁN **11827**
POLONIO *m* **9606**
POLOS *m pl* DE NOMBRE CONTRARIO **13392**
POLOS *m pl* DIFERENTES **13392**
POLOS *m pl* SEMEJANTES **7581**
POLVO *m* **4389**
POLVO *m* ABRASIVO **6110**
POLVO *m* ALEADO **367**
POLVO *m* CARBURANTE **2139**
POLVO *m* DE BRONCE **1652**
POLVO *m* DE BRONCE **1652**
POLVO *m* DE CARBÓN **5469**
POLVO *m* DE CARBÓN **9984**
POLVO *m* DE CARBONILO **1979**
POLVO *m* DE CINC OXIDADO **1374**
POLVO *m* DE COQUE **2659**
POLVO *m* DE CORCHO **6144**
POLVO *m* DE DIAMANTE **3863**
POLVO *m* DE DIAMANTE **3863**
POLVO *m* DE ESMERIL **4697**

POLVO *m* DE ESMERIL **5453**
POLVO *m* DE ESTAÑO **12098**
POLVO *m* DE HIERRO **7145**
POLVO *m* DE HUESOS **1448**
POLVO *m* DE HULLA **2563**
POLVO *m* DE MADERA **13916**
POLVO *m* DE ORO **5998**
POLVO *m* DE PÓMEZ **9727**
POLVO *m* DE TURBA **9726**
POLVO *m* DENTIFRICO **3749**
POLVO *m* GLOBULAR **5979**
POLVO *m* GRUESO **2580**
POLVO *m* IMPALPABLE **6789**
POLVO *m* MOLIDO GROSERAMENTE **2580**
POLVO *m* NEGRO **6181**
POLVOS *m pl* **2024**
POLVOS *m pl* DE GAS DE ALTO HORNO **5469**
PÓMEZ *f* **9988**
PONDERABLE **9619**
PONER A DIGERIR **3937**
PONER BRIDA **5324**
PONER DE NUEVO EN MARCHA **10508**
PONER EN CERO **14030**
PONER EN CERO **14032**
PONER EN CIRCUITO **12555**
PONER EN EXPLOTACIÓN UN INVENTO **13938**
PONER EN MARCHA **12114**
PONER EN MARCHA UNA MÁQUINA **12114**
PONER EN MOVIMIENTO **4289**
PONER EN TIERRA **4410**
PONER ENHIESTO **4805**
PONER FUERA DE CIRCUITO **12554**
PONER UNA MÁQUINA FUERA DE SERVICIO **11406**
PONTÓN *m* **1603**
POR DESCANSOS **1594**
POR PAROS **1594**
POR PISTOLA NEUMÁTICA **5361**
POR TORNILLO ELEVADOR **7206**
PORCELANA *f* **9625**
PORCENTAJE *m* DE CARBÓN **1965**
PORCENTAJE *m* DE CENIZAS **758**
PÓRFIRO *m* **9632**
PÓRFIRO *m* CUARCÍFERO **10081**
PORO *f* **9627**
PORÓGENO **9628**
POROSIDAD **9629**
POROSIDAD *f* DE COMUNICACIÓN INTERNA **7029**
POROSIDADES *f* SUPERFICIALES **9178**
POROSO *m* **9630**
PORTACHAPALETA *m* **4008**

# POR

1102

PORTACHICLER *m* **7219**
PORTACORREA *m* **1159**
PORTAELECTRODO *m* **4575**
PORTAESTAMPA *m* **3884**
PORTAESTAMPAS *m* **8033**
PORTAFUSIBLES *m* **5752**
PORTAINYECTOR *m* **8682**
PORTALÁPIZ *m* DE UN COMPÁS **9165**
PORTAMANDRILADOR *m* **10264**
PORTAMICRÓMETRO *m* **8250**
PORTAMOSQUETÓN *m* **11691**
PORTAOBJETO *m* **12047**
PORTAPUNZONES *m* **8033**
PORTAÚTIL *m* **13003**
PORTAÚTIL *m* PARA VARIOS ÚTILES **5801**
PORTAÚTILES *m* **13012**
PORTAÚTILES *m* **13005**
PORTEZUELA *f* TRASERA **891**
PÓRTICO **9641**
PÓRTICO DE RODAMIENTO **13224**
POSIBILIDAD *f* **5755**
POSICIÓN *f* **3940**
POSICIÓN *f* BINARIA **1249**
POSICIÓN *f* DE ARRANQUE **12126**
POSICIÓN *f* DE CERO **14028**
POSICIÓN *f* DE EQUILIBRIO **9647**
POSICIÓN *f* DE LA MANIVELA **9645**
POSICIÓN *f* DE LA PISTOLA DE SOLDADURA **13782**
POSICIÓN *f* DE REPOSO **9648**
POSICIÓN *f* EN PUNTO MUERTO **9646**
POSICIÓN *f* FINAL **5187**
POSICIÓN *f* INTERMEDIA **8265**
POSICIÓN *f* INTERMEDIA **8265**
POSICIÓN *f* MEDIA **8265**
POSICIÓN *f* POR COORDENADAS **3099**
POSTCALDEO *m* **9668**
POSTE *m* **9311**
POSTE *m* **12062**
POSTE *m* DE LÍNEA ELÉCTRICA **7608**
POSTPROCESOR *m* **9665**
POTASA *f* **9679**
POTASA *f* CÁUSTICA **9687**
POTASA *f* NITROSA **9691**
POTASA *f* NITROSA **9691**
POTASA *f* NITROSA **9691**
POTASIO *m* **9672**
POTENCIA *f* **9730**
POTENCIA *f* **7308**
POTENCIA *f* **1917**
POTENCIA *f* **1917**

POTENCIA *f* ABSORBENTE **42**
POTENCIA *f* ABSORBIDA **4747**
POTENCIA *f* AL FRENO **4458**
POTENCIA *f* AL FRENO **151**
POTENCIA *f* AL FRENO **1535**
POTENCIA *f* AL FRENO **1540**
POTENCIA *f* CALORÍFICA **6392**
POTENCIA *f* DE ATRACCIÓN DE UN IMÁN **13090**
POTENCIA *f* DE FRENADO **1551**
POTENCIA *f* EFECTIVA **1540**
POTENCIA *f* EFECTIVA **1540**
POTENCIA *f* EFECTIVA **4458**
POTENCIA *f* EFECTIVA EN CABALLOS **151**
POTENCIA *f* FISCAL **10233**
POTENCIA *f* INDICADA **6875**
POTENCIA *f* INDICADA (O FISCAL) **6874**
POTENCIA *f* (MATEMÁTICAS) **9729**
POTENCIA *f* MÁXIMA **8066**
POTENCIA *f* MOTRIZ **8409**
POTENCIA *f* NECESARIA **3746**
POTENCIA *f* NOMINAL **10233**
POTENCIA *f* RECOGIDA **4747**
POTENCIA/ALIMENTACIÓN *f* **4546**
POTENCIAL *m* **9708**
POTENCIAL *m* DE CONTACTO **3007**
POTENCIAL *m* DE ELECTRODO **4577**
POTENCIÓMETRO *m* **9711**
POZO *m* DE AERACIÓN **291**
POZO *m* DE GRANULACIÓN DE LA ESCORIA **6056**
POZO *m* (DE MINA) **9398**
PRACTICAR UNA ENTALLADURA EN UNA PIEZA **8554**
PRASEODIMIO *m* **9750**
PREALEACIÓN *f* **5594**
PRECALDEO *m* **9776**
PRECALENTAR **9774**
PRECARGA *f* **9782**
PRECAUCIONES *f pl* **9753**
PRECESIÓN *f* **9754**
PRECINTADO **7479**
PRECINTAR **11077**
PRECINTO *m* DE PLOMO **7480**
PRECIO *m* DE COSTE **3210**
PRECIO *m* DE LA MANO DE OBRA **7346**
PRECIO *m* POR DÍA **3594**
PRECIPITABLE **9757**
PRECIPITACIÓN *f* **9761**
PRECIPITACIÓN *f* **9091**
PRECIPITACIÓN *f* **1934**
PRECIPITADO *m* **9759**
PRECIPITANTE **9758**

PRECIPITANTE *m* **11130**
PRECIPITAR **9760**
PRECIPITARSE **9760**
PRECISIÓN *f* **9763**
PRECISIÓN *f* **82**
PRECISIÓN *f* DE MECANIZACIÓN **83**
PREFILTRO *m* **9751**
PREFORMA *f* **9772**
PREFORMADO *m* **9773**
PREFORMADO *m* **1341**
PREMODELO *m* **4370**
PRENSA *f* **9795**
PRENSA *f* PLEGADORA **9481**
PRENSA *f* BRINELL **1553**
PRENSA *f* DE CALIBRAR **11525**
PRENSA *f* DE CARPINTERO **2451**
PRENSA *f* DE COLADA **3370**
PRENSA *f* DE COLLAR **2451**
PRENSA *f* DE COMPRIMIR LOS POLVOS **9718**
PRENSA *f* DE CUÑA **13734**
PRENSA *f* DE DESBASTE **13211**
PRENSA *f* DE ESTAMPAR **12060**
PRENSA *f* DE ESTIRAR **4972**
PRENSA *f* DE EXCÉNTRICA **4430**
PRENSA *f* DE FORJAR **5562**
PRENSA *f* DE FORJAR HIDRÁULICA **6687**
PRENSA *f* DE PALANCA **7534**
PRENSA *f* DE PASTILLAS **9310**
PRENSA *f* DE RÓTULA **12980**
PRENSA *f* DE TORNILLO **11040**
PRENSA *f* DE TORNILLO **2452**
PRENSA *f* HIDRÁULICA **6693**
PRENSA *f* HIDRÁULICA DE CUELLO DE CISNE **8828**
PRENSA *f* HIDRÁULICA DE CUELLO DE CISNE **8828**
PRENSA *f* HIDRÁULICA DE EMBUTIR **6682**
PRENSA *f* HIDRÁULICA DE MARTILLO PILÓN **6687**
PRENSA *f* MECÁCINA CON PLATO REVOLVER **3839**
PRENSA *f* MECÁNICA DE ARCADA **4157**
PRENSA *f* MECÁNICA DE BASTIDOR EN CUELLO DE CISNE **8814**
PRENSA *f* MECÁNICA DE CALIBRAR Y ESTAMPAR **1864**
PRENSA *f* MECÁNICA DE MONTANTE **12316**
PRENSA *f* MECÑICA PARA GOLPEAR **9182**
PRENSA *f* MONETARIA **2653**
PRENSA *f* PARA CHAPAS FUERTES **6411**
PRENSA *f* ROTATIVA **10757**
PRENSADO *m* **9806**
PRENSADO *m* EN FRÍO **2690**
PRENSADO *m* PROFUNDO **7158**
PRENSAESTOPA *m* **12405**

PRENSAESTOPA *m* **5953**
PRENSAESTOPAS *m* **12405**
PRENSAESTOPAS *m* **9001**
PRENSAESTOPAS *m* **9000**
PRENSAESTOPAS *m* **9008**
PRENSAESTOPAS *m* **9008**
PRENSAESTOPAS *m* **9008**
PRENSAS *f pl* DE TRANSFERENCIA DE PUNZONES MÚLTIPLES **8461**
PREPARACIÓN *f* **9784**
PREPARACIÓN *f* **12130**
PREPARACIÓN *f* DE LOS BORDES **4449**
PREPARACIÓN *f* DE LOS MINERALES **8861**
PREPARACIÓN *f* DE UNA SOLUCIÓN **9785**
PREPARAR UNA SOLUCIÓN **9788**
PRESA *f* **3597**
PRESA *f* **13753**
PRESA *f* **13753**
PRESA *f* DE SALIDA **8904**
PRESELECCIÓN *f* **9789**
PRESERVADOR *m* CONTRA LA OXIDACIÓN **10869**
PRESERVADOR *m* DE LA OXIDACIÓN **10868**
PRESINTERIZACIÓN *f* **9794**
PRESIÓN *f* **10194**
PRESIÓN *f* **11355**
PRESIÓN *f* **9808**
PRESIÓN *f* **10194**
PRESIÓN *f* **13434**
PRESIÓN *f* ABSOLUTA **4459**
PRESIÓN *f* ABSOLUTA **33**
PRESIÓN *f* ATMOSFÉRICA **794**
PRESIÓN *f* BAROMÉTRICA **794**
PRESIÓN *f* (CALDERA) **6314**
PRESIÓN *f* CONSTANTE **2976**
PRESIÓN *f* CRÍTICA **3348**
PRESIÓN *f* DE AGUA **13669**
PRESIÓN *f* DE COMPRESIÓN **2859**
PRESIÓN *f* DE LA CORRIENTE **9825**
PRESIÓN *f* DE PRUEBA **12786**
PRESIÓN *f* DE PRUEBA **12786**
PRESIÓN *f* DE RÉGIMEN **13957**
PRESIÓN *f* DE REGLAJE **9832**
PRESIÓN *f* DE SATURACIÓN **10944**
PRESIÓN *f* DE SERVICIO **13957**
PRESIÓN *f* DE X CM DE MERCURIO **794**
PRESIÓN *f* DEBIDA AL ROZAMIENTO **9816**
PRESIÓN *f* DEL FRENO **1549**
PRESIÓN *f* DEL GAS **5837**
PRESIÓN *f* DEL VAPOR **12181**
PRESIÓN *f* DEL VIENTO **13858**

# PRE

1104

PRESIÓN  f  EN KG POR UNIDAD DE SUPERFICIE **11853**
PRESIÓN  f  EN UNA CALDERA **1417**
PRESIÓN  f  ESTÁTICA **12137**
PRESIÓN  f  ESTÁTICA **12136**
PRESIÓN  f  EXPLOSIVA **4936**
PRESIÓN  f  FINAL **5188**
PRESIÓN  f  HIDRÁULICA **13669**
PRESIÓN  f  HIDROSTÁTICA **6726**
PRESIÓN  f  INICIAL **6929**
PRESIÓN  f  INTERIOR EN UNA CONDUCCIÓN **9822**
PRESIÓN  f  LATERAL **7422**
PRESIÓN  f  LÍMITE **7593**
PRESIÓN  f  MANOMÉTRICA **9809**
PRESIÓN  f  MANOMÉTRICA **5771**
PRESIÓN  f  MEDIA **8075**
PRESIÓN  f  NOMINAL **8613**
PRESIÓN  f  NORMAL **8657**
PRESIÓN  f  OSMÓTICA **8891**
PRESIÓN  f  PARCIAL **9087**
PRESIÓN  f  REAL **4459**
PRESIÓN  f  RELATIVA **5882**
PRESIÓN  f  SOBRE EL ÉMBOLO **9377**
PRESIÓN  f  SOBRE LAS ARISTAS **9826**
PRESIÓN  f  SOBRE LAS SUPERFICIES DE APOYO **1110**
PRESIÓN  f  SUPERFICIAL **12517**
PRESIÓN  f  SUPERIOR A LA PRESIÓN AUTORIZADA **8955**
PRESIÓN  f  TOTAL **13065**
PRESIÓN  f  VARIABLE **13491**
PRESIÓN EJERCIDA SOBRE LAS PLANCHAS  f  **8046**
PRESSIÓN-REACCIÓN  f  SOBRE LOS MUÑONES **7259**
PRESSPAHN  m  **9801**
PRESUPUESTO  m  **4838**
PRESUPUESTO  m  **4838**
PRETENSADO  m  **9782**
PRETENSADO  m  DEL HORMIGÓN **2899**
PRETIL  m  **6259**
PRIMER FILTRO  m  **5265**
PRIMERA CABEZA  f  DE REMACHE **5266**
PRIMERA CAPA  f  DE PINTURA **9864**
PRIMERA MANO  f  **9864**
PRISIONERO  m  **11220**
PRISIONERO  m  **12399**
PRISIONERO  m  **12399**
PRISIONERO  m  ROSCADO **12399**
PRISMA  f  **9875**
PRISMA  f  CUADRANGULAR **10055**
PRISMA  f  DE IGUAL RESISTENCIA **1396**
PRISMA  f  DE SECCIÓN OBLICUA **9876**
PRISMA  f  EXAGONAL **6460**
PRISMA  f  PENTAGONAL **9173**

PRISMA  f  POLARIZADOR **9586**
PRISMA  f  RECTANGULAR **13192**
PRISMÁTICO  m  **9879**
PRISMOIDE  m  **9880**
PROBADOR DE DUCTILIDAD  m  **3462**
PROBETA  f  **12791**
PROBETA  f  **12780**
PROCEDENTE DE FUNDICIÓN **2054**
PROCEDENTE DE FUNDICIÓN **2054**
PROCEDIMIENTO  m  **9883**
PROCEDIMIENTO  m  A PARTIR DE LOS PRODUCTOS RESULTANTES DE LA DESCOMPOSOCIÓN DEL HIDRURO **6699**
PROCEDIMIENTO  m  ÁCIDO **120**
PROCEDIMIENTO  m  BÁSICO **1050**
PROCEDIMIENTO  m  BÁSICO **1043**
PROCEDIMIENTO  m  BAYER **1073**
PROCEDIMIENTO  m  BESSEMER **1214**
PROCEDIMIENTO  m  BETTS **1220**
PROCEDIMIENTO  m  CHAPMAN **2254**
PROCEDIMIENTO  m  CON OXÍGENO **8982**
PROCEDIMIENTO  m  DE ACABADO QUÍMICO DE SUPERFICIE **2309**
PROCEDIMIENTO  m  DE AFINADO **10380**
PROCEDIMIENTO  m  DE AMALGACIÓN **448**
PROCEDIMIENTO  m  DE FABRICACIÓN **8218**
PROCEDIMIENTO  m  DE MECANIZACIÓN **9887**
PROCEDIMIENTO  m  DE MOLDEADO INVERSO **11656**
PROCEDIMIENTO  m  DE MOLDEADO POR MEDIO DEL SACO SACO DE CAUCHO **923**
PROCEDIMIENTO  m  DE REVESTIMIENTO EN BAÑO CALIENTE **6659**
PROCEDIMIENTO  m  DUPLEX **4380**
PROCEDIMIENTO  m  EN CRISOL **3404**
PROCEDIMIENTO  m  HANSGIRG **6272**
PROCEDIMIENTO  m  HORNO KALDO **7271**
PROCEDIMIENTO  m  OLD **8793**
PROCEDIMIENTO  m  POR ASPERSIÓN **11972**
PROCEDIMIENTO  m  QUÍMICO **2291**
PROCEDIMIENTO  m  SIEMENS-MARTÍN **8830**
PROCEDIMIENTO  m  THOMAS **1043**
PROCEDIMIENTO  m  'UNIONMELT' **684**
PROCEDIMIENTO BESSEMER CON CONVERTIDOR PROVISTO DE ÁCIDO **106**
PROCEDIMIENTO DE KYAN **7340**
PROCEDIMIENTOS  m pl  QUÍMICOS DE TRATAMIENTOS DE SUPERFICIE **2314**
PROCESO  m  **9883**
PROCESO  m  DE RECARGA **1696**
PROCESOR  m  **9889**
PRODUCCIÓN  f  **10462**
PRODUCCIÓN  f  **8028**

PRODUCCIÓN *f* DE CALOR **9896**
PRODUCCIÓN *f* DE CORRIENTE **9894**
PRODUCCIÓN *f* DE ENERGÍA **9737**
PRODUCCIÓN *f* DE ENERGÍA **5922**
PRODUCCIÓN *f* DE FRÍO **9895**
PRODUCCIÓN *f* EN SERIE **11198**
PRODUCIDO EN LA COLADA **2054**
PRODUCIR UNA CORRIENTE ELÉCTRICA **5917**
PRODUCIR (VAPORGAS) **5916**
PRODUCIRSE UNA FUGA *f* **7487**
PRODUCTIVIDAD *f* **9897**
PRODUCTO *m* **9892**
PRODUCTO *m* **9784**
PRODUCTO *m* ACABADO **5730**
PRODUCTO *m* ACABADO **5218**
PRODUCTO *m* ANTIOXIDANTE **3189**
PRODUCTO *m* ANTIOXIDANTE **10866**
PRODUCTO *m* ANTIOXIDANTE **10870**
PRODUCTO *m* DE COMBUSTIÓN **9893**
PRODUCTO *m* DE DESTILACIÓN **4071**
PRODUCTO *m* DE LIMPIEZA **2471**
PRODUCTO *m* DE REFINADO **10374**
PRODUCTO *m* DE REVESTIMIENTO **2589**
PRODUCTO *m* ESCALARIO **10966**
PRODUCTO *m* ESPECIAL **11849**
PRODUCTO *m* FINAL **5189**
PRODUCTO *m* FORMAND POROSIDADES **9628**
PRODUCTO *m* HIDRÓFUGO **13674**
PRODUCTO *m* INTERMEDIO **7043**
PRODUCTO *m* MANUFACTURADO **7989**
PRODUCTO *m* (MATEMÁTICAS) **9891**
PRODUCTO *m* PRIMARIO **9852**
PRODUCTO *m* SECUNDARIO **1820**
PRODUCTO *m* SEMIELABORADO **11174**
PRODUCTO *m* VECTORIAL **13509**
PRODUCTOS *m pl* DE ACERO DE RAÍL **10177**
PRODUCTOS *m pl* DE LIMPIEZA Y PULIMENTO **2475**
PRODUCTOS *m pl* DE PRIMERA CALIDAD **9862**
PRODUCTOS *m pl* QUÍMICOS **2320**
PROFUNDIDAD *f* **3779**
PROFUNDIDAD *f* DE CORTE **3782**
PROFUNDIDAD *f* DE CORTE **3526**
PROFUNDIDAD *f* DE ENGRANAJE **13952**
PROFUNDIDAD *f* DE LA CAPA CEMENTADA **2020**
PROFUNDIDAD *f* DE LA ROSCA **3784**
PROFUNDIDAD *f* DEL CUELLO DE CISNE **3783**
PROGRAMA *m* **9902**
PROGRAMA *m* DE COMPUTADOR **10811**
PROGRAMA *m* DE FABRICACIÓN **7994**
PROGRAMA *m* DIAGNÓSTICO **3830**

PROGRAMACIÓN *f* **9904**
PROGRAMACIÓN *f* AUTOMÁTICA **850**
PROGRAMACIÓN *f* DE PIEZA **9084**
PROGRAMACIÓN *f* MANUAL DE PIEZA **6242**
PROGRESIÓN *f* **11203**
PROGRESIÓN *f* ARITMÉTICA **704**
PROGRESIÓN *f* GEOMÉTRICA **5930**
PROLONGACIÓN *f* DE VALIDEZ DE UNA PATENTE **9919**
PROMETEO *m* **6771**
PROPAGACIÓN *f* DE ONDAS **9926**
PROPANO *m* **9927**
PROPIEDAD *f* CORRIENTE **1393**
PROPIEDAD *f* DE CUBRIR DE UN COLOR **1393**
PROPIEDAD *f* REFRACTARIA **10405**
PROPIEDADES *f pl* **2295**
PROPIEDADES *f pl* ANTIFRICCIÓN **617**
PROPIEDADES *f pl* FÍSICAS **9283**
PROPIEDADES QUÍMICAS *f pl* **2295**
PROPILENO *m* **9939**
PROPORCIÓN *f* **9934**
PROPORCIÓN *f* **3011**
PROPORCIÓN *f* **3011**
PROPORCIÓN *f* DE AGUA **13645**
PROPORCIÓN *f* DE AGUA **13645**
PROPORCIÓN *f* DE CARBONO **1947**
PROPORCIÓN *f* DE CARBONO **1947**
PROPORCIÓN *f* DE CENIZAS **758**
PROPORCIÓN *f* DE SAL **10906**
PROPORCIÓN (MATEMÁTICAS) **9933**
PROPORCIONAL **9935**
PROPORCIONALIDAD *f* **9938**
PROPORCIONES *f pl* DEFINIDAS **2771**
PROPULSIÓN *f* **4297**
PROPULSIÓN *f* CON 4 RUEDAS MOTRICES **5601**
PROPULSOR *m* **11041**
PROSPERIDAD *f* ECONÓMICA DE UNA EMPRESA **9462**
PROTACTINIO *m* **9940**
PROTECCIÓN *f* **9943**
PROTECCIÓN *f* **11346**
PROTECCIÓN *f* **11346**
PROTECCIÓN *f* CATÓDICA **2109**
PROTECCIÓN *f* CONTRA LA CORROSIÓN **3191**
PROTECCIÓN *f* CONTRA LA OXIDACIÓN **10871**
PROTECCIÓN *f* CONTRA LA OXIDACIÓN **9945**
PROTECCIÓN *f* DE LA PROPIEDAD INDUSTRIAL **9946**
PROTECCIÓN *f* POR EL CINC **11341**
PROTECTOR *m* CORTACIRCUITOS **5758**
PROTEGER POR EL CINC **11340**

**PRO**

1106

PROTOCARBURO *m* DE HIDROCARBURO DE HIDRÓGENO 8215
PROTOCLORURO *m* DE ESTAÑO 12100
PROTOCLORURO *m* DE MERCURIO 8159
PROTÓN *m* 9954
PROTOSULFURO *m* 627
PROTOTIPO *m* 9955
PROTÓXIDO *m* DE BARIO 1020
PROTÓXIDO *m* DE HIERRO 5125
PROTÓXIDO *m* DE MAGNESIO 7973
PROTÓXIDO *m* DE MERCURIO 8161
PROTÓXIDO *m* DE NITRÓGENO 8597
PROTÓXIDO *m* DE PLOMO 7663
PROTÓXIDO DE NÍQUEL 8565
PROYECCIÓN *f* 11968
PROYECCIÓN *f* 11842
PROYECCIÓN *f* 9912
PROYECCIÓN *f* 6326
PROYECCIÓN *f* CENTRAL 10137
PROYECCIÓN *f* DE UN PLANO 10611
PROYECCIÓN *f* DIMÉTRICA 3961
PROYECCIÓN *f* HORIZONTAL 11124
PROYECCIÓN *f* ISOMÉTRICA 7188
PROYECCIÓN *f* OBLICUA 2501
PROYECCIÓN *f* ORTOGONAL 8870
PROYECCIÓN *f* PARALELA 9058
PROYECCIÓN *f* TRIMÉTRICA 13208
PROYECCIÓN *f* VERTICAL 4659
PROYECCIÓN HORIZONTAL 11124
PROYECCIÓNG GNOMÓNICA 5990
PROYECTAR 9909
PROYECTAR EN... 6934
PROYECTO *m* 3794
PROYECTOR *m* DE LUZ 11091
PROYECTOR *m* DE SOMBRA 11238
PRUEBA *f* 9921
PRUEBA *f* 9921
PRUEBA *f* 12792
PRUEBA *f* 12770
PRUEBA *f* 12792
PRUEBA *f* 12770
PRUEBA *f* A ALTA TEMPERATURA 6499
PRUEBA *f* A LA COMPRESIÓN 2872
PRUEBA *f* A LA FLEXIÓN 1189
PRUEBA *f* A LA FLEXIÓN 10010
PRUEBA *f* A LA GOTA 11958
PRUEBA *f* A LA TORSIÓN 13059
PRUEBA *f* ACÚSTICA 11815
PRUEBA *f* AL CHOQUE (DE CAÍDA) 4328
PRUEBA *f* AL FRENO 1546

PRUEBA *f* CON AIRE COMPRIMIDO 2846
PRUEBA *f* CON CHISPA 11840
PRUEBA *f* DE CAPACIDAD DE FUNDICIÓN 2065
PRUEBA *f* DE CARGA CONSTANTE 2974
PRUEBA *f* DE CHOQUE DE CHARPY (O EN BARRA ENTALLADA) 2270
PRUEBA *f* DE CHOQUE EN BARRA ENTALLADA 8673
PRUEBA *f* DE COMBADURA 1189
PRUEBA *f* DE COMBADURA EN FRÍO 2667
PRUEBA *f* DE COMPRESIÓN 2865
PRUEBA *f* DE COMPRESIÓN 13416
PRUEBA *f* DE CORROSIÓN PROFUNDA 3684
PRUEBA *f* DE CORTE 11949
PRUEBA *f* DE CORTE 11287
PRUEBA *f* DE DESGASTE 13714
PRUEBA *f* DE DESGASTE 16
PRUEBA *f* DE DUREZA 6300
PRUEBA *f* DE DUREZA 3865
PRUEBA *f* DE DUREZA A LA LIMA 5152
PRUEBA *f* DE DUREZA POR IMPRESIÓN DE BOLA 6861
PRUEBA *f* DE DUREZA ROCKWELL 10659
PRUEBA *f* DE EMBUTIDO 10184
PRUEBA *f* DE EMBUTIDO ERICKSEN 8797
PRUEBA *f* DE ESTAMPADO 12061
PRUEBA *f* DE FATIGA / DE RESISTENCIA 4743
PRUEBA *f* DE FLEXIÓN 1177
PRUEBA *f* DE FLEXIÓN AL CHOQUE EN BARRAS NO ENTALLADAS 4328
PRUEBA *f* DE FLEXIÓN AL CHOQUE EN ENTALLADURA 1190
PRUEBA *f* DE FLEXIÓN ALTERNADA 12774
PRUEBA *f* DE FLEXIÓN ALTERNADA 12774
PRUEBA *f* DE FLEXIÓN CONSTANTE 2972
PRUEBA *f* DE FLEXIÓN DE LA CARA DE SOLDADURA 1178
PRUEBA *f* DE FLEXIÓN EN PIEZA ENTALLADA 8555
PRUEBA *f* DE FLEXIÓN INVERTIDA 10535
PRUEBA *f* DE FLEXIÓN POR CHOQUE 4328
PRUEBA *f* DE FLEXIÓN POR CHOQUE EN BARRAS ENTALLADAS 1190
PRUEBA *f* DE FORJADO 5545
PRUEBA *f* DE LA CALDERA 12182
PRUEBA *f* DE LA CALDERA A PRESIÓN 1421
PRUEBA *f* DE MANDRINADO 4911
PRUEBA *f* DE MICRODUREZA 8246
PRUEBA *f* DE PERCUSIÓN CON LA BOLA (APARATO SHORE) 11367
PRUEBA *f* DE PÉRDIDA TÉRMICA 1403
PRUEBA *f* DE PERFORACIÓN 1475
PRUEBA *f* DE PERFORACIÓN 10010
PRUEBA *f* DE PLEGADO 1189
PRUEBA *f* DE PLEGADO 1177

PRUEBA *f* DE PLEGADO **4173**
PRUEBA *f* DE PLEGADO AL REVÉS **1179**
PRUEBA *f* DE PLEGADO EN CALIENTE **6618**
PRUEBA *f* DE PLEGADO EN FRÍO **2667**
PRUEBA *f* DE PRESIÓN **9836**
PRUEBA *f* DE PRESIÓN A VAPOR DE LA CALDERA **12182**
PRUEBA *f* DE PULVERIZACIÓN SALINA **10909**
PRUEBA *f* DE REBORDEADO **5347**
PRUEBA *f* DE REBOTE BRUSCO **7254**
PRUEBA *f* DE RECALCAMIENTO **11949**
PRUEBA *f* DE RECALCAMIENTO **13416**
PRUEBA *f* DE RECALCAMIENTO **1561**
PRUEBA *f* DE RECALCAMIENTO (O DE APLASTAMIENTO) **4374**
PRUEBA *f* DE RECALCAMIENTO (O DE APLASTAMIENTO) **7262**
PRUEBA *f* DE RECEPCIÓN **71**
PRUEBA *f* DE RESISTENCIA **5049**
PRUEBA *f* DE RESISTENCIA **12356**
PRUEBA *f* DE RESISTENCIA A LA FATIGA **5054**
PRUEBA *f* DE RESISTENCIA A LOS CHOQUES **8673**
PRUEBA *f* DE RESISTENCIA AL CALOR AZUL **1372**
PRUEBA *f* DE RESISTENCIA AL CALOR ROJO **10331**
PRUEBA *f* DE RESISTENCIA AL CHOQUE **6786**
PRUEBA *f* DE RESISTENCIA EN CALIENTE **6646**
PRUEBA *f* DE ROTURA **5619**
PRUEBA *f* DE ROTURA AL CHOQUE **6786**
PRUEBA *f* DE SACUDIDAS Y TRAQUETEO **7249**
PRUEBA *f* DE SOLDADURA **13792**
PRUEBA *f* DE TORSIÓN **13306**
PRUEBA *f* DE TRACCIÓN **12751**
PRUEBA *f* DE TRACCIÓN **12748**
PRUEBA *f* EN BANCO **1170**
PRUEBA *f* EN FRÍO **2709**
PRUEBA *f* ESCLEROMÉTRICA **11017**
PRUEBA *f* FÍSICA **9284**
PRUEBA *f* HIDRÁULICA **6695**
PRUEBA *f* NEGATIVA **8524**
PRUEBA *f* OFICIAL **8740**
PRUEBA *f* POR CHOQUE **6786**
PRUEBA *f* POR IMPRESIÓN DE BOLA **1618**
PRUEBA *f* POR INMERSIONES ALTERNADAS **405**
PRUEBA *f* POR LA BOLA DE BRINELL **1618**
PRUEBA *f* PRELIMINAR **9779**
PRUEBA *f* SIMULTÁNEA DE TORSIÓN Y FLEXIÓN **13310**
PRUEBA A LOS ULTRASONIDOS **12480**
PRUEBA CONTRARIA *f* **10522**
PRUEBA CONTRARIA *f* **4384**
PRUEBA CONTRARIA *f* **4384**
PRUEBA (DE DUREZA) BRINELL **1620**

PRUEBA DE ENSANCHAMIENTO **4911**
PRUEBAS *f pl* MECÁNICAS **8112**
PRUSIATO *m* AMARILLO **9685**
PRUSIATO *m* ROJO **9684**
PSICRÓMETRO *m* **9960**
PÚA *f* **11904**
PÚA *f* **4260**
PUDELAR **9964**
PUDINGA *f* **8490**
PUDRIR **10036**
PUDRIRSE **10036**
PUENTE *m* **3667**
PUENTE *m* **1735**
PUENTE *m* BASCULANTE **13745**
PUENTE *m* DE CALDEO **5308**
PUENTE *m* DE CORREDERA DESMOLDEADOR **12383**
PUENTE *m* DE WHEATSTONE **13809**
PUENTE *m* SUSPENDIDO **12528**
PUENTE *m* TRANSBORDADOR **13141**
PUENTE *m* TRASERO (MOTOR) **10265**
PUENTE *m* VOLANTE **7260**
PUENTE GRÚA *m* DE CORREDERA **13156**
PUENTE GRÚA *m* DE FÁBRICA **8942**
PUENTE GRÚA *m* DE OBRA/DE ESTACIÓN **5804**
PUERTA *f* **5242**
PUERTA *f* **891**
PUERTO *m* DE DESCARA (DE NAVÍOS MERCANTES) **8736**
PUESTA *f* A PUNTO **8419**
PUESTA *f* A PUNTO DE UNA HERRAMIENTA **1621**
PUESTA *f* A TIERRA **4417**
PUESTA *f* A TIERRA **6149**
PUESTA *f* EN CIRCUITO **12560**
PUESTA *f* EN ESTADO DE LOS DIENTES DE UNA SIERRA **10958**
PUESTA *f* EN MANOJOS **1772**
PUESTA *f* EN MARCHA **12118**
PUESTA *f* EN MARCHA **12118**
PUESTA *f* EN MARCHA **12130**
PUESTA *f* EN MARCHA DE UNA MÁQUINA **12130**
PUESTA *f* EN SERVICIO **12118**
PUESTA *f* FUERA DE CIRCUITO **12559**
PUESTA *f* FUERA DE SERVICIO DE UNA MÁQUINA **11410**
PUESTA A PUNTO DE UN INSTRUMENTO DE ÓPTICA **5505**
PUESTA FUERA DE SERVICIO *f* **7100**
PUESTO *m* **8839**
PUESTO *m* DE PRUEBA **12773**
PUESTO *m* DE SOLDADURA CON CORRIENTE ALTERNA **2**
PUESTO *m* DE SOLDADURA CON CORRIENTES ALTERNA Y CONTINUA **59**
PUESTO *m* DEL OBRERO **8839**
PULGADA *f* CUADRADA INGLESA **12021**

**PUL** 1108

PULGADA *f* CÚBICA INGLESA **3454**
PULGADA *f* INGLESA **6830**
PULIDO *m* **5408**
PULIDO *m* **1755**
PULIDO *m* **1755**
PULIDO *m* (CAPAZ DE TOMAR UN) **9599**
PULIDO *m* (CAPAZ DE UN BUEN) **9599**
PULIDO *m* PERFECTO **1755**
PULIDO *m* (QUE TOMA BIEN EL) **9599**
PULIDOR *m* **10263**
PULIDOR *m* **1757**
PULIDOR *m* **1686**
PULIDOR A MANO *m* **6247**
PULIDORA *f* **4006**
PULIDORA *f* **4010**
PULIDORA *f* **1471**
PULIDORA *f* **12372**
PULIMENTAR **11679**
PULIMENTAR **1756**
PULIMENTO *m* **1755**
PULIMENTO *m* **1755**
PULIMENTO *m* **5408**
PULIMENTO *m* **11686**
PULIMENTO *m* **9600**
PULIMENTO *m* **9605**
PULIMENTO *m* A MANO **6228**
PULIMENTO *m* CON BOLAS **956**
PULIMENTO *m* CON ESMERIL **4695**
PULIMENTO *m* DE LA SUPERFICIE **3527**
PULIMENTO *m* ELÉCTRICO **4605**
PULIMENTO *m* EN TAMBOR **1012**
PULIMENTO *m* POR RODILLOS **1758**
PULIR **1756**
PULIR **9598**
PULIR **11679**
PULIR CON BRILLO **1756**
PULIR CON ESMERIL **4694**
PULSADOR *m* **12672**
PULSADOR *m* **9797**
PULSADOR *m* **9797**
PULSADOR *m* **9797**
PULSADOR *m* **10029**
PULSADOR *m* DE ROLDANA **10692**
PULSADOR *m* DE VÁLVULA **13466**
PULSÓMETRO *m* **9980**
PULVERIZABLE **9981**
PULVERIZACIÓN *f* **9985**
PULVERIZACIÓN *f* **11968**
PULVERIZACIÓN *f* **12001**
PULVERIZACIÓN *f* **2226**

PULVERIZACIÓN *f* **811**
PULVERIZACIÓN *f* **6117**
PULVERIZACIÓN *f* **2226**
PULVERIZACIÓN *f* **2786**
PULVERIZACIÓN *f* **811**
PULVERIZACIÓN *f* DE UN LÍQUIDO **810**
PULVERIZADO **9983**
PULVERIZADOR *m* **11967**
PULVERIZADOR *m* **809**
PULVERIZADOR *m* **809**
PULVERIZADORES *m pl* DE DISCOS **4007**
PULVERIZAR **6103**
PULVERIZAR **6103**
PULVERIZAR **9982**
PULVERIZAR (UN LÍQUIDO) **808**
PULVERULENTO *m* **9728**
PUNTA *f* ANÓDICA **591**
PUNTA *f* DE ELECTRODO **4579**
PUNTA *f* DE PARÍS **13895**
PUNTA *f* DE RECAMBIO **3006**
PUNTA *f* DE TRAZAR **11068**
PUNTA *f* DE UNA CLAVIJA **6318**
PUNTA *f* DE UNA HERRAMIENTA **8666**
PUNTA *f* DEL ÁNODO **591**
PUNTA *f* DEL ELECTRODO **4578**
PUNTA *f* TRAZADORA DEL PLANIMETRO **13079**
PUNTAL *m* **12402**
PUNTAL **12396**
PUNTAL *m* **12396**
PUNTAL *m* **688**
PUNTAL *m* **898**
PUNTAL *m* **1516**
PUNTAL *m* DE REFUERZO **9925**
PUNTAS *f pl* ABRASIVAS **24**
PUNTAS *f pl* PARA FUNDICIÓN **5598**
PUNTO *m* **9559**
PUNTO *m* CALIENTE **6642**
PUNTO *m* CERO **14027**
PUNTO *m* CRÍTICO **3347**
PUNTO *m* DE APLICACIÓN **9561**
PUNTO *m* DE APOYO **9567**
PUNTO *m* DE ARTICULACIÓN **5717**
PUNTO *m* DE COMBUSTION **5368**
PUNTO *m* DE COMBUSTIÓN **5247**
PUNTO *m* DE CONCURSO **9565**
PUNTO *m* DE CONDENSACIÓN **3824**
PUNTO *m* DE CONGELACIÓN **5656**
PUNTO *m* DE CONTACTO **3005**
PUNTO *m* DE CONTACTO **3009**
PUNTO *m* DE CONTACTO **9562**

QUE

PUNTO *m* DE CRUCE **3393**
PUNTO *m* DE CURIE **7920**
PUNTO *m* DE DESPLOME **11750**
PUNTO *m* DE EBULLICIÓN **1424**
PUNTO *m* DE ENCENDIDO **6759**
PUNTO *m* DE ENCUENTRO **9565**
PUNTO *m* DE FUEGO (ACEITE) **5247**
PUNTO *m* DE FUSIÓN **5759**
PUNTO *m* DE FUSIÓN **8141**
PUNTO *m* DE GUÍA DE LOS NÚCLEOS **3144**
PUNTO *m* DE IGNICIÓN **6759**
PUNTO *m* DE IMAGEN **6780**
PUNTO *m* DE INFLAMABILIDAD **5368**
PUNTO *m* DE INFLAMACIÓN **5363**
PUNTO *m* DE INFLAMACIÓN **6764**
PUNTO *m* DE INFLEXIÓN **9564**
PUNTO *m* DE INTERSECCIÓN **9565**
PUNTO *m* DE LLAMA **6764**
PUNTO *m* DE LLAMA **5363**
PUNTO *m* DE MEDIDA **8091**
PUNTO *m* DE OBJETO **8706**
PUNTO *m* DE PARTIDA DE UN MOVIMIENTO **12124**
PUNTO *m* DE REFERENCIA **9566**
PUNTO *m* DE REFERENCIA **10368**
PUNTO *m* DE REFERENCIA ABSOLUTO **34**
PUNTO *m* DE RETORNO **3502**
PUNTO *m* DE RUPTURA **9563**
PUNTO *m* DE SOLIDIFICACIÓN **11800**
PUNTO *m* DE SOLIDIFICACIÓN **11804**
PUNTO *m* DE SOLIDIFICACIÓN **5656**
PUNTO *m* DE SUSPENSIÓN **9568**
PUNTO *m* DE TANGENCIA **9562**
PUNTO *m* DE TOMA **11804**
PUNTO *m* DE TRANSFORMACIÓN **718**
PUNTO *m* DE TRANSFORMACIÓN **3347**
PUNTO *m* DE TRANSICIÓN **13122**
PUNTO *m* EN EL ESPACIO **9560**
PUNTO *m* FIJO **5295**
PUNTO *m* ISOELÉCTRICO **7175**
PUNTO *m* LUMINOSO **7823**
PUNTO *m* MUERTO **3626**
PUNTO *m* MUERTO **3635**
PUNTO *m* MUERTO ALTO (P.M.A.) **13032**
PUNTO *m* MUERTO ALTO (P.M.A.) **13411**
PUNTO *m* MUERTO BAJO **1491**
PUNTO *m* QUE LUBRIFICAR **8789**
PUNTO *m* TRIPLE **13216**
PUNTO DE FUSIÓN ELEVADO (DE) *m* **6308**
PUNTOS *m pl* BRILLANTES **6472**
PUNZÓN *m* **3162**

PUNZÓN *m* **3162**
PUNZÓN *m* **1560**
PUNZÓN *m* **11068**
PUNZÓN *m* **8522**
PUNZÓN *m* **11904**
PUNZÓN *m* **9997**
PUNZÓN *m* **9544**
PUNZÓN *m* **11068**
PUNZÓN *m* **7332**
PUNZÓN *m* DE CENTRADO **2172**
PUNZÓN *m* (DE INSPECCIÓN) **3893**
PUNZÓN *m* DE TRAZAR **9844**
PUNZÓN *m* INFERIOR **7794**
PUNZÓN *m* SACABOCADOS **6545**
PUNZÓN *m* SACABOCADOS **6545**
PUNZONADO *m* **10008**
PUNZONADO *m* **10006**
PUNZONADO *m* **10012**
PUNZONADO *m* DE LAS CHAPAS **3894**
PUNZONADORA *f* **10001**
PUNZONADORA *f* **10009**
PUNZONADORA-CIZALLADORA *f* **10007**
PUNZONADORA-RECORTADORA *f* **10009**
PUNZONAR **9998**
PUNZONAR **9999**
PUNZONAR **8011**
PURGA *f* **4206**
PURGADOR *m* **1318**
PURGADOR *m* **10020**
PURGADOR *m* DE AGUA CONDENSADA **12188**
PURGADOR *m* DE AGUA CONDENSADA DE DILATACIÓN **12839**
PURGADOR *m* DE AGUA CONDENSADA DE FLOTADOR **5432**
PURGAR **4204**
PURIFICACIÓN *f* ANÓDICA **592**
PURIFICACIÓN *f* DE AGUAS RESIDUALES **13638**
PURIFICACIÓN *f* DE LOS GASES **10018**
PURIFICACIÓN *f* DE LOS GASES **5839**
PURIFICACIÓN *f* DEL AGUA **10019**
PURIFICADO **10372**
PURIFICAR **10370**
PURIFICAR EL AGUA POTABLE POR VÍA QUÍMICA **11748**
PURIFICAR LAS AGUAS DE ALIMENTACIÓN POR VÍA QUÍMICA **11748**
PÚSTULA *f* **1327**
PÚSTULAS *f pl* **1330**
PUTREFACCIÓN (ACCIÓN) *f* **10035**
PUZOLANA *f* **9748**
PUZOLANA *f* **9748**
QUE AUMENTA LA TENSIÓN **1456**

**QUE**

1110

QUE ENCIERRA RESINA **10479**
QUE IMPRIME **9872**
QUE PUEDE COLARSE **1914**
QUE REPOSA **8432**
QUE REPOSA LIBREMENTE **5650**
QUE REPOSA LIBREMENTE SOBRE SUS DOS APOYOS **11474**
QUE RUEDA **9635**
QUEBRADIZO *m* **1627**
QUEBRADIZO EN CALIENTE *m* **6658**
QUEBRADIZO EN CALIENTE *m* **10337**
QUEBRADO *m* IMPROPIO **6807**
QUEBRANTADORAS *f pl* **8296**
QUELATO *m* **11195**
QUEMADO *m* **1750**
QUEMADOR *m* **1749**
QUEMADOR *m* DE GAS **5811**
QUEMADOR *m* DE GAS **5811**
QUEMAR **1745**
QUICIONERA *f* **12905**
QUÍMICA *f* **2290**
QUÍMICA *f* **2322**
QUÍMICA ANALÍTICA *f* **495**
QUÍMICA APLICADA *f* **648**
QUÍMICA FÍSICA *f* **9281**
QUÍMICA INDUSTRIAL O TECNOLÓGICA *f* **9286**
QUÍMICA MINERAL O INORGÁNICA *f* **6958**
QUÍMICA ORGÁNICA *f* **8865**
QUÍMICAMENTE COMBINADO *m* **2317**
QUÍMICAMENTE PURO *m* **2319**
QUÍMICO **2321**
QUINCALLA *f* **11660**
QUINCALLERÍA *f* **11660**
QUINIDRONA *f* (SEMICÉLULA A LA) **10110**
QUINTAL *m* (50 KGS APROXIMADAMENTE) **6668**
QUINTAL *m* MÉTRICO **10111**
QUITAR LA CORREA **12895**
RACOR **13368**
RACOR **5280**
RACOR **2965**
RACOR **3254**
RACOR *m* ATORNILLADO **11058**
RACOR *m* CÓNICO **10352**
RACOR *m* CÓNICO **12647**
RACOR *m* DE ACERO FORJADO **5549**
RACOR *m* DE TUERCAS **1442**
RACOR *m* DE UNIÓN **13369**
RACOR *m* EN T **1559**
RACOR *m* MACHO **8578**
RACOR *m* PARA SOLDAR **13781**
RACOR *m* PARA TUBOS **9350**

RACOR *m* PARA TUBOS FLEXIBLES **6612**
RACOR *m* ROSCADO **11061**
RACOR *m* TRES PIEZAS **13369**
RADIACIÓN **10143**
RADIACIÓN *f* **10143**
RADIADOR *m* **10148**
RADIADOR *m* DE CALEFACCIÓN **10150**
RADIADOR *m* ALFA **401**
RADIADOR *m* DE ALETAS **5233**
RADIADOR *m* DE REFRIGERACIÓN **10149**
RADIADOR *m* EN NIDO DE ABEJA **2129**
RADIAL **10125**
RADIÁN *m* **10138**
RADICAL *m* **10154**
RADIO *m* **10166**
RADIO *m* **10165**
RADIO *m* VECTOR **10170**
RADIO *m* DE CURVATURA **10168**
RADIO *m* DE CURVATURA **1176**
RADIO *m* DE GIRO **10169**
RADIO *m* DE LOS NUDOS DE SOLDADURA **7097**
RADIO *m* DE ROTACIÓN **10169**
RADIO *m* DE SEPARACIÓN ENTRE LOS BORDES **10728**
RADIO *m* DE SEPARACIÓN ENTRE LOS BORDES **6132**
RADIO *m* POLAR **9580**
RADIO *m* POLAR **8128**
RADIOACTIVIDAD *f* **10160**
RADIOACTIVO **10157**
RADIOCRISTALOGRAFÍA *f* **13996**
RADIOGRAFÍA *f* **10161**
RADIOGRAFÍA *f* **10163**
RADIOGRAFÍA *f* **10164**
RADIOGRAFÍA *f* **10664**
RADIOMETALOGRAFÍA *f* **10155**
RADIOS *m* **10242**
RADIÓS *m* DE UNA RUEDA **13811**
RADIOTELEFONÍA *f* **13908**
RADIOTELEGRAFÍA *f* **13907**
RADÓN *m* **10159**
RAEDERA *f* **11009**
RAÍ *f* CUADRADA **12027**
RAÍL **10175**
RAÍL *m* DE CONTACTO **1770**
RAÍL *m* DE GUÍA **6162**
RAÍL *m* DE PUENTE GRÚA **3293**
RAÍL *m* TENSOR **12756**
RAÍLES *m* DE PESTAÑA **1715**
RAÍZ *f* **1028**
RAÍZ *f* **10720**
RAÍZ *f* BICUADRADA **5609**

**1111**        **RAY**

RAÍZ *f* CÚBICA **3447**
RAÍZ *f* DE LA SOLDADURA **10726**
RAÍZ *f* DEL DIENTE **1036**
RAÍZ *f* QUINTA **5147**
RAÍZ (METAMÁTICAS) **10714**
RAJA *f* **5274**
RAJA *f* EN LOS BORDES **3281**
RAJADURA *f* **11250**
RAJAMIENTO *m* **11622**
RALENTI *m* **6755**
RALENTÍ *m* ACELERADO **5038**
RAMA *f* **11845**
RAMA *m* DE UNA CURVA **1555**
RAMAL *m* CONDUCIDO **5516**
RAMAL *m* CONDUCTOR **4316**
RAMAL *m* CONDUCTOR **4316**
RAMAL *m* CONDUCTOR **4316**
RAMAL *m* CORRIENTE **10851**
RAMAL *m* DE UNA CORREA **11413**
RAMAL *m* DE UNA CORREA **11413**
RAMAL *m* FIADOR DEL CABLE **5023**
RAMAL *m* INMÓVIL (O FIJO) **12092**
RAMAL *m* SUELTO **5516**
RAMAL *m* SUELTO **5516**
RAMAL *m* SUELTO **5516**
RAMAL *m* SUELTO **5516**
RAMAL *m* TIRANTE **4316**
RAMAL *m* TIRANTE **4316**
RAMAL LIBRE DE UN APAREJO *m* **10851**
RAMIO *m* **10192**
RAMO *m* **11845**
RAMO *m* **11845**
RAMPA *f* **11627**
RAMPA *f* **2395**
RAMPA *f* **757**
RANGUA *f* **12902**
RANURA *f* **11629**
RANURA *f* **11937**
RANURA *f* **8672**
RANURA *f* **7282**
RANURA *f* **7282**
RANURA *f* **6127**
RANURA *f* **3278**
RANURA *f* **2122**
RANURA *f* **6127**
RANURA *f* **4372**
RANURA *f* ANULAR **2415**
RANURA *f* CIRCULAR **2415**
RANURA *f* DE ENGRASE **7810**
RANURA *f* DE UNA POLEA **6131**

RANURA *f* (O FISURA) SUPERFICIAL **6834**
RANURA *f* PARA CHAVETA **7291**
RANURA *f* PARA CHAVETA **7282**
RANURA CERRADA *f* **2526**
RANURA DE PASO *f* **4455**
RANURA ENCAJADA *f* **2526**
RANURAS CERRADAS *f pl* **2527**
RASCADOR **11009**
RASCADOR **11009**
RASCADOR *m* **11009**
RASCAR **11008**
RASILLA *f* **245**
RASPADO *m* **4802**
RASPADO *m* **11011**
RASPADO *m* **11011**
RASPADO (RESULTADO) **4803**
RASPADOR *m* **11009**
RASPADOR *m* **11009**
RASPADOR *m* **11009**
RASPADOR *m* **11009**
RASPADOR *m* DE DELINEANTE **4800**
RASPADOR *m* DE DESPACHO **4800**
RASPADOR *m* DE OFICINA **4800**
RASPAR **4799**
RASPAR **11008**
RASPAR **11008**
RASTRILLADORAS RECOGEDORAS *f pl* **6311**
RASTRILLOS *m pl* **6312**
RASTRILLOS *m pl* CON VERTIMIENTO LATERAL **11411**
RASTRILLOS *m pl* DE ATRESNALAR **1683**
RAYA *f* **7597**
RAYA *f* DEL SODIO **11723**
RAYAS *f pl* DE FRAUNHOFER **5631**
RAYO *m* CALORÍFICO **6369**
RAYO *m* EMERGENTE **4691**
RAYO *m* INCIDENTE **6832**
RAYO *m* LUMINOSO **7824**
RAYO *m* REFLEJADO **10384**
RAYO *m* REFRACTADO **10397**
RAYO *m* REFRACTADO **10397**
RAYOS *m* ACTÍNICOS **140**
RAYOS *m* ALFA **402**
RAYOS BETA **1218**
RAYOS *m* CATÓDICOS **2104**
RAYOS *m* DE LENARD **7515**
RAYOS *m* GAMMA **5796**
RAYOS *m* INFRARROJOS **7103**
RAYOS *m* ULTRAVIOLETAS **13333**
RAYOS *m* ULTRAVIOLETAS **13332**
RAYOS *m* X **14003**

**RAZ** 1112

RAZÓN DIRECTA (EN) **6815**
RAZÓN INVERSA (EN) **6816**
REACCIÓN *f* **10248**
REACCIÓN *f* ÁCIDA **122**
REACCIÓN *f* ALCALINA **337**
REACCIÓN *f* ELECTROLÍTICA IRREVERSIBLE **7171**
REACCIÓN *f* EN LOS APOYOS **1110**
REACCIÓN *f* EUTECTOIDE **4860**
REACCIÓN *f* MONOTECTOIDE **8386**
REACCIÓN *f* PERITÉCTICA **9199**
REACCIÓN *f* QUÍMICA **2312**
REACTANCIA *f* **10247**
REACTIVO *m* **10257**
REACTIVO *m* **4844**
REACTIVO *m* DE ATAQUE CON ÁCIDO **4847**
REACTIVO *m* INDICADOR **6879**
REACTOR *m* **10251**
REACTOR *m* DE RADIOQUÍMICA **2323**
REALIZAR **7950**
REBABA *f* **7489**
REBABA *f* **10836**
REBABA *f* **1764**
REBABA *f* **1764**
REBABA *f* **1764**
REBABA *f* **1764**
REBABA *f* **1764**
REBABA *f* **5357**
REBABA *f* **5357**
REBABA *f* DE SOLDADURA **8949**
REBABA *f* DE UNA PIEZA FUNDIDA **5184**
REBABAS *f pl* **10856**
REBAJA DE LA CONCENTRACIÓN *f* **3767**
REBAJAMIENTO *m* **4196**
REBAJAMIENTO *m* **1387**
REBAJAR **893**
REBAJAR **13204**
REBAJAR METAL (AL SOPLETE) **10993**
REBAJO *m* **10269**
REBAJO *m* **12646**
REBASAMIENTO *m* **8959**
REBASAMIENTO *m* **8948**
REBLANDECER **12717**
REBORDE *m* **5332**
REBORDE *m* **4441**
REBORDE *m* **3322**
REBORDE *m* **1088**
REBORDE *m* DE ESTANQUEIDAD **13854**
REBORDE *m* DE TIERRA ARCILLOSA (O DE TIERRA GRASA) **2468**
REBORDEAMIENTO **5345**

REBORDEAR **5324**
REBOSADERO *m* **6185**
REBOSADERO *m* **1492**
REBOSADERO *m* **8931**
REBOSADERO *m* **8931**
REBOSADERO *m* **8932**
REBOTAR **10273**
REBOTE **10272**
RECALCADOR *m* **6246**
RECALCADURA *f* **2115**
RECALCADURA *f* **7954**
RECALCAMIENTO *m* **7265**
RECALCAMIENTO *m* DE LOS REMACHES **2490**
RECALCAR **2113**
RECALCAR **7263**
RECALCAR **9712**
RECALCAR LOS REMACHES **2489**
RECALENTADOR *m* **12472**
RECALENTADOR *m* DE AGUA DE ALIMENTACIÓN **5078**
RECALENTADOR *m* DE AIRE **287**
RECALENTAMIENTO *m* **1754**
RECALENTAMIENTO *m* **12473**
RECALENTAMIENTO *m* **12460**
RECALENTAMIENTO *m* **12473**
RECALENTAMIENTO *m* **10274**
RECALENTAMIENTO *m* **10425**
RECALENTAMIENTO *m* **10425**
RECALENTAR **10424**
RECALENTAR **9775**
RECALENTAR **12468**
RECALENTAR **1746**
RECALENTAR **6385**
RECALENTAR **6334**
RECALENTIMIENTO *m* **8946**
RECALESCENCIA *f* **10274**
RECAMBIAR **10463**
RECAMBIO *m* DE UN ÓRGANO DE MÁQUINA **10464**
RECANTEAR **2230**
RECARGA *f* DE UNA SOLDADURA **13762**
RECARGA *f* DURA **6283**
RECEPCIÓN *f* **67**
RECEPCIÓN *f* (DE MÁQUINAS) **68**
RECEPTOR *m* HIDRÁULICO **13692**
RECHAZAR **7263**
RECHAZO *m* **10272**
RECHAZO *m* **13414**
RECHAZO *m* **7265**
RECHAZO *m* **7265**
RECHAZO *m* **4452**
RECHAZO *m* DE CRIBADO **9548**

RECHAZO *m* DE RECEPCIÓN **10431**
RECIBIR UNA FUERZA **12601**
RECIPIENTE *m* **10277**
RECIPIENTE *m* **3010**
RECIPIENTE *m* A PRESIÓN **9839**
RECIPIENTE *m* LLANO **9029**
RECIPIENTE *m* PARA RECOCER **566**
RECIPIENTE (O DEPÓSITO) FORJADO A PRESIÓN *m* **9839**
RECIPIENTE (O DEPÓSITO) FORJADO (O TRABAJADO EN CALIENTE) *m* **4982**
RECOCER **12719**
RECOCER **12717**
RECOCER EL ACERO **12719**
RECOCER EL ACERO **560**
RECOCIDO *m* **562**
RECOCIDO *m* AZUL **572**
RECOCIDO *m* COMPLETO **576**
RECOCIDO *m* CON LLAMA **5319**
RECOCIDO *m* CON SOPLETE **575**
RECOCIDO *m* CONTINUO **574**
RECOCIDO *m* DE GRANO GRUESO **5719**
RECOCIDO *m* DE PUESTA EN SOLUCIÓN **11812**
RECOCIDO *m* DE RELAJACIÓN **12363**
RECOCIDO *m* DE RELAJACIÓN **583**
RECOCIDO *m* DEL ACERO **581**
RECOCIDO *m* DEL ACERO **12733**
RECOCIDO *m* EN CAJA **5371**
RECOCIDO *m* EN EL HORNO ELÉCTRICO **4508**
RECOCIDO *m* EN NEGRO **571**
RECOCIDO *m* ESCALONADO **12240**
RECOCIDO *m* INTERMEDIO **577**
RECOCIDO *m* INTERMEDIO DE MECANIZACIÓN **9884**
RECOCIDO *m* INTERMEDIO ENTRE DOS ESTIRADOS **7085**
RECOCIDO *m* INVERSO **578**
RECOCIDO *m* ISOTÉRMICO **579**
RECOCIDO *m* PARA EMPLEO NORMAL **8664**
RECOCIDO *m* PERIÓDICO **582**
RECOCIDO *m* REDUCTOR DE TENSIÓN **584**
RECOCIDO *m* REDUCTOR DE TENSIÓN **12362**
RECOCIDO *m* REDUCTOR DE TENSIÓN **12044**
RECOCIDO *m* REDUCTOR DE TENSIÓN **9667**
RECOCIDO *m* ROJO BLANCO **573**
RECOCIDO *m* SELECTIVO **580**
RECOCIDO *m* SELECTIVO **11142**
RECOGEDORA *f* DE CASCABILLO **946**
RECOGEDORA *f* DE HENO **12541**
RECOGEDORAS *f pl* DE FORRAJE **6091**
RECOGEDORAS *f* DE GUISANTES **9141**
RECOGEDORAS *f* DE PATATAS **9704**
RECOGEDORAS *f* DE REMOLACHAS **12439**

RECORRIDO *m* **12387**
RECORRIDO *m* **10810**
RECORRIDO *m* **4063**
RECORRIDO *m* O CARRERA DE VÁLVULA O PISTÓN **10611**
RECORRIDO *m* (O DESVIACIÓN *f*) DE LA AGUJA **3699**
RECORRIDO O DESPLAZAMIENTO TRANSVERSAL DE LA MESA *m* **12585**
RECORTADURA *f* **13209**
RECORTAR **13204**
RECORTAR **9998**
RECORTAR CON CIZALLA O CON TIJERAS **11280**
RECORTE *m* **10012**
RECORTE DE CHAPA *m* **9493**
RECORTES *m pl* DE CINC **14040**
RECORTES *m pl* DE CORCHO **6144**
RECORTES *m pl* DE CUERO **7497**
RECORTES *m pl* DE HIERRO **11007**
RECRISTALIZACIÓN **10297**
RECTA *f* **12310**
RECTÁNGULO *m* **10310**
RECTÁNGULO *m* **10299**
RECTIFICACIÓN *f* **10511**
RECTIFICACIÓN *f* **11275**
RECTIFICACIÓN *f* **12319**
RECTIFICACIÓN *f* **6106**
RECTIFICACIÓN *f* AL CHORRO DE VAPOR **7653**
RECTIFICACIÓN *f* CON MANDRILADORA **10271**
RECTIFICACIÓN *f* CON MUELA **11275**
RECTIFICACIÓN *f* CON MUELA EN MÁQUINA **7849**
RECTIFICACIÓN *f* DE ASIENTO (DE UN COJINETE) **12606**
RECTIFICACIÓN *f* DE DIÁMETRO INTERIOR **10271**
RECTIFICACIÓN *f* DE DIÁMETRO INTERIOR **10270**
RECTIFICACIÓN *f* DE SUPERFICIE **12506**
RECTIFICACIÓN *f* EXTERIOR **4957**
RECTIFICACIÓN *f* INTERIOR **6564**
RECTIFICACIÓN *f* INTERIOR **7069**
RECTIFICACIÓN *f* (QUÍMICA) **10311**
RECTIFICACIÓN *f* SEMIONDA **6212**
RECTIFICACIÓN *f* SIN PUNTA(S) **2156**
RECTIFICADO EN FINO *m* **6793**
RECTIFICADOR *m* **13002**
RECTIFICADOR *m* **4254**
RECTIFICADOR *m* **6105**
RECTIFICADOR *m* DE CORRIENTE **10314**
RECTIFICADOR *m* DE VAPOR DE MERCURIO **8164**
RECTIFICADOR *m* ELECTRÓNICO **4634**
RECTIFICADOR *m* ELECTROQUÍMICO **4572**
RECTIFICADOR *m* (O DETECTOR) ELECTROLÍTICO **4606**
RECTIFICADORA *f* **6105**
RECTIFICADORA *f* PAR SUPERFICIES PLANAS **12507**

**REC** 1114

RECTIFICADORA *f* PARA SUPERFICIES DE REVOLUCIÓN EXTERIORES **4953**

RECTIFICADORA *f* PARA SUPERFICIES DE REVOLUCIÓN SIN CENTRO **2155**

RECTIFICAR **10318**

RECTIFICAR **11273**

RECTIFICAR **6790**

RECTIFICAR CON LA MANDRILADORA **10270**

RECTIFICAR CON MUELA **11273**

RECTIFICAR EL ACERO CON UN REVENIDO **6808**

RECTILÍNEO **10319**

RECTO **10577**

RECUBIERTO **8952**

RECUBRIMIENTO *m* **8951**

RECUBRIMIENTO *m* **8948**

RECUBRIMIENTO *m* **8951**

RECUBRIMIENTO *m* **2590**

RECUBRIMIENTO *m* DE CHAPAS **9501**

RECUBRIMIENTO *m* DE TUBOS **7369**

RECUBRIMIENTO *m* DE UN METAL POR VÍA ELECTROQUÍMICA **4562**

RECUBRIMIENTO *m* DEL DISTRIBUIDOR **7399**

RECUBRIMIENTO *m* POR DESCOMPOSICIÓN DE UN GAS **13482**

RECUBRIR **7598**

RECUBRIR LA CABEZA DEL REMACHE **3246**

RECUBRIR LA CABEZA DEL TORNILLO **3246**

RECUPERACIÓN *m* **10296**

RECUPERADOR *m* **10412**

RECUPERADOR *m* **10322**

RECUPERAR **10295**

RED *f* **7940**

RED *f* **2782**

RED *f* A GRAN DISTANCIA **7728**

RED *f* CRISTALINA **7429**

RED *f* DE CONDUCTORES ELÉCTRICOS **4080**

RED *f* DE DIFRACCIÓN **3925**

RED *f* DE DISTRIBUCIÓN ELÉCTRICA **4080**

RED *f* DE ELECTRIFICACIÓN **6096**

RED *f* DE REFLEXIÓN **10388**

RED *f* DE TRANSLACIÓN **13120**

RED *f* DE TUBERIAS **12579**

RED *f* ELÉCTRICA **6096**

RED *f* ESPACIAL **11828**

RED *f* PROTECTORA **6157**

RED *f* RECÍPROCA **10281**

RED *f* WULFF (ESTEREOGRÁFICO) **13992**

REDONDEADO *m* **6537**

REDONDEADO *m* DEL FILETE **10809**

REDONDEADORA *f* **5729**

REDONDEAMIENTO *m* **5728**

REDONDEAR UNA ARISTA **10793**

REDONDOS *m pl* DE ACERO ALEADO **377**

REDUCCIÓN *f* **4196**

REDUCCIÓN *f* **10357**

REDUCCIÓN *f* **13121**

REDUCCIÓN *f* CONICIDAD **4196**

REDUCCIÓN *f* DE LA MARCHA **11649**

REDUCCIÓN *f* DE LA SECCIÓN TRANSVERSAL **10362**

REDUCCIÓN *f* DE LOS EMPLAZAMIENTOS **5774**

REDUCCIÓN *f* DE POTENCIA **7762**

REDUCCIÓN *f* DE TEMPLE **4**

REDUCCIÓN *f* DE VELOCIDAD **10363**

REDUCCIÓN *f* ELECTROLÍTICA **4607**

REDUCCIÓN *f* HEMBRA-HEMBRA **10348**

REDUCCIÓN *f* MACHO-HEMBRA **1773**

REDUCCIÓN *f* POR CONTRACCIÓN **11394**

REDUCCIÓN *f* (QUÍMICA) **10356**

REDUCCIÓN DE LA SECCIÓN *f* **13707**

REDUCIR EN POLVO **6103**

REDUCIR LA MARCHA DE UNA MÁQUINA **11645**

REDUCIR LA VELOCIDAD **3678**

REDUCIR POR LAMINACIÓN **10666**

REDUCIR (QUÍMICA) **10342**

REDUCTOR *m* **10346**

REDUCTOR *m* **10345**

REDUCTOR *m* **10355**

REDUCTOR *m* DE VELOCIDAD **11873**

REDUCTOR *m* DE VELOCIDAD **11872**

REDUCTORA **10345**

REDUNDANCIA *f* **10364**

REEMPLAZAR **10463**

REFINADO **10372**

REFINADO *m* **10377**

REFINADO *m* DE UN METAL **10378**

REFINADO *m* EN EL VACÍO **13447**

REFINAR **10370**

REFINERÍA *f* **10375**

REFINO *m* **10377**

REFLECTOR *m* **10394**

REFLEJAR **10382**

REFLEJAR **10382**

REFLEXIÓN *f* **10387**

REFLEXIÓN *f* **10387**

REFLEXIÓN *f* DE LA LUZ **10390**

REFLEXIÓN *f* DE RETORNO **896**

REFLEXIÓN *f* TOTAL **13060**

REFORZAMIENTO *m* **12153**

REFORZAMIENTO *m* TUBULAR **13258**

REFORZAR **12358**

REFORZAR **12150**

REFRACCIÓN  f **10399**
REFRACCIÓN  f DE LA LUZ **10400**
REFRACTARIO **5257**
REFRACTARIO PLÁSTICO **9473**
REFRACTARIOS BÁSICOS **1051**
REFRACTO  m **10398**
REFRACTÓMETRO  m **10404**
REFRENTADO  m **12522**
REFRENTAR **12497**
REFRIGERACIÓN **3085**
REFRIGERADOR **10409**
REFRIGERANTE **10409**
REFRIGERANTE **3083**
REFRIGERAR **3081**
REFRINGENTE **10401**
REFRINGENTE **10402**
REFUERZO  m **10429**
REFUERZO  m **10569**
REFUERZO  m **12359**
REFUERZO  m **12359**
REFUERZO  m **1082**
REFUERZO  m **1516**
REFUERZO  m CON NERVADURAS **12152**
REFUERZO  m DE LA SOLDADURA **10427**
REFUERZO  m EN TUBOS **13258**
REFUNDICIÓN  f **10447**
REFUNDIR **10446**
REGADERA  f **13687**
REGADORA  f **13687**
REGAR **12000**
REGENERACIÓN  f DE PIEZAS DESCARBURIZADAS **1953**
REGENERADOR  m **10412**
RÉGIMEN  m **10558**
RÉGIMEN  m **8857**
RÉGIMEN  m DE ROTACIÓN **10558**
RÉGIMEN  m DE UTILIZACIÓN **4395**
RÉGIMEN  m DE VELOCIDAD **8663**
REGIÓN  f HULLERA **2562**
REGISTRADOR  m **10289**
REGISTRADOR  m DE DESENROLLADO CONTINUO **12380**
REGISTRADOR  m DE DIAGRAMA CIRCULAR **2408**
REGISTRADOR  m DE TAMBOR **3573**
REGISTRADOR  m MAGNÉTICO **12644**
REGISTRAR **10288**
REGISTRO  m **11427**
REGISTRO  m **9158**
REGISTRO  m DE HUMOS **3603**
REGISTRO  m DE TIRO **3603**
REGLA  f CURVA **5660**
REGLA  f DE AFORO **12303**

REGLA  f DE CÁLCULO **11591**
REGLA  f DE CONTRACCIÓN **3047**
REGLA  f DE DIBUJANTE **10831**
REGLA  f DE FASES **9236**
REGLA  f DIVIDIDA DE PRECISIÓN **9767**
REGLA  f GRADUADA **8085**
REGLA  f PARA TRAZAR PARALELAS **9059**
REGLAJE  m **195**
REGLAJE  m CON TORNILLO **190**
REGLAJE  m CONSECUTIVO **10256**
REGLAJE  m DE LA PRESIÓN **10419**
REGLAJE  m DEL ENCENDIDO **6768**
REGLAMENTOS  m pl DE FÁBRICA **11209**
REGLAR **182**
REGLAS  f pl DE ESCOPLADURA **7290**
REGLAS  f pl DE SERVICIO **8835**
REGUERO  m **6185**
REGUERO  m CANAL  m **2251**
REGULABLE **183**
REGULABLE **183**
REGULADOR  m **6013**
REGULADOR  m **12890**
REGULADOR  m ASTÁTICO **775**
REGULADOR  m AUTOMÁTICO **843**
REGULADOR  m CENTRÍFUGO **2181**
REGULADOR  m CÓNICO **2943**
REGULADOR  m DE BOLAS **2185**
REGULADOR  m DE BRAZOS CRUZADOS **3386**
REGULADOR  m DE CORRIENTE **3491**
REGULADOR  m DE CORRIENTE **13595**
REGULADOR  m DE DEPRESIÓN **12431**
REGULADOR  m DE FUERZA CENTRÍFUGA **2185**
REGULADOR  m DE GASTO **13600**
REGULADOR  m DE GASTO **8909**
REGULADOR  m DE GASTO DE AIRE **3465**
REGULADOR  m DE INTENSIDAD **3491**
REGULADOR  m DE INTENSIDAD **7020**
REGULADOR  m DE INTENSIDAD **13595**
REGULADOR  m DE MANGUITO **11578**
REGULADOR  m DE MANGUITO **11578**
REGULADOR  m DE MASA CENTRAL **13752**
REGULADOR  m DE NIVEL **7654**
REGULADOR  m DE POTENCIA **8909**
REGULADOR  m DE RESORTE **11984**
REGULADOR  m DE TEMPERATURA **12840**
REGULADOR  m DE TENSIÓN **13595**
REGULADOR  m DE VELOCIDAD **11874**
REGULADOR  m DE VELOCIDAD **10421**
REGULADOR  m DE WATT **2185**
REGULADOR  m ELÉCTRICO **4527**

**REG** 1116

REGULADOR  *m*  ELECTRÓNICO **4635**
REGULADOR  *m*  ESTÁTICO **12135**
REGULADOR  *m*  FARCOT **3386**
REGULADOR  *m*  ISÓCRONO **7180**
REGULADOR  *m*  PENDULO **9168**
REGULADOR  *m*  PLAN **11242**
REGULADOR  *m*  PORTER **13752**
REGULADOR  *m*  SEUDOESTÁTICO **9957**
REGULADOR  *m*  SOBRE EL ÁRBOL **11242**
REGULADOR DE GOLPO DE ARIETE  *m*  **246**
REGULAR **182**
REGULAR **5276**
REGULARIDAD  *f*  CÍCLICA **3719**
REGULARIDAD  *f*  DEL MOVIMIENTO **10417**
RÉGULO  *m*  DE ANTIMONIO **10423**
REJALGAR  *m*  **10262**
REJILLA  *f*  **6096**
REJILLA  *f*  CON SACUDIDAS **10655**
REJILLA  *f*  DE DESMOLDEO **7334**
REJILLA  *f*  (DE UN TAMIZ) **8170**
REJILLA  *f*  DE UNA TELA METÁLICA **8170**
REJILLA  *f*  GIRATORIA **10559**
REJILLA  *f*  HORIZONTAL **6584**
REJILLA  *f*  INCLINADA **6837**
REJILLA  *f*  ONDULADA **3200**
REJILLA  *f*  OSCILANTE **10655**
REJILLA  *f*  PARA CALIBRAR LA GRAVA **6075**
REJILLA  *f*  PROTECTORA DE LAS PIEDRAS **12275**
REJILLA  *f*  ROTATIVA **10559**
REJILLA DE RADIADOR  *f*  **10152**
REJILLA (DE UNA CRIBA)  *f*  **8169**
RELACIÓN  *f*  **10226**
RELACIÓN  *f*  **10234**
RELACIÓN  *f* : LÍMITE  *f*  DE FATIGA **4742**
RELACIÓN  *f*  DE ABSORCIÓN **53**
RELACIÓN  *f*  DE COMPRESIÓN **2860**
RELACIÓN  *f*  DE COMPRESIÓN **2860**
RELACIÓN  *f*  DE CONVEXIDAD **3079**
RELACIÓN  *f*  DE CORRIENTE PRIMARIA **9850**
RELACIÓN  *f*  DE DENSIDAD **3759**
RELACIÓN  *f*  DE DISTRIBUCIÓN DEL METAL **3777**
RELACIÓN  *f*  DE DISTRIBUCIÓN DEL METAL **8179**
RELACIÓN  *f*  DE EVAPORACIÓN **1402**
RELACIÓN  *f*  DE LANZAMIENTO **11582**
RELACIÓN  *f*  DE REDUCCIÓN **10360**
RELACIÓN  *f*  DE REFLEXIÓN **10391**
RELACIÓN  *f*  DE VELOCIDADES **13522**
RELACIÓN  *f*  ENTRE ENGRANAJES **5897**
RELACIÓN  *f*  ENTRE LOS BRAZOS DE PALANCA **7536**
RELACIÓN  *f*  VOLUMÉTRICA **2860**

RELACIONADO **1705**
RELACIONES  *f*  ENTRE ENGRANAJES **5896**
RELAJACIÓN  *f*  **10435**
RELAJACIÓN  *f*  **10435**
RELATIVO A LA TRACCIÓN **13098**
RELIEVE  *m*  **9913**
RELIEVE  *m*  **9917**
RELIEVE  *m*  **4684**
RELIEVE  *m*  **2093**
RELLENAR **6153**
RELLENAR CON MASILLA **2134**
RELLENO  *m*  DEL PRENSAESTOPAS **12406**
RELOJ  *m*  REGULADOR **3843**
RELOJ DE PUNTEO  *m*  **12946**
RELUCTANCIA  *f*  **10444**
REMACHADO  *m*  **10643**
REMACHADOR  *m*  **10641**
REMACHADORA  *f*  **10644**
REMACHADORA  *f*  **10642**
REMACHAR **10629**
REMACHAR **2692**
REMACHAR **2516**
REMACHAR **6634**
REMACHAR LA ESPIGA DEL ROBLÓN **2489**
REMACHE  *m*  **10621**
REMACHE  *m*  **10639**
REMACHE  *m*  **10628**
REMACHE  *m*  AL TRESBOLILLO **14034**
REMACHE  *m*  CADENA **2215**
REMACHE  *m*  CON BANDA DE RECUBRIMIENTO **1781**
REMACHE  *m*  CON CUBREJUNTAS SIMPLE **11478**
REMACHE  *m*  CON CUBREJUNTAS SIMPLE **11478**
REMACHE  *m*  CON DOBLE CUBREJUNTAS **4130**
REMACHE  *m*  CON DOS CORTES **4155**
REMACHE  *m*  CON DOS CUBREJUNTAS **4130**
REMACHE  *m*  CON RECUBRIMIENTO **7400**
REMACHE  *m*  CON TRES CORTES **13178**
REMACHE  *m*  CON UN CORTE **11489**
REMACHE  *m*  CON UNA SOLA BANDA DE RECUBRIMIENTO **11478**
REMACHE  *m*  DE DOS HILERAS **4152**
REMACHE  *m*  DE ENSAMBLADO DE FUERZA **9740**
REMACHE  *m*  DE FUERZA **9740**
REMACHE  *m*  DE TRES HILERAS **13177**
REMACHE  *m*  DE UNA HILERA **11487**
REMACHE  *m*  DE UNA HILERA **11487**
REMACHE  *m*  DOBLE **4152**
REMACHE  *m*  EN CALIENTE **6635**
REMACHE  *m*  EN FRÍO **2693**
REMACHE  *m*  EN ROMBO **7799**

**1117**      **RES**

REMACHE *m* SIMPLE **11487**
REMACHE *m* TRIPLE DE TRIPLE HILERA **13177**
REMACHES *m pl* **10646**
REMACHES *m pl* **1241**
REMANENCIA *f* **10473**
REMANENCIA *f* **10445**
REMENDAR **9110**
REMIENDO *m* **9109**
REMIENDO *m* **9111**
REMIENDO *m* (ACCIÓN) **9111**
REMIENDO *m* (RESULTADO) **9109**
REMOJAR **8347**
REMOJO *m* **8348**
REMOLINO *m* **13606**
REMOLINO *m* **13606**
REMOLINO *m* **13827**
REMOLQUES *m pl* **13102**
REMOVER CON LA PALA **13283**
RENDIMIENTO *m* **14010**
RENDIMIENTO *m* **4463**
RENDIMIENTO *m* ANÓDICO **597**
RENDIMIENTO *m* CATÓDICO **2101**
RENDIMIENTO *m* CUÁNTICO **10071**
RENDIMIENTO *m* DE CORRIENTE **3489**
RENDIMIENTO *m* ECONÓMICO **2781**
RENDIMIENTO *m* ELECTROTÉRMICO **4649**
RENDIMIENTO *m* FINAL **5194**
RENDIMIENTO *m* HIDRÁULICO **6684**
RENDIMIENTO *m* INDICADO **6872**
RENDIMIENTO *m* INDUSTRIAL **2781**
RENDIMIENTO *m* MANOMÉTRICO **7984**
RENDIMIENTO *m* MECÁNICO **8100**
RENDIMIENTO *m* ORGÁNICO **8100**
RENDIMIENTO *m* TÉRMICO **12806**
RENDIMIENTO *m* TOTAL **8927**
RENDIMIENTO *m* VOLUMÉTRICO **13602**
RENDIMIENTO COMERCIAL **2781**
RENTABILIDAD *f* **9462**
RENUNCIA **13615**
RENUNCIACIÓN *f* **13615**
REOLOGÍA *f* **10562**
REOSTATO *m* **10563**
REOSTRICCIÓN *f* **9329**
REOSTRICCIÓN *f* **12975**
REPARACIÓN *f* **10459**
REPARAR **10460**
REPARTICIÓN *f* DE CARGAS **7684**
REPARTICIÓN *f* DE MASAS **4082**
REPARTICIÓN *f* DE UNA CARGA **4081**
REPARTIR **1266**

REPASAR **8937**
REPISA *f* **3140**
REPLIEGUE *m* **7395**
REPLIEGUE *m* DE LAMINACIÓN **7395**
REPLIEGUE *m* DE LAMINACIÓN **5510**
REPLIEGUE *m* (TRABAJO DE LAS CHAPAS) **5511**
(REPOSICIÓN) **915**
REPOSO *m* **7100**
REPRESENTACIÓN *f* EXACTA **8872**
REPRESENTACIÓN *f* GEOMÉTRICA **5926**
REPRODUCCIÓN *f* **8481**
REPRODUCCIÓN *f* **10465**
REPRODUCCIÓN *f* AL FERROPRUSIATO EN AZUL SOBRE
   FONDO BLANCO **1373**
REPRODUCCIÓN *f* AL FERROPRUSIATO EN BLANCO SOBRE
   FONDO AZUL **1375**
REPRODUCCIÓN *f* (EN AMPLIACIÓN) **10970**
REPRODUCCIÓN *f* EN PLOMO FUNDIDO **7457**
REPRODUCCIÓN *f* FOTOGRÁFICA **9263**
REPRODUCCIÓN *f* (RESULTADO) **10467**
REPRODUCIR **8484**
REPUJADO *m* **8189**
REPUJADO **8189**
REPUJADO *m* **4684**
REPULSIÓN *f* **10468**
REPULSIÓN *f* MAGNÉTICA **7915**
RESALTO *m* **9917**
RESBALADERA *f* **11587**
RESBALADERO *m* **11585**
RESBALADURA *f* **11611**
RESBALAMIENTO *m* DE LA CORREA **11620**
RESBALAR **11612**
RESBALAR **11612**
RESERVA (DE) **12068**
RESERVAS *f pl* **12294**
RESERVAS *f pl* **12263**
RESIDUO *m* **10475**
RESIDUO *m* DE CALCINACIÓN **6765**
RESIDUO *m* DE LA COMBUSTIÓN **10476**
RESIDUOS *m pl* **12598**
RESÍDUOS *m pl* **13637**
RESIDUOS *m pl* **4331**
RESIDUOS *m* DE FABRICACIÓN **3696**
RESILIENCIA *f* **1918**
RESILIENCIA *f* **6785**
RESILIENCIA *f* **6788**
RESILIENCIA *f* **8671**
RESILIENCIA *f* **10477**
RESILIENCIA *f* **13071**
RESINA *f* **10478**
RESINA *f* **10927**

**RES** 1118

RESINA *f* DAMMAR **3598**
RESINA *f* ELEMÍ **4656**
RESISTENCIA *f* **4738**
RESISTENCIA *f* **11015**
RESISTENCIA *f* **10484**
RESISTENCIA *f* **10502**
RESISTENCIA *f* **13327**
RESISTENCIA *f* **12352**
RESISTENCIA *f* A LA DEFORMACIÓN **10521**
RESISTENCIA *f* A LA DEFORMACIÓN **3328**
RESISTENCIA *f* AL PANDEO **1682**
RESISTENCIA *f* A LA COMPRESIÓN **2870**
RESISTENCIA *f* A LA COMPRESIÓN **13328**
RESISTENCIA *f* A LA CORROSIÓN **3194**
RESISTENCIA *f* A LA DEFORMACIÓN EN UN PERIODE
DETERMINADO **3327**
RESISTENCIA *f* A LA EXTENSIÓN **13331**
RESISTENCIA *f* A LA FATIGA **5052**
RESISTENCIA *f* A LA FLEXIÓN **5424**
RESISTENCIA *f* A LA FLEXIÓN TRANSVERSAL **1192**
RESISTENCIA *f* A LA RODADURA **10703**
RESISTENCIA *f* A LA RUPTURA **13327**
RESISTENCIA *f* A LA RUPTURA TRANSVERSAL **13330**
RESISTENCIA *f* A LA TORSIÓN **13057**
RESISTENCIA *f* A LA TRACCIÓN **13331**
RESISTENCIA *f* A LA TRACCIÓN **12749**
RESISTENCIA *f* A LAS VARIACIONES DE TEMPERATURA O
AL CHOQUE TÉRMICO **12813**
RESISTENCIA *f* A LOS CHOQUES REPETIDOS **12353**
RESISTENCIA *f* AL ACORTAMIENTO **13328**
RESISTENCIA *f* AL ALARGAMIENTO **13331**
RESISTENCIA *f* AL APLASTAMIENTO **13328**
RESISTENCIA *f* AL ARRANQUE **12128**
RESISTENCIA *f* AL CHOQUE **1918**
RESISTENCIA *f* AL CHOQUE **6785**
RESISTENCIA *f* AL CIMBREO **1188**
RESISTENCIA *f* AL DESGASTE **13717**
RESISTENCIA *f* AL DESGASTE **10499**
RESISTENCIA *f* AL DESLIZAMIENTO **10498**
RESISTENCIA *f* AL DESLIZAMIENTO TRANSVERSAL **13330**
RESISTENCIA *f* AL ESFUERZO CORTANTE **13330**
RESISTENCIA *f* AL ESFUERZO CORTANTE **11285**
RESISTENCIA *f* AL ESTADO DE RECOCIDO **569**
RESISTENCIA *f* AL FRENADO **1552**
RESISTENCIA *f* AL MOVIMIENTO **10497**
RESISTENCIA *f* AL PANDEO **3340**
RESISTENCIA *f* AL PLEGADO **1188**
RESISTENCIA *f* APARENTE **6794**
RESISTENCIA *f* COMPLEJA **2822**
RESISTENCIA *f* COMPUESTA **2822**
RESISTENCIA *f* DE AISLAMIENTO **7005**

RESISTENCIA *f* DE BUJÍA DE PRECALDEO **6388**
RESISTENCIA *f* DE MATERIALES **12355**
RESISTENCIA *f* DE ROZAMIENTO **5686**
RESISTENCIA *f* DE RUPTURA POR FRACCIÓN **4742**
RESISTENCIA *f* DE UN CONDUCTOR **10491**
RESISTENCIA *f* DEL AIRE **10492**
RESISTENCIA *f* DIELÉCTRICA O DISRUPTIVA **3900**
RESISTENCIA *f* DISRUPTIVA **4057**
RESISTENCIA *f* EFECTIVA **10261**
RESISTENCIA *f* ELÉCTRICA **4528**
RESISTENCIA *f* EN LA MARCHA EN VACÍO **8600**
RESISTENCIA *f* ESPECÍFICA **4548**
RESISTENCIA *f* ESPECÍFICA ELÉCTRICA **10503**
RESISTENCIA *f* INTERNA **7072**
RESISTENCIA *f* LÍMITE DE CONSISTENCIA **5053**
RESISTENCIA *f* MAGNÉTICA **10444**
RESISTENCIA *f* MOLECULAR **8351**
RESISTENCIA *f* PASIVA **10497**
RESISTENCIA *f* PRIMITIVA **9854**
RESISTENCIA *f* SEGÚN LA TANGENTE **9197**
RESISTENCIA *f* ÚTIL **13426**
RESISTENCIA *f* VIVA **10477**
RESISTIVIDAD *f* **10503**
RESISTIVIDAD *f* **4548**
RESISTIVIDAD *f* EQUIVALENTE **4798**
RESOLUCIÓN *f* **10504**
RESOLVER **11813**
RESONANCIA *f* **10506**
RESORTE *m* **11974**
RESORTE *m* AMORTIGUADOR DE CHOQUES **1688**
RESORTE *m* ANTAGONISTA **11974**
RESORTE *m* ANTAGONISTA **10526**
RESORTE *m* CALIBRADO **1866**
RESORTE *m* CARGADO **11983**
RESORTE *m* CÓNICO **2942**
RESORTE *m* CÓNICO DE LÁMINA PLANA **13605**
RESORTE *m* CÓNICO DE SECCIÓN RECTANGULAR **13605**
RESORTE *m* DE COCHE **2008**
RESORTE *m* DE COMPRESIÓN **2862**
RESORTE *m* DE ÉMBOLO CON CUBETA **9547**
RESORTE *m* DE FLEXIÓN **11993**
RESORTE *m* DE FLEXIÓN ENROLLADO **2649**
RESORTE *m* DE FLEXIÓN RECTO **12312**
RESORTE *m* DE HOJAS **7485**
RESORTE *m* DE HOJAS SUPERPUESTAS **2834**
RESORTE *m* DE INYECTOR **8686**
RESORTE *m* DE LÁMINA **9495**
RESORTE *m* DE LÁMINA RECTANGULAR DE PERFIL
PARABÓLICO **10307**
RESORTE *m* DE REGULADOR **6019**

RESORTE _m_ DE SUSPENSIÓN **1114**
RESORTE _m_ DE TORSIÓN **11994**
RESORTE _m_ DE TRACCIÓN **12759**
RESORTE _m_ DE VÁLVULA **13470**
RESORTE _m_ DE VARIAS HOJAS **2834**
RESORTE _m_ DIAFRAGMA **3875**
RESORTE _m_ EN C **1823**
RESORTE _m_ ESPIRAL **5396**
RESORTE _m_ HELICOIDAL **6427**
RESORTE _m_ HELICOIDAL **6427**
RESORTE _m_ HELICOIDAL **2647**
RESORTE _m_ HELICOIDAL CILÍNDRICO **3585**
RESORTE _m_ RECTANGULAR DE HOJAS SUPERPUESTAS
  **7380**
RESORTE _m_ RECTANGULAR DE LÁMINA PLANA **10306**
RESORTE _m_ TENSO **11983**
RESORTE _m_ TRAPEZOIDAL **13151**
RESORTE _m_ TRIANGULAR **13191**
RESORTE _m_ TRIANGULAR DE HOJAS SUPERPUESTAS **7381**
RESORTE _m_ TRONCOCÓNICO **13236**
RESORTE _m_ ZUNCHADO **11983**
RESPALDO _m_ **12012**
RESPALDO _m_ **917**
RESPALDO _m_ (O ARO _m_) DE UNA RUEDA DE
  ENGRANAJE **11400**
RESPIRACIÓN _f_ PURGADOR _m_ **1593**
RESPIRADERO _m_ **1591**
RESPIRADERO _m_ **3307**
RESPIRADERO _m_ **10614**
RESPIRADERO _m_ **11694**
RESPIRADERO _m_ **13528**
RESPIRADERO _m_ AUTOMÁTICO **1320**
RESPIRADERO _m_ DE ESTANQUEIDAD **10597**
RESPIRADERO _m_ LIBRE **5642**
RESPLANDOR _m_ **6213**
RESQUEBRAJADURA _f_ **5304**
RESQUEBRAJADURA _f_ **5273**
RESQUEBRAJADURA _f_ **3282**
RESQUEBRAJADURA _f_ SUPERFICIAL **12501**
RESQUEBRAJAMIENTO _m_ **5274**
RESQUEBRAJAMIENTO _m_ DE LA MADERA **11948**
RESQUEBRAJAMIENTO _m_ DE LOS AGUJEROS DE REMACHE
  **3286**
RESTAR **12424**
RESTAURACIÓN _f_ **10296**
RESULTADO _m_ DE UNA PRUEBA **10512**
RESULTANTE _f_ **10513**
RETACAR **2113**
RETALLO _m_ **12239**
RETÉN _m_ **11692**
RETENCIÓN _f_ DE AGUA **10182**

RETICULO _m_ **3383**
RETOCAR **5214**
RETOCAR **2113**
RETOCAR EL REGLAJE **10255**
RETOQUE _m_ **11682**
RETOQUE _m_ DE REGLAJE **10256**
RETOQUES _m_ VISIBLES **7407**
RETORNO _m_ DE LA LLAMA **892**
RETORNO _m_ DE LLAMA **906**
RETORNO _m_ RÁPIDO **10106**
RETORNO _m_ VUELTA _f_ **10530**
RETORTA _f_ **10523**
RETORTA TUBULADA _f_ **10525**
RETRACCIÓN _f_ **11397**
RETRACCIÓN _f_ **2437**
RETRACCIÓN _f_ **2437**
RETRASAR **7366**
RETRASAR **6926**
RETRASO _m_ **3730**
RETRASO _m_ DEL CIERRE DE LA VÁLVULA **10519**
RETRASO _m_ EN LA EBULLICIÓN **10517**
RETRASO _m_ EN LA ENTREGA **3731**
RETRASO _m_ EN LA SOLDADURA **12038**
RETROCESO _m_ **919**
RETROVISOR _m_ **10266**
REUNIR POR EMBUTIDO **2957**
REVENIDO _m_ **4230**
REVENIDO _m_ **12731**
REVENIDO _m_ **12733**
REVENIDO _m_ DEFORMACIÓN _f_ POSTERIOR **221**
REVENTÓN _m_ **1767**
REVENTÓN _m_ (DE UN TUBO) **1768**
REVERSIBILIDAD _f_ **10538**
REVERSIBILIDAD _f_ **10537**
REVERSIÓN _f_ **10554**
REVÉS (AL) _m_ **138**
REVESTIDO _m_ DE SUELO **5450**
REVESTIMIENTO _m_ **3274**
REVESTIMIENTO _m_ **2587**
REVESTIMIENTO _m_ **2587**
REVESTIMIENTO _m_ **2590**
REVESTIMIENTO _m_ **2447**
REVESTIMIENTO _m_ **9386**
REVESTIMIENTO _m_ **7623**
REVESTIMIENTO _m_ **7623**
REVESTIMIENTO _m_ **7986**
REVESTIMIENTO _m_ **8999**
REVESTIMIENTO _m_ ANÓDICO **2588**
REVESTIMIENTO _m_ ANTIOXIDANTE **2601**
REVESTIMIENTO _m_ BÁSICO **7584**

**REV** 1120

REVESTIMIENTO *m* CALORÍFUGO **7367**
REVESTIMIENTO *m* CATÓDICO **2102**
REVESTIMIENTO *m* CON BARNIZ FINO **7214**
REVESTIMIENTO *m* DE ALEACIÓN **364**
REVESTIMIENTO *m* DE ANTIFRICCIÓN **7624**
REVESTIMIENTO *m* DE ESTAÑO **2602**
REVESTIMIENTO *m* DE MADERA **13915**
REVESTIMIENTO *m* DE MADERA **13927**
REVESTIMIENTO *m* DE ÓXIDO **2598**
REVESTIMIENTO *m* DE TUBOS **7369**
REVESTIMIENTO *m* DE UN CABLE **715**
REVESTIMIENTO *m* DEL HORNO **5748**
REVESTIMIENTO *m* EXTERIOR **3274**
REVESTIMIENTO *m* FUNDIDO **2032**
REVESTIMIENTO *m* GALVÁNICO EN TAMBOR **1016**
REVESTIMIENTO *m* INTERIOR **7623**
REVESTIMIENTO *m* METÁLICO **8194**
REVESTIMIENTO *m* METÁLICO **2596**
REVESTIMIENTO *m* METÁLICO POR GALVANOPLASTIA **9503**
REVESTIMIENTO *m* METALIZADO **8200**
REVESTIMIENTO *m* NO METÁLICO **8641**
REVESTIMIENTO *m* NO METÁLICO **2597**
REVESTIMIENTO *m* POR COMPOSICIÓN KB TI **7583**
REVESTIMIENTO *m* POR PINTURA **2595**
REVESTIMIENTO *m* PROTECTOR **9949**
REVESTIMIENTO *m* QUÍMICO **2297**
REVESTIMIENTO *m* (RECUBRIMIENTO) ANÓDICO **599**
REVESTIMIENTO *m* REFRACTARIO ÁCIDO **123**
REVESTIMIENTO *m* VÍTREO **2603**
REVESTIMIENTOS *m pl* DE DIFUSIÓN **3930**
REVESTIMIENTOS *m pl* DE PROTECCIÓN **9792**
REVESTIMIENTOS *m pl* ELECTROLÍTICOS O GALVANOPLÁSTICOS **2593**
REVESTIMIENTOS *m pl* ESMALTADOS **2594**
REVESTIMIENTOS *m pl* POR TEMPLE **2592**
REVESTIR **7598**
REVESTIR **7598**
REVESTIR DE COBRE **3124**
REVESTIR UN TUBO **3263**
REVESTIR UN TUBO **3263**
REVESTIR UNA CALDERA DE MAMPOSTERÍA **11215**
REVISAR **8937**
REVISIÓN *f* **10287**
REVOCAR **9464**
REVOCAR **1909**
REVOCO *m* **9463**
REVOLUCIÓN *f* **10557**
REVOLUCIÓN *f* **13279**
REVOLUCIÓN *f* MINUTO **10814**
REVOLUCIÓNES *f pl* POR MINUTO **10814**

REVOLUCIONES *f pl* POR MINUTO **8690**
REVOLVEDOR *m* **12260**
REVUELTA *f* (EN CARRETERAS) **7741**
REZUMAMIENTO *m* **12540**
RIESGO *m* **3608**
RIGIDEZ *f* **10591**
RIGIDEZ **10591**
RIGIDEZ *f* A LA FLEXIÓN **5423**
RIOSTRA *f* **12396**
RIZADO *m* **13985**
RIZO *m* **14014**
ROBLADURA *f* **10639**
ROBLADURA *f* **10628**
ROBLÓN *m* **10621**
ROBLÓN *m* DE CABEZA ACHAFLANADA **2946**
ROBLÓN *m* DE CABEZA AVELLANADA **10635**
ROBLÓN *m* DE CABEZA AVELLANADA ABOMBADA **3249**
ROBLÓN *m* DE CABEZA CILÍNDRICA **10632**
ROBLÓN *m* DE CABEZA CÓNICA **2946**
ROBLÓN *m* DE CABEZA DE GOTA DE SEBO **10633**
ROBLÓN *m* DE CABEZA HEMISFÉRICA **10637**
ROBLÓN *m* DE CABEZA IGUALADA **10635**
ROBLÓN *m* DE CABEZA METIDA **10635**
ROBLÓN *m* DE CABEZA PERDIDA **10635**
ROBLÓN *m* DE CABEZA PLANA **10634**
ROBLÓN *m* DE CABEZA REDONDA **10636**
ROBLÓN *m* DE CABEZA TRONCOCÓNICA **9030**
ROBLÓN *m* DE CADENA **2214**
ROBLÓN *m* DE CORREAS **1155**
ROBLÓN *m* DE ESTANQUEIDAD **12922**
ROBLÓN *m* EN EL BORDE DE LA CHAPA **10622**
ROBLONADO *m* **10643**
ROBLONADO *m* A MANO **6248**
ROBLONADO *m* CON ESPIGA **9321**
ROBLONADO *m* CON MARTILLO **6248**
ROBLONADO *m* CON ROBLÓN SIN CABEZA **9321**
ROBLONADO *m* EN ESPIRAL **11918**
ROBLONADO *m* MECÁNICO **7854**
ROBLONADO *m* PARA CONSTRUCCIONES METÁLICAS **9740**
ROBLONAR **10629**
ROBLONAR **2516**
ROBLONAR EN CALIENTE **6634**
ROBLONAR EN FRÍO **2692**
ROBLONES *m pl* **1241**
ROBLONES *m pl* **10646**
ROBLONES (DISTANCIA ENTRE ROBLONES) ENTRE CENTROS DE UNA LÍNEA A OTRA REMACHADOR *m pl* **13145**
ROCA *f* **10651**
ROCA *f* ERRÁTICA **4821**
ROCA *f* HENDIBLE EN CAPAS **2486**

ROCA _f_ MADRE **5802**
ROCE _m_ **5668**
ROCE _m_ INTERIOR DE LOS LÍQUIDOS **5473**
ROCE _m_ INTERNO **7065**
RODADURA _f_ **10696**
RODAJE _m_ **10855**
RODAJE _m_ **7407**
RODAJE _m_ **6106**
RODAJE _m_ CON ESMERIL **6111**
RODAJE _m_ CON LÍQUIDO **6564**
RODAJE _m_ (DE UN COCHE) **1587**
RODAMIENTO _m_ **1117**
RODAMIENTO _m_ **954**
RODAMIENTO _m_ DE AGUJAS **8518**
RODAMIENTO _m_ DE BOLAS **954**
RODAMIENTO _m_ DE BOLAS **618**
RODAMIENTO _m_ DE BOLAS DE CARGA AXIAL **12901**
RODAMIENTO _m_ DE BOLAS DE CARGA RADIAL **10130**
RODAMIENTO _m_ DE BOLAS DE CARGAS RADIAL Y AXIAL COMBINADAS **538**
RODAMIENTO _m_ DE BOLAS DE EMPUJE RADIAL Y AXIAL COMBINADOS **538**
RODAMIENTO _m_ DE PRESIÓN LATERAL **10130**
RODAMIENTO _m_ DE RODILLOS **10680**
RODAMIENTO _m_ DE RODILLOS **618**
RODAMIENTO _m_ DE RODILLOS CILÍNDRICOS **10682**
RODAMIENTO _m_ DE RODILLOS CÓNICOS **10683**
RODAMIENTO _m_ DE RÓTULA SOBRE RODILLOS **10681**
RODAMIENTO _m_ LISO **9424**
RODAR **10665**
RODAR UN MOTOR **10835**
RODILLO _m_ **8436**
RODILLO _m_ **12334**
RODILLO _m_ **12334**
RODILLO _m_ **10679**
RODILLO _m_ **10671**
RODILLO _m_ **10671**
RODILLO _m_ **10679**
RODILLO _m_ **10671**
RODILLO _m_ **1895**
RODILLO _m_ **1112**
RODILLO _m_ **2645**
RODILLO _m_ **2645**
RODILLO _m_ ABULTADO **1017**
RODILLO _m_ CILÍNDRICO **3589**
RODILLO _m_ CÓNICO **12660**
RODILLO _m_ CÓNICO **12660**
RODILLO _m_ DE CONTACTO **3008**
RODILLO _m_ DE FRICCIÓN **5679**
RODILLO _m_ DE LEVA **12674**
RODILLO _m_ DE RODAMIENTO **10844**

RODILLO _m_ DE RODAMIENTO (RUEDA PORTADORA) **10854**
RODILLO _m_ DE UNA CADENA **10688**
RODILLO _m_ EMPUJADOR **1885**
RODILLO _m_ GUÍA **6161**
RODILLO _m_ GUIADOR **6161**
RODILLO _m_ PARA RODAMIENTOS **1112**
RODILLO _m_ PROPULSOR **1885**
RODILLO _m_ TENSOR **4910**
RODILLO _m_ TENSOR **12334**
RODILLO _m_ TENSOR LENIX **13750**
RODILLO CÓNICO _m_ **2941**
RODILLOS _m pl_ **10695**
RODILLOS _m pl_ DE PULIMENTO DRAPEADOS **2539**
RODIO _m_ **10564**
ROEDERA _f_ **8553**
ROEDURA _f_ **8552**
ROJO _m_ **10329**
ROJO _m_ AL FUEGO **10330**
ROJO _m_ CEREZA **2326**
ROJO _m_ CLARO **1613**
ROJO _m_ CONGO **2935**
ROJO _m_ DE CROMO **2374**
ROJO _m_ DE INGLATERRA **3355**
ROJO _m_ DE PRUSIA **7148**
ROJO _m_ DE PULIR **7148**
ROJO _m_ INGLÉS **7148**
ROJO _m_ NACIENTE **1295**
ROJO _m_ OSCURO **4367**
ROJO _m_ VIVO **1613**
ROLLIZOS _m pl_ (MADERA) **7723**
ROLLO _m_ DE FLEJE **1738**
ROMBO _m_ **10568**
ROMBO _m_ **10568**
ROMBOEDRO _m_ **10566**
ROMBOIDE _m_ **10567**
ROMPEDIZO _m_ **1627**
ROMPEDOR DE CARBÓN _m_ **2658**
ROMPEDOR DE HIERRO _m_ **631**
ROSA _f_ DE LOS VIENTOS **2800**
ROSCA _f_ **3535**
ROSCA _f_ **5092**
ROSCA _f_ **11045**
ROSCA **12857**
ROSCA _f_ BASTA **2575**
ROSCA _f_ DE PASO ALARGADO **10105**
ROSCA _f_ DE PASO ALARGADO **10105**
ROSCA _f_ DE PASO PEQUEÑO **11647**
ROSCA _f_ EXTERIOR **7955**
ROSCA _f_ EXTERIOR **4961**

**ROS** 1122

ROSCA  *f*  EXTERIOR **4960**
ROSCA  *f*  FINA **5201**
ROSCA  *f*  FINA **5204**
ROSCA  *f*  GASTADA **13981**
ROSCA  *f*  GASTADA **13981**
ROSCA  *f*  HEMBRA **5092**
ROSCA  *f*  INTERIOR **5092**
ROSCA  *f*  INTERNA **7078**
ROSCA  *f*  MACHO **7955**
ROSCA  *f*  PLANA (O RECTANGULAR) **12030**
ROSCA  *f*  REDONDA **10802**
ROSCA  *f*  TRAPEZOIDAL **1814**
ROSCA  *f*  TRIANGULAR **545**
ROSCA DERECHA **10585**
ROSCADO  *m*  **11045**
ROSCADO  *m*  **12857**
ROSCADO  *m*  **12868**
ROSCADO  *m*  **3535**
ROSCADO  *m*  CILÍNDRICO **9065**
ROSCADO  *m*  CÓNICO **12666**
ROSCADO  *m*  EXTERIOR **7955**
ROSCADO  *m*  EXTERIOR **4961**
ROTA  *f*  **10236**
ROTACIÓN  *f*  **10765**
ROTACIÓN  *f*  A LA DERECHA **2507**
ROTACIÓN  *f*  A LA IZQUIERDA **3238**
ROTOR  *m*  **707**
ROTOR  *m*  **10767**
ROTOR  *m*  **6795**
RÓTULA  *f*  **7336**
ROTURA  *f*  **10858**
ROTURA  *f*  **10861**
ROTURA  *f*  **10858**
ROTURA  *f*  **5620**
ROTURA  *f*  DE UN TUBO **9353**
ROTURA LAMINAR  *f*  **7378**
ROTURA LISA  *f*  **4871**
ROTURA SEDOSA  *f*  **11454**
ROTURA TRANSCRISTALINA  *f*  **13117**
ROZAMIENTO  *m*  DE LOS MUÑONES **7258**
ROZAMIENTO  *m*  DE RESBALADURA **11601**
ROZAMIENTO  *m*  EN LOS COJINETES **1105**
RUBIDIO  *m*  **10829**
RÚBRICA  *f*  **10340**
RUDLA  *f*  **19**
RUEDA  *f*  **9402**
RUEDA  *f*  **13692**
RUEDA  *f*  **13810**
RUEDA  *f*  ATMOSFÉRICA **13861**
RUEDA  *f*  CENTRAL DE UN TREN PLANETARIO **12457**

RUEDA  *f*  CILÍNDRICA **3591**
RUEDA  *f*  CONDUCIDA **4300**
RUEDA  *f*  CONDUCTORA **4318**
RUEDA  *f*  CÓNICA **1229**
RUEDA  *f*  DE AGRIMENSURA **8092**
RUEDA  *f*  DE ÁNGULO **1229**
RUEDA  *f*  DE CANGILONES **8960**
RUEDA  *f*  DE CENTRO LLENO **4012**
RUEDA  *f*  DE COSTADO (HIDRÁULICA) **7769**
RUEDA  *f*  DE DIENTES DE DOBLE ÁNGULO **13176**
RUEDA  *f*  DE DIENTES DE MADERA **8400**
RUEDA  *f*  DE DIENTES PERPENDICULARES **3399**
RUEDA  *f*  DE DIENTES TALLADOS **3508**
RUEDA  *f*  DE DIENTES TALLADOS **3508**
RUEDA  *f*  DE DIFERENCIAL **3917**
RUEDA  *f*  DE DISCO **4012**
RUEDA  *f*  DE DISCO **4012**
RUEDA  *f*  DE DISCO ABOMBADA **4037**
RUEDA  *f*  DE DISCO PLANA **5379**
RUEDA  *f*  DE ENGRANAJE BRUTA **10773**
RUEDA  *f*  DE ENGRANAJE INTERIOR **7079**
RUEDA  *f*  DE ESPIGAS **4143**
RUEDA  *f*  DE FRICCIÓN **5682**
RUEDA  *f*  DE FRICCIÓN CILÍNDRICA **12007**
RUEDA  *f*  DE FRICCIÓN (CON LLANTA EN FORMA DE CUÑA) **13732**
RUEDA  *f*  DE FRICCIÓN CÓNICA **1225**
RUEDA  *f*  DE FUERZA (MOTRIZ) **6402**
RUEDA  *f*  DE FUERZA (MOTRIZ) **6402**
RUEDA  *f*  DE GRES **6118**
RUEDA  *f*  DE MANDO **4318**
RUEDA  *f*  DE MUELA **6115**
RUEDA  *f*  DE PALETAS **13479**
RUEDA  *f*  DE PALETAS **13479**
RUEDA  *f*  DE RADIOS **11951**
RUEDA  *f*  DE RECAMBIO **2243**
RUEDA  *f*  DE REPUESTO **2243**
RUEDA  *f*  DE REPUESTO **11835**
RUEDA  *f*  DE TORNILLO SIN FIN **13975**
RUEDA  *f*  DE TRACCIÓN PARA CADENAS O CABLES **11662**
RUEDA  *f*  DE TRANSMISIÓN **13128**
RUEDA  *f*  DE TRANSPORTE **6754**
RUEDA  *f*  DE TRINQUETE **1061**
RUEDA  *f*  DE TRINQUETE **2495**
RUEDA  *f*  DE TRINQUETE **10225**
RUEDA  *f*  DE TRINQUETE **10225**
RUEDA  *f*  DE TRINQUETE **10225**
RUEDA  *f*  DE UNA TURBINA **13823**
RUEDA  *f*  DENTADA **9444**
RUEDA  *f*  DENTADA **5903**

1123          **SAL**

RUEDA *f* DENTADA **5903**
RUEDA *f* DENTADA BRUTA DE FUNDICIÓN **10773**
RUEDA *f* DENTADA CILÍNDRICA **12009**
RUEDA *f* DENTADA CON DISCOS LATERALES **11402**
RUEDA *f* DENTADA CON PESTAÑA **11402**
RUEDA *f* DENTADA INTERRUMPIDA **7975**
RUEDA *f* DENTADA RECTA **12009**
RUEDA *f* DENTADA Y FUNDIDA EN BRUTO **10773**
RUEDA *f* ELÍPTICA **4677**
RUEDA *f* ELÍPTICA **4677**
RUEDA *f* ESTRELLADA **12109**
RUEDA *f* HELICOIDAL **6425**
RUEDA *f* HIDRÁULICA DE ATAQUE FRONTAL **6465**
RUEDA *f* HIPERBÓLICA **11534**
RUEDA *f* HIPERBÓLICA **11534**
RUEDA *f* INTERMEDIA **6754**
RUEDA *f* LIBRE **5644**
RUEDA *f* LIBRE **5651**
RUEDA *f* LIBRE **4318**
RUEDA *f* MOTRIZ **2217**
RUEDA *f* MOTRIZ **5889**
RUEDA *f* MOTRIZ **4318**
RUEDA *f* PLANETARIA **9444**
RUEDA *f* POR DEBAJO **13355**
RUEDA *f* POR ENCIMA **8960**
RUEDA *f* PORTADORA **10854**
RUEDA *f* PULIDORA **9604**
RUEDA *f* RECEPTORA **4300**
RUEDA *f* RECTA **3591**
RUEDA *f* SATÉLITE **9444**
RUEDA DENTADA *f* **3399**
RUEDA GUIADA *f* **4300**
RUEDAS *f pl* **7027**
RUEDAS *f pl* DE CONJUNTO **7027**
RUEDECILLA *f* DEL PLANÍMETRO **13817**
RUGOSIDAD *f* **9011**
RUGOSIDAD *f* **10792**
RUGOSIDAD *f* **10792**
RUGOSIDAD *f* DE SUPERFICIE **12518**
RUGOSÍMETRO *m* **12509**
RUGOSÍMETRO *m* REGISTRADOR **12498**
RUIDO *m* **8608**
RUIDO *m* DE UNA BOMBA **7331**
RULETA *f* **10697**
RUPTOR *m* **7949**
RUPTURA *f* **9353**
RUPTURA *f* **10861**
RUPTURA *f* **10861**
RUPTURA *f* **10858**
RUPTURA *f* **10858**

RUPTURA *f* **3278**
RUPTURA *f* **5617**
RUPTURA *f* BRUSCA DEL CUERPO DE UN TORNILLO **13309**
RUPTURA *f* DE FATIGA / DE CONSISTENCIA **4740**
RUPTURA *f* DE LA CAPA DE ESCORIAS **5354**
RUPTURA *f* DE LAS CABEZAS DE ROBLÓN **11999**
RUPTURA *f* DE UN TUBO **1768**
RUPTURA *f* DEL ROBLÓN POR CIZALLADURA **11293**
RUPTURA *f* EN CALIENTE **6621**
RUPTURA *f* POR FLEXIÓN **5488**
RUTENIO *m* **10874**
SACABOCADOS *m* **10000**
SACADORES *m pl* DE CONOS **2929**
SACAR LOS REMACHES **3511**
SACUDIDA *f* **4529**
SACUDIDA *f* **11359**
SACUDIDA *f* ELÉCTRICA **4529**
SAGITA *f* **10613**
SAL *f* ALCALINA **338**
SAL *f* AMONIACAL **462**
SAL *f* COMÚN **2790**
SAL *f* DE ACEDERAS **10907**
SAL *f* DE EPSON **7889**
SAL *f* DE ESTAÑO **12100**
SAL *f* DE FÓSFORO **8241**
SAL *f* DE GLAUBER **5967**
SAL *f* DE SEDLITZ **7889**
SAL *f* DE SIEGNETTE **11729**
SAL *f* DE SOSA **551**
SAL *f* DOBLE **4153**
SAL *f* GEMA **10653**
SAL *f* INGLESA **7889**
SAL *f* MARINA **2790**
SAL *f* MICROCÓSMICA **8241**
SAL *f* NEUTRA **8546**
SAL *f* (QUÍMICA) **10904**
SAL *f* SOLVAY **455**
SAL *f* VOLÁTIL **461**
SALA *f* DE CALDERAS **1418**
SALA *f* DE CALDERAS **1418**
SALA *f* DE DIBUJO Y PROYECTOS **3800**
SALA *f* DE MÁQUINAS **4753**
SALA *f* DE MÁQUINAS **4757**
SALA *f* DE MÁQUINAS **7855**
SALA *f* DE MÁQUINAS **7855**
SALA DE CALDERAS *f* **12270**
SALA DE CALDERAS *f* **1418**
SALA DE MÁQUINAS *f* **4757**
SALARIO *m* **3594**

**SAL** 1124

SALARIO *m* **13613**
SALARIO *m* **10897**
SALARIO *m* **10897**
SALARIO *m* A DESTAJO **9295**
SALARIO *m* A DESTAJO **9295**
SALES *m pl* DE PULIMENTO **1690**
SALES *m pl* PARA BAÑOS **9506**
SALES *m pl* QUE AUMENTAN LA CONDUCTIBILIDAD DE UNA SOLUCIÓN **2915**
SALIDA *f* **8900**
SALIDA *f* DE COLADA (AGUJERO) **12645**
SALIDA *f* DEL AGUA **8899**
SALIDA *f* DEL MATERIAL **5465**
SALIDA *f* EN LINGOTERA **9717**
SALIENTE *m* **9910**
SALIENTE **9917**
SALIENTE **9913**
SALIENTE **2093**
SALIENTE *m* **4301**
SALIENTE *m* DE ENSAMBLADO RECTIFICADO (DE UNA PIEZA DE FUNDICIÓN) **5007**
SALIR **4832**
SALITRE **2330**
SALITRE **10903**
SÁLMER *m* **57**
SALMUERA *f* **1617**
SALPICADURA *f* **11842**
SALPICADURAS *f pl* DE METAL **11929**
SALSERILLA *f* **10946**
SALTADORA *f* **5665**
SALTAR **10273**
SALTO *m* (O GOLPEO *m*) DE LA CORREA **13825**
SÁMAGO *m* **10936**
SAMARIO *m* **10914**
SANDÁRACA *f* **10927**
SANGRAR **8554**
SANGRE *f* DE DRAGO **4203**
SANGRÍA *f* **1321**
SANGRÍA DE HIERRO FUNDIDO **12004**
SANGUINA *f* **8720**
SAPONIFICABLE **10933**
SAPONIFICABLE **10932**
SAPONIFICAR **10934**
SAPONITA *f* **10935**
SAPONITA *f* **10935**
SARRO *m* ANTIMONIAL **9675**
SATÉLITE *m* **9444**
SATÉLITE *m* **9447**
SATÉLITE *m* **6168**
SATÉLITE *m* DE DIFERENCIAL **3918**
SATINADO *m* **5408**

SATINAR **11679**
SATURACIÓN *f* **10943**
SATURACIÓN *f* MAGNÉTICA **7916**
SATURAR **10939**
SEÄNL *f* **5879**
SEBO *m* **12608**
SEBO *m* DE BUEY **1128**
SEBO *m* VEGETAL DE CHINA **2342**
SECADERO *m* **4355**
SECADERO *m* **4256**
SECADERO *m* **4256**
SECADEROS *m* DE FORRAJES **4259**
SECADEROS *m pl* DE GRANOS **4258**
SECADO *m* **4359**
SECADO *m* **928**
SECADOR *m* **4356**
SECADORA *f* CENTRÍFUGA **6703**
SECANTE *m* **4257**
SECANTE *m* **4256**
SECANTE *f* **11099**
SECAR **4338**
SECAR LA MADERA AL AIRE LIBRE **11094**
SECAR POR CENTRIFUGACIÓN **6702**
SECCIÓN *f* **697**
SECCIÓN *f* **7717**
SECCIÓN *f* **12511**
SECCIÓN *f* **11122**
SECCIÓN *f* **11122**
SECCIÓN *f* **11111**
SECCIÓN *f* **11122**
SECCIÓN *f* ANULAR **587**
SECCIÓN *f* CARGADA **4460**
SECCIÓN *f* CIRCULAR **2410**
SECCIÓN *f* CON NERVIOS **6550**
SECCIÓN *f* CÓNICA **2940**
SECCIÓN *f* CÓNICA **13735**
SECCIÓN *f* CUADRADA **12017**
SECCIÓN *f* DE MEDIACAÑA **11170**
SECCIÓN *f* DE PASO **3374**
SECCIÓN *f* DE PASO DE UNA VÁLVULA **11121**
SECCIÓN *f* DE RUPTURA **3373**
SECCIÓN *f* DE RUPTURA **5620**
SECCIÓN *f* DEL ORIFICIO DE SALIDA **4020**
SECCIÓN *f* EFICAZ **3371**
SECCIÓN *f* ELÍPTICA **4674**
SECCIÓN *f* ESTRELLADA **12110**
SECCIÓN *f* LIBRE **3374**
SECCIÓN *f* MACROSCÓPICA **7875**
SECCIÓN *f* NORMAL **8654**
SECCIÓN *f* OBLICUA **8711**

1125     **SEN**

SECCIÓN *f* OVAL **8917**
SECCIÓN *f* PELIGROSA **3609**
SECCIÓN *f* PRINCIPAL **9868**
SECCIÓN *f* RECTA **8654**
SECCIÓN *f* RECTANGULAR **10302**
SECCIÓN *f* RECTANGULAR **6550**
SECCIÓN *f* SEMICIRCULAR **11170**
SECCIÓN *f* SOMETIDA A UN ESFUERZO **3375**
SECCIÓN *f* SOMETIDA A UN ESFUERZO **3376**
SECCIÓN *f* TÉCNICA **3800**
SECCIÓN *f* TRANSVERSAL **3378**
SECCIÓN *f* TRAPEZOIDAL **13183**
SECCIÓN *f* TRIANGULAR **13188**
SECCIÓN *f* ÚTIL **13422**
SECCIÓN DE PASO DE UNA VÁLVULA *f* **11121**
SECCIÓN DE UN DIBUJO *f* **11112**
SECCIÓN (RECTA U OBLICUA) DE UNA VIGA **11116**
SECCIÓN TRANSVERSAL *f* **11111**
SECCIÓN TRANSVERSAL *f* **3377**
SECTOR *m* CIRCULAR **11126**
SECTOR *m* DE UN CÍRCULO **11126**
SECTOR *m* DENTADO **13024**
SECTOR *m* ESFÉRICO **11127**
SECTOR *m* GRADUADO **6867**
SECUENCIA *f* DE CALIBRES **9097**
SECUENCIAL **11194**
SEDA *f* **11452**
SEDA *f* **12614**
SEDA *f* ARTIFICIAL **736**
SEDÁN *m* **10902**
SEDÁN *m* **11128**
SEDÁN *m* DE CUATRO PUERTAS **5599**
SEDIMENTACIÓN *f* **11228**
SEDIMENTACIÓN *f* **11228**
SEDIMENTARSE **11227**
SEDIMENTO *m* **3773**
SEGADORAS *f pl* ARRASTRADAS POR TRACTOR **8439**
SEGADORAS *f pl* DE HIERBA **5525**
SEGMENTO *m* **11135**
SEGMENTO *m* DE CHAPA (DE INDUCIDO) **3160**
SEGMENTO *m* DE CÍRCULO **11136**
SEGMENTO *m* DE COMPRESIÓN **2861**
SEGMENTO *m* DE CORONA CIRCULAR **10603**
SEGMENTO *m* DE ÉMBOLO CON JUNTA SOLAPADA **9382**
SEGMENTO *m* DE ÉMBOLO CON RANURA EN ÁNGULO RECTO **9380**
SEGMENTO *m* DE ÉMBOLO DE JUNTA EN BISEL **9381**
SEGMENTO *m* DE ÉMBOLO PARTIDO **11944**
SEGMENTO *m* DE ESTANQUEIDAD **2867**
SEGMENTO *m* DE FRENO **1542**

SEGMENTO *m* DE FUEGO **13034**
SEGMENTO *m* DE PISTÓN **9379**
SEGMENTO *m* DE PISTÓN EXCÉNTRICO **4429**
SEGMENTO *m* DE RECTA **11118**
SEGMENTO *m* DEL PISTÓN **9379**
SEGMENTO *m* ESFÉRICO DE DOS BASES **14051**
SEGMENTO *m* ESFÉRICO DE UNA BASE **11137**
SEGMENTO *m* (O ANILLO *m*) DE TENSIÓN (O DE FONDO) **1565**
SEGMENTO *m* RASCADOR **8750**
SEGMENTO *m* RASCADOR **8775**
SEGMENTO ESFÉRICO *m* **11137**
SEGREGACIÓN *f* **11139**
SEGREGACIÓN *f* **7635**
SEGREGACIÓN *f* **3172**
SEGREGACIÓN *f* MAYOR **6925**
SEGREGACIÓN *f* MAYOR **8660**
SEGREGACIÓN *f* MENOR **8235**
SEGUNDO FILTRO *m* **11101**
SEGUNDO VACIADO *m* **4383**
SEGURIDAD *f* DE BUEN FUNCIONAMIENTO **10439**
SEGURIDAD *f* DE FUNCIONAMIENTO **10439**
SEGURIDAD *f* DE SERVICIO **10439**
SEGURO *m* (O BLOQUEO *m*) DE LAS TUERCAS **7707**
SELENIO *m* **11146**
SELFINDUCCIÓN *f* **11156**
SELLAR **5872**
SELLO DE GOMA *m* **13722**
SEMBRADORA *f* AL VOLEO **11129**
SEMICÉLULA *f* **6204**
SEMICIRCULAR **11169**
SEMICÍRCULO *m* **11179**
SEMICOJINETE *m* **1773**
SEMICOJINETE *m* INFERIOR **1487**
SEMICOJINETE *m* SUPERIOR **13030**
SEMICOJINETE SUPERIOR *m* **13030**
SEMICOJINETES *m pl* **11947**
SEMIDIESEL **11171**
SEMIEJE *m* **11167**
SEMIESFERA *f* **6438**
SEMIPERFORADORA *f* DE PRECISIÓN **11172**
SEMIRREMOLQUE *m* **11178**
SEÑAL *f* **8012**
SEÑAL *f* ACÚSTICA **816**
SEÑAL *f* DE ALARMA **306**
SEÑAL *f* ÓPTICA **13580**
SEÑALAR **8008**
SENO *m* **11475**
SENSIBILIDAD *f* AL ESPESOR **8027**
SENSIBILIDAD *f* DE UN INSTRUMENTO **11188**

**SEN** 1126

SENSIBILIDAD *f* MAGNÉTICA **7918**
SENSIBLIDAD *f* AL EFECTO DE ENTALLADURA **8670**
SENSOR DE POSICIÓN *m* **9649**
SENTIDO *m* DE LAMINADO **10698**
SENTIDO *m* DE MARCHA **11183**
SENTIDO *m* DE ROTACIÓN **3992**
SENTIDO *m* DE UNA FUERZA **11182**
SENTIDO *m* DEL MOVIMIENTO **11183**
SENTIDO OPUESTO A LAS AGUJAS DE UN RELOJ (EN) **3237**
SEPARACIÓN *f* **4063**
SEPARACIÓN *f* DE UNA MEZCLA **11192**
SEPARACIÓN *f* ELECTROLÍTICA **4602**
SEPARACIÓN *f* ELECTROMAGNÉTICA **4618**
SEPARACIÓN *f* ELECTROSTÁTICA **4646**
SEPARACIÓN *f* MAGNÉTICA **7917**
SEPARACIÓN *f* NEUMÁTICA **290**
SEPARACIÓN *f* (QUÍMICA) **11191**
SEPARADOR *m* **11973**
SEPARADOR *m* **7620**
SEPARADOR *m* **4067**
SEPARADOR *m* **4068**
SEPARADOR *m* DE ACEITE **8778**
SEPARADOR *m* DE AGUA **12188**
SEPARADOR *m* DE VAPOR **12184**
SEPARADOR DE ACEITE PARA VAPOR **8779**
SEPARADOR DE AGUJEROS *m* **9187**
SEPARADOR DE RANURAS *m* **11639**
SEPARADOR SIN TALADRAR *m* **1306**
SEPARADOR TALADRADO *m* **4272**
SEPARADORES *m pl* DE POLVO **4391**
SEPARAR (QUÍMICA) **11189**
SEPARARSE **9760**
SERIE *f* **10462**
SERIE *f* **11219**
SERIE *f* **11213**
SERIE *f* **11203**
SERIE *f* BINOMIAL **1260**
SERIE *f* CONVERGENTE **3065**
SERIE *f* DE ENGRANAJES **5907**
SERIE *f* DE ENGRANAJES **7050**
SERIE *f* DE MÁQUINAS **11213**
SERIE *f* DE OPERACIONES **2222**
SERIE *f* DE PESOS **11219**
SERIE *f* DIVERGENTE **4094**
SERIE *f* EXPONENCIAL **4943**
SERIE *f* FINITA **5232**
SERIE *f* HOMÓLOGA **6562**
SERIE *f* INFINITA **6909**
SERIE *f* LOGARÍTMICA **7719**
SERPENTÍN *m* **12161**

SERPENTÍN *m* **9346**
SERPENTÍN *m* **2645**
SERPENTÍN *m* **2645**
SERPENTÍN *m* DE REFRIGERACIÓN **13978**
SERPENTINA *f* **11204**
SERRAR **10951**
SERRERÍA *f* **10956**
SERRÍN **10953**
SERRUCHO *m* **11659**
SERRUCHO *m* **2802**
SERVICIO *m* **8837**
SERVICIO *m* CONTINUO **9209**
SERVICIO *m* CONTINUO **3038**
SERVICIO *m* INTERMITENTE **7056**
SERVIR DE APOYO **12491**
SERVODIRECCIÓN *f* **9743**
SERVODIRECCIÓN *f* **9743**
SERVOFRENO *m* **9731**
SERVOFRENO *m* **1457**
SERVOMECANISMO *m* **11210**
SERVOMOTOR *m* **11211**
SERVOMOTOR *m* DE ARRANQUE **1018**
SERVOMOTOR *m* LANZADOR **1018**
SESQUICLORURO *m* DE CROMO **2381**
SESQUIÓXIDO *m* DE COBALTO **2611**
SESQUIÓXIDO *m* DE CROMO **2382**
SESQUIÓXIDO *m* DE HIERRO **7148**
SESQUIÓXIDO *m* DE MANGANESO **7970**
SHUNT *m* (DERIVACIÓN) **11403**
SIDEROSA *f* **11421**
SIDERURGIA *f* **8209**
SIENTA *f* **12565**
SIERRA *f* **10950**
SIERRA *f* A LO LARGO **10609**
SIERRA *f* CIRCULAR **2428**
SIERRA *f* CIRCULAR **2427**
SIERRA *f* CIRCULAR **2427**
SIERRA *f* DE BASTIDOR **5629**
SIERRA *f* DE CADENA **2216**
SIERRA *f* DE CINTA **978**
SIERRA *f* DE CINTA **977**
SIERRA *f* DE CONTORNEAR **1505**
SIERRA *f* DE ENCHAPADO **13526**
SIERRA *f* DE ENRASAR **12741**
SIERRA *f* DE ESCOPLEAR **8193**
SIERRA *f* DE ESPIGAS **12741**
SIERRA *f* DE ESPIGAS **12741**
SIERRA *f* DE HENDER DE NUEVO **5628**
SIERRA *f* DE HOJA SIN FIN **978**
SIERRA *f* DE MADERA **13917**

**1127**    **SIS**

SIERRA *f* DE MANO **6249**
SIERRA *f* DE METALES **6196**
SIERRA *f* DE METALES **8186**
SIERRA *f* DE METALES CON MANGO DE PISTOLA **9369**
SIERRA *f* DE MONTURA METÁLICA **8186**
SIERRA *f* DE RECORTAR **5665**
SIERRA *f* DE RECORTAR **3108**
SIERRA *f* DE TRONZONAR **3365**
SIERRA *f* EN CALIENTE **6630**
SIERRA *f* EN FRÍO **2688**
SIERRA *f* INVERTIDA **897**
SIERRA *f* MECÁNICA **9747**
SIERRA *f* OSCILANTE **4337**
SIERRA *f* PARA METALES AL ROJO **6630**
SIERRA DE BASTIDOR (O DE BALLESTA) *f* **5629**
SIERRA DE MANO *f* **5629**
SIERRAS *f pl* DE LEÑOS **10963**
SIFÓN *m* **11517**
SIFÓN *m* **11517**
SIFÓN *m* (DE MANÓMETRO) **11514**
SIGNO *m* **11429**
SIGNO *m* NEGATIVO **8532**
SIGNO *m* POSITIVO **9661**
SILBATO *m* **13829**
SILBATO *m* AVISADOR **307**
SILBATO *m* DE ALARMA **307**
SILBATO *m* DE VAPOR **12190**
SILENCIADOR *m* **8448**
SILENCIADOR *m* **8448**
SILENCIADOR *m* **11431**
SILENCIADOR *m* **11431**
SILEX *m* **5427**
SILEX *m* PIRÓGENO **5427**
SILICATO *m* **11437**
SILICATO *m* DE ALÚMINA **425**
SILICATO *m* DE HIERRO **7149**
SILICATO *m* DE MAGNESIO **7888**
SILICATO *m* DE POTASA **9698**
SILICATO *m* DE SOSA **11731**
SÍLICE *f* **11436**
SILÍCEO **10082**
SILICIO *m* **11434**
SILICIO *m* **11436**
SILICIO *m* **11442**
SILICIO *m* FARINÁCEO **7292**
SILICIO-ARRABIO ESPECULAR *m* **11440**
SILICIURO *m* DE CARBONO **1980**
SILICONO *m* **11456**
SILLAREJO **761**
SÍMBOLO (QUÍMICA) **2315**

SÍMBOLOS *m pl* DE SOLDADURA **13791**
SIMETRÍA *f* **12567**
SIMÉTRICO *m* **12566**
SIMIENTE *f* **12588**
SIMILITUD *f* **11470**
SIMILOR *m* **10326**
SIMILOR *m* **1658**
SIMPLE EFECTO (DE) *m* **11493**
SIN ÁCIDO **5635**
SIN ESCORIAS **5638**
SIN FRAGILIDAD *f* **13342**
SIN MECANIZAR **3406**
SIN ROZAMIENTO **5688**
SINCRÓNICO *m* **12568**
SINCRONISMO *m* **12569**
SÍNCRONO *m* **12570**
SINTERIZACIÓN *f* **7990**
SINTERIZACIÓN *f* **5690**
SINTERIZAR **11509**
SÍNTESIS *f* **12572**
SINTÉTICO **12573**
SINTONÍA *f* **12574**
SINUSOIDE *f* **11513**
SIRENA *f* DE ALARMA **11518**
SISTEMA *m* ANTIDESLIZANTE **8645**
SISTEMA *m* ARTICULADO **7628**
SISTEMA *m* CASI BINARIO **9958**
SISTEMA *m* CENTIMETRO-GRADO-SEGUNDO **2159**
SISTEMA *m* C.G.G. **2159**
SISTEMA *m* DE ALIMENTACIÓN (DEL MOLDE) **10845**
SISTEMA *m* DE CIRCUITO DE RETORNO **2533**
SISTEMA *m* DE COLADA Y DE ALIMENTACIÓN **5870**
SISTEMA *m* DE CONJUNTO DE PALANCAS **12577**
SISTEMA *m* DE COORDENADAS **12575**
SISTEMA *m* DE LAS ALEACIONES **381**
SISTEMA *m* DE LENTES **12576**
SISTEMA *m* DE LOS CRISTALES **3431**
SISTEMA *m* DE MANDO EN CIRCUITO ABIERTO **8817**
SISTEMA *m* DE MANDO NUMÉRICO **8695**
SISTEMA *m* DE MEDIDA **12578**
SISTEMA *m* DE MEDIDA ABSOLUTA **31**
SISTEMA *m* DE PESOS **12580**
SISTEMA *m* DE PINTURA DE DOS COMPONENTES **13311**
SISTEMA *m* DECIMAL **3665**
SISTEMA *m* MÉTRICO **8229**
SISTEMA *m* MÚLTIPLE **8472**
SISTEMA *m* OBJETIVO **8708**
SISTEMA *m* OCULAR **4977**
SISTEMA *m* ÓPTICO **8848**
SISTEMA *m* PIRAMIDAL **10040**

**SIS** 1128

SISTEMA *m* SIEMENS 10412
SISTEMA *m* TERNARIO 12766
SISTEMA *m* TRICLÍNICO 13199
SISTEMA DE CONTROL DE CONTORNO *m* 3039
SISTEMA DE FRENOS *m* 1545
SISTEMA DE REFRIGERACIÓN *m* 3093
SOBRE ENFRIAMIENTO *m* 12465
SOBRE ESPESOR *m* 9948
SOBRE ESPESOR *m* 1695
SOBRE ESPESOR *m* DE MECANIZACIÓN 358
SOBRE ESPESOR *m* DE MECANIZACIÓN 7865
SOBREALIMENTACIÓN *f* DE AIRE BESSEMER 1211
SOBRECARGA *f* 8962
SOBRECARGA *f* 8953
SOBRECARGA *f* 8963
SOBRECARGAR 8954
SOBREDORADO 10673
SOBREDORADO 5999
SOBREENVEJECIMIENTO *m* 8923
SOBREFUSIÓN *f* 12465
SOBREPASAR 8928
SOBRETENSIÓN *f* 8967
SOBRETENSIÓN *f* 4881
SODIO *m* 11714
SOFISTICACIÓN *f* 205
SOGA *f* 12369
SOLADO *m* 5450
SOLAPAR 8950
SOLAPE *m* 8951
SOLAPE *m* 8948
SOLAR *m* PARA CONSTRUIR 1699
SOLAR *m* PARA LA EDIFICACIÓN 1699
SOLDABLE 13769
SOLDADOR *m* 13778
SOLDADOR *m* AL GAS 5824
SOLDADOR *m* DE CALENTAMIENTO *m* AUTOMÁTICO 11155
SOLDADOR *m* DE PUNTA 9573
SOLDADOR *m* ELÉCTRICO 4530
SOLDADOR *m* EN FORMA DE MARTILLO 2350
SOLDADOR ELÉCTRICO *m* 4496
SOLDADURA *f* 1576
SOLDADURA *f* 11083
SOLDADURA *f* 10911
SOLDADURA *f* 11762
SOLDADURA *f* 11762
SOLDADURA *f* 13776
SOLDADURA *f* 13767
SOLDADURA *f* 13779
SOLDADURA *f* 13767

SOLDADURA *f* 13779
SOLDADURA *f* A FUEGO 1576
SOLDADURA *f* A LA DERECHA 907
SOLDADURA *f* A TOPE 1784
SOLDADURA *f* A TOPE 1809
SOLDADURA *f* A TOPE POR CHISPORROTEO 1806
SOLDADURA *f* A TOPE POR RESISTANCIA 1807
SOLDADURA *f* A TOPE POR RESISTENCIA 10488
SOLDADURA *f* A TOPE POR RESISTENCIA 13413
SOLDADURA *f* A TOPE POR RESISTENCIA 1799
SOLDADURA *f* A TOPE (POR RESISTENCIA) 1805
SOLDADURA *f* A TOPE SIN SOBREESPESOR 5481
SOLDADURA *f* AEROACETILÉNICA 295
SOLDADURA *f* AL ACETILENO 96
SOLDADURA *f* AL APLASTAMIENTO 8024
SOLDADURA *f* AL ARCO BAJO PROTECCIÓN GASEOSA 5852
SOLDADURA *f* AL ARCO CON CORRIENTE ALTERNA 685
SOLDADURA *f* AL ARCO CON CORRIENTE CONTINUA 686
SOLDADURA *f* (AL ARCO) ELÉCTRICA 4533
SOLDADURA *f* AL ARCO ELÉCTRICO 681
SOLDADURA *f* AL ARCO ELÉCTRICO 8176
SOLDADURA *f* AL ARCO ELECTRODO DE CARBONO 1943
SOLDADURA *f* AL ARCO EN ATMÓSFERA INERTE 683
SOLDADURA *f* AL ARCO METÁLICO BAJO GAS PROTECTOR 11345
SOLDADURA *f* AL ARCO METÁLICO BAJO PROTECCIÓN DE GAS INERTE 11428
SOLDADURA *f* AL ARCO METÁLICO SIN GAS PROTECTOR 13397
SOLDADURA *f* AL ARCO SUMERGIDO 12414
SOLDADURA *f* AL ARCO SUMERGIDO 684
SOLDADURA *f* AL BISMUTO 1274
SOLDADURA *f* ALUMINOTÉRMICA 12818
SOLDADURA *f* ALUMINOTÉRMICA 9837
SOLDADURA *f* AMARILLA 11880
SOLDADURA *f* AUTÓGENA 8979
SOLDADURA *f* AUTÓGENA 834
SOLDADURA *f* AUTÓGENA 831
SOLDADURA *f* AUTÓGENA 834
SOLDADURA *f* AUTÓGENA 835
SOLDADURA *f* AUTÓGENA 5847
SOLDADURA *f* AUTÓGENA POR PRESIÓN 8978
SOLDADURA *f* AUTOMÁTICA 849
SOLDADURA *f* BAJO POLVO 9722
SOLDADURA *f* BIEN HECHA 6005
SOLDADURA *f* BLANDA 12958
SOLDADURA *f* CLARA 7475
SOLDADURA *f* (COMPOSICIÓN FUSIBLE) 11755
SOLDADURA *f* CON ALEACIÓN DE PLATA 11460
SOLDADURA *f* CON AÑADIDO DE HIERRO-TERMITA 12818

| | | |
|---|---|---|
| SOLDADURA | f | CON ENTALLADURA **11635** |
| SOLDADURA | f | CON ESTAÑO **11743** |
| SOLDADURA | f | CON ESTAÑO **11742** |
| SOLDADURA | f | CON HORNO **5740** |
| SOLDADURA | f | CON LATÓN **1576** |
| SOLDADURA | f | CON PINZA **10027** |
| SOLDADURA | f | CON PINZA **9576** |
| SOLDADURA | f | CON PLATA **11466** |
| SOLDADURA | f | CON PLATA **1576** |
| SOLDADURA | f | CON SOLDADOR **11769** |
| SOLDADURA | f | CON SOPLETE **11768** |
| SOLDADURA | f | CON SOPLETE **5810** |
| SOLDADURA | f | CÓNCAVA **1792** |
| SOLDADURA | f | CONTINUA **3016** |
| SOLDADURA | f | CONTINUA **3037** |
| SOLDADURA | f | CONTINUA **11086** |
| SOLDADURA | f | CONTINUA POR RECUBRIMIENTO **7401** |
| SOLDADURA | f | DE ACABADO **5216** |
| SOLDADURA | f | DE AGUJEROS DE ROBLONES **9537** |
| SOLDADURA | f | DE ALAMBRES EN CRUZ **3385** |
| SOLDADURA | f | DE ÁNGULO ABIERTA **8809** |
| SOLDADURA | f | DE ÁNGULO CON HILERAS ALTERNADAS SIMÉTRICAS **2210** |
| SOLDADURA | f | DE ÁNGULO CÓNCAVA **2878** |
| SOLDADURA | f | DE ÁNGULO CÓNCAVA **7561** |
| SOLDADURA | f | DE ÁNGULO CONVEXA **3077** |
| SOLDADURA | f | DE ÁNGULO DE CORDÓN PLANO **12075** |
| SOLDADURA | f | DE ÁNGULO DISCONTINUA CON HILERAS ALTERNADAS **12049** |
| SOLDADURA | f | DE BORDE **6133** |
| SOLDADURA | f | DE BORDE EN DOBLE U CERRADA **2524** |
| SOLDADURA | f | DE BORDE EN DOBLE V SIN SEPARACIÓN **2525** |
| SOLDADURA | f | DE BORDE EN U CERRADA **2530** |
| SOLDADURA | f | DE BORDE EN V SIN SEPARACIÓN **2531** |
| SOLDADURA | f | DE ENTALLADURA **11636** |
| SOLDADURA | f | DE PASADAS MÚLTIPLES **8455** |
| SOLDADURA | f | DE PLOMO **7476** |
| SOLDADURA | f | DE REFUERZO **10428** |
| SOLDADURA | f | DE ROBLONES **10631** |
| SOLDADURA | f | DE SOSTÉN **12357** |
| SOLDADURA | f | DE UN TUBO **11085** |
| SOLDADURA | f | DE UNA PASADA **11485** |
| SOLDADURA | f | DEPOSITADA A MANO **7988** |
| SOLDADURA | f | DISCONTINUA **7055** |
| SOLDADURA | f | DOBLE ABIERTA **8812** |
| SOLDADURA | f | DOBLE CERRADA **1788** |
| SOLDADURA | f | DOBLE J CERRADA **2523** |
| SOLDADURA | f | EJECUTADA EN LA OBRA **5146** |
| SOLDADURA | f | ELÉCTRICA A FUEGO **4498** |
| SOLDADURA | f | EN ÁNGULO **5162** |

| | | |
|---|---|---|
| SOLDADURA | f | EN ÁNGULO EN PLANO **6583** |
| SOLDADURA | f | EN BAÑO DE SAL **11762** |
| SOLDADURA | f | EN BISEL **7405** |
| SOLDADURA | f | EN CAVETO **7561** |
| SOLDADURA | f | EN CAVETO **5162** |
| SOLDADURA | f | EN CAVETO **2878** |
| SOLDADURA | f | EN CORNISA **6591** |
| SOLDADURA | f | EN EL TALLER **11362** |
| SOLDADURA | f | EN EL TECHO **7113** |
| SOLDADURA | f | EN EL TECHO **8944** |
| SOLDADURA | f | EN ESPIRAL **11921** |
| SOLDADURA | f | EN FRÍO **2712** |
| SOLDADURA | f | EN FRÍO **2712** |
| SOLDADURA | f | EN I CON SEPARACIÓN **8824** |
| SOLDADURA | f | EN I SIN SEPARACIÓN **2532** |
| SOLDADURA | f | EN I SIN SEPARACIÓN DE LOS BORDES **1791** |
| SOLDADURA | f | EN J CON SEPARACIÓN **1798** |
| SOLDADURA | f | EN J CON SEPARACIÓN **8823** |
| SOLDADURA | f | EN J SIN SEPARACIÓN **2529** |
| SOLDADURA | f | EN K CON SEPARACIÓN **1796** |
| SOLDADURA | f | EN K CON SEPARACIÓN **8811** |
| SOLDADURA | f | EN K SIN SEPARACIÓN **1787** |
| SOLDADURA | f | EN K SIN SEPARACIÓN **2522** |
| SOLDADURA | f | EN LA FORJA **6218** |
| SOLDADURA | f | EN LA FORJA **5546** |
| SOLDADURA | f | EN LÍNEA CONTINUA CON LA MOLETA **11086** |
| SOLDADURA | f | EN MEDIA V CON SEPARACIÓN **8822** |
| SOLDADURA | f | EN MEDIA V CON SEPARACIÓN **1797** |
| SOLDADURA | f | EN MEDIA V SIN SEPARACIÓN **1789** |
| SOLDADURA | f | EN MEDIA V SIN SEPARACIÓN **2528** |
| SOLDADURA | f | EN PASADAS SUPERPUESTAS **13757** |
| SOLDADURA | f | EN PASO DE PEREGRINO **901** |
| SOLDADURA | f | EN PASO DE PEREGRINO **918** |
| SOLDADURA | f | EN POSICIÓN PLANA **4190** |
| SOLDADURA | f | EN POSICIÓN TECHO **8941** |
| SOLDADURA | f | EN POSICIÓN VERTICAL ASCENDENTE **13419** |
| SOLDADURA | f | EN POSICIÓN VERTICAL DESCENDENTE **4192** |
| SOLDADURA | f | EN TAPÓN **9536** |
| SOLDADURA | f | (ENSAMBLADO) EN T **1795** |
| SOLDADURA | f | (ENSAMBLADO) EN T **1801** |
| SOLDADURA | f | FUERTE **1576** |
| SOLDADURA | f | FUERTE AL ARCO **666** |
| SOLDADURA | f | FUERTE (COMPOSICIÓN FUSIBLE) **6279** |
| SOLDADURA | f | FUERTE HORIZONTAL **5948** |
| SOLDADURA | f | FUERTE POR INMERSIÓN **3969** |
| SOLDADURA | f | HERMÉTICA **11076** |
| SOLDADURA | f | INTERIOR **7080** |

**SOL** 1130

SOLDADURA *f* INTERMITENTE **7054**
SOLDADURA *f* LINEAL DE FRACCIÓN **1085**
SOLDADURA *f* LLEVADA HACIA LA DERECHA **5539**
SOLDADURA *f* LONGITUDINAL **7737**
SOLDADURA *f* MAL HECHA **920**
SOLDADURA *f* MAL HECHA **920**
SOLDADURA *f* MECÁNICA (AUTOMÁTICA) **8115**
SOLDADURA *f* OXHÍDRICA **8988**
SOLDADURA *f* OXIACETILÉNICA **8979**
SOLDADURA *f* POR ALUMINOTERMIA **12819**
SOLDADURA *f* POR APROXIMACIÓN **1802**
SOLDADURA *f* POR APROXIMACIÓN **1784**
SOLDADURA *f* POR APROXIMACIÓN **1805**
SOLDADURA *f* POR BOMBARDEO ELECTRÓNICO **4627**
SOLDADURA *f* POR CHISPORROTÉO **5358**
SOLDADURA *f* POR CHISPORROTEO **1794**
SOLDADURA *f* POR CONTACTO **682**
SOLDADURA *f* POR ENCOLADO **1802**
SOLDADURA *f* POR FUSIÓN **5762**
SOLDADURA *f* POR FUSIÓN **8643**
SOLDADURA *f* POR HAZ DE ELECTRONES **4630**
SOLDADURA *f* POR IMMERSIÓN **2304**
SOLDADURA *f* POR INDUCCIÓN **4619**
SOLDADURA *f* POR INDUCCIÓN **6893**
SOLDADURA *f* POR INDUCCIÓN PROGRESIVA **9908**
SOLDADURA *f* POR PERCUSIÓN **9183**
SOLDADURA *f* POR PERCUSIÓN CON CONDENSADOR **4645**
SOLDADURA *f* POR PERCUSIÓN ELECTROMÁGNETICA **4617**
SOLDADURA *f* POR PRESIÓN **9842**
SOLDADURA *f* POR PULSACIÓN **9978**
SOLDADURA *f* POR PUNTOS **11959**
SOLDADURA *f* POR PUNTOS CON PISTOLA **9576**
SOLDADURA *f* POR PUNTOS CON RECUBRIMIENTO **7402**
SOLDADURA *f* POR PUNTOS EN SERIE POR RESISTENCIA **11200**
SOLDADURA *f* POR PUNTOS MÚLTIPLES **8464**
SOLDADURA *f* POR PUNTOS POR RESISTENCIA **10493**
SOLDADURA *f* POR RECUBRIMIENTO **7405**
SOLDADURA *f* POR RECUBRIMIENTO **7403**
SOLDADURA *f* POR RESALTES **9916**
SOLDADURA *f* POR RESALTES MÚLTIPLES **8468**
SOLDADURA *f* POR RESISTENCIA **10500**
SOLDADURA *f* POR RESISTENCIA **10487**
SOLDADURA *f* POR ULTRASONIDOS **13338**
SOLDADURA *f* PROVISIONAL POR PUNTOS **12590**
SOLDADURA *f* PROVISIONAL POR PUNTOS DE REFERENCIA **12589**
SOLDADURA *f* RESISTENTE A LA PRESIÓN **9838**
SOLDADURA *f* SEMIAUTOMÁTICA AL ARCO **11166**
SOLDADURA *f* SOBRE BORDES LEVANTADOS **5335**
SOLDADURA *f* SOBRE BORDES RECTOS **12032**

SOLDADURA *f* T.I.G. (AL ARCO DE TUNGSTENO BAJO GAS INERTE) **6906**
SOLDADURA *f* (TRABAJO HECHO SOLDANDO CON INTERPOSICIÓN DE UNA ALEACIÓN) **11761**
SOLDADURA ARCATOM (AL ARCO PROTEGIDO CON HIDRÓGENO ATÓMICO) **801**
SOLDADURA CON LATÓN *f* **1576**
SOLDAR **11756**
SOLDAR **13755**
SOLDAR A LA AUTÓGENA **13758**
SOLDAR CON ESTAÑO **11741**
SOLDAR CON LATÓN **1573**
SOLDAR EN BISEL **7404**
SOLDAR FUERTE **1573**
SOLDAR POR CONTACTO **1785**
SOLDAR POR ENCOLADO **1785**
SOLENOIDE *m* **11774**
SOLENOIDE *m* **11773**
SOLERA *f* **6331**
SOLERA *f* ÁCIDA **108**
SOLERA *f* DE ALTO HORNO **9011**
SOLERA *f* DE LOS ALTOS HORNOS **9011**
SOLERA *f* Y ALIMENTACIÓN BÁSICAS **1045**
SOLICITACIONES *f pl* **7679**
SOLICITACIONES *f pl* **12331**
SOLICITANTE *m* DE PATENTE **645**
SOLICITAR UNA PATENTE **651**
SOLICITUD *f* (DE PATENTE) **646**
SOLICITUD *f* DE PATENTE **646**
SOLIDIFICACIÓN *f* **3483**
SOLIDIFICACIÓN *f* **6292**
SOLIDIFICACIÓN *f* **6292**
SOLIDIFICACIÓN *f* **11797**
SOLIDIFICACIÓN *f* DE LA MASA FUNDIDA EN LA BOLSA **7360**
SOLIDIFICACIÓN *f* DE UN LÍQUIDO **11799**
SOLIDIFICARSE EN EL AGUA **6287**
SOLIDIFICARSE EN EL AGUA (CEMENTO) **6287**
SOLIDIFICARSE EN EL AIRE (CEMENTO) **6286**
SOLIDIFICARSE POR ENFRIAMIENTO **11803**
SOLIDIFICATIÓN *f* **5653**
SÓLIDO *m* **11775**
SÓLIDO *m* ELÁSTICO **4484**
SÓLIDOS *m pl* **11805**
SOLUBILIDAD *f* **11806**
SOLUBILIZAR **10456**
SOLUBLE **11807**
SOLUBLE EN EL AGUA **11809**
SOLUCIÓN *f* **11811**
SOLUCIÓN *f* ÁCIDA **9290**
SOLUCIÓN *f* ACUOSA **661**

1131      **SOS**

SOLUCIÓN  *f*  ADHERENTE **4201**
SOLUCIÓN  *f*  ALCALINA **339**
SOLUCIÓN  *f*  ALCOHÓLICA **315**
SOLUCIÓN  *f*  AMONIACAL **457**
SOLUCIÓN  *f*  AMONIACAL **660**
SOLUCIÓN  *f*  ANÓDICA **606**
SOLUCIÓN  *f*  ARRASTRADA **4202**
SOLUCIÓN  *f*  CONCENTRADA **2883**
SOLUCIÓN  *f*  DE CLORURO DE CINC **7293**
SOLUCIÓN  *f*  DE DECAPADO **9289**
SOLUCIÓN  *f*  DE POTASA CÁUSTICA **9671**
SOLUCIÓN  *f*  DE SOSA CÁUSTICA **2120**
SOLUCIÓN  *f*  DÉBIL **13706**
SOLUCIÓN  *f*  DILUIDA **3953**
SOLUCIÓN  *f*  DILUIDA **3953**
SOLUCIÓN  *f*  FUERTE **2883**
SOLUCIÓN  *f*  GRÁFICA **6060**
SOLUCIÓN  *f*  NO SATURADA **13394**
SOLUCIÓN  *f*  PARA ABRILLANTAR **1609**
SOLUCIÓN  *f*  POR EL CÁLCULO **8694**
SOLUCIÓN  *f*  SALINA **10908**
SOLUCIÓN  *f*  SATURADA **10941**
SOLUCIÓN  *f*  SÓLIDA **11794**
SOLUCIÓN  *f*  SUPERSATURADA **12478**
SOMBRA  *f* **11236**
SOMBRA  *f*  ARROJADA **13339**
SOMBREADO  *m* **11237**
SOMBREAR **11234**
SOMBREAR **6304**
SOMETER UN CUERPO A UNA CARGA **12323**
SONDA  *f*  DE MOLDEADOR **8357**
SONDADORA  *f*  SOBRE CAMIÓN **13614**
SONDEO  *m* **12778**
SONDEO  *m* **12778**
SOPLADOR  *m* **12172**
SOPLADOR  *m* **1361**
SOPLADOR  *m* **242**
SOPLADOR  *m*  DE VAPOR **12172**
SOPLADURA  *f*  MAGNÉTICA AL ARCO **665**
SOPLADURAS  *f* **1330**
SOPLETE  *m* **3539**
SOPLETE  *m* **5307**
SOPLETE  *m* **1355**
SOPLETE  *m* **1749**
SOPLETE  *m* **13042**
SOPLETE  *m* **13042**
SOPLETE  *m*  DE CORTE AUTÓGENO **3537**
SOPLETE  *m*  DE HELIO **6424**
SOPLETE CORTADOR  *m* **5312**
SOPLETE DE BOCA  *m* **8433**

SOPLETE DE CALDEO  *m* **6399**
SOPLETE DE CALDEO PREVIO  *m* **6391**
SOPLETE DE CORTE  *m* **3216**
SOPLETE DE OXÍGENO COMPRIMIDO  *m* **2848**
SOPLETE DESOXIDADOR  *m* **5311**
SOPLETE EXHÍDRICO  *m* **8986**
SOPORTAR **12491**
SOPORTAR **12491**
SOPORTE  *m* **12490**
SOPORTE  *m* **10876**
SOPORTE  *m* **57**
SOPORTE  *m* **3288**
SOPORTE  *m* **6586**
SOPORTE  *m* **1117**
SOPORTE  *m* **1522**
SOPORTE  *m* **57**
SOPORTE  *m* **57**
SOPORTE  *m* **57**
SOPORTE  *m* **1118**
SOPORTE  *m* **1041**
SOPORTE  *m* **3288**
SOPORTE  *m*  ANGULAR **3058**
SOPORTE  *m*  CON ANILLO DE ENGRASE **10602**
SOPORTE  *m*  CON COJINETES LISOS **9424**
SOPORTE  *m*  CONSOLA **1523**
SOPORTE  *m*  (CONSTRUCCIÓN) **1118**
SOPORTE  *m*  DE ALMA **2253**
SOPORTE  *m*  DE ASIENTO EN EL SUELO **9154**
SOPORTE  *m*  DE CUCHILLA **7325**
SOPORTE  *m*  DE EXTREMO **4720**
SOPORTE  *m*  DE HUSO **11910**
SOPORTE  *m*  DE INFORMACIÓN **12289**
SOPORTE  *m*  DE INFORMACIÓN DE ENTRADA **6960**
SOPORTE  *m*  DE MANGUETA **12230**
SOPORTE  *m*  DE PIEZA A ESTAMPAR **1305**
SOPORTE  *m*  DE RODILLOS **10690**
SOPORTE  *m*  DE UN MUÑÓN **11905**
SOPORTE  *m*  DESLIZANTE **11596**
SOPORTE  *m*  EN ESCUADRA **510**
SOPORTE  *m*  MOTOR **4754**
SOPORTE  *m*  MURAL **1523**
SOPORTE DE COJINETE  *m* **1103**
SOPORTE DE EXTREMO  *m* **4726**
SOPORTE EN U  *m* **9166**
SOSA  *f* **11713**
SOSA  *f*  AL AMONIACO **455**
SOSA  *f*  CÁUSTICA **11722**
SOSA  *f*  LEBLANC **12445**
SOSA  *f*  NITROSA **11725**
SOSA  *f*  NITROSA **11725**

# SOS

SOSA  *f* NITROSA **11725**
SOSA  *f* SOLVAY **455**
SOSTÉN  *m* **12153**
SOSTÉN  *m* **12493**
SOSTENER **12491**
SOSTENER **12150**
SOSTENER **12150**
SOSTENER EL MONTÓN **6524**
SOSTENIDO LÍBREMENTE EN SUS DOS APOYOS **11474**
SOSTENIMIENTO **12153**
SOSTENIMIENTO **12493**
SOTAVENTO  *m* **7505**
STOCK  *m* **12263**
SUAVIZACIÓN  *f* **11749**
SUAVIZAR **12717**
SUBACETATO  *m* **7450**
SUBDIVISIÓN  *f* **12409**
SUBENFRIAMIENTO  *m* **13347**
SUBESTRUCTURA  *f* **12423**
SUBIDA  *f* **1925**
SUBIDA  *f* DE LA CORREA **2499**
SUBIDA  *f* DE UNA CARGA **7559**
SUBIDA  *f* DEL PISTÓN **13409**
SUBLIMACIÓN  *f* **12412**
SUBLIMADO  *m* CORROSIVO **8153**
SUBLIMAR **12411**
SUBPRODUCTO  *m* **1820**
SUBPROGRAMA  *m* **12415**
SUBSTANCIA  *f* **12419**
SUBSTANCIA  *f* ACTIVADORA **148**
SUBSTANCIA  *f* ACTIVADORA **4744**
SUBSTANCIA  *f* ADHESIVA **177**
SUBSTANCIA  *f* AGLUTINANTE **1253**
SUBSTANCIA  *f* ANTIINCRUSTANTE **10978**
SUBSTANCIA  *f* CALORÍFUGA **6352**
SUBSTANCIA  *f* CORROSIVA **3197**
SUBSTANCIA  *f* DE DESGASTE **6107**
SUBSTANCIA  *f* EN POLVO FINO **6789**
SUBSTANCIA  *f* ESPESATIVA **12842**
SUBSTANCIA  *f* HOMOGÉNEA **6558**
SUBSTANCIA  *f* MOLIDA FINAMENTE **6489**
SUBSTANCIAS  *f pl* ESTRAÑAS **6813**
SUBSTANCIAS  *f pl* FOSFORESCENTES **9251**
SUBSTANCIAS  *f pl* RADIOACTIVAS **10158**
SUBSTITUCIÓN (MATEMÁTICAS) **12421**
SUBSTRACCIÓN  *f* **12425**
SUBSTRACCIÓN  *f* DEL CALOR **4666**
SUBSTRAER **12424**
SUBSTRAER EL CALOR **13910**
SUCCIÓN  *f* **12428**

SUCEDÁNEO  *m* **12420**
SUCESIÓN  *m* DE LAS OPERACIONES DE SOLDADURA **13790**
SUCESIÓN  *f* DE NUMEROS **11203**
SUCESIVO  *m* **449**
SUCIEDAD  *f* **4331**
SUELDO  *m* **10897**
SUELO **9136**
SUELO  *m* **5450**
SUELO  *m* ACUÍFERO **13642**
SUELO  *m* DEL COCHE **5446**
SUELO  *m* PAVIMENTADO **6101**
SUJECIÓN  *f* **13740**
SUJECIÓN  *f* DE MOHR **8345**
SUJETABARRAS  *m* **12981**
SUJETAMODELOS  *m* **3887**
SULFATO  *m* **1244**
SULFATO  *m* ÁCIDO DE SOSA **11717**
SULFATO  *m* ANHIDRO **549**
SULFATO  *m* D CALCIO **1856**
SULFATO  *m* DE ALUMINIO **426**
SULFATO  *m* DE AMONIO **471**
SULFATO  *m* DE BARIO **1003**
SULFATO  *m* DE CALCIO **6190**
SULFATO  *m* DE CINC **14046**
SULFATO  *m* DE COBALTO **2615**
SULFATO  *m* DE COBRE **3475**
SULFATO  *m* DE COBRE **1376**
SULFATO  *m* DE HIERRO **6093**
SULFATO  *m* DE MAGNESIO **7889**
SULFATO  *m* DE NÍQUEL **8571**
SULFATO  *m* DE PLATA **11467**
SULFATO  *m* DE PLOMO **7473**
SULFATO  *m* DE POTASA **9699**
SULFATO  *m* DOBLE DE NÍQUEL Y AMONIACO **8558**
SULFATO  *m* FÉRRICO **5103**
SULFATO  *m* MANGANOSO **7974**
SULFATO  *m* MERCÚRICO **8158**
SULFATO  *m* MERCÚRIOSO **8162**
SULFATO  *m* NEUTRO DE SODIO **11733**
SULFATO DE CALCIO ANHIDRO  *m* **549**
SULFATO DE COBRE  *m* **1376**
SULFATO DE HIERRO  *m* **6093**
SULFIDRATO  *m* DE AMONIO **464**
SULFITO  *m* **12448**
SULFITO  *m* ÁCIDO **11718**
SULFITO  *m* DE SOSA **11734**
SULFOCIANURO  *m* DE POTASIO **9701**
SULFURO  *m* **12446**
SULFURO  *m* DE AMONIO **472**

SULFURO *m* DE BARIO **1004**
SULFURO *m* DE CARBONO **1964**
SULFURO *m* DE HIERRO **12447**
SULFURO *m* DE POTASA **9700**
SULFURO *m* DORADO DE ANTIMONIO **625**
SULFURO *m* EN CADENA **2221**
SULFURO *m* ESTÁÑICO **12099**
SULFURO *m* ESTÁNNICO **12099**
SULFURO *m* ESTAÑOSO **12103**
SULFURO *m* FERROSO/FÉRRICO **7153**
SULFURO *m* NATURAL DE ARSÉNICO **728**
SULFURO *m* NATURAL DE COBRE **12796**
SULFURO *m* ROJO DE MERCURIO **13535**
SULFURO DE HIDRÓGENO *m* **6717**
SUMA *f* **12454**
SUMAR **162**
SUMERGIR **3968**
SUMERGIR **12413**
SUMINISTRAR CALOR **12485**
SUMINISTRAR NUEVAS CALORÍAS **12485**
SUMINISTRO *m* **7940**
SUMINISTRO *m* DE CALOR **12488**
SUMISIÓN A UNA TENSIÓN PREVIA **830**
SUPERCOMPRESOR *m* **1456**
SUPERCOMPRESOR *m* **1456**
SUPERESTRUCTURA *f* **12475**
SUPERESTRUCTURA *f* **12475**
SUPERFICIE *f* **12496**
SUPERFICIE *f* **12521**
SUPERFICIE *f* **11120**
SUPERFICIE *f* **2019**
SUPERFICIE *f* **697**
SUPERFICIE *f* **694**
SUPERFICIE *f* ALABEADA **11535**
SUPERFICIE *f* CARGADA **12368**
SUPERFICIE *f* CÁUSTICA **2121**
SUPERFICIE *f* CURVA **3498**
SUPERFICIE *f* DE APOYO **1115**
SUPERFICIE *f* DE APOYO **1101**
SUPERFICIE *f* DE APOYO **1115**
SUPERFICIE *f* DE APOYO DE UN EJE **1107**
SUPERFICIE *f* DE APOYO DE UN MODELO **3161**
SUPERFICIE *f* DE APOYO DE UN MUÑON **1116**
SUPERFICIE *f* DE APOYO DE UNA MANIVELA **1116**
SUPERFICIE *f* DE CALDEO **6398**
SUPERFICIE *f* DE CONTACTO **2998**
SUPERFICIE *f* DE CONTACTO **12510**
SUPERFICIE *f* DE DESLIZAMIENTO **11585**
SUPERFICIE *f* DE DESLIZAMIENTO **11608**
SUPERFICIE *f* DE ENFRIAMIENTO **3092**

SUPERFICIE *f* DE ENGRANAJE **696**
SUPERFICIE *f* DE GUÍA **6166**
SUPERFICIE *f* DE IMPRESIÓN **12512**
SUPERFICIE *f* DE LA SECCIÓN **12511**
SUPERFICIE *f* DE LA SOLDADURA **4998**
SUPERFICIE *f* DE LICUACIÓN **7634**
SUPERFICIE *f* DE NIVEL **7257**
SUPERFICIE *f* DE NIVELACIÓN **5058**
SUPERFICIE *f* DE REFRIGERACIÓN (DE ENFRIAMIENTO) **3092**
SUPERFICIE *f* DE REJILLA **6068**
SUPERFICIE *f* DE REVOLUCIÓN **12513**
SUPERFICIE *f* DE RODADURA **10705**
SUPERFICIE *f* DE RODADURA DE UNA RUEDA **13173**
SUPERFICIE *f* DE ROZAMIENTO **5687**
SUPERFICIE *f* DEL BLANCO (OFRECIDA A LAS RADIACIONES) **12683**
SUPERFICIE *f* DESARROLLABLE **3817**
SUPERFICIE *f* DESARROLLABLE **3817**
SUPERFICIE *f* DIFUSIBLE **3935**
SUPERFICIE *f* EQUIPOTENCIAL **7527**
SUPERFICIE *f* FILTRANTE SATURADA **2360**
SUPERFICIE *f* HELICOIDAL **6428**
SUPERFICIE *f* INTERIOR DE UN TUBO **6954**
SUPERFICIE *f* IRREGULAR DE LAS PIEZAS FUNDIDAS **6008**
SUPERFICIE *f* LATERAL DE UN CILINDRO **3590**
SUPERFICIE *f* LATERAL DE UN CONO **2949**
SUPERFICIE *f* MATE **8060**
SUPERFICIE *f* METÁLICA DECAPADA **2470**
SUPERFICIE *f* METÁLICA PULIDA **1611**
SUPERFICIE *f* MUY POROSA **6644**
SUPERFICIE *f* PERIFÉRICA DEL NEUMÁTICO **13172**
SUPERFICIE *f* PICADA DE LA FUNDICIÓN **9134**
SUPERFICIE *f* PLANA **9441**
SUPERFICIE *f* PULIDA **6142**
SUPERFICIE *f* RADIANTE **10142**
SUPERFICIE *f* REFLECTANTE **10385**
SUPERFICIE *f* REFRIGERANTE **3092**
SUPERFICIE *f* RELUCIENTE **11866**
SUPERFICIE *f* RUGOSA **10784**
SUPERFICIE *f* RUGOSA **10779**
SUPERPOSICIÓN *f* **8948**
SUPERPOSICIÓN *f* DE VIBRACIONES **12476**
SUPERPRESIÓN *f* **8955**
SUPERSATURACIÓN *f* **12461**
SUPERSATURACIÓN *f* **12479**
SUPERSATURAR **12477**
SUPLEMENTO *m* DE UN ÁNGULO **12482**
SUPRESIÓN *f* **1337**
SUPRESIÓN *f* **1337**

# SUP

1134

SUPRESIÓN *f* DE LOS CEROS **14033**
SUPRESIÓN *f* DEL HUMO **11977**
SURTIDO *m* **11213**
SURTIDOR *m* **7218**
SURTIDOR *m* **196**
SURTIDOR *m* DE MARCHA LENTA **11646**
SURTIDOR *m* PRINCIPAL **7942**
SURTIR **8042**
SUSCEPTIBILIDAD DE PODERSE TRABAJAR **13946**
SUSPENDIDO **6321**
SUSPENDIDO LIBREMENTE **5649**
SUSPENDIDO SOBRE UN GORRÓN **8432**
SUSPENDIDO SOBRE UNA CUCHILLA **6669**
SUSPENSIÓN *f* **12526**
SUSPENSIÓN *f* BIFILAR **1240**
SUSPENSIÓN *f* DE CARDÁN **1998**
SUSPENSIÓN *f* DE CUCHILLA **7326**
SUSPENSIÓN *f* DE GORRÓN **9570**
SUSPENSIÓN *f* DE RÓTULA **958**
TABIQUE *m* **1726**
TABIQUE *m* **4110**
TABIQUE ANTIFUEGO *m* **5251**
TABIQUERÍA *f* **1602**
TABLA *f* **9032**
TABLA *f* DE CONVERSIÓN (DE REDUCCIÓN) **3069**
TABLA *f* DE LOGARITMOS **7721**
TABLERO *m* **9032**
TABLERO *m* **5692**
TABLERO *m* **655**
TABLERO *m* DE CORCHO **3175**
TABLERO *m* DE CORCHO AGLOMERADO **9802**
TABLERO *m* DE DIBUJO **4231**
TABLERO *m* DEL MOTOR **5251**
TABLÓN *m* **9457**
TACHUELA *f* **12588**
TACO DE CORREDERA *m* **10188**
TACO DE MANGO *m* **6529**
TACÓMETRO *m* **10556**
TACÓMETRO *m* **10556**
TACÓMETRO *m* **12587**
TACÓN *m* **8667**
TACÓN *m* DE CHAVETA **7286**
TACÓN *m* DE UNA CHAVETA **6318**
TAJADERA *f* **2114**
TAJAR **3515**
TALADRADO *m* **4277**
TALADRADO *m* **3855**
TALADRADO *m* **1468**
TALADRADO *m* **12675**
TALADRADORA *f* **1471**

TALADRADORA *f* **4279**
TALADRADORA *f* DE BANCO **1168**
TALADRADORA *f* DE CALDERAS **1409**
TALADRADORA *f* DE COLUMNA **9312**
TALADRADORA *f* EN BASTIDOR O MONTANTE **2755**
TALADRADORA *f* EN COLUMNA ESTANDARD **13412**
TALADRADORA *f* MÚLTIPLE **5799**
TALADRADORA *f* PARA CAJA DE GRASA EJES **878**
TALADRADORA *f* PORTÁTIL **9636**
TALADRADORA *f* RADIAL **10134**
TALADRADORA DE PRECISIÓN *f* PULIDORA DE PRECISIÓN *f* **5196**
TALADRADORA-ESCARIADORA DE COORDENADAS **3098**
TALADRADORAS *f* RÍGIDAS **10590**
TALADRAR **10771**
TALADRAR **9186**
TALADRAR **4264**
TALADRAR **4264**
TALADRO *m* **4265**
TALADRO *m* **4263**
TALADRO *m* **818**
TALADRO *m* **1636**
TALADRO *m* **7332**
TALADRO *m* **9732**
TALADRO *m* PARA CHAPA **9997**
TALADRO *m* PARA PERFORACIÓN PROFUNDA **3686**
TALCO *m* **5659**
TALCO *m* **12608**
TALCO *m* EN POLVO **12607**
TALIO *m* **12801**
TALLADOR *m* DE LIMAS **5151**
TALLADORA *f* DE ENGRANAJES **5891**
TALLAR EN BISEL **1222**
TALLER *m* **773**
TALLER *m* **5013**
TALLER *m* **11364**
TALLER *m* **13943**
TALLER *m* **13968**
TALLER *m* DE CALDERERÍA DE HIERRO **1420**
TALLER *m* DE CARROCERÍA **1398**
TALLER *m* DE CONSTRUCCIÓN DE MÁQUINAS **773**
TALLER *m* DE DESARENADO **5130**
TALLER *m* DE DESBARBADO **5130**
TALLER *m* DE DESCOSTRADO **5130**
TALLER *m* DE FORJA **5547**
TALLER *m* DE MANTENIMIENTO **10461**
TALLER *m* DE MAQUINARIA **7856**
TALLER *m* DE MONTAJE **4811**
TALLER *m* DE TORNEAR **13290**
TALLER DE AJUSTE *m* **5282**

**TAP**

TALLER DE CHAPISTERÍA  *m* **1398**
TALLER DE CONSTRUCCIÓN MECÁNICA  *m* **4764**
TALLER DE FRESADO  *m* **8293**
TALLER DE MÁQUINAS  *m* **7855**
TALLER DE REPARACIONES  *m* **10461**
TALLERES  *m pl* (ESTABLECIMIENTO) DE CONSTRUCCIÓN
  DE MAQUINARIA **4764**
TALÓN  *m* DE CHAVETA **6318**
TALUD  *m* **11627**
TAMAÑO  *m* **7939**
TAMAÑO  *m* **10065**
TAMAÑO  *m* DEL GRANO **6039**
TAMAÑO NATURAL (DE) **5723**
TAMAÑO NATURAL (DE) **5723**
TAMBOR  *m* **3579**
TAMBOR  *m* **4333**
TAMBOR  *m* **1532**
TAMBOR  *m* **10671**
TAMBOR  *m* **10290**
TAMBOR  *m* **13817**
TAMBOR  *m* DE CADENA **2202**
TAMBOR  *m* DE ENROLLAMIENTO **10737**
TAMBOR  *m* DE FRENO **1533**
TAMBOR  *m* DE LIMPIEZA **13261**
TAMBOR  *m* (O CILINDRO  *m*) DE RANURAS **3579**
TAMBOR  *m* PARA CADENA CABLE **2202**
TAMIZ  *m* **10572**
TAMIZ  *m* **11422**
TAMIZ  *m* **11422**
TAMIZ  *m* **11018**
TAMIZADO  *m* **11424**
TAMIZAR **11423**
TAMPÓN  *m* **12785**
TAMPÓN  *m* **1686**
TANATO  *m* **12633**
TANATO  *m* DE SODIO **11735**
TANGENTE  *f* **12615**
TANGENTE  *f* EN EL VÉRTICE **12617**
TANGENTE  *f* (GEOMETRÍA) **12616**
TANINO  *m* **5780**
TANQUE  *m* **13228**
TANQUE  *m* DE DECANTACIÓN **11229**
TANQUE  *m* DE FILTRACIÓN **5178**
TANQUE  *m* (O CUBA  *f*) DE ALIMENTACIÓN **5075**
TÁNTALO  *m* **12634**
TAPA  *f* **12639**
TAPA  *f* **3269**
TAPA  *f* **1910**
TAPA  *f* **1912**
TAPA  *f* **1910**

TAPA  *f* **1451**
TAPA  *f* **1451**
TAPA  *f* **1454**
TAPA  *f* DE AGUJERO DE INSPECCIÓN **7977**
TAPA DE ARCO  *f* **14015**
TAPA DE BISAGRA  *f* **6510**
TAPA DE CHAPA  *f* **11310**
TAPA DE COJINETE  *f* **1104**
TAPA DE CORREDERA  *f* **11604**
TAPA DE GRIFO  *f* **3266**
TAPA DE LA CAJA DE ESTOPA  *f* **5953**
TAPA DE PROTECCIÓN  *f* **9944**
TAPA (DE UNA ESFERA)  *f* **1911**
TAPA DEL PALIER  *f* **1912**
TAPA DEL POTAEQUIPAJES  *f* **13240**
TAPA-ENTRADA  *f* **4835**
TAPACUBOS  *m* **13815**
TAPACUBOS  *m* DE RUEDA **6662**
TAPADER DEL CILINDRO  *f* **3567**
TAPADERA  *f* **3262**
TAPADERA  *f* **3267**
TAPADERA  *f* **1910**
TAPADERA  *f* **1910**
TAPADERA DEL CILÍNDRO  *f* **3567**
TAPADERA DEL CILINDRO  *f* **7266**
TAPARSE **2358**
TAPÓN  *m* **1910**
TAPÓN  *m* **1483**
TAPÓN  *m* **9529**
TAPÓN  *m* **12285**
TAPÓN  *m* **9011**
TAPÓN  *m* DE CALIBRE **5883**
TAPÓN  *m* DE CARGA **5158**
TAPÓN  *m* DE COLADA **12284**
TAPÓN  *m* DE CORCHO **3173**
TAPÓN  *m* DE CORCHO **3176**
TAPÓN  *m* DE GOMA **10824**
TAPÓN  *m* DE LLENADO **5158**
TAPÓN  *m* DE RADIADOR **10151**
TAPÓN  *m* DE ROSCA **11060**
TAPÓN  *m* DE VACIADO **4208**
TAPÓN  *m* DE VÁLVULA **13464**
TAPÓN  *m* DE VAPOR **13481**
TAPÓN  *m* ESMERILADO **6146**
TAPÓN  *m* OBTURADOR **1326**
TAPÓN  *m* ROSCADO **11060**
TAPÓN  *m* ROSCADO **11060**
TAPÓN  *m* ROSCADO **11060**
TAPÓN  *m* ROSCADO **11025**
TAPÓN  *m* ROSCADO **11025**

**TAP** 1136

TAPÓN *m* ROSCADO **11025**
TAPÓN *m* Y MEDIA LUNA DE CALIBRE **3581**
TAPONAR UNA FUGA **12279**
TAPONARSE **2358**
TAQUÍMETRO *m* **12587**
TAQUÍMETRO *m* **11869**
TAQUÍMETRO *m* **11877**
TAQUÍMETRO *m* **10556**
TAQUÍMETRO *m* REGISTRADOR **12586**
TARJETA *f* **1999**
TARJETA PERFORADA *f* **10002**
TÁRTARO *m* EMÉTICO **9675**
TARTRATO *m* **12691**
TARTRATO *m* **473**
TARTRATO *m* DE POTASA Y ANTIMONIO **9675**
TARTRATO *m* DE POTASA Y SOSA **11729**
TARTRÍFUGO *m* **4041**
TARUGO *m* **4180**
TARUGO DE MADERA *m* **13179**
TASA *f* **10226**
TE *f* **12697**
TE *f* DE DIBUJO **12581**
TE *f* DE TRES DIRECCIONES **12699**
TECHO *m* **10708**
TECHO *m* **3667**
TECHO *m* ABOMBADO **4120**
TECHO *m* ABOMBADO **4039**
TECHO *m* CÓNICO **2947**
TECHO *m* FIJO **5296**
TECHO *m* REBAJADO **13046**
TECHO *m* SUSPENDIDO **12524**
TECLARORURO *m* DE CARBONO **1960**
TECNECIO *m* **8040**
TÉCNICO **12695**
TÉCNICO **12694**
TEJA *f* **12934**
TEJA *f* DE VIDRIO **5964**
TEJIDO *m* DE YUTE **6449**
TEJUELO *m* **12241**
TEJUELO *m* ANULAR **2722**
TELA *f* CAUCHUTADA **10818**
TELA *f* DE AMIANTO **748**
TELA *f* ENCAUCHUTADA **10818**
TELA *f* FILTRANTE **5176**
TELA *f* IMPERMEABLE **13690**
TELA *f* METÁLICA **5888**
TELA *f* METÁLICA **13893**
TELA *f* METÁLICA **13893**
TELARAÑA *f* **2616**
TELEAFOR *m* **10449**

TELECALIBRADO **10449**
TELEFONÍA *f* **12712**
TELEFONÍA *f* SIN FILOS **13908**
TELÉFONO *m* **12710**
TELEGRAFÍA *f* **12709**
TELEGRAFÍA *f* SIN FILOS **13907**
TELÉGRAFO *m* **12707**
TELEGRAMA *m* **1830**
TELEMANDO *m* **10448**
TELEMANDO *m* **10448**
TELESCOPIO *m* **10386**
TELESCOPIO *m* DE REFRACCIÓN **10398**
TELETERMÓMETRO *m* **4069**
TELURIO *m* **12716**
TEMPERATURA *f* **12726**
TEMPERATURA *f* **12721**
TEMPERATURA *f* ABSOLUTA **35**
TEMPERATURA *f* AMBIENTE **12729**
TEMPERATURA *f* AMBIENTE **10713**
TEMPERATURA *f* CONSTANTE **2977**
TEMPERATURA *f* CRECIENTE **10618**
TEMPERATURA *f* CRÍTICA **3352**
TEMPERATURA *f* DE ACABADO **5227**
TEMPERATURA *f* DE AFINADO **10381**
TEMPERATURA *f* DE CÁLCULO **3798**
TEMPERATURA *f* DE EBULLICIÓN **1427**
TEMPERATURA *f* DE ENCENDIDO **6767**
TEMPERATURA *f* DE ENVEJECIMIENTO **230**
TEMPERATURA *f* DE EQUILIBRIO **4791**
TEMPERATURA *f* DE ESTUDIO **3798**
TEMPERATURA *f* DE EVAPORACIÓN **4865**
TEMPERATURA *f* DE FORJA **5565**
TEMPERATURA *f* DE FORJA **5560**
TEMPERATURA *f* DE FORJA **2744**
TEMPERATURA *f* DE FUSIÓN **6360**
TEMPERATURA *f* DE IGNICIÓN (O DE INFLAMACIÓN) **6767**
TEMPERATURA *f* DE INFLAMACIÓN **12727**
TEMPERATURA *f* DE LA PASADA INTERMEDIA **7086**
TEMPERATURA *f* DE NUEVA CRISTALIZACIÓN **10298**
TEMPERATURA *f* DE RECOCIDO **11700**
TEMPERATURA *f* DE REDUCCIÓN **10354**
TEMPERATURA *f* DE REFERENCIA **10369**
TEMPERATURA *f* DE SATURACIÓN **10945**
TEMPERATURA *f* DE SERVICIO **8836**
TEMPERATURA *f* DE TRABAJO **8836**
TEMPERATURA *f* DE TRANSFORMACIÓN **13114**
TEMPERATURA *f* DEL AIRE **12728**
TEMPERATURA *f* DESCENDENTE **5025**
TEMPERATURA *f* ELEVADA **4658**

TEMPERATURA *f* EUTÉCTICA **4858**
TEMPERATURA *f* FINAL **5191**
TEMPERATURA *f* INICIAL **6931**
TEMPERATURA *f* MÁXIMA **8068**
TEMPERATURA *f* MEDIA **855**
TEMPERATURA *f* MÍNIMA **8306**
TEMPERATURA *f* NORMAL **10713**
TEMPERATURA *f* NORMAL DE LA SALA **10713**
TEMPERATURA *f* REDUCIDA **10344**
TEMPERATURA *f* SUPERFICIAL MÁXIMA **6654**
TEMPLA *m* AL AGUA SEGUIDO DE REVENIDO **13673**
TEMPLA *m* EN BAÑO DE SAL **10913**
TEMPLA *m* NEGATIVO **8527**
TEMPLADO (NO) **13359**
TEMPLADOR *m* DE UTILLAJE **13008**
TEMPLAR **12717**
TEMPLAR **2332**
TEMPLAR (FUNDICIÓN) **2332**
TEMPLAR UN METAL **6285**
TEMPLE *m* **6291**
TEMPLE *m* **6291**
TEMPLE *m* **2338**
TEMPLE *m* **3975**
TEMPLE *m* **3978**
TEMPLE *m* **10094**
TEMPLE *m* AL ACEITE **8760**
TEMPLE *m* AL ACEITE **8772**
TEMPLE *m* AL AGUA **13672**
TEMPLE *m* AL AGUA **13654**
TEMPLE *m* AL AGUA **285**
TEMPLE *m* AL AIRE **280**
TEMPLE *m* AL AIRE **267**
TEMPLE *m* AL GAS **5840**
TEMPLE *m* CON SOPLETE **5315**
TEMPLE *m* CONTINUO EN CALIENTE **3028**
TEMPLE *m* DE LOS ALAMBRES DE ACERO **9124**
TEMPLE *m* DE METALES **6293**
TEMPLE *m* DE SUPERFICIE **2021**
TEMPLE *m* DIFERENCIAL **3914**
TEMPLE *m* DULCE **8760**
TEMPLE *m* EN BAÑO CALIENTE **8021**
TEMPLE *m* EN BAÑO DE SAL **7651**
TEMPLE *m* EN SUPERFICIE **2023**
TEMPLE *m* ESCALONADO **6633**
TEMPLE *m* ESCALONADO **12242**
TEMPLE *m* ESCALONADO BAINÍTICO **824**
TEMPLE *m* ESCALONADO MARTENSÍTICO **12243**
TEMPLE *m* ININTERRUMPIDO **12249**
TEMPLE *m* INVERSO **7109**
TEMPLE *m* ISOTÉRMICO **7195**

TEMPLE *m* LOCALIZADO **3914**
TEMPLE *m* MARTENSÍTICO **8021**
TEMPLE *m* PARCIAL **7697**
TEMPLE *m* PARCIAL **11145**
TEMPLE *m* POR ETAPAS **824**
TEMPLE *m* POR INDUCCIÓN **6896**
TEMPLE *m* POR NITRURACIÓN **8582**
TEMPLE *m* POR PULVERIZACIÓN **11966**
TEMPLE *m* PRODUCIDO POR ESTIRADO EN FRÍO **6274**
TEMPLE *m* SECUNDARIO **11105**
TEMPLE *m* SUPERFICIAL **12508**
TEMPLE *m* Y REVENIDO **10092**
TEMPLE *m* Y REVENIDO **10095**
TENACIDAD *f* **12737**
TENACIDAD *f* **13071**
TENACIDAD *f* A LA ENTALLADURA **8671**
TENACIDAD *f* DE LOS BARROTES ENTALLADOS **12738**
TENACIDAD *f* EXTREMA **13327**
TENACILLA *f* **5536**
TENAZ **13067**
TENAZA *f* PERFORADORA DE CORREAS **1153**
TENAZAS *f pl* **1298**
TENAZAS *f pl* **12987**
TENAZAS *f pl* **9328**
TENAZAS *f pl* ACHAFLANADAS **13565**
TENAZAS *f pl* CORTANTES **3532**
TENAZAS *f* DE CRISOL **3405**
TENAZAS *f* DE FUNDIDOR **7548**
TENAZAS *f pl* DE HERRERO **1298**
TENAZAS *f pl* DE REMACHAR **10630**
TENAZAS *f pl* DE SOLDAR **11767**
TENAZAS *f pl* (LAS) **12987**
TENAZAS *f pl* PARA TUBOS **9362**
TENAZAS *f pl* SACABOCADOS **10000**
TENDENCIA (CURVA) *f* **13181**
TENDIDO *m* AÉREO **212**
TENSAR DE NUEVO UNA CORREA **12602**
TENSAR UN MUELLE **2838**
TENSAR UN RESORTE **10032**
TENSIÓN *f* **10591**
TENSIÓN *f* **9808**
TENSIÓN *f* **12367**
TENSIÓN *f* **12367**
TENSIÓN *f* **12322**
TENSIÓN *f* **12753**
TENSIÓN *f* **12764**
TENSIÓN *f* CONSTANTE **2978**
TENSIÓN *f* CRÍTICA **3351**
TENSIÓN *f* DE CIZALLADURA **11286**
TENSIÓN *f* DE COLADA **2081**

**TEN**                                    1138

TENSIÓN  f  DE COMPRESIÓN **2871**
TENSIÓN  f  DE CORRIENTE **13593**
TENSIÓN  f  DE DESCOMPOSICIÓN **3675**
TENSIÓN  f  DE EQUILIBRIO **4789**
TENSIÓN  f  DE EQUILIBRIO DE UNA REACCIÓN **4790**
TENSIÓN  f  DE ESTIRADO **12370**
TENSIÓN  f  DE FLEXIÓN **5425**
TENSIÓN  f  DE FLEXIÓN **1193**
TENSIÓN  f  DE FORMACIÓN **5576**
TENSIÓN  f  DE LA CORREA **1162**
TENSIÓN  f  DE PANDEO **3341**
TENSIÓN  f  DE PERFORACIÓN **1582**
TENSIÓN  f  DE SERVICIO **13957**
TENSIÓN  f  DE SERVICIO DEL ARCO **679**
TENSIÓN  f  DE SOLUCIÓN ELECTROLÍTICA **4609**
TENSIÓN  f  DE TORSIÓN **13058**
TENSIÓN  f  DE TRACCIÓN **12750**
TENSIÓN  f  DE UNA CORREA **12258**
TENSIÓN  f  DE UNA CUERDA **12258**
TENSIÓN  f  DE VACIADO **2078**
TENSIÓN  f  EN LOS ELECTRODOS **9709**
TENSIÓN  f  EN VACÍO **8808**
TENSIÓN  f  INTERNA **7074**
TENSIÓN  f  PRINCIPAL **9869**
TENSIÓN  f  SUPERFICIAL **12519**
TENSIÓN  f  SUPERFICIAL **7033**
TENSIÓN  f  TÉRMICA **12814**
TENSIÓN  f  (VOLTAJE) DEL ARCO **676**
TENSIÓN ADMISIBLE  f  **353**
TENSIÓN CIRCULAR O PERIFÉRICA  f  **6576**
TENSIÓN DE UNA CORREA  f  **12605**
TENSIÓN DINÁMICA  f  **4398**
TENSIÓN O FUERZA DE TRACCIÓN  f  **12750**
TENSIÓN RESIDUAL  f  **10474**
TENSIÓN SECUNDARIA  f  **11109**
TENSIÓN TANGENCIAL **11296**
TENSIÓNES  f pl  INTERNAS EN LA FUNDICIÓN **7075**
TENSOR  m  **12334**
TENSOR  m  **6187**
TENSOR  m  DE CADENA **2218**
TENSOR  m  DE CADENA **2219**
TENSOR  m  DE CORREAS **1161**
TENSOR  m  DE POLEA **12334**
TENSOR  m  DE TORNILLO **13285**
TENSOR  m  DE VIGAS DE CHAPA **9489**
TENSOR  m  INTERMEDIO **7047**
TEORÍA  f  ATÓMICA **805**
TEORÍA  f  DE LA DISTORSIÓN DE LA RED **7434**
TEORÍA  f  DE LAS FRACTURAS **5616**
TERBIO  m  **12760**

TERMINACIÓN  f  **11682**
TERMINAL  m  **12762**
TERMINAL  m  BORNE **12762**
TERMINAL DE CABLE  m  **1827**
TERMINALES  m  **12765**
TERMINAR **5214**
TÉRMINO  m  MEDIO ARITMÉTICO **703**
TÉRMINO  m  MEDIO GEOMÉTRICO **5929**
TERMITA  f  DE FUNDICIÓN **2036**
TERMODINÁMICA  f  **12828**
TERMODINÁMICA  f  **12829**
TERMOELECTRICIDAD  f  **12826**
TERMOELÉCTRICO **12823**
TERMÓGRAFO  m  **12832**
TERMÓGRAFO  m  **10293**
TERMOMETALURGIA  f  **4349**
TERMÓMETRO  m  **12833**
TERMÓMETRO  m  **12726**
TERMÓMETRO  m  AGITADOR **13826**
TERMÓMETRO  m  CENTÍGRADO **2186**
TERMÓMETRO  m  DE ALCOHOL **11922**
TERMÓMETRO  m  DE GAS **265**
TERMÓMETRO  m  DE MÁXIMA Y MÍNIMA **8063**
TERMÓMETRO  m  DE MERCURIO **8152**
TERMÓMETRO  m  DIFERENCIAL **3920**
TERMÓMETRO  m  FAHRENHEIT **5020**
TERMÓMETRO  m  GRADUADO EN TUBO **12235**
TERMÓMETRO  m  PATRÓN **12085**
TERMÓMETRO  m  RÉAUMUR **10268**
TERMÓMETRO  m  REGISTRADOR **10293**
TERMOPAR  m  **12821**
TERMOQUÍMICA **12822**
TERMOSCOPIO  m  **12837**
TERMOSTATO  m  **12838**
TERMOSTATO  m  **12722**
TERRACOTA  f  **12767**
TERRAJA  f  **12640**
TERRAJA  f  **11044**
TERRAJA  f  **3883**
TERRAJA  f  A MANO **6257**
TERRAJA  f  A MÁQUINA **7858**
TERRAJA  f  CILINDRICA **9534**
TERRAJA  f  CÓNICA **5268**
TERRAJA  f  DE ACABADO **1499**
TERRAJA  f  DE ACABADO **9534**
TERRAJA  f  DE COJINETES **12266**
TERRAJA  f  DE OJO CENTRAL **12638**
TERRAJA  f  DESBASTADORA **5268**
TERRAJA  f  EN FORMA DE PALETA **11039**
TERRAJA  f  EN FORMA DE PALETA **11039**

1139      **TIR**

TERRAJA *f* INTERMEDIA **11102**
TERRAJA *f* PARA ACABAR **5221**
TERRAJA *f* PARA TUBOS **1121**
TERRAJA *f* REDONDA EN UN SOLO BLOQUE **11781**
TERRAJA *f* SEMICÓNICA **11102**
TERRAJADO *m* DE UN FILETE **11030**
TERRAPLÉN *m* **900**
TERRAPLÉN *m* HIDRÁULICO **6686**
TERRAPLENADO *m* **900**
TERRAZO *m* **12768**
TERRENO *m* ARCILLOSO **2466**
TERRENO *m* ARENOSO **10930**
TERRENO *m* GUIJOSO **6076**
TERRERO *m* **1735**
TERREROS *m* **3946**
TEST *m* **12770**
TEST *m* **12770**
TEST *m* **12792**
TEST *m* DE AJUSTE **6006**
TEST *m* DE MCQUAID-EHN **8071**
TESTERA *f* **12012**
TESTIGO *m* DE ENCENDIDO **6769**
TETRACLORURO *m* **12096**
TETRAEDRO *m* **12797**
TETRATÓMICO **12798**
TETRAVALENTE **12798**
T.H. **7997**
THERMINOL *m* **12817**
TIEMPO *m* **12943**
TIEMPO *m* **12387**
TIEMPO *m* ACTIVO **13410**
TIEMPO *m* DE ADMISIÓN **7008**
TIEMPO *m* DE CAMBIO DE ÚTIL **12999**
TIEMPO *m* DE CIRCULACIÓN DE CORRIENTE **6382**
TIEMPO *m* DE COLOCACIÓN **4944**
TIEMPO *m* DE COLOCACIÓN **9651**
TIEMPO *m* DE COMPRESIÓN **2864**
TIEMPO *m* DE ENFRIAMIENTO **3082**
TIEMPO *m* DE EVACUACIÓN **5459**
TIEMPO *m* DE INVERSIÓN **10533**
TIEMPO *m* DE MANTENIMIENTO DEL ESFUERZO **6523**
TIEMPO *m* DE REPOSO **8734**
TIEMPO *m* DE SOLDADURA EFECTIVO **6382**
TIEMPO *m* MUERTO **6753**
TIEMPO *m* MUERTO **4191**
TIERRA *f* **4409**
TIERRA *f* ARCILLOSA **7691**
TIERRA *f* DE BATÁN **5727**
TIERRA *f* DE DIATOMEAS **3880**
TIERRA *f* DE INFUSORIOS **7292**

TIERRA *f* DE LADRILLOS **1598**
TIERRA *f* DE MODELAR **7691**
TIERRA *f* DE TUBO **9367**
TIERRA *f* (ELECTRICIDAD) **4415**
TIERRA *f* PODRIDA **7292**
TIERRA *f* REFRACTARIA **5241**
TIERRA *f* ROJA **10340**
TIERRA *f* VEGETAL **8423**
TIERRAS *f pl* ALCALINAS **336**
TIERRAS *f pl* RARAS **10210**
TIJERA *f* **13886**
TIJERAS *f pl* **11297**
TIJERAS ARTICULADAS *f pl* **856**
TIJERAS DE BANCO *f pl* **12264**
TIJERAS DE GUILLOTINA *f pl* **6170**
TIJERAS DE MANO *f pl* **6251**
TIJERAS PARA PAQUETES *f pl* **1246**
TIJERAS PARA PAQUETES *f pl* **11554**
TIJERAS PARA PAQUETES Y PLETINAS *f pl* **1244**
TIJERAS ROTATIVAS *f pl* **10759**
TIMBRADO *m* **9828**
TIMBRAR **5872**
TIMBRE *m* **5886**
TIMBRE *m* **1137**
TIMBRE *m* AVISADOR **1137**
TIMBRE *m* DE UN DEPÓSITO (A PRESIÓN) **8614**
TIMBRE *m* DE UNA VÁLVULA **9828**
TINA *f* **13228**
TINA *f* **13228**
TINGLADO *m* **11302**
TINTA *f* DE CHINA **6871**
TINTE *m* DE RECOCIDO **12732**
TINTE *m* DE REVENIDO **12732**
TIOSULFATO *m* **12852**
TIPO *m* **13320**
TIPO *m* **10226**
TIPO *m* DE TRABAJO **13958**
TIPO *m* ESTANDARD **12086**
TIRADOR *m* **5772**
TIRAFONDO *m* **11043**
TIRAFONDOS *m pl* **11575**
TIRALÍNEAS *m* **4241**
TIRALÍNEAS *m* DE PUNTEAR **4126**
TIRANTE *m* **1516**
TIRANTE *m* **6187**
TIRANTE *m* **12151**
TIRANTE *m* **12917**
TIRANTE *m* **9489**
TIRANTE *m* **10663**
TIRANTE *m* DE LEVANTAMIENTO **5772**

# TIR

1140

TIRANTES *m pl* **6186**
TIRANTES *m* DE ESFERA **12919**
TIRANTES *m pl* (DE UNA ESFERA) **1520**
TIRAR **4215**
TIRAS *f pl* **980**
TIRISTOR *m* **12913**
TIRO *m* **4196**
TIRO *m* ARTIFICIAL **8098**
TIRO *m* CON SOPLADURA **8098**
TIRO *m* DE AIRE **257**
TIRO *m* DE AIRE DE LOS MACHOS **3166**
TIRO *m* DE UNA CHIMENEA **4212**
TIRO *m* FORZADO **5533**
TIRO *m* INDUCIDO **6890**
TIRO *m* NATURAL **8501**
TITANIO *m* **12970**
TIXOTROPÍA *f* **12854**
TIZA *f* **13842**
TIZÓN *m* **6324**
TOBA *f* **13260**
TOBA *f* CALCÁREA **1838**
TOBA *f* DE NATURALEZA DE PÓMEZ **9989**
TOBA *f* PORFÍRICA **9631**
TOBA *f* VOLCÁNICA **13590**
TOBERA *f* **12966**
TOBERA *f* **8685**
TOBERA *f* **8679**
TOBERA *f* **8685**
TOBERA *f* **196**
TOBERA *f* **2769**
TOBERA *f* CONVERGENTE **2769**
TOBERA *f* CONVERGENTE **3066**
TOBERA *f* DE AIRE COMPRIMIDO **275**
TOBERA *f* DE EXPULSIÓN **3738**
TOBERA *f* DE PULVERIZACIÓN **11964**
TOBERA *f* DE PULVERIZACIÓN **11963**
TOBERA *f* DE TRAÍDA DE AIRE A PRESIÓN **13299**
TOBERA *f* DE VAPOR **12175**
TOBERA *f* DIVERGENTE **3738**
TOBERA *f* DIVERGENTE **4096**
TOBERA CILÍNDRICA *f* **3576**
TOBERA CONVERGENTE *f* **3066**
TOBERA CONVERGENTE *f* **2769**
TOBERA DE ESCAPE *f* **196**
TOBERA DIVERGENTE *f* **4096**
TOBERA DIVERGENTE *f* **3738**
TOBOGÁN *m* **11914**
TOCAR (GEOMETRÍA) **13066**
TOCHO *m* **1243**
TOCHO *m* **1243**

TOCHO *m* LAMINADO **8441**
TOCHO *m* PARA PRENSA DE ESTIRAR **4971**
TOCHO *m* PRELAMINADO **1346**
TOCHO PARA EXTRUSIÓN **4971**
TOCHOS *m pl* PRELAMINADOS DE ACERO AL CARBONO **1955**
TOLERANCIA *f* **358**
TOLERANCIA *f* **2483**
TOLERANCIA *f* **12982**
TOLERANCIA *f* ADMITIDA **359**
TOLERANCIA *f* DE MECANIZACIÓN **359**
TOLERANCIA *f* DIMENSIONAL **2483**
TOLERANCIA *f* EN LA FABRICACIÓN **358**
TOLERANCIA *f* LIMITE **7587**
TOLERANCIAS *f pl* DE MECANIZACIÓN **4988**
TOLUENO *m* **12983**
TOLUOL *m* **12983**
TOLVA *f* **6577**
TOMA *f* **3483**
TOMA *f* **6943**
TOMA *f* DE AGUA **6672**
TOMA *f* DE AIRE **289**
TOMA *f* DE AIRE **270**
TOMA *f* DE FUERZA **9745**
TOMA *f* DE POLVO **3997**
TOMA *f* DE UNA MUESTRA **10916**
TOMA *f* DEL CEMENTO **11226**
TOMA *f* (DEL CEMENTO) **3484**
TOMA *f* DIRECTA **3983**
TOMA DE AIRE **13530**
TONEL *m* DE ACABADO **13261**
TONEL *m* DE LIMPIEZA **13261**
TONEL *m* DE PULIR **9602**
TONELADA *f* (1000 KG) **12986**
TOPACIO *m* **13038**
TOPE *m* **12278**
TOPE *m* **12278**
TOPE *m* **12278**
TOPE *m* **12278**
TOPE *m* **1686**
TOPE *m* DE LA VÁLVULA **13461**
TOPE *m* DE PARACHOQUES **8956**
TOPE *m* PARA LOS PIES **12977**
TOPE DEL PASADOR DEL PISTÓN *m* **2405**
TOPOQUÍMICA *f* **13039**
TORCEDURA *f* **13629**
TORCER **13628**
TORCER **1173**
TORCER(SE) **13628**
TORCIDO **13305**

TORCIDO **1197**
TORIO *m* **12856**
TORNAPUNTA *f* **12396**
TORNAPUNTA *m* **1516**
TORNEADO *m* **13287**
TORNEADO *m* A PERFIL **1387**
TORNEADO *m* CÓNICO **12668**
TORNEADO *m* DE SUPERFICIES ABOMBADAS **13288**
TORNEADO *m* DE SUPERFICIES CON FIGURAS **8869**
TORNEADO *m* DE SUPERFICIES CÓNICAS **12668**
TORNEADO *m* DE SUPERFICIES ESFÉRICAS **13291**
TORNEADO DE INTERIORES *m* **1473**
TORNEADO INTERIOR *m* **3855**
TORNEADURAS **13293**
TORNEAR **13286**
TORNEAR **13276**
TORNEAR **10763**
TORNEAR **1466**
TORNEAR CUERPOS REDONDOS **13281**
TORNEAR EN FALSA PASADA **10840**
TORNEAR INTERIORMENTE **1462**
TORNEAR SUPERFICIES ABOMBADAS **13277**
TORNEAR SUPERFICIES CON FIGURAS **13280**
TORNEAR SUPERFICIES ESFÉRICAS **13281**
TORNEAR SUPERFICIES OBLICUAS **13282**
TORNEAR UNA SUPERFICIE CILÍNDRICA *f* **13162**
TORNILLO *m* **11021**
TORNILLO *m* **6457**
TORNILLO *m* **2453**
TORNILLO *m* A LA DERECHA **10584**
TORNILLO *m* A LA DERECHA **10580**
TORNILLO *m* A LA IZQUIERDA **7510**
TORNILLO *m* A LA IZQUIERDA **7506**
TORNILLO *m* ATERRAJADOR **11162**
TORNILLO *m* CON CABEZA DE MARTILLO **12701**
TORNILLO *m* CON TUERCA **1441**
TORNILLO *m* CONTINUO **1441**
TORNILLO *m* DE ALETAS **12912**
TORNILLO *m* DE ARQUÍMEDES **13970**
TORNILLO *m* DE BANCO **13579**
TORNILLO *m* DE BANCO **13561**
TORNILLO *m* DE BANCO **1171**
TORNILLO *m* DE BANCO ORDINARIO **6511**
TORNILLO *m* DE BANCO ORDINARIO **6511**
TORNILLO *m* DE BLOQUEO **2453**
TORNILLO *m* DE BLOQUEO **7708**
TORNILLO *m* DE BLOQUEO DE ANILLO **11222**
TORNILLO *m* DE BRIDA **5269**
TORNILLO *m* DE CABEZA **1913**
TORNILLO *m* DE CABEZA CILÍNDRICA **5165**

TORNILLO *m* DE CABEZA CUADRADA **12033**
TORNILLO *m* DE CABEZA CUADRADA **12033**
TORNILLO *m* DE CABEZA HENDIDA **11637**
TORNILLO *m* DE CABEZA HEXAGONAL **6457**
TORNILLO *m* DE CABEZA OCULTA **3248**
TORNILLO *m* DE CABEZA PLANA **5385**
TORNILLO *m* DE CABEZA REDONDA **11051**
TORNILLO *m* DE DOBLE ROSCA **13315**
TORNILLO *m* DE ELEVACIÓN **7556**
TORNILLO *m* DE FIJACIÓN **2453**
TORNILLO *m* DE FIJACIÓN **2553**
TORNILLO *m* DE GANCHO **6569**
TORNILLO *m* DE HUSILLO **1930**
TORNILLO *m* DE MANO **6254**
TORNILLO *m* DE METALES **8187**
TORNILLO *m* DE OREJAS **12912**
TORNILLO *m* DE PALANCA **1930**
TORNILLO *m* DE PRESIÓN **193**
TORNILLO *m* DE PRESIÓN **9831**
TORNILLO *m* DE PURGA **1319**
TORNILLO *m* DE REGLAJE **192**
TORNILLO *m* DE ROSCA CUADRADA **12034**
TORNILLO *m* DE ROSCA MÚLTIPLE **8474**
TORNILLO *m* DE ROSCA REDONDA **10807**
TORNILLO *m* DE ROSCA TRAPEZOIDAL **1815**
TORNILLO *m* DE ROSCA TRIANGULAR **547**
TORNILLO *m* DE TENSIÓN **12758**
TORNILLO *m* DE TOPE **12909**
TORNILLO *m* DE TRANSLACIÓN **10852**
TORNILLO *m* DE TRES ROSCAS **12879**
TORNILLO *m* DE TUBERO **13256**
TORNILLO *m* DE UNA ROSCA **11502**
TORNILLO *m* DIFERENCIAL **2833**
TORNILLO *m* ESFÉRICO **5978**
TORNILLO *m* GIRATORIO **12562**
TORNILLO *m* INCLINABLE **535**
TORNILLO *m* METÁLICO PARA MADERA **13918**
TORNILLO *m* MICROMÉTRICO **8255**
TORNILLO *m* NIVELADOR **7529**
TORNILLO *m* O PERNO DE FIJACIÓN **5043**
TORNILLO *m* O PERNO DE MONTAJE **5043**
TORNILLO *m* ORDINARIO **6511**
TORNILLO *m* ORIENTABLE **12562**
TORNILLO *m* PARA AFILAR SIERRAS **10955**
TORNILLO *m* PARA MADERA DE CABEZA CUADRADA **2552**
TORNILLO *m* PARA TUBOS **9363**
TORNILLO *m* PARA TUBOS **13256**
TORNILLO *m* PARA TUBOS **13256**
TORNILLO *m* PARALELO **9066**

**TOR** 1142

TORNILLO *m* SENCILLO **9429**
TORNILLO *m* SIN CABEZA **6156**
TORNILLO *m* SIN FIN **12619**
TORNILLO *m* SIN FIN **13969**
TORNILLO *m* SIN FIN **13979**
TORNILLO *m* TORNEADO **1607**
TORNILLO *m* TRANSPORTADOR **13970**
TORNILLO *m* UNIVERSAL **13389**
TORNILLO *m* VIOLÍN **12911**
TORNILLOS *m pl* DE CABEZA PLANA **5386**
TORNIQUETE *m* HIDRÁULICO (PARA MEDIR EL CAUDAL DE UNA CORRIENTE DE AGUA) **11027**
TORNO *m* **10557**
TORNO *m* **7427**
TORNO *m* **13851**
TORNO *m* A MANO **6256**
TORNO *m* ACCIONADO POR TUERCA MATRIZ **7428**
TORNO *m* AUTOMÁTICO **846**
TORNO *m* AUTOMÁTICO DE HUSILLOS MÚLTIPLES **8469**
TORNO *m* AUTOMÁTICO TRABAJANDO EN BARRA **983**
TORNO *m* DE AFINADO DE ÚTILES **10443**
TORNO *m* DE ÁRBOL ACODADO **3316**
TORNO *m* DE ÁRBOL DE LEVAS **1897**
TORNO *m* DE ATERRAJAR **3540**
TORNO *m* DE ATERRAJAR **11584**
TORNO *m* DE ATERRAJAR TUERCAS **8699**
TORNO *m* DE BRIDAS **5334**
TORNO *m* DE CARRO **11590**
TORNO *m* DE CICLOS AUTOMÁTICOS **840**
TORNO *m* DE CILINDRAR **11590**
TORNO *m* DE CILINDRAR **9428**
TORNO *m* DE COPIAR **3138**
TORNO *m* DE CRÁCKING **3287**
TORNO *m* DE DESBASTAR **10788**
TORNO *m* DE EJES **11246**
TORNO *m* DE EJES DE RUEDAS **881**
TORNO *m* DE ENFRIAMIENTO **3094**
TORNO *m* DE ENGRANAJE **10014**
TORNO *m* DE FRACCIONAMIENTO **5614**
TORNO *m* DE LINGOTES **6922**
TORNO *m* DE LLANTAS **13321**
TORNO *m* DE MADERA **13922**
TORNO *m* DE MANIVELA **6256**
TORNO *m* DE METALES **8191**
TORNO *m* DE PEDAL **5520**
TORNO *m* DE PIEZAS DE ENSAYO **12771**
TORNO *m* DE PLATOS **13171**
TORNO *m* DE PUNTA **2150**
TORNO *m* DE RELOJERO **13639**
TORNO *m* DE REPRODUCIR **3138**

TORNO *m* DE REPUJAR Y ALISAR **11911**
TORNO *m* DE REVÓLVER **1931**
TORNO *m* DE ROBLONES **12401**
TORNO *m* DE ROSCAR **12859**
TORNO *m* DE ROSCAR **11029**
TORNO *m* DE UN HUSILLO AUTOMÁTICO CON TORRETA **13298**
TORNO *m* DE UNA HÉLICE **13278**
TORNO *m* ELEVADOR **1929**
TORNO *m* (MÁQUINA HERRAMIENTA) **13289**
TORNO *m* PARA MANGUETA DE EJE **880**
TORNO *m* PARA METALES LIGEROS **7565**
TORNO *m* PARA ÓVALOS **8919**
TORNO *m* PARA RUEDAS **13816**
TORNO *m* PARALELO **9428**
TORNO *m* REVÓLVER **13297**
TORNO *m* SIMPLE **13863**
TORNO *m* VERTICAL **13545**
TORNO DE DESPOJAR *m* **913**
TORNO PARA DESTALONAR *m* **913**
TORNOS *m pl* **13852**
TORNOS *m pl* DE DESNUDAR **913**
TORO *m* **13043**
TORO *m* CIRCULAR **3588**
TORRE DE AGUA *f* **13680**
TORRETAS *f* POTAÚTILES **13004**
TORSIÓN *f* **13054**
TORSIÓN *f* **13051**
TORSIÓN *f* ALTERNATIVA **10414**
TORSIÓN *f* DE UNA CUERDA **13305**
TORSIÓN *f* LANG **7389**
TOSTADO *m* **5690**
TOSTADOR *m* **3821**
TOSTAR **11509**
TOSTAR LOS MINERALES **10648**
TOTALIZAR LOS DIAGRAMAS **2765**
TRABAJADOR *m* **13960**
TRABAJAR **13937**
TRABAJAR **5571**
TRABAJAR A LA COMPRESIÓN **1075**
TRABAJAR A LA TRACCIÓN **1075**
TRABAJAR AL ESFUERZO CORTANTE **1078**
TRABAJAR CON PALA **11386**
TRABAJAR EN EL TORNO **13276**
TRABAJO *m* **12331**
TRABAJO *m* **13936**
TRABAJO *m* **13959**
TRABAJO *m* A DESTAJO **9294**
TRABAJO *m* A DESTAJO **9294**
TRABAJO *m* A LA COMPRESIÓN **2869**

| | | |
|---|---|---|
| TRABAJO | *m* | A LA FLEXIÓN **1191** |
| TRABAJO | *m* | A LA TORSIÓN **13056** |
| TRABAJO | *m* | A LA TRACCIÓN **12747** |
| TRABAJO | *m* | A MANO **6240** |
| TRABAJO | *m* | A MÁQUINA **7850** |
| TRABAJO | *m* | ABSORBIDO **4747** |
| TRABAJO | *m* | AL ESFUERZO CORTANTE **11295** |
| TRABAJO | *m* | AL PANDEO **9597** |
| TRABAJO | *m* | CON GUBIA **6011** |
| TRABAJO | *m* | CON LA MOLETA **8287** |
| TRABAJO | *m* | DE COMPRESIÓN **13941** |
| TRABAJO | *m* | DE DÍA **3620** |
| TRABAJO | *m* | DE LA MADERA **13924** |
| TRABAJO | *m* | DE LOS METALES **8192** |
| TRABAJO | *m* | DE NOCHE **8575** |
| TRABAJO | *m* | DEL ROZAMIENTO **13942** |
| TRABAJO | *m* | EFECTUADO **13940** |
| TRABAJO | *m* | ELÉCTRICO **4539** |
| TRABAJO | *m* | EN CADENA **3034** |
| TRABAJO | *m* | EN CALIENTE **6650** |
| TRABAJO | *m* | EN (DOS O TRES) TURNOS **11350** |
| TRABAJO | *m* | EN EL TORNO **13287** |
| TRABAJO | *m* | EN FRÍO **2713** |
| TRABAJO | *m* | EN FRÍO **2713** |
| TRABAJO | *m* | EN GRAN SERIE **8028** |
| TRABAJO | *m* | EN SERIE **10462** |
| TRABAJO | *m* | EN VACÍO **8601** |
| TRABAJO | *m* | EXTERIOR **4962** |
| TRABAJO | *m* | INDICADO **6876** |
| TRABAJO | *m* | INTERIOR **7081** |
| TRABAJO | *m* | MANUAL **6237** |
| TRABAJO | *m* | MECÁNICO **8117** |
| TRABAJO | *m* | MECÁNICO (TRABAJO HECHO A MÁQUINA) **7860** |
| TRABAJO | *m* | MOTOR **8117** |
| TRABAJO | *m* | NOCTURNO **8575** |
| TRABAJO | *m* | POR DÍAS **3621** |
| TRABAJO | *m* | RESISTENTE **13944** |
| TRABAJO | *m* | ÚTIL **13428** |
| TRABAJO EN SERIE | *m* | **10462** |
| TRABAJOS | *m pl* | PRELIMINARES **9787** |
| TRABAJOS | *m pl* | PREPARATORIOS **9787** |
| TRACCÍON | *f* | **9970** |
| TRACCIÓN | *f* | DE LOS VEHÍCULOS **13088** |
| TRACCIÓN | *f* | DELANTERA **5699** |
| TRACCIÓN | *f* | EN LA DIRECCIÓN DE LAS FIBRAS **9968** |
| TRACCIÓN | *f* | NORMALMENTE A LA DIRECCIÓN DE LAS FIBRAS **9967** |
| TRACTIVA **13098** | | |
| TRACTOR | *m* | **13091** |
| TRACTOR | *m* | **13097** |

| | | |
|---|---|---|
| TRACTOR | *m* | **9859** |
| TRACTOR | *m* | AGRÍCOLA DE RUEDAS **13095** |
| TRACTOR | *m* | AGRÍCOLA ORUGA **13094** |
| TRACTOR | *m* | AGRÍCOLA SEMIARRASTRADO **13093** |
| TRACTOR | *m* | HORTENSE **13096** |
| TRADUCCIÓN | *f* | **13123** |
| TRADUCTOR | *m* | DE CLAVE **3670** |
| TRAÍDA DE AGUA | *f* | **13678** |
| TRAÍDO **1705** | | |
| TRAMA | *f* | **13743** |
| TRAMO | *m* | **7256** |
| TRAMO | *m* | AUTOMOTOR **6081** |
| TRAMPA | *f* | DE INSPECCIÓN CON TAPA **13168** |
| TRANSBORDADOR | *m* | **13141** |
| TRANSDUCTOR | *m* | **13108** |
| TRANSDUCTOR | *m* | **13108** |
| TRANSFERENCIA | *f* | DE CALOR **6372** |
| TRANSFERENCIA | *f* | POR CORTOCIRCUITO **11370** |
| TRANSFERENCIA | *f* | POR VENA LÍQUIDA **7659** |
| TRANSFORMACIÓN | *f* | **3067** |
| TRANSFORMACIÓN | *f* | ALOTRÓPICA **355** |
| TRANSFORMACIÓN | *f* | CONGRUENTE **2939** |
| TRANSFORMACIÓN | *f* | DE ENERGÍA **3070** |
| TRANSFORMACIÓN | *f* | DEL HIERRO EN ACERO **3068** |
| TRANSFORMACIÓN | *f* | EN COQUE **2666** |
| TRANSFORMACIÓN | *f* | EN RESINA **10480** |
| TRANSFORMACIÓN | *f* | ISOTERMA **7196** |
| TRANSFORMACIÓN | *f* | QUÍMICA **2296** |
| TRANSFORMADOR | *m* | **13115** |
| TRANSFORMADOR | *m* | AMPLIFICADOR DE POTENCIA **12245** |
| TRANSFORMADOR | *m* | DE DISMINUCIÓN DE VOLTAJE **12244** |
| TRANSFORMADOR | *m* | DE POTENCIAL **13115** |
| TRANSFORMADOR | *m* | ELEVADOR DE VOLTAJE **12245** |
| TRANSFORMADOR | *m* | REDUCTOR DE POTENCIAL **12244** |
| TRANSFORMAR EN COQUE **2656** | | |
| TRANSFORMAR LA ENERGÍA **13112** | | |
| TRANSFORMARSE EN RESINA **10481** | | |
| TRANSISTOR | *m* | **13119** |
| TRANSLACIÓN | *f* | **13123** |
| TRANSLACIÓN | *f* | **13158** |
| TRANSLACIÓN | *f* | PRIMITIVA **9865** |
| TRANSLUCIDEZ | *f* | **13124** |
| TRANSLÚCIDO **13125** | | |
| TRANSMISIÓN | *f* | **11248** |
| TRANSMISIÓN | *f* | **4294** |
| TRANSMISIÓN | *f* | **6372** |
| TRANSMISIÓN | *f* | A LAS RUEDAS **5186** |
| TRANSMISIÓN | *f* | CON REDUCCIÓN DE LA VELOCIDAD **5908** |
| TRANSMISIÓN | *f* | CON SACUDIDAS **7231** |

**TRA** 1144

TRANSMISIÓN *f* CORREAS DE IMPULSIÓN **3141**
TRANSMISIÓN *f* DE ÁNGULO **1149**
TRANSMISIÓN *f* DE ELECTRICIDAD **13133**
TRANSMISIÓN *f* DE ENERGÍA ELÉCTRICA **13129**
TRANSMISIÓN *f* DE MOVIMIENTO **3244**
TRANSMISIÓN *f* DE POTENCIA **13134**
TRANSMISIÓN *f* DE POTENCIA **9746**
TRANSMISIÓN *f* DE UN MOVIMIENTO **13130**
TRANSMISIÓN *f* DEL CALOR **13111**
TRANSMISIÓN *f* DEL CALOR **6374**
TRANSMISIÓN *f* EN EL TECHO **8940**
TRANSMISIÓN *f* FIJADA EN EL SUELO **5444**
TRANSMISIÓN *f* FIJADA EN UN MURO **13619**
TRANSMISIÓN *f* FLEXIBLE **5420**
TRANSMISIÓN *f* FUNICULAR **10734**
TRANSMISIÓN *f* HIDRÁULICA **5472**
TRANSMISIÓN *f* INTERMEDIA **3244**
TRANSMISIÓN *f* MURAL **13619**
TRANSMISIÓN *f* POR CABLE TELEDINÁMICO **12706**
TRANSMISIÓN *f* POR CABLES **10734**
TRANSMISIÓN *f* POR CADENA **2207**
TRANSMISIÓN *f* POR CONOS DE FRICCIÓN **1224**
TRANSMISIÓN *f* POR CORREA **7045**
TRANSMISIÓN *f* POR CORREAS **1144**
TRANSMISIÓN *f* POR CUERDAS CORREAS **10734**
TRANSMISIÓN *f* POR ENGRANAJE (O POR RUEDAS DENTADAS) **13021**
TRANSMISIÓN *f* POR ENGRANAJES **13131**
TRANSMISIÓN *f* POR ENGRANAJES **7050**
TRANSMISIÓN *f* POR FRICCIÓN **5684**
TRANSMISIÓN *f* POR PALANCA **13132**
TRANSMISIÓN *f* POR PLATOS **4005**
TRANSMISIÓN *f* POR POLEAS DE GARGANTAS MÚLTIPLES **8473**
TRANSMISIÓN *f* POR RUEDAS DE FRICCIÓN **13736**
TRANSMISIÓN *f* POR RUEDAS DE LLANTA CUNEIFORME **13736**
TRANSMISIÓN *f* PRINCIPAL **7944**
TRANSMISIÓN *f* SOBRE POLEAS MÚLTIPLES **3015**
TRANSMUTACIÓN *f* (QUIMICA) **13136**
TRANSPARENCIA *f* **13137**
TRANSPARENTE **13138**
TRANSPONTÍN *m* **7261**
TRANSPORTADOR *m* **11253**
TRANSPORTADOR *m* **9956**
TRANSPORTADOR *m* **3080**
TRANSPORTADOR *m* **3080**
TRANSPORTADOR *m* **1675**
TRANSPORTADOR *m* AÉREO **213**
TRANSPORTADOR *m* CON SACUDIDAS **11253**
TRANSPORTADOR *m* DE CANGILÓNES **1675**

TRANSPORTADOR *m* DE CINTA **1164**
TRANSPORTADOR *m* DE CÍRCULO COMPLETO **2426**
TRANSPORTADOR *m* DE CORREA **1164**
TRANSPORTADOR *m* DE HÉLICE **13970**
TRANSPORTADOR *m* DE PALETAS **11570**
TRANSPORTADOR *m* DE RASCADORES **11010**
TRANSPORTADOR *m* DE TABLERO METÁLICO **11570**
TRANSPORTADOR *m* EN FORMA DE ESCUADRA **10308**
TRANSPORTADOR *m* EN SEMICÍRCULO **11180**
TRANSPORTADOR *m* FIJO **10366**
TRANSPORTADOR *m* POR CABLE **213**
TRANSPORTADOR *m* POR GRAVEDAD DE RODILLO **6082**
TRANSPORTE *m* **13140**
TRANSPORTE *m* DE CALOR **6374**
TRANSPORTE *m* DE ENERGÍA A GRAN DISTANCIA **13135**
TRANSPORTE *m* DE ENERGÍA ELÉCTRICA A GRAN DISTANCIA **13133**
TRANSPORTE *m* DE LA ENERGÍA **13134**
TRANSPOSICIÓN (QUIM) **8388**
TRAPECIO *m* **13148**
TRAPEZOIDE *m* **13149**
TRAPO PARA LIMPIAR *m* **11952**
TRAPO PARA SECAR *m* **11952**
TRAQUITA *f* **13081**
TRASIEGO **4225**
TRASLADO *m* **13123**
TRASLADO *m* LATERAL **7423**
TRASPLANTADORA *f* **11133**
TRASS *m* **13152**
TRASTOCAR **2241**
TRASTORNO *m* (CÁLCULO SOBRE SEÍSMOS) **8965**
TRATAMIENTO *m* **13959**
TRATAMIENTO *m* ANÓDICO **605**
TRATAMIENTO *m* CON BICROMATO **1236**
TRATAMIENTO *m* CON CHORRO DE ARENA **2540**
TRATAMIENTO *m* DE LOS METALES EN FRÍO **2710**
TRATAMIENTO *m* DE LOS MINERALES **11666**
TRATAMIENTO *m* DE RECOCIDO **568**
TRATAMIENTO *m* DE REPOSO DESPUÉS DE LA SOLDADURA **9666**
TRATAMIENTO *m* DIRECTO **8799**
TRATAMIENTO *m* INDIRECTO **8735**
TRATAMIENTO *m* ISOTERMO **7194**
TRATAMIENTO *m* MECÁNICO **8861**
TRATAMIENTO *m* PRELIMINAR **9780**
TRATAMIENTO *m* PREPARATORIO **9780**
TRATAMIENTO *m* TÉRMICO **12815**
TRATAMIENTO *m* TÉRMICO **6377**
TRATAMIENTO *m* TÉRMICO **6375**
TRATAMIENTO *m* TÉRMICO EN VACÍO **13443**
TRATAMIENTO *m* ULTERIOR **12417**

1145       **TRI**

TRATAR **13937**
TRATAR LOS MINERALES **11664**
TRATAR MECÁNICAMENTE LOS MINERALES **4253**
TRAVERTINO *m* **13166**
TRAVESAÑO *m* **13243**
TRAVESAÑO *m* **7734**
TRAVESAÑO *m* **3361**
TRAVESAÑO *m* **3367**
TRAVESAÑO *m* DE UNA CADENA **12402**
TRAVESAÑO *m* DE UNA CADENA **12402**
TRAVESAÑO *m* DELANTERO **5693**
TRAVIESA *f* **7734**
TRAVIESA *f* DE HIERRO **7150**
TRAVIESA *f* DE MADERA **12941**
TRAVIESA *f* DE VÍA **11574**
TRAYECTO *m* **4063**
TRAYECTO *m* **4063**
TRAYECTO *m* **4063**
TRAYECTORIA *f* **13104**
TRAYECTORIA *f* **10810**
TRAZADO *m* **8017**
TRAZADO *m* **8017**
TRAZADO *m* **13076**
TRAZADO *m* **3794**
TRAZADO *m* DE CHAPAS **8018**
TRAZADO *m* DE UN DIAGRAMA **9521**
TRAZADOR **8013**
TRAZADOR *m* **9161**·
TRAZAR **8010**
TRAZAR **3795**
TRAZAR **4195**
TRAZAR GRÁFICAMENTE **9519**
TRAZAR UN DIAGRAMA **9520**
TRAZO *m* DE UNA ESCALA **8009**
TRAZO *m* PUNTEADO **4125**
TRAZOS *m* DE SOMBREAR (DELINEANTE) **6306**
TREFILADO *m* **4230**
TREFILADO *m* **13906**
TREFILADO *m* EN CALIENTE **6624**
TREFILAR **4220**
TREFILAR **4220**
TREFILERÍA *f* **13888**
TREFILERÍA *f* (FÁBRICA) **13905**
TREMENTINA *f* **3415**
TREMENTINA *f* DE VENECIA **13527**
TREN *m* CONTINUO LAMINADOR **3030**
TREN *m* DE ACABADO **5229**
TREN *m* DE CINTAS **11321**
TREN *m* DE ENGRANAJES **5901**
TREN *m* DE RODILLOS DE SALIDA **10838**

TREN *m* DESBASTADOR **10789**
TREN *m* DESBASTADOR **1348**
TREN *m* DIFERENCIAL **3913**
TREN *m* EPICICLOIDAL **4778**
TREN *m* LAMINADOR **10670**
TREN *m* LAMINADOR **10669**
TREN *m* LAMINADOR **10701**
TREN *m* LAMINADOR DE CHAPAS FINAS **11324**
TREN *m* LAMINADOR EN FRÍO **2708**
TREN *m* PLANETARIO **9446**
TREN *m* PLANETARIO **12456**
TREN *m* REDUCTOR **10353**
TRENES *m* DE LINGOTES APLASTADOS **11556**
TRENZA *f* **751**
TRENZA *f* **5863**
TRENZA *f* DE ALGODÓN **3220**
TRENZA *f* DE CÁÑAMO **6441**
TRENZA *f* DE CÁÑAMO ENSEBADA **6442**
TRENZADO *m* **12340**
TRENZADO *m* DE UNA CUERDA **12339**
TRENZADO *m* METÁLICO **13902**
TRENZADORA *f* **12341**
TRENZADOS *m pl* DE ACERO PARA CABLES **12217**
TRENZAR **12337**
TRÉPANO *m* **5494**
TRÉPANO **4265**
TREPIDACIÓN *f* OSCILANTE **11353**
TREPIDACIONES *f pl* **13559**
TREPIDACIONES *f pl* **13559**
TRIÁNGULO *m* **13185**
TRIÁNGULO *m* ACUTÁNGULO **157**
TRIÁNGULO *m* DE ENLACE **2962**
TRIÁNGULO *m* DE FUERZAS **13186**
TRIÁNGULO *m* EQUILÁTERO **4785**
TRIÁNGULO *m* ESCALENO **10984**
TRIÁNGULO *m* ESFÉRICO **11891**
TRIÁNGULO *m* ISÓSCELES **7192**
TRIÁNGULO *m* OBTUSÁNGULO **8718**
TRIÁNGULO *m* POLAR **9581**
TRIÁNGULO *m* RECTÁNGULO **10582**
TRIATÓMICO **13197**
TRIBÁSICO **13198**
TRIBROMURO *m* DE FÓSFORO **9255**
TRICLORURO *m* DE ANTIMONIO **626**
TRICLORURO *m* DE ARSÉNICO **724**
TRICLORURO *m* DE BISMUTO **1270**
TRICLORURO *m* DE FÓSFORO **9256**
TRICLORURO *m* DE ORO **821**
TRIEDRO *m* **13202**
TRIGONOMETRÍA *f* **13201**

**TRI** 1146

TRIGONOMÉTRICO  *m* **13200**
TRILLADORAS  *f pl* MECÁNICAS **12884**
TRINITRINA  *f* **8593**
TRINITRINA  *f* **8593**
TRINQUETE  *m* **2496**
TRINQUETE  *m* DE FRICCIÓN **5676**
TRINQUETE DE FLEJE  *m* **11987**
TRINQUETE DE PASADA  *m* **2094**
TRINQUETE DE ROCE  *m* **5675**
TRINQUETE (MECANISMO PARA TRANSFORMAR UN
  MOVIMIENTO ALTERNO EN CONTINUO) **10218**
TRIPODE  *m* **13219**
TRÍPOLI  *m* **13220**
TRÍPOLI  *m* SILÍCEO **7292**
TRISCADO  *m* DE UNA SIERRA **10958**
TRISCAR LOS DIENTES DE UNA SIERRA **11224**
TRISCAR UNA SIERRA **11224**
TRISULFURO  *m* DE ANTIMONIO **627**
TRISULFURO  *m* DE ARSÉNICO **728**
TRITURACIÓN  *f* **6117**
TRITURACIÓN  *f* **6117**
TRITURACIÓN  *f* **8287**
TRITURACIÓN  *f* FINA **6106**
TRITURACIÓN  *m* MOLIENDA  *f* **2786**
TRITURADOR  *m* **3419**
TRITURADOR  *m* **3419**
TRITURADOR  *m* **4045**
TRITURADOR  *m* **8451**
TRITURADOR DE CARBÓN  *m* **2559**
TRITURADOR DE COQUE  *m* **2658**
TRITURAR **6103**
TRITURAR **13222**
TRITURAR **9712**
TRITURAR **9712**
TRIVALENTE **13197**
TROCOIDE **13223**
TROLEBÚS  *m* **13225**
TROMEL  *m* **13226**
TROMPA  *f* **11518**
TRONCO  *m* DE CONO **13235**
TRONCO  *m* DE PARALELEPÍPEDO **13237**
TRONCO  *m* DE PIRÁMIDE **13238**
TRONZADO  *m* **3533**
TRONZADO  *m* **3533**
TRONZADO  *m* DE LA MADERA **4718**
TRONZADORA  *f* **3541**
TRONZAR **3510**
TRONZONADOR  *m* **3365**
TROQUEL  *m* **3883**
TROQUELADO  *m* **2651**

TROQUELAR **12056**
TROSTITA  *f* **13227**
TROZO  *m* **1301**
TROZO  *m* DE ÁRBOL **9643**
TROZO  *m* DE TUBO **9292**
TRUNCAMIENTO  *m* DE UN FILETE **5389**
TUBERÍA  *f* **2845**
TUBERÍA  *f* **9339**
TUBERÍA  *f* **9357**
TUBERÍA  *f* **13666**
TUBERÍA  *f* **13666**
TUBERÍA  *f* **12178**
TUBERÍA  *f* DE DERIVACIÓN **1818**
TUBERÍA CIRCULAR  *f* **2418**
TUBERÍA DE AIRE  *f* **281**
TUBERÍA DE AIRE  *f* **281**
TUBERÍA DE AIRE O VIENTO  *f* **1367**
TUBERÍA DE AIRE O VIENTO  *f* **1314**
TUBERÍA DE AIRE O VIENTO CÁLIDO  *f* **6651**
TUBERÍA DE BAJADA  *f* **3791**
TUBERÍA DE GAS  *f* **5834**
TUBERÍA DE SUBIDA  *f* **756**
TUBERÍA DE VAPOR  *f* LÍNEA DE VAPOR  *f* **12178**
TUBERÍA MARÍTIMA  *f* **11080**
TUBERÍA O TUBO DE DESCARGA **4022**
TUBERÍA VERTICAL  *f* **2753**
TUBERÍAS  *f pl* **2845**
TUBERÍAS  *f pl* **3736**
TUBERÍAS  *f pl* **9357**
TUBERÍAS  *f pl* **9357**
TUBERÍAS  *f pl* **12178**
TUBO  *m* **13257**
TUBO  *m* **13257**
TUBO  *m* **9339**
TUBO  *m* **9339**
TUBO  *m* **4183**
TUBO  *m* ACODADO DE DOS RAMAS COMUNICANTES ENTRE
  SÍ **13325**
TUBO  *m* AISLADOR **7002**
TUBO  *m* ATASCADO **2361**
TUBO  *m* CAPILAR **1921**
TUBO  *m* CAPILAR **13255**
TUBO  *m* CATÓDICO **2105**
TUBO  *m* CILÍNDRICO **3586**
TUBO  *m* CILÍNDRICO GRADUADO **5960**
TUBO  *m* COLADO HORIZONTAL **9342**
TUBO  *m* COLADO VERTICAL **9343**
TUBO  *m* COLECTOR **2725**
TUBO  *m* COMPENSADOR **4913**
TUBO  *m* COMPENSADOR DE DILATACIÓN **4913**

| | | | | | | |
|---|---|---|---|---|---|---|
| TUBO | *m* | CON NERVIOS LONGITUDINALES **7740** | TUBO | *m* | DE FUERZA **13253** |
| TUBO | *m* | CON NERVIOS TRANSVERSALES **13147** | TUBO | *m* | DE FUNDICIÓN **2035** |
| TUBO | *m* | CURVADO **1194** | TUBO | *m* | DE GAS **5833** |
| TUBO | *m* | DE ACERO **12219** | TUBO | *m* | DE GAS DE PAPEL IMPREGNADO DE ASFALTO **6803** |
| TUBO | *m* | DE ACERO **12212** | | | |
| TUBO | *m* | DE ACERO (PARA GASES LICUADOS) **12204** | TUBO | *m* | DE GRES **12277** |
| TUBO | *m* | DE AGUA **13681** | TUBO | *m* | DE HIERRO **13989** |
| TUBO | *m* | DE ALETAS **10571** | TUBO | *m* | DE HOGAR **1412** |
| TUBO | *m* | DE ALETAS **10571** | TUBO | *m* | DE HUMO **5248** |
| TUBO | *m* | DE ALETAS **5234** | TUBO | *m* | DE INYECTOR **13532** |
| TUBO | *m* | DE ALETAS EXTERIORES **4963** | TUBO | *m* | DE JUNTA ESFÉRICA **5418** |
| TUBO | *m* | DE ALETAS INTERIORES **7082** | TUBO | *m* | DE LATÓN **1570** |
| TUBO | *m* | DE ALIMENTACIÓN **5070** | TUBO | *m* | DE LONA DE CÁÑAMO **1908** |
| TUBO | *m* | DE ALUMINIO **427** | TUBO | *m* | DE MADERA **13928** |
| TUBO | *m* | DE ARCILLA (O DE TIERRA) COCIDA **4416** | TUBO | *m* | DE NERVIOS LONGITUDINALES **7740** |
| TUBO | *m* | DE ASPIRACIÓN **12433** | TUBO | *m* | DE PITOT **9415** |
| TUBO | *m* | DE BAJADA **4183** | TUBO | *m* | DE PLOMO **7468** |
| TUBO | *m* | DE BAJADA **4185** | TUBO | *m* | DE PLOMO ESTAÑADO INTERIORMENTE **7469** |
| TUBO | *m* | DE BAJADA **3593** | TUBO | *m* | DE PRESIÓN **3736** |
| TUBO | *m* | DE BARRO **4416** | TUBO | *m* | DE RAYOS CATÓDICOS **2105** |
| TUBO | *m* | DE BORDE VUELTO **1087** | TUBO | *m* | DE RAYOS X **12684** |
| TUBO | *m* | DE BRIDAS **5343** | TUBO | *m* | DE RAYOS X **14002** |
| TUBO | *m* | DE BRONCE **1653** | TUBO | *m* | DE REBOSADERO **8932** |
| TUBO | *m* | DE CALDERA **1422** | TUBO | *m* | DE RECUBRIMIENTO **7406** |
| TUBO | *m* | DE CALEFACCIÓN CENTRAL **6396** | TUBO | *m* | DE REDUCCIÓN **10352** |
| TUBO | *m* | DE CAMBIADOR TÉRMICO **6350** | TUBO | *m* | DE SALIDA **4207** |
| TUBO | *m* | DE CÁTODO CALIENTE **6652** | TUBO | *m* | DE SUBIDA **10615** |
| TUBO | *m* | DE CEMENTO **2898** | TUBO | *m* | DE TOMA DE AGUA **12066** |
| TUBO | *m* | DE CEMENTO ARMADO **5109** | TUBO | *m* | DE TRAÍDA DE AGUAS **12489** |
| TUBO | *m* | DE CHAPA **11312** | TUBO | *m* | DE VAPOR **12177** |
| TUBO | *m* | DE CINC **14047** | TUBO | *m* | DE VAPOR **12177** |
| TUBO | *m* | DE COBRE **3132** | TUBO | *m* | DEL TERMÓMETRO **13255** |
| TUBO | *m* | DE COLLAR VUELTO **1087** | TUBO | *m* | (ELECTRON.) **13453** |
| TUBO | *m* | DE COMUNICACIÓN **2960** | TUBO | *m* | ELEVADOR **10615** |
| TUBO | *m* | DE CONDUCCIÓN **9357** | TUBO | *m* | EN CRUZ DE CUATRO PASOS **3368** |
| TUBO | *m* | DE CONDUCCIÓN **13665** | TUBO | *m* | EN HORQUILLA **1595** |
| TUBO | *m* | DE CONTACTO **1804** | TUBO | *m* | ESTIRADO **11782** |
| TUBO | *m* | DE CRISTAL **5965** | TUBO | *m* | ESTIRADO EN FRÍO **2714** |
| TUBO | *m* | DE CUERO **7499** | TUBO | *m* | EXPANSIONADO **4905** |
| TUBO | *m* | DE DERIVACIÓN **1558** | TUBO | *m* | FLEXIBLE **6609** |
| TUBO | *m* | DE DESAGÜE **4207** | TUBO | *m* | FLEXIBLE **6614** |
| TUBO | *m* | DE DESCARGA **4207** | TUBO | *m* | FLEXIBLE **6614** |
| TUBO | *m* | DE DISTRIBUCIÓN DE AGUA **13665** | TUBO | *m* | FLEXIBLE *m* RODEADO DE ACERO **714** |
| TUBO | *m* | DE EMPALME **2960** | TUBO | *m* | FLEXIBLE CON ARMADURA DE ALAMBRE **714** |
| TUBO | *m* | DE ENTRADA **12489** | TUBO | *m* | (FLEXIBLE) DE CAUCHO **10821** |
| TUBO | *m* | DE ESCAPE **4894** | TUBO | *m* | LAMINADO **10677** |
| TUBO | *m* | DE ESCAPE DE VAPOR **4897** | TUBO | *m* | LISO **11684** |
| TUBO | *m* | DE ESTAÑO **12960** | TUBO | *m* | MANNESMANN **7983** |
| TUBO | *m* | DE EVACUACIÓN **4207** | TUBO | *m* | METÁLICO FLEXIBLE **5419** |
| TUBO | *m* | DE EXPULSIÓN **3736** | TUBO | *m* | METÁLICO FLEXIBLE **5421** |

**TUB** 1148

TUBO *m* PARA ENCAJAR **11707**
TUBO *m* PLEGADO **3199**
TUBO *m* PROTEGIDO CON ALQUITRÁN **12687**
TUBO *m* PROTEGIDO CON CUBIERTA DE YUTE ASFALTADO **766**
TUBO *m* PROTEGIDO CON PINTURA **9016**
TUBO *m* RECTIFICADOR **10317**
TUBO *m* RECTO **12309**
TUBO *m* ROBLONADO **10640**
TUBO *m* ROSCADO **11059**
TUBO *m* ROSCADO **11059**
TUBO *m* RUGOSO **10780**
TUBO *m* SIN SOLDADURA **11089**
TUBO *m* SOLDADO **13775**
TUBO *m* SOLDADO **13777**
TUBO *m* SOLDADO A LA AUTÓGENA **9364**
TUBO *m* SOLDADO A TOPE **1803**
TUBO *m* SOLDADO CON ALEACIÓN **11760**
TUBO *m* SOLDADO EN ESPIRAL **11920**
TUBO *m* SOLDADO EN HÉLICE **11920**
TUBO *m* SOLDADO POR CONTACTO **1804**
TUBO *m* SOLDADO POR RECUBRIMIENTO **7406**
TUBO *m* TAPONADO **2361**
TUBO *m* TRITURADOR **13252**
TUBO *m* VERTICAL **10615**
TUBO ACODADO *m* **1194**
TUBO DE DERIVACIÓN *m* **1818**
TUBO DE PASO DEL COMBUSTIBLE *m* **12489**
TUBOS *m pl* DE EMPALMES **9365**
TUBOS *m pl* DE NERVIOS **10571**
TUBOS *m pl* ELECTRÓNICOS **4636**
TUBOS *m pl* EN CONTACTO **2512**
TUBOS *m pl* ESTIRADOS EN FRÍO **2678**
TUBULADURA *f* **8679**
TUBULADURA *f* AUTOREFORZADA **9012**
TUBULADURA *f* DE ADMISIÓN **6948**
TUBULADURA *f* DE ALIMENTACIÓN **5084**
TUBULADURA *f* DE BRIDA **5337**
TUBULADURA *f* DE BRIDA **5341**
TUBULADURA *f* DE COLLAR **8514**
TUBULADURA *f* DE COLLAR **8683**
TUBULADURA *f* DE DERRAME **3736**
TUBULADURA *f* DE EMPALME **1557**
TUBULADURA *f* DE EMPALME **5337**
TUBULADURA *f* DE ENTRADA **6946**
TUBULADURA *f* DE ENTRADA **6946**
TUBULADURA *f* DE ESCAPE **4894**
TUBULADURA *f* DE FONDO **1495**
TUBULADURA *f* DE PURGA CON CUBETA PERIFÉRICA **4226**
TUBULADURA *f* DE SALIDA **8901**

TUBULADURA *f* DE SALIDA/DE ASPIRACIÓN **4705**
TUBULADURA *f* DE TECHO **10711**
TUBULADURA *f* EMPOTRADA **6969**
TUBULADURA *f* FLEXIBLE DE PURGA **6613**
TUERCA *f* **8698**
TUERCA *f* ALMADENADA **2085**
TUERCA *f* ALMENADA **2085**
TUERCA *f* ALMENADA **2085**
TUERCA *f* CIEGA **1512**
TUERCA *f* CIEGA **4118**
TUERCA *f* CON REBORDE **2085**
TUERCA *f* CUADRADA **12024**
TUERCA *f* DE AJUSTE (O DE REGULACIÓN) **191**
TUERCA *f* DE BLOQUEO **7702**
TUERCA *f* DE CORONA **2085**
TUERCA *f* DE HUSILLO **11907**
TUERCA *f* DE INMOVILIZACIÓN DE DISCO (DE VÁLVULA) **4009**
TUERCA *f* DE MARIPOSA **12911**
TUERCA *f* DE RETENCIÓN **10514**
TUERCA *f* DE SEGURIDAD **7702**
TUERCA *f* DE VOLANTE **6268**
TUERCA *f* DE YUGO (O DE CABALLETE) **14018**
TUERCA *f* EN BLANCO (A SOLDAR) **1307**
TUERCA *f* ENTALLADA **6533**
TUERCA *f* ENTALLADA **11942**
TUERCA *f* ENTALLADA **11942**
TUERCA *f* HEXAGONAL **6455**
TUERCA *f* HEXAGONAL CON REBORDE **5340**
TUERCA *f* MARIPOSA **12911**
TUERCA *f* MATRIZ **7471**
TUERCA *f* MATRIZ **6165**
TUERCA *f* MOLETEADA **8280**
TUERCA *f* MÓVIL **13159**
TUERCA *f* NEGRA **1290**
TUERCA *f* PRENSADA **8700**
TUERCA *f* PULIDA **1612**
TUERCA *f* (REDONDA) DE DOS O MÁS AGUJEROS **6533**
TUERCA *f* SIN ROSCA **1308**
TUERCA *f* TAPÓN **1512**
TUERCA *f* TAPÓN **1512**
TUERCA ALMADENADA **2085**
TUERCA CON ANILLO **2085**
TUERCA CON ENTALLAS **2085**
TUERCA DE ALETAS **12911**
TUERCA DE ALETAS **12911**
TUERCA DE CORONA **2085**
TUERCA DE CORONA **2085**
TUERCA DE CORONA **2085**
TUERCA DE CUBO **1512**

1149     **URA**

TUERCA DE DOS O MÁS AGUJEROS **6533**
TUERCA DE EMPAQUETADURA **9005**
TUERCA DE PRENSAESTOPA **9005**
TUERCA EN BRUTO **1290**
TUESTE *m* DE MINERALES **10650**
TUESTE *m* DEL MINERAL **8862**
TULIO *m* **12910**
TUMBAGA *f* AMARILLA **12984**
TUNGSTATO *m* DE SOSA **11737**
TUNGSTATO NATURAL DE CALCIO *m* **10997**
TUNGSTATO NATURAL DE CALCIO *m* **10997**
TUNGSTENO *m* **13262**
TURBA *f* **9147**
TURBA *f* ATERRONADA **4364**
TURBA *f* COMPRIMIDA **9804**
TURBA *f* MENUDA **9726**
TURBA *f* PARA QUEMAR **9151**
TURBINA *f* **6795**
TURBINA *f* **13267**
TURBINA *f* A PRESIÓN INTERIOR **10250**
TURBINA *f* AMERICANA **8330**
TURBINA *f* AXIAL **862**
TURBINA *f* DE ACCIÓN **6810**
TURBINA *f* DE ADMISIÓN PARCIAL **9085**
TURBINA *f* DE ADMISIÓN TOTAL **5718**
TURBINA *f* DE AIRE **13859**
TURBINA *f* DE ALTA PRESIÓN **6494**
TURBINA *f* DE BAJA PRESIÓN **7788**
TURBINA *f* DE BOMBA CENTRÍFUGA **6795**
TURBINA *f* DE EXPANSIÓN **4925**
TURBINA *f* DE GAS **5844**
TURBINA *f* DE IMPULSIÓN **6810**
TURBINA *f* DE LIBRE DESVIACIÓN **6810**
TURBINA *f* DE REACCIÓN **10250**
TURBINA *f* DE RETORNO DE ACEITE **8763**
TURBINA *f* DE VAPOR **12189**
TURBINA *f* HIDRÁULICA **6696**
TURBINA *f* MIXTA **8330**
TURBINA *f* PARALELA **862**
TURBINA *f* RADIAL **10136**
TURBINA *f* TANGENCIAL **12621**
TURBIO **1378**
TURBIO **1347**
TURBOCOMPRESOR *m* **2178**
TURBOCOMPRESOR *m* **13272**
TURBOGENERADOR *m* **13271**
TURBOVENTILADOR *m* **13270**
TURBULENCIA *f* **13273**
TURMALINA *f* **13072**
U *f* DE MONTAJE **12388**

ULTRAMICROSCOPIO *m* **13335**
ULTRAPASAR **8928**
UÑA *f* **4301**
UÑETA *f* **3364**
UNIDAD *f* DE CALOR **12816**
UNIDAD *f* DE DISTRIBUCIÓN **2229**
UNIDAD *f* DE LONGITUD **13373**
UNIDAD *f* DE LUZ **9270**
UNIDAD *f* DE MASA **13374**
UNIDAD *f* DE MEDIDA **13375**
UNIDAD *f* DE PERFORACIÓN **10011**
UNIDAD *f* DE PESO **13378**
UNIDAD *f* DE SUPERFICIE **13372**
UNIDAD *f* DE SUPERFICIE NUCLEAR **1006**
UNIDAD *f* DE TIEMPO **13376**
UNIDAD *f* DE TRABAJO **13379**
UNIDAD *f* DE VOLUMEN **13377**
UNIDAD *f* FOTOMÉTRICA **9270**
UNIDAD *f* TÉRMICA **12816**
UNIDAD *f* TÉRMICA INGLESA **1626**
UNIDAD *f* VIOLLE (DE INTENSIDAD LUMÍNICA) **13569**
UNIFICACIÓN *f* **12091**
UNIFICAR **12090**
UNIÓN *f* **13368**
UNIÓN *f* **5416**
UNIÓN *f* **3254**
UNIÓN *f* **1778**
UNIÓN *f* A BISEL **8324**
UNIÓN *f* A COLA DE MILANO **7396**
UNIÓN *f* CON CHAVETA (TRANSVERSAL) **7285**
UNIÓN *f* DE LAS CORREAS CON REMACHES **10555**
UNIÓN *f* DE LAS CORREAS POR TIRAS DE CUERO **7348**
UNIÓN *f* EN ÁNGULO **2519**
UNIÓN *f* EN T **12702**
UNIÓN *f* EXTREMO CON EXTREMO **1778**
UNIÓN *f* FRÍA **2705**
UNIÓN *f* HOMOGÉNEA **6556**
UNIÓN *f* POR MANGUITO Y TUERCA **7726**
UNIÓN *f* POR ROBLONADO **10639**
UNIÓN *f* ROSCADA (DE TUBOS) **13369**
UNIÓN *f* SOLDADA **13772**
UNIÓN F **1500**
UNIÓN POR CLAVIJAS *f* **7288**
UNIÓN POR CLAVO *f* **10639**
UNIÓN POR SOLDADURA *f* **11759**
UNIÓN POR SOLDADURA DE PIEZAS FUNDIDAS *f* **2060**
UNIVALENTE **8377**
UNTUOSIDAD *f* DEL LUBRIFICANTE **7813**
URANIO *m* **13420**
URANITA *f* **9411**

**URA** 1150

URANITA  f 9411
URDIMBRE DEL TEJIDO  f 13627
USO 13982
ÚTIL  m  PARA TRISCAR 10957
ÚTIL PARA TRISCAR UNA SIERRA 10957
UTILIZACIÓN  f 13429
UTILIZAR 13430
UTILIZAR DE NUEVO 10246
UTILLAJE  m 13015
UTILLAJE  m 4794
UTILLAJE  m DEL MONTADOR 4817
UTILLAJE  m EN ESPINA 1143
UTILLAJE  m PARA DELINEANTE 4236
UTILLAJE  m PARA MONTAJE 4812
VACANTE  f 13585
VACANTE  f 13433
VACIADO  m 13326
VACIADO  m 8428
VACIADO  m 4225
VACIADO  m 4024
VACIADO  m 4024
VACIADO  m DE UNA CALDERA 1364
VACIADO  m EN ESCAYOLA 6188
VACIADO  m EN ESCAYOLA 9465
VACIADOR  m DE CAJAS PARA SIN ELLAS LOGRAR EL
    MOLDE DE ARENA 2012
VACIAR 4018
VACIAR 4018
VACIAR 4204
VACIAR 4204
VACIAR 4204
VACÍO  m 6530
VACÍO 13434
VACIO  m ACTIVADO 6477
VACÍO  m ENTRE LAS ONDAS 6543
VACÍO  m LIBRE 2481
VACUIDAD  f 13585
VACUÓMETRO  m 13442
VAGÓN  m CISTERNA 12626
VAGÓN  m DEPÓSITO 12626
VAGONETA  f PARA CALDERO DE COLADA 2072
VAINA  f 11576
VAIVÉN  m 13725
VALENCIA  f 13452
VALOR  m APROXIMADO 653
VALOR  m CALCULADO 1858
VALOR  m DE EQUILIBRIO 4792
VALOR  m DE REGLAJE 11221
VALOR  m FINAL 5192
VALOR  m INICIAL 6932

VALOR  m INSTANTÁNEO 6990
VALOR  m INTERMEDIO 7051
VALOR  m LÍMITE 7594
VALOR  m MÁXIMO 8069
VALOR  m MEDIO 8073
VALOR  m MÍNIMO 8307
VALOR  m NOMINAL 8616
VALOR  m NUMÉRICO 8697
VALOR  m REAL 153
VALOR  m TEÓRICO 1858
VÁLVULA  f 2617
VÁLVULA  f 2617
VÁLVULA  f 2284
VÁLVULA  f 5353
VÁLVULA  f 13472
VÁLVULA  f 13453
VÁLVULA  f 13453
VÁLVULA  f 13453
VÁLVULA  f 12436
VÁLVULA  f ANULAR 10605
VÁLVULA  f AUTOMÁTICA 852
VÁLVULA  f AUTOMÁTICA 852
VÁLVULA  f CON ENVUELTA TERMÓGENA 7205
VÁLVULA  f CON ETAPAS 8475
VÁLVULA  f CON MANGUITO 11579
VÁLVULA  f DE ADMISIÓN 6949
VÁLVULA  f DE ADMISIÓN 201
VÁLVULA  f DE AIRE 259
VÁLVULA  f DE ALIMENTACIÓN 5076
VÁLVULA  f DE ARRANQUE 12131
VÁLVULA  f DE ASIENTO CÓNICO 2951
VÁLVULA  f DE ASIENTO PLANO 4011
VÁLVULA  f DE ASIENTO SIMPLE 11497
VÁLVULA  f DE ASIENTOS OBLICUOS 12662
VÁLVULA  f DE ASIENTOS PARALELOS 9060
VÁLVULA  f DE BLOQUEO MECÁNICO 9062
VÁLVULA  f DE BOLA 968
VÁLVULA  f DE BOLA 968
VÁLVULA  f DE CAMPANA 1136
VÁLVULA  f DE CAMPANA INTERIOR 11579
VÁLVULA  f DE CHARNELA 5353
VÁLVULA  f DE COMPUERTA 5867
VÁLVULA  f DE COMPUERTA 11652
VÁLVULA  f DE COMPUERTA GIRATORIA 10760
VÁLVULA  f DE COMPUERTA GIRATORIA 10760
VÁLVULA  f DE CONTRAPRESIÓN 895
VÁLVULA  f DE CONTROL 3872
VÁLVULA  f DE CORNOUAILLES 1136
VÁLVULA  f DE CUÁDRUPLE ASIENTO 10060
VÁLVULA  f DE DERIVACIÓN 1819

**1151**                                                                          **VAP**

VÁLVULA *f* DE DESCARGA **1358**
VÁLVULA *f* DE DESCARGA **10441**
VÁLVULA *f* DE DETENCIÓN **12282**
VÁLVULA *f* DE DETENCIÓN DE VAPOR **12186**
VÁLVULA *f* DE DISCO **4011**
VÁLVULA *f* DE DOBLE ASIENTO **4166**
VÁLVULA *f* DE DOS PASOS **13318**
VÁLVULA *f* DE EMISIÓN **4899**
VÁLVULA *f* DE ERUPCIÓN **1360**
VÁLVULA *f* DE ESCAPE **797**
VÁLVULA *f* DE ESCAPE **4899**
VÁLVULA *f* DE EVACUACIÓN **1358**
VÁLVULA *f* DE EXPANSIÓN **4926**
VÁLVULA *f* DE EXTRACCIÓN **1359**
VÁLVULA *f* DE FLOTADOR **5433**
VÁLVULA *f* (DE GRIFO O DE LLAVE) **4016**
VÁLVULA *f* DE INJECCIÓN **6937**
VÁLVULA *f* DE LIBRE DILATACIÓN **9061**
VÁLVULA *f* DE MANDO HIDRÁULICO **6697**
VÁLVULA *f* DE MANDO NEUMÁTICO **9557**
VÁLVULA *f* DE MANIOBRA RÁPIDA **10103**
VÁLVULA *f* DE MARIPOSA **12890**
VÁLVULA *f* DE MARIPOSA **1811**
VÁLVULA *f* DE NÚCLEO GIRATORIO **968**
VÁLVULA *f* DE PASO **5867**
VÁLVULA *f* DE PRESIÓN DEPRESIÓN **9843**
VÁLVULA *f* DE REBOSADERO **8933**
VÁLVULA *f* DE REDUCCIÓN **10355**
VÁLVULA *f* DE REPULSIÓN **3739**
VÁLVULA *f* DE RETENCIÓN **5353**
VÁLVULA *f* DE RETENCIÓN **12642**
VÁLVULA *f* DE RETENCIÓN **7547**
VÁLVULA *f* DE RETENCIÓN **7547**
VÁLVULA *f* DE SEGURIDAD **10891**
VÁLVULA *f* DE SEGURIDAD **1593**
VÁLVULA *f* DE SEGURIDAD DE CARGA DIRECTA **3632**
VÁLVULA *f* DE SEGURIDAD DE CARGA DIRECTA DE
  RESORTE **3987**
VÁLVULA *f* DE SEGURIDAD DE CONTRAPESO **13749**
VÁLVULA *f* DE SEGURIDAD DE GRAN RECORRIDO **10890**
VÁLVULA *f* DE SEGURIDAD DE PALANCA Y CONTRAPESO
  **7535**
VÁLVULA *f* DE SEGURIDAD DE PALANCA Y RESORTE
  **11985**
VÁLVULA *f* DE SEGURIDAD DE RESORTE **11998**
VÁLVULA *f* DE SEGURIDAD DE RESORTE **11986**
VÁLVULA *f* DE SUPRESIÓN DE VACÍO **13437**
VÁLVULA *f* DE TOMA DE VAPOR **12187**
VÁLVULA *f* DE TORNILLO EXTERIOR **8914**
VÁLVULA *f* DE TORNILLO INTERIOR **6980**
VÁLVULA *f* DE TRES PASOS **12882**

VÁLVULA *f* DE VACIADO **1358**
VÁLVULA *f* DE VÁSTAGO ASCENDENTE **10617**
VÁLVULA *f* DE VÁSTAGO FIJO **8624**
VÁLVULA *f* ELÉCTRICA **4549**
VÁLVULA *f* ELÉCTRICA **4549**
VÁLVULA *f* ELECTROMAGNÉTICA **11774**
VÁLVULA *f* ELECTROMAGNÉTICA **11774**
VÁLVULA *f* EN ESCUADRA **534**
VÁLVULA *f* EQUILIBRADA **934**
VÁLVULA *f* EQUILIBRADA **934**
VÁLVULA *f* MANDADA **8120**
VÁLVULA *f* MARIPOSA REGULADORA DEL GAS **12890**
VÁLVULA *f* MOTORIZADA **8416**
VÁLVULA *f* MÚLTIPLE **8476**
VÁLVULA *f* OSCILANTE **10760**
VÁLVULA *f* RECTA **12317**
VÁLVULA *f* ÚNICA **11491**
VÁLVULA ANTIHIELO *f* **8633**
VÁLVULA BALASTO *f* **970**
VÁLVULA COMPUERTA *f* **2617**
VÁLVULA DE ASPIRACIÓN *f* **12436**
VÁLVULA DE CHAPELETA *f* **5353**
VÁLVULA DE CHEQUE **2283**
VÁLVULA DE COMPUERTA *f* **11592**
VÁLVULA DE DESCARGA *f* **3739**
VÁLVULA DE DESCARGA *f* VÁLVULA DE PURGA *f*
  **10441**
VÁLVULA DE FONDO *f* **5523**
VÁLVULA DE FONDO *f* **5523**
VÁLVULA DE INVERSIÓN *f* VÁLVULA DE RENVÍO *f*
  **10553**
VÁLVULA DE REDUCCIÓN (DE REGULACIÓN) DE PRESIÓN
  **10420**
VÁLVULA DE REDUCCIÓN (DE REGULACIÓN) DE PRESIÓN
  **10355**
VÁLVULA DE RETENCIÓN *f* **2284**
VÁLVULA DE RETENCIÓN *f* **2283**
VÁLVULA DE RETENCIÓN DE BATIENTE *f* **12545**
VÁLVULA DE RETENCIÓN DE CHAPELETA *f* **7543**
VÁLVULA FILTRO *f* **5523**
VÁLVULAS *f pl* EN CABEZA **8943**
VANADIO *m* **13475**
VAPOR *m* **13484**
VAPOR *m* **12155**
VAPOR *m* A ALTA PRESIÓN **7785**
VAPOR *m* A ALTA PRESIÓN **6491**
VAPOR *m* DE AGUA **12192**
VAPOR *m* DE CALEFACCIÓN **6397**
VAPOR *m* DE EBULLICIÓN **1404**
VAPOR *m* DE ESCAPE **4896**
VAPOR *f* DE UN LÍQUIDO EN EBULLICIÓN **1404**

# VAP

1152

VAPOR *m* FRESCO **7673**
VAPOR *m* HÚMEDO **13805**
VAPOR *m* RECALENTADO **12471**
VAPOR *m* RECALENTADO **12469**
VAPOR *m* SATURADO **10942**
VAPOR *m* SATURANTE **10942**
VAPOR *m* SECO **4351**
VAPORES *m pl* ÁCIDOS **127**
VAPORIZACIÓN *f* **4867**
VAPORIZACIÓN *f* **13483**
VAPORIZAR **4862**
VARIABLE *f* **13488**
VARIABLE *f* **13494**
VARIABLE *f* COMPLEJA **2814**
VARIACIÓN *f* **13495**
VARIACIÓN *f* BRUSCA DE TEMPERATURA **12437**
VARIACIÓN *f* DE TEMPERATURA **13498**
VARIACIÓN *f* (DIÁMETRO *m*) ADMISIBLE SOBRE EL BANCO **12547**
VARIACIÓN *f* (MATEMÁTICAS) **13496**
VARIACIÓN *f* PROGRESIVA DE TEMPERATURA / DE VELOCIDAD **6024**
VARIACIONES *f pl* DE NIVEL DE AGUA **13500**
VARIACIONES *f pl* DE PRESIÓN **13497**
VARIACIONES *f pl* DE VELOCIDAD **13499**
VARIADOR *f* DE VELOCIDAD **13493**
VARIANTE *f* **410**
VARILLA *f* **5211**
VARILLA *f* **12237**
VARILLA *f* **11257**
VARILLA *f* **10663**
VARILLA *f* **10663**
VARILLA *f* **10663**
VARILLA *f* **10660**
VARILLA *f* AGITADORA **12260**
VARILLA *f* ASCENDENTE **10616**
VARILLA *f* DE CREMALLERA **10124**
VARILLA *f* DE GUÍA **6164**
VARILLA *f* DE GUÍA **6164**
VARILLA *f* DE RETENCIÓN **10516**
VARILLA *f* ELÁSTICA **1196**
VARILLA *f* FIJA **8623**
VARILLA *f* ROSCADA **11062**
VARILLA *f* ROSCADA DE CAPÓ **1453**
VARILLA *f* VERTICAL **6018**
VASELINA *f* **13508**
VASELINA *f* **13508**
VASO *m* DE PRECIPITACIÓN **1092**
VASO *m* DEL ACUMULADOR **1067**
VASOS *m pl* COMUNICANTES **13553**
VÁSTAGO *m* **12237**

VÁSTAGO *m* **11257**
VÁSTAGO *m* **11472**
VÁSTAGO *m* **10660**
VÁSTAGO *m* **10663**
VÁSTAGO *m* DE BALANCÍN **10026**
VÁSTAGO *m* DE BALANCÍN **10031**
VÁSTAGO *m* DE ÉMBOLO **9383**
VÁSTAGO *m* DE ÉMBOLO ATRAVESADOR **9387**
VÁSTAGO *m* DE ENLACE **2962**
VÁSTAGO *m* DE EXCÉNTRICA **4431**
VÁSTAGO *m* DE REMACHE **11263**
VÁSTAGO *m* DE TORNILLO EXTERIOR **8915**
VÁSTAGO *m* DE TORNILLO INTERIOR **6981**
VÁSTAGO *m* DE VÁLVULA **12236**
VÁSTAGO *m* DEL ÉMBOLO BILATERAL **9387**
VATÍMETRO *m* **13698**
VATIO *m* **13694**
VATIO-HORA *m* **13695**
VATIO-MINUTO *m* **13696**
VATIO-SEGUNDO *m* **13697**
VECTOR *m* **13510**
VECTOR *m* UNITARIO **13380**
VEHÍCULO *m* ARTICULADO **13092**
VEHÍCULO *m* DE TRES EJES **12871**
VEHÍCULO *m* DE VOLQUETE **12967**
VEHÍCULO *m* TODO TERRENO **3362**
VEHÍCULO *m* UTILITARIO **2784**
VELA *f* **3667**
VELADO **1378**
VELADO **1347**
VELARSE **13628**
VELETA *f* **13860**
VELOCIDAD *f* **11875**
VELOCIDAD *f* **11868**
VELOCIDAD *f* **10226**
VELOCIDAD *f* A LA LLEGADA **6950**
VELOCIDAD *f* A LA SALIDA **8903**
VELOCIDAD *f* ANGULAR **546**
VELOCIDAD *f* CIRCULAR **9198**
VELOCIDAD *f* CRECIENTE **6852**
VELOCIDAD *f* CRÍTICA **3353**
VELOCIDAD *f* DE CIRCULACIÓN **5462**
VELOCIDAD *f* DE CIRCULACIÓN **8903**
VELOCIDAD *f* DE CIRCULACIÓN DE ACEITE **10232**
VELOCIDAD *f* DE COMBUSTIÓN **10227**
VELOCIDAD *f* DE CORRIENTE **13516**
VELOCIDAD *f* DE CORROSIÓN **3193**
VELOCIDAD *f* DE CORTE CONSTANTE **2971**
VELOCIDAD *f* DE CRUCERO **3417**
VELOCIDAD *f* DE DEFORMACIÓN **3326**

VELOCIDAD *f* DE DEFORMACIÓN **5459**
VELOCIDAD *f* DE DEFORMACIÓN **12330**
VELOCIDAD *f* DE DEPÓSITO **10229**
VELOCIDAD *f* DE ENTRADA **6950**
VELOCIDAD *f* DE FUSIÓN **8144**
VELOCIDAD *f* DE HUSILLO **11909**
VELOCIDAD *f* DE INFLAMACIÓN **11870**
VELOCIDAD *f* DE LA LUZ **13517**
VELOCIDAD *f* DE LA LUZ **7569**
VELOCIDAD *f* DE LLEGADA **6950**
VELOCIDAD *f* DE PASO **13518**
VELOCIDAD *f* DE PROPAGACIÓN **13519**
VELOCIDAD *f* DE PROPAGACIÓN DE LA LLAMA **10230**
VELOCIDAD *f* DE RÉGIMEN **8663**
VELOCIDAD *f* DE ROTACIÓN **11876**
VELOCIDAD *f* DE SALIDA **8903**
VELOCIDAD *f* DE TRANSFORMACIÓN **13521**
VELOCIDAD *f* DECRECIENTE **3679**
VELOCIDAD *f* DEL ÉMBOLO **9388**
VELOCIDAD *f* DEL HILO **13900**
VELOCIDAD *f* DEL SONIDO **13520**
VELOCIDAD *f* FINAL **5193**
VELOCIDAD *f* INICIAL **6933**
VELOCIDAD *f* LINEAL **7617**
VELOCIDAD *f* MÁXIMA **8067**
VELOCIDAD *f* MULTIPLICADA **8930**
VELOCIDAD *f* NORMAL DE FUNCIONAMIENTO **8663**
VELOCIDAD *f* PERIFÉRICA **9198**
VELOCIDAD *f* TANGENCIAL **12623**
VELOCIDAD *f* UNIFORME CONSTANTE **13363**
VELOCIDAD *f* VARIABLE **13494**
VELOCIDAD *f* VIRTUAL **13573**
VELOCIDAD DE UNA MÁQUINA *f* **10850**
VENCER UNA RESISTENCIA **8929**
VENTAJA *f* DE TRABAJO **8094**
VENTANA *f* **13864**
VENTANILLA *f* DE INSPECCIÓN **2721**
VENTEADURA *f* **1353**
VENTEADURA *f* **1351**
VENTEADURA *f* **5836**
VENTEADURA *f* **5825**
VENTEADURA *f* **7523**
VENTEADURAS *f pl* **11903**
VENTEADURAS *f pl* **1362**
VENTEADURAS *f pl* **1330**
VENTILACIÓN *f* **13530**
VENTILACIÓN **13530**
VENTILACIÓN **13530**
VENTILACIÓN *f* **13528**
VENTILACIÓN *f* ARTIFICIAL **738**

VENTILACIÓN *f* NATURAL **8508**
VENTILACIÓN *f* POR ASPIRACIÓN **13450**
VENTILACIÓN *f* POR IMPULSIÓN **9517**
VENTILACIÓN DEL AGUA *f* **210**
VENTILADOR *m* **211**
VENTILADOR *m* **5033**
VENTILADOR *m* ASPIRANTE **12429**
VENTILADOR *m* ASPIRANTE E IMPELENTE **2768**
VENTILADOR *m* DE ENFRIAMIENTO **3088**
VENTILADOR *m* DE FUERZA CENTRÍFUGA **2179**
VENTILADOR *m* DE HÉLICE **9929**
VENTILADOR *m* DE IMPULSIÓN **9817**
VENTILADOR *m* DE IMPULSIÓN **9817**
VENTILADOR *m* DE PISTÓN **9372**
VENTILADOR *m* DE PISTÓN ROTATIVO **10751**
VENTILADOR *m* SISTEMA ROOT **10729**
VERDE DE SCHEELE **10996**
VERDE DE SCHWEINFURT **11000**
VERDE ESMERALDA **2372**
VERDETE **13533**
VERDÍN *m* **13533**
VERDÍN *m* **220**
VERIFICACIÓN *f* **13534**
VERIFICACIÓN *f* DE LA COMPOSICIÓN QUÍMICA **2280**
VERIFICACIÓN *f* DEL PARALELISMO **13086**
VERIFICADOR *m* **5871**
VERIFICADOR *m* DE INCITACIÓN A LA RESISTENCIA **12329**
VERIFICADOR *m* DE RESISTENCIA AL ESFUERZO **10494**
VERIFICADOR *m* (METROLOGÍA) **5871**
VERIFICADOR DIMENSIONAL **1867**
VERIFICAR LAS MEDIDAS **2279**
VERNIER *m* **13536**
VERTEDERO *m* **8931**
VERTEDERO *m* **2251**
VERTEDERO *m* DE LOS PLATILLOS **4188**
VERTER EL HORMIGÓN **2895**
VERTICAL *f* **9217**
VERTICAL **13551**
VERTICALMENTE **9217**
VÉRTICE *m* **12455**
VÉRTICE *m* **638**
VÉRTICE *m* **638**
VÉRTICE *m* DE LA ROSCA **3333**
VÉRTICE *m* DE UN POLÍGONO **13543**
VÉRTICE *m* DE UNA ROSCA **12455**
VÉRTICE *m* DEL DIENTE **12514**
VERTIDO *m* **4376**
VERTIMIENTO *m* **4376**
VÍA *f* **13085**

**VIA** 1154

VÍA  *f*  DECAUVILLE **9639**
VÍA  *f*  FÉRREA **7606**
VÍA  *f*  FÉRREA DE TALLER **13965**
VÍA  *f*  PORTÁTIL **9639**
VÍA FÉRREA  *f*  **7606**
VIAJERO  *m*  **7625**
VIBRACIÓN  *f*  **8884**
VIBRACIÓN  *f*  **13146**
VIBRACIÓN  *f*  **13554**
VIBRACIÓN  *f*  **3600**
VIBRACIÓN  *f*  DEBIDA A LOS ESFUERZOS DE FLEXIÓN **13556**
VIBRACIÓN  *f*  DEBIDA A LOS ESFUERZOS DE TORSIÓN **13557**
VIBRACIÓN  *f*  FUNDAMENTAL **5736**
VIBRACIÓN  *f*  LUMINOSA **7825**
VIBRACIÓN  *f*  MECÁNICA **8114**
VIBRACIÓN  *f*  NO AMORTIGUADA **13346**
VIBRACIÓN  *f*  PROPIA **5736**
VIBRACIÓN  *f*  SONORA **11818**
VIBRACIONES  *f pl*  **13560**
VIBRACIONES  *f pl*  **13559**
VIBRACIONES  *f pl*  **13559**
VIBRACIONES  *f pl*  **2277**
VIBRACIONES  *f pl*  DEBIDAS A LA RESONANCIA **8883**
VIBRAR **8877**
VIBROCULTORES  *m pl*  **3457**
VICIO  *m*  **3692**
VICIO  *m*  DE CONCEPCIÓN **3694**
VICIO  *m*  DE CONSTRUCCIÓN **3693**
VICIO  *m*  DE FUNCIONAMIENTO **3695**
VICIO  *m*  DE MATERIA **3680**
VIDRIADO  *m*  **3264**
VIDRIADO  *m*  **5968**
VIDRIADO  *m*  **5972**
VIDRIADO  *m*  **5968**
VIDRIO **5956**
VIDRIO **8708**
VIDRIO  *m*  SOLUBLE **11808**
VIDRIO  *m*  SOPLADO **1365**
VIENTO  *m*  **1315**
VIENTO  *m*  **6187**
VIENTO  *m*  RICO EN OXÍGENO **4770**
VIENTO DE LA MÁQUINA SOPLANTE  *m*  **243**
VIENTO INYECTADO  *m*  **243**
VIENTRE  *m*  **1720**
VIENTRE DE PESCADO (CON)  *m*  **5272**
VIGA  *f*  **5946**
VIGA  *f*  **1099**
VIGA  *f*  **1093**
VIGA  *f*  **986**

VIGA  *f*  **1522**
VIGA  *f*  APOYADA EN SUS DOS EXTREMOS **1098**
VIGA  *f*  COMPUESTA **9490**
VIGA  *f*  COMPUESTA **9488**
VIGA  *f*  CONTINUA **3018**
VIGA  *f*  DE ALAS ANCHAS **1639**
VIGA  *f*  DE HIERRO **12199**
VIGA  *f*  DE MADERA **949**
VIGA  *f*  DE PUENTE GRÚA **13157**
VIGA  *f*  DE RIGIDEZ **13856**
VIGA  *f*  DE TEJADO **1581**
VIGA  *f*  EMPOTRADA **1702**
VIGA  *f*  EMPOTRADA **5286**
VIGA  *f*  EMPOTRADA **6968**
VIGA  *f*  EMPOTRADA EN SUS DOS EXTREMOS **1703**
VIGA  *f*  EMPOTRADA EN UN EXTREMO Y APOYADA EN EL OTRO **1097**
VIGA  *f*  EMPOTRADA POR UN EXTREMO **1904**
VIGA  *f*  EN ENREJADO **7431**
VIGA  *f*  EN VOLADIZO **1905**
VIGA  *f*  EN VOLADIZO **1904**
VIGA  *f*  ENVUELTA **4714**
VIGA  *f*  INCORPORADA **7010**
VIGA  *f*  MIXTA O COMPUESTA **2831**
VIGA  *f*  RADIAL **10131**
VIGA  *f*  SIN ENTRELAZAR **1905**
VIGA  *f*  TIRANTE **13856**
VIGILANCIA  *f*  **12481**
VIGILANCIA  *f*  DE LAS CALDERAS **9193**
VIGILANTE  *m*  **8958**
VIGILAR **12474**
VIGUETA  *f*  **1093**
VIGUETA  *f*  **986**
VIGUETA  *f*  **986**
VIGUETA  *f*  DE ALAS ANCHAS **13849**
VIGUETA  *f*  EN I **6748**
VIGUETA  *f*  EN U **2249**
VIGUETAS  *f pl*  DE ALAS ANCHAS **1641**
VINAGRE  *m*  RADICAL **86**
VIRGEN (MINERAL) **5647**
VIROLA  *f*  **5128**
VIROLA  *f*  DE UNA CALDERA **3260**
VIRUTA  *f*  **2346**
VIRUTA  *f*  **2343**
VIRUTA  *f*  **2343**
VIRUTA  *f*  **12536**
VIRUTA  *f*  DE HIERRO **11953**
VIRUTA  *f*  DE HIERRO **6217**
VIRUTA ADHERENTE  *f*  **1707**
VIRUTAS  *f pl*  **3543**

1155      **XEN**

VIRUTAS  *f pl* **13293**
VIRUTAS  *f pl* **11278**
VIRUTAS DE FIBRAS DE MADERA  *f pl* **13923**
VIRUTAS (DE MADERA)  *f pl* **13919**
VIRUTAS DE METAL  *f pl* **2348**
VIRUTAS DE SONDEO  *f pl* **1476**
VIRUTAS DEL MANDRINADO  *f pl* **11277**
VISCOSIDAD  *f* **13576**
VISCOSÍMETRO  *m* **13574**
VISCOSO **13575**
VISCOSO **13577**
VISTA  *f* **13567**
VISTA  *f* A VUELO DE PÁJARO **1264**
VISTA  *f* ANTERIOR **5694**
VISTA  *f* ANTERIOR POSTERIOR **4717**
VISTA  *f* DE ABAJO ARRIBA **1498**
VISTA  *f* DE ARRIBA ABAJO **13037**
VISTA  *f* DE CONJUNTO **9430**
VISTA  *f* DE CONJUNTO **9430**
VISTA  *f* DISGREGADA **4934**
VISTA  *f* EN PERSPECTIVA O CABALLERA **1264**
VISTA  *f* LATERAL **11420**
VISTA  *f* POR DEBAJO **1498**
VISUALIZACIÓN  *f* **10253**
VÍTREO **13582**
VITRIFICACIÓN  *f* **13584**
VITRIFICADO  *m* **5972**
VITRIOLO  *m* **12453**
VITRIOLO  *m* AZUL **1376**
VITRIOLO  *m* BLANCO **14046**
VITRIOLO  *m* MARCIAL **6093**
VITRIOLO  *m* VERDE **6093**
VIVIENDA  *f* **6660**
VOCABLO  *m* **13934**
VOLADIZO **8936**
VOLADIZO **8934**
VOLANTE  *m* **13810**
VOLANTE  *m* A MANO **6267**
VOLANTE  *m* DE CADENA **2223**
VOLANTE  *m* DE CADENA ADAPTABLE **2220**
VOLANTE  *m* DE DIRECCIÓN **12233**
VOLANTE  *m* DE DISCO **4004**
VOLANTE  *m* DE DOS SEGMENTOS **5497**
VOLANTE  *m* DE GARGANTAS **10738**
VOLANTE  *m* DE MANIOBRA **6255**
VOLANTE  *m* DE TORNEADO **13163**
VOLANTE  *m* DE UNA SOLA PIEZA **11784**
VOLANTE  *m* DE VARIOS SEGMENTOS **11138**
VOLANTE  *m* DENTADO **5906**
VOLANTE  *m* EN DISCO **4004**

VOLANTE  *m* HENDIDO **11941**
VOLANTE  *m* MOTOR **5496**
VOLANTE  *m* POLEA **1147**
VOLATILIDAD  *f* **13589**
VOLATILIZACIÓN  *f* **13587**
VOLATILIZAR **13588**
VOLCABLE **6835**
VOLCADOR  *m* DE VAGONETAS **1932**
VOLFRAMIO  *m* **13912**
VOLQUETE  *m* **13812**
VOLQUETE  *m* **2017**
VOLTAJE  *m* **13593**
VOLTAJE  *m* EN LOS BORNES **12764**
VOLTAJE  *m* EN LOS BORNES (EN LOS TERMINALES)
   **12764**
VOLTAJE  *m* NORMAL **8659**
VOLTÁMETRO  *m* **3227**
VOLTEADOR  *m* **10654**
VOLTEADOR  *m* DE LINGOTES **7982**
VOLTEADORA  *f* DE HENO **12537**
VOLTÍMETRO  *m* **13597**
VOLTIO  *m* **13591**
VOLTIO-AMPERIO  *m* **13592**
VOLTIO-CULOMBIO  *m* **7255**
VOLUMEN  *m* **13598**
VOLUMEN  *m* **13598**
VOLUMEN  *m* ATÓMICO **806**
VOLUMEN  *m* CRÍTICO **3354**
VOLUMEN  *m* DESPLAZADO **4053**
VOLUMEN  *m* ENGENDRADO POR EL DESPLAZAMIENTO DEL
   ÉMBOLO **13599**
VOLUMEN  *m* ESPECÍFICO **11854**
VOLUMEN  *m* MOLECULAR **8362**
VOLUMEN  *m* (PORCENTAJE DEL) **9179**
VOLUMEN  *m* QUE PASA A TRAVÉS DE UN ORIFICIO POR
   SEGUNDO **4023**
VOLVEDOR  *m* **1818**
VOLVER A MOLDEAR **6105**
VOLVER A MONTAR **10244**
VUELTA  *f* A LA TEMPERATURA AMBIENTE **3096**
VUELTA  *f* DE ESPIRA **2646**
VUELTA  *f* EN EL AIRE **5005**
VUELTA  *f* EN EL AIRE **5001**
VUELTA  *f* EN EL AIRE EN PLATO HORIZONTAL **1469**
VUELTA  *f* FRONTAL (VUELTA EN EL AIRE) **5697**
VUELTA DEL CUERO  *f* **5414**
VULCANIZACIÓN  *f* **3484**
VULCANIZACIÓN  *f* **13607**
VULCANIZAR **13608**
WULFENITA  *f* **13991**
XENÓN  *m* **14004**

# XER

1156

XEROGRAFÍA  *f* **14005**
XILENO  *m* **14006**
XILOIDINA  *f* **6176**
XILOL **14006**
YACIMIENTO  *m* MINERAL **8303**
YACIMIENTO  *m* MINERO **8303**
YARDA  *f* **14007**
YARDA  *f* CUADRADA **12031**
YESO  *m* **9466**
YESO  *m* DE VACIAR **6190**
YODO  *m* **7120**
YODURO  *m* DE MERCURIO **8155**
YODURO  *m* DE POTASIO **9689**
YODURO DE PLATA **11464**
YUNQUE  *m* **630**
YUNQUE  *m* CON SUFRIDERA DE REMACHAR **11032**
YUNQUE  *m* INFERIOR **633**
YUNQUE  *m* PEQUEÑO **4116**
YUTE  *m* **7268**
ZAMAK  *m* **14021**
ZAMBULLIRSE **3968**
ZANCA  *f* **12052**
ZANCA  *f* DE ESCALERA **12377**
ZAPATA  *f* **11587**
ZAPATA  *f* **11360**
ZAPATA  *f* DE FRENO **1543**
ZAPATA  *f* DE FRENO **1531**
ZAPATA  *f* MAGNÉTICA **8188**
ZAPATA  *f* PARA DISPOSITIVO DE ELEVACIÓN **7207**
ZINGAJE  *m* ELECTROQUÍMICO ELECTROLÍTICO **4566**
ZIRCONIO  *m* **14049**
ZÓCALO  *m* **1026**
ZÓCALO  *m* **9011**
ZÓCALO  *m* **12490**
ZÓCALO  *m* DE FUNDICIÓN **1037**
ZONA  *f* DE DIFUSIÓN **3934**
ZONA  *f* DE FUSIÓN **5763**
ZONA  *f* DE FUSIÓN **5761**
ZONA  *f* DE GUINTER-PRESTON **6171**
ZONA  *f* DE SOLIDIFICACIÓN **5658**
ZONA  *f* DE SUPERFICIE DE SEPARACIÓN **7034**
ZONA  *f* DE TRANSFORMACIÓN **13113**
ZONA  *f* DEFICIENTE EN PERLITA **5105**
ZONA  *f* ESFÉRICA **14051**
ZONA  *f* INFLUENCIADA POR EL CALOR **6380**
ZONA  *f* IONIZADA **7128**
ZONA  *f* NEUTRA **8547**
ZUNCHADO  *m* **11398**
ZUNCHADO  *m* EN CALIENTE **11398**
ZUNCHAR EN CALIENTE **11390**

ZUNCHO  *m* **7203**
ZUNCHO  *m* **1252**
ZUNCHO  *m* **2931**
ZUNCHO  *m* COLOCADO EN CALIENTE **11391**

# ÍNDICE REMISSIVO PORTUGUÊS

# 1159

| | | | |
|---|---|---|---|
| 1 | CORRENTE ALTERNADA (C.A.) | 40 | ABSORVEDOR |
| 2 | MÁQUINA DE SOLDAR DE C.A. | 41 | CAPACIDADE DE ABSORÇÃO CALORIFICA |
| 3 | CORRENTE ALTERNADA DE ALTA FREQÜÊNCIA | 42 | PODER OU POTÊNCIA DE ABSORÇÃO |
| | | 43 | ABSORCIÔMETRO |
| 4 | REDUÇÃO DA TÊMPERA | 44 | ABSORÇÃO |
| 5 | ABERRAÇÃO DA LUZ | 45 | FAIXA DE ABSORÇÃO |
| 6 | DESTRUTIBILIDADE | 45 | RAIA DE ABSORÇÃO |
| 7 | CRESCIMENTO ANORMAL DOS CRISTAIS | 46 | COEFICIENTE DE ABSORÇÃO |
| 8 | AÇO ANORMAL | 47 | CONSTANTE DE ABSORÇÃO |
| 9 | FERRO FORJADO ANORMAL | 48 | DINAMÔMETRO DE ABSORÇÃO |
| 10 | AFIAR | 49 | BORDA DE ABSORÇÃO |
| 10 | AMOLAR | 50 | LIMITE DE ABSORÇÃO |
| 10 | ESMERILHAR | 51 | ABSORÇÃO DE CALOR |
| 11 | MATÉRIA PARA AMOLAR | 52 | ABSORÇÃO DE ÁGUA |
| 12 | ENDIREITADOR DE TUBOS | 53 | RELAÇÃO OU PROPORÇÃO DE ABSORÇÃO |
| 13 | ABRASÃO | 54 | ESPECTRO DE ABSORÇÃO |
| 14 | DUREZA À ABRASÃO | 55 | DINAMÔMETRO DE FREIO |
| 15 | MARCAS DE ABRASÃO | 55 | DINAMÔMETRO DE ABSORÇÃO |
| 16 | ENSAIOS DE DESGASTE POR ABRASÃO | 56 | ABSORVÊNCIA |
| 17 | ABRASIVO | 57 | SUPORTE |
| 18 | FITA DE LIXAR | 57 | APOIO |
| 18 | CORREIA ABRASIVA | 57 | ENCOSTO |
| 19 | PEDRA DE AMOLAR | 57 | ESCORA |
| 20 | DISCO ABRASIVO | 58 | BRONZE DE ALUMÍNIO |
| 20 | DISCO DE ESMERILHAR | 59 | MÁQUINA DE SOLDAR DE C.A. E C.C. |
| 21 | GRÂNULO OU GRÃO ABRASIVO | 60 | MOVIMENTO ACELERADO |
| 22 | SUBSTÂNCIA ABRASIVA | 61 | BOMBA DE ACELERAÇÃO |
| 22 | LIMALHA | 62 | ACELERAÇÃO |
| 23 | ESPESSURA DOS GRÃOS ABRASIVOS | 63 | ACELERAÇÃO DA VELOCIDADE DE UM CORPO QUE CAI |
| 24 | PONTAS ABRASIVAS | | |
| 25 | GRANALHA ABRASIVA | 64 | ACELERAÇÃO DE GRAVIDADE |
| 26 | RODA DE ESMERIL | 65 | ACELERAÇÃO DA GRAVIDADE |
| 26 | DISCO DE ESMERILHAR | 66 | ACELERADOR |
| 26 | REBOLO | 67 | RECEBIMENTO |
| 27 | ABSCISSA | 67 | RECEPÇÃO |
| 28 | ÁLCOOL QUIMICAMENTE PURO | 67 | ACEITAÇÃO |
| 28 | ÁLCOOL ABSOLUTO | 68 | RECEPÇÃO DE MÁQUINAS |
| 28 | ÁLCOOL ANIDRO | 69 | LIMITE DE ACEITAÇÃO |
| 29 | DIMENSIONAMENTO ABSOLUTO | 70 | CERTIFICADO DE RECEBIMENTO |
| 30 | UMIDADE ABSOLUTA DO AR | 70 | CERTIFICADO DE RECEPÇÃO |
| 31 | SISTEMA DE MEDIÇÃO ABSOLUTA | 71 | ENSAIO DE ACEITAÇÃO |
| 32 | MOVIMENTO ABSOLUTO | 71 | TESTE DE RECEBIMENTO |
| 33 | PRESSÃO ABSOLUTA | 72 | ACESSIBILIDADE |
| 34 | PONTO ABSOLUTO DE REFERÊNCIA | 73 | ACESSÍVEL |
| 35 | TEMPERATURA ABSOLUTA | 74 | ACESSÓRIOS |
| 36 | ZERO ABSOLUTO | 75 | ACIDENTE DE TRABALHO |
| 37 | NEUTRALIZAR | 76 | ACUMULADOR |
| 37 | ABSORVER | 77 | BATERIA DE ACUMULADORES |
| 38 | ABSORVÍVEL | 78 | ELEMENTO DE ACUMULADOR |
| 39 | ABSORVENTE | 79 | LOCOMOTIVA ELÉTRICA DE ACUMULADORES |
| 40 | AMORTECEDOR | 80 | METAL DE ACUMULADOR |

| | | | |
|---|---|---|---|
| 81 | PLACA OU CHAPA DE ACUMULADOR | 113 | AÇO ELÉTRICO (ÁCIDO) |
| 82 | EXATIDÃO | 114 | FUNDENTE ÁCIDO |
| 83 | PRECISÃO DE USINAGEM | 115 | ELEMENTO ACIDÍFERO |
| 84 | ACETALDEÍDO | 116 | ÁCIDO SIEMENS MARTIN POR PROCESSO ÁCIDO |
| 84 | ALDEÍDO | | |
| 84 | ALDEÍDO ACÉTICO | 117 | FERROGUSA ÁCIDO |
| 84 | HIDRATO DE ACETILO | 118 | OXALATO ÁCIDO DE POTÁSSIO |
| 84 | ÁCIDO ALDEÍTICO | 119 | BITARTRATO |
| 84 | ETANOL | 119 | CREMOR TÁRTARO |
| 84 | ÓXIDO DE ETILIDENO | 119 | CRISTAIS |
| 84 | ALDEÍDO ETILICO | 120 | PROCESSO BESSEMER |
| 84 | HIDRATO DE VINIL | 120 | PROCESSO ÁCIDO |
| 85 | ACETATO | 121 | BOMBA DE ÁCIDOS |
| 86 | ÁCIDO ACÉTICO | 122 | REAÇÃO ÁCIDA |
| 87 | ANIDRIDO ACÉTICO | 123 | REVESTIMENTO REFRATÁRIO ÁCIDO |
| 88 | ACETATO DE ETILO | 124 | À PROVA DE ÁCIDO |
| 88 | ÉTER ACÉTICO | 124 | ANTIÁCIDO |
| 89 | ACETÍMETRO | 125 | LIGAS RESISTENTES AO ÁCIDO |
| 89 | PESA-ÁCIDOS | 125 | LIGAS ANTIÁCIDO |
| 89 | ACIDÍMETRO | 126 | BICARBONATO DE SODA |
| 89 | ACETÔMETRO | 126 | CARBONATO ÁCIDO DE SÓDIO |
| 90 | ACETONA | 127 | VAPORES ÁCIDOS |
| 90 | ACETONA DIMETÍLICA | 128 | À PROVA DE ÁCIDO |
| 90 | DIMETILCETONA | 128 | INATACÁVEL AO ÁCIDO |
| 91 | ACETATO | 129 | ÁCIDO |
| 91 | ACETATO DE CELULOSE, ACETILCELULOSE | 129 | ACIDÍFERO |
| 92 | CLORETO DE ACETILO | 130 | ACIDÍFERO |
| 93 | ACETILENO | 130 | ACIDIFICANTE |
| 94 | CORTE POR CHAMA DE ACETILENO | 131 | ACIDOMETRIA |
| 95 | BICO DE ACETILENO | 131 | ACIDIMETRIA |
| 95 | LÂMPADA DE ACETILENO | 132 | ÁCIDOS |
| 96 | SOLDAGEM A ACETILENO | 133 | ACIDULAR |
| 97 | FORNO DE ACHESON | 134 | ÁGUA ACIDULADA |
| 98 | ACROMÁTICO | 135 | ACERAGEM |
| 99 | ACROMATIZAÇÃO | 136 | ACÚSTICO |
| 100 | ACROMATIZAÇÃO | 137 | ACÚSTICA |
| 101 | SEM COR | 138 | A CONTRAFIO |
| 101 | ACROMATISMO | 139 | ACTÍNICO |
| 102 | ACICULADO | 140 | RAIOS ACTÍNICOS |
| 102 | ACICULAR | 141 | ACTÍNIO |
| 103 | MARTENSITA ACIDULAR | 142 | ACTINÔMETRO |
| 104 | ÁCIDO | 143 | AÇÃO DE UMA FORÇA |
| 105 | FERROGUSA BESSEMER | 144 | CATALIZAÇÃO |
| 106 | PROCESSO BESSEMER ÁCIDO | 144 | ATIVAÇÃO |
| 107 | AÇO BESSEMER ÁCIDO | 145 | ADIÇÃO DE CARBONO |
| 108 | BASE ÁCIDA | 146 | ATUADOR |
| 109 | FRAGILIDADE POR DECAPAGEM | 146 | ATIVADOR |
| 110 | SOLDA COM NÚCLEO DE ÁCIDO | 147 | ENERGIA DE ATIVAÇÃO |
| 111 | BANHO ÁCIDO | 148 | SUBSTÂNCIA ATIVADORA |
| 111 | MERGULHO ÁCIDO | 149 | DEPÓSITO RADIOATIVO |
| 112 | DECAPAGEM COM BANHO ACIDULADO | 149 | DEPÓSITO ATIVO |

| | |
|---|---|
| 150 | HIDROGÊNIO RADIOATIVO |
| 150 | HIDROGÊNIO ATÔMICO |
| 151 | POTÊNCIA EFETIVA NO FREIO EM CAVALOS |
| 151 | POTÊNCIA EFETIVA EM CAVALO VAPOR (C.V.) |
| 151 | CAVALO EFETIVO |
| 152 | DIMENSÃO REAL |
| 153 | VALOR REAL |
| 154 | ACUTANGULAR |
| 154 | ACUTÂNGULO |
| 155 | ÂNGULO AGUDO |
| 155 | ÂNGULO VIVO |
| 156 | BISSETRIZ AGUDA |
| 157 | TRIÂNGULO ACUTÂNGULO |
| 158 | BRILHO OU LUSTRO ADAMANTINO |
| 159 | LINGUAGEM DE PROGRAMAÇÃO ADAPT |
| 160 | AJUSTADOR |
| 160 | ADAPTADOR |
| 161 | COMANDO ADAPTATIVO |
| 162 | AUMENTAR |
| 162 | ADICIONAR |
| 162 | SOMAR |
| 162 | ACRESCENTAR |
| 163 | ADICIONAR ÁGUA |
| 164 | APÊNDICE |
| 164 | ADENDO |
| 164 | ALTURA DA FRENTE |
| 164 | ALTURA DA CABEÇA DE UM DENTE |
| 164 | COMPLEMENTO |
| 165 | ÂNGULO DE CABEÇA DE ENGRENAGEM |
| 166 | CÍRCULO DE CABEÇA |
| 166 | CÍRCULO DE TOPO |
| 166 | CÍRCULO EXTERNO |
| 167 | PERIFERIA DE ENGRENAGEM |
| 168 | ADITIVO |
| 168 | ELEMENTO DE ADIÇÃO |
| 169 | ADJUVANTE |
| 169 | ADIÇÃO |
| 170 | PERDA ADICIONAL |
| 171 | ENDEREÇO |
| 172 | TESTE DE ADESÃO |
| 172 | CONTROLE DE ADERÊNCIA |
| 173 | ADESÃO |
| 174 | ADERÊNCIA |
| 175 | ADERENTE |
| 175 | ADESIVO |
| 176 | PROPRIEDADE ADESIVA |
| 176 | PODER ADESIVO |
| 176 | PROPRIEDADE ADERENTE |
| 177 | SUBSTÂNCIA ADESIVA |
| 178 | ADIABÁTICO |

| | |
|---|---|
| 179 | CURVA ADIABÁTICA |
| 179 | LINHA ADIABÁTICA |
| 180 | ÂNGULO ADJACENTE |
| 181 | ADJACENTE |
| 181 | CONTÍGUO |
| 181 | PRÓXIMO |
| 182 | ADAPTAR |
| 182 | REGULAR |
| 182 | AFINAR |
| 182 | AJUSTAR |
| 183 | GRADUÁVEL |
| 183 | REGULÁVEL |
| 183 | AJUSTÁVEL |
| 184 | ALARGADOR DE EXTENSÃO MANUAL AJUSTÁVEL |
| 184 | ESCAREADOR MANUAL AJUSTÁVEL |
| 185 | CUNHA DE APERTO |
| 185 | CHAVETA AJUSTÁVEL |
| 185 | CUNHA |
| 186 | CALIBRE DE BOCA REGULÁVEL |
| 187 | BATENTE REGULÁVEL |
| 187 | ESPERA REGULÁVEL |
| 188 | ESCAREADOR DE EXPANSÃO REGULÁVEL |
| 188 | ALARGADOR DE EXPANSÃO DE LÂMINAS MÓVEIS |
| 189 | FILEIRAS REGULÁVEIS |
| 189 | MATRIZES REGULÁVEIS |
| 190 | REGULAGEM COM PARAFUSO |
| 191 | PORCA REGULADORA |
| 191 | PORCA DE AJUSTE |
| 192 | PARAFUSO DE REGULAGEM |
| 192 | PARAFUSO DE AJUSTE |
| 193 | PARAFUSO DE PRESSÃO |
| 194 | LUVA DE REGULAGEM |
| 195 | AJUSTAGEM |
| 195 | REGULAGEM |
| 196 | TUBO DE ESCAPE |
| 196 | BOCAL |
| 197 | BRONZE DE CANHÃO |
| 198 | METAL NAVAL |
| 198 | LATÃO DE MARINHA |
| 199 | LINHA DE ADMISSÃO OU ADUÇÃO DO VAPOR |
| 200 | CANAL DE ADMISSÃO |
| 200 | ABERTURA DE ADMISSÃO |
| 201 | VÁLVULA DE ADMISSÃO |
| 202 | FIXAR POR ADSORÇÃO |
| 202 | ADSORVER |
| 203 | ADSORÇÃO |
| 204 | ADULTERAR |
| 204 | FALSIFICAR |
| 205 | ADULTERAÇÃO |

| | |
|---|---|
| 205 | FALSIFICAÇÃO |
| 205 | FRAUDE |
| 206 | AVANÇO |
| 207 | ENXÓ |
| 207 | MACHADINHA DE TANOEIRO |
| 208 | AERAR (AREIA) |
| 209 | ELEMENTO DE AERAÇÃO |
| 209 | CÉLULA DE AERAÇÃO |
| 210 | AERAÇÃO DA ÁGUA |
| 211 | VENTILADOR |
| 211 | AERADOR |
| 212 | LINHA AÉREA |
| 213 | TRANSPORTADOR AÉREO |
| 213 | TRANSPORTADOR AÉREO POR CABO |
| 214 | AERODINÂMICO |
| 215 | AERODINÂMICA |
| 216 | DE BRONZE |
| 217 | AEROSTÁTICO |
| 218 | AEROSTÁTICA |
| 219 | AZINHAVRADO |
| 219 | ERUGINOSO |
| 220 | AZINHAVRE |
| 220 | VERDETE |
| 221 | DEFORMAÇÃO POSTERIOR |
| 221 | ESCOAMENTO PLÁSTICO POSTERIOR |
| 222 | ÁGATA |
| 223 | TEMPERADO POR ENVELHECIMENTO |
| 223 | ENDURECIMENTO POR ENVELHECIMENTO |
| 224 | ENDURECIMENTO ESTRUTURAL |
| 225 | CURA |
| 225 | ENVELHECIMENTO |
| 226 | ENVELHECIMENTO ARTIFICIAL |
| 227 | AGREGADO |
| 227 | CONJUNTO |
| 228 | MATÉRIA PARA MISTURA |
| 229 | AGREGAÇÃO |
| 229 | AGREGADO |
| 230 | TEMPERATURA DE CURA |
| 230 | TEMPERATURA DE ENVELHECIMENTO |
| 231 | CURA COMPLETA |
| 231 | ENVELHECIMENTO COMPLETO |
| 232 | CURA GRADUADA |
| 232 | ENVELHECIMENTO GRADUADO |
| 233 | CURA NATURAL |
| 233 | ENVELHECIMENTO NATURAL |
| 234 | CURA PROGRESSIVA |
| 234 | ENVELHECIMENTO PROGRESSIVO |
| 235 | CURA POR TRABALHO A FRIO |
| 235 | ENVELHECIMENTO POR TRABALHO A FRIO |
| 236 | AGITADOR |
| 237 | REBAIXO DE AGITADOR |

| | |
|---|---|
| 237 | RECESSO DE AGITADOR |
| 238 | AGITADOR MECÂNICO |
| 239 | VERNIZ DO JAPÃO |
| 240 | AR |
| 241 | CÂMARA DE AR |
| 241 | ANEL DE VENTO |
| 242 | INJEÇÃO DE AR |
| 242 | JATO DE AR |
| 242 | SOPRO DE AR |
| 243 | VENTO INJETADO |
| 244 | LIMPEZA POR JATO ABRASIVO |
| 244 | LIMPEZA POR JATO DE AR |
| 245 | TIJOLO VAZADO |
| 245 | TIJOLO PERFURADO |
| 246 | CÂMARA DE AR |
| 246 | ANEL DE VENTO |
| 246 | CÂMARA PNEUMÁTICA |
| 247 | CANAIS DE AR |
| 247 | CONDUTOS DE AR |
| 248 | CLASSIFICAÇÃO POR CORRENTE GASOSA |
| 248 | CLASSIFICAÇÃO GRANULOMÉTRICA POR JATO DE AR CONTRACORRENTE |
| 249 | BOMBA DE AR |
| 249 | COMPRESSOR DE AR |
| 250 | CONDICIONADOR DE AR |
| 251 | MOTOR RESFRIADO A AR |
| 252 | REFRIGERAÇÃO A AR |
| 252 | ESFRIAMENTO DE AR |
| 253 | CORRENTE DE AR |
| 254 | ALMOFADA PNEUMÁTICA |
| 254 | COLCHÃO DE AR |
| 254 | CAMADA DE AR |
| 255 | AMORTECEDOR DE AR PNEUMÁTICO |
| 256 | AMORTECEDOR PNEUMÁTICO |
| 257 | TIRAGEM DE AR |
| 257 | EXAUSTÃO DO AR |
| 258 | PERFURADORA PNEUMÁTICA |
| 258 | FURADEIRA PNEUMÁTICA |
| 258 | BROCA PNEUMÁTICA |
| 259 | VÁLVULA DE ESCAPE DE AR |
| 260 | PURIFICADOR DE AR |
| 260 | FILTRO DE AR |
| 261 | FORNO DE REVÉRBERO |
| 261 | FORNO DE TIRAGEM NATURAL |
| 262 | FOLGA |
| 262 | ESPAÇO DE AR |
| 262 | VÃO LIVRE |
| 262 | LUZ |
| 262 | ENTREFERRO |
| 262 | INTERSTÍCIO |
| 263 | ENTREFERRO DE ÍMÃ |

| | |
|---|---|
| 264 MISTURA DE GÁS E AR | 290 SEPARAÇÃO PNEUMÁTICA |
| 264 GÁS DE AR | 291 POÇO DE AERAÇÃO |
| 265 TERMÔMETRO DE GÁS | 291 CHAMINÉ DE AR |
| 266 RESPIRADOURO | 292 PASSAGEM DE AR |
| 266 CORRENTE DE AR | 293 TORNEIRA DE AR |
| 267 TÉMPERA AO AR | 294 RESERVATÓRIO DE AR |
| 267 ENDURECIMENTO AO AR | 295 SOLDAGEM AEROACETILÊNICA |
| 268 CALEFATOR DE AR | 296 CONDENSADOR DE SUPERFÍCIE POR |
| 268 AQUECEDOR DE AR | REFRIGERAÇÃO DE AR |
| 268 AQUECIMENTO POR AR QUENTE | 297 MADEIRA SECADA AO AR |
| 268 CALEFAÇÃO A AR AQUECIDO | 298 AÇO AUTOTEMPERÁVEL |
| 269 RESPIRADOURO | 299 MÁQUINA DE INJEÇÃO PNEUMÁTICA |
| 269 ORIFÍCIO DE AR | 300 PROCESSO BESSEMER |
| 270 ENTRADA DE AR | 301 AGLUTINANTE DE PEGA AO AR |
| 270 ADMISSÃO DE AR | 302 CIMENTO DE PEGA AO AR |
| 271 EJETOR PNEUMÁTICO | 303 HERMÉTICO |
| 272 PULVERIZADOR | 303 IMPERMEÁVEL AO AR |
| 272 ATOMIZADOR | 304 ALABASTRO |
| 272 PISTOLA DE AR COMPRIMIDO | 305 ALARME |
| 273 BOMBA ASPIRANTE | 305 APARELHO DE ALARME |
| 273 BOMBA DE ELEVAÇÃO DE AR | 306 SINAL DE ALARME |
| 274 CÂMARA DE COMPRESSÃO | 307 APITO DE ALARME |
| 274 COMPARTIMENTO ESTANQUE | 308 ALBEDO |
| 275 BOCAL DE SAÍDA DE AR | 308 COEFICIENTE DE REFLEXÃO |
| 276 PISTOLA DE AR COMPRIMIDO | 309 CABO DE CABLAGEM ALBERT |
| 277 AR COMBURENTE | 310 ALBUMINA |
| 277 COMBURENTE | 311 PAPEL ALBUMINADO |
| 278 AFASTAMENTO DAS BARRAS DA GRELHA | 312 MOTOR A ÁLCOOL |
| 278 INTERVALO ENTRE AS GRELHAS | 313 ÁLCOOL COMUM |
| 279 MANDRIL PNEUMÁTICO | 313 ÁLCOOL DE VINHO |
| 280 PATENTEAMENTO AO AR | 313 ÁLCOOL ETÍLICO |
| 280 TÉMPERA AO AR | 313 HIDRATO DE ETILO |
| 281 CANALIZAÇÃO DE AR | 314 ALCOÓLICO |
| 281 ENCANAMENTO DE AR | 315 SOLUÇÃO ALCOÓLICA |
| 281 LINHA DE AR | 316 ALCOÔMETRO |
| 281 AERODUTO | 317 ALDEÍDO |
| 281 TUBULAÇÃO DE AR | 318 ALNO |
| 282 ÉMBOLO DE AR | 319 ÁLAMO PRETO |
| 282 PISTÃO PNEUMÁTICO | 319 ALFAMETRO |
| 283 MANÔMETRO DE AR | 320 ÁLGEBRA |
| 283 CALIBRADOR PNEUMÁTICO | 321 ALGÉBRICO |
| 284 BOMBA DE AR | 322 EQUAÇÃO ALGÉBRICA |
| 284 BOMBA DE VÁCUO | 323 CALIBRAR |
| 284 BOMBA PNEUMÁTICA | 323 ALINHAR |
| 285 TÉMPERA AO AR | 323 AJUSTAR |
| 286 SOCADOR PNEUMÁTICO | 323 NIVELAR |
| 287 REAQUECEDOR DE AR | 324 ALINHAMENTO |
| 288 CAREPA FORMADA AO AR | 324 CENTRALIZAÇÃO |
| 289 COLETOR DE AR | 324 PARALELISMO |
| 289 ENTRADA DE AR | 325 ALINHAMENTO |
| 290 SEPARAÇÃO DE AR | 326 COMPOSTO ALIFÁTICO |

1164

| | | | |
|---|---|---|---|
| 327 | ALIZARINA | 367 | LIGA EM PÓ |
| 328 | ÁLCALI | 368 | AÇO-LIGA |
| 329 | METAIS ALCALINOS | 369 | ÂNGULOS DE AÇO-LIGA |
| 330 | ALCALIZAR | 370 | LINGOTES DE AÇO-LIGA |
| 330 | ALCALINIZAR | 371 | TIRAS DE AÇO-LIGA |
| 331 | ALCALÍMETRO | 372 | FUNDIÇÕES DE AÇO-LIGA |
| 332 | ALCALIMÉTRICO | 373 | PLANOS DE AÇO-LIGA |
| 333 | ALCALIMETRIA | 374 | BARRAS DE AÇO-LIGA |
| 334 | LIMPEZA ALCALINA | 375 | BARRAS OCTAGONAIS DE AÇO-LIGA |
| 335 | METAIS ALCALINO-TERROSOS | 376 | ARAME DE AÇO-LIGA |
| 336 | TERRAS ALCALINAS | 377 | BARRAS REDONDAS DE AÇO-LIGA |
| 337 | REAÇÃO ALCALINA | 378 | CHAPAS DE AÇO-LIGA |
| 338 | SAL ALCALINO | 378 | BARRAS DE AÇO-LIGA |
| 339 | SOLUÇÃO ALCALINA | 379 | BARRAS QUADRADAS DE AÇO-LIGA |
| 340 | ALCALICIDADE | 380 | CHAPAS FINAS DE AÇO-LIGA |
| 340 | ALCALINIDADE | 381 | SISTEMA DE LIGAS |
| 341 | ALCALÓIDE | 382 | AÇO COM POUCA LIGA |
| 342 | PAPEL DE ALCANA | 383 | LIGA RESISTENTE AO DESGASTE |
| 343 | CABO CONDUTOR DE ALUMÍNIO | 384 | LIGA RESISTENTE AOS ÁCIDOS |
| 344 | FLOTAÇÃO | 385 | LIGA PARA MANCAIS |
| 345 | TODO DE FERRO | 385 | LIGA ANTIFRICÇÃO |
| 346 | GUSA DE PRIMEIRA FUSÃO | 386 | LIGAS DE SOLDA FORTE |
| 346 | FERRO VIRGEM | 387 | LIGA RESISTENTE À CORROSÃO |
| 347 | AMOSTRA DE METAL PURO | 387 | LIGA INOXIDÁVEL |
| 348 | PELE DE JACARÉ | 388 | LIGA PARA FUNDIÇÃO EM MATRIZES |
| 349 | ALOMÉRICO | 389 | LIGA DE FUNDIÇÃO EM MOLDE |
| 350 | ALOMERIA | 390 | LIGA RESISTENTE AO CALOR E À CORROSÃO |
| 351 | ALOMORFISMO | 391 | LIGA REFRATÁRIA |
| 352 | ALOMORFO | 391 | LIGA RESISTENTE AO CALOR |
| 353 | TENSÃO PERMISSÍVEL | 392 | LIGA PARA IMÃ |
| 353 | MARGEM DE ESFORÇO | 392 | LIGA MAGNÉTICA |
| 354 | AEOTRIOMÓRFICO | 393 | LIGA REFRATÁRIA |
| 355 | TRANSFORMAÇÃO ALOTRÓPICA | 394 | ADIÇÃO |
| 356 | ALOTRÓPICO | 394 | ALIAGEM |
| 357 | ISOMERIA | 394 | FORMAÇÃO DE LIGAS |
| 358 | FOLGA | 395 | ELEMENTOS DE LIGA |
| 358 | TOLERÂNCIA | 396 | LIGAS RESISTENTES À ABRASÃO E À CORROSÃO |
| 358 | MARGEM | | |
| 358 | DIFERENÇA ADMISSÍVEL | 397 | AMÁLGAMA |
| 359 | TOLERÂNCIA ADMITIDA | 398 | ALNICO |
| 359 | TOLERÂNCIA DE USINAGEM | 399 | LATÃO ALFA |
| 360 | LIGA | 400 | PARTÍCULA ALFA |
| 361 | MISTURAR | 401 | IRRADIADOR ALFA |
| 361 | LIGAR | 401 | RADIADOR ALFA |
| 361 | AMALGAMAR | 402 | RAIOS ALFA |
| 362 | BALANÇA PARA ELEMENTOS DE LIGA | 403 | LATÃO ALFA-BETA |
| 363 | FUNDIÇÃO DE LIGA | 404 | PAR DE CONES LISOS |
| 364 | REVESTIMENTO DE LIGA | 404 | CONE E CONTRACONE |
| 364 | CAMADA DE LIGA | 405 | ENSAIO POR IMERSÕES E EMERSÕES ALTERNADAS |
| 365 | CONTAMINAÇÃO DA LIGA | | |
| 366 | GALVANIZAR | 406 | CORRENTE ALTERNADA |

| | |
|---|---|
| 407 | DÍNAMO |
| 407 | GERADOR DE C.A. |
| 407 | MÁQUINA DE CORRENTE ALTERNADA |
| 407 | ALTERNADOR |
| 408 | MOTOR DE C.A. |
| 409 | ALTERNADO |
| 409 | ALTERNATIVO |
| 410 | VARIANTE |
| 411 | GERADOR DE C.A. |
| 411 | ALTERNADOR |
| 412 | ALUMINA |
| 413 | ALUMINA |
| 413 | ÓXIDO DE ALUMÍNIO |
| 414 | ALUMINATO |
| 415 | ALUMINÍFERO |
| 416 | ALUMÍNIO |
| 417 | ACETATO DE ALUMÍNIO |
| 418 | LIGA DE ALUMÍNIO |
| 419 | LATÃO DE ALUMÍNIO |
| 420 | BRONZE DE ALUMÍNIO |
| 421 | CLORETO DE ALUMÍNIO |
| 422 | LIMA DE ALUMÍNIO |
| 423 | HIDRÓXIDO DE ALUMÍNIO |
| 424 | ALUMÍNIO EM LINGOTE |
| 425 | SILICATO DE ALUMÍNIO |
| 426 | SULFATO DE ALUMÍNIO |
| 427 | TUBO DE ALUMÍNIO |
| 428 | FIO, ARAME OU CONDUTOR DE ALUMÍNIO |
| 429 | ALUMINIZAÇÃO |
| 429 | ALUMINAÇÃO |
| 430 | ALUMINO |
| 431 | ALUMINOTERMIA |
| 432 | ALUMÍNIO |
| 433 | LIGA DE ALUMÍNIO FORJÁVEL |
| 434 | BRONZE DE ALUMÍNIO |
| 435 | LIGA DE ALUMÍNIO PARA FUNDIÇÕES |
| 436 | FOLHA OU CHAPA DE ALUMÍNIO |
| 437 | LIGA DE ALUMÍNIO PARA FORJA |
| 438 | ÓXIDO DE ALUMÍNIO |
| 438 | ALUMINA |
| 439 | LIGA À BASE DE ALUMÍNIO |
| 440 | LIGA DE ALUMÍNIO BERÍLIO |
| 441 | CHAPA REVESTIDA DE ALUMÍNIO |
| 442 | AÇO ACALMADO COM ALUMÍNIO |
| 443 | CIMENTO REFRATÁRIO AO SILICATO DE ALUMÍNIO |
| 444 | ALUMÍNIO |
| 445 | AMÁLGAMA |
| 446 | AMALGAMAR |
| 447 | AMALGAMAÇÃO |
| 448 | PROCESSO DE AMALGAMAÇÃO |
| 449 | ÂMBAR |
| 450 | AR AMBIENTE |
| 451 | PASSO DO SISTEMA DE ROSCAS SELLERS |
| 452 | AMPERÍMETRO |
| 453 | AMONÍACO |
| 453 | GÁS AMONÍACO |
| 454 | AMONÍACO |
| 454 | AMÔNIA |
| 455 | SODA DE AMÔNIA |
| 455 | SODA SOLVAY |
| 455 | SAL SOLVAY |
| 456 | LICOR AMONIACAL |
| 456 | ÁGUA AMONIACAL DO GÁS |
| 457 | SOLUÇÃO AMONIACAL |
| 458 | ACETATO DE AMÔNIO |
| 459 | BICARBONATO DE AMÔNIO |
| 460 | BISSULFETO DE AMÔNIO |
| 461 | CARBONATO DE AMÔNIO |
| 461 | SAL VOLÁTIL |
| 462 | CLORETO DE AMÔNIO |
| 462 | SAL AMONÍACO |
| 462 | HIDROCLORATO |
| 462 | MURIATO DE AMONÍACO |
| 463 | FLUORETO DE AMÔNIO |
| 464 | SULFIDRETO DE AMÔNIO |
| 465 | NITRATO DE AMÔNIA |
| 466 | NITRITO DE AMÔNIO |
| 467 | OXALATO DE AMÔNIO |
| 468 | PERSULFATO DE AMÔNIO |
| 469 | FOSFATO DE AMÔNIO |
| 470 | CLORETO DUPLO DE ESTANHO E AMÔNIO |
| 470 | SAL DE PINK |
| 471 | SULFATO DE AMÔNIO |
| 472 | SULFETO DE AMÔNIO |
| 473 | TARTRATO DE AMÔNIO |
| 474 | MUNIÇÃO |
| 475 | AMORFO |
| 476 | ENXOFRE AMORFO |
| 477 | COEFICIENTE DE RETRAÇÃO |
| 478 | AMPERAGEM |
| 478 | INTENSIDADE DA CORRENTE ELÉTRICA |
| 478 | NÚMERO DE AMPÈRES |
| 479 | AMPÈRE |
| 480 | AMPÈRE-VOLTA |
| 481 | AMPÈRE-HORA |
| 482 | AMPÈRE-MINUTO |
| 483 | AMPÈRE-SEGUNDO |
| 484 | METAL ANFÓTERO |
| 485 | AMPLIFICADOR |
| 485 | AMPLIFICADOR |
| 486 | AMPLITUDE |

| | |
|---|---|
| 487 | ACETATO DE AMILO |
| 488 | ÁLCOOL AMÍLICO |
| 489 | ANAERÓBICO |
| 490 | ANALÓGICO |
| 491 | ANALISAR |
| 492 | VERIFICADOR |
| 492 | ANALISADOR |
| 493 | ANÁLISE |
| 494 | ANALÍTICO |
| 495 | QUÍMICA ANALÍTICA |
| 496 | DETERMINAÇÃO ANALÍTICA |
| 497 | LENTE ANASTIGMÁTICA |
| 498 | LIGA OSTEOPLÁSTICA |
| 499 | ANCORAGEM |
| 500 | ÁNCORA |
| 501 | CHUMBADOR |
| 501 | CAVILHA DE FIXAÇÃO |
| 501 | GANHO DE FIXAÇÃO |
| 502 | CONTRAPLACA |
| 502 | PLACA DE FIXAÇÃO |
| 503 | ANEMÔMETRO |
| 504 | BARÔMETRO ANERÓIDE |
| 504 | BARÔMETRO METÁLICO |
| 505 | ÁNGULO |
| 506 | CANTONEIRA |
| 507 | ÁNGULO CENTRAL |
| 508 | MANCAL EM ÁNGULO |
| 508 | MANCAL OBLÍQUO |
| 508 | MANCAL COM LINHA DIVISÓRIA INCLINADA |
| 509 | CHAVE DE BOCA CURVA |
| 510 | CANTONEIRA |
| 510 | SUPORTE ANGULAR |
| 511 | TORNEIRA DE ÁNGULO |
| 512 | FLANGE ANGULAR |
| 513 | GONIÔMETRO |
| 513 | CALIBRE DE ÁNGULO |
| 514 | CANTONEIRA DE FERRO |
| 514 | FERRO EM L |
| 514 | FERRO ANGULAR |
| 515 | ÁNGULO DE ALIMENTAÇÃO |
| 515 | ÁNGULO DE AVANÇO |
| 516 | ÁNGULO DE CHANFRO |
| 517 | ÁNGULO DE CONTATO |
| 518 | ÁNGULO DE DESVIO |
| 519 | ÁNGULO DE FLEXÃO |
| 520 | ÁNGULO DE INCIDÊNCIA |
| 521 | ÁNGULO DE INCLINAÇÃO |
| 522 | ÁNGULO DE ATRASO |
| 523 | ÁNGULO DE ATRASO DE FASE |
| 524 | ÁNGULO DE AVANÇO DE FASE |
| 525 | ÁNGULO DE REFLEXÃO |
| 526 | ÁNGULO DE REFRAÇÃO |
| 527 | ÁNGULO DE REPOUSO |
| 527 | ÁNGULO DE ATRITO |
| 528 | ÁNGULO DE ROTAÇÃO |
| 529 | ÁNGULO DE CONICIDADE |
| 530 | ÁNGULO DE ROSCA |
| 530 | ÁNGULO DE FILETE |
| 531 | ÁNGULO DE INCLINAÇÃO DO FILETE |
| 532 | ÁNGULO DE TORÇÃO |
| 533 | CANTONEIRA |
| 533 | CHAPA EM ÁNGULO |
| 534 | VÁLVULA ANGULAR |
| 534 | VÁLVULA EM ESQUADRIA |
| 535 | TORNO INCLINÁVEL |
| 536 | ANGSTRÖM |
| 537 | ACELERAÇÃO ANGULAR |
| 538 | ROLAMENTO DE ESFERAS OBLÍQUO |
| 539 | CORTE ANGULAR |
| 540 | FRESAS ANGULARES |
| 541 | DESLOCAMENTO ANGULAR |
| 542 | CONTRAÇÃO ANGULAR |
| 543 | FRESA CÔNICA |
| 543 | FRESA ANGULAR |
| 544 | MOVIMENTO ANGULAR |
| 545 | ROSCA OU FILETE TRIANGULAR |
| 546 | VELOCIDADE ANGULAR |
| 547 | PARAFUSO DE ROSCA TRIANGULAR |
| 548 | ANIDRIDO |
| 549 | ANIDRITA |
| 549 | SULFATO DE CAL ANIDRA NATURAL |
| 550 | ANIDRO |
| 551 | CARBONATO DE SÓDIO ANIDRO |
| 551 | SAL DE SODA |
| 552 | FENILAMINA |
| 553 | ÓLEO DE ANILINA |
| 554 | CARVÃO ANIMAL |
| 555 | ÓLEO ANIMAL |
| 556 | ANION |
| 557 | FLOTAÇÃO ANIÔNICA |
| 558 | ANISÓTROPO |
| 559 | ANISOTROPIA |
| 560 | RECOZER O AÇO |
| 560 | DESTEMPERAR O AÇO |
| 561 | ARAME RECOZIDO |
| 562 | RECOZIMENTO |
| 563 | CAIXA OU CÂMARA DE RECOZIMENTO |
| 564 | FORNO DE RECOZIMENTO |
| 565 | INSTALAÇÃO DE RECOZIMENTO |
| 566 | CADINHO DE RECOZIMENTO |
| 567 | CAIXAS DE RECOZIMENTO |
| 568 | PROCESSO DE RECOZIMENTO |

| | |
|---|---|
| 569 | RESISTÊNCIA AO ESTADO DE RECOZIMENTO |
| 570 | MACLA DE RECOZIMENTO |
| 571 | RECOZIMENTO PRETO OU SIMPLES |
| 571 | RECOZIMENTO EM CAIXA OU FORNO ABERTO |
| 572 | RECOZIMENTO AZULADO |
| 573 | RECOZIMENTO BRILHANTE |
| 574 | RECOZIMENTO CONTÍNUO |
| 575 | RECOZIMENTO A FOGO |
| 576 | RECOZIMENTO COMPLETO |
| 577 | RECOZIMENTO INTERMEDIÁRIO |
| 578 | RECOZIMENTO INVERSO |
| 579 | RECOZIMENTO ISOTÉRMICO |
| 580 | RECOZIMENTO LOCALIZADO |
| 581 | RECOZIMENTO DO AÇO |
| 582 | RECOZIMENTO PERIÓDICO |
| 583 | RECOZIMENTO REDUTOR DE TENSÕES |
| 584 | RECOZIMENTO REDUTOR DE TENSÕES |
| 585 | CONSTRUÇÃO ANEXA |
| 585 | DEPENDÊNCIA |
| 586 | CAMADA ANUAL |
| 586 | ANEL ANUAL |
| 586 | CÍRCULO ANUAL |
| 587 | SEÇÃO ANULAR |
| 588 | ANULAR |
| 589 | ANEL |
| 589 | COROA CIRCULAR OU ANULAR |
| 590 | ÂNODO |
| 590 | ELÉTRODO POSITIVO |
| 591 | CABO DE ÂNODO GASTO |
| 591 | PONTA DE ÂNODO |
| 592 | LIMPEZA ANÓDICA |
| 593 | COBRE ANÓDICO |
| 594 | COEFICIENTE DE CORROSÃO ANÓDICA |
| 595 | QUEDA DE TENSÃO NO ÂNODO |
| 596 | EFEITO ANÓDICO |
| 597 | RENDIMENTO ANÓDICO |
| 598 | ÂNODO INSOLÚVEL |
| 599 | CAMADA ANÓDICA |
| 599 | REVESTIMENTO ANÓDICO |
| 600 | LAMA ANÓDICA |
| 600 | LODO ANÓDICO |
| 601 | DECAPAGEM ANÓDICA |
| 602 | ÂNODO |
| 602 | ELÉTRODO POSITIVO |
| 603 | ANÓDICO |
| 604 | POLARIZAÇÃO ANÓDICA |
| 605 | ANODIZAÇÃO |
| 605 | OXIDAÇÃO ANÓDICA |
| 605 | TRATAMENTO ANÓDICO |
| 606 | ANÓLITO |

| | |
|---|---|
| 606 | SOLUÇÃO ANÓDICA |
| 607 | ANTRACENO |
| 608 | ÓLEO DE ANTRACENO |
| 609 | ANTRACITO |
| 610 | CANHÃO ANTIAÉREO |
| 611 | ANTICÁTODO |
| 612 | ANTICONGELANTE |
| 613 | COMBUSTÍVEL ANTIDETONANTE |
| 614 | ANTIMAGNÉTICO |
| 615 | REVESTIMENTO |
| 615 | COMPOSTO EXOTÉRMICO |
| 616 | ADITIVO ANTI-PITE |
| 617 | PROPRIEDADES DE ANTIFRICÇÃO |
| 618 | MANCAL ANTIFRICÇÃO |
| 618 | ROLAMENTO DE ROLOS |
| 618 | ROLAMENTO DE ESFERAS |
| 619 | METAL ANTIFRICÇÃO |
| 619 | METAL BRANCO |
| 619 | METAL PATENTE |
| 620 | COMPLEMENTO DE UM LOGARITMO |
| 620 | ANTILOGARITMO |
| 621 | CHUMBO ANTIMONIAL |
| 622 | ESTIBINA |
| 623 | ANTIMÔNIO |
| 624 | PENTACLORETO DE ANTIMÔNIO |
| 625 | PENTASSULFETO DE ANTIMÔNIO |
| 626 | TRICLORETO DE ANTIMÔNIO |
| 627 | TRISSULFETO DE ANTIMÔNIO |
| 627 | PROTOSSULFETO |
| 628 | ANTI-SÉPTICO |
| 628 | DESINFETANTE |
| 628 | ANTIPUTRESCENTE |
| 629 | AGENTE ANTI-SÉPTICO |
| 629 | AGENTE ANTIPUTRESCENTE |
| 630 | BIGORNA |
| 631 | TALHADEIRA DE FERREIRO |
| 632 | ASSENTADOR PARA BIGORNA |
| 633 | BLOCO DE PORTA-BIGORNA |
| 633 | BIGORNA INFERIOR |
| 634 | APERIÓDICO |
| 635 | INSTRUMENTO APERIÓDICO |
| 636 | MOVIMENTO APERIÓDICO |
| 637 | APERIODICIDADE |
| 638 | VÉRTICE |
| 638 | TOPO |
| 638 | ÁPICE |
| 638 | CUME |
| 639 | LENTE APLANÉTICA |
| 640 | APOCROMÁTICO |
| 641 | APARELHO |
| 641 | DISPOSITIVO |

1168

| | | | |
|---|---|---|---|
| 641 | INSTRUMENTO | 676 | TENSÃO (VOLTAGEM) DO ARCO |
| 642 | DENSIDADE APARENTE | 677 | INÍCIO DO ARCO NA SOLDA |
| 643 | CONSTANTE DE RADIAÇÃO APARENTE | 678 | ESPESSURA DO ARCO |
| 644 | FORMAÇÃO DE RUPTURAS | 679 | TENSÃO DE SERVIÇO DO ARCO |
| 644 | FORMAÇÃO DE FISSURAS | 680 | MÁQUINA DE SOLDAGEM A ARCO |
| 645 | SOLICITANTE DE PATENTE | 680 | SOLDADOR A ARCO VOLTAICO |
| 646 | SOLICITAÇÃO DE PATENTE | 680 | SOLDADOR A ARCO ELÉTRICO |
| 646 | REQUISIÇÃO DE PATENTE | 681 | SOLDAGEM A ARCO ELÉTRICO |
| 647 | APLICAÇÃO DE UMA FORÇA | 682 | SOLDAGEM A ARCO POR CONTATO |
| 648 | QUÍMICA APLICADA | 683 | SOLDAGEM A ARCO EM ATMOSFERA INERTE |
| 649 | PESQUISA APLICADA | 684 | SOLDAGEM A ARCO SUBMERSO |
| 650 | APERTAR O FREIO | 684 | PROCESSO "UNION MELT" |
| 650 | PISAR NO FREIO | 685 | SOLDAGEM A ARCO COM C.A. |
| 650 | FREIAR | 686 | SOLDAGEM A ARCO COM C.C. |
| 651 | SOLICITAR UMA PATENTE | 687 | TIJOLO EM CUNHA |
| 652 | CÁLCULO APROXIMADO | 688 | ARCOBOTANTE |
| 653 | VALOR APROXIMADO | 688 | ARQUIVOLTA |
| 654 | FÓRMULA APROXIMADA | 689 | BOCA ESPIRAL |
| 654 | FÓRMULA DE APROXIMAÇÃO | 689 | PUA ESPIRAL |
| 655 | TABLIER | 690 | ESPIRAL DE ARQUIMEDES |
| 656 | LINGUAGEM DE PROGRAMAÇÃO APT | 691 | ARQUITETO |
| 657 | ÁGUA-FORTE | 692 | BRONZE PARA ARQUITETURA |
| 657 | ÁGUA E ÁCIDO AZÓTICO | 693 | DESENHO DE ARQUITETURA |
| 658 | ÁGUA-RÉGIA | 694 | SUPERFÍCIE |
| 658 | ÁCIDO NÍTRICO-CLORÍDRICO | 694 | ÁREA |
| 659 | ÁLCOOL DILUÍDO | 694 | ZONA |
| 659 | ÁLCOOL AQUOSO | 695 | ÁREA DO CÍRCULO |
| 660 | SOLUÇÃO DE AMÔNIA DILUÍDA | 696 | SUPERFÍCIE DE ENGRENAGEM |
| 660 | ÁLCALI VOLÁTIL | 697 | SUPERFÍCIE |
| 660 | AMONÍACO | 697 | EXTENSÃO |
| 661 | SOLUÇÃO AQUOSA | 698 | COORDENADAS PLANAS |
| 662 | ÁRVORE | 699 | MARGA ARGILOSA |
| 662 | EIXO | 700 | XISTO ARGILOSO |
| 662 | SEMI-EIXO | 700 | ARGILITO |
| 663 | FRESAS COM FUSO | 701 | ARGÔNIO |
| 664 | ARCO DE CURVA | 702 | ARITMÉTICA |
| 665 | SALTO DE ARCO VOLTAICO | 703 | MÉDIA ARITMÉTICA |
| 666 | SOLDAGEM A ARCO | 704 | PROGRESSÃO ARITMÉTICA |
| 667 | FORNO ELÉTRICO DE ARCO DIRETO | 705 | BRAÇO DE VOLANTE |
| 668 | FORNO DE ARCO VOLTAICO | 705 | BRAÇO DE POLIA |
| 668 | FORNO DE ARCO ELÉTRICO | 706 | BRAÇO DE ALAVANCA |
| 669 | FORNO DE ARCO INDIRETO | 707 | INDUZIDO |
| 670 | FORNO A ARCO DE CARVÃO | 707 | ROTOR |
| 671 | FORNO ELÉTRICO DE ARCO DIRETO | 707 | ARMADURA |
| 672 | LÂMPADA DE ARCO | 708 | CHAPA PARA NÚCLEO DE INDUZIDO |
| 673 | LUZ DE ARCO ELÉTRICO | 709 | MECANISMO DE ENROLAMENTO DE INDUZIDO |
| 673 | LUZ DE ARCO VOLTAICO | 709 | MÁQUINA BOBINADORA DE INDUZIDO |
| 674 | ARCO DE CÍRCULO | 710 | PROTETOR DO ÍMÃ |
| 675 | ARCO DE CONTATO | 710 | CONTATO DO ÍMÃ |
| 675 | ARCO ABRANGENTE | 711 | LINGOTE DE FERRO ARMCO |
| 675 | CURVA DE CONTATO | | |

| | | | |
|---|---|---|---|
| 712 | CHAPA OU PLACA PARA COURAÇAS | 750 | FELTRO DE AMIANTO |
| 712 | CHAPA OU PLACA DE BLINDAGEM | 751 | TRANÇA DE AMIANTO |
| 713 | CABO ARMADO | 752 | PAPEL DE AMIANTO |
| 714 | TUBO FLEXÍVEL COM ARMAÇÃO DE ARAME | 753 | ANEL DE AMIANTO |
| 715 | BLINDAGEM DE CABO | 754 | TIRA DE AMIANTO |
| 715 | REVESTIMENTO DE CABO | 755 | AMIANTO |
| 716 | COMPOSTOS AROMÁTICOS | 755 | ASBESTO |
| 717 | DISTRIBUIÇÃO DOS REBITES | 756 | TUBULAÇÃO ASCENDENTE |
| 718 | PONTO DE TRANSFORMAÇÃO | 756 | ENCANAMENTO ASCENDENTE |
| 719 | SETA | 757 | ACLIVE |
| 719 | FLECHA | 757 | LADEIRA |
| 720 | ARSENIATO | 757 | RAMPA |
| 721 | ARSÊNICO | 757 | SUBIDA |
| 721 | ARSÊNIO | 758 | TEOR DE CINZA |
| 722 | ÁCIDO ARSÊNICO | 758 | PORCENTAGEM DE CINZA |
| 723 | PENTÓXIDO DE ARSÊNICO | 759 | CINZEIRO |
| 724 | TRICLORETO DE ARSÊNICO | 760 | CINZAS |
| 725 | COBRE ARSENICAL | 761 | CANTARIA |
| 726 | ARSENIATO | 761 | PEDRA BRUTA DE ALVENARIA |
| 727 | ÓXIDO ARSENIOSO | 761 | SILHAR |
| 727 | ANIDRIDO ARSENIOSO | 762 | CONSTRUÇÃO COM SILHAR |
| 727 | ÁCIDO ARSENIOSO | 763 | BETUMINAR |
| 727 | ARSÊNICO BRANCO | 763 | ASFALTAR |
| 728 | SULFETO ARSENIOSO | 764 | MÁSTIQUE DE ASFALTO |
| 729 | ARSENITO | 765 | FELTRO BETUMINADO |
| 730 | ARSINE | 765 | FELTRO ASFALTADO |
| 730 | HIDROGÊNIO ARSENIURADO | 766 | TUBO ASFALTADO |
| 731 | ENVELHECIMENTO ARTIFICIAL | 767 | ASFALTAGEM |
| 731 | TRATAMENTO ARTIFICIAL | 768 | BETUME |
| 732 | COMBUSTÍVEL ARTIFICIAL | 768 | ASFALTO |
| 733 | ILUMINAÇÃO ARTIFICIAL | 769 | APARELHO DE SUCÇÃO |
| 734 | LUZ ARTIFICIAL | 769 | ASPIRADOR |
| 735 | ÍMÃ ARTIFICIAL | 770 | ÁREA DE MONTAGEM |
| 736 | SEDA ARTIFICIAL | 771 | CAVILHA DE MONTAGEM |
| 737 | PEDRA SINTÉTICA | 771 | PINO DE LIGAÇÃO |
| 737 | PEDRA ARTIFICIAL | 772 | DESENHO DE MONTAGEM |
| 738 | VENTILAÇÃO ARTIFICIAL | 773 | OFICINA DE MONTAGEM |
| 739 | EM ESTADO BRUTO DE FUSÃO | 774 | ASTÁTICO |
| 740 | EM ESTADO BRUTO | 775 | REGULADOR ASTÁTICO |
| 741 | EM ESTADO DE ENTREGA | 776 | ASTERISMO |
| 742 | EM ESTADO BRUTO DE FORJA | 777 | ELEMENTO ASSIMÉTRICO |
| 743 | EM ESTADO BRUTO DE TÊMPERA | 778 | ASSIMÉTRICO |
| 744 | EM ESTADO BRUTO DE LAMINAÇÃO | 778 | DISSIMÉTRICO |
| 745 | EM ESTADO BRUTO DE SOLDAGEM | 779 | ASSIMETRIA |
| 746 | AMIANTO | 779 | DISSIMETRIA |
| 746 | ASBESTO | 780 | ASSÍNTOTA |
| 747 | PAPELÃO DE AMIANTO | 781 | ASSINTÓTICO |
| 748 | TELA DE AMIANTO | 782 | ASSINCRONISMO |
| 748 | TECIDO DE AMIANTO | 783 | MOTOR ASSÍNCRONO |
| 749 | CORDA DE AMIANTO | 784 | ASSÍNCRONO |
| 749 | FIBRA DE AMIANTO | 785 | ADIATERMIA |

| | |
|---|---|
| 785 | ATERMIA |
| 786 | ATÉRMICO |
| 786 | ATÉRMANO |
| 786 | ADIATÉRMICO |
| 787 | ATMOSFERA |
| 788 | ATMOSFERA (ATM) |
| 789 | ATMOSFERA ARTIFICIAL |
| 790 | ATMOSFERA DE PROTEÇÃO |
| 791 | ATMOSFERA DE USO ESPECIAL |
| 792 | AÇÕES ATMOSFÉRICAS |
| 793 | AGENTES ATMOSFÉRICOS |
| 794 | PRESSÃO BAROMÉTRICA |
| 794 | PRESSÃO ATMOSFÉRICA |
| 795 | CORROSÃO ATMOSFÉRICA |
| 796 | ELETRICIDADE ATMOSFÉRICA |
| 797 | VÁLVULA DE ESCAPE |
| 798 | LINHA ATMOSFÉRICA |
| 799 | ALTURA DA PRESSÃO ATMOSFÉRICA |
| 800 | ÁTOMO |
| 801 | SOLDAGEM A ARCO COM PROTEÇÃO DE HIDROGÉNIO ATÔMICO |
| 802 | CALOR ATÔMICO |
| 803 | NÚMERO ATÔMICO |
| 804 | PLANO RETICULAR |
| 805 | TEORIA ATÔMICA |
| 806 | VOLUME ATÔMICO |
| 807 | PESO ATÔMICO |
| 808 | ATOMIZAR UM LÍQUIDO |
| 808 | VAPORIZAR UM LÍQUIDO |
| 808 | PULVERIZAR UM LÍQUIDO |
| 809 | PULVERIZADOR |
| 809 | VAPORIZADOR |
| 809 | ATOMIZADOR |
| 810 | PULVERIZAÇÃO DE LÍQUIDOS |
| 811 | ATOMIZAÇÃO |
| 811 | PULVERIZAÇÃO |
| 812 | UNIÃO |
| 812 | ACESSÓRIO |
| 812 | PERTENCE |
| 812 | FIXAÇÃO |
| 813 | ATAQUE |
| 814 | FUNCIONAMENTO DE MÁQUINAS |
| 815 | ATRAÇÃO |
| 816 | SINAL ACÚSTICO |
| 817 | LIGA DE AUER |
| 818 | PUA |
| 818 | BROCA |
| 819 | AUGITA |
| 820 | AUGITA SIENITA |
| 821 | TRICLORETO ÁURICO |
| 822 | AURÍFERO |

| | |
|---|---|
| 823 | CLORETO ÁURICO |
| 824 | AUSTÉMPERA |
| 825 | AUSTENITA |
| 826 | AÇO AUSTENÍTICO |
| 827 | AUSTENITIZAÇÃO |
| 828 | MOTOR DE ARRANQUE AUTOMÁTICO |
| 829 | AUTOCLAVE |
| 829 | DIGESTOR |
| 830 | PROTENSÃO DE CILINDRO METÁLICO OCO |
| 830 | SUJEIÇÃO A UMA TENSÃO PRÉVIA |
| 830 | ESTIRAGEM A FRIO |
| 831 | SOLDAGEM AUTÓGENA |
| 832 | CORTE AUTOGÉNEO |
| 833 | MÁQUINA PARA CORTE AUTOGÉNEO |
| 834 | SOLDA AUTÓGENA |
| 834 | SOLDAGEM AUTÓGENA |
| 835 | SOLDAGEM AUTÓGENA |
| 836 | ACELERAÇÃO AUTOMÁTICA |
| 837 | AUTOMATIZAÇÃO |
| 838 | REATÂNCIA AUTOMÁTICA |
| 838 | AFOGADOR AUTOMÁTICO |
| 839 | CICLO AUTOMÁTICO |
| 840 | TORNO DE CICLO AUTOMÁTICO |
| 841 | DESACELERAÇÃO AUTOMÁTICA |
| 842 | ALAVANCA DE ALIMENTAÇÃO AUTOMÁTICA |
| 842 | ALAVANCA DE AVANÇO AUTOMÁTICO |
| 843 | REGULADOR AUTOMÁTICO |
| 844 | IGNIÇÃO AUTOMÁTICA |
| 845 | REGISTRO DE ISOLAMENTO |
| 846 | TORNO AUTOMÁTICO DE PARAFUSOS |
| 846 | TORNO AUTOMÁTICO |
| 847 | COMANDO AUTOMÁTICO DO NÍVEL |
| 847 | ESTABILIZADOR AUTOMÁTICO |
| 848 | LUBRIFICAÇÃO AUTOMÁTICA |
| 849 | SOLDAGEM AUTOMÁTICA |
| 850 | PROGRAMAÇÃO AUTOMÁTICA |
| 851 | LUBRIFICADOR AUTOMÁTICO |
| 852 | VÁLVULA AUTOMÁTICA |
| 853 | MOTOR AUXILIAR |
| 853 | MÁQUINA AUXILIAR |
| 854 | FUNÇÃO AUXILIAR |
| 855 | TEMPERATURA MÉDIA |
| 856 | TESOURAS ARTICULADAS |
| 857 | MACHADO |
| 858 | EIXOS CORTADOS EM ÂNGULO RETO |
| 859 | COMPONENTE AXIAL |
| 860 | DESLOCAMENTO AXIAL |
| 860 | DESLOCAMENTO LONGITUDINAL |
| 860 | DESLOCAMENTO PARALELO AO EIXO |
| 861 | BOMBA DE CIRCULAÇÃO AXIAL |
| 861 | BOMBA PROPULSORA |

| | |
|---|---|
| 862 | TURBINA DE CIRCULAÇÃO AXIAL |
| 863 | EIXO DE SIMETRIA DOS CRISTAIS |
| 864 | EIXO |
| 865 | EIXO DE UM CRISTAL |
| 866 | EIXO DE UM TUBO |
| 867 | EIXO DE OSCILAÇÃO |
| 868 | EIXO DE ROTAÇÃO |
| 869 | EIXO DE SIMETRIA |
| 870 | EIXO DE SOLDAGEM |
| 871 | EIXO DO CORDÃO DE SOLDAGEM |
| 872 | EIXO DOS X |
| 872 | EIXO DAS ABSCISSAS |
| 873 | EIXO DAS ORDENADAS |
| 874 | EIXO DOS Y |
| 875 | EIXO GEOMÉTRICO |
| 875 | EIXO DE RODA |
| 876 | MANCAL DE EIXO |
| 877 | CAIXA DE GRAXA |
| 877 | CAIXA DE MANCAL DE EIXO |
| 877 | CAIXA DE LUBRIFICAÇÃO |
| 878 | FURADEIRA PARA CAIXA DE MANCAL DE EIXO |
| 879 | GRAXA PARA EIXO |
| 880 | TORNO |
| 881 | TORNO DE MANCAL DE EIXO |
| 881 | TORNO PARA PONTAS DE EIXO |
| 882 | MANGA DO EIXO |
| 883 | CHAVE DE EIXOS |
| 883 | CHAVE DE CAIXA PARA EIXOS |
| 884 | EIXO |
| 885 | PERSPECTIVA AXONOMÉTRICA |
| 886 | AZURITA |
| 886 | CARBONATO AZUL DE COBRE |
| 887 | INSTITUTO BRITÂNICO DE NORMALIZAÇÃO |
| 888 | BABIT |
| 888 | METAL ANTIFRICÇÃO |
| 889 | METAL BRANCO |
| 889 | METAL BRANCO |
| 889 | METAL PATENTE |
| 890 | CURVA EXTERNA DE ARCO |
| 890 | DORSO |
| 890 | COSTAS |
| 890 | PARTE TRASEIRA |
| 890 | AVESSO |
| 891 | PORTA TRASEIRA |
| 891 | PORTA DE FUNDO |
| 891 | .PORTA FALSA |
| 892 | RETORNO DA CHAMA |
| 892 | TIRO PELA CULATRA |
| 892 | RETROCESSO |
| 893 | REBAIXAR |

| | |
|---|---|
| 893 | CERCEAR |
| 894 | MARCHA EM CONTRAPRESSÃO |
| 895 | VÁLVULA DE CONTRAPRESSÃO |
| 895 | VÁLVULA DE REPERCUSSÃO |
| 896 | RETRORREFLEXÃO |
| 897 | SERROTE DE COSTAS |
| 898 | BATENTE |
| 898 | ESPERA |
| 898 | ESCORA |
| 899 | VIDRO TRASEIRO |
| 899 | JANELA TRASEIRA |
| 900 | ATERRO |
| 900 | ENCHIMENTO |
| 900 | TERRAPLENAGEM |
| 901 | SOLDA DE RETROCESSO |
| 901 | SOLDA A "PASSO DE PEREGRINO" |
| 901 | SOLDA PASSO-A-PASSO |
| 902 | TIRA-SUPORTE |
| 903 | CILINDROS DE ENCOSTO |
| 904 | CORDÃO SUPORTE (AO CONTRÁRIO) |
| 905 | FRESA DE PERFIL CONSTANTE |
| 906 | TIRO PELA CULATRA |
| 906 | RETORNO DE CHAMA |
| 906 | EXPLOSÃO PREMATURA |
| 907 | SOLDAGEM EM SENTIDO CONTRÁRIO AO DA CHAMA |
| 908 | FARÓIS DE MARCHA À RÉ |
| 909 | METAL DE SUPORTE |
| 910 | CERCEAMENTO |
| 910 | DESAFOGO |
| 910 | DESPOJO |
| 911 | ANEL DE APOIO |
| 911 | ANEL DE ENCOSTO |
| 912 | AREIA DE CARGA |
| 912 | AREIA DE ENCHIMENTO |
| 913 | TORNO DE DESPOJAR |
| 914 | FOLGA |
| 914 | ESPAÇO MORTO |
| 914 | MOVIMENTO PERDIDO |
| 914 | RETROCESSO |
| 915 | RETIFICADOR DE FOLGA |
| 915 | ELIMINADOR DE FOLGA |
| 916 | PERDA DE CURSO |
| 916 | MOVIMENTO PERDIDO |
| 917 | SUPORTE TRASEIRO |
| 917 | DESCANSO TRASEIRO |
| 918 | SOLDA DE RETROCESSO |
| 919 | MOVIMENTO RETRÓGRADO |
| 919 | RECUO |
| 919 | RETROCESSO |
| 920 | SOLDAGEM MAL FEITA |

| | |
|---|---|
| 921 | DEFLETOR |
| 921 | CHAPA DEFLETORA |
| 921 | CHICANA |
| 921 | SEPTO |
| 921 | ANTEPARO |
| 922 | CHICANA |
| 922 | PLACA DEFLETORA |
| 923 | PROCESSO DE MOLDAGEM POR SACO DE BORRACHA |
| 924 | BAGAÇO |
| 925 | BAINITA |
| 926 | ARGILA COZIDA (GORDA) |
| 927 | NÚCLEO SECO |
| 927 | MACHO ESTUFADO |
| 928 | COZIMENTO |
| 928 | SECAGEM |
| 928 | ESTUFAGEM |
| 929 | EQUILÍBRIO |
| 930 | EQUILIBRAR |
| 930 | COMPENSAR |
| 930 | CONTRABALANÇAR |
| 931 | BALANÇA |
| 932 | ECONOMIA SÃ |
| 932 | ECONOMIA EM EQUILÍBRIO |
| 933 | FILTROS SIMÉTRICOS |
| 934 | VÁLVULA EQUILIBRADA |
| 935 | COMPENSAÇÃO |
| 936 | DESCARGA DE UMA VÁLVULA |
| 937 | APARELHO EQUILIBRADOR |
| 938 | CILINDRO DE EQUILÍBRIO |
| 939 | CILINDRO DE EQUILÍBRIO |
| 939 | TAMBOR DE EQUILÍBRIO |
| 940 | MÁQUINA DE COMPENSAR |
| 940 | MÁQUINA DE EQUILIBRAR |
| 941 | EQUILÍBRIO DAS MASSAS |
| 942 | EQUILÍBRIO |
| 942 | COMPENSAÇÃO |
| 943 | BALATA |
| 944 | CORREIA DE BALATA |
| 945 | FARDO |
| 945 | PACOTE |
| 945 | BALA |
| 946 | RECOLHEDOR DE FARDOS |
| 947 | CARRINHO DE ARMAZÉM |
| 947 | CARRINHO PARA TRANSPORTAR FARDOS |
| 948 | ENFARDADEIRA |
| 948 | ENFARDADOR |
| 949 | TRAVE DE MADEIRA |
| 949 | VIGA DE MADEIRA |
| 950 | BOLA |
| 950 | ESFERA |
| 951 | ESFERA DE AÇO |
| 951 | BOLA DE AÇO |
| 951 | LINGOTE DE AÇO |
| 952 | MANCAL DE ARTICULAÇÃO ESFÉRICA |
| 952 | MANCAL DE RÓTULA ESFÉRICA |
| 953 | ARTICULAÇÃO ESFÉRICA OU DE RÓTULA |
| 953 | ARTICULAÇÃO UNIVERSAL |
| 954 | ROLAMENTO DE ESFERAS |
| 954 | MANCAL DE ROLAMENTO DE ESFERAS |
| 955 | ALVÉOLO |
| 955 | CAIXA DE ROLAMENTO DE ESFERAS |
| 956 | BRUNIDURA EM TAMBOR DE ESFERAS |
| 956 | POLIMENTO POR BOLAS |
| 957 | GAIOLA DE ESFERAS |
| 957 | PORTA-ESFERAS |
| 958 | SUSPENSÃO DE RÓTULA |
| 959 | MOINHO DE ESFERAS |
| 960 | MARTELO DE BOLA |
| 961 | MARTELO DE PENA REDONDA |
| 962 | MARTELO DE PENA REDONDA |
| 963 | PENA ESFÉRICA DO MARTELO |
| 964 | ANEL DE ROLAMENTO |
| 964 | PISTA DE ESFERAS |
| 965 | ANEL DE ROLAMENTO DAS ESFERAS |
| 966 | ROLAMENTO DE ESFERAS AXIAL |
| 967 | DURÔMETRO DE ESFERA |
| 968 | VÁLVULA ESFÉRICA |
| 969 | BALASTRO |
| 969 | LASTRO |
| 970 | VÁLVULA DE LASTRO |
| 971 | BALASTRO |
| 971 | LASTRO |
| 972 | BAMBU |
| 973 | ESTANHO DE BANCA |
| 974 | CINTA |
| 974 | BANDA |
| 974 | FAIXA |
| 974 | LIGADURA |
| 974 | FITA |
| 975 | POLIA DE CORREIA PLANA |
| 976 | INDICADOR DE TENSÃO DA FITA |
| 977 | SERRA DE FITA |
| 978 | SERRA CONTÍNUA |
| 978 | SERRA DE FITA |
| 978 | SERRA SEM-FIM |
| 979 | ESTRUTURA BANDEADA |
| 980 | FITAS |
| 980 | CINTAS |
| 980 | TIRAS |
| 981 | BARRA |
| 982 | MÁQUINA PARA ESTIRAR BARRAS E TUBOS |

| | |
|---|---|
| 983 | TORNO AUTOMÁTICO DE BARRA |
| 984 | FERRO EM BARRAS |
| 984 | AÇO EM BARRAS |
| 985 | ÍMÃ RETO |
| 985 | ÍMÃ DE BARRA |
| 986 | BARRA |
| 986 | VIGA |
| 987 | ARAME FARPADO |
| 988 | MÁQUINA DE ARAME FARPADO |
| 989 | ELÉTRODO NU |
| 990 | ARAME SEM REVESTIMENTO |
| 990 | ARAME NU |
| 991 | BATELÃO |
| 991 | BARCAÇA |
| 991 | BATELADA |
| 992 | BÁRIO |
| 993 | ACETATO DE BÁRIO |
| 994 | ALUMINATO DE BÁRIO |
| 995 | CARBURETO DE BÁRIO |
| 996 | CARBONATO DE BÁRIO |
| 997 | CLORETO DE BÁRIO |
| 998 | BIÓXIDO DE BÁRIO |
| 999 | FLUORETO DE BÁRIO |
| 1000 | HIDRATO DE BARITA |
| 1000 | HIDRATO DE BÁRIO |
| 1001 | AZOTATO DE BÁRIO |
| 1001 | NITRATO DE BÁRIO |
| 1002 | PLATINOCIANETO DE BÁRIO |
| 1003 | SULFATO DE BÁRIO |
| 1003 | BRANCO DE BARITA |
| 1003 | BRANCO FIXO |
| 1004 | SULFETO DE BÁRIO |
| 1005 | CASCA DE ÁRVORE |
| 1005 | CORTIÇA |
| 1005 | CASCA ABAIXO DA CAREPA |
| 1006 | BARNE |
| 1006 | UNIDADE DE SUPERFÍCIE NUCLEAR |
| 1007 | BARÓGRAFO |
| 1007 | BARÔMETRO REGISTRADOR |
| 1008 | BARÔMETRO |
| 1009 | BAROMÉTRICO |
| 1009 | BARÔMETRO |
| 1010 | CONDENSADOR BAROMÉTRICO |
| 1011 | BAROSCÓPIO |
| 1012 | POLIMENTO EM TAMBOR |
| 1013 | MÁQUINA DE ESCAREAR EM OCO |
| 1014 | ACABAMENTO EM TAMBOR |
| 1015 | CORPO DE BOMBA |
| 1015 | CILINDRO |
| 1016 | GALVANOPLÁSTICA EM TAMBOR |
| 1016 | REVESTIMENTO GALVANIZADO EM TAMBOR |

| | |
|---|---|
| 1017 | ROLO APIPADO |
| 1018 | SERVOMOTOR LANÇADOR |
| 1018 | SERVOMOTOR DE ARRANQUE |
| 1018 | VIRADOR A MOTOR |
| 1018 | MOTOR AUXILIAR |
| 1019 | ÁGUA DE BARITA |
| 1020 | MONÓXIDO DE BÁRIO |
| 1020 | BARITA |
| 1021 | BARITINA |
| 1021 | BARITITA |
| 1021 | ESPATO PESADO |
| 1022 | BASALTO |
| 1023 | BASÁLTICO |
| 1024 | BASE |
| 1024 | INGREDIENTE PRINCIPAL |
| 1025 | SOLEIRA |
| 1025 | ASSENTO |
| 1025 | PÉ |
| 1025 | PEDESTAL |
| 1026 | FUNDO |
| 1026 | FUNDAMENTO |
| 1026 | SOCO |
| 1027 | BASE |
| 1028 | BASE DE ROSCA |
| 1029 | CHUMBO NÃO REFINADO |
| 1029 | CHUMBO IMPURO |
| 1030 | CÍRCULO DE BASE |
| 1030 | CÍRCULO PRIMITIVO |
| 1031 | METAL NÃO PRECIOSO |
| 1031 | METAL COMUM |
| 1032 | METAL DE BASE |
| 1033 | BASE DE LOGARITMO |
| 1034 | PATIM DE MANCAL |
| 1035 | BASE DE COLUNA |
| 1036 | RAIZ DE DENTE |
| 1037 | PLACA DE BASE |
| 1037 | PLACA DE ASSENTAMENTO |
| 1037 | PLACA DE FUNDO |
| 1037 | PLACA DE APOIO |
| 1038 | ELEMENTO BÁSICO |
| 1039 | AMOSTRA DE METAL DE BASE |
| 1040 | PLACA DE ASSENTO |
| 1040 | PLACA DE BASE |
| 1041 | PÉ |
| 1041 | PERNA |
| 1041 | SUPORTE |
| 1042 | BÁSICO |
| 1043 | PROCESSO BESSEMER BÁSICO |
| 1044 | AÇO THOMAS |
| 1045 | BASE E REVESTIMENTO BÁSICOS |
| 1046 | FLUXO BÁSICO |

| | |
|---|---|
| 1047 | AÇO SIEMENS-MARTIN BÁSICO |
| 1048 | AÇO SIEMENS-MARTIN BÁSICO |
| 1049 | GUSA BÁSICO |
| 1049 | FERRO GUSA THOMAS |
| 1050 | PROCESSO BÁSICO |
| 1051 | REFRATÁRIOS BÁSICOS |
| 1052 | INVESTIGAÇÃO PURA |
| 1052 | INVESTIGAÇÃO FUNDAMENTAL |
| 1053 | DIMENSÃO BÁSICA |
| 1054 | ESCÓRIA BÁSICA |
| 1054 | FOSFATO THOMAS |
| 1054 | ESCÓRIA THOMAS |
| 1055 | BASICIDADE |
| 1056 | PALHA DE JUNCO |
| 1056 | LÍBER |
| 1056 | FLOEMA |
| 1057 | LIMA BASTARDA |
| 1058 | CORTE LONGITUDINAL DA MADEIRA |
| 1058 | SERRAGEM AO LONGO |
| 1058 | CORTE PARALELO DA MADEIRA |
| 1059 | MASSA |
| 1059 | LOTE |
| 1059 | FORNADA |
| 1060 | FORNO DE CARREGAR |
| 1060 | FORNO INTERMITENTE |
| 1061 | RODA DE LINGÜETA |
| 1062 | BANHO |
| 1063 | TORNEIRA DE BANHEIRA |
| 1064 | TENSÃO DE BANHO |
| 1065 | INCLINAÇÃO |
| 1065 | OBLIQÜIDADE |
| 1066 | BATERIA |
| 1067 | CAIXA DE BATERIA |
| 1068 | REGISTRO DA BATERIA |
| 1069 | CONJUNTO DE CALDEIRAS |
| 1069 | BATERIA DE CALDEIRAS |
| 1070 | EFEITO BAUSCHINGER |
| 1071 | BAUXITA |
| 1072 | BAÍA |
| 1072 | OGIVA |
| 1072 | COMPARTIMENTO |
| 1072 | VÃO |
| 1072 | PAINEL |
| 1073 | PROCESSO BAYER |
| 1074 | JUNTA A BAIONETA |
| 1075 | FUNCIONAR SOB TRAÇÃO |
| 1075 | FUNCIONAR SOB COMPRESSÃO |
| 1076 | EQUILIBRAR-SE |
| 1076 | ESTAR EM EQUILÍBRIO |
| 1077 | ENGRENAR–SE |
| 1078 | CISALHAR |

| | |
|---|---|
| 1078 | CORTAR |
| 1078 | ESTAR SUJEITO A ESFORÇO CORTANTE |
| 1078 | OPERAR SOB ESFORÇO CORTANTE |
| 1079 | FUNCIONAR A PLENA CARGA |
| 1079 | OPERAR COM CARGA MÁXIMA |
| 1080 | FUNCIONAR A CARGA INCOMPLETA |
| 1081 | FUNCIONAR EM VAZIO |
| 1082 | MEIO-FIO |
| 1082 | BOLHA |
| 1082 | CORDÃO DE SOLDA |
| 1082 | FILETE |
| 1083 | REBORDO |
| 1084 | REVIRAR AS BORDAS |
| 1084 | DOBRAR O FLANGE DOS TUBOS |
| 1084 | SOLDAR EM SOBREPOSTA |
| 1085 | CORDÃO DE SOLDA EM SUPERFÍCIE PLANA |
| 1085 | SOLDAGEM LINEAR DE FRAÇÃO |
| 1086 | FERRO BORDEADO |
| 1087 | TUBO COM REBORDO |
| 1087 | TUBO DE BORDA REVIRADA |
| 1088 | REVIRAMENTO DA BORDA |
| 1088 | MOLDURA |
| 1088 | REVIRAMENTO DO FLANGE DOS TUBOS |
| 1088 | DOBRA DAS BORDAS DA CHAPA |
| 1089 | FERRAMENTA DE REVIRAR TUBOS |
| 1089 | MÁQUINA DE FAZER BORDAS |
| 1090 | BRAÇO DE BIGORNA |
| 1091 | BIGORNA |
| 1092 | COPO DE BOCA LARGA |
| 1092 | TAÇA DE LABORATÓRIO |
| 1093 | FEIXE ELETRÔNICO |
| 1093 | RAIO LUMINOSO |
| 1093 | VIGA |
| 1093 | BARROTE |
| 1093 | VIGOTA |
| 1093 | TRAVE |
| 1093 | TRAVESSÃO |
| 1094 | DISPOSITIVO BIELA E MANIVELA |
| 1095 | BALANÇA COM TRAVESSÃO |
| 1096 | COMPASSO DE LANÇA OU VARA |
| 1096 | CINTEL |
| 1097 | VIGA FIXADA EM UMA PONTA E APOIADA NA OUTRA |
| 1098 | VIGA APOIADA DOS DOIS LADOS |
| 1099 | VIGA |
| 1100 | MANCAL |
| 1100 | ROLAMENTO |
| 1100 | CHUMACEIRO |
| 1100 | COXINETE |
| 1100 | BRONZINA |
| 1100 | APOIO |

## 1175

| | | | | |
|---|---|---|---|---|
| 1101 | SUPERFÍCIE DE APOIO | 1131 | ALAVANCA ARTICULADA |
| 1102 | ESFERA PARA ROLAMENTO | 1132 | FORNO DE RESISTÊNCIA EM FORMA DE |
| 1103 | CONSOLO | | CAMPÂNULA |
| 1103 | SUPORTE DE ROLAMENTO | 1133 | CAPA DE EMBREAGEM |
| 1104 | TAMPA DE CHUMACEIRA | 1134 | BRONZE DE SINO |
| 1104 | CAPA DE MANCAL | 1134 | CAMPANIL |
| 1105 | ATRITO DOS MANCAIS | 1135 | FORNO DE CÂMARA LEVADIÇA |
| 1106 | METAL PATENTE | 1136 | VÁLVULA DE SINO |
| 1106 | METAL ANTIFRICÇÃO | 1137 | CAMPAINHA |
| 1106 | LIGA DE METAL PARA MANCAL | 1137 | CAMPAINHA DE ALARME |
| 1107 | SUPERFÍCIE DE APOIO DE EIXO | 1138 | VÁLVULA DE FOLE |
| 1107 | MOENTE DE EIXO | 1139 | FOLE |
| 1108 | AGULHAS PARA ROLAMENTO | 1139 | FOLE DE FORJA |
| 1109 | CHAPA DE APOIO | 1140 | CINTA |
| 1109 | CHAPA DE MANCAL | 1140 | CORREIA |
| 1109 | CHAPA DE ASSENTO | 1141 | CARGA DE CORREIA TRANSPORTADORA |
| 1110 | PRESSÃO NO APOIO | 1142 | ACOPLAMENTO POR CORREIAS |
| 1110 | REAÇÃO DO APOIO | 1142 | UNIÃO POR CORREIAS |
| 1111 | PISTA DE ESFERAS DE ROLAMENTO | 1143 | FERRAMENTA DE LOMBO |
| 1112 | ROLO PARA ROLAMENTO | 1144 | TRANSMISSÃO POR CORREIA |
| 1113 | CASCO DE MANCAL | 1145 | MÁQUINA ACIONADA POR CORREIA |
| 1114 | MOLA DE SUSPENSÃO | 1146 | COLCHETE DE CORREIA |
| 1115 | SUPERFÍCIE SUSTENTADORA | 1146 | GRAMPO DE CORREIA |
| 1115 | SUPERFÍCIE DE ENCOSTO | 1147 | VOLANTE DE CORREIA |
| 1116 | SUPERFÍCIE DE APOIO DE MUNHÃO | 1148 | FORNO DE TRANSPORTADOR |
| 1116 | SUPERFÍCIE DE APOIO DE MANIVELA | 1149 | TRANSMISSÃO DE ÂNGULO |
| 1117 | MANCAL | 1150 | GUIA DE CORREIA |
| 1117 | ROLAMENTO | 1151 | JUNTA DE CORREIA |
| 1118 | SUPORTE | 1151 | ACOPLAMENTO DE CORREIAS |
| 1118 | APOIO | 1152 | POLIA COMUM |
| 1119 | VIBRAÇÃO | 1153 | ALICATE VAZADOR PARA CORREIAS |
| 1119 | BATIDA | 1153 | SACA-BOCADOS PARA CORREIAS |
| 1120 | MARTELAGEM | 1154 | MECANISMO DE INVERSÃO DE CORREIA |
| 1120 | LAMINAÇÃO A MARTELO | 1155 | REBITE PARA CORREIAS |
| 1121 | TARRAXA DE ABRIR ROSCA | 1156 | PARAFUSO PARA CORREIAS |
| 1122 | CENTRAR-SE | 1157 | DESLOCADOR DE CORREIA |
| 1123 | DESMAGNETIZAR-SE | 1158 | DESLOCAMENTO DA CORREIA |
| 1123 | DESIMANTAR-SE | 1159 | GARFO MUDA CORREIA |
| 1124 | ELETRIZAR-SE | 1160 | MONTAGEM DA CORREIA |
| 1125 | ALONGAR-SE | 1161 | ESTICADOR OU TENSOR DE CORREIA |
| 1125 | ESTENDER-SE | 1162 | TENSÃO DA CORREIA |
| 1126 | IMANTAR-SE | 1163 | CORREIA MOTRIZ |
| 1126 | MAGNETIZAR-SE | 1163 | CORREIA DE COMANDO |
| 1127 | CHAPA DE ASSENTO | 1164 | CORREIA TRANSPORTADORA |
| 1127 | PLACA DE FUNDAÇÃO | 1164 | ESTEIRA TRANSPORTADORA |
| 1127 | ESCORA | 1164 | ESTEIRA SEM-FIM |
| 1128 | SEBO DE BOI | 1165 | ESPESSURA DE CORREIA |
| 1129 | CERA DE ABELHA | 1166 | CORREIA DE VÁRIAS ESPESSURAS |
| 1130 | CAMADA DE BEILBY | 1167 | BANCO |
| 1131 | ALAVANCA ANGULAR | 1167 | BANCADA |
| 1131 | ALAVANCA EM COTOVELO | 1167 | BANQUETA |

| | | | |
|---|---|---|---|
| 1167 | PLATAFORMA | 1196 | MADEIRA CURVA |
| 1168 | FURADEIRA DE BANCADA | 1197 | TORTO |
| 1169 | MOLDAGEM DE BANCADA | 1197 | DESALINHADO |
| 1170 | TESTE DE BANCADA | 1198 | BENZALDEÍDO |
| 1170 | PROVA DE BANCADA | 1199 | BENZENO |
| 1171 | MORSA DE BANCADA | 1199 | BENZOL |
| 1171 | TORNO DE BANCADA | 1200 | ÁCIDO BENZÊNICO-SULFÔNICO |
| 1172 | CURVATURA | 1200 | ÁCIDO FENILSULFUROSO |
| 1172 | COTOVELO | 1201 | BENZIDINA |
| 1173 | CURVAR | 1202 | ÁCIDO BENZÓICO |
| 1173 | ARQUEAR | 1203 | BENJOIM |
| 1173 | DOBRAR | 1204 | BENZOL |
| 1173 | EMPENAR | 1205 | BENZONA |
| 1174 | ENVERGAR | 1205 | BENZOFENONA |
| 1175 | CURVAR UM TUBO | 1206 | AZUL DE BERLIM |
| 1175 | DOBRAR UM TUBO | 1206 | AZUL DA PRÚSSIA |
| 1176 | RAIO DE CURVATURA | 1207 | BERÍLIO |
| 1177 | ENSAIO DE DOBRAMENTO | 1208 | BRONZE AO BERÍLIO |
| 1177 | TESTE DE FLEXÃO | 1209 | LIGA DE COBRE E BERÍLIO |
| 1178 | PROVA DE FLEXÃO DO LADO DA SOLDAGEM | 1209 | COBRE AO BERÍLIO |
| | | 1210 | GLUCÍNIO |
| 1179 | PROVA DE FLEXÃO AO CONTRÁRIO | 1211 | SOPRO PROLONGADO DO CONVERSOR BESSEMER |
| 1180 | JOELHO DE TUBO | | |
| 1181 | MÁQUINA DE DOBRAR | 1212 | CONVERSOR BESSEMER |
| 1182 | CURVATURA | 1213 | FERRO GUSA PARA CONVERSOR BESSEMER |
| 1182 | FLEXÃO | 1213 | FUNDIÇÃO BESSEMER |
| 1183 | VIRADEIRA (PRENSA DE CURVAR CHAPAS) | 1214 | PROCESSO BESSEMER |
| 1184 | PRENSA DE CURVAR | 1215 | AÇO BESSEMER |
| 1184 | MÁQUINA DE CURVAR | 1216 | LATÃO BETA |
| 1185 | MOMENTO FLETOR | 1217 | PARTÍCULA BETA |
| 1185 | MOMENTO DE FLEXÃO | 1218 | RAIOS BETA |
| 1186 | MÁQUINA DE DESEMPENAR CHAPAS | 1219 | ESTRUTURA BETA |
| 1186 | ROLO DE CURVAR | 1220 | PROCESSO BETTS |
| 1186 | JOGO DE CILINDROS PARA BOBINAR OU DESBOBINAR ARAME | 1221 | CHANFRO |
| | | 1221 | BISEL |
| 1187 | ESFORÇO DE FLEXÃO OU DE CURVATURA | 1222 | CHANFRAR |
| 1187 | DEFORMAÇÃO DE FLEXÃO | 1222 | BISELAR |
| 1188 | RESISTÊNCIA À FLEXÃO | 1223 | ÂNGULO OBLÍQUO |
| 1189 | ENSAIO DE FLEXÃO | 1224 | TRANSMISSÃO POR CONES DE FRICÇÃO |
| 1190 | TESTE DE FLEXÃO POR CHOQUE EM BARRAS ENTALHADAS | 1225 | CONE DE FRICÇÃO |
| | | 1225 | RODA DE FRICÇÃO CÔNICA |
| 1190 | TESTE DE FLEXÃO AO CHOQUE EM ENTALHE | 1226 | COROA DE DENTES RETOS |
| | | 1226 | PINHÃO CÔNICO |
| 1191 | ESFORÇO DE FLEXÃO | 1227 | ENGRENAGEM DE ÂNGULO |
| 1191 | ESFORÇO TRANSVERSAL | 1227 | ENGRENAGEM CÔNICA |
| 1192 | RESISTÊNCIA À FLEXÃO TRANSVERSAL | 1228 | SUTA |
| 1193 | TENSÃO DE FLEXÃO | 1228 | ESQUADRO MÓVEL DE TRAÇAR ÂNGULOS |
| 1194 | CANO CURVO | 1229 | RODA CÔNICA |
| 1194 | TUBO CURVO | 1229 | ENGRENAGEM CÔNICA |
| 1195 | CHAVE CURVA | 1230 | TRANSMISSÃO POR ENGRENAGEM CÔNICA |
| 1195 | CHAVE ARTICULADA | 1231 | BISELAGEM |

| | |
|---|---|
| 1231 CHANFRADURA | 1267 BISSEÇÃO |
| 1232 BISEL | 1268 BISSETRIZ |
| 1232 ENGASTE | 1269 BISMUTO |
| 1233 ELÉTRODO BIPOLAR | 1270 CLORETO DE BISMUTO |
| 1234 TORNEIRA DE PONTA CURVA | 1270 TRICLORETO DE BISMUTO |
| 1235 TUBO DE TORNEIRA | 1271 NITRATO DE BISMUTO |
| 1236 TRATAMENTO COM BICROMATO | 1272 ÓXIDO DE BISMUTO |
| 1237 LENTE BICÔNCAVA | 1273 NITRATO DE BISMUTO |
| 1238 LENTE BICONVEXA | 1274 SOLDA DE BISMUTO |
| 1239 CORRENTE DE BICICLETA | 1275 BISMUTINA |
| 1240 SUSPENSÃO BIFILAR | 1275 SULFETO NATURAL DE BISMUTO |
| 1241 REBITES FENDIDOS | 1276 PORCELANA FOSCA |
| 1242 MANCAL DE CABEÇA DE BIELA | 1277 ÂNGULO DE ACUNHAMENTO |
| 1242 MANCAL DE PINO DE MANIVELA | 1277 ÂNGULO DE ATAQUE |
| 1243 LINGOTE | 1277 ÂNGULO CORTANTE |
| 1243 PALANQUILHA | 1278 ENCAIXE DE CORDA NA RANHURA |
| 1244 TESOURAS PARA LINGOTES | 1279 GRANULAÇÃO |
| 1245 LAMINADOR DE LIGOTES | 1280 BETUME |
| 1246 TESOURAS PARA LINGOTES | 1281 BETUMINOSO |
| 1247 LIGA BINÁRIA | 1282 CARVÃO BETUMINOSO |
| 1248 CÓDIGO BINÁRIO DECIMAL | 1282 CARVÃO GORDO |
| 1249 POSIÇÃO BINÁRIA | 1282 HULHA BETUMINOSA |
| 1249 DÍGITO OU ALGARISMO BINÁRIO | 1283 VERNIZ DO JAPÃO |
| 1249 BIT | 1283 VERNIZ BETUMINOSO |
| 1250 ELEMENTO AGLUTINANTE | 1284 ARAME PRETO RECOZIDO |
| 1251 MÁQUINAS DE SEGAR E CEIFAR | 1285 CORPO OPACO |
| 1252 BRAÇADEIRA | 1285 CORPO NEGRO |
| 1252 CHAVETA ANULAR CÔNICA | 1286 PINO NÃO MECANIZADO |
| 1253 AGLOMERANTE | 1287 COBRE PRETO |
| 1253 MATERIAL AGLUTINANTE | 1287 COBRE EM BRUTO |
| 1253 AGLUTINANTE | 1288 RUBRO NASCENTE |
| 1253 CIMENTO | 1289 CHAPAS NEGRAS |
| 1254 BORNE DE LIGAÇÃO | 1290 PORCA EM BRUTO |
| 1254 TERMINAL | 1291 ÓLEO PRETO |
| 1255 ARAME OU FIO DE JUNÇÃO | 1292 FERRO GUSA GRAFÍTICO |
| 1256 MICROSCÓPIO BINOCULAR | 1292 FUNDIÇÃO GRAFÍTICA |
| 1257 COEFICIENTE BINOMIAL | 1293 PINHO LARIÇO |
| 1258 DISTRIBUIÇÃO DE BERNOUILLI | 1293 PINHEIRO DA CÓRSEGA |
| 1258 LEI BINOMIAL | 1293 PINHEIRO PRETO |
| 1259 EQUAÇÃO BINOMIAL | 1294 CHAPA FINA PRETA |
| 1260 SÉRIE BINOMIAL | 1295 CALOR RUBRO |
| 1261 BIPLANO | 1295 RUBRO NASCENTE |
| 1262 EQUAÇÃO BIQUADRÁTICA | 1296 CHAPA PRETA |
| 1262 EQUAÇÃO DE QUARTO GRAU | 1297 GRAXA PRETA |
| 1263 MICROFISSURA | 1297 PRETO DE FUNDIÇÃO |
| 1264 PERSPECTIVA | 1298 TENAZES DE FERREIRO |
| 1264 VISTA AÉREA | 1299 PALHETA |
| 1265 BIRREFRINGENTE | 1299 LÂMINA |
| 1266 BISSEGMENTAR | 1299 FOLHA |
| 1266 SECIONAR | 1300 FOLHA CORTANTE |
| 1266 DIVIDIR EM DUAS PARTES | 1300 LÂMINA CORTANTE |

| | | | | |
|---|---|---|---|
| 1300 | LÂMINA DE FERRAMENTA CORTANTE | 1332 | BLOCO |
| 1301 | PEÇA EM BRUTO | 1333 | POLIA DE TALHA |
| 1301 | PEÇA EM BRANCO | 1333 | PLAINA |
| 1302 | PARAFUSO POR ROSCAR | 1333 | SAPATA |
| 1303 | PONTA DE TUBO TAMPADO | 1333 | CALÇO |
| 1304 | MANILHA CEGA | 1333 | CEPO |
| 1304 | FLANGE CEGO | 1333 | MOITÃO |
| 1305 | SUPORTE DE PEÇA A ESTAMPAR | 1333 | CADERNAL |
| 1306 | SEPARADOR SEM PERFURAÇÃO | 1333 | BLOQUEIO |
| 1307 | PORCA VIRGEM | 1333 | TRAVA |
| 1307 | PORCA SEM ROSCA | 1334 | FORMATO DE BLOCO DE ENDEREÇO |
| 1308 | PORCA SEM ROSCA | 1335 | FREIO DE SAPATA |
| 1309 | CORTE | 1336 | CORRENTE PLANA ARTICULADA |
| 1309 | ESTAMPAGEM | 1337 | SUPRESSÃO |
| 1310 | MATRIZ DE ESTAMPAR | 1338 | |
| 1311 | ALTO-FORNO | 1339 | LINGOTE DE ESTANHO |
| 1311 | FORNO DE FUNDIÇÃO | 1339 | ESTANHO EM BLOCOS |
| 1312 | ESCÓRIA DE ALTO-FORNO | 1340 | CLICHÊ TIPOGRÁFICO |
| 1313 | GÁS DE ALTO-FORNO | 1341 | BLOQUEIO |
| 1314 | TUBULAÇÃO PORTA-VENTO | 1342 | CONDENSADOR DE BLOQUEIO |
| 1315 | CORRENTE DE AR | 1343 | DESBASTADOR |
| 1315 | VENTO | 1344 | GRUA TELEFÉRICA |
| 1316 | EXPLOSÃO | 1345 | LUPA |
| 1316 | DETONAÇÃO | 1346 | EFLORESCÊNCIA |
| 1317 | PÓ DE BRANQUEAR | 1347 | DE OU PARA BLOCOS |
| 1317 | CLORETO DE CAL | 1348 | LAMINADOR DE DESBASTAR |
| 1318 | PURGADOR | 1348 | DESBASTADOR DE LINGOTES |
| 1319 | PARAFUSO SANGRADOR | 1349 | LUPAS |
| 1320 | RESPIRADOURO AUTOMÁTICO | 1350 | MATA-BORRÃO |
| 1321 | DRENAGEM | 1351 | GOLPE |
| 1321 | TRANSVAZAMENTO | 1351 | PANCADA |
| 1321 | SANGRIA | 1351 | JATO |
| 1322 | CONTRAÇÃO NO MOLDE | 1351 | SOPRO |
| 1323 | DOSAR | 1352 | FUNDIR |
| 1323 | MISTURAR | 1352 | SOPRAR |
| 1323 | COMBINAR | 1352 | QUEIMAR |
| 1324 | BLENDA | 1352 | INSUFLAR |
| 1324 | ESFALERITA | 1353 | CAVIDADE |
| 1325 | DOSAGEM | 1353 | BOLHA |
| 1325 | COMBINAÇÃO | 1354 | DESPRENDIMENTO |
| 1325 | MISTURA | 1355 | TUBO DE SOLDAR |
| 1326 | OBTURADOR | 1355 | MAÇARICO |
| 1326 | FLANGE CEGO | 1355 | FERRO DE SOLDAR |
| 1327 | EMPOLA | 1356 | ANÁLISE DE MAÇARICO |
| 1327 | VESÍCULA | 1357 | TORNEIRA DE DESCARGA |
| 1327 | BOLHA | 1359 | VÁLVULA DE DESCARGA |
| 1328 | BARRA DE AÇO CEMENTADO | 1359 | VÁLVULA DE ESGOTO |
| 1329 | COBRE VESICULADO | 1359 | PURGADOR |
| 1329 | COBRE EMPOLADO | 1360 | PROTETOR ANTIEXPLOSIVO |
| 1330 | EMPOLAMENTO | 1361 | VENTOINHA |
| 1331 | INCHAÇÃO | 1361 | INSUFLADOR |

| | |
|---|---|
| 1361 VENTILADOR | 1391 MÁQUINA DE MODELAR |
| 1362 BOLHA DE GÁS | 1391 MÁQUINA DE DOBRAR |
| 1363 COMPRESSOR | 1392 CORPO MÓVEL |
| 1363 MÁQUINA ASSOPRADORA | 1392 CORPO EM MOVIMENTO |
| 1363 BROQUE | 1393 PROPRIEDADE DE PIGMENTAR |
| 1364 ESVAZIAMENTO DE UMA CALDEIRA | 1394 NÚCLEO DO PARAFUSO |
| 1365 VIDRO SOPRADO | 1394 SEÇÃO DE ROSCA DO PARAFUSO |
| 1366 METAL LÍQUIDO SOPRADO | 1395 CONSISTÊNCIA DE ÓLEO |
| 1367 TUBO DE SOPRAR | 1396 PRISMA DE IGUAL RESISTÊNCIA |
| 1368 RECOZER O AÇO | 1397 ASSENTO DE CORPO DE VÁLVULA |
| 1368 AZULAR O AÇO | 1398 OFICINA DE CARROCERIAS |
| 1369 BANHO MERCURIOSO | 1399 CENTRO CÚBICO |
| 1369 BANHO AZUL | 1400 VIDRO BRANCO DA BOÊMIA |
| 1370 CALOR AZUL | 1401 FERVER |
| 1371 AQUECIDO AO AZUL | 1402 TAXA DE EVAPORAÇÃO |
| 1372 ENSAIO DE RUPTURA AO AZUL | 1403 ENSAIO DE PERDA TÉRMICA |
| 1372 TESTE DE RUPTURA AO AZUL | 1404 EVAPORAÇÃO |
| 1373 CÓPIA HELIOGRÁFICA AZUL | 1404 VAPOR DE EBULIÇÃO |
| 1374 PÓ DE ZINCO OXIDADO | 1405 EVACUAÇÃO DO VAPOR DE EBULIÇÃO |
| 1375 CÓPIA HELIOGRÁFICA | 1406 CALDEIRA |
| 1375 CÓPIA DE FERROPRUSSIATO | 1407 ALAMBIQUE |
| 1376 VITRÍOLO AZUL | 1407 CUCÚRBITA |
| 1376 SULFATO DE COBRE | 1408 REVESTIMENTO CALORÍFICO PARA |
| 1376 SULFATO CÚPRICO | CALDEIRAS |
| 1376 PEDRALIPES | 1409 PERFURATRIZ DE CALDEIRAS |
| 1377 SOLUÇÃO DE ANIL | 1410 EXPLOSÃO DE CALDEIRA |
| 1377 AZULAGEM | 1411 ACESSÓRIOS PARA CALDEIRAS |
| 1378 VELAME | 1411 APARELHAGEM AUXILIAR PARA |
| 1378 VÉU | CALDEIRAS |
| 1379 TÁBUA | 1412 TUBO DE FORNALHA |
| 1379 PRANCHA | 1412 TUBO DE CALDEIRA |
| 1379 QUADRO | 1413 CASA DE CALDEIRAS |
| 1380 MARTELO DE QUEDA COM PRANCHA | 1414 INSPEÇÃO DE CALDEIRA |
| 1380 MARTINETE DE PRANCHA | 1415 CALDEIREIRO |
| 1380 MARTELO PILÃO COM PRANCHA | 1416 CHAPA OU PLACA DE CALDEIRA |
| 1381 CARTÃO COMPRIMIDO | 1417 PRESSÃO DE CALDEIRA |
| 1381 PAPELÃO | 1418 SALA OU CASA DE CALDEIRAS |
| 1382 PREGO DE EMBARCAÇÃO | 1419 CORPO DE CALDEIRA |
| 1383 ASSENTO SUSPENSO | 1419 CARCAÇA DE CALDEIRA |
| 1384 BOBINA | 1419 CASCO DE CALDEIRA |
| 1385 CORPO | 1420 CALDEIRARIA (DE FERRO) |
| 1385 CHASSI | 1421 PROVA DE CALDEIRA SOB PRESSÃO |
| 1385 CARROCERIA | 1422 TUBO DE CALDEIRA |
| 1386 CORPO EM REPOUSO | 1423 FÁBRICA DE CALDEIRAS |
| 1387 REBAIXAMENTO | 1423 CALDEIRARIA |
| 1387 CERCEAMENTO | 1424 PONTO DE EBULIÇÃO |
| 1387 TORNEAMENTO EM PERFIL | 1425 COM ALTO PONTO DE EBULIÇÃO |
| 1388 ÂNGULO DE PROFUNDIDADE DO | 1426 COM BAIXO PONTO DE EBULIÇÃO |
| TORNEAMENTO | 1427 TEMPERATURA DE EBULIÇÃO |
| 1389 COR OPACA | 1428 ÁGUA EM EBULIÇÃO |
| 1390 LIMA—FRESA | 1428 ÁGUA FERVENTE |

| | |
|---|---|
| 1429 | EBULIÇÃO |
| 1430 | ARGILA FRIÁVEL |
| 1430 | ARGILA CALCÁRIO-FERRUGINOSA |
| 1430 | ARGILA ESMÉTICA |
| 1431 | BOLÔMETRO |
| 1432 | PINO |
| 1432 | PERNO |
| 1432 | PARAFUSO |
| 1432 | CAVILHA |
| 1432 | TRANQUETA |
| 1432 | FERROLHO |
| 1433 | CÍRCULO DOS ORIFÍCIOS DOS PINOS |
| 1434 | DIÂMETRO DE PINO |
| 1435 | PARAFUSAR |
| 1436 | CABEÇA DE CAVILHA |
| 1436 | CABEÇA DE PARAFUSO |
| 1437 | FURO DE CAVILHA |
| 1437 | FURO PARA PARAFUSO |
| 1438 | DIÂMETRO DE PERFURAÇÃO |
| 1439 | DIÂMETRO DE PERFURAÇÃO |
| 1440 | DIÂMETRO DE FURO PARA PARAFUSO |
| 1441 | PARAFUSO COM PORCA |
| 1442 | UNIÃO COM PINOS |
| 1442 | UNIÃO COM PARAFUSOS |
| 1443 | AFERROLHAMENTO |
| 1443 | TRAVAMENTO |
| 1444 | LIGAÇÃO |
| 1444 | UNIÃO |
| 1444 | JUNTURA |
| 1444 | APARELHO DE CONSTRUÇÃO (OU DE TIJOLOS) |
| 1445 | AGLUTINANTE |
| 1446 | CABOS INJETADOS |
| 1447 | NEGRO ANIMAL |
| 1448 | FARINHA DE OSSOS |
| 1449 | COLA DE OSSOS |
| 1450 | ÓLEO DE MOCOTÓ |
| 1451 | CAPOTA |
| 1451 | CAPÔ |
| 1451 | CAPOTA |
| 1451 | COBERTURA DE MOTOR |
| 1451 | TAMPÃO |
| 1451 | CHAPÉU |
| 1452 | FLANGE DE TAMPA |
| 1453 | VARETA ROSCADA DO CAPÔ |
| 1454 | TAMPA |
| 1455 | CAMPÂNULA DA CHAMINÉ |
| 1455 | CANO DE CHAMINÉ |
| 1456 | SUPRESSOR |
| 1456 | SOPRADOR |
| 1456 | SOBREVOLTADOR |

| | |
|---|---|
| 1456 | INTENSIFICADOR |
| 1456 | ELEVADOR DE TENSÃO |
| 1457 | FREIO AUXILIAR |
| 1457 | SERVOFREIO |
| 1458 | POÇO DE ELEVADOR |
| 1458 | BAÚ |
| 1458 | COFRE |
| 1459 | BÓRAX |
| 1459 | TINCAL |
| 1459 | BORATO DE SÓDIO |
| 1460 | CURVA LIMITE |
| 1461 | FURO |
| 1461 | CALIBRE |
| 1461 | DIÂMETRO INTERNO |
| 1462 | FURAR |
| 1462 | BROQUEAR |
| 1462 | SONDAR |
| 1462 | VERRUMAR |
| 1463 | FURO DE SONDAGEM |
| 1464 | DIÂMETRO INTERNO DE UM TUBO |
| 1465 | CAMISA DE CILINDRO |
| 1466 | TORNEAR |
| 1467 | ÁCIDO BÓRICO |
| 1468 | PERFURAÇÃO |
| 1468 | BROQUEAMENTO |
| 1468 | ALESAGEM |
| 1468 | SONDAGEM |
| 1469 | MÁQUINA DE BROQUEAR E TORNEAR |
| 1469 | TORNO VERTICAL DE PRATO HORIZONTAL |
| 1470 | BARRA DE BROQUEAR OU DE SONDAR |
| 1470 | PORTA-BROCA |
| 1471 | BROQUEADEIRA |
| 1471 | SONDA |
| 1471 | MÁQUINA PERFURADEIRA |
| 1472 | FRESA DE BROQUEAR |
| 1473 | ALESAGEM COM TORNO |
| 1473 | MANDRILAGEM |
| 1474 | LUNETAS DE ALESAGEM |
| 1475 | ENSAIO DE PERFURAÇÃO |
| 1476 | APARAS DE FURAGEM |
| 1477 | BORO |
| 1478 | LIGAS DE BORO |
| 1479 | CARBURETO DE BORO |
| 1479 | CARBONETO DE BORO |
| 1480 | DIAMANTE NEGRO |
| 1480 | CARBONADO |
| 1481 | CUBO DE RODA |
| 1482 | ENTALHAMENTO |
| 1482 | EMBUTIMENTO |
| 1483 | TAMPA |
| 1484 | VIDRO CÔNCAVO |

**1181**

| | |
|---|---|
| 1484 | VIDRO DE GARRAFA |
| 1485 | MACACO A GARRAFA |
| 1486 | PLACA OU CHAPA DE ASSENTO |
| 1486 | CHAPA DE FUNDO |
| 1487 | BRONZE INFERIOR |
| 1488 | ENCHIMENTO PELO FUNDO |
| 1489 | FOLGA NA BASE DOS DENTES DE ENGRENAGEM |
| 1490 | CANTONEIRA DE FUNDO DE TANQUE |
| 1491 | PONTO MORTO INFERIOR |
| 1492 | DRENO DE FUNDO |
| 1493 | REGISTRO DE PURGA DE FUNDO |
| 1494 | FUNDO DO CILINDRO |
| 1495 | TUBULAÇÃO DE FUNDO |
| 1496 | PANELA DE VAZAR PELO FUNDO |
| 1497 | MATRIZ INFERIOR |
| 1497 | ESTAMPA INFERIOR |
| 1498 | VISTA POR BAIXO |
| 1499 | MACHO PARA FURO CEGO |
| 1499 | MACHO CILÌNDRICO |
| 1499 | MACHO PARA ACABAMENTO |
| 1500 | LIMITE |
| 1500 | CONTÉRMINO |
| 1500 | CONFIM |
| 1500 | UNIÃO DE JUNTA |
| 1501 | MANÔMETRO BOURDON |
| 1502 | BURNONITA |
| 1503 | COMPASSO DE MOLA |
| 1504 | RABECA |
| 1504 | PUA DE ARCO E CORDA |
| 1505 | SERRA DE VOLTEAR |
| 1505 | SERRA DE ARCO |
| 1505 | SERRA DE CONTORNAR |
| 1506 | ABAULAMENTO |
| 1506 | ARQUEAMENTO |
| 1507 | CAIXA |
| 1508 | FUNDIÇÃO EM CAIXA |
| 1509 | CABEÇA DE BIELA DE CAIXA FECHADA |
| 1510 | ACOPLAMENTO DE LUVA |
| 1511 | CHASSI-CAIXA |
| 1512 | PORCA CEGA |
| 1512 | PORCA DE CAPA |
| 1513 | CAVILHA DE CENTRAGEM |
| 1514 | ÉMBOLO OCO |
| 1514 | PISTÃO OCO |
| 1515 | CHAVE DE CAIXA |
| 1515 | CHAVE DE ENCAIXE |
| 1516 | REFORÇO |
| 1516 | BRAÇADEIRA |
| 1516 | ESTEIO |
| 1516 | PONTALETE |

| | |
|---|---|
| 1516 | TIRANTE |
| 1516 | CONTRAFIXA |
| 1516 | ARCO DE PUA |
| 1517 | CONTRAVENTAR |
| 1517 | FIRMAR |
| 1517 | ESTEIAR |
| 1517 | ESCORAR |
| 1518 | VIRABREQUIM COM PARAFUSO DE PRESSÃO |
| 1519 | VIRABREQUIM |
| 1519 | ARCO DE PUA |
| 1520 | BRAÇOS |
| 1520 | CRUZETAS DE ARMAÇÃO |
| 1521 | TRELIÇA |
| 1521 | CONTRAVENTAMENTO |
| 1521 | ESCORAMENTO |
| 1522 | CANTONEIRA |
| 1522 | SUPORTE |
| 1522 | CONSOLO |
| 1523 | SUPORTE MURAL |
| 1524 | ÁGUA SALOBRA |
| 1525 | MÉTODO DE BRAGG |
| 1525 | LEI DE BRAGG |
| 1526 | GUARNIÇÃO TRANÇADA |
| 1527 | CORDA TRANÇADA |
| 1528 | ARAME TRANÇADO |
| 1528 | FIO TRANÇADO |
| 1529 | FREIO |
| 1529 | PRENSA VIRADEIRA |
| 1530 | FREAR |
| 1531 | BLOCO DE FREIO |
| 1531 | SAPATA DE FREIO |
| 1532 | CILINDRO DE FREIO |
| 1532 | TAMBOR |
| 1533 | TAMBOR DE FREIO |
| 1534 | DEPÓSITO DE ÓLEO DE FREIO |
| 1535 | POTÊNCIA DO FREIO |
| 1536 | MORDAÇA DO FREIO |
| 1537 | ALAVANCA DO FREIO |
| 1538 | LONA DE FREIO |
| 1539 | ARTICULAÇÃO DO FREIO |
| 1540 | POTÊNCIA DE FRENAGEM |
| 1540 | POTÊNCIA EFETIVA DO FREIO |
| 1541 | ANEL DE FRENAGEM |
| 1542 | BLOCO DO FREIO |
| 1542 | SAPATA DO FREIO |
| 1543 | BLOCO DO FREIO |
| 1543 | SAPATA DO FREIO |
| 1544 | CINTA DE FREIO |
| 1545 | SISTEMA DE FREIOS |
| 1546 | VERIFICAÇÃO DO FREIO |
| 1546 | PROVA DE FREIO |

| | |
|---|---|
| 1547 | PESO DO FREIO |
| 1547 | CONTRAPESO DO FREIO |
| 1548 | POLIA DO FREIO |
| 1548 | VOLANTE DO FREIO |
| 1548 | RODA DO FREIO |
| 1549 | FRENAGEM |
| 1549 | FRENAÇÃO |
| 1550 | AÇÃO DO FREIO |
| 1550 | FRENAÇÃO |
| 1551 | ESFORÇO DE FRENAÇÃO |
| 1551 | FORÇA DE FRENAÇÃO |
| 1551 | POTÊNCIA DE FRENAÇÃO |
| 1552 | RESISTÊNCIA À FRENAÇÃO |
| 1553 | PRENSA BRINELL |
| 1554 | DERIVAÇÃO |
| 1555 | DERIVAÇÃO DE UMA CURVA |
| 1556 | RAMIFICAR-SE |
| 1556 | BIFURCAR-SE |
| 1557 | TUBULAÇÃO DE DERIVAÇÃO |
| 1558 | TUBO RAMAL |
| 1558 | CANO DE DERIVAÇÃO |
| 1559 | LIGAÇÃO EM T |
| 1560 | MARCA |
| 1560 | MARCA REGISTRADA |
| 1560 | MARCA DE FÁBRICA |
| 1560 | FERRETE |
| 1561 | TESTE DE RECALQUE DE CILINDRO |
| 1562 | LATÃO |
| 1562 | METAL AMARELO |
| 1562 | BRONZE |
| 1563 | LINGOTE DE LATÃO |
| 1564 | BANHO DE LUSTRO |
| 1565 | SEGMENTO DE FUNDO |
| 1565 | ANEL DE FUNDO |
| 1566 | FUNDIÇÃO DE LATÃO |
| 1567 | LATONAGEM |
| 1568 | FIO LAMINADO DE LATÃO |
| 1569 | LATÃO EM FOLHA |
| 1569 | LÂMINA DE LATÃO |
| 1569 | CHAPA DE LATÃO |
| 1570 | CONDUTO DE LATÃO |
| 1570 | TUBO DE LATÃO |
| 1571 | FIO DE LATÃO |
| 1571 | ARAME DE LATÃO |
| 1572 | BRONZES DE MANCAL |
| 1572 | MANCAL DE DUAS PEÇAS |
| 1573 | SOLDAR FORTE |
| 1573 | BRASAR |
| 1573 | ESTANHAR |
| 1574 | IMPLANTAÇÕES DE SOLDA FORTE |
| 1575 | COBRE EM FOLHA PARA CALDEIREIROS |

| | |
|---|---|
| 1575 | COBRE DE SOLDAGEM |
| 1576 | BRASAGEM |
| 1576 | SOLDA FORTE |
| 1577 | FORNO DE SOLDA FORTE |
| 1578 | INSERÇÕES DE SOLDA |
| 1579 | LARGURA OU COMPRIMENTO DE DENTE |
| 1580 | QUEBRAR |
| 1580 | INTERROMPER |
| 1580 | ROMPER |
| 1580 | FRATURAR |
| 1581 | PANE |
| 1581 | ENGUIÇO |
| 1581 | RUPTURA |
| 1581 | AVARIA |
| 1581 | FALHA |
| 1582 | VOLTAGEM DE RUPTURA |
| 1582 | TENSÃO DE RUPTURA |
| 1582 | TENSÃO MÍNIMA DE FUNCIONAMENTO |
| 1583 | DESBASTE INTERMEDIÁRIO |
| 1584 | COMPRIMENTO DE RUPTURA |
| 1585 | CARGA DE RUPTURA |
| 1586 | CARGA LIMITE DE ELASTICIDADE |
| 1587 | RODAGEM DE VEÍCULO |
| 1588 | RUPTURA |
| 1588 | ESMAGAMENTO |
| 1589 | ROMPIMENTO |
| 1589 | PERFURAÇÃO |
| 1590 | PORTA DE FERRO (DE FORNO CUBILÔ) |
| 1590 | PEITORIL DE ENCOSTO |
| 1591 | RESPIRADOURO |
| 1592 | DEPÓSITO DE TAMPA |
| 1593 | VÁLVULA DE ALÍVIO |
| 1593 | VÁLVULA DE SEGURANÇA |
| 1594 | PERDA POR PAUSA |
| 1595 | FORQUILHA |
| 1595 | TUBO BIFURCADO |
| 1595 | TUBO EM Y |
| 1596 | LADRILHO |
| 1596 | TIJOLO |
| 1597 | REVESTIR COM TIJOLO |
| 1597 | LADRILHAR |
| 1598 | BARRO OU ARGILA DE FABRICAR TIJOLOS |
| 1599 | ALICERCE DE TIJOLOS |
| 1600 | ENCAIXADO EM OBRA DE ALVENARIA |
| 1601 | ASSENTAMENTO DE TIJOLO |
| 1602 | ALVENARIA DE TIJOLO |
| 1603 | ACESSO |
| 1603 | PONTÃO |
| 1603 | PONTE SOBRE ESTACAS |
| 1604 | FORMAÇÃO DE VAZIOS EM CARGA DE PÓ |
| 1604 | FORMAÇÃO DE PONTE |

# 1183

| | | | |
|---|---|---|---|
| 1605 | PASSO DO SISTEMA BRIGGS DE TUBOS | 1644 | PEDRA BRITADA |
| 1606 | ARAME RECOZIDO BRILHANTE | 1645 | BROMETO DE PRATA |
| 1607 | PARAFUSO POLIDO | 1645 | BROMITA |
| 1608 | BANHO POLIDOR | 1646 | BROMATO |
| 1608 | BANHO ABRILHANTADOR | 1647 | ÁCIDO BRÔMICO |
| 1609 | ACABAMENTO LUSTROSO | 1648 | BROMETO |
| 1610 | FIO DE FERRO CLARO CRU | 1648 | BROMURETO |
| 1611 | SUPERFÍCIE METÁLICA POLIDA | 1649 | BRÔMIO |
| 1612 | PORCA POLIDA | 1649 | BROMO |
| 1613 | RUBRO CEREJA | 1650 | BRONZE |
| 1613 | RUBRO CLARO | 1651 | REVESTIR DE BRONZE |
| 1613 | RUBRO VIVO | 1651 | BRONZEAR |
| 1614 | QUENTE AO RUBRO CEREJA | 1652 | LIMALHA DE BRONZE |
| 1615 | AGENTE ABRILHANTADOR | 1652 | BRONZE EM PÓ |
| 1616 | POLIMENTO | 1652 | PURPURINA |
| 1616 | BRILHO | 1653 | TUBO DE BRONZE |
| 1616 | LUSTRO | 1654 | ARAME DE BRONZE |
| 1617 | ÁGUA SALGADA | 1654 | FIO DE BRONZE |
| 1617 | SALMOURA | 1655 | BRONZE ANTIÁCIDO |
| 1618 | TESTE DE DUREZA BRINELL | 1656 | BRONZE ALFA |
| 1618 | ENSAIO DE DUREZA BRINELL | 1657 | BRONZE COMUM |
| 1619 | ÍNDICE DE DUREZA BRINELL | 1657 | BRONZE COMERCIAL |
| 1620 | ENSAIO BRINELL | 1658 | BRONZE DURO |
| 1621 | REGULAGEM DE UMA FERRAMENTA | 1659 | BRONZE AO ESTANHO |
| 1622 | BRIQUETA | 1659 | BRONZE PARA FERRAGEM |
| 1623 | COMPACTADO | 1659 | BRONZE PARA PARAFUSOS |
| 1623 | PASTILHA DE PÓ COMPRIMIDO | 1660 | BRONZE PLÁSTICO |
| 1624 | METAL BRITÂNIA OU BRETANHA | 1660 | BRONZE DE MANCAL |
| 1625 | UNIDADE TÉRMICA INGLESA (BTU) | 1661 | BRONZE DE MOLA |
| 1626 | UNIDADE TÉRMICA INGLESA (BTU) | 1662 | BRONZE PARA ESTÁTUAS |
| 1627 | FRÁGIL | 1663 | BRONZE COMERCIAL BRUNIDO |
| 1627 | QUEBRADIÇO | 1663 | BRONZE ORNAMENTAL |
| 1628 | FRAGILIDADE | 1664 | BRONZEAMENTO |
| 1629 | FRAGILIDADE DE FERRO | 1665 | LINHITA |
| 1630 | FRAGILIDADE DE ÁCIDO | 1666 | AGLOMERADO DE LINHITA |
| 1631 | FRAGILIDADE AO AZUL | 1667 | ALCATRÃO DE LINHITA |
| 1632 | FRAGILIDADE DE ENTALHE | 1668 | ÓLEO DE ALCATRÃO DE LINHITA |
| 1633 | FRAGILIDADE REOTRÓPICA | 1669 | COBRE PARA ESCOVAS ELÉTRICAS |
| 1634 | FRAGILIDADE DE REVENIDO | 1670 | BOLHA DE AR |
| 1635 | ALARGAR OS FUROS DE REBITES | 1671 | BOLHA DE GÁS |
| 1636 | ESCAREADOR | 1672 | FORMAÇÃO DE BOLHAS |
| 1636 | DESBASTADOR | 1673 | PISTÃO DE VÁLVULA |
| 1637 | MANDRILAGEM | 1673 | PANELA |
| 1637 | ESCAREAÇÃO | 1674 | CAÇAMBA |
| 1637 | USINAGEM COM BROCHA | 1674 | BALDE |
| 1638 | ALARGAMENTO DOS FUROS DOS REBITES | 1674 | ALCATRUZ |
| 1639 | TRAVE DE ABA LARGA | 1675 | TRANSPORTADOR DE CAÇAMBA |
| 1640 | FERRO EM T DE ABA LARGA | 1676 | ELEVADOR DE CAÇAMBA |
| 1641 | VIGOTAS DE ABA LARGA | 1677 | PALHETA DE RODA HIDRÁULICA |
| 1642 | LAMINADOR TRANSVERSAL | 1678 | ASSENTO INDIVIDUAL |
| 1643 | CILINDROS TRANSVERSAIS PARA LAMINAÇÃO | 1679 | CHAPA EMBUTIDA |

| | |
|---|---|
| 1679 | CHAPA ABAULADA |
| 1680 | PREGAS |
| 1681 | FLAMBAGEM |
| 1681 | CAMBAGEM |
| 1682 | RESISTÊNCIA À FLAMBAGEM |
| 1683 | ANCINHO |
| 1684 | DISCO DE POLIR |
| 1685 | COURO DE BÚFALO |
| 1686 | AMORTECEDOR |
| 1686 | PÁRA-CHOQUE |
| 1686 | TAMPA |
| 1686 | POLIDOR |
| 1687 | BATERIA COMPENSADORA |
| 1688 | MOLA AMORTECEDORA OU COMPENSADORA |
| 1689 | MEMÓRIA INTERMEDIÁRIA |
| 1690 | SAIS DE POLIMENTO |
| 1691 | POLIMENTO |
| 1692 | COMPOSTO PARA POLIMENTO |
| 1693 | DISCO OU RODA DE POLIR |
| 1694 | CONSTRUIR |
| 1695 | EXCEDENTE |
| 1695 | INCREMENTO |
| 1695 | DESENVOLVIMENTO |
| 1696 | PROCESSO DE RECARREGAMENTO |
| 1697 | BLOCOS DE CONSTRUÇÃO |
| 1697 | PERPIANHOS |
| 1697 | TIJOLO PERFURADO |
| 1698 | EMPREITEIRO DE OBRA |
| 1699 | LOCAL DE CONSTRUÇÃO |
| 1700 | PEDRA DE CONSTRUÇÃO |
| 1701 | REFORÇO |
| 1701 | INTENSIFICAÇÃO |
| 1701 | DEPOSIÇÃO DE METAL PARA AUMENTAR PEÇAS |
| 1701 | ACELERAÇÃO GRADUAL |
| 1702 | VIGA EMBUTIDA |
| 1703 | VIGA EMBUTIDA NAS PONTAS |
| 1704 | ELEMENTO DE ARMAÇÃO INCORPORADO |
| 1705 | COMPOSTO |
| 1705 | ARMADO |
| 1705 | ACUMULAÇÃO |
| 1706 | MANIVELA COMPOSTA |
| 1707 | LASCA ADERENTE |
| 1708 | FLANGE MÓVEL |
| 1708 | FLANGE SOLTO |
| 1709 | PISTÃO DE DUAS PEÇAS |
| 1710 | PLACA MOLDADA |
| 1711 | EMPOLA |
| 1711 | LÂMPADA |
| 1711 | GLOBO DE TERMÔMETRO |
| 1712 | CANTONEIRA DE BULBO |
| 1713 | CANTONEIRAS |
| 1714 | FERRO CHATO COM BULBO |
| 1715 | TRILHOS DE FLANGE |
| 1716 | FERRO DE BULBO |
| 1717 | AMPOLA DE TERMÔMETRO |
| 1718 | PIPETA DE CILINDRO |
| 1719 | FERRO DE BULBO EM T |
| 1720 | SALIÊNCIA |
| 1720 | PROTUBERÂNCIA |
| 1720 | CONVEXIDADE |
| 1720 | ABAULAMENTO |
| 1721 | INCHAR |
| 1721 | ABAULAR-SE |
| 1722 | ABAULADO |
| 1723 | EXPANSÃO INTERNA DE UM CORPO |
| 1723 | ALARGAMENTO |
| 1723 | AMPLIAÇÃO |
| 1724 | DENSIDADE APARENTE |
| 1725 | PESO ESPECÍFICO DA MASSA |
| 1725 | PESO ESPECÍFICO APARENTE |
| 1726 | TABIQUE |
| 1726 | ANTEPARO |
| 1727 | ESTIRAGEM EM GROSSO |
| 1727 | SARILHO DE ESTIRAR ARAME GROSSO |
| 1728 | PANELA DE VAZAR PELA BICA |
| 1728 | CUBA PORTÁTIL DE FUNDIÇÃO |
| 1729 | METAL PRECIOSO EM BARRAS |
| 1730 | BARRA DE METAL PRECIOSO |
| 1731 | MALACATO |
| 1731 | CARROCEL |
| 1732 | PÁRA-CHOQUE |
| 1732 | AMORTECEDOR |
| 1732 | ESPERA |
| 1732 | BATENTE |
| 1733 | PENEIRA DE SACUDIR |
| 1734 | FERRAMENTA DE MARTELAGEM A MÃO |
| 1735 | CAVALETE |
| 1736 | PACOTE |
| 1736 | EMBRULHO |
| 1736 | FEIXE |
| 1737 | ATAR |
| 1737 | ENFEIXAR |
| 1737 | EMPACOTAR |
| 1738 | CINTA DE FERRO |
| 1739 | BELICHE |
| 1739 | ARMÁRIO-CAMA |
| 1740 | CARVOEIRA |
| 1740 | PAIOL DE CARVÃO |
| 1741 | BICO DE BUNSEN |
| 1742 | FLUTUABILIDADE |

| | |
|---|---|
| 1742 | FORÇA ASCENDENTE |
| 1742 | IMPULSO DE BAIXO PARA CIMA |
| 1743 | BURETA |
| 1743 | CONTA-GOTAS DE PRECISÃO |
| 1744 | TUBULAÇÃO SUBTERRÂNEA |
| 1745 | QUEIMAR |
| 1745 | CALCINAR |
| 1746 | AQUECER O FERRO |
| 1747 | COMBUSTÃO NUCLEAR |
| 1748 | LINGOTE QUEIMADO |
| 1749 | QUEIMADOR |
| 1749 | MAÇARICO |
| 1749 | CÂMARA DE COMBUSTÃO |
| 1749 | COMBUSTOR |
| 1749 | BICO DE GÁS |
| 1750 | QUEIMA |
| 1750 | COMBUSTÃO |
| 1750 | CALCINAÇÃO |
| 1750 | COZIMENTO |
| 1751 | CALEFAÇÃO A GÁS |
| 1752 | CALEFAÇÃO A ÓLEO |
| 1752 | CALEFAÇÃO A COMBUSTÍVEL |
| 1753 | CALEFAÇÃO A CARVÃO PULVERIZADO |
| 1754 | AQUECIMENTO DO FERRO |
| 1755 | LUSTRO |
| 1755 | BRILHO |
| 1756 | BRUNIR |
| 1756 | POLIR |
| 1756 | LUSTRAR |
| 1757 | BRUNIDOR |
| 1757 | LUSTRADOR |
| 1757 | POLIDOR |
| 1758 | BRUNIMENTO |
| 1758 | POLIMENTO |
| 1759 | ESFERAS DE BRUNIMENTO |
| 1760 | TIJOLO COZIDO |
| 1761 | DEPÓSITO QUEIMADO |
| 1762 | FERRO QUEIMADO |
| 1763 | AÇO QUEIMADO |
| 1764 | REBARBA |
| 1764 | RESSALTO |
| 1765 | FRESA REMOVEDORA DE REBARBA |
| 1766 | REBARBAÇÃO |
| 1767 | ESTOURO |
| 1767 | EXPLOSÃO |
| 1768 | RUPTURA DE UM TUBO |
| 1769 | RUPTURA DE POLIA |
| 1769 | RUPTURA DE VOLANTE |
| 1770 | BARRAMENTO |
| 1770 | BARRA COLETORA |
| 1770 | BARRA ÔNIBUS |

| | |
|---|---|
| 1770 | TRILHO DE CONTATO |
| 1771 | MANCAL DE UMA SÓ PEÇA |
| 1772 | SEGUNDA PUDLAGEM |
| 1772 | REFINAÇÃO DE FERRO FORJADO |
| 1773 | BUCHA |
| 1773 | EMBUCHAMENTO |
| 1773 | MANGUITO |
| 1773 | REDUTOR MACHO-FÊMEA |
| 1773 | CASQUILHO |
| 1773 | ANEL |
| 1774 | TUBO PORTA-VENTO DE ALTO-FORNO |
| 1774 | CONDUTOR CIRCULAR DE VENTO QUENTE |
| 1775 | BUTANO |
| 1776 | JUNTA DE TOPO |
| 1776 | JUNTA COM COBREJUNTA |
| 1777 | JUNTA SOLDADA DOS DOIS LADOS |
| 1778 | JUNTA DE TOPO A TOPO |
| 1778 | JUNTA DE ENCONTRO |
| 1779 | JUNTA SOLDADA DE UM SÓ LADO |
| 1780 | COURO OU CABEDAL DE PRIMEIRA QUALIDADE |
| 1781 | JUNTA REBITADA POR COBREJUNTA |
| 1782 | TIRA OU FITA DE TOPO |
| 1782 | JUNTA SOLDADA |
| 1782 | UNIÃO COM COBREJUNTAS |
| 1783 | TIRA OU FITA DE TOPO |
| 1783 | COBREJUNTA |
| 1784 | SOLDA DE TOPO |
| 1784 | SOLDA POR CONTATO |
| 1785 | SOLDAR PELO TOPO |
| 1785 | SOLDAR POR CONTATO |
| 1786 | ESPESSURA DE SOLDA DE TOPO |
| 1787 | SOLDAGEM EM K SEM SEPARAÇÃO |
| 1788 | SOLDAGEM DUPLA FECHADA |
| 1789 | SOLDAGEM EM MEIO V SEM SEPARAÇÃO |
| 1790 | JUNTA DE SOLDAGEM EM J FECHADA |
| 1791 | SOLDAGEM EM I SEM SEPARAÇÃO DAS BORDAS |
| 1792 | SOLDAGEM CÔNCAVA |
| 1793 | CHANFRO (SOLDAGEM) EM K |
| 1794 | SOLDAGEM POR CENTELHA |
| 1795 | SOLDAGEM EM T |
| 1796 | SOLDAGEM EM K COM SEPARAÇÃO |
| 1797 | SOLDAGEM EM MEIO V COM SEPARAÇÃO |
| 1798 | SOLDAGEM EM J COM SEPARAÇÃO |
| 1799 | SOLDAGEM DE TOPO POR RESISTÊNCIA |
| 1800 | CHANFRO EM MEIO V |
| 1801 | SOLDAGEM EM T |
| 1802 | SOLDAGEM POR APROXIMAÇÃO |
| 1803 | TUBO SOLDADO A TOPO |
| 1804 | TUBO SOLDADO POR CONTATO |

| | |
|---|---|
| 1805 | SOLDAGEM DE TOPO |
| 1805 | SOLDAGEM POR CONTATO |
| 1806 | SOLDAGEM A TOPO POR CENTELHA |
| 1807 | SOLDAGEM A TOPO POR RESISTÊNCIA |
| 1808 | |
| 1809 | SOLDAGEM A TOPO |
| 1810 | ORIFÍCIOS A SOLDAR (NA PONTA, POR DENTRO) |
| 1811 | VÁLVULA DE ESTRANGULAMENTO |
| 1811 | VÁLVULA BORBOLETA |
| 1812 | BOTÃO |
| 1813 | CABEÇA REDONDA DE PARAFUSO |
| 1814 | ROSCA TRAPEZOIDAL |
| 1815 | PARAFUSO DE ROSCA TRAPEZOIDAL |
| 1816 | BUTILENO |
| 1817 | ÁCIDO BUTÍRICO |
| 1818 | BY-PASS |
| 1818 | PASSAGEM AUXILIAR |
| 1818 | PASSAGEM LATERAL |
| 1818 | TUBO DE DERIVAÇÃO |
| 1819 | VÁLVULA AUXILIAR |
| 1819 | VÁLVULA DE DESVIO |
| 1819 | VÁLVULA DE DESCARGA |
| 1820 | PRODUTO DERIVADO |
| 1820 | SUBPRODUTO |
| 1821 | DERIVAÇÃO |
| 1821 | BY-PASS |
| 1822 | CHAVE DE GANCHO |
| 1823 | MOLA EM C |
| 1824 | CABINA ADIANTADA |
| 1825 | CABO |
| 1826 | VIA FÉRREA DE TRAÇÃO A CABO |
| 1826 | FUNICULAR |
| 1827 | TERMINAL DO CABO |
| 1827 | BORNE DO CABO |
| 1828 | CABLAGEM |
| 1829 | CABO CALABROTEADO |
| 1830 | TELEGRAMA |
| 1830 | CABOGRAMA |
| 1831 | CÁDMIO |
| 1832 | CADMIAÇÃO |
| 1833 | CÉSIO |
| 1834 | LINGOTE DE SAÍDA |
| 1835 | CARVÃO FUSÍVEL |
| 1835 | HULHA GORDA |
| 1835 | CARVÃO BETUMINOSO |
| 1836 | ESMITSONITA |
| 1836 | CALAMINA |
| 1837 | TRAVERTINO |
| 1837 | CONCREÇÃO CALCÁRIA |
| 1838 | TUFO CALCÁRIO |
| 1839 | CALCINAÇÃO |
| 1840 | CALCINAÇÃO DE MINERAIS |
| 1841 | CALCINAR OS MINERAIS |
| 1842 | MAGNÉSIA CALCINADA |
| 1843 | FORNO DE CALCINAÇÃO |
| 1844 | CALCITA |
| 1845 | ESPATO CALCÁRIO |
| 1846 | CÁLCIO |
| 1847 | BICARBONATO DE CÁLCIO |
| 1848 | CARBURETO DE CÁLCIO |
| 1849 | CARBONATO DE CÁLCIO |
| 1850 | CLORETO DE CÁLCIO |
| 1851 | HIDRÓXIDO DE CÁLCIO |
| 1851 | CAL HIDRATADA |
| 1851 | CAL APAGADA |
| 1851 | HIDRATO DE CAL |
| 1852 | MONOSSULFURETO DE CAL |
| 1853 | OXALATO DE CÁLCIO |
| 1854 | ÓXIDO DE CÁLCIO |
| 1854 | CAL VIRGEM |
| 1854 | CAL VIVA |
| 1855 | FOSFATO DE CÁLCIO |
| 1856 | SULFATO DE CÁLCIO |
| 1856 | GESSO DE PARIS |
| 1857 | CALCULAR |
| 1858 | VALOR TEÓRICO |
| 1858 | VALOR CALCULADO |
| 1859 | MÁQUINA CALCULADORA |
| 1860 | CÁLCULO |
| 1861 | CALIBRAR |
| 1861 | CALCULAR A CAPACIDADE |
| 1862 | CADEIAS OU CORRENTES CALIBRADAS |
| 1863 | CALIBRAGEM (DE UM DEPÓSITO) |
| 1864 | PRENSA MECÂNICA DE CALIBRAR E ESTAMPAR |
| 1865 | MÁQUINA DE CALIBRAR |
| 1866 | MOLA DE CALIBRAR |
| 1867 | GRADUAÇÃO |
| 1867 | CALIBRAÇÃO |
| 1868 | CONDENSADOR-PADRÃO |
| 1869 | ERRO DE CALIBRAGEM |
| 1870 | CALIBRE |
| 1870 | CALIBRADOR |
| 1870 | COMPASSO |
| 1871 | CALIBRE COM RÉGUA DE PROFUNDIDADE |
| 1872 | MACETE DE CALAFETAR |
| 1872 | MARTELO DE ENCALCAR |
| 1873 | COMPASSO DE ESPESSURA |
| 1874 | COMPASSO DE CALIBRE |
| 1875 | MICRÔMETRO |
| 1876 | ELÉTRODO DE CALOMEL |

| | |
|---|---|
| 1877 | CALORÍMETRO |
| 1878 | CALORIMÉTRICO |
| 1879 | BOMBA CALORIMÉTRICA |
| 1880 | ANÁLISE CALORIMÉTRICA |
| 1881 | CALORIMETRIA |
| 1882 | CALORIZAÇÃO |
| 1883 | CAME |
| 1883 | EXCÊNTRICO |
| 1884 | CARREIRA DO CAME |
| 1884 | AÇÃO DO CAME |
| 1884 | LEVANTAMENTO DO CAME |
| 1885 | ROLETE DO CAME |
| 1885 | SEGUIDOR DO CAME |
| 1885 | PROPULSOR DO CAME |
| 1886 | MECANISMO DE CAME |
| 1887 | PASSADOR DE CAME |
| 1888 | EIXO DE CAMES |
| 1888 | ÁRVORE DE CAMES |
| 1889 | CAMBAMENTO |
| 1889 | ABAULAMENTO |
| 1889 | CAMBAGEM |
| 1889 | ÂNGULO DE QUEDA |
| 1890 | PÊLO DE CAMELO |
| 1891 | CORREIA DE PÊLO DE CAMELO |
| 1892 | TIRA DE RECAUCHUTAGEM |
| 1893 | CÂNFORA |
| 1894 | ÓLEO DE CÂNFORA |
| 1895 | ROLO DE CAME |
| 1895 | SEGUIDOR DE CAME |
| 1896 | EIXO DE CAMES |
| 1896 | ÁRVORE DE CAMES |
| 1897 | TORNO DE ÁRVORE OU EIXO DE CAMES |
| 1898 | AMIANTO DO CANADÁ |
| 1899 | CANDELA |
| 1899 | VELA |
| 1900 | POTÊNCIA LUMINOSA |
| 1901 | CARVÃO DE PEDRA GORDO |
| 1901 | CARVÃO DE GÁS |
| 1902 | CHANFRO |
| 1902 | ESQUINA |
| 1902 | ÂNGULO SALIENTE |
| 1902 | BISEL |
| 1902 | CANTO |
| 1902 | PLANO INCLINADO |
| 1903 | LIMA TRIANGULAR ACHATADA |
| 1903 | LIMA LANCETEIRA TRIANGULAR |
| 1904 | CANTILÉVER |
| 1905 | TRAVESSÃO CANTILÉVER |
| 1905 | VIGA CANTILÉVER |
| 1906 | LONA |
| 1907 | CORREIA DE LONA |

| | |
|---|---|
| 1908 | MANGUEIRA DE LONA |
| 1909 | REVESTIR |
| 1909 | ENCAPAR |
| 1910 | CALOTA |
| 1910 | CAPITEL |
| 1910 | TAMPA |
| 1910 | CAPA |
| 1910 | COBERTA |
| 1911 | CALOTA DE ESFERA |
| 1912 | TAMPA DE MANCAL |
| 1913 | PARAFUSO DE REMATE |
| 1913 | PARAFUSO DE CABEÇA |
| 1914 | APTO PARA FUSÃO |
| 1915 | APTO PARA LAMINAÇÃO |
| 1916 | CONDENSADOR |
| 1916 | CAPACITOR |
| 1917 | CAPACIDADE |
| 1917 | POTÊNCIA |
| 1917 | ALCANCE |
| 1918 | CAPACIDADE DE RESISTÊNCIA AO CHOQUE |
| 1919 | BEDAME |
| 1920 | CAPILARIDADE |
| 1920 | AÇÃO CAPILAR |
| 1921 | TUBO CAPILAR |
| 1922 | ASPIRAÇÃO POR CAPILARIDADE |
| 1923 | CONSTANTE CAPILAR |
| 1924 | DEPRESSÃO CAPILAR |
| 1925 | ASCENSÃO CAPILAR |
| 1925 | ELEVAÇÃO CAPILAR |
| 1926 | CAPITEL DE COLUNA |
| 1927 | FORMAÇÃO DE CROSTA |
| 1928 | TIRAS DE METAL DE REVESTIMENTO |
| 1929 | CABRESTANTE |
| 1930 | PARAFUSO COM CABO |
| 1930 | PARAFUSO COM BRAÇO |
| 1931 | TORNO-REVÓLVER |
| 1932 | BASCULADOR DE VAGONETE |
| 1932 | BASCULADOR DE CARRINHO |
| 1933 | CARBURETO |
| 1934 | PRECIPITAÇÃO DE CARBURETO |
| 1935 | ESCAREADOR DE PONTA DE CARBONETO |
| 1936 | BROCA DE PONTA DE CARBONETO |
| 1937 | HIDRATO DE CARBONO |
| 1937 | CARBOIDRATO |
| 1938 | ÁCIDO CARBÓLICO |
| 1938 | ÁCIDO FÉNICO |
| 1938 | FENOL |
| 1939 | CARBOLEÍNA |
| 1940 | CARVÃO |
| 1940 | CARBONO |

| | | | |
|---|---|---|---|
| 1941 | ARCO COM ELÉTRODO DE CARBONO | 1982 | CARBURADOR |
| 1942 | CORTE POR ARCO DE CARBONO | 1983 | ÁLCOOL CARBURADO |
| 1943 | SOLDAGEM COM ARCO DE CARBONO | 1984 | CARBURADOR |
| 1944 | ARCO NÃO PROTEGIDO POR ELÉTRODO DE CARBONO | 1985 | CARBURAÇÃO DO FERRO |
| 1945 | ARCO PROTEGIDO POR ELÉTRODO DE CARBONO | 1986 | CARBURAR O FERRO |
| 1946 | ESCOVA DE CARVÃO | 1987 | CARBURAÇÃO |
| 1947 | PORCENTAGEM DE CARBONO | 1988 | CARBURANTES |
| 1947 | TEOR DE CARBONO | 1989 | CAIXA DE CEMENTAÇÃO |
| 1947 | PROPORÇÃO DE CARBONO | 1990 | CHAMA CARBURANTE |

1941 ARCO COM ELÉTRODO DE CARBONO
1942 CORTE POR ARCO DE CARBONO
1943 SOLDAGEM COM ARCO DE CARBONO
1944 ARCO NÃO PROTEGIDO POR ELÉTRODO DE CARBONO
1945 ARCO PROTEGIDO POR ELÉTRODO DE CARBONO
1946 ESCOVA DE CARVÃO
1947 PORCENTAGEM DE CARBONO
1947 TEOR DE CARBONO
1947 PROPORÇÃO DE CARBONO
1948 GÁS CARBÔNICO
1948 ANIDRIDO CARBÔNICO
1949 ÁCIDO CARBÔNICO
1950 ELÉTRODO DE CARBONO
1951 LÂMPADA DE FILAMENTO DE CARVÃO
1952 ÓXIDO DE CARBONO
1952 MONÓXIDO DE CARBONO
1953 RECARBURAÇÃO
1954 AÇO AO CARBONO
1955 BARRAS DE AÇO AO CARBONO
1956 CHAPAS DE AÇO AO CARBONO
1957 AÇO DURO DE ALTO TEOR EM CARBONO
1958 AÇO DOCE
1959 AÇO SEMI-DOCE
1960 TETRACLORETO DE CARBONO
1961 SEM CARBONO
1961 ISENTO DE CARBONO
1962 CARBONO COMBINADO
1963 CARBONO DISSOLVIDO
1964 SULFETO DE CARBONO
1965 PORCENTAGEM DE CARBONO
1966 CARBONÍFERO
1967 DIAMANTE NEGRO
1968 CARBONATO
1969 PEDRA CALCÁRIA CARBONÍFERA
1970 CARBONIZAÇÃO
1971 CARBONIZAR
1971 CARBONAR
1972 CARBONITRIFICAÇÃO
1973 ATMOSFERA DE CARBONITRURAÇÃO
1974 CARBONIZAÇÃO
1975 CARBONIZAÇÃO
1975 COQUIFICAÇÃO
1976 CARBONILO
1977 FERRO DE CARBONILO
1978 NÍQUEL DE CARBONILO
1979 PÓ DE CARBONILO
1980 CARBORUNDO
1981 GARRAFÃO
1981 BOMBONA

1982 CARBURADOR
1983 ÁLCOOL CARBURADO
1984 CARBURADOR
1985 CARBURAÇÃO DO FERRO
1986 CARBURAR O FERRO
1987 CARBURAÇÃO
1988 CARBURANTES
1989 CAIXA DE CEMENTAÇÃO
1990 CHAMA CARBURANTE
1991 FORNO DE CARBURAÇÃO
1992 CEMENTAÇÃO POR GÁS
1993 CEMENTAÇÃO HOMOGÊNEA
1994 BANHO DE CEMENTAÇÃO
1995 CEMENTAÇÃO SELETIVA
1996 CEMENTAÇÃO EM CAIXA
1997 ACOPLAMENTO CARDAN
1998 SUSPENSÃO CARDAN
1999 CARTOLINA
1999 PAPELÃO
2000 DEFORMAÇÃO PRINCIPAL
2001 CARDIÓIDE
2002 PAPEL CARMIM
2003 CERA DE CARNAÚBA
2004 CICLO DE CARNOT
2005 CARPINTEIRO
2006 CARPINTARIA
2007 MÁQUINA DE APLAINAR EQUIPADA COM CARRO
2008 MOLA DE CARRO
2009 BROCA CÔNICA
2009 PERNO CÔNICO
2010 EIXO DE SUPORTE
2010 EIXO PORTADOR
2011 CAPACIDADE DE CARGA
2012 CHAPA SECA
2012 ESVAZIADOR DE CAIXAS
2013 CARRO
2013 CARROÇA
2014 COORDENADAS CARTESIANAS
2015 CARTUCHO
2016 LATÃO PARA CARTUCHOS
2017 CARRO AGRÍCOLA
2018 CASCATA
2019 CAIXA
2019 INVÓLUCRO
2019 CAPA
2019 CAMADA CEMENTADA
2020 PROFUNDIDADE DE CEMENTAÇÃO
2021 CEMENTAÇÃO
2021 TÊMPERA DE SUPERFÍCIE
2022 CEMENTO

| | |
|---|---|
| 2023 | CEMENTAÇÃO PARCIAL |
| 2023 | TÊMPERA DE SUPERFÍCIE |
| 2023 | CEMENTAÇÃO DAS PEÇAS DE AÇO DOCE |
| 2024 | MATERIAIS PARA CEMENTAÇÃO |
| 2025 | CASEÍNA |
| 2026 | CÁRTER |
| 2026 | CARCAÇA |
| 2026 | ARMAÇÃO |
| 2026 | CAIXA |
| 2027 | CALIBRE PARA TUBOS |
| 2028 | CASSETTE |
| 2029 | OVAL CASSINIANA |
| 2029 | CASSINÓIDE |
| 2030 | VAZAR |
| 2030 | MOLDAR |
| 2030 | FUNDIR |
| 2030 | LINGOTAR |
| 2031 | LATÃO FUNDIDO |
| 2032 | REVESTIMENTO FUNDIDO |
| 2033 | FUROS ORIGINADOS DA FUNDIÇÃO |
| 2034 | FERRO FUNDIDO |
| 2035 | TUBO DE FERRO FUNDIDO |
| 2035 | CARRO DE FERRO FUNDIDO |
| 2035 | TUBO CENTRIFUGADO |
| 2036 | TERMITA PARA FUNDIÇÃO |
| 2037 | LIGA DE FERRO FUNDIDO |
| 2038 | FERRO FUNDIDO BRANCO |
| 2038 | FERRO FUNDIDO EM COQUILHA |
| 2039 | FUNDIÇÃO RESISTENTE À CORROSÃO |
| 2040 | FERRO FUNDIDO DÚCTIL |
| 2040 | FERRO MODULAR |
| 2041 | FERRO-GUSA |
| 2041 | FERRO FUNDIDO CINZENTO |
| 2042 | FERRO FUNDIDO DE ALTA RESISTÊNCIA |
| 2043 | FERRO FUNDIDO MALEÁVEL |
| 2044 | FERRO FUNDIDO MOSQUEADO |
| 2045 | FERRO DÚCTIL |
| 2045 | FERRO MODULAR |
| 2046 | FERRO FUNDIDO PERLÍTICO |
| 2047 | FERRO FUNDIDO PERLÍTICO MALEÁVEL |
| 2048 | FERRO FUNDIDO RESISTENTE AO DESGASTE |
| 2049 | FUNDIÇÃO BRANCA |
| 2050 | METAL FUNDIDO |
| 2051 | PREGO FUNDIDO |
| 2052 | PLACA MODELO |
| 2053 | PROCESSO DE FUNDIÇÃO TUBULAR |
| 2054 | COADO EM UMA SÓ PEÇA |
| 2054 | PROCEDENTE DA FUNDIÇÃO |
| 2055 | AÇO FUNDIDO |
| 2056 | CENTRO DE RODA DE AÇO FUNDIDO |
| 2057 | AÇO FUNDIDO |
| 2057 | AÇO DE CADINHO |
| 2058 | ESTRUTURA DE LIGAS |
| 2059 | DENTE BRUTO DE FUNDIÇÃO |
| 2060 | MONTAGEM POR SOLDA DE PEÇAS FUNDIDAS |
| 2061 | CRESCIMENTO DE FERRO FUNDIDO |
| 2062 | CANO DE FERRO FUNDIDO |
| 2063 | FLANGE FUNDIDO COM A PEÇA |
| 2064 | FUSIBILIDADE |
| 2064 | FUNDIBILIDADE |
| 2065 | PROVA DE CAPACIDADE DE FUSÃO |
| 2066 | RODÍZIO |
| 2066 | FUNDIDOR |
| 2067 | ÂNGULO DE AVANÇO |
| 2068 | FUNDIÇÃO |
| 2069 | PEÇA FUNDIDA |
| 2069 | LINGOTE |
| 2070 | FUSÃO (OPERAÇÃO) |
| 2071 | PÁTIO DE VAZAMENTO |
| 2071 | ÁREA DE VAZAMENTO |
| 2072 | VAGONETES PARA FUNDIÇÃO |
| 2073 | COBRE PARA FUNDIÇÃO |
| 2074 | FUNDIÇÃO SEM TENSÕES INTERNAS |
| 2075 | FUNDIÇÃO SEM BOLSAS DE SEGREGAÇÃO |
| 2076 | FUNDIÇÃO (LOTE DE...) |
| 2077 | PÁTIO DE FUNDIÇÃO |
| 2078 | DEFORMAÇÕES DE PEÇAS FUNDIDAS |
| 2079 | PEÇA DE FUNDIÇÃO |
| 2080 | PEÇAS FUNDIDAS |
| 2081 | TENSÃO DE FUNDIÇÃO |
| 2082 | PEÇAS FUNDIDAS ANTICORROSIVAS |
| 2083 | PEÇAS MOLDADAS EM FUNDIÇÃO GRIS |
| 2084 | PEÇAS FUNDIDAS RESISTENTES AO CALOR |
| 2085 | PORCA DE ENTALHES |
| 2085 | PORCA AMEADA |
| 2085 | PORCA ENTALHADA |
| 2085 | PORCA ACASTELADA |
| 2086 | ÓLEO DE RÍCINO |
| 2087 | TURCO |
| 2087 | LUVA DE CENTRAGEM |
| 2088 | OLHO DE GATO |
| 2089 | CURVA CATACÁUSTICA |
| 2090 | CATALISAÇÃO |
| 2090 | CATÁLISE |
| 2091 | CATALISADOR |
| 2092 | CATALÍTICO |
| 2093 | ESPERA |
| 2093 | FECHO |
| 2093 | GARRA |
| 2093 | ALDRAVA |

| | | | |
|---|---|---|---|
| 2094 | DETENTOR | 2125 | ESPAÇO VAZIO |
| 2094 | ESPERA | 2126 | CÉLULA |
| 2094 | BATENTE | 2126 | PILHA ELÉTRICA |
| 2094 | TRINCO | 2127 | CAVIDADE DE CÉLULA |
| 2094 | LINGÜETA | 2128 | CONSTANTE DE CÉLULA ELETROLÍTICA |
| 2094 | ARGOLA | 2129 | RADIADOR ALVEOLADO |
| 2095 | CATENÁRIA | 2129 | RADIADOR DE COLMEIA |
| 2096 | CATETÔMETRO | 2130 | CELULÓIDE |
| 2097 | CÁTODO | 2131 | CELULOSE |
| 2098 | LIMPEZA ELETROLÍTICA DO CÁTODO | 2132 | ACETATO DE CELULOSE |
| 2099 | COBRE ELETROLÍTICO | 2133 | CIMENTO |
| 2100 | QUEDA CATÓDICA | 2133 | CEMENTO |
| 2100 | QUEDA DE TENSÃO NO CÁTODO | 2133 | ARGAMASSA |
| 2101 | EFICIÊNCIA CATÓDICA | 2134 | CIMENTAR |
| 2101 | RENDIMENTO CATÓDICO | 2134 | CEMENTAR |
| 2102 | CAMADA CATÓDICA | 2134 | ARGAMASSAR |
| 2103 | DECAPAGEM CATÓDICA | 2135 | CONCRETO DE CIMENTO |
| 2104 | RAIOS CATÓDICOS | 2136 | COBRE CIMENTADO |
| 2105 | VÁLVULA DE RAIOS CATÓDICOS | 2136 | COBRE REGENERADO |
| 2105 | TUBO LENARD DE RAIOS CATÓDICOS | 2136 | CIMENTO DE COBRE |
| 2106 | CÁTODO | 2137 | ARGAMASSA DE CIMENTO |
| 2106 | ELÉTRODO NEGATIVO | 2138 | AÇO CEMENTADO |
| 2107 | CORROSÃO CATÓDICA | 2138 | AÇO DE CEMENTAÇÃO |
| 2108 | POLARIZAÇÃO CATÓDICA | 2139 | CEMENTAÇÃO |
| 2109 | PROTEÇÃO CATÓDICA | 2139 | AÇÃO DE CEMENTAR |
| 2110 | ATAQUE POR BOMBARDEIO ATÔMICO | 2139 | PÓ CARBURANTE |
| 2110 | GRAVAÇÃO CATÓDICA | 2140 | COLA DE COUROS CURTIDOS |
| 2111 | CATÓLITO | 2140 | COLA PARA CORREIAS |
| 2112 | CÁTION | 2141 | CEMENTAÇÃO |
| 2113 | CALAFETAR | 2142 | CEMENTAÇÃO (DO FERRO) |
| 2113 | RECALCAR | 2143 | JUNTA DE CORREIA COLADA |
| 2113 | RETOCAR | 2144 | FERRAMENTAS COM INCLUSÕES DE |
| 2114 | FERRO DE ENCALCAR | | CARBURETO |
| 2114 | FERRAMENTA DE CALAFETAR | 2145 | CORREIA COLADA |
| 2115 | CALAFETO | 2146 | CIMENTAÇÃO |
| 2115 | ENCALQUE | 2146 | CEMENTAÇÃO |
| 2116 | CURVA CÁUSTICA | 2147 | CEMENTITA |
| 2117 | BANHO DE SODA CÁUSTICA | 2148 | CENTRO |
| 2118 | FRAGILIDADE CÁUSTICA | 2149 | CAVILHA DA MOLA |
| 2119 | SOLUÇÃO CÁUSTICA | 2149 | PARAFUSO DE FIXAÇÃO |
| 2119 | SOLUÇÃO CORROSIVA | 2150 | TORNO DE PONTAS |
| 2120 | LIXÍVIA | 2151 | EIXO GEOMÉTRICO |
| 2120 | SOLUÇÃO DE SODA CÁUSTICA | 2151 | LINHA CENTRAL |
| 2121 | SUPERFÍCIE CÁUSTICA | 2151 | FIBRA NEUTRA |
| 2122 | CAVETO | 2152 | CENTRADOR (TORNO) |
| 2123 | CAVITAÇÃO | 2152 | LUNETA FIXA |
| 2124 | CAVIDADE | 2152 | APOIO CENTRAL |
| 2124 | COVA | 2153 | PINO CENTRAL |
| 2124 | BURACO | 2153 | PINO DE GUIA |
| 2125 | CAVIDADE | 2154 | ANEL CENTRADOR |
| 2125 | ESPAÇO OCO | 2154 | ARO DE CENTRAGEM |

| | |
|---|---|
| 2155 | RETIFICADORA ACÊNTRICA |
| 2156 | RETIFICAÇÃO ACÊNTRICA |
| 2157 | ESCALA CENTÍGRADA |
| 2157 | ESCALA DE CELSIUS |
| 2158 | CENTÍMETRO |
| 2159 | SISTEMA CENTÍMETRO-GRAMA-SEGUNDO (CGS) |
| 2159 | SISTEMA CEGESIMAL |
| 2160 | AQUECIMENTO CENTRAL |
| 2160 | CALEFAÇÃO CENTRAL |
| 2161 | CARGA CENTRAL |
| 2162 | CENTRO |
| 2163 | CENTRAR |
| 2164 | TRADO DE GUIA |
| 2164 | VERRUMA DE TRÊS PONTAS |
| 2164 | BROCA DE CENTRO |
| 2165 | DISTÂNCIA CENTRAL |
| 2166 | INSTRUMENTO PARA CENTRAR |
| 2167 | CENTRO DE CURVATURA |
| 2167 | CENTRO DE CURVA |
| 2168 | CENTRO DE GRAVIDADE |
| 2169 | CENTRO DE MOVIMENTO |
| 2169 | EIXO DE ROTAÇÃO |
| 2170 | CENTRO DE OSCILAÇÃO |
| 2171 | CENTRO DE REBITE |
| 2172 | PUNÇÃO DO BICO |
| 2172 | PUNÇÃO DE MARCADOR |
| 2173 | ESQUADRO PARA TRAÇAR CENTROS |
| 2173 | ESQUADRO DE CENTRALIZAÇÃO |
| 2174 | RETIFICADORA ACÊNTRICA |
| 2175 | FREIO CENTRÍFUGO |
| 2176 | FUNDIÇÃO CENTRÍFUGA |
| 2177 | EMBREAGEM CENTRÍFUGA |
| 2178 | TURBOCOMPRESSOR |
| 2178 | COMPRESSOR CENTRÍFUGO |
| 2179 | VENTILADOR CENTRÍFUGO |
| 2180 | FORÇA CENTRÍFUGA |
| 2181 | REGULADOR CENTRÍFUGO |
| 2182 | LUBRIFICADOR CENTRÍFUGO |
| 2183 | MOMENTO CENTRÍFUGO |
| 2184 | BOMBA CENTRÍFUGA |
| 2185 | REGULADOR DE FORÇA CENTRÍFUGA |
| 2185 | REGULADOR DE WATT |
| 2185 | REGULADOR DE BOLAS |
| 2186 | TERMÔMETRO CENTÍGRADO |
| 2187 | CENTRAGEM |
| 2187 | CENTRALIZAÇÃO |
| 2188 | MÁQUINA DE CENTRAR E RETIFICAR |
| 2189 | ACELERAÇÃO CENTRÍPETA |
| 2190 | FORÇA CENTRÍPETA |
| 2191 | CENTRO DE GRAVIDADE |
| 2191 | CENTRÓIDE |
| 2192 | CERMET (CERÂMICA + METAL) |
| 2192 | CERAMET |
| 2193 | CERÂMICA |
| 2194 | CERASINA |
| 2194 | CERESINA |
| 2194 | CERA ARTIFICIAL |
| 2195 | CÉRIO |
| 2196 | CERUSITA |
| 2197 | CÉSIO |
| 2198 | NÚMERO DE CETANO |
| 2198 | ÍNDICE DE CETANO |
| 2199 | CORTA-PALHA |
| 2199 | CORTA-FENO |
| 2200 | FADIGA POR ATRITO |
| 2201 | CADEIA |
| 2201 | CORRENTE |
| 2202 | TAMBOR PARA CADEIA-CABO |
| 2203 | FREIO DE CADEIA |
| 2204 | CÁRTER DE CADEIA |
| 2205 | LINHA DE UM TRAÇO |
| 2206 | TRANSMISSÃO POR CORRENTE |
| 2206 | ACIONAMENTO POR CORRENTE |
| 2207 | ACIONAMENTO POR CORRENTE |
| 2208 | ACIONAMENTO POR CORRENTE |
| 2209 | GRELHA DE CADEIA |
| 2210 | SOLDA INTERMITENTE DE PEQUENOS FILETES |
| 2211 | ELO DE CORRENTE |
| 2211 | ELO DE CADEIA |
| 2212 | LUBRIFICAÇÃO POR CORRENTE |
| 2213 | BLOCO DE POLIA A CADEIA |
| 2214 | REBITE EM CADEIA |
| 2215 | JUNTA REBITADA EM CADEIA |
| 2216 | SERRA DE CADEIA |
| 2217 | POLIA DE CORRENTE |
| 2217 | POLIA DE CADEIA |
| 2217 | RODA MOTRIZ |
| 2218 | TENSOR DE CADEIA |
| 2219 | ESTICADOR DE CORRENTE |
| 2220 | VOLANTE DE CADEIA ADAPTÁVEL |
| 2221 | SULFETO EM CADEIA |
| 2222 | SÉRIE DE OPERAÇÕES |
| 2222 | CADEIA DE OPERAÇÕES |
| 2223 | RODA DE CORRENTE |
| 2224 | GIZ |
| 2225 | MARGA CALCÁRIA |
| 2226 | PULVERIZAÇÃO DE GIZ |
| 2227 | ÁGUA CALCÁRIA |
| 2228 | ÁCIDO DE CÂMARA |
| 2229 | CAIXA DE VÁLVULAS |

| | |
|---|---|
| 2229 | CÂMARA DE DISTRIBUIÇÃO |
| 2230 | CHANFRAR |
| 2230 | ACANALAR |
| 2230 | BISELAR |
| 2230 | ESTRIAR |
| 2231 | CANTO CHANFRADO |
| 2231 | CHANFRO |
| 2231 | BISEL |
| 2232 | MARTELO CHANFRADO |
| 2233 | CHANFRADURA |
| 2233 | CHANFRO |
| 2234 | CAMURÇA |
| 2235 | CHAMOTE |
| 2235 | TIJOLO REFRATÁRIO |
| 2236 | MUDANÇA DE DIREÇÃO |
| 2237 | MUDANÇA DE PRESSÃO |
| 2238 | MUDANÇA DE ESTADO |
| 2239 | MUDANÇA DE TEMPERATURA |
| 2240 | MUDANÇA DE VOLUME |
| 2241 | INVERTER |
| 2241 | COMUTAR |
| 2242 | CAIXA DE MUDANÇAS |
| 2242 | MECANISMO DE MUDANÇA DE VELOCIDADE |
| 2243 | RODA SOBRESSALENTE |
| 2244 | COMUTADOR |
| 2244 | INTERRUPTOR INVERSÍVEL |
| 2245 | MUDANÇA DE VELOCIDADE |
| 2246 | COMUTAÇÃO |
| 2247 | VESTIÁRIO |
| 2248 | CANAL |
| 2248 | CALHA |
| 2248 | CONDUTO |
| 2248 | MEIA CANA |
| 2248 | FERRO EM U |
| 2249 | BARROTE DE FERRO EM U |
| 2250 | FERRO EM U |
| 2250 | FERRO EM CANALETAS |
| 2250 | FERRO EM E |
| 2251 | CANAL |
| 2251 | VERTEDOURO |
| 2252 | CHAPA ACANALADA |
| 2252 | CHAPA ESTRIADA |
| 2253 | SUPORTE DO MACHO |
| 2253 | COLAR |
| 2254 | PROCESSO CHAPMAN |
| 2255 | CARÁTER |
| 2256 | CURVA CARACTERÍSTICA |
| 2257 | CARACTERÍSTICA DE UM LOGARITMO |
| 2258 | FERRO GUSA AO CARVÃO VEGETAL |
| 2259 | CARGA |
| 2260 | CARREGAR UM FORNO METALÚRGICO |

| | |
|---|---|
| 2261 | CARREGAR UM ACUMULADOR |
| 2262 | CILINDRADA |
| 2263 | CARGA |
| 2263 | ALIMENTAÇÃO |
| 2264 | CARREGAMENTO DE UM FORNO METALÚRGICO |
| 2265 | CARREGAMENTO DE UM ACUMULADOR |
| 2266 | CORRENTE DE CARGA |
| 2267 | INDICADOR DE CARGA |
| 2268 | GERADOR DE CARGA |
| 2268 | MÁQUINA DE CARREGAR |
| 2269 | CARREGAMENTO |
| 2270 | TESTE DE IMPACTO CHARPY |
| 2271 | PÊNDULO DE CHARPY |
| 2272 | COURO QUEIMADO |
| 2272 | COURO CARBONIZADO |
| 2273 | QUADRO |
| 2273 | MAPA |
| 2273 | TABELA |
| 2273 | GRÁFICO |
| 2273 | DIAGRAMA |
| 2274 | CINZELADOR |
| 2274 | GRAVADOR |
| 2274 | PENTE DE ABRIR ROSCAS |
| 2274 | COXINETE |
| 2275 | CHASSI |
| 2276 | MARCAS DO REBOLO |
| 2276 | MARCAS DA FERRAMENTA NA PEÇA USINADA |
| 2276 | MARCAS DE VIBRAÇÃO |
| 2277 | VIBRAÇÕES DA VÁLVULA |
| 2278 | FENDA |
| 2278 | GRETA |
| 2278 | TRINCA |
| 2278 | RACHADURA |
| 2279 | VERIFICAR AS MEDIDAS |
| 2280 | ANÁLISE COMPROBATÓRIA |
| 2280 | ANÁLISE DE CONTROLE |
| 2280 | CONTRA-ANÁLISE |
| 2281 | PARAFUSO DE RETENÇÃO |
| 2281 | PARAFUSO DE BLOQUEIO |
| 2282 | MARCAS DE TREFILAÇÃO EM FORMA DE V |
| 2283 | VÁLVULA DE RETENÇÃO |
| 2283 | VÁLVULA DE REPERCUSSÃO |
| 2284 | VÁLVULA DE RETENÇÃO |
| 2284 | VÁLVULA DE PRESSÃO |
| 2285 | CHAPA ESTRIADA |
| 2285 | CHAPA ENXADREZADA |
| 2286 | QUEBRA DE REVESTIMENTO |
| 2286 | TRINCA |
| 2286 | FENDIMENTO |

| | |
|---|---|
| 2287 | CAIXA DE MOLDAGEM INTERMEDIÁRIA |
| 2287 | MORDENTE |
| 2287 | PARTE CENTRAL |
| 2288 | TALAGARÇA |
| 2288 | MUSSELINA |
| 2289 | AGENTE QUELIFERO |
| 2290 | QUÍMICO |
| 2291 | AÇÃO QUÍMICA |
| 2292 | AFINIDADE QUÍMICA |
| 2293 | ANÁLISE QUÍMICA |
| 2294 | BALANÇA DE LABORATÓRIO |
| 2295 | COMPORTAMENTO QUÍMICO |
| 2295 | CARACTERÍSTICAS QUÍMICAS |
| 2295 | PROPRIEDADES QUÍMICAS |
| 2296 | TRANSFORMAÇÃO QUÍMICA |
| 2296 | ALTERAÇÃO QUÍMICA |
| 2297 | REVESTIMENTO QUÍMICO |
| 2298 | COMPONENTE QUÍMICO |
| 2299 | COMPOSIÇÃO QUÍMICA |
| 2300 | COMPOSTO QUÍMICO |
| 2301 | CONSTITUIÇÃO QUÍMICA |
| 2302 | CORROSÃO QUÍMICA |
| 2303 | FLUIDOS DE CORTE QUÍMICOS |
| 2303 | FLUIDOS DE CORTE SINTÉTICOS |
| 2304 | SOLDA POR IMERSÃO |
| 2305 | ENERGIA QUÍMICA |
| 2306 | ENGENHEIRO QUÍMICO |
| 2307 | EQUILÍBRIO QUÍMICO |
| 2308 | EQUIVALENTE QUÍMICO |
| 2309 | PROCESSO DE ACABAMENTO QUÍMICO |
| 2310 | FÓRMULA QUÍMICA |
| 2311 | CHUMBO QUÍMICO |
| 2311 | CHUMBO COMERCIALMENTE PURO |
| 2312 | REAÇÃO QUÍMICA |
| 2313 | ESTABILIDADE QUÍMICA |
| 2314 | PROCESSOS QUÍMICOS DE TRATAMENTO DE SUPERFÍCIE |
| 2315 | SÍMBOLO QUÍMICO |
| 2316 | CELULOSE DE MADEIRA |
| 2317 | QUIMICAMENTE COMBINADO |
| 2318 | ÁGUA COMBINADA QUIMICAMENTE |
| 2318 | ÁGUA DE CONSTITUIÇÃO |
| 2319 | QUIMICAMENTE PURO |
| 2320 | PRODUTOS QUÍMICOS |
| 2321 | QUÍMICO |
| 2322 | QUÍMICA |
| 2323 | REATOR QUIMIONUCLEAR |
| 2323 | REATOR RADIOQUÍMICO |
| 2324 | ESTANHO QUIMICAMENTE PURO |
| 2325 | CHAPA ESTRIADA |
| 2326 | RUBRO CEREJA |

| | |
|---|---|
| 2326 | CALOR RUBRO CEREJA |
| 2327 | AQUECIDO AO RUBRO CEREJA |
| 2328 | ANTRACITO |
| 2329 | ENGENHEIRO CHEFE DA CONSTRUÇÃO |
| 2330 | SALITRE |
| 2330 | SALITRE DO CHILE |
| 2330 | NITRATO DE SÓDIO |
| 2331 | COQUILHA |
| 2332 | TEMPERAR |
| 2332 | COQUILHAR |
| 2332 | RESFRIAR |
| 2333 | FERRO GUSA VASADO EM COQUILHAS |
| 2334 | VAZAMENTO EM COQUILHA |
| 2334 | FUNDIÇÃO DURA |
| 2334 | FUNDIÇÃO EM COQUILHA |
| 2335 | FUNDIÇÃO COQUILHADA |
| 2336 | FERRO FUNDIDO EM CÔQUILHA |
| 2337 | METAL FUNDIDO EM COQUILHA |
| 2338 | COQUILHAMENTO |
| 2338 | TÊMPERA |
| 2339 | CHAMINÉ |
| 2340 | CAULIM |
| 2340 | PORCELANA CHINESA |
| 2341 | CARACTERES CHINESES |
| 2342 | SEBO VEGETAL DA CHINA |
| 2343 | APARA |
| 2343 | LASCA |
| 2343 | CAVACO |
| 2344 | CINZELAR |
| 2344 | GOIVAR |
| 2344 | BURILAR |
| 2345 | ENSAIO DE CAVACO |
| 2346 | APARA |
| 2347 | REBARBAÇO |
| 2347 | CINZELAMENTO |
| 2348 | APARAS DE METAL |
| 2349 | BURIL |
| 2349 | CINZEL |
| 2349 | FORMÃO |
| 2349 | TALHADEIRA |
| 2349 | ESCOPRO |
| 2350 | SOLDADOR EM FORMA DE CINZEL |
| 2351 | CLORATO |
| 2352 | CLORETO |
| 2353 | CLORAÇÃO |
| 2354 | CLORO |
| 2355 | MONÓXIDO DE CLORO |
| 2356 | CLOROFÓRMIO |
| 2357 | AFOGADOR |
| 2357 | DIFUSOR |
| 2358 | AFOGAR |

| | |
|---|---|
| 2358 | OBSTRUIR |
| 2358 | ENTUPIR |
| 2359 | DIFUSOR |
| 2359 | BOCAL |
| 2360 | SUPERFÍCIE FILTRANTE SATURADA |
| 2361 | TUBO ENTUPIDO |
| 2362 | OBSTRUÇÃO |
| 2363 | BORRACHA ENDURECIDA |
| 2363 | EBONITE |
| 2363 | VULCANITE |
| 2364 | CORDA DE UM CÍRCULO |
| 2365 | ESPESSURA DO DENTE À CORDA |
| 2366 | CROMATO |
| 2367 | CROMATIZAÇÃO |
| 2368 | CROMÁTICO |
| 2369 | ABERRAÇÃO CROMÁTICA |
| 2370 | ALÚMEN DE CROMO |
| 2371 | TIJOLO DE CROMITA |
| 2372 | VERDE DE CROMO |
| 2373 | CROMITA |
| 2373 | MINÉRIO DE CROMO |
| 2374 | VERMELHO DE CROMO |
| 2375 | AMARELO DE CROMO |
| 2375 | CROMATO DE CHUMBO |
| 2376 | AÇO CROMO-NÍQUEL |
| 2377 | COURO CURTIDO AO CROMO |
| 2378 | AÇO CROMO-TUNGSTÊNIO |
| 2379 | ÁCIDO CRÓMICO |
| 2380 | ANODIZAÇÃO A ÁCIDO CRÓMICO |
| 2381 | CLORETO DE CRÓMIO |
| 2382 | ÓXIDO CRÓMICO |
| 2383 | ANIDRIDO CRÓMICO |
| 2384 | CROMITA |
| 2384 | SIDEROCROMO |
| 2385 | CROMO |
| 2386 | AÇO AO CROMO-NÍQUEL |
| 2387 | CORANTE À BASE DE CROMO |
| 2388 | CROMAGEM |
| 2388 | CROMEAÇÃO |
| 2388 | REVESTIMENTO DE CROMO |
| 2389 | AÇO CROMO |
| 2390 | CEMENTAÇÃO PELO CROMO |
| 2390 | CROMAGEM |
| 2391 | CLORETO CROMOSO |
| 2392 | CRISOLITA |
| 2393 | MANDRIL |
| 2393 | PLACA DE TORNO |
| 2394 | MORDENTES DE MANDRIL |
| 2395 | CALHA DE ESCOAMENTO |
| 2395 | TUBO INCLINADO |
| 2395 | PLANO INCLINADO |

| | |
|---|---|
| 2395 | ESCOEDOURO |
| 2395 | CANALETA DE DESCARGA |
| 2396 | ISQUEIRO |
| 2396 | ACENDEDOR DE CIGARROS |
| 2397 | CINZA |
| 2397 | ESCÓRIA |
| 2397 | CARVÃO APAGADO |
| 2398 | RESFRIADOR DO FURO DE ESCÓRIA |
| 2398 | ESFRIADOR DE CINZA |
| 2399 | FURO DE ESCÓRIA |
| 2400 | MINÉRIO DE MERCÚRIO |
| 2400 | CINABRE |
| 2401 | CÍRCULO |
| 2402 | CÍRCULO DE CURVATURA |
| 2402 | CÍRCULO DE ARCO |
| 2403 | TESOURAS CIRCULARES |
| 2404 | CÍRCULO |
| 2404 | CIRCUNFERÊNCIA |
| 2405 | TRAVA DE PINO DE PISTÃO |
| 2406 | CIRCUITO |
| 2406 | GIRO |
| 2406 | VOLTA |
| 2406 | PERÍMETRO |
| 2407 | DISJUNTOR |
| 2408 | REGISTRADOR DE DIAGRAMA CIRCULAR |
| 2409 | CONE CIRCULAR |
| 2409 | CONE DE BASE CIRCULAR |
| 2410 | SEÇÃO CIRCULAR |
| 2411 | CILINDRO CIRCULAR |
| 2412 | ELÉTRODO GIRATÓRIO |
| 2413 | FUNÇÃO CIRCULAR |
| 2413 | FUNÇÃO CÍCLICA |
| 2414 | VIDRO REDONDO |
| 2415 | RASGO REDONDO |
| 2415 | RANHURA CIRCULAR |
| 2415 | RANHURA ANULAR |
| 2416 | INTERPOLAÇÃO CIRCULAR |
| 2417 | LÂMINA CIRCULAR |
| 2417 | GUILHOTINA CIRCULAR |
| 2417 | NAVALHA CIRCULAR |
| 2418 | TUBULAÇÃO CIRCULAR |
| 2419 | MEDIDA CIRCULAR |
| 2420 | FRESADORA CIRCULAR OU ANULAR |
| 2421 | MOVIMENTO CIRCULAR |
| 2422 | PÊNDULO CIRCULAR |
| 2423 | PASSO CIRCUNFERENCIAL |
| 2424 | PRATOS CIRCULARES |
| 2425 | ESCOVA DE DISCO |
| 2426 | TRANSFERIDOR CIRCULAR |
| 2427 | SERRA CIRCULAR |
| 2428 | SERRA MECÂNICA CIRCULAR |

| | |
|---|---|
| 2429 | TESOURA CIRCULAR |
| 2430 | NÍVEL ESFÉRICO |
| 2431 | ESPESSURA CIRCULAR DO DENTE |
| 2432 | GIRAR |
| 2432 | CIRCULAR |
| 2433 | CIRCULAÇÃO |
| 2434 | CIRCULAÇÃO DA ÁGUA |
| 2435 | CÍRCULO CIRCUNSCRITO |
| 2435 | CIRCUNFERÊNCIA CIRCUNSCRITA |
| 2436 | POLÍGONO CIRCUNSCRITO |
| 2437 | CONTRAÇÃO |
| 2437 | RETRAÇÃO |
| 2438 | CISSÓIDE |
| 2439 | CISTERNA |
| 2440 | BARÔMETRO |
| 2440 | BARÔMETRO DE CALHA |
| 2441 | ÁCIDO CÍTRICO |
| 2442 | ARQUITETURA |
| 2443 | ENGENHEIRO CIVIL |
| 2444 | ENGENHARIA CIVIL |
| 2444 | CONSTRUÇÃO CIVIL |
| 2445 | CHAPA BLINDADA |
| 2446 | AÇO DUPLEX |
| 2446 | AÇO CHAPEADO |
| 2446 | AÇO REVESTIDO |
| 2447 | PLACAGEM |
| 2447 | RECOBRIMENTO |
| 2447 | REVESTIMENTO |
| 2448 | GRAMPO |
| 2448 | GATO |
| 2448 | BRAÇADEIRA |
| 2448 | PREGADOR |
| 2448 | PRESILHA |
| 2448 | SARGENTO |
| 2449 | ACOPLAMENTO DE COMPRESSÃO |
| 2450 | PINÇA |
| 2450 | ESTRIBO |
| 2450 | BRAÇADEIRA |
| 2450 | GRAMPO |
| 2450 | PINO EM U |
| 2451 | GRAMPO |
| 2451 | PRENSA DE CARPINTEIRO |
| 2451 | PRENSA DE GRAMPO |
| 2452 | GRAMPO |
| 2452 | SARGENTO |
| 2452 | PRENSA DE PARAFUSO |
| 2453 | PARAFUSO DE APERTO OU DE SUJEIÇÃO |
| 2453 | GRAMPO COM ROSCA |
| 2453 | GRAMPO ROSCADO |
| 2454 | CAIXA PORTA-FERRAMENTAS |
| 2455 | PURIFICAÇÃO |

| | |
|---|---|
| 2455 | CLARIFICAÇÃO |
| 2456 | PURIFICAR |
| 2456 | CLARIFICAR |
| 2456 | CLAREAR |
| 2457 | CRAVO SEM CABEÇA |
| 2458 | CLASSE DE FERRO |
| 2458 | CATEGORIA DE FERRO |
| 2458 | ESPÉCIE DE FERRO |
| 2459 | CATEGORIA DE AÇO |
| 2460 | CLASSIFICAÇÃO |
| 2461 | EMBREAGEM DE GARRAS |
| 2461 | ACOPLAMENTO DENTADO |
| 2462 | MARTELO DE UNHA |
| 2462 | MARTELO COM GARRA DE EXTRAIR PREGOS |
| 2463 | ORELHA DE MARTELO |
| 2464 | GARRA |
| 2464 | GARFO |
| 2464 | DENTE |
| 2465 | ARGILA |
| 2465 | BARRO |
| 2466 | TERRENO ARGILOSO |
| 2467 | SIDERITA |
| 2467 | GANGA ARGILÁCEA |
| 2468 | ARGOLA DE ARGILA |
| 2469 | APARAR AS PEÇAS FUNDIDAS |
| 2469 | LIMPAR AS PEÇAS FUNDIDAS |
| 2469 | POLIR AS PEÇAS FUNDIDAS |
| 2470 | SUPERFÍCIE METÁLICA APARADA |
| 2471 | DETERGENTE |
| 2471 | LIMPADOR |
| 2472 | DETERGENTE ALCALINO |
| 2472 | LIMPADOR ALCALINO |
| 2473 | SOLVENTE |
| 2474 | LIMPEZA |
| 2474 | OPERAÇÃO DE ACABAMENTO |
| 2475 | PRODUTOS DE LIMPEZA E DE POLIMENTO |
| 2476 | BANHO DE POLIMENTO INICIAL |
| 2477 | ÓLEO DE LIMPEZA |
| 2478 | APARA |
| 2478 | REBARBAÇÃO |
| 2479 | IMAGEM NÍTIDA |
| 2480 | ÓLEO CLARO |
| 2480 | ÓLEO TRANSPARENTE |
| 2481 | ESPAÇO LIVRE |
| 2481 | FOLGA |
| 2481 | VÃO |
| 2481 | ABERTURA |
| 2481 | LUZ |
| 2482 | LUZ |
| 2482 | ESPAÇO LIVRE |

| | | | |
|---|---|---|---|
| 2482 | ESPAÇAMENTO | 2508 | ENROLADO NO SENTIDO HORÁRIO |
| 2482 | FOLGA | 2509 | MOVIMENTO DE RELÓGIO |
| 2482 | INTERVALO | 2509 | MECANISMO DE RELÓGIO |
| 2483 | JOGO | 2510 | ENTUPIMENTO |
| 2483 | TOLERÂNCIA | 2511 | FERRO DE GRANULAÇÃO COMPACTA |
| 2484 | ÂNGULO DE AFASTAMENTO | 2511 | FERRO DE GRANULAÇÃO FINA |
| 2484 | ÂNGULO DE ATAQUE | 2512 | TUBOS EM CONTATO |
| 2485 | CHAPUZ | 2513 | CABO FECHADO |
| 2485 | CALÇO | 2514 | ESTRUTURA COMPACTA |
| 2485 | TRAVA | 2515 | FECHAR O CIRCUITO ELÉTRICO |
| 2485 | GANCHO | 2516 | REBITAR |
| 2485 | PRESILHA | 2517 | ESPUMA DE CÉLULAS FECHADAS |
| 2485 | GRAMPO | 2518 | HIDROCARBURETOS DE SÉRIE AROMÁTICA |
| 2485 | CLITE | 2519 | UNIÃO EM ÂNGULO |
| 2485 | PRENSA-FIO | 2520 | CURVA FECHADA |
| 2486 | ROCHA CLIVÁVEL | 2520 | CÍRCULO |
| 2487 | FENDILHAMENTO | 2521 | MATRIZES FECHADAS |
| 2487 | LAMINAÇÃO | 2522 | SOLDAGEM EM K SEM SEPARAÇÃO |
| 2487 | CLIVAGEM | 2523 | SOLDAGEM DUPLA FECHADA EM J |
| 2488 | PLANO DE CLIVAGEM | 2524 | SOLDAGEM DE BORDA FECHADA EM DUPLO U |
| 2489 | RECALCAR OS REBITES | | |
| 2490 | RECALQUE DOS REBITES | 2525 | SOLDAGEM DE BORDA FECHADA EM DUPLO V SEM SEPARAÇÃO |
| 2491 | GRAMPO EM U | | |
| 2491 | ENGATE EM U | 2526 | PASSE FECHADO |
| 2491 | MANILHA | 2527 | PASSES FECHADOS |
| 2491 | FORQUILHA | 2528 | SOLDAGEM EM MEIO V SEM AFASTAMENTO |
| 2492 | CAVIRÃO | 2529 | SOLDAGEM EM J SEM AFASTAMENTO |
| 2492 | PASSADOR DE FORQUILHA | 2530 | SOLDAGEM DE BORDA FECHADA EM V |
| 2493 | LINGÜETA | 2531 | SOLDAGEM DE BORDA EM V SEM AFASTAMENTO |
| 2493 | TRINQUETE | | |
| 2493 | GATILHO | 2532 | SOLDAGEM EM I SEM AFASTAMENTO |
| 2494 | MECANISMO DE LINGÜETA DUPLA | 2533 | SISTEMA DE MALHA FECHADA |
| 2495 | CATRACA | 2533 | SISTEMA DE CIRCUITO DE RETORNO |
| 2496 | LINGÜETA DE CATRACA | 2534 | MANÔMETRO A AR COMPRIMIDO |
| 2497 | FRESAMENTO COM MOVIMENTO NA MESMA DIREÇÃO | 2535 | PISTÃO DE FECHAMENTO DO MOLDE |
| | | 2536 | LINHA DE FECHAMENTO |
| 2498 | CAPACIDADE DE SUBIDA | 2537 | FECHAMENTO DA VÁLVULA |
| 2499 | SUBIDA DA CORREIA | 2538 | ESFREGÃO DE PANO |
| 2500 | CLÍNQUER | 2539 | ROLOS DE POLIMENTO DE PANO |
| 2500 | ESCÓRIA | 2540 | TRATAMENTO A JATO DE AREIA |
| 2501 | PROJEÇÃO OBLÍQUA | 2541 | TURVAÇÃO |
| 2502 | PINÇA | 2541 | DISTÚRBIO |
| 2502 | GRAMPO | 2542 | ZONAS GUINIER PRESTON |
| 2502 | CLIPE | 2543 | LAMINADOR DE SEIS CILINDROS |
| 2503 | POLIA DE GARRAS | 2544 | EMBREAGEM |
| 2504 | APARAS | 2545 | GUARNIÇÃO DA EMBREAGEM |
| 2505 | LATÃO DE RELOJOARIA | 2545 | REVESTIMENTO DA EMBREAGEM |
| 2506 | SENTIDO HORÁRIO | 2545 | LONA DA EMBREAGEM |
| 2507 | ROTAÇÃO NO SENTIDO HORÁRIO | 2546 | CÁRTER DA EMBREAGEM |
| 2507 | ROTAÇÃO PARA A DIREITA | 2546 | CAIXA DA EMBREAGEM |
| 2508 | ENROLADO PARA A DIREITA | 2547 | PEDAL DA EMBREAGEM |

| | | | |
|---|---|---|---|
| 2548 | LIVRADOR DA EMBREAGEM | 2578 | DE MALHA GROSSA |
| 2548 | DESEMBREAGEM | 2579 | CABO METÁLICO DE FIOS GROSSOS |
| 2549 | MANCAL DA EMBREAGEM | 2580 | PÓ GROSSO |
| 2550 | LAVAR OS MINERAIS | 2581 | CAMADA DE LACA |
| 2551 | CHAVE INGLESA | 2582 | DEMÃO DE PINTURA A ÓLEO |
| 2552 | TIRAFUNDO DE PONTA CÔNICA | 2583 | DEMÃO DE PINTURA |
| 2552 | PARAFUSO DE CABEÇA QUADRADA PARA MADEIRA | 2584 | ELÉTRODO REVESTIDO |
| 2553 | PARAFUSO FRANCÊS OU TIRAFUNDO | 2585 | PARTÍCULAS DE METAL RECOBERTAS POR OUTRO METAL |
| 2554 | PARAFUSO DE CARROCERIA | 2586 | FOLHAS DE METAL RECOBERTAS |
| 2555 | COAGULAR | 2586 | CHAPAS DE METAL REVESTIDAS |
| 2556 | COAGULAÇÃO | 2587 | CAMADA |
| 2557 | COÁGULO | 2587 | REVESTIMENTO |
| 2558 | HULHA | 2587 | DEMÃO |
| 2558 | CARVÃO DE PEDRA | 2588 | REVESTIMENTO ANÓDICO |
| 2558 | CARVÃO FÓSSIL | 2589 | PRODUTO DE REVESTIMENTO |
| 2558 | CARVÃO | 2590 | CAMADAS |
| 2559 | BRITADOR DE CARVÃO | 2591 | CAMADA DE CROMATO |
| 2560 | BRIQUETE DE CARVÃO | 2592 | REVESTIMENTOS POR TÊMPERA |
| 2560 | AGLOMERADO DE HULHA | 2593 | REVESTIMENTOS ELETROLÍTICOS OU GALVANOPLÁSTICOS |
| 2561 | PAIOL DE CARVÃO | 2594 | REVESTIMENTOS ESMALTADOS |
| 2561 | CARVOEIRA | 2595 | REVESTIMENTOS POR PINTURA |
| 2562 | REGIÃO CARVOEIRA | 2596 | REVESTIMENTOS METÁLICOS |
| 2563 | PÓ DE CARVÃO | 2597 | REVESTIMENTOS NÃO METÁLICOS |
| 2563 | CARVÃO PULVERIZADO | 2598 | REVESTIMENTOS DE ÓXIDO |
| 2563 | MOINHA DE CARVÃO | 2599 | PINTURAS |
| 2564 | AQUECIMENTO A CARVÃO | 2600 | FOSFATAÇÃO |
| 2564 | CALEFAÇÃO A CARVÃO | 2601 | REVESTIMENTOS ANTIFERRUGINOSOS |
| 2565 | FORNALHA DE CARVÃO | 2602 | REVESTIMENTOS DE ESTANHO |
| 2566 | MINA DE CARVÃO | 2603 | REVESTIMENTOS VÍTREOS |
| 2566 | HULHEIRA | 2604 | ZINCAGEM |
| 2566 | MINA DE HULHA | 2604 | GALVANIZAÇÃO |
| 2567 | MATÉRIA CORANTE DERIVADA DO ALCATRÃO DE HULHA | 2605 | COAXIAL |
| 2568 | NAFTA DISSOLVENTE | 2606 | PEDAÇOS GRANDES DE CARVÃO |
| 2568 | ÓLEO DE ALCATRÃO DA HULHA | 2607 | COBALTO |
| 2569 | BREU DE ALCATRÃO DE HULHA | 2608 | CARBONILO DE COBALTO |
| 2570 | COLTAR | 2609 | CLORETO DE COBALTO |
| 2570 | ALCATRÃO MINERAL | 2610 | NITRATO DE COBALTO |
| 2570 | PÊZ DE HULHA | 2611 | SESQUIÓXIDO DE COBALTO |
| 2571 | COBRE DE BRIQUETES SINTERIZADOS | 2612 | AÇO AO COBALTO |
| 2572 | COALESCÊNCIA | 2613 | AÇO AO COBALTO E CROMO |
| 2572 | FUSÃO | 2614 | COBALTITA |
| 2573 | DE TEXTURA GROSSA | 2614 | COBALTINA |
| 2573 | GRANULAÇÃO GROSSA | 2615 | SULFATO DE COBALTO |
| 2573 | GRÃO BRUTO | 2616 | TEIA DE ARANHA |
| 2574 | AREIA GROSSA | 2617 | TORNEIRA |
| 2575 | ROSCA DE PASSO GROSSO | 2617 | REGISTRO |
| 2576 | ROSCA SEM PRECISÃO | 2617 | VÁLVULA |
| 2576 | ROSCA LARGA OU BRUTA | 2618 | CHAVE DE COMANDO |
| 2577 | AÇO DE GRANULAÇÃO GROSSA | 2619 | RUGAS |

| | | | |
|---|---|---|---|
| 2620 | ÓLEO DE COCO | 2658 | BRITADOR DE COQUE |
| 2621 | COEFICIENTE | 2658 | TRITURADOR DE COQUE |
| 2622 | COEFICIENTE DE CONDUTIBILIDADE TÉRMICA | 2659 | PÓ DE COQUE |
| | | 2659 | MOINHA DE COQUE |
| 2623 | COEFICIENTE DE CONTRAÇÃO | 2660 | FILTRO DE COQUE |
| 2624 | COEFICIENTE DE CORROSÃO | 2661 | FORNO DE COQUE |
| 2625 | COEFICIENTE DE DILATAÇÃO CÚBICA | 2662 | COQUE DE FORNO |
| 2626 | COEFICIENTE DE DESCARGA | 2662 | COQUE METALÚRGICO |
| 2627 | COEFICIENTE DE RESISTIVIDADE ELÉTRICA | 2663 | GÁS DE FORNO DE COQUE |
| 2628 | COEFICIENTE DE EXPANSÃO | 2664 | FERRO GUSA AO COQUE |
| 2628 | COEFICIENTE DE DILATAÇÃO | 2664 | FUNDIÇÃO COM COQUE DE MADEIRA |
| 2629 | COEFICIENTE DE ATRITO OU DE FRICÇÃO | 2665 | FÁBRICA DE CARBONIZAÇÃO DE HULHA |
| 2630 | COEFICIENTE DE DILATAÇÃO LINEAR | 2666 | COQUEIFICAÇÃO |
| 2631 | COEFICIENTE DE PROPORCIONALIDADE | 2667 | ENSAIO DE ENVERGAMENTO A FRIO |
| 2632 | COEFICIENTE DE RESISTÊNCIA | 2667 | PROVA DE FLEXÃO A FRIO |
| 2633 | COEFICIENTE DE ROLAMENTO | 2668 | FLEXÃO A FRIO |
| 2634 | COEFICIENTE DE DESLIZAMENTO | 2668 | DOBRAMENTO A FRIO |
| 2635 | COEFICIENTE DE DILATAÇÃO SUPERFICIAL | 2669 | FERRO FUNDIDO AO AR FRIO |
| 2636 | COEFICIENTE DE DILATAÇÃO TÉRMICA | 2670 | MÁQUINA DE CÂMARA FRIA |
| 2637 | COEFICIENTE DE EFEITO TERMOELÉTRICO | 2671 | FUNDIÇÃO EM CÂMARA FRIA |
| 2638 | COEFICIENTE DE VELOCIDADE | 2672 | CORTA-FERRO |
| 2639 | FORÇA COERCIVA | 2672 | CORTA-FRIO |
| 2640 | COERCIVO | 2672 | TALHADEIRA DE CORTAR METAL |
| 2641 | COERCIVIDADE | 2673 | CUNHAGEM A FRIO |
| 2642 | LAMINAÇÃO | 2673 | ESTAMPAGEM A FRIO |
| 2642 | DESBASTE DE LINGOTES | 2674 | RUPTURA A FRIO |
| 2643 | COESÃO | 2675 | ESTIRAR A FRIO |
| 2644 | COESÃO | 2676 | ESTIRAGEM A FRIO |
| 2644 | PODER COESIVO | 2677 | ESTIRADO A FRIO |
| 2644 | FORÇA DE COESÃO | 2678 | TUBOS ESTIRADOS A FRIO |
| 2645 | ROLO | 2679 | ACABAMENTO A FRIO |
| 2645 | ENROLAMENTO | 2680 | DEFORMAÇÃO A FRIO |
| 2645 | BOBINA | 2680 | CIRCULAÇÃO A FRIO |
| 2645 | SERPENTINA | 2681 | FORJA A FRIO |
| 2646 | ESPIRA | 2681 | CUNHAGEM A FRIO |
| 2647 | MOLA HELICOIDAL | 2682 | FORMAÇÃO A FRIO |
| 2648 | BOBINA | 2682 | MOLDAGEM A FRIO |
| 2648 | ENROLAMENTO DE BOBINA | 2683 | GALVANIZAÇÃO A FRIO |
| 2648 | BOBINAGEM | 2684 | MARTELAR A FRIO |
| 2649 | MOLA DE FLEXÃO AO ENROLAMENTO | 2685 | MARTELAGEM A FRIO |
| 2650 | ENROLAMENTO | 2686 | FORMAÇÃO DE CABEÇAS A FRIO (DE PREGOS, PARAFUSOS, ETC.) |
| 2650 | BOBINAGEM | | |
| 2651 | CUNHAGEM | 2687 | EXAME A FRIO |
| 2651 | ESTAMPAGEM | 2687 | INSPEÇÃO A FRIO |
| 2652 | MATRIZ DE ESTAMPAGEM | 2688 | SERRA A FRIO |
| 2653 | PRENSA DE CUNHAR | 2689 | PENETRAÇÃO A FRIO |
| 2654 | FIBRA DE COCO | 2690 | ACETINAGEM A FRIO |
| 2654 | CORDAME DE FIBRA DE COCO | 2690 | COMPRESSÃO A FRIO |
| 2655 | COQUE | 2690 | PRENSAGEM A FRIO |
| 2656 | COQUEIFICAR | 2691 | REDUÇÃO A FRIO |
| 2657 | FUNDIÇÃO COM COQUE DE ALTO-FORNO | 2692 | REBITAR A FRIO |

| | |
|---|---|
| 2693 | REBITAGEM A FRIO |
| 2694 | LAMINAR A FRIO |
| 2695 | BARRAS LAMINADAS A FRIO |
| 2696 | CHAPA OU PLACA LAMINADA A FRIO |
| 2697 | AÇO LAMINADO A FRIO |
| 2698 | LAMINAÇÃO A FRIO |
| 2699 | SERRAÇÃO A FRIO |
| 2699 | SERRA A FRIO |
| 2700 | ISOLAMENTO A FRIO |
| 2701 | TALHADEIRA PARA CORTE A FRIO |
| 2702 | FERRO QUEBRADIÇO A FRIO |
| 2702 | FERRO FRÁGIL A FRIO |
| 2703 | FRAGILIDADE A FRIO |
| 2704 | FRAGILIDADE DO FERRO |
| 2705 | SOLDADO A FRIO |
| 2706 | GOTA FRIA |
| 2707 | REMOÇÃO A FRIO |
| 2707 | DECAPAGEM A FRIO |
| 2708 | TREM DE LAMINAÇÃO A FRIO |
| 2709 | TESTE A FRIO |
| 2709 | PROVA A FRIO |
| 2709 | ENSAIO A FRIO |
| 2710 | TRATAMENTO DOS METAIS A FRIO |
| 2711 | REBARBAÇÃO A FRIO |
| 2711 | APARA A FRIO |
| 2712 | SOLDAGEM A FRIO |
| 2713 | USINAGEM A FRIO |
| 2713 | BENEFICIAMENTO A FRIO |
| 2714 | TUBULAÇÃO ESTIRADA A FRIO |
| 2715 | FIO OU ARAME ESTIRADO A FRIO |
| 2716 | LAMINADO A FRIO |
| 2717 | FORMÃO PARA CORTE A FRIO |
| 2718 | FLEXIBILIDADE |
| 2718 | RETRATIBILIDADE |
| 2719 | CAPOTA CONVERSÍVEL |
| 2720 | ESTRIBO |
| 2720 | ALÇA |
| 2720 | COLAR |
| 2720 | ANEL |
| 2721 | ANEL CALIBRADOR |
| 2722 | SUPORTE DE BASE ANULAR |
| 2722 | RELA COM PIVÔ ANULAR |
| 2723 | FLANGE DO MANCAL AXIAL |
| 2724 | ANEL OU COLAR FIXO |
| 2724 | ARRUELA DE UMA ÁRVORE |
| 2724 | COLAR DE BASE |
| 2725 | CANO COLETOR |
| 2726 | PLACAS COLETORAS |
| 2727 | MANDRIL DE FIXAÇÃO |
| 2727 | MANDRIL |

| | |
|---|---|
| 2727 | BUCHA |
| 2728 | LUVA DE APERTO |
| 2728 | MANGUITO DE FIXAÇÃO |
| 2729 | ENCABADOUROS |
| 2729 | BUCHAS |
| 2730 | COLIMAR |
| 2731 | COLIMAÇÃO |
| 2732 | COLIMADOR |
| 2733 | COLÓDIO |
| 2734 | COLÓIDE |
| 2735 | COLOIDAL |
| 2736 | PARTÍCULAS COLOIDAIS |
| 2737 | COLOFÔNIA |
| 2738 | METALOGRAFIA A CORES |
| 2739 | ESPECTROSCOPIA COLORIMÉTRICA |
| 2740 | COLORAÇÃO |
| 2741 | COR |
| 2742 | LAVAR UM DESENHO |
| 2743 | PINCEL |
| 2744 | TEMPERATURA DE FORJA |
| 2744 | CALOR DE FORJA |
| 2745 | LÁPIS DE COR |
| 2746 | VIDRO INCOLOR |
| 2747 | NIÓBIO |
| 2747 | COLÔMBIO |
| 2748 | POSTE |
| 2748 | COLUNA |
| 2748 | PILAR |
| 2749 | CABEÇA DE POSTE |
| 2750 | COLUNA LÍQUIDA |
| 2751 | COLUNA BAROMÉTRICA |
| 2751 | COLUNA DE MERCÚRIO |
| 2752 | COLUNA DE ÁGUA |
| 2753 | COLUNA MONTANTE |
| 2753 | ENCANAMENTO VERTICAL |
| 2753 | TUBULAÇÃO VERTICAL |
| 2754 | ARMAÇÃO SUSTENTADA POR COLUNAS |
| 2755 | PERFURADORA TIPO COLUNA |
| 2756 | COLUNA COM AS DUAS PONTAS ENGASTADAS |
| 2757 | CRISTAIS BASÁLTICOS |
| 2758 | ESTRUTURA BASÁLTICA |
| 2759 | ARMAÇÃO DE POSTES |
| 2760 | CALIBRE DE ROSCA |
| 2761 | COMBINAÇÃO |
| 2762 | MATRIZ COMBINADA |
| 2763 | BROCA DE CENTRAR |
| 2764 | ALICATE MOTORISTA |
| 2765 | TOTALIZAR OS DIAGRAMAS |
| 2765 | ORDENAR OS DIAGRAMAS SEGUNDO O MÉTODO RANKIN |

| | | | |
|---|---|---|---|
| 2766 | COMBINAÇÃO DE MÁQUINAS DE CEIFAR E DEBULHAR | 2798 | COMPARTIMENTO |
| 2767 | CARBONO EM COMBINAÇÃO QUÍMICA | 2799 | BÚSSOLA |
| 2768 | VENTILADOR E EXAUSTOR | 2800 | ROSA-DOS-VENTOS |
| 2769 | BOCAL CONVERGENTE | 2801 | CEPILHO CIRCULAR |
| 2769 | BOCAL | 2801 | PLAINA REDONDA |
| 2770 | ORGANIZAÇÃO DE DIAGRAMAS CONFORME O MÉTODO DE RANKIN | 2802 | SERRA OU SERROTE DE PONTA |
| | | 2802 | SERRA DE CERCEAR |
| 2771 | PROPORÇÕES DEFINIDAS | 2803 | COMPASSO COM TIRA-LINHAS |
| 2772 | COMBUSTÍVEL | 2804 | COMPASSOS COM PONTA DE LÁPIS |
| 2773 | COMBUSTIBILIDADE | 2805 | COMPASSOS COM PONTAS DE REPOSIÇÃO |
| 2774 | COMBUSTÃO | 2806 | COMPATIBILIDADE |
| 2775 | CURSO DE COMBUSTÃO | 2807 | EQUILIBRAR |
| 2775 | CURSO DE EXPANSÃO E EXPLOSÃO | 2807 | COMPENSAR |
| 2776 | CÂMARA DE COMBUSTÃO | 2808 | PÊNDULO COMPENSADOR |
| 2777 | CÂMARA DE COMBUSTÃO DE UM FORNO | 2808 | PÊNDULO COMPENSADO |
| 2778 | CÂMARA DE COMBUSTÃO DE MOTOR | 2809 | COMPENSAÇÃO |
| 2778 | CÂMARA DE EXPLOSÃO DE MOTOR | 2810 | COMPLEMENTO DE UM ÂNGULO |
| 2779 | COMBUSTÃO COMPLETA | 2811 | ÂNGULO COMPLEMENTAR |
| 2780 | CONTROLE | 2812 | COR COMPLEMENTAR |
| 2780 | COMANDO | 2813 | NÚMERO COMPOSTO |
| 2781 | RENDIMENTO COMERCIAL | 2813 | NÚMERO COMPLEXO |
| 2781 | RENDIMENTO ECONÔMICO | 2814 | VARIÁVEL COMPOSTA |
| 2782 | REDE | 2814 | VARIÁVEL COMPLEXA |
| 2782 | SETOR | 2815 | COMPONENTE |
| 2783 | APLICAÇÃO INDUSTRIAL DE UMA INVENÇÃO | 2816 | FORÇA COMPONENTE |
| | | 2817 | COMPONENTE DE UMA FORÇA |
| 2784 | VEÍCULO UTILITÁRIO | 2818 | MATRIZ COMPOSTA |
| 2785 | ZINCO COMERCIAL | 2819 | ELÉTRODO COMPOSTO |
| 2785 | ZINCO BRUTO | 2820 | NÚMERO MISTO |
| 2786 | PULVERIZAÇÃO | 2820 | NÚMERO COMPOSTO |
| 2786 | TRITURAÇÃO | 2821 | DEPÓSITO ELETROLÍTICO DE VÁRIAS CAMADAS |
| 2787 | ALÚMEN COMUM (POTÁSSICO) | | |
| 2788 | LOGARITMO DE BRIGGS | 2822 | RESISTÊNCIA COMPLEXA |
| 2788 | LOGARITMO COMUM | 2822 | RESISTÊNCIA COMPOSTA |
| 2788 | LOGARITMO DECIMAL | 2823 | SÍNTESE |
| 2789 | DENOMINADOR COMUM | 2823 | COMPOSIÇÃO |
| 2790 | SAL COMUM | 2824 | LATÃO VERMELHO |
| 2790 | CLORETO DE SÓDIO | 2825 | COMPOSIÇÃO DE FORÇAS |
| 2791 | DENSO | 2826 | PLANO DE COMPOSIÇÃO |
| 2791 | COMPACTO | 2827 | PREPARADO |
| 2791 | SÓLIDO | 2827 | COMPOSTO |
| 2791 | MACIÇO | 2828 | COMPACTO COMPOSTO |
| 2791 | AGLOMERADO | 2829 | MÁQUINA COMPOSTA |
| 2792 | COQUE COMPACTO | 2829 | MÁQUINA COMPOUND |
| 2793 | COTAS DE UNIÃO | 2830 | MANOVACUÔMETRO |
| 2794 | COMPARADOR | 2831 | VIGA COMPOSTA |
| 2795 | COMPARADORES | 2831 | VIGA SAMBLADA |
| 2796 | BLOCOS DE COMPARAÇÃO | 2832 | ÓLEO MISTO |
| 2797 | MEDIDA DE COMPARAÇÃO | 2832 | ÓLEO COMPOSTO |
| 2798 | CAIXA | 2833 | ROSCA DIFERENCIAL |
| | | 2833 | PARAFUSO COMPOSTO |

| | | | |
|---|---|---|---|
| 2834 | MOLA DE LÂMINAS MÚLTIPLAS | 2874 | COMPRESSOR |
| 2834 | MOLA DE LÂMINAS SOBREPOSTAS | 2875 | COMANDO DIRETO POR COMPUTADOR |
| 2835 | MOTOR DE ENROLAMENTO "COMPOUND" | 2876 | CONSUMO DE ENERGIA |
| 2836 | COMPRESSOR "COMPOUND" | 2877 | CÔNCAVO |
| 2837 | PRENSAR | 2878 | SOLDAGEM DE ÂNGULO CÔNCAVO |
| 2837 | COMPRIMIR | 2879 | ESPELHO CÔNCAVO |
| 2838 | COMPRIMIR UMA MOLA | 2880 | CONCAVIDADE |
| 2839 | AR COMPRIMIDO | 2881 | CONCENTRADO |
| 2840 | FREIO PNEUMÁTICO | 2882 | CONCENTRAR |
| 2840 | FREIO A AR COMPRIMIDO | 2883 | SOLUÇÃO CONCENTRADA |
| 2841 | CILINDRO A AR COMPRIMIDO | 2884 | ÁCIDO SULFÚRICO CONCENTRADO |
| 2841 | CILINDRO PNEUMÁTICO | 2885 | CONCENTRAÇÃO DE SOLUÇÃO POR EVAPORAÇÃO |
| 2842 | ACIONAMENTO PNEUMÁTICO | | |
| 2842 | TRANSMISSÃO PNEUMÁTICA | 2886 | CONCENTRAÇÃO |
| 2843 | MOTOR A AR COMPRIMIDO | 2887 | ELEMENTO DE DOIS LÍQUIDOS |
| 2843 | MOTOR PNEUMÁTICO | 2887 | PILHA DE DOIS LÍQUIDOS |
| 2844 | LOCOMOTIVA A AR COMPRIMIDO | 2888 | CORROSÃO DA PILHA DE CONCENTRAÇÃO |
| 2845 | TUBULAÇÃO A AR COMPRIMIDO | 2889 | POLARIZAÇÃO DE ELÉTRODO POR QUEDA DE CONCENTRAÇÃO |
| 2846 | TESTE A AR COMPRIMIDO | | |
| 2847 | GÁS COMPRIMIDO | 2890 | CÍRCULOS CONCÊNTRICOS |
| 2848 | MAÇARICO A OXIGÊNIO COMPRIMIDO | 2891 | CONCENTRICIDADE |
| 2849 | AÇO COMPRIMIDO | 2892 | CONCÓIDE |
| 2850 | EIXO DE AÇO COMPRIMIDO | 2893 | FRATURA CONCOIDAL |
| 2851 | COMPRESSIBILIDADE | 2894 | CONCRETO |
| 2852 | COMPRESSIBILIDADE | 2895 | CONCRETAR |
| 2853 | COMPRESSÍVEL | 2895 | LANÇAR CONCRETO |
| 2854 | COMPRESSÃO | 2896 | MACIÇO DE ALVENARIA |
| 2855 | BARRA SOB COMPRESSÃO | 2896 | ALICERCE DE CONCRETO |
| 2856 | CÂMARA DE COMPRESSÃO | 2896 | FUNDAÇÃO |
| 2857 | LINHA DE COMPRESSÃO | 2897 | CORTADORA DE FERRO PARA CONCRETO |
| 2858 | COMPRESSÃO DO AR | 2898 | TUBO DE CIMENTO |
| 2859 | PRESSÃO DE COMPRESSÃO | 2899 | PROTENSÃO DO CONCRETO |
| 2860 | COEFICIENTE DE COMPRESSÃO | 2900 | LAJE DE CONCRETO |
| 2860 | TAXA DE COMPRESSÃO | 2901 | OBRAS DE CONCRETO |
| 2860 | RELAÇÃO DE COMPRESSÃO | 2902 | CONCRETAGEM |
| 2861 | ANEL DE SEGMENTO | 2903 | FORÇAS CONCORRENTES |
| 2861 | ANEL DE COMPRESSÃO | 2904 | CALEFAÇÃO ADICIONAL |
| 2862 | MOLA DE COMPRESSÃO | 2905 | CONDENSAÇÃO |
| 2863 | TENSÃO DE COMPRESSÃO | 2906 | CONDENSAÇÃO |
| 2863 | ESFORÇO DE COMPRESSÃO | 2907 | CONDENSAR |
| 2864 | TEMPO DE COMPRESSÃO | 2908 | CONDENSADOR |
| 2864 | CURSO OU MOVIMENTO DE COMPRESSÃO | 2909 | LENTE CONVERGENTE |
| 2865 | TESTE DE COMPRESSÃO | 2910 | LENTE CONVERGENTE |
| 2866 | MOTOR DIESEL | 2910 | LENTE CONVEXA |
| 2867 | SEGMENTO DE VEDAÇÃO | 2911 | MÁQUINA A VAPOR DE CONDENSAÇÃO |
| 2868 | FORÇA DE COMPRESSÃO | 2912 | ELIMINAÇÃO DA CAMADA SUPERFICIAL |
| 2869 | ESFORÇO DE COMPRESSÃO | 2913 | CONDUZIR (ELETRICIDADE, CALOR, ETC.) |
| 2870 | RESISTÊNCIA À COMPRESSÃO | 2914 | MEIO CONDUTOR |
| 2871 | TENSÃO DE COMPRESSÃO | 2915 | SAIS CONDUTORES |
| 2872 | TESTE OU ENSAIO DE COMPRESSÃO | 2916 | CONDUÇÃO |
| 2873 | LIMITE DE RUPTURA | 2917 | CONDUÇÃO DE CALOR |

| | |
|---|---|
| 2918 | CONDUTOR |
| 2919 | CONDUTIVIDADE |
| 2920 | CONDUTIBILIDADE TÉRMICA |
| 2921 | CONDUTOR |
| 2922 | FIO OU ARAME CONDUTOR |
| 2923 | ABAFADOR (LOCOMOTIVA) |
| 2924 | CONE |
| 2925 | CORREIA TRAPEZOIDAL |
| 2926 | FREIO DE CONES |
| 2927 | EMBREAGEM CÔNICA |
| 2928 | ACOPLAMENTO DE CONES |
| 2929 | EXTRATORES DE CONES |
| 2930 | EMBREAGEM CÔNICA |
| 2931 | CHAVETA CÔNICA |
| 2932 | CONE LUMINOSO |
| 2933 | CONFOCAL |
| 2934 | CONGLOMERADO |
| 2935 | VERMELHO CONGO |
| 2936 | PAPEL VERMELHO CONGO |
| 2937 | CONGRUÊNCIA |
| 2937 | COINCIDÊNCIA |
| 2938 | FUSÃO CONGRUENTE |
| 2939 | TRANSFORMAÇÃO CONGRUENTE |
| 2940 | SEÇÃO CÔNICA |
| 2941 | CONE DE GUIA |
| 2942 | MOLA CÔNICA |
| 2943 | REGULADOR CÔNICO |
| 2944 | PISTÃO CÔNICO |
| 2945 | ANEL CÔNICO |
| 2946 | REBITE DE CABEÇA CÔNICA |
| 2947 | TETO CÔNICO |
| 2947 | TELHADO CÔNICO |
| 2948 | CONICIDADE |
| 2948 | FORMA CÔNICA |
| 2949 | SUPERFÍCIE CÔNICA |
| 2949 | SUPERFÍCIE LATERAL DO CONE |
| 2950 | ELEMENTOS DE REDUÇÃO EM FORMA DE CONE TRUNCADO |
| 2951 | VÁLVULA CÔNICA |
| 2952 | CONJUGADO |
| 2953 | EIXO CONJUGADO DE HIPÉRBOLE |
| 2953 | EIXO NÃO TRANSVERSAL DE HIPÉRBOLE |
| 2954 | DIÂMETRO CONJUGADO |
| 2955 | LIGAR |
| 2955 | CONECTAR |
| 2956 | LIGAR EM PARALELO |
| 2957 | LIGAR EM SÉRIE |
| 2958 | LIGAÇÃO |
| 2959 | PINO DE UNIÃO |
| 2959 | CAVILHA DE LIGAÇÃO |
| 2959 | PARAFUSO DE UNIÃO |

| | |
|---|---|
| 2960 | TUBO DE COMUNICAÇÃO |
| 2960 | TUBO DE LIGAÇÃO |
| 2961 | ANEL DE LIGAÇÃO |
| 2962 | BIELA |
| 2962 | TRIÂNGULO DE LIGAÇÃO |
| 2962 | TIRANTE DE LIGAÇÃO |
| 2962 | BARRA DE LIGAÇÃO |
| 2963 | CABEÇA DE BIELA |
| 2964 | PASSARELA DE LIGAÇÃO |
| 2965 | LIGAÇÃO |
| 2966 | LIGAÇÃO (ELETRICIDADE) |
| 2967 | CONSERVAÇÃO DA ENERGIA |
| 2967 | MANUTENÇÃO DA ENERGIA |
| 2968 | CONSISTÊNCIA |
| 2969 | CONSTANTE |
| 2970 | FONTE DE CORRENTE DE SOLDAGEM CONSTANTE |
| 2971 | VELOCIDADE DE CORTE CONSTANTE |
| 2972 | TESTE OU PROVA DE FLEXÃO CONSTANTE |
| 2973 | FORÇA CONSTANTE |
| 2974 | TESTE OU PROVA DE CARGA CONSTANTE |
| 2975 | INTENSIDADE DA GRAVIDADE |
| 2976 | PRESSÃO CONSTANTE |
| 2977 | TEMPERATURA CONSTANTE |
| 2978 | VOLTAGEM CONSTANTE |
| 2978 | TENSÃO CONSTANTE |
| 2979 | FONTE DE CORRENTE DE TENSÃO CONSTANTE PARA SOLDAGEM |
| 2980 | CONSTANTAN |
| 2981 | CONSTITUINTE |
| 2981 | COMPONENTE |
| 2982 | METAL COMPONENTE DE UMA LIGA |
| 2983 | COMPONENTE |
| 2984 | DIAGRAMA DE FASES |
| 2985 | MOVIMENTO DE COMANDO POSITIVO |
| 2985 | DISPOSITIVO DE COMANDO MECÂNICO |
| 2986 | CONSTRUÇÃO |
| 2986 | MONTAGEM |
| 2986 | EDIFICAÇÃO |
| 2987 | BARRACÃO DO CANTEIRO DE OBRAS |
| 2988 | METAIS DE CONSTRUÇÃO |
| 2989 | ENGENHEIRO CONSULTOR |
| 2990 | ELÉTRODO FUSÍVEL |
| 2991 | JUNTA FUSÍVEL |
| 2992 | PESO CONSUMIDO |
| 2993 | CONSUMO DE CORRENTE |
| 2994 | CONSUMO DE COMBUSTÍVEL |
| 2995 | CONSUMO DE VAPOR |
| 2995 | GASTO DE VAPOR |
| 2996 | CONTATO |
| 2997 | ARCO DE CONTATO |

| | | | | |
|---|---|---|---|
| 2998 | SUPERFÍCIE DE CONTATO | 3039 | SISTEMA DE COMANDO DE CONTORNO |
| 2999 | BARRA DE CONTATO | 3040 | FRESAGEM DE PERFIS |
| 3000 | INTERRUPTOR | 3041 | FORMAÇÃO DO MODELO |
| 3001 | ELÉTRODO DE CONTATO | 3042 | CONTRAÍDO |
| 3002 | CORROSÃO POR CONTATO | 3043 | RETRAÇÃO |
| 3003 | PLACA DE CONTATO | 3043 | CONTRAÇÃO |
| 3004 | DEPÓSITO POR CONTATO | 3044 | CONTRAÇÃO DO JATO |
| 3005 | PLATINADO | 3045 | CONTRAÇÃO |
| 3005 | PONTA DE CONTATO | 3045 | ENCURTAMENTO |
| 3006 | PONTA DE REPOSIÇÃO | 3046 | CONTRAÇÃO DO CORPO DO REBITE |
| 3007 | POTENCIAL DE CONTATO | 3047 | REGRA DE CONTRAÇÃO |
| 3008 | ROLETE DE CONTATO | 3048 | COMANDO |
| 3009 | PONTO DE CONTATO | 3048 | CONTROLE |
| 3010 | RECIPIENTE | 3049 | CONTROLAR |
| 3010 | RESERVATÓRIO | 3049 | MANOBRAR |
| 3010 | DEPÓSITO | 3049 | COMANDAR |
| 3011 | CONTEÚDO | 3050 | BRAÇO DE COMANDO |
| 3011 | TEOR | 3050 | BRAÇO DE SUSPENSÃO |
| 3011 | PROPORÇÃO | 3051 | CABO DE COMANDO |
| 3012 | LUBRIFICAÇÃO CONTÍNUA | 3052 | DISPOSITIVO DE CONTROLE |
| 3013 | PAPEL CONTÍNUO | 3053 | MANÔMETRO DE CONTROLE |
| 3014 | SINTERIZAÇÃO CONTÍNUA | 3053 | CALIBRE DE CONTROLE |
| 3015 | TRANSMISSÃO POR POLIAS MÚLTIPLAS | 3054 | PAINEL DE CONTROLE |
| 3016 | SOLDAGEM CONTÍNUA | 3054 | PAINEL DE COMANDO |
| 3017 | CONTINUIDADE | 3055 | FORNO DE ATMOSFERA CONTROLADA |
| 3018 | VIGA CONTÍNUA | 3056 | RESFRIAMENTO CONTROLADO |
| 3019 | FUNDIÇÃO CONTÍNUA | 3056 | REFRIGERAÇÃO CONTROLADA |
| 3020 | ELEVADOR CONTÍNUO | 3057 | CONTROLADOR |
| 3021 | DÍNAMO | 3057 | CONTROLER |
| 3021 | GERADOR DE CORRENTE CONTÍNUA | 3058 | CANTONEIRA |
| 3022 | MOTOR DE CORRENTE CONTÍNUA | 3058 | SUPORTE ANGULAR |
| 3023 | CORRENTE CONTÍNUA | 3059 | TRANSMISSÃO |
| 3024 | DESTILAÇÃO CONTÍNUA | 3059 | CONVECÇÃO |
| 3025 | FUNÇÃO CONTÍNUA | 3060 | CONVECÇÃO |
| 3026 | FORNO CONTÍNUO | 3061 | FRESAGEM CLÁSSICA (TRADICIONAL) |
| 3027 | GALVANIZAÇÃO CONTÍNUA | 3062 | CONVERGIR |
| 3028 | TÊMPERA CONTÍNUA A QUENTE | 3063 | CONVERGÊNCIA |
| 3029 | LINGOTAMENTO CONTÍNUO | 3064 | CONVERGENTE |
| 3030 | LAMINADOR CONTÍNUO | 3065 | SÉRIE CONVERGENTE |
| 3031 | MOVIMENTO CONTÍNUO | 3066 | BOCAL CONVERGENTE |
| 3032 | COMANDO CONTÍNUO | 3067 | CONVERSÃO |
| 3033 | FASE CONTÍNUA | 3068 | TRANSFORMAÇÃO DE FERRO EM AÇO |
| 3033 | FASE DISPERSIVA | 3069 | TABELA OU TÁBUA DE CONVERSÃO |
| 3034 | PRODUÇÃO CONTÍNUA | 3070 | TRANSFORMAÇÃO DE ENERGIA |
| 3034 | FABRICAÇÃO EM SÉRIE | 3071 | TRANSFORMADOR |
| 3035 | LAMINAÇÃO CONTÍNUA | 3071 | CONVERSOR |
| 3036 | ESPECTRO CONTÍNUO | 3072 | CONE DO CONVERSOR |
| 3037 | SOLDA CONTÍNUA | 3073 | CARRO CONVERSÍVEL |
| 3037 | SOLDAGEM CONTÍNUA | 3074 | FORNO DE CEMENTAÇÃO |
| 3038 | SERVIÇO CONTÍNUO | 3075 | CAIXA DE CEMENTAÇÃO |
| 3038 | FUNCIONAMENTO CONTÍNUO | 3076 | CONVEXO |

| | | | |
|---|---|---|---|
| 3077 | SOLDAGEM DE ÂNGULO CONVEXO | 3113 | BARRA DE COBRE |
| 3078 | ESPELHO CONVEXO | 3114 | MOEDAS DE COBRE |
| 3079 | RELAÇÃO DE CONVEXIDADE | 3115 | CIANETO DE COBRE |
| 3080 | TRANSPORTADOR | 3116 | FIO OU ARAME PLANO (OU CHATO) DE COBRE |
| 3081 | RESFRIAR | | |
| 3081 | REFRIGERAR | 3117 | FOLHA FINA DE COBRE |
| 3082 | TEMPO DE REFRIGERAÇÃO | 3118 | PROTO-SULFURETO NATURAL DE COBRE |
| 3083 | REFRIGERANTE | 3118 | CALCOSITA |
| 3083 | ESFRIADOR | 3119 | MARTELO DE COBRE |
| 3083 | FLUIDO DE RESFRIAR | 3120 | LINGOTE DE COBRE |
| 3084 | PISTÃO ESFRIADO | 3121 | MATE DE COBRE |
| 3085 | RESFRIAMENTO | 3122 | MINÉRIO DE COBRE |
| 3085 | REFRIGERAÇÃO | 3123 | LÂMINA OU FOLHA DE COBRE |
| 3086 | AGENTE DE REFRIGERAÇÃO | 3123 | PLACA OU CHAPA DE COBRE |
| 3087 | CURVA DE RESFRIAMENTO | 3124 | REVESTIR DE COBRE |
| 3088 | VENTILADOR DE REFRIGERAÇÃO | 3124 | FOLHEAR DE COBRE |
| 3089 | INSTALAÇÃO PARA RESFRIAMENTO DAS ÁGUAS DE CONDENSAÇÃO | 3124 | COBREAR |
| | | 3125 | COBREAÇÃO |
| 3090 | DEPÓSITO DE RESFRIAMENTO | 3125 | REVESTIMENTO COM COBRE |
| 3091 | ESFORÇOS DE ESFRIAMENTO | 3126 | CALCOPIRITA |
| 3092 | SUPERFÍCIE DE ESFRIAMENTO | 3126 | PIRITA DE COBRE |
| 3092 | SUPERFÍCIE DE REFRIGERAÇÃO | 3127 | CHAPA OU PLACA DE COBRE |
| 3093 | SISTEMA DE REFRIGERAÇÃO | 3128 | GRÂNULOS DE COBRE PURO |
| 3093 | SISTEMA DE RESFRIAMENTO | 3128 | GRANALHA DE COBRE |
| 3094 | TORRE DE ESFRIAMENTO | 3129 | PLACA DE COBRE FUNDIDO |
| 3095 | ÁGUA REFRIGERANTE | 3129 | LINGOTE PLANO DE COBRE |
| 3095 | ÁGUA DE REFRIGERAÇÃO | 3130 | AÇO AO COBRE |
| 3096 | VOLTA À TEMPERATURA AMBIENTE | 3131 | LÂMINA DE COBRE |
| 3097 | COTAÇÃO ABSOLUTA | 3132 | TUBO DE COBRE |
| 3098 | PERFURADEIRA E ESCAREADORA DE COORDENADAS | 3133 | FIO OU ARAME DE COBRE |
| | | 3134 | JUNTA DE METAL E PLÁSTICO |
| 3099 | POSIÇÃO POR COORDENADAS | 3135 | CALDEIREIRO DE COBRE |
| 3100 | COORDENADAS | 3136 | CALDEIRARIA DE COBRE |
| 3101 | COPAÍBA | 3137 | SOLDA DE COBRE |
| 3102 | GOMA COPAL | 3138 | TORNO DUPLICADOR |
| 3102 | RESINA COPAL | 3138 | TORNO DE COPIAR |
| 3103 | VERNIZ DE COPAL | 3139 | MÁQUINA COPIADORA |
| 3104 | ABÓBADA | 3139 | MÁQUINA DE REPRODUZIR |
| 3104 | PARTE DE CIMA | 3140 | CONSOLO |
| 3104 | CÚPULA | 3140 | MODILHÃO |
| 3105 | MODELO EM DUAS PARTES | 3141 | TRANSMISSÃO POR CORREIAS DE IMPULSÃO |
| 3106 | FIO OU ARAME DE COBRE | | |
| 3107 | CUMEEIRA | 3142 | CONDUTOR |
| 3108 | SERRA DE CONTORNAR | 3142 | NÚCLEO |
| 3108 | SERRA DE RECORTAR | 3142 | MADRE |
| 3108 | SERRA TICO-TICO | 3142 | MACHO |
| 3109 | PÁRA-RAIOS | 3142 | ALMA |
| 3109 | PÁRA-FAÍSCAS | 3143 | BARRA DE REFORÇO DE MACHO |
| 3110 | COBRE | 3143 | ARMADURA DE NÚCLEO |
| 3111 | LIGA DE COBRE | 3144 | PONTO DE GUIA DOS NÚCLEOS |
| 3112 | ÁNODO DE COBRE | 3145 | AGLOMERANTE PARA MACHOS |

| | | | |
|---|---|---|---|
| 3146 | MÁQUINA DE MOLDAR OS MACHOS | 3182 | CORROER |
| 3147 | CAIXA DE MACHOS | 3183 | CORROSÃO |
| 3148 | COQUILHA DE SECAGEM | 3184 | AÇOS RESISTENTES À CORROSÃO E AO CALOR |
| 3149 | BROCA OCA | | |
| 3149 | PERFURADORA DE SOLO | 3184 | AÇOS ANTICORROSIVOS E ANTITÉRMICOS |
| 3150 | MÁQUINA DE RETIFICAÇÃO DE MACHOS | 3185 | CORROSÃO FISSURANTE |
| 3151 | AGLOMERANTE PARA MACHOS | 3186 | FRAGILIDADE POR CORROSÃO |
| 3152 | GANCHO DE NÚCLEOS | 3187 | FADIGA POR CORROSÃO |
| 3153 | MÁQUINA DE REMOÇÃO DE MACHOS DE AREIA | 3188 | LIMITE DE FADIGA POR CORROSÃO |
| | | 3189 | INIBIDOR DE CORROSÃO |
| 3153 | MÁQUINA DE EXTRAIR OS NÚCLEOS | 3189 | PRODUTO ANTICORROSIVO |
| 3154 | MÁQUINA DE MOLDAR MACHOS | 3190 | PICADURA POR CORROSÃO |
| 3155 | NÚCLEO DE UMA GAXETA | 3191 | PREVENÇÃO CONTRA A CORROSÃO |
| 3156 | NÚCLEO DA SEÇÃO | 3192 | SOLVENTES PARA CORROSIVOS |
| 3157 | ÓLEO DE MACHOS | 3193 | VELOCIDADE DE CORROSÃO |
| 3157 | ÓLEO DE NÚCLEOS | 3194 | RESISTÊNCIA À CORROSÃO |
| 3158 | FORNO PARA MACHOS | 3195 | CORROSÃO SOB TENSÃO |
| 3159 | JUNTA DE INSERÇÃO | 3196 | CÁUSTICO |
| 3160 | PLACA PARA MACHOS DE MOLDAGEM | 3196 | CORROSIVO |
| 3160 | DISCO DE CHAPA (DE INDUZIDO) | 3197 | SUBSTÂNCIA CORROSIVA |
| 3160 | ALMA (DE PILHA) | 3198 | CHAPA DE FERRO CORRUGADA |
| 3161 | PORTA-MACHO | 3198 | CHAPA ONDULADA |
| 3161 | MARCA DO MACHO | 3199 | TUBO CORRUGADO OU ONDULADO |
| 3162 | SALIÊNCIA NA MATRIZ QUE FURA O COMPACTADO DE PÓ | 3200 | TELA ONDULADA |
| | | 3201 | CORINDO |
| 3163 | AREIA PARA MACHOS | 3201 | CORÍNDON |
| 3164 | NÚLEO DE FILTRO | 3201 | ESMERIL |
| 3165 | ESTRUTURA DO NÚCLEO | 3202 | CO-SECANTE |
| 3166 | EXTRAÇÃO DO AR DOS MACHOS | 3203 | CO-SENO |
| 3167 | ALMA (DE CABO) | 3204 | GASTOS DE MANUTENÇÃO |
| 3168 | BARRA DE MACHO FUSÍVEL | 3205 | GASTOS DE EMBALAGEM |
| 3169 | CRISTAL ZONADO | 3206 | GASTOS DE FORÇA MOTRIZ |
| 3169 | CRISTAL INOMÓGENO | 3207 | GASTOS DE PRODUÇÃO |
| 3170 | ESTRUTURA CRISTALINA ZONADA | 3208 | GASTOS DE REPARAÇÕES |
| 3170 | HETEROGENEIDADE | 3209 | GASTOS DE TRANSPORTES |
| 3171 | REVESTIMENTO PARA MACHOS | 3209 | GASTOS DE FRETE |
| 3172 | SEGREGAÇÃO | 3210 | PREÇO DE CUSTO |
| 3172 | MICROSSEGREGAÇÃO | 3211 | CO-TANGENTE |
| 3173 | CORTIÇA | 3212 | PASSADOR |
| 3173 | ROLHA DE CORTIÇA | 3212 | CHAVE |
| 3174 | TIJOLO DE CORTIÇA | 3212 | CHAVETA |
| 3175 | PLACA OU CHAPA DE CORTIÇA | 3213 | PASSADOR DE RETENÇÃO |
| 3176 | TAMPA DE CORTIÇA | 3213 | CAVILHA DE CHAVETA |
| 3177 | MAQUINÁRIA DE CLASSIFICAÇÃO E DE LIMPEZA DE MILHO E SEMENTES | 3213 | CONTRAPINO |
| | | 3214 | FURO DO PASSADOR |
| 3178 | MÁQUINA DE ABRIR FUROS EM ÂNGULO | 3215 | CHAVETA TRANSVERSAL |
| 3179 | JUNTA ANGULAR | 3215 | CAVILHA DE CUNHA |
| 3180 | ESTABILIDADE NA ESTRADA EM CURVA | 3216 | MAÇARICO DE CORTE |
| 3181 | CORREÇÃO | 3217 | ALGODÃO |
| 3182 | DESGASTAR | 3218 | CORREIA OU CINTA DE ALGODÃO |
| 3182 | ATACAR | 3219 | ARAME REVESTIDO DE ALGODÃO |

| | | | |
|---|---|---|---|
| 3219 | FIO REVESTIDO DE ALGODÃO | 3253 | UNIR |
| 3219 | FIO COM ENCAPAMENTO DE ALGODÃO | 3253 | ACOPLAR |
| 3220 | TRANÇA DE ALGODÃO | 3253 | JUNTAR |
| 3221 | CORDA DE ALGODÃO | 3254 | ACOPLAMENTO |
| 3222 | ÓLEO DE SEMENTE DE ALGODÃO | 3254 | UNIÃO |
| 3223 | ESTOPA DE ALGODÃO | 3254 | JUNÇÃO |
| 3224 | BARREIRA DE COTTRELL | 3255 | FLANGE DE ACOPLAMENTO |
| 3225 | COULOMB | 3255 | DISCO DE UNIÃO |
| 3226 | MÓDULO DE COULOMB | 3256 | BIELA DE ACOPLAMENTO |
| 3227 | COULÔMETRO | 3256 | TIRANTE DE ACOPLAMENTO |
| 3228 | DÍNAMO COMPOUND | 3257 | LUVA DE ACOPLAMENTO |
| 3229 | CONTADOR | 3258 | ACOPLAMENTO |
| 3230 | CONTRACORRENTE | 3258 | ACOPLAGEM |
| 3231 | FORÇA CONTRA ELETROMOTRIZ | 3259 | ASSENTO DE TIJOLOS |
| 3232 | CONTRAPRESSÃO | 3259 | CARREIRA DE TIJOLOS |
| 3233 | CONTRAVEIO | 3260 | VIROLA DE CALDEIRA |
| 3233 | CONTRA-EIXO | 3261 | CO-VARIÂNCIA |
| 3233 | EIXO INTERMEDIÁRIO | 3262 | CHAPA PROTETORA |
| 3234 | ESCAREAMENTO | 3262 | TAMPA |
| 3235 | EIXO DE MANIVELAS A CONTRAPESO | 3263 | REVESTIR UM TUBO |
| 3235 | VIRABREQUIM A CONTRAPESO | 3264 | CAMADA DE ACABAMENTO |
| 3236 | ESCAREAMENTO | 3264 | LUSTRE DE ACABAMENTO |
| 3236 | REBAIXAMENTO | 3265 | VIDRO DE TAMPA |
| 3237 | MOVIMENTO PARA A ESQUERDA | 3266 | TAMPA DE VÁLVULA |
| 3237 | SENTIDO ANTI-HORÁRIO | 3266 | TAMPA DE TORNEIRA |
| 3238 | ROTAÇÃO NO SENTIDO ANTI-HORÁRIO | 3267 | CHAPA DE REFORÇO |
| 3238 | ROTAÇÃO PARA A ESQUERDA | 3267 | TAMPA |
| 3239 | BOBINADO PARA A ESQUERDA | 3268 | CHAPA METÁLICA PROTETORA |
| 3240 | CONTRAVEIO | 3268 | TIRA METÁLICA DE PROTEÇÃO |
| 3240 | CONTRA-EIXO | 3269 | TAMPA |
| 3241 | PERFURAÇÃO | 3270 | CAME COM RANHURA |
| 3241 | ESCAREAMENTO | 3271 | ELÉTRODO REVESTIDO |
| 3242 | ESCAREAMENTO | 3272 | FIO OU ARAME ENCAPADO |
| 3243 | MOVIMENTO EM SENTIDO CONTRÁRIO | 3273 | PODER DE COBRIR |
| 3244 | TRANSMISSÃO INTERMEDIÁRIA | 3274 | REVESTIMENTO |
| 3244 | TRANSMISSÃO DE MOVIMENTO | 3274 | ENVOLTÓRIO |
| 3245 | FRESADORA | 3274 | COBERTURA |
| 3245 | ESCAREADOR | 3275 | COURO DE BOI |
| 3246 | ESCAREAR A CABEÇA DE UM PARAFUSO, DE UM REBITE | 3275 | COURO DE VACA |
| 3247 | ESCAREAR UM FURO PARA PARAFUSO, PARA REBITE | 3276 | CAPÔ |
| 3248 | PARAFUSO DE CABEÇA EMBUTIDA | 3276 | TAMPA |
| 3249 | REBITE DE CABEÇA ESCAREADA | 3276 | CAPOTA |
| 3249 | REBITE DE CABEÇA EMBUTIDA | 3277 | INSTALAÇÕES PARA ESTÁBULOS |
| 3250 | CABEÇA ESCAREADA DE PARAFUSO | 3278 | RUPTURA |
| 3251 | CONTRAPESO | 3278 | FENDA |
| 3252 | BINÁRIO (DE FORÇA) | 3278 | GRETA |
| 3252 | PAR (DE FORÇA) | 3278 | RACHADURA |
| 3252 | TORQUE | 3278 | BRECHA |
| | | 3278 | FISSURA |
| | | 3278 | FALHA |
| | | 3279 | RACHAR |

| | |
|---|---|
| 3279 | QUEBRAR |
| 3279 | FENDER-SE |
| 3280 | DETECTOR DE RACHADURAS E FENDAS |
| 3281 | FENDILHAMENTO NAS BORDAS |
| 3282 | FISSURA DO AÇO TEMPERADO |
| 3282 | RACHADURA DO AÇO TEMPERADO |
| 3283 | MICROFISSURA |
| 3284 | ESTAMPIDO |
| 3284 | FISSURAÇÃO |
| 3284 | CRAQUEAMENTO |
| 3285 | PROCESSO DE "CRACKING" |
| 3286 | FISSURAÇÃO DOS FUROS DE REBITES |
| 3287 | TORNO DE "CRACKING" |
| 3288 | CAVALETE |
| 3288 | BERÇO |
| 3288 | SUPORTE |
| 3289 | TÉCNICO |
| 3289 | OPERÁRIO PROFISSIONAL |
| 3289 | ARTÍFICE |
| 3290 | GRUA |
| 3290 | GUINDASTE |
| 3291 | BRAÇO DE GUINDASTE |
| 3291 | LANÇA DE GUINDASTE |
| 3292 | COLHER DE GRUA |
| 3293 | VIGA DE ROLAMENTO DE GRUA |
| 3293 | TRILHO DE GUINDASTE |
| 3294 | GRUAS AGRÍCOLAS |
| 3295 | MANIVELA |
| 3296 | BRAÇO DE MANIVELA |
| 3297 | CUBO DE MANIVELA |
| 3298 | CÍRCULO DESCRITO PELA MANIVELA |
| 3299 | CABEÇA GRANDE DE BIELA |
| 3300 | CABO DA MANIVELA |
| 3301 | BRAÇO DA MANIVELA |
| 3302 | PINO DA MANIVELA |
| 3302 | ESPIGA DA MANIVELA |
| 3303 | MANCAL DO EIXO DE MANIVELAS |
| 3303 | MANCAL PRINCIPAL |
| 3304 | BRAÇO DA MANIVELA |
| 3305 | MANIVELA COM LUVA |
| 3306 | CÁRTER |
| 3306 | CAIXA DE EIXO DE MANIVELA |
| 3307 | RESPIRADOURO |
| 3308 | ÓLEO DE PURGA DO CÁRTER |
| 3309 | EIXO DE COTOVELO |
| 3309 | EIXO DE MANIVELA |
| 3310 | MOTOR DE PARTIDA |
| 3310 | MOTOR DE ARRANQUE |
| 3311 | PINO DE BIELA |
| 3311 | MOENTE DO VIRABREQUIM |
| 3312 | ANÉIS DE TORNEAR |

| | |
|---|---|
| 3313 | EIXO DE MANIVELA |
| 3313 | VIRABREQUIM |
| 3314 | MANCAL DO EIXO DE MANIVELAS |
| 3315 | ENGRENAGEM DO EIXO DE MANIVELAS |
| 3315 | PINHÃO DO EIXO DE MANIVELAS |
| 3316 | TORNO DE EIXOS DE MANIVELAS |
| 3317 | CRATERA |
| 3318 | GRETA CAPILAR |
| 3319 | FISSURAÇÃO SUPERFICIAL |
| 3320 | DOBRA |
| 3320 | PREGA |
| 3321 | MARTELO DE ESTRIAR |
| 3321 | MARTELO DE ACANALAR |
| 3322 | BIGORNA |
| 3323 | MÁQUINA DE ESTRIAR |
| 3324 | FLUÊNCIA |
| 3324 | DEFORMAÇÃO |
| 3325 | LIMITE DE FLUÊNCIA |
| 3326 | VELOCIDADE (RITMO) DE FLUÊNCIA |
| 3327 | RESISTÊNCIA À FLUÊNCIA DEPENDENDO DO TEMPO |
| 3328 | RESISTÊNCIA À FLUÊNCIA |
| 3329 | CONTRAÇÃO DA CORREIA |
| 3330 | FLUÊNCIA DE UMA SOLUÇÃO |
| 3331 | ÓLEO DE CREOSOTO |
| 3332 | CREOSOTAGEM |
| 3333 | CRISTA |
| 3333 | VÉRTICE |
| 3333 | CUME |
| 3333 | CUMEEIRA |
| 3334 | CRISTA DA ONDA |
| 3335 | FOLGA NA CRISTA |
| 3335 | ESPAÇO LIVRE ENTRE VÉRTICE E FUNDO |
| 3336 | ENRUGAR |
| 3336 | PREGUEAR |
| 3336 | ONDULAR |
| 3337 | FLAMBAGEM |
| 3337 | DEFORMAÇÃO PERMANENTE |
| 3338 | CARGA DE RUPTURA À FLAMBAGEM |
| 3339 | ESFORÇO DE FLAMBAGEM |
| 3340 | RESISTÊNCIA À FLAMBAGEM |
| 3341 | ESFORÇO DE FLAMBAGEM POR UNIDADE DE SEÇÃO |
| 3342 | TESTE DE FLAMBAGEM |
| 3342 | ENSAIO DE FLAMBAGEM |
| 3343 | FLAMBAGEM |
| 3343 | CAMBAMENTO |
| 3344 | ENVELHECIMENTO COMPLETO |
| 3344 | ENVELHECIMENTO CRÍTICO |
| 3345 | ÂNGULO LIMITE |
| 3345 | ÂNGULO CRÍTICO |

| | |
|---|---|
| 3346 | UMIDADE CRÍTICA |
| 3347 | TEMPERATURA DE TRANSFORMAÇÃO |
| 3347 | PONTO CRÍTICO |
| 3348 | PRESSÃO CRÍTICA |
| 3349 | ESTADO CRÍTICO |
| 3350 | DEFORMAÇÃO CRÍTICA |
| 3351 | TENSÃO CRÍTICA |
| 3352 | TEMPERATURA DE TRANSFORMAÇÃO |
| 3352 | TEMPERATURA CRÍTICA |
| 3353 | VELOCIDADE CRÍTICA |
| 3354 | VOLUME CRÍTICO |
| 3355 | AÇAFRÃO |
| 3356 | AFLORAMENTO |
| 3356 | PONTAS DE REFUGO |
| 3357 | DESBASTE |
| 3357 | APARA |
| 3358 | TESOURA DE CORTE DE PONTAS |
| 3358 | TESOURA PARA RECORTE |
| 3359 | CRUZ |
| 3360 | ESTRUTURA DE CRUZETAS |
| 3361 | BARRA TRANSVERSAL |
| 3361 | TRAVESSA |
| 3361 | PONTALETE |
| 3361 | TIRANTE |
| 3362 | VEÍCULO PARA TODO TERRENO |
| 3363 | CORRENTE CRUZADA |
| 3363 | CORRENTE TRANSVERSAL |
| 3364 | BEDAME |
| 3365 | SERROTE GRANDE |
| 3265 | TRAÇADOR |
| 3366 | APLICAÇÃO DE PICADURAS CRUZADAS |
| 3367 | TRAVESSÃO |
| 3368 | PEÇA EM CRUZ |
| 3368 | CRUZ DE QUATRO DIREÇÕES |
| 3369 | PENA CRUZADA |
| 3370 | PRENSA DE FUNDIÇÃO |
| 3371 | SEÇÃO TRANSVERSAL |
| 3371 | PERFIL TRANSVERSAL |
| 3371 | CORTE TRANSVERSAL |
| 3372 | FERRO EM CRUZ |
| 3373 | SEÇÃO DE RUPTURA |
| 3373 | PLANO DE RUPTURA |
| 3374 | SEÇÃO DE PASSAGEM |
| 3374 | SEÇÃO LIVRE |
| 3375 | SEÇÃO SUJEITA A UM ESFORÇO DE COMPRESSÃO |
| 3376 | SEÇÃO SUJEITA A ESFORÇO DE TRAÇÃO |
| 3377 | SEÇÃO TRANSVERSAL |
| 3377 | PERFIL TRANSVERSAL |
| 3378 | SEÇÃO TRANSVERSAL |
| 3379 | CARRO DE ESPERA TRANSVERSAL |

| | |
|---|---|
| 3379 | CARRINHO PORTA-FERRAMENTA TRANSVERSAL |
| 3380 | DESVIO |
| 3381 | AÇO EM CRUZ |
| 3382 | CORDÃO DE ESMAGAMENTO |
| 3383 | CRUZ RETICULAR |
| 3383 | RETÍCULO |
| 3384 | LAMINAÇÃO TRANSVERSAL |
| 3385 | SOLDAGEM DE FIOS EM CRUZ |
| 3386 | REGULADOR FARCOT |
| 3386 | REGULADOR DE BRAÇOS CRUZADOS |
| 3387 | CORREIA CRUZADA |
| 3387 | CORREIA INVERTIDA |
| 3388 | CRUZETA |
| 3389 | PÉ DA BIELA |
| 3390 | MANCAL DE PÉ DE BIELA |
| 3391 | PINO DA CRUZETA |
| 3391 | MUNHÃO GIRATÓRIO PARA FORQUILHA |
| 3391 | MUNHÃO DA CRUZETA |
| 3392 | LIMA OVALADA |
| 3392 | LIMA CRUZADA |
| 3393 | PONTO DE CRUZAMENTO |
| 3394 | ALÇAPREMA |
| 3394 | PÉ-DE-CABRA |
| 3394 | ALAVANCA DE UNHA |
| 3395 | MARCAS DE TREFILAÇÃO |
| 3395 | ARANHA |
| 3396 | COROA |
| 3396 | CONTORNO |
| 3396 | CONVEXIDADE |
| 3396 | TETO |
| 3396 | VÉRTICE |
| 3397 | VIDRO LEVE |
| 3397 | CROWN-GLASS |
| 3398 | ABAULAMENTO DO ARO DE UMA POLIA |
| 3399 | ENGRENAGEM DE COROA |
| 3399 | COROA DENTADA |
| 3399 | RODA DENTADA |
| 3400 | POLIA CONVEXA |
| 3401 | CADINHO |
| 3401 | CRISOL |
| 3402 | FORNALHA DE CADINHO |
| 3402 | FORNO DE CRISOL |
| 3403 | LEVANTADOR DE CRISOL |
| 3404 | PROCESSO DE CRISOL |
| 3405 | TORQUÊS DE CADINHO |
| 3405 | TENAZES DE CRISOL |
| 3406 | CRU |
| 3406 | BRUTO |
| 3406 | SEM USINAGEM |
| 3407 | TANQUE DE PETRÓLEO BRUTO |

| | |
|---|---|
| 3408 | BENZINA BRUTA |
| 3408 | GASOLINA BRUTA |
| 3409 | CHUMBO BRUTO |
| 3410 | METAL NÃO REFINADO |
| 3410 | METAL BRUTO |
| 3411 | ÓLEO CRU |
| 3411 | PETRÓLEO BRUTO |
| 3412 | PETRÓLEO BRUTO |
| 3412 | ÓLEO CRU |
| 3413 | BORRACHA CRUA OU BRUTA |
| 3413 | BORRACHA VIRGEM |
| 3414 | AÇO NÃO REFINADO |
| 3414 | AÇO BRUTO |
| 3415 | TEREBINTINA NÃO RETIFICADA |
| 3415 | TEREBINTINA BRUTA |
| 3416 | AUTONOMIA DE CRUZEIRO |
| 3417 | VELOCIDADE DE CRUZEIRO |
| 3418 | DESAGREGAÇÃO |
| 3418 | DESINTEGRAÇÃO |
| 3418 | DESMORONAMENTO |
| 3419 | TRITURADOR |
| 3419 | BRITADOR |
| 3419 | PILÃO |
| 3420 | MOEDURA |
| 3420 | BRITAGEM |
| 3420 | TRITURAÇÃO |
| 3420 | ESMAGAMENTO |
| 3421 | CROSTA |
| 3421 | CASCA |
| 3421 | INCRUSTAÇÃO |
| 3422 | CRIOIDRATO |
| 3422 | MISTURA EUTÉTICA |
| 3423 | CRIOLITA |
| 3424 | CRISTAL |
| 3425 | ANÁLISE DE ESTRUTURA CRISTALINA |
| 3426 | ALONGAMENTO DOS CRISTAIS |
| 3427 | PLANO CRISTALINO |
| 3427 | FACE DE UM CRISTAL |
| 3427 | PLANO DE CRISTAL |
| 3428 | CRISTAL ARTIFICIAL |
| 3428 | CRISTAL |
| 3429 | MANCHAS POR CRISTAIS |
| 3430 | ESTRUTURA CRISTALINA |
| 3431 | SISTEMA CRISTALINO |
| 3431 | SISTEMA DOS CRISTAIS |
| 3432 | UNIDADE CRISTALINA |
| 3432 | CRISTAL OSCILANTE |
| 3433 | CRISTALINO |
| 3434 | TEXTURA CRISTALINA |
| 3435 | ENXOFRE CRISTALINO |
| 3435 | ENXOFRE CRISTALIZADO |

| | |
|---|---|
| 3436 | CRISTALIZABILIDADE |
| 3747 | CRISTALIZÁVEL |
| 3438 | CRISTALIZAÇÃO |
| 3439 | CRISTALIZAR |
| 3440 | CRISTALITO |
| 3441 | CRISTALOGRAMA |
| 3441 | DIAGRAMA DE DIFRAÇÃO A RAIOS X |
| 3442 | CRISTALOGRAFIA |
| 3443 | CRISTALÓIDE |
| 3444 | CUBAGEM |
| 3444 | CUBATURA |
| 3445 | CUBO |
| 3446 | ELEVAR AO CUBO |
| 3447 | RAIZ CÚBICA |
| 3448 | CILINDRADA |
| 3448 | CAPACIDADE CÚBICA |
| 3449 | CENTÍMETRO CÚBICO |
| 3450 | CRISTAIS CÚBICOS |
| 3451 | DECÍMETRO CÚBICO |
| 3452 | EQUAÇÃO CÚBICA |
| 3452 | EQUAÇÃO DO TERCEIRO GRAU |
| 3453 | PÉ CÚBICO |
| 3454 | POLEGADA CÚBICA |
| 3455 | METRO CÚBICO |
| 3456 | MILÍMETRO CÚBICO |
| 3457 | CULTIVADORES |
| 3458 | COURO EMBUTIDO |
| 3459 | GAXETA DE COURO EMBUTIDO |
| 3460 | FIBRAS TORCIDAS DE MADEIRA |
| 3461 | ARRUELA BELLEVILLE |
| 3462 | MÁQUINA DE ENSAIO DE ESTAMPAGEM PROFUNDA |
| 3462 | APARELHO DE TESTE DE DUCTILIDADE |
| 3463 | COPELAÇÃO |
| 3464 | CUBILÔ |
| 3464 | CÚPULA |
| 3465 | REGULADOR DE POTÊNCIA DE AR |
| 3466 | FORNO DE CUBILÔ |
| 3467 | FUNDIÇÃO DE CUBILÔ MALEÁVEL |
| 3468 | METAL DE CUBILÔ |
| 3469 | ESTAMPAGEM PROFUNDA |
| 3469 | EMBUTIMENTO |
| 3470 | CARBONATO DE COBRE |
| 3471 | ÓXIDO CÚPRICO HIDRATADO |
| 3472 | NITRATO DE COBRE |
| 3473 | NITRETO DE COBRE |
| 3474 | ÓXIDO DE COBRE |
| 3475 | SULFATO DE COBRE |
| 3476 | CUPRITA |
| 3477 | CUPRONÍQUEL |
| 3478 | CLORETO CÚPRICO |

| | |
|---|---|
| 3479 | CUPRITA |
| 3479 | ÓXIDO CÚPRICO |
| 3480 | PESO EM ORDEM DE MARCHA |
| 3481 | CURCUMINA |
| 3482 | SABÃO DOMÉSTICO |
| 3482 | SABÃO BRANCO COMUM |
| 3483 | CURA |
| 3483 | PEGA |
| 3483 | ENDURECIMENTO |
| 3483 | SOLIDIFICAÇÃO |
| 3484 | PEGA DO CIMENTO |
| 3484 | VULCANIZAÇÃO |
| 3485 | CONJUNTO DE MATRIZES DE REBORDEAR |
| 3485 | FERRAMENTA DE DOBRAR CHAPAS |
| 3486 | CORRENTE |
| 3487 | COORDENADAS CORRENTES |
| 3488 | DENSIDADE DA CORRENTE |
| 3489 | EFICIÊNCIA DA CORRENTE |
| 3489 | RENDIMENTO DA CORRENTE |
| 3490 | MEDIDOR DE CORRENTE |
| 3490 | AMPERÍMETRO |
| 3491 | REGULADOR DE CORRENTE |
| 3492 | CORTINAS |
| 3493 | CICLÓIDE ENCURTADA |
| 3494 | CURVATURA |
| 3494 | ARQUEAMENTO |
| 3495 | CURVA DE UM DIAGRAMA |
| 3496 | CURVA |
| 3497 | BRAÇO PARABÓLICO DE POLIA |
| 3498 | SUPERFÍCIE CURVA |
| 3498 | LADO CURVO |
| 3499 | CURVILÍNEO |
| 3500 | MOVIMENTO CURVILÍNEO |
| 3501 | CURVÍMETRO |
| 3502 | VÉRTICE DE UMA CURVA |
| 3502 | PONTO DE REVERSÃO DA CURVA |
| 3503 | CORTE |
| 3503 | GRAVURA |
| 3503 | CLICHÉ |
| 3503 | INCISÃO |
| 3504 | CORTAR |
| 3504 | TALHAR |
| 3504 | LAVRAR |
| 3505 | CORTAR POR PROCESSO AUTÓGENO |
| 3505 | CORTAR COM MAÇARICO |
| 3506 | GUME |
| 3507 | LAVRAR AS LIMAS |
| 3508 | RODA DE DENTES FRESADOS |
| 3509 | CORTAR NAS DIMENSÕES EXATAS |
| 3510 | DESLIGAR |
| 3510 | CORTAR |
| 3511 | ESTAMPAR OS REBITES |
| 3512 | CORTAR ROSCAS |
| 3513 | CORTAR CHAPAS |
| 3514 | DENTE FRESADO |
| 3515 | CORTAR COM TALHADEIRA |
| 3516 | DISJUNTOR |
| 3517 | CORTE DE SERRA |
| 3518 | CORTE DE LIMA |
| 3519 | FRESA |
| 3520 | EIXO DE FRESAR |
| 3521 | CORREÇÃO DE FRESA |
| 3522 | FRESAS |
| 3523 | CORTE |
| 3524 | ÂNGULO DE CORTE |
| 3524 | ÂNGULO DE ATAQUE |
| 3525 | DISPOSITIVO DE CORTE |
| 3526 | PROFUNDIDADE DE CORTE |
| 3527 | REBAIXO COM ESMERIL |
| 3527 | POLIMENTO DA SUPERFÍCIE |
| 3528 | ARESTA DE CORTE |
| 3528 | GUME DA FERRAMENTA |
| 3529 | LAVRA DE LIMAS |
| 3530 | FLUIDO CORROSIVO |
| 3530 | FLUIDO DE CORTE |
| 3531 | CABEÇA DE CORTE |
| 3532 | ALICATE DE CORTE |
| 3532 | TENAZ PARA CORTE |
| 3533 | CORTE |
| 3533 | INTERRUPÇÃO |
| 3534 | ÓLEO DE CORTE |
| 3535 | ROSQUEAMENTO |
| 3536 | CURSO DE CORTE |
| 3536 | MOVIMENTO DE CORTE |
| 3537 | BICO DE MAÇARICO |
| 3537 | PONTA DE CORTE |
| 3538 | FERRAMENTA DE CORTE |
| 3539 | MAÇARICO |
| 3540 | TORNO MECÂNICO DE TALHAR OU SANGRAR |
| 3541 | MÁQUINA DE TALHAR |
| 3542 | DISCO DE CORTAR |
| 3543 | APARAS |
| 3544 | CIANATO |
| 3545 | ÁCIDO CIÂNICO |
| 3546 | EXTRAÇÃO DE OURO POR CIANURAÇÃO |
| 3547 | CIANETO |
| 3548 | PRECIPITADOS DE METAIS NOBRES |
| 3548 | PARTÍCULAS DE METAIS NOBRES |
| 3549 | CIANURETAÇÃO |
| 3549 | ENDURECIMENTO COM CIANETO |
| 3549 | CIANOGENAÇÃO |

## 1211

| | | | |
|---|---|---|---|
| 3550 | FORNO DE CIANURETAÇÃO | 3587 | CALIBRES MACHOS CILÍNDRICOS |
| 3551 | CIANOGÊNIO | 3588 | ANEL CILÍNDRICO |
| 3552 | ÁCIDO CIANÚRICO | 3589 | ROLO CILÍNDRICO |
| 3553 | CICLO | 3590 | SUPERFÍCIE CILÍNDRICA |
| 3554 | CICLO DE FUNCIONAMENTO | 3591 | RODA CILÍNDRICA |
| 3554 | CICLO DE OPERAÇÕES | 3592 | GAVETA EM D |
| 3555 | CURVA CÍCLICA | 3593 | TUBO DE DESCIDA |
| 3556 | PERMUTAÇÃO CÍCLICA | 3594 | SALÁRIO |
| 3557 | CICLÓIDE | 3594 | DIÁRIA |
| 3558 | ENGRENAGEM CICLOIDAL | 3595 | MAQUINARIA DE LACTICÍNIO |
| 3559 | CICLÔMETRO DE ALGARISMOS | 3596 | CHAPA DE ESCÓRIA |
| 3559 | CONTADOR DE JANELA | 3596 | PLACA DE DAMA DO CADINHO |
| 3560 | CICLONE | 3597 | BARRAGEM OU REPRESA DE VALE |
| 3561 | CILINDRO | 3598 | RESINA DAMMAR |
| 3562 | CAMISA DE CILINDRO | 3598 | COPAL |
| 3562 | CORPO DE CILINDRO | 3599 | AR ÚMIDO |
| 3563 | BITE MEIA CANA | 3600 | VIBRAÇÃO AMORTECIDA |
| 3563 | BROCA DE CANHÃO | 3601 | AMORTECEDOR |
| 3564 | BLOCO DE CILINDROS | 3602 | AMORTECEDOR |
| 3564 | BLOCO DO MOTOR | 3603 | REGISTRO DE TIRAGEM DE CHAMINÉ |
| 3565 | MANDRILAGEM DE CILINDRO | 3604 | ATENUAÇÃO |
| 3565 | ALESAGEM DO CILINDRO | 3604 | AMORTECIMENTO |
| 3565 | RETIFICAÇÃO DE CILINDRO | 3605 | CAPACIDADE DE AMORTECIMENTO |
| 3565 | CALIBRE DO CILINDRO | 3606 | AMORTECIMENTO DE VIBRAÇÕES |
| 3565 | DIÂMETRO INTERNO DO CILINDRO | 3607 | A PRIMEIRA DE DUAS SOLEIRAS |
| 3566 | CILINDRADA | 3607 | FORNO DE LIGA INICIAL |
| 3567 | TAMPA DO CILINDRO | 3608 | PERIGO DE INCÊNDIO |
| 3568 | RETIFICADOR DE CILINDRO | 3608 | RISCO DE INCÊNDIO |
| 3569 | CABEÇA OU CABEÇOTE DO CILINDRO | 3609 | SEÇÃO PERIGOSA |
| 3569 | CULATRA DO CILINDRO | 3610 | PAINEL DE INSTRUMENTOS |
| 3570 | JUNTA DA CULATRA OU DO BLOCO DE CILINDROS | 3611 | AMORTECEDOR A ÊMBOLO |
| 3571 | CAMISA DO CILINDRO | 3612 | ELEMENTOS |
| 3571 | FORRO DO CILINDRO | 3612 | DADOS |
| 3572 | ÓLEO PARA CILINDROS | 3613 | CADERNO DE DADOS |
| 3573 | REGISTRADOR DE TAMBOR | 3614 | DOCUMENTAÇÃO TÉCNICA |
| 3574 | CABEÇA CILÍNDRICA DE PARAFUSO | 3615 | FOLHA DE DADOS |
| 3575 | TORNEIRA DE GARRAFA DE GÁS COMPRIMIDO | 3615 | FICHAS TÉCNICAS |
| 3576 | BOCAL CILÍNDRICO | 3616 | DATA DE REGISTRO DO REQUERIMENTO DE UMA PATENTE |
| 3577 | CILÍNDRICO | 3617 | DATA DE CONCESSÃO DA PATENTE |
| 3578 | CALDEIRA CILÍNDRICA | 3618 | BONECA |
| 3579 | CAME CILÍNDRICO | 3618 | GUINDASTE GIRATÓRIO |
| 3579 | TAMBOR CILÍNDRICO | 3619 | ALAVANCA DE MOVIMENTO GIRATÓRIO |
| 3580 | COORDENADAS CILÍNDRICAS | 3620 | TURNO DE DIA |
| 3581 | CALIBRE MACHO-FÊMEA | 3621 | TRABALHO DIÁRIO |
| 3582 | CILINDRO GRADUADO | 3622 | LUZ DO DIA |
| 3583 | RETIFICADORA DE CILINDROS | 3622 | LUZ NATURAL |
| 3584 | GUIA CILÍNDRICA | 3623 | DESAERAÇÃO DA ÁGUA |
| 3585 | MOLA HELICOIDAL CILÍNDRICA | 3624 | EIXO PASSIVO |
| 3586 | TUBO CILÍNDRICO | 3624 | EIXO FIXO |
| | | 3625 | PONTO MORTO |

| | | | | |
|---|---|---|---|---|
| 3625 | CENTRO FIXO | | 3663 | VELA DECIMAL |
| 3626 | PONTO MORTO | | 3664 | NÚMERO DECIMAL |
| 3627 | CONDUTOR DESLIGADO | | 3665 | SISTEMA DECIMAL |
| 3627 | CONDUTOR SEM CORRENTE | | 3666 | DECÍMETRO |
| 3628 | DECAPAGEM FOSCA | | 3667 | CONVÉS |
| 3629 | BÓIA DE MADEIRA | | 3667 | PONTE |
| 3630 | FURO CEGO | | 3667 | TETO |
| 3630 | FURO SEM SAÍDA | | 3668 | DECLINAÇÃO DA AGULHA MAGNÉTICA |
| 3631 | CARGA MORTA | | 3669 | COZIMENTO |
| 3631 | CARGA IMÓVEL | | 3669 | DECOCÇÃO |
| 3631 | PESO MORTO | | 3670 | DECIFRADOR |
| 3631 | CARGA ESTÁTICA | | 3670 | DECODIFICADOR |
| 3632 | VÁLVULA DE SEGURANÇA DE CARGA DIRETA | | 3671 | SUSCETÍVEL DE DECOMPOSIÇÃO |
| 3633 | CARGA PERMANENTE | | 3672 | DECOMPOR |
| 3634 | AQUECIMENTO ACIMA DO PONTO DE FUSÃO | | 3673 | DECOMPOR-SE |
| 3635 | PONTO MORTO | | 3674 | DECOMPOSIÇÃO |
| 3636 | CALCINAÇÃO TOTAL | | 3675 | VOLTAGEM DE DECOMPOSIÇÃO ELETROLÍTICA |
| 3637 | PESO MORTO | | 3676 | DECOMPOSIÇÃO DA LUZ |
| 3637 | CONTRAPESO | | 3677 | DIMINUIÇÃO DE VELOCIDADE |
| 3638 | FREIO A ALAVANCA E CONTRAPESO | | 3678 | REDUZIR A VELOCIDADE |
| 3639 | MAGNESITA MORTA | | 3679 | VELOCIDADE DECRESCENTE |
| 3640 | AMORTECER UM GOLPE | | 3680 | DEFEITO DA SUBSTÂNCIA |
| 3641 | SUBSTÂNCIA IMPERMEÁVEL AO SOM | | 3681 | DEDENDUM |
| 3642 | REBARBAÇÃO | | 3681 | DISTÂNCIA ENTRE O PASSO CIRCULAR E A RAIZ DO DENTE DE ENGRENAGEM |
| 3643 | MÉTODO DE DEBYE-SCHERRER | | | |
| 3644 | DECÁGONO | | 3682 | DESEMPOEIRAMENTO |
| 3645 | DECAGRAMA | | 3682 | EXTRAÇÃO DO PÓ |
| 3646 | DECALESCÊNCIA | | 3683 | ESTAMPAGEM PROFUNDA |
| 3647 | DECALITRO | | 3683 | EMBUTIMENTO PROFUNDO |
| 3648 | DECÂMETRO | | 3684 | TESTE DE ATAQUE PROFUNDO |
| 3649 | DECANTAR | | 3684 | ENSAIO DE CORROSÃO PROFUNDA |
| 3650 | DECANTAÇÃO | | 3685 | CAUSTICAÇÃO PROFUNDA |
| 3651 | DESCARBURAÇÃO | | 3685 | ATAQUE PROFUNDO |
| 3651 | DESCARBONETAÇÃO | | 3686 | FURADEIRA DE ABRIR FUROS PROFUNDOS |
| 3652 | DESCARBONETAR | | 3687 | MÁQUINA DE FURAR E ESCAREAR FUROS PROFUNDOS |
| 3652 | DESCARBONIZAR | | | |
| 3653 | DESCARBURAÇÃO DO FERRO | | 3688 | AÇO PARA EMBUTIMENTO PROFUNDO |
| 3654 | DESCARBURAR O FERRO | | 3689 | BOMBA PARA POÇO PROFUNDO |
| 3655 | DESCARBURAÇÃO | | 3690 | LATÃO APROPRIADO PARA EMBUTIMENTO PROFUNDO |
| 3656 | DESINTEGRAÇÃO | | | |
| 3656 | DETERIORAÇÃO | | 3691 | DEFEITO |
| 3656 | QUEDA | | 3691 | FALHA |
| 3656 | ESTRAGO | | 3691 | IMPERFEIÇÃO |
| 3656 | CORRUPÇÃO | | 3692 | FALHA DO MATERIAL |
| 3657 | DECIGRAMA | | 3693 | DEFEITO DE FABRICAÇÃO |
| 3658 | DECILITRO | | 3694 | PROJETO DEFEITUOSO |
| 3659 | DECIMAL | | 3695 | DEFEITO DE FUNCIONAMENTO |
| 3660 | BALANÇA DECIMAL | | 3696 | PEÇAS DEFEITUOSAS |
| 3661 | CÓDIGO DECIMAL | | 3696 | TRABALHO DEFEITUOSO |
| 3662 | FRAÇÃO DECIMAL | | 3697 | INTEGRAL DEFINIDA |

1213

| | | | |
|---|---|---|---|
| 3698 | AFASTAMENTO | 3736 | TUBO DE PRESSÃO |
| 3698 | DESVIO | 3737 | CONDIÇÕES DE ENTREGA |
| 3698 | DEFORMAÇÃO | 3738 | TUBO DIVERGENTE |
| 3698 | FLECHA | 3738 | TUBO DE RECALQUE |
| 3698 | FLEXÃO | 3738 | TUBO DE DISTRIBUIÇÃO |
| 3699 | DESVIO DO PONTEIRO | 3738 | TUBO DE DESCARGA |
| 3700 | FLEXÃO TRANSVERSAL | 3739 | VÁLVULA DE RECALQUE |
| 3701 | FLECHA | 3740 | FERRO DELTA |
| 3701 | FLEXÃO | 3741 | METAL DE LIGA DELTA |
| 3702 | DEFLETOR | 3742 | DESIMANTAÇÃO |
| 3703 | GRAFITE DESFLOCULADA | 3742 | DESMAGNETIZAÇÃO |
| 3704 | ELIMINAÇÃO DO EMBAÇAMENTO DO VAPOR | 3743 | DESMAGNETIZAR |
| | | 3744 | DESMAGNETIZADORES |
| 3705 | DEFORMABILIDADE | 3744 | DESIMANTADORES |
| 3706 | FAIXA DE DEFORMAÇÃO | 3745 | COMBUSTÍVEL NECESSÁRIO |
| 3707 | MUDANÇA DE FORMA | 3746 | FORÇA NECESSÁRIA |
| 3708 | DESCONGELADOR | 3746 | POTÊNCIA REQUERIDA |
| 3709 | LIGA NEUTRALIZADORA DE GASES | 3747 | AGENTE DESNATURANTE |
| 3710 | DESTILAÇÃO SECA | 3748 | DENDRITA |
| 3710 | DEGASEIFICAÇÃO | 3749 | PÓ DENDRÍTICO |
| 3711 | EMULSÃO PARA PELES | 3750 | ESTRUTURA DENTRÍTICA |
| 3712 | DESENGORDURAMENTO | 3751 | DESNIQUELAÇÃO |
| 3712 | DESENGRAXAMENTO | 3752 | DENOMINADOR |
| 3713 | COMPOSIÇÃO DE DESENGORDURAMENTO | 3753 | DENSIFICADOR |
| 3713 | COMPOSIÇÃO DE DESENGRAXAMENTO | 3754 | DENSIFICADOR |
| 3714 | GRAU | 3754 | MEIO DE HOMOGENEIZAÇÃO |
| 3715 | GRAU BAUMÉ | 3755 | DENSÍMETRO |
| 3716 | GRAU CENTÍGRADO | 3756 | DENSIDADE |
| 3717 | GRAU ENGLER | 3757 | DENSIDADE DE UM GÁS |
| 3718 | GRAU FAHRENHEIT | 3758 | DENSIDADE DE UM LÍQUIDO |
| 3719 | COEFICIENTE DE REGULARIDADE | 3759 | RELAÇÃO DE DENSIDADE |
| 3720 | GRAU DE DUREZA | 3760 | MOSSA |
| 3721 | GRAU DE PRECISÃO | 3760 | ENTALHE |
| 3722 | GRAU DE SATURAÇÃO | 3760 | MARCA |
| 3723 | COEFICIENTE DE SENSIBILIDADE | 3761 | DENTE E ENTALHE |
| 3724 | GRAU RÉAUMUR | 3762 | DESOXIDAÇÃO |
| 3725 | GRAU TWADDELL | 3763 | DESOXIDAR |
| 3726 | GRAUS DE LIBERDADE | 3764 | COBRE DESOXIDADO |
| 3727 | DESIDRATAR | 3765 | DESOXIDANTE |
| 3728 | DESIDRATAÇÃO | 3766 | DESOXIDAÇÃO |
| 3729 | DESIONIZAÇÃO | 3767 | ESGOTAMENTO |
| 3730 | RETARDAMENTO | 3767 | REBAIXAMENTO DA CONCENTRAÇÃO |
| 3730 | ATRASO | 3768 | DESPOLARIZAÇÃO |
| 3730 | RETARDO | 3769 | DESPOLARIZAR |
| 3731 | ATRASO NA ENTREGA | 3770 | DESPOLARIZANTE |
| 3732 | DERRETER-SE | 3770 | DESPOLARIZADOR |
| 3732 | DELIQÜESCER | 3771 | DESPOLARIZAÇÃO |
| 3733 | DELIQÜESCÊNCIA | 3772 | DESPOLARIZADOR |
| 3734 | DELIQÜESCENTE | 3773 | SEDIMENTO |
| 3735 | TRANSMISSÃO DE CALOR | 3774 | CORROSÃO CAUSADA POR SEDIMENTAÇÃO |
| 3736 | TUBO DE RECALQUE | 3775 | METAL ELETROLÍTICO |

| | |
|---|---|
| 3776 | METAL FUNDIDO APLICADO |
| 3777 | RELAÇÃO DE DISTRIBUIÇÃO DO METAL |
| 3778 | DEPRESSÃO |
| 3779 | PROFUNDIDADE |
| 3780 | PERFURAÇÃO PROFUNDA |
| 3781 | CALIBRE DE PROFUNDIDADE |
| 3782 | PROFUNDIDADE DE CORTE |
| 3783 | PROFUNDIDADE DO VÃO |
| 3784 | PROFUNDIDADE DA ROSCA |
| 3785 | ALTURA DO DENTE |
| 3786 | DERIVATIVO |
| 3787 | BARCAÇAS DE TRANSPORTE |
| 3788 | GUINDASTE DERRIQUE |
| 3788 | GRUA DERRIQUE |
| 3788 | GUINDASTE DE BRAÇO |
| 2789 | DESATIVAÇÃO |
| 3790 | BANHO DE DECAPAGEM |
| 2790 | BANHO DE DESENCRUSTRAÇÃO |
| 3791 | TUBULAÇÃO EM DECLIVE |
| 3791 | ENCANAMENTO DESCENDENTE |
| 3792 | DESCIDA |
| 3792 | DECLIVE |
| 3792 | ENCOSTA |
| 3792 | RAMPA |
| 3792 | GRADIENTE |
| 3793 | ESCARVA |
| 3793 | REBARBAÇÃO |
| 3794 | TRAÇADO |
| 3794 | CONCEITO |
| 3794 | PLANO |
| 3794 | PROJETO |
| 3795 | PROJETAR |
| 3795 | ESBOÇAR |
| 3795 | CALCULAR |
| 3796 | ESCRITÓRIO TÉCNICO |
| 3796 | ESCRITÓRIO DE ESTUDOS |
| 3797 | ESBOÇO |
| 3798 | TEMPERATURA DE CÁLCULO |
| 3799 | DESENHO |
| 3799 | ESTUDO |
| 3799 | PLANEJAMENTO |
| 3799 | PROJETO |
| 3800 | DEPARTAMENTO DE ESTUDOS |
| 3800 | SALA DE PROJETOS |
| 3801 | DESPRATEAR |
| 3802 | DESPRATEAMENTO |
| 3803 | ELIMINAÇÃO DA ESCÓRIA |
| 3804 | DESSECADOR |
| 3805 | DESTILAÇÃO COM DECOMPOSIÇÃO |
| 3806 | TESTE OU ENSAIO DESTRUTIVO |
| 3807 | ELIMINAÇÃO DAS CAMADAS SUPERFICIAIS |

| | |
|---|---|
| 3808 | REMOVÍVEL |
| 3808 | DESMONTÁVEL |
| 3809 | DESENHO EM DETALHE |
| 3810 | PROJETO DE CONSTRUÇÃO |
| 3811 | PEÇA SOLTA |
| 3812 | PLANO DETALHADO |
| 3813 | DETERGENTE |
| 3814 | DETERMINANTE |
| 3815 | DESENVOLVER |
| 3816 | REVELÁVEL |
| 3817 | SUPERFÍCIE REVELÁVEL |
| 3818 | DESPRENDIMENTO DE GASES |
| 3819 | AFASTAMENTO |
| 3819 | DESVIO |
| 3819 | DIVERGÊNCIA |
| 3820 | DISPOSITIVO |
| 3820 | MECANISMO |
| 3821 | TOSTADOR |
| 3821 | BRASEIRO |
| 3822 | GANCHO DE CADEIA |
| 3823 | DESVITRIFICAÇÃO |
| 3824 | PONTO DE ORVALHO |
| 3824 | PONTO DE CONDENSAÇÃO |
| 3825 | DEXTRINA |
| 3826 | ÁCIDO DEXTROTARTÁRICO |
| 3827 | DEXTRORROTATÓRIO |
| 3827 | DEXTRÓGIRO |
| 3828 | DIABASE |
| 3829 | CURVA DIACÁUSTICA |
| 3829 | LENTE BICONVEXA |
| 3830 | ROTINA DE DIAGNÓSTICO |
| 3830 | PROGRAMA DE DIAGNÓSTICO |
| 3831 | DIAGONAL |
| 3832 | PINÇA OU ALICATE DE CORTE DIAGONAL |
| 3833 | ESCALA TRANSVERSAL (UNIVERSAL) |
| 3834 | DIAGRAMA |
| 3834 | ESQUEMA |
| 3835 | DIAGRAMA DE FORÇAS |
| 3836 | DESENHO DIAGRAMÁTICO |
| 3836 | DESENHO ESQUEMÁTICO |
| 3836 | CROQUIS |
| 3837 | DISCO |
| 3837 | QUADRANTE |
| 3837 | INDICADOR GRADUADO |
| 3837 | ESCALA GRADUADA |
| 3838 | COMPARADOR DE DISCO PARA ESCAREAÇÃO |
| 3839 | PRENSA MECÂNICA COM PRATO REVÓLVER |
| 3840 | INDICADOR |
| 3840 | QUADRANTE INDICADOR |
| 3840 | CALIBRADOR DE QUADRANTE |

| | |
|---|---|
| 3841 ESCALA ANULAR | 3881 BIATÔMICO |
| 3842 PALPADOR DE QUADRANTE | 3881 BIVALENTE |
| 3843 CRONÔMETRO | 3882 BIBÁSICO |
| 3844 DIALISAR | 3883 MOLDE |
| 3845 DIALISADOR | 3883 ESTAMPA |
| 3846 DIÁLISE | 3883 MATRIZ |
| 3847 DIAMAGNÉTICO | 3884 BLOCO PORTA-MATRIZ |
| 3848 DIAMAGNETISMO | 3885 CORPO DE MATRIZ |
| 3849 DIÂMETRO | 3886 PEÇA FUNDIDA SOB PRESSÃO |
| 3850 DIÂMETRO DO NÚCLEO DE UM PARAFUSO | 3886 FUNDIÇÃO MATRIZADA |
| 3851 COMPLEMENTO DIAMETRAL | 3887 AMORTECEDOR DA MATRIZ |
| 3852 DIÂMETRO EXTERNO DE ROSCA | 3888 MARCA DE ESTAMPA |
| 3853 DIÂMETRO DE PERFURAÇÃO | 3889 METAL PARA MATRIZES |
| 3854 DIÂMETRO DO FURO DO PERNO | 3890 JOGO DE MATRIZES |
| 3855 DIÂMETRO DE PERFURAÇÃO | 3890 ALINHAMENTO DA MATRIZ |
| 3855 DIÂMETRO DO FURO | 3891 DESLOCAMENTO DA MATRIZ |
| 3856 DIÂMETRO DE UM ELO DE CORRENTE | 3892 GRAVAÇÃO DE MATRIZES |
| 3857 DIÂMETRO DO FURO | 3892 FRESAGEM DE MATRIZES |
| 3858 DIÂMETRO DE CANO | 3893 PUNÇÃO (DE FISCALIZAÇÃO) |
| 3858 DIÂMETRO DO TUBO | 3894 ESTAMPAGEM DAS MATRIZES |
| 3859 DIÂMETRO DE REBITE | 3894 DEFEITO NA CHAPA A MATRIZAR |
| 3860 ESPESSURA DE FIO | 3895 PORTA-COXINETES |
| 3860 ESPESSURA DE ARAME | 3895 PORTA-TARRAXA |
| 3861 PASSO DIAMETRAL | 3896 COXINETE |
| 3861 MÓDULO DIAMETRAL (DE DENTES DE ENGRENAGEM) | 3896 TARRAXA |
| | 3897 MATRIZ DE FERREIRO |
| 3862 DIAMANTE | 3898 DIELÉTRICO |
| 3863 PÓ DE DIAMANTE | 3898 ISOLANTE |
| 3864 RODA DE ESMERIL A DIAMANTE | 3898 NÃO CONDUTOR DE ELETRICIDADE |
| 3864 DISCO DE RETIFICAR A DIAMANTES | 3899 CONSTANTE DIELÉTRICA |
| 3864 REBOLO A DIAMANTES | 3900 RESISTÊNCIA DIELÉTRICA |
| 3865 TESTE DE DUREZA | 3901 MOTOR DIESEL |
| 3865 ENSAIO (PROVA) DE DUREZA | 3902 DIFERENÇA |
| 3866 FERRAMENTA A DIAMANTE | 3903 CALIBRE DE TOLERÂNCIA |
| 3867 ESMERIL A DIAMANTE | 3904 DIFERENÇA DE TEMPERATURA |
| 3868 DIAFANIDADE | 3905 CALIBRE DE TOLERÂNCIA |
| 3869 DIÁFANO | 3906 SELETIVO |
| 3870 DIAFRAGMA | 3906 DIFERENCIAL |
| 3870 MEMBRANA | 3907 FREIO DIFERENCIAL |
| 3871 DIAFRAGMA | 3908 CÁLCULO DIFERENCIAL |
| 3872 VÁLVULA REGULADORA DE MEMBRANA | 3909 COEFICIENTE DIFERENCIAL |
| 3873 MANÔMETRO DE DIAFRAGMA | 3910 COROA GRANDE DO DIFERENCIAL |
| 3874 BOMBA DE DIAFRAGMA | 3911 DINAMÔMETRO DIFERENCIAL |
| 3875 MOLA DE DIAFRAGMA | 3912 EQUAÇÃO DIFERENCIAL |
| 3876 VÁLVULA DE DIAFRAGMA | 3913 ENGRENAGEM DIFERENCIAL |
| 3876 REGISTRO DE MEMBRANA | 3914 TÊMPERA DIFERENCIAL |
| 3877 DIAFRAGMAR | 3914 TÊMPERA SELETIVA |
| 3878 DIATERMÂNCIA | 3915 AQUECIMENTO SELETIVO |
| 3879 DIATÉRMICO | 3916 QUOCIENTE DIFERENCIAL |
| 3880 DIATÔMITO | 3917 RODA DE DIFERENCIAL |
| 3880 TERRA DIATOMÁCEA | 3918 SATÉLITE DE DIFERENCIAL |

| | |
|---|---|
| 3919 | ANÁLISE TÉRMICA SELETIVA |
| 3920 | TERMÔMETRO DIFERENCIAL |
| 3921 | MANÔMETRO DIFERENCIAL |
| 3922 | DIFERENCIAR |
| 3923 | DIFERENCIAÇÃO |
| 3924 | DIFRAÇÃO |
| 3925 | REDE DE DIFRAÇÃO |
| 3926 | FIGURA DE DIFRAÇÃO |
| 3926 | DIAGRAMA DE DIFRAÇÃO RX |
| 3927 | LUZ DIFUSA |
| 3928 | DIFUSOR |
| 3929 | DIFUSÃO |
| 3930 | REVESTIMENTOS DE DIFUSÃO |
| 3931 | COEFICIENTE DE DIFUSÃO |
| 3932 | DIFUSÃO DOS GASES |
| 3933 | DIFUSÃO DA LUZ |
| 3934 | ZONA INTERFACIAL |
| 3934 | ZONA DE DIFUSÃO |
| 3935 | SUPERFÍCIE DIFUSÍVEL |
| 3936 | DIFUSIBILIDADE |
| 3937 | COZER |
| 3937 | DIGERIR |
| 3938 | DIGESTOR |
| 3939 | DIGESTÃO |
| 3939 | COZIMENTO A CALOR BRANDO |
| 3940 | DÍGITO |
| 3940 | ALGARISMO |
| 3940 | CIFRA |
| 3941 | DIGITAL |
| 3941 | NUMÉRICO |
| 3942 | INFORMAÇÃO DE ENTRADA NUMÉRICA |
| 3943 | CODIFICADOR NUMÉRICO |
| 3944 | ÂNGULO EM V |
| 3944 | ÂNGULO DIEDRO |
| 3945 | DIQUE |
| 3945 | REPRESA |
| 3945 | LEVANTAMENTO DE TERRA |
| 3946 | ALICATE DE CORTE DIAGONAL |
| 3947 | DILATABILIDADE |
| 3948 | DILATÁVEL |
| 3949 | DILATAÇÃO |
| 3950 | DILATÔMETRO |
| 3951 | DILUENTE |
| 3952 | DILUIR |
| 3953 | SOLUÇÃO DILUÍDA |
| 3954 | DILUIÇÃO DE UMA SOLUÇÃO |
| 3955 | LUZ DIFUNDIDA |
| 3956 | COTA |
| 3957 | LINHA DE COTA |
| 3958 | ESTABILIDADE DIMENSIONAL |
| 3959 | DESENHO COM INDICAÇÃO DAS DIMENSÕES |
| 3960 | DIMENSÕES |
| 3960 | MEDIDAS |
| 3961 | PROJEÇÃO DIMÉTRICA |
| 3962 | REDUTOR DE ESCAREAÇÃO |
| 3962 | LUVA DE REDUÇÃO DO ALARGAMENTO |
| 3963 | INTERRUPTOR DO REDUTOR DA LUZ |
| 3964 | DIODO |
| 3965 | LÂMPADA DE DIODO |
| 3966 | DIORITA |
| 3967 | IMERSÃO |
| 3967 | BANHO |
| 3968 | SUBMERGIR |
| 3968 | MERGULHAR |
| 3968 | IMERGIR |
| 3969 | SOLDAGEM FORTE POR IMERSÃO |
| 3970 | REVESTIMENTO POR IMERSÃO |
| 3970 | APLICAÇÃO DE REVESTIMENTO POR TÊMPERA |
| 3971 | FURO DE MEDIDA |
| 3972 | FURO DE MEDIDA COMBINADO COM RESPIRADOURO |
| 3973 | TANQUE DE IMERSÃO |
| 3974 | DIFENILAMINA |
| 3975 | MERGULHO |
| 3975 | IMERSÃO |
| 3976 | CESTA DE IMERSÃO |
| 3977 | PROCESSO DE MERGULHO OU IMERSÃO |
| 3978 | TÊMPERA |
| 3978 | IMERSÃO |
| 3979 | VARETA DE MEDIR O NÍVEL DO ÓLEO |
| 3980 | DE AÇÃO DIRETA |
| 3981 | COMANDO DIRETO POR COMPUTADOR |
| 3982 | MÁQUINA DE ACOPLAMENTO DIRETO |
| 3983 | ACIONAMENTO DIRETO |
| 3983 | TOMADA DIRETA |
| 3984 | EXTRUSÃO DIRETA |
| 3985 | COMANDO DIRETO POR COMPUTADOR |
| 3986 | CALIBRE DE CORREDIÇA COM ESCALA |
| 3987 | VÁLVULA DE SEGURANÇA DE CARGA DIRETA DE MOLA |
| 3988 | CONDENSADOR POR MISTURA |
| 3989 | PISCA-PISCA |
| 3989 | LANTERNAS INDICADORAS DE DIREÇÃO |
| 3990 | DIREÇÃO DE UMA FORÇA |
| 3991 | DIREÇÃO DO MOVIMENTO |
| 3992 | SENTIDO DE ROTAÇÃO |
| 3993 | DIREÇÃO DAS FIBRAS |
| 3994 | ORIENTAÇÃO DOS CRISTAIS |
| 3995 | DIRETOR |
| 3996 | DIRETRIZ |
| 3997 | TOMADA DE PÓ |

| | | | |
|---|---|---|---|
| 3997 | RECOLHIMENTO DE PÓ | 4030 | DESENGATAR |
| 3998 | GRÃOS DA FUNDIÇÃO | 4031 | DESENGATE |
| 3999 | DESINTEGRAR | 4031 | ESCAPAMENTO DE UMA MOLA |
| 3999 | DESAGREGAR | 4031 | DESLIGAMENTO |
| 4000 | DESINTEGRAÇÃO | 4032 | ACOPLAMENTO DE DESEMBREAGEM |
| 4000 | DESAGREGAÇÃO | 4033 | ACOPLAMENTO DE DESEMBREAGEM |
| 4001 | FREIO DE DISCO | 4034 | ENGRENAGEM DESENGATADORA |
| 4002 | EMBREAGEM DE DISCO | 3034 | MECANISMO DE DESEMBREAGEM |
| 4003 | MANIVELA DE DISCO | 4035 | ALAVANCA DESENGATADORA |
| 4004 | VOLANTE DE DISCO | 4035 | ALAVANCA DE DESEMBREAGEM |
| 4005 | TRANSMISSÃO A DISCO | 4036 | FUNDO CÔNCAVO |
| 4006 | DISCO DE ESMERIL | 4037 | RODA DE DISCO ABAULADA |
| 4006 | POLIDORA | 4038 | FUNDO EMBUTIDO |
| 4007 | GRADE OU ARADO DE DISCO | 4038 | FUNDO ABAULADO |
| 4007 | ATOMIZADORES A DISCO | 4039 | TETO ABAULADO |
| 4008 | PRENDEDOR DO DISCO | 4040 | ESTAMPAGEM |
| 4009 | PORCA DE TRAVAMENTO DO DISCO DE VÁLVULA | 4040 | ABAULAMENTO |
| | | 4040 | CONVEXIDADE |
| 4010 | DISCO LIXADOR | 4041 | DESINCRUSTANTE |
| 4010 | POLIDORA | 4042 | DESINFETANTE |
| 4011 | VÁLVULA DE ASSENTO PLANO | 4043 | DESINTEGRAR-SE |
| 4011 | VÁLVULA DE DISCO | 4043 | DESAGREGAR |
| 4012 | RODA DE DISCO | 4043 | DECOMPOR-SE |
| 4012 | RODA MACIÇA | 4044 | DESINTEGRAÇÃO |
| 4013 | CENTRO DA RODA | 4045 | PULVERIZADOR |
| 4013 | DISCO PLANO DE VOLANTE | 4045 | TRITURADOR |
| 4013 | DISCO DE RODA | 4046 | EMBREAGEM A DISCO |
| 4014 | DISCO DE VÁLVULA | 4047 | DESLOCAMENTO |
| 4015 | DISCO | 4048 | CALIBRE DESMONTÁVEL |
| 4016 | CONE | 4049 | FASE DISPERSA |
| 4017 | DESCARGA | 4050 | AGENTE DE DISPERSÃO |
| 4018 | DESCARREGAR | 4051 | DISPERSÃO |
| 4018 | ESVAZIAR | 4052 | DESLOCÁVEL |
| 4019 | DESCARREGAR UM ACUMULADOR | 4053 | DESLOCAMENTO |
| 4020 | SEÇÃO DO ORIFÍCIO DE SAÍDA | 4054 | DESLOCAMENTO DE LÍQUIDO |
| 4021 | ALTURA DE DESCARGA DE UMA BOMBA | 4055 | DESLOCAMENTO DO EIXO |
| 4022 | ENCANAMENTO DE DESCARGA | 4056 | DISPOSIÇÃO |
| 4022 | TUBULAÇÃO DE DESCARGA | 4056 | ARRANJO |
| 4023 | VOLUME DE PASSAGEM POR SEGUNDO POR UM ORIFÍCIO | 4057 | LIMITE DE RESISTÊNCIA À DISRUPÇÃO |
| | | 4058 | DISSOCIAÇÃO |
| 4024 | ESVAZIAMENTO | 4059 | DISSOLUÇÃO |
| 4024 | DESCARGA | 4060 | DISSOLUÇÃO |
| 4025 | DESCARGA DE UM ACUMULADOR | 4061 | DECOMPOR |
| 4026 | DESCOLORAÇÃO | 4061 | DISSOLVER |
| 4026 | ALTERAÇÃO DA COR | 4061 | FUNDIR |
| 4027 | DESMONTÁVEL | 4061 | DERRETER |
| 4028 | DESCONEXÃO | 4062 | PODER DISSOLVENTE |
| 4028 | DESLIGAMENTO | 4062 | PODER DE DISSOLUÇÃO |
| 4029 | DISCRIMINANTE | 4063 | AFASTAMENTO |
| 4029 | DISCRIMINADOR | 4063 | DISTÂNCIA |
| 4030 | DESEMBREAR | 4063 | TRAJETO |

| | |
|---|---|
| 4064 | DISTÂNCIA ENTRE MANCAIS |
| 4065 | DISTÂNCIA ENTRE CENTROS |
| 4065 | DISTÂNCIA ENTRE EIXOS |
| 4066 | DISTÂNCIA DO CENTRO DO REBITE À BORDA DA CHAPA |
| 4067 | DISTANCIADOR |
| 4067 | SEPARADOR |
| 4068 | PEÇA SEPARADORA |
| 4069 | TELETERMÔMETRO |
| 4070 | DESTILAR |
| 4071 | PRODUTO DE DESTILAÇÃO |
| 4071 | DESTILADO |
| 4072 | DESTILAÇÃO |
| 4073 | DESTILAÇÃO COM VAPOR DE ÁGUA |
| 4074 | DESTILAÇÃO DA HULHA |
| 4075 | DESTILAÇÃO NO VÁCUO |
| 4076 | ÁGUA DESTILADA |
| 4077 | DEFORMAÇÃO |
| 4077 | DISTORÇÃO |
| 4078 | CARGA DISTRIBUÍDA |
| 4079 | CONDUTOR DE REDE |
| 4079 | CABO DE DISTRIBUIÇÃO |
| 4080 | REDE DE DISTRIBUIÇÃO ELÉTRICA |
| 4080 | REDE DE CONDUTORES ELÉTRICOS |
| 4081 | DISTRIBUIÇÃO DE UMA CARGA |
| 4082 | DISTRIBUIÇÃO DE MASSAS |
| 4083 | DISTRIBUIÇÃO DA TEMPERATURA |
| 4084 | DISTRIBUIDOR |
| 4085 | BRAÇO DA PLATINA DA DISTRIBUIÇÃO |
| 4085 | BRAÇO DO DISTRIBUIDOR DO ROTOR |
| 4086 | DISTRIBUIDOR |
| 4086 | CAIXA DO DISTRIBUIDOR |
| 4087 | DISTRIBUIDORES DE FERTILIZANTES |
| 4088 | MECANISMOS PARA ENGATE DE REBOQUES |
| 4089 | DISTRIBUIDORES DE CAL |
| 4090 | ARADOS DE SUBSOLO E ARADOS DE VERTEDOURO |
| 4091 | DIVERGIR |
| 4092 | DIVERGÊNCIA |
| 4093 | DIVERGENTE |
| 4094 | SÉRIE DIVERGENTE |
| 4095 | LENTE DIVERGENTE |
| 4096 | BOCAL DIVERGENTE |
| 4097 | DIVIDIR |
| 4098 | MANCAIS DE COQUILHAS |
| 4099 | DIVIDENDO |
| 4100 | DIVISOR |
| 4101 | DIVISORES |
| 4101 | COMPASSO DIVISOR |
| 4101 | COMPASSO DE BICOS |
| 4102 | MÁQUINA DE DIVIDIR OU DE SECIONAR |
| 4103 | MÁQUINA DE SECIONAMENTO DE CÍRCULOS |
| 4104 | MÁQUINA PARA DIVIDIR LINHAS RETAS |
| 4105 | APARELHO DIVISOR |
| 4106 | CHAPA OU PLACA DIVISÓRIA |
| 4106 | DISCO DIVISOR |
| 4107 | DIVISÃO |
| 4108 | DIVISÃO DO CÍRCULO |
| 4109 | DISCO DIVISOR |
| 4110 | DIAFRAGMA |
| 4110 | DIVISÓRIA |
| 4111 | DIVISOR |
| 4112 | DODECAEDRO |
| 4113 | EMBREAGEM DE GARRAS |
| 4114 | DOLERITA |
| 4115 | ENCONTRO |
| 4115 | CONTRA-REBITADOR |
| 4115 | MAÇACOTE |
| 4116 | MALHO |
| 4116 | MÁQUINA DE LAVAR MINÉRIOS |
| 4117 | CALCÁRIO DOLOMÍTICO |
| 4117 | DOLOMITA |
| 4118 | PORCA CEGA |
| 4119 | LÂMPADA DE TETO |
| 4120 | TETO ABAULADO |
| 4121 | RESERVATÓRIO DE COBERTA ABAULADA |
| 4122 | CAIXILHOS |
| 4123 | FECHADURA DE PORTA |
| 4124 | SUCATA INDUSTRIAL |
| 4124 | FERRAGENS DE PROTEÇÃO PRÓPRIA |
| 4125 | LINHA PONTILHADA |
| 4126 | TIRA-LINHAS PARA FAZER PONTOS |
| 4127 | POLIAS DE BRAÇO DUPLO |
| 4128 | CORREIA DUPLA |
| 4129 | FREIO DE DUPLA SAPATA |
| 4130 | REBITE COM DUPLA COBREJUNTA |
| 4131 | ALAVANCA DE TRÊS BRAÇOS |
| 4132 | PICAGEM EM CRUZ |
| 4132 | CORTE DUPLO |
| 4133 | LIMA DE DUPLA PICAGEM |
| 4133 | LIMA DE PICADO DUPLO |
| 4134 | LIMA DE CORTE DUPLO |
| 4135 | DUPLO DECÍMETRO |
| 4136 | DECOMPOSIÇÃO DUPLA |
| 4137 | CALIBRADOR DE LIMITE COM DUAS PONTAS |
| 4138 | ALIMENTAÇÃO DUPLA |
| 4139 | REBORDO DUPLO |
| 4139 | FLANGE DUPLO |
| 4140 | MARTELO PNEUMÁTICO DE ARMAÇÃO DUPLA |
| 4141 | JUNTA DE DUPLA SOLDAGEM |
| 4142 | ENGRENAGEM DUPLA |

| | | | |
|---|---|---|---|
| 4142 | TREM DUPLO DE ENGRENAGENS | 4177 | SAMBLADO |
| 4143 | ENGRENAGEM HIPOIDAL | 4178 | JUNTA SAMBLADA |
| 4144 | DENTE EM V | 4179 | MÁQUINA DE SAMBLAR |
| 4145 | INTEGRAL DUPLA | 4180 | TARUGO DE MADEIRA |
| 4146 | PLAINA DE CONTRAFERRO | 4180 | ESPIGÃO |
| 4147 | ALAVANCA INTERFIXA | 4180 | CAVILHA |
| 4147 | ALAVANCA DE DOIS BRAÇOS | 4181 | CAVILHA |
| 4148 | CALIBRE DE TOLERÂNCIAS | 4181 | PINO DE TRAVA |
| 4149 | NIPLE DUPLO | 4182 | FRESAGEM DESCENDENTE |
| 4150 | ARMAÇÃO DENTADA | 4183 | ALGEROZ |
| 4150 | ARMAÇÃO DE CREMALHEIRA | 4183 | TUBULAÇÃO DE DESCIDA |
| 4151 | DUPLA REFRAÇÃO | 4184 | A JUSANTE |
| 4152 | JUNTA DE REBITAGEM DUPLA | 4185 | CANO DE DESCIDA |
| 4153 | SAL DUPLO | 4186 | CANAL DE VAZAMENTO |
| 4154 | VÁLVULA DE SEDE DUPLA | 4186 | DESCIDA DE FUNDIÇÃO |
| 4154 | REGISTRO DE DUPLA VÁLVULA | 4187 | CURSO DESCENDENTE DO PISTÃO |
| 4155 | JUNTA REBITADA DE DUPLO CORTE | 4187 | DESCIDA DO PISTÃO |
| 4155 | REBITE COM DOIS CORTES | 4188 | DESAGUADOURO |
| 4156 | AÇO CEMENTADO E REFINADO DUAS VEZES | 4189 | CARBURADOR INVERTIDO |
| 4156 | AÇO DE PACOTE DUPLO | 4190 | SOLDAGEM PLANA |
| 4157 | PRENSA MECÂNICA DE DOIS LADOS | 4191 | TEMPO MORTO |
| 4158 | JUNTAS PARA LIGAR DOIS TUBOS CORTADOS | 4192 | SOLDAGEM EM POSIÇÃO VERTICAL DESCENDENTE |
| 4159 | SOQUETE DUPLO | 4193 | MATRIZAGEM POR DESCIDA ACIONADA |
| 4160 | BROCA AMERICANA | 4194 | GÁS POBRE |
| 4160 | BROCA DE GUME INVERTIDO | 4195 | DESENHAR |
| 4161 | TANQUE DE PAREDE DUPLA | 4195 | TRAÇAR |
| 4162 | OPÉRCULO DUPLO | 4196 | TIRAGEM |
| 4163 | DE DUPLO EFEITO | 4196 | REBAIXAMENTO |
| 4164 | PISTÃO DE DUPLO EFEITO | 4196 | REDUÇÃO |
| 4165 | MÁQUINA DE DUPLO EFEITO | 4197 | ÂNGULO DE TIRAGEM |
| 4166 | VÁLVULA DE DUPLO ASSENTO | 4198 | ATELIER |
| 4167 | CHAVE DE DUAS BOCAS | 4198 | SALA DE DESENHO |
| 4167 | CHAVE DE FORQUILHA DUPLA | 4199 | SEÇÃO INFERIOR DA CAIXA DO MOLDE DE FUNDIÇÃO |
| 4168 | MÁQUINA COM DUPLA EXPANSÃO | | |
| 4169 | MARTELO DE DUAS CABEÇAS | 4200 | COEFICIENTE DE ARRASTO |
| 4169 | MARTELO DE DUAS FACES | 4201 | SOLUÇÃO ADERENTE |
| 4170 | DE PAREDE DUPLA | 4202 | SOLUÇÃO ARRASTADA |
| 4171 | JUNTA DE COBERTURA SOLDADA PELOS DOIS LADOS | 4203 | SANGUE DE DRAGÃO (RESINA) |
| | | 4204 | ESCOAR |
| 4172 | LENTE DUPLA | 4204 | PURGAR |
| 4172 | DIPOLO | 4204 | DRENAR |
| 4173 | ENSAIO DE CURVATURA | 4204 | DESAGUAR |
| 4173 | TESTE DE DOBRAMENTO | 4204 | ESVAZIAR |
| 4174 | PLACA METÁLICA | 4205 | TORNEIRA DE PURGA |
| 4175 | SAMBLADURA | 4205 | REGISTRO DE PURGA |
| 4175 | RABO DE ANDORINHA | 4205 | REGISTRO DE ESVAZIAMENTO |
| 4175 | PRISMA | 4206 | PURGA |
| 4175 | RABO DE POMBO | 4206 | TUBO DE DESCARGA |
| 4176 | FRESAS PARA CORTAR EM RABO DE ANDORINHA | 4207 | CANO DE DESCARGA |
| | | 4207 | CANO DE PURGA |

| | | | | |
|---|---|---|---|---|
| 4208 | BUJÃO DE ESCOAMENTO | | 4239 | DISPOSITIVO A RETIRAR |
| 4209 | DRENAR O SOLO | | 4240 | PAPEL DE DESENHO |
| 4210 | DRENAGEM | | 4241 | TIRA-LINHAS |
| 4211 | REGISTRADOR DE TIRAGEM | | 4242 | PERCEVEJO |
| 4211 | MANÔMETRO PARA DETERMINAÇÕES ANEMOMÉTRICAS | | 4243 | MESA DE DESENHO |
| | | | 4244 | FERRAMENTA DE ESTIRAR |
| 4212 | TIRAGEM DE CHAMINÉ | | 4244 | FERRAMENTA DE TREFILAR |
| 4213 | DESENHISTA | | 4245 | CROQUI |
| 4214 | MECÂNICO CONSTRUTOR | | 4246 | DESENHO (ARTE) |
| 4214 | DESENHISTA | | 4247 | ESTIRADO |
| 4215 | ARRASTAR | | 4248 | BARRAS DE AÇO ESTIRADAS |
| 4215 | TIRAR | | 4249 | FERROS DE MEIA CANA ESTIRADOS |
| 4215 | ESTIRAR | | 4250 | CHAPAS ESTIRADAS |
| 4215 | DESENHAR | | 4251 | AÇO ESTIRADO |
| 4216 | TRAÇAR UMA PERPENDICULAR | | 4252 | ARAME TREFILADO |
| 4217 | BARRA DE ENGATE | | 4252 | ARAME ESTIRADO |
| 4217 | BARRA DE TRAÇÃO | | 4253 | TRATAR OS MINERAIS MECANICAMENTE |
| 4218 | BANCO DE ESTIRAR | | 4254 | REBARBADOR |
| 4219 | TIRAR | | 4254 | DESBASTADOR |
| 4219 | PUXAR | | 4255 | AREIA SECA |
| 4219 | ARRASTAR | | 4256 | ESTUFA |
| 4220 | ESTIRAR | | 4256 | ENSECADEIRA |
| 4220 | TREFILAR | | 4256 | SECADOR |
| 4221 | GARLOPA (PLAINA) | | 4257 | SECANTE |
| 4222 | AJUSTAR UMA RODA | | 4258 | SECADORES DE GRÃOS |
| 4223 | FIEIRA DE TREFILAR | | 4259 | SECADORES DE FORRAGEM |
| 4224 | ESTIRAR TUBOS | | 4260 | MANDRIL |
| 4225 | DECANTAR | | 4260 | PUA |
| 4225 | ESVAZIAR | | 4261 | PUNÇÃO |
| 4226 | BOCAL DE ESCOAMENTO COM CUBA PERIFÉRICA | | 4261 | TUFO |
| | | | 4262 | ALARGAR FUROS COM O MANDRIL |
| 4227 | CAIXA DE ESCOAMENTO | | 4263 | PUA |
| 4228 | DUCTILIDADE | | 4263 | VERRUMA |
| 4228 | ESTIRABILIDADE | | 4263 | BROCA |
| 4229 | DESENHO | | 4264 | BROCAR |
| 4229 | PLANO | | 4264 | PERFURAR |
| 4230 | TREFILAÇÃO | | 4265 | BROCA |
| 4230 | REVENIMENTO | | 4265 | PUA |
| 4230 | ESTIRAGEM DE ARAME | | 4266 | PINÇA PARA BROCAS |
| 4231 | PRANCHETA DE DESENHO | | 4266 | PORTA-BROCAS |
| 4232 | LATÃO DE ESTIRAGEM | | 4267 | CALIBRE DE BROCAS |
| 4233 | COMPOSTO LUBRIFICANTE DE TREFILAR | | 4268 | GABARITOS DE PERFURAÇÃO |
| 4233 | GRAXA DE ESTIRAGEM | | 4269 | DIÂMETRO DA PONTA DA BROCA |
| 4234 | MATRIZ PARA ESTIRAR | | 4270 | AÇO PARA BROCA |
| 4235 | REDUÇÃO MECÂNICA DE SEÇÃO | | 4271 | BROCA |
| 4235 | MARTELAGEM | | 4271 | PUA |
| 4236 | OBJETOS PARA DESENHO | | 4272 | PERFURATRIZ |
| 4237 | MÁQUINA DE DESENFORNAR | | 4273 | FURO BROQUEADO |
| 4237 | MÁQUINA DE EMBUTIR | | 4273 | FURO RETIFICADO |
| 4237 | MÁQUINA DE ESTIRAR | | 4274 | CHAPA DE FUROS PERFURADOS |
| 4238 | ATELIER | | 4275 | FURO DE REBITE PERFURADO |

| | | | | |
|---|---|---|---|---|
| 4276 | SONDA | 4303 | ACIONAMENTO |
| 4276 | PERFURADOR | 4304 | ACIONAMENTO POR FRICÇÃO |
| 4277 | BROQUEAMENTO | 4305 | CORRENTE DE TRANSMISSÃO |
| 4277 | PERFURAÇÃO | 4306 | CADEIA DE TRANSMISSÃO |
| 4277 | SONDAGEM | 4307 | AJUSTE |
| 4278 | CABEÇOTE DE PERFURAÇÃO | 4307 | MONTAGEM |
| 4279 | ESCAREADOR | 4307 | ACOPLAMENTO |
| 4279 | FURADEIRA | 4308 | FRASCO SECADOR |
| 4279 | MÁQUINA DE PERFURAR | 4309 | MECANISMO DE COMANDO |
| 4280 | ÓLEO DE LUBRIFICAR BROCAS | 4309 | ENGRENAGEM PROPULSORA |
| 4280 | ÓLEO PARA PERFURAR | 4310 | EMBUTIMENTO DE CHAVETA |
| 4281 | ÁGUA POTÁVEL | 4310 | BLOQUEIO DE CHAVETA |
| 4282 | GOTA | 4311 | MECANISMO PROPULSOR OU MOTOR |
| 4283 | APANHA-GOTAS | 4312 | RETIRADA DA CHAVETA |
| 4283 | COLETOR DE ÓLEO | 4313 | POLIA MOTRIZ |
| 4284 | LUBRIFICAÇÃO POR CONTA-GOTAS | 4313 | POLIA DE TRANSMISSÃO |
| 4285 | GOTEIRA | 4313 | POLIA DE COMANDO |
| 4285 | CALHA | 4313 | POLIA PROPULSORA |
| 4286 | PINÇA DE MANGUEIRA | 4314 | CABO DE TRANSMISSÃO |
| 4287 | ALIMENTAÇÃO DE ÓLEO POR GOTEJAMENTO | 4315 | EIXO MOTOR |
| 4287 | INTRODUÇÃO DE ÓLEO POR GOTAS | 4315 | ÁRVORE DE COMANDO |
| 4288 | ACIONAMENTO | 4316 | PARTE CONDUTORA |
| 4288 | TRANSMISSÃO | 4316 | PARTE ACIONADORA |
| 4288 | MARCHA | 4316 | RAMAL CONDUTOR |
| 4288 | DIREÇÃO | 4317 | BIELA DE COMANDO |
| 4289 | ACIONAR | 4318 | RODA MOTRIZ |
| 4289 | CONDUZIR | 4318 | RODA PROPULSORA |
| 4289 | COLOCAR EM MOVIMENTO | 4318 | RODA ACIONADORA |
| 4290 | EIXO-MOTOR | 4319 | ACIONAMENTO POR CORREIA |
| 4291 | ACIONAR POR FRICÇÃO | 4319 | TRANSMISSÃO POR CORREIA |
| 4292 | CRAVAR UM PREGO | 4320 | DEIXAR CAIR |
| 4293 | CAVILHAR | 4321 | CONTA-GOTAS |
| 4293 | COLOCAR UM CALÇO | 4322 | ARO DE BASE CÔNCAVA |
| 4294 | TRANSMISSÃO | 4323 | LUBRIFICADOR POR CONTA-GOTA |
| 4294 | ACIONAMENTO | 4324 | PEÇA MATRIZADA |
| 4295 | RETIRAR UMA CHAVETA | 4325 | MARTINETE DE QUEDA |
| 4296 | EIXO MOTOR | 4325 | MARTELO PILÃO |
| 4296 | ÁRVORE DE TRANSMISSÃO | 4326 | MARTINETE DE QUEDA |
| 4297 | COMANDO | 4326 | BATE-ESTACAS |
| 4297 | ACIONAMENTO | 4326 | MARTELO PILÃO |
| 4297 | PROPULSÃO | 4327 | MARTELO DE QUEDA LIVRE |
| 4298 | POLIA ACIONADA | 4328 | ENSAIO OU TESTE DE QUEDA |
| 4299 | EIXO ACIONADO | 4328 | PROVA OU ENSAIO DE FLEXÃO POR CHOQUE |
| 4299 | EIXO RECEPTOR | 4329 | PESO DE QUEDA |
| 4300 | RODA ACIONADA | 4329 | CONTRAPESO |
| 4301 | CONDUTOR | 4329 | PESO DO MARTINETE |
| 4301 | MOTORISTA | 4330 | ENSAIO DE QUEDA DO PESO |
| 4301 | ACIONADOR | 4331 | ESCÓRIA |
| 4302 | CARTEIRA DE MOTORISTA | 4331 | RESÍDUOS |
| 4302 | CARTEIRA DE HABILITAÇÃO | 4332 | FURO DE ESCÓRIA |

| | |
|---|---|
| 4333 | TAMBOR |
| 4334 | FREIO DE TAMBOR |
| 4335 | LIMPEZA EM TAMBOR |
| 4336 | PANELA BARRIL |
| 4337 | SERRA CIRCULAR OSCILANTE |
| 4338 | SECAR |
| 4338 | DESSECAR |
| 4339 | AR SECO |
| 4340 | BOMBA DE AR SECO |
| 4341 | ANÁLISE POR VIA SECA |
| 4342 | AGLUTINANTE SECO |
| 4343 | PILHA SECA |
| 4344 | CARVÃO SECO (MAGRO) |
| 4345 | COMPRESSOR SECO |
| 4346 | DESTILAÇÃO SECA |
| 4347 | ESTIRAGEM BRILHANTE |
| 4348 | CAMISA SECA |
| 4349 | TERMOMETALURGIA |
| 4350 | OXIDAÇÃO OU CORROSÃO SECA |
| 4351 | VAPOR SECO |
| 4352 | RESISTÊNCIA A SECO |
| 4352 | ESTABILIDADE EM SECO |
| 4353 | FUNDIÇÃO EM MOLDE DE AREIA SECA |
| 4354 | MOLDAGEM EM AREIA SECA |
| 4355 | APARELHO DE SECAR |
| 4355 | SECADOR |
| 4356 | CÂMARA DE SECAGEM |
| 4357 | ÓLEO SICATIVO |
| 4358 | ESTUFA DE SECAGEM |
| 4359 | SECAGEM |
| 4360 | CARBURADOR DE DUPLO CORPO |
| 4361 | MALEÁVEL |
| 4361 | FLEXÍVEL |
| 4361 | DÚCTIL |
| 4362 | FERRO DÚCTIL |
| 4362 | FUNDIÇÃO COM GRAFITE ESFEROIDAL |
| 4363 | DUCTILIDADE |
| 4364 | TURFA ESCAVADA À MÃO |
| 4365 | ARESTA CORTANTE REBAIXADA |
| 4366 | CROMEAÇÃO MATE (FOSCA) |
| 4367 | RUBRO ESCURO |
| 4368 | AQUECIDO AO RUBRO ESCURO |
| 4369 | EMBACIAMENTO |
| 4370 | MAQUETE |
| 4371 | PACOTE PARA LAMINAR |
| 4372 | PASSE CEGO (LAMINAÇÃO) |
| 4372 | PASSAGEM EM VAZIO |
| 4373 | CILINDRO EM VAZIO |
| 4374 | TESTE DE RECALQUE |
| 4375 | CAMINHÃO BASCULANTE |
| 4376 | DESPEJO |

| | |
|---|---|
| 4376 | DESCARREGAMENTO |
| 4377 | FISSURA |
| 4378 | LIGA DÚPLEX |
| 4379 | FRESADORA DE DOIS CABEÇOTES |
| 4379 | FRESADORA DÚPLEX DE GRANDE POTÊNCIA |
| 4380 | PROCESSO DÚPLEX |
| 4381 | BOMBA DE DOIS CILINDROS |
| 4381 | BOMBA DÚPLEX |
| 4382 | MÁQUINA DE SOLDAR DE PONTO DUPLO |
| 4383 | MOLDAGEM DUPLA |
| 4384 | CONTRA-PROVA |
| 4385 | DURABILIDADE |
| 4386 | DURÁVEL |
| 4387 | DURALUMÍNIO |
| 4388 | FUNDIÇÃO TRANQÜILA |
| 4389 | PÓ |
| 4390 | ASPIRADOR DE PÓ |
| 4391 | COLETORES DE PÓ |
| 4392 | EXAUSTÃO DE GÁS E POEIRA |
| 4393 | À PROVA DE PÓ |
| 4394 | COBERTURA PROTETORA DE ENXOFRE |
| 4394 | PULVERIZAÇÃO |
| 4395 | CICLO ATIVO |
| 4395 | REGIME DE UTILIZAÇÃO |
| 4396 | REPOUSO |
| 4397 | CORANTE |
| 4398 | TENSÃO DINÂMICA |
| 4399 | DINÂMICO |
| 4400 | DINÂMICA |
| 4401 | DINAMITE |
| 4402 | DÍNAMO |
| 4403 | DINAMÔMETRO |
| 4404 | DINAMOMÉTRICO |
| 4405 | DINA |
| 4406 | DÍNODO |
| 4407 | DISPRÓSIO |
| 4408 | ORELHA |
| 4408 | PREGA |
| 4408 | ALHETA |
| 4408 | ASA |
| 4409 | TERRA |
| 4409 | SOLO |
| 4409 | MASSA |
| 4410 | LIGAR À TERRA OU À MASSA |
| 4411 | FIO TERRA |
| 4412 | CORANTE MINERAL |
| 4413 | OZOQUERITA |
| 4413 | CERA FÓSSIL |
| 4414 | EQUIPAMENTO DE TERRAPLENAGEM |
| 4414 | EQUIPAMENTO PARA NIVELAMENTO DE SOLO |

| | | | |
|---|---|---|---|
| 4415 | CONTATO TERRA | 4448 | ARESTA DE REGRESSÃO |
| 4415 | TERRA | 4449 | PREPARAÇÃO DAS BORDAS |
| 4416 | TUBO DE BARRO | 4450 | MÓ VERTICAL |
| 4416 | MANILHA | 4450 | MOINHO COM MÓ VERTICAL |
| 4417 | ATERRAMENTO | 4451 | LAMINADOR DE BORDAS |
| 4417 | LIGAÇÃO À TERRA | 4452 | RECALQUE |
| 4418 | RESSALTO DE ATERRAMENTO | 4452 | IMPULSÃO |
| 4419 | CALÇO DE ATERRAMENTO | 4452 | REPULSÃO |
| 4420 | ESCAVAÇÕES | 4453 | MÁQUINAS DE CHANFRAR |
| 4420 | ATERRO | 4454 | LAMINADOR DE BORDAS |
| 4421 | FRATURA TERROSA | 4455 | RANHURA DE PASSO |
| 4422 | ÁGUA DE LABARRAQUE | 4456 | CILINDRO REGULADOR |
| 4423 | ÉBANO | 4457 | CALOR ÚTIL |
| 4424 | DESCENTRADO | 4457 | CALOR EFETIVO |
| 4424 | EXCÊNTRICO | 4458 | POTÊNCIA EFETIVA |
| 4425 | EXCÊNTRICO | 4459 | PRESSÃO DE REGIME |
| 4426 | CÍRCULOS EXCÊNTRICOS | 4459 | PRESSÃO EFETIVA |
| 4427 | MECANISMO DE MANIVELA EXCÊNTRICA | 4459 | PRESSÃO ÚTIL |
| 4428 | CARGA EXCÊNTRICA | 4459 | PRESSÃO ABSOLUTA |
| 4429 | SEGMENTO DE PISTÃO EXCÊNTRICO | 4460 | SEÇÃO EFETIVA |
| 4430 | PRENSA EXCÊNTRICA | 4461 | EFERVESCÊNCIA |
| 4431 | HASTE EXCÊNTRICA | 4461 | EBULIÇÃO |
| 4431 | BIELA EXCÊNTRICA | 4461 | FORMAÇÃO DE ESPUMA |
| 4432 | CABEÇA DE BIELA EXCÊNTRICA | 4462 | AÇO EFERVESCENTE |
| 4433 | ROLDANA EXCÊNTRICA | 4463 | RENDIMENTO |
| 4433 | EXCÊNTRICO | 4463 | EFICIÊNCIA |
| 4434 | POLIA DE ROLDANA EXCÊNTRICA | 4464 | EFLORESCÊNCIA |
| 4434 | DISCO DE EXCÊNTRICO | 4465 | EFUSÃO |
| 4435 | ANEL OU COLAR DE EXCÊNTRICO | 4466 | EFUSÃO DE GASES |
| 4436 | EXCENTRICIDADE | 4467 | COTOVELO A 1/2 |
| 4437 | ECONOMIZADOR | 4468 | EXPELIR |
| 4438 | CORRENTE PARASITA | 4468 | EXPULSAR |
| 4438 | CORRENTE PARASITA | 4468 | LANÇAR FORA |
| 4438 | CORRENTE DE FOUCAULT | 4469 | EJETOR |
| 4439 | FREIO A CORRENTE DE FOUCAULT | 4470 | CONDENSADOR DO EJETOR |
| 4440 | CORRENTES DE FOUCAULT | 4471 | EJETOR POR EXTRATOR DE BRAÇOS |
| 4441 | BEIRA | 4472 | EJETOR |
| 4441 | BORDA | 4472 | EXAUSTOR |
| 4441 | FIO | 4473 | ELÁSTICO |
| 4441 | ARESTA | 4474 | FLUÊNCIA ELÁSTICA |
| 4441 | MARGEM | 4474 | EFEITO ELÁSTICO SECUNDÁRIO |
| 4441 | ÂNGULO | 4475 | CONSTANTE OU MÓDULO ELÁSTICO |
| 4442 | CAME | 4476 | ACOPLAMENTO ELÁSTICO |
| 4442 | EXCÊNTRICO | 4476 | LUVA ELÁSTICA |
| 4442 | CAME DE DISCO CURVO | 4476 | MANGUITO ELÁSTICO |
| 4443 | DISCORDÂNCIA DE CUNHA | 4477 | FLEXÃO ELÁSTICA |
| 4444 | DISPOSITIVO DE MARCAÇÃO DAS BORDAS | 4478 | DEFORMAÇÃO ELÁSTICA |
| 4445 | JUNTA DE ARESTAS PARALELAS | 4479 | DIAFRAGMA ELÁSTICO |
| 4446 | FRESA ESTREITA AXIAL | 4479 | MEMBRANA ELÁSTICA |
| 4447 | ARESTA DE UM ORIFÍCIO | 4480 | FORÇA ELÁSTICA DE UM GÁS |
| 4448 | ARESTA DE RETROCESSO | 4481 | LIMITE DE ELASTICIDADE |

| | |
|---|---|
| 4482 | JUNTA PLÁSTICA |
| 4483 | MÓDULO DE ELASTICIDADE |
| 4484 | SÓLIDO ELÁSTICO |
| 4485 | DEFORMAÇÃO ELÁSTICA |
| 4486 | ARRUELA ELÁSTICA |
| 4487 | ELASTICIDADE |
| 4488 | ELASTICIDADE DE COMPRESSÃO |
| 4489 | ELASTICIDADE DE FLEXÃO |
| 4490 | ELASTICIDADE DE TORÇÃO |
| 4491 | ELASTICIDADE DE TRAÇÃO |
| 4492 | DEPÓSITO ELEVADO |
| 4493 | ÂNGULO |
| 4493 | COTOVELO |
| 4494 | ARCO ELÉTRICO |
| 4494 | ARCO VOLTAICO |
| 4495 | FORNO A ARCO |
| 4496 | MAÇARICO ELÉTRICO |
| 4497 | CALDEIRA ELÉTRICA |
| 4498 | SOLDA ELÉTRICA (FORTE) |
| 4499 | BOBINA |
| 4500 | CORRENTE ELÉTRICA |
| 4501 | DENSIDADE DE CORRENTE |
| 4501 | DENSIDADE ELÉTRICA |
| 4502 | DESCARGA ELÉTRICA |
| 4503 | COMANDO ELÉTRICO |
| 4504 | CAMPO ELÉTRICO |
| 4505 | CAMPO ELÉTRICO |
| 4506 | INTENSIDADE DO CAMPO ELÉTRICO |
| 4507 | FORNO ELÉTRICO |
| 4508 | RECOZIMENTO EM FORNO ELÉTRICO |
| 4509 | FUNDIÇÃO ELÉTRICA |
| 4510 | FUNDIÇÃO EM FORNO ELÉTRICO |
| 4511 | AÇO DE FORNO ELÉTRICO |
| 4511 | AÇO ELÉTRICO |
| 4512 | CENTRAL ELÉTRICA |
| 4513 | CALEFAÇÃO ELÉTRICA |
| 4513 | AQUECIMENTO ELÉTRICO |
| 4514 | IGNIÇÃO ELÉTRICA |
| 4515 | FORNO ELÉTRICO DE INDUÇÃO |
| 4516 | LÂMPADA ELÉTRICA |
| 4517 | LUZ ELÉTRICA |
| 4518 | ILUMINAÇÃO ELÉTRICA |
| 4519 | LINHA DE ILUMINAÇÃO |
| 4520 | LOCOMOTIVA ELÉTRICA |
| 4521 | LINHA DE TRANSMISSÃO ELÉTRICA A GRANDE DISTÂNCIA |
| 4522 | MÁQUINA ELÉTRICA |
| 4523 | REDE ELÉTRICA |
| 4523 | LINHA DE ELETRICIDADE |
| 4524 | MOTORES ELÉTRICOS |
| 4524 | GERADOR DE ELETRICIDADE |

| | |
|---|---|
| 4525 | ENERGIA ELÉTRICA |
| 4526 | LINHAS DE TRANSMISSÃO DE ENERGIA ELÉTRICA |
| 4526 | LINHAS DE TRANSMISSÃO |
| 4527 | REGULADOR ELÉTRICO |
| 4528 | RESISTÊNCIA ELÉTRICA |
| 4529 | CHOQUE |
| 4530 | FERRO PARA SOLDA ELÉTRICA |
| 4531 | FAÍSCA ELÉTRICA |
| 4532 | AÇO DE FORNO ELÉTRICO |
| 4533 | SOLDA ELÉTRICA |
| 4534 | ACUMULADOR ELÉTRICO |
| 4535 | COMPARADOR ELÉTRICO |
| 4536 | CONDUTIBILIDADE ELÉTRICA |
| 4537 | CONDUTOR ELÉTRICO |
| 4538 | METAIS PARA CONTATOS ELÉTRICOS |
| 4539 | ENERGIA ELÉTRICA |
| 4540 | ENGENHEIRO ELETRICISTA |
| 4541 | ENGENHARIA ELÉTRICA |
| 4541 | ELETRICIDADE INDUSTRIAL |
| 4542 | EQUIPAMENTO ELÉTRICO |
| 4543 | MONTADOR ELETRICISTA |
| 4544 | CHAPA DE TRANSFORMADOR |
| 4545 | ISOLAMENTO ELÉTRICO |
| 4546 | CARGA ELÉTRICA |
| 4547 | OSCILAÇÃO ELÉTRICA |
| 4548 | RESISTIVIDADE |
| 4548 | RESISTÊNCIA ESPECÍFICA |
| 4549 | VÁLVULA ELÉTRICA |
| 4550 | FUNDIÇÃO ELÉTRICA |
| 4551 | ELETRICISTA |
| 4552 | ELETRICIDADE |
| 4553 | CONTADOR DE LUZ |
| 4553 | CONTADOR ELÉTRICO |
| 4554 | ELETRIFICAÇÃO |
| 4555 | ELETRIFICAR |
| 4556 | FURADEIRA ELÉTRICA |
| 4556 | BROCA ELÉTRICA |
| 4556 | PUA ELÉTRICA |
| 4557 | MOLDE ELÉTRICO |
| 4558 | REFINAÇÃO ELETROLÍTICA |
| 4559 | CORTE POR ELETROEROSÃO |
| 4560 | ELETROQUÍMICO |
| 4561 | ELETROQUÍMICA |
| 4562 | DEPOSIÇÃO ELETROLÍTICA DE METAIS |
| 4563 | ELETRODINÂMICO |
| 4564 | ELETRODINAMÔMETRO |
| 4565 | ELETROEROSÃO |
| 4566 | ELETROGALVANIZAÇÃO |
| 4566 | ZINCAGEM ELETROLÍTICA |
| 4567 | ELETROÍMA |

| | | | |
|---|---|---|---|
| 4568 | ELETROSTÁTICO | 4616 | DISPERSÃO ELETROMAGNÉTICA |
| 4569 | ELETROTIPIA | 4617 | SOLDAGEM A IMPACTO ELETROMAGNÉTICO |
| 4570 | ELETROANÁLISE | 4618 | SEPARAÇÃO ELETROMAGNÉTICA |
| 4571 | EQUIVALENTE ELETROQUÍMICO | 4619 | SOLDAGEM POR INDUÇÃO |
| 4572 | RETIFICADOR ELETROQUÍMICO | 4620 | ELETROMAGNETISMO |
| 4573 | ELETROQUÍMICA | 4621 | ELETROMETALURGIA |
| 4574 | ELÉTRODO | 4622 | FORÇA ELETROMOTRIZ F.E.M. |
| 4575 | PORTA-ELÉTRODO | 4623 | MOTOR ELÉTRICO |
| 4576 | METAL DE ELÉTRODO | 4624 | ELÉTRON |
| 4577 | POTENCIAL ELETROLÍTICO | 4625 | FEIXE DE ELÉTRONS |
| 4578 | PONTA DE ELÉTRODO | 4626 | LENTE DE CONCENTRAÇÃO DOS ELÉTRONS |
| 4579 | PONTA DE ELÉTRODO | 4627 | SOLDAGEM POR FEIXE DE ELÉTRONS |
| 4580 | DEPOSIÇÃO ELETROLÍTICA | 4628 | CANHÃO ELETRÔNICO |
| 4581 | DISSOLUÇÃO ELETROLÍTICA | 4629 | MICROSCÓPIO ELETRÔNICO |
| 4582 | EXTRAÇÃO ELETROLÍTICA | 4630 | SOLDAGEM POR FEIXE DE ELÉTRONS |
| 4583 | GALVANIZAÇÃO ELETROLÍTICA | 4631 | ELETRONEGATIVO |
| 4584 | CALIBRE DE TOLERÂNCIAS | 4632 | COMPARADOR ELETRÔNICO |
| 4585 | ELETROLISAR | 4633 | IGNIÇÃO ELETRÔNICA |
| 4586 | ELETRÓLISE | 4634 | RETIFICADOR ELETRÔNICO |
| 4587 | ELETRÓLITO | 4635 | REGULADOR ELETRÔNICO |
| 4588 | CÉLULA ELETROLÍTICA | 4636 | TUBOS ELETRÔNICOS |
| 4589 | LIMPEZA ELETROLÍTICA | 4637 | ELETRÔNICA |
| 4590 | CONDENSADOR ELETROLÍTICO | 4638 | ELETRO OSMOSE |
| 4591 | COBRE ELETROLÍTICO | 4639 | CATAFORESE |
| 4592 | DEPÓSITO GALVANIZADO | 4639 | ELETROFORESE |
| 4593 | DEPOSIÇÃO ELETROLÍTICA | 4640 | ELETROGALVANIZAÇÃO |
| 4594 | ANÁLISE ELETROLÍTICA | 4640 | GALVANOPLASTIA |
| 4595 | DISSOCIAÇÃO ELETROLÍTICA | 4640 | GALVANOPLÁSTICA |
| 4596 | DECOMPOSIÇÃO ELETROLÍTICA | 4641 | ELETROPOSITIVO |
| 4596 | IONIZAÇÃO | 4642 | FORÇA ELETROSTÁTICA |
| 4597 | FORNO DE ELETRÓLISE ÍGNEA | 4643 | GERADOR ELETROSTÁTICO |
| 4598 | OURO ELETROLÍTICO | 4644 | INDUÇÃO ELETROSTÁTICA |
| 4599 | MANGANÉS ELETROLÍTICO | 4645 | SOLDAGEM POR PERCUSSÃO COM |
| 4600 | NÍQUEL ELETROLÍTICO | | CONDENSADOR |
| 4601 | OXIDAÇÃO ELETROLÍTICA | 4646 | SEPARAÇÃO ELETROSTÁTICA |
| 4602 | SEPARAÇÃO ELETROLÍTICA | 4647 | ELETROTÉCNICO |
| 4602 | DIVISÃO ELETROLÍTICA | 4648 | ELETROTÉCNICA |
| 4603 | DECAPAGEM ELETROLÍTICA | 4649 | RENDIMENTO ELETROTÉRMICO |
| 4604 | POLARIZAÇÃO ELETROLÍTICA | 4649 | EFICIÊNCIA ELETROTÉRMICA |
| 4605 | POLIMENTO ELETROLÍTICO | 4650 | ELETROTERMIA |
| 4606 | RETIFICADOR ELETROLÍTICO | 4651 | GALVANOPLASTIA |
| 4607 | REDUÇÃO ELETROLÍTICA | 4652 | EXTRAÇÃO ELETROLÍTICA |
| 4608 | PRATA ELETROLÍTICA | 4653 | ÁMBAR AMARELO |
| 4609 | TENSÃO DE SOLUÇÃO ELETROLÍTICA | 4653 | ELETRO |
| 4610 | COBRE ELETROLÍTICO DE ÓXIDO CÚPRICO | 4654 | ELEMENTO |
| 4611 | ELETROÍMA | 4654 | CORPO SIMPLES |
| 4612 | ELETROMAGNÉTICO | 4655 | ANÁLISE ELEMENTAR |
| 4613 | FREIO ELETROMAGNÉTICO | 4656 | ELEMI |
| 4614 | ANALISADOR ELETROMAGNÉTICO DE | 4657 | ELETROANÁLISE |
| | DUREZA | 4658 | TEMPERATURA ELEVADA |
| 4615 | INDUÇÃO ELETROMAGNÉTICA | 4659 | ELEVAÇÃO |

| | | | | |
|---|---|---|---|---|
| 4660 | ELEVADOR | 4701 | POTÊNCIA EMISSIVA |
| 4661 | ELEVADORES DE FENO E DE PALHA | 4702 | EMISSIVIDADE |
| 4662 | ELIMINAR | 4703 | IRRADIAR |
| 4662 | SUPRIMIR | 4703 | EMITIR RAIOS |
| 4663 | ELIMINAR CALOR | 4704 | FÓRMULA EMPÍRICA |
| 4664 | ELIMINAÇÃO | 4705 | TUBULAÇÃO DE SAÍDA DE ASPIRAÇÃO |
| 4665 | ESVAZIAMENTO DO AR DE UM CONDUTO | 4706 | ÓLEO EMULSIONADO |
| 4666 | SUBTRAÇÃO DO CALOR | 4707 | EMULSIONAR |
| 4667 | ELIMINAÇÃO | 4708 | EMULSÃO |
| 4668 | ELINVAR (LIGA) | 4709 | ESMALTE |
| 4669 | ELIPSE | 4710 | ESMALTAR |
| 4670 | ELIPSÓGRAFO | 4711 | PINTURA A ESMALTE |
| 4671 | ELIPSÓIDE | 4712 | ESMALTAGEM |
| 4672 | ELIPSÓIDE DE ROTAÇÃO | 4713 | ENANTIOTRÓPICO |
| 4673 | CABEÇA ELIPSOIDAL | 4714 | VIGA REVESTIDA |
| 4674 | SEÇÃO ELÍPTICA | 4715 | MOTOR BLINDADO |
| 4675 | CILINDRO ELÍPTICO | 4716 | CODIFICAÇÃO |
| 4676 | INTEGRAL ELÍPTICA | 4717 | VISTA POSTERIOR |
| 4677 | ENGRENAGEM ELÍPTICA | 4718 | SERRAGEM VERTICAL DA MADEIRA |
| 4677 | RODA ELÍPTICA | 4718 | SERRAGEM CONTRA-VEIO DA MADEIRA |
| 4678 | ARAME OVAL | 4719 | MADEIRA CORTADA CONTRA A FIBRA |
| 4678 | FIO ELÍPTICO | 4720 | MANCAL DE EXTREMIDADE |
| 4679 | ALONGAMENTO | 4721 | MUNHÃO DE PONTA |
| 4680 | EXTENSÃO | 4722 | FRESA FRONTAL |
| 4681 | ELUTRIAÇÃO | 4722 | FRESA DE TOPO |
| 4681 | DECANTAÇÃO | 4722 | FRESA RADIAL |
| 4682 | EMBUTIR NO CONCRETO | 4723 | FRESAS DE TOPO |
| 4683 | GRAU DE PENETRAÇÃO | 4724 | FIM DE PROGRAMA |
| 4683 | GRAU DE EMBUTIMENTO | 4725 | FINAL DE FITA |
| 4684 | GRAVAÇÃO EM RELEVO | 4726 | SUPORTE DE PONTA |
| 4685 | FRAGILIDADE | 4727 | FOLGA AXIAL OU LONGITUDINAL |
| 4686 | EMBRIÃO | 4728 | PAREDE FRONTAL |
| 4687 | FREIO DE EMERGÊNCIA | 4729 | DE BASES CENTRADAS |
| 4688 | ILUMINAÇÃO AUXILIAR | 4730 | FIM DE BLOCO |
| 4688 | ILUMINAÇÃO DE EMERGÊNCIA | 4731 | FINAL DE LINHA |
| 4689 | LUZES DE EMERGÊNCIA | 4732 | CORRENTE SEM-FIM |
| 4690 | LINHA DE EMERGÊNCIA | 4733 | CABO SEM-FIM |
| 4691 | RAIO EMERGENTE | 4734 | IMPULSO LONGITUDINAL |
| 4692 | ESMERIL NATURAL | 4734 | IMPULSO AXIAL |
| 4693 | TELA DE ESMERIL | 4735 | FOLGA LATERAL DOS EIXOS |
| 4693 | LIXA DE ESMERIL | 4736 | ENDOSMOSE |
| 4694 | ESMERILHAR | 4737 | ENDOTÉRMICO |
| 4694 | POLIR COM ESMERIL | 4738 | DURAÇÃO |
| 4695 | POLIMENTO COM ESMERIL | 4738 | RESISTÊNCIA |
| 4696 | LIXA DE ESMERIL | 4739 | FISSURA POR FADIGA |
| 4697 | PÓ DE ESMERIL | 4740 | RUPTURA POR FADIGA |
| 4698 | RODA DE ESMERIL | 4741 | LIMITE DE RESISTÊNCIA |
| 4698 | REBOLO DE ESMERIL | 4742 | RELAÇÃO DO LIMITE DE RUPTURA |
| 4699 | CORINDO | 4743 | TESTE DE RESISTÊNCIA |
| 4699 | ESMERIL | 4743 | ENSAIO DE FADIGA |
| 4700 | EMISSÃO | 4743 | TESTE DE FADIGA |

| | | | |
|---|---|---|---|
| 4744 | EXCITADOR | 4788 | DIAGRAMA DE EQUILÍBRIO |
| 4744 | ATIVADOR | 4789 | POTENCIAL ELETROLÍTICO ESTÁTICO |
| 4745 | ENERGIA | 4790 | VOLTAGEM MÁXIMA DE REAÇÃO ELETROQUÍMICA |
| 4746 | EFICÁCIA ENERGÉTICA | | |
| 4747 | CONSUMO DE ENERGIA | 4791 | TEMPERATURA DE EQUILÍBRIO |
| 4747 | POTÊNCIA ABSORVIDA | 4792 | VALOR DE EQUILÍBRIO |
| 4748 | ENERGIA DE DESCARGA | 4793 | EQUILÍBRIO |
| 4749 | ENGATAR | 4794 | EQUIPAMENTO |
| 4750 | ENGRENAR | 4794 | ACESSÓRIOS |
| 4751 | ENGATE | 4794 | APARELHAGEM |
| 4752 | ENGRENAGEM | 4795 | EQUIVALÊNCIA |
| 4753 | CASA DAS MÁQUINAS | 4796 | EQUIVALENTE |
| 4754 | SUPORTE MOTOR | 4797 | CONDUTIBILIDADE EQUIVALENTE |
| 4755 | ÓLEO PARA MÁQUINAS | 4798 | RESISTIVIDADE EQUIVALENTE |
| 4756 | PEÇA DE MÁQUINA | 4799 | RASPAR |
| 4757 | SALA DAS MÁQUINAS | 4799 | APAGAR |
| 4758 | EIXO DO MOTOR OU DA MÁQUINA | 4799 | DESFAZER |
| 4759 | MÁQUINA DE VAPOR SUPERAQUECIDA | 4800 | RASPADOR |
| 4760 | FREIO MOTOR | 4800 | LÂMINA PARA RASPAR |
| 4761 | ENGENHEIRO | 4801 | BORRACHA DE APAGAR |
| 4762 | ENGENHEIRO CHEFE | 4802 | RASPAGEM |
| 4763 | FUNDIÇÃO MECÂNICA | 4803 | RASPAGEM |
| 4764 | OFICINA DE CONSTRUÇÃO MECÂNICA | 4804 | ÉRBIO |
| 4765 | MAQUINISTA | 4805 | MONTAR |
| 4766 | MOTORES (GASOLINA, QUEROSENE E DIESEL) | 4805 | ERIGIR |
| | | 4805 | EDIFICAR |
| 4767 | COBRE PARA GRAVURAS | 4806 | LEVANTAR UMA PERPENDICULAR |
| 4768 | ALARGAMENTO DE UM CANO | 4807 | MONTADO SIMULTANEAMENTE OU SUBSEQÜENTEMENTE |
| 4769 | AMPLIAÇÃO DE UM DESENHO | | |
| 4770 | JATO DE AR ENRIQUECIDO DE OXIGÊNIO | 4808 | MONTAGEM |
| 4771 | AR FALTO (INFILTRADO) | 4808 | EDIFICAÇÃO |
| 4771 | ENTRADA DE AR | 4808 | INSTALAÇÃO |
| 4772 | INCLUSÃO DE ESCÓRIA | 4809 | EQUIPAMENTO DE MONTAGEM |
| 4773 | ENTROPIA | 3810 | MATERIAL DE MONTAGEM |
| 4774 | LADO DE ENTRADA | 4811 | OFICINA DE MONTAGEM |
| 4775 | LINHA DE ENTRADA | 4812 | FERRAMENTAS DE MONTAGEM |
| 4776 | INVÓLUCRO | 4813 | MONTAGEM |
| 4776 | ENVOLVENTE | 4813 | INSTALAÇÃO |
| 4777 | LUSTRO | 4813 | EDIFICAÇÃO |
| 4778 | TREM EPICICLOIDAL | 4814 | PLANO DE MONTAGEM |
| 4779 | EPICICLÓIDE | 4815 | INSTALAÇÃO |
| 4780 | ENGRENAGEM EPICICLOIDAL | 4816 | INSTALADOR |
| 4780 | DENTES EPICICLOIDAIS | 4817 | FERRAMENTAS DE MONTADOR |
| 4781 | CANTONEIRA DE LADOS IGUAIS | 4818 | ERG (UNIDADE DE ENERGIA DO SISTEMA CGS) |
| 4782 | EQUAÇÃO | | |
| 4783 | EQUAÇÃO DE ESTADO | 4819 | MÁQUINA PARA TESTES OU ENSAIOS DE DUCTILIDADE ERICHSEN |
| 4784 | CRISTAIS EQUIAXIAIS | | |
| 4784 | CRISTAIS DE EIXOS IGUAIS | 4820 | EROSÃO |
| 4785 | TRIÂNGULO EQUILÁTERO | 4821 | ERRÁTICO |
| 4786 | EQUILÍBRIO | 4821 | BLOCO ERRANTE |
| 4787 | CONSTANTE DE EQUILÍBRIO | 4821 | OCASIONAL |

| | |
|---|---|
| 4822 | ERRO |
| 4823 | DETETOR DE ERROS |
| 4824 | ERRO DE CÁLCULO |
| 4825 | ERRO DE PROJETO |
| 4826 | ERRO DE LEITURA |
| 4827 | ERRO DE APRECIAÇÃO |
| 4828 | ERRO DE COLIMAÇÃO |
| 4829 | ERRO DE OBSERVAÇÃO |
| 4830 | REGISTRADOR DE ERROS |
| 4831 | ERITROSINA |
| 4832 | ESCAPAR |
| 4832 | SAIR |
| 4833 | ESCAPAMENTO DE GASES, VAPOR |
| 4834 | CIRCUNFERÊNCIA TANGENTE |
| 4835 | GUARDA-PÓ |
| 4835 | PROTEÇÃO |
| 4836 | ÓLEO VOLÁTIL |
| 4836 | ÓLEO ESSENCIAL |
| 4837 | ÉSTER |
| 4838 | ORÇAMENTO DE CUSTO |
| 4839 | CAUSTICAR |
| 4839 | ATACAR COM ÁCIDO |
| 4840 | LINHAS DE CORROSÃO |
| 4841 | FISSURAS DE ATAQUE QUÍMICO |
| 4842 | FIGURAS DE CORROSÃO |
| 4843 | PITES DE CORROSÃO |
| 4844 | REAGENTE CÁUSTICO |
| 4845 | FIGURA DE CORROSÃO |
| 4846 | ATAQUE POR REATIVO QUÍMICO |
| 4846 | CAUSTIFICAÇÃO |
| 4847 | CORROSIVO |
| 4848 | ETANO |
| 4849 | CLORETO DE ETILO |
| 4850 | ETILO NÍTRICO |
| 4851 | ETILENO |
| 4852 | EUDIÔMETRO |
| 4853 | CLORETO DE COBRE |
| 4854 | EURÓPIO |
| 4855 | EUTÉTICO |
| 4856 | FUSÃO EUTÉTICA |
| 4857 | MISTURA EUTÉTICA |
| 4858 | TEMPERATURA EUTÉTICA |
| 4859 | EUTECTÓIDE |
| 4860 | REAÇÃO EUTECTÓIDE |
| 4861 | EVAPORÁVEL |
| 4862 | EVAPORAR |
| 4863 | EVAPORAR AO AR LIVRE |
| 4863 | VAPORIZAR-SE AO AR LIVRE |
| 4864 | CÁPSULA |
| 4864 | EVAPORADOR |
| 4865 | TEMPERATURA DE EVAPORAÇÃO |

| | |
|---|---|
| 4866 | PERDA POR EVAPORAÇÃO |
| 4867 | VAPORIZAÇÃO |
| 4868 | CONDENSADOR DE EVAPORAÇÃO |
| 4869 | EVAPORADOR |
| 4870 | CAIXA OU CORPO DE UM EVAPORADOR |
| 4871 | RUPTURA LISA |
| 4872 | NÚMERO PAR |
| 4873 | EVOLUTA |
| 4874 | DESPRENDIMENTO DE CALOR |
| 4875 | MEDIÇÃO PRECISA |
| 4875 | MEDIÇÃO EXATA |
| 4876 | CONTROLE |
| 4876 | EXAME |
| 4877 | INSPEÇÃO POR SECIONAMENTO |
| 4878 | EXCESSO |
| 4879 | VÁLVULA REGULADORA DE VAZÃO |
| 4880 | CHAMA DE ACETILENO |
| 4880 | EXCESSO DE TRABALHO |
| 4881 | SOBRETENSÃO |
| 4882 | CHAMA REDUTORA |
| 4883 | CHAMA OXIDANTE |
| 4884 | INTERCÂMBIO DE CALOR |
| 4885 | EXCITAÇÃO |
| 4886 | ÂNODO DE EXCITAÇÃO |
| 4887 | EXCITAR |
| 4888 | EXCITADOR |
| 4889 | ESFOLIAÇÃO |
| 4890 | ESCAPAMENTO |
| 4891 | GÁS DE ESCAPAMENTO |
| 4892 | LINHA DE ESCAPAMENTO DO VAPOR |
| 4892 | TUBO DE ESCAPAMENTO DE VAPOR |
| 4892 | MANGUEIRA DE ESCAPAMENTO DO VAPOR |
| 4893 | COLETOR DE ESCAPAMENTO |
| 4894 | TUBO DE ESCAPE |
| 4895 | ORIFÍCIO DE ESCAPE |
| 4896 | VAPOR DE ESCAPE |
| 4897 | TUBO DE ESCAPE DE VAPOR |
| 4898 | CURSO DE ESCAPE OU EXAUSTÃO |
| 4899 | VÁLVULA DE ESCAPE |
| 4900 | EXAUSTOR |
| 4901 | EXOTÉRMICO |
| 4902 | DILATAR-SE |
| 4902 | EXPANDIR-SE |
| 4903 | ALARGAR UM TUBO |
| 4904 | METAL ESTIRADO |
| 4905 | TUBO ALARGADO |
| 4906 | MANDRIS DE EXPANSÃO |
| 4907 | MANDRIL EXPANSÍVEL |
| 4908 | DILATAÇÃO DE TUBOS |
| 4909 | POLIA DE DIÂMETRO VARIÁVEL |
| 4910 | ROLO TENSOR |

| | | | |
|---|---|---|---|
| 4911 | PROVA DE MANDRILAGEM | 4949 | EXTENSÔMETRO |
| 4912 | EXPANSÃO | 4950 | ÂNGULO EXTERNO |
| 4912 | DILATAÇÃO | 4951 | FRESA DE REMOVER APARAS DE TUBOS |
| 4912 | AUMENTO DE VOLUME | 4952 | PENTE DE ABRIR MACHOS |
| 4913 | TUBO COMPENSADOR | 4953 | RETIFICADORA DE SUPERFÍCIES EXTERNAS |
| 4913 | COMPENSADOR DE DILATAÇÃO | 4954 | FORÇA EXTERNA |
| 4913 | CURVA DE EXPANSÃO | 4954 | ESFORÇO EXTERNO |
| 4914 | COEFICIENTE DE DILATAÇÃO | 4954 | CARGA EXTERNA |
| 4915 | LUVA DE DILATAÇÃO | 4955 | CALIBRE EXTERNO |
| 4916 | CURVA DE EXPANSÃO | 4956 | ENGRENAGEM EXTERNA |
| 4917 | ESCAREADOR MANUAL EXTENSÍVEL | 4957 | RETIFICAÇÃO EXTERNA |
| 4918 | JUNTA DE DILATAÇÃO | 4958 | DIÂMETRO EXTERNO |
| 4919 | DILATAÇÃO DE METAL | 4959 | DENTES EXTERNOS |
| 4920 | EXPANSÃO DOS GASES | 4960 | ROSCA EXTERNA |
| 4921 | EXPANSÃO DE VAPOR | 4961 | ROSQUEAMENTO EXTERNO |
| 4922 | PEÇA DE COMPENSAÇÃO | 4962 | TRABALHO EXTERNO |
| 4923 | ESCAREADOR REGULÁVEL | 4963 | TUBO DE ALHETAS EXTERNAS |
| 4924 | MÁQUINA DE EXPANSÃO | 4964 | EXTRATO |
| 4925 | TURBINA DE EXPANSÃO | 4965 | REAGENTE HIDROMETALÚRGICO |
| 4926 | VÁLVULA DE EXPANSÃO | 4965 | LÍQUIDO DE EXTRAÇÃO |
| 4927 | ESPERANÇA MATEMÁTICA | 4966 | EXTRAÇÃO DOS METAIS |
| 4928 | ENSAIAR | 4967 | EXTRATOR |
| 4928 | FAZER EXPERIÊNCIA | 4968 | LEI DOS VALORES EXTREMOS |
| 4929 | DETERMINAÇÃO EXPERIMENTAL | 4969 | MOLDURAS EXTRUDADAS |
| 4930 | PERITO | 4970 | EXTRUSÃO |
| 4930 | ESPECIALISTA | 4971 | LINGOTE DE EXTRUSÃO |
| 4930 | TÉCNICO | 4972 | PRENSA DE EXTRUSÃO |
| 4931 | APRECIAÇÃO DE PERITO | 4973 | OLHAL (PARAFUSO, PINO, ETC.) |
| 4932 | EXPIRAÇÃO DE UMA PATENTE | 4974 | OLHAL (GANCHO) |
| 4933 | EXPLODIR | 4975 | OLHO DO MARTELO |
| 4933 | ESTOURAR | 4976 | OLHO DA BIELA |
| 4933 | DETONAR | 4977 | OCULAR |
| 4934 | VISTA DETALHADA | 4978 | ESCAREAÇÃO DE UMA RODA, DE UMA POLIA |
| 4934 | DESENHO DETALHADO | 4979 | REBITADORA COM OLHAL |
| 4935 | EXPLOSÃO | 4980 | ILHÓ |
| 4936 | PRESSÃO EXPLOSIVA | 4981 | CORREIA DE FIBRAS TÊXTEIS |
| 4937 | EXPLOSIVO | 4982 | RECIPIENTE FORJADO |
| 4938 | MISTURA DETONADORA | 4982 | RECIPIENTE TRABALHADO A QUENTE |
| 4938 | MISTURA EXPLOSIVA | 4983 | FABRICAÇÃO |
| 4939 | EXPOENTE | 4984 | PLANTA DE EXECUÇÃO |
| 4940 | EXPOENTE DE DESCARGA | 4984 | DESENHO DE FABRICAÇÃO |
| 4941 | DISTRIBUIÇÃO EXPONENCIAL | 4985 | BASTIDOR DE MONTAGEM |
| 4942 | FUNÇÃO EXPONENCIAL | 4986 | NÚMERO DE FABRICAÇÃO |
| 4943 | SÉRIE EXPONENCIAL | 4987 | REQUISITOS DE FABRICAÇÃO |
| 4944 | EXPOSIÇÃO | 4988 | TOLERÂNCIAS DE FABRICAÇÃO |
| 4945 | ALARGADORA COM CABO | 4989 | FACE |
| 4946 | ALONGAMENTO | 4989 | LADO |
| 4946 | AMPLIAÇÃO | 4989 | SUPERFÍCIE |
| 4946 | EXTENSÃO | 4990 | ÂNGULO DE POLIEDRO |
| 4947 | BARRA DE EXTENSÃO | 4991 | CUBO DE FACE CENTRADA |
| 4948 | DILATAÇÃO POR CALOR | 4992 | FRESA DE TOPO |

| | |
|---|---|
| 4992 | FRESA AXIAL OU RADIAL |
| 4993 | CABEÇA DE MARTELO |
| 4994 | LADO DE UMA PORCA |
| 4995 | MESA DE BIGORNA |
| 4996 | FRENTE DE VÁLVULA DE GAVETA |
| 4997 | PERFIL DE DENTE |
| 4998 | SUPERFÍCIE DA SOLDA |
| 4999 | PLACA FRONTAL |
| 4999 | CHAPA OU PLACA UNIVERSAL |
| 4999 | PLACA DE TORNO |
| 5000 | TELA DE SOLDAGEM |
| 5001 | TORNO DE FACEAR |
| 5001 | TORNO PLANO |
| 5002 | DE FACES CENTRADAS |
| 5003 | FLANGE GUARNECIDO |
| 5004 | TIJOLO DE FACHADA |
| 5004 | TIJOLO DE PARAMENTO |
| 5005 | TORNO DE FACEAR |
| 5006 | AREIA DE MOLDAGEM |
| 5007 | TIRA DE FACES TORNEADAS |
| 5007 | CALÇO DE AJUSTE |
| 5008 | COEFICIENTE |
| 5008 | FATOR |
| 5009 | FATOR DE SEGURANÇA |
| 5009 | COEFICIENTE DE SEGURANÇA |
| 5010 | FÁBRICA |
| 5011 | CALIBRE DE REVISÃO |
| 5012 | EDIFÍCIO INDUSTRIAL |
| 5013 | FÁBRICA |
| 5014 | DESCOLORAÇÃO |
| 5015 | FEIXE (DE FUSÃO) |
| 5015 | PACOTE (DE FERRO) |
| 5016 | PACOTE DE SUCATA |
| 5017 | PACOTE |
| 5018 | PACOTAGEM |
| 5019 | ESCALA FAHRENHEIT |
| 5020 | TERMÔMETRO FAHRENHEIT |
| 5021 | FALHA DE MOTOR |
| 5022 | QUEDA DA TEMPERATURA |
| 5023 | PONTA LIVRE |
| 5024 | QUEDA LIVRE |
| 5025 | TEMPERATURA DECRESCENTE |
| 5026 | FUNDO DUPLO |
| 5026 | FALSO FUNDO |
| 5027 | FALSO NÚCLEO |
| 5028 | FEIXE DE CURVAS |
| 5029 | CORREIA DE VENTILADOR |
| 5030 | PÁS DO VENTILADOR |
| 5031 | FREIO A MOLINETE |
| 5032 | POLIA DE VENTILADOR |
| 5033 | VENTILADOR |

| | |
|---|---|
| 5034 | CONDUTO AFUNILADO |
| 5034 | CONDUTO DE UNIÃO |
| 5035 | FARAD |
| 5036 | GAIOLA FARADAY |
| 5037 | ACOPLAMENTO RÍGIDO |
| 5037 | ACOPLAMENTO FIXO |
| 5038 | MARCHA REDUZIDA |
| 5039 | FLANGE FIXO |
| 5040 | POLIA FIXA |
| 5041 | APERTAR |
| 5041 | FIXAR |
| 5042 | FIXADOR |
| 5042 | PEÇA DE APERTO |
| 5043 | PARAFUSO DE FIXAÇÃO |
| 5043 | PARAFUSO DE APERTO |
| 5044 | FIXAÇÃO |
| 5045 | GORDO |
| 5045 | GRAXA |
| 5046 | CAL GORDA |
| 5047 | FADIGA |
| 5048 | FISSURA POR FADIGA |
| 5049 | TESTE OU PROVA DE RESISTÊNCIA |
| 5050 | LIMITE DE RESISTÊNCIA À FADIGA |
| 5051 | FADIGA DO MATERIAL |
| 5052 | RESISTÊNCIA À FADIGA |
| 5053 | LIMITE DE FADIGA |
| 5053 | RESISTÊNCIA LIMITE DE CONSISTÊNCIA |
| 5054 | TESTES DE RESISTÊNCIA À FADIGA |
| 5055 | ÁCIDO GORDUROSO |
| 5056 | DEFEITO DA FUNDIÇÃO |
| 5057 | DEFEITUOSO |
| 5057 | DETERIORADO |
| 5058 | SUPERFÍCIES DE ATRITO |
| 5058 | SUPERFÍCIES DE NIVELAMENTO |
| 5059 | CHAVETA RETANGULAR |
| 5059 | LINGÜETA |
| 5060 | ALHETA DE VÁLVULA |
| 5061 | LINGÜETA |
| 5061 | ESTRIA |
| 5061 | RANHURA |
| 5062 | PINO OU PARAFUSO COM RESSALTO |
| 5063 | ADMISSÃO |
| 5063 | INTRODUÇÃO |
| 5063 | ALIMENTAÇÃO |
| 5063 | AVANÇO |
| 5064 | ALIMENTAR |
| 5064 | INTRODUZIR |
| 5064 | AVANÇAR |
| 5065 | ALAVANCA SELETORA DOS AVANÇOS |
| 5066 | TORNEIRA DE ADMISSÃO |
| 5066 | REGISTRO DE ALIMENTAÇÃO |

| | |
|---|---|
| 5067 | MECANISMO DE AVANÇO |
| 5068 | AVANÇO DE UMA FERRAMENTA |
| 5068 | PENETRAÇÃO DE UMA FERRAMENTA |
| 5069 | AVANÇO POR DENTE |
| 5070 | TUBO DE ALIMENTAÇÃO |
| 5071 | BOMBA DE ALIMENTAÇÃO |
| 5072 | REGULADOR DE AVANÇO |
| 5072 | ALIMENTADOR AUTOMÁTICO |
| 5073 | ALAVANCA DE INVERSÃO DO AVANÇO |
| 5074 | ROLO ALIMENTADOR |
| 5074 | CILINDRO DE ALIMENTAÇÃO |
| 5075 | TANQUE DE ALIMENTAÇÃO |
| 5076 | VÁLVULA DE ADMISSÃO |
| 5077 | ÁGUA DE ALIMENTAÇÃO |
| 5078 | PREAQUECEDOR DE ÁGUA DE ALIMENTAÇÃO |
| 5079 | CORREÇÃO DA VELOCIDADE DE AVANÇO |
| 5080 | MALHA DE REALIMENTAÇÃO |
| 5081 | CABO DE ALIMENTAÇÃO |
| 5081 | CABO PRINCIPAL |
| 5081 | ARTÉRIA |
| 5081 | CONDUTO PRINCIPAL |
| 5082 | ALIMENTAÇÃO |
| 5083 | APARELHO DE AVANÇO OU DE ENCHIMENTO |
| 5083 | ALIMENTADOR |
| 5084 | TUBULAÇÃO DE ALIMENTAÇÃO |
| 5085 | CÓDIGO DE VELOCIDADE DE AVANÇO |
| 5086 | CALIBRE APALPADOR |
| 5086 | MEDIDOR DE ESPESSURA |
| 5087 | FELDSPATO |
| 5088 | ARO DE RODA |
| 5089 | FELDSPATO |
| 5090 | FELTRO |
| 5091 | CALIBRE EXTERNO |
| 5092 | ROSCA FÊMEA |
| 5092 | ROSCA INTERNA |
| 5093 | CUNHA DE PLAINA |
| 5094 | CERCA |
| 5094 | CERCADO |
| 5095 | PÁRA-LAMA |
| 5096 | ARRUELA DE PÁRA-LAMA |
| 5097 | FERMENTO |
| 5098 | FERMENTAÇÃO |
| 5099 | ACETATO FÉRRICO |
| 5100 | CLORETO DE FERRO |
| 5101 | HIDRÓXIDO DE FERRO |
| 5102 | ÓXIDO DE FERRO |
| 5103 | SULFATO DE FERRO |
| 5104 | FERRITA |
| 5105 | FAIXA DE FERRITA LIVRE |

| | |
|---|---|
| 5106 | FERRO-ALUMÍNIO |
| 5107 | FERROBORO |
| 5108 | FERROCROMO |
| 5109 | TUBO OU CANO DE CIMENTO ARMADO |
| 5110 | FERROMANGANÊS |
| 5111 | FERROMOLIBDÊNIO |
| 5112 | FERRONÍQUEL |
| 5113 | FERROSSILÍCIO |
| 5114 | FERROTITÂNIO |
| 5115 | FERROTUNGSTÊNIO |
| 5116 | FERROVANÁDIO |
| 5117 | LIGAS DE FERRO |
| 5118 | FERROMAGNÉTICO |
| 5119 | PAPEL FERROPRUSSIATO |
| 5120 | ACETATO FERROSO |
| 5121 | CLORETO FERROSO |
| 5122 | MINÉRIO DE MANGANÊS FERROSO |
| 5123 | SIDERURGIA |
| 5123 | METALURGIA DO FERRO |
| 5124 | OXALATO DE FERRO |
| 5125 | ÓXIDO FERROSO |
| 5125 | PROTÓXIDO DE FERRO |
| 5126 | FERRO VELHO |
| 5126 | SUCATA DE FERRO E AÇO |
| 5127 | FERRUGINOSO |
| 5128 | CASQUILHO |
| 5128 | VIROLA |
| 5129 | DESBARBAGEM |
| 5129 | REBARBAÇÃO |
| 5129 | ESMERILHAMENTO |
| 5130 | OFICINA DE REBARBAÇÃO |
| 5131 | FIBRA |
| 5132 | EIXO DE FIBRA |
| 5133 | DIREÇÃO DAS FIBRAS |
| 5133 | SENTIDO DAS FIBRAS |
| 5134 | TENSÃO DE FIBRA |
| 5135 | ESTRUTURA FIBROSA |
| 5136 | FIBRA |
| 5137 | FIBROSO |
| 5138 | FRATURA FIBROSA |
| 5139 | FERRO FIBROSO |
| 5140 | MATERIAL FIBROSO |
| 5141 | ESTRUTURA FIBROSA |
| 5142 | CARROÇA |
| 5143 | CAMPO VISUAL |
| 5143 | HORIZONTE VISUAL |
| 5144 | DENSIDADE MAGNÉTICA |
| 5144 | INTENSIDADE DO CAMPO |
| 5145 | SUPERVISOR DE CANTEIRO DE OBRAS |
| 5146 | SOLDA DE MONTAGEM NO LOCAL |
| 5147 | RAIZ QUINTA |

| | |
|---|---|
| 5148 | LIMA |
| 5149 | LIMAR |
| 5150 | ESCOVA DE ARAME PARA LIMAS |
| 5150 | CARDA DE LIMPAR LIMA |
| 5151 | PICADOR DE LIMA |
| 5152 | TESTE DE DUREZA À PROVA DE LIMA |
| 5153 | LIMADURA |
| 5154 | MÁQUINA DE LIMAR |
| 5155 | LIMALHAS |
| 5155 | LIMADURAS |
| 5156 | OBTURAR |
| 5156 | ENCHER |
| 5156 | CARREGAR |
| 5157 | CARGA QUÍMICA |
| 5158 | TAMPA DE CARGA |
| 5159 | METAL DE ENCHIMENTO |
| 5160 | GUIA DE OBTURAÇÃO |
| 5161 | FILETE |
| 5161 | COLAR |
| 5161 | NERVURA |
| 5161 | MEIA-CANA |
| 5161 | MOLDURA |
| 5162 | SOLDAGEM EM FILETE |
| 5163 | PERDA POR ENCHIMENTO |
| 5164 | MATERIAL DE ENCHIMENTO |
| 5165 | PARAFUSO DE FENDA COM CABEÇA CILÍNDRICA |
| 5166 | CAMADA |
| 5166 | PELÍCULA |
| 5166 | MEMBRANA |
| 5167 | PELÍCULA DE ÓLEO |
| 5167 | CAMADA FINA DE ÓLEO |
| 5168 | PELÍCULA DE ÓXIDO |
| 5169 | CAMADA DE ÁGUA |
| 5170 | ESPESSURA DE PELÍCULA |
| 5171 | PELÍCULA |
| 5171 | CAMADA FINA |
| 5172 | FILTRO |
| 5173 | FILTRAR |
| 5174 | COADJUVANTE DE FILTRAÇÃO |
| 5175 | CARTUCHO FILTRANTE |
| 5176 | TECIDO FILTRANTE |
| 5177 | PAPEL DE FILTRAR |
| 5178 | TANQUE DE FILTRAÇÃO |
| 5179 | MATERIAL FILTRANTE |
| 5180 | FILTRO-PRENSA |
| 5181 | FILTRADO |
| 5181 | LÍQUIDO FILTRADO |
| 5182 | FILTRAÇÃO |
| 5183 | ALHETA |
| 5183 | ASA |
| 5183 | BARBATANA |
| 5183 | NERVURA |
| 5184 | REBARBA DE FUNDIÇÃO |
| 5185 | DESENHO FINAL |
| 5185 | PLANO DEFINITIVO |
| 5186 | ACIONAMENTO FINAL |
| 5186 | TRANSMISSÃO ÀS RODAS |
| 5187 | POSIÇÃO FINAL |
| 5188 | PRESSÃO FINAL |
| 5189 | PRODUTO FINAL |
| 5190 | ESTADO FINAL |
| 5191 | TEMPERATURA FINAL |
| 5192 | VALOR FINAL |
| 5193 | VELOCIDADE FINAL |
| 5194 | RENDIMENTO FINAL |
| 5195 | MULTA |
| 5196 | MANDRILADORA DE PRECISÃO |
| 5196 | MÁQUINA DE BROQUEAR DE PRECISÃO |
| 5197 | ESCAREADOR DE ESTRIAS FINAS |
| 5198 | OURO FINO |
| 5199 | AREIA DE GRÃO FINO |
| 5200 | ESTRUTURA DE GRÃO FINO |
| 5201 | ROSCA DE PASSO FINO |
| 5202 | PRATA FINA |
| 5203 | ESTRUTURA FINA |
| 5204 | ROSCA FINA |
| 5205 | ARAME OU FIO FINO |
| 5206 | DE MALHA ESTREITA |
| 5207 | CABO METÁLICO DE FIOS FINOS |
| 5208 | FINURA |
| 5209 | GRAU DE PUREZA DE UMA LIGA |
| 5210 | ESTRUTURA FINA |
| 5211 | BARRA REGULADORA |
| 5211 | CUNHA |
| 5211 | LINGÜETA |
| 5211 | PASSADOR |
| 5212 | DEFORMAÇÕES EM MEIA-LUA |
| 5213 | REVESTIMENTO |
| 5213 | ACABAMENTO |
| 5214 | ACABAR |
| 5214 | RETOCAR |
| 5214 | EFETUAR O ACABAMENTO |
| 5215 | LAMINAÇÃO DE ACABAMENTO |
| 5216 | SOLDAGEM DE ACABAMENTO |
| 5217 | CAMADA SUPERFICIAL (DE PINTURA) |
| 5218 | PRODUTO ACABADO |
| 5219 | ACABADOR |
| 5219 | REMATADOR |
| 5220 | APERFEIÇOAMENTO DO ACABAMENTO |
| 5221 | MATRIZ DE ACABAMENTO |
| 5222 | LAMINADOR DE ACABAMENTO |

| | |
|---|---|
| 5223 | OPERAÇÃO DE ACABAMENTO |
| 5224 | ACABAMENTO AO ESMERIL |
| 5224 | ACABAMENTO POR POLIMENTO |
| 5225 | CILINDROS DE ACABAMENTO |
| 5225 | LAMINADORES DE EFETUAR ACABAMENTO |
| 5226 | ESCAREADOR DE ACABAMENTO CÔNICO |
| 5227 | TEMPERATURA DE ACABAMENTO |
| 5228 | FERRAMENTA DE ACABAMENTO |
| 5229 | TREM DE ACABAMENTO |
| 5230 | ARRUELA DECORATIVA |
| 5231 | FRAÇÃO DECIMAL FINITA |
| 5232 | SÉRIE FINITA |
| 5233 | RADIADOR DE ALETAS |
| 5234 | TUBO COM NERVURAS |
| 5234 | TUBO COM ALETAS |
| 5235 | AQUECER |
| 5235 | ESQUENTAR |
| 5236 | ACENDER A FORNALHA DA CALDEIRA |
| 5237 | BARRA DE GRELHA |
| 5238 | CAIXA DE FOGO |
| 5238 | CÂMARA DE COMBUSTÃO DE CALDEIRA |
| 5239 | TIJOLO REFRATÁRIO |
| 5240 | RACHADURA A QUENTE |
| 5241 | ARGILA REFRATÁRIA |
| 5241 | TERRA REFRATÁRIA |
| 5242 | PORTA DA FORNALHA |
| 5242 | PORTA CORTA-FOGO |
| 5243 | DOURADO A QUENTE |
| 5244 | BOCA DE INCÊNDIO |
| 5244 | HIDRANTE DE INCÊNDIO |
| 5245 | REFINAMENTO AO FOGO |
| 5246 | CAMADA DE ÓXIDO CÚPRICO |
| 5247 | ENSAIO DE RESISTÊNCIA AO FOGO |
| 5247 | PONTO DE COMBUSTÃO |
| 5248 | TUBO DE FUMAÇA |
| 5249 | CALDEIRA DE TUBOS DE FUMAÇA |
| 5249 | CALDEIRA FLAMOTUBULAR |
| 5250 | COBRE REFINADO AO FOGO |
| 5251 | PAREDE CORTA-FOGO |
| 5251 | MURO REFRATÁRIO |
| 5252 | TIJOLO REFRATÁRIO |
| 5253 | ARGILA REFRATÁRIA |
| 5254 | TIJOLO REFRATÁRIO ALUMINOSO |
| 5255 | CIMENTO REFRATÁRIO |
| 5256 | LOCOMOTIVA SEM CALDEIRA |
| 5257 | À PROVA DE FOGO |
| 5257 | IGNÍFUGO |
| 5258 | LENHA |
| 5258 | LENHA PARA QUEIMAR |
| 5259 | AQUECIMENTO |
| 5259 | CALEFAÇÃO |
| 5260 | SEQÜÊNCIA DE EXPLOSÃO |
| 5260 | ORDEM DE IGNIÇÃO |
| 5261 | ATIÇADOR |
| 5261 | ESPADETA |
| 5262 | CARGA DE FORNALHA |
| 5262 | ALIMENTAÇÃO DE UMA FORNALHA |
| 5263 | IGNIÇÃO DE FORNALHA DE CALDEIRA |
| 5264 | FORMÃO GROSSO |
| 5265 | PRIMEIRO FILTRO |
| 5266 | PRIMEIRA CABEÇA DE REBITE |
| 5267 | CABEÇA DE DESTILAÇÃO |
| 5268 | TARRAXA CÔNICA |
| 5268 | TARRAXA DESBASTADORA |
| 5269 | PARAFUSO DE TALA DE JUNÇÃO |
| 5270 | TALA DE JUNÇÃO (DE TRILHO) |
| 5271 | CAVIDADE EM V |
| 5272 | EM FORMA DE VENTRE DE PEIXE |
| 5273 | RUPTURA |
| 5273 | FISSUA |
| 5274 | FISSURAMENTO |
| 5274 | FENDILHAMENTO |
| 5275 | AJUSTE |
| 5275 | ENCAIXE |
| 5275 | MONTAGEM |
| 5275 | JUNÇÃO |
| 5276 | AJUSTAR |
| 5276 | ENCAIXAR |
| 5276 | REGULAR |
| 5277 | ENCAIXAR OS TUBOS |
| 5278 | ADAPTADOR |
| 5278 | AJUSTADOR |
| 5278 | AJUSTADOR MECÂNICO |
| 5279 | MARTELO DE AJUSTADOR |
| 5280 | AJUSTAGEM |
| 5280 | ACERTO |
| 5280 | ENCAIXE |
| 5280 | CONEXÃO |
| 5281 | ENCAIXE DE TUBOS |
| 5282 | OFICINA DE AJUSTAGEM |
| 5283 | PEÇAS AUXILIARES |
| 5283 | ACESSÓRIOS |
| 5284 | EMBUTIDO PELAS DUAS PONTAS |
| 5285 | EMBUTIDO POR UMA PONTA |
| 5286 | VIGA ENGASTADA |
| 5286 | VIGA EMBUTIDA |
| 5287 | POLIA FIXA |
| 5288 | FORMATO DE BLOCO FIXO |
| 5289 | CARBONO FIXO |
| 5290 | CÍRCULO FIXO |
| 5291 | GRUA FIXA |
| 5291 | GUINDASTE FIXO OU ESTACIONÁRIO |

| | |
|---|---|
| 5292 | CICLO FIXO |
| 5293 | CALIBRE FIXO |
| 5294 | ÓLEO FIXO |
| 5295 | PONTO FIXO |
| 5296 | TETO FIXO |
| 5297 | FORMATO DE SEQÜÊNCIA FIXA |
| 5298 | FRESADORA DE BANCADA FIXA |
| 5299 | MORDAÇA FIXA DE TORNO DE BANCADA |
| 5300 | FIXAÇÃO DA PROVETA |
| 5301 | MONTAGEM |
| 5301 | ARMAÇÃO |
| 5301 | LUMINÁRIA |
| 5302 | LAJE |
| 5303 | LÂMINA |
| 5303 | FLOCO |
| 5304 | FISSURA |
| 5304 | GRETA |
| 5305 | GRAFITA EM LÂMINA |
| 5306 | ESFOLIAÇÃO |
| 5307 | MAÇARICO |
| 5308 | ALTAR DE FORNALHA |
| 5309 | LIMPAR COM MAÇARICO |
| 5310 | LIMPEZA COM CHAMA DE MAÇARICO |
| 5311 | MAÇARICO DESOXIDANTE |
| 5312 | MAÇARICO DE CORTAR |
| 5313 | DECAPAGEM À CHAMA |
| 5314 | CONTROLADOR DE CHAMA |
| 5315 | TÊMPERA COM MAÇARICO |
| 5316 | IGNIÇÃO POR CHAMA |
| 5317 | GALVANIZAÇÃO A CHAMA |
| 5318 | CORTE COM CHAMA |
| 5319 | RECOZIMENTO POR CHAMA |
| 5320 | ESPECTROSCOPIA DA CHAMA |
| 5321 | PÁRA-CHAMAS |
| 5322 | À PROVA DE CHAMAS |
| 5322 | ANTIDEFLAGRANTE |
| 5323 | REBORDO |
| 5323 | FLANGE |
| 5324 | FLANGEAR |
| 5324 | REBORDAR |
| 5325 | ADAPTADOR DE FLANGE |
| 5326 | LADO CONTRÁRIO DO FLANGE |
| 5327 | FACE DO FLANGE |
| 5328 | FUROS DE FLANGE |
| 5329 | CUBO DE FLANGE |
| 5330 | ABA DE FERRO EM T |
| 5331 | ARO DE RODA |
| 5332 | FLANGE DE POLIA |
| 5333 | MÁQUINA DE MANDRILAR FLANGE |
| 5334 | TORNO DE FLANGES |
| 5335 | SOLDAGEM EM BORDAS LEVANTADAS |
| 5336 | POLIA DE ABAS |
| 5336 | POLIA COM REBORDOS |
| 5337 | BOCAL DE LIGAÇÃO COM FLANGE |
| 5338 | UNIÃO DE FLANGES |
| 5339 | ORIFÍCIOS COM FLANGES |
| 5340 | PORCA HEXAGONAL COM COLAR |
| 5341 | BOCAL COM FLANGE |
| 5342 | PORCA COM COLAR |
| 5343 | TUBO COM FLANGE |
| 5344 | JUNTA DE TUBO POR FLANGES |
| 5345 | REVIRAMENTO |
| 5345 | FORMAÇÃO DE FLANGES |
| 5346 | MÁQUINA PARA REVIRAR BORDAS |
| 5347 | TESTE DE REVIRAMENTO |
| 5347 | PROVA OU ENSAIO DE FLANGEAMENTO |
| 5348 | FLANCO |
| 5348 | LADO |
| 5349 | FOLGA ENTRE OS DENTES |
| 5350 | FLANCO DA ROSCA |
| 5351 | FLANCO DO DENTE |
| 5352 | FLANELA |
| 5353 | VÁLVULA DE REPERCUSSÃO |
| 5353 | VÁLVULA DE CHARNEIRA |
| 5353 | CHAPELETA |
| 5354 | TRAPEAMENTO DA ESCÓRIA |
| 5355 | CHAMA |
| 5355 | LABAREDA |
| 5355 | AFUNILAMENTO |
| 5356 | BRILHAR |
| 5356 | ALARGAR |
| 5356 | AFUNILAR |
| 5356 | TER SALIÊNCIA |
| 5357 | RAIO |
| 5357 | JATO DE LUZ |
| 5357 | JORRO DE LUZ |
| 5357 | CLARÃO |
| 5357 | CENTELHA |
| 5358 | SOLDAGEM A ARCO |
| 5359 | LANÇAR CHAMA |
| 5360 | ESTUFA DE SECAGEM RÁPIDA |
| 5361 | USINAGEM POR PULVERIZADOR |
| 5362 | AQUECIMENTO RÁPIDO |
| 5363 | PONTO DE INCANDESCÊNCIA |
| 5363 | PONTO DE CHAMA |
| 5364 | APARAR |
| 5364 | REBARBAR |
| 5365 | ENTRADA DA CHAMA |
| 5366 | LUZ INTERMITENTE |
| 5366 | PISCA-PISCA |
| 5366 | LANTERNA MANUAL |
| 5367 | INCRUSTRAÇÃO DE RESÍDUOS DE CARVÃO |

| | | | |
|---|---|---|---|
| 5368 | PONTO DE INFLAMABILIDADE | 5409 | TESTE OU ENSAIO DE ACHATAMENTO |
| 5369 | CAIXA DE MOLDAGEM | 5410 | ALISADOR |
| 5370 | BALÃO | 5410 | APLAINADOR |
| 5370 | FRASCO | 5411 | RACHADURA |
| 5371 | RECOZIMENTO EM CAIXA | 5411 | DEFEITO |
| 5372 | PASSADOR DE CHASSI | 5411 | FALHA |
| 5373 | ARCO REBAIXADO | 5411 | FENDA |
| 5374 | BARRA CHATA | 5411 | GRETA |
| 5375 | FERRO PLANO | 5412 | LINHO |
| 5376 | FERO CHATO COM BULBO | 5413 | ESTOPA DE LINHO |
| 5377 | FORMÃO PLANO | 5414 | LADO AVESSO DO COURO |
| 5377 | TALHADEIRA CHATA | 5414 | LADO AVESSO DA PELE |
| 5378 | CURVA ABERTA | 5415 | FLEXIBILIDADE |
| 5379 | RODA DE DISCO PLANO | 5416 | FIXAÇÃO |
| 5380 | BROCA CHATA | 5416 | LIGAÇÃO FLEXÍVEL |
| 5381 | LIMA CHATA | 5417 | ACOPLAMENTO FLEXÍVEL |
| 5382 | FLANGE APLANADO | 5418 | TUBO DE JUNTA ESFÉRICA |
| 5383 | MOTOR DE QUATRO CILINDROS OPOSTOS HORIZONTAIS | 5419 | TUBO METÁLICO FLEXÍVEL |
| | | 5420 | EIXO FLEXÍVEL |
| 5384 | CORREDIÇA CHATA | 5420 | TRANSMISSÃO FLEXÍVEL |
| 5385 | PARAFUSO DE CABEÇA CHATA | 5421 | TUBO FLEXÍVEL |
| 5386 | PARAFUSOS DE CABEÇA PLANA | 5422 | FLEXÃO |
| 5387 | MISTURADORA DE SOLEIRA PLANA | 5423 | RIGIDEZ À FLEXÃO |
| 5388 | CHAVETA PLANA OU LISA | 5424 | RESISTÊNCIA À FLEXÃO |
| 5389 | TRUNCAMENTO DE ROSCA | 5425 | TENSÃO DE FLEXÃO |
| 5390 | LIMA CHATA | 5426 | FLEXÃO |
| 5391 | CILINDRO LISO | 5427 | PEDERNEIRA |
| 5392 | AÇOS LAMINADOS PLANOS | 5427 | SEIXO |
| 5393 | CABOS PLANOS | 5427 | CALHAU |
| 5394 | CABEÇA CHATA DE PARAFUSO | 5428 | CRISTAL DE ROCHA |
| 5395 | CHAPA PLANA | 5429 | MULTIVIBRADOR BIESTÁVEL |
| 5396 | MOLA ESPIRAL | 5430 | FLUTUADOR |
| 5397 | CORREIA DE TECIDO TUBULAR | 5431 | CÂMARA DE BÓIA |
| 5398 | MOTOR DE DOIS CILINDROS OPOSTOS HORIZONTAIS | 5431 | RESERVATÓRIO DE NÍVEL CONSTANTE |
| | | 5432 | PURGADOR DE FLUTUADOR |
| 5399 | ARRUELA CHATA | 5433 | VÁLVULA DE FLUTUADOR |
| 5400 | CUNHA PLANA | 5433 | VÁLVULA DE BÓIA |
| 5401 | SOLDADURA PLANA | 5434 | FLUTUAÇÃO |
| 5402 | ARAME OU FIO CHATO | 5434 | BÓIA |
| 5403 | ALICATE DE ARAME CHATO | 5434 | NADANTE |
| 5404 | POLIA RETA | 5435 | EIXO FLUTUANTE OU OSCILANTE |
| 5404 | POLIA CILÍNDRICA | 5436 | CORPO FLUTUANTE |
| 5405 | REBAIXAR | 5437 | MATRIZ FLUTUANTE |
| 5405 | ACHATAR | 5438 | MANDRIL FLUTUANTE |
| 5405 | APLAINAR | 5439 | COBERTURA FLUTUANTE |
| 5405 | ENDIREITAR | 5440 | ZERO FLUTUANTE |
| 5406 | APLAINADO | 5441 | FLOCULAÇÃO |
| 5407 | CABO METÁLICO DE FIOS PLANOS | 5442 | LUBRIFICAÇÃO POR BOMBEAMENTO DE ÓLEO |
| 5408 | ACHATAMENTO | | |
| 5408 | ALISAMENTO | 5443 | ALAGAMENTO |
| 5408 | POLIMENTO | 5443 | VAZAMENTO |

| | |
|---|---|
| 5444 | TRANSMISSÃO FIXA AO SOLO |
| 5445 | MOLDAGEM NO SOLO |
| 5446 | PISO DO AUTOMÓVEL |
| 5447 | CHAPA PARA REVESTIMENTO DE PISOS |
| 5448 | COLUNA DE MANOBRA |
| 5449 | CHAPA PARA PISOS |
| 5450 | PAVIMENTO |
| 5451 | PAVIMENTO |
| 5452 | FLOTAÇÃO |
| 5453 | PÓ DE ESMERIL |
| 5454 | VAZÃO |
| 5454 | FLUXO |
| 5454 | CORRENTE |
| 5454 | FLUÊNCIA |
| 5454 | DESCARGA |
| 5454 | ESCOAMENTO |
| 5455 | MEDIDOR DE VAZÃO |
| 5455 | AFERIDOR DE DESCARGA |
| 5456 | LIMITE DE VAZÃO |
| 5457 | LINHA DE CIRCULAÇÃO |
| 5458 | FLUXÍMETRO |
| 5459 | VELOCIDADE DE ESCOAMENTO |
| 5460 | ESFORÇO DE FLUXO |
| 5461 | ESTRUTURA DE DEFORMAÇÃO PLÁSTICA |
| 5462 | VELOCIDADE DE CIRCULAÇÃO |
| 5463 | FLUIDEZ |
| 5464 | FLOR DE ENXOFRE |
| 5464 | ENXOFRE SUBLIMADO |
| 5465 | FLUÊNCIA DO MATERIAL |
| 5465 | SAÍDA DO MATERIAL |
| 5466 | ÁGUA CORRENTE |
| 5467 | CONDUTO DE GASES |
| 5468 | CALDEIRA DE TUBOS DE FUMAÇA |
| 5469 | POEIRAS DE GÁS DE ALTO-FORNO |
| 5470 | GÁS DE COMBUSTÃO |
| 5471 | FLUIDO |
| 5472 | TRANSMISSÃO HIDRÁULICA |
| 5473 | ATRITO FLUIDO |
| 5473 | TRITO INTERNO DOS LÍQUIDOS |
| 5474 | FLUIDEZ |
| 5475 | FLUIDIZADOR |
| 5476 | FLUORESCÊNCIA |
| 5477 | QUADRO FLUORESCENTE |
| 5478 | FLÚOR |
| 5479 | FLUORITA |
| 5479 | ESPATOFLÚOR |
| 5480 | FAROL EMBUTIDO |
| 5481 | CORDÃO DE SOLDA LISA |
| 5482 | AFLORADO |
| 5483 | ESTRIA |
| 5483 | CANELADURA |

| | |
|---|---|
| 5484 | ACANALADO |
| 5484 | ESTRIADO |
| 5485 | ALARGADOR ACANALADO |
| 5485 | ESCAREADOR ACANALADO |
| 5486 | CILINDRO ACANALADO |
| 5487 | ESPECTRO ACANALADO |
| 5488 | RUPTURA POR FLEXÃO |
| 5489 | FLUXO |
| 5489 | FUNDENTE |
| 5490 | FUNDENTE PARA SOLDA |
| 5491 | ÓLEO DERRETIDO |
| 5492 | ELÉTRODO REVESTIDO |
| 5493 | CINZAS VOLANTES |
| 5494 | CORTADOR GIRATÓRIO OU VOLANTE |
| 5495 | TESOURA VOLANTE |
| 5496 | VOLANTE |
| 5497 | VOLANTE DE DOIS SEGMENTOS |
| 5498 | FOSSO DO VOLANTE |
| 5499 | ESPUMA |
| 5500 | DISTÂNCIA OU COMPRIMENTO FOCAL |
| 5501 | PLANO FOCAL |
| 5502 | FOCO |
| 5503 | DISTÂNCIA FOCAL |
| 5504 | FEIXE CONCENTRADO |
| 5505 | FOCAGEM |
| 5505 | FOCALIZAÇÃO |
| 5506 | FAROL ANTINEBLINA |
| 5506 | FAROL DE MILHA |
| 5507 | EMBACIAMENTO |
| 5507 | ESCURECIMENTO |
| 5508 | FOLHA |
| 5508 | LÂMINA |
| 5509 | FOLHA METÁLICA FINA |
| 5510 | DOBRA |
| 5510 | PREGA |
| 5511 | VINCO |
| 5512 | METRO OU RÉGUA DE DOBRAR |
| 5513 | FÓLIO DE DESCARTES |
| 5514 | LUNETA DE ACOMPANHAMENTO |
| 5515 | ARESTA DE SAÍDA |
| 5516 | RAMAL SOLTO |
| 5517 | INDÚSTRIA DE PRODUTOS ALIMENTÍCIOS |
| 5517 | INDÚSTRIA DE PROCESSAMENTO DE ALIMENTOS |
| 5518 | PÉ (MEDIDA INGLESA) |
| 5519 | FREIO DE PEDAL |
| 5520 | TORNO DE PEDAL |
| 5521 | ALAVANCA DE PEDAL |
| 5522 | PÉ-LIBRA (MEDIDA INGLESA DE PESO) |
| 5523 | VÁLVULA INFERIOR |
| 5523 | VÁLVULA DE PEDAL |

| | | | |
|---|---|---|---|
| 5524 | MANCAL AXIAL | 5562 | PRENSA DE FORJAR |
| 5524 | MANCAL VERTICAL | 5563 | CILINDROS DE FORJAR |
| 5524 | MANCAL DE PÉ | 5564 | DEFORMAÇÕES DE FORJAMENTO |
| 5525 | SEGADORAS DE FENO | 5564 | ESFORÇOS DE FORJA |
| 5526 | DIAGRAMA DE ESFORÇOS | 5565 | TEMPERATURA DE FORJAMENTO |
| 5527 | AJUSTE PRENSADO | 5566 | FERROS FORJADOS |
| 5527 | MONTAGEM POR PRENSA | 5567 | JUNTA DE FORQUILHA |
| 5528 | FORÇA DE MOLA | 5568 | PÉ DE BIELA EM FORQUILHA |
| 5529 | FORÇA DE ATRAÇÃO | 5569 | ALAVANCA DE FORQUILHA |
| 5530 | FORÇA REPULSIVA | 5570 | FORMA |
| 5531 | BOMBA DE RECALQUE | 5570 | MOLDE |
| 5531 | BOMBA DE COMPRESSÃO | 5571 | FORMAR |
| 5532 | FORÇA | 5571 | CONFIGURAR |
| 5532 | ESFORÇO | 5571 | MOLDAR |
| 5533 | TIRAGEM FORÇADA | 5571 | LAVRAR |
| 5533 | TIRAGEM MECÂNICA | 5571 | MODELAR |
| 5534 | FLUXO FORÇADO | 5572 | FATOR DE FORMA |
| 5535 | OSCILAÇÕES FORÇADAS | 5573 | FORMALDEÍDO |
| 5536 | PINÇA PEQUENA | 5573 | METANOL |
| 5536 | ALICATE DE MOLA | 5574 | FORMATO |
| 5537 | FORÇAS INVERSAS | 5575 | FORMAÇÃO DE MOFO |
| 5538 | FORÇAS DA MESMA DIREÇÃO | 5575 | CRIAÇÃO DE BOLOR |
| 5539 | SOLDAGEM PUXANDO PARA A ESQUERDA | 5576 | TENSÃO DE FORMAÇÃO |
| 5540 | PATENTE ESTRANGEIRA | 5577 | FRESAS PERFILADAS |
| 5541 | CONTRAMESTRE | 5578 | ÁCIDO FÓRMICO |
| 5541 | CAPATAZ | 5579 | FORMAÇÃO |
| 5542 | FORJAR | 5579 | MODELAÇÃO |
| 5543 | CARVÃO DE FORJA | 5580 | MATRIZ DE ESTAMPAGEM |
| 5544 | FUNDIÇÃO AFINADA | 5580 | MATRIZ DE MODELAR |
| 5544 | FERRO GUSA DE FORJA | 5580 | MATRIZ DE EMBUTIR |
| 5545 | TESTE (ENSAIO) DE FORJAMENTO | 5581 | FORMAÇÃO |
| 5546 | SOLDAGEM NA FORJA | 5581 | MODELAGEM |
| 5547 | FORJA | 5581 | ESTAMPAGEM |
| 5547 | OFICINA DE FORJA | 5581 | DOBRAGEM |
| 5548 | FORJA | 5582 | FÓRMULA |
| 5548 | FERRARIA | 5583 | FÓRMULA DE CONSTITUIÇÃO |
| 5549 | AÇO-CARBONO FORJADO | 5584 | AVANÇO |
| 5550 | MANIVELA FORJADA | 5584 | MOVIMENTO DE AVANÇO |
| 5551 | BARRA COM ILHÓS | 5585 | CURSO DE AVANÇO DO PISTÃO |
| 5552 | FORJA DE UMA PEÇA NA MASSA | 5586 | COMBUSTÍVEL FÓSSIL |
| 5553 | SUCATA | 5587 | BLOQUEAR |
| 5553 | FERRO VELHO | 5588 | ELETRÓLITO SUJO |
| 5554 | AÇO FORJADO | 5589 | ALICERCE |
| 5555 | FORJAMENTO | 5589 | FUNDAÇÃO |
| 5556 | PEÇA FORJADA | 5589 | BASE |
| 5557 | FORJAMENTO | 5589 | FUNDAMENTO |
| 5558 | LATÃO PARA FORJADOS | 5590 | CAVILHA DE BASE |
| 5559 | MARTELO DE QUEDA | 5590 | PARAFUSO DE ASSENTAMENTO |
| 5559 | MARTELO DE FORJAR MECÂNICO | 5590 | PARAFUSO CHUMBADOR |
| 5560 | TEMPERATURA DE FORJAMENTO | 5591 | FUNDIDOR |
| 5561 | MÁQUINA DE FORJAR | 5592 | FUNDIÇÃO |

| | |
|---|---|
| 5593 | FUNDIÇÃO |
| 5593 | OFICINA DE FUNDIÇÃO |
| 5594 | LIGA DE FUNDIÇÃO |
| 5595 | COQUE PARA FUNDIÇÃO |
| 5596 | FUNDIÇÃO CINZENTA |
| 5596 | FERRO GUSA DE FUNDIÇÃO |
| 5597 | INSTALAÇÕES DE FUNDIÇÃO |
| 5598 | PONTAS PARA FUNDIÇÃO |
| 5599 | SEDAN DE QUATRO PORTAS |
| 5600 | MOTOR A QUATRO TEMPOS |
| 5601 | TRAÇÃO NAS QUATRO RODAS |
| 5602 | ASTERÓIDE |
| 5603 | MOTOR A QUATRO TEMPOS |
| 5604 | MANDRIL DE QUATRO MORDAÇAS INDEPENDENTES |
| 5605 | TORNEIRA DE QUATRO VIAS |
| 5606 | VÁLVULA DE QUATRO ENTRADAS OU SAÍDAS |
| 5606 | VÁLVULA EM CRUZ |
| 5607 | ARAME DE BRONZE FOSFÓRICO |
| 5608 | QUARTA POTÊNCIA |
| 5609 | RAIZ BIQUADRADA |
| 5610 | MADEIRA PODRE |
| 5611 | FRAÇÃO |
| 5612 | DESTILAÇÃO FRACIONADA |
| 5613 | NÚMERO FRACIONÁRIO |
| 5613 | FRAÇÃO |
| 5614 | TORRE FRACIONÁRIA |
| 5615 | FRACIONAR |
| 5616 | TEORIA DAS RUPTURAS |
| 5617 | FRATURA |
| 5617 | RUPTURA |
| 5618 | TENSÃO DE RUPTURA |
| 5619 | PROVA OU ENSAIO DE RUPTURA |
| 5620 | SUPERFÍCIE DE FRATURA OU RUPTURA |
| 5621 | FRÁGIL |
| 5622 | FRAGILIDADE |
| 5623 | FRAGMENTAÇÃO DE GRÃOS |
| 5624 | CHASSI |
| 5624 | ARMAÇÃO |
| 5624 | BASTIDOR |
| 5624 | CARCAÇA |
| 5624 | FUSELAGEM |
| 5624 | QUADRO |
| 5625 | PADIOLA |
| 5626 | CHASSI DE MÁQUINA |
| 5627 | VIGA DE ESTRUTURA DE CAPOTA |
| 5628 | ARCO DE SERRA |
| 5628 | SERRA MANUAL |
| 5629 | SERRA DE VAIVÉM |
| 5629 | SERRA DE CAIXILHO |

| | |
|---|---|
| 5629 | SERRA TICO-TICO |
| 5630 | VIGAMENTO |
| 5630 | ESTRUTURA |
| 5630 | ARMAÇÃO |
| 5631 | LINHAS DE FRAUNHOFER |
| 5632 | CIANETO LIVRE |
| 5633 | QUEDA LIVRE |
| 5634 | CURSO LIVRE |
| 5634 | CORRENTE LIVRE |
| 5635 | SEM ÁCIDO |
| 5636 | SEM CINZA |
| 5637 | DESEMPOEIRAR |
| 5638 | SEM ESCÓRIAS |
| 5639 | AÇO DE FÁCIL USINAGEM |
| 5640 | MAGNETISMO LIVRE |
| 5641 | ACESSO LIVRE |
| 5642 | VENTO LIVRE |
| 5642 | RESPIRO LIVRE |
| 5643 | OSCILAÇÃO LIVRE |
| 5644 | RODA LIVRE |
| 5645 | LATÃO DE FÁCIL USINAGEM |
| 5646 | ESCADA DIRETA |
| 5647 | NATIVO (MINERAL) |
| 5648 | DESENHO A MÃO LIVRE |
| 5649 | LIVREMENTE SUSPENSO |
| 5650 | APOIADO LIVREMENTE |
| 5651 | RODA LIVRE |
| 5652 | MECANISMO DE RODA LIVRE |
| 5653 | CONGELAMENTO |
| 5653 | SOLIDIFICAÇÃO |
| 5654 | MISTURA REFRIGERANTE |
| 5655 | CONGELAMENTO DO FORNO |
| 5656 | PONTO DE CONGELAMENTO |
| 5656 | PONTO DE SOLIDIFICAÇÃO |
| 5657 | ANTICONGELANTE |
| 5658 | INTERVALO DE SOLIDIFICAÇÃO |
| 5658 | ZONA DE SOLIDIFICAÇÃO |
| 5659 | ESTEATITA |
| 5659 | TALCO |
| 5660 | PISTOLÉ CURVILÍNEO |
| 5660 | RÉGUA DE CURVAS |
| 5661 | FREQÜÊNCIA |
| 5662 | FREQÜÊNCIA EMPÍRICA |
| 5663 | ÁGUA DOCE |
| 5664 | CALCÁRIO DE ÁGUA DOCE |
| 5665 | SERRA TICO-TICO |
| 5666 | CORROSÃO POR ATRITO |
| 5667 | CORROSÃO DAS SUPERFÍCIES DE CONTATO |
| 5668 | FRICÇÃO |
| 5669 | FREIO DE ATRITO |
| 5669 | FREIO DE FRICÇÃO |

| | |
|---|---|
| 5670 | COEFICIENTE DE ATRITO |
| 5671 | CONE DE FRICÇÃO |
| 5672 | EMBREAGEM DE FRICÇÃO |
| 5673 | DISCO OU PRATO DE FRICÇÃO |
| 5674 | TRANSMISSÃO POR ATRITO |
| 5674 | ENGRENAGEM DE FRICÇÃO |
| 5675 | LINGÜETA DE FRICÇÃO |
| 5675 | LINGÜETA DE APERTO |
| 5676 | LINGÜETA DE APERTO |
| 5677 | ATRITO CINÉTICO |
| 5677 | ATRITO EM MOVIMENTO |
| 5678 | ATRITO DE ARRANQUE |
| 5679 | ROLO DE FRICÇÃO |
| 5680 | SERRAÇÃO POR ATRITO |
| 5681 | FREIO DE FITA |
| 5681 | FREIO DE CINTA |
| 5682 | RODA DE FRICÇÃO |
| 5683 | FORÇA DE ATRITO |
| 5684 | TRANSMISSÃO POR FRICÇÃO |
| 5685 | PERDA POR ATRITO |
| 5686 | RESISTÊNCIA DE ABRASÃO |
| 5686 | RESISTÊNCIA DE ATRITO |
| 5687 | SUPERFÍCIE DE ATRITO |
| 5688 | SEM ATRITO |
| 5688 | SEM FRICÇÃO |
| 5689 | LINHAS LIMITE |
| 5690 | SINTERIZAÇÃO |
| 5691 | EIXO DIANTEIRO |
| 5692 | PAINEL DIANTEIRO |
| 5693 | TRAVESSA DIANTEIRA |
| 5694 | VISTA DE FRENTE |
| 5694 | VISTA ANTERIOR |
| 5695 | CONJUNTO DO CAPÔ E TABLADO |
| 5696 | GEOMETRIA DE EIXO DIANTEIRO |
| 5697 | TORNO DE OPERAÇÃO FRONTAL |
| 5698 | ÂNGULO DE CORTE |
| 5698 | ÂNGULO DE ATAQUE OU DE FRENTE |
| 5699 | ACIONAMENTO DIANTEIRO |
| 5699 | TRAÇÃO DIANTEIRA |
| 5700 | GRETAS DA MADEIRA DEVIDAS A CONGELAÇÃO |
| 5701 | VIDRO FOSCO |
| 5702 | FOSCAGEM |
| 5703 | FORMAÇÃO DE ESPUMA |
| 5704 | MÁQUINAS DE LAVAR E CLASSIFICAR FRUTAS E VEGETAIS |
| 5705 | COMBUSTÍVEL |
| 5706 | PAIOL DE COMBUSTÍVEL |
| 5707 | ECONOMIA DE COMBUSTÍVEL |
| 5708 | FILTRO DE COMBUSTÍVEL |
| 5709 | GÁS PARA CALEFAÇÃO |
| 5709 | GÁS COMBUSTÍVEL |
| 5710 | INDICADOR OU MEDIDOR DO NÍVEL DE COMBUSTÍVEL |
| 5711 | BOMBA DE INJEÇÃO DE COMBUSTÍVEL |
| 5712 | CÁRTER DE BOMBA DE INJEÇÃO |
| 5713 | BOMBA DE ALIMENTAÇÃO |
| 5714 | ÓLEO COMBUSTÍVEL |
| 5715 | BOMBA DE COMBUSTÍVEL |
| 5715 | BOMBA DE ALIMENTAÇÃO |
| 5716 | DEPÓSITO DE COMBUSTÍVEL |
| 5717 | CENTRO DE ROTAÇÃO |
| 5718 | TURBINA DE ADMISSÃO TOTAL |
| 5719 | RECOZIMENTO COMPLETO |
| 5720 | JUNTA SOLDADA COM UM SÓ FILETE |
| 5721 | ENDURECIMENTO COMPLETO |
| 5721 | TÊMPERA COMPLETA |
| 5722 | PLENA CARGA |
| 5723 | DE TAMANHO NATURAL |
| 5723 | DE ESCALA NORMAL |
| 5724 | DESENHO DE TAMANHO NATURAL |
| 5725 | LINHA CHEIA |
| 5726 | ESTAMPA DE ESTIRAR |
| 5727 | GREDA DE PISOEIRO |
| 5727 | TERRA DE FULLER |
| 5728 | DESBASTE |
| 5728 | ARREDONDAMENTO |
| 5729 | FERRO DE CALCAR |
| 5730 | PRODUTO ACABADO |
| 5730 | PEÇA ACABADA |
| 5731 | ÁCIDO FULMÍNICO |
| 5732 | FUMAÇA |
| 5732 | VAPORES |
| 5732 | GASES |
| 5733 | ÁCIDO DE NORDHAUSEN |
| 5734 | FUNÇÃO |
| 5735 | INVESTIGAÇÃO FUNDAMENTAL |
| 5736 | VIBRAÇÃO PRÓPRIA |
| 5737 | POLÍGONO FUNICULAR |
| 5738 | FUNIL |
| 5739 | FORNO |
| 5739 | FORNALHA |
| 5740 | SOLDA FORTE EM FORNO |
| 5741 | CROMO PARA FORNO |
| 5742 | ESFRIAMENTO DO FORNO |
| 5743 | CONDUTO DE FUMAÇA |
| 5744 | FORNALHA DE GÁS |
| 5745 | FORNALHA DE ÓLEO PESADO |
| 5746 | FORNALHA DE CARVÃO PULVERIZADO |
| 5747 | FORNO DE CALDEIRA |
| 5748 | REVESTIMENTO DO FORNO |
| 5749 | CARCAÇA DO FORNO |

| | |
|---|---|
| 5749 | CAMISA DO FORNO |
| 5750 | USINAGEM ULTERIOR |
| 5750 | TRATAMENTO ULTERIOR DE USINAGEM |
| 5751 | FUSÍVEL |
| 5752 | CAIXA DE FUSÍVEIS |
| 5753 | ALUMINA FUNDIDA |
| 5753 | ELETROCORÍNDON |
| 5754 | ÓLEO DE BATATA |
| 5755 | FUSIBILIDADE |
| 5756 | FUSÍVEL |
| 5757 | LIGA FUSÍVEL |
| 5758 | BUJÃO FUSÍVEL |
| 5759 | PONTO DE FUSÃO |
| 5760 | FUSÃO |
| 5761 | ZONA DE FUSÃO |
| 5762 | SOLDAGEM POR FUSÃO |
| 5763 | ZONA DE FUSÃO |
| 5764 | FUSÃO ÍGNEA |
| 5765 | GABRO |
| 5766 | DISPOSITIVO ACESSÓRIO |
| 5767 | GADOLÍNIO |
| 5768 | MANÔMETRO |
| 5768 | INDICADOR |
| 5768 | CALIBRE |
| 5768 | CALIBRADOR |
| 5768 | GABARITO |
| 5769 | BLOCO CALIBRADOR |
| 5769 | GABARITOS |
| 5770 | CALIBRAÇÃO |
| 5771 | PRESSÃO MANOMÉTRICA |
| 5772 | GANCHO |
| 5772 | AFERIDOR |
| 5773 | GANHO |
| 5773 | LUCRO |
| 5774 | REDUÇÃO DE ESPAÇO |
| 5775 | GALENA |
| 5776 | GALERIA |
| 5776 | PLATAFORMA |
| 5776 | PASSARELA |
| 5777 | ÁCIDO GÁLICO |
| 5778 | DESGASTE POR ATRITO |
| 5778 | GRIPAGEM |
| 5779 | GÁLIO |
| 5780 | ÁCIDO TÂNICO |
| 5780 | TANINO |
| 5781 | GALÃO |
| 5782 | PILHA GALVÂNICA |
| 5783 | CORROSÃO ELETROLÍTICA |
| 5783 | CORROSÃO GALVÂNICA |
| 5784 | GALVANIZAR |
| 5785 | CHAPA GALVANIZADA |
| 5785 | CHAPA ZINCADA |
| 5786 | ARAME GALVANIZADO |
| 5787 | GALVANIZAÇÃO |
| 5788 | TIRAS GALVANIZADAS |
| 5789 | GALVANIZAÇÃO |
| 5789 | ZINCAGEM |
| 5790 | FRAGILIDADE À ZINCAGEM |
| 5791 | GALVANÔMETRO |
| 5792 | GALVANOPLÁSTICO |
| 5793 | GOMA-GUTA |
| 5794 | FUNÇÃO GAMA |
| 5795 | FERRO GAMA |
| 5796 | RAIOS GAMA |
| 5797 | ESTRUTURA GAMA |
| 5798 | GAMÁGRAFO |
| 5798 | REGISTRADOR GAMA |
| 5799 | FURADEIRA DE TRADOS MÚLTIPLOS |
| 5800 | FRESAGEM CONJUGADA |
| 5800 | FRESAGEM DE CORTE MÚLTIPLO |
| 5801 | PORTA-FERRAMENTA MÚLTIPLO |
| 5802 | GANGA |
| 5803 | GANISTRO |
| 5803 | CAMADA REFRATÁRIA |
| 5804 | PONTE ROLANTE-PÓRTICO |
| 5804 | GUINDASTE DE CAVALETE |
| 5805 | MISTURA DE GRÃOS |
| 5806 | JUNTA FENDIDA |
| 5807 | GRANADA |
| 5808 | GÁS |
| 5809 | ANÁLISE DE GÁS |
| 5810 | SOLDA FORTE COM MAÇARICO |
| 5811 | BICO DE GÁS |
| 5811 | QUEIMADOR DE GÁS |
| 5812 | COQUE |
| 5812 | CARVÃO DE RETORTA |
| 5813 | CARVÃO DE GÁS |
| 5814 | TORNEIRA DE GÁS |
| 5815 | CONSTANTE DE UM GÁS |
| 5816 | CORRENTE DE GÁS |
| 5817 | CORTE AUTÓGENO |
| 5817 | CORTE A GÁS |
| 5818 | CIANETAÇÃO A GÁS |
| 5819 | MOTOR A GASOLINA |
| 5820 | CHAMA DE GÁS |
| 5821 | CONDUTO DE GÁS |
| 5822 | RANHURA COM CHAMA |
| 5823 | ONDULAÇÕES FEITAS PELO GÁS |
| 5824 | SOLDADOR AQUECIDO A GÁS |
| 5825 | ORIFÍCIO PRODUZIDO POR BOLHA DE GÁS |
| 5826 | LÂMPADA A GÁS |
| 5827 | LUZ DE GÁS |

| | |
|---|---|
| 5828 | ILUMINAÇÃO A GÁS |
| 5829 | MARCADOR OU REGISTRO DE GÁS |
| 5830 | NITRURAÇÃO GASOSA |
| 5831 | ÓLEO DIESEL |
| 5832 | DECAPAGEM A GÁS |
| 5833 | TUBO DE GÁS |
| 5834 | CONDUTO DE GÁS |
| 5835 | ALICATE DE GASISTA |
| 5836 | BOLHA DE GÁS |
| 5837 | PRESSÃO DE GÁS |
| 5838 | GASOGÊNIO |
| 5838 | GERADOR DE GÁS |
| 5839 | PURIFICAÇÃO DE GÁS |
| 5839 | DEPURAÇÃO DE GÁS |
| 5840 | TÊMPERA A GÁS |
| 5841 | RECUPERAÇÃO DO GÁS SEM COMBUSTÃO |
| 5842 | COLETOR DE GÁS |
| 5843 | ROSCA DE TUBOS DE GÁS |
| 5844 | TURBINA A GÁS |
| 5845 | GARRAFA PARA LAVAGEM A GÁS |
| 5846 | AQUECEDOR DE ÁGUA A GÁS |
| 5847 | SOLDA AUTÓGENA |
| 5848 | USINA DE GÁS |
| 5849 | COQUE DE USINA DE GÁS |
| 5850 | GERADORA DE GÁS |
| 5851 | FORNO AQUECIDO A GÁS |
| 5852 | SOLDAGEM A ARCO SOB PROTEÇÃO GASOSA |
| 5853 | À PROVA DE GÁS |
| 5853 | IMPERMEÁVEL AO GÁS |
| 5854 | COMBUSTÍVEL GASOSO |
| 5855 | INCLUSÃO GASOSA |
| 5856 | MISTURA GASOSA |
| 5857 | ESTADO GASOSO |
| 5858 | ABERTURA |
| 5858 | ENTALHAMENTO |
| 5858 | CORTE INICIAL |
| 5859 | GASÔMETRO |
| 5860 | GASEIFICÁVEL |
| 5861 | GASEIFICAÇÃO |
| 5862 | GASEIFICAR |
| 5863 | GAXETA |
| 5863 | VEDAÇÃO |
| 5863 | JUNTA |
| 5863 | EMPANQUE |
| 5864 | GASOLINA |
| 5865 | GASEIFICAÇÃO |
| 5866 | PORTA |
| 5866 | COMPORTA |
| 5867 | REGISTRO DE GAVETA |
| 5867 | ADUFA |

| | |
|---|---|
| 5867 | COMPORTA |
| 5867 | REGISTRO |
| 5868 | MODELO DE FUNDIÇÃO |
| 5869 | AUMENTO DA SEÇÃO TRANSVERSAL |
| 5870 | SISTEMA DE FUNDIÇÃO E DE ALIMENTAÇÃO |
| 5871 | BITOLA |
| 5871 | CALIBRE |
| 5871 | AFERIDOR |
| 5871 | INDICADOR DE PRESSÃO |
| 5872 | CALIBRAR |
| 5872 | AFERIR |
| 5872 | MARCAR |
| 5873 | BLOCO CALIBRADOR |
| 5874 | CALIBRAGEM DE UMA MEDIDA |
| 5875 | TORNEIRA DE MANÔMETRO |
| 5876 | BÓIA DE CALIBRE |
| 5877 | CABEÇA DE CALIBRE |
| 5878 | COMPRIMENTO DE REFERÊNCIA |
| 5879 | MARCA |
| 5880 | NÚMERO DE CALIBRE DE UMA CHAPA |
| 5881 | NÚMERO DE CALIBRE DE UM ARAME |
| 5882 | PRESSÃO MANOMÉTRICA |
| 5882 | PRESSÃO RELATIVA |
| 5883 | TAMPA DE CALIBRE |
| 5884 | MONTAGEM DE CUNHAS CALIBRADORAS |
| 5885 | PLATAFORMA DE CALIBRAGEM |
| 5886 | MEDIÇÃO |
| 5886 | CALIBRAGEM |
| 5886 | AFERIÇÃO |
| 5886 | GRADUAÇÃO |
| 5887 | DISTRIBUIÇÃO GAUSSIANA |
| 5888 | GAZE |
| 5888 | TECIDO METÁLICO |
| 5889 | ENGRENAGEM |
| 5889 | PINHÃO |
| 5889 | RODA DENTADA |
| 5890 | CAIXA DE ENGRENAGENS |
| 5890 | CAIXA DE MUDANÇAS |
| 5890 | CAIXA DE MARCHAS |
| 5891 | FRESADORA DE ENGRENAGENS |
| 5892 | ACIONAMENTO POR ENGRENAGEM |
| 5893 | MÁQUINA ACIONADA POR ENGRENAGEM |
| 5894 | FRESADORA DE ENGRENAGENS |
| 5895 | BOMBA A ENGRENAGEM |
| 5896 | RELAÇÃO DE ENGRENAGEM |
| 5897 | RELAÇÃO DE ENGRENAGEM |
| 5898 | FRESA DE TALHAR DENTES DE ENGRENAGENS |

| | |
|---|---|
| 5899 | VERNIER OU NÔNIO DE DENTES DE ENGRENAGENS |
| 5900 | CALIBRE VERNIER PARA DENTES DE ENGRENAGENS |
| 5901 | CONJUNTO DE ENGRENAGENS |
| 5901 | TREM DE ENGRENAGENS |
| 5902 | BANCADA DE VERIFICAÇÃO DE ENGRENAGENS |
| 5903 | RODA DE ENGRENAGEM |
| 5903 | RODA DENTADA |
| 5904 | AÇO DE RODA DE ENGRENAGEM |
| 5905 | VIRABREQUIM DE ENGRENAGEM |
| 5906 | VOLANTE DENTADO |
| 5906 | VOLANTE DE ENGRENAGEM |
| 5907 | ENGRENAGEM |
| 5908 | REDUÇÃO OU DESMULTIPLICAÇÃO |
| 5909 | MULTIPLICAÇÃO |
| 5910 | ENGATE DE RODAS DENTADAS |
| 5911 | MEDIDOR GEIGER |
| 5912 | GEL |
| 5913 | GELATINA |
| 5914 | DISPOSIÇÃO GERAL |
| 5914 | TRAÇADO GERAL |
| 5915 | DIRETOR GERAL |
| 5916 | DESENVOLVER |
| 5916 | GERAR |
| 5916 | PRODUZIR |
| 5917 | PRODUZIR CORRENTE ELÉTRICA |
| 5918 | CONE GERADOR |
| 5918 | CONE COMPLEMENTAR |
| 5919 | FUNÇÃO GERATRIZ |
| 5920 | CENTRAL ELÉTRICA |
| 5921 | CÍRCULO MÓVEL |
| 5922 | PRODUÇÃO DE ENERGIA |
| 5923 | PRODUÇÃO DE VAPOR |
| 5924 | DÍNAMO |
| 5924 | GERADOR DE CORRENTE |
| 5925 | GERATRIZ (GEOM.) |
| 5926 | REPRESENTAÇÃO GEOMÉTRICA |
| 5927 | GEOMÉTRICO |
| 5928 | DESENHO GEOMÉTRICO |
| 5929 | MÉDIA GEOMÉTRICA |
| 5930 | PROGRESSÃO GEOMÉTRICA |
| 5931 | GEOMETRIA |
| 5932 | PRATA ALEMÃ |
| 5932 | ARGENTÃO |
| 5933 | GERMÂNIO |
| 5934 | GERMINAÇÃO |
| 5935 | CONDIÇÃO CRÍTICA DE DEFORMAÇÃO |
| 5936 | GÊISER (AQUECEDOR PARA BANHOS) |
| 5937 | CONTRACHAVETA |
| 5937 | CALÇO |
| 5937 | CUNHA |
| 5938 | CHAVETA DUPLA |
| 5938 | CHAVETA E CONTRACHAVETA |
| 5939 | CHAVETA COM CABEÇA |
| 5940 | CHAVETA |
| 5941 | DOURAR |
| 5942 | DOURAÇÃO |
| 5943 | LIGA COBRE E ZINCO |
| 5944 | VERRUMA |
| 5945 | TRIPÉ |
| 5946 | TRAVE |
| 5946 | VIGA |
| 5947 | ESCORA DE VIGA |
| 5948 | SOLDAGEM FORTE HORIZONTAL |
| 5949 | CEDER |
| 5949 | DAR |
| 5949 | DAR DE SI |
| 5950 | DESPRENDER CALOR |
| 5951 | DADO |
| 5951 | QUANTIDADE CONHECIDA |
| 5952 | ÁCIDO ACÉTICO CRISTALIZÁVEL |
| 5953 | PRENSA-ESTOPA |
| 5953 | BUCHA |
| 5953 | CHUMACEIRO |
| 5953 | GAXETA DE VEDAÇÃO |
| 5954 | TORNEIRA DE ENGAXETAMENTO |
| 5955 | FLANGE DA GAXETA |
| 5956 | COPO |
| 5956 | VASO |
| 5956 | VIDRO |
| 5957 | PEDRA OU TIJOLO DE VIDRO |
| 5958 | PAPEL DE LIXA (DE VIDRO) |
| 5959 | ELÉTRODO DE VIDRO |
| 5960 | TUBO CILÍNDRICO GRADUADO |
| 5961 | PAPEL DE VIDRO |
| 5961 | LIXA |
| 5962 | VIDRO EM PÓ |
| 5963 | CHAPA DE VIDRO |
| 5964 | TELHA DE VIDRO |
| 5965 | TUBO DE VIDRO |
| 5966 | LÃ DE VIDRO |
| 5967 | SAL DE GLAUBER |
| 5968 | LUSTRO |
| 5968 | ACETINAGEM |
| 5968 | BRILHO |
| 5968 | VERNIZ |
| 5969 | VIDRAR |
| 5969 | ESMALTAR |
| 5969 | ENVERNIZAR |
| 5970 | TIJOLO VIDRADO |

| | |
|---|---|
| 5971 | MASSA DE VIDRACEIRO |
| 5971 | MÁSTIQUE |
| 5972 | VITRIFICAÇÃO |
| 5972 | LUSTRO |
| 5973 | DESLIZAMENTO |
| 5974 | COEFICIENTE DE ELASTICIDADE DE CISALHAMENTO |
| 5975 | PLANO DE DESLIZAMENTO |
| 5976 | CURVA DE DESLIZE |
| 5977 | VÁLVULA ESFÉRICA |
| 5978 | PARAFUSO ESFÉRICO |
| 5979 | PÓ GLOBULAR |
| 5980 | PORTA-LUVAS |
| 5981 | CALOR |
| 5981 | INCANDESCÊNCIA |
| 5982 | AQUECER AO RUBRO |
| 5983 | INCANDESCENTE |
| 5984 | COLA |
| 5984 | GOMA |
| 5985 | COLAR |
| 5986 | JUNTA COLADA |
| 5987 | COLAGEM |
| 5988 | GLICERINA |
| 5989 | GNEISSE |
| 5990 | PROJEÇÃO GNOMÔNICA |
| 5991 | CALIBRE PASSA-NÃO-PASSA |
| 5992 | ÓCULOS DE PROTEÇÃO |
| 5993 | OURO |
| 5994 | BATIDA DO OURO |
| 5995 | BRONZE DE OURO |
| 5996 | OURO DE MOEDA |
| 5997 | CIANETO DE OURO |
| 5998 | PÓ DE OURO |
| 5999 | CHAPEADO DE OURO |
| 5999 | FOLHEADO A OURO |
| 6000 | FOLHA DE OURO |
| 6001 | TINTA DE DOURAR |
| 6002 | GALVANOSTEGIA A OURO |
| 6002 | DOURAÇÃO |
| 6003 | OURIVESARIA |
| 6004 | GONIÔMETRO |
| 6005 | SOLDAGEM BEM FEITA |
| 6006 | TESTE DE AJUSTAGEM |
| 6007 | MONTA-CARGA |
| 6008 | SUPERFÍCIE IRREGULAR DAS PEÇAS FUNDIDAS |
| 6009 | COLO DE CISNE |
| 6009 | PESCOÇO DE GANSO |
| 6010 | GOIVA |
| 6010 | ESCOPRO |
| 6011 | TRABALHO COM ESCOPRO |

| | |
|---|---|
| 6012 | MÁQUINA DE RECORTAR |
| 6013 | REGULADOR |
| 6014 | BRAÇO DO REGULADOR |
| 6015 | ESFERA DO REGULADOR |
| 6016 | CÁRTER DO REGULADOR |
| 6016 | CAIXA DO REGULADOR |
| 6017 | LUVA DO REGULADOR |
| 6018 | HASTE DO REGULADOR |
| 6019 | MOLA DO REGULADOR |
| 6020 | FRANQUIA |
| 6021 | GRAU |
| 6021 | NÍVEL |
| 6021 | QUALIDADE |
| 6022 | QUALIDADE DO AÇO |
| 6023 | ANÁLISE GRANULOMÉTRICA |
| 6024 | MUDANÇA GRADUAL DE TEMPERATURA/ VELOCIDADE |
| 6025 | GRADUAR |
| 6026 | CÍRCULO GRADUADO |
| 6026 | LIMBO |
| 6027 | DISCO GRADUADO |
| 6028 | PIPETA GRADUADA |
| 6029 | GRÃO (MEDIDA INGLESA) |
| 6030 | GRÃO |
| 6030 | CRISTAL |
| 6031 | FIBRAS |
| 6032 | GRANULOMETRIA |
| 6033 | CONTORNO DE GRÃO |
| 6033 | LIMITE DA SUPERFÍCIE DE GRÃOS |
| 6034 | ELEVADORES DE CEREAIS |
| 6035 | ENGROSSAMENTO DOS GRÃOS |
| 6035 | CRESCIMENTO DOS GRÃOS |
| 6036 | CHAPA DE GRANULAÇÃO ORIENTADA |
| 6037 | REFINO DO GRÃO |
| 6038 | LADO DO PÊLO DO COURO |
| 6039 | TAMANHO DO GRÃO |
| 6040 | GRANULOMETRIA |
| 6041 | ESTRUTURA DO GRÃO |
| 6042 | ESTANHO GRANULADO |
| 6043 | GRANULAÇÃO |
| 6044 | MOLÉCULA-GRAMA |
| 6045 | CALORIA GRAMA |
| 6045 | BAIXA CALORIA |
| 6046 | GRAMA |
| 6047 | GRANITO |
| 6048 | MÁRMORE |
| 6049 | CONCESSÃO DE PATENTE |
| 6050 | GRANULAR |
| 6051 | FRATURA GRANULAR |
| 6052 | ESTRUTURA GRANULAR |
| 6053 | TEXTURA GRANULAR |

| | | | |
|---|---|---|---|
| 6054 | METAL EM GRANALHA | 6095 | GRAUVAQUE |
| 6054 | METAL GRANULADO | 6096 | REDE |
| 6055 | ESCÓRIA GRANULADA | 6096 | GRADE |
| 6056 | POÇO DE GRANULAÇÃO DA ESCÓRIA | 6097 | ACUMULADOR DE GRELHA |
| 6057 | GRANULAÇÃO | 6098 | FERRO PARA BARRAS DE GRELHA |
| 6058 | AÇÚCAR DE UVA | 6099 | QUADRICULADO |
| 6058 | GLICOSE | 6100 | VÁLVULA DE GRELHA |
| 6059 | CARBONO GRAFÍTICO | 6101 | ESTRADO |
| 6060 | SOLUÇÃO GRÁFICA | 6102 | PISO DE ESTRADO |
| 6061 | GRAFOSTÁTICO | 6103 | TRITURAR |
| 6062 | GRAFITE | 6103 | PULVERIZAR |
| 6063 | ÓLEO GRAFITADO | 6103 | MOER |
| 6063 | GRAXA GRAFITADA | 6103 | ESMERILHAR |
| 6064 | CRISOL DE GRAFITE | 6103 | RETIFICAR |
| 6065 | PIRÔMETRO DE GRAFITE | 6104 | ESMERILHAR |
| 6066 | GRAFITIZAÇÃO | 6105 | REBOLO |
| 6067 | GRAFITIZANTE | 6105 | PEDRA DE AMOLAR |
| 6068 | SUPERFÍCIE DE GRELHA | 6105 | ESMERILHADORA |
| 6069 | BARRAS PARA GRELHAS | 6105 | RETIFICADORA |
| 6070 | GRELHA | 6106 | TRITURAÇÃO |
| 6071 | GRADE | 6106 | ESMERILHAMENTO |
| 6071 | GRADEAMENTO | 6106 | PULVERIZAÇÃO |
| 6072 | AERÔMETRO DE PESO CONSTANTE | 6107 | MATÉRIA PARA AMOLAR |
| 6073 | CASCALHO | 6108 | PASTA PARA ESMERIL |
| 6073 | PEDREGULHO | 6109 | LÍQUIDO ESFRIADOR DE ESMERILHAMENTO |
| 6074 | FILTRO DE CASCALHO OU PEDREGULHO | 6110 | PÓ DE ABRASIVO |
| 6075 | GRADE PARA CALIBRAR O CASCALHO | 6111 | ESMERILHAÇÃO |
| 6076 | TERRENO PEDREGOSO | 6112 | LUBRIFICANTE DE ESMERILHAMENTO |
| 6077 | ANÁLISE GRAVIMÉTRICA | 6113 | MÁQUINA DE ESMERILHAR |
| 6077 | GRAVIMETRIA | 6113 | RETIFICADORA |
| 6078 | GRAVIDADE | 6114 | DISCO DE MOER |
| 6079 | FUNDIÇÃO POR GRAVIDADE | 6115 | REBOLO |
| 6080 | MARTELO PILÃO | 6115 | RODA DE ESMERIL |
| 6081 | PLANO INCLINADO | 6116 | BALANCEADOR DE REBOLO |
| 6082 | TRANSPORTADOR A ROLO POR GRAVIDADE | 6117 | TRITURAÇÃO |
| 6083 | CORPO CINZENTO | 6117 | ESMERILHAÇÃO |
| 6084 | LUBRIFICAR | 6117 | PULVERIZAÇÃO |
| 6084 | ENGRAXAR | 6118 | MÓ |
| 6085 | CAIXA DE GRAXA | 6118 | PEDRA DE AMOLAR |
| 6086 | ENGRAXADOR | 6118 | REBOLO |
| 6087 | LUBRIFICAÇÃO COM GRAXA | 6119 | PODER DE OPACIDADE INSUFICIENTE |
| 6088 | VERDE | 6120 | GRAMPO |
| 6089 | CARBONATO BÁSICO DE COBRE | 6120 | CABO |
| 6089 | MALAQUITA | 6120 | MORDAÇA |
| 6090 | COMPACTADO VERDE | 6120 | TENAZ |
| 6090 | COMPACTO NÃO ACABADO | 6120 | GARRA |
| 6091 | RECOLHEDORAS DE FORRAGEM | 6121 | MORDENTE |
| 6092 | OURO VERDE | 6121 | MANDRIL DE APERTO |
| 6093 | CAPARROSA | 6122 | MORDAÇA DE TORNO |
| 6093 | SULFATO DE FERRO | 6123 | AREIA |
| 6094 | FERRO GUSA CINZENTO | 6123 | CASCALHO |

| | | | |
|---|---|---|---|
| 6123 | LIMADURA | 6158 | PINO DE PISTÃO |
| 6124 | GRANALHA | 6158 | PINO DE CRUZETA |
| 6125 | MATERIAL CALCINADO | 6159 | PINO DE FORQUILHA |
| 6125 | MASSA REFRATÁRIA | 6160 | GUIA |
| 6126 | ARGAMASSA REFRATÁRIA | 6161 | POLIA DE GUIA |
| 6127 | RANHURA | 6162 | TRILHO DE GUIA |
| 6127 | SULCO | 6163 | ANEL DE GUIA |
| 6127 | ESTRIA | 6164 | BARRA OU TIRANTE DE GUIA |
| 6127 | GARGANTA | 6165 | PARAFUSO DE AVANÇO |
| 6128 | ENTALHAR | 6166 | SUPERFÍCIE DE GUIA |
| 6128 | RANHURAR | 6167 | PALHETA DIRETRIZ |
| 6128 | CHANFRAR | 6168 | RODA DIRETRIZ |
| 6129 | ÂNGULO DE BISEL | 6168 | SATÉLITE |
| 6129 | ÂNGULO DE ABERTURA DA RANHURA | 6168 | COROA FIXA |
| 6130 | LADO DE SOLDA | 6169 | GUIA DA CRUZETA |
| 6130 | LADO DA JUNTA | 6170 | TESOURA GUILHOTINA |
| 6131 | GARGANTA DE POLIA | 6171 | ZONAS GUINIER-PRESTON |
| 6132 | RAIO DE AFASTAMENTO ENTRE AS BORDAS | 6172 | GOMA-ARÁBICA |
| 6133 | SOLDAGEM EM CHANFRO | 6173 | GOMA-RESINA |
| 6134 | CAME DE RANHURA | 6174 | GOMA ADRAGANTO |
| 6135 | POLIA DE RANHURA | 6175 | REPARO DE PEÇA |
| 6136 | CILINDRO COM RANHURA | 6176 | ALGODÃO-PÓLVORA |
| 6137 | RANHURA | 6176 | ALGODÃO FULMINANTE |
| 6137 | CHANFRADURA | 6176 | PIROCILINA |
| 6138 | MÁQUINA DE CHANFRAR | 6177 | BROCA DE CANHÃO |
| 6138 | MÁQUINA DE ABRIR RANHURAS | 6178 | BRONZE DE CANHÃO |
| 6139 | JUNTEIRA | 6179 | PINTURA A PISTOLA |
| 6139 | GUILHERME | 6180 | PISTOLA DE SOLDAR POR PONTOS |
| 6139 | GOIVETE | 6181 | PÓLVORA |
| 6140 | POLIA DE GARGANTA | 6182 | CANTONEIRA |
| 6140 | TAMBOR DE GORNES | 6183 | CORREIA DE TRIPA |
| 6141 | PESO BRUTO | 6184 | GUTA-PERCHA |
| 6142 | SUPERFÍCIE POLIDA E RETIFICADA | 6185 | CALHA |
| 6143 | ALTURA LIVRE (VEÍCULOS) | 6185 | SARJETA |
| 6144 | FARINHA DE CORTIÇA | 6185 | GOTEIRA |
| 6145 | VIDRO FOSCO | 6186 | TIRANTE DE CABO |
| 6146 | TAMPA ESMERILHADA | 6187 | CABO DE RETENÇÃO |
| 6147 | ÁGUA SUBTERRÂNEA | 6188 | MOLDE DE GESSO |
| 6147 | LENÇOL FREÁTICO | 6189 | MODELO DE GESSO |
| 6148 | NÍVEL DO LENÇOL FREÁTICO | 6190 | SULFATO DE CÁLCIO |
| 6149 | LIGAÇÃO EM TERRA | 6190 | GESSO |
| 6150 | ACIONAMENTO COLETIVO | 6191 | GIROSCÓPIO |
| 6150 | COMANDO POR GRUPOS | 6192 | AÇÃO GIROSCÓPICA |
| 6151 | GRUPO DE MÁQUINAS | 6193 | MOVIMENTO GIROSCÓPICO |
| 6152 | MASSA DE CIMENTO | 6194 | VIGA I |
| 6153 | INJETAR CIMENTO | 6194 | VIGA DUPLO T |
| 6153 | COAR CIMENTO | 6194 | FERRO EM H |
| 6154 | CIMENTAÇÃO | 6195 | FRATURA ESTRIADA |
| 6155 | AUMENTO | 6196 | SERRA PARA METAL |
| 6156 | PARAFUSO SEM CABEÇA | 6197 | LÂMINA DE SERRA PARA METAL |
| 6157 | REDE PROTETORA | 6198 | MÁQUINA DE SERRAR ALTERNATIVA |

| | |
|---|---|
| 6199 | HÁFNIO |
| 6200 | CORREIA DE CRINA |
| 6201 | COMPASSO DE PRECISÃO |
| 6202 | TRINCA CAPILAR |
| 6202 | GRETAS CAPILARES |
| 6203 | FORMAÇÃO DE HALO |
| 6204 | SEMICÉLULA |
| 6205 | METADE DE ACOPLAMENTO |
| 6206 | FRESAS DE CORTE LATERAL |
| 6207 | CORREIA SEMICRUZADA |
| 6208 | LIMA MEIA-CANA |
| 6209 | FERRO MEIA-CANA |
| 6210 | MADEIRA MEIA-CANA |
| 6211 | CAMADA DE SEMI-ESPESSURA |
| 6212 | RETIFICAÇÃO DE MEIA ONDA |
| 6213 | HALO |
| 6214 | HALOGÊNIO |
| 6215 | MARTELO |
| 6216 | MARTELAR |
| 6217 | APARAS DE FERRO |
| 6217 | ESCÓRIA DE FORJA |
| 6218 | SOLDAGEM A FORJA |
| 6219 | ENDURECIMENTO A MARTELO |
| 6219 | MARTELAGEM A FRIO |
| 6220 | MARTELADO |
| 6221 | METAL MARTELADO |
| 6222 | AÇO BATIDO |
| 6223 | MARTELAGEM |
| 6224 | GOLPE DA VÁLVULA |
| 6225 | FERREIRO MANUAL |
| 6226 | MÃO |
| 6226 | PONTEIRO |
| 6227 | FREIO DE MÃO |
| 6228 | BRUNIDURA MANUAL |
| 6228 | POLIMENTO MANUAL |
| 6229 | CABRESTANTE A ALMANJARRAS |
| 6230 | CARRINHO DE MÃO |
| 6231 | MANIVELA MANUAL |
| 6232 | CORTE MANUAL |
| 6233 | ACIONAMENTO MANUAL |
| 6234 | LIMA MANUAL |
| 6235 | MARTELO DE MÃO |
| 6236 | FURO PARA PÔR A MÃO |
| 6237 | TRABALHO MANUAL |
| 6238 | COLHER DE FUNDIÇÃO |
| 6238 | PANELA DE FUNDIÇÃO MANUAL |
| 6239 | ALAVANCA MANUAL |
| 6240 | FEITO À MÃO |
| 6241 | DE COMANDO MANUAL |
| 6242 | PROGRAMAÇÃO MANUAL DE PEÇA |
| 6243 | ESCRITURA RETA |

| | |
|---|---|
| 6243 | ESCRITURA PERPENDICULAR |
| 6244 | BOMBA MANUAL |
| 6245 | FERRO DE CORRIMÃO |
| 6246 | CALCADEIRA MANUAL |
| 6247 | ESCAREADOR MANUAL |
| 6248 | REBITAGEM MANUAL |
| 6249 | SERRA DE MÃO |
| 6250 | PANELA DE MÃO COM CABO |
| 6251 | TESOURA DE MÃO |
| 6252 | LUVA PROTETORA |
| 6253 | FERRAMENTA DE MÃO |
| 6254 | TORNO DE MÃO |
| 6255 | VOLANTE DE MÃO |
| 6255 | VOLANTE DE MANOBRA |
| 6256 | GUINCHO MANUAL |
| 6257 | TARRAXA MANUAL |
| 6258 | BROCA MANUAL |
| 6259 | CORRIMÃO |
| 6260 | DESINTUMESCIMENTO (PRÉ-AQUECIMENTO ANTES DE SOLDAR) |
| 6261 | FORJADO À MÃO |
| 6262 | CABO |
| 6263 | CABO DE FERRAMENTA |
| 6264 | ORIFÍCIOS DE MANIPULAÇÃO |
| 6265 | FERRO PARA CORRIMÃO |
| 6266 | MONTANTE DE CORRIMÃO |
| 6267 | VOLANTE DE MÃO |
| 6268 | PORCA DE RETENÇÃO DO VOLANTE |
| 6269 | MANEJÁVEL |
| 6269 | À MÃO |
| 6270 | MANCAL PENDENTE FECHADO |
| 6271 | MANCAL PENDENTE ABERTO |
| 6272 | PROCESSO HANSGIRG |
| 6273 | TIJOLO DURO |
| 6274 | TÊMPERA POR ESTIRAGEM A FRIO |
| 6275 | GRAXA CONSISTENTE |
| 6276 | CHUMBO ANTIMONIOSO |
| 6276 | METAL BRANCO DURO |
| 6277 | METAL DURO |
| 6278 | COLOCAÇÃO DE PLACAS PARA CORTE DE METAL DURO |
| 6279 | SOLDAGEM FORTE |
| 6280 | AÇO DURO |
| 6281 | ÁGUA DURA |
| 6283 | ENDURECIMENTO DA SUPERFÍCIE |
| 6284 | LIGA DE ENDURECIMENTO DA SUPERFÍCIE |
| 6285 | TEMPERAR UM METAL |
| 6286 | ENDURECER AO AR |
| 6286 | SOLIDIFICAR-SE AO AR |
| 6287 | ENDURECER SOB A ÁGUA |
| 6287 | SOLIDIFICAR-SE SOB A ÁGUA |

| | |
|---|---|
| 6288 | APTIDÃO PARA A TÊMPERA |
| 6289 | AÇO TEMPERADO |
| 6290 | ENDURECEDOR |
| 6291 | TÊMPERA |
| 6291 | ENDURECIMENTO |
| 6292 | ENDURECIMENTO |
| 6292 | SOLIDIFICAÇÃO (DO CIMENTO, ETC.) |
| 6293 | TÊMPERA |
| 6294 | BANHO DE TÊMPERA |
| 6295 | ÓLEO DE TÊMPERA |
| 6296 | QUALIDADE DE TÊMPERA DO METAL |
| 6297 | DUREZA |
| 6298 | DUREZA DA ÁGUA |
| 6299 | GRAU DE TÊMPERA DO AÇO |
| 6300 | TESTE OU PROVA DE DUREZA |
| 6301 | MADEIRA DE LEI |
| 6302 | MOVIMENTO PENDULAR |
| 6303 | GRADE (DE CORRENTE ZIGUEZAGUE, ETC.) |
| 6304 | SOMBREAR |
| 6305 | MACHADINHA |
| 6306 | SOMBREADO A TRAÇO |
| 6307 | GANCHOS DE TRAÇÃO |
| 6308 | PONTO ELEVADO DE FUSÃO |
| 6309 | CABO CALABROTEADO |
| 6310 | FORCADOS |
| 6310 | DESCARREGADOR DE GARRAS |
| 6311 | RASTELOS COMBINADOS COM RECOLHEDORES |
| 6312 | ANCINHOS |
| 6313 | NEBLINA |
| 6313 | NEVOEIRO |
| 6313 | BRUMA |
| 6314 | CABEÇOTE |
| 6314 | CABEÇA |
| 6314 | EXTREMIDADE |
| 6314 | PRESSÃO |
| 6315 | PERDA DE CARGA |
| 6316 | FUNDO DE TAMBOR |
| 6317 | CABEÇA DO MARTELO |
| 6318 | PONTA DE CHAVETA |
| 6319 | CANAL ADUTOR |
| 6320 | CABECEIRA |
| 6321 | MANCAL PENDENTE |
| 6322 | NASCENTE |
| 6323 | QUEDA |
| 6323 | PRESSÃO DA ÁGUA |
| 6323 | CARGA DA ÁGUA |
| 6324 | TUBO DE COMUNICAÇÃO |
| 6324 | TRAVESSÃO |
| 6325 | FERRAMENTA DE FORMAR CABEÇAS |
| 6326 | FAROL |

| | |
|---|---|
| 6326 | PROJETAR |
| 6326 | HOLOFOTE |
| 6327 | FAROL DIANTEIRO DO AUTOMÓVEL |
| 6327 | REFLETOR |
| 6327 | HOLOFOTE |
| 6328 | CABEÇOTE FIXO |
| 6329 | CAME CODRIFORME |
| 6330 | SAPATILHO OVAL |
| 6331 | SOLEIRA |
| 6331 | CADINHO |
| 6331 | CUBILÔ |
| 6331 | LAR |
| 6331 | CRISOL |
| 6332 | SOLEIRA DE FORNO |
| 6333 | CALOR |
| 6334 | AQUECER |
| 6334 | ESQUENTAR |
| 6335 | CAPACIDADE CALORÍFICA |
| 6336 | ACUMULADOR DE CALOR |
| 6337 | EQUILÍBRIO TÉRMICO |
| 6338 | AQUECIMENTO INTERNO |
| 6339 | CAPACIDADE CALORÍFICA |
| 6340 | CONDUTOR DE CALOR |
| 6341 | CONSTANTE CALORÍFICA |
| 6342 | TEOR TÉRMICO |
| 6342 | CAPACIDADE CALORÍFICA |
| 6343 | CALOR PROVOCADO POR ATRITO |
| 6344 | ENERGIA TÉRMICA OU CALORÍFICA |
| 6345 | MÁQUINA TÉRMICA |
| 6345 | MOTOR TÉRMICO |
| 6346 | DIAGRAMA ENTRÓPICO |
| 6347 | EQUIVALENTE CALORÍFICO DO TRABALHO |
| 6348 | NÚMERO DE CALORIAS DESPRENDIDAS EM UMA REAÇÃO |
| 6349 | PERMUTADOR DE CALOR |
| 6350 | TUBO DE PERMUTADOR TÉRMICO |
| 6351 | AQUECER EM CONTATO COM A ATMOSFERA |
| 6352 | ISOLADOR TÉRMICO |
| 6353 | PERDA TÉRMICA |
| 6354 | CALOR DE ABSORÇÃO |
| 6355 | CALOR DE CARBURAÇÃO |
| 6356 | CALOR DE COMBUSTÃO |
| 6357 | CALOR DE DECOMPOSIÇÃO |
| 6358 | CALOR DE DISSOCIAÇÃO |
| 6359 | CALOR DE EVAPORAÇÃO |
| 6360 | CALOR DE FUSÃO |
| 6361 | CALOR DE OXIDAÇÃO |
| 6362 | CALOR DE REDUÇÃO |
| 6363 | CALOR DE SUBLIMAÇÃO |
| 6364 | CALOR DE TRANSFORMAÇÃO |
| 6365 | CALOR DE TRANSIÇÃO |

| | |
|---|---|
| 6366 | CALOR DE VAPORIZAÇÃO |
| 6367 | AQUECER EM RECIPIENTE FECHADO |
| 6368 | PENETRAÇÃO DO CALOR |
| 6369 | RAIO CALORÍFICO |
| 6370 | CALOR DESPRENDIDO |
| 6371 | COLORAÇÃO TÉRMICA |
| 6372 | TRANSFERÊNCIA TÉRMICA |
| 6373 | COEFICIENTE DE CONDUTIBILIDADE TÉRMICA |
| 6374 | TRANSMISSÃO DE CALOR |
| 6375 | TRATAMENTO TÉRMICO |
| 6376 | INSTALAÇÃO DE TRATAMENTO TÉRMICO |
| 6377 | TRATAMENTO TÉRMICO |
| 6378 | PODER OU VALOR CALORÍFICO |
| 6379 | ONDA CALORÍFICA |
| 6380 | ZONA INFLUENCIADA PELO CALOR |
| 6381 | PERDAS TERMÓGENAS |
| 6382 | TEMPO DE CIRCULAÇÃO DE CORRENTE |
| 6383 | LIGA DE TRATAMENTO PELO CALOR |
| 6384 | PISTÃO AQUECIDO |
| 6385 | CALEFATOR |
| 6385 | AQUECEDOR |
| 6386 | FILAMENTO |
| 6387 | VELA DE PRÉ-AQUECIMENTO |
| 6388 | RESISTÊNCIA DE VELA DE PRÉ-AQUECIMENTO |
| 6389 | COMUTADOR DE VELAS DE PRÉ-AQUECIMENTO |
| 6390 | CALEFAÇÃO |
| 6390 | AQUECIMENTO |
| 6391 | MAÇARICO DE PRÉ-AQUECIMENTO |
| 6392 | POTÊNCIA CALORÍFICA |
| 6393 | ABERTURA DE AQUECIMENTO |
| 6394 | INSTALAÇÃO DE CALEFAÇÃO OU AQUECIMENTO CENTRAL |
| 6395 | CALEFAÇÃO DE PRÉDIOS |
| 6396 | TUBO DE AQUECIMENTO CENTRAL |
| 6397 | VAPOR DE AQUECIMENTO |
| 6398 | SUPERFÍCIE DE AQUECIMENTO |
| 6399 | MAÇARICO DE AQUECER |
| 6400 | AQUECIMENTO DOS MANCAIS |
| 6401 | CORRENTE DE GRANDE INTENSIDADE |
| 6402 | ENGRENAGEM DE FORÇA |
| 6402 | RODA DE FORÇA MOTRIZ |
| 6403 | ÓLEO PESADO |
| 6403 | ÓLEO ESPECIAL |
| 6404 | FRESAS SIMPLES PARA TRABALHO PESADO |
| 6405 | CAMINHÃO PESADO |
| 6406 | PEÇA DE FORJA PESADA |
| 6407 | METAL PESADO |
| 6408 | ÓLEO PESADO |

| | |
|---|---|
| 6409 | CHAPA FORTE |
| 6410 | LAMINADOR DE CHAPAS PESADAS |
| 6311 | PRENSA PARA CHAPAS FORTES |
| 6412 | MARCHA PESADA |
| 6413 | PERFIS PESADOS |
| 6414 | ÁGUA PESADA |
| 6415 | HECTOLITRO |
| 6416 | HECTOWATT |
| 6417 | HECTO-WATT/HORA |
| 6418 | MÁQUINA PARA PODAR AS SEBES |
| 6419 | VELA HEFNER |
| 6420 | ALTURA |
| 6421 | ALTURA DE QUEDA |
| 6422 | NÍVEL BAROMÉTRICO |
| 6423 | ALTURA SOB TRAVESSÃO |
| 6424 | MAÇARICO DE HÉLIO |
| 6425 | ENGRENAGEM HELICOIDAL |
| 6426 | MOVIMENTO HELICOIDAL |
| 6427 | MOLA HELICOIDAL |
| 6427 | MOLA ESPIRAL |
| 6428 | SUPERFÍCIE HELICOIDAL |
| 6429 | HÉLIO |
| 6430 | HÉLICE |
| 6431 | ÂNGULO DE AVANÇO |
| 6431 | ÂNGULO HELICOIDAL |
| 6432 | MÁSCARA DE SOLDADOR |
| 6433 | CABO DE MACHADO |
| 6434 | HEMATITA |
| 6435 | FERRO GUSA DE HEMATITA |
| 6436 | CRISTAL HEMIÉDRICO |
| 6437 | CRISTAL HEMIMÓRFICO |
| 6438 | HEMISFÉRIO |
| 6439 | CÂNHAMO |
| 6440 | NÚCLEO DE CÂNHAMO |
| 6441 | GAXETA DE CÂNHAMO |
| 6442 | GAXETA DE CÂNHAMO ENGRAXADA |
| 6443 | CORDA DE CÂNHAMO |
| 6444 | ESTOPA DE CÂNHAMO |
| 6445 | LONA DE CÂNHAMO |
| 6446 | ÓLEO DE CÂNHAMO |
| 6447 | HERMETICAMENTE FECHADO |
| 6447 | VEDADO |
| 6448 | ENGRENAGEM HIPOIDAL |
| 6449 | JUTA |
| 6449 | TECIDO DE EMBALAGEM |
| 6450 | RAIOS X HETEROCROMÁTICOS |
| 6451 | HETEROGÊNEO |
| 6452 | CONTEXTURA HETEROGÊNEA |
| 6453 | HEXÁGONO |
| 6454 | BARRA HEXAGONAL OU SEXTAVADA |
| 6455 | PORCA HEXAGONAL |

| | |
|---|---|
| 6456 | GONIÔMETRO SEXTAVADO |
| 6457 | PARAFUSO SEXTAVADO |
| 6458 | ESTRUTURA HEXAGONAL COMPACTA |
| 6459 | CRISTAL HEXAGONAL |
| 6460 | PRISMA HEXAGONAL |
| 6461 | CABEÇA SEXTAVADA DE PARAFUSO |
| 6462 | ARAME SEXTAVADO |
| 6463 | HEXAEDRO |
| 6464 | IMPERFEIÇÕES DE SUPERFÍCIE |
| 6465 | RODA DE PEITO |
| 6466 | MÁQUINA DE GRANDE POTÊNCIA |
| 6467 | ALTA FREQÜÊNCIA |
| 6468 | CORRENTE DE ALTA FREQÜÊNCIA |
| 6469 | FORNO DE ALTA FREQÜÊNCIA |
| 6470 | BROCA DE HÉLICE APERTADA |
| 6471 | FRESAS SIMPLES DE HÉLICE RÁPIDA |
| 6472 | PONTOS BRILHANTES |
| 6473 | ALTA PRESSÃO |
| 6474 | AÇO RÁPIDO |
| 6475 | FERRAMENTAS PARA AÇO DE CORTE RÁPIDO |
| 6476 | ALTA TEMPERATURA |
| 6477 | VÁCUO ELEVADO |
| 6478 | ALTA TENSÃO |
| 6479 | ALTA TENSÃO |
| 6480 | LATÃO DE ELEVADA PERCENTAGEM DE ZINCO |
| 6481 | LIGA DE ALTA DENSIDADE |
| 6482 | METAL DE ALTA DENSIDADE |
| 6483 | DE ALTO GRAU |
| 6483 | DE ALTO TEOR |
| 6484 | COMBUSTÍVEL DE BOA QUALIDADE |
| 6485 | MINÉRIO RICO |
| 6486 | AÇO DE QUALIDADE SUPERIOR |
| 6487 | CALDEIRA DE ALTA PRESSÃO |
| 6488 | CILINDRO DE ALTA PRESSÃO |
| 6489 | CALEFAÇÃO POR ÁGUA QUENTE A ALTA PRESSÃO |
| 6490 | TUBULAÇÃO DE ALTA PRESSÃO |
| 6491 | VAPOR DE ALTA PRESSÃO |
| 6492 | MÁQUINA A VAPOR DE ALTA PRESSÃO |
| 6493 | AQUECIMENTO POR VAPOR A ALTA PRESSÃO |
| 6494 | TURBINA DE ALTA PRESSÃO |
| 6495 | PERFURATRIZ DE ALTA VELOCIDADE |
| 6496 | MOTOR DE ALTA VELOCIDADE |
| 6497 | AÇO RÁPIDO |
| 6498 | OXIDAÇÃO A ALTA TEMPERATURA |
| 6499 | TESTE A ALTA TEMPERATURA |
| 6500 | CORRENTE DE ALTA TENSÃO |
| 6501 | LINHA DE ALTA TENSÃO |
| 6502 | MOTOR DE ALTA TENSÃO |
| 6503 | ALTAMENTE INFLAMÁVEL |
| 6504 | CONTRAÇÃO ESTORVADA |
| 6505 | DOBRADIÇA |
| 6505 | GONZO |
| 6505 | ARTICULAÇÃO |
| 6505 | CHARNEIRA |
| 6506 | ALÇA DE DOBRADIÇA |
| 6507 | PILAR DOBRADIÇO |
| 6508 | PINO OU PERNO DA CHARNEIRA |
| 6509 | PARAFUSO DE CHARNEIRA |
| 6510 | TAMPA DE DOBRADIÇA |
| 6511 | TORNO ARTICULADO |
| 6512 | FRESA HELICOIDAL |
| 6512 | FRESA-MÃE |
| 6513 | ACABAMENTO FEITO NA FRESA-MÃE |
| 6514 | CAVIDADE FRESADA |
| 6515 | ENXADAS (ARRASTADAS PELO TRATOR OU NELE MONTADAS) |
| 6516 | MONTA-CARGAS |
| 6516 | ELEVADOR |
| 6516 | GUINCHO |
| 6516 | GUINDASTE |
| 6517 | IÇAR |
| 6517 | ELEVAR |
| 6517 | LEVANTAR |
| 6518 | CORRENTE DE IÇAR |
| 6519 | MECANISMO DE LEVANTAR |
| 6519 | APARELHO ELEVADOR |
| 6520 | CABO DE IÇAR |
| 6521 | SUSPENSÃO |
| 6521 | PARADA |
| 6522 | DISPOSITIVO DE SUJEIÇÃO |
| 6522 | GRAMPO |
| 6522 | ANCORAGEM |
| 6523 | TEMPO DE MANUTENÇÃO DE ESFORÇO |
| 6524 | APOIAR |
| 6524 | SUSTENTAR |
| 6524 | ESCORAR |
| 6525 | MECANISMO DE RETENÇÃO EM POSIÇÃO ABERTA |
| 6526 | RETENÇÃO |
| 6526 | SUJEIÇÃO |
| 6527 | FORNO DE ESPERA |
| 6528 | MANUTENÇÃO DA TEMPERATURA |
| 6529 | CONTRAMARTELO |
| 6530 | ORIFÍCIO |
| 6530 | FURO |
| 6530 | BURACO |
| 6530 | ABERTURA |
| 6530 | OLHO |

| | |
|---|---|
| 6530 | VÃO |
| 6531 | BITOLA MACHO |
| 6531 | MACHO CALIBRADOR |
| 6532 | CALIBRE DE MATRIZ |
| 6533 | PORCA REDONDA DE DOIS OU MAIS ORIFÍCIOS |
| 6534 | ESCOVA ELÉTRICA |
| 6535 | ENSAIO OU TESTE DE ESCOVA ELÉTRICA |
| 6536 | LACUNAS (AFNOR) |
| 6536 | FALHAS (AFNOR) |
| 6537 | VAZADO |
| 6537 | OCO |
| 6537 | CÔNCAVO |
| 6538 | CORPO OCO |
| 6539 | PEÇA DE FUNDIÇÃO OCA |
| 6540 | CILINDRO OCO |
| 6541 | FERRO OCO DE MEIA-CANA |
| 6542 | CHAVE FÊMEA |
| 6543 | ONDA CÔNCAVA |
| 6543 | CÔNCAVO DA ONDA |
| 6544 | PLAINA CÔNCAVA |
| 6545 | SACA-BOCADOS |
| 6545 | VAZADOR |
| 6546 | GOIVA DE FERREIRO |
| 6547 | EIXO OCO |
| 6548 | ESPAÇO OCO ENTRE OS DENTES |
| 6549 | ESFERA OCA |
| 6550 | SEÇÃO RETANGULAR OCA |
| 6551 | HÓLMIO |
| 6552 | CRISTAL HOLOÉDRICO |
| 6553 | LEVANTAMENTO |
| 6554 | FERRAGEM DE FABRICAÇÃO PRÓPRIA |
| 6555 | HOMOGÊNEO |
| 6556 | UNIÃO HOMOGÊNEA |
| 6557 | EQUAÇÃO HOMOGÊNEA |
| 6558 | SUBSTÂNCIA HOMOGÊNEA |
| 6559 | RADIAÇÃO HOMOGÊNEA |
| 6560 | TEXTURA HOMOGÊNEA |
| 6561 | HOMOGENEIZAÇÃO |
| 6562 | SÉRIE HOMÓLOGA |
| 6563 | FERRO GUSA COM ALVÉOLOS |
| 6564 | RETIFICAÇÃO INTERNA |
| 6565 | MÁQUINA DE ESMERILHAR |
| 6566 | CAPÔ DE AUTOMÓVEL |
| 6567 | CASCOS DE ANIMAIS |
| 6568 | GATO (GUINDASTE) |
| 6568 | GANCHO |
| 6569 | CAVILHA DE GANCHO |
| 6570 | CORRENTES DE GANCHOS |
| 6571 | CHAVE DE GANCHO |
| 6572 | JUNTA UNIVERSAL ARTICULADA |

| | |
|---|---|
| 6573 | CARDAN |
| 6573 | JUNTA CARDAN |
| 6573 | ARTICULAÇÃO CARDAN |
| 6573 | JUNTA UNIVERSAL |
| 6574 | LEI DE HOOKE |
| 6575 | FERRO EM ARCOS OU CINTAS |
| 6575 | ARCO DE FERRO |
| 6575 | CINTA DE FERRO |
| 6576 | TENSÃO CIRCUNFERENTE |
| 6577 | TREMONHA |
| 6578 | HORIZONTAL |
| 6579 | CALDEIRA HORIZONTAL |
| 6580 | DEPÓSITO HORIZONTAL |
| 6581 | MÁQUINA DE FURAR HORIZONTAL |
| 6582 | MÁQUINA HORIZONTAL |
| 6583 | SOLDA EM ÂNGULO EM PLANO |
| 6584 | GRELHA HORIZONTAL |
| 6585 | LINHA HORIZONTAL |
| 6586 | APOIO INTERMEDIÁRIO DE EIXO |
| 6587 | EIXO HORIZONTAL |
| 6588 | MÁQUINA DE AMOLAR DE EIXO HORIZONTAL |
| 6589 | FRESADORA HORIZONTAL |
| 6590 | IMPULSO HORIZONTAL |
| 6591 | SOLDAGEM HORIZONTAL |
| 6592 | BRAÇO DE PRESSÃO |
| 6592 | BUZINA |
| 6593 | CHAPA DE PROTEÇÃO |
| 6594 | CENTRO DE COMPASSO |
| 6595 | APARAS DE CHIFRES |
| 6596 | DISTÂNCIA ENTRE OS BRAÇOS |
| 6597 | PONTA DO SUPORTE |
| 6598 | HORNBLENDA |
| 6599 | AMIANTO |
| 6600 | ENTRADA EM FORMA DE CHIFRE |
| 6601 | CRAVO DE FERRADURA |
| 6602 | CAVALO VAPOR (CV) |
| 6603 | CAVALO/HORA (CV/H) |
| 6604 | CRINA DE CAVALO |
| 6605 | FERRO DE FERRADURA |
| 6606 | IMÃ EM FORMA DE FERRADURA |
| 6607 | CALIBRE DE BOCA PARA DIMENSÕES MÍNIMA E MÁXIMA |
| 6608 | CALIBRE DE MORDAÇA |
| 6609 | MANGUEIRA |
| 6610 | CINTA PARA MANGUEIRA |
| 6611 | BRAÇADEIRA PARA MANGUEIRA |
| 6612 | UNIÃO PARA MANGUEIRAS |
| 6613 | MANGUEIRA DE PURGA |
| 6614 | MANGUEIRA |
| 6614 | TUBO FLEXÍVEL |

| | | | |
|---|---|---|---|
| 6615 | MOTOR DE AR QUENTE | 6660 | CARCAÇA |
| 6616 | CALEFAÇÃO A AR QUENTE | 6660 | CÁRTER |
| 6617 | LEITO OU MESA DE ESFRIAMENTO | 6661 | CUBO DE RODA |
| 6618 | TESTE OU PROVA DE DOBRAMENTO A QUENTE | 6662 | CALOTA DE RODA |
| | | 6663 | FLANGE DE CUBO |
| 6619 | DOBRAMENTO A QUENTE | 6664 | UMEDECEDOR |
| 6620 | FUNDIÇÃO A AR QUENTE | 6665 | ÁCIDO HÚMICO |
| 6621 | RUPTURA A QUENTE | 6666 | ESTADO HIGROMÉTRICO DO AR |
| 6622 | CORTE A QUENTE | 6666 | UMIDADE DO AR |
| 6623 | ESTIRAR A QUENTE | 6667 | HÚMUS |
| 6624 | ESTIRAGEM A QUENTE | 6668 | QUINTAL (APROXIMADAMENTE 50 KG) |
| 6624 | TREFILAGEM A QUENTE | 6669 | SUSPENSO POR UMA LÂMINA |
| 6625 | FRAGILIDADE A QUENTE | 6670 | RECALQUE |
| 6626 | FORJAMENTO A QUENTE | 6670 | BOMBEAMENTO |
| 6627 | FORMAÇÃO A QUENTE | 6670 | RECALQUE |
| 6628 | GALVANIZAÇÃO A QUENTE | 6671 | OSCILAÇÕES DO REGULADOR |
| 6629 | DUREZA A QUENTE | 6672 | HIDRANTE |
| 6630 | SERRA A QUENTE | 6673 | HIDRATO |
| 6630 | SERRA PARA METAL A QUENTE | 6673 | HIDRÓXIDO |
| 6631 | METAL EM ESTADO DE FUSÃO | 6674 | HIDRATADO |
| 6632 | ESTAMPAGEM A QUENTE | 6675 | ÁGUA DE HIDRATAÇÃO |
| 6633 | TÊMPERA EM MEIO QUENTE | 6676 | HIDRÁULICO |
| 6634 | REBITAR A QUENTE | 6677 | ACUMULADOR HIDRÁULICO |
| 6635 | REBITAGEM A QUENTE | 6678 | FREIO HIDRÁULICO |
| 6636 | LAMINAR A QUENTE | 6679 | MANDRIS HIDRÁULICOS |
| 6637 | CHAPA LAMINADA A QUENTE | 6680 | COMPRESSOR HIDRÁULICO |
| 6638 | LAMINAÇÃO A QUENTE | 6681 | EMBREAGEM HIDRÁULICA |
| 6639 | ISOLAMENTO TÉRMICO | 6681 | ACOPLAMENTO HIDRÁULICO |
| 6640 | DECEPADOR A QUENTE | 6682 | PRENSA HIDRÁULICA DE EMBUTIR |
| 6641 | FRAGILIDADE EM QUENTE | 6683 | ACIONAMENTO HIDRÁULICO |
| 6642 | PONTO QUENTE | 6684 | RENDIMENTO HIDRÁULICO |
| 6643 | ESTAMPAGEM A QUENTE | 6685 | ENGENHARIA HIDRÁULICA |
| 6644 | SUPERFÍCIE MUITO POROSA | 6686 | TERRAPLENAGEM HIDRÁULICA |
| 6645 | RACHADURA POR CONTRAÇÃO | 6687 | PRENSA DE FORJAR HIDRÁULICA |
| 6646 | ENSAIO DE RESISTÊNCIA A QUENTE | 6688 | MACACO HIDRÁULICO |
| 6647 | REBARBAÇÃO EM QUENTE | 6689 | CAL HIDRÁULICA |
| 6648 | CALEFAÇÃO A ÁGUA QUENTE | 6690 | ARGAMASSA HIDRÁULICA |
| 6649 | TUBULAÇÃO DE ÁGUA QUENTE | 6691 | MOTOR HIDRÁULICO |
| 6650 | TRABALHO A QUENTE | 6692 | CENTRAL HIDRÁULICA |
| 6651 | TUBULAÇÃO DE AR QUENTE | 6692 | USINA HIDRÁULICA |
| 6652 | TUBO DE CÁTODO QUENTE | 6693 | PRENSA HIDRÁULICA |
| 6653 | GALVANIZAÇÃO A QUENTE | 6694 | ARIETE HIDRÁULICO |
| 6654 | TEMPERATURA SUPERFICIAL MÁXIMA | 6695 | PROVA OU ENSAIO HIDRÁULICO |
| 6655 | ACABAMENTO A QUENTE | 6695 | TESTE DE PRESSÃO DE ÁGUA |
| 6656 | LAMINAÇÃO A QUENTE | 6696 | TURBINA HIDRÁULICA |
| 6657 | CORTE POR SERRA A QUENTE | 6697 | VÁLVULA ACIONADA HIDRAULICAMENTE |
| 6658 | QUEBRADIÇO A QUENTE | 6698 | HIDRÁULICA |
| 6659 | PROCESSO DE REVESTIMENTO EM BANHO QUENTE | 6699 | PROCESSO HIDRICO |
| | | 6700 | GERADOR HIDRELÉTRICO |
| 6660 | ALOJAMENTO | 6701 | CENTRAL HIDRELÉTRICA |
| 6660 | CAIXA | 6702 | CENTRIFUGAR |

| | |
|---|---|
| 6703 | MÁQUINA CENTRÍFUGA |
| 6704 | ÁCIDO BROMÍDRICO |
| 6705 | HIDROCARBONATO |
| 6706 | ÁCIDO CLORÍDRICO |
| 6706 | ÁCIDO MURIÁTICO |
| 6707 | ÁCIDO CIANÍDRICO |
| 6707 | ÁCIDO PRÚSSICO |
| 6708 | HIDRODINÂMICO |
| 6709 | FREIO HIDRÁULICO |
| 6710 | HIDRODINÂMICA |
| 6711 | ÁCIDO FLUORÍDRICO |
| 6712 | HIDROGÊNIO |
| 6713 | FRAGILIZAÇÃO PELO HIDROGÊNIO |
| 6713 | FRAGILIDADE À DECAPAGEM |
| 6714 | CHAMA DE HIDROGÊNIO |
| 6715 | CONCENTRAÇÃO HIDROGENIÔNICA |
| 6715 | CONCENTRAÇÃO DE ÍONS DE HIDROGÊNIO |
| 6716 | PERÓXIDO DE HIDROGÊNIO |
| 6716 | ÁGUA OXIGENADA |
| 6717 | ÁCIDO SULFÍDRICO |
| 6718 | CORROSÃO COM DESPRENDIMENTO DE HIDROGÊNIO |
| 6719 | HIDRÓLISE |
| 6720 | HIDROMECÂNICA |
| 6721 | HIDROMETALURGIA |
| 6722 | HIDRÔMETRO |
| 6722 | DENSÍMETRO |
| 6723 | HIDRÔMETRO DE PESO VARIÁVEL |
| 6724 | HIDRÓFILO |
| 6725 | BALANÇA HIDROSTÁTICA |
| 6726 | PRESSÃO HIDROSTÁTICA |
| 6727 | TESTE OU PROVA HIDROSTÁTICA |
| 6728 | HIDROSTÁTICA |
| 6729 | HIGRÔMETRO |
| 6730 | HIGROSCÓPICO |
| 6731 | UMIDADE HIGROSCÓPICA |
| 6732 | HIGROMETRICIDADE |
| 6733 | HIPEREUTECTÓIDE |
| 6734 | HIPÉRBOLE |
| 6735 | HIPERBÓLICO |
| 6736 | CILINDRO HIPERBÓLICO |
| 6737 | FUNÇÃO HIPERBÓLICA |
| 6738 | ESPIRAL HIPERBÓLICA |
| 6739 | HIPERBOLÓIDE DE UMA FOLHA |
| 6740 | HIPERBOLÓIDE DE DUAS FOLHAS |
| 6741 | HIPOEUTECTÓIDE |
| 6742 | ÁCIDO HIPOCLOROSO |
| 6743 | HIPOCICLÓIDE |
| 6744 | ENGRENAGEM HIPOCICLOIDAL |
| 6745 | ENGRENAGENS HIPÓIDES |
| 6746 | HIPOTENUSA |

| | |
|---|---|
| 6747 | HISTERESE |
| 6748 | VIGA EM I |
| 6748 | VIGA EM DUPLO T |
| 6749 | CALORÍMETRO DE GELO |
| 6750 | MÁQUINA DE FAZER GELO |
| 6751 | CRISTAL IDIOMÓRFICO |
| 6752 | MARCHA EM VAZIO |
| 6753 | TEMPO MORTO |
| 6754 | RODA INTERMEDIÁRIA |
| 6754 | POLIA LOUCA |
| 6755 | MARCHA LENTA |
| 6755 | MARCHA REDUZIDA |
| 6756 | EIXO INTERMEDIÁRIO |
| 6756 | CONTRA-EIXO |
| 6757 | ACENDER |
| 6757 | INFLAMAR |
| 6758 | ACENDEDOR |
| 6759 | PONTO DE IGNIÇÃO |
| 6760 | IGNIÇÃO |
| 6761 | BOBINA DE IGNIÇÃO |
| 6762 | DISTRIBUIDOR DE IGNIÇÃO |
| 6763 | PERDAS NO FOGO |
| 6764 | PONTO DE IGNIÇÃO OU INFLAMAÇÃO |
| 6765 | RESÍDUO DE CALCINAÇÃO |
| 6766 | INTERRUPTOR DE IGNIÇÃO |
| 6767 | PONTO DE INFLAMAÇÃO |
| 6767 | TEMPERATURA DE IGNIÇÃO |
| 6768 | REGULAGEM DE IGNIÇÃO |
| 6769 | LUZ DE AVISO DE IGNIÇÃO |
| 6770 | IGNIÇÃO |
| 6771 | ILÍNIO |
| 6772 | ILUMINADOR |
| 6772 | LUMINÁRIA |
| 6773 | CORPO ILUMINADO |
| 6774 | DISPOSITIVO DE ILUMINAÇÃO |
| 6775 | GÁS DE ILUMINAÇÃO |
| 6776 | PODER DE ILUMINAÇÃO |
| 6777 | ILUMINAÇÃO |
| 6778 | ILUSTRAÇÃO |
| 6778 | FIGURA |
| 6779 | IMAGEM |
| 6780 | PONTO DE IMAGEM |
| 6781 | NÚMERO IMAGINÁRIO |
| 6782 | FUSÃO INCOMPLETA |
| 6783 | IMPACTO |
| 6783 | CHOQUE |
| 6784 | EXTRUSÃO POR IMPACTO |
| 6784 | EXTRUSÃO POR CHOQUE |
| 6785 | RESISTÊNCIA AO CHOQUE |
| 6786 | ENSAIO OU PROVA DE RESISTÊNCIA AO CHOQUE |

| | | | |
|---|---|---|---|
| 6787 | MÁQUINA DE TESTAR IMPACTOS | 6831 | INCIDÊNCIA |
| 6788 | VÁLVULA DE IMPACTO | 6832 | RAIO DE INCIDÊNCIA |
| 6789 | PÓ IMPALPÁVEL | 6833 | RACHADURA INCIPIENTE |
| 6789 | SUBSTÂNCIA PULVERIZADA | 6834 | FRATURA SUPERFICIAL |
| 6790 | AFIAR | 6835 | INCLINÁVEL |
| 6790 | AMOLAR | 6835 | BASCULANTE |
| 6791 | APLICAR CAMADA DE PROTEÇÃO | 6836 | INCLINAÇÃO |
| 6792 | APLICAÇÃO DE CAMADA DE PROTEÇÃO | 6837 | GRELHA INCLINADA |
| 6793 | AFIAÇÃO | 6838 | PLANO INCLINADO |
| 6794 | IMPEDÂNCIA | 6839 | EMBREAGEM DE DENTE CÔNICO |
| 6794 | RESISTÊNCIA APARENTE | 6840 | INCLUSÃO |
| 6795 | PROPULSOR | 6841 | INCLUSÕES EM FILEIRAS |
| 6795 | ROTOR | 6842 | INCOMBUSTIBILIDADE |
| 6796 | IMPERMEABILIDADE À ÁGUA | 6843 | INCOMBUSTÍVEL |
| 6797 | IMPERMEABILIDADE | 6844 | ALIMENTAÇÃO DE ENTRADA |
| 6798 | IMPERMEÁVEL | 6845 | COMBUSTÃO INCOMPLETA |
| 6799 | CORROSÃO POR EROSÃO | 6846 | INCOMPRESSIBILIDADE |
| 6800 | IMPONDERÁVEL | 6847 | INCOMPRESSÍVEL |
| 6801 | EMPOBRECIMENTO | 6848 | AUMENTO DE PRESSÃO |
| 6802 | IMPREGNAR | 6849 | AUMENTO DE VELOCIDADE |
| 6802 | EMBEBER | 6850 | AUMENTO DE RESISTÊNCIA |
| 6803 | TUBO DE GÁS EM PAPEL BETUMINADO | 6851 | ACELERAR |
| 6804 | AGENTE DE IMPREGNAÇÃO | 6851 | AUMENTAR A VELOCIDADE |
| 6805 | IMPREGNAÇÃO | 6852 | VELOCIDADE CRESCENTE |
| 6806 | IMPRESSÃO | 6853 | DEFORMAÇÃO PROGRESSIVA |
| 6807 | EXPRESSÃO FRACIONÁRIA | 6854 | COTA INCREMENTAL |
| 6808 | CORRIGIR O AÇO POR TRATAMENTO TÉRMICO | 6855 | AUMENTO DE PRESSÃO |
| 6809 | IMPULSO | 6856 | INCRUSTAÇÃO |
| 6810 | TURBINA A IMPULSÃO | 6857 | INCRUSTADO |
| 6811 | FORÇA IMPULSIVA | 6858 | INTEGRAL INDEFINIDA |
| 6812 | CARGA PERIÓDICA | 6859 | ENTALHE |
| 6813 | IMPUREZAS | 6859 | PENETRAÇÃO |
| 6814 | IMPUREZA | 6859 | MOSSA |
| 6815 | EM RAZÃO DIRETA | 6860 | DUREZA VICKERS |
| 6816 | EM RAZÃO INVERSA | 6861 | TESTE DE DIREZA POR IMPRESSÃO DE BOLA |
| 6817 | SOB FORMA DE VAPOR | 6862 | ENTALHADO |
| 6818 | EM ESTADO LIVRE | 6863 | MÁQUINA DE ACIONAMENTO INDEPENDENTE |
| 6819 | EM ORDEM DE SERVIÇO | 6864 | INDICADOR |
| 6820 | INACESSIBILIDADE | 6864 | ÍNDICE |
| 6821 | INACESSÍVEL | 6865 | MANIVELA COM DIVISOR |
| 6822 | INCANDESCÊNCIA | 6866 | ÍNDICE DE REFRAÇÃO |
| 6823 | CALOR BRANCO | 6867 | DISCO GRADUADO |
| 6823 | BRANCO INCANDESCENTE | 6868 | ÍNDICE |
| 6824 | INCANDESCENTE | 6868 | PONTEIRO |
| 6825 | LÂMPADA INCANDESCENTE | 6869 | MECANISMO DE AVANÇO |
| 6826 | LUZ DE LÂMPADA INCANDESCENTE | 6869 | CABEÇOTE DIVISOR |
| 6827 | GÁS INCANDESCENTE | 6870 | DISCOS DIVISORES |
| 6828 | LÂMPADA A GÁS | 6871 | TINTA NANQUIM |
| 6829 | LUZ DE GÁS DE INCANDESCÊNCIA | 6872 | RENDIMENTO INDICADO |
| 6830 | POLEGADA | 6873 | CAVALO VAPOR INDICADO |

| | |
|---|---|
| 6874 | POTÊNCIA INDICADA |
| 6875 | FORÇA OU POTÊNCIA INDICADA |
| 6876 | TRABALHO INDICADO |
| 6877 | MICRÔMETRO DE MOSTRADOR |
| 6878 | INDICADOR |
| 6879 | INDICADOR |
| 6880 | CARTÃO INDICADOR |
| 6881 | DIAGRAMA DE INDICADOR |
| 6881 | DIAGRAMA DE TRABALHO |
| 6882 | EQUILÍBRIO INDIFERENTE |
| 6883 | DE AÇÃO INDIRETA |
| 6884 | EXTRUSÃO INDIRETA OU INVERTIDA |
| 6885 | ÍNDIO |
| 6886 | ACIONAMENTO INDIVIDUAL |
| 6887 | ILUMINAÇÃO INTERNA |
| 6888 | INDUZIR |
| 6889 | CORRENTE DE INDUÇÃO |
| 6890 | TIRAGEM POR INDUÇÃO |
| 6891 | INDUTÂNCIA |
| 6892 | INDUÇÃO |
| 6893 | SOLDA FORTE POR INDUÇÃO |
| 6894 | BOBINA DE INDUÇÃO |
| 6895 | FORNO DE INDUÇÃO |
| 6896 | TÊMPERA POR INDUÇÃO |
| 6897 | CALEFAÇÃO POR INDUÇÃO |
| 6898 | INDUTOR |
| 6899 | FUMAÇA INDUSTRIAL |
| 6900 | FORNO INDUSTRIAL |
| 6901 | ORGANIZAÇÃO INDUSTRIAL |
| 6901 | ADMINISTRAÇÃO INDUSTRIAL |
| 6902 | EFLUENTES INDUSTRIAIS |
| 6903 | INDÚSTRIA |
| 6904 | INELÁSTICO |
| 6905 | GÁS INERTE |
| 6906 | SOLDAGEM A ARCO DE TUNGSTÊNIO SOB GÁS INERTE |
| 6907 | INÉRCIA |
| 6908 | MORTALIDADE INFANTIL |
| 6909 | SÉRIE INFINITA |
| 6910 | INFINITAMENTE GRANDE |
| 6911 | INFINITAMENTE PEQUENO |
| 6912 | CÁLCULO INFINITESIMAL |
| 6913 | INFLAMABILIDADE |
| 6914 | INFLAMÁVEL |
| 6915 | ENTRADA DE ÁGUA |
| 6916 | INFRAÇÃO AOS DIREITOS DE UMA PATENTE |
| 6917 | INFUSIBILIDADE |
| 6918 | INFUSÍVEL |
| 6919 | LINGOTE |
| 6920 | CARRINHO DE LINGOTES |
| 6921 | FERRO FUNDIDO |

| | |
|---|---|
| 6921 | FERRO GUSA |
| 6921 | FERRO EM LINGOTES |
| 6922 | TORNO DE LINGOTES |
| 6923 | LINGOTEIRA |
| 6924 | AÇO FUNDIDO |
| 6924 | AÇO EM LINGOTES |
| 6925 | SOLIDIFICAÇÃO DENDRÍTICA |
| 6926 | LIMITAR |
| 6926 | INIBIR |
| 6926 | IMPEDIR |
| 6927 | INIBIDOR |
| 6928 | FRENAÇÃO INICIAL |
| 6929 | PRESSÃO INICIAL |
| 6930 | ESTADO INICIAL |
| 6931 | TEMPERATURA INICIAL |
| 6932 | VALOR INICIAL |
| 6933 | VELOCIDADE INICIAL |
| 6934 | INJETAR |
| 6935 | INJEÇÃO |
| 6936 | ORDEM DE INJEÇÃO |
| 6937 | VÁLVULA DE INJEÇÃO |
| 6938 | INJETOR |
| 6939 | BORRACHA DE APAGAR TINTA |
| 6940 | PASSAR A TINTA |
| 6941 | DESENHO A TINTA |
| 6942 | PASSAGEM DE TINTA |
| 6943 | ENTRADA |
| 6943 | ADMISSÃO |
| 6943 | TOMADA |
| 6944 | TERMINAL DE ENTRADA |
| 6945 | TUBO DE ADMISSÃO MÚLTIPLA |
| 6945 | COLETOR DE ADMISSÃO |
| 6946 | BOCAL DE ADMISSÃO |
| 6947 | ORIFÍCIO DE ADMISSÃO |
| 6947 | ORIFÍCIO DE INTRODUÇÃO |
| 6948 | TUBO DE ADMISSÃO |
| 6949 | VÁLVULA DE ADMISSÃO |
| 6950 | VELOCIDADE À ENTRADA |
| 6951 | CONE INTERNO |
| 6952 | CONE INTERNO DA CHAMA |
| 6953 | ANEL INTERNO DO ROLAMENTO DE ESFERAS |
| 6954 | SUPERFÍCIE INTERNA DE TUBO |
| 6955 | CÂMARA DE AR |
| 6956 | INOCULAÇÃO |
| 6957 | SUBSTÂNCIA INORGÂNICA |
| 6958 | QUÍMICA MINERAL OU INORGÂNICA |
| 6959 | INOXIDÁVEL |
| 6960 | SUPORTE DE INFORMAÇÃO DE ENTRADA |
| 6961 | QUADRILÁTERO INSCRITO |
| 6962 | ÂNGULO INSCRITO |

| | |
|---|---|
| 6963 | CÍRCULO INSCRITO |
| 6964 | POLÍGONO INSCRITO |
| 6965 | INSERÇÃO |
| 6965 | SUPLEMENTO |
| 6965 | ENCAIXE |
| 6966 | MATRIZ MÓVEL |
| 6967 | PÔR OS REBITES |
| 6968 | VIGA ENCAIXADA |
| 6969 | BOCAL ENCAIXADO |
| 6970 | PEÇA ENCAIXADA |
| 6971 | FRESA DE DENTES FIXOS |
| 6971 | FRESA DE LÂMINAS FIXAS |
| 6972 | COLOCAÇÃO DOS REBITES |
| 6973 | BORRACHA COM INSERÇÃO |
| 6974 | INTERIOR |
| 6974 | LADO INTERNO |
| 6974 | DENTRO |
| 6975 | CALIBRE INTERNO |
| 6975 | COMPASSO PARA DIÂMETRO INTERNO |
| 6976 | MANIVELA DO VIRABREQUIM |
| 6977 | DIÂMETRO INTERNO |
| 6978 | PASSO DE CORRENTE |
| 6979 | MICRÔMETRO PARA MEDIDA INTERNA |
| 6980 | VÁLVULA DE ROSCA INTERNA |
| 6981 | HASTE DE ROSCA INTERNA |
| 6982 | LARGURA INTERNA DE ELO DE CORRENTE |
| 6983 | INSOLUBILIDADE |
| 6984 | INSOLÚVEL |
| 6985 | FISCALIZAÇÃO |
| 6986 | LINHA DE FISCALIZAÇÃO |
| 6987 | INSPEÇÃO OU CONTROLE |
| 6988 | INSTALAÇÃO |
| 6989 | CENTRO INSTANTÂNEO DE ROTAÇÃO |
| 6990 | VALOR INSTANTÂNEO |
| 6991 | INSTRUÇÃO |
| 6992 | MODO DE EMPREGO |
| 6992 | INSTRUÇÕES PARA USO |
| 6993 | PAINEL DE INSTRUMENTOS |
| 6994 | ISOLAR |
| 6995 | TANQUE CALORÍFUGO |
| 6996 | FIO OU ARAME ISOLADO |
| 6997 | COMPOSTO ISOLANTE |
| 6998 | MATERIAL ISOLANTE |
| 6998 | ISOLANTE |
| 6999 | ÓLEO ISOLANTE |
| 7000 | PODER ISOLANTE |
| 7001 | FITA ISOLANTE |
| 7002 | TUBO ISOLANTE |
| 7003 | ISOLAMENTO TÉRMICO |
| 7004 | ISOLAMENTO ACÚSTICO |
| 7005 | RESISTÊNCIA AO ISOLAMENTO |
| 7006 | ISOLANTE |
| 7007 | COLETOR DE ADMISSÃO |
| 7008 | TEMPO DE ADMISSÃO |
| 7009 | INTEGRAL |
| 7010 | VIGA INCORPORADA |
| 7011 | CÁLCULO INTEGRAL |
| 7012 | NÚMERO INTEIRO |
| 7013 | INTÉGRAFO |
| 7014 | INTEGRAR |
| 7015 | INTEGRAÇÃO |
| 7016 | INTEGRADOR |
| 7017 | TELA REFORÇADORA |
| 7018 | INTENSIDADE |
| 7019 | INTENSIDADE DE RADIAÇÃO |
| 7019 | INTENSIDADE LUMINOSA |
| 7020 | REGULADOR DE INTENSIDADE |
| 7021 | INTENSIDADE DE CORRENTE |
| 7022 | INSERIR |
| 7022 | INTERCALAR |
| 7023 | INSERÇÃO |
| 7023 | INTERCALAÇÃO |
| 7024 | INTERCEPTAR RAIOS |
| 7025 | INTERCAMBIABILIDADE |
| 7026 | INTERCAMBIÁVEL |
| 7027 | ENGRENAGENS INTERMUTÁVEIS |
| 7028 | FABRICAÇÃO SERIADA |
| 7028 | INTERCAMBIABILIDADE DE FABRICAÇÃO |
| 7029 | POROSIDADE INTERCOMUNICANTE |
| 7030 | CORROSÃO INTERCRISTALINA |
| 7030 | CORROSÃO INTERGRANULAR |
| 7031 | CORROSÃO INTERDENDRÍTICA |
| 7032 | INTERFACE |
| 7033 | TENSÃO INTERFACIAL |
| 7034 | ZONA INTERFACIAL |
| 7035 | INTERFERÊNCIA |
| 7036 | FAIXA DE INTERFERÊNCIA |
| 7037 | COR DE INTERFERÊNCIA |
| 7038 | COMPARADOR INTERFERENCIAL |
| 7039 | FIGURA OU IMAGEM DE INTERFERÊNCIA |
| 7040 | FRANJA DE INTERFERÊNCIA |
| 7041 | CORROSÃO INTERGRANULAR |
| 7042 | FRATURA INTERGRANULAR |
| 7043 | PRODUTO INTERMEDIÁRIO |
| 7044 | MANCAL AUXILIAR OU SECUNDÁRIO |
| 7045 | TRANSMISSÃO POR CORREIA |
| 7046 | ESFRIADOR INTERMÉDIO |
| 7047 | VIGA INTERMEDIÁRIA |
| 7047 | TENSOR INTERMEDIÁRIO |
| 7048 | MANCAL INTERMEDIÁRIO |
| 7049 | EIXO INTERMEDIÁRIO |
| 7050 | ENGRENAGEM INTERMEDIÁRIA |

| | |
|---|---|
| 7050 | TRANSMISSÃO POR ENGRENAGEM |
| 7051 | VALOR INTERMEDIÁRIO |
| 7052 | COMPOSTO INTERMETÁLICO |
| 7053 | MOVIMENTO INTERMITENTE |
| 7054 | SOLDA POR PONTOS |
| 7054 | SOLDAGEM INTERMITENTE |
| 7055 | SOLDAGEM DESCONTÍNUA |
| 7056 | FUNCIONAMENTO INTERMITENTE |
| 7057 | ÂNGULO INTERNO |
| 7058 | ENGRENAGEM INTERNA |
| 7059 | FRESA DE INTERIOR PARA TUBOS |
| 7060 | PENTE PARA ABRIR ROSCA FÊMEA |
| 7061 | MOTOR DE COMBUSTÃO INTERNA |
| 7062 | MOTOR DE COMBUSTÃO INTERNA |
| 7063 | DESLOCAMENTO INTERNO |
| 7064 | FORÇA INTERNA |
| 7065 | HISTERESE |
| 7065 | ATRITO INTERNO |
| 7066 | CALIBRE DE INTERIORES |
| 7067 | ENGRENAGEM INTERNA |
| 7068 | RETIFICADOR INTERNO |
| 7069 | RETIFICAÇÃO INTERNA |
| 7070 | AQUECIMENTO INTERNO |
| 7071 | DIÂMETRO INTERNO |
| 7072 | RESISTÊNCIA INTERNA |
| 7073 | CAVIDADE POR CONTRAÇÃO |
| 7074 | TENSÃO INTERNA |
| 7075 | TENSÕES INTERNAS EM FUNDIÇÕES |
| 7076 | CALIBRE DE TAMPA CÔNICA |
| 7077 | DENTES INTERNOS |
| 7078 | ROSCA INTERNA |
| 7079 | RODA DE DENTES INTERNOS |
| 7080 | SOLDAGEM INTERNA |
| 7081 | TRABALHO INTERNO |
| 7082 | TUBO DE ALETAS INTERNAS |
| 7083 | ROSCA MÉTRICA INTERNACIONAL |
| 7084 | ROSCA DE PASSO MILIMÉTRICO |
| 7085 | RECOZIMENTO INTERMEDIÁRIO ENTRE DUAS ESTIRAGENS |
| 7086 | TEMPERATURA DA PASSAGEM INTERMEDIÁRIA |
| 7087 | DISTÂNCIA RETICULAR |
| 7088 | INTERPOLAR |
| 7089 | INTERPOLAÇÃO |
| 7090 | INTERROMPER O CIRCUITO ELÉTRICO |
| 7090 | CORTAR A CORRENTE |
| 7091 | ENVELHECIMENTO INTERROMPIDO OU POR ESTÁGIOS |
| 7092 | INTERRUPÇÃO DO TRABALHO |
| 7093 | INTERRUPÇÃO DA CORRENTE ELÉTRICA |
| 7093 | CORTE DA ELETRICIDADE |

| | |
|---|---|
| 7094 | CORTAR |
| 7094 | CRUZAR |
| 7095 | PLANO DE INTERSEÇÃO |
| 7096 | EIXOS CONCORRENTES |
| 7096 | EIXOS CONVERGENTES |
| 7097 | CONTROLE RADIOGRÁFICO DE INTESEÇÃO |
| 7078 | GAIOLA MÉDIA |
| 7099 | ÔNIBUS INTERURBANO |
| 7100 | INTERVALO |
| 7101 | INTERVALO |
| 7102 | MISTURA ÍNTIMA |
| 7103 | RAIOS INFRAVERMELHOS |
| 7104 | INTENSIDADE LUMINOSA POR UNIDADE DE SUPERFÍCIE |
| 7105 | METAL INVAR |
| 7106 | INVARIANTE |
| 7107 | INVENÇÃO |
| 7108 | INVENTOR |
| 7109 | TÊMPERA INVERSA |
| 7110 | INVERSÃO |
| 7111 | VÁLVULA DE ENCAIXE INVERTIDA |
| 7112 | FERRO PARA PLATAFORMA DE PONTE |
| 7113 | SOLDAGEM NO TETO |
| 7114 | EXAME MICROSCÓPICO |
| 7115 | FUNDIÇÃO PELO PROCESSO DE CERA PERDIDA |
| 7116 | MODELO DE CERA PERDIDA |
| 7117 | EVOLVENTE |
| 7117 | CURVA EVOLVENTE |
| 7118 | EVOLVENTE DO CÍRCULO |
| 7119 | DENTES INVOLUTOS |
| 7120 | IODO |
| 7121 | ÍON |
| 7122 | CONCENTRAÇÃO DE ÍONS |
| 7123 | MIGRAÇÃO DE ÍONS |
| 7124 | IONIZAÇÃO |
| 7125 | CÂMARA DE IONIZAÇÃO |
| 7126 | CORRENTE DA CÂMARA DE IONIZAÇÃO |
| 7127 | MÉTODO DE IONIZAÇÃO |
| 7128 | ZONA IONIZADA |
| 7129 | IONÓGENO |
| 7130 | SOLVENTE IONÓGENO |
| 7131 | IRÍDIO |
| 7132 | DIAFRAGMA ÍRIS |
| 7133 | FERRO |
| 7134 | ACETATO DE FERRO |
| 7135 | ALÚMEN DE FERRO |
| 7136 | MÁQUINA DE CORTAR FERROS E PERFIS |
| 7137 | CANTONEIRAS EM PACOTE |
| 7138 | CARBONETO DE FERRO |
| 7138 | CEMENTITA |

| | |
|---|---|
| 7139 | DIAGRAMA FERRO CARBONO |
| 7140 | FERROCARBONILO |
| 7140 | CARBONILO DE FERRO |
| 7141 | MÁSTIQUE DE FERRO |
| 7141 | MÁSTIQUE PARA FUNDIÇÃO |
| 7142 | FUNDIÇÃO DE FERRO |
| 7143 | MINÉRIO DE FERRO |
| 7144 | ÓXIDO DE FERRO |
| 7145 | PÓ DE FERRO |
| 7146 | PIRITA DE FERRO |
| 7146 | SULFURETO DE FERRO |
| 7147 | CABO DE ARAME |
| 7148 | PERÓXIDO DE FERRO |
| 7148 | SESQUIÓXIDO DE FERRO |
| 7148 | RUBRO DA PRÚSSIA |
| 7149 | SILICATO DE FERRO |
| 7150 | DORMENTE DE FERRO |
| 7151 | ESPONJA DE FERRO |
| 7152 | CONSTRUÇÃO METÁLICA |
| 7152 | ARMAÇÃO METÁLICA |
| 7153 | SULFURETO DE FERRO |
| 7154 | DENTE DE FERRO FUNDIDO |
| 7155 | FIO DE FERRO |
| 7155 | ARAME DE FERRO |
| 7156 | LIGA À BASE DE FERRO |
| 7157 | FERRO FUNDIDO |
| 7158 | PRENSAGEM PROFUNDA |
| 7158 | EMBUTIMENTO PROFUNDO |
| 7159 | OBRA DE FERRO |
| 7159 | FERRAGEM |
| 7160 | FUNDIÇÃO |
| 7160 | FORJARIA |
| 7161 | IRRADIAÇÃO |
| 7162 | NÚMERO IRRACIONAL |
| 7162 | NÚMERO INCOMENSURÁVEL |
| 7163 | IRREGULAR |
| 7164 | POLÍGONO IRREGULAR |
| 7165 | ACIONAMENTO IRREGULAR |
| 7165 | FUNCIONAMENTO IRREGULAR |
| 7165 | MARCHA IRREGULAR |
| 7166 | LINHA QUEBRADA |
| 7167 | IRREGULARIDADE DE MOVIMENTO |
| 7168 | IRREVERSIBILIDADE |
| 7169 | IRREVERSÍVEL |
| 7170 | MUDANÇA IRREVERSÍVEL DE ESTADO |
| 7171 | PROCESSO ELETROLÍTICO IRREVERSÍVEL |
| 7172 | INSTALAÇÕES DE IRRIGAÇÃO |
| 7173 | LINHA ISENTRÓPICA |
| 7174 | COLA DE PEIXE |
| 7175 | PONTO ISOELÉTRICO |
| 7176 | ISÓBARO |

| | |
|---|---|
| 7177 | CURVA ISOBÁRICA |
| 7178 | ISOCRONISMO |
| 7179 | ISÓCRONO |
| 7180 | REGULADOR ISÓCRONO |
| 7181 | LINHA ISOCLÍNICA OU ISÓCLINA |
| 7182 | LINHA ISODINÂMICA |
| 7183 | CARGA ISOLADA |
| 7184 | ISOLAMENTO |
| 7185 | ISÔMERO |
| 7186 | ISOMERISMO |
| 7186 | ISOMERIA |
| 7187 | LINHA ISOMÉTRICA |
| 7188 | PROJEÇÃO ISOMÉTRICA |
| 7189 | ISOMORFISMO |
| 7190 | ISOMORFO |
| 7191 | MISTURA ISOMORFA |
| 7192 | TRIÂNGULO ISÓSCELES |
| 7193 | CURVA ISOTÉRMICA |
| 7194 | TRATAMENTO ISOTÉRMICO |
| 7195 | TÉMPERA ISOTÉRMICA |
| 7196 | TRANSFORMAÇÃO ISOTÉRMICA |
| 7197 | ISÓTOPOS |
| 7198 | ISOTRÓPICO |
| 7199 | MARFIM |
| 7200 | TESTE OU ENSAIO DE IZOD |
| 7201 | PLAINA DE DESBASTAR |
| 7201 | GARLOPA |
| 7202 | EIXO OU ÁRVORE INTERMEDIÁRIA |
| 7203 | CAMISA |
| 7203 | ENVOLTURA |
| 7203 | INVÓLUCRO |
| 7204 | ESFRIAMENTO POR CAMISA DE ÁGUA |
| 7205 | VÁLVULA COM CAMISA TÉRMICA |
| 7206 | PÉ DE LEVANTAMENTO POR MACACO |
| 7207 | SAPATA PARA DISPOSITIVO DE ELEVAÇÃO |
| 7208 | MANDRIL DILATÁVEL JACOBS |
| 7209 | CHUMBADOR FARPADO |
| 7210 | ENCRAVAR |
| 7210 | ENGASTAR |
| 7210 | ENTUPIR |
| 7210 | OBSTRUIR |
| 7211 | OMBREIRA |
| 7211 | UMBRAL |
| 7211 | MONTANTE LATERAL DE ENTRADA |
| 7212 | CONVERGÊNCIA |
| 7212 | BLOQUEIO |
| 7213 | CERA DO JAPÃO |
| 7214 | ENVERNIZAMENTO COM CHARÃO |
| 7215 | MÁQUINA DE CALCAR |
| 7216 | BOCA DE CHAVE |
| 7217 | VIDRO DE JENA |

| | | | | |
|---|---|---|---|---|
| 7218 | JATO | 7256 | MUNHÃO |
| 7218 | ESGUICHO | 7256 | MOENTE |
| 7218 | GICLÊ | 7257 | MANCAL RADIAL |
| 7219 | PORTA-PULVERIZADOR | 7258 | ATRITO DE MUNHÃO |
| 7219 | BOCAL INJETOR | 7259 | PRESSÃO SOB OS MUNHÕES |
| 7220 | CONDENSADOR POR INJEÇÃO | 7260 | CADAFALSO (ANDAIME) |
| 7221 | JATO LÍQUIDO | 7261 | ASSENTO BASCULANTE |
| 7222 | PERFURAÇÃO POR CHAMA | 7262 | TESTE DE ESMAGAMENTO |
| 7223 | BOMBA DE JATO | 7263 | RECALCAR |
| 7224 | GUINDASTE DE LANÇA | 7263 | ESMAGAR |
| 7225 | COMPRIMENTO DA LANÇA | 7264 | CABO VOLANTE |
| 7226 | LANÇA DE GUINDASTE | 7265 | RECALQUE |
| 7227 | GABARITO | 7265 | ESMAGAMENTO |
| 7227 | DISPOSITIVO DE APERTAR | 7266 | TAMPA DE CILINDRO |
| 7228 | MÁQUINA DE BURILAR | 7266 | TAMPA DE PISTÃO |
| 7229 | OBRA | 7267 | CALCÁRIO JURÁSSICO |
| 7229 | TRABALHO | 7268 | JUTA |
| 7230 | FUNDIÇÃO COM MODELOS | 7268 | CÁNHAMO |
| 7231 | TRANSMISSÃO POR SACUDIDELAS | 7269 | COEFICIENTE CALORÍFICO |
| 7232 | MÁQUINA DE CONTRACURVAR | 7269 | COEFICIENTE DE CONDUTIBILIDADE TÉRMICA |
| 7233 | MARCENEIRO | | |
| 7234 | BANCO DE MARCENEIRO | 7270 | FERRO KAHLBAUM |
| 7235 | MARCENARIA | 7271 | PROCESSO DE FORNO KALDO |
| 7236 | MARCENARIA | 7272 | CORTA-NABOS |
| 7237 | JUNTA | 7273 | LINGOTE-PROVETA |
| 7238 | JUNTA | 7274 | CORTE |
| 7238 | ARTICULAÇÃO | 7274 | INCISÃO |
| 7239 | FUNÇÃO DE DISTRIBUIÇÃO COMPOSTA | 7275 | ÓLEO DE QUEROSENE |
| 7240 | GEOMETRIA DA JUNTA | 7275 | ÓLEO PARA LÂMPADAS |
| 7241 | JUNTA DE SEPARAÇÃO DO MANCAL | 7276 | CHAVE |
| 7242 | PINO DE ARTICULAÇÃO OU DE JUNTA | 7276 | CHAVETA |
| 7242 | PASSADOR DE ARTICULAÇÃO | 7276 | CUNHA |
| 7243 | LIGAR TUBOS POR FLANGES | 7277 | CHAVETAR |
| 7244 | LIGAR TUBOS | 7277 | CALÇAR |
| 7245 | GARLOPA | 7278 | TOCA PINOS |
| 7246 | JUNTADEIRA | 7278 | DESENCHAVETADEIRA |
| 7246 | GARLOPA | 7279 | CHAVETAR |
| 7247 | MATERIAL PARA FAZER FUNTA | 7280 | GARRA DE FIXAÇÃO |
| 7248 | LIGAÇÃO DE TUBOS | 7281 | MÁQUINA DE ABRIR RASGOS NAS CHAVETAS |
| 7249 | TESTE DE SACUDIDELAS E ENROLAMENTO | | |
| 7250 | MÁQUINA DE MOLDAR A SACUDIDELA | 7282 | RASGO DE CHAVETA |
| 7251 | MÁQUINA DE MOLDAR A SACUDIDELAS COM CHAPA REVERSÍVEL | 7282 | RANHURA DE CHAVETA |
| | | 7283 | CALIBRE PARA RANHURA DE CHAVETA |
| 7252 | MÁQUINA DE APERTO POR SACUDIDELA E PRESSÃO SEM DESMOLDAGEM | 7284 | CHAVE DE CALIBRE |
| | | 7284 | CHAVE DE FORQUILHA |
| 7253 | MÁQUINA DE MOLDAR A SACUDIDELA E DE APERTO EM COMBINAÇÃO COM DESMOLDAGEM | 7285 | JUNTA CHAVETADA |
| | | 7286 | CABEÇA DE CHAVETA |
| | | 7287 | RASGO DE CHAVETA |
| 7254 | TESTE OU ENSAIO JOMINY | 7287 | BURACO DA FECHADURA |
| 7255 | JOULE (UNIDADE DE TRABALHO ELÉTRICO) | 7288 | CHAVETAMENTO |
| 7256 | PINO | 7289 | BLOCO ACESSÓRIO PARA RÉGUAS DE AÇO |

| | |
|---|---|
| 7290 RÉGUA PARA SUPERFÍCIES CILÍNDRICAS | 7325 SUPORTE DE LÂMINA |
| 7291 RASGO DE CHAVETA | 7326 SUSPENSÃO DE CUTELO |
| 7292 DIATOMITO | 7327 COLISÃO DE NÊUTRONS COM ÁTOMOS |
| 7292 KIESELGUHR | 7328 EXTRAÇÃO |
| 7292 TERRA INFUSÓRIA | 7329 DESARMADO |
| 7292 FARINHA FÓSSIL | 7329 DESMONTADO |
| 7293 ÁGUA PARA SOLDAR | 7330 DETONAÇÃO |
| 7293 SOLUÇÃO DE CLORETO DE ZINCO | 7331 RUÍDO DE BOMBA |
| 7294 AÇO ACALMADO | 7332 PUNÇÃO EJETOR |
| 7295 FORNO DE CALCINAÇÃO | 7333 PASSADOR EXTRATOR |
| 7296 QUILODINA | 7334 CHAPA EXTRATORA |
| 7297 QUILOGRAMA | 7335 QUANTIDADE CONHECIDA |
| 7298 QUILOCALORIA | 7336 ARTICULAÇÃO DE PINO |
| 7299 QUILOGRÁMETRO | 7337 TRANSMISSÃO POR PARAFUSO |
| 7300 QUILÔMETRO | SERRILHADO |
| 7301 QUILOVOLT | 7338 SERRILHADO |
| 7302 QUILOVOLT AMPÈRE | 7338 RECARTILHAMENTO |
| 7303 QUILOWATT | 7339 CRÍPTON |
| 7304 QUILOWATT-HORA | 7340 CIANIZAÇÃO |
| 7305 CINEMÁTICO | 7340 IMPREGNAÇÃO DA MADEIRA PELO |
| 7306 CINEMÁTICA | PROCESSO KYANG |
| 7307 CINÉTICO | 7341 PERDA POR REVENIDO |
| 7308 ENERGIA CINÉTICA | 7341 PERDA NO FOGO |
| 7309 ATRITO CINÉTICO | 7342 GÁS LIQUEFEITO |
| 7310 CINÉTICA | 7343 LÁBIL |
| 7311 PINO CENTRAL | 7343 INSTÁVEL |
| 7311 PINO DE DIREÇÃO | 7343 VARIÁVEL |
| 7312 ÂNGULO DE INCLINAÇÃO DOS PIVÔS | 7344 LABORATÓRIO |
| 7313 FLEXÃO | 7345 JOGO DE LABORATÓRIO |
| 7313 PREGA | 7346 PREÇO DE MÃO-DE-OBRA |
| 7313 DOBRA | 7346 CUSTO DE MÃO-DE-OBRA |
| 7314 TIRA DE VOLTA | 7347 GUARNIÇÃO |
| 7315 DEFORMAÇÃO POR DOBRA | 7347 JUNTA DE LABIRINTO |
| 7316 KIP = 1000 LIBRAS = 453,59 KG | 7348 JUNÇÃO DE CORREIAS COM TIRAS DE |
| 7317 ESCÓRIA GRAFITOSA | COURO |
| 7318 AMIANTO VULCANIZADO | 7349 MANGUITO COM TIRAS DE CORREIA |
| 7318 CLINGERITE | 7350 CORREIA COSTURADA |
| 7319 FRESADORA DE CONSOLO E COLUNA | 7351 FALTA DE FUSÃO |
| 7320 JOELHO | 7352 FALTA DE HOMOGENEIDADE DO |
| 7320 ESQUADRO | MATERIAL |
| 7320 COTOVELO | 7353 ENVERNIZAR |
| 7320 ÂNGULO | 7353 LAQUEAR |
| 7320 CURVA | 7354 VERNIZ DE LACA |
| 7321 JOELHO | 7354 CHARÃO |
| 7321 OMBRO | 7355 ÁCIDO LÁCTICO |
| 7322 FRESADORA DE CONSOLO | 7356 PANELA DE FUNDIÇÃO |
| 7323 NAVALHA | 7357 ADIÇÃO EM PANELA DE FUNDIÇÃO |
| 7323 FACA | 7358 ANÁLISE NA PANELA (DE FUNDIÇÃO) |
| 7323 LÂMINA | 7359 TIJOLO REFRATÁRIO PARA PANELA DE |
| 7324 LIMA FACA | FUNDIÇÃO |
| 7325 LÂMINA | 7360 SOLIDIFICAÇÃO DO METAL NA PANELA |

1260

| | |
|---|---|
| 7361 | BICO DA PANELA |
| 7362 | FUNDIDOR |
| 7363 | BICO DA PANELA |
| 7364 | ÁCIDO LEVOTARTÁRICO |
| 7365 | LEVOGIRO |
| 7366 | RETARDAR |
| 7367 | REVESTIMENTO OU FORRO ISOLANTE |
| 7368 | DEFASAGEM |
| 7369 | REVESTIMENTO DE TUBOS |
| 7370 | COBRE DO ESTADO DE MICHIGAN |
| 7371 | LAMELA |
| 7372 | LAMELAR |
| 7373 | ESTRUTURA LAMELAR OU LAMINAR |
| 7374 | CONTEXTURA LAMELAR |
| 7375 | LAMINADO |
| 7376 | CORREIA MÚLTIPLA |
| 7376 | CORREIA DE VÁRIAS CAMADAS |
| 7377 | IMÃ DE LÂMINAS SOBREPOSTAS |
| 7378 | FRATURA LAMELOSA |
| 7379 | METAL DÚPLEX |
| 7379 | METAL ESTRATIFICADO |
| 7380 | MOLA RETANGULAR DE FOLHAS SOBREPOSTAS |
| 7381 | MOLA TRIANGULAR DE FOLHAS SOBREPOSTAS |
| 7382 | LAMINAGEM |
| 7383 | RUPTURA DE LAMINAGEM |
| 7384 | LÂMPADA |
| 7385 | LÂMPADA |
| 7386 | NEGRO DE FUMO |
| 7387 | CORTE COM MAÇARICO A OXIGÉNIO |
| 7388 | PATAMAR |
| 7388 | PLATAFORMA |
| 7389 | ACABAMENTO LANG |
| 7390 | CABO DE CABLAGEM LANG |
| 7391 | LANOLINA |
| 7392 | ANEL DE LANTERNA |
| 7392 | ANEL DE FECHAMENTO HIDRÁULICO |
| 7393 | ENGRENAGEM LANTERNA |
| 7393 | LANTERNIM |
| 7394 | LANTÂNIO |
| 7395 | SUPERPOSIÇÃO |
| 7395 | SOBREPOSIÇÃO |
| 7395 | RECOBRIMENTO |
| 7396 | JUNTA SOBREPOSTA |
| 7397 | JUNTA COM RECOBRIMENTO |
| 7398 | FLANGE DE JUNTA SOBREPOSTA |
| 7399 | RECOBRIMENTO DE VÁLVULA GAVETA |
| 7400 | JUNTA SOBREPOSTA REBITADA |
| 7401 | SOLDAGEM CONTÍNUA POR RECOBRIMENTO |
| 7402 | SOLDA POR PONTOS COM RECOBRIMENTO |
| 7403 | SOLDA SOBREPOSTA |
| 7404 | SOLDAR COM SOBREPOSIÇÃO |
| 7405 | JUNTA DE SOLDA SOBREPOSTA |
| 7406 | TUBO SOLDADO POR SOBREPOSIÇÃO |
| 7407 | ESMERILHAMENTO |
| 7407 | POLIMENTO |
| 7407 | EXPIRAÇÃO DE UMA PATENTE |
| 7409 | ÓLEO DE GRAXA |
| 7410 | MOTOR DE GRANDE POTÊNCIA A GASOLINA |
| 7411 | GRANDE INCLINAÇÃO DE CORTE EFETIVO |
| 7412 | CALDEIRA DE GRANDE VOLUME |
| 7413 | RESTOS DE DESTILAÇÃO |
| 7414 | ALDRAVA |
| 7414 | LINGÜETA |
| 7414 | TRINCO |
| 7415 | CALOR LATENTE |
| 7416 | CALOR LATENTE DE VAPORIZAÇÃO |
| 7417 | MAGNETISMO LATENTE |
| 7418 | CAMBAGEM LATERAL |
| 7419 | DESVIO LATERAL |
| 7420 | DESLOCAMENTO LATERAL |
| 7421 | DILATAÇÃO LATERAL |
| 7422 | PRESSÃO LATERAL |
| 7423 | TRANSLAÇÃO LATERAL |
| 7424 | CONTRAÇÃO LATERAL |
| 7425 | LÁTEX |
| 7426 | RIPA |
| 7427 | TORNO |
| 7428 | TORNO DE TRANSMISSÃO POR PARAFUSO DE GUIA |
| 7429 | TRELIÇA |
| 7429 | RETÍCULO CRISTALINO |
| 7430 | PARÂMETRO DO RETICULADO |
| 7430 | CONSTANTES DA REDE |
| 7431 | VIGA EM TRELIÇA |
| 7431 | VIGA TRELIÇADA |
| 7432 | PLANO RETICULAR |
| 7433 | TRELIÇA |
| 7433 | GRADEAMENTO |
| 7434 | TEORIA DE DISTORÇÃO DA REDE |
| 7435 | DIAGRAMA DE LAUE |
| 7436 | CALHA |
| 7437 | LAVA |
| 7438 | MÉTODO DE LAVE |
| 7439 | CORTADOR OU APARADOR DE GRAMA |
| 7440 | BARCAÇAS DE COLOCAÇÃO |
| 7441 | INSTALAR TUBOS OU CANOS |
| 7442 | ESTRATO |
| 7442 | CAMADA |
| 7443 | CORROSÃO POR INFILTRAÇÃO ESTRATIFICADA |

| | |
|---|---|
| 7444 | ESTRATO |
| 7445 | PLANTA |
| 7445 | TRAÇADO |
| 7445 | PLANO |
| 7445 | DESENHO |
| 7446 | LIXIVIAÇÃO |
| 7447 | CHUMBO |
| 7448 | AVANÇAR |
| 7448 | REVESTIR DE CHUMBO |
| 7449 | PAPEL COM ACETATO DE CHUMBO |
| 7450 | ACETATO DE CHUMBO |
| 7451 | LIGA DE CHUMBO |
| 7452 | FEIXE DE ARAME |
| 7453 | LIGA À BASE DE CHUMBO |
| 7454 | BANHO DE CHUMBO |
| 7455 | ACUMULADOR DE CHUMBO |
| 7456 | BRONZE AO CHUMBO |
| 7457 | REPRODUÇÃO EM CHUMBO FUNDIDO |
| 7458 | CLORETO DE CHUMBO |
| 7459 | FIO REVESTIDO DE CHUMBO |
| 7460 | CHAPA DE FERRO COBERTA DE CHUMBO |
| 7461 | DIÓXIDO DE CHUMBO |
| 7462 | FOLHA DE CHUMBO |
| 7463 | MARRETA DE CHUMBO |
| 7464 | JUNTA VEDADA COM CHUMBO PARA CANOS |
| 7465 | GALENA |
| 7465 | MINÉRIO DE CHUMBO |
| 7466 | TINTA COM BASE DE CHUMBO |
| 7467 | DESENHO A LÁPIS |
| 7468 | TUBO DE CHUMBO |
| 7469 | TUBO DE CHUMBO ESTANHADO |
| 7470 | ANEL DE CHUMBO |
| 7471 | PARAFUSO DE AVANÇO |
| 7472 | GRANALHA DE CHUMBO |
| 7473 | BALAS DE CHUMBO |
| 7473 | SULFATO DE CHUMBO |
| 7474 | TIOSSULFATO DE CHUMBO |
| 7474 | HIPOSSULFITO DE CHUMBO |
| 7475 | SOLDAGEM CLARA |
| 7476 | SOLDAGEM COM CHUMBO |
| 7477 | FIO DE CHUMBO |
| 7478 | LÁPIS |
| 7479 | COM ADIÇÃO DE CHUMBO |
| 7480 | SELO DE CHUMBO |
| 7481 | DADOS PRINCIPAIS |
| 7482 | CAPATAZ |
| 7483 | DEFASAGEM |
| 7484 | TRABALHO DE ENCANADOR |
| 7485 | MOLA DE LÂMINAS |
| 7486 | FUGA |
| 7486 | PERDA |

| | |
|---|---|
| 7486 | ESCAPAMENTO |
| 7486 | VAZAMENTO |
| 7487 | VAZAR |
| 7487 | ESCAPAR |
| 7488 | FUGA |
| 7489 | DERRAME |
| 7489 | ESCAPAMENTO |
| 7490 | CORRENTE DE DISPERSÃO |
| 7491 | PERMEABILIDADE |
| 7492 | VAZAMENTO |
| 7493 | NÃO ESTANQUE |
| 7493 | QUE VAZA |
| 7494 | COURO |
| 7495 | CORREIA DE COURO |
| 7496 | CORREIA DE COURO DE ELOS |
| 7497 | RECORTES DE COURO |
| 7498 | DIAFRAGMA DE COURO |
| 7499 | MANGUEIRA DE COURO |
| 7500 | CORREIA DE COSTURA |
| 7501 | ACOPLAMENTO FLEXÍVEL DE ELOS DE COURO |
| 7502 | GUARNIÇÃO DE COURO |
| 7502 | GAXETA DE COURO |
| 7503 | TIRA DE COURO |
| 7504 | LEDEBURITA |
| 7505 | SOTAVENTO |
| 7506 | PARAFUSO DE ROSCA À ESQUERDA |
| 5707 | DESVIO PARA A ESQUERDA |
| 7508 | ROSCA À ESQUERDA |
| 7509 | DENTES À ESQUERDA |
| 7510 | PARAFUSO DE ROSCA À ESQUERDA |
| 7511 | CABO COCHADO À ESQUERDA |
| 7512 | LADO DE ÂNGULO |
| 7513 | LEGENDA |
| 7514 | LEMNISCATA |
| 7515 | RAIOS DE LENARD |
| 7516 | COMPRIMENTO |
| 7517 | COMPRIMENTO DE ARCO |
| 7518 | COMPRIMENTO LIVRE |
| 7519 | CURSO DO PISTÃO |
| 7520 | COMPRIMENTO DO CORDÃO |
| 7521 | ALONGAMENTO DO COMPASSO |
| 7522 | LENTE |
| 7523 | EFEITO LEONARD |
| 7524 | INDICAÇÕES DE UM DESENHO |
| 7525 | NÍVEL |
| 7526 | INDICADOR DE NÍVEL |
| 7527 | SUPERFÍCIE PLANA |
| 7527 | SUPERFÍCIE DE NÍVEL |
| 7528 | EFEITO DE NIVELAÇÃO |
| 7529 | PARAFUSO DE NIVELAÇÃO |

| | | | | |
|---|---|---|---|---|
| 7530 | ALAVANCA | 7569 | VELOCIDADE DA LUZ |
| 7531 | BRAÇO DE ALAVANCA | 7570 | ÓLEO LEVE |
| 7532 | FREIO DE ALAVANCA | 7571 | ONDA LUMINOSA |
| 7533 | MACACO DE ALAVANCA | 7572 | À PROVA DE LUZ |
| 7534 | PRENSA DE ALAVANCA | 7572 | IMPERMEÁVEL À LUZ |
| 7535 | VÁLVULA DE SEGURANÇA DE ALAVANCA E CONTRAPESO | 7573 | FOGUETE LUMINOSO |
| | | 7574 | ILUMINAÇÃO |
| 7536 | FORÇA DE ALAVANCA | 7575 | PÁRA-RAIOS |
| 7536 | BRAÇO DE POTÊNCIA DE ALAVANCA | 7576 | PÁRA-RAIOS |
| 7537 | LEVIGAÇÃO | 7577 | LENHINA |
| 7538 | BANHO DE DECOMPOSIÇÃO DE ELETRÓLITO | 7578 | LINHITA |
| 7539 | PERMISSÃO | 7579 | CERA DE LINHITA |
| 7539 | LICENÇA | 7580 | LIGROÍNA |
| 7540 | LICENCIADO | 7581 | PÓLOS SEMELHANTES |
| 7540 | CONCESSIONÁRIO DE LICENÇA | 7582 | CAL |
| 7541 | DURAÇÃO | 7583 | REVESTIMENTO TIPO CAL E TITÂNIA |
| 7542 | LEVANTAR UM FARDO | 7584 | REVESTIMENTO BÁSICO |
| 7543 | VÁLVULA HORIZONTAL DE RETENÇÃO | 7585 | ÁGUA DE CAL |
| 7544 | TRAJETO ASCENDENTE DA VÁLVULA | 7586 | CALCÁRIO |
| 7545 | BOMBA ELEVATÓRIA | 7587 | LIMITE |
| 7545 | BOMBA DE RECALQUE | 7588 | LIMITE DE ELASTICIDADE |
| 7546 | CABO DE ASCENSOR | 7589 | LIMITE DE ERRO |
| 7547 | VÁLVULA DE DESLOCAMENTO VERTICAL | 7590 | LIMITE DE ELASTICIDADE PROPORCIONAL |
| 7548 | IÇADOR | 7591 | LIMITE DE SATURAÇÃO |
| 7548 | ELEVADOR | 7592 | LIMITE DE TEMPERATURA |
| 7549 | LEVANTAMENTO | 7593 | PRESSÃO LIMITE |
| 7549 | IÇAMENTO | 7594 | VALOR LIMITE |
| 7550 | CILINDRO DE LEVANTAMENTO | 7595 | LIMITES DE TOLERÂNCIA |
| 7551 | ALTURA DE LEVANTAMENTO DE GRUA | 7596 | LIMONITO |
| 7552 | GATO | 7506 | HEMATITA PARDA |
| 7552 | GANCHO DE SUSPENSÃO | 7597 | LINHA |
| 7553 | ALAVANCA DE PURGA LIVRE | 7598 | FORRAR |
| 7554 | ELETROÍMÃ DE LEVANTAMENTO | 7598 | ALINHAR |
| 7555 | PISTÃO DE LEVANTAMENTO | 7598 | REVESTIR |
| 7556 | ROSCA DE ELEVAÇÃO | 7599 | FONTE LINEAR |
| 7556 | SACA-MODELO | 7600 | INTEGRAL LINEAR |
| 7557 | TENAZ DE LEVANTAR | 7601 | LINHA DE COLIMAÇÃO |
| 7558 | MUNHÃO GIRATÓRIO COM GANCHO DE ELEVAÇÃO | 7602 | LINHA DE ENGRENAGEM |
| | | 7603 | LINHA DE FORÇA |
| 7559 | LEVANTAMENTO DE UM FARDO | 7604 | LINHA DE GRAMINHO |
| 7560 | LUZ | 7605 | LINHA DE INTERSEÇÃO |
| 7561 | SOLDAGEM DE ÂNGULO CÔNCAVO | 7606 | VIA FÉRREA |
| 7562 | CARGA INCOMPLETA | 7607 | LINHA DE EIXOS |
| 7562 | CARGA ABAIXO DA NORMAL | 7607 | LINHA DE TRANSMISSÃO |
| 7563 | CAMIONETA | 7608 | POSTE DE LINHAS |
| 7564 | METAL LEVE | 7609 | ACIONAMENTO POR EIXO DE TRANSMISSÃO |
| 7565 | TORNO PARA METAIS LEVES | 7610 | ESPECTRO DESCONTÍNUO |
| 7566 | FENÔMENO LUMINOSO | 7611 | ACELERAÇÃO LINEAR |
| 7567 | MARCHA SUAVE | 7612 | DILATAÇÃO LINEAR |
| 7568 | FONTE DE LUZ | 7613 | INTERPOLAÇÃO LINEAR |
| 7568 | FONTE LUMINOSA | 7614 | PERSPECTIVA LINEAR |

| | |
|---|---|
| 7615 | PASSO LINEAR |
| 7616 | EQUAÇÃO DE PRIMEIRO GRAU |
| 7616 | EQUAÇÃO LINEAR |
| 7617 | VELOCIDADE LINEAR |
| 7618 | PANELA GUARNECIDA |
| 7619 | LINHO |
| 7620 | FORRO |
| 7620 | CALÇO DE CHAPA |
| 7620 | REVESTIMENTO |
| 7621 | CHAPA DE AJUSTE |
| 7622 | LINHAS DE LUDERS |
| 7623 | REVESTIMENTO INTERNO |
| 7623 | FORRO |
| 7624 | REVESTIMENTO PARA MANCAIS |
| 7624 | GUARNIÇÃO DE METAL ANTIFRICÇÃO |
| 7625 | DADO DO SETOR |
| 7625 | BLOCO PORTA-MATRIZ |
| 7626 | DISTRIBUIÇÃO DE SETOR |
| 7627 | ANEL OU ELO DE CORRENTE |
| 7628 | ENCADEAMENTO |
| 7628 | ARTICULAÇÃO |
| 7629 | ENCADEADO |
| 7629 | ARTICULADO |
| 7630 | LINÓLEO |
| 7631 | ÓLEO DE LINHAÇA |
| 7632 | LÁBIO |
| 7632 | BEIÇO |
| 7632 | BORDA |
| 7632 | BICO DE PANELA |
| 7633 | BORDAS DE CORTE |
| 7634 | EXSUDAÇÕES |
| 7635 | LIQUAÇÃO |
| 7635 | SEGREGAÇÃO |
| 7636 | LIQUEFAÇÃO DE GÁS |
| 7637 | GÁS LIQUEFEITO |
| 7638 | GÁS LIQUEFEITO DE PETRÓLEO |
| 7639 | LIQUEFICÁVEL |
| 7640 | LIQUEFAZER UM GÁS |
| 7641 | LÍQUIDO |
| 7642 | LÍQUIDO |
| 7643 | AR LÍQUIDO |
| 7644 | AMONÍACO |
| 7645 | ÁCIDO CARBÔNICO LÍQUIDO |
| 7646 | CEMENTAÇÃO EM BANHO DE SAL |
| 7647 | CARGA LÍQUIDA |
| 7648 | CONTRAÇÃO NO ESTADO LÍQUIDO |
| 7649 | AMORTECIMENTO POR LÍQUIDO |
| 7650 | COMBUSTÍVEL LÍQUIDO |
| 7651 | TÊMPERA EM BANHO DE SAL |
| 7652 | CARGA HIDROSTÁTICA |
| 7653 | POLIMENTO POR JATEAMENTO DE VAPOR |

| | |
|---|---|
| 7654 | REGULADOR DE NÍVEL |
| 7655 | CONTROLADOR DE NÍVEL |
| 7656 | EXAME POR RESSUDAÇÃO |
| 7657 | ESTADO LÍQUIDO |
| 7658 | CAIXÕES ESTANQUES |
| 7659 | TRANSFERÊNCIA POR VEIA LÍQUIDA |
| 7660 | LÍQUIDOS |
| 7661 | LIQUIDUS |
| 7662 | LISTA DE PEÇAS |
| 7663 | LITARGÍRIO |
| 7664 | LÍTIO |
| 7665 | CARBONATO DE LÍTIO |
| 7666 | CLORETO DE LÍTIO |
| 7667 | FLUORETO DE LÍTIO |
| 7668 | PAPEL DE TORNASSOL |
| 7669 | LITRO |
| 7670 | CONDUTOR LIGADO |
| 7671 | CARGA VIVA |
| 7671 | CARGA MÓVEL |
| 7672 | CARGA VARIÁVEL |
| 7672 | CARGA INTERMITENTE |
| 7673 | VAPOR VIVO OU SOB PRESSÃO |
| 7674 | FÍGADO DE ENXÔFRE |
| 7675 | ENGROSSAMENTO DE TINTA |
| 7676 | LIXIVIAR |
| 7677 | LIXIVIAÇÃO |
| 7678 | TANQUE DE GNL (GÁS NATURAL LIQUEFEITO) |
| 7679 | CARGA |
| 7679 | SOLICITAÇÃO |
| 7679 | ESFORÇO EXTERNO |
| 7680 | CARREGAR |
| 7681 | FREIO DE RETENÇÃO |
| 7682 | CAPACIDADE DE CARGA |
| 7683 | DIAGRAMA DE CARGA |
| 7684 | DISTRIBUIÇÃO DE CARGA |
| 7685 | CARGA SEM CHOQUE |
| 7686 | MOTOR SOB TENSÃO |
| 7687 | CARREGADORES PARA PASTO VERDE |
| 7688 | CARREGADORES E LEVANTADORES DE SACOS E BETERRABAS |
| 7689 | CARREGADORES DE ESTERCO |
| 7690 | MATÉRIA DE CARGA |
| 7691 | GREDA |
| 7691 | BARRO |
| 7692 | TIJOLO CRU |
| 7693 | MOLDE DE BARRO |
| 7694 | ELEMENTO GALVÂNICO LOCALIZADO |
| 7695 | CORROSÃO LOCAL |
| 7696 | AQUECIMENTO PARCIAL |
| 7697 | TÊMPERA PARCIAL |

| | | | |
|---|---|---|---|
| 7698 | FECHO | 7741 | VOLTA DE UMA CURVA |
| 7698 | COMPORTA | 7742 | LAÇO DE UMA CORDA |
| 7698 | ECLUSA | 7743 | ANEL DE FIXAÇÃO |
| 7699 | TRAVAR | 7743 | COLAR DE RETENÇÃO AMOVÍVEL |
| 7699 | FIXAR | 7744 | MODELO INDIVIDUAL |
| 7700 | BLOQUEAR UMA PORCA | 7745 | PARTE DESMONTÁVEL |
| 7701 | ÂNGULO DE VIRAGEM | 7746 | FLANGE LOUCO |
| 7702 | CONTRAPORCA | 7747 | POLIA LOUCA |
| 7702 | PORCA DE PRESSÃO | 7748 | BUCHA DE POLIA LOUCA |
| 7703 | ARRUELA DE PRESSÃO | 7749 | MONTADO FROUXAMENTE NO EIXO |
| 7704 | FIXAÇÃO DE CUNHA DE APERTO | 7750 | AFROUXAR UMA CHAVETA |
| 7705 | DISPOSITIVO DE TRAVA | 7751 | AFROUXAMENTO DE UMA CHAVETA |
| 7706 | ALAVANCA DE BLOQUEIO | 7752 | CAMINHÃO |
| 7707 | BLOQUEIO DE PORCAS E PARAFUSOS | 7753 | CAMINHÃO |
| 7708 | PARAFUSO DE APERTO | 7754 | PERDA |
| 7708 | PARAFUSO FIXADOR | 7755 | PERDA DE ATRITO |
| 7709 | MECANISMO DE PARADA | 7756 | PERDA POR VAZAMENTO |
| 7710 | TRAVAMENTO | 7757 | PERDA POR CHOQUE |
| 7711 | BLOQUEIO | 7758 | PERDA DE ENERGIA |
| 7712 | LOCOMOÇÃO | 7759 | PERDA DE ALTURA (HIDRÁULICA) |
| 7713 | LOCOMOTIVA | 7760 | PERDA TÉRMICA |
| 7714 | CALDEIRA DE LOCOMOTIVA | 7761 | PERDA DE IGNIÇÃO |
| 7715 | PONTO GEOMÉTRICO | 7762 | PERDA DE POTÊNCIA |
| 7716 | LOESS | 7763 | PERDA DE PRESSÃO |
| 7717 | GRÁFICO | 7764 | PERDA DE PESO |
| 7717 | DIAGRAMA | 7765 | PERDA DE TRABALHO |
| 7717 | PERFIL | 7766 | PORÇÃO |
| 7718 | LOGARITMO | 7766 | LOTE |
| 7719 | SÉRIE LOGARÍTMICA | 7767 | CONTORNO DE PEQUENO ÂNGULO |
| 7720 | ESPIRAL LOGARÍTMICA | 7768 | LATÃO COMUM |
| 7721 | TÁBUA DE LOGARITMOS | 7769 | RODA HIDRÁULICA COM ENTRADA LATERAL |
| 7722 | CURVA LOGOCÍCLICA | 7770 | AÇO DE BAIXO TEOR DE CARBONO |
| 7722 | ESTROFÓIDE | 7771 | BAIXA FREQÜÊNCIA |
| 7723 | TRONCOS | 7772 | FORNO DE INDUÇÃO DE BAIXA |
| 7724 | CARVÃO DE CHAMA LONGA | | FREQÜÊNCIA |
| 7725 | BIMBARRA | 7773 | LIGAS FUSÍVEIS |
| 7726 | UNIÃO COM LUVA E PORCA | 7774 | BAIXA PRESSÃO |
| 7727 | FABRICAÇÃO EM GRANDE SÉRIE | 7775 | BAIXA TEMPERATURA |
| 7728 | REDE DE GRANDE DISTÂNCIA | 7776 | DESTILAÇÃO DE COMBUSTÍVEIS EM BAIXA |
| 7729 | EFEITO DE LINHA DE TRANSMISSÃO | | TEMPERATURA |
| 7730 | CADEIA DE ELOS COMPRIDOS | 7776 | CARBONIZAÇÃO A BAIXA TEMPERATURA |
| 7731 | MÁQUINA DE GRANDE CURSO | 7777 | CORRENTE DE BAIXA TENSÃO |
| 7732 | MANIVELA DE GRANDE RAIO | 7778 | BAIXA TENSÃO |
| 7733 | EIXO LONGITUDINAL | 7779 | METAL LEVE |
| 7734 | LONGARINA | 7780 | COMBUSTÍVEL INFERIOR |
| 7735 | DUCTILIDADE NO SENTIDO DAS FIBRAS | 7781 | MINÉRIO DE BAIXO TEOR |
| 7736 | PASSO LONGITUDINAL DOS REBITES | 7781 | MINÉRIO POBRE |
| 7737 | SOLDA DE COSTURA LONGITUDINAL | 7782 | CALDEIRA DE BAIXA PRESSÃO |
| 7738 | PERFIL OU SEÇÃO LONGITUDINAL | 7783 | CILINDRO DE BAIXA PRESSÃO |
| 7739 | OSCILAÇÃO LONGITUDINAL | 7784 | AQUECIMENTO POR ÁGUA QUENTE A BAIXA |
| 7740 | TUBO DE ESTRIAS LONGITUDINAIS | | PRESSÃO |

| | |
|---|---|
| 7785 | VAPOR DE BAIXA PRESSÃO |
| 7786 | MÁQUINA A VAPOR DE BAIXA PRESSÃO |
| 7787 | CALEFAÇÃO A VAPOR DE BAIXA PRESSÃO |
| 7788 | TURBINA DE BAIXA PRESSÃO |
| 7789 | MOTOR LENTO |
| 7789 | MÁQUINA DE BAIXA VELOCIDADE |
| 7790 | UNIÃO A BAIXA TEMPERATURA |
| 7791 | MOTOR A BAIXA TENSÃO |
| 7792 | PASSO DE ROSCA LOWENHERTZ |
| 7793 | ABAIXAR UMA CARGA |
| 7793 | DESCER UMA CARGA |
| 7794 | PUNÇÃO INFERIOR |
| 7794 | FUNDO DE MATRIZ |
| 7795 | GRADE INFERIOR |
| 7796 | GUIA DA FITA DE SERRA INFERIOR |
| 7797 | DESCIDA DE UM FARDO |
| 7798 | DESNIVELAMENTO DA ÁGUA |
| 7799 | JUNTA DE REBITAGEM EM LOSANGO |
| 7800 | LUBRIFICANTE |
| 7801 | LUBRIFICAR |
| 7801 | ENGRAXAR |
| 7802 | VÁLVULA DE ENCAIXE LUBRIFICADA |
| 7803 | LUBRIFICAÇÃO |
| 7804 | GRAXA PARA LUBRIFICAÇÃO |
| 7805 | ÓLEO LUBRIFICANTE |
| 7806 | QUALIDADE DE LUBRIFICAÇÃO |
| 7807 | MECHA DE LUBRIFICAÇÃO |
| 7808 | LUBRIFICAÇÃO |
| 7809 | LUBRIFICAÇÃO POR ÓLEO COMPRESSOR |
| 7810 | RANHURA OU RASGO DE LUBRIFICAÇÃO |
| 7811 | PARAFUSO LUBRIFICADOR |
| 7812 | LUBRIFICADOR |
| 7813 | VISCOSIDADE DO LUBRIFICADOR |
| 7814 | LUBRIFICAÇÃO |
| 7815 | LINHAS DE LUDERS |
| 7816 | ALÇA |
| 7816 | ORELHA |
| 7816 | ASA |
| 7816 | ARGOLA |
| 7816 | LINGÜETA |
| 7817 | ORELHA |
| 7817 | FLANGE |
| 7817 | PÉ |
| 7818 | LÚMEN |
| 7819 | LUMINESCÊNCIA |
| 7820 | CHAMA LUMINOSA |
| 7821 | FLUXO LUMINOSO |
| 7822 | INTENSIDADE LUMINOSA |
| 7823 | PONTO LUMINOSO |
| 7824 | RAIO LUMINOSO |
| 7825 | VIBRAÇÃO LUMINOSA |

| | |
|---|---|
| 7826 | CARVÃO GRAÚDO |
| 7827 | COMBUSTÍVEL A GRANEL |
| 7828 | NITRATO DE PRATA |
| 7828 | PEDRA INFERNAL |
| 7829 | LÚNULA |
| 7829 | CRESCENTE |
| 7830 | BRILHO |
| 7831 | VEDAR JUNTAS COM LUTO |
| 7832 | FLANGE DE CANO |
| 7833 | LUTÉCIO |
| 7834 | LUX |
| 7835 | LIXÍVIA |
| 7836 | MACERAR |
| 7837 | MACERAÇÃO |
| 7838 | USINABILIDADE |
| 7839 | MÁQUINA |
| 7840 | PARAFUSO MECÂNICO |
| 7841 | PREGO CORTADO À MÁQUINA |
| 7842 | CORTE MECÂNICO |
| 7842 | FRESAGEM |
| 7843 | DESENHO DE MÁQUINA |
| 7844 | ACABAMENTO MECÂNICO |
| 7845 | MÁQUINA PARA TESTES DE FLEXÃO |
| 7846 | DINAMÔMETRO |
| 7847 | FORJAMENTO MECÂNICO |
| 7848 | FUNDAÇÃO DE UMA MÁQUINA |
| 7849 | RETIFICAÇÃO MECÂNICA |
| 7850 | FEITO À MÁQUINA |
| 7851 | MOLDAGEM MECÂNICA |
| 7852 | PEÇA DE MÁQUINA |
| 7853 | ALARGADOR DE ESPIGA CÔNICA |
| 7854 | REBITAGEM MECÂNICA |
| 7855 | OFICINA MECÂNICA |
| 7856 | OFICINA |
| 7857 | AÇO PARA MÁQUINA |
| 7858 | MACHO DE ACIONAMENTO MECÂNICO |
| 7859 | MÁQUINA-FERRAMENTA |
| 7860 | TRABALHO MECÂNICO |
| 7861 | TRABALHADO |
| 7861 | USINADO |
| 7862 | MAQUINARIA |
| 7863 | FUNDIÇÃO MECÂNICA |
| 7864 | USINAGEM |
| 7865 | SUPERESPESSURA PARA USINAGEM |
| 7866 | GRAU DE USINAGEM |
| 7867 | LARGURA DE USINAGEM |
| 7868 | MAQUINISTA |
| 7868 | MECÂNICO |
| 7868 | AJUSTADOR MECÂNICO |
| 7869 | MACROESTRUTURA |
| 7870 | ATAQUE MACROGRÁFICO |

| | | | |
|---|---|---|---|
| 7871 | MACROGRAFIA | 7914 | PIRROTITA |
| 7872 | MACROSCÓPICO | 7914 | PIRITA MAGNÉTICA |
| 7873 | OBSERVAÇÃO MACROSCÓPICA | 7915 | REPULSÃO MAGNÉTICA |
| 7874 | ESFORÇO MACROSCÓPICO | 7916 | SATURAÇÃO MAGNÉTICA |
| 7875 | SEÇÃO MACROSCÓPICA | 7917 | SEPARAÇÃO MAGNÉTICA |
| 7876 | MACROSSEGREGAÇÃO | 7918 | SUSCETIBILIDADE MAGNÉTICA |
| 7877 | MAGNETOSCOPIA | 7919 | FITA MAGNÉTICA |
| 7878 | MAGNÁLIO | 7920 | PONTO CURIE |
| 7879 | ÓXIDO DE MAGNÉSIA | 7921 | MARTELO IMANTADO |
| 7879 | MAGNÉSIA | 7922 | MAGNETIZÁVEL |
| 7880 | GIOBERTITA | 7923 | MAGNETIZAÇÃO |
| 7880 | MAGNESITA | 7924 | MAGNETIZAR |
| 7881 | TIJOLO DE MAGNESITA | 7924 | IMANTAR |
| 7882 | MAGNÉSIO | 7925 | FORÇA MAGNETIZANTE |
| 7883 | BICARBONATO DE MAGNÉSIO | 7926 | MAGNETISMO |
| 7884 | CARBONATO DE MAGNÉSIA | 7927 | MAGNETITA |
| 7885 | CLORETO DE MAGNÉSIO | 7927 | FERRO OXIDULADO |
| 7886 | FLUORETO DE MAGNÉSIO | 7927 | MINÉRIO DE FERRO MAGNÉTICO |
| 7887 | HIDRÓXIDO DE MAGNÉSIO | 7928 | MAGNETIZAÇÃO |
| 7887 | HIDRATO DE MAGNÉSIO | 7928 | IMANTAÇÃO |
| 7888 | SILICATO DE MAGNÉSIO | 7929 | FORÇA MAGNETIZANTE |
| 7889 | SULFATO DE MAGNÉSIO | 7930 | MÁQUINA MAGNETOELÉTRICA |
| 7889 | SAL INGLÊS | 7931 | EXAME MAGNETOGRÁFICO |
| 7890 | LIGA À BASE DE MAGNÉSIO | 7932 | FORÇA MAGNETOMOTRIZ (FMM) |
| 7891 | ÍMÃ | 7933 | MAGNETOSTRIÇÃO |
| 7891 | MAGNETO | 7934 | EMBREAGEM MAGNÉTICA |
| 7892 | AÇO PARA ÍMÃS | 7935 | AMPLIAÇÃO |
| 7893 | MAGNÉTICO | 7936 | LENTE DE AUMENTO |
| 7894 | ANÁLISE MAGNÉTICA | 7936 | LUPA |
| 7895 | ATRAÇÃO MAGNÉTICA | 7937 | POTÊNCIA AMPLIATIVA |
| 7896 | FREIO MAGNÉTICO | 7938 | POTÊNCIA DE AMPLIAÇÃO DA LENTE |
| 7897 | CALÇOS MAGNÉTICOS DE FIXAÇÃO | 7939 | INTENSIDADE DE UMA FORÇA |
| 7898 | MANDRIS MAGNÉTICOS | 7940 | ALIMENTAÇÃO |
| 7899 | DENSIDADE MAGNÉTICA | 7940 | REDE DE ALIMENTAÇÃO |
| 7900 | ENERGIA MAGNÉTICA | 7941 | MANCAL PRINCIPAL |
| 7901 | CAMPO MAGNÉTICO | 7942 | JATO PRINCIPAL |
| 7902 | ESPECTRO MAGNÉTICO | 7943 | EIXO PRIMÁRIO OU PRINCIPAL |
| 7903 | FLUXO MAGNÉTICO | 7944 | TRANSMISSÃO PRINCIPAL |
| 7904 | FORÇA MAGNÉTICA | 7944 | EIXO DE TRANSMISSÃO |
| 7905 | INDICADOR MAGNÉTICO | 7945 | CUSTO DE MANUTENÇÃO |
| 7906 | HISTERESE MAGNÉTICA | 7946 | MANUTENÇÃO |
| 7906 | MAGNETIZAÇÃO | 7947 | EIXO MAIOR DA ELIPSE |
| 7907 | PERDAS POR HISTERESE MAGNÉTICA | 7948 | FABRICAR |
| 7907 | PERDAS DE MAGNETIZAÇÃO | 7948 | MANUFATURAR |
| 7908 | INDUÇÃO MAGNÉTICA | 7949 | INTERRUPTOR AUTOMÁTICO |
| 7909 | AGULHA MAGNÉTICA | 7950 | ESTABELECER O CONTATO |
| 7909 | AGULHA IMANTADA | 7950 | LIGAR |
| 7910 | MAGNETOSCOPIA | 7951 | AFLORAR |
| 7911 | PERMEABILIDADE MAGNÉTICA | 7952 | MALEABILIZAR A FUNDIÇÃO |
| 7912 | DISCOS MAGNÉTICOS | 7953 | VEDAR |
| 7913 | PÓLO MAGNÉTICO | 7953 | IMPERMEABILIZAR |

| | |
|---|---|
| 7954 | VEDAÇÃO |
| 7954 | IMPERMEABILIZAÇÃO |
| 7955 | ROSCA EXTERNA |
| 7956 | CALIBRE MACHO |
| 7957 | ENCAIXE MACHO-FÊMEA |
| 7958 | MALEABILIDADE |
| 7959 | FERRO FUNDIDO MALEÁVEL |
| 7960 | MALEÁVEL |
| 7961 | MALEABILIZAÇÃO |
| 7962 | MACHO DE MADEIRA |
| 7963 | PORTINHOLA OU JANELA DE INSPEÇÃO |
| 7964 | MANDRIL |
| 7964 | ESPIGA |
| 7965 | CRINA DE CAVALO |
| 7966 | MANGANÊS |
| 7967 | BRONZE-MANGANÊS |
| 7968 | AÇO-MANGANÊS |
| 7969 | AÇO ACALMADO AO MANGANÊS |
| 7970 | SESQUIÓXIDO DE MANGANÊS |
| 7971 | MANGANÍFERO |
| 7972 | CLORETO DE MANGANÊS |
| 7973 | PROTÓXIDO DE MANGANÊS |
| 7974 | SULFATO DE MANGANÊS |
| 7975 | RODA DENTADA INTERROMPIDA |
| 7976 | ABERTURA DE INSPEÇÃO |
| 7977 | TAMPA DE ABERTURA DE INSPEÇÃO |
| 7978 | UNIÃO DA ABERTURA DE INSPEÇÃO |
| 7979 | COLETOR |
| 7980 | MANILHA |
| 7981 | CABO DE CÂNHAMO |
| 7982 | MANIPULADOR |
| 7982 | MANIPULAÇÃO |
| 7983 | TUBO MANNESMANN |
| 7984 | RENDIMENTO MANOMÉTRICO |
| 7985 | MANTISSA |
| 7986 | CAPA |
| 7986 | CAMISA |
| 7987 | ENTRADA MANUAL DE DADOS |
| 7988 | SOLDA MANUAL |
| 7989 | MANUFATURA |
| 7989 | FABRICAÇÃO |
| 7989 | CONSTRUÇÃO |
| 7990 | FABRICAÇÃO DE AGLOMERADOS |
| 7991 | FABRICAÇÃO DE COQUE |
| 7992 | INDUSTRIAL |
| 7992 | FABRICANTE |
| 7993 | ESTADO DESCRITIVO DO CONSTRUTOR |
| 7994 | GAMA DE FABRICAÇÃO |
| 7994 | PROGRAMA DE FABRICAÇÃO |
| 7995 | ESPALHADOR DE ADUBO |
| 7996 | MANUSCRITO |
| 7997 | REGISTRO DE INSPEÇÃO |
| 7998 | CAIXILHO DE REGISTRO DE INSPEÇÃO |
| 7999 | PENA DE DESENHO |
| 8000 | AÇOS "MARAGING" |
| 8001 | MÁRMORE |
| 8002 | CHAPA LATERAL |
| 8003 | CALDEIRA NAVAL |
| 8004 | CADEIAS DE MARINHA |
| 8005 | MOTOR DE NAVIO |
| 8006 | COLA MARINHA |
| 8007 | CABEÇA DE BIELA DE CAIXA ABERTA |
| 8008 | ASSINALAR |
| 8008 | MARCAR |
| 8009 | GRAU DE ESCALA |
| 8010 | TRAÇAR |
| 8010 | RISCAR |
| 8011 | FAZER MARCA |
| 8012 | MARCA |
| 8013 | MARCADOR |
| 8014 | CHUMBO DOCE |
| 8015 | MARCAÇÃO |
| 8016 | GRAMINHO |
| 8017 | TRAÇADO |
| 8018 | TRAÇADO DE CHAPAS |
| 8019 | MARGA |
| 8020 | SABÃO DE MARSELHA |
| 8021 | MARTÊMPERA |
| 8022 | MARTENSITA |
| 8023 | AÇO SIEMENS-MARTIN |
| 8024 | SOLDA DE PONTOS MÚLTIPLOS EM UMA SÓ OPERAÇÃO |
| 8025 | ALVENARIA |
| 8026 | MASSA |
| 8027 | EFEITO DE MASSA |
| 8028 | PRODUÇÃO EM SÉRIE |
| 8029 | ESPECTRÔMETRO DE MASSA |
| 8030 | COEFICIENTE DE ABSORÇÃO MÁSSICA |
| 8031 | PROTÓXIDO DE CHUMBO |
| 8031 | MASSICOTE |
| 8032 | PRINCIPAL |
| 8032 | MESTRE |
| 8033 | PORTA-PUNÇÕES |
| 8034 | MODELO PADRÃO |
| 8035 | CONTRA-CALIBRE |
| 8035 | CALIBRE PADRÃO |
| 8036 | JOGO DE MEDIDAS PARA CONTRASTE |
| 8037 | CILINDRO PRINCIPAL |
| 8038 | MÁSTIQUE |
| 8039 | MÁSTIQUE EM GRÃOS |
| 8040 | MASÚRIO |
| 8041 | ÓLEO PESADO |

| | |
|---|---|
| 8042 | AJUSTAR |
| 8042 | COMBINAR |
| 8042 | EQUIPARAR |
| 8043 | LINHA DE BASE |
| 8044 | PLACA-MODELO |
| 8045 | AJUSTAR AS PLACAS |
| 8046 | AJUSTE DE PLACAS |
| 8047 | CANTIL DE CARPINTEIRO |
| 8048 | AJUDANTE |
| 8049 | PREÇO DE MATERIAL |
| 8049 | PREÇO DE CONSUMO |
| 8050 | MATERIAL DE CONSTRUÇÃO |
| 8051 | INSTRUMENTOS DE MATEMÁTICA |
| 8052 | TABUADA |
| 8053 | MATEMÁTICA |
| 8054 | CONTRA-FLANGE |
| 8055 | MATRIZ |
| 8056 | LATÃO DE BASE DE LINOTIPO |
| 8057 | METAL MATRIZ |
| 8057 | METAL DE BASE |
| 8058 | MATE |
| 8059 | BANHO DE ACABAMENTO MATE |
| 8060 | SUPERFÍCIE MATE OU FOSCA |
| 8061 | SUBSTÂNCIA EM DISSOLUÇÃO |
| 8062 | SUBSTÂNCIAS EM SUSPENSÃO |
| 8063 | TERMÔMETRO DE MÁXIMA E MÍNIMA |
| 8064 | FLECHA MÁXIMA |
| 8065 | CARGA MÁXIMA |
| 8066 | RENDIMENTO MÁXIMO |
| 8066 | POTÊNCIA MÁXIMA |
| 8067 | VELOCIDADE MÁXIMA |
| 8068 | TEMPERATURA MÁXIMA |
| 8069 | VALOR MÁXIMO |
| 8070 | PESO MÁXIMO |
| 8071 | TESTE DE MCQUAID-EHN |
| 8072 | MÉDIO |
| 8073 | VALOR MÉDIO |
| 8074 | DESVIO MÉDIO |
| 8075 | PRESSÃO MÉDIA |
| 8076 | CALOR ESPECÍFICO MÉDIO |
| 8077 | MEDIDA |
| 8078 | MEDIR |
| 8079 | MEDIDA DE CAPACIDADE |
| 8080 | MEDIDA LINEAR |
| 8081 | MEDIDA DE SUPERFÍCIE |
| 8082 | MEDIDA DE VOLUME |
| 8083 | MEDIR A POTÊNCIA DO FREIO |
| 8084 | MEDIR COM O PLANÍMETRO |
| 8085 | RÉGUA GRADUADA |
| 8086 | MEDIDA DE TEMPERATURA |
| 8087 | MEDIDA COM O PLANÍMETRO |

| | |
|---|---|
| 8088 | MEDIÇÃO |
| 8089 | ERRO DE MEDIDA |
| 8090 | INSTRUMENTO DE MEDIDA |
| 8091 | PONTO DE MEDIDA |
| 8092 | TRENA |
| 8092 | FITA MÉTRICA |
| 8093 | MECÂNICO |
| 8094 | RENDIMENTO MECÂNICO |
| 8095 | MANDRIS MECÂNICOS |
| 8096 | LIMPEZA MECÂNICA |
| 8097 | COMPARADOR MECÂNICO |
| 8098 | TIRAGEM ARTIFICIAL |
| 8099 | DESENHO INDUSTRIAL |
| 8100 | RENDIMENTO MECÂNICO |
| 8101 | ENERGIA MECÂNICA |
| 8102 | ENGENHEIRO MECÂNICO |
| 8103 | CONSTRUÇÃO MECÂNICA |
| 8103 | ENGENHARIA MECÂNICA |
| 8104 | EQUIVALENTE MECÂNICO DO CALOR |
| 8105 | LUBRIFICADOR DE PRESSÃO MECÂNICA |
| 8106 | MANUTENÇÃO MECÂNICA |
| 8107 | METALURGIA MECÂNICA |
| 8108 | ELETRODEPOSIÇÃO COM MANEJO MECÂNICO |
| 8109 | CARACTERÍSTICAS OU PROPRIEDADES MECÂNICAS |
| 8110 | CARREGADOR MECÂNICO (FORNALHA) |
| 8111 | AQUECIMENTO MECÂNICO |
| 8112 | TESTAGEM MECÂNICA |
| 8113 | MACLA MECÂNICA |
| 8114 | VIBRAÇÃO MECÂNICA |
| 8115 | SOLDA MECÂNICA |
| 8116 | PASTA MECÂNICA DE MADEIRA |
| 8117 | TRABALHO MECÂNICO |
| 8118 | COMPARADOR ÓPTICO-MECÂNICO |
| 8119 | ACIONADO MECANICAMENTE |
| 8120 | VÁLVULA ACIONADA |
| 8121 | MECÂNICA |
| 8122 | MECANISMO |
| 8122 | MOVIMENTO |
| 8123 | DIVISÃO DE UMA LINHA EM RAZÃO MÉDIA E EXTREMA |
| 8124 | LINHA MEDIANA |
| 8125 | ÓLEO MÉDIO |
| 8126 | CALDEIRA DE CAPACIDADE MÉDIA |
| 8127 | CALDEIRA DE PRESSÃO MÉDIA |
| 8128 | RAIO MEDULAR |
| 8129 | MEGADINA |
| 8130 | MEGAVOLT |
| 8131 | MEGERG |
| 8132 | MEGOHM |

| | | | |
|---|---|---|---|
| 8133 | BASALTITE | 8174 | ARCO METÁLICO |
| 8133 | MELÁFIRO | 8175 | CORTE A ARCO METÁLICO |
| 8134 | FUSÃO | 8176 | SOLDA A ARCO ELÉTRICO |
| 8135 | FUNDIR | 8177 | CABO BLINDADO |
| 8135 | DERRETER | 8177 | CABO DE CAPA METÁLICA |
| 8136 | DERRETIMENTO | 8178 | MÁQUINA DE CORTAR METAL |
| 8136 | FUSÃO | 8179 | RELAÇÃO DE DISTRIBUIÇÃO DO METAL |
| 8137 | BANHO DE FUSÃO | 8180 | ELÉTRODO METÁLICO |
| 8138 | FORNO DE FUSÃO | 8181 | LÂMPADA DE FILAMENTO METÁLICO |
| 8139 | GELO EM FUSÃO | 8182 | NÉVOA METÁLICA |
| 8140 | PERDAS DE FUSÃO | 8183 | BRONZE DE MOEDAS |
| 8141 | PONTO DE FUSÃO | 8184 | FOLHA METÁLICA |
| 8142 | CADINHO | 8185 | METAL PULVERIZADO |
| 8143 | INTERVALO DE FUSÃO | 8186 | SERROTE PARA METAL |
| 8144 | VELOCIDADE DE FUSÃO | 8187 | PARAFUSO PARA METAL |
| 8145 | COMPONENTE | 8188 | SAPATA METÁLICA |
| 8145 | ELEMENTO | 8189 | REPUXAMENTO DE METAL |
| 8146 | MEMÓRIA | 8190 | METALIZAÇÃO A JATO |
| 8147 | LENTE CONVEXO-CÔNCAVA | 8191 | TORNO DE METAIS |
| 8148 | FERRO COMERCIAL | 8192 | USINAGEM DE METAIS |
| 8149 | PERFIS COMERCIAIS | 8193 | SERRA PARA RANHURAR METAIS |
| 8150 | BARÔMETRO DE MERCÚRIO | 8194 | REVESTIMENTO METÁLICO |
| 8151 | MANÔMETRO DE MERCÚRIO | 8195 | LUSTRO METÁLICO |
| 8152 | TERMÔMETRO DE MERCÚRIO | 8196 | GUARNIÇÃO METÁLICA |
| 8153 | CLORETO DE MERCÚRIO | 8197 | METALÍFERO |
| 8153 | BICLORETO DE MERCÚRIO | 8198 | MINA DE METAL |
| 8154 | FULMINATO DE MERCÚRIO | 8199 | PAPEL METALIZADO |
| 8155 | IODETO DE MERCÚRIO | 8200 | REVESTIMENTO METALIZADO |
| 8156 | NITRATO DE MERCÚRIO | 8201 | METALIZAÇÃO |
| 8156 | AZOTATO MERCÚRICO | 8202 | METALOGRÁFICO |
| 8157 | ÓXIDO DE MERCÚRIO | 8203 | METALOGRAFIA |
| 8158 | SULFATO MERCÚRICO | 8204 | ATAQUE METALOGRÁFICO |
| 8159 | MURIATO DE MERCÚRIO | 8205 | METALÓIDE |
| 8159 | CALOMELANOS | 8206 | METALÚRGICO |
| 8160 | NITRATO MERCURIOSO | 8207 | FORNO METALÚRGICO |
| 8161 | ÓXIDO MERCURIOSO | 8208 | METALURGIA |
| 8162 | SULFATO MERCURIOSO | 8209 | SIDERURGIA |
| 8163 | BOMBA A MERCÚRIO | 8210 | ÁCIDO METAFOSFÓRICO |
| 8164 | RETIFICADOR (A VAPOR) DE MERCÚRIO | 8211 | ÁCIDO METASSILÍCICO |
| 8165 | CÉLULA A MERCÚRIO | 8212 | METAESTÁVEL |
| 8166 | CONTADOR A MERCÚRIO | 8213 | ÁGUA METEÓRICA |
| 8167 | LÂMPADA A VAPOR DE MERCÚRIO | 8214 | CONTADOR |
| 8168 | MERCÚRIO | 8215 | METANO |
| 8169 | MALHA | 8215 | GRISU |
| 8170 | MALHA DE PENEIRA | 8215 | GÁS DE PÂNTANOS |
| 8170 | MALHA DE TELA METÁLICA | 8216 | MÉTODO |
| 8171 | ENGATADO | 8217 | MÉTODO DE ENGRENAGEM |
| 8171 | ENGRENADO | 8218 | MÉTODO DE FABRICAÇÃO |
| 8171 | ACOPLADO | 8219 | MÉTODO DE MEDIDA |
| 8172 | METACENTRO | 8220 | MÉTODO DE TRABALHO |
| 8173 | METAL | 8220 | MODO DE OPERAÇÃO |

| | | | |
|---|---|---|---|
| 8221 | CLORETO DE METILO | 8267 | INTERMEDIÁRIOS DE MINERAÇÃO |
| 8222 | ÉTER METÍLICO | 8268 | MIGRAÇÃO |
| 8223 | METILORANGE | 8269 | ABRASIVO DOCE OU BRANDO |
| 8223 | ALARANJADO DE METILO | 8270 | AÇO DOCE |
| 8224 | ÁLCOOL DESNATURADO | 8270 | AÇO DE BAIXO TEOR DE CARBONO |
| 8225 | METRO | 8271 | MÍLDIO |
| 8226 | METRO RETO | 8271 | MOFO |
| 8227 | MEDIDA MÉTRICA | 8271 | BOLOR |
| 8228 | MICRÔMETRO MÉTRICO | 8272 | MILHA |
| 8229 | SISTEMA MÉTRICO | 8273 | VIDRO OPACO |
| 8230 | CALIBRE DE TAMPA DE CONE MÉTRICO | 8274 | LEITE DE CAL |
| 8231 | MICA | 8275 | MÁQUINA ORDENHAR |
| 8232 | MICAXISTO | 8276 | ESMERILHAR |
| 8233 | MICANITE | 8276 | FRESAR |
| 8234 | MICROFISSURAS | 8276 | POLIR |
| 8235 | MICROSSEGREGAÇÃO | 8277 | MARTELAR CABEÇA DE PARAFUSO |
| 8236 | CONTRAPONTA MICROMÉTRICA | 8278 | ACABAMENTO NO LAMINADOR |
| 8237 | MICROAMPERÔMETRO | 8279 | CAREPA DE LAMINAÇÃO |
| 8238 | MICROAMPÈRE | 8280 | PORCA SERRILHADA |
| 8239 | MICRORRAIO | 8281 | CABEÇA DE PARAFUSO ESTRIADA |
| 8240 | BARRA DE ESCAREAÇÃO MICROMÉTRICA | 8282 | ÍNDICES DE MILLER |
| 8241 | FOSFATO DE SÓDIO E AMÔNIO | 8283 | MILIAMPERÔMETRO |
| 8241 | SAL DE FÓSFORO | 8284 | MILIAMPÈRE |
| 8241 | SAL MICROCÓSMICO | 8285 | MILIGRAMA |
| 8242 | MICROFARAD | 8286 | MILÍMETRO |
| 8243 | MICROGRÁFICO | 8287 | FRESAGEM |
| 8244 | MICROGRAFIA | 8287 | RECARTILHAMENTO |
| 8245 | MICRODUREZA | 8288 | FRESAGEM DE CABEÇA DE PARAFUSO |
| 8246 | TESTE DE MICRODUREZA | 8289 | FRESA |
| 8246 | ENSAIO DE MICRODUREZA | 8290 | PASSADORES DE FRESAGEM |
| 8247 | MICROHM | 8290 | MESAS DE FIXAÇÃO |
| 8248 | MICROPOLEGADA | 8291 | FRESADORA |
| 8249 | MICRÔMETRO | 8292 | FRESADOR |
| 8250 | PORTA-MICRÔMETRO | 8293 | OFICINA DE FRESAGEM |
| 8251 | CALIBRES MICROMÉTRICOS | 8294 | MILIVOLT |
| 8252 | MICRÔMETRO DE PROFUNDIDADE | 8295 | COMBINAÇÃO DE MOINHOS |
| 8253 | ESCALA MICROMÉTRICA | 8296 | MOINHOS DE ESMAGAR E MOER |
| 8254 | MICRÔMETRO OCULAR | 8297 | MOINHOS E TRITURADORES |
| 8255 | PARAFUSO MICROMÉTRICO | 8298 | MÓ |
| 8256 | CALIBRADOR MICROMÉTRICO | 8298 | GALGA |
| 8257 | MÍCRON | 8299 | PEDRA MOLAR |
| 8258 | MICROFOTOGRAFIA | 8300 | JAZIDA |
| 8259 | MICROSCÓPIO | 8300 | MINA |
| 8260 | EXAME MICROSCÓPICO | 8301 | MINERAL |
| 8261 | CORPO DE PROVA PARA MICROSCOPIA | 8302 | ÁCIDO INORGÂNICO |
| 8262 | MICROESTRUTURA | 8302 | ÁCIDO MINERAL |
| 8263 | MICRÓTOMO | 8303 | JAZIDA DE MINERAL |
| 8264 | MICROVOLT | 8304 | ÓLEO MINERAL |
| 8265 | POSIÇÃO INTERMÉDIA | 8305 | MINETA |
| 8266 | LIMA MEIO-MURÇA | 8305 | FERRO OOLÍTICO |
| 8267 | FRAGMENTOS MIÚDOS | 8306 | TEMPERATURA MÍNIMA |

| | | | |
|---|---|---|---|
| 8307 | VALOR MÍNIMO | 8352 | MOLDE |
| 8308 | LIMITE ELÁSTICO MÍNIMO GARANTIDO | 8352 | COQUILHA |
| 8309 | COMPRIMENTO DE ONDA MÍNIMO | 8352 | LINGOTEIRA |
| 8310 | PESO MÍNIMO | 8353 | CAVIDADE DO MOLDE |
| 8311 | EXPLORAÇÃO DE MINAS | 8354 | CAIXA DE REFORÇO DE MOLDAGEM |
| 8311 | MINERAÇÃO | 8355 | SUSPENSÃO AQUOSA PARA FACEAMENTO |
| 8312 | ENGENHEIRO DE MINAS | | DO MOLDE |
| 8313 | EIXO MENOR DE ELIPSE | 8356 | PESO DE CARGA DO MOLDE |
| 8314 | DIÂMETRO INTERNO | 8357 | ESCALA DE CONTRAÇÃO |
| 8315 | DETERMINANTE MENOR | 8358 | MÁQUINA DE MOLDAR |
| 8316 | MINUENDO | 8359 | ATRAÇÃO MOLECULAR |
| 8317 | GROSSURA MÍNIMA DO GRÃO | 8360 | FORÇA MOLECULAR |
| 8318 | CALEFAÇÃO POR VAPOR A PRESSÃO | 8361 | ESTRUTURA MOLECULAR |
| | INFERIOR À ATMOSFÉRICA | 8362 | VOLUME MOLECULAR |
| 8319 | FUNÇÃO AUXILIAR | 8363 | PESO MOLECULAR |
| 8320 | LIGA DE CÉRIO, LANTÁNIO E DIDÍMIO | 8364 | MOLÉCULA |
| 8320 | "MISCH METAL" | 8365 | METAL EM FUSÃO |
| 8321 | ENCHIMENTO INCOMPLETO DO MOLDE | 8366 | MOLIBDENITA |
| 8321 | FUNDIÇÃO FALHA | 8367 | MOLIBDÊNIO |
| 8322 | PEÇA FORJADA MAL APARADA | 8368 | AÇO-MOLIBDÊNIO |
| 8323 | ENGRENAGENS CÔNICAS | 8369 | AÇO MOLÍBDICO |
| 8324 | JUNTA DE MEIA-ESQUADRIA | 8370 | MOMENTO DE UMA FORÇA |
| 8325 | SUTA | 8371 | MOMENTO DE ATRITO |
| 8326 | MEIA-ESQUADRIA | 8372 | MOMENTO DE INÉRCIA |
| 8327 | MISTURA | 8373 | MOMENTO DA QUANTIDADE DE MOVIMENTO |
| 8328 | MISTURAR | 8374 | MOMENTO DE RESISTÊNCIA |
| 8329 | CRISTAIS MISTOS | 8375 | MOMENTO DE ESTABILIDADE |
| 8330 | TURBINA DE ADMISSÃO MISTA | 8376 | MOMENTO |
| 8331 | MISTURADOR | 8376 | QUANTIDADE DE MOVIMENTO |
| 8332 | MISTURADORES | 8377 | MONATÔMICO |
| 8333 | PANELA DE MISTURAR | 8378 | GÁS MOND |
| 8334 | MISTURADORA | 8379 | METAL MONEL |
| 8335 | VÁLVULA MISTURADORA | 8380 | RESFRIADOR DO ORIFÍCIO DE ESCÓRIA |
| 8336 | MISTURA | 8381 | PAREDE DA GARGANTA DO FORNO |
| 8337 | MISTURA DE AR E COMBUSTÍVEL | 8382 | EMISSIVIDADE MONOCROMÁTICA |
| 8338 | "MODEM" (MODULADOR-DESMODULADOR) | 8383 | RADIAÇÃO MONOCROMÁTICA |
| 8339 | MÓDULO | 8384 | CRISTAL MONOCLÍNICO |
| 8340 | COEFICIENTE DE RESISTÊNCIA AO | 8385 | REVESTIMENTO MONOLÍTICO |
| | ALONGAMENTO | 8386 | REAÇÃO MONOTECTÓIDE |
| 8340 | MEDIDA DE ELASTICIDADE | 8387 | MONOTRON |
| 8341 | MÓDULO DE ELASTICIDADE | 8388 | MONOTRÓPICO |
| 8342 | MÓDULO DE CISALHAMENTO | 8389 | MONTA CALDO |
| 8343 | MÓDULO DE RUPTURA | 8390 | AMARRA |
| 8344 | ARADO DE SUBSOLO | 8390 | ATADOURO |
| 8345 | GRAMPO DE MOHR | 8391 | CORROSIVO |
| 8346 | ESCALA DE MOHS | 8391 | MORDENTE |
| 8347 | UMEDECER | 8392 | CALIBRE DE CONE MORSE |
| 8348 | UMEDECIMENTO | 8393 | CALIBRE DE CONICIDADE NORMAL |
| 8349 | À PROVA DE UMIDADE | 8394 | ARGAMASSA |
| 8350 | CONDUTIVIDADE MOLECULAR | 8395 | ALMOFARIZ |
| 8351 | RESISTÊNCIA MOLECULAR | 8396 | GRAL |

| | | | |
|---|---|---|---|
| 8397 | CARRETA DE ARGAMASSA | 8440 | INTUMESCÊNCIA |
| 8398 | BEDAME | 8441 | BARRA DE FERRO CRU |
| 8398 | FORMÃO DE ENTALHAR | 8442 | BOCA DE PURGA |
| 8399 | GRAMINHO DE MORTAGEM | 8443 | PÁRA-LAMA |
| 8400 | RODA DE DENTES DE MADEIRA | 8444 | LAMA |
| 8401 | ENCAIXE | 8444 | LODO |
| 8401 | MALHETE | 8445 | LAMACENTO |
| 8401 | MORTAGEM | 8446 | ÁGUA LODOSA |
| 8402 | MÁQUINA DE MALHETAR | 8447 | FORNO DE MUFLA |
| 8403 | ESTRUTURA MOSAICA | 8447 | MUFLA |
| 8404 | ZINCO GRANULADO | 8448 | SILENCIOSO |
| 8405 | LICOR PRINCIPAL | 8448 | ABAFADOR |
| 8405 | ÁGUA-MÃE | 8449 | MISTURADORA |
| 8406 | MOVIMENTO | 8450 | OPERAÇÃO DE TRITURAR AREIA |
| 8407 | MOVIMENTO DE TRANSLAÇÃO | 8451 | MISTURADORA DE AREIA |
| 8408 | AGENTE MOTOR | 8452 | INJETOR DE ORIFÍCIOS |
| 8409 | FORÇA MOTRIZ | 8453 | MOTOR POLICILÍNDRICO |
| 8410 | ÔNIBUS ELÉTRICO | 8454 | FREIO A DISCO |
| 8411 | AUTOMÓVEL | 8455 | SOLDAGEM DE MÚLTIPLOS PASSOS |
| 8412 | ÔNIBUS | 8456 | MÁQUINA DE UTILIZAÇÃO MÚLTIPLA |
| 8413 | MOTOR-GERADOR | 8457 | MÁQUINA DE PERFILAR DE ROLOS MÚLTIPLOS |
| 8414 | CAMINHÃO INDUSTRIAL | | |
| 8415 | ÓLEO DE MOTOR | 8458 | CABEÇOTE DE PUA DE BROCAS MÚLTIPLAS |
| 8416 | VÁLVULA DE GAVETA MOTORIZADA | 8459 | CABEÇOTE DE BROCAS MÚLTIPLAS |
| 8417 | VÁLVULA MOTORIZADA | 8460 | PERFURADORA DE BROCAS MÚLTIPLAS EM LINHA |
| 8418 | MOTOR DE ARRANQUE | | |
| 8419 | REGULAGEM DO MOTOR | 8461 | PRENSAS DE FASES MÚLTIPLAS |
| 8420 | FERRO FUNDIDO MOSQUEADO | 8462 | CORRENTE POLIFÁSICA |
| 8421 | MOSQUEAGEM | 8463 | CORREIA MÚLTIPLA |
| 8422 | CALIBRE PARA PERFIS | 8464 | SOLDAGEM POR PONTOS MÚLTIPLOS |
| 8422 | LINGOTEIRA | 8465 | INTEGRAL MÚLTIPLA |
| 8423 | MOLDE | 8466 | MOLDE MÚLTIPLO |
| 8424 | MOLDAR | 8467 | REGISTRO DE DISTRIBUIÇÃO |
| 8425 | TIJOLO PERFILADO | 8468 | SOLDAGEM POR RESSALTOS MÚLTIPLOS |
| 8426 | CONCRETO MOLDADO | 8469 | TORNO AUTOMÁTICO DE BROCAS MÚLTIPLAS |
| 8427 | MOLDADOR | | |
| 8427 | FUNDIDOR | 8470 | FURADEIRA DE BROCAS MÚLTIPLAS |
| 8428 | MOLDAGEM | 8471 | FRESADORA MÚLTIPLA |
| 8429 | MÁQUINA DE MOLDAR | 8472 | SISTEMA MÚLTIPLO |
| 8430 | AREIA DE MOLDAGEM | 8473 | TRANSMISSÃO POR POLIA DE GARGANTAS MÚLTIPLAS |
| 8430 | AREIA DE FUNDIÇÃO | | |
| 8431 | FAZER UM DECALQUE | 8474 | PARAFUSO DE ROSCAS MÚLTIPLAS |
| 8432 | SUSPENSO POR PIVÔ | 8475 | VÁLVULA ESCALONADA |
| 8433 | MAÇARICO DE BOCA | 8475 | VÁLVULA MÚLTIPLA |
| 8434 | BOCA DE PLAINA | 8476 | VÁLVULA MÚLTIPLA |
| 8435 | POLIA MÓVEL | 8477 | MÁQUINA DE EXPANSÃO MÚLTIPLA |
| 8436 | PRATO MÓVEL | 8477 | MÁQUINA COMPOUND |
| 8437 | MORDAÇA MÓVEL DE TORNO | 8478 | EIXO DE VÁRIAS MANIVELAS |
| 8438 | MOVIMENTO | 8479 | MULTIPLICANDO |
| 8439 | SEGADORAS MONTADAS E ARRASTADAS POR TRATOR | 8480 | MULTIPLICAÇÃO |
| | | 8481 | REPRODUÇÃO |

| | | | | |
|---|---|---|---|---|
| 8482 | MULTIPLICADOR | 8519 | LIMA LANCETEIRA |
| 8483 | MULTIPLICAR | 8520 | LUBRIFICADOR DE AGULHA |
| 8484 | REPRODUZIR | 8521 | PONTIAGUDO |
| 8484 | MULTIPLICAR | 8522 | VÁLVULA DE AGULHA |
| 8485 | TORNO MÚLTIPLO DE ACABAMENTO | 8523 | AÇO BORETADO |
| 8486 | METAL PATENTE | 8523 | AÇO DE ESTRUTURA ACICULAR |
| 8486 | METAL MUNTZ | 8524 | NEGATIVO (DE FOTOGRAFIA) |
| 8487 | CALCÁRIO DE COQUILHA | 8525 | ACELERAÇÃO NEGATIVA |
| 8488 | ESTÁGIO PASTOSO | 8525 | RETARDAMENTO |
| 8489 | INDUÇÃO MÚTUA | 8526 | ELETRICIDADE NEGATIVA |
| 8490 | CONGLOMERADO | 8527 | TÊMPERA NEGATIVA |
| 8491 | PREGO | 8528 | CALOR DE DECOMPOSIÇÃO |
| 8491 | CRAVO | 8529 | MATRIZ NEGATIVA |
| 8492 | CRAVAR | 8530 | PLACA NEGATIVA |
| 8492 | PREGAR | 8531 | PÓLO NEGATIVO |
| 8493 | NAFTA | 8532 | SINAL NEGATIVO |
| 8494 | NAFTALINA | 8533 | NEODÍMIO |
| 8495 | NAFTOL | 8534 | NEODÍMIO |
| 8496 | FRESA CIRCULAR | 8535 | NÉON |
| 8496 | FRESA A DISCO | 8536 | LÂMPADA DE NÉON |
| 8497 | NASCENTE | 8537 | ANÁLISE NEFELOMÉTRICA |
| 8498 | LIGA NATURAL | 8538 | FEIXE DE TUBOS |
| 8499 | ABRASIVO NATURAL | 8539 | ESTRUTURA CRISTALINA RETICULAR |
| 8500 | ENVELHECIMENTO NATURAL OU ESPONTÂNEO | 8540 | ESTRIAS DE NEUMANN |
| | | 8541 | EIXO NEUTRO |
| 8501 | TIRAGEM NATURAL | 8542 | FIBRA NEUTRA |
| 8502 | EVAPORAÇÃO NATURAL | 8543 | CHAMA NEUTRA |
| 8503 | COMBUSTÍVEL NATURAL | 8544 | CAMADA DE FIBRAS INVARIÁVEIS |
| 8504 | GÁS NATURAL | 8545 | LINHA NEUTRA |
| 8505 | ILUMINAÇÃO NATURAL | 8546 | SAL NEUTRO |
| 8506 | ÍMÃ NATURAL | 8547 | ZONA NEUTRA |
| 8506 | MAGNETO NATURAL | 8548 | NEUTRALIZAÇÃO |
| 8507 | PEDRA NATURAL | 8549 | NEUTRALIZAR |
| 8508 | VENTILAÇÃO NATURAL | 8550 | LINHO DA NOVA ZELÂNDIA |
| 8509 | LOGARITMO NATURAL | 8551 | BICO |
| 8510 | CONSTRUÇÃO NAVAL | 8551 | PONTA AGUDA |
| 8511 | LATÃO NAVAL | 8551 | COMPACTADO DE PÓ ACABADO |
| 8511 | LATÃO ALFA-BETA | 8552 | CORTE IRREGULAR |
| 8512 | COLO | 8553 | MÁQUINA DE EFETUAR CORTE IRREGULAR |
| 8512 | PESCOÇO | 8554 | ENTALHAR |
| 8512 | GARGANTA | 8555 | ENSAIO DE RUPTURA A ENTALHE |
| 8513 | PINO DE SUPORTE DE EIXO | 8556 | NÍQUEL |
| 8514 | BOCAL DE COLAR | 8557 | LIGA DE NÍQUEL |
| 8515 | REDUÇÃO | 8558 | SULFATO DUPLO DE NÍQUEL E AMONÍACO |
| 8515 | ESTRICÇÃO | 8559 | LATÃO AO NÍQUEL |
| 8516 | ESTRICÇÃO | 8560 | BRONZE AO NÍQUEL |
| 8517 | AGULHA | 8561 | CARBONILO DE NÍQUEL |
| 8517 | PONTEIRO | 8562 | CLORETO DE NÍQUEL |
| 8517 | PARTÍCULA ACICULAR | 8563 | MATE DE NÍQUEL |
| 8518 | ROLAMENTO DE AGULHAS | 8564 | MINÉRIO DE NÍQUEL |
| 8519 | LIMA AGULHA | 8565 | ÓXIDO DE NÍQUEL |

| | |
|---|---|
| 8566 | NIQUELAR |
| 8567 | NIQUELAMENTO |
| 8568 | ESFÉRULAS DE NÍQUEL |
| 8569 | ARGENTÃO |
| 8569 | PRATA ALEMÃ |
| 8570 | AÇO NÍQUEL |
| 8571 | SULFATO DE NÍQUEL |
| 8572 | BRONZE DE NÍQUEL E ALUMÍNIO |
| 8573 | AÇO NIQUELADO |
| 8574 | ÓXIDO DE NÍQUEL |
| 8575 | TURNO DA NOITE |
| 8576 | NIÓBIO |
| 8577 | ÂNGULO DE ACUNHAMENTO |
| 8578 | BICO |
| 8578 | NIPLE |
| 8578 | BOCAL COM ROSCA |
| 8579 | NITRATO |
| 8579 | AZOTO |
| 8580 | ÁGUA FORTE |
| 8580 | ÁCIDO NÍTRICO |
| 8581 | ÓXIDO AZÓTICO OU NÍTRICO |
| 8582 | TÊMPERA POR NITRURAÇÃO |
| 8583 | ATMOSFERA DE NITRURAÇÃO |
| 8584 | FORNO DE NITRURAÇÃO |
| 8585 | AÇO DE NITRURAÇÃO |
| 8586 | NITRITO |
| 8587 | NITROBENZINA |
| 8588 | NITROGÊNIO |
| 8589 | NITRETAÇÃO |
| 8590 | ANIDRIDO NÍTRICO |
| 8591 | PERÓXIDO DE NITROGÊNIO |
| 8592 | ANIDRIDO NITROSO |
| 8593 | NITROGLICERINA |
| 8594 | NITRÔMETRO |
| 8595 | ÁCIDO NITROSSULFÔNICO |
| 8596 | ÁCIDO NITROSO |
| 8597 | ÓXIDO NITROSO |
| 8598 | MARCHA EM VAZIO |
| 8599 | PERDA EM VAZIO |
| 8600 | RESISTÊNCIA NA MARCHA EM VAZIO |
| 8601 | TRABALHO EM VAZIO |
| 8602 | METAL NOBRE OU PRECIOSO |
| 8603 | METAL PRECIOSO |
| 8604 | CÍRCULO DE PONTO NEUTRO |
| 8605 | NÓ DE VIBRAÇÃO |
| 8606 | ESFEROIDAL |
| 8607 | FERRO DÚCTIL |
| 8608 | RUÍDO |
| 8609 | MARCHA SILENCIOSA |
| 8610 | MARCHA RUIDOSA |
| 8611 | DIÂMETRO NOMINAL |

| | |
|---|---|
| 8612 | DIMENSÃO NOMINAL |
| 8613 | PRESSÃO NOMINAL |
| 8614 | TIMBRE DE TANQUE A PRESSÃO |
| 8615 | TAMANHO NOMINAL |
| 8616 | VALOR NOMINAL |
| 8617 | NOMOGRAMA (ÁBACO) |
| 8618 | ELÉTRODO NÃO CONSUMÍVEL |
| 8619 | LIGA NÃO FERROSA |
| 8620 | INCLUSÕES NÃO METÁLICAS |
| 8621 | NÃO REATIVO |
| 8621 | INERTE |
| 8622 | LIGA NÃO REFRATÁRIA |
| 8623 | HASTE FIXA |
| 8624 | VÁLVULA DE HASTE FIXA |
| 8625 | CALIBRADOR FIXO |
| 8626 | CARVÃO NÃO AGLUTINANTE |
| 8627 | MÁQUINA SEM CONDENSAÇÃO |
| 8628 | CALORÍFUGO |
| 8629 | MOVIMENTO DE ACIONAMENTO ELÁSTICO |
| 8630 | TESTE NÃO DESTRUTIVO |
| 8631 | NÃO FERROSO |
| 8632 | METAL NÃO FERROSO |
| 8633 | CHAPELETA ANTIGELO |
| 8634 | INCONGELABILIDADE |
| 8635 | INCONGELÁVEL |
| 8636 | CHAMA INCOLOR |
| 8636 | CHAMA OXIDANTE |
| 8637 | AMAGNÉTICO |
| 8637 | NÃO MAGNÉTICO |
| 8638 | AÇO NÃO MAGNÉTICO |
| 8639 | NÃO METÁLICO |
| 8640 | METALÓIDE |
| 8641 | REVESTIMENTO NÃO METÁLICO |
| 8642 | ACIONAMENTO ELÁSTICO |
| 8643 | SOLDA SEM PRESSÃO MECÂNICA |
| 8643 | SOLDAGEM POR FUSÃO |
| 8644 | AÇO INOXIDÁVEL |
| 8645 | SISTEMA DIFERENCIAL ANTIDERRAPANTE |
| 8646 | CABO ANTIGIRATÓRIO |
| 8647 | MOVIMENTO IRREGULAR |
| 8647 | MOVIMENTO NÃO UNIFORME |
| 8648 | MOVIMENTO NÃO UNIFORMEMENTE ACELERADO |
| 8649 | MOVIMENTO NÃO UNIFORMEMENTE RETARDADO |
| 8650 | MOLDE NÃO METÁLICO |
| 8651 | NÓ CORREDIÇO |
| 8652 | NORMAL |
| 8653 | ACELERAÇÃO NORMAL |
| 8654 | SEÇÃO NORMAL |
| 8655 | CARGA NORMAL |

| | |
|---|---|
| 8656 | FOSFATO DE MAGNÉSIA |
| 8657 | PRESSÃO NORMAL |
| 8658 | POTÊNCIA NORMAL |
| 8659 | TENSÃO NORMAL |
| 8660 | SEGREGAÇÃO NORMAL |
| 8661 | CARGA NORMAL |
| 8661 | TENSÃO NORMAL |
| 8662 | NORMAL DE UMA CURVA |
| 8663 | MARCHA OU VELOCIDADE DE REGIME |
| 8664 | NORMALIZAÇÃO |
| 8665 | PÓLO NORTE DO ÍMÃ |
| 8666 | BICO DE FERRAMENTA |
| 8667 | NARIZ |
| 8668 | ENTALHE |
| 8668 | RANHURA |
| 8668 | RECORTE |
| 8669 | FRAGILIDADE AO ENTALHE |
| 8670 | SENSIBILIDADE AO ENTALHE |
| 8671 | RESISTÊNCIA AO ENTALHE |
| 8672 | ENTALHE |
| 8673 | ENSAIO DE IMPACTO EM BARRA COM ENTALHE |
| 8674 | LINGOTE ÉNTALHADO |
| 8675 | PROVETA COM ENTALHE |
| 8676 | ENTALHADURA |
| 8676 | MALHETE |
| 8677 | ESCATELADORA |
| 8677 | MÁQUINA DE RANHURAR |
| 8678 | MACHARRÃO |
| 8678 | CAIXA DE MOLDAR DE BAIXO |
| 8679 | BOCAL |
| 8679 | ESGUICHO |
| 8679 | TUBEIRA |
| 8680 | ALTURA DE BOCAL |
| 8681 | MÁQUINA DE PERFURAR TUBOS |
| 8682 | PORTA-BOCAL |
| 8683 | BOCAL DE COLAR |
| 8684 | AGULHA DE INJETOR |
| 8685 | BOCAL |
| 8686 | MOLA DE INJETOR |
| 8687 | NUCLEAÇÃO |
| 8688 | NÚCLEO |
| 8689 | NÚMERO DE UM LOGARITMO |
| 8690 | NÚMERO DE ROTAÇÕES POR MINUTO (RPM) |
| 8691 | NÚMERO DE DENTES |
| 8692 | NÚMERO DE ROSCAS |
| 8693 | NUMERADOR |
| 8694 | SOLUÇÃO POR CÁLCULO |
| 8695 | SISTEMA DE CONTROLE NUMÉRICO |
| 8696 | DADOS NUMÉRICOS |
| 8697 | VALOR NUMÉRICO |

| | |
|---|---|
| 8698 | PORCA |
| 8699 | TORNO DE ATARRAXAR PORCAS |
| 8700 | PORCA EMBUTIDA |
| 8701 | TRAVA DE PORCA |
| 8701 | CONTRAPORCA |
| 8702 | NUTAÇÃO |
| 8703 | JUNTA TÓRICA |
| 8704 | COURO CURTIDO A CORTIÇA |
| 8705 | OBELISCO |
| 8706 | PONTO DE OBJETO |
| 8707 | OBJEÇÃO CONTRA UMA PATENTE |
| 8708 | OBJETIVO |
| 8709 | CONE OBLÍQUO |
| 8710 | COORDENADAS OBLÍQUAS |
| 8711 | SEÇÃO OBLÍQUA |
| 8712 | CILINDRO OBLÍQUO |
| 8713 | PARALELEPÍPEDO OBLÍQUO |
| 8714 | ORIFÍCIO ALONGADO |
| 8715 | OBLONGO |
| 8716 | OBSIDIANA |
| 8717 | ÁNGULO OBTUSO |
| 8718 | TRIÂNGULO OBTUSÁNGULO |
| 8719 | ABSORÇÃO |
| 8719 | OCLUSÃO |
| 9720 | OCRE |
| 8721 | OCTÁGONO |
| 8722 | OCTAEDRO |
| 8723 | ÍNDICE DE OCTANA |
| 8724 | OCTANTE |
| 8725 | NÚMERO ÍMPAR |
| 8726 | ODONTÓGRAFO |
| 8727 | DE UMA DIMENSÃO |
| 8728 | TRIDIMENSIONAL |
| 8729 | BIDIMENSIONAL |
| 8730 | DESCENTRADO |
| 8731 | DESCENTRADO |
| 8732 | CORRIDA QUE NÃO ATINGIU AS ESPECIFICAÇÕES |
| 8733 | GUSA FORA DE ANÁLISE |
| 8734 | TEMPO DE REPOUSO |
| 8734 | CORTE DE CORRENTE |
| 8735 | TRATAMENTO INDIRETO |
| 8736 | PORTO DE DESCARGA |
| 8737 | DESVIO |
| 8738 | AO LARGO |
| 8739 | AÇO PARA PLATAFORMA NO MAR |
| 8740 | TESTE OFICIAL |
| 8741 | ARCO DECIMÁCIO |
| 8741 | ARCO DE GOLA |
| 8742 | OHM |
| 8743 | ÓLEO |

| | |
|---|---|
| 8744 | LUBRIFICAR |
| 8745 | BANHO DE ÓLEO |
| 8746 | FILTRO DE AR DE BANHO DE ÓLEO |
| 8747 | INDICADOR COM RETORNO AO BANHO DE ÓLEO |
| 8748 | DEPÓSITO DE ÓLEO |
| 8749 | AZEITEIRA |
| 8749 | ALMOTOLIA |
| 8750 | ANEL DE LUBRIFICAÇÃO (PISTÃO) |
| 8751 | REFRIGERADOR A ÓLEO |
| 8752 | REFRIGERAÇÃO A ÓLEO |
| 8753 | COPO DE LUBRIFICAÇÃO |
| 8754 | ALMOFADA DE ÓLEO |
| 8755 | AMORTECEDOR A ÓLEO |
| 8756 | MOTOR A ÓLEO |
| 8757 | FILTRO A ÓLEO |
| 8758 | GÁS RICO |
| 8758 | GÁS DE ÓLEO |
| 8759 | RANHURA DE LUBRIFICAÇÃO |
| 8760 | TÊMPERA EM ÓLEO |
| 8761 | ORIFÍCIO DE LUBRIFICAÇÃO |
| 8762 | PERFURADOR DE CONDUTO DE ÓLEO |
| 8763 | TURBINA DE RETORNO DE ÓLEO |
| 8764 | INDICADOR DE NÍVEL DE ÓLEO |
| 8765 | ESSÊNCIA DE TEREBINTINA |
| 8765 | AGUARRÁS |
| 8766 | PINTURA A ÓLEO |
| 8767 | BANDEJA DE ÓLEO |
| 8768 | INDICADOR DA PRESSÃO DO ÓLEO |
| 8769 | BOMBA DE LUBRIFICAÇÃO |
| 8769 | BOMBA HIDRÁULICA |
| 8769 | BOMBA A ÓLEO |
| 8770 | COADOR DE ÓLEO |
| 8771 | MÁSTIQUE COM ÓLEO |
| 8772 | TÊMPERA A ÓLEO |
| 8773 | RESERVATÓRIO DE ÓLEO |
| 8774 | ANEL DE LUBRIFICADOR |
| 8775 | SEGMENTO RASPADOR |
| 8776 | VEDAÇÃO A ÓLEO |
| 8777 | SEPARAÇÃO DE ÓLEO |
| 8778 | SEPARADOR OU CLASSIFICADOR DE ÓLEO |
| 8779 | SEPARADOR DE ÓLEO PARA VAPOR |
| 8780 | XISTO BETUMINOSO |
| 8781 | PEDRA DE AFIAR COM ÓLEO |
| 8782 | CÁRTER INFERIOR |
| 8783 | SUPRIMENTO DE ÓLEO |
| 8784 | SERINGA PARA LUBRIFICAÇÃO |
| 8785 | MÁQUINA DE TESTAR ÓLEO |
| 8786 | VERNIZ A ÓLEO DE LINHAÇA |
| 8787 | ÍNDICE DE VISCOSIDADE |
| 8788 | PAPEL OLEADO |

| | |
|---|---|
| 8789 | PONTO DE LUBRIFICAÇÃO |
| 8790 | ANEL DE LUBRIFICAÇÃO |
| 8791 | LUBRIFICAÇÃO A ÓLEO |
| 8792 | À PROVA DE ÓLEO |
| 8793 | PROCESSO OLD |
| 8794 | JUNTA DE OLDHAM |
| 8795 | ÁCIDO OLÉICO |
| 8796 | OLIVINA |
| 8796 | PERIDOTO |
| 8797 | TESTE DE EMBUTIMENTO OLSEN |
| 8798 | DESPESAS GERAIS |
| 8799 | OPERAÇÃO DIRETA |
| 8799 | TRATAMENTO DIRETO |
| 8800 | MONTAGEM NO LOCAL |
| 8801 | CALCÁRIO OOLÍTICO |
| 8802 | OPACIDADE |
| 8803 | OPACO |
| 8804 | CORREIA ABERTA |
| 8805 | EXCÊNTRICO PLANO |
| 8806 | HIDROCARBONETOS DE CADEIA ABERTA |
| 8807 | CANAL ABERTO |
| 8808 | TENSÃO EM VAZIO |
| 8809 | SOLDAGEM DE ÂNGULO ABERTO |
| 8810 | MATRIZ ABERTA |
| 8811 | SOLDAGEM EM K COM SEPARAÇÃO |
| 8812 | SOLDAGEM DUPLA ABERTA |
| 8813 | FOGO NU |
| 8814 | PRENSA MECÂNICA DE FRENTE ABERTA |
| 8815 | FORNO SIEMENS-MARTIN |
| 8816 | AÇO SIEMENS-MARTIN |
| 8817 | SISTEMA DE CONTROLE DE CIRCUITO ABERTO |
| 8818 | MOTOR ABERTO |
| 8819 | FERRO DE GRANULAÇÃO GROSSA |
| 8820 | MOLDAGEM A DESCOBERTO |
| 8821 | PLAINA MECÂNICA DE UMA COLUNA |
| 8822 | SOLDAGEM EM MEIO V COM SEPARAÇÃO |
| 8823 | SOLDAGEM EM J COM SEPARAÇÃO |
| 8824 | SOLDAGEM EM I COM SEPARAÇÃO |
| 8825 | AÇO NÃO ACALMADO |
| 8826 | ABRIR O CIRCUITO |
| 8827 | MANÔMETRO DE AR LIVRE |
| 8828 | PRENSA HIDRÁULICA DE COLO DE CISNE |
| 8829 | FORNO SIEMENS-MARTIN |
| 8830 | PROCESSO SIEMENS-MARTIN |
| 8831 | PASSAGEM |
| 8831 | ABERTURA |
| 8832 | ABERTURA DA VÁLVULA |
| 8833 | ALAVANCA DE MANOBRA |
| 8834 | CONDIÇÕES DE OPERAÇÃO |
| 8835 | INSTRUÇÕES DE OPERAÇÃO |

| | |
|---|---|
| 8836 | TEMPERATURA OPERACIONAL |
| 8837 | FUNCIONAMENTO |
| 8837 | OPERAÇÃO |
| 8838 | NÚMERO DE OPERAÇÕES |
| 8839 | POSTO DE OPERAÇÃO |
| 8839 | POSTO DO OPERADOR |
| 8840 | ÓPTICO |
| 8841 | EIXO ÓPTICO |
| 8842 | COMPARADOR ÓPTICO |
| 8843 | PLANO ÓPTICO |
| 8844 | INSTRUMENTO ÓPTICO |
| 8845 | PIRÔMETRO ÓPTICO |
| 8846 | PIROMETRIA ÓPTICA |
| 8847 | LEITORES ÓPTICOS |
| 8848 | SISTEMA ÓPTICO |
| 8849 | ÓPTICA |
| 8850 | PARADA FACULTATIVA |
| 8851 | EFEITO DE "CASCA DE LARANJA" |
| 8852 | ORDEM DE GRANDEZA |
| 8853 | ÉTER COMUM |
| 8854 | ARGAMASSA DE CAL |
| 8855 | CORRENTE COMUM |
| 8856 | ÁCIDO SULFÚRICO COMERCIAL |
| 8857 | CONDIÇÕES ORDINÁRIAS DE TRABALHO |
| 8857 | REGIME DE TRABALHO |
| 8858 | ORDENADA |
| 8859 | MINÉRIO |
| 8860 | BRIQUETE DE MINÉRIO |
| 8861 | BENEFICIAMENTO MECÂNICO DO MINÉRIO |
| 8862 | USTULAÇÃO DE MINÉRIOS |
| 8863 | MINÉRIOS E FUNDENTES |
| 8864 | ÁCIDO ORGÂNICO |
| 8865 | QUÍMICA ORGÂNICA |
| 8866 | MATÉRIA ORGÂNICA |
| 8867 | ORIENTAÇÃO |
| 8868 | ORIGEM DAS COORDENADAS |
| 8869 | TORNEAMENTO DE SUPERFÍCIES ORNAMENTAIS |
| 8870 | PROJEÇÃO ORTOGONAL |
| 8871 | EIXOS CRISTALINOS ORTO-HEXAGONAIS |
| 8872 | REPRESENTAÇÃO CONFORME |
| 8873 | ÁCIDO ORTOFOSFÓRICO |
| 8874 | CRISTAIS ORTORRÔMBICOS |
| 8875 | ÁCIDO ORTO-SILÍCICO |
| 8876 | ÁCIDO TÚNGSTICO |
| 8877 | OSCILAR |
| 8877 | VIBRAR |
| 8878 | CAME OSCILANTE |
| 8879 | MÉTODO DE CRISTAL OSCILANTE |
| 8880 | MÁQUINA DE CILINDRO OSCILANTE |
| 8881 | MOVIMENTO OSCILATÓRIO |

| | |
|---|---|
| 8882 | PISTÃO OSCILANTE |
| 8883 | VIBRAÇÕES DE RESSONÂNCIA |
| 8884 | OSCILAÇÃO |
| 8885 | OSMIRÍDIO |
| 8889 | ÓSMIO |
| 8890 | OSMOSE |
| 8891 | PRESSÃO OSMÓTICA |
| 8892 | DESENGRENADO |
| 8893 | DESALINHADO |
| 8894 | EXCENTRICIDADE |
| 8895 | FORA DE ESQUADRIA |
| 8896 | POTÊNCIA |
| 8896 | RENDIMENTO |
| 8897 | ILUMINAÇÃO EXTERNA |
| 8898 | PISTA EXTERNA DE ROLAMENTO DE ESFERAS |
| 8899 | DESCARGA DE ÁGUA |
| 8900 | SAÍDA |
| 8901 | BOCAL DE SAÍDA |
| 8902 | ORIFÍCIO DE DESCARGA |
| 8903 | VELOCIDADE DE SAÍDA |
| 8904 | BARRAGEM DE SAÍDA |
| 8905 | DESENHO EM PERFIL |
| 8906 | PERFIL DE CAME |
| 8907 | CONTORNO |
| 8908 | POTÊNCIA |
| 8909 | REGULADOR DE POTÊNCIA |
| 8910 | EIXO SECUNDÁRIO |
| 8911 | LADO EXTERNO |
| 8912 | COMPASSO DE ESPESSURA |
| 8913 | DIÂMETRO EXTERNO |
| 8914 | VÁLVULA DE PARAFUSO EXTERNO |
| 8915 | HASTE DE PARAFUSO EXTERNO |
| 8916 | BARRA DE FERRO OVALADO |
| 8917 | SEÇÃO OVAL |
| 8918 | FLANGE OVAL |
| 8919 | TORNO DE OVALAR |
| 8920 | FORNO |
| 8921 | MULTIPLICADOR DE VELOCIDADE |
| 8921 | SOBREMARCHA |
| 8921 | OVERDRIVE |
| 8922 | DIMENSÕES EXTERNAS |
| 8923 | SUPERENVELHECIMENTO |
| 8924 | ALTURA TOTAL |
| 8925 | COMPRIMENTO TOTAL |
| 8926 | LARGURA TOTAL |
| 8927 | RENDIMENTO TOTAL |
| 8928 | PREPONDERAR |
| 8929 | VENCER A RESISTÊNCIA |
| 8930 | VELOCIDADE SOBREMULTIPLICADA |
| 8930 | OVERDRIVE |

| | | | |
|---|---|---|---|
| 8931 | VERTEDOURO | 8978 | SOLDAGEM AUTÓGENA POR PRESSÃO |
| 8932 | TUBO LADRÃO | 8979 | SOLDAGEM A OXIACETILENO |
| 8933 | VÁLVULA LADRÃO | 8980 | OXIGÊNIO |
| 8934 | SACADA | 8981 | LANÇA DE OXIGÊNIO |
| 8935 | CILINDRO EM BALANÇO | 8982 | PROCESSO A OXIGÊNIO |
| 8936 | SACADA | 8983 | COBRE DE ALTA CONDUTIBILIDADE ISENTO |
| 8937 | FAZER REVISÃO | | DE OXIGÊNIO |
| 8938 | CABO AÉREO | 8984 | OXIGENAÇÃO |
| 8939 | EIXO DE CAMES SUSPENSO | 8984 | OXIDAÇÃO |
| 8940 | TRANSMISSÃO INTERMEDIÁRIA SUPERIOR | 8985 | GÁS OXÍDRICO |
| 8941 | SOLDAGEM SUPERIOR EXECUTADA | 8986 | MAÇARICO OXÍDRICO |
| | POR BAIXO | 8987 | LUZ OXÍDRICA |
| 8942 | PONTE ROLANTE DE USINA | 8988 | SOLDAGEM OXÍDRICA |
| 8943 | VÁLVULAS SUSPENSAS | 8989 | OZÔNIO |
| 8944 | SOLDAGEM SOBRE A CABEÇA | 8990 | EMPACOTAR |
| 8945 | AÇO SUPERAQUECIDO | 8990 | GUARNECER |
| 8946 | SUPERAQUECIMENTO | 8990 | VEDAR |
| 8947 | MANIVELA FRONTAL | 8991 | EMBALAR |
| 8948 | SOBREPOSIÇÃO | 8992 | CEMENTAÇÃO EM CAIXA |
| 8949 | SOBREPOSIÇÃO DE SOLDA | 8993 | PELÍCULA RÍGIDA |
| 8950 | SOBREPOR | 8994 | LAMINAÇÃO DE PACOTE |
| 8951 | SOBREPOSIÇÃO | 8995 | ACONDICIONAMENTO |
| 8952 | CAMADA | 8995 | EMBALAGEM |
| 8952 | REVESTIMENTO | 8996 | ÓLEOS EMBALADOS |
| 8953 | SOBRECARGA | 8997 | VÁLVULA MACHO DE CAIXA |
| 8954 | SOBRECARREGAR | 8998 | EMPANQUE |
| 8955 | SOBREPRESSÃO | 8998 | GAXETA |
| 8956 | ENCOSTO DE PÁRA-CHOQUE | 8998 | ENGAXETAMENTO |
| 8957 | EMBREAGEM DE RODA LIVRE | 8999 | EMPACOTAMENTO |
| 8958 | SUPERINTENDENTE | 9000 | GAXETA |
| 8959 | ULTRAPASSAGEM | 9000 | PRENSA-ESTOPA |
| 8960 | RODA HIDRÁULICA POR CIMA | 9001 | SOBREPOSTA DE ENGAXETAMENTO |
| 8961 | TAMANHO ACIMA DO NORMAL | 9002 | FLANGE DE SOBREPOSTA DE |
| 8962 | SOBRECARREGAR UM MATERIAL | | ENGAXETAMENTO |
| 8963 | SOBRECARGA | 9003 | ROMANEIO |
| 8964 | HORA EXTRA | 9004 | MATERIAL PARA SINTERIZAÇÃO |
| 8965 | DERRUBAMENTO | 9005 | PORCA DE APERTO DO ENGAXETAMENTO |
| 8965 | TOMBAMENTO | 9006 | PEÇA DE AJUSTE |
| 8966 | MOMENTO DE TOMBAMENTO | 9007 | ANEL DE GUARNIÇÃO |
| 8967 | SOBRETENSÃO | 9008 | CÂMARA DE GAXETA |
| 8968 | OXALATO | 9009 | GAXETA |
| 8969 | ÁCIDO OXÁLICO | 9009 | JUNTA |
| 8970 | OXIDAÇÃO | 9009 | GUARNIÇÃO |
| 8971 | ÓXIDO | 9010 | VÁLVULA SEM GAXETA |
| 8972 | OXIDÁVEL | 9011 | COXIM |
| 8973 | OXIDAR | 9011 | ALMOFADA |
| 8974 | OXIDANTE | 9012 | BOCAL AUTO-REFORÇADO |
| 8975 | CHAMA OXIDANTE | 9013 | PINTURA |
| 8976 | ELIMINAÇÃO DE DEFEITOS DE SUPERFÍCIE | 9014 | PINTAR |
| | COM MAÇARICO | 9015 | COR |
| 8977 | OXICORTE | 9015 | PINTURA |

| | | | |
|---|---|---|---|
| 9016 | TUBO PROTEGIDO POR PINTURA | 9057 | PARALELOGRAMO ARTICULADO |
| 9017 | CADAFALSO | 9058 | PROJEÇÃO PARALELA |
| 9017 | PLATAFORMA PARA PINTAR | 9059 | RÉGUA DE TRAÇAR PARALELAS |
| 9018 | PINTURA | 9060 | VÁLVULA DE ASSENTOS PARALELOS |
| 9019 | PINCEL | 9061 | VÁLVULA DE LIVRE DILATAÇÃO |
| 9020 | PINTURA A PISTOLA | 9062 | VÁLVULA DE BLOQUEIO MECÂNICO |
| 9021 | DEFEITOS DE PINTURA | 9063 | ASSENTOS PARALELOS |
| 9022 | COMPASSO | 9064 | EIXOS PARALELOS |
| 9023 | PALÁDIO | 9065 | ROSCAMENTO PARALELO |
| 9024 | PALHETA | 9066 | TORNO DE BANCADA PARALELA |
| 9024 | ESTRADO | 9067 | LIMA PARALELA |
| 9025 | CAMINHÕES DE TRANSPORTE COM ESTRADO | 9068 | PARALELEPÍPEDO |
| | | 9069 | PARALELISMO |
| 9026 | COLOCAÇÃO DE ESTRADOS | 9070 | PARALELOGRAMO |
| 9027 | ÓLEO DE COCO | 9071 | PARALELOGRAMO DAS FORÇAS |
| 9028 | ÁCIDO PALMÍTICO OU CETÍLICO | 9072 | PARALELOGRAMO DAS VELOCIDADES |
| 9029 | RECIPIENTE | 9073 | PARAMAGNÉTICO |
| 9029 | PANELA | 9074 | PARAMAGNETISMO |
| 9029 | TACHO | 9075 | PARÂMETRO |
| 9030 | REBITE DE CABEÇA TRAPEZOIDAL | 9076 | GALVANIZAÇÃO PARCIAL |
| 9031 | PENA DO MARTELO | 9077 | PERGAMINHO |
| 9032 | PAINEL | 9078 | PAPEL PERGAMINHO |
| 9032 | PRANCHA | 9079 | METAL DE BASE |
| 9033 | PANTÓGRAFO | 9080 | FORMÃO DE CARPINTEIRO |
| 9034 | POLIA DE CARTÃO | 9081 | CONTROLE DE PARIDADE |
| 9035 | PASTA DE PAPEL | 9082 | FREIO DE MÃO |
| 9035 | CELULOSE | 9083 | PEÇA |
| 9036 | PAPIER-MÂCHÉ | 9084 | PROGRAMAÇÃO DE PEÇA |
| 9037 | BORRACHA DO PARÁ | 9085 | TURBINA DE ADMISSÃO PARCIAL |
| 9038 | PARÁBOLA | 9086 | EQUAÇÃO DIFERENCIAL PARCIAL |
| 9039 | CILINDRO PARABÓLICO | 9087 | PRESSÃO PARCIAL |
| 9040 | INTERPOLAÇÃO PARABÓLICA | 9088 | PARTÍCULA |
| 9041 | ESPELHO PARABÓLICO | 9089 | GROSSURA DE PARTÍCULA |
| 9042 | PARABOLÓIDE DE ROTAÇÃO | 9090 | COMPOSIÇÃO GRANULOMÉTRICA |
| 9043 | PARAFINA | 9091 | PRECIPITAÇÃO |
| 9044 | ÓLEO PESADO DE PARAFINA | 9092 | LUBRIFICANTE PARA MOLDE |
| 9045 | CERA DE PARAFINA | 9093 | PLANO DE JUNTA |
| 9046 | MOTOR A PETRÓLEO | 9094 | AREIA ISOLANTE |
| 9047 | PARALAXE | 9095 | LISTA DE PEÇAS |
| 9048 | ERRO DE PARALAXE | 9096 | PASSE |
| 9049 | PARALELA | 9096 | CAMADA |
| 9050 | PARALELO | 9097 | SEQÜÊNCIA DE CALIBRES |
| 9051 | MONTAGEM EM PARALELO | 9098 | PASSAGEM DO CALOR |
| 9051 | LIGAÇÃO EM PARALELO | 9099 | PASSAGEM DA LUZ |
| 9052 | OPÉRCULO PARALELO COM APERTO DE MOLA | 9100 | ORIFÍCIO DE PASSAGEM |
| | | 9101 | ASCENSOR |
| 9053 | OPÉRCULO PARALELO COM APERTO MECÂNICO | 9102 | LUZ DE ULTRAPASSAGEM |
| | | 9103 | BANHO DE PASSIVAÇÃO |
| 9054 | ENTRADA EM PARALELO | 9104 | PELÍCULA PASSIVANTE |
| 9055 | CORRENTE DE FILETES PARALELOS | 9105 | PASSIVAÇÃO |
| 9056 | FORÇAS PARALELAS | 9106 | PASSIVADOR |

| | |
|---|---|
| 9107 | PASSIVIDADE |
| 9108 | PASTA DE SOLDAR |
| 9109 | REMENDO |
| 9109 | MANCHÃO |
| 9110 | REMENDAR |
| 9111 | REPARAÇÃO |
| 9111 | REMENDAGEM |
| 9112 | PATENTE |
| 9113 | PATENTEAR |
| 9114 | AGENTE DE PATENTES |
| 9115 | TAXAS DE PATENTE |
| 9116 | LEI SOBRE PATENTES |
| 9117 | VERNIZ (COURO) |
| 9118 | APLAINAMENTO |
| 9119 | ESPECIALIDADE FARMACÊUTICA |
| 9120 | REPARTIÇÃO DE PATENTES |
| 9121 | DIREITOS DE PATENTE |
| 9122 | INVENÇÃO PATENTEÁVEL |
| 9123 | PROPRIETÁRIO DA PATENTE |
| 9124 | DE PATENTE |
| 9125 | TRAJETO SEGUIDO POR UM FLUXO |
| 9126 | MICRÓBIO PATOGÊNICO |
| 9127 | PÁTINA |
| 9128 | PADRÃO |
| 9128 | MODELO |
| 9129 | MODELO PARA FUNDIÇÃO |
| 9130 | MODELADOR |
| 9131 | MODELAGEM |
| 9132 | OFICINA DE MOLDES |
| 9133 | MODELO |
| 9134 | CASCA DE LARANJA (AFNOR) |
| 9135 | MODELAGEM |
| 9136 | CALÇAMENTO |
| 9136 | PAVIMENTAÇÃO |
| 9137 | PARALELEPÍPEDO |
| 9137 | PEDRA PARA PAVIMENTAÇÃO |
| 9138 | MOVIMENTO DE CATRACA COM LINGÜETA |
| 9139 | CARGA ÚTIL |
| 9140 | CARVÃO MIÚDO |
| 9140 | GRÃOS PARA GASOGÊNIO |
| 9141 | RECOLHEDORAS DE ERVILHA |
| 9142 | FRASCO CUNEIFORME |
| 9143 | PERLASCO |
| 9143 | CARBONATO DE POTÁSSIO |
| 9144 | PERLITA |
| 9145 | AÇO PERLÍTICO |
| 9146 | BRILHO NACARADO |
| 9147 | TURFA |
| 9148 | TIJOLO DE TURFA |
| 9149 | AGLOMERADO DE TURFA |
| 9150 | PLACA DE TURFA |

| | |
|---|---|
| 9151 | TURFA PARA QUEIMAR |
| 9152 | SEIXO |
| 9152 | CASCALHO |
| 9153 | COLETOR DE SEIXOS |
| 9154 | SUPORTE DE MANCAL |
| 9155 | CASCA |
| 9156 | ESFOLIAÇÃO |
| 9156 | DESCASCADURA |
| 9157 | MARTELAGEM |
| 9158 | VIGIA |
| 9158 | POSTIGO DE INSPEÇÃO |
| 9159 | CAVILHA |
| 9159 | TARUGO |
| 9160 | TIRA-LINHAS |
| 9161 | LÁPIS |
| 9162 | FEIXES LUMINOSOS |
| 9163 | BORRACHA DE LÁPIS |
| 9164 | FEIXE LUMINOSO |
| 9165 | PORTA-MINAS |
| 9165 | PORTA-LÁPIS |
| 9166 | CADEIRA EM U |
| 9167 | PÊNDULO |
| 9168 | REGULADOR PENDULAR |
| 9169 | LÍQUIDO PENETRANTE |
| 9170 | PENETRAÇÃO |
| 9171 | PENETRÔMETRO |
| 9172 | PENTÁGONO |
| 9173 | PRISMA PENTAGONAL |
| 9174 | PIRÂMIDE PENTAGONAL |
| 9175 | PENTAEDRO |
| 9176 | PENTANA (NORMAL) |
| 9177 | PENUMBRA |
| 9178 | POROSIDADES SUPERFICIAIS |
| 9179 | PORCENTAGEM POR VOLUME |
| 9180 | PORCENTAGEM POR PESO |
| 9180 | ÁGUA DE INFILTRAÇÃO |
| 9182 | PRENSA MECÂNICA DE PERCUSSÃO |
| 9183 | SOLDAGEM POR PERCUSSÃO |
| 9184 | COMBUSTÃO PERFEITA |
| 9185 | GÁS PERFEITO |
| 9186 | PERFURAR |
| 9187 | SEPARADOR DE ORIFÍCIOS |
| 9188 | POLIA COM ARO FURADO |
| 9189 | CHAPA PERFURADA |
| 9190 | PERÍMETRO |
| 9191 | PERIÓDICO |
| 9192 | FRAÇÃO DECIMAL PERIÓDICA |
| 9193 | INSPEÇÃO PERIÓDICA DE CALDEIRAS |
| 9194 | MOVIMENTO PERIÓDICO |
| 9195 | LUBRIFICAÇÃO INTERMITENTE |
| 9196 | PERIODICIDADE |

| | | | |
|---|---|---|---|
| 9197 | RESISTÊNCIA TANGENCIAL | 9245 | REVESTIMENTO DE FOSFATO |
| 9198 | VELOCIDADE PERIFÉRICA | 9246 | BRONZE FOSFÓRICO |
| 9199 | REAÇÃO PERITÉCTICA | 9247 | FOSFORESCÊNCIA |
| 9200 | FUNDIÇÃO PERLÍTICA | 9248 | FOSFORESCENTE |
| 9201 | PERMALLOY | 9249 | ÓXIDO FOSFÓRICO |
| 9202 | DEFORMAÇÃO PERMANENTE | 9250 | COBRE FOSFÓRICO |
| 9203 | DUREZA PERMANENTE DA ÁGUA | 9251 | SUBSTÂNCIAS FOSFORESCENTES |
| 9204 | ÍMÃ PERMANENTE | 9252 | FÓSFORO |
| 9205 | DISCO DE ÍMÃ PERMANENTE | 9253 | COBRE FOSFÓRICO |
| 9206 | MAGNETISMO PERMANENTE | 9254 | PENTACLORETO DE FÓSFORO |
| 9207 | MOLDE PERMANENTE | 9255 | TRIBROMETO DE FÓSFORO |
| 9207 | COQUILHA | 9256 | TRICLORETO DE FÓSFORO |
| 9208 | FUNDIÇÃO EM COQUILHA | 9257 | PAPEL HELIOGRÁFICO |
| 9209 | SERVIÇO CONTÍNUO | 9258 | FOTODIODO |
| 9210 | DEFORMAÇÃO PERMANENTE | 9259 | PILHA FOTOELÉTRICA |
| 9211 | PERMEABILIDADE | 9259 | CÉLULA FOTOELÉTRICA |
| 9212 | PERMEÁVEL AO AR | 9260 | FOTOCÉLULA |
| 9213 | PERMEÁVEL | 9261 | CÉLULA FOTOCONDUTORA |
| 9214 | PERMEÂMETRO | 9262 | FOTOGRAFAR |
| 9215 | CARGA ADMITIDA | 9263 | FOTOGRAFIA |
| 9216 | PERMUTAÇÃO | 9264 | MÁQUINA FOTOGRÁFICA |
| 9217 | PERPENDICULAR | 9265 | FOTOGRAFIA |
| 9218 | LADO PERPENDICULAR DO TRIÁNGULO RETÁNGULO | 9266 | MACROFOTOGRAFIA |
| | | 9267 | FOTÔMETRO |
| 9219 | PERPENDICULARIDADE | 9268 | BANCO FOTOMÉTRICO |
| 9220 | PERSPECTIVA | 9269 | FOTOMÉTRICO |
| 9221 | PILÃO | 9270 | UNIDADE FOTOMÉTRICA |
| 9222 | GASOLINA | 9271 | FOTOMETRIA |
| 9223 | MOTOR A GASOLINA | 9272 | MICROFOTOGRAMA |
| 9224 | LÂMPADA DE GASOLINA | 9273 | CÉLULA FOTOEMISSIVA |
| 9225 | LOCOMOTIVA A GASOLINA | 9274 | FOTOMULTIPLICADOR |
| 9226 | PETRÓLEO | 9275 | FÓTON |
| 9227 | LÂMPADA A QUEROSENE | 9276 | FOTOCÓPIA |
| 9228 | ÉTER DE PETRÓLEO | 9276 | CÓPIA HELIOGRÁFICA |
| 9229 | PETRÓLEO | 9277 | CÉLULA FOTOVOLTAICA |
| 9230 | PELTRE | 9278 | FILITO |
| 9231 | PH | 9279 | FÍSICO |
| 9232 | FASE | 9280 | ALTERAÇÃO DE ESTADO FÍSICO |
| 9233 | ÂNGULO DE ATRASO | 9281 | FÍSICO-QUÍMICA |
| 9233 | ÂNGULO DE DEFASAGEM | 9282 | METALURGIA FÍSICA |
| 9234 | DEFASAGEM | 9283 | PROPRIEDADES FÍSICAS |
| 9235 | INDICADOR DE FASE | 9284 | ENSAIOS FÍSICOS |
| 9236 | LEI DAS FASES | 9285 | FÍSICA |
| 9237 | MUDANÇA DE FASE | 9286 | QUÍMICA INDUSTRIAL OU TECNOLÓGICA |
| 9238 | FENOLFTALEÍNA | 9287 | CORDA DE PIANO |
| 9239 | PAPEL DE FENOLFTALEÍNA | 9288 | DESOXIDAÇÃO |
| 9240 | FENÔMENO | 9288 | DECAPAGEM |
| 9241 | FERRO EM QUARTO DE CÍRCULO CONVEXO | 9289 | BANHO DE DECAPAGEM |
| 9242 | FONAUTÓGRAFO | 9290 | SOLUÇÃO ÁCIDA |
| 9243 | FONÓLITO | 9291 | ÁCIDO PÍCRICO |
| 9244 | FOSFATO | 9292 | SEÇÃO DE TUBO |

| | |
|---|---|
| 9293 | PEÇA A TRABALHAR |
| 9294 | TRABALHO POR PEÇA |
| 9294 | EMPREITADA |
| 9295 | SALÁRIO DE EMPREITADA |
| 9296 | MÁQUINA DE PERFURAR |
| 9297 | PIEZOELETRICIDADE |
| 9298 | GUSA |
| 9298 | FERRO GUSA |
| 9299 | FERRO GUSA |
| 9300 | COURO DE PORCO |
| 9301 | GANCHO EM RABO DE PORCO |
| 9302 | GUSA |
| 9303 | PIGMENTO |
| 9303 | CORANTE |
| 9304 | PILHA |
| 9304 | ESTACA |
| 9305 | CABEÇOTE DE CRAVAÇÃO (ESTACAS) |
| 9306 | CRAVAÇÃO DE ESTACA |
| 9307 | EMPILHAR MADEIRA |
| 9308 | FORNO DE AQUECIMENTO EM PACOTES |
| 9309 | EMPILHAMENTO DE MADEIRA |
| 9310 | PRENSA DE PASTILHAS |
| 9311 | PILAR |
| 9312 | PERFURADORA DE COLUNA |
| 9313 | CORPO DE MANCAL |
| 9313 | COXIM DE MANCAL |
| 9314 | GRANULAÇÃO SUPERFICIAL |
| 9315 | PINO |
| 9315 | CAVILHA |
| 9315 | PASSADOR |
| 9315 | FUSO |
| 9315 | ALFINETE |
| 9316 | BROCA DE CABEÇA CILÍNDRICA |
| 9317 | CABEÇA DE ALFINETE |
| 9318 | ARTICULAÇÃO COM PINOS |
| 9319 | BOTÃO DE VIRABREQUIM |
| 9319 | CABEÇA DO EIXO DE MANIVELAS |
| 9320 | PIVÔ DE CORRENTE DE ROLOS |
| 9321 | REBITAGEM COM REBITES SEM CABEÇA |
| 9322 | CHAVE DE FORQUETA |
| 9323 | PIVÔ DE ENGRENAGEM DE LANTERNA |
| 9324 | PINHÃO DE ESPIGAS |
| 9325 | ENGRENAGEM DE ESPIGAS |
| 9326 | EXTRATOR |
| 9327 | PINACÓIDE |
| 9328 | TORQUÊS |
| 9328 | TENAZ |
| 9329 | CONSTRIÇÃO POR FORÇA MAGNÉTICA |
| 9330 | LAMINAÇÃO COM PRESSÃO FRACA |
| 9331 | DENDRITA |
| 9332 | FURO DE PINO |

| | |
|---|---|
| 9333 | POROSIDADE DO FURO DO PINO |
| 9334 | ABERTURA DE FURO DE PINO |
| 9335 | PINHÃO |
| 9336 | ATAQUE DE PINHÃO |
| 9336 | ACIONAMENTO POR PINHÃO |
| 9337 | PINTO (0,473 l) |
| 9338 | BOCAL TIPO AGULHA |
| 9339 | CANO |
| 9339 | TUBO |
| 9340 | CAVIDADE POR CONTRAÇÃO |
| 9341 | CURVATURA DE CANO |
| 9342 | TUBO FUNDIDO HORIZONTALMENTE |
| 9343 | TUBO FUNDIDO DE PÉ |
| 9344 | GRAMPO DE FIXAÇÃO PARA CANOS |
| 9344 | COLAR DE TUBOS |
| 9345 | GRAMPO |
| 9345 | BRAÇADEIRA |
| 9346 | SERPENTINA |
| 9347 | UNIÃO DE TUBOS |
| 9348 | CORTA-TUBOS |
| 9349 | MÁQUINA DE CORTAR TUBOS |
| 9350 | LIGAÇÕES PARA TUBOS |
| 9351 | FLANGE DE TUBOS |
| 9352 | MÁQUINA DE ALARGAR TUBOS |
| 9353 | RUPTURA DE TUBO |
| 9354 | GANCHO PARA TUBOS |
| 9355 | JUNTA PARA TUBOS |
| 9356 | COLOCAÇÃO DE TUBOS |
| 9357 | TUBULAÇÃO |
| 9358 | LAMINADOR DE TUBOS |
| 9359 | PADRÕES DE TUBULAÇÃO |
| 9360 | ROSCA DE TUBOS |
| 9361 | MÁQUINA DE FAZER ROSCAS DE TUBOS |
| 9362 | TORQUÊS DE TUBOS |
| 9363 | TORNO DE TUBOS |
| 9364 | TUBO SOLDADO POR PROCESSO AUTÓGENO |
| 9365 | TUBO COM LIGAÇÕES |
| 9366 | CHAVE GRIFO |
| 9366 | CHAVE DE TUBOS |
| 9367 | ARGILA BRANCA PLÁSTICA |
| 9368 | PIPETA |
| 9369 | SERRA MANUAL DE CABO PARA METAIS |
| 9370 | PISTÃO |
| 9371 | ACELERAÇÃO DO PISTÃO |
| 9372 | VENTILADOR DE PISTÃO |
| 9373 | CABEÇA DE CORPO DE PISTÃO |
| 9374 | COMPRESSOR DE PISTÃO |
| 9375 | GAXETA DE PISTÃO |
| 9376 | PINO DO PISTÃO |
| 9377 | PRESSÃO SOBRE O PISTÃO |
| 9378 | BOMBA DE PISTÃO |

| | |
|---|---|
| 9379 | ANEL DE SEGMENTO |
| 9379 | ANEL DE PISTÃO |
| 9380 | SEGMENTO DE PISTÃO COM JUNTA E COBREJUNTA |
| 9381 | SEGMENTO DE PISTÃO COM JUNTA INCLINADA |
| 9382 | SEGMENTO DE PISTÃO COM JUNTA SUPERPOSTA |
| 9383 | HASTE DO PISTÃO |
| 9383 | PICOTA |
| 9384 | PONTA DA HASTE DO PISTÃO |
| 9385 | GUIA DA HASTE DO PISTÃO |
| 9386 | EMPANQUE DA HASTE DO PISTÃO |
| 9387 | HASTE DE PISTÃO TRANSVERSAL (BILATERAL) |
| 9388 | VELOCIDADE DO PISTÃO |
| 9389 | CURSO DO PISTÃO |
| 9390 | VÁLVULA DE PISTÃO |
| 9390 | DISTRIBUIDOR CILÍNDRICO |
| 9391 | PISTÃO DE DUPLA HASTE |
| 9392 | PISTÃO DE HASTE ÚNICA |
| 9393 | PITE |
| 9393 | COVA |
| 9393 | POÇO |
| 9393 | FOSSO |
| 9394 | FUNDIÇÃO EM POÇO |
| 9395 | PLAINA MECÂNICA DE VALETA |
| 9396 | AREIA DE MINA |
| 9397 | ÁGUA DE POÇO DE MINA |
| 9398 | POÇO DE MINA |
| 9399 | PASSO |
| 9400 | PEZ |
| 9400 | BREU |
| 9400 | PICHE |
| 9401 | ÂNGULO PRIMITIVO |
| 9402 | RODA DENTADA PARA CORRENTE |
| 9403 | CÍRCULO PRIMITIVO |
| 9404 | CÍRCULO PRIMITIVO |
| 9404 | CIRCUNFERÊNCIA PRIMITIVA |
| 9405 | HULHA BETUMINOSA |
| 9406 | CONE PRIMITIVO |
| 9407 | DIÂMETRO EFETIVO |
| 9408 | PASSO DE ENGRENAGEM |
| 9409 | PASSO DE REBITES |
| 9410 | PASSO DE ROSCA |
| 9410 | PASSO DE PARAFUSO |
| 9411 | URANINITA |
| 9412 | CORRENTE CALIBRADA |
| 9413 | MEDULA DE MADEIRA |
| 9414 | ALAVANCA DE COMANDO |
| 9414 | BRAÇO PITMAN |

| | |
|---|---|
| 9415 | TUBO DE PITOT |
| 9416 | PICADURAS |
| 9417 | MICROFISSURAÇÃO |
| 9417 | PICADURAS |
| 9418 | CORROSÃO LOCALIZADA |
| 9419 | PIVÔ |
| 9420 | PIVÔ |
| 9421 | PINO |
| 9421 | PIVÔ |
| 9422 | PIVOTADO |
| 9423 | LOCAL DE MONTAGEM |
| 9423 | LUGAR DE INSTALAÇÃO |
| 9424 | ROLAMENTO LISO |
| 9425 | MANDRIL DE MONTAGEM LISA |
| 9426 | DISTRIBUIDOR PLANO |
| 9427 | AÇO COMUM |
| 9428 | TORNO PARALELO |
| 9429 | TORNO SIMPLES |
| 9430 | VISTA DE CONJUNTO |
| 9431 | CALIBRE FÊMEA LISO |
| 9432 | PLAINA |
| 9433 | PLANO |
| 9434 | APLAINAR |
| 9435 | CURVA PLANA |
| 9436 | FACA DE PLAINA |
| 9437 | ESPELHO PLANO |
| 9438 | PLANO DE PROJEÇÃO |
| 9439 | PLANO DE REFRAÇÃO |
| 9440 | PLANO DE SIMETRIA |
| 9441 | SUPERFÍCIE PLANA |
| 9442 | MÁQUINA DE NIVELAR E RETIFICAR |
| 9443 | PLAINA MECÂNICA |
| 9444 | RODA SATÉLITE |
| 9444 | RODA PLANETÁRIA |
| 9445 | PLANETÁRIO |
| 9446 | ENGRENAGEM EPICÍCLICA |
| 9446 | ENGRENAGEM PLANETÁRIA |
| 9446 | EIXO PLANETÁRIO |
| 9447 | MOVIMENTO PLANETÁRIO |
| 9448 | PLANÍMETRO |
| 9449 | PLANIMETRIA |
| 9450 | APLAINAMENTO |
| 9451 | MÁQUINA DE APLAINAR |
| 9452 | PLAINA |
| 9453 | PLAINA-FRESADORA |
| 9454 | ALISAMENTO |
| 9454 | APLAINAMENTO |
| 9455 | MARTELO DE APLAINAR |
| 9456 | LAMINADOR DE POLIR |
| 9457 | PRANCHA |
| 9458 | LENTE PLANO-CÔNCAVA |

| | | | | |
|---|---|---|---|---|
| 9459 | LENTE PLANO-CONVEXA | | 9503 | ELETRODEPOSIÇÃO |
| 9460 | FRESADORA-APLAINADORA | | 9504 | PLANO DE CHAPEAMENTO |
| 9461 | USINA | | 9505 | PORTA-PEÇAS NO ELETRÓLITO |
| 9461 | FÁBRICA | | 9506 | SAIS ELETROLÍTICOS |
| 9461 | INSTALAÇÃO INDUSTRIAL | | 9507 | CLORETO PLATÍNICO |
| 9462 | RENTABILIDADE | | 9508 | PLATINITE |
| 9463 | REBOCO | | 9509 | CLORETO PLATINOSO |
| 9463 | REBOCAR | | 9510 | PLATINA |
| 9463 | GESSO | | 9511 | PÓ DE PLATINA |
| 9464 | REVESTIR COM GESSO | | 9512 | CADINHO DE PLATINA |
| 9465 | MOLDE DE GESSO | | 9513 | FIO DE PLATINA |
| 9466 | GESSO | | 9514 | PÓ DE PLATINA |
| 9467 | CORPO PLÁSTICO | | 9515 | PLATINA IRIDIADA |
| 9468 | FIO REVESTIDO COM PLÁSTICO | | 9516 | JOGO |
| 9469 | DEFORMAÇÃO PLÁSTICA | | 9516 | FOLGA |
| 9470 | ARGILA PLÁSTICA | | 9517 | VENTILAÇÃO POR IMPULSÃO |
| 9471 | DEFORMAÇÃO PLÁSTICA | | 9518 | FLEXÍVEL |
| 9472 | CABO ISOLADO COM P.V.C. | | 9519 | PLOTAR |
| 9473 | REFRATÁRIO PLÁSTICO | | 9520 | TRAÇAR UM DIAGRAMA |
| 9474 | PLASTICIDADE | | 9521 | TRAÇADO DE UM DIAGRAMA |
| 9475 | PLASTIFICADOR | | 9522 | ARADO |
| 9476 | MATÉRIA PLÁSTICA | | 9522 | GUILHERME DE CARPINTEIRO |
| 9477 | PLACA | | 9523 | ARADO DE DISCOS |
| 9477 | CHAPA | | 9524 | ARADOS MONTADOS |
| 9478 | CHAPA PARA EMBUTIMENTO | | 9525 | ARADOS ARRASTADOS |
| 9479 | COBRIR COM CHAPA | | 9526 | ARADOS |
| 9479 | CHAPEAR | | 9527 | ARADO DE LOMBADA |
| 9480 | MÁQUINA DE CURVAR CHAPAS | | 9528 | AÇO PARA ARADO |
| 9481 | PRENSA DE CURVAR CHAPAS | | 9529 | BUJÃO |
| 9482 | CAME DE DISCO | | 9529 | TAMPA |
| 9483 | BORDA DE CHAPA | | 9529 | TOMADA |
| 9484 | MÁQUINA DE CHANFRAR CHAPAS | | 9530 | MACHO DE TORNEIRA |
| 9485 | MÁQUINA DE DESEMPENAR CHAPAS | | 9531 | VERIFICADOR MACHO |
| 9486 | EMBREAGEM A DISCO | | 9531 | MACHO CALIBRADOR |
| 9487 | CALIBRE PARA CHAPAS | | 9532 | CHAVE DE TORNEIRA |
| 9488 | VIGA DE ALMA CHEIA | | 9533 | ESQUADRO PARA TORNEIRA |
| 9489 | TIRANTE | | 9534 | MACHO MATRIZ |
| 9490 | VIGA COMPOSTA | | 9535 | VÁLVULA DE MACHO |
| 9491 | VIDRO-CRISTAL | | 9536 | SOLDA DE BUJÃO |
| 9492 | FOLHA DE MOLA | | 9537 | SOLDAGEM DE FUROS DE REBITE |
| 9493 | RECORTE DE CHAPA | | 9538 | PESO DE PRUMO |
| 9494 | TESOURA PARA CHAPAS | | 9539 | FIO DE PRUMO |
| 9495 | MOLA DE FOLHA | | 9540 | RÉGUA OU NÍVEL DE PRUMO |
| 9496 | APARA DE CHAPA | | 9541 | GRAFITA |
| 9497 | CAMES DE DISCO | | 9541 | PLUMBAGINA |
| 9498 | PLAQUETA | | 9542 | PLUMBAGINA |
| 9499 | CHAPA DE FIXAÇÃO | | 9543 | CHUMACEIRA |
| 9500 | CHAPAS (ORDEM DE COLOCAÇÃO DAS) | | 9544 | PUNÇÃO |
| 9501 | RECOBRIMENTO COM CHAPAS | | 9545 | MERGULHADOR |
| 9502 | PLATAFORMA | | 9545 | PICOTA |
| 9503 | CHAPEAMENTO | | 9546 | BOMBA DE ÊMBOLO MERGULHADOR |

| | | | |
|---|---|---|---|
| 9547 | MOLA DE PISTÃO COM FIXADOR | 9597 | TRABALHO DE VISADA |
| 9548 | REFUGO DE PENEIRAMENTO | 9598 | POLIR |
| 9549 | PNEUMÁTICO | 9599 | POLÍVEL |
| 9550 | MANDRIS PNEUMÁTICOS | 9600 | POLIMENTO |
| 9551 | MARTELO PNEUMÁTICO | 9601 | MATÉRIA ABRASIVA |
| 9552 | MARTELO-PILÃO | 9602 | TAMBOR DE POLIR |
| 9553 | MARTELO PNEUMÁTICO | 9603 | MÁQUINA DE POLIR |
| 9554 | EJETOR PNEUMÁTICO | 9604 | RODA DE POLIR |
| 9555 | REBITADOR PNEUMÁTICO | 9605 | POLIMENTO |
| 9556 | FERRAMENTA PNEUMÁTICA | 9606 | POLÔNIO |
| 9557 | VÁLVULA DE COMANDO PNEUMÁTICO | 9607 | POLICRÔMICO |
| 9558 | PNEUMÁTICA | 9608 | METAL POLICRISTALINO |
| 9559 | PONTO | 9609 | POLÍGONO |
| 9560 | PONTO NO ESPAÇO | 9610 | POLÍGONO DE FORÇAS |
| 9561 | PONTO DE APLICAÇÃO | 9611 | LINHA POLIGONAL |
| 9562 | PONTO DE CONTATO | 9612 | POLIEDRO |
| 9563 | PONTO DE RUPTURA | 9613 | POLÍMERO |
| 9564 | PONTO DE INFLEXÃO | 9614 | POLIMERIZAÇÃO |
| 9565 | PONTO DE INTERSEÇÃO | 9615 | POLIMERIZAR (SE) |
| 9566 | PONTO DE REFERÊNCIA | 9616 | POLIMERIA |
| 9567 | PONTO DE APOIO | 9617 | POLIMORFISMO |
| 9568 | PONTO DE SUSPENSÃO | 9618 | CURVA POLITRÓPICA |
| 9569 | CABEÇA DE DENTE | 9619 | PONDERÁVEL |
| 9570 | SUSPENSÃO DE PIVÔ | 9620 | ABERTURA OU REGISTRO DE INSPEÇÃO |
| 9571 | GUILHERME | 9621 | TELHADO DE PONTÃO |
| 9571 | BURIL BISELADO | 9622 | GAIOLA AFINADORA |
| 9572 | CONTROLE PONTA-A-PONTA | 9623 | CAL MAGRA |
| 9573 | FERRO DE SOLDAR RETO | 9624 | ÓLEO DE PAPOULA |
| 9574 | CONTATOS | 9625 | PORCELANA |
| 9575 | ATIÇAR O FOGO | 9626 | CADINHO DE PORCELANA |
| 9576 | SOLDAGEM POR PONTOS A RESISTÊNCIA | 9627 | PORO |
| 9577 | POLAR | 9628 | MATERIAL POROSO |
| 9578 | COORDENADAS POLARES | 9629 | POROSIDADE |
| 9579 | DISTÂNCIA POLAR | 9630 | POROSO |
| 9580 | RAIO POLAR | 9631 | TUFO PORFIRÍTICO |
| 9581 | TRIÂNGULO POLAR | 9632 | PÓRFIRO |
| 9582 | POLARIZAÇÃO | 9633 | ORIFÍCIO |
| 9583 | MICROSCÓPIO POLARIZANTE | 9634 | ORIFÍCIO DE PASSAGEM |
| 9584 | POLARISCÓPIO | 9635 | MÓVEL |
| 9585 | LUZ POLARIZADA | 9636 | PUA PORTÁTIL |
| 9586 | PRISMA POLARIZADOR | 9637 | FORJA PORTÁTIL |
| 9587 | POLARIDADE | 9638 | BOMBA PORTÁTIL |
| 9588 | INDICADOR DE POLARIDADE | 9639 | LINHA FÉRREA DECAUVILLE |
| 9589 | POLARIZAÇÃO | 9640 | LOCOMÓVEL |
| 9590 | POLAROGRAFIA | 9641 | GRUA DE PÓRTICO |
| 9591 | PÓLO | 9642 | FRESADORA DE PÓRTICO |
| 9592 | PÓLO | 9643 | PARTE DE EIXO |
| 9593 | MASSAS POLARES | 9644 | CIMENTO PORTLAND |
| 9594 | PAPEL POLAR | 9645 | POSIÇÃO DA MANIVELA |
| 9595 | PÓLO DE ÍMÃ | 9646 | POSIÇÃO EM PONTO MORTO |
| 9596 | FORÇA POLAR | 9647 | POSIÇÃO DE EQUILÍBRIO |

| | | | | |
|---|---|---|---|
| 9648 | POSIÇÃO DE REPOUSO | 9695 | PERMANGANATO DE POTÁSSIO |
| 9649 | CAPTADOR DE POSIÇÃO | 9696 | FOSFATO DE POTÁSSIO |
| 9650 | COMANDO DE POSICIONAMENTO | 9697 | POLISSULFETO DE POTÁSSIO |
| 9651 | TEMPO DE POSICIONAMENTO | 9698 | SILICATO DE POTÁSSIO |
| 9652 | ACELERAÇÃO POSITIVA | 9699 | SULFATO DE POTÁSSIO |
| 9653 | BOMBA VOLUMÉTRICA | 9700 | SULFETO DE POTÁSSIO |
| 9654 | ACIONAMENTO POSITIVO | 9701 | SULFOCIANETO DE POTÁSSIO |
| 9655 | ELETRICIDADE POSITIVA | 9702 | ENXADA LATERAL PARA BATATAS |
| 9656 | CALOR DE FORMAÇÃO | 9703 | ARRANCADORA DE BATATAS |
| 9657 | ÍON POSITIVO | 9704 | CEIFADORA DE RAMA DE BATATA |
| 9657 | CÁTION | 9705 | SEPARADORA DE BATATA |
| 9658 | PLACA POSITIVA | 9706 | CLASSIFICADORES DE BATATA |
| 9659 | PÓLO POSITIVO | 9707 | ARRANCADORES DE BATATA |
| 9660 | LUZ ANÓDICA | 9708 | POTENCIAL |
| 9661 | SINAL POSITIVO | 9709 | DIFERENÇA DE POTENCIAL |
| 9662 | POSITRON | 9709 | TENSÃO NOS ELÉTRODOS |
| 9663 | MANCAL CONSOLO EM COLUNA | 9710 | ENERGIA POTENCIAL |
| 9664 | VERRUMAS | 9710 | ENERGIA LATENTE |
| 9665 | PÓS-PROCESSADOR | 9711 | POTENCIÔMETRO |
| 9666 | TRATAMENTO DE REPOUSO APÓS SOLDAGEM | 9712 | PISAR |
| | | 9712 | BATER |
| 9667 | RECOZIMENTO REDUTOR DE TENSÃO | 9712 | ESMAGAR |
| 9668 | PÓS-AQUECIMENTO | 9712 | RECALCAR |
| 9669 | FORNO DE CADINHO | 9712 | TRITURAR |
| 9670 | CEMENTAÇÃO COM CIANETO DE POTÁSSIO | 9713 | ASFALTO LANÇADO |
| 9671 | LIXÍVIA DE POTASSA | 9714 | CONCRETO LANÇADO |
| 9672 | POTÁSSIO | 9715 | LANÇAMENTO |
| 9673 | ACETATO DE POTÁSSIO | 9715 | VAZAMENTO |
| 9674 | ALUMINATO DE POTÁSSIO | 9716 | FUNIL DE LANÇAMENTO |
| 9675 | TARTRATO DE POTÁSSIO E ANTIMÔNIO | 9717 | SAÍDA EM LINGOTEIRA |
| 9676 | BICARBONATO DE POTÁSSIO | 9718 | PRENSA DE COMPRIMIR PÓ |
| 9677 | BICROMATO DE POTÁSSIO | 9719 | CORTE COM PÓ |
| 9678 | BROMETO DE POTÁSSIO | 9720 | METALURGIA DO PÓ |
| 9679 | CARBONATO DE POTÁSSIO | 9721 | MÉTODO DOS PÓS |
| 9679 | POTASSA | 9722 | SOLDAGEM SOB PÓ |
| 9680 | CLORATO DE POTÁSSIO | 9723 | ASFALTO EM PÓ |
| 9681 | CLORETO DE POTÁSSIO | 9724 | TIJOLO EM PÓ |
| 9682 | CROMATO NEUTRO DE POTÁSSIO | 9725 | MAGNÉSIA EM PÓ |
| 9683 | CIANETO DE POTÁSSIO | 9726 | TURFA MIÚDA |
| 9684 | CIANETO DE POTÁSSIO E FERRO | 9727 | PEDRA-POMES EM PÓ |
| 9685 | CIANETO DE POTÁSSIO E FERRO | 9728 | POEIRENTO |
| 9686 | FLUORETO DE POTÁSSIO | 9729 | POTÊNCIA |
| 9687 | POTASSA CÁUSTICA | 9730 | POTÊNCIA |
| 9687 | HIDRATO DE POTÁSSIO | 9730 | FORÇA |
| 9688 | CLORETO DE POTÁSSIO | 9730 | PODER |
| 9689 | IODETO DE POTÁSSIO | 9731 | SERVO-FREIOS |
| 9690 | PAPEL AMIDADO COM IODETO DE POTÁSSIO | 9731 | FREIOS ASSISTIDOS |
| 9691 | NITRITO DE POTÁSSIO | 9732 | PUA ELÉTRICA |
| 9692 | OXALATO NEUTRO DE POTÁSSIO | 9733 | FORÇA MECÂNICA |
| 9693 | PERCARBONATO DE POTÁSSIO | 9733 | FORÇA MOTRIZ |
| 9694 | PERCLORATO DE POTÁSSIO | 9734 | ACIONAMENTO MECÂNICO |

| | | | |
|---|---|---|---|
| 9735 | FATOR DE POTÊNCIA | 9781 | DISPOSITIVO DE PROTENSÃO |
| 9736 | GÁS INDUSTRIAL | 9782 | PROTENSÃO |
| 9737 | PRODUÇÃO DE ENERGIA | 9783 | FORRO REVESTIDO PREVIAMENTE DE |
| 9738 | FORÇA BRAÇAL | | PEDREGULHO |
| 9739 | USINA ELÉTRICA | 9784 | PREPARAÇÃO |
| 9740 | REBITAGEM PARA CONSTRUÇÕES | 9785 | PREPARAÇÃO DE UMA SOLUÇÃO |
| | METÁLICAS | 9786 | FUNÇÃO PREPARATÓRIA |
| 9741 | ASSENTO DE REGULAGEM AUTOMÁTICA | 9787 | TRABALHO PREPARATÓRIO |
| 9742 | USINA ELÉTRICA | 9788 | PREPARAR UMA SOLUÇÃO |
| 9743 | SERVO-DIREÇÃO | 9789 | PRÉ-SELETOR |
| 9744 | DISTRIBUIÇÃO DE ENERGIA | 9790 | CONSERVAÇÃO DA MADEIRA |
| 9744 | FORNECIMENTO DE CORRENTE | 9791 | PRESERVATIVO |
| | INDUSTRIAL | 9792 | REVESTIMENTOS DE PROTEÇÃO |
| 9745 | TOMADA DE FORÇA | 9793 | CAMADA PROTETORA |
| 9746 | TRANSMISSÃO DE FORÇA | 9794 | PRÉ-SINTERIZAÇÃO |
| 9747 | MÁQUINA DE SERRAR | 9795 | PRENSA |
| 9747 | SERRA MECÂNICA | 9796 | PISTOLAS DE AR COMPRIMIDO |
| 9748 | POZOLANA | 9797 | PULSADOR |
| 9749 | CIMENTO DE POZOLANA | 9797 | BOTÃO DE APERTAR |
| 9750 | PRASIODÍMIO | 9798 | FORJA A PRENSA |
| 9751 | PRÉ-FILTRO | 9799 | SINTERIZAÇÃO SOB PRESSÃO |
| 9752 | USINAGEM PRÉ-REGULADA | 9799 | ESTAMPAGEM A QUENTE |
| 9753 | PRECAUÇÕES | 9800 | FORJAR COM PRENSA |
| 9754 | PRECESSÃO | 9801 | CARTÃO ACETINADO |
| 9755 | RETIFICAÇÃO DE PRECISÃO | 9801 | PRESSPAN |
| 9756 | METAL PRECIOSO | 9802 | PLACA DE CORTIÇA AGLOMERADA |
| 9757 | PRECIPITÁVEL | 9803 | FLANGE BORDEADO |
| 9758 | PRECIPITANTE | 9804 | TURFA COMPRIMIDA |
| 9759 | PRECIPITADO | 9805 | POLIA DE AÇO PRENSADO |
| 9760 | PRECIPITAR | 9806 | COMPRESSÃO |
| 9761 | PRECIPITAÇÃO | 9806 | PRENSAGEM |
| 9762 | ENDURECIMENTO POR PRECIPITAÇÃO | 9807 | FORJA A PRENSA |
| 9763 | PRECISÃO | 9808 | PRESSÃO |
| 9764 | BALANÇA DE PRECISÃO | 9808 | TENSÃO |
| 9765 | MODELAGEM DE PRECISÃO | 9809 | PRESSÃO MANOMÉTRICA |
| 9766 | CALIBRE DE PRECISÃO | 9810 | ÂNGULO DE PRESSÃO |
| 9767 | REGRA DIVIDIDA DE PRECISÃO | 9811 | DEPRESSÃO |
| 9768 | CALIBRE DE ALTURA DE PRECISÃO | 9812 | FUNDIÇÃO SOB PRESSÃO |
| 9769 | DIVISOR DE PRECISÃO | 9813 | CONTROLADOR DE PRESSÃO |
| 9770 | MÁQUINA DE PRECISÃO | 9814 | DIFERENÇA DE PRESSÃO |
| 9771 | ORIENTAÇÃO PREFERENCIAL | 9815 | QUEDA DE PRESSÃO |
| 9772 | PRÉ-FORMA | 9816 | PRESSÃO POR ATRITO |
| 9773 | PREFORMAÇÃO | 9817 | VENTILADOR CALCANTE |
| 9774 | PREAQUECER | 9818 | LUBRIFICAÇÃO SOB PRESSÃO |
| 9775 | PREAQUECEDOR | 9819 | GASOGÊNIO DE AR SOPRADO |
| 9776 | PREAQUECIMENTO | 9820 | MANÔMETRO |
| 9777 | FORNO DE PREAQUECIMENTO | 9821 | MANÔMETRO |
| 9778 | PRÉ-IGNIÇÃO | 9822 | PRESSÃO INTERNA EM TUBULAÇÃO |
| 9778 | IGNIÇÃO PREMATURA | 9823 | PRESSÃO REQUERIDA |
| 9779 | TESTE PRELIMINAR | 9823 | CARGA DE FORJA |
| 9780 | TRATAMENTO PRELIMINAR | 9824 | LUBRIFICAÇÃO SOB PRESSÃO |

| | |
|---|---|
| 9825 | PRESSÃO DE FLUXO |
| 9826 | PRESSÃO NAS ARESTAS |
| 9827 | TUBO DE PRESSÃO |
| 9828 | AFERIÇÃO DE VÁLVULA |
| 9829 | DISPOSITIVO DE CONTROLE DE PRESSÃO |
| 9830 | ANEL DE PRESSÃO |
| 9831 | PARAFUSO DE PRESSÃO |
| 9832 | PRESSÃO DE REGULAGEM |
| 9833 | GRAU DE PRESSÃO |
| 9834 | CURSO DE PRESSÃO |
| 9835 | CHAVE DE PRESSÃO |
| 9836 | TESTE DE PRESSÃO |
| 9837 | SOLDAGEM TÉRMICA COM PRESSÃO MECÂNICA |
| 9838 | SOLDAGEM RESISTENTE À PRESSÃO |
| 9839 | VASO DE PRESSÃO |
| 9840 | CONDUTO FORÇADO |
| 9841 | ÁGUA SOB PRESSÃO |
| 9842 | SOLDAGEM A PRESSÃO |
| 9843 | VÁLVULA DE PRESSÃO-DEPRESSÃO |
| 9844 | PUNÇÃO DE BICO |
| 9844 | PUNÇÃO DE MARCAR |
| 9845 | BATERIA PRIMÁRIA |
| 9845 | BATERIA DE PILHA |
| 9846 | PILHA PRIMÁRIA |
| 9847 | COR SIMPLES |
| 9848 | ELEMENTO PROEUTETÓIDE |
| 9848 | CONSTITUINTE PRIMÁRIO |
| 9849 | CRISTALIZAÇÃO PRIMÁRIA |
| 9850 | TAXA DE CORRENTE PRIMÁRIA |
| 9851 | GRAFITE PRIMÁRIA |
| 9852 | PRODUTO PRIMÁRIO |
| 9853 | METAL VIRGEM |
| 9854 | RESISTÊNCIA PRIMITIVA |
| 9855 | PRINCIPAL |
| 9855 | DE PRIMEIRA QUALIDADE |
| 9856 | ESCORVAR UMA BOMBA |
| 9857 | PRIMEIRA CAMADA DE REVESTIMENTO |
| 9857 | PRIMEIRA MÃO |
| 9858 | PREÇO DE FÁBRICA |
| 9859 | FORÇA MOTRIZ |
| 9859 | PRINCÍPIO MOTOR |
| 9860 | NÚMERO PRIMO |
| 9861 | LIGA DE COBRE E ZINCO |
| 9862 | PRODUTOS DE PRIMEIRA QUALIDADE |
| 9863 | ESCORVA |
| 9863 | SUCÇÃO DE ÁGUA POR VAPOR |
| 9864 | PRIMEIRA MÃO |
| 9864 | PRIMEIRA CAMADA DE TINTA |
| 9865 | TRANSLAÇÃO PRIMITIVA |
| 9866 | EIXO PRINCIPAL |

| | |
|---|---|
| 9867 | DÍNAMO |
| 9868 | SEÇÃO PRINCIPAL |
| 9869 | TENSÃO PRINCIPAL |
| 9870 | CÓPIA |
| 9871 | CIRCUITO IMPRESSO |
| 9872 | QUE IMPRIME |
| 9873 | MÁQUINA DE MARTELAR OS CILINDROS IMPRESSORES |
| 9874 | IMPRESSÃO |
| 9875 | PRISMA |
| 9876 | PRISMA DE SEÇÃO OBLÍQUA |
| 9877 | PLANO PRISMÁTICO |
| 9878 | ESPECTRO PRODUZIDO POR PRISMA |
| 9879 | PRISMÁTICO |
| 9880 | PRISMÓIDE |
| 9880 | PRISMATÓIDE |
| 9881 | FUNÇÃO DE DISTRIBUIÇÃO |
| 9882 | SONDA |
| 9883 | VARETA |
| 9884 | RECOZIMENTO INTERMEDIÁRIO |
| 9885 | MANUAL DE FABRICAÇÃO |
| 9886 | METALURGIA DE EXTRAÇÃO |
| 9887 | PROCESSO DE USINAGEM |
| 9888 | INDÚSTRIA DE TRANSFORMAÇÃO |
| 9889 | PROCESSADOR |
| 9890 | GÁS DE GASOGÊNIO |
| 9891 | PRODUTO |
| 9892 | PRODUTO |
| 9893 | PRODUTO DE COMBUSTÃO |
| 9894 | PRODUÇÃO DE CORRENTE |
| 9895 | PRODUÇÃO DE FRIO |
| 9896 | PRODUÇÃO DE CALOR |
| 9897 | PRODUTIVIDADE |
| 9898 | PERFIL |
| 9899 | FRESA PERFILADA |
| 9900 | FRESADORA DE PERFILAR |
| 9900 | FRESADORA DESBASTADORA |
| 9901 | TUPIA |
| 9902 | PROGRAMA |
| 9903 | PARADA PROGRAMADA |
| 9904 | PROGRAMAÇÃO |
| 9905 | PROGRESSO |
| 9906 | ENVELHECIMENTO PROGRESSIVO |
| 9907 | CALIBRE DE TOLERÂNCIAS GRADUADAS |
| 9908 | SOLDAGEM FORTE POR INDUÇÃO PROGRESSIVA |
| 9909 | PROJETAR |
| 9910 | EM FALSO |
| 9910 | EM SACADA |
| 9910 | FORA DE PRUMO |
| 9910 | SALIENTE |

| | |
|---|---|
| 9911 | CHAPA EM RELEVO |
| 9912 | PROJEÇÃO |
| 9913 | SALIÊNCIA |
| 9914 | LENTE DIVERGENTE |
| 9915 | SOLDA A RESISTÊNCIA DE RESSALTOS |
| 9916 | SOLDAGEM POR RESSALTOS |
| 9917 | PROJEÇÃO |
| 9917 | RESSALTO |
| 9917 | RELEVO |
| 9918 | CICLÓIDE ALONGADO |
| 9919 | PROLONGAMENTO DE DURAÇÃO DE PATENTE |
| 9920 | FREIO DE PRONY |
| 9920 | FREIO DINAMOMÉTRICO |
| 9921 | PROVA |
| 9922 | RESISTÊNCIA DE PROVA |
| 9923 | LIMITE DE ESCOAMENTO |
| 9923 | LIMITE ELÁSTICO CONVENCIONAL |
| 9924 | TESTE ANTIDESTRUTIVO |
| 9924 | PROVA |
| 9924 | EXPERIÊNCIA |
| 9925 | ESTEIO |
| 9925 | PONTALETE |
| 9925 | ESPEQUE |
| 9925 | SUPORTE |
| 9926 | PROPAGAÇÃO DE ONDAS |
| 9927 | PROPANA |
| 9928 | PÁ DE HÉLICE |
| 9929 | VENTILADOR DE HÉLICE |
| 9930 | EIXO TRANSMISSOR |
| 9930 | EIXO DE HÉLICE |
| 9931 | MISTURADOR DE HÉLICE |
| 9932 | FRAÇÃO PRÓPRIA |
| 9933 | PROPORÇÃO |
| 9934 | PROPORÇÃO DE MISTURA |
| 9934 | DOSAGEM DE MISTURA |
| 9935 | PROPORCIONAL |
| 9936 | LIMITE PROPORCIONAL |
| 9937 | COMPASSO REDUTOR |
| 9938 | PROPORCIONALIDADE |
| 9939 | PROPILENO |
| 9940 | PROTATÍNEO |
| 9941 | MOTOR PROTEGIDO |
| 9942 | LUVA PROTETORA |
| 9943 | PROTEÇÃO |
| 9944 | TAMPA DE PROTEÇÃO |
| 9945 | PROTEÇÃO CONTRA FERRUGEM |
| 9945 | PROTEÇÃO ANTIOXIDANTE |
| 9946 | PROTEÇÃO DE PROPRIEDADE INDUSTRIAL |
| 9947 | ATMOSFERA PROTETORA |
| 9948 | CAIXA PROTETORA |
| 9949 | REVESTIMENTO PROTETOR |
| 9950 | CAMADA PROTETORA |
| 9950 | PELÍCULA PROTETORA |
| 9951 | GRADE DE PROTEÇÃO |
| 9952 | MATERIAL DE PROTEÇÃO |
| 9953 | PAREDE DE PROTEÇÃO |
| 9953 | MURO DE ARRIMO |
| 9954 | PRÓTON |
| 9955 | PROTÓTIPO |
| 9956 | TRANSFERIDOR |
| 9957 | REGULADOR PSEUDO-ASTÁTICO |
| 9958 | LIGA TERNÁRIA PSEUDOBINÁRIA |
| 9959 | CEMENTAÇÃO BRILHANTE |
| 9960 | PSICRÓMETRO |
| 9961 | PUDLAR |
| 9961 | CIMENTO HIDRÁULICO |
| 9961 | BANHO DE FUSÃO |
| 9962 | FERRO PUDLADO |
| 9963 | AÇO PUDLADO |
| 9964 | PUDLAGEM |
| 9965 | FORNO DE PUDLAR |
| 9966 | MAXALADEIRA DE ARGILA |
| 9966 | MOINHO DE AMASSAR |
| 9967 | TRAÇÃO NORMAL NO SENTIDO DAS FIBRAS |
| 9968 | TRAÇÃO NA DIREÇÃO DAS FIBRAS |
| 9969 | FAZER COINCIDIR OS FUROS DE REBITE |
| 9970 | TRAÇÃO |
| 9971 | ROLDANA |
| 9971 | POLIA |
| 9972 | CADERNAL |
| 9972 | MOITÃO |
| 9973 | MOITÕES |
| 9974 | POLIAS DEFEITUOSAS |
| 9975 | TORNO COM POLIAS |
| 9976 | POLIA DE BRAÇOS CURVOS |
| 9977 | POLIA DE BRAÇOS RETOS |
| 9978 | SOLDAGEM POR PULSAÇÃO |
| 9979 | PULSO |
| 9979 | IMPULSO |
| 9980 | PULSÔMETRO |
| 9981 | PULVERIZÁVEL |
| 9982 | PULVERIZAR |
| 9983 | PULVERIZADO |
| 9984 | CARVÃO PULVERIZADO |
| 9985 | PULVERIZAÇÃO |
| 9986 | PEDRA-POMES |
| 9987 | POLIR COM PEDRA-POMES |
| 9988 | PEDRA-POMES |
| 9989 | TUFO DE POMES |
| 9990 | POLIMENTO COM PEDRA-POMES |
| 9991 | BOMBA |

| | |
|---|---|
| 9992 | CILINDRO DA BOMBA |
| 9993 | INJETOR DE BOMBA |
| 9994 | LUBRIFICADOR A BOMBA |
| 9995 | PISTÃO DE BOMBA |
| 9996 | BOMBAS |
| 9997 | FURADOR |
| 9997 | PUNÇÃO |
| 9998 | PUNCIONAR |
| 9998 | PERFURAR |
| 9999 | PUNCIONAR |
| 10000 | ALICATE VAZADOR |
| 10001 | PRENSA DE FURAR OU DE ESTAMPAR |
| 10002 | CARTÃO PERFURADO |
| 10003 | CHAPA DE FUROS PUNCIONADOS |
| 10004 | ORIFÍCIO DE REBITE PUNCIONADO |
| 10005 | FITA PERFURADA |
| 10006 | PERFURAÇÃO |
| 10007 | MÁQUINA DE PUNCIONAR E CISALHAR |
| 10008 | PUNCIONAMENTO |
| 10009 | MÁQUINA DE PUNCIONAR |
| 10010 | TESTE DE PUNCIONAMENTO |
| 10011 | UNIDADE DE PUNCIONAMENTO |
| 10012 | PUNCIONAMENTO |
| 10013 | PERFURAÇÃO POR DESCARGA DISRUPTIVA |
| 10014 | GUINCHO DE ENGRENAGEM |
| 10015 | CALIBRE DE RECEPÇÃO |
| 10016 | PESQUISA PURA |
| 10017 | PURGA |
| 10018 | PURIFICAÇÃO DO GÁS |
| 10019 | PURIFICAÇÃO DA ÁGUA |
| 10020 | DEPURADOR |
| 10020 | PURIFICADOR |
| 10021 | COMPRESSÃO NO SENTIDO DAS FIBRAS |
| 10022 | COMPRESSÃO NORMAL NO SENTIDO DAS FIBRAS |
| 10023 | BANCO DE ESTIRAGEM |
| 10024 | FORNO POR PERCUSSÃO |
| 10025 | AJUSTE COM FOLGA |
| 10026 | HASTE DE IMPULSO |
| 10027 | SOLDAGEM DE MONOPONTO A RESISTÊNCIA |
| 10028 | IMPULSO |
| 10028 | COMPRESSÃO |
| 10029 | PROPULSOR |
| 10030 | FORNO CONTÍNUO TIPO PROPULSOR |
| 10031 | HASTE DE IMPULSO |
| 10032 | ESTICAR UMA MOLA |
| 10033 | EMBREAR |
| 10034 | DESEMBREAR |
| 10035 | PUTREFAÇÃO |

| | |
|---|---|
| 10036 | APODRECER |
| 10037 | MASSA DE VIDRACEIRO |
| 10037 | MÁSTIQUE |
| 10038 | PIRÂMIDE |
| 10039 | DUREZA VICKERS |
| 10040 | SISTEMA PIRAMIDAL |
| 10041 | PIRIDINA |
| 10042 | PIROELÉTRICO |
| 10043 | PIROELETRICIDADE |
| 10044 | PIROCONDUTIVIDADE |
| 10044 | CONDUTIVIDADE TERMOELÉTRICA |
| 10045 | ÁCIDO PIROGÁLICO |
| 10046 | ÁCIDO PIROLENHOSO |
| 10047 | BIÓXIDO DE MANGANÊS |
| 10047 | PIROLUSITA |
| 10048 | PIROMETALURGIA |
| 10049 | PIRÔMETRO |
| 10050 | CONE PIROMÉTRICO |
| 10051 | EQUIVALENTE DO CONE PIROMÉTRICO |
| 10052 | PIROMETRIA |
| 10053 | LIGA PIROFÓRICA |
| 10054 | ÁCIDO PIROFOSFÓRICO |
| 10055 | PRISMA QUADRANGULAR |
| 10056 | QUADRANTE |
| 10057 | EQUAÇÃO DO SEGUNDO GRAU |
| 10057 | EQUAÇÃO QUADRÁTICA |
| 10058 | QUADRILÁTERO |
| 10059 | MOTOR DE EXPANSÃO QUÁDRUPLA |
| 10060 | VÁLVULA DE ASSENTO QUÁDRUPLO |
| 10061 | PENETRÔMETRO |
| 10062 | ANÁLISE QUALITATIVA |
| 10063 | CONTROLE DE QUALIDADE |
| 10064 | ANÁLISE QUANTITATIVA |
| 10065 | GRANDEZA |
| 10065 | QUANTIDADE |
| 10066 | QUANTIDADE DE CALOR |
| 10067 | QUANTIDADE DE ELETRICIDADE |
| 10068 | QUANTIDADE DE MOVIMENTO |
| 10069 | VAZÃO |
| 10069 | DÉBITO |
| 10070 | QUANTIDADE A SER MEDIDA |
| 10071 | RENDIMENTO QUÂNTICO |
| 10072 | COMPRIMENTO CRÍTICO DE ONDAS |
| 10073 | PEDREIRA |
| 10074 | CURVA DE 90° |
| 10075 | CORTE RADIAL DA MADEIRA |
| 10076 | MADEIRA EM QUARTOS |
| 10077 | QUARTZO |
| 10078 | FIO OU FIBRA DE QUARTZO |
| 10079 | VIDRO DE QUARTZO |
| 10080 | LÂMPADA DE MERCÚRIO EM QUARTZO |

| | |
|---|---|
| 10081 | PÓRFIRO QUARTZOSO |
| 10082 | AREIA QUARTZÍFERA |
| 10083 | QUARTZITA |
| 10084 | LIGA QUATERNÁRIA |
| 10085 | LIGA QUATERNÁRIA EUTÉTICA |
| 10086 | QUADRIFÓLIO |
| 10087 | ENVELHECIMENTO POR ESFRIAMENTO RÁPIDO |
| 10088 | FLEXÃO EM AÇOS TRATADOS COM TÊMPERAS |
| 10089 | ENDURECIMENTO POR TÊMPERA |
| 10090 | TANQUE DE TÊMPERA |
| 10091 | ESFRIAR BRUSCAMENTE O AÇO |
| 10092 | TEMPERADO E REVENIDO |
| 10093 | AÇO ACALMADO E TEMPERADO |
| 10094 | RESFRIAMENTO BRUSCO |
| 10095 | TÊMPERA E REVENIDO |
| 10096 | BANHO DE TÊMPERA |
| 10097 | FRATURA DE TÊMPERA |
| 10098 | MEIO DE TÊMPERA |
| 10099 | ÓLEO DE TÊMPERA |
| 10100 | RESFRIAMENTO BRUSCO DO AÇO |
| 10101 | QUESTIONÁRIO |
| 10102 | CURVA ACENTUADA |
| 10103 | COMPORTA DE MANOBRA RÁPIDA |
| 10104 | VÁLVULA DE MANOBRA RÁPIDA |
| 10105 | FILETE OU ROSCA DE PASSO RÁPIDO |
| 10106 | MECANISMO DE RETORNO RÁPIDO |
| 10107 | CIMENTO DE PEGA RÁPIDA |
| 10108 | ADAPTADOR PARA MUDANÇA RÁPIDA |
| 10109 | FUNDIÇÃO TRANQÜILA |
| 10110 | QUINIDRONA (SEMICÉLULA À) |
| 10111 | QUINTAL (MÉTRICO) |
| 10112 | EQUAÇÃO DE QUINTO GRAU |
| 10113 | CITAR |
| 10114 | QUOCIENTE |
| 10115 | REBAIXADEIRA |
| 10115 | PLAINA DE RANHURAR |
| 10116 | BARRA DE BATER A ESCÓRIA |
| 10117 | DISPARAR |
| 10117 | ACELERAR |
| 10117 | PRECIPITAR-SE |
| 10118 | VELOCIDADE EXCESSIVA DE UM MOTOR |
| 10118 | DISPARO |
| 10119 | CREMALHEIRA |
| 10120 | CREMALHEIRA E PINHÃO |
| 10121 | MACACO DE CREMALHEIRA |
| 10122 | COMPASSO DE CREMALHEIRA |
| 10123 | MECANISMO DE AVANÇO POR CREMALHEIRA |
| 10124 | HASTE DE CREMALHEIRA |

| | |
|---|---|
| 10125 | RADIAL |
| 10126 | PNEU DE LONA RADIAL |
| 10127 | ACELERAÇÃO CENTRÍFUGA |
| 10128 | BRAÇO RADIAL |
| 10129 | PERFURATRIZ DE BRAÇO RADIAL |
| 10130 | MANCAL DE ESFERAS RADIAL |
| 10131 | FEIXE RADIAL |
| 10131 | VIGA RADIAL |
| 10132 | COMPONENTE RADIAL |
| 10133 | DESLOCAMENTO RADIAL |
| 10134 | PERFURATRIZ RADIAL |
| 10135 | MOTOR RADIAL |
| 10135 | MOTOR ESTRELADO |
| 10136 | TURBINA RADIAL |
| 10137 | PROJEÇÃO CENTRAL |
| 10138 | RADIANO |
| 10139 | ENERGIA DE IRRADIAÇÃO |
| 10140 | CALOR RADIANTE |
| 10141 | RADIAR |
| 10141 | IRRADIAR |
| 10142 | SUPERFÍCIE IRRADIANTE |
| 10143 | RADIAÇÃO |
| 10144 | CONSTANTE DE RADIAÇÃO |
| 10145 | PERDA DE CALOR POR IRRADIAÇÃO |
| 10146 | IRRADIAÇÃO DE CALOR |
| 10147 | IRRADIAÇÃO DE LUZ |
| 10148 | RADIADOR |
| 10149 | RADIADOR DE ESFRIAR |
| 10150 | RADIADOR DE AQUECER |
| 10151 | TAMPA DE RADIADOR |
| 10152 | CALANDRA DE RADIADOR |
| 10153 | VÁLVULA DE RADIADOR |
| 10154 | RADICAL |
| 10155 | RADIOMETALURGIA |
| 10156 | ANTIPARASITA |
| 10157 | RADIOATIVO |
| 10158 | SUBSTÂNCIAS RADIOATIVAS |
| 10159 | EMANAÇÃO RADIOATIVA |
| 10160 | RADIOATIVIDADE |
| 10161 | RADIOGRAFIA |
| 10162 | EXAME RADIOGRÁFICO |
| 10163 | RADIOGRAFIA |
| 10164 | RADIOLOGIA |
| 10165 | RÁDIO |
| 10166 | RAIO |
| 10167 | ESTRIAMENTO |
| 10168 | RAIO DE CURVATURA |
| 10169 | RAIO DE ROTAÇÃO |
| 10170 | RAIO VETOR |
| 10171 | TRAPO |
| 10172 | CHUMBADOR FARPADO |

| | |
|---|---|
| 10173 | RODA DE TRAPOS |
| 10174 | CILINDRO PICADO |
| 10175 | TRILHO |
| 10176 | MÁQUINA DE PERFURAR TRILHOS E TALAS |
| 10177 | PRODUTOS EM AÇO PARA TRILHO |
| 10178 | MANCHAS DE ÁGUA (DE CHUVA) |
| 10179 | ÁGUA DE CHUVA |
| 10180 | ELEVAR A UMA POTÊNCIA |
| 10181 | CHAPA PADRÃO ELEVADA |
| 10182 | RETENÇÃO DE ÁGUA |
| 10183 | FLANGE DE FACE ELEVADA |
| 10184 | TESTE DE BRUNIDURA |
| 10184 | TESTE DE SUSPENSÃO |
| 10185 | AUMENTO DE VELOCIDADE |
| 10186 | ÂNGULO DE INCLINAÇÃO |
| 10186 | ÂNGULO DE CORTE |
| 10187 | DENTES ALTERNADOS |
| 10188 | PISTÃO HIDRÁULICO |
| 10188 | ARÍETE |
| 10188 | MACACO DE BATE-ESTACA |
| 10189 | SOCAR |
| 10189 | CALCAR |
| 10189 | PISAR |
| 10190 | FRESA RADIAL DE CORREDIÇA |
| 10191 | GANCHO DUPLO |
| 10192 | RAMI |
| 10193 | CONCRETO BATIDO |
| 10194 | OPERAÇÃO DE CALCAR OU PISAR |
| 10195 | OPERAÇÃO DE SOCAR |
| 10196 | PISTÃO RAMSBOTTOM |
| 10197 | ÓLEO RANÇOSO |
| 10198 | ACESSO ALEATÓRIO |
| 10198 | ACESSO DIRETO |
| 10199 | ORIENTADO AO ACASO |
| 10200 | ALCANCE |
| 10200 | GAMA |
| 10201 | FAIXA DE ESCALA DE UM INSTRUMENTO |
| 10202 | ALCANCE DO SOM |
| 10203 | DIAGRAMA RANKINE |
| 10204 | ÓLEO DE COLZA |
| 10205 | COMBUSTÃO VIVA |
| 10206 | BROCA DE CORTE RÁPIDO |
| 10207 | AÇO-FERRAMENTA RÁPIDO |
| 10208 | AVANÇO RÁPIDO |
| 10209 | EIXO DE ALTA VELOCIDADE |
| 10210 | TERRAS RARAS |
| 10211 | RAREFAÇÃO DE UM GÁS |
| 10212 | RAREFAÇÃO DO AR |
| 10213 | AR RAREFEITO |
| 10214 | RAREFAZER O GÁS |

| | |
|---|---|
| 10215 | LIMA |
| 10215 | GROSA |
| 10215 | GROSA |
| 10216 | LIMA CAUDA DE RATO |
| 10217 | FLUTUADOR DE ESTACAGEM E DE CHEGADA |
| 10218 | CATRACA |
| 10219 | ROQUETE |
| 10219 | ARCO DE PUA DE CATRACA |
| 10220 | EFEITO DE CATRACA |
| 10221 | ENGRENAGEM DE CATRACA |
| 10222 | MACACO A CATRACA |
| 10223 | ALAVANCA A CATRACA |
| 10224 | CHAVE DE CATRACA |
| 10225 | RODA DE CATRACA |
| 10226 | TAXA |
| 10226 | GRAU |
| 10226 | VELOCIDADE |
| 10226 | RITMO |
| 10227 | GRAU DE COMBUSTÃO |
| 10228 | POTÊNCIA DE UMA BOMBA |
| 10229 | QUANTIDADE DE DEPOSIÇÃO DE METAL |
| 10230 | VELOCIDADE DA PROPAGAÇÃO DA CHAMA |
| 10231 | GRAU DE AQUECIMENTO |
| 10232 | VELOCIDADE DA VAZÃO DO ÓLEO |
| 10233 | CAVALO-FORÇA NOMINAL |
| 10234 | PROPORÇÃO |
| 10234 | RAZÃO |
| 10234 | RELAÇÃO |
| 10235 | NÚMERO RACIONAL |
| 10236 | TORIM |
| 10236 | JUNCO |
| 10237 | COURO CRU |
| 10238 | PINHÃO DE COURO CRU |
| 10239 | MATÉRIA-PRIMA |
| 10240 | ÁGUA NATURAL |
| 10240 | ÁGUA NÃO TRATADA |
| 10241 | IRRADIAÇÃO |
| 10242 | RAIOS |
| 10243 | ÂNGULO DE REENTRÂNCIA |
| 10244 | TORNAR A MONTAR |
| 10245 | REEREÇÃO |
| 10245 | REMONTAGEM |
| 10246 | REUTILIZAÇÃO |
| 10247 | REATÂNCIA |
| 10248 | REAÇÃO |
| 10249 | LIMITE DE REAÇÃO |
| 10250 | TURBINA A REAÇÃO |
| 10251 | REATOR |
| 10252 | LER |

| | |
|---|---|
| 10253 | VISUALIZAÇÃO |
| 10254 | LEITURA |
| 10255 | REAJUSTAR |
| 10256 | REAJUSTE |
| 10257 | REAGENTE |
| 10258 | FOCO REAL |
| 10259 | IMAGEM REAL |
| 10260 | NÚMERO REAL |
| 10261 | RESISTÊNCIA EFETIVA |
| 10262 | ÓXIDO DE ARSÊNIO |
| 10262 | REALGAR |
| 10263 | ALARGADOR |
| 10263 | ESCAREADOR |
| 10264 | PORTA-ESCAREADOR |
| 10265 | EIXO TRASEIRO |
| 10266 | ESPELHO RETROVISOR |
| 10267 | ESCALA DE REAUMUR |
| 10268 | TERMÔMETRO REAUMUR |
| 10269 | REBAIXO |
| 10269 | ENTALHE |
| 10269 | ESTRIA |
| 10270 | RETIFICAR |
| 10271 | ESCAREAÇÃO |
| 10272 | RESSALTO |
| 10272 | REPERCUSSÃO |
| 10273 | RESSALTAR |
| 10274 | RECALESCÊNCIA |
| 10275 | RECARBURIZAÇÃO DO FERRO |
| 10276 | RECARBURANTE |
| 10277 | RECIPIENTE |
| 10277 | RECEPTOR |
| 10277 | CARREGADOR |
| 10278 | POSTO RECEPTOR |
| 10279 | VÃO |
| 10279 | REBAIXO |
| 10279 | RECESSO |
| 10280 | RECÍPROCO |
| 10281 | REDE RECÍPROCA |
| 10282 | FRESAGEM RECÍPROCA |
| 10283 | MOVIMENTO ALTERNATIVO |
| 10283 | MOVIMENTO DE VAIVÉM |
| 10284 | BOMBA-PISTÃO |
| 10285 | MÁQUINA DE PISTÃO |
| 10286 | RETROCESSO |
| 10287 | REACONDICIONAMENTO |
| 10288 | REGISTRAR |
| 10288 | GRAVAR |
| 10289 | REGISTRADOR |
| 10289 | GRAVADOR |
| 10290 | CILINDRO GIRATÓRIO DE REGISTRADOR |
| 10291 | DINAMÓGRAFO |

| | |
|---|---|
| 10292 | MANÔMETRO REGISTRADOR |
| 10293 | TERMÓGRAFO |
| 10294 | APARELHO REGISTRADOR |
| 10295 | RECUPERAR |
| 10296 | RESTAURAÇÃO |
| 10296 | RECUPERAÇÃO |
| 10297 | RECRISTALIZAÇÃO |
| 10298 | TEMPERATURA DE RECRISTALIZAÇÃO |
| 10299 | RETÂNGULO |
| 10300 | MÁQUINA DE BURILAR POR FAÍSCAS EM COORDENADAS RETANGULARES |
| 10301 | COORDENADAS RETANGULARES |
| 10301 | COORDENADAS ORTOGONAIS |
| 10302 | SEÇÃO RETANGULAR |
| 10303 | CARGA RETANGULAR |
| 10304 | MALHA RETANGULAR |
| 10305 | PARALELEPÍPEDO RETANGULAR |
| 10306 | MOLA DE FOLHA RETANGULAR |
| 10307 | MOLA DE FOLHA RETANGULAR DE PERFIL PARABOLÓIDE |
| 10308 | TRANSFERIDOR RETANGULAR |
| 10309 | CABEÇA QUADRADA DE PARAFUSO |
| 10310 | RETANGULAR |
| 10311 | RETIFICAÇÃO |
| 10312 | RETIFICAÇÃO |
| 10313 | ÁLCOOL RETIFICADO |
| 10314 | RETIFICADOR |
| 10315 | ÂNODO DE RETIFICADOR |
| 10316 | CÁTODO DE RETIFICADOR |
| 10317 | TUBO RETIFICADOR |
| 10318 | RETIFICAR |
| 10319 | RETILÍNEO |
| 10320 | MOVIMENTO RETILÍNEO |
| 10321 | FORNO RECUPERATIVO |
| 10322 | RECUPERADOR |
| 10323 | RENOVAR AS LIMAS |
| 10324 | RENOVAÇÃO DA LIMA |
| 10325 | LATÃO VERMELHO |
| 10326 | LIGA DE BRONZE E ZINCO |
| 10326 | BRONZE VERMELHO |
| 10327 | FUMAÇA VERMELHA |
| 10328 | DUREZA AO RUBRO |
| 10329 | RUBRO |
| 10329 | CALOR AO RUBRO |
| 10330 | DE CALOR AO RUBRO |
| 10331 | ENSAIO DE RUPTURA AO RUBRO |
| 10332 | MÁSTIQUE VERMELHO |
| 10332 | MÁSTIQUE AO MÍNIO |
| 10333 | MÍNIO |
| 10333 | ZARCÃO |
| 10334 | FÓSFORO VERMELHO |

| | | | |
|---|---|---|---|
| 10335 | FERRUGEM | 10381 | TEMPERATURA DE REFINAÇÃO |
| 10336 | ARENITO VERMELHO | 10382 | REFLETIR |
| 10337 | QUEBRADIÇO AO RUBRO | 10383 | LUZ REFLETIDA |
| 10337 | FRÁGIL AO RUBRO | 10384 | RAIO REFLETIDO |
| 10338 | FERRO FRÁGIL AO RUBRO | 10385 | SUPERFÍCIE REFLETORA |
| 10339 | FRAGILIDADE AO RUBRO | 10386 | TELESCÓPIO |
| 10340 | OCRE VERMELHO | 10387 | REFLEXÃO |
| 10340 | GIZ VERMELHO | 10388 | REDE DE REFLEXÃO |
| 10341 | ZINCO REFUNDIDO | 10389 | PERDA POR REFLEXÃO |
| 10342 | REDUZIR | 10390 | REFLEXÃO DA LUZ |
| 10343 | ESCALA REDUZIDA | 10391 | RELAÇÃO DE REFLEXÃO |
| 10344 | TEMPERATURA REDUZIDA | 10392 | PODER DE REFLEXÃO |
| 10345 | REDUTOR | 10393 | REFLEXIVIDADE |
| 10346 | AGENTE REDUTOR | 10394 | REFLETOR |
| 10347 | ATMOSFERA REDUTORA | 10395 | INDICADOR A REFRAÇÃO |
| 10348 | LUVA DE REDUÇÃO | 10396 | VIDRO DE REFRAÇÃO |
| 10348 | REDUTOR MACHO-FÊMEA | 10397 | RAIO REFRATADO |
| 10349 | CHAMA REDUTORA | 10398 | TELESCÓPIO DE REFRAÇÃO |
| 10350 | FLANGE DE REDUÇÃO | 10398 | LUNETA DE APROXIMAÇÃO |
| 19351 | LUVA DE REDUÇÃO | 10398 | REFRATOR |
| 10352 | TUBO DE REDUÇÃO | 10399 | REFRAÇÃO |
| 10353 | CILINDROS DE DESBASTAR | 10400 | REFRAÇÃO DA LUZ |
| 10354 | TEMPERATURA DE REDUÇÃO | 10401 | MEIO REFRATÁRIO |
| 10355 | VÁLVULA DE REDUÇÃO DE PRESSÃO | 10402 | REFRINGENTE |
| 10356 | REDUÇÃO | 10403 | REFRATIVIDADE |
| 10357 | REDUÇÃO | 10403 | REFRINGÊNCIA |
| 10357 | DESMULTIPLICAÇÃO | 10404 | REFRACTÔMETRO |
| 10358 | CONE DE REDUÇÃO | 10405 | PROPRIEDADE REFRATÁRIA |
| 10359 | FORNO REDUTOR | 10406 | ARGAMASSA REFRATÁRIA |
| 10360 | RELAÇÃO DE REDUÇÃO | 10407 | REFRIGERADOR |
| 10361 | REDUÇÃO DA SUPERFÍCIE | 10407 | FRIGORÍFICO |
| 10362 | DIMINUIÇÃO DA SEÇÃO TRANSVERSAL | 10408 | INSTALAÇÃO DE REFRIGERAÇÃO |
| 10363 | REDUÇÃO DA VELOCIDADE | 10409 | REFRIGERADOR |
| 10364 | REDUNDÂNCIA | 10409 | GELADEIRA |
| 10365 | COMPARADOR DE LÂMINAS | 10410 | FORNO DE RECUPERAÇÃO DE CALOR |
| 10366 | CALIBRE PADRÃO | 10411 | CALEFAÇÃO REGENERATIVA |
| 10366 | CALIBRE DE REFERÊNCIA | 10412 | REGENERADOR |
| 10367 | ÍNDICE DE REFERÊNCIA | 10412 | RECUPERADOR |
| 10368 | PONTO DE REFERÊNCIA | 10413 | REGISTRO |
| 10369 | TEMPERATURA DE REFERÊNCIA | 10414 | ACOCHAMENTO DIAGONAL |
| 10370 | REFINAR | 10414 | CABLAGEM ALTERNATIVA |
| 10371 | REFINAR UM METAL | 10415 | CABO METÁLICO TRANÇADO |
| 10372 | REFINADO | | ALTERNADAMENTE |
| 10373 | ÓLEO REFINADO | 10416 | POLÍGONO REGULAR |
| 10374 | PRODUTO DE REFINAÇÃO | 10417 | REGULARIDADE DO MOVIMENTO |
| 10375 | REFINARIA | 10418 | DISPOSITIVO REGULADOR |
| 10376 | CHAMA DE REFINARIA | 10419 | REGULAGEM DA PRESSÃO |
| 10377 | REFINAÇÃO | 10420 | REGULADOR |
| 10378 | REFINAÇÃO DE UM METAL | 10421 | REGULADOR |
| 10379 | FORNO DE REFINAÇÃO | 10422 | RÉGULO |
| 10380 | PROCESSO DE REFINAÇÃO | 10423 | RÉGULO DE ANTIMÔNIO |

| | | | |
|---|---|---|---|
| 10424 | REAQUECER | 10467 | REPRODUÇÃO |
| 10425 | REAQUECIMENTO | 10468 | REPULSÃO |
| 10426 | FORNO DE REAQUECIMENTO | 10469 | GRANDEZA DESEJADA |
| 10426 | FORNO DE RECOZER | 10469 | QUANTIDADE REQUERIDA |
| 10427 | REFORÇO DA SOLDA | 10470 | RELAMINAÇÃO |
| 10428 | SOLDA DE REFORÇO | 10471 | RESERVATÓRIO |
| 10429 | REFORÇO | 10472 | ELASTICIDADE RESIDUAL |
| 10430 | CHAPA DE REFORÇO | 10473 | INDUÇÃO RESIDUAL |
| 10431 | REJEIÇÃO | 10474 | ESFORÇO RESIDUAL |
| 10432 | UMIDADE RELATIVA | 10475 | RESÍDUO |
| 10433 | UMIDADE RELATIVA DO AR | 10476 | RESÍDUO DE COMBUSTÃO |
| 10434 | MOVIMENTO RELATIVO | 10477 | ELASTICIDADE |
| 10435 | AFROUXAMENTO | 10477 | RESILIÊNCIA |
| 10436 | SOLTAR O FREIO | 10478 | RESINA |
| 10437 | GATILHO | 19479 | RESINOSO |
| 10437 | LINGÜETA DE DISPARO | 10480 | RESINIFICAÇÃO |
| 10438 | ALAVANCA DE DISPARO OU DESENGATE | 10481 | RESINIFICAR |
| 10439 | SEGURANÇA DE FUNCIONAMENTO | 10482 | MASSA RESINOSA |
| 10440 | SEGURO | 10483 | MADEIRA RESINOSA |
| 10441 | VÁLVULA DE EMERGÊNCIA | 10484 | RESISTÊNCIA |
| 10441 | VÁLVULA DE DESCARGA | 10485 | FORNO A ARCO DE RESISTÊNCIA |
| 10442 | ARCO DE DESCARGA | 10486 | LIGAS PARA RESISTÊNCIAS |
| 10443 | TORNO DETALONADOR OU REBAIXADOR | 10487 | SOLDAGEM FORTE POR RESISTÊNCIA |
| 10444 | RESISTÊNCIA MAGNÉTICA | 10488 | SOLDAGEM DE TOPO À RESISTÊNCIA |
| 10444 | RELUTÂNCIA | 10489 | DIAGRAMA DE RESISTÊNCIA |
| 10445 | MAGNETISMO RESIDUAL | 10490 | FORNO ELÉTRICO À RESISTÊNCIA |
| 10446 | REFUNDIR | 10491 | RESISTÊNCIA DE UM CONDUTOR |
| 10447 | REFUNDIÇÃO | 10492 | RESISTÊNCIA DO AR |
| 10448 | COMANDO À DISTÂNCIA | 10493 | SOLDAGEM POR PONTOS À RESISTÊNCIA |
| 10448 | CONTROLE REMOTO | 10494 | VERIFICADOR DE RESISTÊNCIA AO |
| 10449 | CALIBRAGEM À DISTÂNCIA | | ESFORÇO |
| 10450 | MANIVELA REMOVÍVEL | 10495 | PIRÔMETRO DE RESISTÊNCIA |
| 10451 | REMOÇÃO E REMONTAGEM | 10496 | RESISTÊNCIA AOS ÁCIDOS |
| 10452 | EVACUAÇÃO DO PÓ | 10497 | RESISTÊNCIA AO MOVIMENTO |
| 10453 | ESCOAMENTO DE ÁGUAS RESIDUAIS | 10498 | RESISTÊNCIA AO DESLIZAMENTO |
| 10454 | ELIMINAÇÃO DE FERRO DA ÁGUA | 10498 | RESISTÊNCIA À DERRAPAGEM |
| 10455 | EVACUAR OS GASES | 10499 | RESISTÊNCIA AO DESGASTE |
| 10456 | SOLUBILIZAR | 10500 | SOLDAGEM POR RESISTÊNCIA |
| 10456 | TORNAR SOLÚVEL | 10501 | FIO PARA RESISTÊNCIA |
| 10457 | RENOVAR PEÇAS DE MÁQUINA | 10502 | RESISTÊNCIA |
| 10458 | RENOVAÇÃO DE PEÇA DE MÁQUINA | 10503 | RESISTIVIDADE |
| 10459 | REPARAÇÃO | 10504 | DECOMPOSIÇÃO |
| 10459 | CONSERTO | 10505 | DECOMPOSIÇÃO DE FORÇAS |
| 10460 | REPARAR | 10506 | RESSONÂNCIA |
| 10460 | CONSERTAR | 10507 | REESQUADRAMENTO |
| 10461 | OFICINA DE CONSERTO | 10507 | CISALHAMENTO |
| 10462 | FABRICAÇÃO EM SÉRIE | 10508 | REPOR EM MOVIMENTO |
| 10463 | SUBSTITUIR | 10508 | REINICIAR |
| 19464 | SUBSTITUIÇÃO DE PEÇA | 10509 | REINÍCIO |
| 10465 | RÉPLICA | 10510 | INIBIDOR |
| 10466 | MATERIAIS REFRATÁRIOS | 10511 | RETIFICAÇÃO |

| | | | |
|---|---|---|---|
| 10512 | RESULTADO DE TESTE | 10556 | TAQUÍMETRO |
| 10513 | RESULTANTE | 10557 | ROTAÇÃO |
| 10514 | PORCA DE RETENÇÃO | 10557 | GIRO |
| 10515 | ANEL DE RETENÇÃO | 10558 | ROTAÇÕES POR MINUTO (RPM) |
| 10516 | HASTE DE RETENÇÃO | 10559 | GRELHA GIRATÓRIA |
| 10517 | ATRASO DE EBULIÇÃO | 10560 | CONTRAPONTO GIRATÓRIO |
| 10518 | MOVIMENTO RETARDADO | 10561 | MASSA GIRATÓRIA |
| 10519 | ATRASO DO FECHAMENTO DA VÁLVULA | 10562 | REOLOGIA |
| 10520 | DUREZA APÓS REVENIDO | 10563 | REOSTATO |
| 10521 | RESISTÊNCIA À DEFORMAÇÃO | 10564 | RÓDIO |
| 10522 | CONTRA-TESTE | 10565 | CRISTAL ROMBOÉDRICO |
| 10523 | RETORTA | 10566 | ROMBOEDRO |
| 10524 | FORNO DE RETORTA | 10567 | ROMBÓIDE |
| 10525 | RETORTA COM TUBO | 10568 | ROMBO |
| 10526 | MOLA DE CHAMADA | 10568 | LOSANGO |
| 10527 | MONTAGEM ULTERIOR | 10569 | NERVURA |
| 10528 | CONTRAMANIVELA | 10569 | FRISO |
| 10529 | CURSO EM VAZIO | 10569 | ABA |
| 10530 | CURSO DE RETORNO DO PISTÃO | 10570 | NERVURA DE UM TUBO |
| 10530 | RETORNO DO PISTÃO | 10571 | TUBO ALADO |
| 10531 | ORNAMENTAÇÕES | 10572 | CRIVO |
| 10532 | FORNO DE REVÉRBERO | 10572 | PENEIRA |
| 10533 | TEMPO DE INVERSÃO | 10573 | CHARRUA DE ALPORCAR |
| 10534 | INVERTER | 10574 | CHAPA ESTRIADA |
| 10535 | TESTE DE FLEXÃO ALTERNADA | 10575 | LANCETEIRA CURVA |
| 10536 | CONTRA-REAÇÃO | 10575 | LIMA DE ENTRAR |
| 10537 | REVERSIBILIDADE | 10576 | ESTRIAS |
| 10538 | REVERSÍVEL | 10577 | ÂNGULO RETO |
| 10539 | MUDANÇA REVERSÍVEL DE ESTADO | 10578 | CONE VERTICAL OU RETO |
| 10540 | MOTOR REVERSÍVEL | 10579 | CILINDRO RETO |
| 10541 | INVERSÃO DE MARCHA | 10580 | PARAFUSO COM ROSCA À DIREITA |
| 10542 | DISPOSITIVO DE MUDANÇA DE SENTIDO DE MARCHA | 10581 | PARALELEPÍPEDO RETO |
| | | 10582 | TRIÂNGULO RETÂNGULO |
| 10543 | MÁQUINA A VAPOR REVERSÍVEL | 10583 | DESVIO À DIREITA |
| 10544 | MECANISMO DE INVERSÃO DE MARCHA | 10584 | PARAFUSO À DIREITA |
| 10545 | MECANISMO DE INVERSÃO DE MARCHA MEDIANTE ENGRENAGENS CÔNICAS | 10585 | ROSCA À DIREITA |
| | | 10586 | ENGRENAGEM HELICOIDAL À DIREITA |
| 10546 | DISPOSITIVO DE INVERSÃO DE MARCHA MEDIANTE DISCOS DE FRICÇÃO | 10587 | CABO TRANÇADO À DIREITA |
| | | 10588 | CORPO RÍGIDO |
| 10547 | DISPOSITIVO DE INVERSÃO DE MARCHA MEDIANTE ENGRENAGENS DE DENTES RETOS | 10589 | FIXAÇÃO RÍGIDA |
| | | 10590 | BROCAS RÍGIDAS |
| | | 10591 | RIGIDEZ |
| 10548 | INVERSOR DE MARCHA | 10592 | ARO |
| 10549 | ALAVANCA DE MUDANÇA DE MARCHA | 10593 | ARO DE VOLANTE |
| 10550 | EIXO DE MUDANÇA DE MARCHA | 10594 | ARO DE RODA DE ENGRENAGEM |
| 10551 | POLIA DE TRANSMISSÃO | 10595 | ARO DE POLIA |
| 10552 | INVERSÃO DO MOVIMENTO | 10596 | COROA DE RODA |
| 10553 | VÁLVULA INVERSORA | 10597 | RESPIRO DE VEDAÇÃO |
| 10554 | REVERSÃO | 10598 | AÇO EFERVESCENTE |
| 10555 | JUNÇÃO DE CORREIAS POR REBITES | 10599 | AÇO EM FUSÃO |
| 10556 | CONTA-GIROS | 10599 | AÇO EFERVESCENTE |

| | | | |
|---|---|---|---|
| 10600 | ARO | 10642 | MÁQUINA DE REBITAR |
| 10600 | ANEL | 10643 | REBITAGEM |
| 10601 | LUBRIFICAÇÃO POR ANEL | 10644 | MARTELO DE REBITAR |
| 10602 | MANCAL LUBRIFICADOR POR ANEL | 10645 | MÁQUINA DE REBITAR |
| 10603 | SEGMENTO DE ANEL | 10646 | REBITES |
| 10604 | JUNTA ANULAR | 10647 | ASFALTO LÍQUIDO |
| 10605 | VÁLVULA ANULAR | 10648 | TORRAR OS MINÉRIOS |
| 10606 | PIVÔ ANULAR | 10649 | FORNO DE TORREFAÇÃO |
| 10607 | LAVAR COM JATO DE ÁGUA | 10650 | TORREFAÇÃO DE MINÉRIOS |
| 10607 | ENXAGUAR | 10651 | ROCHA |
| 10608 | ENXAGUADURA | 10652 | CRISTAL DE ROCHA |
| 10609 | SERRA DE FENDER | 10653 | SAL-GEMA |
| 10609 | SERRA CIRCULAR | 10654 | BALANCIM |
| 10610 | GUIA PARA SERRAR EM REDOR | 10654 | BRAÇO OSCILANTE |
| 10611 | ALTA | 10654 | BRAÇO MÓVEL |
| 10611 | SUBIDA | 10655 | GRELHA OSCILANTE |
| 10611 | ELEVAÇÃO | 10656 | ALAVANCA OSCILANTE |
| 10612 | ALTA TEMPERATURA | 10657 | EIXO OSCILANTE |
| 10613 | FLECHA | 10658 | TESOURA BASCULANTE |
| 10614 | ESPELHO | 10659 | TESTE OU ENSAIO DE DUREZA ROCKWELL |
| 10614 | MONTANTE | 10660 | BARRA |
| 10614 | TUBO DE SUBIDA | 10660 | HASTE |
| 10614 | CANO ASCENDENTE | 10660 | VARETA |
| 10615 | CANO ASCENDENTE | 10661 | CALIBRE DE ALESAGEM |
| 10616 | HASTE ASCENDENTE | 10662 | BRAÇO DE PLANÍMETRO |
| 10617 | VÁLVULA DE HASTE ASCENDENTE | 10663 | HASTE |
| 10618 | TEMPERATURA ASCENDENTE | 10664 | RADIOGRAFIA |
| 10619 | AREIA DE RIO | 10665 | ROLAR |
| 10620 | ÁGUA DOCE | 10665 | LAMINAR |
| 10620 | ÁGUA FLUVIAL | 10666 | REDUZIR POR LAMINAÇÃO |
| 10621 | REBITE | 10667 | FILME EM ROLO |
| 10622 | REBITE NA BORDA DA CHAPA | 10668 | FORJA POR ROLOS |
| 10623 | FORJA DE AQUECER REBITES | 10669 | TREM DE LAMINADOR |
| 10624 | CABEÇA DE REBITE | 10670 | TREM DE LAMINADOR |
| 10625 | FURO DE REBITE | 10671 | CILINDRO |
| 10626 | PUNÇÃO PARA CONTRA-REBITES | 10671 | ROLO |
| 10627 | AÇO PARA REBITES | 10671 | TAMBOR |
| 10628 | CABEÇA REBITADA | 10672 | FLANGE LAMINADO |
| 10629 | REBITAR | 10673 | OURO LAMINADO |
| 10630 | TENAZ OU TORQUÊS PARA REBITES | 10674 | CHAPA LAMINADA |
| 10631 | SOLDAGEM DOS REBITES | 10675 | PERFIL LAMINADO |
| 10632 | REBITE DE CABEÇA CILÍNDRICA | 10676 | FERRO LAMINADO |
| 10633 | REBITE DE CABEÇA DE GOTA DE SEBO | 10676 | AÇO LAMINADO |
| 10634 | REBITE DE CABEÇA CHATA | 10677 | TUBO LAMINADO |
| 10635 | REBITE DE CABEÇA AMENDOADA | 10678 | FIO LAMINADO |
| 10636 | REBITE DE CABEÇA REDONDA | 10679 | ROLO |
| 10637 | REBITE DE CABEÇA HEMISFÉRICA | 10679 | ROLETE |
| 10638 | FLANGE REBITADO | 10680 | MANCAL DE ROLAMENTO |
| 10639 | JUNTA REBITADA | 10680 | ROLAMENTO DE ROLOS |
| 10640 | TUBO REBITADO | 10681 | ROLAMENTO DE RÓTULA SOBRE ROLOS |
| 10641 | REBITADOR | 10682 | ROLAMENTO DE ROLOS CILÍNDRICOS |

| | | | | |
|---|---|---|---|---|
| 10683 | ROLAMENTO DE ROLOS CÔNICOS | | 10729 | VENTILADOR DE SISTEMA ROOT |
| 10684 | CORRENTE A ROLOS | | 10730 | CABO |
| 10685 | DESEMPENADEIRA DE ROLOS | | 10730 | CORDA |
| 10686 | ALAVANCA ROLANTE | | 10731 | MOITÃO |
| 10687 | BRITADEIRA DE CILINDROS | | 10732 | FREIO DE CORDA |
| 10688 | ROLO DE CORRENTE | | 10733 | DIÂMETRO DE CABO |
| 10689 | PISTA DOS ROLOS DE ROLAMENTO | | 10734 | TRANSMISSÃO POR CABO |
| 10690 | SUPORTE DE ROLOS | | 10735 | ACIONAMENTO POR CABO |
| 10691 | MANCAL DE ROLOS | | 10736 | MÁQUINA DE ACIONAMENTO POR CABO |
| 10692 | TUCHO DE ROLO | | 10737 | TAMBOR DE GORNES PARA CABOS |
| 10693 | CALIBRE DE MORDAÇA PARA ROLOS | | 10738 | VOLANTE DE CABO |
| 10694 | SUPORTE DE ROLOS | | 10739 | CABLAGEM |
| 10695 | ROLOS | | 10740 | CORDÃO DE CABO |
| 10696 | ROLAMENTO | | 10741 | TALHA DE CORDA |
| 10696 | LAMINAÇÃO | | 10742 | POLIA DE CABO |
| 10697 | CURVA ROLANTE | | 10743 | FIO PARA CABOS |
| 10698 | SENTIDO DE LAMINAÇÃO | | 10744 | FILÁSTICA |
| 10699 | FLANGE DE LAMINAÇÃO | | 10745 | CORDAME |
| 10700 | ATRITO DE ROLAMENTO | | 10746 | ROSA |
| 10701 | TREM DE LAMINADOR | | 10746 | CRIVO DE REGADOR |
| 10701 | USINA DE LAMINAÇÃO | | 10747 | ALARGADOR TIPO ROSETA |
| 10702 | MOVIMENTO ROLANTE | | 10748 | COBRE ROSETA |
| 10703 | RESISTÊNCIA AO ROLAMENTO | | 10749 | ÓLEO DE RESINA |
| 10704 | CAIXA DE CILINDROS | | 10750 | ÁCIDO ROSÓLICO |
| 10705 | SUPERFÍCIE DE ROLAMENTO | | 10751 | VENTILADOR DE PISTÃO ROTATIVO |
| 10706 | CARGA ROLANTE | | 10752 | RESFRIADOR CIRCULAR |
| 10707 | CIMENTO ROMANO | | 10753 | MOTOCULTIVADORES |
| 10708 | TELHADO | | 10754 | MOTOR DE PISTÕES ROTATIVOS |
| 10708 | TETO | | 10755 | LIMA ROTATIVA |
| 10709 | LÂMPADA DE TETO | | 10756 | PISTÃO ROTATIVO |
| 10710 | PORTINHOLA DE INSPEÇÃO DE TETO | | 10757 | PRENSA ROTATIVA |
| 10711 | BOCAL DE TETO | | 10758 | BOMBA ROTATIVA |
| 10712 | PAPELÃO BETUMINADO | | 10759 | TESOURAS ROTATIVAS |
| 10713 | TEMPERATURA AMBIENTE | | 10760 | VÁLVULA DISTRIBUIDORA ROTATIVA |
| 10714 | RAIZ | | 10761 | MÁQUINA A VAPOR ROTATIVA |
| 10715 | CORTA-RAÍZES | | 10762 | MESA GIRATÓRIA |
| 10716 | ÂNGULO DE BASE | | 10763 | GIRAR |
| 10717 | CIRCULO DE RAIZ | | 10763 | RODAR |
| 10718 | CONE DE BASE | | 10764 | EIXO GIRATÓRIO |
| 10719 | DIÂMETRO DE PÉ | | 10765 | ROTAÇÃO |
| 10720 | ARESTA DE RAIZ | | 10766 | MOVIMENTO DE ROTAÇÃO |
| 10721 | FLANCO DE RAIZ | | 10767 | ROTOR |
| 10722 | LEVANTADORES DE RAÍZES | | 10768 | MADEIRA PODRE |
| 10723 | CIRCULO DE RAIZ | | 10769 | DECOMPOSIÇÃO |
| 10723 | CIRCULO DE FUNDO | | 10770 | DECOMPOSIÇÃO DA MADEIRA |
| 10724 | RAIZ DE DENTE | | 10771 | PERFURAR EM BRUTO |
| 10725 | RAIZ DE DENTE | | 10772 | CÁLCULO APROXIMADO OU ESTIMATIVO |
| 10726 | RAIZ DE SOLDA | | 10773 | RODA DE ENGRENAGEM FUNDIDA EM BRUTO |
| 10727 | VÃO DA RAIZ | | | |
| 10728 | RAIO DA RAIZ | | 10774 | LIMA GROSSA |
| 10728 | RAIO DE AFASTAMENTO DAS BORDAS | | 10775 | DESBASTAR |

| | |
|---|---|
| 10776 | FLANGE BRUTO DE FUNDIÇÃO |
| 10777 | RETIFICAÇÃO |
| 10778 | LAMINADO EM BRUTO |
| 10779 | SUPERFÍCIE RUGOSA |
| 10780 | TUBO ÁSPERO |
| 10781 | PESO BRUTO |
| 10782 | FURO PRÉVIO |
| 10783 | TORNAR ÁSPERO |
| 10784 | SUPERFÍCIE ÁSPERA |
| 10785 | DESBASTE EM BRUTO |
| 10786 | DESBASTE |
| 10787 | CILINDRO DESBASTADOR |
| 10788 | TORNO DE DESBASTAR |
| 10789 | FRESA DE DESBASTE |
| 10789 | TREM DESBASTADOR |
| 10790 | ALARGADOR CÔNICO |
| 10791 | FERRAMENTA PARA DESBASTAR |
| 10792 | RUGOSIDADE |
| 10792 | ASPEREZA |
| 10793 | ARREDONDAR UMA ARESTA |
| 10794 | CANTONEIRA DE ÂNGULO INTERNO ARREDONDADO |
| 10795 | FERRO REDONDO |
| 10796 | LIMA REDONDA |
| 10797 | FLANGE REDONDO |
| 10798 | BALÃO CÔNCAVO |
| 10799 | LETRA REDONDA |
| 10800 | PLAINA CONVEXA |
| 10801 | CABO REDONDO |
| 10802 | ROSCA REDONDA |
| 10803 | MADEIRA EM TOROS |
| 10804 | FIO OU ARAME REDONDO |
| 10805 | ALICATE DE FIO REDONDO |
| 10806 | PENA REDONDA |
| 10807 | PARAFUSO DE ROSCA REDONDA |
| 10808 | CANTO ARREDONDADO |
| 10809 | ARREDONDAMENTO DE ROSCA |
| 10810 | PERCURSO |
| 10810 | ROTA |
| 10811 | PROGRAMA DE COMPUTADOR |
| 10812 | LINHA |
| 10812 | SÉRIE |
| 10812 | FILEIRA |
| 10813 | LINHA DE REBITES |
| 10814 | RPM (ROTAÇÕES POR MINUTO) |
| 10815 | DESENFERRUJAR |
| 10816 | BORRACHA |
| 10817 | CORREIA DE BORRACHA |
| 10818 | TELA RECAUCHUTADA |
| 10819 | DIAFRAGMA DE BORRACHA |
| 10820 | JUNTA OU GAXETA DE BORRACHA |
| 10821 | MANGUEIRA DE BORRACHA |
| 10822 | FITA COM ISOLAMENTO DE BORRACHA |
| 10823 | ANEL DE BORRACHA |
| 10824 | TAMPA OU ROLHA DE BORRACHA |
| 10825 | BORRACHA |
| 10826 | DESENFERRUJAMENTO |
| 10827 | PEDREGULHO |
| 10827 | PEDRA GRANDE |
| 10828 | ALVENARIA DE PEDRA BRUTA |
| 10829 | RUBÍDIO |
| 10830 | BOBINA DE RUHMKORFF |
| 10831 | RÉGUA |
| 10832 | CAMADA |
| 10833 | CORRER A ALTA VELOCIDADE |
| 10834 | CORRER A BAIXA VELOCIDADE |
| 10835 | AMACIAR UM MOTOR |
| 10836 | ROMPIMENTO |
| 10837 | FUNDIR-SE |
| 10838 | MESA DE SAÍDA |
| 10838 | TREM DE ROLOS DE SAÍDA |
| 10839 | COLETOR |
| 10840 | ESTAR DESCENTRADO |
| 10841 | HULHA NÃO CLASSIFICADA |
| 10842 | CHAPA TECNOLÓGICA |
| 10843 | DEPÓSITO DE RECEBIMENTO |
| 10844 | CANAL DE ENTRADA (FUNDIÇÃO) |
| 10845 | FUNDIÇÃO |
| 10845 | VAZAMENTO |
| 10846 | MARCHA À RÉ |
| 10847 | AJUSTAGEM DESLIZANTE |
| 10848 | MARCHA À FRENTE |
| 10849 | METRO CORRENTE |
| 10850 | MARCHA DO MOTOR |
| 10851 | RAMAL LIVRE DE UM APARELHO |
| 10852 | PARAFUSO DE TRANSLAÇÃO |
| 10853 | LADO INTERNO DE UMA CORREIA |
| 10854 | RODA MOTRIZ |
| 10854 | RODA DE ROLAMENTO |
| 10855 | RODAGEM |
| 10855 | AMACIAMENTO |
| 10856 | FUNCIONAMENTO |
| 10857 | RAMPA |
| 10857 | PISTA |
| 10857 | CALHA |
| 10858 | RUPTURA |
| 10859 | ROMPER |
| 10859 | QUEBRAR |
| 10859 | RASGAR |
| 10860 | DISCO DE RUPTURA |
| 10861 | FRATURA |
| 10861 | ROMPIMENTO |

| | | | |
|---|---|---|---|
| 10861 | RUPTURA | 10903 | NITRO |
| 10862 | ÓLEO DE MADEIRAS RESINOSAS | 10904 | SAL |
| 10863 | FERRUGEM | 10905 | BANHO DE SAL |
| 10864 | ENFERRUJAR | 10906 | TEOR DE SAL |
| 10865 | FORMAÇÃO DE FERRUGEM | 10907 | BIOXALATO DE POTÁSSIO |
| 10866 | PRODUTO ANTIFERRUGEM | 10907 | SAL OXÁLICO |
| 10867 | JUNTA FEITA COM PASTA OXIDANTE | 10908 | SOLUÇÃO SALINA |
| 10868 | ANTIFERRUGINOSO | 10909 | TESTE DE PULVERIZAÇÃO SALINA |
| 10869 | SUBSTÂNCIA ANTIFERRUGINOSA | 10910 | ÁGUA SALGADA |
| 10870 | PRODUTO ANTIFERRUGINOSO | 10911 | SOLDAGEM FORTE EM BANHO DE SAL |
| 10871 | PROTEÇÃO ANTIFERRUGINOSA | 10912 | FORNO DE BANHO DE SAL |
| 10872 | BANHO DE DESENFERRUJAMENTO | 10913 | TÊMPERA EM BANHO DE SAL |
| 10873 | ENFERRUJADO | 10914 | SAMÁRIO |
| 10874 | RUTÊNIO | 10915 | AMOSTRA |
| 10875 | FITA DE AÇO INOXIDÁVEL | 10916 | AMOSTRAGEM |
| 10876 | SELA | 10917 | AREIA |
| 10876 | SELIM | 10918 | BANHO DE AREIA |
| 10877 | SUPORTE | 10919 | LIMPAR COM JATO DE AREIA |
| 10878 | LIMA DE BORDAS LISAS | 10920 | MÁQUINA DE JATO DE AREIA |
| 10879 | CARGA ADMISSÍVEL | 10921 | LIMPEZA A JATO DE AREIA |
| 10879 | CARGA LIMITE | 10922 | FUNDIÇÃO EM AREIA |
| 10880 | ESFORÇO ADMISSÍVEL | 10923 | FILTRO DE AREIA |
| 10881 | DISPOSITIVO PROTETOR | 10924 | MOLDE DE AREIA |
| 10882 | CINTO DE SEGURANÇA | 10925 | LIXA |
| 10883 | FREIO DE SEGURANÇA | 10926 | MÁQUINA DE LIXAR |
| 10884 | ACOPLAMENTO DE SEGURANÇA | 10927 | SANDARACA |
| 10885 | COEFICIENTE DE SEGURANÇA | 10928 | GRÉS |
| 10886 | FUSÍVEL DE CORTA-CIRCUITO | 10928 | ARENITO |
| 10887 | DISCO DE SEGURANÇA CONTRA RUPTURA | 10929 | LAMINAÇÃO POR CHAPAS SUPERPOSTAS |
| 10888 | GANCHO DE SEGURANÇA | 10930 | TERRENO ARENOSO |
| 10889 | NORMAS DE SEGURANÇA | 10931 | INSTALAÇÕES SANITÁRIAS |
| 10890 | VÁLVULA DE SEGURANÇA DE GRANDE ALCANCE | 10932 | SAPONIFICÁVEL |
| | | 10933 | SAPONIFICAÇÃO |
| 10891 | VÁLVULA DE SEGURANÇA | 10934 | SAPONIFICAR |
| 10892 | ARQUEAMENTO | 10935 | PEDRA-SABÃO |
| 10892 | CURVATURA | 10935 | SAPONITA |
| 10892 | FLEXÃO | 10936 | CERNE |
| 10893 | CURVAR | 10936 | ALBURNO |
| 10893 | DOBRAR | 10937 | CAIXILHO DE FERRO |
| 10894 | FLEXÃO | 10938 | ACABAMENTO ACETINADO |
| 10895 | FLEXÕES | 10939 | SATURAR |
| 10896 | SALAMANDRA | 10940 | HIDROCARBONETOS SATURADOS |
| 10897 | SALÁRIO | 10941 | SOLUÇÃO SATURADA |
| 10898 | ENGENHEIRO DE VENDAS | 10942 | VAPOR SATURADO |
| 10899 | ÁCIDO SALICÍLICO | 10943 | SATURAÇÃO |
| 10900 | ÂNGULO SALIENTE | 10944 | PRESSÃO DE SATURAÇÃO |
| 10901 | SALINÔMETRO | 10945 | TEMPERATURA DE SATURAÇÃO |
| 10901 | PESA-SAL | 10946 | PIRES |
| 10902 | CONDUTO INTERNO | 10946 | GODÉ |
| 10903 | SALITRE | 10947 | ECONOMIA DE MÃO-DE-OBRA |
| 10903 | NITRATO DE POTÁSSIO | 10948 | ECONOMIA DE FORÇA ELÉTRICA |

| | | | |
|---|---|---|---|
| 10949 | ECONOMIA DE TEMPO | 10991 | ESCÂNDIO |
| 10950 | SERRA | 10992 | VARREDURA |
| 10951 | SERRAR | 10992 | EXPLORAÇÃO |
| 10952 | FOLHA DE SERRA | 10993 | SAMBLADURA |
| 10953 | SERRAGEM | 10994 | DISPERSÃO |
| 10953 | PÓ DE SERRA | 10994 | DIFUSÃO |
| 10954 | LIMA TRIANGULAR | 10995 | ELIMINADOR DE IMPUREZAS |
| 10954 | LIMA PARA SERRA | 10996 | ARSENIATO ÁCIDO DE COBRE |
| 10955 | TORNO PARA AFIAR SERRAS | 10996 | VERDE DE SCHEELE |
| 10956 | SERRARIA | 10997 | XILITA |
| 10957 | TRAVADEIRA | 10998 | VERNIZ DE GOMA-LACA |
| 10958 | TRAVADEIRA DE DENTES DE SERRA | 10999 | XISTO |
| 10959 | DENTE DE SERRA | 11000 | VERDE IMPERIAL |
| 10960 | EMBREAGEM DE DENTE DE SERRA | 11000 | VERDE DE SCHWEINFURT |
| 10961 | SERRAÇÃO | 11001 | ORGANIZAÇÃO CIENTÍFICA |
| 10962 | MADEIRA SERRADA | 11002 | ESCLERÔMETRO |
| 10963 | SERRAS E BANCAS DE SERRA | 11003 | DUREZA SHORE |
| 10964 | ESCAMA | 11003 | DUREZA ESCLEROSCÓPICA |
| 10964 | COBREJUNTA | 11004 | ESCORIFICAÇÃO |
| 10965 | ANDAIME | 11005 | POLIR |
| 10966 | PRODUTO ESCALAR | 11005 | DECAPAR |
| 10967 | QUANTIDADE ESCALAR | 11006 | DECAPAGEM |
| 10968 | ESCALA | 11007 | SUCATA |
| 10969 | DEPÓSITOS CALCÁRIOS | 11007 | FERRO-VELHO |
| 10969 | TÁRTARO DE CALDEIRAS | 11008 | RASPAR |
| 10970 | ESCALA (REPRODUÇÃO EM AMPLIAÇÃO) | 11008 | APLANAR |
| 10971 | DESINCRUSTAR | 11009 | RASPADOR |
| 10972 | TRAVESSÃO DE BALANÇA | 11010 | RASPADOR |
| 10973 | ESCALA DE UMA PLANTA | 11011 | RASPAGEM |
| 10974 | ESCALA DE DUREZA | 11012 | MÁQUINA DE RASPAR |
| 10975 | DESCAMAR | 11013 | RISCO |
| 10976 | PRATO DE BALANÇA | 11013 | VINCO |
| 10977 | POÇO DE CAREPA | 11013 | ARRANHÃO |
| 10978 | SUBSTÂNCIA ANTI-INCRUSTANTE | 11014 | ESCOVA DE AÇO |
| 10979 | DECAPAGEM | 11015 | RESISTÊNCIA À ABRASÃO |
| 10980 | INOXIDABILIDADE | 11016 | ACABAMENTO COM ESCOVA DE AÇO |
| 10981 | DIVISÃO | 11017 | TESTE OU ENSAIO ESCLEROMÉTRICO |
| 10981 | ESCALA | 11018 | CRIVO |
| 10981 | GRADUAÇÃO | 11018 | PENEIRA |
| 10982 | ESCALA (RELAÇÃO DE DIMENSÕES) | 11018 | COADOR |
| 10983 | DESENHO ESCALA | 11019 | ÉCRAN |
| 10984 | TRIÂNGULO ESCALENO | 11020 | ANÁLISE GRANULOMÉTRICA |
| 10985 | DESCAMAÇÃO | 11021 | PARAFUSO |
| 10986 | MARTELO PICADOR | 11022 | PARAFUSAR |
| 10986 | MARTELO DESCROSTADOR | 11023 | PUA |
| 10987 | DESINCRUSTAÇÃO | 11023 | VERRUMA |
| 10988 | RASPAGEM | 11024 | EIXO DE SIMETRIA |
| 10988 | DESCASCAMENTO | 11025 | TAMPA ROSCADA |
| 10988 | GRAFITA ESCAMADA | 11026 | LUVA ROSCADA |
| 10990 | VARRER | 11027 | MOLINETE HIDRÁULICO |
| 10990 | EXPLORAR | 11028 | ABERTURA DE ROSCAS |

| | | | | |
|---|---|---|---|---|
| 11029 | TORNO DE ABRIR ROSCAS | | 11074 | BACIA COLETORA |
| 11030 | ABERTURA DE ROSCA | | 11075 | CHAPA DE VEDAÇÃO |
| 11031 | DISCORDÂNCIA EM PARAFUSO | | 11076 | SOLDA ESTANQUE |
| 11032 | PUXADEIRA DE PARAFUSO | | 11077 | CHUMBAR |
| 11033 | TORNEIRA COM PARAFUSO DE PRESSÃO | | 11078 | VEDADOR |
| 11034 | CALIBRE DE ROSCA | | 11079 | MONOBLOCO |
| 11035 | MACACO DE PARAFUSO | | 11080 | CANALIZAÇÃO MARÍTIMA |
| 11036 | MÁQUINA DE FRESAR PARAFUSOS | | 11081 | VEDAÇÃO |
| 11037 | PARAFUSAR | | 11082 | LÍQUIDO DE VEDAÇÃO |
| 11038 | MEDIDOR PARA PASSO DE ROSCA | | 11083 | COSTURA |
| 11039 | TARRAXA DE PALMATÓRIA | | 11084 | LINHA DA COSTURA DAS CHAPAS |
| 11040 | PRENSA DE PARAFUSO | | 11085 | SOLDAGEM DE TUBOS |
| 11041 | HÉLICE | | 11086 | SOLDAGEM CONTÍNUA |
| 11041 | PROPULSOR | | 11087 | MÁQUINA DE DOBRAR |
| 11042 | BOMBA HELICOIDAL | | 11088 | MÁQUINA DE COSTURAR |
| 11043 | TIRAFUNDO | | 11089 | TUBO SEM SOLDADURA |
| 11044 | MACHO DE ABRIR ROSCA | | 11090 | APALPADOR |
| 11045 | FILETE OU ROSCA DE PARAFUSO | | 11091 | PROJETOR DE LUZ |
| 11046 | ABRIR ROSCA DE PARAFUSO | | 11092 | FENDA DE SECAGEM |
| 11047 | CALIBRE DE ROSCA | | 11093 | FENDAS DE ENVELHECIMENTO |
| 11048 | COMPARADOR MICROMÉTRICO PARA ROSCAS | | 11093 | CORROSÃO INTERCRISTALINA |
| | | | 11094 | SECAR A MADEIRA AO AR LIVRE |
| 11049 | CALIBRE MACHO DE ROSCA | | 11095 | SECAGEM DE MADEIRA AO AR LIVRE |
| 11050 | ANEL ROSCADO DO CALIBRE DE ROSCAS | | 11096 | CINTO DE SEGURANÇA |
| 11051 | PARAFUSO DE CABEÇA REDONDA | | 11097 | ASSENTO DE VÁLVULA |
| 11052 | CHAVE INGLESA | | 11098 | ASSENTO |
| 11053 | ORIFÍCIOS ATARRAXADOS (FÊMEAS) | | 11099 | SECANTE |
| 11054 | ORIFÍCIOS ROSCADOS (MACHOS) | | 11100 | LIMA BASTARDINHA |
| 11055 | FLANGE ROSCADO | | 11101 | FILTRO SECUNDÁRIO |
| 11056 | ORIFÍCIO COM ROSCA | | 11102 | MACHO INTERMEDIÁRIO |
| 11057 | GANCHO COM PARAFUSO | | 11103 | COR COMPOSTA OU SECUNDÁRIA |
| 11058 | JUNTA DE ROSCA PARAFUSADA | | 11104 | FLUÊNCIA SECUNDÁRIA |
| 11059 | TUBO ROSCADO | | 11105 | TÊMPERA SECUNDÁRIA |
| 11060 | TAMPA DE ROSCA | | 11106 | INCLUSÃO SECUNDÁRIA |
| 11060 | BUJÃO DE ROSCA | | 11107 | METAL DE RECUPERAÇÃO |
| 11061 | UNIÃO DE ROSCA | | 11108 | ESPECTRO SECUNDÁRIO |
| 11062 | HASTE ROSCADA | | 11109 | TENSÃO SECUNDÁRIA |
| 11063 | FLANGE PARAFUSADO | | 11110 | CORRENTE SECUNDÁRIA DE SOLDAGEM |
| 11064 | FLANGE ROSCADO | | 11111 | SEÇÃO |
| 11065 | PARAFUSAMENTO | | 11111 | CORTE TRANSVERSAL |
| 11066 | MÁQUINA DE ABRIR ROSCAS | | 11112 | CORTE |
| 11066 | MÁQUINA DE PARAFUSAR | | 11112 | VISTA EM SEÇÃO |
| 11067 | MONTAGEM A PARAFUSO | | 11113 | SEÇÃO PARA PESQUISA MICROSCÓPICA |
| 11068 | AGULHA | | 11114 | PERFIS |
| 11068 | PONTEIRO | | 11115 | MÓDULO DE INÉRCIA |
| 11068 | RISCADOR | | 11116 | SEÇÃO DE UMA VIGA |
| 11069 | GRAMINHO COM PÉ | | 11117 | ELEMENTO DE RECIPIENTE A PRESSÃO |
| 11070 | NÍVEL DO MAR | | 11118 | SEGMENTO DE RETA |
| 11071 | AREIA DO MAR | | 11119 | FERRO PERFILADO |
| 11072 | ÁGUA SALGADA | | 11120 | ÁREA DA SEÇÃO |
| 11073 | COLETOR VEDADO | | 11121 | SEÇÃO DE PASSAGEM DE UMA VÁLVULA |

1303

| | | | |
|---|---|---|---|
| 11122 | DESENHO EM CORTE | 11167 | SEMI-EIXO |
| 11123 | CALIBRE DE PERFILAGEM | 11168 | CARVÃO MAGRO |
| 11124 | PROJEÇÃO HORIZONTAL | 11169 | SEMICIRCULAR |
| 11125 | AÇO PERFILADO | 11170 | SEÇÃO HEMISFÉRICA |
| 11126 | SETOR DE CÍRCULO | 11171 | MOTOR SEMIDIESEL |
| 11127 | SETOR ESFÉRICO | 11172 | SEMIPERFURADORA DE PRECISÃO |
| 11128 | SEDAN | 11173 | AÇO SEMI-ACALMADO |
| 11129 | MÁQUINA DE SEMEAR AO LARGO | 11174 | PRODUTO SEMI-ACABADO |
| 11130 | AGENTE PRECIPITANTE | 11175 | MÁQUINA SEMIFIXA A VAPOR |
| 11131 | GOMA-LACA EM GRÃOS | 11176 | BOMBA DE PISTÃO OSCILANTE |
| 11132 | MÁQUINAS SEMEADORAS | 11177 | AÇO DE MEIA TÊMPERA |
| 11133 | TRANSPLANTADORAS | 11177 | SEMI-AÇO |
| 11134 | CONE PIROMÉTRICO DE SEGER | 11178 | SEMI-REBOQUE |
| 11135 | SEGMENTO | 11179 | SEMICÍRCULO |
| 11136 | SEGMENTO DE CÍRCULO | 11180 | TRANSFERIDOR HEMISFÉRICO |
| 11137 | CALOTA ESFÉRICA | 11181 | LAMINADOR SENDZIMIR |
| 11138 | VOLANTE SEGMENTÁRIO | 11182 | SENTIDO DE UMA FORÇA |
| 11139 | SEGREGAÇÃO | 11183 | SENTIDO DO MOVIMENTO |
| 11140 | GRIMPAR | 11184 | CALOR TERMOMÉTRICO |
| 11140 | AGARRAR | 11184 | CALOR SENSÍVEL |
| 11141 | GRIPAGEM | 11185 | MÁQUINAS ELETRÔNICAS DE |
| 11142 | RECOZIMENTO SELETIVO | | CLASSIFICAR |
| 11143 | CEMENTAÇÃO SELETIVA | 11186 | PERFURATRIZ DE PRECISÃO |
| 11144 | FLOTAÇÃO SELETIVA | 11187 | CHAPA SENSÍVEL |
| 11145 | TÊMPERA PARCIAL | 11187 | CHAPA FOTOGRÁFICA |
| 11146 | SELÊNIO | 11188 | SENSIBILIDADE DE UM INSTRUMENTO |
| 11147 | CORPO LUMINOSO | 11189 | SEPARAR |
| 11148 | AUTOMÁTICO | 11190 | EXCITAÇÃO ISOLADA |
| 11149 | EMBREAGEM AUTOMÁTICA | 11191 | SEPARAÇÃO |
| 11150 | MANCAL AUTO-REGULADOR | 11192 | SEPARAÇÃO DE UMA MISTURA |
| 11151 | MÁQUINA INDEPENDENTE | 11193 | NÚMERO DE SEQÜÊNCIA |
| 11152 | MANDRIS AUTOMÁTICOS | 11194 | SUBSEQÜENTE |
| 11153 | AUTO-EXCITAÇÃO | 11195 | SEQÜESTRO |
| 11154 | AÇO AUTOTEMPERANTE | 11196 | EM SÉRIE |
| 11155 | FERRO DE SOLDAR DE AQUECIMENTO | 11197 | NÚMERO DE FABRICAÇÃO |
| | AUTOMÁTICO | 11198 | FABRICAÇÃO EM SÉRIE |
| 11156 | AUTO-INDUÇÃO | 11199 | MONTAGEM OU LIGAÇÃO EM SÉRIE |
| 11157 | BLOQUEIO AUTOMÁTICO | 11200 | SOLDAGEM POR PONTOS EM SÉRIE POR |
| 11158 | MANCAL AUTOLUBRIFICANTE | | RESISTÊNCIA |
| 11159 | CONE AUTODESMONTÁVEL | 11201 | DÍNAMO ENROLADO EM SÉRIE |
| 11160 | RESERVATÓRIO DE TETO CÔNICO | 11202 | MOTOR ENROLADO EM SÉRIE |
| | AUTO-SUSTENTADO | 11203 | SÉRIE |
| 11161 | ESTRUTURA INDEPENDENTE | 11203 | SEQÜÊNCIA |
| 11162 | PARAFUSO MACHO | 11203 | PROGRESSÃO |
| 11162 | PARAFUSO DE ROSQUEAMENTO | 11204 | SERPENTINA |
| | AUTOMÁTICO | 11205 | CRISOTILO |
| 11163 | ARRUELA DE ROSQUEAMENTO | 11206 | CILINDRO ESTRIADO |
| | AUTOMÁTICO | 11207 | ALBUMINA DO SORO |
| 11164 | ACOPLAMENTO SELLERS | 11208 | CONDIÇÕES DE EMPREGO |
| 11165 | SEMI-ANTRÁCITO | 11209 | INSTRUÇÕES RELATIVAS AO TRABALHO |
| 11166 | SOLDAGEM A ARCO SEMI-AUTOMÁTICA | 11210 | SERVOMECANISMO |

| | |
|---|---|
| 11211 | SERVOMOTOR |
| 11212 | ÓLEO DE SÉSAMO |
| 11213 | JOGO |
| 11213 | CONJUNTO |
| 11213 | SÉRIE |
| 11213 | GRUPO |
| 11214 | AJUSTAR |
| 11214 | FIXAR |
| 11214 | ENCAIXAR |
| 11214 | LIGAR |
| 11215 | CERCAR UMA CALDEIRA COM ALVENARIA |
| 11216 | TARAR UMA VÁLVULA |
| 11217 | CORTA-FERRO |
| 11218 | MARTELO EMBUTIDOR |
| 11219 | JOGO DE PESOS |
| 11220 | CONTRAPINO |
| 11220 | PINO DE AJUSTE |
| 11221 | PONTA DE FIXAÇÃO |
| 11222 | PARAFUSO DE RETENÇÃO |
| 11222 | PARAFUSO DE AJUSTE |
| 11223 | ESQUADRO |
| 11224 | ACERTAR OS DENTES DA SERRA |
| 11225 | CALIBRE DE AJUSTE |
| 11226 | PEGA DO CIMENTO |
| 11227 | DEPOSITAR-SE |
| 11227 | ASSENTAR |
| 11228 | DECANTAÇÃO |
| 11228 | SEDIMENTAÇÃO |
| 11229 | TANQUE DE DECANTAÇÃO OU SEDIMENTAÇÃO |
| 11230 | ÁGUA DE ESGOTO |
| 11231 | OLHO DE UM MACHADO |
| 11232 | BRAÇADEIRA |
| 11233 | FORQUILHAS |
| 11234 | SOMBREAR |
| 11235 | DESENHO SOMBREADO |
| 11236 | SOMBRA |
| 11237 | SOMBREADO |
| 11238 | PROJETOR DE SOMBRA |
| 11239 | EIXO |
| 11239 | ÁRVORE |
| 11239 | POÇO |
| 11240 | ACOPLAMENTO DE EIXOS |
| 11241 | FORNO DE CUBA |
| 11242 | REGULADOR AXIAL |
| 11243 | FUSTE DE COLUNA |
| 11244 | CABO DE MARTELO |
| 11245 | MÁQUINA DE RETIFICAR EIXOS |
| 11246 | TORNO DE EIXOS |
| 11247 | EIXO COM SALIÊNCIA DOS DOIS LADOS |
| 11248 | TRANSMISSÃO |
| 11249 | EIXOS EM ÂNGULO RETO |

| | |
|---|---|
| 11250 | RACHADURA DA MADEIRA |
| 11251 | DESMOLDAGEM |
| 11252 | PENEIRA OSCILANTE |
| 11253 | TRANSPORTADOR VIBRATÓRIO |
| 11254 | AGITAÇÃO DO BANHO |
| 11255 | ÓLEO DE XISTO BETUMINOSO |
| 11256 | ÓLEO DE XISTO |
| 11257 | ESPIGA |
| 11257 | CORPO |
| 11257 | HASTE |
| 11258 | PANELA DE FUNDIÇÃO COM ASA |
| 11259 | FRESA COM HASTE |
| 11260 | ESPIGA DE PARAFUSO |
| 11261 | CORPO DE BIELA |
| 11262 | CORPO DE CHAVETA |
| 11263 | CORPO DE REBITE |
| 11264 | FORMA |
| 11265 | PEÇA MOLDADA |
| 11266 | CHAPAS PERFILADAS |
| 11267 | TORNO LIMADOR |
| 11268 | MODELAGEM |
| 11269 | TORNO LIMADOR |
| 11270 | CHAGRÉM |
| 11271 | CANTONEIRA EM ÂNGULO AGUDO |
| 11272 | ARESTA VIVA |
| 11273 | AFIAR |
| 11273 | AGUÇAR |
| 11274 | MÁQUINA DE AFIAR |
| 11275 | AFIAMENTO |
| 11275 | AGUÇAMENTO |
| 11276 | NITIDEZ DA IMAGEM |
| 11277 | APARAS |
| 11278 | APARAS |
| 11279 | CISALHAMENTO |
| 11280 | CISALHAR |
| 11281 | ÂNGULO DE CISALHAMENTO |
| 11282 | FOLHA DE TESOURA |
| 11283 | PINO DE CISALHAMENTO |
| 11284 | PLANO DE CISALHAMENTO |
| 11285 | RESISTÊNCIA AO CISALHAMENTO |
| 11286 | TENSÃO DE CISALHAMENTO |
| 11287 | TESTE DE CISALHAMENTO |
| 11288 | CISALHAMENTO |
| 11289 | ABSORÇÃO |
| 11290 | CISALHAMENTO |
| 11291 | ESFORÇO CORTANTE |
| 11291 | FORÇA DE CISALHAMENTO |
| 11292 | TESOURA MECÂNICA |
| 11293 | RUPTURA DO REBITE POR CISALHAMENTO |
| 11294 | PINO DE CISALHAMENTO |
| 11295 | ESFORÇO DE CISALHAMENTO |

| | |
|---|---|
| 11296 | ESFORÇO CORTANTE |
| 11296 | TENSÃO DE CISALHAMENTO |
| 11297 | TESOURAS |
| 11298 | CHAPA |
| 11299 | ELÉTRODO BLINDADO |
| 11300 | FIO ENCAPADO |
| 11301 | POLIA DE GARGANTA |
| 11302 | HANGAR |
| 11303 | CONCHA |
| 11303 | ARMAÇÃO |
| 11303 | REVESTIMENTO |
| 11304 | FOLHA |
| 11304 | LÂMINA |
| 11305 | CHAPA |
| 11306 | BARRA PARA LIMINAÇÃO |
| 11307 | CHAPA DE LATÃO |
| 11308 | COBRE EM FOLHA |
| 11309 | CHAPA DE FERRO |
| 11310 | REVESTIMENTO DE CHAPA |
| 11311 | CALIBRE PARA CHAPAS |
| 11312 | TUBO DE CHAPAS |
| 11313 | FOLHA DE FERRO |
| 11314 | FOLHA DE CHUMBO |
| 11315 | CHAPA METÁLICA |
| 11316 | MÁQUINA DE APLAINAR E RETIFICAR AS CHAPAS |
| 11317 | MÁQUINAS DE PERFURAR CHAPAS METÁLICAS |
| 11318 | MÁQUINAS DE APLAINAR CHAPAS METÁLICAS |
| 11319 | MÁQUINA DE ENTALHAR CHAPAS METÁLICAS |
| 11320 | MÁQUINAS DE TRABALHAR CHAPAS METÁLICAS |
| 11321 | LAMINADOR DE TIRAS |
| 11322 | FOLHA DE FELTRO |
| 11323 | MÁQUINA DE CISALHAR METAIS EM FOLHAS |
| 11324 | LAMINADOR DE CHAPAS |
| 11325 | CHAPA DE AÇO |
| 11326 | ESTANHO EM FOLHAS |
| 11327 | FOLHA DE ZINCO |
| 11328 | ESFOLIAÇÃO |
| 11329 | FOLHA DE BORRACHA |
| 11329 | FOLHA DE NEOPRENE |
| 11330 | CONCHA |
| 11330 | CAMISA |
| 11331 | LEVANTAMENTO DE TETO FLUTUANTE |
| 11332 | REGISTRO DE PAREDE |
| 11333 | MOLDAGEM EM COQUILHA |
| 11334 | CORPO DE TORNEIRA |

| | |
|---|---|
| 11335 | CHAPA DE REVESTIMENTO |
| 11336 | ESCAREADOR OCO |
| 11337 | FRESAS COM PONTA CÔNCAVA |
| 11338 | GOMA-LACA |
| 11339 | ESFOLIAÇÃO |
| 11340 | XERARDIZAR |
| 11341 | XERARDIZAÇÃO |
| 11342 | ANTEPARO |
| 11342 | ESCUDO PROTETOR |
| 11342 | COURAÇA |
| 11343 | CHAPA DE BLINDAGEM |
| 11344 | ELÉTRODO REVESTIDO |
| 11345 | SOLDAGEM METÁLICA A ARCO |
| 11346 | PROTEÇÃO |
| 11346 | BLINDAGEM |
| 11347 | TURNO |
| 11348 | EQUIPE DE TURNO |
| 11349 | DESLOCAR A CORREIA |
| 11350 | TRABALHO EM EQUIPE |
| 11351 | CUNHA |
| 11351 | CALÇO |
| 11352 | CALÇO DE ESPESSURA |
| 11353 | SHIMMY |
| 11353 | OSCILAÇÃO |
| 11354 | RIPA |
| 11354 | CASCALHO |
| 11354 | TELHA DE MADEIRA |
| 11355 | COMPRESSÃO |
| 11355 | APERTO |
| 11356 | CHAPA PARA EMBARCAÇÕES |
| 11357 | INSTALAR A CORREIA |
| 11358 | AMORTECEDOR DE CHOQUES |
| 11359 | CHOQUE |
| 11359 | COLISÃO |
| 11359 | IMPACTO |
| 11360 | SAPATA |
| 11361 | DESENHO DE OFICINA |
| 11362 | SOLDA DE OFICINA |
| 11363 | DESENHO DE UMA PEÇA MECÂNICA |
| 11364 | OFICINA |
| 11365 | ESCORA |
| 11365 | PONTALETE |
| 11366 | ESCLEROSCÓPIO |
| 11367 | TESTE DE ESCLEROSCÓPIO |
| 11368 | FERRO QUEBRADIÇO |
| 11369 | CURTO-CIRCUITO |
| 11370 | TRANSFERÊNCIA POR CURTO-CIRCUITO |
| 11371 | CARVÃO DE CHAMA CURTA |
| 11372 | CURTO-CIRCUITO |
| 11373 | CADEIA DE ELOS CURTOS |
| 11374 | MOTOR DE PISTÃO DE PEQUENO CURSO |

| | |
|---|---|
| 11375 | MANIVELA DE PEQUENO CURSO |
| 11376 | REDUÇÃO |
| 11376 | ENCURTAMENTO |
| 11377 | ENCURTAMENTO DE UM CABO |
| 11378 | FRAGILIDADE |
| 11379 | GRANALHA |
| 11379 | TIRO |
| 11380 | JATEAMENTO COM GRANALHA |
| 11381 | JATOPERCUSSÃO |
| 11382 | JATEAMENTO COM GRANALHA |
| 11383 | REBORDO |
| 11383 | OMBRO |
| 11383 | RESSALTO |
| 11383 | REBAIXO |
| 11384 | ANEL DE EIXO |
| 11385 | PÁ |
| 11386 | PADEJAR |
| 11387 | VÁLVULA DE CHUVEIRO |
| 11388 | CONTRAIR |
| 11388 | ENCOLHER |
| 11389 | AJUSTAMENTO A QUENTE |
| 11390 | ENCAIXAR A QUENTE |
| 11391 | ANEL ENFIADO A QUENTE |
| 11392 | RETRAÇÃO |
| 11392 | CONTRAÇÃO |
| 11393 | CAVIDADE DE CONTRAÇÃO |
| 11394 | REDUÇÃO POR CONTRAÇÃO |
| 11395 | FISSURA DE CONTRAÇÃO |
| 11396 | CONTRAÇÃO DA MADEIRA |
| 11397 | CONTRAÇÃO |
| 11397 | RETRAÇÃO |
| 11397 | ENCOLHIMENTO |
| 11398 | ENCAIXE A QUENTE |
| 11398 | EMBUTIMENTO A QUENTE |
| 11399 | ENRUGAMENTO |
| 11400 | FACE DE RODA DE ENGRENAGEM |
| 11401 | CABO FORMADO DE QUATRO PONTAS |
| 11402 | RODA DE ENGRENAGEM COM FACE LATERAL |
| 11403 | DESVIO |
| 11403 | DERIVAÇÃO |
| 11404 | DÍNAMO EM DERIVAÇÃO |
| 11405 | MOTOR EM DERIVAÇÃO |
| 11406 | DESLIGAR UMA MÁQUINA |
| 11407 | OBTURAR A ENTRADA DE UMA TUBULAÇÃO |
| 11408 | VÁLVULA DE FECHAMENTO |
| 11409 | PARALISAÇÃO DO TRABALHO |
| 11410 | PARALISAÇÃO DE UMA MÁQUINA |
| 11411 | RASTELOS COM DESPEJO LATERAL |
| 11412 | FRESA FRONTAL |
| 11413 | RAMAL DE CORREIA |
| 11414 | LADO DE UM POLÍGONO |
| 11415 | MÁQUINA LATERAL DE APLAINAR |
| 11416 | TALA DE UMA CORRENTE DE ROLOS |
| 11417 | PLAINA LATERAL |
| 11418 | ÂNGULO DE INCLINAÇÃO LATERAL |
| 11419 | ONDULAÇÕES |
| 11420 | VISTA LATERAL |
| 11420 | PERFIL |
| 11421 | SIDERITA |
| 11422 | PENEIRA |
| 11422 | CRIVO |
| 11423 | PENEIRAR |
| 11423 | JOEIRAR |
| 11424 | PENEIRAMENTO |
| 11425 | LUBRIFICADOR DE FLUXO VISÍVEL |
| 11426 | CONTROLADOR DE CIRCULAÇÃO |
| 11427 | ABERTURA OU REGISTRO DE INSPEÇÃO |
| 11427 | VIGIA |
| 11428 | SOLDAGEM A ARCO METÁLICO COM PROTEÇÃO DE GÁS INERTE |
| 11429 | SINAL |
| 11430 | MÁQUINA DE ENSILAGEM |
| 11431 | SILENCIOSO |
| 11432 | CORRENTE SILENCIOSA |
| 11433 | MOVIMENTO DE CATRACA SILENCIOSO |
| 11434 | SÍLICA |
| 11435 | TIJOLO DE SÍLICA |
| 11436 | SÍLICA |
| 11436 | ÁCIDO SILÍCICO |
| 11437 | SILICATO |
| 11438 | CALAMITA |
| 11439 | MARGA SILICIOSA |
| 11440 | FERRO MANGANÊS SILICIOSO |
| 11441 | ÁCIDO SÍLICO-FLUORÍDRICO |
| 11442 | SILÍCIO |
| 11443 | LATÃO SILICIOSO |
| 11444 | BRONZE SILICIOSO |
| 11445 | CARBONETO DE SILÍCIO |
| 11446 | COBRE SILICIOSO |
| 11447 | AÇO AO SILÍCIO |
| 11448 | CHAPA ELÉTRICA |
| 11449 | AÇO AO SILÍCIO |
| 11450 | AÇO MANGANÊS SILICIOSO |
| 11451 | CALCÁRIO SILICIOSO |
| 11452 | SEDA |
| 11453 | MATIZADO |
| 11453 | ENFEITADO |
| 11454 | FRATURA SEDOSA |
| 11455 | BRILHO SEDOSO |
| 11456 | SILICONE |

| | |
|---|---|
| 11457 | ENLAMEAMENTO DE UM CANO |
| 11458 | PRATA |
| 11459 | PRATEAR |
| 11460 | SOLDA FORTE COM LIGA DE PRATA |
| 11461 | CLORETO DE PRATA |
| 11462 | CIANETO DE PRATA |
| 11463 | FULMINATO DE PRATA |
| 11464 | IODETO DE PRATA |
| 11465 | PRATEAÇÃO |
| 11465 | BANHO DE PRATA |
| 11466 | SOLDAGEM COM PRATA |
| 11467 | SULFATO DE PRATA |
| 11468 | COBRE ARGENTÍFERO |
| 11469 | PRATEAÇÃO |
| 11470 | SEMELHANÇA |
| 11471 | INTEGRAL SIMPLES |
| 11472 | HASTE DE PISTÃO UNILATERAL |
| 11473 | AÇO AO CARBONO |
| 11474 | SUSTENTADO LIVREMENTE NAS DUAS PONTAS |
| 11475 | SENO |
| 11476 | CURVA SINUOSA |
| 11477 | CORREIA SIMPLES |
| 11478 | REBITE COM COBREJUNTA SIMPLES |
| 11479 | MANCAL AXIAL DE UM SÓ APOIO |
| 11480 | MONOCRISTAL |
| 11481 | LIMA MURÇA |
| 11481 | LIMA DE PICADO SIMPLES |
| 11482 | PICADO SIMPLES DE LIMA |
| 11483 | FORÇA ÚNICA |
| 11484 | PEÇA DESPRENDIDA |
| 11484 | PEÇA SOLTA |
| 11485 | SOLDAGEM DE PASSE ÚNICO |
| 11486 | MÁQUINA PARA TRABALHOS ESPECIAIS |
| 11487 | REBITAGEM DE UMA FILEIRA |
| 11488 | VÁLVULA DE ASSENTO SIMPLES |
| 11489 | REMATE DE UM CORTE |
| 11490 | AÇO DE PACOTE SIMPLES |
| 11491 | VÁLVULA ÚNICA |
| 11492 | OPÉRCULO SIMPLES |
| 11493 | DE SIMPLES EFEITO |
| 11494 | PISTÃO DE SIMPLES EFEITO |
| 11495 | MÁQUINA DE EFEITO SIMPLES |
| 11496 | FERRAMENTA DE EFEITO SIMPLES |
| 11497 | VÁLVULA DE ASSENTO SIMPLES |
| 11498 | MÁQUINA MONOCILÍNDRICA |
| 11499 | CHAVE DE CALIBRE SIMPLES |
| 11500 | MOTOR DE EXPANSÃO SIMPLES |
| 11501 | CORRENTE MONOFÁSICA |
| 11502 | PARAFUSO DE ROSCA SIMPLES |
| 11503 | EIXO DE MANIVELAS SIMPLES |
| 11504 | JUNTA DE RECOBRIMENTO SOLDADA DE UM SÓ LADO |
| 11505 | CAVIDADE POR CONTRAÇÃO |
| 11506 | CABEÇA DE PEÇA DE FUNDIÇÃO |
| 11507 | PENETRAÇÃO |
| 11508 | LAMINADOR REDUTOR |
| 11509 | SINTERIZAR |
| 11509 | CONCRECIONAR |
| 11510 | LIGA DE METAL DURO |
| 11511 | SINTERIZAÇÃO |
| 11512 | FORNO DE SINTERIZAR |
| 11513 | SENÓIDE |
| 11514 | SIFÃO |
| 11515 | BARÔMETRO DE SIFÃO |
| 11516 | LUBRIFICADOR POR MECHA |
| 11517 | SIFÃO |
| 11518 | SIRENA |
| 11519 | BARRACA DE CANTEIRO |
| 11520 | MESTRE-DE-OBRAS |
| 11521 | LIMUSINE |
| 11522 | ESPESSURA DE GRÃO |
| 11523 | TAMANHO DA MALHA |
| 11524 | CLASSIFICAÇÃO |
| 11525 | PRENSA DE CALIBRAR |
| 11526 | GABARITO CIRCULAR |
| 11527 | TIRAS PARA FABRICAÇÃO DE TUBOS |
| 11528 | ESBOÇO |
| 11529 | ESBOÇAR |
| 11530 | PAPEL QUADRICULADO |
| 11531 | PLACA DE RECORTE ESPECIAL |
| 11532 | CROQUI |
| 11533 | ESBOÇO |
| 11533 | ESBOÇAR |
| 11534 | ENGRENAGEM HIPERBOLÓIDE |
| 11535 | SUPERFÍCIE OBLÍQUA |
| 11536 | ESCUMADEIRA |
| 11537 | CARÊNCIA |
| 11538 | CROSTA |
| 11538 | PELE |
| 11539 | COLA DE PELE |
| 11540 | EMBALAGEM PELICULAR |
| 11541 | LAMINAÇÃO DE ACABAMENTO |
| 11542 | LAMINAÇÃO DE ACABAMENTO |
| 11543 | LAMINAÇÃO DE DESBASTE |
| 11544 | PELÍCULA |
| 11545 | FORMAÇÃO DE PELES |
| 11546 | INTERRUPÇÃO |
| 11547 | ABA |
| 11547 | SAIA |
| 11548 | ABA DE UMA TAMPA |
| 11548 | SAIA DE UMA COBERTURA |

| | | | |
|---|---|---|---|
| 11549 | ABA DE RESERVATÓRIO | 11592 | VÁLVULA DE GAVETA |
| 11550 | DEFEITO DE FABRICAÇÃO | 11593 | DIAGRAMA DE DISTRIBUIÇÃO |
| 11551 | LINTOTE | 11594 | DISTRIBUIÇÃO POR REGISTRO |
| 11551 | LAJE | 11595 | DESLIZAMENTO |
| 11552 | FRESA PARALELA | 11596 | MANCAL DESLIZANTE |
| 11553 | DOBRAMENTO DE LINGOTES | 11597 | PAQUÍMETRO |
| 11554 | TESOURA PARA PACOTES | 11598 | ENGRENAGEM DESLIZANTE |
| 11555 | LAMINADOR PARA PLACAS | 11599 | LUVA DE EMBREAGEM |
| 11556 | LAMINADOR DE PLACAS | 11600 | AJUSTAGEM DESLIZANTE |
| 11557 | MIÚDOS DE CARVÃO | 11601 | ATRITO DE ESCORREGAMENTO |
| 11558 | AFOUXAR UMA PORCA | 11602 | TREM CORREDIÇO |
| 11559 | DESAPERTAR | 11603 | TORNO CORREDIÇO |
| 11560 | AFOUXAMENTO | 11604 | TAMPA CORREDIÇA |
| 11561 | ESCÓRIA | 11605 | MOVIMENTO DESLIZANTE |
| 11562 | PORTADOR DE ESCÓRIAS | 11606 | BERÇO DE DESLIZAMENTO |
| 11563 | TIJOLO DE ESCÓRIA | 11607 | ESCALA MÓVEL |
| 11564 | CIMENTO DE ESCÓRIA | 11608 | SUPERFÍCIE DE DESLIZAMENTO |
| 11565 | CONCRETO DE ESCÓRIA | 11609 | VASA |
| 11566 | LÃ DE ESCÓRIA | 11609 | LODO |
| 11566 | LÃ MINERAL | 11609 | LIMO |
| 11567 | INCLUSÃO DE ESCÓRIA | 11610 | LINGA |
| 11568 | APAGAR A CAL | 11610 | ESLINGA |
| 11569 | EXTINÇÃO DA CAL | 11611 | ESCORREGAMENTO |
| 11570 | TRANSPORTADOR DE FITA | 11612 | DESLIZAR |
| 11571 | ARDÓSIA | 11612 | PATINAR |
| 11572 | MARTELO DE FORJA | 11613 | PLANOS DE DESLIZAMENTO |
| 11572 | MALHO | 11614 | EMBREAGEM DE FRICÇÃO |
| 11573 | MALHO | 11615 | FENDA POR ESCORREGAMENTO |
| 11574 | DORMENTE | 11616 | MOLDE OU FORMA DESLIZANTE |
| 11575 | TIRA-FUNDOS | 11617 | JUNTA DESLIZANTE |
| 11576 | BUCHA | 11618 | ANEL COLETOR |
| 11576 | LUVA | 11619 | EMBREAGEM PROGRESSIVA DE FRICÇÃO |
| 11577 | UNIÃO DE MANGUITO | 11620 | DESLIZAMENTO DA CORREIA |
| 11578 | REGULADOR DE LUVA | 11621 | PATINAÇÃO DAS RODAS |
| 11579 | VÁLVULA TUBULAR | 11622 | FENDIMENTO |
| 11579 | VÁLVULA DE LUVAS | 11622 | CORTE LONGITUDINAL |
| 11580 | DELGADEZ | 11623 | LIMA-FACA DUPLA |
| 11581 | DELGADEZA DE UMA VIGA | 11624 | CROSTA |
| 11582 | RELAÇÃO ENTRE O COMPRIMENTO E A SEÇÃO DE UM CORPO DE PROVA | 11624 | LASCA |
| | | 11625 | MINÉRIO DE PRATA |
| 11583 | GUINDASTE GIRATÓRIO | 11626 | IMPULSOS |
| 11584 | TORNO DE CERCEAR | 11627 | TALUDE |
| 11585 | PATIM | 11627 | INCLINAÇÃO |
| 11585 | CURSOR | 11628 | PENEIRA PARA AREIA E TERRA |
| 11585 | PEÇA CORREDIÇA | 11629 | FENDA |
| 11586 | DESLIZAR | 11629 | RANHURA |
| 11587 | PATIM DE CRUZETA | 11629 | RASGO |
| 11588 | CORREDIÇA | 11630 | ESCATELAR |
| 11589 | LÂMINA DE VIDRO | 11630 | RANHURAR |
| 11590 | TORNO COM CARRINHO | 11630 | ABRIR CHANFRO |
| 11591 | RÉGUA DE CÁLCULO | 11631 | MANIVELA E CORREDIÇA |

| | | | |
|---|---|---|---|
| 11632 | FRESAS DE RANHURAR | 11679 | ALISAR |
| 11633 | ELO INVERSOR | 11680 | LIMA MURÇA |
| 11634 | FRESA DE ESCATELAR | 11681 | MARCHA UNIFORME |
| 11634 | FRESA DE RANHURAR | 11682 | RETOQUE |
| 11635 | SOLDA POR ENTALHE | 11682 | ACABAMENTO LISO |
| 11636 | SOLDAGEM POR ENTALHE | 11683 | FRATURA NÍTIDA |
| 11637 | PARAFUSO DE CABEÇA ENTALHADA | 11684 | TUBO LISO |
| 11638 | ALAVANCA COM CORREDIÇA | 11685 | ARRANQUE SUAVE |
| 11639 | SEPARADOR DE RANHURAS | 11686 | ALISAMENTO |
| 11640 | ESCATELADORES | 11686 | SUAVIZAÇÃO |
| 11641 | AÇÃO DE ENTALHAR | 11687 | REBOTE |
| 11642 | APARELHO DE ESCATELAR | 11688 | QUEIMAR SEM CHAMA |
| 11643 | MÁQUINA DE ABRIR RANHURAS | 11689 | ESMERILHAMENTO DE REBARBAS |
| 11644 | COMBUSTÃO LENTA | 11690 | INTERRUPTOR DE AÇÃO INSTANTÂNEA |
| 11645 | DIMINUIR A VELOCIDADE DE UM MOTOR | 11691 | GANCHO DE MOSQUETÃO |
| 11646 | VAPORIZADOR DE MARCHA LENTA | 11692 | ANEL DE PRESSÃO |
| 11647 | ROSCA DE PASSO PEQUENO | 11693 | CALIBRADOR DE BOCA |
| 11648 | CIMENTO DE PEGA LENTA | 11693 | CALIBRE EM FORMA DE FERRADURA |
| 11649 | REDUÇÃO DA VELOCIDADE | 11694 | VÁLVULA DE ASPIRAÇÃO |
| 11650 | EIXO DE BAIXA VELOCIDADE | 11695 | CARGA DE NEVE |
| 11651 | PENEIRA GIRATÓRIA | 11696 | CORRENTES DE PNEUS PARA NEVE |
| 11652 | COMPORTA | 11697 | LIMPEZA POR IMERSÃO |
| 11652 | ECLUSA | 11698 | FORNO-POÇO |
| 11653 | REGISTRO DE GAVETA | 11699 | FORNO PROFUNDO |
| 11654 | LAMA | 11700 | TEMPERATURA DE RECOZIMENTO |
| 11654 | PASTA FLUIDA | 11701 | SABÃO |
| 11655 | ARGAMASSA AGUADA | 11702 | ÁGUA DE SABÃO |
| 11656 | PROCESSO DE MOLDAGEM INVERSA | 11703 | ESTEATITA |
| 11657 | RESÍDUOS DE COQUE | 11703 | PEDRA-SABÃO |
| 11658 | MOTOR DE BAIXA POTÊNCIA | 11704 | FORMÃO DE ESPIGA OCA |
| 11659 | SERRA MANUAL PEQUENA | 11705 | ENCAIXE DE TUBO |
| 11660 | PEÇAS METÁLICAS | 11705 | JUNTA DE UNIÃO |
| 11661 | MOTOR DE BAIXA POTÊNCIA | 11706 | GARRA DE UNIÃO DE CABOS |
| 11662 | PINHÃO PARA CORRENTE | 11707 | TUBO COM PONTA E BOLSA |
| 11663 | CALDEIRA DE POUCO VOLUME | 11708 | TUBO PARA ENCAIXAR |
| 11664 | TRATAR OS MINERAIS | 11709 | CHAVE DA CAIXA |
| 11665 | FORNO DE FUNDIR | 11710 | PONTA FÊMEA DE UM TUBO |
| 11666 | FUSÃO DE METAIS | 11711 | CRISTAIS DE SODA |
| 11667 | FORNO DE FUSÃO | 11712 | LIXÍVIA DE SODA |
| 11668 | USINA METALÚRGICA | 11713 | SODA |
| 11669 | FORJA MANUAL | 11713 | CARBONATO DE SÓDIO |
| 11670 | PEÇA FORJADA A MARTELO | 11714 | SÓDIO |
| 11671 | FERREIRO | 11715 | ACETATO DE SÓDIO |
| 11672 | FUMAÇA | 11716 | ALUMINATO DE SÓDIO |
| 11673 | FUMÍVORO | 11717 | BISSULFATO DE SÓDIO |
| 11674 | FORNO FUMÍVORO | 11718 | BISSULFETO DE SÓDIO |
| 11675 | FORMAÇÃO DE FUMAÇA | 11719 | CITRATO DE SÓDIO |
| 11676 | INCÔMODO CAUSADO PELA FUMAÇA | 11720 | CIANETO DE SÓDIO |
| 11677 | SUPRESSÃO DE FUMAÇA | 11721 | FLUORETO DE SÓDIO |
| 11678 | CHAMA FULIGINOSA | 11722 | HIDRÓXIDO DE SÓDIO |
| 11679 | POLIR | 11722 | SODA CÁUSTICA |

| | |
|---|---|
| 11723 | RAIA DE SÓDIO |
| 11724 | MONÓXIDO DE SÓDIO |
| 11725 | NITRITO DE SÓDIO |
| 11726 | OXALATO DE SÓDIO |
| 11727 | BIÓXIDO DE SÓDIO |
| 11728 | FOSFATO DE SÓDIO |
| 11729 | TARTRATO DE POTÁSSIO E SODA |
| 11730 | PIROFOSFATO DE SÓDIO |
| 11731 | SILICATO DE SÓDIO |
| 11732 | ESTANATO DE SÓDIO |
| 11733 | SULFATO NEUTRO DE SÓDIO |
| 11734 | SULFITO DE SÓDIO |
| 11735 | TANATO DE SÓDIO |
| 11736 | HIPOSSULFITO DE SÓDIO |
| 11737 | TUNGSTATO DE SÓDIO |
| 11738 | METAL DOCE |
| 11739 | GAXETA MOLE |
| 11740 | SABÃO DE POTASSA |
| 11741 | SOLDA BRANCA |
| 11741 | SOLDA FRACA |
| 11741 | SOLDA DE ESTANHO |
| 11742 | SOLDA DE ESTANHO |
| 11743 | SOLDAGEM A ESTANHO |
| 11744 | AÇO DOCE |
| 11745 | ÁGUA PURA |
| 11745 | ÁGUA DOCE |
| 11746 | MADEIRA BRANDA |
| 11747 | MARTELO DE CABEÇA DE PLÁSTICO |
| 11748 | PURIFICAR A ÁGUA POR PROCESSO QUÍMICO |
| 11749 | ABRANDAMENTO |
| 11750 | PONTO DE AMOLECIMENTO |
| 11751 | CONSISTÊNCIA DO SOLO |
| 11752 | ESTUDO DO TERRENO |
| 11753 | ÓLEO SOLAR |
| 11754 | ESPECTRO SOLAR |
| 11755 | SOLDA |
| 11756 | SOLDAR |
| 11757 | FRAGILIDADE POR PENETRAÇÃO DA SOLDA |
| 11758 | FLANGE SOLDADO |
| 11759 | MONTAGEM POR SOLDA |
| 11760 | TUBO SOLDADO |
| 11761 | SOLDAGEM |
| 11762 | SOLDAGEM |
| 11763 | FORNO DE SOLDAR |
| 11764 | FERRO DE SOLDAR |
| 11765 | FERRO DE SOLDAR |
| 11766 | MAÇARICO DE SOLDAR |
| 11767 | ALICATE DE SOLDAR |
| 11768 | SOLDAGEM COM MAÇARICO |

| | |
|---|---|
| 11769 | SOLDAGEM COM FERRO DE SOLDAR |
| 11770 | SOLA DE COURO |
| 11771 | PLACA DE PLAINA |
| 11772 | PLACA DE FUNDAÇÃO |
| 11773 | SOLENÓIDE |
| 11774 | VÁLVULA ELETROMAGNÉTICA |
| 11775 | SÓLIDO |
| 11776 | ÂNGULO SÓLIDO |
| 11777 | MANCAL INTEIRIÇO |
| 11778 | BARRA SÓLIDA DE PERFURAR |
| 11779 | CUBO INTEIRIÇO |
| 11780 | TIJOLO MACIÇO |
| 11781 | MATRIZ ÚNICA |
| 11781 | TARRAXA INTEIRIÇA |
| 11782 | TUBO ESTIRADO |
| 11783 | FRESAS DE HASTE MACIÇA |
| 11784 | VOLANTE DE UMA SÓ PEÇA |
| 11785 | COMBUSTÍVEL SÓLIDO |
| 11786 | FERRO SEMI-REDONDO MACIÇO |
| 11787 | JATO COMPACTO |
| 11788 | MANCAL DE UMA SÓ PEÇA |
| 11789 | MANDRIL LISO |
| 11790 | CORPO DE ROTAÇÃO |
| 11791 | PISTÃO MACIÇO |
| 11792 | POLIA DE UMA SÓ PEÇA |
| 11793 | EIXO MACIÇO |
| 11794 | SOLUÇÃO SÓLIDA |
| 11795 | ESTADO SÓLIDO |
| 11796 | OPÉRCULO MONOBLOCO |
| 11797 | SOLIDIFICAÇÃO |
| 11798 | FRENTE DE SOLIDIFICAÇÃO |
| 11799 | SOLIDIFICAÇÃO DE UM LÍQUIDO |
| 11800 | PONTO DE SOLIDIFICAÇÃO |
| 11801 | INTERVALO DE SOLIDIFICAÇÃO |
| 11802 | CONTRAÇÃO DE SOLIDIFICAÇÃO |
| 11803 | SOLIDIFICAR |
| 11804 | PONTO DE PEGA |
| 11804 | PONTO DE SOLIDIFICAÇÃO |
| 11805 | SÓLIDO |
| 11806 | SOLUBILIDADE |
| 11807 | SOLÚVEL |
| 11808 | VIDRO SOLÚVEL |
| 11809 | SOLÚVEL NA ÁGUA |
| 11810 | ÓLEO SOLÚVEL |
| 11811 | SOLUÇÃO |
| 11812 | RECOZIMENTO POR SOLUÇÃO |
| 11813 | SOLVER |
| 11813 | RESOLVER |
| 11814 | DISSOLVENTE |
| 11814 | SOLVENTE |
| 11815 | TESTE OU ENSAIO ACÚSTICO |

## 1311

| | |
|---|---|
| 11816 | FULIGEM |
| 11817 | SORBITA |
| 11818 | VIBRAÇÃO SONORA |
| 11819 | ONDA SONORA |
| 11820 | MADEIRA SÃ |
| 11821 | HOMOGENEIDADE DE UMA SOLDAGEM |
| 11822 | PETRÓLEO BRUTO SULFUROSO |
| 11823 | FONTE DE CORRENTE ELÉTRICA |
| 11824 | FONTE DE ENERGIA |
| 11825 | FONTE DE ERRO |
| 11826 | FONTE DE LUZ |
| 11827 | PÓLO SUL DE ÍMÃ |
| 11828 | RETICULADO CRISTALINO |
| 11829 | ESPAÇO OCUPADO |
| 11830 | LASCAMENTO |
| 11831 | OLHAL |
| 11831 | VÃO |
| 11832 | ABERTURA DE CHAVE |
| 11833 | CHAVE DE PARAFUSO |
| 11834 | PEÇA DE REPOSIÇÃO |
| 11835 | RODA SOBRESSALENTE |
| 11836 | FAÍSCA |
| 11837 | AVANÇO DE FAÍSCA |
| 11838 | VELA DE IGNIÇÃO |
| 11839 | BUJÃO PORTA-VELA |
| 11840 | ENSAIO DE FAÍSCA |
| 11841 | VELA DE IGNIÇÃO |
| 11842 | BORRIFO |
| 11843 | PERDAS POR BORRIFO |
| 11844 | ESPÁTULA |
| 11845 | RAMO ESPECIAL |
| 11846 | CHAPA PERFILADA |
| 11847 | FIO PERFILADO |
| 11848 | AÇO ESPECIAL |
| 11849 | ESPECIALIDADE |
| 11850 | DENSIDADE RELATIVA |
| 11850 | PESO ESPECÍFICO |
| 11851 | PICNÔMETRO |
| 11852 | CALOR ESPECÍFICO |
| 11853 | PRESSÃO ESPECÍFICA |
| 11854 | VOLUME ESPECÍFICO |
| 11855 | ESPECIFICAÇÃO |
| 11856 | ESPECIFICAÇÃO DE UMA PATENTE |
| 11857 | DIMENSÃO NOMINAL |
| 11858 | CORPO DE PROVA |
| 11858 | AMOSTRA |
| 11859 | CORES ESPECTRAIS |
| 11860 | ESPECTRÓGRAFO |
| 11861 | ANÁLISE ESPECTROGRÁFICA |
| 11862 | ESPECTROSCÓPIO |
| 11863 | ESPECTRO |
| 11864 | ANÁLISE ESPECTRAL |
| 11865 | OLIGISTO |
| 11865 | HEMATITA |
| 11866 | ESPELHO |
| 11867 | LIGA ESPECULAR |
| 11868 | VELOCIDADE |
| 11869 | TAQUÍMETRO |
| 11869 | VELOCÍMETRO |
| 11869 | TAQUÍMETRO |
| 11870 | VELOCIDADE DE IGNIÇÃO |
| 11871 | POLIA MÚLTIPLA |
| 11872 | REDUTOR DE VELOCIDADE |
| 11873 | ENGRENAGEM DESMULTIPLICADORA |
| 11873 | REDUTOR DE VELOCIDADE |
| 11874 | REGULADOR DE VELOCIDADE |
| 11875 | VELOCIDADE |
| 11876 | VELOCIDADE DE ROTAÇÃO |
| 11877 | VELOCÍMETRO |
| 11878 | RÉGULO DOS MINÉRIOS ARSENICAIS E ANTIMONIAIS |
| 11879 | ZINCO COMERCIAL |
| 11880 | SOLDAGEM AMARELA |
| 11881 | ÓLEO DE ESPERMACETE |
| 11882 | ESPERMACETE |
| 11883 | ESFERA |
| 11883 | GLOBO |
| 11884 | ESFÉRICO |
| 11885 | ABERRAÇÃO DE ESFERICIDADE |
| 11886 | ÂNGULO ESFÉRICO |
| 11887 | CALOTA ESFÉRICA |
| 11888 | ESPELHO ESFÉRICO |
| 11889 | MOVIMENTO ESFÉRICO |
| 11890 | MANCAL AXIAL DE ESFERAS |
| 11891 | TRIÂNGULO ESFÉRICO |
| 11892 | UNHA ESFÉRICA |
| 11892 | CUNHA ESFÉRICA |
| 11893 | PINO ESFÉRICO |
| 11894 | FERRO FUNDIDO NODULAR |
| 11895 | FERRO DÚCTIL |
| 11895 | FERRO NODULAR |
| 11896 | COALESCIMENTO |
| 11897 | ESFERÔMETRO |
| 11898 | FERRO SPIEGEL |
| 11899 | FERRO ESPECULAR |
| 11900 | LIGAÇÃO DE BOCA E CORDÃO |
| 11900 | JUNTA DE CAIXA |
| 11900 | JUNTA DE BOCA |
| 11901 | PONTA MACHO DE UM CANO |
| 11902 | CRAVOS |
| 11902 | PREGOS |
| 11903 | DERRAMAMENTOS |

# 1312

| | |
|---|---|
| 11904 | MANDRIL |
| 11904 | EIXO |
| 11904 | HASTE |
| 11904 | FUSO MESTRE |
| 11904 | VEIO |
| 11904 | BROCA |
| 11905 | MANCAL DO EIXO MOTOR |
| 11906 | DIÂMETRO INTERNO DO EIXO MOTOR |
| 11907 | PORCA EIXO |
| 11908 | ÓLEO PARA FUSOS OU EIXOS |
| 11909 | VELOCIDADE DE EIXO |
| 11910 | SUPORTE DE EIXO |
| 11911 | TORNO DE REPUXAR E ALISAR |
| 11912 | ESPIRAL |
| 11913 | CAME DE DISCO CURVO |
| 11914 | CONDUTO ESPIRAL |
| 11915 | ALARGADOR DE ESTRIAS EM ESPIRAL |
| 11916 | ENGRENAGEM HELICOIDAL |
| 11917 | FRESA DE DENTES HELICOIDAIS |
| 11918 | REBITADO EM ESPIRAL |
| 11919 | ESCADA CARACOL |
| 11920 | TUBO SOLDADO EM ESPIRAL |
| 11921 | SOLDAGEM EM ESPIRAL |
| 11922 | TERMÔMETRO A ÁLCOOL |
| 11923 | LÂMPADA A ÁLCOOL |
| 11924 | CONE DEFLETOR (EM DEPÓSITO) |
| 11925 | LUBRIFICAÇÃO POR SALPIQUE |
| 11926 | PAINEL PROTETOR |
| 11927 | GUARDA-LAMA |
| 11928 | ÓLEO DERRAMADO |
| 11929 | SALPICADURAS DE METAL |
| 11930 | EMENDA |
| 11930 | JUNÇÃO |
| 11930 | UNIÃO |
| 11931 | ENTRANÇAR UMA CORDA |
| 11932 | ELEMENTOS DE COBREJUNTAS |
| 11933 | AÚSTE DE CABO |
| 11934 | ENTRANÇADURA DE UM CABO |
| 11935 | EIXO ACANALADO |
| 11936 | FRATURA ESTILHADA |
| 11937 | FENDA |
| 11937 | DIVISÃO |
| 11938 | CUBO BIPARTIDO |
| 11939 | ANEL DE APERTO |
| 11940 | CONTRAPINO FENDIDO |
| 11940 | CHAVETA FENDIDA |
| 11941 | VOLANTE BIPARTIDO |
| 11942 | PORCA BIPARTIDA |
| 11943 | CHAVETA FENDIDA |
| 11944 | ANEL FENDIDO DE PISTÃO |
| 11945 | POLIA DE DUAS PEÇAS |
| 11946 | DISSOCIAR |
| 11946 | CINDIR |
| 11947 | MANCAIS BIPARTIDOS |
| 11948 | RACHADURA DE MADEIRA |
| 11949 | TESTE OU ENSAIO DE CISALHAMENTO |
| 11950 | DESDOBRAMENTO |
| 11951 | RODA DE RAIOS |
| 11952 | PANO DE ESPONJA |
| 11952 | TRAPO PARA LIMPEZA |
| 11953 | FERRO-ESPONJA |
| 11954 | CHUMBO ESPONJOSO |
| 11955 | ESPONJA DE PLATINA |
| 11956 | COMBUSTÃO ESPONTÂNEA |
| 11957 | VERRUMA DE COLHER |
| 11958 | TESTE NA GOTA |
| 11959 | SOLDA POR PONTOS |
| 11960 | ACABAMENTO PARCIAL |
| 11961 | FORMAÇÃO DE MANCHAS |
| 11962 | PISTOLA DE PULVERIZAÇÃO |
| 11963 | BOCAL DE ATOMIZAR |
| 11964 | BOCAL DE PULVERIZAÇÃO |
| 11965 | PINTURA À PISTOLA |
| 11966 | TÊMPERA POR ATOMIZAÇÃO |
| 11967 | ATOMIZADOR |
| 11967 | PULVERIZADOR |
| 11968 | PULVERIZAÇÃO |
| 11968 | ATOMIZAÇÃO |
| 11969 | PULVERIZADOR PORTÁTIL |
| 11970 | PULVERIZADORES SULFUROSOS |
| 11971 | PULVERIZADORES |
| 11972 | PROCESSO POR ASPERSÃO |
| 11973 | ESPALHADOR |
| 11974 | MOLA |
| 11975 | MÁQUINA DE TESTAR MOLAS E FIOS |
| 11976 | BALANÇA DE MOLAS |
| 11977 | LÂMINA DE MOLA |
| 11978 | LATÃO DE MOLA |
| 11979 | CASQUILHO COM MOLA |
| 11980 | AMORTECEDOR DE MOLA |
| 11980 | CAIXA DE MOLA |
| 11981 | FATOR DE VIBRAÇÃO |
| 11982 | COMPRESSOR A GRAXA |
| 11983 | MOLA SOB TENSÃO |
| 11984 | REGULADOR A MOLA |
| 11985 | VÁLVULA DE SEGURANÇA DE ALAVANCA E MOLA |
| 11986 | VÁLVULA DE SEGURANÇA DE MOLA |
| 11987 | LINGÜETA DE MOLA |
| 11988 | FOLHA DE MOLA |
| 11989 | MANÔMETRO METÁLICO |
| 11990 | ANEL ELÁSTICO |

| | | | |
|---|---|---|---|
| 11991 | BRAÇADEIRA DE MOLA | 12036 | QUADRATURA |
| 11992 | AÇO DE MOLA | 12037 | TESOURA DE ESQUADRIAR |
| 11993 | MOLA DE FLEXÃO | 12038 | ATRASO NA SOLDAGEM |
| 11994 | MOLA DE TORÇÃO | 12039 | ESPREMER |
| 11995 | ARRUELA DE PRESSÃO | 12040 | GAIOLA DE ROLAMENTO DE ROLOS |
| 11995 | ARRUELA GROWER | 12041 | ESTABILIDADE |
| 11996 | ÁGUA DE FONTE | 12042 | EIXO ESTABILIZADOR |
| 11997 | FIO PARA MOLA | 12043 | ESTABILIZAÇÃO |
| 11998 | VÁLVULA DE SEGURANÇA DE MOLA | 12044 | RECOZIMENTO DE ESTABILIZAÇÃO |
| 11999 | RUPTURA DAS CABEÇAS DOS REBITES | 12045 | EQUILÍBRIO ESTÁVEL |
| 12000 | REGAR | 12046 | CUBA |
| 12000 | BORRIFAR | 12046 | CHAMINÉ |
| 12001 | REGA | 12046 | PILHA |
| 12001 | BORRIFO | 12047 | PORTA-OBJETO |
| 12002 | CORRENTE ARTICULADA | 12048 | ALTERNADO |
| 12003 | GITO | 12048 | EM ZIGUEZAGUE |
| 12003 | FUNIL | 12048 | DESENCONTRADO |
| 12004 | FUNIL DE FUNDIÇÃO | 12049 | SOLDAGEM ALTERNADA |
| 12005 | MEALHAR | 12050 | ÁGUA ESTAGNADA |
| 12006 | MÁQUINA PARA CORTAR AS ENGRENAGENS RETAS E HELICOIDAIS | 12051 | AÇO INOXIDÁVEL |
| | | 12052 | PERNA DE ESCADA |
| 12007 | RODA DE FRICÇÃO CILÍNDRICA | 12053 | ESCADA |
| 12008 | ENGRENAGEM RETA | 12054 | ESTALAGMOMETRIA |
| 12009 | RODA DE ENGRENAGEM RETA | 12055 | PILÃO |
| 12010 | TRANSMISSÃO POR ENGRENAGEM RETA | 12055 | MATRIZ |
| 12011 | MOITÃO DE ENGRENAGEM RETA | 12056 | CUNHAR |
| 12012 | ESPALDAR | 12056 | ESTAMPAR |
| 12013 | QUADRADO | 12057 | MOINHO DE MINÉRIOS |
| 12014 | ESQUADRO | 12058 | CORRENTE ESTAMPADA |
| 12015 | FERRO QUADRADO | 12059 | ESTAMPAGEM |
| 12016 | CENTÍMETRO QUADRADO | 12060 | MÁQUINA DE ESTAMPAR |
| 12017 | SEÇÃO QUADRADA | 12060 | PRENSA DE ESTAMPAR |
| 12018 | DECÍMETRO QUADRADO | 12061 | TESTE OU ENSAIO DE ESTAMPAGEM |
| 12019 | LIMA QUADRADA | 12062 | ESCORA |
| 12020 | PÉ QUADRADO | 12062 | PONTALETE |
| 12021 | POLEGADA QUADRADA | 12063 | MONTANTE |
| 12022 | METRO QUADRADO | 12064 | ASSENTO NO SOLO |
| 12023 | MILÍMETRO QUADRADO | 12065 | CÂMARA DE LAMINADOR |
| 12024 | PORCA QUADRADA | 12066 | TUBO DE TOMADA DE ÁGUA |
| 12025 | PEÇA QUADRADA | 12067 | PIEZÔMETRO |
| 12026 | PIRÂMIDE QUADRANGULAR | 12068 | DE RESERVA |
| 12027 | RAIZ QUADRADA | 12069 | COMPRESSOR AUXILIAR |
| 12028 | CABO DE SEÇÃO QUADRADA | 12070 | MOTOR DE RESERVA |
| 12029 | EIXO QUADRADO | 12071 | NORMA |
| 12030 | ROSCA PLANA | 12071 | PADRÃO |
| 12030 | ROSCA QUADRADA | 12072 | PÉ CÚBICO PADRÃO |
| 12031 | JARDA QUADRADA | 12073 | MODELO PADRÃO |
| 12032 | SOLDA EM BORDAS RETAS | 12074 | DESVIO PADRÃO |
| 12033 | PARAFUSO DE CABEÇA QUADRADA | 12075 | SOLDA DE ÂNGULO DE CORDÃO PLANO |
| 12034 | PARAFUSO DE ROSCA QUADRADA | 12076 | CALIBRE PADRÃO |
| 12035 | MADEIRA ESQUADREJADA | 12077 | MEDIDA PADRÃO |

| | |
|---|---|
| 12078 | MONTANTE DE UMA MÁQUINA |
| 12079 | MODELO DE REFERÊNCIA |
| 12080 | MANÔMETRO PADRÃO |
| 12081 | METRO PADRÃO |
| 12082 | AMOSTRA PADRÃO |
| 12083 | PERFIL NORMAL |
| 12084 | LICOR NORMAL |
| 12084 | SOLUÇÃO TITULADA |
| 12084 | SOLUÇÃO NORMAL |
| 12085 | TERMÔMETRO PADRÃO |
| 12086 | TIPO PADRÃO |
| 12087 | CALIBRE COM TAMPA NORMAL |
| 12088 | CALIBRE DE BOCA NORMAL |
| 12089 | BITOLA NORMAL PARA ARAME |
| 12090 | PADRONIZAR |
| 12090 | UNIFICAR |
| 12091 | PADRONIZAÇÃO |
| 12092 | CORDA FIXA DE MOITÃO |
| 12093 | CANALIZAÇÃO ASCENDENTE |
| 12094 | PARADA DE UM MOTOR |
| 12095 | ESTANATO |
| 12096 | CLORETO ESTÁNICO |
| 12097 | ÁCIDO ESTÁNICO |
| 12098 | ÓXIDO ESTÁNICO |
| 12099 | SULFETO ESTÁNICO |
| 12100 | CLORETO ESTANHOSO |
| 12101 | HIDRATO ESTANHOSO |
| 12102 | ÓXIDO ESTANHOSO |
| 12103 | SULFETO ESTANHOSO |
| 12104 | GRAMPO EM U |
| 12105 | GRAMPO |
| 12106 | GRAMPO |
| 12107 | POLÍGONO EM ESTRELA |
| 12108 | FENDAS DA MADEIRA |
| 12109 | RODA ESTRELADA |
| 12110 | SEÇÃO ESTRELADA |
| 12111 | FÉCULA |
| 12111 | GOMA |
| 12111 | AMIDO |
| 12111 | POLVILHO |
| 12112 | GOMA DE AMIDO |
| 12113 | ARRANCAR |
| 12113 | DAR PARTIDA |
| 12113 | COMEÇAR |
| 12114 | DAR PARTIDA AO MOTOR |
| 12114 | COLOCAR O MOTOR EM FUNCIONAMENTO |
| 12115 | BOTÃO DE FUNCIONAR E PARAR |
| 12116 | MOTOR DE ARRANQUE |
| 12116 | MOTOR DE PARTIDA |
| 12117 | CONTROLE DO MOTOR DE ARRANQUE |
| 12118 | ARRANQUE |

| | |
|---|---|
| 12118 | COLOCAÇÃO EM FUNCIONAMENTO |
| 12119 | APARELHO DE COLOCAÇÃO EM FUNCIONAMENTO |
| 12120 | ALAVANCA DE ARRANQUE |
| 12121 | MOTOR DE ARRANQUE |
| 12122 | ARRANQUE DE UM MOTOR |
| 12123 | PERÍODO DE PARTIDA |
| 12124 | PONTO DE PARTIDA DE UM MOVIMENTO |
| 12125 | HIPÓTESES DE BASE |
| 12126 | POSIÇÃO DE ARRANQUE |
| 12127 | PUNÇÃO TOCADORA |
| 12128 | RESISTÊNCIA DE PARTIDA |
| 12129 | BINÁRIO DE ARRANQUE |
| 12130 | COLOCAÇÃO DE UM MOTOR EM FUNCIONAMENTO |
| 12130 | LIGAÇÃO DO MOTOR |
| 12131 | VÁLVULA DE ARRANQUE |
| 12132 | ESTADO DE EQUILÍBRIO |
| 12133 | ESTÁTICO |
| 12134 | ATRITO ESTÁTICO |
| 12135 | REGULADOR ESTÁTICO |
| 12136 | PRESSÃO ESTÁTICA |
| 12137 | PRESSÃO ESTÁTICA |
| 12138 | CARGA ESTÁTICA |
| 12139 | MOMENTO ESTÁTICO |
| 12140 | ESTÁTICA |
| 12141 | CAMIONETA |
| 12141 | AUTOMÓVEL UTILITÁRIO |
| 12142 | FORNO FIXO |
| 12143 | CALDEIRA INDUSTRIAL |
| 12144 | MÁQUINA A VAPOR FIXA |
| 12145 | ONDA ESTACIONÁRIA |
| 12146 | ESTATOR |
| 12147 | BRONZE PARA ESTÁTUAS |
| 12148 | LUBRIFICADOR STAUFFER |
| 12149 | ADUELA |
| 12150 | ESTEIAR |
| 12150 | ESCORAR |
| 12150 | SUSTENTAR |
| 12151 | TIRANTE |
| 12152 | REFORÇO COM NERVURAS |
| 12153 | ESCORAMENTO |
| 12154 | LUNETA FIXA (DE TORNO) |
| 12155 | VAPOR |
| 12156 | ACUMULADOR DE VAPOR |
| 12157 | BANHO DE VAPOR |
| 12158 | CALDEIRA A VAPOR |
| 12159 | FREIO A VAPOR |
| 12160 | CALORÍMETRO A VAPOR |
| 12161 | SERPENTINA DE AQUECER POR VAPOR |
| 12162 | CILINDRO A VAPOR |

| | |
|---|---|
| 12163 | CÚPULA DE VAPOR |
| 12164 | MOTOR A VAPOR |
| 12164 | MÁQUINA A VAPOR |
| 12165 | MÁQUINA A PLENA PRESSÃO |
| 12166 | MARTELO PILÃO A VAPOR |
| 12167 | CALEFAÇÃO OU AQUECIMENTO A VAPOR |
| 12168 | CAMISA DE VAPOR |
| 12169 | GERADOR A VAPOR |
| 12170 | JATO DE VAPOR |
| 12171 | INJETOR DE VAPOR |
| 12172 | EJETOR |
| 12173 | LOCOMOTIVA A VAPOR |
| 12174 | INDICADOR DE VAPOR |
| 12175 | BOCAL DE SAÍDA DE VAPOR |
| 12176 | CANAL DE VAPOR |
| 12177 | TUBO A VAPOR |
| 12178 | CANALIZAÇÃO OU TUBULAÇÃO DE VAPOR |
| 12179 | PISTÃO A VAPOR |
| 12180 | INSTALAÇÃO DE MÁQUINAS A VAPOR |
| 12181 | PRESSÃO DE VAPOR |
| 12182 | TESTE A QUENTE DE CALDEIRA |
| 12183 | BOMBA A VAPOR |
| 12184 | SEPARADOR DE VAPOR |
| 12185 | CÂMARA DE VAPOR DE CALDEIRA |
| 12186 | VÁLVULA DE FECHAMENTO DO VAPOR |
| 12187 | VÁLVULA DE ENTRADA DO VAPOR |
| 12188 | SEPARADOR DE ÁGUA DE CONDENSAÇÃO |
| 12189 | TURBINA A VAPOR |
| 12190 | APITO A VAPOR |
| 12191 | GERADOR A VAPOR |
| 12192 | VAPOR DE ÁGUA |
| 12193 | À PROVA DE VAPOR |
| 12194 | ÁCIDO ESTEÁRICO |
| 12195 | ESTEARINA |
| 12196 | AÇO |
| 12197 | FITA DE AÇO |
| 12198 | FERRO PARA ARMAÇÃO DE CONCRETO |
| 12199 | VIGA DE FERRO OU AÇO |
| 12200 | CORREIA DE AÇO |
| 12201 | CABO DE AÇO |
| 12202 | AÇO FUNDIDO |
| 12203 | CONCRETO ARMADO |
| 12204 | CILINDRO DE AÇO |
| 12205 | REVESTIR DE AÇO |
| 12205 | ACERAR |
| 12206 | ACERAÇÃO |
| 12206 | CALDEAMENTO |
| 12207 | FUNDIÇÃO DE AÇO |
| 12208 | ARMAÇÃO METÁLICA |
| 12209 | AÇO SEM BOLHAS |
| 12210 | LINGOTE DE AÇO |

| | |
|---|---|
| 12211 | ACIARIA |
| 12212 | TUBO DE AÇO |
| 12213 | CHAPA DE AÇO |
| 12214 | ELABORAÇÃO DO AÇO |
| 12215 | CABO DE AÇO |
| 12216 | FOLHA DE AÇO |
| 12217 | AÇO TRANÇADO PARA CABOS |
| 12218 | CONSTRUÇÃO DE AÇO |
| 12218 | CONSTRUÇÃO METÁLICA |
| 12219 | TUBO DE AÇO |
| 12220 | AROS DE AÇO PARA LOCOMOTIVAS |
| 12221 | FIO OU ARAME DE AÇO |
| 12222 | ACIARIA |
| 12223 | AÇO |
| 12224 | AÇO EXTRA-DOCE |
| 12225 | BALANÇA ROMANA |
| 12226 | MANOBRA |
| 12226 | DIREÇÃO |
| 12227 | BRAÇO DE DIREÇÃO |
| 12228 | COLUNA DE DIREÇÃO |
| 12229 | MECANISMO DE DIREÇÃO |
| 12230 | PONTA DE EIXO DIANTEIRO DO VEÍCULO |
| 12231 | BIELA DA PONTA DO EIXO DIANTEIRO DO VEÍCULO |
| 12232 | LIAME DE DIREÇÃO |
| 12233 | VOLANTE DE DIREÇÃO |
| 12234 | ESTELITA |
| 12235 | TERMÔMETRO GRADUADO |
| 12236 | HASTE DE VÁLVULA |
| 12237 | HASTE |
| 12238 | ESTÊNCIL |
| 12239 | DEGRAU |
| 12239 | PASSO |
| 12240 | RECOZIMENTO POR ESTÁGIOS |
| 12241 | MANCAL ESCALONADO |
| 12242 | TÊMPERA RETARDADA |
| 12243 | TÊMPERA POR ESTÁGIO |
| 12244 | TRANSFORMADOR REDUTOR |
| 12245 | TRANSFORMADOR ELEVADOR |
| 12246 | ESCALONADO |
| 12247 | ENGRENAGEM DE DENTES CRUZADOS |
| 12248 | GRELHA ESCALONADA |
| 12249 | TÊMPERA POR ESTÁGIOS |
| 12250 | ESTEREOMÉTRICO |
| 12251 | ESTEREOMETRIA |
| 12252 | ESTERILIZAÇÃO DA ÁGUA |
| 12253 | PRATA DE LEI |
| 12254 | GOMA-LACA EM RAMOS |
| 12255 | ENXOFRE EM BASTÃO |
| 12256 | ESTICADOR |
| 12256 | REFORÇO |

| | |
|---|---|
| 12256 | CONTRAFORTE |
| 12257 | CHAPA DE REFORÇO |
| 12258 | ESTICADOR DE CORREIA |
| 12259 | ALAMBIQUE |
| 12260 | AGITADOR |
| 12261 | ESTRIBO |
| 12262 | CEPO DE PLAINA |
| 12263 | ESTOQUE DE MATERIAL |
| 12264 | TESOURA DE BANCO |
| 12265 | DEPÓSITO |
| 12265 | CANTEIRO |
| 12266 | TARRAXAS |
| 12267 | ESTEQUIOMÉTRICO |
| 12268 | ESTEQUIOMETRIA |
| 12269 | CARREGAR A FORNALHA |
| 12269 | ALIMENTAR A FORNALHA |
| 12270 | SALA DAS CALDEIRAS |
| 12271 | FOGUISTA |
| 12271 | CARREGADOR MECÂNICO |
| 12272 | FOGUISTA |
| 12273 | BRITADOR DE PEDRA |
| 12274 | CIMENTO DE PEDRA |
| 12275 | POLAINA |
| 12275 | PROTETOR CONTRA PEDRAS |
| 12276 | LOUÇA DE PÓ DE PEDRA |
| 12277 | TUBO DE LOUÇA |
| 12278 | ESBARRO |
| 12278 | BATENTE |
| 12278 | PARADA |
| 12278 | ESPERA |
| 12278 | DESCANSO |
| 12278 | LINGÜETA |
| 12279 | TAPAR UM VAZAMENTO |
| 12280 | PARAR UMA MÁQUINA |
| 12281 | TORNEIRA DE PASSAGEM |
| 12282 | VÁLVULA DE PASSAGEM |
| 12283 | CRONÔMETRO |
| 12284 | BUJÃO |
| 12284 | TAMPA |
| 12285 | TAMPA |
| 12286 | PARADA DE MOTOR |
| 12287 | REVESTIMENTO ISOLADOR |
| 12288 | ARMAZENAMENTO |
| 12289 | SUPORTE DE INFORMAÇÃO |
| 12290 | ACUMULAÇÃO DE ENERGIA |
| 12291 | ACUMULAÇÃO DE CALOR |
| 12292 | TANQUES DE RESERVA |
| 12293 | DEPÓSITO |
| 12293 | ARMAZÉM |
| 12294 | ARMAZENAR |
| 12295 | ARMAZENAR ENERGIA |

| | |
|---|---|
| 12296 | ACUMULAR CALOR |
| 12297 | ALMOXARIFADO |
| 12297 | DEPÓSITO |
| 12298 | ALMOXARIFE |
| 12299 | ARMAZENAMENTO |
| 12300 | ESTUFA |
| 12300 | FORNO |
| 12300 | FOGÃO |
| 12301 | FRESA COM GUME LATERAL |
| 12302 | BRAÇO DIREITO DE UMA POLIA |
| 12303 | CALIBRE DE CONFRONTO |
| 12304 | BROCA PARALELA |
| 12305 | ALARGADOR PARALELO |
| 12306 | ALAVANCA RETA |
| 12307 | FRESA DE DENTES RETOS |
| 12308 | MARTELO DE PENA LONGITUDINAL |
| 12309 | TUBO RETO |
| 12310 | LINHA RETA |
| 12310 | RETA |
| 12311 | DENTES RETOS |
| 12312 | MOLA DE FLEXÃO RETA |
| 12313 | EMBREAGEM DE DENTES RETOS |
| 12314 | CONTROLE PARAXIAL |
| 12315 | MOVIMENTO RETILÍNEO |
| 12316 | PRENSA MECÂNICA A MONTANTE |
| 12317 | VÁLVULA RETA |
| 12318 | ALINHAR |
| 12318 | ENDIREITAR |
| 12318 | RETIFICAR |
| 12319 | ENDIREITAMENTO |
| 12319 | RETIFICAÇÃO |
| 12319 | ALINHAMENTO |
| 12320 | MÁQUINA DE ALINHAR |
| 12321 | CHAPA DE ALINHAR |
| 12322 | ESFORÇO |
| 12322 | TENSÃO |
| 12322 | DEFORMAÇÃO |
| 12323 | SUBMETER UM CORPO A CARGA |
| 12324 | ENVELHECIMENTO POR ESFORÇOS |
| 12325 | EXTENSÔMETRO |
| 12326 | ENCRUAMENTO |
| 12327 | ENVELHECIMENTO POR DEFORMAÇÃO |
| 12328 | ENVELHECIMENTO POR DEFORMAÇÃO |
| 12329 | MEDIDOR DE DEFORMAÇÃO |
| 12330 | VELOCIDADE OU TAXA DE DEFORMAÇÃO |
| 12331 | ESFORÇO |
| 12331 | SOLICITAÇÃO |
| 12332 | COADOR |
| 12333 | FILTRO |
| 12333 | SEPARADOR DE SEDIMENTOS |
| 12334 | TENSOR |

1317

| | | | |
|---|---|---|---|
| 12335 | ESTANHO DA MALACA | 12378 | FITA |
| 12336 | COCHA | 12379 | DEFORMAR A ROSCA |
| 12336 | CORDÃO | 12380 | REGISTRADOR DE DESENROLAMENTO CONTÍNUO |
| 12337 | TRANÇAR | | |
| 12337 | COCHAR | 12381 | SOLVENTES DE DECAPAGEM |
| 12338 | FIO DE UM CABO | 12382 | BANHO DE DECAPAGEM |
| 12339 | FIO DE UMA CORDA | 12383 | GUINDASTE PARA SACAR LINGOTES |
| 12340 | ACOCHAMENTO | 12384 | PRATO DE MÁQUINA DE DESMOLDAR |
| 12341 | MÁQUINA DE ACOCHOAR CABOS | 12385 | ESTROBOSCÓPIO |
| 12342 | DISPOSITIVO DE ESTRANGULAMENTO | 12386 | MÉTODO ESTROBOSCÓPICO |
| 12343 | CORDÃO | 12387 | TEMPO |
| 12344 | FREIO DE PARAFUSO | 12387 | CURSO |
| 12345 | FORQUILHA DE CABEÇA DE BIELA | 12388 | U DE MONTAGEM |
| 12346 | FORQUILHA DE GUIA | 12389 | ESTRÔNCIO |
| 12347 | CHARNEIRA DE SUPERFÍCIE | 12390 | FLUORETO DE ESTRÔNCIO |
| 12348 | FIBRA DE PALHA | 12391 | ELEMENTO ESTRUTURAL |
| 12349 | CORRENTE PARASITA | 12393 | AÇO PARA ESTRUTURAS |
| 12350 | CORROSÃO POR CORRENTE PARASITA | 12394 | ESTRUTURA |
| 12351 | LINHA AERODINÂMICA | 12395 | CONTEXTURA |
| 12352 | FORÇA | 12395 | ESTRUTURA |
| 12352 | RESISTÊNCIA | 12395 | CONSTRUÇÃO |
| 12353 | RESISTÊNCIA AOS CHOQUES REPETIDOS | 12396 | ESCORA |
| 12354 | GRAU DE UMA SOLUÇÃO | 12396 | ESTEIO |
| 12355 | RESISTÊNCIA DE MATERIAIS | 12396 | ESPEQUE |
| 12356 | TESTE DE RESISTÊNCIA | 12397 | PERNO |
| 12357 | SOLDA POR RESISTÊNCIA | 12397 | PINO |
| 12358 | REFORÇAR | 12398 | PINO ROSCADO |
| 12359 | REFORÇO | 12399 | PINO PRISIONEIRO |
| 12360 | CONCENTRAÇÃO DA TENSÃO | 12400 | PISTOLA PARA ENFIAR CAVILHAS |
| 12361 | CORROSÃO SOB TENSÃO | 12401 | TORNO PARA PERNOS |
| 12362 | RECOZIMENTO COM REDUÇÃO DE TENSÃO | 12402 | TRAVESSA DE CORRENTE |
| 12363 | ALÍVIO DE TENSÕES RESIDUAIS | 12403 | CORRENTE COM TRAVESSA |
| 12364 | FISSURAS DEVIDAS À CORROSÃO SOB TENSÃO | 12404 | PNEU COM GARRAS |
| | | 12405 | ENGAXETAMENTO |
| 12365 | CURVA ESFORÇO-DEFORMAÇÃO | 12405 | CAIXA DE VEDAÇÃO |
| 12366 | DIAGRAMA DA RESISTÊNCIA MECÂNICA | 12405 | PRENSA-ESTOPAS |
| 12367 | CARGA POR UNIDADE DE SEÇÃO | 12406 | GUARNIÇÃO DE CAIXA DE PREME-GAXETA |
| 12367 | TENSÃO INTERNA | 12407 | MÁQUINA STUMPF |
| 12368 | SUPERFÍCIE SOLICITADA | 12408 | JUNTA INFERIOR |
| 12368 | SUPERFÍCIE CARREGADA | 12409 | SUBDIVISÃO |
| 12369 | TENSOR | 12410 | DIVISÃO DO TRABALHO |
| 12370 | TENSÃO DE ESTIRAGEM | 12411 | SUBLIMAR |
| 12371 | LINHAS DE LUDERS | 12412 | SUBLIMAÇÃO |
| 12372 | DESEMPENADEIRA POR TRAÇÃO | 12413 | SUBMERGIR |
| 12373 | ESFORÇO DE TENSÃO | 12414 | SOLDA DE ARÇO SUBMERSO |
| 12374 | ALONGAMENTO DE CORREIA, DE CABO | 12415 | SUBPROGRAMA |
| 12375 | GOLPE | 12416 | OXIDAÇÃO SUBSUPERFICIAL |
| 12376 | CORDÃO DE SOLDA RETILÍNEA | 12417 | TRATAMENTO ULTERIOR |
| 12377 | LONGARINA | 12418 | ENFRAQUECIMENTO |
| 12377 | PERNA DE ESCADA | 12418 | SUBSIDÊNCIA |
| 12378 | TIRA | 12419 | MATÉRIA |

| | |
|---|---|
| 12419 SUBSTÂNCIA | 12465 SUPERFUSÃO |
| 12420 SUBSTITUTO | 12465 SUPER-RESFRIAMENTO |
| 12421 SUBSTITUIÇÃO | 12466 DILATAÇÃO SUPERFICIAL |
| 12422 METAL DE BASE | 12467 LIMA MURÇA FINA |
| 12423 SUBESTRUTURA | 12468 SUPERAQUECER |
| 12424 SUBSTRATO | 12469 VAPOR SUPERAQUECIDO |
| 12425 SUBTRAÇÃO | 12470 ÁGUA SUPERAQUECIDA |
| 12426 SUBTRAENDO | 12471 VAPOR SUPERAQUECIDO |
| 12427 ASPIRAR | 12472 SUPERAQUECEDOR |
| 12428 ASPIRAÇÃO | 12473 SUPERAQUECIMENTO |
| 12428 SUCÇÃO | 12474 SUPERVISIONAR |
| 12429 EXAUSTOR | 12475 SUPERESTRUTURA |
| 12430 GASOGÊNIO A ASPIRAÇÃO | 12476 SUPERPOSIÇÃO DE VIBRAÇÕES |
| 12431 REGULADOR A DEPRESSÃO | 12477 SUPERSATURAR |
| 12432 ALTURA DE ASPIRAÇÃO DE UMA BOMBA | 12478 SOLUÇÃO SUPERSATURADA |
| 12433 TUBO DE ASPIRAÇÃO | 12479 SUPERSATURAÇÃO |
| 12434 BOMBA ASPIRANTE | 12480 INSPEÇÃO ULTRA-SÔNICA |
| 12435 CURSO DE ASPIRAÇÃO | 12481 SUPERVISÃO |
| 12436 VÁLVULA DE ASPIRAÇÃO | 12482 SUPLEMENTO DE UM ÂNGULO |
| 12437 VARIAÇÃO BRUSCA DE TEMPERATURA | 12483 ÂNGULO SUPLEMENTAR |
| 12438 MÁQUINA SEPARADORA DE BETERRABA DE AÇÚCAR | 12484 CABOS DE ALIMENTAÇÃO |
| | 12485 FORNECER CALOR |
| 12439 COLHEDORES DE BETERRABA | 12486 ADMISSÃO DE AR |
| 12440 LEVANTADORES DE BETERRABA | 12487 FORNECIMENTO DE ENERGIA ELÉTRICA |
| 12441 MÁQUINAS PARA PREPARO DE BETERRABA | 12488 FORNECIMENTO DE CALOR |
| | 12489 TUBO ADUTOR |
| 12442 FRAGILIDADE PELO ATAQUE DE SULFETO | 12490 SUPORTE |
| 12443 CAMADA DE ÓXIDO FERROSO | 12490 APOIO |
| 12444 SULFATO | 12491 APOIAR |
| 12445 SODA LEBLANC | 12491 SUSTENTAR |
| 12446 SULFETO | 12492 ANEL DE SUPORTE |
| 12447 SULFETO DE FERRO | 12493 APOIO |
| 12448 SULFITE | 12494 DADOS JUSTIFICATIVOS |
| 12449 ENXOFRE | 12495 CHAPA DE SUPORTE |
| 12450 ANIDRIDO SULFUROSO | 12496 SUPERFÍCIE |
| 12450 ÓXIDO SULFUROSO | 12497 POLIR |
| 12451 CLORETO DE ENXOFRE | 12497 APLANAR |
| 12452 ANIDRIDO SULFÚRICO | 12498 ANALISADOR DE SUPERFÍCIE |
| 12453 ÁCIDO SULFÚRICO | 12499 CONDENSADOR POR SUPERFÍCIE |
| 12454 SOMA | 12500 ESTADO DA SUPERFÍCIE |
| 12455 PONTA DE ROSCA | 12501 FISSURA SUPERFICIAL |
| 12456 MOVIMENTO PLANETÁRIO | 12502 DEFEITO DE SUPERFÍCIE |
| 12457 RODA CENTRAL DE TREM PLANETÁRIO | 12503 IRREGULARIDADE DE SUPERFÍCIE |
| 12458 CHAVETA EMBUTIDA | 12504 ACABAMENTO DE SUPERFÍCIE |
| 12459 LIGA DE ALTA TEMPERATURA | 12505 ESMERIL DE SUPERFÍCIES PLANAS |
| 12460 SUPERAQUECIMENTO | 12506 RETIFICAÇÃO DE SUPERFÍCIE |
| 12461 SUPERSATURAÇÃO | 12507 RETIFICADORA DE SUPERFÍCIES PLANAS |
| 12462 AÇO FINO | 12508 TÊMPERA SUPERFICIAL |
| 12463 SUPERFUNDIR | 12509 RUGOSÍMETRO |
| 12463 SUPER-REFRIGERAR | 12510 SUPERFÍCIE DE CONTATO |
| 12464 LÍQUIDO SUPERFUNDIDO | 12511 SUPERFÍCIE DE CORTE |

## 1319

| | | | |
|---|---|---|---|
| 12512 | SUPERFÍCIE DE IMPRESSÃO | 12556 | MUDANÇA DE VIA |
| 12513 | SUPERFÍCIE DE ROTAÇÃO | 12557 | QUADRO DE DISTRIBUIÇÃO DE LIGAÇÕES |
| 12514 | PONTA DO DENTE | 12558 | APARELHAMENTO DE COMANDO |
| 12515 | APLAINADORA | | ELÉTRICO |
| 12516 | PLACA DE DESEMPENO | 12559 | DESLIGAMENTO |
| 12517 | PRESSÃO SUPERFICIAL | 12560 | LIGAÇÃO |
| 12518 | RUGOSIDADE DA SUPERFÍCIE | 12561 | TORNEL |
| 12519 | TENSÃO SUPERFICIAL | 12561 | TORNIQUETE |
| 12520 | ÁGUA SUPERFICIAL | 12562 | TORNO DE PLACA DE INVERSÃO |
| 12521 | SUPERFÍCIE | 12563 | MANCAL DE RÓTULA |
| 12522 | ACABAMENTO | 12564 | GANCHO DE RÓTULA |
| 12522 | ALISAMENTO | 12565 | SIENITO |
| 12523 | AGENTE DE TRATAMENTO DE SUPERFÍCIE | 12566 | SIMÉTRICO |
| 12524 | TETO SUSPENSO | 12567 | SIMETRIA |
| 12525 | RESERVATÓRIO DE TETO SUSPENSO | 12568 | SINCRO |
| 12526 | SUSPENSÃO | 12569 | SINCRONISMO |
| 12527 | GANCHO DE SUSPENSÃO | 12570 | SÍNCRONO |
| 12528 | PONTE SUSPENSA | 12570 | SINCRÔNICO |
| 12529 | UMEDECIMENTO | 12571 | MOTOR SÍNCRONO |
| 12530 | ESTAMPAR | 12572 | SÍNTESE |
| 12531 | ESTAMPA | 12573 | SINTÉTICO |
| 12532 | ESTAMPAGEM | 12574 | SINTONIA |
| 12533 | MÁQUINA DE RECALCAR OU ESTAMPAR | 12575 | SISTEMA DE COORDENADAS |
| 12534 | ESTAMPAGEM | 12576 | SISTEMA DE LENTES |
| 12535 | COLO DE CISNE | 12577 | SISTEMA DE ALAVANCAS |
| 12535 | TUBO EM S | 12578 | SISTEMA DE MEDIDAS |
| 12536 | DETRITOS DE USINAGEM | 12579 | SISTEMA DE TUBOS |
| 12537 | MÁQUINA PARA REVIRAR O FENO | 12580 | SISTEMA DE PESOS |
| 12538 | OSCILAR | 12581 | ESQUADRO OU RÉGUA EM T |
| 12539 | BARRA ESTABILIZADORA | 12582 | FRESAS PARA RANHURAS EM T |
| 12540 | LAVAGEM | 12583 | FORMATO DE TUBULAÇÃO |
| 12540 | EXUDAÇÃO | 12584 | MESA |
| 12541 | RECOLHEDORA DE FENO | 12584 | QUADRO |
| 12542 | DILATAR | 12585 | CURSO TRANSVERSAL DA MESA |
| 12542 | INCHAR | 12586 | TACÓGRAFO |
| 12543 | INCHAÇO | 12587 | CONTA-GIROS |
| 12543 | ENCHIMENTO | 12587 | TAQUÍMETRO |
| 12544 | DILATAÇÃO DA MADEIRA | 12588 | TACHA |
| 12545 | VÁLVULA DE CHARNEIRA | 12589 | SOLDA POR PONTOS |
| 12546 | UNIÃO GIRATÓRIA | 12590 | SOLDAGEM POR PONTOS |
| 12547 | DIÂMETRO ADMISSÍVEL DO BANCO | 12591 | VISCOSIDADE |
| 12548 | OSCILAÇÃO DE PÊNDULO | 12592 | REBITE PROVISÓRIO |
| 12549 | BRAÇO OSCILANTE | 12593 | FOLHA MUITO FINA |
| 12550 | FURADEIRA DE BRAÇO MÓVEL | 12594 | CRINA DE CAVALO |
| 12551 | CÂMARA DE TURBULÊNCIA | 12595 | LUZES TRASEIRAS |
| 12552 | PASSO DO SISTEMA THURY | 12596 | CANAL DE FUGA |
| 12553 | INTERRUPTOR | 12596 | CANAL DE DESCARGA |
| 12553 | CHAVE | 12597 | ÁGUA DE DESCARGA |
| 12554 | DESLIGAR | 12598 | RESÍDUOS |
| 12555 | LIGAR | 12599 | CABEÇOTE MÓVEL |
| 12556 | AGULHA DE CHAVE | 12600 | DESMONTAR |

| | | | |
|---|---|---|---|
| 12601 | RECEBER UMA FORÇA | 12646 | CONICIDADE |
| 12602 | CORRIGIR A FOLGA DE UMA CORREIA | 12647 | UNIÃO CÔNICA |
| 12603 | COMPENSAR A FOLGA DE UM MANCAL | 12648 | LIMA TRIANGULAR |
| 12604 | DESMONTAGEM | 12649 | ASSENTO CÔNICO |
| 12605 | CORREÇÃO DA FOLGA DE UMA CORREIA | 12650 | ALARGADOR MANUAL CÔNICO |
| 12606 | COMPENSAÇÃO DA FOLGA DE UM MANCAL | 12651 | MANDRIL CÔNICO |
| 12607 | PÓ DE TALCO | 12652 | MICRÔMETRO DE CONICIDADE |
| 12608 | TALCO | 12653 | AJUSTE DE CHAVETA |
| 12609 | SEBO | 12654 | CONICIDADE DE CHAVETA |
| 12610 | ASFALTO COMPRIMIDO | 12655 | PINO OU TARUGO CÔNICO |
| 12611 | ATACADOR | 12656 | CALIBRE MACHO CÔNICO |
| 12611 | CALCADEIRA | 12657 | CALIBRE MACHO CÔNICO COM PONTA |
| 12612 | CASCA COMPRIMIDA | 12658 | ALARGADOR CÔNICO |
| 12613 | MÁQUINA TANDEM | 12659 | CALIBRES FÊMEAS CÔNICOS |
| 12614 | ESPIGA | 12660 | ROLO CÔNICO |
| 12615 | TANGENTE (DE UM ÂNGULO) | 12661 | CABO DE SEÇÃO CÔNICA |
| 12616 | TANGENTE (DE UMA CURVA) | 12662 | VÁLVULA DE ASSENTOS OBLÍQUOS |
| 12617 | TANGENTE NO VÉRTICE | 12663 | ASSENTOS OBLÍQUOS |
| 12618 | CHAVETA TANGENCIAL | 12664 | ESPIGA OU HASTE CÔNICA |
| 12619 | PARAFUSO DE CHAMADA | 12665 | CHAVETA CÔNICA |
| 12619 | PARAFUSO TANGENTE | 12666 | ROSCAS CÔNICAS |
| 12620 | ACELERAÇÃO TANGENCIAL | 12667 | MANDRIL DE ESPIGA CÔNICA |
| 12621 | TURBINA TANGENCIAL | 12668 | TORNEAMENTO CÔNICO |
| 12622 | FORÇA TANGENCIAL | 12669 | POLIA CÔNICA |
| 12623 | VELOCIDADE TANGENCIAL | 12670 | BARRA DE SEÇÃO DECRESCENTE |
| 12624 | ESFORÇO TANGENCIAL | 12671 | AFINAMENTO DE UMA CHAPA |
| 12625 | TANQUE | 12672 | TUCHO |
| 12625 | RESERVATÓRIO | 12673 | FOLGA DAS VÁLVULAS |
| 12626 | VAGÃO-CARRO | 12674 | ROLETE DE TUCHO |
| 12627 | PARQUE DE TANQUES | 12675 | VAZAMENTO |
| 12628 | BASE DE DEPÓSITO | 12676 | APARELHO DE ABRIR ROSCA |
| 12629 | POÇO DE RETENÇÃO DE UM DEPÓSITO | 12677 | MÁQUINA DE ABRIR ROSCAS |
| 12630 | INVÓLUCRO DO DEPÓSITO | 12678 | ABERTURA DE ROSCAS |
| 12631 | RESERVATÓRIO DE FUNDO CÔNCAVO | 12679 | ALCATRÃO |
| 12632 | RESERVATÓRIO DE FUNDO CONVEXO | 12680 | ALCATROAR |
| 12633 | TANATO | 12681 | ÓLEO DE ALCATRÃO |
| 12634 | TÂNTALO | 12682 | ALVO |
| 12635 | CASCA ESGOTADA | 12683 | SUPERFÍCIE DO ALVO (OFERECIDA ÀS RADIAÇÕES) |
| 12636 | TARRAXAR | | |
| 12636 | ABRIR ROSCA | 12684 | TUBO DE RAIOS X |
| 12636 | PUNCIONAR | 12685 | EMBACIAR |
| 12637 | FURO DE CORRIDA | 12686 | CAMINHÃO COM TOLDO |
| 12638 | DESANDADOR DE MACHOS | 12687 | TUBO ALCATROADO |
| 12639 | BICA | 12688 | CORDA BREADA |
| 12639 | TORNEIRA | 12689 | ALCATROAMENTO |
| 12640 | MACHO DE TARRAXA | 12690 | ÁCIDO TARTÁRICO |
| 12641 | FITA | 12691 | TARTRATO |
| 12642 | VÁLVULA DE RETENÇÃO | 12692 | LER |
| 12643 | ENTRADA DE DADOS POR FITA | 12693 | PANELA SINFONADA |
| 12644 | GRAVADOR | 12694 | TÉCNICO |
| 12645 | FURO DE CORRIDA | 12695 | TÉCNICA |

| | |
|---|---|
| 12696 | MÁQUINA DE ESPALHAR FENO |
| 12697 | T |
| 12698 | FERRO EM T |
| 12699 | CANO EM T |
| 12700 | FERRO T |
| 12701 | PARAFUSO EM T |
| 12702 | UNIÃO EM T |
| 12703 | VAZAMENTO |
| 12703 | LINGOTAMENTO |
| 12704 | DENTES |
| 12705 | CABO TELEDINÁMICO |
| 12706 | TRANSMISSÃO TELEDINÁMICA |
| 12707 | TELÉGRAFO |
| 12708 | FIO TELEGRÁFICO |
| 12709 | TELEGRAFIA |
| 12710 | TELEFONE |
| 12711 | FIO TELEFÔNICO |
| 12712 | TELEFONIA |
| 12713 | CALIBRES TELESCÓPICOS |
| 12714 | PIRÔMETRO À DISTÁNCIA |
| 12715 | ABERTURA DE INSPEÇÃO |
| 12716 | TELÚRIO |
| 12717 | REVENIR |
| 12718 | MISTURAR |
| 12719 | REVENIR |
| 12720 | LAMINAÇÃO A FRIO |
| 12721 | TEMPERATURA |
| 12722 | TERMOSTATO |
| 12723 | CURVAS DE TEMPERATURA |
| 12724 | QUEDA DE TEMPERATURA |
| 12725 | RELEVOS DE TEMPERATURA |
| 12726 | INDICADOR DE TEMPERATURA |
| 12727 | TEMPERATURA DE IGNIÇÃO |
| 12728 | TEMPERATURA DO AR |
| 12729 | TEMPERATURA DO AR AMBIENTE |
| 12730 | FAIXA DE TEMPERATURA |
| 12731 | REVENIDO |
| 12732 | COLORAÇÃO DO REVENIDO |
| 12733 | REVENIDO |
| 12734 | GABARITO |
| 12735 | DUREZA PROVISÓRIA DA ÁGUA |
| 12736 | MEMÓRIA PROVISÓRIA |
| 12737 | TENACIDADE |
| 12738 | TENACIDADE DE BARRAS ENTALHADAS |
| 12739 | CABOS |
| 12740 | ESPIGA |
| 12741 | SERRA DE SAMBLAR |
| 12742 | MÁQUINA DE FAZER ESPIGAS |
| 12743 | DÚCTIL |
| 12744 | DEFORMAÇÃO POR TENSÃO |
| 12745 | FORÇA DE TRAÇÃO |
| 12746 | CARACTERÍSTICAS MECÁNICAS |
| 12747 | ESFORÇO DE TRAÇÃO |
| 12748 | TESTE DE RESISTÊNCIA À TRAÇÃO |
| 12749 | RESISTÊNCIA À TRAÇÃO |
| 12750 | ESFORÇO DE TRAÇÃO |
| 12751 | TESTE DE TRAÇÃO |
| 12752 | MÁQUINA DE ENSAIO DE TRAÇÃO |
| 12753 | TENSÃO |
| 12754 | BARRA DE TRABALHO A TENSÃO |
| 12755 | PINO DE TRAÇÃO |
| 12756 | CARRO-TENSOR |
| 12757 | ENERGIA DE CHOQUE |
| 12758 | PARAFUSO DE TENSÃO |
| 12759 | MOLA DE TRAÇÃO |
| 12760 | TÉRBIO |
| 12761 | DURAÇÃO DE UMA PATENTE |
| 12762 | TERMINAL |
| 12763 | POSTE DE LIGAÇÃO DE TERMINAIS |
| 12764 | TENSÃO DE TERMINAIS |
| 12765 | TERMINAIS |
| 12766 | SISTEMA TERNÁRIO |
| 12767 | TERRACOTA |
| 12768 | MOSAICO |
| 12769 | CHAPA ENXADREZADA |
| 12770 | TESTE |
| 12770 | ENSAIO |
| 12770 | PROVA |
| 12771 | TORNO DE CORPO DE PROVA |
| 12772 | CORPO DE PROVA |
| 12773 | BANCO DE ENSAIO |
| 12774 | TESTE DE FLEXÃO ALTERNADA |
| 12775 | ATESTADO DE ENSAIO |
| 12776 | TORNEIRA DE PROVA |
| 12777 | AMOSTRA PARA ENSAIO |
| 12778 | SONDAGEM POR PERFURAÇÃO |
| 12779 | CALIBRE DE CONTROLE |
| 12780 | TUBO DE ENSAIO |
| 12781 | CARGA DE TESTE |
| 12782 | ENSAIO DE MATERIAIS |
| 12783 | PAPEL REAGENTE |
| 12784 | CORPO DE PROVA |
| 12785 | BUJÃO DE PROVA |
| 12786 | PRESSÃO DE PROVA |
| 12787 | BOMBA DE PROVA |
| 12788 | AMOSTRA PARA ENSAIO |
| 12789 | CORPO DE PROVA |
| 12790 | DEPÓSITO DE PROVA |
| 12791 | TUBO DE ENSAIO |
| 12792 | EXPERIÊNCIA |
| 12792 | TESTE |
| 12793 | APARELHO DE TESTE |

| | | | |
|---|---|---|---|
| 12794 | PISTA DE TESTE | 12841 | DE PAREDE ESPESSA |
| 12795 | TETRAGONAL | 12842 | ESPESSADOR |
| 12796 | TETRAEDRITA | 12843 | ESPESSURA |
| 12796 | PANABÁSIO | 12844 | ESPESSURA DE TUBO |
| 12797 | TETRAEDRO | 12845 | ESPESSURA DE CHAPA |
| 12798 | TETRATÔMICO | 12846 | ESPESSURA DE DENTE |
| 12799 | FIBRA TÊXTIL | 12847 | MÁQUINA DE APLAINAR MADEIRA DESBASTANDO A ESPESSURA |
| 12800 | ESTRUTURA | | |
| 12800 | TEXTURA | 12848 | DEDAL |
| 12801 | TÁLIO | 12849 | FIO METÁLICO FINO |
| 12802 | QUE PODE SER MANUFATURADO | 12850 | CHAPA FINA |
| 12803 | CAPACIDADE TÉRMICA | 12851 | DE PAREDE FINA |
| 12804 | CONDUTIVIDADE TÉRMICA | 12852 | TIOSSULFATO |
| 12805 | CONTRAÇÃO TÉRMICA | 12853 | ÁCIDO HIPOSSULFUROSO |
| 12806 | RENDIMENTO TÉRMICO | 12854 | TIXOTROPIA |
| 12807 | FORÇA ELETROMOTRIZ TÉRMICA | 12855 | AÇO BESSEMER BÁSICO |
| 12808 | DILATAÇÃO TÉRMICA | 12855 | AÇO THOMAS |
| 12809 | COEFICIENTE DE DILATAÇÃO TÉRMICA | 12856 | TÓRIO |
| 12810 | ISOLAMENTO TÉRMICO | 12857 | ROSCA |
| 12811 | RADIAÇÃO TÉRMICA | 12858 | FOLGA DE FUNDO DE ROSCA |
| 12812 | CHOQUE TÉRMICO | 12859 | TORNO DE ABRIR ROSCA |
| 12813 | RESISTÊNCIA AO CHOQUE TÉRMICO | 12860 | CALIBRE PARA ROSCAS |
| 12814 | TENSÃO TÉRMICA | 12861 | CALIBRE NORMAL |
| 12815 | TRATAMENTO TÉRMICO | 12862 | CALIBRES MACHOS PARA ROSCA |
| 12816 | CALORIA | 12863 | CALIBRE NORMAL |
| 12816 | UNIDADE DE CALOR | 12864 | RAIZ DE FILETE DE ROSCA |
| 12817 | TÉRMITA | 12864 | GABARITO PARA FERRAMENTAS DE ROSCAR |
| 12818 | SOLDAGEM COM ACRÉSCIMO DE FERRO-TERMITA | | |
| | | 12866 | FLANGE ROSCADO |
| 12819 | SOLDAGEM ALUMINOTÉRMICA | 12867 | MANDRIL ROSCADO |
| 12820 | PILHA TERMOELÉTRICA | 12868 | ROSQUEAMENTO |
| 12821 | BINÁRIO TERMOELÉTRICO | 12869 | MÁQUINA DE ABRIR ROSCA |
| 12822 | TERMOQUÍMICA | 12870 | LIMA TRIANGULAR DE QUINAS VIVAS |
| 12823 | TERMOELÉTRICO | 12871 | VEÍCULO DE TRÊS EIXOS |
| 12824 | CORRENTE TERMOELÉTRICA | 12872 | ASA DE CESTO |
| 12825 | PIRÔMETRO TERMOELÉTRICO | 12873 | MOTOR DE TRÊS CILINDROS |
| 12826 | TERMOELETRICIDADE | 12874 | MANDRIL UNIVERSAL DE TRÊS MORDENTES |
| 12827 | PAR TERMOELÉTRICO | | |
| 12828 | TERMODINÂMICO | 12875 | GERADOR TRIFÁSICO |
| 12829 | TERMODINÂMICA | 12876 | MOTOR TRIFÁSICO |
| 12830 | EFEITO TERMOELÉTRICO | 12877 | CORRENTE TRIFÁSICA |
| 12831 | FORÇA TERMOELÉTRICA | 12878 | CORREIA TRIPLA |
| 12832 | TERMÓGRAFO | 12879 | PARAFUSO DE TRÊS ROSCAS |
| 12833 | TERMÔMETRO | 12880 | EIXO MOTOR DE TRÊS MANIVELAS |
| 12834 | INDICADOR DE TEMPERATURA | 12881 | TORNEIRA DE TRÊS SAÍDAS |
| 12835 | ESCALA TERMOELÉTRICA | 12882 | VÁLVULA DE TRÊS VIAS |
| 12836 | PILHA TERMOELÉTRICA | 12883 | MÉTODO TRIFILAR |
| 12837 | TERMOSCÓPIO | 12884 | DEBULHADORA |
| 12838 | TERMOSTATO | 12885 | ESPESSURA DA SOLDA |
| 12839 | PURGADOR TERMOSTÁTICO | 12886 | ESPESSURA DE SOLDA EM ÂNGULO |
| 12840 | VÁLVULA TERMOSTÁTICA | 12887 | LARGURA DE SOLDA |

| | |
|---|---|
| 12888 | BORBOLETA |
| 12888 | AFOGADOR |
| 12889 | AFOGAR |
| 12890 | VÁLVULA BORBOLETA |
| 12890 | VÁLVULA DO AFOGADOR |
| 12891 | AFOGAMENTO |
| 12891 | ENTRANGULAMENTO |
| 12892 | ENDURECIMENTO DE FORA A FORA |
| 12893 | FURO ATRAVESSANTE |
| 12894 | CURSO DO EXCÊNTRICO |
| 12895 | DESCER A CORREIA |
| 12896 | PLAQUETAS DE UM SÓ USO |
| 12897 | EMBREAGEM |
| 12898 | DESEMBREAGEM |
| 12899 | AÇÃO DE PROFUNDIDADE |
| 12900 | ROLAMENTO AXIAL DE ESFERAS |
| 12901 | ROLAMENTO AXIAL DE ESFERAS |
| 12902 | MANCAL AXIAL |
| 12903 | CHUMACEIRA DE IMPULSO AXIAL |
| 12904 | ANEL DE ESCORA |
| 12904 | COLAR DE MANCAL DE EMPUXO |
| 12905 | COXIM DE PÉ |
| 12906 | PINO MOENTE COM ANÉIS |
| 12907 | IMPULSO DE TERRAS |
| 12908 | IMPULSO NO VÉRTICE |
| 12909 | PARAFUSO DE IMPULSO |
| 12909 | ROSCA DE BATENTE |
| 12910 | TÚLIO |
| 12911 | PORCA BORBOLETA |
| 12912 | PARAFUSO ALADO |
| 12912 | PARAFUSO DE BORBOLETA |
| 12912 | PARAFUSO DE APERTO MANUAL |
| 12913 | TIRISTOR |
| 12914 | LIGAR |
| 12914 | PRENDER |
| 12915 | TIRANTE |
| 12916 | TIRANTE |
| 12917 | TIRANTE |
| 12918 | AÇÃO DE ATAR |
| 12918 | ANCORAGEM |
| 12919 | TIRANTES DE ESFERA |
| 12920 | HERMÉTICO |
| 12920 | IMPERMEÁVEL |
| 12921 | JUNTA VEDADA |
| 12922 | REBITAGEM DE VEDAÇÃO |
| 12923 | CABO TENSO |
| 12924 | APERTAR UMA CUNHA |
| 12925 | APERTAR UMA PORCA |
| 12926 | APERTAR A CAIXA DE PREME-GAXETA |
| 12927 | APERTAR A FUNDO UMA PORCA |
| 12928 | APERTO DE UMA CHAVETA |
| 12929 | APERTO POR CUNHAS |
| 12930 | APERTO POR PARAFUSOS |
| 12931 | TORQUE DE APERTO |
| 12932 | VEDAÇÃO |
| 12932 | IMPERMEABILIDADE |
| 12933 | TELHA |
| 12933 | LADRILHO |
| 12933 | AZULEJO |
| 12934 | TELHA |
| 12935 | PANELA DE FUNDIÇÃO COM INVERSÃO |
| 12936 | MOMENTO BASCULANTE |
| 12937 | MADEIRA DE CONSTRUÇÃO |
| 12938 | MADEIRA CORTADA RADIALMENTE |
| 12939 | MADEIRA CORTADA NA DIREÇÃO DA FIBRA |
| 12940 | MADEIRA SEM NÓS |
| 12941 | DORMENTE DE MADEIRA |
| 12942 | VIGAMENTO |
| 12942 | ARMAÇÃO DE MADEIRA |
| 12943 | TEMPO |
| 12944 | CONSTANTE DE TEMPO |
| 12945 | DURAÇÃO DE UMA OSCILAÇÃO |
| 12946 | RELÓGIO REGISTRADOR |
| 12947 | CÁRTER DE DISTRIBUIÇÃO |
| 12948 | CORREIA DE DISTRIBUIÇÃO |
| 12949 | PINHÃO DE DISTRIBUIÇÃO |
| 12950 | CORRENTE DE DISTRIBUIÇÃO |
| 12951 | MARCAS DE REGULAGEM |
| 12952 | REGULAGEM DE DISTRIBUIÇÃO |
| 12953 | ESTANHO |
| 12954 | ESTANHAR |
| 12955 | PAPEL DE ESTANHO |
| 12955 | FOLHA DE ESTANHO |
| 12956 | MINÉRIO DE ESTANHO |
| 12957 | FOLHA DE FLANDRES |
| 12957 | CHAPA ESTANHADA |
| 12958 | SOLDA BRANCA COMUM |
| 12959 | CASSITERITA |
| 12960 | TUBO DE CHUMBO |
| 12961 | LATA |
| 12962 | ARAME ESTANHADO |
| 12963 | ESTANHAGEM |
| 12964 | FUNILEIRO |
| 12965 | DESENHO A NANQUIM |
| 12966 | BOCAL |
| 12967 | CAMINHÃO BASCULANTE |
| 12968 | TITULAÇÃO |
| 12968 | GRADUAÇÃO |
| 12969 | PAPEL DE SEDA |
| 12970 | TITÂNIO |
| 12971 | RUTILO |

| | |
|---|---|
| 12971 | BIÓXIDO DE TITÂNIO |
| 12972 | AÇO AO TITÂNIO |
| 12973 | TITULAR |
| 12973 | GRADUAR |
| 12974 | GRADUAÇÃO |
| 12974 | TITULAGEM |
| 12975 | CONVERGÊNCIA DAS RODAS DO VEÍCULO |
| 12976 | DIVERGÊNCIA DAS RODAS DO VEÍCULO |
| 12977 | ENCOSTO PARA OS PÉS |
| 12978 | FREIO DE ALAVANCA ARTICULADA |
| 12979 | ARTICULAÇÃO DE RÓTULA |
| 12979 | JUNTA EM COTOVELO |
| 12980 | PRENSA DE ALAVANCA DE COTOVELO |
| 12981 | ALAVANCAS ARTICULADAS |
| 12982 | TOLERÂNCIA |
| 12983 | TOLUENO |
| 12984 | TOMBAQUE |
| 12984 | AURICALCO |
| 12985 | ALAVANCA DE PARAFUSO |
| 12986 | TONELADA (MÉTRICA) |
| 12987 | TENAZ |
| 12987 | PINÇA |
| 12987 | TORQUÊS |
| 12988 | RANHURAR |
| 12989 | LINGÜETA E RANHURA |
| 12989 | MACHO E FÊMEA |
| 12990 | ENCAIXE MACHO E FÊMEA |
| 12991 | UNIÃO DE LINGÜETA E RANHURA |
| 12992 | MÁQUINA DE FAZER ENCAIXE MACHO E FÊMEA |
| 12993 | GUILHERME |
| 12994 | FERRAMENTA |
| 12995 | ÂNGULO DE CORTE |
| 12996 | BOLSA DE FERRAMENTAS |
| 12997 | CAIXA DE FERRAMENTAS |
| 12998 | ARMÁRIO DE FERRAMENTAS |
| 12999 | TEMPO DE TROCA DE FERRAMENTA |
| 13000 | TROCADOR DE FERRAMENTAS |
| 13001 | FUNÇÃO DE FERRAMENTA |
| 13002 | RETIFICADOR OU ESMERIL DE FERRAMENTAS |
| 13003 | PORTA-FERRAMENTAS |
| 13004 | TORNO PORTA-FERRAMENTA |
| 13005 | PORTA-FERRAMENTAS |
| 13006 | FABRICAÇÃO DE FERRAMENTAS |
| 13007 | CORREÇÃO DA POSIÇÃO DA FERRAMENTA |
| 13008 | TEMPERADOR DE FERRAMENTAS |
| 13009 | AÇO DE FERRAMENTAS |
| 13010 | PERNO PORTA-FERRAMENTAS |
| 13011 | LÂMINA |
| 13012 | PORTA-FERRAMENTAS |

| | |
|---|---|
| 13013 | FLANGES DE USINAGEM |
| 13014 | MARTELO DE FABRICANTE DE FERRAMENTAS |
| 13015 | FERRAMENTAS |
| 13015 | INSTRUMENTOS |
| 13016 | DENTE |
| 13017 | ALTURA DE DENTE |
| 13018 | FLANCO DE DENTE |
| 13019 | PERFIL DE DENTE |
| 13020 | PERFIL DE DENTE |
| 13021 | ENGRENAGEM |
| 13022 | CREMALHEIRA |
| 13023 | COROA DENTADA |
| 13024 | SETOR DENTADO |
| 13025 | COMANDO OU ACIONAMENTO POR ENGRENAGENS |
| 13026 | DENTES |
| 13026 | DENTEADO |
| 13027 | PLAINA COM FERRO DENTADO |
| 13028 | CANTONEIRA DE TETO |
| 13029 | PLANO DE SUSTENTAÇÃO |
| 13030 | BRONZE SUPERIOR DE MANCAL |
| 13031 | VAZAMENTO POR CIMA |
| 13032 | PONTO MORTO SUPERIOR (PMS) |
| 13033 | CONTRAFERRO DE PLAINA |
| 13034 | SEGMENTO DE FOGO |
| 13035 | TRAVESSA SUPERIOR DE PORTA |
| 13036 | ESTAMPA SUPERIOR |
| 13037 | VISTA DO ALTO |
| 13038 | TOPÁZIO |
| 13039 | TOPOQUÍMICA |
| 13040 | PETRÓLEO RESIDUAL |
| 13041 | LIMA PLANA COM PARTES ARREDONDADAS |
| 13042 | MAÇARICO |
| 13043 | PÉ DE COLUNA |
| 13044 | FUNDO TORICÔNICO |
| 13045 | FUNDO TIPO ALÇA DE CESTO |
| 13046 | TETO REBAIXADO |
| 13047 | RESERVATÓRIO DE TETO REBAIXADO |
| 13048 | TORQUE |
| 13048 | BINÁRIO |
| 13048 | CONJUGADO |
| 13048 | PAR DE FORÇAS |
| 13049 | CHAVE DE BOCA |
| 13050 | TORCÍMETRO |
| 13051 | TORÇÃO |
| 13052 | BALANÇA DE TORÇÃO |
| 13053 | BARRA DE TORÇÃO |
| 13054 | TORÇÃO |
| 13055 | FORÇA DE TORÇÃO |

| | | | |
|---|---|---|---|
| 13056 | ESFORÇO DE TORÇÃO | 13099 | BALANÇA DE COMÉRCIO EXTERNO |
| 13057 | RESISTÊNCIA À TORÇÃO | 13100 | MARCA REGISTRADA |
| 13058 | ESFORÇO DE TORÇÃO POR UNIDADE DE SEÇÃO | 13101 | NOME COMERCIAL |
| | | 13102 | CARRO REBOQUE |
| 13059 | ENSAIO DE TORÇÃO | 13102 | TRAILERS |
| 13059 | TESTE OU PROVA DE TORÇÃO | 13103 | ÓLEO DE BALEIA |
| 13060 | REFLEXÃO TOTAL | 13104 | TRAJETÓRIA |
| 13061 | ALTURA DE ELEVAÇÃO DE UMA BOMBA | 13104 | CURSO |
| 13062 | CARGA TOTAL | 13104 | ROTA |
| 13063 | MOVIMENTO TOTAL PERDIDO | 13104 | TRAJETO |
| 13064 | POTÊNCIA TOTAL | 13104 | PERCURSO |
| 13065 | PRESSÃO TOTAL | 13105 | COMPASSO DE VARA |
| 13066 | TOCAR | 13106 | FERRO RESIDUAL |
| 13067 | RESISTENTE | 13107 | EQUAÇÃO TRANSCENDENTAL |
| 13068 | FERRO TENAZ | 13108 | TRANSDUTOR |
| 13069 | COBRE TENAZ | 13109 | TRANSFERÊNCIA |
| 13070 | COBRE REFINADO | 13110 | PANELA DE BALDEAÇÃO |
| 13071 | TENACIDADE | 13111 | TRANSMISSÃO DE CALOR |
| 13072 | TURMALINA | 13112 | TRANSFORMAR A ENERGIA |
| 13073 | ESTOPA | 13113 | DOMÍNIO DE TRANSFORMAÇÃO |
| 13073 | PANO ESFIAPADO | 13114 | TEMPERATURA DE TRANSFORMAÇÃO |
| 13074 | LIXO | 13115 | TRANSFORMADOR |
| 13075 | ÁGUA ENCANADA | 13116 | CHAPA PARA TRANSFORMADORES |
| 13076 | VESTÍGIO | 13117 | FRATURA INTRACRISTALINA |
| 13076 | TRAÇO | 13118 | FLUÊNCIA PLÁSTICA OU TRANSITÓRIA |
| 13077 | TRAÇAR | 13119 | TRANSÍSTOR |
| 13078 | TRAÇADOR | 13120 | RETICULADO DE TRANSIÇÃO |
| 13079 | TRAÇADOR DO PLANÍMETRO | 13121 | REDUÇÃO |
| 13080 | FRESA ACIONADA POR DISPOSITIVO DE CÓPIA | 13122 | PONTO DE TRANSIÇÃO |
| | | 13123 | DESLOCAMENTO |
| 13081 | TRAQUITO | 13123 | TRANSLAÇÃO |
| 13082 | DECALQUE | 13124 | TRANSLUCIDEZ |
| 13082 | DESENHO | 13125 | TRANSLÚCIDO |
| 13083 | TELA DE DESENHO | 13126 | ÓRGÃOS DE TRANSMISSÃO |
| 13084 | PAPEL DE DECALQUE | 13127 | DINAMÔMETRO DE TRANSMISSÃO |
| 13084 | PAPEL TRANSPARENTE | 13128 | ENGRENAGEM DE TRANSMISSÃO |
| 13085 | PISTA | 13129 | TRANSMISSÃO DE ENERGIA ELÉTRICA |
| 13085 | VIA | 13130 | TRANSMISSÃO DO MOVIMENTO |
| 13086 | VERIFICAÇÃO DE PARALELISMO | 13131 | TRANSMISSÃO POR ENGRENAGEM |
| 13087 | GUIA DE CENTRAGEM | 13132 | TRANSMISSÃO POR ALAVANCA |
| 13088 | TRAÇÃO | 13133 | TRANSMISSÃO DE ELETRICIDADE A GRANDES DISTÂNCIAS |
| 13089 | ESFORÇO DE TRAÇÃO | | |
| 13090 | FORÇA DE TRAÇÃO DE ÍMÃ | 13134 | TRANSMISSÃO DE ENERGIA |
| 13091 | TRATOR | 13135 | TRANSMISSÃO DE ENERGIA A GRANDES DISTÂNCIAS |
| 13092 | VEÍCULO ARTICULADO | | |
| 13093 | TRATOR AGRÍCOLA | 13136 | TRANSMUTAÇÃO |
| 13094 | TRATOR AGRÍCOLA MOVIDO A LAGARTA | 13137 | TRANSPARÊNCIA |
| 13095 | TRATOR AGRÍCOLA DE RODAS | 13138 | TRANSPARENTE |
| 13096 | TRATOR DE HORTICULTURA | 13139 | MEIO TRANSPARENTE |
| 13097 | TRATOR | 13140 | TRANSPORTE |
| 13098 | TRATIVA | 13141 | TRANSPORTADOR |

| | | | |
|---|---|---|---|
| 13142 | EIXO TRANSVERSAL | 13186 | TRIÂNGULO DE FORÇAS |
| 13143 | EIXO FOCAL DE HIPÉRBOLE | 13187 | COMPASSO DE TRÊS PONTAS |
| 13144 | ELASTICIDADE DE CISALHAMENTO | 13188 | SEÇÃO TRIANGULAR |
| 13145 | PASSO TRANSVERSAL DOS REBITES | 13189 | LIMA TRIANGULAR |
| 13146 | VIBRAÇÃO TRANSVERSAL | 13190 | CARGA TRIANGULAR |
| 13146 | OSCILAÇÃO TRANSVERSAL | 13191 | MOLA TRIANGULAR |
| 13147 | TUBO DE NERBURAS TRANSVERSAIS | 13192 | PRISMA TRIANGULAR |
| 13148 | TRAPÉZIO | 13193 | PIRÂMIDE TRIANGULAR |
| 13149 | TRAPEZÓIDE | 13194 | CABO DE SEÇÃO TRIANGULAR |
| 13150 | CARGA TRAPEZOIDAL | 13195 | CABOS DE FIOS DE PERFIL TRIANGULAR |
| 13151 | MOLA TRAPEZOIDAL | 13196 | FIO TRIANGULAR |
| 13152 | TRASS | 13197 | TRIVALENTE |
| 13153 | INDICADOR DE ABERTURA | 13198 | TRIBÁSICO |
| 13154 | FOLGA DE VÁLVULA | 13199 | SISTEMA TRICLÍNICO |
| 13155 | CARRINHO DE PONTE | 13200 | TRIGONOMÉTRICO |
| 13156 | PONTE ROLANTE | 13201 | TRIGONOMETRIA |
| 13157 | VIGA DE PONTE ROLANTE | 13202 | TRIEDRO |
| 13158 | TRANSLAÇÃO | 13203 | COORDENADAS NO ESPAÇO |
| 13158 | TRAVESSA DE PONTE ROLANTE | 13204 | APARAR |
| 13159 | PORCA MÓVEL | 13204 | REBARBAR |
| 13160 | CURSOR | 13204 | RECORTAR |
| 13161 | GRUA OU GUINDASTE MÓVEL | 13205 | APARAR UMA CHAPA |
| 13162 | ATRAVESSAR | 13206 | TIRAR AS REBARBAS |
| 13162 | CRUZAR | 13207 | ÓXIDO SALINO DE MANGANÊS |
| 13163 | VOLANTE DE TORNEAR | 13208 | PROJEÇÃO TRIMÉTRICA |
| 13164 | TORNEAMENTO PARALELO | 13209 | RECORTE |
| 13165 | MACACO DE PÉ CORREDIÇO | 13209 | REBARBAÇÃO |
| 13166 | TRAVERTINO | 13210 | RASPAGEM DAS REBARBAS |
| 13167 | BANDEJA | 13211 | PRENSA DE APARAR |
| 13167 | TABULEIRO | 13212 | ASFALTO DE TRINIDAD |
| 13167 | PLATAFORMA | 13213 | EQUAÇÃO TRINÔMICA |
| 13168 | ABERTURA DE INSPEÇÃO DE PLATAFORMA | 13214 | GARRAS DE LIGAR E DESLIGAR |
| | | 13215 | INTEGRAL TRIPLA |
| 13169 | DISTÂNCIA ENTRE AS PLACAS | 13216 | PONTO TRIPLO |
| 13170 | COROA SUPORTE DE DISCOS | 13217 | MOTOR DE TRIPLA EXPANSÃO |
| 13171 | TORNO DE DISCOS | 13218 | MACACO DE TRIPÉ |
| 13172 | FACE DE ROLAMENTO | 13219 | TRIPÉ |
| 13173 | SUPERFÍCIE DE ROLAMENTO DE RODA | 13220 | TRIPOLO |
| 13174 | PEDAL | 13221 | DISCO DE CAMES |
| 13175 | MALEABILIZAÇÃO DO FERRO FUNDIDO | 13222 | TRITURAR |
| 13176 | RODA DE DENTES DE DUPLO ÂNGULO | 13223 | TROCÓIDE |
| 13177 | REBITAGEM DE TRÊS FILEIRAS | 13224 | PÓRTICO DE ROLAMENTO |
| 13178 | REBITE COM TRÊS CORTES | 13225 | TRÓLEBUS |
| 13179 | CAVILHA DE MADEIRA | 13226 | TROMMEL |
| 13180 | GRADEAMENTO | 13226 | PENEIRA CILÍNDRICA GIRATÓRIA |
| 13181 | INCLINAÇÃO | 13227 | TROOSTITA |
| 13181 | TENDÊNCIA | 13228 | TANQUE |
| 13182 | MÁQUINA DE PERFURAR | 13229 | CABINA DE CAMINHÃO |
| 13183 | SEÇÃO TRAPEZOIDAL | 13230 | CAMINHÃO |
| 13184 | MONTAGEM EXPERIMENTAL | 13231 | CARRINHO DE MÃO |
| 13185 | TRIÂNGULO | 13232 | ENDIREITAR |

| | |
|---|---|
| 13232 | RETIFICAR |
| 13232 | CONSERTAR |
| 13233 | APARELHOS PARA DIAMANTAR |
| 13234 | RETIFICAÇÃO |
| 13235 | CONE TRUNCADO |
| 13236 | MOLA TRONCÔNICA |
| 13237 | PARALELEPÍPEDO TRUNCADO |
| 13238 | TRONCO DE PIRÂMIDE |
| 13239 | COFRE |
| 13239 | MALA |
| 13240 | TAMPA DE MALA |
| 13241 | PISTÃO OCO |
| 13242 | MUNHÃO |
| 13242 | MOENTE |
| 13242 | PINO GIRATÓRIO |
| 13243 | TRELIÇAS |
| 13244 | ARMAÇÃO EM TRELIÇA |
| 13245 | ESQUADRO DE ENCOSTO |
| 13246 | CÂMARA DE AR |
| 13247 | ROSCA-TUBOS |
| 13248 | CORTA-TUBOS |
| 13249 | ESTIRAGEM DE TUBOS |
| 13250 | ABRE-TUBOS |
| 13250 | MANDRIL DE ALARGAR TUBOS |
| 13251 | IGNIÇÃO POR INCANDESCÊNCIA |
| 13252 | LAMINADOR DE TUBOS |
| 13253 | TUBO DE FORÇA |
| 13254 | PLACA OU PAREDE PARA TUBOS |
| 13255 | TUBO CAPILAR DE TERMÔMETRO |
| 13256 | TORNO DE TUBOS |
| 13257 | TUBO |
| 13257 | CANO |
| 13258 | REFORÇO DE TUBOS |
| 13259 | NÍVEL DE BOLHA |
| 13260 | TUFO |
| 13261 | TAMBOR DE LIMPEZA |
| 13262 | TUNGSTÊNIO |
| 13263 | BRONZE AO TUNGSTÊNIO |
| 13264 | LÂMPADA A FILAMENTO DE TUNGSTÊNIO |
| 13265 | AÇO AO TUNGSTÊNIO |
| 13266 | TRIÓXIDO DE TUNGSTÊNIO |
| 13267 | TURBINA |
| 13268 | PALHETAS DE TURBINA |
| 13269 | BOMBA CENTRÍFUGA |
| 13270 | TURBOVENTILADOR |
| 13271 | TURBOGERADOR |
| 13272 | TURBOCOMPRESSOR |
| 13273 | TURBULÊNCIA |
| 13274 | CORRENTE OU CIRCULAÇÃO TURBULENTA |
| 13275 | PAPEL REATIVO |
| 13275 | PAPEL DE CURCUMA |
| 13276 | TORNEAR |
| 13276 | MODELAR AO TORNO |
| 13277 | TORNEAR SUPERFÍCIES CURVAS |
| 13278 | VOLTA DE HÉLICE |
| 13279 | GIRO DE ROSCA |
| 13280 | TORNEAR SUPERFÍCIES COM FIGURAS |
| 13281 | TORNEAR SUPERFÍCIES ESFÉRICAS |
| 13282 | TORNEAR SUPERFÍCIES CÔNICAS |
| 13283 | REVOLVER COM A PÁ |
| 13284 | TURN-KEY (EM NEGÓCIOS) |
| 13285 | TENSOR |
| 13285 | ESTICADOR |
| 13286 | TORNEADOR |
| 13286 | TORNEIRO |
| 13287 | TORNEAMENTO |
| 13288 | TORNEAMENTO DE SUPERFÍCIES ABAULADAS |
| 13289 | TORNO MECÂNICO |
| 13290 | TORNEARIA |
| 13291 | TORNEAMENTO DE SUPERFÍCIES ESFÉRICAS |
| 13292 | FERRAMENTA DE TORNEAR |
| 13293 | APARAS DE TORNO |
| 13294 | CHAVE DE PARAFUSO |
| 13294 | CHAVE DE DESATARRAXAR PARAFUSOS |
| 13295 | PLATAFORMA GIRATÓRIA |
| 13296 | VERNIZ DE TEREBINTINA |
| 13297 | TORNO REVÓLVER |
| 13298 | TORNO REVÓLVER SEMI-AUTOMÁTICO |
| 13299 | VENTANEIRA |
| 13300 | DUPLO |
| 13300 | EMPARELHADO |
| 13300 | CONJUGADO |
| 13300 | GÊMEO |
| 13301 | MOTOR DE CILINDROS EM V |
| 13302 | MACLAÇÃO |
| 13303 | TORCER |
| 13304 | BROCA HELICOIDAL |
| 13304 | BROCA AMERICANA |
| 13305 | TORCEDURA DE CORDA |
| 13306 | ENSAIO DE TORÇÃO |
| 13307 | CURVA NO ESPAÇO |
| 13308 | MOMENTO DE TORÇÃO |
| 13309 | RUPTURA BRUSCA DO CORPO DE UM PARAFUSO |
| 13310 | PROVA OU ENSAIO DE TORÇÃO |
| 13311 | SISTEMA DE PINTURA DE DOIS COMPONENTES |
| 13312 | MOTOR DE DOIS TEMPOS |
| 13313 | MÁQUINA DE DOIS CILINDROS |

| | |
|---|---|
| 13313 | MOTOR DE DOIS CILINDROS |
| 13314 | CORRENTE BIFÁSICA |
| 13315 | PARAFUSO DE DUAS ROSCAS |
| 13316 | EIXO MOTOR DE MANIVELAS DOBRADAS |
| 13317 | TORNEIRA DE DUAS VIAS |
| 13318 | VÁLVULA DE DUAS VIAS |
| 13319 | METAL DE TIPO |
| 13319 | METAL PARA FABRICAÇÃO DE TIPO |
| 13320 | TIPO |
| 13320 | MODELO |
| 13321 | TORNO DE RODAS |
| 13322 | PNEUMÁTICO |
| 13323 | CURVA EM U (TUBO) |
| 13324 | PINO EM U |
| 13325 | TUBO EM U |
| 13326 | VAZIO |
| 13326 | MÍNGUA |
| 13327 | RESISTÊNCIA À RUPTURA |
| 13328 | RESISTÊNCIA À COMPRESSÃO |
| 13329 | ALONGAMENTO PROPORCIONAL AO LIMITE ELÁSTICO |
| 13330 | RESISTÊNCIA AO CISALHAMENTO |
| 13331 | LIMITE DE RESISTÊNCIA À TRAÇÃO |
| 13332 | RAIOS ULTRAVERMELHOS |
| 13333 | RAIOS ULTRAVIOLETA |
| 13334 | ULTRAMARINO |
| 13335 | ULTRAMICROSCÓPIO |
| 13336 | EXAME FEITO NO ULTRAMICROSCÓPIO |
| 13337 | CONTROLE ULTRA-SÔNICO |
| 13338 | SOLDAGEM ULTRA-SÔNICA |
| 13339 | CONE DE SOMBRA |
| 13339 | SOMBRA PROJETADA |
| 13340 | ARAME CLARO |
| 13341 | DESEQUILÍBRIO |
| 13342 | FRAGILIDADE |
| 13343 | INQUEBRÁVEL |
| 13344 | NÃO QUEIMADO |
| 13345 | GRAFITA |
| 13345 | CARBONO NÃO COMBINADO |
| 13346 | VIBRAÇÃO NÃO AMORTECIDA |
| 13347 | ARREFECIMENTO ABAIXO DA TEMPERATURA NORMAL |
| 13348 | FALTA DE ENCHIMENTO |
| 13349 | TAMANHO ABAIXO DO NORMAL |
| 13350 | FISSURA SOB CORDÃO |
| 13351 | CORTE INFERIOR REBAIXADO |
| 13352 | CORROSÃO SUBJACENTE |
| 13353 | LINHA SUBTERRÂNEA |
| 13354 | TUBULAÇÃO SUBTERRÂNEA |
| 13355 | RODA HIDRÁULICA |
| 13356 | CANTONEIRA DE LADOS DESIGUAIS |
| 13357 | FRATURA DESIGUAL |
| 13358 | CUNHA ESFÉRICA |
| 13359 | NÃO TEMPERADO |
| 13360 | CORRENTES DO MESMO SENTIDO |
| 13361 | ACELERAÇÃO UNIFORME |
| 13362 | MOVIMENTO UNIFORME OU CONSTANTE |
| 13363 | VELOCIDADE UNIFORME OU CONSTANTE |
| 13364 | UNIFORMIDADE DO MATERIAL |
| 13365 | MOVIMENTO UNIFORMEMENTE ACELERADO |
| 13366 | CARGA UNIFORMEMENTE DISTRIBUÍDA |
| 13367 | MOVIMENTO UNIFORMEMENTE RETARDADO |
| 13368 | UNIÃO |
| 13369 | UNIÃO |
| 13369 | JUNÇÃO |
| 13369 | LIGAÇÃO |
| 13370 | ALONGAMENTO RELATIVO |
| 13371 | CARGA POR UNIDADE DE SUPERFÍCIE |
| 13372 | UNIDADE DE SUPERFÍCIE |
| 13373 | UNIDADE DE COMPRIMENTO |
| 13374 | UNIDADE DE MASSA |
| 13375 | UNIDADE DE MEDIDA |
| 13376 | UNIDADE DE TEMPO |
| 13377 | UNIDADE DE VOLUME |
| 13378 | UNIDADE DE PESO |
| 13379 | UNIDADE DE TRABALHO |
| 13380 | VETOR UNITÁRIO |
| 13381 | CARROCERIA UNIFICADA |
| 13382 | MANDRIL UNIVERSAL |
| 13383 | RETIFICADORA UNIVERSAL DE SUPERFÍCIES DE ROTAÇÃO |
| 13384 | RETIFICADORA UNIVERSAL |
| 13385 | JUNTA CARDAN |
| 13385 | JUNTA UNIVERSAL |
| 13386 | LAMINADOR UNIVERSAL |
| 13387 | FRESADORA UNIVERSAL |
| 13388 | MÁQUINA UNIVERSAL DE TESTES |
| 13389 | TORNO UNIVERSAL |
| 13390 | CABEÇA DE SOLDA UNIVERSAL |
| 13391 | INCÓGNITA |
| 13392 | PÓLOS OPOSTOS |
| 13393 | HIDROCARBONETOS NÃO SATURADOS |
| 13394 | SOLUÇÃO NÃO SATURADA |
| 13395 | DESAPARAFUSAR |
| 13396 | DESAPARAFUSAMENTO |
| 13397 | SOLDAGEM A ARCO METÁLICO SEM GÁS PROTETOR |
| 13398 | OPERÁRIO NÃO ESPECIALIZADO |
| 13398 | MÃO-DE-OBRA NÃO ESPECIALIZADA |
| 13399 | DESSOLDAR |

| | |
|---|---|
| 13400 | DESSOLDAGEM |
| 13401 | EQUILÍBRIO INSTÁVEL |
| 13402 | DE MANEJO DIFÍCIL |
| 13403 | REGULAGEM DE FOLGA |
| 13404 | DESENROLAR |
| 13405 | DESENROLAMENTO |
| 13406 | CURSO COMPLETO DO PISTÃO |
| 13407 | A MONTANTE |
| 13408 | FRESAGEM ASCENDENTE |
| 13409 | SUBIDA DO PISTÃO |
| 13410 | TEMPO ATIVO |
| 13411 | PONTO MORTO SUPERIOR (PMS) |
| 13412 | FURADEIRA VERTICAL |
| 13413 | SOLDAGEM DE TOPOS RECALCADOS |
| 13414 | RECALQUE |
| 13414 | IMPULSO |
| 13415 | REPULSÃO |
| 13415 | MÁQUINA DE RECALCAR |
| 13416 | ENSAIO DE RECALCAMENTO |
| 13417 | RECALCAMENTO COM AQUECIMENTO DE EFEITO JOULE |
| 13418 | FUMEIRO |
| 13419 | POSIÇÃO VERTICAL ASCENDENTE |
| 13420 | URÂNIO |
| 13421 | ÔNIBUS URBANO |
| 13422 | SEÇÃO ÚTIL |
| 13423 | DIÂMETRO ÚTIL |
| 13424 | COMPRIMENTO ÚTIL |
| 13425 | CARGA ÚTIL |
| 13426 | RESISTÊNCIA ÚTIL |
| 13427 | LARGURA ÚTIL DE LAMINAÇÃO |
| 13428 | TRABALHO ÚTIL |
| 13429 | UTILIZAÇÃO |
| 13430 | UTILIZAR |
| 13431 | CORREIA TRAPEZOIDAL |
| 13432 | GOIVA TRIANGULAR |
| 13433 | LACUNA |
| 13434 | VÁCUO |
| 13435 | CAIXA EM VAZIO |
| 13436 | FREIO A VÁCUO |
| 13437 | VÁLVULA DE SUPRESSÃO A VÁCUO |
| 13438 | CAIXA EM VAZIO |
| 13439 | FUNDIÇÃO A VÁCUO |
| 13440 | CÂMARA DE VÁCUO |
| 13441 | ATMOSFERA RAREFEITA |
| 13442 | VACUÔMETRO |
| 13443 | TRATAMENTO TÉRMICO A VÁCUO |
| 13444 | FUSÃO A VÁCUO |
| 13445 | METALIZAÇÃO A VÁCUO |
| 13446 | METALURGIA A VÁCUO |
| 13447 | REFINAÇÃO A VÁCUO |
| 13448 | SINTERIZAÇÃO A VÁCUO |
| 13449 | CÂMARA DE VÁCUO |
| 13450 | VENTILAÇÃO POR ASPIRAÇÃO |
| 13451 | TANQUE A VÁCUO |
| 13452 | VALÊNCIA |
| 13453 | VÁLVULA |
| 13454 | CORPO DE VÁLVULA |
| 13455 | TORNEIRA DE VÁLVULA |
| 13456 | CONTROLE DE VÁLVULA |
| 13457 | DIAGRAMA DE ABERTURA E FECHAMENTO DE VÁLVULA |
| 13458 | EFEITO DE VÁLVULA |
| 13459 | CHAPELETA DE VÁLVULA |
| 13460 | DISTRIBUIÇÃO POR VÁLVULA |
| 13461 | LIMITADOR DE VÁLVULA |
| 13462 | GUIA DE VÁLVULA |
| 13463 | CABEÇA DE VÁLVULA |
| 13464 | TAMPA DE VÁLVULA |
| 13465 | ALAVANCA DE VÁLVULA |
| 13466 | TUCHO DE VÁLVULA |
| 13467 | LUBRIFICADOR DE VÁLVULA |
| 13468 | ASSENTO OU SEDE DE VÁLVULA |
| 13469 | REGULAGEM DE VÁLVULA |
| 13470 | MOLA DE VÁLVULA |
| 13471 | REGULAGEM DE VÁLVULA |
| 13472 | VÁLVULA |
| 13473 | CALIBRE DE REGULAGEM DE VÁLVULA |
| 13474 | CARROÇÃO |
| 13474 | FURGÃO |
| 13475 | VANÁDIO |
| 13476 | AÇO AO VANÁDIO |
| 13477 | CATA-VENTO |
| 13477 | PÁ |
| 13477 | PALHETA |
| 13478 | BOMBA DE PALHETAS |
| 13479 | RODA DE PALHETAS |
| 13480 | PALHETA DE TURBINA |
| 13481 | BOLSA DE AR |
| 13482 | RECOBRIMENTO POR DECOMPOSIÇÃO DE UM GÁS |
| 13483 | VAPORIZAÇÃO |
| 13484 | VAPOR |
| 13485 | INSTALAÇÃO DE EVAPORAÇÃO |
| 13486 | DESENGORDURAMENTO A VAPOR |
| 13487 | DEPOSIÇÃO A VAPOR |
| 13488 | VARIÁVEL |
| 13489 | FORMATO DE BLOCO VARIÁVEL |
| 13490 | MOVIMENTO VARIÁVEL |
| 13491 | PRESSÃO VARIÁVEL |
| 13492 | CONJUNTO DE CONTROLE DE VELOCIDADE VARIÁVEL |

| | |
|---|---|
| 13493 | VARIADOR DE VELOCIDADE |
| 13494 | VELOCIDADE VARIÁVEL |
| 13495 | VARIAÇÃO |
| 13496 | VARIAÇÃO |
| 13497 | VARIAÇÃO DE PRESSÃO |
| 13498 | VARIAÇÃO DE TEMPERATURA |
| 13499 | VARIAÇÃO DE VELOCIDADE |
| 13500 | VARIAÇÕES DE NÍVEL DE ÁGUA |
| 13501 | BORNITA |
| 13502 | ARENITO MATIZADO |
| 13503 | ESPÉCIES DE MADEIRA |
| 13504 | VERNIZ |
| 13505 | ENVERNIZAMENTO |
| 13506 | PAPEL GOMA-LACA |
| 13507 | ACELERAÇÃO NÃO UNIFORME |
| 13508 | VASELINA |
| 13509 | PRODUTO VETORIAL |
| 13510 | VETOR |
| 13511 | CORREIA EM V |
| 13512 | ÓLEO VEGETAL |
| 13513 | CURVA DE VELOCIDADE |
| 13514 | DIAGRAMA DE VELOCIDADE |
| 13515 | CARGA DE VELOCIDADE |
| 13516 | VELOCIDADE DE FLUXO |
| 13517 | VELOCIDADE DA LUZ |
| 13518 | VELOCIDADE DE PASSAGEM |
| 13519 | VELOCIDADE DE PROPAGAÇÃO |
| 13520 | VELOCIDADE DO SOM |
| 13521 | VELOCIDADE DE TRANSFORMAÇÃO |
| 13522 | RELAÇÃO DE VELOCIDADES |
| 13523 | ESTÁGIO DE VELOCIDADE |
| 13524 | FOLHA PARA CHAPEAR |
| 13525 | MÁQUINA DE FAZER FOLHAS PARA CHAPEAR |
| 13526 | SERRA BRAÇAL |
| 13527 | TEREBINTINA DE VENEZA |
| 13528 | ESCAPE |
| 13528 | RESPIRADOURO |
| 13529 | MOTOR VENTILADO |
| 13530 | VENTILAÇÃO |
| 13531 | DEFLETOR |
| 13532 | TUBO VENTURI |
| 13533 | AZINHAVRE |
| 13533 | VERDETE |
| 13534 | VERIFICAÇÃO |
| 13535 | VERMELHÃO |
| 13535 | CINABRE |
| 13536 | NÔNIO |
| 13536 | VERNIER |
| 13537 | PAQUÍMETRO |
| 13538 | CALIBRE DE CORREDIÇA DE PROFUNDIDADE |
| 13539 | CALIBRE DE CORREDIÇA DE PROFUNDIDADE COM FIXAÇÃO MICROMÉTRICA |
| 13540 | MICRÔMETRO VERNIER |
| 13541 | ESCALA VERNIER |
| 13542 | EM COMPARAÇÃO A |
| 13543 | VÉRTICE DE UM POLÍGONO |
| 13544 | CALDEIRA VERTICAL |
| 13545 | TORNO VERTICAL |
| 13546 | MOTOR VERTICAL |
| 13547 | MANCAL INTERMEDIÁRIO DE EIXOS VERTICAIS |
| 13548 | FRESADORA VERTICAL |
| 13549 | CURSO VERTICAL |
| 13550 | EIXO VERTICAL |
| 13551 | VERTICAL |
| 13552 | MÁQUINA DE PERFURAR VERTICAL |
| 13553 | VASOS COMUNICANTES |
| 13554 | VIBRAÇÃO |
| 13554 | OSCILAÇÃO |
| 13555 | AMORTECEDOR DE VIBRAÇÕES |
| 13556 | VIBRAÇÃO CAUSADA POR ESFORÇOS DE FLEXÃO |
| 13557 | VIBRAÇÃO CAUSADA POR ESFORÇOS DE TORÇÃO |
| 13558 | OSCILAÇÃO DE UMA MOLA |
| 13559 | VIBRAÇÕES |
| 13560 | VIBRAÇÕES DO ÉTER |
| 13561 | TORNO |
| 13562 | MORDAÇA ARTICULADA |
| 13563 | MORDAÇA DE TORNO |
| 13564 | MORDAÇA DE TORNO |
| 13565 | MORDENTE PARA MONTAGEM DE PNEUS |
| 13566 | DUREZA VICKERS |
| 13567 | VISTA |
| 13568 | TELA DE PROJEÇÃO |
| 13569 | UNIDADE VIOLLE |
| 13569 | PADRÃO VIOLLE |
| 13570 | METAL VIRGEM |
| 13570 | METAL PURO |
| 13571 | FOCO VIRTUAL |
| 13572 | IMAGEM VIRTUAL |
| 13573 | VELOCIDADE VIRTUAL |
| 13574 | VISCOSÍMETRO |
| 13575 | VISCOSO |
| 13576 | VISCOSIDADE |
| 13577 | VISCOSO |
| 13578 | FLUXO VISCOSO |
| 13579 | TORNO |
| 13580 | SINAL VISÍVEL |
| 13581 | ÂNGULO VISUAL |

| | |
|---|---|
| 13582 | VÍTREO |
| 13583 | BRILHO VÍTREO |
| 13584 | VITRIFICAÇÃO |
| 13585 | LACUNA |
| 13586 | PARTE CONSTITUINTE VOLÁTIL |
| 13587 | VOLATILIZAÇÃO |
| 13588 | VOLATILIZAR |
| 13589 | VOLATILIDADE |
| 13590 | TUFO VULCÂNICO |
| 13591 | VOLT |
| 13592 | VOLT-AMPÈRE |
| 13593 | TENSÃO |
| 13593 | VOLTAGEM |
| 13594 | QUEDA DE TENSÃO |
| 13594 | BAIXA DA TENSÃO |
| 13595 | REGULADOR DE TENSÃO |
| 13596 | PILHA VOLTÁICA |
| 13597 | VOLTÍMETRO |
| 13598 | VOLUME |
| 13599 | VOLUME DO CURSO |
| 13600 | REGULADOR DO VOLUME |
| 13601 | ANÁLISE VOLUMÉTRICA |
| 13602 | RENDIMENTO VOLUMÉTRICO |
| 13603 | DILATAÇÃO CÚBICA |
| 13603 | EXPANSÃO CÚBICA |
| 13604 | VOLÚMETRO |
| 13605 | MOLA HELICOIDAL CÔNICA |
| 13606 | REMOINHO |
| 13607 | VULCANIZAÇÃO |
| 13608 | VULCANIZAR |
| 13609 | FIBRA VULCANIZADA |
| 13610 | BORRACHA VULCANIZADA |
| 13611 | FRAÇÃO ORDINÁRIA |
| 13612 | ALGODÃO HIDRÓFILO |
| 13613 | SALÁRIO |
| 13614 | PERFURADORA ROLANTE |
| 13615 | RENÚNCIA |
| 13615 | DESISTÊNCIA |
| 13616 | PASSARELA |
| 13617 | CAIXA DE PAREDE |
| 13618 | CONSOLO |
| 13619 | TRANSMISSÃO INTERMEDIÁRIA MURAL |
| 13620 | MÁQUINA A VAPOR MURAL |
| 13621 | CONTRAPLACA |
| 13621 | FRECHAL |
| 13622 | TOMADA DE PAREDE |
| 13623 | GRUA TIPO FORCA |
| 13623 | GUINDASTE DE MODELO DE FORCA |
| 13624 | PAREDE DE UM FURO |
| 13625 | LIMA PONTIAGUDA |
| 13626 | ORDEM DE OPERAÇÃO |

| | |
|---|---|
| 13626 | ORDEM DE FUNCIONAMENTO |
| 13627 | URDIDURA |
| 13627 | EMPENAMENTO |
| 13627 | ENVERGADURA |
| 13627 | DEFORMAÇÃO |
| 13628 | EMPENAR |
| 13629 | EMPENAMENTO |
| 13630 | TORNEIRA DE LAVATÓRIO |
| 13631 | ARRUELA |
| 13632 | LAVAGEM |
| 13633 | FRASCO LAVADOR |
| 13634 | GÁS PERDIDO |
| 13635 | CALOR PERDIDO |
| 13636 | ÓLEO EM EXCESSO |
| 13637 | RESÍDUOS |
| 13637 | DESPEJOS |
| 13638 | PURIFICAÇÃO DE ÁGUAS RESIDUAIS |
| 13639 | TORNO DE RELOJOEIRO |
| 13640 | ÁGUA |
| 13641 | BANHO-MARIA |
| 13642 | SOLO AQÜÍFERO |
| 13643 | CALORÍMETRO A ÁGUA |
| 13644 | TORNEIRA DE ÁGUA |
| 13645 | TEOR DE ÁGUA |
| 13646 | REFRIGERAÇÃO A ÁGUA |
| 13647 | DECAPAGEM A ÁGUA |
| 13648 | PELÍCULA À PROVA DE ÁGUA |
| 13649 | ÁGUA INDUSTRIAL |
| 13650 | ÁGUA ESTERILIZADA |
| 13651 | GÁS DE ÁGUA |
| 13652 | INDICADOR DE NÍVEL DE ÁGUA |
| 13653 | MARTELO HIDRÁULICO |
| 13653 | ARÍETE HIDRÁULICO |
| 13654 | TÊMPERA A ÁGUA |
| 13655 | CAMISA DE ÁGUA |
| 13656 | JATO DE ÁGUA |
| 13657 | INJETOR HIDRÁULICO |
| 13658 | EJETOR HIDRÁULICO |
| 13659 | NÍVEL DE ÁGUA |
| 13660 | MARCA DO NÍVEL DE ÁGUA |
| 13661 | CONTADOR DE ÁGUA |
| 13662 | ÁGUA DE CONDENSAÇÃO |
| 13663 | ÁGUA DE CRISTALIZAÇÃO |
| 13664 | PINTURA A AQUARELA |
| 13664 | PINTURA A ÁGUA |
| 13665 | TUBO OU CANO DE ÁGUA |
| 13666 | CANALIZAÇÃO DE ÁGUA |
| 13666 | ENCANAMENTO DE ÁGUA |
| 13667 | PISTÃO HIDRÁULICO |
| 13668 | FORÇA HIDRÁULICA |
| 13669 | PRESSÃO DE ÁGUA |

| | |
|---|---|
| 13670 | MOTOR MOVIDO A PRESSÃO DE ÁGUA |
| 13671 | À PROVA DE ÁGUA |
| 13671 | IMPERMEÁVEL |
| 13672 | TÊMPERA EM ÁGUA |
| 13673 | TÊMPERA A ÁGUA SEGUIDA DE REVENIDO |
| 13674 | PRODUTO HIDRÓFUGO |
| 13675 | JUNTA HIDRÁULICA |
| 13676 | DEPURAÇÃO QUÍMICA DA ÁGUA |
| 13676 | PURIFICAÇÃO QUÍMICA DA ÁGUA |
| 13677 | CÂMARA DE ÁGUA DE UMA CALDEIRA |
| 13678 | DISTRIBUIÇÃO DE ÁGUA |
| 13678 | FORNECIMENTO DE ÁGUA |
| 13679 | RESERVATÓRIO DE ÁGUA |
| 13679 | DEPÓSITO DE ÁGUA |
| 13680 | TORRE DE ÁGUA |
| 13681 | TUBO DE AR |
| 13682 | CALDEIRAS DE TUBO DE AR |
| 13683 | REFRIGERADO A ÁGUA |
| 13684 | CONDENSADOR POR SUPERFÍCIE POR MEIO DE ÁGUA |
| 13685 | HIDRÓFUGO |
| 13686 | À PROVA DE ÁGUA |
| 13686 | IMPERMEÁVEL |
| 13687 | REGADOR |
| 13688 | À PROVA DE ÁGUA |
| 13689 | IMPERMEABILIZAR |
| 13689 | VEDAR |
| 13690 | TECIDO IMPERMEÁVEL |
| 13691 | IMPERMEABILIZAÇÃO |
| 13692 | RODA HIDRÁULICA |
| 13693 | INSTALAÇÃO DE ABASTECIMENTO DE ÁGUA |
| 13694 | WATT |
| 13695 | WATT/HORA |
| 13696 | WATT/MINUTO |
| 13697 | WATT/SEGUNDO |
| 13698 | WATTÍMETRO |
| 13699 | ONDA |
| 13700 | COMPRIMENTO DE ONDA |
| 13701 | ONDULAÇÃO |
| 13702 | CERA |
| 13703 | MODELO DE CERA |
| 13704 | LINHOL |
| 13705 | CORRENTE DE FRACA INTENSIDADE |
| 13706 | SOLUÇÃO FRACA |
| 13707 | ENFRAQUECIMENTO DA SEÇÃO |
| 13708 | ENFRAQUECIMENTO DO MATERIAL |
| 13709 | DESGASTE |
| 13710 | DESGASTE NORMAL |
| 13711 | CUNHAS DE DESGASTE |
| 13712 | GASTO POR ATRITO |

| | |
|---|---|
| 13712 | DESGASTE DE FRICÇÃO |
| 13713 | DESGASTAR-SE |
| 13714 | TESTE DE DESGASTE |
| 13715 | ENDURECIMENTO DE DESGASTE |
| 13716 | CHAPA OU PLACA DE DESGASTE |
| 13717 | RESISTÊNCIA AO DESGASTE |
| 13718 | AÇO RESISTENTE AO DESGASTE |
| 13719 | OVALIZAÇÃO DE UM MANCAL |
| 13720 | JUNTA SECUNDÁRIA DE VEDAÇÃO |
| 13721 | LADO DO VENTO |
| 13722 | BORRACHA DE VEDAÇÃO |
| 13723 | INALTERÁVEL ÀS INTEMPÉRIES |
| 13724 | PASSADA AMPLA |
| 13725 | MOVIMENTO ALTERNATIVO |
| 13726 | ALMA |
| 13727 | DEFORMAÇÃO PERMANENTE DA ALMA DE UMA VIGA |
| 13728 | BRAÇO DE CANTONEIRA |
| 13729 | ALMA DE VIGA |
| 13730 | ALMA |
| 13731 | CUNHA |
| 13731 | CALÇO |
| 13732 | RODA DE ATRITO |
| 13732 | RODA DE FRICÇÃO |
| 13733 | CUNHA DE PLAINA |
| 13734 | PRENSA COM CUNHA |
| 13735 | SEÇÃO CÔNICA |
| 13736 | TRANSMISSÃO POR RODAS DE FRICÇÃO |
| 13737 | CUNEIFORME |
| 13738 | TIJOLO DE CUNHA |
| 13739 | CHAVETA |
| 13739 | CUNHA |
| 13740 | CALÇAMENTO |
| 13741 | CORTADOR DE CARDO E SAMAMBAIA |
| 13742 | SACHADORES |
| 13743 | TECIDO |
| 13743 | TRAMA |
| 13743 | ENTRELAÇAMENTO |
| 13743 | REDE |
| 13744 | PESAR |
| 13745 | PONTE BASCULANTE |
| 13746 | PESAGEM |
| 13747 | PESO |
| 13748 | PESO POR METRO |
| 13749 | VÁLVULA DE SEGURANÇA DE CONTRAPESO |
| 13750 | BOBINADOR DE POLIAS TIPO LENIX |
| 13751 | ALAVANCA DE CONTRAPESO |
| 13752 | REGULADOR DE MASSA CENTRAL |
| 13753 | BARRAGEM |
| 13753 | REPRESA |

| | |
|---|---|
| 13754 | CRISTA DA REPRESA |
| 13755 | SOLDAR |
| 13756 | CORDÃO DE SOLDA |
| 13757 | SOLDAGEM POR PASSADAS SOBREPOSTAS |
| 13758 | SOLDAGEM AUTÓGENA |
| 13759 | CORROSÃO DA SOLDA |
| 13760 | DEFEITOS DA SOLDAGEM |
| 13761 | METAL DEPOSITADO |
| 13762 | RECARREGAMENTO DE UMA SOLDA |
| 13763 | METAL DE SOLDAGEM |
| 13764 | PEPITA DE SOLDA |
| 13765 | AÇO SOLDADO |
| 13766 | FERRO SOLDADO |
| 13767 | SOLDAGEM |
| 13768 | SOLDABILIDADE |
| 13769 | SOLDÁVEL |
| 13770 | CORRENTE DE ELOS SOLDADOS |
| 13771 | ANEL SOLDADO |
| 13772 | LIGAÇÃO SOLDADA |
| 13773 | FLANGE SOLDADO |
| 13774 | JUNTA SOLDADA |
| 13775 | TUBO SOLDADO |
| 13776 | JUNTA SOLDADA |
| 13777 | TUBO SOLDADO |
| 13778 | SOLDADOR |
| 13779 | SOLDAGEM |
| 13779 | SOLDADURA |
| 13780 | INTENSIDADE DA CORRENTE DE SOLDAGEM |
| 13781 | LIGAÇÃO A SOLDAR |
| 13782 | POSIÇÃO DA PISTOLA DE SOLDAR |
| 13783 | CABEÇA DE SOLDAGEM |
| 13784 | TEMPERATURA DE SOLDAR |
| 13785 | GUIA DE SOLDAR |
| 13786 | MÁQUINA DE SOLDAR |
| 13787 | PARÂMETROS DE SOLDAGEM |
| 13788 | DURAÇÃO DO CICLO DE SOLDAGEM |
| 13789 | ELÉTRODO DE SOLDAR |
| 13790 | SEQÜÊNCIA DE SOLDAGEM |
| 13791 | SÍMBOLOS DE SOLDAGEM |
| 13792 | TESTE DE SOLDABILIDADE |
| 13793 | FIO DE SOLDAR |
| 13794 | FLANGE DE SOLDAR |
| 13795 | CONJUNTO SOLDADO |
| 13796 | ÁGUA DE POÇO |
| 13797 | MASSA DE ENCANADOR |
| 13798 | POLIA WESTON |
| 13799 | BOMBA A AR ÚMIDO |
| 13800 | ANÁLISE POR VIA ÚMIDA |
| 13801 | COMPRESSOR ÚMIDO |
| 13802 | CORROSÃO ÚMIDA |

| | |
|---|---|
| 13803 | TREFILAÇÃO POR VIA ÚMIDA |
| 13804 | CAMISA ÚMIDA |
| 13805 | VAPOR ÚMIDO |
| 13806 | UMIDADE DO VAPOR |
| 13807 | UMEDECIMENTO |
| 13808 | AGENTE UMIDIFICANTE |
| 13809 | PONTE DE WHEATSTONE |
| 13810 | RODA |
| 13811 | RAIOS DE RODA |
| 13812 | CARRINHO DE MÃO |
| 13813 | DISTÂNCIA ENTRE EIXOS |
| 13814 | CENTRO DE RODA |
| 13815 | COBRE-RODAS |
| 13816 | TORNO PARA RODAS |
| 13817 | TAMBOR DE PLANÍMETRO |
| 13818 | ARO DE RODA |
| 13819 | DENTE DE ENGRENAGEM |
| 13820 | PALHETA MÓVEL DE TURBINA |
| 13821 | JOGO DE RODAS |
| 13822 | MÁQUINA DE PERFILAR OS AROS DE RODAS |
| 13823 | COROA MÓVEL DA TURBINA |
| 13824 | PEDRA DE AFIAR |
| 13825 | OSCILAÇÃO DE UMA CORREIA |
| 13826 | TERMÔMETRO CLÍNICO |
| 13827 | VOLTEIO |
| 13828 | FIO MONOCRISTALINO |
| 13829 | APITO |
| 13830 | FERRO FUNDIDO BRANCO |
| 13831 | OURO BRANCO |
| 13832 | INCANDESCÊNCIA |
| 13833 | PAU FERRO |
| 13834 | ALVAIADE DE CHUMBO |
| 13835 | METAL BRANCO DEFLOCULADO |
| 13836 | METAL BRANCO |
| 13837 | GUARNIÇÃO ANTIFRICÇÃO |
| 13838 | ÓLEOS BRANCOS |
| 13839 | CORDA NÃO ALCATROADA |
| 13840 | PNEUS DE FLANCOS BRANCOS |
| 13841 | GIZ PULVERIZADO |
| 13842 | CARGA NEUTRA |
| 13843 | MÁQUINA WHITWORTH DE MEDIR |
| 13844 | ROSCA WHITWORTH |
| 13845 | ALTURA DE DENTE |
| 13846 | MECHA |
| 13846 | PAVIO |
| 13847 | LUBRIFICAÇÃO POR MECHA |
| 13848 | FRESA CILÍNDRICA |
| 13849 | VIGOTA DE ABAS LARGAS |
| 13850 | LARGURA |
| 13851 | GUINCHO |

1334

| | | | |
|---|---|---|---|
| 13852 | GUINCHOS | 13896 | TELA DE ARAME |
| 13853 | ENROLAR | 13897 | MÁQUINA DE FAZER TELA DE ARAME |
| 13854 | BORDA DE VEDAÇÃO | 13898 | CARRETEL PARA ARAME |
| 13855 | MOTOR A VENTO | 13899 | CABO METÁLICO |
| 13855 | MOINHO DE VENTO | 13900 | VELOCIDADE DO FIO |
| 13856 | VIGA DE RIGIDEZ | 13901 | MÁQUINA DE ENROLAR MOLAS HELICOIDAIS |
| 13857 | CARGA CAUSADA PELO VENTO | | |
| 13858 | PRESSÃO DO VENTO | 13902 | CORDOALHA DE ARAME |
| 13859 | TURBINA A AR | 13903 | MÁQUINA DE ENROLAR ARAME |
| 13860 | CATA-VENTO | 13904 | MÁQUINA DE TRABALHAR OS FIOS METÁLICOS |
| 13861 | RODA ATMOSFÉRICA | | |
| 13862 | ENROLAMENTO | 13905 | TREFILARIA |
| 13862 | BOBINAGEM | 13906 | TREFILAGEM |
| 13863 | MOLINETE | 13907 | TELEGRAFIA SEM FIO |
| 13864 | JANELA | 13908 | TELEFONIA SEM FIO |
| 13865 | CAIXILHO DE JANELA | 13909 | INSTALAÇÃO ELÉTRICA |
| 13866 | VIDRAÇA | 13909 | COLOCAÇÃO DE ARAMES |
| 13867 | REGULADOR DE JANELA | 13910 | SUBTRAIR CALOR |
| 13868 | CORREDIÇA DE JANELA | 13911 | CARBONATO NATURAL DE BÁRIO |
| 13869 | DEBULHADORAS | 13911 | VITERITA |
| 13870 | LAVADOR DE PÁRA-BRISA | 13912 | VOLFRÂMIO |
| 13871 | LIMPADOR DE PÁRA-BRISA | 13913 | MADEIRA |
| 13872 | PÁRA-BRISA | 13914 | CARVÃO DE LENHA |
| 13873 | JOGO | 13914 | CARVÃO VEGETAL |
| 13874 | ASA | 13915 | REVESTIMENTO DE MADEIRA |
| 13875 | PLATAFORMA EM SACADA | 13916 | PÓ DE MADEIRA |
| 13876 | COMPASSOS DE QUADRANTE | 13917 | SERRA DE MADEIRA |
| 13877 | EXTRAÇÃO DO CARVÃO | 13918 | PARAFUSO DE MADEIRA |
| 13878 | ENXUGADOR | 13919 | MARAVALHAS |
| 13878 | LIMPADOR | 13919 | APARAS DE MADEIRA |
| 13879 | ANEL COLETOR DE ÓLEO | 13919 | SERRAGEM |
| 13880 | FIO METÁLICO | 13920 | ÁLCOOL METÍLICO |
| 13881 | LIGAR UM FIO CONDUTOR | 13921 | ALCATRÃO DE MADEIRA |
| 13882 | BARRA A TREFILAR | 13921 | PICHE VEGETAL |
| 13883 | MÁQUINA DE DOBRAR FIOS | 13922 | TORNO PARA MADEIRA |
| 13884 | ESCOVA DE ARAME | 13923 | LÃ DE MADEIRA |
| 13885 | MÁQUINA DE FAZER CORRENTES DE ARAME | 13924 | TRABALHO DE MADEIRA |
| | | 13925 | MÁQUINA-FERRAMENTA DE TRABALHAR MADEIRA |
| 13886 | ALICATE DE CORTE | | |
| 13886 | CORTA-FIO | 13926 | MACETE DE MADEIRA |
| 13887 | FIEIRA A TREFILAR | 13927 | FORRO DE MADEIRA |
| 13888 | TREFILAÇÃO DE ARAME | 13928 | TUBO DE MADEIRA |
| 13889 | MÁQUINA DE TREFILAR | 13929 | CHAVETA SEMI-REDONDA |
| 13890 | PARTÍCULAS MIÚDAS DE AÇO (FR. MORFIL) | 13930 | FRESAS DE RANHURAR WOODRUFF |
| | | 13931 | MÁQUINAS DE LAVRAR MADEIRA |
| 13891 | FORJADOR DE PREGOS | 13932 | LÃ |
| 13892 | FIEIRA | 13933 | GRAXA |
| 13893 | TELA DE ARAME FINO | 13934 | PALAVRA |
| 13894 | VIDRO ARMADO | 13935 | FORMATO DE ENDEREÇOS |
| 13895 | PONTAS DE PARIS | 13936 | TRABALHO |
| 13895 | PREGOS DE ARAME | 13937 | TRABALHAR |

| | |
|---|---|
| 13937 | TRATAR |
| 13937 | USINAR |
| 13938 | EXPLORAR UMA INVENÇÃO |
| 13939 | DISTRIBUIÇÃO DO TRABALHO |
| 13940 | TRABALHO EFETUADO |
| 13941 | TRABALHO DE COMPRESSÃO |
| 13942 | TRABALHO DE ATRITO |
| 13943 | LUGAR DE TRABALHO |
| 13944 | TRABALHO RESISTENTE |
| 13945 | MORDENTE DE BLOQUEIO |
| 13946 | USINABILIDADE |
| 13947 | TRABALHÁVEL |
| 13948 | EXPLORAÇÃO DE UMA INVENÇÃO |
| 13949 | CONDIÇÕES DE SERVIÇO |
| 13950 | GASTOS DE EXPLORAÇÃO |
| 13951 | ALTURA DE AÇÃO |
| 13952 | PROFUNDIDADE DE ENGRENAGEM |
| 13953 | ÓRGÃO QUE FUNCIONA |
| 13954 | CILINDRO MOTOR |
| 13955 | CALIBRE DE FABRICAÇÃO |
| 13956 | CARGA ADMISSÍVEL |
| 13957 | PRESSÃO DE REGIME |
| 13958 | TAXA DE TRABALHO |
| 13959 | TRABALHO |
| 13959 | TRATAMENTO |
| 13959 | USINAGEM |
| 13960 | OPERÁRIO |
| 13960 | TRABALHADOR |
| 13961 | MÃO-DE-OBRA |
| 13962 | OPERARIADO |
| 13963 | DIREÇÃO DE TRABALHO |
| 13964 | CHEFE DE FABRICAÇÃO |
| 13964 | CHEFE DE SERVIÇO |
| 13964 | CHEFE DE OFICINA |
| 13965 | VIA FÉRREA DE OFICINA |
| 13966 | LIGAÇÃO DE VIA INDUSTRIAL |
| 13967 | CALIBRE DE FABRICAÇÃO |
| 13968 | ATELIER |
| 13968 | OFICINA |
| 13969 | PARAFUSO SEM-FIM |
| 13970 | ELEVADOR DE ROSCA SEM-FIM |
| 13971 | FRESA-MÃE |
| 13972 | FRESA DE CORTAR ENGRENAGENS HELICOIDAIS |
| 13973 | POLIA DE PARAFUSO TANGENTE |
| 13973 | POLIA DE PARAFUSO SEM-FIM |
| 13974 | ENGRENAGEM HELICOIDAL |
| 13974 | ENGRENAGEM SEM-FIM |
| 13975 | RODA DE PARAFUSO SEM-FIM |
| 13976 | CARUNCHOSO |
| 13976 | CARCOMIDO |
| 13977 | MADEIRA CARUNCHOSA |
| 13978 | SERPENTINA DE RESFRIAMENTO |
| 13979 | PARAFUSO SEM-FIM |
| 13980 | MANCAL GASTO |
| 13981 | ROSCA DESGASTADA |
| 13982 | DESGASTADO |
| 13983 | CORREIA TORCIDA |
| 13984 | PAPEL DE EMBRULHO |
| 13985 | ENRUGAMENTO |
| 13986 | PINO DE CRUZETA |
| 13987 | LATÃO BRUTO |
| 13988 | FERRO DOCE |
| 13988 | FERRO FORJADO |
| 13989 | CANO DE FERRO |
| 13990 | PREGO FORJADO |
| 13991 | VULFENITA |
| 13992 | REDE DE WULF |
| 13993 | ANÁLISE RADIOGRÁFICA |
| 13994 | APARELHO DE RAIO X |
| 13995 | FEIXE DE RAIO X |
| 13996 | CRISTALOGRAFIA DE RAIO X |
| 13997 | DIAGRAMA DE DIFRAÇÃO DE RAIO X |
| 13998 | CONTROLE RADIOGRÁFICO |
| 13999 | ANÁLISE FLUORESCENTE |
| 14000 | ESPECTRÔMETRO DE RAIOS X |
| 14001 | ESPECTRO DE RAIO X |
| 14002 | TUBO DE RAIO X |
| 14003 | RAIOS-X |
| 14004 | XÊNON |
| 14005 | XEROGRAFIA |
| 14006 | XILOL |
| 14006 | XILÊNIO |
| 14007 | JARDA |
| 14008 | LATÃO AMARELO |
| 14009 | FÓSFORO AMARELO |
| 14010 | RENDIMENTO |
| 14011 | PONTO DE RUPTURA |
| 14012 | LIMITE ELÁSTICO |
| 14013 | LIMITE ELÁSTICO |
| 14014 | CULATRA |
| 14014 | BRIDA |
| 14014 | BRAÇADEIRA |
| 14014 | ESTRIBO |
| 14014 | FORQUILHA |
| 14015 | TAMPA DE ARCO |
| 14016 | LUVA DE ARCO |
| 14017 | CULATRA DE ÍMÃ |
| 14018 | PORCA DE CAVALETE |
| 14019 | ITÉRBIO |
| 14020 | ÍTRIO |
| 14021 | ZAMAK |

| | | | | |
|---|---|---|---|
| 14022 | VERNIZ ZAPON | 14038 | CLORETO DE ZINCO |
| 14023 | FERRO EM Z | 14039 | CROMATO DE ZINCO |
| 14024 | DESVIO NULO | 14040 | LIMALHA DE ZINCO |
| 14025 | LINHA ZERO | 14041 | CIANETO DE ZINCO |
| 14026 | DESLOCAMENTO DO PONTO DE ORIGEM | 14042 | MINÉRIO DE ZINCO |
| 14027 | PONTO ZERO | 14043 | ÓXIDO DE ZINCO |
| 14028 | POSIÇÃO DE ZERO | 14044 | GALVANIZAÇÃO |
| 14029 | LINHA DE PRESSÃO NULA | 14044 | ZINCAGEM |
| 14030 | COLOCAÇÃO EM ZERO | 14045 | ZINCAGEM |
| 14031 | DESLOCAMENTO DO PONTO DE ORIGEM | 14046 | SULFATO DE ZINCO |
| 14032 | SINCRONIZAÇÃO DO PONTO ZERO | 14047 | TUBO DE ZINCO |
| 14033 | SUPRESSÃO DOS ZEROS | 14048 | ARAME DE ZINCO |
| 14034 | REBITE EM QUINCÔNCIO | 14049 | ZIRCÔNIO |
| 14035 | ZINCO | 14050 | FUSÃO POR ZONA |
| 14036 | ACETATO DE ZINCO | 14051 | ZONA ESFÉRICA |
| 14037 | CARBONATO DE ZINCO | 14051 | SEGMENTO ESFÉRICO DE DUAS BASES |

Este livro DICIONÁRIO TÉCNICO INDUSTRIAL de Michel Feutry, Robert M. de Mertzenfeld, Agnès Dollinger é o volume 10 da coleção Dicionários Garnier. Capa Cláudio Martins. Impresso na Editora Gráfica Líthera Maciel Ltda, Rua Simão Antônio, 157, Contagem, para Livraria Garnier, à Rua São Geraldo, 53 - Belo Horizonte - MG. No catálogo geral leva o número 3116/6B. ISBN. 85-7175-064-5.

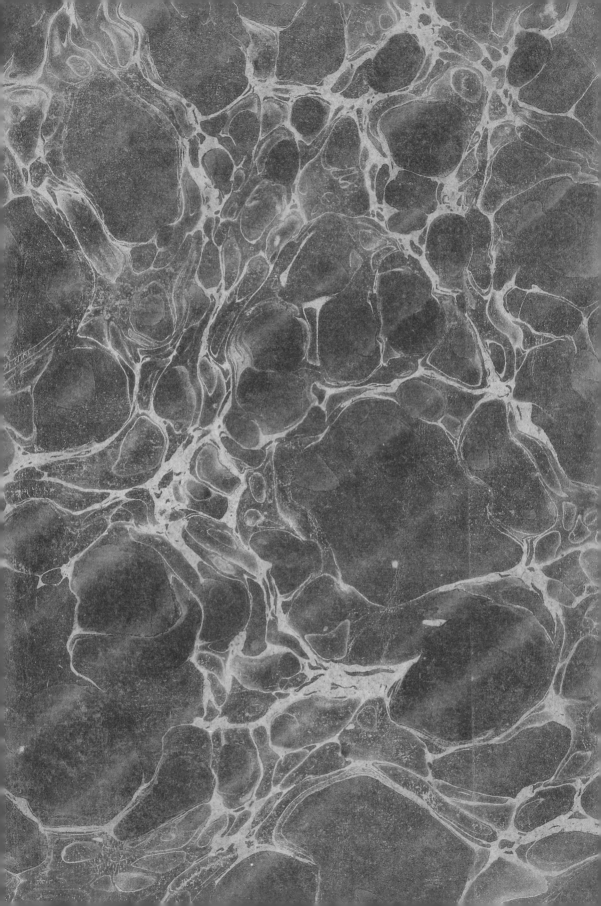